T5-AFZ-433

WHO'S WHO
IN AMERICAN MUSIC:
CLASSICAL

WHO'S WHO IN AMERICAN MUSIC:

CLASSICAL

First Edition

Edited by JAQUES CATTELL PRESS

R. R. BOWKER COMPANY
New York & London

Published by the R. R. Bowker Company
205 East 42nd Street, New York, New York 10017
Copyright© 1983 by Xerox Corporation.
All rights reserved. Reproduction of this work in whole or in part,
without written permission of the publisher is prohibited.
International Standard Book Number: 0-8352-1725-6
International Standard Serial Number: 0737-9137
Printed and bound in the United States of America

The publishers do not assume and hereby disclaim any liability to
any party for any loss or damage caused by errors or omissions in
Who's Who in American Music: Classical, whether such errors
or omissions result from negligence, accident or any other cause.

Notice: This book has no connection with *Who's Who in America*
or its publisher, Marquis-Who's Who, Inc.

841599

Contents

LIBRARY
ALMA COLLEGE
ALMA, MICHIGAN

Advisory Committee

Catherine French, Chief Executive Officer
American Symphony Orchestra League
633 E Street, N.W.
Washington, DC 20004

Karen Monson
Author and Critic
6634 Majorea Way East
Phoenix, AZ 85016

Margaret Jory, Director of Symphonic
   & Concert Department
American Society of Composers,
   Authors & Publishers
One Lincoln Plaza
New York, NY 10023

Maria Rich, Executive Director
Central Opera Service
Metropolitan Opera
Lincoln Center
New York, NY 10023

D. W. Krummel, Professor of Library &
   Information Science and of Music
University of Illinois at Urbana-Champaign
410 David Kinley Hall
1407 West Gregory Drive
Urbana, IL 60801

Susan T. Sommer, Head
Rare Books & Manuscript-Music Division
The New York Public Library
111 Amsterdam Avenue
New York, NY 10023

Arlys L. McDonald, Music Librarian
Music Library
Arizona State University
Tempe, AZ 85287

James W. Pruett, Chairman &
   Professor of Music
University of North Carolina
Chapel Hill, NC 27514

Preface

The need for a biographical directory covering Americans in all areas of serious music first surfaced during a publication planning meeting between R. R. Bowker editors and library and media representatives. It was the concensus of the group that although other areas of American contemporary music were represented in biographical directories, performers of classical and concert music, music educators, and other music professionals, with few exceptions, were not. This focus group determined the general direction and content of the directory. With the help of Dr. D. W. Krummel of the University of Illinois, a member of the original group, an advisory committee of distinguished members of the music and academic communities was then assembled. With their help the editors designed the entry format and compiled a list of prospective entrants. The result of these labors, *Who's Who in American Music: Classical,* is the first edition of a work planned to become a permanent member of the Bowker/Cattell biographical publications family. Revision is scheduled at two year intervals.

The directory provides biographical data on 6,800 members of the music community who are currently active and influential contributors to the creation, preservation, performance, or promotion of serious music in America. In addition to composers and performers, there are included educators, librarians, writers, editors, organization administrators and executives, directors, patrons, and managers. The majority of those who appear in the directory are American citizens, but a small number of non-citizens can be found, and are included because they are U.S. residents, hold positions with American organizations, or have performed extensively in this country.

Questionnaires were sent to prospective entrants during the winter and spring of 1983. The editors reviewed all that were returned and composed entries for those who qualified for inclusion. If no information was forthcoming from an artist whose achievements mandated representation in a directory of leaders in American music, an entry was compiled from other published sources. In all such cases, however, a copy proof was provided to the entrant for approval and verification.

It is not the purpose of *Who's Who in American Music: Classical* to provide detailed biographical information, but rather to give a brief accounting of background, major achievements and current location or representation. Entrants are limited as to the number of compositions, publications, memberships and certain other data they may list in entries. The editors have made every effort to assure accurate reproduction of the material submitted, but in some cases have had to edit such material to conform to format, content, and space requirements. All entrants were provided with copy proofs prior to publication.

Who's Who in American Music: Classical could not have been compiled without the cooperation of many individuals and organizations. The advisory committee was generous with support and encouragement. Professional organizations and societies provided publicity, mailing lists or mailing services. Managers and artist's representatives forwarded mail or supplied information. To all of them we say a heartfelt "thank you." In addition, the Jaques Cattell Press was fortunate to have the services of a group of dedicated editorial assistants and researchers who made the success of the book a personal goal.

Because this is a first edition we must assume that in spite of time and effort expended and the best of intentions, we have failed to include some worthy representatives of the music world. If such omissions have occurred they are unintentional, and we urge our users to bring them to our attention. We are also interested in suggestions for improvement in content and style — anything that will increase the value of *Who's Who in American Music: Classical* to its users. Please address all comments to The Editors, Biographical Directories, Jaques Cattell Press, P.O. Box 25001, Tempe, Arizona, 85282.

Carol Borland, Editor
Renee Lautenbach, Managing Editor
Terence Basom, General Manager
JAQUES CATTELL PRESS

November, 1983

Sample Entry

SMITH, CAROL JOAN
[1]SOPRANO, COMPOSER
[2]b Paducah, Ky, June 7, 41. [3]*Study:* Ind Univ, BA, 61; Cargill Sch Music, with Deborah Weiss & Jill Standish. [4]*Works:* Five Songs (sop & flute), 72 & Raise Your Eyes (sop voice), 75, Special Music Co. [5]*Rec Perf:* Carol Smith Sings, Classical Record Co, 82. [6]*Roles:* Violetta in La Traviata, Mimi in La Boheme, Cio Cio San in Madama Butterfly, Donna Elvira in Don Giovanni, Dorinda in Orlando & Pomina in The Magic Flute, Nat Opera Theatre. [7]*Pos:* Mem, Am Opera Co, 65-72; prin sop, Nat Opera Theatre, 73-; soloist with major US & Europ Orch, 73-; recitalist, US, Europe & South Am, 73- [8]*Teaching:* Instr voice, Cargill Sch Music, 80- [9]*Awards:* Winner, Mid-Am Voice Compt, 65; Deanna Lowder Award, Am Opera Soc, 68; Becker Prize, 71. [10]*Bibliog:* James Pennypacker (auth), Carol Smith, Singer and Composer, Music Mag, summer 81. [11]*Mem:* Am Asn Authors & Comp; Am Opera Soc. [12]*Interests:* Women composers. [13]*Publ:* Auth, Caro Roma, Am Comp, April 78; Women With Vision, Musica Publ Co, 80. [14]*Rep:* JRW Agency 88 Oak Ave Washington DC 20017 [15]*Mailing Add:* 672 Whitt St Bethesda MD 21044

[1]Professional Classification. Limited to two.

[2]Birth Data.

[3]Study and Training: degrees; years of study; prominent instructors.

[4]Works: titles of original compositions; by whom published, performed, or commissioned. Limited to seven.

[5]Recorded Performances: titles of recordings or programs; name of recording company or broadcasting station. Limited to seven.

[6]Roles: representative roles or vocal selections; companies or groups with which performed. Limited to seven.

[7]Positions: past and present professional experience; career outline.

[8]Teaching: past and present teaching or coaching experience.

[9]Honors and Awards: prizes, grants, scholarships. Limited to three.

[10]Bibliography: articles or books written about the entrant. Limited to three.

[11]Memberships: current memberships in music organizations; offices held. Limited to five.

[12]Research Interests: areas of scholarly study.

[13]Publications: articles or books authored, edited or translated; name of publisher or publication. Limited to five.

[14]Representative: manager or artist's representative; address.

[15]Mailing Address.

Abbreviations

ABC— American Broadcasting Company
abstr—astract(s)
acad—academic, academy
accad—accademia
accmp—accompanist, accompaniment
acct—account, accountant, accounting
acoust—accoustic(s), acoustical
actg—acting
activ—activities, activity
add—address
addn—addition(s), additional
adj—adjunct, adjutant
adjust—adjustment
admin—administration, administrative
adminr—administrator(s)
admis—admissions
adv—adviser(s), advisor(s), advisory, advocate
advan—advance(d), advancement
advert—advertisement, advertising
aesthet—aesthetics
AFB—Air Force Base
affil—affiliate(s), affiliation
agt—agent(s)
Agy—Agency
AHA—American Historical Association
Ala—Alabama
alt—alternate
Alta—Alberta
Am—America, American
ann—annal(s), annual, annually
APO—Army Post Office
app—appoint, appointed, appointment
appl—applied
appln—application
approx—approximate, approximately
Apr—April
apt—apartment(s)
arch—archive(s)
Arg—Argentina, Argentine
Ariz—Arizona
Ark—Arkansas
arr—arranged, arrangement, arranger, arranging
ASCAP—American Society of Composers,
   Authors and Publishers
asn(s)—association(s)
assoc—associate(s), associated
asst—assistant
attend—attendant, attending
Aug—August
auth—author
Ave—Avenue

b—born
bar—baritone
BC—British Columbia
bd—board(s)
behav—behavior, behavioral, behaviour,
   behavioural

bibliog—bibliographic, bibliographical,
   bibliographies, bibliography
bibliogr—bibliographer
bk(s)—book(s)
bldg—building
Blvd—Boulevard
BMI—Broadcast Music Incorporated
bor—borough
br—branch
Brit—Britain, British
bs—bass
bur—bureau
bus—business
BWI—British West Indies

Calif—California
Can—Canada, Canadian
cand—candidate
cath—catholic
CBS—Columbia Broadcasting System
Cent Am—Central America
cent—central
cert—certificate(s), certification, certified
chap—chapter
chg—charge
chmn—chairman
class—classical
cmndg—commanding
c/o—care of
co—companies, company, county
coauth—coauthor
co-chmn—co-chairman
co-dir—co-director
co-ed—co-editor
col(s)—college(s), collegiate
collab—collaboration, collaborative
collabr—collaborator
Colo—Colorado
commun—communicable, communication(s)
comn(s)—commission(s), commissioned
comnr—commissioner
comp—compose, composer, composition(s)
   composed
compt—competition
comput—computation, computer(s), computing,
   computational
comt(s)—committee(s)
conct—concert
cond—conductor, conducting
conf—conference
Cong—Congress(es), Congressional
Conn—Connecticut
consult(s)—consultant, consulting,
   consultanship(s)
consv—conservatory
cont—contest
contemp—contemporary
contr—contralto
contrib—contribute, contributing, contribution,

contribr—contributor
conv—convention
coop—cooperation, cooperative, cooperating
coord—coordinate, coordinated,
   coordination, coordinating
coordr—coordinator
corp—corporate, corporation
corresp—correspondence, correspondent,
   corresponding
coun—council, counsel, counselling
counr—councillor, counselor(s)
ct—court
ctr—center
cult—cultural, culture
cur—curator
curric—curriculum

DC—District of Columbia
Dec—December
Del—Delaware
dep—deputy
dept—department, departmental
develop—developed, developing,
   development, developmental
dict—dictionaries, dictionary
Dig—Digest
dipl—diploma
dir—director(s), directory
distrib—distributive, distributed, distribution
distribr—distributor(s)
div—division, divisional
doc—document(s), documentation, documentary
Dr—Doctor, Drive

E—East
ed—edition(s), editor, editorial, edit,
   editing, edited
educ—education, educational, educate,
   educated, educating
educr—educator(s)
elem—elementary
emer—emeritus
employ—employment
encycl—encyclopedia(s)
ens—ensemble(s)
espec—especially
estab—established, establishment(s)
ethnomusicol—ethnomusicology
Europ—European
eval—evaluation
Evangel—Evangelical
exam—examination(s), examining
examr—examiner(s)
except—exceptional
exec—executive(s)
exhib—exhibition(s)
exten—extension

fac—faculty
facil—facilities, facility
Feb—February
fed—federal
fedn—federation
fel(s)—fellow(s), fellowship(s)
fest—festival
Fla—Florida
found—foundation
FPO—Fleet Post Office
Fri—Friday
Ft—Fort

Ga—Georgia
gen—general
geog—geographic, geographical, geography
Ger—Germany
gov—governing, governor(s)
govt—government, governmental
grad—graduate, graduated
Gt Brit—Great Britain
Gtr—Greater
guid—guidance

handbk(s)—handbook(s)
hist—historical, history
hon—honor(s), honorable, honorary
hq—headquarters
Hwy—Highway

Ill—Illinois
imp—imperial
improv—improvement
Inc—Incorporated
incl—include(s), included, including
Ind—Indiana
indust—industrial, industries, industry
info—information
inst(s)—institute(s), institution(s)
instnl—institutional, institutionalized
instr—instruction, instructor(s), instruct
instrm—instrument, instrumental
int—international
introd—introduction
invest—investigation(s), investigative
investr—investigator
Ital—Italian

J—Journal
Jan—January
jour—journal, journalism
jr—junior
juv—juvenile(s)

Kans—Kansas
Ky—Kentucky

La—Louisiana
lab—laboratories, laboratory
lang—language(s)
lect—lecture(s)
lectr—lecturer(s)
legis—legislation, legislative, legislature
lett—letter(s)
lib—liberal
libr—libraries, library
librn—librarian(s)
lic—license, licensed
ling—linguistic(s)
lit—literary, literature
Ltd—Limited

lyr—lyric

mag—magazine
maj—major
Man—Manitoba
Mar—March
Mass—Massachusetts
Md—Maryland
Mediter—Mediterranean
mem—member(s), memorial, membership, memoirs
Mex—Mexican, Mexico, Mexicano
mfr(s)—manufacture(s), manufacturer(s)
mgr—manager
mgt—management
Mich—Michigan
mid—middle
mil—military
Minn—Minnesota
Miss—Mississippi
mkt—market, marketing
Mo—Missouri
mod—modern
monogr—monograph
Mont—Montana
ms—mezzo-soprano
mt—mount
munic—municipal, municipalities
musicol—musicological, musicology

N—North
nac—nacional
nat—national, naturalized
NB—New Brunswick
NBC—National Broadcasting Company
NC—North Carolina
NDak—North Dakota
Nebr—Nebraska
Neth—Netherlands
Nev—Nevada
Nfld—Newfoundland
NH—New Hampshire
NJ—New Jersey
NMex—New Mexico
no—number
nonres—nonresident
norm—normal
Norweg—Norwegian
Nov—November
NS—Nova Scotia
NSW—New South Wales
NT—Northwest Territories
NY—New York
NZ—New Zealand

observ—observatory
occas—occasional
occup—occupation, occupational
Oct—October
off—office, officials(s)
Okla—Oklahoma
Ont—Ontario
oper—operation(s), operational, operative
op—opus
orch(s)—orchestra(s), orchestral, orchestration
Ore—Oregon
orgn—organization(s), organizational
orient—oriental, orientalist

Pa—Pennsylvania
Pac—Pacific
Pan-Am—Pan-American
PBS—Public Broadcast System

PEI—Prince Edward Island
perc—percussion, percussionist
perf—performs, performing, performance
phil—philharmonic
phys—physical
Pkwy—Parkway
Pl—Place
polit—political, politics
Pontif—Pontifical
pop—population
Port—Portugal, Portuguese
pos—position
PR—Puerto Rico
pract—practice
practr—practitioner
prehist—prehistoric, prehistory
prem—premiere
prep—preparation, preparative, preparatory
pres—president
Presby—Presbyterian
preserv—preservation
prev—prevention, preventive
prin—principal(s)
prob(s)—problem(s)
proc—proceedings
prod—product(s), production, productive
prof—professor, professorial, professional
prog—program(s), programmed, programming
proj—project(s), projectional, projective
prom—promotion
prov—province, provincial
Pt—Point
pub—public
publ—publication(s), publisher, publishing, published

qual—qualitative, quality
quant—quantitative
quart—quarterly
Que—Quebec

Rd—Road
RD—Rural Delivery
rec—record(s), recording
ref—reference
regist—registration, register, registered
registr—registrar
relig—religion, religious
Rep—Representative, Republican(s), represent
repty—repertory
Repub—Republic
req—requirements
res—residence, research
ret—retired
rev—review, revision(s), revised, revista, revue
RFD—Rural Free Delivery
rhet—rhetoric, rhetorical
RI—Rhode Island
rm—room
RR—Railroad, Rural Route
Rte—Route
Russ—Russian
rwy—railway

S—South
Sask—Saskatchewan
sax—saxophone
SC—South Carolina
Scand—Scandinavia, Scandinavian
sch—school(s)
scholar—scholarship
sci—science(s), scientific
SDak—South Dakota
sec—secondary
sect—section

secy—secretary
sem—seminar, seminary
Sept—September
ser—serial, series
serol—serologic, serological, serology
serv—service(s), serving
soc—societies, society
sop—soprano
spec—special
sq—square
sr—senior
St—Saint, Street
sta—station(s)
Ste—Sainte
struct—structure(s), structural
subj—subject
subsid—subsidiary
substa—substation
Sun—Sunday
super—superior
suppl—supplement, supplemental, supplementary
supt—superintendent
supv—supervising, supervision
supvr—supervisor
supvry—supervisory
Swed—Swedish
Switz—Switzerland
symph(s)—symphonies, symphony
syst—system(s), systematic(s), systematical

tech—technic(s), technical, technique(s)
technol—technologic, technological, technology
temp—temporary
ten—tenor
Tenn—Tennessee
Terr—Terrace
Tex—Texas
textbk(s)—textbook(s)
theol—theologic, theological, theology
theoret—theoretic, theoretical
Thurs—Thursday
trans—transactions
transl—translation(s)
translr—translator
treas—treasurer, treasury
Tues—Tuesday
TV—television
Twp—Township

UK—United Kingdom
UN—United Nations
univ—universities, university
US—United States
USSR—Union of Soviet Socialist Republics

Va—Virginia
var—various

vchmn—vice chairman
VI—Virgin Islands
vis—visiting
voc—vocational
vocab—vocabulary
vol—volume(s), voluntary, volunteer(s)
vpres—vice president
Vt—Vermont

W—West
Wash—Washington
Wed—Wednesday
WI—West Indies
Wis—Wisconsin
wkshp(s)—workshop(s)
WVa—West Virginia
Wyo—Wyoming

yearbk(s)—yearbook(s)
YMCA—Young Men's Christian Association
YMHA—Young Men's Hebrew Association
yr(s)—year(s)
YWCA—Young Women's Christian Association
YWHA—Young Women's Hebrew Association

Who's Who in American Music

A

AAHOLM, PHILIP EUGENE
CLARINET, EDUCATOR
b Sheboygan, Wis, Apr 3, 37. *Study:* Univ Wis, Madison, BA, 64, MM, 68; Univ Ariz, AMusD, 72. *Pos:* Clarinetist, Colo Wind Quintet, Boulder, 80- & Colo Music Fest, Boulder, 82- *Teaching:* Asst prof woodwinds, Lamar Univ, 66-70; teaching assoc clarinet & theory, Univ Ariz, 70-72; assoc prof clarinet & hist, Univ Colo, Boulder, 72- *Mem:* Int Clarinet Soc (vpres, 76-78); Clarinetwork Int Inc; Colo Music Educr Asn. *Interests:* Wind chamber music. *Publ:* Auth, Forum, Tonal Development, 77, Forum, Breathing While Standing, 77 & Forum, Relaxation in Clarinet Performance, 78, Clarinet. *Mailing Add:* 8464 W Fork Rd Boulder CO 80302

AARONS, MARTHA IRENE
FLUTE & PICCOLO
b Los Angeles, Calif, June 14, 51. *Study:* Cleveland Inst Music, with Sharp Hebert, MM; Juilliard Sch, with Baker & Marcel Moyse. *Pos:* First flute, NC Symph, 75-; second flute, Cleveland Orch, 81- *Mailing Add:* Cleveland Orch Severance Hall Cleveland OH 44106

ABBADO, CLAUDIO
CONDUCTOR & MUSIC DIRECTOR
b June, 26, 33. *Study:* Consv G Verdi, Milan; Musical Acad, Vienna. *Pos:* Guest cond prin orchs in Europe & Am, currently; cond prin festivals & opera houses, 61-; music dir, La Scala, Milan, 68- & Europ Community Youth Orch, 77-; prin cond, Vienna Phil Orch, 71- & London Symph Orch, 79- *Awards:* Sergei Koussewitzky Prize, Berkshire Music Ctr, 58; Dimitri Mitroupoulos Prize, 63; Mozart-Medaille, Mozart-Gemiende, Vienna, 73. *Mailing Add:* Piazetta Bossi 1 20121 Milan Italy

ABBATE, CAROLYN
EDUCATOR
b New York, NY, Nov 20, 55. *Study:* Yale Univ, BA & MA, 77; Princeton Univ, MFA, 79, PhD, 83. *Teaching:* Vis lectr, Univ Calif, Berkeley, 82; asst prof, Princeton Univ, 82- *Awards:* Martha Baird Rockefeller Award, 80-81. *Mem:* Am Musicol Soc; Geselschaft Musikforschung. *Interests:* Opera; 19th century music; 20th century music. *Publ:* Auth, Tristan in the Composition of Pelleas, 19th Century Music, 81; The Parisian Venus and the Paris Tannhäuser, J Am Musicol Soc, 83; Der Junge Wagner Malgre Lui, Wagner-Studien (in prep). *Mailing Add:* Dept Music Princeton Univ Princeton NJ 08540

ABBOTT, MICHAEL
PIANO, EDUCATOR
Study: Cleveland Inst Music, BM; Univ Mich, MM; studied with Victor Babin, Marianne Mastics, Marian Owen, and Vitya Vronsky. *Pos:* Soloist, Univ Circle Orch; recitalist, Ann Arbor & Cleveland. *Teaching:* Mem fac piano, Cleveland Inst Music, 71- *Mem:* Pi Kappa Lambda. *Mailing Add:* Cleveland Inst Music 11021 East Blvd Cleveland OH 44106

ABEL, PAUL LOUIS
EDUCATOR, COMPOSER
b Clarksdale, Miss, Nov 23, 26. *Study:* Eastman Sch Music, Univ Rochester, BMus, 48, MMus, 50. *Works:* Cyrano de Bergerac, perf by Mont State Univ Band, 54; Vignette for Orchestra, Rochester Phil, 62; In Memoriam Astronautarun, New Orleans Phil, 66; Fantasia on Gregarian Thames, perf by La State Univ Symph, 72; Requiem (chorus & orch), comn & perf by Baton Rouge Choral Soc, 79; Fantasia for Cello, comn & perf by Thaddus Buys, 82. *Teaching:* Instr, Univ Mont, Missoula, 50-54; prof, La State Univ, Baton Rouge, 54- *Awards:* Benjamin Award, Eastman Sch Music, 62; Herb Catton Award, La State Univ, 76. *Mem:* Music Teachers Nat Asn (brass chmn, 64-65); Am Soc Univ Comp (conf & prog dir, 83). *Mailing Add:* 760 Dartmoor Dr Baton Rouge LA 70815

ABER, ALICE LAWSON See Lawson, Alice

ABER, MARGERY VINIE
EDUCATOR, ADMINISTRATOR
b Racine, Wis, Feb 15, 14. *Study:* Oberlin Col, BM, 37; Columbia Univ, MA, 46; Colorado Univ, Wayne State Univ, Univ NY, Oakland Univ & Univ Hawaii, 37-; study with Dr Shinchi Suzuki in Japan & US, 67- *Pos:* Dir, Am Suzuki Inst, 71- *Teaching:* Instr string, Detroit Pub Sch, 37-67; mem fac, Wayne St Univ, 47-59; prof, Univ Wis, Stevens Pt, 67- *Mem:* Am Suzuki Inst; Music Educr Nat Conf; Music Teachers Nat Asn; Am String Teachers Asn; Suzuki Asn Am. *Publ:* Auth, Pedagogy of Violin Teaching, Delta Omicron, 74; Toshio Takahashi—Flutist, Instrumentalist, 80; The Story of the First Am Suzuki Institute, Am Suzuki J, 80; China Dolls, Suzuki World, 83. *Mailing Add:* 511 Michigan Ave Stevens Point WI 54481

ABERTS, EUNICE DOROTHY
CONTRALTO, EDUCATOR
b Boston, Mass. *Study:* With Cleora Wood & Rosalie Miller; New England Consv Music, studied dramatics with Boris Goldovsky; studied cond with Nadia Boulanger. *Rec Perf:* On CRI. *Roles:* Suzuki in Madama Butterfly, 51 & Rebecca Nurse in The Crucible, 61, New York City Opera; Mrs Herring in Albert Herring; Mere in Louise; Abuela in La Vida Breve; Baba the Turk in The Rake's Progress; Maurya in Riders to the Sea. *Pos:* Singer with maj opera co in US. *Teaching:* Mem fac, Boston Univ, formerly; adj mem fac voice, Univ Lowell, currently. *Mailing Add:* 7 Sherbourne Rd Lexington MA 02173

ABRAHAMS, FRANK E
EDUCATOR, ADMINISTRATOR
b Philadelphia, Pa, Nov 8, 47. *Study:* Temple Univ, with Robert Page, BME, 69; New England Consv, with Lorna Cooke de Varon, MM, 72. *Teaching:* Prof music educ & music theatre, New England Consv, 72-; prof supvr fine arts, Stoneham Pub Sch, Mass, 75- *Publ:* Auth various articles in Mass Music News, Md Music News & Philadelphia Orch Prog. *Mailing Add:* 20 Dana Rd West Peabody MA 01960

ABRAM, BLANCHE SCHWARTZ
PIANO, EDUCATOR
b Brooklyn, NY. *Study:* Brooklyn Col, BA, 45; NY Univ, 45-46; study piano with Isabelle Vengerova, Heida Hermanns & Alexander Kelberine. *Rec Perf:* Sonora (Marga Richter), Orion, 82. *Pos:* Co-dir & pianist, Am Chamber Ens, 77-; pianist, Drucker Trio, 78- *Teaching:* Fac mem, Y Sch Music of Ninety Second St, New York, 45-; adj sr prof, Hofstra Univ, Hempstead, NY, 68- *Awards:* Young Am Artist Award, Brooklyn Acad Music, 46. *Mem:* New York State Music Teachers Asn; European Piano Teachers Asn; Int Soc for Study of Tension in Perf; Col Music Soc. *Publ:* Auth, Educating Young Musicians—A Guide for Students, Teachers and Parents, Y Sch Music of Ninety Second St, New York, 60; Training Musicianship Through Structural Awareness, Clavier, 77. *Mailing Add:* 2320 Surrey Lane Baldwin NY 11510

ABRAMS, RICHARD
DIRECTOR — OPERA
b Cincinnati, Ohio, Jan 13, 42. *Study:* Ind Univ; studied in Cincinnati, Hamburg & Cologne. *Pos:* Asst stage dir, New York City Opera, formerly; dir & producer opera for maj co in US. *Teaching:* Lectr, col. *Awards:* Chicago Lyr Stage Dir Compt, 64. *Mailing Add:* 325 Riverside Dr New York NY 10025

ABRAMSON, ROBERT U
EDUCATOR, COMPOSER
b Philadelphia, Pa, Aug 23, 28. *Study:* Dalcroze Sch Music, lic, 53; Manhattan Sch Music, BM, 65, MM, 68; L'Inst Jaques-Dalcroze, Geneva, Switzerland, dipl, 74. *Works:* Dance Variations For Piano and Orchestra, Serenus Music Publ, 68; Thee Old Songs Resung, Mercury Music. *Pos:* Dir, Dalcroze Inst, Manhattan Sch Music, 83- *Teaching:* Prof theory dept, Manhattan Sch Music, 72- *Mem:* Dalcroze Soc Am (pres, 71-73). *Publ:* Auth, Rhythm Games for Perception & Cognition, Columbia Pictures, 69; Improvisation as Synthesis, Music Educr Nat Conf J, 71. *Mailing Add:* 250 W 94th St New York NY 10025

ABRAVANEL, MAURICE
MUSIC DIRECTOR, EDUCATOR
b Salonica, Greece, Jan 6, 03; US citizen. *Study:* Univ Lausanne, Switzerland, 19-21; studied with Kurt Weill, 22-23; Westminster Col, Univ Utah, Hon

PhD, 54; Cleveland Inst Music, Hon PhD, 82. *Rec Perf:* Complete Orchestral Works (Brahms), Symphonies (Sibelius) & Symphonies (Mahler), Vanguard; Complete Orchestral Works (Tchaikovsky) & Complete Orchestral Works (Grieg), Vox; Judas Maccabaeus (Handel), Westminster; Satie Complete, Varese Ameriques; over 100 records. *Pos:* Cond, Metropolitan Opera, 36-38; music dir, Utah Symph, 47-79 & Music Acad West, 54-80; actg artistic dir & artist in res, Berkshire Music Ctr, 82-; guest conductor with leading symphony orchestras in US, Europe & Australia. *Awards:* Kilenyi Mahler Medal, 65; Ditson Cond Award, 71; Gold Baton, Am Symph Orch League, 81. *Mem:* Nat Coun Arts; Am Arts Alliance (bd mem, 77-); Am Symph Orch League; Int Gustav Mahler Soc. *Mailing Add:* 1235 E 7th S Salt Lake City UT 84102

ACORD, THOMAS WADSWORTH
TENOR, CONDUCTOR
b Houston, Tex, Sept 26, 43. *Study:* Tex Tech Univ, with Gene Kenney & Robert Deahl, BMus, 67; Univ Tex, Austin, with Jess Walters & Walter Ducloux, MMus, 69, DMA, 81. *Roles:* Jenik in The Bartered Bride, Fresno Opera Asn, 73; Ferrando in Cosi fan tutte, Sao Paulo Opera, Brasil, 74; Eisenstein in Die Fledermaus, Portland Opera, 76; Don Jose in Carmen, 79; Don Ramiro, Scholar Opera, 80; Curly, Nevada Opera Asn, 80; Duke of Mantua in Rigoletto, 83. *Pos:* Artistic adv, Oakland Opera, Calif, currently. *Teaching:* Prof music, Calif State Univ, Hayward, 72- *Awards:* Artist Award, Calif Nat Asn Teachers Singing, 73. *Mem:* Nat Asn Teachers Singing; Nat Opera Asn; Cent Opera Serv; Calif Fedn Music Clubs. *Publ:* Auth, The Making of a Magic Potion, 75, A Family Affair, 76, A Higher and a Nether World, 76 & Olga, To Your Memory, 80, San Francisco Opera; An Examination of Leos Janacek's Compositions for Solo Voice & Piano, Univ Tex, 81. *Mailing Add:* 24657 Leona Dr Hayward CA 94542

ACOSTA, ADOLOVNI P
ADMINISTRATOR, PIANO
b Manila, Philippines. *Study:* Studied with Zenon Fishbein & Claude Frank; Univ Philippines, TDM, 65, BM, 66, MM, 68; Juilliard Sch, studied piano with Mieczyslaw Munz, MS, 71; NY Univ, study with Eugene List, currently. *Rec Perf:* Andalucia Suite (Ernesto Lecuona), 82 & Danzas Afro Cubanas (Ernesto Lecuona), 82, Orion Master Rec. *Pos:* Founder & dir, East & West Artists, 71- *Awards:* First Prize, Nat Piano Compt, Music Prom Found Philippines, 65. *Bibliog:* John Rockwell (auth), East & West Artists Presents Its Winners, New York Times, 2/1/76; Max Harrison (auth), Adolovni Acosta, Times, London, 4/23/80; Claude Lully (auth), Musique Adolovni Acosta, Parisien Libere, 12/9/82. *Mem:* Piano Teachers Cong NY; Col Music Soc; Phi Kappa Phi. *Mailing Add:* 310 Riverside Dr Apt 313 New York NY 10025

ADAM, CLAUS
COMPOSER, EDUCATOR
b Sumatra, Indonesia, Nov 5, 17; nat US. *Study:* Salzburg Mozarteum; Nat Orch Asn, studied cond with Leon Barzin, 35-40; studied cello with Joseph Emonts, 35-38, with Emanuel Feuermann, 38-43 & with D C Dounis; studied comp with Joseph Blatt & Stefan Wolpe. *Works:* Piano Sonata, Saltzburg Fest, 52; String Trio, 68; Herbstgesänge (song cycle for sop & piano), 69; Concerto for Piano and Orchestra, 73; String Quartet, 75; Concerto Variations (cello & orch), 76. *Pos:* Asst first cellist, Minneapolis Symph, 40-43; first cellist, Sta WOR, 46-48; cellist & organizer, New Music String Quartet, 48-54; mem, Juilliard String Quartet, 55-74; comp in res, Am Acad, Rome, 76; participant & performer, Aspen Music Sch & Fest & Santa Fe Chamber Music Fest; adminr, Nat Orch Asn, NY. *Teaching:* Mem fac cello & string ens, Juilliard Sch, 55-, Mannes Col Music, 55-, Philadelphia Col Perf Arts, 55- & NY Univ. *Awards:* Gabrilowitsch Mem Award, 39; grants, Nat Endowment Arts & Guggenheim Found, 75-76; Third Prize, Friedheim Comp Cont, Kennedy Ctr, 79. *Mem:* ASCAP; League Comp, Int Soc Contemp Music. *Mailing Add:* Juilliard Sch Lincoln Ctr New York NY 10023

ADAMS, ALAN EUGENE
ADMINISTRATOR, MUSIC DIRECTOR
b Stamford, Conn, July 12, 39. *Study:* State Univ NY, Potsdam, BS, 61; Ill Wesleyan Univ, MM, 66; studied voice with Henry Charles, Robert Weede, Iride Pilla & cond with Brock McElheran. *Pos:* Asst to pres, Boston Consv, 82-; dean students, Peabody Consv, 80-82. *Mem:* Phi Mu Alpha Sinfonia (exec dir, 67-78); Am Choral Dir Asn; Music Educr Nat Conf; Col Music Soc. *Publ:* Auth, Culture by the Pound, Scripps Howard Newspapers, 74; The Greek Connection, Nat Asn Sch Music, 76; European Music Festivals, Memphis Commercial Appeal, 77. *Mailing Add:* Boston Consv 8 The Fenway Boston MA 02215

ADAMS, (JOHN) CLEMENT
COMPOSER
b Attleboro, Mass, Nov 28, 47. *Study:* Boston Consv Music, BM & MM, 71; Harvard Univ, AM & PhD, 82. *Works:* Ibidem (piano, four hands), John Adams & Alfred Lee, 74; Variation (piano & orch), perf by Alfred Lee with Buffalo Phil, 76; Cello Sonata, 79 & Wind Quintet, 81, E C Schirmer Co, 81; Dream Dances, Comp in Red Sneakers, 81. *Teaching:* Fac mem, Boston Consv Music, 72-; vis lectr, Harvard Univ, 83-84. *Awards:* BMI Award, 70; Margaret Grant Prize, Berkshire Music Fest, 74. *Mailing Add:* 223 White St Belmont MA 02178

ADAMS, ELWYN ALBERT
EDUCATOR, VIOLIN
b Cleveland, Ohio, Aug 4, 33. *Study:* New England Consv Music, with Richard Burgin, BM, 56; Brussels Royal Consv, with Arthur Grumaux, 57. *Rec Perf:* Violin Recital, BRT, Brussels, Belgium, 70; Caprice No 24

(Paganini), Positively Black, NBC TV, 74; violin recital, Nat Gallery Art, 76. *Pos:* First violinist, Quebec Symph Orch, 61-63; concertmaster, Bordeaux Symph Orch, 63-70; conct violinist & recitalist, US & Europe. *Teaching:* Asst prof violin, Fla A&M Univ, 60-61; assoc prof, Univ Fla, 70- *Awards:* First prize, Int Compt, Munich, 55; Third Prize, Int Youth Compt, Moscow, 59; Ysaye Found Award, 67. *Mem:* Am String Teachers Asn. *Mailing Add:* c/o Albert Kay Assoc Inc 58 W 58th St New York NY 10019

ADAMS, JOHN (LUTHER)
COMPOSER, PERCUSSION
b Meridian, Miss, Jan 23, 53. *Study:* Mercer Univ & Wesleyan Col, study comp with Fred Coulter, 69-70; Calif Inst Arts, with James Tenney & Leonard Stein, BFA(comp), 73; Ga State Univ, with Charles Knox, 73-74. *Works:* Floating Petals, perf by Cal Arts New Music Group, 73 & Memphis State Ens, 74; Green Corn Dance, Memphis State Univ Perc Ens, 74; Wind Garden, perf by James Atwood & Patti Adams, 76; Night Peace, 77, Songbirdsongs, 79 & A Northern Suite, 81, Op One Rec; Rainbow Snow, Greats Winds of Alaska, 82. *Pos:* Comp in res, Hambidge Ctr & Ossabaw Island Proj, 75-77; prin perc & timpanist, Fairbanks Symph Orch & Arctic Chamber Orch, 80-; instr comp & perc, Univ Alaska, 82- *Teaching:* Instr comp & perc, Univ Alaska, 82- *Awards:* Fels, Nat Endowment Arts, 74, Idaho Comn Arts, 78 & Alaska State Coun Arts, 80 & 82. *Bibliog:* Stephen D Chawkin (auth), Guide to Records, Am Rec Guide, 10/81; Eric Salzman (auth), Two John Adamses, Stereo Rev, 10/81; Stefani Starin (auth), Earplugs, Ear Mag East, spring 1983. *Mem:* Am Music Ctr. *Mailing Add:* Star Rte 10739 Old Nenana Rd Fairbanks AK 99701

ADAMS, LESLIE
COMPOSER
b Cleveland, Ohio, Dec 30, 32. *Study:* Oberlin Consv, Oberlin Col, BME, 55; Calif State Univ, Long Beach, MA, 67; Ohio State Univ, PhD, 73. *Works:* For You There Is No Song (song), perf by Hilda Harris & Wayne Sanders, 80; Creole Girl (song), perf by Barbara Conrad (ms) & Israela Margalit Maazel (pianist), 80; Dunbar Songs, Rarities for Strings Publ, 83; Prelude and Fugue, perf by Leonard Raver (organist), 83; Blake, perf by William Appling Singers & Orch, 83; Ode to Life, perf by Buffalo Phil Orch, 83. *Pos:* Comp in res, Karamu House, Cleveland, Ohio, 79-81; YADDO Artists Colony, Saratoga Springs, NY, 80 & Cleveland Music Sch Settlement, 81- *Teaching:* Assoc prof, Univ Kans, 69-77. *Awards:* Nat Winner Choral Compt (for Psalm 121), Christian Arts Inc, 75; Nat Endowment Arts Award, 78; fel, Rockefeller Found, 79. *Bibliog:* Kenneth Fain (auth), Artists and Their Art: Composers, Cul Post/Nat Endowment Arts, May-June 79; Karen Green-Crocheron (auth), Meet Composer Leslie Adams, Galore Mag, Cleveland, 5/82; Robert Finn (auth), Slave Rebellion Before Civil War Stirs Work on Opera, Plain Dealer, Cleveland, 1/1/83. *Mem:* Am Music Ctr; Am Choral Dir Asn; Kans Comp Forum; Fortnightly Musical Club Cleveland. *Mailing Add:* 9409 Kempton Ave Cleveland OH 44108

ADAMS, RICHARD ELDER
ADMINISTRATOR, LECTURER
b Miami, Fla, June 10, 36. *Study:* Fla State Univ, BM(theory), 58; Berkshire Music Ctr, cert merit, 60; Manhattan Sch Music, MM(French horn), 61. *Pos:* French horn, New Orleans Phil, 61-62 & L'Orch Symph, Quebec, 62-64; mgr staff, Colbert Artists Mgt, 64-70. *Teaching:* Dir placement serv & career coun, Manhattan Sch Music, 78- & instr music business, 81-; guest lectr, Yale Univ, 81- & Rutgers Univ, NJ, 81- *Awards:* Grant, Josephine Bay Paul & C Michael Paul Found, New York, 83. *Mem:* Chamber Music Am; Music Indust Educr Asn; Asn Arts Admin Educr; Asn Class Music; Col Music Soc. *Mailing Add:* Manhattan Sch Music 120 Claremont Ave New York NY 10027

ADAMSON, JANIS JOHN
CELLO
b Timosov, Russia, Oct 10, 24. *Study:* Latvian State Consv; studied with Atis Teichmanis. *Pos:* Mem, Latvian Nat Opera, Riga, Latvian Ballet Co Orch, Stuttgart, Indianapolis Symph Orch, currently & Starlight Musicals, Ind. *Mem:* Am Fedn Musicians. *Mailing Add:* 820 N Graham Indianapolis IN 46219

ADDISON, ANTHONY
CONDUCTOR, DIRECTOR — OPERA
b Bournemouth, England, Sept 28, 26. *Study:* Royal Acad Music, 43-45 & 48. *Pos:* Dir music, Univ Col, London, 49-52 & 60-62; chorus master & cond, Carl Rosa Opera Co, 52-59; freelance cond, ballet, musicals & opera, Europe, 59-62; assoc dir, Goldovsky Opera Inst, 62-64; cond, Univ Circle Youth Orch, Cleveland, 68-75. *Teaching:* Chmn opera theater dept, Cleveland Inst Music, 64-81; mem fac, Univ Tex, Austin, 81- *Mem:* Cent Opera Serv; Nat Opera Asn; Metropolitan Guild; Pi Kappa Lambda. *Mailing Add:* Dept Music Univ Tex Austin TX 78712

ADDISS, STEPHEN
COMPOSER, EDUCATOR
b New York, NY, Apr 2, 35. *Study:* Harvard Univ, BA, 57; New Sch Social Res, with John Cage, 58-60; Mannes Col Music, dipl, 59; Univ Mich, MA, 73, PhD, 77. *Works:* Score for Yeats Play, Living Theater, New York, 60; numerous songs, BMI, 64-77; In the Year of the Pig (musical score), 69; Serenade Nocture and Albada, Kaw Valley Dance Theater, 83; Three Duets for Solo Cello, John Talleur, 83. *Rec Perf:* Addiss and Crofut, Columbia, 66; Thuong Binh, Song Nhac, Vietnam, 67; Summit Sessions, 68 & Eastern Ferris Wheel, 68, Columbia. *Pos:* Conct perf, Columbia Artists Mgmt, US Dept State, 61-77; cur Japanese art, New Orleans Museum Art, 79- *Teaching:* Asst prof art hist & music, Univ Kans, 77-79, assoc prof, 79- *Awards:* Grants, Southern Ill Univ, 72, John D Rockefeller III Fund, 75 & Univ Kans Res

Fund, 82-83. *Mem:* Soc Ethnomusicol. *Interests:* Music of Uragami Gyokudo (1745-1820). *Publ:* Auth, Music of the Cham People, Asian Music, 71; Theater Music Vietnam, SE Asia, 71; Hat a Dao, the Sung Poetry of North Vietnam, J Am Oriental Soc, 74; Gyokudo no ongaku (The Music of Gyokudo), Gyokudo, 80; A Kaleidoscope on the Art of John Cage, Triquarterly, 82. *Mailing Add:* Spencer Museum Univ Kans Lawrence KS 66045

ADKINS, ALDRICH WENDELL
ADMINISTRATOR, CONDUCTOR
b Alexandria, Va, July 22, 22. *Study:* Howard Univ, BM, 48, MM, 53; Univ Tex, Austin, DMA, 71. *Teaching:* Asst prof voice, Va State Col, 54-65; chmn music dept voice & choir, Spelman Col, 70-71 & Southern Univ, 71- *Mem:* Music Educr Nat Conf; Am Choral Dir Asn; Nat Asn Teachers Singing; Col Music Soc; Music Teachers Nat Conf. *Mailing Add:* Music Dept Southern Univ Baton Rouge LA 70813

ADKINS, PAUL SPENCER
TENOR
Study: WVa Univ, with Rose Crain, dipl; Philadelphia Col Perf Arts; Acad Vocal Arts. *Roles:* The Hero & Moses, 81, Opera Co Philadelphia; Rodolfo in La Boheme, Asolo Opera; Duke in Rigoletto, Tri Cities Opera; Faust in Faust, Wilmington Opera Soc; Lucia di Lammermoor, Pittsburgh Opera Co; Abduction from the Seraglio, Opera South. *Pos:* Perf with New York Choral Soc, Am Symph Orch, Savannah Symph Orch, Syracuse Symph & New Orleans Symph Orch. *Awards:* Winner, First Luciano Pavarotti Int Voice Compt & Philadelphia & Princeton Metropolitan Opera Auditions. *Mailing Add:* c/o Tornay Mgt 127 W 72nd St New York NY 10023

ADLER, BARBARA JO See Bucker, B J

ADLER, JAMES R
COMPOSER, PIANO
b Chicago, Ill, Nov 19, 50. *Study:* With Rose Willits, Mollie Margolies, Rudolph Ganz & Olga Barabini, 60-; Curtis Inst Music, BMus(piano perf), 73, MMus(comp), 76. *Works:* Classic Ragtime Suite (orch), Chautauqua Fest Orch, 73; Piano Concerto in G, 80 & Suite Moderne for Strings, 82, Belwin-Mills Publ Corp; Songs of Innocence And of Experience, premiere at Alice Tully Hall, 82; Carols of Splendour (choral & instrm), comn by New York City Gay Men's Chorus, 82; We Celebrate Ourselves (choral), comn by Stonewall Awards Found, 83; What About Tomorrow? (choral), perf at Carnegie Hall, 83. *Rec Perf:* Young Musical Artists, PBS, 69-70; Artists Showcase, WGN-TV, Chicago, 69; The Hat Act (filmscore), 75; Grant Park Concerts, 81. *Pos:* Conct pianist/comp, 77- *Awards:* Chicago Symph Orch Audition, 68; Women's Asn Symph Orch, 69; Comp Achievement, ASCAP, 76- *Bibliog:* Stan Leventhal (auth), Our Songs, Ourselves, New York Native, 6/83; Peter Brabson (auth), article, Michael's Thing, 8/83; Terry Payton (auth), James Adler: Pianist/Composer, WUHY-FM. *Mem:* Am Fedn Musicians; ASCAP; Dramatists Guild, New York. *Mailing Add:* c/o Maxim Gershunoff Attractions Inc 502 Park Ave New York NY 10022

ADLER, KURT HERBERT
CONDUCTOR, ADMINISTRATOR
b Vienna, Austria, Apr 2, 05; US citizen. *Study:* Vienna Acad Music, 23-28; Vienna Consv Music, 23-28; Vienna Univ, 23-28. *Rec Perf:* O Holy Night (L Pavarotti), 76 & Verismo Arias (M Chiara), 72, London Rec; Operatic Duet (R Scotto & P Domingo), CBS, 78; Adler at the Opera, 78, Operatic Recital (L Mitchell), 79 & Royal Gala (L Pavarotti & Royal Phil), 82, London Rec. *Pos:* Cond, opera houses in Germany, Italy & Czechoslovakia, 28-38; asst to A Toscanini, Salzburg, 36; cond & chorus dir, Chicago Opera, 38-42; chorus dir, San Francisco Opera, 43-52, artistic dir, 53-56, gen dir, 57-81 & gen dir emer, 82- *Teaching:* Orch, Univ Calif, Berkeley, 49-50; teacher orch & band, Univ Pac, 50-60; teacher opera, Merola Prog, San Francisco Opera, 58-83. *Awards:* Commandeur Arts & Lett, Govt France, 78; Commander Brit Empire, Queen Elizabeth II, 80; Hon Prof, Govt Austria. *Mem:* Nat Coun Arts. *Mailing Add:* PO Box 1446 Ross CA 94957

ADLER, MARVIN STANLEY
EDUCATOR, CRITIC
b Bronx, NY, Feb 25, 38. *Study:* City Col, City Univ New York, BA, 60, MA, 62; Teachers Col, Columbia Univ, PD, 67, EdD, 70; studied with Harry Wilson, Robert Pace & Gladys Tipton. *Works:* Brock's Place (comic opera), Community Opera Inc. *Pos:* Music Sub-Leader, Kreel Prod, 65- *Teaching:* Proj dir music, Columbia Univ, 69-70, instr, 70. *Awards:* Area Studies Grant, NY State Regents, 66; Coop Res Act, US Off Educ, 68. *Bibliog:* Joan Frye (auth), Elementary Speaking, Sch Music News, 5/83. *Mem:* ASCAP; Music Educr Nat Conf; Am Fedn Musicians; Music Belongs Inc (treas, 79-81); Kings Co Music Educr Asn (pres, 82). *Interests:* Developing understanding of 20th century compositions, styles and techniques. *Publ:* Auth, What Next, 4/70 & H H Stuckenschmidt, 20th Century Music, 9/70, Music Educr J; Music & Art in Elementary Educ, Kendall/Hunt, 76; Elementary Teachers Music Almanac, 79 & Making Music Fun, 81, Parker, Prentice-Hall. *Mailing Add:* 308 E Euclid St Valley Stream Valley Stream NY 11580

ADLER, RICHARD
COMPOSER
b New York, NY, Aug 3, 21. *Study:* Univ NC, AB, 43. *Works:* The Pajama Game, 54 & Damn Yankees, 55, Frank Music Co/Richard Adler Music; Kwamina, Sahara Music/Chappell, 61; Memory of a Childhood, 78, Retrospectrum, 79, Yellowstone Overture, 80 & Wilderness Suite, 83, Richard Adler Music. *Awards:* Tony for Pajama Game (music & lyrics), 54 & Damn Yankees (music & lyrics), 55. *Mem:* ASCAP (bd dir, 64-69); Am Guild Auth & Comp (bd dir, 60-70); New Dramatists (bd dir, 73-). *Mailing Add:* Eight E 83rd St New York NY 10028

ADLER, SAMUEL H
COMPOSER, CONDUCTOR & MUSIC DIRECTOR
b Mannheim, Ger, Mar 4, 28; US citizen. *Study:* Boston Univ, BM, 48; Harvard Univ, MA, 50; Southern Methodist Univ, DMus, 69; Wake Forest Univ, DFA, 83. *Works:* Symphony No 1, Theodore Presser, 53; Sonata for Violin and Piano #3, Boosey & Hawkes, 72; The Wrestler (opera), Oxford Univ Press, 73; Concerto (flute & orch), Southern Music Publ, 77; String Quartet #6, Carl Fischer, 78; Joi, Amor, Cortezia, 82 & String Quartet #7, 83, G Schirmer. *Pos:* Dir music, Temple Emanu-El, Dallas, Tex, 53-66. *Awards:* Grants, Ford Found, 68, Nat Endowment Arts, 69, 72, 77 & 81 & Rockefeller Found, 83. *Publ:* Auth, Choral Conducting, An Anthology, Holt, Rinehart & Winston, 71; Sightsinging, 79 & The Study of Orchestration, 82, W W Norton. *Mailing Add:* 54 Railroad Mills Rd Pittsford NY 14534

ADOLPHUS, MILTON
COMPOSER
b New York, NY, Jan 27, 13. *Study:* Curtis Inst Music, 35-36. *Works:* War Sketches, Philadelphia Orch, 38; String Quartet No 23, Los Angeles String Quartet, 53; Elegy, CRI, 66; Christmas Carol: Spain 1936, Hershey Symph Orch, 80; Ulalume, 80 & David's Dream, 82, Orch Soc Philadelphia; Interlude, Harrisburg Symph Orch, 82. *Pos:* Dir, Philadelphia Music Ctr, Pa, 35-38. *Awards:* Pa Comp of Yr, Orch Soc Philadelphia, 80 & 82. *Bibliog:* Paul B Beers (auth), The Evening News, Harrisburg, Pa, 5/22/78 & 10/22/82. *Mem:* Am Comp Alliance; Wednesday Club; BMI. *Mailing Add:* 3920 Chambers Hill Rd Harrisburg PA 17111

ADONAYLO, RAQUEL
PIANO, SOPRANO
b Uruguay. *Study:* With Wilhelm Kolischer, Enrique Casal Chapi & Lazare-Levy; W Kolischer Consv Music, dipl; studied voice with Ninon Vallin. *Rec Perf:* On Columbia. *Pos:* Conct pianist, 41-; sop opera, oratorio, chamber music & lieder, France, US, Israel & South Am, 52-; soloist with maj orchs in US, Argentina, Uruguay & Israel. *Teaching:* Private instr piano, Uruguay, 47-62, Israel, 63-75 & Rosemont, Pa, 76-; dir, Ninon Vallin Sch Singing, 53-58; mem fac, W Kolischer Consv Music, seven yrs & Rubin Acad, Jerusalem, 63-64; vocal coach, 66-; mem fac voice, Curtis Inst Music, 75-; coach chamber music & dir sem, Israel & US. *Awards:* Grand Prize, Rec Circle Critics, 66. *Mailing Add:* Curtis Inst Music 1726 Locust St Philadelphia PA 19103

AGARD, DAVID LEON
CONDUCTOR & MUSIC DIRECTOR, VIOLIN
b Binghamton, NY, Aug 31, 41. *Study:* Ithaca Col, BS, 64; State Univ NY, Binghamton; Am Symph Orch League Cond Symposium, with Dr Richard Lert, 66. *Pos:* Asst cond, Tri-Cities Opera, Binghamton, NY, 67-71, concertmaster, 83-; artistic dir & founder, B C Pops Inc, 75-; prin second violin, Catskill Symph, Oneonta, NY, 80-82. *Teaching:* Instr string, Union-Endicott Pub Sch, NY, 65-66, Amsterdam Pub Sch, NY, 66-68 & Maine-Endwell Pub Sch, NY, currently. *Mem:* Am Fedn Musicians (pres local 380, 80-). *Mailing Add:* c/o B C Pops Orch 233 Main St Vestal City NY 13850

AGAY, DENES
COMPOSER, EDUCATOR
b Kiskunfelegyhaza, Hungary, June 10, 11; US citizen. *Study:* Liszt Acad Music, Budapest, with Albert Siklos dipl(comp & cond), 33; Univ Budapest, PhD, 34. *Works:* Five Dances (woodwind quintet), Theodore Presser, 56; Sonatina No 3, Samfot, 63; Sonatina Hungarica, MCA Music, 67; Serenata Burlesca, Boosey & Hawkes, 68; Seven Piano Pieces, G Schirmer, 69; Old Irish Blessing (choral), Warner Brothers, 70; The Piano Music of Denes Agay, Yorktown Music Press, 80. *Pos:* Comp, ed & consult with several publ firms, 52-76. *Teaching:* Lectr on a wide range of subjects at various col & univ. *Awards:* Best of Yr Citation, Piano Quart. *Mem:* ASCAP; Am Liszt Soc; Piano Teachers Cong NY. *Publ:* Auth, The Joy of Piano, 64, Best Loved Songs of the American People, 75, The Baroque Period: Masters of the 17th & 18th Centuries, 81, The Classic Period: Haydn, Mozart, Beethoven & Their Contempories, 81 & Teaching Piano, two vol, 81, Music Sales. *Mailing Add:* 1391 Madison Ave New York NY 10029

AGLER, DAVID
CONDUCTOR
b South Bend, Ind, Apr 12, 47. *Study:* Westminster Choir Col, BMus, 65-70; Philadelphia Col Perf Arts, 73-75. *Pos:* Admin dir, Spoleto Fest, 74-75, gen mgr & assoc music dir, 75-76; music dir, Syracuse Opera Theatre, 78-79; music supvr & res cond, San Francisco Opera, 79-; dir, Am Opera Proj. *Teaching:* Mem fac, Westminster Choir Col, 70-72, Acad Vocal Arts, Philadelphia, 70-72, Philadelphia Col Perf Arts, 73-75 & San Francisco Consv Music, 80- *Awards:* Exxon Arts Endowment Cond Award, 79. *Mailing Add:* San Francisco Consv Music 1201 Ortega St San Francisco CA 94122

AHNELL, EMIL GUSTAVE
COMPOSER, EDUCATOR
b Erie, Pa, June 4, 75. *Study:* New England Consv, BM, 51; Northwestern Univ, MM, 52; Univ Ill, PhD, 57. *Works:* Nanas Songs, Northwestern Univ Ens, 81; We Praise Thy Name, Ky Wesleyan Choir, 82; Scenerios for Orch, Owensboro Symph Orch, 83; In Shaded Sun-Song Cycle, Owensboro Trio, 83; Six Preludes for Piano, 83. *Teaching:* Prof theory & hist, Ky Wesleyan Col, 58- *Mem:* ASCAP. *Mailing Add:* Music Dept Ky Wesleyan Col Owensboro KY 42301

AHRENDT, KARL F
COMPOSER, ADMINISTRATOR
b Toledo, Ohio, Mar 7, 04. *Study:* Cincinnati Consv Music, BM, 36; Eastman Sch Music, MM, 37, PhD, 46. *Works:* 67th Psalms (womens' voices), Witmark, 45; Johnny Applesead (orch), Carl Fischer, 54; Dance Overture, perf by Cleveland Orch, 68; Montage for Orchestra, Ludwig Music Publ Co, 74; Affirmations (wind ens), Opus Music Publ Co, 77; Pastorale for Strings, 81 & 7 Miniatures (flute & perc), 83, Ludwig Music Publ Co. *Pos:* Dir, Sch Music, Augustana Col, 46-50 & Ohio Univ, 50-67. *Teaching:* Assoc prof violin, Fla State Univ, 37-44; prof music, Sch Music, Ohio Univ, 67-74. *Awards:* First Prize, Philadelphia Arts Alliance Comp Compt, 44; first prize, Ohio Music Teachers Asn Comp Compt, 72; Roth Award, 73. *Mailing Add:* 5 Old Peach Ridge Athens OH 45701

AHROLD, FRANK
COMPOSER, PIANO
b Long Beach, Calif, Dec 12, 31. *Study:* Univ Calif, Los Angeles, studied comp with Lukas Foss & John Vincent, BA, 53 & 55-56. *Works:* The View (one act opera); The Spider and the Fly (ballet); Second Coming (ten & orch); Three Poems of Sylvia Plath (sop & chamber orch); Behold the Joy (chorus); The Canticle of Judith (chorus); Song Without Words (orch), 71. *Rec Perf:* With CRI. *Pos:* Cond, Long Beach Civic Chorus, 61-65 & Camarata de Musici, 64-68; asst musical dir, Long Beach Civic Light Opera, 65-68; pianist, Oakland Symph Orch, 73-78 & currently. *Publ:* Auth, Music Calendar Datebook. *Mailing Add:* 1430 Hawthorne Terr Berkeley CA 94708

AIRD, DONALD BRUCE
COMPOSER, MUSICAL DIRECTOR
b Provo, Utah, May 24, 24. *Study:* Univ Calif, Berkeley, studied with Roger Sessions & Bukofzer; San Francisco State Univ, MM; Univ Southern Calif, comp with Ingolf Dahl, 58-60. *Works:* Songs for Carol (two flutes, piano, viola & cello), Carol Aird, 67; Chamber Concerto, 67; The Silver Swan (sop, clarinet & piano), Samela Aird, 67; Para Praise (organ, 14 winds & perc), comn by Ted Flath, 79; Night Voyagess (counter ten, two ten, bass & piano), comn by Hillard Ens, London, 80; Sinfonia Concertant (violin, viola & orch), San Jose Symph Orch, 82; Fantasia (sop, oboe & piano), comn by Nancy Middleton, Anna Carol Dudley & Herb Bielawa, 83. *Rec Perf:* Lobet Den Herrn (Bach), Missa Hercules (Des Prez) & Six Chansons (Hindemith), Music Libr Rec, 56. *Pos:* Dir, Berkeley Chamber Singers, 20 years, Glee Club & Treble Clef Soc, Univ Calif, Berkeley, two years. *Teaching:* Asst prof music, Univ Minn, Minneapolis, 60-63, San Francisco State Univ & Univ Calif, Berkeley, formerly. *Awards:* Helen S Anstead Comp Award. *Mem:* Am Guild Organists; ASCAP. *Mailing Add:* 252 Stanford Ave Kensington CA 94708

AITAY, VICTOR
VIOLIN
b Budapest, Hungary. *Study:* Franz Liszt Royal Acad, dipl; study with Bela Bartok, Ernst von Dohnanyi, Zolton Kodaly & Leo Weiner. *Pos:* Concertmaster, Metropolitan Opera Co, Hungarian Royal Opera, Phil Orch, formerly & Chicago Symph, 54-; founder, Aitay String Quartet; recitalist & soloist (violin), with leading orch in US & Europe; music dir & cond, Lake Forest Symph, currently; leader, Chicago Symph String Quartet, currently. *Teaching:* Prof violin, DePaul Univ, currently. *Mailing Add:* 212 Oak Knoll Terr Highland Park IL 60035

AITKEN, HUGH
COMPOSER, EDUCATOR
b New York, NY, Sept 7, 24. *Study:* Juilliard Sch Music, MS(comp), 50. *Works:* Piano Fantasy, 68 & six solo cantatas, Oxford Univ Press; Trios (11 instrm), 70, Fables, (chamber opera), 76, In Praise of Ockeghem (string orch), 82 & Felipe (opera), 82, Theodore Presser Co; Tromba, Trumpet & String Quartet, perf by Gerard Schwarz, Concord Quartet, 79. *Teaching:* Fac mem, Juilliard Sch Music, 60-70; prof, William Paterson Col, 70- *Awards:* Grant, Nat Endowment for Arts, 81. *Mem:* ASCAP; Am Music Ctr. *Mailing Add:* Music Dept William Paterson Col Wayne NJ 07470

AJEMIAN, ANAHID M
VIOLIN
b New York, NY. *Study:* Juilliard Sch Music, artist dipl, 48. *Rec Perf:* On RCA Victor, Columbia, CRI, Golden Crest & Musical Heritage Soc. *Pos:* Mem, Comp String Quartet, 69- *Teaching:* Asst prof violin, Columbia Univ, 76- *Awards:* Walter W Naumberg Award, 48; Laurel Leaf Award, Am Comp Alliance, 50. *Mailing Add:* 285 Central Park W New York NY 10024

AJMONE-MARSAN, GUIDO
CONDUCTOR
b Turin, Italy, Mar 24, 47; US citizen. *Study:* Eastman Sch Music, BM, 68; Consv St Cecilia, Rome, Italy, with Franco Ferrara, cond degree, 71. *Pos:* Chief cond, Gelders Orch, Arnhem, Holland, 82-; music adv, The Orch Ill, 82- *Awards:* Cantelli Cond Compt Award, La Scala, Milan, Italy, 69; Rupert Found Cond Compt Award, 73; George Solti Cond Compt Award, 73. *Mailing Add:* c/o ICM Artists 40 W 57th St New York NY 10019

AKI, SYOKO
VIOLIN, EDUCATOR
Study: Toho Acad Music, Japan; Hartt Col Music; Yale Sch Music. *Pos:* Performer, Yale Summer Sch & Fest, 83; soloist, Philharmonia Orch Yale; soloist & chamber musician. *Teaching:* Instr, Eastman Sch Music, formerly & State Univ NY, Purchase, formerly; mem fac, Yale Sch Music, 68- *Mailing Add:* Sch Music Yale Univ New Haven CT 06520

AKOS, FRANCIS
VIOLIN, CONDUCTOR & MUSIC DIRECTOR
b Budapest, Hungary; US citizen. *Study:* Gymnasium, Baccalaureat; Franz Liszt Acad Music, Budapest, Master Dipl, Teachers Dipl. *Pos:* Concertmaster, Budapest Symph Orch, Phil Soc & Budapest Opera House, Gothenburg, Sweden & Staedtische Oper, Berlin, WGer, formerly; cond & founder, Chicago Strings, formerly; cond & music dir, Fox River Valley Symph, Chicago Heights Symph, formerly & Highland Park Strings, currently; asst concertmaster, Chicago Symph Orch, currently. *Awards:* Hubay Prize, 39 & Remenyi Prize, 39, Music Acad Budapest. *Mem:* Cond Guild; String Teacher's Asn. *Mailing Add:* 5650 N Sheridan Chicago IL 60660

ALAVEDRA, MONTSERRAT
SOPRANO, EDUCATOR
b Terrasa-Barcelona, Spain. *Study:* Mozarteum, Salzburg, Austria, 66-69; Escuela Superior De Canto, Madrid, Spain, 69-72. *Rec Perf:* Works by Purcell, Mozart, Beethoven, Schubert, Wolf, Faure, Brahms, Falla, Mompou & Toldra, on RCA, Dischopon, Spain & Crystal. *Roles:* Bastienne in Bastien und Bastienne; Suzanna & Countess in Le Nozze di Figaro; Pamina in Die Zauberflöte; Despina & Fiordiligi in Cosi fan tutte; Zerlina in Don Giovanni; Mimi in La Boheme; Lauretta in Gianni Schicchi; & others. *Pos:* Sop soloist, Orquesta de la RTVE, Madrid, & Orquesta Ciudad De Barcelona; recitalist, with Erik Werba, Miguel Zanetti, Felix Lavilla, J Marchwinski & Federico Mompou, in Europe, SAfrica, Can & US. *Teaching:* Assoc prof voice, Univ Wash, 79- *Rep:* Felicitas Keller Vitoria Alcala 30 Madrid Spain. *Mailing Add:* Music DN-10 Univ Wash Seattle WA 98115

ALBAM, MANNY
COMPOSER, EDUCATOR
b Samana, Dominican Republic, June 24, 22. *Study:* Studied with Tibor Serly. *Works:* Nostalgico for Saxophone & Orchestra, Phil Woods Orch Am Music, 77; Trio for Brass, 77; Rhapsody for Trumpet, Clarinet & Strings, 78; Duet for Tubas & Brass Ensemble, Harvey Phillips & Owen Metcalf, 79; Trio for Brass & Wind Ensemble, Philadelphia, 80; Quintet for Tuba & Strings, Prima Vera Quintet, 81; Quintet for Trombone & Strings, Eastman Sch Music, 83. *Rec Perf:* The Blues Is Everybody's Business, Decca Rec, 58; The Soul of the City, United Artists Rec, 68; Rhapsody for Tuba, Strings & Harp, Michael Lind with Danish Radio Symph, 82. *Pos:* Co-dir, Eastman Summer Comp Prog, 63- & Arr Lab Wkshp, Eastman Sch Music; music dir, Solid State Rec. *Teaching:* Assoc prof comp, Eastman Sch Music, 63-; assoc prof & proj specialist, Glassboro State Col, 71- *Awards:* Nat Endowment Arts Grant, 77, 79 & 83. *Mem:* BMI; Am Comp Alliance; Nat Acad Rec Arts & Sci (nat trustee, 68-71). *Mailing Add:* 7 Glengary Rd Croton-on-Hudson NY 10520

ALBERS, BRADLEY GENE
COMPOSER, EDUCATOR
b Houston, Tex, Aug 26, 52. *Study:* Sam Houston State Univ, BM(theory & comp), 75; Univ Ill, MM(comp), 76; Univ Ill, with Thomas Frederickson, Salvatore Martirano, John Melby & Paul Zonn, DMA(comp), 78. *Works:* Nexus for Oboe & Computer Generated Tape, 83, Aggregate for Symphonic Band, 83, Exegeses for Clarinet & Computer Generated Tape, 83 & Martial Cadenza for Voice & Tape, 83, ACA. *Pos:* Dir, Syst Complex Studio & Perf Arts, Univ SFla, 78- *Teaching:* Asst prof electronic music & comp, Univ SFla, 78- *Awards:* Sound Studio Grant, 80-81 & Sound Synthesis Grant, 83, Univ SFla; Sound Sources Comn Award, Nat Pub Radio, 83. *Bibliog:* Kurt Loft (auth), Better Music Through Science, Tampa Tribune, 12/80; Technology—The New Artistic Pallet, WTVT News, 12/81; Ken Hall (auth), SYCOM: A Revolutionary System for Teaching the Technical Side of Composition, Music Mag, 3/82. *Mem:* BMI; Comp Forum Inc; Am Comp Alliance; Pi Kappa Lambda. *Mailing Add:* PO Box 271226 Tampa FL 33688

ALBERT, DONNIE RAY
BASS-BARITONE
Rec Perf: Porgy and Bess, RCA. *Pos:* Conct performer, New York Phil, Los Angeles Phil, Chicago Symph, Dallas Symph & Seattle Symph. *Awards:* Nat Opera Inst Grant, 76. *Publ:* Porgy in Porgy and Bess, Houston Grand Opera, 76 & Baltimore Opera, 82-83; Jake Wallace in La Fanciulla del West, New York City Opera, 78-79 & Houston Grand Opera; Monterone in Rigoletto, Chicago Lyr Opera, 79-80; La Cenerentola, Vancouver Opera, 81-82; I Due Foscari, Opera Orch New York, 81-82; Ernani, Boston Conct Opera, 82-83; Colline in La Boheme, Baltimore Opera, 83 & Vancouver Opera, 83. *Mailing Add:* c/o Harold Shaw 1995 Broadway New York NY 10023

ALBERT, JONES ROSS
TEACHER, VIOLA
b Cleona, Pa, Sept 1, 22. *Study:* Lebanon Valley Col, BS(music educ), 47; Converse Col, MM(music educ), 64; Univ NC, Greensboro, EdD, 76. *Works:* Cantata: The Beginning, Lebanon High Sch Choir, Pa, 61; Five Songs of the Dark, 69 & Trombone Sonata, 73, NC Comp Conct. *Pos:* Prin violist, Wilson Symph Orch, 79-; pres, Arts Coun Wilson, 83- *Teaching:* Dir music educ, Atlantic Christian Col, 64-72, chmn, Dept Music, 72- *Mem:* Music Educr Nat Conf; Music Teachers Nat Asn; Nat Asn Teachers Singing. *Mailing Add:* 2215 Arbor Rd Wilson NC 27893

ALBERT, STEPHEN JOEL
COMPOSER
b New York, NY, Feb 6, 41. *Study:* With Elie Siegmeister, 56-58 & Darius Milhaud, summer 58; Eastman Sch Music, with Wayne Barlow, A I McHose & Bernard Rogers, 58-60; Philadelphia Musical Acad, with Joseph Castaldo, BMus, 62; Univ Pa, with George Rochberg, 63. *Works:* Wolf Time (sop,

chamber orch & amplification), comn by Seattle Players, Univ Wash; Leaves From the Golden Notebook (orch), comn by Chicago Symph Orch; Imitations (string quartet), 64; Supernatural Songs (sop & chamber orch), 64; Winter Songs (tenor & orch), 65; Voices Within (concertino ens), comn by Berkshire Music Fest & Fromm Found, 75; To Wake the Dead (sop & chamber ens), 77. *Pos:* Performer with many orchs & insts. *Teaching:* Instr, Philadelphia Musical Acad, 68-70, Stanford Univ, 70-71 & Smith Col, 74-76. *Awards:* Ford Found CMP Grant, 67-68; Martha Baird Rockefeller Grants, 66, 69 & 74; ASCAP Awards. *Mem:* ASCAP; Am Music Ctr. *Mailing Add:* c/o Shaw Concerts 1995 Broadway New York NY 10023

ALBERT, THOMAS RUSSEL
COMPOSER, EDUCATOR
b Lebanon, Pa, Dec 14, 48. *Study:* Atlantic Christian Col, AB(music educ), 70; Univ Ill, Urbana-Champaign, MMus(comp), 72, DMA(comp), 74. *Works:* Lizbeth (opera), perf by Shenandoah Consv Music Opera Co, 76; Ancren Chronicles, comn & perf by Cantus Singers Shenandoah Consv, 80; A Maze (with Grace), perf by Res Musica Baltimore, 81; Winter Monarch, Media Press, 82; Lullaby, perf by Contemp Music Forum, 82; The Gift (film score), Shenandoah Nat Park, 82; Big Bend Portrait (film score), Big Bend Nat Park, 83. *Teaching:* Lectr music, Univ Ill, 73-74; assoc prof music theory & comp & chmn theory div, Shenandoah Consv Music, Va, 74- *Awards:* Comp Fel, Nat Endowment for Arts, 76. *Mem:* ASCAP; Am Soc Univ Comp; Tubists' Universal Brotherhood Asn. *Mailing Add:* 405 Green St Winchester VA 22601

ALBIN, WILLIAM ROBERT
EDUCATOR, PERCUSSION
b New Albany, Ind, June 16, 48. *Study:* Ind Univ, with George Gaber, BM, BME, 71, with Robert Klotman, DMusEd, 79; Wichita State Univ, MM(perc), 74. *Pos:* Mem, Colo Summer Phil, 70, Toledo Symph, 71 & Wichita Symph, 72-74; prin perc & timpanist, Richmond Ind Symph, 75-82; prin perc, Cincinnati Ballet Orch, 80- & Middletown Ohio Symph, 82- *Teaching:* Assoc instr perc, Ind Univ, 74-75; assoc prof perc & jazz hist, Miami Univ, 75- *Mem:* Phi Mu Alpha Sinfonia; Pi Kappa Lambda; Percussive Arts Soc; Am Fedn Musicians; Music Educr Nat Conf. *Publ:* Auth, Keyboard Percussion Mallets, Comp Mag, 77; The Development of Videotaped Instructional Units for Teaching Selected Aspects of Mallet-Played, Latin American, and Accessory Percussion Instruments, Triad, Ohio Music Educr Asn, 82. *Mailing Add:* 616 French Dr Oxford OH 45056

ALBISTON, MARION H
TROMBONE, TEACHER
b Preston, Idaho, Sept 20, 30. *Study:* Univ Utah, BS, 59. *Pos:* Second trombone, Utah Symph Orch, 58- *Mailing Add:* Utah Symph Symph Hall 123 W South Temple Salt Lake City UT 84101

ALBRECHT, OTTO EDWIN
EDUCATOR, LIBRARIAN
b Philadelphia, Pa, July 8, 1899. *Study:* Univ Pa, AB, 21, MA, 25, PhD, 31. *Pos:* Cur, Albrecht Music Libr, 35- *Teaching:* From lectr to asst prof music, Univ Pa, Philadelphia, 38-60, prof, 60-70 & emer prof, 70- *Bibliog:* John W Hill (ed), Studies in Musicology in Honor of Otto E Albrecht, Kassel, Bärenreiter Verlag, 80; Lorraine Hanaway (auth), Bibliographer-Musicologist Otto E Albrecht, Philadelphia Ctr for Study Aging Newsletter, 83. *Mem:* Hon mem, Am Musicol Soc (treas, 54-70); Music Libr Asn (vpres, 40-45 & 51-52); Int Asn Music Libr; Int Musicol Soc; hon mem, Sonneck Soc. *Interests:* Music in United States to 1860; history of art song; bibliography. *Publ:* Ed, Catalogue of Music for Small Orchestra, Music Libr Asn, 47; auth, Census of Autograph Music Manuscript of European Composers, Univ Pa Press, 53; ed, Richard Strauss, Drei Liebeslieder, CF Peters, 58; coauth, The M F Cary Music Collection, Pierpont Morgan Libr, 70; co-ed, Marian Anderson, A Catalog of the Collection, Univ Pa Libr, 81. *Mailing Add:* Univ Pa 201 S 34th St Philadelphia PA 19104

ALBRECHT, THEODORE JOHN
MUSIC DIRECTOR, EDUCATOR
b Jamestown, NY, Sept 24, 45. *Study:* St Mary's Univ, BME, 67; NTex State Univ, MM, 69, PhD, 75; cond study with George Yaeger, 65-67 & Anshel Brusilow, 73-75. *Pos:* Music librn, Case Western Reserve Univ, Cleveland, 76-80; music dir, Northland Symph Orch, Kansas City, 80- *Teaching:* Vis asst prof, Appalachian State Univ, Boone, NC, 75-76; lectr, Case Western Reserve Univ, Cleveland, 76-80; assoc prof & chmn dept music, Park Col, Kansas City, Mo, 80- *Mem:* Am Musicol Soc; Col Music Soc (ed, Symposium, 83-); Sonneck Soc. *Interests:* Beethoven, German romanticism, music in Mid and Southwest United States. *Publ:* Auth, Julius Weiss, Scott Joplin's Teacher Symposium, 79; Bruckner and the Liedertafel Movement, Am Choral Rev, 80; Schumann, Fallersleben & In Beiden Welten, Opera J, 80; Program Notes, Tucson Symph Orch, 80-; A New Wagner Letter, to a Friend, April 4, 1875, Musical Quart, 82. *Mailing Add:* 11206 Lema Dr Kansas City MO 64152

ALBRIGHT, PHILIP H
EDUCATOR, DOUBLE BASS
b Winfield, Kans, July 7, 27. *Study:* Eastman Sch Music, BMus, 49, DMA, 69; Wash Univ, MA, 59. *Pos:* Double bassist, Rochester Phil, 45-49, Nat Symph Orch, 49-50 & St Louis Symph Orch, 50-58; solo double bass, Lake Placid Sinfonietta, 48-; prin double bass, Muncie Symph Orch, 59- *Teaching:* Prof double bass, Ball State Univ, 59-; instr, Eastman Sch Music, 65-66. *Mem:* Int Soc Bassists; Am String Teachers Asn (pres, 78-80); Music Educr Nat Conf; Ind String Task Force (chmn, 81-). *Publ:* Auth, Serge Koussevitzky, String Bass Virtuoso, Instrumentalist, 67; Concerto for Double Bass and Orchestra—Proto, 69 & Yohanen by Robert Rohe, 79, Int Soc Bassists Newsletter. *Mailing Add:* 2400 W Berwyn Rd Muncie IN 47304

ALBRIGHT, WILLIAM HUGH
COMPOSER, ORGAN
b Gary, Ind, Oct 20, 44. *Study:* Univ Mich, BM, 66, MM, 67, DMA, 70. *Works:* Take That, 72, Stipendium Peccati, 73, Jobert; Seven Deadly Sins, 74, Chichester Mass, 74, Five Chromatic Dances, 76, Organbook III, 78 & Bacchanal, 81, C F Peters. *Rec Perf:* The Symphonic Jazz of James P Johnson, Albright Plays Albright, Ragtime Back to Back & Sweet Sixteenths, Musical Heritage Soc; New Music for Organ, Nonesuch; Masquerades (Curtis-Smith) & Megaliths (Hodkinson), CRI. *Pos:* Music dir, First Unitarian Church, Ann Arbor, 66- *Teaching:* Prof music & music dir, Univ Mich, 70- *Awards:* Queen Marie-Jose Prize, 69; fels, Guggenheim Found, 76 & Koussevitzky Found, 82. *Bibliog:* Douglas Reed (auth), Organ Music of William Albright, Eastman Sch Music, 75; David Burge (auth), Five Chromatic Dances, Contemp Keyboard, 79. *Mem:* ASCAP; Am Music Ctr; Comp Forum. *Rep:* Murtagh McFarlane Inc 3269 W 30th St Cleveland OH 44109. *Mailing Add:* 608 Sunset Ann Arbor MI 48103

ALCANTARA, THEO
MUSIC DIRECTOR & CONDUCTOR, ARTISTIC DIRECTOR
b Cuenca, Castile, Spain, 1941; US citizen. *Study:* Real Consv Musica, Madrid, dipl(piano & comp), 56; Akad Mozarteum, Salzburg, dipl(cond), 64. *Pos:* Cond, Frankfurt Opera Theatre Orch, 64-66; guest cond, San Diego Opera, New York City Opera, Can Opera Co, 82 & Europ & North & South Am orchs, festivals & opera co; music dir & prin cond, Grand Rapids Symph, 73-78 & Phoenix Symph, 78-; artistic dir & cond, Music Acad West & Summer Fest, 80- *Teaching:* Mem fac & dir orchs, Univ Mich, 68-73. *Awards:* Lili Lehman Medal; Silver Medal, Dimitri Mitropoulos Int Cond Compt, 66; Distinguished Serv Award, Mich Found Arts, 77. *Mailing Add:* Phoenix Symph Orch 6328 N 7th St Phoenix AZ 85014

ALCH, MARIO
TENOR, EDUCATOR
b Highland, Ill, Mar 20, 20. *Study:* Wash Univ; Juilliard Sch Music, BS(music); Columbia Univ, MA(music). *Pos:* Tenor, Bern, Aachen, Cologne, Dusseldorf, Kassel, Braunschweig, Hannover, Hamburg, Frankfurt, Munich, Stuttgart, Zurich, Graz, Linz, Salzburg, Klagenfurt, Innsbruck & Vienna opera co; TV & radio appearances, Graz, Vienna, Salzburg, Hamburg, Hannover & Munich. *Teaching:* Prof music, Ohio State Univ, currently. *Mem:* Am Guild Musical Artists; Am Asn Univ Prof; Nat Asn Teachers Singing; Music Teachers Nat Asn. *Mailing Add:* 1298 Bryden Columbus OH 43205

ALDERDICE, MARY
PIANO, HARPSICHORD
b Pasadena, Calif. *Study:* Eastman Sch Music, BM, 68; spec studies with Rosalyn Tureck, Leon Fleisher, Joseph Silverstein & Jens Nygaard, 68-80. *Pos:* Soloist & chamber musician in major halls throughout country with groups such as Marlboro Fest, Mostly Mozart Fest, NY String Orch, Brandenburg Ens, Jupiter Symph & Opera Ens; music dir & co-founder, Jupiter Symph, 80-; producer, Naumburg Orch, 80-; music dir & founder, Calisto Chamber Players, 80- *Teaching:* Private piano & harpsichord, New York, 70- *Mem:* Am Fedn Musicians. *Mailing Add:* 600 W 111th St New York NY 10025

ALDERSON, RICHARD M
EDUCATOR
Study: Millsaps Col, AB, 59; ETex State Univ, MEd, 63; Northwestern Univ, DM, 69. *Teaching:* Prof & chmn, Voice Dept, Sch Music, Northwestern Univ, 70- *Awards:* Jane Hamilton Fisk Award; Fredrik A Chramer Award; Nat Found Humanities Grant. *Mem:* Pi Kappa Lambda; Nat Opera Asn; Nat Asn Teachers Singing; Chicago Singing Teachers Guild. *Interests:* Musical ornaments in opera from 1700-1850; French opera from 1850-1900; translation of opera librettos into English. *Publ:* Auth, Complete Handbook of Voice Training, 79. *Mailing Add:* Sch Music Northwestern Univ Evanston IL 60201

ALDWELL, EDWARD
PIANO, EDUCATOR
Study: Juilliard Sch, BS, MS; studied piano with Adele Marcus & theory & analysis with Carl Schachter. *Pos:* Recitalist throughout US. *Teaching:* Mem fac piano, Greenwich House Music Sch, 64-70; instr keyboard studies, Juilliard Sch, 66-70; mem fac piano, Prep Sch, Mannes Col Music, 69-73, mem fac techniques music & piano, 69-; mem fac, Curtis Inst Music, 71- *Publ:* Coauth (with Carl Schachter), Harmony and Voice Leading, two vol, Harcourt Brace Jovanowich, 79. *Mailing Add:* Curtis Inst Music 1726 Locust St Philadelphia PA 19103

ALEKSANDRUK, LINDA (MARIE)
SOPRANO, TEACHER
b Sanford, Maine, July 29, 56. *Study:* Univ Maine, Orono, BMus, 79, BS(music educ), 79. *Roles:* Despina in Cosi fan tutte, Haydn Co Fest Opera Co, Lamoine, Maine, 77. *Pos:* Singer, Philadelphia Singers, 82- *Teaching:* Voice instr, Philadelphia, 82- *Mem:* Am Guild Musical Artists; Nat Asn Teachers Singing; Am Fedn TV & Radio Artists. *Mailing Add:* 950 Walnut St #703 Philadelphia PA 19107

ALETTE, CARL
COMPOSER, EDUCATOR
b Philadelphia, Pa, May 31, 22. *Study:* Eastman Sch Music, with Wayne Barlow, A I McHose & Bernard Rogers. *Works:* Resurgence (orch); Symphony (chamber orch); Trombone Sonata; Suite for Clarinet Choir; Scherzo (brass quintet); 4 Songs. *Teaching:* Mem fac, Univ Tenn, 51-54, State

Univ NY, Brockport, 54-57 & Univ Miss, 57-68; vis prof, Univ Calif, Los Angeles, 64-65; prof theory & analysis, orchestration & comp, Univ Southern Ala, 68- *Awards:* Louisville Symph Award, 55. *Mailing Add:* 4584 Hawthorne Pl Mobile AL 36608

ALEXANDER, BRAD
PERCUSSION, EDUCATOR
b Brooklyn, NY, Mar 14, 53. *Study:* Queens Col, City Univ New York, with Bradley Spinney, Raymond Des Roches & Doug Allan, BA, 77; NY Univ, with Dave Samuels & Sashi Nyak, MA(perf), 83. *Rec Perf:* New Composers Ensemble, Opus I Rec, 81. *Pos:* Solo timpanist, Ens Trombone Paris, 76-77; solo perc & founding mem, New Repty Ens NY, 77-; rec artist, films, radio & TV, NY, 79-; perc, Broadway shows, 80- *Teaching:* Adj lectr perc, Queens Col, City Univ New York, 77-; adj lectr perc & perc ens, NY Univ, 79- *Awards:* John F Kennedy Award, 72; Philadelphia Orch Award, 73. *Mailing Add:* 11 Island Plaza Bellmore NY 11710

ALEXANDER, JOHN
TENOR, EDUCATOR
b Meridian, Miss. *Study:* Col Consv Music, Univ Cincinnati, BM; Duke Univ; Col Consv Music, Univ Cincinnati, Hon DMus, 67. *Rec Perf:* Norma; Anna Bolena; rec on London. *Roles:* Faust in Faust, Cincinnati Summer Opera, 52; Pallione in Pallione; Florestan in Fidelio; Don Jose in Carmen; Canio in I Pagliacci; Ferrando in Cosi fan tutti; Des Grieux in Manon Lescaut; and many others. *Pos:* Lyr ten, New York City Opera, Covent Garden, Vienna Volksoper, Vienna Staatsoper & others; res mem, Metropolitan Opera, currently. *Teaching:* Vis distinguished prof voice & opera, Col Consv Music, Univ Cincinnati, 74- *Mem:* Am Guild Musical Artists. *Rep:* Columbia Artists Mgt 165 W 57th St New York NY 10019. *Mailing Add:* Metropolitan Opera Lincoln Ctr New York NY 10023

ALEXANDER, JOHN ALLEN
CONDUCTOR, EDUCATOR
b Monroe, La, July 20, 44. *Study:* Oberlin Consv, Oberlin Col, BMus, 65; Univ Ky, MMus, 67; Univ Ill, 67-69. *Rec Perf:* Blanco y Negro, 73 & Music of Mario Castelnuovo-Tedesco, 82, Klavier Rec. *Pos:* Artistic dir, Perf Arts Asn Orange Co, 72-; cond, Pac Chorale & Pac Singers, 72- *Teaching:* Prof music & dir choral activ, Calif State Univ, Northridge, 70- *Awards:* Sigma Alpha Iota Radio-TV Award, 76; Distringuished Prof Award, Calif State Univ, Northridge, 77. *Mem:* Am Choral Dir Asn; Choral Cond Guild Calif; Nat Music Educr Conf. *Mailing Add:* 2847 Lambert Dr Los Angeles CA 90068

ALEXANDER, JOSEF
COMPOSER, EDUCATOR
b Boston, Mass, May 15, 07. *Study:* New England Consv Music, dipl, 25 & artist degree, 26; Harvard Univ, AB, 38, MA, 41. *Works:* Clockwork (Symphony #1), Little Orch Soc, 49; Epitaphs (orch), New York Phil, 51; Symphony #2, Orch Am, 64; Quiet Music for Strings, Denver Symph, 66; Symphony #3, Dallas Symph Orch, 72; Symphony #4, Nat Orch Asn, 76; Salute to the Whole World, Symph New World, 77. *Pos:* Contribr, Reprint Bulletin-Book Review, Glanville Publ, 65- *Teaching:* Prof music, Brooklyn Col, City Univ New York, 43- *Awards:* Fulbright Award, 55; Comp Grant, Int Humanities, 60; Comp Asst Grant, Nat Endowment Arts, 69. *Bibliog:* Joseph Machlis (auth), Contemporary Music, W W Norton, 79; Arthur Cohn (auth), Recorded Am Music, Macmillan, 81. *Mem:* Nat Asn Comp (pres, NY chap, 80-); Bohemians (bd Gov, 78-); New York Fedn Music Clubs (bd dir, 70-); ASCAP; Am Soc Univ Comp. *Mailing Add:* 229 W 78th St New York NY 10024

ALEXANDER, PETER MARQUIS
ADMINISTRATOR, WRITER
b Tyler, Tex, Mar 6, 45. *Study:* Ind Univ Sch Music, BME, 67, MM, 76. *Pos:* Music critic, Bloomington Herald-Telephone, 75-79; dir publicity, Ind Univ Sch Music, 83- *Awards:* Fulbright Fel, 79-81. *Mem:* Am Musicol Soc; Col Music Soc; Music Libr Asn. *Interests:* Late Classic and early Romantic period; Carl Maria von Weber; works of Franz Danzi. *Publ:* Coauth, Franz Danzi, Works List, In: New Grove Dict of Music & Musicians, 80; ed, Franz Danzi: Three Symphonic Works, In: The Symphony: 1720-1840, Garland Press (in prep). *Mailing Add:* 3201 Valleyview Dr Bloomington IN 47401

ALEXANDER, ROBERTA LEE
SOPRANO
b Lynchburg, Va, Mar 3, 49. *Study:* Cent State Univ, Ohio, BSME, 69; Univ Mich, MMus(voice), 71; Royal Consv, Hague, studied voice with Herman Woltman. *Roles:* Pamina in Die Zauberflöte, Houston Grand Opera, 80 & Netherlands Opera, 81; Daphne, Santa Fe Opera, 81; Elletra in Idomeneo, Zurich Opera, 82; Mimi in La Boheme, Der Komische Opera, Berlin, 82; Micaëla in Carmen, 82 & Vitellia, 83, Netherlands Opera; Zerlina, Metropolitan Opera, 83. *Rep:* Columbia Artists 165 W 57th New York NY 10019. *Mailing Add:* 50 Von Liebiweg Amsterdam Netherlands

ALEXANDER, WILLIAM PEDDIE
COMPOSER, EDUCATOR
b Lompoc, Calif, Nov 8, 27. *Study:* Univ Calif, Santa Barbara, BA, 49; Peabody Col, Vanderbilt Univ, studied comp with Roy Harris, MA, 51, PhD, 57. *Works:* Prologue & Repartee, Erie Phil, 69; Symphonic Suite, 75 & Sinfonietta, 76, Pittsburgh Symph; The Morning Trumpet, 76; Suite for Small Orchestra, Orch Soc Philadelphia, 81; Symphony No 2, comn by York Symph, 83. *Pos:* Music adv comt, Pa Coun on Arts, 80- *Teaching:* Asst prof, Shepherd Col, 57-62; prof music hist & chmn music dept, Edinboro Univ Pa,

62- *Awards:* Ostwald Band Comp Award, Am Bandmasters Asn, 60. *Mem:* Am Musicol Soc; Col Music Soc; Am Music Ctr. *Publ:* Auth, Music Heard Today, William C Brown, 66, 69. *Mailing Add:* 116 Terrace Dr Edinboro PA 16412

ALLANBROOK, DOUGLAS PHILLIPS
COMPOSER, HARPSICHORD
b Melrose, Mass, Apr 1, 21. *Study:* Studied with Nadia Boulanger, 40-42 & 48-50; Harvard Col, BA, 48; studied harpsichord with Ruggero Gerlin, 50-52. *Works:* Symphony #1, comn by Ford Found, perf by Nat Symph, 57; Four Orchestra Landscapes (Symphony #3), Oakland Symph, 65, Forty Changes for Piano, 73 & Twelve Preludes for All Seasons, 73, Boosey & Hawkes; Symphony for Brass Quintet, Annapolis Symph & Munich Radio Orch, 77; Music from the Country (Symphony #7), New Phil, 79. *Teaching:* Tutor, St John's Col, 52-; prof comp & theory, Peabody Consv, 56-58. *Awards:* Am Acad & Inst Arts & Lett Ann Awards, 82; ASCAP Yearly Award, 76- *Mem:* ASCAP; Yaddo. *Mailing Add:* 6 Revell St Annapolis MD 21401

ALLANBROOK, WYE JAMISON
WRITER, EDUCATOR
b Hagerstown, Md, Mar 15, 43. *Study:* Vassar Col, BA, 64; Stanford Univ, PhD, 75. *Teaching:* Prof, lib arts, St John's Col, Annapolis, Md, 69- *Mem:* Am Musicol Soc. *Interests:* Classical music—Mozart. *Publ:* Auth, Dance, Gesture, and The Marriage of Figaro, St John's Rev, 74; Metric Gesture as a Topic in Le Nozze di Figaro & Don Giovanni, Musical Quart, 81; Pro Marcellina: The Shape of Figaro, Act IV, Music & Lett, 83; Rhythmic Gesture in Mozart: Le Nozze di Figaro & Don Giovanni, Univ Chicago Press, 83; Opera Seria Borrowings in Le Nozze di Figaro, In: Studies in Hist Music, Vol II, Broude Bros (in prep). *Mailing Add:* 6 Revell St Annapolis MD 21401

ALLARD, JOSEPH
SAXOPHONE, CLARINET
b Lowell, Mass. *Study:* New England Consv Music; studied clarinet with Gaston Hamelin, Daniel Bonade & Ralph MacLean; studied sax with Chester Hazlett. *Pos:* Clarinet & bass clarinet, NBC Symph, formerly; mem, WOR Symph, formerly & Symph Air, formerly; solo sax, New York Phil, NBC Symph, Symph Air & RCA Victor, formerly; solo clarinetist, Bell Telephone Hour, formerly. *Teaching:* Mem fac clarinet & bass clarinet, Juilliard Sch, 56-; instr sax, clarinet, bass clarinet & jazz, New England Consv Music, currently; asst prof sax, Brooklyn Col, City Univ New York, currently; instr sax, Manhattan Sch Music, currently. *Mailing Add:* New England Consv Music 290 Huntington Rd Boston MA 02115

ALLEN, COREY LEE
COMPOSER, TEACHER
b Jan 13, 58. *Study:* Berklee Col Music, BM; Boston Consv, master class cond with Atillio Potto; private study with Dr Tom Lee. *Works:* Since First I Saw Your Face (choral), European Symposium of Choral Masterworks, 80; For Parker K, 81, C'est Bon, 81, Child's Play, 81, White Karat Music; Waldon Suite, perf by Portland Symph Orch, Maine, 83. *Teaching:* Fac mem, theory & arr, Berklee Col Music, 80-; lectr comp, Univ Duisburg, WGer, 82- *Mailing Add:* Berklee Col Music 1140 Boylston St Boston MA 02215

ALLEN, JANE
PIANO, EDUCATOR
b Dallas, Tex, June 15, 28. *Study:* With Paul van Katwijk, 41-47; Sch Music, Southern Methodist Univ, 44-46. *Pos:* Mem, Ritter Allen Duo, 59-; off pianist, St Louis Symph, 61-64; soloist, St Louis Symph & Baltimore Symph; conct tours, US, Can & Europe. *Teaching:* Privately, St Louis, 52-; head piano dept, Sewanee Summer Music Ctr, Tenn, 63, 64 & 68; artist in res & mem fac piano, Stephens Col, 66-75, St Louis Consv Music, 75-, Am Acad Arts in Europe, Verona, Italy, formerly & Univ Mo, St Louis, 76; mem fac piano & chamber music, St Louis Consv, currently. *Awards:* Artists Presentation Soc Award, St Louis, 58; Mason & Hamlin Teacher Award, 70. *Mem:* Sigma Alpha Iota; Nat Music Teachers Asn. *Rep:* Albert Kay Assoc 58 W 58th St New York NY 10019. *Mailing Add:* 7471 Kingsbury Blvd St Louis MO 63130

ALLEN, JUDITH S
COMPOSER, EDUCATOR
b Brookline, Mass, Nov 21, 49. *Study:* Douglass Col, AB, 71; Juilliard Sch, MM, 74; Princeton Univ, MFA, 76, PhD, 79. *Works:* Arche for Viola and Orchestra, 76, Follies and Fancies, 81-82 & Aura for Orchestra, 82, Am Comp Alliance; Sursum Corda (cello), perf by Piccolo Spoleto & British Embassy, 82. *Teaching:* Asst prof (comp & theory), Univ Va, 79- *Awards:* NJ State Coun Arts Comp Fel, 76; Mem Found Jewish Cult Grant, 78; Nat Endowment Arts Comp Fel, 81. *Mem:* League Comp, Int Soc Contemp Music (mem bd dir, 74-82); Am Women Comp Inc (secy & mem exec bd, 81); Am Music Ctr. *Mailing Add:* 2415 Kerry Lane Charlottesville VA 22903

ALLEN, NANCY
HARP, EDUCATOR
Study: Juilliard Sch, BM, MM. *Rec Perf:* On Angel, CRI & RCA. *Pos:* Soloist, Affiliated Artists; concerts throughout US. *Teaching:* Head harp dept, Aspen Music Fest, 79-; fac mem, Manhattan Sch Music, 82-; asst prof harp, NY Univ, currently. *Awards:* First Prize, Fifth Int Harp Compt. *Mailing Add:* c/o Columbia Artists Mgt 165 W 57th St New York NY 10019

ALLEN, ROBERT E
COMPOSER
b Minneapolis, Minn, Feb 1, 20. *Study:* Comp with Frances Richter & Kurt George Roger. *Works:* Partita (piano); Introduction & Allegro (cello & piano); The Ascension (chorus); Cantata (ms, chorus, trumpets, harp, timpani & organ); Quartet for Strings; Cecily (Broadway show score); One More Spring (Broadway show score). *Pos:* Coordr publ, Carl Fisher Inc; ed, Franco Columbo Inc. *Mem:* ASCAP. *Mailing Add:* 37 Charles St New York NY 10011

ALLEN, ROBIN PERRY
ADMINISTRATOR, WRITER
b State College, Pa, Jan 27, 52. *Study:* Calif State Univ, Humboldt, BA, 74; Univ Calif, Riverside, MPA, 76. *Pos:* Ed, Symph Mag, Am Symph Orch League, 79-, dir commun, 80- *Publ:* Coauth, The Fun Run: From Start to Finish, Am Symph Orch League & Symph News, 79; ed, The Best of Black Notes, 83. *Mailing Add:* Am Symph Orch League 633 E St NW Washington DC 20004

ALLEN, SUSAN ELIZABETH
HARP, TEACHER
b Monrovia, Calif, May 10, 51. *Study:* Music Acad of West, with Suzanne Balderston, cert, 71; Calif Inst Arts, with Catherine Gotthoffer, BFA, 73; private study with Marcella DeCray, 74-75 & Susann McDonald, 75-76. *Rec Perf:* Women's Orchestral Works, Galaxia, 79; New Music for Harp, Vol I, Arch Rec, 81. *Pos:* Conct harpist, 70-; has premiered over 35 works for the harp; has appeared on radio & TV. *Teaching:* Instr harp, Community Serv Div, New England Consv Music, 80 & Walnut Hill Sch Perf Arts, 79. *Awards:* Maurice Abravanel Award for Outstanding Achievement, Music Acad of West, 71; grants, Gaudeamus Found, 76 & Martha Baird Rockefeller Fund for Music, 81. *Mem:* Am Harp Soc Inc (pres Boston chap, 75-81, New England regional dir, 81-). *Mailing Add:* 185 Chapel St Newton MA 02158

ALLERS, FRANZ
CONDUCTOR
b Carlsbad, Czechoslovaka, Aug 6, 05; US citizen. *Study:* Acad Music, Prague, 19-23; Hochschule Musik, Berlin, 23-26. *Rec Perf:* My Fair Lady, 56, Camelot, 60 & Show Boat, 62, Columbia; La Vie Parisienne, Eurodisc, 66. *Pos:* Music dir, My Fair Lady, 56-60, Camelot, 60-62 & Gaertnerplatz-State Theatre, Munich, 73-76; cond, major US orch & many European orch. *Awards:* Antoinette Perry Award, Am Theatre Wing, 57 & 61; Grand Cross Honor, Austrian Govt, 82. *Mailing Add:* c/o Columbia Artists Mgt 165 W 57th St New York NY 10019

ALLEY, EDWARD L
ADMINISTRATOR, CONDUCTOR
b San Angelo, Tex, June 1, 35. *Study:* Angelo State Univ, 52-53; NTex State Univ, BME, 56, MM, 57. *Pos:* Cond & gen mgr, Goldovsky Opera Theater, New York, 60-69; vpres prog, Affiliate Artists, Inc, New York, 69-79; exec dir, Martha Baird Rockefeller Fund Music, 79-81; orch mgr, New York Phil, 81-83. *Awards:* Commendation Medal, Seventh Army Symph, US Army, 60. *Mem:* Am Symph Orch League. *Mailing Add:* 181 Chittenden Ave Crestwood NY 10707

ALLGOOD, WILLIAM THOMAS
COMPOSER, EDUCATOR
b Raleigh, NC, Dec 28, 39. *Study:* ECarolina Univ, with Martin Mailman, BM; Univ Ill, with Ben Johnston, MM; Cath Univ, with Emerson Myers; Univ Mich, DMA. *Works:* Trio (trumpet, bassoon & cello), 64; Brass Quintet, 64; 2 Woodwind Quintets, 64 & 65; Pentacycle (bassoon & tape), 69; Vectors (tuba & electronic sounds), 70; Music da Camera, Repetitions (oboe, trumpet, string bass, perc, tape, slides & film), 71; Anthem (choir & tape). *Teaching:* Mem fac, Univ Ill, 65-66 & Univ Md, 66-69; assoc prof music, Western Mich Univ, 69- *Mailing Add:* Music Dept Western Mich Univ Kalamazoo MI 49008

ALMEIDA, LAURINDO
GUITAR, COMPOSER
b Brazil, Sept 2, 17; nat US. *Study:* Escola Nacional Musica, Rio de Janeiro. *Works:* Maracaibo (film score), 56; Goodbye My Lady (film score), 57; Lament in Tremolo Form; First Concerto for Guitar & Orchestra, Concord Rec; and other compositions & film scores. *Rec Perf:* For Capitol, World Pacific, Decca & Orion. *Pos:* Soloist, Stan Kenton Orch, Chicago Opera House & Carnegie Hall, 47-50 & Modern Jazz Quartet; guitarist, motion picture prod, 49-; owner & operator, Brazilliance Music Publ Co, 52- *Awards:* Cert Appreciation, Am String Teachers Asn; Grammy (five), Nat Acad Rec Arts & Sci; Cert Hon, Achievement Recognition Inst. *Mem:* ASCAP; Am Songwriters Asn; Comp Guild Am; Nat Acad Rec Arts & Sci; Am Fedn TV & Radio Artists. *Mailing Add:* c/o Ray Lawrence Ltd PO Box 1987 Studio City CA 91604

ALPER, CLIFFORD DANIEL
EDUCATOR, CRITIC-WRITER
b New York, NY. *Study:* Univ Miami, BM, 54, MM, 56; Univ Md, PhD, 72. *Teaching:* Music, Dade County Sch, Miami, Fla, 54-60; prof music & music educ, Towson State Univ, 60-; lectr opera, Baltimore Opera Guild & Harford Opera Theatre, 75-82. *Awards:* Grant, Nat Endowment Humanities, 80. *Mem:* Am Inst Verdi Studies; Nat Opera Asn; life mem, Music Educr Nat Conf; life mem, Phi Mu Alpha Sinfonia. *Interests:* Relationships of Verdi's melodic structure with the dramatic aspects of his work; implications of Froebel for 20th century early childhood music education. *Publ:* Auth, Family Resemblance, Opera News, 67; The Oneness of Wozzeck, Pelleas, and Bomarzo, Music J, 72; Verdi's Luisa Miller: Her Ancestors and Descendants, Opera J, 80; Froebelian Implications in Texts of Early Childhood Songs, J Res Music Educ, 82; Thematic Similarities in Early & Middle Period Verdi, Verdi Newsletter, 83. *Mailing Add:* Music Dept Towson State Univ Baltimore MD 21204

ALSTADTER, JUDITH R
PIANO, TEACHER-COACH
b New York, NY. *Study:* Juilliard Sch, with Rosina Lhevinne & Sascha Gorodnitzki, BS; Sch Music, Yale Univ, with Ward Davenny, DMA; studied with Jeanne-Marie Darre & Volya Cossack. *Rec Perf:* Piano Music of Clara Schumann & Fanny Mendelssohn, Musical Heritage Soc, 80; Judith Alstadter Plays Music by Romantic Women Composers, 83 & Music Inspired by Children, 83, Educo Rec. *Pos:* Conct pianist, solo recitals, lecture-recitals, chamber music & soloist with orch; dir, Judith Alstadter Piano Studios; dir & founder, Minnewaska Chamber Music Soc, 79- *Teaching:* Asst prof, Five Towns Col, Seaford, NY, 74-; adj prof & lectr, CW Post Ctr, Long Island Univ, Greenvale, NY, 80-; Clinician music, teachers & civic group wkshps. *Mem:* Mu Phi Epsilon (pres New York alumni, 77-80); Piano Teachers Cong New York; Asn Piano Teachers Long Island; Musicians Club New York. *Interests:* Women comp; music inspired by children; Faure. *Publ:* Auth, Gabriel Faure—The Man & His Music, Music J, 71; French Music I Like To Play and Teach, 77 & Keeping in Keyboard Shape, 78, Mu Phi Epsilon Triangle; The Piano Works of Gabriel Faure, Keynote, 78; Piano Music of Romantic Women Composers, Mu Phi Epsilon, 80. *Mailing Add:* 25 Red Maple Dr N Wantagh NY 11793

ALTMAN, LUDWIG
ORGAN, COMPOSER
b Breslau, Germany, Sept 2, 10. *Study:* Univ Breslau; State Acad Church & Sch Music Berlin; Univ Berlin; Hon Dr Music, 82. *Works:* Sabbath Music, Transcontinental Music Publ, 63; Psalm 13, Lawson-Gould, 67; Psalm 47, Transcontinental Music Publ, 71; The Beloved of the Lord, Lawson-Gould, 72; The Blessing of Moses, 77, Prelude for Organ on Leoni, 77 & Organ Prelude on Avinu, Malkenu, 80, Transcontinental Music Publ. *Pos:* Organist & choir dir, Temple Emanu-El, San Francisco, 37-; staff organist, Palace Legion of Honor (museum), San Francisco, 52-; off organist, San Francisco Orch, 39-72. *Teaching:* Instr organ music hist, Univ Calif, Berkeley, exten, 48-63. *Awards:* First Ann Isadore Freed Award, Temple Israel, Lawrence, NY, 66. *Publ:* Ed, Organ Works of Beethoven, Hinrichsen-Peters, 62; Wellington's Victory at Vittoria, H W Gray, 77. *Mailing Add:* 1656 18th Ave San Francisco CA 94122

ALTMEYER, JEANNINE THERESA
SOPRANO
b Pasadena, Calif, May 2, 48. *Study:* With Betty Olssen, Martial Singher, Lotte Lehmann & George London. *Roles:* Voce dal cielo from Don Carlo, Metropolitan Opera, 71; Gräfin in Capriccio; Elsa in Lohengrin; Eva in Die Meistersinger von Nürnburg; Gutrune in Götterdämmerung; Elisabeth in Tannhäuser; Agathe in Der Freischutz. *Pos:* Res mem, Zurich Opera, currently. *Awards:* First Prize, Metropolitan Coun Auditions, 70; WGN Opera Auditions Prize. *Mem:* Nat Opera Inst Grant. *Mailing Add:* c/o Columbia Artists Mgt 165 W 57th St New York NY 10019

ALTON, ARDYTH
CELLO, EDUCATOR
Study: Oberlin Col, BM; Juilliard Sch. *Pos:* Perf trio conct & soloist throughout North Am. *Teaching:* Mem fac, Prep Div, Manhattan Sch Music, 65-, mem fac violoncello, 69-; mem fac, Meadowmount Sch Strings, summers & Pre-Col Div, Juilliard Sch; affil artist, State Univ NY Col, Purchase. *Mailing Add:* Manhattan Sch Music 120 Claremont Ave New York NY 10027

ALVARADO, MARILU (MRS ALAN H RAPOPORT)
PIANO
b Rio Piedras, PR; US citizen. *Study:* New England Consv Music, BM(piano), 60; special studies with Joseph Prostakoff, New York. *Rec Perf:* Moods and Contrasts, 81 & Puerto Rican and European Classics for Two Pianos, 83. *Pos:* Conct pianist, Whitney-Alvarado Piano Duo, currently. *Awards:* Three grants, Puerto Rican Govt, 70's. *Rep:* Albert Kay Assoc Inc 58 W 58th St New York NY 10019. *Mailing Add:* Himalaya 225 Urb Monterrey Rio Piedras PR 00926

AMACHER, MARYANNE
COMPOSER, ELECTRONIC
b Kane, Pa, Feb 25, 42. *Study:* Philadelphia Consv Music, 55-62; Univ Pa, with George Rochberg & K Stockhausen, BFA(music), 59-64; Univ Ill, Urbana-Champaign, 65-66. *Works:* Remainder, comn by Merce Cunningham Dance Co, 75; Lecture on the Weather (comp with John Cage), C F Peters, 76; Close Up, perf by comp & John Cage, 79; Research & Development: Living Sound (Patent Pending, St Paul, 80), comn by Walker Art Ctr, 80; Research & Development: Music for the Webern Car, comn by Galerie Nachst St Stephan, Vienna, 81; Intelligent Life, comn by Stichting de Appel, Amsterdam, 82; Intercept, comn by Kitchen Ctr Video & Music, 83. *Pos:* Fel, Ctr Advanced Visual Studies, Mass Inst Technol, 72-76 & Bunting Inst, Radcliffe Col, 78-79. *Teaching:* Res assoc, Studio Experimental Music, Sch Engineering, Univ Ill & Moore Sch Electrical Engineering, Univ Pa, 64-66; creative assoc, Ctr Creative & Perf Arts, State Univ NY Col, Buffalo, 66-67. *Awards:* Multi Media Award, NY State Coun Arts, 78-79; Musical Comp Award, Nat Endowment Arts, 78-79 & Beards Fund Arts, 80. *Bibliog:* Christina Kubisch (auth), Time into Space/Space into Time, Flash Art, 3/79; Alberto Dentice (auth), Concerto per Idraulico e Pettiroso, L'Expresso, 3/80; Tom Hight (auth), Music: The Arts, Omni Mag, 11/81. *Mailing Add:* 80 Marius St Kingston NY 12401

AMARA, LUCINE
SOPRANO
b Hartford, Conn, Mar 1, 27. *Study:* Music Acad West, 47; Univ Southern Calif, 49-50. *Rec Perf:* Pagliacci, 51 & 60; recorded for Columbia, RCA Victor, Metropolitan Opera Rec Club & Angel. *Roles:* Princess Turandot in Turandot, Toledo Opera Co, 79 & Dayton Opera Co, 79; Aida in Aida, Seattle Opera Co, 80; Amelia in Un Ballo in maschera, Metropolitan Opera, 81; Tosca in Tosca, St Petersburg Opera, 81; Princess Turandot in Turandot, Stamford Opera Co, 81. *Pos:* Soloist, San Francisco Symph, 49-50 & Metropolitan Opera, 50-; soprano in operas & concerts worldwide. *Awards:* First Prize, Atwater-Kent Radio Auditions, 48. *Mem:* Sigma Alpha Iota. *Mailing Add:* c/o Riva Mgt 260 West End Ave Suite 7A New York NY 10023

AMATO, BRUNO
COMPOSER, EDUCATOR
b Hartford, Conn, Oct 21, 36. *Study:* Hartt Col Music, BM, 58; Manhattan Sch Music, MM, 63; Accad Santa Cecilia, dipl, 67; Princeton Univ, MFA, 69, PhD, 73; studied with Arnold Frachetti, Goffredo Petrassi, Milton Babbitt, Edward Cone, Peter Westergaard, Gunther Schuller & Luciano Berio. *Works:* Music for Emily (sop & brass quintet), 72; Larghetto (strings), 73; Soliloquy III (cello), 73; Five Bagatelles (tenor sax & piano), 73; Hommage (organ), 73; Pezzetto (three tubas), 73; Psalmody (antiphonal orchs), 76. *Teaching:* Mem fac, Ball State Univ, 70-71, Ind Univ, 71-78 & Peabody Consv, currently; assoc prof theory & comp, Calif State Univ, Fullerton, formerly. *Awards:* Sinfonia Found Award, 69 & 70; Serge Koussevitzky Award, 69. *Mem:* Nat Endowment Arts Grant, 77. *Mailing Add:* 1217 St Andrews Way Baltimore MD 21239

AMELING, ELLY (ELISABETH SARA)
SOPRANO
b Rotterdam, Holland, Feb 8, 38. *Study:* Consv Dipl in Hague, Holland; Univ BC, Hon Dr, 81. *Pos:* Conct artist, specializing in the art of song: German lied & French melodie, currently. *Awards:* Edison Award; Ridder in De Orde Van Oranje Nassau, 71; Japan Grand Prix Du Disque, 81. *Mailing Add:* c/o Sheldon Soffer Mgt 130 W 56th St New York NY 10019

AMES, F(RANK) ANTHONY
ADMINISTRATOR, PERCUSSION
b Oct 12, 42; US citizen. *Study:* Eastman Sch Music, BM, 64; Carnegie-Mellon Univ, MFA, 66. *Rec Perf:* The Transfiguration of Christ (Oliver Messiaen), Decca, London, 78; Twentieth Century Consort, Vol I, 80 & Vol II, 82, Smithsonian Rec. *Pos:* Prin perc, Nat Symph Orch, 68-; pres, 20th Century Consort, 75-, Millennium Ens Inc, 80- & Potomac Prod Inc, 82- *Bibliog:* David Deutsch (producer), 20th Century Consort Presents (film), 76, Clark Santee (producer), Music Is (film), 78 & Jackson Front (producer), Copland (film), 83, WETA TV. *Mailing Add:* 1235 Potomac St NW Washington DC 20007

AMIRKHANIAN, CHARLES BENJAMIN
COMPOSER, CRITIC-WRITER
b Fresno, Calif, Jan 19, 45. *Study:* Calif State Univ, Fresno, BA, 67; San Francisco State Univ, MA, 69; Mills Col, MFA(electronic music), 80. *Works:* Symphony I, 64, Just, 72, Heavy Aspirations, 73, Seatbelt Seatbelt, 73, Dutiful Ducks, 77, Egusquiza to Falsetto (chamber orch, comp with Margaret Fisher), 79, Spoilt Music (comp with Carol Law), 79, The Putts, 81 & Andas, 83, Arts Plural Publ. *Pos:* Comp in res, Ann Halprin's Dancers Wkshp, San Francisco, 68-69; music dir, KPFA Radio, Berkeley, Calif, 69- *Teaching:* Lectr mixed media, perf & sound, San Francisco State Univ, 77-79. *Bibliog:* Richard Kostelanetz (auth), Text-Sound Art, Perf Arts J, Vol II, No 3; Stephen Ruppenthal & Larry Wendt (auth), American Text-Sound Composition and the Works of Charles Amirkhanian, Arch Rec, 80; Paul Kresh (auth), An Art between Speech & Music, New York Times, 4/3/83. *Mem:* Am Music Ctr; BMI. *Publ:* Auth, Applications of a Visual Transduction Notation System to Art & Life Experience, KPFA Folio, 9/69; Radical Aesthetics & Sound Sensitivity Information, KPFA Folio, 7/73 & Ararat Mag, winter 73; 10 Plus 2 Equals 12 American Text-Sound Pieces, 74 & New Music for Electronic & Recorded Media, 77, Arch Rec; Introduction to re-issue of Bad Boy of Music, Da Capo Press, 81. *Mailing Add:* 7722 Lynn Ave El Cerrito CA 94530

AMLIN, MARTIN DOLPH
PIANO, COMPOSER
b Dallas, Tex, June 12, 53. *Study:* Ecoles Normale Musique Paris, 73; Southern Methodist Univ, BM, 74; Eastman Sch Music, MM, 77, DMA, 77. *Works:* Lintrigue Des Accords Oublies, 77 & The Black Riders, 77, Seesaw Music; Quatrains From the Rubaiyat, Pro Arte Chamber Orch, 80; Israfel, Alea III, 82; Fifth Piano Sonata, Composer, 82-83; The Three Marias, Mimmi Fulmer, 82-83; Shadowdance, Pro Arte Chamber Orch, 83. *Rec Perf:* I Just Want to Go Back and Start This Whole Thing Over, Sine Qua Non, 78; Computer Music, Folkways, 83. *Pos:* Freelance pianist, Boston, 77-83. *Teaching:* Instr piano & comp, Phillips Exeter Acad, 78-; affil artist piano, Mass Inst Technol, 80-; instr comp, Boston Univ, 83- *Awards:* Comp asst grants, Am Music Ctr, 80 & 83; MacDowell Colony Fel, 80-83; young comp grants, ASCAP, 82. *Mem:* ASCAP; Am Music Ctr. *Mailing Add:* 51 Park Dr Boston MA 02215

AMMER, CHRISTINE
WRITER, LECTURER
b Vienna, Austria, May 25, 31; nat US. *Study:* Swarthmore Col, BA, 52. *Mem:* Assoc mem, Int League Women Comp. *Publ:* Ed, Harvard Dict of Music, Harvard Univ Press, 68; auth, Musician's Handbook of Foreign Terms, Schirmer, 71; Harper's Dict of Music, Harper & Row, 72; Unsung: A History of Women in American Music, Greenwood Press, 80. *Mailing Add:* 5 Tricorne Rd Lexington MA 02173

AMOAKU, WILLIAM KOMLA
EDUCATOR, ADMINISTRATOR
b Ho, Ghana, June 26, 40. *Study:* Univ Ill, MM, 71; Univ Ghana, PhD, 73; Univ Pittsburgh, PhD, 75. *Teaching:* Asst prof, Univ Ghana, Ho, 71-73 & Howard Univ, 76-78; instr, Univ Pittsburgh, 73-75; prof & chmn, Cent State Univ, Ohio, 78- *Mem:* Am Fedn Musicians; Soc Ethnomusicol; Nat Assoc Smithsonian Inst; Nat Orff-Shulwerk Asn. *Interests:* African retentions in Afro-American music; traditional religion and music of the Ewe of Ghana. *Publ:* Auth, Parallelisms in Orff-Schulwerk and Traditional African Methods of Music Education, DC Music Educ Asn Newsletter, 1/79; Polyrhythmn in the Classroom: A Simple Approach, Sch Musician, 5/83. *Mailing Add:* Dept Music Cent State Univ Wilberforce OH 45384

AMPER, LESLIE RUTH
PIANO, EDUCATOR
b Pittsburgh, Pa, Mar 26, 54. *Study:* Oberlin Col; New England Consv, BM, 76, MM, 80. *Rec Perf:* Liebeslieder Waltzes (Brahms), Sail Rec, 82. *Pos:* Solo piano recitalist contemp music, Alea 3, Composers in Red Sneakers; concertos, performances, Pittsburgh Symph & Mckeesport Pa Symph. *Teaching:* Piano teacher, Longy Sch Music, 76-; music tutor, Harvard Univ, 82- *Awards:* Jordan Hall Hon Compt, New England Consv, 79, Concerto Compt, 80; Scholar, Crescendo Club, 83. *Bibliog:* Marvin Hightower (auth), Pianist Couple Bring Contemporary Touch to Currier House, Harvard Univ Gazette, 10/22/82. *Mem:* Boston Musicians Asn. *Mailing Add:* Longy Sch Music One Follen St Cambridge MA 02138

AMRAM, DAVID WERNER
COMPOSER, FRENCH HORN
b Philadelphia, Pa, Nov 17, 30. *Study:* Consv Music, Oberlin Col, studied French horn with Martin Morris, 48; George Washington Univ, studied French horn with William Klang & Abe Kniaz, BA, 52; Manhattan Sch Music, studied comp with Vittorio Giannini & Ludmilla Ulehla, 55; studied comp with Jonel Perlea; Moravian Col, LLD, 79. *Works:* Sacred Service for Sabbath Eve, comn by Park Ave Synagogue, NY, 61; Let Us Remember (soloists, chorus & orch), comn by Union Am Hebrew Congregations, 65; The Final Ingredient (opera, libretto by Arnold Weinstein), ABC TV, 65; King Lear Variations (woodwinds, brass, perc & piano), perf by New York Phil, 67; Twelfth Night (opera, libretto with Joseph Papp), Lake George Opera Fest, 68; Concerto for Wind, Brass, Jazz Quintets and Orchestra, comn by Am Symph, 71; The Trail of Beauty (ms, oboe & orch), comn by Philadelphia Orch, 77. *Rec Perf:* Triple Concerto, Para Los Papiues, No More Walls, King Lear Variations, Eastern Scene, Broadway Reunion & Autobiography for Strings, Flying Fish Rec Inc. *Pos:* Perf at Cafe Bohemia, Birdland & with Amram Barrow Quartet, formerly; French horn, Nat Symph Orch, 51-52; comp in res, New York Phil, 66-67; cond, Corpus Christi, Tex, 67; musical ambassador of goodwill, Cuba, 77, Cent Am, 77 & Mid East, 78. *Awards:* Rockefeller Found Grant, New York Phil, 66-67. *Bibliog:* World of David Amram, Nat Educ TV, 69; documentary, PBS, 78. *Mailing Add:* c/o Barna Ostertag 501 Fifth Ave Apt 1410 New York NY 10017

AMSTUTZ, A KEITH
TRUMPET, EDUCATOR
b Saginaw, Mich, May 3, 41. *Study:* Mich State Univ, with Byron L Autrey, BS, 63, MM, 64; studied with Earl D Irons, 64-67; NTex State Univ, with John J Haynie, 65-67; Univ Okla, DME, 70. *Rec Perf:* Solos for Trumpet, Coronet Rec, 69. *Pos:* Asst ed, Int Trumpet Guild, 78- *Teaching:* Instr, Univ Tex, Arlington, 64-67; NTex State Univ, 67-70; asst prof, Univ Kans, 70-73; asst prof, Univ SC, 73-77, assoc prof, 77- *Mem:* Music Teachers Nat Asn; Phi Mu Alpha (prov gov, 75-81); Int Trumpet Guild. *Publ:* Auth, The Multiple Tongue, Nat Asn Col Wind & Perc Instrm J, 75; A Videofluorographic Study of the Teeth Aperture, Instrument Pivot and Tongue Arch and Their Influence on Trumpet Performance, 77 & coauth, Orthodontics and the Trumpeter's Embouchure—A Practical Solution, 83, Int Trumpet Guild J. *Mailing Add:* Music Dept Univ SC Columbia SC 29208

ANDERS, (BARBARA) LYNNE
SOPRANO
b Jackson, Miss. *Study:* Belhaven Col, 56-57; studied with Paul Berl. *Rec Perf:* The Messiah, Tri-Con Prod, 65; Lynne Anders, Soprano, Golden Age Rec, 74. *Roles:* Mercedes in Carmen, Jackson Opera Guild, Miss, 56; Marsinah in Kismet, 65 & Margot in Desert Song, 66, Am Light Opera Co; Sandman in Dew Fairy, Washington Civic Opera, 67; Lia in L'Enfant Prodique, Friends of Music, 70; Mother in Amahl and the Night Visitors, Richmond Civic Opera, 77. *Pos:* Soloist, with Gulf Coast Symph, Montgomery Chamber Orch & Georgetown Symph & appeared at Kennedy Ctr, Wolf Trap, Brevard Music Ctr, Piccolo Spoleto Fest & others. *Teaching:* Master class voice, Haverford Col, 9/11/76; vocal workshop, Gardner-Webb Col, 3/1/83. *Awards:* Marie Morrisey Keith Award, Nat Fedn Music Clubs, 56. *Mem:* DC Fedn Music Clubs (pres, 78-80); Am Opera Scholar Soc (pres, 80-81); Friday Morning Music Club, Washington, DC (pres, 83-85); Am Guild Musical Artists (mem nat bd gov, 80-83); Am Fedn TV & Radio Artists. *Rep:* Springer-Auty Assoc 1001 Rolandvue Rd Towson Md 21204. *Mailing Add:* 3216 Prince William Dr Fairfax VA 22031

ANDERSEN, ELNORE C (MARJORIE)
VIOLIN
b Detroit, Mich. *Study:* Sch Music, Univ Mich, Ann Arbor, BMus, 55, MMus, 56. *Pos:* Concertmaster, Peninsula Symph Va, 81-; first violinist & violin soloist, Colonial Williamsburgs Gov Palace Orch. *Interests:* Identification and location of music listed in Thomas Jefferson's Catalogue of Library dated 1783. *Mailing Add:* 116 Caran R1 Williamsburg VA 23185

ANDERSON, ADRIAN DAVID
COMPOSER
b Palo Alto, Calif, Dec 27, 52. *Study:* San Francisco Consv Music, BM, 75; Boston Univ Sch Arts, MMus, 77; Inst Sonology, Netherlands, 78. *Works:* String Quartet, perf by Alea III, 80 & Boston Musica Viva, 80; Piano Quintet, perf by Tanglewood/Berkshire Chamber Music Ens, 83. *Awards:* ASCAP Found Grant, 80; Comp Fel Grant, Nat Endowment Arts, 82-83. *Mem:* ASCAP; Am Music Ctr; MacDowell Colony Fel. *Mailing Add:* 22 Ortalon Ave Santa Cruz CA 95060

ANDERSON, ALFRED LAMAR
BARITONE, EDUCATOR
b Smith Co, Miss, Aug 28, 42. *Study:* Miss Col, BME, 65; Ind Univ, MM, 69. *Rec Perf:* Dr Heidegger's Fountain of Youth (J Beeson), CRI, 78. *Roles:* Escamillo in Carmen, Cincinnatti Opera, 76; Don Giovanni in Don Giovanni, Royal Opera, Ghent, Belgium, 78; Scarpia in Tosca, 78, Tonio in I Pagliacci, 79 & Alfio in Cavalleria rusticana, 79, Hong Kong Opera; Carlo in Forza del Destino, Palm Beach Opera, 82; Sharpless in Madama Butterfly, 83 & Escamillo in Carmen, 83, New York City Opera. *Teaching:* Assoc prof voice, Univ Southern Miss, 79- *Awards:* Wm M Sullivan Award, Sullivan Found for Music, 72-; Churchill Fel, English Speaking Union, New York, 74; Martha Baird Rockefeller Grant, 75. *Mem:* Nat Asn Teachers Singing; Am Guild Musical Artists. *Rep:* Eric Semon Assoc 111 W 57th St New York NY 10019. *Mailing Add:* 544 W Fouth St Hattiesburg MS 39401

ANDERSON, ALLEN LOUIS
COMPOSER, EDUCATOR
b Palo Alto, Calif, Mar 13, 51. *Study:* Univ Calif, Berkeley, BA, 73; Brandeis Univ, MFA, 77. *Works:* Skies, The Quake, APNM, 76; Arcade, Johnson State Comp Conf, 76 & 80; Aria di Notte, Dinosaur Annex, 77; Zephyro, Zephyro, 78, Supra Rosa, 78 & Measure of Terraine, 79, APNM. *Teaching:* Instr music, Brandeis Univ, 77- *Awards:* Comn, Am Music Ctr, 79. *Mem:* BMI. *Mailing Add:* 73 Glen Ave Newton Center MA 02159

ANDERSON, BETH (BARBARA ELIZABETH)
COMPOSER, PIANO
b Lexington, Ky, Jan 3, 50. *Study:* Univ Ky, 66-68; Univ Calif, Davis, BA(music), 71; Mills Col, MFA(piano), 73, MA(comp), 74; NY Univ, 77-78. *Works:* Tulip Clause, 73 & Joan, 74, Am Comp Alliance; The Eighth Ancestor, Joshua Corp, 81; Manos Inquietas, 82, Network, 82, Suite for Winds & Percussion, 82 & Quilt Music, 83, Am Comp Alliance. *Rec Perf:* Torero Piece, Arch Rec, 74; If I Were A Poet, Watershed Found Tape, 77; I Can't Stand It, Dial-A-Poem Poets, 80; Ocean Motion Mildew Mind, New Music Distrib, 80; Yes Sir Ree, 83, Country Time, 83 & The People Rumble Louder Than The Poet Speaks, 83, Widemouth Tapes. *Pos:* Dance accmp, Martha Graham Sch Dance, 75-78; res comp, New York Young Audiences, 82- *Teaching:* Adj prof women comp, New Sch Social Res, 76; adj prof listening skills music theory, NY Univ, 78; adj prof music theory, Col New Rochelle Sch New Resources, 78-; vis spec speech & theatre depts, Montclair State Col, 83- *Awards:* Award, Found Contemp Perf Arts, 75; Award of Merit, Nat Fedn Music Clubs, 77. *Bibliog:* Julie Cheever (auth), Composing From Life, San Francisco Chronicle Mag, 6/23/74; Joan Malone (auth), Working Hard For Music Success, Mt Sterling Advocate, Ky, 1/5/83. *Mem:* BMI; Sonneck Soc; Am Comp Alliance; Int League Women Comp; Am Music Ctr. *Publ:* Auth, Copyright Amazement, Ear Mag, 5/75; Report From the Front, 6/27/79 & What's Happening In New Music?, 12/20/79, Soho Weekly News; My Personal Approach to Music, Heresies Mag, No 10, 80; Beauty Is Revolution, Am Women Comp News, 1/82. *Rep:* Am Comp Alliance 170 W 74th St New York NY 10023. *Mailing Add:* 26 Second Ave #2B New York NY 10003

ANDERSON, DEAN
PERCUSSION, EDUCATOR
Study: Univ Miami, BM; New England Consv Music, MM, studied perc with Fred Wickstrom, Stanley Leonard, Al Payson & Everett Firth. *Pos:* Clinician, Ludwig Int Symposium; performer, Am Wind Symph, Gtr Miami Phil, Boston Pops, Boston Symph, Boston Opera Co & Boston Ballet. *Teaching:* Instr perc, Univ Miami, formerly & Atlantic Union Col, formerly; chmn dept, Berklee Col Music, currently. *Mailing Add:* Berklee Col Music 1140 Boylston St Boston MA 02215

ANDERSON, DONNA K
EDUCATOR, PIANO
b Underwood, NDak, Feb 16, 35. *Study:* MacPhail Col Music, BM, 57, MM, 59; Ind Univ, PhD, 66. *Teaching:* Asst prof music hist, State Univ NY, Cortland, 67-70, assoc prof, 70-78 & prof, 78- *Mem:* Music Libr Asn; Sonneck Soc; Am Musicol Soc; Col Music Soc. *Interests:* Music of Charles T Griffes; film music. *Publ:* Auth, Charles T Griffes: An Annotated Bibliography-Discography, Info Coordr, 77; Griffes, Charles T(omlinson), In: New Grove Dict of Music & Musicians, 80; The Griffes Poem: A New Perspective, Nat Flute Asn Newsletter, 82; The Works of Charles T Griffes: A Descriptive Catalogue, UMI Res Press, 83. *Mailing Add:* 14 Pleasant St Cortland NY 13045

ANDERSON, FLETCHER CLARK
EDUCATOR
b Birmingham, Ala, Dec 7, 39. *Study:* Birmingham Southern Col, AB & BME, 63; Univ Ill, MS, 67; Univ GA, EdD, 78. *Teaching:* Music, Atlanta pub schs, Ga, 63-65; choral dir, Elizabethtown High Sch, Ky, 65-66; asst prof music, Edinboro State Col, 67-70; assoc prof & chmn, Fine Arts, Wesleyan Col, Ga, 70- *Mem:* Music Educr Nat Conf; Ga Music Educr Asn (col div chmn, 80-81);

Am Choral Dir Asn (res chmn, 77-79); Am Guild Organists. *Publ:* Coauth, Toward a Musical Classroom, Kendall/Hunt, 69; auth, Foundations of a Musical Culture in Birmingham, Ala, 1871-1900, J Birmingham Hist Soc, 80. *Mailing Add:* Dept Music Wesleyan Col Macon GA 31297

ANDERSON, GARLAND (LEE)
COMPOSER, WRITER
b Union City, Ohio, June 10, 33. *Study:* Univ Edinburgh, studied comp with Hans Gal, 54-55; Ind Univ, studied comp with Roy Harris, 59-60; Earlham Col, BA, 75. *Works:* Sonata for Alto Saxophone & Piano, Southern Music Co, 68; Concertino for Pianoforte & Orch, Am Music Ed, 69; Sonata for Tenor Saxophone & Piano, 74 & Sonata for Baritone Saxophone & Piano, 76, Southern Music Co; Soyazhe (opera in one act), Cent City Opera House Asn, 79; Concerto for Viola & Winds, comn by Robert Slaughter, 81; Sonata No 2 for Alto Saxophone & Piano, Southern Music Co, 82. *Pos:* Music dir, WGLM Radio, Richmond, Ind, 62-64; fac adv, WECI Radio, Earlham Col, 65-66. *Teaching:* Private piano instr, Richmond, Ind, 60-76. *Awards:* Fel, Nat Endowment for Arts, 76; Standard Award, ASCAP, 80, 81 & 82. *Bibliog:* J Londeix (auth), 125 Ans de Music Pour Saxophone, Alphonse Leduc, Paris, France. *Mem:* ASCAP. *Interests:* Early American music before 1800. *Publ:* Auth, American Piano Music, Showcase Music Clubs Mag, 62; The Music of Ned Rorem, Music J, 63; Early American Music, Showcase Music Clubs Mag, 64; Alexander Reinagle and the Philadelphia Sonatas, Music J, 66. *Rep:* George Hayduk & Assoc 108 S Walnut PO Box 785 Muncie IN 47305. *Mailing Add:* 316 N Mulberry #103 Muncie IN 47305

ANDERSON, GILLIAN BUNSHAFT
MUSIC DIRECTOR, LIBRARIAN
b Brookline, Mass, Nov 28, 43. *Study:* Harvard Summer Sch, studied choral cond with Iva Dee Hyatt, 63; Bryn Mawr Col, with Isabelle Cazeaux, BA, 65; Univ Vienna, cert, 66; Univ Ill, with Charles Hamm & Nicholas Temperley, MM(musicol), 69. *Rec Perf:* Music of the American Revolution, Vol 1, CSP; Francis Hopkinson (1737-1791), America Independent, or, The Temple of Minerva & Daniel Bayley, A New Royal Harmony, Musical Heritage Soc. *Pos:* Dir, Colonial Singers & Players, 71-; dir, producer & writer, Nat Pub Radio shows, 76; proj dir & prod, Voluptuous Variety: Am Music from 1750-1900, Nat Pub Radio, 77-; choir dir, St Mark's Church, Washington, DC, 78-81 & St James Church, 82; ref libr, Music Div, Libr Cong, 78- *Mem:* Am Musicol Soc; Sonneck Soc; Music Libr Asn (mem bd dir, 82-); Int Asn Music Librn; Int Asn Study Popular Music. *Interests:* American music; colonial music; movie music; music periodicals; the copyright records. *Publ:* Auth, Political and Patriotic Music of the American Revolution, twenty ed, C T Wagner, 75 & 81; The Temple of Minerva and Francis Hopkinson: A Reappraisal of America's First Poet-Composer, Proc Am Philosophical Soc, 6/76; The Funeral of Samuel Cooper, New England Quart, 12/77; compiler & ed, Freedom's Voice in Poetry and Song, Scholarly Resources Inc, 77; auth, Eighteenth Century Evaluations of William Billings: A Reappraisal, Quart J Libr Cong, 1/78. *Mailing Add:* 1320 North Carolina Ave NE Washington DC 20002

ANDERSON, GLENN ALAN
LIBRARIAN
b Philipsburg, Pa, Apr 3, 48. *Study:* State Univ NY, Albany, BA, 70, MA, 76; Fla State Univ, MLS, 78. *Pos:* Humanities ref librn, Ralph Brown Draughon Libr, Auburn Univ, 78- *Mailing Add:* 1123 Old Mill Rd Auburn AL 36830

ANDERSON, JUNE
SOPRANO
b Boston, Mass. *Rec Perf:* Egitto, Philips Rec. *Roles:* Queen of the Night in The Magic Flute, New York City Opera, 78; Lucia in Lucia di Lammermoor, Milwaukee Florentine Opera, 82; Gulnara in Il Corsaro, San Diego Opera Verdi Fest, 82; I Puritani, Edmonton Opera, 82-83; Semiramide, Rome Opera, 82-83; Rosina in The Barber of Seville, Seattle Opera & Teatro Massimo, 82-83. *Pos:* Conct & oratorio vocalist, Chicago Pops Orch, Handel Fest Kennedy Ctr, Denver Symph, St Louis Symph, Cincinnati Symph & Maracaibo Symph, Venezuela. *Awards:* Richard Tucker Found Grant, 83. *Mailing Add:* c/o Columbia Artists 165 W 57th St New York NY 10019

ANDERSON, KAREN
VIOLA
b Cardston, Alta, May 25, 45. *Study:* Mannes Col Music, BS, 70. *Pos:* Rehearsal pianist, Perf Arts Ctr, St Paul, Minn, 71-72; sect violist, Civic Orch Minneapolis, 71-72; prin violist, 72 & 73; temp sect violist, Westchester Symph, NY, formerly; sect violist, Edmonton Symph Orch, Alta, 72-73; asst prin violist, 73-75; sect violist, Milwaukee Symph, 75. *Mailing Add:* 2211 E Kenwood Blvd Milwaukee WI 53211

ANDERSON, NEIL
GUITAR, EDUCATOR
b Jamestown, NY, Aug 27, 52. *Study:* Hartt Col Music, Univ Hartford, BM(guitar perf), 74; private study with Aaron Shearer, Eli Kassner & Manuel Barrueco. *Rec Perf:* The Boston Guitar Project, SAIL Records, 83. *Teaching:* Fac, Chautauqua Summer Music Fest, NY, 74-, Univ Lowell, 75-, Boston Consv, 77-, Manhattan Sch Music, 80-82 & New England Consv, 80- *Awards:* Symposium Performer's Award, Am String Teacher's Asn, 79 & 81. *Mem:* Am String Teacher's Asn; Boston Class Guitar Soc; Music Teachers Nat Asn; Guitar Found Am. *Publ:* Auth, Aim-Directed Movement, Guitar Player, 79. *Mailing Add:* 284 Arlington St Watertown MA 02172

ANDERSON, PENNY
VIOLA
b Seattle, Wash, May 11, 49. *Study:* Aspen, with Lillian Fuchs, 70; Smith Col, with E Wallfisch, BA, 71; Juilliard Sch, with W Lincer, MA; Ind Univ, with T Wronski, 75. *Pos:* Mem, Buffalo Phil, 79-80 & Pittsburgh Symph, 80- *Teaching:* Asst, Juilliard Sch, 76; fac mem viola, Consv Music, Oberlin Col, 77-79. *Mailing Add:* Pittsburgh Symph Heinz Hall 600 Penn Ave Pittsburgh PA 15222

ANDERSON, ROBERT (THEODORE)
ORGAN, EDUCATOR
b Chicago, Ill, Oct 5, 34. *Study:* Am Consv, Chicago, with Mary Ruth Craven; Ill Wesleyan Univ, with Lillian Mecherle McCord, BSM, 55; Staatliche Hochschule Musik, Frankfurt, Ger, with Helmut Walcha, 57-59; Union Theol Sem, New York, with Robert Baker, MSM, 57, DSM, 61. *Works:* Lord, Thou Hast Searched Me, 64 & Hodie, Christus Natus Est, 69, Lawson Gould; Communion Prelude on Kingdom, Abingdon, 78; Rejoice, The Lord is King, Hope, 82. *Rec Perf:* Organ Music of the Classic Period, 70, Organ Music of the Romantic Period, 70 & Organ Music of the 20th Century, 71, Aeolian-Skinner; Organ Concert at Southern Methodist Univ, KERA-TV, Dallas, 81. *Teaching:* Prof organ & sacred music, Southern Methodist Univ, Dallas, 60- *Awards:* First Meadows Found Distinguished Prof Award, 81-82. *Bibliog:* Robert Anderson as Performer and Teacher (film), KERA-TV, Dallas, 79. *Mem:* Pi Kappa Lambda; Am Guild Organists (mem nat coun, 67-69 & dean Dallas chap, 68-70); Phi Mu Alpha Sinfonia (pres Alpha Lambda chap, 54-55). *Interests:* Organ literature, organ history, organ building, and performance. *Publ:* Auth, The Art of Helmut Walcha, 59 & An Organist's View Through the Music Rack, 76, Diapason; The FAGO Test Pieces, 73 & Reflections on Organ Teaching-Gradus ad Parnassum, 78, Music, Am Guild Organists Mag. *Mailing Add:* 6810 Stichter Dallas TX 75230

ANDERSON, ROBERT PETER
DOUBLE BASS
b Hartford, Conn, Jan 22, 47. *Study:* Ind Univ, BMus, 69; Hochschule Musik, München, 69-70; Catholic Univ Am, MMus, 73. *Pos:* Bassist, Ft Wayne Phil, 73-74 & Minn Orch, 74- *Teaching:* Double bass, Univ Wis, Eau Claire, 74-75 & MacPhail Ctr Arts, Minneapolis, 77- *Awards:* Fulbright Grant, 69. *Mailing Add:* 4744 Lyndale Ave S Minneapolis MN 55409

ANDERSON, RONALD K
ADMINISTRATOR, EDUCATOR
b Kansas City, Mo, Aug 19, 34. *Study:* Cent Mo State Col, Warrensburg, BME, 55; Juilliard Sch Music, BS, 57, MS, 58; Columbia Univ, MA, 62, EdD, 70. *Rec Perf:* Numerous solo & chamber phonorecordings in US & Europe. *Pos:* Mem, Renaissance Band, New York Pro Musica, 60-63; first trumpet, Am Brass Quintet, 60-65; staff-trumpet, Comp Conf, 61- & Group Contemp Music, 62-; Europe solo recital tours, 67, 69, 70 & 74; prin trumpet, New York City Ballet Orch, 75-; music adv, Cent Phil Orch China, Beijing, 81- *Teaching:* Fac mem, State Univ NY, Stony Brook, 69-, State Univ NY, Purchase, 72-, NY Univ, 78- & Teachers Col, 83- *Awards:* Grant, Martha Baird Rockefeller Found, 71. *Mem:* Stefan Wolpe Soc Inc (pres, 82-); Int Soc Contemp Music (mem bd dir, 73-76 & 77-80). *Publ:* Ed, Solo Piece for Trumpet, Josef Marx Music, 69. *Mailing Add:* 251 W 92 St Apt 11-B New York NY 10025

ANDERSON, RUTH
COMPOSER, EDUCATOR
b Kalispell, Mont, March 21, 28. *Study:* Univ Wash, BA(flute), 49, MA(comp), 51; Manhattan Sch Music, 52-53; Mannes Col Music, 53-55; Princeton Univ, 62-63; studied comp with Darius Milhaud, 51, 53 & 59-60 & Nadia Boulanger, 58-59 & flute with Jean-Pierre Rampal, 58-59. *Works:* Prelude and Rondo (flute & strings), 56; Feather Song (women's or mixed chorus), Warner Brothers, 58; Richard Cory (women's voices & pianoforte), G Schirmer, 60; Morning Prayer (mixed chorus), Boosey & Hawkes, 60; SUM (State of the Union Message) (tape), 74, 2 Movements for Strings, 79 & Dump (two channel tape), 79, Am Comp Ed. *Pos:* Solo flutist, Totenberg Instrm Ens, 51-58 & Boston Pops Orch, 58; orchestrator & choral arranger, NBC-TV, 60-66, Lincoln Ctr Theatre, 66 & freelance; electronic music studio consult, New York cols & univ, 70- *Teaching:* Grad asst musical analysis & cond comp orch, Univ Wash, 49-51; instr flute, Westchester Consv, 51-52; prof music, Hunter Col, 66-, founder & dir, Electronic Music Studio, 68- *Awards:* MacDowell Colony Fels, 57-73; Ingraham-Merrill Grant, 63-64; Res Found Grant, City Univ New York, 74. *Publ:* Compiler, Contemporary American Composers, G K Hall & Co, 82. *Mailing Add:* Baron de Hirsch Rd Crompond NY 10517

ANDERSON, SHIRLEY PATRICIA
PERCUSSION, EDUCATOR
b Aberdeen, Wash, Oct 10, 33. *Study:* Philadelphia Musical Acad, studied perc with Fred Hinger & Charles Owen, BMus(perc), 59; Combs Col Music, with Michael Bookspan, MMus(perc), 60, DMus(perc), 63. *Works:* Flight Pattern for Three (fugue for perc), perf by Perc Group, Guam Symph, 68. *Rec Perf:* Sonatina for Three Tympano & Piano (Alexander Tcherepnin), Denver, 74. *Pos:* First chair perc, Guam Symph, 66-68; freelance musician, Philadelphia, 68- *Teaching:* Instr perc, Combs Col Music, 60-63; instr music in action, Philadelphia Col Perf Arts, 82- *Bibliog:* Gordon Peters (auth), Notation for Percussion Instruments, Percussive Arts Soc, 64. *Mem:* Philadelpha Musical Soc; Am Musicol Soc; Music Educr Nat Conf; Percussive Arts Soc. *Publ:* Auth, Anderson's Animals. *Mailing Add:* 2101 Chestnut St #1017 Philadelphia PA 19103

ANDERSON, SYLVIA
MEZZO-SOPRANO
b Denver, Colo. *Study:* Eastman Sch Music, with Anna Kaskas; Hochschule Musik, Cologne, with Ellen Bosenius; MacMurry Col, Hon DM. *Roles:* Feodor in Boris Godunov, Cologne Opera, 62; Ophelia in Hamlet, Hamburg Opera, 68; Carmen in Carmen; Giovanna in Anna Bolena; Dorabella in Cosi fan tutte; Octavian in Der Rosenkavalier; Eboli in Don Carlo. *Pos:* Singer with maj opera co in Europe & US. *Mailing Add:* c/o Thea Dispeker 59 E 54th St New York NY 10022

ANDERSON, THOMAS JEFFERSON, JR
COMPOSER, CONDUCTOR
b Coatesville, Pa, Aug 17, 28. *Study:* WVa State Col, BMus, 50; Pa State Univ, MMusEd, 51; Univ Iowa, PhD, 58; Col Holy Cross, Hon Dr Musical Arts. *Works:* Messages, a Creole Fantas (orch), Carl Fischer, Inc, 79; Vocalise (violin & harp), 80, Soldier Boy, Soldier (opera), 82, Inaugural Piece (three trumpets & three trombones), 82, Jonestown (children's choir & piano), 82, Call & Response (solo piano), 82, Thomas Jefferson's Minstrels, 82, Comp Facsimile Ed. *Teaching:* Instr, WVa State Col, 55-56; prof music & chmn dept, Langston Univ, 58-63; prof, Tenn State Univ, 63-69; Danforth vis prof, Danforth Found, Morehouse Col, 71-72; Fletcher prof, Tufts Univ, 72- *Awards:* Award, Fromm Found, 64; comp-in-res, Rockefeller Found & Atlanta Symph Orch, 69-71; award, Nat Endowment for Arts, 76. *Mem:* Founder, Black Music Caucus (chmn, 76-78); Col Music Soc (coun mem, 78-79); Mass Coun on Arts & Humanities (coun mem, 78-80); Kodaly Inst (mem bd, 78-79). *Publ:* Contribr, Black Music in Our Culture, Kent State Univ Press, 70; Readings in Black American Music, W W Norton & Co, Inc, 71; Reflections on Afro-American Music, Kent State Univ Press, 73; The Black Composer Speaks, Scarecrow Press, Inc, 78; ed, Racial & Ethnic Directions in American Music, Col Music Soc, 82. *Rep:* Meet the Composer 250 W 57th St Suite 2532 New York NY 10107. *Mailing Add:* 34 Grove St Winchester MA 01890

ANDERSON, WALDIE ALFRED
TENOR, EDUCATOR
b Aberdeen, Wash, Feb 5, 30. *Study:* Cent Wash Univ, BA, 52; Univ Mich, MM, 54. *Teaching:* Fac mem, Davenport Pub Sch, Iowa, 56-60; asst prof, Cent Wash Univ, 60-65; fac mem & admnr, Interlochen Arts Acad, 65-80; vis assoc prof, Univ Tex, Austin, 77-78, Fla State Univ, 81-82 & Univ Mich, 82- *Mem:* Nat Asn Teachers Singing; Music Educr Nat Conf. *Mailing Add:* Sch Music Univ Mich Ann Arbor MI 48109

ANDERSON, WARREN DEWITT
WRITER, EDUCATOR
b Brooklyn, NY, Mar 19, 20. *Study:* Haverford Col, BA, 42; Harvard Univ, MA, 47, PhD, 54; Oxford Univ, BA, 49. *Works:* Mass for Three Voices, perf by Grace Church Choir, Amherst, Mass, 75 & St James by Pkwy Choir, Minneapolis, Minn, 82. *Teaching:* From instr to prof, Col Wooster, 50-67; prof, Univ Iowa, 67-70 & Univ Mass, Amherst, 70- *Mem:* Am Musicol Soc. *Interests:* Ancient Greek music. *Publ:* Auth, Ethos and Education in Greek Music, Harvard Univ Press, 66; Word-Accent and Melody in Ancient Greek Musical Texts, J Music Theory, 73; What Song the Sirens Sang: Problems & Conjectures ..., 79 & Musical Developments in the School of Aristotle, 80, Royal Musical Asn Res Chronicle; Seventy-two articles, In: New Grove Dict of Music & Musicians, Macmillan, 82. *Mailing Add:* 27 High Point Dr Amherst MA 01002

ANDERSON, WILLIAM MILLER
ADMINISTRATOR, EDUCATOR
b Pulaski, Va, Nov 26, 40. *Study:* Eastman Sch Music, BM, 63, MM, 64; Univ Mich, PhD, 70. *Pos:* Dir, Ctr for Study World Musics, Kent State Univ, 80. *Teaching:* Prof music educ & world musics, Kent State Univ, 71-, asst dean, grad col, 78- *Mem:* Music Educr Nat Conf (ed bd Music Educr J); Soc Ethnomusicol (chmn, music educ comt, 71-73 & instr resources comt, 73-75); Soc Asian Music. *Publ:* Auth, Teaching Asian Musics in Elementary and Secondary Schools, Leland Press, 75; coauth, Music and Related Arts for the Classroom, Kendall-Hunt, 78; contribr, Segments on World Musics, In: Silver Burdett Music, Silver-Burdett, 81. *Mailing Add:* Sch Music Kent State Univ Kent OH 44240

ANDRADE, ROSARIO
SOPRANO
b Veracruz, Mex, Apr 6, 51. *Study:* Consv Santa Cecilia, Italy, 73; Veracruz Consv; Mexico City Consv. *Roles:* Cio Cio San in Madama Butterfly, Teatro Bellas Artes, Mexico City, 74; Donna Anna in Don Giovanni, Royal Opera Theatre Monnaie, Belgium, 72; Donna Elvira in Don Giovanni, Glyndebourne Fest, England, 77 & 78; Mimi in La Boheme, Warsaw Opera, 81; Asteria in Nerone, Carnegie Hall, 82; Antonia in The Tales of Hoffmann, Metropolitan Opera, 82; Violeta in La Traviata, Warsaw Opera, 83. *Awards:* Greatest Artist Mex Award, Union Mex Cronistas Teatro Musica, 80. *Mailing Add:* c/o Robert Lambardo Assoc 1 Harkness Plaza 61 W 62nd Ste 6F New York NY 10023

ANDREWS, GEORGE
COMPOSER, MUSIC DIRECTOR
b Winnipeg, Man, Jan 24, 27; US citizen. *Study:* Tufts Univ, with Kenneth McKillop, 55; Univ Southern Calif, with Halsey Stevens, 59-60; Calif State Univ, Fullerton, with Donal Michalsky, BA, 65, MA, 66. *Works:* Sextet for Brass, Calif State Univ Long Beach Brass Sextet, 63; Expansions & Contractions for Clarinet Alone, comn by Edward Casem, Los Angeles, 64; Solipsism for Soprano & String Trio, Calif State Univ, Fullerton, 65; 344 for

String Quartet, Nat Asn Comp, USA, 76; Four Bagatelles for Piano, comn by Natalie Field, 81; Periodicities for Flute & Piano, 83 & Periodicities II For Double String Quartet, 83, SBay Chamber Music Soc Conct, Los Angeles. *Pos:* Freelance composer & arranger, 52-66. *Teaching:* Comp, privately, 55-; teacher music, South High Sch, Torrance, Calif, 66-, chmn dept, 66- *Mem:* Calif Band Dir Asn; Nat Asn Comp, USA; SBay Chamber Music Soc (mem bd, 71-83, pres, 78-79); Southern Calif Sch Band & Orch Asn. *Mailing Add:* 3810 Shad Pl San Pedro CA 90732

ANDRIX, GEORGE PAUL
COMPOSER, VIOLA
b Chicago, Ill, June 15, 32. *Study:* Univ Ill, BM, 56, MM, 57; Trinity Col Music, London, 58-60. *Works:* Free Forms (four pieces for bass trombone & strings), G Schirmer; Five Pieces for Orchestra, Structures for Brass Quintet & others, Seesaw Music. *Pos:* Violist, Ithaca String Quartet, 60-66; concertmasterr, Great Falls Symph Orch, Mont, 69-70; prin viola, Edmonton Symph Orch, Canada, 76-77 & Ohio Chamber Orch, 81- *Teaching:* Asst prof music, Ithaca Col, 60-67 & Morehead State Univ, 67-68; instr violin, Nat Music Camp, Interlochen, Mich, 81- *Mailing Add:* 2812 Corydon Rd Cleveland OH 44118

ANDRUS, DONALD GEORGE
COMPOSER, EDUCATOR
b Seattle, Wash, Sept 13, 35. *Study:* Univ Wash, with John Verrall, MA(music), 60; Univ Ill, with Kenneth Gaburo & Lejaren Hiller, DMA, 68; Inst Sonologie, Rijksuniv, Utrecht, Holland, 63-64; Ctr Comput Res Music & Acoustics, Stanford Univ, 76. *Works:* PSSSH, perf by Univ Ill, 65 & 69; The Aardvark Shuffle, comn by Bertram Turetzky, 74 & 79; Space Dust ... with Bird?, perf by Univ Ill, 77; Imbrications for Four Performers, Lingua Press, 77; Undersokelser, 80 & Searchings II, 82-83, comn by Shanley; Dedication Clang, NY Univ Fest, 83. *Teaching:* Instr music, Univ Ill, 66-68; assoc prof music & dir electronic music studio, Calif State Univ, Long Beach, 68- *Awards:* Fulbright Grant, Inst Sonologie, Utrecht, Holland, 63-64. *Mem:* Am Soc Univ Comp (region co-chmn & mem nat coun, 83-); Nat Asn Comp. *Publ:* Contribr, Notes, Music Libr Asn, 83. *Mailing Add:* 21516 Encina Rd Topanga CA 90290

ANDY, KATJA
PIANO
Study: Hochschule Musik, Cologne; studied theory & comp with Wilhelm Mahler & with Alfred Cortot; Sorbonne. *Pos:* Soloist & mem, Edwin Fischer's Chamber Orch. *Teaching:* Prin asst, Edwin Fischer's master classes, Berlin & Lucerne; chmn piano dept, DePaul Univ, formerly; mem fac piano, New England Consv, currently. *Mailing Add:* New England Consv 290 Huntington Rd Boston MA 02115

ANELLO, JOHN-DAVID
CONDUCTOR & MUSIC DIRECTOR
Study: With Otto Semper, 27-30; Univ Wis, 31-35; studied with Foca di Leo, 31-33 & Giuseppe Balestrieri, 31-40; Wis Consv Music, teacher's cert, 35; studied with Nicolai Malko, 47-49 & Arthur Rodzinski, 50. *Pos:* Founder, artistic dir & cond, Florentine Opera Co, Milwaukee, 33-75, consult, currently; founder, Milwaukee Pops Orch, 48, cond, Music Under the Stars, Summer Series, Milwaukee Symph Orch, 68-; admin positions, Milwaukee Opera Theatre, 48-52, Nat Opera Fest, 48-49; Jackson Opera Co, Mich, 50-52 & Int Friendship Gardens, Michigan City, 51-52; dir, UN People to People Concerts, 62-; guest cond, Teatr Wielki, Lodz, Poland, 75-76 & Panstowa Opera, Wrockloaw, Poland, 78. *Teaching:* Pub sch, Milwaukee, 33-50. *Awards:* Civic Music Asn Award, 71; Pro Mundi Dipl & Medal, Brazilian Acad Humanities, 75. *Mem:* Nat Civic Music Asn; Milwaukee Musicians Asn. *Mailing Add:* 4420 W Vliet St Milwaukee WI 53208

ANGARANO, ANTHONY
CRITIC, ADMINISTRATOR
b Winsted, Conn, Nov 30, 38. *Study:* Boston Univ, BA, 61; Univ Conn, MA, 65; Berkshire Music Ctr, with Phyllis Curtin, 70; private piano studies for 14 yrs. *Pos:* Prog writer, Conn Opera Asn, 79-; music critic, The Hartford Courant, 82-; mgr, Arioso String Ens. *Mem:* Chamber Music Am. *Mailing Add:* PO Box 136 New Hartford CT 06057

ANGELINI, LOUIS A
COMPOSER, EDUCATOR
b Utica, NY, June 13, 35. *Study:* Ithaca Col, BM, 59; Eastman Sch Music, with Bernard Rogers, MM, 60, PhD, 68; Domaine Sch Cond, with Pierre Monteux, cert, 61; Berkshire Music Ctr, with Witold Lutoslawski & Lucas Foss, cert, 62; Inst Int Educ, with Luigi Nono & Franco Evangelisti, cert, 65. *Works:* Music for Chamber Orchestra, Eastman Summer Symph, 58; Poems & Dances, Utica Symph Orch, 65; Two Graphs for Strings, Lincoln Youth Orch Strings, Nebr, 67-68; Silver Fountain (flute), Syracuse Symph Orch, 77; The Death and Resurrection of BJCM, Utica Col Prog Original Musical Theatre, 78; Do Not Go Gentle Into That Good Night, Mount Union Col Choir, 81; FESTA!, Utica Col Prog Original Musical Theatre, 82. *Teaching:* From asst prof to prof music, Utica Col, Syracuse Univ, 70- *Awards:* Koussevitsky Prize Comp, Berkshire Music Ctr, 62; Contemp Music Proj Fel Comp, Ford Found, 67-68; Utica Col Fac Grants Comp, 73, 75 & 79. *Mem:* Col Music Soc. *Mailing Add:* Snowden Hill Rd New Hartford NY 13413

ANIEVAS, AGUSTIN
PIANO, EDUCATOR
b New York, NY. *Study:* Juilliard Sch Music, with Adele Marcus, BS, 58, MS, 59. *Teaching:* Prof & chmn piano music, Consv Music, Brooklyn Col, 74. *Awards:* Dimitri Mitropoulos Int First Prize; Michaels Mem Award; Conct Artists Guild Debut Award. *Mailing Add:* 142 Rugby Rd Brooklyn NY 11226

ANNIS, ROBERT LYNDON
CLARINET, EDUCATOR
Study: New England Consv, BM; Univ Southern Calif, MM. *Pos:* Clarinet, San Antonio Symph, 71-73; clarinet, Collage Inc, Boston, 76-, exec dir, 79-82. *Teaching:* Instr clarinet, Brown Univ, 77-; instr clarinet, New England Consv, 78-, dir, Summer Sch, 78-80. *Mem:* Nat Acad Rec Arts & Sci. *Mailing Add:* 2350 Broadway #419 New York NY 10024

ANSBACHER, CHARLES ALEXANDER
CONDUCTOR & MUSIC DIRECTOR, EDUCATOR
b Burlington, Vt, Oct 5, 41. *Study:* Brown Univ, BA(music), 65; Col-Consv Music, Univ Cincinnati, MM & DMA, 79. *Pos:* Cond & music dir, Middletown Symph Orch, Ohio, 67-70, Ball State Univ Symph, 68-70, Colorado Springs Symph Orch, 70- & Young Artists Orch Denver, 81- *Teaching:* Asst prof music, Univ Colo, Colorado Springs, 77- *Awards:* White House Fel, 76-77. *Mem:* Am Symph Orch League (bd mem, 79-81 & pres, Cond Guild, 79-81); Colo Coun Arts & Humanities. *Rep:* Colorado Springs Symph Box 1692 Colorado Springs CO 80901. *Mailing Add:* 1431 N Tejon St Colorado Springs CO 80907

ANSTINE, GEORGIA REBECCA
HARP
b York, Pa, Dec 5, 55. *Study:* Dickinson Col, BA, 77; Tanglewood Inst, with Lucile Lawrence; Peabody Consv, with Jeanne Chalifoux, MM(harp), 79; Salzedo Summer Harp Colony, with Alice & Jeanne Chalifoux. *Pos:* Prin harp, Kennedy Ctr Opera House Orch, 80-, Washington Opera, 80- & New World Players, Washington, DC, 82. *Mailing Add:* 5850 Cameron Run Terr #107 Alexandria VA 22303

ANTHONY, JAMES RAYMOND
EDUCATOR, WRITER
b Providence, RI, Feb 18, 22. *Study:* Columbia Univ, BS, 46, MA, 48; Univ Paris, La Sorbonne, dipl, 51; Univ Southern Calif, PhD, 64. *Teaching:* Instr, Univ Mont, 48-50; from asst prof to prof harpsichord & musicol, Univ Ariz, 52-; vis prof musicol, Ind Univ, 81. *Awards:* Creative Teaching Award, Univ Ariz, 80. *Mem:* Am Musicol Soc; Soc Francaise Musicol. *Interests:* French baroque music. *Publ:* Auth, French Baroque Music, W W Norton, 74, French transl, Flammarion, 81; Church Music in France: 1661-1750, In: New Oxford Hist Music, 75; over 40 articles, In: New Grove Dict of Music & Musicians, 81; ed, Michel-Richard Delalande's De Profundis, NC Press, Chapel Hill, 81. *Mailing Add:* 800 N Wilson Ave Tucson AZ 85719

ANTOKOLETZ, ELLIOTT MAXIM
EDUCATOR
b Jersey City, NJ, Aug 3, 42. *Study:* Juilliard Sch Music, studied violin with Delay & Galamian, 60-65; Hunter Col, City Univ New York, studied musicol with H W Hitchcock, BA, 68, MA, 70; Grad Ctr, City Univ New York, studied musicol with George Perle, PhD, 75. *Teaching:* Lectr theory & chamber music, Queens Col, City Univ New York, 73-76; assoc prof musicol, Univ Tex, Austin, 76- *Awards:* Nat Endowment Humanities Grant, 80; Bela Bartok Mem Award, Hungary, 81; Am Musicol Soc Grant, 82. *Mem:* Am Musicol Soc; Int Alban Berg Soc; Music Theory Soc; Soc Ethnomusicol; Col Music Soc. *Publ:* Auth, Principles of Pitch Organization in Bartok's Fourth String Quartet, 77 & Verdi's Dramatic Use of Harmony and Tonality in Macbeth, 79, In Theory Only; The Musical Language of Bartok's 14 Bagatelles for Piano, Tempo, 81; Pitch-Set Derivations from the Folk Modes in Bartok's Music, Studia Musicol, 82; The Music of Bela Bartok: A Study of Tonality and Progression in 20th Century Music, Univ Calif Press, 83. *Mailing Add:* 2802 Horseshoe Bend Cove Austin TX 78704

ANTONIOU, THEODORE
COMPOSER, CONDUCTOR & MUSIC DIRECTOR
b Athens, Greece, Feb 10, 35; US citizen. *Study:* Nat Consv Greece, dipl(violin), 56, dipl(theory), 58; Greek Consv, with Manolis Kalomiris & Yannis A Papaioannou, dipl(comp & orch), 61; Hochschule Musik, Munich, with Adolph Mennerich & Günther Bialas, dipl(comp & cond), 64; Siemens Studio Electronic Music, with Josef Riedl, dipl, 65; Int Music Courses, Darmstadt, with Boulez, Berio, Stockhausen & Ligeti. *Works:* Events II (orch), 69, Casandra (dancers & orch), 70, Nenikikamen (sop, bar, choir & orch), 72, Fluxus I (orch), Double Concerto for Percussion and Orchestra, 78, Circle of Thanatos and Genesis (tenor, choir & orch), 81 & Periander (opera), 83, Bärenreiter. *Pos:* Dir orch, City Athens, Greece, 66-67; cond, Philadelphia Musical Acad Symph Orch, 70 & 75; dir, Alea III, Boston, 79. *Teaching:* Comp in res & vis prof comp & orch, Stanford Univ, 69-70, prof drama, 76; comp in res, Berkshire Music Ctr, 69, comp, cond & asst dir contemp activ, 74-; comp in res, Univ Utah, 70 & 72; prof comp & dir, New Music Group, Philadelphia Col Perf Arts, 70-; guest prof comp, Univ Pa, 78; prof, Boston Univ, 79- *Awards:* Richard Strauss Prize, City Munich, 64; Premio Ondas (for Cassandra), Radio-TV, Barcelona, 70; Prix, Councours Int Guitare (for Stichomythia II), 78. *Bibliog:* Nickolas Slonimsky (auth), New Music in Greece, In: Contemporary Music in Europe, W W Norton, 68; D Chittum (auth), Antoniou Roads to Philadelphia, Sunday Star, Washington, DC, 4/16/72; D & B Rosenberg (auth), The Music Makers, Columbia Univ Press, 79. *Mailing Add:* 855 Commonwealth Ave Boston MA 02215

ANWYL, MARGERY MACKAY See MacKay, Margery

APOSTLE, NICHOLAS
OBOE & ENGLISH HORN
b Kenton, Ohio, May 24, 30. *Study:* Ohio State Univ, BS, 52; Columbia Teachers Col, MA, 55; Nat Orch Asn, 54-55; Berkshire Music Ctr, 55. *Pos:* First oboist, Boston Pops Tour, 55- & Radio City Music Hall Orch, 56-62; Broadway Theatre, Westbury Music Fair, 62-75; oboist & English horn, Long Island Symph, 76-82. *Teaching:* Music consult instrm music, Oyster Bay East Norwich Sch Dist, NY, 63-; private oboe instr, Nassau Community Col, 70- *Mailing Add:* 84 Muttontown Rd Syosset NY 11791

APPELMAN, RALPH
BASS, EDUCATOR
b Eau Claire, Wis, Feb 9, 08. *Study:* Northwestern Univ, BME, 34, MMus, 40; Ind Univ, PhD, 53. *Roles:* Gurnemahz in Parsifal, Ind Univ Opera Theatre (18 perf), 52-73; Tohy in Happy Fella, Ind Univ Opera Theatre, Memphis Opera Theatre & Texas State, Lubbock, 67; King Phillipe in Don Carlos, Ind Univ Opera Theatre, 68; Boris in Boris Godunov, Memphis Opera Theatre & Ind Univ Opera Theatre, 68; Pizarro in Fidelio, Cincinnati Symph Orch, 69; Mefistofele in Mefistofele, 71 & Hans Sachs in Meistersinger, 73, Ind Univ Opera Theatre. *Teaching:* Dir music, State Teachers Col, Kearney, Nebr, 34-39; head consv music, Westminster Consv, 40-42; assoc prof voice, NTex State, Denton, 45-51; prof voice, Ind Univ, Bloomington, 51-78, emer prof, 79- *Mem:* Nat Asn Teachers Singing (chmn vocal res, 60-68); Am Acad Teachers Singing. *Publ:* Auth, Science of Vocal Pedagogy, Ind Univ Press, 67; Is It So, Why Is It So, To What Extent Is It So? 68 & Whither Vocal Pedagogy? 69, Nat Asn Teachers Singing. *Mailing Add:* 5168 Sunnybrook Ct Cape Coral FL 33904

APPERT, DONALD LAWRENCE
TROMBONE, TEACHER
b Moses Lake, Wash, Jan 2, 53. *Study:* New England Consv, trombone with Ronald Barron & John Coffey, cond with Richard Pittman, BMus, 75, MMus, 77. *Pos:* Prin trombone, Va Orch Asn, 78-83 & Va Orch Group, 79-83; second trombone, Kansas City Symph, 83- *Teaching:* Instr music, Hampton Inst, 78- *Mem:* Int Trombone Asn; ASCAP; Col Music Soc; Tidewater Comp Guild (secy, 79-82, pres, 82-83). *Mailing Add:* 2500 W 6th St #305 Lawrence KS 66044

APPLEBAUM, EDWARD
COMPOSER, EDUCATOR
b Los Angeles, Calif, Sept 28, 37. *Study:* Univ Calif, Los Angeles, with Henri Lazarof & Lukas Foss; studied with Ingvar Lidholm. *Works:* The Frieze of Life (one-act opera); Times Three (flute choir & perc); Foci (viola & piano), 71; Piano Trio, 72; Face in the Cameo (clarinet & piano); Stemmen (sop, cello & piano); When Dreams Do Show Thee Me (clarinet, cello, piano, chamber chorus & orch), 72. *Teaching:* Mem fac, Calif State Univ, Long Beach, 68-71; assoc prof theory & analysis & comp, Univ Calif, Santa Barbara, 71- *Awards:* Grants, Am-Scand Found & Rockefeller Found; ASCAP Awards. *Mailing Add:* 226 Selrose Lane Santa Barbara CA 93109

APPLEBAUM, SAMUEL
LECTURER, VIOLIN
b Passaic, NJ, Jan 15, 04. *Study:* Inst Musical Art; Juilliard Sch Music, BM, 23; Columbia Univ; Gettysburgh Col, Hon Dr Music, 76; Southwestern Univ, Hon Dr Music, 78. *Rec Perf:* Ten lectures, Golden Crest; film ser, Belwin-Mills & Univ Wis. *Pos:* Ed, Strad Mag London, 40-74. *Teaching:* Fac mem, Manhattan Sch Music, 56-, Fairleigh Dickinson Univ, 68- & Kean Col, 73-75. *Awards:* Teacher of Yr, Am String Teachers Asn, 67. *Mem:* Music Educr Asn (pres NJ chap, 50-58); Am Fedn Music Clubs (vpres NJ chap, 45-49); Soc Music Arts (pres NJ chap, 81-). *Publ:* Auth, over 450 study books & coauth, twelve text books, Paganiniana Press, 54- *Mailing Add:* 23 N Terr Maplewood NJ 07040

APPLEBAUM, STAN (STANLEY S)
COMPOSER, WRITER
b Newark, NJ. *Study:* Studied comp with Stephan Wolpe, Wallingford Reigger & Tibor Serly; studied cond with Leon Barzin. *Works:* Creative Rhythmic Reading at the Piano, Schroeder & Gunther, 72; Marrakech Bazaar (suite), 73 & Toboggan Ride (symph band), 74, Chappell Inc; Sound World (piano folio), Schroeder & Gunther, 74; Double play, (piano four hands), 76 & Frenzy (piano conct piece), 78, Alexander Broude, 78. *Pos:* Artist & repertoire dir, Warner Brothers Rec, 58-62. *Awards:* Clio Award, 58; Int Broadcasting Award, Hollywood Radio & TV Soc, 59. *Publ:* Coauth, A Not So Ugly Friend, Holt, Reinhardt & Winston, 73; The Flying Janitor, 73, Nature's Carpet Sweeper, 73 & The Knight in Crusty Armor, 73, Golden Press; Going My Way?, Harcourt, Brace & Jovanovich, 75. *Mailing Add:* 330 W 58th St New York NY 10019

APPLEBY, DAVID P
EDUCATOR, PIANO
b Belo Horizonte, Brazil, Oct 16, 25; US citizen. *Study:* Univ NC, BA; Southern Methodist Univ, with Paul van Katwijk, BM, 48, MA, 49; Ind Univ, with Bela Boszormenyi Nagy, PhD, 56. *Teaching:* Chmn piano dept, Houston Baptist Univ, 65-69; mem fac theory & piano, Morehead State Univ, 69-71; prof music & piano, Eastern Ill Univ, 71- *Awards:* Outstanding Fac Merit Award, Eastern Ill Univ, 82; Nat Endowment for Humanities Grant, 83. *Mem:* Music Teachers Nat Asn; Ill Music Teachers Asn. *Interests:* Music of Brazil. *Publ:* Auth, History of Church Music, Moody Press, 66; The Music of Brazil, Univ Tex Press, 83; articles on Brazilian music in Latin Am Music Rev, Piano Quart & others. *Mailing Add:* 1020 Williamsburg Dr Charleston IL 61920

APPLETON, CLYDE ROBERT
EDUCATOR
b Climax Springs, Mo, Nov 21, 28. *Study:* Park Col, BA, 54; Univ Ariz, MMusEd, 57; NY Univ, PhD, 71. *Teaching:* Asst prof music, Shaw Univ, 62-66, Western Carolina Univ, 66-70; Purdue Univ, 73-78; assoc prof creative arts, Univ NC, Charlotte, 78- *Mem:* Music Educr Nat Conf; Soc Ethnomusicol; Col Music Soc. *Publ:* Auth, Black and White in the Music of American Youth, New York Univ Educ Quart, 73; Where Do We Start? We Start at the Beginning, NAJE Educ, 74; Singing in the Streets of Raleigh, 1963, Black Perspective Music, 75. *Mailing Add:* 2010-3 Canterwood Dr Charlotte NC 28213

APPLETON, JON H
COMPOSER, EDUCATOR
b Los Angeles, Calif, Jan 4, 39. *Study:* Reed Col, BA, 61; Univ Ore, MA, 65; Columbia-Princeton Electronic Music Ctr, 66. *Works:* Chef d'Oeuvre, Folkway Rec, 67; Human Music, Flying Dutchman Rec, 70; Winesburgh, Ohio, Philadelphia Comp Forum, 73; String Quartet, 76; In Medias Res, Dartmouth Rec, 78; Sashasonjon (synclavier), Folkway Rec, 82; The Lament of Kamuela, 83. *Pos:* Dir, Stiftelsen Elektronmusikstudion, Sweden, 76-77. *Teaching:* Prof, Dartmouth Col, 67- *Awards:* Fels, Guggenheim, 70, Fulbright, 70 & Nat Endowment Arts, 76 & 80. *Mem:* ASCAP; Col Music Soc; founding mem, Int Confederation Electroacoust Music. *Interests:* Music and computers; digital performance instruments. *Publ:* Auth, Re-evaluating the Principle of Expectation, Perspectives New Music, 69; co-ed, The Development and Practice of Electronic Music, Prentice-Hall, 75; auth, A Special Purpose Digital System for Music, Comput & Humanities, 76; Electronic Music: Questions of Style, Musical Quart, 79. *Mailing Add:* PO Box 50 Hanover NH 03755

ARAD, ATAR
VIOLA, EDUCATOR
b Tel Aviv, Israel, Mar 8, 45. *Study:* Israel Acad Music, artist dipl, 66; La Chapelle Musicale Reine Elisabeth, Belgium, dipl, 72; Consv Royal Musique Bruxelles, dipl superieur, 73. *Rec Perf:* Sonata for Grand Viola and Orch (Paganini), 75, Hoffmeister and Stamitz Concerto, Virtuoso Chamber Music for Viola, 76, Hindemith Sonata Op No 4 76, Mozart Symphonie Concertante, 79 & Schubert Trout, 81, Telefunken. *Pos:* Violist, Cleveland Quartet, 80- *Teaching:* Sr lectr, Royal Northern Col Music, Gt Brit, 75-80; prof viola, Eastman Sch Music, 80- *Awards:* First Prize, Geneva Int Compt Viola, 72. *Mailing Add:* 210 Devonshire Dr Rochester NY 14625

ARAGALL, GIACOMO (JAIME)
TENOR
b Barcelona, Spain, June 6, 39. *Study:* Barcelona Consv; studied with Francisco Puig & Waldimiro Badiali. *Rec Perf:* On Decca. *Roles:* Gaston in Gerusalemmo, Teatro la Fenice, 63; Fritz in L'amico Fritz, La Scala, 63-64; Duke of Mantua in Rigoletto, Covent Garden, 66; Rodolfo in La Boheme; Pinkerton in Madama Butterfly; Cavaradossi in Tosca; Alfredo Germont in La Traviata. *Pos:* Appeared with maj co incl Milan La Scala, Covent Garden, Munich Staatsoper, Vienna Staatsoper, Metropolitan Opera, Philadelphia Lyr Opera & San Francisco Opera. *Awards:* Winner, Busseto Singing Compt, 63; Medallia de oro, Teatro del Liceo, Barcelona; Prize Piemonte, Teatro Regio, Turin. *Mailing Add:* c/o Lombardo Assoc 1 Harkness Plaza 61 W 62nd Suite 6F New York NY 10023

ARANT, (EVERETT) PIERCE, JR
MUSIC DIRECTOR, TENOR
b Orangeburg, SC, Dec 3, 38. *Study:* Wofford Col, AB, 61; Converse Col, 61-62; Yale Univ, MMus, 64; Univ Ga, EdD, 70. *Rec Perf:* Gates of Justice (Dave Brubeck), SC Educ TV, 76; Community Christmas Celebration, Ga Educ TV & SECA-TV, 77-82; Concert Choir in Concert, Crest Rec, 80; Univ Ga Men's Glee Club in Concert, 81 & Heaven is Music, 82, Ga Educ TV & Crest Rec. *Teaching:* Assoc prof voice, dir choral activ & dir, Men's Glee Club Conct Choir, Univ Ga, 66- *Awards:* Fac Serv Award, Univ Ga Alumni Soc, 83. *Mem:* Nat Asn Teachers Singing (state vpres, 72-74, state pres, 74-76); Intercol Musical Coun (mem bd dir, 72-81, vpres, 81-); Music Educr Nat Conf; Am Choral Dir Asn; Ga Music Educr Asn. *Publ:* Auth, Report of the American Choral Directors Association Committee on the Male Chorus—Objective: To Increase the Participation of Boys and Men In Singing, Choral J, 83. *Mailing Add:* 500 Brookwood Dr Athens GA 30605

ARBIZU, RAY LAWRENCE
TENOR, EDUCATOR
b Phoenix, Ariz, Aug 10, 29. *Study:* Ariz State Univ, BA, 52, MA, 55; Univ Southern Calif, 56-60; Acedemie Musik, Vienna, 60-61. *Roles:* Othello, Bonn Opera Co, 62; Canio in Pagliacci, Köln Oper, 63; Lucia di Lammermoor, Essen Oper, 65; Cavaradossi in Tosca, Am Nat Opera, 67; Duke in Rigoletto, Deutsche Oper Am Rhine, 67; Il Trovatore, Bremen Oper, 67; Don Jose in Carmen, Chicago Grant Park Series, 68. *Pos:* Lead tenor, Bonn Opera Co, 62-65, Essen Opera Co, 65-67 & Am Nat Opera Co, 67-68. *Teaching:* Asst prof voice, Northern Ariz Univ, 68-70; assoc prof, Brigham Young Univ, 70- *Awards:* Fulbright Scholar, 60. *Mem:* Nat Asn Teachers Singing; Music Educr Nat Conf. *Mailing Add:* 661 W 700 N Orem UT 84057

ARBTITER, ERIC A
BASSOON, EDUCATOR
b Yonkers, NY, July 1, 50. *Study:* Oberlin Consv Music, BM, 72; Cleveland Inst Music, MM, 74. *Pos:* Solo bassoon, Ohio Chamber Orch, 72-75; prin bassoon, Ft Wayne Phil, 73-74; assoc prin bassoon, Houston Symph Orch, 74- *Teaching:* Artist-teacher bassoon, Shepherd Sch Music, Rice Univ, 76- *Awards:* Pi Kappa Lambda. *Mailing Add:* c/o Shepherd Sch Music Rice Univ Houston TX 77251

ARCHER, MARY ANN
FLUTE & PICCOLO
b Coco Solo, Panama Canal Zone, Oct 23, 49. *Study:* Col Consv Music, Univ Cincinnati, BMus, 72; Cath Univ Am, MMus, 77; study with Julius Baker, Jack Wellbaum, James Pappoutsakis, Britten Johnson & William Herbert. *Pos:* Prin flute, Va Phil, 72-77; second flute & piccolo, Metropolitan Opera Orch, 77- *Mailing Add:* 418 Van Buren St Ridgewood NJ 07450

ARCHIBALD, BRUCE
COMPOSER, EDUCATOR
b White Plains, NY, May 2, 33. *Study:* Cornell Univ, with Robert Palmer, Hunter Johnson & Karel Husa, 51-57; Berkshire Music Ctr, with Aaron Copland, 58; Harvard Univ, with Walter Piston & Leon Kirchner, PhD, 65. *Works:* 4 songs on poems of e e cummings (sop, string quartet & piano), 54; String Quartet, Variations, 57; God's Grandeur (male chorus & piano, four hands), 61; What the Thunder Said (cantata for solo bar & eight instrm), 60; Chemquasabamticook, Variations (organ), 71; and works for orch, small ensembles, chorus & piano. *Pos:* Wassataquoik Song (oboe & piano), 71. *Teaching:* Mem fac, Amherst Col, 63-67; prof theory & analysis & comp, Temple Univ, 67- *Awards:* BMI Prize, 54; Friends of Music Award, 56; Fels Found Grant, 62-63. *Mem:* Am Musicol Soc (coun mem, 71-73); Col Music Soc; Soc Music Theory; Int Alban Berg Soc (secy-treas, 73-77). *Publ:* Articles & reviews in Musical Quart, Perspectives of New Music, Opera News, Notes of the Music Libr Asn, The Music Rev & Grove Dict of Music & Musicians. *Mailing Add:* 421 Wyndon Rd Ambler PA 19002

ARCHIBEQUE, CHARLENE P
CONDUCTOR & MUSIC DIRECTOR, EDUCATOR
b Mt Sterling, Ohio, July 15, 35. *Study:* Consv Music, Oberlin Col; Univ Mich, BME, 57; San Diego State Col, MA, 65; Univ Colo, DMA, 69. *Rec Perf:* Den Haag Int Choral Fest, 73; New York Int Choral Fest, 74; seven rec with San Jose State Univ Choir & Choraliers, 70-80. *Pos:* Cond, Calif Bay Area Chorales, formerly; dir music, First Presby Church, Burlingame, Calif, 73-82; choral dir, San Jose Symph, Calif, 75- *Teaching:* Prof choral cond & lit & dir choral activ, San Jose State Univ, 70-; staff mem, Aspen Music Fest, 78 & 80. *Awards:* First place, Int Choral Fest, Den Haag, 73; Gold Medal, Int Collegiate Choral Fest, Mexico City, 80. *Mem:* Music Educr Nat Conf; Am Choral Dir Asn. *Mailing Add:* 1201 Weymoth Dr Cupertino CA 95104

ARDEN, DAVID MITCHELL
MUSIC DIRECTOR, PIANO
b Los Angeles, Calif, Sept 6, 49. *Study:* Peabody Inst Music, with Lucy Brown, 69-71; Royal Flemish Music Consv, with Frederic Gevers, prem prix & conct dipl, 74; Musikhochschule, Cologne, with Aloys Kontarsky, 76-78. *Rec Perf:* Piano Recital, NHK, Tokyo, 80; Music by Kienman and Crumb, British Broadcasting Corp, London, 82. *Pos:* Music dir, NY Shakespeare Fest Prod, Wake Up, It's Time to Go to Bed, 78-79; piano soloist, Am Ballet Theater, New York, 81- *Teaching:* Prof piano, Univ Calif, San Diego, 79-80. *Awards:* Tento-Young Virtuoso's Prize, Belgian Radio & TV Compt, Brussels, 74; Kranichsteiner Prize, Darmstadt Summer Course Mod Music, Germany, 76; First Prize, Gandeamus Compt Interpreters Mod Music, Rotterdam, Holland, 81. *Mailing Add:* 4255 54th Pl San Diego CA 92115

ARDOYNO, DOLORES
ADMINISTRATOR
b Mobile, Ala, Sept 23, 21. *Study:* Webster Col, 39-41; Springhill Col, 44; St Louis Univ, 44-45; Loyola Univ, 51-52. *Pos:* Asst prod coordr western div, ABC-TV, Los Angeles, 50-54; publicity dir, Petit Theatre, 55-58; dir radio & TV div, Whitlock, Swigart & Evans Advert Co, New Orleans, 57-60; owner & dir, PR Serv New Orleans, 60-68; mgr, New Orleans Summer Pops Orch, 60-66; dir pub relations, New Orleans Opera, 68-71; gen mgr, Opera South, Jackson, Miss, 71-80 & Baton Rouge Opera, 81- *Mailing Add:* Baton Rouge Opera PO Box 103 Baton Rouge LA 70821

ARGANBRIGHT, NANCY (NANCY WEEKLEY)
PIANO, EDUCATOR
b Georgetown, Ind. *Study:* Sch Music, Ind Univ, BM(piano), 57; Univ Wis, MS, 71. *Pos:* Mem, Weekley & Arganbright, conct tours, 65. *Teaching:* Instr piano, Huntington Col, 57-64; lectr music, Univ Wis, La Crosse, 74- *Interests:* Original music for one piano, four hands; transcription for four hands. *Rep:* Karlsrud Concerts 948 The Parkway Mamaroneck NY 10543. *Mailing Add:* 1532 Madison St La Crosse WI 54601

ARGENTO, DOMINICK
COMPOSER, EDUCATOR
b York, Pa, Oct 27, 27. *Study:* Peabody Consv Music, studied comp with Nicolas Nabakov, Vittorio Rietti & Henry Cowell, BM, 51, MM, 54; Consv Cherubini, Florence, 51-52; Eastman Sch Music, studied comp with Bernard Rogers, Howard Hanson & Alan Hovhaness, PhD, 57. *Works:* Divertimento (piano & strings), 54; Masque of Angels (opera), 63; Homage to the Queen of Tonga (small orch), 64; Trio Carmina Paschalia (women's voices, guitar & harp), 70; Jonah and the Whale (opera), 74; The Voyage of Edgar Allan Poe (opera), 76; A Ring of Time: In Praise of Music, Seven Songs for Orchestra, 77; and others. *Pos:* Co-founder, Ctr Opera, Minneapolis & Hilltop Opera, Baltimore. *Teaching:* Fac mem, Hampton Inst, 52-55; Regents prof music, Univ Minn, Minneapolis, 58- *Awards:* ASCAP Award, 73; Nat Endowment Arts Grant, 74, 75 & 76; Pulitzer Prize, 75. *Mem:* ASCAP; Am Acad & Inst Arts & Lett. *Mailing Add:* Dept Music Univ Minn Minneapolis MN 55455

ARLEN, WALTER
EDUCATOR, CRITIC
b Vienna, Austria; US citizen. *Study:* Peabody Consv Music, BS(music educ), 51; Univ Calif, Los Angeles, MA(music), 55; study with Leo Sowerby, 3 yrs & Roy Harris, 4 yrs. *Pos:* Asst music critic, Los Angeles Times, 52-70, staff writer music, 70- *Teaching:* Prof music hist & criticism, Loyola Marymount Univ, Los Angeles, 68-; dir, Am Acad Arts, Veroria, Italy, 74-75. *Mem:* Nat Asn Comp & Cond (first vpres, 60-); Nat Fedn Music Clubs. *Interests:* Twentieth-century music. *Publ:* Articles in Musical Am, 50's & Opera News, 60's; reviews in Los Angeles Times, 50's, 60's, 70's & 80's. *Mailing Add:* Loyola Blvd at W 80th St Los Angeles CA 90045

ARLIN, MARY IRENE
EDUCATOR, VIOLA
b Lyons, NY, June 26, 39. *Study:* Ithaca Col, BS, 61; Ind Univ, MM, 65, PhD, 72. *Pos:* Prin viola, Elmira Symph, 77-81; viola, Binghamton Symph, 79. *Teaching:* Grad asst theory, Ind Univ, 63-66; prof, Ithaca Col, 66- *Mem:* Music Theory Soc NY (secy, 73-); Sigma Alpha Iota (Eta province vpres, 75-); Pi Kappa Lambda (mem bd regents, 80-84); Soc Music Theory; Am Viola Soc. *Publ:* Coauth & ed, Music Sources, Prentice-Hall, 79; auth, Fetis' Contribution to Historical & Practical Theory, Revue Belge Musicologie, 72-73; Francois-Joseph Fetis: Esquisse de l'Histoire de l'Harmonie, Inst Mediaeval Music. *Mailing Add:* 623 Utica St Ithaca NY 14850

ARMER, ELINOR FLORENCE
COMPOSER, TEACHER
b Oakland, Calif, Oct 6, 39. *Study:* Mills Col, comp with Darius Milhaud & Leon Kirchner & piano with Alexander Libermann, BA, 61; Calif State Univ, San Francisco, studied comp with Roger Nixon, MA, 72. *Works:* Spin Earth (SATB & organ), Lawson-Gould, Inc, 74; Thaw (piano solo), comn & perf by Lois Brandy, 75-83; Denim Blues (ms & eight instrm), comn & perf by Bettina Jonic, 78; The Golden Ring (tenor & nine instrm), comn & perf by John Duykers & Port Costa Players, 78; Recollections & Revel (cello & piano), comn & perf by Bonnie Hampton & Nathan Schwartz, 78-82; Proportions (SAA, flute & bassoon), perf by Veil of Isis, 81-83; String Quartet, comn by San Francisco Chamber Music Soc, 83. *Teaching:* Dir music prog, Katherine Branson Sch, Ross, Calif, 65-68; instr musicianship, comp & piano, Prep Dept, San Francisco Consv, 69-75, comp, harmony & orch, Undergrad & Grad Dept, 76-; lectr, musicianship, harmony & piano, Univ Calif, Berkeley, 74-76. *Awards:* Standard Awards, ASCAP, 74-; Norman Fromm Comp Award, San Francisco Chamber Music Soc, 81; Edward MacDowell Found Res, 83. *Mem:* ASCAP. *Mailing Add:* San Francisco Consv Music 1201 Ortega St San Francisco CA 94122

ARMS, MARGARET FAIRCHILD
SOPRANO, TEACHER
b Princeton, NJ, Nov 26, 42. *Study:* Wash Music Inst, 67-73; Sch Music, Cath Univ, 73-75; studied voice with Winifred Hartman, 77-82. *Pos:* Solo recitalist, womansong, 82- *Teaching:* Private instr voice, 73-; instr, Wash Musical Inst, 74-75. *Mem:* Nat Asn Teachers Singing; Am Women Comp; Int League Women Comp. *Mailing Add:* 7275 Swan Rd Colorado Springs CO 80908

ARMSTRONG, ANTON EUGENE
CONDUCTOR, EDUCATOR
b New York, NY, Apr 26, 56. *Study:* St Olaf Col, with Kenneth Jennings, BMus, 78; Univ Ill, with Harold A Decker, MMus, 80; Mich State Univ, with Charles K Smith. *Pos:* Dir, Albemarle, Princeton, NJ, 80-; cond, Calvin Col Alumni Choir, 81-, St Cecilia Youth Chorale, Grand Rapids, Mich, 81- & Grand Rapids Symph Choir, 82-; guest cond, Univ Ill Summer Youth Music Jr High Chorus, 82. *Teaching:* Instr music, Calvin Col, 80- *Mem:* Am Choral Dir Asn; Col Music Soc; Choristers Guild. *Mailing Add:* 3441 Newcastle SE Grand Rapids MI 49508

ARMSTRONG, HELEN (HELEN ARMSTRONG GEMMELL)
VIOLIN, TEACHER & COACH
b Rockford, Ill. *Study:* Juilliard Sch, with Ivan Galamian & Dorothy DeLay, BS, 65, MS, 66. *Rec Perf:* Sonata (William Walton), 78, Sonata and Concertante (Alan Rawsthorne), 78, Musical Heritage Soc. *Pos:* Soloist, Boston Symph, 76-, Indianapolis Symph, 77- & Martha Graham Dance Co, 77- *Teaching:* Coach & teacher violin, Mozartina Musical Arts Consv, 77 & State Univ NY, Purchase, 80- *Awards:* Young Artist Award, Soc Am Musicians, 57 & Nat Fedn Music Clubs, 76; prize winner, Tibor Varga Int Violin Compt, 76. *Mem:* Mu Phi Epsilon (vpres, 77); Am Fedn Musicians; Am Women Comp. *Mailing Add:* c/o ICA Mgt 2219 Eastridge Rd Timonium MD 21093

ARMSTRONG, PETER MCKENZIE
PIANO
b Suffern, NY, Mar 12, 40. *Study:* Harvard Col; Longy Sch Music, dipl, 64; Emerson Col, BMus, 68; Yale Sch Music, MMus(arts), 72, DMA. *Rec Perf:* With Olga Averino. *Pos:* Soloist, Philadelphia Symph Orch, 55; radio broadcasts, Boston; recitalist, Boston, Hartford & various cols. *Teaching:* Lectr music, Trinity Col & Harvard Univ; assoc prof music & Dolores P Bolin chair piano, Midwestern State Univ, 81- *Awards:* Winner, New York Music Educ League Piano Compt, 52. *Rep:* Int Artist Alliance PO Box 131 Springfield VA 22150. *Mailing Add:* Dept Music Midwestern State Univ Wichita Falls TX 76308

ARNATT, RONALD (KENT)
MUSIC DIRECTOR, COMPOSER
b London, England, Jan 16, 30. *Study:* Trinity Col, London, FTCL, 50; Am Guild Organists, FAGO, 52; Durham Univ, England, BMus, 54; Westminister Choir Col, DMus, 70. *Works:* More than 100 compositions for chorus, organ, chorus & brass, organ & brass, publ by Basil Ramsey, Augsburg, Concordia, GIA, Presser, Agape, Belwin-Mills, Flammer & Walton; more than 70 comn works. *Rec Perf:* King of Instruments, Aeolian-Skinner, 68; The Liturgical Year, Christ Church Cathedral Rec, 74. *Pos:* Dir music, Christ Church Cathedral, St Louis, Mo, 54-80; music dir & cond, Bach Soc St Louis, Mo, 74-80. *Teaching:* Instr & lectr, Am Univ, 51-54; dir music, Mary Inst, St Louis, Mo, 54-68; prof music, Univ Mo, St Louis, 74-80. *Awards:* ASCAP Standard Awards, 11 yr; Danforth Found Grant, 67; Kindler Found Award, 82. *Mem:* Am Guild Organists (nat counr, 68-71, vpres, 79-); Asn Anglican Musicians (vpres, 71-72, pres, 72-73, mem exec comt, 73-74); Music Comn Diocese Mo (chmn 59-68); ASCAP; Col Music Soc. *Mailing Add:* 417 Lafayette St Salem MA 01970

ARNOLD, CORLISS RICHARD
EDUCATOR, ORGAN
b Monticello, Ark, Nov 7, 26. *Study:* Hendrix Col, BMus, 46; Univ Mich, Ann Arbor, MMus, 48; Union Theol Sem, SMD, 54. *Works:* Fantasy, Chorale and Toccata on Veni Emmanuel, Summy-Birchard, 59; A Child This Day Is Born; Magnificat. *Pos:* Dir music, First Methodist Church, El Dorado, Ark, 48-52 & First Methodist Church, Oak Park, Ill, 54-59. *Teaching:* Instr, Hendrix Col, 46-47; prof music, Mich State Univ, East Lansing, 59- *Awards:* Fulbright Fel, 56-57; fel & choirmaster cert, Am Guild Organists, 59 & 83. *Mem:* Am Guild Organists (nat dir guild student groups, 76-81, regional chmn nat coun, 77-82); Hymn Soc Am; Phi Mu Alpha Sinfonia. *Publ:* Auth, Organ Literature: A Comprehensive Study, Scarecrow Press, 73; A Bird's Eye View of Organ Composition Since 1960, Am Organist, 5/75. *Mailing Add:* 1114 Sunset Lane East Lansing MI 48823

ARNOLD, DAVID
BARITONE
b Atlanta, Ga. *Rec Perf:* Gurrelieder, Philips; Full Moon in March, CRI; The Magic World, Leonarda Rec. *Roles:* Enrico in Lucia di Lammermoor, Metropolitan Opera, 83; Zurga in Pearl Fishers, New York City Opera; Amonasro in Aida, Opera Co Boston; Escamillo in Carmen, Tulsa Opera; Creon in Oedipus Rex, San Francisco Symph; Dandini in La Cenerentola, Va Opera; King in Winter's Tale, San Francisco Opera. *Pos:* Solo baritone with Boston, Chicago, San Francisco, Baltimore, Detroit, Atlanta, Houston & Pittsburgh Symph Orchs; appeared with Spoleto Fest, Italy; toured Austria & Yugaslavia in concert. *Awards:* Gold Debut Award, New York City Opera, 80; Career Grant, Nat Opera Inst. *Mailing Add:* PO Box 345 Roosevelt NJ 08555

ARNOLD, LOUIS
GUITAR, EDUCATOR
Study: Lake Forest Col; Longy Sch Music, studied guitar with John Mavras, Guy Simeone & Hopkinson Smith, sr dipl; Hartt Sch Music, with Oscar Ghiglia, 72; studied guitar & vihuela with Emilio Pujol, 73 & 74; Sch Fine Arts, Banff Ctr, with Alirio Diaz, 77. *Pos:* Performer solo & chamber recitals, Midwest, Spain & Boston. *Teaching:* Instr guitar, Longy Sch Music, Wellesley Col & Boston Consv, currently. *Mailing Add:* Wellesley Col Wellesley MA 02181

ARNOLD, (DONALD) THOMAS
TENOR
b Columbia, Mo, Sept 6, 55. *Study:* Cent Methodist Col, BMus, 79; Univ Mo, Columbia, MM, 82; Peabody Inst Music, currently. *Roles:* Town Crier in Naughty Marietta, Blossom Fest Sch & Cleveland Symph, 80; Romeo in Maddelena, 82 & Torquemada in L'Heure Espagnole, 82, Opera Theatre St Louis. *Pos:* Soloist, Opera Theatre St Louis, 80-; singer, Baltimore Opera Co, 82- *Mem:* Am Guild Musical Artists; Phi Mu Alpha. *Mailing Add:* Peabody Inst Music 1 E Mt Vernon Baltimore MD 21201

ARNON, BARUCH
PIANO, TEACHER
b Novi Sad, Yugoslavia, Aug 26, 31; US citizen. *Study:* Israel Acad Music, dipl, 60; Juilliard Sch Music, MS, 65. *Pos:* Music dir & pianist, Musica da Camera, Westchester Co, NY, 72-80. *Teaching:* Fac mem piano, Israel Acad Music, 60-62; fac mem keyboard studies, Juilliard Sch, 71- *Publ:* Auth, Keyboard Studies at the Juilliard School, Piano Quart, 82. *Mailing Add:* Juilliard Sch Lincoln Ctr New York NY 10023

ARONOFF, FRANCES WEBBER
EDUCATOR, LECTURER
b Columbia, SC, Sept 30, 15. *Study:* Juilliard Sch Music, dipl, 38; Dalcroze Sch Music, New York, lic, 45; Ohio State Univ, BA, 44; Teachers Col, Columbia Univ, MA, 64, EdD, 68. *Teaching:* Fac mem, Juilliard Sch Music, 38-43, 46-47 & 63-67; Dalcroze Sch Music, 50-52; McGill Univ, Montreal, summer 69 & Mills Col Educ, 67-69; prof, NY Univ, 69- *Mem:* Col Music Soc; Music Educr Nat Conf; Int Soc Music Educ; Union Int des Prof de la Rhythmique Jaques-Dalcroze. *Publ:* Auth, Music-Movement Game Strategies, 2/71 & No Age Is Too Early to Begin, 3/74, Music Educ J; Music and Young Children: Expanded Edition, 79 & Move With the Music, 82, Turning Wheel Press. *Mailing Add:* 4 Washington Sq Village New York NY 10012

ARRAU, CLAUDIO
PIANO
b Chillan, Chile, Feb 6, 03. *Study:* Stern Consv, Berlin, with Martin Krause, 12-18. *Rec Perf:* Recorded major piano works of Beethoven, Brahms, Debussy, Liszt, Chopin, Schubert & Schumann. *Pos:* Soloist & pianist with major orchestras worldwide. *Awards:* Liszt Prize, 13 & 14; Ibach Prize, 17; Grand Int Prize, Geneva, 27. *Bibliog:* Donal Henahan (auth), Philadelphians with Arrau, Pianist, New York Times, 2/10/83; Allan Kozin (auth), Arrau, Stagebill, 83. *Mailing Add:* c/o Int Creative Mgt Artists 40 W 57th St New York NY 10019

ARROYO, MARTINA
SOPRANO
b New York, NY, Feb 2, 40. *Study:* With Marinka Gurewich & Martin Rich; Kathryn Long Course, Metropolitan Opera; Opera Wkshp, Hunter Col, City Univ New York, with Josef Turnau, Rose Landver, Hon Dr, 81. *Rec Perf:* Requiem (Verdi), CBS; Les Huguenots, London; La Forza del Destino, Angel; Don Giovanni, Deutsche Grammophon & Philips; I Vespri Siciliani, RCA; Symphony No 8 (Mahler), DGG; Cavalleria Rusticana (in prep); other rec on Columbia, EMI, Decca, Philips, London, Angel, RCA & DGG. *Roles:* First Corifea in L'Assassinio nella cattedrale, Carnegie Hall, 58; Voice from Heaven in Don Carlos, 59; Elsa in Lohengrin, 68 & Santuzza in Cavalleria Rusticana, 78, Metropolitan Opera; Amelia in Un Ballo in maschera, Munich; Liu in Turandot, Can Opera Co, Toronto, 83; Leonora in Il Trovatore, Miami Opera, 83; and others. *Pos:* Sop with maj orchs & opera co in Arg, Australia, Czechoslovakia, France, Germany, Italy, Poland, Switz, UK, US, Yugoslavia, South Am & South Africa; leading sop, Metropolitan Opera, 58-78; soloist & recitalist; trustee, Carnegie Hall, New York. *Teaching:* Mem fac, Music Acad West, currently; teacher master classes, Mozarteum, Salzburg, summer 83. *Awards:* Metropolitan Opera Auditions Winner, 58. *Bibliog:* John Gruen (auth), Martina Arroyo is Back After a Five Year Absence, New York Times, 4/17/83. *Mailing Add:* c/o Thea Dispeker 59 E 54th St New York NY 10022

ARTLEY, MALVIN NEWTON
EDUCATOR
b Newark, NJ, Aug 17, 21. *Study:* Shenandoah Consv Music, BMus, 43; Cincinnati Consv Music, MMus, 47; Chicago Musical Col Roosevelt Univ, DFA, 55. *Teaching:* Assoc prof theory & orch, Bethany Col, 49-53; fac mem, WLiberty State Col, 53-54; dir instr music & orch, Burlington City Sch, 55-65; prof theory, orch & music ed, Elon Col, 65- *Mem:* Nat Sch Orch Asn (treas, 65-69, pres 69-71); charter mem, Am String Teachers Asn (state pres, 68-71); Music Educr Nat Conf; Am Musicol Soc. *Publ:* Auth, Teaching Theory Through the Orchestra, Instrumentalist, 67; String Instrument Repair-Problems and Solutions, Am String Teachers Asn Journal, 73. *Mailing Add:* PO Box 865 Elon College NC 27244

ARTYMIW, LYDIA (TAMARA)
PIANO
b Philadelphia, Pa, Sept 9, 54. *Study:* Philadelphia Col Perf Arts, BM, 73; study with Freda Pastor Berkowitz & Gary Graffman. *Rec Perf:* Variations by Haydn, Mozart, Beethoven & Mendelssohn, 80, Davidsbündlertänze & Humoreske (Schumann), 80, Sonata, Op 58, Rondo, Op, 16, Andante Spianato & Grand Polonaise, Op 22 (Chopin), 81, The Seasons, Op 37a (Tchaikowsky), 82 & Sonata, Op 6 (Mendelssohn), Three Caprices, Op 16 (Mendelssohn), Fantasy, Op 28 (Mendelssohn) & Rondo Capriccioso, Op 14 (Mendelssohn), 83, Chandos, England. *Pos:* Pianist, currently. *Teaching:* Artist in res, Harvard Univ, 76-79. *Awards:* First prize, Chopin Compt, Kosciuszko Found, 72; third prize, Leeds Int Compt, 78. *Bibliog:* Deena Rosenberg (auth), The Music Makers, Columbia Univ Press, 79. *Mailing Add:* c/o Harry Beal Mgt 119 W 57th St New York NY 10019

ARTZT, ALICE JOSEPHINE
GUITAR & LUTE, WRITER
b Philadelphia, Pa, Mar 16, 43. *Study:* Columbia Univ, BA, 65; studied comp with Darius Milhaud & guitar with Julian Bream, Ida Presti & Alexandre Lagoya. *Pos:* Concert guitarist, performing worldwide, 69- *Teaching:* Mannes Col Music, 66-69 & Trenton State Univ, 77-80; Trenton State Univ, 77-80; teach privately, currently. *Bibliog:* M Summerfield (auth), The Classical Guitar, Ashley Mark Publ, 82. *Mem:* Guitar Found Am (mem bd dir, 77-80 & 82-); New York Guitar Soc; Am Lute Soc. *Interests:* Performance practice, Renaissance through the 19th century; use of historic instruments for recordings and concerts. *Publ:* Auth, The Art of Practicing, Musical New Serv, 78; numerous articles in guitar periodicals. *Rep:* H S Green 51 Hawthorne Ave Princeton NJ 08540. *Mailing Add:* 180 Claremont Ave Apt 31 New York NY 10027

ARZRUNI, SAHAN
PIANO, ETHNOMUSICOLOGIST
b Armenian descent, June 8, 43; US citizen. *Study:* Juilliard Sch Music, BM, 67, MS, 68; NY Univ. *Rec Perf:* Children's Music (Khachaturian), 72, Music for Children (Kabalevsky), Music for Children (Bartok), 76, Toccatas for Piano, 76, Complete Sonatas for Piano with Violin (Haydn), 79 & An Anthology of Armenian Piano Music, 81, Musical Heritage Soc; Sonata for Piano Duet & String Quartet (Moross), Varese Sarabande, 81. *Pos:* Chmn, Khachaturian Music Compt, 78- *Awards:* AGBU Manoogian Award, 80. *Mem:* Soc Asian Music (vpres, 80-). *Publ:* Contrib, Armenia, In: The Dict of the Middle Ages, Scribner's Sons, 82; ed, Songs by Women Composers, G Schirmer, 83; contrib, Armenian Music in America, In: New Grove Dict of Music in US, Macmillan, 83. *Rep:* Gurtman & Murtha Assoc 162 W 56 St New York NY 10019. *Mailing Add:* 215 E 80th St #LD New York NY 10021

ASCHAFFENBURG, WALTER (EUGENE)
COMPOSER, EDUCATOR
b Essen, Germany, May 20, 27; US citizen. *Study:* Oberlin Col, BA, 51; Eastman Sch Music, MA, 52; studied comp with Herbert Elwell, Bernard Rogers & Luigi Dallapiccola. *Works:* Ozymandias for Orchestra, MS, 52; The 23rd Psalme, 63, Bartleby (opera), 64 & Three Dances for Orchestra, 67, Theodore Presser Co; Conversations, Six Pieces for Piano, 73, Libertatem Appellant for Tenor, Baritone & Orchestra, 76 & Concertino for Violin, Ten Winds & CB, 82, MS. *Teaching:* Prof comp & music theory, Consv Music, Oberlin Col, 52- *Awards:* Fromm Music Found Award, 53; Guggenheim Fel, 55 & 73; Nat Inst Arts & Lett Award, 66. *Mem:* ASCAP; Am Music Ctr; Am Soc Univ Comp; Soc Music Theory; Cleveland Comp Guild. *Mailing Add:* 49 Shipherd Circle Oberlin OH 44074

ASH, RODNEY P
COMPOSER, EDUCATOR
b Reading, Pa, Jan 2, 31. *Study:* Eastman Sch Music, with Louis Mennini, BM, AMD; Ind Univ, with Bernhard Heiden, MM; Acad Music, Vienna; Univ Ark, with John Cowell. *Works:* Okanagan in Tempera (piano suite); Songs of Experience (song cycle on poems of Blake); Piano Sonata. *Teaching:* Mem fac, Okla State Univ, 58-60; prof music, Western State Col Colo, 60- *Mailing Add:* 3 Commanche Rd Gunnison CO 81230

ASHBROOK, WILLIAM SINCLAIR, JR
EDUCATOR, WRITER
b Philadelphia, Pa, Jan 28, 22. *Study:* Univ Pa, AB, 46; Harvard Univ, AM, 47. *Teaching:* Asst prof humanities, Stephens Col, 49-55; prof, Ind State Univ, Terre Haute, 55-73, chmn humanities dept, 73-74; prof opera & humanities, Philadelphia Col Perf Arts, 74- *Awards:* Prize in Biography, Ind State Auth Day, 65. *Interests:* Nineteenth century Italian opera. *Publ:* Auth, Donizetti, Cassell, 65; The Operas of Puccini, Oxford & Cassell, 69; Donizetti & His Operas, Cambridge Univ Press, 82; contribr, New Grove Dict of Music & Musicians, 6th ed, 82; Opera News & Opera. *Mailing Add:* 310 Barberry Lane Wayne PA 19087

ASHENS, ROBERT J, III
CONDUCTOR, COACH
b Kansas City, Mo, Mar 10, 55. *Study:* Springfield Consv Music, cert, 73; studied piano with Anne Koscielny & Donald Currier, 73-79; Hartt Sch Music, BM, 77; studied cond with Vytautas Marijosius, 76-77 & coaching with Martin Katz, Kurt Klippstatter & Stephen Lord, 80-83. *Pos:* Assoc cond, A Chorus Line, Int Touring Co, 81-82; music dir, Troupers Light Opera, Conn, 82- & Manchester G & S Players, Conn. *Teaching:* Assoc opera coaching, Hartt Sch Music, 77-, music dir, Hartt Musical Theatre, 82- *Mem:* Am Fedn Musicians. *Mailing Add:* 146 Whitman Ave West Hartford CT 06107

ASHFORTH, ALDEN
COMPOSER, EDUCATOR
b New York, NY, May 13, 33. *Study:* Oberlin Col, AB, 58, Consv Music, BMus, 58; Princeton Univ, MFA, 60, PhD, 71; studied comp with Channing Lefebrve, Edward Burlingame Hill, Joseph Wood, Richard Hoffmann, Roger Sessions, Earl Kim & Milton Babbitt. *Works:* Piano Sonata (piano solo), 55; Variations for Orchestra (large orch), 58; Fantasy-Variations (violin & piano), 59; Episodes (chamber concerto for eight instrm), 62-68; Pas Seul (flute solo), 74; The Quintessential Zymurgistic Waffle (electronic music comedy with Paul Reale), 75; Sentimental Waltz (piano solo), C F Peters, 77. *Teaching:* Instr, Princeton Univ, 61, Oberlin Col, 61-65, NY Univ, 65-66 & Manhattan Sch Music, 65; lectr, City Col, City Univ New York, 66-67; asst prof, Univ Calif, Los Angeles, 67-, assoc prof, 72-, coordr, Electronic Music Studio, 69-, prof, 80- *Bibliog:* Malcolm S Cole (auth), Philip Batstone: A Mother Goose Primer and Alden Ashforth (auth), The Unquiet Heart (A Study in Contrast), Perspectives New Music, fall-winter 70; Royal S Brown (auth), Byzantia: Two Journeys After Yeats, High Fidelity Mag, 10/75. *Publ:* Auth, Is Music Just Around the Corner?, Cult Affairs, winter 70; The Relationship of the Sixth in Beethoven's Piano Sonata, Op 110, Music Rev, 5/71; Linear and Textural Aspects of Schoenberg's Cadences, Perspectives New Music, spring-summer 78; Marching with Doc Paulin, Footnote, 12/80-1/81. *Mailing Add:* Dept Music Col Fine Arts Univ Calif Los Angeles CA 90024

ASHKENAZY, VLADIMIR D
PIANO, CONDUCTOR
b Gorky, USSR, July 6, 37; Icelandic citizen. *Study:* Moscow Central Sch Music, 45-55; Moscow Consv, 55-63. *Rec Perf:* Piano Concertos (Rachmaninoff), 71, Five Piano Concertos (Beethoven), 74, Five Piano Concertos (Prokofiev), 77, Symphonies No 4, 5 & 6 (Tchaikovsky), 81, Piano Sonatas (Beethoven), 82, Three Piano Concertos (Bartok), 83 & Symphonies No 5 & 6 (Beethoven), 83, Decca, UK. *Pos:* Concert pianist, worldwide; cond & pianist, Philharmonia Orch; violin & piano duo with Itzhak Perlman. *Awards:* Second Prize, Int Chopin Compt, Warsaw, 55; Gold Medal, Queen Elizabeth Int Piano Compt, Brussels, 56; Co-winner, Tchaikovsky Piano Compt, Moscow, 62. *Rep:* ICM Artists 40 W 57th St New York NY 10019. *Mailing Add:* c/o Harrison Parrott Ltd 12 Penzance Pl London W11 4PA England United Kingdom

ASHLEY, DOUGLAS DANIELS
PIANO, EDUCATOR
b Kansas City, Mo. *Study:* Northwestern Univ, BM, MM, PhD; Consv Vienna, with Viola Thern, piano dipl; study piano with Maria Curcio-Diamand, London. *Works:* The Seasons (solo piano), Bradley Publ, 83. *Pos:* Artist in res, Rome Fest Orch, 75-; recitalist, Spoleto Fest, 80, Carnegie

Recital Hall, 81, Berlin, 83 & Rome, 83; ed consult, Bradley Publ, currently. *Teaching:* Assoc prof, Col Charleston, 72- *Awards:* Fel, Nat Piano Found, 81- *Bibliog:* Was Häschen nicht lernt, Sonnabend, Berlin, 6/12/82; Gertrud Firnkees, Bei den Ersten Internationalen Tagen neuer Klaviermusik fürkinder in Berlin. *Mem:* Music Teachers Nat Asn; SC Music Teachers Asn; Am Musicol Soc; ASCAP; Contemp Rec Soc. *Publ:* Auth & ed, teaching pieces for piano, In: Bradley's Contemp Levels, Books I-V, 80-81; Maria Curcio-Diamand, Portrait of an Artist-Teacher, Clavier, 11/81. *Mailing Add:* c/o Atlanta Conct Artists 1323 Weston Dr Decatur GA 30032

ASHMEAD, ELIZABETH
FLUTE & PICCOLO
b Calif. *Study:* Eastman Sch Music, with Paul Renzi & Joseph Mariano, BM, 75. *Pos:* Flute & piccolo, San Diego Symph Orch, 75-; mem, San Diego Opera Orch, currently & La Jolla Chamber Orch, currently. *Mailing Add:* San Diego Opera Orch Box 988 San Diego CA 92112

ASHTON, JACK SCHRADER
VIOLIN, CONDUCTOR
b Salt Lake City, Utah, Sept 3, 38. *Study:* Univ Utah, BA, 65. *Pos:* Music dir & perf, Salt Lake Young Audience String Quartet, 66-76; asst prin second violin, Utah Symph, 68-; guest clinician violin perf, Utah State Univ, 83. *Teaching:* Private instr violin, 68-; Chamber Music Coordr, Am String Teachers Asn Strong Wkshps, 74-79; dir strings cond orch, Olympus High Sch, 74- *Mem:* Nat Fed Music Clubs; Utah Music Teachers Asn. *Mailing Add:* 980 S 1300 E Salt Lake City UT 84102

ASHTON, JOHN HOWARD
TRUMPET, COMPOSER
b Pittsburgh, Pa, July 11, 38. *Study:* Carnegie Mellon Univ, with Nikolai Lopatnikoff, MFA, 61; Cath Univ Am, with Lloyd Geisler, 62-66. *Works:* Songs from the Unknown Eros, Fairmont Chamber Players, 74; Sonata (trumpet & piano), 77, Piano Variations, 77 & Dialogues, Discourses, 77, Seesaw Music; Variations, Songs of the Sea, Baylor Univ Band, 80; Music for Community Orchestra, Carnegie Symph Orch, 81. *Pos:* Trumpet, US Naval Acad Band, Annapolis, Md, 62-66; prin trumpet, RTE Symp Orch, Dublin, Ireland, 67-68; trumpet, New Orleans Phil, 68-89; mus dir & cond, Fairmont Col Community Symph, 72- *Teaching:* Asst prof trumpet, Univ Nebr, 69-70; assoc prof theory & brass, Fairmont State Col, 70- *Awards:* First prize, WVa Univ Am Comp Cont, 61 & Nat Asn Col Wind & Perc Instr Comp Cont, 64. *Mem:* Am Fedn Musicians; Int Trumpet Guild; WVa Trumpet guild (pres, 80-82); Am Symph Orch League; Pittsburgh Asn Comp. *Mailing Add:* 1109 Alexander Pl Fairmont WV 26554

ASHTON, WENDELL JEREMY
PATRON
Study: Univ Utah, BS, 33; Westminster Col, LLD, 80. *Pos:* Pres & chief exec officer, Utah Symph, 66-; mem bd gov, Deseret Utah Art Found, 74-; publ, Deseret News Publ Co, Salt Lake City, 78- *Mailing Add:* Deseret News PO Box 2220 Salt Lake City UT 84110

ASHWORTH, JACK S
EDUCATOR
b Colfax, Wash, Jan 20, 49. *Study:* Whitman Col, BA(organ), 71; Stanford Univ, MM, 74, DMA(hist perf pract), 77. *Teaching:* Asst prof, Univ Louisville, 77-83, dir, Consort, 77-, assoc prof & chmn dept music hist, 83- *Mem:* Am Musicol Soc; Viola da Gamba Soc Am; Am Recorder Soc. *Publ:* Coauth, Two Elizabethan Stage Jigs, Musica Sacra et Profana, 78. *Mailing Add:* Sch Music Univ Louisville Louisville KY 40292

ASLANIAN, RICHARD
CONDUCTOR & MUSIC DIRECTOR
b Jersey City, NJ, Dec 30, 34. *Study:* New England Consv Music, BMusEd, 57; Mannes Col Music, dipl, 59; Cologne Consv Music, Germany, dipl, 62. *Pos:* Cond, Saarbrücken Opera, Germany, 65-69; music dir, Univ Ill Opera Theatre, 69-76, Baton Rouge Ballet Theatre, 81- & Gilbert and Sullivan Fest, Boulder, 83-; assoc cond, Cent City Opera, Colo, 74-78; dir, La State Univ Opera Theatre 76- *Teaching:* Assoc prof cond, & opera coaching, La State Univ, 76-80. *Awards:* Walter Damrosch Cond Award, Mannes Col Music, 59; Fulbright Grant, 60 & 61. *Mailing Add:* Opera Theatre La State Univ Baton Rouge LA 70803

ASLANIAN, VAHE
CONDUCTOR, EDUCATOR
b Dorchester, Mass, Mar 13, 18. *Study:* Boston Univ, MusB, 40; Claremont Grad Sch, MA, 50; Stanford Univ, DMA, 65. *Works:* In Monte Oliveti (Leonardo Leo), 62, Ecce Vidimus (Leonardo Leo), 62 & Tristis Est Anima Mea (Leonardo Leo), 62, Concordia Press; Chamber Mass (Antonio Vivaldi), 64, Mass in F Major (Leonardo Leo), 70, O Magnum Mysterium (Jacob Handl), 77, Te Deum Laudamus (Leonardo Leo), 77, Mission Music of San Juan Bautista, 77 & Nigra Sum (Tomas Luis de Victoria), Lawson-Gould; *Pos:* Cond, Men's Glee Club, Stanford Univ, 62-63; founder & cond, Camerata Singers, Salinas, Calif, 80- *Teaching:* Prof music & cond choral orgn, Hartnll Col, 50-80, founder & dir, Consv Music, 74-80. *Awards:* Ann Gannett Award, Berkshire Music Fest, 55; Fulbright Grant, 58-59; Martha Baird Rockefeller Grant, 58. *Mem:* Northern Calif Music Educr Asn (pres, 68-70); Nat Educ Asn; Music Educr Nat Conf; Col Music Soc; Calif Teachers Asn. *Interests:* California mission music; sacred & folk music in Armenian culture; sacred choral music of 18th century in Italy. *Publ:* Auth, A New Discovery of an Old Master (Antonio Vivaldi), Music J, 69; George Enescu, A Romanian Genius, Romanian Rev, 82. *Mailing Add:* 181 San Benancio Rd Salinas CA 93908

ATAMIAN, DICKRAN HUGO
PIANO
b Chicago, Ill, Mar 14, 55. *Study:* Oberlin Consv, studied with John Perry, 71-72; Univ Tex, 72-78, BA, 75; studied with Jorge Bolet. *Rec Perf:* Young-Uck Kim and Dickran Atamian, PBS, 79; Rite of Spring (solo piano), RCA Red Seal Digital, 80; An Evening With Dickran Atamian, PBS, 80; Festival of Chopin, Pearldiver Rec, 81; Atamian Salutes Kapell, PBS, 82; Atamian Plays Pictures, 82 & Bach and Prokofiev, 82, Pearldiver Rec. *Pos:* Artistic dir, Austin Fest Music, 79- & Kerville Summer Music Fest, summer 81. *Awards:* First Prize, Boyd Piano Compt, 74 & 50th Anniversary Naumburg Piano Compt, 75; grant, Rockefeller Found, 78. *Bibliog:* Andrew Porter (auth), Music of Three Seasons, New Yorker, 72; Robert Silverman (auth), Five Remarkable Talents, Piano Quart, 82. *Rep:* Price, Rubin & Partners Inc 133 W 69th St New York NY 10023. *Mailing Add:* c/o Price Rubin & Partners Inc 133 W 69th St New York NY 10023

ATHERTON, DAVID
CONDUCTOR & MUSIC DIRECTOR, PIANO
b Blackpool, Lancaster, England, Jan 3, 44. *Rec Perf:* Complete Ensemble Works (Schoenberg), Complete Ensemble Works (Janacek), King Priam (Tippett), Punch & Judy (Birtwistle), Serenade for 13 Wind Instruments (Mozart), Mass In C (Schubert) & Clarinet Concertos (Spohr), Decca/Argo. *Pos:* Music dir & founder, London Sinfonietta, 67-73; res cond, Royal Opera House, Covent Garden, 68-80; artistic dir, London Stravinsky Fest, 79-82; prin cond & artistic adv, Royal Liverpool Phil Orch, 80-83; music dir & prin cond, San Diego Symph Orch, 80- *Awards:* Grand Prix Du Disque, 77; Int Rec Critic's Award, 82; Koussevitsky Int Award, 82. *Mem:* Inc Soc Musicians; Royal Soc Arts; Royal Phil Soc. *Publ:* Ed, Ensemble Works of Schoenberg & Gerhard, Sinfonietta Publ, 73; contribr, Musical Companion, Gollancz, 80; New Grove Dict of Music & Musicians, Macmillan, 82. *Rep:* Shaw Concts Inc 1995 Broadway New York NY 10023. *Mailing Add:* San Diego Symph Orch House of Hospitality Balboa Park San Diego CA 92103

ATHERTON, JAMES PEYTON, JR
TENOR
b Montgomery, Ala, Apr 27, 43. *Study:* Peabody Consv Music, BMus, 65, MMus, 66. *Pos:* Mem, Santa Fe Opera, 73-78 & Metropolitan Opera, 77-; ten, Holland Fest, 76, Glyndebourne Fest, 79, San Francisco Opera, Houston Grand Opera, Miami Opera, Dallas Opera & Can Opera. *Awards:* Nat Opera Inst Award, 72. *Mailing Add:* c/o Columbia Artists 165 W 57th St New York NY 10019

ATHERTON, PETER L
BASS, TEACHER
b Louisville, Ky, Nov 4, 53. *Study:* Juilliard Sch, BMus, 75; Univ Southern Calif, MMus, 79. *Roles:* Figaro in The Marriage of Figaro, 82 & Colline in La Boheme, 82, Western Opera Theatre; Zebul in Jephtha, Basel Chamber Orch, 82; Bass Arias in St Matthew Passion, Swiss Romande Orch, 82; Ishmael in Moby Dick, Symph by the Sea Fest, 82; Giove in La Calisto, 83 & Colline in La Boheme, 83, Wolftrap Opera Co. *Teaching:* Lectr voice & diction, Univ Southern Calif, Los Angeles, 78-80. *Awards:* Artist of Yr, Nat Asn Teachers Singing, 79. *Mailing Add:* 37 W 74th St New York NY 10023

ATZMON, MOSHE
CONDUCTOR & MUSIC DIRECTOR
b Budapest, Hungary, July 30, 31; Israeli citizen. *Study:* Rubin Acad, Tel-Aviv; Guildhall Sch Music, London. *Rec Perf:* Overtures (Mozart) & Seventh Symphony (Bruckner), Ex Libris; Overtures (Mendelssohn), EMI; Symphony No 2 (Sibelius) & Music for Strings (Bartok), Columbia, Japan. *Pos:* Chief cond, Sydney Symph Orch, 69-72, Basel Symph Orch, 72- & Am Symph, 82-; music dir, NDR, Hamburg, Germany, 72-76. *Awards:* Second Prize, Mitropolous Compt, 63; First Prize, Liverpool Cond Compt, 64. *Mailing Add:* Concerto Winderstein Munich Germany, Federal Republic of

AUERBACH, CYNTHIA
DIRECTOR-OPERA
b Nyack, NY. *Study:* Crane Sch Music, State Univ NY, Potsdam, BM(piano educ), 60; Manhattan Sch Music, MMus. *Pos:* Founder, stage dir & cond, Manhattan Sch Music Children's Opera, 69-; stage dir, New York City Opera, 76- & guest stage dir, Houston, New Orleans, Pittsburgh, Vancouver & others, 76-; artistic dir, Chautauqua Opera, 81- *Teaching:* Prof music theory & instr opera, Manhattan Sch Music, 63-82; instr opera, Univ Conn, formerly. *Rep:* Columbia Artist Mgt 165 W 57th St New York NY 10019. *Mailing Add:* 315 W 70th St New York NY 10023

AULD, LOUIS EUGENE
ADMINISTRATOR, EDUCATOR
b Conneaut, Ohio, Nov 12, 35. *Study:* Oberlin Col, BA, 57; Univ Calif, Los Angeles, MA, 59; Bryn Mawr Col, PhD, 68. *Pos:* Dir, Rec Libr, Music Dept, Duke Univ, 76-80. *Teaching:* Instr French, Smith Col, 65-70 & Duke Univ, 70-74; asst to dean, Yale Sch Music, 81- *Mem:* Founder, Lyrica Soc Word-Music Relations (pres, 83-); Am Musicol Soc; Modern Language Asn. *Publ:* Auth, The Music of the Spheres in the Comedy Ballets, Esprit Createur, fall 66; Music in the Secular Theatre of Marguerite de Navarre, Renaissance Drama VII, 70; Pierre Perrin's Pomone: or, First Fruits of French Opera, French Lit & Arts, 78; ed, Ars Lyrica Newsletter, spring 81-; auth, The Lyric Art of Pierre Perrin, Founder of French Opera, Inst Medieval Music (in press). *Mailing Add:* 90 Church St Guilford CT 06437

AURAND, CHARLES HENRY, JR
CLARINET, EDUCATOR
b Battle Creek, Mich, Sept 6, 32. *Study:* Mich State Univ, BM, 54, MM, 58; Univ Mich, PhD, 71. *Pos:* Mem, Battle Creek Symph, formerly, Youngstown Symph, formerly, Flagstaff Symph, formerly & Shreveport Symph, formerly; Bd dir, Youngstown Symph Soc, 60-73, Flagstaff Symph Soc, 73- & Flagstaff Fest Arts, 73-; chamber music & recital soloist in Ohio & Ariz, currently. *Teaching:* Asst prof & actg chmn, Dept Music, Hiram Col, 58-60; prof & dean, Dana Sch Music, Youngstown State Univ, 60-73 & Col Creative Arts, Northern Ariz Univ, 73- *Mem:* Phi Mu Alpha (Ohio gov, 75-78). *Publ:* Auth, Selected Solos, Ensembles Instrumental Conducting, Youngstown Univ Press, 63; Career Patterns and Job Mobility of College and University Music Faculty, J Res Music Educ, summer 73; Recruitment and Its Relationship to Some Characteristics of the Typical Academic Musician On Our Campuses, Proceedings, Nat Asn Sch Music, 6/73. *Mailing Add:* 3251 S Little Dr Flagstaff AZ 86011

AUSTIN, ALTEOUISE DEVAUGHN See DeVaughn, Alteouise

AUSTIN, ARTHUR WILLIAM See Ostrovsky, Arthur

AUSTIN, JOHN (BRADBURY)
COMPOSER
b Mt Vernon, NY, June 8, 34. *Study:* Studied with Roy Harris, 52-56; Harvard Col, AB, 56; Harvard Law Sch, LLB, 60; Roosevelt Univ, with Robert Lombardo, MM, 73; Univ Chicago, with Ralph Shapey, PhD, 81. *Works:* Two Piano Pieces, 73 & Designs with Refrain, 76, Am Comp Alliance; In Memoriam, Needham, 80; The Moon Wears a Wax Moustache, 80, The Wicked and Unfaithful Song of Marcell Duchamp to His Queen, 81, Requiem, 81, The Writer, 82, The Poem that Took the Place of a Mountain & The Planet on the Table, 83, Am Comp Alliance. *Awards:* Winner, Nat Compt Percussive Arts Soc, 77-78. *Mem:* Am Comp Alliance; founding mem, Chicago Soc Comp; BMI. *Mailing Add:* 1209 Astor St Chicago IL 60610

AUSTIN, LARRY DON
COMPOSER
b Duncan, Okla, Sept 12, 30. *Study:* NTex State Univ, with Violet Archer, BME(music), 51, MM(theory), 52; San Antonio Col, 52-55; Mills Col, studied comp with Darius Milhaud, 55; Univ Calif, Berkeley, studied comp & musicol with Andrew Imbrie, 55-58; Stanford Univ, 69; Mass Inst Tech, MS(computer music), 78. *Works:* Piano Set in Open Style & Piano Variations, 69, Caritas (electronic), 70, Current, 74, Maroon Bells, Catalogo Voce, Quadrants: Event/Complex No 1 & Second Fantasy on Ives' Universe Symphony, 80 & Canadian Coastlines: Canonic Fractals for Musicians and Computer Band, 81, Peer-Southern. *Pos:* Co-dir, New Music Ens, 63-68; ed & publ, Source, 66-71. *Teaching:* Teaching asst & assoc, Univ Calif, Berkeley, 56-58; asst prof music, Univ Calif, Davis, 58-64, assoc prof, 64-70, prof, 70-72; prof, Trinity Univ, 70, Univ SFla, 72-78 & NTex State Univ, 78- *Awards:* Grant, Nat Endowment Arts, 80-81 & 81; res, MacDowell Colony, 81 & 82. *Bibliog:* Walter Zimmerman (auth), Desert Plants: Conversations with 23 American Composers, ARC Publ, 76; Joseph Machlis (auth), Introduction to Contemporary Music, 2nd ed, Norton, 79; Roger Johnson (auth), Scores: An Anthology of New Music, Macmillan, 80; also many others. *Mem:* Am Comp Alliance; Am Soc Univ Comp; Am Music Ctr; Comp Forum; Computer Music Asn. *Publ:* Auth, New Romanticism: An Emerging Aesthetic for Electronic Music, Part 1, Vol VI, No 1, 73 & Part 2, Vol VI, No 2, 73, Mundus Artium, J Int Lit & Arts; SYCOM—Systems Complex for the Studio and Performing Arts, Numus West, 5/74; coauth (with Larry Bryant), A Computer-Synchronized, Multi-Track Recording System, Second Ann Music Comput Conf, 75; Composing Hybrid Music with an Open, Interactive System, Proc Third Ann Music Comput Conf, 76. *Mailing Add:* 2109 Woodbrook Denton TX 76201

AUSTIN, LOUISE FAVILLE
TEACHER, RECORDER
b Menomonie, Wis, Aug 22, 30. *Study:* Beloit Col, 48-59; Triton Col, 55-56. *Pos:* Dir, Early Music Fest, Whitewater, Wis, 73-; music rev ed, Am Recorder Mag, 74- *Teaching:* Instr recorder & dir, Am Recorder Soc Wkshps, 63- & Oak Park Recorder Sch, 76-; private recorder instr, 63- *Mem:* Am Recorder Soc (bd mem, 72-80); Chicago Chap Am Recorder Soc (pres 72 & music consult, 73-83); MacDowell Artists Asn (prog dir, 81); Am Fedn Musicians. *Mailing Add:* 706 N Main St Lake Mills WI 53551

AUSTIN, WILLIAM WEAVER
EDUCATOR, WRITER
b Lawton, Okla, Jan 18, 20. *Study:* Harvard Univ, AB, 39, AM, 40, PhD, 51. *Teaching:* From asst prof to Goldwin Smith prof musicol, Cornell Univ, 47-; vis assoc prof, Princeton Univ, 57-58. *Awards:* Kinkeldey Award, Am Musicol Soc, 67; Dent Award, Int Musicol Soc, 67; Clark Award, Cornell Univ, 82. *Mem:* Am Musicol Soc; Int Musicol Soc; Am Ethnomusicol; Col Music Soc (pres, 60); Music Educr Nat Conf. *Interests:* Music in 20th century; American music; philosophy of music. *Publ:* Auth, Espressivo, J Aesthetics, 54; Music in the 20th Century, W W Norton, 66; ed, New Looks at Italian Opera, Cornell Univ Press, 68; auth, Susanna, 75, Jeanie, 75 & The Old Folks, 75, Macmillan; translr, Carl Dahlhaus's Aesthetics of Music, Cambridge Univ Press, 82. *Mailing Add:* Music Dept Cornell Univ Ithaca NY 14853

AVERITT, WILLIAM EARL
COMPOSER, MUSIC DIRECTOR

b Paducah, Ky, Nov 14, 48. *Study:* Murray State Univ, with James Woodard, BM(comp), 70; Fla State Univ, with John Boda, MM, 72, DM, 73; Berkshire Music Ctr, with Betsy Jolas. *Works:* O Vos Omnes, Hinshaw Music, 79; Elegy (flute, strings & perc), 83, Partita (eight instrm), 83, Fantasia (solo flute), 83, Trio (flute, clarinet & bassoon), 83, Permutations (flute & harpsichord), 83 & Night Piece (flute & piano), 83, Dorn Publ. *Pos:* Music dir, Front Royal Oratorio Soc, Va, 75-81; founder & music dir, Winchester Musica Viva, Va, 81- *Teaching:* Assoc prof music, Shenandoah Consv Music, 73- *Awards:* Fel, Nat Endowment Arts, 76 & 78. *Mailing Add:* 568 Fredericktonne Dr Stephens City VA 22655

AVSHALOMOV, JACOB DAVID
COMPOSER, CONDUCTOR & MUSIC DIRECTOR

b Tsingtao, China, Mar 28, 19; US citizen. *Study:* With Ernst Toch, 37; Reed Col, 39-41; Eastman Sch Music, BM, 41, MA, 43; studied with Aaron Copland, 46. *Works:* Taking of Tung Kuan, perf by Detroit Symph, 52; Tom o' Bedlam, E C Schirmer, 53; Phases of the Great Land, Galaxy Press, 59; Symphony: The Oregon, comn by Ore State, 60; Praises from the Corners of the Earth, MCA, 63; The 13 Clocks, comn & perf by Portland Jr Symph, 74; Raptures for Orchestra on Madrigals of Gesualdo, perf by Spokane Symph, 82. *Rec Perf:* Chameleon Variations (Bergsma), 59, World of Paul Klee, 59, Capriccio and Epilogue (B Lees), 59, Reverie and Dance (Roy Harris), 59, Divertimento (Robert Ward), 64, Peking Hutungs, Piano Concerto in G (Aaron Avshalomov), 68, Suite Symphonique and Symphony for Trombone (Ernest Bloch), 76, CRI. *Teaching:* Asst prof, Columbia Univ, 46-54; vis prof, Reed Col, summer 48 & Univ Wash, 55; guest cond, Northwestern Univ, summer 62 & Aspen Music Sch, summer 71. *Awards:* Award Comp, 46 & Cond Award, 64, Ditson Found; Guggenheim Fel, 52; NY Music Critics Circle Award, 53. *Publ:* Auth, Music Is Where You Make It, Portland Jr Symph Asn, 79. *Mailing Add:* 1133 SW Park Ave Portland OR 97205

AX, EMANUEL
PIANO

b Lvov, Poland, 1949. *Study:* Columbia Univ; Juilliard Sch Music, with Mieczyslaw Munz. *Rec Perf:* Beethoven, Chopin & Ravel albums; Brahms Quintet (in prep); Mozart Concerto (in prep); Brahms Sonatas (in prep). *Pos:* Solo pianist, worldwide. *Awards:* First Rubinstein Int Piano Compt Winner, 74; Young Concert Artist's Michaels Award, 75; Avery Fisher Prize, 79. *Mailing Add:* c/o ICM Artists Ltd 40 W 57th St New York NY 10019

AYBAR, FRANCISCO (RENE)
PIANO, EDUCATOR

b Santo Domingo, Dominican Repub, Oct 29, 40; US citizen. *Study:* Fordham Univ, AB, 65; Manhattan Sch Music, with Dora Zaslavsky, MM, 69; work with Ilona Kabos, London & NY & Peter Feuchtnanger, London, 69-73. *Rec Perf:* Iberia (Isaac Albeniz), 74 & Goyescas (Enrique Granados), 75, Connoisseur Soc; many solo recitals & concerts broadcast on NPR, PBS, BBC & Norwegian Radio. *Teaching:* Prof music & humanities, Lamont Sch Music, Univ Denver, 73-; residencies in cols in Colo, Mont, Wyo, Calif, Kans, Conn & elsewhere. *Awards:* Grants, Nat Endowment for Arts & Sears-Roebuck, 70-72; Martha Baird Rockefeller Grant, 71. *Mem:* Solo Recitalists Music Panel, Nat Endowment for Arts. *Rep:* Rosalie Lampl 16 Cherry Lane Dr Englewood CO 80110. *Mailing Add:* 7250 Eastmoor Dr Denver CO 80237

AYOTTE, JEANNINE MARIE
LIBRARIAN

b Lowell, Mass, May 28, 49. *Study:* Univ Lowell, BM, 72; Simmons Col, MS, 76. *Pos:* Librn, New England Consv Music, 73-77; music ref librn, Boston Pub Libr, 77. *Mem:* Music Libr Asn. *Mailing Add:* 15 Colbourne Crescent Brookline MA 02146

B

BABAK, RENATA
MEZZO-SOPRANO

b Kharkiv, Ukraine, Feb 4, 34; stateless. *Study:* Rimsky-Korsakov Consv, Leningrad, 58; P I Tchaikovsky Consv, Kiev, dipl, 61. *Roles:* Carmen in Carmen, Santuzza in Cavalleria Rusticana & Laura in La Gioconda, Lviv State Opera, 61-64; Amneris in Aida, Eboli in Don Carlos, Azucena in Il Trovatore & Charlotte in Werther, Bolshoi Theatre Opera, 64-73; and many others. *Pos:* Maj artist, Lviv State Opera, 61-64 & Bolshoi Opera Theatre, Moscow, 64-73; ms, Carnegie Hall, 75 & various opera houses throughout North Am, currently. *Awards:* Winner, Leningrad Opera Theater, 58. *Mailing Add:* c/o Maxim Gershunoff Attractions 502 Park Ave New York NY 10022

BABBITT, MILTON BYRON
COMPOSER, EDUCATOR

b Philadelphia, Pa, May 10, 16. *Study:* NY Univ, BA, 35; studied comp with Roger Sessions, 35-58; Princeton Univ, MFA, 42. *Works:* Three Compositions for Piano, Boelke-Bomart, 48; Compositons for Four Instruments, Theodore Presser, 48; String Quartet No 2, Assoc Music Publ, 54; Post-Partitions, 66, String Quartet No 4, 70, Arie Da Capo, 74 & Phonemena, 75, C F Peters. *Teaching:* Conant Prof, Princeton Univ, 38-; prof comp, Juilliard Sch, 71-; vis prof, Rubin Acad, Jerusalem, 77-78 & Univ Wis, Madison, 83. *Awards:* Pulitzer Prize Spec Citation, Columbia Univ, 82; Gold Medal, Brandeis Univ; George Peabody Medal, Johns Hopkins Univ, 83. *Bibliog:* Mark Zuckerman (auth), On Milton Babbitt's String Quartet No 2, 76 & S Arnold & G Hair (auth), String Quartet No 3, 76, Perspectives New Music. *Mem:* Am Acad & Inst Arts & Lett; fel, Am Acad Arts & Sci; Int Soc Comtemp Music; Meet the Comp; Stefan Wolpe Soc. *Publ:* Auth, Set Structure as a Compositional Determinant, J Music Theory, 61; The Structure and Function of Musical Theory, Col Music Symposium, 65; On Relata I, Orch Comp Point of View, 70; Contemporary Musical Composition and Music Theory, W W Norton, 71; Since Schoenberg, Perspectives New Music, 74. *Mailing Add:* Woolworth Ctr Princeton Univ Princeton NJ 08544

BABCOCK, MICHAEL
EDUCATOR

b Centralia, Wash, June 12, 40. *Study:* Ind Univ, with Iannis Xenakis, Juan Orrego-Salas, Roque Cordero & John Eaton, MM, 71. *Works:* Inflexaleus (five perc), 71; Minutia (cello & piano). *Pos:* Res fel, Ctr Mathematical & Automated Music, Ind Univ, 69-71; dir, Studio for Electronic & Experimental Music, Chicago Musical Col, Roosevelt Univ, 72-76. *Teaching:* Mem fac, Univ Wis, 76- *Mailing Add:* 3070 Cambridge Ave Milwaukee WI 53211

BABER, JOSEPH (WILSON)
COMPOSER, EDUCATOR

b Richmond Va, Sept 11, 37. *Study:* Univ Miami, with Renee Longy, 56; Mich State Univ, with Mario Castelnuovo-Tedesco, BMus, 62; Eastman Sch Music, with Howard Hanson, MMus, 65. *Works:* Rhapsody for Viola & Orchestra, Eastman Rochester Orch, 65; Frankenstein (opera, suite), Lexington Phil, 66; Concerto No 2 (viola & orch), Tokyo Phil, 68; String Quartet Op 30, Ill Quartet, 68; Rumpelstiltskin, Philadelphia Opera Co, 76; Landscapes (sop & cello), Nebr Cello Ens, 77; Rhapsody for Cello & Orchestra, Nebr Sinfonia, 77. *Pos:* Prin violist, Tokyo Phil Orch, 65-67; violist, Ill String Quartet, 67-70. *Teaching:* Comp in res, Kans Coop Col Comp Proj, 70-71, Univ Ky, Lexington, 71- *Mem:* ASCAP; life mem, Phi Mu Alpha. *Mailing Add:* 138 Arcadia Park S Lexington KY 40503

BABINI, ITALO (S)
CELLO

b Nov 20, 28; Brazil citizen. *Study:* Acad Music, Rio de Janeiro, with Lorenzo Fernandez; Munich Acad Music, 57; Yale Univ, 59; studied cello with Pablo Casals. *Rec Perf:* W Walton Cello Concerto, Samuel Barber Cello Concerto, Brahms Double Concerto with Mische Michakof & Rococo Variation (Tchaikovsky), broadcast rec; Lalo Cello Concerto, broadcast rec; Music of Ornstein and Hayef, Serenus. *Pos:* Prin cellist, New Haven Symph Orch, 59-60, Conn Symph Orch, 59-60 & Detroit Symph Orch, 60- *Teaching:* Instr cello, Wayne State Univ. *Awards:* First Prize, Brazilian Compt, Brazilian Ministry Educ, 56; First Prize, Berkshire Music Ctr, 59. *Mailing Add:* c/o Detroit Symph Orch Ford Auditorium Detroit MI 48226

BACAL, HARVEY
MUSICOLOGIST, EDUCATOR

b Quebec, May 24, 15. *Study:* Philadelphia Col Perf Arts, studied comp & music with Jaromir Weinberger, Frederick Schleider & William Happich; New York Inst Finance; La Salle Col Law. *Works:* Orch Suite—5 Pieces for Children, I'm Afraid to Remember, Pianino, Shadow Tango & Good Humor, Arcot Music Publ Co; A'La Parisienne, Mitchell Publ Co. *Pos:* Musicologist, Stop the Music, TV & radio networks, formerly, Yours for a Song, TV, formerly, Music Bingo, TV, formerly & Name That Tune, TV, formerly & 77-; arr, comp & cond, TV & radio shows, formerly; arr & mgr, Raymond Scott Orch, formerly; freelance musicol consult, rec co, music publ & advertising agencies. *Teaching:* Adj prof musicol, Pepperdine Univ, 81- *Mem:* Calif Copyright Conf; Choral Soc Southern Calif (pres, 82-). *Publ:* Auth, ABC's of Modern Arranging, Roslyn Publ Co, 55; Key to Modern Dance Band Arranging, New Sounds in Modern Music, 60; Fun with Music, Arcot Music Publ Co, 70. *Mailing Add:* 7244 Hillside Ave Suite 309 Hollywood CA 90046

BACH, JAN (MORRIS)
COMPOSER, EDUCATOR

b Forrest, Ill, Dec 11, 37. *Study:* Univ Ill, Urbana-Champaign, BM(comp), 59, MM(comp), 61, DMA(comp), 71. *Works:* Four Two-Bit Contraptions, Media Press, 71; Dirge for a Minstrel, Assoc Music Publ, 74; Laudes, Mentor Music, 76; Three Bagatelles, Assoc Music Publ, 79; Rounds and Dances, 82 & Skizzen, 83, Galaxy Music Corp; My Wilderness, Boosey & Hawkes, 83. *Teaching:* Instr music, Univ Tampa, 65-66; from instr to asst prof, Northern Ill Univ, 66-71, assoc prof, 71-78, prof, 78- *Awards:* Student Comp Awards First Prize, BMI, 57; Chamber Orch Compt Award, Nebr Sinfonia, 80; Am One-Act Opera Compt Award, New York City Opera, 80. *Bibliog:* Dorle J Soria (auth), An American Trilogy, Musical Am, 10/80; Peter G Davis (auth), Three American Composers, New York Times, 10/5/80; Robert C Marsh (auth), Modern-day Bach, Chicago Sun-Times, 7/12/81. *Mem:* BMI; Am Music Ctr; Col Music Soc. *Mailing Add:* 9 Moraine Terr De Kalb IL 60115

BACH, P D Q See Schickele, Peter

BACHMANN, GEORGE THEODORE
VIOLA, LIBRARIAN

b Annapolis, Md, Mar 31, 30. *Study:* Studied theory with Phyllis Olson, 78-80 & viola da gamba with Gian Lyman & Carol Rowan. *Works:* Recorder Trio, Am Recorder Soc, Washington, DC, 80. *Pos:* Recorder, Gettysburg Baroque Ens, 61-64; viola da gambist, Annapolis Baroque Ens, 68-69 & Ars Antiqua of Baltimore, 76-77; clarinetist, Essex Conct Band, 82- *Teaching:* Assoc prof recorder, Western Md Col, 72- *Mem:* Viola da Gamba Soc Am (asst ed jour, 64-69, ed newsletter, 73-75, treas, 81-); Am Recorder Soc. *Publ:* Auth, List of Doctoral Dissertations Accepted by American Universities on the Viola da Gamba, Its Music & Composers, Viola da Gamba Soc Am, 67. *Mailing Add:* 71 Pennsylvania Ave Westminster MD 21157

BACON, DAVID
PIANO, EDUCATOR
Study: Yale Univ, cert music; studied piano with Egon Petri, James Friskin & Mieczyslaw Horszowski. *Pos:* Chamber music & solo recitals, Calif Inst Technol, Town Hall, Jordan Hall, Boston Univ, Harvard Univ & Gardner Museum; appearances with members of Gordon Quartet & Stradivarius Quartet; guest artist, Berkshire String Quartet; pianist with Maurice Eisenberg, New England; soloist, Boston Pops, Albany Symph & Curtis String Orch. *Teaching:* Head piano dept, South End Music Ctr, 50-54; mem fac, Cummington Sch Arts, 54-57 & New England Consv, 59-63; mem fac piano, Longy Sch Music, currently. *Awards:* Ditson Fugue Prize. *Mailing Add:* Longy Sch Music One Follen St Cambridge MA 02138

BACON, DENISE
EDUCATOR, ADMINISTRATOR
b Newton, Mass, Mar 20, 20. *Study:* Longy Sch Music, soloist dipl, 43; studied with Mieczyslaw Horszowski, 44-52; New England Consv Music, BM, 52, MM, 54. *Works:* Let's Sing Together for 3, 4 & 5 Year Olds, Boosey & Hawkes, 71; 46 Two-Part American Folk Songs, Kodaly Ctr Am, 73; 50 Easy Two-Part Exercises, European Am, 77; 185 Unison Pentatonic Exercises, Kodaly Ctr Am, 78. *Pos:* Founder & dir, Dana Sch Music, 57-69, Kodaly Musical Training Inst, 69-77 & Kodaly Ctr Am, Inc, 77- *Teaching:* Fac mem piano, music lit & theory, Pine Manor Jr Col, 48-53; head dept piano, Dana Hall Sch, 48-69. *Awards:* Braitmayer Fel, Nat Asn Independent Sch, 67-68. *Bibliog:* The Children are Singing (film), MaFilm, Budapest, 70; Philip Tacka (auth), Denise Bacon—Musician and Educator: Contributions to the Adaptation of the Kodaly Concept in the US, Cath Univ, 82. *Mem:* Music Educr Nat Conf; Orgn Kodaly Educr; Int Kodaly Soc; Nat Asn Sch Music. *Publ:* Auth, Can We Afford to Ignore the Kodaly Method?, Nat Asn Independent Sch Bulletin, 68; The Why of Kodaly, Music J, 71; Tribute to Kodaly, Muzsika, 72; The Kodaly Concept in the United States, Hungarian Quart, 78; Hungary Will Never Outgrow Kodaly, Music Educr J, 79. *Mailing Add:* 15 Denton Rd Wellesley MA 02181

BACON, ERNST
PIANO, COMPOSER
b Chicago, Ill, May 26, 1898. *Study:* Northwestern Univ; Univ Chicago; Univ Calif, MA, 37. *Works:* From These States (suite), Assoc Music Publ; Sonata for Cello and Piano, C F Peters; A Life (cycle for cello & piano), Columbia Univ Press; From Emily's Diary (cycle for women's voices & piano), G Schirmer; Nature (cycle for women's voices & piano), E C Schirmer; The Hootenanny (piano), Chappell; Sassafras (piano), Lawson-Gould; and hundreds more. *Pos:* Cond, San Francisco Jr Symph, 31-33; founder & cond, Bach Fest, Carmel, Calif, 35; supvr & orch cond, Fed Music Proj, 35-37; guest cond, San Francisco, Detroit, Southern, Chicago, Los Angeles & Oakland Fed orchs; founder & dir, Carmel Bach Fest & Spartanburg Fest. *Teaching:* Opera coach & piano instr, Eastman Sch, 25-27; instr, San Francisco Consv, 27-30; actg prof, Hamilton Col, 38, Stanford Univ, 40 & Univ Wyo, 42; dean & prof piano, Converse Col, 38-45; dir sch music & comp in res, Syracuse Univ, 45-62; fel, Ctr Advan Studies, Wesleyan Univ, 63. *Awards:* Pulitzer Fel, 32; Guggenheim Fel; Nat Acad Arts & Lett Award. *Mem:* ASCAP; Nat Acad Arts & Lett. *Publ:* Auth, Words on Music, 60 & Notes on the Piano, 63, Syracuse Univ Press. *Mailing Add:* 57 Claremont Ave Orinda CA 94563

BACON, MADI
CONDUCTOR & MUSIC DIRECTOR
b Chicago, Ill, Feb 15, 06. *Study:* Univ Chicago, PhB, 27, MA, 41; San Francisco Consv Music, studied with Ernest Bloch & Giulio Silva, 28-30; Northwestern Univ, 39; Berkshire Music Ctr, with Koussevitzky, 40. *Pos:* Cond, NShore Choral Soc, Winnetka, Ill, 31-41; founder & cond, Elizabethan Madrigal Singers, Chicago, 31-42 & San Francisco Boys Chorus, 48-73; mem staff, San Francisco Opera, 48-72; numerous radio & TV appearances, Chicago & San Francisco. *Teaching:* Supvr music, Glencoe Pub Sch, 33-35; dean & choral cond, Roosevelt Univ, 41-46; lectr & head, Music Exten Div, Univ Calif, Berkeley, 46-54. *Mailing Add:* 1120 Keith Ave Berkeley CA 94708

BACON, VIRGINIA PAYTON
EDUCATOR
Study: Inst Musical Art, Juilliard Sch, dipl; Mannes Sch, studied cello with Willem Willeke, Lieff Rosanoff & Maurice Eisenberg. *Pos:* Solo & chamber music perf, Calif, New York & New England, formerly; mem, San Diego Symph, formerly. *Teaching:* Mem fac, Groton Sch, 41-56, Cummington Sch Arts, 54-56 & New England Consv Music, 50-73; instr violoncello & chamber music, Longy Sch Music, currently. *Mailing Add:* Longy Sch Music One Follen St Cambridge MA 02138

BACON-SHONE, FREDERIC
PIANO, TEACHER
b London, England, Nov 30, 24. *Study:* Guildhall Sch Music, LGSM(perf), 46; London Univ, BA, 49; Columbia Univ, MA, 53; Univ Southern Calif, PhD, 76. *Works:* Psalm 121; Easter. *Rec Perf:* Chamber Mass (Vivaldi). *Pos:* Pianist, concerts & recitals in London, US & Can; dir, Blomstedt & Wilcocks Wkshps, Loma Linda, Calif, 75-76. *Teaching:* Vis prof, Columbia Univ, 59; instr, Covina-Valley Unified Sch Dist, Covina, Calif, 60- *Mem:* Am Musicol Soc; Am Guild Organists; Music Educr Nat Conf. *Publ:* Auth, Form in the Chamber Music of Frederick Delius, 76. *Mailing Add:* 6940 Abel Stearns Ave Riverside CA 92509

BADEA, CHRISTIAN
CONDUCTOR, DIRECTOR—OPERA
b Romania. *Study:* Bucharest Consv Music; Juilliard Sch. *Pos:* Opera dir, Spoleto Fest Two Worlds, Charleston & Italy, Theatre Royal Monnaie, Brussels, Netherlands Opera & Atlanta Civic Opera; music dir & cond, Savannah Symph, Ga, 78-; guest cond, Columbus Symph, Ohio, 83, Miami Phil, 83 & various symphs in Europe & North Am; Brit, Ital & Am TV perfs; cond, Kentucky Opera, 83. *Mailing Add:* c/o ICM Artists 40 W 57th St New York NY 10019

BAE, IK-HWAN
VIOLIN, TEACHER
b Seoul, Korea, Nov 19, 56. *Study:* Juilliard Sch, studied with Ivan Galamian & Dorothy DeLay, 71-76. *Rec Perf:* Tashi, RCA, 82. *Pos:* Soloist with Chamber Music Northwest, 77-, Chamber Music Soc Lincoln Ctr, 80-82, Seattle Chamber Music Fest, 82- & Theater Chamber Players, 83. *Teaching:* Artist in res violin & chamber music, Univ Conn, 76-79. *Mailing Add:* 251 W 97th New York NY 10025

BAER, (DOLORES) DALENE
VIOLIN, EDUCATOR
b Gary, Ind, Apr 10, 35. *Study:* Am Consv Music, BM, 57, MM, 59; Ariz State Univ. *Pos:* First violinist, Atlanta Symph, 61-63, Phoenix Symph, 64-65 & Monroe Symph Orch, 79-; concertmistress, SArk Symph, 65- *Teaching:* Instr strings & theory, SDak State Univ, 63-64; grad asst strings, Ariz State Univ, 64-65; assoc prof, Southern Ark Univ, 65- *Mem:* Am String Teachers Asn; Music Educr Nat Conf; Ark State Music Teachers Asn. *Mailing Add:* Music Dept Southern Ark Univ Magnolia AR 71753

BAGGER, LOUIS S
PIANO, EDUCATOR
Study: Yale Univ, BA; Princeton Univ, MFA; studied harpsichord with Kirkpatrick & Leonhardt, organ with Weinrich, Noss & Vignanelli & piano with Loesser & Steuermann. *Rec Perf:* On Monitor, Music Heritage & Vox. *Pos:* Performer, solo recitals, chamber music concerts & radio broadcasts in Europe & North Am. *Teaching:* Fulbright Scholar, Univ Rome, 49; mem fac, Music Dept, Brandeis Univ 66-75; artist in res, Univ Calif, Davis, spring 76; mem fac music hist, Manhattan Sch Music, 76-, mem fac harpsichord, 82- *Rep:* Del Rosenfield Assocs 714 Ladd Rd Bronx NY 10471. *Mailing Add:* Manhattan Sch Music 120 Claremont Ave New York NY 10027

BAHMANN, MARIANNE ELOISE
COMPOSER, MEZZO-SOPRANO
b McKeansburg, Pa, Dec 1, 33. *Study:* Drake Univ, BMus, 54, MM, 57; Staatliche Hochschule Musik, 54-55; vocal & operatic study with Rose Bampton & Wilfrid Pelletier, 57-58. *Works:* The Altar of God (choral), Carl Fischer, Inc, 62; Pastorale on Greensleeves (organ), Broadman, 70; Voluntary on a Theme of Tchaikovsky (organ), Hope Publ Co, 72; Meditation for Chimes (organ), Abingdon Press, 77; Behold, a Host (organ), Arvon Publ, 78; Christ Church Carol, Christ Church, Bethlehem, Pa, 78; A Service of Commitment (music & liturgy), perf by Univ Lutheran Church, 80-82. *Rec Perf:* The Medium (Menotti), 80, Les Noces (Stravinsky), 80 & Mass in E Flat (Schubert), 81, Stanford Univ Dept Music. *Roles:* Popova in The Bear, 76 & Suzuki in Madama Butterfly, 77, West Bay Opera; Mrs Gobineau in The Medium, Stanford Opera Theater, 80. *Pos:* Choir dir, Univ Lutheran Church, Palo Alto, Calif, 74-80; rehearsal accmp & chorus trainer, West Bay Opera, 75-77. *Teaching:* Private teacher voice, 73-; support staff supvr & ref specialist, Stanford Univ Music Libr, 78-82. *Awards:* Fulbright Award, 54-55. *Mem:* Soc Europ Stage Authors & Comp, Inc; Mu Phi Epsilon. *Mailing Add:* Bethaniendamm 23 D1000 Berlin 36 Germany, Federal Republic of

BAILEY, BARBARA ELLIOTT
LECTURER, PIANO
b Philadelphia, Pa, May 25, 22. *Study:* Curtis Inst Music, BMus, 43; Northwestern Univ, MMus, 70, PhD, 80. *Rec Perf:* Eighth and Eleventh Sonatas of Vincent Persichetti, Contemp Rec Studios, 83. *Pos:* Lectr & recitalist, 63- *Teaching:* Asst piano, Curtis Inst Music, 41-57; vis instr music hist, Beloit Col, 74-76. *Awards:* Youth Award, Philadelphia Orch, 42. *Bibliog:* Robert D Schick (auth), The Vengerova System of Piano Playing, Pa State Univ Press, 82. *Mem:* Am Musicol Soc; Col Music Soc; Sonneck Soc; Am Music Ctr. *Interests:* Examination, evaluation and listing of published American piano music. *Mailing Add:* 200 W Willow Grove Ave Philadelphia PA 19118

BAILEY, DAVID WAYNE
CONDUCTOR & MUSIC DIRECTOR, EDUCATOR
b Johnson City, NY, May 17, 49. *Study:* Eastman Sch Music, BMus, 71; Boston Consv Music, MMus, 81; studied cond with Attilio Poto. *Pos:* Cond & music dir, Torrington Civic Symph, Conn, 78- *Teaching:* Fac mem instrm music, Kent Sch, Conn, 75-79; fac mem music educ, Boston Consv Music, 80- *Mem:* Am Symph Orch League; Music Educr Nat Conf; Nat Sch Orch Asn. *Mailing Add:* 82 Fitchburg Turnpike Concord MA 01742

BAILEY, DENNIS FARRAR
TENOR
b Tupelo, Miss, Nov 20, 43. *Study:* Univ Southern Miss; Loyola Univ, La. *Rec Perf:* Fidelio, 82 & Katya Kabanowa, 82, BBC Broadcast, TV. *Roles:* Siegfried, Chicago Symph, Orch, 81; Bacchus, Glyndebourne Fest Opera, 81 & Hamburg Staatsoper, 82; Florestan in Fidelio, Welsh Nat Opera, 82; Midas, Santa Fe Opera, 82; Don Jose in Carmen & Pinkerton in Madama Butterfly, Wash Opera. *Mem:* Am Guild Musical Artists; Can Actors Equity; UK Musical Artists Equity. *Mailing Add:* c/o Columbia Artists Mgt Inc 165 W 57th New York NY 10019

BAILEY, ELDEN C
PERCUSSION, EDUCATOR
b Portland, Maine. *Study:* New England Consv Music, 41-42; Juilliard Sch, dipl, 49. *Pos:* Perc, New York Phil, 49-; mem, Little Orch Soc, formerly & Sauter-Finegan Conct Jazz Orch, 53. *Teaching:* Mem fac, Greenwich House Music Sch, formerly, New York Col Music, formerly & NY Univ, formerly; mem fac perc, Juilliard Sch, 69- *Publ:* Auth, Mental and Manual Calisthenics for the Modern Mallet Player. *Mailing Add:* New York Phil Avery Fisher Hall New York NY 10023

BAILEY, EXINE MARGARET ANDERSON
SOPRANO, EDUCATOR
b Cottonwood, Minn, Jan 4, 22. *Study:* Univ Minn, BS, 44; Columbia Univ, MA, 45, prof dipl, 51. *Rec Perf:* On RCA Victor. *Pos:* Sop, NBC Symph, ABC Symph & CBS Symph; solo, recital & orch appearances on West Coast. *Teaching:* Instr, Columbia Univ, 47-51; mem fac, Univ Ore, 51-66, prof voice, 66-; vis prof & head vocal instr, Columbia Univ, summers 52 & 59. *Awards:* Young Artists Award, New York City Singing Teachers, 45; Kathryn Long Scholar, Metropolitan Opera, 45; Hon Award, Music Fedn Club, New York, 51. *Mem:* Nat Asn Teachers Singing (lieutenant gov, 68-72); Ore Music Teachers Asn (pres, 74-76); Music Teachers Nat Asn; Am Asn Univ Prof; Sigma Alpha Iota. *Mailing Add:* 17 Westbrook Way Eugene OR 97405

BAILEY, JAMES
CONDUCTOR, CELLO
b Wheatland, Wyo, Sept 29, 46. *Study:* Univ Northern Colo, BMA, 68; Univ Colo, MM, 73; Univ Kans, DMA, 83. *Pos:* Cond, Hays Symph, 76-79 & Univ Northern Colo Symph, 82- *Teaching:* Prof cello, Ft Hays State Univ, 76-79 & Univ Northern Colo, 80- *Mem:* Colo Music Educr Asn; Music Educr Nat Conv; Am String Teachers Asn; Music Teachers Nat Asn. *Mailing Add:* 2420 29th Ave Greeley CO 80631

BAILEY, ROBERT
MUSICOLOGIST, EDUCATOR
b Flint, Mich, June 21, 37. *Study:* Dartmouth Col, BA, 59; Staatliche Hochschule Musik, Munich, studied piano with Friedrich Wührer, 59-60; Juilliard Sch Music, studied piano with Edward Steuermann; Princeton Univ, 60-62, MFA, 62, PhD, 69. *Teaching:* Mem fac music, Princeton Univ, 62-63 & NY Univ, 77; mem fac, Yale Univ, 64-77, assoc prof, formerly; vis mem fac, Univ Calif, Berkeley, 70-71; assoc prof musicol, Eastman Sch Music, 77- *Awards:* Travel Grant, Am Philosophical Soc, 70; Younger Humanist Fel, Nat Endowment Humanities, 72-73. *Mem:* Am Musicol Soc; Int Musicol Soc. *Publ:* Auth, Critical Edition of Wagner's Tristan & Isolde, Neue Wagner-Gesamtausgabe (in prep); contrib to Music Libr Asn Notes, Musical Times & New Grove Dict of Music & Musicians. *Mailing Add:* Eastman Sch Music 26 Gibbs St New York NY 14604

BAILY, DIETTE (DEE) MARIE
LIBRARIAN, WRITER
b Mitchell, SDak, May 10, 49. *Study:* Sch Music, Univ Mich, BM, 71, Sch Libr Sci, AMLS, 72; Grad Sch Arts & Sci, NY Univ, MA(musicol), 77. *Pos:* Asst librn, Harry Scherman Libr, Mannes Col Music, 72-74; ref librn, Music Div, New York Pub Libr, 74-76; head music libr, Brooklyn Col, City Univ New York, 76- *Teaching:* Music bibliog, Brooklyn Col Consv, 76- *Mem:* Music Libr Asn (NY chap secy-treas, 77-79 & chair, 79-81); Am Musicol Soc (chair AMS-MLA Transl Ctr, 76-); Int Asn Music Libr; Mu Phi Epsilon; Asn Col & Res Libr. *Interests:* Music bibliography. *Publ:* Auth, A Report on the AMS-MLA Translations Center, Music Libr Asn Notes, 9/78; numerous articles & liner notes for Musical Heritage Society, 80-; ed, A Checklist of Music Bibliographies & Indexes in Progress & Unpublished, 4th ed, Music Libr Asn, 82; contribr, J Haydn, Works, J Haydn Inst (in prep); numerous articles, In: New Grove Dict of Music in US (in prep). *Mailing Add:* Brooklyn Col Music Libr Bedford Ave & Ave H Brooklyn NY 11210

BAIRD, EDWARD ALLEN
EDUCATOR, BASS
b Kansas City, Kans, Mar 18, 33. *Study:* Univ Mo, Kansas City, BA(music), 55, MA(music), 56; Univ Mich, DMA(perf), 62. *Roles:* Bartolo in The Barber of Seville, St Louis Opera Theater, 65 & Kansas City Lyr Theater, 67; Don Pasquale in Don Pasquale, Kansas City Lyr Theater, 66 & Jacksonville Opera, Fla, 83; High Priest in The Magic Flute, Houston Grand Opera, 66; King in Aida, San Diego Opera, 66; Leporello in Don Giovanni, Kansas City Lyr Theater, 67; Bartolo in The Marriage of Figaro, Ft Worth Opera Asn, 68; Figaro in The Marriage of Figaro, Beaumont Civic Opera, 74; and many others. *Teaching:* Supvr music, Recreation Div, Kansas City, 54-56; asst prof, Midland Lutheran Col, 56-60; grad fel, Univ Mich, Ann Arbor, 60-62; from asst prof to prof, NTex State Univ, 62- *Awards:* Regional Winner, Metropolitan Opera Auditions, 62; Outstanding Prof, NTex State Univ, 64. *Mem:* Nat Asn Teachers Singing (regional gov, 70-74, nat dir wkshps, 77-, nat vpres, 79-83); Int Asn Res Singing (dir conf, 81-); Am Guild Musical Artists; Actors Equity. *Publ:* Coauth, Studies of the Male High Voice Mechanisms, J Res Singing, 80; auth, Summer Vocal Workshops—A 1981 Retrospective, 81, Summer Vocal Workshops, 1982, 82, Last Call for Summer Vocal Workshops!, 82 & Summer Workshops in Review, 82, Nat Asn Teachers Singing Bulletin. *Mailing Add:* PO Box 5095 NTex State Univ Denton TX 76203

BAISLEY, ROBERT WILLIAM
EDUCATOR, PIANO
b New Haven, Conn, Apr 5, 23. *Study:* Yale Univ, BMus, 49; Columbia Univ, MA, 50. *Rec Perf:* Music of Charles Cadman, Cambria Rec, 82. *Teaching:* Instr music, Cherry Lawn Sch, Darien, Conn, 50-51; dir, Neighborhood Music Sch, New Haven, 51-56; asst prof piano, Yale Univ, 56-65; prof music, Pa State Univ, 65- *Mem:* Col Music Soc; Music Educr Nat Asn; Music Teachers Nat Asn; Pa Music Teachers Asn. *Publ:* Coauth, They Who Speak in Music, Neighborhood Music Sch, 57; auth, Charles Wakefield Cadman—Strictly American, Music Educr J, 75. *Mailing Add:* 454 Park Ln State College PA 16801

BAKER, ALAN
BARITONE
b Kansas City, Mo. *Study:* Juilliard Sch, with Sergius Kagen & Mack Harrell; Hochschule Musik, Stuttgart, with Alfred Paulus & Hermann Reutter. *Rec Perf:* On Decca. *Roles:* Angel in Sarah, CBS-TV, 58; Dandini in La Cenerentola, 59 & Clown in Goodbye to the Clown, 60, Turnau Opera, NY; Max in The Final Ingredient, ABC-TV, 65; Marcello in La Boheme; Figaro in Il Barbiere di Siviglia; Germont in La Traviata. *Pos:* Mem, New York City Opera, currently; recitalist & appearances with maj opera co. *Mailing Add:* c/o David Schiffman 333 West End Ave New York NY 10023

BAKER, CLAUDE
COMPOSER
b Lenoir, NC, Apr 12, 48. *Study:* Eastman Sch Music, with Samuel Adler, Wayne Barlow & Warren Benson. *Works:* Rest, Heart of the World (orch & sop solo); Four Songs on Poems of Kenneth Patchen (sop solo); Capriccio (band); Speculum Musicae (string quartet, woodwind quartet, brass trio, perc & piano); Banchetto Musicale (clarinet, violin, piano & perc), perf at Kennedy Ctr, Washington, DC, 79. *Pos:* Four Songs on Poems of Kenneth Patchen (sop & orch); Capriccio (band). *Teaching:* Mem fac, Univ Ga, 74-76; W Claude Baker assoc prof theory & comp, Univ Louisville, 76- *Awards:* ASCAP Awards; MacDowell Fel; BMI Award for Rest, Heart of the World, 73; Kennedy Ctr Friedheim Award; Rockefeller Found Fel. *Mailing Add:* Dept Music Univ Louisville Louisville KY 40292

BAKER, DON RUSSELL
PERCUSSION, TEACHER
b Edgerton, Ohio, Apr 10, 48. *Study:* Adrian Col, BA, 70; Indiana Univ Pa, MEd, 72; Univ Ill. *Pos:* Prin perc, Greensboro Symph Orch, 78- *Teaching:* Instr music, Western Mich Univ, Kalamazoo, 72-76 & Univ NC, Greensboro, 78-; instr perc, Nat Music Camp, Interlochen, Mich, 79. *Mem:* Percussive Arts Soc; NC Percussive Arts Soc; Nat Asn Col Wind & Perc Instrm; Soc Ethnomusicol. *Interests:* Lou Harrison's percussion ensemble music; music education; percussion. *Publ:* Auth, Several articles on percussion education including music reviews, Instrumentalist, 74- *Mailing Add:* 320 N Oak St Edgerton OH 43517

BAKER, JAMES M
EDUCATOR, WRITER
b Nashville, Tenn, June 21, 48. *Study:* Yale Univ, BA, 70, MPhil, 74, PhD, 77. *Pos:* Ed, J Music Theory, 74-75. *Teaching:* Actg asst prof music, Univ Va, 75-76; asst prof music, Columbia Univ, 77-83 & Brown Univ, 83- *Awards:* Carnegie Teaching Fel, 70-71; Mellon Found Grant, 81; Am Coun Learned Soc Fel, 82-83. *Mem:* Am Musicol Soc; Soc Music Theory. *Interests:* Origins of atonality in late 19th century music. *Publ:* Auth, Scriabin's Implicit Tonality, 80 & Coherence in Webern's Six Pieces for Orchestra Op 6, 82, Music Theory Spectrum; Schenkerian Analysis and Post-Tonal Music, In: Aspects of Schenkerian Theory, 83 & The Music of Scriabin (in press), Yale Univ Press. *Mailing Add:* Dept Music Brown Univ Providence RI 02912

BAKER, JANET ABBOTT
MEZZO-SOPRANO
b Aug 21, 33. *Study:* Col Girls, York, England; Wintringham, Grimsby, England; hon degrees from various Brit univ. *Pos:* Co-dir, Kings Lynn Fest; concert artist throughout Europe. *Teaching:* Fel, St Anne's Col, Oxford Univ, 75. *Awards:* Shakespeare Prize, Hamburg, 71; Sonning Prize, Copenhagen, 79; Dame, Brit Empire. *Mem:* Fel, Royal Soc Arts. *Mailing Add:* c/o Harold Shaw 1995 Broadway New York NY 10023

BAKER, JULIUS
FLUTE, EDUCATOR
b Cleveland, Ohio, Sept 23, 15. *Study:* Eastman Sch Music, 32-33; Curtis Inst Music, dipl, 37. *Rec Perf:* For RCA Victor, Decca, Vanguard, Westminster & Desmar. *Pos:* Mem, Cleveland Orch, 37-41 & Bach Aria Group, 47-65; first flutist, Pittsburgh Symph, 41-43, CBS Symph, 43-51 & Chicago Symph, 51-51; solo flutist, New York Phil Orch, 65- & throughout US, Canada, Europe & Japan. *Teaching:* Mem fac flute, Juilliard Sch, 54-, Curtis Inst Music, 80-, Manhattan Sch Music, 82- & New England Consv Music. *Mailing Add:* Enoch Crosbie Rd RFD 1 Brewster NY 10509

BAKER, LARRY A
COMPOSER, CONDUCTOR & MUSIC DIRECTOR
b Ft Smith, Ark, Sept 7, 48. *Study:* Okla Univ, with Spencer Norton, BMEd & BM(comp), 71; Cleveland Inst Music with Donald Erb, MM(comp), 73. *Works:* Before Assemblages III, Crystal Rec, 78; Childness, Fortnightly Music Club, 79; Chairs, Case Western Reserve Univ Surrealism Fest, 79; Reason, Cleveland Museum Art Fest, 81; Scaffolds, Cleveland Inst Music Symph Orch, 82; Pri-, Reconnaissance, 83. *Rec Perf:* Margins (David Cope), Orion Rec, 75; Embarking For Cythera (Eugene O'Brien), CRI, 82. *Pos:* Cond, Perf Group, 71-73; dir, New Music Ens, Cleveland Inst Music, 73-; cond, Reconnaissance, 78- *Teaching:* Fac mem, Cleveland Inst Music, 73- *Awards:* Grants, Nat Endowment Arts, 76 & 79 & Ohio Arts Coun, 79, 80 & 83; Cleveland Arts Prize, 83. *Mailing Add:* 2496 Derbyshire #11 Cleveland Heights OH 44106

BAKER, NANCY KOVALEFF
EDUCATOR, WRITER
b New York, NY, Oct 29, 48. *Study:* Smith Col, BA, 69; Yale Univ, MA & MPhil, 72, PhD(music hist), 75. *Teaching:* Asst prof music hist, Columbia Univ, 76- *Awards:* Res Humanities Grant, Columbia Univ, 77 & 78. *Mem:* Am Musicol Soc. *Interests:* Eighteenth century music theory; 18th and 19th century aesthetics of music. *Publ:* Auth, Heinrich Koch and the Theory of Melody, J Music Theory, 20: 1-48; The Aesthetic Theories of Heinrich Christoph Koch, Int Rev of the Aesthetics and Sociology of Music, VIII: 183-209; coauth, Expression, In: New Grove Dict of Music & Musicians, 78. *Mailing Add:* 25 Claremont Ave 4C New York NY 10027

BAKER, NORMAN LOUIS
CLARINET
b Milwaukee, Wis, Dec 8, 41. *Study:* Juilliard Sch Music, BMus, 64; Cleveland Inst Music, MMus, 68. *Pos:* Prog coordr, Atlanta Symph, three yrs, assoc prin clarinet, currently. *Teaching:* Mem fac, Ga State Univ, formerly. *Awards:* Nat Endowment Arts Chamber Music Grant, 70-72. *Mailing Add:* 4307 Rickenbacker Way NE Atlanta GA 30342

BAKER, ROBERT HART
CONDUCTOR & MUSIC DIRECTOR, COMPOSER
b Bronxville, NY, Mar 19, 54. *Study:* Mozarteum Consv, Salzburg, Austria, dipl, 71; Harvard Col, with Leonard Bernstein, AB, 74; Sch Music, Yale Univ, with Otto-Werner Mueller, MMA, 78. *Works:* Tombling Day Songs, perf by Betty Allen with RI Phil, 78; Sinfonietta, comn by Conn Comn Arts, 79. *Pos:* Music dir & cond, Youth Symph Orch NY, 77-81 & York Symph Orch, Pa, 83-; music dir & res cond, Asheville Symph Orch, NC, 81-; cond, St Louis Phil, 82- *Teaching:* Instr choral music, State Univ NY, Purchase, 77-78; lectr music hist, Univ NC, Asheville, 81- *Awards:* Devora Nadworney Young Comp Award, Nat Fedn Music Clubs, 75; Contemp Music Programming Award, ASCAP, 81. *Mem:* Am Symph Orch League; Int Double Reed Soc; ASCAP; Am Inst Verdi Studies; Ernest Bloch Soc. *Rep:* ICA Mgt 2219 Eastridge Rd Timonium MD 21093. *Mailing Add:* 129 Evelyn Pl Asheville NC 28801

BAKER, WARREN LOVELL
EDUCATOR, TROMBONE
b San Diego, Calif, Jan 22, 25. *Study:* Whitworth Col, Spokane, Wash, BA, 53; Ind Univ, Bloomington, MMEd, 54. *Pos:* Prin trombone, Ore Symph Orch, Portland, 64- *Teaching:* Prof music, Linfield Col, McMinnville, 57- *Mem:* Int Trombone Asn; Music Educr Nat Conf. *Mailing Add:* Dept Music Linfield Col McMinnville OR 97128

BAKKEGARD, (BENJAMIN) DAVID
HORN, EDUCATOR
b Austin, Tex, Jan 19, 51. *Study:* Calif State Univ, Fresno, BA(music); Northwestern Univ, MM; studied horn with Dale Clevenger, James Winter, James Decker, John Keene, Phillip Farkas, Wendell Hoss & Arnold Jacobs. *Pos:* Assoc co-prin horn, Baltimore Symph Orch, 76-80, prin horn, currently; mem, Chicago Opera Studio, formerly, Fresno Phil Orch, formerly, Towson Chamber Players, currently & Baltimore Wind Quintet, currently. *Teaching:* Mem fac horn, Peabody Consv Music, currently. *Awards:* Los Angeles Horn Club Compt Award, 71; Music Acad West Award, 73; Am Wind Symph Orch Award, 74. *Mem:* Phi Mu Alpha Sinfonia. *Mailing Add:* Horn Dept Peabody Consv Music Baltimore MD 21202

BAKSA, ROBERT (FRANK)
COMPOSER
b Bronx, NY, Feb 7, 38. *Study:* Univ Ariz, BA(comp), 59. *Works:* Aria de Capo (opera), Red Carnations (opera), Nonet for Winds and Strings, Songs to Poems of Emily Dickinson (two vols), Quintet for Oboe and Strings & Bagatelles for Piano, Alexander Broude, Inc. *Awards:* Standard Award, ASCAP, 64- *Mailing Add:* 625 West End Ave New York NY 10024

BALADA, LEONARDO
COMPOSER, EDUCATOR
b Barcelona, Spain, Sept 22, 33. *Study:* Consv Liceo, studied piano, 53; Juilliard Sch Music, dipl(comp), 60. *Works:* Guernica (orch), 67 & Maria Sabina (oratorio), 69; Gen Music Publ; Homage to Casals & to Sarasate, 75, Sardana (orch), 79, Quasi un Pasodoble (orch), 81, Hangman, Hangman! (chamber opera), 82 & Concerto for Violin & Orchestra, 82, G Schirmer. *Teaching:* Music, Walden Sch, New York, 62-63; head music dept, UN Int Sch, New York, 63-70; prof comp, Carnegie-Mellon Univ, 70- *Awards:* ASCAP Awards; Nat Endowment Arts Prize, Barcelona. *Bibliog:* Peter E Stone (auth), He writes for the audience, but on his own terms, New York Times, 11/21/82; Joseph Machlis (auth), Leonardo Balada, In: Introduction to Contemporary Music, Norton, 79. *Mem:* ASCAP; Am Music Ctr. *Publ:* Balada at 50, Madimina, A Chronicle of Musical Catalogues (in prep). *Rep:* G Schirmer Inc 866 Third Ave New York NY 10022. *Mailing Add:* Music Dept Carnegie-Mellon Univ Pittsburgh PA 15213

BALAZS, FREDERIC
CONDUCTOR, VIOLIN
b Budapest, Hungary. *Study:* Royal Acad Music, Budapest, dipl(violin, comp & cond); two year study at Univ Budapest; New York Col Music, DMus(perf). *Works:* Cello Concerto, Gabor Rejto, 64; Two Dances After David, Phil Hungarica, 66; A Statement of Faith, Victoria Symph, 66; Passacaglia, San Gabriel Symph, 80; Concerto (women's voices & orch), Los Angeles Phil; String Quartet #4 & #5, Portland String Quartet & Alban Berg String Quartet; An American Symphony After Walt Whitman, New York Phil and others. *Rec Perf:* Two Dances After David, CRI. *Pos:* Conct violinist & chamber music perf, nationwide; concertmaster, Budapest Symph Orch, various East Coast seasonal festivals, Victoria Fest Orch, Honolulu & NC Symph, also various motion picture & recording productions; music dir, Wichita Falls Symph, Tex & Tucson Symph Soc, Ariz; guest dir, numerous symph orch in US, Mex, Can, Asia & Europe; founder & dir, Vt Inst & Hawaii Inst Orch & Ens, 74- *Teaching:* Head, Instrm Div, Midwestern Univ, Wichita Falls, Tex; dir orch & opera dept, Col Consv Music, Univ Cincinnati; vis prof numerous colleges; also gives seminars & masterclasses. *Awards:* Remenyi Prize; Alice M Ditson Award for promotion of new Am music; hon mem, Int Mark Twain Lit Soc. *Mem:* Am Comp Alliance; BMI; Nat Fedn Music Clubs; Am Fedn Musicians. *Mailing Add:* 1314 Palm St #6 San Luis Obispo CA 93401

BALDASSARRE, JOSEPH ANTHONY
GUITAR & LUTE, EDUCATOR
b Cleveland, Ohio, Oct 16, 50. *Study:* Baldwin-Wallace Col Consv, BME, 72; Kent State Univ, MA(music hist & lit), 79; Cleveland Inst Music; Case Western Reserve Univ. *Teaching:* Lectr guitar, Baldwin-Wallace Col, 74-75; assoc prof music hist, guitar & lute, Boise State Univ, 75- *Bibliog:* Blake Bonnabeau (auth), His Music is Magic, Woodrover J, 7/22/81. *Mem:* Am Lute Soc; Guitar Soc. *Interests:* Lute technique. *Publ:* Auth, A Discussion of the Contents of Robert Dowland's Varietie of Lute-lessons (1610), Kent State Univ, 79. *Mailing Add:* Dept Music Boise State Univ Boise ID 83725

BALDERSTON, SUZANNE
HARP, EDUCATOR
Study: Juilliard Prep Sch; Consv Music, Oberlin Col; studied with Lucy Lewis & Edward Vito. *Pos:* Mem, NBC Symph, formerly; conct performer throughout US. *Teaching:* Head, Harp Dept, Univ Ala, formerly & Univ Calif, Santa Barbara, formerly; mem fac, Music Acad West, summer 83 & Calif State Univ, Northridge, currently. *Mem:* Am Harp Soc. *Mailing Add:* Dept Music Calif State Univ Northridge CA 91330

BALDWIN, DAVID
EDUCATOR, COMPOSER
b Alliance, Ohio, Dec 6, 46. *Study:* Baldwin-Wallace Col, BM, 68; Yale Univ, with Robert Morris, MMA, 74. *Works:* Notes (brass quintet), 73; Divertimento (flute & tuba); The Last Days (horn & tuba); This New Man (brass trio); Absurdities (brass trio); Time: Friend or Foe (brass choir); Time: A Confrontation (brass choir). *Teaching:* Asst prof brass, Univ Minn, Minneapolis, 74- *Mailing Add:* 589 Lincoln Ave St Paul MN 55102

BALDWIN, JOHN
EDUCATOR, PERCUSSION
b Arkansas City, Kans, Apr 12, 40. *Study:* Univ Wichita, BME, 63; Wichita State Univ, MME, 65; Mich State Univ, PhD, 70. *Works:* Odo, Idaho Bicentennial Choir, 76; Allegro, Boise State Keyboard Perc Ens. *Pos:* Mem, Boise Phil, Boise Opera, Treasure Valley Wind Ens, Music from Bear Valley & Boise City Band, currently. *Teaching:* Instr, Mich State Univ, 65-68 & Wis State Univ, 68-71; grad asst, Lawrence Univ, 69-71; prof, Boise State Univ, 71- *Mem:* Music Educr Nat Conf; Percussive Arts Soc; Music Teachers Nat Asn; Nat Asn Col Wind & Perc Instr. *Publ:* Ed, Percussion Clinical Column, Sch Musician; Newsline/On the Move, Percussive Notes. *Mailing Add:* Dept Music 1910 University Dr Boise ID 83725

BALDWIN, MARCIA
MEZZO-SOPRANO, EDUCATOR
b Milford, Nebr, Nov 5, 39. *Study:* Northwestern Univ; studied with Marinka Gurewich; Opera Wkshp, Hunter Col, with Rose Landver & Ludwig Donath; Kathryn Long Opera Sch; studied with Ellen Faull, Esther Andreas, Jan Behr, Madeline Saunders & Martin Rich. *Rec Perf:* On DG. *Roles:* Mercedes in Carmen, Santa Fe Opera, 61; Viola in Twelfth Night, Lake George Opera, 68; Leonore in Fidelio, Kaiserslautern, WGer, 77; Suzuki in Madama Butterfly; Magdalene in Die Meistersinger von Nürnberg; Siebel in Faust; Stephano in Romeo et Juliette. *Pos:* Mem, Metropolitan Opera, 63-76; leading roles with San Francisco, Philadelphia, Ft Worth, Santa Fe, Central City, Cincinnati & Lake George opera co; recitalist, symph & oratorio appearances throughout US. *Teaching:* Private lessons voice, 70-; mem fac, Am Inst Musical Studies, Graz, Austria, summers 76-78 & Ind Univ, 78-81; prof voice, Eastman Sch Music, 80- *Awards:* Rockefeller Found Grant; Ford Fel; Winner, Int Music Compt, Munich. *Mailing Add:* Eastman Sch Music 26 Gibbs St Rochester NY 14604

BALDWIN, NICHOLAS G
CRITIC
b Florence, Italy, Oct 6, 28; US citizen. *Study:* Wesleyan Univ, BA, 51; Univ Manchester, England, MA, 55. *Pos:* Music critic, Des Moines Register, Iowa, 68- *Mailing Add:* Des Moines Register 715 Locust Des Moines IA 50304

BALDWIN, SHIRLEE EMMONS See Emmons, Shirlee

BALES, RICHARD HENRY HORNER
COMPOSER, CONDUCTOR & MUSIC DIRECTOR
b Alexandria, Va, Feb 3, 15. *Study:* Eastman Sch Music, MusB, 36; Berkshire Music Ctr, studied cond with Serge Koussevitzky, 40; Juilliard Sch, dipl(cond), 41; studied with Albert Stoessel, Abram Chasins & Bernard Rogers. *Works:* The Great American Fishing Industry (music for four doc films), US Dept Commerce, 76; In Memory of Leopold Stokowski, 77; God's Presence (a cappella choir); four National Gallery Suites; Episodes From a

Lincoln Ballet; Stony Brook (strings); The Republic (chorus, soloists, speaker & orch). *Pos:* Cond, Va-NC Symph, 36-38 & Washington Cathedral Choral Soc, 45-46; music dir & cond, Nat Gallery Orch, Nat Gallery Art, 43-; music dir, Nat Symph Orch, summer 47; guest cond, Philadelphia Little Symph Orch, New York Fest, Rochester Phil, Nat Symph Orch, San Antonio, Oklahoma Symph; and others. *Teaching:* Instr, Mass State Teachers Col, summer 41, George Washington Univ, 53 & Eastman Sch Music, summers 65, 66 & 67. *Awards:* Award Merit, Nat Asn Comp & Cond, 59; Alice M Ditson Award, 60; First Annual Arts Award, Washington Times, 83. *Mem:* Life fel, Int Inst Arts & Lett; Am Fedn Musicians; Bruckner Soc Am. *Mailing Add:* Nat Gallery Art Constitution Ave at 6th NW Washington DC 20565

BALEY, VIRKO
CONDUCTOR, COMPOSER
b Radechiv, Ukraine, USSR, Oct 21, 38. *Study:* Los Angeles Consv, BM, 60, MM, 62. *Works:* Tropes (cello & piano), comn by Nev Teachers Asn, 72; Pentat (trombone & string quartet), comn by Nat Endowment Arts, 78; Words VII, perf by Carol Plantamura & Sonor, 79; Partita for Trombone, Piano & Tape, Lamentation of Adrian Leverkuehn, 79 & Sculptured Birds, 82, comn by Nev State Coun on Arts. *Rec Perf:* Dragonetti Lives!, Takoma Rec, 75; 20th Century Ukrainian Violin Music, Orion Rec, 79; The Music of Morton Subotnick: The Wild Beasts, Nonesuch Rec, 81. *Pos:* Asst cond, 52nd Army Band, Fort Ord, Calif, 63; assoc cond, 84th Army Band, Fulda, Germany, 63-65; music dir, Ann Contemp Music Fest, Las Vegas, Nev, 70-74 & Las Vegas Symph Orch, 80-; music dir & cond, Las Vegas Chamber Players, 74- *Teaching:* Instr piano, theory & comp, Calif Inst Arts, 66-70; prof piano, hist & comp, Univ Nev, 70- *Awards:* Nat Endowment Arts Music Fel, 79; Musician of Year, Nev Gov Award, 83. *Mem:* Nat Acad Rec Arts & Sci. *Interests:* 20th century Soviet music. *Publ:* Auth, The Kiev Avant-Garde, Numus-West, 74; Die Avantgarde con Kiew: Ein Retrospective auf halbem Weg, Melos, 76; A Retrospective: The Soviet Avant-Garde, Perf Arts, Los Angeles Phil, 82. *Mailing Add:* Dept Music Univ Nev Las Vegas NV 89154

BALK, H WESLEY
DIRECTOR—OPERA, EDUCATOR
Study: Yale Univ. *Pos:* Res theater dir, Minn Opera, 65-; dir, New York City Opera, formerly, Santa Fe Opera, formerly, Houston Grand Opera, formerly, Aspen Music Fest, formerly, Juilliard Sch, formerly & others; supvr, San Francisco Opera Merola Prog, currently. *Teaching:* Assoc prof theater arts, Univ Minn, currently. *Awards:* Nat Opera Inst Hon, 82. *Mem:* Nat Asn Sch Music. *Publ:* Auth, The Complete Singer-Actor: Training for Music-Theater, Univ Minn Press; Performing Power (in press). *Mailing Add:* Minn Opera 850 Grand Ave St Paul MN 55105

BALK, LEO FREDERICK
ADMINISTRATOR, EDITOR
b El Paso, Tex, Feb 3, 53. *Study:* Univ Chicago, with Philip Gossett & Howard M Brown, BA, 74; Univ Pa, MA, 79. *Pos:* Music ed, Garland Publ Inc, 81- *Awards:* Martha Baird Rockefeller Fund Grant, 80-81; Lurcy Fel, 80-81. *Mem:* Am Musicol Soc; Music Libr Asn. *Interests:* Nineteenth century French opera. *Mailing Add:* c/o Garland Publ Inc 136 Madison Ave New York NY 10016

BALKIN, ALFRED
COMPOSER, EDUCATOR
b Boston, Mass, Aug 12, 31. *Study:* Ind Univ, Bloomington, AB, 52, MA, 53; Columbia Univ, EdD, 68. *Works:* We Live in the City (song cycle for children), Theodore Presser Co, 70; America's About ... , 76, City Scene (song cycle for children), 77 & The Musicians of Bremen, 82, Now View Music. *Teaching:* Asst prof music, Eastern Conn State Col, 66-68; assoc prof, Fla State Univ, 63-71 & Western Mich Univ, 71- *Mem:* Music Educr Nat Conf; ASCAP; Am Fedn Musicians. *Publ:* Auth, Educators Must Face Reality, Music J, 72; coauth (with Jack Taylor), Involvement with Music, Houghton Mifflin Co, 74; auth, What Kind of MCP Are You?, Selmer Bandwagon, 80, Arts Educ, 80 & Fla Music Dir, 81; Computer-assisted Instruction ... Hi-Tech for Higher Achievement, Selmer Educ Serv, 83. *Mailing Add:* 2506 Frederick Ave Kalamazoo MI 49008

BALL, LOUIS OLIVER, JR
EDUCATOR, ADMINISTRATOR
b Knoxville, Tn, May 15, 29. *Study:* Univ Tenn, BA, 51, MS, 53; Southern Baptist Theol Sem, Louisville, MSM, 57, DMA, 62. *Works:* The Heavens Are Telling (organ & piano), 79, Lift Thine Eyes (organ & piano), 83 & Duo Deo Gloria, A Wedding Album (organ & piano; in prep), Broadman Press. *Rec Perf:* The Tennessee Baptist Chorale, SBC-TV, 68; Volunteer Choral on Tour, Smith Studios, 72. *Pos:* Choral dir, Fulton High Sch, Tenn, 51-53. *Teaching:* Prof cond & church music, Carson-Newman Col, 61- *Awards:* Teacher of Year, Knoxville Music Teachers Asn, 76. *Mem:* Music Teachers Nat Asn; Hymn Soc Am; Nat Guild Piano Teachers; Tenn Asn Music Exec (pres, 75); Southern Baptist Church Music Conf (vpres, 80-82). *Publ:* Auth, Hymn Playing Kit, 79 & Five Lessons in Hymn Playing (in prep), Convention. *Mailing Add:* 405 E Ellis St Jefferson City TN 37760

BALLAM, MICHAEL L
TENOR
b Logan, Utah, Aug 21, 51. *Study:* Utah State Univ, BMus, 72; Ind Univ, MMus, 74, DMus, 76. *Roles:* Beelzebub in Paradise Lost, Lyr Opera Chicago, 78; Duke of Mantua in Rigoletto, Providence Opera, 80; Elemer in Arabella, San Francisco Opera, 81; Rodolfo in La Boheme, 81 & Eisenstein in Fledermaus, 82, Miss Opera; Don Jose in Carmen, Mich Opera, 82; Babylas in Monsieur Choufleuri, Washington Opera, 82 & 83; Pinkerton in Madame

Butterfly, Ark Opera Theatre & Chattanooga Opera, 82 & 83. *Teaching:* Artist in res voice, Ind Univ, Bloomington, 76-77; master voice & opera, Univ Utah, 82- *Awards:* Nat Opera Inst Perf Grant, 80 & 81. *Publ:* Auth, History of Music Through Ten European Cities, Universal/Princeton, 74. *Rep:* ICM Artists Ltd 40 W 57th New York NY 10019. *Mailing Add:* 116 W 72nd #12D New York NY 10023

BALLARD, GREGORY
COMPOSER, PIANO
b Battle Creek, Mich, July 18, 54. *Study:* Univ Mich, BMus, 76; spec study & res, WBerlin, Germany, 76-77. *Works:* Piano Music 2, perf by Robert Black, 76, Robert Miller, 78 & Donna Coleman, 79; Mercury (oboe & piano), C F Peters, 82; Construction I (piano solo), 82; Suite No 2, Rockit, comn & perf by Current & Modern Consort, 82; Construction VII, South Wind, comn by Danza Una Costa Rica. *Pos:* Comp & pianist, Morelli Ballet Sch, New York, 79-81; comp & pianist in res, New Perf Gallery, San Francisco, 83- *Teaching:* Music dir, comp, pianist & asst prof, Sch Music, Univ Mich, 80-83. *Awards:* Piano Comp Cont Winner, Int Soc Contemp Music, 76; Charles Ives Award, Am Acad & Inst Arts & Lett, 77. *Mailing Add:* 285 Downey St San Francisco CA 94117

BALLARD, LOUIS WAYNE
COMPOSER, EDUCATOR
b Miami, Okla, July 8, 31. *Study:* Northeast Okla A&M Col, Miami, AA, 51; Univ Tulsa, BA, 53, BMusEd, 54, MMus, 62; Col Santa Fe, Hon DMus, 73. *Works:* The Gods Will Hear (cantata), Bourne Music Co, 64; Koshare (ballet), 66 & The Four Moons (ballet), 67, New Southwest Music Publ; Scenes From Indian Life, 68, Ritmo Indio (woodwind quintet), 69 & Why the Duck Has a Short Tail, 69, Bourne Music Co; Incident at Wounded Knee, Belwin Mills Publ Corp, 74; Portrait of Will Rogers (cantata with narrator), New Southwest Music Publ, 76. *Pos:* Music dir, Nelagoney Consolidated Sch, Okla, 54-56 & Webster High Sch, 56-58; dir music & perf arts, Inst Am Indian Arts, Santa Fe, 62-69; prog dir music, US Dept Interior, Cent Off, Washington, DC, 69-79. *Awards:* Standard Awards, ASCAP, 66-82; First Prize, Marion Nivens MacDowell, 69; Educr Press Award, Syracuse Univ, 70. *Bibliog:* William Farrington (auth), Louis Ballard, American Composer, Vol V, No 1, Sunstone Press, Santa Fe, 76; Jane B Katz (auth), This Song Remembers, Houghton Mifflin Co, 80. *Mem:* Am Music Ctr; ASCAP; Music Educr Nat Conf. *Publ:* Auth, The American Indian Sings, Southwest Music Publ, 70; Oklahoma Indian Chants for the Classroom (disc), Murbo Rec, 70; Discovering American Indian Music (film), BFA Educ Media, 70; American Indian Music for the Classroom (text), Canyon Rec, 73; Music and Dance of North American Indians, Arete Publ, 75. *Mailing Add:* 3956 Old Santa Fe Trail Santa Fe NM 87501

BALLARD, MARY ANNE
VIOLA DA GAMBA, EDUCATOR
b Louisville, Ky, Feb 27, 42. *Study:* Wellesley Col, BA, 64; Univ Pa, MA, 75. *Rec Perf:* Fantasies of Henry Purcell (in prep), William Lawes (in prep) and John Jenkins (in prep), Gasparo. *Pos:* Mem, Oberlin Consort Viols, 77-, Baltimore Consort, 79-, Serenata, 82- *Teaching:* Dir collegium musicum, Univ Pa, 71-; instr viola da gamba, Peabody Inst Music, 81-; dir musica alta & instr viola da gamba, Princeton Univ, 82- *Mem:* Am Musicol Soc; Viola da Gamba Soc Am. *Publ:* Auth, Music of the French Baroque, Vox Prod, 77. *Mailing Add:* 8871 Norwood Ave Philadelphia PA 19118

BALLENGER, KENNETH LEIGH
EDUCATOR, BARITONE
b Des Moines, Iowa, July 28, 21. *Study:* Hardin-Simmons Univ, BM, 47; Eastman Sch Music, MM, 48. *Works:* 150 Years—A Celebration, perf by First Presby Choir & Orch, 80; Harps of Gold, perf by First Presby Choir & Instrm, 82. *Teaching:* Assoc prof voice & opera, Stetson Univ, 48-53; prof, Univ Ark, Fayetteville, 53-, dir, Univ Arkettes, currently. *Mem:* Music Teachers Nat Asn. *Mailing Add:* 506 Hawthorn Fayetteville AR 72701

BALLINGER, CATHRYN (FLUELLEN)
MEZZO-SOPRANO, ADMINISTRATOR
b New Castle, Ala, Feb 16, 40. *Study:* Calif Inst Arts, with Charles Brausz, 58-59; Univ Calif, Los Angeles, with Martial Singher, Dr Jan Popper & Dr Natalie Limonick, 59-60; Los Angeles City Col, with John Biggs, cert, 60. *Works:* Cease Sorrow, 74 & I Believe in Love, 74, perf by Cathryn Ballinger & Tony Williams, 74; Requiem for the Children, perf by Cathryn Ballinger, Emme Kemp & others, 81. *Rec Perf:* A Vivaldi, Crystal Rec, 75; Il Tramonto (O Respighi), Orion Master Rec, 78 & PBS, 81. *Roles:* Serena, San Bernardino Civic Light Opera, 72; Azucena in Il Trovatore, Santa Monica Opera Co, 79; Monisha, Los Angeles Opera Co, 79. *Pos:* Soloist, Los Angeles Jubilee Singers, 65-70; soloist & mem, Los Angeles Camerata, 72-; mem, NY Opera Ebony, 83. *Teaching:* Instr voice, Eubanks Consv Music, Los Angeles, 76-78. *Awards:* Nat Winner, Cleveland Symph Orch Blossom Fest, 70. *Bibliog:* Article, Univ Calif, Los Angeles Bruin, 78; George Jellinek (auth), article, Stereo Rev, spring 79; Luigi Smaldino (auth), article, L'Italo Am Los Angeles, 79. *Mem:* Nat Asn Negro Musicians (vpres western region, 74-75); founder, Los Angeles Coun Arts (pres, 72-). *Publ:* Auth, Musicians Convention in Atlanta, Lyr Mag, 74. *Mailing Add:* c/o John Copage of Hollywood 5875 Verdun Ave Los Angeles CA 90043

BALOGH, ENDRE
VIOLIN
b Los Angeles, Calif, June 28, 54. *Study:* Univ Calif, Los Angeles; studied with Joseph Borisoff Piastro, Manuel Compinsky; Yehudi Menuhin Sch, London, 64; studied with Mehli Mehta. *Pos:* Soloist, various Am symph incl Los

Angeles Phil, Denver Symph, Wash Nat Symph & Seattle Symph; recitalist, throughout US & Europe with Berlin Phil, Rotterdam Phil, Frankfurt Symph, Tonhalle Orch & Basel Symph; violinist, Pac Soloists Trio. *Teaching:* Fac mem, Univ Southern Calif. *Awards:* First Prize & Grand Prize, Denver Symph Solo Compt; Top Violin Prize, Merriweather Post Cont; and numerous others. *Publ:* Contribr, Los Angeles Times. *Mailing Add:* 318 N Detroit St Los Angeles CA 90036

BALOGH, OLGA MITANA
VIOLIN
b Budapest, Hungary, Oct 19, 17. *Study:* Southwestern Col Music; Muzart Consv Music; studied with Vlado Kolitsch & Joesph Piastro. *Pos:* Violinist, NBC & CBS; mem, Los Angeles Phil & Hollywood Bowl Symph Orch, 43-77; performed throughout Asia, Europe, Can & US. *Mem:* Hollywood Wilshire Community Conct Asn; Calif String Teachers Asn. *Mailing Add:* 318 N Detroit St Los Angeles CA 90036

BALSAM, ARTUR
PIANO, TEACHER
b Warsaw, Poland, 06; US citizen. *Study:* Consv Lodz, Poland; Music Acad, Berlin, 28-31. *Rec Perf:* Piano music of Mozart & Haydn; chamber music with several great artists. *Pos:* Perf, solo piano & chamber music pub concts. *Teaching:* Instr, Eastman Sch Music, Boston Univ & Manhattan Sch Music, 68- *Awards:* First prize, piano compt, Berlin, 30 & 31. *Mem:* Bohemians. *Mailing Add:* 258 Riverside Dr New York NY 10025

BALSHONE, CATHY S (CATHY S BALSHONE-BECZE)
COMPOSER, LIBRARIAN
b Columbus, Ohio, Apr 1, 46. *Study:* Sarah Lawrence Col, studied comp with Meyer Kupferman, BA, 68; Sch Libr Serv, Columbia Univ, MS, 70; Longy Sch Music, studied music kindergarten method with Minnetta Kessler, cert, 80 . *Works:* Nikstlitslepmur (ballet), 67, Androcles & the Lion (cabaret song), 67 & Echo & Narcissus (opera), 68, Sarah Lawrence Col; Invitation to a Concert (series), Broward Co Pub Sch Syst, Fla, 74; For You, Jazz Trio, Hyatt Regency, Cambridge, Mass, 82; Eleanor, Benjamin Balshone, Ohio State Univ, 82. *Pos:* Librn II, Fine & Perf Arts, Ft Lauderdale Pub Libr, 70-72; librn & asst to cur educ, Ft Lauderdale Museum Arts, 74-77; head librn, Boston Consv, 77-, ed, Trichordon, 81- *Teaching:* Instr Music, Maumee Valley Co Day Sch, 68-69; private instr piano, 68-; chair educ dept, Ft Lauderdale Jr Symph Guild, 74-76. *Awards:* Sarah Parker Award, Am Symph Orch League, 76. *Mem:* Music Libr Asn; Boston Area Music Libr (chmn, 82-, co-secy, 80); Mass Music Teachers Asn. *Publ:* Auth, The Museum Experience for Children, Ft Lauderdale Museum Arts, 75. *Mailing Add:* 24 Concord Ave #116 Cambridge MA 02138

BALTER, ALAN (NEIL)
CONDUCTOR, CLARINET
b New York, NY, Mar 17, 45. *Study:* Juilliard Sch Music, 61-62; Oberlin Col, BA & BMus, 66; Cleveland Inst Music, MMus, 67. *Pos:* Princ clarinet, 67-75, Atlanta Symph Orch, cond asst, 72-75; cond, San Francisco Consv Music, 75-79; Exxon/Arts Endowment Cond, 79-82; assoc cond, Baltimore Symph Orch, 82-; music dir & cond, Akron Symph Orch, 83- & Memphis Symph Orch, 84- *Teaching:* Instr orch & clarinet, Ga State Univ, 70-75; instr orch, cond & clarinet, San Francisco Consv Music, 75-79. *Awards:* Award Grant, Nat Endowment Arts, 66; Exxon/Arts Endowment Cond Fel, 79. *Mem:* Am Symph Orch League Cond Guild; Int Clarinet Soc; Clarinetwork, (mem bd dir, 81-). *Publ:* Self Expression & Conducting: The Humanities, Harcourt Brace Jovanovich, 78. *Rep:* Herbert Barrett Mgt 1860 Broadway New York NY 10023. *Mailing Add:* 327 Dumbarton Rd Baltimore MD 21212

BAMBERGER, DAVID
DIRECTOR—OPERA, WRITER
b Albany, NY, Oct 14, 40. *Study:* Sch Drama, Yale Univ; Univ Paris; Swarthmore Col, BA. *Pos:* Stage dir & producer, New York City Opera, Nat Opera, Santiago, Chile, Cincinnati Summer Opera, Pittsburgh Opera, Hartford Opera Co & Oberlin Music Theater, Ohio; gen mgr & artistic dir, Cleveland Opera Co, currently; producer & dir many operas; contribr, Opera News. *Awards:* H H Powers Travel Award, 79. *Mailing Add:* 1289 Andrews Ave Cleveland OH 44107

BAMPTON, ROSE E (PELLETIER)
SOPRANO
b Cleveland, Ohio. *Study:* Curtis Inst Music, BM, 32; Hobart & William Smith Col, 80; Drake Univ, LHD, 40. *Rec Perf:* Gurdelieder (Schönberg), 31 & Album Operatic Arias, 32-35, RCA Victor. *Roles:* Aida, Trovatore, Parsifal, Tannhäuser, Lohengren & Alceste, Metropolitian Opera, 32-50; Aida, Covent Garden, London, 35; Parsifal, Tannhauser, Lohengren, Meistersinger, Rosenkavalier, Ariadne, Daphne & Armide, Teatro Colon, Beunos Aires, Argentina, 45-50. *Pos:* Pres, Bagby Found, 79- *Teaching:* Voice fac, Manhattan Sch Music, 63-79, NC Sch Arts, 64-69; Juilliard Sch, 74- *Mem:* Nat Asn Teachers Singing; New York Singing Teachers Asn. *Mailing Add:* 322 E 57th St New York NY 10022

BANAT, GABRIEL JEAN
VIOLIN, CONDUCTOR
b Timisoara, Romania, Sept 23, 26; US citizen. *Study:* Royal Hungarian Acad Music, MA(perf), 44; studied with Ede Zathureczky, Leo Weiner, Zoltan Kodaly, George Enesco, Galamian & Milstein. *Rec Perf:* Violin Show Pieces, Decca, London, 65; Bartok Solo Sonata & Sonata II (violin & piano), Cutty Wren, 68; The Advantgarde Violin, 70 & Pendereczky Album, Vox; Toccata (R H Lewis), CRI, 71. *Pos:* Charter mem, Marlborough Fest Young

Audiences, 51-62; concertmaster, Hartford Symph,, 61-62; music dir, Westchester Consv Symph, 68-81; violinist, New York Phil, 70- *Teaching:* Asst prof violin, Smith Col, 56-64; head violin & orch, Westchester Consv, 64-81; affiliate, State Univ NY, Purchase. *Awards:* Bronze Medal, Concours Int Consv, Geneva, 46; winner, Concert Artists Guild, 50. *Publ:* Ed, Masters of the Violin, 6 vols, Johnson Reprint Corp, 80-82. *Mailing Add:* c/o Diana Stevenson 26 Magnolia Dr Dobbs Ferry NY 10522

BANDUCCI, ANTONIA
EDUCATOR
b Apr 3, 45. *Study:* Univ Colo, BA; Adams State Col, MA; Wash Univ. *Pos:* Mem, Collegium Musicum, Wash Univ; staff mem, Am Recorder Soc—Amherst Summer Wkshp. *Teaching:* Lectr music, Univ Col, Wash Univ; guest lectr, St Louis Symph Orch; mem fac music hist, St Louis Consv Music, currently. *Mem:* Col Music Soc; Am Musicol Soc. *Mailing Add:* St Louis Consv Music 560 Trinity Ave St Louis MO 63130

BANOWETZ, JOSEPH MURRAY
PIANO, EDUCATOR
b Muskogee, Okla, Dec 5, 34. *Study:* Juilliard, studied piano with Carl Friedberg, 52-53; Vienna State Acad Music & Dramatic Arts, artist dipl, 56; Univ Mich, studied piano with Gyorgy Sandor, 63-66. *Rec Perf:* 12 Transcendental Etudes (Liszt), 72, Miniatures (Liszt), 73, Piano Works, 73 & Sonata No 3 (De Almeida), 75, Educo Rec; Kinderszenen (Schumann), 75 & Sonatas, Op 13, Op 27, No 2 (Beethoven), 75, Gen Words & Music; Four Mephisto Waltzes (Liszt), Orion Master Rec, 80. *Pos:* Rec ed, Piano Quart, Wilmington, Vt, 81- *Teaching:* Guest lectr piano, Nat Music Camp, Interlochen, Mich, 68-73; prof, NTex State Univ, 73-; artist & teacher, Nat Piano Found, Chicago, Ill, 77-; vis prof, Canton Consv Music, People's Rep China, summer 83. *Awards:* Pan Am Prize, Orgn Am States, Washington, DC, 66. *Mem:* Am Liszt Soc; Am Asn Univ Prof; Music Teachers Nat Asn; Col Music Soc; Tex Music Teachers Asn (keyboard chmn, 75, 76 & 80). *Publ:* Contribr, How to Teach Piano Successfully, 73, ed, Scarlatti: An Introduction to the Composer and His Music, 78, Bach: An Introduction to the Well-Tempered Clavier, 79 & Liszt: Forgotten Masterpieces, 80, Kjos; contrib, Teaching Piano: A Comprehensive Guide, Yorktown Press, 81. *Rep:* 130 Social Hall Ave Salt Lake City UT 84111. *Mailing Add:* PO Box 955 Denton TX 76201

BARACH, DANIEL PAUL
EDUCATOR, VIOLA
b Weirton, WVa, Feb 8, 31. *Study:* Mich State Univ, BMus, 53; Univ Ill, MMus, 57; Eastman Sch Music, with Francis Tursi; private study with Primrose, Lillian Fuchs, Renzo Sabatini & Bela Katona. *Pos:* Violist, Houston Symph Orch, 54-55, Minneapolis Symph Orch, 57-64, Marlboro Music Fest, summer 59 & Sheldon String Trio, 77- *Teaching:* Prof viola, State Univ New York, Oswego, 64-; instr viola, Nat Music Camp, summer 74; teacher Alexander tech, Eastman Sch Music, 83. *Mem:* Music Educr Nat Conf; Viola Soc Am; Viola D'Amore Soc Am; Soc Teachers of Alexander Tech, England; New York State Sch Music Asn. *Publ:* Auth, Conversation with Feodor Drushynin, Am Viola Soc Newsletter No 21, 81. *Mailing Add:* 160 West 4th St Oswego NY 13126

BARATI, GEORGE
COMPOSER, CONDUCTOR & MUSIC DIRECTOR
b Gyor, Hungary, Apr 3, 13; US citizen. *Study:* Franz Liszt Consv Music, Budapest, grad, teacher's & state artist dipl, 35-38; Princeton Univ, study comp with Roger Sessions, 39-43. *Works:* Symphony, The Dragon and the Phoenix, Chamber Concerto & Harpsichord Quartet (flute, oboe & double bass), Peters Ed; Confluence for Orchestra, Am Comp Alliance; Cello Concerto, London, San Francisco & Honolulu; Branches of Time (two pianos & orch), Aptos, Calif, Grand Rapids & Berkeley. *Rec Perf:* Masses No 4 & No 12 (Haydn), 63, Masses No 1 & No 4 (Schubert), 65 & St Luke Passion (Bach), Lyrichord Disks; Works by Halsey Stevens, Ulysses Kay & Dai-Keong Lee, Works by Gordon Binkerd, Tcherepnin & Saint-Saens & Cello Concerto, CRI; Music of Hawaii, Decca. *Pos:* Music dir, Barati Chamber Orch San Francisco, 47-52, Honolulu Symph & Opera, 50-68 & Santa Cruz Co Symph, 71-81; exec dir, Montalvo Ctr for Arts, Saratoga, Calif, 68-78. *Teaching:* Lectr, Univ Hawaii, 50-57 & Univ Calif, Santa Cruz, 72-73. *Awards:* Ditson Award; Naumburg Award, 59; Guggenheim Fel, 65. *Mem:* Am Comp Alliance. *Publ:* Auth, A Composer Looks at the Arts (film), made in Korea for US agencies, 71; Mathematics and Music, Univ Hawaii, 65, 2nd ed, Musical Am, 66. *Mailing Add:* 230 Sunset Lane Soquel CA 95073

BARBAGALLO, JAMES ANGELO
PIANO
b Pittsburg, Calif, Nov 3, 52. *Study:* Juilliard Sch, BM, 74, MM, 76. *Rec Perf:* Concerto in Slendro (Lou Harrison), Westminster, 72; Sonatas (Beethoven), Nimbus, 80; Sonata K570 (Mozart), Melodiya, 82. *Pos:* Piano soloist, San Francisco Symph, 70, Baltimore Symph, 77, Moscow State Orch, 82, and others. *Teaching:* Asst to Sascha Gorodnitzki, Juilliard Sch, 80- *Awards:* Second Prize, Univ Md Int Piano Compt, 77 & Gina Bachauer Int Piano Compt, 80; Bronze Medal Winner, Tschaikovsky Int Piano Compt, Moscow, 82. *Bibliog:* William Fertik (dir), III Int Tschaikovsky Piano Compt (film), Johnston Films, 82; The Pianists Progress, New Yorker. *Rep:* Am Artists Mgt Inc 300 West End Ave New York NY 10023. *Mailing Add:* 50-12 Vernon Blvd Long Island City NY 11101

BARBASH, LILLIAN
ADMINISTRATOR
b Brooklyn, NY, Aug 10, 27. *Study:* Hunter Col, AB, 47; Hofstra Univ, 77. *Pos:* Exec dir, Islip Arts Coun, 76- & Long Island Phil, 80- *Mem:* Chamber Music Am; Asn Col, Univ & Community Arts Adminr. *Mailing Add:* 30 Bayway Ave Brightwaters NY 11718

BARBEAU, BERNARD
TEACHER, BARITONE
b Peabody, Mass. *Study:* New England Consv Music, with William L Whitney, BM, 48, MM, 50; Aspen Music Sch, with Martial Singher. *Roles:* Fat in Second Hurricane, Jordan Hall, Boston, Mass, 47; Rigoletto in Rigoletto, Arundel Opera Theater, Maine, 53. *Pos:* Soloist, Boston Pops, 68; baritone, The Cavaliers (male quartet), 54-70. *Teaching:* Voice, New England Consv Music, 52- *Mailing Add:* 17 Amherst Rd Beverly MA 01915

BARBER, DANIEL ROWLAND *
PIANO
b Cleveland, Ohio, Apr 30, 48. *Study:* Oberlin Col Consv, BM, 70; Ind Univ, MM, 72. *Teaching:* Asst to Jorge Bolet, Ind Univ, 75-77; asst prof piano, Ill State Univ, 78-80; fac mem piano, Cleveland Music Sch Settlement, 82- & Cleveland Inst Music, 82- *Mailing Add:* 3541 Normandy Rd Shaker Heights OH 44120

BARBER, GAIL (GUSEMAN)
HARP, COMPOSER
b New Iberia, La. *Study:* Baylor Univ, 54-56; Eastman Sch Music, with Eileen Malone, BM(harp), 56-59, perf cert. *Works:* Windmill Sketches, perf by comp, 70 & Salvi Publ, 83; Improvisation on a Familiar Melody, perf by comp, 71 & Salvi Publ, 83; Visions (harp solo), perf by comp, 74; Duets for Harp, 76 & 83 & Prelude in E Minor (Bach), 83, comn & perf by Tex Tech Harp Ens. *Rec Perf:* Poeme, 76, Harp Concerto (Gliere), 80 & Sonate (Damase), 83, Am Harp Soc Tape Libr; Gail Barber—Harpist, Caldwell Studios (in prep). *Pos:* Second harp, Rochester Phil Orch & Eastman Rochester, 57-59; prin harp, Peninsula Fest Orch, 59-61; harp soloist & prin harp, Cleveland Little Symph, 60-61; concerto performer, Community Concerts & Civic Music, 60-61; ed, Am Harp J, Am Harp Soc, 71-79. *Teaching:* Instr harp & music theory, Baylor Univ, 61-66; assoc prof music, Tex Tech Univ, 66- *Awards:* Citation for Outstanding Serv, Am Harp Soc, 70 & 79. *Mem:* Am Harp Soc (mem bd dir, 70-76 & 80-84). *Mailing Add:* PO Box 64189 Lubbock TX 79464

BARBIERI, FEDORA
MEZZO-SOPRANO, CONTRALTO
b Trieste, Italy, June 4, 19. *Study:* Consv Trieste, with Luigi Toffolo; Centro Avviamento Teatro Lirico, Florence; studied with Bugamelli. *Rec Perf:* On His Master's Voice, RCA Victor, Cetra & Philips. *Roles:* Fidalma in Il Matrimonio segreto, Teatro Comunale, Florence, 40; Dariola in Don Giovanni Manara, 43 & Celestina, 63, Maggio M, Florence; Governante in Il Linguaggio dei fiori, La Scala, 63; Lizaveta in La Idiota, Rome, 70; Anfissa in Il Esculapio al Neon, Caligari, 72; Angelina in La Cenerentola; Azucena in Il Trovatore; and many others. *Pos:* Ms & contr, Teatro Colon, Buenos Aires, 47-, Royal Opera House Covent Garden, 50-, Metropolitan Opera House, 50-, La Scala, 52- & with other maj co in Europe, North Am & South Am. *Awards:* Citation, Repub Italy. *Mailing Add:* c/o Robert Lombardo Assoc 1 Harkness Plaza 61 W 62 St Suite 6F New York NY 10023

BARBIERI, SAVERIO
BASS
b New York, NY. *Study:* Univ Fla. *Roles:* Colline in La Boheme; Pimen in Boris Godunov; Osmin in Die Entführung aus dem Serail; Hunding in Die Walküre; Marti in A Village Romeo and Juliet; Raimondo in Lucia di Lammermoor; Basilio in Il Barbiere di Siviglia. *Pos:* Performer, St Paul Opera, Mich Opera Theater, Metropolitan Opera Studio, Opera Orch New York, Opera Co Boston, New York Phil, Pittsburgh Symph, Handel Opera Fest, Boston Symph & Pittsburgh Symph. *Mailing Add:* c/o Int Artists Mgt 58 W 72nd St New York NY 10023

BARBOSA, ANTONIO (G)
PIANO
b Paraiba, Brazil, Dec 9, 46. *Study:* Brazilian Consv, Rio de Janeiro, MA, 69. *Rec Perf:* Chopin Sonatas, 72, Chopin Polonaises, 73, Chopin Waltzes, 74, Chopin Scherzi, 76, Beethoven Sonatas op 53 & 109, 78 & Schubert-Liszt songs, 80, Connoisseur Soc. *Pos:* Solo pianist with major orchs. *Teaching:* Prof, NY Univ, 81-83. *Rep:* Barrettt Mgt 1860 Broadway New York NY 10023. *Mailing Add:* 329 W 71st St Apt 4 New York NY 10023

BARBOSA-LIMA, CAROLOS
GUITAR, EDUCATOR
b São Paulo, Brazil, Dec 17, 44. *Study:* With Benedito Moreira, Isaias Savio, Andres Segovia & Abel Carlevaro. *Rec Perf:* Barbosa-Lima in a Scarlatti Guitar Recital, ABC/ATS; The Twelve Etudes by Francisco Mignone, Philips Brazil. *Pos:* Guitarist, São Paulo, 57 & extensive tours North Am, South Am, England, France & Sweden; performer with Pro-Arte Orch Munich, Mexico City, 81. *Teaching:* Guitar, Hartford, Conn, 73-74 & Manhattan Sch Music, currently; artist in res & prof, Carnegie-Mellon Inst. *Rep:* Shaw Conct Inc 1995 Broadway New York NY 10023. *Mailing Add:* Manhattan Sch Music 120 Claremont Ave New York NY 10027

BARCZA, PETER (JOSEPH)
BARITONE
b Stockholm, Sweden, June 23, 49, Can citizen. *Study:* Univ Toronto, opera perf dipl, 71; Villa Schifanoia Grad Sch Fine Arts, Florence, Italy, 71. *Roles:* Valentin in Faust, Manitoba Opera & Can Opera Co, 76; Papageno in The Magic Flute, Can Opera Co, 77; Blondel in Richard, Coeur de Lion, Theatre Royale de Wallonie, Belgium, 78; Enrico in Lucia di Lammermoor, Ky Opera, Opera Memphis & Southern Alberta Opera, Calgary, 79; Silvio in I Pagliacci, Rochester Opera, Can Opera & Manitoba Opera, 80; soloist in Le Bal

Masque, Paris Opera, 81; Marcello in La Boheme, Conn Opera, 83. *Awards:* Regional Winner, Metropolitan Opera Auditions, 72; Bruce Yarnell Mem Award, San Francisco Opera, 76; Floyd Chalmers Award, Ontario Arts Coun, 82. *Mem:* Asn Can TV & Radio Artists; Am Guild Musical Artists; Can Actors Equity Asn. *Mailing Add:* c/o Harry Beall Mgt 119 W 57th St New York NY 10019

BAR-ILLAN, DAVID J
PIANO
b Haifa, Israel, Feb 7, 30; Israeli & US citizen. *Study:* Juilliard Sch Music, dipl, 50; Mannes Col Music, 52; studied with Rosina Lhevinne, Hans Neumann & Dora Zaslansky. *Rec Perf:* Eroica Variations, RCA, 68; Concerto in E, 80, Sonata in A Flat, 81, Sonatas (Waldstein), Op 2 No 3, 83 & Eroica Variations, 83, Audiof; Schubert Wanderer Fantasy & Sonata in g (Schumann), Connoisseur Soc, 80. *Pos:* Numerous solo perf with all major Am & European orch. *Teaching:* Prof piano & artist in res, Southern Methodist Univ, 72-74 & Col Consv Music, Univ Cincinnati, 74-80; prof piano, Mannes Col Music, 81- *Mailing Add:* 924 West End Ave New York NY 10025

BARKER, EDWIN BOGUE
DOUBLE BASS, TEACHER-COACH
b Tucson, Ariz, Apr 14, 54. *Study:* New England Consv Music, study double bass with Henry Portnoi, BM, 76. *Pos:* Mem, Chicago Symph Orch, 76-77; prin double bassist, Boston Symph Orch, 77-; bassist, Col Contemp Music Ens, currently. *Teaching:* Coach chamber music & double bass, Berkshire Music Ctr, 77-; instr double bass, New England Consv Music, 77- & Boston Consv Music, 81- *Awards:* Benjamin H Delson Mem Prize, Berkshire Music Ctr, 75; Chadwick Medal, New England Consv, 76. *Mailing Add:* 134 Fuller St Brookline MA 02146

BARKIN, ELAINE RADOFF
COMPOSER, EDUCATOR
b New York, NY, Dec 15, 32. *Study:* Queens Col, City Univ New York, BA, 54; Brandeis Univ, MFA, 56, PhD, 71. *Works:* String Quartet, Comp Rec Inc, 69; Mixed Modes, 75 & Plein Chant, 77, Mobart Music Publ; Two Dickinson Choruses, CRI, 77; The Supple Suitor, Asn Prom New Music, 78; De Amore, Oberlin Col Opera Wkshp, 80; N B Suite, Bertram & Nancy Turetzky, 82. *Pos:* Ed, Perspectives New Music, 65- *Teaching:* Lectr music, Queens Col, City Univ New York, 64-70; asst prof music theory, Univ Mich, 70-74; prof comp, Univ Calif, Los Angeles, 74- *Awards:* Fulbright Fel, 56-57; Nat Endowment for Arts Grant, 76-78; Rockefeller Found Grant, 80. *Bibliog:* Eleanor Cory (auth), Elaine Barkin: String Quartet, Musical Quart, 76. *Mem:* Am Comp Alliance; Am Soc Univ Comp. *Mailing Add:* 12533 Killion St North Hollywood CA 91607

BARLOW, WAYNE BREWSTER
COMPOSER, ORGAN
b Elyria, Ohio, Sept 6, 12. *Study:* Eastman Sch Music, with Bernard Rogers, Howard Hanson & Arnold Schoenberg, BM, 34, MM, 35, PhD(comp), 37; Univ Toronto, studied electronic music with Myron Schaeffer, 63-64. *Works:* Dialogues (harp & tape), 69; Saxophone Concerto, 70; Soundscapes (orch & tape), 72; Vocalize and Canon (tuba & piano), Rochester, NY, 76; Voices of Faith (narrator & orch), Augusta, Ga, 76; Voices of Darkness (perc, piano, reader & tape), 76; Out of the Cradle Endlessly Rocking (tenor solo, clarinet, viola, piano & tape), Rochester, NY, 78. *Pos:* Organist & choir dir, St Thomas Episcopal Church, formerly & Christ Church, formerly. *Teaching:* Mem fac, Eastman Sch Music, 37-78, emer prof, 78-; Fulbright sr lectr, Royal Univ, Consv Copenhagen & Univ Aarhus, Denmark, 55-56. *Awards:* Fulbright Res Grant, Belgium & Holland, 64-65; Musician of Year Award, Mu Phi Epsilon, 72. *Mem:* ASCAP; Phi Mu Alpha Sinfonia. *Publ:* Auth, Foundations of Music, 53. *Mailing Add:* 95 Elmcroft Rd Rochester NY 14609

BARLOWE, AMY
STRINGS, EDUCATOR
b Copiague, NY, Jan 20, 52. *Study:* Juilliard Pre-Col, 69-70; Juilliard Sch, BM, 75, MM, 76; Meadowmount Sch Music, 69-76. *Pos:* Asst concertmaster, Juilliard Pre-Col Orch, 69-70 & Great Neck Symph, NY, 70-76; from assoc concertmaster to co-concertmaster, Salem Symph, Ore, 80-82. *Teaching:* Fel, Meadowmont Sch Music, 73-75; asst prof violin, viola & chamber music, Willamette Univ, 76-82, founder & dir, Pre-Col Div Music, 81-83, assoc prof, 83- *Awards:* Helena Rubinstein Found Scholar, 75; NW Area Grant, 82; Atkinson Grant, 82, 83. *Mem:* Am String Teachers Asn; Ore Music Teachers Asn; Am Fedn Musicians; Col Music Soc. *Publ:* Auth, String Thing on a Shoestring, Am String Teachers Asn J, 83; A Guide for Enjoyable Listening, Panther Press, 83. *Mailing Add:* Music Dept Willamette Univ Salem OR 97301

BARNEA, URI
MUSIC DIRECTOR, COMPOSER
b Petah-Tikvah, Israel, May 29, 43; US citizen. *Study:* Oranim Music Inst, Tivon, Israel, teaching cert, 66; Rubin Acad Music & Hebrew Univ, Jerusalem, BMus, 71; Univ Minn, Minneapolis, MA, 74, PhD, 77. *Works:* Passacaglia for Orchestra, Minn Orch & Knox-Galesburg Symph, 72; Ruth (music for ballet), Univ Minn Symph & Knox-Galesburg Symph, 72; America, comn by Col St Thomas & St Catherine, 76; Fantasy for Organ and Orchestra, comn by Unitarian Orch, 76; String Quartet, Kronos Quartet, 76; Variations on a Theme by Stravinsky, Kenwood Chamber Orch & Peoria Symph, 78; A Festive Overture, comn by Knox-Galesburg Symph & Rockford Symph, 81. *Pos:* Music dir, Kenwood Chamber Orch & Unitarian Chorus & Orch, 73-78; music dir, Knox-Galesburg Symph, 78-83. *Teaching:* Asst orch, Univ Minn, Minneapolis, 72-77; asst prof music, Knox Col, 78-83; vis asst prof string tech

& violin, Monmouth Col, 79-80. *Awards:* Dipl, G B Viotti Int Music Compt, Vercelli, Italy, 75; First Prize, Aspen Fest Comp Cont, 76 & First Annual Oberhoffer Comp Cont, Univ Minn, 76. *Mem:* Ill Arts Coun; ASCAP; Am String Teachers Asn; Cond Guild; Minn Comp Forum. *Mailing Add:* 253 N Chambers St Galesburg IL 61401

BARNES, DARREL
VIOLA, EDUCATOR
Pos: Viola, Rochester Phil, currently. *Teaching:* Asst prof viola, Music Dept, Ithaca Col, currently. *Mailing Add:* 249 N Main PO Box 249 Interlaken NY 14847

BARNES, LARRY JOHN
COMPOSER, PIANO
b Cleveland, Ohio, July 17, 50. *Study:* Cleveland Inst Music, BMus, 72, MMus, 73; Eastman Sch Music, DMA, 79. *Works:* Solar Winds, perf by Cleveland Orch, 72; The 800th Lifetime, perf by Comp Theater, New York, 73; The Devil Tree, Seesaw Music Corp, 78; Music for Solo Percussion, Southern Music Corp, 82; The River of Heaven, perf by Voices of Change, 83; Behind the Golden Door, Int Fest Arts, San Antonio, Tex, 83. *Pos:* Res musical dir, Luzerne Music Ctr, NY, summer 82. *Teaching:* Asst prof, Heidelberg Col, 73-77; asst prof theory & comp, Univ Tex, San Antonio, 79- *Awards:* Nat Endowment Arts Fel, 77; ASCAP Awards, 79-82. *Mem:* ASCAP; Am Soc Univ Comp; Comp & Perf Alliance of San Antonio (vpres, 80-81). *Rep:* 7151 Spring Grove San Antonio TX 78249. *Mailing Add:* Div Music Univ Tex San Antonio TX 78285

BARNES, MARSHALL H
EDUCATOR, COMPOSER
b Fairfield, Iowa. *Study:* Univ Iowa, BM, 42, MA, 44, PhD, 51. *Works:* A Scrapbook for Julie (male chorus), E C Kerby, 74; Four Piano Pieces, Op Music, 79; Salt Water Ballads, Consv Music, Univ Cincinnati, 81; Old Worthington Suite (flute, clarinet & piano), Col Arts, Ohio State Univ, 82; Variations on an Island Tune, Pro Musica Orch, 83; As Lately We Watched (mixed chorus & string orch), Lorenz, Dayton, 83. *Teaching:* Prof, Ohio State Univ, 57- & chmn music theory & comp, 68-76. *Mem:* Ohio Music Educr Asn; Music Educr Nat Conf. *Mailing Add:* 33 Wilson Dr Worthington OH 43085

BARNETT, CAROL EDITH
COMPOSER
b Dubuque, Iowa, May 23, 49. *Study:* Univ Minn, studied comp with Paul Fetler & Dominick Argento, BA, 72, MA, 76. *Works:* Sonata for Horn & Piano, perf by Charles McDonald, 73; Adon Olam Variations, comn by First Unitarian Soc Minn, 76; Overture to the Midnight Spectacle, perf by St Paul Chamber Orch, 78; Gyri, comn by Andrew Rist, 79; Cinco Poemas de Becquer, comn by Harry L Bratnober Family, 79; Nocturne for Chamber Orch, perf by St Paul Chamber Orch, 80; Four Chorale Meditations (solo violin), comn by Jean Marker, 82. *Mem:* Minn Comp Forum; Int League Women Comp; Am Fedn Musicians. *Publ:* Coauth, La musica nell'opera di Aleksandr Solzenicyn, Nuova Rivista Musicale Ital, 75; contribr, AGO Minnesota Anthem Anthology, Colwell Press, 79. *Mailing Add:* 3008 42nd Ave S Minneapolis MN 55406

BARNETT, DAVID
PIANO, COMPOSER
b New York, NY, Dec 1, 07. *Study:* Juilliard Sch Music, dipl, 25; Columbia Univ, BA, 27; Ecole Normale Musique, dipl, 28. *Works:* Fantasy for Clarinet & Piano, Salabert, Paris, 50; Ballade for Viola & Piano, Oxford Univ Press, 59; Trio for Violin, Cello & Piano, comn by Harvard Musical Asn, 63; Gallery (children's pieces), Assoc Music Publ, 72; Sonatina for Oboe & Piano, 77 & Rhapsody & Scherzo for Violin & Piano, 79, Ledgebrook Assoc Publ; Arioso for Trombone & Orchestra, perf by Univ Bridgeport Orch, 83. *Rec Perf:* Three Cycles of Robert Schumann, 79 & The Complete Etudes and Preludes of Chopin, 81, Cook Lab, South Norwalk, Conn. *Teaching:* Instr, Wellesley Col, 35-65; instr counterpoint, Columbia Univ, summers 46-62; instr piano lit & pedagogy, New England Consv, 46-65; preceptor, Harvard Univ, 55-59; prof, Univ Bridgeport, 67- *Mem:* Conn State Music Teachers Asn (pres, 81-); Am Music Ctr; Am & Brit Soc Aesthetics; Col Music Soc. *Publ:* Auth, Living With Music, G Stewart Co, 44; Harmonic Rhythm and Mother Goose, Music Educr J, 69; The Performance of Music, Ledgebrook Assoc Publ, 72. *Rep:* Ledgebrook Assoc Box 1304 Weston CT 06883. *Mailing Add:* 3 Ledgebrook Ct Weston CT 06883

BARNEWITZ, A WILLIAM
FRENCH HORN
b Reno, Nev, Dec 21, 58. *Study:* Juilliard Sch Music; NC Sch Arts. *Rec Perf:* Alexander's Bach Time Band, 79 & Macbeth, 80, PBS. *Pos:* Solo horn, New York String Orch, 79-80; sect horn & solo horn, New York Chamber Soloists, 80-82; sect horn, New York City Opera, 80-82; prin horn, Sacramento Symph, 81- *Teaching:* Assoc prof horn, Cal State Univ, Sacramento, 82- *Awards:* Los Angeles Phil Inst Fel, 83. *Mem:* Sacramento Players Asn. *Mailing Add:* Sacramento Symph Asn 2848 Arden Way Suite 210 Sacramento CA 95825

BARON, CAROL K
ADMINISTRATOR, MUSICOLOGIST
b New York, NY, June 29, 34. *Study:* Queens Col, BA, 57, MA, 77; Yale Univ, 57-58; Grad Col, City Univ New York, MPh, 80; studied piano with Dorothy Taubman. *Rec Perf:* New American Music for Flute and Piano, Desto Rec; Deconcertant et Sublime, Serenus Rec. *Pos:* Conct pianist &

harpischordist, US, Can & Israel, 66-; music ed, Margun Music, 78 & Holt, Rinehart & Winston, 78-80; admin dir, Bach Aria Group, Stony Brook & New York, NY, 80- *Teaching:* Coach & teacher piano & chamber music, privately, New York & Great Neck, NY, 50-79; adj lectr music, York Col, 74-75, Hunter Col, 79-80 & Adelphi Univ, 80-82. *Awards:* Alfred P Sloan Found Fel, 79. *Mem:* Am Musicol Soc; Col Music Soc; Chamber Music Am. *Interests:* Twentieth century music; analytical studies. *Publ:* Auth, An Analysis of the Pitch Organization in Boulez's Sonatine for Flute and Piano, Current Musicol, 75; The Composer as Poet: Meaning in the Music of Luigi Dallapicolla (1904-1975), Centerpoint: J Interdisciplinary Studies, 75; contribr, Charles Ives, Oxford Univ Press, 77; auth, Varese's Explication of Debussy's Syrinx in Density 21.5: A Secret Model Revealed, Music Rev, 82. *Mailing Add:* 321 Melbourne Rd Great Neck NY 11021

BARON, JOHN HERSCHEL
WRITER, EDUCATOR
b Milwaukee, Wis, May 7, 36. *Study:* Harvard Univ, BA, 58, MA, 59; Berkshire Music Ctr, 58-59; Brandeis Univ, PhD, 67; studied with Bernice S Baron, Ruth Posselt, Charlotte Chambers & Alexander Schneider. *Works:* Background music to films, 74-80; Cantata, Univ Wis Milwaukee Chamber Players, 81. *Pos:* Founder & cond, Tulane Chamber Orch, 70-75; music critic, Vieux Carre Courier, 72-79. *Teaching:* Instr, Boston Univ, 64-65; asst prof, Univ Calif, Los Angeles, 67-68 & Univ Calif, Davis, 68-69; assoc prof, Tulane Univ, 69-; mem fac, Am Recorder Soc Summer Workshop, Amherst, Mass, 82. *Awards:* Am Coun Learned Soc Res Grant, Spain, 75-76; Mellon Summer Res Grant, 82; Fulbright Res Scholar, Holland, 83. *Mem:* Am Musicol Soc; Sonneck Soc (mem bd, 79-80); Int Musicol Soc; Am Soc Jewish Music; Gesellschaft Musikforschung. *Publ:* Auth, 40 articles, In: New Grove Dict of Music & Musicians, 6th ed, 80; ed, Piano Music from New Orleans 1851-1898, Da Capo, 81; The Brasov Tablature, A-R Ed, 82; Obras Completas de Cristobal Galan (vol I), Medieval Inst Music, 82. *Mailing Add:* Music Dept Newcomb Col Tulane Univ New Orleans LA 70118

BARON, SAMUEL
FLUTE, CONDUCTOR
b Brooklyn, NY, Apr 27, 25. *Study:* Music Sch of Henry St Settlement; Juilliard Sch Music, BS, 48; studied flute with Georges Barrere & Arthur Lora & cond with Edgar Schenkman. *Rec Perf:* Woodwind Quintets (Hindemith, Francaix, Etler, Schuller, Fine & Carter), Concert-Disc, 56-68; Flute & Harp Concerto (Mozart), Decca, 63; Contemporary Flute Sonatas (Laderman, Wolpe, Sydeman & Blackwood), Desto, 69; Flute Sonatas (J S Bach), Musical Heritage, 70; Music for Solo Flute by American Composers (Kupferman, Riegger, Hovhaness, Perle, Wigglesworth, Mamlok & Martino), CRI. *Pos:* Flutist, New York City Symph, formerly, New York City Opera, formerly, Minneapolis Symph, formerly, NY Woodwind Quintet, 49-69 & 80-, NY Chamber Soloists, 58-65 & Contemp Chamber Ens, 62-65; flutist, Bach Aria Group, 65-80, dir, 80-; consult music prog, Nat Endowment Arts, 73-76; performer, New Col Summer Music Fest, 74-; founder, Bach Aria Fest & Inst, Stony Brook, NY, 80; flutist & asst cond, Musica Aeterna, Metropolitan Museum Art, 80- *Teaching:* Lectr flute, Yale Univ, 65-67; instr chamber music, Univ Wis, Milwaukee, summers 54-67; lectr flute, State Univ NY, Stony Brook, 66-71, asst prof flute & chamber music, 66-67, assoc prof, 72-74, prof, 74-; perf artist in res, Harpur Col, State Univ NY, Binghamton, 67-69; prof chamber music, Juilliard Sch, 71-, teacher flute, 74-; vis prof, Eastman Sch Music, 74-75 & Sibelius Acad, Helsinki, Finland, summer 75. *Awards:* Distinguished Perf Arts Award, Sch Fine Arts, Univ Wis, Milwaukee, 64. *Bibliog:* Pilar Estevan (auth), Talking With Flutists, Edutainment, 73; Eleanor Lawrence (auth), interview, Nat Flute Asn J, 80. *Mem:* Nat Flute Asn (pres, 77). *Mailing Add:* 321 Melbourne Rd Great Neck NY 11021

BARR, JOHN GLADDEN
COMPOSER, EDUCATOR
b Myrtle Point, Ore, July 24, 38. *Study:* Manchester Col, Ind, BS(music educ), 60; Union Theol Sem, SMM, 62, SMD, 77. *Works:* Magnificat and Nunc Dimittis (unison voice & organ), Mercury Music, 65; How Brightly Shines the Morning Star (organ chorale prelude), 72 & Two Preludes on Hymn Tunes: Converse & Simple Gifts (organ), H W Gray, 82. *Teaching:* Music, Hillcrest Sch, Jos, Nigeria, 62-65; prof organ & piano, Bridgewater Col, 68- *Mem:* Am Guild Organists; Hymn Soc Am. *Mailing Add:* 101 Broad St Bridgewater VA 22812

BARR, RAYMOND ARTHUR
EDUCATOR, WRITER
b Pitcairn, Pa, Jan 1, 32. *Study:* Pa State Univ, BS, 53; Univ Wis, MS, 61, PhD, 68. *Teaching:* Music, Scotland Sch, Pa, 57-60 & Arnold High Sch, Wiesbaden, Germany, 64-66; asst prof musicol, State Univ NY, Geneseo, 68-72; prof, Univ Miami, 72- *Mem:* Col Music Soc (Southern region pres, 80-82, mem nat coun, 82-85); Am Musicol Soc (pres, 78-80, chap rep, 80-83). *Interests:* Eighteenth century art song. *Publ:* Auth, numerous articles, In: New Grove Dict of Music & Musicians, Vol VI, Macmillan, 80. *Mailing Add:* 5840 SW 57 Ave #127 Miami FL 33143

BARRA, DONALD PAUL
CONDUCTOR & MUSIC DIRECTOR, WRITER
b Newark, NJ, Aug 21, 39. *Study:* Eastman Sch Music, AB, 61; Juilliard Sch Music, MS, 63; Columbia Univ, EdD, 75. *Pos:* Cond, Columbia Univ Symph Band, 66-73; music dir, Johnstown Symph Orch, Pa, 73-83; music adv, Pa Coun Arts, 83-84. *Teaching:* Dir orch, San Diego State Univ, 83- *Mem:* Am Symph Orch League; Col Music Soc. *Interests:* Psychology of perception and musical performance. *Publ:* Auth, Sonographs: An Audio-Visual Teaching System for Music, Electra Publ, 69; The Dynamic Performance: A Performer's Guide to Musical Expression and Interpretation, Prentice-Hall, 83. *Mailing Add:* 372-A Bonair St La Jolla CA 92037

BARRETT, OREEN
TEACHER, SOPRANO
b Chicago, Ill. *Study:* Univ Ill, Urbana, BMEd, 70; Hochschule Musik Mozarteum, Salzburg, cert, 73; Eastman Sch Music, 74. *Roles:* Dorabella in Cosi fan tutte, Chicago Opera Theatre & Grant Park Fest; Florence in Albert Herring, Schwertleite in Die Walküre & Bianca in The Rape of Lucretia, Chautauqua Fest. *Pos:* Artistic dir & sop, Kinnor Chamber Players, 74-; sop, Harp, Flute & Voice Ens. *Teaching:* Private instr voice & English diction, New York, 80- *Awards:* Bellinger Mem Award, Chautauqua Inst, 75. *Mem:* Mu Phi Epsilon; Chamber Music Am. *Interests:* Sephardic Songs. *Mailing Add:* 180 West End #3H New York NY 10023

BARRETT, PAUL H
BASSOON, EDUCATOR
b Los Angeles, Calif, Aug 17, 54. *Study:* Interlochen Arts Acad; Eastman Sch Music; Cleveland Inst Music, BM, 78. *Pos:* Second bassoonist, Louisville Orch, 72-73; prin bassoonist, Honolulu Symph, 77- *Teaching:* Lectr bassoon, Univ Hawaii, 78- *Mailing Add:* 3633 Sierra Dr Honolulu HI 96816

BARRETT, WALTER EDMUND
TROMBONE, EUPHONIUM
b New York, NY, Oct 8, 54. *Study:* Manhattan Sch Music; private study with Wayne Andre, Fred Snyder & Alan Raph. *Rec Perf:* Capriccio Furioso (Walter Ross), Boosey & Hawkes Publ, 81. *Pos:* Euphonium soloist, NY Univ Conct Band, 80 & White Plains Pops Band, 80-; prin trombone, Phil Symph Westchester, Mt Vernon, NY, 81- *Mem:* Int Trombone Asn; Chamber Music Am; Am Fedn Musicians. *Mailing Add:* 55 N Perkins Ave Elmsford NY 10523

BARROW, REBECCA ANNE
PIANO, TEACHER-COACH
b Mattoon, Ill, Feb 12, 42. *Study:* Millikin Univ, BMus; Juilliard Sch Music, MSc; studied with Elizabeth Travis, Irwin Freundlich, Jacob Lajeiner & Mo Agosti. *Rec Perf:* The Twentieth Century Double Bass (with Lynn Peters). *Pos:* Soloist, Austin Symph, Chicago Businessmen's Orch & in Mex, formerly; mem recitalist duo, currently. *Teaching:* Mem fac piano & group piano, NC Sch Arts, currently. *Awards:* Brewster-Allison Award, 62; Fulbright Grant Italy, 68-69. *Mem:* Pi Kappa Lambda. *Mailing Add:* NC Sch Arts PO Box 12189 Winston-Salem NC 27107

BARRUECO, MANUEL
GUITAR, TEACHER
b Cuba, Dec 16, 52; US citizen. *Study:* Peabody Consv Music, BM, 75. *Rec Perf:* Manuel Barrueco Plays Solo Guitar, 76, Works for Guitar By Albgniz and Granados, 79 & Manuel Barrueco Plays Sonatas, 80, Vox-Turnabout; Bach Lute Suites Nos 2 & 4, Vox-Cum Laude, 81. *Pos:* Guitarist, currently. *Teaching:* Instr guitar, Manhattan Sch Music, 75-82; artist in res guitar, Peabody Consv Music, 82- *Rep:* Columbia Artists Mgt Inc 165 W 57 St New York NY 10019. *Mailing Add:* PO Box 341 Union NJ 07083

BARRUS, CHARLES LAMAR, JR
EDUCATOR, CONDUCTOR
b Sugar City, Idaho, July 22, 35. *Study:* Vienna Acad Music, 58-59; Univ Utah, BA, 64, MMus, 66, PhD, 68. *Works:* Trio for Two Violins & Viola, many perf in Idaho, Utah & Vienna, Austria, 65; Elegy for Viola & Piano, many perf by Clyn Barrus & others, 65; Ode to Libertad, A Choral Symphony, perf by Brigham Young Univ & Idaho Falls Symph, 68; Berceuse and Soliloquy for Organ, 72 & Three Songs of Faith, 75, Harold Flammer; The Song of the Righteous, perf by Ricks Col A Cappella Choir, 82. *Pos:* First violin, Utah Symph Orch, 53-65; cond, Ricks Col Symph Orch, Rexburg, Idaho, 60- & Idaho Falls Symph Orch, 65-70. *Teaching:* Prof music theory & orch, Ricks Col, Rexburg, Idaho, 60-, chmn music dept, 72-80. *Mem:* Music Educr Nat Conf; Am String Teachers Asn. *Publ:* Auth, A Week of Inspiration with Kato Havas, Am String Teacher, 78. *Mailing Add:* 260 S 3rd East Rexburg ID 83440

BARRY, JEROME
BARITONE, ADMINISTRATOR
b Boston, Mass, Nov 16, 39. *Study:* Northeastern Univ, BA, 61; Tufts Univ, MA, 63; St Cecilia Consv, Rome; Sch Fine & Applied Arts, Boston Univ. *Roles:* Germont in La Traviata & Gypsy Baron, Israel Nat Opera, 71 & 72; Gianni Schicchi in Gianni Schicchi, Israel Phil Orch, 74; Aeneus in Dido and Aeneas, Jerusalem Symph Orch, 74; Don Bartolo in Marriage of Figaro, Long Island Opera Co, 75; Mandarin in Turandot, Baltimore Opera, 80. *Pos:* Managing dir, Washington Music Ens, 81- *Teaching:* Instr German, Tufts Univ, 61-63 & Northeastern Univ, 70; instr voice, Tel Aviv Univ, 72-74 & Univ Md, 75-76. *Awards:* Ford Award, Northeastern Univ, 61. *Mem:* Nat Asn Teachers Singing; Am Guild Musical Artists. *Rep:* Guy Freedman 37 Robins Crescent New Rochelle NY 10801. *Mailing Add:* 9517 Seminole St Silver Spring MD 20901

BARTHELSON, JOYCE HOLLOWAY
COMPOSER, CONDUCTOR
b Yakima, Wash. *Study:* Univ Calif, Berkeley; Manhattan Sch Music; studied piano with Harold Bauer; studied orch & comp with Nicholas Flagello. *Works:* Feathertop, perf by Community Opera, 66; Chanticleer, comn by Hoff-Barthelson Music Sch & Folger Shakespeare Theatre, Washington, DC, 66; The King's Breakfast, perf by Manhattan Sch, 72; Greenwich Village, 1910, comn by New York Music Libr, 72; The Devil's Disciple, perf by White Plains Opera House, 76; Lysistrata, comn by NY Univ Music Dept, 82. *Pos:* Pianist, Arion Trio, NBC San Francisco, 30-45; co-founder & co-dir, Hoff-Barthelson Music Sch, 44-74; lectr, Colston Leigh Lectr Bureau, 40-50; asst cond, Womesn Symph, New York 45-50. *Teaching:* Supv, piano & theory, Hoff-Barthelson Music Sch, 44-74. *Awards:* Contemp Opera Award, ASCAP, 67. *Mem:* Am Music Ctr. *Mailing Add:* Chateau Touraine 7Y Scarsdale NY 10583

BARTHOLOMEW, LYNNE
PIANO, EDUCATOR
b Sellersville, Pa, Dec 17, 41. *Study:* Univ Mich, BMus, 63, MMus, 65; Hochschule Musik, Freiburg, 65-66; Univ Southern Calif, 79-80. *Teaching:* Instr, Univ Mich, Ann Arbor, 66-69, asst prof 69-76 & assoc prof, 76-; piano fac, Univ Mich, Interlochen, Mich, 80- *Awards:* Fulbright Scholar, 65. *Mem:* Nat Music Teachers Asn; Mich Music Teachers Asn; Women Arts (prog chair, 82-83); Pi Kappa Lambda. *Mailing Add:* Sch Music Univ Mich Ann Arbor MI 48109

BARTLETT, LOREN W
EDUCATOR, BASSOON
b Dallas, Ore, Feb 7, 32. *Study:* Eastern Wash State Univ, BA, 54; Oberlin Consv Music, MM, 55; Univ Iowa, PhD, 61. *Pos:* First bassoonist, Greeley Phil Orch, 65-; bassoonist, Ginsberg Arts Woodwind Quintet, 65- *Teaching:* Assoc prof music, Ark Tech Univ, 55-65; prof music & chmn woodwind dept, Univ Northern Colo, 65- *Mem:* Nat Asn Col Wind & Perc Instr (Ark state chmn, 63-65, Southwest chmn, 65-67); Int Double Reed Soc; Music Educr Nat Conf; NAm Sax Alliance. *Mailing Add:* Sch Music Univ Northern Colo Greeley CO 80631

BARTOLETTI, BRUNO
CONDUCTOR
b Sesto Fiorentino, Italy, June 10, 26. *Study:* Consv Florence, Italy. *Rec Perf:* On DG, RCA, EMI & Decca. *Pos:* Artistic dir & cond, Lyr Opera Chicago, currently; cond, maj opera co in US & Europe & maj orchs in Europe. *Mailing Add:* Lyr Opera Chicago 20 N Wacker Dr Chicago IL 60606

BARTOLINI, LANDO
TENOR
b Prato, Italy. *Study:* Acad Vocal Arts Philadelpha, 60-74. *Roles:* Many roles with NY State Theater, 75-80; Andrea Cheinier, NJ Opera Co; La Boheme, Venezuela Opera Co, 80; Ernani, Teatro alla Scala, Milan, 82; Calaf in Turandot, Verona Arena, 83; Tabarro, Teatro alla Scala, Milan, 82; Aida, Buenos Aires, 83. *Awards:* Mario Lawna Scholar, 69. *Mailing Add:* c/o Robert Lombardo Assoc 1 Harkness Plaza 61 W 62 Ste 6F New York NY 10023

BARTOLOWITS, DAVID JOHN
VIOLIN
b Milford, Conn, Oct 16, 57. *Study:* Duquesne Univ, 75-77; Meadowmount Sch Music, 78-79; Carnegie-Mellon Univ, BFA(music perf), 80. *Pos:* Violinist, Pittsburgh Ballet Orch, 77-81 & Pittsburgh New Music Ens, 80-81; concertmaster, New Pittsburgh Chamber Orch, 80-81; assoc prin second violin, Indianapolis Symph, 81- *Mailing Add:* 6137 A Robin Run Indianapolis IN 46254

BARWICK, STEVEN
EDUCATOR, PIANO
b Lincoln, Nebr, Mar 2, 21. *Study:* Coe Col, BM & BA, 42; Eastman Sch Music, with Cecile Genhart, MMus, 43; Harvard Univ, MA, PhD, 49; Ecole Normale, Paris, with Claudio Arrau & Jules Gentil; Coe Col, Hon Dr Fine Arts, 69. *Teaching:* Asst prof music appreciation, Univ Pittsburgh, 49-51; assoc prof piano & theory, Western Ky Univ, 51-55; prof piano & music lit, Southern Ill Univ, 55- *Mem:* Am Musicol Soc; Music Teachers Nat Asn. *Interests:* Music in Mexico in the early colonial period. *Publ:* Auth & ed, The Franco Codex, Southern Ill Univ Press, 65; auth, A Recently Discovered Miserere of Fernando Franco, Yearbook Inter-Am Musical Res, 70; auth & ed, Two Mexico City Choirbooks of 1717, Southern Ill Univ Press, 82. *Mailing Add:* 709 W Elm Carbondale IL 62901

BARZENICK, WALTER
EDUCATOR, WRITER
b Maywood, Ill, Nov 23, 22. *Study:* Northwestern Univ, BMus, 49, MMus, 50; studied clarinet with Wesley Shepard, Tony Sirmarco, Dominco De Caprio, Sidney Forest & Simon Bellison. *Pos:* Performer with symph orchs in Ill & La; prin clarinet, Baton Rouge Symph, 50-; clinician, recitalist, consult & adjudicator throughout South & Southwest US. *Teaching:* Prof music, Southeastern La Univ, currently. *Mem:* La Music Educr Asn; La Bandmasters Asn; Am Fedn Musicians; Nat Asn Col Wind & Perc Instr; Int Clarinet Soc. *Publ:* Auth, The Clarinet, 69; Interesting Events in the History of the Clarinet, 72; Symphonic Works Played by Baton Rouge Symphony, 1950-79, 79; contribr to Instrumentalist. *Mailing Add:* 100 Elm Dr Hammond LA 70401

BASART, ANN PHILLIPS
LIBRARIAN, WRITER
b Denver, Colo, Aug 26, 31. *Study:* Univ Calif, Los Angeles, BA(music), 53; Univ Calif, Berkeley, MLS, 58, MA(music), 61. *Pos:* Ref libr, Music Libr, Univ Calif, Berkeley, 60-61 & 70-, ed newsletter, Cum notis variorum, 76- *Teaching:* Instr, San Francisco Col Women, 64-67. *Awards:* Fulbright Fel, 56-57. *Mem:* Music Libr Asn (mem bd dir, 78-80); Int Asn Music Libr (mem bd, 82-). *Publ:* Auth, Serial Music: A Classified Bibliography of Writings ..., Univ Calif Press, 61; coauth, Listening to Music, McGraw-Hill, 71; auth, various articles, interviews & bibliographies in Cum notis variorum, 76-; auth, entries on Burrill Phillips, Arnold Elston & Andrew Imbrie, In: New Grove Dict of Music & Musicians, 81. *Mailing Add:* Music Libr 240 Morrison Hall Univ Calif Berkeley CA 94720

BASART, ROBERT
EDUCATOR, COMPOSER
b Watertown, SDak, Nov 17, 26. *Study:* Univ Calif, Berkeley, MA, PhD. *Works:* Fantasy (flute & piano), Salabert, 63; Kansas City Dump (four instrm & tape), San Francisco Symph Musica Viva, 68; Excursion from or into the Wilderness (chorus & tape), 70; Variations (cello & piano), Salbert, 71; Stem, Leaf, Leaves, Small Flower, Francesco Trio, 76; Imaginary Song (string quartet), Lenox String Quartet, 79; Now Venus, Turning (orch) Nat Endowment for Arts, 81. *Teaching:* Prof comp & theory, Calif State Univ, Hayward, 68- *Awards:* Martha Baird Rockefeller Found Grant, 74; Nat Endowment for Arts Grant, 76 & 81; Norman Fromm Comp Award, 80. *Mem:* ASCAP. *Mailing Add:* 2419 Oregon St Berkeley CA 94705

BASKERVILLE, DAVID
COMPOSER, EDUCATOR
b Freehold, NJ, Aug 15, 18. *Study:* Univ Wash, BA, 40; Univ Calif, Los Angeles, MA(comp), 55, PhD(hist musicol), 65; studied orch with Mario Castelnuovo-Tedesco. *Works:* Night Song; Grand Entry Swing March; Ventura Venture; Moonride; Hollywood Swing March; Monograph for Orchestra, perf by Denver Symph Orch. *Pos:* Trombonist, Seattle Symph Orch, 40-47 & Los Angeles Phil, 47-48; staff comp & cond, NBC, Hollywood, 47-51; orch arr, Paramount Pictures & 20th Cent Fox; TV producer, BBC, London, 61; pres, Sherwood Rec Studios, Los Angeles, 64-67; exec vpres, Ad-Staff, Hollywood; contribr, Instrumentalist, Music J, Music Educr J & Downbeat. *Teaching:* Mem fac, Westlake Col Music, 47-48 & Univ Calif, Los Angeles, 51-56; prof music, Univ Colo, Denver, 69-83. *Awards:* Music Award, Lord Mayor of London, 61; Deems Taylor Award, ASCAP, 80. *Mem:* ASCAP; Nat Asn Jazz Educr; Music Educr Nat Conf; Am Fedn Musicians; Col Music Soc. *Publ:* Auth, Music Business Handbook and Career Guide, 79. *Mailing Add:* Col Music Univ Colo Denver CO 80202

BASNEY, ELDON E
COMPOSER, TEACHER & COACH
b Port Huron, Mich, June 14, 13. *Study:* Peabody Consv Music, 32-39; studied comp with Gustav Strube, violin with Stanislaw Schapiro & Frank Gittleson. *Works:* Essay for Strings, Baltimore Women's String Symph, 36; Seventh String Quartet, Peabody Fac String Quartet, 38; Marriage of the Rivers, Estelle Dennis Dance Group with Martha Graham soloists, 39; Fall River, Buffalo Chamber Orch, 55; Seventeenth String Quartet, Comp Forum, NY, 68; String Trio, Am Comp Fest, Eastman Sch Music, 68. *Pos:* Cond with various orch incl Baltimore String Symph, Kanakee Civic Orch & Chorus; guest cond, Chicago Women's Symph Strings & Buffalo Phil. *Teaching:* Private teacher & coach, 27-; music theory & appl music at various col, 46-78. *Awards:* Thomas Prize, 39; MacDowell Colony Fel, 68. *Mem:* ASCAP. *Mailing Add:* Rte 1 Box 43 Houghton NY 14744

BASQUIN, PETER JOHN
PIANO, EDUCATOR
b New York, NY, June 19, 43. *Study:* Carleton Col, BA, 63; Manhattan Sch Music, MM, 67. *Rec Perf:* Sonata for Piano (M Richter) & New People (M Colgrass), Grenadilla Rec, 54; Works by Arthur Farwell, Preston Ware Orem & Charles Wakefield Cadman & Where Home Is, New World Rec; Piano Sonata (K Husa), Clarinet Sonata (I Dahl) & Vocalises (D Diamond), Grenadilla Rec, 75; Concerto for Piano, Clarinet & String Quartet (R Harris) & Quintet for Clarinet, Two Violas & Two Cellos (D Diamond), Grenadilla Rec; Concerto for Clavier & Orchestra, Op 7, No 5 & Op 13, No 4 (Bach), Peters Int. *Pos:* Pianist, Am Chamber Trio, 72- & Aeolian Chamber Players, 81- *Teaching:* Fac mem, Hunter Col, City Univ New York, 69-75, assoc prof, 76- *Awards:* Highest award, Montreal Int Music Compt, 71. *Mem:* Col Music Soc. *Publ:* Coauth, Explorations in the Arts, Holt, Rinehart & Winston (in prep). *Rep:* American Chamber Concerts 890 West End Ave New York NY 10025. *Mailing Add:* 101 W 78th St New York NY 10024

BASS, CLAUDE LEROY
TEACHER, COMPOSER
b Gainesville, Tex, Oct 31, 35. *Study:* Okla Baptist Univ, BMusEd, 57; Univ Okla, with Violet Archer, MMus, 60; NTex State Univ, with Samuel Adler, PhD, 72. *Works:* The Messiah Has Come, Broadman Press, 77; We Have Seen The Lord, Word Inc, 77; Jesus, The Very Thought, Hinshaw Music, 79; The Father's Love, Broadman Press, 79; Sing to the Lord, Triune Music, 82; Praise, My, Soul the King, Hinshaw Music, 82; The Holy Light, Broadman Press, 83. *Teaching:* Choral music, various high sch, 57-65; prof music theory & comp, Okla Baptist Univ, 65-77; Southwestern Baptist Theol Sem, 77- *Mem:* Soc Music Theory; Tex Soc Music Theory (treas, 79-83); Southern Baptist Church Music Leadership Conf. *Publ:* Auth, Five Practical Lessons in Music Reading, Convention Press, 82. *Mailing Add:* Music Dept Southwestern Baptist Sem Ft Worth TX 76122

BASS, WARNER SEELEY
COMPOSER, EDUCATOR
b Brandenburg, Germany, Oct 6, 15. *Study:* Berlin Univ, MA; Berlin State Acad Music, MM; New York Col Music, MusB; NY Univ, MA. *Works:* Song of Hope (overture & fugue for orch); Suite for String Orchestra; Taps (adagio for string orch with trumpet & perc); Serenata Concertante (viola & string orch); Psalm 96 (solo ten, women's chorus & organ); Sonata for Viola and Piano; Sonatinetta for Trumpet and Piano. *Rec Perf:* On RCA Victor. *Pos:* Cond, State Theatre & Kulturbund Theatre, Berlin, Germany; assoc cond, Am Symph Orch, 62-64. *Teaching:* Vis prof, Southampton Col, Long Island Univ, 65; assoc prof, NY Univ, 67-69; prof & music dir, New York Col Music; asst prof music, Kingsborough Community Col, City Univ New York, 69-71, assoc prof, 71-75, prof, 75-81, emer prof, 81- *Awards:* Outstanding Educr Am Award, 71 & 72. *Mem:* ASCAP; Am Symph Orch League. *Mailing Add:* 260 W 72nd St New York NY 10023

BASSETT, LESLIE RAYMOND
COMPOSER, EDUCATOR
b Hanford, Calif, Jan 22, 23. *Study:* Fresno State Col, BA, 47; Univ Mich, MMus, 49, AMusD, 56; Ecole Normale Musique, Paris, France, 50-51; studied with Ross Lee Finney, Arthur Honegger, Nadia Boulanger, Roberto Gerhard, Mario Davidovsky. *Works:* Variations for Orchestra, 63, Moon Canticle (chorus), 69, Sextet for Piano & Strings, 71, Echoes From An Invisible World, 76 & Concerto for Two Pianos & Orchestra, 76, C F Peters; Fourth String Quartet, Merion Music, 78; Concerto Grosso (brass quintet with wind ens), C F Peters, 82. *Pos:* Albert A Stanley Distinguished Univ Prof music, Univ Mich, 52- *Awards:* Fulbright Fel to Paris, France, 50-51; Prix de Rome, Am Acad in Rome, 61-63; Pulitzer Prize, 66. *Bibliog:* Roger Scanlon (auth), Spotlight on Contemporary Composers, Bulletin Nat Asn Teachers Singing, 75; Bicentennial Report, BMI Mag, spring 76; Anthony Brown (auth), The Music of Leslie Bassett, Asterisk, Vol 2, 2. *Mem:* Am Acad & Inst Arts & Lett; Am Comp Alliance; Am Soc Univ Comp. *Mailing Add:* 1618 Harbal Dr Ann Arbor MI 48105

BASSETT, RALPH EDWARD
BASS-BARITONE
b Long Beach, Calif, Dec 25, 44. *Study:* Merola Opera Prog, with Allan Lindquest; studied with Ernest St John Metz. *Pos:* Bass-bar, New York City Opera, 78; Community Concts, Western Opera Theatre, Kansas City Lyr Opera, San Diego Opera, Nev Opera Co, Augusta Opera Asn & Miami Beach Opera Co. *Awards:* Martha Baird Rockefeller Grants, 76 & 78; Euterpe Opera Singer of Yr, 79. *Mem:* Am Guild Musical Artists. *Rep:* Cond Int Mgt 95 Cedar Rd Ringwood NJ 07456. *Mailing Add:* c/o Kazuko Hillyer Int Inc 250 W 57th St New York NY 10107

BASTIAN, JAMES
EDUCATOR, PIANO
b Chicago, Ill, June 2, 26. *Study:* Doane Col, AB, 50; Northwestern Univ, MMus, 55; Univ Mich, PhD, 67. *Teaching:* Prof music hist & theory, Doane Col, 55-; vis prof music hist, Univ Denver, 67 & Univ Mo, 70-71. *Mem:* Nebr Music Teachers Asn (pres, 64-66); Music Teachers Nat Asn (mem nat exec bd, 67-68); Music Libr Asn; Am Musicol Soc. *Interests:* The life and works of Claudio Meralo; sacred music of J C Bach. *Publ:* Auth, The Masses of Claudio Meralo, 70 & The Cappella Musicale at San Marco in the Late Sixteenth Century, 70, Am Choral Rev; ed, J C Bach's Dies Irae, Universal Ed, 72; The Sacred Works of Claudio Meralo, Am Inst Musicol, 6 vol, 70-83. *Mailing Add:* 1015 Longwood Dr Crete NE 68333

BATES, LEON
PIANO, EDUCATOR
b Philadelphia, Pa. *Study:* Studied with Irene Beck; studied piano with Natalie Hinderas. *Rec Perf:* Sonata No 4 (MacDowell), Orion; rec on Perf Rec. *Pos:* Pianist, worldwide concerts. *Teaching:* Assoc prof piano, Univ Del, currently. *Awards:* Winner, Nat Asn Music Teachers Col Artists Compt; Winner, RI New World Compt; Solo Recitalist Fel, Nat Endowment Arts. *Mailing Add:* Sch Music Univ Del Newark DE 19711

BATTIPAGLIA, DIANA MITTLER
PIANO, TEACHER
b New York, NY, Oct 19, 41. *Study:* Juilliard Sch Music, BS & MS; Eastman Sch Music, DMA. *Rec Perf:* Best of Offenbach. *Pos:* Piano soloist, New York Phil, New Haven Symph, New York Symph & various solo & chamber recitals. *Teaching:* Chmn music & choral dir, Flushing High Sch, NY. *Mem:* Music Educr Nat Conf. *Publ:* Auth, Franz Mittler—Composer, Pedagogue & Practical Musician, 74. *Mailing Add:* 108-57 66th Ave Forest Hills NY 11375

BATTISTI, FRANK LEON
CONDUCTOR, EDUCATOR
b Ithaca, NY, June 27, 31. *Study:* Ithaca Col, BS, 53, MS, 64. *Rec Perf:* New England Consv Wind Ens, 70, Anthology of Circus Music, 70, Be Glad Then America, 78 & Stravinsky Festival, 82, Golden Crest Rec. *Pos:* Cond, Symph Wind Ens, Baldwin Wallace Col Consv Music, Beria, Ohio, 67-69, Wind Ens, New England Consv, 69- & Mass Youth Wind Ens, Boston, 70-78; vis cond, Harvard Univ Band, 71-72 & Ithaca Col Wind Ens, 81-82. *Teaching:* Dir bands, Ithaca High Sch, 55-67; chmn, Instrm Music Dept, Ithaca Pub Sch, 61-67; instr cond & music educ, New England Consv, 69- *Mem:* Col Band Dir Nat Asn; Wind Ens Nat Conf; World Asn Wind Bands & Ens; New England Col Band Asn; Music Educr Nat Conf. *Mailing Add:* 214 Causeway St Medfield MA 02052

BAULT, DIANE LYNN
GUITAR, EDUCATOR
b Kearney, Nebr, June 14, 37. *Study:* Univ Fla, BA; Concordia Consv Music, NDak; studied with Manuel Lopez Ramos, 70-76. *Pos:* Performer guitar concerts, Ala & Fla; founder, Guitar Perf Ens, southern US, 75. *Teaching:* Instr music, Univ SAla, currently. *Mem:* Clara Schumann Club; Int Soc Class Guitar; Sigma Alpha Iota; Guitar Found Am. *Mailing Add:* Dept Music Univ SAla 9 Faculty Court East Mobile AL 36605

BAUMAN, JON WARD
COMPOSER, CONDUCTOR
b Big Rapids, Mich, June 7, 39. *Study:* Univ Colo, BMus, 61; Univ Ill, MMus, 63, DMA, 72. *Works:* Seven Songs of the City: Chicago, Univ Ill, 64; Quintet for Trumpet, Guitar, and Three Double Basses, WGer Radio, Cologne, 67; Aphorisms, Memphis State Perc Ens, 68; The Pineapple Story, Univ Ill, 69; Contrasts, Brooklyn Ctr, Long Island Univ Orch, 71; Concerto for Oboe d'Amore, Ft Worth Chamber Orch, 75; Inscape, New Music Group,

Frostburg State Col, 82. *Teaching:* Instr music, Chicago Pub Sch, 69-70; assoc prof comp & theory, Frostburg State Col, 70- *Awards:* Fulbright Grant, 65. *Bibliog:* Peter Christ (ed), Composium, Crystal Rec Co, 73- *Mem:* Am Soc Univ Comp; Southeastern Comp League; Md State Arts Coun; Am Music Ctr. *Mailing Add:* 273 Welsh Hill Frostburg MD 21532

BAUMGARTNER, PAUL LLOYD
EDUCATOR, PIANO
b Berne, Ind, Feb 21, 29. *Study:* Heidelberg Col, BM, 51; Eastman Sch Music, MM, 55; Univ Ariz, MusAD, 74; studied piano with Sidney Foster & Ozan Marsh; Ind Univ. *Pos:* Mem, Baumgartner Piano Duo, currently. *Teaching:* Instr piano, Wis State Univ, Stevens Point, 59-61 & Chowan Col, 62-64; assoc prof, Miyagi Col, Japan, 55-58; prof, Gustavus Adolphus Col, 64- *Awards:* Touring Grant, Nat Endowment Arts & SDak Arts Coun, 80. *Mem:* Minn Music Teachers Asn. *Mailing Add:* 607 N Minnesota Ave St Peter MN 56802

BAUR, JOHN WILLIAM
COMPOSER, EDUCATOR
b St Louis, Mo, Feb 27, 47. *Study:* Col Consv Music, Univ Cincinnati, with Jeno Takacs & Paul Cooper; studied with Thea Musgrave & Richard Rodney Bennett, London, 71-72. *Works:* Symphony No 1, 76; String Quintet No 2 (guitar & quartet), 77; The Moon and the Yew Tree (sop, flute, cello & piano), 77; Shadow Rites (ballet, chorus & orch), 78; Songs of Livingdying II (sop & chamber ens), 78; Patterns of Love (tenor & tape), 78; Impressions II (clarinet & tape), 78. *Teaching:* Fac mem, Shenandoah Consv, 73-74 & Tulane Univ, formerly; assoc prof music, Memphis State Univ, currently. *Awards:* Fulbright Grant; Nat Endowment Arts Grant, 74 & 78. *Mailing Add:* Dept Music Memphis State Univ Memphis TN 38152

BAUSTIAN, ROBERT
CONDUCTOR, EDUCATOR
b Storm Lake, Iowa, June 4, 21. *Study:* Eastman Sch Music, BMus, 42, MMus, 48; Zurich Consv, studied piano with Walter Frey & cond with Paul Mueller, 48-49. *Pos:* Coach & cond, Zurich Opera, 49-53; second cond, Hessian State Opera, Wiesbaden, Ger, 53-57; cond & music dir, Santa Fe Opera, formerly; guest cond, US & Europe. *Teaching:* Prof orch, Univ Kans, 57-66; prof cond, Consv Music, Oberlin Col, 66- *Mem:* Am Symph Orch League; Music Educr Nat Conf; Nat Opera Asn; Pi Kappa Lambda. *Mailing Add:* Consv Music Oberlin Col Oberlin OH 44074

BAVEL, ZAMIR
COMPOSER, VIOLIN
b Tel-Aviv, Israel, Feb 8, 29. US citizen. *Study:* Shulamit Consv, Tel Aviv, dipl, 47; Southern Ill Univ, BS, BA, BSEd, 54, MA, 55; Univ Ill, PhD, 65; studied comp with Roy Harris, Ben Haiim & Boskovitz. *Works:* Israeli Rhapsody, perf by Voice of Israel Symph, Southern Ill Univ Symph, Lawrence Symph, Topeka Symph & several other orch; Erev Bakfar, Vanguard; Taltalon & Bat Midbar. *Pos:* Concertmaster, Lawrence Symph & Lawrence Chamber Players, currently; first violin, Topeka Symph, currently. *Mailing Add:* Dept Electrical Eng & Comput Sci Polytechnic Inst NY 333 Jay St Brooklyn NY 11201

BAVICCHI, JOHN ALEXANDER
CONDUCTOR, COMPOSER
b Boston, Mass, Apr 25, 22. *Study:* New England Consv Music, BM, 52; Harvard Univ, with Walter Piston, 52-55. *Works:* Trio No 4, Op 33 & Violin Sonata #3, Op 39, CRI, 60; Six Duets for Flute & Clarinet, Op 27, 62, Clarinet Concerto, Op 11, 67, Corley's March, Op 54, 71, Violin Sonata No 4, Op 63, 74 & Mont Blanc Overture, Op 74, 78, Oxford Univ Press; Trio No 8, Op 77, Cardiff Fest Music, Wales, 83. *Pos:* Music dir, Am Fest Ballet, 62-65; cond, Sharon Symph Orch, 63-67; dir, Boston Community Ctr, 67-68; cond, Arlington Phil Soc, 68- *Teaching:* Mem fac theory, Cape Cod Consv, 56-58; lect lectr, Cambridge Ctr Adult Educ, 60-73; mem fac comp, Berklee Col Music, 64- *Awards:* Nat Inst Arts & Lett Award, 59; Am Symph Orch League Rec Grant, 61. *Bibliog:* James Gillespie (auth), The Clarinet Music of John Bavicchi, Clarinet, 2/75; Jeffrey Bishop (auth), John Bavicchi at the Cardiff Fest, Oxford Press, 4/6/82. *Mem:* ASCAP; Am Symph Orch League; Am Music Ctr. *Mailing Add:* Box 377 Newton MA 02161

BAXTER, CHARLES ALLEN
FRENCH HORN
b Lexington, Ky, Aug 30, 43. *Study:* Univ Louisville, BM, 65, BMusEd, 66; Yale Univ, MM, 71, MMA, 72. *Rec Perf:* Baroque Brass, 75, Rags and Other American Things, 76 & Classical Brass, 78, Klavier. *Pos:* Asst prin, Louisville Orch, 61-66; prin French horn, Pierre Monteaux Fest Orch, 63-69, US Military Acad Band, 66-69, New Haven Symph, 69-79, New York City Ballet & Opera, 72-74 & Eastern Brass Quintet, 70-81. *Teaching:* Artist in res, Univ Conn, 75-79. *Mailing Add:* 53 Stanton Rd Clinton CT 06413

BAXTER, LINCOLN ARTHUR
COMPOSER, EDUCATOR
b Winchester, Mass, July 6, 51. *Study:* Conn Col, with Charles R Shackford, BA, 75; Temple Univ, with Robert P Morgan, MM, 77, with Robert P Morgan & Maurice Wright, DMA, 83. *Works:* Movement for String Orchestra, perf by Orch Soc Philadelphia, 76 & Concerto Soloist Philadelphia, 78; Land Blowing Out to Sea, perf by Temple Univ Players & Singer, 78; Three Pieces for Unaccompanied Cello, perf by David Cowley, 78; Cantata on Psalm 100, comn by Northfield Hermon Sch, 80; Ice, a symphonic cycle for mezzo soprano and orchestra, 82. *Pos:* Music collection intern, Fleisher Collection Orch Music, 76-78. *Teaching:* Adj fac mem, univ fel & grad asst, Temple Univ, 76-80; asst prof music, Haverford Col, 82-83. *Mem:* Am Musicol Soc; Am Soc Aesthet. *Publ:* Auth, New Music, The Intentional Fallacy Restored, J Aesthet, fall 1980. *Mailing Add:* 1517 S Corlies St Philadelphia PA 19146

BAXTER, ROBERT T S
CRITIC & WRITER
b Fresno, Calif, Oct 15, 40. *Study:* Stanford Univ, BA, 62, PhD, 68. *Pos:* Music critic, Camden Courier-Post, 79- *Publ:* Auth, Zubin Mehta, Fugue, 79; Katia Ricciarelli, Ovation, 81; Conductors, Horizon, 82; Claudio Arrau on Singers and Singing, 83 & Oliviero de Fabritus, 83, Opera News. *Mailing Add:* 1200 E Marlton Pike Cherry Hill NJ 08034

BAXTER, WILLIAM HUBBARD, JR
EDUCATOR, BARITONE
b Birmingham, Ala, Nov 14, 21. *Study:* Birmingham-Southern Col, BA, 42; Birmingham Consv Music, BM, 47; Union Theol Sem, New York, SMM, 49; Univ Rochester, PhD, 57. *Teaching:* Asst prof music, WKy State Col, 49-51; prof music, Birmingham-Southern Col, 53- *Awards:* Fel, Southern Found, 56-57; Internship Acad Admin, Am Coun Educ, 67-68. *Mem:* Music Libr Asn; Hymn Soc Am; Music Teachers Nat Asn. *Interests:* Study of hymn texts in their original form. *Publ:* Auth, Basic Studies in Music, Allyn and Bacon, 68. *Mailing Add:* 1244 Greensboro Rd Birmingham AL 35208

BAYARD, CAROL ANN
SOPRANO, EDUCATOR
b Glens Falls, NY, June 22, 34. *Roles:* Rosalinda in Die Fledermaus, New York City Opera, 64-74; Curley's Wife in Of Mice and Men, Seattle Opera, 70; Manon, New York City Opera, 70; Nedda in Pagliacci, Houston Opera, 72; Grand Duchess of Gerolstein, San Francisco Opera, 74; Donna Anna in Don Giovanni, New York City Opera, Dayton Opera & Toledo Opera, 78. *Pos:* Leading sop, New York City Opera Co, 64-74. *Teaching:* Voice, Queens Col, City Univ New York, 77-80. *Mailing Add:* 400 W 43rd Apt 30-G New York NY 10036

BAYLOR, HUGH MURRAY
EDUCATOR, COMPOSER
b What Cheer, Iowa, Apr 8, 13. *Study:* Univ Iowa, BA, 34, MA, 36, PhD, 50; Consv Am, Fontainebleau, France, dipl, 38; private study New York & Paris, 36-37, 63 & 69. *Works:* By Gemini Comic Opera, Knox Col, 50; Songs, 60 & Chamber Music, 65, Galesburg, Ill; By Gemini Comic Opera, New York private sch, 83. *Teaching:* Asst in music, Univ Iowa, 34-; chmn music dept, William Penn Col, Oskaloosa, Iowa, 37-42; prof music & chmn, Knox Col, Galesburg, Ill, 42-80 & emer prof music, 80- *Mem:* Music Teachers Nat Asn; Ill Music Teachers Asn; Col Music Soc; Soc Music Theory. *Interests:* Piano music of Scriabin; Rachmaninoff & Satie. *Publ:* Auth, various short articles in jour. *Mailing Add:* 1187 N Cherry St Galesburg IL 61401

BAYNE, PAULINE SHAW
LIBRARIAN
b Berwyn, Ill, Feb 15, 46. *Study:* Morton Col, AA, 66; Millikin Univ, BM, 68; Northwestern Univ, MM, 70; Univ NC, Chapel Hill, MS(libr sci), 73. *Pos:* Music librn, Univ Tenn, Knoxville, 73- *Teaching:* Music, pub sch, Chicago, 68-72; assoc prof, Univ Tenn, Knoxville, 73- *Mem:* Music Libr Asn (pres Southeast Chap, 74-76). *Publ:* Auth, The Gottfried Galston Music Collection & the Galston-Busoni Archive, Univ Tenn Libr, 78; ed, A Basic Music Library: Essential Scores & Books, 78 & co-ed, 2nd ed, 83, Am Libr Asn; coauth, Access to Songs in Collections, Tenn Librn, 81. *Mailing Add:* 7209 Stockton Dr Knoxville TN 37919

BAYS, ROBERT EARL
ADMINSTRATOR, EDUCATOR
b Bonne Terre, Mo, Apr 8, 21. *Study:* Emporia State Univ, BS, 46; Teachers Col, Columbia Univ, MA, 49; George Peabody Col, PhD, 53. *Pos:* Dir, Sch Music, George Peabody Col, 65-69 & Sch Music, Univ Ill, Urbana, 49-; chmn, Dept Music, Univ Tex, Austin, 69-74. *Mem:* Nat Asn Sch Music (pres, 79-82); Col Music Soc (vpres, 74-76); Music Educr Nat Conf (pres Southern div, 67-69). *Mailing Add:* 56 Lake Park Champaign IL 61820

BAZELON, IRWIN ALLEN
COMPOSER, CONDUCTOR
b Evanston, Ill, June 4, 22. *Study:* DePaul Univ, BA & MA, 45; Mills Col, with Darius Milhaud, 45-47. *Works:* Short Symphony, 62 & Symphony No 5, 67, Boosey & Hawkes; Duo—Viola & Piano, 73, Woodwind Quintet, 78, Cross-Currents, 80, De-Tonations, 81, Imprints for Piano, 83 & Fusions (chamber ens), 83, Novello. *Rec Perf:* Short Symphony, Louisville Rec, 66; Symphony No 5, 67, Propulsions for Percussion, 75, Brass Quintet, 75 & Duo for Viola and Piano, 75, CRI; Woodwind Quintet, Orion, 78; Sound Dreams, Comp Rec Inc, 83. *Pos:* Comp-in-res, Univ Akron, 10/80 & Royal Northern Col Music, Manchester, England, 10/82. *Awards:* S Koussevitsky Found Award, 82. *Bibliog:* David Cox (auth), Bazelon's Violent Silence, London Musical Times, 82. *Mem:* ASCAP; Am Music Ctr. *Publ:* Auth, Knowing the Score... Notes on Film Music, Arco Publ, 80. *Mailing Add:* 142 E 71 New York NY 10021

BEACH, DAVID WILLIAMS
EDUCATOR, ADMINISTRATOR
b Hartford, Conn, Sept 5, 38. *Study:* Brown Univ, BA, 61; Yale Univ, MMus, 64, PhD, 74. *Teaching:* Instr, Yale Univ, 64-67; asst prof, 67-71; asst prof, Brooklyn Col, City Univ New York, 71-72; assoc prof, Eastman Sch Music, 74- *Mem:* Am Musicol Soc; Soc Music Theory. *Publ:* Auth, The Origins of Harmonic Analysis, J Music Theory, 74; Pitch Structure and the Analytic Process in Atonal Music, Music Theory Spectrum, 79; co-transl, Kirnberger's The Art of Strict Musical Compositions, 82 & ed, Aspects of Schenkerian Theory, 83, Yale Univ Press. *Mailing Add:* 17 Country Corner Lane Fairport NY 14450

BEACRAFT, ROSS (ORTON)
TRUMPET, LECTURER
b Pottstown, Pa, Nov 11, 47. *Study:* Eastman Sch Music, BMA, 69; Civic Orch Chicago, 70-73; studies with Adolph Herseth, 70-74. *Rec Perf:* Chicago Brass Quintet, Crystal Rec, 81. *Pos:* Prin trumpet, Norwegian Opera & Ballet Orch, 74-75, Chicago Brass Quintet, 75-, Chicago Opera Theater, 75-, Am Chamber Symph, 75- & Chicago Ballet, 82- *Teaching:* Lectr trumpet & brass dept chmn, DePaul Univ, 78- *Mem:* Int Trumpet Guild; Am Symph Orch League. *Rep:* Herbert Barrett Mgt 1860 Broadway New York NY 10023. *Mailing Add:* 6346 N Spokane Chicago IL 60646

BEADELL, ROBERT MORTON
COMPOSER, EDUCATOR
b Chicago, Ill, June 18, 25. *Study:* Northwestern Univ, Evanston, Ill, BM, 49, MM, 50; study with Leo Sowerby, 51 & Darius Milhaud, 62. *Works:* Introduction and Allegro (brass & timpani), Music for Brass Publ, 51; Elegy For A Dead Soldier (baritone), Univ Nebr Singers & Orch, 58; Number of Fools (opera), comn by Northwestern Univ Opera Wkshp, 66; Trilogy (SATB & brass), AMP Music Publ, 73; Improvisation and Dance, comn & perf by Minn Orch, 74; Holy Sonnet (SATB), Shawnee Press, 75; Variations for Jazz Trio (flugelhorn & strings), comn by Nat Endowment Arts. *Teaching:* Prof theory & comp, Univ Nebr, Lincoln, 54- *Awards:* Standard Award, ASCAP, 67-82. *Mem:* ASCAP. *Mailing Add:* 7541 Old Post Rd #9 Lincoln NE 68506

BEADLE, ANTHONY
DOUBLE BASS, EDUCATOR
b Brookline, Mass, Apr, 22, 52. *Study:* Boston Univ, BMus, 74. *Pos:* Mem, Boston Ballet Orch, 77- & Harvard Univ Chamber Orch, 78-; prin bass, Pro Arte Chamber Orch Boston, 78-; mgr, Boston Musica Viva, 78-79. *Teaching:* Instr double bass, Longy Sch Music, 79- & Northeastern Univ, 82- *Mailing Add:* 28 Nottinghill Rd Brighton MA 02135

BEALE, EVERETT MINOT
PERCUSSION, EDUCATOR
b Rockland, Mass, July 7, 39. *Study:* New England Consv Music, BM, 62. *Pos:* Prin perc, Boston Ballet Orch, 61-; asst timpanist, Boston Opera Orch, 61-78; solo timpanist, Boston Pops Esplanade Orch, 68-; perc, Boston Symph Orch & Boston Pops Orch. *Teaching:* Head perc dept, Congregation Arts, Dartmouth Col, 63-68, Univ Lowell, 64- & Keene State Col, 75-78. *Awards:* Mem, World Symph Orch, 71; John Philip Souza Band Award. *Mem:* Phi Mu Alpha Sinfonia; Percussive Arts Soc. *Publ:* Auth, The Playing and Teaching of Percussion Instruments, 75. *Rep:* Mgt in the Arts 551 Tremont St Boston MA 02116. *Mailing Add:* 104 Redgate Rd Tyngsboro MA 01879

BEALE, JAMES
EDUCATOR, COMPOSER
b Wellesley Hills, Mass, Jan 20, 24. *Study:* Harvard Univ, AB, 45; Yale Univ, BMus, 46, MMus, 47. *Works:* Trio, Op 5 (violin, violoncello & piano), 47, Symphony for Chamber Orchestra, 50, Seventh Piano Sonata, 52, Cressay Symphony, Op 26, 59, Three Pieces for Vibraphone, 60, Sextet for Winds & Piano, Op 39, 76, How Like a Winter (SATB), 82, Comp Facsimile Ed. *Pos:* Asst dir, Univ Wash Sch Music, 82- *Teaching:* Prof, Univ Wash Sch Music, 48-; vis prof theory & comp, Carnegie-Mellon Univ, 69-70. *Awards:* Woods-Chandler Prize, Yale Univ, 47; Newsmaker of Tomorrow, Time Mag, 52; Guggenheim Fel, 58-59. *Mem:* Am Comp Alliance; Soc Music Theory. *Publ:* Auth, The Music of John Verrall, Am Comp Alliance Bulletin, Spring 58; Webern's Musikalischer Nachlass, Melos, Oct 64, reprinted in English as Webern's Musical Estate, In: Anton Von Webern, Perspectives, Univ Wash Press, 66. *Mailing Add:* 7508 42nd NE Seattle WA 98115

BEALL, JOHN OLIVER
COMPOSER, EDUCATOR
b Belton, Tex, June 12, 42. *Study:* Baylor Univ, BM, 64, MM, 66; Eastman Sch Music, PhD, 73. *Works:* Concerto (piano & wind orch), 79, Concerto (brass quintet & winds), 79 & Lament for Those Lost In the War, 79, Carl Fischer Inc; Piano Fantasy, comn by Steven Smith, 81; String Quartet, WVa Grad Quartet, 82; Sextet (woodwind quintet & piano), Dorn Inc, 83; On Chestnut Ridge, Aeolian Chamber Players, 83. *Teaching:* Asst prof music, Southwest Tex State Univ, San Marcos, 75-76 & Eastern Ill Univ, Charleston, 76-78; assoc prof, WVa Univ, Morgantown, 78- *Awards:* Louis Lane Prize, 72; Howard Hanson Prize, 73; ASCAP Award, 79-82. *Mem:* ASCAP; Pittsburgh Alliance Comp (bd mem, 83-); Am Soc Univ Comp. *Mailing Add:* Creative Arts Ctr WVa Univ PO Box 6111 Morgantown WV 26506

BEALL, LEE MORRETT
EDUCATOR, ORGAN
b Washington, DC. *Study:* Am Univ, BA, 56, EdD, 58; Univ Md, College Park, MEd, 57. *Pos:* Dir, Mayland Choral Soc, Spruce Pine, NC, 70- *Teaching:* Prof music, Winston-Salem State Univ, 70- *Mem:* Am Guild Organists; Am Orff-Schulwerk Asn; Music Educr Nat Conf; Nat Asn Music Therapy; Am Asn Music Therapy. *Publ:* Auth, Who's Afraid of PL 94-142, NC Music Educr, 82. *Mailing Add:* 117 Gloria Ave Winston-Salem NC 27107

BEAN, SHIRLEY ANN
EDUCATOR
b Kansas City, Mo, Oct 30, 38. *Study:* Univ Kansas City, BME, 60, MM(theory), 63; Univ Mo, Kansas City, DMA(hist & lit), 73. *Teaching:* Instr music, Shawnee Mission High Sch District, Kans, 63-65; instr music theory, Univ Mo, Kansas City, 69-74, asst prof, 75- *Awards:* Excellence in Undergraduate Teaching, Amoco Found, 73 & 80. *Mem:* Am Musicol Soc;

Pi Kappa Lambda; Sigma Alpha Iota. *Publ:* Auth, The Missouri Harmony, 1820-1858: The Refinement of a Southern Tunebook, Mo J Res Music Educ, 73. *Mailing Add:* Consv Music Univ Mo 4420 Warwick Kansas City MO 64111

BEARDSLEE, BETHANY E
SOPRANO, TEACHER
b Lansing, Mich. *Study:* Mich State Univ, BMus; Juilliard Sch Music, dipl; Princeton Univ, Hon Dr Music, 76. *Rec Perf:* Seven Early Songs (Berg), 61 & Altenberg Lieder (Berg), 61, Columbia Rec; Eighteenth Century Vocal Recital, Monitor Rec, 66; Vision and Prayer, CRI Rec, 75; Philomel, New World Rec, 80; Second String Quartet (Schoenberg), 80 & Little Companion Pieces (Powell), 80, Nonesuch Rec. *Roles:* Premiered many 20th Century works by Stravinsky, Berg, Webern, Babbitt, Krenek & maj Am comp. Also Boulez, Peter Maxwell Davies, Monod, Godfrey Winham & Dallapiccola; maj work in recitals, 50- *Teaching:* Prof voice, Univ Tex, Austin, 80-81. *Awards:* Laurel Leaf Award, Am Comp Alliance, 61; Ford Found Award, 63. *Mem:* NY Guild Comp (pres, 82-83). *Mailing Add:* 315 W 106 St New York NY 10025

BEARDSLEE, SHEILA MARGARET
RECORDER, TEACHER
b Biddeford, Maine, Mar 28, 50. *Study:* New England Consv, studied recorder with Nancy Joyce Roth, musicol with Anne Hallmark & historic dance with Julia Sutton, MM(perf early music), 78. *Pos:* Founder & co-dir, Much Ado (Renaissance consort), Boston, 75-81 & New England Baroque Ens, Boston, 77-83; mem, Greenwood Consort, 83- *Teaching:* Fac mem recorder & chamber music, Tufts Univ, 77-; fac mem recorder, ens & historic dance, Am Recorder Soc Wkshp, Boston, 81- & Mountain Collegium, Brasstown, NC, 81- *Mem:* Am Musicol Soc; Am Recorder Soc (Boston chap music dir, 78, newsletter ed, 82). *Interests:* Sixteenth-eighteenth century music, dance and theater. *Mailing Add:* 20 Milton St Arlington MA 02174

BEARER, ELAINE LOUISE
COMPOSER, CONDUCTOR
b Morristown, NJ, Apr 1, 47. *Study:* Manhattan Sch Music, BMus, 70; NY Univ, MA & PhD, 73; Fountainebleau Am Consv, Cert d'Assist. *Works:* Five Pieces for Organ, 74; Three Songs of Innocence, 74. *Teaching:* Instr music, San Francisco State Univ, 73-75; asst prof, Lone Mountain Col, 73-74. *Awards:* NY Univ Fel. *Mem:* Am Musicol Soc. *Mailing Add:* 61 Parnassus Ave San Francisco CA 94117

BEASER, ROBERT HARRY
COMPOSER, CONDUCTOR & MUSIC DIRECTOR
b Boston, Mass, May 29, 54. *Study:* Sch Music, Yale Col, with Jacob Druckman & Yehudi Wyner, BA, 76; Berkshire Music Ctr, with Betsy Jolas, MM, 77, MMA, 80; private study with Gofreddo Petrassi & Arnold Franchetti, Rome. *Works:* Canti Notturni, European Am Music Corp, 75; String Quartet, perf by Berkshire Fest Orch, 76; Symphony (sop & orch), perf by Rome Radio Orch, 77; The Seven Deadly Sins, 79, Shadow and Light (woodwind quintet), 82, Notes On A Southern Sky, 82 & Variations (flute & piano), 83, European Am Music Corp. *Pos:* Asst cond, Norwalk Symph Orch, 75-77; co-music dir & cond, Musical Elements, New York, 79- *Awards:* Prix de Rome, Am Acad, 77-78; Charles Ives Scholar, Am Acad Inst Arts & Lett, 79; Guggenheim Fel, 83-84. *Mem:* BMI; Am Music Ctr. *Mailing Add:* 35 W 90th St 11C New York NY 10024

BEASLEY, RULE CURTIS
EDUCATOR, BASSOON
b Texarkana, Ark, Aug 12, 31. *Study:* Southern Methodist Univ, BA, 52; Juilliard Sch Music, 53; Univ Ill, MM, 58. *Works:* Divertimento (bassoon, harp & strings), Kurhaus Orch, St Moritz, Switz, 62; Lyric Prelude (orch), Oklahoma City Symph Orch, 63; First String Quartet, Bennington Comp Conf, Vt, 64; Psalm 48 (chorus & perc), Cleveland Inst Music, 64; Concerto (tuba & winds), State Univ NY, Potsdam, 69; Elegy (orch), NMex State Univ Orch, 80. *Pos:* Prin bassoon, Ft Worth Symph Orch, 68-73 & Ft Worth Opera Asn, 68-73; alt bassoon, Dallas Symph Orch, 66-67. *Teaching:* Assoc prof music, Centenary Col La, Shreveport, 58-66 & NTex State Univ, Denton, 66-73; prof, Santa Monica Col, 73- *Awards:* Best Orch Comp, Southeastern Comp League, 63. *Mem:* Am Soc Univ Comp. *Publ:* Coauth, Practical Re-Scoring Tips, Instrumentalist, 8/78. *Mailing Add:* 1127 Pacific St Santa Monica CA 90405

BEATTIE, HERBERT (WILSON)
BASS, EDUCATOR
b Chicago, Ill, Aug 23, 26. *Study:* Am Consv Music, with John C Wilcox; Colo Col, BA, 48; Westminster Choir Col, MA, 50; Mozarteum, Salzburg, Austria, 55; studied with Josef Krips; Colo Col, Hon PhD, 78. *Rec Perf:* Andrew Bordon in Lizzie Borden, NET TV; rec on Columbia, Desto & Cambridge. *Roles:* Baron Douphol in La Traviata, 58 & Andrew Borden in Lizzie Borden, 65, New York City Opera; Don Alfonso in Cosi fan tutte; Sarastro in Zauberflöte; Kezal in The Bartered Bride; Boris, Varlaam & Pimen in Boris Godunov; King of Clubs in The Love of the Three Oranges. *Pos:* Mem, New York City Opera, 58-69 & 80-81, Central City Colo Opera, 59-65 & San Francisco Opera, 60-66; dir, Colo Opera Fest, 70-75, stage dir, currently; perf artist, concerts in US, Can, Netherlands, Brussels & Amsterdam. *Teaching:* Instr, Syracuse Univ, 50-52; asst prof music, Pa State Univ, 52-53 & Buffalo Univ, 53-59; prof, Hofstra Univ, 59- *Awards:* Sullivan Found Award, 59; Rockefeller Scholar, 59-60. *Mem:* Am Guild Musical Artists; Am Asn Univ Prof; Phi Mu Alpha. *Rep:* Lew & Benson Moreau-Neret Inc 204 W 10th St New York NY 10014. *Mailing Add:* Dept Music Hofstra Univ Fulton St Hempstead NY 11550

BEATY, DANIEL JOSEPH
COMPOSER, PIANO
b Sapulpa, Okla, Apr 25, 37. *Study:* Univ Tulsa, BM, 59, MM, 60; NTex State Univ, PhD, 64. *Works:* Many songs, piano & choral pieces, perf by various groups & individuals in US, 60-; Woodbugs & Watersprites, 72 & Seven Bagatelles, 79, Kjos West; East Texas Landscape, perf at several fest in Southwest, 80-; Vietnam Suite, perf at several art galleries in Southwest, 80-; Toccatas for Tape, Voice & Instruments, perf at several Southwestern sch & fest, 80-83. *Teaching:* Asst prof music, Bishop Col, Dallas, 60-64; prof, Stephen F Austin State Univ, 64- *Bibliog:* Robert Blocker (auth), Seven Bagatelles, Keynotes, 80. *Mem:* Fine Arts Soc Tex; Tex Music Educr Asn; Am Soc Univ Comp; Tex Soc Music Theory; Tex Music Libr Asn. *Publ:* Auth, A Marriage of Music and English, Music Educr J, 72; coauth, Texas Folk Music, Encino Press, 77; auth, A Composer Speaks, Kjos West, 80; coauth, Singin' Texas, Encino Press, 83; auth, Research and Creativity, Artes Liberales, 83. *Mailing Add:* Music Dept Stephen F Austin State Univ Nacogdoches TX 75962

BEAUCHAMP, JAMES W
EDUCATOR
b Highland Park, Mich, Oct 17, 37. *Study:* Univ Mich, BS, 60, MS, 61; Univ Ill, Urbana-Champaign, PhD, 65. *Teaching:* Asst prof music, Univ Ill, Urbana-Champaign, 69-70, assoc prof, 70- *Mem:* Fel, Audio Engineering Soc; Computer Music Asn (mem bd dir, 80-, pres, 81-). *Publ:* Auth, Additive Synthesis of Harmonic Musical Tones, J Audio Engineering Soc, 66; A Computer System for Time-Variant Harmonic Analysis and Synthesis of Musical Tones, In: Music by Computers, McGraw Hill, 69; co-ed, Music by Computers, McGraw Hill, 69; auth, Electronic Music: Apparatus and Technology, In: Dict Contemp Music, 74; Time-Variant Spectra of Violin Tones, J Acoustic Soc Am, 74; Analysis and Synthesis of Cornet Tones Using Nonlinear Interharmonic Relationships, 75 & Synthesis by Spectral Amplitude and Brightness Matching of Analyzed Musical Instrument Tones, 82, J Audio Engineering Soc. *Mailing Add:* 2136 Music Bldg 1114 W Nevada Univ Ill Urbana IL 61801

BEAUREGARD, CHERRY NIEL
TUBA
b Filmore, Utah, Oct 6, 33. *Study:* Staatliche Hochschule Musik, Munich, 56-68; Brigham Young Univ, BA, 59; Eastman Sch Music, MMus, 64, DMus 70. *Rec Perf:* German & English Music of the Late Renaissance for Brass; Canto VII for Tuba Solo (Samuel Adler). *Pos:* Tubist, Bavarian State Opera Orch, Munich, 60-62, Rochester Phil Orch, 62- & Eastman Brass Quintet, 64-; mem tours US, Can, Mex, Peru, Chile, Ecuador & Israel. *Teaching:* Assoc prof tuba, Eastman Sch Music, 71- *Mailing Add:* Eastman Sch Music 26 Gibbs St Rochester NY 14604

BECERRIL, ANTHONY RAYMOND
BARITONE
b Flagstaff, Ariz, Feb 8, 45. *Study:* With Robert Lawrence, Feliz Popper & Nicolosi. *Roles:* Silvio in Pagliacci, Salmaggi Opera, New York, 67; Escamillo in Carmen; Malatesta in Don Pasquale; Marcello in La Boheme; Figaro in Il Barbiere di Siviglia; Wolfram in Tannhäuser; Masetto in Don Giovanni. *Pos:* Recitalist & appearances with maj orchs in US & Austria. *Teaching:* Private lessons voice. *Awards:* Dramatic Musical Comedy Scholar, Am Music Dir Asn. *Mailing Add:* c/o Matthews-Napal 270 West End Ave New York NY 10023

BECK, FREDERICK ALLAN
TRUMPET, EDUCATOR
b Newport, Vt, July 3, 46. *Study:* Univ Vt, BS, 69; Eastman Sch Music, MM, 73, DMA, 79. *Works:* Vocalise for Unaccompanied Flugelhorn, Int Nat Trumpet Guild, 77; Snake Rag for Brass Quintet, Accura Music, 81; Jazz Suite, 82. *Pos:* Third asst first trumpet, Portland Symph Orch, Maine, 73-76; co-prin trumpet, Greensboro Symph Orch, 80- *Teaching:* Chmn music dept, Mt Ararat Sch, Topsham, Maine, 73-76; instr trumpet, Mansfield Col, 79-80; asst prof, Univ NC, Greensboro, 80- *Awards:* Fac Excellence Fund, Univ NC, Greensboro, 82. *Mem:* Music Educr Nat Conf; Nat Asn Col Wind & Perc Instr; Int Trumpet Guild; Nat Asn Jazz Educr; Pi Kappa Lambda. *Publ:* Auth, The Flugelhorn as an Orchestral Instrument, 78 & The Flugelhorn as a Recital Instrument, 79, Woodwind World, Brass & Perc; The Flugelhorn: Its History & Development, Int Trumpet Guild J, 80. *Mailing Add:* 901 King George Dr Greensboro NC 27410

BECK, JOHN H
PERCUSSION, COMPOSER
b Lewisburg, Pa, Feb 16, 33. *Study:* Eastman Sch Music, BM, MM, perf cert. *Works:* Concerto (drum set & perc ens), comn & perf by Univ Okla Perc Ens, 78; Rhapsody for Percussion and Band; Jazz Variants (perc ens); Sonata Timpani; Colonial Drummer; Colonial Capers; Episode (solo perc); publ by Boston Music, Kendor Music, MCA, Wimbledon Music & Studio 4 Prod. *Pos:* Perc, timpanist & marimba soloist, US Marine Band, 55-59; prin perc, Rochester Phil, 59-62, prin timpanist, 62-; cond, Eastman Perc Ens, 62-; perc columnist, Nat Asn Col Wind & Perc Instr J, 65-72; performer, Aeolean Consort, 77; solo appearances with Syracuse Wind Ens, Chautauqua Band, Rochester Chamber Orch, Rochester Phil Orch & others. *Teaching:* Mem fac, Eastman Sch, 59- *Awards:* Musician of Yr, Mu Phi Epsilon, 76. *Mem:* NY State Sch Music Asn (chmn perc, 70-); NY State Percussive Arts Soc (pres, 76-82, second vpres, 82-). *Publ:* Contribr to Music J, Instrumentalist, Woodwind World, Brass & Perc Mag & Percussive Notes. *Mailing Add:* Rochester Phil Orch 108 East Ave Rochester NY 14604

BECK, MARTHA DILLARD (MRS G HOWARD CARRAGAN)
COMPOSER, TEACHER
b Sodaville, Ore, Jan 19, 02. *Study:* Univ Chicago; Columbia Sch Music; Oberlin Col, with George Whitfield Andrews, BM, 24; Am Consv Music, with Adolf Weidig, MM, 27; Juilliard Sch, with Silvio Scionti, 27-29; studied with Hugo Leichtentritt & Frances Frothingham. *Works:* Piano and String Quintet, 27; Fantasy for Chamber Orchestra, 27; A Legend of Tamarac (cantata for mixed chorus & small orch), 66; Michael and Cornelia: A Saga of the Hudson Valley Dutch (cantata), 75; American Pageant (two pianos), Schnectady, NY, 76; Psalm 122 (chorus, organ, brass quintet & perc), perf by Fest Chorus, Saratoga, NY, 76; Prelude for Orchestra, comn by Albany Symph, 77. *Teaching:* Mem fac, Am Consv Music, 24-29; NCent Col, 24-29 & Emma Willard Sch, Troy, NY, 32-48; private teacher piano, Troy, NY. *Awards:* Adolf Weidig Gold Medal, 27; First Prize, Mu Phi Epsilon Nat Cont, 27 & Maxine Schreiver Compt, 27 & 28. *Mem:* ASCAP. *Publ:* Auth, The Martha Beck Rhythm Rule Method, 61. *Mailing Add:* Tamarac Rd Troy NY 12180

BECKEL, JAMES A, JR
TROMBONE, EDUCATOR
b Marion, Ohio, July 16, 48. *Study:* Ind Univ, BM, 72. *Works:* Three Sketches for Orchestra, 78 & Celebrations, 80, Indianapolis Symph. *Pos:* Prin trombonist, Indianapolis Symph Orch, 69- *Teaching:* Instr trombone, DePauw Univ, 71- & Ind Cent Univ, 80- *Mailing Add:* 6039 Harlescott Rd Indianapolis IN 46220

BECKER, BONITA RUTH
VIOLIN, PIANO
b West Allis, Wis, Oct 29, 42. *Study:* Nat Music Camp, summer 79; Young Artists Instrm Prog, Tanglewood, studied violin with Ikuko Mizuno, summer 80; studied violin with Max Mandel & piano with Ruth Kolb Smith; Univ Mich, Ann Arbor, violin studies with Angel Reyes, 80- *Pos:* Solo pianist, Mesa Symph Orch, Ariz, 78; concertmaster, Phoenix Symph Youth Orch, 78-79; mem first violin sect, Univ Philharmonia, Univ Mich, Ann Arbor, 80-82, Univ Symph Orch, 82- *Teaching:* Piano, privately, 78-80. *Awards:* First Place Piano, Mesa Music Guild Compt, Ariz, 78; First Place Violin, Phoenix Symph Guild Concerto Compt, 80; Nat Symph Orch Asn Award, 80. *Rep:* E C Cargill 8108 E Buena Terra Way Scottsdale AZ 85253. *Mailing Add:* 9459 E Jenan Dr Scottsdale AZ 85260

BECKER, C(ECIL) WARREN
EDUCATOR, ORGAN
b St Maries, Idaho, May 25, 23. *Study:* Walla Walla Col, Wash, BA(music), 45; Eastman Sch Music, MMus, 51, DMus Arts, 63. *Teaching:* Instr music, Pac Union Col, Calif, 45-59; prof music, Andrews Univ, Mich, 59- *Awards:* C E Weniger Award, 82; J N Andrews Award, 82. *Mem:* Am Guild Organists; Seventh-Day Adventists Church Musician Guild; Hymn Soc Am; Am Musicol Soc. *Publ:* Coauth (with Harold Gleason), Music Literature Outlines, Vol 1-5, Frangipani Press, 80-81. *Mailing Add:* 295 University Blvd Berrien Springs MI 49103

BECKER, EUGENE
VIOLA, EDUCATOR
b New York, NY, Aug 2, 29. *Study:* Manhattan Sch Music, 39-48; Syracuse Univ, BM, 51, MM, 52; studied with William Lincer, 55-57. *Pos:* Violist, Krasner String Quartet, 49-53 & Gramercy String Quartet, 64-76; asst prin violist, New York Phil, 57- *Teaching:* Adj assoc prof music hist & chamber music, Herbert Lehman Col, City Univ New York, 70-80; mem fac, Precol Div, Juilliard Sch Music, 75- *Mailing Add:* 303 W 66th St Apt 11GE New York NY 10023

BECKER, RICHARD
EDUCATOR, COMPOSER
b White Plains, NY, Sept 27, 43. *Study:* Eastman Sch Music, with Samuel Adler; Boston Univ, with Gardner Read & Alan Schindler. *Works:* Sonata for 2 Pianos, 75; The Cat and the Moon (vocal quartet, trumpet, horn, oboe & trombone), 79; Mavromata (piano), 79; Five Mementos (piano solo), 80; In Praise of Spring (piano solo), 82; Der Panther (sop voice & woodwind quintet), 83. *Teaching:* Instr piano, Univ Tex, 67-71 & Boston Univ, 71-75; asst prof hist, lit & piano, Univ Richmond, 75- *Awards:* Comp Grant, Univ Richmond. *Mailing Add:* 4301 Wythe Ave Richmond VA 23221

BECKERMAN, MICHAEL BRIM
EDUCATOR, CRITIC & WRITER
b New York, NY, Aug 2, 51. *Study:* Hofstra Univ, with Elie Siegmeister, BA, 69-73; Columbia Univ, MA, 76, MPhil, 78, PhD, 82. *Works:* Czech Journey, 79; Sheva Brachot, 79 & Song of Songs, 83, New Calliope Singers. *Pos:* Critic, St Louis Globe Democrat, 83- *Teaching:* Preceptor, Barnard Col, Columbia Univ, 75-81; instr, Fordham Univ, 81-82; asst prof musicol, Washington Univ, 82- *Awards:* Long Island Piano Soc Award, 73; Czech Music Fund Award, 78; Fulbright Award, 79. *Interests:* Leos Janacek's writings; Czech music. *Publ:* Auth, Janacek and the Herbartians, 83 & Janacek's Kata Kabanova, 83, Musical Quart; Smetana's Bartered Bride, Notes, 83. *Mailing Add:* Music Dept Washington Univ St Louis MO 63112

BECKLER, S R (STANWORTH RUSSELL)
COMPOSER, EDUCATOR
b Escondido, Calif, Dec 26, 23. *Study:* Col of Pac, BA & BM, 50, MA, 51; Eastman Sch Music, with Wayne Barlow, 61; Univ Southern Calif, with George Perle, 65. *Works:* Seven Ages of Man (orch), comn & perf by Stockton Symph, 72; Seven Little Wind Sonatas, Op 49, 80, Nine Little Piano Pieces, Op 45, 80, Five Little String Sonatas, Op 53, 80, Little Suite Woodwind

Quintet, Op 59, 80 & Little Suite Contrabass Quartet, Op 73, 80, Seesaw Music Corp; Bust, Lawson-Gould, 83. *Teaching:* Instr music hist, Col of Pac, 51-53, from asst prof to prof theory, Univ of Pac, 55-, chmn dept theory, Music Consv, currently. *Mem:* Am Asn Univ Prof; ASCAP; Soc Music Theory; Col Music Soc; Am Soc Univ Comp. *Publ:* Contribr to four columns on theory, Voice, 80. *Mailing Add:* Consv Annex Univ of Pac Stockton CA 95211

BECKON, LETTIE MARIE
COMPOSER, PIANO
b Detroit, Mich, Apr 13, 53. *Study:* Bailey Temple Sch Music; studied pipe & electronic organ with William Wise, clarinet with Al Green & piano with Pearl McCullom; Wayne State Univ, studied piano with Frank Murch & Mischa Kottler & comp with James Hartway, BM(comp & piano), 76, MM(comp & piano), 78; Univ Mich, studied comp with Leslie Bassett, William Bolcom, Eugene Kurzt & George Wilson. *Works:* Head a Woe (two violins & cello), 75; Three Implied Jesters (solo clarinet), 75; Composition I (12 tones; clarinet ens), 76; Effigy (oboe, piano & perc), 76; Symphonic Essay (string orch & perc), 77; Visions (marimba & piano), 77; Integrated Concerto (piano & orch), 78. *Pos:* Concert artist, Wayne State Univ, part-time. *Teaching:* Piano, several private sch & studios, 75-; teaching asst, Univ Mich, 82. *Awards:* Ida K Smokler Award, 76. *Mailing Add:* 16849 Asbury Park Detroit MI 48235

BEDFORD, JUDITH EILEEN
BASSOON, EDUCATOR
b Johnstown, NY, July 16, 43. *Study:* New England Consv Music, BM, 65, MM, 67 & 71, artist dipl, 75. *Pos:* Freelance bassoonist, Boston, Mass, 69-; bassoon consult, Brown Univ, 74- *Teaching:* Instr bassoon, clarinet & chamber music, Belmont Music Sch, Mass, 69-; instr woodwind minor instrm, New England Consv, 75. *Mailing Add:* 138 Renfrew St Arlington MA 02174

BEDNAR, STANLEY
VIOLIN, EDUCATOR
Study: Eastman Sch Music; Univ Minn; Juilliard Sch; Manhattan Sch Music, MM; studied violin with Gordon, Mischakoff, Kortschak & Bronstein. *Pos:* Mem, Rochester Phil Orch, formerly, Dallas Symph, formerly, Chamber Music Circle, formerly, Casals Fest Orch, formerly, Columbia Rec Orch, formerly & Am Chamber Orch, formerly; piano accmp tours with violinists & singers; performer chamber music, Budapest Quartet. *Teaching:* Mem violin fac, Manhattan Sch Music, 54-, dir admis, 56-81, chmn string dept, 68-82. *Mailing Add:* Manhattan Sch Music 120 Claremont Ave New York NY 10027

BEEGLE, RAYMOND BRUCE
MUSIC DIRECTOR, PIANO
b Los Angeles, Calif, Jan 17, 42. *Study:* Univ Calif, Los Angeles, BA, 64; Univ Southern Calif; Vienna Acad Music. *Pos:* Accmp, Licia Albanese, Martial Singher, Eugene Conley & Teresa Zylis-Gara, formerly; artistic dir, New York Vocal Arts Ens, 71- *Awards:* First place, Artists of Future, Los Angeles Bur Music, 63; 1st place chamber music, Geneva Int Comp, 80. *Rep:* Columbia Artists Mgt 165 W 57th St New York NY 10019. *Mailing Add:* 12 W 72nd St New York NY 10023

BEELER, CHARLES ALAN
EDUCATOR, COMPOSER
b St Louis, Mo, Feb 10, 39. *Study:* Ill Wesleyan Univ, BMus, 61; Wash Univ, St Louis, MA, 65, PhD, 73. *Works:* Evolving Shapes (flute, clarinet, viola & pianoforte), perf by Les Scott, Jan Scott, Rosemary Goldsmith & Barton Weber, 65; Quintessence II, Webster Groves Symph Orch, 66; Sonata (oboe & piano), perf by Alan Beeler & Bruce Bennet, 75; Serial Sonata, perf by Earl Thomas, Richard Bremley, Roy Houser & Alan Beeler, 76; 1st Scene: The Bald Soprano, perf by Wayne Gebb, Eastern Ky Univ Opera Wkshp, 80. *Teaching:* Instr, Wis State Univ, Stevens Point, 67-70; asst prof music theory & comp, Eastern Ky Univ, 70-75, assoc prof, 75-80, prof, 80- *Mem:* Col Music Soc; Soc Music Theory; Int Double Reed Soc. *Mailing Add:* 123 Hager Ave Richmond KY 40475

BEER, HANS L
CONDUCTOR, EDUCATOR
b Munich, Germany, May 5, 27. *Study:* Music Acad, Munich, with Carl Orff, 55. *Pos:* Assoc cond, Univ Southern Calif Symph, 58-68, dir, Opera Theater, 68-74; assoc cond, San Diego Opera, 67; guest cond, US & Europe, 74- *Teaching:* Prof opera, opera hist & cond, Univ Southern Calif, 58- *Awards:* Fulbright Fel, 55-56. *Mailing Add:* Sch Music Univ Southern Calif Los Angeles CA 90089

BEERMAN, BURTON
COMPOSER, CLARINET
b Atlanta, Ga, June 12, 43. *Study:* Fla State Univ, BM, 66; Univ Mich, MM, 68, DMA, 71. *Works:* Four in Six (quartet), Gaudeamus String Quartet, 76; Dance for Celeste (tape), Electronic Music Plus, 81; Night Calls (clarinet, dance & tape), Piccolo Spoleto, 82; Moments—1981 (quintet), AKI Fest, Cleveland, Ohio, 82; Concerto I (sax & tape), perf by John Sampen, 82; Secret Gardens (ens), Baylor Univ Wind & Perc Fac, 83; Romance (piano & tape), perf by Frances Burnett, 83. *Pos:* Clarinet soloist & recitalist, US & Can, 82-83. *Teaching:* Prof music comp, Bowling Green State Univ, 70-; guest lectr, Univ Utah, 75-76. *Awards:* Pittsburgh Flute Comp Award, Pittsburgh Flute Club, 71; Martha K Cooper Orch Prize, Ohioana Found, 82. *Mem:* BMI; Am Comp Alliance; Am Soc Univ Comp. *Mailing Add:* 713 Champagne Ave Bowling Green OH 43402

BEESON, JACK (HAMILTON)
COMPOSER, EDUCATOR
b Muncie, Ind, July 15, 21. *Study:* Univ Toronto, cert (piano & theory), 38; Eastman Sch Music, Univ Rochester, BM, 42, MM, 43; private study with Bela Bartok, 44-45. *Works:* Hello Out There, Belwin-Mills, 54; The Sweet Bye and Bye, 57 & Lizzie Borden, 65, Boosey & Hawkes; Symphony #1 in A, MCA & Belwin-Mills, 66; My Heart's in the Highlands, 70, Captain Jinks of the Horse Marines, 75 & Dr Heidegger's Fountain of Youth, 78, Boosey & Hawkes. *Pos:* Music publ comt chmn, Columbia Univ Press, 71- *Teaching:* Fac mem, Columbia Univ, 45- & Juilliard Sch Music, 61-63; MacDowell prof music, Columbia Univ. *Awards:* Rome Prize, 48-50; Guggenheim Fel, 58-59; Gold Medal, Nat Arts Club, 76. *Mem:* Am Acad Inst Arts & Lett (treas, 80-83); Comp Rec Inc (bd mem, 67-, vpres, 67-75, coactg pres, 75-76); Am Acad Rome (bd trustees, 75-). *Rep:* Boosey & Hawkes 24 W 57th St New York NY 10019. *Mailing Add:* Seaforth Lane Lloyd Neck NY 11743

BEGLARIAN, GRANT
COMPOSER, ADMINISTRATOR
b Tiflis, Georgia, USSR, Dec 1, 27; US citizen. *Study:* Univ Mich, BM, 50, MM, 54, DMA, 58; Berkshire Music Ctr with Aaron Copland, 59. *Works:* Divertimento for Orchestra, 59, A Hymn for Our Times, 66, And All the Hills Echoed, 68, Fables (voice & narration), 71, Diversions (voice & orch), 72, Sinfonia for Strings, 74 & To Manitou, 76, Piedmont Music. *Pos:* Ed, Prentice Hall Inc, 60-61; dir, Contemp Music Proj, 61-69; dean, Sch Perf Arts, Univ Southern Calif, 69-82; pres, Nat Found Adv Arts, 82- *Teaching:* Instr comp, Univ Mich, 51-52; US Army Music Sch, Germany, 52-54. *Awards:* Gershwin Award, 58; Young Comp Award, Ford Found, 59; ASCAP Award, 63- *Mem:* ASCAP; Int Coun Fine Arts Deans (pres 80-82); Calif Alliance Arts Educ (chmn, 72-74); Am Music Ctr. *Mailing Add:* 100 N Biscayne Blvd Suite 1800 Miami FL 33132

BEHAGUE, GERARD HENRI
EDUCATOR
b Montpellier, France, Nov 2, 37. *Study:* Nat Sch Music, Univ Brazil, Rio de Janeiro, Curso de Formacao Profissional, 56; Brazilian Consv Music, Curso de Formacao Profissional, 58; Inst Musicol, Sorbonne, dipl, 63; Tulane Univ, PhD, 66. *Pos:* Ed, Ethnomusicol, 74-78 & Latin Am Music Rev, 80-; ed, RILM, 75- *Teaching:* Grad asst, Tulane Univ, 64-65; res asst, 65-66; instr, Univ Fla, Gainesville, summers 64 & 65; instr, Univ Ill, Urbana, 67-69, asst prof, 66-67, assoc prof, 69-74; prof, Univ Tex, Austin, 74-, actg chmn dept music, 80-81, chmn, 81- *Awards:* Guggenheim Fel, 72; Foreign Area Fel, Ford Found, 72. *Bibliog:* Gerald Benjamin (auth), Review, Ethnomusicol, 80; Juan A Orrego-Salas (auth), Review, Latin Am Music Rev, 80. *Mem:* Soc Ethnomusicol (pres, 79-81); Am Musicol Soc (counr, 71-73); Latin Am Study Asn; Int Musicol Soc; Col Music Soc. *Interests:* Ethnomusicology; music and ritual; Afro-Brazilian religious music; art and popular music of Brazil and Andean countries. *Publ:* Auth, The Beginnings of Musical Nationalism in Brazil, Info Coordr, 71; Music in Latin America: An Introduction, Prentice-Hall, 79; 110 entries in New Grove Dict of Music & Musicians, Macmillan, London, 80; America Latina e Caribi, Verona, 82; Performance Practice: Ethnomusicological Perspectives, Greenwood Press, 83. *Mailing Add:* 6106 Highland Hills Dr Austin TX 78731

BEHNKE, MARTIN KYLE
EDUCATOR, CONDUCTOR
b Yreka, Calif, Jan 19, 46. *Study:* San Jose State Univ, BM, 67, MM, 71; Univ Colo, Boulder, PhD(music educ), 75. *Teaching:* Prof music, Cochise Col, 71-73; asst prof, Univ Mo, 74-76 & Seattle Pac Univ, 76-79; assoc prof & dir bands, Willamette Univ, 79- *Mem:* Music Educr Nat Conf; Col Music Soc; Col Band Dir Nat Asn (pres Ore chap, 81-83); Nat Asn Jazz Educr (pres Ore chap, 83-). *Mailing Add:* 820 Ironwood Dr SE Salem OR 97306

BEHR, JAN
CONDUCTOR
b Krnov, Czechoslovakia, Apr 1, 11. *Study:* Acad Music, Prague, studied piano with Franz Langer & cond with George Szell; German Opera House, Prague, 33-38; German Univ Prague, LLD. *Rec Perf:* On Columbia & Urania. *Pos:* Cond, Traviata Opera House, Prague, 36, Orch Nat, Brussels, 46 & other opera co in US & Europe; res cond, Metropolitan Opera, currently. *Mailing Add:* 514 West End Ave New York NY 10024

BEHREND, JEANNE
PIANO, EDUCATOR
b Philadelphia, Pa, May 11, 11. *Study:* Curtis Inst, dipl, 34; studied with Josef Hofmann & Rosario Scalero. *Rec Perf:* Piano Music by American Composers, RCA Victor, 40; Piano Music by L M Gottschalk, MGM, 58. *Teaching:* Instr, Curtis Inst, 36-43; Juilliard Sch, 46-52, New Sch Music, 69-74, Philadelphia Col Perf Arts, 74-; assoc prof, Western Col, 46-52. *Awards:* Order Southern Cross, Brazil, 65. *Mem:* Am Musicol Soc; Sonneck Soc. *Interests:* Music of the Western Hemisphere. *Publ:* Ed, Notes of a Pianist, Knopf, 64. *Mailing Add:* Suite 4A1 2401 Pennsylvania Ave Philadelphia PA 19130

BEHRENS, JACK
COMPOSER, ADMINISTRATOR
b Lancaster, Pa, Mar 25, 35. *Study:* Juilliard Sch, BSc, 58, MSc, 59; Harvard Univ, PhD(comp), 73. *Works:* In a Manger, Elkan-Vogel, 62; Soundings, comn by Can Coun, 65; The Feast of Life, Op One, 76; Music for Two Pianos, comn by Ont Arts Coun, 78; String Quartet, comn by Can Broadcasting Corp, 80; Fiona's Flute, 83 & Dialogue, 83, Orion. *Rec Perf:* Ballade for Flute & Piano, Op 68 (Peter Racine Fricker), 83 & Bagatelles for Clarinet & Piano, Op 83 (Peter Racine Fricker), 83, Orion. *Pos:* Head theory dept, Consv Univ

Regina, 62-66. *Teaching:* Actg chmn, Ctr Commun & Arts, Simon Fraser Univ, 66-67; chmn, Fine Arts Dept, Calif State Col, Bakersfield, 73-76; dean fac music, Univ Western Ont, London, Ont, 80- *Mem:* ASCAP; Am Soc Univ Comp; Can League Comp; Can Univ Music Soc . *Publ:* Auth, Recent Piano Works of Christian Wolff, 77 & Peter Racine Fricker on His 60th Birthday, 80, Studies in Music, Univ Western Ont; Restoring the Soul, Instnl Vitality, Siena Heights Col, 81. *Mailing Add:* Dept Music Univ Western Ont London ON N6A 3K7 Canada

BELCHER, DEBORAH JEAN
PIANO, EDUCATOR
b Greenville, SC, Oct 21, 49. *Study:* Eastman Sch Music, with Eugene List, 70; Ind Univ, with Karen Shaw, MM(piano), 74; Manhattan Sch Music, with Robert Goldsand. *Teaching:* Fac mem piano, Interlochen Arts Acad, Mich, 74-79; coordr piano dept, Northwestern Mich Col, 75-82 & Cleveland Inst Music, 82- *Awards:* Scholar, Presser Found, 68-69 & 69-70; Mich Coun Arts Touring Grant, 76. *Mem:* Chamber Music Am; Ohio Music Teachers Asn; NE Ohio Music Teachers Asn; Music Teachers Nat Asn; Pi Kappa Lambda. *Mailing Add:* 2331 Scholl Rd University Heights OH 44118

BELFORD, MARVIN L
EDUCATOR, TRUMPET
b Beatrice, Nebr, Aug 15, 33. *Study:* Drake Univ, BME, 55, MME, 57; Univ Iowa, PhD, 67. *Teaching:* Instr, Fresno City Col, 57-64; asst prof, Millikin Univ, 66-68; assoc prof, Southern Ore State Col, 68- *Mem:* Music Educr Nat Conf; Ore Music Educr Asn; Nat Asn Col Wind & Perc Instr; Int Trumpet Guild; Phi Mu Alpha Sinfonia. *Publ:* Auth, Sputnik Vs Notenik, Instrumentalist, 58; Are Your Musicians Educated?, Holton Fanfare, 59; Electronic Music, F E Olds, 65; coauth, Acoustic Flexibility in Concert Halls, Instrumentalist, 77. *Mailing Add:* 385 Kearney St Ashland OR 97520

BELIAVSKY, YURI
VIOLIN, TEACHER
b Moscow, USSR, Feb 15, 32, Israeli & US citizen. *Study:* Moscow Consv with I Yampolsky, BA, 51; Moscow Gnesin State Music Inst, with A Yampolsky, MA, 56. *Rec Perf:* Concerto for Violin and Orchestra in G No 3 (Mozart), Concerto for Violin and Orchestra No 1 (Bartok) & Kol Nidre (Bruch), Jerusalem Symph. *Pos:* First Violinist, State Symph Orch of Cinema 55-62, Grand Symph Radio, USSR, 62-71 & Milwaukee Symph, 78-; asst concert master, Jerusalem Symph, Israel, 72-75. *Teaching:* Instr violin, Jerusalem Music Acad Rubin, 72-75, Wis Consv Music, 76 & NShore Music Ctr Chicago, 82. *Mailing Add:* 907 E Calumet Rd Fox Point WI 53217

BELISLE, JOHN M
DIRECTOR—OPERA, EDUCATOR
b Morris, Okla, May 31, 27. *Study:* Sch Music, Okla City Univ, BMus(voice), 54; Sch Music, Ind Univ, with Paul Matthen, M Taylor & Ralph Appleman, MMusEd, 57, MusD, 65; Oglebay Inst Opera, studied opera directing with Boris Goldovsky, 71. *Pos:* Managing dir & founder, San Marcos Summerfest Theater & Fest, 80- *Teaching:* Dir opera ens, SW Tex State Univ, 62- *Interests:* Directing and acting for opera theater. *Publ:* Auth, Some Factors Influencing Diction in Singing, 64 & Carmen: A Director's View, 78, Nat Asn Teachers Singing Bulletin; ed, Voice-Piano, Vol I, 82 & Voice, Piano and Obbligato Instrument, Vol II, 83, In: American Artsong Anthology, Galaxy Music Co. *Mailing Add:* 1604 Stokes St San Marcos TX 78666

BELL, (S) AARON
COMPOSER, DOUBLE BASS
b Muskogee, Okla, Apr 24, 24. *Study:* Xavier Univ, BA, 42; NY Univ, MA, 51; Columbia Univ, MEd, 76, EDd, 77. *Works:* Hobbitt Suite, 73, Rondo-Schizo (clarinet & piano), 76, Watergate Piano Sonata, 76, Bicentennial Symphony, 76, Farewell Fugue, 81 & Memorial Suite for Orchestra, 83, Caaron Music. *Rec Perf:* The Aaron Bell Trio, Herald, 56; Victory at Sea, 60, Sunset Strip, 62 & Peter Gunn, 63, MGM; The Party's Over, 64 & The Hobbitt Suite, 66. *Pos:* First chair bassist, MBL Studio Band, 62-64; res comp, La Mama Theatre, 64-74; res comp & cond, Richard Allen Theatre, 80-81. *Teaching:* Prof music, Essex County Col, 69-, chmn fine & perf arts & dir stage band, 78-81. *Awards:* ASCAP Comp Award Winner, 73-; Ford Found Fel, 75-77. *Mem:* ASCAP; Comp Guild NJ; Am Soc Lit & Arts; Int Platform Assoc. *Mailing Add:* 444 S Columbus Ave Mt Vernon NY 10553

BELL, CHARLES E
FRENCH HORN
b Norfolk, Va, June 3, 56. *Study:* New England Consv; Col-Consv Music, Univ Cincinnati, BA, 78, MM, 80. *Pos:* Third horn, Louisville Orch, 81-82; asst first & utility horn, Cincinnati Symph Orch, 82-; horn, Queen City Brass Quintet, 83- *Rep:* Cincinnati Symph Orch 1241 Elm St Cincinnati OH 45210. *Mailing Add:* 729 Edgecliff Rd C-32 Covington KY 41014

BELL, LARRY THOMAS
COMPOSER, PIANO
b Wilson, NC, Jan 17, 52. *Study:* Appalachian State Univ, BM, 74; Juilliard Sch, MM, 77, DMA, 82. *Works:* String Quartet No 1, Juilliard String Quartet, 76; The Idea of Order at Key West, Juilliard Phil, 82; Prologue & the End of the World, Juilliard Pre-Col Chorus, 82; Fantasia on an Imaginary Hymn, Joel Krosnick (in prep). *Pos:* Fel, Am Acad Rome, 82-83. *Teaching:* Instr solfege & theory, Juilliard Sch Pre-Col, 79-; prof comp, Boston Consv, 80- *Awards:* Charles Ives Award, Am Acad Nat Inst Arts & Lett, 77; John Simon Guggenheim Mem Found Fel, 82; Prix de Rome, Am Acad Rome, 82 & 83. *Mem:* Am Music Ctr; Am Soc Univ Comp; Sonneck Soc. *Mailing Add:* 255 Massachusetts Ave Apt 305 Boston MA 02115

BELL, WINSTON A
EDUCATOR, PIANO
b Winchester, Ky, Mar 24, 30. *Study:* Fisk Univ, BA, 51; Univ Mich, MM, 55; Columbia Univ, EdD, 64; Gen Theol Sem, STB. *Pos:* Mem bd dirs, Winston-Salem Symph. *Teaching:* Instr piano, Elizabeth City State Univ, 55-59; assoc prof music, Winston-Salem State Univ, 72-77, prof, 77-, chmn dept, 77-82. *Mem:* Phi Mu Alpha Sinfonia; Suzuki Asn Am; NC Piedmont Orff Soc; Keyboard Artists; Music Educr Nat Conf. *Mailing Add:* Music Dept Winston-Salem State Univ Winston-Salem NC 27102

BELLING, SUSAN
SOPRANO
b Bronx, NY. *Study:* Chatham Sq Music Sch; Manhattan Sch Music. *Rec Perf:* Mavra (Stravinsky), Canciones (Nono) & Elephant Steps (Silverman), Columbia Rec. *Roles:* Various roles with major co including, Second Quarter, Boston Orch; Belinda in Dido and Aeneas, Metropolitan Opera; Zerlina in Don Giovanni, Hollywood Bowl; Papagena in The Magic Flute, Cleveland Conct Assoc; soloist in Midsummer Night's Dream & Fourth Symphony (Mahler), Chicago Symph; Susanna in Marriage of Figaro, Atlanta Symph Orch; Melusine in Melusine, Santa Fe Opera; Rosina in The Barber of Seville, Miami Opera; Arcena in Gypsy Baron, Little Orch Conct at Avery Fisher Hall & Pamina in The Magic Flute, Cleveland Opera. *Pos:* Guest soloist, major US symph & opera co, 77- *Mailing Add:* c/o Thea Dispeker 59 E 54th St New York NY 10022

BELNAP, NORMA LEE MADSEN See Madsen, Norma Lee

BELOW, ROBERT CLAUDE
PIANO, COMPOSER
b Louisville, Ky, Jan 3, 34. *Study:* Univ Louisville, BMus, 54, MMus, 58; Hochschule Musik, Köln Rhein, WGermany, with Dwight Anderson, George Perle & Heinz Schröter, konzertdipl, 60. *Works:* Te Deum (first setting), St Francis Episcopal Church, Louisville, 58; Second Piano Sonata, perf by comp, 60; Duo (flute & piano), perf by Nan Orthman & comp, 69; Symphonic Movement, perf by Lawrence Univ Wind Ens, 81; To the Holy Spirit, All Saints Episcopal Church, 81-82; Trio (clarinet, cello & piano), perf by comp, C McCreery & D Sparks, 82; With Rue My Heart, perf by Lawrence Univ Conct Choir, 83. *Teaching:* Asst prof, Univ Calif, Davis, 59-64; prof, Lawrence Univ, 64- *Mailing Add:* 115 Park Ave Appleton WI 54911

BELSOM, JACK (JOHN ANTON)
CRITIC-WRITER, ADMINISTRATOR
b Roaring Spring, Pa, June 21, 33. *Study:* Tulane Univ, BA, 55; La State Univ, Baton Rouge, MA, 72. *Pos:* Critic-writer, Opera News, New York, 62-73 & Opera, London, 63-; archivist, New Orleans Opera Asn, 74- *Interests:* History of opera in New Orleans, 1800 to the present. *Publ:* Ed, Settlement of the German Coast of Louisiana, Genealogical Publ Co, Baltimore, 69. *Mailing Add:* 721 Barracks St New Orleans LA 70116

BENAGLIO, ROBERTO
CHORUS MASTER
Pos: Chorus master, Dallas Opera, 59-61 & 74- & La Scala, Milan, 62-73; prepared choruses for Teatro Regio, Turin, Teatro San Carlo, Naples, Teatro Bellini, Catania, Vienna Staatsoper & Salzburg Fest. *Mailing Add:* Dallas Opera Majestic Theatre 1925 Elm St Dallas TX 75201

BENDELL, CHRISTINE J
EDUCATOR, PIANO
b Minneapolis, Minn, Nov 12, 48. *Study:* McPhail Sch Music, Minneapolis, 62-66; Wis State Univ, 66-67; Gustavus Adolphus Col, BA, 70; Univ Ill, Champaign, MM, 72; Northwestern Univ, 74, 75, 77 & 78; Univ Northern Colo, DA, 82. *Pos:* Educ dir, Baldwin Piano & Organ Co, 72-73; adjudicator, Wis Music Scholar Fund, Morraine Area Jr Music Club Compt, 72-74, Barkl & Ringley Scholar SDak, 74-75, Kans State High Sch Activ Asn Piano Fest, 79-, Kans Fedn Women's Clubs District Compt, 79 & Nat Fedn Music Clubs Compt, 83; pianist & harpsichordist, Topeka Symph Orch, 76-78; group piano coordr, Melody Brown Found, 77-78. *Teaching:* Lectr wrkshps & clinics, Music Educr Nat Conf, 73, Topeka Music Teachers Asn, 76 & 83, Melody Brown Found, 78, Kans Music Teachers Asn, 78, Sigma Alpha Iota, 78, Kans Christian Women's Auxiliary, 8, NCent Piano Teachers League Clinic, 82 & The Value of Live Perf Sem, 83; fac mem, Univ SDak, 74-75, Harper Col, 75-76 & Washburn Univ, 76-; teaching asst, Univ Northern Colo, 79-80. *Awards:* Danforth Found Assoc, 78; Nat Cert Piano Pedagogy, Music Teachers Nat Asn, 83. *Mem:* Music Educr Nat Conf; Music Teachers Nat Asn; Sigma Alpha Iota (mem exec bd); Am Symph Orch League. *Interests:* Frederico Mompou: an analytical and stylistic study of the Canciones y Danzas for Piano. *Publ:* Auth, articles in Music Educr J, Keyboard Consult & Kans Music Rev. *Mailing Add:* Dept Music Washburn Univ Topeka KS 66621

BENEDETTI, EVANGELINE
CELLO, EDUCATOR
Study: Manhattan Sch Music, MM; studied cello with Greenhouse, Britt & Nelsova; studied Alexandre Technique. *Pos:* Cello, New York Phil, 67- *Teaching:* Mem fac, Manhattan Prep Div, New York Col Music, formerly; mem fac violoncello, Manhattan Sch Music, 70- *Mailing Add:* New York Phil Avery Fisher Hall New York NY 10023

BENEFIELD, RICHARD DOTSON
BARITONE, CONDUCTOR
b Birmingham, Ala, Feb 8, 54. *Study:* Baylor Univ, BM, 76, MM, 80; Boston Univ; voice study with Richard Robinson, Berton Coffin & Shirlee Emmons. *Roles:* Don Alfonso in Cosi fan tutte, Georgia Opera Inc, 79; Mr Ford in Merry Wives of Windsor, Baylor Opera Theater, 80; Figaro in Barber of Seville, 82, Malatesta in Don Pasquale, 82 & Belcore in L'Elisir d'amore, 82, Goldovsky Opera Inst. *Pos:* Founder & music dir, Paris Motet Choir, Tex. *Awards:* Nat Endowment for Humanities Grant, 81. *Mem:* Nat Asn Teachers Singing; Am Musicol Soc. *Mailing Add:* 5520 56th St #804 Lubbock TX 79414

BENFIELD, WARREN A
DOUBLE BASS, EDUCATOR
b Allentown, Pa, Feb 12, 13. *Study:* Interlochen Music Camp, 30-31; Curtis Inst Music, 32-34. *Pos:* String bassist, Minn Symph, 34-37; string bass, St Louis Symph Orch, 37-38, prin, 38-42; string bass, Philadelphia Orch, 42-48, co-prin, 48-49; string bass, Chicago Symph Orch, 49-, prin, 49-51. *Teaching:* Prof string bass, Northwestern Univ, 54-79; teacher & artist, Am Fedn Musicians, Cong of Strings, 59-72; teacher, DePaul Univ, 67- *Publ:* Auth, The Responsibility of the Professional Musician-Teacher, Instrumentalist, 6/69; 20th Century Orchestra Studies, For Double Bass, G Schirmer, 72; coauth, The Art of Double Bass Playing, Summy-Birchard Co, 73. *Mailing Add:* 357 W Grove St Lombard IL 60148

BENGTSON, F DALE
COMPOSER, EDUCATOR
b Des Moines, Iowa, Oct 22, 34. *Study:* Anderson Col, BA, 57; State Univ Wichita, MMus, 60; Univ Mo, DMA, 72. *Works:* Ricercare (brass quintet), Robert King Publ; Gloria in Excellsis Deo (SATB choral), There is Christmas (SATB & organ), Speak Words of Praise (SATB choral) & Create and Celebrate (SATB choral), Theodore Presser Publ. *Pos:* Cond, Anderson Col Choir, Ind, 63-73 & Europ Concert Tour, Am Choral Dir Asn & Coun Inter-cult Relations, 73. *Teaching:* Mem fac, Anderson Col, Ind, 60-, prof & chmn, Dept Music, 69- *Mem:* Ind State Higher Educ Music Adminr; Am Musicol Soc; Phi Mu Alpha Sinfonia; Pi Kappa Lambda; Nat Asn Sch Music. *Publ:* Auth, A Baroque Study Ich Hoffe Darauf Dass Du So Gnadig Bist, 72. *Mailing Add:* Dept Music Anderson Col E 5th & College Dr Anderson IN 46012

BENHAM, HELEN WHEATON
PERFORMER, PIANO
b New York, NY, Dec 4, 41. *Study:* Oberlin Consv Music, BMus, 62; Oberlin Col, BA, 63; Juilliard Sch, MS, 65. *Pos:* Accmp & soloist piano & harpsichord, Monmouth Symph Orch, 76-; Eisner-Benham Duo, 77-80; pianist & harpsichordist, Albert Kay Assoc Conct Wkshp Mgt, 80-; soloist, ens US & Europe, currently. *Teaching:* Piano & ens fac mem, Prep Sch, Mannes Col Music, 66-; fac piano, Monmouth Consv, Little Silver, NJ, 67-; assoc prof music, Brookdale Community Col, Lincraft, NJ, 73- *Mem:* Mu Phi Epsilon; Nat Guild Piano Teachers; Shore Music Educr Asn; Comp Guild NJ; Pi Kappa Lambda. *Publ:* Auth, Piano for the Adult Beginner, Books I & II, Brookdale Community Col Instr Develop Lab, 77. *Mailing Add:* 960 Elberon Ave Elberon NJ 07740

BENI, GIMI (JAMES J)
BASS-BARITONE
b Philadelphia, Pa. *Study:* Acad Vocal Arts, Philadelphia, with Clytie Mundy; studied with Stuart Ross & Julia Drobner; Am Theatre Wing, New York. *Roles:* Don Pasquale in Don Pasquale, Rome Opera, 55; Papa Gonzalez in Summer and Smoke, St Paul Opera, Minn, 71; Dr Dulcamara in The Elixir of Love, Washington Opera; Gianni Schicchi in Gianni Schicchi, Palm Beach Opera; Bartolo in The Barber of Seville; Sharpless in Madama Butterfly; Alcindoro & Benoit in La Boheme, Baltimore Opera, 82. *Pos:* Bass-baritone & basso-buffo with major opera co & symph orchs in US, Italy & Israel, currently; libretto translr, currently. *Teaching:* Voice, currently; guest artist in res opera, various col & univ, currently. *Awards:* Fulbright Scholar, Italy. *Mailing Add:* c/o James Scovotti Mgt 185 West End Ave New York NY 10023

BENJAMIN, THOMAS EDWARD
COMPOSER, EDUCATOR
b Bennington, Vt, Feb 17, 40. *Study:* Bard Col, BA, 61; Harvard Univ, MA, 63; Brandeis Univ, MFA, 65; Eastman Sch Music, PhD, 68. *Works:* Articulations, Ludwig, 76; Freu' dich sehr, Galaxy, 76; Te Deum, Mark Foster, 78; Postludium, Shawnee, 80; The Message, Mark Foster, 81; Night Songs, Hinshaw, 82; Le Son du Cor, Lawson-Gould, 83. *Teaching:* Prof, Univ Houston Sch Music, 68-; instr, Nat Music Camp, Interlochen, Mich, 69. *Awards:* Res fel, MacDowell Colony, 75 & 82; Comp-librettist Award, Nat Endowment Arts, 77-78; First Prize, Mars Hill Compt, 78. *Mem:* Am Soc Univ Comp; Col Music Soc; ASCAP; Am Music Ctr; Pi Kappa Lambda. *Publ:* Auth, The Craft of Modal Counterpoint, Macmillan, 78; coauth, Techniques of Materials of Tonal Music, 78, Music for Analysis, 78 & Music for Sight Reading, 83, Houghton Mifflin; auth, The Learning Process and Teaching, Symposium, 83. *Mailing Add:* 2629 Cason St Houston TX 77005

BENNETT, HAROLD
FLUTE & PICCOLO, EDUCATOR
Study: Curtis Inst Music, dipl; studied flute with Sharp & Kincaid. *Rec Perf:* With many maj rec co. *Pos:* Solo flute, Nat Symph Orch, formerly, Pittsburgh Symph Orch, formerly, Radio Symph Orch, formerly & Metropolitan Opera, 44-65; asst first flute & piccolo, Philadelphia Symph Orch, formerly. *Teaching:* Mem fac flute, Manhattan Sch Music, 62-; coach flute, Nat Orch Asn, 63; mem fac, Teachers Col, Columbia Univ, 63. *Mailing Add:* Manhattan Sch Music 120 Claremont Ave New York NY 10027

BENOIT, KENNETH ROGER
COMPOSER, LIBRARIAN
b Coral Gables, Fla, Oct 12, 52. *Study:* Miami-Dade Community Col, AA(music educ), 72; Univ WFla, BA(music educ), 74; Univ Miami, MM(theory & comp), 78; Fla State Univ, MLS, 79. *Works:* String Quartet in A Minor, perf by Fla State Univ student quartet, 80; Variations on a Theme by Robert Schumann, perf by La State Univ students, 81; Trio for Piccolo, Trumpet & String Bass, perf by Univ Ala students, 82; Missa Brevis in F, comn by York Mem United Methodist Church, 82; Fanfare and Anthem, comn by North Miami Community Conct Band, 83; The Librarians March, perf by NMiami Community Conct Band, 83. *Pos:* Music Librn, Miami-Dade Pub Libr, 79- *Mem:* ASCAP; Am Soc Univ Comp; Am Symph Orch League; Soc for Music Theory; Music Libr Asn. *Publ:* Auth, Updating Basic Record Lists, Libr J, (in press); The Miami-Dade Public Library Art & Music Dept, Breve Notes, 82. *Mailing Add:* 1475 NE 111th St #109 Miami FL 33161

BENSON, JOAN
CLAVICHORD & FORTEPIANO, LECTURER
b St Paul, Minn. *Study:* Univ Ill, BMus, MMus; Sch Music, Ind Univ, perf cert; study with Edwin Fischer, Europe, 3 yrs; study clavichord & early music with Fritz Neumeyer, Ger & Santiago Kastner, Portugal; advan studies in London, France, Italy, Ger, Austria, Switz & Port, incl consv Luzern, Vienna, Lisbon, Freiburg & Sienna. *Rec Perf:* Joan Benson—Clavichord, Repertoire Rec, 62; Music of C P E Bach (early piano & clavichord), Orion Master Rec, 73; Joan Benson: Works of Haydn and Pasquini, on Boston Museum of Fine Arts Clavichords, Titanic Rec, 82. *Pos:* Conct artist & lectr, Am, Europe, Middle E, Far E & SPac, 62- *Teaching:* Lectr clavichord & fortepiano, Dept Music, Stanford Univ, 70, 75 & 83; asst prof early keyboard, Sch Music, Univ Ore, 76-82. *Awards:* Kate Neal Kinley Award. *Mem:* Am Musicol Soc. *Publ:* Auth, Vienna Haydn 250th Anniversary Congress Book (1982): The Use of the Clavichord in Haydn's Music, Vienna, 83. *Rep:* Beverly Simmons 15706 Hazel Rd East Cleveland Ohio 44112. *Mailing Add:* Dept Music Stanford Univ Stanford CA 94305

BENSON, WARREN F
COMPOSER, EDUCATOR
b Detroit, Mich, Jan 26, 24. *Study:* Univ Mich, BM, 49, MM, 51. *Works:* Songs For the End of the World, perf by, Jan DeGaetani & Verne Reynolds, 81; The Man With the Blue Guitar, 81 & Beyond Winter: Sweet Aftershowers, 82, Rochester Phil Orch; Symphony II: Lost Songs, Mich State Univ Symph Band & Larvik Wind Ens, Norway, 83; Hills, Woods Brook: Three Love Songs, Doris Yarick-Cross, Univ Conn Chamber Players, 83; Moon Rain and Memory Jane, perf by Lucy Shelton, 84. *Teaching:* Fulbright instr music, Anatolia Col, Salonica, Greece, 50-52; prof music & comp in res, Ithaca Col, 53-67; prof comp, Eastman Sch Music, Univ Rochester, 67- *Awards:* Kilbourn Distinguished Prof, Eastman Sch Music, 80-81; fel, John Simon Guggenheim Found, 81-82. *Mailing Add:* Univ Rochester 26 Gibbs St Rochester NY 14604

BENT, MARGARET
EDUCATOR
b St Albans, England, Dec 23, 40. *Study:* Cambridge Univ, BA, 62, MusB, 63, MA, 65, PhD, 69. *Pos:* Dir summer sem, Nat Endowment for Humanities, 79 & 81. *Teaching:* Lectr music, Goldsmiths' Col, Univ London, 72-75; Ziskin vis prof, Brandeis Univ, 75-76 & prof, 76-81; prof music, Princeton Univ, 81- *Awards:* Dent Medal, 79; Guggenheim Fel, 83. *Mem:* Am Musicol Soc. *Interests:* Late-medieval music; notation and manuscript studies; compositional and performance problems. *Publ:* Auth, Sources of the Old Hall Music, Proc Royal Music Asn, 67-68; New and Little-Known Fragments of English Medieval Polyphony, 68 & Dufay, Dunstable, Plummer—A New Source, 69, J Am Musicol Soc; co-ed, The Old Hall Manuscript, Am Inst Musicol, Rome, 69-73; auth, Musica Recta and Musica Ficta, Musica Disciplina, 72; The Transmission of English Music 1300-1500: Some Aspects of Repertory and Presentation, In: Studien zur Tradition in der Musik: Kurt Von Fischer zum 60 Geburtstag, Munich, 73. *Mailing Add:* 25 Mercer Princeton NJ 08540

BENTLEY, JOHN E
EDUCATOR, OBOE
b Florence, Ala, Dec 5, 37. *Study:* Univ Ala, BS, 60; Peabody Col, MA, 63; Univ Mich, oboe with Florian Mueller, DMA, 67. *Pos:* Prin oboe, Knoxville Symph, 67-72. *Teaching:* Asst prof, Wartburg Col, 63-65; asst prof woodwinds, Univ Tenn, 67-71; prof oboe & chamber music, Bowling Green State Univ, 72-; teacher oboe, Nat Music Camp, 74-75. *Mem:* Int Double Reed Soc; Nat Asn Col Wind & Perc Instr; Music Educrs Nat Conf; Ohio Music Educr Asn; Col Music Soc. *Mailing Add:* 405 Normandie Blvd Bowling Green OH 43402

BENTON, WALTER BRADFORD
HICHIRIKI
b Stillwater, Okla, July 12, 50. *Study:* Sam Houston State Univ, BM, 73; Univ Tex, Austin, with Leeman Perkins & James Reid. *Works:* Normal Approximations, Fermata, 79; Fremde Reihe, Kappa Kappa Psi, Sam Houston State Univ. *Rec Perf:* Songs of the Endless Earth, Folkways Rec. *Pos:* Hichiriki solo, Austin Gagaku Group, 80- *Mem:* Soc Ethnomusicol; Am Musicol Soc. *Interests:* Gagaku style, history and performance; uses of the computer to aid musicological studies. *Mailing Add:* 3107 Jeanette Ct Austin TX 78745

BERBERIAN, ARA
BASS-BARITONE
b Detroit, Mich. *Study:* Univ Mich, AB, LLB; studied with Kenneth Westerman, Themy Georgi & Beverley Johnson. *Rec Perf:* B Minor Mass; three albums of works by Alan Hovhaness. *Roles:* Don Magnifico in La Cenerentola, Turnau Opera, NY, 58; Rocco in Fidelio; Mephistopheles in Faust; Don Alfonso in Cosi fan tutte; Creon in Oedipus Rex; Ramfis in Aida; König Heinrich in Lohengrin. *Pos:* Conct performer, New York City Opera, 62-; San Francisco Opera, 66-, Metropolitan Opera, 79 & others. *Mailing Add:* c/o Robert Lombardo Assoc 61 W 62nd St Suite 6F New York NY 10023

BERBERIAN, HRATCH
VIOLIN, EDUCATOR
b Athens, Greece, Jan 13, 27. *Study:* Ecole Superieure Musique, Paris, with Cesar Franck, dipl; Boston Consv Music, MMus; Univ Iowa. *Pos:* Violinist, recitals & chamber music performances, Middle East, France & US, formerly, with Boston Pops Orch, formerly, Pablo Casals Fest Orch, formerly & Goldowski Opera Orch, 61-66; radio appearance, Commentary on the Classics. *Teaching:* Prof music, SDak State Univ, 67- *Awards:* First Prize, Nicola Dale Middle East Violin Compt, 45. *Mem:* Am String Teachers Asn. *Mailing Add:* Lincoln Music Hall SDak State Univ Brookings SD 57007

BERDES, JANE L
WRITER
b Marion, Ohio, Sept 13, 31. *Study:* Mount St Joseph, 49-51; Marquette Univ, BA, 53; Univ Md, MM, 79. *Awards:* Nat Music Critics Asn Fel, 72, 74 & 79; Nat Endowment for Humanities Grant, 83. *Mem:* Am Musicol Soc; Nat Music Critics Asn; Am Soc 18th Century Studies; Washington Independent Writers. *Interests:* Venetian conservatories in music history; Maddalena Lombardini-Sirmen (1745-1818), Venetian composer. *Publ:* Ed, The Works of Maddalena Lombardi-Sirmen, A-R Ed, 83. *Mailing Add:* 6025 Berkshire Dr Bethesda MD 20814

BERENDES, M BENEDICTA
EDUCATOR
b New York, NY, Nov 28, 27. *Study:* Marywood Col, BM, 55; Univ Notre Dame, MM, 62; Univ Pittsburgh, PhD, 73. *Pos:* Music specialist, church sch, 48-70. *Teaching:* Assoc prof musicol, Marywood Col, Scranton, Pa, 73- *Awards:* First Prize Musicol, Nat Catholic Music Educr, 62; grant, Nat Endowment Humanities, 82. *Mem:* Am Asn Univ Prof; Am Musicol Soc; Nat Pastoral Musicians. *Interests:* Medieval Monophonic sources; complete transcription of CADEAC. *Publ:* Auth, Operation: Polyphony, Musart, 62. *Mailing Add:* Box 864 Marywood Col Scranton PA 18509

BERG, CHRISTOPHER (PAUL)
COMPOSER, PIANO
b Detroit, Mich, June 30, 49. *Study:* Manhattan Sch Music, with Robert Helps, 71-72; Centre Musical Font'neuve, 76. *Works:* Last Letter, Galaxy Music Corp, 77; Mass, perf by NMex Music Fest, 78; Distant Episodes, comn by Chorus of Santa Fe, NMex, 80; Not Waving But Drowning, comn by Chamber Orch Albuquerque, 80; Four Nobokov Songs, comn by Iris Hiskey, 82; Hidden Instruction, comn by Am Ctr Electronic Music, 82. *Rec Perf:* Piano Sonata, Op 40 (Noel Farrand), 79 & Six Songs (Christopher Berg), 79, Opus One Rec; Tidal (Michael Byron), Neutral Rec, 83. *Pos:* Music dir, Greer Garson Theatre Ctr, Santa Fe, NMex, 78-82. *Awards:* Rec Grant, Martha Baird Rockefeller Fund Music, 79; grant, Am Music Ctr, 80; fel, Am Ctr Electronic Music, 82. *Mem:* Assoc mem, Dramatists Guild, Inc; Am Fedn Musicians. *Mailing Add:* 195 12th St Brooklyn NY 11215

BERG, DARRELL MATTHEWS
MUSICOLOGIST
b Marianna, Fla. *Study:* Juilliard Sch Music, BS, 55; Smith Col, MA, 57; State Univ NY, Buffalo, PhD, 75. *Pos:* Violinist, Kansas City Phil, 57-60, Cincinnati Symph Orch, 60-62 & Buffalo Phil, 63-65. *Teaching:* Prof music hist, St Louis Consv Music, 77- *Interests:* Editions of works of C P E Bach; aesthetics in North Germany in the 18th century. *Publ:* Auth, Towards a Catalogue of the Keyboard Sonatas of C P E Bach, J Am Musicol Soc, 79; C P E Bach's Harp Sonata, Am Harp J, 80; C P E Bach's Embellishments and Variations for His Keyboard Sonatas, J Musicol, spring 83; ed, Selected Keyboard Sonatas by C P E Bach, G Henle (in press). *Mailing Add:* St Louis Consv Music 560 Trinity Ave St Louis MO 63130

BERG, JACOB
FLUTE
Study: Curtis Inst Music, artist's dipl; Peabody Consv Music, teacher's cert; studied flute with William Kincaid & Britton Johnson. *Rec Perf:* On Vox & Telarc Rec. *Pos:* Prin flute, Buffalo Phil Orch, formerly, Cincinnati Symph Orch, formerly, Kansas City Phil, formerly & Seventh Army Orch, formerly; mem, Baltimore Symph Orch, formerly; prin flute & soloist, St Louis Symph Orch, currently. *Teaching:* Mem fac, State Univ NY, Buffalo, formerly, St Louis Consv Music, currently & Washington Univ, St Louis, currently. *Mem:* Nat Flute Asn (pres, 81-82). *Mailing Add:* 6334 Waterman St Louis MO 63130

BERGELL, AARON
TENOR
b Bayonne, NJ, Nov 13, 43. *Study:* NY Univ, with Raymond Buckingham & Carolina Segrera, BS(music ed), 59; Am Opera Ctr, Juilliard Sch, 76. *Roles:* Rodolfo in La Boheme, Israel Opera, Tel Aviv, 71; Don Jose in Carmen; Nadir in Pecheurs de perles; Nemorino in L'Elisir d'amore; Edgardo in Lucia di Lammermoor; Faust in Faust; Turiddu in Cavalleria rusticana. *Pos:* Appearances with maj opera co & symph orchs in US, Brazil & Can. *Awards:* William Mattheus Sullivan Music Found Award, 75-77. *Mem:* Am Guild Musical Artists. *Mailing Add:* Rutherford NJ

BERGER, ARTHUR VICTOR
COMPOSER, CRITIC-WRITER
b New York, NY, May 15, 12. *Study:* NY Univ, BMus, 34; Longy Sch Music, 34-36; Harvard Univ, MA, 36. *Works:* Woodwind Quartet, 41, Serenade Concertante, 44 & Chamber Music for 13 Players, 56, Peters Ed; Polyphony, comn by Louisville Symph, 56; Ideas of Order, 58 & Septet, 66, Peters Ed; Trio (guitar, violin & piano), Boelke-Bomart, 72. *Pos:* Music reviewer, Boston Transcript, 34-37 & New York Sun, 43-46; assoc music critic, New York Herald Tribune, 46-53. *Teaching:* Instr music, Mills Col, 39-41; prof music, Brandeis Univ, 53-80, prof emer, 80-; fac mem comp, New England Consv Music, 80- *Awards:* Grants, Fulbright, 60 & Nat Found Arts & Humanities, 66; Guggenheim Fel, 75. *Bibliog:* Festschrift, Perspectives New Music, fall 78; J M Perkins (auth), Arthur Berger: The Composer as Mannerist, In: Perspectives on American Composers, W W Norton. *Mem:* Fel, Am Acad & Inst Arts & Lett; fel, Am Acad Arts & Sci; ASCAP. *Publ:* Auth, Aaron Copland, Oxford Univ Press, 53; contribr, Plight of the American Composer, Van Nostrand, 61 & Beacon, 64; Introduction to Aesthetic Analysis, Crowell-Apollo, 67; Perspectives on Schoenberg & Stravinsky, Princeton Univ, 68 & W W Norton, 72; Perspectives on Contemporary Music Theory, W W Norton, 72. *Mailing Add:* 9 Sparks St Cambridge MA 02138

BERGER, KAROL
EDUCATOR, WRITER
b Bytom, Poland; US citizen. *Study:* Yale Univ, PhD, 75. *Teaching:* Asst prof, Boston Univ, 75-82; assoc prof, Stanford Univ, 82- *Awards:* Nat Endowment Humanities Fel, 80-81. *Mem:* Am Musicol Soc; Int Musicol Soc. *Interests:* History of music theory and aesthetics. *Publ:* Auth, Prospero's Art, Shakespeare Studies, 77; Theories of Chromatic and Enharmonic Music in Late 16th Century Italy, UMI Res Press, 80; Tonality and Atonality in The Prologue to Orlando di Lasso's Prophetiae, Musical Quart, 80; The Hand and the Art of Memory, Musica Disciplina, 81. *Mailing Add:* Dept Music Stanford Univ Stanford CA 94305

BERGER, MELVIN
WRITER, LECTURER
b New York, NY, Aug 23, 27. *Study:* Eastman Sch Music, BM, 50; Columbia Univ, MA, 51; London Univ, cert, 65. *Works:* Music in Perspective, Sam Fox, 62; Three 14th Century Dances, 64 & Basic Viola Technique, 66, MCA Music; Viola Solos, 67 & Dource Memoire, 68, MCA Music. *Rec Perf:* Viola Suite (Vaughan Williams), Pye Rec, 66; Viola Concerto (Starer), 78. *Pos:* Violist, Res Quartet, City Col New York, 51-54, Forum String Quartet, 68-, Connoisseur Chamber Ens, 73- *Teaching:* Lectr music, Post Col, 79-82 & Manhattan Marymount Col, 82- *Interests:* Chamber music; orchestral music. *Publ:* Auth, Science and Music, McGraw-Hill, 61; Program Notes—Am Symph & Long Island Phil, 79-; Stereo Hi-Fi Handbook, William Morrow, 79; Photo Dictionary of the Orchestra, Methuen, 81; Listener's Guide to Chamber Music, Dodd, Mead (in press). *Rep:* Brandt & Brandt 1501 Broadway New York NY 10036. *Mailing Add:* 18 Glamford Rd Great Neck NY 11023

BERGERON, THOMAS MARTIN
PERCUSSION
b Nashua, NH, Jan 7, 54. *Study:* Univ NH, BSMus Ed, 76; Western Mich Univ, MM(perf), 81. *Pos:* Prin tympanist, Twin Cities Symph, Mich, 80-; prin perc & asst tympanist, Kalamazoo Symph, 81-; perc, Battle Creek Symph, 82- *Mem:* Nat Asn Col Wind & Perc Instr; Percussive Arts Soc; Nat Fedn Musicians. *Mailing Add:* 4635 S 6th Kalamazoo MI 49009

BERGERSEN, CHARLOTTE (CHARLOTTE B CHEVALIER)
PIANO, TEACHER-COACH
b Chicago, Ill. *Study:* Am Consv Music, BMus(piano), 49, MMus(piano), 52, BMus(theory & comp), 72; Univ Chicago; Northwestern Univ. *Teaching:* Teacher-coach, Am Consv Music, 50-, dir, Robyn Children's Dept, 70- *Awards:* Lyon & Healy Young Artist Award, 56; Cordon Club Jr Award, 60-62. *Mem:* Soc Am Musicians; Musicians Club Women; Highland Park Music Club (vpres, 70-72 & 75-76 & pres, 79-81). *Mailing Add:* Am Consv Music 116 S Michigan Ave Chicago IL 60603

BERGINC, CHARLES DAVID
TRUMPET
b Cleveland, Ohio, Feb 6, 52. *Study:* Baldwin-Wallace Col, BM, 76; Boston Univ & Univ Tex, San Antonio, MM, 79. *Rec Perf:* Dallas Trumpets, Crystal Rec, 80. *Pos:* Second trumpet, San Antonio Symph, 77-79; prin trumpet, State Orch Mex, 80-82 & Phoenix Symph, 82- *Mailing Add:* 3033 N 42nd Ave Phoenix AZ 85019

BERGMAN, JANET LOUISE MARX
FLUTE, EDUCATOR
b St Louis, Mo, June 15, 20. *Study:* With John F Kiburz & Laurent Torno. *Pos:* Mem, St Louis Woman's Symph, 37-38, St Louis Opera Co, 42 & St Louis Symph, 43-47; first flutist & soloist, St Louis Little Symph, 43-47; flutist & soloist, Oklahoma City Symph, 44-45, City Symph Chicago, 63- & Aeolian Woodwind Ens, Chicago, 65-76; flutist, New Orleans Symph & Opera Co, 45-47, Chicago Women's Sinfonietta, 48, Chicago Park Band Concts, 47-, Chicago Chamber Orch, 54-58 & Lyr Opera Orch, Chicago, 64-71; adjudicator, Ill High Sch Solo Asn, 73-79, Flute Concourse, Univ Quebec,

Montreal, 74-77 & others; founder & cond, Flute Sinfonietta, 75-; soloist, Artists Assoc, 76-77. *Teaching:* Fac mem, Niles E & Niles W high sch, 64- & New Trier E & W high sch, 77-; prof flute, Chicago Consv Col, 68-78, Northeastern Ill Univ, 78- & Am Consv Music, 78-81. *Awards:* First Place, Solo Comp, Nat Cont; First Place, Solo Comp, State Cont, 39. *Mem:* Chicago Fedn Musicians; Nat Flute Asn; Soloist Artists Asn; Chicago Flute Soc (pres, 77-); Soc Am Musicians. *Publ:* Auth, Do's and Dont's of Flute Playing, 67. *Mailing Add:* 1817 GW Hood St Chicago IL 60660

BERGQUIST, PETER
EDUCATOR, WRITER
b Sacramento, Calif, Aug 5, 30. *Study:* Eastman Sch Music, 48-51; Mannes Col Music, BS, 58; Columbia Univ, MA, 58, PhD, 64. *Rec Perf:* New Music for Woodwind Quintet, 72. *Teaching:* Asst prof music, Sch Music, Univ Ore, Eugene, 64-68, assoc prof, 68-73, prof, 73- *Awards:* Ersted Award Distinguished Teaching, Univ Ore, 72. *Mem:* Am Musicol Soc; Col Music Soc; Music Libr Asn; Int Musicol Soc; Soc Music Theory. *Publ:* Transl, Pietro Aaron's Toscanello in Musica, Colo Col Music Press, 70; auth, The Poems of Lasso's Prophetiae Sibyllarum and Their Sources, J Am Musicol Soc, 79; The First Movement of Mahler's Symphony No 10: An Analysis and an Examination of the Sketches, Music Forum, 80; Ed, Lasso, Motet Cycles on Readings from the Prophet Job, 83 & Lasso, Penitential Psalms (in prep), A-R Ed Inc. *Mailing Add:* Sch Music Univ Ore Eugene OR 97403

BERGSMA, WILLIAM LAURENCE
COMPOSER, EDUCATOR
b Oakland, Calif, Apr 1, 21. *Study:* Stanford Univ, 38-40; Eastman Sch Music, with Howard Hanson & Bernard Rogers, BA, 42, MA, 43. *Works:* Blatent Hypotheses (trombone & perc), 77; Sweet Was the Song the Virgin Sung/Tristan Revisited, Seattle, Wash, 78; Four All (three instrm & perc), 79; Quintet for Flute & String Quartet, 79; The Voice of the Coelacanth, 80; In Campo Aperto (oboe concertante, two bassoons & strings), 81; Four Songs (medium voice, clarinet, bassoon & piano), 81. *Teaching:* Instr, Juilliard Sch Music, 46-63, chmn comp dept, chmn lit & materials music dept & assoc dean, 61-63; dir, Sch Music, Univ Wash, Seattle, 63-71, prof, 63-; vis prof, Brooklyn Col, City Univ New York, 72-73. *Awards:* Soc Publ Am Music Award, 45; Guggenheim Fel, 46 & 51; Nat Endowment Arts Fel, 79. *Mem:* Am Acad & Inst Arts & Lett. *Mailing Add:* 2328 Delmar Dr E Seattle WA 98102

BERGT, ROBERT ROLAND
CONDUCTOR, TEACHER-COACH
b Schuyler, Nebr, Jan 7, 30. *Study:* Concordia Sem, St Louis, STM, 57; Domaine Sch Cond, Hancock, Maine, cert, 64; studied cond with Walter Susskind, 68. *Works:* The Royal Banners Forward Go (SATB), Concordia Publ House, 58. *Rec Perf:* The Best of Lutheran Hymns, Am Lutheran Publ, 62; From Bach to Bender, Schola Cantorum Rec, 65; Schütz Tercentinary, Am Kantorei Rec, 72; Motets of H Schütz, Vox-Turnabout, 73. *Pos:* Cond, Southern Ill Univ Symph Orch & Choirs, 73-; cond & music dir, Am Kantorei, St Louis, 69-; cond & guest artist, Musashino Acad Musicae, Tokyo, 81-82; cond & admin dir, Concordia Sem, Chorus, Chapel Choir & Schola Cantorum, 56-73. *Teaching:* Prof music, Southern Ill Univ, Carbondale, 73- *Mem:* Am Choral Dir Asn; Am Guild Organists; Int Heinrich Schütz Gesellschaft; Int J S Bach Gesellschaft; Am Symph Soc Cond. *Interests:* Modern performance editions of A C G Bergt scores, motets, cantatas, oratorios, orchestral works and chamber music. *Mailing Add:* 2005 W Freeman Carbondale IL 62901

BERK, ADELE L
COMPOSER, EDUCATOR
b New York, NY. *Study:* Berkshire Music Ctr, 49; Columbia Univ, MA, 50; studied with Norman Lockwood, Irving Fine, Edgard Varese & David Diamond. *Works:* The Lord Bless Thee and Keep Thee (SATB with piano), perf at Contemp Choral Fest, Mars Hill Col, 80; I Will Lift Up Mine Eyes, 81 & Alleluia is Our Song (SA with piano), 81, Belwin-Mills Publ Corp; O Praise the Lord (SA with piano), Plymouth Music Co Inc, 81; Three Pieces for Clarinet & Piano, Timbrel Music, 82; Holy is the Lord of Hosts (SA with piano), Plymouth Music Co Inc, 83; Divertimento (clarinet, viola, bassoon & piano), perf by Long Island Comp Alliance, 83. *Teaching:* Instr music, Nassau Community Col, 70-72; comp in res, Wantagh Publ Sch, 71-73; adj asst prof music, Dowling Col, 73-80. *Mem:* ASCAP; Long Island Comp Alliance; Int League Women Comp. *Mailing Add:* 254 Twin Lane E Wantagh NY 11793

BERK, LEE ELIOT
ADMINISTRATOR
Study: Brown Univ, AB; Boston Univ, JD; studied piano with Margaret Chaloff; Sch Law, Harvard Univ. *Pos:* Legal adv, Nat Asn Jazz Educr; consult to munic agencies sponsoring mod music prog; pres, Berklee Col Music, currently. *Awards:* First Prize, Deems Taylor Award Best Bk in Music for Legal Protection for the Creative Musician, ASCAP. *Mem:* Mass Asn Jazz Educr (pres, formerly). *Mailing Add:* Berklee Col Music 1140 Boylston St Boston MA 02215

BERK, MAYNARD
ORGAN, COMPOSER
b Bucyrus, Ohio, July 27, 13. *Study:* Univ Redlands, BM; Union Theol Sem, NY, SMM; NY Univ, with Philip James & Edwin Stringham, PhD; Univ Southern Calif, with Ernest Kanitz & Halsey Stevens; studied with Henk Badings, Netherlands. *Works:* Kyrie Eleison (chorus); Sanctus (chorus); Vocalise (unison choir, instrm & organ); many organ, piano & vocal works. *Teaching:* Prof organ, Sioux Falls Col, 49- *Mailing Add:* Dept Music Sioux Falls Col Sioux Falls SD 57101

BERKENSTOCK, JAMES TURNER
BASSOON, EDUCATOR
b Joliet, Ill, Oct 9, 42. *Study:* George Peabody Col for Teachers, BS(music educ), 64; Northwestern Univ, MM, 66, PhD, 75. *Pos:* Prin bassoon, Lyric Opera Chicago, 68- & Grant Park Symph Orch, 79-; prin bassoon, Orch Ill, 78-, vpres bd dirs, 81- *Teaching:* Asst prof music, Northern Ill Univ, 78- *Mem:* Int Conf Symph & Opera Musicians; Rec Musicians of Am. *Interests:* The smaller sacred compositions of Joseph Haydn. *Publ:* Coauth, Joseph Haydn in Literature: A Bibliography, Haydn Studien, G Hence Verlag, 74. *Mailing Add:* 3626 Thayer St Evanston IL 60201

BERKOWITZ, RALPH
PIANO, ADMINISTRATOR
b New York, NY, Sept 5, 10. *Study:* Curtis Inst Music, with Isabelle Vengerova, 35. *Works:* A Telephone Call (voice & orch), Orquestra Sinfonica Brasileira, Rio de Janerio, 57. *Rec Perf:* Recorded Sonatas for Piano and Cello (Bach, Brahms, Chopin, Barber, Hindemith, Prokofieff & others) with RCA & Columbia. *Pos:* Lectr, The Substance of Music, Radio Prog, formerly, Boston Symph Intermission Talks the Arts, TV, formerly & pub lectures; solo pianist, Boston Symph Orch, formerly; exec asst, Serge Koussevitzky, 47-51; pianist with cellist Gregor Piatigorsky, formerly; tours in US, Can, Latin Am, Middle East & the Orient, 53-72. *Teaching:* Dean, Berkshire Music Ctr. *Mem:* ASCAP. *Publ:* Auth, What Every Accompanist Knows, Penguin Bks, 51; various articles for Etude & Juilliard Rev. *Mailing Add:* 523 14th St NW Albuquerque NM 87104

BERKOWITZ, SOL
EDUCATOR, COMPOSER
b Warren, Ohio, Apr 27, 22. *Study:* Queens Col, with Karol Rathaus, BA, 42; Columbia Univ, with Otto Luening, MA, 47; studied with Abby Whiteside. *Works:* Miss Emily Adams, 60 & Nowhere To Go But Up 62, Chappel Publ; Intro & Scherzo (viola), 70 & Suite (wood winds), 75, Theo Presser Co; four ballet scores, Eliot Feld Ballet Co, 75-82; Dialogue (cello), 80 & Dance Suite (strings), 82, Theo Presser Co. *Pos:* Staff comp, Gary Moore Show, CBS TV, 64. *Teaching:* Prof comp & orch, Queens Col, 47- *Awards:* Grant, Ford Found, 55-56; Comp Awards, ASCAP, 61-82. *Mem:* ASCAP; Am Fedn Musicians. *Publ:* Auth, A New Approach to Sight Singing, W W Norton, 59; Improvisation Through Keyboard Harmony, Prentice-Hall, 75. *Mailing Add:* 46-36 Hanford St Douglaston NY 11362

BERKY, CARL R
COMPOSER, PIANO
b Boyertown, Pa. *Study:* Philadelphia Consv Music, MM, 57; Univ Pa, MA, 62; studied piano with Ed Steuermann & comp with V Persichetti, K Stockhausen & G Rochberg. *Works:* Gedicht, 63, Auras (piano), 65, Sonatina (piano), 67, Symphony of Chorales, 73, Songs of Nostalgia, 75 & Concerto (two pianos), 80, W-House Press. *Pos:* Pianist, Pa Players, 63-65. *Teaching:* Asst, Swarthmore Col, 62-66 & Berkshire Music Fest, 64. *Mailing Add:* RD2 Box 202E New Milford PA 18834

BERL, CHRISTINE
PIANO, COMPOSER
b New York, NY. *Study:* Mannes Col Music, piano with Nadia Reisenberg, BS, 64; Queens Col, City Univ New York, comp with George Perle, Henry Weinberg & Yehudi Wyner, MA, 70; Manhattan Sch Music, piano with John Browning & Constance Keene, DMA. *Works:* Two Movements in Memoriam, perf by Andre-Michel Schub, 76; Ab la Dolchor (secular cantata sop, chr and orch), comn by Susan Davenny Wyner, 79; Three Pieces for Chamber Ensemble, Am Soc Univ Comp, 80. *Teaching:* Lectr, Queens Col, 68-70; piano fac, tech music, Mannes Col, 74-80. *Awards:* High Fidelity Mag Award, 62. *Mailing Add:* 110 W 96 St New York NY 10025

BERLIN, DAVID
COMPOSER, EDUCATOR
b Jan 23, 43; US citizen. *Study:* Carnegie Inst Technol, with Forrest Standley, BFA(French horn), 65, BFA(music educ), 65; Duquesne Univ, 65; Carnegie-Mellon Univ, MFA(music educ), 69, with Leonardo Balada, Nikolai Lopatnikoff, James Beale & Roland Leich, MFA(comp), 72; Am Univ, Wolf Trap Acad Perf Arts Comp Wkshp, 74; studied comp with Leonardo Balada, 72-77; Allegheny Intermediate Unit, 76; WVa Univ, with John Beall & Gerald Lefkoff, 78- *Works:* Quintet for Bassoon and Strings, perf by Pittsburgh New Music Ens, 79; Synergism #1, Los Alamos Wind & String Chamber Music Awards Fest, 79; Structures for Chamber Orchestra, perf by Franklin Sinfonia, 79; Three Miniatures for Guitar, 82 & Trio for Flute, Oboe and Guitar, 82, Guitar Found Am; A Work for Solo Tuba and Solo Clarinet and Orchestra, comn by James Patterson for William Winkle, 82; Cheyt-M, perf by David Satterfield, 83. *Pos:* Perf with Carnegie-Mellon Univ Kiltie Band, 60-65, Carnegie-Mellon Univ Brass Choir, 60-65, Carnegie-Mellon Col-Community Symph Orch, 60-65, Wilkinsburg Symph Orch, 61-64, Carnegie Civic Symph Orch, 64-73, Butler Co Symph Orch, 66-72 & Am Youth Symph Band & Chorus, 73 & 76. *Teaching:* Instr music, Carnegie Inst Technol Pre-Col Prog, 62; asst marching band dir, Baldwin Whitehall Sch District, 62-64; instr comp & French horn, privately, Pittsburgh, 63 & WVa Univ, 79 & 81-82; teacher instrm music, Pittsburgh Pub Sch, 64-65; teacher music, North Allegheny Sch District, 65-; instr French horn & music theory, Volkwein Sch Music, 73-75. *Awards:* ASCAP Standard Awards, 77-82; Salop-Slates Award, Southeastern Comp League, 81; Phi Mu Alpha Comp Cont, 71. *Bibliog:* Michael Caruso (auth), Davison First Symphony Given Its Area Premiere, News Del Co, 12/20/79; Marcia Bennett (auth), Teen-agers Compose Music on Winning Note, Pittsburgh Post-Gazette, 3/31/83; Lance W Brunner (auth), Electronic Music Plus, High Fidelity, 4/83. *Mem:* ASCAP; Am Soc Univ Comp; Music Educr Nat Conf; Pittsburgh Alliance Comp (mem exec bd, 75-, vchmn, 83-); Phi Mu Alpha Sinfonia. *Mailing Add:* 4809 Baptist Rd Pittsburgh PA 15227

BERLINGHOFF, DAN A
PIANO, CONDUCTOR & MUSIC DIRECTOR
b Buffalo, NY, Aug 29, 51. *Study:* Villa Maria Inst Music, dipl, 68; Juilliard Sch Music, studied piano with Irwin Freundlich & Beveridge Webster, BM, 73, MM, 74. *Pos:* Artistic dir & pianist, The Music Project, New York, 77-; musical dir & cond, Pirates of Penzance, Broadway, 80-82. *Rep:* Kazuko Hillyer Int Inc 250 W 57th St New York NY 10107. *Mailing Add:* 825 West End Ave New York NY 10025

BERLINSKI, HERMAN
COMPOSER, ORGAN
b Leipzig, Ger, Aug 18, 10; US citizen. *Study:* Staats Konservatorium, Leipzig, artist dipl, 32; Ecole Normale Musique, Paris, with Cortot & Boulanger, dipl d'exec, 37; Jewish Theol Sem, New York, DSM, 60. *Works:* The Burning Bush, H W Gray, 57; Kol Nidre, Mercury Music Corp, 61; Elegy, Transcontinental Music Publ, 66; Sinfonia I: Litanies for the Persecuted, HB Facsimile Ed, 67; Shovas Vayeenofash: Prelude for the Sabbath, Transcontinental Music Publ, 68; Sinfonia V, 68 & Sinfonia X (cello & organ), 75, HB Facsimile Ed. *Rec Perf:* Sinfonia VIII: Eliyahu, 65, Music from the Synagogue & Frescobaldi, Kohs, Liszt, Berlinski, Musical Heritage Soc. *Pos:* Organist, Temple Emmanu-el, New York, 54-63; minister music, Washington Hebrew Congregation, 63-77; music critic, Jewish Week, Washington, DC, currently. *Awards:* ASCAP Yearly Award, 75- *Mem:* Music Critics Asn. *Mailing Add:* 4000 Tunlaw Rd NW Washington DC 20007

BERMAN, JANET ROSSER
VIOLIN
b Vass, NC, Oct 3, 28. *Study:* Oberlin Consv, 45-47; Philadelphia Consv Music, BM, 51, MM, 53. *Pos:* Asst prin second violin, Princeton Chamber Orch, 65-69; first violin sect, Am Symph Orch, 69-72; prin second violin, NJ Symph Orch, 72-74; co-prin second violin, New York City Ballet Orch, 74- *Mailing Add:* 180 West End Ave New York NY 10023

BERMAN, LYNN HOWELL
TRUMPET, EDUCATOR
b Miami, Fla, Oct 21, 29. *Study:* Paris Consv, France, 51; Univ Miami, BM, 52; Manhattan Sch Music, MM, 56. *Pos:* Prin trumpet, Israel Phil, 50-51; solo stage trumpet, Metropolitan Opera, 57-, second trumpet, 73-; first & second trumpet, Sante Fe Opera, 60-66. *Teaching:* Prof trumpet, New York Col Music, 67-68. *Mailing Add:* 180 West End Ave New York NY 10023

BERMAN, MARSHA F
LIBRARIAN, EDUCATOR
b Los Angeles, Calif, Feb 23, 35. *Study:* Univ Calif, Los Angeles, BA(music), 57; Univ Calif, Berkeley, MLS, 63. *Pos:* Librn, Brooklyn Pub Libr, 59-62 & 63-64 & art & music dept, San Francisco Pub Libr, 62-63; assoc music librn, Music Libr, Univ Calif, Los Angeles, 66-; ed, Music Libr Asn Newsletter, 81- *Teaching:* Supvr music libr internship prog, Grad Sch Libr & Info Science, Univ Calif, Los Angeles, 73- *Mem:* Music Libr Asn (Southern Calif chap chairperson, 74-75); Int Asn Music Libr; Educ Media Assoc (treas & mem bd, 79-). *Publ:* Auth, Current Bibliography ... J Arnold Schoenberg Inst, 10/74, 2/77 & 6/77. *Mailing Add:* 2417 4th St Santa Monica CA 90405

BERMAN, RUTH (RUTH BERMAN HARRIS)
HARP, COMPOSER
b New Haven, Conn, Nov 3, 16. *Study:* Juilliard Sch, 34-37; State Univ NY, Purchase, 78-81; studied harp with Marie Miller, Carlos Salzedo, Lucille Lawrence & Casper Reardon, 29-42; studied comp with Ronald Herder, 78-81. *Works:* Miniatures No 1, 2 & 3, 78, O Holy Night (Adolphe Adam), 78, Requiem Mark Sumner Harris, 81, Nightsong (small orch & voices), 81, String Quartet, 82, Passacaglia (two pianos), 82 & Winter (flute, harp & clarinet), 82, Sumark Press. *Rec Perf:* String Time, Liberty Music Shoppe, New York, 44; Ruth Berman & Orchestra, Standard Transcription Co, Hollywood, 47 & 48. *Pos:* Freelance orch harpist & soloist, NBC radio & TV networks, 38-42, CBS radio & TV networks, 42-50 & NBC, CBS, ABC TV networks plus Symph Orch, Movie & Rec Cos, 53-82; staff orch harpist & soloist, ABC, 50-53. *Teaching:* Instr harp, Westchester Music Consv, 69- *Awards:* Madrigal Award, Musical Soc, 33; Meet The Composer Grant, 82. *Mem:* Am Harp Soc; Music Teachers Coun Westchester (treas, 81-); Purchase Music Ens Inc (vpres, 83-); Int League Women Comp; Nat Acad Rec Arts & Sci. *Mailing Add:* 25 Ria Dr White Plains NY 10605

BERNARDO, JOSE RAUL
COMPOSER, CONDUCTOR & MUSIC DIRECTOR
b Havana, Cuba, Oct 3, 38; US citizen. *Study:* Havana Consv, Cuba, BMus, 58; Miami Univ, Fla, MMus, 69; Columbia Univ, PhD, 72. *Works:* Sonata for Amplified Piano, 73 & Canciones Negras, 73, JBBJ Music Inc; The Child (opera), Lake George Opera, NY, 74; Of Things Past (ballet & concerto), JBBJ Music Inc, 75; Something for the Palace (opera), Cent City Opera, 81; That Night of Love (filmscore for Fat Chance), 82; Unavoidable Consequences (opera), 83. *Pos:* Comp in res, Cent City Opera, summer 81. *Awards:* Prod grants for The Child (operatic poem), Nat Opera Inst, NY State Coun Arts & Am Music Ctr, 74. *Mailing Add:* 240 W 98th St New York NY 10025

BERNHEIMER, MARTIN
CRITIC, LECTURER
b Munich, Ger, 1936. *Study:* Brown Univ, BA, 58; Munich Consv, 58-59; NY Univ, MA(music), 61. *Pos:* Music staff, New York Herald Tribune, 59-62; temp music critic, New York Post, 61-65; contrib ed, Musical Courier, 61-64; asst music ed, Saturday Rev, 62-65; managing ed, Phil Hall Prog Mag, 62-65;

music critic, Los Angeles Times, 65- *Teaching:* Lectr music, NY Univ, 59-62; guest lectr, Univ Southern Calif, Univ Calif, Los Angeles, Calif Inst Arts, Calif State Univ, Northridge & Rockefeller Prog for Training Music Critic. *Awards:* Pulitzer Prize for Criticism, 81; Deems Taylor Award, ASCAP, 74 & 78. *Mem:* Pi Kappa Lambda; Nat Opera Inst. *Publ:* Published articles in Music Quart, Critic, Opera News, Musical Am, Christian Sci Monitor, New York Times, New York Times Mag, Hi Fidelity, Hi Fi Stereo Rev, Am Rec Guide, Reporter, Nation, Commonwealth, Aufbau, Opera, Metropolitan Opera Prog Mag, State Theater Prog, Music J. *Mailing Add:* c/o Los Angeles Times Times Mirror Sq Los Angeles CA 90053

BERNSTEIN, DAVID STEPHEN
EDUCATOR, COMPOSER
b Boston, Mass, Jan 6, 42. *Study:* Fla State Univ, with Carlisle Floyd & John Boda; Ind Univ, with Juan Orrego-Salas. *Works:* Dialogue (double orch & perc); Sonata for Chamber Orch; Quartet for Clarinet, Trumpet, Cello & Harpsichord; 4 Songs (tenor & 14 instrm); Ziz (six perc); Sette (piano). *Teaching:* Mem fac, Ind Univ, 69-71; asst prof music, Univ Akron, 72- *Mailing Add:* 3327 Overlook Dr Akron OH 44312

BERNSTEIN, JACOB
CELLO, EDUCATOR
b Kaunas, Lithuania, Sept 4, 05. *Study:* Consv Moscow; Consv Leipzig; studied cello with Julius Klengel. *Pos:* Mem, NBC Symph, formerly; solo cellist, Israel Phil; soloist & mem chamber music ens throughout USSR, Far East, Europe & US; arr various transcriptions cello; comp cadenzas for maj conct. *Teaching:* Mem fac cello, Manhattan Sch Music, 66- *Awards:* Citation Outstanding Contrib, Far East Tour, 59. *Mem:* Cello Soc. *Mailing Add:* Manhattan Sch Music 120 Claremont Ave New York NY 10027

BERNSTEIN, LAWRENCE F
MUSICOLOGIST, EDUCATOR
b New York, NY, Mar 25, 39. *Study:* Hofstra Univ, BS, 60; NY Univ, PhD(musicol), 69. *Teaching:* From instr to asst prof music & humanities, Univ Chicago, 65-70; assoc prof music, Univ PA, 70-80, prof, 80- *Mem:* Am Musicol Soc; Int Musicol Soc; Music Libr Asn; Am Asn Univ Prof. *Interests:* French secular music of the Renaissance; 18th century symphony; stylistic analysis. *Publ:* Auth, The Cantus-Firmus Chansons of Tylman Susato, 69 & La Courone et Fleur des Chansons a Troys, 73, J Am Musicol Soc; The Bibliography of Music in Conrad Gesner's Pandectae, 1548, Acta Musicologica, 73. *Mailing Add:* Dept Music Univ Pa Philadelphia PA 19104

BERNSTEIN, LEONARD
CONDUCTOR & MUSIC DIRECTOR, COMPOSER
b Lawrence, Mass, Aug 25, 18. *Study:* Harvard Univ, AB, 39; Curtis Inst Music, 41; studied cond with Fritz Reiner & Serge Koussevitzky, comp with Walter Piston & Edward Burlingame Hill, piano with Helen Coates, Isabelle Gebhard & Isabelle Vengerova; several hon degrees. *Works:* Facsimile (ballet), 46; Trouble in Tahiti (opera), 52; Westside Story, 57; Four Anniversaries (piano), 64; Mass (theater), JFK Ctr Perf Arts, 71; Meditations (solo cello & orch), 76; 1600 Pennsylvania Avenue (musical), 76. *Pos:* Asst cond, New York Phil Symph, 43-44; cond, New York City Symph, 45-48, La Scala, Metropolitan Opera & Vienna Staatsoper; guest cond, major US & European orch, 46-; guest cond, Israel Phil Orch, 47-, music adv, 48-49; co-cond, New York Phil, 57-58, music dir, 58-69, laureate cond, 69-; host & cond, Young People's Series, CBS-TV. *Teaching:* Mem fac, Berkshire Music Ctr, 48-55, head cond dept, 51-55; prof music, Brandeis Univ, 51-56; Charles Eliot Norton prof poetry, Harvard Univ, 72-73; inst lect, Mass Inst Technol, 74- *Awards:* Emmy Award, Nat Acad TV Arts & Sci, 60; Handel Medallion, 77; Sonning Prize, Denmark. *Publ:* Auth, The Joy of Music, 59; Leonard Bernstein's Young Peoples Concerts for Reading and Listening, 62 & 70; The Infinite Variety of Music, 66; The Unanswered Question: Six Talks at Harvard, 76. *Mailing Add:* 1414 Avenue of the Americas New York NY 10019

BERNSTEIN, MARTIN
EDUCATOR, ADMINISTRATOR
b New York, NY, Dec 14, 04. *Study:* NY Univ, ScB, 25, MusB, 27. *Pos:* Double bs, NY Phil Orch, 26-28; cond, Am Bach Soc, 51-53; Lectr, weekly program, WCBS, NY, 55-57. *Teaching:* From instr to prof music, NY Univ, 26-72, head dept, 57-72, emer prof, 72-; guest lectr, Harvard Univ, Univ Calif, Rutgers Univ, Univ Kent, Univ Pa & Univ Ind, 50- *Awards:* Great Teachers Award, NY Univ, 68. *Mem:* Am Musicol Soc; Col Music Soc; Neue Bach Gesellschaft. *Publ:* Auth, Score Reading, Witmark, 32-49; contrib, An Intellectual and Cultural Hist of the Western World, Dover, 37, 41 & 65; coauth, An Introduction to Music, Prentice Hall, 37, 51 & 56. *Mailing Add:* 1 Blackstone Pl Bronx NY 10471

BERNSTEIN, SEYMOUR ABRAHAM
COMPOSER, PIANO
b Newark, NJ, Apr 24, 27. *Study:* Mannes Col Music, with Felix Salzer, 48; Juilliard Sch, 49; Fontainebleau Consv, France, with Nadia Boulanger; studied comp with Ben Weber & piano with Alexander Brailowsky & Clifford Curzm. *Works:* Toccata Francaise (piano), 69; Birds (piano), Bk 1, 72 & Bk 2, 73; Concerto for Our Time (piano), 73; New Pictures at an Exhibition, 74; Raccoons, Books 1 & 2 (piano), 75; Insects (two bks for piano), 76; Interrupted Waltz (piano). *Pos:* Conct performer, NJ Symph, Chicago Symph, Tokyo Phil & throughout Europe, Asia, Can, South Am & US; Mem, Philomusica Ens & Alsop-Bernstein Trio. *Teaching:* Mem fac, Chatham Sq Music Sch, formerly, Hoff-Barthelson Music Sch, formerly & State Univ NY Col, Purchase, currently. *Awards:* Griffith Artists Award, 45; State Dept Grants, 55, 60, 61 & 67; ASCAP Award, 78-80. *Mem:* ASCAP; Assoc Music Teachers League; Bohemians; Nat Fedn Music Teachers; Music Teachers Nat Asn. *Mailing Add:* 10 W 76th St New York NY 10023

BERRY, CORRE IVEY
EDUCATOR, TEACHER & COACH
b Bastrop, Tex, Mar 27, 29. *Study:* Baylor Univ, BA, 50, MA, 52, BMus, 53; New England Consv Music, MMus, 58; NTex State Univ, PhD, 75; studied with Thomas Houser, Oren Brown, Allan Rogers Lindquest, Marie Sundelius & Fritz Lehmann. *Teaching:* Asst prof, Baylor Univ, 62-65 & Southwestern Univ, Tex, 65-69; assoc prof voice & musicol, Sam Houston State Univ, 72- *Mem:* Nat Asn Teachers Singing (Texoma Region gov, 83-); Am Musicol Soc (chmn, Southwest Chap, 77-79). *Interests:* Vocal duets. *Publ:* Auth, The Secular Dialogue Duet: 1600-1900, Music Rev, 11/79; Airs from the British Isles and Airs from Moravia: Duets Incorporating Diverse Folk Materials, Vol XXXVI, No 2, Chamber Duets by Schumann, Cornelius, and Brahms, Vol XXXVI, No 5 & Salon Duets by Operatic Composers, Vol XXXVII, No 1, Nat Asn Teachers Singing Bulletin; Vocal Chamber Duets: An Annotated Bibliography, Nat Asn Teachers Singing, Inc, 81. *Mailing Add:* 1425 Ave O Huntsville TX 77340

BERRY, LEMUEL, JR
EDUCATOR, WRITER
b Oneonta, NY, Oct 11, 46. *Study:* Livingstone Col, BA, 69; Univ Iowa, MA & PhD, 73. *Pos:* Dir black music prog, Sta KOKC, Guthrie, Okla, formerly; conct performer, US, Can, Mex, Panama & Bahamas; adjudicator & consult; brass clinician; German acad res scholar, Saarbrucken, WGermany, 81; chmn media comt, Okla Arts Coun, 82- *Teaching:* Chmn dept music, Fayetteville State Univ, 73-75, chmn div humanities, 73-75; chmn dept music, Langston Univ, 76-81, chmn dept music & art, 81-83; dean, Sch Music, Ala State Univ, 83- *Mem:* Am Choral Dir Asn; Music Educr Nat Conf; Nat Black Music Colloquium; Nat Asn Col Wind & Perc Instr; Int Soc Music Educr. *Publ:* Auth, Biographical Dictionary of Black Musicians and Black Educators, 78; Afro-American Resource Guide and Dictionary: A Bibliographic Source Guide, 78; African Instruments, 80; Popular Music, Perspectives in Jazz. *Mailing Add:* PO Box 120 Langston OK 73050

BERRY, PAUL
EDUCATOR, TENOR
b Granite City, Ill, Feb 15, 38. *Study:* Simpson Col, studied voice with Hadley Crawford & comp with Sven Lekberg, BS(music educ), 59; Miami Univ, Ohio, studied voice with George Barron & musicol with Winifred Cummings, MM(voice & musicol), 64; State Univ NY, Buffalo, with J Bruce Francis, R O Berdahl, W C Hobbs & I J Spitzberg, PhD(curricular theory), 80. *Teaching:* Asst, Miami Univ, Ohio, 54-61 & 63-64; prof fine arts, Roberts Wesleyan Col, 64- *Mem:* Am Asn Higher Educ; Am Asn Univ Prof; Am Musicol Soc; Asn Gen & Lib Studies; Nat Asn Teachers Singing. *Interests:* Philosophical and theoretical foundations of aesthetic awareness. *Mailing Add:* 11 Brentwood Dr Rochester NY 14624

BERRY, WALLACE TAFT
EDUCATOR, COMPOSER
b La Crosse, Wis, Jan 10, 28. *Study:* Univ Southern Calif, BMus, 49, PhD, 56; Consv Nat Music, Paris, 53-54. *Works:* Duo for Violin and Piano, Carl Fischer, Inc, 63; String Quartet No 2, Elkan-Vogel Co, 67; Canto Lirico for Viola and Piano, 70 & Fantasy in Five Statements for Clarinet and Piano, 71, Carl Fischer; Duo for Flute and Piano, Southern Music Co, 72; Fantasy for Organ on Von Himmel Hoch, 78 & Trio for Piano, Violin, and Cello, 78, Carl Fischer, Inc. *Rec Perf:* Works rec by CRI & Opus I. *Pos:* Mem ed bd, Perspectives New Music, currently. *Teaching:* From instr to prof, Univ Mich, Ann Arbor, 57-77; prof & head dept, Univ BC, 78- *Awards:* Distinguished Fac Serv Award, Univ Mich, 63; Outstanding Music Alumnus, Univ Southern Calif, 73; Composer Award, Am Acad & Inst Arts & Lett, 78. *Mem:* Soc Music Theory (pres, 82-); ASCAP. *Publ:* Auth, Form in Music, Prentice-Hall, 66; coauth (with Edward Chudacoff), Eighteenth-Century Imitative Counterpoint: Music for Analysis, Appleton-Century-Crofts, 69; auth, Structural Functions in Music, Prentice-Hall, Inc, 75; On Structural Levels in Music, Spectrum, J Soc Music Theory, 80; Symmetrical Interval Sets and Derivative Pitch Materials in Bartok's String Quartet No 3, Perspectives New Music, Vol XVIII, No 1 & 2. *Mailing Add:* Dept Music VBC 6361 Memorial Rd Vancouver BC V6T 1W5 Canada

BERRY, WALTER
BARITONE
b Vienna, Austria. *Study:* Akad Musik & darstellende Kunst, 47-49. *Rec Perf:* Kezal in The Bartered Bride, Bavarian TV; recorded for CBS, Electrola, Philips, Decca, EMI, Polydor, Angel & Seraphim; baritone in films of Cosi fan tutte, Don Giovanni, Tosca & Wildschütz. *Roles:* Bass solo in Jeanne d'Arc, Vienna Staatsoper, 50; Escamillo in Carmen; Alfio in Cavalleria rusticana; Guglielmo & Don Alfonso in Cosi fan tutte; Figaro in Le Nozze di Figaro; Scarpia in Tosca; Wotan in Die Walküre; and other roles with major Europ opera co. *Pos:* Leading bar, Vienna Staatsoper, 50-, Metropolitan Opera, Grand Opera, Paris, Teatro Colon, Buenos Aires, Covent Garden, Lyric Opera Chicago & Deutsche Opera, Berlin; guest perf, Salzburg Fest, 52-, Lucerne Fest, Saratoga Fest & others. *Awards:* First Prize, Llangollen, Wales, 48; Mozart Compt Prize, Vienna, 49; Second Prize, Concours Musical, Verviers, Belguim, 49. *Mailing Add:* c/o Thea Dispeker 59 E 54th St New York NY 10022

BERTA, JOSEPH MICHEL
EDUCATOR, CLARINET
b Glendale, Calif, May 5, 40. *Study:* Univ Calif, Santa Barbara, BA(music), 62, MA(music), 65; studied clarinet with Mitchell Lurie, Rudolf Jettel in Vienna, Austria & Clayton Wilson. *Pos:* Soloist, Rochester Phil Orch, formerly; prin clarinetist, Bear Valley Music Fest & Santa Barbara Symph

Orch, formerly; clarinetist, Berta Vehr Duo, currently. *Teaching:* Fac mem music, Prarie View A & M Col, Tex, 67-69 & Allen Hancock Col, Calif, 69-71; assoc prof music, Hobart & William Smith Col, 71-; inst music, Northwest Music Camp, Ware, Mass, 75-80. *Awards:* Phillsbury Found Award, 65. *Mem:* Am Musicol Soc; Col Music Soc; Int Clarinet Soc; Clarinetwork Int Inc; Music Educr Nat Conf. *Mailing Add:* 55 Ver Planck St Geneva NY 14456

BERTHELOT, JOHN (MENARD), JR
ADMINISTRATOR, COMPOSER
b New Orleans, La, Oct 8, 42. *Study:* Loyola Univ, La, with John Butler & Patrick McCarthy, BMEd, 65; La State Univ, with Kenneth Klaus, MMus(comp), 67; Univ New Orleans, MEd, 77. *Works:* The Roach, 71 & The Streetcar, 71, rec by Alvin Thomas; Dap, rec by Porgy Jones, 72; I'm from the South, rec by Jerry Byrne, 72; Louisiana Boys, rec by Tucker McDaniel, 79; Cityscape, rec by Urban Spaces Jazz Orch, 81. *Pos:* Music arr, US Air Force 502nd Band, 67-70 & Cosimo's Rec Studio, Jazz Studio, 70-75; rec producer, GNP Crescendo Rec, Rounder, Instant & Bandy, currently; cond, Urban Spaces Jazz Orch, currently. *Teaching:* Instrm music, New Orleans Pub Sch, 70-; instr music bus, Univ New Orleans, 79- *Awards:* First Place, Jazz Compt Cont, Sam Houston State Univ, 67. *Mem:* Sonneck Soc; Nat Acad Rec Arts & Sci; ASCAP; Am Music Ctr; Ctr Develop New Orleans Music. *Interests:* Consumer demand patterns in music in a changing technology intersecting with evolving world cultures. *Publ:* Auth, The Making of Clifton Chenier in New Orleans, Wavelength, 79; An Overview of Federal Grant Programs Available to Local School Districts, Fed Res Report, 79. *Rep:* Creative Assoc 524 S Olympia St New Orleans LA 70119. *Mailing Add:* PO Box 13977 New Orleans LA 70185

BERTHOLD, SHERWOOD FRANCIS
TIMPANI, PERCUSSION
b Utica, NY, Oct 27, 56. *Study:* Manhattan Sch Music, perc study with Fred D Hinger, BMus, 79; Manhattan Sch Music, with Walter E Rosenberger, MMus, 80; private study with Leigh Howard Stevens, 79-81. *Pos:* Timpanist & perc, Am Symph Wind Ens, 79-81; prin timpanist, Jackson Symph Orch, 81- *Mem:* Perc Arts Soc (pres, 73-); Am Fedn Musicians. *Mailing Add:* 3948 Willo-run Dr Jackson MS 39212

BERTINI, GARY
MUSIC DIRECTOR, COMPOSER
b Birzewo, Bessarabia, May 1, 27. *Study:* Verdi Consv, Milan, 46-47; Tel-Aviv Col Music Educ, 50; Nat Consv Music & Inst Musicol, Univ Paris, 54; Normal Sch Music, with Arthur Honneger, 51-54. *Works:* Horn Concerto; Violin Sonata; stage music for Wozzeck, King Lear, Twelfth Night & Blood Wedding; ballet & film music. *Rec Perf:* Cantata No 1 (Webern); Five Pieces Op 10; Concerto for Violin & Orch (Shostakovitch); L'Apres-midi d'un Faune & Printemps (Debussy). *Pos:* Founder & music adv, Rinat Chamber Choir, 55; founder & music dir, Israel Chamber Orch, 65; music adv, Batsheva Dance Co, formerly & Detroit Symph Orch, currently. *Mailing Add:* Detroit Symph Orch Ford Auditorium Detroit MI 48226

BERTOLINO, MARIO ERCOLE
BASS-BARITONE
b Palermo, Italy, Sept 10, 34. *Study:* Consv V Bellini, Palermo, Italy; Consv G Verdi, Milan; studied with Mario Basiola & Giuseppe Danise. *Roles:* Marcello in La Boheme, Teatro Nuovo, Milan, 55; Enrico & Raimondo in Lucia di Lammermoor, Philadelphia Lyr Opera; Beaupertuis in Italian Straw Hat, Catania, Italy, 77; Dulcamara in L'Elisir d'amore, Melitone in La Forza del destino, Sonora in La Fanciulla del West & Bonzo in Madama Butterfly, 82, NJ State Opera. *Pos:* Bass-baritone, Metropolitan Opera, currently; appearances in North & South Am, Europe & Far East. *Awards:* First Place, Int Voice Cont, Asn Lirica Concertistica, Milan, 55. *Mem:* Am Guild Musical Artists; Am Fedn TV & Radio Artists; Am Guild Variety Artists; Soc Ital Autore & Editore. *Rep:* Robert Lombardo Assoc 61 W 62nd St Suite 6F New York NY 10023. *Mailing Add:* c/o Int Artists Mgt 111 W 57th St New York NY 10019

BERV, HARRY
FRENCH HORN, EDUCATOR
b New Brunswick, NJ. *Study:* Curtis Inst Music, grad. *Rec Perf:* Extensive jazz & classical with maj rec co. *Pos:* French hornist, Philadelphia Orch, formerly & NBC Symph, formerly; soloist, NBC radio, CBC radio, Montreal, NBC-TV, CBS-TV & WNDT-TV. *Teaching:* Mem fac French horn, coach & cond, Consv Musique d'Art Dramatique, Montreal & Quebec, formerly; McGill Univ, formerly & Columbia Univ, formerly; mem fac, Univ Mich, summers formerly & inst orch repertoire classes, 72; mem fac, White Plains Consv, formerly & State Univ NY, Purchase; mem fac & woodwind coach, NJ State Col, formerly; instr orch repertoire class, Univ Bridgeport, formerly; mem fac French horn, Juilliard Sch, 73- *Publ:* Auth, A Creative Approach to the French Horn, Chappell Music Co. *Mailing Add:* Juilliard Sch Lincoln Ctr New York NY 10023

BESTOR, CHARLES L
COMPOSER, EDUCATOR
b New York, NY, Dec 21, 24. *Study:* Yale Univ, with Paul Hindemith, 43-44; Swarthmore Col, BA, 48; Juilliard Sch Music, with Vincent Persichetti & Peter Mennin, BS, 51; Univ Ill, with Burrill Phillips, MM, 52; Univ Colo, DMA, 74. *Works:* Twelve Short Movements for String Quartet & Tape, comn by Comp String Quartet, 76; Piano Sonata, Gen Music, 77; Until A Time, comn by Utah Symph, 77; Lyric Variations for Oboe with Viola & Tape, comn by Charles Lehrer, 78; Suite for Winds & Trumpet from Incidental Music for

Play, "J B", Gen Music, 80; Overture to a Romantic Comedy (orch), G Schirmer, 83. *Teaching:* Fac mem lit & materials music & asst dean, Juilliard Sch Music, 51-59; asst prof theory & comp, Univ Colo, 59-64; prof theory & comp & dean, Col Music, Willamette Univ, 64-71; chmn dept music, Univ Ala, 71-73; prof electronic music & head dept music, Utah Univ, 73-77; prof & head dept music & dance, Univ Mass, 77- *Mem:* Col Music Soc; ASCAP; Nat Asn Sch Music; Nat Asn Comp; Snowbird Arts Found. *Mailing Add:* 19 Birchcroff Lane Amherst MA 01002

BETJEMAN, PAUL
COMPOSER, TEACHER
b London, England, Nov 26, 37. *Study:* Oxford Univ, BA; Berklee Col Music; Harvard Univ, MAT; studied comp with Stefan Wolpe; Columbia Univ, studied electronic music with Mario Davidowsky, Vladimir Ussachevsky & Charles Dodge. *Works:* Pueblo (electronic music & concrete sound for play), prod at Arena Stage, Washington, DC, 71; Hawthorn, 72; Forbidden (electronic score for ballet), comn by Harkness Ballet Co, 74; Hawthorn 2 (two pianos & two perc), 75; Hawthorn 3 (piano & string quartet), 75; Slow Burn (clarinet, string quartet & bass viol); Paces (organ & trumpet). *Awards:* Nat Endowment Arts Fel Grant, 75. *Mem:* Am Music Ctr. *Mailing Add:* Riverdale Sch Music West 253 & Past Rd Bronx NY 10471

BEUDERT, MARK
TENOR
b Mineola, NY, June 4, 57. *Study:* Columbia Univ, BA(theater-music), 82. *Roles:* Hoffman in Contes de Hoffman, Brit-Am Opera Exchange, 79; Fritz in Grand Duchesse de Gerolstein, Village Light Opera, 80; Frederic in Pirates of Penzance, NY Shakespeare Fest, 81; Rodolfo in La Boheme, Ctr Opera Perf, 82; Edgardo in Lucia di Lammermoor, Santo Domingo Opera, 83; Frederic in Pirates of Pensance, 83 & Alfredo in La Traviata, 83, Philadelphia Lyric Opera. *Mem:* Am Fedn TV & Radio Artists; Screen Actors Guild. *Rep:* Warden Assoc 45 W 60th St New York NY 10023. *Mailing Add:* 299 E Tenth St #4 New York NY 10009

BEVERS, MICHAEL EARL
BASSOON, TEACHER
b Atlanta, Ga, July 20, 57. *Study:* Cleveland Inst Music, BMus, 79, MMus, 82; bassoon studies with George Goslee & comp with Donald Erb. *Pos:* Second bassoon, Caracas Phil, Venezuela, 79-81 & Ohio Chamber Orch, 81-; prin bassoon, Cleveland Ballet Orch, 81- & Cleveland Opera Orch, 82- *Teaching:* Instr bassoon, Cleveland Inst Music, 83- *Mailing Add:* 1716 E 115th St Cleveland OH 44106

BEYER, FREDERICK H
COMPOSER, EDUCATOR
b Chicago, Ill, Dec 3, 26. *Study:* Columbia Univ, studied with Otto Luening & Jack Beeson; Fla State Univ, with John Boda. *Works:* Overture (band), 65; Vision of Time and the River (third symph), Eastern Music Fest, 78; Conversations (brass trio); Man with the Blue Guitar (chorus & piano). *Teaching:* Assoc prof music, Greensboro Col, 66- *Awards:* Ostwald Band Comp Award, 65. *Mailing Add:* 5006 Forest Oaks Dr Greensboro NC 27406

BIALOSKY, MARSHALL H
EDUCATOR, COMPOSER
b Cleveland, Ohio, Oct 30, 23. *Study:* Syracuse Univ, BMus, 49; Northwestern Univ, MMus, 50. *Works:* Two Movements for Brass Trio, Robert King Music Co; Five Western Scenes (piano), Galaxy Music Co; Little Ghost Things (choral), Walton Music Co; An Old Picture (vocal), Summy-Birchard Music Co; Suite for Flute, Oboe and Clarinet, Fantasy Scherzo for Saxophone and Piano & Sonatina for Oboe and Piano, Western Int Music Co; There is a Wisdom That is Woe (choral), A Song of Degrees (choral), Of Music and Musicians (choral) & Be Music, Night (choral), Theodore Presser Co; Seven Academic Graffiti (choral), Starting Over (solo flute), Three Canzonets (choral), At Last (choral) & An Album for the Young (piano), Seesaw Music Corp. *Teaching:* Asst prof music, Milton Col, 50-54; asst prof humanities & music, Univ Chicago, 56-61; assoc prof music, State Univ NY, Stony Brook, 61-64; prof & chmn dept fine arts, Calif State Univ, Dominguez Hills, 64- *Awards:* Calif State Univ, Dominguez Hills Outstanding Prof, 77; Wurlitzer Found Grant, 79; first prize, Int Horn Soc Comp Cont, 80. *Mem:* Am Soc Univ Comp (nat chmn, 74-77); Nat Asn Comp (pres, 78-); Col Music Soc (mem nat coun, 79-81); ASCAP. *Publ:* Auth, A Brief History of Composers' Groups in the US, Col Music Soc Symposium, fall 80; Remembering Dallapiccola, Proc 11 & 12, Am Soc Univ Comp & Some Late 19th Century Members of ASUC; Roy Harris: In Memoriam (But Keep Your Hats On), Col Music Soc Symposium, fall 82. *Mailing Add:* 84 Cresta Verde Dr Rolling Hills Estates CA 90274

BIANCO, ANTHONY
DOUBLE BASS
b New Haven, Conn, Sept 3, 17. *Study:* Samuel Levitan, 37-44; studied with D C Dounis, 48-52 & Solfeggio with N Lapatnikoff, Rosolino DeMaria & Francesco Riggio. *Pos:* Prin bass, Pittsburgh Symph, 44-70; prin bass, Chautauqua Symph, 44-55; mem, Casals Fest, San Juan, PR, 60-63. *Teaching:* Sr lectr bass, Carnegie-Mellon Univ, 45-; adj assoc prof, Kent State Univ, 80- *Mailing Add:* Pittsburgh Symph Heinz Hall 600 Penn Ave Pittsburgh PA 15222

BIBLE, FRANCES LILLIAN
MEZZO-SOPRANO
b Sackets Harbor, NY. *Study:* Inst Musical Art; Juilliard Sch Music, dipl, 47; studied with Queena Mario. *Roles:* Cherubino in Le Nozze di Figaro, New York City Opera, 48; Angelina in La Cenerentola; Herodias in Salome; Jocasta in Oedipus Rex; Augusta in The Ballad of Baby Doe, Central City Opera, Colo, 56; Amneris in Aida; Elizabeth Proctor in The Crucible, New York City Opera, 61. *Pos:* Ms with opera co & orchs throughout US, Can, Australia & Europe. *Teaching:* Adj artist in res voice, Shepherd Sch Music, Rice Univ, 75- *Awards:* Alice Breen Mem Prize & Fel, Juilliard Sch. *Mem:* Sigma Alpha Iota. *Rep:* Robert M Gewald Mgt 58 W 58 St New York NY 10019. *Mailing Add:* 2225 Bolsover Houston TX 77005

BICK, DONALD ALAN
EDUCATOR, PERCUSSION
b Wilkes-Barre, Pa, July 18, 48. *Study:* Eastman Sch Music, BM, 70; Univ Md, MM, 74. *Rec Perf:* Toot Sweet, (Moss), 77 & Sonata for Piano with Flute and Percussion, (Grahn), 77, Opus One Rec. *Pos:* Perc, Rochester Phil Orch, 69-70 & US Marine Band, 70-71; prin perc, Richmond Symph Orch, 75- *Teaching:* Asst prof applied music, Va Commonwealth Univ, 74- *Mem:* Am Fedn Musicians; Percussive Arts Soc; Col Music Soc; Nat Asn Col Wind & Perc Instr; Music Teachers Nat Asn. *Mailing Add:* 3967 Fauquier Ave Richmond VA 23227

BICKLEY, THOMAS FRANK
COMPOSER, RECORDER
b Houston, Tex, Sept 13, 54. *Study:* Univ Houston, BMus(theory), 77; NTex State Univ, with Larry Austin & Merrill Ellis, 78-79; Am Univ, with Ruth Steiner & Edward Lowinsky, MA(musicol), 83. *Works:* 21 Zones to Help You Find Your Best Frequency, perf by Chamber Orch, Houston & Denton, 75 & 76; A Liturgy (speech choirs, tape, organ & congregation), 79 & In Praise of Dialectic, 80, perf by Univ Ministry Ctr Choir, Denton, 80; Gloria: In the Beginning, perf by Bethany Univ Presby Choir, Dallas, 80; Gloria: Night Visions, perf by Protestant Choir, Kay Chapel, Am Univ, 82; Psalm 114 (electronic tape & congregation), perf by Dumbarton United Methodist Church, Washington, DC, 83. *Pos:* Chmn, Classical Music Collective, KPFT-FM 90 Pacifica, Houston, 75-78; music dir protestant choir, Univ Ministry Ctr, Denton, 79 & Campus Ministry, Am Univ, 81- *Teaching:* Music, Solomon Schechter Acad, Dallas, 80. *Mem:* Hymn Soc Am; Am Musicol Soc; Tex Music Educr Asn; Denton Comp Forum. *Interests:* American Methodist hymn tunes, 1780-1830. *Mailing Add:* 5111 Connecticut Ave NW #3 Washington DC 20008

BIDDLECOME, ROBERT EDWARD
TROMBONE, ADMINISTRATOR
b Somerville, NJ, May 9, 30. *Study:* Juilliard Sch, dipl, 52, BM, 67, MS, 71. *Pos:* Bass trombone, Am Brass Quintet, 63-, Music Aeterna Orch, 63-, New York City Ballet Orch, 64-, Am Symph Orch, 65-, Aspen Fest Orch, 70- & Am Comp Orch, 76-; exec dir, Am Brass Chamber Music Asn, 72-; pres, Am Symph Orch, 77-80 & 82- *Teaching:* Asst dean, Aspen Music Fest & Sch, 72- *Bibliog:* Koichi Akiyama (auth), interview, Band J, Japan, 1/83; Leslie Rubenstin (auth), Profile, CMA Board Member, Am Ens, spring 83. *Mem:* Chamber Music Am (treas, 79-); Bohemians. *Mailing Add:* 210 W 70th St Apt 804 New York NY 10023

BIELAWA, HERBERT WALTER
COMPOSER, EDUCATOR
b Chicago, Ill, Feb 3, 30. *Study:* Univ Ill, BM, 54, BA, 54, MM, 58; Univ Southern Calif, DMA, 69. *Works:* Quodlibet SF 42569, Belwin Mills Inc, 69-83; Emily Dickinson Album, comn by Calif Music Teachers Asn, 73; Divergents for Orchestra, perf by San Francisco Symph, 76; Monophonies for Organ, Sandra Soderlund, 79-83; Warp for Flute and Piano, perf by San Francisco Contemp Music Players, 82; Binaries for French Horn and Tape, perf by Barry Tuckwell, 83; Spectrum for Band and Tape, Shawnee Press Inc. *Teaching:* Instr, Bethany Col, Kans, 58-60; comp in res, Spring Branch Independant Sch District & Ford Found, 64-66; San Francisco Symph, 76 & San Francisco Sch District Summer Music Wkshp, 76; prof music, San Francisco State Univ, 66- *Awards:* Ingram Merrill Comp Prize, Aspen Music Sch, 58. *Mem:* ASCAP; Am Soc Univ Comp; Minneapolis Comp Forum; New York Comp Forum. *Mailing Add:* 81 Denslowe Dr San Francisco CA 94132

BIERLEY, PAUL EDMUND
WRITER
b Portsmouth, Ohio, Feb 3, 26. *Study:* Ohio State Univ, BAeroEng, 53; studied with William J Bell, 61-62. *Pos:* Asst cond, NAm Aviation Conct Band, 61-76; tubist, Columbus Symph Orch & Brass Quintet, 64-81, World Symph Orch, 72 & Detroit Conct Band, 73- *Awards:* Edwin Franko Goldman Mem Citation, 74. *Mem:* Assoc mem, Am Bandmasters Asn; assoc mem, Am Sch Band Dir Asn; Nat Band Asn; charter mem, Tubists Universal Brotherhood Asn; Sonneck Soc. *Interests:* Band subjects. *Publ:* Auth, John Philip Sousa, American Phenomenon, Prentice-Hall, 73; John Philip Sousa, A Descriptive Catalog of His Works, Univ Ill Press, 73; Hallelujah Trombone!—The Story of Henry Fillmore, 82 & The Music of Henry Fillmore and Will Huff, 82, Integrity Press. *Mailing Add:* 3888 Morse Rd Columbus OH 43219

BIESTER, ALLEN GEORGE
COMPOSER, MUSIC DIRECTOR
b Philadelphia, Pa, June 18, 40. *Study:* Univ Md, BA, 63, MA, 65; Univ Va, PhD, 74. *Works:* O Vos Omnes, 70, Quem Vidistis Pastores, 73, Wir Danken Dir, 73, Buccinate, 74, Two Baroque Pieces for Kazoos, 73, Dirinum Mysterium, 83 & Quem Pastores, 85, Lawson-Gould. *Pos:* Chapel organist, Univ Md, College Park, 58-63; dir glee club & brass ens, Va Mil Inst, Lexington, 65-73. *Teaching:* Adj prof music, Gloucester Co Col, Sewell, NJ, 81- *Mem:* Am Guild Organists. *Mailing Add:* 1347 Cooper St Deptford NJ 08096

BIGGS, JOHN JOSEPH
COMPOSER, MUSIC DIRECTOR
b Los Angeles, Calif, Oct 18, 32. *Study:* Univ Calif, Los Angeles, MA(comp), 63; Royal Flemish Acad, Antwerp, Belguim, 64-65; Univ Southern Calif, 65-66. *Works:* Triple Concerto (trumpet, horn, trombone & strings), 62, Symphony No 1, 65, Concerto for Viola, Woodwinds & Percussion, 66, Am Fold Song Suite (men's chorus & orch), 67, Canticle of Life (chorus, solos, chamber orch & dancers), 75, Variations on a Theme of Shostakovich (piano & orch), 78 & Little Suite (two violins & chamber orch), 79, Consort Press. *Pos:* Dir, John Biggs Consort, 63- & Early Music Ser, 79-; chief ed, Consort Press, 80- *Teaching:* Comp in res, Kans State Teachers Col, 67-70. *Awards:* Excellence in Comp, Atwater Kent, 63; Standard Award in Serious Music, ASCAP, 74-; Work of Exceptional Merit, Nat Flute Asn, 81. *Mem:* ASCAP. *Mailing Add:* 1738 Rocky Rd Fullerton CA 92631

BIGHAM, WILLIAM MARVIN
ADMINISTRATOR, EDUCATOR
b Paris, Tenn, June 6, 34. *Study:* Murray State Univ, BMusEd, 56; Univ Miami, MMus, 57; Fla State Univ, PhD, 65. *Teaching:* Prof music, Morehead State Univ, Ky, 65-, head dept music, 80- *Mem:* Ky Music Educr Asn; Music Educr Nat Conf; Int Clarinet Soc; Soc Res Music Educ; Col Music Soc. *Publ:* Auth, 25 bk reviews, Choice, 70-83. *Mailing Add:* Music Dept Morehead State Univ Morehead KY 40351

BIGLER, CAROLE L
LECTURER, EDUCATOR
b Kingston, Pa, Oct 16, 40. *Study:* Syracuse Univ, BME, 62; Ithaca Col, 63; Cornell Univ, 71. *Pos:* Organist, First Congregational Church, 68-; Suzuki piano specialist-pedagogue, throughout Can & US, 73- *Teaching:* Suzuki piano, Emporia State Univ, Univ Wis, Stevens Pt, Queens Univ, State Univ, Kingston, Ont, George Mason Univ & Pacific Univ, summers 76-; adj prof music, Emporia State Univ, 80-; fac mem, Ithaca Col, 82- *Mem:* Suzuki Asn Am (bd dir 79-81). *Publ:* Coauth, A Suzuki Piano Celebration, Am Suzuki J, 78; Studying Suzuki Piano More Than Music, Ability Develop Assoc Inc, 79; Kato Havas and Shinicki Suzuki, Strad Mag, England, 80; Teaching a Bach Minuet the Suzuki Way, Clavier Mag, 80. *Mailing Add:* Churchill Pl R D # 1 Big Flats NY 14814

BILGER, DAVID VICTOR
CONDUCTOR, SAXOPHONE
b Reading, Pa, Apr 16, 45. *Study:* Ithaca Col, BM, 67; studied with Sigurd Rascher, 69-79; Univ Hartford, 70. *Rec Perf:* Bilger Duo, Vol I, Dimension 5 Studios, 76; Bilger Duo Plays Recital Favorites, Trutone Rec, 77; Saxophone Sinfonia Playing Selections from its Lincoln Center Concert Program, Golden Crest, 82. *Pos:* Cond, Sax Sinfonia, 82- *Teaching:* Instr sax, Lebanon Valley Col, 74- *Bibliog:* Ron Caravan (auth), The Saxophone Sinfonia is Warmly Received in New York's Alice Tully Hall Concert, Sax Symposium, 82; Harry Gee (auth), 18 Saxophonists Give Unique Recital, Sch Musician, 83. *Mem:* Reading Music Teachers Asn (treas, 73-79); World Saxophone Cong, NAm Sax Alliance (region eight coordr, 72-78). *Mailing Add:* 1200 Bedford Ave Shillington PA 19607

BILLINGS, CHARLES W
ADMINISTRATOR, MUSIC DIRECTOR
b Memphis, Tenn, July 17, 55. *Study:* Memphis State Univ. *Pos:* Announcer & prod, WKNO-FM, Memphis, 79-; events chmn, Opera Memphis, 81-; exec dir, Concts Int, 82- *Mailing Add:* WKNO 900 Getwell Rd Memphis TN 38111

BILLINGS, DAVID ARTHUR
TEACHER, ORGAN
b Montrose, Pa, Aug 9, 55. *Study:* Pa State Univ, BFA, 77; Eastman Sch Music, MM, 79, 80-. *Pos:* Music dir, Parkwood United Presby Church, Allison Park, Pa, 81- *Teaching:* Organ, harpsichord & organ lit, Duquesne Univ, 81- *Mem:* Am Guild Organists. *Mailing Add:* 431 Browns Lane Pittsburgh PA 15237

BILLINGSLEY, WILLIAM ALLEN
COMPOSER, TRUMPET
b Glasgow, Mont, June 28, 22. *Study:* Trumpet with John Egan, 47-48; Drake Univ, BM, 52, MM, 53. *Works:* Mr Nobody (treble voices & piano), Carl Fischer, 62; The Paradox, comn & perf by Spokane Symph, 74; Requiem (ballet), perf by Ballet Folk Moscow, Idaho, 76; Six Solos for Young Flutist with Piano Accompaniment, Belwin-Mills, 77-78; Concerto for Orchestra, comn & perf by Wash Idaho Symph, 81; Sonata for Flute and Piano, Third Annual New Music Fest, Bowling Green State Unv, 82; Landscape Sketches for Two Pianos, comn & perf by Univ Idaho, 83. *Pos:* Trumpet, Drake-Des Moines Symph, 50-53; staff trumpeter & arranger, WHO Radio Sta, Des Moines, 53-54; first trumpet, Spokane Symph, 60-61. *Teaching:* Prof trumpet & comp, Sch Music, Univ Idaho, 54- *Awards:* Spec Three Star Award Merit Comp, Nat Fedn Music Clubs, 78; Prizewinner, Comp Cont Int Double Reed Soc, 79. *Mem:* Am Soc Univ Comp; Am Fedn Musicians; ASCAP. *Mailing Add:* 108 N Monroe Moscow ID 83843

BILLMEYER, DEAN WALLACE
ORGAN, EDUCATOR
b Wilmington, Del, June 2, 55. *Study:* Eastman Sch Music, BMus, 77, DMA, 82; Southern Methodist Univ, MMus, 79; Hochschule Musik, Vienna, 79-80. *Teaching:* Asst prof music, Univ Minn, Minneapolis, 82- *Awards:* Inst Int Educ Fulbright-Hays Grant, 79; Second Prize, Dublin Int Organ Playing Compt, Ireland, 80. *Mem:* Am Guild Organists. *Mailing Add:* 3414 Grand Ave S Minneapolis MN 55408

BILSON, MALCOLM
PIANO, EDUCATOR
Los Angeles, Calif, Oct 24, 35. *Study:* Bard Col, BA, 57; Vienna Acad Music, Reifezeugnis, 59; Univ Ill, DMA, 68. *Rec Perf:* Mozart Sonatas, 81 & Beethoven Sonatas, 82, Nonesuch Rec; Mozart Piano Concertos (with J E Gardiner), Deutsche Grammophon, 83. *Teaching:* Instr music, Univ Ill, 62-68; prof, Cornell Univ, 68-; Fortepiano summer wkshps, Wellesley Col, 76-78, Univ Calif, 80, Oberlin Col, 81 & Eszterhaza, Hungary, 82. *Awards:* Fulbright Grant, 59. *Mailing Add:* Dept Music Lincoln Hall Cornell Univ Ithaca NY 14853

BILYEU, LANDON ALAN
EDUCATOR, PIANO
b Lufkin, Tex, Dec 30, 39. *Study:* Centenary Col, BM(piano), 62; Univ Tulsa, study with Bela Rozsa, MM(piano), 64; Boston Univ, study with Bela Nagy, 65 & 69. *Works:* Piano soli & chamber music, 62-76. *Pos:* About 500 perf as pianist (solo, chamber music, concert soloist & accompanist). *Teaching:* Asst prof piano, music theory & comp, Midwestern Univ, Wichita Falls, Tex, 64-71 & Univ Idaho, Moscow, 71-74; assoc prof, Va Commonwealth Univ, 74- *Publ:* Auth, Note Whiz, 82, Pitch Master, 82, Chord Speller, 83 & Harmonia, 83, Comput Assisted Instr Music, MECA Inc. *Mailing Add:* 431 N Stafford Richmond VA 23220

BINKERD, GORDON WARE
COMPOSER
b Lynch, Nebr, May 22, 16. *Study:* Dakota Wesleyan Univ, BM, 37; Univ Rochester, with Bernard Rogers, MM, 41; Harvard Univ, with Walter Piston, MA, 52. *Works:* Symphony #1, 54, Symphony #2, 56, Symphony #4, 62 & Sonata (violin & piano), 68, Boosey & Hawkes. *Awards:* Nat Inst Arts & Lett Award, 60; Comp Prize, Chicago Symph Orch, 62. *Mem:* ASCAP. *Rep:* Boosey & Hawkes, 24 W 57th St New York NY 10019. *Mailing Add:* 1705 Highcross Rd Urbana IL 61801

BINKLEY, THOMAS E
EDUCATOR, ADMINISTRATOR
b Cleveland, Ohio, Dec 26, 31. *Study:* Univ Colo, Boulder; Univ Ill, Urbana, BM, 54; Univ Munich, Ger. *Rec Perf:* Carmina Burana & Chansons der Trouveres, 64, Telefunken; Peter Abelard, Ludi Sancti Nicolai, Estampie & Vox Humana, 81, EMI Reflexe; Greater Passion Play from Carmina Burana, Focus Rec, Ind Univ, 83. *Pos:* Dir, Studio der frühen Musik, Munich, Early Music Quartet, Ger, 59-79. *Teaching:* Fac mem, Sch Cantorum Basiliensis, Basel, Switz, 73-77; dir & prof, Early Music Inst, Sch Music, Ind Univ, Bloomington, 79- *Awards:* Edison Prize, Holland, 66 & 82; Preis Deutschen Schallplatten Industrie, 68, 70 & 81; Dickenson Col Arts Award, 83. *Mem:* Am Musicol Soc. *Interests:* Medieval music—secular, liturgical, music drama, organology. *Publ:* Transl, Fritz Winchel, Music Sound and Sensation, Dover Press, 62; auth, Le Luth et sa Technique, Pars NRS, 63; Electronic Processing of Musical Materials, Gustav Bosse, Regensburg, 67; Zur Afführungspraxis der ... Musik der Mittelalters, 77 & The Greater Passion Play from Carmina Burana, 83, Basler Jahrbuch Historische Musikpraxis. *Mailing Add:* Early Music Inst Ind Univ Bloomington IN 47405

BIRDWELL, EDWARD RIDLEY
FRENCH HORN
b Houston, Tex, Apr 20, 36. *Study:* Houston Consv Music, BMus; Univ Houston, MMus. *Pos:* Dep dir, Carnegie Hall, New York, formerly; mem, Am Brass Quintet; mem, treas & bd dir, Am Symph Orch, New York. *Teaching:* Asst dean, Aspen Music Sch & Fest, formerly. *Bibliog:* Article, New York Times Weekly Mag, 1/74. *Mem:* Am Brass Chamber Music Asn. *Rep:* Melvin Kaplan Mgt 1860 Broadway Suite 401 New York NY 10023. *Mailing Add:* 210 Riverside Dr New York NY 10025

BIRDWELL, FLORENCE (GILLAM-HOBIN)
MEZZO-SOPRANO, EDUCATOR
b Douglas, Ariz, Sept 3, 22. *Study:* Okla City Univ, BM, 47, MA, 70; studied with Vera Nielson, Inez Silberg, Elizabeth Parham, Chloe Owen, Marlena Malas, Seth Riggs & Boris Goldovsky. *Pos:* Performer, Lyr Theater, Oklahoma City, 69-82; solo recitals in the Southwest & Mont, 69-; narrator, Okla Symph Orch, 80-82 & Okla Art Museum, 80-82. *Teaching:* Assoc instr, Okla City Univ, 60-69, instr, 69-75, asst prof, 75-82, assoc prof, 83- *Mem:* Nat Asn Teachers Singing; Nat Music Teachers Asn; Okla Music Teachers Asn; Sigma Alpha Iota; Nat Opera Asn. *Mailing Add:* Music Dept Oklahoma City Univ Oklahoma City OK 73106

BISCARDI, CHESTER
COMPOSER, EDUCATOR
b Kenosha, Wis, Oct 19, 48. *Study:* Univ Bologna & Consv Musica G B Martini, 69-70; Univ Wis, Madison, studied comp with Les Thimmig, BA, 70, MA, 72, MM, 74; Sch Music, Yale Univ, MMA(comp), 76, DMA(comp), 79; study with Robert Morris, Krzysztof Penderecki, Toru Takemitsu & Yehudi Wyner. *Works:* Tenzone (2 flutes & piano), Merion Music Inc & Theodore Presser Co, 75 & Music Today, 76; Trio (violin, violoncello & piano), 76 & At The Still Point (orch), 77, Merion Music Inc & Theodore Presser Co; Eurydice (chorus & orch), Am Comp Alliance, 78; Mestiere (piano), Merion Music Inc & Theodore Presser Co, 79; Trasumanar (12 perc & piano), 80 & Di Vivere (clarinet & piano with flute, violin & violoncello), 81, Am Comp Alliance. *Teaching:* Asst theory, Univ Wis, Madison, 73-74; fel, Sch Music, Yale Univ, 75-76; music fac, Sarah Lawrence Col, 77- *Awards:* Charles E Ives Scholar, Am Acad & Inst Arts & Lett, 75-76; Prix de Rome, Am Acad, 76-77; John Simon Guggenheim Mem Found Fel, 79-80. *Mem:* Am Acad Rome; Am Comp Alliance; Am Music Ctr; BMI; Guild Comp. *Mailing Add:* 542 Ave of the Americas 4R New York NY 10011

BISER, LARRY GENE
CONDUCTOR & MUSIC DIRECTOR, TENOR
b Woolrich, Pa, Aug 21, 43. *Study:* Westminster Choir Col, BM, 65. *Rec Perf:* Works for Cathedral Spaces (organ & choir), River City Studios, 83, Wicks Organ Series. *Pos:* Organist & choirmaster, Epworth United Methodist Church, Norfolk, Va, 67-69 & E Congregational Church, Grand Rapids, Mich, 69-; music dir & cond, Chamber Choir Grand Rapids, Mich, 81-; dir choruses, Opera Grand Rapids, Mich, 82- *Mem:* Am Choral Dir Asn; Am Guild Organists; Choristers' Guild; Westminster Choir Col Alumni Asn; Am Fedn Musicians. *Rep:* Brandon Assoc 1110 Giddings Ave SE Grand Rapids MI 49506. *Mailing Add:* 1005 Giddings Ave SE Grand Rapids MI 49506

BISHOP, ADELAIDE
EDUCATOR, DIRECTOR—OPERA
b New York, NY. *Study:* Private study with Louis Polanski, Paul Breisach, Rose Landuer, Ludwig Donath, Thais Lawton. *Pos:* Artistic dir, Wolf Trap Opera Co, 80- *Teaching:* Assoc prof & dir opera dept, Sch Arts, Boston Univ, 69-82; prof, chmn opera dept & artistic dir, Hartt Sch Music, Univ Hartford, 82- *Rep:* 240 E 76th St New York NY 10021. *Mailing Add:* 55 Baldwin St Nashua NH 03060

BISHOP, MARTHA (JANE)
VIOLA DA GAMBA, EDITOR
b North Wilkesboro, NC, July 31, 37. *Study:* Univ NC, Greensboro, BMus, 59; Univ NC, Chapel Hill, MMus, 62. *Pos:* Mem, Atlanta Symph Orch, 65-70; Emory String Quartet, 70-78; Pied Pipers Renaissance Mus, 75-; Westminister String Quartet, 78- *Teaching:* Asst prof music history, WGa Col, 71-73; numerous early music & viola da gamba wkshp in US. *Bibliog:* Carol Herman, review, 80 & Molly Johnston, review, 82, Viola da Gamba Soc Am News; Joan Wess, review, Early Music, Oxford Univ Press, 82. *Mem:* Pi Kappa Lambda; Viola da Gamba Soc Am (pres, 78-80). *Publ:* Auth, Method, Bishop Publ, 79; ed, Tablature for Two, 80, Tabulature for Three, 80 & Vade Mecum, 81, Bishop Publ; Schwartzkopf Trio Sonata, Dove House Ed, 83. *Mailing Add:* 1859 Westminister Way NE Atlanta GA 30307

BISHOP, RONALD TAYLOR
TUBA, EDUCATOR
b Rochester, NY, Dec 21, 34. *Study:* Eastman Sch Music, BMus, perf cert(tuba); Univ Ill, Urbana-Champaign, MMusEd; studied with Arnold Jacobs. *Rec Perf:* Highlights from the Ring (Wagner); Romeo & Juliet (Prokofiev); Porgy & Bess (Gershwin); Carmina Burana (Orff). *Pos:* Soloist, San Francisco Symph Orch, 65; tubist, Eastman Symph Wind Ens, formerly, Am Wind Symph, formerly, Buffalo Phil Orch, formerly, US Army Field Band, formerly, Eastman Brass Quintet, formerly, San Francisco Symph, formerly, San Francisco Opera Orch, formerly, Camara Brass Quintet, formerly & Cleveland Brass Quintet, formerly, mem, Severance Brass Quintet, Reconnaissance, Cleveland, currently; prin tuba, Cleveland Orch, 67- *Teaching:* Mem fac, Eastman Sch Music, formerly, Univ Buffalo, formerly, San Francisco State Col, formerly, Youngstown State Univ, formerly, Univ Akron, formerly & Cleveland Inst Music, 68- *Mem:* Tubist Universal Brotherhood Asn. *Mailing Add:* Cleveland Inst Music 11021 East Blvd Cleveland OH 44106

BISKIN, HARVEY
TIMPANI, ADMINISTRATOR
b Schenectady, NY, Sept 2, 25. *Study:* Berkshire Music Ctr, 47; Eastman Sch Music, BMus, 49; Eastman Sch Music, MMus, 50. *Pos:* Perc, Rochester Phil, 48-50; Prin timpanist, Chautauqua Symph, 50-; prin timpanist, San Antonio Symph, 50-; educ dir, 55-, asst cond, 73- *Teaching:* Instr, Trinity Univ, 55-76; lectr timpani & perc, Univ Tex, Austin, 57-65 & Univ Tex, San Antonio, 76- *Mailing Add:* 615 Patterson Ave San Antonio TX 78209

BITGOOD, ROBERTA (ROBERTA BITGOOD WIERSMA)
ORGAN, COMPOSER
b New London, Conn, Jan 15, 08. *Study:* Conn Col Women, AB, 28; Guilmant Organ Sch, cert, 30; Teachers Col, Columbia Univ, MA, 32; Sch Sacred Music, Union Theol Sem, MSM, 35, SMD, 45. *Works:* My Heart Is Ready, O God (unison, chorus & flute), Broadman Press, 81; Great Is God (solo sop & ATB), 82 & Happy the People (SATB), 82, Sacred Music Press; The Lord's My Shepherd (SA), H W Gray, 83; Sound Over All Waters (unison & descant), Westminster Press; Rejoice, Give Thanks (organ & four brass), Hope Publ Co; Meditation on Kingsfold (organ solo), Hinshaw Music, Inc. *Pos:* Organist & dir, Westminster Presby Church, Bloomfield, NJ, 32-47, Holy Trinity Lutheran Church, Buffalo, 47-52, Calvary Presby Church, Riverside, Calif, 52-60, Redford Presby Church, Detroit, 60-63, First Presby, Bay City, Mich, 63-68 & First Congregational Church, Battle Creek, 69-76. *Teaching:* Dir music, Bloomfield Col & Sem, 35-47; instr private organ. *Awards:* Teacher of Yr, Mich Fedn Music Clubs, 64. *Bibliog:* Calvert Shenk (auth), article, Am Organist, 7/81. *Mem:* Am Guild Organists (nat pres, 75-81); Choristers Guild (mem nat bd, 62-76); Hymn Soc Am (mem nat bd, 75-79). *Mailing Add:* 13 Best View Rd Quaker Hill CT 06375

BIXLER, MARTHA HARRISON
RECORDER, EDUCATOR
b Springfield, Mass, Aug 9, 27. *Study:* Smith Col, BA, 48; Yale Univ, MusB, 51; Brooklyn Col, MA, 75. *Rec Perf:* Recorder Music of the 20th Century, 58, Medieval, Renaissance and Baroque Recorder Music, 58, A Day in the Park, 59, The Music of Georg Philipp Telemann, 59, Solo Music from the 18th Century, 60, Baroque Arias with Recorders, 60 & The Medieval Jazz Quartet, 60, Classic Ed. *Teaching:* Instr, Dwight Sch, Lenox Sch & Dalton Sch, 55-75 & NY Col Music, 58-62; Prof, Wagner Col, 79- *Bibliog:* Rhoda Weber (auth),

Martha Bixler: A Profile, Am Recorder, summer 70; Edgar Hunt (auth), Martha Bixler: An Interview, Recorder & Music, 12/74. *Mem:* Hon life mem, Am Recorder Soc (pres, 76-80); Am Musicol Soc; Viola da Gamba Soc Am. *Mailing Add:* 670 West End Ave New York NY 10025

BJERREGAARD, CARL
EDUCATOR
Study: Western Mich Univ, BM; Mich State Univ, BM. *Teaching:* Dir instrm music, pub sch, Montague, Mich & Muskegan Mich, formerly; mem fac, Eastern Mich Univ, Mich State Univ & Blue Lake Fine Arts Camp, formerly; dir bands, Western Mich Univ, formerly; prof chamber winds, flute & cond, Fla State Univ, currently. *Mailing Add:* 2918 Coldstream Dr Tallahassee FL 32312

BLACK, C ROBERT
SAXOPHONE, EDUCATOR
b Sentinel, Okla, Oct 21, 51. *Study:* Northwestern Univ, BMus(perf), 73; Consv Nat Music, Bordeaux, France, 72. *Rec Perf:* Concert Repertoire for Saxophone, Brewster Rec, 76; The Final Alice, DGG, 78; New Music Series, 82 & Concert Repertoire for Saxophone, 83, Brewster Rec. *Pos:* Pres & chmn bd, Sax Shop, Ltd, Evanston, Ill, 74-; first call sax, Chicago Symph Orch, 74- & Grant Park Symph, Chicago, Ill, 74- *Teaching:* Instr sax, DePaul Univ, 78- *Awards:* First Prize Sax, Consv Nat Musique, Bordeaux, France, 72. *Publ:* Auth, The Saxophone Retrospect and Perspective, Instrumentalist, 76; Saxophonists Unite, Accent Mag, 79; Exploring the Altissimo, Instrumentalist, 80. *Mailing Add:* 922 Noyes St Evanston IL 60201

BLACK, RALPH
ARTIST MANAGER
b July 11, 19. *Study:* Houghton Col, 41. *Pos:* Gen mgr, Chattanooga Symph, 50-51, Buffalo Phil, 51-55, Nat Symph Orch, 55-60, Baltimore Symph Orch, 60-63 & Nat Ballet Washington DC, 63-73; exec dir, Am Symph Orch League, 73-80, vpres, 80- *Awards:* Silver Baton, Bell Syst, 78; Louis Sudler Award, 82. *Mem:* Asn Am Dance Co; Am Arts Alliance; Nat Music Coun. *Publ:* Auth, The Best of Black Notes, Am Symph Orch League, 6/83. *Mailing Add:* 633 E Street NW Washington DC 20004

BLACK, ROBERT CARLISLE
CONDUCTOR, PIANO
b Dallas, Tex, Apr 28, 50. *Study:* Oberlin Consv, BM, 72; Juilliard Sch Music, MM, 74, DMA, 77. *Rec Perf:* From Variations (Ralph Shapey), 79, Piano Works of Sessions, Weber & Gideon, 83 & Piano Works of Erich Itor Kahn, 83, CRI; Epic Poem (Dane Rudhyar), CP2, 83; Piano Works (Liszt), Orion, 83. *Pos:* Artistic dir & cond, NY New Music Ens, 75-; cond & pianist, Speculum Musicae, 78- *Teaching:* Fac piano, Princeton Univ, 76-83 & Univ Calif, Santa Barbara, 81-82; assoc musical perf, Columbia Univ, 82- *Awards:* Edward Steuermann Mem Prize, Juilliard Sch Music, 74; Nat Endowment Arts Solo Recitalists Fel, 81. *Mem:* Lincoln Ctr Chamber Music Soc; League Comp, Int Soc Contemp Music; Am Liszt Soc. *Publ:* Auth, Symphonic Genesis in Wagner's Götterdämmerung, Juilliard Sch Music, 77; ... And Each Harmonical Has a Point of Its Own ... , 78 & Boulez's Third Sonata: Surface and Sensibility, 82, Perspectives New Music. *Rep:* Judith Finell Music Services 155 W 68th St New York NY 10023. *Mailing Add:* 23 W 73rd St #607 New York NY 10023

BLACKBURN, WALTER WESLEY
CONDUCTOR & MUSIC DIRECTOR, EDUCATOR
b Norristown, Pa, Feb 19, 39. *Study:* State Col, West Chester, Pa, BS(music educ), 61; Univ Ind, Bloomington, MM(cond), 62. *Rec Perf:* Anthology of Moravian Music, 72. *Pos:* Choral dir & cond, Lancaster Opera Wkshp, 77- *Teaching:* Dir music, Penns Grove Sch District, NJ, 62-64; asst prof music, Drexel Univ, 64-71; assoc prof & dir, Univ Choir, Millersville Univ, 71- *Mem:* Am Fedn Musicians; Am Choral Dir Asn; Pa Collegiate Choral Dir Asn (pres, 72-76). *Mailing Add:* 1410 Millersville Pike Lancaster PA 17603

BLACKHAM, RICHARD ALLAN
WRITER
b Winchester, Mass, Feb 19, 29. *Study:* Harvard Univ, 46-48; Longy Sch Music, theory with Melville Smith & hist with Erwin Bodky, 48-52; Boston Univ, musicol with Karl Geiringer, MusB, 56. *Pos:* Rec librn, Music Libr, Harvard Univ, 56-61; class ed, Schwann Rec & Tape Guide, Boston, 61- *Interests:* Discography, current and historical. *Mailing Add:* ABC Schwann Publ 535 Boylston St Boston MA 02116

BLACKWELDER, STEPHEN DWIGHT
CONDUCTOR & MUSIC DIRECTOR
b Concord, NC, Oct 16, 56. *Study:* Univ NC, Chapel Hill, BMus, 78; Northwestern Univ, MMus, 79. *Pos:* Asst cond, Harford Opera Theater, Baltimore, 77, Hinsdale Opera Theater, Ill, 80-82 & Chicago Opera Theater, 82-; music dir & cond, Hinsdale Chamber Orch, Ill, 83- *Mem:* Am Guild Musical Artists; Am Symph Orch League Cond Guild. *Mailing Add:* 305 Custer Ave #1 Evanston IL 60202

BLACKWOOD, EASLEY
COMPOSER, PIANO
b Indianapolis, Ind, Apr 21, 33. *Study:* Piano study; Berkshire Music Ctr, studied comp with Olivier Messiaen, 48-50; Ind Univ, with Bernard Heiden; Yale Univ, with Paul Hindemith, PhD, 54; studied with Nadia Boulanger, Paris, 54-56. *Works:* Symphony No 1, 55; Chamber Symphony for 14 Wind Instruments, 55; Fantasy for Cello and Piano, 60; Symphony No 2, comn by G Schirmer, 60; Pastorale and Variations (wind quintet), 61; Concerto for

Oboe and String Orchestra, 66; Un Voyage d Cythere (sop & ten players), 66; and others. *Pos:* Piano soloist, Indianapolis Symph, 47. *Teaching:* Mem fac, Univ Chicago, 58- & Webster Col, 78-79. *Awards:* Koussevitzky Music Found Prize, 58; Fulbright Grant. *Mailing Add:* 5300 South Shore Dr Chicago IL 60615

BLAIN, ALBERT VALDES
GUITAR, EDUCATOR

b Havana, Cuba, Apr 10, 21; US citizen. *Study:* Studied with Marinez & Oyanguren, 36-69; Juilliard Sch Music, 46; Greenwich House Sch Music, teachers dipl, 50; studied with Andres Segovia, 56. *Pos:* Conct guitarist, 55-65. *Teaching:* Asst prof class guitar, NY Univ, 67- & Consv Music, Brooklyn Col, 74-; prof, Mannes Col Music, 73- *Awards:* Fels, New York Soc Class Guitar, 54, Philadelphia Soc Class Guitar, 57 & Cincinatti Soc Class Guitar, 60. *Bibliog:* Arnie Berle (auth), Albert Valdes Blain, Guitar Player Mag, 11/79; Maurice Summerfield (auth), Albert Valdes Blain, Class Guitar, 82. *Publ:* Auth of articles on music & guitar technique, Guitar News, London, 50-55; The Guitar, The Beginner & The Teacher, Guitar Rev, 55; 700 Years of Music for Classical Guitar, Hansen Publ, 67. *Mailing Add:* 25 W 13th St New York NY 10011

BLAIR, WILLIAM P
ADMINISTRATOR

b Canton, Ohio. *Study:* Ohio State Univ, Columbus, BA, MA, JD. *Pos:* Attorney at law, Canton, Ohio, currently; founding pres & mem bd, Ohio Found Arts, formerly; pres, Ohio Citizens Comt for Arts, currently; founding chmn, WKSU Adv Bd, Kent State Univ, formerly, mem bd & Kent Found. *Mem:* Ohio Orgn Orch; Canton Symph Orch Asn (pres, currently); Am Symph Orch League (vchmn, currently); Am Arts Alliance (mem bd trustees & secy, currently); Metropolitan Opera Nat Coun. *Mailing Add:* 636 Citizens Savings Bldg Canton OH 44702

BLAKE, RAN
PIANO, COMPOSER

b Springfield, Mass, Apr 20, 35. *Study:* Lenox Sch Jazz, 57-60; Bard Col, BA, 60; studied with Ray Cassarino, Willis Lawrence James, Oscar Peterson, Bill Russo, Mal Waldron, Gunther Schuller & Mary Lou Williams. *Works:* Wende, 48, Vanguard, 53, Breakthru, 59, Thursday, 59 & Arline, 63, MJQ Music, Inc & BMI; Touch of Evil, 80 & Garden of Delight, 80, Margun Music, Inc & BMI. *Rec Perf:* Field Cry, 76, How 'Bout That, 76 & Eve, 80, Dimension Sound Studios, Boston. *Teaching:* Mem fac third stream music & jazz, New England Consv Music, 68-, prod mgr & music dir, Commun Serv Dept, 69-72, chairperson, Dept Third Stream Studies, 73-; mem fac third stream music, Hartford Consv, 72-75. *Awards:* Guggenheim Found Fel, 82; Mass Artists Found Fel, 82; Nat Endowment Arts Fel, 82. *Bibliog:* Len Lyons (auth), The Great Jazz Pianist, Quill, Ran Blake: Pianist & Teacher from the Third Stream, Keyboard Mag, 10/78; Michael Ullman (auth), Jazz Lives, New Repub Bks, 80; Gianni Gualberto (auth), Il Jazz Degli Anni '70, Gammalibri Milano, 80. *Mem:* BMI; Music Critics Asn; Col Music Soc. *Publ:* Auth, Chris Connor, Down Beat Mag, 69; Teaching Third Stream, Music Educr J, 76; Anthony Braxton, Bay State Banner, 79; Third Stream and the Importance of the Ear, Symposium, 81; The Monk Piano Style, Keyboard Mag, 82. *Rep:* Gregory Silberman 11 Chestnut Pl Brookline MA 02146. *Mailing Add:* 290 Huntington Ave Boston MA 02115

BLAKE, ROCKWELL
TENOR

Roles: Count Almaviva in The Barber of Seville, Houston Opera Co, Hamburg Opera, Vienna Opera, Dallas Opera Co, Ft Worth Opera Co, Tex & Nat Arts Ctr, Ottawa; Count Ory in Count Ory, New York City Opera, 79-80 & City Opera Los Angeles, 79-80; La Cenerentola, Dallas Civic Opera, 79-80 & Houston Grand Opera, 79-80; The Magic Flute, Columbus Symph, 79-80 & Pittsburgh Opera, 79-80; Il Furioso del Isola San Domingo, Kennedy Ctr Summer Opera, 79; Lindoro in L'Italiana in Algeri, Hamburg State Opera, 79-80 & Metropolitan Opera, 80-81; Daughter of the Regiment, Nat Arts Ctr, Ottawa, 80. *Pos:* Mem, Wolf Trap Co, 75; tenor, Wash Opera, Mich Opera Theatre, Washington, DC, Baltimore Symph, Houston Grand Opera, Brussels Theatre Monnaie, Omaha Opera, Fest Ottawa & others, formerly. *Awards:* Richard Tucker Award, 78. *Mailing Add:* c/o Columbia Artists 165 W 57th St New York NY 10019

BLAKELY, LLOYD GEORGE
ADMINISTRATOR, EDUCATOR

b Mountain Grove, Mo, March 4, 21. *Study:* Northwestern Univ, MM, 47; Boston Univ, DMA, 58. *Teaching:* Prof & head dept music, Southern Ill Univ, Edwardsville, 58-70 & Southwest Mo State Univ, Springfield, 70- *Awards:* Fulbright Fel, Ger, 64. *Mem:* Music Educr Nat Asn; Nat Asn Sch Music; Sonneck Soc. *Interests:* Music of the Ephrata, Pennsylvania cloister. *Mailing Add:* Dept Music Southwest Mo State Univ Springfield MO 65802

BLAKEMAN, VIRGINIA (VIRGINIA BLAKEMAN LENZ)
VIOLA

b Sandusky, Ohio, Aug 1, 49. *Study:* New England Consv Music, with Eugene Lehner, BM, 71; Yale Sch Music, with J Silverstein, MM, 74. *Pos:* Participant, Marlboro Music Fest, Vt, 73-74; prin violist, Rochester Phil, 74-80, violist, 80- *Awards:* Benjamin H Delson Award, Tanglewood Fest, 70; Munich Int Compt Scholar, Inst Int Educ, 75. *Mailing Add:* 63 Avondale Pk Rochester NY 14620

BLAND, WILLIAM KEITH
COMPOSER, PIANO

b WVa, Nov 17, 47. *Study:* Peabody Inst, John Hopkins Univ, with Ernst Krenek & Earle Brown, DMA(comp), 73. *Works:* Like a Mad Animal ... (solo double bass & ens), Yorke Ed, Galaxy Music, 72; An Impression by Arp, perf by Orpheus Chamber Ens, 77; Concerto for Amplified Guitar & Orchestra, comn by Bennington Community Orch, Vt, 79; Untitled Duo (perc & amplified piano), comn by Gordon & Jay Gottlieb, perf by Hartt Sch Music, 80; Quongngai-4 (solo piano), perf by Mona Golabeck, 80; Six Pieces for Guitar, Two Songs & Four Etudes on Spanish Subjects, perf by David Starobin, 81; Untitled Composition in 2 Movements: Moto Perpetuo & Adagio (flute, clarinet, violin & piano), comn by Lincoln Ctr Chamber Music Soc, 82. *Pos:* Pianist & comp, Baltimore Group Experimental Music, 70-73. *Teaching:* Comp & artist in res, Catskill Fest, NY, 78; artist in res piano, Contemp Music Fest, Bowdoin Col, 79-80; private teacher piano, currently. *Awards:* Creative Artist Pub Serv Award, State of NY, 76; Edward McDowell Found Fel, 75 & 77; Troisieme Prix Award, Concours Int Guitare, France, 80. *Bibliog:* David Cope (auth), New Directions in Music, W C Brown & Co, 71. *Publ:* Auth, Earle Brown, Morton Feldman & Christian Wolff, In: New Grove Dict of Music & Musicians, London, 80. *Mailing Add:* Rt 1 Shepherdstown WV 25443

BLANK, ALLAN
COMPOSER, EDUCATOR

b Bronx, NY, Dec 27, 25. *Study:* Juilliard Sch Music, 45-47; Wash Square Col, NY Univ, BA, 48; Univ Minn, MA, 50. *Works:* Aria da Capo (chamber opera), Theodore Presser & Co, 60; Concert Piece for Band, Assoc Music Publ, 61; Two Ferlinghetti Songs (sop & bassoon), 64 & Thirteen Ways of Looking at a Blackbird, 65, CRI; Excitement at the Circus (children's opera), Seesaw Music Corp, 68; Diversions (solo clarinet), Assoc Music Publ, 74; Divertimento for Tuba & Symph Band, perf by Jack Robinson & Univ Northern Colo Band, 83. *Pos:* Violinist, Pittsburgh Symph Orch, 50-52. *Teaching:* Asst prof music, Paterson State Col, 66-70 & 77-78; assoc prof, Herbert H Lehman Col, City Univ New York, 70-77 & Va Commonwealth Univ, 78- *Awards:* Cond fel, Juilliard Sch Music, 45-47; First Prize, Phi Mu Alpha Sinfonia, 54; George Eastman Prize, 83. *Mem:* Am Comp Alliance (mem bd gov, 66-68); Am Music Ctr; Va Comp Guild (mem exec bd, 83-). *Publ:* Auth, Student Composers on the High School Program, Va Music Educ Asn Notes, Vol XXXI, No 4. *Mailing Add:* 2920 Archdale Rd Richmond VA 23235

BLANKERS, LAURENS A(RTHUR)
CELLO, ORGAN

b O'Brien Co, Iowa, Jan 20, 33. *Study:* Univ Northern Iowa, BA(music educ), 55; Univ Colo, Boulder, MMusEd(orch), 69; George Peabody Col, MLS(music), 74. *Pos:* Cond, Sheridan Summer Community Orch, Wyo, 70-72; chorus mem & librn, Nashville Symph Chorus, 73-; cellist & violist, Jackson Symph Orch, 78-; pres, librn, cellist & violist, Nashville Community Orch, 80-; organist, St Matthias Episcopal Church, 83-; owner & mgr, Better Music Type, currently. *Teaching:* Orch dir, N Platte, Nebr Pub Sch, 65-68 & Sheridan, Wyo Pub Sch, 69-72. *Mem:* Nat Sch Orch Asn; Am Guild Organists; Music Educr Nat Conf; Phi Mu Alpha Sinfonia. *Mailing Add:* 1100 16th Ave S Nashville TN 37212

BLANKSTEIN, MARY FREEMAN
VIOLIN

b Rutherfordton, NC. *Study:* Juilliard Sch Music, dipl, 55, BS, 58; Brussels Consv, 58-59; Univ Maine, MM, 75; Jstudied with Emmett Gore, Christine & Edouard Dethier, Arthur Grumiaux, Joseph Fuchs, Erica Morini & others. *Rec Perf:* On Musical Heritage Soc Rec. *Pos:* Violin soloist, Little Orch Soc, New York, 55; asst concertmaster, Am Symph, 65-68, concertmaster, 68-72; co-founder & mem, New York Lyr Arts Trio, 74-; co-founder, Downeast Chamber Music Ctr, Castine, Maine, 77; solo recitalist in US & Europe. *Teaching:* Violin, Prep Div, Juilliard Sch Music, 68-69 & Manhattan Sch Music, 69-; private teacher violin & chamber music, 70-; head instrm dept, Chapin Sch, New York, 73- *Mem:* Am String Teachers Asn. *Mailing Add:* 116-37 Union Turnpike Forest Hills NY 11375

BLATTER, ALFRED WAYNE
EDUCATOR, COMPOSER

b Litchfield, Ill, Dec 24, 37. *Study:* Univ Ill, BM, 61, MM, 65, DMA, 74. *Works:* Fusions, Eugene Ore Symph, 69; A Study in Time and Space, 70, Five Sketches, 70 & A Dream Within A Dream, 72, Media Press Inc; Reflections, Eastern Ill Univ, 74; Suite for Brasses, M M Cole, 75; Fanfare, Brass Press, 77. *Pos:* Hornist & arr, US Army Band, 62-65. *Teaching:* Asst prof music, Marshall Univ, Huntington, WVa, 66-69; asst prof, Univ Ill, 69-76, dir sch music, 76-79; head music dept, Drexel Univ, Philadelphia, 79- *Mem:* Nat Asn Sch Music; Col Music Soc. *Interests:* Music theory, especially instrumentation. *Publ:* Auth, Instrumentation/Orchestration, Longman Inc, 80. *Mailing Add:* 153 Latches Lane Media PA 19063

BLAUSTEIN, SUSAN
COMPOSER

b Palo Alto, Calif, Mar 22, 53. *Study:* Pomona Col, with Karl Kohn, BA(piano & comp), 75; Consv Royal Liege, Belgium, with Henri Pousseur, premiers prix, 76; Brandeis Univ, studied comp with Seymour Shifrin, 77; Yale Sch Music, with Jacob Druckman & Betsy Jolas, MM, 79, MMA, 80. *Works:* The Moon Has Nothing to Be Sad About, 77, Canzo: Due Madrigali di Torquato Tasso, 79, Fantasie (piano solo), 80, Commedia (eight players), 80, APNM; Ricercate: String Quartet #1, comn by Group Contemp Music, 81; To Orpheus: Four Sonnets (SSATB, a cappella), APNM, 82. *Teaching:* Lectr comp, Yale Col, 80-81 & Yale Sch Music, 80-81. *Awards:* Charles Ives Scholar, Am Acad Arts & Lett, 79; BMI Award Student Comp, 79; Harvarad Jr Fel, Soc Fel, Harvard Univ, 82- *Mem:* Guild Comp (mem bd, 82-). *Mailing Add:* 339 Willow St New Haven CT 06511

BLEECKER, RUTH (MERCER)
LIBRARIAN
b Philadelphia, Pa, Mar 18, 21. *Study:* Colo State Univ, BMus, 43; Kans Univ, MMusEd, 48; Rutgers Univ, MLS, 63. *Pos:* Secy & librn music dept, Rutgers Univ, 58-63; cur music, Boston Pub Libr, 63- *Teaching:* Private violin, various Colo & NH towns, 37-58; teacher music, Ordway, Cortex & Monte Vista, Colo Pub Sch, 43-48. *Interests:* Elementary string teaching. *Mailing Add:* 4 Pheasant Circle Milford MA 01757

BLEGEN, JUDITH
LYRIC COLORATURA SOPRANO
b Missoula, Mont. *Study:* Curtis Inst Music; Music Acad West. *Rec Perf:* La Boheme (Puccini); Carmina Burana (Orff); Symphony No 4 (Mahler); Harmonienmesse (Haydn); A Midsummer Night's Dream (Mendelssohn); Peer Gynt Suite (Grieg); Lieder Recital (Richard Strauss & Hugo Wolf). *Roles:* Rosina in The Barber of Seville, Vienna Staatsoper; Melisande in Pelleas et Melisande, Spoleto Fest & Metropolitan Opera; Susanna in The Marriage of Figaro, San Francisco Opera & Edinburgh Fest; Despina in Cosi fan tutte, Covent Garden; Blondchen in The Abduction from the Seraglio, Salzburg Fest; Marzelline in Fidelio & Sophie in Der Rosenkavalier, 83, Metropolitan Opera. *Pos:* Leading sop, Staatsoper, Vienna, 68-70, Metropolitan Opera, San Francisco Opera, Chicago Opera, Hamburg State Opera, Munich State Opera & Paris Opera. *Awards:* Fulbright Scholar; Two Grammy Awards; Grand Prix du Disque, 81. *Mailing Add:* c/o Thea Dispeker 59 E 54th St New York NY 10022

BLEWETT, QUENTIN H
COMPOSER
b Galena, Ill, Apr 11, 27. *Study:* Am Consv, with Leo Sowerby, BM, 51; Manhattan Sch Music, with Nicolas Flagello & Wallingford Riegger, MM, 55. *Works:* Symphony No 1 (orch), 55; Ballad for Orchestra, 57; Dramatic Overture, 60; String Quartet No 2, 69; Cello Sonata, 71; Three Songs for Soprano and Piano, New England Comp Conf, Johnson Col, Vt, 72; Revolutionary Suite (orch), 76. *Mailing Add:* 171 S Broadway Nyack NY 10960

BLICE, CAROLYN MACDOWELL
FRENCH HORN, MANAGER
b Camden, NJ, Mar 18, 39. *Study:* Trenton State Col, BA, 61; Temple Univ, MM, 64. *Pos:* Second horn, Fla Symph Orch, 66-71, third & asst prin horn, 71-83, asst prin horn, 83-; mgr, Orlando Brass Quintet, 71-83. *Teaching:* Music, Pennsauken Pub Sch, NJ, 61-66; adj prof horn, Seminole Community Col, Fla, 67-83, Rollins Col, Fla, 74-83 & Valencia Community Col, Fla, 76-83. *Mailing Add:* Fla Symph Orch PO Box 782 Orlando FL 32802

BLICKHAN, (CHARLES) TIMOTHY
COMPOSER, EDUCATOR
b Quincy, Ill, June 9, 45. *Study:* Northeast Mo State Univ, with Leon Karel & Tom V Ritchie, 63-67; Univ Ill, with Paul Zonn & Ben Johnston, 73-76. *Works:* Nonet Three (perc), 74; Hymn (winds), 74; Variations/Permutations (winds, perc & piano), 74; Speak Softly (sop flute & vibraphone), 74; Bon Mot Finesse (trombone), 75; Dialectics for Orchestra, 75; State of the Art (alto sax), 77. *Teaching:* Asst prof theory, analysis & comp, Northern Ill Univ, 76- *Awards:* Nat Fedn Music Clubs Award, 72. *Mailing Add:* Music Dept Northern Ill Univ De Kalb IL 60115

BLISS, ANTHONY ADDISON
ADMINISTRATOR
b New York, NY, Apr 19, 13. *Study:* Harvard Univ, BA, 36; Univ Va, LLB, 40; Long Island Univ, DFA, 79. *Pos:* Mem law firm, Milbank, Tweed, Hadley & McCloy, New York; exec dir, mem bd dir & exec comt, Metropolitan Opera Asn, pres, 56-67, managing dir & gen mgr, 81-; mem, Nat Coun Arts, 65-68; trustee, US Trust Co & Portledge Sch; chmn bd, Found Am Dance Inc-City Ctr Joffrey Ballet; mem bd dir, NY Found Arts Inc & Am Arts Alliance; co-chmn, Nat Corp Fund for Dance Inc. *Mailing Add:* Met Opera Asn Lincoln Ctr Plaza New York NY 10023

BLISS, MARILYN
COMPOSER, FLUTE & PICCOLO
b Cedar Rapids, Iowa, Sept 30, 54. *Study:* Coe Col, BM, 76; Univ Pa, studied comp with George Crumb & George Rochberg, MA, 78; Berkshire Music Ctr, study with Jacob Druckman. *Works:* Shadowflowers, perf at Tanglewood Fest, 74; Huatzu Hill, perf at Comp Conf, 79; Trio (piano & strings), comn by Philadelphia Art Alliance, 79; Encounter (flute solo), Zalo Publ, 79. *Pos:* Index ed, RILM, Abstr Music Lit, 79- *Awards:* Charles Ives Prize, Am Acad & Inst Arts & Lett, 79; ASCAP Found Grant, 79. *Mem:* BMI; Nat Flute Asn; Col Music Soc; Nat Asn Comp; League Women Comp. *Publ:* Ed, RILM English-language Thesaurus, 83 & RILM Cumulative Index, No 2, 83, RILM Abstr. *Mailing Add:* 34-40 79th St Apt 5E Jackson Heights NY 11372

BLOCH, BORIS
PIANO
b Odessa USSR, Feb 12, 51. *Study:* Odessa Stoliarsky Sch, dipl, 68; Moscow Tchaikovsky Consv, MA, 73, studied with Dm Bashkiros; studied with V L Ashkenazy & W Kempff. *Rec Perf:* Piano Recital, Works of Beethoven, Busoni, Rachmaninov & Liszt, Deutsche Grammophon, 80; Piano Recital,

Works of Schuman, Fouit Cetra, 83. *Pos:* Mem, New York City Young Conct Artists, 76-79. *Teaching:* Piano instr, San Diego State, 78-79, Ariz State Univ, 78 & Sherman Clay, Los Angeles, 78-83. *Awards:* First Prize, Young Conct Artists Int Auditions, 76; Silver Medal Prize, Arthur Rubinstein Compt, 77; Grand prize, Busoni Int Compt, 78. *Bibliog:* Harris Goldsmith (auth), Young Pianist in Debut Recording, High Fidelity, 1/81; Bernard Holland (auth), Recital: Boris Bloch, Pianist, 1/19/81 & Joe Goldberg (auth), To Be Young and a Concert Pianist, 10/18/81, New York Times. *Publ:* Contribr, Gedanken zur Stellung des Pianisten Einst und Jetzt, Berliner Festspiele, 79. *Mailing Add:* 225 Cent Park W New York NY 10024

BLOCH, JOSEPH
PIANO, LECTURER
b Indianapolis, Ind, Nov 6, 17. *Study:* Chicago Musical Col, BMus, 39; Harvard Univ, MA, 46. *Rec Perf:* Moevs (piano sonato), 60, De Menasce (piano), 62 & Seeger (piano), 70, CRI. *Teaching:* Fac mem piano lit, Juillard Sch Music, 48- & Johannesen Int Sch of Arts, 78- *Mem:* Am Liszt Soc (mem adv bd, 75-); Musicians Club New York (mem bd dirs, 82-); European Piano Teachers Asn (mem adv bd, 78-); Delta Omicron. *Mailing Add:* 19 Avon Rd Larchmont NY 10538

BLOCH, ROBERT SAMSON
VIOLIN, COMPOSER
b Evanston, Ill, June 2, 34. *Study:* Univ Chicago, AB, 56, MA, 60; Consv Royal Musique, Brussels, premier prix, 62. *Works:* Improvisings (orch), Minn Civic Orch, 75. *Rec Perf:* Rebel Sonatas, Pathe-Marconi; Schubert & Janacek, Redwood Rec. *Pos:* Violinist, San Francisco Symph, 59-61; violinist & violist, San Francisco Opera, 59-63; prin second violin, Minn Orch, 71-74. *Teaching:* Asst prof music, Cornell Univ, 69-71; prof, Univ Calif, Davis, 64-69 & 74- *Awards:* First Prize, Young Artists Cont, 56; Alfred Herz Mem Fel, Univ Calif, 61; Kranichsfeiner Musikpreis, Darmstadt, Germany, 62. *Mem:* Am Musicol Soc. *Mailing Add:* 4060 Vista Way Davis CA 95616

BLOCK, ADRIENNE FRIED
WRITER
b New York, NY, Mar 11, 21. *Study:* Dalcroze Sch Music, NY, teaching cert, 48; Hunter Col, BA, 59, MA, 69; City Univ New York, PhD, 79. *Pos:* Asst cond, St George's Episcopal Church, 63-69; choral cond, Dalcroze Sch Music, 63- *Teaching:* Mem fac, Dalcroze Sch Music, 48-63; asst prof music, Col Staten Island, 74-79. *Awards:* Award of Merit, Nat Fedn Music Clubs, 79. *Mem:* Col Music Soc; Am Musicol Soc; Women in Music. *Interests:* Women's studies; American music; French 16th century music. *Publ:* Co-ed, Women in American Music: A Bibliography of Music & Literature, Greenwood Press, 79; auth, The Early French Parody Noël, UMI Res Press, 83; Timbre, texte et melodie, Rev Musicol, 83; contribr, New Grove Dict of Music in US (in prep); Introd to Amy Beach's Quintet in F Sharp Minor, Capo. *Mailing Add:* 420 E 23rd St New York NY 10010

BLOCK, GEOFFREY HOLDEN
EDUCATOR, COMPOSER
b Oakland, Calif, May 7, 48. *Study:* Univ Calif, Los Angeles, BA, 70; Harvard Univ, AM, 73, PhD, 79. *Works:* Element of Doubt, Thacher Sch, Ojai, Calif, 80; Tony Lumpkin, Sch Music, Univ Puget Sound, 83. *Pos:* Dir music, Thacher Sch, Ojai, Calif, 77-80. *Teaching:* Asst prof, Sch Music, Univ Puget Sound, 80- *Awards:* Atwater Kent Award in musicol, Univ Calif, Los Angeles, 70; Fulbright Fel, 75-76. *Mem:* Am Musicol Soc. *Interests:* Beethoven's compositional process; American musical theater. *Mailing Add:* 816 N Anderson St Tacoma WA 98406

BLOCK, ROBERT PAUL
EDITOR
b Cincinnati, Ohio, Aug 17, 42. *Study:* Chicago Music Col with Karel Jirak, Roberto Lombardo & Robert Muczynaski, BMus, 64, MMus, 65; Univ Iowa, with Richard Harvig, PhD, 68. *Works:* Incantation & Canzone, 73 & Homage to DS, 73, WIM; Fantasy for Viola Alone, 74, Fantasy for Cello Alone, 74 & Fantasy for Double Bass Alone, 74, Musica Rara. *Teaching:* Priv instr recorder, early music, baroque flutes & renaissance winds, 68- *Mailing Add:* 629 N Linn Iowa City IA 52240

BLOCK, STEVEN D
COMPOSER, CRITIC-WRITER
b New York, NY, Nov 5, 52. *Study:* Antioch Col, BA, 73; Accademia Musicale Chigiana, Italy; Univ Iowa, MA, 75; Stanford Univ, 75-76; Univ Pittsburgh, PhD(comp), 81; Berkshire Music Ctr, Tanglewood, 82. *Works:* Fire Tiger, 77, Darkness Songs, 80, The Tumbler of God, 81, Players, 82, Thelonious Rex, 82, Piano Sonata No 1, 82 & Two Trees: An American Indian Music Drama, 83, Am Comp Alliance. *Pos:* Music critic, Market Square News, 81- *Teaching:* Adj fac theory, Queens Col, 77-78, Univ Pittsburgh, 79-81. *Awards:* Leonard Bernstein Fel, Berkshire Music Ctr, Tanglewood, 82. *Mem:* Pittsburgh Alliance Comp; Soc Music Theory; Am Musicol Soc; Col Music Soc; Am Soc Univ Comp. *Publ:* Auth, George Rochberg: Progressive or Master Forger?, Perspectives, 82-83; The Making of a New Music Ensemble, Perspectives New Music, 82-83 & Musical Am, 83. *Mailing Add:* 524 Pine Line Dr Pittsburgh PA 15237

BLOCKER, ROBERT L
ADMINISTRATOR, PIANO
b Charleston, SC, Sept 4, 46. *Study:* Furman Univ, BA(music), 68; NTex State Univ, MA(music), 70, DMA, 72. *Teaching:* Chmn div fine arts, Brevard Col, 74-76; chmn dept music, Stephen F Austin State Univ, 76-81; dean sch music, Univ NC, Greensboro, 81-83, Baylor Univ, 83- *Mem:* Nat Asn Sch Music;

Tex Asn Music Sch (pres, 80); NC Asn Music Sch (pres, 82); Pi Kappa Lambda (mem bd regents, 81-); Nat Asn Music Exec State Univ. *Publ:* Auth, The Arts: A Basic Component of Education, Am Music Teacher, 81. *Mailing Add:* Sch Music Baylor Univ Waco TX 76798

BLODGETT, DAVID MURRAY
ADMINISTRATOR

b Chicago, Ill, May 13, 44. *Study:* Oberlin Col, BA, 66; Univ Chicago, JD, 69. *Pos:* Pres, Sherwood Music Sch, 82- *Mailing Add:* Sherwood Music Sch 1014 S Michigan Ave Chicago IL 60605

BLOOD, ESTA (DAMESEK)
COMPOSER

b New York, NY, Mar 25, 33. *Study:* Manhattan Sch Music, 42-47; Bennington Col Comp Wkshps with Vivian Fine, Louis Calabro & Henry Brant, summer, 77 & 79. *Works:* Balkan Suite (piano), G Schirmer, 70; A Psalm of David (ten, chor, piano), comn by Cantor Stahl, Temple Beth-Emeth, 73; Jack & the Beanstalk (four instrm, narrator), 73 & Improvisations on Shaker Tunes (three instrm & sop), 75, comn by Winds & Strings; Three Variations for Two Pianos, Eight Hands, Sine Music Co, 78; The Three Sillies (harp & cello with narration), comn by Winn & Creighton, 78; If ... (class guitar), Guitar Found Am, 82. *Teaching:* Private lessons piano, 50- *Awards:* Winner, Int Wind & String Chamber Music Comp Compt for Bulgarian Trio, 79. *Bibliog:* Coral Crosman (auth), Ssh! Mom's at the Piano, Schenectady Union-Star, 1/16/68; Richard Vincent (auth), From Folkdancing to Composing, Albany Times-Union, 1/30/73; Richard Edwards (auth), The Music of Esta Blood, KITE, 1/23/80. *Mem:* ASCAP; Am Music Ctr. *Mailing Add:* 1218 Regent St Schenectady NY 12309

BLOOM, JULIUS
ADMINISTRATOR

b Brooklyn, NY, Sept 23, 12. *Study:* Rutgers Univ, BA, 33; NY Univ, 34-36. *Pos:* Exec dir, Brooklyn Acad Music, 36-57; pres, Brooklyn Music Sch, 56-62; dir conct & lectr, Rutgers Univ, 54-72; exec dir, Nat Inst Music, New York, 57-59 & Carnegie Hall Corp, New York, 60-77; dir corporate develop, Carnegie Hall Corp, 77-79; consultant to univ, conct hall construction & prog, 77- *Teaching:* Dir, Busoni Archives, 83- *Publ:* Auth, The Year in American Music, 1946-47, Allen, Towne & Heath, 47; Cultural Exchange in the American Symphony Orchestra, Basic Books, 67; The Concert World: Where Is It At?, Music & Artists, Vol 2, No 3. *Mailing Add:* 1207 Dorchester Rd Brooklyn NY 11218

BLOOM, LAWRIE
CLARINET, EDUCATOR

b Buffalo, NY, Aug 20, 52. *Study:* Temple Univ, with Anthony M Gigliotti, BM, 74; Ariz State Univ, MM, 76. *Pos:* Clarinet & bass clarinet, Phoenix Symph Orch, 74-76, Lyric Opera Chicago, 76-77, Vancouver Symph Orch, 78-79, Cincinnati Symph Orch, 79-80 & Chicago Symph Orch, 80- *Teaching:* Instr clarinet, DePaul Univ, 80- *Mailing Add:* 1838 Wesley Evanston IL 60201

BLOOM, ROBERT
OBOE & ENGLISH HORN, EDUCATOR

b Pittsburgh, Pa. *Study:* Curtis Inst Music, studied oboe with Marcel Tabuteau. *Pos:* Asst first oboe & solo English horn, Philadelphia Orch, formerly; first oboe, Rochester Phil Orch, formerly; solo oboist, NBC Symph, six yrs; soloist, Bach Aria Group, 47. *Teaching:* Mem fac, Philadelphia Col Perf Arts, currently & New Col Music Fest, Fla, currently; emer prof, Yale Sch Music, currently; mem fac oboe & chamber music, Juilliard Sch, 73- *Mailing Add:* Juilliard Sch Lincoln Ctr New York NY 10023

BLUMENFELD, AARON JOEL
COMPOSER, WRITER

b Newark, NJ, Apr 18, 32. *Study:* Sch Music Educ, NY Univ, 50-52; Juilliard Sch Music, 52-54; Rutgers Univ, Newark, BA, 62; studied jazz piano improvisation with John Mehegan, 68; Rutgers Univ, New Brunswick, MA, 74. *Works:* Ten Blues Pieces for Piano, Or Tav, Israel, 76; Ezk'roh, perf by Berkeley Chamber Orch, 80; Barrelhouse Piano Concerto, perf by Prometheus Orch, 81. *Teaching:* Instr blues improvisation, Rubin Acad, Jerusalem, 76-77; instr piano improvisation, Univ Calif, Berkeley, 79- *Bibliog:* Bob Doerschuk (auth), article, Keyboard Mag, 11/80; Kathy Sheehy (auth), article, Ear Mag W, 7/81; George Estrada (auth), Oakland Tribune, 8/23/82. *Mem:* Am Music Ctr. *Interests:* The improvisation techniques of blues and barrelhouse piano; techniques of avant-garde free improvisation at the piano based on a new perspective of 12 tone harmony. *Publ:* Auth, A Proposal for Spiritual Discipline, Sh'Ma Mag, 73; The Art of Blues & Barrelhouse Piano Improvisation, P-F Publ, 79. *Mailing Add:* 935 Talbot Ave Albany CA 94706

BLUMENFELD, HAROLD
COMPOSER, WRITER

b Seattle, Wash, Oct 15, 23. *Study:* Eastman Sch Music, 41-43; Yale Sch Music, BM, 48, MMus, 49. *Works:* Rilke for Voice & Guitar, Berlin Amerikahaus, 75; Fritzi: Opera-Bagatelle in One Act, 79; Circle of the Eye: Cycle of Eleven Poems after Tom McKeown, Carnegie Recital Hall, 79 & Galaxy, 81; La Vie Anterieure, Spatial Cantata in Three Parts after Baudelaire, New Music Day, St Louis, 81; La Voix Reconnue, Cantata after Verlaine (ten, sop & 12 players), Monday Evening Conct, Los Angeles, 83; La Face Cendree, Cantata after Rimbaud, Voices of Change, Dallas, 83. *Pos:* Dir, Wash Univ Opera Studio, 63-71; artistic dir, Opera Theatre St Louis, 64-68. *Teaching:* Prof music, Wash Univ, St Louis, 51-; vis prof, Queens Col, City Univ New York, 71-72. *Awards:* Award, Am Acad & Nat Inst Arts &

Lett, 77; grant, Nat Endowment Arts, 79. *Bibliog:* David Ewen (auth), American Composers, Putnam, 83. *Mem:* ASCAP; Nat Opera Asn; Am Soc Univ Comp. *Publ:* Auth, Hugo Weisgall and His Gardens of Adonis, Perspectives New Music, 78; English transl, Michael Praetorius, Syntagma Musicum, Vol II, De Capo Press, 81; Postman and the St Louis Season, Opera, Gt Brit, 10/82; Ad Vocem Adorno, Musical Quart, fall 84; many other critical pieces for Opera, Opera J, Los Angeles Times Calendar & Sunday St Louis Post-Dispatch. *Mailing Add:* 34 Washington Terr St Louis MO 63112

BLUMENTHAL, DANIEL HENRY
PIANO

b Landstuhl, WGermany, Sept 23, 52. *US citizen. Study:* Univ Mich, BMus, 75; Juilliard Sch, MMus, 76. *Rec Perf:* Hungarian Dances (Brahms), 75 & Slavonic Dances (Dvorak), 75, Musical Heritage Soc; Rhapsody in Blue & Concerto in F (Gershwin), EMI, 83. *Pos:* Pianist in res, Bargemusic, Brooklyn, NY, 77-83. *Teaching:* Artist in res, Elder Consv, Univ Adelaide, Australia, 82- *Awards:* Fourth Prize, Leeds Int Piano Compt, 81; Second Prize, Geneva Int Music Compt, 82; Fourth Prize, Queen Elizabeth Int Piano Compt Belgium, 83. *Rep:* Judith Kurz Enterprises 215 W 91st St New York NY 10024. *Mailing Add:* 200 W 70th St 921 New York NY 10023

BLUMFIELD, COLEMAN
PIANO

b Chicago, Ill. *Study:* DePaul Univ, with Serge Tarnowsky & Katja Andy; Curtis Inst Music, with Isabella Vengerova, 56; studied with Vladimir Horowitz, 56-58. *Pos:* Artist in res, City of Flint, 62-65; cult officer & perf artist, Off Economic Opportunity, 65-69; perf artist, Ford Motor Co, 69-73; conct pianist, 73- *Awards:* Businessmens Coun Arts Award, Esquire Mag, 70. *Bibliog:* G Plaskin (auth), Secret Career of Vladimir Horowitz, Sunday New York Times Mag, 5/11/80; G Plaskin (auth), Horowitz—A Bibliography, Morrow, 83. *Mem:* Am Fedn Musicians; Cuntis Inst Music Alumni Asn. *Publ:* Auth, Artist Sparked by Flint, Musical J, 63; Study With Horowitz, Clavier, 66. *Rep:* Maxim Gershunoff Attractions Inc 502 Park Ave at 59th St New York NY 10022. *Mailing Add:* 2821 28th St NW Washington DC 20008

BOAL, DEAN
ADMINISTRATOR

b Longmont, Colo, Oct 20, 31. *Study:* Univ Colo, studied piano with Storm Bull, BMus, 53, DMA, 58; Ind Univ, with Bela Nagy, MMus, 56. *Pos:* Dean, Peabody Consv Music, 66-70; pres, St Louis Consv Music, 73-76; dir, KWMU, St Louis, 76-78; vpres & gen mgr, WETA-TV-FM, Washington, DC, 78-83; dir arts & perf, Nat Pub Radio, Washington, DC, 82- *Teaching:* Assoc prof piano, Bradley Univ, 60-66; prof & chmn music dept, State Univ NY, Fredonia, 70-73. *Mem:* Col Music Soc. *Publ:* Coauth, Concepts and Skills for the Piano, Bk I, 69, Bk II, 70, Canyon Press. *Mailing Add:* 6601 Virginia View Ct Bethesda MD 20816

BOARDMAN, DAVID ROBESON
PERCUSSION, COMPOSER

b Houston, Tex, May 15, 56. *Study:* Sch Music, Fla State Univ, BMEd, 78. *Works:* Contortionic Continuum, perf by Fla State Perc Ens, 76 & Univ Ga Perc Ens, 77; Recent Acquisitions, 79, Field Spores, 79, Cowboy Swift Fit, 81, Sandstone Portrait, 81, Lambent Stiletto, 82 & Dance of the Banshees, 82, Jeffco. *Pos:* Dir & perf, Bizarre Arte Ens, Athens, Ga, 75-; timpanist, Athens Symph, 79-; perc, Savannah Symph, 81- *Teaching:* Instr perc, Clarke Cent High Sch, Athens, Ga, 76- *Mem:* Percussive Arts Soc (secy & treas Ga chap, 82-83); Music Teachers Nat Asn; Music Educr Nat Conf; Chamber Music Am. *Mailing Add:* PO Box 6071 Athens GA 30604

BOATWRIGHT, HOWARD LEAKE, JR
COMPOSER, WRITER

b Newport News, Va, Mar 16, 18. *Study:* Sch Music, Yale Univ, MusB, 47, MMus, 48; studied comp with Paul Hindemith. *Works:* Quartet for Clarinet & Strings, Oxford Univ Press, 63; Canticle of the Sun, 63 & The Passion According to St Matthew, 67, E C Schirmer; Serenade for Two Strings & Two Winds, 74 & Variations for Small Orchestra, 77, Oxford Univ Press; Symphony, perf by Syracuse Symph, 79; String Quartet No 2, CRI, 83. *Rec Perf:* Passio D N Jesu Christi (Scarlatti), Overtone, 52 & Lumen, Paris, 58; Four Cantatas (Buxtehude), 54 & Four Cantatas (Rosenmüller), 56, Overtone. *Teaching:* Assoc prof violin, Univ Tex, Austin, 43-45; asst prof music theory, Yale Univ, 48-56; assoc prof, 56-64; prof music, Syracuse Univ, 64-, dean sch music, 64-71. *Awards:* Grand Prix du Disque, Acad Charles le Gros, 58; Fulbright Grants, 59-60 & 71-72; Cert Merit, Yale Sch Music Alumni Asn, 70. *Bibliog:* Janet Knapp (auth), Howard Boatwright, An American Master of Choral Music, Am Choral Rev, 63. *Mem:* ASCAP; Soc Asian Music (bd mem, 60-77); Col Music Soc. *Publ:* Auth, Introduction to the Theory of Music, W W Norton, 56; A Handbook on Staff Notation for Indian Music, Bharatiya Vidya Bhavan, Bombay, 60; ed, Essays Before a Sonata & Other Writings, W W Norton, 62; auth, Paul Hindemith as a Teacher, Musical Quart, 64. *Mailing Add:* 7153 W Genesee St Fayetteville NY 13066

BOBBITT, RICHARD
ADMINISTRATOR, WRITER

Study: Davidson Col, BS; Boston Consv Music, BM; Boston Univ, MM(comp), PhD(music hist & theory); studied comp & theory with Alan Hovhaness, Nicolas Slonimsky, Stefan Wolpe & Walter Piston, musicol with Karl Geiringer & Otto Kinkeldy & arr & comp with Eddie Sauter. *Pos:* Mem exam bd, Schillinger Inst. *Teaching:* Assoc dean, Boston Consv Music, 60-61; vis lectr theory, Northeastern Univ, formerly; dean, Berklee Col Music, currently. *Mem:* Pi Kappa Lambda; Am Musicol Soc. *Publ:* Auth, Harmonic Technique in the Rock Idiom, Wadsworth; contribr to Yale J Music Theory, Music Rev, Music Educr J & J Res in Music Educ. *Mailing Add:* Berklee Col Music 1140 Boylston St Boston MA 02215

BOBERG, ROBERT MARTIN
EDUCATOR, COMPOSER
b Brooklyn, NY, Nov 7, 33. *Study:* Brooklyn Col, BA, 54; Univ Mich, Ann Arbor, MMus, 58. *Works:* Christ Is Born (SATB & SSA), Carl Fischer, 65; The Computer (SAA, SA & SATB), 68, Take Me To The Moon (musical), 69 & Didn't My Lord Deliver Daniel (SATB), 71, Alfred Music Co; Kyrie (SSA), Pro Art, 77; Chromatic Waltz (two pianos), perf by James & Marlane Fairleigh, 78; Introits, Amens and Benedictions (SATB), Boston Music Co, 81. *Teaching:* Instr vocal & gen music, Jr High Sch, Walled Lake, Mich, 58-66; from asst to assoc prof music, RI Col, 66- *Mem:* Music Educr Nat Conf; RI Music Educr Asn ; Am Choral Dir Asn; Col Music Soc; Am Asn Univ Prof. *Publ:* Auth, Ear Opening Experiences With Rhythm and Pitch, Music Educr Nat Conf J, 12/75. *Mailing Add:* 12 Midway Dr Warwick RI 02886

BOBROW, SANCHIE
COMPOSER, TEACHER
b Brooklyn, NY, Oct 3, 60. *Study:* Douglass Col, Rutgers Univ, BA(music), 81; Aaron Copland Sch Music, Queens Col, City Univ New York, MA(comp), 83; studied with Noel DaCosta, Hugo Weisgall, George Perle, Henry Weinberg & Carl Schachter. *Works:* Little Black Fish, On Stage Children Theatre Co, 81; Our Town (Thornton Wilder) & As You Like It (Shakespeare), Camden Shakespeare Co, 82; Memories and Time (three songs for sop & cello), perf at Buttenwieser Hall, New York, 82. *Pos:* Librn, Int League Women Comp, 79-80; asst to ed, Am Music Ctr Newsletter, 81-82; comp in res, Camden Shakespeare Co, 82. *Teaching:* Instr, Princeton High Sch, 81; adj mem fac music, Aaron Copland Sch, Queens Col, City Univ New York, 82-83. *Mem:* Am Music Ctr; Am Jewish Music. *Interests:* Jewish Music. *Publ:* Auth, The Composers Recording, Am Music Ctr, 81; The Art of Orchestration, Music ... Alive!, Cherry Lane Music Co. *Rep:* 170 Heffernan St Staten Island NY 10312. *Mailing Add:* 170 Heffernan St Staten Island NY 10312

BOCK, EMIL WILLIAM
EDUCATOR, MUSICOLOGIST
b Chicago, Ill, June 25, 17. *Study:* Northwestern Univ, BMus, 38, MMus, 39; State Univ Iowa, PhD(musicol), 56. *Pos:* Concertmaster, Waterloo Symph, currently. *Teaching:* Assoc prof, Univ Northern Iowa, 56-61, prof violin & music hist, 61- *Mem:* Am Musicol Soc; Am String Teachers Asn; Music Libr Asn. *Interests:* Renaissance and baroque music; American and contemporary music; ethnic music, non-western. *Publ:* Auth, The String Fantasies of John Hingeston. *Mailing Add:* Dept Music Univ Northern Iowa Cedar Falls IA 50613

BOCK, RICHARD C
CELLO
b New York, NY, Jan 4, 47. *Study:* City Univ New York, BA, 69. *Rec Perf:* Three Intamezzi for Solo Cello (Bresnick), CRI Rec, 81. *Pos:* Prin solo cellist, Am Symph Orch, 68-70, Maggio Musicale Orch, Florence, Italy, 72-78 & Buffalo Phil Orch, 81- *Mailing Add:* 15 Hodge Buffalo NY 14222

BODA, JOHN
COMPOSER, EDUCATOR
b Boyceville, Wis, Aug 2, 22. *Study:* Kent State Univ, BS; Eastman Sch Music, MM & DMA(comp). *Works:* Sinfonia (orch), 60; Prelude, Scherzo, Postlude (brass quartet), 64; Four Byzantine Etudes (guitar, cornet sonatina & clarinet sonatina); Introduction and Dance (guitar); and many others. *Pos:* Apprentice cond, George Szell & Cleveland Orch, 46-47. *Teaching:* Prof theory & comp, Fla State Univ, 47- *Mailing Add:* 1904 Greenwood Dr Tallahassee FL 32303

BODINE, WILLIS (RAMSEY), JR
ORGAN, EDUCATOR
b Austin, Tex, Nov 15, 35. *Study:* Univ Tex, Austin, with John Boe & Kent Kennan, BMus, 57, with Paul Pisk, MMus, 60; Nordwestdeutsche Musikakademie, Detmold, Ger, 57-59. *Works:* Music for the Parish Eucharist, 58; Break Forth, O Beauteous, Heavenly Light, 66 & Christ, Our Passover (canticle), 70, H W Gray; Kyrie, Sanctus and Benedictus, Agnus Dei, Protestant Episcopal Church, 60. *Pos:* Dir music & organist, First Presby Church, Gainesville, Fla, 61- *Teaching:* Prof music, Univ Fla, Gainesville, 59- *Awards:* Fulbright Fel, Germany, 57-59. *Bibliog:* Lee Prater Yost (auth), Carillon: Colossus of Keyboard Instruments, Clavier, 11/81. *Mem:* Am Musicol Soc; Organ Hist Soc; Guild Carillonneurs North Am; Am Music Teachers Asn; Presby Asn Musicians. *Mailing Add:* 326 Music Bldg Univ Fla Gainesville FL 32607

BOE, DAVID S
EDUCATOR, ORGAN
b Duluth, Minn, Mar 11, 36. *Study:* St Olaf Col, BA, 58; Syracuse Univ, MMus, 60; Hochschule Musik, Frankfurt am Main, 60-61; study organ with Arthur Poister & Helmut Walcha & harpsichord with Maria Jaeger & Gustav Leonhardt. *Rec Perf:* The Organs of Oberlin, Gasparo, 82. *Teaching:* Asst prof music, Univ Ga, 61-62; from asst prof to prof & dean, Consv Music, Oberlin Col, 62- *Mem:* Pi Kappa Lambda (nat vpres, 82-); Nat Asn Sch Music (secy, 82-). *Mailing Add:* Consv Music Oberlin Col Oberlin OH 44074

BOEHLE, WILLAM RANDALL
EDUCATOR
b Waxahachie, Tex, July 1, 19. *Study:* Hardin-Simmons Univ, BM, 41; La State Univ, MM, 48; Univ Iowa, PhD, 54. *Teaching:* Prof theory & comp, Chadron State Col, 49-60 & Univ NDak, 60- *Mem:* Soc Music Theory; Col Music Soc; Music Teachers Nat Asn (Nebr state pres, 56-60, nat chmn student activ, 59-65); Music Educr Nat Conf. *Mailing Add:* 406 22nd Ave S Grand Forks ND 58201

BOEHM, MARY LOUISE
PIANO, LECTURER
b Sumner, Iowa, July 25, 28. *Study:* Northwestern Univ, BM; Univ Nebr, Lincoln, MM; private study with Robert Casadesus, Paris & Walter Gieseking, Saarbrücken, Germany. *Rec Perf:* Concerto C# minor (piano & orch), Prelude & Fugue (piano & orch), Concerto C major (Moscheles), Effusio Musica (Kalkbrenner), Concerto (violin & piano) (Pixis), Etudes Op 125 (Hummel), Quintet & Foote Quintet (Beach) & Nocturnes (John Field), Vox/Turnabout. *Pos:* Pianist, concerts in Am, Europe, South Am, currently. *Teaching:* Asst prof piano, Peabody Col, formerly; assoc prof piano, Wesleyan Col, currently. *Awards:* Woolley Fel; Fulbright Travel Grant, Inst Int Educ. *Mem:* Sonneck Soc; Am Liszt Soc; Bohemians; Sigma Alpha Iota. *Interests:* Music for the early pianofortes; performance practices of classic-early romantic; American music at the turn of the century. *Rep:* Artist Mgt 84 Prospect Ave Douglaston NY 11363. *Mailing Add:* 210 Riverside Dr New York NY 10025

BOERLAGE, FRANS T
STAGE DIRECTOR, EDUCATOR
b Bussum, Netherlands, Oct 1, 30. *Study:* Univ Amsterdam, BLL, 50; Webber Douglas Sch Singing & Dramatic Art, London, dipl, 54. *Rec Perf:* Perf, opera co in Holland, Spain, Poland, S Africa, South Am, Can, Seattle, Portland, Cincinnati, Philadelphia, Honolulu, Milwaukee, San Antonio & others. *Pos:* Res stage dir, Netherlands Opera, 52-69; TV dir, AVRO TV, Holland, 63-70; res stage dir, Seattle Opera, 63-72. *Teaching:* Stage dir & coach, Studio Netherlands Opera, 63-70; stage dir & prof, Univ Southern Calif Opera, Los Angeles, 74- *Mem:* Am Guild Musical Artists. *Publ:* Auth, The Lobby, Chanteleer Theater, London, 62; The Enemy Moves In, 63 & Der Schauspieldirektor, 64; AVRO TV, Holland; Chambre Sepazee, Holland, 67; La Clemenza di Tito, 83, Univ Southern Calif Opera. *Mailing Add:* 427 Ocean Ave #7 Santa Monica CA 90402

BOGARD, CAROLE CHRISTINE
SOPRANO
b Cincinnati, Ohio, June 25, 36. *Study:* Univ Calif, Berkeley; studied with Amy C MacMurray. *Rec Perf:* Songs (Dominic Argento), Holland, 78; Songs (John Duke), 79; rec on RCA, Vox & Cambridge. *Roles:* Despina in Cosi fan tutte, San Francisco Opera, 65; Poppea in Coronation of Poppea, Netherlands Opera, 71; Trial of Mary Lincoln, NET Opera, New York, 72; Micaela in Carmen; Aldimira in L'Erismena; Violante in Finta giardiniera; Susanna & Cherubino in Le Nozze di Figaro. *Pos:* Conct appearances throughout Europe & with Smithsonian Chamber Players, 76- *Mailing Add:* c/o Cambridge Artists 124 Irving St Framingham MA 01701

BOGDANOFF, LEONARD
VIOLA
b Philadelphia, Pa, June 14, 30. *Study:* Settlement Music Sch, Philadelphia. *Pos:* Violist, Air Force Symph Washington, DC, 51-53; asst first violist, New Orleans Symph, 54-55; violist, Philadelphia Orch, 55- *Mailing Add:* Philadelphia Orch 1420 Locust St Philadelphia PA 19102

BOGGS, MARTHA DANIEL
EDUCATOR, CLARINET
b Abilene, Tex, July 4, 28. *Study:* Hardin-Simmons Univ, BM, 48, MM, 61; Univ Tex, Austin, 67-74. *Pos:* Prin clarinet, Abilene Phil Orch, 51- *Teaching:* Asst prof woodwinds & music lit, Hardin-Simmons Univ, 61- *Mem:* Int Clarinet Soc; Nat Asn Col Wind & Perc Instr; Tex Music Educr Asn. *Publ:* Auth, Program Notes, Abilene Phil Orch, 81- *Mailing Add:* 2654 Garfield Abilene TX 79601

BOGIN, ABBA
MUSIC DIRECTOR, PIANO
b New York, NY, Nov 11, 25. *Study:* Curtis Inst Music, prof dipl, 49. *Rec Perf:* Complete Sonatas for Cello & Piano (Beethoven), 55 & Complete Sonatas for Cello & Piano (Brahms), 56, Period Records; Original Cast Album (Greenwillow), RCA Rec, 80; Sonata for Viola & Piano (Bax), Musical Heritage Rec, 79. *Pos:* Conct pianist, soloist, 47-; res cond, Am Symph Orch, 72-77; music dir, Tappan Zee Chamber Players, 72-; dir music prog, NY State Coun Arts, 73-75; assoc music dir, Mohawk Trail Conct, Mass, 76- *Awards:* Walter W Naumburg Found Award, 47; Philadelphia Orch Youth Award, 47. *Mem:* Am Guild Musical Artists (nat treas, 50-55); Bohemians; Mohawk Trail Conct, Mass, (assoc music dir, 76-). *Rep:* Raymond Weiss Artists Mgt 300 W 55th St New York NY 10019. *Mailing Add:* 838 West End Ave New York NY 10025

BOGIN, MASAKO YANAGITA See Yanagita, Masako

BOGNAR, DOROTHY MCADOO
EDUCATOR, LIBRARIAN
b Atlanta, Ga, June 23, 44. *Study:* Univ Calif, Santa Barbara, BM, 66; Univ Calif, Berkeley, MM, 68, MLS, 69. *Pos:* Head music librn, Univ Conn, 69- *Mem:* Music Libr Asn (vpres New England chap, 71-72, pres, 72-74, mem-at-lg, 82-84); Int Asn Music Libr. *Publ:* Coauth, Management Review and Analysis Program Report, Univ Conn, 74; The Management Review and Analysis Program at the University of Connecticut, J Acad Librarianship, 7/75; ed, What's the Score on New England Music Library Association?, 80 & Directory of Music Libraries and Collections in New England, 6th ed, 81, Music Libr Asn New England Chap. *Mailing Add:* PO Box 309 Storrs CT 06268

BOGORAD, JULIA (ANNE)
FLUTE & PICCOLO
b Washington, DC, Jan 22, 55. *Study:* Oberlin Consv, 72-74; Ind Univ, BMus, 74-76; Yale Univ, with Marcel Moyse, 76-77. *Pos:* Prin flute, St Paul Chamber Orch, 77- *Awards:* Best Rec Chamber Music, Grammy Award, 78. *Mailing Add:* 797 Lincoln Ave St Paul MN 55105

BOGUE, LAWRENCE
EDUCATOR
Study: Univ Wash, BFA; Juilliard Sch Music, MS; studied voice with Carlo Tagliabue, Lina Pagliughi, Mack Harrell, John Anello, Richard de Young & operatic act with Hans Wolmut. *Roles:* Impresario in Impresario, Educ TV. *Pos:* Performer, conct, recital, oratorio, opera & contemp music prog throughout US, Europe & Japan; soloist, Stravinsky Fest, Lincoln Ctr, Marlboro Music Fest & Bach Fest Buffalo. *Teaching:* Mem fac, Univ Buffalo, State Univ NY, Am Acad Vocal & Dramatic Art & privately, Japan, formerly; mem fac voice, New England Consv Music, currently. *Mailing Add:* New England Consv Music 290 Huntington Rd Boston MA 02115

BOGUSZ, EDWARD
BASS, EDUCATOR
Roles: Dr Bartolo in The Barber of Seville, 79, Dr Bartolo in The Marriage of Figaro, 81 & Sir Toby Belch in Twelfth Night, 81, Philadelphia Opera Theater. *Pos:* Bass, Des Moines Opera, Wilmington Opera, Philadelphia Music Theatre, Pennsylvania Opera Theatre, Fest Lirico Int Barga, San Francisco Opera, Miss Opera & Wolf Trap Fest. *Teaching:* Mem fac voice, Temple Univ, currently. *Mailing Add:* Music Dept Temple Univ Philadelphia PA 19122

BOHRNSTEDT, WAYNE R
COMPOSER, EDUCATOR
b Onalska, Wis, Jan 19, 23. *Study:* Univ Wis; Univ Mich; Northwestern Univ, with Albert Noelte & Robert Delaney, BM, MM; Eastman Sch Music, with Herbert Elwell & Howard Hanson, PhD. *Works:* Romantic Overture, 51; The Necklace (chamber opera); Mass for the People; Trumpet Concerto; Symphony No 1; Concertino for Timpani, Xylophone and Orchestra; Concertino for Trombone and Strings. *Teaching:* Fac mem, Northwestern Univ, 46-47; from asst prof to assoc prof, Bowling Green State Univ, 47-53; from assoc prof to prof, Univ Redlands, dir sch music, 68-, dean div fine arts, 72-79. *Awards:* First Prize, Oppenheimer Cont Ohio Comp, 51 & Nat Fedn Music Clubs, 51. *Mailing Add:* Sch Music Univ Redlands Redlands CA 92373

BOILES, CHARLES LAFAYETTE
EDUCATOR, WRITER
b Ada, Okla, June 15, 32. *Study:* Juilliard Sch Music, BS, 56; Tulane Univ, PhD, 69. *Works:* El Hechicero, Ballet Nac Mex, 64. *Pos:* Ethnomusicologist, Inst Antropologia Univ Veracruzana, Jalapa, Veracruz, Mex, 63-67; contribr, LaPalabra Hombre, Yearbk for Inter-Am Musical Res, J Soc Ethnomusicol & Musique Jeu. *Teaching:* Assoc prof ethnomusicol, Ind Univ, Bloomington, 69-76; prof, Univ Montreal, 76- *Awards:* Jaap Kunst, Soc Ethnomusicol, 66. *Mem:* Soc Ethnomusicol; Int Coun Traditional Music. *Interests:* Ethnomusicology of the Americas; comparitive semiology of world music. *Publ:* Auth, Tepehua Thought-song, Ethnomusicol, 67; Man, Magic & Musical Occasions, Col Press, 78; A Paradigmatic Test of Acculturation, Cross-cultural Perspectives Music, 82; Processes of Musical Semiosis, Int Coun Trad Music Yearbk, 83. *Mailing Add:* 590 Bloomfield #27 Outremont PQ H2V 3R8 Canada

BOLCOM, WILLIAM ELDEN
EDUCATOR, COMPOSER
b Seattle, Wash, May 26, 38. *Study:* Univ Wash, 49-55, BA, 58; Paris Consv, 59-61 & 64-65; Mills Col, MA, 61; Stanford Univ, DMA, 64. *Works:* Black Host (organ, tape & perc), Jobert, 67; Sessions I-IV (chamber music), perf in Berlin, Paris & New York, 65-67; Frescoes (two pianos), CBC, Toronto; Commedia, perf by St Paul Chamber Orch, 71; Piano Concerto, E B Marks, 76; Symphony for Chamber Orch, perf by St Paul Chamber Orch, 79; Songs of Innocence and of Experience, perf by Stuttgart Opera. *Rec Perf:* 12 Etudes (Bolcom), Advance, 66; Heliotrope Bouquest, 70 & Piano Music of George Gershwin, 73, Nonesuch; Accompaniment to wife Joan Morris (ms), Nonesuch, CBS, RCA & Arabeske, 74-; Pastimes and Piano Rags, 74 & Piano Music (Milhaud), Nonesuch; Piano Quartet, CRI, 81; Piano Concerto (Bolcom), Pantheon, 82; Violin & Piano Works, Nonesuch, 83. *Teaching:* Adj asst prof, Univ Wash, 65-66; from lectr to asst prof, Queens Col, City Univ New York, 66-68; vis critic in musical theater, Yale Drama Sch, 68-69; freelance comp, arr & writer, New York, 69-73; from asst prof to prof, Univ Mich, Ann Arbor, 73- *Awards:* Guggenheim Fel, 64 & 68; Nat Endowment Arts Grant, 71, 74, 78 & 82; Koussevitzky Found Grant, 74; and others. *Mem:* Am Music Ctr (mem bd dir, 81-83); Am Comp Alliance. *Publ:* Coauth (with R Kimball), Reminiscing with Sissle and Blake, Viking, 73; auth, Ragtime, 73 & coauth (with R Kimball), James P Johnson & Fats Waller, 73, In: New Grove Dict of Music & Musicians; auth, articles in Musical Newsletter, 78 & 80. *Rep:* Shaw Concts 1995 Broadway New York NY 10024. *Mailing Add:* 3080 Whitmore Lake Rd Ann Arbor MI 48103

BOLDREY, RICHARD (LEE)
CONDUCTOR, PIANO
b Richmond, Ind, Dec 12, 40. *Study:* Chicago Musical Col, Roosevelt Univ, BMus, 63; studied piano with Dr Rudolph Ganz & Mollie Margolies. *Pos:* Asst cond, Chicago Symph Chorus, 72-77; Opera Midwest, Ill, 79-80; Lyr Opera Chicago, 81-83. *Teaching:* Asst prof, NPark Col, 74-79. *Mailing Add:* 5152 N Lowell Chicago IL 60630

BOLEN, CHARLES WARREN
EDUCATOR, ADMINISTRATOR
b West Frankfort, Ill, Sept 27, 23. *Study:* Northwestern Univ, BME, 48; Univ Rochester, MM, 50; Ind Univ, PhD(music), 54. *Pos:* Consult, Nat Asn Schs Music, 62-, Chancellor's Panel, State Univ NY, 70-72 & Asn State Cols & Univs, 72-; chmn, Mont Arts Coun, 65-; mem arts & humanities comt, Fedn Rocky Mountain States, 66-; mem, President's Adv Comt Arts, 76-81; mem adv bd, Kennedy Ctr Perf Arts, 70- *Teaching:* Instr theory & woodwinds, Eastern Ill State Col, 50-51; assoc prof music & chmn dept, Ripon Col, 54-62; dean sch fine arts, Univ Mont, 62-70; prof music & dean col fine arts, Ill State Univ, 70- *Mem:* Am Musicol Soc; Music Teachers Nat Asn; Music Educr Nat Conf. *Interests:* Baroque music; instrumental wind music. *Publ:* Auth, Equestrian Ballets of the Baroque, Am Music Teacher; Aristocrat or Peasant Musician, J Res Music Educ; What You Can Expect From a College Education, Wis Sch Musician. *Mailing Add:* Col Fine Arts Ill State Univ Normal IL 61761

BOLEN, JANE MOORE
EDUCATOR, CONDUCTOR
b Montgomery Punjab, India, Mar 17, 28; US citizen. *Study:* Erskine Col, AB, 48; Converse Col, MMus, 70; Fla State Univ, PhD(musical), 74. *Works:* Suite for Two Pianos, perf by Beverly Barrs & Jane Bolen, 67; Ballet Suite for Chamber Orchestra, Converse Col Chamber Ens, 70; Dance Suite for Woodwinds, Fla State Univ Ens, 72; Easter Alleluia, Assoc Reformed Presby Choir, 80-81. *Pos:* Exec dir, Greenwood Coun Arts, 76-81. *Teaching:* Piano, privately, 48-66; instr piano & theory, Prep Dept, Converse Col, 66-70; instr theory, Lander Col, 74-77. *Awards:* Pi Kappa Lambda Award, Converse Col, 74. *Mem:* Am Musicol Soc; SC Music Teachers Asn. *Interests:* Johann Christian Bach. *Mailing Add:* 210 W Cambridge Ave Greenwood SC 29646

BOLET, JORGE
PIANO, EDUCATOR
b Havana, Cuba, 1914. *Study:* Curtis Inst Music, with David Saperton, MusB. *Rec Perf:* Piano soundtrack of Song Without End, 60; Carnegie Hall recital, RCA; rec on Remington, Everest, Oiseau Lyre & Vox Rec. *Pos:* Music dir, Gen Hq, US Army, Tokyo, 46. *Teaching:* Instr, Curtis Inst Music, 38-42, head, Piano Dept, 77-; prof music, Sch Music, Ind Univ, 68. *Awards:* Naumberg Prize, 37; Josef Hofmann Award, 38. *Rep:* Columbia Artists 165 W 57th St New York NY 10019. *Mailing Add:* Curtis Inst Music 1726 Locust St Philadelphia PA 19103

BOLITHO, ALBERT GEORGE
EDUCATOR, ORGAN
b Highland Park, Mich, Jan 6, 29. *Study:* Wayne State Univ, BM, 50, MM, 52; Mich State Univ, PhD, 68. *Teaching:* Chmn music dept, Henry Ford Community Col, 56-67; prof music, Albion Col, 67- *Publ:* Auth, Organ Tour, 1977, Music—Am Guild Organists-Royal Can Col Organist Mag, 78; The Quality of Music, J Church Music, 80; coauth, Ann Arbor Keyboard Institute, Music—Am Guild Organists-Royal Can Col Organists Mag, 81; ed, Worship, Music and the Arts, Mag Mich Methodist Musicians and Clergy, 83. *Mailing Add:* 917 Maple Albion MI 49224

BOLLE, JAMES D
COMPOSER, CONDUCTOR
b Evanston, Ill, July 26, 31. *Study:* Harvard Univ, 49-51; studied with Darius Milhaud, 50-52; Antioch Univ, BA, 57; Northwestern Univ, MM, 68; Franklin Pierce Col, DHL, 83. *Works:* Cantata (based on texts of Christopher Smart), 68 & Oil of Dog (opera), 72, Monadnock Music; God Forbid That Those Who Have Sucked Bostonian Breasts (vocal work), Evening Length, Boston, 78; Woodwind Quintet (capriccio), 80; Brass Quintet (capriccio), 80. *Rec Perf:* Serenade No 10 (Mozart), 71 & Concerti Grossi (Geminiani-Corelli), 74, Musical Heritage Soc; Symphonies (Haydn), Titanic, 81-; Armide (Lully), Centaur, 83. *Pos:* Dir, Univ Saskatchewan Jubilee Fest, 59; dir & founder, Chicago Community Music Found, 61-67; Monadnock Music, 66- & NH Symph, 73- *Mailing Add:* Main St Francestown NH 03043

BOLTER, NORMAN HOWARD
TROMBONE, EDUCATOR
Study: New England Consv Music; Berkshire Music Ctr; studied trombone with John Swallow & Steven Zellmer. *Rec Perf:* On Sine Qua Non, Columbia & Nonesuch. *Pos:* Prin trombone, Springfield Symph, formerly, Boston Ballet, formerly & Opera Co Boston Orchs, formerly; mem, Cambridge Brass Quintet, formerly, Empire Brass Quintet, 75-80, Boston Symph Orch, 75- & Boston Pops, 75- *Teaching:* Mem fac, Boston Univ, currently; instr trombone, New England Consv Music, currently. *Awards:* C D Jackson Prize, Berkshire Music Ctr, 74; Naumberg Chamber Music Prize, 76. *Mailing Add:* New England Consv Music 290 Huntington Rd Boston MA 02115

BOLZ, HARRIETT (HALLOCK)
COMPOSER, WRITER
b Cleveland, Ohio. *Study:* Cleveland Inst Music, 28; Case Western Reserve Univ, BA(music), 33; Ohio State Univ, MA(comp), 58; private study comp with Leo Sowerby & Paul Creston. *Works:* That I May Sing! (with organ), Sam Fox Publ Co, 70; Duo Scherzando (for trumpet & piano), Harold Branch Publ Inc, 76; Episode For Organ, 79 & Narrative Impromptu For Harp, 79, Arsis Press; Floret—A Mood Caprice for Piano, 80, Capital Pageant (piano four-hands), 80 & How Shall We Speak? (SATB with organ), 81, Sisra Publ. *Teaching:* Private piano and organ teaching. *Awards:* First Prize, Comp Cont, Phi Beta Nat, 68, Bicentennial Music Comp, 76 & Mary Haubiel Comp, 80, Nat League Am Pen Women. *Mem:* Nat League Am Pen Women; ASCAP; life mem, Ohio Fedn Music Clubs; Int League Women Comp. *Publ:* Auth, Sing Unto the Lord A New Song!, 12/78, Old and Ever New, 1/79, Music Markets, 11/79, Notational Nuance, 1/80 & Orchestral Polyphony, 2/80, Pen Woman Mag. *Mailing Add:* 3097 Herrick Rd Columbus OH 43221

BONACINI, RENATO
VIOLIN, EDUCATOR
Study: Paganini Consv, Genoa, Italy, MMus, dipl(comp). *Pos:* Asst cond & concertmaster, Hartford Symph; concertmaster, RCA Victor Orch & Brooklyn Phil; soloist with orchs in US, Europe, South Am & Can; cond, Conn String Orch, 68- *Teaching:* Mem fac, Palestrina Consv, Escuela Superior Musica, Brooklyn Sch Music & Quartet Prog, Troy, NY, summers 75-; prof violin & ens, Hartt Sch Music, Univ Hartford, 62-; vis lectr chamber groups, Univ Conn, currently. *Mailing Add:* Hartt Sch Music Univ Hartford West Hartford CT 06117

BONAZZI, ELAINE
MEZZO-SOPRANO
b Endicott, NY. *Study:* Eastman Sch Music, BM; studied with Jennie Tourel & Aldo Di Tullio. *Rec Perf:* Le Rossignol (Stravinsky) & Cantata 198 (Bach), Columbia; Songs of Erik Satie, Candide; Silver Lake (K Weil), Nonesuch; La Pietra dal Pakagone (Rossini), Vanguard; New People (Colgrass), Grenadilla; Hera Hung From the Sky (Ivey), CRI. *Roles:* Baba the Turk in The Rake's Progress, Santa Fe Opera, 68; Dorabella in Cosi fan tutte, Opera Int de Bellas Artes, Mexico City, 70; Foreign Singer in Postcard from Morocco, Washington Opera, 79; Lulu in Countess Geschwitz, Netherlands Opera, 79; Frau von Luber in Silverlake, New York City Opera Co, 80; Lulu in Countess Geschwitz, 81 & Pique Dame in Pique Dame, 82, Netherlands Opera; Mother Marie in Dialogue of the Carmelites, Baltimore Opera, 84. *Pos:* Performer, New York City Opera Co, Dallas Opera, Washington Opera, Cincinnati Opera, Netherlands Opera & others & Spoleto, Mostly Mozart, Caramoor & Berlin Festivals; soloist with major US symph incl New York Phil, Philadelphia Orch, Cleveland Orch & Am Symph; recitals & operas on PBS, CBS, ABC & NBC. *Teaching:* Mem fac voice, Peabody Consv, 72- *Awards:* William Matheus Sullivan Grant. *Rep:* Lew & Benson Artists Rep 204 W 10th St New York NY 10014. *Mailing Add:* 650 West End Ave New York NY 10025

BOND, VICTORIA
COMPOSER, CONDUCTOR
b Los Angeles, Calif. *Study:* Univ Calif, with Ingolf Dahl & Ellis Kohs, BM; Juilliard Sch, with Roger Sessions & Vincent Persichetti, MM, 75, DMA, 77. *Works:* Recitative for English Horn & String Trio, 75 & Suite Miniature, 75, Theodore Front; Conversation Piece (viola & vibraphone), 75 & From an Antique Land (song cycle), 76, Seesaw Music; Equinox (suite), Evergreen, Colo, 78; Tarot (chorus & perc), Fairmont Col, 78; Peter Quince at the Clavier (voice & piano), New York, 78. *Rec Perf:* Two American Contemporaries; Twentieth Century Cello; Sonata for Cello. *Pos:* Asst cond, Contemp Music Ens, Juilliard Sch, 73-77, orch, 75-77; music dir & cond, New Amsterdam Symph, 77-78 & Pittsburgh Youth Orch, 78-80; asst cond, Pittsburgh Symph, 78-80; guest cond with maj orchs in US. *Awards:* Victor Herbert Cond Award, Juilliard Sch, 75; ASCAP Awards, 77-82. *Mem:* ASCAP; Mu Phi Epsilon; Am Symph Orch League; Am Fedn Musicians. *Mailing Add:* 349 W 71st St New York NY 10023

BONDE, ALLEN
COMPOSER, EDUCATOR
b Newton, Wis, Nov 22, 36. *Study:* Lawrence Univ, with James Ming; Cath Univ Am, with George Thaddeus Jones & Robert Hall Lewis. *Works:* Fantasia (piano & orch); Romance (viola & piano), 61; Contrasts (violin & piano), 61; Romance (violin & piano), 65; Umore, 71; Five Preludes (guitar), 72; Sonus II (two pianos), 73. *Teaching:* Fac mem, Hood Col, 63-71; assoc prof theory, analysis & comp, Mt Holyoke Col, 71- *Awards:* Rockefeller Found Grant, 68; Mt Holyoke Col Fac Grant, 72. *Mailing Add:* Dept Music Mt Holyoke Col South Hadley MA 01075

BONINO, MARYANN
ADMINISTRATOR, EDUCATOR
b Los Angeles, Calif. *Study:* Mt St Mary's Col, Calif, BA, 61; Univ Southern Calif, MA, 63, PhD, 71. *Pos:* Prog Producer, KUSC-FM, Los Angeles, 79-; exec dir, DaCamera Soc & Chamber Music Historic Sites. *Teaching:* Prof music hist, theory & piano, Mt St Mary's Col, Calif, 66- *Awards:* Woodrow Wilson Found Fel, 61-62. *Mem:* Am Musicol Soc; Asn Col, Univ & Community Arts Adminr; Western Alliance Arts Adminr; Chamber Music Am. *Interests:* Early 17th century Italian vocal music; life and works of Don Severo Bonino. *Publ:* Auth, Polemic & Compromise: Bonini's View of the Camerata, Ressegna del Rinascimento Musicale, 77; ed, Severo Bonini's Discorsi E Regole, Bringham Young Univ Press, 79; auth, Severo Bonini, In: New Grove Dict of Music & Musicians, 6th ed, 80. *Mailing Add:* Mt St Mary's Col 12001 Chalon Rd Los Angeles CA 90049

BONTRAGER, CHARLES E
MUSIC DIRECTOR & CONDUCTOR
Study: Studied with Schippers, Louis Lane, Michael Semanitzky, Richard Lert & Elmer Thomas. *Pos:* Orch & choral preparer, Manon Lescaut, Spoleto Fest, Italy, 73 & 74, co-cond, Beethoven Marathon Concert, 73 & 74; music dir, Hamilton Symph, Ohio, 73-78 & Cent Ky Youth Music Soc, 76-79; founder & cond, Camarata Singers, Cincinnati, formerly; guest cond, Trieste Symph, Spoleto Fest Orch, Nat Orch Asn, New York, Cincinnati Chamber Orch, Lafayette Symph, Ind, Mansfield Symph, Ohio & Mod Music Master's 25th Anniversary Nat Conv; music dir & cond, Springfield Symph Orch & Springfield Regional Opera Co, 78- *Teaching:* Adj prof instrm cond, Col-Consv Music, Univ Cincinnati, 72-76. *Mailing Add:* 1675 E Seminole Suite G200 Springfield MO 65804

BOOKSPAN, MARTIN
ADMINISTRATOR, WRITER
b Boston, Mass. *Study:* Boston Music Sch; Harvard Col, BS, 47. *Pos:* Music dir, sta WBMS, Boston, 46-51; dir serious music, sta WCOP & WBZ, Boston, 51-56; music & prog dir, sta WQXR, New York, 56-67; freelance writer & broadcaster, 68-; vpres & A&R dir, Moss Music Group, 83- *Teaching:* Adj asst prof symph, NY Univ, 76- *Awards:* Distinguished Serv to Music, Nat Asn Am Comp & Cond, 74; Lett Distinction, Am Music Ctr, 77; Citation of Merit, Nat Asn Comp USA, 82. *Mem:* Bohemians; Nat Music Coun; Am Music Ctr. *Publ:* Auth, 101 Masterpieces of Music & Their Composers, Doubleday, 68 & Dolphin, 73; contribr, The New York Times Guide to Recorded Music, Macmillan, 68; auth, Consumer Reports Reviews Classical Records, Consumer Reports, 72 & 80; coauth, Zubin: The Zubin Mehta Story, Harper & Row, 78; Andre Previn: A Biography, Doubleday, 81. *Mailing Add:* c/o ASCAP 1 Lincoln Plaza New York NY 10023

BOOKSPAN, MICHAEL L
PERCUSSION, EDUCATOR
b Brooklyn, NY, Sept 7, 29. *Study:* Juilliard Sch, with Morris Goldenberg, BS, 53; private study with Jimmie Lent, Fred Albright & Saul Goodman. *Rec Perf:* Concerto for Solo Percussionist, comn by Robert Sudernurg & perf by Philadelphia Orch, 79 & 80. *Pos:* Timpanist & xylophone soloist, US Air Force Band, San Antonio, Tex, 46-48; perc, Little Orch Soc New York, 51-53 & New York City Ballet Orch, 51-53; perc & timp, Philadelphia Orch, 53-, prin perc & assoc timp, 72- *Teaching:* Instr perc, Philadelphia Col Performing Arts, 59-; instr orch repertoire, Curtis Inst Music, 80- *Awards:* C Hartman Kuhn Award, Philadelphia Orch Asn, 81. *Mem:* Percussive Arts Soc. *Mailing Add:* 300 Valley Rd Havertown PA 19083

BOONE, CHARLES N
COMPOSER
b Cleveland, Ohio, June 21, 39. *Study:* Acad Music, Vienna, studied with Karl Schiske, 60-61; Univ Southern Calif, BM, 63; San Francisco State Col, MA, 68; with Ernst Krenek & Adolf Weiss. *Works:* 2 Landscapes (orch) & The Yellow Bird (orch), 67; The Edge of the Land (orch) & Shadow (orch & solo oboe), 68; Chinese Texts (orch & solo sop), 70; Raspberries (three drummers), 74; Linea Meridiana (eight instrm), 75; Shunt (three drummers), 78; Streaming (solo flute), San Francisco, 79; and many others;. *Pos:* Music writer, San Francisco Examiner, 65 & Oakland Tribune, 70; coordr, Mills Col Perf Group & Tape Music Ctr, 66-68; founder, BYOP Conct. *Teaching:* Comp in res, City Berlin, German Acad Exchange Serv, 75-76. *Awards:* Grant, Nat Endowment Arts. *Mem:* San Francisco Comp Forum (chmn, 64-66). *Mailing Add:* 2340 Pacific Ave Apt #204 San Francisco CA 94115

BOONE, CLARA LYLE See de Bohun, Lyle

BOONSHAFT, PETER LOEL
MUSIC DIRECTOR
b Abington, Pa, Feb 7, 58. *Study:* Hartt Sch Music, BMus, 79, MMusEd, 81; Kodaly Musical Training Inst, cert, 81. *Pos:* Music dir, Conn Valley Youth Wind Ens, 80- & Metropolitan Wind Symph Boston, 82-; adjudicator, Fiesta Int Music Fest, 82- *Teaching:* Fac mem, Hartt Sch Music. *Awards:* Conn Gen Corp Fel, 80. *Mem:* Nat Band Asn; Nat Asn Col Wind & Perc Instr; Music Educr Nat Conf; NY Brass Conf Scholarships; Conn Music Educr Asn. *Publ:* Auth, Repertoire for Rent, Instrumentalist, 82. *Mailing Add:* 236 Oxford St Hartford CT 06105

BOORMAN, STANLEY HAROLD
EDUCATOR
b Croydon, England, Aug 28, 39. *Study:* Royal Col Music, London, ARCM; King's Col, Univ London, AKC, 67, BMus, 67, MMus, 68, PhD, 76; Cambridge Univ, MA, 72. *Teaching:* Lectr music, Univ Nottingham, England & Univ Cambridge, England; assoc prof, Univ Wis, Madison, formerly & NY Univ, currently. *Awards:* Fel, Villa I Tatti, Florence, 83-84. *Mem:* Am Musicol Soc; Int Musicol Soc; Royal Musical Asn. *Publ:* Auth, The first edition of the Odhecation A, J Am Musicol Soc, 77; ed, New Edition of Guillaume de Machaut, Oiseau-Lyre, 78; auth, Petrucci at Fossombrone: Some New Editions & Cancels, In: Source Materials and the Interpretation of Music, 81; Limitations and Extensions of Filiation Technique, In: Music in Medieval and Early Modern Europe, 81; ed, Studies in the Performance of Late Medieval Music, Cambridge Univ Press, 83. *Mailing Add:* 227 Highbrook Ave Pelham NY 10803

BOOTH, NANCY
SOPRANO
Roles: Kate in The Ballad of Baby Doe & Frasquita in Carmen, 83, Ariz Opera; La Traviata, Fiordiligi in Cosi fan tutte, 82 & Lauretta in Gianni Schicchi, Univ Ariz Opera Theatre; First Lady in The Magic Flute; Mother in Amahl and the Night Visitors. *Pos:* Featured soloist, Tucson Pops Orch, currently, Univ Ariz Symph & others; performer, chamber music, plays & musicals. *Awards:* Ariz Metropolitan Opera Auditions Winner. *Mailing Add:* Ariz Opera 3501 N Mountain Ave Tucson AZ 85719

BOOTH, PHILIP (SAFFERY EVANS)
BASS
b Washington, DC, May 6, 42. *Study:* Wash & Lee Univ, Va, AB; Eastman Sch Music, with Julius Huehn, 65-66; studied with Todd Duncan & Daniel Ferro. *Rec Perf:* Le Testament De Villon (Ezra Pound) & The Mother of Us All (Virgil Thompson), Fantasy Rec. *Roles:* Stranger in Young Goodman Brown, Lake George Fest, 70; King of Scotland in Ariodante, Kennedy Ctr, 71; Ramfis in Aida; Le Coq d'Or, New York City Opera, 78; Eugene Onegin

& The Magic Flute, Santa Fe Opera Co; The Ring of the Nibelung, Seattle Opera Co; Colline in La Boheme, Florentine Opera, Milwaukee, 83. *Pos:* Soloist, US Army Chorus, formerly; mem, San Francisco Opera, 71-74 & Metropolitan Opera, 75-, Cincinnati Opera Asn, formerly, Houston Opera Studio, formerly & San Diego Opera, formerly. *Awards:* Gramma Fisher Award, Metropolitan Opera Nat Coun Auditions, 70; Kansas City Lyric Award, 70; Nat Opera Inst Award, 72-73. *Mailing Add:* c/o Herbert Barrett Mgt 1860 Broadway New York NY 10023

BOOZER, BRENDA LYNN
MEZZO-SOPRANO
b Atlanta, Ga, Jan 25, 48. *Study:* Sch Music, Fla State Univ, BA & BM, 71; Juilliard Sch Music, 76-79. *Rec Perf:* Falstaff, Deutsche Grammophon, 82. *Roles:* Hansel in Hansel & Gretel, Metropolitan Opera, 79 & 81; Meg Page in Falstaff, Covent Garden Royal Opera House, 82, Paris Opera, 82 & Teatro Communale, Florence, 83; Lola in Cavalleria rusticana, Chicago Opera; Cenerentola in La Cenerentola, Houston Grand Opera; Anna Bolena in Henry VIII, San Diego Opera. *Awards:* Liederkranz winner, 79. *Mem:* Am Guild Musical Artists. *Mailing Add:* c/o Columbia Artists Mgt Inc 165 W 57th St New York NY 10019

BOR, CHRISTIAAN
VIOLIN
b Amsterdam, Netherlands, May 23, 50. *Study:* Private lessons with Tan Bor; Muzieklyceum, Amsterdam, with Herman Krebbers, 64-69; Univ Southern Calif, with Jascha Heifetz, 71-77. *Rec Perf:* Grieg & Saint Saens Sonatas, 79, Saint Saens & Faure Trios, 79 & Piano Trio, Violin & Cello Sonata, Violin & Piano Sonata (Ravel), 81, Pelican Rec; Sonata No 1 and Sonata for Solo Violin (Bartok), CBS, 81. *Pos:* Soloist in recital & chamber music throughout Europe, Middle & Far East, South Am & US, 66- *Awards:* Prix d'Excellance, Muzieklyceum, 69. *Mem:* Reizend Muziekgezelschap Found. *Mailing Add:* PO Box 907 Sitka AK 99835

BORDA, DEBORAH A
ADMINISTRATOR
b New York, NY, July 15, 49. *Study:* Bennington Col, BA, 71; Royal Col Music, 72. *Pos:* Dir tech assistance prog, Mass Coun Arts & Humanities, 73-75; mgr, Boston Musica Viva, 75-77; gen mgr, Handel & Haydn Soc, 77-79; artistic adminr, San Francisco Symph, 79- *Mailing Add:* c/o San Francisco Symph Davies Symph Hall San Francisco CA 94102

BORDEN, DAVID
COMPOSER
b Boston, Mass, Dec 25, 38. *Study:* Boston Univ, with Klaus George Roy; Eastman Sch Music, with Louis Mennini, Bernard Rogers & Howard Hanson, BM, 61, MM, 62; Hochschule Musik, Berlin with Boris Blacher, 65; Berkshire Music Ctr, with Wolfgang Fortner & Gunther Schuller, 66; Harvard Univ, MA, 67; studied with Jimmy Giuffre, Jaki Byard & Robert Moog. *Works:* Concertino for Piano and Orchestra, 60; The Force (orch & sop solo), 62; Trudymusic (orch & piano solo), 67; All-American (band), 67; Variations (band), 68; Counterpoint (harp, cello & flute), 78; and many electronic pieces. *Pos:* Founder, Mother Mallard's Portable Masterpiece Co, 69, Earthquack Rec, 74 & Lameduck Publ Co, 74. *Awards:* Fulbright Scholar; Ford Found Grants; ASCAP Fel; and others. *Mailing Add:* 1191 E Shane Dr Ithaca NY 14850

BORETZ, BENJAMIN AARON
CRITIC-WRITER, EDUCATOR
b New York, NY, Oct 3, 34. *Study:* Brooklyn Col, BA, 54; Brandeis Univ, MFA, 54; Princeton Univ, MFA, 60, PhD, 70. *Works:* Concerto Grosso, perf by Boston Chamber Orch, 55; Violin Concerto, perf by Aspen Fest Orch, 56; String Quartet, perf by Comp String Quartet, 59; Group Variations for Orchestra, Group Contemp Music, 67 & 68; Group Variations for Computer, CRI, 70 & 74; My Chart Shines High Where the Blue Milk's Upset, 78 & Language as a Music, 78-80, Lingua Press. *Pos:* Ed & co-founder, Perspectives New Music, 61-; music critic, The Nation, 62-69. *Teaching:* Asst prof music, NY Univ, 64-69 & Columbia Univ, 69-72; prof & chmn music dept, Bard Col, 73- *Awards:* Award, Ingram Merrill Found, 66; Fels, Fulbright, 71-72 & Coun Humanities, Princeton Univ, 72-73. *Mem:* Founding mem, Am Soc Univ Prof (chmn, 66-68). *Interests:* Criticism, theory, philosophy and social commentary. *Publ:* Co-ed, Perspectives on New Music (four bks), W W Norton, 69-79; Meta-Variations: Studies in the Foundations of Musical Thought, Perspectives New Music, 69-74; Language as a Music, Six Marginal Pretexts for Composition, Lingua Press, 78; If I am a Musical Thinker ..., Station Hill Press, 83. *Mailing Add:* River Rd Barrytown Red Hook NY 12571

BORISHANSKY, ELLIOT (DAVID)
COMPOSER, EDUCATOR
b New York, NY, Mar 17, 30. *Study:* Queens Col, City Univ New York, BA, 51; Columbia Univ, with Otto Luening & Jack Beeson, MA, 58; Univ Mich, with Ross Lee Finney, DMA, 70; Staatliche Hochschule Musik, Hamburg, with Phillipp Jarnach . *Works:* Music for Orchestra, New York Phil, 58; Two Pieces for Unaccompanied Clarinet, 76 & Silent Movie, 76, Media Press; Three Pieces for Piano Solo, Schirmer, 81; Three Mosquitoes Find They Are Reunited After a Convention in Atlantic City, New Jersey, Brass Press & Am Soc Univ Comp J Music Scores, 82. *Rec Perf:* Two Pieces for Unaccompanied Clarinet, Advance Rec. *Teaching:* Prof music theory & comp, Denison Univ, 68- *Awards:* George Gershwin Mem Award, B'nai Brith Hillel Found, 58; Fulbright Grant, 59; MacDowell Colony Fel, 62-64. *Mem:* Am Soc Univ Comp; Am Comp Alliance; BMI. *Publ:* Auth, The Sense of Musical Humor, Am Soc Univ Comp, 83. *Mailing Add:* 403 W Broadway Granville OH 43023

BORNSTEIN, CHARLES ZACHARY
CONDUCTOR & MUSIC DIRECTOR, COMPOSER
b Buffalo, NY, Jan 12, 51. *Study:* Juilliard Sch, BM, 74; Mozarteum, Salzburg, Austria, dipl, 74; studied with Hans Swarowsky, Wien, 74-75; Wiener Meisterkors, dipl, 75. *Works:* Seven songs on Poems by Carl Sandburg (sop & orch), 79-81 & Symphony, John Fitzgerald Kennedy & Martin Luther King in Memoriam (symph orch & two speakers), 78-81, Vandenburg. *Pos:* Asst cond, Am Symph, New York, 71-72 & Juilliard Chamber Orch, summer 73; music dir & prin cond, Newfoundland Symph Orch, Can, 82- *Bibliog:* Boulez & Students, PBS film, WNET, New York, 70; Paula Adamick, interview, Music Mag, Toronto, 8-9/83. *Mem:* ASCAP. *Mailing Add:* Unit 205 693 Windermere London ON N5X 2P1 Canada

BOROK, EMANUEL
VIOLIN
b Tashkent, Russia, July 15, 44; nat US. *Study:* Darzinya Music Sch, Riga; Gnessin Music Sch & Gnessin Inst Music, Moscow, with Michael Garlitsky, MusM, 69. *Rec Perf:* On Advent & Sine Qua Non. *Pos:* Mem, Orch Bolshoi Theater, 69-71; String Quartet Moscow Phil, formerly; asst concertmaster, Moscow Phil, 71-73 & Boston Symph Orch, 74-; concertmaster, Israel Chamber Orch, 73-74 & Boston Pops Orch, currently; soloist, Berkshire Music Ctr, 75, Carnegie Hall, formerly. *Teaching:* Instr violin, Boston Consv, currently & Longy Sch Music, Mass, currently; assoc, Boston Univ, currently. *Awards:* Second Prize, Violin Compt Russ Soviet Repub, 65; Fourth Prize, Violin Compt Soviet Union, 65. *Mem:* Boston Musicians Asn Club. *Mailing Add:* Boston Symph Orch 251 Huntington Ave Boston MA 02215

BOROUCHOFF, ISRAEL
FLUTE & PICCOLO, EDUCATOR
US citizen. *Study:* Juilliard Sch Music. *Rec Perf:* Quintets (Villalobos, Francaix & Downey), 72, Solo Sonatas (Prokofiev & Reinecke), 73, Song for a Dolphin (Downey), 76, Orion Rec; Quintets (Muller), Crystal Recs, 76; Quintets (Reicha), Musical Heritage Recs, 77. *Pos:* Prin flute, St Louis Symph, 58-66 & Chamber Symph Philadelphia, 66-68. *Teaching:* Adj instr flute, Temple Univ, 66-68; assoc prof flute, Univ Wis, Milwaukee, 68-74; prof flute, Mich State Univ, 74- *Awards:* Israel-Am Cultural Found Grant, 55. *Mem:* Nat Flute Asn; Pi Kappa Lambda; Fontana Ens Mich; founder, Flute Guild Mich. *Mailing Add:* 5467 Maple Ridge Dr Haslett MI 48840

BORROFF, EDITH
COMPOSER, EDUCATOR
b New York, NY, Aug 2, 25. *Study:* Am Consv Music, BMus, 46, studied comp with Irwin Fischer, MMus 48; Univ Mich, studied musicol with Louise Cuyler, PhD, 58. *Works:* Sonata for Horn & Piano, King, 66 & Fox, 68; Song Cycle: Modern Love, 80; Marimba Concerto, State Univ NY, 81; Game Pieces (woodwind quintet), perf by Wingra Woodwind Quintet, 82; Piano Trio, perf by Western Arts Trio, 83. *Teaching:* Instr music, Milwaukee-Downer Col, 50-54; teaching fel, Univ Mich, 55-58; from assoc prof to prof & assoc dean, Hillsdale Col, 58-62; assoc prof, Univ Wis, Milwaukee, 62-66; prof, Eastern Mich Univ, 66-72 & State Univ NY, Binghamton, 73-; vis prof, Univ NC, 72-73. *Awards:* Univ Wis Res Grant, 64 & 66; State Univ NY Res Grant, 75-76. *Mem:* Col Music Soc; Am Musicol Soc (midwest chap secy & treas, 68-72); Sonneck Soc; Music Teachers Nat Asn. *Interests:* General history; baroque and American music; liberal arts. *Publ:* Music of the Baroque, Da Capo, 70; Music in Europe & the United States, Prentice-Hall, 71; Notations and Editions, Da Capo, 72. *Mailing Add:* 900 Lehigh Ave Binghamton NY 13903

BORROR, RONALD ALLEN
TROMBONE, EDUCATOR
b Columbus, Ohio, Feb, 18, 42. *Study:* Ohio State Univ, BMus & BScEd, 65; Yale Univ, MusM, 67, MMA, 73, DMA, 78. *Rec Perf:* Music of Mid-1800's, Titanic, 80; Tashi Plays Takemitsu, RCA, 80; Parnassus Plays Works by Wolpe, Davidovsky, Wuorinen, 80 & The Yankee Brass Band, 81, New World; Virgil Thomson: A Portrait Album, Nonesuch, 82; Parnassus Plays Babbitt and Korf, CRI, 83; Trombone Recital (music by American composers), Crystal Rec, 83. *Pos:* Trombone & euphonium, New York City Ballet Orch, 75-; trombonist, Am Brass Quintet, 77-83 & Parnassus, New York, NY, 78-; co-prin trombonist, Am Comp Orch, 78- *Teaching:* Vis instr trombone, NC Sch Arts, 78-; vis lectr, Hartt Sch Music, 80-; lectr, State Univ NY, Stony Brook, 81- *Mailing Add:* 251 W 97th St #1F New York NY 10025

BORTNICK, EVAN N
TENOR
b Jersey City, NJ, May 28, 54. *Study:* Consv Music, Oberlin Col, BM, 77. *Roles:* Rodolfo in La Boheme, Des Moines Metro Summer Fest, 78; Ferrando in Cosi fan tutte, Houston Grand Opera, 79; Tonio in Fille du regiment, Augusta Opera, 80; Cherubino in Rosina, Minn Opera, 80; Nemorino in L'elisir d'amore, Kansas City Lyr Opera, 81; Camille in Merry Widow, Rochester Opera, 82; Uronsky in Anna Varenina, Los Angeles Opera Theater, 83. *Awards:* Sullivan Found Grant, 82. *Mailing Add:* c/o Munro Artists Mgt 344 W 72nd St New York NY 10023

BORWICK, SUSAN HARDEN
ADMINISTRATOR, EDUCATOR
b Dallas, Tex, Feb 12, 46. *Study:* Baylor Univ, BMus(theory & comp), 68, BME, 68; Univ NC, Chapel Hill, with William S Newman, Howard Smither & James W Pruett, PhD(musicol), 72. *Teaching:* Asst prof music, Sch Music, Baylor Univ, Waco, Tex, 72-77, coordr div music lit, hist & church music, 76-77; asst prof theory, Eastman Sch Music, Rochester, 77-82; assoc prof &

chmn dept music, Wake Forest Univ, Winston-Salem, NC, 82- *Awards:* Outstanding Woman Musician, Baylor Univ, 68; Nat Defence Educ Act Fel, 68-71. *Mem:* Am Musicol Soc (secy & treas, 74-); Col Music Soc; Soc Music Theory; Music Libr Asn. *Interests:* Lotte Lenya, Kurt Weill, and Bertolt Brecht; aural perception. *Publ:* Auth, Weill's and Brecht's Theories on Music in Drama, J Musicol Res, 82. *Mailing Add:* 4101 Mill Creek Rd Winston-Salem NC 27106

BÖSZÖRMENYI-NAGY, BELA
PIANO, EDUCATOR
b Satoraljaujhely, Hungary, Apr 9, 12; US citizen. *Study:* Liszt Ferenc Acad, artist dipl, 37; Cath Univ, Szeged, Hungary, PhD, 37; studied piano with Imre Keeri-Szanto & Erno Dohnanyi, comp with Zoltan Kodaly & chamber music with Leo Weiner. *Rec Perf:* Dohnanyis's Variations, Rome, 43; Bartok's 3rd Concerto, Budapest, Prague, Firenze & Chicago, 47; Concerto (Sir Arthur Bliss), Budapest, 48; Concerto I (Rawsthorne), Toronto, 50; Bartok's 3rd Concerto, Toronto, 51; Concerto (Veress), Vancouver, 60. *Teaching:* Prof piano & chamber music, Liszt Acad, 37-48, Royal Consv Toronto, 48-53, Ind Univ, 53-62, Boston Univ, 62-82 & Cath Univ Am, 77-83. *Awards:* Liszt Award, City Budapest, 35-37; Bartok Mem Award, Govt Hungary, 81. *Mem:* Music Teachers Nat Asn; Am Liszt Soc; Artaria Int (pres, currently). *Publ:* Auth, Evaluating Piano Performance, Music J, 59; Federal Aid to the Arts, Portland Rev, 60; Study Abroad?, 64 & Kodaly's Legacy, 67, Clavier. *Mailing Add:* 27 Sunset Dr Sharon MA 02067

BOTTJE, WILL GAY
COMPOSER, FLUTE & PICCOLO
b Grand Rapids, Mich, June 30, 25. *Study:* Juilliard Sch Music, BS, 47, MS, 48; Eastman Sch Music, DMA, 55. *Works:* Altgeld (opera), comn by Southern Ill Univ, 68; Symphony No 7 (tangents), 70, comn by Ill State Univ; Metaphors (wind ens & tape), comn by Wash Univ, 71; Root (chamber opera), comn by Southern Ill Univ Opera Workshop, 72; Chiaroscuros (orch), Indianapolis Symph, 75; From the Winds and Farthest Spaces (multi media), comn by Grand Valley State Col, 76; Scene Changes (13 flutes), comn by Calvin Col, 82. *Teaching:* Private teacher, Grand Rapids, Mich, 47-52; assoc prof, Univ Miss, 55-57; prof theory & comp, Southern Ill Univ, 57-81, emer prof, 81- *Mem:* Am Soc Univ Comp; Am Comp Alliance; Am Soc Univ Prof. *Mailing Add:* 12871 Lakeshore Rd Grand Haven MI 49417

BOUCHARD, LINDA
COMPOSER, CONDUCTOR
b Val-D'or, Que, Can, May 21, 57. *Study:* Vanier Col, Montreal, DEC, 76; Bennington Col, BA(flute & comp), 79; Manhattan Sch Music, MA(comp), 82. *Works:* Before the Cityset (eight violas with oboe, French horn & perc), comn by New Music Viola Series, 81; Revealing of Men (six trombones & string quintet), comn by Bay Bones Trombone Choir San Francisco, 82; Web-Trap & Cherchell, comn by Chamber Music Conf Comp Forum of East, 82; Triskelion (concert-drama), perf by Open Circle, 83; Pourtinade, perf by Musicians Accord & New Music Consort, 82. *Pos:* Comp in res, Chamber Music Conf & Composers Forum of East, 82. *Teaching:* Comp, Schumiatcher Music Sch, 82-; instr theory, Bronx Music Sch, 82- *Awards:* First Prize, Nat Asn Comp USA, 82; Comp Assistance Prog Award, Meet the Comp, 82; Can Coun Comn Award, 82. *Mailing Add:* 223 W 105th St #5FW New York NY 10025

BOUCHER, (CHARLES) GENE
BARITONE, ADMINISTRATOR
b Tagbilaren, Bohol, Philippine Islands, Dec 6, 33; US citizen. *Study:* Westminister Col, BA, 55; Consv de Lille, France, dipl du chant, 56. *Rec Perf:* Psalms for Baritone and Strings (Hanson), Mercury Rec, 64. *Roles:* Schaunard in La Boheme, 65-78, Ned Keene in Peter Grimes, 67 & Haly in L'Italiana, 71, Metropolitan Opera; DeBecque in South Pacific, Pittsburgh Civic Light Opera, 82. *Pos:* Bar soloist, Metropolitan Opera Asn, 65-; nat exec, Am Guild Muiscal Artists, 82- *Mem:* Am Guild Musical Artists (pres, 77-82). *Mailing Add:* 1841 Broadway New York NY 10023

BOULEYN, KATHRYN
SOPRANO
b Maga Vista, Md, May 3, 47. *Study:* Ind Univ, BA(music), 70; Curtis Inst Music, cert, 73. *Roles:* Desdemona in Otello, Miami Opera Co, 78; The Fox in The Cunning Little Vixen, Netherlands Opera Co, 81; Countess in The Marriage of Figaro, New York City Opera, 82; Manon Lescaut, Boston Conct Opera, 83; Elvira in Don Giovanni, Opera Theatre St Louis, 83; Tatyana in Eugene Onegin, Nat Arts Ctr, Ottawa, 83; Fennimore in Fennimore and Gerda, Edinburgh Fest, Scotland, 83. *Awards:* Third Prize, Metropolitan Opera Auditions, 73; Rockefeller Grant, 75; Nat Opera Inst Grant, 82. *Mailing Add:* c/o Columbia Artists Mgt 165 W 57th St New York NY 10019

BOURY, ROBERT WADE
COMPOSER, EDUCATOR
b Wheeling, WVa, Dec 28, 46. *Study:* Manhattan Sch Music, BMus, 68; Univ Mich, MMus, 69; Rackham Sch Grad Studies, DMus, 72. *Works:* Piano Concerto, comn & perf by Wheeling Symph Soc, WVa, 75; Time Steals Softly (operetta), comn & perf by Oglebay Inst, Wheeling, WVa, 76; Piano Trio, comn & perf by Arden Trio, 83; Fiddle Concerto, comn & perf by Ark Pops Orch, 83. *Pos:* Prog developer, Lansing Community Col, 77-80; coordr theory prog, Univ Ark, Little Rock, 81- *Teaching:* Lectr counterpoint & comp, West Liberty State Teachers Col, 76-77; lectr theory & comp, Lansing Community Col, 77-80; asst prof, Univ Ark, Little Rock, 81- *Awards:* Award to Student Comp, BMI, 70; II Fest Guanabara, Brazil, 70; Joseph H Bearns Prize, Columbia Univ, 70. *Mem:* Ark Music Teachers Asn; Am Music Ctr. *Mailing Add:* Music Dept Univ Ark Little Rock AR 72204

BOWDER, JERRY LEE
COMPOSER, EDUCATOR
b Portland, Ore, July 7, 28. *Study:* Univ Wash, with George F McKay, BA, 52; Lewis & Clark Col, with Robert Stoltze, MM, 56; Eastman Sch Music, with Howard Hanson, PhD, 60. *Works:* Symphony No 2, perf by Eastman-Rochester Phil, 59; Woodwind Quintet, Accura Music Publ, 63; Symphony No 3, Portland Symph Orch & RI Phil, 68; String Quartet No 1, Portland String Quartet, 72; Symph No 4 (celebration music), Portland Symph Orch & Bangor Symph Orch, 76; Three Pieces for Clarinet & Bassoon, Portland Chamber Players, 78; Tracings for String Orchestra, Univ Southern Maine Chamber Orch, 81. *Teaching:* Prof music, Univ Southern Maine, 60- *Awards:* Fel, Nat Endowment Arts & Humanities, 72. *Mem:* Am Soc Univ Comp; Soc Music Theory. *Mailing Add:* RFD 3 Box 25 Gorham ME 04038

BOWEN, EUGENE EVERETT
COMPOSER
b Biloxi, Miss, July 30, 50. *Study:* Calif Inst Arts, BFA, 72. *Works:* Longbow Angels, Int Soc Bassists, 73; Jewelled Settings, San Francisco Consv New Music Ens, 80; Steal Away, E G Rec, 80; Bourgeois Magnetic, Cantil Rec-Sespe Music, 81. *Mem:* ASCAP. *Mailing Add:* RR 2 Filmore CA 93015

BOWEN, JEAN
LIBRARIAN, ADMINISTRATOR
b Albany, NY, Mar 23, 27. *Study:* Berkshire Music Ctr, 46; Smith Col, AB, 48, AM, 56; studied voice with Anna Hamlin, 48-62; Columbia Univ, MS, 57. *Pos:* Consult, Rockefeller Brothers Fund, New York, 63-67; head Rodgers & Hammerstein Collection Recorded Sound, New York Pub Libr, Lincoln Ctr, 63-67, asst chief music div, 67-; cur music collection, New York Hist Soc, 79- *Mem:* Music Libr Asn; Int Music Libr Asn; Sonneck Soc. *Publ:* Auth, Buried in the Stacks, Opera News, 61; Voice and Voice Production, Encycl Am, 63; Holcman Collection, Sat Rev, 67; Women in Music—Their Fair Share?, High Fidelity, 74; Music, Funk & Wagnalls New Enclyc Yearbk, 79, 80 & 81. *Mailing Add:* 111 Amsterdam Ave New York NY 10023

BOWERS, JANE MEREDITH
WRITER, MUSICOLOGIST
b Minneapolis, Minn, Sept 17, 36. *Study:* Wellesley Col, studied flute with James Pappoutsakis, BA, 58; Univ Calif, Berkeley, MA, 62, PhD, 71; Royal Consv Music, Hague, Netherlands, studied flute with Frans Vester & baroque flute & recorder with Frans Brüggen, 65-66. *Pos:* Performer baroque flute, US, 71-; conct tour, Bowers/Wolf Duo, summer 75. *Teaching:* Instr flute, Univ NC, Chapel Hill, 68-72; asst prof music hist & musicol, Eastman Sch Music, Rochester, 72-73 & 74-75 & Univ Wis, Milwaukee, 81-; instr women's studies & music, Ore, 77-81. *Awards:* Fel, Am Asn Univ Women, 73-74 & 78-79 & Nat Endowment Humanities, 80. *Mem:* Col Music Soc; Am Musicol Soc (mem coun, 81-); Am Musical Instr Soc; Soc Ethnomusicol. *Interests:* French 18th century flute music; history of the flute and flute-playing; history of women in Western music; women musicians cross-culturally. *Publ:* Auth, New Light on the Development of the Transverse Flute Between About 1650 and About 1770, J Am Mus Inst Soc, 77; ed, Michel de la Barre, Pieces pour la Flute Traversiere avec la basse continue, Heugel & Cie, Paris, 78; auth, A Catalogue of French Works for the Transverse Flute, 1692-1761, Recherches Musique Francaise Classique, 78; Flaüste Traverseinne and Flute d'Allemagne—The Flute in France from the Late Middle Ages up through 1702, Recherches, 79; co-ed & contribr, Women Making Music: Essays on the History of Women in Western Music from the Middle Ages to the Present, Univ Ill Press (in press). *Mailing Add:* Dept Music Univ Wis Milwaukee WI 53201

BOWLES, GARRETT H
LIBRARIAN, EDUCATOR
b San Francisco, Calif, Feb 3, 38. *Study:* Univ Calif, Davis, AB, 60; Univ Calif, Berkeley, MLS, 65; Stanford Univ, PhD, 78. *Pos:* Head music cataloger, Stanford Univ, 65-79. *Teaching:* Music librn, Univ Calif, San Diego, 79-, asst adj prof, 80-; vis music librn, Univ Exeter, England, 83. *Bibliog:* Donald Seibert (auth), The MARC Music Format, Music Libr Asn Tech Reports, 83. *Mem:* Music Libr Asn ; Asn Rec Sound Collections (pres, 79-81); Int Asn Music Librn. *Interests:* Automation in music libraries; thematic catalog of Marin Marais; music printing in France, 1680-1720. *Publ:* Auth, Directory of Music Library Automation Projects, Music Libr Asn, 73 & 79; coauth, Music a MARC Format, Libr Cong, 76; auth, The AAA Project: a Report, Asn Rec Sound Collections J, Vol 9, 77; A Computer Produced Thematic Catalog: The Pieces de Viola of Marin Marais, Fontes Artis Musicae 26, 79; Sound Recordings, Am Libr Asn, 83. *Mailing Add:* 14290 Mango Dr Del Mar CA 92014

BOWLES, PAUL FREDERICK
COMPOSER, CRITIC
b New York, NY, Dec 30, 10. *Study:* With Aaron Copland, 29-31. *Works:* Yankee Clipper, perf by Philadelphia Orch, 37; Music for a Farce, Columbia, 38; The Wind Remains, MGM, 43; Sonata (two pianos), 45 & Songs, 40's, Schirmer; Concerto (two pianos, winds & perc), 47. *Pos:* Music critic, New York Herald Tribune, 43-46. *Awards:* Fel, Guggenheim Found, 41; grant, Rockefeller Found, 59. *Mem:* ASCAP. *Mailing Add:* 2117 Tanger Socco Tangier Morocco

BOWLES, RICHARD WILLIAM
COMPOSER, CONDUCTOR
b Rogers, Ark, June 30, 18. *Study:* Ind Univ, BPSM, 40; Univ Wis, MS, 50. *Works:* Burst of Flame (conct march), 54, Heat Lightning (conct march), 55, Marching the Blues (swing march), 56 & The Brigadier (overture), 58,

Fitzsimons; Sword and Shield (conct march), Hal Leonard, 69; more than 100 comp for band, orch, ens & solos. *Pos:* Band & orch dir, Culver Pub Sch, Ind, 40-42 & 47-53; dir music, Lafayette City Sch, Ind, 53-58. *Teaching:* Dir bands, Univ Fla, 58-73; prof music, 73- *Mem:* Am Bandmasters Asn; Col Band Dir Nat Asn; ASCAP; Outdoor Writers Asn Am. *Publ:* Auth, Singing Achievement Test, Belwin Mills, 69. *Mailing Add:* 827 NW 15th Ave Gainesville FL 32601

BOWMAN, CARL BYRON
COMPOSER, EDUCATOR
b Philomath, Ore, Dec 14, 13. *Study:* Willamette Univ, BMus, 42; Juilliard Sch Music, 44-46; Columbia Univ, 45-47; Univ Wash, MA in Mus, 52; NY Univ, PhD, 71. *Works:* Trio (trombone, viola & cello), comn by Davis Shuman, 56; Fantasy On A Carol Tune, perf by Brooklyn Phil, 61; Symphonic Statement (strings), perf by Portland Chamber Orch, 62; The Lamb, John T Benson, 69; Festival of Praise, Celebration Press, 73; Suite for Brass Ensemble and Piano, perf by Manhattan Brass Ens, 78; Ballad, perf by Guggenheim Conct Band, 82. *Teaching:* Instr music, King's Col, Briarcliff Manor, 61-64; asst prof, Shelton Col, Cape May, NJ, 64-65; prof, Manhattan Community Col, City Univ New York, 66- *Mem:* Am Music Ctr; Am Soc Univ Comp; ASCAP; Am Fedn Musicians. *Publ:* Ed, Banchieri—Truth Has Risen, 72 & Sang All Israel, 72, Music 70. *Mailing Add:* 140 W 69 St New York NY 10023

BOWMAN, JACK WALTER
EDUCATOR, MUSIC DIRECTOR
b Youngstown, Ohio, Feb 27, 45. *Study:* Ohio Wesleyan Univ, BM, 67; Univ Mich, MM, 68, DMA, 74. *Teaching:* Dir instrm music, Alma Col, 68-78; chmn, Dept Perf Arts, Cameron Univ, 80-83, prof music, 82-, div head, 83- *Awards:* Teacher of Arts, Lawton Arts & Humanities Coun, 81. *Mem:* Am Symph Orch League; Col Band Dir Nat Asn; Okla Bandmasters Asn; Okla Music Educ Asn; Nat Band Asn. *Publ:* Auth, The Present State of Research on Construction of the Clarinet, J Band Res, 73; Changes That Improve Rehearsal Atmosphere, 77 & The Musical Circus, 83, Instrumentalist. *Mailing Add:* Music Dept Cameron Univ Lawton OK 73505

BOWMAN, PETER
OBOE, EDUCATOR
Study: New England Consv Music; studied oboe with Ralph Gomberg & John Mack. *Pos:* Prin oboe, Montreal Symph Orch, formerly, Can Broadcasting Orch, formerly, McGill Chamber Orch, formerly & St Louis Symph Orch, currently; performer, Boston Symph Orch, formerly, Boston Pops, formerly, Boston Opera, formerly & Boston Ballet, formerly; mem, St Louis Woodwind Quintet, currently; soloist, Fest Winds Soloists, Toronto, Ont. *Teaching:* Mem fac oboe & chamber music, McGill Univ, formerly, Dalhousie Univ, formerly & St Louis Consv Music, currently; instr master classes, Eastman Sch Music & Univ Mich, Ann Arbor; instr oboe, Banff Fest Fine Arts. *Awards:* Albert Spaulding Award, Berkshire Music Ctr, 71. *Mailing Add:* 7225 Shaftsbury St Louis MO 63130

BOYADJIAN, HAYG
COMPOSER, PIANO TECHNICIAN-TUNER
b Paris, France, May 15, 38, US citizen. *Study:* Liszt Consv, Buenos Aires, Arg, BA, 58; Northeastern Univ, BA, 67; Brandeis Univ, 69. *Works:* Movement No 1 and 4, Darryl Rosenberg, 72-81; Sonata (viola solo), Steve Spackman, Scotland, 80; Mobile (harp, flute & cello), Susan Allen, Chris Krueger & T Rutishauser, 81; Dialogues (two clarinets), Abgar Muradian & Vlachislav Manooshagian, USSR, 82; Symphonia No 2, Armenian Chamber Orch, 83; Work for Tuba Solo, comn by Samuel Pilafian, Empire Brass Quintet, 83; Work for Chamber Orchestra, comn by Cambridge Little Orch, 83. *Pos:* Comp mem, The Annex Players, 72-76. *Bibliog:* Phyllis Whitman (auth), The Joy of an Unfolding Talent, 1/26/78, & Paul Ciano (auth), Contemporay Works by H Boyadjian, 10/11/79, Lexington Minute-Man; Cecilia Proudian (auth), National Reverberations, Voice of the Nation, Armenia, USSR, 4/6/83. *Mem:* Am Music Ctr; Biblioteques Int Musique Contemp. *Publ:* Auth, A Composer's Journey to Erevan, Am Music Ctr Newsletter, spring 82; A Composer's Impressions of Contemporary Armenia, Armenian Mirror-Spectator, 83. *Mailing Add:* 43 Fern St Lexington MA 02173

BOYAJIAN, ARMEN
COACH, PIANO
b Paterson, NJ, June 28, 31. *Study:* Juilliard Sch Music, 50; Montclair State Teacher's Col, BS(music), 55; private piano study with Grace Castagnetta, 55-58. *Pos:* Dir, Paterson Lyr Opera Theatre, 58-73. *Teaching:* Private vocal coach, New York & Paterson, NJ, 58-; fac mem, William Paterson Col, 72-75. *Mailing Add:* 825 West End Ave 3B New York NY 10025

BOYARSKY, TERRY LINDA
EDUCATOR, PIANO
b Nuremberg, Germany, Aug 17, 49; US citizen. *Study:* Duke Univ, 66-68; Reed Col, BA, 70; Aspen Music Sch, studied piano with Jeaneane Dowis, 70 & 73; studied piano with Rebecca Penneys, Milwaukee, Wis, 74-77; Macphail Ctr Perf Arts, studied eurhythmics with Martha Baker, 75; Dalcroze Soc Am Wkshp, Kent State Univ, 75; Cleveland Inst Music, BA(eurhythmics), 77; Dalcroze Sch Music, with Dr Hilda Schuster & Johanna Gjerulff, 78; studied piano with James Tannebaum, Cleveland, Ohio, 80- *Pos:* Accmp for various string & wind players of St Paul Chamber Orch & Minn Orch, 72-76; chamber music recitals, Macalester Col, 72-75; harpsichord, Baroque Trio, 75-77; chamber music recitals in Cleveland & Akron area, currently. *Teaching:* Private piano instr, 73-; instr eurhythmics, Cleveland Inst Music, 76- & Cleveland Inst Dance, 77- *Mem:* Dalcroze Soc Am; Alliance Francaise. *Mailing Add:* 2990 Warrington Rd Shaker Heights OH 44120

BOYD, BONITA K
FLUTE, EDUCATOR
b Pittsburgh, Pa, Aug 1, 49. *Study:* Eastman Sch Music, BM(theory) & perf cert, 71; studied with Roger Stevens, Maurice Sharp & Joseph Mariano. *Rec Perf:* Music for Solo Flute, 80 & Paganini Caprices, 80, Spectrum Rec; Flute Music of Les Six, Tioch Rec, 82; Concerto (Adler), 83 & Suite for Flute and Marimba (Wilder), 83, Pantheon Rec. *Pos:* US East & West Coast, Mex & Cent Am tours; performer, Marlboro Fest, formerly & Nat Pub Radio, formerly; prin flute, Rochester Phil, 71-, Chautauqua Symph, 71-77 & Filamonica de las Americas, Mexico City, 77; soloist, Nat Gallery Orch, Washington, DC & Nat Symph Dominican Repub; soloist, Rochester Phil, formerly, prin flute & Charlotte Whitney Allen chair, 71- *Teaching:* Assoc prof flute, Eastman Sch Music, 76- *Awards:* UN Fel Comp; Rec of Yr Award, Stereo Rev Mag, 82. *Mem:* Nat Flute Asn (mem bd, 78-80 & 82-). *Rep:* Thea Dispecker 59 E 54th New York NY 10022. *Mailing Add:* 84 Adams St Rochester NY 14608

BOYD, GERARD
TENOR
b Glasgow, Scotland, June 17, 42; US citizen. *Study:* Univ Toronto, Can, dipl(operatic perf), 70. *Roles:* Valzacchi in Der Rosenkavalier, 78 & Don Basilio in Marriage of Figaro, 79, Can Opera Co; Monsieur Triquet in Eugene Onegin, Philadelphia Opera Co, 81; Sancho Panza in Man of La Mancha, Lake George Opera Fest, 81; Vashek in Bartered Bride, Ky Opera Asn, 82; Kaspar in Amahl Night & The Visitors, Avery Fisher Hall, 82. *Pos:* Singer, Germany, 72-78; performer, various repty & opera co incl Edinburgh Int Fest, Can Opera Co, Nat Arts Ctr, Ottawa & Spring Fest, Guelph, Ont & on TV. *Mailing Add:* c/o Thea Dispeker 59 E 54th St New York NY 10022

BOYD, JACK ARTHUR
WRITER, COMPOSER
b Indianapolis, Ind, Feb 9, 32. *Study:* Abilene Christian Univ, BMusEd, 55; NTex State Univ, MMus(comp), 59; Univ Iowa, PhD(choral lit), 71. *Works:* One hundred-twenty choral works by 14 publishers, including original works, scholarly editions of older music, and choral arrangements; background score for 13 episodes of Tales From The Great Book religious films, 70. *Pos:* Choral dir, Paducah High Sch, 57-63, Univ Dubuque, 64-67 & Abilene Christian Univ, 68-69; ed, Choral J, 78-81; fine arts critic, KRBC-TV (NBC affil), Abilene, Tex, 79- *Teaching:* Prof musicology, Abilene Christian Univ, 79- *Mem:* Life mem, Am Choral Dir Asn. *Interests:* Choral literature of the 19th century. *Publ:* Auth, Rehearsal Guide for the Choral Director, Parker Publ, 70; Teaching Choral Sight Reading, Parker Publ & Mark Foster Music, 82. *Mailing Add:* 541 Col Dr Abilene TX 79601

BOYD, ROBERT FERRELL
TROMBONE
b Chicago, Ill, Nov 22, 21. *Study:* Eastman Sch Music. *Pos:* Trombone & marimba soloist, US Navy Band, Washington, 42-45; co-prin trombonist, New York Phil, 45-46; prin trombonist, Metropolitan Opera Orch, 46-48 & Cleveland Orch, 48- *Teaching:* Chmn, Trombone Dept, Cleveland Inst Music, 48-, chmn, Brass Dept, 82-83; chmn, Trombone Dept, Blossom Fest Sch, Kent State Univ, 83. *Mailing Add:* Cleveland Orch Severance Hall Cleveland OH 44106

BOYD, RODNEY CARNEY
EDUCATOR, BASSOON
b Baton Rouge, La, Sept 27, 43. *Study:* La State Univ, BMusEd, 65; Ill State Univ, MS(music educ), 66; Boston Univ, currently; studied with Leonard Sharrow, Sherman Walt & Louis A Skinner. *Pos:* Solo bassoonist, Topeka Symph Orch, 68-; bassoonist, Washburn Arts Quintet, 73. *Teaching:* Assoc prof music double reeds, Washburn Univ, 68- *Mem:* Int Double Reed Soc; Nat Asn Col Wind & Perc Instr (state chmn, 73-75); Col Music Soc; Phi Mu Alpha Sinfonia; Nat Flute Asn. *Publ:* Auth, Making the Bassoon Playable, Woodwind World. *Mailing Add:* 3856 SW Atwood Topeka KS 66610

BOYKAN, MARTIN
COMPOSER, PIANO
b New York, NY, Apr 12, 31. *Study:* Harvard Univ, with Walter Piston, BA, 51; Univ Zurich, with Paul Hindemith, 51-52; Yale Univ, MM, 52. *Works:* String Quartet No 0, Juilliard Quartet, 50; String Quartet No 1, Comp String Quartet, 67; Concerto for 13 Players, Boston Symph Chamber Players, 71; String Quartet No 2, Pro Arte Quartet, 73; Piano Trio, Wheaton Col Trio, 76; Psalm 128 for Chorus, Mobart Press, 76; Elegy for Soprano and Six Instruments, Musica Viva, 81. *Teaching:* Prof comp, Brandeis Univ, 58- *Awards:* Jeunesses Musicale Award, 67; Fromm Found Comn, 75; Martha Baird Rockefeller Found Rec Award, 76. *Bibliog:* John Harbison & Eleanor Cory (auth), Martin Boykan: Two Views, Perspectives New Music, 73; Eleanor Cory (auth), American String Quartets, Musical Quart, 10/76. *Mem:* Perspectives New Music; Am Music Ctr. *Mailing Add:* Music Dept Brandeis Univ Waltham MA 02154

BOYKIN, ANNIE HELEN
COMPOSER, TEACHER
b River Falls, Ala, Nov 5, 04. *Study:* Ala Col, BM 27; Akad Tonkunst, Munich, Ger, 30-33; Yale Univ, summer 52 & 53. *Works:* Piano Concerto in F Major, Schroeder & Gunther; over 40 piano solos. *Teaching:* Piano & theory, Ala Col, 27-30 & privately, Atlanta, Ga, 34-65 & Montgomery, Ala, 65- *Mailing Add:* 3207 Carter Hill Rd Montgomery AL 36111

BOYLAN, PAUL C
ADMINISTRATOR, EDUCATOR
b Portage, Wis, Oct 2, 39. *Study:* Univ Wis, with Johansen, Ehlers & Kohlisch, BM(piano), 61, MM(theory), 62; Univ Mich, with Sandor, David & Cuyler, PhD(musicol), 68. *Teaching:* Asst prof theory, Sch Music, Univ Mich, 69-71, assoc prof, 72-74, prof, 75-, assoc dean, 75-79, dean, 79-; dir univ div, Nat Music Camp, Interlochen, Mich, 72-75. *Awards:* Rackham Endowment Res Fel, 69. *Mem:* Music Teachers Nat Asn; Nat Asn Sch Music; Int Coun Fine Arts Deans. *Interests:* Late 19th century harmony. *Publ:* Auth, Revitalizing the Summer Session, 77 & Evaluation of Teaching and Research, 79, Nat Asn Sch Music. *Mailing Add:* 1722 Shadford Rd Ann Arbor MI 48104

BOYLE, J DAVID
EDUCATOR, ADMINISTRATOR
b Gravette, Ark, Sept 1, 34. *Study:* Univ Ark, BS, 56; Univ Kans, MME, 60, PhD, 68. *Teaching:* Asst prof music, Moorhead State Col, 67-68; from asst prof to prof, Pa State Univ, 68-81; prof & chmn music educ, Univ Miami, Fla, 81- *Mem:* Music Educr Nat Conf; Soc Res Music Educ; Int Soc Music Educ; Col Music Soc; Am Educ Res Asn. *Publ:* Ed, Instructional Objectives in Music, Music Educr Nat Conf, 74; coauth, Psychological Foundations of Musical Behavior, C C Thomas, 79; Contextual Influences on Pitch Judgement, Psychology Music, Vol 8, No 2; auth, Selecting Music Tests for Use in Schools, Update, Vol 1, No 1; coauth, Music Education, In: Encycl Educ Res, 5th ed, Free Press, 82. *Mailing Add:* Sch Music Univ Miami Coral Gables FL 33214

BOZARTH, GEORGE S
MUSICOLOGIST
b Trenton, NJ. *Study:* Princeton Univ, MFA, 70, PhD, 78. *Pos:* Dir, Int Brahms Conf, Libr Cong, 83; founding mem ed bd, Johannes Brahms, Gesamtausgabe der musikalischen Werke, 83-; exec dir, Am Brahms Soc, 83- *Teaching:* Asst prof hist musicol, Univ Wash, Seattle, 78- *Awards:* Am Coun Learned Soc Fel, 82; Nat Endowment Humanities Res Conf Grant, 83. *Mem:* Am Brahms Soc; Am Musicol Soc. *Interests:* Johannes Brahms: manuscript studies & compositional process; lieder and piano music; editing. *Publ:* Ed, Bach, Cantata Ach Gott vom Himmel sieh darein, Neue Bach Ausgabe, 81; auth, Synthesizing Word and Tone: Brahms's Setting of Hebbel's Vorüber, Brahms Studies, Cambridge Univ Press, 83; Brahms's Lieder Inventory of 1859-60 and Other Documents of His Life and Work, Fontes Artis Musicae, 83; Johannes Brahms und die Liedersammlungen von Corner, Meister und Arnold, Die Musikforschung, 83; Brahms's Duets for Soprano and Alto Op 61, Studia Musicol, 83. *Mailing Add:* Sch Music Univ Wash Seattle WA 98195

BOZEMAN, GEORGE LEWIS, JR
ORGAN
b Pampa, Tex, Nov 10, 36. *Study:* NTex State Univ, 55-59; studied organ with Helen Hewitt. *Pos:* Apprentice, Otto Hofmann, organbuilder, 59-60; vpres, Robert L Sipe Inc, 64-67; voicer, Noack Organ Co Inc, 68-70; co-owner, Bozeman-Gibson & Co, 71-82; owner, Geo Bozeman & Co Inc, 82-; active recitalist, US, currently; mem (with J Bryan Dyker), Hot Air Duo, currently. *Awards:* Fulbright Award, 67-68. *Mem:* Int Soc Organbuilders; Am Guild Organists; Organ Hist Soc (counr, 72- & vpres, 77-). *Publ:* Auth, The Organ in Matthews Memorial Presbyterian Church, Organ, 10/62; The Nature of the Organ and Its Future, Diapson, 4/79; History of International Society of Organbuilders, Am Organist, 5/79. *Mailing Add:* RFD 1 Deerfield NH 03037

BOZICEVICH, RONALD RAYMOND
DOUBLE BASS
b Wheeling, WVa, Feb 8, 48. *Study:* Double bassist, Wheeling Symph, 64-67 & Cincinnati Symph, 70- *Pos:* Electric bassist, Cincinnati Pops, currently. *Mailing Add:* c/o Cincinnati Symph 1241 Elm St Cincinnati OH 45210

BRACALI, GIAMPAOLO
COMPOSER, CONDUCTOR
b Rome, Italy, May 24, 41. *Study:* St Cecilia Consv, Rome, dipl(piano), 60, dipl(comp), 65-67; studied with N Boulanger, 65-67. *Works:* Musica per Fiati, Ricordi, Milan, 65; Concerto per Organo, 66, Cyrano Ballet, 68 & Concerto per Piano, 69, Sonzogno, Milan; 3 Salmi, Edizioni RAI, 72; Quintetts (guitar & string quartet), Suvini/Zer, 74. *Pos:* Assoc cond, Acad Filarmonica Romana, 61-65 & Manhattan Sch Music, 69-77. *Teaching:* Prof comp & cond, Manhattan Sch Music, 69- *Awards:* First prize, F M Napolitano, 64 & Lili Boulanger Award, 67; Prince Pierre de Monaco Comp Compt Award, 68 & 78. *Mailing Add:* 601 Kappock Riverdale NY 10463

BRACCHI-LE ROUX, MARTA N
PIANO
b Montevideo, Uruguay, Feb 7, 32. *Study:* Univ Montevideo, BM, 54. *Pos:* Pianist, freelance, 60 & San Francisco Contemp Music Players, 75- *Teaching:* Instr piano & chamber music, San Francisco Consv Music, 64-70. *Awards:* Bach Award, Univ Uruguay, 53. *Mailing Add:* 2874 Washington St San Francisco CA 94115

BRADETICH, JEFF
DOUBLE BASS, EDUCATOR
b McMinneville, Ore, Feb 3, 57. *Study:* Northwestern Univ, BM, 80. *Pos:* Sect mem, Lyr Opera Chicago Orch, 76-79; exec dir, Int Soc Bassists, 82-; co-ed, Int Soc Bassists Mag, 82- *Teaching:* Instr double bass, Univ Mich, Ann Arbor, 80-83 & Northwestern Univ, 83- *Awards:* Young Artists Compt Winner, Civic Orch Chicago, 80 & Lansing Symph Orch, 80. *Mem:* Int Soc Bassists (exec dir, 82-); Am String Teacher Asn; Col Music Soc; Am Symph Orch League; Chamber Music Am. *Publ:* Auth, The Contrabass as a Musical Instrument ..., Am String Teachers Asn, Winter, 83. *Mailing Add:* Sch Music Northwestern Univ Evanston IL 60201

BRADLEY, CAROL JUNE
LIBRARIAN, EDUCATOR
b Huntingdon, Pa, Aug 12, 34. *Study:* Lebanon Valley Col, BS, 56; Western Res Univ, MS, 57; Fla State Univ, PhD, 78. *Pos:* Librn, Drinker Libr Choral Music, Free Libr Philadelphia, 57-59; music librn, US Mil Acad Libr, 59-60; music cataloguer, Vassar Col, 60-67; assoc dir, Music Libr, State Univ NY, Buffalo, 67- *Teaching:* Prof music librarianship, State Univ NY, Buffalo, 78- *Mem:* Music Libr Asn; Int Asn Music Libr; Oral Hist Asn. *Interests:* History of music librarianship; history of music libraries; biographies of music librarians. *Publ:* Ed, Manual of Music Librarianship, Music Libr Asn, 66; auth, The Dickinson Classification: A Cataloguing & Classification Manual for Music, Carlisle Bks, 68; Reader in Music Librarianship, Microcard Ed, 73; Music Libraries in North America, In: Encycl of Library and Information Science, 76; Music Collections in American Libraries: A Chronology, Info Coordr, 81. *Mailing Add:* 818 Delaware Rd Kenmore NY 14223

BRADSHAW, DAVID RUTHERFORD
EDUCATOR, PIANO
b Washington, DC, Oct 31, 37. *Study:* Juilliard Sch Music, BS, 60; Arrigo Boito Consv, Parma, Italy, Hon PhD, 78. *Rec Perf:* On Educo Rec, 78. *Pos:* Conct pianist throughout US, England, Italy, Can, Austria & Mex; recitalist, White House, 60; performer, BBC Symph, London, Nat Symph, Washington, DC, Mex Nat Symph, Baltimore Symph, San Francisco Symph & Cincinnati Symph; co-founder & pres, Alton Jones Assoc Ltd, 70-74, vpres, 76. *Teaching:* Assoc dir, Nassau Consv, 65-75 & Am Acad, 70-75; head piano dept, Molloy Col, 75-; mem fac, Mozartina Musical Arts Consv, Tarrytown, NY, 76- *Awards:* Helen Kline Mem Award, 59; winner, Nat Soc Arts & Lett Int Compt, 60. *Mem:* Nat Guild Piano Teachers; Am Asn Univ Prof; Bohemians. *Mailing Add:* 170 W 73rd St New York NY 10023

BRADSHAW, MERRILL KAY
EDUCATOR, COMPOSER
b Lyman, Wyo, June 18, 29. *Study:* Brigham Young Univ, BA, 54, MA, 55; Univ Ill, MMus, 56, DMus, 62. *Works:* Third Symphony, perf by Utah Symph, 68; Facets, perf by Phoenix Symph, 69; The Restoration, perf by Brigham Young Univ Oratorio Choir & Phil Orch, 74; Four Mountain Sketches, San Diego Symph, Detroit Symph & many others, 74; Fifth Symphony, Auckland Symph, 79; Homages for Viola & Orchestra, perf by Jun Takahira & US Air Force Orch, 79e; Concerto for Vioilin & Orchestra, perf by Brigham Young Univ & Elizabeth Matesky, 81. *Teaching:* From instr to assoc prof music, Brigham Young Univ, 57-72, prof music & comp in res, 72-, distinguished fac lectr, 81; prof, Univ Ind, 74. *Awards:* Karl G Maeser Creative Arts Award, 67-68. *Publ:* Auth, Spirit and Music, 77 & contribr, Arts and Inspiration, 80, Brigham Young Univ Press. *Mailing Add:* 248 E 3140 N Provo UT 84604

BRADSHAW, MURRAY CHARLES
WRITER, ORGAN
b Hinsdale, Ill, Sept 25, 30. *Study:* Am Consv Music, MMus(organ), 55, MMus(organ), 59; Univ Chicago, PhD, 69. *Teaching:* Prof music, Univ Calif, Los Angeles, 66- *Mem:* Am Inst Musicol (pres, pac SW chap, 78-80); Am Guild Organists; Int Soc Musicol. *Interests:* Falsobordone; toccata; embellishment; sacred monody. *Publ:* Auth, The Origin of the Toccata, Am Inst Musicol, 72; The Falsobordone, A Study in Renaissance and Baroque Music, Hänssler, 78; Francesco Severi, Salmi Passaggiati (1615), A-R Publ, 81; Giovanni Luca Conforti, Salmi Passaggiati (1601-1603), Hänssler (in prep); coauth, Girolamo Diruta, Il Transilvano, Mediaeval Inst (in prep). *Mailing Add:* 6173 Le Sage Ave Woodland Hills CA 91364

BRADSHAW, RICHARD JAMES
CONDUCTOR & MUSIC DIRECTOR
b Rugby, England, Apr 26, 44. *Study:* Univ London, BA, 65; studied cond with Adrian Boult, Charles Groves & John Pritchard. *Rec Perf:* Saltarello Choir (Brahms, Bruckner & Verdi), CRD, 75. *Pos:* Dir, New London Ens, England, 72-77; chorus dir, Glyndebourne Fest Opera, Sussex, England, 75-77; cond & chorus dir, San Francisco Opera, 77- *Rep:* Allied Artists 42 Montpelier Sq London SW7 1JZ England. *Mailing Add:* 957 The Alameda Berkeley CA 94707

BRAHINSKY, HENRY JOSEPH
VIOLIN, TEACHER
b Kansas City, Mo, Jan 6, 17. *Study:* Univ Nebr, BM(music educ), 40; NTex State Univ, MMusEd, 59. *Pos:* Asst concertmaster, Dallas Symph Orch, 40-41; concertmaster, Ft Worth Symph Orch, 61-63 & Ft Worth Summer Musicals, 62-64; second concertmaster, Ft Worth Opera Orch, 81- *Teaching:* Instr orch, Dallas Independent Sch District, 46-81; instr violin, Tex Womens Univ, 66-68. *Awards:* Presser Found Scholar, 38-40. *Mem:* Am Fedn Musicians (mem Dallas bd, 53); Dallas Music Teachers Asn; Dallas Music Educr Asn (pres, 61-62); Tex Music Educr Asn; Nat Music Teachers Asn. *Mailing Add:* Ft Worth Opera Orch 3505 W Lancaster Ft Worth TX 76107

BRAITHWAITE, JAMES ROLAND
EDUCATOR, ORGAN
b Boston, Mass, Feb 28, 27. *Study:* Col Music, Boston Univ, MusB, 48, MA, 50, PhD, 67. *Teaching:* Assoc prof music, Talladega Col, 52-, head music dept, 69-76, chair humanities div, 67-71, dean of col, 74-81 & Buell Gordon Gallagher Prof Humanities, 73- *Mem:* Am Guild Organists; Am Musicol Soc; Phi Mu Alpha Sinfonia; Am Asn Univ Prof. *Interests:* Franco-Netherlandish music in early Tudor England; Afro-American religious music; minorities in liberal education. *Publ:* Coauth, Inquiry Centered Teaching, Focus on Curric, 72; ed, The Administration of a Curriculum Experiment, Inst Serv to Educ, 74; auth, A Minority Perception of Liberal Education, Lib Educ, 81. *Mailing Add:* Dept Music Talladega Col Talladega AL 35160

BRAM, MARJORIE
EDUCATOR, WRITER
b Philadelphia, Pa, June 28, 19. *Study:* Temple Univ, BS, 40; Juilliard Sch Music, summer 45; Berkshire Music Ctr, 50; Columbia Univ, MA, 51; Mozarteum, Salzburg, cert cond, 57. *Pos:* First chair viola, NJ Symph Orch, 45-48 & Am Symph Orch League Wkshp Cond & Comp, Asilomar, Calif, 59; cond, South Orange Community Orch, 49-69 & Sewanee Summer Music Ctr, Tenn, 59; founder & dir, Friends Early Music, NJ, 64-74 & Fla Friends Early Music, 75- *Teaching:* Instr instrm music, Maplewood Sch Dist, South Orange, NJ, 42-74; mem fac applied music, Manatee Jr Col, currently. *Awards:* First Prize Comp, Temple Univ, 39 & 40. *Mem:* Viola da Gamba Soc Am (dir 66-, pres, 70-72); Am Symph Orch League; Int Soc Music Educr; Music Educr Nat Conf; Am String Teachers Asn. *Publ:* Auth, Sound Dimensions for New Players, 71; contribr to Music Educr J, Instrumentalist, J Viola da Gamba Soc & Strad Mag, UK. *Mailing Add:* 3614 22nd Ave W Bradenton FL 33505

BRAND, MANNY
EDUCATOR
b Coral Gables, Fla, July 27, 50. *Study:* Fla State Univ, BME, 71; Univ Miami, MM, 74, PhD, 76. *Teaching:* Asst prof music educ, State Univ NY, Potsdam, 76-79; assoc prof, Univ Houston, 79-; vis prof, Ithaca Col & Saratoga-Potsdam Choral Inst. *Bibliog:* Hildegard C Froehlich (auth), A Study of the Effectiveness of Simulation Techniques in Teaching Behavior Management Skills to Music Education Majors, Bulletin Coun Res Music Educ, 78. *Mem:* Music Instr Strategies Res Interest Group (nat chair, 83-); mem coun, Bulletin Coun Res Music Educ; Tex State Music Educ Res Comt (chair, 80-82); Music Educr Nat Conf. *Publ:* Auth, How to Improve Rehearsals, Instrumentalist, 80; Toward Greater Teaching Effectivenes, Col Music Symposium, 80; The First-Year of Music Teaching, Music Educr J, 81; Effects of Student Teaching on the Classroom Management Beliefs of Music Student Teachers, J Res Music Educ, 82; coauth, Music in the Early Childhood Curriculum, Childhood Educ, 83. *Mailing Add:* Dept Music Educ Farish Hall Univ Houston Houston TX 77004

BRAND, MYRA JEAN
EDUCATOR, SOPRANO
b Dallas, Ore, Sept 4, 36. *Study:* Willamette Univ, BM, 58; Univ Ore, MM, 71, DMA, 79. *Roles:* Adele in Die Fledermaus, Portland Opera Co, 65; Norina in Don Pasquale, Eugene Opera Co, 76. *Teaching:* Asst prof, Western Ore State Col, 71-79, assoc prof, 79- *Mem:* Am Choral Dir Asn; Nat Asn Teachers Singing (state gov, 80-); Mu Phi Epsilon (treas, 69-81); Music Teachers Nat Asn; Ore Music Teachers Asn. *Publ:* Auth, Lady Dean Paul (Poldowski) Composer ..., Triangle, Mu Phi Epsilon, 79; Songs of Poldowski (Lady Dean Paul), Nat Asn Teachers Singing Bulletin, 80. *Mailing Add:* 720 McGilchrist SE Salem OR 97302

BRANDON, ROBERT EUGENE
GUITAR & LUTE
b Minneapolis, Minn, Nov 21, 46. *Study:* Univ Calif, Berkeley, 67; El Estudio de Arte Guitarristico, Mexico, dipl, 69-72; studied with Rey de la Torre & Manuel Lopez Ramos. *Pos:* Conct artist, US cols & univ, 72- *Teaching:* Instr master classes, US cols & univ, 72- *Rep:* Albert Kay & Assoc Inc 58 W 58th St New York NY 10019. *Mailing Add:* 173 Santa Rita Ct Los Altos CA 94022

BRANDSTADTER, EUGENE J
VIOLA, VIOLIN
b New York, NY. *Study:* Columbia Univ, with Herbert Dittler, BA, 32; Ariz State Univ, with William Magers, 76-77; New York Col Music, with Sigmund Feuermann. *Pos:* Prin viola, Northeastern Pa Phil, 46-76, Bach Fest, 46-76 & Mesa Symph, 76-77; organizer, mgr & violist, Phil String Quartet, Wilkes Barre & Scranton, Pa, 55-65 & Phoenix String Quartet, 78-79; sect viola, Sun City Symph, 76-77, Phoenix Symph, 77-, Summer Fest Music, Eugene, Ore, 79 & Fla Fest Music, 80; asst prin viola, Alaska Fest Music, 79; organizer & violist, Phil String Quartet, 79- *Awards:* Gold Baton Award, Northeastern Pa Phil Soc, 76. *Mem:* Am Fedn Musicians. *Mailing Add:* 6023 E Harvard Scottsdale AZ 85257

BRANDT, BARBARA JEAN
SPINTO, TEACHER
b Battle Creek, Mich, Feb 18, 42. *Study:* Mich State Univ; studied with Gean Greenwell, Oren Brown, & Thelma Halverson. *Roles:* Socrate, 66-67, Sphinx in Oedipus and the Sphinx, 69-70, Birdwoman in The Wanderer, 69-70, Margherita in Faust Counter Faust, 70-71, Lady with a Hatbox in Postcard from Morocco, 71-72, Ann Sexton in Transformation, 72-73 & Lois in Newest Opera in the World, 73-74, Minn Opera Co. *Pos:* Res mem, Minn Opera Co; recitalist with symph orchs. *Teaching:* Voice & music in pub sch. *Mailing Add:* 2630 Irving Ave S Minneapolis MN 55408

BRANDT, WILLIAM EDWARD
COMPOSER, EDUCATOR
b Butte, Mont, Jan 14, 20. *Study:* Wash State Col, BA, 42; Eastman Sch Music, MM(comp), 48, PhD(comp), 50. *Works:* String Quartet No 3, perf by Kilbourn Hall String Quartet, 49; King Lear, Suite for Orchestra, Eastman Sch Music, 50; No Neutral Ground, perf by Chamber Opera, Wash State Univ, 61; Symphony No 1, perf by Spokane Phil Orch, Wash, 71; Toccata for Piano, Hope Publ Co, 73; Canzona Prismatica (band), comn by Wash State Univ Found, 82-83. *Teaching:* From instr to prof hist music & music theory, Wash State Univ, 56- *Awards:* Wash State Univ Libr Award, 81; Fac Enrichment Award, Wash State Univ Found, 82. *Mem:* Am Musicol Soc (pac northwest chap pres, 69); Int Webern Soc (secy/treas, 81-). *Interests:* Nineteenth century festivals; piano concertos of Steibelt; piano concertos in early 19th century. *Publ:* Auth, The Way of Music, Allyn & Bacon, 68; Elliott Carter: Simultaneity & Complexity, Music Educr J, 74; The Comprehensive Study of Music: Anthologies II & III, Harper & Row, 77. *Mailing Add:* NE 1115 Indiana St Pullman WA 99163

BRANNING, GRACE
TEACHER, COMPOSER
b Washington, DC, Oct 10, 12. *Study:* Univ Pittsburgh, BM, 37; studied piano, organ & voice with Homer Wickline & comp with Mildred Gardner & Nicolai Lopatnikoff. *Works:* Gethsemane (voice & pianoforte); God's World (women's voices); Capriccio (piano duet); Ballade (piano); Arioso and Dance (flute); Allegro Risoluto (violin); Scene for Icelandic Saga (opera for sop, ten & chorus). *Teaching:* Instr piano, privately, 37-, Pittsburgh Musical Inst, 37-60 & Fillion Studios, 60- *Awards:* Three comp awards, Pittsburgh Piano Teachers Asn. *Mailing Add:* 160 Montclair Ave Pittsburgh PA 15237

BRANSFORD, MALLORY WATKINS
EDUCATOR
b Smoot, WVa, Mar 9, 19. *Study:* Oberlin Consv Music, BM(organ); Butler Univ, BMusEd & MM; Walden Univ, PhD, 76. *Pos:* Organist & choirmaster, Court St United Methodist Church, Rockford, Ill, 36-42 & Zion United Church of Christ, Indianapolis, Ind, 44- *Teaching:* Music specialist, Indianapolis Pub Sch, 44-64; chmn organ dept, Jordan Col Fine Arts, Butler Univ, 60- *Awards:* Distinguished Service Award, Ind Music Educr Asn. *Mem:* Phi Mu Alpha. *Mailing Add:* 4705 Melbourne Rd Indianapolis IN 46208

BRANT, BORIS
TEACHER, VIOLIN
b Odessa, USSR, Jan 10, 26. *US citizen. Study:* Odessa State Consv, 49; Moscow Consv Music, with David Oistrach, 50; Univ Mich, MA, 78. *Teaching:* Prof violin, Stolarsky Sch, Odessa, USSR, 50-74 & Odessa State Consv, USSR, 50-74; artist in res, Mich Coun Arts, 77-80; assoc prof, Bowling Green State Univ, 80- *Awards:* Minister Cult Excellence in Teaching Award, 70; Ukranian Union Cult Workers, Teaching Excellence Award, 73. *Mailing Add:* 1022 Melrose Bowling Green OH 43402

BRANT, HENRY DREYFUS
COMPOSER, EDUCATOR
b Montreal, Que, Sept 15, 13. *US citizen. Study:* Inst Musical Art, with Leopold Mannes; Juilliard Sch Music, with Rubin Goldmark, 30-34; studied with Wallingford Riegger, Aaron Copland & George Antheil. *Works:* Antiphonal Responses, 77; Everybody, Inc (operatic spectacle), 78; Trinity of Spheres, 78; Spatial Concerto: Questions from Genesis (piano, women's chorus, orch & instrm), Cambridge, Mass, 79; Orbits (80 trombones & organ), San Francisco, 79; The Secret Calendar, 80; The Glass Pyramid, 80. *Pos:* Comp & cond doc films, US Govt, 40-47; comp & cond, NBC, CBS & ABC radio, 42-46. *Teaching:* Mem fac, Columbia Univ, 43-53, Juilliard Sch Music, 47-55 & Bennington Col, 57-80. *Awards:* Thorne Fel, 72; NY Coun Arts Grant, 74; Nat Endowment Arts Grant, 76. *Mem:* Life mem, Am Acad-Inst Arts & Lett. *Mailing Add:* Santa Barbara CA

BRATT, C(HARLES) GRIFFITH
COMPOSER, ORGAN
b Baltimore, Md, Nov 21, 14. *Study:* Peabody Consv Music, artists dipl, 39, MMus, 43; Univ Utah; NW Nazarene Col, Hon Dr Mus, 60. *Works:* Symphony #1, Boise Phil Orch; Symphony #2, 58 & A Season For Sorrow (opera), 62, comn by Nat Fedn Music Clubs; Organ Voluntaries For Church Year, World Libr Sacred Music, 58-62; Rachel (opera), Boise Opera Co, 72; Academic Rhapsody, comn by Boise State Univ, 82. *Pos:* Organist & choirmaster, St John's Lutheran & Grace Lutheran Church, Baltimore, Md, 35-43 & St Michael's Episcopal Cathedral, Boise, Idah, 46-; minister music, Luther Place Church, Washington, DC, 43-44 & 46. *Teaching:* Prof music & dept head, Boise State Univ, 46-76. *Awards:* Distinguished Alumni Award, Peabody Consv Music, 71; Idaho Gov Silver Medal (for contributions to the arts), 72. *Bibliog:* Jeanne MacNeil (auth), Idaho in Concert, KAID TV, 77. *Mem:* Am Guild Organist (dean, Les Bois chap, 47-52, state chmn, 52-79); life mem, Nat Fedn Music. *Mailing Add:* 1020 N 17th St Boise ID 83702

BRAUCHLI, BERNARD MARC
CLAVICHORD, ORGAN
b Lausanne, Switzerland, May 2, 44. *Study:* Inst Ribaupierre, Lausanne, 67; New England Consv, MA(musicol), 76. *Rec Perf:* The Renaissance Clavichord, 76, The Renaissance Clavichord II, 78 & Keyboard Sonatas of A Soler, 79, Titanic Rec; Keyboard Sonatas of C Seixas, EMI, 82; Eighteenth Century Basque Keyboard Music, Titanic Rec, 83. *Teaching:* Instr clavichord, Boston Museum Fine Arts, 77-; prof, New England Consv, 83. *Awards:* Julius Adams Stratton Prize for Intercult Achievement, Friends of Switz, Boston, 83. *Mem:* Cambridge Soc Early Music (vpres, 81-). *Interests:* The clavichord—history, technical development, social and musical role. *Publ:* Auth, Le Clavichorde, cet instrument meconnu, Revue Musicale Suisse Romande, 78; Comments on the Lisbon Collection of Clavichords, Galpin Soc J, 80; Le Clavichord dans la Peninsule Jberique, Revue Musicale Suisse Romande, 83; The Clavichord in Thon's Ueber Klavierinstrumente, J Am Musicol Soc, Vol VIII, 83. *Mailing Add:* 82 Oakley Rd Belmont MA 02178

BRAUER, CECILIA GNIEWEK
PIANO, CELESTE
b Detroit, Mich, Nov 17, 23. *Study:* Curtis Inst Music, studied with Isabelle Vengerova, 38-40; studied with Muriel Kerr, 42-48 & Edwin Hughes, 58-62. *Pos:* Soloist & accmp, Nat Music League, 47-49; celeste, Metropolitan Opera Orch, 72- *Mailing Add:* 2267 Hewlett Ave Merrick NY 11566

BRAUGHT, EUGENE A
CONDUCTOR, EDUCATOR
b Stuart, Iowa, Dec 22, 18. *Study:* Simpson Col, Iowa, BMus, 41; Drake Univ, MSE(music), 54; Southern Col Fine Arts, Hon Dr Music, 60. *Pos:* Band & orch dir, East High Sch, Des Moines, Iowa, 41-43; band dir, McAllen, Tex High Sch, 44-48, Bloomfield, Iowa High Sch, 48-52 & Weslaco, Tex High Sch, 52-58; percussionist, Corpus Christi, Tex Symph Orch, 58-62; cond & dir cond & perc wkshps in over 30 states. *Teaching:* Prof music & dir band, Del Mar Col, 58-62; prof & dir band, Univ Okla, 62-71, assoc dir sch music, 71- *Awards:* Okla Bandmasters Hall of Fame, 75. *Mem:* Phi Mu Alpha Sinfonia; Pi Kappa Lambda; Music Educr Nat Conf; Okla Music Educr Asn; Nat Educr Asn. *Publ:* Auth, Yes, We Have Low Bleachers, Instrumentalist, 62; Percussion: Its Application to the Concert Band, Myers, 63; The Balanced Sound of the Concert Band, Sch Musician, 64. *Mailing Add:* Music Dept Univ Okla Norman OK 73069

BRAUN, EDGAR J
MUSIC DIRECTOR & CONDUCTOR, VIOLA
Study: L'Ecole Monteux, studied cond with Pierre Monteux; Univ Calif, studied chamber music with Griller Quartet, MMus, DMus; studied comp & musicianship with Ernst Bloch & Roger Sessions. *Pos:* Guest cond, Netherlands, Mex, Argentina, Vienna, Paris, Lisbon, Poland, Dublin, Germany, Sao Paulo, Rio de Janiero, Czechoslovakia, Rome & Hong Kong; music dir & cond, San Francisco Chamber Orch, 66-; cond, Lake Tahoe Summer Music Fest, currently. *Mailing Add:* San Francisco Chamber Orch San Francisco CA 94111

BRAUN, VICTOR
BARITONE
b Canada. *Rec Perf:* Wolfram in Tannhauser, Decca/London Rec. *Roles:* Goulaud in Pelleas et Melisande & Dr Shon in Lulu, Nat Arts Ctr, Ottawa; Councillor Lindorf, Coppelius, Dapertutto & Dr Miracle in The Tales of Hoffmann, Cologne Opera, 80; Kurwenal in Tristan und Isolde, New Orleans Opera Asn, 83; Ford in Falstaff, Eugene Onegin in Eugene Onegin & Heathcliffe in Wuthering Heights, 83, Portland Opera Asn. *Pos:* Performer, Cologne Opera, Royal Opera House Covent Garden, La Scala & opera co & symphonies throughout North Am & Europe; res mem, Bayerische Staatsoper, Munich. *Awards:* Mozart Compt Winner, 63. *Mailing Add:* c/o Shaw Concerts Inc 1955 Broadway New York NY 10023

BRAUNINGER, EVA JEANNINE
EDUCATOR, DOUBLE BASS
b Fredonia, Kans, July 8, 31. *Study:* Wichita State Univ, BMus, 54; Eastman Sch Music, 55; Ind Univ, Bloomington, 60-62. *Pos:* String bass, Wichita Symph, 50-53; mem orch & chorus, Hormel All-Girl Orch, 54; prin string bass, Des Moines Symph, 63- *Teaching:* Strings, West Des Moines Pub Sch, 73- *Mem:* Suzuki Asn Am. *Mailing Add:* 3108 Giles St West Des Moines IA 50265

BRAUNINGER, JAMES EDWARD
VIOLIN, TEACHER
b Kansas City, Mo, Mar 2, 27. *Study:* Eastman Sch Music, with Andre de Ribaupierre, BM, 51; Univ Tulsa, MM, 55; Univ Ind, studied Daniel Guilet. *Pos:* Asst concertmaster, Des Moines Symph, 63-72 & 73-, concertmaster, 72-73. *Teaching:* Asst prof, Phillips Univ, 53-57 & Bethany Col, Kans, 59-63; string specialist, Des Moines Pub Sch, Iowa, 63- *Mem:* Am String Teachers Asn (Iowa state pres, 70-72). *Mailing Add:* 3108 Giles West Des Moines IA 50265

BRAUNLICH, HELMUT
EDUCATOR, COMPOSER
b Brünn, Czechoslovakia, May 19, 29; US citizen. *Study:* Salzburg Mozarteum, with Kornauth & Keller; Cath Univ Am, with George Thaddeus Jones; Berkshire Music Ctr, with Leon Kirchner. *Works:* Duo for Violin and Trombone, 77; Concerto for Oboe, Strings and Brass; Concerto for 10 Instruments; Wind Quintet; Quartet for Flute, Viola, Bassoon and Piano; Viola Sonatina (trio for clarinet, cello & piano). *Pos:* Violinist & dir personnel, Contemp Music Forum. *Teaching:* Assoc prof music, Cath Univ Am, 61- *Mailing Add:* Sch Music Cath Univ Am Washington DC 20064

BRAVENDER, PAUL EUGENE
EDUCATOR, ADMINISTRATOR
b Flint, Mich, July 17, 36. *Study:* Western Mich Univ, BS, 60; Roosevelt Univ, MM, 70; Mich State Univ, PhD, 77. *Teaching:* Asst prof, Eastern Mich Univ, 75-81; assoc prof & coordr voice div, Memphis State Univ, 81- *Mem:* Nat Asn Teachers Singing (chap pres, 81-); Int Asn Experimental Res Singing; Nat Opera Asn; Nat Asn Music Teachers. *Interests:* Physical damage to female singing voice from hyperfunctional use other than singing. *Publ:* Auth, Oral Interpretation: An Aid in Developing Singing Skill, Nat Asn Teachers Singing Bulletin, 74; Cheerleading and Singing, Univ Mich, 77; Phonational Properties of Choral Blend, Tenn Musician, 80; The Effect of Cheerleading Female Singing Voice, Nat Asn Teachers Singing Bulletin, 80; The Bernoulli Effect and Choral Blend, Am Music Teacher (in prep). *Mailing Add:* 6970 Stout Rd Memphis TN 38119

BRAVERMAN, SAUL
EDUCATOR, ADMINISTRATOR
b New York, NY, Aug 7, 35. *Study:* Columbia Col, NY, 52-54; Juilliard Sch, BS, 57, MS, 59. *Teaching:* Fac, Juilliard Sch, 59-70; prof theory, Manhattan Sch Music, 66-; dir degree studies. *Mem:* Music Theory Soc. *Publ:* Auth, Josef Hofmann, 79 & Fritz Kreisler, 80, Scribners. *Rep:* Dict Am Biography Charles Scribners' Sons 597 5th Ave New York NY. *Mailing Add:* Manhattan Sch Music 120 Claremont Ave New York NY 10027

BRAYNARD, DAVID O
TUBA, EDUCATOR
b Glen Cove, NY, Apr 27, 51. *Study:* Manhattan Sch Music, BM, 76. *Pos:* Soloist, recordings of Parnassus, Group Contemp Music, 75-; outside player, Metropolitan Opera Orch, 75-; freelance tuba, New York Yankees Dixieland Jazz Band & others, 77-; prin tuba, Am Ballet Theater Orch, 82- *Teaching:* Prof tuba, Brooklyn Col, 78- *Bibliog:* Review, New York Times, 11/80. *Mem:* Chamber Music Am. *Mailing Add:* 233 W 99th St 11D New York NY 10025

BREAM, JULIAN
GUITAR & LUTE
b London, England, July 15, 33. *Study:* Royal Col Music; Univ Surrey, hon degree, 68. *Rec Perf:* Guitar Concerto (Malcolm Arnold) & other recordings, RCA Victor. *Pos:* Guitarist worldwide, 46-; Founder, Julian Bream Consort, 60. *Awards:* Order Brit Empire. *Interests:* Elizabethan lute music. *Mailing Add:* c/o Harold Shaw 1995 Broadway New York NY 10023

BRECKNOCK, JOHN LEIGHTON
TENOR
b Derby, UK, Nov 29, 37. *Study:* Birmingham Sch Music, with Frederic Sharp; studied with Denis Dowling. *Rec Perf:* Alfredo Germont in La Traviata; Duke of Mantua in Rigoletto; Edgardo Ravenswood in Lucia di Lammermoor. *Roles:* Alfred in Die Fledermaus, Sadler's Wells Opera, London, 66; Don Ottavio in Don Giovanni, Nat Arts Ctr, Ottawa, 73 & Metropolitan Opera, 78; Vasco da Gama in Story of Vasco, Sadler's Wells Opera, London, 74; Tonio in Daughter of the Regiment, Baltimore Opera, 78; Count Almaviva in The Barber of Seville, 82-83. *Pos:* Tenor, Covent Garden, Teatro Colon, Paris Opera & many other Europe & North Am opera co. *Mailing Add:* c/o Dorothy Cone Inc 250 W 57th St New York NY 10019

BREDA, MALCOLM JOSEPH
EDUCATOR, CONDUCTOR
b Alexandria, La, Aug 14, 34. *Study:* Xavier Univ La, BS, 56; Ind Univ, MMusEd, 62; Univ Southern Miss, PhD, 75; Univ Nebr; Harvard Univ; Atlanta Univ; Eastman Sch Music; Western Wash State; Westminster Choir Col. *Rec Perf:* Christmas at Boys Town, 65 & Nat Cath High Sch Chorus, 72, Capital La. *Pos:* Accmp, pianist & organist, Father Flanagan's Home for Boys, Nebr, 64-67. *Teaching:* Asst prof music, Ala Agricultural & Mechanical Univ, 56 & 58-64; from assoc prof to prof, Xavier Univ La, 67- *Awards:* Fel, Nat Fel Fund, 73-75. *Mem:* Music Educr Nat Conf; Nat Asn Schs Music. *Mailing Add:* 7325 Palmetto St New Orleans LA 70125

BREESKIN, BARNETT
CONDUCTOR
b New York, NY, Feb 20, 14. *Study:* Long Island Univ, 31-32; Brooklyn City Col, 32-34. *Pos:* Mem violin sect, Nat Orch, 39-45; cond & mgr, Miami Beach Symph Orch, 55-; chmn, Miami Beach Social Serv Adv Bd. *Teaching:* Private lessons, Md & Washington. *Mem:* Cult Exec Coun Dade Co. *Mailing Add:* 420 Lincoln Rd Miami Beach FL 33139

BREHM, ALVIN
COMPOSER
b New York, NY, Feb 8, 25. *Study:* Studied string bass with Fred Zimmerman, 38-43; studied orch with Vittorio Giannini, 42-43; Juilliard Sch, dipl, 43; Columbia Univ, BS, 46, MA, 50; studied comp with Wallingford Riegger, 48-51. *Works:* Violin Concertino, 76; Concerto for Piano and Orch, 78; Metamorphy, 79; A Pointe at His Pleasure (chamber music for Renaissance instrm), comm by Walter W Naumberg; Quintet for Brass, comm by Am Brass Quintet; Concerto for Contrabass and Orchestra, YMHA Symph, 83. *Pos:* Personnel mgr, RCA Victor Rec, 58-63, Robert Shaw Chorale, 59-65, Masterworks Chorus, 60-68 & Vanguard Rec, 65-72; double bassist, Lincoln Ctr Chamber Music Soc, 70-83; chmn music panel, NY State Coun Arts, 82-83; guest artist with Lincoln Ctr Chamber Music Soc, 70-; Budapest Quartet, Lenox Quartet, Comp Quartet, NY Woodwind Quintet, White House, Speculum Musicae, NY Phil & others. *Teaching:* Mem fac, State Univ NY, Plattsburgh, 51-53, Mannes Sch, 68-70, Manhattan Sch, 69-75 & Queens Col, 72-75; artist in res, State Univ NY, Stony Brook, 68-75; prof, State Univ NY, Purchase, 72-, dean music div, 82-; instr comp sem & cond conct, Ind Univ, NC Sch Fine Arts, Swarthmore Col, Bennington Col, Columbia Col & others. *Awards:* Grants, NY State Coun Arts, 72 & Naumberg Found, 77. *Mem:* Am Music Ctr (mem bd dir, 80); ASCAP. *Mailing Add:* 302 W 86th St New York NY 10024

BRENDE, ALFRED
PIANO, WRITER
b Wiesenberg, Czechoslovakia, Jan 5, 31; Austrian citizen. *Study:* Piano with Sofija Deselic, Ludovika von Kaan, Paul Baumgartner, Edward Steuermann & Edwin Fischer, comp with A Michl & harmony with Franjo Dugan; Univ London, Hon DMus, 78. *Rec Perf:* Complete piano works of Beethoven; Schubert's piano works 1822-28; works by Mozart & Liszt; rec on Turnabout & Philips. *Pos:* Conct tours throughout Europe, Latin Am, North Am, & Australia; performer with maj orchs in Europe & US; appearances at maj festivals worldwide. *Awards:* Grand Prix des Disquaires, France, 75; Deutscher Schallplattenpreis, 76; Wiener Flötenuhr, 76. *Bibliog:* Manuela Hoelterhoff (auth), Alfred Brendel: Today's Most Formidable Pianist, Wall St J, 2/26/82. *Publ:* Auth, Musical Thoughts and Afterthoughts, 76; contribr to Phono, Fono Forum, Österreichische Muzikzeitschrift, New Grove Dict of Music & Musicians, Hi-Fi Stereophone & others. *Mailing Add:* c/o Colbert Artist Mgt 111 W 57th St New York NY 10019

BRENNER, ROSAMOND DROOKER
COMPOSER, ORGAN

b Cambridge, Mass, Mar 23, 31. *Study:* Radcliffe Col, AB, 53, AM(teaching), 54; Vienna Acad Music, Austria, 54-56; Geneva Consv Music, Switzerland, cert(organ), 59; Brandeis Univ, PhD, 68. *Works:* The Choice (cantata), Trinity Church, Wheaton, Ill, 75 & 76; Love and Unity, The Desire & Be Not Grieved, perf by Simon Estes & Rosamond Brenner, 76; Darkness Hath Fallen, Baha'i World, Vol XVI, 78; Healing, Gladness, Gratitude & Exaltation (meditations), Baha'i Publ Trust (in prep). *Pos:* Organist & choir dir, Trinity Episcopal Church, Wheaton, Ill, 71-78. *Teaching:* Fac mem, Brandeis Univ, 64-66 & Columbia Col, Chicago, 72-74; prof music hist, Boston Consv Music, 67-70; prof musicol & organ, Am Consv Music, 71-75; private teacher organ, piano & harpsichord, currently. *Awards:* Fulbright Grant, 54-56. *Mem:* Glen Ellyn Musicians' Club; Ill State Music Teachers' Asn; Am Women Comp Inc. *Interests:* Baroque music. *Publ:* Auth, Emotional Expression in Keiser's Operas, Music Rev, England, 72. *Mailing Add:* 726 North Park Blvd Glen Ellyn IL 60137

BRESNICK, MARTIN
COMPOSER, EDUCATOR

b New York, NY, Nov 13, 46. *Study:* Hartt Sch Music, Univ Hartford, AB, 67; Stanford Univ, MA, 68, DMA, 72; Akad Musik, Vienna, 69-70. *Works:* Ocean of Storms, 70 & 3 Intermezzi, 71, Bote & Bock; B's Garlands, 73, Wir Weben, Wir Weben, 78, Conspiracies, 79, Der Signal, 82 & High Art, 83, Alexander Broude Inc Publ. *Teaching:* Instr, San Francisco Consv Music, 71-72; lectr, Stanford Univ, 72-75; asst prof, Dept Music, Yale Univ, 76-81; assoc prof, Yale Sch Music, 81- *Awards:* Prize, Am Acad Rome, 75; Awards, Nat Endowment Arts, 72, 75 & 79; Premio Ancona, Italy, 80. *Mem:* Conn Comp Inc (mem bd dir, 81-); ASCAP; Am Music Ctr. *Publ:* Auth, Cage's Unexpected Offspring, Mosaic, 73; Today's Music, In: How Music Works, Macmillan, 81. *Mailing Add:* Yale Sch Music 96 Wall St New Haven CT 06520

BRESSLER, CHARLES
TENOR, EDUCATOR

b Kingston, Pa, Apr 1, 26. *Study:* Juilliard Sch Music, dipl, 50, post-grad dipl, 51; studied voice with Lucia Dunham, Sergius Kagen & Marjorie Schloss. *Rec Perf:* On Decca, Columbia, Cambridge, Project 3 & Nonesuch. *Pos:* Mem, New York Pro Musica, 53-60, Santa Fe Opera, formerly & Wash Opera Soc, formerly; ten soloist, New York Chamber Soloists; frequent appearances with Boston Symph, Chicago Symph, San Francisco Symph Orch, Los Angeles Symph Orch, Minneapolis Symph & New York Phil; recitalist, London & New York. *Teaching:* Mem fac, Mannes Col Music, 66-, mem fac voice, 78-; mem fac, NC Sch Arts, 78- & Manhattan Sch Music, 78- *Awards:* Best Male Singer, Nat Fest Paris, 60. *Mailing Add:* c/o Melvin Kaplan Inc 1860 Broadway New York NY 10023

BRETT, PHILIP
CRITIC-WRITER, EDUCATOR

b Edwinstowe, England, Oct 17, 37; US citizen. *Study:* King's Col, Cambridge, England, BA, 58, BMus, 61, MA, 62, PhD, 65. *Teaching:* Fel & asst lectr, King's Col, Cambridge, Univ, 63-66; asst prof, Univ Calif, Berkeley, 66-71, assoc prof, 71-78, prof, 78- *Awards:* Archibald T Davison Medal, Harriet Cohen Int Awards, 70; Noah Greenberg Perf Award, Am Musicol Soc, 80. *Mem:* Am Musicol Soc; Royal Musical Asn; Plainsong & Medieval Music Soc. *Interests:* Early English music; performance practice; William Byrd; Benjamin Britten. *Publ:* Ed, Consort Songs, Musica Britannica, Vol XXII, Royal Music Asn, 69, 74; William Byrd: Consort Songs, Byrd Ed, Vol XV, 70, William Byrd: Madrigals, Songsand Canons, Byrd Ed, Vol XVI, 75 & William Byrd: The Masses, Byrd Ed, Vol IV, 81, Stainer & Bell; Benjamin Britten: Peter Grimes, Cambridge Univ Press, 83. *Mailing Add:* 980 Middlefield Rd Berkeley CA 94708

BREUNINGER, TYRONE
TROMBONE, EDUCATOR

b Red Hill, Pa, Jan 9, 39. *Study:* West Chester State Col, BS(music educ), 61; Temple Univ, MMus(trombone), 66. *Pos:* Co-first trombone, Philadelphia Symph Orch, 67- *Teaching:* Instr music, Folcroft Borough Sch Dist, Pa, 61-64; instr lower brass instrm, West Chester State Col, 64-82; instr trombone, Temple Univ, 75-82, New Sch Music, 69-82 & Philadelphia Col Perf Arts, 72-82. *Mem:* Phi Mu Alpha Sinfonia. *Mailing Add:* Philadelphia Orch 1420 Locust St Philadelphia PA 19102

BREVIG, PER (ANDREAS)
TROMBONE, EDUCATOR

Halden, Norway, Sept 7, 36. *Study:* Studied trombone with Palmer Traulsen, 58 & cond with Leopold Stokowski, 66-67; Juilliard Sch, BM, 68, MM, 69, DMA, 71. *Rec Perf:* Trombone Concerto (Egil Hovland), Philips; rec on Philips, CRI, MMO, DMLP & Desto. *Pos:* Mem, Bergen Symph Orch, Norway, 57-65; first trombone, Am Symph Orch, 65-68; prin trombone, Metropolitan Opera Orch, 68-; prin trombone & cond, Aspen Music Fest, 70- *Teaching:* Mem fac & cond chamber music, Juilliard Sch, 66-; teacher, Aspen Music Fest, 70-; mem fac & cond trombone, Mannes Col Music, 76- *Awards:* S Koussevitzky Fel, Tanglewood Music Fest, 61 & 66; First Prize, XIV Int Music Compt, Prague, 62; Henry B Cabot Award, Boston Symph Orch, 66. *Mem:* Bohemians; Nat Soc Lit & Arts. *Publ:* Auth, Avant-Garde Techniques in Solo Trombone Music, Problems of Notation and Execution, 71. *Mailing Add:* Juilliard Sch Lincoln Ctr New York NY 10023

BREWER, CHRISTINE
SOPRANO

b Springfield, Ill, Oct 26, 55. *Study:* McKendree Col, Ill, BA(perf), 76; vocal instr with Edmund LeRoy, 79- & Margaret Harshaw, 82- *Pos:* Soloist & section leader, St Louis Symph Chorus, 77-; soloist & chorister, Opera Theatre of St Louis, 80-; soloist, Bach Soc of St Louis, 81- & Opera on the Road, Opera Theatre of St Louis, 82- *Awards:* Thomas Peck Award for Most Promising Young Singer, St Louis Symph, 82. *Mailing Add:* c/o Opera Theatre of St Louis PO Box 13148 St Louis MO 63119

BREWER, EDWARD
HARPSICHORD, ORGAN

b Erie, Pa, Aug 31, 37. *Study:* Oberlin Consv Music, BM & AB, 60; Staatliche Hochschule Musik, Frankfurt am Main, with H Walcha, 61-63; Univ Ill, Champaign, MusM, 63. *Rec Perf:* On Nonesuch, VSM & Musical Heritage, 74-80; Art of the Trumpet, Vox, 80; Bach Inventions, Pantheon, 83. *Pos:* Harpsichordist & organist, freelance solo & chamber music, 63- *Mailing Add:* 110 Leonia Ave Leonia NJ 07605

BREWER, LINDA JUDD
CELLO, EDUCATOR

b Arkansas City, Kans, Nov 13, 45. *Study:* Chamber music with Raymond Cerf & Karel Blaas; Univ Kans, studied cello with Raymond Stuhl, BM; Univ Tex, studied cello with Adolphe Frezan, George Neikrug & Phyllis Young, chamber music with Andor Toth & Leonard Shure & bass with Stuart Sankey, MM, 69, DMA, 78. *Pos:* Prin cellist & soloist, Kans Univ Orch, 64-65 & 65-66; mem, Aspen Fest Orch, 71 & 72; soloist, Oklahoma City Symph, formerly & Aspen Phil Orch, 72. *Teaching:* Asst prof, Univ Wis, 74- *Awards:* Regional Winner, NMTA Col Artists Auditions, 70; First Pl, Aspen Cello Comp, 72; First Prize, Holtzschue String Award. *Mailing Add:* Dept Music Univ Wis La Crosse WI 54601

BREWER, RICHARD H
MUSIC DIRECTOR, EDUCATOR

b San Diego, Calif, Aug 12, 21. *Study:* San Jose State Univ, BA(music), 43; Columbia Univ, 43; Ind Univ, Bloomington, MMus, 49; Westminster Choir Col, 51-52; Univ Calif, Los Angeles; Summer Choral Inst, San Diego State Col, with Robert Shaw & Julius Herford, 53-55; Univ Southern Calif, DMA, 64. *Works:* My Sheep Hear My Voice, 63, Sing to the Lord of Harvest, 63 & Rejoice and Be Merry, 63, Brodt Music Co; The Resurrection and Ascension of Jesus (oratorio), Shawnee Press, 68; Away in a Manger (SATB children), Theodore Presser. *Rec Perf:* Testament of Freedom (Randall Thompson), Gloria (John Rutter), Te Deum (Verdi) & Mozart Mass in F, K 192, Pfeiffer Choir & Orch. *Pos:* Dir music, Highland Park Presby Church, Los Angeles, 58-60, Wilshire Methodist Church, Los Angeles, 61-62 & First Methodist Church, Salisbury, NC, 72-79. *Teaching:* Grad asst, Ind Univ, 48-49; asst prof choral music, Minot State Col, NDak, 49-51; assoc prof choral voice theory, Omaha Univ, 52-55; prof music & dir choral activities, Pfeiffer Col, Misenheimer, NC, 62-, chmn, Dept Music & Div Fine Arts, 62-73. *Awards:* Alumni Merit Award, Westminster Choir Col, 68. *Mem:* Pi Kappa Lambda; Am Choral Dir Asn; Phi Mu Alpha; Music Educr Nat Conf; Nat Asn Teachers Singing. *Publ:* Auth, The Processional in the Non-Liturgical Church, Music Minstry, 62; The Polychoral Works of Michael Praetorius, 66 & The Two Oratorios of C P E Bach in Relation to Performance, 82, Choral J. *Mailing Add:* Dept Music Pfeiffer Col Misenheimer NC 28109

BREZNIKAR, JOSEPH (JOHN)
GUITAR, EDUCATOR

b Cleveland, Ohio. *Study:* Cleveland State Univ, BA; Univ Akron, MMus; studied with Sophocles Papas, 73-74, Carlos Barbose Lima, 75-78, Abel Carlevard, 78 & Guido Santorsola, 79. *Rec Perf:* The Contemporary Classical Guitar! Music From Two Continents, Coronet Rec, 82. *Teaching:* Lectr class guitar, Cleveland State Univ, 73-80; instr, Univ Akron, 73-80; asst prof, Southern Ill Univ, Carbondale, 80- *Awards:* Cert Excellence, Music Educr Nat Conf, 80. *Mem:* New York Soc Classic Guitar; Guitar Found Am; Music Educr Nat Conf; Am String Teachers Asn. *Mailing Add:* Sch Music Southern Ill Univ Carbondale IL 62901

BRICARD, NANCY (NANCY BRICARD WOODS)
PIANO, TEACHER

b San Francisco, Calif, Feb 17, 33. *Study:* Univ Southern Calif, with Lillian Steuber, BMus, 55; Nat Consv Music, Paris, France, with Marcel Ciampi, 57-63; Univ Southern Calif, MMus, 65. *Rec Perf:* Sonata for Horn and Piano (Halsey Stevens), Entracte Rec, 76. *Teaching:* Assoc prof piano, Univ Southern Calif, 72- *Mem:* Music Teachers Nat Asn; Calif Asn Prof Music Teachers; Am Fedn Musicians. *Publ:* Coauth, Memory Problems in Concert Performers, Col Music Symposium, 78. *Mailing Add:* 5284 Los Diegos Way Los Angeles CA 90027

BRICCETTI, THOMAS BERNARD
MUSIC DIRECTOR, COMPOSER

b Mt Kisco, NY, Jan 14, 36. *Study:* Studied with Jean Dansereau, 48-60; Eastman Sch Music, with Bernard Rogers, 53-55; Grad Sch Fine Arts, Columbia Univ, 54-55; studied with Richard Lert, 63-64, with Samuel Barber, Peter Mennin & Alan Hovhaness. *Works:* Three Songs, Op 2 (voice & chamber orch); Violin Concerto, comn by Nat Endowment Arts, 67; Roman Sketches (violin, viola & cello trio); Turkey Creek March (band); Fountain of Youth (overture for orch), 72; Five Love Poems (mixed chorus & orch); Sonata for Flute & Piano, Op 14. *Pos:* Pianist & comp, 55-62; music dir & cond, Pinellas Co Youth Symph, Fla, 62-68, St Petersburg Symph Orch, Fla, 63-68, St Petersburg Civic Opera Co, 63-68 & Ft Wayne Phil, Ind, 70-78;

assoc cond, Indianapolis Symph, 68-72; music dir, Univ Circle Orch, Cleveland Inst Music, 72-75, Omaha Symph, 75- & Fest Thousand Oaks, 78-; guest cond, various orchs in North Am & Europe, 72-; founder & music dir, Nebr Sinfonia, 77- *Teaching:* Mem fac, Univ Nebr, Omaha, 76- *Awards:* Prix de Rome, Ital govt, 58-59; Ford Found Comp Fels, 60-61; Yaddo Grant, 63. *Mem:* ASCAP; Phi Mu Alpha Sinfonia. *Rep:* Grapa Concerts USA 1995 Broadway Suite 204 New York NY 10023. *Mailing Add:* 603 N 38th St Omaha NE 68131

BRICKMAN, JOEL IRA
COMPOSER, TEACHER

b New York, NY, Feb 6, 46. *Study:* Manhattan Sch Music, BMus, 68, MMus, 70. *Works:* Sonata for Saxophone, perf by Paul Eisler, 71; Thousands of Days, perf by Manhattan Orch, Manhattan Sch Music, 72; Of Wonder (SATB), 72 & Suite for Woodwind Quintet, Assoc Music Co, G Schirmer, Inc; Prelude & Caprice, Pietro Deiro Music, 73; Three Songs for Voice & Orch, perf by Ridgewood Chamber Orch, 77; Prelude & Dithyramb, perf by Ridgewood Symph Orch, 79. *Teaching:* Instr comp & orch, Manhattan Sch Music, 71-81; instr theory & comp, Marymount Col, 72-78. *Awards:* Comp Contest, Manhattan Sch Music, 72; US Test Comp, Am Accordionists' Asn, 73; World Test Comp, Accordion Coupe Mondiale, Vichy, France, 73. *Mem:* Col Music Soc; ASCAP. *Mailing Add:* 90 Edison Ct Monsey NY 10952

BRICKMAN, MIRIAM
PIANO, CONDUCTOR & MUSIC DIRECTOR

b Gt Barrington, Mass, Dec 6, 33. *Study:* Queens Col, BA, 56; Juilliard Sch Music, with Alton Jones, MS, 67; Berkshire Music Ctr; Columbia Univ, study cond with Hound Shanet & chamber music with F Galimeve & W Trampler; study piano with Ray Lav. *Pos:* Southeast Asian tours, incl Hong Kong, Indonesia, Singapore, Philippines & Japan, 77, 80 & 83; guest artist, Bronx Arts Ens, 79-; music dir & solo recitalist, Australia, NZ & SPac, 73; guest artist, major groups & orch in US & Europe; freelance musician & staff accmp, Juilliard Sch Music. *Teaching:* Adj prof music, Baruch Col, Queensborough Community Col, LaGuardia Community Col & Col Staten Island, City Univ New York, 69-75; private coaching chamber groups & singers, currently. *Awards:* Scholar, Rockefeller Found, 66-67. *Mem:* Bohemians; Alton Jones Asn (vpres, 78). *Publ:* Auth, Use of Multiple Key Approach With Creative Methods to Piano Playing, Yamaha Music Sch, 78. *Mailing Add:* 210 Lakeview Pl Riverdale NY 10471

BRIDE, KATHLEEN
HARP, TEACHER

b Plainfield, NJ. *Study:* Marywood Col, with Marcel Grandjany, BMus, 67; Juilliard Sch, with Marcel Grandjany, MSci, 70. *Rec Perf:* New Music (Berio), 68 & Contemporary Music, 68, Philips; New Music (Berio), RCA Victor, 68; Ascension Voluntaries, Church of Ascension, New York, 77. *Pos:* Solo harpist, Juilliard Ens Contemp Music, 67-70; assoc ed, Am Harp J, 80- *Teaching:* Fac mem harp, Prep Div, Manhattan Sch Music, 75-; Instr music theory & functional piano, William Paterson Col NJ, 76-82. *Awards:* Award of Appreciation, Am Harp Soc Inc, 78 & 83. *Mem:* Am Harp Soc (dir mid-Atlantic region, 77-83). *Publ:* Auth, How To Ship a Harp, Am Harp J, summer 82. *Mailing Add:* 13 Schuyler Ave Pequannock NJ 07440

BRIDGER, CAROLYN
EDUCATOR, PIANO

Study: Oberlin Consv, BM; Ind Univ, MM; Univ Iowa, DMA; Mozarteum Akad, Salzburg; Boston Univ, studied with Bela Nagy. *Pos:* Soloist with major orchs in US, formerly & with Bela Trio, SAm, formerly. *Teaching:* Instr, Emory Univ, Univ NC & Delta State Univ, formerly; Assoc prof piano, Fla State Univ, 76- *Awards:* Schubert Prize Accompanying, Schubert Inst, Austria. *Mailing Add:* Sch Music Fla State Univ Tallahassee FL 32306

BRIEF, TODD L
COMPOSER

b New York, NY, Feb 53. *Study:* New England Consv Music, BM, 76, MM, 78; Harvard Univ, AM, 81, PhD, 83. *Works:* Fantasy (violin & piano), Stroud Fest, 79; Concert Etude (piano), Michael Dewart, 81; Cantares (sop & large orch), Dutch Phil Orch, 82 & Rome Radio Orch, 83; Moments (harp), Susan Jolles, 83; Canto (flute), Am Comp Alliance, 83; Slow Lament (ms & piano), comn by Fromm Music Found, 83. *Awards:* Joseph H Bearns Prize, Columbia Univ, 76; Prix de Rome, Am Acad in Rome, 81-82; Guggenheim Fel, 83-84. *Mem:* BMI; Am Comp Alliance. *Rep:* Am Comp Alliance 170 W 74th St New York NY 10012. *Mailing Add:* 100 Bleeker St #18D New York NY 10012

BRILL, HERBERT M
ASSISTANT CONCERTMASTER, VIOLIN

b Portland, Maine, Mar 31, 17. *Study:* Eastman Sch Music, BA & perf cert violin, 39. *Pos:* Asst concertmaster, Rochester Phil Orch, 63- *Mailing Add:* 84 Rockhill Rd Rochester NY 14618

BRILL, MICHELLE MATHEWSON
VIOLA

b San Francisco, Calif, Nov 29, 56. *Study:* Col Consv Music, Univ Cincinnati, BMus, 79, MMus, 81; viola perf studies with Donald McInnes, Peter Kamnitzer & Karen Tuttle. *Pos:* Viola sect mem, Cincinnati Chamber Orch, 74-81; substitute mem, Cincinnati Symph, 81; prin viola, Omaha Symph, 81- *Mailing Add:* 4730 Chicago St #10 Omaha NE 68132

BRINDEL, BERNARD
COMPOSER, EDUCATOR

b Chicago, Ill, Apr 23, 12. *Study:* Chicago Musical Col, BM, MM, 46; studied with Isaac Levin & Paul Held, 26-31 & Max Wald, 44-48. *Works:* Two Songs for Soprano, Grace Bumbry, 65; String Quartet No 2, Contemp Arts String Quartet, 66; The Lonely, Nat Music Camp Chorus, 66; Sonata for Violin & Piano, Elaine Skorodin & Ruth Greene, 73; Music for Strings No 4, Sinfonia Musicale, 82; Cello Concertino No 1, Jill Brindel & Carolyn Pope Kobler, 82; String Quartet No 3, San Francisco Symph String Quartet, 83. *Pos:* Dir music & choral cond, Beth Hillel, Wilmette, Ill, 58-62 & Temple Sholom, Chicago, 64-78. *Teaching:* Theory & comp, Chicago Musical Col, 46-54, Morton Col, Ill, 54-79, Nat Music Camp, Interlochen, 55-67 & New Trier Exten, Ill, 80- *Awards:* Am Fedn Music Award, 73; William C Byrd Artists Award, 76. *Mailing Add:* 2740 Lincoln Lane Wilmette IL 60091

BRINGS, ALLEN STEPHEN
COMPOSER, PIANO

b New York, NY, Feb 24, 34. *Study:* Queens Col, BA, 55; Columbia Univ, with Otto Luening, MA, 57; Boston Univ, with Gardner Read, MusAD, 64; Princeton Univ, with Roger Sessions. *Works:* Sonata (solo violin), 59 & Capriccio & Notturno (orch), 77, Seesaw Music Corp; Sonata (piano), 77, Concerto (orch), 78 & Quintet (strings), 79, Mira Music Assoc; Quintet (brass), 81 & Lamentationes Jeremiae Prophetae (chr & perc), 81, Seesaw Music Corp. *Rec Perf:* Saccade (Helps), 78, Three Pieces (Pleskow), 78 & Metamorphosis (Moore), 78, CRI; Antiphonies (Leo Kraft), 80 & Three Sonatas (Clementi), 80, Orion Master Rec. *Teaching:* Instr music, Bard Col, 59-60; teaching fel, Boston Univ, 60-62; lectr to prof, Queens Col, City Univ New York, 63- *Awards:* ASCAP Award, 74- *Mem:* Am Soc Univ Comp (chmn, region II, 68-72); ASCAP; Am Musicol Soc; Col Music Soc. *Mailing Add:* 199 Mountain Rd Wilton CT 06897

BRINK, EMILY RUTH
EDUCATOR, COMPOSER

Grand Rapids, Mich, Oct 21, 40. *Study:* Calvin Col, BA, 62; Univ Mich, MM, 64; Northwestern Univ, PhD, 80. *Works:* Four Preludes on Genevan Psalm Tunes, Geneva Music Press, 74; Eight Heidelberg Catechism Songs, CRC Bd Publ, 78. *Pos:* Music ed, CRC Bd Publ, Mich, 83- *Teaching:* Asst prof music theory, State Univ NY, New Paltz, 66-67, Trinity Christian Col, 67-72 & Univ Ill, Urbana-Champaign, 74-83. *Mem:* Col Music Soc; Soc Music Theory. *Interests:* Cognitive approach to the teaching of aural skills viewed as applied music theory. *Publ:* Auth, A Look at E Gordon's Theories, Coun Res Music Educ, 83; Ed, Psalter Hymnal Sampler, CRC Bd Publ, 83. *Mailing Add:* 81 Maryland NE Grand Rapids MI 49503

BRINK, ROBERT
EDUCATOR, VIOLIN

Study: New England Consv Music; Harvard Univ; studied violin with Jaques Malkin & Albert Spaulding. *Rec Perf:* Over 30. *Pos:* Violin, chamber music & orch appearances throughout North Am, Europe, Scand & Iceland; concertmaster, US & Can tour, Boyd Neel Chamber Orch, formerly & Boston Classical Orch, currently; TV appearances on PBS, CBS & CBC. *Teaching:* Mem fac, Boston Univ, formerly; mem fac violin, New England Consv Music, currently. *Mailing Add:* New England Consv Music 290 Huntington Rd Boston MA 02115

BRINKMAN, ALEXANDER R
ELECTRONIC, EDUCATOR

Study: Eastman Sch Music, BA, MA, PhD; studied comput music synthesis with Leland Smith & Barry Vercoe. *Works:* Systenarius, Mass Inst Technol, 78. *Teaching:* Mem fac, Eastman Sch Music, 73-75, asst prof music, 76- *Awards:* Nat Defense Educ Act Fel, 66-69. *Mem:* Soc Music Theory; Am Musicol Soc; Col Music Soc; New York Theory Soc; Comput Music Asn. *Interests:* Computer applications in music; coding, languages and data structures for computer analysis of music. *Publ:* Contribr to Music Theory Spectrum & Proc Int Comput Music Conf. *Mailing Add:* Eastman Sch Music 26 Gibbs St Rochester NY 14604

BRION, (K) KEITH
CONDUCTOR & MUSIC DIRECTOR, EDUCATOR

b Philipsburg, Pa, July 9, 33. *Study:* West Chester State Col, BS(music educ), 55; Rutgers Univ, MEd, 61. *Rec Perf:* Wind Music (Alan Hovhaness), Mace Rec, 69; Stars & Stripes Forever & Marching Along With Sousa, 83, Bainbridge Rec. *Pos:* Founder & dir, NJ Wind Symph, 63-71; band dir & cond in res, Yale Sch Music, 73-80; asst dir, Waterloo Music Fest, 76-80; freelance orch pops cond, 80-; music dir, New Sowa Band, 83- *Mem:* Am Symph Orch League. *Mailing Add:* 57 Mill Rock Rd New Haven CT 06511

BRISCOE, JAMES ROBERT
EDUCATOR, CRITIC & WRITER

b Decatur, Ala, Dec 24, 49. *Study:* Univ Ala, BMus, 72; Univ NC, MA(music), 74, PhD(musicol), 79. *Teaching:* Asst prof music hist, Meredith Col, Raleigh, NC, 76-80; assoc prof, Butler Univ, Indianapolis, 80- *Awards:* Fels, French Govt, 76, Danforth Found, 79-85 & Nat Endowment Humanities, 81. *Mem:* Am Musicol Soc; Music Libr Asn; Col Music Soc. *Interests:* Music of Debussy; women composers and the 19th century. *Publ:* Auth, The Practical Sources of Early Organum, Current Musicol, 76; Debussy d'apres Debussy, 19th-Century Music, 81; Debussy Festival, Indianapolis 1982, J Musicol, 83. *Mailing Add:* c/o Jordan Col Fine Arts Butler Univ 4600 Sunset Ave Indianapolis IN 46208

BRISMAN, HESKEL
COMPOSER, TEACHER
b New York, NY, May 12, 23. *Study:* Juilliard Sch; Yale Sch Music; Columbia Univ; Berkshire Music Ctr; studied with Ernst Toch, Luigi Dallapiccola, Richard Donovan, Quincy Porter & Paul Hindemith. *Works:* Sinfonia Breve, Carl Fischer; Whirligig (one act opera), Theodore Presser; Concerto for Horn & Orchestra, perf by William Kuyper, with Masterwork Chamber Orch; Concerted Music for Piano & Percussion, perf by Elizabeth Marshall, with Paul Price Perc Ens; Don't Listen to the Wind (cantata), perf by Ars Musica Chorale & Orch; Dialogue for Flute & Percussion, perf by Paul Price Perc Ens; Andante Sostenuto for Strings, perf by Garden State Chamber Orch. *Pos:* Comp, Sermi Film Music, Rome, Italy, 59-62; ed, Carl Fischer, Inc, 67-69. *Teaching:* Dir, Joseph Achron Consv, Petakh-Tikva, Israel, 64-67. *Awards:* Fel, Nat Endowment Arts, 75 & NJ State Coun Arts, 81; ASCAP Award, 81 & 82. *Mem:* ASCAP; Nat Asn Comp USA; Musicians Club New York (mem bd dir, 79-); Comp Guild NJ. *Mailing Add:* 961 E Lawn Dr Teaneck NJ 07666

BRITAIN, RADIE
COMPOSER
b Silverton, Tex. *Study:* Am Consv, BM, 25; Musical Arts Consv, DM, 58. *Works:* Drums of Africa (SATB & TTBB), Witmark & Son, 34; Noontide (SSAA), Heroico Music Publ, 35; Heroic Poem (orch), Juilliard Publ, 38; Prison (chamber orch), 40; Nisan (SSAA & strings), 63, Brothers of the Clouds (TTBB & orch), 64 & Epiphyllum for Piano, 71, Heroico Music Publ. *Teaching:* Piano & comp, private studios, Amarillo, Tex, 26-28 & Hollywood, Calif, 40-60; instr comp, Chicago Musical Col, 35-40. *Awards:* First Nat Prize, Suite for Strings, Sigma Alpha Iota, 41; First Nat Prize, Light Orchestra, Boston Womans Symph, 45; First Nat Prize, Cosmic Mist Symphony, Nat League Am Pen Women, 65. *Mem:* ASCAP; Nat League Am Pen Women; MacDowell Club. *Mailing Add:* 1945 N Curson Ave Hollywood CA 90046

BRITTON, ALLEN PERDUE
EDUCATOR
b Elgin Ill, May 25, 14. *Study:* Univ Ill, BSc, 37, MA, 39; Univ Mich, PhD, 50. *Pos:* Ed, J Res Music Educ, Music Educr Nat Conf, 53-72; Am Music Quart J, Univ Ill Press, 81- *Teaching:* Music, Griffith Ind Public Sch, 38-41; instr music, Eastern Ill Univ, 41-43; prof music, Univ Mich, 49-, dean, Sch Music, 69-79. *Bibliog:* A H Goodman (auth), Music Education Perspectives and Perceptions, Kendall-Hunt, 82. *Mem:* Am Musicol Soc (coun mem, 64-65); Music Educr Nat Conf (pres, 60-62); Soc Ethnomusicol; Sonneck Soc (ed, 80-). *Interests:* Early American sacred music. *Publ:* Auth, Singing School in the United States, Int Soc Music, 62; Music: A New Start, In: Britannica Review of American Education, 69; coauth, Bibliography of American Sacred Music, Am Antiquarian Soc, 83. *Mailing Add:* 1475 Warrington Dr Ann Arbor MI 48103

BRITTON, DAVID
TENOR
b Louisville, Ky. *Study:* NTex State Univ, BMus; Juilliard Sch; Manhattan Sch Music. *Rec Perf:* St Matthew Passion, 83 & Maestro di Musica, 83, EMI, Angel. *Roles:* Shepherd in La Dafne, Fest Two Worlds, Spoleto, Italy, 73; St Stephen in Four Saints in Three Acts, Metropolitan Opera Mini-Met, 73; Belmonte in The Abduction From The Seraglio, San Francisco Opera, 75; Prince in Cinderella, Dallas Civic Opera, 79; Tamino in The Magic Flute, Caracas Opera, 79; Bastien in Bastien und Bastienne, Mostly Mozart Fest, 81; Count Almaviva in The Barber of Seville, Opera Lyon, 82. *Pos:* Guest soloist with Am & European orch & groups including New York Phil Orch, Chicago Symph, Detroit Symph, Baltimore Symph, Dallas Symph, L'Orch France, Mexico City Symph & Spoleto Fest Two Worlds, Italy. *Mem:* Am Guild Musical Artists; Am Fedn TV & Radio Artists; Actor's Equity Asn; Phi Mu Alpha. *Mailing Add:* c/o Colbert Artists Mgt 111 W 57th St New York NY 10019

BROCK, KARL
TENOR, EDUCATOR
b Great Bend, Kans, June 17, 30. *Study:* With Paul Althouse & Alice Nichols; studied dramatics with Rose Landver. *Roles:* Tamino in Die Zauberflöte, Basel Opera, 57; Florestan in Fidelio, Don Jose in Carmen; Christoph in Verlobung in San Domingo; Canio in Pagliacci; Rodolfo in La Boheme; Bacchus in Ariadne auf Naxos. *Pos:* Tenor with maj opera co in US & Europe. *Teaching:* Mem fac, Univ Wis, Oshkosh, formerly; prof opera & voice, Univ Southern Miss, currently. *Mailing Add:* Dept Music Univ Southern Miss Hattiesburg MS 39401

BROCKETT, CLYDE WARING, JR
EDUCATOR, WRITER
b Norfolk, Va, Aug 30, 34. *Study:* Columbia Univ, MA, 62, PhD(musicol), 65. *Teaching:* Asst prof musicol, Ohio Univ, 66-68, Univ Wis, Milwaukee, 68-70, Univ Ky, 70-72 & Christopher Newport Col, 78- *Mem:* Am Musicol Soc; Int Musicol Soc; Music Libr Asn; Medieval Acad Am; Renaissance Soc Am. *Interests:* Latin liturgical chant; liturgical drama; music in the humanities. *Publ:* Auth, Antiphons, Responsories and Other Chants of the Mozarabic Rite, Inst Medieval Music, 68; Noeane and Neuma- A Theoretical and Musical Equation, Int Musicol Soc Cong Report, 74; Saeculorum Amen and Differentia: Practical Versus Theoretical Tradition, Musica Disciplina, 76; Easter Monday Antiphons and the Peregrinus Play, Kirchenmusikalishces Jahrbuch, 78; The Role of the Office Antiphon in Tenth-Century Liturgical Drama, Musicaq Dicsiplina, 80; Guido's Monochord, Current Musicol, 81. *Mailing Add:* 6160 Westwood Terr Norfolk VA 23508

BROCKMAN, JANE ELLEN
COMPOSER, LECTURER
b Schenectady, NY, Mar 17, 49. *Study:* Univ Mich, Ann Arbor, with Leslie Bassett, Eugene Kurtz, George Balch Wilson & Wallace Berry, BM, 71, MM, 73, DMA, 77; studied with Max Deutsch, 75-76. *Works:* Eventail for Orchestra, Fargo-Moorhead Symph Orch, 73; Tower Music (carillon), Hudson-Ladd, World Conf Carillonneurs, France, 74; Music for Clarinet and Piano, David Harman, 81; Metamorphosis (four channel electronic work), Lawrence Goodridge, 82; Tell-Tale Fantasy, Arsis Press, 82; Autumnal Contrasts for Wind Ensemble, Larry Rachleff, 82. *Pos:* Advance rev, G Schirmer Books, 80 & 82. *Teaching:* Asst prof music, Univ RI, Kingston, 77-78, Univ Conn, 78-83, Hartt Sch Music, 83- *Awards:* Fulbright-Hays & Alliance Francaise Fel, 75-76; Johnson Comp Conf Fel, 81; MacDowell Colony Residencies, 82 & 83. *Bibliog:* Ruth Anderson (auth), Am Women Comp, A Biographical Dict, 78 & 82; Composium, Dir New Music, Crystal Music Works, 83. *Mem:* Comp Forum; Col Music Soc; BMI. *Rep:* Clara Lyle Boone 1719 Bay St SE Washington DC 20003. *Mailing Add:* 448 W 37th St #6H New York NY 10018

BRODY, CLARK L
CLARINET, EDUCATOR
b Three Rivers, Mich, June 9, 14. *Study:* Mich State Univ, BA, 34; Eastman Sch Music, BA, 36, perf cert, 37. *Rec Perf:* Trio for Clarinet, Viola and Piano (Mozart), Oxford Rec Co, 48; Serenade Op 24 (Schönberg), Counterpoint, 49; Mozart Quintet in E Flat for Piano & Winds (Mozart), 78 & L'Histoire du Soldat (Stravinsky), 78, RCA. *Pos:* Solo clarinetist, CBS Symph Orch, NY, 41-51; prin clarinet, Chicago Symph Orch, 51-78. *Teaching:* Prof clarinet, Northwestern Univ, 78- *Mailing Add:* Sch Music Northwestern Univ Evanston IL 60201

BRODY, ELAINE
EDUCATOR, CRITIC-WRITER
b Apr 21, 23; US citizen. *Study:* Wash Sq Col, New York Univ, AB, 44; Columbia Univ, AM(musicol), 60; New York Univ, PhD(music), 64. *Teaching:* Instr music, Wash Sq Col, New York Univ, 63-65; asst prof, Univ Col, New York Univ, 65-66, asst prof & chmn, 66-67, assoc prof & chmn, 67-70, prof & chmn, 70-73, prof grad sch, 70- *Awards:* John Dewey Award, 71; Six grants, William Randolph Hearst Found, 72-77. *Mem:* Am Musicol Soc (coun mem, 71-73); Col Music Soc; Music Libr Asn; Int Music Libr Asn. *Interests:* Music in a socio-historical context; culture of cities; French music 1870-1925. *Publ:* Auth, Music in Opera, Prentice Hall, 70; The German Lied and Its Poetry, New York Univ Press, 71; The Music Guide to Austria and Germany, 75, The Music Guide to Great Britain, 75, The Music Guide to Belgium, Luxembourg, Holland and Switzerland, 78 & Music Guide to Italy, 78, Dodd Mead & Co. *Mailing Add:* 35 E 84th St New York NY 10028

BROEKEMA, ANDREW J
ADMINISTRATOR, EDUCATOR
b Grand Rapids, Mich, Apr 21, 31. *Study:* Univ Mich, BMus, 53, MMus, 54; Univ Tex, Austin, DPhil, 62. *Teaching:* Instr music, Univ Tex, Austin, 57-62; asst prof & asst dir, Sch Music, Ohio State Univ, 62-65, prof & dean, Col Arts, 76-; prof & chmn, Dept Music, Eastern Ky Univ, 65-68; chmn, Dept Music, Ariz State Univ, 68-76. *Mem:* Int Coun Fine Arts Deans (pres, 82-); Comn on Arts, Nat Asn State Univ & Land Grant Col (chmn, 81-82); Music Teachers Nat Asn (chmn higher educ, 81-83); Phi Mu Alpha Sinfonia; Pi Kappa Lambda. *Publ:* Auth, The Music Listener, William C Brown, 78. *Mailing Add:* 3048 Leeds Rd Columbus OH 43221

BROEMEL, ROBERT W
BASSOON
b Chicago, Ill. *Study:* Northwestern Univ, BM, 60; studied with Willard Elliot. *Pos:* Prin bassoonist, Lyr Opera Chicago, 66, Grant Park Symph, Chicago, 66-78 & Indianapolis Symph, 70- *Mailing Add:* 5458 Michigan Rd Indianapolis IN 46208

BROFSKY, HOWARD
EDUCATOR, TRUMPET
b New York, NY. *Study:* Studied comp with Nadia Boulanger, 54-55; NY Univ, PhD, 63. *Teaching:* Instr, NY Univ, 55-59; asst prof, Univ Chicago, 60-67; assoc prof, Queens Col, 67-70, prof, 70- *Mem:* Am Musicol Soc; Int Musicol Soc; Col Music Soc; Nat Asn Jazz Educr. *Interests:* Eighteenth century; jazz history. *Publ:* Auth, The Symphonies of Padre Martini, Musical Quart, 65; The Keyboard Sonatas of Padre Martini, Quadrivium, 67; Jommelli e Padre Martini, Rivista Ital di Musicol, 73; Doctor Burney and Padre Martini, Musical Quart, 79; coauth, The Art of Listening: Developing Musical Perception, Harper & Row, 4th ed, 79. *Mailing Add:* 186 Riverside Dr New York NY 10024

BROIDO, ARNOLD PEACE
ADMINISTRATOR, PIANO
b New York, NY, Apr 8, 20. *Study:* Ithaca Col, BS, 41; Columbia Univ, MA, 54. *Pos:* Ed & prod mgr, Boosey & Hawkes Inc, 45-55; vpres & gen mgr, Century Music & Mercury Music Corp, 55-57; educ dir, Edward B Marks Music Corp, 57-62; dir publs & sales, Frank Music Corp, 62-69; vpres, Boston Music Co, 68-69; pres, Theodore Presser Co, 69-; pres, Oliver Ditson Co, 69-; chmn, Elkan-Vogel Inc, 70- *Teaching:* Teacher instrm music, East Jr High Sch, Binghamton, NY, 41-42. *Mem:* ASCAP (dir, 72-); Am Music Ctr (mem bd dir, 68-72 & 78-83); Music Publ Asn US (secy & mem bd dir, 65-70, first vpres, 70-72, pres, 72-73 & 80-82 & dir, 83-); Int Publ Asn (vpres music sect, 72-80); Music Indust Coun (pres, 66-68, vpres, 69-70). *Publ:* Coauth, Music Dictionary, 56 & Invitation to the Piano, 59. *Mailing Add:* c/o Theodore Presser Co Presser Place Bryn Mawr PA 10910

BROILES, MELVYN
TRUMPET, EDUCATOR
b Coquille, Ore. *Study:* Juilliard Sch; studied with Vacchiano. *Works:* Chamber pieces for woodwind & brass ens. *Pos:* Prin trumpet, Metropolitan Opera Orch, 58- *Teaching:* Mem fac trumpet, Manhattan Sch Music, 63-, Juilliard Sch Music, 71- & Mannes Col Music, currently. *Mem:* Metropolitan Opera Asn. *Mailing Add:* 243 W 70th St #9F New York NY 10023

BROMLEY, RICHARD H
EDUCATOR, COMPOSER
b Charleston, Ill, July 18, 38. *Study:* Lawrence Col, with James Ming, BM, 60; Am Consv, with Leo Sowerby & Stella Roberts, MM, 67; Univ Colo, with Philip Batstone, Charles Eakin & David Diamond, DMA, 74. *Works:* Tensegrity, 67; Synergia No 4, 71; Texture of Time, 73. *Teaching:* Assoc prof music, Eastern Ky Univ, 74- *Awards:* Nat Endowment Arts Grant, 71. *Mailing Add:* Music Dept Eastern Ky Univ Richmond KY 40475

BRONFMAN, YEFIM
PIANO
b Tashkent, Russia, 1958. *Study:* Studied with Arie Vardi, 73-76; Juilliard Sch Music & Curtis Inst Music, 76-78. *Pos:* Guest soloist, Montreal Symph, 75; Israel Phil Orch, 76 & 78-82, New York Phil, 77 & 81-82, Toronto Symph, 81-82, Los Angeles Phil, Philadelphia Orch, Jerusalem Symph Orch, Mostly Mozart Fest, New York, Hollywood Bowl, Spoleto Fest, Charleston & Italy & many others; participant, Marlboro Music Fest, 76; soloist & recitalist, Australia, 78, South Am, 79-82 & Europe, 81-82. *Awards:* Am-Israel Cult Found Fel, 76. *Mailing Add:* c/o ICM Artists 40 W 57th St New York NY 10019

BRONS, MARTHA (PARKER)
CELLO, ADMINISTRATOR
b Chicago, Ill, Apr 16, 34. *Study:* Univ Ill, BMus, 55; Phil Acad, MMus, 65. *Pos:* First chair cello & soloist, Haddonfield Symph, 59-75; freelance cellist, Philadelphia, NJ & Del, 59-75; cellist & pres, Heritage Chamber Players, 76- *Teaching:* Cello, privately, NJ & SC, 61-; instr string methods, Phil Musical Acad, 63-69. *Mailing Add:* 302 Hermitage Rd Greenville SC 29615

BRONSON, BERTRAND HARRIS
WRITER, MUSICOLOGIST
b Lawrenceville, NJ, June 22, 02. *Study:* Univ Mich, AB, 21; Harvard Univ, MA; Univ Oxford, BA, MA; Yale Univ, PhD; Univ Leval, D es L; Univ Chicago, LHD; Univ Calif, LLD; Univ Mich, LHD. *Awards:* Guggenheim Fel, 43, 44 & 48; Am Coun Learned Soc Award, 59; Wilbur Cross Medal, Yale Univ, 70. *Mem:* Am Acad Arts & Science; Int Folk Music Coun; Am Folklore Soc; Brit Acad. *Publ:* Auth, The Ballad as Song, Univ Calif Press, 69; ed, The Traditional Tunes of Child's Ballads (four vol), 59-72 & The Singing Tradition of Child's Popular Ballads, 75, Princeton Univ Press. *Mailing Add:* 927 Oxford St Berkeley CA 94707

BRONSTEIN, RAPHAEL
VIOLIN, EDUCATOR
Study: Petrograd Imp Consv; studied violin with Leopold Auer & chamber music with Alexander Glazounov. *Pos:* Leader, Glazounov Quartet; performer, concerts in Russia & Europe; ed & analyst, Bach's works. *Teaching:* Mem fac, Teachers Col, Columbia Univ, formerly & Boston Univ, formerly; mem fac violin, Manhattan Sch Music, 68- & Kniesel Hall Sch Chamber Music, currently; vis prof, Hartt Sch Music, 48-; Mannes Col Music, currently; guest lectr, Leningrad Consv, 66 & US cols & univ. *Awards:* Artist-Teacher Award, Am String Teachers Asn, 76. *Publ:* Auth, The Science of Violin Playing, Paganiniana Publ. *Mailing Add:* Manhattan Sch Music 120 Claremont Ave New York NY 10027

BROOK, BARRY SHELLEY
MUSICOLOGIST, EDUCATOR
b New York, NY, Nov 1, 18. *Study:* City Col, City Univ New York, BSS, 39; Columbia Univ, MA, 42; Univ Paris, Dr l'Univ, 59; Univ Adelaide, Hon PhD. *Pos:* Ed in chief, RILM Abstracts Music Lit Quart, 67- & Symphony 1720-1840, 79- *Teaching:* Prof music, Queens Col, City Univ New York, 45-, co-dir, Res Ctr Music Iconography; vis prof, Grad Sch Arts & Sci, NY Univ, 60-61; lectr, Univ Paris, 67-68; distinguished vis prof, Eastman Sch Music, 73; vis centenary prof, Univ Adelaide, 74; mem fac, Juilliard Sch, 77- *Awards:* Guggenheim Fel, 61-62 & 66-67; Dent Medal, Royal Music Asn, 65; Chevalier Order Arts & Lett, French govt, 72. *Mem:* Int Asn Music Libr (pres, 77-80); Int Music Coun, UNESCO (pres, 82-); Am Coun Learned Soc. *Publ:* Auth, La Symphonie Francaise Dans la Seconde Moitie du XVIIIe Siecle, 62; ed, Breitkopf Thematic Catalogue, 1762-1787, 66; Musicology 1960-2000: A Practical Program, Three Symposia, 70; Music, 18th Century: A Current Bibliography, Philology Quart, 71; auth, Thematic Catalogues in Music: An Annotated Bibliography, 72; contribr to many prof publ. *Mailing Add:* 50 Central Park W New York NY 10023

BROOK, CLAIRE
ADMINISTRATOR, WRITER
b New York, NY. *Study:* Queens Col, City Univ New York, BA, 45; Columbia Univ, MA, 47; study with Nadia Boulanger, Paris, 47-48. *Pos:* Managing ed, RILM Abstr Music Lit, 68-69; assoc music ed, W W Norton, 69-73, music ed, 73- & vpres, 79- *Awards:* Distinguished Alumni Award, Aaron Copland Sch Music, Queens Col, 82. *Mem:* Am Music Ctr (coun mem, 71-82, vpres, 75-82); Col Music Soc (coun mem, 75-78); Am Inst Verdi Studies (secy, 76-82); Am Musicol Soc; Music Libr Asn. *Publ:* Coauth (with E Blody), Music Guide to Austria and Germany, 75, Music Guide to Great Britain, 75, Music Guide to Belgium, Luxembourg, Holland & Switzerland, 76 & Music Guide to Italy, 77, Dodd, Mead; co-ed (with E Clinkscale), A Musical Offering: Essays in Honor of Martin Bernstein, Pendragon Press, 77. *Mailing Add:* 50 Central Park W New York NY 10023

BROOK, STEVEN HENRY
VIOLA, VIOLIN
b Grand Haven, Mich, Aug 28, 56. *Study:* Mich State Univ, BM, 78. *Pos:* Prin second violin, Grand Rapids Symph Orch, 79-; violist, Fontana Ens, Mich, 79- *Mailing Add:* 1316 Atlantic NW Grand Rapids MI 49504

BROOKS, RICHARD J
COMPOSER, WRITER
b Syracuse, NY, Dec 26, 42. *Study:* Crane Sch Music, State Univ NY, Potsdam, BS, 66; State Univ NY, Binghamton, studied theory with William Mitchell & comp with Karl Korte, MA, 71; New York Univ, with Ursula Mamlok & Michael Czajkowski, PhD, 81. *Works:* Rapunzel (opera), 69, Sonata (violin & piano), 73, Last Night I Was the Wind (bar & wind quintet), 76, Chorale Variations, 80, Symphony in One Movement, 81, Collage (wind ens), 81 & trio (piano, violin & violoncello), 81, Am Comp Alliance. *Teaching:* Asst prof music, Nassau Community Col, 75- *Awards:* Res grant, State Univ NY, 77; arts in soc fel, Community Col Proj, City Univ New York, 82; comp fel, Nat Endowment for Arts, 82-83. *Mem:* Am Soc Univ Comp (chmn exec comt, 77-82); Music Theory Soc NY (mem bd dir, 75-80); Am Comp Alliance (mem bd gov, currently); Soc Music Theory; Am Music Ctr. *Interests:* Theory of music. *Publ:* Coauth, Layer Dictation: A New Approach to the Bach Chorales, Longman Inc, 78. *Mailing Add:* 107 W 86th St New York NY 10024

BROOKS, WILLIAM F
COMPOSER, WRITER
b New York, NY, Dec 17, 43. *Study:* Wesleyan Univ, BA, 65; Univ Ill, MMus, 71, DMA, 76. *Works:* Madrigals, Schott, 77-78; Medley, comn by British Arts Coun, 78; Wallpaper Pieces, perf by Neely Bruce, 79-83; Footnotes, perf by Michael Cedric Smith, 81-83; The Legacy, comn by Gulbenkian Found, 83. *Pos:* Freelance comp & scholar, 77- *Teaching:* Asst prof, Univ Calif, Santa Cruz, 73-75 & Univ Calif, San Diego, 75-77; sr lectureship, Int Coun Exchange Scholars, 77-78. *Awards:* Sr Fel, Inst Studies Am Music, 83; fel, Nat Endowment Arts, 83. *Mem:* ASCAP; Sonneck Soc; Int Asn Study Popular Music. *Interests:* Popular music; all aspects of music in the United States. *Publ:* Auth, Ives Today, In: An Ives Celebration, Univ Ill Press, 77; Maledette Competenza, Perspectives New Music, 79; The American Piano, In: The Book of the Piano, Phaidon, 81; Choice and Change in Cage's Recent Music, TriQuarterly 54, 82; On Being Tasteless, Popular Music 2, Cambridge Univ Press, 82. *Mailing Add:* 714 Ridge Rd Orange CT 06477

BROTHERS, LESTER D
EDUCATOR, WRITER
b Hanford, Calif, July 10, 45. *Study:* Calif State Univ, Fresno, BA, 67; Univ Calif, Los Angeles, MA, 70, PhD, 73. *Teaching:* Lectr musicol, Calif State Univ, Long Beach, 73-74; asst prof musicol, NTex State Univ, 74-79, assoc prof, 79-, coordr musicol, 81- *Mem:* Am Musicol Soc (chmn, Southwest chap, 79-81, coun, 83-); South-Cent Renaissance Conf (vpres, 81, pres, 82). *Interests:* Sacred vocal music of 16th & 17th centuries; colonial Latin American music; 20th century American Music. *Publ:* Auth, A New World Hexachord Mass by Francisco Lopez Capillas, In: Yearbook Inter-Am Musical Research, 73; Avery Burton and His Hexachord Mass, Musica Disciplina, 74; Sixteenth Century Spanish Musicians in the New World, Explorations in Renaissance Cult, 78; New Light on an Early Tudor Mass, Musica Disciplina, 78; Ten biographical entries on American composers, In: Die Musik in Geschichte und Gegenwart, 79. *Mailing Add:* 2608 Sherwood Lane Denton TX 76201

BROUWER, MARGARET LEE
VIOLIN, COMPOSER
b Ann Arbor, Mich. *Study:* Consv Music, Oberlin Col, BM(perf), 52; Mich State Univ, MM(perf), 63; studied with Andor Toth & Stuart Canin. *Works:* Dream Drifts, comn & perf by Ellen Rose, 83. *Pos:* First violin, Tex Little Symph, 72-79 & Gallery String Quartet Kimball Art Museum, Tex, 73-77; assoc concertmaster, Ft Worth Opera Orch, 79- *Teaching:* Instr violin, Elmhurst Col, 64-69. *Mailing Add:* Ft Worth Opera Orch 3505 W Lancaster Ft Worth TX 76107

BROWN, A PETER
CRITIC, EDUCATOR
b Chicago, Ill, Apr 30, 43. *Study:* Domaine Sch, 65; Northwestern Univ, BM, 65, MM, 66, PhD, 70; NY Univ, 70. *Teaching:* Lectr, Ind Univ NW, 67-69; asst prof, Univ Hawaii, Honolulu, 69-74; prof, Ind Univ, Bloomington, 74- *Awards:* Am Council Learned Soc Fel, 72-73; John Simon Guggenheim Mem Found Fel, 78-79. *Mem:* Am Musicol Soc; Music Libr Asn; Int Musicol Soc. *Interests:* Music in Vienna 1700-1830; history of orchestral music; style analysis, Joseph Haydn. *Publ:* Coauth, Joseph Haydn in Literature, Henle Publ, 74; auth, Carlo d'Ordonez: A Thematic Catalogue, Info Coordr, 78; Approaching Musical Classicism, Col Music Symph, 80; The Symphonies of Carlo d'Ordonez, Haydn Yearbk, 81; Traetta and the Genesis of Haydn Aria, Haydn Studien, 83. *Mailing Add:* Music Dept Ind Univ Bloomington IN 47405

BROWN, BEATRICE
CONDUCTOR, VIOLA
b Leeds, England, May 17, 17; US citizen. *Study:* Music Sch Settlement, artists dipl, 37; Hunter Col, with Louise Talma, BA, 37; Sch Arts & Sci, New York Univ, with Philip James & Curt Sachs, MA, 43. *Pos:* Prin viola, Am Symph Orch, 62-63; music dir & cond, Scranton Phil Orch & NE Pa Phil, 63-72, Ridgefield Orch, 70-, Western Conn Symph Orch, 81-82 & Housatonic Chamber Orch, 81- *Teaching:* Tutor music, Hunter Col, 37-43; instr, Bronx High Sch Sci, 70-79; asst prof, Lehman Col, 72-73. *Awards:* Hall of Fame, Hunter Col, 72; United Nations Peace Medal, 80; Contemporary Music Award, Nat League Am Penwomen, 81. *Bibliog:* Carolyn Eisele (auth), Beatrice Brown, Hunter Alumni Quart, 69; Beatrice Brown, Conn Pub TV, 79. *Mem:* Cond Guild (mem bd dirs, 81-); Am Symph Orch League; Am Fed Musicians. *Mailing Add:* 39 Glenbrook Rd Stamford CT 06902

BROWN, CORRICK LANIER
CONDUCTOR & MUSIC DIRECCTOR
b Santa Rosa, Calif, Mar 8, 30. *Study:* Stanford Univ, BA, 51; Univ Calif, Berkeley; Acad Musik, Vienna; study with Richard Lert, Hans Swarowsky & Adolph Baller. *Rec Perf:* Sacre du Printemps (Stravinsky), S C Rec, 76. *Pos:* Cond & music dir, Santa Rosa Symph, 57-; guest cond, Los Angeles, Fresno, San Francisco, Vienna & Seville. *Rep:* Pietro Menci Kincora New Beer Rd Seaton Devon England. *Mailing Add:* PO Box 1766 Santa Rosa CA 95402

BROWN, DAVID AULDON
COMPOSER, EDUCATOR
b Birmingham, Ala, Feb 6, 43. *Study:* Curtis Inst, with Myron Fink. *Works:* Toccata (piano), 71; Sonatina (piano), 72; Piano Trio, 75; Woodwind Quintet; Suite for Flute & Piano; Rondo Fantasy; Variations (string orch). *Teaching:* Mem fac, Wilmington Music Sch, 67- & Univ Del, 72- *Awards:* First Prize, Comp Guild Cont, Salt Lake City, 72. *Mailing Add:* 2220 Marsh Rd Wilmington DE 19810

BROWN, DONALD CLAYTON
ADMINISTRATOR, EDUCATOR
b Little Rock, Ark, Sept 18, 38. *Study:* Univ SC, BA, 61; Sch Church Music, Southwestern Baptist Sem, MMus, 64, DMA, 73. *Teaching:* From asst prof to prof music hist, choral & church music, William Jewell Col, 67-83, chmn dept music, 81- *Mem:* Southern Baptist Church Music Conf (pres, 74-75); Music Educr Nat Conf; Hymn Soc Am; Am Choral Dir Asn. *Interests:* Hymnody, particularly English hymnody. *Publ:* Auth, Practical Lessons in Conducting, Conv Press, 82. *Mailing Add:* 431 Monterey Liberty MO 64068

BROWN, EARLE
COMPOSER
Study: Northeastern Univ, 44-45; Schillinger House Sch Music, 46-50; studied with Dr Kenneth McKillop, Jesse Smith & Dr Roslyn Brogue Henning, 47-50. *Works:* Syntagm III (8 instrm), Fondation Maeght, Fest St Paul Vence, France, 70; New Piece Loops (large orch & chorus), Venice Bienale Musica, Int, 71-72; Time Spans (large orch), City Kiel, West Germany, 72; Sign Sounds (chamber orch), State Univ NY, Albany, 72; Centering (solo violin & chamber orch), London Sinfonietta, 73; Cross Sections and Color Fields (large orch), Denver Symph Orch, 75; Windsor Jambs (soprano & chamber orch), Fromm Music Found, 80. *Pos:* Guest cond, Contemp Music Fest, St Lawrence Univ, 70, Oberlin Consv Summer Fest & Inst, 71 & 81, Aspen Summer Music Fest, 71 & 81, Contemp Music Fest, Capital Univ Consv Music, 72 & Saarbrucken Rundfunk, 81. *Teaching:* Guest comp & lectr, Darmstadt Summer Courses, 64-65, Univ Wide Student Comp Fest, State Univ NY, 72 & Contemp Music Fest, Capital Univ Consv Music, 72; comp, Berkshire Music Ctr, 68; comp in res, Peabody Inst Consv Music, 68-73, Rotterdam Phil & Consv, 74, Calif Inst Arts, 74-, Aspen Summer Music Fest, 75 & 81, Berkshire Music Ctr, 75 & Am Dance Fest, NC, 81; featured guest comp, Contemp Music Fest, St Lawrence Univ, 70, Oberlin Consv Summer Fest & Inst, 71 & Saarbrucken Rundfunk, 81; exterior examr, doctorate prog, York Univ, England, 70-71; guest prof, Basel Consv, Switzerland, 75; vis prof, State Univ NY, Buffalo, 75, Univ Calif, Berkeley, 76, Calif Inst Arts, 77, Univ Southern Calif, 78 & Yale Univ, 80-81. *Awards:* NY State Coun Arts Award, 74; Nat Endowment Arts Award, 74; Brandeis Univ Creative Arts Award, 77. *Bibliog:* Joan La Barbara (auth), Earle Brown's Homage to Alexander Calder, Musical Am, 7/80; Virgil Thomas (auth), Sculpture in Sound, Time Mag, 1/24/69; Michael Nyman (auth), Experimental Music, Schirmer Books. *Mem:* Am Music Ctr (mem bd trustees, 83-). *Publ:* Notation, 64 & Form in New Music, 65, Darmstuden Beitrage; Auth, Serial Music Today, Breaking the Sound Barrier, Dutton, 81. *Mailing Add:* c/o ICI 799 Broadway Suite 642 New York NY 10003

BROWN, FRANK NEIL
TROMBONE, EDUCATOR
b Nevada, Tex, Sept 14, 42. *Study:* NTex State Univ, BM, 64, DMA, 78. *Rec Perf:* The Ithaca Brass Quintet, Golden Crest Rec, 73. *Pos:* Prin trombone, Ft Worth Opera Orch, 65-68 & 79-, Ft Worth Symph Orch, 65-68 & Richardson Symph Orch, Tex, 80-; trombonist, Ithaca Brass Quintet, 70-76. *Teaching:* Assoc prof trombone, Ithaca Col, 70-76; asst prof, Univ Tex, Austin, 76-77 & Tex Christian Univ, 79- *Mem:* Tex Music Educr Asn; Int Trombone Asn; Tuba Universal Brotherhood Asn. *Mailing Add:* 2940 Furneaux Ln Carrollton TX 75007

BROWN, HOWARD MAYER
EDUCATOR, MUSICOLOGIST
b Los Angeles, Calif, Apr 13, 30. *Study:* Harvard Univ, AB, 51, MA, 54, PhD, 59. *Teaching:* Instr, Wellesley Col, 58-60; from asst prof & prof, Univ Chicago, 60-76, Ferdinand Schevill Distinguished Serv Prof, 76-; King Edward Prof, Univ London, 72-74. *Awards:* Guggenheim Fel, 63-64; Villa I Tatti Fel, Harvard Univ, 69-70. *Mem:* Int Musicol Soc (vpres, 82-88); Am Musicol Soc (pres, 78-80); fel, Am Acad Arts & Sci. *Interests:* Music in Renaissance and late Middle Ages. *Publ:* Auth, Music in the French Secular Theater, 1400-1550, 63 & Instrumental Music Printed Before 1600, 65, Harvard Univ; Embellishing Sixteenth-Century Music, Oxford, 74; Music in the Renaissance, Prentice-Hall, 78; ed, Florentine Chansonnier from the Time of Lorenzo the Magnificent (2 vols), Chicago Press, 83. *Mailing Add:* 1415 E 54th St Chicago IL 60615

BROWN, JONATHAN BRUCE
COMPOSER
b Highland, Ill, June 18, 52. *Study:* Cent Mich Univ, BA, 74; Univ Hawai, Manoa, MM, 76; NTex State Univ. *Works:* Laminations (brass quintet), 75 & Strata (tuba & perc quartet), 75, Seesaw Music Corp; Warmth of Distant Suns (three pieces for orch), Honolulu Symph, 76; Lyric Variations (tuba, strings & orch), Seesaw Music Corp, 80; Energies (clarinet, perc & piano), 82, Of Gifts, The Highest and the Best (a cappella choir), 83 & For Celebration (choral ens), 83, Quadrivium Music Press. *Teaching:* Asst prof music, Pikeville Col, 76-79; teaching fel, NTex State Univ, 81-83. *Mem:* ASCAP; Phi Mu Alpha Sinfonia. *Mailing Add:* 1005 Monterey Denton TX 76201

BROWN, KEITH
EDUCATOR, CONDUCTOR & MUSIC DIRECTOR
b Colorado Springs, Colo, Oct 21, 33. *Study:* Univ Southern Calif, studied trombone with Robert Marsteller & cond with Ingolf Dahl, BM, 57; Manhattan Sch Music, MM, 64. *Rec Perf:* Three Italian Masques (Franchetti), 59 & Serenade (Wyner), 59, CRI; New York Brass Quintet in Concert, Golden Crest Rec Inc, 59; Igor Stravinsky Conducts 1961 (octet), Columbia Rec, 61; Keith Brown Solo Recording, Golden Crest Rec Inc, 71; Keith Brown (three solo albums), Music Minus One, 73; Footlifters (Incredible Columbia All-Star Band), Columbia Rec, 75. *Pos:* Trombonist, New York Brass Quintet, 58-59; assoc first trombonist, Philadelphia Orch, 59-62; prin trombonist, Metropolitan Opera Orch, 62-65 & Fest Casals Orch, San Juan, PR, 58-80; trombonist, Chamber Music Soc Lincoln Ctr, 69- *Teaching:* Dir instrm activ & prof music, Temple Univ, 65-71; prof, Ind Univ, Bloomington, 71- *Awards:* Sch Music Alumni Award, Univ Southern Calif, 57; special award, Asoc Musical, Caracas, Venezuela, 79; hon fac mem, Cent Consv Music, Beijing, China & Shanghai Consv, China, 82. *Bibliog:* Harold C Schonberg (auth), Musical Softball, New York Times, 7/24/62; Hurshelene Journey-McCarty (auth), There's More Pub, Etc, Sch Musician, 64; Harold C Schonberg (auth), And No Busted Fingers, New York Times, 5/30/65. *Mem:* Int Trombone Asn. *Publ:* Edited numerous works originally for other instruments & voice for use on trombone, for study or solo as well as ten volumes of orchestra excerpts for trombone and tuba. *Rep:* Int Music Co 545 Fifth Ave New York NY 10017. *Mailing Add:* Sch Music Ind Univ Bloomington IN 47405

BROWN, LEON FORD
EDUCATOR, TROMBONE
b Taylorsville, NC, Jan 14, 18. *Study:* Okla State Univ, BFA, 40; Catholic Univ Am, MA, 45; NTex State Univ. *Teaching:* Fac mem brass instrm, US Navy Sch Music, 42-46; prof trombone, NTex State Univ, 46-83. *Mem:* Tex Music Educr Asn; Tex Asn Col Teachers; Int Trombone Asn (mem bd dir, 72-80). *Publ:* Auth, The Trombone Legato, 55 & The Brass Choir in the Sch Music Program, 56, Southwestern Musician; The Brass Choir, 57 & Study Literature for F-Attachment Trombone, 69, Instrumentalist; Trombone Forum—Trombone Past and Present, Southwestern Brass J, 57. *Mailing Add:* 2907 Nottingham Denton TX 76201

BROWN, MALCOLM HAMRICK
EDUCATOR, WRITER
b Carrollton, Ga, Nov 9, 29. *Study:* Sch Music, Converse Col, BMus, 51; Sch Music, Univ Mich, MMus, 56; Sch Music, Fla State Univ, PhD, 67. *Teaching:* Head piano dept, Dept Music, Mt Union Col, 56-59; prof musicol, Sch Music, Ind Univ, Bloomington, 62-, chmn, 72-79. *Awards:* Res grants, Am Coun Learned Soc, 69-70, Rockefeller Found, 69-70, Lilly Endowment, 81-82 & Am Coun Learned Soc & Acad Sci USSR, 82. *Mem:* Am Musicol Soc (mem coun, 81-83); Am Asn Advan Slavic Studies (mem ed bd, Slavic Rev, 82-84). *Interests:* Russian and Soviet-Russian music; the life and works of Prokofiev. *Publ:* Ed, Papers of the Yugoslav-American Seminar on Music, Ind Univ, 70; auth, Prokofiev's War and Peace: A Chronicle, Musical Quart, 7/77; Skriabin and Russian Mystic Symbolism, 19th Century Music, 7/79; ed, Musorgsky: In Memoriam, 1881-1981, UMI Res Press, 82; contribr, Art and Society in 19th Century Russia, Ind Univ Press, 83. *Mailing Add:* 6701 E Bender Rd Bloomington IN 47401

BROWN, MERRILL EDWIN
EDUCATOR, WRITER
b Council Bluffs, Iowa, Mar 10, 26. *Study:* Simpson Col, Iowa, BM, 49; Drake Univ, MME, 54; Univ Iowa, PhD, 67. *Teaching:* Dir band & orch, Council Bluffs, Iowa, 54-59; instrm music dir, Carthage Col, Wis, 59-67; chmn fine & applied arts dept, Dakota State Col, SDak, 67-73; prof music, Univ Toledo, 73- *Mem:* Music Educr Nat Conf; Nat Asn Col Wind & Perc Instr; Am Musical Instr Soc. *Interests:* Wind and percussion literature in college recitals. *Publ:* Auth, Wind and Percussion Ensembles Most Often Performed in College Student Recitals, Nat Asn Col Wind & Perc Instr J, 75; An Established Repertoire for Chamber Ensembles, Instrumentalist, 77; Guide for Developing a Woodwind Solo Repertoire, Woodwind World—Brass & Perc, 79; Don't Lose Your Band or Orchestra Because of Dropouts, Instrumentalist, 80; Teaching the Successful High School Brass Section, Parker Publ Co, 81. *Mailing Add:* 5718 Candlestick Ct E Toledo OH 43615

BROWN, MERTON LUTHER
COMPOSER, PIANO
b Berlin, Vt, May 5, 13. *Study:* Study comp with Wallingford Riegger & Carl Ruggles. *Works:* Catabile, New Music Soc, 46; Consort (four voices), perf by William Masselous & Maro Ajamian, 47; Sonata (piano), Grete Sultan, Times Hall, NY, 48; Concerto Breve, perf by L'orch Allesandro Scalatti da Napoli, Naples, 60; Suite Per Archi, 62; Divertimento, Bicentennial Conct, 75; Concerto Grosso (conct band), comn by Mass Inst Tech, Cambridge, 78. *Mailing Add:* 48 Washington St Charlestown MA 02129

BROWN, MYRNA WEEKS
FLUTE, EDUCATOR
b Gridley, Calif, July 4, 37. *Study:* Brigham Young Univ, 54-56; Univ Utah, with Eugene Foster, BM, 58; NTex State Univ, with George Morey, MM, 73, DMA, 81; private study with William Kincaid, John Wummer & Geoffrey Gilbert. *Pos:* Second flutist, Ark Orch Soc, 67-70; prin flute, Wichita Falls Symph, 74-80; exec coordr, Nat Flute Asn, 76- *Teaching:* Instr flute, NTex State Univ, 74-80, Midwestern State Univ, 74-80 & Univ Tex, Arlington, 81- *Mem:* Mu Phi Epsilon (pres, 77-79); Tex Flute Club (pres, 76-77); Nat Flute Asn; Music Teachers Nat Asn; Am Fedn Musicians. *Publ:* Auth, Programmatic Elements in Carl Reinecke's Sonata, Opus 167, Undine, Newsletter Nat Flute Asn, 82. *Mailing Add:* 805 Laguna Dr Denton TX 76201

BROWN, NEWEL KAY
COMPOSER, EDUCATOR
b Salt Lake City, Utah, Feb 29, 32. *Study:* Univ Utah, BFA, 53, MFA, 55; Eastman Sch Music, PhD, 67. *Works:* Saxophone Sonata, 68, Trombone Sonata, 69, Postures (bass trombone & piano), 72, Windart II (euphonium, 6 clarinets, vibes & perc), 80, Four Meditations (bass voice, alto sax & perc), 81 & Dejeuner sur l'herb (soprano voice, flute, alto sax & piano), 82, Seesaw Music Corp. *Teaching:* Instr music, Centenary Col for Women, NJ, 61-67; instr theory, comp & orch, Henderson State Col, Ark, 67-70; prof comp & theory, NTex State Univ, 70- *Mem:* ASCAP; Am Soc Univ Comp; NY Musicians Club; Col Music Soc; Music Teachers Nat Asn. *Mailing Add:* Music Dept North Tex State Univ Denton TX 76203

BROWN, OREN LATHROP
EDUCATOR, VOICE
b Somerville, Mass. *Study:* Boston Univ, BM(voice), MA(comp). *Pos:* Consult otolaryngology, St Louis City Hospital, formerly; musical adv, USO, formerly. *Teaching:* Private voice, Boston, 32; mem fac, Principia Col, formerly, Southern Ill Univ, formerly, Mo Univ, formerly, Washington Univ, formerly, Mannes Col Music, formerly & Union Theol Sem, formerly; prof voice & chmn music dept, Shurtleff Col, 47-54; lectr voice therapy, Sch Med, Washington Univ, 52-68; mem fac voice, Juilliard Sch, 72-; dir, Oren Brown Voice Sem, Zuoz, Switz, summers & Amherst, Mass, summers; lectr & clinician, col clinics & vocal pedagogy wkshps. *Mem:* Int Asn Experimental Res Singing. *Mailing Add:* 160 W 73rd St 9G2 New York NY 10023

BROWN, RAYMOND
EDUCATOR, VOICE
b Hope Mills, NC, June 20, 20. *Study:* Univ NC; Juilliard Sch Music; Peabody Consv Music; Johns Hopkins Univ. *Pos:* Opera, oratorio & recital performer in eastern US; choir dir, tours throughout US, Europe & Israel. *Teaching:* Prof & dir choral music, Pa State Univ, currently. *Awards:* Alpha Phi Omega Distinguished Serv Award, 75. *Mem:* Nat Asn Teachers Singing; Col Music Soc; Am Choral Dir Asn. *Mailing Add:* 1359 Penfield Rd State College PA 16801

BROWN, RAYNER
COMPOSER, ORGAN
b Des Moines, Iowa, Feb 23, 12. *Study:* Univ Southern Calif, BMus, 38, MMus, 47. *Works:* Over 100 works published. *Pos:* Church organist, 28-77. *Teaching:* Prof music, Biola Univ, 48-77, emer prof, 77- *Awards:* ASCAP Award, 67-77. *Mem:* Am Guild Organists (dean Los Angeles chap, 61-63). *Mailing Add:* 2423 Panorama Terr Los Angeles CA 90039

BROWN, RICHARD S
PERCUSSION, EDUCATOR
b Philadelphia, Pa, Sept 10, 47. *Study:* Temple Univ, BMusEd; Cath Univ Am, MMus, 69-72. *Rec Perf:* With Houston Symph, US Army Band & Chamber Symph Philadelphia. *Pos:* Mem, US Army Band, Washington DC, 69-72 & Chamber Symph Philadelphia, formerly; perc, Grand Teton Music Fest Orch, Wyo, formerly, Houston Symph Orch, formerly, Houston Grand Opera, formerly & Houston Ballet, formerly. *Teaching:* Asst prof perc, Shepherd Sch Music, Rice Univ, currently; mem fac, Univ St Thomas, formerly. *Mem:* Percussive Arts Soc. *Mailing Add:* 4231 Tennyson Houston TX 77005

BROWN, WILLIAM ALBERT
EDUCATOR, TENOR
b Jackson, Miss, Mar 29, 38. *Study:* Jackson State Univ, BME, 59; Ind Univ, MM, 62; Peabody Consv Music. *Rec Perf:* On Columbia Rec, CRI, London Rec, Musical Heritage & Nonesuch. *Roles:* Don Ottavio in Don Giovanni, Goldvsky Opera Co, 69; Don Ottavio in Don Giovanni, 69, Fenton in Die Lustigen Weiber von Windsor, 69 & LySander, 70, Lake George Opera; Belmonte in Entfuhrung aus dem Serail, Bel Aix Music Fest, 70; Calaf in Turandot, Little Orch Soc, 70; Faust, Jacksonville Opera Co, 73. *Pos:* Perf with maj symph orchs, opera co & chamber ens throughout US. *Teaching:* Prof voice, Univ NFla, 72- *Awards:* William M Sullivan Found Award, 69. *Publ:* Coauth, article, In: Blues Encyclopedia of Black America, McGraw-Hill. *Rep:* Joanne Rile Mgt Box 27539 Philadelphia PA 19118. *Mailing Add:* 8865 Yorkshire Jacksonville FL 32217

BROWN, WILLIAM JAMES
VIOLIN
b Council Grove, Kans, Dec 13, 18. *Study:* Southwestern Col, Kans, BM, 40; Univ Okla, MM, 41; studied with Raphael Bronstein, 45-46. *Pos:* Violinist—tutti, Cleveland Orch, 46- *Teaching:* Priv instr violin, 46- *Mailing Add:* c/o Cleveland Orch Severence Hall Cleveland OH 44106

BROWNE, JOHN P, JR
EDUCATOR, TROMBONE
Study: Northwestern Univ, BME, 49, MM, 50; Univ Calif, Los Angeles. *Teaching:* Instr music educ & band dir, Univ Hawaii, 50-53 & Manchester Col, 53-55; prof music educ & band dir, Calif State Univ, Chico, 57-83. *Mem:* Music Educr Nat Conf; Calif Music Educr Asn; Nat Asn Col Wind & Perc Instr; Nat Asn Jazz Educr. *Mailing Add:* Music Dept Calif State Univ Chico CA 95926

BROWNE, PHILIP R
COMPOSER, EDUCATOR
b Norman, Okla, July 27, 33. *Study:* Aspen Sch Music, with Darius Milhaud; Ariz State Univ, BA(music), 56; Eastman Sch Music, with Bernard Rogers & Wayne Barlow, MMus(comp), 59; Univ Calif, Los Angeles, with Roy Harris, 64. *Works:* Sonoro and Brioso, Summy-Birchard Publ Co, 67; Suite No 2 for Winds, 74 & Windroc Overture, 75, Belwin Mills; Serenade (orch), Forest R Etling, 76; Concerto (strings), 77 & Carousel from Windfair Suite, 78, Joseph Boonin Publ Co; Skyride from Windfair Suite, Neil Kjos Publ Co, 82. *Teaching:* Prof & band cond, Calif State Polytechnic Univ, Pomona, 63-, chmn music dept, 67-78. *Awards:* ASCAP Award, 73-82; Outstanding Comp for Band, Col Band Dir Nat Asn, 73; Outstanding Comp for Orch, Nat Sch Orch Asn, 75. *Mem:* ASCAP; Col Band Dir Nat Asn; Music Educr Nat Conf; Calif Music Educr Asn. *Mailing Add:* 1857 Olivewood St La Verne CA 91750

BROWNE, RICHMOND
THEORIST, COMPOSER
b Flint, Mich, Aug 8, 34. *Study:* Mich State Univ, studied comp with H Owen Reed, BMus(theory & comp), 55; Yale Univ, studied comp with Richard Donovan & Quincy Porter, BMus(comp), 57, MMus(theory & comp), 58. *Works:* Reri Velocitatem (any three instrm), 62; Translations (orch), 64; 2 Introductions, 3 Cadenzas and 6 Maps (sextet), 64; Klasmata (organ), 64; Trio for Solo Viola, 65; Chortos I (speech chorus), 67; Chortos II (speech chorus), 70. *Teaching:* Mem fac theory & comp, Yale Univ, 60-68; prof music theory, Univ Mich, 68- *Awards:* BMI Awards, 57 & 58; Yale Morse Grant, 64; Mich Kackham Fel, 70. *Mem:* Col Music Soc; founding mem, Soc Music Theory (nat secy, currently). *Interests:* Schenkerian theory; linguistics; metatheories of music. *Mailing Add:* Sch Music Univ Mich Ann Arbor MI 48109

BROWNING, JAMES FRANCIS
ADMINISTRATOR
b Tonawanda, NY. *Study:* Univ Buffalo, BA, 46. *Pos:* Asst mgr, Pittsburgh Symph, 57-59; adminr, Metropolitan Opera Nat Coun, 59-62; freelance critic, 62-; consult to arts councils, 63-; gen mgr, Am Music Ctr, 63-72; ed, Music Today Newslett, 63-72 & Nat Music Coun Bulletin, 65-72; exec secy, Nat Music Coun, 65-72 & Nat Asn Teachers Singing, 73- *Mailing Add:* 114 W 70th St Apt 2D New York NY 10023

BROWNING, JOHN (S), JR
PIANO, TEACHER
b Denver, Colo, May 23, 33. *Study:* Occidental Col, with Lee Pattison; Juilliard Sch Music; studied with Rosina Lhevinne; Ithaca Col, Hon Dr Music; Occidental Col, Hon Dr Music, 70. *Rec Perf:* Chopin Etudes, Ravel Left Hand Concerto, Tschaikovsky Concerto, Prokofiev Concertos, Barber Concerto # 1 & piano solos of Bach & Debussy, recorded on RCA, Columbia, Desco, Capital & Masterworks. *Pos:* Concert pianist with New York Phil & leading orchestras in US, Europe, Mex & USSR, currently. *Teaching:* Prof piano, Northwestern Univ, 75-80 & Manhattan Sch Music, 80- *Awards:* Steinway Centennial Award, Nat Fedn Music Clubs, 54; Queen Elizabeth Int Councours Award, Brussels, Belgium, 56. *Mailing Add:* c/o Columbia Artists Mgt 165 W 57 New York NY 10019

BROWNING, ZACK DAVID
COMPOSER, TRUMPET
b Atlanta, Ga, Aug 10, 53. *Study:* Fla State Univ, BM, 75; Univ Ill, MM, 76, DMA, 80. *Works:* Concerto, Univ Ill Brass Ens, 77; Zece for Piano, Sever Tipei, Univ, 80; Crossings, NC Arts Coun, 81; Quintet for Winds, ALEA III, Boston Univ, 81; Dialogue, Meet the Composer, 81; Variables, La State Univ Contemp Players, 82; In Garden of Thedas, Ga Arts Coun, 83. *Rec Perf:* Mobile Jazz Fest, Univ Ala publ TV, 83. *Pos:* Fourth trumpet, Atlanta Symph Orch, 79-80; prin trumpet, Johnson City Symph Orch, 82- *Teaching:* Asst theory, Univ Ill, Urbana, 77-79; vis artist, NC Arts Coun, 80-81; instr trumpet, jazz & theory, Atlanta Sch Music, 81-82; asst prof, ETenn State Univ, 82-83; asst prof, Univ Ill, 83- *Awards:* Raymond Hubbell Scholar, ASCAP, 78; Ga Coun for Arts Comp Grant, 83. *Mem:* Am Soc Univ Comp; Int Trumpet Guild; Col Music Soc. *Publ:* Auth, Trumpet Techniques in the Performance of Microtones, Int Trumpet Guild Newsletter, 79. *Mailing Add:* 5980 River Chase Circle Atlanta GA 30328

BROYLES, MICHAEL E
EDUCATOR, WRITER
b Houston, Tex, Sept 29, 39. *Study:* Austin Col, BA, 61; Univ Tex, Austin, MM, 64, PhD, 67. *Teaching:* Asst prof, Univ Md, Baltimore, 67-71, assoc prof, 71- *Mem:* Am Musicol Soc (pres Capitol Chap, 83); Am Soc 18th Century Studies. *Interests:* Classical period, especially Beethoven; early 19th

century American music. *Publ:* Auth, Beethoven's Sonata Op 14 No 1, J Am Musicol Soc, 70; Rhythm, Metre and Beethoven, Music Rev, 72; coauth, Meyer, Meaning and Music, J Aesthetics & Art Criticism, 73; auth, Organic Form and the Binary Repeat, Musical Quart, 80; The Two Instrumental Styles of Classicism, J Am Musicol Soc, 83. *Mailing Add:* 5401 Wilkens Ave Baltimore MD 21228

BROZEN, MICHAEL
COMPOSER, WRITER
b New York, NY, Aug 5, 34. *Study:* Bard Col, with Paul Nordoff, 50-52; Berkshire Music Ctr, with Lukas Foss, 52; Juilliard Sch Music, with Vincent Persichetti, BS & MS, 52-57. *Works:* Canto (orch), Dark Night, Gentle Night (sop, tenor & orch), Five Alleluias (chorus), Fantasy (piano), The Bugle Moon (bar & nine instrm), Caliban (musical play) & In Memoriam (sop & string orch), Theodore Presser Co. *Awards:* Nat Inst & Am Acad Arts & Lett Grant & Rec Award, 69; Guggenheim Fel, 71; Wurlitzer Found Res Grant, 75. *Mem:* ASCAP; Am Music Ctr; Am Fedn Musicians. *Mailing Add:* 86 Horatio St New York NY 10014

BRUCE, FRANK NEELY
COMPOSER, EDUCATOR
b Memphis, Tenn, Jan 21, 44. *Study:* Univ Ala, with Thomas Canning, J F Goossen & David Cohen, BM, 65; Univ Ill, with Ben Johnston & Hubert Kessler, MM, 66, DMA, 71. *Works:* The Trials of Psyche (one act opera), 71; Piano Sonata, No 6, 73; Concerto for Violin & Chamber Orchestra, 74; Grand Duo (trumpet & piano), 74; Rondo for Flute, Tuba & Piano, 76; Grand Duo (flute & piano), 77; Grand Duo (cello & piano), 77. *Pos:* Mem, Contemp Chamber Players, Univ Ill, formerly; founder & dir, Am Music Group, formerly; pianist & harpsichordist. *Teaching:* Prof, Sch Music, Univ Ill, Urbana-Champaign, 68-74; prof choral music, Wesleyan Univ, 74- *Awards:* Martha Baird Rockefeller Grant, 76; Nat Endowment Humanities Grant, 77. *Mem:* Am Musicol Soc; ASCAP. *Mailing Add:* Music Dept Wesleyan Univ Middletown CT 06457

BRUCH, DELORES RUTH
ORGAN, EDUCATOR
b Independence, Mo, Sept 22, 34. *Study:* Cent Mo State Univ, BS, 56; Univ Mo, Kansas City, MM, 69; Univ Kans, DMA, 79. *Teaching:* Asst prof organ, music theory & music hist, Park Col, 78-79; from asst prof to assoc prof organ & church music, Univ Iowa, 79- *Awards:* Int Res & Exchanges Bd Grant, 83. *Mem:* Am Guild Organists (chap dean 79-81); Organ Hist Soc; Am Musicol Soc; Hymn Soc Am; Col Music Soc. *Publ:* Auth, Creativity and the New Organ, Am Organist, 80; Kansas Organ Institute, 81, 1982 Organ Academies, Germany and Italy, 82 & Frescobaldi Quadrocentennial Conference, 83, Diapason; Summer in Europe 1982, Am Organist, 83. *Mailing Add:* 410 Hawaii Ct Iowa City IA 52240

BRUCK, CHARLES
CONDUCTOR, EDUCATOR
b Timisoara, Rumania; French citizen. *Study:* Ecole Normale Musique, Paris; Univ Paris, Doctorate, 33; P Monteux Sch Cond, Paris, MA, 35. *Rec Perf:* The Fire Angel (Prokofieff), Vega; Symphony No 1, No 2 & No 3 (Prokofieff), Columbia; Orpheus (Gluck), EMI; Terretektorrh Nomos Gamma (Xenakis), Erato; 2d Suite 2 Portraits (Bartok), His Masters Voice; Violin Concerto (S Nigg), Deutsche Grammophon; Violin Concerto (Brahms), Columbia. *Teaching:* Master, P Monteux Sch Cond, Maine, 69-; dir orch activ, Hartt Sch Music, Univ Hartford, 81- *Awards:* Chevalier de la Legion d'Honneur, Govt France, 67. *Rep:* 5 square Mignot 75016 Paris France. *Mailing Add:* Hartt Sch Music 200 Bloomfield Ave West Hartford CT 06117

BRUMIT, J(OSEPH) SCOTT
BARITONE, TEACHER
b Kansas City, Mo, Sept 7, 49. *Study:* Occidental Col, Los Angeles, BA, 71; New England Consv, MM, 73. *Roles:* Nick Shadow in Rake's Progress, New England Consv, 73; Magistrate in Signor Deluso, Wolf Trap Opera, 74; Nick Bottom in Midsummer Night's Dream, Harvard Opera, 77; Dr Dulcamara in L'Elisir d'Amore, Artists Int, 77; Gianni Schicchi in Gianni Schicchi, Harvard Opera, 78; Dr Bartolo in Il Barbiere di Siviglia, Marlboro Symph, 83; Sam in American Passion, Musical Theater Lab, 83. *Teaching:* Instr voice, privately, 75-; asst dir opera dept, Boston Consv, 75-80; mem fac voice, Anna Maria Col, 78-79. *Mem:* Am Guild Musical Artists (mem exec comt, 80-); Actors' Equity Asn. *Rep:* Rivera Mgt 251 W 98th St Suite 7B New York NY 10025. *Mailing Add:* 66 Elm St Medford MA 02155

BRÜN, HERBERT
COMPOSER, EDUCATOR
b Berlin, Germany, July 9, 18; US citizen. *Study:* Jerusalem Consv, Israel, with Stefan Wolpe & Frank Pelleg; Columbia Univ. *Works:* Mobile (orch), 58; Gestures for 11 (chamber ens), 64; Sonoriferous Loops (instrm & tape), 64; Gesto (piccolo & piano), 65; 6 for 5 by 2 in Pieces (oboe & clarinet), 71; At Loose Ends (perc), 74; In and ... and Out (chamber ens), 74; and others. *Pos:* Researcher electroacoustics & electronic sound prod, Paris, Cologne & Munich, 55-61. *Teaching:* Mem staff res electronic music, Sch Music, Univ Ill, formerly, prof, currently; distinguished vis prof, Col Arts, Ohio State Univ, 69-70. *Awards:* ESCO Found Award, 48; first prize, Int Bassist's Comp Compt, 77. *Mailing Add:* 307 S Busey Urbana IL 61801

BRUNELLE, PHILIP CHARLES
CONDUCTOR & MUSIC DIRECTOR, ORGAN
b Faribault, Minn, July 1, 43. *Study:* study organ with Arthur B Jennings, 60-65; Univ Minn, BA, 65; study with George Schick, Metropolitan Opera, 68.

Rec Perf: Postcard from Morocco, Desto, 75; Jonah and the Whale, CRI, 82; In A Winter Garden, Pro Arte, 83; Irene Gubrud solo album, Augsburg, 83; On Christmas Night, Pro Arte, 83. *Pos:* Music dir & prin cond, Minn Opera, 68-; music dir & founder, Plymouth Music Series, Minneapolis, 69-; choirmaster & organist, Plymouth Congregational Church, 69-; music adv, Walker Art Ctr, 78-, Choral Panel, Nat Endowment Arts, 83- *Teaching:* Adj prof sacred music, United Theol Sem, New Brighton, Minn, 78-; adj prof choral music, Westminster Choir Col, Princeton, NJ, summers 81- *Awards:* Grant, Martha Baird Rockefeller Found, 68; summer fel, Bush Found, 75; Kodaly Medal, Hungarian Govt, 83. *Mem:* Am Guild Organists; Am Choral Dir Asn; Minn State Arts Bd. *Publ:* Auth, Choral Music—Old and New, Am Organist, 82- *Mailing Add:* 4211 Glencrest Rd Golden Valley MN 55416

BRUNELLI, LOUIS JEAN
ADMINISTRATOR, COMPOSER
b New York, NY, June 24, 25. *Study:* Guildhall Sch Music, London, cert, 46; NY Univ, BA(music), 49; Manhattan Sch Music, MM(comp), 50. *Works:* In Memoriam, Chappell & Co, Inc, 71; Arlecchino, Southern Music Co, Inc, 74; Essay for Cyrano, 74 & Chronicles, 77, Boosey & Hawkes, Inc. *Rec Perf:* Longines Symphonette, WCBS, 49-54. *Pos:* Educ dir, Chappell & Co, Inc, 54-71. *Teaching:* Dir perf & mem fac theory, orch & calligraphy, Manhattan Sch Music, 72-77; asst dean, Juilliard Sch, 77-81, assoc dean, 82- *Awards:* Rec Repertoire, Am Symph League, 60. *Mem:* ASCAP. *Mailing Add:* 32-43 90 St Jackson Heights NY 11369

BRUNNER, RICHARD
TENOR
Roles: Don Ramiro in La Cenerentola, 78 & Eisenstein in Die Fledermaus, 78, Opera Co Philadelphia; Mime in Das Rheingold, 81, Salome, 82 & The Merry Widow, 82, Cincinnati Opera; Gerald in Lakme, Opera South; Mime in Das Rheingold, Dallas Opera. *Pos:* Mem, Cincinnati Opera's Young Am Artists Program; performer, Cincinnati Opera, Pittsburgh Opera, Can Opera Co & Pa Opera Theatre. *Mailing Add:* c/o Robert Lombardo Assoc 1 Harkness Plaza 61 W 62nd #6F New York NY 10023

BRUNSMA, DONNA LOUISE
VOCAL COACH
b Indianapolis, Ind. *Study:* Eastman Sch Music, BM, 55; Juilliard Sch Music, Columbia Univ & Union Theol Sem, 55-58; Nat Music Camp, Interlochen, Mich, four summers. *Pos:* Asst cond & vocal coach, Maggio Musicale Fiorentino, Florence, Italy, 69-79; Teatro Sao Carlos, Lisbon, Portugal, 73-81; Fest Two Worlds, Spoleto, Italy, 77-82; Lyr Opera Chicago & Lyr Opera Ctr Am Artists, 78- & Theatre Royal de la Monnaie, Brussels, 81- *Teaching:* Vocal coach, Sarah Lawrence Col, Bronxville, NY, 58-61; Villa Schifanoia Grad Sch Fine Arts, Florence, Italy, 67-72 & Vocal Inst, Graz, Austria, 77-78. *Mailing Add:* Patargnone Cetona 53040 Italy

BRUNYATE, ROGER
EDUCATOR, DIRECTOR—OPERA
Study: Trinity Col, Cambridge, BA, MA; studied with Peter Ebert, Colin Graham, Rudolf Hartmann, Franco Enriquez, Mario Bolognini & Margherita Wallmann. *Pos:* Dir & designer theatre, 64- & opera, 68-; with Scottish Opera, Edinburgh Fest Opera, Glyndebourne Fest Opera & English Opera Group, formerly. *Teaching:* Lectr, Glasgow Univ, 63-67; dir opera prod, Fla State Univ, 72-74; asst dean, Univ Tex, 74-76; coordr opera, Col-Consv Music, Cincinnati, 76-80; vis prof, Univ Mo, 78-79; mem fac, Brevard Music Ctr, 80; dir opera prog, Peabody Consv Music, currently. *Mailing Add:* Peabody Consv Music 1 E Mt Vernon Pl Baltimore MD 21202

BRUSH, RUTH DAMARIS
COMPOSER, PIANO
b Fairfax, Okla. *Study:* Consv Music, Kansas City, BMus, 46. *Works:* Valse Joyeuse, Comp Press, 59; Two Expressive Pieces, J Fischer & Bro, 62; Pastorale, Lorenz Publ, 64; Playtime Piano Pieces, Dee Publ, 70; This Same Jesus, 72 & The Lord Is My Shepherd, 74, Bartlesville Publ Co. *Pos:* Studio pianist & prog chmn, WHB, Kansas City, 55-60. *Teaching:* Instr piano & organ, Frank Phillips Col, Borger, Tex, 60-65, head piano dept, currently. *Awards:* Publ Award, Comp Press, 59. *Bibliog:* Judith Lang Zaimont & Karen Famera (auth), Contemporary Concert Music by Women, League Women Comp, 81. *Mem:* ASCAP; Nat Asn Am Comp & Cond; Am Women Comp Inc. *Interests:* Music history; classical music and composers twentieth-century music. *Publ:* Auth, Junior Composers, Nat Fedn Music Clubs, 68-74. *Mailing Add:* 3413 Wildwood Ct Bartlesville OK 74003

BRUSILOW, ANSHEL
CONDUCTOR & MUSIC DIRECTOR, EDUCATOR
b Philadelphia, Pa, Aug 14, 28. *Study:* Curtis Inst Music, 39-43; Philadelphia Musical Acad, dipl, 47. *Rec Perf:* The Seasons (solo violin; Vivaldi), Columbia Rec, 60; Serenade No 1 (Brahms), LeBourgeois Gentilhomme (Strauss), Suite No 4, Mozartiana (Tchaikowsky), Le Tombeau de Couperin (Ravel) & Symphony No 60, Il Distratto (Haydn), 67, RCA Victor; Borodin, Rimsky-Korsakov & Balakiev, EMI, 74. *Pos:* Assoc concertmaster, Cleveland Orch, 55-59; concertmaster, Philadelphia Orch, 59-66; cond & music dir, Chamber Symph Philadelphia, 66-68; cond & exec dir, Dallas Symph Orch, 70-73; dir orch, NTex State Univ, 73-82; dir orch activ, Southern Methodist Univ, 82- *Teaching:* Prof cond, NTex State Univ, 73-82 & Southern Methodist Univ, 82- *Mailing Add:* Music Dept Southern Methodist Univ Dallas TX 75275

BRUSTADT, MARILYN
SOPRANO

b Mentor, Minn, Mar 19, 51. *Study:* Moorhead State Univ, BA(philosophy), 74. *Rec Perf:* PDQ Bach Music You Can't Get Out of Your Head, Vanguard, 82. *Roles:* Lisetta in La Gazzetta, Wiener Kammeroper, 77; Queen of Night, New York City Opera, 77; Berthe in Le Prophete, Metropolitan Opera, 79; Lucia di Lammermoor, Opera Theatre of Rochester, 80; Leonoro in Trovatore, Opera Theater of Syracuse, 82; Maria in Maria Padilla, Opera Soc Long Island, 83; Violetta, Central City Opera Co, 83. *Mem:* Am Guild Musical Artists. *Mailing Add:* c/o Janina K Burns Assoc 136 Kingsland St Nutley NJ 07110

BRYAN, KEITH (WALBURN)
FLUTE

b Knoxville, Tenn, Dec 21, 31. *Study:* Eastman Sch Music, BM & perf cert, 53; studied with Joseph Mariano, 49-53 & William Kincaid, 53-55. *Rec Perf:* 20th Century Music, Vol I & II & Variations (Schubert), Lyrichord Rec; Sonata (Walter Piston), Duo (A Copland), Sonata (Kuhlau), Op 69 & Sonata (Hoffmeister), Op 13, Orion Rec; Duo (Wallace Berry), CRI. *Pos:* Asst first & second flute, Nat Symph Orch, 53-61; solo flute, Seventh Army Symph, Stuttgart, Ger, 55-57; conct flutist, The Bryan & Keys Duo, 61- *Teaching:* Prof flute, Sch Music, Univ Mich, 65- *Rep:* Anne J O'Donnell 1776 Boradway New York NY 10019. *Mailing Add:* 1050 Wall St Ann Arbor MI 48105

BRYAN, PAUL ROBEY, JR
EDUCATOR, WRITER

b Pittsburgh, Pa, Mar 7, 20. *Study:* Univ Mich, BM(music educ), 41, MM(theory), 48 & PhD(music), 56; studied with Thor Johnson, Vittorio Giannini, Simone Mantia, Donald S Reinhardt, Gardell Simons, William Revelli, Louise Cuyler & Hans David. *Pos:* Trombonist, Brevard Symph Orch, 49-54, 56 & 57; cond, Duke Wind Symph, 51-83 & Durham Youth Symph, 72-76; cond & mem bd dir, Durham Civic Choral Soc, 56-67, Durham Savoyards, 61-67, 69 & 74-75 & Triangle Symph Inc. *Teaching:* Vis instr theory, Univ Mich, 48-51 & 54-55 & vis prof, 62; staff cond & head theory dept, Brevard Music Ctr, 49-57; asst prof music, Duke Univ, 51-58, assoc prof, 58-75, prof, 75-; vis prof music & acting dir, Univ Conct Band, Univ Calif, Davis, summer 83. *Awards:* Duke Univ Res Coun Grant, 67-68; Chapelbrook Found Grant, 67-68; Silver Medal Honor, Dank & Anerkennung Förderung Volksmusik Niederösterreich, 78. *Mem:* Am Bandmasters Asn; Gesellschaft zur Erforschung Förderung Blasmusik (mem praesidium, 75-); Col Band Dir Nat Asn. *Interests:* Eighteenth century symphonies in western and central Europe; music of Mozart and Haydn; music for wind instruments. *Publ:* Auth, The Horn in the Works of Mozart and Haydn: Some Observations, Haydn Jahrbuch, Bd IX, 75; Carl Franz, Eighteenth Century Virtuoso: A Reappraisal, Alta Musica IV, 79; A Look at Some 18th Century Source Material for the Trombone, J Int Trombone Asn, Vol IV, 1/76; contribr, The College and University Band 1941-75, Music Educr Nat Conf, 77; ed, Five Symphonies: Em1, Cm2, Bb1, C11, Dm2 by Joh Krtitel Vanhal, The Symphony 1720-1840, Garland Publ, 81 & many others. *Mailing Add:* Dept Music Duke Univ Durham NC 27706

BRYANT, ALLAN CHARLES
COMPOSER

b Detroit, Mich, July 12, 31. *Study:* Princeton Univ, BA, 53; Köln State Music Sch, Germany, dipl, 64. *Works:* Quadruple Play, 66 & Masses, 67, Musica Elettronica Viva; Pitch Out, Univ Calif, 68; Space Guitars, CRI, 77. *Mailing Add:* 682 Lincoln Rd Grosse Pointe MI 48230

BRYANT, CAROLYN FRANCES
WRITER

b Washington, DC, July 26, 44. *Study:* Dickinson Col, BA, 66; NY Univ, MA, 73. *Pos:* Quart contribr, Music Quart & G Schirmer, 74-; writer prepared exhibit & catalog, Smithsonian Inst, Washington, DC, 74-75; writer & ed, New Grove Dict of Music & Musicians, London, 75-76. *Mem:* Am Musicol Soc; Sonneck Soc; Am Musical Instrm Soc; Am Recorder Soc. *Interests:* History of American music. *Publ:* Auth, And the Band Played On, 1776-1976: A History of Band Music in America, Smithsonian Inst Press, 75. *Mailing Add:* 141 D St SE Washington DC 20003

BUBALO, RUDOLPH DANIEL
COMPOSER

b Duluth, Minn, Oct 21, 27. *Study:* Chicago Musical Col, Roosevelt Univ, studied comp with Ernst Krenek, John Becker & Vittorio Rieti, cond & piano with Rudolph Ganz, musicol with Hans Tischler & Hans Rosenwald, BM, 54, MM, 56. *Works:* Spacescape for Orchestra & Tape, Galaxy Music, 76; Trajectories (tape & orch), Nat Endowment for Arts, 78; Strands (orch), Ohio Arts Coun Grant, 80; Symmetricality (piano & orch), comn by Ohio Chamber Orch, 83; Adagio & Allegro (clarinet & orch), comn by Cleveland Chamber Symph, 83. *Teaching:* Prof comp & dir electronic music studio, Cleveland State Univ, 69- *Awards:* Rockefeller Found Award, 60; Nat Endowment for Arts Grant, 78; Ohio Arts Coun Grant, 80. *Mem:* Cleveland Comp Guild (pres, 64-68); Am Soc Univ Comp; Comp Forum; Am Music Ctr; Nat Asn Comp. *Mailing Add:* 3764 Glenwood Rd Cleveland OH 44121

BUCCHERI, ELIZABETH
PIANO, TEACHER-COACH

b Chester, SC, Sept 26, 42. *Study:* Winthrop Col, BS, 64; Eastman Sch Music, MM, 66, DMA, 78. *Rec Perf:* Variations on Obiter Dictum (Karlins), CRI, 78; Nineteenth Century Music for Piano Four Hands, 79 & Songs of Les Six, 81, Spectrum. *Pos:* Pianist & accmp, Chicago Symph Chorus, 69-; freelance coach, Chicago Symph Orch, 82- *Teaching:* Assoc prof piano & theory, North Park Col, Chicago, 69-; pianist & coach, Am Choral Found, 69-75 & Brevard Music Ctr, 72. *Mem:* Am Fedn Musicians; Soc Am Musicians (mem bd dir, 79-81); Col Music Soc; Music Teachers Nat Asn. *Mailing Add:* Music Dept North Park Col Chicago IL 60625

BUCCHERI, JOHN
EDUCATOR

Study: Tufts Univ, BA, 62; Eastman Sch Music, MA, 65, PhD, 75. *Teaching:* Assoc prof & chmn dept theory & comp, Northwestern Univ, 67- *Awards:* Teaching fels, Phi Mu Alpha & Eastman Sch Music. *Mem:* Phi Mu Alpha. *Interests:* Rhythmic analysis. *Mailing Add:* Sch Music Northwestern Univ Evanston IL 60201

BUCCI, MARC LEOPOLD
COMPOSER, WRITER

b New York, NY, Feb 26, 29. *Study:* Juilliard Sch Music, BS(music), 51. *Works:* Sweet Betsy from Pike, 58 & Tale for a Deaf Ear, 58, Frank Music Corp; The Dress, Chappell/Frank Music, 58; The 13 Clocks, Music Theatre Int, 60; Concerto for a Singing Instrument, Frank Music Corp, 62; The Hero, comn & perf by Lincoln Ctr, 65; The Wondrous Kingdom (unaccmp choral cycle), MCA Music, 68. *Awards:* Fel, J S Guggenheim Mem Found, 53 & 57; grant comp, Nat Inst Arts & Lett, 60. *Mem:* BMI. *Publ:* Coauth, Days on End, Samuel French, 60; Diary of Adam and Eve, 72, The Cop and the Anthem, 73, Court of Stone Children, 78 & Paul's Case, 81, Dramatic Publ. *Rep:* Jasper Vance 1680 N Vine St Hollywood CA 90028. *Mailing Add:* 5625 Beck Ave North Hollywood CA 91601

BUCCI, THOMAS VINCENT
COMPOSER, PIANO

b Providence, RI, Sept 7, 26. *Study:* New England Consv Music, BM, 51, MM, 61. *Works:* Concertante (viola), Young World Publ Co, 75; Brass Quintet & Electronic Tape, comn by RI Phil Brass Quintet, 76; Mass (chorus & orch), Ed Musicus Publ, 78; Sing Joyfully to God (SATB), Music 70 Publ, 79; Dinner Anyone (SATB), 79 & Trio for Trumpets, 79, Ed Musicus Publ; Jazz Fugue (SATB), Plymouth Music Co, 81. *Pos:* Supvr music, City of Portland, Maine, 52-81. *Teaching:* Fac appl music, Univ Maine, 70- *Mem:* Music Educr Nat Conf; Maine Music Educr Asn; Am Fedn Musicians. *Mailing Add:* 140 Abby Lane Portland ME 04103

BUCHBINDER, RUDOLF
PIANO

b Czechoslovakia, 1947. *Study:* Studied with Bruno Seidlhofer. *Rec Perf:* Complete piano music of Haydn; complete Beethoven sonatas. *Pos:* Concert pianist, Corinthian Summer Fest, Ossiach, 79-; piano soloist, New York Phil, 83; pianist, worldwide performances. *Awards:* First Prize, ARD Radio Compt, Munich & Harriet Cohen Compt; Special Prize, Van Cliburn Compt, 67. *Mailing Add:* c/o Colbert Artists Mgt 111 W 7th St New York NY 10019

BUCHTEL, FORREST LAWRENCE
COMPOSER, EDUCATOR

b St Edward, Nebr, Dec 9, 99. *Study:* Simpson Col, AB, 21; Univ Chicago, summer 23 & 24; Columbia Univ, summer 28; Northwestern Univ, MS(educ), 31; VanderCook Col Music, BMusEd, 32, MMusEd, 33. *Works:* Thirty sets of band books, 30 marches, 30 overtures & 800 solos & ens for sch bands. *Teaching:* Music, South High Sch, Grand Rapids, Mich, 21-25; assoc prof, Kans State Col, 25-30; teacher, Lane Tech High Sch, Chicago, Ill, 30-34 & Amundsen High Sch, Chicago, Ill, 34-54; teacher, VanderCook Col Music, 31-81, dean 70-81. *Mem:* ASCAP; Am Bandmasters Asn; Phi Mu Alpha Sinfonia. *Publ:* Auth, Melody Fun Method for the Tonette, 38 & Buchtel Recorder Method, 67, Neil A Kjos Music Co. *Mailing Add:* 1116 Cleveland St Evanston IL 60202

BUCK, DAVID A
CONDUCTOR, EDUCATOR

b San Jose, Calif. *Study:* Univ Pac, studied violin with Emanuel Zetlin, Noumi Fischer & Ralph Matesky, BM, 66; Univ Wash, studied cond with Dr Richard Lert & Dr Stanley Chapple, MM, 68, DMus, 70. *Pos:* Concertmaster, Fest Opera Co, 68-70; guest cond, Contemp Group, Seattle, 69-70 & Baltimore Symph, 75; Coordr, Arts in Educ, RI State Coun Arts, 71-73; second violin, Colonial String Quartet, 73-76; organizer & dir, RI Int Master Pianist Compt, 73-76; cond, Calif State Univ Los Angeles Symph, 76-; dir string prog, NMex Music Fest Taos, 80-82, guest cond, 81-82; mem bd dir, Music at Angel Fire, NMex. *Teaching:* Asst prof music, Univ RI, 70-76; assoc prof music & head string dept, Calif State Univ, Los Angeles, 76- *Awards:* Danforth Found Award, 62; Boise Found Award, 62-66; grant, Rockefeller Found, 66-67. *Mem:* Am Symph Orch League Cond Guild; Am Fedn Musicians; Am Asn Univ Prof; Phi Mu Alpha Sinfonia. *Mailing Add:* Music Dept Calif State Univ Los Angeles CA 90032

BUCKER, B J (BARBARA JO ADLER)
ADMINISTRATOR

b St Louis, Mo, July 29, 49. *Study:* Univ Mo, Kansas City, BA, 71, MA, 75. *Pos:* Exec dir, Kansas City Young Audiences, 76-81 & Chamber Music Am, 82-; assoc dir, Young Audiences, 81-82. *Mailing Add:* 215 Park Ave S New York NY 10003

BUCKLEY, EMERSON
CONDUCTOR & MUSIC DIRECTOR, ADMINISTRATOR

b New York, NY, Apr 14, 16. *Study:* Columbia Univ, BA, 36; Univ Denver, LHD, 59; Nova Univ, Hon MusD, 80. *Rec Perf:* Tagarazuka Dance Theatre, Columbia Rec, 58; The Ballad of Baby Doe, Deutsche Grammophon Rec, 59;

The Crucible, CRI, 62; Yes Giorgio, MGM-London Rec, 81. *Pos:* Music dir, Columbia Grand Opera, 36-38, Palm Beach Symph & Chorus, Fla, 38-41, New York City Symph, 41-42, San Carlo Opera, 43-45, WOR-MBS, New York, 45-54, Marquis de Cuevas Ballet, 50, Mendelssohn Glee Club, New York, 54-63, PR Opera Fest, 54-58, Chicago Opera, 56, Tagarazuka Dance Theatre & Greek Theatre, Los Angeles, 58 & Chautauqua Fest, New York, 60; music & artistic dir, Miami Opera Guild, Fla, 50- & Central City Opera, Colo, 56-69; music dir & cond, Ft Lauderdale Symph, 63-; music dir, Seattle Opera, 64-; cond, New York City Opera, 55-78, Duluth Opera, 70-, New Orleans Opera, 70-, Baltimore Opera, 70, Philadelphia Lyric Opera, 75-, San Francisco Opera, 75-, Houston Opera, 76- Milwaukee Opera, 76-, Tulsa Opera, 76-, Metropolitan Opera of Caracas, Venezuela, 77-81, New World Fest Arts, 82 & Opera de Madrid, Spain, 83; guest appearances with numerous orchestras; art dir & res cond, Gtr Miami Opera Asn & Fla Family Opera, USA, 73- *Teaching:* Fac mem, Univ Denver, 56, Columbia Univ, 57-58, Manhattan Sch Music, 58-70, Temple Univ, 70 & NC Sch Arts, 71. *Awards:* Alice M Ditson Cond Award, 64; Gold Chair Award, Central City Opera, 65; Chevalier Order Arts & Lett, 70. *Interests:* A combination of ideas and ideals of creativity and interpretation, adapted pragmatically to the maelstrom of life surrounding us. *Rep:* Herbert Barrett Mgt 1860 Broadway New York NY 10023. *Mailing Add:* 19640 NE 20th Ave North Miami Beach FL 33179

BUCKLEY, MARY HENDERSON
TEACHER, SOPRANO

b Longueuil, Que, Dec 17, 12; US citizen. *Study:* Univ McGill, Montreal, licentiate music, 32. *Rec Perf:* On Allegro Rec. *Roles:* Lisa in Pique Dame, New Opera Co, 42; Fiordiligi in Cosi fan tutte, Montreal Opera Guild, 43; Marguerite in La Traviata, San Carlo Opera Co, 43-45; Micaela in Carmen, Metropolitan Opera Co, 46; Madama Butterfly, Wagner Opera Co, 48; Nedda in Pagliacci, Miami Opera Co, 50. *Teaching:* From prof to emer prof, Univ Miami, 64-78; teacher voice, privately, currently. *Mem:* Am Guild Musical Artists. *Mailing Add:* 19640 NE 20th Ave North Miami Beach FL 33162

BUELOW, GEORGE JOHN
EDUCATOR, ADMINISTRATOR

b Chicago, Ill, Mar 31, 29. *Study:* Chicago Musical Col, BM, 50, MM, 51; Univ Hamburg, 54-55; NY Univ, PhD(musicol), 61. *Pos:* Am ed, Acta Musicologica, 67-; mem exec comt, New Grove Dict of Music & Musicians, 6th ed, 72-80; gen ed, Studies in Musicol, Univ Microfilms Res Press, 77-; consult, Martha Baird Rockefeller's Fund Music, 79-80; co-chmn, Int Johann Mattheson Symph, Wolfenbuttal, Germany, 81; co-ed, New Mattheson Studies, Cambridge Univ Press, 83. *Teaching:* Instr music hist, Chicago Consv Music, 59-61; assoc prof, Univ Calif, Riverside, 61-68; prof & chmn, Dept Music, Univ Ky, 68-69; prof music, coord chmn music dept & dir grad studies, Rutgers Univ, 69-77, fac res fel, 74-75; prof musicol, Ind Univ, Bloomington, 77- *Awards:* Fels, Fulbright, 54-55 & Guggenheim, 67. *Publ:* Coauth, Thorough-bass Accompaniment According to Johann David Heinichen, Univ Calif, Berkeley, 66; The Adriadne auf Naxos' by H von Hofmannsthal and R Strauss, Univ NC, Chapel Hill, 75; auth, A Lesson in Operatic Performance Practice by Madam Faustina Bordoni, In: A Musical Offering, Essays in Honor of M Bernstein, Pendragon, 76; In Defense of J A Scheibe Against J S Bach, Proc Royal Musical Asn, 77; Symbol and Structure in the Kyrie of Bach's B Minor Mass, In: Essays on Bach and Other Matters: A Tribute to G Herz, Univ Ky, 78 & 82; The Concept of Melodielehre: A Key to the Definition of Classic Musical Style, In: Mozart Jahrbuch, Salzburg, 79; 100 articles in The New Grove, London, 80. *Mailing Add:* Sch Music Ind Univ Bloomington IN 47405

BUFF, IVA MOORE
LIBRARIAN

b Port Arthur, Tex, Aug 28, 32. *Study:* Eastman Sch Music & Col Arts & Sci, Univ Rochester, BMus, BA, 53; Smith Col, MA, 54; Univ Rochester, PhD, 73. *Pos:* Res assoc musicol, Eastman Sch Music, 73-75, head acquisitions & collection develop, Sibley Music Libr, 79- *Awards:* J T Massa Fel, 73, NY State Endowed Fel, 74 & Am Asn Univ Women. *Mem:* Am Musicol Soc; Music Libr Asn; Int Asn Music Libr; Mu Phi Epsilon (pres, 68). *Interests:* Sacred and secular vocal music of the 17th century. *Publ:* Auth, A Thematic Catalog of the Sacred Works of Giacomo Carissimi, European Am Music Corp, 79; contribr, Notes & RILM, Currently. *Mailing Add:* 90 Roby Dr Rochester NY 14618

BUGGERT, ROBERT W
EDUCATOR, COMPOSER

b Chicago, Ill, July 25, 18. *Study:* Vandercook Sch Music, BM, 38; Univ Mich, MMEd, 47, PhD, 56. *Works:* Toccata #1, 69; Short Overture, 69; Dialogue (solo perc & piano), 69; Fanfare, Song and March (perc & piano), 69; J-21557, 69; Didiptich #1 and #2, 70; The Night Thoreau Spent in Jail (theater), 70. *Pos:* Perc ed, Instrumentalist, 55-59; ed, Contemp Perc Libr. *Teaching:* Pub sch, 39-43; mem fac, Univ Wichita, formerly, Univ Okla, formerly & Boston Univ, formerly; dean & prof, Northern Ill Univ, 64- *Mailing Add:* 1712 Judy Lane De Kalb IL 60115

BUHL, KEITH ROBERT
TENOR

b Granite City, Ill, May 14, 55. *Study:* Manhattan Sch Music, BM, 80. *Roles:* Tonio in Daughter of the Regiment, 82 & Count Almaviva in Il Barbiere di Siviglia, 83, Tex Opera Theatre; Mayor in Albert Herring, Houston Opera Studio, 83. *Mailing Add:* 928 N Sleight St Naperville IL 60540

BUKETOFF, IGOR
CONDUCTOR & MUSIC DIRECTOR, ADMINISTRATOR

b Hartford, Conn, May 29, 15. *Study:* Univ Kans, 31-32; Juilliard Inst Musical Art, BS, 35, MS, 41, Grad Sch, 39-42; Los Angeles Consv Music & Art, Hon MusD, 49. *Rec Perf:* On RCA. *Pos:* Cond US & Europ tours, Broadway Co, 47-48; cond, Young People's Concerts, New York Phil Orch, 48-53, music dir, 50-53; guest cond, symph orchs in Europe, US & South Am, 57-; founder & chmn, Int Contemp Music Exchange, 59-; music dir, Iceland State Symph, 64-65; dir, Contemp Comp Proj, Inst Int Educ, 67-70; music dir & cond, St Paul Opera Asn, 68-74; artistic dir, Tex Chamber Orch, 80-81. *Teaching:* Mem fac, Juilliard Sch, 35-45, Chautauqua Sch Music, summers 41-47 & Columbia Univ, 43-47; assoc prof music, Butler Univ, 53-63; vis prof, Univ Houston, 77-79. *Awards:* Alice M Ditson Grants, 56, 70 & 72; Rockefeller Found Grant, 59; State Dept Cult Exchange Grant USSR, 72. *Mem:* Bax Soc; Am Symph Orch League (mem bd dir, 59-62). *Mailing Add:* 500 E 85th St New York NY 10028

BULL, STORM
EDUCATOR, PIANO

b Chicago, Ill, Oct 13, 13. *Study:* Am Consv Music; Chicago Musical Col; Ecole Normale Musique Superieur, Paris; Sorbonne, Paris; Liszt Acad Music, Budapest; Univ Budapest; studied with Bela Bartok, Percy Grainger, Lazare Levi & Louise Robyn. *Works:* Tone Poem (Dawn), Nat Youth Orch, 34; Nocturne, Interlochen Symph Band, 37; Risen Is the Good Shepherd, Univ Choir & Chamber Orch, 51. *Pos:* Conct pianist, 35-42. *Teaching:* Asst prof, Baylor Univ, 45-47; prof music & head div piano, Col Music, Univ Colo, Boulder, 47-77, prof emer & vis prof, 77-83; guest prof musicol, Univ Oslo, 56-57. *Mem:* Am Musicol Soc. *Interests:* Contemporary composers and music; Bartok and his music; Johan Sebastian Bach. *Publ:* Co-ed, North Am Ed Musikkens Verden, A S, Oslo, 51, rev ed, 63; auth, J S Bach, In: New Century Cyclopedia of Names, Appleton-Century-Crofts, 54; Index to Biographies of Contemporary Composers, Vol I, 64, Vol II, 74, Scarecrow Press; numerous articles in professional periodicals. *Mailing Add:* Sunshine Canyon Boulder CO 80302

BULLARD, TRUMAN CAMPBELL
EDUCATOR, MUSIC DIRECTOR

b Rochester, NY, Sept 17, 38. *Study:* Haverford Col, BA, 60; Harvard Univ, MA, 63; Eastman Sch Music, PhD, 71. *Works:* Six Russian Folk Songs, European Am Press, 76; Wreath of French Noels, perf by Dickinson Col Chamber Choir, 78; Spirit of Life, perf by Harrisburg Fest Choir, 83. *Teaching:* Instr music, Lakeside Sch, 63-65; instr, Dickinson Col, 65-68, asst prof, 68-71, assoc prof, 71-79, prof, 79- *Awards:* Distinguished Teaching Award, Lindback Found, 71. *Mem:* Am Musicol Soc; Int Double Reed Soc; Am Choral Dir Asn. *Interests:* Stravinsky's music, 1910-1918; Russian music. *Publ:* Ed, Canticles of the Eastean Church, Albert Bridge Press, 73; auth, The Riot at the Rite: Not So Surprising After All, In: Essays on Music, 79. *Mailing Add:* Music Dept Dickinson Col Carlisle PA 17013

BULLAT, GEORGE J NICHOLAS
ORGAN, EDUCATOR

b Chicago, Ill, Mar 10, 43. *Study:* Aquinas Inst, Ill, BA, 64, MA(philosophy), 66, MA(theology), 69; Am Consv Music, BMus, 68, MMus, 69, DMA, 74; studied organ with E Eigenschenk, R Lodine & K Paukert. *Pos:* Dir music, Emmanuel Episcopal Church, La Grange, Ill, 71-74; minister music, First United Church, Oak Park, Ill, 74- *Teaching:* Prof organ, Am Consv Music, 71-, dean grad div, 78- *Awards:* Fel, Am Guild Organists, 66; First Place, Soc Am Musicians Organ Compt, 67; fel & Healey Willan Prize, Royal Can Col Organists, 75. *Mem:* Am Guild Organists (dean Chicago chap, 76-78); Royal Can Col Organists. *Mailing Add:* Am Consv Music 116 S Michigan Ave Chicago IL 60603

BULLEN, SARAH
HARP

b Glen Cove, NY, May 1, 56. *Study:* Juilliard Sch, BMus, 78, MMus, 79. *Pos:* Prin harp, Greenwich Phil, 77-81, Am Phil, New York, 80-81 & Utah Symph, 81-; second harp, NJ Symph, 79-81. *Awards:* Walter E Naumberg Award, 78; First Place Nat Harp Compt, Ruth Lorraine Close Award, 80. *Mem:* Am Harp Soc; Am Fedn Musician. *Mailing Add:* 52 E 200 North Salt Lake City UT 84103

BULLIN, CHRISTINE NEVA
ADMINISTRATOR

b New Plymouth, New Zealand, Apr 13, 48; US citizen. *Pos:* Dir, Opera New England, Boston, 75-78; adminr, several San Francisco Opera affil prog, 78-79; mgr, San Francisco Opera Ctr, 81- *Mailing Add:* 301 Vanness Ave San Francisco CA 94102

BULLOCK, WILLIAM JOSEPH
CONDUCTOR, EDUCATOR

b Crawfordsville, Ind, Dec 25, 43. *Study:* Fla State Univ, BME, 66, MA, 68, PhD, 71. *Rec Perf:* Luigi Zaninelli: For Spacious Skies, Spectrum, 80; Univ Southern Miss Singers, Crest Rec, 80. *Pos:* Cond, Columbus Civic Chorale Inc, 82- *Teaching:* Prof music & coordr vocal & choral music, Tarrant Co Jr Col, Ft Worth, 68-77; assoc prof music & dir choral activ, Univ Southern Miss, 77-82 & Columbus Col, 82- *Mem:* Am Choral Dir Asn (Miss pres, 81-83); Am Choral Found; Col Music Soc; Music Educr Nat Conf; Van Cliburn Int Quadrennial Piano Compt (mem bd dir, 74-77). *Publ:* Auth, A Review of Measures of Musico-Aesthetic Attitude, J Res Music Educ, 73; ed, Liszt's Inno a Maria Vergine, Lawson-Gould, 81; auth, Sacred Choral Works with Small Instrumental Ensemble: An Annotated List of Selected Twentieth-Century Works, Am Choral Found, 82; ed, Schubert's Al par del ruscello, 83 & Schubert's Wer wird Zähren from Stabat Mater, 83, Lawson-Gould. *Mailing Add:* 3720 Mote Rd Columbus GA 31907

BULLOUGH, JOHN FRANK
EDUCATOR, MUSIC DIRECTOR
b Washington, DC, Oct 15, 28. *Study:* George Washington Univ, BA, 54; Union Theol Sem, SMM, 58; studied voice with Dolf Swing & Reinald Werrenrath, organ with Claire Coci, comp with Seth Bingham. *Pos:* Organist & choirmaster, St Paul's Episcopal Church, Englewood, NJ, 73- *Teaching:* Instr music & speech, Hartford Theol Sem Found, 58-60, asst prof, 61-64; Asst prof, Fairleigh Dickinson Univ, 64-70, assoc prof, 70-74, prof, 74- *Mem:* Am Guild Organists (dean, Hartford, Conn chap, 63-64, NValley, NJ chap, 75-77); Col Music Soc. *Interests:* History of the British Chapel Royal and the Anglican cathedral tradition in music. *Mailing Add:* 488 Fairidge Terr Teaneck NJ 07666

BULMER, STEVEN ROBERT
TUBA, ELECTRIC BASS
b New London, Conn, June 15, 60. *Study:* Eastman Sch Music, BM, 82, BMusEd, 82; Northwestern Univ, MM, 83. *Rec Perf:* Ventures for Orchestra, Eastman Sch Music, 81; Lyric Piece for Tuba & Orchestra, William Billings Inst Am Music, 83. *Pos:* Tubist, Eastern Conn Symph Orch, 76-78; assoc tubist, Civic Orch Chicago, 82- *Mem:* Tubist Universal Brotherhood Asn; Phi Mu Alpha Sinfonia Am. *Mailing Add:* 99 Lovers Lane East Lyme CT 06333

BUMBRY, GRACE
MEZZO-SOPRANO
b St Louis, Mo, Jan 4, 37. *Study:* Boston Univ, 54-55; Music Acad West, 56-59; studied with Lotte Lehman; Chicago Univ; Northwestern Univ; Univ St Louis, Hon DH; Rockhurst Col, Hon DMus. *Rec Perf:* For Deutsche Grammophon, Angel, London & RCA; perf in film of Carmen. *Roles:* Amneris in Aida, 60 & Carmen in Carmen, Paris Opera; Elvira in Ernani; Santuzza in Cavalleria rusticana; Olga in Eugene Onegin; Ulrica in Ballo in maschera; Venus in Tannhäuser und der Sängerkrieg auf Wartburg. *Pos:* Ms, Basle Opera, 60-63, Bayreuth Fest, 62, Vienna Staatsoper, 63, Covent Garden, 63, 68, 69 & 76, Salzburg Fest, 64, Metropolitan Opera, 65, La Scala, 66 & other opera companies in US & Europe. *Awards:* Richard Wagner Medal, 63; Nat Marian Anderson Award; Grammy Award. *Bibliog:* Harold C Schonberg (auth), Opera's Black Voices, New York Times, 1/17/82. *Mem:* Sigma Alpha Iota. *Mailing Add:* c/o Columbia Artists Mgt Inc 165 W 57th St New York NY 10019

BUMGARDNER, THOMAS ARTHUR
EDUCATOR
b Houston, Tex, Sept 30, 42. *Study:* NTex State Univ, BA, 64; Univ Minn, Minneapolis, MFA, 66; Univ Tex, Austin, DMA, 73. *Teaching:* Prof music, Univ Wis, Superior, 66-, dept head, 78- *Mem:* Nat Asn Teachers Singing; Nat Asn Schs Music; Int Asn Encouragement Res in Singing. *Publ:* Norman Dello Joio, Twayne Publ (in prep). *Mailing Add:* 5803 John Ave Superior WI 54880

BUNCH, MERIBETH ANN
VOICE CONSULTANT, EDUCATOR
b Aulander, NC, Apr 20, 38. *Study:* Salem Col, NC, voice with Joan Jacobowsky, BM, 60; Union Theol Sem, NY, SMM, 62; vocal coaching with Martin Katz, 73-79; Univ Southern Calif, voice with William Vennard, PhD, 74; studied dance & movement with John O'Brien, 79-; voice with Audrey Langford, 80-; Alexander technique with Bill Williams, 80- *Pos:* Consult voice, Dynamic Communication, Ltd, 82-; private consult opera, music theatre & bus, currently. *Teaching:* Assoc prof voice & anatomy, Univ Del, 74-82; prof anatomy, Royal Acad Dancing, London, England, 80-; prof voice, Cent Sch Speech & Drama, London, 83- *Awards:* Res Fel, Royal Col Surgeons England, Nat Inst Health, 79-81. *Mem:* Nat Asn Teachers Singing; Collegium Theatri Medici. *Interests:* Vocal anatomy and physiology; relationship of sound, body and mind. *Publ:* Auth, You, Too, Can Read Scientific Materials, Nat Asn Teachers Singing Bulletin, 75; A Cephalometric Study of Structures of the Head and Neck during Sustained Phonation of Covered and Open Qualities, Folia Phoniatrica, 76; A Survey of the Research on Covered and Open Voice Qualities & coauth, Some Further Observations on Covered and Open Vocal Qualities, Nat Asn Teachers Singing Bulletin, 77; auth, Dynamics of the Singing Voice, Springer-Verlag, 82. *Mailing Add:* 100 Christiana Med Ctr Newark DE 19702

BUNGER, RICHARD JOSEPH
COMPOSER, EDUCATOR
b Allentown, Pa, June 1, 42. *Study:* Consv Music, Oberlin Col, BM, 64; Univ Ill, MM, 66. *Works:* Oedipus Rex (singers & tape); Good Woman of Setzuan (singers, perc, tape & slides); Variations on a Sonata (string quartet); Twice 5 for 2 (violin & cello); Hommage (a suite); Pianography, Fantasy on a Theme by Fibonacci (prepared piano & electronics); 3 Bolts Out of the Blues (prepared piano). *Pos:* Performer 20th century music throughout US & Europe. *Teaching:* Mem fac, Queens Col, 65-68 & Oberlin Col, 68-69; prof & dir, Electronic Music & Rec Prog, Calif State Univ, Dominguez Hills, 70- *Awards:* Grants, Martha Baird Rockefeller Fund, Bennington Comp Conf, Toyota Corp & Nissan Corp. *Mem:* Am Soc Univ Comp; Nat Asn Am Comp & Cond; Int Soc Contemp Music; Pi Kappa Lambda; Am Fedn Musicians. *Publ:* Auth, The Well-Prepared Piano, Vol 1-10, 76, Japanese ed, 78. *Mailing Add:* Dept Music Calif State Univ Carson CA 90747

BUNKE, JEROME SAMUEL
CLARINET
b Albany, NY, Sept 8, 45. *Study:* Juilliard Sch, BMus, MMus; NY Univ, PhD. *Rec Perf:* Concerto for Clarinet (Robert Keys Clark); Clarinet Sonata No 1 (Brahms); Fantasiestucke & Romances (Schumann); Grand Duo Concertant (Weber); Studies in English Folksong (Vaughn Williams); Concerto (Mozart);

Sonatine (Wilson). *Pos:* TV & radio appearances, New York, Kansas City & Tokyo; conct clarinetist, Carnegie Hall, Japan Phil Symph Orch, NHK Ymiuri Nippon Symph Orch, Chautauqua Fest & others. *Awards:* Conct Artists Guild Award, 68. *Publ:* Contrib to Maine Music Educr J & Conn Music Educr Asn Mag. *Mailing Add:* c/o Joanne Rile Mgt Box 27539 Philadelphia PA 19118

BUNTING, MELODY
ARTIST REPRESENTATIVE
b Los Angeles, Calif, Apr 21, 46. *Study:* Univ Calif, Los Angeles, BMus, 70. *Pos:* Artist rep, New York, 81- *Mem:* Am Symph Orch League; Chopin Soc US. *Mailing Add:* 118 W 72nd St Suite 1002 New York NY 10023

BURANSKAS, KAREN
EDUCATOR, CELLO
b Allen Park, Mich. *Study:* Ind Univ, with Janos Starker & Fritz Magg, BM, 73; Univ Southern Calif, with Gregor Piatigorsky, 73-75; Yale Univ, with Aldo Parisot, MM, 77. *Teaching:* Asst instr cello, Ind Univ, Bloomington, 76-77; assoc prof music & cello, Notre Dame Univ, Ind, 79- *Awards:* Leta Snow String Compt Award, 73; Conct Artists Guild Award, 77; Aldo Parisot Int Cello Compt Award, 80. *Rep:* Albert Kay Assoc Inc 58 W 58th St New York NY 10019. *Mailing Add:* 1522 Rosemary Lane A South Bend IN 46637

BURCHINAL, FREDERICK
BARITONE
Rec Perf: A Christmas Carol. *Roles:* Paolo in Simon Boccanegra, San Francisco Opera, 80; Scrooge in A Christmas Carol, Covent Garden, 81; Lescaut in Manon Lescaut, Baltimore Opera, 82; Jack Rance in La Fanciulla del West, 83, Enrico in Lucia di Lammermoor, 83 & Marcello in La Boheme, 83, New York City Opera; Scarpia in Tosca, Conn Grand Opera, 83; and others. *Pos:* Performer, New York City Opera, San Francisco Opera, Philadelphia Opera & others. *Mailing Add:* c/o Harold Shaw 1995 Broadway New York NY 10023

BURDA, PAVEL
CONDUCTOR, EDUCATOR
b Bohemian Budweis, Czechoslovakia, Apr 7, 42. *Study:* Prague Consv Music, adv dipl; State Univ NY, MMus; State Acad Music, Hamburg. *Works:* Incidental Music for Vysinuta Hrdicka, Theatre on Balustrade, Prague, 63-65. *Rec Perf:* On JEM Rec, Orion & Supraphon. *Pos:* Timpanist, Symph Orch Vit Nejedly, TV shows & toured with orchs in Eastern & Western Europe & NAfrica; solo timpanist, Brazilian Symph Orch & Fest Casals Orch, PR, 76; prin timpanist & perc, Orch de Camera, NY; dir & cond, Music with Percussion Ens; founder, dir & cond, Milwaukee 20th Century Ens, Inc. *Teaching:* Assoc prof mus, Univ Wis, Milwaukee, currently. *Awards:* Tanglewood Fel, 70. *Mem:* Am Fedn Musicians. *Mailing Add:* 3003 N Farwell Ave Milwaukee WI 53211

BURGANGER, JUDITH
PIANO, EDUCATOR
b Buffalo, NY. *Study:* State Consv Music, Stuttgart, Germany, studied piano with Wladimir Horbowski & chamber music with Hubert Giesen, 57-62. *Rec Perf:* Various rec, USA, West Germany & Switzerland, 65-; Virtuose Klaviermusik, Eurocord, 65. *Pos:* Pianist with numerous orchs throughout Europe, North Am & Japan; mgr, Fla Atlantic Chamber Music Ser, 80- *Teaching:* Assoc prof, Carnegie-Mellon Univ, formerly & Tex Tech Univ, formerly; prof, Fla Atlantic Univ, currently. *Awards:* First Prize, Merriweather Post Compt, 56; Medallion & Dipl, Int Compt, Geneva, Switz, 59; First Prize, Munich Int Piano Compt, 65. *Mem:* Nat Soc Arts & Lett; Boca Raton Music Guild; Coral Springs Soc Perf Arts; Am Music Scholar Asn; Fla State Music Teachers Asn. *Mailing Add:* Music Dept Fla Atlantic Univ 500 NW 20th St Boca Raton FL 33432

BURGESS, GARY ELLSWORTH
TENOR, EDUCATOR
b Devonshire, Bermuda, May 31, 38; US citizen. *Study:* Ind Univ, with Margaret Harshaw; Curtis Inst Music, with Dino Yannopoulos & Margaret Harshaw. *Roles:* Male Chorus in The Rape of Lucretia, Kentucky Opera, 69; Edgardo in Lucia di Lammermoor; Turiddu in Cavalleria rusticana; Rodolfo in La Boheme; Pinkerton in Madama Butterfly; Cavaradossi in Tosca; Bacchus in Ariadne auf Naxos. *Pos:* Lyr ten, Jackson Opera South, Kentucky Opera & Philadelphia Lyr Opera; res mem, San Francisco Opera & Greek Nat Opera, Athens. *Teaching:* Prof opera & voice, State Univ NY, Buffalo, currently. *Rep:* Teilesco Artists 5-31 50th Ave Long Island City NY 11101. *Mailing Add:* Opera Dept State Univ NY Buffalo NY 14214

BURGESS, MARY MINOTT
SOPRANO
b Anderson, SC. *Study:* Curtis Inst Music, BMus, 63. *Rec Perf:* Moravian Duets Op 20 (Dvorak), Columbia, 66; Cantata No 30 (Bach), Ars Nova, 70; Night Conjure Verse (Del Tredici), CRI, 71; Gloria (Vivaldi), CBS, 76; Choral Fantasy (Beethoven), Telarc, 82. *Roles:* Fiordiligi in Cosi fan tutte, Fest Ottawa, 79 & Nev Opera, 81; Countess in Marriage of Figaro, Shreveport Opera, 81 & St Petersburg Opera, 82; Governess in Turn of the Screw, Baltimore Chamber Opera, 82; Martha in Martha, oder Der Markt von Richmond, Dublin Grand Opera Soc, 82; Madama Butterfly in Madama Butterfly, Nev Opera, 82; Gilda in Rigoletto, Santa Barbara Symph, 83; Mimi in La Boheme, Nev Opera, 83. *Rep:* Thea Dispeker Artists Mgt 59 E 54th St New York NY 10024. *Mailing Add:* 124 W 79th St New York NY 10024

BURGIN, JOHN
EDUCATOR
b White Pine, Tenn, Jan 7, 32. *Study:* Carson-Newman Col, BA, 52; Ind Univ, MM, 58; George Peabody Col, PhD, 71. *Teaching:* Prof music, Northeast La Univ, 65- *Mem:* Nat Asn Teachers Singing (nat vpres, 79-81, pres, 82-); Am Choral Dir Asn; Music Educr Nat Conf; Presby Asn Musicians. *Interests:* Comparative vocal pedagogy bibliography. *Publ:* Auth, Teaching Singing, Scarecrow Press, 73; The Hope for a New Golden Age, Vol 39, No 2, Of Value to Art, Vol 39, No 3, Me, You and the NATS Code of Ethics, Vol 39, No 4, & Contributions to Vocal Pedagogy, 1972-75, Vol 33, No 3, Nat Asn Teachers Singing Bulletin; Of Value to Art, Vol 39, No 3. *Mailing Add:* 19 Elmwood Dr Monroe LA 71203

BURGSTAHLER, ELTON EARL
EDUCATOR, COMPOSER
b Orland, Calif, Sept 16, 24. *Study:* Univ Pac, Stockton, Calif, AB, BMus, 47; James Millikin Univ, Decatur, Ill, MMus, 50; Fla State Univ, Tallahassee, Fla, PhD, 66. *Works:* Three Anthems, Carl Fischer, 56; Deep Waters—Band Overture, 58, Folk Christmas (cantata), 69 & The Truth About Christmas (cantata), 72, Pro Art Publ, Belwin; Spectrum (ten flutes), Music Educr Nat Conf, 80; Seven Modal Settings of the Lord's Prayer, Chamber Singers, Southwest Mo State Univ, 81; Dorian Gray (opera), Southwest Mo State Univ, 83. *Teaching:* Instr music, Westwood, Calif, Springfield, Mo & Manteca, Calif High Sch, 47-49 & Millikin Univ, Decatur, Ill, 50-56; prof music, Southwest Mo State Univ, 56- *Mem:* Nat Theory Asn; Col Music Soc; ASCAP. *Mailing Add:* 1948 E Sunset Springfield MO 65804

BURK, JAMES MACK
EDUCATOR
b Muskogee, Okla, July 1, 31. *Study:* Oklahoma City Univ, BM, 53; Univ Okla, MMusEd, 60, MMus, 63, DMusEd, 67; Ind Univ, Bloomington. *Teaching:* Instr music theory, Okla Col Liberal Arts, 63-66 & Oklahoma City Univ, 65-67; assoc prof, Univ Mo, Columbia, 67- *Awards:* Sinfonia Found Grant, 69; Nat Endowment Humanities Grant, 77. *Mem:* Col Music Soc; Soc Music Theory; Sonneck Soc. *Interests:* Charles Ives and his music; American music; musical analysis. *Publ:* Auth, The Wind Music of Charles Ives, Instrumentalist, 10/69; Ives Innovations in Piano Music, Clavier, 10/74; Schillinger's Double Equal Temperament System, Symposium Res Psychology & Acoustics Music, 79; articles, In: New Grove Dict of Music & Musicians, 80; articles, In: New Grove Dict of Music in US (in prep); coauth & ed, A Charles Ives Bibliography, Col Music Soc (in prep). *Mailing Add:* 3111 Crawford St Columbia MO 65201

BURKAT, LEONARD
WRITER, ADMINISTRATOR
b Boston, Mass, July 21, 19. *Study:* Boston Latin Sch; Boston Univ; Columbia Univ; Harvard Univ; study with R S Angell, E Ballantine, O Kinkeldey, A T Merritt & W Piston. *Pos:* From page to asst dept head, Music Dept, Boston Pub Libr, 37-47; librn & adminr, Berkshire Music Ctr, 46-63; asst librn, asst to music dir & artistic adminr, Boston Symph Orch, 47-63; vpres, CBS-Columbia Rec, 63-73; prog note writer & proprietor, Leonard Burkat, Prog Note Serv. *Bibliog:* Leadership in the Arts: A Study on the Relocation of Authority, Harvard Inst Arts Admin, 75; C Nelson & A Nesnow (auth), The Burkat Collection, Yale Univ Music Libr Arch Collection, 79. *Mem:* Am Musicol Asn; Am Symph Orch League; Chamber Music Am; Music Critics Asn; Music Libr Asn; Nat Acad Rec Arts & Sci. *Interests:* Concert repertoire studies; American topics, especially Boston. *Publ:* Auth, articles & rev in Boston Globe & Transcript, 38-44, Notes, 42-53, Libr J, 44-50, Musical Quart, 48-53 & many others; ed & translr, C Munch, IAmConductor, Oxford Univ Press, 55; many short articles in New Grove Dict of Music in US (in prep); program notes for numerous orchestras, festivals & other concert organizations. *Mailing Add:* 1 Lake Crest Dr Danbury CT 06810

BURKAT, MARION F (GUMNER)
EDITOR
b Boston, Mass, Sept 26, 19. *Study:* Radcliffe Col, with Archibald T Davison, Donald J Grout & Stephen D Tuttle, AB, 40. *Pos:* Managing ed, Program Note Serv, 75- *Mem:* Bohemians; Am Musicol Soc. *Mailing Add:* 1 Lake Crest Dr Danbury CT 06810

BURKH, DENNIS
CONDUCTOR
b San Francisco, Calif. *Rec Perf:* Rhapsody in Blue—American In Paris (Gershwin); rec on Opus, Victor & Musical Heritage. *Pos:* Cond, Mich Opera Theatre, currently; artistic dir, Opera Co Gtr Lansing, currently; music dir, Mich State Univ Orch Int Season, currently; guest cond, London New Philharmonia Orch, Prague Symph, Radio Symph Orch Trieste, Milan & Turin, Seoul Phil, Teatro Nuovo & others. *Mailing Add:* Opera Co Greater Lansing 919 E Grand River Lansing MI 48906

BURKHOLDER, J PETER
EDUCATOR, WRITER
b Chapel Hill, NC, June 17, 54. *Study:* Earlham Col, AB, 75; Univ Chicago, MA, 80, PhD, 83. *Teaching:* Lectr music, Univ Chicago, 79 & 81; instr music hist, Univ Wis, 82-83; asst prof, 83- *Awards:* Fel, Danforth Found, 75; grant, Martha Baird Rockefeller Fund, 82. *Mem:* Am Musicol Soc; Soc Music Theory; Col Music Soc. *Interests:* Charles Ives and his music; modernism as a musical concept; 20th century music, especially American. *Publ:* Auth, Museum Pieces: The Historicist Mainstream in Music of the Last Hundred Years, J Musicol, 83; Quotation and Emulation: Charles Ives' Use of His Models, Music Quart (in prep). *Mailing Add:* Sch Music Univ Wis Madison WI 53706

BURKLEY, BRUCE
COMPOSER, VIOLA
b Allentown, Pa, Aug 16, 36. *Study:* Houghton Col, NY, MusB, 58; Peabody Consv, MusM & artist dipl, 62; WVa Univ; Univ Minn. *Works:* Image for Flute and Orchestra (string); Concert Piece for Orchestra; String Quartet, perf by Fine Arts Quartet; Rainy Day (chorus & orch), perf by Cincinnati Symph; chamber works incl sonatas for violin, viola, violoncello, song cycles & suites. *Pos:* Ford Found comp in res, Cincinnati, 62-63; choral cond & violist, Lydian Music Teaching Studio, Minn, currently. *Teaching:* Instr, Peabody Consv & Prep Dept, formerly; asst prof, West Liberty State Col, WVa, 64-68 & St Paul Bible Col, Minn, 70-77; grad asst, WVa Univ, formerly. *Awards:* Gustav Klemm Prize, Peabody Consv. *Mem:* Nat Asn Comp USA. *Mailing Add:* PO Box 378 Lester Prairie MN 55354

BURLESON, SPENCER (J), III
GUITAR, COMPOSER
b Brownwood, Tex, Feb 15, 49. *Study:* San Francisco Consv Music, BM, 71; Consv Antonio Vivaldi, with Alirio Diaz, 72-73; study with Jose Tomas, Spain, 72-74 & Leo Brouwer, France, 74. *Works:* Improvisation I, Collective Invention, 71; Spaces, comn by class guitarists, 79; Sonorities, 81 & Inner Voices, 82, comn by Meet the Comp. *Rec Perf:* Chronica Italiana, Italian Nat TV, 72; Morning Scene, KOVR-TV, Sacramento & Stockton, Calif, 75; 1750 Arch Street, KPFA, Berkeley, 76; Black Unlimited, WTVD-TV, NC, 78; Harambe, WRAL-TV, Raleigh, NC, 78; Spoleto Festival 81, PBS; Westside Workshop, Ch C, cable TV, New York, 82. *Pos:* Vis artist, NC State Arts Coun, 79-80; musician in res, NC State Univ, Raleigh, 79-80. *Teaching:* Instr, guitar, City Col San Francisco, 75-78. *Awards:* Grants, San Francisco Consv Scholar Fund, 70 & Meet the Comp, 75-78. *Publ:* Auth, The Evolution of the Electronic Guitar, Guitar Player Mag, Vol X, 76; Abel Carlevaro, Gendai Guitar, Vox XII, No 3. *Mailing Add:* c/o Gerald Arbee PO Box 714 New York NY 10002

BURMAN-HALL, LINDA CAROL
EDUCATOR, HARPSICHORD
b Los Angeles, Calif, Apr 5, 45. *Study:* Univ Calif, Los Angeles, BA, 66; Princeton Univ, MFA, 68, PhD, 74. *Rec Perf:* Antonio Vivaldi, Sonic Arts, 78; Messe des Morts (Jean Gilles), Musical Heritage, 81. *Pos:* Music dir, Santa Cruz Fest Living Music, 72- *Teaching:* Lectr music, Univ Calif, Los Angeles, 73-74; asst prof, Univ Calif, Santa Cruz, 76-82, assoc prof, 82-, chair, 83- *Mem:* Soc Ethnomusicol (chmn northern Calif chap, 83-). *Interests:* Baroque chamber and keyboard works; Indonesian and American traditional music. *Mailing Add:* Music Dept Univ Calif Santa Cruz CA 95064

BURNETT, HENRY
EDUCATOR, SHAMISEN & KOTO
b New York, NY, Nov 21, 44. *Study:* Queens Col, City Univ New York, BA(music), 68, MA(music), 71, Grad Ctr, City Univ New York, PhD(musicol), 78. *Rec Perf:* The Works of Matsuura Kengyo, Vol 1, Hogaku Soc Rec, 82. *Pos:* Mem, NY Sankyoku Kai, 80-; exec dir, Traditional Japanese Music Soc, City Univ New York, 82- *Teaching:* Assoc prof musicol & ethnomusicol, Queens Col, City Univ New York, 80-, fac mem, Grad Ctr, currently. *Awards:* Staff expansion grant, Japan Found, 78-80. *Mem:* Asian Music Soc; Am Musicol Soc; Soc Ethnomusicol; Col Music Soc. *Interests:* Eighteenth century Western music & traditional Japanese chamber music. *Publ:* Auth, An Introduction to the History & Aesthetics of Japanese Jiuta-Tegotomono, Asian Music, 80; Boris Schwarz, New Grove Dict of Music & Musicians, 80; The Evolution of Shamisen Tegotomono: A Study of the Development of Voice-Shamisen Relationship, Hogaku Soc J, Vol 1, 83. *Mailing Add:* 42-16 147th St Flushing NY 11355

BURNHAM, JAMES
VIOLIN, EDUCATOR
b Asheville, NC. *Study:* Manhattan Sch Music, with A Bronne & R Bronstein, BM, 71, MM, 72. *Rec Perf:* Heller-Burnham Violin Duo, Music Heritage Soc, 81. *Pos:* Prin violinist, Hartford Symph, 74-76 & NJ Symph, 76-78; violinist, Heller-Burnham Violin Duo, 76- *Teaching:* Violin & viola, Prep Div, Manhattan Sch Music, 78-; vis teacher violin, viola & chamber music, Wesleyan Univ, 80- *Mem:* Chamber Music Am. *Mailing Add:* 150 West End Ave New York NY 10023

BURNS, JUDITH CAPPER
CONDUCTOR, EDUCATOR
b Petersburg, Va, Oct 2, 52. *Study:* Cent Mich Univ, BME, 74; Mich State Univ, MM(voice), 80. *Teaching:* Choral dir, Western Sch Dist, 75-79; dir women's glee club, Mich State Univ, 80-82; dir choral activities, Cent Wash Univ, 82- *Mem:* Nat Asn Teachers Singing; Music Educr Nat Conf; Am Choral Dir Asn; Mich Sch Vocal Asn. *Mailing Add:* Music Dept Cent Wash Univ Ellensburg WA 98926

BURNSWORTH, CHARLES CARL
CONDUCTOR, EDUCATOR
b Niagara Falls, NY, June 27, 31. *Study:* State Univ NY, Fredonia, BS(music educ), 53; Univ Ill, MS(music educ), 56; Boston Univ, with Karl Geiringer & Richard Burgin, DMA, 65. *Rec Perf:* Missa Brevis in C Major (Mozart) & Messe in C Major, Op 48 (Schubert), 78, Rico Sonderegger, St Gallen, Switz; Messe No 1 in F Major (Schubert) & Magnificat (Schubert), 81, Sonographic, Schlieren, Switz. *Pos:* Cond, New York Chamber Choir, 78- *Teaching:* Prof music, State Univ NY, Oneonta, 57- *Mem:* Music Educr Nat Conf; NY State Sch Music Asn; NY State Choral Dir Guild (secy, 70-). *Publ:* Auth, The Self-Contained Classroom Reconsidered, In: Perspectives in Music Education, Music Educr Nat Conf, 66; Choral Music for Women's Voices, Scarecrow Press, 68. *Mailing Add:* 14 Suncrest Terr Oneonta NY 13820

BURROWS, JAMES STUART
TENOR

b Cilfynydd, Wales, Feb 7, 35. *Study:* Trinity Col, SWales, degree educ, 55-57. *Rec Perf:* Anna Bolena (Donizetti), ABC/ATS; Requiem (Berlioz), CBS Masterworks; Don Giovanni (Mozart), Phillips & Decca; Die Zauberflote (Mozart), Decca; Stuart Burrows (operetta), L'oiseau Lyre; La Clemenza Ditito (Mozart), Phillips; Tales of Hoffman (Offenbach), ABC/ATS. *Roles:* Faust & The Magic Flute, Metropolitan Opera; Don Giovanni & The Magic Flute, Vienna State Opera; Entfuhrung, Paris Opera; Idomeneo & Don Pasquale, Royal Opera House; Manon, San Francisco Opera; Tales of Hoffman, Buenos Aires Opera; also perf with La Scala, Milan. *Awards:* Hon Doctorate, Univ Wales, 82. *Mailing Add:* c/o Columbia Artists 165 W 57th St New York NY 10019

BURROWS, JOHN
MUSIC DIRECTOR, EDUCATOR

b Newcastle, Staffordshire, England, Aug 3, 41. *Study:* Manchester Univ, England, with Humphrey Proctor-Gregg, MusB, 62; Royal Manchester Col Music, with Eric Chadwick & Clifton Helliwell, 62; London Opera Centre, with Edward Downes, Jani Strasser & Joan Cross, 62-63. *Pos:* Music staff, asst chorusmaster & prompter, English Nat Opera, London, 63-73; musical dir, Mermaid Theatre, London, 73-76 & Theatre Royal Drury Lane, London, 76-78; artistic dir, Pub Opera Dallas, 83- *Teaching:* Prof opera, Southern Methodist Univ, Tex, 80-83; Prof vocal instr, Temple Univ, 83- *Awards:* Ivor Novello Award, 73 & 74. *Mailing Add:* Col Music Temple Univ Philadelphia PA 19122

BURT, GEORGE
COMPOSER, EDUCATOR

b San Francisco, Calif, Oct 7, 29. *Study:* Univ Calif, Berkeley, with Andrew Imbrie; Mills Col, with Darius Milhaud & Leon Kirchner; Princeton Univ, with Roger Sessions, Milton Babbit & Edward Cone; studied with György Ligeti. *Works:* Introduction (orch), 62; Canzona (viola & cello), 65; Threnody (double men's chorus), 67; Exit Music (12 players), 68; Improvization II (synthesizer, piano & tape), 72; Time Passes (chorus & piano), 72; Sam's Story (synthesizer, piano, tape & film), 73; publ by Alexander Broude Inc, Valley Music Press & Jobert Publ. *Teaching:* Instr, Smith Col, 63-69; assoc prof theory & orch, Univ Mich, 69- *Awards:* Horace H Rackham Grant. *Interests:* Electronic production and manipulation of sound. *Mailing Add:* Sch Music Univ Mich Ann Arbor MI 48109

BURT, MICHAEL ROBERT
BASS-BARITONE

b Guildford, Surrey, England. *Roles:* Ratcliffe in Billy Budd, Royal Opera, Covent Garden, 79; Mephistopheles in Faust, San Antonio Opera Co, 81; bass soloist in Messiah, Philadelphia Orch, 81 & 82; bass soloist in Mahler 8th, Seattle Symph Orch, 82; Pizarro in Fidelio, Städtische Bühnen, Frankfurt, Germany, 82; The Flying Dutchman & Der Ring Des Nibelungen, Marin Symph Orch, 83; Figaro in Marriage of Figaro, Seattle Opera, 83. *Rep:* Columbia Artists 165 W 57 New York NY 10019. *Mailing Add:* 530 Park Ave New York NY 10021

BURT, WARREN ARNOLD
COMPOSER, WRITER

b Baltimore, Md, Oct 10, 49. *Study:* State Univ NY, Albany, with Joel Chadabe, BA, 71; Univ Calif, San Diego, with Kenneth Gaburo & Robert Erickson, MA, 75. *Works:* Aardvarks I (piano solo), 76; Nighthawk I (solo reader), 76; Five Adventures of a Stunned Mullet, Just Improvisations (computer), 79 & Penguino Lunaire (solo voice), 79, Lingua Press; Four Pieces for Synthesizer (electronic), 81 & Studies for Synthesizer (electronic), 82, Scarlet Aardvark Tapes; Song-Dawn-Chords (electronics), RASH, 82. *Pos:* Fel res, Ctr Music Experiment, Univ Calif, San Diego, 73-75; music educ officer, Coun Adult Educ, Melbourne, 82-83. *Teaching:* Sr tutor theory, hist & electronics, La Trobe Univ, Melbourne, 75-78; lectr, 81; lectr comp, Sidney Consv, Australia, 79. *Publ:* Auth, Musical Perception and Exploratory Music, Art Text, Melbourne, 81; Seven Composers in Three Parts, Art Network, Sydney, 81; On Sound and Image in Moods, Cantrills Filmnotes, Melbourne, 81; Music Art and a Repudiation of Irony in Post-Modernism, Virgin Press, Melbourne, 82; How To Be a Great Composer, New Music Articles, Melbourne, 82. *Mailing Add:* 30 Third St Waterford NY 12188

BURTON, STEPHEN DOUGLAS
COMPOSER, EDUCATOR

b Whittier, Calif, Feb 24, 43. *Study:* Consv Music, Oberlin Col, with Richard Hoffmann, 60-62; Mozarteum Acad, Salzburg, studied comp with Hans Werner Henze, 62-64; Peabody Consv Music, with Jean Elvey, MM, 74. *Works:* Duchess of Malfi (three-act opera), 75; Americana (three one-act operas), 75; Ariel Symph No 2 (baritone), Wash, 76; Songs of the Tulpehocken (ten & orch), 76; Finisterre (ballet), 77; String Quartet No 2 (chamber music), 77; Piano Trio (chamber music), 77. *Rec Perf:* On Louisville Masterworks & Peter's Int. *Pos:* Music dir, Munich Kemmerspiele, 63-64. *Teaching:* Instr, Cath Univ Am, 70-74; assoc prof music, George Mason Univ, 74- *Awards:* Nat Endowment Arts Grant, 74 & 77; Nat Opera Inst Grant, 75; ASCAP Awards, 76- *Mailing Add:* 9477 Arlington Blvd Fairfax VA 22031

BUSBY, GERALD
COMPOSER, TEACHER

b Abilene, Tex, Dec 16, 35. *Study:* Yale Sch Music, Yale Univ, BA, 60. *Works:* Runes (ballet), comn by Paul Taylor, 76; 3 Women (filmscore), comn by Robert Altman, 77; Oberndorf Revisited (TV filmscore), C F Peters, 79; Court Dances (ballet), C F Peters, 80; Glyphs (quartet), comn by Speculum Musicae, 81; Old World (theatre score), comn by Philadelphia Drama Guild, 81; Cellosuite (ballet), comn by Nancy Meehan Dance Co, 82. *Teaching:* Instr piano, Princeton Univ, 72-76 & privately, 72- *Awards:* Fels, Nat Endowment Arts, 76 & 81 & John Simon Guggenheim Found, 81-82. *Mem:* ASCAP; Am Fedn Musicians; Screen Actors Guild. *Rep:* C/o Walter Gidaly 750 3rd Ave New York NY 10022. *Mailing Add:* 222 W 23 New York NY 10011

BUSH, DOUGLAS EARL
EDUCATOR, ORGAN

b Butte, Mont, Mar 1, 47. *Study:* Brigham Young Univ, BA, 72, MM, 74; Univ Tex, Austin, PhD, 82. *Works:* Hymn Harmonizations, 80, Organ Preludes on Children's Hymns, 81, Hymn Harmonizations and Descants, 83 & An Organ Book, 83, Sonos Music Resources Inc. *Pos:* Music dir, Utah Bach Choir, 78- *Teaching:* Musicol, Brigham Young Univ, 78-, asst prof music. *Mem:* Am Musicol Soc (chap secy, 80); Int Schütz Soc; Am Guild Organists (chap dean, 82-). *Interests:* Musical-liturgical matters of Renaissance and Baroque; organ historical research. *Publ:* Auth, J S Bach's Art of Fugue, Music, 74; Nicolas DeGrigny's Livre d'Orgue, Diapason, 74. *Mailing Add:* 418 N 500 W Provo UT 84601

BUSH, MILTON LOUIS
EDUCATOR, TROMBONE

b New Orleans, La, July 22, 25. *Study:* Southeastern La Col, BA & BMus, 47; La State Univ, MMusEd, 48; Juilliard Sch Music, 48. *Works:* Ballad for Trombone; Mill Mountain Roanoke. *Rec Perf:* Trombones Beaucoup, Swing Low Album. *Pos:* Mem, New Orleans Opera Orch, 48-68; mem, New Orleans Summer Pops Orch, 49-, pres, 57-77; co-cond, 60-; mem, New Orleans Opera Orch, 48-68; arr staff educ div, Warner Brothers, 74-82; reviewer new band publ, La Musician, 80- *Teaching:* Instrm music elem pub sch, New Orleans, 48-49; dir band, Behrman High Sch, New Orleans, 49-66 & Kennedy High Sch, New Orleans, 66-68; prof music, Univ New Orleans, 68- *Mem:* Col Band Dir Asn (La state chmn, 76-78 & 80-83); Community Concerts Asn; La Bandmasters' Asn; Music Educr Nat Conf; La Music Educr Asn (pres, 72-74). *Mailing Add:* 1932 Wildair Dr New Orleans LA 70122

BUSHMAN, IRVIN
CANTOR, EDUCATOR

Study: Oberlin Consv, BM, 39, MM, 47; Curtis Inst Music, 39-40. *Roles:* The Crucible & Gianni Schicchi, Cleveland Orch. *Pos:* Cantor & dir music, Temple Emanu-El, 47-; performer recitals, oratorios & operas. *Teaching:* Instr voice, Oberlin Consv, 40-42 & Cleveland Inst Music, 46- *Mem:* Nat Asn Teachers Singing (pres, 79-82). *Mailing Add:* 4388 Greenway Rd Cleveland OH 44121

BUSHOUSE, M DAVID
FRENCH HORN, EDUCATOR

b Kalamazoo, Mich, Jan 12, 41. *Study:* Univ Mich, with Louis Stout, Harry Berv & William Revelli, BM, 65, MM, 66. *Teaching:* Instr French horn, Morehead State Univ, Ky, 66-69; from asst prof to prof, Univ Kans, 69-; dir, Midwestern Music Camp, 79- *Mem:* Int Horn Soc (Kans coordr, 78-); Nat Asn Col Wind & Perc Instr (Kans chairperson, 80-); Music Educr Nat Conf. *Publ:* Auth, Practical Hints on Playing the French Horn, Belwin Mills (in prep). *Mailing Add:* Dept Music Univ Kans Lawrence KS 66045

BUSSE, BARRY L
TENOR

b Gloversville, NY, Aug 18, 46. *Study:* Consv Music, Oberlin Col, BM, 68; Manhattan Sch Music, MM, 70. *Rec Perf:* Postcard from Morroco (Argento), Desto Rec, 72; Mary, Queen of Scots (Musgrave), EMC Rec, 80. *Roles:* Alwa in Lulu, Santa Fe Opera, 79; Don Jose in Carmen, Netherlands Opera, 82; Florestan in Fidelio, Florentine Opera, 83; Cavaradossi in Tosca, Orlando Opera, 83; Pollione in Norma, Hawaii Opera, 83; Des Grieux in Manon Lescaut, Chautauqua Opera, 83. *Awards:* Nat Opera Inst Career Grant, 73. *Mem:* Am Guild Musical Artists. *Mailing Add:* 650 W 204th St New York NY 10034

BUSWELL, JAMES OLIVER
EDUCATOR, VIOLIN

b Ft Wayne, Ind, Dec 4, 46. *Study:* Harvard Univ, BA; Juilliard Sch. *Pos:* Recitalist & soloist, orchs & chamber music groups throughout US, Can, UK & Italy. *Teaching:* Prof music, Ind Univ, Bloomington, currently. *Rep:* Columbia Artists Mgt 165 W 57th St New York NY 10019. *Mailing Add:* 3930 E 10th St Bloomington IN 47401

BUTLER, BARBARA
TRUMPET, EDUCATOR

Study: Northwestern Univ, with Vincent Cichowicz, Adolph Herseth, Gerard Schwarz, Armando Ghitalla & Roger Voisin, BM. *Rec Perf:* With Vancouver Symph & Chicago Symph. *Pos:* Leader, Aulos Brass Quintet, 72-75; performer, Contemp Chamber Players Chicago, 74; prin trumpet, Grant Park Symph Orch, 75-80; co-prin trumpet, Vancouver Symph, 76-80; solo recitalist, BBC, 76-80; mem, Eastman Brass, 80-; soloist, Grant Park Symph Orch, Montana Symph Orch, Chicago Brass Ens, Masterpiece Music Series & Music of Baroque Series; guest artist, Chicago Symph Orch Brass Ens, Mostly Mozart Series, Minn Symph Rug Conct Series; participant, Tanglewood Fest, Aspen Fest & Pierre Monterey Fest. *Teaching:* Fac mem, Vancouver Community Col, 76-77; Univ British Columbia, 76-80 & Vancouver Acad Music, 76-80; assoc prof trumpet, Eastman Sch Music, 80-, Kilbourn prof, 82-83. *Mailing Add:* Music Dept Eastman Sch Music Rochester NY 14604

BUTTERLY, MARGARET PARDEE See Pardee, Margaret

BUYS, DOUGLAS
EDUCATOR, PIANO

Study: Juilliard Sch Music, BM, MM; Peabody Consv; studied piano with Rudolf Firkusny, Walter Hautzig, John Perry & Lilian Kallir; studied in Paris & Fountainbleau with Nadia Boulanger, Robert Casadesus, Jean Casadesus & Gaby Casadesus. *Pos:* Pianist, recitals & orch perf in Fountainbleau, Paris, New York, Aspen & Baltimore. *Teaching:* Instr theory & ear training, Aspen Music Sch; instr music theory, New England Consv, currently. *Mailing Add:* New England Consv 290 Huntington Rd Boston MA 02115

BUYSE, LEONE KARENA
FLUTE & PICCOLO, EDUCATOR

b Oneida, NY, Feb 7, 47. *Study:* Eastman Sch Music, with Joseph Mariano, BM & perf cert, 68; studied with Michel Debost, Paris, France, 68-70; Paris Consv, with Jean-Pierre Rampal, cert, 70; Emporia State Univ, MM, 80. *Rec Perf:* Vivaldi Piccolo Concerto in C, Op 44, No 11, Sonar, 76. *Pos:* Second flute & piccolo, Rochester Phil Orch, 71-78; asst prin flute, San Francisco Symph, 78-83 & Boston Symph Orch, 83-; prin flute, Boston Pops, 83- *Teaching:* Privately, 66-; instr flute, Prep Dept, Eastman Sch Music, 66-68; Nazareth Col Rochester, 73-78, State Univ NY Col Geneseo, 73-76 & San Francisco State Univ, 79. *Awards:* Fulbright Grant for study in France, 68-69; Winner, Mu Phi Epsilon Int Compt, 70. *Publ:* Auth, The French Rococo Flute Style Exemplified in Selected Chamber Works of Joseph Bodin de Boismortier (1689-1755), Emporia State Res Studies, spring 79. *Mailing Add:* c/o San Francisco Symph Davies Symph Hall San Francisco CA 94102

BYBEE, ARIEL (ARIEL BYBEE MCBAINE)
MEZZO-SOPRANO

b Reno, Nev, Jan 9, 43. *Study:* Brigham Young Univ, BS, 65; Univ Southern Calif, with William Vennard, 70; study with Daniel Ferro, formerly & Cornelius Reid, currently. *Rec Perf:* Luisa Miller, La Traviata, Elektra & Lucia di Lammermoor, Live at Lincoln Ctr Metropolitan Opera. *Roles:* Jenny in Mahagonny, 72, Carmen, 73 & Musetta in La Boheme, 74, San Francisco Opera; Hansel in Hansel & Gretel, 80-81, Suzuki in Madame Butterfly, 80, 82 & 83, Jenny in Mahagonny, 81 & Nicklause in Hoffmann, 82 & 83, Metropolitan Opera Co. *Mem:* Am Guild Musical Artists; Am Fedn TV & Rec Artists. *Rep:* Lew & Benson Moreau-Neret Inc 204 W 10th St New York NY 10014. *Mailing Add:* 44 W 62nd St New York NY 10023

BYCHKOV, SEMYON
CONDUCTOR & MUSIC DIRECTOR

b Leningrad, USSR, Nov 30, 52. *Study:* Leningrad Consv, acad ref, 74; Mannes Col Music, dipl, 76. *Pos:* Music dir, Mannes Col Music Orch, 76-80 & Grand Rapids Symph, 80-; prin guest cond, Buffalo Phil, 79- *Awards:* First Prize, Rachmaninoff Cond Compt, 73; Second Prize, Gino Marinuzzi Int Cond Compt, 76. *Bibliog:* John Guinn (auth), Musician of the Month, Musical Am, 9/81. *Mailing Add:* c/o Columbia Artists Mgt 165 W 57th St New York NY 10019

BYERS, HAROLD RALPH
VIOLIN, EDUCATOR

b Portland, Ore, Aug 16, 44. *Study:* Oberlin Consv Music, studied violin with David Cerone, BM, 66; Juilliard Sch, studied violin with Ivan Galamian & Paul Makanowitzky, 68; studied chamber music with members of Juilliard, Cleveland & Guarneri Quartets. *Pos:* Violinist, Chamber Symph, Philadelphia, 68, Cazenovia String Quartet & Syracuse Symph, 68-70, Atlanta String Quartet & Symph, 71-72, Columbus String Quartet & Symph, 72-74 & Cincinnati Symph Orch, 74- *Teaching:* Instr violin, Miami Univ, Oxford, Ohio, 80- *Mailing Add:* c/o Cincinnati Symph Orch 1241 Elm St Cincinnati OH 45210

BYO, DONALD WILLIAM
EDUCATOR, BASSOON

b Youngstown, Ohio, June 22, 32. *Study:* Youngstown State Univ, BM, 54; Kent State Univ, MM, 58; studied bassoon with William Polisi. *Pos:* Music supvr, Vernon Sch, Ohio, 54-55; bassoonist, US Army Band, 55-56; dir music, Niles Sch, Ohio, 57-63. *Teaching:* Prof music, Youngstown State Univ, 63- *Mem:* Music Educr Nat Conf; Int Double Reed Soc; Col Music Soc; Am Fedn Musicians. *Mailing Add:* Music Dept, Youngstown State Univ 410 Wick Ave Youngstown OH 44555

BYRD, SAMUEL (TURNER)
BARITONE

US citizen. *Study:* Birmingham Southern Col, BM; Univ Tex, Austin, MM. *Roles:* Figaro in The Barber of Seville, Western Opera, Charlotte Opera & Utah Opera, 75; Shaunard in La Boheme, San Francisco Opera & Ft Worth Opera; Dandini in Cenerentola, Can Opera; Faulke in Die Fledermaus, St Petersburg Opera Co & Miss Opera; Guglielmo in Cosi, Charlotte Opera; David in L'Amico Fritz, Boston Concert Opera; Escamillo in Carmen, Tuscon Opera. *Awards:* Young Singer Award, Nat Opera Inst. *Mem:* Am Guild Musicol Artists. *Rep:* Munro Artists Mgt 344 W 72nd New York NY 10023. *Mailing Add:* 162 W 81st New York NY 10024

BYRNES, KEVIN MICHAEL
VIOLA, COMPOSER

b Jersey City, NJ, Nov 4, 51. *Study:* New England Consv, studied viola with Burton Fine & comp with Robert Helps, 69-71; Hartt Sch Music, studied viola with Rafael Bronstein & comp with Norman Dinerstein, BMus, 71-73; Inst Hautes Etudes Musicales, studied viola with Brund Pasquier. *Works:* String Quartet #1, Manhattan Summer Chamber Ctr, 72; Whorls for Piano, comn by Byrd Hoffman, Sch Byrds, perf by Brooklyn Acad, 74; Four Songs, Ilga

Paups & Kevin Byrnes, 75; The Terrible Crystal, Arioso, 81. *Pos:* Asst prin violist, Arioso, 80-83, Hartford Symph Orch, 81-83 & Hartford Chamber Orch, 81-83; prin violist, New Britain Symph, 82- *Teaching:* Prof piano, viola, violin & theory, Alband Sch Arts, 80-83. *Mailing Add:* 197 Sisson Ave Hartford CT 06105

C

CABALLE, MONTSERRAT FOLCH
SOPRANO

b Barcelona, Spain, Apr 12, 33. *Study:* Consv Liceo; studied with Eugenia Kemeny, Conchita Badia & Napoleone Annovazi. *Rec Perf:* Lucrezia Borgia, La Traviata, Salome & Aida. *Roles:* Mimi in La Boheme, State Opera Basel, Switzerland, 56; Manon in Manon, Mexico City, 64; Lucrezia in Lucrezia Borgia, Carnegie Hall, 65; Marschallin in Der Rosenkavalier, 65 & Countess in The Marriage of Figaro, 65, Glyndebourne Fest; Marguerite in Faust, Metropolitan Opera, 65; Violetta in La Traviata. *Pos:* Guest soprano with Metropolitan Opera and many other opera houses throughout US & Europe. *Awards:* Cross of Lazo de Dama; Order of Isabel the Catholic, Spain; Most Excellent and Illustrious Dona. *Mailing Add:* c/o Columbia Artists 165 W 57th St New York NY 10019

CABOT, EDMUND BILLINGS
ADMINISTRATOR, PATRON

b Waltham, Mass, July 21, 34. *Study:* Harvard Col, AB, 65; Harvard Medical Sch, MD, 72. *Pos:* Benefactor, Boston Symph Orch, 81- & Opera Co Boston, 81-; corporator, Handel & Haydn Soc, 82- *Mailing Add:* 130 Marsh St Belmont MA 02178

CACIOPPO, GEORGE EMANUEL
COMPOSER, TEACHER

b Monroe, Mich, Sept 24, 26. *Study:* Univ Mich, with Ross Lee Finney, BMus, 51, MMus, 52, with Roberto Gerhard, 59-60; Berkshire Music Ctr, with Leon Kirchner, 59. *Works:* Bestiary I: Eingang, Perc Music, Inc, 61; Pianopiece #1, 62, Pianopiece #2, 62, Cassiopeia, 62, Time On Time In Miracles, 65 & Holy Ghost Vacuum, or American Faints, 66, Berandol Press, Ltd. *Pos:* Co-founder, Once Fest, Ann Arbor, Mich, 61-68; producer & host, New Music Prog, WUOM, Univ Mich, Ann Arbor, 68- *Teaching:* Lectr comp, Univ Mich, Ann Arbor, 68-73 & 79-80; private teacher, Ann Arbor, Mich, 73- *Awards:* Koussevitsky Grant, 59. *Bibliog:* Gordon Mumma (auth), The ONCE Festival, Arts in Soc, Vol IV, No 2; Gregory Battock (auth), Breaking the Sound Barrier, E P Dutton, 81. *Publ:* Auth, Apteryx Paper, Generation, Univ Mich, Vol XVIII, No 2. *Mailing Add:* 1291 King George Blvd Ann Arbor MI 48104

CADY, HENRY LORD
EDUCATOR, WRITER

b Quincy, Mass, July 6, 21. *Study:* Middlebury Col, AB, 47; Westminster Choir Col, 47-48; Teachers Col, Columbia Univ, MA, 52; Univ Kans, PhD, 62. *Teaching:* Instr, Pembroke Co Day Sch, Kansas City, Mo, 48-55; prof & head, Dept Music, William Jewell Col, 55-62; asst prof, Ohio State Univ, 62-66, assoc prof, 66-70, prof, 70-75; prof, Univ Del, 75-, chmn, Dept Music, 75-80. *Mem:* Music Educr Nat Conf; Col Music Soc (gov NC region, 63-66); Del Music Educ Asn; Pi Kappa Lambda; Phi Mu Alpha Sinfonia. *Interests:* Philosophy of music education. *Publ:* Coauth, Evaluation and Synthesis of Research in Music Education, 65 & ed, A Conference on Research in Music Education, 67, US Off Educ; auth, Tests and Measures in Higher Education—School Music Teacher, J Res Music Educ, 67; ed, Contributions to Music Education, Ohio Music Educ Asn J, 73-75; auth, Seeking a Theory of Music Education, Music Educ J, 79. *Mailing Add:* 24 Minquil Dr Newark DE 19713

CAGE, JOHN
COMPOSER, LECTURER

b Los Angeles, Calif, Sept 5, 12. *Study:* Studied privately with Henry Cowell, Adolph Weiss, Richard Buhlig & Arnold Schoenberg. *Works:* Sonatas and Interludes, 48, Music of Changes, 51, Etudes Australes, 75, Etudes Borealis, 78, Freeman Etudes, 78, Thirty Pieces for Five Orchestras, 81 & Dance/4 Orchestras, 81. *Pos:* Musical adv, Merce Cunningham Dance Co, 51- *Awards:* Commandeur l'Ordre Arts & Lett, French Minister Cult, 82; Notable Achievement Award, Brandeis Univ, 83. *Bibliog:* Richard Kostelanetz (auth), John Cage, Praeger, 70; Daniel Charles (auth), For the Birds, Boyars, 81. *Mem:* Nat Acad & Inst Arts & Lett; Am Acad Arts & Sci. *Publ:* Auth, Silence, 61 & A Year From Monday, 67, Wesleyan Univ Press; Notations, Something Else Press, 69; M, 73 & Empty Words, 79, Wesleyan Univ Press; Themes and Variations, Station Hill Press, 82. *Rep:* Mimi Johnson Artservices 325 Spring St New York NY 10013. *Mailing Add:* 101 W 18th New York NY 10011

CAIN, JAMES NELSON
ADMINISTRATOR

b Arcadia, Ohio, Jan 6, 30. *Study:* Ohio State Univ, AB, 55. *Pos:* Dir, Prestige Concts Inc, Columbus, 48-62; music critic, Columbus Citizen, 55-62; exec dir, Music Assoc Aspen Inc, 62-68; from asst mgr to mgr, St Louis Symph Orch, 68-80; found, St Louis Symph Youth Orch & St Louis Symph Chorus, formerly; vpres, St Louis Consv & Sch Arts, 80- *Mailing Add:* 2 Nantucket Lane St Louis MO 63132

CALABRO, LOUIS
COMPOSER, MUSIC DIRECTOR
b Brooklyn, NY, Nov 1, 26. *Study:* Juilliard Sch, dipl, 53 & 54. *Works:* Eighteen works published by Elkan Vogel of Theodore Presser & 81 works composed and premiered, 52- *Pos:* Musical dir, Sage City Symph, 72- *Teaching:* Fac mem, Bennington Col, 55- *Awards:* Fel, Guggenheim Found, 55 & 59, Nat Endowment Arts, 70, 76 & 80 & Vt Coun Arts, 71, 77 & 81. *Mem:* ASCAP. *Mailing Add:* Dept Music Bennington Col Bennington VT 05201

CALDERON, JAVIER FRANCISCO
GUITAR, EDUCATOR
b La Paz, Bolivia, May 26, 46; US citizen. *Study:* Musica en Compostela, with Andres Segovia, dipl, 68; NC Sch Arts, BM, 70; Univ NC, Greensboro, MM, 71; Univ Ind, Bloomington, artist dipl, 76. *Rec Perf:* Calderon at the OAS, Washington, DC, 74; Calderon in Recital, WPBS Bloomington, Ind, 75; Javier Calderon Eximio Guitarrista, Lyra, 78. *Pos:* Conct guitarist, SRO Artists, Wis, 71- *Teaching:* Instr guitar, Ind Univ, Bloomington, 71-76; artist in res, Col-Consv Music, Univ Cincinnati, 74-76; assoc prof, Del Mar Col, Tex, 76- & Corpus Christi State Univ, 76- *Awards:* Musico Distinguido, Sociedad Filarmonica de La Paz, 75. *Mem:* Tex Comn Arts; Col Music Soc; Am String Teachers Asn. *Mailing Add:* 5901 Weber #2003 Corpus Christi TX 78413

CALDWELL, JAMES BOONE
OBOE, EDUCATOR
b Gladewater, Tex, Dec 3, 38. *Study:* Curtis Inst Music, dipl, 61. *Rec Perf:* Le Tombeau de Coupeim (Ravel), RCA, 68; Music of the French Baroque, Vox Box, 76; Handel Solo & Trio Sonatas, Smithsonian, 81; Schoenberg Wind Quintet, 82, Telemann, 300th Anniversary, 82 & Chamber Music of C P E Bach, 82, Gasparo. *Pos:* Soloist & oboist, Casals Fest Orch, San Juan, PR, 61-65; soloist & first oboist, Nat Symph, 65-66 & 68-71 & Chamber Symph, Philadelphia, 66-68. *Teaching:* Prof oboe, Consv Musica PR, San Juan, 61-65; prof oboe & dir, Baroque Perf Inst, Consv Music, Oberlin Col, 71- *Awards:* Albert Spaulding Award, Berkshire Music Ctr, 58; Title Recognition, Fest Casals, 67. *Mem:* Int Double Reed Soc; Am Musical Instrm Soc (mem bd gov, 80); Viola da gamba Soc Am; Am Musicol Soc. *Publ:* Ed, publications in Facsimile, Marin Marais, Forqueray, Schenk, Roland Marais & Louis de Cai d'Hervelois, 72. *Mailing Add:* c/o Consv Music Oberlin Col Oberlin OH 44074

CALDWELL, JOHN TIMOTHY
EDUCATOR, TENOR
b Ashland, Ky. *Study:* Univ Mich, with John McCollum, BM, 67, with John McCollum, MM, 69. *Roles:* Hippolytus, Pa Opera Fest, 83 & Contemp Opera Co Am, Philadelphia, 83. *Teaching:* Instr voice, Univ Maine, Orono, 72-74; assoc prof voice, Cent Mich Univ, 74- *Mem:* Nat Asn Teachers Singing. *Mailing Add:* 8020 E Pickard Mt Pleasant MI 48858

CALDWELL, SARAH
CONDUCTOR, DIRECTOR—OPERA
b Maryville, Mo, Mar 6, 24. *Study:* Hendrix Col; Univ Ark; New England Consv Music, with Richard Burgin; Berkshire Music Ctr; Harvard Univ, Hon DM; Simmons Col, Hon DM; Bates Col, Hon DM; Bowdoin Univ, Hon DM. *Rec Perf:* Don Pasquale, Angel, 78. *Pos:* Asst dir, New England Opera Co; founder, Boston Opera Group (now Opera Co Boston), 57, artistic dir & cond, 57-; cond, Am Symph Orch, 74, Cent Opera Theatre of Beijing, 78, maj opera co incl NY Metropolitan Opera, Dallas Civic Opera, Houston Grand Opera & New York City Opera & maj symph incl Indianapolis Symph, Pittsburgh Symph, Milwaukee Symph & New York Phil; music dir, Wolf Trap Fest, Washington, DC, formerly. *Teaching:* Mem fac, Berkshire Music Ctr; head, Opera Dept, Boston Univ, formerly, founder, music theater dept, dir, Boston Univ Opera Wkshp, 53-57. *Awards:* Rogers & Hammerstein Award. *Mem:* Mass Coun on Arts. *Mailing Add:* Opera Co Boston 539 Washington St Boston MA 02111

CALLAHAN, ANNE
ADMINISTRATOR, EDUCATOR
b Des Moines, Iowa. *Study:* St Mary Col, Kans, BMus, 59; DePaul Univ, MMus, 65. *Teaching:* Instr music, St Pius X High Sch, Kansas City, Mo, 64 & Immaculata High Sch, Leavenworth, Kans, 72-76; asst prof & dept chmn, St Mary Col, Kans, 76- *Mem:* Nat Asn Sch Music; Music Teachers Nat Asn; Kans Music Teacher's Asn; Music Educr Nat Conf; Nat Asn Pastoral Musicians. *Mailing Add:* Music Dept St Mary Col Leavenworth KS 66048

CALLAHAN, JAMES PATRICK
EDUCATOR, COMPOSER
b Fargo, NDak, Jan 15, 42. *Study:* St John's Univ, Minn, BA, 64; Vienna Acad Music, with Anton Heiller, 64-65; Salzburg Mozarteum, with Hans Leygraf & Stanley Pope, 64, 65, 67, & 71; Univ Minn, MFA, 67, PhD, 71. *Works:* Six Pieces for Organ Based on Gregorian Themes, Gregorian Inst Am, 64; Parish Worship, McLaughlin & Reilly Co, 66; Metamorphosis—An Overture, Pueblo Orch, 73; Variations for Organ, Belwin Mills, 74; Toccata-Veni Creator Spiritus, Abingdon Press, 78; Three Fantasies, comn by CCP, perf by Musical Offering, 79; Duo for Violin and Piano, Daws-Faricy Duo, 83. *Teaching:* Prof piano, organ & music theory, Col St Thomas, 68- *Mem:* Minn Comp Forum; Am Guild Organists. *Mailing Add:* Music Dept Col St Thomas St Paul MN 55105

CALLAWAY, ANN MARIE
EDITOR, COMPOSER
b Washington, DC, Oct 28, 49. *Study:* Smith Col, with Alvin Etler, BA, 71; Univ Pa, with George Crumb & George Rochberg, MA, 74. *Works:* Seven Dramatic Episodes for Flute, Cello and Piano, comn by Walden Trio, 76; Agnus Dei, Arsis Press, 80; Four Elements for Horn & Piano, New Valley Music Press, Smith Col, 81; A Dream within a Dream, perf by Jerome Barry & Alan Mandel, 83. *Pos:* Asst music ed, Garland Publ Inc, 82- *Mem:* Am Music Ctr; Am Comp Alliance; BMI; Am Women Comp (chmn New York chap, 82-83); Am Musicol Asn. *Mailing Add:* 3111 Broadway Apt 1-C New York NY 10027

CALLEO, RICCARDO
TENOR
b Endicott, NY. *Study:* Yale Univ, BA, 61; Consv G Verdi, Milan, with Guiseppe Pais, 61-64; Curtis Inst Music, with Martial Singher, dipl, 67; Hochschule Musik, Stuttgart; Music Acad West; studied with Ken Neate. *Roles:* Duke of Mantua in Rigoletto, Cincinnati Opera, 79 & Mich Opera; Don Jose in Carmen, Houston Grand Opera, 81; Pinkerton in Madama Butterfly, Dayton Opera, 82; Rodolfo in La Boheme, Baltimore Opera, 83; Hoffmann in The Tales of Hoffmann, Houston Opera, 83; Cavaradossi in Tosca, Los Angeles Opera, 83; Edgardo in Lucia di Lammermoor, Washington Opera; and many others. *Pos:* First ten, Bonn Opera, Ger, formerly; leading ten, New York City Opera, 79-; performer, opera co & symph orchs in US & Europe. *Awards:* Fulbright Grant, 68. *Bibliog:* Carl Cunningham (auth), Opera: Bizet's Carmen, Houston Post, 1/26/81. *Mailing Add:* c/o Thea Dispeker 59 E 54th St New York NY 10022

CAMAJANI, GIOVANNI
CONDUCTOR, EDUCATOR
b New York, NY, May 5, 15. *Study:* NY Univ, BS(music), 37, MA, 41, PhD, 45; Trinity Col Music, London, FTCM, 45. *Rec Perf:* Music of Ernest Bascon. *Pos:* Am asst, Verona Opera Fest, Italy; guest cond, Tuskegee Choir, Ala; assoc cond, Pac Opera Co, San Francisco; cond, Bach Circle, Los Angeles; founder & dir, Schola Cantorum & Brass Ens San Francisco; contrib ed, Encycl Am, 45-50; contribr, Ramparts, Music Mag, New Grove Dict of Music in US & Liturgical Quart. *Teaching:* Assoc prof & head, Vocal Dept, Opera Repty Theatre, San Francisco State Univ. *Mailing Add:* 124 Presideo Ave San Francisco CA 94115

CAMERON, ANDRE
VIOLA, LECTURER
b Greensboro, NC, Dec 22, 57. *Study:* NC Sch Arts, dipl, 76; Verdi Consv, Turin, Italy, studied chamber music with Piero Farulli, 79; New England Consv Music, BM, 83. *Pos:* Violist, Teatro Regio, Turin, Italy, 78-79 & La Scala, Milan, Italy, 79-82; solo recitalist, Europe & US, 82- *Teaching:* Guest clinician string, Summer String Inst, Greensboro, NC, currently. *Awards:* First Prize, Concerto Compt, Rome Fest, 77. *Mailing Add:* c/o Luca De Perini Via Alzaia Nav Pavese 10 Milano 27406 Italy

CAMERON, CHRISTOPHER
TENOR
Roles: Duke in Rigoletto, Seattle Opera, 83, Manitoba Opera, 83 & Eastern Opera Theater; Ferrando in Cosi fan tutte, Opera Theater Rochester; Rodolfo in La Boheme & Ernesto in Don Pasquale, Western Opera Theater; Jenik in The Bartered Bride, Central City Opera. *Pos:* Tenor with opera co in US & Can. *Mailing Add:* c/o Robert Lombardo Assoc 1 Harkness Plaza 61 W 62nd #6F New York NY 10023

CAMERON, WAYNE
EDUCATOR, TRUMPET
Study: ECarolina Univ, BM; Peabody Consv, MM; studied with William Long, Howard Snell & James Hustis. *Pos:* First trumpet, Fla Int Music Fest Orch, Annapolis Symph, NC Symph & Chesapeake Brass Quintet; solo perf throughout southeastern US; dir & soloist, Belvedere Players. *Teaching:* Dir instrm music, Friends Sch, Baltimore, 75-76; vis instr, Towson State Univ, 75; mem fac, Peabody Consv Music, currently. *Mailing Add:* Peabody Consv Music 1 E Mt Vernon Pl Baltimore MD 21202

CAMERON-WOLFE, RICHARD G
COMPOSER, PIANO
b Cleveland, Ohio, Sept 23, 43. *Study:* Oberlin Col; Ind Univ, BA, 68, MA, 72. *Works:* Kyrie/Mantra (three flutes), Zalo Publ, 76; Listen to Me, comn for Gertrude Stein Play, 81; Reconciliation, NMex Music Fest Chamber Orch, 81; Transcendental Etude, comn by William Kapell Found, 82; Aetherwind (piano), Crystal Springs Music Publ, 82; Scanning Sagas, comn by L'esprit Chamber Ens, 83. *Pos:* Found co-dir, Friends Am Music Inc, 74- *Teaching:* Asst prof, Univ Wis, Milwaukee, 74-75 & State Univ NY, Col Purchase, 78-; co-dir & dean fac, NMex Music Fest, 78- *Mem:* Am Comp Alliance; BMI; Friends Am Music, Inc (bd dir, 74-). *Mailing Add:* Winkler's Farm Towners Rd Carmel NY 10512

CAMESI, DAVID See Champion, David

CAMP, MAX W
EDUCATOR, PIANO
US citizen. *Study:* Univ Ala, with Roy McAllister, BM(piano perf), 57; Peabody Col, Vanderbilt Univ, MM(piano perf), 65; Ind Univ, with Sidney Foster; Univ Okla, with Celia Mae Bryant, DME(piano pedagogy), 77. *Teaching:* Dir piano, Camp Sch Music, 59-70; prof piano & piano pedagogy, Univ SC, 70-; prof piano, Interlochen Nat Music Camp, summer 79. *Mem:*

Music Teachers Nat Asn (nat exec bd, 74-82); SC Music Teachers Asn (Southern div pres, 74-76, pres, 73-75). *Publ:* Auth, The Right Principles, 67 & The Teaching of Bartok, 69, Clavier; coauth, Criteria for Performance Degrees, Col Music Soc Symposium, 80; auth, Developing Piano Performance, Hinshaw Music, 82. *Mailing Add:* Dept Music Univ SC Columbia SC 29208

CAMPBELL, ARTHUR M
COMPOSER
b Lexington, Mo, Apr 4, 22. *Study:* Studied with Alec Rowley, London; Park Col, BA, 44; Kansas City Consv Music, studied with David Van Vactor, BM, 47; Eastman Sch Music, studied with Howard Hanson & Bernard Rogers, PhD, 59. *Works:* Gods Grandeur (song cycle), Donald Hoiness & Arthur Campbell, 65; Whither Shall I Go (anthem; SATB), Schmitt, Hall & McCreary, 66; Romance & Caprice for Horn & Piano, Miles Johnson, 67; Chameleon Variations, St Olaf Col Orch, 78; Music for Piano and Computer Generated Voices, 79 & Hammered Sugar, 81 & Homage to Fibonacci, 81, private publ; Evening Prayer (anthem; SATB), St Olaf Choir, 83. *Teaching:* Asst prof music, Monmouth Col, 49-52; prof, St Olaf Col, 52- *Awards:* Winner, Harvey Gaul Compt, 58. *Mem:* Am Soc Univ Comp. *Mailing Add:* Music Dept St Olaf Col Northfield MN 55057

CAMPBELL, BRUCE
EDUCATOR
Study: Brandeis Univ, BA(music); Juilliard Sch Music, MS; Yale Univ, MA, PhD; studied organ with Anthony Newman, harpsichord with Fernando Valente, Ralph Kirkpatrick & Albert Fuller, comp with Frank Lewin & Leonard Stein, Schenker theory with Ernst Oster & Oswald Jonas, & baroque keyboard with Louis Bagger. *Works:* Publ by Transcontinental Music & Shawnee Press. *Rec Perf:* On Musique Int. *Pos:* Recital tours, 64-; soloist, Brandeis Chamber Players & Boston Pops. *Teaching:* Fac mem, Calif Inst Arts, 71-72, Yale Univ, 74-75 & Conn Col, 76-77; asst prof theory, Eastman Sch Music, 79- *Mailing Add:* Eastman Sch Music Rochester NY 14604

CAMPBELL, CHARLES JOSEPH
COMPOSER, EDUCATOR
b Cleveland, Ohio, Aug 8, 30. *Study:* Cleveland Inst Music, with Herbert Elwell & Marcel Dick; Western Reserve Univ; Univ Miami. *Works:* 2 Symphonies (orch); 2 Overtures (orch); song cycles; piano works; Solo Etudes (trombone & tuba); and pieces for woodwind & brass ens. *Teaching:* Mem fac & admin, Cleveland Inst Music, 55-57, Cleveland Music Sch Settlement, 58-61, Wilmington Music Sch, 61-66, Auburn Univ, 66-68 & Va Commonwealth Univ, 70-72; prof music, Univ Miami, 72- *Mailing Add:* 9781 SW 160th St Miami FL 33157

CAMPBELL, FRANK CARTER
LIBRARIAN, ADMINISTRATOR
b Winston-Salem, NC, Sept 26, 16. *Study:* Salem Col, BMus(piano), 38; Eastman Sch Music, MMus(musicol), 43. *Pos:* Cataloger, Sibley Libr, Eastman Sch Music, 43; librn music div, Libr Cong, 43-59; assoc ed, Notes, Quart J Music Libr Asn, 50-67, ed, 71-74; asst chief music div, New York Pub Libr, 59-66, chief, 66- *Awards:* Fels, Hattie M Strong, 40-41, musicol, 41-42 & piano pedagogy, 42-43, Univ Rochester; Citation, Music Libr Asn, 83. *Mem:* Music Libr Asn (secy, 48-50, pres, 67-69); Am Musicol Soc; Int Asn Music Libr; Clarion Music Soc. *Publ:* The Musical Scores of George Gershwin, Libr Cong, Quart J Current Acquisitions; Some Manuscripts of George Gershwin, Manuscripts, J Manuscripts Soc; The Music Library Association, Music Publ J, 5-6/46; The Music Division of the New York Public Library, Fontes Artis Musicae, 3/69; coauth (with Philip L Miller), How the Music Division of the New York Public Library Grew—A Memoir, Part 1 & 2, Vol 35, No 3, Part 3, Vol 36, No 1, Notes, J Music Libr Asn. *Mailing Add:* Nevada Towers 1 Nevada Plaza New York NY 10023

CAMPBELL, HENRY C
COMPOSER, EDUCATOR
b Osceola, Nebr, Nov 13, 26. *Study:* Eastman Sch Music, with Burrill Phillips & Bernard Rogers, BM, 48, MM, 49; Univ Wash, with George McKay; studied with Julius Gold. *Works:* Sinfonia non Troppo Serioso (orch); Waltz—Then March (orch & piano); Diversion (clarinet, viola & piano); Many Happy Returns (string quartet); Grass Roots Ballad (tenor or bar & piano); Folk Song Suite (chorus); Make We Joy (chorus). *Teaching:* Prof theory & analysis, orch & piano, Mont State Univ, 49- *Awards:* Mont String Teachers Asn, J Fischer Brothers Centennial Comp Cont & Music Teachers Nat Asn. *Mem:* ASCAP. *Mailing Add:* 515 S Grand Ave Bozeman MT 59715

CAMPBELL, JOHN COLEMAN
EDUCATOR, ORGAN
b Hereford, Tex, July 1, 35. *Study:* Univ Okla, with Mildred Andrew Boggess, MMus, 64; Eastman Sch Music, with Russell Saunders, DMA, 75; Hochschule Musik, Cologne, West Germany, with Michael Schneider. *Teaching:* Asst prof organ & theory, Berea Col, 65-71; prof, Hardin-Simmons Univ, 71-, dept head appl music, 74- *Mem:* Am Guild Organists. *Mailing Add:* 1609 Wishbone Abilene TX 79603

CAMPBELL, LARRY BRUCE
EDUCATOR, TROMBONE
b Charlotte, NC, July 20, 40. *Study:* Eastman Sch Music, BM, 62; Southwest Tex State Univ, MEd, 68. *Pos:* Prin euphoniumist, US Coast Guard Band, 62-66; prin trombonist, San Antonio Symph, 68-69 & Baton Rouge Symph, 69-; consult Hirsbrunner Compensating Euphonium, Peter Hirshbrunner & Co, Sumiswald, Switz, 78. *Teaching:* From asst prof to assoc prof, La State

Univ, 69- *Awards:* Cert appreciation, Tubists Universal Brotherhood Asn, 78 & 80. *Mem:* Tubists Universal Brotherhood Asn; Int Trombone Asn; Am Fedn Musicians; Music Educr Nat Conf. *Publ:* Auth, Fingering Comparison for Brass Instruments, Selmer Bandwagon, No 80, 11-13; Master Solos-Intermediate Level for Baritone Horn, Hal Leonard, 78; Why Double on Trombone and Euphonium, Tubists Universal Brotherhood Asn J, spring 83; coauth, Brass Solo and Study Material Music Guide, 2nd ed (in press). *Mailing Add:* 373 College Hill Dr Baton Rouge LA 70808

CAMPBELL, ROBERT GORDON
EDUCATOR, PIANO
b Camden, Ark, May 24, 22. *Study:* Hendrix Col, BA, 43; Univ Tex, Austin, BMus, 48, MMus, 50; Ind Univ, Bloomington, PhD, 66. *Teaching:* Instr music, Univ Tex, Austin, 50-52; prof music, Southern Ark Univ, 52- & chmn, Div Fine Arts, 63-79. *Awards:* Outstanding Col Teacher, Ark State Music Teachers Nat Asn, 80. *Mem:* Music Teachers Nat Asn (exec bd, 68-72); Ark State Music Teachers Asn (pres, 67 & 68); Am Musicol Soc; Col Music Soc; Music Libr Asn. *Interests:* Piano sonatas of Schubert; Johann Gottfried Muethel, 1728-1788. *Rep:* Robert G Campbell 508 Margaret St Magnolia AR 71753. *Mailing Add:* Box 1398 Southern Ark Univ Magnolia AR 71753

CAMPBELL, TERESA HICKS
VIOLIN, TEACHER
b Salt Lake City, Utah, Apr 4, 52. *Study:* Santa Barbara Music Acad, with Oscar Chausow, 70-71; Blossom Music Fest, with Daniel Majesky, 72; Univ Utah, BA, 75. *Pos:* First violin, Utah Symph, 71- & Utah Chamber Orch, 73-81. *Teaching:* Private violin, Salt Lake City, 70-80. *Mailing Add:* 680 East 2000 South Bountiful UT 84010

CAMPIONE, CARMINE
CLARINET, EDUCATOR
b Elizabeth, NJ, May 7, 37. *Study:* Consv Music, Oberlin Col, with George Waln, 55-56; Curtis Inst Music, with Anthony Gigliotti, BM, 61; studied with Joe Allard & Daniel Bonade. *Pos:* Clarinetist, Cincinnati Symph Orch, 61- *Teaching:* Adj prof clarinet & coordr clarinet studies, Col Consv Music, Univ Cincinnati, 61- *Awards:* Outstanding Instrumentalist, High Fidelity Mag, 59. *Mem:* Phi Mu Alpha. *Mailing Add:* 5541 Whispering Way Cincinnati OH 45247

CAMPO, FRANK PHILIP
COMPOSER
b New York, NY, Feb 4, 27. *Study:* Univ Southern Calif, with Ingolf Dahl & Leon Kirchner, BM, 50, MM, 53, DMA, 68; Ecole Normal Musique, Paris, France, with Arthur Honegger, 51; studied in Rome with Goffredo Petrassi, 58. *Works:* Madrigals for Brass Quintet, comn & perf by Los Angeles Phil Brass Quintet, 71; Partita for Two Chamber Orchestras, comn & perf by Los Angeles Chamber Orch, 73; Five Pieces for Five Winds, perf by Los Angeles Phil Woodwind Quintet, 73; Capriccio for Wind Orchestra, Univ Southern Calif Wind Orch, 76; Alpine Holiday Overture, Pasadena Symph Orch, 78; Preludes (flute, clarinet & guitar), Belwin-Mills Publ, 78; Concerto for Bassoon & String Orchestra, perf by Kenneth Meyes with Pasadena Chamber Orch, 82. *Awards:* Fulbright Scholar, Italy, 57; Comp Prize, BMI, 58; Spec Merit Award, Nat Asn Comp, USA, 80. *Mem:* Am Fedn Musicians; Nat Asn Comp, USA (pres, 71-73, mem bd dir, 74-); Int Soc Contemp Music; ASCAP. *Mailing Add:* c/o Dario Music 12336 Milbank Studio City CA 91604

CAMUS, RAOUL FRANCOIS
EDUCATOR
b Buffalo, NY, Dec 5, 30. *Study:* Queens Col, City Univ New York, BA, 52; Columbia Univ, MA, 56; NY Univ, PhD, 69. *Teaching:* Orch music, Martin Van Buren & Newtown High Schools, New York, NY, 59-70; from asst to assoc prof, Univ NY, 70-79; prof music, Queensborough Community Col, 79- *Awards:* Fel, Nat Endowment Humanities, 80. *Mem:* Sonneck Soc (treas, 77-81 & pres, 81-); Am Musicol Soc; Int Musicol Soc; Col Band Dir Nat Asn. *Interests:* Bands in America. *Publ:* Auth, Military Music of the American Revolution, Univ NC, 76; Military Music of Colonial Boston, In: Music in Colonial Massachusetts, 1630-1820, Colonial Soc Mass, 80; A Source for Early American Band Music, NOTES, Music Libr Asn, 82. *Mailing Add:* 14-34 155th St Whitestone NY 11357

CANAFAX, LOUISE TERRY
EDUCATOR, VIOLA
b Bryson, Tex. *Study:* Tex Wesleyan Col, BM; Tex Christian Univ, MME; Eastman Sch Music, with Francis Tursi; Univ Southern Calif, with Milton Thomas; Wellesley Col, Sam Houston State Univ; Univ Tex, San Antonio. *Rec Perf:* Mercury Rec. *Pos:* Viola, San Antonio Symph, 63-69 & NH Music Fest Orch, 69-; prin viola, Ft Worth Opera & Symph, 71-78 *Teaching:* Chmn music dept, Trinity Valley Sch, Ft Worth, 72-; instr, Tex Wesleyan Col, 80-82. *Mem:* Orgn Am Kodaly Educr; Kodaly Educr Tex (pres, 83-85); Sigma Alpha Iota. *Mailing Add:* 6101 McCart Ave Ft Worth TX 76133

CANARINA, JOHN BAPTISTE
CONDUCTOR & MUSIC DIRECTOR, EDUCATOR
b New York, NY, May 19, 34. *Study:* Studied cond with Pierre Monteux, summers 53-58 & 61; Juilliard Sch Music, studied cond with Jean Morel, BS, 57, MS, 58. *Rec Perf:* Trois Petites Liturgies de la Presence Divine (Messiaen), Columbia Rec, 61. *Pos:* Cond, Seventh US Army Symph Orch, Ger, 59-60; asst cond, New York Phil, 61-62; cond & music dir, Jacksonville Symph Orch, Fla, 62-69; guest cond, Oberlin Consv, 72-73; dir orchestral activ, Drake Univ, 73-; auth, monthly rev, High Fidelity, ABC Leisure, 80- *Awards:* ASCAP Award, 76, 78, 79 & 80. *Mem:* Am Symph Orch League;

Cond Guild. *Publ:* Auth, Will the Real Colin Wilson Please Stand Up?, High Fidelity, ABC Leisure, 81; The Enigma of English Music, Keynote, 81; Dame Ethel Smyth, Composer, Helicon Nine, 81. *Mailing Add:* 36 Verdi Ave Tuckahoe NY 10707

CANELLAKIS, MARTIN
CONDUCTOR & MUSIC DIRECTOR, EDUCATOR
b Tientsin, China, Jan 10, 42; US citizen. *Study:* Ecole Normale de Musique, Paris, 57-60; Juilliard Sch, BS, 64, MS, 65; Teachers Col, Columbia Univ, dipl, 68; Mannes Col Music, dipl (orchestral cond), 69; studied with Jorge Mester, Sixten Ehrling, Walter Susskind & Carl Bamberger. *Pos:* Founder & cond, Peabody Chamber Orch, 66-67; guest cond, Baltimore Symph, Eglevsky Ballet Ens, Jerusalem Symph Orch, formerly; cond concts, Meadow Brook Music Fest, Mich, Aspen Music Fest & Southern Vt Music Fest, formerly; music dir, Brooklyn Symph Orch, 68-77, Queensborough Orch, 71-, Queens Col Orch Soc, 75- & Westchester Symph Orch, 82- *Teaching:* Prof music & orch, Queensborough Community Col, City Univ New York, 71-; adj prof orch, Queens Col, City Univ New York, 75-, exchange prof cond, 79-82. *Awards:* Piano fel, Peabody Consv, 66-67; Perera Mem Award, Mannes Col Music, 68; cond fel, Nat Orch Asn, 71-72. *Bibliog:* Al Cohn (auth), Giving Queens A Musical Build-Up, Newsday, 1/21/79; Robert Sherman (auth), A Look At New Baton of the Symphony, New York Times, 3/28/82; Lou Civetello (auth), Martin Canellakis Leads Westchester Symphony, Gannett Press, 12/13/82. *Mailing Add:* 452 Riverside Dr New York NY 10027

CANIN, MARTIN
PIANO, EDUCATOR
b New York, NY. *Study:* Piano with Aurelio Giorni, Robert Scholz, Olga Samaroff & musical analysis with Stefan Wolpe; Juilliard Sch Music, with Rosina Lhevinne, BS, MS; studied chamber music with Felix Salmond. *Pos:* Soloist & recitalist with orchs in US & Europe. *Teaching:* Mem fac, Teachers Col, Columbia Univ, 59-76 & Summer Music Sch, Bowdoin Col, 71-; asst to Rosina Lhevinne, Juilliard Sch, 59-76, mem fac piano, 59-; teacher master classes, Univ Calif, 63-64; perf artist fac, Summer Congregation Arts, Dartmouth Col, 65-67; artist in res, State Univ NY, Stony Brook, 65- *Awards:* Loeb Prize; Nat Music League Award. *Publ:* Contrib ed, Piano Quart. *Mailing Add:* 875 West End Ave New York NY 10025

CANIN, STUART V
VIOLIN, EDUCATOR
b New York, NY, Apr 5, 26. *Study:* Studied violin with Ivan Galamian, 39-44 & 46-49; Juilliard Sch Music, 46-49. *Pos:* Concertmaster, Chamber Symph Philadelphia, 66-68, San Francisco Symph, 70-80 & 20th Century Fox Studios, Los Angeles, 81- *Teaching:* Assoc prof violin, Univ Iowa, 53-61; prof, Consv Music, Oberlin Col, 61-66; head string dept, San Francisco Consv Music, 71-80. *Awards:* First Prize Winner, Paganini Int Violin Compt, Genoa, Italy, 59; Handel Medal, New York City, 60. *Publ:* Forward to Edward Bachmann's Encyclopedia of the Violin, Da Capo Press. *Mailing Add:* 1302 Holmby Ave Los Angeles CA 90024

CANNON, ALLEN E
VIOLIN, EDUCATOR
b Crystal Falls, Mich, June 24, 20. *Study:* Univ Ill, Urbana-Champaign, BM & BMus, 41, MMus, 42; Am Consv Music, violin with Scott Willits, 45-49; Chicago Musical Col, Roosevelt Univ, DMusEd, 54. *Pos:* Concertmaster, Peoria Symph Orch, Ill, 46- *Teaching:* Instr violin, music hist, lit & music appln, Bradley Univ, 45-57, prof music hist & string tech, 45-, dir, Sch Music, 57- *Mem:* Phi Mu Alpha. *Interests:* Use of violin literature to develop techniques instead of using etudes. *Publ:* Auth, Video-Tape Improves Teaching, 7/70 & School Music, European Style, 12/71, Music J; Handel Sonatas: Why Not?, Am String Teacher, spring 81. *Mailing Add:* 2721 W Parkridge Dr Peoria IL 61604

CANNON, DWIGHT
EDUCATOR, COMPOSER
b Pomona, Calif, July 6, 32. *Study:* DePaul Univ, with Alexander Tcherepnin & Leon Stein, BM, 59; San Jose State Univ, MA, 66; Univ Calif, San Diego, with Bob Erickson, Pauline Oliveros & Ken Gaburo, 71. *Pos:* Dir, Ctr Creative Arts & Sci, San Francisco, 78-82; music coordr, San Jose Civic Light Opera, 79- *Teaching:* Prof music, San Jose State Univ, 65- *Interests:* Energy fields and communication in performing environments with improvisation (multi-sensory perception). *Mailing Add:* Music Dept San Jose State Univ San Jose CA 95192

CANTOR, OWEN POLK
ADMINISTRATOR, FRENCH HORN
b Pittsburgh, Pa, July 8, 47. *Study:* Studied French horn with Forrest Standley, Sid Kaplan & Betty K Levine, 63-73; Univ Pittsburgh, DMD, 73. *Pos:* Founder & artistic dir, Summerfest Chamber Music Fest, 80-; trustee, Pittsburgh Chamber Music Soc, 80-, Pittsburgh New Music Ens, 81- & Y-Music Soc, 83- *Mem:* Chamber Music Am; Music Libr Asn. *Interests:* Performance and publication of rare music for wind ensemble, especially harmonie music, 1750-1850. *Mailing Add:* 1225 Farragut St Pittsburgh PA 15206

CANTRELL, BYRON
COMPOSER, MUSICOLOGIST
b Brooklyn, NY, Nov 14, 19. *Study:* Third St Settlement, dipl, 35; Nat Orch Asn, New York, 37-38; NY Univ, with Marion Bauer & Philip James, BA(music), 39; Berkshire Music Sch, 41; studied with Paul Emerich, 42-44; Univ Calif, Los Angeles, with Lukas Foss & John Vincent, MA(comp), 55, PhD(musicol), 57; studied cond with Leon Barzin, Emerson Buckley & Serge Koussevitzky. *Works:* A Jubilee Overture (orch); Piano Concerto (with orch); What Child is This (chorus); A Tooth for Paul Revere (opera); The Land of Heart's Desire (opera); Sacred Service (choral); Raisins and Almonds (Broadway show score). *Rec Perf:* A Mark Twain Album. *Pos:* Cond, Hampton Roads Civic Orch, Los Virtuosos de Los Angeles, Young Peoples' Opera Asn, Culver City, 66- & New York Little Symph; prog annotator, Ambassador Int Cult Found, ABC Westminster Rec, MCA Rec & Capitol Rec; music reviewer, New York Post, Newport News Daily Press, Hicks-Deal Newspapers, Los Angeles Times & Los Angeles Herald-Examr; music ed, Summit Publ Co & Western Periodicals Co. *Teaching:* Mem fac, Tahoe Paradise Col, 67-69, Calif State Univ, Fullerton, 69-70 & El Camino Col, 71-72; adj mem fac theory & analysis, hist & lit, Int Col, 72- *Awards:* Second Prize, Los Angeles Phil Comp Cont, 44. *Mem:* ASCAP. *Mailing Add:* Dept Music International Col Westwood CA 90024

CANTRICK, ROBERT B
EDUCATOR, CRITIC
b Adrian, Mich, Dec 8, 17. *Study:* Univ Rochester, studied flute with Joseph Mariano, AB, 38, MA(aesthetics), 46; Univ Iowa, PhD(comp), 59. *Works:* String Trio (violin, viola & violoncello), Music in Our Time, 59; Sonorities (flute & orch), Southeastern Comp League, 62; Three Mimes (flute & voice), Contemp Chamber Players, 67 & Creative Assoc, 70; Friendly Beasts (voice & orch), Harbison, Buffalo Phil Wkshp, 75; Local II (flute & four sound syst), Robert Dick, 80. *Rec Perf:* Hammersmith (Holst), Carnegie Inst Technol, 54. *Teaching:* Asst prof cond, Juilliard Sch, Furman Univ, Carnegie-Mellon Univ & Cornell Col, 46-59; dean & dir, Jacksonville Ala State Univ, Wis State Univ, Stevens Pt & State Univ NY Col, Buffalo, 59-69; prof, State Univ NY Col, Buffalo, 69- *Awards:* Ford Found Fel, 51-52; State Univ NY Res Found Fel, 70-71. *Bibliog:* Sur & Schuller (ed), Music Education for Teen-Agers, Harper, 58; Nancy Toff (auth), The Development of the Modern Flute, Taplinger, 79. *Mem:* Am Music Ctr; Music Educr Nat Conf; Am Soc Aesthetics; Nat Flute Asn; Semiotics Soc Am. *Publ:* Auth, A Pragmatic Test of Thorndike's GG, Am Sociological Rev, 41; Hammersmith and Two Worlds of Gustav Holst, Music Lett, 56; The Blind Men and the Elephant, Ethnomusicol, 65; Creation and Necessity, Proc, IX Int Cong Aesthetics, 80; contribr, Semiotics 1980, Plenum Press, 82. *Mailing Add:* 159 Bidwill Pkwy Buffalo NY 14222

CAPANNA, ROBERT
COMPOSER, ADMINISTRATOR
b Camden, NJ, July 7, 52. *Study:* Philadelphia Musical Acad, with Joseph Castaldo & Theodore Antoniov, BM, 73, MM, 75; Berkshire Music Ctr, Tanglewood, with Jacob Druckman, 74. *Works:* Concerto for Chamber Orchestra, Fleisher Collection, 74; Phorminx for Solo Harp, 75 & Rota for Percussion Quartet, 76, G Schirmer; Three Songs for Chorus, Orchestra and Tenor and Viola Soloists, 77 & Reliquaries for Soprano and Chamber Orchestra, Part I, 80, Fleisher Collection; Reliquaries, Part II, comn by Samuel S Fels Fund, 82. *Pos:* Dir admis, Philadelphia Musical Acad, Pa, 74-76; dir, Kardon-ne Branch, Settlement Music Sch, Philadelphia, Pa, 76-82, asst exec dir, 79-82 & exec dir, 82- *Teaching:* Instr theory, comp & musicianship, Philadelphia Musical Acad, 73-76; dir musical studies, Amherst Summer Music Ctr, Raymond, Maine, 76-78. *Awards:* Koussevitsky Comp Prize, Berkshire Music Ctr, 74; Koss Music Teachers Nat Asn Comp Prize, 76. *Mem:* ASCAP; Nat Guild Community Sch Arts. *Publ:* Co-ed, Guide to the Selection of Musical Instruments with Respect to Physical Ability and Disability, Magnamusic-Baton Inc, 82. *Mailing Add:* PO Box 25120 Philadelphia PA 19147

CAPLIN, MARTHA J
VIOLIN
b Cleveland, Ohio, Nov 9, 51. *Study:* Cleveland Inst Music, with Margaret Randall, Donald Weilerstein & David Cerone, BM, 73; Juilliard Sch, with Joseph Fuchs, MM, 75. *Rec Perf:* String Quartets (David Loeb & Justin Dello Joio), Grenadilla, 78; String Quartet (Elie Sigmeister), CRI, 80; Symphonies No 44 & No 77 (Haydn), Pro Arte, 83. *Pos:* Violinist & soloist, Orpheus Chamber Ens, New York, 73-; first violinist, Primavera String Quartet, New York, 75-; guest artist, Chamber Music Soc Lincoln Ctr, 82- *Awards:* Jerome Gross Award, Cleveland Inst Music, 73; Michael Rabin Award, Juilliard Sch, 75; Naumburg Chamber Music Award, 77. *Bibliog:* Raymond Ericson (auth), Return of Springtime with Primavera Quartet, New York Times, 9/12/80; David Roberts (auth), Primavera, Horizon Mag, 7/81 & 8/81; Robert Finn (auth), Musician's Road Unexpectedly Easy, Cleveland Plain Dealer, 2/22/81. *Mem:* Chamber Music Am. *Rep:* Herbert Barrett Mgt 1860 Broadway New York NY 10023. *Mailing Add:* 11 Riverside Dr #10KW New York NY 10023

CAPOBIANCO, TITO
DIRECTOR-OPERA, EDUCATOR
b La Plata, Arg, Aug 28, 31. *Study:* Univ Buenos Aires, MA(music). *Pos:* Tech dir, Teatro Colon, 58-62; gen dir, La Plata, Arg, 59-61, Chile Opera Co, 67-70, San Diego Opera, 75-83 & Pittsburgh Opera, 83-; artistic dir, Cincinnati Opera Fest, 61-65 & Cincinnati Opera, 62-65; founder, San Diego Opera Ctr, 77, Verdi Opera Fest, San Diego, 78 & Young Am Opera Cond Prog, 80; dir & prod, major opera companies in Americas & Europe. *Teaching:* Prof, Univ Chile, 54-56; prof acting & interpretation, Acad Vocal Arts, Philadelphia, 62-68; founder & dir, Am Opera Ctr, Juilliard Sch Music, 67-69; dir opera studies & fest stage dir, Music Acad West, 83-; dir, Opera Inst, San Diego State Univ, currently. *Awards:* One of Ten Best Talents, Arg, 68; Cavaliere Award, Italy. *Bibliog:* New Director Vows to Build Reputation of Pittsburgh Opera, Ariz Repub, 3/24/83. *Mailing Add:* Pittsburgh Opera 600 Penn Ave Pittsburgh PA 15222

CAPPS, FERALD BUELL, JR
OBOE & ENGLISH HORN, COMPOSER
b Phoenix, Ariz, Sept 2, 43. *Study:* Ariz State Univ, BA; Temple Univ, MM. *Works:* Deux (duet for oboe & clarinet); 3 Sketches (oboe, bassoon, clarinet & piano); Sonata in 2 Movements (clarinet & piano). *Rec Perf:* Complete Orchestral Works of Ravel. *Pos:* Solo English horn, Aspen Fest Orch; prin oboe, Santa Fe Opera Co & Philadelphia Lyr Opera Co; solo English horn, Chamber Symph Philadelphia; John Gilman Ordway chair English horn, Minn Orch, currently. *Mem:* Phi Mu Alpha. *Mailing Add:* 301 Janalyn Circle Golden Valley MN 55416

CAPPS, WILLIAM
FRENCH HORN, EDUCATOR
b St Louis, Mo, Mar 21, 41. *Study:* Curtis Inst Music, BMus & perf dipl; Hochschule Musik, Berlin; Cath Univ, MMus, DMA. *Pos:* Prin horn, Spoleto Fest Orch, formerly, Spoleto Woodwind Quintet, formerly, Berlin Radio Orch, formerly, Tokyo Phil Orch, formerly, Philadelphia Little Symph, formerly & US Marine Corps Orch & Band, Washington, DC, formerly; soloist & mem horn sect, Robin Hood Dell Concerts, Philadelphia Orch, formerly. *Teaching:* Assoc prof French horn, Sch Music, Fla State Univ, 71- *Mem:* Int Horn Soc. *Mailing Add:* Sch Music Fla State Univ Tallahassee FL 32306

CARABO-CONE, MADELEINE
VIOLIN, EDUCATOR
b St Louis, Mo, June 2, 15. *Study:* Studied with Mischa Mischakoff, George Enesco & Nathan Milstein; studied sonata lit with Carl Friedberg; Juilliard Grad Sch, 38. *Pos:* Conct violinist, recitalist & soloist, Chicago Symph, 37; first violin sect, Cleveland Orch, 43-45; recitalist, Town Hall, New York, 39 & 47. *Teaching:* Guest fac mem, Eastman Sch Music, 68; lectr, Univ Calif, Berkeley, 69, Univ Winnipeg & York Univ, Toronto, 73; instr, Univ Fla, 72, Northern Mont Col, 74, Trenton State Col, summer 74 & State Univ NY, Buffalo, summer 75; guest lectr, Music Educ Dept, BC, Alta, Sask, Regina & Saskatoon campuses, Univ NC, Chapel Hill & Greensboro, Northwestern Ill State, Univ Rochester, Temple Univ, San Francisco State Univ & many others. *Awards:* Frederick Stock Award, Nat Fedn Music Clubs; Eminent Scholar, Va State Univ, 83. *Mem:* Mu Phi Epsilon; Bohemians. *Interests:* Carabo-Cone pedagogic system. *Publ:* Auth, How to Help Children Learn Music, 53 & The Playground as Music Teacher, 55, Harper & Row; Concepts for Strings, Carabo-Cone Found, 66; A Sensory-Motor Approach to Music Learning, MCA & Belwin-Mills, 71. *Mailing Add:* 1 Sherbrooke Rd Scarsdale NY 10583

CARAHER, JAMES H
CONDUCTOR & MUSIC DIRECTOR, PIANO
b Seneca Falls, NY, Dec 19, 50. *Study:* Hamilton Col, BA, 73; Grad Sch Music, Ithaca Col. *Pos:* Rehearsal accmp & asst, Tri Cities Opera, Binghamton, NY, 74-78; chorus master & asst cond, Opera Theater Syracuse, 78-79, music dir, 79-; music dir, Indianapolis Opera Co, 82. *Mem:* Am Fedn Musicians. *Mailing Add:* 251 W 97th St New York NY 10025

CARAVAN, RONALD L
COMPOSER, EDUCATOR
b Pottsville, Pa, Nov 20, 46. *Study:* State Univ NY, Fredonia, BS(music educ), 68; Eastman Sch Music, MA(music theory), 73, DMA(music educ), 74. *Works:* Montage I (oboe, clarinet & cello), 73 & Montage II (bassoon & piano), 75, Ethos Publ; Paradigms I (sax), Dorn Publ, 76; Polychromatic Diversions (clarinet), 79, Canzona (four sax & AATB), 79, Quiet Time (sax & piano), 80 & Jubilate! A Concert Prelude for Saxophones, 82, Ethos Publ. *Rec Perf:* Jubilate! A Concert Prelude for Saxophones, Golden Crest, 82. *Pos:* Ed, Sax Symposium, J NAm Sax Alliance, 75-; sop saxophonist & founder, Aeolian Sax Quartet, 77-; concertmaster, Sax Sinfonia, 82- *Teaching:* Prof music, State Univ NY, 75-79; prof clarinet & sax, Syracuse Univ, 80- *Mem:* Int Clarinet Soc; NAm Sax Alliance; Col Music Soc; Music Educr Nat Conf; NY State Sch Music Asn. *Publ:* Auth, Structural Aspects of Paul Creston's Sonata for Alto Saxophone, Op 19, 76, Some Thoughts on Mastering & Teaching Articulation, 80 & Coming to Grips with the Single-Reed Embouchure, 82, Sax Symposium. *Mailing Add:* Phoenix NY

CARDAMONE, DONNA See Jackson, Donna Cardamone

CARDELL, VICTOR THOMAS
LIBRARIAN
b Hartford, Conn, Oct 31, 51. *Study:* Trinity Col, BA, 73; Columbia Univ, MSLS, 75; NY Univ, MA. *Pos:* Cataloger & asst to Virgil Thomson, New York, 74-79; asst music librn, Music Libr, Cornell Univ, 79-81, actg music librn, 81-82; asst music librn, Music Libr, Yale Univ, 82- *Mem:* Music Libr Asn (chmn New York/Ont chap, 80-81, chmn Marc 048 subcomt, 82-); Res Libr Group; Sonneck Soc; Int Asn Music Libr. *Publ:* Contribr, New Grove Dict of Music in US. *Mailing Add:* 100 York St 9M New Haven CT 06511

CARDENES, ANDRES JORGE
VIOLIN
b Habana, Cuba, May 2, 57, US citizen. *Study:* Ind Univ, 75-81. *Rec Perf:* Sonata for Violin & Piano (David Canfield), Enharmonic Rec, 81. *Pos:* Concertmaster, Utah Symph, 82- *Teaching:* Asst prof, Indiana Univ, Bloomington, 80-82; prof music, Univ Utah, 82- *Awards:* Laureate, Queen Elizabeth Int Violin Compt, Brussels, Belgium, 80; Third Prize, Sibelius Int Violin Compt, Helsinki, 80 & Tchaikovsky Int Violin Compt, Moscow, 82. *Bibliog:* Canadian Broadcasting (film), Tchaikovsky Compt, Tom Deacon, 82; BBC (film), Tchaikovsky Compt, 82. *Rep:* C/o Am Int Artists 275 Madison Ave New York NY 10019. *Mailing Add:* 658 Columbus St Salt Lake City UT 84103

CARELLI, GABOR P
EDUCATOR, TENOR
b Budapest, Hungary, Mar 20, 15; US citizen. *Study:* Liszt Ferenc Acad, Budapest, 34; private tenor study in Rome with Beniamino Gigli. *Rec Perf:* Falstaff, 50, Psalmus Hungaricus, 50 & Nozze di Figaro, 58, RCA Victor; Requiem (Verdi), Deutsche Grammofon, 60; Opera Arias, 60 & Neapolitan Songs, 61, Qualiton. *Roles:* Rodolfo in La Boheme, Tamino in The Magic Flute, Pinkerton in Madame Butterfly, Don Pasquale in Don Pasquale, Don Basilio in The Marriage of Figaro, Duke in Rigoletto & Alfredo in La Traviata, Metropolitan Opera Asn, 50-74. *Pos:* Tenor soloist, Dallas Symph Orch, 48-52, NBC Falstaff, 50, Metropolitan Opera Asn, 50-74 & Minneapolis Symph Orch, 52-56 ; mem, Israel Phil Orch, 56-57. *Teaching:* Prof voice, Manhattan Sch Music, 64-; instr, Consv Peking & Sangai, China, 82. *Mem:* Life mem, Am Guild Musical Artists. *Publ:* Auth, My Way to the Metropolitan, Editio Musica Budapest, 81. *Mailing Add:* 23 W 73 St Apt 908 New York NY 10023

CAREY, THOMAS D
BARITONE, EDUCATOR
b Bennettsville, SC, Dec 29, 31. *Study:* City Col, City Univ New York, 54-58; Stuttgart Musikhochschule, 60-62; Musikhochschule Munich, 62-65. *Roles:* Giorgio Germont in La Traviata, Nederland Opera Co, 62; Absolom in Lost in the Stars, Stuttgart Opera, 63; Mel in The Knot Garden, London Royal Opera, 71; Joe in Show Boat, 71. *Pos:* Conct artist, 57-; founder, Church Circuit Opera Co, 76; bd dir, Okla Arts & Humanities Coun, formerly. *Teaching:* Fac mem, Univ Okla, 69-, assoc prof voice, 71-77, prof, 77-; fac mem, Am Inst Musical Studies, Graz, Austria, 79- *Awards:* Marian Anderson Award, Munich Int Compt, 61; winner, Hertogenbosch Int Compt, 61; Okla Musician of Yr, 77. *Mem:* Nat Asn Teachers Singing; Okla Music Teachers Asn; Am Guild Musical Artists; Music Educr Nat Conf; Pi Kappa Lambda. *Mailing Add:* 801 Jona Kay Terr Norman OK 73069

CARIAGA, DANIEL PHILIP
CRITIC
b Long Beach, Calif, May 10, 35. *Study:* Univ Calif, Los Angeles, 53-56; Calif State Univ, Long Beach, 54-59; Music Acad West, Santa Barbara, 55-57. *Pos:* Pianist & cond, Lola Montes Spanish Dancers, 61-71; pianist & asst cond, Norman Luboff Choir, 63; music critic, Long Beach Independent, Press Telegram, 64-72; from music stringer to ed, Los Angeles Times, 72- *Awards:* Award, Am Guild Organists, 70. *Mem:* Music Critics Asn. *Mailing Add:* Los Angeles Times Los Angeles CA 90053

CARIAGA, MARVELLEE M
SOPRANO
b Huntington Park, Calif, Aug 11, 42. *Study:* State Univ Calif, Long Beach, BA, 60. *Rec Perf:* The Consul (Gian Carlo Menotti), Great Perf, PBS, 78. *Roles:* Fricka in Die Walküre, Northwest Wagner Fest, Seattle, 75-81; Brunnhilde in Siegfried, San Diego Opera, 76; Magda Sorel in Consul, Spoleto Fest USA, 77; Santuzza in Cavalleria Rusticana, Rio de Janeiro, 79 & Netherlands Opera, 82; Isolde in Tristan und Isolde, Hawaii Opera, 83; Ortrud in Lohengrin, Portland Opera, 83. *Awards:* Regional First Place, Nat Fedn Music Clubs, 68. *Mailing Add:* c/o Regency Artists 9200 Sunset Blvd Los Angeles CA 90069

CARILLO, NANCY
VIOLIN, EDUCATOR
Study: Mannes Col Music; Manhattan Sch Music. *Rec Perf:* On CRI, Delos, Nonesuch & Orion. *Pos:* Violinist, touring with Music from Marlboro, Manhattan Trio, New Art Trio & Boston Musica Viva; recitalist, New York & Boston. *Teaching:* Fac mem, Brandeis Univ & Wheaton Col, formerly; instr chamber groups, string ens & violin, Wellesley Col, currently; fac mem violin, New England Consv, currently. *Awards:* Naumburg Award. *Mailing Add:* New England Consv 290 Huntington Rd Boston MA 02115

CARLIN, MARYSE
PIANO, EDUCATOR
Study: Univ Paris, MM; Ecole Normale Musique, lic(piano); studied harpsichord with Ruth Nurmi & Sylvia Marlowe. *Pos:* Recital & chamber music performer, Carnegie Hall, Boston Museum Fine Arts, Hunter Col, Cornell Univ & others; guest artist, Marlboro Fest, formerly & Blue Hill Fest, formerly; soloist, Mass Inst Technol Chamber Orch, formerly & Brandeis Bach Soc, formerly; TV appearances, French Nat TV & US sta. *Teaching:* Mem fac, New England Consv Music, formerly, Philipps-Exeter Acad, formerly, Hiram Col, formerly & Ecole Normale Musique, formerly; mem fac solfege, harpsichord & chamber music, St Louis Consv Music, currently. *Awards:* First Prize Piano, Solfege & Chamber Music, Bordeaux Consv. *Mailing Add:* St Louis Consv Music 560 Trinity Ave St Louis MO 63130

CARLSON, CLAUDINE (CLAUDINE H CARLSON-RUBIN)
MEZZO-SOPRANO
b Mulhouse, Alsace, France, Feb 26. *Study:* Manhattan Sch Music, with Pierre Bernac, Jennie Tourel, Aksel Schiotz, Gertrude Gruenberg, Marta Spoël & Esther Andreas. *Rec Perf:* Mrs Nolan in The Medium, Columbia Rec, 68; The Music of William Grant Still, Orion Rec, 72; Two Songs for Viola, Piano & Voice (Brahms), Sheffield Rec, 74; Alexander Nevsky, Vox cum Laude, 77; Isadora in Le Fou, Erato Rec, 78; Ivan the Terrible, Vox cum Laude, 79; Nocturnes (Carlos Chavez), RCA Mex, 80. *Roles:* Cornelia in Julius Caesar, New York City Opera, 67; Mrs Nolan in The Medium, Opera Soc Wash, 68; Suzuki in Madama Butterfly, Portland Opera, 72; Genevieve in Pelleas et Melisande, 77 & Le Patre La tasse chinoise in L'enfant et les sortileges, 81, Metropolitan Opera. *Pos:* Soloist, currently. *Mailing Add:* 16566 Bosque Dr Encino CA 91436

CARLSON, JANE E
TEACHER-COACH, PIANO
b Hartford, Conn, Nov 19, 18. *Study:* Shenandoah Consv Music, Dayton, Va, BMus, 40; Juilliard Sch Music, dipl, 46; Shenandoah Consv Music, Winchester, Va, Hon Dr Music, 82. *Rec Perf:* Ludus Tonalis (Paul Hindemith), Odeon, EMI, 65. *Pos:* Conct pianist, US, Europe & Asia, 52-78; performer, BBC Radio, 63-70. *Teaching:* Piano, Juilliard Sch Music, 46-; instr master classes, Blonay, Switzerland, Seoul, Korea & Hong Kong, 74- *Awards:* Naumburg Found Award, 47. *Mailing Add:* 257 W 86th St New York NY 10024

CARLSON, JON O
EDUCATOR, MUSIC DIRECTOR
b Harrisburg, Pa, Jan 19, 42. *Study:* Messiah Col, Pa, 59-61; Westminster Choir Col, BM, 63, MM, 64; Univ Ill, Urbana, DMA, 74. *Pos:* Organist & dir music, Lakewood Presby Church, Jacksonville, Fla, 78- *Teaching:* Asst prof music, Alaska Methodist Univ, 71-75 & Ind State Univ, Evansville, 75-78; assoc prof & dir choral activ, Jacksonville Univ, 78- *Mem:* Life mem, Am Choral Dir Asn (Alaska state pres, 74-75); Fla Vocal Asn; Col Music Soc; Am Guild Organists; Music Educr Nat Conf. *Publ:* Auth, Five Anthems with New Sounds, Church Music Bulletin, Brethren in Christ Church, 71; The Performance of Choral Music in America, 74 & Televising an Elizabethan Christmas Dinner, 79, Choral J. *Mailing Add:* 3213 Hermitage Rd Jacksonville FL 32211

CARLSON, LENUS JESSE
BARITONE, TEACHER
b Jamestown, NDak, Feb 11, 45. *Study:* Jamestown Col, 63-64; Central City Opera Apprentice Prog, Colo; Moorhead State Univ, with Dwayne Jorgenson, BA, 67; Juilliard Sch Music, with Oren Brown, 70-73; Tanglewood Opera Theatre Wkshp. *Roles:* Demetrius in A Midsummer's Night Dream, Ctr Opera, Minneapolis, 67; Thomas Moore in Lord Byron, Juilliard Am Opera Ctr, 72; Silvio in I Pagliacci, Metropolitan Opera, 74; Marcello in La Boheme, Netherlands Opera, 74 & Opera Co Boston; Archie Weir in Hermiston, Scottish Opera, Edinburg Fest, 75; Valentin in Faust, Royal Opera House, London, 76; Count Almaviva in The Marriage of Figaro, Santa Fe Opera Fest, 76. *Pos:* Baritone soloist, Minneapolis Symph, 66-68, Dallas Opera House, 72-73, San Antonio Opera House, 72-73, Wash Opera House, 73-74 & others in US & Europe; bar soloist, Metropolitan Opera, 74, 76 & 79-80, res mem, currently. *Teaching:* Private voice, Minneapolis, 65-70, New York, 70- *Mailing Add:* c/o Columbia Artists Mgt Inc 165 W 57th St New York NY 10019

CARLTON, STEPHEN EDWARD
EDUCATOR, WRITER
b Beloit, Wis, Dec 26, 52. *Study:* Lawrence Univ, BMus, 75; Univ Pittsburgh, PhD, 81. *Teaching:* Asst prof music hist, Carnegie-Mellon Univ, 81. *Awards:* Fulbright Fel, 78-80. *Mem:* Am Musicol Soc; Int Musicol Soc; Col Music Soc. *Interests:* Autographs & working methods of Franz Schubert. *Publ:* Auth, Schubert and Sacred Music, 80, Schubert: The Instrumental Composer, 81, The Chamber Music of Schubert and Schumann, 82, Schubert and the Concerto, 82 & Schubert's Early Symphonies, 83, Musical Heritage. *Mailing Add:* Dept Music Carnegie-Mellon Univ Pittsburgh PA 15213

CARLYSS, EARL
VIOLIN, EDUCATOR
b Chicago, Ill. *Study:* Paris Consv; Juilliard Sch Music, BM & MS, 64. *Pos:* Recitalist, Scandinavia, 56 & 63; concertmaster, New York City Ballet Orch, 65; violinist, Juilliard String Quartet, 66- *Teaching:* Mem fac chamber music, Juilliard Sch, 66- *Awards:* Morris Loeb Mem Prize, 64. *Mailing Add:* Juilliard Sch Lincoln Ctr Pl New York NY 10023

CARLYSS, GERALD
TIMPANI, EDUCATOR
Study: Juilliard Sch Music, with Saul Goodman, BMus, MS; Paris Consv Music, with Felix Passerone. *Pos:* Solo timpanist, Cincinnati Symph, 65-67 & Philadelphia Orch, 67- *Teaching:* Mem fac timpani & perc, Curtis Inst Music, 68- *Mailing Add:* Curtis Inst Music 1726 Locust St Philadelphia PA 19103

CARMEN, MARINA (CARMEN MANTECA GIOCONDA)
COMPOSER, GUITAR
b Santander, Spain, July 17, 42. *Study:* Santander Consv, with Saez de Adana; Royal Consv Music, Madrid, studied class guitar with Sainz de la Maza & harmony, counterpt, fugue & comp with Rafael Brubeck de Burgos, grad; studied music appreciation & cond with Andres Segovia & chamber music with Gaspar Cassado. *Works:* Suite Amatoria (orch), 60; Oriente-Ocidente, Fantasy (orch), 61; The Old Man and the Sea (opera), 62-64; Trio (guitar, flute & cello), 63-75; Prelude and Fugue (two guitars), 76; Seis Caprichos (ms, guitar & chamber ens), 76-77; You are My Man, Aren't You? (voice & guitar), 77. *Rec Perf:* XIX Century Music for the Guitar. *Pos:* Performer, Radio TV Espanola, Radio WAXR & Radio WNYC; conct performer in Spain, France, Italy, Morocco, Japan, NAfrica & US. *Mem:* Am String Teachers Asn. *Publ:* Contribr to Ritmo. *Mailing Add:* 333 Pearl St Apt 17K New York NY 10038

CARNOVALE, A NORBERT
ADMINISTRATOR, EDUCATOR
b Biloxi, Miss, July 20, 32. *Study:* La State Univ, BM, 54; Teachers Col, Columbia Univ, MA, 68; Univ Iowa, with Paul Anderson & John Beer, DMA, 73. *Teaching:* Instr brass, NMex State Univ, 57-58; dir bands, Univ Tex, El Paso, 58-62; instr trumpet, Univ Southern Miss, 62-74, chmn music dept, 75-80, coordr music indust & prof music, currently. *Mem:* Music Libr Asn; Music Indust Educr Asn; Int Trumpet Guild. *Publ:* Auth, articles on brass music, Notes, 71; Twentieth Century Music for Trumpet & Orch, Brass Press, 75. *Mailing Add:* 102 Brentwood Place Hattiesburg MS 39401

CAROL, NORMAN
VIOLIN, EDUCATOR
b Philadelphia, Pa. *Study:* Curtis Inst Music, with Efrem Zimbalist, dipl. *Pos:* Concertmaster, Tanglewood Fest Orch, formerly & Philadelphia Orch, 66-; first violin, Boston Symph Orch, formerly. *Teaching:* Mem fac strings, Curtis Inst Music, 79- *Mailing Add:* Curtis Inst Music 1726 Locust St Philadelphia PA 19103

CARPENTER, HOWARD RALPH
ADMINISTRATOR, VIOLIN
b Natural Bridge, NY, Oct 11, 19. *Study:* State Normal Sch, BS, 42; Univ Ala, BM, 47; Eastman Sch Music, MM, 48, PhD, 53; Western Ky Univ, BA, 80. *Works:* Wind Quintet, Col Quintet, 41; Symphony No 1, Southeastern Comp League, 54; Allegro for Piano, perf by comp, 58. *Pos:* Second violin, Cadek String Quartet, 44-46; violin-celeste, Rochester Phil Orch, 47-49; prin violist, Nashville Symph, 55-61; mem ed bd, Am Music Mag, 77- *Teaching:* Head, Dept Music, Univ Richmond, 53-61; prof, Western Ky Univ, 53-, head, Dept Music, 65-75. *Mem:* Nat Asn Rec Artists. *Publ:* Auth, A Russian Defector Speaks, 1/81 & Kentucky Minstrel, 4/82, Am Music Teacher Mag. *Mailing Add:* 1730 Chestnut St Bowling Green KY 42101

CARPENTER, HOYLE DAMERON
EDUCATOR, WRITER
b Stockton, Calif, Aug 8, 09. *Study:* Univ Pacific, MusB, 30; Eastman Sch Music, organ with Harold Gleason, MusM, 32; Univ Calif, musicol with Boyden & Bukofzer, 45; Univ Chicago, PhD, 57. *Teaching:* Instr, Fort Hays Kans State Col, 41-43; asst prof music, Grinnell Col, 43-57; prof music, Glassboro State Col, 57-76, prof emer, 76- *Mem:* Music Teachers Nat Asn (secy eastern div, 62-64); NJ Music Teachers Asn (pres, 61-63); Int Musicol Soc; Am Musicol Soc; Am Guild Organists. *Interests:* Portuguese and Spanish music; 17th, 18th and 19th century American music; relationship of music to other fields. *Publ:* Auth, Salon Music in the Mid-19th Century, Civil War Hist, 9/58; Teaching Elementary Music Without a Supervisor, J Weston Walch, 59; co-ed, Pieces From Instrument at Assistant of Samuel Holyoke, Elkan-Vogel, 59; auth, Microtones in a 16th Century Portuguese Manuscript, Acta Musicologia, 3/60; Tempo and Tactus in the Age of Cabezon, Anuario Musical, 68. *Mailing Add:* 512 S Woodbury Rd Pitman NJ 08071

CARR, BRUCE ALAN
ADMINISTRATOR, CRITIC-WRITER
b Des Moines, Iowa, Oct 17, 38. *Study:* Harvard Col, AB, 60; State Univ NY, Buffalo, MA, 67. *Pos:* Prog ed, Detroit Symph, 71-77, asst mgr, 77-81; music adminr, Pittsburgh Symph, 82- *Interests:* American and 19th century music. *Publ:* Auth, The First All-Sung English 19th Century Opera, Musical Times, 74; co-ed, Beethoven, Performers and Critics, Wayne State Univ Press, 80; auth, Theatre Music, 1800-34, In: Athlone History Vol V, Athlone London, 82. *Mailing Add:* 600 Penn Ave Pittsburgh PA 15222

CARR, EUGENE V
CELLO, ADMINISTRATOR
b New York, NY, Jan 3, 59. *Study:* Oberlin Consv, BM, 82; Oberlin Col, BA, 82. *Pos:* Cellist & orch mgr, Am Symph Orch, 83- *Mailing Add:* 40 W 77 St #11F New York NY 10024

CARR, MAUREEN ANN
EDUCATOR
b Teaneck, NJ, Aug 23, 39. *Study:* Marywood Col, Pa, BA(music), 61; Rutgers Univ, MFA(music theory), 64; Univ Wis, Madison, PhD(music theory), 72. *Pos:* Mem, Music Comt, Grad Rec Exam, Educ Testing Serv, 78- & Undergrad Comn, Nat Asn Sch Music, 81- *Teaching:* Chmn dept music, Montclair State Col, NJ, 75-79; prof music, Pa State Univ, 79-, dir sch music, 79-83. *Awards:* Ford Found Fel, 67-68 & 68-69; Nat Endowment Humanities Fel, 79; Pa State Univ Inst Arts & Humanistic Studies Fac Res Fel, 80. *Mem:* Col Music Soc (secy, 84-); Soc Music Theory; Am Musicol Soc. *Interests:* Musical analysis of motivic process in the dramatic works of Stravinsky, from Firebird to The Flood. *Publ:* Auth, The Sound of Mussorgsky, Opera News, 1/25/75; Abstract of The Motivic Structure of Stravinsky's Firebird, Proc Col Music Symposium 21, 81. *Mailing Add:* 37 Abby Pl State College PA 16801

CARRA, DALMO
PIANO, EDUCATOR
b New York, NY, Sept 11, 31. *Study:* Oberlin Consv; Manhattan Sch Music, BM, 58, MM, 60. *Teaching:* Fac mem piano & chmn, Piano Minor Dept, Manhattan Sch Music, 68- *Mailing Add:* 120 Claremont Ave New York NY 10027

CARRERAS, JOSE
TENOR
b Barcelona, Spain, Dec 5, 46. *Rec Perf:* Don Carlos, Aida, Werther, Ballo in Maschera, Turandot, La Boheme, Lucia di Lammermoor & others on Philips, RCA & Vanguard. *Roles:* Gennaro in Lucrezia Borgia, Teatro del Liceo, Barcelona, 70; Faust in Mefistofele; Edgardo in Lucia di Lammermoor; Des Grieux in Manon; Hoffmann in Tales of Hoffmann; Don Carlo in Don Carlo; Alfredo in La Traviata. *Pos:* Sang with maj co worldwide incl Vienna Staatsoper, Deutsche Oper, Milan La Scala, London Royal Opera, Metropolitan Opera, San Francisco Opera, Philadelphia Lyric Opera & New York City Opera; appearances on radio & TV in Italy, France, Spain, Austria & US. *Awards:* Verdi Singing Compt, 71; Palcoscenico d'oro, Italy. *Mailing Add:* c/o Columbia Artists Mgt 165 W 57th St New York NY 10019

CARROLL, CHARLES MICHAEL
EDUCATOR, CRITIC-WRITER
b Otterbein, Ind, Mar 5, 21. *Study:* Ind Univ, with Paul Nettl, BM, 49; Fla State Univ, with Warren D Allen & Ernst Dohnanyi, MM, 51, PhD, 60. *Pos:* Music critic, Tallahassee Democrat, 50-53 & St Petersburg Independent, 76-; asst mgr, Nat Symph Orch, 55-56. *Teaching:* Instr music, Fla State Univ, 50-53; prof music, Pensacola Jr Col, 60-64 & St Petersburg Jr Col, 64- *Mem:* Am Musicol Soc (nat coun 74-77, chmn southern chap, 74-76); Col Music Soc (nat coun 77-80 & ed symposium, 79-83); Southeastern Am Soc 18th Century Studies (pres, 79-80). *Publ:* Auth, Philidor & Bagge, MGG; The History of Berthe—A Comedy of Errors, Music & Lett, 7/63; The Great Chess Automaton, Dover, 75; A Beneficent Poseur, Recherches Musique Francaise XVI, 76; Eros on the Operatic Stage, Opera Quart, spring 83. *Mailing Add:* 1701 80th St N St Petersburg FL 33710

CARROLL, CHRISTINA
EDUCATOR, SINGER
b Tinca, Rumania, Dec 9, 20; nat US. *Study:* Univ Southern Calif, 39. *Rec Perf:* With opera co. *Pos:* Singer, St Louis, Metropolitan, Glyndebourne & Royal Operas, Edinburgh Fest, radio & TV. *Teaching:* Mem fac, Ariz State Univ, 66-; prof music, 72-; lectr, Am Acad Ophthalmology & Otolaryngology, 71- *Awards:* Ariz State Univ Grants, 72 & 73. *Mem:* Collegium Medicorum Theatri; Music Teachers Nat Asn; Nat Asn Teachers Singing; Sigma Alpha Iota. *Publ:* Auth, Improving Voice Training Techniques, 72; Longevity of Vocal Careers, 74. *Mailing Add:* Music Dept Ariz State Univ Tempe AZ 85281

CARROLL, FRANK MORRIS
EDUCATOR, ADMINISTRATOR
b Norfolk, Va, Mar 19, 28. *Study:* Shenandoah Consv, BM, 50; Col Music Cincinnati, MM, 52; Eastman Sch Music, PhD, 60. *Works:* Old Woman and Pig (opera), Salisbury State Col, 66, Centenary Col Opera, 72 & Shreveport Opera, 83; Suite for Violin & Piano, perf by Diane Spognorki, 68; Concerto for Piano & Orchestra, perf by Constance Carroll & Wis State Univ Orch, 69. *Teaching:* Asst prof, Salisbury State Col, 63-66; assoc prof, Wis State Univ, Superior, 65-69; instr theory, Centenary Col, 69-, dean, Sch Music, 69-74 & 79-; chmn music dept, Appalachian State Univ, 74-79. *Mem:* Music Teachers Nat Asn; Greater Shreveport Music Teachers Asn (pres, 80-82); La Music Teachers Asn (first vpres, 79); Nat Fedn Music Clubs (orch chmn, 83-85). *Mailing Add:* 518 Sophia Lane Shreveport LA 71115

CARROLL, GREGORY DANIEL
EDUCATOR, COMPOSER
b Waterloo, Iowa, Sept 7, 49. *Study:* St John's Univ, Minn, BA, 67; Univ Iowa, MA, 77, PhD, 79. *Works:* Symphonic Fantasy, Minneapolis Metropolitan Youth Symph Orch, 68 & Austin Symph, Minn, 68; Med Ethics Soundtrack, Med Ethics Wkshp, Univ Iowa, 77; Elegy (harpsichord), comn & perf by Sven Hansell, 79; Threesome for Clarinet, perf by Jeff Flolo, 82. *Teaching:* Instr music hist, Col St Teresa, Minn, 73-74; vis asst prof theory & lit, Ind State Univ, 80-81; asst prof theory & comp, Univ NC, Greensboro, 81- *Mem:* Am Musicol Soc; Am Soc Univ Comp; Soc Music Theory; Col Music Soc; Monroe Inst Appl Sci. *Interests:* Consciousness research and musical arts; application of hemispheric synchronization of the brain in accelerated learning; stress-tension control and enhanced creativity. *Mailing Add:* 1002 Jefferson Rd Greensboro NC 27410

CARROLL, JOSEPH ROBERT
COMPOSER, EDUCATOR
b Haverhill, Mass, Jan 31, 27. *Study:* New England Consv, BMus, 49, MMus, 50; Univ Paris, Doctorat L'Univ, 52. *Works:* Missa Pastoralis, Op 1, 60, Wedding Music, Op 3, 65 & Four Offertories, Op 5, 65, Gregorian Inst Am; Songs of the Heart, Op 4, G Schirmer, 68; Byzantine Anthems, Op 2, 72 & Three Christmas Carols, Op 7, 75, Gregorian Inst Am; Introit for Christ the King, Op 6, World Libr Sacred Music. *Rec Perf:* The Tones and Tongues of Christmas, Gregorian Inst Am, 71. *Pos:* Ed, Gregorian Inst Am, 53-58; organist, St Catherine's Parish, 54-73. *Teaching:* Prof music, Mary Manse Col, 59-64; assoc prof, Univ Toledo, 64- *Awards:* Fulbright Fel, 50. *Publ:* Auth, The Chironomy of Gregorian Chant, 55, ed, A Method of Gregorian Chant, 56, auth, Compendium of Liturgical Terms, 64, ed, The Grail Gelineau Psalter, 72 & contribr, The Gelineau Gradual, 77, Gregorian Inst. *Mailing Add:* 3098 Smith Rd Lambertville MI 48144

CARROLL, MARIANNE
ADMINISTRATOR, VIOLIN
b Edmonton, Alta, June 20, 53. *Study:* Univ Alta, Can, 71; studied violin with Carroll Glenn & Patinka Kopec, 72-77; Philadelphia Musical Acad, BMus, 75; Manhattan Sch Music, 75-77. *Pos:* Adminr, Southern Vt Music Fest, 77-78; violinist, CHIC, 78-79; publicist & adminr, Colucci & Ruggieri Music Mime Theater, 78-79; exec dir, Aston Magna Found Music, 79- *Mailing Add:* 65 W 83rd St New York NY 10024

CARRON, ELISABETH (ELISABETTA CARADONNA)
SOPRANO
US citizen. *Study:* With Mrs Rodney Saylor & piano with Rodney Saylor. *Rec Perf:* On Columbia & RCA. *Roles:* Cio-Cio-San in Madama Butterfly, New York City Opera; Micaela in Carmen; Medea in Medea; Susanna in Le Nozze di Figaro; Mimi & Musetta in La Boheme; Violetta in La Traviata; Birdie in Regina. *Pos:* Singer with maj opera co in Mex & US. *Mailing Add:* c/o Matthews-Napal 270 West End Ave New York NY 10023

CARSON, MARGARET
ARTIST REPRESENTATIVE
b Salt Lake City, Utah. *Study:* Univ Toledo, BA; Ohio State Univ, MA. *Pos:* Owner, Carson Off, 44- *Mem:* Asn Class Music (mem bd dir, currently); Asn Theatrical Press Agt & Mgr. *Publ:* Auth, numerous articles in Town & Country, Holiday, Harper's & others. *Mailing Add:* 1414 Ave of the Americas New York NY 10019

CARTER, CHARLES
COMPOSER
b Ponca City, Okla, July 10, 26. *Study:* Ohio State Univ, BA, with Norman Phelps & Kent Kennan; Eastman Sch Music, MA, with Bernard Rogers & Wayne Barlow. *Works:* Sinfonia, Overture in Classic Style, Metropolis, Seminole Song, Overture for Winds, Queen City Suite, Motet for Band, Cakewalk & many more. *Pos:* Composer & arranger band lit. *Teaching:* Instr brass, Ohio State Univ, 52-53 & Fla State Univ, 53- *Mailing Add:* Sch Music Fla State Univ Tallahassee FL 32306

CARTER, ELLIOTT COOK
COMPOSER
b New York, NY, Dec 11, 08. *Study:* Harvard Univ, with Walter Piston & Gustav Holst, AB, 30, AM, 32; Ecole Normale Musique, Paris, with Nadia Boulanger, DMus, 35; Swarthmore Col, Hon MusD, 56; New England Consv, Hon MusD, 61; Princeton Univ, Hon MusD, 67; Boston Univ, Hon MusD; Yale Univ, Hon MusD; Oberlin Col, Hon MusD, 70; Harvard Univ, Hon MusD, 70; Cambridge Univ, Hon MusD, 83. *Works:* Holiday Overture, 44, String Quartet No 1, 53, Variations for Orchestra, 54, String Quartet No 2, 60, Concerto for Orchestra, 69, String Quartet No 3, 73 & Brass Quintet, 74, Assoc Music Publ. *Pos:* Musical dir, Ballet Caravan, 37-39; critic, Modern Music, 37-42. *Teaching:* Tutor, St John's Col, Md, 39-41; mem fac comp, Peabody Consv, 46-48; Columbia Univ, 48-50, Queen's Col, 55-56; prof music, Yale Univ, 60; Andrew White Prof at large, Cornell Univ, 67-; mem fac, Juilliard Sch, 66- *Awards:* Handel Medallion, New York, 78; Siemens Prize for Music, Munich, 80; MacDowell Colony Gold Medal, 83. *Bibliog:* Allen Edwards (auth), Flawed Words and Stubborn Sounds, 71; John Rockwell (auth), article in New York Times, 12/17/74; David Schiff (auth), Elliott Carter, Da Capo Press, 83. *Mem:* Nat Inst Arts & Lett; Akad Künste; Am Acad Arts & Lett; League Comp; Int Soc Contemp Music. *Mailing Add:* Box L Waccabuc NY 10597

CASCARINO, ROMEO
EDUCATOR, COMPOSER
b Philadelphia, Pa, Sept 28, 22. *Study:* Philadelphia Consv Music, with Paul Nordoff, BMus, 43; Hon DMus, Combs Col Music, 60. *Works:* Spring Pastoral, 45; Prospice (ballet), 49; Sonata for Bassoon and Piano, 50; The Acadian Land (woodwinds & strings), 60; William Penn (opera), 75; Blades of Grass (English horn & strings); Portrait of Galatea (tone poem). *Pos:* Orch & chief arr, Armed Forces Spec Serv Orch, NBC & CBS, 40-45; commercial arr, 47-63; cond & music dir, Co-Opera Co, 50-57; arr, Somerset Rec 101 Strings, 56-63. *Teaching:* Head theory & comp dept, Combs Col Music, 55- *Awards:* Guggenheim Fel, 48 & 49; Benjamin Award, 60; Orpheus Award, Phi Mu Alpha, 75. *Mailing Add:* 17 Zummo Way Norristown PA 19401

CASIELLO, MARIANNE
SOPRANO, EDUCATOR
Study: Philadelphia Musical Acad; Curtis Inst Music; vocal study with Euphemia G Gregory. *Roles:* Mimi in La Boheme; Violetta in La Traviata; Leonora in Il Trovatore; Giorgetta in Il Tabarro; Micaela in Carmen; Nedda in Pagliacci; Marguerite in Faust. *Teaching:* Mem fac voice, Philadelphia Col Perf Arts, currently, Settlement Music Sch, currently & Curtis Inst Music, 74- *Mailing Add:* Curtis Inst Music 1726 Locust St Philadelphia PA 19103

CASS, LEE
EDUCATOR, BASS-BARITONE
b New York, NY, May 11, 24. *Study:* Juilliard Sch Music, BS(music), 52, MS(music), 57; Univ Pittsburgh, PhD, 74. *Rec Perf:* Jud in Oklahoma, 53, Ali-ben-Ali in Desert Song, 53 & Postman & Cashier in Most Happy Fella, 56, Columbia Rec; Thomas Clegg in Greenwillow (Frank Loesser), RCA Victor, 60; Anthony Absolute in All in Love (Jacques Urbont), Mercury Rec, 61. *Roles:* Gremin in Eugene Onegin, Frankfurt Opera, 57; Pizarro in Fidelio, NBC-TV Opera, 59; Basilio in Barber of Seville, Metropolitan Opera Studio, 62; Schigolch in Lulu, Santa Fe Opera, 63; Frank in Fledermaus, 64, Varlaam in Boris Godunov, 64 & Pooh-Bah in Mikado, 64, New York City Opera; Basilio in Barber of Seville, Houston Opera, 68. *Teaching:* Instr, Nat Acad Vocal Arts, 45-48; prof music, voice & English diction, Carnegie-Mellon Univ, Pittsburgh, 66- *Awards:* Walter W Naumburg Award, 53; Marian Anderson Award, 54 & 55; Martha Baird Rockefeller Grant, 57. *Mem:* Nat Asn Teachers Singing; Music Teachers Nat Asn; Bohemians; Col Music Soc. *Mailing Add:* 920 College Ave Pittsburgh PA 15232

CASS, RICHARD BRANNAN
EDUCATOR, PIANO
b Greenville, SC, May 3, 31. *Study:* Furman Univ, BA, 53; Ecole Normale Musique Paris, lic conct, 54. *Rec Perf:* Piano Recital, Am Cablevision, 83; Governor's School (doc), ETV, SC, 83. *Teaching:* Assoc prof piano, NTex State Univ, 67-75; prof, Consv Music, Univ Mo, Kansas City, 75- *Awards:* Young Artists Award, Nat Fedn Music Clubs, 53; Sullivan Award, NY Southern Soc, 53; Fulbright Scholar France, 53, 54 & 55. *Bibliog:* Homer Ulrich (auth), Convention Artist, Am Music Teacher, 81. *Mem:* Music Teachers Nat Asn; Pi Kappa Lambda; life mem, Nat Fedn Music Clubs. *Mailing Add:* 4949 Cherry Kansas City MO 64110

CASSEL, WALTER JOHN
BARITONE, EDUCATOR

b Council Bluffs, Iowa, May 15, 20. *Study:* With Frank LaForge. *Rec Perf:* On MGM. *Roles:* Bretigny in Manon, Metropolitan Opera, 44; Horace Tabor in The Ballad of Baby Doe, Cent City Fest, Colo, 56; Petrucchio in The Taming of the Shrew, New York City Opera, 58; Escamillo in Carmen; Tonio in I Pagliacci; Jack Rance in La Fanciulla del West; Wolfram in Tannhäuser; and many others. *Pos:* Dramatic bar with maj opera co in Austria, Can, WGermany, Italy, Mex, Spain & US; res mem, Metropolitan Opera. *Teaching:* Prof voice, Ind Univ, Bloomington, currently. *Rep:* Sardos Artists Mgt 180 West End Ave New York NY 10023. *Mailing Add:* Sch Music Ind Univ Bloomington IN 47401

CASSILLY, RICHARD
TENOR

b Washington, DC, Dec 14, 27. *Study:* Peabody Consv Music, 46-52. *Rec Perf:* Aaron (Schoenberg), Hamburg, 74; Otello; Wozzeck; Fidelio; Die Meistersinger von Nürnberg; rec on Deutsche Grammophon, CBS, EMI, Westminster & Columbia. *Roles:* Michele in The Saint of Bleecker Street, Broadway Co, 55; German Soldier in Tale for a Deaf Ear, New York City Opera, 58; Laca in Jenufa, Chicago Lyr Opera, 59 & Covent Garden, 68; Peter Grimes in Peter Grimes, Scottish Opera, Edinburgh Fest, 68; Tannhäuser in Tannhäuser, Vienna Staatsoper, 70; Mog Edwards in Unter dem Milchwald, Staatsoper, Hamburg, 73; Radames in Aida, Metropolitan Opera, 73; and many others. *Pos:* Ten, New York City Opera, 55-66, Chicago Lyr Opera, 59-, Deutsche Opera Berlin, 65-, San Francisco Opera, 66-, Hamburgische Staatsoper, 66-, Covent Garden, 68-, La Scala, Milan, 70, Wiener Staatsoper, 70, Staatsoper München, 70, Paris Opera, 72 & Metropolitan Opera, 73- *Awards:* Kammersinger, Hamburg, 73; Voice of Achievement Prizes (two), Peabody Consv Music. *Mailing Add:* c/o Robert Lombardo Assoc 1 Harkness Plaza 61 W 62 Suite 6F New York NY 10023

CASSUTO, ALVARO LEON
CONDUCTOR

b Oporto, Portugal. *Study:* Univ Libson, MA, 64; Vienna Consv, Kapellmeister, 65. *Works:* In Memoriam, 63 & Cro(mo-no)fonia, 67, G Schirmer; Evocations, Tonos, Darmstadt, 69; Circles, 70 & To Love and Peace, 73, G Schirmer. *Pos:* Cond, Gulben Orch, 65-68; substitute dir, Nat Portuguese Radio Symph, 70-75, music dir, 75-; gen dir, Nat Portuguese Opera, 81-82. *Teaching:* Prof music, Univ Calif, Irvine, 74-79. *Awards:* Koussevitzky Prize, Berkshire Music City, 69. *Mailing Add:* RI Phil 334 Westminister Mall Providence RI 02903

CASTALDO, JOSEPH F
EDUCATOR, COMPOSER

b New York, NY, Dec 23, 27. *Study:* Santa Cecilia Acad, Rome; studied with Dante Fiorello; Manhattan Sch Music, with Hugh Ross & Vittorio Giannini; Philadelphia Consv, with Vincent Persichetti, BM, MM. *Works:* Flight (cantata for chorus, winds, perc, narrator & sop), Temple Univ, 60; At Her Feet (a cappella choir); Cycles (orch), Philadelphia, 70; Askesis (chamber ens), Athens, 71; Protogenesis (15 instrm, lights, film, slides & Zeiss planetarium instrm), perf at May Fest, Fels Planetarium, Philadelphia, 73; Theoria (winds, piano & perc), Philadelphia, 73; Kannon (chamber ens), Boston, 76. *Teaching:* Jr High Sch Art Ctr, formerly & Philadelphia Consv, formerly; head, Comp & Theory Dept, Philadelphia Col Perf Arts, 60-66, pres, 66- *Mem:* ASCAP; Philadelphia Comp Forum (chmn, currently); Music Teachers Nat Asn. *Mailing Add:* Philadelphia Col Perf Arts 1617 Spruce St Philadelphia PA 19103

CASTEL, NICO
TENOR, EDUCATOR

b Lisbon, Portugal, Aug 1, 31; US citizen. *Study:* Consv Nac, Caracas, Venezuela, 46-48; Temple Univ, BA, 52. *Roles:* Goro in Madame Butterfly, 66 & Guillot in Manon, 68, New York City Opera; Magician in Consul, Spoleto Fest & Maggio Musicale Florentino, 70; Monostatos in Magic Flute, 72, Majordomo in Ariadne, 74 & Marquis in Lulu, 80, Metropolitan Opera; Guillot in Manon, Chicago Lyric Opera, 83. *Pos:* Prin singer, New York City Opera, 65-69, Metropolitan Opera, 69- *Teaching:* Prof diction, 92nd St Y Sch Music, 76-, Am Inst Musical Studies, Graz, Austria, 78- & Mannes Col Music, 79- *Mem:* Am Guild Musical Artists (bd mem, 75-78); Am Fedn TV & Radio Artists. *Publ:* Auth, The Nico Castel Ladino Song Book, Tara, 80. *Rep:* Kazuko Hillyer Int 250 W 57th St New York 10019. *Mailing Add:* 170 W End Ave New York NY 10023

CASTIGLIONE, RICHARD B
CONDUCTOR, ADMINISTRATOR

b Kingston, NY, Nov 12, 28. *Study:* Studied trumpet with Ernest Williams, 44-45; State Univ NY, Potsdam, BS, 49; Columbia Univ, MA, 56. *Pos:* Cond, ABC TV, New York, 52-56; pres, Amherst Summer Music Ctr, 76- *Teaching:* Cond chamber music, Manhattan Sch Music, 58-61; cond wind ens & dean, Philadelphia Musical Acad, 68-76; cond wind ens, Boston Univ, 82-83. *Awards:* Award for Excellence, Music Educr Nat Conf, 71. *Publ:* Co-ed, Essentials of Music, Philadelphia Sch Dist, 66. *Mailing Add:* 855 Commonwealth Ave Boston MA 02215

CASTLEMAN, CHARLES MARTIN
VIOLIN, EDUCATOR

b Quincy, Mass, May 22, 41. *Study:* Curtis Inst Music, BMus; Harvard Univ, AB; Univ Pa, MA; studied with Emmanuel Ondricek, Ivan Galamian, Josef Gingold, David Oistrakh & Henryk Szeryng. *Rec Perf:* String Trios (Reger); Trios (Martin); Solo Sonatas (Ysaye); on BASF, Desmar, Sonar, Nonesuch

& Melodya. *Pos:* Conct violinist throughout North Am, South Am & Europe; soloist, Boston Symph, Brussels Symph, New York Phil, Chicago Symph, Philadelphia Orch, Moscow State Orch & Belgian Nat Orch; founder & dir, The Quartet Prog, Emma Willard Sch, Troy, NY; mem bd dir, Curtis Inst Music, 75-77; violinist, Raphael Trio, New York & Round Top Chamber Players, currently. *Teaching:* Prof violin, Philadelphia Musical Acad, 67-76 & State Univ NY Col, Purchase, 72-76; prof violin, Eastman Sch Music, 75- *Awards:* Silver Medal, Queen Elisabeth of Belgium Cont, 63; Laureate, Tchaikovsky Cont, 66. *Mem:* Chamber Music Am. *Publ:* Contribr to Anvario Musicale & Music J. *Rep:* Hamlen/Landau Mgt Inc 140 W 79th St Suite 2A New York NY 10024; Francis Crociata Swan St Rochester NY 14604. *Mailing Add:* Eastman Sch Music 26 Gibbs St Rochester NY 14604

CASTLEMAN, HEIDI WALDRON
VIOLA, EDUCATOR

b Suffern, NY. *Study:* Wellesley Col, BA, 64; Univ Pa, MA, 66. *Pos:* Co-dir, Quartet Prog, Troy, NY, 70-; violist, NY String Sextet, 72-76. *Teaching:* Prof viola, Eastman Sch Music, 76-, New England Consv, 79-83 & Shepherd Sch Music, Rice Univ, 83- *Mem:* Chamber Music Am (vpres, 77-83, pres, 83-). *Mailing Add:* 261 Shoreham Dr Rochester NY 14618

CATHCART, KATHRYN
CONDUCTOR & MUSIC DIRECTOR, COACH

b Tracy, Minn. *Study:* St Olaf Col, BA; Northwestern Univ, MM. *Pos:* Cond & coach, Cologne Opera, WGer, 73-81 & San Francisco Opera, 81-; cond, Opera Columbia, 79; music dir, Conct Opera Asn San Francisco, 83. *Rep:* Robert Lombardo 61 W 62nd New York NY 10023. *Mailing Add:* 2635 Lyon St San Francisco CA 94123

CAVE, MICHAEL
COMPOSER, PIANO

b Springfield, Mo, May 17, 44. *Study:* Washington Univ, St Louis, 1 yr; Calif Inst Arts, BMus, 68; Sch Perf Arts, USC, MMus, 72. *Works:* Pandora's Box (childrens opera), Music Dept, Westlake Sch, 71; Ecclesiastes (two sop & chamber ens), Univ Southern Calif Ens, 71; By the Waters of Babylon (cantata for sop, flute, oboe & piano), Li Trobador, Siena, Italy & Calif, 73; Elegy (sop, oboe & piano), Schönberg Inst Recital, Los Angeles, 82; Piano Sonatas #1 & #2, Dutch Radio, 82 & 83; Five New Age Songs, perf by Delcina Stevenson, 83; Valse, DC, perf by Gervase de Peyer, 83. *Rec Perf:* Cave Plays Mozart on Fortepiano, Orion Rec, 72; Cave Compositions, Dalton Rec, 76; Cave Plays Debussy & Schumann, Creative Soc, 78. *Teaching:* Masterclasses & privately piano & comp, Venice, Calif, 68-; head music dept, Choral & Instrm Ens, Musical Prod, Westlake Sch, 68-72; lectr piano, Univ Calif, Los Angeles, 71-76. *Awards:* First Place Piano, Nat Soc Arts & Lett, 68 & Denver Symph Compt, 72. *Rep:* Jacquolene Young Hursey PO Box 513 Pacific Palisades CA 90272; Nanette de Freese PO Box 1037 1400 BA Bussum Holland. *Mailing Add:* 1525 Walnut Ave Venice CA 90291

CAVIANI, RONALD JOSEPH
COMPOSER, EDUCATOR

b Iron Mountain, Mich, Mar 12, 31. *Study:* Northern Mich Univ, BMusEd, 62; Notre Dame Univ, Ind, MMus, 64; Univ Mich; Mich State Univ, 70-72. *Works:* The Darkling Thrush, Lawson-Gould; Stopping By Woods ... & When You Are Old and Grey, Mark Foster Music Co; Piece for Trumpet and Tape, A & O, Tromba Publ Co; Pity This Busy Monster ..., Mark Foster Music Co, 70; Dance Suite (clarinet & piano), 82 & Five Scenes for Viola and Piano, 82, Dorn Publ. *Teaching:* Head dept music, Brandywine Pub Sch, Niles, Mich, 63-66; assoc prof music, Northern Mich Univ, 66-68 & Consv Music, Univ of Pac, 78- *Mailing Add:* Consv Music Univ of Pac Stockton CA 95211

CAWOOD, (ELIZABETH) MARION
SOPRANO

b Harlan, Ky, Sept 14, 41. *Study:* Ind Univ, Bloomington, BM(voice), 68; Univ Ky, MM(voice), 71; Fla State Univ, DM(voice), 79. *Roles:* Rosalinda in Die Fledermaus, 62, Mimi in La Boheme, 63, Fiordiligi in Cosi fan tutte, 64 & Donna Anna in Don Giovanni, 64, Ind Univ; Gretchen in Wildschütz, Cologne Opera House, 70; Violetta in La Traviata, 77 & Antonia in Tales of Hoffmann, 78, Fla State Univ. *Pos:* Soloist soprano, Cologne Opera House, Ger, 68-70. *Teaching:* Asst vocal studies, Univ Ky, 70-71 & Fla State Univ, 77-79; asst prof, David Lipscomb Col, 72- *Awards:* Fulbright Scholar, 66. *Mem:* Nat Asn Teachers Singing (treas & secy, 80-82); Nat Music Teachers Asn. *Mailing Add:* Music Dept David Lipscomb Col Nashville TN 37203

CAZEAUX, ISABELLE ANNE-MARIE
EDUCATOR, CRITIC-WRITER

b New York, NY, Feb 24, 26. *Study:* Hunter Col, BA, 45; Smith Col, MA, 46; Consv Nat Musique, Paris, prem medaille, 50; Ecole normale musique, Paris, lic d'enseignement, 50; Columbia Univ, MS(libr sci), 59, PhD(musicol), 61. *Pos:* Asst, music libr, Columbia Univ, 56-57; sr music cataloger & head music & phonorec cataloging, New York Publ Libr, 57-63. *Teaching:* Private teaching violin, piano, theory, counterpoint, 46-56; prof & chairman music dept, Bryn Mawr Col, 63-; fac musicol, Manhattan Sch Music, 69-82; vis prof musicol, Douglass Col, Rutgers Univ, 78. *Awards:* Libby van Arsdale Prize, Hunter Col, 45; grants, Martha Baird Rockefeller Fund, 71-72 & Herman Goldman Found, 80. *Mem:* Am Musicol Soc (coun, 68-70); Soc francaise musicol; Int Musicol Soc; Music Libr Asn; Pomerium Musices (adv coun, 80-). *Interests:* French Renaissance music; music criticism; French music and letters. *Publ:* Co-ed, Anthologie de la chanson parisienne au XVI siecle, L'Oiseau-lyre, 53; contribr, on Music Cataloging and Classification, In: Manual of Music, Librarianship, Music Libr Asn, 66; ed, Sermisy: Chansons (two vols), Corpus Mensurabilis Musicae, Am Inst Musicol, 74; auth, French Music in the Fifteenth and Sixteenth Centuries, Blackwell & Praeger, 75; Outdoor Music in the French Renaissance, J Japanese Musicol Soc, 82. *Mailing Add:* 415 E 72nd St New York NY 10021

CECCATO, ALDO
CONDUCTOR & MUSIC DIRECTOR

b Milan, Italy, Feb 18, 34. *Study:* Verdi Consv, Milan; Musikhochschule, Berlin; Accad Chigiana, Siena. *Rec Perf:* La Traviata; Maria Stuarda; Grace Bumbry Italia Album; John Ogdon, Mendelssohn Piano Concertos. *Pos:* Music dir & cond, Detroit Symph Orch, formerly & Hamburg Phil, formerly; guest cond, maj symph orchs & opera houses throughout world. *Mailing Add:* c/o Herbert Barrett Mgt 1860 Broadway New York NY 10023

CECCHINI, PENELOPE C
PIANO, EDUCATOR

b Kokomo, Ind. *Study:* Jordan Col Music, Butler Univ, BM, 65; Inst Music, Aspen, 65; Mich State Univ, with Luboshutz, Nemenoff & Ralph Votapek, MM(piano perf), 66, dipl(perf), 79. *Teaching:* Head keyboard div dept music, Univ Wis, Eau Claire, 66- *Awards:* Ruby Sword of Honor, Sigma Alpha Iota, 65. *Mem:* Sigma Alpha Iota (chap pres, 65); Phi Kappa Phi; Pi Kappa Lambda. *Mailing Add:* 515 Lincoln Ave Eau Claire WI 54701

CECCONI-BATES, AUGUSTA N
COMPOSER, LECTURER

b Syracuse, NY, Aug 9, 33. *Study:* Syracuse Univ, AB, 56, MA(musicol) 60; Cornell Univ, 76-77. *Works:* Sonata No 2 (violin & piano), Warick Lister, 78; Pasticcio, Chicago Symph Wind Ens, 80; War is Kind, comn by State Univ NY, Oswego, 81; Willie Was Different, Derek Coleman, 81; For Ilya, Max Lifchitz, 82; The Touch of Christmas, Children's Chorale, Syracuse Univ, 82; Sonnino 1982, Band Sonnino, Italy, 83. *Pos:* Music specialist, Syracuse Sch District, 68-; comp in res, Vt Music & Arts Ctr, summers 77-81; asst cond, Music Int, summer 82. *Teaching:* Instr, Maria Regina Col, 64-65. *Awards:* Several grants, Meet The Comp. *Mem:* ASCAP; Asn Conct Bands Inc; Soc New Music; Racine Munic Band; Nat League Pen Women. *Publ:* Auth, Percussion is Important in Pasticcio, 81, Cor Anglais in Bits o' Scotland, 82, Percussion Patterns in War is Kind, 82 & Cor Anglais in Paragraphs & Fugue, 83, Woodwind Brass Perc. *Mailing Add:* Toad Harbor 816 Shaw Dr West Monroe NY 13167

CECERE, ANTHONY ROBERT
FRENCH HORN

b New York, NY, July 20, 52. *Study:* Univ Mich, BMus, 74, MMus, 76; Berkshire Music Ctr, 74-75; Aspen Music Fest, 76-77. *Rec Perf:* Concerto K495 No 4 (Mozart), 76 & Concerto No 1 in D (Haydn), 76, Peters Int Rec. *Pos:* Second horn, NJ Symph, 76-78, third horn, 78-80; prin horn, New Orleans Symph, 80-; third horn, First Monday Contemp Group, Tulane Univ, 83- *Awards:* C D Jackson Prize, Berkshire Music Ctr, 76. *Bibliog:* C Leuba (auth), Records in Review, Horn Call Mag, 80. *Mem:* Am Fedn Musicians; Int Horn Soc. *Mailing Add:* 1238 Cambronne St New Orleans LA 70118

CEDEL, MARK
VIOLA, MUSIC DIRECTOR

Study: Curtis Inst Music. *Pos:* Mem, Guarneri String Quartet, formerly & Philadelphia Orch, formerly; violist, Quarteto Univ Fed Rio Grande Norte, Brazil, formerly; guest cond, Orch Camera, formerly; prin viola, Charleston Symph Orch, 79-, asst cond, 81-82, actg music dir, 82- *Teaching:* Distinguished vis prof, Univ Fed Rio Grande Norte, Brazil, formerly. *Mailing Add:* Charleston Symph Orch 3 Chisolm St Charleston SC 29401

CEDRONE, FRANK JOSEPH
PIANO, EDUCATOR

b Brighton, Mass, Aug 2, 34. *Study:* Boston Consv Music, BMus, 56; studied piano with Ernest Bacon, David Barnett, Georg Fior & David Saperton. *Works:* Melpomene (ballet), Jan Veen Dance Co, Boston, 56; numerous two-piano conct arrangements. *Pos:* Pianist, Markowski & Cedrone Duo-Pianists, 58- *Teaching:* Asst dir, Boston Consv Music, 56-59, instr piano & theory, 58-60; instr, New York Col Music, 65-66; artist in res, piano & piano ens, Univ Southern Colo, 69- *Awards:* Conct Artist Guild Award Winner, New York, 58. *Mem:* Colo State Music Teachers Asn (pres, 72-73); Pueblo Area Music Teachers Asn (pres, 83-84); Music Teachers Nat Asn; Am Col Musicians; Phi Mu Alpha. *Publ:* Auth, The Well-Tempered Hanon, M & C Publ, 78; How Fast is Fast? Understanding the Metronome, Piano Guild Notes, 78; Profile of a Piano Team, Piano Quart, 78. *Mailing Add:* M & C Mgt 2723 6th Ave Pueblo CO 81003

CEELY, ROBERT PAIGE
COMPOSER

b Torrington, Conn, Jan 17, 30. *Study:* New England Consv Music, BMus, 54; Princeton Univ, with Roger Sessions & Milton Babbitt, 57-59; Mills Col, with Darius Milhaud, MA, 61. *Rec Perf:* Logs for 2 Double Basses, Hymn for Cello & Bass, Les Fleurs for Magnetic Tape, Stratti for Magnetic Tape, CRI; Piano Variations & Totems for Oboe & Tape, Beep. *Teaching:* Dir music, Lawrenceville Sch, NJ, 60-61; prof, Robert Col, Istanbul, Turkey, 61-63; tech suprv, Harvard Univ, 65-66; prof comp, New England Consv, 66- *Awards:* Fromm Music Found Award, 69; Fel, Nat Endowment Arts, 79 & Mass Coun Arts, 79. *Bibliog:* Joan Higgins (auth), Such Shocking Music, WCRB Prog Guide, 7/74; Steve Robinson (auth), Robert Ceely A Contemporary Composer, Rec Buyer's Guide, 8/75. *Mem:* BMI; Am Comp Alliance; Col Music Soc; Audio Engineering Soc (pres, 79-80). *Publ:* Auth, Electronic Music Three Ways, Electronic Music Rev, 67; Thoughts About Electronic Music, Comp Mag, 73; Electronic Music Resource Book, BEEP Sounds, 81. *Mailing Add:* 33 Elm St Brookline MA 02146

CELESTINO, THOMAS
TENOR

b Tuckahoe, NY, Mar 17, 50. *Study:* Bridgeport Univ, BA; Colgate Univ, MA. *Roles:* Mario Cavaradossi in Tosca, 82; Lt Pinkerton in Madame Butterfly, 82; Rodolfo in La Boheme, 82; Rinuccio in Gianni Schicchi, Tarrytown Music Hall, 82; Turriddu in Cavalleria Rusticana, 83; tenor soloist in Verdi Requiem, 83. *Mailing Add:* c/o European Am Artists Inc 27 Pine St New Canaan CT 06840

CELLI, JOSEPH ROBERT
OBOE, LECTURER

b Bridgeport, Conn, Mar 19, 44. *Study:* Hartt Sch Music, BME, 67; Northwestern Univ Chicago, MM, 71. *Works:* Snare Drum for Camus, Ringing for Antique Cymbals, Improvisations for Oboe, Final Phase (chamber ens) & Sky: S for J (five English horns without reeds), J Celli. *Rec Perf:* Organic Oboe No 1, 80; Celli Plays Niblock, Niblock for Celli, 83; The Seasons: Vermont, 83; Duo Improvisations, 83. *Pos:* Dir, Organic Oboe, Hartford, Conn, 71- & Real Art Ways, Hartford, 75-; artist in res, Star Island Conf Arts, 81 & Yellow Springs Arts Conf, 83. *Teaching:* Oboe instr, Hartt Sch Music, 72-78 & Univ Bridgeport, 75-77. *Awards:* Grant, Conn Comm Arts, 80. *Mem:* Conn Comp Inc; Comn Cult Affairs; Meet the Comp; Conn Adv Arts; New Music Alliance. *Mailing Add:* Box 3313 Hartford CT 06103

CELONA, JOHN ANTHONY
COMPOSER, COMPUTER MUSIC

b San Francisco, Calif, Oct 30, 47. *Study:* San Francisco State Univ, BMus, 70, studied with Henry Onderdonk, MA, 71; Univ Calif, San Diego, with Ken Gaburo, PhD, 77. *Works:* Proportions (Networks), Lingua Press, 77; Player Piano V, Jeu Publ, 78; Moving Points, perf by Johannesen Int Sch Arts, 79; Music on One Timbre, 79 & Arpeggio, 81, Days, Months & Years to Come; Instrument Flying, perf by Salvatore Ferreras, percussionist, 83; Music in Circular Motions, Folkways Rec, 83. *Pos:* Res fel, Ctr Music Experiment, Univ Calif, San Diego, 73-75, assoc music, 76-77. *Teaching:* Asst prof music comp, Univ Victoria, 77- *Awards:* BMI Award, 71-72. *Bibliog:* Roscoe Mitchell (auth), Jazz Music, Coda, 74; Virginia Gaburo (auth), Notation, Lingua Press, 77. *Mem:* Comput Music Asn; Perf Rights Orgn, Can; Comp Forum Inc. *Publ:* Auth, Structural Aspects of Contemporary Music Notation and Command-String Notation, A New Music Notational System, Univ Microfilms Inc. *Mailing Add:* 2317 Belmont Ave Victoria BC V8R 4A2 Canada

CERA, STEPHEN CHARLES
CRITIC, PIANO

b Winnipeg, Man, Can, Oct 6, 51. *Study:* Pomona Col, BA, 72; Univ Southern Calif, MM(piano), 73; private study with Rosina Lhevinne & Martino Tirimo. *Pos:* Music staff mem, Los Angeles Times, 72-77; music ed, Baltimore Sun, 77- *Teaching:* Fac music, Pierce Col, 77. *Awards:* William Lincoln Honnold Found Fel, 72; fel, Music Critics Asn US & Can, 77. *Mem:* Music Critics Asn (mem comt on educ music critics, 79-82); Pi Kappa Lambda. *Mailing Add:* 500 W University Pkwy Baltimore MD 21210

CERNY, WILLIAM JOSEPH
PIANO, EDUCATOR

b New York, NY, Dec, 28. *Study:* Yale Univ, BA, 51; Yale Sch Music, BMus, 52, MMus, 54. *Rec Perf:* Scott Joplin Rags, 75; Music Saxophone & Piano. *Pos:* Pianist & accmp for leading conct artists, 54-59. *Teaching:* Fac mem, Eastman Sch Music, 59-72; prof music, Univ Notre Dame, 72- *Awards:* Music Educ League NY Award, 51. *Mem:* Phi Mu Alpha; Am Musicol Soc; Col Music Soc. *Publ:* Contribr, Notes. *Mailing Add:* 2918 Caroline St South Bend IN 46614

CERVETTI, SERGIO
COMPOSER, EDUCATOR

b Uruguay, Nov 9, 40; US citizen. *Study:* Peabody Consv, BM, 67. *Works:* Prisons, Akad Kunste, Berlin, 69; Plexus, comn by OEA, perf by Nat Symph, 70; Madrigal III, San Francisco Contemp Music Players, 76; Forty second-42nd Variations, 79, Cantata '84, 80, Generation Pieces, 81 & Fable (in four fugues), 82, Kenneth Rinker Dance Co. *Teaching:* Asst prof, Brooklyn Col, 70-71; asst prof electronic music, Sch of Arts, NY Univ, 72- *Awards:* DAAD Comp in Res, WBerlin, 69; second prize, Civdad de Maracaibo, Venezuela, 77; Nat Endowment for Arts Fel, 78. *Mem:* BMI. *Mailing Add:* 96 Park Pl Brooklyn NY 11217

CERVONE, D(OMENIC) DONALD
COMPOSER, EDUCATOR

b Meadville, Pa, July 27, 32. *Study:* Eastman Sch Music, BM, 55, PhD, 70; Univ Ill, MM, 60. *Works:* Prelude on a Shaped-Note Hymn, Wedlock, Milwaukee Civic Orch, 62; Canzone II, Eastman-Rochester Symph Orch, 64; Arioso & Allegro, Rochester Phil Orch, 68; Two Elegies, Rochester Phil Orch, 68 & Buffalo Phil Orch, 70; These Are the Times, Northwest Symph Orch, Pa, Choir Allegheny Col & Meadville Chorale. *Pos:* Founder & cond, Amici della Musica, 67-, Brockport Singers, 67-83, Brockport Pro Musica Consort, 67-77, Brockport Sinfonia Pro Musica, 70-76 & Ragazzi Consort, 73- *Teaching:* Comp in res, pub sch, Mont, 60-61 & Milwaukee, 61-62; asst prof, State Univ NY, Brockport, 66-71, assoc prof, 71-83. *Awards:* Young Comp Award, Ford Found & Nat Music Coun, 60 & 61; Comp Forum Award, Ford Found & New York City Opera Co, 60. *Interests:* Performance practices of music before 1800; iconography and construction of keyboard instruments. *Publ:* Contribr, Introduction to Music, Force, 78; ed, J Brockport Int Keyboard Fest, State Univ NY, Brockport, 80. *Mailing Add:* 3318 Brockport-Spencerport Rd Spencerport NY 14559

CHADABE, JOEL A
COMPOSER, EDUCATOR
b New York, NY, Dec 12, 38. *Study:* Univ NC, Chapel Hill, BA, 59; studied comp with Elliott Carter, 61-64; Yale Univ, MM, 62. *Works:* Ideas of Movement at Bolton Landing, Op One Rec, 71; Echoes, perf by Paul Zukofsky on CP2 Rec, 72; From the 14th On (solo cello), perf by David Gibson, 73; Flowers, perf by Paul Zukofsky on CP2 Rec, 75; Settings for Spirituals, with Irene Oliver, 77; Rhythms (comput & perc), perf by comp & Jan Williams on Lovely Music Rec, 81. *Teaching:* From assoc prof to prof comp & electronic music, State Univ NY, Albany, 65-; consult electronic music, Bennington Col, 71- *Bibliog:* Tom Johnson, interview, High Fidelity, Musical Am, 75. *Mem:* Comp Forum Inc (pres, 79-); ASCAP; Comput Music Asn; Am Music Ctr. *Publ:* Auth, New Approaches to Analog Studio Design, Perspectives New Music, 67; Le Principe du Voltage-Controle, Musique en Jeu, 72; The Voltage-Controlled Synthesizer, In: The Development & Practice of Electronic Music, 75; Some Reflections on the Nature of the Landscape, 77 & An Introduction to the Play Program, 78, Comput Music J. *Mailing Add:* PO Box 8748 Albany NY 12208

CHAJES, JULIUS T
COMPOSER, CONDUCTOR & MUSIC DIRECTOR
b Lwow, Poland, Dec 21, 10; US citizen. *Study:* Vienna Consv Music, Austria, 26-28; Vienna Univ, Austria, 29-30. *Works:* Cello Concerto, 29, 2nd String Quartet, 30, 142nd Psalm, 32, Sonata in A Minor, 45, Piano Concerto, 52, Eros Symphonic Poem, 60 & Out of the Desert Opera, 66, Transcontinental Music Publ. *Pos:* Music dir, Jewish Community Ctr, Detroit, Mich, 40- *Teaching:* Head piano dept, Beit Leviim Music Sch, Tel Aviv, Israel, 34-36; adj prof, Wayne State Univ, 50- *Mailing Add:* 6820 E Dartmoor West Bloomfield MI 48033

CHALIFOUX, ALICE (ALICE CHALIFOUX RIDEOUT)
HARP, EDUCATOR
b Birmingham, Ala, Jan 22, 08. *Study:* Curtis Inst Music, BM, 34. *Pos:* Prin harp, Cleveland Orch, 31-74. *Teaching:* Head harp dept, Cleveland Inst Music, 31-, Consv Music, Oberlin Col, 70- & Baldwin-Wallace Consv, 72-; dir, Summer Harp Colony, Camden, Maine, 62- *Mem:* Pi Kappa Lambda. *Mailing Add:* Cleveland Inst Music 11021 E Blvd Cleveland OH 44106

CHALKER, MARGARET
SOPRANO, EDUCATOR
Study: Studied with Helen Boatwright. *Roles:* Antonia in The Tales of Hoffmann, Opera Theatre Syracuse; Anna in The Merry Widow, Artpark; Nyade in Ariadne auf Naxos, Chautauqua Opera Asn; Rosalinda in Die Fledermaus & Kate Pinkerton in Madama Butterfly, Tex Opera Theatre. *Pos:* Sop, Tex Opera Theatre, currently. *Teaching:* Instr voice, State Univ NY, Fredonia, currently. *Awards:* First Prize, Baltimore Opera Auditions, 80. *Mailing Add:* c/o Tornay Mgt Inc 127 W 72nd St New York NY 10023

CHALMERS, BRUCE ABERNATHY
ADMINISTRATOR
b Turriff, Scotland, May 3, 15. *Study:* Edinburgh Univ, MA, 36, LLB, 38. *Pos:* Admin dir, Can Opera Co, 72-76; gen mgr, Portland Opera Asn, Ore, 76-82; gen dir, Charlotte Opera, currently. *Mem:* Opera Am. *Mailing Add:* Charlotte Opera 110 E 7th St Charlotte NC 28202

CHAMBERLIN, ROBERT CHARLES
COMPOSER, EDUCATOR
b Hershey, Pa, Sept 1, 50. *Study:* St Olaf Col, BMus, 71; Southern Ill Univ, with Alan Oldfield, MM, 73; Univ Ill, with Ben Johnston. *Works:* 3 Pastimes 3, perf by Jacques & Gail Israelievitch, 81-82; Trio for Winds, perf by New Music Circle Perf Ens, 82; Duet Concertante, perf by Webster Symph Orch, 74. *Pos:* Mem, Ed Adv Bd, Music Business Handbk & Career Guide, 81- *Teaching:* Asst prof theory & comp, Webster Univ, 73- *Bibliog:* William Duckworth & Edward Brown (auth), Theoretical Foundations of Music, Wadsworth Publ Co, 78; Jane Berdes (auth), Webster: Arts School, Nat Cath Reporter, 10/26/79; Earl Henry (auth), Music Theory, Vol 2, Prentice Hall (in prep). *Mem:* Col Music Soc; Am Soc Univ Comp; New Music Circle St Louis (chmn music comt, 80-82). *Mailing Add:* 1036 Lancover Kirkwood MO 63122

CHAMBERS, JAMES
FRENCH HORN, EDUCATOR
b Trenton, NJ. *Study:* Curtis Inst Music, with Anton Horner, 38-41. *Pos:* Mem, Am Youth Orch, 40-41 & Pittsburgh Symph, 41-42; solo horn, Philadelphia Orch, 42-46; solo horn, New York Phil, 46-69, personnel mgr, 69-; performer, Aspen Fest, 57-58 & 74. *Teaching:* Mem fac, Curtis Inst Music, 42-46 & Manhattan Sch Music, 56-63; mem fac French horn & chamber music, Juilliard Sch, 46-; teacher, Aspen Music Sch, 57-58 & 74; woodwind & brass coach & cond, Stratford Shakespearean Fest, Ont, 66. *Mailing Add:* Juilliard Sch Lincoln Ctr New York NY 10023

CHAMBERS, VIRGINIA ANNE
EDUCATOR
b Middlesboro, Ky, Jan 28, 31. *Study:* Sch Music, Univ Louisville, BME, 52; Eastman Sch Music, MM, 64; Sch Music, Univ Mich, PhD, 70. *Teaching:* Elem gen music, Oak Ridge, Tenn, 52-63; instr, State Univ NY Col, Geneseo, 64-66 & Univ Wis, Madison, 68-75; prof theory & music educ, Univ Toledo, 75- *Mem:* Music Educr Nat Conf; Ohio Music Educr Asn. *Publ:* Auth, Words and Music: An Introduction to Music Literary, 76; coauth, Tometics: Reading Rhythm Patterns, 79, Tometics: Reading Tonal Patterns, 82, Reading Rhythm Patterns: Computerized Version, 82 & auth, Piano Accompaniments for A Nichol's Worth, Vols 3 & 4, 82, Tometic Assoc Ltd. *Rep:* Tometic Assoc Ltd 8545 Main St Suite 12 Buffalo NY 14221. *Mailing Add:* Ctr Perf Arts Univ Toledo 2801 W Bancroft St Toledo OH 43606

CHAMBERS, WENDY MAE
COMPOSER
Study: Barnard Col, with J Beeson, Charles Wuorinen & Nicholas Roussakis, BA, 75; State Univ NY, Stony Brook, with David Lewin, MA, 78; Univ Calif, San Diego, 79-80; study piano with Kenneth Cooper. *Pos:* Pres, Artmusic Inc, 80- *Works:* Real Music For 9 Cars, Potsdam, 78; Street Music, Washington Sq Park, 78; Music for Choreographed Rowboats, Central Park Lake, 79; The Village Green, Norwood, 80; Busy Box Quartet, La Jolla, 80; One World Percussion, World Trade Ctr Fountain Plaza, 81; Car Horn Organ Performances, Brooklyn Bride Centennial, 83. *Awards:* Alice M Ditson Fund Award, 79; New York State Coun Arts Grant, 80; Nat Endowment Arts Grant, 83. *Bibliog:* Howard Smith (auth), Scenes Column, Village Voice, 7/16/79; Irvin Molotsky (auth), New York Times, 7/20/79; Edward Rothstein (auth), Music Critic, New York Times, 9/29/81. *Mem:* Comp Forum. *Mailing Add:* 248 Sackett St Brooklyn NY 11231

CHAMBLEE, JAMES MONROE
EDUCATOR, MUSIC DIRECTOR
b Raleigh, NC, Jan 10, 35. *Study:* Univ NC, Chapel Hill, BA, PhD; Columbia Univ, MA. *Pos:* Dir, Raleigh Oratorio Soc; choir dir, Murfreesboro Baptist Church, NC. *Teaching:* Prof music, Gardner-Webb Col; dir, Summer Sch Chorus, Univ NC, Chapel Hill; prof music & chmn dept fine arts, Chowan Col, currently. *Mem:* Am Musicol Soc; Col Music Soc; Music Libr Asn; Asn Choral Cond; Music Teachers Nat Asn. *Publ:* Contribr, Am Music Teacher & Current Musicol. *Mailing Add:* 112 Springlake Dr Murfreesboro NC 27855

CHAMPION, DAVID (DAVID CAMESI)
EDUCATOR, TRUMPET
b Pittsburgh, Pa, June 14, 37. *Study:* Juilliard Sch Music, BS, 61; Columbia Univ, MA, 65. *Teaching:* Prof music, Calif State Univ, Dominguez Hills, 69- *Mem:* Col Music Soc; Am Musicol Soc; Music Educr Nat Conf; Am Symph Orch League. *Publ:* Auth, Eighteenth Century Conducting, J Res Music Educ, 70. *Mailing Add:* 229 15th St Manhattan Beach CA 90266

CHAMPLIN, TERRY (ARTHUR DOYLE), III
COMPOSER, GUITAR
b New Haven, Conn, Mar 2, 48. *Study:* Studied guitar with Garcia-Renart & comp with David Loeb. *Works:* Passeavase (violin & guitar), perf by comp & Mary Lou Saetta & comp & Carol Marie Harris, 80-83; Chamber Concerto (nine guitars), perf by Purchase Guitar Ens, 81 & 82; Children Playing (sop, alto, viola, perc & guitar), 82; Capitol Chamber Music (flute, string trio & guitar), comn & perf by Capitol Chamber Artists, 82 & 83; Solaris (two guitars), 83. *Teaching:* Fac mem guitar, Vassar Col, 76-; fac mem music tech & chamber music, Mannes Col Music, 80- *Mailing Add:* 23 Bowers Rd Rock Hill NY 12775

CHAN, TIMOTHY TAI-WAH
VIOLIN, CONDUCTOR & MUSIC DIRECTOR
b Hong Kong, Aug 31, 45; US citizen. *Study:* San Francisco Consv Music, BMus, 70; Calif State Univ, San Francisco, MA, 72. *Pos:* Concertmaster & soloist, San Francisco Consv Music Orch, 69-70; violinist, Marin Symph Orch, Calif, 71-72, San Francisco Symph Pops Orch, 71 & Oakland Symph Orch, Calif, 72- *Teaching:* Instr violin, privately, 64-, San Francisco Consv Music, 69-71; asst cond orch, Calif State Univ, San Francisco, 71-72. *Mem:* Am Fedn Musicians. *Mailing Add:* 2366 45th Ave San Francisco CA 94116

CHANCE, NANCY LAIRD
PIANO, COMPOSER
b Cincinnati, Ohio, Mar 19, 31. *Study:* Bryn Mawr Col, 49-50; Columbia Univ, 59-67, comp & comp with Vladimir Ussachesky, Otto Luening & Chou Wen-Chung; studied piano with Lilias MacKinnon & William R Smith. *Works:* Movements (string quartet), Am Music Ctr, 67; Motet (double chorus, a cappella), 69, Lyric Essays, 72, Edensong (sop, flute, clarinet, cello, harp & three perc), 73, Duos (sop & flute), 75, Ritual Sound (brass quintet & three perc), 75, Ceremonial (perc quartet), 76, Seesaw. *Teaching:* Piano, Kenya, 74-78. *Awards:* ASCAP Special Award, 78-79. *Bibliog:* Women Composers: Summergarden Concert, High Fidelity, Musical Am, Vol 25, 27-28. *Mem:* ASCAP; League Women Comp; Am Music Ctr Inc. *Mailing Add:* c/o Judith Finell 155 W 68th St New York NY 10023

CHANEY, SCOTT CLAY
VIOLA, VIOLIN
b Joliet, Ill, Apr 7, 41. *Study:* Drake Univ, with George Perlmman & Maya Vukovic, BME, 67. *Pos:* Violinist, Des Moines Symph Orch, 59-68 & Cabrillo Music Fest Orch, Calif, 67-; violinist & violist, Tulane Summer Lyric Theater Orch, 68-; violist, New Orleans Phil, 68- *Mailing Add:* 4201 St Charles Ave New Orleans LA 70115

CHANG, LYNN
VIOLIN, EDUCATOR
Study: New England Consv Prep Div, studied violin with Alfred Krips, 68; Juilliard Sch Pre-Col, studied with Ivan Galamian, 71; Harvard Univ, studied with Leon Kirchner, BA, 75. *Pos:* Participant, Marlboro Fest; solo & chamber music appearances throughout US & Far East. *Teaching:* Vis prof, Music Dept, Cornell Univ, 78-79; fac mem, Kneisel Hall, Maine, 79-; instr, Dept Music, Harvard Univ, 79-; fac mem, Boston Consv, 83- *Awards:* First Prize, Buffalo Phil Young Artists Compt, 72; Int Paganini Comp Prize, 74; Conct Artist Guild Award. *Mailing Add:* 1534 Cambridge St Cambridge MA 02139

CHAPIN, SCHUYLER GARRISON
ADMINISTRATOR, EDUCATOR
b New York, NY, Feb 13, 23. *Study:* Longy Sch Music. *Pos:* Vpres, Lincoln Ctr for Perf Arts, 64-68; exec prod, Amberson Prod, 68-71; gen mgr, Metropolitan Opera Coun, 72-75; dean, Sch Arts, Columbia Univ, 76- *Awards:* Emmy Awards, 71, 75 & 79; Gold Medal Music, Nat Arts Club New York, 83. *Mem:* Bagby Found Musical Arts (chmn, 80); Walter W Naumburg Found (bd mem, 60-); Nat Music Coun (bd mem, 76-); Am Symph Orch League (mem bd, 75-, chmn, 82-). *Publ:* Auth, Musical Chairs, A Life in the Arts, G P Putnam Sons, 77; Arts in China, Horizon, 79; Being Fired at Fifty, Prime Time, 80; Beverly Sills in China, New York Times, 81; Culture and the Tube, TV Quart, 81. *Mailing Add:* 901 Lexington Ave New York NY 10021

CHAPMAN, BASIL
CLARINET, EDUCATOR
Study: Trinity & Royal Sch Music, London, teachers dipl; Univ SAfrica, artists dipl; New England Consv Music, BM, MM; studied clarinet with Gino Cioffi & Peter Hadcock, comp with Donald Martino & chamber music with Gunther Schuller, Rudolf Kolisch & Harold Wright. *Pos:* Prin clarinet, Boston Civic Symph, formerly; chamber music perf, Boston; solo perf, SAfrica. *Teaching:* Fac mem clarinet, wind ens & chamber music, Longy Sch Music, currently. *Publ:* Auth, Impressions for Solo Trumpet and Electronic Tape. *Mailing Add:* Longy Sch Music One Follen St Cambridge MA 02138

CHAPMAN, CHARLES WAYNE
EDUCATOR, COMPOSER
b Ardmore, Okla, Oct 7, 36. *Study:* Univ Okla, BME, 58, MME, 62; Univ Tex, Austin, PhD, 71. *Works:* Peter Gray (opera), Southwestern Okla State Univ Opera Wkshp, 78; Why Aren't They in Cages (film score), Bingham Prod, 79; Sky Dancers (film score), Shawnee Britton Prod, 80. *Teaching:* Prof music, Southwestern Okla State Univ, 62- *Mem:* Music Educr Nat Conf (state pres, 81-82); Am Choral Dir Asn (state pres, 81-82); Alliance for Arts Educ (state chair, 83-); Nat Asn Teachers Singing; Am Guild Organists. *Publ:* Auth, Words, Music, and Translations, Nat Asn Teachers Singing, 77; How to Avoid Singing in a Vulgar Manner, J Am Choral Dir Asn, 80; Counterpoint, Nat Asn Teachers Singing, 81. *Mailing Add:* 621 N Broadway Weatherford OK 73096

CHAPMAN, ERIC JOHN
VIOLIN DEALER, VIOLIST
b Hartford, Conn, Sept 10, 42. *Study:* Hobart Col, BA, 64; Trinity Col, MA, 69; studied with Frederick William & Marion Eleanor. *Pos:* Violist, NH Phil Orch, 66-68, Ann Arbor Symph, 73-75 & Sarah Lawrence Chamber Orch, 78-; field services coordr, High Score Educ Res Found, 70-75; bd dir, Ann Arbor Symph, 73-75, Thoreau Sch, Eastern Conn State Col, 76-80, Sea Cliff Chamber Players, 80-; founder & exec dir, Ann Arbor Summer Symph, 74-77; pres, Eric Chapman Violins Inc 78- *Teaching:* Instr hist, St Paul Sch, 64-68; fel, Univ Mich, 68-70. *Mem:* Violin Soc Am (pres, 75-82 & hon dir, 82-); Am Viola Soc. *Mailing Add:* 37 Watkins Pl New Rochelle NY 10801

CHAPMAN, KEITH (RONALD)
ORGAN, COMPOSER
b San Mateo, Calif, July 16, 45. *Study:* Studied with Richard Purvis; Curtis Inst Music, with Alexander McCurdy, BM, 68; Temple Univ, MM, 71; Combs Col Music, DMA, 78. *Works:* Hearken All!, 76, The Learn'd Astronomer, 77, Which Way to Turn, 77, Psalm 121, 77, Let Us Now Praise Famous Men, 78 & Improvisations for Organ, McAfee Music Corp; Welcome Happy Morning, Richard Bradley Publ, 82. *Rec Perf:* Thus Spake Zarathustra, Philadelphia Orch, 72; Grand Court Organ, 72, Pictures at an Exhibition, 74, Airs and Arabesques, 76 & The Armory Organ, 77, Stentorian Prod. *Pos:* Head organist, John Wanamaker Grand Court Organ, Philadelphia, 66-; guest organist, Philadelphia Orch, 67- *Teaching:* Instr organ, Glassboro State Col, 77-79 & Combs Col Music, 78- *Bibliog:* Samuel Singer (auth), Music in Philadelphia, Philadelphia Inquirer, 76; Jean Garland (auth), The Chapman Classique, Keyboard World, 79. *Mem:* Am Guild Organists; Am Fedn Musicians; Musical Fund Soc, Philadelphia. *Publ:* Auth, Pastoral Musicians, 80- *Mailing Add:* 8525 Seminole St Philadelphia PA 19118

CHAPUIS, ISABELLE
FLUTE, EDUCATOR
b Dijon, France, Sept 6, 49. *Study:* Consv Nat Versailles, with Roger Bourdin, dipl(flute), 68; Consv Nat Paris, with Jean-Pierre Rampal & Pierre Pierlot, dipl(flute), 70, dipl(chamber music), 72. *Pos:* Prin flute, San Francisco Chamber Orch, 77- & San Jose Community Opera Theater, 81-; solo artist, Young Audiences Bay Area, 80-; substitute prin flute, San Jose Symph, 80-82; flute soloist with orchs in US & Europe incl Calif Bach Soc, Berkeley, L'Orch Chambre L'ORTF, Paris, Milwaukee Civic Symph Orch, Pac Phil, San Mateo, L'Orch Symphonique Jeunesse Musicale Belgique & Bach-to-Mozart Fest Orch, Mill Valley; ed, J Calif Music Teachers Asn, currently. *Teaching:* Asst prof flute, San Jose State Univ, 75-; instr, Col Notre Dame, Calif, 81- *Awards:* Premier Prix Flute, Consv Nat Versailles, 69; Premier Prix, Flute, 69 & Chamber Music, 72, Consv Nat Paris, 72. *Mem:* Am Fedn Musicians; Nat Flute Asn; Calif Music Teachers Asn. *Publ:* Auth, Using Time Effectively for Flute Study, 80 & How Flutists Breathe, 83, J Calif Music Teachers Asn. *Rep:* Albert Kay Assoc 58 W 58th St New York NY 10019. *Mailing Add:* 132 Loucks Ave Los Altos CA 94022

CHARKEY, STANLEY
GUITAR & LUTE, EDUCATOR
b Brooklyn, NY, July 8, 48. *Study:* Hartt Col Music, BM, 70; Univ Mass, MM, 72. *Works:* Ephemera, 83 & Night Call, 83, perf by Jane Bryden, Memphis State Univ. *Rec Perf:* Ma Daphne, Musical Heritage, 72; Dances of Orchesography, Arabesque, 83. *Pos:* Lutanist, New York Pro Musica, 70-72, New York Renaissance Band, 78- & Jones-Charkey Duo, 80- *Teaching:* Artist in res, Sarah Lawrence Col, 75-78; prof music theory & hist, Marlboro Col, 78- *Awards:* Bodky Award Perf Early Music, Cambridge Soc, 70. *Mem:* Am Musicol Soc; Col Music Soc. *Mailing Add:* 98 Prospect St Brattleboro VT 05301

CHARRY, MICHAEL (RONALD)
CONDUCTOR & MUSIC DIRECTOR
b New York, NY, Aug 28, 33. *Study:* Oberlin Consv Music, 50-52; Juilliard Sch Music, orch cond with Jean Morel, BS, 55, MS, 56. *Pos:* Apprentice & asst cond, Cleveland Orch, 61-72; music dir & cond, Canton Symph, 61-74, Nashville Symph, 76-82 & Peninsula Music Fest, 78-82. *Teaching:* Assoc prof orch cond, Sch Music, Syracuse Univ, 83- *Awards:* Fulbright Scholar, Hamburg, Germany, 56-57; Grant in Aid, Martha Baird Rockefeller Found, 73; Alice M Ditson Award, Columbia Univ, 81. *Mailing Add:* Two Lincoln Sq Apt 6E New York NY 10023

CHASE, ALLAN STUART
EDUCATOR, SAXOPHONE
b Willimantic, Conn, June 22, 56. *Study:* Ariz State Univ, BMus, 78; Creative Music Studio, Woodstock, NY, study with Roscoe Mitchell & Anthony Braxton, 78 & 79; New England Consv Music, study with Joe Allard, 80-81. *Works:* Songs (ms, cello & piano), 78; Opening (alto sax & piano), comn by James Ferrell, 79; Song for What's Gone, 82 & One Breath (four women's voices & four sax), 82, Your Neighborhood Sax Quartet. *Pos:* Saxophonist, Charles Lewis Quintet, Phoenix, Ariz, 75-80 & Prince Shell Big Band, Phoenix, 77-80; co-leader, Lewis Nash-Allan Chase Duo, Phoenix, 79-80 & Your Neighborhood Saxophone Quartet, Boston, 81- *Teaching:* Dept assoc, Berklee Col Music, 81- *Mailing Add:* 25 Wendell St Apt 1 Cambridge MA 02138

CHASE, JOSEPH RUSSELL
EDUCATOR
b Eastham, Mass, Mar 9, 22. *Study:* Calvin Coolidge Col, BSc, MEd. *Pos:* Music therapist for 20 yrs. *Teaching:* Co-founder, Cape Cod Consv Music, instr piano & theory, 63-70; studio & conct accmp, music therapist; piano teacher for 40 yrs; instr, Kingsley Sch, Boston & Parents Sch for Atypical Children, Chatham, Mass. *Awards:* George B Baker Scholar Music, 40; Founders Medal, Nat Guild Piano Teachers, 70. *Mem:* Nat Asn Music Therapy; Nat Guild Piano Teachers; Int Soc Musical Educ; Music Teachers Nat Asn; Nat Asn Teachers Singing. *Mailing Add:* Salt Pond Rd PO Box 228 Eastham MA 02642

CHASE, SAM
WRITER, ADMINISTRATOR
b New York, NY. *Pos:* Ed in chief & assoc publ, Billboard Mag; ed & publ, Music Bus Mag; pres, Chase Assocs, Inc; founder, publ & ed, Ovation Mag, 80- *Awards:* Deems Taylor Award, ASCAP, 81. *Mem:* Bohemians. *Mailing Add:* Ovation Mag 320 W 57th St New York NY 10019

CHASE, STEPHANIE ANN
VIOLIN, EDUCATOR
b Evanston, Ill, Oct 1, 57. *Study:* Studied with Fannie Chase, 59-66, Sally Thomas, 66-76, Arthur Grumiaux, 76- & chamber music with Josef Gingold. *Pos:* Violinist with major US & Europ orchs & on TV & radio. *Teaching:* Fac mem, Boston Consv, currently. *Awards:* First Prize, G B Dealey Award, 78; Ima Hogg Young Artists Compt Award, 78; Bronze Medal, Tchaikovsky Compt, 82. *Mailing Add:* Boston Consv 8 The Fenway Boston MA 02215

CHASINS, ABRAM
COMPOSER, PIANO
b New York, NY, Aug 17, 03. *Study:* Juilliard Found, studied piano with Ernest Hutcheson & comp with Rubin Goldmark, 22-26; Curtis Inst, with Josef Hofmann, 26-36; studied with Donal F Tovey, London, 31. *Works:* 105 publ works for orch, piano, two pianos, songs & others, 25-50; First Piano Concerto, Philadelphia Orch; three Chinese pieces, 24 preludes, narrative & others perf by Hofmann, Moiseiewitsch, Bachaus, Serkin, Hess & others, 25-; Parade (orch), perf by New York Phil, 31. *Rec Perf:* All Chopin, All Bach, All Brahms, HMV, 31; perf own comp, rec by Protone, Mercury, Kapp & Philips, 50-; Three Chinese Pieces, RCA Victor, 60-73. *Pos:* Recitalist & soloist with leading orch in Am & Europe, 25-46; found & dir, WQXR, radio station of New York Times, 46-71; adjudicator, Leventritt Found, Metropolitan Opera Auditions, New York Phil Youth Conct, Chopin Prize, Rachmaninoff Award & Van Cliburn Compt, formerly. *Teaching:* Piano, Third St Settlement, 17-20; asst to Ernest Hutcheson, Juilliard Sch, 23-26; mem fac, Curtis Inst, 25-36, Berkshire Music Ctr, 39-40; emer prof, Univ Southern Calif, 72-77. *Awards:* Three Distinguished Serv on Behalf of World War II, US Treas Dept, 42-44; Peabody Award, 61; Serv to USA Music, Nat Fedn Music Clubs, 76. *Publ:* Auth, Speaking of Pianists, Knopf, 57; The Van Cliburn Legend, Doubleday, 59; The Appreciation of Music, Crown, 66; Music At The Crossroads, Macmillan, 72; Leopold Stokowski—A Profile, Hawthorne-Dutton, 79. *Mailing Add:* 10717 Wilshire Blvd Los Angeles CA 90024

CHATHAM, RHYS
COMPOSER
b New York, NY, Sept 19, 52. *Study:* NY Univ, 68-70; studied with Morton Subotnick & LaMonte Young. *Works:* For Brass, comn by Paris Opera, 82; Drastic Classicism, Antartica Label, 82; Guitar Ring, Moers Music Label, 83; Guitar Trio, Lovely Music Label, 83; Battery 1-3, comn by Creative Time,

Inc, 83. *Pos:* Music dir & co-founder, Kitchen Ctr, 71-73 & 77-80. *Awards:* Intermedia Grants, Meet the Comp, Inc, 80 & Creative Artists Pub Serv, 81; Inter-Arts Grant, Nat Endowment for Arts, 82. *Bibliog:* John Rockwell (auth), Classical Road to Rock, New York Times, 4/81; Gregory Sandow (auth), The New New Music, Village Voice, 5/81; Steve Rogers (auth), Minimalist Headbangers, Perf Mag, 1/83. *Mem:* BMI. *Rep:* Performing Arts Serv 325 Spring St New York NY 10012. *Mailing Add:* 129 First Ave #3A New York NY 10003

CHAUDOIR, JAMES EDWARD
COMPOSER, CONDUCTOR
b Baton Rouge, La, July 24, 46. *Study:* La State Univ, BM, 70, MM, 74; Univ Md, DMA, 77. *Works:* Textures, Dorn Publ Inc, 79; Ave Maria (SSAA), comn by Tex Woman's Univ, 79; String Quartet, New Times String Quartet, 80; Conjunctive Parallels, Contemp Music Forum, 80; Three Dance Interludes, Dorn Publ Inc, 81; Nuages, Autumn Fest Contemp Music, 80; Concerto (tuba & wind ens), Ohio Univ Wind Ens, 83. *Teaching:* Asst prof theory & comp, Tex Woman's Univ, 78-81; asst prof comp, Ohio Univ, 81- *Mem:* ASCAP; Am Soc Univ Comp; Southeastern Comp League; Nat Asn Comp; Tubist Universal Brotherhood Asn. *Mailing Add:* 257 Highland Ave Athens OH 45701

CHAULS, ROBERT N
COMPOSER, CONDUCTOR
b Port Chester, NY, July 18, 42. *Study:* Royal Col Music, London, 63; Antioch Col, BA, 64; Univ Mich, MMus, 66; Univ Southern Calif, DMA, 72. *Works:* Sonata-Fantasy (piano trio), Willamette Univ Trio, 66; Nasherei (sop & brass quintet), Neva Pilgrim-Modern Brass Quintet, 69; Nicholas Christmas (children's choir), J T Dye Sch Choir, 74; Alice in Wonderland (opera), Belwin-Mills, 74. *Pos:* Artistic dir & cond, Valley Opera, 77- *Teaching:* Asst prof music, Willamette Univ, 66-70; prof, Los Angeles Valley Col, 73- *Awards:* Northern Bavarian Critics Award, 63; Compt Award, Nat Fedn Music Clubs, 65 & 68 & O'Neill Opera-Music Theatre Conf, 83. *Mem:* Nat Opera Asn; Musicians Union; Cent Opera Serv. *Mailing Add:* 3457 Valley Meadow Rd Sherman Oaks CA 91403

CHAUNCEY, BEATRICE ARLENE
EDUCATOR, FLUTE
b Akron, Ohio. *Study:* Univ Akron, BS; Columbia Univ, MA. *Teaching:* Prof music, ECarolina Univ, 49- *Mem:* Nat Flute Asn; Music Educr Nat Conf; NC Music Educr Conf. *Mailing Add:* 1405 N Overlook Dr Greenville NC 27834

CHAZANOFF, DANIEL
LECTURER, CELLO
b New York, NY, Mar 1, 23. *Study:* Ohio State Univ, BSc, 49; Columbia Univ, MA, 51, EdD, 64. *Pos:* Asst prin cellist, Ohio State Univ Symph, 46-49; cellist, Berkshire Music Fest, Tanglewood, summer 50; prin cellist, Columbia Univ Little Symph, 50-51; asst prin cellist, Birmingham Symph, Ala, 51-52. *Teaching:* Asst prof music, Northern State Col, 57-59; lectr music appreciation, Bronx Community Col, City Univ New York, 59-64; supvr music, City Sch District, Rochester, NY, 64-76. *Awards:* Res grant, Nat Found Jewish Cul, 69. *Mem:* Col Music Soc; Music Educr Nat Conf; Am String Teachers Asn. *Interests:* String literature; music history; music education. *Publ:* Ed, Music Round the School Year, Hargail Music Press, 66; auth, Musical Instruments for 1971—Violins & Guitars, Consumer Guide, 70; Articulating Music and Foreign Language Study, Language Asn Bulletin, 76; Salamone Rossi and the Baroque Sonata in Italy, The Strad, London, 81. *Mailing Add:* 114 Penarrow Rd Rochester NY 14618

CHEADLE, LOUISE M
PIANO, ADMINISTRATOR
b Donora, Pa, July 4, 36. *Study:* Studied with Sascha Gorodnitzki, 55-59; Juilliard Sch, artist dipl, 59. *Pos:* Performer & wkshps cond, Louise & William Cheadle, Piano-Duettists & Duo-Pianists, 59-; dir prep div, Westminster Choir Col, 72-77, dir Consv, 77-82; ed & publ newsletter, Piano for Two, Nat Publ, 82- *Teaching:* Instr piano, Westminster Choir Col, 72-82; adj instr, Mercer Co Col, 77-78; freelance piano, Princeton, NJ, 82- *Mem:* Piano Teachers Cong New York; Music Educr Asn NJ; Am Col Musicians; Music Club Princeton (secy, 72-73). *Publ:* Coauth, Piano Ensemble—From Memory or from the Score, Clavier, 79; contribr, chap on duets, In: Teaching Piano, Bk II, Yorktown Publ, 81; ed, Piano for Two Quarterly Newsletter & Directory, private publ, 82-83. *Rep:* C & C Mgt PO Box 109 Kingston NJ 08528. *Mailing Add:* 338 Hamilton Ave Princeton NJ 08540

CHEADLE, WILLIAM G
PIANO, COMPOSER
b Detroit, Mich, Dec 11, 38. *Study:* Juilliard Sch, with Sascha Gorodnitzki, BM(piano), 56-61, with Adele Marcus, MS(piano), 64-65. *Works:* Skip To My Lou and Others Too (piano quartet), 79, Picture Postcards Set I (piano duet), 80, Set II, 81 & Six for Three (6 pieces for piano trio), 81, Myklas Press. *Teaching:* Instr piano, Music Sch, Henry St Settlement, New York, 57-65; Bronx House Music Sch, 61-65; assoc prof piano, Westminster Choir Col, Princeton, 65- *Awards:* Kresge Found Grants, 56-61; Kosciuszko Found, Chopin Scholar Award, 59. *Mem:* ASCAP; Piano Teachers Cong New York; NJ Comp Guild. *Publ:* Coauth, Piano Ensemble Performance: From Memory or From the Score? Clavier Mag, 12/78; contribr, The Repertory of Piano Duets/Duos, Teaching Piano, 81; auth, Musicately (and Piano-Ately), A Look At Musical Stamp Collecting, Piano Quart, winter 81-82. *Mailing Add:* c/o C & C Mgt PO Box 109 Kingston NJ 08528

CHECCHIA, ANTHONY PHILLIP
ADMINISTRATOR, MUSIC DIRECTOR
b Philadelphia, Pa, June 4, 30. *Study:* New Sch Music, 47-48; Curtis Inst, 50-51. *Pos:* First bassoonist, New York City Ctr Ballet Orch, 57-62; mgr, Marlboro Sch & Fest, 58-; music dir, Philadelphia Chap Young Audiences, 62-68; asst dir, Curtis Inst Music, 68-77. *Mem:* Musical Fund Soc (mem bd dir, 83). *Mailing Add:* 135 S 18th St Philadelphia PA 19103

CHEEK, JOHN TAYLOR
BASS-BARITONE
b Greenville, SC, Aug 17, 48. *Study:* NC Sch Arts, BM, 70; Accad Chigiana, Siena, Italy, dipl merito, 69; Manhattan Sch Music, 71. *Rec Perf:* Mass John K Paine, New World, 78; Mefistofele Prologue, Telarc, 79; Tosca (Angelotti), EMI, 80; Messiah, RCA, 82. *Roles:* Pimen in Boris Godunov, 77, Oroveso in Norma, 82 & Alvise in La Gioconda, 82, Metropolitan Opera. *Mailing Add:* 201 W 77th St New York NY 10024

CHELSI, LAWRENCE G
BARITONE, TEACHER-COACH
b Portland, Ore, July 2, 30. *Study:* Juilliard Sch; Columbia Univ; Univ Calif, Los Angeles; Univ Ore, MA(music, voice, piano & repertoire), 56; study with Giuseppe DeLuca, Giovanni Martinelli, Martial Singher & Eva Gauthier. *Rec Perf:* American Songs (Robert Shaw), RCA Victor Rec; Songs of the American Revolution, CBS Masterworks Rec; French Art Songs & Offenbach Operettas, Magic-Tone Rec; Shakespearian Songs, Rondo Rec; Chelsi Sings, London Rec; The Housewives' Cantata, Original Cast Rec. *Teaching:* Prof voice & coach, NY Univ, 80- *Bibliog:* Emmons & Sonntag (auth), The Art Of The Song Recital, Schirmer Books, 79; New York Times Theatre Directory, New York Times/ARNO; Miller, P L (auth), Guide To Long Playing Records, Alfred A Knopf Inc. *Mem:* New York Singing Teachers Asn (bd mem, 78-82 & vpres, 82-); Nat Asn Teachers Singing; BMI; Am Fedn TV & Radio Asn. *Interests:* Intensive operatic research; performance history. *Publ:* Coauth, Metropolitan Opera Broadcast Scripts, Int Broadcasts, 76-77. *Mailing Add:* 17 Park Ave New York NY 10016

CHENETTE, LOUIS FRED
EDUCATOR, ADMINISTRATOR
b Powersville, Iowa, Apr 2, 31. *Study:* Wheaton Col, BA, 53; Northwestern Univ, MM, 56; Ohio State Univ, PhD, 67. *Teaching:* Dir music, Antioch Twp High Sch, Ill, 53-58; dir bands, Bemidji State Col, 58-59; head dept music, asst to pres & actg pres, Findlay Col, 60-72; dean, Jordan Col Fine Arts, Butler Univ, 72- *Mem:* Am Musicol Soc; Int Musicol Soc; Phi Kappa Lambda; Phi Mu Alpha Sinfonia. *Interests:* Music theory in the British Isles during the Enlightenment. *Publ:* Auth, Establishing a Standard for Articulation Markings, Instrumentalist, 61; Perceptive Listening, Key to Improved Performance, Sch Musician, 65; The Harmonic Art of Giorgio Antoniotto, 71; Notes on a Noble Cellist, 81. *Mailing Add:* 45 Dickson Rd Indianapolis IN 46226

CHENOWETH, VIDA
EDUCATOR, MARIMBA
b Enid, Okla. *Study:* William Woods Col, AA, 49; Northwestern Univ, BM, 51; Am Consv Music, MM, 53; Univ Aukland, PhD, 74. *Rec Perf:* Vida Chenoweth, Marimbist, Epic Rec, 56-66. *Pos:* Conct artist, Columbia Conct Bur, 56-66; int consult ethnomusicol, Summer Inst Linguistics, 56- *Teaching:* Prof ethnomusicol, Wheaton Col, 77- *Mem:* Soc Ethnomusicol. *Publ:* Auth, Marimbas of Guatemala, Univ Ky Press, 65; Informatin on the Marimba, Christian Communications, 76; The Usarufas & Their Music, 77 & Music for the Eastern Highlands, 78, SIL; New Testament in Usarufa, Park Press, 81. *Mailing Add:* Music Dept Wheaton Col Wheaton IL 60187

CHERKASSKY, SHURA
PIANO
b Odessa, USSR, Oct 7, 11; US citizen. *Study:* With Lydia Schlemenson; Curtis Inst Music, with Josef Hofmann. *Rec Perf:* Russian music, notably Tchaikovsky, Rachmaninov & Prokofiev on Deutsche Grammophon, Philips & Decca. *Pos:* Concert pianist touring worldwide. *Mailing Add:* c/o Sheldon Soffer Mgt 130 W 56th St New York NY 10019

CHERRY, KALMAN
PERCUSSION, EDUCATOR
b Philadelphia, Pa, Apr 9, 37. *Study:* Curtis Inst Music, dipl, 58. *Pos:* Timpanist, Dallas Symph Orch, 58-; performer, Marlboro Music Fest & Bethlehem Bach Fest, Pa. *Teaching:* Mem fac, NTex State Univ; adj prof perc, Southern Methodist Univ, currently; private instr & clinician. *Mem:* Percussive Arts Soc. *Mailing Add:* Music Dept Southern Methodist Univ Dallas TX 75275

CHERRY, PHILIP
CELLO
b Philadelphia, Pa, July 31, 23. *Study:* Juilliard Sch Music, with Felix Salmond, BS, 50; Teachers Col, Columbia Univ, MA, 51. *Pos:* Prin cello, St Louis Symph, 51-52; Buffalo Phil, 52-53; Casals Fest Orch, 57-80 & Metropolitan Opera Orch, 61- *Teaching:* Instr music theory, Colo Col, 53-54. *Mailing Add:* 70 W 95th St Apt 19C New York NY 10025

CHEVALIER, CHARLOTTE BERGERSEN See Bergersen, Charlotte

CHEVALLARD, (PHILIP) CARL
CONDUCTOR & MUSIC DIRECTOR, EDUCATOR
b Columbus, Ohio, June 17, 50. *Study:* Ohio State Univ, BME, 72; Univ Iowa, MA, 76, PhD, 82. *Rec Perf:* Tenor tuba & euphonium soloist, San Jose Symph, 79-82 & munic bands in Ohio, Iowa & Calif, 72-83. *Pos:* Asst dir bands, Mich State Univ, 77-79; dir bands, San Jose State Univ, 79-83; asst cond, US Air Force Band, 83- *Mem:* Col Band Dir Nat Asn (state chmn, 81-83); Nat Band Asn (state chmn, 82-83); Music Educr Nat Conf; Am Fedn Musicians. *Interests:* Psychoacoustics; pitch perception. *Mailing Add:* US Air Force Band Bolling AFB Washington DC 20332

CHIHARA, PAUL SEIKO
COMPOSER
b Seattle, Wash, July 9, 38. *Study:* Univ Wash, BA, 60; Cornell Univ, with Robert Plamer, MA, 61, DMA, 65; studied with Nadia Boulanger, Paris, 61-62, Ernst Pepping, Berlin, 65-66; Berkshire Music Ctr, with Gunther Schuller, 66-68. *Works:* Symphony in Celebration, 75; Shin-Ju (ballet), 76, Two Symphonies, 76-82, Saxophone Concerto, 80 & The Tempest (ballet in 2 acts), 80, C F Peters; Prince of the City (movie), Warner Brothers. *Pos:* Comp in res, San Fransisco Ballet, 79-; appeared as performer, cond & comp in concts in US, Japan & Mex. *Teaching:* Prof music, Univ Calif, Los Angeles, 66-73; instr comp, Calif Inst Arts, 75. *Awards:* Fulbright Fel, 65; Nat Endowment Arts Grant, 73; Guggenheim Fel, 75. *Mem:* ASCAP. *Mailing Add:* 11734 Tennessee Pl Los Angeles CA 90064

CHIHUARIA, ERNESTINE (ELIZABETH) RIEDEL
VIOLIN
b Oakland, Calif. *Study:* San Francisco Consv Music, 54; Univ Calif, Los Angeles, master class with Jascha Heifetz, 59; Mozarteum, Salzburg, 61. *Rec Perf:* Violin solos & sonatas for Rias, Berlin; Works of Dello-Joio & Walton Violin Sonata, Nord Deutsche Rundfunk, Köln; Walton Violin Concerto, BBC. *Pos:* First violin, Oakland Symph, 62-63 & San Francisco Symph, 64-; recitalist, US, Mex & Europe, 63- *Mailing Add:* San Francisco Symph Davies Symph Hall San Francisco CA 94102

CHILD, PETER BURLINGHAM
COMPOSER
b Great Yarmouth, England, May 6, 53. *Study:* Reed Col, BA, 75; Berkshire Music Ctr, study with Jacob Druckman, 78; Brandeis Univ, study with Arthur Berger, Martin Boykan & Seymour Shifrin, PhD, 81. *Works:* Sonata for Piano, 77 & Heracliti Reliquiae, 78, Asn for Prom New Music; Duo for Flute & Percussion, Mobart Music Publ, 79; Ensemblance, comn by Boston Musica Viva, 82; Wind Quintet, Emmanuel Wind Quintet, 83; Teneramente, League Int Soc Comtemp Music, Boston, 83; Embers, comn by Alea III (in prep). *Teaching:* Asst prof music, Brandeis Univ, Waltham, 79- *Awards:* Margaret Grant Mem Prize, Berkshire Music Ctr, 78; First Prize, East & West Artists, 79; New Works Prize, New England Consv Music, 83. *Mem:* BMI. *Mailing Add:* 13 Worcester St Belmont MA 02178

CHILDS, BARNEY SANFORD
COMPOSER, WRITER
b Spokane, Wash, Feb 13, 26. *Study:* Deep Springs Col, 43-45; Univ Nev, BA, 49; Oxford Univ, BA, 51, MA, 55; Stanford Univ, PhD, 59; studied with Carlos Chavez, Aaron Copland & Elliott Carter. *Works:* Music for Two Flute Players, Merion Music Inc, 69; Concerto for Clarinet and Orchestra, comn & perf by Milwaukee Symph Orch, 70-71; Keet Seel (a capella choir), Am Comp Alliance, 76; Any Five (any five of the eight parts provided), Smith Publ, 77; Music for Piano and Strings, Pembroke Music Co, 79; Welcome to Whipperginny (perc 9 players), Music Perc, 80; Four Pieces for Six Winds, Dorn Publ, 81. *Pos:* Comp in res, Wis Consv Music, 69-71; dir, new music ens, Univ Redlands, 71-; co-ed, The New Instrumentation Series, Univ Calif, 74- *Teaching:* Instr English, Univ Ariz, 56-61, asst prof, 61-65; dean, Deep Springs Col, 65-69; fac fel music & lit, Johnston Col, Univ Redlands, 71-73; prof comp & music lit, Univ Redlands, 73- *Mem:* Am Comp Alliance; Am Soc Univ Comp (nat coun, 67-70, 74-77 & exec comt 70-73); Am Music Soc, England; Charles Ives Ctr Am Music. *Publ:* Auth, Some Anniversaries, Proc Am Soc Univ Comp, 75; Time and Music: A Composer's View, Perspectives of New Music, 77; Poetic and Musical Rhythm: One More Time, Music Theory: Spec Topics, 81. *Mailing Add:* Sch Music Univ Redlands Redlands CA 92373

CHILDS, EDWIN T
EDUCATOR, COMPOSER
b Plymouth, NH, Jan 7, 45. *Study:* Wheaton Col, with Jack Goode, BMus, 67; Eastman Sch Music, with Samuel Adler & Wayne Barlow, PhD, 74; studied with Alice Parker. *Works:* Two Communion Meditations (organ), H W Gray Co, 80; Fantasia on Leoni (organ), Harold Flammer Music, 81; Joyful Songs (SATB with organ), Augsburg Publ House, 82. *Teaching:* Asst prof theory & comp, Philadelphia Col Bible, 73-78; adj fac theory, Temple Univ, 77-78; prof theory & comp, Biola Univ, 78- *Mem:* Am Guild Organists; ASCAP; Hymn Soc Am. *Mailing Add:* 14757 Fairvilla Dr La Mirada CA 90638

CHILDS, GORDON BLISS
EDUCATOR, VIOLA
b Springville, Utah, Oct 22, 27. *Study:* Brigham Young Univ, BA(music educ), 50, MA(musicol), 53; Univ Mont, EdD(music admin), 76. *Rec Perf:* Ancient Instruments Ensemble in Concert, Adams State Col, 75. *Pos:* Soloist & lectr, viola d'amore, most Western states, 53-; founding mem & second violin, Montana String Quartet, Missoula, 56-60; violinist & dir, Adams State Col Fac Trio, 67-72; string specialist, Ancient Instrm Ens, Alamosa, Colo, 71-81. *Teaching:* Asst prof string & music theory, Univ Mont, 56-60; prof orch & music hist & head music dept, Adams State Col, 60-81; prof chamber music & coordr music educ, Univ Wyo, 81- *Biblog:* Bob Swerengin (auth), Reviving the Viola d'Amore, Wyo Horizons Mag, 6/82. *Mem:* Music Educr Nat Conf (chmn Northwest orch, 83); Am String Teachers Asn (pres Colo unit, 62-66); Am Musicol Soc (secy Rocky Mountain chap, 67); Viola d'Amore Soc Am (chmn first int cong, 82); Viola Res Soc. *Interests:* The history, technique and literature of the Viola d'Amore. *Publ:* Auth, An Interview with Sergiu Luca, Colo Am String Teachers Asn Newslett, 78; The Lack of People that Showed Up, Colo Music Educ J, 79 & Wyo Music Educ J, 81; Bow Tips, Wyo Music Educ J, 82; John Hilgendorf and Utah's First Baby Orchestra, Am String Teachers Asn J, 83. *Mailing Add:* 1552 N 18th Laramie WY 82070

CHOBANIAN, LORIS OHANNES
COMPOSER, GUITAR & LUTE
b Mosul, Iraq, Apr 17, 33; US citizen. *Study:* La State Univ, with Kenneth Klaus, BM, 64, MM, 66; Mich State Univ, with H Owen Reed, PhD, 70. *Works:* Sonics (four guitars), comn by Cleveland Area Arts Coun; Sumer and Akkad (chamber ens, perc & dancers), WMSB-TV, East Lansing, 69; The Gift (Christmas ballet); Guitar Concerto, East Lansing, 71; Soliloquy—Testament of a Madman (bar & orch); Capriccio (wind ens with piano solo), Berea, 74; Music for Brass and Timpani, 78. *Pos:* Guitarist in concerts & on TV. *Teaching:* Prof lute, Consv Music, Oberlin Col, formerly; mem fac, Muskegon Community Col, 68-70; assoc prof orch, comp & guitar, Baldwin-Wallace Col, 70- *Awards:* ASCAP Awards, 74-79; Cleveland Area Arts Coun Grant, 77; Am String Teachers Asn Award, 77. *Mem:* ASCAP; Am String Teachers Asn. *Mailing Add:* 26716 Redwood Dr Olmsted Falls OH 44138

CHODOS, GABRIEL
PIANO, EDUCATOR
b White Plains, NY, Feb 7, 39. *Study:* Studied with Aube Tzerko, Los Angeles, 55-63; Univ Calif, Los Angeles, BA, 59, MA, 64; Akad Musik, Vienna, dipl, 66. *Rec Perf:* Sonata (Bartok), Vision & Prophecies (Bloch) & Prelude, Aria et Final (Franck), 73 & Sonata in B-flat major (Schubert), 76, Orion Rec; Various Composers: Encore Favorites (two rec), Japan Victor, 77 & 78. *Teaching:* From instr to asst prof piano, Univ Ore, 63-68; asst prof, State Univ NY, Buffalo, 68-70; from assoc prof to prof music, Dartmouth Col, 70-78; mem fac piano, New England Consv, 74-80, chmn piano dept, 80- *Awards:* Fulbright Scholar, 65; Conct Artists Guild Award, 70; Martha Baird Rockefeller Grant, 70 & 74. *Rep:* Aaron & Gorden Conct Mgt 25 Huntington Ave Boston MA 02116. *Mailing Add:* 245 Waban Ave Waban MA 02168

CHORBAJIAN, JOHN
COMPOSER
b New York, NY, June 2, 36. *Study:* Manhattan Sch Music, BMus, 57, MMus, 59. *Works:* Four Christmas Psalms (sop solo, mixed chorus & orch), 61; Bitter for Sweet, 69, When David Heard That His Son Was Slain, 73, Vital Spark of Heavenly Flame, 76, In the Bleak Mid-Winter, 79, A Dream Within a Dream, 79 & Three Poems From A Shropshire Lad, 80, G Schirmer. *Teaching:* Private instr comp & piano. *Awards:* Ford Found Comp in Res Award, 61-62. *Mem:* ASCAP; Am Music Ctr. *Mailing Add:* 57-36 138th St Flushing NY 11355

CHOSET, FRANKLIN
CONDUCTOR, DIRECTOR—OPERA
b New York, NY, Feb 15, 34. *Study:* New England Consv Music, with Boris Goldovsky. *Rec Perf:* For Israel Broadcasting. *Pos:* Cond, US Army Orch, Stuttgart, Israel Nat Opera, Tel Aviv, Romanian State Opera, Bucharest, Oak Ridge Fest Grand Opera & Caracas Opera Ctr, formerly; guest cond, Jerusalem Symph Orch, New York City Opera, Maracaibo Symph Orch & Univ Ala Ann Contemp Music Forum, formerly; gen mgr & musical dir, Miss Opera, currently; dir, Miss Opera Chorus, currently. *Awards:* Fulbright-Hays Grant, Austria. *Mailing Add:* Miss Opera PO Box 1551 Jackson MS 39205

CHOU, WEN-CHUNG
COMPOSER, EDUCATOR
b Chefoo, China, July 28, 23, nat US. *Study:* Nat Chunking Univ, BS, 45; New England Consv Music, 46-49; Columbia Univ, MA, 54; studied with Edgard Varese, 49-54. *Works:* Metaphors (wind symph orch), 60-61, Cursive (flute & piano), 63, The Dark and The Light (piano, perc, & strings), 64, Riding the Wind (wind symph orch), 64 & Yü Ko (Nine Players), 65, C F Peters. *Pos:* Comp in res, Fest Arts of This Century, East-West Ctr, Honolulu, 67; dir, Ctr US-China Arts Exchange, 78- *Teaching:* Res assoc music, Univ Ill, 58-59; lectr, Brooklyn Col 61-62; Hunter Col, 63-64; asst prof Columbia Univ, 64-68; assoc prof, 68-72, prof, 72-, chmn music div, Sch Arts, 69-, assoc dean, 75-76 & vdean, 76-; chmn comp comt, music dept, Columbia Univ, 69-74 & music div, Sch Arts, 69- *Awards:* William & Mona Copley Found Award, 66; Alice M Ditson Fund Grant, 69; Nat Endowment Arts Grant, 75. *Biblog:* Hugh Miller (auth), History of Music, 3rd ed, 60; Nicolas Slonimsky (auth), Chou Wen-chung, Am Comp Alliance Bulletin, Vol 9, No 4, 61; Gilbert Chase (auth), America's Music, rev ed, 66. *Mem:* Soc Asian Music (bd mem, 67-); found mem, Am Soc Univ Comp; Am Comp Alliance; Int Soc Contemp Music; Soc Ethnomusicol. *Publ:* Chinese Historiography and Music; Some Observations, Musical Quart, 4/76; Chinese Historiography and Music: The Use and Misuse of Historical and Musical Information, Occas Papers, No 7, Ariz State Univ, 10/76; A Half Century of Varese, Musical Heritage Rev, Vol 1, No 18, 1/78; Ionisation, Die Reihe Musik-Konzepte 6, Müchen, 78; Ionisation: The Function of Timbres in its Formal and Temporal Organization, Monogr, Inst Studies Am Music, Brooklyn Col, 78. *Mailing Add:* Deans Off Sch Arts Columbia Univ 615 Dodge New York NY 10027

CHOUINARD, JOSEPH JEROD
LIBRARIAN, BASS
b Middletown, Conn, May 7, 26. *Study:* Univ Conn, Storrs, BA, 50, MA, 51; voice study in Fontainebleau, France; private study in Paris, 57-58; State Univ NY, Geneseo, MLS, 70. *Roles:* Soloist in opera (oratorio), Aspen, Interlochen & Berkshire Music Ctr, formerly; Operetta & supporting roles, Atlanta Theatre Under The Stars, summer 54; supporting roles, Chattanooga Opera Co, Tenn, 55; bass roles, Tri-Cities Opera, Binghamton, NY, 56-66; soloist, Summer Sch Singers, Oxford, 61, Fla Int Fest opera, Daytona Beach, 65 & Allegheny Summer Music Fest, Pa, 79; various roles, Arundel Opera, Maine, formerly. *Pos:* Music & art librn, Calif State Col, San Bernardino, 70-74; asst music librn, State Univ NY, Buffalo, 74-78; music librn, State Univ NY, Fredonia, 78- *Mem:* Nat Asn Teachers Singing; Am Musicol Soc; Music Libr Asn. *Mailing Add:* 71 Central Ave Fredonia NY 14063

CHRIST, PETER
OBOE, ADMINISTRATOR
b Teaneck, NJ, Feb 22, 38. *Study:* Univ Calif, Los Angeles, BA, 60, 61-64; San Diego State Univ, MS, 61. *Rec Perf:* Westwood Wind Quintet, Columbia Rec, 64 & Crystal Rec, 66-83; Oboist Peter Christ, Crystal Rec, 80. *Pos:* Oboist, various motion picture & freelance orch, 59-83; leader & oboist, Westwood Wind Quintet, 59-; first oboist, San Diego Symph, 60-62; pres, Crystal Rec Inc, 66- *Teaching:* Calif State Univ, Los Angeles, 61-70. *Mem:* Int Double Reed Soc; Nat Acad Rec Arts & Sci (mem bd gov, 73-74). *Mailing Add:* 2235 Willida Lane Sedro Woolley WA 98284

CHRIST, WILLIAM B
EDUCATOR, ADMINISTRATOR
b Marion, Ill, Nov 22, 19. *Study:* Ill Wesleyan Univ, BMus, 41; Ind Univ, MMus, 49, PhD, 53. *Pos:* District dir, South Ind District Metropolitan Opera Auditions, 67-; mem, Ind State Arts Comn, 69-77, chmn, 71-72. *Teaching:* Dir music, asst prof music educ & dir choral music, Col Consv Music, Univ Cincinnati, 53-55; asst prof theory, Sch Music, Ind Univ, 55-59, asst dean & prof, 63, assoc dean, 68-, dir grad studies, currently. *Awards:* Orchestral Comp Prize, 52. *Mem:* Pi Kappa Lambda; Phi Mu Alpha; Am Asn Univ Prof; Ind Music Teachers Asn; Soc Music Theory. *Publ:* Auth, The Materials & Structure of Music, 67; The Comprehensive Study of Music (four vol); Anthologies of Music from Plainchant to Stockhausen, 76-79; Piano Reductions for Harmonic Study, 79; Basic Principles of Music Theory, 79. *Mailing Add:* Sch Music Ind Univ Bloomington IN 47401

CHRISTENSEN, BETH ELAINE
LIBRARIAN
b Mendota, Ill, May 10, 54. *Study:* Ill State Univ, BMus, 76; Univ Ill, MS(libr sci), 77. *Pos:* Music & ref librn, St Olaf Col, Minn, 77- *Mem:* Music Libr Asn; Music OCLC Users Group; Am Libr Asn. *Publ:* Co-ed, A Directory of Music Library Instruction Programs in the Midwest, Ind Univ, 82; Bibliographic Instruction in Music at St Olaf College, Music Libr Asn Newsletter, 82; book reviewer for Libr.J. *Mailing Add:* Music Libr St Olaf Col Northfield MN 55057

CHRISTENSEN, DIETER
EDUCATOR, ADMINISTRATOR
b Berlin, Germany, Apr 17, 32. *Study:* Berlin State Consv, studied violoncello with Klemm, cert, 52; Free Univ Berlin, PhD(musicol), 57. *Pos:* Curator & dir, Dept Ethnomusicol, State Museums, Berlin, Germany, 58-72; dir, Ctr Studies Ethnomusicol, Columbia Univ, 71-; ed, Yearbook for Traditional Music, Int Coun Traditional Music, 82- *Teaching:* Lectr musicol, Free Univ Berlin, 62-70; vis prof, Wesleyan Univ, 70; prof, Columbia Univ, 71- *Mem:* Int Musicol Soc; Soc Ethnomusicol; Int Coun Traditional Music (mem bd, 71-; secy gen, 81-); US Coun Traditional Music (pres, 82-). *Interests:* History & methodology of comparative musicology & ethnomusicology. *Publ:* Auth, Die Musik der Kate und Sailum, FU Berlin, 57; coauth, Die Musik der Ellice-Inseln, Staatl Museen 64; El Anillo de Tlalocan, Mann Berlin, 76; co-ed, Hornbostel Opera Omnia, Nijhoff, 75. *Mailing Add:* Dept Music Columbia Univ New York NY 10027

CHRISTENSEN, JEAN MARIE
EDUCATOR, WRITER
b San Bernardino, Calif. *Study:* Pomona Col, BA, 62; Maitre au Consv, with Vlado Perlmutter, 64-66; Univ Calif, Riverside, MA, 78; Univ Calif, Los Angeles, PhD, 79; studied with Jan Maegaard, Univ Copenhagen. *Teaching:* Instr piano, Univ Calif, Fullerton, 66-67; asst prof musicol, Univ Louisville, 79- *Awards:* George C Marshal Mem Found Grant, 75-77 & 83; Martha Baird Rockefeller Musicol Award, 78-79; Am Philosophical Soc Grant, 81. *Bibliog:* Bonnie Hough (auth), Arnold Schoenberg's Herzgewachse, Univ Wash, 81; Ivan Hansen (ed), Per Nørgaard: Artikler 1962-1982, Hansen, 82. *Mem:* Am Musicol Soc; Int Soc Contemp Music; Soc Music Theory; Arnold Schoenberg Inst; Louisville Jazz Soc (bd dir, 83-). *Interests:* Arnold Schoenberg's music and documentation; the music & thought of Per Nørgaard; jazz in Louisville. *Publ:* Auth, Ernst Krenck Fest Concerts, Musical Quart, 75; Sketches for Arnold Schoenberg's Die Jakobsleiter, J Arnold Schoenberg Inst, 78; Per Nørgaards 3 Symfoni, Ballade, 79; Arnold Schoenberg as Advocate of the Arts, Sinfonia, 83; Carl Nielsen's Piano Works: Review of Complete Editions, Notes, 83. *Mailing Add:* 616 Camp St Louisville KY 40203

CHRISTENSEN, ROY HARRY
ADMINISTRATOR, CELLO
b Racine, Wis, June 3, 41. *Study:* New Sch Music, Philadelphia, 59-60; Northwestern Univ, 60-62. *Rec Perf:* Schuller, Crumb, Hindemith & Dallapiccola, 76, Bach, Sessions & Penderecki, 78, Bassoon & Cello Duos

(Mozart & Hindemith), 79, Il Concerto (Parris & Sydeman), 79, Caprices (Piatti), 80, Bach & Arma Sonatas, 81 & Rolla & Loeb, 82, Gasparo Studios. *Pos:* Prin cellist, Atlanta Symph Orch, 62-64 & Cincinnati Symph Orch, 64-74; freelance cellist, 74-; owner, producer, adminr & performer, Gasparo Rec, 74- *Teaching:* Mem fac, Col Consv Music, Univ Cincinnati, 66-68 & Int Cong Strings, 72-74. *Mem:* Am Fedn Musicians. *Mailing Add:* 1807 Tyne Blvd Nashville TN 37215

CHRISTIANSEN, LARRY ARTHUR
COMPOSER, EDUCATOR
b Chicago, Ill, Oct 10, 41. *Study:* Ohio Wesleyan Univ, BM, 63; Northwestern Univ, MM, 64. *Works:* Echo (SATB), Summy-Birchard Co, 64; Fragments for Orchestra, Chicago Chamber Orch, 68; Fragments for Percussion, Cole Publ Co, 73; Come Live With Me (SATB), 73, Exultate Justi, 73, Three Choral Songs, 73 & Gloria, 73, G Schirmer. *Teaching:* Prof music, Culver-Stockton Col, 64-66; Concord Col, 66-67; Chicago City Col, 67-68 & Southwestern Col, Calif, 68- *Mem:* Am Soc Univ Comp; Am Choral Dir Asn. *Mailing Add:* 4696 E Talmadge Dr San Diego CA 92116

CHRISTIANSEN, TICHO PARLY FREDERIK See Parly, Ticho

CHRISTIE, JAMES DAVID
ORGAN, HARPSICHORD
b La Cross, Wis, July 8, 52. *Study:* Oberlin Consv, BMus, 75; New England Consv, MMus, 77, artist dipl, 78; New England Sch Law, hon DFA, 80. *Rec Perf:* Symphony #8 (Mahler), Philips Rec, 81; B Minor Mass (Bach), Nonesuch Rec, 82; Organ Works (Pinkham), Northeastern Rec, 82; Organ Works (McLennan), GunMar Rec, 83. *Pos:* Organist, Boston Symph Orch, 78- & Mass Inst Technol, 82-; artist adv, John Oliver Chorale, currently. *Teaching:* Chmn organ & harpsichord, Boston Consv, 82. *Awards:* First prize, Mass Young Artist Compt, 76 & Int Organ Compt, Bruges, Belgium, 79. *Mem:* Am Guild Organists; Boston Early Music Fest; Am Musicol Soc; Wellesley Bach Fest. *Mailing Add:* c/o Concert Mgt Inc 13408 Flagstone Lane Dallas TX 75240

CHRISTIN, JUDITH
MEZZO-SOPRANO
b Providence, RI, Feb 15, 48. *Study:* Ind Univ, BM, 70, MM, 72. *Rec Perf:* Madama Butterfly, Live from Lincoln Center, PBS, 82; Albert Herring, PBS & BBC. *Pos:* Appearances with New York City Opera, Dallas Opera, Washington Opera, Santa Fe Opera, Wolf Trap Co, Tulsa Opera & others, 72- *Teaching:* Instr voice, Ill State Univ, 72-73. *Awards:* Grants, Sullivan Found & Rockefeller Found. *Mailing Add:* 220 W 98 New York NY 10025

CHRISTMAN, SHARON
SOPRANO, TEACHER-COACH
US citizen. *Study:* Coach with Joan Dornemann, 79; coach with Carolina Segrera, 80; Centro di Culturo Stranieri, 80. *Roles:* Lakme in Lakme, Opera Orch New York, 80; Countess Adele, Pa Opera Theatre, 81; Pisana in I Due Foscari, Opera Orch New York, 81; Marianne in Der Rosenkavalier, Dallas Civic Opera, 82; Rosalinda in Der Fledermaus, Mississippi Opera, 82; The Queen of the Night in The Magic Flute, New York City Opera, 83; First Lady in The Magic Flute, Pittsburgh Opera, 83. *Pos:* Guest artist, Pa Opera Theatre, 81; Dallas Civic Opera, 82 & Opera Orch New York, 81-83; prin artist, New York City Opera, 83- *Awards:* Puccini Found Award, NJ State Opera Compt, 80 & Baltimore Opera Compt, 81; Asbach-Uralt Award, Int Liederkranz Compt, 80. *Mem:* Am Guild Musical Artists. *Rep:* Robert Lombardo Assoc Suite 6F 61 W 62nd St New York NY 10023. *Mailing Add:* 158-18 Riverside Dr 1E New York NY 10032

CHRISTNER, PHILIP JOSEPH
TRUMPET
b Buffalo, NY, Aug 30, 54. *Study:* State Univ NY, Buffalo, BA(music educ), 77, BFA(music perf), 77. *Pos:* Prin trumpet, Charleston Symph Orch, 78-80; assoc prin trumpet, Buffalo Phil Orch, 80-; dir wind ens, Col Charleston, 79-80. *Mem:* Am Fedn Musicians. *Mailing Add:* 545 Cleveland Dr Cheektowaga NY 14225

CHRISTOFF, BORIS
BASS
b Plovdiv, Bulgaria, May 18, 19; Ital citizen. *Study:* Univ Sofia; studied with Riccardo Stracciari. *Rec Perf:* Numerous recordings incl more than 500 Russian songs, EMI. *Roles:* Colline in La Boheme, Rome, 46; King Marke in La Venice, 47; Boris Godunov, San Francisco Opera, 56, Rome Opera & Covent Garden; Don Carlos, Lyr Opera, Chicago, 57; King Philip in Don Carlos, Metropolitan Opera; perf with major co in Argentina, Australia, Brazil, Denmark, France, Germany, Holland, Hungary, Italy, Spain, US & others; many perf with Wagner Repty. *Pos:* Soloist, Bulgarian Gussla Choir; mem, Sofia Cathedral Choir. *Awards:* Sonning Prize; Edison Prize, Acad Charles Cros, Paris; Award Acad Francaise. *Bibliog:* Lanfranco Rasponi (auth), Czar Boris, Opera News, 1/24/83. *Mailing Add:* c/o Columbia Artists 165 W 57th St New York NY 10019

CHRISTOPHER, KAREN MARY
PIANO, TEACHER-COACH
b New York, NY, Apr 6, 52. *Study:* Manhattan Sch Music, BM, 75, MM, 77; piano study with Isabelle Yalkowsky Byman; chamber music study with Raphael Bronstein & Lillian Fuchs. *Pos:* Recitalist, accmp, chamber musician & guest soloist, New Amsterdam Symph Orch. *Teaching:* Fac mem piano, Manhattan Sch Music, 77-, Lenox Sch, 80- & NY Univ, 83- *Mem:* Assoc Music Teachers League; Nat Guild Piano Teachers; Bohemians (NY Musicians Club). *Mailing Add:* 4701 90th St Elmhurst NY 11373

CHRISTOPHER, RUSSELL LEWIS
BARITONE
b Grand Rapids, Mich, Mar 12, 30. *Study:* Grand Rapids Jr Col, AA, 50; Univ Mich, MusB, 53, MusM, 54. *Roles:* Emperor in Turando, New York City Opera, 59; Maecenas in Antony & Cleopatra, Metropolitan Opera, 66; Tonio in I Pagliacci; Marcello in La Boheme; Sharpless in Madama Butterfly; Alberich in Siegfried; Germont in La Traviata; and others. *Pos:* Music librn, NBC, 55-58; prin artist, New York City Opera Co, 58-60, San Francisco Opera Co, 62 & 63, Metropolitan Opera Asn, 63-; soloist with symph orchs in Los Angeles, Montreal, Chicago & Richmond, 63-; lyr bar with maj opera co in US, Can & Japan; conct soloist, Spoleto Fest, Italy, 77. *Awards:* Martha Baird Rockefeller Fund Music Award, 61; Winner, Metropolitan Opera Auditions, 62; Mrs Frederick K Weyerhaeuser Award, 63. *Mailing Add:* 314 W 77th St New York NY 10024

CHRISTOS, MARIANNA
SOPRANO
b Beaver Falls, Pa. *Roles:* Leila in The Pearl Fishers, 81-82, Mimi & Musetta in La Boheme, 81-82, Micaela in Carmen, 81-82 & Antonia in The Tales of Hoffmann, New York City Opera; Adina in L'Elisir d'Amore, Washington Opera, 82 & Houston Grand Opera, 82; Violetta in La Traviata, Chautauqua Fest, 82; Marguerite in Faust, Hawaii Opera, 82 & Pittsburgh Opera, 83. *Pos:* Leading artist, New York City Opera, currently; performer, Chicago, San Francisco, Boston, Santa Fe & Pittsburgh Operas & other US opera co. *Awards:* Metropolitan Opera Nat Auditions Winner, 75. *Mailing Add:* c/o Columbia Artists 165 W 57th St New York NY 10019

CHUGG, M DAVID
EDUCATOR
b Ogden, Utah, Nov 3, 34. *Study:* Utah State Univ, BS, 55, MS, 58; Univ Ore, EdD, 64. *Teaching:* Chmn, Music Dept, Ricks Col, 63- *Mem:* Music Educr Nat Conf; Nat Asn Col Wind & Perc Instr; Int Clarinet Soc. *Mailing Add:* 368 West Fourth South Rexburg ID 83440

CHUNG, MI-HEE
VIOLIN
b Seoul, Korea, Mar 6, 56. *Study:* Sch Music, Univ Mich, BMus, 79; Juilliard Sch, with Ivan Galamian, MMus, 81. *Pos:* First violin, Houston Symph, 81- *Mailing Add:* 4633 Wild Indigo #551 Houston TX 77027

CHUSID, MARTIN
MUSICOLOGIST, EDUCATOR
b Brooklyn, NY, Aug 19, 25. *Study:* Univ Calif, Berkeley, AB, 50, AM, 55, PhD, 61; Ctr Col Ky, DHL, 77. *Teaching:* From instr to asst prof music hist, Univ Southern Calif, 59-63; assoc prof music, NY Univ, 63-68, chmn dept music, 67-70, prof, 68-, assoc dean grad sch arts & sci, 70-72, dir, Am Inst Verdi Studies, 76- *Awards:* Grants, Nat Endowment Humanities, 77-81, Martha Baird Rockefeller, 78-83 & Ford Found, 79-83. *Mem:* Am Musicol Soc; Int Musicol Soc; Col Music Soc; Music Libr Asn; Int Music Libr Asn. *Publ:* Schubert's Cyclic Compositions of 1824, Acta Musicol, 64; The Significance of D Minor in Mozart's Dramatic Music, Mozart-Jahrbuch, 65, 66 & 67; auth & ed, Schubert's Symphony in B Minor (Unfinished): Essays in History and Analysis, a Critical Edition, Norton, 68 & 71; Rigoletto and Monterone: A Study in Musical Dramaturgy, Report XI Cong, Int Musicol Soc, 72 & Hansen, 74; coauth, The Verdi Companion, Norton, 79. *Mailing Add:* 4 Washington Sq Village New York NY 10012

CIANI, SUZANNE E
COMPOSER, ELECTRONIC
b Indianapolis, Ind, June 4, 46. *Study:* Longy Sch Music, with Nicholas Van Slyck; Wellesley Col, with Hubert Lamb, BA(music), 68; Stanford Univ, with John Chowning, 68-70; Univ Calif, Berkeley, with Andrew Imbrie, MA(comp), 70. *Works:* Koddesh-Koddehim (buchla synthesizer), 72; Lixiviation (film score), 72; New York, New York (buchla synthesizer), 74; New York, New York II (buchla synthesizer), 75; Have a Coke and a Smile; The Stepford Wives; The Incredible Shrinking Woman. *Rec Perf:* Seven Waves, JVC. *Pos:* Pres, Electronic Ctr New Music, 74-76; founder & pres, Ciani Musica Inc, 77-; pioneer electronic music & perf. *Teaching:* Instr, Univ Calif, 71-72. *Awards:* Grants, Ford Found & Nat Endowment Arts, 76; Clio, Golden Globe. *Mem:* ASCAP; Screen Actors Guild; Am Fedn TV & Radio Artists; Soc Advert Musicians, Producers, Arrangers & Composers. *Mailing Add:* 40 Park Ave New York NY 10016

CIANNELLA, YVONNE
EDUCATOR, VOICE
Study: Queen's Col, NY, BA. *Rec Perf:* With Vox Turnabout, RCA & Philips. *Roles:* Soloist in War Requiem (Britten), Houston Symph. *Pos:* Vis soloist opera & conct, US, Germany & Austria, currently. *Teaching:* Voice, Am Inst Musical Studies, Austria, 82; prof voice, Sch Music, Fla State Uiv, currently. *Mailing Add:* Sch Music Fla State Univ Tallahassee FL 32306

CIARLILLO, MARJORIE ANN
EDUCATOR, PIANO
b Cleveland, Ohio, Nov 1, 40. *Study:* Univ di Pisa, Italy, cert, 60; Lake Erie Col, BA, 62; Univ London, cert, 62; Case Western Reserve Univ, MA, 71; Ind Univ; Shanghai Consv Music, piano study with Grant Johannesen, 82-83. *Pos:* Dir, China Music Proj, 81- *Teaching:* Fac mem piano, Cleveland Inst Music, 71- *Awards:* Various awards for res & study in China, Sept 78, Aug 79, June 80 & 82-83. *Mem:* Am Musicol Soc; Soc for Asian Music; Chinese Music Soc NAm. *Interests:* Western influences on traditional Chinese music and instruments; gugin (ancient horozontal Chinese instrument with seven strings). *Publ:* Auth, On China—Music, Lifelong Learning, 79; coauth, Music of China: Thirty Years of Change (video tape), Northern Ohio Live, 81; auth, Review—Phases of the Moon, Northern Ohio Live, 81 & US-China Rev, 81; Music Mirrors China's Growth, US-China Rev, 82. *Mailing Add:* 334 Claymore Blvd Cleveland OH 44143

CICHOWICZ, VINCENT M
EDUCATOR, TRUMPET
Works: Galliard and Fugue for Brass Quartet, Crown Press, 72. *Pos:* Mem, Houston Symph, 44-45, Fifth Army Band, 45-46, Grant Park Symph, 47-58, Chicago Symph Orch, 51-74 & Chicago Symph Brass Quintet, 61-74. *Teaching:* Prof trumpet & cornet, Northwestern Univ, 59- *Mem:* Phi Mu Alpha; Pi Kappa Lambda. *Publ:* Auth, The Piccolo Trumpet, Selmer, 72. *Mailing Add:* Sch Music Northwestern Univ Evanston IL 60201

CIECHANSKI, ALEKSANDER
CELLO, EDUCATOR
Study: Acad Music, Cracow, artist's dipl; studied cello with Joseph Mikulski. *Rec Perf:* On Muza, Polish Radio & Archiv. *Pos:* Prin cello, Warsaw Nat Orch, formerly; assoc prin cello, Poznan Symph Orch, formerly; mem, Cracow Radio Orch, formerly, Chopin Piano Trio, formerly, Wronski's Quartet, formerly, Capella Soloists, formerly & St Louis Symph Orch, currently; soloist, US & Europe; mem, Warsaw Piano Quintet tours Europe, India, Hong Kong, Japan, Can, Mex & US, formerly; mem bd dir, New Music Circle St Louis, currently & Univ City Symph Orch, currently. *Teaching:* Mem fac cello & chamber music, Acad Music, Warsaw, formerly & St Louis Consv Music, currently. *Mailing Add:* St Louis Consv Music 560 Trinity Ave St Louis MO 63130

CIESINSKI, KATHERINE
MEZZO-SOPRANO
b Del. *Study:* Temple Univ; Curtis Inst Music. *Rec Perf:* Vanessa (Barber), Spoleto Fest USA, PBS; Messiah (Handel), RCA, 83. *Roles:* Countess Geschwitz in Lulu, Santa Fe Opera; Prince Orlovsky in Die Fledermaus, Minn Orch; Requiem, France, 83; Nuits d'ete, Graz, 83; Lyric Suite, Cologne, 83; Bluebeard's Castle, Dallas Symph Orch, 83; Octavian in Der Rosenkavalier, Dallas Opera, 83. *Pos:* Recitalist & conct artist, Lyr Opera Chicago, formerly, Santa Fe Opera, formerly, Chicago Symph, 83, Houston Symph, 83, Boston Symph, 83 & other symph orchs; duet recitalist with Kristine Ciesinski, Peabody-Mason Found, Boston, Lincoln Ctr Chamber Music Soc, NY & throughout US. *Awards:* First Prize, Geneva Int Compt & Concours Int Chant Paris. *Mailing Add:* c/o Columbia Artists New York NY 10019

CIESINSKI, KRISTINE F
SOPRANO
b Wilmington, Del. *Study:* Boston Univ, BFA(appl voice), 74; private study with Todd Duncan, Margaret Hoswell, Margaret Harshaw & Michael Warren. *Roles:* Elvira in Don Giovanni, Des Moines Metropolitan Opera, 82; Rosalinde in Die Fledermaus, Va Opera Asn, 82; Tosca in Tosca, Opera Del, 82; Manon in Manon Lescaut, Chautauqua Opera, 83; Fiordiligi in Cosi fan tutte, Ky Opera Asn, 83; Eva in Die Meistersinger von Nürnberg, Cincinnati Opera, 83; Salome in Salome, Florentine Opera, 83. *Pos:* Leading sop, Salzburg Opera, 78-82; concert singer with major orchs & chamber music with major orgn & soloists; solo & duet recital artist. *Awards:* First Prize, Geneva Int Music Compt, 77, Salzburg Opera Compt, 77. *Rep:* Columbia Artist Mgt 164 W 57th St New York NY 10019. *Mailing Add:* 148 W 77th St Apt C New York NY 10024

CIMINO, JOHN
BARITONE, LECTURER
b New York, NY, July 15, 49. *Study:* Rensselaer Polytechnic Inst, BS, 71; Manhattan & Juilliard Sch Music, with Daniel Ferro, 76-79; studied with Ettore Campogalliani, Mantova, Italy, 77. *Roles:* Sharpless in Madama Butterfly, NJ State Opera, 79; Silvio in Pagliacci, New York City Opera Touring Co, 79-80; Enrico in Lucia di Lammermoor, 80 & Germont in La Traviata, 81, Am Opera Ctr; Marcello in La Boheme, Opera Co Philadelphia, 82; Rigoletto in Rigoletto, San Francisco Opera & Western Opera Theater, 82. *Pos:* Pres & dir, Assoc Solo Artists Inc, New York, 72-; artist & consult, Capital Region Inst Arts Educ, 83-; artist in sch, NC Arts Coun, 83- *Awards:* Silver medal, Amici Della Lirica, Mantova, Italy, 77; winner, Int Verdi Compt, Busseto, Italy, 77 & Pavarotti Int Singing Compt, Opera Co Philadelphia, 81-82. *Bibliog:* Nancy Cain (ed), Affiliate Artist Cimino is a Renaissance Man, World's Fair: Knoxville Daily Times, 82. *Mem:* Am Guild Musical Artists; Affil Artists Inc. *Interests:* Creativity, human values and the shaping of reality in the arts and sciences. *Rep:* Tornay Mgt 127 W 72nd St New York NY 10023. *Mailing Add:* RD 6 Box 21 Sweetmilk Creek Rd Troy NY 12180

CIOFFARI, RICHARD JOHN
EDUCATOR, COMPOSER
b Detroit, Mich, Dec 27, 43. *Study:* Univ Mich, BMus, 66, MMus, 67. *Works:* Sonata for Bassoon & Piano, comn & perf by Robert Moore, 73; Rhapsody for Tuba & Orchestra, comn & perf by Ivan Hammond, 75; Sonata for Horn & Piano, comn & perf by Herbert Spencer, 75; Fantasy for Flute, Strings & Harp, comn & perf by Lima Symph Orch, Ohio, 76; Five for Five (brass quintet), comn & perf by Bowling Green State Univ Brass Quintet, 78; Sonatina for Tuba Trio, comn & perf by Toledo Tuba Ens, Ohio, 79; Badinage (trumpet sextet), comn & perf by Bowling Green State Univ Grad Trumpet Ens, 80. *Pos:* Prin double bass, NC Symph, 67. *Teaching:* Instr music, Bowling Green State Univ, 67-73, asst prof, 73-79, assoc prof, 79- *Awards:* First Prize, Roth Comp Cont, Nat Sch Orch Asn, 72. *Mem:* Int Soc Bassists; Music Educr Nat Conf; Am String Teachers Asn. *Mailing Add:* Col Musical Arts Bowling Green State Univ Bowling Green OH 43403

CIOLEK, LYNDA L
ARTIST MANAGER, ADMINISTRATOR
b Chicago, Ill, June 24, 52. *Study:* Ind Univ, Bloomington, BS, 74; Manhattan Sch Music, MMus, 76; NY Univ. *Pos:* Pres, Steorra Enterprises, 78- *Teaching:* Asst to dir perf, Manhattan Sch Music, 76-78. *Awards:* Yale Univ Fel. *Mailing Add:* 243 West End Ave Suite 907 New York NY 10023

CIOMPI, GIORGIO
VIOLIN, EDUCATOR
b Florence, Italy, Jan 27, 18. *Study:* Paris Consv, dipl & perf artist dipl; studied with George Enesco & Diran Alexanian. *Rec Perf:* Chamber music & piano trios. *Pos:* Recitalist & soloist with maj orchs in Europe & US; mem, Albeneri Trio, 16 yrs & Toscanini NBC Orch, formerly; first violinist, Ciompi Quartet, Duke Univ; participant, Casals Fest & Aspen Fest. *Teaching:* Head string dept, Cleveland Inst Music, formerly; artist in res string ens & viola, Duke Univ, currently. *Awards:* Premier Prix, Consv Paris, 34; Fedn Music Clubs Award, 68; Recognition of Hon, PR Govt, 70. *Mem:* Bohemians; Am Fedn Musicians; Am String Teachers Asn. *Mailing Add:* 3614 Westover Rd Durham NC 27707

CIPOLLA, FRANK J
CONDUCTOR, EDUCATOR
b Buffalo, NY, Mar 31, 28. *Study:* Eastman Sch Music, BM, 52, MM, 56; Vienna Acad Music, 60; Univ Southern Calif, with Ingolf Dahl, 68. *Pos:* Trumpet, Kansas City Phil Orch, 52-56. *Teaching:* Instr, Univ Mo, 56-61; prof music, State Univ NY, Buffalo, 61- *Bibliog:* Robert Garofola & Mark Elrod (auth), Heritage Americana, Vol 17, No 1 & Lavern John Wagner (auth), Ms Band Books in the W H Shipman Collection, Vol 18, No 1, J Band Res. *Mem:* Col Band Dir Nat Asn (pres eastern div, 78-80); NY State Band Dir Asn (secy, 81-83 & pres, 83-); World Asn Symphonic Bands & Ens; NY State Sch Music Asn; Sonneck Soc. *Interests:* Patrick S Gilmore, Irish-American bandmaster, 1829-1892. *Publ:* Auth, Annotated Bibliography for the Study of 19th Century Band Music, 78 & Bibliography of Dissertations Relative to the Study of Bands, 79 & 80, J Band Res; The Music of Patrick Gilmore, 78 & Francesco Fanciulli, Turn of the Century Bandmaster, 79, Instrumentalist; coauth, Oom-Pah-Pah, The Great Am Band, New York Hist Soc, 82. *Mailing Add:* Music Dept State Univ NY Buffalo NY 14260

CIPOLLA, WILMA REID
LIBRARIAN, PIANO
b Moberly, Mo, Oct 18, 30. *Study:* Pomona Col, BA, 51; Eastman Sch Music, MM, 52; Vienna Acad Music, studied piano with Hans Graf, 59-60; State Univ NY, Buffalo, MLS, 74. *Pos:* Pianist, Kansas City Phil, 54-56; serials librn, State Univ NY, Buffalo, 74-82, dir, Undergrad Libr, 83- *Teaching:* Instr piano & music hist, Southwest Mo State Univ, 52-53; instr organ & music hist, Columbia Col, Mo, 57-59. *Mem:* Sonneck Soc; Music Libr Asn; Am Guild Organists. *Interests:* American music publishing, especially the Arthur P Schmidt Co; the Boston Group of 19th century composers. *Publ:* Auth, Music Subject Headings: A Comparison, Libr Res Tech Serv, 74; ed, Arthur Foote, 1853-1937: An Autobiography, Da Capo Press, 79; auth, A Catalog of the Works of Arthur Foote, 1853-1937, Info Coordrs, 80. *Mailing Add:* 79 Roycroft Blvd Buffalo NY 14226

CIRONE, ANTHONY J
COMPOSER, PERCUSSION
b Jersey City, NJ, Nov 8, 41. *Study:* Juilliard Sch, studied perc with Saul Goodwin & comp with Vincent Persichetti, BS, MS. *Works:* 50 Studies for Marimba; Percussionality (perc); A Sacred Mass for Chorus & Percussion; Cairo Suite (concerto for Middle Eastern instrm & perc); Sonata No 4 (violin, piano & perc); Japanese Impressions (perc quintet); 4/4 for Four (perc quartet). *Rec Perf:* 76 Pieces of Explosive Percussion by Sonic Arts Symph, Perc Consortium. *Pos:* Perc, San Francisco Symph, 65- *Teaching:* Assoc prof music, San Jose State Univ, 65-; Lectr, Stanford Univ. *Mem:* ASCAP; Percussive Arts Soc (mem bd dir, 70-72). *Publ:* Contribr to Instrumentalist, Percussive Arts Soc & Brass & Perc World. *Mailing Add:* PO Box 612 Menlo Park CA 94025

CITRON, MARCIA JUDITH
EDUCATOR, WRITER
b Brooklyn, NY, Dec 24, 45. *Study:* Brooklyn Col, BA, 66; Univ NC, MA, 68; PhD, 71. *Teaching:* Asst prof musicol & theory, Va Commonwealth Univ, Richmond, 71-73 & Brooklyn Col, 73-76; assoc prof, Rice Univ, Houston, 76- *Mem:* Am Musicol Soc. *Interests:* Fanny Mendelssohn Hensel. *Publ:* Auth, Corona Schröter: Singer, Actress, Composer, Music & Lett, 80; The Lieder of Fanny Mendelssohn Hensel, Musical Quart, 83; Fanny Hensel's Letters to Felix Mendelssohn in Oxford's Green Books Collection, In: Mendelssohn & Schumann Essays, Duke Univ Press (in prep); Women as Lieder Composers: 1775-1850, In: Women Making Music, Univ Ill (in prep); Letters of Fanny Hensel to Felix Mendelssohn, Pendragon, 84. *Mailing Add:* 2700 Bellefontaine B-29 Houston TX 77025

CLAPP, LOIS STEELE
MUSIC DIRECTOR, ORGANIST
b Newburgh, NY, Sept 28, 40. *Study:* New England Consv Music; Camerata Sch Music & Fine Arts; studied piano with Hans Graf. *Works:* St Mary's Mass. *Rec Perf:* With New England Consv Chorus & Boston Symph Orch. *Pos:* Organist & choir dir, St Mary's Episcopal Church, Rockport, Mass; accmp, Rockport Community Chorus. *Teaching:* Perf & instr wkshps, Univ Maine; private lessons, organ & harpsichord. *Mem:* Am Guild Organists; Am Musicol Soc. *Interests:* Baroque music. *Mailing Add:* 90 Main St PO Box 270 Rockport MA 01966

CLAPP, STEPHEN H
VIOLIN, EDUCATOR
b Tallmann, NY, Nov 27, 39. *Study:* Consv Music, Oberlin Col, BMus, 61; Juilliard Sch Music, MSc, 65. *Rec Perf:* Cuatro Caprichos (Donald Grantham), Orion, 77; Dimensions I (Barton McLean), Advance, 79. *Pos:* Concertmaster, Aspen Fest Chamber Symph, 71-79. *Teaching:* Assoc prof music, George Peabody Col Teachers, 67-72 & Univ Tex, Austin, 72-79; fac mem violin & chamber music, Aspen Music Fest, 71-; prof violin, Consv Music, Oberlin Col, 78- *Awards:* First Chamber Music Award, Walter W Naumburg Found, 65. *Mem:* Am String Teachers Asn; Music Teachers Nat Asn; Music Educr Nat Conf; Am Fedn Musicians. *Publ:* Auth, Putting Myself Out of a Job, Instrumentalist, 78-82, Will Your Students Be Employable?, 79, Creating An Atmosphere, 81 & Tension in Violin Playing, 82, Am String Teacher. *Mailing Add:* 123 Forest St Oberlin OH 44074

CLAREY, CYNTHIA
MEZZO-SOPRANO
b Smithfield, Va, Apr 25, 49. *Study:* Howard Univ, BMus, 70; Juilliard Sch Music, dipl, 72. *Roles:* Countess in Voice of Ariadne, New York City Opera, 77; Rosina in Il barbiere di Siviglia, Tri-Cities Opera, Binghamton, NY, 79; Hannah in The Ice Break, Boston Opera Theatre, 79; Carmen in Carmen, Houston Grand Opera, 81; Namiji in Actor's Revenge, St Louis Opera Theatre, 81; Diana in L'Orione, Santa Fe Opera, 83. *Mem:* Sigma Alpha Iota. *Mailing Add:* 132 Leroy St Binghamton NY 13905

CLARK, J BUNKER
EDUCATOR, WRITER
b Detroit, Mich, Oct 19, 31. *Study:* Univ Mich, BMus, 54, MMus, 57, PhD, 64; Cambridge Univ, 62-63. *Pos:* Ed, Bibliographies in Am Music 75-; gen ed, Info Coordr, 82- *Teaching:* Instr organ & theory, Stephens Col, 57-59; lectr music, Univ Calif, Santa Barbara, 64-65; prof music hist, Univ Kans, 65- *Awards:* Fulbright Scholar to England, 62-63; grant, National Endowment Humanities, 72-73. *Mem:* Am Asn Univ Prof (pres, Univ Kans chap, 71-72); Am Musicol Soc (chmn Midwest chap, 74-76); Sonneck Soc (bd, 79-82, secy, 83-85); Col Music Soc. *Interests:* Early American keyboard music to 1830; early 17th-century English church music. *Publ:* Auth, Transpositions in 17th Century English Organ Accompaniments, Detroit Monogr Musicol, 74; ed, Anthology of Early American Keyboard Music, 1787-1830, A-R Ed, 77; Nathaniel Giles: Anthems, Early English Church Music, Vol 23, 79; auth, American Musical Tributes of 1824-25 to Lafayette, Fontes Artis Musicae, 79; American Organ Music Before 1830, Diapason, 11/81. *Mailing Add:* Dept Music Univ Kans Lawrence KS 66045

CLARK, JOHN FREDERICK
DOUBLE BASS, EDUCATOR
b Omaha, Nebr, Aug 31, 53. *Study:* Sch Music, Univ Nebr with Priscilla Parson, BMus, 74; Music Acad West, with Peter Mercurio; Northwestern Univ, with Warren Benfield; private study with Michael Krasnopolsky. *Pos:* Double bass, Omaha Symph & Lincoln Symph, 71-74; prin double bass, Nebr Chamber Orch, 73-74; asst prin double bass, Utah Symph, 74-77, prin double bass, 77- *Teaching:* Instr applied bass, Brigham Young Univ, 77-78, Utah State Univ, 78-; adj asst prof applied bass, Univ Utah, 78- *Mem:* Int Soc Bassists; Am Fedn Musicians; Am String Teachers Asn. *Mailing Add:* 1246 E Parkway Ave Salt Lake City UT 84106

CLARK, SONDRA RAE
MUSICOLOGIST, CRITIC
b Breckenridge, Minn, Jan 20, 41. *Study:* Juilliard Sch, BM; Calif State Univ, San Jose, MA; Stanford Univ, PhD. *Pos:* Critic, Oakland Tribune, San Francisco; annotator, San Jose Symph; pianist, Am Sampler Ens. *Teaching:* Instr musicol & thesis writing, Calif State Univ, San Jose. *Awards:* Ella Moore Shiel Fel, 67-68. *Mem:* Am Musicol Soc; Music Critics Asn. *Publ:* Contribr to newspapers & journals. *Mailing Add:* 208 Diablo Ave Mountain View CA 94043

CLARK, THOMAS SIDNEY
COMPOSER, EDUCATOR
b Highland Park, Mich, Aug 23, 49. *Study:* Univ Mich, with George Balch Wilson, Eugene Kurtz & Leslie Bassett, DMA. *Works:* Microscopic Episodes (band), 73; Animated Landscapes #1 (orch), 72 & #2 (orch), 74; A New Dusk (chamber ens), 74; Shores of Infinity (choir & tape), 74; Celestial Ceremonies (tape), 75; Illuminations: 3 Refractions of Time (orch), 76; Diag Dreams (viola & tape), 78. *Teaching:* Mem fac, Ind Univ, 73, Pac Luth Univ, 73-74 & Interlochen Nat Music Camp, summers 75-78; assoc prof theory & analysis, orch & comp, NTex State Univ, 76- *Mailing Add:* Sch Music NTex State Univ Denton TX 76203

CLARK, THOMAS TERRENCE
ORGAN, MUSIC DIRECTOR
b Gary, Ind, Aug 9, 30. *Study:* Ill Benedictine Col, BA, 53; Ind Univ, MS(educ), 55; Am Consv Music, BMus, 70 & MMus(organ), 72. *Works:* Hodie, Plymouth Music Corp, 65. *Pos:* Organist & choirmaster, Holy Angels Cathedral, Gary, Ind, 57-60; chmn fine arts dept, Gavit High Sch, Hammond, Ind, 60-80; dir music, Nativity Our Savior Church, Portage, Ind, currently. *Teaching:* Instr organ, Am Consv Music, currently. *Mem:* Choristers Guild; Piano Guild; Royal Sch Church Am; Int Fedn Pueri Cantores; Church Music Asn Am. *Publ:* Auth, The Coir Rehearsal Procedures, Our Sunday Visitor, 58. *Mailing Add:* 1834 Oriole Dr Munster IN 46321

CLARKE, GARRY EVANS
EDUCATOR, ADMINISTRATOR
b Moline, Ill, Mar 19, 43. *Study:* Cornell Col, BMus, 65; Yale Univ, MMus, 68. *Works:* Tryptich (piano), Judith Solomon, 67; Westchester Limited (opera), Washington Col, 73; Peck Hill Holiday (orch), Aberdeen High Sch Orch, 74; Epitaphs (choral), Washington Col Chorale, 77; Magnificat and Nunc Dimittis (chorus, chamber ens), Washington Col Chorus, 82. *Teaching:* Asst prof music, Washington Col, 68-73, chmn dept, 69-77, assoc prof, 73-79, prof, 79-, dean, 77-83, actg pres, 81-82. *Mem:* Soc Music Theory; Sonneck Soc; Nat Asn Sch Music. *Publ:* Co-ed, Ives, Varied Air and Variations, Merian, 71; auth, Essays in American Music, Greenwood, 77; The Introduction to Music Course, Nat Asn Sch Music, 78. *Mailing Add:* Kentmere-Quaker Neck Chestertown MD 21620

CLARKE, HENRY LELAND
EDUCATOR, COMPOSER
b Dover, NH, Mar 9, 07. *Study:* Harvard Univ, AB, 28, AM, 29, PhD, 47; comp study with Nadia Boulanger, Paris, 29-31; comp study with Gustov Holst, Hans Weisse & Otto Luening, 31, 34 & 36-38. *Works:* Danza de la muerte, Bennington Sch Dance, 37; No Man is an Island, Harvard Glee Club, 52-56; Monograph, Univ Calif, Los Angeles Orch, 55; Gloria in the Five Languages of the United Nations, Roger Wagner Chorale & mem Los Angeles Phil, 55; The Loafer and the Loaf, Univ Calif, Los Angeles Opera Wkshp, 56; Danza de la vida, Univ Wash Wkshp, 76; Drastic Measures for Trombone Alone, Stuart Dempster, 82. *Pos:* Asst, Music Div, New York Pub Libr, 32-36. *Teaching:* Fac mem & chmn grad fac, Westminster Choir Col, Princeton, NJ, 38-42; asst prof theory & musicol, Univ Calif, Los Angeles, 47-48 & 49-58; asst prof comp, Vassar Col, 48-49; from assoc prof musicol to prof, Univ Wash, Seattle, 58-77 & prof emer, 77- *Awards:* Fels, John Harvard Traveling, Harvard Univ, 29-30 & MacDowell Colony, 66 & 67; State Prize Comp, Wash Music Educr, 64. *Bibliog:* John Verrall (auth), Henry Leland Clarke, Am Comp Alliance Bulletin, 60; Oliver Daniel (auth), Henry Leland Clarke, BMI, 70. *Mem:* Charter mem, Am Comp Alliance; Soc Music in Lib Arts Col (secy, 56-57); Col Music Soc (vpres, 61-63); Am Musicol Soc (chap pres, 67-68); Am Soc for Aesthet (chap pres, 67-68). *Interests:* John Blow, last composer of an era; baroque and American music. *Publ:* Auth, Toward a Musical Periodization of Music, Musicol Soc, Vol IV, 25-30; Moll Davies, First Lady of English Opera, In: Essays in Honor of Archibald Thompson Davison by His Associates, Dept Music, Harvard Univ, 57; The Abuse of the Semitone in Twelve-Tone Music, Musical Quart, Vol XLV, 295-301; Musicians of the Northern Renaissance, In: Aspects of Medieval and Renaissance Music, A Birthday Offering to Gustave Reese, W W Norton, 66; The Habitat of Homing Melody, In: Festival Essays for Pauline Alderman, Brigham Young Univ Press, 76. *Mailing Add:* One Wapping Rd Deerfield MA 01342

CLARKE, KAREN
VIOLIN, EDUCATOR
Study: Peabody Consv Music, with Robert Gerle, BM, MM; Yale Sch Music, with Joseph Silverstein. *Rec Perf:* On Leonarda Rec. *Pos:* Mem, Baltimore Symph, Aspen Fest Orch & Rogeri Trio, formerly; concertmistress, Berkshire Music Fest & Wis Chamber Orch, formerly; soloist, Buffalo Phil & NC Symph. *Teaching:* Asst prof violin, Fla State Univ, 80- *Mailing Add:* Sch Music Fla State Univ Tallahassee FL 32306

CLARKE, ROSEMARY
COMPOSER, EDUCATOR
b Daytona Beach, Fla, June 23, 21. *Study:* Stetson Univ, studied comp with Robert Bailey, BM, MM, 41; Philadelphia Musical Acad, with Rollo Maitland, MM & organ dipl, 42; Eastman Sch Music, studied comp with Bernard Rogers & Herbert Elwell, PhD(comp), 50. *Works:* Fantasy (piano & band); To Beat or Not to Beat (tape, visuals & dancer), 72-73; The Cat and the Moon (opera); Cynthia (vocal madrigal), 74; Continuum (horn, alto sax & vibraphone), 77; Nonet (four brasses, four woodwinds & perc), 78; Sieben (seven trombones), 78. *Pos:* Founder & dir, Rosemary Clarke Consv Music Fla, 49-57. *Teaching:* Assoc prof music, Stetson Univ, 42-57; artist in res, Univ Dubuque, 57-62; prof, Univ Wis, Platteville, 62-, comp in res, 69-75. *Mem:* Fel, Am Guild Organists. *Mailing Add:* 1925 Loras Dubuque IA 52001

CLARKE, WILLIAM (JAY)
CONDUCTOR & MUSIC DIRECTOR, EDUCATOR
b Wichita, Kans, July 6, 39. *Study:* Univ Fla, BFA, 62; Univ Ill, MS(music educ), 69; studied cond with Harold Decker, Elwood Keister & Colleen Kirk. *Pos:* Cond, Choral Soc Pensacola, Fla, 71-; assoc cond, Pensacola Symph Orch, Fla, 72- *Teaching:* Choral & dir choral activ, Augustana Col, 69-70, Millikin Univ, 70-71, Pensacola Jr Col, Fla, 71- & Univ WFla, 79- *Mem:* Am Choral Dir Asn; Music Educr Nat Conf; Fla Music Educr Asn; Fla Vocal Asn. *Mailing Add:* 4494 Whisper Dr Pensacola FL 32504

CLAUSER, DONALD R
VIOLA
b Ft Worth, Mar 2, 41. *Study:* Studied with Donald Milton & Selina Almira; Univ NMex, BFA, 62; Boston Univ, MusM, 64; Curtis Inst Music, dipl, 67. *Pos:* Mem viola sect, Philadelphia Orch, 66- *Mailing Add:* Philadelphia Orch 1420 Locust St Philadelphia PA 19102

CLAYSON, LOUIS O
EDUCATOR, ADMINISTRATOR
b Walla Walla, Wash, June 23, 34. *Study:* Whitman Col, AB(music), 56; Eastman Sch Music, MMus, 58. *Roles:* Abelson in Intervals, Northwest Opera Co, 61; Rinuccio in Gianni Schicchi, San Francisco Opera Co, 62;

Gonsalve in Spanish Hour, 62, Duke in Rigoletto, 63, Ferrando in Cosi fan tutte, 64 & Eisenstein in Die Fledermaus, 65, Sacramento Opera Co. *Pos:* Musical dir, Westminster Presby Church, 78- *Teaching:* Prof music, Ore State Univ, 58-59; prof music, Calif State Univ, 59-78, dept chmn, 78- *Mem:* Nat Asn Sch Music; Calif Music Exec; Nat Asn Teachers Singing; Am Choral Dir Asn. *Publ:* Auth, Contemporary American Music, Ore Syst Higher Educ, 58. *Mailing Add:* 1015 Dunbarton Circle Sacramento CA 95825

CLAYTON, LAURA
COMPOSER, EDUCATOR
b Lexington, Ky, Dec 8, 43. *Study:* Ohio State Univ, BMus(piano perf), 66; New England Consv Music, MMus(comp), 71; Univ Mich, DM(comp), 83. *Works:* Cree Songs to the Newborn, C F Peters, 79; Simichai-Ya (sax & tape), Sixth World Sax Conf, 79; Passaggio (solo piano), Renee Hostetler, 82; Herself the Tide, League Comp, 82; work for dance (untitled), Am Dance Fest, 83. *Teaching:* Guest comp, State Univ NY, Fredonia, 82. *Awards:* Charles Ives Fel, Am Acad Arts & Lett, 80; MacDowell Colony Fel, 81; Walter B Hinrichsen Award, Columbia Univ & C F Peters, 82. *Bibliog:* David Burge (auth), Passaggio for Solo Piano, Contemp Keyboard, 5/79. *Mem:* BMI. *Mailing Add:* 565 Norway Hill Hancock NH 03449

CLEMAN, THOMAS
EDUCATOR, COMPOSER
b Ellensburg, Wash, Jan 5, 41. *Study:* Whitman Col, with William Bailey, BA; Univ Calif, Berkeley, with David Lewin, Charles Cushing, Arnold Elston & Seymour Shifrin, MA; Stanford Univ, with Marius Constant & Leland Smith, DMA. *Works:* Variations (piano, four hands), 65; Music for Percussion, 67; Music for Large Orchestra, 69; For Clarinet and Piano, 69; Under the Winter Moon (solo flute), 72; Words for the Wind (bar & chamber ens). *Pos:* Ed, Am Soc Univ Comp Newsletter; founder & co-dir, Northern Ariz Soc Contemp Music. *Teaching:* Macalester Col, 68-69; assoc prof humanities, Northern Ariz Univ, 69- *Mailing Add:* Dept Humanities & Religious Studies Northern Ariz State Univ Flagstaff AZ 86011

CLEMENS, EARL L
EDUCATOR, OBOE
b Dover, Ohio, June 11, 25. *Study:* Yale Univ; Worcester Polytechnic Inst; Univ Wis; Mt Union Col, BPSM, 49; Northwestern Univ, MM, 59; Ind Univ, 61-67. *Works:* Soaring, 77, Andantino, 77, Menuet, 77, Adagio, 78, Minuet, 78, Waltz, 79 & Grand March, 79, Belwin Mills. *Pos:* First oboe, civic & semi-prof orgn incl Tuscarawas Symph Orch, Coshocton Symph Orch, Youngstown Symph Orch, Lorain VFW Band, All Am Bandmasters Band, 56-61, Rockford Symph Orch, Aurora Symph, Elgin Orch & Ill Chamber Orch. *Teaching:* Instrm music, Constantine, Mich, 49-50 & Bolivar, Ohio, 50-51; music supvr, Erie Co Pub Sch, Ohio, 52-59; asst prof educ, Northern Ill Univ, 59-; instr music, Int Music Camp, 60- & Lakeland Music Camp, 79- *Bibliog:* Vergil Moberg (auth), The Oboist, Turtle Mt Star, Rolla, NDak, 7/17/80. *Mem:* Int Double Reed Soc (vpres, 74-75 & pres, 75-78); Int Music Camp (mem bd dir, 70-). *Publ:* Auth, Remedies for Reeds, Int Music Camp, 60 & 71; Pre-Method Book Oboe Teaching, Instrumentalist, 77; contribr, many articles on oboe, Instrumentalist, 77-; auth, Hints on Playing the Oboe, Belwin-Mills, 83. *Mailing Add:* 220 W Royal Dr De Kalb IL 60115

CLEMENT, ROGER
ADMINISTRATOR
b Manchester, NH, July 25, 50. *Study:* Cath Univ Am, BA, MA, 72; NY Univ, studied with Jan LaRue & James Haar, MA(musicol), 75. *Pos:* Asst ed contemp music, Musikverlage Hans Gerig, Cologne, 77-80 & Breitkopf & Härtel, Wiesbaden, 80-81; chief ed, Ahn & Simrock, Munich, 81- *Teaching:* Instr style analysis, Laval Univ, Quebec City, Quebec, 75. *Mem:* Int Soc Contemp Music. *Publ:* Auth, 1957-1977: 20 Jahre Dokumentation Über ... Neue Musik ..., Int Soc Contemp Music, Bonn, 80. *Mailing Add:* Steinsdorf Str 5 8000 Munich 22 Germany, Federal Republic of

CLEMENT, SHEREE JEAN
COMPOSER, EDUCATOR
b Baltimore, Md, Aug 12, 55. *Study:* Univ Mich, BMus, 77, MMus, 78; Columbia Univ, DMA, 83. *Works:* Glinda Returns, Columbia-Princeton Electronic Music Ctr, 79; Belladonna Dreams, Borealis Ens, 80; Five Preludes (piano), Allen Shawn, 81; Chamber Concerto, Comp Conf Ens, 82; String Quartet, Atlantic String Quartet, 82. *Teaching:* Preceptor musicianship, Columbia Univ, 81-83. *Awards:* Winner, League Int Soc Contemp Music Nat Comp Comt, 81; Margaret Grant Award, Berkshire Music Ctr, 81; Guggenheim Fel, 83-84. *Mem:* League Int Soc Contemp Music (vpres, 83); Am Soc Univ Comp; Col Music Soc. *Mailing Add:* 949 West End Ave Apt 7F New York NY 10025

CLEMENTS, JOY
SOPRANO, TEACHER-COACH
b Dayton, Ohio. *Study:* Studied with Marinka Gurewich; Univ Miami; Acad Vocal Arts. *Roles:* Musetta in La Boheme, Opera Gtr Miami, 56; Mary Warren in The Crucible, New York City Opera, 61; Micaëla in Carmen; Norina in Don Pasquale; Despina in Cosi fan tutte; Olympia & Antonia in Les Contes d'Hoffmann; Gilda in Rigoletto; and many others. *Pos:* Sop with maj opera co in Can, Israel & US. *Teaching:* Instr voice & coach repertoire, currently. *Mailing Add:* c/o Ludwig Lustig Mgt 41 W 72nd New York NY 10023

CLEVE, GEORGE
CONDUCTOR & MUSIC DIRECTOR
b Vienna, Austria, 1936. *Study:* Mannes Col Music; studied with Pierre Monteux, George Szell & Franco Ferrara; Univ Santa Clara, Hon DFA. *Pos:* Co-founder & music dir, Midsummer Mozart Fest, Calif; music dir, Winnipeg Symph; music dir & cond, San Jose Symph, 72-; guest cond with major US & Europ orchs. *Awards:* First Community Arts Program Award, San Jose. *Mailing Add:* San Jose Symph 170 Park Ctr Pl San Jose CA 95113

CLIBURN, VAN (HARRY LAVAN, JR)
PIANO
b Shreveport, La, July 12, 34. *Study:* Studied with Rildia Bee Cliburn, 37-51; Juilliard Sch Music, with Rosina Lhevinne, 54; Baylor Univ, HHD, 58. *Rec Perf:* For RCA Victor. *Pos:* Performer, Shreveport Symph, 40, Houston Symph Orch, 47, Dallas Symph Orch, 52, New York Phil Orch, 54 & 58, Symph of Air, 58, Brussels Fair, 58 & many others; conct pianist on tour US, 55-, USSR, 58. *Awards:* Nat Music Fest Award, 48; Kosciuszko Found Chopin Award, 52; First Prize, Int Tschaikovsky Piano Compt, Moscow, 58. *Mem:* Am Guild Musical Artists. *Mailing Add:* 455 Wilder Pl Shreveport LA 71104

CLICKNER, SUSAN FISHER
MEZZO-SOPRANO, EDUCATOR
b Buffalo, NY, Apr 15, 34. *Study:* Ind Univ, BM(voice), 55; Curtis Inst Music, artist's dipl, 59; studied under Martial Singher & Herbert Graf. *Teaching:* Affil assoc prof, Clark Univ, 69-83; founding mem fac, Worcester Community Sch Perf Arts, 71-74; mem fac voice, New England Consv, 72- *Mem:* Nat Asn Teachers Singing (mem bd dir Boston chap, 77-81). *Mailing Add:* 64 Eastwood Rd Shrewsbury MA 01545

CLINTON, MARIANNE HANCOCK
ADMINISTRATOR
b Dyersburg, Tenn, Dec 7, 33. *Study:* Cincinnati Consv Music, BMus, 56; Univ Cincinnati, BS, 56; Miami Univ, Ohio, MMus, 71. *Pos:* Mem admin bd, Middletown First United Methodist Church, Ohio, 68-72; managing dir, Am Music Teacher, 77-; exec dir, Music Teachers Nat Asn, 77- *Teaching:* Music, Hamilton Co Pub Sch, Ohio, 56-57; instr voice & piano, Butler Co, Ohio, 64; instr music, Miami Univ, Ohio, 72-74. *Mem:* Pi Kappa Lambda; Music Educr Nat Conf; Am Educ Res Asn; Am Soc Asn Exec; Nat Fedn Music Clubs. *Mailing Add:* 2113 Carew Tower Cincinnati OH 45202

CLOUD, LEE VERNELL
EDUCATOR
b Winston-Salem, NC, May 24, 50. *Study:* Morehouse Col, BA, 72; Bowling Green State Univ, MMus, 73; Univ Iowa, PhD, 78. *Teaching:* Instr theory, Winston-Salem State Univ, 74-75; asst prof theory & cond, Grinnell Col, 78-; vis prof Afro-Am music, Univ Iowa, 82-83. *Mem:* Phi Mu Alpha; Am Soc Univ Comp; Am Musicol Soc. *Publ:* Coauth, A Selected Annotated Bibliography of Twentieth Century Choral Music Suggested for Colleges and Universities, Am Choral Dir Asn (in prep). *Mailing Add:* 1215 Elm St Grinnell IA 50112

CLOUGH, JOHN L
WRITER, EDUCATOR
b Boston, Mass, Feb 11, 30. *Study:* Univ Del, 48-49; Oberlin Col, 49-51; Yale Univ, MusM, 55. *Teaching:* From instr to assoc prof music, Oberlin Col, 55-70; from assoc prof to prof music, Univ Mich, 70-81; Slee prof music theory, State Univ NY, Buffalo, 81- *Mem:* Soc Music Theory; Col Music Soc. *Publ:* Auth, Aspects of Diatonic Sets, J Music Theory, 79; Diatonic Interval Sets and Transformational Structures, Perspectives New Music, 79-80; Profiling of Pitch Class Sets: The Exclusion Relation, J Music Theory, 83; coauth, Scales, Intervals, Keys, Triads, Rhythm and Meter, 83 & Basic Harmonic Progressions (in press), W W Norton & Co. *Mailing Add:* Dept Music State Univ NY Buffalo NY 14260

CLYNE, MALCOLM EDWARD
COMPOSER
b Tunja, Boyaca, Colombia, Sept 6, 43; Brit citizen. *Study:* Consv Nat De Musica, Bogota, Colombia, 56-59; Bethel Col, BA, 66; NTex State Univ, study comp with William P Latham & musicol with Dika Newlin, MM, 75. *Works:* Ricercare For Brass Trio, 74 & Carterian Variations for Unaccompanied Clarinet, 75, Quadrivium Music Press. *Mem:* Phi Mu Alpha; Am Musicol Soc; Am Soc Univ Comp. *Mailing Add:* 3330 Rosedale Dallas TX 75205

COATES, GLORIA (KANNENBERG)
COMPOSER, LECTURER
b Wausau, Wis. *Study:* Monticello Col, DePaul Univ, with David Itkin; Mozarteum Salzburg, Austria, with Alexander Tcherepnin, cert(comp), 62; La State Univ, with Helen Gunderson & Kenneth Klaus, BA & BM(voice & comp), 63, MM(comp & musicol), 65; Columbia Univ, with Otto Luening & Jack Beeson, 66-68. *Works:* Five Pieces for Four Wind Players, Ahn & Simrock Publ, 76; Music on Open Strings, Polish Chamber Orch, Warsaw Autumn Fest, 78 & St Paul Chamber Orch, 82; Nonette, Rome, Italy, 79; Ecology No 2, East Berlin Fest, 79; Waltz Triste, comn by Warsaw Autumn Fest, 80; Sinfonia della Notte, perf by Wilde Gungle, Munich, Ger, 82; Fourth String Quartet, Bombay String Quartet, 82; and many others. *Pos:* Orgnr & producer, Ger-Am Music Concts, Munich, 71-84; writer & moderator, Open House Broadcast, WDR Cologne Radio, Ger, 78- *Teaching:* Guest lectr opera & oratorio Univ Wis & various conct in Calcutta, New Delhi, Bombay, India, Munich, Ger, & London, England, 75-; private teacher voice & comp,

currently. *Awards:* Munich Ministry of Cult Grant, 71-83; Alice M Ditson Grant, 74-83; MacDowell Found Fel, 82. *Bibliog:* Orzysztof Baculewski (auth), Warsaw Autumn, Ruch Muzyczny, Poland, 12/78; Dr Uwe Kramer (auth), Warten auf die ersti Beethovena, Fono Forum, 11/79; Grisela Glagla (auth), Eine Wilde mit System, Music Medicine, WGer, No 25, 12/3/82. *Mem:* Am Music Ctr; Gesellschaft Musikalische Auffuhrung; Int League Women Comp (mem bd dir, 76-80); German Comp Union; UN Educ, Sci, Cult Orgn World Music Days, Prague, (rep, 77). *Mailing Add:* Postfach 430661 8 Munich 43 Germany, Federal Republic of

COBB, A(LFRED) WILLARD
TENOR, EDUCATOR
b Baltimore, Md, Dec 19, 29. *Study:* Tusculum Col, BA, 51; Consv Music, Oberlin Col, BMus, 55, MMus, 57; Royal Acad Music, LRAM, 62; Trinity Col Music, London, FTCL(voice), 62, LTCL(recorder), 63. *Rec Perf:* Songs (John Dowland), Carmina Burana & others on Telefunken, Odeon, EMI & Musical Heritage Soc. *Pos:* Mem, Early Music Quartet, 63-70, Baroque Ens St Louis, St Louis Consv Early Music Ens, St Louis Madrigal Singers & Am Kantorei; soloist, Temple Israel & Grace Methodist Church, St Louis; conct singer in England & Europe. *Teaching:* Instr music, Fairmont State Col, 57-60; teaching fel, Boston Univ, 60-61; instr voice & early music, St Louis Consv, 73- *Awards:* Fulbright Scholar, 62; Elizabeth Schumann Prize. *Mem:* Pi Kappa Lambda; Nat Asn Teachers Singing. *Interests:* Vocal music from the Renaissance and Baroque periods. *Publ:* Contribr, KWMU radio mag. *Mailing Add:* 5112 Westminster Pl St Louis MO 63108

COBB, DONALD LORAIN
COMPOSER, MUSIC DIRECTOR
b Oakland, Calif, Nov 13. *Study:* Rollins Col, 54-56; Sch Music, Yale Univ, BMus, 59; Mills Col, MA, 63. *Works:* Heaven Conserve Thy Course in Quietness (SSAA & viola), Galaxy Music Corp, 73; The Springfield of the Far Future (SATB & piano), 76 & The Town of American Visions (SATB & piano), 77, Lawson-Gould Inc; Exultation (SATB), Music 70, 77; Red River Valley (SATB), J Fischer, 78; Begone Dull Care (SATB), Lawson-Gould Inc, 81. *Pos:* Dir, Lodestar Music Camp, Jackson, Calif, 68-69; music dir, Oakland Museum Conct, 71-72. *Teaching:* Lectr, Mills Col, Oakland, 68-73; instr, Athenian Sch, Danville, Calif, 76-78 & Black Pine Circle Sch, Berkeley, 79- *Publ:* Auth, Roy Harris, In: New Grove Dict of Music & Musicians, 80. *Mailing Add:* PO Box 324 San Leandro CA 94577

COCHRAN, J PAUL
COMPOSER, EDUCATOR
b Pittsburgh, Pa, May 25, 46. *Study:* Hanover Col, BA, 68; Univ Redlands, MM, 72; Northwestern Univ, DM, 82. *Works:* Drone/Fantasy B flat (clarinet & piano), Seesaw; The Sun By Day (SATB choir), Northwestern Univ Chapel Choir, 77; This Will Be A Sign (SATB choir & organ), comn by First Presby Church, Ft Wayne, Ind, 81. *Teaching:* Instr, Chicago Consv Col, 77-81 & Sherwood Music Sch, 82- *Mem:* Col Music Soc; Am Soc Univ Comp. *Mailing Add:* 2321 Cedar St Des Plaines IL 60018

CODISPOTI, NORMA (CONSTANCE)
MEZZO-SOPRANO, TEACHER-COACH
b Cleveland, Ohio, Oct 10, 38. *Study:* Baldwin-Wallace Col & Conv, Berea, Ohio, BMusEd, 74, BMus, 78; Ohio State Univ, MMus, 79. *Roles:* Prince Orlofsky in Die Fledermaus, 75 & Principessa in Suor Angelica, Cleveland Opera Theater, 76; Berthe in Barber of Seville, Columbus Symph Opera, 79; Giovanna in Rigoletto, New Cleveland Opera, 80; Martha in Faust, 81 & Alisa in Lucia di Lammermoor, 82, Youngstown Opera; Annina in La Traviata, Youngstown Opera, 82 & Opera Columbus, 83. *Teaching:* Instr voice, Koch Sch Music, Rocky River, Ohio, 74-; adj fac mem, Baldwin-Wallace Conv Music, 80- *Mem:* Cent Opera Serv; Nat Opera Asn; Nat Asn Teachers Singing (secy & treas Ohio chap, 81-83); life mem, Mu Phi Epsilon; life mem, Pi Kappa Lamda. *Interests:* Vocal pedagogy . *Publ:* Auth, The Singing Voice—Its Care and Function, Gamut Mag, Cleveland State Univ Press, 6/83. *Mailing Add:* 2570 Northview Rd Rocky River OH 44116

CODY, JUDITH (ANN)
COMPOSER, LECTURER
b Troy, NY. *Study:* Japanese music, 68-69. *Works:* Dances, Op 8 (flute & guitar), 78, Seven Concert Etudes, Op 10, 11, 13-15 & 18 (guitar), 78, Nocturne, Op 9 (guitar), 78, Flute Poems, Op 19, 78-79, Sonata, Op 22 (flute & guitar), 78-82, Looking Under Footprints (opera), 83 & Theme & Variations, Op 27 (piano), 83, Kikimora Publ Co. *Teaching:* Officer & lectr, Bay Area Cong Women in Music, San Francisco State Univ, 80-81; lectr, San Francisco Consv Music, 81. *Awards:* Nat Cont Winner, New Times Conct, La State Univ, 79. *Mem:* Comp mem, Am Music Ctr; Soc Univ Comp; Int League Women Comp; fel, Int Acad Poets; Int Platform Asn. *Publ:* Coauth, Foreground, Foothill Col, 75; Amphichroia, Fault Press, 78; ed, Resource Guide on Women in Music, Kikimora Publ Co, 81. *Mailing Add:* PO Box 1107 Los Altos CA 94022

COE, KENTON
COMPOSER
b Tenn, Nov 12, 32. *Study:* Yale Univ, with Quincy Porter & Paul Hindemith, BA, 53; Paris Consv, with Nadia Boulanger, 53-56. *Works:* Birds in Peru (film score), 68; South (opera adapted from play by Julien Green), perf by Paris Opera, 72; Le Grand Siecle (one act opera with text by Ionesco), perf by Opera Nantes, 72; The White Devil (opera on play by John Webster); Rachel (opera with libretto by Anne Howard Bailey), comn by Tenn Arts Comn & Tenn Perf Arts Found, 76; The Handwriting on the Wall (cantata for chorus, four brasses, timpani & two pianos), Nashville, 78. *Awards:* Comp Prize, Fontainebleau Consv, 53; French Govt Grants, 54 & 55; MacDowell Fels, 60 & 63. *Mailing Add:* 1309 Lynnwood Dr Johnson City TN 37601

COE, ROBERT M
ADMINISTRATOR, EDUCATOR
b Saltville, Va, Aug 28, 31. *Study:* Appalachian State Univ, BS, 52; Eastern Ky Univ, MA, 53; Univ Northern Colo, EdD(music), 61; Eastman Sch Music; Mozarteum, Salzburg, 71. *Pos:* Orch mem, Greeley Phil, Colo, 56-58; organist & choirmaster, St Margaret's Episcopal Church, Carrollton, 64- *Teaching:* Asst prof, Hastings Col, Nebr, 58-63; prof & chmn dept fine arts, WGa Col, Carrollton, 63- *Mem:* Am Asn Univ Prof; Music Teachers Nat Asn; Ga Music Teachers Asn; Music Educr Nat Conf; Ga Music Educr Asn. *Mailing Add:* Music Dept West Georgia Col Carrollton GA 30118

COFFEY, DENISE (DENISE COFFEY PATE)
SOPRANO
b Rockville Centre, NY, Apr 22, 50. *Study:* Hofstra Univ, Hempstead, NY, BA, 72; Acad Vocal Arts, 78. *Roles:* Gretel in Hansel & Gretel, Opera Co of Philadelphia, 76; Pauline in The Toyshop, New York City Opera, 78; Gilda in Rigoletto, Opera Del, 79; Norina in Don Pasquale, Mich Opera Theatre, 80; Miss Hope in The Boy Who Grew Too Fast, Opera Del, 82; Gilda in Rigoletto, 82 & Despina in Cosi Fan Tutte, 83, Cincinnati Opera; Oscar in Un Ballo in Maschera, Ft Worth Opera, 84. *Mailing Add:* 30 N Lecato Ave Audubon NJ 08106

COFFIN, (ROSCOE) BERTON
EDUCATOR, WRITER
b Fairmont, Ind, Apr 11. *Study:* Earlham Col, BA, 32; Chicago Musical Col, BM, 34; Eastman Sch Music, MM, 48; Columbia Univ, AM, 46, EdD, 50. *Roles:* Baritone, conct, oratorio & guest in several operas in Chicago, Denver & Boulder, 36-66. *Teaching:* Prof voice, Univ Colo, Boulder, 46-77, chmn voice dept, 59-77, emer prof, 77-; teacher voice & vocal pedagogy, US, Europe & Nat Asn Teachers Singing Workshops, 50-; teacher singing, private studio, Vienna, Austria, 77-79 & 79-; vis prof voice, Col-Consv Music, Univ Cincinnati, 81-82 & Southern Methodist Univ, 82- *Mem:* Nat Asn Teachers Singing (pres, 68-69); Am Acad Teachers Singing. *Interests:* Vocal pedagogy; the pitch of vowels (acoustical labs in US & Europe); vocal repertoire; phonetics; translations; vocal acoustics. *Publ:* Auth, The Singer's Repertoire (1 vol, later into 4 vol), 60 & coauth, Program Notes, Word for Word Translation, Part I, 62 & 66, Scarecrow Press; Phonetic Readings of Songs & Arias, Pruett Press, 64 & Scarecrow Press, 82; auth, Sounds of Singing, 77 & Overtones of Bel Canto, 80, Scarecrow Press. *Mailing Add:* c/o D K Schwartz PO Box 1483 Boulder CO 80306

COFFMAN, PHILLIP HUDSON
ADMINISTRATOR, EDUCATOR
b Lincoln, Nebr, Nov 27, 36. *Study:* Univ Nebr, BME,, 58; Univ Idaho, MM, 62; Univ Toledo, PhD, 71; studied perc with Bradley Spinney, 60 & William Kraft, 64. *Teaching:* Instr, Pub Schs, Ruchville, Nebr, 58-59 & Doane Col, 59-60; teaching asst, Univ Idaho, Moscow, 60-62, instr, 62-65; assoc prof & head music, Jamestown Col, 65-68; assoc prof & head music, Univ Minn, Duluth, 71-76, prof & dean, Fine Arts, 76- *Awards:* First Place Award, F E Olds Scholarship in Music, 63. *Mem:* Int Coun Fine Arts Deans. *Publ:* Auth, Perfection in Drumming, Percussive Notes, 69; Articulation in the Percussion & String Families, Perc Arts, 79; Economic Impact of the Arts, Perf Arts Rev, 79. *Mailing Add:* 4601 Woodland Ave Duluth MN 55803

COGAN, ROBERT DAVID
COMPOSER, EDUCATOR
b Detroit, Mich, Feb 2, 30. *Study:* Univ Mich, with Ross Lee Finney, BMus, 51, MMus, 52; Princeton Univ, with Roger Sessions, MFA, 56; Staatliche Hochschule Musik, Hamburg, 58-60; studied with Aaron Copland, Nadia Boulanger & Philipp Jarnach. *Works:* Fantasia (orch), 51; Violin Sonata, 53; Sounds and Variants (piano), 61; Spaces and Cries (five brasses), 64; Whirl ... ds I (voice, 44 instrm & microphonist), 67; Whirl ... ds II (two solo voices or chorus), 73; No Attack of Organic Metals (organ & tape), 73. *Pos:* Prog head & mem eastern regional exec bd, Inst Music Contemp Educ, 66-69, ed, Sonus, 80- *Teaching:* Grad asst music, Univ Mich, 51-52 & Princeton Univ, 54-55; private instr comp, New York, 61-63; instr comp, New England Consv Music, 63-, chmn theoret studies, 63-68, chmn grad theoret studies, 68-, dir, Sonic Analysis Lab, currently; vis fac mem, Berkshire Music Ctr, State Univ NY, Purchase, IBM Watson Res Ctr & others. *Mem:* Int Soc Contemp Music (dir US sect, currently). *Publ:* Coauth (with Pozzi Escot), Sonic Design: The Nature of Sound and Music, 76; (with Pozzi Escot), Sonic Design: Practice and Problems, 81; New Images of Musical Sound, 84. *Mailing Add:* 24 Avon Hill St Cambridge MA 02140

COGGINS, WILLIS ROBERT
EDUCATOR, CLARINET
b Winston-Salem, NC, Aug 20, 26. *Study:* Davidson Col, BS, 49; Univ Ill, MS, 57. *Works:* Aria (alto saxophone), 70 & Andantino (baritone saxophone), 70, Belwin Mills Publ Co. *Pos:* Dir bands, Conway Pub Sch, 49-53. *Teaching:* Prof appl music, clarinet & sax, Univ Ill, Urbana, 53- *Mem:* NAm Saxophone Alliance; ClariNetwork Int, Inc; Am Fedn Musicians. *Publ:* Auth, The Saxophone Student, Books 1, 2 & 3, 71, Studies and Melodious Etudes for Saxophone, Books 1, 2 & 3, 71, The Saxophone Soloist, Book 1, 71 & Tunes for Technic for Saxophone, Book 3, 71, Belwin Mills Publ Co. *Mailing Add:* Sch Music Univ Ill Urbana IL 61801

COGLEY, MARK
PIANO, CONDUCTOR
b Rockville Centre, NY, Mar 24, 53. *Study:* Oberlin Col, BA(music), 76. *Pos:* Music staff, Florentine Opera, Milwaukee, Wis, 78-79; asst chorusmaster, Metropolitan Opera Asn, New York, 79- *Teaching:* Fac mem, Music Acad West, 75-76 & Univ Wis, Milwaukee, 77-79. *Mailing Add:* 166 W 76 St #4A New York NY 10023

COHEN, ALBERT
EDUCATOR, WRITER
b New York, NY, Nov 16, 29. *Study:* Juilliard Sch Music, BS(violin), 51; NY Univ, AM(musicol), 53, PhD(musicol), 59; Univ Paris, France, 56-57. *Teaching:* Mem fac music, Univ Mich, Ann Arbor, 60-64, assoc prof, 64-67, prof, 67-70; prof & chmn dept music, State Univ NY, Buffalo, 70-73; prof & chmn dept, Stanford Univ, 73-, William H Bonsall prof, 74- *Awards:* Fulbright Fel, 59; Guggenheim Fel, 68-69; Nat Endowment Humanities Grant, 75-76. *Mem:* Int Musicol Soc; Am Musicol Soc; French Musicol Soc; Galpin Soc; Music Libr Asn. *Publ:* Auth, Treatise on the Composition of Music, 62 & Elements or Principles of Music, 65, Inst Mediaeval Music; coauth (with J D White), Anthology of Music for Analysis, Norton, 65; (with L E Miller), Music in the Paris Academy of Sciences, 1666-1793, An Index, 79; auth, Music in the French Royal Academy of Sciences, 81; articles in J Am Musicol Soc, J Music Theory & others. *Mailing Add:* Dept Music Stanford Univ Stanford CA 94305

COHEN, DAVID
COMPOSER, EDUCATOR
b Pulaski, Tenn, Oct 14, 27. *Study:* Philadelphia Consv; Juilliard Sch; studied with Vincent Persichetti; Univ Southern Calif, with Ingolf Dahl. *Works:* Piano Trio, 60; Divertimento (four flutes), 67; Symphony #2 (orch), 70; Rhinoceros Variations (band); La Maison Construite par Jean (chorus with small orch), 71; Sound Image I (rec synthesizer), 71; Beauty is Fled (children's opera), Phoenix, 77. *Teaching:* Mem fac, Univ Ala, 55-67; prof theory & analysis, comp & electronic studio, Ariz State Univ, 67- *Awards:* Coolidge Chamber Music Prize, Juilliard Sch, 52; Fulbright Scholar, 53; IBM Grad Res Grant, 65. *Mailing Add:* 1045 E Loyola Dr Tempe AZ 85282

COHEN, EDWARD
EDUCATOR, COMPOSER
b 1940. *Study:* Univ Calif, Berkeley, with Seymour Shifrin & Luigi Dallapiccola; studied with Max Deutsch, Paris. *Works:* Nocturne (orch), 73; Madrigal for 5 Instruments (chamber music); Elegy (sop & chamber ens), Berkshire Music Ctr, 77. *Teaching:* Fac mem, Brandeis Univ; lectr theory & analysis, Mass Inst Technol, 78- *Mailing Add:* Music Dept Mass Inst Technol Cambridge MA 02139

COHEN, FRANKLIN R
CLARINET, EDUCATOR
b New York, NY, July 28, 46. *Study:* Juilliard Sch Music, BM, 70. *Pos:* Solo clarinetist, Am Symph, 67-69, Baltimore Symph, 69-75, Cleveland Orch, 75- & Casals Fest Orch, 77. *Teaching:* Clarinet & chamber music, Peabody Inst, 69-76 & Cleveland Inst Music, 75- & Blossom Music Sch. *Awards:* First Prize, Int Music Compt, Munich, 68; Star of Week, Munich Newspaper, 68 & 79. *Mailing Add:* 2632 Exeter Rd Cleveland OH 44118

COHEN, FREDRIC THOMAS
OBOE, EDUCATOR
b Philadelphia, Pa, May 14, 48. *Study:* Philadelphia Musical Acad, BMus & BMusEd, 70; studied oboe with Stevens Hewitt, Jerry Sirucek & John DeLancie & chamber music with Marcel Moyse & Sol Shoenbach. *Pos:* Prin oboe, Concerto Soloists, Philadelphia, 69-73 & Springfield Symph, Mass, currently; solo oboist, Apple Hill Chamber Players, 69-74 & other chamber ens; chmn woodwinds & dir chamber music, Amherst Music Ctr, Maine, 74-80; instr oboe, coach chamber music & cond, Chamber Wind Ens, New England Consv Music, 75- *Teaching:* Mem fac, Ctr Chamber Music, Apple Hill, 69-74, Worcester Community Sch, formerly, Keene State Col, formerly, Settlement Music Sch, Philadelphia, formerly & Smith Col, 78-79. *Mem:* Am Fedn Musicians. *Mailing Add:* New England Consv Music 290 Huntington Rd Boston MA 02115

COHEN, ISIDORE
VIOLIN, EDUCATOR
Study: Juilliard Sch Music, studied violin with Ivan Galamian & chamber music with Felix Salmond & Hans Lety, BS. *Pos:* Mem, Schneider & Juilliard Quartets, formerly & Beaux Arts Trio, currently; solo appearances, Fest Casals, Music Aeterna, Am Symph Orch, Flagstaff Fest, Cranbrook Fest, Mostly Mozart Lincoln Ctr & recitals. *Teaching:* Mem fac violin, Mannes Col Music, 70- *Mailing Add:* Mannes Col Music 157 E 74th St New York NY 10021

COHEN, JEROME D
ADMINISTRATOR, MUSIC DIRECTOR
b Spokane, Wash, Feb 6, 36. *Study:* New England Consv Music, cond with Richard Burgin, BMus, 59, MMus, 63. *Works:* Concert Overture No 1, comn by Gtr Boston Youth Symph Orch, 59; Cape Ann Concert Overture No 2, 73 & The Girl with the Flaxen Hair (Debussy), 81, Boston Pops Orch. *Pos:* Music dir, Cape Cod Symph Orch, 70-80; consult, New England Found for Arts, 77- & Evening at Pops, 81-; music asst, Boston Pops Orch, 80-82. *Awards:* ASCAP Award, 73, 78 & 79. *Mem:* ASCAP. *Publ:* Auth, Prog notes for conct, Boston Pops Orch, 81. *Mailing Add:* 12 Pat Rd Hanover MA 02339

COHN, JAMES (MYRON)
COMPOSER, MUSICOLOGIST
b Newark, NJ, Feb 12, 28. *Study:* Studied with Wayne Barlow, 40-41, Roy Harris, 41-43 & Bernard Wagenaar, 43-50; Juilliard Sch Music, BS(comp), 49, MS(comp), 50. *Works:* Symphony No 2, Franz-Andre & Belgian Nat Radio Orch, 53; The Fall of the City (opera), Ohio Univ Opera Workshop, 55; Symphony No 3, Paul Paray & Detroit Symph Orch, 59; Symphony No 4, Ferruccio Scaglia & Orch Asn Ital Diffuzione Educ Musica, Florence, Italy,

60; Variations on The Wayfaring Stranger, Paul Paray & Detroit Symph, 62; Concerto da Camera, comn by McKim Fund, 82; Piano Sonata No 4, comn by Morton Estrin, 82. *Pos:* Musicologist, ASCAP, 55- *Awards:* Young Comp Award, Nat Fedn Music Clubs, 44 & 46; Bronze Medal, Queen Elisabeth of Belgium Prize, 53; Asn Ital Diffuzione Educ Music Award, 60. *Mem:* ASCAP; Am Guild Authors & Comp; Am Fedn Musicians; B'nai B'rith Music & Perf Arts Lodge; Asn Class Music. *Interests:* Eastern Asiatic music; electronic music. *Mailing Add:* c/o ASCAP 1 Lincoln Plaza New York NY 10023

COHRS, ARTHUR LOTHAR
EDUCATOR, PIANO
b Merrill, Wis, Aug 13, 37. *Study:* Univ Wis, Madison, BMus, 59; Eastman Sch Music, MMus, 61; Northwestern Univ. *Teaching:* Asst prof music, Concordia Teachers Col, Ill, 61-66; instr music, Univ Wis Ctr Syst, 66-69; asst prof to prof music, Univ Wis, Green Bay, 69- *Mailing Add:* CC-331 Univ Wis Green Bay WI 54301

COKER, WILSON
COMPOSER, EDUCATOR
b Pinckneyville, Ill, Nov 26, 28. *Study:* St Louis Inst Music, BM, 49; Yale Univ, BM, 51, MM, 54; Univ Ill, DMA, 54; Berkshire Music Ctr, with Milton Babbitt & Aaron Copland. *Works:* Trombone Concerto (with band), 61; Woodwind Quintet, 64; Concertino for Bassoon and String Trio, 64; Paean (large chorus & orch), 66; Lyric Statement (orch), 67; Polyphonic Ode (band), 69; Declarative Essay (orch), 70. *Pos:* Mem staff, Lincoln Ctr, 62-64. *Teaching:* Mem fac, Hartwik Col, 58-60, San Jose State Col, 64-68 & Fresno State Col, 68-75; prof theory & analysis, orch & comp, Southern Ill Univ, 76- *Awards:* John Day Jackson Prize, 54; Koussevitzky Prize, 59; Music Educr Nat Conf & Ford Found Grant, 60-63. *Publ:* Auth, Music and Learning, 71. *Mailing Add:* Sch Music Southern Ill Univ Carbondale IL 62901

COKKINIAS, PETER LEONIDAS
CONDUCTOR & MUSIC DIRECTOR, CLARINET
b Springfield, Mass, May 24, 45. *Study:* Hartt Sch Music, BM, 67, BMEd, 68; studied opera with Boris Goldovsky, 74-; Manhattan Sch Music, MM, 71; Col-Consv Music, Univ Cincinnati, DMA, 76. *Rec Perf:* Gurrelieder (Schoenberg), Deutsche Grammophon, 79; Yes Giorgio, MGM Film Studio, 81. *Pos:* Soloist, Boston Symph Orch, 62; Springfield Symph Orch, 72 & Boston Pops, 83; music dir, St Nicholas Greek Church, Newburgh, NY, 68-71 & Holy Trinity, St Nicholas Greek Church, Cincinnati, Ohio, 71-74; asst cond, Univ Cincinnati Wind Ens, 72-74; cond, Eastern Inst Orch Studies, Va, 74 & Southeastern Mass Univ Opera Inst, 75-79; artistic dir & cond, Community Opera Tufts, 76-78 & Tufts Opera Theater, 79-80; music dir & cond, Cambridge Opera Wkshp, 76 & Gtr Marlboro Symph Orch, Mass, 80-; vis cond, Mass Youth Wind Ens, New England Consv Music, 78-79; guest cond, Boston Pops, 79 & Cent Mass District Music Fest, 80 & 81; clarinet, Scarborough Chamber Players, 83-; clarinet, E-flat clarinet & bass clarinet, Boston Symph Orch, Boston Pops, Boston Ballet, Opera Co Boston, Boston Repty Ballet, Cincinnati Symph Orch, Cincinnati Opera Co, US Mil Acad Band West Point, Hartford Symph Orch, Conn Opera Co & Goodspeed Opera Co. *Teaching:* Dir instrm prog, Holy Trinity Elem & Jr High Sch, Poughkeepsie, NY, 68-71 & Our Lady Lourdes Elem & Jr High Sch, Cincinnati, Ohio, 72-74; lectr clarinet, Univ Cincinnati, 72; lectr clarinet, music educ, & perc tech, Anna Maria Col, Mass, 77-78; asst prof music & dir chamber music, bands & opera, Tufts Univ, 74-81; mem fac cond & clarinet, Boston Consv, 80- *Mem:* Cond Guild, Am Symph Orch League; Col Band Dir Nat Asn; Am Fedn Musicians. *Mailing Add:* Boston Consv 8 The Fenway Boston MA 02215

COLANERI, JOSEPH
CONDUCTOR, COACH
b Jersey City, NJ, Dec 14, 55. *Study:* NY Univ, BA, 77; Westminster Choir Col, MM, 80. *Pos:* Chorusmaster, New York City Opera, 83- *Awards:* Hanna von Vollenhallen Prize in Music, 77. *Mem:* Am Choral Dir Asn; Phi Beta Kappa. *Mailing Add:* 61 Danforth Ave Jersey City NJ 07305

COLBURN, DANIEL NELSON, II
ADMINISTRATOR
b Minneapolis, Minn, Sept 17, 47. *Study:* Macalester Col, AB, 69. *Pos:* Asst to gen mgr, St Paul Opera Co, 69-70; proj assoc, Arts Develop Assoc Inc, Minneapolis, 70-72; dir commun, Affil Artists Inc, 73-78; arts prog analyst, NY State Coun Arts, 78-80; exec dir, Am Guild Organists, 80- *Mem:* Am Guild Organists; Interfaith Forum Religion, Art & Architecture. *Mailing Add:* 815 Second Ave New York NY 10017

COLBY, EDWARD E(UGENE)
LIBRARIAN, TEACHER
b Oakland, Calif, July 5, 12. *Study:* Univ Calif, Berkeley, BA(music), 35, cert(librarianship), 41; Stanford Univ, MA(music), 56. *Pos:* Actg chief music div, Oakland Pub Libr, Calif, 46-49; music librn, Stanford Univ, 49-78; archivist recorded sound, 58-78. *Teaching:* Lectr music bibliog, Stanford Univ, 51-79. *Bibliog:* Marcia Tanner (auth), Colby Retires, Campus Report, Stanford Univ, 9/20/78. *Mem:* Music Libr Asn (pres, 50-52); Int Asn Music Libr; Asn Recorded Sound Collections; Int Asn Sound Archives; Am Musicol Soc. *Interests:* Use of sound recordings in scholarly research. *Publ:* Auth, prog notes, Carmel Bach Fest, 57-72; Sound Recordings in the Music Library: With Special Reference to Record Archives, 4/60 & Sound Scholarship: Scope, Purpose, Function and Potential of Phonorecord Archives, 7/72, Libr Trends; Early Days of Music Librarianship in the San Francisco Bay Area, Cum Notis Variorum, Univ Calif, Berkeley, 7-8/83. *Mailing Add:* 1749 Duvall Dr San Jose CA 95130

COLE, GERALD E
COMPOSER, EDUCATOR
b Topeka, Kans, Aug 29, 17. *Study:* Univ Kans; Oberlin Col, with Normand Lockwood; Eastman Sch Music, with Wayne Barlow. *Works:* String Quartet; harp pieces; organ pieces; 2-Piano Sonata; mass; motets; songs. *Teaching:* Mem fac, Tarkio Col, 40-44, Phillips Univ, 44-49 & Univ Western Ontario, 51-55; chmn & prof theory & analysis, comp & organ, Western Md Col, 55- *Mailing Add:* Music Dept Western Md Col Westminster MD 21157

COLE, MALCOLM STANLEY
EDUCATOR, ORGAN
b San Francisco, Calif, Apr 15, 36. *Study:* Univ Calif, Berkeley, BA, 58; Princeton Univ, MFA, 60, PhD, 64. *Pos:* Music dir, St Francis' Episcopal Church, San Francisco, 64-67. *Teaching:* Dean, San Francisco Consv Music, 64-67; asst prof musicol, Univ Calif, Los Angeles, 67-74, assoc prof, 74-82, prof, 82- *Awards:* Humanities Inst App, 71-72 & Fac Fel Humanities, 74-75, Univ Calif, Los Angeles; summer stipend, Nat Endowment Humanities, 76. *Mem:* Am Guild Organists (mem Los Angeles chap exec bd, 76-79); Am Musicol Soc (Pac SW chap secy-treas, 70-73, vpres, 80-82 & pres, 83-84); Am Soc 18th Century Studies; Int Musicol Soc. *Interests:* Viennese classicism; Austro-German emigre studies; opera. *Publ:* Auth, The Vogue of the Instrumental Rondo in the Late Eighteenth Century, J Am Musicol Soc, 69; Techniques of Surprise in the Sonata-Rondos of Beethoven, Studia Musicologica, 70; Afrika singt: Austro-German Echoes of the Harlem Renaissance, J Am Musicol Soc, 77; Eric Zeisl: The Rediscovery of an Emigre Composer, Musical Quart, 78; Haydn's Symphonic Rondo Finales: Their Structural and Stylistic Evolution, Haydn Yearbook, 82. *Mailing Add:* Dept Music Schoenberg Hall Univ Calif Los Angeles CA 90024

COLE, ORLANDO T
CELLO, EDUCATOR
b Philadelphia, Pa, Aug 16, 08. *Study:* Curtis Inst Music, BMus, 34. *Rec Perf:* Dover Beach (Samuel Barber), 31, Sonata for Cello-Piano (Samuel Barber), 32 & String Quartet (Samuel Barber), 36, First Perf. *Pos:* Cellist, Curtis String Quartet, 27-80. *Teaching:* Instr cello, Curtis Inst Music, 39-; prof, New Sch Music. *Mem:* Violoncello Soc NY (mem bd, 65-); Musical Fund Soc Philadelphia; Phildelphia Art Alliance. *Mailing Add:* 1017 Keystone Ave Upper Darby PA 19082

COLE, ULRIC
COMPOSER, PIANO
b New York, NY, Sept 9, 05. *Study:* Inst Music Arts, with Boyle and Goetschius, 23-24; Juilliard Grad Sch, with Josef Lhevinne & Rubin Goldmark, 24-27 & 30-32. *Works:* Sonata for Violin & Piano, Soc Publ Am Music, 30; Two Pieces for String Orchestra, perf by Wallenstein String Orch, 38; Divertimento for String Orchestra & Piano, J Fischer & Brother, 39; Quintet for Piano & Strings, Soc Publ Am Music, 41; Concerto No 2 for Piano & Orchestra, Cincinnati Symph, 46; Nevada (orch), perf by Scranton Phil, 49; Sunlight Channel (orch), perf by Sydney Symph, Australia, 55. *Teaching:* Piano & comp, Masters Sch, Dobbs Ferry, NY, 36-42. *Awards:* Fel, Juilliard Grad Sch, 24-27 & 30-32. *Bibliog:* Ewen (auth), American Composers Today, H W Wilson Co, 49; John Tasker Howard (auth), Our Contemporary Composers, Crowell Publ Co, 49; William Phemister (auth), 100 Years of American Piano Concertos, Col Music Soc (in prep). *Mem:* ASCAP; Am Music Ctr. *Mailing Add:* PO Box 284 Southport CT 06490

COLE, VINCENT L
COMPOSER, EDUCATOR
b Los Angeles, Calif, 1946. *Study:* Univ Calif, Los Angeles, with Alden Ashforth, Roy Travis & Henri Lazarof, BA, 69, PhD, 79; Calif State Univ, Northridge, with Aurelio de la Vega, MA, 75. *Works:* Lamentation (oboe & tape), 73; Meditation (piano & tape), 74; Cantata (sop & orch), 75; Distillations (solo cello), 77; Chronikos (chamber ens), 77; Wind Quintet, 78; Songs of the Sea (chorus & orch), 79. *Pos:* Mem staff, Electronic Music Lab, Calif State Univ, Northridge, 73-75. *Teaching:* Mem fac, Moorpark Col, currently. *Awards:* Atwater-Kent Comp Award. *Mem:* Nat Asn Comp; Am Musicol Soc. *Mailing Add:* 16823 McKeever St Granada Hills CA 91344

COLEMAN, RANDOLPH E
COMPOSER, EDUCATOR
b Charlottesville, Va, July 20, 37. *Study:* Northwestern Univ, with Anthony Donato, BM, 60, MM, 61, DM, 63. *Works:* Soundprint I (orch), 71; Event I, 71; Format I, 71; Format II, 71; Soundprint II (four pianos), 72; String Quartet, 73; Format III (musicians, dancers & lights), 73. *Teaching:* Asst prof, Winthrop Col, 63-65; asst prof music theory, Univ Tex, summer 65; prof comp & music theory, Consv Music, Oberlin Col, 65-; asst prof music theory & comp, Univ Mich, Interlochen, summers 69 & 70. *Awards:* William Faricy Award, 60; Int Soc Contemp Music Awards, 62-63; Fromm Found Grant, 64. *Mem:* Am Soc Univ Comp. *Mailing Add:* Consv Music Oberlin Col Oberlin OH 44074

COLF, HOWARD
CELLO, TEACHER
b Cincinnati, Ohio, July 6, 36. *Study:* Studied cello with Edgar Lustgarten, 49-56 & Gabor Rejto, 56-58; Univ Calif, Los Angeles, BA, 57. *Rec Perf:* Time Cycle, Columbia, 63; Solo Album (with Lincoln Mayorga), Sheffield-Town Hall, 72. *Pos:* Solo cellist, St Louis Symph, 62-63, Cincinnati Symph, 63-64, Buffalo Phil, 64-67 & Ojai Fest, 59, 61, 62, 63, 65 & 82. *Teaching:* Instr cello, State Univ NY, Buffalo, 64-68. *Mailing Add:* 8306 Wilshire Blvd #6048 Beverly Hills CA 90211

COLGRASS, MICHAEL CHARLES
COMPOSER, LECTURER
b Chicago, Ill, Apr 22, 32. *Study:* Berkshire Music Ctr, studied with Lukas Foss, 52-54; Aspen Music Ctr, studied with Darius Milhaud, 53; Univ Ill, BMus, 56. *Works:* As Quiet As, comn by Fromm Music Found, 66; New People, comn by Lincoln Ctr Chamber Music Soc, 69; The Earth's a Baked Apple, comn by Boston Symph, 69; Concertmasters, comn by Detroit Symph Orch, 75; Letter from Mozart, comn by Musica Aeterna Orch, 76; Deja Vu, comn by New York Phil, 77; Memento, comn by New World Fest, 82. *Awards:* Guggenheim Fel, 64-68; Pulitzer Prize, 78; Emmy, Nat Acad TV Arts & Sci, 82. *Bibliog:* Joseph Horowitz (auth), Musician of the Month: Michael Colgrass, Musical Am, 11/78; Mary Lou Humphrey (auth), Michal Colgrass: Music's Pulitzer Prize Winning Pitcher, Music J, 12/78; Soundings: The Music of Michael Colgrass, WGBH TV, Boston, 2/80. *Mem:* ASCAP; Am Music Ctr. *Publ:* Auth, A Composer Who'll Try Anything—Once, 68, Wanted: Music for the Young, 69, Then I Stood On My Head, 72 & Catch 22 for Composers: You Need Another Job to Support Yourself, 74, New York Times ; Living With the Demon, Music Mag, 83. *Mailing Add:* 583 Palmerston Ave Toronto ON M6G 2P6 Canada

COLLIER, CHARLES R
INSTRUMENT MAKER
b Washington, DC, Sept 10, 35. *Study:* Swarthmore Col; Univ Chicago; Chicago Art Inst; Art Students League, New York. *Pos:* Maker of early wind instruments including mute cornettos & cornettinos & Renaissance flutes, recorders & shawms, 72- *Mailing Add:* PO Box 9442 Berkeley CA 94709

COLLIER, GILMAN FREDERICK
COMPOSER, CONDUCTOR
b New York, NY, Apr 14, 29. *Study:* Harvard Univ, study with Walter Piston, AB, 50; Yale Sch Music, with Hindemith; Mannes Col, with Martinu; study piano with Nadia Reisenberg & cond with Pierre Monteux. *Works:* Sonata for Piano & Violin, perf by Editha Braham & Arlene Zallman, 58; Four Chicago Psalms, comn & perf by Chicago Children's Choir, 66; Three Piano Sonatas, perf by Helen Benham, 76-; Palindrome—A Dance Piece, comn & perf by Brookdale Community Col, 78; Almande Smedelyn (double reed quartet), perf by New York Kammermusiker, 78; Divertimento (double reed quintet), perf by Josef Marx Ens, 79; Xaipe (five E E Cummings songs) perf by Anne Runyon Hurd & G Collier, 82 & Judith Otten & Kevin Wood, 83. *Pos:* Music dir & cond, Monmouth Symph Orch, 64-72. *Teaching:* Fac mem theory, New Sch Social Res, 54-60; fac mem piano, theory & comp, Westchester Consv Music, 54-74; asst dir, Monmouth Consv Music, 69- *Mem:* Comp Guild NJ (treas, 81-); BMI. *Mailing Add:* 65 Larchwood Ave Oakhurst NJ 07755

COLLIER, NATHAN MORRIS
EDUCATOR, VIOLIN
b Clinton, Okla, July 23, 24. *Study:* Univ Okla, study violin with Margaret Farish, BMus, 49; Eastman Sch Music, study violin with Millard Taylor, MMus, 51; Univ Nebr, Lincoln, studied violin & cond with Emanuel Wishnow, 52-55 & 80-81; coaching with Janos Starker, David Dawson, Paul Rolland & Zvi Zeitlin, 70-75; Kans State Univ, study hist with Chappell White, 81. *Works:* Sarabande, perf by Charles Moon, 48-49; Ballade, perf by Frank Williams & Charles Moon, 49; Duo, perf by Richard Ferrin & Robert Dean, 51 & Morris and Aleta Collier, 74. *Pos:* First violinist, Lincoln String Quartet, 51-83 & Res String Quartet, Kans State Univ, 80-81; asst concertmaster, Lincoln Symph Orch, 53-; asst concertmaster, Nebr Chamber Orch, 74-83, concertmaster, 81-83; assoc concertmaster, Omaha Symph & Nebr Sinfonia, 76-77; actg concertmaster, Omaha Symph Orch, 77; concertmaster, Lincoln Little Symph, 77-78 & Lincoln Symph Orch, 78; co-concertmaster, Lincoln Civic Orch, 79-80 & 82-83. *Teaching:* Instr & consult string music, Lincoln Pub Sch, 51-68; private instr violin & viola, 51-; asst prof violin, strings & theory, Nebr Wesleyan Univ, 68-; asst prof music, Kans State Univ, 80-81. *Mem:* Am String Teachers Asn (pres Nebr unit, 66-68); Music Teachers Nat Asn (Nebr strings chmn, 66-74); Music Educr Nat Conf (Nebr orch chmn, 66-68); Nat Sch Orch Asn; Violin Soc Am. *Mailing Add:* 4544 Mohawk Lincoln NE 68510

COLLINS, DAVID EDWARD
VIOLIN, TEACHER
b Chicago, Ill, Nov 19, 49. *Study:* Eastman Sch Music, BMus, 71, perf cert, 71; studied with Josef Gingold & Carroll Glenn. *Pos:* First violin section, Milwaukee Symph Orch, 71-73, asst concertmaster, 73-74; first violin section, Indianapolis Symph Orch, 80-82, actg asst concertmaster, 82- *Teaching:* Private teaching. *Mailing Add:* 2733 Barbary Lane Indianapolis IN 46205

COLLINS, DON L
EDUCATOR, CONDUCTOR & MUSIC DIRECTOR
b Lamesa, Tex, Apr 25, 39. *Study:* Wayland Baptist Col, BA, 61; New Orleans Baptist Theol Sem, MCM, 63; Fla State Univ, MME, 68, PhD, 70. *Works:* On Independence (SSCB), 74, Praise Thee, Lord (SSCB), 75, Be Strong and Wise in the Lord (CCBB), 76, Three Proverbial Loves (SCB), 80, All for One World (SCB), 80, There is a Ladye (SCB), 80 & Come All Ye Fair and Tender Ladies (SCB), 80, Cambiata Press. *Rec Perf:* Man's Music, 76 & Choral Fantasy on Huckleberry Finn, 78, Pinnacle Sounds. *Pos:* Music minister, Date St Baptist Church, Plainview, Tex, 58-60, First Baptist Churches, Tex, 60-61, Miss, 61-63 & Fla, 63-67 & Dawson St Baptist Church, Thomasville, Ga, 67-70; cond, Univ Cent Ark Chorale & Bel Cantos, 70-75; founder & owner, Cambiata Press, 72-; founder & dir, Ark Boys Choir, 75-79 & Cambiata Vocal Music Inst Am, 79-; founder, Cambiata Studios for Gifted Singers, 82-; guest cond, 17 hon choirs. *Teaching:* Prof music, Univ Cent Ark, 70-; freelance lectr, 73- *Awards:* Cert Excellence, Music Educr Nat Conf, 78; Ten Yrs Serv Award,

Univ Cent Ark. *Bibliog:* John Cooksey (auth), The Development of a Contemporary Eclectic Theory of Training and Cultivation of the Junior High School Male Changing Voice, Part I, Choral J. *Mem:* Am Choral Dir Asn; Music Educr Nat Conf; Phi Mu Alpha Sinfonia. *Publ:* Auth, The Cambiata Concept of Boys Changing Voices, Church Musician, 69; The Adolescent Reading Singer, 77, ed, Music for Changing Voices Choral Library, 79 & The Cambiata Concept, A Comprehensive Philosophy and Methodology of Teaching Music to Adolescents, 81, Cambiata Press; auth, The Cambiata Concept, A Comprehensive Philosophy and Methodology of Teaching Music to Adolescents, Choral J, 82. *Mailing Add:* 1806 Bruce Conway AR 72032

COLLINS, MICHAEL B
EDUCATOR, MUSICOLOGIST
b Turlock, Calif, July 26, 30. *Study:* Stanford Univ, BA, 54, MA, 58, PhD, 63. *Teaching:* Asst prof, Eastman Sch Music, 64-68; prof, NTex State Univ, 68- *Awards:* Fulbright Fel, 63. *Mem:* Am Musicol Soc. *Interests:* Baroque performance practice. *Publ:* Auth, A Reconsideration of French Over-dotting, Music & Lett, 68; In Defense of the French Trill, J Am Musicol Soc, 73; Improvisation and Ornamentation (1600-1750), In: New Grove Dict Music & Musicians, 80; The Literary Background of I Capuleti ed i Montecchi, J Am Musicol Soc, 82; Tigrane, Harvard Univ Press, 83. *Mailing Add:* Sch Music NTex State Univ Denton TX 76203

COLLINS, PHILIP MICHAEL
COMPOSER, MUSIC DIRECTOR
b San Mateo, Calif, Nov 13, 51. *Study:* Univ Calif, Berkeley, with Edwin Dugger, summers 73-74; San Francisco State Univ, with Henry Onderdonk, BMus, 76. *Works:* Hymn to the City, San Francisco State Univ & San Francisco Museum, 75-76; Fast Food Worker Opera, 80-81 & Seven Haiku, 80-82, New Music Works; Sappho Songs, Sets I & II, Santa Cruz Women's Chorus & Veils of Isis, 81-83; Symphony No 1, perf by Santa Cruz Chamber Orch, 82; Concentrations I, comn by Rachel Rudich & Cory Grossman, 83; Clarinet Concertino, comn by Eternal Youth Orch, 83. *Pos:* Co-dir & adminr, New Music Works Santa Cruz, 79-; copyist & asst, Lou Harrison, 79-; accmp & comp, Pac Coast Prod, 81-; music rev, Santa Cruz Sentinel, 82- *Bibliog:* David Heckler (auth), Speaking on Writing, Santa Cruz Express, 7/83. *Mem:* Nat Asn Comp, USA. *Mailing Add:* 700 Spring St Santa Cruz CA 95060

COLLINS, RICHARD L
EDUCATOR, BARITONE
b Louisville, Ky. *Study:* Univ Louisville, BA, 45; Cincinnati Consv Music, BMus, 48; Columbia Univ, MA, 53; Ind Univ, DMus, 75. *Roles:* Gianni Schicchi, Birmingham Civic Opera, 64; Sharpless in Madama Butterfly, Lake George Opera, 65; Count in Marriage of Figaro, Birmingham Civic Opera, 66; Iago in Otello, 68 & Amonasro in Aida, 69, State Opera Fla; Rigoletto, 74 & Valentin in Faust, 75, Opera Co Jacksonville. *Pos:* Prin stage dir, Birmingham Civic Opera, 63-79; stage dir, Opera Co Jacksonville, 70- & Opera Memphis, 78-79; dir opera, Bayview Fest, Mich, 82. *Teaching:* Dir opera & prof voice, Auburn Univ, Ala, 48-56 & Fla State Univ, Tallahassee, 57-70; head vocal div, Millikin Univ, Decatur, Ill, 70-76, Memphis State Univ, 76-78, Houston Baptist Univ, 80- *Awards:* Gold Key Award, Fla State Univ, 70. *Mem:* Nat Opera Asn (vpres, 63-65 & pres, 66-67); Nat Asn Teachers Singing. *Mailing Add:* 8722 Reamer Houston TX 77074

COLLINS, WALTER STOWE
WRITER, EDUCATOR
b West Hartford, Conn, Jan 12, 26. *Study:* Yale Univ, AB, 48, BMus, 51; Univ Mich, MA, 53, PhD, 60; Oxford Univ, England, 57-58. *Pos:* Dir choral music, Auburn Univ, 51-55 & Univ Minn, Minneapolis, 58-60. *Teaching:* Chmn dept music, Oakland Univ, Rochester, Mich, 60-71; found, Meadow Brook Fest & Sch Music; prof music & assoc dean, Univ Colo, Boulder, 71- *Awards:* Fulbright Scholar, 57-58; Res Fel, Am Coun Learned Soc, 61; Cert Merit, Yale Sch Music, 80. *Mem:* Am Choral Dir Asn (pres, 77-79); Col Music Soc (pres, 71-74); Am Musicol Soc; charter mem, Int Fedn Choral Music (mem bd dir, 81-). *Interests:* Editing early choral music; bibliography and literature of choral music. *Publ:* Auth & ed, numerous articles and editions of music, 58-; co-ed, Thomas Weelkes: Collected Anthems, Musica Britannica, 66; coauth, Choral Conducting: A Symposium, Prentice-Hall, 73; ed, International Choral Bulletin, Int Fedn Choral Music, 81-; Familiar Choral Masterworks in Authoritative Editions, Hinshaw Music, 81- *Mailing Add:* Box 301 Univ Colo Boulder CO 80309

COLON, EVANGELINA
SOPRANO
b Guayama, PR; US citizen. *Study:* PR Music Consv, BM, 68; Sch Music, Fla State Univ, MM, 70, DM, 72; vocal studies with Elena Nikolaidi, Eleanor Steber & Rita Patane. *Roles:* Micaela in Carmen, Opera PR, 75; Mimi in La Boheme, New York City Opera Theater, 78; Giorgetta in Tabarro, Pan Am Opera, 78; Nedda in I Pagliacci, New York City Opera Theater, 78 & Pan Am Opera, 79; Marguerite in Faust, Singers Theater, 79; Elvira in Macias, 81 & Rosalinda in Die Fledermaus, 83, Opera San Juan. *Pos:* Distinguished interpreter of Spanish Zarzuela. *Awards:* Winner, Int Sing Comp, Chilean Govt, 75; Opera Singer of Year, Inst PR, 76; Award for Young Am Singer, Nat Opera Inst, 81. *Bibliog:* Kathleen Golden (auth), Opera Star's Leap from Crib to Stage in Record Time, Dateline PRUSA, 3-4/81; Edmundo Lopez (auth), Los Valores de Colon, La Voz, 6/10/82; Michelle Berberena (auth), Opera Star, Arbutus, 2/83. *Mem:* Am Guild Musical Artists. *Rep:* Robert Lombardo Assoc 61 W 62nd St New York NY 10023. *Mailing Add:* 201 W 70th St New York NY 10023

COLUMBRO, MADELINE MARY
EDUCATOR
b Aurora, Ohio, Mar 16, 34. *Study:* Notre Dame Col, Ohio, BA, 56; Catholic Univ Am, MA, 66; Case Western Reserve Univ, PhD, 74. *Teaching:* Head music dept, Notre Dame Col, 63-; adj prof music & humanities, Lakeland Community Col, 79-81; prof music hist, Borromeo Col, 82. *Awards:* Fel, Newberry Libr, 73; Ranney Found Scholar, 73-74; Grant, Nat Endowment Humanities, 77 & 80. *Mem:* Am Musicol Soc; Renaissance Soc Am; Cleveland Medieval Soc; Am Rec Soc. *Interests:* Medieval and Renaissance motet repertory. *Publ:* Auth, The Chanson-Motet: A Remnant of the Courtly Love Tradition, Music and Man, 74; Schools, Music and Liturgy, Not Enough Hours, Pastoral Music, 76; Courtly Love Themes in the Franco-Flemish Chanson Motet, Studies in Med Culture, 76; Special Teachers for Special Children, Am Music Teacher, 78; Dropping the Arts ... A Betrayal of Liturgy, Today's Catholic Teacher, 79. *Mailing Add:* 4545 College Rd Cleveland OH 44121

COLVIG, DAVID
FLUTE
b Medford, Ore, Apr 8, 19. *Study:* San Francisco State Col; Curtis Inst Music, dipl, 48. *Pos:* Second flute & solo alto flute, Houston Symph Orch, 48- *Mailing Add:* 6426 Sewanee Houston TX 77005

COLVIN, (OTIS) HERBERT, JR
EDUCATOR, COMPOSER
b El Dorado, Ark, Mar 18, 23. *Study:* Baylor Univ, BA, 44, BMus, 48; Univ Colo, MMus, 50; Eastman Sch Music, PhD, 58. *Works:* Organ Voluntaries on American Hymn Tunes, 64 & Short Pieces for Organ, 71, Carl Fischer, Inc; For Sunday (six chorale preludes), Word, Inc, 72; Editions of five sacred choruses by William Billings, Elkan-Vogel, Inc, 75-79; Gloria (anthem for mixed voices, accmp), Triune Music, Inc, 76; Nine Hymn Settings for Organ, Broadman Press, 76; Make a Joyful Noise (anthem for mixed voices, accmp), Word, Inc, 82. *Teaching:* Instr piano, Tex Technol Col, 50-55; grad asst, Eastman Sch Music, 55-57; asst prof piano, Baylor Univ, 57-62, chmn dept, 58-64, assoc prof theory, 62-64, prof & coordr theory div, 64- *Mem:* Am Guild Organists (dean, Waco chap, 58-60, 68-69); Music Teachers Nat Asn; Tex Soc Music Theory (treas, 83-); ASCAP. *Publ:* Auth, Contemporary American Piano Music, Am Music Teacher, 1-2/65; The Educated Guess, 8/67, The Organist's Theory Background, 6/69 & The Organist's Theory Background: Improvisation, 8/69; Church Musician; Organ Techniques (The Organist's Theory Background), Music Ministry, 2/73. *Mailing Add:* 80 Cottonwood St Waco TX 76706

COLWELL, RICHARD JAMES
EDUCATOR
b Sioux Falls, SDak, May 27, 30. *Study:* Univ SDak, BFA, 53, MM, 53; Univ Ill, EdD, 61. *Teaching:* Sioux Falls Pub Sch, 53-55; assoc prof, Eastern Mont Col, 55-61; prof, Univ Ill, Urbana, 61- *Awards:* John Guggenheim Found Fel, 75. *Mem:* Music Educr Nat Conf; Coun Res in Music Educ; Col Music Soc. *Interests:* Evaluation of perceptual abilities. *Publ:* Auth, The Teaching of Instrumental Music, Appleton Century, 69; Music Achievement Tests, Follett Publ Co, 70; The Evaluation of Music Teaching and Learning, Prentice-Hall, 70; coauth, Concepts for a Musical Found, Prentice-Hall, 75; auth, Silver Burdett Competing Tests, Silver Burdett, 79. *Mailing Add:* Music Dept Ill Univ Urbana IL 61801

COMBERIATI, CARMELO PETER
EDUCATOR
b New York, NY, June 10, 52. *Study:* NY Univ, BS(music), 74; State Univ NY, MA(music), 76; Univ Vienna, with Walter Pass, 80-82; Univ Mich, PhD(musicol), 83. *Pos:* Book rev ed, J Musicol Res, 81-, assoc ed, 83- *Teaching:* Instr music hist, Univ Mich, Ann Arbor, 82-83; asst prof, Manhattanville Col, 83- *Awards:* Fulbright-Hays Fel, 80-82. *Mem:* Am Musicol Soc; Oesterreichische Gesellschaft Musikwissenschaft; Friends Hill Monastic Ms Libr. *Interests:* Renaissance and Medieval music, particularly settings of the Mass, early Organum, and lute music. *Publ:* Auth, The Modal Implications in Two Pieces of Organum, 81 & On The Threshold of Homophony: Some Aspects of Texture in 16th Century Lute Music, 83, J Musicol Res; Late Renaissance Music at the Habsburg Court: Masses at the Court of Rudolf II (1576-1612), Gordon & Breach, 83; co-ed, Essays in Honor of Gwynn S McPeek, Gordon & Breach (in prep). *Mailing Add:* Dept Music Manhattanville Col Purchase NY 10577

COMBOPIANO, CHARLES ANGELO
DIRECTOR—OPERA, MUSIC DIRECTOR
b Rome, NY, Aug 8, 35. *Study:* Syracuse Univ, BMus, 57; NY Univ; private cond study with Laszlo Halasz. *Pos:* Gen mgr & art dir, Whitewater Opera Co Inc, Richmond, Ind, 72-; music dir, Peterloon Opera Fest, Cincinnati, 82- *Teaching:* Instr music, State Univ NY, Stony Brook, 69-70; asst prof, Earlham Col, Richmond, Ind, 70-76. *Bibliog:* Sharon Little (auth), Combopiano Brings Opera to Richmond, Ft Wayne News Sentinel, 10/10/81; Joanne Douglass (auth), Whitewater Opera: Spirit of Business Arts, Ind Arts Insight, 4/83; Stephen Stroff (auth), News From: Indiana-Whitewater Opera, Opera News Mag, 1/29/83. *Mem:* Consortium Ind Advocates Opera (pres, 82-); Ind Assembly Arts Coun (bd mem, 77-); Ind Presenters Network (bd mem, 83-); Ind Arts Comn Music Gen Panel (chmn, 82-); Nat Opera Asn (Ind gov, 83-). *Rep:* Whitewater Opera Co Inc PO Box 633 805 Promenade Richmond IN 47374. *Mailing Add:* 861 Hidden Valley Lane Richmond IN 47374

COMBS, F MICHAEL
COMPOSER, EDUCATOR
b Hazard, Ky, May 30, 43. *Study:* Univ Ill, with Jack McKenzie & Thomas Siwe, BS; Univ Mo, MA. *Works:* Concert Snare Drum Solos, 68; Gesture (solo perc), 69; Mano Dance, 71; Leatherwood, 71. *Pos:* Prin timpanist, Knoxville Symph, currently. *Teaching:* Mem fac, Univ Tenn, Knoxville, 72-; instr perc, Knoxville Col, currently. *Mailing Add:* 501 Kendall Rd Knoxville TN 37919

COME, ANDRE
TRUMPET, EDUCATOR
Study: Trumpet with Marcel LaFosse. *Rec Perf:* On RCA, Polydor, Deutsche Grammophon & Columbia. *Pos:* Mem, Baltimore Symph Orch, formerly & US Air Force Band, formerly; mem trumpet sect, Boston Symph Orch, 57-; prin trumpet, Boston Pops, currently. *Teaching:* Mem fac, Boston Univ, formerly, Boston Consv Music, formerly, Brown Univ, currently & New England Consv Music, currently. *Mailing Add:* New England Consv Music 290 Huntinton Rd Boston MA 02115

COMET, CATHERINE
CONDUCTOR & MUSIC DIRECTOR
b France. *Study:* Juilliard Sch Music, MMus(orch cond); studied with Pierre Boulez, Nadia Boulanger & Igor Markevich. *Pos:* Music dir & cond, Symph & Chamber Orch, Univ Wis, Madison, formerly; Exxon-Arts Endowment cond, St Louis Symph Orch, currently; music dir, St Louis Youth Orch, currently; guest cond, BBC Symph Orch, London, Paris Orch Phil & Orch Nat de l'Opera; vis cond, Chamber Orch, Nat Radio, Iran. *Awards:* First Prize, Int Young Cond Compt, France, 66; Dimitri Mitroupolos Int Cont Prize, 68. *Mailing Add:* St Louis Symph 718 N Grand St Louis MO 63103

COMISSIONA, SERGIU
MUSIC DIRECTOR & CONDUCTOR, EDUCATOR
b Bucharest, Romania, June 16, 28. *Study:* Consv Romania, Bucharest, with E Lindenberg & C Silvestri; Peabody Consv Music, Hon MusD, 72; Loyola Col, LHD, 73; Western Md Col, Hon DFA, 77; Towson State Univ, LHD, 80; Washington Col, Hon DFA, 80; Univ Md, Hon DFA, 81. *Rec Perf:* Maestro di cappella, Swedish TV video; rec with Haifa Symph Orch, Israel, Stockholm Phil, Suisse Romande, London Symph Orch, Baltimore Symph Orch & Houston Symph. *Pos:* Violinist, Bucharest, 46-48; music dir, Rumanian State Ens Orch, 50-55; Haifa Symph Orch, Israel, 59-66; Israel Chamber Orch, 60-65; Göteborg Symph Orch, Sweden, 66-72 & Baltimore Symph Orch, 69-84; music dir, Rumanian State Opera, 55-59; music adv & cond, Ulster Orch, Belfast, Ireland, 67-69; music adv, Music Fest, Temple Univ, 75-76; artistic dir, 76-80; music dir & prin cond, Chautauqua Symph Orch Summer Fest, 76-78; music adv, Am Symph Orch, 78-82; artistic adv, Houston Symph, 80-83; music dir, 83-; permanent guest cond, Radio Phil Orch, Netherlands, 82- *Teaching:* Artist in res & cond orch, Shepherd Sch Music, Rice Univ, currently. *Awards:* Winner, Int Compt Young Cond, Besancon, France, 56; Gold Medal, City of Göteborg, 76; Ditson Cond Award, Columbia Univ, 79. *Rep:* ICM Artists Mgt 40 W 57th St New York NY 10019. *Mailing Add:* c/o Houston Symphony 615 Louisiana Houston TX 77002

COMPTON, CATHERINE LOUISE
VIOLA
b Detroit, Mich, Feb 26, 48. *Study:* Oberlin Col, AB, 69; Univ Mich, MMus, 81. *Pos:* Violist, Detroit Symph Orch, 73- *Mem:* Int Conf Symph & Opera Musicians (cent area vchmn, 81-83). *Interests:* Revised International Conference of Symphony and Opera Musicians conductor evaluation form. *Publ:* Auth, A New Computerized Conductor Evaluation Form, Senza Sordino, Vol 21, No 2. *Mailing Add:* 221 E Boston Blvd Detroit MI 48202

CONABLE, WILLIAM G, JR
CELLO, MUSIC DIRECTOR
b Buffalo, NY, Sept 1, 42. *Study:* Univ Ill, with Peter Farrell, AB, 64; Boston Univ, with Richard Kapuscinski, MM, 65, with Leslie Parnas, DMA, 69. *Pos:* Prin cellist, Youngstown Symph, 68-72 & Columbus Symph, 77-; music dir, Knox Co Symph, Mt Vernon, Ohio, 79-82 & Ohio Light Opera, 81-82. *Teaching:* Asst prof cello, Youngstown State Univ, 68-72 ; assoc prof, Ohio State Univ, 72- *Mem:* Am Fedn Musicians; Am String Teachers Asn; Music Educr Nat Conf. *Interests:* Alexander technique. *Mailing Add:* 1866 N College Rd Columbus OH 43210

CONANT, RICHARD PAUL
EDUCATOR, BASS
b New York, NY, Mar 16, 41. *Study:* Univ Calif, Los Angeles, BA(music), 63; Univ Md, College Park, MM(choral cond), 70; Univ Tex, Austin, DMA(choral cond), 77. *Pos:* Bass singer, Roger Wagner Chorale, 60-65 & US Army Chorus, 66-70; singer & cond, various SE regional co, orch & political events, 73- *Teaching:* Asst instr choral music, Univ Md, College Park, 67-68; grad asst, Univ Tex, Austin, 70-73; assoc prof choral & vocal music, Univ SC, Columbia, 73- *Mem:* Am Choral Dir Asn; Music Educr Nat Conf; Am Choral Found; SC Music Educr Asn. *Mailing Add:* 2716 Diane Dr Columbia SC 29210

CONANT, ROBERT S
HARPSICHORD, EDUCATOR
b Passaic, NJ, Jan 6, 28. *Study:* Yale Univ, studied harpsichord with Ralph Kirkpatrick, BA, 49, MM, 56; Juilliard Sch, 49-50. *Rec Perf:* Elliott Carter Sonata, CBS, 58; Bach Concerti, Decca, 62; Yale Collection of Musical Instruments (solo), Yale Univ, 65. *Pos:* Pres & artistic dir, Found Baroque

Music, 59- *Teaching:* Asst prof ens & curator, Collection Musical Instrm, Sch Music, Yale Univ, 61-66; assoc prof music hist, Chicago Musical Col, Roosevelt Univ, 67-71, prof, 71- *Mem:* Col Music Soc (treas, 71-75); Am Musicol Soc; Am Musical Instrm Soc. *Interests:* Contemporary harpsichord music; history of basso continuo. *Publ:* Coauth, Twentieth Century Harpsichord Music: A Classified Catalog, Joseph Boonin, 74. *Rep:* George Cochran Assoc 225 W 57th St New York NY 10019. *Mailing Add:* 154 Maple Ave Wilmette IL 60091

CONE, EDWARD TONER
CRITIC, WRITER
b Greensboro, NC, May 4, 17. *Study:* Princeton Univ, AB, 39, MFA, 42. *Works:* Let Us Now Praise Famous Men (male chorus), Princeton Choir and Glee Club, 47; Elegy (orch), perf by Princeton Symph Orch, 54; Excursions (mixed chorus), Rongwen, 55; Prelude, Passacaglia, and Fugue (piano), perf by E T Cone, 59; Nocturne and Rondo for Piano and Orch, 62 & Violin Concerto, 64, perf by Princeton Symph; Music for Strings, comn by NJ Bicentennial Fest Orch, 64. *Teaching:* Asst prof, Princeton Univ, 47-52, assoc prof, 52-60, prof comp, theory & analysis, 60-; A D White prof at large, Cornell Univ, 79- *Awards:* Guggenheim Fel, 47; Deems Taylor Award, ASCAP, 75. *Publ:* Co-ed, Perspectives on Schoenberg and Stravinsky, Princeton Univ, 68; auth, Musical Form and Musical Performance, Norton, 68; co-ed, Perspectives on American Composers, Norton, 71; auth, The Composer's Voice, Univ Calif, 74; ed, Roger Sessions on Music, Princeton Univ, 79. *Mailing Add:* 18 College Rd W Princeton NJ 08540

CONLIN, THOMAS (BYRD)
CONDUCTOR & MUSIC DIRECTOR
b Arlington, Va, Jan 29, 44. *Study:* Peabody Consv Music, BMus, 66, MMus, 67; study with Leonard Bernstein, Erich Leinsdorf & Sir Adrian Boult. *Pos:* Artistic dir, Chamber Opera Soc Baltimore, 66-72; assoc cond, NC Symph Orch, 72-74; music dir, Queens Orchestral Soc, New York, 74-76; cond, Amarillo Symph Orch, 76- & Charleston Symph Orch, 83- *Teaching:* Asst prof music, Queens Col, City Univ New York, 74-76. *Mem:* Cond Guild, Am Symph Orch League; Nat Opera Asn; Cent Opera Serv. *Mailing Add:* 4116 Julie Dr Amarillo TX 79109

CONNOLLY, MARTHA (NIXON TAUGHER)
MEZZO-SOPRANO, EDUCATOR
b Mt Vernon, Ohio. *Study:* Univ Mich, BMus, 60; Cath Univ Am, MMus, 71; studied piano with Meyers, voice with Katharine Hansel, Roland Wyatt & Genevieve McGiffert. *Roles:* Cherubino in Le Nozze di Figaro & Marcellina in Fidelio, 69-73, Wash Lyr Opera; Donna Elvira in Don Giovanni & Siebel in Faust; perf works by Walter Ross, Vix Grahm, Robert Johnson & Winifred Hyson. *Pos:* Soloist, Cath Cathedral, Washington Hebrew Congregation & Church of the Annunciation, Washington DC. *Teaching:* Voice, Cath Univ, 70-73; lectr, Mt Vernon Col, 73-79, Univ Va, 78-80 & Col William & Mary, 79- *Mem:* Nat Asn Teachers Singing; Kindler Found; Am Asn Univ Prof; Music Educr Nat Conf; Am Musicol Soc. *Mailing Add:* Music Dept Col William & Mary Williamsburg VA 23185

CONRAD, LAURIE M
COMPOSER
b Manhattan, NY, July 5, 46. *Study:* Ithaca Col, with Karel Husa, BM, MM, 70. *Works:* Voiles (ballet), 79 & Seaglass (ballet), 82, Ithaca Ballet; Pas a Deux (two clarinets), Stanley & Naomi Drucker, 80; Prelude & Dance (solo cello), Chase Morrison, 81; Etoiles, Contemp Players New York City, 81; Preludes, 82 & L'Apparition, 83, Contemp Players, Washington, DC. *Bibliog:* Garden Concert, Ithaca Video Project, 80. *Mem:* ASCAP; Am Women Comp Inc. *Mailing Add:* 113 1/2 W Buffalo St Ithaca NY 14850

CONSOLI, MARC-ANTONIO
COMPOSER, MUSIC DIRECTOR
b Catania, Italy, May 19, 41; nat US. *Study:* New York Col Music, BMus, 66; Peabody Consv, MMus, 67; Yale Univ, MMA, 71, DMA, 77; Warsaw Consv, Poland; Accad Chigiana, Italy; Berkshire Music Ctr; studied with Ernst Krenek, Gunther Schuller & George Crumb. *Works:* Tre Fiori Musical (flute & guitar), 78; Vuci Siculani (ms & chamber ens), 79; Naked Masks (orch), 80; The Last Unicorn (orch), 81; Orpheus Meditation (guitar), 81; Afterimages (orch), 82; Fantasia Celeste (sop & ens), 83. *Pos:* Dir & perf, Yale Players New Music, 69-74, Experiment, Poland, 74 & Musica Oggi, New York. *Awards:* Guggenheim Found Fel, 71-72 & 79-80; Fulbright Fel, 72-74; Nat Endowment Arts Grant, 79. *Mem:* BMI; Am Comp Alliance; Am Music Ctr. *Mailing Add:* 95-27 239th St Bellerose NY 11426

CONSTANTEN, THOMAS CHARLES STURE
COMPOSER, PIANO
b Long Branch, NJ, Mar 19, 44. *Study:* Univ Nev, Las Vegas, 60-61; Kranichsteiner Musikinstitut, Germany, 62-63; Studio di Fonologia Musicale, Italy; studied comp with Luciano Berio, Henri Pousseur, Pierre Boulez & Karlheinz Stockhausen, piano with Mario Feninger & violin with Frank E Iddings. *Works:* Conversation Piece (piano & orch), Antonio Morelli & Orch, 61; Tarot (musical), Chelsea Theater Ctr, New York, & Circle in Square, New York, 70-71; A Giraffe of Wyne (& Thou), perf by Donald Knaack, 74; The Syntax Collector, Capricorn Asunder Gallery, Calif, 76-; Dejavalse, C F Peters, 78; Sonata Desaxificata, comn by Margaret Fabrizio, 81; Lignified Rock Episodes, Kronos String Quartet, 82. *Pos:* Comp & perf, San Francisco Mime Troupe, 64; keyboard, Grateful Dead, 68-70; arr, cond & perf, Incredible String Band, 70; comp & music dir, Tarot, N/R Prod, 70-71; comp in res, Twelfth Ann Mozart Fest, Calif, 82; comp & piano soloist, US & Europe. *Teaching:* Prof comp, State Univ NY, Buffalo, 74-75; instr piano &

theory, Community Music Ctr, San Francisco, 80- *Awards:* Second Place Off-Broadway Comp, New York Critics' Circle Poll, 70-71. *Mem:* ASCAP; Am Fedn Musicians. *Interests:* Harpsichord music of Frederick William Herschel. *Mailing Add:* 314 1/2 49th St Oakland CA 94609

CONSTANTINIDES, DINOS (CONSTANTINE DEMETRIOS)
COMPOSER, VIOLIN
b Ioannina, Greece, May 10, 29; US citizen. *Study:* Greek Consv, Athens, dipl(violin), 50, (theory), 57; Juilliard Sch Music, with Galamian, dipl(violin), 60; Ind Univ, with Gingold, MM(violin), 65; Mich State Univ, with Owen Reed, PhD(comp), 68. *Works:* Four Songs on Poems by Sappho, 68-71, Dedications, 74 & Impressions for Clarinet and Piano, 75, Seesaw; Fantasy for Solo Euphonium, perf by L Campbell, 78; Mountains of Epirus (concerto violin & orch), comn by Atlanta Community Orch, 80; Intimations (one act opera), Brooklyn Col, 81; Reflections II (viola & voice), perf by J Kozmala & R Rees, 82. *Pos:* First violinist, Athens State Orch, Athens Radio Orch, 52-57 & 61-63, Indianapolis Symph Orch, 63-65; concertmaster & assoc cond, Baton Rouge Symph, 66-; concertmaster, Baton Rouge Opera, 82- *Teaching:* Prof comp & violin, Sch Music, La State Univ, 66- *Awards:* Seven ASCAP Awards for serious music, 76-83; 4 grants, Meet the Comp, New York, 79-; First Prize, Brooklyn Col Chamber Opera Comp Cont, 81. *Mem:* Am Soc Univ Comp (mem nat coun, 81-83); Music Teachers Nat Asn; ASCAP; Music Educr Nat Conf; La Music Teachers Asn (chmn instrm div, 83-84). *Publ:* Auth, The Bach Chaconne, La Musician, 11/72; New Audiences and the "New Times" at the LSU Union Art Gallery, In: Monographs on Higher Educ, Nat Asn Sch Music, 2/74 & In: La Musician, 2/75. *Mailing Add:* 947 Daventry Dr Baton Rouge LA 70808

CONTI, JOSEPH JOHN
PERCUSSION
b Providence, RI, July 18, 47. *Study:* New England Consv Music, BM, 70; Berkshire Music Fest; studied with Vic Firth. *Pos:* Perc, Milwaukee Symph Orch, 72- *Mailing Add:* 2656 N 72nd Milwaukee WI 53213

COOK, CARLA
EDUCATOR, MEZZO-SOPRANO
b Salt Lake City, Utah. *Study:* Univ Utah, BMusEd, 74; Boston Univ, MMus, 75; Manhattan Sch Music, 80. *Roles:* Octavian in Der Rosenkavalier, Music Acad West, 77; Composer in Ariadne auf Naxos, Des Moines Metropolitan Opera, 80; Tisbe in La Cenerentola, Miss Opera, 80; Isakella in Wuthering Heights, Portland Opera, 82; Melinda in L'Ormindo, Bianca in The Rape of Lucretia, Siegrune in Die Walküre & Girl No 5 in Rise and Fall of the City of Mahagonny, San Francisco Spring Opera, 83; perf with Metropolitan Opera, San Francisco Opera, Seattle Opera and others. *Awards:* Metropolitan Opera Nat Auditions Winner, 82; Munich Int Vocal Compt Winner, 82; San Francisco Opera Auditions Winner, 82. *Mailing Add:* 1778 Nevada St Salt Lake City UT 84108

COOK, DEBORAH
SOPRANO
b Philadelphia, Pa. *Study:* Private study with Irene Williams & Nicola Palumbo. *Rec Perf:* Prascovia in L'Etoile du Nord, Opera Rara, 74; Nyade in Ariadne auf Naxos, EMI, 77; Dinorah in Dinorah, Opera Rara, 78; Zerbinetta (original version) with BBC Symph, 81. *Roles:* Lucia in Lucia di Lammermoor Buxton Fest; Constanze, Bavarian State Opera; Fiakermilli, Royal Opera, Covent Garden ; Queen of the Night in Die Zauberflöte, Deutsche Oper & Hamburg State Opera; Gilda in Rigoletto, Royal Opera, Covent Garden; Rachel in We Come to the River, Deutsche Oper, Berlin; Zerbinetta in Ariadne auf Naxos, Glyndebourne Opera; all roles between 72-82. *Pos:* Coloratura sop, Bremen Opera, 72-77 & Bavarian State Opera, 79-81; perf with major symphonies in US & Europe. *Mem:* Am Guild Musical Artists. *Mailing Add:* c/o Robert Lombardo Assoc One Harkness Plaza 61 W 62nd St New York NY 10023

COOK, GARY D
PERCUSSION, EDUCATOR
b Jackson, Mich, Jan 20, 51. *Study:* Univ Mich, BM, 72, MM, 75. *Works:* Ode II (perc ens), 72; Time on Time, 76 & Sunrise Ceremonial, 78, Univ Ariz; Idols, Ariz Fac Dance, 80. *Pos:* Timpanist & prin perc, Tucson Symph & Ariz Opera Orch, 75- *Teaching:* Instr music, La Tech Univ, 72-75; assoc prof music, Univ Ariz, 75- *Mem:* Percussive Arts Soc; Am Music Teachers Nat Asn; Nat Asn Col Wind & Perc Instr. *Publ:* Auth, Teaching Percussion, Schirmer Books (in press). *Mailing Add:* Sch Music Univ Ariz Tucson AZ 85721

COOK, JEAN LOUISE
SOPRANO
b Phoenix, Ariz, Mar 6, 37. *Study:* Univ Calif, Santa Barbara, BA, 58; Music Acad West, 58-60; Univ Southern Calif; Univ Calif, Los Angeles, with Lotte Lehmann, 58-60; Univ Southern Calif; Univ Calif, Los Angeles, with Jan Popper; studied with William Eddy & Dixie Neill. *Rec Perf:* On Decca. *Roles:* Pamina in Die Zauberflöte, Operhaus Zurich, 60; Elsa in Lohengrin; Arabella in Arabella; Elizabeth in Tannhauser; Chrysothemis in Eleka. *Pos:* Singer with maj opera co in US & Europe; recitalist & appearances with maj orchs in US & Europe. *Awards:* Rockefeller Grant, 60 & 64; Univ Calif Award for Distinquished Achievement, 75. *Mem:* Am Guild Musical Artists. *Mailing Add:* 1442 12th St Los Osos CA 93402

COOK, JEFF HOLLAND
CONDUCTOR & MUSIC DIRECTOR, COMPOSER
b Chicago, Ill, Aug, 21, 40. *Study:* Northwestern Univ, BM, 62; Berkshire Music Ctr, 63, 64 & 70; Ohio State Univ, MA, 64; New England Consv

Music, MM, 66; Boston Univ, 71-72; studied with Barbirolli, Boulez & Leinsdorf. *Works:* The Herne's Egg, 71 & Electra, 72, Boston Univ Theatre. *Pos:* Asst cond, RI Phil, 66-68; cond, Omnibus Contemp Music Series, Boston, 71-73; guest cond, Greenboro Symph, NC, 75, Orquesta Sinfonica Nac, Dominican Repub, 75, NC Symph, 76, RI Phil, 78, Eastern Music Fest, NC, 80, Inland Empire Symph, Calif, 82 & Anchorage Symph Orch, 82; music dir, Wheeling Symph, WVa, 73- & Mansfield Symph, Ohio, 76- *Teaching:* Mem cond fac, Boston Univ, 71-73. *Awards:* Award for Innovative Prog, ASCAP, 73-74. *Mailing Add:* RD 4 Box 116 Wheeling WV 26003

COOK, PETER FRANCIS
COMPOSER, ORGAN
b Morristown, NJ, Sept 1, 23. *Study:* Oberlin Col, Consv Music, BM, 46, MM, 50; Peabody Consv Music, DMA, 75. *Works:* Forlana (pianoforte), The Paddle Wheel, Vespers in Silvara, Indian Summer, Op Music Publ; Mice in Three Blind Keys, Plaint at Sundown, There's a Cricket in the House, Boston Music Co. *Teaching:* Instr, Fla State Univ, 46-47 & Mont State Univ, 48-49; asst prof, Mason Col, Charleston, WVa, 55-56; assoc prof piano, organ, comp, music appreciation, Austin Peay State Univ, 56- *Mem:* Phi Alpha Sinfonia; Tenn Fedn Music Clubs. *Mailing Add:* Austin Peay State Univ Box 4426 Clarksville TN 37040

COOK, REBECCA
SOPRANO
b Chattanooga, Tenn. *Study:* Univ Tenn, BM; Ind Univ, with Margaret Harshaw, MM(vocal perf). *Roles:* Cio-Cio San in Madama Butterfly, Hidden Valley Opera, 78; Elektra in Elektra, 79, Fiordiligi in Cosi fan tutte, Amelia in Un Ballo in maschera, 82 & Countess in The Marriage of Figaro, 82, San Francisco Opera; Mariane in Tartuffe, Am Opera Project; Mary Seaton in Mary, Queen of Scots. *Pos:* Sop with various opera co. *Awards:* First Prize, Grand Finals San Francisco Opera Auditions, 78. *Mailing Add:* 40 Cliffside Crossing Atlanta GA 30338

COOK, RICHARD G
COMPOSER, EDUCATOR
b Dallas, Tex, Oct 20, 29. *Study:* Tex Christian Univ, with Ralph Guenther; NTex State Univ, with Samuel Adler. *Works:* Concertino for Orchestra; 3 Songs of Hopelessness (sop & piano), 63; String Quartet, 72; Concert Piece (trumpet & piano); Psalm 137 (chorus); The Hydrogen Dog and the Cobalt Cat (sop & tape), 72; Requiem for Mahalia (viola, piano & tape), 72. *Teaching:* Handley High Sch, 57-61 & Univ Tex, Arlington, 62-63; assoc prof music, Kans State Univ, Pittsburg, 66- *Awards:* Rockefeller Found Grants (two). *Mailing Add:* 402 W First Pittsburg KS 66762

COOK, TERRY
BASS
b Tex. *Study:* Tex Tech Univ. *Roles:* Mityukh in Boris Godunov, 80, Macbeth, 81, Fidelio, 81 & Romeo et Juliette, 81, Lyr Opera Chicago; Requiem, Midland-Odessa Symph, Tex, 82; Tosca, 83; Don Fernando in Fidelio, Florentine Opera Milwaukee, 83; Raimondo in Lucia di Lammermoor, Minn Opera Co, 83. *Pos:* Performer, Chicago Symph, formerly, Lyr Opera Chicago, 80-82, Santa Fe Opera, formerly, Midland-Odessa Symph, Tex, 82, Florentine Opera Milwaukee, 83 & Minn Opera Co, 83. *Mailing Add:* c/o Theo Dispeker 59 E 54th St New York NY 10022

COOK, WAYNE EVANS
TRUMPET, CONDUCTOR
b Pearsall, Tex, Dec, 1939. *Study:* NTex State Univ, BMus, 62; Univ Ill, MS(music educ), 64; Eastman Sch Music, 65. *Rec Perf:* NTex State Univ Conct Band, Austin Rec, 60; Univ Ill Conct Band, Columbia Rec, 63; Compositions (John Downey), Orion Master Rec, 70; Band Music of the Confederacy, Heritage Military Music Found, 75. *Teaching:* Asst trumpet, NTex State Univ, 61-62 & Univ Ill, 63-64; instr music, Ind State Univ, 64-66; prof, Univ Wis, Milwaukee, 66- *Mem:* Int Trumpet Guild; Nat Asn Col Wind & Perc Instr; Music Educr Nat Conf; Wis Music Educr Asn; Milwaukee Musicians Asn. *Mailing Add:* 5647 W Glenbrook Rd Milwaukee WI 53223

COOKE, (JOHN) ANTONY
CELLO, COMPOSER
b Sydney, Australia, Aug 3, 48; US citizen. *Study:* Royal Col Music, ARCM, 68; Royal Acad Music, LRAM, 69. *Works:* Sword of Orion (band), perf by Univ SFla Wind Ens, 79; Tomorrow (orch), perf by Univ SFla Orch, 80; Andante (orch), perf by Fla All-State, 80; Western Overture (band), 80 & Herculaneum (band), 80, Kendor Publ; Waltzing Matilda Variations (band), perf by Fla State Univ Wind Ens, 81; Barbara Allen (band), perf by Univ NH, 82. *Rec Perf:* Music for Cello and Wind Orchestra, 79, Locatelli & Kabalevsky Sonatas for Cello and Piano, 80, Music for Violin & Cello, 81 & Music for Cello and Percussion, 82, Golden Crest. *Pos:* Prin cellist, London Mozart Orch, 71-74. *Teaching:* Asst prof cello, Univ SFla, 79-80 & assoc prof, 80; assoc prof cello, Northwestern Univ, 80- *Awards:* Gold Medalist London Music Compt, 64; Outstanding Teacher, Phi Mu Alpha, 77; Young Musicians Award, London, 73. *Mem:* Am Fedn Musicians. *Mailing Add:* 534 Melrose Ave Kenilworth IL 60043

COOLEY, MARILYN GRACE
ADMINISTRATOR, MUSIC DIRECTOR
b Cincinnati, Ohio, Feb 16, 56. *Study:* Miami Univ Ohio, BMus, 78; Northwestern Univ, MMus, 79. *Pos:* Staff announcer, WGUC-FM, Cincinnati, 80-82; music dir, WBJC-FM, Baltimore, 82- *Teaching:* Instr music appreciation, Baltimore Co pub schs, fall 82. *Mem:* Am Musicol Soc. *Mailing Add:* 531 Chisholm Trail Cincinnati OH 45215

COOLIDGE, RICHARD ARD
COMPOSER, EDUCATOR
b Williamsport, Pa, Nov 1, 29. *Study:* Cincinnati Consv Music, BMus, 52, MMus, 53; Fla State Univ, DMus, 63; Peabody Consv Music; Ind Univ. *Works:* Music for a Rhapsody by Shelley, 74, Weeping Dancer, 74 & Curves of Gold, 74, Kendor Music Co; Triptych, Southern Music Co, 78; Three Songs of Night, 79 & Illuminations, 80, Kendor Music Co; Point Silver Point, Southern Music Co, 82. *Teaching:* Asst prof, ETenn State Univ, 57-61; assoc prof, Pensacola Jr Col, 63-67; prof, Stephen F Austin State Univ, 67- *Awards:* Perf Award, 76 & 78 & First Prize, Vocal Music, 77, Delius Comp, Jacksonville, Fla. *Mem:* Pi Kappa Lambda; ASCAP; Phi Mu Alpha Sinfonia; Southeastern Comp League. *Publ:* Auth, Form in the String Quartets of Franz Schubert, Music Rev, England, 71; Owls, Pussycats, Cabbages & Kings, Kendall-Hunt, 72; Aaron Copland's Passacaglia: An Analysis, Musical Analysis, 74; Concertos of Rahkmaninov, Music Rev, England, 79. *Mailing Add:* Stephen F Austin State Univ Box 13043 Nacogdoches TX 75962

COOMBS, DANIEL RAYMOND
COMPOSER, MUSIC DIRECTOR
b Chicago, Ill, Aug 26, 53. *Study:* DePaul Univ, studied comp with Leon Stein & Phil Winsor, BA, 74, MA, 76; private study cond with Leonard Slatkin, 81-83. *Works:* Phillipe de Vitry, perf by Sweet Betsy from Pike Band, 76; Haiku, comn & perf by Chapman Repty Dance, 79; Lifeline (perc), Judy Green Music, 81; Silence of the Sea (guitar), comn by Seigo Yamada, 83; Rappacini's Daughter (opera), comn by St John's Univ, 83; In Paradisum, perf by New Music Chicago, 83; Public Statues (piano), perf by Bryan Shilander, 83. *Pos:* Comp in res, Park Forest Consv, 72-; music dir, New Esterhazy Chamber Orch, 81- *Teaching:* Instr clarinet, Park Forest Consv, 72- *Mem:* Charles Ives Soc Chicago (pres, 80-82); New Music Chicago; Am Music Ctr; BMI. *Publ:* Trends in 20th Century Orchestration, 78. *Mailing Add:* 6436 Maplewood Chicago IL 60629

COOPER, DAVID EDWIN
LIBRARIAN
b Jan 30, 44. *Study:* Univ Mich, BMus, 66; Ohio Univ, MFA, 68; Univ Kans, MA, 72; Kent State Univ, MLS, 73. *Pos:* Librn, Music Libr, Univ Kans, 70-72, Kent State Univ, 72-73, State Univ NY, Buffalo, 73-75, C F Peters Corp, New York, 76- *Mem:* Am Musicol Soc; Music Libr Asn; Asn Rec Sound Collections. *Publ:* Auth, International Bibliography of Discographies, 75; contribr to prof publ. *Mailing Add:* 100 LaSalle St Apt 2F New York NY 10027

COOPER, DAVID S(HEARER)
ADMINISTRATOR, COMPOSER
b Minneapolis, Minn, Oct 3, 22. *Study:* Univ Va, with Randall Thompson, 40-42; Princeton Univ, with Roger Sessions & Oliver Strunk, BA, 44; Univ Calif, Berkeley, with Manfred Bukofzer, MA, 50. *Works:* Time (women's voices & piano), 48; Three Poems for Children (women's voices & piano), 54; 150th Psalm (mixed chorus, organ, brass & perc), 54; Sancta Maria (women's voices a cappella), 55. *Pos:* Chief, Music Branch, US Info Agy, 51-59; dean, Peabody Consv, 59-61; vpres, Assoc Music Publ, 61-65; exec dir, Manhattan Sch Music, 65-69 & Am Comp Alliance, 71-75; dir, Third St Music Sch Settlement, 75-77. *Teaching:* Fac mem, Univ Calif, Berkeley, 48-50 & Mercy Col, 78. *Awards:* Outstanding Service to Am Music Award, Nat Asn Am Comp & Cond, 57. *Mem:* Nat Asn Sch Music; Am Symph Orch League; Am Fedn Musicians; BMI. *Mailing Add:* 101 Gedney St Apt 1E Nyack NY 10960

COOPER, IRMA MARGARET
SINGER, EDUCATOR
b Sturgis, SDak, Sept 28, 12. *Study:* Grinnell Col, BM, 34; Am Consv Music, MM, 37. *Pos:* Prof singer, Chicago, 39-43 & New York, 43-52; performer, leading opera roles, Germany, 52-64; appearances, Handel & Haydn Soc, Boston, Lindsborg Easter Fest, Kans, Miami Opera Guild, Manhattan Opera Co & others. *Teaching:* Prof voice, Ohio State Univ, Columbus, 64- *Awards:* Winner, Chicagoland Music Fest, 40; Distinguished Teaching Award, Ohio State Univ, 68. *Mem:* Metropolitan Opera Nat Coun; Nat Asn Teachers Singing; Music Teachers Nat Asn; Pi Kappa Lambda; Opera-Columbus (mem bd dir). *Mailing Add:* Music Dept Ohio State Univ Columbus OH 43210

COOPER, KENNETH
HARPSICHORD, MUSICOLOGIST
b New York, NY, May 31, 41. *Study:* Mannes Col Music, 60-63; Columbia Col, BA(music), 62; Columbia Univ, MA(musicol), 64, PhD(musicol), 71. *Rec Perf:* Couperin Chamber Music, Serenus, 68; Sonatas, Vols I & II (Scarlatti), Vanguard, 74; Handel—Scarlatti, CBS, 75; Flute & Harpsichord Sonatas, 75 & 76 (Bach & Handel) & Theatre & Outdoor Music, 77 (Handel) Vanguard; Cousins, Nonesuch, 77; Bach Gamba & Harpsichord Sonatas, CBS, 83. *Pos:* Dir, Columbia Univ Collegium Musicum, 67-69 & Mannes Baroque Ens, 76-82; solo performer, works by Vivaldi, Steffani, Scarlatti, Salibri, Galuppi, Handel, Bach, Daniel Paget, George Flynn, Paul Ben-Haim, Noel Lee, Ferruccio Busoni, Gerald Busby, Seymour Barab, & others; harpsichordist in res, Santa Fe Chamber Music Fest & Spoleto Fest, currently. *Teaching:* Instr, Columbia & Barnard Cols, 64-71; asst prof, Brooklyn Col, 71-74; prof harpsichord & baroque perf practice, Mannes Col Music, 74-; vis specialist, Montclair State Col, 76- *Awards:* Rec of Yr Award, Stereo Rev, 77. *Bibliog:* Joseph Horowitz, Kenneth Cooper & the Fortepiano, NY Times. *Mem:* Harpsichord Music Soc (mem bd, 81-). *Interests:* Eighteenth century performance practice. *Publ:* Coauth, Muffat's First Observations, Musical Quart, 67; ed, Monteverdi: Tirsi e Clori, Pa State Univ Press, 67; auth, Scarlatti's Sonatas, Bach's Flute Sonatas, Vanguard Rec Soc, 75-76; The Lyrical Intermezzo, Musik Geshichte & Geganwart, 75; A Mass of Evidence, Messiah, etc, High Fidelity, 81-83. *Rep:* Thea Dispeker 248 E 78 New York NY 10028. *Mailing Add:* 405 W 118 St New York NY 10027

COOPER, LAWRENCE
BARITONE

b Los Angeles, Calif, Aug 14, 46. *Study:* San Fernanco Valley State Col, 71. *Roles:* Valentin in Faust, 79 & Marcello in La Boheme, 80, San Francisco Opera; George in Of Mice & Men, Nevada Opera & Wexford Fest, Ireland, 81; Valentin in Faust, Orlando Opera, 82; Wozzeck in Wozzeck, Houston Grand Opera, 82; George in Of Mice & Men, New York City Opera, 83. *Rep:* Columbia Artists Mgt Inc 165 W 57th St New York NY 10019. *Mailing Add:* 5003 Delacroix Rd Rancho Palos Verdes CA 90274

COOPER, LEWIS HUGH
BASSOON, EDUCATOR

b Pontiac, Mich, Dec 31, 20. *Study:* Sch Music, Univ Mich, BM. *Pos:* Bassoonist, Detroit Symph Orch, 17 yrs, Detroit Little Symph, formerly, Detroit Light Opera Orch, formerly & Leonard Smith's Conct Band, formerly; participant, Ford Sun Evening Hour, Reichold Hour, Edison Hour & many other network radio broadcasts; expert & consult, voicing, repair & design of bassoons. *Teaching:* From mem fac to prof bassoon, Sch Music, Univ Mich, Ann Arbor, 45-, charter mem, Fac Woodwind Quintet. *Mem:* Am Asn Univ Prof; Am Fedn Musicians; Int Double Reed Soc. *Publ:* Auth, Essentials of Bassoon Technique, 68. *Mailing Add:* Sch Music Univ Mich Ann Arbor MI 48109

COOPER, PAUL
COMPOSER, EDUCATOR

b Victoria, Ill, May 19, 26. *Study:* Univ Southern Calif, with Ernest Kanitz, Halsey Stevens & Roger Sessions, BA, 50, MA, 53, DMA, 56; Nat Consv Paris & Sorbonne, with Nadia Boulanger, 53-54. *Works:* Violin Concerto, 67; Variants II (viola & piano), 72; Antiphons (solo oboe & wind ens), 73; Equinox (chorus, flute, cello & piano), 76; Refrains (double chorus, sop, bar & orch), 76; Concert for 3 (clarinet, cello & piano), 77; Requiem (organ & perc), 78; and others. *Pos:* Performer, 53-; music critic, Los Angeles Mirror, 52-55 & Ann Arbor News, 59-65; minister music, St Matthews Lutheran Church, North Hollywood, Calif, 54-55. *Teaching:* Fac mem, Univ Mich, Ann Arbor, 55-68, prof music, 65-68, chmn theory dept, 66-68; guest lectr, cols & univ, 68-; prof, comp in res & head acad div, Univ Cincinnati, 69-74; prof, comp in res & chmn scholar fac, Shepherd Sch Music, Rice Univ, 74- *Awards:* Guggenheim Found Fels, 65 & 72; citation & award, Am Acad & Inst Arts & Lett, 77; Martha Baird Rockefeller Found Grant, 79. *Mem:* Music Teachers Nat Asn (vpres, 75-77, mem exec bd, 77-). *Publ:* Auth, Workbooks for Perspectives in Music, 73-75; Perspectives in Music Theory, 73; Music for Sight Singing, 80. *Mailing Add:* Shepherd Sch Music Rice Univ Houston TX 77251

COOPER, ROSE MARIE (MRS WILLIAM H JORDAN)
COMPOSER

b Cairo, Ill, Feb 21, 37. *Study:* Okla Baptist Univ, with Warren Angell, BMus, 59; Teachers Col, Columbia Univ, with Henry Cowell, MA(music & music educ), 60; Univ NC, Greensboro, PhD, 75. *Works:* Morning Star (unison, two part cantata), Carl Fischer, 70; Tell The Blessed Tidings (unison, two part), Broadman, 70; Hymn of Truth, 70 & Lord, Speak To Me (TTBB), 71, Julian Assoc; Settings of Five Haiku, Byron-Douglas Publ,72; Christ-child Come Below, 75 & This Is The Land That I Love, 76, Hinshaw Music, Inc. *Teaching:* Instr music, Greensboro Col, 65-67. *Awards:* Nat Fedn Music Clubs Award of Merit; ASCAP Awards, 16 yrs. *Mem:* ASCAP; Sigma Alpha Iota; Mortarboard; Nat Fedn Music Clubs. *Publ:* Auth, Tools of the Trade, Choristers Guild, 71; Music and the Two-Year-Olds, Music J, Vol XXXI, No 1. *Mailing Add:* 607 W Greenway N Greensboro NC 27403

COOPER, WILLIAM B(ENJAMIN)
ORGAN, COMPOSER

b Philadelphia, Pa, Feb 14, 20. *Study:* Manhattan Sch Music & Trinity Col Music, 45; Philadelphia Musical Acad, BMus(organ), 51, MMus(organ), 52; Sch Sacred Music, Union Theol Sem, 55; study with Dr Rollo F Maitland & comp with Stefan Wolpe. *Works:* Mass of Thanksgiving, 67 & Rhapsody on the Name—Fela Sowande, 73, Danj Music Co; Psalm 150 (string orch, piano, perc & chorus), perf by Ossining Choral Soc, 76; The Choral Service of the Episcopal Church, Dangerfield Music Co, 78; A Child's Flute Tune (organ), 81 & A Song of Deliverance, 83, Danj Music Co. *Pos:* Organist & choirmaster, St Philip's Episcopal Church, New York, 53-74 & St Martin's Episcopal Church, New York, 74- *Teaching:* Instr organ, Hampton Inst, Va, summers 40-41; instr & organist, Bennett Col, NC, 51-53; instr music, Wadleigh Intermediate Sch, NY, 58- & Mercy Col, White Plains, NY, 80-81; lectr, Trinity Episcopal Church, Mt Vernon, NY, 80-81. *Awards:* Outstanding Music Activ in Harlem Community, Amsterdam News, 56; Musical Achievement Plaque, Nat Asn Negro Musicians, 73. *Bibliog:* Evelyn White (auth), African-American Composers of Choral Music, Scarecrow Press, 81. *Mem:* Nat Asn Negro Musicians; Schomburg Libr Corp (bd mem, 83); Am Guild Organists; West Chester Afro-Am Cult Found (bd mem, 79-81). *Mailing Add:* 61 Manhattan Ave Greenburgh NY 10607

COOVER, JAMES BURRELL
LIBRARIAN, EDUCATOR

b Jacksonville, Ill, June 3, 25. *Study:* Univ Northern Colo, AB, 49, MA, 50; Denver Univ, MA, 53. *Pos:* Asst dir, Bibliog Ctr Res, Denver, Colo, 50-53; head, George Sherman Dickinson Music Libr, Vassar Col, 53-67; dir, Music Libr, State Univ NY, Buffalo, 67- *Teaching:* Ziegel prof music, State Univ NY, Buffalo, 67- *Mem:* Asn Int Bibliot Musicales; Music Libr Asn (pres, 59-60); Asn Recorded Sound Collections; Dict Soc NAm. *Interests:* Lexicography; British music trade; music journalism. *Publ:* Auth, Music Lexicography, 52, 58 & 71; East European Music Periodicals, Fontes Artis Musicae, 56-63;

Music Theory in English Translation, J Music Theory, 59 & 70; coauth, Medieval and Renaissance Music on LP Records, Info Coordr, 64 & 73; auth, Musical Instrument Collections, Info Coordr, 81. *Mailing Add:* 111 Marjann Terr Buffalo NY 14223

COPE, DAVID HOWELL
COMPOSER, EDUCATOR

b San Francisco, Calif, May 17, 41. *Study:* Ariz State Univ, BA(music), 63; Univ Southern Calif, MA(music), 65. *Works:* Arena, 73 & Triplum, 74, Carl Fischer; Requiem for Bosque Redondo, A Broude, 75; Re-Birth, Seesaw, 76; Threshold & Visions, A Broude, 77; Concert for Piano & Orchestra, 80 & The Way, 81, Opus One. *Teaching:* Instr, Kans State Col, 66-68 & Cleveland Inst Music, 70-73; from asst to assoc prof, Miami Univ, Ohio, 73-77; prof, Univ Calif, Santa Cruz, 77- *Awards:* Nat Endowment Arts Grant, 76 & 81. *Bibliog:* Machlis (auth), Contemporary Music, 81. *Mem:* ASCAP; Phi Mu Alpha. *Publ:* Auth, New Directions in Music, William C Brown, 70, 76 & 80; New Music Composition, Macmillan, 76; New Music Notation, Kendall & Hunt, 76. *Mailing Add:* Music Dept Univ of Calif Santa Cruz CA 95064

COPELAND, KEITH LAMONT
PERCUSSION, TEACHER

b New York, NY, April, 18, 46. *Study:* Berklee Col Music, 67-70. *Rec Perf:* Return of the Griffin, Galaxy Rec, 78; Sam Jones the Bassist, Discovery Rec, 79; In Motion, Columbia Rec, 79; Electronic Sonata for Souls Loved by Nature, Soul Note Rec, 80; Where've You Been, Concord Jazz Rec, 80; Once in Every Life, Bee Hive Rec, 80. *Pos:* Drummer, Maggi Scott Trio, 75-78 & Heath Brothers, 78-79; drummer & clinician, Billy Taylor Trio, 80- *Teaching:* Instr drum set & class snare drum, Berklee Col Music, 75-78; instr drum set, Eastman Sch Music, 81-; affil teacher, Long Island Univ & Brooklyn Univ, 82- *Mailing Add:* 160-05 134th Ave Jamaica NY 11434

COPELAND, ROBERT MARSHALL
EDUCATOR, CONDUCTOR & MUSIC DIRECTOR

b Douglas, Wyo, Jan 30, 45. *Study:* Geneva Col, BS, 66; Col Consv Music, Univ Cincinnati, MMus, 70, PhD, 74. *Pos:* Co-ed, Pa Newsletter, Am Choral Dir Asn, 83- *Teaching:* Asst prof music, Mid-Am Nazarene Col, 71-75, assoc prof, 75-79, prof, 79-81; vis lectr music hist, Univ Kans, Lawrence, 77; prof music & chmn dept, Geneva Col, 81- *Mem:* Am Musicol Soc; Sonneck Soc; Col Music Soc; Am Choral Dir Asn. *Interests:* American music of 19th century; Isaac Baker Woodbury; French theory of the 16th century; metrical Psalmody; pedagogy of music history. *Publ:* Co-ed, The Book of Psalms for Singing, RPCNA, 73; contribr, Metrical Psalmody of the Covenanters, Prairie Schooner, 79; auth, Music Historiography in the Classroom, Col Mus Symposium, 79; The Christian Message of Igor Stravinsky, Musical Quart, 82; contribr, Museums, Humanities & Educated Eyes, Univ Kans Museum, 82. *Mailing Add:* 3111 Fifth Ave Beaver Falls PA 15010

COPLAND, AARON
COMPOSER, WRITER

b Brooklyn, NY, Nov 14, 1900. *Study:* Studied piano with Leopold Wolfson, Victor Wittgenstein & Clarence Adler, comp & theory with Rubin Goldmark, 17-21; Fountainebleau Sch Music, 21; studied with Nadia Boulanger, 21-24; various hon degrees from many US univ, 56- *Works:* Appalachian Spring (ballet & orch suite), 44; Twelve Poems of Emily Dickinson (voice & piano), 50; The Tender Land (opera), 54; A Canticle of Freedom (mixed chorus & orch), 55; Dance Panels (ballet), 59; Music for a Great City (orch), 64; Three Latin American Sketches, 72. *Pos:* Co-organizer, Copland-Sessions Concts, 28-31; guest cond, Boston Symph, 60 & New York Phil, 60- *Teaching:* Lectr, New Sch Social Res, 27-37; lectr, Harvard Univ, 35 & 44, Charles Eliot Norton prof poetry, 51-52; head comp dept, Berkshire Music Ctr, 40-65, fac chmn, 57-65. *Awards:* Henry Hadley Medal, Nat Asn Am Comp & Cond, 64; US Pres Medal Freedom, 64; Kennedy Ctr Hon Lifetime Achievement Perf Arts, 79. *Mem:* League Comp, Int Soc Contemp Music; Edward MacDowell Asn; Walter M Naumburg Music Found; Am Music Ctr; founder, Am Comp Alliance. *Publ:* Auth, What to Listen For in Music, 37; Our New Music, 41; Music and Imagination, 52; Copland on Music, 60; The New Music, 1900-1960, rev ed, 68. *Mailing Add:* c/o Boosey & Hawkes 30 W 57th St New York NY 10019

COPLEY, R EVAN
EDUCATOR, COMPOSER

b Liberal, Kans, Mar 22, 30. *Study:* Mich State Univ, with H Owen Reed. *Works:* Toccata (band); Three Symphonies (orch); Symphony (band); twelve preludes & fugues (piano); nine piano sonatas; two suites (band); 48 works for organ. *Teaching:* Fac mem, Iowa Wesleyan Col, 58-64. *Mailing Add:* Music Dept Univ Northern Colo Greeley CO 80639

COPPOCK, BRUCE
EDUCATOR, CELLO

Study: New England Consv Music, BM, MM; studied with David Soyer & Laurence Lesser. *Rec Perf:* With Nonesuch, Delos & CRI. *Pos:* Prin cello, Handel & Haydn Soc Orch, formerly; mem, Boston Musica Viva & Cambridge Chamber Players, formerly; cello solo & chamber music, US & Europe; soloist, Vt Symph & Boston Civic Symph Orch; substitute cellist, Boston Symph Orch. *Teaching:* Mem fac, Longy Sch Music, Brown Univ, Tufts Univ & Univ NH, formerly; chmn string dept & actg chmn music div, Boston Consv, currently. *Mailing Add:* 273 Chestnut Ave Jamaica Plain MA 02130

COPPOLA, CARMINE (CARMEN)
COMPOSER, CONDUCTOR
b New York, NY, June 11, 12. *Study:* Juilliard Sch Music, with Bernard Wagenaard, dipl, 33; studied with Joseph Schillinger, 36-39, Paul Creston, 42-43 & Norman Dello Joio, 45-46; Manhattan Sch Music, MMus, 50. *Works:* Madrigale (sop & piano), 75; Escorial (opera), 79; The Godfather Part I & II (film score); The Black Stallion (film score); Apocalypse Now (film score); Napoleon (film score); Radio City Music Hall, 81; The Outsiders (film score), 83. *Rec Perf:* The Godfather Part II; The Godfather's Wedding Album; Accordeon Concerto; Woodwind Quintet; Symphony Poem; Phantom Calvary. *Pos:* First flutist, Radio City Music Hall, 34-36, arr, 48-56; first flutist, Detroit Symph, 36-41 & NBC Orch, 42-48; opera cond, Brooklyn Acad Music, 48-55; music dir, Merrick Prod, 55-66; comp & cond, Warner Bros & Paramount. *Awards:* Oscar for The Godfather Part II score, 75; First Prize, Pittsburgh Bicentennial Comp Cont; Calif Arts Coun Grant. *Mem:* ASCAP; Acad Motion Pictures Arts & Sci; Phi Mu Alpha Sinfonia. *Publ:* Auth, A Manual of Flute Instruction, 75. *Mailing Add:* 19813 Gilmore St Woodland Hills CA 91367

CORAL, LENORE
LIBRARIAN
b Detroit, Mich, Jan 30, 39. *Pos:* Fine arts librn, Univ Calif, Irvine, 67-72; music librn, Univ Wis, Madison, 72-82 & Cornell Univ, 82- *Awards:* Res fels, Fulbright-Hays, 65-67 & Nat Endowment for Humanities, 79-80; res grant, Nat Endowment for Humanities, 76-77. *Mem:* Music Libr Asn (mem bd, 73-75, ed technic reports, 76-82); Am Musicol Soc (mem coun, 75-77, 82-84); Int Asn Music Libr (secy cat comn, 79-83 & chair, 83-); Royal Musical Asn. *Interests:* Seventeenth-Eighteenth century English music; 19th century American music. *Publ:* Auth, Concordance of the Thematic Indexes to the Instrumental Works of Antonio Vivaldi, Music Libr Asn, 72; The History of Thematic Catalogues, Music Librarianship, 73; coauth, British Book Sale Catalogues 1676-1800, Mansell, 77; auth, Music in Auctions: Dissemination as a Factor of Taste, Source Materials, Thurston Dart, 82. *Mailing Add:* 105 Eastwood Terr Ithaca NY 14850

CORD, (NOEL) EDMUND, II
TRUMPET, EDUCATOR
b Indianapolis, Ind, June 9, 49. *Study:* Sch Music, Ind Univ, with H Mueller, L Davidson & C Gorham, BM(trumpet), 72; Music Acad of West, with Tom Stevens, 72; study with Pierre Thibaud, James Stamp, Vincent Cichowicz & Arnold Jacobs. *Rec Perf:* The Web, Kolinor Studios, Tel Aviv, 75. *Pos:* Prin trumpet, Israel Phil, Tel Aviv, 72-76 & Santa Fe Opera, 78-80; founding mem, Israel Phil Brass Quintet, Tel Aviv, 73-76 & Utah Symph Brass Quintet, 81-; co-prin trumpet, Utah Symph, 76- *Teaching:* Instr trumpet, Acad Music, Tel Aviv, 74-76 & Univ Utah, 82- *Awards:* Music Dir Award, Music Acad of West, 72. *Mem:* Int Trumpet Guild. *Mailing Add:* 3173 Hollyhock Hill Salt Lake City UT 84121

CORDERO, ROQUE
COMPOSER, EDUCATOR
b Panama, Aug 16, 17. *Study:* Comp with Ernst Krenek, 43-47 & cond with Dimitri Mitropoulos, 44-47; Berkshire Music Ctr, studied cond with Stanley Chapple, 46; Hamline Univ, 47. *Works:* Second Symphony, Sinfonica Venezuela, 57; String Quartet No 1, comn by Coolidge Found, 60; Violin Concerto, comn by Koussevitzky Found, 61; Symphony No 3, Philadelphia Orch, 66; String Quartet No 2, comn by Ala Univ, 68; Musica Veinte, comn by Rio de Janeiro Fest, 70; Cantata for Peace, comn by Nat Endowment Arts, 76. *Pos:* Dir, Nat Inst Music, Panama, 53-64; cond, Nat Orch Panama, 64-66; asst dir, Latin Am Music Ctr, 66-69; music consult, Peer-Southern Music Orgn, 69-80. *Teaching:* Prof comp, Nat Inst Music, Panama, 50-66, Ill State Univ, 72-; assoc prof comp, Ind Univ, 66-69. *Awards:* Caro de Boesi Award, Caracas Fest, 57; Koussevitzky Int Rec Award, 74; Chamber Music Award, InterAm Fest, Costa Rica, 77. *Bibliog:* Gilbert Chase (auth), Composed by Cordero, Americas-OAS, 58; Magdalena Vicuna (auth), Entrevista, Revista Musical Chilena, 67; InterAm Music Coun (secy gen, 56-60); Am Music Ctr; BMI; Am Soc Univ Comp; Soc Music Theory. *Interests:* Twentieth century Latin American music; folk music of Panama. *Publ:* Auth, Curso de Solfeo, Ricordi, Buenos Aires, 63; La Musica en Centro America y Panama, J InterAm, 66; El Publico y la Musica Viva, Music Am, 67; Vigencia del Musico Culto, UN Educ, Sci & Cult Orgn, 77; The Folkmusic of Panama, In: New Grove Dict of Music & Musicians, 80. *Mailing Add:* 308 Clay St Normal IL 61761

CORDOVA, RICHARD ALLAN
CONDUCTOR, PIANO
b Los Angeles, Calif, Jan 7, 54. *Study:* Univ Southern Calif, BMus, 75; studied cond with Fritz Zweig, 75-78. *Pos:* Music dir, Den Nat Scene, Bergen, Norway, 76-77 & Music Theater Group, Lenox Arts Ctr, NY, 83; asst cond, Theater der Stadt Bonn, Germany, 78-80, New York City Opera, 80, Los Angeles Phil, 82, Santa Fe Opera, 82 & Dallas Opera, 82; cond, Opera Co Boston, 81-82. *Mem:* Am Fedn Musicians. *Mailing Add:* 202 W 96th St #5W New York NY 10025

CORELLI, FRANCO
TENOR
b Ancona, Italy, 1923. *Study:* Univ Bologna, Italy; Pesaro Consv Music; Maggio Musicale, Florence, Italy. *Rec Perf:* For Angel, London, Columbia & Cetra. *Roles:* Don Jose in Carmen, Spoleto Fest, Italy, 52; Manrico in Il Trovatore, Metropolitan Opera, 61; major parts in Andrea Chenier, La Boheme, Turandot, Tosca, Ernani, Aida, Don Carlos & others throughout US & Europe. *Pos:* Ten, major opera houses in US & Europe; perf on Am TV. *Awards:* Winner vocal compt, Florence Music Fest, Italy, 51; First Prize, Spoleto Nat Compt. *Mailing Add:* c/o Columbia Artists 165 W 57th St New York NY 10019

CORENNE, RENEE
TEACHER, SOPRANO
b Bucharest, Roumania; US citizen. *Study:* Bucharest Acad Music, BMus; studied with Antonio Narducci, Vittorio Aderno & Fausto Cleva. *Roles:* Zerlina in Don Giovanni, Israel Phil, 64; Santa Teodosia (oratorio), Radiodiffusion TV Franchaise, 65; Violetta in La Traviata, Bucharest, 67; Marguerite in Faust, Cluj, Roumania, 70; Musetta in La Boheme, NJ Opera, 72 & Pittsburgh Opera, 74; Manon in Manon, Ohio Opera Co, 75. *Teaching:* Singing technique, New York City. *Mailing Add:* 324 Lantana Ave Englewood NJ 07631

CORIGLIANO, JOHN PAUL
COMPOSER, EDUCATOR
b New York, NY, Feb 16, 38. *Study:* Columbia Col, BA, 59. *Works:* Sonata (violin & piano), 63, The Cloisters (cycle four songs), 65, Concerto (piano & orch), 68, Concerto (oboe & orch), 75, Etude Fantasy for Piano, 76, A Dylan Thomas Trilogy: Fern Hill, Poem in October & Poem On His Birthday (choral symph for chorus, soloists & orch), 76, Concerto (clarinet & orch), 77 & Pied Piper Fantasy (concerto for flute & orch), 82, G Schirmer. *Teaching:* Prof music, Lehman Col, 74-; prof comp, Manhattan Sch Music, 75- *Awards:* Award, Spoleto Fest Chamber Music Compt, 64; Guggenheim Fel, 68. *Bibliog:* William H Hoffmann (auth), John Corigliano on Cracking the Establishment, Village Voice, 2/21/77; Allan Kozinn (auth), The Unfashionably Romantic Music of John Corigliano, Sunday New York Times, 4/27/80; Bernard Holland (auth), Highbrow Music to Hum, New York Times Mag, 1/31/82. *Mem:* ASCAP; Bohemians. *Mailing Add:* 365 West End Ave New York NY 10024

CORINA, JOHN HUBERT
COMPOSER, OBOE
b Cleveland, Ohio, Apr 21, 28. *Study:* Western Reserve Univ, BS, 51, MA, 56; Fla State Univ, with John Boda, DM, 65. *Works:* Dance Figure (ten & ens), 73; Partita for Alto Saxophone & Piano, 74; Sonet (solo oboe & strings), 74; Partita for Oboe & Percussion, 75; Partita for Woodwind Quintet, 76; Song Cycle, Songs of Day (treble chorus & piano), 77; Chamber Opera: The Telling of the North Star, 82. *Pos:* Organist & choirmaster, Emmanuel Episcopal Church, currently; oboist, Ga Woodwind Quintet. *Teaching:* Instr, Emerson Jr High Sch, Lakewood, Ohio, 51-57; instr orch, North Miami Beach Jr High Sch, 57-60; instr theory, band & orch, Dade Co Jr Col, 60-66; prof music, Univ Ga, 68- *Awards:* Am Choral Dir Asn Comp Compt Award; Tex Womens Univ Choral Comp Compt Award; ASCAP Standard Award. *Mem:* Music Educr Nat Conf; ASCAP; Southeastern Comp League; Int Double Reed Soc. *Publ:* Contribr, J Int Double Reed Soc. *Mailing Add:* 396 Hancock Ln Rt 3 Athens GA 30605

CORMIER, RICHARD
CONDUCTOR, ADMINISTRATOR
Study: New England Consv Music, BMus, 51; Columbia Univ, MA, 55, EdD, 63. *Pos:* Music dir, Charlotte NC Symph, 63-67 & Chatanooga Symph, 67-83; dir, Atlantic Ctr Arts, 83- *Teaching:* Dept head & prof music, Park Col, 55-63; instr, Columbia Univ, 60-63. *Mem:* Am Fedn Musicians; Am Symph Orch League. *Mailing Add:* Chattanooga Symph 615 Lindsay St Chattanooga TN 37402

CORNELIUS, JEFFREY MICHAEL
ADMINISTRATOR, EDUCATOR
b Chicago, Ill, Apr 26, 43. *Study:* King Col, AB, 65; Westminster Choir Col, BMus, 70; Temple Univ, studied with Robert Page, MMus, 72. *Pos:* Dir music, Langhorne Presby Church, Pa, 75- *Teaching:* Mem fac, Bristol Pub Sch, Tenn, 65-68; adj instr music, Mercer Co Community Col, 70-71; instr, LaSalle Col, 71-72; from instr to assoc prof choral music & assoc dean, Col Music, Temple Univ, 72- *Mem:* Am Choral Dir Asn Pa (pres, 82-); Music Educr Nat Conf; Am Choral Found; Musical Fund Soc Philadelphia. *Interests:* Choral literature of the Classic period; choral conducting and teaching procedures; faculty development; administration of college and university music programs; church music. *Publ:* Ed, Pennsylvania Newsletter, Am Choral Dir Asn, 79-82; auth & contribr, Chabrier, Charpentier, Covent Garden, Dukas, Hovhaness, Levine & Lully, In: Acad Am Encycl, 80; auth, The Classic Period: Accessible Repertoire for the Church Choir, 81 & The Use of Metaphor in the Choral Rehearsal, 82, Choral J. *Mailing Add:* Col Music Temple Univ Philadelphia PA 19122

CORNELL, GWYNN
MEZZO-SOPRANO
b Concord, NC. *Study:* Westminster Choir Col; Acad Vocal Arts. *Roles:* Azucena in Il Trovatore, Waltrante, Fricka & Erha in Der Ring des Nibelunge, Amneris in Aida, Klytemnestra in Elektra, Nurse in Frau ohne Schatten & Ulrica in Masked Ball, perf with various opera co, 70-; Venus in Tannhäuser, Metropolitan Opera, 81-82. *Pos:* Leading soloist, Deutsche Oper Am Rhein, Düsseldorf, Germany, 70-76 & Metropolitan Opera, 78- *Awards:* Fulbright Scholarship; First Baltimore Opera Compt, 64. *Rep:* Robert Lombardo Assoc 1 Harkness Plaza 61 W 62nd Suite 6F New York NY 10023. *Mailing Add:* 710 Colonial Rd Franklin Lakes NJ 07417

CORNER, PHILIP LIONEL
COMPOSER, CRITIC-WRITER
b New York, NY, Apr 10, 33. *Study:* City Univ New York, BA, 55; Consv Paris, with Messaien, 2nd Prix, 57; Columbia Univ, MA, 59; studied piano with Dorothy Taubman, 61-75. *Works:* Passionate Expanse of the Law, The Four Suits, Something Else Press, 59; Seven Joyous Flashes, 59, Sprouting, 62 & Gong!, 71, C F Peters; Om Entrance, Soundings III, 72; Gamelan

I—VIII, 75-76 & Gamelan IX, XII, 77, Pieces III. *Teaching:* Music, New York City Bd Educ, 61-62 & New Winston High Sch, New York, 66-72; prof, Livingston Col, Rutgers Univ, 72- *Awards:* Berliner Kunstler Residency, Deutsche Akad Anstauch Dienst, 83. *Bibliog:* Tom Johnson (auth), The Changing of the Avant Garde, Boston Phoenix, 77; Dick Higins (auth), A Dialectic of Centuries, Printed Educ, 78; Harry Rube (auth), Fluxus ..., A, Amsterdam, 79. *Mem:* Experimental Intermedia Found. *Mailing Add:* 75 Leonard St New York NY 10013

CORNWELL, RICHARD WARREN
ADMINISTRATOR, CRITIC-WRITER
b Seattle, Wash, July 15, 34. *Study:* Mass Inst Technol, 51-52; Univ Wash, BA, 55. *Pos:* Asst mgr, Seattle Symph Orch, 60-68; exec dir, Pac NW Ballet Asn, 68-70; managing dir, Honolulu Symph & Hawaii Opera Theatre, 70-73; exec dir, Assoc Pac Artists, 73- & Consortium for Pac Arts & Cultures, 83-; writer, Hawaii Music, Arts, Entertainment, Culture & Dining, Off Duty Mag, 75- *Mem:* Int Soc Perf Arts Adminr; Ens Players Guild, Hawaii Chamber Orch; Opera Players of Hawaii; Arts Coun Hawaii; Int Alliance Theatrical & Stage Employees. *Publ:* Auth, articles on Samoan educ, artistic & cultural events, ASOH Newsletter, 82-; coauth, Siapo—Samoan Tapa, Am Samoa Arts Coun, 83; auth, Chamber Music in Hawaii, Cult Climate, 83. *Mailing Add:* 1437 Mokuna Pl Honolulu HI 96816

CORRADO, RONALD ANTHONY
BARITONE
b New York, NY, July 28, 46. *Study:* Juilliard Sch & Am Opera Inst, 72-76. *Rec Perf:* Guido, Tassilone, Clarion Opera, 79. *Roles:* Germont in La traviata, 79 & Figaro in The Marriage of Figaro, 79, Can Opera Co Tour; Silvio in Pagliacci, St Petersburg Opera, 80; Escamillo in Carmen, Shreveport Symph Opera, 82; Solomon Mikhoels, Young Men's Hebrew Asn Opera, 82. *Pos:* Soloist, Spoleto Fest, 72 & with Cincinnati Symph, Detroit Symph, Kalamazoo Fest, Linsborg Fest & Calif Bach Fest. *Rep:* Thea Dispeker 59 E 54th St New York NY 10022. *Mailing Add:* 523 Hudson St New York NY 10014

CORRIGAN, JOHN
EDUCATOR
b Dallas, Tex, Jun 7, 39. *Study:* With Walter Gieseking, 53; Juilliard Sch Music, BS, 61; Columbia Univ, MA, 70. *Rec Perf:* John Corrigan Plays Medtner & Bach, Orion, 83. *Pos:* Conct pianist, currently. *Teaching:* Instr piano, Univ Conn, 68-73 & Jersey City State Col, 81-82. *Mailing Add:* 140 W 79th St New York NY 10024

CORSARO, FRANK ANDREW
DIRECTOR—OPERA
b New York, NY, Dec 22, 24. *Study:* Drama Sch, Yale Univ, grad, 47; Actor's Studio, NY. *Rec Perf:* Rachel, Rachel (film), 67; Prince Igor (video), Col Consv Music, Univ Cincinnati. *Pos:* Dir & actor in many TV prod, 48-; dir, New York City Opera, 58-; Wash Opera Soc, 70-74 & St Paul Opera, 71; dir, Houston Grand Opera, 73-77, assoc artistic dir, 77-; stage dir, Spoleto Fest, Italy, formerly; Cincinnati Opera, formerly, Lake George Opera Co, formerly, San Francisco Spring Opera, formerly, Seattle Opera, formerly, Wolf Trap, 77, Glyndebourne, 82, Deutsches Opera, 82, Nat Arts Ctr Ottawa, Hawaii Opera Theatre, 83 & others. *Teaching:* Prof music & drama, Univ Houston, formerly; teacher actg for singers, privately. *Publ:* Auth, Maverick, A Director's Personal Experience in Opera and Theater, Vanguard, 78. *Rep:* Columbia Artists Mgt Inc 165 W 57th St New York NY 10019. *Mailing Add:* Box 138 Fishers Island NY 06390

CORTES, RAMIRO
COMPOSER, EDUCATOR
b Dallas, Tex, Nov 25, 33. *Study:* Univ Southern Calif, with Halsey Stevens & Ingolf Dahl; Princeton Univ, with Roger Sessions, 59; studied with Henry Cowell & Goffredo Petrassi. *Works:* Divertimento (woodwind trio), 53; Prometheus (one act opera), 60; Homage to Jackson Pollack (solo viola), 68; Charenton (chamber orch), 68-71; Movements in Variation, 72; Piano Concerto, 76; Cello Sonata, 77; and others. *Teaching:* Fac mem, Univ Southern Calif, formerly; assoc prof comp, Univ Utah, 73-, mem, New Music Ens, currently. *Awards:* Steinway Centennial Prize, 54; BMI Awards, 54 & 58; Fulbright Fel, 56-58. *Mailing Add:* Music Dept Univ Utah 204 Gardner Hall Salt Lake City UT 84112

CORTINA, RAQUEL
SOPRANO, EDUCATOR
b Havana, Cuba, Jan 23, 46. *Study:* La State Univ, BA, 68; Fla State Univ, MMus, 70, DMus, 72. *Roles:* Sop in King David & Les Noces, New Orleans Phil Symph Orch. *Pos:* Recitalist, opera & chamber music; conct performer in La, Miss & Fla; participant, radio & TV prog. *Teaching:* Prof music, head voice dept & dir opera theater & vocal activ, Univ New Orleans, currently. *Mem:* Nat Asn Teachers Singing. *Mailing Add:* Music Dept Univ New Orleans New Orleans LA 70148

CORTO, DIANA-MARIA
SOPRANO, EDUCATOR
b Buffalo, NY. *Study:* Juilliard Sch Music, studied voice with Maria Kurenko, Ina Souez & Tina Paggi; Manhattan Sch Music; Hunter Col, BS, 76, MA, 79. *Rec Perf:* Arias and Showtunes, Vanguard Digital Rec, 83. *Roles:* Rosina in Barber of Seville, Lucia in Lucia di Lammermoor, Despina in Cosi fan tutte & Italian in Birthday of the Infanta, Metropolitan Opera Studio; Mimi & Musetta in La Boheme, Palm Springs Opera & City of Angels Opera; Maria in West Side Story, nat tour. *Pos:* Soloist with opera companies, leading

orchestras, in Broadway musicals & with major summer musical theatres throughout US, SAm, Asia & Can, currently. *Teaching:* Prof voice & opera stage dir, Calif State Univ, Los Angeles, 74-76; teacher perf arts, privately, 77- *Awards:* Merwyn Daughtry Award, 74; Gladys Turk Award, 74 & 76; William Matheus Sullivan Award, 82. *Rep:* Mathews-Napal Mgt 270 W End Ave New York NY 10023. *Mailing Add:* 400 W 43rd St 19D New York NY 10036

CORY, ELEANOR THAYER
COMPOSER, EDUCATOR
b Englewood, NJ, Sept 8, 43. *Study:* Sarah Lawrence Col, with Meyer Kupferman, BA, 65; Harvard Univ, MAT, 66; New England Consv Music, with Charles Wuorinen, MusM, 70; Columbia Univ, with Chou Wen-Chung, Bulent Arel & Benjamin Baretz, DMA, 75. *Works:* Ocatons (chamber ens), 76; Trio (flute, oboe & piano), 77; Aria Viva (ten, four woodwinds & guitar), 77; Counterbrass (brass trio, piano & perc), 78; Designs (piano trio), 79; Suite a la Brecque (solo piano), 79; Surroundings (ms & piano), 81. *Pos:* Ed, Contemp Music Newsletter, 72-77. *Teaching:* Preceptor, Columbia Univ, 70-72; adj lectr, Brooklyn Col, 71-72; asst prof, Baruch Col, City Univ New York, 73-78 & Yale Univ, 78- *Awards:* Creative Artist Pub Serv Grant, NY Coun Arts, 76; MacDowell Fel, 77; Am Comp Alliance Rec Award, 81. *Mem:* Am Comp Alliance (mem bd dir, 75-81, second vpres, 72-81); League Comp, Int Soc Contemp Music; Am Music Ctr. *Publ:* Contribr to Perspectives New Music, 73. *Mailing Add:* 945 West End Ave Apt 8B New York NY 10025

CORZINE, MICHAEL
ORGAN, EDUCATOR
b Macomb, Ill, Jan 21, 47. *Study:* Univ Wis, Superior, BMus; Eastman Sch Music, MM, DMA, artists dipl. *Pos:* Organist & choirmaster, First Presby Church, Tallahassee, currently; performer throughout midwestern & eastern US. *Teaching:* Prof organ, Fla State Univ, 73- *Awards:* First Place, Am Guild Organists Regional Compt, NY, 69 & Nat Organ Playing Compt, 73. *Mailing Add:* 2109 Mulberry Blvd Tallahassee FL 32303

COSS, (SARAH) ELIZABETH
COACH, SOPRANO
b Ashland, Ohio. *Study:* Eastman Sch Music, BM, 58, MM(perf), 60; Juilliard Sch Music, 70. *Roles:* High Priestess in Aida, 78, Overseer in Elektra, 78 & Mother in The Bartered Bride, 79, Metropolitan Opera Asn; Kostelnichka in Jenufa, Am Opera Ctr, 79; Marianne in Der Rosenkavalier, 82, Ortlinda in Die Walküre, 82 & 83 & Berta in The Barber of Seville, 83, Metropolitan Opera Asn. *Pos:* Prin artist, Metropolitan Opera Asn, 77- *Teaching:* Prof voice, Univ Bridgeport, 68-70 & Queens Col, City Univ New York, 81-83. *Awards:* Martha Baird Rockefeller Grant, 60-61; First Prize, Nat Arts Club, 70. *Mem:* Am Fedn Radio & TV Artists; Am Guild Musical Artists; Am Guild Variety Artists. *Mailing Add:* 36 Burr Farms Rd Westport CT 06880

COSSA, DOMINIC
BARITONE, TEACHER-COACH
b Jessup, Pa, May 13, 35. *Study:* Univ Scranton, BS, Hon Dr; Univ Detroit, MA. *Rec Perf:* Les Huguenots & Elixir of Love, London Decca; Julius Caesar, RCA; Bernstein Mass, Columbia; When Lilacs Last in (the Dooryard Bloom'd), New World Rec; Chamber Music Soc, Book of Month Club Rec. *Roles:* Figaro, Germont in La Traviata, Yeletsky in The Queen of Spades, Marcello in La Boheme & Valentin, Metropolitan Opera; Zurga, Harlequin in Ariadne, Dr Engel in Student Prince, Germont in La Traviata & Figaro, New York City Opera. *Pos:* Leading baritone, New York City Opera, 61- & Metropolitan Opera & San Francisco Opera, 70-75. *Teaching:* Vis specialist voice, Montclair State Col, 80- *Awards:* First Prize, Metropolitan Nat Council, Metropolitan Opera; First Prize, Auditions, WGN Chicago; First Prize, Liederkrantz. *Mem:* Am Guild Music Artists; Delta Omicron. *Rep:* Colbert Artists Mgt 111 W 57 New York NY. *Mailing Add:* 429 Hegi Dr New Milford NJ 07646

COSSA, JOANNE HUBBARD
ADMINISTRATOR
b Oswego, NY, Nov 5, 46. *Study:* Syracuse Univ, 64-66; Music Dept, Hunter Col, 71-73. *Pos:* Develop dir, Chamber Music Soc Lincoln Ctr, 75-78, asst to exec dir, 78-81, assoc dir, 81-82, exec dir, 82- *Mem:* Int Soc Perf Arts Adminr. *Mailing Add:* Alice Tully Hall 1941 Broadway New York NY 10023

COSTA, MARY
SOPRANO
b Knoxville, Tenn. *Study:* Los Angeles Consv Music, with Mario Chamlee & Ernest St John Metz; Hardin-Simmons Univ, Hon DM, 73. *Rec Perf:* For RCA & BBC TV (video); Sleeping Beauty, Walt Disney Prod; The Great Waltz, 72. *Roles:* Burgundian Lady in Carmina Burana, 59 & Ninette in Blood Moon, 61, San Francisco Opera; Violetta in La Traviata, Metropolitan Opera, 64 & Bolshoi Opera, 70; sop in Candide, John F Kennedy Ctr Perf Arts, 71; Nedda in I Pagliacci; Despina in Cosi fan tutte; Rosalinde in Die Fledermaus; Gilda in Rigoletto. *Pos:* Sop, Glyndebourne Opera House, Royal Opera House Covent Garden, Teatro Nacional de San Carlos & Grand Theatre de Geneve; recitalist on tour US, USSR & England; vpres, Calif Inst Arts. *Awards:* Woman of Yr, Los Angeles, 59. *Mailing Add:* 2404 Wyoming Ave NW Washington DC 20008

COSTA-GREENSPON, MURIEL
MEZZO-SOPRANO
b Detroit, Mich. *Study:* With Sam Morgenstern; Univ Mich, Ann Arbor, with Josef Blatt, BA, 59, MA, 60. *Roles:* Mrs Todd in The Old Maid and the Thief, Detroit Opera Theater, 60; Anna Semyonovna in Natalia Petrovna, New York City Opera, 64; Ilsabill in The Fisherman and His Wife, Boston Opera,

70; Marquise de Birkenfeld in La Fille du regiment; Badessa & Principessa in Suor Angelica; Genevieve in Pelleas et Melisande; and many others. *Pos:* Ms with maj opera co & symph orch in Italy & US; res mem, New York City Opera. *Awards:* Rockefeller Grants; Grinnell Found Award. *Rep:* Maxim Gershunoff Attractions 502 Park Ave New York NY 10022. *Mailing Add:* 321 W 78th St New York NY 10024

COSTELLO, MARILYN
HARP, EDUCATOR
b Cleveland, Ohio. *Study:* Curtis Inst Music, with Carlos Salzedo, dipl. *Rec Perf:* Flute and Harp Concerto (Mozart). *Pos:* Prin harpist, Philadelphia Orch, 46- *Teaching:* Mem fac, Curtis Inst Music, 61- *Awards:* Phonographic Critics Award, Italy, 65. *Mailing Add:* Curtis Inst Music 1726 Locust St Philadelphia PA 19103

COSTINESCU, GHEORGHE
COMPOSER, TEACHER
b Bucharest, Rumania, Dec 12, 34. *Study:* Bucharest Music Consv, comp with Mihail Jora, MA, 61; New Music Courses in Cologne, comp with Karlheinz Stockhausen, 68; Juilliard Sch Music, comp with Luciano Berio, PGD, 71; Columbia Univ, comp with Chou Wen-chung & Vladimir Ussachevsky, electronic music with Mario Davidovsky, DMA, 76. *Works:* Cantec Apelor Tarii, Bucharest Radio Orch & Chorus, 65; Sonata for Violin & Piano, Shiraz-Persepolis Fest, 67; Evolving Cycle of Two-Part Modal Inventions for Piano, Editura Muzicala, Paris, 68; Comme de Longs Nuages, Juilliard Chorus, 70; In Search of Song, French Radio & TV Orch, 72; Invention 5-B, Electronic Music Fest, Univ Va, 78; The Musical Seminar (stage work), Tanglewood Fest Contemp Music, 82. *Pos:* Dir electronic music prog, Herbert H Lehman Col, City Univ New York, 82- *Teaching:* Fel lit & materials, Juilliard Sch Music, 71-72; asst prof theory, comp & electronic music, Kinsborough Community Col, 81-82; asst prof theory, comp & electronic music, Herbert H Lehman Col, City Univ New York, 82- *Awards:* George Enescu Prize, Rumanian Acad, 65; Alexandre Gretchaninoff Prize, Juilliard Sch Music, 70; PSC City Univ New York Res Award, 83. *Mem:* BMI; Am Music Ctr Inc; Col Music Soc; MacDowell Colony Inc. *Interests:* Musical phonology. *Publ:* Auth, The Quintet, Op 4, No 2 for Two Violins, Viola, Cello & Piano by George Enescu; Expression of the Composer's Mature Style, Ed Rumanian Acad, 65; coauth, Vox Maris by George Enescu, Revista Muzica, Bucharest, 65; auth, Olivier Messiaen; Contemporary French Composer, Revista Muzica, 66. *Mailing Add:* 125 Riverside Dr New York NY 10024

COTE, PAUL G
ARTIST MANAGER
b Westbrook, Maine, Jan 3, 42. *Study:* Bentley Col, BS, 65. *Pos:* Artist mgr, Ludwig Lustig & Florian Ltd, 77-81; artist mgr & mgr vocal div, Kazuko Hillyer Int, 81- *Mem:* Opera Mgr Asn (secy/treas, 81-82, vpres, 82-83). *Mailing Add:* 460 W 24th St New York NY 10011

COTEL, MORRIS MOSHE
COMPOSER, PIANO
b Baltimore, Md, Feb 20, 43. *Study:* Peabody Consv; Juilliard Sch Music, BM, 64, MS, 65; Am Acad, Rome, FAAR, 68. *Works:* Piano Concerto, RAI Orch, Italy, 68; Humanoid Ritual Dances, US Cult Ctr, Israel, 71; Piano Sonata, self perf, NY, 77; August 12, 1952: The Night of the Murdered Poets, narrated by Richard Dreyfuss, 78; Harmony of the World, Baltimore Symph Orch, 80; The Fire and the Mountains, Baltimore Holocaust Mem Observance, 80; Yetzirah (two microtonal pianos), Brooklyn Acad Music, 81. *Rec Perf:* August 12, 1952: The Night of Murdered Poets, Pro Sonata, The Fire and the Mountains (choral cantata) & Sonata for Piano 4-hands, Grenadilla. *Teaching:* Fac mem, Rubin Acad Music, Israel, 70-72 & Peabody Consv, 72- *Awards:* Am Acad, Rome Prize, 66; Second prize, Int Arnold Schoenberg Piano Compt, 75; Israel Int Comp Compt Winner, 78. *Mailing Add:* 639 West End Ave New York NY 10025

COTRUBAS, ILEANA
SOPRANO
b Galati, Rumania. *Study:* Scoala speciala Musica, Bucharest; Ciprian Porumbescu Consv, Bucharest; Musikakad, Vienna; studied with Constantin Stroescu. *Rec Perf:* Cantatas (Bach), Masses (Mozart), Requiem (Brahms), Symphonies 2 & 8 (Mahler) & many operas, Phillips & Decca Rec. *Roles:* Yniold in Pelleas et Melisande, Bucharest Opera, 64; Zerlina in Don Giovanni; Norina in Don Pasquale; Mimi in La Boheme; Despina in Cosi fan tutte; Susanna & Cherubino in The Marriage of Figaro; Pamina in The Magic Flute. *Pos:* Sop, Frankfurt Opera, Ger, 68-71; Vienna Staatsoper, 70-, Covent Garden, 71-, Munich Staatsoper, 73-, Lyric Opera Chicago, 73-75, Opera Paris, 74-75, La Scala, 75-, Metropolitan Opera, 77- & San Francisco Opera, 78-; conct perf with major Europ orchs. *Awards:* First Prize, Int Singing Compt, Netherlands, 65; First Prize, Munich Radio Compt, 66. *Mailing Add:* c/o Columbia Artists Mgt 165 W 57 St New York NY 10019

COUSIN, JACK
DOUBLE BASS
b Boston, Mass, Oct 17, 52. *Study:* New England Consv Music, dipl. *Pos:* Appearances with Boston Youth Symph, 70; soloist, Holyoke Symph, 70, Red Fox Music Camp Orch, 71; double bass, Los Angeles Phil Orch, currently; recitalist, Boston & Los Angeles. *Mem:* Int Soc Bassists. *Publ:* Contribr to Los Angeles Bass Club Newsletter. *Mailing Add:* 5010 Timberlake Terr Culver City CA 90230

COVERT, MARY ANN
EDUCATOR, PIANO
b Memphis, Tenn, Sept 24, 36. *Study:* Studied with Mrs Robert Cockcroft, 39-54, Silvio Scionti, 52-54 & Delias Franz, 56-57; Okla Baptist Univ, with Clair McGavern, BMus, 58; Memphis State Univ, with Edwin LaBounty, MA, 65; study with Leon Fleischer, 83- *Rec Perf:* Movement for Quintet and Piano (Malcolm Lewis), Recital Music for Trumpet & Recital Music for Horn, Mark Rec; Concertino for Winds and Piano (Kent Kennan), Rhapsody in Blue (George Gershwin) & Mary Ann Covert Plays Keyboard Works of Karel Husa, Crest Rec. *Pos:* Organist & dir youth choirs, Union Ave Baptist Church, Memphis, 57-60 & Bellevue Baptist Church, Memphis, 60-66; music dir & cond, Front St Theatre, Memphis, 61-66; mem, Muses Delight, Jupiter Ens, Ithaca String Trio, Lenox Quart, Ithaca Brass Quintet, Ithaca Woodwind Quintet & Covert-Mehta Duo; pianist, currently. *Teaching:* Music, White Station High Sch, Memphis, 57-58 & Shelby Co Sch, Memphis, 61-62; teacher, Knight Rd Elem Sch, Memphis, 62-66; McGraw Cent Sch, NY, 66-67 & Lansing Cent Sch, NY, 67-68; instr, Sch Music, Ithaca Col, 67-71, asst prof, 71-76, assoc prof 76-82, chair dept appl music, 80-83, prof music, 82- *Awards:* Young Artist Dipl, Nat Fedn Music Clubs, 58 & 65; Second & Third Prize, Int Rec Compt, Nat Piano Teachers Guild, 79; Dana Scholar, Sch Music, Ithaca Col, 80-81. *Mem:* Am Fedn Musicians; Nat Piano Teachers Guild; Nat Federated Music Clubs (mem NY State bd dir, 79-); Music Teachers Nat Asn (IV vpres eastern div, 82-); Sigma Alpha Iota. *Mailing Add:* 215 N Cayuga St Apt 108 Ithaca NY 14850

COWAN, JOAN YARBROUGH See Yarbrough, Joan

COWAN, ROBERT (HOLMES)
PIANO, TEACHER
b Enid, Okla, Jan 12, 31. *Study:* Juilliard Sch Music, BS, 54, MS, 55; Royal Acad Music, London, LRAM(piano perf), 63; Eastman Sch Music, DMA, 64. *Rec Perf:* Modern Music for Two Pianos, CRI, 74; Yarbrough & Cowen Play Clementi, Schumann & Reizenstein, Orion, 76; Two Piano Concerto and Sonata (Poulenc), Musical Heritage Soc, 77; Two Piano Concerto & Scaramouche & Carnaval a la Nouvelle Orleans (Milhaud), Orion, 78; Milhaud and Poulenc Repertoire, Pantheon, 83. *Teaching:* Instr piano & chamber music, Oklahoma City Univ, 57-60; prof music, Univ Montevallo, 63- *Awards:* All Am Press Assoc Award, 66. *Bibliog:* Dean M Elder (auth), An American Idiom—Two Piano Music, Clavier, 4/75; Miriam Edwards (auth), An Interview with Duo-pianists Joan Yarbrough and Robert Cowan, Ga Music News, 11/76. *Mem:* Nat Fedn Music Clubs; Music Teachers Nat Asn; Ala Music Teachers Asn. *Publ:* Coauth, Have Pianos Will Travel, 66, Another Look at Duo-pianism, 68 & Two Pianos on Tour, 70, Music J; A Primer of Recent Two-Piano Concertos, Symph News, 76. *Rep:* Maxim Gershunoff Attractions Inc 502 Park Ave New York NY 10022. *Mailing Add:* PO Box 465 Montevallo AL 35115

COWAN, SIGMUND SUMNER
BARITONE
b New York, NY, Mar 4, 48. *Study:* Univ Miami, 63-64; Univ Fla, 65-68; Juilliard Sch Music, 69-70; Manhattan Sch Music, 72-73. *Pos:* Bar, New York Opera, Lake George Opera Fest, Wolf Trap Farm Park Perf Arts, Rochester Opera, Miami Opera Guild & San Antonio Grand Opera; conct performer, Baltimore Symph, Spoleto Fest Orch, Nat Symph, Rochester Phil & Fest Chamber Orch. *Awards:* Int Opera & Belcanto, Belgium, 78. *Mem:* Am Guild Musical Artists; Phi Mu Alpha Sinfonia. *Mailing Add:* Sardos Artists Mgt 180 West End Ave New York NY 10023

COWDEN, ROBERT HAPGOOD
EDUCATOR, WRITER
b Warren, Pa, Nov 18, 34. *Study:* Princeton Univ, AB, 56; Univ Rochester, BM, 59, MM, 60, DMA, 66; Hochschule Musik, Frankfurt, dipl, 63. *Pos:* Prin artist, Metropolitan Opera Nat Co, 65-66. *Teaching:* Dir grad opera prog, Wayne State Univ, Detroit, 68-72; Isaacson prof music, Univ Nebr, Omaha, 74-76; chmn & prof music, San Jose State Univ, 76- *Interests:* Bibliographic research on concert and opera singers 1600-1970. *Publ:* Transl, Verdi, Un Ballo In Maschera, Edwin F Kalmus, 70; auth, Acting and Directing in the Lyric Theater, Music Libr Asn Notes, 74; The Chautauqua Opera Association 1929-1958, Nat Opera Asn, 74; Index to the Yearbooks of the Komische Oper, 76 & The Lyric Theater: An Annotated Checklist, 77, Opera J. *Mailing Add:* 18195 Via Encantada Monte Sereno CA 15030

COWDEN, SUSAN JANE
FLUTE & PICCOLO, TEACHER-COACH
b Lancaster, Ohio, Oct 1, 41. *Study:* Univ Mich, with Nelson Hauenstein & Keith Bryan, BMus, 65; Royal Manchester Col Music, with Geoffrey Gilbert, 67-69. *Pos:* Flutist, Cowden & Harriman Flute & Harp Duo, 69-; sonata recitalist, 69- *Teaching:* Coach flute, privately, Columbus, Ohio, 69-; lectr flute, Capital Univ, 74-76. *Awards:* Fulbright Grant, 67-69. *Mem:* Am Fedn Musicians; Am Musicol Soc; Soc Ethnomusicol; Col Music Soc; Ohio Music Teachers Asn. *Mailing Add:* 1110 James Rd Lancaster OH 43130

COWLES, DARLEEN L
COMPOSER, EDUCATOR
b Chicago, Ill, Nov 13, 42. *Study:* De Paul Univ, BM, 66; Northwestern Univ, MM, 67; Univ Chicago, PhD. *Works:* Translucent Unreality No 1-7, Am Comp Alliance, 81; Vox Numina, comn by Univ Redlands, 82; From the King's Chamber, Needham Publ Co, 82; Variants (violin & piano), New Music Fest, Baton Rouge, La, 82; Fragments of a Lost Song, Veil of Isis, San Francisco, Calif, 83; over 45 works, solo, chamber & orchestral, publ Am

Comp Alliance. *Rec Perf:* Translucent Unreality No 1, Capriccio, 83. *Pos:* Secy & performer, Marcel Duchamp Memorial Players, 75- *Teaching:* Instr theory, Elmhurst Col, 71-72; instr theory & comp, DePaul Univ, 72-82; dir develop dept, Am Consv Music, 82- *Awards:* Grants, Meet Comp Inc, 82 & Ill Arts Coun, 83. *Mem:* BMI; Am Comp Alliance; Am Soc Univ Comp; Chicago Soc Com; Col Music Soc. *Mailing Add:* 5913 N Winthrop Chicago IL 60660

COX, CLIFFORD L
EDUCATOR, VIOLA
b New Kensington, Pa, Jan 30, 35. *Study:* Ind Univ of Pa, BS(music), 52, MMus, 58. *Works:* The Cynic (opera), Ind Opera House, 56; PSI, An Overture for Orchestra. *Pos:* Violist, Erie Phil, 68-; asst cond, Erie Phil Youth Orch, 79- *Teaching:* Prof cond & strings, Edinboro Univ, 68- *Awards:* Corrine Menk Wahn Award, 56; Orpheus Award, Phi Mu Alpha, 82. *Mem:* Am Fedn Musicians. *Publ:* Coauth, Toward A Musical Classroom, William C Brown, 70. *Mailing Add:* Rm 219 Admin Bldg Edinboro Univ Edinboro PA 16444

COX, JEFF REEVE
VIOLIN, EDUCATOR
b Denison, Iowa, Jan 20, 53. *Study:* Eastman Sch Music, BM, 75, MM, 76; Yale Univ, MMA, 78, DMA, 83. *Pos:* Mem, Cent Trio, 78-, Waterloo Fest Orch, summers 78-80 & White Mountains Fest Orch, summers 78-80. *Teaching:* Asst prof music, Cent Wash Univ, 78-; instr violin, Nat Music Camp, Interlochen, summer 81. *Mem:* Susuki Asn Am. *Mailing Add:* Music Dept Cent Wash Univ Ellensburg WA 98926

COX, KENNETH
BASS
b Lansing, Mich. *Study:* Wheaton Col; Ind Univ. *Roles:* Sarastro in The Magic Flute, Ariz Opera, 82; Don Basilio in The Barber of Seville, San Diego Opera Ctr, 82 & Indianapolis Opera, 83; Tom in Un Ballo in Maschera, 82, Alidoro in La Cenerentola, 83 & Commendatore in Don Giovanni, 83, San Diego Opera; Sparafucile in Rigoletto, Conn Opera, 83; Mephistopheles in Faust, Opera Theatre Syracuse, 83 & Indianapolis Opera, 83. *Pos:* Performer, New Orleans Opera, Opera Memphis, San Diego Opera & others. *Awards:* James S Copley First Place Honors Award, 82 & Walter Herbert Cert Distinguished Achievement, 82, San Diego Opera Ctr. *Mailing Add:* c/o Kazuko Hillyer Int 250 W 57 St New York NY 10107

COX, RICHARD GARNER
CONDUCTOR, EDUCATOR
b Rocky Mount, NC, Dec 12, 28. *Study:* Univ NC, Chapel Hill, AB, 49, MA, 51; Consv Nat Musique, Paris, France, dipl, 52; Northwestern Univ, PhD, 63. *Teaching:* Asst prof music, High Point Col, 53-58; assoc prof, Univ NC, Greensboro, 60-70, prof, 71- *Awards:* Fulbright scholar, 51-52; grant, Southern Fel Fund, 55. *Mem:* Am Choral Dir Asn (pres, Southern div, 67-71, pres, NC chap, 83-85); Music Educr Nat Conf (chmn choral section, 75-78). *Publ:* Auth, The Singer's Manual of German and French Diction, Schirmer Bks, 70; The Short Secular Piece in Twentieth-Century America, Choral J, 12/75; ed, Domine non sum dignus, Lawson-Gould, 75; Psalm 100, 80 & Talismane, 82, Hinshaw. *Mailing Add:* 1015 Guilford Ave Greensboro NC 27401

COYNER, LOUIS P
COMPOSER, EDUCATOR
b Pittsburgh, Pa, Mar 11, 31. *Study:* Carnegie-Mellon Univ, BFA, 59, MFA, 60; Univ Iowa, PhD, 63. *Works:* South Rampart Street: Revisited, 79 & A Crepuscular Time, 80, Dorn Publ; The Softest Things in the World, Am Comp Alliance Ed, 80; Saxifrage No 2, Dorn Publ, 81; Dawnstone No 2, C F Peters Inc, 82; Echoes Upon the Stilled Air, 82 & A Whorl of Time, 83, Am Comp Alliance Ed. *Teaching:* Comp in res, prof music, chmn dept music & chmn division humanities, Chatham Col, 63- *Awards:* Grants, Nat Endowment Humanities, 82 & Nat Endowment Arts, 82-83. *Mem:* Am Comp Alliance; Pittsburgh Alliance Comp; Opera Workshop Inc; Pa Coun Arts; Am Music Ctr. *Interests:* Ethnomusicology. *Mailing Add:* Chatham Col Music Dept Woodland Rd Pittsburgh PA 15232

COZAD, JOSEPH
GUITAR, TEACHER
b Topeka, Kans, Nov 30, 35. *Study:* Washburn Univ Topeka, BM(violin), 58; studied with Fritschy, 60, Diaz, 61, Romeros, 62, Ghiglia, 63 & Segovia, 64. *Pos:* Concert guitarist & clinician, mid-west; guest soloist, Kansas City Phil. *Teaching:* Instr guitar, Univ Mo, Kansas City, 61-76; vis lectr, Webster Col, Mo, 70 & Washburn Univ Topeka, 75; asst prof guitar, Univ Kans, Lawrence, 77- & Penn Valley Community Col, Kansas City, 77-; instr master classes & clinician, St Louis Guitar Guild, Wichita Guitar Soc, Webster Col, Southern Ill Univ, Univ Mo, St Louis, Washington Univ & others. *Bibliog:* Anthony L Glise (auth), A New Left Hand Position, Soundboard, winter 82-83. *Mem:* Am String Teachers Asn. *Mailing Add:* Dept Music Univ Kans Lawrence KS 66045

COZETTE, CYNTHIA
COMPOSER, ADMINISTRATOR
b Pittsburgh, Pa, Oct 19, 53. *Study:* Carnegie-Mellon Univ, BFA, 75; Univ Pa, Philadelphia, MA, 77; Juilliard Sch Music, 77-78. *Works:* Four Songs on Freedom, comn by Jacksonville Black Am Social & Cult Comt, 74; Colors (women's voices & perc), Carnegie-Mellon Univ Women's Choir, 74; Ebony Reflections (orch), Relache Contemp Music Ens, 77; The Martyr (bar & piano), Opera Ebony Affil, 78; The Black Guitar (opera excerpts), 83 & Adea (opera excerpts), 83, Acad Vocal Arts Affil; Nigerian Treasures for Solo Flute,

Flute Soc Gtr Philadelphia, 83. *Pos:* Radio consult classical music, WUHY Pub Broadcasting Radio, Philadelphia, 76-77; radio producer & commentator, WPEB Educ Radio, Philadelphia, 81- *Teaching:* Instr flute & piano, Epiphany Cath Ctr, Pittsburgh, 69-71; teaching asst orch, Carnegie-Mellon Univ, 74-75; Spanish music dir choir, Laura Wheeling Sch, Philadelphia, 79-80. *Awards:* Third Prize, 75 & Second Prize, 79, Mu Phi Epsilon Nat Comp Cont. *Bibliog:* Ron Suber (auth), Meeting of Two Musical Worlds, Pittsburgh Courier, 4/12/75; Winner Tops Winner, Pittsburgh Courier, 7/75; Barbara Faggins (auth), 5 Centuries on Women in Music, Philadelphia Tribune, 5/15/81. *Mem:* ASCAP; Flute Soc Gtr Philadelphia; Nat Flute Asn; Am Music Ctr; cofounder, Penn Comp Guild, Univ Pa (dir, 76-77). *Publ:* Auth, Classical Music on WPEB Radio, Philadelphia Tribune, 82. *Mailing Add:* PO Box 2074 Philadelphia PA 19103

CRABTREE, PHILLIP D
MUSICOLOGIST, EDUCATOR
b Des Moines, Iowa, Feb 25, 37. *Study:* Cornell Col, AB; Univ Iowa, MA; Univ Cincinnati, PhD. *Teaching:* Cond, pub sch, 59-65; asst prof choral music & musicol, Univ Hawaii, 68-72; assoc prof musicol, Col Consv Music, Univ Cincinnati, 72- *Mem:* Am Musicol Soc; Am Choral Dir Asn; Neue Bach-Gessellschaft; Int Heinrich Schütz Soc; Music Educr Nat Asn. *Interests:* Music of the Guami family. *Mailing Add:* 2622 Cyclorama Dr Cincinnati OH 45211

CRADER, JEANNINE
SOPRANO, EDUCATOR
b Jackson, Mo, May 9, 34. *Study:* St Louis Inst Music, with William Heyne; Merola Training Prog, San Francisco Opera, with Hans Frohlich; studied with Elda Ercole. *Roles:* First Orphan in Der Rosenkavalier, San Francisco Opera, 55; Florinda in Don Rodrigo; Santuzza in Cavalleria rusticana; Fiordiligi in Cosi fan tutte; Donna Anna & Donna Elvira in Don Giovanni; Turandot in Turandot; Leonora in Il Trovatore; and many others. *Pos:* Dramatic sop with maj opera co in Can, Italy, Portugal, UK & US. *Teaching:* Artist in res opera & instr voice, NTex State Univ, currently. *Awards:* Winner, Merola Debut Auditions, San Francisco Opera, 55; Martha Baird Rockefeller Grants (three). *Mailing Add:* Dept Music NTex State Univ Denton TX 76203

CRAFT, BARRY HUNT
TENOR
b McKinney, Tex, Apr 25, 48. *Study:* NTex State Univ, BMus, 70; ETex State Univ, MMus, 74; study with Eugene Conley. *Roles:* Hadji in Lakmé, 80 & Romeo in Romeo & Juliet, 81, Dallas Opera; Ralph in Pinafore, 81 & Alfred in Die Fledermaus, 82, Gold Coast Opera; Beppe in Pagliacci, 82 & Major Domo in Der Rosenkavalier, 82, Dallas Opera; Nemorino in L'Elisir d'amore, High Noon Opera Co, 82. *Mem:* Am Guild Musical Artists. *Mailing Add:* 2017 Rocky Cove Irving TX 75060

CRAFTS, EDWARD JAMES
BARITONE, EDUCATOR
b New York, NY, Nov 11, 46. *Study:* Music Acad West, 64-67; Curtis Inst Music, BM, 68; Ind Univ, MS, 77. *Roles:* Jochanaan, Syracuse Symph, 81; Scarpia, Opera Delaware, 82; Dulcamara, Houston Grand Opera, 82; Escamillo, New York City Opera, 82; Alidoro, Chicago Lyr Opera, 83; Falstaff, Cleveland Opera, 83; Mephistofeles, Opera Omaha, 83. *Teaching:* Asst prof opera, Univ Nebr, 77-79. *Awards:* Grants, Fulbright Comn, 72, Martha Baird Rockefeller Fund, 80 & Bruce Yarnell Compt, 80. *Publ:* Auth, A Tale of Two Cats, Bolletino Centro Studil Rossiniani, 76; Don Giovanni--Directorial Problems & Solutions, 80 & A Case For Opera Comique, 81, Opera J. *Mailing Add:* c/o Columbia Artists 165 W 57th St New York NY 10019

CRAGER, TED J
ADMINISTRATOR, EDUCATOR
b Lockney, Tex, Dec 27, 25. *Study:* Tex Tech Univ, BS, 49, MEd, 50; Teachers Col, Columbia Univ, MA, 54, EdD, 55. *Teaching:* Coord music, Lubbock Pub Schs, 56-58; chmn dept music, WTex State Univ, 58-63; dir music educ, Tex Woman's Univ, 63-65; assoc dean, Sch Music, Univ Miami, Coral Gables, 67- *Mailing Add:* 7305 SW 141 Terrace Miami FL 33158

CRAIG, PATRICIA
SOPRANO
b Queens, NY, July 21, 47. *Study:* Ithaca Col; studied with Don Craig & Marinka Gurewich. *Roles:* Nedda in Pagliacci, Florentine Opera, Milwaukee, 70; Musetta in La Boheme, Metropolitan Opera, 83; Micaela in Carmen; Marguerite in Faust; Susanna in Le Nozze di Figaro; Rosalinde in Die Fledermaus; Violetta in La Traviata. *Pos:* Singer with major opera co in US. *Teaching:* Classroom music, formerly. *Rep:* Robert Lombardo 61 W 62nd St Suite 6F New York NY 10023. *Mailing Add:* 121 W 72nd St New York NY 10023

CRAIGHEAD, DAVID
ORGAN, EDUCATOR
Study: Curtis Inst Music, BM; studied with Clarence Mader, Olga Steib & Alexander McCurdy, Lebanon Valley Col, Hon MusD. *Rec Perf:* On Artisan & Crystal Rec. *Pos:* Annual recital tours incl Am Guild Organists & Int Cong Organists conventions; soloist, St Paul Chamber Orch, Rochester Chamber Orch, Eastman Phil & others. *Teaching:* Fac mem, Westminster Choir Col, 45-46 & Occidental Col, 48-55; prof organ & chmn keyboard dept, Eastman Sch Music, 55- *Awards:* Eisenhart Award for Teaching Excellence, 75. *Mailing Add:* c/o Murtagh McFarland Inc 3269 W 30th St Cleveland OH 44109

CRAMER, EDWARD M
ADMINISTRATOR
b New York, NY, May 27, 25. *Study:* Columbia Univ, AB, 47; Cornell Univ, LLB, 50; NY Univ, LLM, 53. *Pos:* Pres & chief exec officer, BMI Inc, 68- *Mem:* Nat Music Coun; Asn Class Music; Nat Arts Club; Broadcast Pioneers. *Mailing Add:* Broadcast Music Inc 320 W 57th St New York NY 10019

CRANE, FREDERICK BARON
EDUCATOR
b Mt Pleasant, Iowa, Mar 4, 27. *Study:* Carleton Col, BA, 49; Univ Iowa, MA, 56, PhD, 60. *Teaching:* Fac mem, Minot State Col, 57-58 & State Univ NY, Binghamton, 60-63; asst prof, La State Univ, 63-68; prof, Univ Iowa, 68- *Mem:* Am Musicol Soc; Int Musicol Soc; Sonneck Soc; Am Musical Instrm Soc; Galpin Soc. *Interests:* Iowa music, music of Chautauqua and Lyceum; musical instruments; medieval music. *Publ:* Auth, Materials for the Study of the 15th Century Basse Danse, Inst Medieval Music, 68; Extant Medieval Musical Instruments, Univ Iowa Press, 72. *Mailing Add:* Sch Music Univ Iowa Iowa City IA 52242

CRANE, JOHN THOMAS
COMPOSER, OBOE & ENGLISH HORN
b New York, NY, Sept 17, 43. *Study:* Columbia Univ, BA, 65, DMA, 73. *Works:* Aria (flute solo) & Quartet (piano, clarinet, violin & cello), Heron Ed, 83. *Pos:* Dir music, United Methodist Church Sea Cliff, NY, 73- *Teaching:* Instr music, Dalton Sch, New York, 69-71 & Fordham Univ, 70-73; asst prof, Baruch Col, 73-75. *Mem:* Am Fedn Musicians. *Mailing Add:* 782 West End Ave New York NY 10025

CRANE, ROBERT
COMPOSER, EDUCATOR
b Winchester, Mass, Dec 24, 19. *Study:* Consv Music, Oberlin Col, with Normand Lockwood, BMus; Longy Sch Music, with Nadia Boulanger, dipl; Univ Rochester, with Bernard Rogers & Howard Hanson, MMus, PhD. *Works:* Chorale Prelude on Wachet auf (orch); Aleatory Suite (orch); Rotunda Music (brass); Peter Quince at the Clavier (cantata), 50; Piano Sonatina, 52; The Litany (soloists & orch); Missa de Angelis (chorus). *Teaching:* Mem fac music, Univ Wis, Madison, 50- *Awards:* Lili Boulanger Award, 42; Wis Fedn Music Clubs Award. *Mailing Add:* 1615 Adams St Madison WI 53711

CRAWFORD, DAVID EUGENE
WRITER, EDUCATOR
b Ft Scott, Kans, July 16, 39. *Study:* Univ Kans, BA, 61, MA, 64; Univ Vienna, 61-62; Univ Ill, PhD, 67. *Teaching:* Asst prof, Musicol Dept, Univ Mich, 69-71, assoc prof, 71-77, prof, 77- & chmn, 78- *Awards:* Fulbright Scholar, 61-62; Hon Mem for Distinguished Teaching, Phi Eta Sigma, 69; Res Fel, Am Coun Learned Soc, 72. *Mem:* Am Musicol Soc (mem nat coun, 76-78); Int Musicol Soc; Col Music Soc; Music Libr Asn; Renaissance Soc Am. *Interests:* Renaissance sacred music and manuscript studies; computer applications to music research. *Publ:* Auth, Reflections on Some Masses from the Press of Moderne, Musical Quart, Vol XVIII, 72; Sixteenth-Century Choirbooks at Casale Monferrato, Am Int Musicol, 75; Two Choirbooks of Renaisssance Polyphony at Guadalupe, Fontes Artis Musicae, Vol XXIV, 77; ed, Francesco Cellavenia: Collected Works, Am Inst Musicol, 78; coauth, Gregory's Scribe: Inexpensive Graphics for Pre-1600 Music Notation, Comput Music J, 83. *Mailing Add:* 1204 Iroquois Ann Arbor MI 48104

CRAWFORD, DAWN CONSTANCE
EDUCATOR, COMPOSER
b Ellington Field, Tex, Dec 19, 19. *Study:* Rice Univ, BA, 39; Houston Consv Music, BM, 40; Eastman Sch Music, with Bernard Rogers & Herbert Elwell, 41, 46 & 47; Teachers Col, Columbia Univ, MA, 54. *Works:* Incidental music for Love Possessed Juana, Houston Little Theatre, 46; Über Nacht (SSA, piano accmp), Dominican Singers, 65 & 76; The Pearl (chamber opera), Dominican Col, 72; Vermont Requiem (women's chorus, flute, oboe, clarinet, two fagotti), Sigma Alpha Iota Alumnae, 78; Amforsam One (organ & trumpet), A M Flusche, 80 & 82; A Gamut of Badinages (seven songs for sop & piano), Paulina Stark (in prep); Essay for Solo Violoncello, Paula Eisenstein Baker, 83. *Pos:* Music dir, Houston Little Theatre, 46. *Teaching:* Instr theory, comp & piano & asst dir, Houston Consv Music, 38-49; assoc prof & chmn music dept, Dominican Col, 64-75; instr theory, St Agnes Acad, 76- *Publ:* Contribr, Mary Parker Follett, Harvard Univ Press, 71. *Mailing Add:* 13722 Hooper Rd Houston TX 77047

CRAWFORD, H GERALD
EDUCATOR, BARITONE
b West Frankfort, Ill, Apr 18, 37. *Study:* Eastman Sch Music, BM, 59, MM, 71. *Teaching:* Asst prof music, Southeastern La Univ, 66-74; assoc prof, Western Ill Univ, 74-79; assoc prof singing, Consv Music, Oberlin Col, 79- *Mem:* Nat Asn Teachers Singing. *Mailing Add:* Music Dept Oberlin Col Oberlin OH 44074

CRAWFORD, JOHN CHARLTON
COMPOSER, EDUCATOR
b Philadelphia, Pa, Jan 19, 31. *Study:* Yale Sch Music, with Paul Hindemith, BMus, 50, MMus, 53; Consv Nat Musique, Paris, with Nadia Boulanger, 50-51; Harvard Univ, with Walter Piston & Randall Thompson, PhD, 63. *Works:* Magnificat, E C Schirmer, 57; String Quartet No 2, Brandeis Univ String Quartet, 66; Ash Wednesday, 68 & Psalm 98, 71, Oxford Univ Press; Metracollage (symph orch), Buffalo Phil Orch, 73; Don Cristobal and Rosita, Carl Fisher, Inc, 79; Three Palindromes, Univ Southern Calif Contemp Music

Ens, 82. *Teaching:* Asst, Harvard Univ, 56-61; instr music, Amherst Col, 61-63; asst prof music, Wellesley Col, 63-70; prof music, Univ Calif, Riverside, 70- *Awards:* Boott Prize, Choral Compt, Harvard Univ, 56; John Knowles Paine Travelling Fel, 59; Serious Music Award, ASCAP, 69-74. *Bibliog:* William A Herrmann (auth), Premiere of Mr Crawford's Opera, Wellesley Alumnae Mag, spring 1970. *Mem:* ASCAP; Nat Asn Comp USA; Col Music Soc; Am Musicol Soc; Am Music Ctr. *Mailing Add:* 703 11th St Santa Monica CA 90402

CRAWFORD, LISA
EDUCATOR, HARPSICHORD
Study: Radcliffe Col, BA(music), 65; Harvard Univ, MA(musicol), 69; studied harpsichord with Gustav, Leonhardt, Albert Fuller & David Fuller. *Pos:* Solo & ens appearances throughout eastern US. *Teaching:* Fac mem, Longy Sch Music, 70-73; fel, Radcliffe Inst, 71-73; assoc prof harpsichord, Consv Music, Oberlin Col, 73- *Awards:* Fulbright Grant, 65-66. *Mailing Add:* Consv Music Oberlin Col Oberlin OH 44074

CRAWFORD, MARIBETH KIRCHHOFF
CONDUCTOR, EDUCATOR
b Indianapolis, Ind. *Study:* Lawrence Univ, BM, 64; Am Consv, MM, 65; Köln Hochschule Musik, cond cert, 69. *Pos:* Cond, Lawrence Civic Choir, Kans, 74- *Teaching:* Instr voice, Wis State Univ, 66-68, assoc prof, Univ Kans, Lawrence, 70-, dir vocal div, 83- *Mailing Add:* Dept Music Univ Kans Lawrence KS 66045

CRAWFORD, RICHARD
EDUCATOR
b Detroit, Mich, May 12, 35. *Study:* Univ Mich, BMus, 58, MMus, 59, PhD(musicol), 65. *Teaching:* Instr music hist, Univ Mich, 62-66, asst prof, 66-69, assoc prof, 69-75, prof, 75- *Awards:* Otto Kinkeldey Award, Am Musicol Soc, 76; John Simon Guggenheim Fel, 77-78. *Mem:* Am Musicol Soc (bd mem, 76-78, vpres, 78-80, pres, 82-84); Soc Ethnomusicol; Sonneck Soc (bd mem, 75-77, vpres, 81-83); Am Antiquarian Soc; Int Asn Study Popular Music. *Interests:* Music in the United States. *Publ:* Auth, Andrew Law, American Psalmodist, Northwestern Univ Press, 68; American Studies and American Musicology, Inst Studies Am Music, Brooklyn, 75; coauth, William Billings of Boston: 18th Century Composer, Princeton Univ Press, 75; ed, The Civil War Songbook, Dover, 77; auth, A Historian's Introduction to Early American Music, Am Antiquarian Soc, 79. *Mailing Add:* Burtan Tower Univ Mich Ann Arbor MI 48109

CRAY, KEVIN E
COMPOSER, PIANO
b Erie, Pa, Jun 20, 22. *Study:* Cath Univ Am, BMus, 50; St John's Univ, Minn, 51-53; Chautauqua, with George Shearing, 75-80. *Works:* Mass of the Pslams, 51, Three Motets, 51 & Savior of the World, 52, Gregorian Inst. *Teaching:* Instr piano & comp, Cray Studio, Erie, Pa, 68- *Awards:* Outstanding Service, Pa Music Teachers Asn, 76. *Mem:* Am Col Musicians (fac mem, 73-); Pa Music Teachers Asn; Music Teachers Nat Asn. *Mailing Add:* 945 W 38th St Erie PA 16508

CREAMER, ALICE DUBOIS
BAROQUE INSTRUMENTS, MUSICOLOGIST
b Roadstown, NJ, Apr 16, 15. *Pos:* Performer on piano, pipe organ, cello, recorder, krummhorn, kortholt & viola da gamba; organizer & perf, Baroque Chamber Ens, Cumberland Co Hist Soc; cur hist instrm, Cumb Co Hist Soc & Bridgeton Antiquarian League. *Mem:* Am Recorder Soc; Am Viola da Gamba Soc; Int Soc Harpsichord Builders; Galpin Soc England. *Interests:* Old musical instruments. *Mailing Add:* RFD Apt 5 Finley Rd Bridgeton NJ 08302

CREDITOR, BRUCE MITCHELL
CLARINET, TEACHER
b Brooklyn, NY, Nov 4, 53. *Study:* New England Consv Music, BM, 75, MM, 77. *Pos:* Prin clarinet, Boston Phil Orch, 73- & NH Symph Orch, 73-; clarinet & asst cond, New England Ragtime Ens, 73-; clarinet, Emmanuel Wind Quintet, 75-; Gen mgr, Margun Music Inc, 80- *Teaching:* Music hist, New England Consv Music, 75-79; instr clarinet, Boston Consv Music, 83- *Awards:* Grammy Award for New England Ragtime Ens, Nat Acad Rec Arts & Sci, 73; Award Chamber Music, Walter Naumburg Found, 81. *Mem:* Int Clarinet Soc; Nat Acad Rec Arts & Sci; Col Music Soc; Am Music Ctr; Chamber Music Am. *Mailing Add:* 17 Leonard Rd Sharon MA 02067

CREED, KAY
MEZZO-SOPRANO, EDUCATOR
b Oklahoma City, Okla, Aug 19, 40. *Study:* Oklahoma City Univ, BM, 64, MPA, 82. *Roles:* Ulrica in Un Ballo in maschera, Cent City Opera, 69; Dorabella in Cosi fan tutte, 69-71 & Cenerentola in La Cenerentola, 72, New York City Opera; Marina in Boris Godunov, Cincinnati Opera, 73; Cherubino in Le Nozze di Figaro, Hartford Opera, 73; Giulietta in Les Contes d'Hoffman, Memphis Opera, 75; Carmen in Carmen, Nat Opera, 79. *Pos:* Ms, New York City Opera, 65-73. *Teaching:* Asst prof voice, Oklahoma City Univ, 73-, asst prof opera repertoire, themes & plots, 74- *Awards:* Fulbright Grant, 65; grant, Rockefeller Found, 67. *Mem:* Nat Asn Teachers Singing; Music Teachers Nat Asn; Okla Music Teachers Asn; Okla Federated Music Clubs. *Rep:* Ludwig Lustig W 57th St New York NY 10019. *Mailing Add:* 415 W Eubanks Oklahoma City OK 73118

CRESHEVSKY, NOAH EPHRAIM
COMPOSER, EDUCATOR
b Rochester, NY, Jan 31, 45. *Study:* L'Ecole Normale de Musique, with Nadia Boulanger, 63-64; State Univ NY, Buffalo, BFA(comp), 66; Juilliard Sch, with Luciano Berio, MS, 68. *Works:* Circuit, 71, Broadcast, 72 & In Other Words (Portrait of John Cage), 75, Op One Rec; Great Performances, Alexander Broude Inc, 77; Highway, 79 & Sonata, 80, Op One Rec; Nightscape, comn by Nat Endowment Arts, 82; over 150 performances throughout US of taped electronic music. *Teaching:* Fac mem ear-training, Juilliard Sch, 68-70; assoc prof theory & comp, Brooklyn Col, City Univ New York, 69- *Awards:* Fel, Nat Endowment Arts, 81. *Mem:* ASCAP. *Mailing Add:* Consv Music Brooklyn Col City Univ New York Brooklyn NY 11210

CRESPIN, REGINE C
SOPRANO
b Marseilles, France, Feb 23, 27. *Study:* Lycee Francaise, Consv Paris; Consv Nat Musique. *Rec Perf:* For EMI, London, Decca, DG & Erato. *Roles:* Elsa in Lohengrin, Mulhouse Opera, France, 51; Brünnhilde in Die Walküre, First Easter Fest, Salzburg, 67; Marguerite in La Damnation de Faust; Fiordiligi in Cosi fan tutte; Donna Anna in Don Giovanni; Salome in Herodiade; Marschallin in Der Rosenkavalier, Glyndebourne Fest, 61, Metropolitan Opera & Vienna Opera. *Pos:* Sop with major opera co & orch throughout NAm, SAm & Europe. *Awards:* Chevalier Legion d'Honneur; Commandeur Arts & Lett; Chevalier l'Ordre Nat Merite, French govt. *Mailing Add:* c/o Herbert H Breslin Inc 119 W 57th St New York NY 10019

CRESTON, PAUL
COMPOSER, WRITER
b New York, NY, Oct 10, 06. *Study:* Self taught in harmony, orch & comp; studied piano with Carlo Stea, G Aldo Randegger & Gaston Dethier, & organ with Pietro Yon. *Works:* Fantasy for Trombone & Orch, comn by Alfred Wallenstein; Symphony No 3, comn by Eugene Ormandy; Invocation and Dance for Orchestra, comn by Louisville Orch; Toccata for Orch, comn by George Szell; Symphony No 5, comn by Nat Symph Orch; Violin Concerto #2, comn by Ford Found; Sadhana (violoncello & orch), comn by Los Angeles Chamber Orch; Symphony No 6, comn by Am Guild Organists; over 100 maj works incl ten symphonic band works, six symphonies & 15 concertos; 35 works commissioned. *Pos:* Organist, St Malachy's Church, NY, 34-67; music dir, Hour of Faith & Storyland Theatre, ABC; comp, The 20th Century, CBS-TV. *Teaching:* Fac mem, Cummington Sch Arts, 40, Univ Southern Calif, 48 & Swarthmore Col, 56; prof, New York Col Music, 64-68; comp in res & prof, Cent Wash State Col, 68-76. *Awards:* Guggenheim Fel, 38-39; Music Award, Nat Inst Arts & Lett, 43; Nat Arts Club Gold Medal, 63. *Mem:* Nat Music Coun (mem exec comt, 50-68); Col Music Soc; Nat Asn Am Comp & Cond (pres, 56-60); ASCAP (dir, 60-68); Bohemians (gov, 50-68). *Publ:* Auth, Principles of Rhythm, 61 & Rational Metric Notation, 79. *Mailing Add:* Box 28511 San Diego CA 92128

CRIBB, GEORGE ROBERT
EDUCATOR, PIANO
b Nichols, SC, July 21, 27. *Study:* Wake Forest Univ, BA, 50; Teachers Col, Columbia Univ, MA, 51, SpMusEd, 52; NTex State Univ, EdD, 65. *Teaching:* Asst prof music, William Carey Col, 52-57 & Miss Col, 57-63; chmn dept fine arts, Campbellsville Col, 64-69; chmn dept fine arts & cond choral ens, Gardner-Webb Col, 69- *Mem:* Music Educr Nat Conf; Music Teachers Nat Asn; Am Choral Dir Asn; Phi Mu Alpha Sinfonia; Nat Fedn Music Clubs. *Interests:* Comparative effectiveness and programmed learning procedures in teaching fundamentals of music. *Mailing Add:* Music Dept Gardner-Webb Col Boiling Springs NC 28017

CRISS, WILLIAM
OBOE, EDUCATOR
Study: Curtis Inst Music, with Marcel Tabuteau. *Pos:* Solo & first oboe, Metropolitan Opera Orch, formerly; prin oboe, NBC Symph, formerly, Philadelphia Orch, formerly & New York Phil, formerly; performer, Los Angeles ensembles, currently. *Teaching:* Adj assoc prof oboe, Univ Southern Calif, currently; mem fac, Music Acad West, summer 83; adj mem fac, Calif State Univ, Northridge, currently. *Mailing Add:* Dept Music Calif State Univ Northridge CA 91330

CRIST, RICHARD (LEROY)
BASS
b Harrisburg, Pa, Oct 21, 47. *Study:* Messiah Col, Grantham, Pa, BS(music ed), 70; New England Consv Music, Boston, MMus(voice), 72; Goldovsky Opera Inst, 77. *Roles:* Stabat Mater, Washington Choral Arts Soc, 79; Messiah, St Louis Symph, 79; Bartolo in Marriage of Figaro, San Francisco Opera, 81; Osmin in Abduction from Seraglio, Lake George Opera Fest, 81; Bartolo in Barber of Seville, Kalamazoo Symph, 82; Sarastro in Magic Flute, Va Opera Theater, 82; Wesener in Die Soldaten, Opera Co Boston, 82 & Opera de Lyon, France, 83. *Mem:* Am Guild Musical Artists. *Rep:* Thea Dispeker Artists Rep 59 E 54th St New York NY 10022. *Mailing Add:* 484 W 43rd St New York NY 10036

CRITTENDEN, RICHARD RAYMOND
EDUCATOR, STAGE DIRECTOR
b San Diego, Calif, July 23, 38. *Study:* Occidental Col, AB, 60; studied with Boris Goldovsky, 71. *Teaching:* Asst prof opera, Sch Music, Yale Univ, 76-82; stage dir, Curtis Inst Music, 77- & Mannes Col Music, 79-81. *Mem:* Nat Opera Asn. *Mailing Add:* 96 Van Buren Ave Teaneck NJ 07666

CROCHET, EVELYNE
PIANO, EDUCATOR
b Paris, France, Nov 9, 37; US citizen. *Study:* Paris Nat Consv, spec studies with Edwin Fischer & Rudolf Serkin, First Prize, 56. *Pos:* Pianist in res, Brandeis Univ, 59-64; artist in res, Rutgers Univ, 64-70; soloist with Boston Symph, Chicago Orch, Pittsburgh Symph, Detroit Symph, Minn Orch, Baltimore Symph, Buffalo Phil, London Symph, Royal Phil, London Phil, Paris Nat Orch, Bavarian Radio Orch, NGerman Radio Orch & Residency Orch Hague. *Teaching:* Prof music, Boston Univ, 82- *Awards:* First Medal Int Compt Geneva, 56. *Rep:* M Cohen 1 W 64th St #10F New York NY 10023. *Mailing Add:* 215 W 83rd New York NY 10023

CROCIATA, FRANCIS JOSEPH
ARTIST MANAGER, WRITER
b Rochester, NY, Aug 4, 48. *Study:* St John Fisher Col, BA, 70. *Pos:* Dir publ relations, Eastman Sch Music, 75-77; exec dir, Va Orch Group, 77-80; pres & dir, F Crociata Artists Rep, 80- *Interests:* Sergei Rachmaninoff; life and works of Leo Sowerby. *Publ:* Auth, The Complete Rachmaninoff (booklet), RCA Rec, 73; Nina Koshetz, Desmar Music Inc, 77; coauth, Contemporary Musicians in Photographs, Dover, 79. *Mailing Add:* 15 Swan St Rochester NY 14604

CROCKER, RICHARD LINCOLN
EDUCATOR, WRITER
b Roxbury, Mass, Feb 17, 27. *Study:* Yale Univ, BA, 50, PhD(music), 57. *Teaching:* From instr to asst prof music, Yale Univ, 55-62; from asst prof to assoc prof, 63-71; prof music, Univ Calif, Berkeley, 71- *Awards:* Res Humanities Fels, 67 & 73; Guggenheim Fel, 69-70. *Mem:* Am Musicol Soc. *Interests:* Early medieval music; sequences. *Publ:* Auth, A History of Musical Style, McGraw, 66; coauth, Some 9th-Century Sequences, J Am Musicol Soc, winter 67; auth, Shape and Syntax, A Listener's Introduction, 67; coauth, Listening to Music, 71, McGraw; auth, The Early Medieval Sequence, Univ Calif, 77. *Mailing Add:* Dept Music Univ Calif Berkeley CA 94720

CROCKER, RONALD JAY
COMPOSER, TEACHER
b Lincoln, Nebr, Sept 26, 41. *Study:* Nebr Wesleyan Univ, BMusEd, 64; Univ Iowa, MA, 66. *Works:* Tunings, 72, Composition for Winds, 72, Memories of Tomorrow, 76, March April, 77, Syncopolyophony, 78, Demannu, 80 & Dejaview, 81, perf by Kearney State Col Symph Wind Ens. *Teaching:* Music, Mead pub schs, Nebr, 64-65; fac mem & dir bands, Kearney State Col, 66- *Mem:* Nebr Music Educr; Nebr Band Masters. *Mailing Add:* 360 Northview Dr Kearney NE 68847

CROCKETT, DONALD (HAROLD)
COMPOSER, EDUCATOR
b Pasadena, Calif, Feb 18, 51. *Study:* Univ Southern Calif, with Robert Linn, BM, 74, with Halsey Stevens, MM, 76; Univ Calif, Santa Barbara, with Peter Racine Fricker, PhD, 81. *Works:* Trio for Flute, Cello & Harp, comn & perf by Greylock Trio, Boston, Mass, 79; Lyrikos (ten & orch), comn & perf by Pasadena Chamber Orch, 79; Occhi dell'Alma Mia (sop & guitar), Serenissima-Unicorn Music Co, 82; Vox in Rama (chorus & orch), comn & perf by Pasadena Chamber Orch, 83; The Pensive Traveller (high voice & piano), Serenissima-Unicorn Music Co, 83. *Teaching:* Asst prof theory & comp, Univ Southern Calif, currently. *Awards:* Award, BMI, 72. *Mem:* Soc Music Theory. *Mailing Add:* 4393 Bel Air Dr La Canada CA 91011

CROLIUS, NANCY PETERSON
MEZZO-SOPRANO
b Plainfield, NJ, July 31, 50. *Study:* Peabody Consv Music, BMEd(voice), 72; Hope Col. *Pos:* Chorister, Baltimore Opera Chorus, 76-77 & Metropolitan Opera Chorus, 80-; singer, Gregg Smith Singers, 79-80. *Mem:* Am Guild Musical Artists; Am Fedn TV & Radio Artists. *Mailing Add:* 159-00 Riverside Dr W #3K New York NY 10032

CROOM, JOHN (ROBERT)
COMPOSER, EDUCATOR
b Jennings, La, Apr 27, 41. *Study:* La State Univ, with Kenneth Klaus, PhD, 79; McNeese State Univ, with Woodrow James. *Works:* Pentagon for Brass (quintet); Variations for a Dozen Clarinets; Five Subconscious Flights (piano); Metamorphosis (two pianos); Didactic Material (clarinet solo); Mass; Symphony for Brass and Percussion. *Teaching:* Assoc prof music & head dept, Nicholls State Univ, 70- *Mem:* La Music Educr Asn. *Mailing Add:* 503 Willow St Thibodaux LA 70301

CROSBIE, WILLIAM PERRY
ORGAN, MUSIC DIRECTOR
b Exeter, NH, Aug 19, 47. *Study:* Whittier Col, AB, 69; WVa Univ, MM, 79, DMA, 80. *Pos:* Organist & choirmaster, St Margaret's Episcopal Church, 61-65 & St Matthew's Episcopal Cathedral, Wheeling, WVa, 70; asst organist & choirmaster, St Paul's Episcopal Cathedral, Los Angeles, 65-70. *Teaching:* Instr music, Bethany Col, WVa, 77-83. *Mem:* Asn Anglican Musicians; Royal Sch Church Music; Am Guild Organists. *Mailing Add:* 1410 Chapline St Wheeling WV 26003

CROSBY, JOHN O'HEA
ADMINISTRATOR, CONDUCTOR & MUSIC DIRECTOR
b New York, NY, July 12, 26. *Study:* Yale Univ, BA, 50; Columbia Univ, 51-55; Univ NMex, Hon LittD, 67; Col Santa Fe, Hon MusD, 69; Cleveland Inst Music, Hon MusD, 74; Univ Denver, LHD, 77. *Pos:* Accmp, music coach & cond, NY, 51-56; founder, gen dir & mem cond staff, Santa Fe Opera, 57-;

guest cond with Baltimore Opera Co, Can Opera Co, Edmonton Opera Co & New York City Opera Co; pres, Manhattan Sch Music, 76- *Mem:* Opera Am (pres, 75-79); Am Arts Alliance; Metropolitan Opera Club; Century Asn. *Mailing Add:* Manhattan Sch Music 120 Claremont Ave New York NY 10027

CROSS, LOWELL MERLIN
COMPOSER, LASER
b Kingsville, Tex, June 24, 38. *Study:* Tex Tech Univ, BA, 61, BMus, 63; Univ Toronto, MA, 68. *Works:* 0.8 Century (tape music), In: John Cage's Notations, 61; Three Etudes for Magnetic Tape, CRI, 65; Video II (B) & (C) (tape music & TV), 65, Video II (L) (tape music, laser syst), 65 & Musica Instrumentalis (performers & TV), 66, Source, music of the avant garde; Video/Laser I & II, Expo '70, Osaka, Japan, 69-70; Video/Laser III, 71- *Pos:* Res assoc, Univ Toronto Electronic Music Studio, 67-68; consult artist & engineer, Experiments in Art & Technol Inc, 68-70. *Teaching:* Artistic dir, Tape Music Ctr, Mills Col, 68-69; from asst prof to prof art & technol & audio rec, Sch Music, Univ Iowa, 71- *Mem:* Audio Engineering Soc. *Interests:* Laser applications in art and music. *Publ:* Auth, A Bibliography of Electronic Music, Univ Toronto Press, 67; Electronic Music, 1948-1953, Perspectives New Music, Vol 7, No 1; Audio, Video, Laser, Source, music of the avant garde, 70; Laser Deflection System, In: Pavilion, E P Dutton, 72; The Audio Control of Laser Displays, db, The Sound Engineering Mag, Vol 15, No 7. *Mailing Add:* Sch Music Univ Iowa Iowa City IA 52242

CROSS, RICHARD BRUCE
BASS-BARITONE
b Faribault, Minn, Dec 7, 35. *Study:* Cornell Col. *Rec Perf:* For Decca, Westminster & RCA. *Roles:* Postman in Scarf, Spoleto Fest, 58; Colline in La Boheme & Forester in The Cunning Little Vixen, New York City Opera; Sarastro in Die Zauberflote, Washington Opera; Dr Schön in Lulu, Spoleto Fest; Ramfis in Aida; Orest in Elektra. *Pos:* Leading bass-bar, Frankfurt Opera, 73-; perf at Glyndebourne Fest, Spoleto Fest & others & with major US & Europ opera co. *Awards:* Promising Personality, Theater World Mag. *Mailing Add:* c/o Thea Dispeker 59 E 54th St New York NY 10022

CROSS, RONALD
EDUCATOR, ORGAN
b Ft Worth, Tex, Feb 18, 29. *Study:* Centenary Col La, BA, 50; NY Univ, MA, 53, PhD, 61. *Teaching:* Prof musicianship & music hist, dir collegium musicum & chmn music dept, Wagner Col, Staten Island, 68- *Awards:* Fulbright Scholar, 55-57. *Mem:* Am Musicol Soc; Soc Int Musicol; Col Music Soc; Soc Enthnomusicol; Am Guild Organists. *Interests:* Fifteenth-century music. *Publ:* Auth, The Life and Works of Matthaeus Pipelare, Musica Disciplina, 63; ed, Matthaeus Pipelare: Opera Omnia, Vol I, 66, Vol II, 67 & Vol III, 67, Am Inst Musicol; auth, The Chansons of Matthaeus Pipelare, Musical Quart, 10/69. *Mailing Add:* 221 Ward Ave Staten Island NY 10304

CROSSLEY, PAUL CHRISTOPHER RICHARD
PIANO
b Dewsbury, Yorkshire, UK, May 17, 44. *Study:* Mansfield Col, Oxford, MA, 66; private piano studies with Fanny Waterman, Yvonne Loriod & Olivier Messiaen. *Rec Perf:* The Three Piano Sonatas (Tippett), Philips, 73; Prelude, Choral et Fugue & Prelude, Aria et Final (Franck), 74, The Complete Piano Works (Janacek), 79 & Chamber Concerto (Berg), 79, Decca; The Complete Piano Works (Faure), CRD, 82. *Awards:* Fel, Gulbenkian Found, 71-74; Grand Prix du Disque, Acad du Disque Francais, 79. *Mailing Add:* c/o Herbert Barrett Mgt 1860 Broadway New York NY 10023

CROW, TODD
PIANO
b Santa Barbara, Calif, July 25, 45. *Study:* Univ Calif, BA, 67; Juilliard Sch Music, MS, 68; Music Acad West. *Pos:* Pianist, concerts throughout US & Europe; appearances with Composers String Quartet & Concord String Quartet. *Teaching:* Assoc prof theory, analysis & piano & chmn dept, Vassar Col, currently. *Mem:* Am Musicol Soc; Am Liszt Soc. *Publ:* Auth, Bartok Studies, 76; contribr, Notes. *Rep:* New Era Int Concerts Ltd London. *Mailing Add:* 16 Redondo Dr Poughkeepsie NY 12603

CROWDER, ELIZABETH (BETTE HOPE WADDINGTON)
VIOLIN
b San Francisco, Calif, July 27, 21. *Study:* Univ Calif, Berkeley, AB(music & art), 45; San Francisco State Univ, MA(music & art), 53; violin teachers incl Naoum Blinder, Eddy Brown, Melvin Ritter, Frank Gittelson, Dr D C Dounis, Daniel Bonsack, Felix Khuner, Louis Ford, Antonio de Grassi, Dean Donaldson, Joseph Fuchs & Henry Temianka. *Pos:* Violinist, Bach Fest, Carmel, Calif, 46-49 & 51, Erie Orch, Pa, 50-51, Dallas Symph, 57-58 & St Louis Symph Orch, 58- *Teaching:* Violin, Erie Pub Sch, Pa, 50-51. *Mem:* Am String Teachers Asn. *Mailing Add:* 2800 Olive St St Louis MO 63103

CROZIER, CATHARINE (CATHARINE C GLEASON)
EDUCATOR, ORGAN
b Hobart, Okla, Jan 18, 14. *Study:* Eastman Sch Music, artists dipl, 38, MM(music lit), 41; hon deg from Smith Col, Univ Southern Colo, Univ Ill & Baldwin-Wallace Col. *Rec Perf:* Gothic Rec, 78. *Pos:* Conct organist throughout US & Europ; fac mem music dept & organist Knowles Chapel, Rollins Col, 55-69. *Teaching:* Fac mem organ, Eastman Sch Music, 36-55. *Mem:* Am Guild Organists; Am Musicol Soc. *Interests:* Organ literature and performance. *Rep:* Murtagh-MacFarlane Artists Mgt 3269 W 30th St Cleveland OH 44109. *Mailing Add:* 6308 Friends Ave Whittier CA 90601

CRUM, DOROTHY EDITH
EDUCATOR, SOPRANO
b Providence, RI, May 24, 44. *Study:* Coached voice with William Vennard, French with Pierre Bernac & German with John Wustman, 68-69; Bowling Green State Univ, MM(voice), 69; Univ Colo, Boulder, DMA, 77. *Roles:* Mabel in Little Mary, Baltimore Comic Opera, 69; Frasquita & Lucy in The Telephone, Bowling Green State Univ Opera, 70; Frasquita, Wichita Symph Opera, 78. *Pos:* Leading sop, Baltimore Comic Opera, 68-70; soloist, Wichita Choral Soc, 75, Hutchinson Choral Soc, Kans, 77-80 & Chamber Choral, 79-80; sop soloist opera & oratorio, Wichita Symph, 76- *Teaching:* Asst prof voice, diction, choir & opera, Colby Sawyer Col, 70-73, asst prof voice & diction, Wichita State Univ, 73- *Mem:* Nat Asn Teacher's Singing (auditions chmn, 74-76 & regional gov, 76-82); Music Teacher's Nat Asn; Kansas Music Teacher's Asn (auditions chmn, 82-). *Publ:* Auth, Creative Recitaling, Haines Publ, Kans, 78. *Mailing Add:* 554 N Crestway Wichita KS 67208

CRUMB, GEORGE (HENRY)
COMPOSER, EDUCATOR
b Charleston, WVa, Oct 24, 29. *Study:* Mason Col Music, BM, 50; Univ Ill, MM, 52; Univ Mich, DMA, 59; Oberlin Col, Hon Dr; WVa Univ, Hon Dr; New England Consv Music, Hon Dr. *Works:* Eleven Echoes of Autumn, Peters Corp, 66; Echoes of Time and the River (orch), Belwin-Mills, 67; Ancient Voices of Children, 70, Black Angels (string quartet), 70, Vox Balaenae, 71, Music for a Summer Evening, 74 & Celestial Mechanics (Makrokosmos IV), 79, Peters Corp. *Teaching:* Instr piano, Univ Colo, 59-65; prof comp, Univ Pa, 65- *Awards:* Pulitzer Prize Music, 68. *Mem:* BMI. *Mailing Add:* 240 Kirk Lane Media PA 19063

CRUTCHER, FRANCES HILL
EDUCATOR, PIANO
b Nashville, Tenn, Nov 2, 05. *Study:* Cadek Consv, dipl (piano & theory), 26, dipl, 27; Univ Tenn, Chattanooga, BM, 39; studied with Blanche Merriman, Olga Samaroff, James Friskin & Wendell Keeney, 40-52. *Pos:* Accmp, Chattanooga Civic Chorus, 30-50 & Nashville Symph Chorus, 62-75. *Teaching:* Piano & theory, Cadek Consv, 22-42; instr piano, Univ Chattanooga, 42-52, asst prof, 52-62; prof, David Lipscomb Col, 62- *Awards:* Tenn Music Teacher of Year, Tenn Music Teachers Asn, 71. *Mem:* Nashville Area Music Teachers Asn (pres, currently); Tenn Music Teachers Asn; Music Teachers Nat Asn (secy-treas southern div, 73-75). *Mailing Add:* 3401 Granny White Pike #L-229 Nashville TN 37204

CRUZ, ANGELO
BARITONE, EDUCATOR
b Bayamon, PR, Aug 8, 42. *Study:* Juilliard Sch Music, with Elenor Steber, 77; vocal training with Elizabeth Cole, 78-81 & Jay Pohue, 82. *Roles:* Silvio in Pagliacci, Opera de San Juan, 75; Schaunard in La Boheme, Opera de PR Inc, 75; Duke Alfonso in Lucrezia Borgia, Opera Orch NY, 80; Schaunard in La Boheme, Conn Grand Opera Co, 82; Amonasro in Aida, NY Grand Opera Co, 82; Nabucco in Nabucco, Ebony Opera. *Teaching:* Prof music educ, Univ PR, 69-71; prof music appreciation, Inter-Am Univ, 71-72; prof music hist, Hostos Community Col, 77-78. *Mem:* Am Guild Musical Artists. *Rep:* Warden Assoc Ltd Suite 4K 45 W 60th St New York NY 10023. *Mailing Add:* 484 W 43rd Apt 21-0 New York NY 10036

CRUZ-ROMO, GILDA (GILDA CRUZ ROMO)
SOPRANO
b Guadalajara, Jalisco, Mex. *Study:* Consv Nacional Mex, 62. *Rec Perf:* Luisa Miller, RAI, Italy, 74; Aida, Orange Fest, France, 77; Il Trovatore, Florence, Televise over Europe, 77-78; Otello, Metropolitan Opera, 79. *Roles:* Aida in Aida, Donna Leonora di Vargus in Forze del Destino, Leonora in Il Trovatore, Cio-Cio-San in Madama Butterfly, Manon Lescaut, Suor Angelica & Desdemona in Otello, Metropolitan Opera. *Pos:* Mem, Vienna Staatsoper, Austria, perf worldwide. *Awards:* Primio Jalisco, 80; Testimonio de Honor, Excuela Musica Univ, Guadalajara, 80; Merito Cultural, Inst Cult Mexicano-Norteamericano, 80. *Rep:* Columbia Artist Mgt Inc 165 W 57th St New York NY 10019. *Mailing Add:* 397 Warwick Ave Teaneck NJ 07666

CSONKA, MARGARITA (MARGARITA C MONTANARO)
HARP
b Havana, Cuba; US citizen. *Study:* Curtis Inst Music, with Carlos Salzedo & Marilyn Costello, 63. *Pos:* Harp, Philadelphia Orch, 63- *Mailing Add:* 220 Pine St Philadelphia PA 19106

CUCCARO, COSTANZA (CONSTANCE JEAN PENHORWOOD)
SOPRANO
b Toledo, Ohio. *Study:* Univ Iowa, studied voice with Herald Stark, BMus, 68; studied opera with Luigi Ricci, Rome, 68; Acad Santa Cecilia, art song study with Giorgio Favretto, Rome, 69. *Rec Perf:* Der Tod Jesu (H Graun), Schwann Rec, 81; Die Entführung aus dem Serail, Can Broadcasting Co, 82; Mozart Mass in C Minor, Hessischer Rundfunk Frankfurt, 83. *Roles:* Rosina in Barber of Seville, Metropolitan Opera, 75; Gilda in Rigoletto, Munich Staatsoper, 78; Konstanze in Die Entführung aus dem Serail, Vienna Staatsoper, 78; Norina in Don Pasquale, Deutsche Oper Berlin, 80; Lucia in Lucia di Lammermoor, Vancouver Opera, 82; Pamina in Die Zauberflöte, Toronto Opera, 82; Sophie in Der Rosenkavalier, Dallas Opera, 82. *Awards:* First Place, Metropolitan Opera Nat Coun Auditions, 67; Fulbright Scholar, Rome, 68. *Bibliog:* Ekkehard Pluta (auth), Junge Talente, Opera Welt, Imre Fabion Ed, Zurich, 74; Wallace Dace (auth), National Theaters in the Larger German and Austrian Cities, Richards Rosen Press Inc, 80. *Rep:* Colbert Artists Mgt Inc 111 W 57th St New York NY 10019. *Mailing Add:* 745 Austin Dr Lumberton NC 28358

CUCKSON, ROBERT
ADMINISTRATOR, EDUCATOR
Study: New South Wales Consv Music, dipl; Mannes Col Music, MM, MMA; Yale Univ, DMA; studied theory & analysis with Carl Schachter, Ernst Oster & Allen Forte, comp with Georg Tintner, Peter Racine Fricker, Peter Pindar Stearhs & Yehudi Wyner, piano with Ilona Kabos, Carlo Zecchi & Jeaneane Dowis. *Teaching:* Fac mem, Mannes Col Music, 72-, dean fac, 79- *Mailing Add:* Mannes Col Music 157 E 74th Street New York NY 10021

CUDEK, MARK S
EDUCATOR, GUITAR & LUTE
b Buffalo, NY, June 3, 52. *Study:* State Univ NY, Buffalo, BFA, 74; Peabody Inst, Johns Hopkins Univ, MM, 82; studied guitar pedogogy with Aaron Shearer. *Teaching:* Instr guitar, Summer Div Univ Mich, Interlochen, 74-, Col VI, 78-79 & Peabody Inst, Johns Hopkins Univ, 82-; dir guitar dept, Nat Music Camp, Interlochen, Mich, 74- *Mem:* Lute Soc Am. *Mailing Add:* 3025 St Paul St Baltimore MD 21218

CUKRO, GREGORY
BASSOON
b Colo, June 10, 50. *Study:* Manhattan Sch Music, BMus, 75, MMus, 76. *Pos:* Prin bassoon, Jackson Symph, 78- *Mailing Add:* PO Box 1394 Jackson MS 39205

CULLEY, PAMELA OVERSTREET
VIOLIN, CONDUCTOR & MUSIC DIRECTOR
b Peoria, Ill, Mar 11, 53. *Study:* DePaul Univ, BM, 74, MM, 80; studied with Mary K Rosen. *Pos:* Cond & dir, Metropolitan Youth Symph Orch, Chicago, 78- *Teaching:* Orch dir, Niles Sch District #71, Ill, 74-; lectr violin pedagogy, DePaul Univ, 78- *Mailing Add:* 476 N 7th Ave Des Plaines IL 60016

CULP, PAULA N
PERCUSSION, TEACHER
b Ft Smith, Ark, Apr 9, 41. *Study:* Mozarteum, Salzburg, Austria, with Paul Hirsch, 61-62; Oberlin Consv with Cloyd Duff, BME, 63; Indiana Univ, Bloomington, with George Gaber, MME & perf cert, 65. *Pos:* Prin timpanist, Metropolitan Opera Nat Co, 65-67; prin perc, Indianapolis Symph, 67-68; perc & assoc timpani, Minnesota Orch, 68- *Teaching:* Asst teaching perc, Indiana Univ, Bloomington, 63-65; fac perc, DePauw Univ, 64-65; assoc fac perc, Univ Minn, Minneapolis, 69- *Mem:* Perc Arts Soc. *Mailing Add:* 4210 Abbott Ave S Minneapolis MN 55410

CULVER, ROBERT
EDUCATOR, VIOLA
Study: Eastman Sch Music, grad. *Pos:* Violist, Rochester Phil, Detroit Symph & Hughes Quartet, Ohio State Univ; recitalist & clinician. *Teaching:* Cond, pub sch orch, northwest US & regional & all state orch; developer string orchs, pub sch nationwide; mem fac, Sch Music, Univ Mich, Ann Arbor, 77- *Mailing Add:* Sch Music Univ Mich Ann Arbor MI 48109

CUMBERLAND, DAVID
BASS
Study: Ohio Univ; Am Opera Ctr, Juilliard Sch Music. *Roles:* Kasper in Der Freischütz; Rigoletto; L'Amore dei tre re; Fafner in Das Rheingold; Callatinus in Lucrezia Borgia; Ferrando in Il Trovatore; Ramphis in Aida, Miss Opera Asn, 83. *Pos:* Performer, New York Phil, formerly; prin bass, New York City Opera, currently & Cologne Munic Opera, Germany, currently. *Mailing Add:* c/o Dorothy Cone Inc 250 W 57th St New York NY 10019

CUMMING, RICHARD (JACKSON)
COMPOSER, PIANO
b Shanghai, China, June 9, 28, US citizen. *Study:* San Francisco Consv Music, 46-51; study with Rogers Sessions, 45-51 & with Ernest Bloch, 47-51. *Works:* Piano Sonata, J & W Chester, 53; The Crowne (voice & orch), comn by Peninsula Fest, perf by Gramm/Thor Johnson, 56; We Happy Few (voice & piano), 64, 24 Preludes for Piano, 69, Boosey & Hawkes; My Beloved Is Mine, comn & perf by RI Col Chamber Singers, 83. *Pos:* Concert accmp, 50-75; comp in res, Trinity Sq Repty Co, Providence, RI, 66-83. *Awards:* First Prize, Nat Fedn Music Clubs, 54; Ford Found Fel, 62; Comp-Librettist Grant, Nat Endowment Arts, 76. *Mem:* Am Fedn Musicians; ASCAP; Am Music Ctr. *Mailing Add:* 414 Benefit St Providence RI 02903

CUMMINGS, ANTHONY MICHAEL
EDUCATOR
b Worcester, Mass, May 3, 51. *Study:* Williams Col, BA, 73; Princeton Univ, MFA, 75, PhD, 80. *Teaching:* Lectr music, Princeton Univ 80- *Mem:* Am Musicol Soc. *Interests:* Musical patronage in Renaissance, Italy. *Publ:* Auth, Toward an Interpretation of the 16th Century Motet, J Am Musicol Soc, 81; Medici Musical Patronage in the Early 16th Century, Studi Musicali, 81; Bemerkungen Zu Isaacs Motette Ave Ancilla Trinitatis, Die Musikforschung, 81; A Florentine Sacred Repertory From the Medici Restoration, ACTA Musicologica, 83; The Transmission of Some Josquin Motets, Quadrivium (in prep). *Mailing Add:* Music Dept Princeton Univ Princeton NJ 08544

CUMMINGS, CLAUDIA
SOPRANO
b Santa Barbara, Calif, Nov 12, 41. *Study:* San Francisco State Univ; studied with Rue Knapp. *Roles:* Rosina in Il Barbiere di Siviglia, Kansas City Lyr Opera, 71; Siegfried, San Francisco Opera; Miss Schlesen in Satyagraha & four heroines in The Tales of Hoffmann, 83, Netherlands Opera; Ann Trulove in The Rake's Progress, Artpark Fest; Julie in Minutes Till Midnight, Miami

Int Fest; Lucia in Lucia di Lammermoor, Minn Opera Co, 83. *Pos:* Sop, San Francisco Opera, San Diego Opera, Gtr Miami Opera, Houston Grand Opera, Seattle Opera, Can Opera Toronto, San Francisco Spring Opera, Los Angeles Phil, Spoleto USA Fest, Kennedy Ctr Summer Fest & others. *Mailing Add:* PO Box 812 Mill Valley CA 94941

CUMMINGS, CONRAD
COMPOSER, CONDUCTOR
b San Francisco, Calif, Feb 10, 48. *Study:* Yale Univ, BA, 70; State Univ NY, Stony Brook, MA, 73; Columbia Univ, DMA, 77. *Works:* Summer Air (nine instrm), 81 & Eros and Psyche (three act opera), 83, Belwin-Mills; Dinosaur Music, comn by Nat Museum Natural Hist, Smithsonian Inst, 83. *Rec Perf:* Beast Songs & Summer Air, CRI, 83. *Pos:* Staff mem, Columbia Princeton Electronic Music Ctr, New York, 74-77; vis res, Inst Res & Coord Music & Acoustics, Paris, 79-80. *Teaching:* Asst prof, Consv Music, Oberlin Col, 80- *Awards:* Margaret Lee Crofts Fel, Berkshire Music Ctr, 74; Fel, Nat Endowment Arts, 81; Grant, Martha Baird Rockefeller Fund, 81 & 82. *Mem:* Am Music Ctr; Am Comp Alliance; Comput Music Asn; Am Soc Univ Comp; BMI. *Publ:* Auth, An American Composer in Paris, 80 & An American Composer in the Orient, 82, Musical Am; Some Observations on Computer Music, Perspectives New Music, 82. *Mailing Add:* 133 E College St Oberlin OH 44074

CUMMINGS, DIANE M
VIOLIN
b Williams, Ariz, Mar 24, 52. *Study:* Northern Ariz Univ; Ariz State Univ, BMus, 75; studied with Kathleen Gregg, Clarence Shaw, Eugene P Lombardi, Eudice Shapiro, Sydney Harth & Bronstein, 75. *Rec Perf:* Recital of music by Handel, Ibert, Bloch, Kerr & Franck, 75. *Pos:* Soloist, Flagstaff Symph, 70; mem, Ariz All State Orch, formerly & Flagstaff Summer Fest, formerly; first violin, Phoenix Symph, 75-76, mem second violin sect, currently. *Awards:* Gold Medal, State Solo & Ens Fest, 69. *Mem:* Nat Educ Asn; Music Educr Nat Conf; Sigma Alpha Iota. *Mailing Add:* Phoenix Symph 6328 N 7th St Phoenix AZ 85014

CUNDY, RHONDA GAIL
SOPRANO, STAGE DIRECTOR
b St Paul, Minn, Sept 12, 41. *Study:* Cornell Col Iowa, BMus, 63; Ecole Normale Musique, Paris, voice with Pierre Bernac, lic conct, 65; Northwestern Univ, MMus, 66. *Pos:* Recitalist in US & France, 64-; prin lyr sop, Dormund Opera, Ger, 67-68; found & dir, White Heron Opera, Appleton, Wis, 78-; dir opera prog, Blossom Fest, Cleveland Orch, summer 82; freelance opera stage dir, 82-; stage dir, Attic Theatre, Appleton, Wis, summer 83. *Teaching:* Fac mem voice, Univ Wis, Madison, 67- & Northwestern Univ, 68-71; chmn music dept, Univ Wis, Menasha, 75-80; dir opera theatre, Kent State Univ, 81-83. *Awards:* Grant, US Fulbright Comn, 63-65; Prix d'Excellence, Int Compt Interpretation French Melodie, 65. *Mem:* Nat Opera Asn. *Publ:* Auth, Rameau's Platee, Opera J, 82. *Mailing Add:* 1515 S Mason St Appleton WI 54914

CUNNINGHAM, ARTHUR
COMPOSER, DOUBLE BASS
b Piermont, NY, Nov 11, 28. *Study:* Fisk Univ, with John W Work, BA, 51; Juilliard Sch, with Henry Brant, Norman Lloyd & Wallingford Riegger, 51-52; Columbia Teachers Col, with John Mehegan, MA, 57; studied with Margaret Hillis, Teddy Wilson & Peter Wilhousky. *Works:* Dim du Mim (oboe & orch), 69; The Walton Statement (double bass & orch), comn by Ortiz Walton, 71; Eclatette (solo cello), 71; Romp (strings & woodwinds), 71; Covenant (cello & double bass), 72; The Prince (bass baritone & orch), 73; Night Song (chorus & orch), 73. *Pos:* Double bassist, Rockland Co Symph & Suburban Symph; adv, Rockland Co Playhouse, 64; music dir, summer theaters, formerly. *Awards:* Two grants, Nat Endowment Arts; five ASCAP awards. *Mem:* ASCAP. *Mailing Add:* 4 N Pine St Nyack NY 10960

CUNNINGHAM, CAROLINE M
EDUCATOR, STRINGS
b New Haven, Conn, Jan 18, 25. *Study:* Bryn Mawr Col, BA, 46, PhD, 69; Wesleyan Univ, MA, 60. *Teaching:* Vis lectr, Swarthmore Col, 70 & Lafayette Col, 72; instr music hist, Sch Music, Temple Univ, summer 71 & 72 & Manhattan Sch Music, 72-83. *Bibliog:* H M Brown (auth), Music in the Renaissance, Prentice Hall, 78. *Mem:* Am Musicol Soc (secy-treas, 70-72 & coun rep, 80-82); Col Music Soc; Viola da Gamba Soc; Am Musical Instrm Soc; Am Recorder Soc. *Interests:* Renaissance chansons and dances; early Baroque performance practices; history of instruments. *Publ:* Auth, E Dutertre, J D'Estree & Franco-Flemish Chansons & Consort Dances, 71 & Italian 16th Century Ensemble Dances, 80, Musica Disciplina; seven short articles on Renaissance composers, In: New Grove Dict of Music & Musicians, 80; Christopher Simpson, The Months and The Seasons, Dove House Press, 83. *Mailing Add:* 735 Millbrook Lane Haverford PA 19041

CUNNINGHAM, MICHAEL GERALD
COMPOSER, EDUCATOR
b Warren, Mich, Aug 5, 37. *Study:* Wayne State Univ, BMus, 59; Univ Mich, MMus, 61; Ind Univ, DMus, 73. *Works:* Coloratura (clarinet choir), 81 & Starry Visions (band & tape), 81, Dorn Publ; Dorian Gray (2 act opera), Am Music Ctr, 82; Preludes for Harp Op 68, 83, Partitions (string quartet), 83 & Time Frame (chamber orch), 83, Seesaw Music Corp; Divertimento (perc), Dorn Publ, 83. *Teaching:* Instr theory, Wayne State Univ, 67-69; vis lectr, Univ Kans, Lawrence, 72; asst prof theory & comp, Univ Pac, 73; assoc prof, Univ Wis, Eau Claire, 73- *Mem:* ASCAP. *Mailing Add:* Music Dept Univ Wis Eau Claire WI 54701

CUNNINGHAM, WALKER EVANS
ORGAN, HARPSICHORD
b Richmond, Va, July 10, 47. *Study:* Consv Music, Oberlin Col, with Fenner Douglass & Emil Danenberg, AB & BM, 70; Inst Musicol, Univ Fribourg, Switzerland, with Luigi F Tagliavini, 73-74; Univ Calif, Berkeley, with Alan Curtis, MA, 77, PhD, 81. *Pos:* Dir music, St Mark's Espiscopal Church, Berkeley, Calif, 76-79. *Teaching:* Inst arts & humanities, Emma Willard Sch, Troy, NY, 70-73; adj instr music skills, Church Divinity Sch Pac, 76-80. *Awards:* Haskell Fel, Oberlin Col, 79; Eisner Prize, Univ Calif, 80; 2nd prize, Hofhaimer Comp, Austria, 81. *Mem:* Am Musicol Soc; San Francisco Early Music Soc ; Am Guild Organists. *Interests:* Sixteenth and 17th century keyboard music; performance practice; music of Mozart; music of Bartok. *Publ:* Auth, The Keyboard Music of John Bull, UMI Research Press, 83; co-ed, Claudio Merulo Canzoni d'Intavolatura, Societa' Italiana di Musicologia, 83. *Rep:* Melinda Buchanan Conct Mgt 19 Tamalpais Rd Berkeley CA 94708. *Mailing Add:* 3560 19th St San Francisco CA 94110

CUPPERNULL, GEORGE JOSEPH
EDUCATOR
b Oswego, NY, Aug 23, 30. *Study:* State Univ NY Col, Potsdam, BM, 52; Columbia Univ, studied clarinet with Leon Russianoff, 53-54; Syracuse Univ, MM, 59. *Teaching:* Dir music, Potsdam Cent Sch, 55-56 & Bd Coop Educ Serv, Pulaski, NY, 56-63; teacher music, Patchogue Pub Sch, 63-64; prof music, State Univ NY Col, Oswego, 64-, chmn, 80-83. *Mem:* Nat Asn Sch Music Adminr; Col Band Dir Asn; Music Educr Nat Conf; NY United Univ Prof; Am Fedn Musicians. *Mailing Add:* Music Dept State Univ NY Col Oswego NY 13126

CUREAU, REBECCA TURNER
EDUCATOR, LECTURER
b New Orleans, La, Apr 5, 30. *Study:* Bennett Col, BA, 53; Northwestern Univ, MMus, 54. *Teaching:* Instr music, Clark Col, 54-55; from instr to prof, Dillard Univ, 55-61; from asst to assoc prof, Southern Univ, 61- *Mem:* Am Choral Dir Asn; Col Music Soc; Soc Enthomusicol; Am Musicol Soc. *Interests:* Afro-American music; ethnomusicology. *Publ:* Auth, Black Folklore, Musicology, and Willis James, Negro Hist Bulletin, 80; contribr, Alain Locke: A Modern Renaissance Man, La State Univ Press, 83; contribr, Biographical Sketch on Willis Laurence James (in prep) & ed, Willis Laurence James: Stars in De Elements (in prep), Univ Ga Press. *Mailing Add:* 1076 Mayhaw Dr Baton Rouge LA 70807

CURLEY, CARLO
ORGAN
b Monroe, NC, 1952. *Study:* Studied with Virgil Fox & George Thalben-Ball. *Pos:* Organist & choirmaster, Druid Hills Baptist Church, Atlanta, Ga, 69-71 & Girard Col, Philadelphia, 71; organ soloist, Royal Fest Hall, London, formerly; Europ concerts, TV & radio performances; command perf, White House, 80. *Mailing Add:* c/o Columbia Artists 165 W 57th St New York NY 10019

CURRAN, ALVIN S
COMPOSER, ELECTRONIC
b Providence, RI, Dec 13, 38. *Study:* Brown Univ, studied comp with Ron Nelson, BA, 60; Yale Sch Music, with Elliott Carter & Mel Powell, MMus, 63. *Works:* Songs and Views from the Magnetic Garden, 73-77, Light Flowers, Dark Flowers, 75-78, Canti Illuminati, 76- & The Works, 76-, perf by comp; Music for Every Occasion, comn by St Paul Chamber Orch, 80; Maritime Rites, 80-; Monumenti, comn by Alte Oper, Frankfurt. *Rec Perf:* Friday, Horo, 69; Spacecraft, Mainstream, 69; United Patchwork, Horo, 80. *Pos:* Co-founder, Musica Elettronica Viva, 66-; dir, Chorus (vocal improvisation group), 82- *Teaching:* Vocal improvisation, Accad Nazionale Arte Drammatica, Rome, 75-80. *Awards:* BMI Award, 63; Bearns Prize, 63; grant, Nat Endowment Arts, 78. *Publ:* Auth & contribr various articles & lett, Musics, 78-80; auth, The Music of Giacinto Scelsi, Zagreb Fest, 79; Last Thoughts on Soup, Almanacco Musica 2; Twelve Years of American Music in Rome, Soundings 10. *Mailing Add:* via G Vestri 8 Rome 00151 Italy

CURRIE, RUSSELL
COMPOSER, ADMINISTRATOR
b North Arlington, NJ, Apr 3, 54. *Study:* Brooklyn Col, BA(music), 81; Mannes Col Music, studied comp with Robert Starer & piano with John Challener & Paul Jacobs. *Works:* The Heart of the City (soundtrack), comn by Cent Park Community Fund, 79; The Dream (song cycle), comn by Triple Play, 81; Suite for Solo Flute, comn by Antonio Naranjo, 81; Perfect Roses (sound track), comn by Brooklyn Botanic Gardens, 81; The Cask of Amontillado (opera), 82 & The System of Dr Tarr and Prof Fether (opera), 83, comn by Bronx Arts Ens; Night Thoughts, Da Capo Chamber Players, 83. *Pos:* Admin dir, Haydn-Mozart Chamber Orch, 81- *Awards:* Meet the Comp Award, 82. *Mailing Add:* 98 Christopher St #9 New York NY 10014

CURRIER, DONALD ROBERT
PIANO, EDUCATOR
Study: New England Consv Music, grad; Yale Sch Music, grad; Harvard Univ. *Pos:* Solo recitalist, New York, Boston, Paris, Amsterdam & London; performer throughout US. *Teaching:* Mem fac, Yale Sch Music, 51-, prof music, currently. *Mailing Add:* Yale Sch Music Box 2104A Yale Sta New Haven CT 06520

CURRY, DIANE
MEZZO-SOPRANO
b Clifton Forge, Va, Feb 26, 42. *Study:* Westminster Choir Col, BMus, MMus. *Rec Perf:* On Ariel Symph. *Pos:* Mem, New York City Opera, currently; appearances with maj opera co in US & Europe; performer with choral orgn & orchs in US & Italy; conct & oratorio recitalist. *Mailing Add:* c/o Columbia Artists Mgt 165 W 57th St New York NY 10019

CURRY, DONNA (JAYNE)
LUTE, TEACHER-COACH
b Los Angeles, Calif, Jan 26, 39. *Study:* Whittier Col, BA, 58; Schola Cantorum Basiliensis, Basel, Switz, 70-73; study lute with Eugen Dombois, voice with Cornelius Reid & Elsa Cavelti. *Rec Perf:* Since First I Saw Your Face, 72 & Gently, Johnny, My Jingalo, 72, Klavier Rec. *Pos:* Lutanist, singer & solo recitalist, USA & Europe, 70-; musical educ dir, Am Lute Sem, 73- *Teaching:* Instr lute & early vocal tech, Calif State Univ, Los Angeles, 78-83; instr lute, Sch Music, Univ Southern Calif, 76-81 & Claremont Grad Sch, 79-82; private instr voice & lute, currently. *Mem:* Lute Soc Am (mem bd & secy, 69-74); Lute Soc England; Am Fedn Musicians; Am Musicol Soc. *Interests:* The lute song literature of Renaissance and Baroque eras. *Publ:* Ed, An Anthology of Lute Song, Am Lute Sem, 76. *Mailing Add:* c/o Gordon Herritt PO Box 194 Topanga CA 90290

CURTIN, PHYLLIS
SOPRANO, EDUCATOR
b Clarksburg, WVa, Dec 3, 21. *Study:* Wellesley Col, BA, 43; WVa Univ, Marshall Univ & New England Consv, Hon Dr Music; Albertus Magnus Col, LHD. *Roles:* Fiordiligi in Cosi Fan Tutte, New York City Opera, Vienna Staatsoper, La Scala, Metropolitan Opera & NBC Opera; Susannah, New York City Opera; Violetta in La Traviata, New York City Opera, Vienna Staatsoper & Metropolitan Opera; Salome in Salome, New York City Opera, Vienna Staatsoper & Metropolitan Opera; Ellen Orford in Peter Grimes, Metropolitan Opera, Edinburgh Fest; Cio Cio San in Madame Butterfly, Vienna Staatsoper; Manon in Manon, Teatro Colon, Buenos Aires. *Pos:* Sop, New York City Opera, 51-64, Vienna Staatsoper, 59-63, La Scala, Milano, 59 & Metropolitan Opera, 61-74; recitalist in US, Europe, Australia, New Zealand & Israel. *Teaching:* Prof voice, Yale Sch Music, Yale Univ, 74-83; prof voice & dean, Sch Arts, Boston Univ, 83- *Mailing Add:* 24 Cottage Farm Rd Brookline MA 02146

CURTIS, ALAN
EDUCATOR, HARPSICHORD
b Masone, Mich, Nov 17, 34. *Study:* Mich State Univ, BMus, 55; Univ Ill, MMus, 56. *Rec Perf:* L'Incoronazione di Poppea (Monteverdi). *Pos:* Cond & harpsichord, Holland Festivals, 74-75 & Brussels Royal Opera, 74; broadcast & recital performances, Europe, US & Can. *Teaching:* Prof music, Univ Calif, Berkeley, currently. *Mem:* Am Musicol Soc; Vereniging voor Nederlands Muziekgeschiedenis. *Publ:* Auth, Sweelinck's Keyboard Music, 63; contribr, Tijdschrift VNM & Rev Musicol. *Mailing Add:* Dept Music Univ Calif Berkeley CA 94720

CURTIS, (WILLIAM) EDGAR
COMPOSER, CONDUCTOR & MUSIC DIRECTOR
b Aberdeen, Scotland, Mar 11, 14, Gt Brit. *Study:* Univ Edinburgh, with Donald Francis Tovey, BMus, 35, MA, 36; study with Rudolf Serkin & Adolf & Fritz Busch (piano, comp & cond), 36-39; Curtis Inst Music, Philadelphia, study cond with Fritz Reiner, 40-41; Berkshire Music Ctr, with Koussevitzky. *Works:* Fantasia on Billing's Chester, Scottish BBC Orch, 58; Concerto (organ & strings), C F Peters Corp, 60; Sonata for Unaccompanied Flute, London BBC, 61; Three for Stephen—Music for Piano Solo, perf by Stephen Manes, 68; Sonata A Due (flute & guitar), perf by Dwyer & Flower, 74; Quintet for Brass, Brass Quintet of Univ Mass, Amherst, 76; Music for Piano (four hands), perf by Frieda & Stephen Manes, 76. *Pos:* Founder & cond, Curtis String Orch, Boston, 42-44 & Northeastern NY Phil, 67-69; musical dir, Albany Symph Orch, 48-67; guest cond, Boston Symph Orch, BBC, Oslo Phil & Swiss Radio, 45- *Teaching:* Instr, US Navy Sch Music, Washington, DC, 44-46; dir orch dept, Sch Music, Boston Univ, 46-48; prof comp, Union Col, NY, 55-79, chmn arts dept, 66-72. *Awards:* Citation, Am Fedn Musicians, 52. *Mem:* Am Fedn Musicians. *Mailing Add:* Box 12 Berlin NY 12022

CURTIS, JAN (JUDITH ANNE)
MEZZO-SOPRANO
b Colfax, Wash, July 27, 45. *Study:* Univ Wash, BM, 66; New England Consv Music, artist dipl, 68, MM, 71. *Rec Perf:* Monteverdi Scherzi, Vox Rec, 67; Corridors of Memory, Delos Rec, 75; Oleum Canis, Serenus Rec, 76. *Roles:* Mum in Albert Herring, Opera Theatre St Louis, 76; Carolina in Elegy for Young Lovers, San Francisco Spring Opera, 78; Sadie Burke in Willie Stark, Houston Grand Opera, 81; Carmen in Carmen, Cleveland Opera, 82; Witch in Hansel and Gretel, Opera Co Boston, 82; Marquise of Berkenfield in Daughter of the Regiment, Omaha Opera, 82. *Mem:* Mu Phi Epsilon. *Rep:* Regency Artists Ltd 9200 Sunset Blvd Los Angeles CA 90069. *Mailing Add:* 2970 Hidden Valley Lane Santa Barbara CA 93108

CURTIS, WILLIAM H
DOUBLE BASS, EDUCATOR
Study: Boston Univ, BM; Harvard Univ; studied orch with Serge Koussevitzky. *Pos:* Prin bassist, Boston Civic Symph, formerly, New England Phil & Boston Phil, currently; performer, Boston Pops, formerly. *Teaching:* Mem fac double bass, Berklee Col Music, currently. *Mailing Add:* Berklee Col Music 1140 Boylston St Boston MA 02215

CURTIS-SMITH, CURTIS O B
COMPOSER, EDUCATOR
b Walla Walla, Wash, Sept 9, 41. *Study:* Northwestern Univ, with Alan Stout, MMus, 65; Univ Ill, with Kenneth Gaburo; Berkshire Music Ctr, with Bruno Maderna; Whitman Col, with David Burge. *Works:* A Song of Degrees (two pianos & perc), 72-73; Rhapsodies (piano), Ed Salabert, 73; Suite in Four Movements (harpsichord), 75; Unisonics (sax & piano), 76; Bells: Belle du jour (piano & orch), Ed Salabert, 76; Ensembles/Solos (11 players), 77; Masquerades (organ), Universal Ed, 78; The Great American Symphony, comn by Kalamazoo Symph Orch, 82 & perf by Am Comp Orch, 83. *Rec Perf:* Five Sonorous Inventions (Curtis-Smith), 73; Unisonics (Curtis-Smith), CRI. *Teaching:* Prof music, Western Mich Univ, 68-; vis lectr, Univ Mich, 76-77. *Awards:* Salabert Prize, 76; Am Acad & Inst Arts & Lett Grant, 78; Guggenheim Fel, 78. *Publ:* Contribr to Woodwind World & Brass & Perc. *Mailing Add:* 2412 Crest Kalamazoo MI 49008

CURTIS-VERNA, MARY (VIRGINIA)
SOPRANO, EDUCATOR
b Salem, Mass, May 9, 21. *Study:* Abbot Acad; Hollins Col, AB, 43; Harvard Col; Juilliard Sch. *Rec Perf:* Aida, 50, Marchera, 53, Don Giovanni, 55 & L P Recitals, 56, Cetra; Andrea Chenier, 57 & Il Trovatore, 58, Columbia. *Roles:* Aida, Il Trovatore, Un Ballo in maschera, Tosca, Turandot, Don Giovanni & Norma, Metropolitan Opera & San Francisco Opera, Europe. *Pos:* Leading sop, Metropolitan Opera, San Francisco Opera, La Scala, Milan & others, 49-69. *Teaching:* Prof music & chmn voice dept, Univ Wash, 69- *Awards:* Gold Medal, Hollins Col, 55; Outstanding Artist Award, Lyon, France, 60. *Mailing Add:* 1600 E Boston Terr Seattle WA 98112

CUSTER, ARTHUR
ADMINISTRATOR, COMPOSER
b Manchester, Conn, Apr 21, 23. *Study:* Univ Conn, BA(music), 49; Univ Redlands, MMus, 51; Univ Iowa, PhD(music), 59; comp study with Nadia Boulanger, France, 60-61. *Works:* Colloquy for String Quartet, Merion, 61; Symphony, 69, Found Objects No 2 For Orchestra, 70, Comments on This World, 72, Found Objects No 7 For Piano and Tape, 76 & Fables for Ten Instruments, 81, Joshua; Images of William Blake, Sun Group, 82. *Pos:* Supvr music, US Dependent sch, Spain, 59-62; exec dir, Metro Educ Ctr in Arts, St Louis, 67-70 & Arts in Educ Proj, RI Arts Coun, 70-75; comp & prod, Sun Group, New York, 75- *Teaching:* Asst dean, Fine Arts, Univ RI, 62-65; dean, Philadelphia Musical Acad, 65-67. *Awards:* Publ Award, Soc for Publ Am Music; Rec Award, Am Comp Alliance; Comp Assistance Grant, Am Music Ctr. *Mem:* Am Comp Alliance (bd gov, 63-66); BMI; Am Music Ctr; Nat Humanities Fac. *Publ:* Contribr, Contemporary Music in Spain, Musical Quart, 62; Contemporary Music in Europe, Norton, 65; auth, Program Annotations, St Louis Symphony, 68-69; contribr, Current Chronicle: Edwardsville, 68 & New England Music Circuit, 75, Musical Quart. *Mailing Add:* 505 Fifth Ave New York NY 10017

CUSTER, CALVIN H
COMPOSER, CONDUCTOR
b Atlantic City, NJ, July 15, 39. *Study:* Carnegie Mellon Univ, BFA(comp & perf), 62; Syracuse Univ, MFA(comp), 64. *Works:* Variations on a Theme of William Byrd, 72, Fanfare for Percussion, 76, Baroque Suite for Orchestra, 76, Elegy for Yesterday and Tomorrow, 79, Concertino for Horn and Orchestra, 80, Music for Brass with Percussion, 82 & Concertino for Percussion and Strings, 83, comn by Syracuse Symph Orch. *Pos:* Res cond & comp-arr, Syracuse Symph Orch, 72- *Mem:* ASCAP. *Mailing Add:* Syracuse Symph Orch 411 Montgomery St Syracuse NY 13202

CUYLER, LOUISE E
EDUCATOR, WRITER
b Omaha, Nebr, Mar 14, 08. *Study:* Eastman Sch Music, BMus, 29, PhD, 48; Univ Mich, MA, 31. *Teaching:* Prof music & musicol, Univ Mich, 29-75, emer prof, 75-; guest prof, Stanford Univ, 64-65; William Allan Neilson Prof, Smith Col, 75. *Awards:* Fulbright Res Scholar, 53-54; Am Coun Learned Soc Fel, 59-60; Distinguished Fac Award, Univ Mich, 73. *Bibliog:* Edith Borroff (ed), Notations and Editions, William C Brown, 74; The Emperor's Motets, Times Lit Suppl, 73. *Mem:* Am Musicol Asn (nat secy, 55-70); Music Libr Asn; Renaissance Soc Am. *Interests:* Renaissance, low countries and Austria; music of the 19th century. *Publ:* Ed, Choralis Constantinus Book III of H Isaac, 50 & Five Polyphonic Masses of H Isaac, 56, Univ Mich Press; auth, The Emporor Maximilian and Music, Oxford, 73; The Symphony, Harcourt Brace Jovanovich, 73. *Mailing Add:* 8545 Carmel Valley Rd Carmel CA 93923

CYKLER, EDMUND A
EDUCATOR, ADMINISTRATOR
b San Jose, Calif, Sept 2, 03. *Study:* Univ Calif, Berkeley, BA, 26; studied viola with Jindrich Feld, Praque Consv, 26-28; Charles Univ, Prague, Czechoslovakia, PhD, 28; studied analysis with Arnold Schoenberg, 38. *Teaching:* Chmn music dept, Los Angeles City Col, 29-44; prof, Univ Calif, Berkeley, summers, 32-35 & Univ NC, Chapel Hill, summers, 36-38; assoc prof music, Occidental Col, 44-47; prof & assoc dean, Univ Ore, Eugene, 47-72. *Awards:* Fulbright Res Grant, 55-56; US Dept Educ Res Grant, 69-71. *Mem:* Int Soc Music Educ. *Interests:* Comparative Music Educ. *Publ:* Coauth, Introduction to Music & Art in the Western World, seventh ed, 56-83 & Outline History of Music, fifth ed, 63-84, Wm C Brown. *Mailing Add:* 1055 W 17th Ave Eugene OR 97402

CYR, GORDON CONRAD
EDUCATOR, COMPOSER
b Oakland, Calif, Oct 5, 25. *Study:* Univ Calif, Berkeley, with Edwin Dugger, Roger Sessions & William Denny, AB, 66, PhD, 69. *Works:* Lamentations of Jeremiah, perf by Carole Bogard & Ruth Onstadt with Cabrillo Fest Orch, 67; Tabb Songs, perf by Ruth & Arno Drucker, Bicentennial Parade of Am Music, 75; Rhombohedra, perf by F Battisti with New England Consv Wind Ens, 76; Tetramusic, Comtemp Music Forum, 77; The Siren Stream to the Outcast, perf by Ostryniec, Comtemp Music Forum, 81; Two Songs on Poems of Walt Whitman, perf by M Ingham, Chamber Music Soc Baltimore, 82; String Quartet #2, perf by Sequoia String Quartet, Chamber Music Soc Baltimore, 83. *Rec Perf:* Tetramusic, Tabb Songs, Orion Rec. *Teaching:* Lectr, Univ Calif, Berkeley, 70-71 & Calif State Univ, San Francisco, spring 71; from asst prof to assoc prof theory & comp, Towson State Univ, 71- *Awards:* Artists Fel Award, Md State Arts Coun, 78. *Mem:* Am Soc Univ Comp (chmn region III, 73-77); Chamber Music Soc Baltimore (bd mem & prog comnr, 81-); Res Musica Baltimore (bd mem, 81-). *Mailing Add:* 6 Upland Rd Apt G-2 Baltimore MD 21210

CZAJKOWSKI, MICHAEL
COMPOSER, EDUCATOR
b Milwaukee, Wis, June 7, 39. *Study:* Univ Wis, BFA; Am Consv, with Leo Sowerby; Juilliard Sch Music, with Bernard Wagenaar & Vincent Persichetti, MS(comp), 66; NY Univ with Morton Subotnick; Aspen Sch, with Darius Milhaud. *Works:* Toccata, Romance & Sundance (piano); Three Shaker Songs (choral); Serenade (conct band, rock groups, tape, lights & film); People the Sky (tape); String Trio; Woodwind Quartet; A Sunday in Hohocus (oboe & tape). *Teaching:* Fac mem, Juilliard Sch, 66- & Aspen Sch, 66-; dir, Comp Wkshp, NY Univ, 69-, asst prof music, Sch Educ, 71- *Awards:* Gretchaninoff Award, 65 & 66. *Mailing Add:* Juilliard Sch Lincoln Ctr New York NY 10023

D

D'ACCONE, FRANK A
EDUCATOR
b Somerville, Mass, June 13, 31. *Study:* Boston Univ, BM, 52, MM, 53; Harvard Univ, AM, 55, PhD, 60. *Teaching:* Asst prof, State Univ NY, Buffalo, 60-63, assoc prof, 63-68; vis prof, Univ Calif, Los Angeles, 65-66, prof, 68-; vis prof, Yale Univ, 72-73. *Awards:* Fulbright Award, 64-65; Nat Endowment Humanities Fel, 75; Guggenheim Fel, 80-81. *Mem:* Am Musicol Soc (mem bd dir, 73-74); Int Musicol Soc; Col Music Soc. *Interests:* History of music, circa 1450-1700, mainly Italian. *Publ:* Ed, Music of the Florentine Renaissance (10 vol), Am Inst Musicol, 66-81; auth, The Florentine Fra Mauros, Musica Disciplina, 79; Repertory and Performance Practice in S Maria Novella at the Turn of the 17th Century, In: A Festschrift for Albert Seay, Colo Press, 82; ed, Gli Equivoci Nel Sembiante, Harvard Press, 82. *Mailing Add:* Music Dept Univ Calif 405 Hilgard Ave Los Angeles CA 90024

DA COSTA, NOEL
COMPOSER, EDUCATOR
b Lagos, Nigeria, 30; US citizen. *Study:* Queens Col; Columbia Univ; studied with Luigi Dallapiccola. *Works:* In the Circle (four electric guitars, brass, perc), 69; The Confessional Stone (sop & ten instrm, text by Owen Dodson); The Last Judgement (women's chorus, narrator, piano & perc, text by James Weldon Johnson), 70; Blues Mix (contrabass & tape), New York, 71; Fanfare Rhythms, New York, 74; Five Verses with Vamps (cello & piano), 75; Spiritual Set (organ), 77. *Pos:* Cond, Triade Chorale, currently. *Teaching:* Assoc prof music, Rutgers Univ, currently. *Awards:* NY Coun Arts Grant, 74. *Mailing Add:* 250 W 94th St New York NY 10025

DAGON, RUSSELL
CLARINET, EDUCATOR
b Joliet, Ill, Mar 17, 38. *Study:* Northwestern Univ, BMus, 61, MMus, 62; Eastman Sch Music, 65-66. *Pos:* Prin clarinet, Milwaukee Symph Orch, 69-; clarinetist, Milwaukee Chamber Soc, 73- & Wis Chamber Players, 74- *Teaching:* Dir chamber music, Birch Creek Acad, 79-; instr clarinet, Northwestern Univ, 80- *Mailing Add:* W 271 S 2701 Apache Pass Waukesha WI 53186

DAHLGREN, CARL HERMAN PER
ARTIST MANAGER, EDUCATOR
b New York, NY, July 2, 29. *Study:* Westminster Choir Col, BM, 54. *Pos:* Project dir, Benson & Benson, Princeton, NJ, 54-56; dir & co-founder, Westminster Choir Col Alumni Fund Asn, 54-59; asst head spec res & analysis, Gallup & Robinson, Princeton, 56-57; mgr, Princeton Symph Orch, 56-58; vpres & artist mgr, Columbia Artists Mgt, 58-68; vpres & artist mgr, Hurok Concerts, Inc, 68-70, assoc, 70-74; gen mgr & exec dir, Cent City Opera House Asn, 70-72; pres, Dahlgren Arts Mgt, 70-78; exec dir & secy, Colo Celebration Arts, 74-76. *Teaching:* Dir, MA grad prog Arts Admin, Col-Consv Music, Univ Cincinnait, 78-, acting head, Broadcasting Div, 79-80. *Awards:* Insignia Knight First Class Order of Lion Finland, 69; Merit Award, Westminster Choir Col, 79; Ernest N Glover Distinguished Teacher Award, Col-Consv Music, Univ Cincinnati, 83. *Mem:* Cincinnati Chamber Orch (pres, 82-); Am Symph Orch League. *Mailing Add:* Dept Music Univ Cincinnati Cincinnati OH 45221

DAHLMAN, BARBRO
PIANO, TEACHER
b Stockholm, Sweden, Feb 16, 46; US citizen. *Study:* State Col Music, Stockholm, Sweden, 67; Swedish Radio Music Inst, Edsberg Col, Sweden, artist dipl, 71; private study with Emerson Meyers, Washington, DC. *Rec Perf:* Ancient Music (piano & orch; Ulf Grahn), Danish Radio Orch, Copenhagen, Denmark, 70; Numerous solo recordings of Am & Swedish piano music for Swedish Radio, 70; Piano music by Ulf Grahn, Emerson Meyers, Frederick Koch & Joel Naumann, Op One Rec, 77; Three Generations of Swedish Composers, Hans Eklund, Lars-Erik Larsson & Ulf Grahn, STIM, 81. *Pos:* Found mem & pianist, Contemp Music Forum, Washington, DC, 73- *Teaching:* Instr piano, Selma Levine Sch Music, Washington, DC, 76- *Rep:* Virginia Carre-Magee Nordic Arts Exchange 1632A Wisconsin Ave Washington DC 20007. *Mailing Add:* 7229 Deborah Dr Falls Church VA 22046

DAIGLE, ANNE CECILE
EDUCATOR, COMPOSER
b Seattle, Wash, June 25, 08. *Study:* Marylhurst Col, BMus, 36; DePaul Univ, with Leon Stein, Czerwonky & Lieberson, MMus, 49; Univ Southern Calif, with Halsey Stevens, Ingolf Dahl & Muriel Kerr, DMA, 60. *Works:* Chronicle of Creation, Spokane Symph. 53; Quintet for Piano & Strings, Holy Names Centenary, 59; Trumpet Sonata, perf by James Smith, 60-67; Dance Concertino, Marylhurst Symph, Portland State Sinfonietta & North Coast Chamber Orch, 70; Piano Sonata No 2, Bela Nagy, 71; Four Temperaments (two harps & tape), comn by One Music Teachers Asn, 73; Violin Concerto, perf by Marylhurst Symph, 80. *Teaching:* Comp & piano, Holy Names Col, 45-55; prof comp, piano & theory, Marylhurst Col, 62- *Awards:* Comp of Year, Ore Music Teachers Asn, 72; NW Woman Comp of Year, Nat Fedn Music Clubs, 73. *Mem:* Music Teachers Nat Asn (adjudicator, 65-82); Young Audiences of Ore; Nat Fedn Music Clubs; Col Music Soc; Int Soc Contemp Comp. *Mailing Add:* Music Dept Marylhurst Educ Ctr Col Marylhurst OR 97036

DAITZ, MIMI SEGAL
EDUCATOR, CONDUCTOR
b New York, NY, Apr 1, 39. *Study:* Queens Col, City Univ New York, BA, 61; City Col City Univ New York, MA, 64; NY Univ, PhD, 74; studied piano with Alexander Lipskey, voice with Constantine Cassolas, Lois Bove & Yves Tinayre. *Teaching:* Dir City Col Chorus & asst prof music dept, City Col, City Univ New York, 64- *Mem:* Am Musicol Soc; Asn Choral Cond; Soc Francaise Musicol. *Interests:* Vocal music of the late 19th century and early 20th century; songs of Faure. *Publ:* Auth, Grieg & Breville: Nous Parlons de la Jeune Ecole Francaise, 19th Century Music, 78; Pierre Onfroy de Breville, In: New Grove Dict of Music & Musicians, 80; Pierre de Breville (1861-1941), 19th Century Music, 81; Les Manuscrits et les Premieres Editions des Melodies de Faure, Etudes Faureennes, 82. *Mailing Add:* Dept Music City Col City Univ New York New York NY 10031

D'ALBERT, FRANCOIS J
VIOLIN, EDUCATOR
b Györ, Hungary, Sept 17, 18. *Study:* Royal Liszt Acad, Budapest, artist & prof dipl; Peter Pazmany Univ, Budapest, PhD. *Rec Perf:* Over 10. *Pos:* Film, TV, radio & conct appearances in over 50 countries. *Teaching:* Prof music, Sherwood Music Sch, currently. *Awards:* Winner, Geneva Int Compt; Prox Heugel; Hubay Grand Prix. *Mailing Add:* 53 W Jackson Blvd Chicago IL 60604

DALEY, JOSEPH ALBERT
TENOR SAXOPHONE, TEACHER
b Salem, Ohio, July 30, 18. *Study:* Detroit Inst Musical Arts, 38-39; Chicago Musical Col, BM(comp), 53; DePaul Univ, 54-55. *Works:* Sonata Movement for Piano, comn by Columbia Univ & WYNC, NY, 53; Introduction & Rondo for Violin & Piano, perf by Larry Grika with Philadelphia Symph, 53; Quartet for Trumpets, 73 & Fugue for Four Trumpets, 73, Opus Music Inc; Fanfare for Trumpet Quartet, perf by Chicago Forefront Quartet, 75. *Rec Perf:* Joe Daley Trio at Newport, 63, RCA Victor, 63; Charlie Parker Memorial Concert, Cadet Rec, 70; Quartet for Trumpets, 73 & Fanfare for Trumpet Quartet, 76, AFI Rec. *Teaching:* Sax, woodwinds & improvisation, privately, 56-; lectr, DePaul Univ, 82- *Bibliog:* Don Rose (auth), Chicago Sun Times, 8/77; Larry Birnbaum (auth), Profile: Joe Daley, Downbeat Music Mag, 2/79; Larry Kart (auth), Chicago Tribune, 4/79. *Mem:* Am Fedn Musicians. *Mailing Add:* 2955 N Nagle Chicago IL 60634

DALIS, IRENE See Loinaz, Yvonne Dalis

DALLIN, LEON
CRITIC-WRITER, COMPOSER
b Silver City, Utah, Mar 26, 18. *Study:* Eastman Sch Music, BM, 40, MM, 41; Univ Southern Calif, PhD, 49. *Works:* Symphonic Sketches, 40 & Clarinet Concerto, 48, Eastman-Rochester Symph; Film Overture, Utah Symph, 50; String Quartet in D, Paganini Quartet & Fine Arts Quartet, 52; Symphony in D, Utah Symph, 52; Sierra Overture (band), Sam Fox Publ Co, 63; Songs of Praise (choir & orch), MCA Music, 70. *Teaching:* Asst prof theory & comp, Colo State Univ, 46; vis prof, Univ Southern Calif, 46-51; from asst to assoc prof, Brigham Young Univ, 48-55; prof, Calif State Univ, Long Beach, 55- *Mem:* ASCAP; Nat Asn Comp; Col Music Soc; Am Musicol Soc; Am Asn Univ Prof. *Publ:* Auth, Techniques of Twentieth Century Composition, 57-75, coauth, Music Skills for Classroom Teachers, 58-83 & auth, Listeners Guide to Musical Understanding, 59-82, William C Brown; Foundation in Music Theory, Wadsworth, 62-67; Introduction to Music Reading, Scott-Foresman, 66-77. *Mailing Add:* PO Box 2400 Seal Beach CA 90740

DALSCHAERT, CATHLEEN See O'Carroll, Cathleen

DALSCHAERT, STEPHANE
VIOLIN, TEACHER-COACH
b Wezembeek, Brabant, Belgium; US citizen. *Study:* Royal Consv Music, Belgium, 53; studied with Alfred DuBois & Artur Grumiaux. *Pos:* Concertmaster, Musica Viva Chamber Orch, 53-58; first violinist, New Orleans Symph, 58-60 & Cleveland Orch, 60-67; violinist, Philadelphia Orch, 67- *Teaching:* Private lessons, currently. *Awards:* Premier Prix, Royal Consv Music, Belgium, 53. *Mailing Add:* 1230 Forge Rd Cherry Hill NJ 08034

DALVIT, LEWIS DAVID, JR
CONDUCTOR
b Denver, Colo, Dec 11, 25. *Study:* Beloit Col, BA, 50; Vandercook Col, MS, 56. *Pos:* Cond, Beloit Symph Orch, 53-63, 64 & Jackson Symph, Miss, currently; asst cond, Honolulu Symph, 63-64; guest cond, US, Mexico, Germany, Cent Am & Japan, 64-73. *Teaching:* Mem fac, Milton Col, 52-63; mem fac, Beloit Col, 60, artist in res, 64, actg chmn music dept, 65-66. *Awards:* Orpheus Award, Phi Mu Alpha Sinfonia, 73. *Mailing Add:* Jackson Symph PO Box 4584 Jackson MS 39216

D'AMBROSE, JOSEPH LAWRENCE
ADMINISTRATOR, FLUTE
b Brooklyn, NY, Oct 31, 38. *Study:* Henry St Settlement Sch Music, 56; Juilliard Sch Music, flute with Julius Baker, BS, 61. *Pos:* First flutist, Birmingham Symph, Ala, 62-64; prin flutist, Royal Ballet, New York, 67-68; dir prog, BMI, 69-80. *Teaching:* Mem fac, Henry St Settlement Sch Music, 65-67; instr flute, Juilliard Private Teacher Directory, 80- *Awards:* Scholar Incentive Award, Univ State NY, 62. *Mem:* Am Symph Orch League; Am Fedn Musicians. *Mailing Add:* 149 W 72nd St Apt #3C New York NY 10023

DANCZ, ROGER LEE
CONDUCTOR, EDUCATOR
b Ludington, Mich, May 25, 30. *Study:* John B Stetson Univ, BM, 52; George Peabody Col Teachers, MM, 58. *Works:* After the Game, Mark IV Rec. *Pos:* Trumpet soloist, Third Army Band, Ft McPherson, 53-55. *Teaching:* Dir instrm music, Martin Co Sch, Stuart, Fla, 52-53; dir bands & assoc prof music, Univ Ga, 55-, dir jazz studies, 65- *Awards:* Music in Sports Award, BMI, 76; Sandy Beaver Award Superior Teaching, Univ Ga, 81. *Mem:* Ga Music Educr Asn Inc (pres, 64-65); Music Educr Nat Conf (state pres, 64-65); Nat Asn Jazz Educr (pres Ga chap, 65-67); Col Band Dir Nat Asn (pres southern div, 68-72). *Publ:* Auth, Bandwatchers Guide, Athens Banner Herald, 70- *Mailing Add:* Sch Music Univ Ga Athens GA 30602

DANE, JEAN R
VIOLA, EDUCATOR
b Hattiesburg, Miss, Apr 8, 48. *Study:* New England Consv Music, BMus, 73. *Pos:* Violist, Blair String Quartet, formerly & Comp String Quartet, 74-; prin viola, Nashville Symph, 72-74; appearances, US, Can, Europe, Israel & India; radio appearances, Europe, Israel & India; TV appearances, India & Romania. *Teaching:* Mem fac, Blair Acad, formerly, Peabody Col, Tenn, formerly & Columbia Univ, currently. *Mem:* Soc Chamber Music Inc. *Publ:* Contribr, Boston Globe, 70-72. *Mailing Add:* 21 W 86th St Apt 410 New York NY 10024

DANFELT, LEWIS S(EYMOUR)
EDUCATOR, OBOE
b Chambersburg, Pa, June 3, 20. *Study:* Eastman Sch Music, BM, 48; Fla State Univ, MME, 54, EdD, 70. *Pos:* Second oboe, Denver Symph, 47-48. *Teaching:* Asst prof oboe, bassoon & theory, ECarolina State Univ, Greenville, 55-62 & Univ Ky, 62-66; prof oboe, bassoon & music educ, NE Mo State Univ, 66- *Mem:* Music Educr Nat Conf; Nat Asn Col Wind & Perc Instr; Int Double Reed Soc. *Mailing Add:* 1202 E Randolph Kirksville MO 63501

DANFORTH, FRANCES ADAMS
TEACHER, COMPOSER
b Chicago, Ill, June 28, 03. *Study:* Univ Mich, with Joseph Brinkman, BM, 27; Toledo Consv Music, with Otto Sturmer; Eastern Mich Univ, with Edith Borroff & Anthony Iannoccone, MA(music), 73. *Works:* Suite for Piano, perf by Carol Kenney, 78; Variations for Wind Trio, MØE Wind Trio, 79; Karelian Light (piano), British Fedn Music Fest, 79; Into the Vortex (dialogue for timpani & tape), Michael Baker, Ithaca Col, 82; Rain Forest (perc ens), Charles Ives Ctr Am Music, New Milford, Conn, 83. *Teaching:* Private piano, Ann Arbor, Mich, 30- *Awards:* Teacher of Yr Award, Mich Music Teachers Asn, 78. *Bibliog:* J Zaimont & K Famera (ed), Contemporary Concert Music By Women, Greenwood Press, 81. *Mem:* Mu Phi Epsilon (pres alumna Chap, 28-29, historian & publicity chmn, 76-80); Women's Asn Civic Symph (pres, 58-59); Ann Arbor Civic Symph—Women's Asn (pres, 42-45); Nat Guild Piano Teachers (local chmn, 61-70). *Mailing Add:* 1411 Granger Ann Arbor MI 48104

DANIEL, CYRUS CHRISLEY
EDUCATOR, COMPOSER
b Carpenter, Ill, Feb 27, 1900. *Study:* Shurtleff Col, AB, 21; Northwestern Univ, BMus, 24; Yale Univ, BMus, 37;. *Works:* Nocturne (orch), New Haven Symph, 37; Piano Quintet, Lawrence Ens, 43; Psalm 68, First Presby Choir, Nashville, 55; Piano Sonata in G, Mars Hill Fest, NC, 57; Beatitudes (tableaux), Glencliff Presby, Nashville, 76; Toccata-Gloria (organ), Murfressboro Recital, Tenn, 78; Crucifixion (tableaux) First Presby Choir, Leesburg, Fla, 80. *Teaching:* Prof theory & comp, Lawrence Consv, 25-44; dir music, Vanderbilt Univ, 44-68 & emer prof, 68- *Awards:* Am Guild Organists Fel, 27. *Mem:* Am Guild Organists (dean, 46-63); Intercollegiate Musical Coun (treas, 60-). *Mailing Add:* 2416 Abbott Martin Rd Nashville TN 37215

DANIEL, OLIVER
ADMINISTRATOR, MUSICOLOGIST
b De Pere, Wis, Nov 24, 11. *Study:* St Norbert Col, 25-29; studied piano, Amsterdam, Berlin & Boston; New England Consv Music, Hon DMus, 73. *Pos:* Music dir educ div, CBS, 42-44, producer music doc & dramatic prog, 47-54; supvr serious music, ABC, 44-46; vpres conct music admin, BMI, 54-77; founder, CRI, 54, dir, 54-82, mem exec adv bd, currently; mem bd dir, Comp Forum & Nat Music Coun, 57-78, Am Symph Orch, 62-72, Am Music Ctr, 66-78, Soc Asian Music, 67-69 & Thorne Music Fund, 70-74; chmn bd, Comp Conct Inc, 76-; co-chmn bd, New York Young Audiences, 77-79. *Teaching:* Boston Consv, 36-38 & Marot Col, 39-42. *Awards:* Laurel Leaf Award, Am Comp Alliance, 56. *Mem:* Contemp Music Soc (co-founder, 52, pres bd dir, 66-); Charles Ives Soc (vpres bd dir, 73-); life mem, Phi Mu Alpha. *Publ:* Ed, The Music of Williams Billings, 43-67; Down East Spirituals, 49; The Harmony of Maine, 49; auth, Leopold Stokowski: A Counterpoint of View, 81. *Mailing Add:* PO Box 658 Scarsdale NY 10583

DANIEL, SEAN
EDUCATOR, BARITONE
b Scranton Pa, Aug 27, 39. *Study:* Syracuse Univ, BM, 61; Ind Univ, with Margaret Harshaw & Frank St Leger, MME, 63; Goethe Inst, Murnau, WGer, dipl, 64; Hochschule Musik, Stuttgart, with Hermann Reuter, 65. *Rec Perf:* The Bishop of Brindisi, 66 & B minor Mass (Bach), 68, Syracuse Univ Rec Label; B minor Mass (Bach), Bach Bethlehem Fest, 71. *Roles:* Eugene Onegin in Eugene Onegin, Tri-Cities Opera, Binghamton, NY, 65; Sharpless in Madama Butterfly, 65 & Germont in La Traviata, 66, Syracuse Symph; Rigoleto in Rigoleto, Tri-Cities Opera, Binghamton, NY, 66; Marcello in La Boheme, 67 & Figaro in Barber of Seville, 67, Opera Under the Stars, Rochester, NY; Don Giovanni in Don Giovanni, Albuquerque Opera Theatre, 77. *Pos:* Ed, The Bulletin, Univ NMex, 75-77. *Teaching:* Asst prof, Syracuse Univ, 63-69; teacher voice, Ind Univ, Bloomington, 66-67; dir opera & voice, Univ NMex, 73-82; assoc prof, Univ Okla, 82- *Awards:* Career Award, Nat Soc Arts & Lett, 63; Fulbright Fel, 64-65. *Mem:* Nat Asn Teachers Singing; Pi Kappa Lambda; Am Guild Musical Artists; Actors Equity Asn. *Mailing Add:* Sch Music Univ Okla Norman OK 73019

DANIELLE, RUTH
SOPRANO, TEACHER
b Aurora, Ill, Dec 26, 50. *Study:* Chicago Musical Col, Roosevelt Univ, BME, 76; Northwestern Univ. *Pos:* Chorister, Grant Park Symph Chorus, Chicago, 75, Chicago Symph Orch Chorus, 77-, Opera Midwest, 78-80 & Music of Baroque, 80-81. *Teaching:* Instr studio voice, Wright Community Col, Ill, 80-81; dir, Mu Phi Epsilon Sch Music, 81-82. *Mem:* Am Guild Musical Artists; Nat Asn Teachers Singing; Mu Phi Epsilon; Nat Opera Asn. *Mailing Add:* 1129 Pratt Blvd Chicago IL 60626

DANIELS, DAVID WILDER
CONDUCTOR, EDUCATOR
b Penn Yan, NY, Dec 20, 33. *Study:* Oberlin Col, AB, 55; Boston Univ, MA, 56; Univ Iowa, MFA & PhD, 63; Inst Orchestral Studies, 64 & 66. *Rec Perf:* Operatic Arias & Art Songs, Symphonia, 79. *Pos:* Music dir, Warren Symph, 74-, Mich Lyr Opera, 76-80 & Pontiac-Oakland Symph, 77- *Teaching:* Asst prof, Univ Redlands, 63-64 & Knox Col, 65-69; assoc prof, Oakland Univ, 69-, chmn, 82- *Mem:* Mich Orch Asn (pres, 81-); Mich Coun Arts. *Publ:* Auth, Orchestral Music, Scarecrow Press, 2nd ed, 82. *Mailing Add:* 1215 Gettysburg Rochester MI 48063

DANIELS, MELVIN L
COMPOSER, EDUCATOR
b Cleburne, Tex, Jan 11, 31. *Study:* Abilene Christian Univ, BS, 55, MEd, 56; NTex State Univ, studied comp with Samuel Adler, EdD, 64. *Works:* Festique (orch), 71 & Sunfest (orch), 73, Ludwig Music Publ; Concordium (band), Warner Brothers Music, 75; Reflections (band), 77 & Pendleton Suite (strings), 77, Etling Music Publ; Bandante (band), Kjos Music Co, 81; Fanfare Symph (orch), perf by Abilene Phil & Beaumont Symph, 82-83; and others. *Teaching:* Prof music, Abilene Christian Univ, 59-, head dept, 64-79. *Awards:* First prize, Nat Sch Orch Asn Comp Contest, 69, 72 & 79; Piper Prof Tex, Minnie Stevens Piper Found, 82. *Mem:* ASCAP; Am Soc Univ Comp; Tex Music Educr Asn; Tex Orch Dir Asn. *Mailing Add:* 401 E North 23rd St Abilene TX 79601

DANN, ELIAS
EDUCATOR, CONDUCTOR & MUSIC DIRECTOR
b Kingston, NY, Mar 12, 16. *Study:* Bard Col, BA, 37; Juilliard Sch, dipl, 40; Columbia Univ, PhD(musicol), 68. *Pos:* Cond & musical dir, Okla tour, 46-50; dir bands, Columbia Univ, 57-68. *Teaching:* Lectr music hist, Columbia Univ, 57-68; prof musicol, Fla State Univ, 68- *Mem:* Am Musicol Soc; Col Music Soc. *Interests:* Heinrich I F Biber; 17th century instrumental music; history of instruments; the violin and gut strings. *Publ:* Auth, articles in Col Music Symposium, 77, J Am Violin Soc, 77, Musical Quart & Music Libr Asn Notes. *Mailing Add:* 2012 Travis Circle Tallahassee FL 32303

DANNER, DOROTHY
DIRECTOR—OPERA
b St Louis, Mo, July 8, 41. *Pos:* Stage dir, Houston Grand Opera, Lake George, Kansas City, Mich Opera Theatre, Chautauqua Opera, Opera Omaha, Minn Opera, Toledo Opera, Syracuse Opera Theatre, Augusta Opera & Glimmerglass Opera, currently; choreographer, New York Opera, Washington Opera & Philadelphia Opera, currently. *Rep:* Columbia Artists 157 W 57th St New York NY 10019. *Mailing Add:* 52 Hillside Ave Englewood NJ 07631

DANNER, HARRY
TENOR
b Philadelphia, Pa. *Study:* Metropolitan Opera Studio; studied with Beverly Johnson, Sara Lee & Uta Hagen. *Roles:* Rudolpho in La Boheme, Atlanta Opera & Lake George Opera; Painter in Lulu (Berg), Houston Grand Opera; Alfred in Die Fledermaus; Don Ottavio in Don Giovanni; Pinkerton in Madama Butterfly; Almaviva in Il Barbiere di Siviglia; Eisenstein in Die Fledermaus, Glimmerglass Opera Theatre, 83. *Pos:* Recitalist with symph orchs in US. *Awards:* Sullivan Found Award. *Mailing Add:* c/o Matthews-Napal 270 West End Ave New York NY 10023

DANSBY, WILLIAM (ROLAND)
BASS
b Bryan, Tex, May 9, 42. *Study:* Southwestern Univ, BMus, 64; NTex State Univ, 64-67. *Roles:* Escamillo in Carmen, Milwaukee Florentine Opera, 80; Basilio in Barber of Seville, 80 & 81 & Nick Shadow in Rake's Progress, 81, Washington, DC Opera; Doctor in Wozzeck, 82, Timur in Turandot, 82 & Grand Inquisitor in Don Carlo, 82, Houston Grand Opera; Scarpia in Tosca, New York City Opera, 83. *Rep:* Lew & Benson Moreau-Neret Inc 204 W 10th St New York NY 10014. *Mailing Add:* 280 Riverside Dr # 3B New York NY 10025

DARCY, WARREN JAY
COMPOSER, EDUCATOR
b Buffalo, NY, Dec 10, 46. *Study:* Consv Music, Oberlin Col, with Richard Hoffmann & Walter Aschaffenburg, BM(comp & music theory), 68; Univ Ill, with Benjamin Johnston & Edwin London, MM(comp), 69, DMA(comp), 73. *Works:* Grand Sonata (violin & piano), 66; Five Structures for Five Instruments (chamber music), 66; Improvisations I (violin, clarinet & piano), 67; Variations (orch), 67; Episode (string quartet), 68; Dichotomy (flute, horn, cello & piano), 70; Expansions (violin & piano), 70. *Teaching:* Teaching asst, Univ Ill, 69-72, lectr music theory, 72-73; assoc prof music theory, Consv Music, Oberlin Col, 73- *Mailing Add:* Consv Music Oberlin Col Oberlin OH 44074

DARLING, SANDRA (SANDRA DARLING MITCHELL)
SOPRANO, TEACHER
b St Petersburg, Fla. *Study:* Juilliard Sch Music with Mack Harrell; Southern Methodist Univ, with Mack Harrell, BM. *Rec Perf:* Merry Christmas New York from the Radio City Music Hall, 72. *Roles:* Vera in Natalia Petrorna, 64, Miss Wordsworth in Albert Herring & Clorinda in La Cenerentola, New York City Opera; Despina in Cosi fan tutte, Can Opera; Frasquita in Carmen, Nat Am Opera; Violetta in La Traviata, Maine Opera Co, 79; Birdie in Regina, Colo Opera Fest, 80. *Teaching:* Chair vocal dept, Masterwork Sch Arts, 70- *Mailing Add:* 1245 Longfellow Ave Teaneck NJ 07666

DARRENKAMP, JOHN DAVID
BARITONE
b Lancaster, Pa, July 9, 35. *Study:* Acad Vocal Arts, 65-59. *Roles:* Zuane in La Giaconda, Philadelphia Lyr, 66; Sharpless in Madama Butterfly, New York City Opera, 69; Montano in Otello, Metropolitan Opera, 79; Dott Malatesta in Don Pasquale; Alfio in Cavalleria rusticana; Lescaut in Manon. *Pos:* New York City Opera, 69-77 & Metropolitan Opera, 79-; bar with maj opera co in Mex, Spain & US. *Rep:* Kazuko Hillyer Int 250 W 57th St New York NY 10107. *Mailing Add:* 116 Ruby St Lancaster PA 17603

DARTER, THOMAS E
CONDUCTOR, CRITIC-WRITER
b Livermore, Calif, Feb 13, 49. *Study:* Cornell Univ, with Robert Palmer & Karel Husa, BA, 69, MFA, 72, DMA(music comp), 79. *Works:* Piano Sonata, 67; Sonatina (solo trumpet), 70; Quartet for Piano & Strings, 72; Oranges (voice & ens), 74; Fresco (orch), 76; Dual for Electric Guitar & Electric Bass, 76; Clarion for Trumpet & Piano, 79. *Pos:* Ed & contribr, Contemp Keyboard Mag, 75-; keyboardist & specialist 20th century ens work, improvisation & jazz. *Teaching:* Dir, Contemp Music Ens & mem fac, Chicago Musical Col, Roosevelt Univ, 72-75. *Awards:* First Prize, 69 & 71 & Devora Nadworney Award, 71, Nat Fedn Music Clubs; Otto Stahl Award, Cornell Univ, 71. *Publ:* Contribr to Choice, Music J & Guitar Player. *Mailing Add:* 1671 Honfleur Dr Sunnyvale CA 94087

DASHER, RICHARD TALIAFERRO
EDUCATOR, WRITER
b Washington, DC, Feb 10, 33. *Study:* Univ Miami, BM, 55, MM, 60; Univ Mich, EdD, 68. *Teaching:* Elem music teacher, Dade County Sch, Miami, Fla, 57-59; teacher jr high band, St Lucie County Sch, Ft Pierce, Fla, 59-60; high sch band, Broward County Sch, Ft Lauderdale, Fla, 60-65; teaching fel, Univ Mich, 65-68; prof music educ & lit, Edinboro State Col, 68- *Mem:* Col Music Soc; Music Educr Nat Conf; Chinese Music Soc. *Publ:* Auth, Black American Music, 74, Music Around the World, 75, Musical Theory, 78, Applying Musical Theory, 80 & Songs for General Music Class, 81, J Weston Walch. *Mailing Add:* Rd 1 Florex Rd Edinboro PA 16412

DASHNAW, ALEXANDER
EDUCATOR, CONDUCTOR & MUSIC DIRECTOR
Study: Crane Sch Music, BS; State Univ NY, Potsdam; Northwestern Univ, MMus. *Pos:* Cond, Brooklyn Phil Chorus, currently & Manhattan Chorale, currently; artistic dir, Jubilee Fest, Kennedy Ctr, 75-; conct tours of Europe. *Teaching:* Dir choral activ, C W Post Ctr, Long Island Univ, 66- & Hartt Col Music, 81- *Mem:* Am Choral Dir Asn (pres eastern div, 80-82). *Mailing Add:* Hartt Col Music Univ Hartford West Hartford CT 06117

DASHOW, JAMES
COMPOSER, MUSIC DIRECTOR
b Chicago, Ill, Nov 7, 44. *Study:* Princeton Univ, with Babbitt, Cone, Kim & Randall, BA, 66; Brandeis Univ, with Berger & Shifrin, MFA, 69; Accad Nazionale Di Santa Cecilia, with Petrassi, dipl, 71. *Works:* Ashberry Setting (sop, flute & piano), Forum Players, 71-72; Some Dream Songs (sop, violin & piano), Seesaw Music, 75; Second Voyage (tenor voice & comput music), comn by Nat Endowment Arts, 78-79; Conditional Assemblies (comput music), 80 & The Little Prince (opera for voices, comput music, lasers & graphics), 82-, comn by Venice Biennale, 80; Mnemonics I (violin & comput music), comn by Nat Endowment Arts, 82-82; In Winter Shine (comput music), comn by Mass Inst Tech Arts Coun, 83. *Pos:* Organizer & dir, Forum Players New Music End, Rome, 71-75; dir, Studio Di Musica elettronica Sciadoni, Rome, 73- *Teaching:* Assoc prof & comp in res, Centro Di Sonologia Computazionale, Univ Di Padova, Italy, 78-; vis lectr & actg dir, Experimental Music Studio, Mass Inst Tech, Cambridge, 83. *Mem:* Comput Music Asn (vpres, 80-); ASCAP; Am Music Ctr. *Publ:* Auth, 3 Methods for the Digital Synthesis of Non-Harmonic Chords, Interface, 80; Spectra as Chords, Comput Music J, MIT Press, 81; Note Per Conditional Assemblies, Bolletino No 1 Del Limb, 81 & Note Per Il Piccolo Principe, No 2, 83; monthly articles on techniques of computer music in Fare Musica, Roma, Publitarget, SRL, 82- *Mailing Add:* Via Della Luce 66 Roma 00153 Italy

DAUB, PEGGY ELLEN
LIBRARIAN, EDUCATOR
b Bluffton, Ohio, Oct 15, 49. *Study:* Miami Univ, Ohio, BMus, 72; Cornell Univ, MA, 75; Univ Ill, Champaign-Urbana, MSLS, 80. *Pos:* Sub-ed, New Grove Dict of Music & Musicians, Macmillan, London, England, 75-76; asst music libr & rare bk libr, Yale Univ, 80-82; head, Music Libr, Univ Mich, 82- *Teaching:* Asst prof music bibliog & librarianship, Univ Mich, 82- *Mem:* Am Musicol Soc; Music Libr Asn; Am Libr Asn. *Interests:* Patronage of music in 18th century England. *Publ:* Contribr, New Grove Dict of Music & Musicians, Macmillan, 80; auth, From George Grove to the New Grove, Reference Serv Rev, 82; contribr, New Grove Dict of Music in US, Macmillan (in prep). *Mailing Add:* Sch Music Univ Mich Ann Arbor MI 48109

DAVIDOVICH, BELLA
PIANO, TEACHER
b Baku, USSR; US citizen. *Study:* Moscow Consv, BM & MM. *Rec Perf:* Beethoven, 79, Chopin, 79, Schumann, 80 & Chopin 81 & 82, Philips. *Pos:* Conct pianist, US & Europe, currently. *Teaching:* Prof, Moscow Consv, formerly & Juilliard Sch, 82- *Awards:* First Prize, Chopin Compt, Warsaw, 49. *Rep:* Jacques Leises Artists Mgt 155 W 68th St New York NY 10023. *Mailing Add:* 8300 Talbot St Apt 6H Kew Gardens NY 11415

DAVIDOVSKY, MARIO
COMPOSER, EDUCATOR
b Medanos, Argentina, Mar 4, 34; US citizen. *Study:* private music study in Buenos Aires. *Works:* Inflexions (perc, pianoforte & strings) & Scenes From Shir-Ha-Shirim (sop, two tenors, bass & instrm), E B Marks Music Corp; Pennplay (perc, pianoforte & strings), comn by Univ Pa; Electronic Study No 1, No 2 & No 3, Columbia Rec, 64; Consorts for Symphonic Band, 80; String Quartet No 4, comn by Naumburg Found, 80; Romancero (sop, flute, clarinet, violin & cello), 83; and many others. *Teaching:* Vis prof, Univ Mich, 64, Manhattan Sch Music, 68 & Yale Univ, 72; prof music, City Col, formerly & Columbia Univ, 81-; dir Electronic Music Lab, Columbia Univ, 81- & Princeton Univ, 81- *Awards:* Am Acad Arts & Lett, 64 & Walter W Naumburg Found, 72; Pulitzer Prize, 71. *Mem:* Am Inst Acad Arts & Lett; BMI. *Mailing Add:* 490 West End Ave New York NY 10023

DAVIDSON, AUDREY EKDAHL
EDUCATOR, CONDUCTOR
b Willmar, Minn, Aug 7, 30. *Study:* Wayne State Univ, BA, 61, MA, 64; Univ Minn, PhD, 75; New York Pro Musica & Studium Musicae, Brussels, studied voice & early music with Avery Crew. *Works:* Mass in D, St Barnabas Cath Church, Mich, 61. *Pos:* Musical dir, Soc Old Music, Mich, 66- & St Martin Tours Episcopal Church, Kalamazoo, Mich, 78- *Teaching:* From adj to assoc prof humanities, Western Mich Univ, 65-; lectr music hist, Univ Minn, 75. *Bibliog:* P E Schubert (auth), Medieval Music Lives Today Through Dr Audrey Davidson's Efforts, Encore, 2/76. *Mem:* Am Musicol Soc. *Interests:* Early music, especially performance practice; topics in modern music; editing works by medieval and baroque women composers. *Publ:* Auth, I Will Sing Unto the Lord a New Song: The Works of Heinz Werner Zimmerman, Chantry Music Press, 69; Transcendental Unity in the Works of Charles Ives, Am Quart, 70; Substance and Manner, Hiawatha Press, 77; The Performance Practice of Early Vocal Music, EDAM Newsletter, 81; St John Passions from Scandinavia and Their Medieval Background, Medieval Inst Publ, 81. *Mailing Add:* 2006 Argyle Ave Kalamazoo MI 49008

DAVIDSON, JOY ELAINE
MEZZO-SOPRANO
b Ft Collins, Colo, Aug 18, 40. *Study:* Occidental Col, BA, 59; Fla State Univ. *Roles:* Carmen in Carmen, New York City Opera, San Francisco Opera, Lyons Opera & Welsh Nat Opera, 65-; Dalila in Samson et Dalila, La Scala Opera & Ft Worth Opera, 65-; Charlotte in Werther, Turin Opera & Madrid Opera, 65-; Amneris in Aida, Houston Opera & Edmonton Opera, 65-; Adalgisa in Norma, Metropolitan Opera, Edminton Opera, Hartford Opera & Seattle Opera, 65-; Klytemnestra in Elektra, Art Park Opera, 65-; Angelina in Cenerentola, Metropolitan Nat Co, 65- *Awards:* Gold Medal, Int Compt Young Opera Singers, Bulgaria, 69. *Mem:* Sigma Alpha Iota. *Mailing Add:* 5751 SW 74 Ave Miami FL 33143

DAVIDSON, LOUIS
TRUMPET, EDUCATOR
b New York, NY, Mar 16, 12. *Study:* Studied trumpet with Max Schlossberg. *Rec Perf:* Thou Who Sits To The Fathers Right, B minor mass (Bach), Little Fugue in G (four trumpets) & Romance in G (Beethoven), Charles Colin. *Pos:* Second trumpet, Cincinnati Symph, 28-33; first trumpet, Cleveland Orch, 35-58 & Teatro Colon, Buenos Aires, 41. *Teaching:* Instr, Cleveland Inst Music, Oberlin Col & Western Reserve, formerly; Assoc prof trumpet, Ind Univ, 63-65, prof trumpet, 65-82, prof emer, 82- *Mem:* Am Fedn Musicians. *Publ:* Auth, articles in Symph Mag, New York Brass Conf J, Getzen Gazette, Brass-Woodwind Mag & Holton Mag, 55-82; Trumpet Techniques, 70, rev ed, 74 & Trumpet Profiles, 76, private publ. *Mailing Add:* 608 Kerry Dr Bloomington IN 47401

DAVIDSON, LYLE
COMPOSER, EDUCATOR
b 1938. *Study:* New England Consv Music, studied theory & comp with Francis Judd Cooke, Daniel Pinkham & Luise Vosgerchian, BM, MM; Brandeis Univ, studied theory & comp with Arthur Berger; Boston Univ. *Works:* A Certain Gurgling Melodiousness (chamber orch & double bass), 73 & Voices of the Dark (chorus, tape & optional bass instrm), E C Schirmer Music Co. *Pos:* Researcher, Project Zero, Harvard Sch Educ, currently. *Teaching:* Mem fac, Mass Inst Technol, formerly & Harvard Univ, formerly; mem fac music theory, New England Consv Music, currently. *Mailing Add:* 197 Lake View Ave Cambridge MA 02138

DAVIDSON, TINA
COMPOSER, PIANO
b Stockholm, Sweden, Dec 30, 52; US citizen. *Study:* Bennington Col, with Henry Brant, Vivian Fine & Lionel Nowak, BA(piano & comp), 76. *Works:* Dancers (orch), Orch Soc Philadelphia, 80; Seven Macabre Songs (piano solo), Mikrokosmik Rec Label, 81; Two Beasts From the Forest of Imaginary Beings (narrator & orch), 82 & Piano Concerto (pianoforte & orch), 82, Orch Soc Philadelphia; Unicorn-Tapestry (ms & violoncello), Relache, Philadelphia, Pa & Nat Asn Comp USA, Calif, 83; Quintet (flute, clarinet, viola, violoncello & double bass), Pittsburgh New Music Ens, 83; To Understand Weeping (sop), Calisto Rec Label, 83; Other Echos (two violins), Sarah Lawrence Col, 83. *Pos:* Assoc dir, Relache, Ens Contemp Music, Philadelphia, Pa, 78- *Teaching:* Instr, Drexel Univ, 80- *Awards:* Fel, Pa Coun Arts, 83. *Mem:* Int League Women Comp. *Mailing Add:* 508 Woodland Terr Philadelphia PA 19104

DAVIES, BRUCE MACPHERSON
VIOLIN
b Ithaca, NY, May 28, 48. *Study:* Kent State Univ, BMus, 71, MMus, 74; studied with Raymond Montoni, Bernard Goldschmidt, Eugene Altschuler, Jaime Laredo, Ma Si-hon & Howard Weiss. *Pos:* Violinist, Syracuse Symph Orch, 74- *Mailing Add:* 3170 Jane St Caledonia NY 14423

DAVIES, DENNIS
CONDUCTOR & MUSIC DIRECTOR, PIANIST
b Toledo, Ohio, Apr 16, 44. *Study:* Juilliard Sch Music, BA, 66, MA, 68, DMA, 72. *Pos:* Music dir, Norwalk Symph Orch, Conn, 68-72, St Paul Chamber Orch, 72-81, Cabrillo Music Fest, 74- & White Mountains Fest Arts, 75-; cond, Juilliard Ens, 68-74 & Flying Dutchman, Bayreuth Fest, 78-; regular guest cond, Netherlands Opera, 73-; guest cond, Stuttgart Opera, 76-80, music dir, 80- *Mailing Add:* Cabrillo Music Fest 6500 Soquel Dr Aptos CA 95003

DAVINE, ROBERT A
EDUCATOR, CONCERT ACCORDION
b Pueblo, Colo, Apr 5, 24. *Study:* Northwestern Univ, comp with Robert DeLaney & accordion with Andrew Rizzo, BMus, 49, MMus, 50. *Rec Perf:* On Crystal Rec. *Pos:* Mem staff orch, Nat Broadcasting Co, Denver, 52-54. *Teaching:* Instr accordion, San Francisco Consv, 51-52; prof accordion & theory, Lamont Sch Music, Univ Denver, 54- *Awards:* Educ Award, Am Accordionists Asn, 73. *Mem:* Col Music Soc; Accordion Teachers Guild; Am Accordionists Asn. *Mailing Add:* 2500 S Kearney St Denver CO 80222

DAVIS, ALLAN GERALD
COMPOSER, EDUCATOR
b Watertown, NY, Aug 29, 22. *Study:* Sch Music, Syracuse Univ, BM, 44, MM, 45. *Works:* Razorback Reel for Piano, 65 & Festival Concerto for B Flat Clarinet & Orchestra, 74, Oxford Univ Press; Italian Festival Suite for Brass Choir and Percussion, 74 & The Departure (opera in three acts), 75, E C Kerby Ltd; Razorback Reel for Band, 75 & Divertimento for Small Orchestra, 81, Oxford Univ Press. *Teaching:* Prof comp, theory & counterpoint, Herbert H Lehman Col, City Univ New York, 68- *Awards:* Grant, Ala Coun Arts & Nat Endowment Arts, 75. *Mem:* Am Asn Univ Prof; Nat Opera Asn. *Mailing Add:* 210 Riverside Dr New York NY 10025

DAVIS, BARBARA SMITH
SOPRANO
b Harrisburg, Pa. *Study:* Southern Methodist Univ; Boris Goldovskey Opera Wkshp. *Roles:* Alice Ford in Merry Wives of Windsor, Lake George Opera Fest; Gilda in Rigoletto, Corp de Arte Lirico de Sontiago, Chile; Zerlina in Don Giovanni, Goldovsky Opera Theater; Angel More in Mother of Us All, Kansas City Opera; Violetta in La Traviata, Family Opera NJ. *Pos:* Artist, Affil Artists Inc, 82- *Mailing Add:* RD 2 Box 600 Sussex NJ 07401

DAVIS, DEBORAH GRIFFITH
LIBRARIAN

b Rockville Centre, NY, Dec 30, 54. *Study:* Am Univ, BMus, 76; Cath Univ Am, MA, 81; Columbia Univ, MSLS, 82. *Pos:* Asst librn, Juilliard Sch, 82- *Mem:* Music Libr Asn; Am Musicol Soc. *Mailing Add:* 8 Brookside Dr Huntington NY 11743

DAVIS, IVAN
PIANO, EDUCATOR

Study: NTex State Univ, BM, 52; Santa Cecilia Acad, Rome, artist's dipl, 58; studied with Silvio Scionti & Vladimir Horowitz. *Rec Perf:* Piano Concerto No 1 & 2 (Liszt); Piano Concerto No 2 (Rachmaninoff); Piano Concerto No 1 (Tchaikovsky); Fantasie Impromptu (Chopin); Etude No 3 (Chopin); Barcarolle (Chopin); Waltzes No 6 & 7 (Chopin). *Pos:* Performer with maj orchs & recitalist throughout US, UK, Europe, Can & South Am. *Teaching:* Prof applied music & pianist in res, Univ Miami, 66- *Awards:* First prize, Casella Compt, Naples, 58 & Int Liszt Compt, 60-61; Handel Award, New York, 62. *Interests:* History and performance of opera. *Mailing Add:* Sch Music Univ Miami Coral Gables FL 33124

DAVIS, J(AMES) B(ENJAMIN)
BASS

b Louisville, Ky, Aug 6, 35. *Study:* Columbia Univ, BFA, 58. *Rec Perf:* The Taming of the Shrew (Vittorio Gianini), CRI, 70. *Roles:* Basilio in The Barber of Seville, Seattle Opera, 66; Sparafucile in Rigoletto, 73 & Tolomeo in Giulio Cesare, 73, New York City Opera; Daland in The Dutchman, 75 & Pere Laurent in Romeo & Juliet, 75, Miami Opera; Mephisto in Faust, Baltimore Symph, 76; Doctor in Vanessa, 79, Kansas City Lyr Opera. *Pos:* Affiliate artist, Univ Tenn, Chattanooga, 75-78. *Rep:* Tony Hartmann Assoc 250 W 57th St New York NY 10017. *Mailing Add:* RD 2 Box 600 Sussex NJ 07461

DAVIS, JEAN REYNOLDS
COMPOSER

b Cumberland, Md, Nov 1, 27. *Study:* Sch Fine Arts, Univ Pa, BMus, 49. *Works:* The Mirror (chamber opera), Acad Vocal Arts, 53; Shenandoah Holiday, Philadelphia Orch, 61; Yankee Doodle Doodles, Presser Music Co, 62; Slick Tricks, Witmark & Sons, 62; Doors Into Music, Boston Music Co, 66. *Pos:* Ed consult piano educ dept, Music Publ Holding Corp, 59-65. *Teaching:* Private piano, 45-; instr piano & theory, Haverford Friends Sch, 49-55. *Awards:* Benjamin Franklin Medal, 48, Thornton Oakley Medal, 49 & Award of Merit, 53, Univ Pa. *Mem:* ASCAP; Am Col Musicians. *Mailing Add:* Mermont Plaza Apt 104 Bryn Mawr PA 19010

DAVIS, LEONARD
VIOLA, EDUCATOR

b Willimantic, Conn. *Study:* Juilliard Sch, dipl, 41 & post grad study; viola study with Milton Katims, 44-48. *Pos:* Assoc prin viola, New York Phil, 50-; prin violist, New York Phil Chamber Ens, 60-71; perf, Hidden Valley Masters Fest, Carmel, CA, 82- *Teaching:* Asst prof, Brooklyn Col Consv Music, City Univ New York, 74-; vis prof, Ind Univ, Bloomington, 76-79; res, Mannes Col Music, 82- *Mem:* Juilliard Alumni Asn; Am String Teachers Asn. *Publ:* Ed, 30 Major Works for Viola, Int Music Co, 76; auth, Careers, Am String Teacher, 80; The Four Faces of Music, Instrumentalist, 81. *Mailing Add:* 185 W End Ave New York NY 10023

DAVIS, MICHAEL DAVID
VIOLIN, EDUCATOR

b Hull, England, May 29, 37. *Study:* Guildhall Sch Music, London, 54-57; Staatliche Hochschule Musik, Cologne, 57-59; Royal Acad Music, London, LRAM, 55; Royal Col Music, London, ARCM, 55. *Rec Perf:* On Orion. *Pos:* Concertmaster, Scottish Nat Orch, 74-76 & Columbus Symph Orch, 77-; recitalist throughout Europe. *Teaching:* Artist in res, Col Wooster, 60-74; assoc prof violin, Ohio State Univ, 76- *Awards:* First Prize, Int Carl Flesch Compt, 57. *Mem:* NY Musicians Club; Am String Teachers Asn; Pi Kappa Lambda. *Rep:* Great Lakes Perf Artists Assoc 310 E Washington Dr Ann Arbor MI 48104. *Mailing Add:* 1400 Tiehack Ct Columbus OH 43085

DAVIS, PAUL
ORGAN

Study: Peabody Consv, BM, MM, DMA; studied with Arthur Howes, Marilyn Mason, Helmut Walcha & Maria Jaeger. *Pos:* Organist & choirmaster, Christ Lutheran Church, Baltimore, 65-; recitalist, US, England, Germany, Austria, Holland & Sweden, currently. *Teaching:* Mem fac & col organist, Berea Col, 62-65; mem fac, Peabody Consv, currently. *Mailing Add:* Peabody Consv Music 1 E Mt Vernon Pl Baltimore MD 21202

DAVIS, RICHARD
BARITONE

b NMex. *Study:* WTex State Univ; Ind Univ, MMus. *Pos:* Baritone, Augusta Opera Co, Wolf Trap, Chautauqua Opera Co, Rochester Opera Co, Tulane Lyr Opera & other opera co & orchs. *Teaching:* Mem fac voice, Ind Univ, formerly, Columbus Col, Ga, formerly & Eastman Sch Music, formerly. *Mailing Add:* c/o Liegner Mgt 1860 Broadway Suite 1610 New York NY 10023

DAVIS, SHARON (SHARON YVONNE DAVIS SCHMIDT)
COMPOSER, PIANO

b NHollywood, Calif, Sept 30, 37. *Study:* Univ Southern Calif, with John Crown, BMus, 60; Juilliard Sch Music, with Rosina Lhevinne, MS, 62; studied with Nadia Boulanger & Yvonne Lefebure, 62-63. *Works:* Though Men Call Us Free, 76, Three Moods of Emily Dickinson, 76, Three Poems of William

Blake, 78, Suite of Wildflowers, 81, Cocktail Etudes, 81 & Six Songs Set to Poems of William Pillin, 83, WIM Rec. *Pos:* Conct & rec artist piano & harpiscord NAm & Europe, 64-; ed, Western Int Music Inc, 66-; comp, transcriber & arr, 67- *Teaching:* Head piano fac, ETex State Univ, 64-66; staff accmp, Calif State Col, Los Angeles, 66; coach piano & accmp, Univ Southern Calif, 66-66. *Awards:* Fulbright Grant, 62-63; Ford Found Rec Grant, 76. *Mem:* ASCAP. *Mailing Add:* c/o Avant Music WIM 2859 Holt Ave Los Angeles CA 90034

DAVISON, JOHN HERBERT
COMPOSER, EDUCATOR

b Istanbul, Turkey, May 31, 30; US citizen. *Study:* Haverford Col, BA, 51; Harvard Univ, MA, 52; Eastman Sch Music, PhD, 59. *Works:* Sonata for Trombone & Piano, Shawnee Press, 57; Symphony No 2, perf by Eastman-Rochester Orch, 59; Communion Service No 3 in D, Theodore Presser, 72; The American Prophet (cantata), comn & perf by Deerfield Acad, 76; Magnificat & Nunc dimittis, comn & perf by Pro Arte Chorale, 78; Arthur's Return (bagpipes & strings), comn & perf by Concerto Soloists Philadelphia, 83; Windows (oboe, sop & strings), comn & perf by Wayne Rapier, 83. *Teaching:* Ruth Marshall Magill prof music, Haverford Col, 59- *Awards:* Comp in Res, Kansas City, Mo, Ford Found & Music Educr Nat Conf, 62. *Mailing Add:* 3 College Circle Haverford PA 19041

DAVISON, PETER SAUL
COMPOSER, CONDUCTOR

b Los Angeles, Calif, Oct 26, 48. *Study:* Calif State Univ, Northridge, BA(comp), 73, with Aurelia de la Vega & L Christianson, MA(comp), 75; Univ Calif, San Diego, with Roger Reynolds. *Works:* Symphony #1, comn by Nat Endowment Arts, 76; Cascade, 78, Poltergeist, 78, Sitting at La Brea Tar Pits Dreaming of Indonesia, 78 & Summer's Bittersweet Ending, 78, comn by Calif Arts Coun; Kawitan, perf & comn by Calif Perc Ens, 80; Eagle Springs, comn by Found New Am Music, 82. *Rec Perf:* Music on the Way, 80, Glide, 81, Star Gazer, 81, Forest, 82 & Mountain, 83, Avocado Rec. *Pos:* Comp, Comn for Music, 70-; freelance comp, film scoring, 73-; comp, perf & producer, Avocado Rec, Santa Monica, Calif, 80- *Teaching:* Instr music, Calif State Univ, 70-73, Univ Calif, San Diego, 73-75, Glendale Col, 75-76 & East Los Angeles Col, 76- *Awards:* Comp Award, Calif State Univ, Northridge, 75; Nat Endowment Arts Grant, 77; Calif Arts Coun Comn, 78. *Mem:* Am Fedn Musicians. *Mailing Add:* 1924 Euclid Santa Monica CA 90404

DAVYE, JOHN JOSEPH
COMPOSER, EDUCATOR

b Milton, Mass, Oct 19, 29. *Study:* Univ Miami, BM, 52; Ithaca Col, with Warren Benson, MM, 65. *Works:* Sinfonietta (strings); Three Episodes (brass & choir); Canonic Fantasy (two flutes); A Child Is Born to US (treble voices); Missa Brevis; Jerusalem Awake; Tenebrae Factae Sunt. *Pos:* Cond & comp choral, chamber & orchestral music; cond choral group on radio networks, conf & conv throughout US. *Teaching:* Music sec level, pub sch, 55-65; assoc prof music, Old Dominion Univ, 66-79, dir choral activities, 66-, prof music, 80- *Mem:* Am Choral Dir Asn; Am Soc Univ Comp; Music Educr Nat Conf; Phi Mu Alpha Sinfonia; Am Asn Univ Prof. *Mailing Add:* 141 Fayton Ave Norfolk VA 23505

DAW, KURT DAVID
ADMINISTRATOR

b Twin Falls, Idaho, Aug 21, 56. *Study:* Univ Idaho, BA, 74; Southern Methodist Univ, MFA, 81. *Pos:* Stage dir, Dallas Opera & High Noon Ens, 82; gen mgr, Pub Opera Dallas, 82- *Mailing Add:* 3212 Stanford Dallas TX 75225

DAWSON, GEORGE C
COMPOSER, MUSICOLOGIST

b Boise, Idaho. *Study:* Univ Idaho, BA(music); Univ Southern Calif, MMus(comp), PhD(musicol), 69. *Works:* Sonata for Piano, George Dawson, 55; Overture to Antigone, Idaho State Symph Orch, 57; String Quartet, Univ Southern Calif String Quartet, 60; Pas de deux, Studio Orch, Hollywood, 61; Sonata for Clarinet & Piano, Commack & Dawson, 63; Song Cycle, Max Schimsky, 65. *Pos:* Found & dir, Dawson Music Studios, 50-60; freelance comp, Hollywood, 68-72. *Teaching:* Assoc prof musicol & comp, Univ Portland, 62-68; special lectr musicol, Calif State Univ, Long Beach, 72-77; prof music & music hist, Oxnard Col, 77-81. *Mem:* Mahler Soc; Am Musicol Soc; Int Musicol Soc; Calif Music Teachers Asn; Nat Guild Piano Teachers. *Interests:* Works by Bartok involving orchestras, tracing his development as orchestrator. *Publ:* Auth, Di Lasso's Seven Penit Psalms, Univ Southern Calif Monograph, 62. *Mailing Add:* 3729 Amesbury Rd Los Angeles CA 90027

DAWSON, JAMES EDWARD
SAXOPHONE, EDUCATOR

b Waynesburg, Pa, May 20, 44. *Study:* Northwestern Univ, BME, 67, MM, 69; Consv Nat Paris, 69; Univ Mich, AMusD, 74; Royal Col Music, London, 80-82; Guildhall Sch Music & Drama, London, 80-82; Brit Music Information Ctr & Horniman Museum, London, 80-82; Can Music Ctr, Toronto, 82-83; studied with Frederick Hemke, Lawrence Teal & Daniel Deffayet. *Rec Perf:* Chicago Saxophone Quartet, Coronet Rec, 70; Chicago Saxophone Quartet, Brewster Rec, 71; James Dawson, Soprano Saxophone, Crystal Rec, 82; Quartet, Op 22 (Anton Webern), 83 & Music of Charles Dakin, 83, BBC Archive Rec. *Pos:* Guest cond, Tidewater Music Fest, Washington, DC, 77 & Int Fest Music, Dubrovnik, Yugoslavia, 78; artist in res, Oakland Univ, currently; saxophonist, Detroit Symph Orch, currently. *Teaching:* Asst prof sax, Univ Tenn, 70-72; fac mem wind instrument, Univ Mich, Ann Arbor, 72-74; assoc prof sax & theory, Oakland Univ, 74- *Awards:* ASCAP Award (for contemp music), 76. *Bibliog:* Steven Mauk (auth), James Dawson, Soprano Saxophone, Chamber Music Quart, Winter 82; *Mem:* World Sax Cong (exec bd mem, 70-72); Music Educr Nat Conf; Nat Asn Col Wind & Perc Instr; Col Band Dir Nat Asn. *Interests:* Bibliographic research in music reference and resource materials; evolution of musical aesthetics; biography. *Publ:* Auth, Selection, Preparation & Adjustment of Single Reeds, Instrumentalist, 69; Creating Pitch Sensitivity in Saxophone Performance, Woodwind World, 76; Chromatic Fantasy by Gregory Kosteck, Sax Symposium, 81; Music for Saxophone by British Composers, Dorn Publ, 81; Challenge to Aesthetic Perception, Mich Acad Sci, 83. *Mailing Add:* Dept Music Oakland Univ Rochester MI 48063

DAY, RICHARD WRISLEY
CRITIC

b Rhineback, NY, Jan 25, 36. *Study:* Opera with John Nichols & Jean Wells, 48-54; Hartwick Col, 54-56; Acad Minerva, Bari, Italy, BA, 57; Bard Col, 58. *Pos:* Arts critic, The Woodstock Rev, NY, 58; arts ed & critic, Landers Suburban Newspapers, Hudson Valley, NY, 59; chief arts critic & ed, The Post & The Telegram, Bridgeport, Conn, 60-; exec bd, The Conn Grand Opera; mem bd dir, The Bridgeport Symph Orch. *Awards:* Huneker Award for Arts Criticism, 82. *Mem:* Music Critics Asn. *Mailing Add:* 338 Beechwood Ave Bridgeport CT 06604

DEAHL, ROBERT WALDO
EDUCATOR, TROMBONE

b Pittsburgh, Pa, Oct 9, 28. *Study:* Consv Music, Oberlin Col, BM, 50, MM, 52; Akad Mozarteum, Salzburg, Austria. *Pos:* First trombone, US Air Force Band, 54-55; Lubbock Symph Orch, 74- & Roswell Symph Orch, 74-; dir, Consv Music, Salzburg Div, Oberin Col, 59-64. *Teaching:* Prof trombone & humanities, Tex Tech Univ, 64- *Mem:* Tex Music Educr Asn; Southern Humanities Asn; Int Trombone Asn; Phi Mu Alpha; Pi Kappa Lambda. *Mailing Add:* 3212 25th St Lubbock TX 79410

DEAK, JON
DOUBLE BASS, COMPOSER

b Hammond, Ind, Apr 27, 43. *Study:* Juilliard Sch, BM(contrabass), 65; Univ Ill, MM, 68; studied comp with Alcides Lanza. *Works:* Surrealist Studies (solo bass), 70; The Great Plains (ens), 73; Iowa (ens), 74; A December Evening in the Adirondacks (ens), 74, Antrim County, Michigan, 75 & Young Giacometti, 75, New York; Split Rock (chamber music with dance). *Pos:* Solo bassist, Chicago Little Symph, 65-67; assoc bassist, New York Phil, 69- *Teaching:* Instr, Interlochen Arts Acad, 65-67; teaching asst, Univ Ill, 68-69. *Awards:* Fulbright Fel Res Rome, 67. *Mailing Add:* 215 W 98th St #4B New York NY 10025

DEAN, TALMAGE WHITMAN
EDUCATOR, COMPOSER

b Russellville, Tenn, Jan 29, 15. *Study:* Hardin Simmons Univ, BA & BM, 40; Eastman Sch Music, MMus, 41; Univ Southern Calif, PhD, 60. *Works:* Baptist Hour Choral Series, Broadman Press, 57-63; Canticles of Christmas, Southern Music, 63; Behold the Glory of the Lamb (oratorio), 64 & Proclaim the Word (canticle), 65, Broadman Press; The Word Was Made Flesh (canticle), Southern Music, 65; Pax Vobis (oratorio), Ft Worth Symph & Abilene Phil & Chorus, 67; David and Bathsheba (canticle), Hardin Simmons Univ Conct Choir, 83. *Teaching:* Prof theory & comp, Hardin Simmons Univ, Abilene, 41-56 & dean, Sch Music, 67-81; prof theory & chmn grad studies, Southwestern Sem, Ft Worth, 56-67. *Awards:* Award, Nat Conf Church Musicians, 64; Keeter Award, Hardin Simmons Univ, 82. *Mem:* Am Musicol Soc (pres Tex chap, 53-55 & secy-treas, 58-60); Southern Baptist Church Music Conf (pres, 61-63); Tex Music Educr Asn (mem bd dir, 76-68). *Interests:* The organ in eighteenth-century English colonial America; source readings in the history of church music. *Mailing Add:* Rte 3 Box 313 Abilene TX 79605

DEAS, RICHARD RYDER
PIANO, EDUCATOR

b Birmingham, Ala, Jan 19, 27. *Study:* Univ NMex, BFA(music), 49; Juilliard Sch Music, BS(piano), 52, MS(piano), 53; Teachers Col, Columbia Univ, EdD(music), 68. *Rec Perf:* Duets for Piano (Erik Satie), Candide Rec, 69. *Pos:* Chmn bd dir, Community Orch Inc, Univ NC, Wilmington. *Teaching:* Asst prof music, Bennett Col, 60-70; prof, Univ NC, Wilmington, 70-, chmn dept, 73-80, asst to chmn creative arts dept, 80- *Mailing Add:* 510 Upland Dr Wilmington NC 28405

DEASON, WILLIAM DAVID
COMPOSER, EDUCATOR

b Sioux Falls, SDak, May 24, 45. *Study:* Fla State Univ, with John Boda & Harold Schiffman, BMus, 67, MMus, 68; studied cond with Richard Burgin & comp with Lester Trimble; Juilliard Sch, with Roger Sessions. *Works:* Piano Concerto, perf by Columbia Phil Orch, 70; Baleen (guitar, quarter-tone harpsichord & orch); Cello Concertino; Tuba Concerto; Wind Tunnels (brass trio); Quartet for Flute, Bassoon, Violin and Cello; Polarity (two clarinets). *Teaching:* Asst prof music, Caldwell Col, 77-; mem fac, New Sch Social Res, 78- *Awards:* ASCAP Standard Awards (two); Meet the Comp Grant. *Mailing Add:* 380 92nd St #F-1 Brooklyn NY 11209

DEATHERAGE, MARTHA
EDUCATOR, SOPRANO

b Parsons, Kans. *Study:* Stephens Col; Univ Tex, Austin; studied with Maggie Teyte & Lotte Lehmann. *Teaching:* Prof voice & coordr vocal div, Univ Tex, Austin, 62- *Awards:* Artist Presentation Award, St Louis, Mo, 56; Artist Award Winner, Nat Fedn Music Clubs, 57. *Mem:* Nat Asn Teachers Singing (district gov Texhoma region, 72-80); Pi Kappa Lambda; Sigma Alpha Iota. *Mailing Add:* Dept Music Univ Tex Austin TX 78712

DE BLASIS, JAMES MICHAEL
ADMINISTRATOR, DIRECTOR—OPERA

b New York, NY, Apr 12, 31. *Study:* Carnegie Mellon Univ, BFA, 59; MFA, 60; studied with Karl Kritz. *Pos:* Asst dir, Pittsburgh Opera, 58-63, artistic adv, 79-83; adminr opera, Syracuse Symph, 62-71; adv opera, Corbett Found, 71-76; prod dir, Cincinnati Opera, 68-72, gen dir, 73-; freelance int stage dir operas, currently. *Teaching:* Mem fac drama, Carnegie Mellon Univ, 60-62; head dept, Onondaga Community Col, 63-72; head opera wkshp, Syracuse, NY, 69-70. *Mem:* Actors Equity; Am Guild Musical Artists. *Mailing Add:* c/o Thea Dispeker 59 E 54th St New York NY 10022

DE BOHUN, LYLE (CLARA LYLE BOONE)
ADMINISTRATOR, COMPOSER

b Stanton, Ky, Sept 6, 27. *Study:* Asbury Col, Centre Col Ky, BA, 49; Radcliffe Col; Grad Sch Educ, Harvard Univ, MAT, 51; studied comp with Walter Piston & Darius Milhaud. *Works:* Songs of Estrangement (string quartet & soprano), Aspen Music Fest, 58; Annunciation of Spring, perf by Am Univ Orch, 59; Motive and Chorale, perf by Shoestring Orch Capitol Hill, 82; also numerous songs, choral & chamber works. *Pos:* Dir music, Willard Day Sch, Troy, NY, 54-57 & Beauvoir Sch, Washington Cath, DC, 57-59; owner, Arsis Press & Sisra Publ, 74- *Awards:* Paul Revere Awards, Music Publ Asn US, 76. *Bibliog:* Zita Dressner (auth), A Talk with Clara Lyle Boone, Am Women Comp News, 80; Barbara Feinman (auth), New Women Composers, Washington Post, 83. *Mem:* Music Publ Asn US; Am Women Comp; publ affiliate, Int League Women Comp. *Publ:* Contribr, The Musical Woman: An International Perspective, Greenwood Press, 83. *Mailing Add:* 1719 Bay St SE Washington DC 20003

DEBOLT, DAVID ALBERT
BASSOON, EDUCATOR

b Charleston, WVa. *Study:* Ohio State Univ, BMus, 60, MA, 63; bassoon study with Bernard Garfield & Harold Goltzer. *Works:* Adagio & Fugue (flute, violin, bassoon & piano), CRS Rec, 82. *Rec Perf:* Quartet for Bassoon and Strings (Bernard Garfield), 82, Adagio and Fugue (David DeBolt), 82, Concerto in G Minor F VIII, No 11 (Vivaldi), 82, Concerto in C Major F VIII, No 3 (Vivaldi), 82 & Concerto in B flat Major (Capel Bond), 82, CRS Rec. *Pos:* Prin bassoonist, Birmingham Symph, 62-63, Tulsa Phil Orch, 64-66, Kansas City Phil Orch, 66-82 & Santa Fe Opera, formerly; bassoonist, Kent Wind Quintet, 82-; recitalist, 82- *Teaching:* Res artist quintet & bassoon, Univ Kans, 70-74; asst prof bassoon & lit, Kent State Univ, 82- *Mem:* Am Musicol Soc; Int Double Reed Soc; Am Fedn Musicians. *Publ:* Coauth, Tension and Musical Behavior, Nat Asn Teachers Singing Bulletin, 62 & Am String Teacher, 63; auth, Bassoonists View of the 1979 IDRS Convention, 79 & The Bassoon at Lubbock 1981, 81, Double Reed. *Mailing Add:* 1227 Fairview Dr Kent OH 44240

DE BRANT, CYR (JOSEPH VINCENT HIGGINSON)
COMPOSER, WRITER

b Irvington, NJ, May 17, 1896. *Study:* NY Univ, BMus, 29, MMus, 38. *Works:* Songs, Bamberger Symph, 33; There Will Be Rest, Choir Invisible, 33; Pie Jesu, Cathedral Choir, 40- *Pos:* Organist & choirmaster, Blessed Sacrament Church, New York, 50-53 & Transfiguration Church, Brooklyn, 53-58; assoc ed, Hymn Soc Am, 66-76. *Awards:* Knight Commander St Gregory, Pope John XXIII, 61. *Bibliog:* Article, Hymn, Hymn Soc Am, 10/76. *Mem:* Nat Pastoral Musicians; Hymn Soc Am; Church Music Soc; Am Musicol Soc. *Publ:* Auth, Revival of Gregorian Chant—Influence on English Hymnody, Paper XV, 49 & Hymnody in the American Indian Missions, Paper XVIII, 54, Hymn Soc Am; Mediator Del Hymnal, Gregorian Inst, 55; Handbook for American Catholic Hymnals, 76 & History of American Catholic Hymnals—Survey & Backgrounds, 82, Hymn Soc Am. *Mailing Add:* 21-10 33 Rd Long Island City NY 11106

DE CARLO, RITA FRANCES
MEZZO-SOPRANO

b Aug 15, 38; US citizen. *Study:* Studied with John Daggett Howell & David Bender. *Roles:* Zita in Gianni Schicchi, Chautauqua Opera Fest, NY, 63; Suzuki in Madama Butterfly, Marina in Boris Godunov, Zita in Gianni Schicchi, 83; Madame Larina in Eugene Onegin, 83; Frugolo in Il Tabarro, 83; Maddalena in Rigoletto, 83. *Pos:* Mezzo-soprano with Can & US opera co. *Mailing Add:* c/o Sardos Artists Mgt 180 West End Ave New York NY 10023

DE CESARE, RUTH
EDUCATOR, COMPOSER

b New York, NY, July 2, 23. *Study:* Hunter Col, City Univ New York, AB, 43; Queens Col, City Univ New York, MS, 60; NY Univ, PhD, 72. *Works:* Songs for the French (Italian, Spanish, German & Russian) Classes, 59-62 & Latin American (French) Game Songs, 59 & 62, Belwin-Mills; They Came Singing, Sam Fox Music, 63; American Tunes & Tales, Witmark, 61; Piano Games, Marks Music, 61; Music for Every Child, I-IV, Educ Activ Inc, 79. *Pos:* Music specialist, New York City Bd Educ, 66-69. *Teaching:* Instr music, Mills Col Educ, 60-62; music specialist, Union Free Sch District #3, Levittown, NY, 62-65; prof music, Ind Univ Pa, 69- *Mem:* Music Educr Nat Conf; Soc Ethnomusicol. *Interests:* Music and related heritage arts of the Cocopah Indians of southwest Arizona. *Publ:* Auth, Of Musical Translation, Music J, 61; The New Music Teacher: Guideposts to a Good Start, 74, Music in the Life of the Exceptional Student, 76 & The Gifted and Talented in the Elementary Music Class, 79, Pa Music Educr Asn News; Labeling & Its Impact on the Music Education of Exceptional Students, Pa Music Educr Asn Bulletin Res Music Educ, 81. *Mailing Add:* 545 Grandview Ave Indiana PA 15701

DECHARIO, TONY HOUSTON
ADMINISTRATOR
b Girard, Kans, Sept 25, 40. *Study:* Wichita State Univ, 58-60; Eastman Sch Music, with Emory Remington, BM(trombone), 62, MM(trombone), 63. *Pos:* Prin Trombone, Dallas Symph, 64-71; second trombone, Rochester Phil Orch, 65-71, personnel mgr, 72-75, general mgr, 75- *Mailing Add:* 108 East Ave Rochester NY 14604

DECIMA, TERRY
PIANO, EDUCATOR
Study: Oberlin Col, BM; New England Consv Music, MM; Mozarteum, Salzburg, cert. *Pos:* Pianist, Mozarteum, Salzburg & throughout Boston area; organist, First Parish Weston, Mass. *Teaching:* Mem fac, Boston Commonwealth Sch, formerly, Allegheny Music Fest, formerly & Berkshire Music Ctr, currently; head vocal accmp & coaching, New England Consv Music, currently. *Awards:* Martha Baird Rockefeller Grant Opera Study. *Mailing Add:* New England Consv Music 290 Huntington Ave Boston MA 02115

DECK, WARREN
TUBA, EDUCATOR
b Baltimore, Md, Feb 20, 54. *Study:* Univ Mich, BM, 75. *Pos:* Artist in res, Grand Rapids Symph, 74-76; solo tuba, Houston Symph, 77-79; prin tuba, New York Phil, 79- *Teaching:* Artist instr, Rice Univ, 77-79; mem fac tuba, Mannes Col Music, 81- *Mailing Add:* Mannes Col Music 157 E 74th St New York NY 10021

DECKER, GERALDINE
CONTRALTO
Roles: Erda & First Norn in Der Ring des Nibelungen, Pacific NW Fest, 75-84; Filipeuna in Eugene Onegin, Seattle Opera, 75 & Portland Opera, 81; Azucena in Il Trovatore, Seattle Opera, 75 & Hawaii Opera, 78; Marthe in Faust, Lyr Opera & Seattle Opera, 79; Innkeeper & Nurse in Boris Gudonov, Metropolitan Opera, 83; Schwerlleite in Die Walküre, Metropolitan Opera, 83; Auntie in Peter Grimes, Metropolitan Opera, 83. *Pos:* Soloist with Opera Orch NY, Portland Symph, Anchorage Symph, Seattle Youth Symph, Long Beach, Calif Symph & Am Youth Symph; appeared in Franco Zefferelli film prod of La Traviata; performer, major Am opera co. *Mailing Add:* c/o Tony Hartmann Assoc 250 W 57th St Suite 1120 New York NY 10107

DECKER, HAROLD A
EDUCATOR, CONDUCTOR
b Belleville, Kans, May 13, 14. *Study:* Morningside Col, AB, 34, MusB, 34; Consv Music, Oberlin Col, with Olaf Christiansen, MMus, 38; study with Thomas MacBurney, 41, Sydney Dietch, 44-45 & Nadia Boulanger, 53; Morningside Col, Hon Dr Music, 57. *Teaching:* Vis prof choral music, Oberlin Col, 39-40 & Calif State Univ, Fullerton, 81-83; prof & chmn vocal & choral depts, Wichita State Univ, 44-57; prof & chmn choral div, Univ Ill, Urbana-Champaign, 57-81. *Awards:* Outstanding Cond, Ecole Beaux Artes, Fontainebleau, France, 53; Distinguished Serv Award, Am Choral Dir Asn, 76; Harold A Decker Award, Ill State Chap, Am Choral Dir Asn, 81. *Mem:* Am Choral Dir Asn (pres, 66-68); Music Educr Nat Conf; Coun Intercultural Relations, Vienna, Austria (mem exec bd, 68-76); Int Fedn Choral Music. *Publ:* Coauth, Choral Conducting: A Symposium, 73 & Choral Conducting: A Focus on Communication (in prep), Prentice-Hall. *Rep:* 3300 A via Carrizo Laguna Hills CA 92653. *Mailing Add:* 1204 S Vine Urbana IL 61801

DECKER, JAMES
EDUCATOR, HORN
Pos: First horn, Nat Symph, Washington, DC, Kansas City Phil, Calif Chamber Orch, Robert Wagner Symph & Los Angeles Phil, formerly; prin horn, rec & studio orchs, Los Angeles, currently. *Teaching:* Assoc prof horn, Univ Southern Calif, currently; mem fac, Music Acad West, currently. *Mailing Add:* 1 Sicilian Walk Long Beach CA 90803

DECRAY, MARCELLA
HARP
b Philadelphia, Pa. *Study:* Univ Pa, BA, 58; studied with Henriette Reme. *Rec Perf:* Harp Aujord'hui, Coronet, 72; San Francisco Contemporary Music Players, Grenadilla, 83. *Pos:* Second harp, Philadelphia Orch, 56-63; first & second harp, San Francisco Opera, 63-; exec dir, San Francisco Contemp Music Players, 74-; first harp, San Francisco Ballet, 80- *Teaching:* Prof harp, San Francisco Consv Music, 64- *Awards:* Citation, Am Harp Soc, 80. *Bibliog:* Walter Blum (auth), Marcella De Cray, Calif Living, 9/72. *Mem:* Am Harp Soc (nat treas, 78-82). *Mailing Add:* 30 Commonwealth Ave San Francisco CA 94118

DEDEE, EDWARD A
ADMINISTRATOR
b Rochester, NY, Nov 11, 49. *Study:* State Univ NY Col, Fredonia, BMus, 71. *Pos:* Co mgr, Hawaii Perf Arts Co, 72-73; asst managing dir, Michael C Rockefeller Arts Ctr, State Univ NY Col, Fredonia, 73-74; managing dir, 74-78; dir concerts, Eastman Sch Music, 78- *Mem:* Am Symph Orch League; Chamber Music Am; Asn Col Univ & Community Arts Adminr. *Mailing Add:* 5 Lonran Dr Rochester NY 14624

DEDEL, PETER J D
ADMINISTRATOR, WRITER
b Nyack, NY, Nov 30, 48. *Study:* Lehigh Univ, BA, 70; Aspen Music Sch, 71, 72 & 74; Wesleyan Univ; Columbia Univ, MA, 73, MPhil, 75. *Pos:* Prog ed, Carnegie Hall Corp, 78-79. *Mem:* Am Musicol Soc; Manuscript Soc.

Interests: Nineteenth century sources. *Publ:* Auth, J S Bach's Art of Fugue: Dissemination and Dispute, Current Musicol, 75; Johannes Brahms: A Guide to His Autograph in Facsimile, Music Libr Asn, 78. *Mailing Add:* Summit Ave Spring Valley NY 10977

DEDERER, WILLIAM BOWNE
ADMINISTRATOR, TRUMPET
b Poughkeepsie, NY, July 15, 45. *Study:* State Univ NY Col, Fredonia, BS(music educ), 67; Univ Mich, MM(music educ), 68, DMA(music perf), 75. *Teaching:* Assoc prof trumpet, State Univ NY Col, Fredonia, 69-82; teaching asst, Univ Mich, 74-75; dean, Boston Consv, 82- *Mem:* Phi Mu Alpha Sinfonia; Int Trumpet Guild; Pi Kappa Lambda. *Mailing Add:* Lofty Pines 3 Cifre Lane Plaistow NH 03865

DE FILIPPI, AMEDEO
COMPOSER
b Ariano, Italy, Feb 20, 1900. *Study:* Juilliard Sch Music, 26-29; studied violin with Arthur Lichenstein, piano with Stanley Haschek & comp with Rubin Goldmark. *Works:* Robert E Lee (incidental music), 25; The Green Cuckatoo (one-act opera), 27; Serenade for Strings (orch), 30; Leatherneck (film score), 30; Les Sylphides (ballet), 33; Carnaval (ballet), 33; Dances of Manfredonia (12 pieces), 75; and others. *Pos:* Comp, arr & orchestrator, Pathe Films, Judson Radio Prog Co, Victor Phonograph Co & var theatres & publ, 24-30; mem staff, CBS, 30-; orchestrator ballets, Ballet Russe & Ballet Theatre. *Mem:* ASCAP; Bohemians; Am Music Ctr; Nat Asn Am Comp & Cond. *Mailing Add:* 4101 Wilkinson Ave Studio City CA 91604

DEFORD, RUTH I
EDUCATOR
b Lawrence, Kans, Dec 8, 46. *Study:* Oberlin Col & Consv Music, BA & BMus, 68; Harvard Univ, PhD, 75. *Pos:* Asst prof, State Univ NY, Geneseo, 75-77; asst prof, Hunter Col, City Univ New York, 77- *Mem:* Am Musicol Soc. *Publ:* Auth, The Evolution of Rhythmic Style in Italian Secular Music of the Late 16th Century, Studi Musicali, 81; ed, Giovanni Ferretti, Il secondo libro delle canzoni a sei voci (1575), A-R Ed, 83. *Mailing Add:* 118 Edgars Ln Hastings NY 10706

DEFOREST, JUNE
VIOLIN
b Pittsburgh, Pa . *Study:* Carnegie-Mellon Univ, 57-60; Manhattan Sch Music, BM, 60, MM, 73, studied with Rophael Browstein. *Pos:* Concertmaster, Joffrey Ballet, 66 & Can Opera, 68; violinist, Chicago Lyric Opera, 68-; asst concertmaster, Am Ballet Theatre, 69-70. *Mailing Add:* c/o Am Chamber Conct 890 West End Ave New York NY 10025

DE FRANK, VINCENT
CONDUCTOR & MUSIC DIRECTOR, EDUCATOR
b Long Island City, NY, June 18, 15. *Study:* Violin with George Frenz, 20-33 & cello with Percy Such, 33-37; Juilliard Sch Music, cond with Albert Stoessel, 34-36; Ind Univ, 50-52; Southwestern Memphis, Hon DMus, 74. *Pos:* Cellist, Detroit Symph Orch, 39-40 & St Louis Symph, 47-50; founder, cond & music dir, Memphis Symph Orch, 52-, Memphis Little Symph & Memphis Chamber Orch; dir three serv bands, US Army, formerly; guest cond, Memphis Civic Ballet, Memphis Opera Theatre, Sewanee Summer Music Ctr & various southern US orchs. *Teaching:* Music supvr, Memphis-Hebrew Acad, 69-; vis prof music, Southwestern Memphis, 77- *Awards:* ASCAP Award, 67; Memphis Symph Award, 73; Gov Outstanding Tennessean Award, 81. *Mem:* Memphis Music Inc; Am Symph Orch League; Violoncello Soc; Cond Guild; Nat Soc Lit & Arts. *Mailing Add:* 3100 Walnut Grove Rd Memphis TN 38111

DEGAETANI, JAN
MEZZO-SOPRANO, TEACHER
b Massillon, Ohio, July 10, 33. *Study:* Juilliard Sch, with Sergius Kagen, BS(voice), 55; Mt Holyoke Col, Hon Dr, 81; Calif Inst Arts, Hon Dr, 83. *Rec Perf:* Punch and Judy (Harrison Birtwhistle), Decca Head; Songs from the Spanisches Liederbuch (Wolf), Schubert Songs, Book of the Hanging Gardens (Schoenberg), Stephen Foster Songs, Charles Ives Songs, Ancient Voices of Children (George Crumb) & Chausson and Rachmaninoff Songs, Nonesuch. *Roles:* Apparition (George Crumb); Black Pentecost (Peter Maxwell Davies); Phaedre (Benjamin Britten); Ancient Voices of Children (George Crumb); Lamia (Jacob Druckman); Visions of Terror and Wonder (Richard Wernick); Syringa (Elliott Carter). *Pos:* Soloist, currently. *Teaching:* Prof voice, Eastman Sch Music, 72- *Publ:* Coauth, The Complete Sightsinger, Harper & Row, 80. *Mailing Add:* c/o Norma Hurlburt 2248 Broadway New York NY 10024

DE GASTYNE, SERGE
COMPOSER, EDUCATOR
b Paris, France, July 27, 30; US citizen. *Study:* Univ Portland,BA,50; Eastman Sch Music, studied comp with Howard Hanson, 51; Univ Md, MM, 68, DMA, 71. *Works:* Two Chansons Francaises, 68; Four Musical Moments (trumpet & piano), 69; Bassoon Sonata (chamber music), 69; Symphony No 5 (orch), 70; Cantique de Joie (organ), 72; Symphony No 6 (orch), 73; Hayasdan (orch with chorus), Yerevan, Armenia, 76; and many others. *Pos:* Comp in res, US Air Force Symph Orch & Band, 53-73. *Teaching:* Prof, Northern Va Community Col, 72- *Awards:* Annual ASCAP Awards, 61-77; Cert Merit, Nat Band Asn, 78. *Mailing Add:* Music Dept Northern Va Community Col 8333 Little River Turnpike Annandale VA 22003

DEGEN, BRUCE N
EDUCATOR, BASSOON
b Floral Park, NY, July 2, 32. *Study:* State Univ NY, Potsdam, BS, 54; Eastman Sch Music, MMus, 59, DMA, 71. *Pos:* Prin bassoon, Des Moines Symph Orch, 68- *Teaching:* Prof music, Simpson Col, Iowa, 59- *Mem:* Int Double Reed Soc (librn, 74-81); Sonneck Soc; Am Fedn Musicians. *Interests:* The life and work of the American composer, Oliver Shaw (1779-1848). *Publ:* Auth, First Lessons on the Bassoon, Fanfare, 61. *Mailing Add:* 1006 N Howard St Indianola IA 50125

DEGROOT, DAVID JOSEPH
PERCUSSION, EDUCATOR
b Green Bay, Wis, June 27, 46. *Study:* St Norbert Col, 64-66; Univ Wis, Milwaukee, BFA, 70; New England Consv Music, MMus, 72. *Pos:* Sect perc, Milwaukee Symph, summers 70-; second perc, New Orleans Phil, 72- *Teaching:* Lectr perc, Xavier Univ La, 76-, Southeastern La Univ, 80-81 & Loyola Univ, 81- *Mem:* Percussive Arts Soc; Int Conf Symph & Opera Musicians; Am Fedn Musicians. *Mailing Add:* 109 Harding St Jefferson LA 70121

DEHNERT, EDMUND JOHN
WRITER, COMPOSER
b Chicago, Ill, Feb 15, 31. *Study:* St Mary of Lake Univ, AB, 52; De Paul Univ, with Alexander Tcherepnin, MMus, 56; Univ Chicago, PhD(musicol), 63. *Works:* Pentatonic Sketches for Orchestra, Chicago Fest Orch, 75-76; For the Dead Children of Auschwitz, Jagiellonian Univ, Cracow, Poland, 75; Dance on Nine Tones, comn by TV Station WTTW, Chicago, 68. *Teaching:* Chmn humanities dept, Truman Col, 64-; prof humanities, City Cols Chicago, 70- *Awards:* City of Cracow Award, Poland, 75; Bicentennial Award for Composer, Ill Arts Coun, 76; Myth of Sisyphus, Northwestern Univ, 79. *Mem:* Am Musicol Soc; Am Folklore Soc; Am Soc Univ Comp. *Interests:* Interface between technology and culture; Polish-American folklore. *Publ:* Auth, Parsifal as Will & Idea, J Aesthetics & Art Criticism, 61; The Theory of Games, Information Theory & Value Criterias, J Value Inquiry, 67; Music as Liberal in Augustine & Boethius, Vrin, Paris, 68; The Consciousness of Music Wrought by Musical Notation, Long Island Univ Press, 83; The Dialectic of Technology & Culture, Univ Del Press, 83. *Mailing Add:* 1121 Harvard Terr Evanston IL 60202

DEIBLER, ARLO C I
MUSIC DIRECTOR, ADMINISTRATOR
b Berrysburg, Pa, Jan 2, 30. *Study:* St Louis Inst Music, BMus, 56; Washington Univ, St Louis, MM, 58; Acad Rome, MusD, 73. *Pos:* Cond & music dir, SW Fla Symph & Chorus Asn, 60-; admin dir music, Int Fest Perf Arts, London, England, 69-79; dir music, Cape Coral First United Methodist Church, 79-; assoc dir, York Music Ctr Young Musicians, Pa, 80- *Awards:* Ordre Haut Dignitaire, Acad Royale Lett d'Or France, 72; Dipl Cert Klas, Nederlands Laureaat Van De Arbeid, 72; Cavaliere-Commendatore con Placca, Int Legion d'Onore Immacolata, Italy, 72. *Mem:* Am Fedn Musicians; Fla Asn Symph Orch; Am Symph Orch League. *Mailing Add:* PO Box 1534 Ft Myers FL 33902

DE INTINIS, RANIER
FRENCH HORN, EDUCATOR
b Steubenville, Ohio. *Study:* Juilliard Sch, BS; Dalcroze Sch Music, 46-47; Berkshire Music Ctr, 46 & 47. *Pos:* Fourth horn, New York Phil, 50-57, second horn, 57-60, third horn, 60-; mem, Phil Chamber Ens, currently. *Teaching:* Mem fac French horn, Juilliard Sch, 61- & Mannes Col Music, 82- *Mailing Add:* New York Phil Avery Fisher Hall New York NY 10023

DE JONG, CONRAD JOHN
COMPOSER, EDUCATOR
b Hull, Iowa, Jan 13, 34. *Study:* NTex State Univ, BM, 54; Ind Univ, with Bernhard Heiden, MM, 59; Univ Mich, summer 68; Univ Denver, summer 68; Amsterdam Consv, Ton de Leeuw, summer 69; studied in Montreaux, Switz, 74. *Works:* Quarter Break Bit (activ), 72; Four Songs (high voice & piano), 73; Kaleidoscopic Vision: With Flashbacks (tape & synchronized swimmers), 73; Resound (flute, guitar, perc, tape delay syst & 35 mm slide), 74; Song and Light (high voice & perc), 75; A Prayer (piano, brass, wind chimes & audience), 75; Heliotrope (one or two melody instrm or voices, keyboard, electric bass & perc), 76. *Pos:* Participating comp, Bennington Comp Conf, Vt, 65; guest rehearsal cond, Civic Orch Minneapolis, 71; guest comp, Fine Arts Ctr, Univ Minn, 75. *Teaching:* Prof music, Univ Wis, River Falls, 59- *Awards:* ASCAP Annual Awards, 70-75. *Mem:* Am Soc Univ Comp; League Comp, Int Soc Contemp Music; Col Music Soc; Nat Asn Wind & Perc Instr (state chmn, 69-72); Phi Mu Alpha Sinfonia. *Mailing Add:* 404 S Falls St River Falls WI 54022

DE LA FUENTE, LUIS HERRERA
CONDUCTOR & MUSIC DIRECTOR
b Mexico City, Mex. *Study:* Bach Acad, Mex; Univ Mex; studied comp with Rodolfo Halffter & cond with Herman Scherchen. *Pos:* Music dir & cond, Orquesta Camara Mex, Orquesta Sinfonica Nac, Mex, Orquesta Filarmonica Am, Mex & Okla Symph Orch, currently; guest cond, Dallas Symph, Montreal Symph, San Diego Symph, Athens Phil, London Royal Phil, Phil Orch, Leningrad, USSR, Orch Nat, Paris, Orch Nat Nelge, Brussels & many others; cond, Athens Fest, Casals Fest, Montreux Fest, Switzerland & others. *Awards:* Knight Order King Leopold, Belgium; Gold Medal, Jewish Group Peru; dipl, Mex Soc Theater & Music Critics. *Mem:* Manuel M Ponce Chamber Music Soc. *Mailing Add:* Okla Symph Orch 512 Civic Ctr Music Hall Oklahoma City OK 73102

DE LANCIE, JOHN
ADMINISTRATOR, OBOE
b Berkeley, Calif. *Study:* Curtis Inst Music, studied oboe with Marcel Tabuteau, 40, Hon Dr Music, 80. *Rec Perf:* Several concerti for oboe and orchestra with Philadelphia Orch & London Symph. *Pos:* Mem, Pittsburgh Symph, Robin Hood Dell Orch & European Theater, formerly; assoc solo oboist & prin oboist, Philadelphia Orch, formerly; dir, Curtis Inst Music, currently. *Teaching:* Instr oboe & woodwinds, Curtis Inst Music, currently. *Mailing Add:* Curtis Inst Music 1726 Locust St Philadelphia PA 19103

DELANEY, CHARLES OLIVER
COMPOSER, EDUCATOR
b Winston-Salem, NC, May 21, 25. *Study:* Davidson Col, BS, 47; Consv Lausanne, Switz, virtuosity degree, 49; Univ Colo, MMus, 50. *Works:* Marshes of Glynn (film), Univ Ill Orch & Chorus, 54; Sonatina for Oboe and Piano, Southern Publ Co, 54; American Waltzes, Univ Ill Symph Orch, 60; Flower of Love (film), Univ Ill Orch & Chorus, 63; Concerto for Flute and Orchestra, Brevard Music Fest Orch, 65; Suite for Woodwind Quintet, Southern Publ Co, 66; Etudes for Orchestra, Ill Summer Youth Sr Orch, 74. *Rec Perf:* Flute Contest Music Vols I-III, Lanier Rec, 54-74; A Concert by the Fleury Trio, Audiophile Rec, 56. *Teaching:* Instr music, Earlham Col, 50-52; prof music, Univ Ill, 52-76 & Fla State Univ, 76- *Mem:* Nat Flute Asn (mem bd dir, 82-). *Publ:* Auth, Fundamentals of Flute Playing, Lanier Press, 60; The Teacher's Guide to the Flute, H & A Selmer, 68. *Mailing Add:* 914 Ivanhoe Rd Tallahassee FL 32312

DE LARROCHA, ALICIA (DE LA CALLE)
PIANO
b Barcelona, Spain, May 23, 23. *Study:* Acad Marshall, Barcelona; studied with Serracant, R Lamonte de Grignon, J Zamacois & Frank Marshall. *Rec Perf:* On Hispavox, CBS, EMI & Decca-London. *Pos:* Solo recital & conct pianist, Europe, US, Can, Cent Am, SAm, SAfrica, NZ, Australia & Japan; dir, Acad Marshall, Barcelona, 59- *Awards:* Edison Award, Amsterdam, 68; Grammy Award, 74 & 75; Musician of Year, US, 78. *Bibliog:* Harold C Schonberg (auth), Miss De Larrocha Rules as the Queen of Pianists, New York Times, 82. *Mem:* Musica Compostela; Int Piano Archives. *Mailing Add:* Harry Beall Mgt Inc 119 W 57th St New York NY 10019

DELAY, DOROTHY (MRS EDWARD NEWHOUSE)
EDUCATOR, VIOLIN
b Medicine Lodge, Kans, Mar 31, 17. *Study:* Oberlin Col, 33-34; Mich State Univ, BA, 37; Juilliard Sch, artist dipl, 41; Oberlin Col, Hon DMus, 81. *Teaching:* Prof violin, Juilliard Sch, 48-, Sarah Lawrence Col, 48- & Aspen Music Sch, 70-; Starling prof violin, Univ Cincinnati, 75-; vis prof violin, New England Consv, Boston, 77- *Awards:* Artist Teacher Award, Am String Teachers Asn, 75; Citation, Nat Fedn Music Clubs, 83. *Bibliog:* Joseph Deitch (auth), She Teaches Violin the American Way, New York Times, 6/22/80; Myriam Anissimov (auth), D D Connection, Le Monde de la Musique, Paris, 1/82; Ellen Freilich (auth), Dorothy DeLay, Am Arts, 9/80. *Mailing Add:* 349 N Broadway Upper Nyack NY 10960

DEL BORGO, ELLIOT ANTHONY
COMPOSER, CONDUCTOR
b Port Chester, NY, Oct 27, 38. *Study:* State Univ NY, BS, 60; Temple Univ, MEd, 62; Philadelphia Consv, MM, 62. *Works:* Declarations, Do Not Go Gentle into That Good Night & Rituale, Shawnee; Prologue and Dance, March Laureate and Chant Variants, Jenson; Canticle (three solo flutes), Alfred; & many other works for symphonic band. *Teaching:* Instr instrm music, Philadelphia sch, 60-65; prof music, State Univ NY, Potsdam, 65- *Awards:* Standard Award, ASCAP, 80-82. *Mem:* Hon mem, Sigma Alpha Iota; ASCAP; Music Educr Nat Conf. *Mailing Add:* RD #1 Potsdam NY 13676

DE LEMOS, JURGEN HERMANN
CELLO, CONDUCTOR & MUSIC DIRECTOR
b Leipzig, Germany, Oct 10, 37; US citizen. *Study:* Private studies with Pablo Casals, 58-60 & 73; Hochschule Musik, Munich, Staatsexamen(cello & comp), 61; Ecole Normale, Paris, with Andre Navarra, Lic Conct, 63; Juilliard Sch, studied with Leonard Rose & cond with Jean Morel & Jorge Mester 63-64; Univ Southern Calif, with Gregor Piatigorski, 64; Aspen, studied cond with Walter Susskind, 64. *Rec Perf:* Ives Trio & Brahms C Major Trio, Auris Rec, 79; St Mathew Passion, EMI Rec, 82. *Pos:* Cellist, New York Phil, 64-68; prin cellist, Denver Symph, 68-; mem, Pablo Casals Trio, 69-; music dir & cond, Arvada Chamber Orch, Colo, 79-; solo cellist, NGerman Radio Symph, 81-82; assoc prin cellist, Richard Wagner Fest, Bayreuth, Germany, 82. *Teaching:* Assoc prof adj cello & chamber music, Univ Colo, Boulder, 69- *Awards:* First Prize, Baglioni Int Cello Compt, Siena, Italy, 61; Second Prize, Casals Int Cello Compt, Israel, 61; Dipl, Tchaikovski Int Cello Compt, Moscow, 62. *Rep:* Konzertagentur Franz Buescher Postfach 101424 Heidelberg D-6900 West Germany. *Mailing Add:* 5000 S Emporia St Englewood CO 80111

DE LERMA, DOMINIQUE-RENE
EDUCATOR, WRITER
b Miami, Fla, Dec 8, 28. *Study:* Univ Miami, BM, 52; Ind Univ, PhD, 58; Berkshire Music Ctr; Curtis Inst Music; Univ Okla; Col Notre Dame. *Teaching:* From instr to assoc prof, Univ Miami, 51-61; asst prof, Univ Okla, 62-63 & Ind Univ, Bloomington, 63-76; prof & grad music coordr, Morgan State Univ, 76- *Awards:* Outstanding Achievement Award, Nat Black Music Caucus Music Educr Nat Conf, 82. *Mem:* Inst Res Black-Am Music (Fisk Univ chmn, nat adv bd, 79-); Music Libr Asn (mem bd dir, 69-71); Col Music

Soc (mem coun, 80-82); Soc Ethnomusicol. *Interests:* Various aspects of Black music. *Publ:* Auth, Händel-Spuren im Notenbuch Leopold Mozarts, Acta Mozartiana, 58; The Chevalier de Saint-Georges, Rev-Rev Interamericana, 78; Olly Wilson, In: Die Musik in Geschichte und Gegenwart, 79; Concert Music and Spirituals, A Discography, Fisk Univ, 81; Bibliography of Black Music, Greenwood Press, 81- *Rep:* Pat Springer 3721 Collier Rd Randallstown MD 21207. *Mailing Add:* 711 Stoney Springs Dr Baltimore MD 21210

DEL FORNO, ANTON
GUITAR, TEACHER-COACH
b Dumont, NJ, Aug 17, 50. *Study:* Mannes Col Music, with Leonid Bolotine, BM, 72. *Rec Perf:* Impressies, CBS Europe, 79. *Pos:* Concert guitarist, US and Europe, 72- *Teaching:* Fac mem class guitar, St John's Univ, New York, 73-75; private coaching, currently. *Rep:* Raymond Weiss 300 W 55th St New York NY 10019. *Mailing Add:* 604 79th North Bergen NJ 07047

DELLA PERUTI, CARL MICHAEL
COMPOSER, TROMBONE
b Plainfield, NJ, Apr 1, 47. *Study:* Eastman Sch Music, studied trombone with Emory Remington, 66-67; Ithaca Col, BFA, 69; Cleveland Inst Music, studied comp with Don Erb, MM, 71. *Works:* Four Movements for Winds & Bass, perf by Monadnock Music, 72; Quartet for New Violins, perf by Catgut Accoust Soc, 74; Endgame, Dorn Publ, 82; Fantasia for Brass, perf by Solid Brass, 83; Capriccio, comn & perf by Rutgers Univ Wind Ens, 83. *Pos:* Music dir, New Music Coalition, Plainfield, NJ, 73-79 & Solid Brass, Chatham, NJ, 82- *Teaching:* Instr trombone, Tidewater Music Fest, St Mary's Col, Md, 74 & The Pingry Sch, Hillside, NJ, currently. *Bibliog:* Liz Matt (producer), State of the Arts, NJ Network TV, 5/83. *Mem:* Comp Guild NJ; Int Trombone Asn. *Mailing Add:* 1315 E 7th St Plainfield NJ 07062

DELLA PICCA, ANGELO ARMANDO
COMPOSER, EDUCATOR
b Udine, Italy, Jan 6, 23; US citizen. *Study:* Pontifical Inst Music, Rome, with H Angles, D Bartolucci & F Vignanelli, BMus, 47, MMus, 49, DMus, 53; Villanova Univ, MA, 64; Univ Pa; Col Consv Music, Univ Cincinnati. *Works:* Hymn of Praise (Te Deum) for Soli, Chorus & Orchestra, comn by Archdiocese, Philadelphia, 71; Sonata for Flute & Piano, 80, Konzertstück (piano & cello), 81, Rondo Capriccioso (piano), 81 & Dialogue for Flute & Piano, 82, Col Mt St Joseph; Litanie Nostalgiche, Coro Candotti, Italy, 82; Dance Suite, six sets, Univ Wis, 83. *Pos:* Dir music & choirmaster, St Francis de Sales, Philadelphia, 56-61 & Diocese Allentown, 61-65. *Teaching:* Assoc prof music, Seminario Maggiore, Udine, Italy, 53-56; prof music, Col Mt St Joseph, 66- *Mem:* Phi Mu Alpha; Nat Asn Comp USA; Am Soc Univ Comp; Am Asn Univ Prof. *Interests:* Italian Ars Antiqua and Ars Nova. *Mailing Add:* Delhi and Neeb Rd Mt St Joseph OH 45051

DELLI, (HELGA) BERTRUN
EDITOR, TEACHER
b Dresden, Germany, July 17, 28. *Study:* State Acad Music & Theatre, Dresden; Free Univ, Berlin, PhD(musicol), 57; lang dipl, 67 & 68; Pratt Inst, MSc(libr & info), 78. *Pos:* Ed music & art publ, Germany, 57- & US, 60-; asst ed, Art Index, H W Wilson Co, 73-76, ed, Biography Index, 77- *Teaching:* Piano lang, music & art hist at jr sch & cols, Germany & US, 58-; asst prof, Concordia Teachers Col, 72-73. *Awards:* Clawson Mills Res Fel, Metropolitan Museum Art, 69-70. *Mem:* Am Musicol Soc; Am Libr Asn; Int Biographical Asn. *Publ:* Auth, Dances From Igoo, 68. *Mailing Add:* 408 W 34th St Apt 1A New York NY 10001

DELLO JOIO, NORMAN
COMPOSER, EDUCATOR
b New York, NY, Jan 24, 13. *Study:* City Col, City Univ New York, 32-34; Inst Musical Art, 36; Juilliard Sch, 39-41; Yale Univ, comp with Paul Hindemith, 41; five hon degrees. *Works:* Lyric Fantasies for Viola and Strings, 73; Mass to the Blessed Virgin (organ & chorus), 74; Satiric Dances (band), 74; Mass in Honour of Pope John XXIII (organ, brass, strings & chorus), 75; Southern Echoes (orch), 76; The Psalmist's Meditation (chorus & piano), 78; Ballabili (dances for orch), 81. *Pos:* Commentator, Metropolitan Opera broadcasts; comp TV scores, CBS, NBC & ABC. *Teaching:* Mem fac comp, Sarah Lawrence Col, 44-50 & Mannes Col Music, 52-; dean & prof music, Sch Arts, Boston Univ, 72-78. *Awards:* New York Music Critics Circle Award, 49 & 58; Pulitzer Prize, 57; Emmy, 64; Lancaster Symph Comp Award, 67. *Mem:* Nat Inst Arts & Lett; Century Asn; Am Music Ctr; League Comp; BMI. *Mailing Add:* Box 154 East Hampton NY 11937

DELOGU, GAETANO
MUSIC DIRECTOR & CONDUCTOR
Rec Perf: Symphonies (Haydn & Mahler), Classics for Pleasure, EMI; rec on Prague Supraphon; Capuleti e Montecchi (Bellini), Erato (in prep). *Pos:* Guest cond, Czech Phil, 75-, Prague Spring Fest & many orchs of Europe, Japan, Hong Kong & US; cond, Teatro Massimo Palermo, 75-78; music dir, Denver Symph Orch, 78- *Teaching:* Adj prof music, Univ Colo, 81-82. *Awards:* Winner, Dimitri Mitropoulos Compt, 68. *Mailing Add:* Denver Symph Orch 1245 Champa Denver CO 80204

DEL TREDICI, DAVID
COMPOSER
b Cloverdale, Calif, Mar 16, 37. *Study:* Piano with Bernhard Abramowitsch, 54-60; Univ Calif, Berkeley, studied comp with Seymour J Shifrin, Andrew Imbrie & Arnold Elston, BA, 59; studied piano with Robert Helps, 60-63; Princeton Univ, studied comp with Roger Sessions & Earl Kim, MFA, 64.

Works: Scherzo (piano, four hands), 60, Pop-pourri, 68, An Alice Symphony (orch), 69 & 76, Vintage Alice, 72, Final Alice, 76 & Acrostic Paraphrase, 83, Boosey & Hawkes. *Pos:* Recital & symph pianist, incl appearances with San Francisco Symph Orch, currently; comp in res, Tanglewood, Marlboro & Aspen Music Fest & Ind Univ, Eastman Sch Music, Dominican Col & Univ Southern Calif, formerly. *Teaching:* Prof music, Harvard Univ, 68-72, State Univ NY, Buffalo, 73 & Boston Univ, 73- *Awards:* Guggenheim Fel, 66; Naumberg Rec Award, 72; Pulitzer Prize for In Memory of a Summer Day, 80. *Mem:* ASCAP. *Rep:* Boosey & Hawkes Inc 24 W 57th St New York NY 10019; Lynn Garon 11099 Park Ave New York NY 10028. *Mailing Add:* 463 West St Apt G121 New York NY 10014

DEMAIN, JOHN LEE
CONDUCTOR & MUSIC DIRECTOR, PIANO
b Youngstown, Ohio, Jan 11, 44. *Study:* Juilliard Sch Music, studied piano with Adele Marcus, BM, 66, studied cond with Jorge Mester, MS, 68. *Rec Perf:* Piano Concerto (Francis Thorne), CRI, 75; Porgy and Bess, RCA, 76; Nocturnes (Miriam Gideon), CRI, 78. *Pos:* Assoc cond, St Paul Chamber Orch, 72-74; music dir, Tex Opera Theater, 74-76; Houston Grand Opera, 79- & Opera Omaha, 83- *Awards:* Julius Rudel Award, 71; Grammy Award, 77; Grand Prix, 77. *Rep:* Columbia Artists Mgt 165 W 57th St New York NY 10019. *Mailing Add:* 1714 W Alabama Houston TX 77098

DEMAREE, ROBERT WILLIAM, JR
ADMINISTRATOR, EDUCATOR
b Indianapolis, Ind, Apr 10, 37. *Study:* Ind Univ, Bloomington, BM(comp), 62, MM(choral cond), 63, PhD(music theory), 73. *Works:* String Quartet in A, perf by Berkshire Quartet, Bloomington, Ind, 62; Three Visions of Light, Spokane, Wash, 66; Festival Mass, Episcopal Conv, South Bend, Ind, 69. *Pos:* Mem, US Army Chorus, Washington, DC, 58-61. *Teaching:* Prof music theory, Ind Univ, South Bend, 65-, chmn music div, currently. *Mem:* Music Educr Nat Conf; Am Choral Dir Asn; Pi Kappa Lambda; Phi Mu Alpha. *Interests:* Franz Joseph Haydn. *Publ:* Auth, Introduction to the Haydn Quartets, Harper & Row, 76; The Significance of Music (in prep). *Mailing Add:* Div Music Indiana Univ South Bend IN 46615

DEMAS, TERRANCE LOUIS
ADMINISTRATOR
b Barre, Vt, Feb 1, 45. *Study:* Ohio Univ, 70; Univ Vt, BA, 73. *Pos:* Dir, George Bishop Lane Ser, Univ Vt, 76- *Mem:* New England Presentors (pres, 80-); Green Mountain Consortium for Perf Arts (pres, 77-80); Asn Col Univ & Community Arts Adminrs; Int Soc Perf Arts Adminrs; Chamber Music Am. *Mailing Add:* Univ Vt Grasse Mt 411 Main St Burlington VT 05401

DEMBO, ROYCE
COMPOSER
b Troy, NY. *Study:* Eastman Sch Music; Syracuse Univ; Ithaca Col, BSMEd; Univ Wis, Madison, MM(comp), 70; studied with Warren Benson, Boris Lazarof, Robert Crane, Burt Levy & Renato Premezzi. *Works:* Quintet No 1 (woodwinds), Tamarack Chamber Group, 78; Song Cycle (text) Anna Akhmatova, comn by Penina Schwartz & Florence Moore, 78; The Story of Beowulf (early instrument & narrator), comn & perf by Encore, 79; Four Songs for Soprano, Horn and Piano, comn & perf by Douglas Hill, Karen Hill & Ilono Kombrink, 80; The Audience (chamber opera), Golden Fleece, 82; Four Songs for Soprano, Flute and Harp, comn & perf by Lois Dick, Bernice Kliebard & Mary Ann Harr, 82; Variations on Transformations, perf by Warren Downs & Ed Walters, 83. *Teaching:* Piano, theory & comp, privately, 69- *Awards:* First Prize for Trio No 1 (flute, oboe & bassoon), Adult Comp Cont, Nat Fedn Music Clubs, 78; grants, Wis Arts Bd & Nat Endowment for Arts, 79 & Meet the Comp, 82. *Mem:* Am Music Ctr; Int League Women Comp; Am Women Comp (Wis chmn, 79-80); Am Col Musicians; Nat Fedn Music Clubs. *Mailing Add:* 5 Beach St Madison WI 53705

DEMBSKI, STEPHEN MICHAEL
COMPOSER, EDUCATOR
b Boston, Mass, Dec 13, 49. *Study:* Antioch Col, with John R Ronsheim, BA, 73; State Univ NY, Stony Brook, with Bülent Arel, MA, 75; Princeton Univ, with Milton Babbitt, MFA, 77, PhD, 80. *Works:* Of Mere Being (sop & piano), Am Comp Alliance, 74; Sunwood (guitar), Ed Musicales Transatlantiques, Paris, 78; Digit (clarinet & computer-synthesized sound), 78, Hard Times (piano), 78, Alba (flute, clarinet, perc, violin & viola), 80 & Alta (piano), 81, Am Comp Alliance; Pterodactyl & Tender Buttons, Philo Rec, 81. *Pos:* Prin flute, Orch Grandes Concerts Sorbonne, Paris, 71; dir, Cambium Music Publ, 75-; mem bd adv, CRI, 79-; asst to dir, Comp Conf, Johnson, Vt, 79- *Teaching:* Fac mem, New Sch, New York, 77-78; vis asst prof, Dartmouth Col, 78-81 & Bates Col, 82; prin instr comp & asst prof, Univ Wis, Madison, 82- *Awards:* Comp-librettist fel, Nat Endowment Arts, 79; comp fel, Nat Endowment Arts, 81; Goddard Lieberson Fel, Am Acad & Inst Arts & Lett, 82. *Bibliog:* John Rockwell (auth), Music Review, New York Times, 2/2/71; Andrew Porter (auth), Music Review, New Yorker, 4/24/78; Frank Hoffman (auth), In Performance, WVPR, Nat Pub Radio, Vt, winter 80. *Mem:* Int Soc Contemp Music (mem bd dir, 77-); Am Comp Alliance; New York New Music Ens; Am Music Ctr; BMI. *Publ:* Coauth & co-ed, International Musical Lexicon, Ed Musicales Transatlantiques, Paris, 80. *Mailing Add:* 96 Perry St #B-22 New York NY 10014

DE MOURA CASTRO, LUIZ
PIANO, EDUCATOR
b Rio de Janeiro, Brazil. *Study:* Acad Music Lorenzo Fernandez, dipl, 63; Nat Sch Music, Fed Univ, Rio de Janeiro, 64; Liszt Acad Music, Budapest, cert,

66. *Rec Perf:* Brazilian Music, Chanticler Rec, Brazil, 63; Liszt & Villa-Lobos, Educo Rec, 79; Marlos Novae, EMI Rec, 81. *Pos:* Founder, Int Piano Fest & Summer Course, Gorizia, Italy, 77 & 78 & Bartok Ens, Geneva, 78-; soloist, Brazilian Symph Orch, Nat Symph Rio de Janeiro, Dallas Symph Orch & Ft Worth Symph; concerts & chamber music recitals in North & South Am & Europe. *Teaching:* Prof piano, Pro Arte Sch Music, Rio de Janeiro, 66-68; assoc prof music, Tex Christian Univ, 69-80; assoc prof piano, Hartt Col Music, 79-, head piano dept, 84-; master classes piano, Lisbon Consv, Fribourg Consv, Barcelona Consv & others. *Awards:* First Prize, Brazilian Symph Orch, 58; Second Prize, Nat Liszt Compt, Brazil, 61; Teacher of Year, Ft Worth Music Teachers Asn, 73 & 75. *Mem:* Pi Kappa Lambda; Music Teachers Nat Asn; Nat Guild Piano Teachers; Am Liszt Soc; Brazilian Musicians Union. *Rep:* Maxim Gershonoff Attractions Inc Delmonico's 521 Park 57th New York NY. *Mailing Add:* 12 Old Village Rd Bloomfield CT 06002

DEMPSEY, JOHN D
EDUCATOR, VIOLIN
b Akron, Ohio, Jan 14, 42. *Study:* Baldwin-Wallace Col, BM, 63; Eastman Sch Music, MM, 64. *Pos:* First violinist, RI Phil, 73-78. *Teaching:* Asst prof music, Kent State Univ, 64-73; prof, Univ RI, Kingston, 73- *Mem:* Am String Teachers Asn (pres RI chap, 82-). *Mailing Add:* Music Dept Univ RI Kingston RI 02881

DEMPSTER, STUART
COMPOSER
b Berkeley, Calif, July 7, 36. *Study:* San Francisco State Col, with Wendall Otey & Roger Nixon; Univ Ill, 71-72. *Works:* Ten Grand Hosery (trombone), 75-76; Standing Waves 1976 (trombone); Didjeridervish, 76; Standing Waves 1978 (trombone); Monty (didjeridu technique), 79; Gone with the Wind, 80. *Teaching:* Creative assoc, State Univ NY, Buffalo, 67-68; mem fac, Univ Wash, 68- *Awards:* Paul Masson Comp Award, 63; Nat Endowment Arts Grant, 78. *Mailing Add:* Dept Music Univ Wash Seattle WA 98195

DENGEL, EUGENIE (LIMBERG)
VIOLIN, VIOLA
b Austin, Tex, Apr 19, 10. *Study:* Bush Consv, Chicago, BM, 29; Cincinnati Consv, MM, 32; Juilliard Grad Sch, with Louis Persinger, dipl, 38; Barnard Col, Columbia Univ, BA, 41. *Rec Perf:* Add-A-Part Series (with Rothschild String Quartet), Columbia, 41-44; also with Kohon String Quartet on Vox, CRI & Desto Rec. *Pos:* Violist, Rothschild String Quartet, 41-44 & Kohon String Quartet, 54-; staff violinist & violist, ABC, 44-54; prin violist, Orch of Am, 54-64. *Teaching:* Instr violin, viola & chamber music, Dalcroze Sch Music, 55-; mem summer fac, Southampton Col, Long Island Univ & Trinity Col, Conn; adj prof viola, Jersey City State Col; mem fac prep dept, Mannes Col Music. *Mem:* Am Fedn Musicians; Music Teachers Nat Asn; Sigma Alpha Iota; Musicians Club New York. *Mailing Add:* 165 W 82 ST New York NY 10024

DENMAN, JOHN ANTHONY
EDUCATOR, CLARINET
b London, England, July 23, 33. *Study:* Royal Mil Sch Music, cert, 50. *Works:* Skye Boat Song, Cramer's, 70. *Rec Perf:* Concerto No 2 (Spohr) & Concerto No 3 (Stamitz), Oryx Rec, 72; Concerto (Finzi), Lyrita Rec, 76; Sonatas (Brahms), Vocalise Rec, 79; Concerto No 3 (Spohr), 80 & Clarinet Concerto (Mozart), 80, BBC; Solo Recital, China Nat TV Network, 81; Virtuoso Solos, China Rec Co, 82. *Pos:* Prin clarinet, MGM Films, 63-76, Guildford Phil, 63-76, London Symph, formerly & English Nat Opera, formerly. *Teaching:* Prof clarinet & sax, Trinity Col Music, London, 68-76; prof clarinet, Univ Ariz, 76- *Awards:* John Denman Trust, Int Clarinet Soc, 80. *Bibliog:* M Livingood, Man With the Gold Clarinets, 78, J Gillespie (auth), Interview with J Denman, 78 & Paula Fan (auth), China, 81, Clarinet. *Mem:* Int Clarinet Soc. *Interests:* Discovery of lost orchestra material for Spohr Concerto Numbers Two, Three and Four. *Publ:* Auth, Denmania, Clarinet. *Mailing Add:* 1542 E Lester Tucson AZ 85719

DENNING, DARRYL (L)
GUITAR
b Palmdale, Calif, May 29, 39. *Study:* Univ Calif, Santa Barbara, BA, 61; Univ Calif, Berkeley, 61-62; Univ Calif, Los Angeles, 62-64. *Works:* Crisis (film suite for guitar), Santa Fe Film Fest, 82. *Rec Perf:* Music of Spain and South America, Pelican Rec, 76; Miklos Rozsa, 79 & Crisis (film suite for guitar), 79, Citadel Rec; Two Worlds of the Classical Guitar, Glendale Rec, 82. *Pos:* Conct classical guitarist, tours in Europe, 71, Mex, 71 & 72, London, 75 & Am, 79- *Teaching:* Prof applied music, Occidental Col, 68-; instr guitar, Univ Calif, Los Angeles, 69-76 & Calif Inst Technol, 74- *Publ:* Auth, The Vihuela—The Royal Guitar of 16th Century Spain, Music J, 77. *Rep:* New Era Conct Box 171 Hollywood CA 90028. *Mailing Add:* 6116 Glen Tower Dr Los Angeles CA 90068

DENNISON, SAM MELVIN
COMPOSER, LIBRARIAN
b Geary, Okla, Sept 26, 26. *Study:* Univ Okla, BMus, 50; Univ Southern Calif, MMus, 63; Drexel Univ, MSLS, 66. *Works:* History of Delaware (film score), comn by State of Del, 64-66; Cirrus, comn by Huntingdon Trio, 78; Adagio for Horn and Orchestra, Fleisher Collection, 80; Kaleidoscope Overture, comn by Kaleidoscope, 81; Lyric Piece and Rondo, Edwin F Kalmus, 82; In Nomine Variations, comn by Huntingdon Trio, 82. *Pos:* Music librn, Free Libr Philadelphia, 64-75, curator, Fleisher Collection, 75- *Teaching:* Instr music, InterAm Univ, San German, PR, 60-64. *Awards:* Comp Award, Sigma Alpha Iota, 49; Carolyn Alchin Award, Univ Southern Calif, 50 & 51. *Bibliog:*

Jeanette Drone (auth), American Composer Update, Pan Pipes, Sigma Alpha Iota, 78. *Mem:* Musical Fund Soc Philadelphia; Sonneck Soc. *Interests:* Black imagery in American popular music; early American music history. *Publ:* Auth, Catalog of Orchestral & Choral Compositions Published and in Manuscript Between 1790 and 1840, Musical Fund Soc Philadelphia, 74; Scandalize My Name: Black Imagery In American Popular Music, Garland, 82; contribr, Coon Song, New Grove Dict of Music in US (in prep). *Mailing Add:* 4608 Wilbrock St Philadelphia PA 19136

DENOV, SAM
PERCUSSION, LECTURER
b Chicago, Ill, Dec 11, 23. *Study:* Studied perc & timpani with Roy C Knapp, 38-41; US Navy Sch Music, dipl, 43; Roosevelt Univ, BGS, 73. *Pos:* Perc, San Antonio Symph Orch, 47-50 & Pittsburgh Symph Orch, 50-52; perc & asst timpanist, Chicago Symph Orch, 54- *Teaching:* Master classes at various univ; clinician, Avedis Zildjian Co, 58- *Awards:* Twenty-four Grammy Awards, Nat Acad Rec Arts & Sci, 71-82. *Bibliog:* James Blades (auth), Percussion Instruments and Their History, Frederick A Praeger, Inc, 70; William Barry Furlong (auth), Season with Solti, Macmillan Publ Co, Inc, 74. *Mem:* Am Fedn Musicians; Int Conf Symph & Opera Musicians (chmn, 69-70); Am Symph Orch League; Percussive Arts Soc. *Publ:* Auth, Art of Playing the Cymbals, Belwin-Mills, 63; ed, Senza Sordino, Int Conf Symph & Opera Musicians, 68-69; auth, Hunting For Your Cymbals, Percussive Arts Soc, 83. *Mailing Add:* 3200 Lake Shore Dr Chicago IL 60657

DE PASQUALE, JOSEPH
VIOLA, EDUCATOR
b Philadelphia, Pa, Oct 14, 19. *Study:* Curtis Inst Music, 42; studied with Louis Bailly, Max Aronoff & William Primrose. *Rec Perf:* On RCA, Columbia & Boston Rec. *Pos:* Mem, All-Am Youth Orch, 41, ABC Symph Orch, 45-47 & various chamber music groups, Boston, 48-60; first violist, Boston Symph Orch, 47-64; co-founder & mem, de Pasquale String Quartet, 63-; prin violist, Philadelphia Orch, 64-; solo & recital performer in North Am, South Am, Europe & Japan; mem quartet in res, Haverford Col, 77- *Teaching:* Viola, Hartt Sch Music, 47-50, Boston Consv, 47-48, New England Consv Music, 48-64, Tanglewood Summer Music Sch, 47-64, Curtis Inst Music, 64-, Philadelphia Col Perf Arts, 76-, Temple Univ, currently & Haverford Col, currently. *Mem:* Philadelphia Music Soc; Inst Italian Cult Philadelphia. *Mailing Add:* 532 General Lafayette Rd Merion Station PA 19066

DEPONTE, NIEL BONAVENTURE
CONDUCTOR & MUSIC DIRECTOR, PERCUSSION
b New York, NY, May 3, 53. *Study:* State Univ NY, Col Fredonia, perf cert(perc), 74, BMusEd, 74; Eastman Sch Music, perf cert(perc), 76, MM(perf), 76. *Works:* Forest Rain, Music Perc, 76; Concertino for Marimba, Studio 4 Prod, 79; Celebration and Chorale, Music Perc, 80. *Pos:* Prin perc, Ore Symph Orch, 77-; music dir & cond, WCoast Chamber Orch, Portland, Ore, 80- *Teaching:* Asst prof perc, Univ Mass, 76-77; instr, Interlochen Ctr Arts, 76-79 & Lewis & Clark Col, 77- *Mem:* Percussive Arts Soc. *Publ:* Auth, Zyklus; How and Why, Perc Mag, 76; Janissary Music, Woodwind, Brass & Perc Mag, 77. *Mailing Add:* 5826 NE 28th Ave Portland OR 97211

DE PREIST, JAMES ANDERSON
CONDUCTOR & MUSIC DIRECTOR
b Philadelphia, Pa, Nov 21, 36. *Study:* Univ Pa, BS, 58, MA, 61, LHD, 76; Philadelphia Consv Music, 59-61. *Rec Perf:* With Stockholm Phil. *Pos:* Cond in res, Bangkok, Thailand, 63-64; asst cond to Leonard Bernstein, New York Phil Orch, 65-66; prin guest cond, Symph New World, 68-70; assoc cond, Nat Symph, 71-75; prin guest cond, 75-76; music dir, Quebec Symph Orch, 76- & Ore Symph, 80-; guest cond, major US & Europ orch including Philadelphia Orch, Boston Symph, New York Phil, Chicago Symph, Cleveland Orch, Rotterdam Phil, Radio Symph Orchs Berlin, Munich, Stuttgart & Helsinki, Stockholm Phil, Amsterdam Phil & others. *Awards:* First Prize Gold Medal, Dimitri Mitropoulos Int Music Compt Cond, 64; Merit Citation, Philadelphia, 69; Martha Baird Rockefeller Found Grant, 69. *Rep:* Hurok Concerts 1370 Ave of the Americas New York NY 10019. *Mailing Add:* 142 West End Ave Apt 3U New York NY 10023

DEPUE, WALLACE EARL
COMPOSER, EDUCATOR
b Columbus, Ohio, Oct 1, 32. *Study:* Capital Univ, BMus(comp), 55, BMusEd, 56; Ohio State Univ, MA(theory), 56; Mich State Univ, PhD(comp & theory), 65. *Works:* Toccatina, Mills Music, 64; Hold My Hand (SATB), Lawson-Gould Publ, 69; Hosanna (SATB), Walton Music Corp, 72; A Great Light (SATB), Neil Kjos Publ, 72; Serenade, HaMar Publ, 75; Sonata Primitif, Music Perc Publ, 76; O Be Joyful, Alex Broude Inc, 83. *Pos:* Supvr music & choral dir, Toledo Museum Art, Ohio, 64-66. *Teaching:* Supvr music, Leetonia High Sch, Ohio, 57-58; dir choral activ, Dover High Sch, Ohio, 59-60; prof theory & comp, Bowling Green State Univ, 66- *Awards:* Winner, Arthur Shepherd Comp Cont, 68 & Univ Denver Nat String Orch Comp Cont, 72; Distinguished Teaching Award, 74 & Fac Achievement Award, 75, Bowling Green State Univ. *Mem:* ASCAP. *Mailing Add:* Music Dept Bowling Green State Univ Bowling Green OH 43402

DERBY, RICHARD WILLIAM
COMPOSER, EDUCATOR
b Indianapolis, Ind, Jan 23, 51. *Study:* Univ Calif, Santa Barbara, BA, 73, PhD, 78. *Works:* To Everything There Is a Season, 71 & Adoramus Te & Resurrexi, 74, Lawson-Gould Music Publ; Symphony, Royal Col Music, London, 78. *Teaching:* Lectr comp & 20th century music, Col Creative Studies, Univ Calif, Santa Barbara, 74-76 & 78-79. *Awards:* BMI Award Student Comp, 75;

Fulbright Fel London, 77-78; United Music Publ Ltd Prize, Royal Col Music, London, 78. *Mem:* Col Music Soc. *Publ:* Auth, Elliott Carter's Duo for Violin and Piano, Perspectives New Music 20: 149-68. *Mailing Add:* 1280 SE Walnut Ave #54 Tustin CA 92680

DE RENZI, VICTOR
CONDUCTOR & MUSIC DIRECTOR
b NY. *Pos:* Head, Apprentice Prog, Des Moines Metro Opera, 81; artistic dir & cond, Sarasota Opera, currently; cond, New York City Opera, Nat Opera Touring Co, Opera Theatre St Louis, New Orleans Opera & Opera Grand Rapids. *Mailing Add:* 210 W 101 St 9E New York NY 10025

DERNESCH, HELGA
SOPRANO
b Vienna, Austria, Feb 3, 39. *Study:* Consv Vienna. *Roles:* Marina in Boris Godunov, Stadttheater Bern, Switzerland, 61; Elisabeth Tudor, Deutsche Oper, Berlin, 72; Leonore in Fidelio; Fiordiligi in Cosi fan tutte; Donna Anna & Donna Elvira in Don Giovanni; Mimi in La Boheme; Marschallin in Die Rosenkavalier; and many others. *Pos:* Sop, Berne, 61-63, Weisbaden, 63-66, Bayreuth Fest, 65-69, Cologne, 66-69 & Salzburg Easter Fest, 69-73; guest sop, Deutsche Oper, Berlin; performer in operas & concerts throughout US & Europe. *Mailing Add:* c/o Columbia Artists 165 W 57th St New York NY 10019

DERR, ELLWOOD S
LECTURER, EDUCATOR
b Danville, Pa, May 7, 32. *Study:* Eastman Sch Music, BM, 54; Univ Ill, MM, 58, DMA, 68; Staatliche Hochschule Musik, Munich, 59-61. *Works:* One-in-five-in-one, 76 & I Never Saw Another Butterfly, 77, Dorn Prod. *Teaching:* Prof music, Univ Mich, Ann Arbor, 62- *Mem:* Soc Music Theory; Int Johannes Brahms-Gesellschaft; Am Brahms Soc. *Interests:* Eigthteenth century music; compositional process; 18th century performance practices. *Publ:* Auth, The Two-Part Inventions: Bach's Composers' Vademecum, Music Theory Spectrum, 81; Beethoven's Long-Term Memory of C P E Bach's Rondo in E-flat in the Variations, Op 35, Musical Quart, 83; Zur Zierpraxis im spaeten 18 Jahrhundert, Musikzeitschrift, 77; Handel's Use of Materials by Telemann in Solomon, Haendel-Beitraege (in prep); A Foretaste of Beethoven's Borrowings From Haydn in Op 2, Kongressbericht Wien 1982 (in prep). *Mailing Add:* 929 Olivia Ave Ann Arbor MI 48104

DERTHICK, THOMAS V(INTON)
DOUBLE BASS, EDUCATOR
b Charlotte, NC, Oct 7, 59. *Study:* Calif State Univ, Long Beach, with Abe Luboff, 77-80; Aspen Music Fest, with Stuart Sankey, 79-80; Calif State Univ, Sacramento, with Murray Grodner, BM, 81. *Pos:* Prin bass, Aspen Conct Orch, 80 & Sacramento Symph & Chamber Orch, 82-; sect bass, Sacramento Symph, 80-82 & Colo Music Fest, 83. *Teaching:* Instr double bass, Los Angeles Harbor Col, 79-80, Calif State Univ, Sacramento, 82- & Univ Calif, Davis, 82- *Mem:* Int Soc Bassists; Am Fedn Musicians. *Mailing Add:* 1850 Ethan Way #9 Sacramento CA 95825

DE RUGERIIS, JOSEPH CARMEN
CONDUCTOR, ADMINISTRATOR
b Philadelphia, Pa, July 16, 48. *Study:* Columbia Col, New York, BA, 69; Mannes Col Music, cert, 69; Consv Santa Cecilia, Rome, cert, 70. *Pos:* Asst cond, San Francisco Opera, 76 & asst cond & music adminr, San Diego Opera, 77-82; guest cond, Chicago Opera Theater, 1/82-2/82 & 3/83-4/83. *Teaching:* Lectr opera, San Diego State Univ, 81-82. *Mem:* Am Symph Orch League. *Publ:* Auth, L'Amore Dei Tre Re: Expressionism in Opera, 81 & Boheme's Bittersweet Act III, Washington Opera, 82. *Rep:* Calif Artists 23 Liberty St San Francisco CA 94110. *Mailing Add:* 755 7th Ave San Francisco CA 94118

DERUSHA, STANLEY EDWARD
MUSIC DIRECTOR, EDUCATOR
b Fond du Lac, Wis, Dec 7, 45. *Study:* Univ Wis, Milwaukee, BS(music educ), 68; Univ Wis, Madison, MM(cond), 72. *Rec Perf:* Music of John Downey, Orion, 76; Music of H Owen Reed, Mark Rec, 81. *Teaching:* Dir bands, Univ Wis, Milwaukee, 73-78; dir bands & orch, Mich State Univ, East Lansing, 78- *Mem:* Col Band Dir Nat Asn; Music Educr Nat Conf. *Publ:* Coauth, Wind Ensemble Literature, Univ Wis Bands, 72. *Mailing Add:* 5243 Park Lane Rd East Lansing MI 48823

DES MARAIS, PAUL
COMPOSER, EDUCATOR
b Menominee, Mich, June 23, 20. *Study:* Harvard Univ, with Walter Piston, BA, 49, MA, 53; studied with Nadia Boulanger. *Works:* Piano Sonatas (two), 47 & 52; Theme and Changes (harpsichord), 53; Psalm 121 (a cappella chorus), 59; Motet (chorus, cellos & double basses), 59; Capriccio (two pianos, perc & celeste), 62; Epiphanies (chamber opera with film sequences), 64-68; Songs of Love and Fear (cycle for high voice), 77. *Teaching:* Prof, Univ Calif, Los Angeles, 60- *Awards:* John Knowles Paine Traveling Fel, 49-51; Thorne Music Fund Award, 70-73; MacDowell Fel for Songs of Love and Fear, 77. *Interests:* Plant responses to various stimuli and measuring the results with electronic equipment. *Mailing Add:* Dept Music Col Fine Arts Univ Calif Los Angeles CA 90024

DESTWOLINSKI, GAIL
EDUCATOR
b Sidney, Mont, Nov 8, 21. *Study:* Univ Mont, MusB, 43; Eastman Sch Music, MM(music theory), 46, PhD(music theory), 66. *Teaching:* Instr, Univ Okla,

46, asst prof music theory, 49-55, chmn dept music theory & comp, 53-60, assoc prof, 55-66, prof, 66- distinguished prof, 70- *Awards:* Regents Award Superior Teaching, Univ Okla, 66. *Mem:* Soc Music Theory; Mu Phi Epsilon; Music Teachers Nat Asn; Music Educr Nat Conf; Col Music Soc. *Publ:* Auth, Form and Content in Instrumental Music. *Mailing Add:* Music Dept Univ Okla Norman OK 73019

DETURK, WILLIAM N
CARILLON, TEACHER
b Sellersville, Pa, May 15, 45. *Study:* Heidelberg Col, BMus, 67; Univ Mich, MMus, 69. *Pos:* Dir music & carillonneur, Grosse Pointe Mem Church, Mich, 77- *Teaching:* Carillonneur & adj asst prof, Univ Mich, 81- *Mem:* Guild Carillonneurs NAm (pres, 79-83); Am Guild Organists; Am Guild English Handbell Ringers; Choristers Guild. *Interests:* American bellfounding, especially the American chime. *Publ:* Ed, Bicentennial Book of Carillon Music, Guild Carillonneurs NAm, 76; auth, The Centennial Bell, 76, 1974 Carillon Scholar at the Bok Singing Tower, 76, Meneely Bells, an American Heritage, 78 & President's Message, 80, Guild Carillonneurs NAm. *Mailing Add:* 2057 Hyde Park Detroit MI 48207

DEUTEKOM, CRISTINA
SOPRANO
b Amsterdam. *Study:* Studio Netherlands Opera. *Rec Perf:* Attila (Verdi), I Lombardi & Arias (Mozart), Angel/EMI, Decca, Philips & London; Die Zauberflöte, Hamburg TV. *Roles:* Königin der Nacht in Die Zauberflöte, Netherlands Opera, 63 & Metropolitan Opera, 67; Giselda in I Lombardi, 79 & Abigaille in Nabucco, 81, Verdi Fest; Lucia in Lucia di Lammermoor; Turandot in Turandot, 82 & Catherine of Aragon in Henry VIII, 83, San Diego Opera. *Pos:* Sop with major opera co in Europe, US, Can & South Am. *Awards:* Grand Prix du Disque, 69 & 72; Singer of Year, Milan, 73. *Mailing Add:* c/o Columbia Artists 165 W 57th St New York NY 10019

DEUTSCH, HERBERT ARNOLD
ELECTRONIC, EDUCATOR
b Baldwin, NY, Feb 9, 32. *Study:* Hofstra Univ, BS, 56; Manhattan Sch Music, BMus, 60, MMus, 61. *Works:* Fantasia on Es Ist Genug, H Branch Publ Co, 71; Sonorities (tape & orch), comn by Nat Sch Orch Asn, 71; Mutima, an African Tale of Creation, World Libr, 73; Moon Ride (tape & band), Alfred Publ Co, 74; Fantasia on the New Jerusalem, comn by Am Concert Band, 76; Man You Loved to Hate (film score), Brit Broadcasting Corp, 79. *Pos:* Product consult, Norlin Music, Inc, 76-80; dir mkt, Moog Music, Inc, Buffalo, NY, 80-83; asst to pres, Moog Music, 83. *Teaching:* Chmn music dept, Hofstra Univ, 73-80, prof music merchandising & electronic music, 82- *Mem:* ASCAP; NY State Sch Music Asn; NY State Coun Adminr Music; co-founder, Long Island Composer's Alliance (co-dir, 72-76). *Publ:* Auth, A Workshop in Electronic Music, J Audio Engineering Soc, 65; Electronic Music in the School, Nat Sch Orch Asn, 71; Synthesis, an Introduction to Electronic Music, Alfred Publ Co, 76; various owner's manuals & technical manuals for Moog Music, 80-83; Moog—The First Decade, NY State Mus J, 81. *Mailing Add:* 19 Crossman Pl Huntington NY 11743

DEUTSCH, ROBERT LARRY
CELLO, EDUCATOR
b Miami, Fla, July 2, 46. *Study:* New England Consv Music, BM, 68, MM, 69; Col Music, Yale Univ, 68. *Pos:* Prin cello, Tulsa Phil Orch, 69-72, Greater Miami Opera, 75-76 & Ft Lauderdale Symph, 75-76; assoc prin cello, Miami Phil, 72-75; cellist, Houston Symph Orch, 76- *Teaching:* Instr cello, New England Consv Music, 67-69; instr cello & chamber music, Univ Tulsa, 69-72. *Mem:* Int Conf Symph Orch Musicians. *Mailing Add:* 801 Merrill St Houston TX 77009

DE VALE, SUE CAROLE
HARP, EDUCATOR
b Chicago, Ill, Nov 30, 42. *Study:* Mundelein Col, BA, 71; Northwestern Univ, MM, 72, PhD, 77. *Pos:* Harpist, Chicago Symph Orch & Lyr Opera Chicago; gamelan prog dir, Field Museum Nat Hist, 76-78, curator ethnomusicol, 78- *Teaching:* Harp, ethnomusicol & music hist, Valparaiso Univ, 72, Northwestern Univ, 72-76 & Univ Wis, Madison, 76-77. *Awards:* Charles Seeger Award, 76; Grants, Nat Endowment Arts, 76 & Walter E Heller Found, 77. *Mem:* Soc Ethnomusicol; Int Folk Music Coun; Am Musicol Soc. *Publ:* Auth, A Sudanese Gamelan: A Gestalt Approach to Organology, 77; contribr to Grove Dict Music in the US & Field Museum Bulletin. *Mailing Add:* 3750 N Lakeshore Dr Chicago IL 60613

DEVAN, WILLIAM LEWIS, JR
PIANO, EDUCATOR
b Tuscaloosa, Ala, Aug 26, 49. *Study:* Aspen Music Sch, with Jeaneane Dowis, summers, 68-82; Juilliard Sch, BM, 71, MM, 72; Hochschule Music & Theater, Hannover, WGermany, konzertexamen, 79. *Pos:* Conct pianist, US, 80- *Teaching:* Asst to Jeaneane Dowis, Aspen Music Sch, 79-82, instr piano, 79-83; asst prof, Birmingham-Southern Col, Ala, 80- *Awards:* First Place, Vianna Motta, Lisbon, Portugal, 75. *Mem:* Ala Music Teachers Asn; Birmingham Music Teachers Asn; Nat Fedn Music Clubs; Music Teachers Nat Asn; Birmingham Music Club (bd mem, 82-83). *Mailing Add:* PO Box 39028 Birmingham AL 35208

DEVARON, LORNA COOKE
CONDUCTOR, EDUCATOR
b Western Springs, Ill, Jan 17, 21. *Study:* Wellesley Col, AB, 42; Radcliffe Col, AM, 45; studied with Nadia Boulanger, Robert Shaw & Wallace Woodworth.

Rec Perf: Requiem (Berlioz), RCA Victor, 60; Copland Choral Works, Columbia Rec, 66; Requiem (Brahms), RCA Victor, 70; Paradiso Chorus (Martino), Crest Rec, 73; Romeo & Juliette (Berlioz), Boston Symph, 76; Missa Carmina (Chihara), 77 & Modern Choral Works, 82, CRI. *Pos:* Cond, Bryn Mawr Col Chorus, 44-45 & New England Consv choruses, 47-, chmn choral dept, currently. *Teaching:* Asst prof music, Bryn Mawr Coll, 44-47; mem choral dept, Berkshire Music Ctr, 53-66; guest cond in many choral festivals & workshops. *Mem:* Pi Kappa Lambda; Mu Phi Epsilon. *Mailing Add:* New England Consv 290 Huntington Ave Boston MA 02115

DEVAUGHN, ALTEOUISE (ALTEOUISE DEVAUGHN AUSTIN)
MEZZO-SOPRANO
b Compton, Calif, Feb 7, 57. *Study:* Eastman Sch Music, dipl, 77; Juilliard Sch, BM, 81. *Roles:* Suzuki in Madame Butterfly, Lake George Opera, 80; Susan B Anthony, Am Opera Ctr, 80; Third Lady, Washington Opera, 81, Houston Grand Opera, 81 & Omaha Opera, 82; Addie, Chautauqua Opera, 82; Mercedes, New York City Opera, 83. *Awards:* Winner, Int Youth Fest, Vienna, Austria, 75; David Lloyd Award, Lake George Opera, 80. *Mem:* Am Guild Musical Artists. *Rep:* Sullivan & Lindsey Assoc 133 W 87th St New York NY 10024. *Mailing Add:* 1606 Hammersley Ave Bronx NY 10469

DEVITO, ALBERT KENNETH
COMPOSER, TEACHER
b Hartford, Conn, Jan 17, 19. *Study:* NY Univ, BS, 48, MA, 50; Columbia Univ; Midwestern Univ, PhD, 75; Eastern Nebr Christian Col, Hon MusD. *Works:* Piano Sonata #1, Kenyon Publ. *Pos:* Mgr, G Schirmer Inc, 48-52; owner, Kenyon Publ, 60- *Teaching:* Instr music, Westburg Pub Sch, 52-55 & Albert DeVito Piano & Organ Studio, 50- *Awards:* Panel Awards, ASCAP; Parade of Am Music Award, Am Fedn Music Clubs, 74. *Bibliog:* Roberta Oborne (auth), Albert DeVito, Musician, Reaches Out for Life, Sun Storm, 1/82; People, Western Line, 78; Personalities in News, Keyboard World, 9-10/81. *Mem:* Piano Teachers Cong New York Inc (pres, 79-83); ASCAP; Music Educr Nat Conf; Assoc Musicians Greater NY; NY Fedn Music Clubs (bd mem, 80-). *Publ:* Auth, Chord Dictionary, 61, The Chord Approach to Pop Piano Players, 62, Chord Encyclopedia, 63 & The Modern Organ Course, 64, Kenyon Publ; contribr, Techniques for the Modern Pianist, Kenyon Publ, 78. *Mailing Add:* 361 Pin Oak Lane Westbury NY 11590

DEVLIN, MICHAEL COLES
BARITONE
b Chicago, Ill, Nov 27, 42. *Study:* La State Univ, BMus, 65; Santa Fe Apprentice Prog, with Norman Treigle & Daniel Ferro. *Roles:* Don Giovanni in Don Giovanni, Covent Garden, 77 & Munich Opera, 77; Julius Caesar in Julius Caesar, New York City Opera, 77; Eugene Onegin in Eugene Onegin, Metropolitan Opera, 80; Escamillo in Carmen, Paris Opera, 81; Four Villians in The Tales of Hoffmann, Metropolitan Opera, 82; Wotan in Das Rheingold, San Francisco Opera, 83; Julius Caesar in Julius Caesar, New York City Opera, 77. *Pos:* Soloist, Covent Garden, 76-, Munich Opera, 77-, Metropolitan Opera, 78- & Paris Opera, 80- *Mailing Add:* c/o Columbia Artists 165 W 57th St New York NY 10019

DEVOLL, RAY
EDUCATOR, VOICE
Rec Perf: On Decca & Columbia. *Pos:* Soloist, Bethlehem Bach Fest, formerly; Bach Fest, Fla, formerly & New York Pro Musica, 62-; mem, Liederkreis Vocal Quartet, currently; solo recital, opera & oratorio performer throughout Eastern US. *Teaching:* Mem fac voice, New England Consv Music, currently. *Mailing Add:* New England Consv Music 290 Huntington Rd Boston MA 02115

DE VOLT, ARTISS
HARP, EDUCATOR
b Iowa City, Iowa. *Study:* New England Consv Music, Boston, 30; study with Alfred Holy, Vienna, Austria, 30-37. *Pos:* Harpist, solo recitals in US & abroad; harp, Mozarteum Symph, formerly; soloist, Salzburg Fest, formerly. *Teaching:* Instr harp, New England Consv, Boston, 32-42, Mozarteum, Salzburg, Austria, 35-54, Boston Univ, 35-45 & Jacksonville Univ, 53-80. *Mem:* Mu Phi Epsilon; Pi Kappa Lambda. *Interests:* Alfred Holy. *Mailing Add:* Box 202 Sea Island GA 31561

DE VOLT, CHARLOTTE (CHARLOTTE DE VOLT ELDER)
VIOLIN
b Iowa City, Iowa. *Study:* Violin with Leopold Auer, Victor Kuzdo & Charles Martin Loeffler, 17-22; Longy Sch Music, dipl, 19; Univ Vienna, Austria, 30, Coe Col, BM, 34. *Pos:* Violinist, Harp-Violin Chamber Music Recitals (with Artiss de Volt), US & Europe, 44- *Teaching:* Instr violin & orch, Winthrop Col, 23-25 & Erskine Col, 26-29; instr violin, solfege & orch, Univ Vt, 29-40; head, Music Dept, Lynchburg Col, 40-44. *Mailing Add:* 114 Arthur J Moore Dr St Simons Island GA 31522

DEVOTO, MARK BERNARD
COMPOSER, EDUCATOR
b Cambridge, Mass, Jan 11, 40. *Study:* Harvard Col, AB, 61; Princeton Univ, MFA, 63, PhD, 67. *Teaching:* Instr, Reed Col, 64-66 & asst prof, 66-68; asst prof, Univ NH, 68-74 & assoc prof, 74-71; prof, Tufts Univ, 81- *Mem:* Perspectives New Music (mem ed bd, 72-); Int Alban Berg Soc (mem bd dir, 75-); Am Musicol Soc (mem nat coun, 80-83, New England chap chmn, 82-83); Soc Music Theory. *Interests:* Late 19th and early 20th century harmony & form; Alban Berg; Debussy; Ravel; Schubert. *Publ:* Auth, Some Notes on the Unknown Altenberg Lieder, Perspectives New Music, 66; coauth (with Walter Piston), Harmony, 4th Ed, W W Norton, 78; auth, Alban Bergs Drei Orchesterstücke Op 6, Vol 2, Universal Ed, Berg-Studien, 82. *Mailing Add:* 33 West St Medford MA 02155

DE WAART, EDO
MUSIC DIRECTOR & CONDUCTOR
b Amsterdam, Netherlands, June 1, 41. *Study:* Amsterdam Music Lyceum, with Haakon Stotijn & Jaap Spaanderman, grad(oboe), 62. *Rec Perf:* With Netherlands Wind Ens, New Philharmonia, English Chamber Orch, Royal Phil Orch, Dresden State Orch & Leipzig Gewandhaus Orch; rec on Philips. *Pos:* Oboist, Concertgebouw Orch, Amsterdam, 63-64, asst cond, 66-67, guest cond, formerly; asst cond to Leonard Bernstein, New York Phil, 64-65; cond, Rotterdam Phil, Netherlands, 67-73, prin cond & music dir, 73-79; founding cond, Netherlands Wind Ens, 67-71; prin guest cond, San Francisco Symph, 74-77, music dir & cond, 77-, creator, New & Unusual Music Ser, 81-, creator, San Francisco Youth Orch & Beethoven Fest; guest cond, Berlin Phil, Boston Symph Orch, Chicago Symph Orch, London Symph Orch, Cleveland Orch, New York Phil, Philadelphia Orch, Royal Opera House, Covent Garden, Bayreuth Fest, summer 79, Bavarian State Opera, Spoleto Fest, Monte Carlo Opera, Houston Grand Opera, Santa Fe Opera Asn & Netherlands Opera. *Awards:* First prize, Dimitri Mitropoulos Compt, New York, 64; Edison Rec Awards, 69 & 71. *Rep:* Columbia Artists 165 W 57th St New York NY 10019. *Mailing Add:* San Francisco Symph 107 War Mem Veterans Bldg San Francisco CA 94102

DEWITT, ANDREW RANSOM
DOUBLE BASS
b Chicago, Ill, Nov 20, 59. *Study:* Studied with Eugene Levinson & Bruce Bransby. *Pos:* Prin bassist, Omaha Symph Orch, 81- *Mailing Add:* 2508 W 88th St Leawood KS 66206

DEXTER, BENNING
PIANO, EDUCATOR
b Oakland, Calif, Mar 11, 15. *Study:* Juilliard Grad Sch, dipl, 39, MS, 49; Univ Calif, Berkeley; San Jose State, BA, 41. *Rec Perf:* Solos of Chopin, Schubert, Rachmaninoff & Gershwin & accompaniments of Bach, Beethoven & Kreisler for Columbia Rec, Nipponaphone, Tokyo. *Teaching:* From instr to assoc prof, San Jose State, 39-48; from assoc prof to prof, Univ Mich, 49-, chmn piano dept, 61-73. *Mem:* Pi Kappa Lambda. *Publ:* Coauth, Editions of Piano Music, Univ Mich, 51 & 59, Am Music Teacher, 52 & Clavier, 68; Another Look at Editions, Piano Quart, 82. *Mailing Add:* 928 Aberdeen Ann Arbor MI 48104

DE YOUNG, LYNDEN EVANS
COMPOSER, EDUCATOR
b Chicago, Ill, Mar 6, 23. *Study:* Roosevelt Univ, BMus(comp), 50, MMus(comp), 51; Northwestern Univ, DMus(comp), 66. *Works:* Direntissement (brass choir), Music Brass, 53; Texture: Organ, Harp, Celesta, 75 & Homage to Dixieland (perc ens), 76, Seesaw Music; Blues (ens, dance & actors), 81, Chorus (chorus, dance & ens), 81 & Transformation (alto sax), 81, Dorn Publ. *Pos:* Jazz trombonist, various ens, 43- *Teaching:* Instr music theory, Roosevelt Univ, 51-59; teacher, Ill Pub Sch, 53-60; prof music theory & comp, Northwestern Univ, 66- *Mem:* Am Asn Univ Prof; Nat Asn Comp, USA; ASCAP; Am Soc Univ Comp; Am Musicol Soc. *Publ:* Auth, Fugue: The Treatment of Thematic Materials, Clavier Mag, 68; Six Miniatures for Piano & Violin, *Asterisk, 75; Pitch Order & Duration Order in Boulez' Structure La, Perspectives of New Music, 78. *Mailing Add:* 664 Pine Ct Lake Bluff IL 60044

DIACONOFF, THEODORE A
COMPOSER, EDUCATOR
b Akron, Ohio, Oct 7, 28. *Study:* New Sch Music, with George Rochberg; Juilliard Sch, with Vincent Persichetti & Rosina Lhevinne; Univ Calif, Los Angeles, with Lucas Foss, Roy Harris & John Vincent. *Works:* Wind Quintet (chamber music), 47; String Quartet (chamber music), 52; Toccata (piano), 52; Piano Sonata (chamber music), 61; Piano Concerto (orch), 62; Incidental Music to Ibsen's Enemy of the People (theatre), 78; Incidental Music to Agatha Cristie's Ten Little Indians, 83. *Pos:* Recitalist, 24 preludes of Chopin, 83. *Teaching:* Mem fac, Calif Inst Arts, 47-53, Univ Calif, 61-62, Los Angeles Trade Technol Jr Col, 66-69, Mich Technol Univ, 72-77 & Northern Ky Univ, formerly; asst prof music, Univ Sci & Arts Okla, currently. *Awards:* First Prize, Comp Cont, Univ Calif, Los Angeles, 47; Young Artist Piano Prize, Hollywood Bowl, 48; fel, Northern Ky Univ, 78. *Mailing Add:* Dept Music Univ Sci & Arts Okla Chickasaw OK 73018

DIAMOND, ARLINE R
COMPOSER
b New York, NY, Jan 17, 28. *Study:* Eastman Sch Music; Univ Miami, BA(music), 53; Teachers Col, Columbia Univ, MA, 54. *Works:* Clarinet Composition, Theodore Presser, 63; Portraits of 5 Artists (violin, cello & film), 78; This Beautiful World (piano solo), 79 & Trio for Flute, Clarinet & Trumpet, 79, Gen Music; and many others. *Rec Perf:* Clarinet Composition, Advan Rec, 64. *Teaching:* Piano comp & theory, currently; teacher music, Friends World Col, 66-76. *Mem:* Am Soc Univ Comp; Long Island Comp Asn; Am Women Comp; Piano Teachers Cong Assoc Music Teachers League. *Mailing Add:* 186 Birch Dr New Hyde Park NY 10040

DIAMOND, DAVID (LEO)
COMPOSER, EDUCATOR
b Rochester, NY, July 9, 15. *Study:* Cleveland Inst Music, with Andre de Ribaupierre, 27-29; Eastman Sch Music, with Bernard Rogers, 33-34; New Music Sch & Dalcroze Inst, with Roger Sessions & Paul Boepple, 34-35; Consv Am Fountainebleau; studied with Nadia Boulanger, 37, 38 & 39 & Hermann Scherchern, Neuchatel, 38 & 39. *Works:* Symphony No 4, G Schirmer, 45; Romeo & Juliet, Boosey & Hawkes, 47; Symphony No 6, Broude Bro, 54; Symphony No 7, 61, Symphony No 8, 61, To Music (choral

symph), 63 & Symphony No 5, 64, Southern Music Publ Co; and many others. *Rec Perf:* Rec with Columbia, CRI, Grenadilla, Peters, Vox-Turnabout, Nonesuch, Odyssey-Epic & Capitol. *Pos:* Cond, New York Phil & other major orch, 65-66. *Teaching:* Comp, Metropolitan Sch, New York, NY, 42-44 & Manhattan Sch Music, 66-67; prof comp & lectr, State Univ NY, Buffalo, 61 & 63 & Juilliard Sch, 73- *Awards:* Guggenheim Fel, 38, 41 & 58; Prix de Rome, Am Acad Rome, 42; Stravinsky Award, ASCAP, 67. *Bibliog:* Madeleine Goss (auth), David Diamond, Mod Music Makers, 50. *Mem:* Am Acad Nat Inst Arts & Lett (vpres, 67); ASCAP. *Mailing Add:* 249 Edgerton St Rochester NY 14607

DIAMOND, HAROLD J
LIBRARIAN, CRITIC-WRITER
b New York, NY, Feb 16, 34. *Study:* Hunter Col, BA(music), 56; NY Univ, with Gustave Reese & Jan LaRue, MA(musicol), 65. *Pos:* Music librn, New York Pub Libr, 56-59 & Herbert H Lehman Col, 59-; co-ed, Notes, Music Libr Asn, 75-81. *Teaching:* Assoc prof, Herbert H Lehman Col, 59- *Mem:* Music Libr Asn (treas, 81-); Asn Rec Sound Collections; Am Musicol Soc; Int Asn Music Libr. *Publ:* Auth, Music Criticism, Scarecrow, 79; contribr, Music Insider, Olga Lewando, 81- *Mailing Add:* 17 Calumet Ave Hastings-on-Hudson NY 10706

DIAMOND, JODY
COMPOSER, EDUCATOR
b Pasadena, Calif, Apr 23, 53. *Study:* Calif Inst Arts; Univ Calif, Los Angeles; Univ Calif, Berkeley, AB, 77; San Francisco State Univ, MA, 79. *Works:* In That Bright World, 81, Sabbath Bride, 82 & Gending Chelsea: on a theme by Virgil Thomson, 82, Mills Col Gamelan; Dance Music, The Diamond Bridge: An American Gamelan, 83. *Pos:* Dir, Am Gamelan Inst, Berkeley, 81- *Teaching:* Lectr Javanese music, Univ Calif, Berkeley, 76-; asst prof, Mill Col, 83- *Mem:* Soc Ethnomusicol. *Publ:* Auth, From the Cross-Cultural to the Creative: Gamelan Programs for Children, Ear Mag East, 83. *Mailing Add:* Music Dept Mills Col Oakland CA 94613

DIAMOND, STUART SAMUEL
COMPOSER, LYRICON
b New York, NY, Jan 15, 50. *Study:* Haverford Col, BA, 71; Sarah Lawrence Col, MFA, 73. *Works:* Macha, SLC Symph Orch, 78; Macbeth (rock opera film), 78; Lyric Images (live electronic symph), Guggenheim Museum, 80; Journey (video ballet), 81; Beauty and the Beast (electronic medium), 82; Master of the Astral Plane, Brooklyn Col Consv Music, 83; Greatest Hits of 2150. *Awards:* Outstanding Comp, Nat Found Arts & Sci, 73; fel, Criterion Found, 77-82. *Mem:* ASCAP. *Mailing Add:* 202 W 85 New York NY 10024

DIARD, WILLIAM
EDUCATOR, VOICE
Study: Juilliard Sch Music; Hartt Sch Music; Naples Consv; studied with Samuel Margolies, Pasquale Rubino & Daniel Wolf. *Rec Perf:* On RCA-Victor. *Pos:* Solo & duet recitalist throughout Europe & North Am; soloist, Robert Shaw Chorale; performer, New York City Opera, Miami Opera Guild, New Orleans Opera, San Antonio Opera & Hartt Opera-Theater. *Teaching:* Mem fac, Miami Consv, formerly; prof & chmn voice, Hartt Sch Music, 67- *Mailing Add:* Hartt Sch Music Univ Hartford 200 Bloomfield Ave West Hartford CT 06117

DI CHIERA, DAVID
DIRECTOR—OPERA, ADMINISTRATOR
b McKeesport, Pa, Apr 8, 37. *Study:* Univ Calif, Los Angeles, BA(music), 56, MA(comp), 58, PhD(musicol), 62; Naples Consv Music, cert (comp & piano), 59. *Works:* Concerto for Piano & Orchestra, 58; Piano Sonata, 59; Fantasy for Violin & Piano, 65; Four Sonnets (sop & piano), 65; Black Beads (ms & piano), Pan Am Union Publ, 66; Thirteenth Psalm (a cappella chorus), 68; Rumpelstiltskin (one act opera), 77. *Pos:* Producer & dir, Overture to Opera Ser, Detroit Grand Opera Series, 63-71; founder & gen dir, Mich Opera Theatre, 71-; founding dir, Music Hall Ctr Perf Arts, Detroit, 73-; artistic dir, Dayton Opera Asn, 81- *Teaching:* Instr music, Univ Calif, Los Angeles, 60-61; asst prof, Oakland Univ, 62-65; dept chmn, 66-73. *Awards:* George Gershwin Fel, 58; Fulbright Res Grant, 59; Mich Found Arts Award, 81. *Mem:* Opera Am; Arts Task Force City Detroit; Cent Opera Serv; Am Arts Alliance. *Publ:* A Producer Looks At Kurt Weill, Impresario, 69; Opera and Its Future, Am Arts, 83. *Mailing Add:* 5030 Chain Bridge Rd Bloomfield Hills MI 48013

DICK, ROBERT J
ALTO & BASS FLUTE, COMPOSER
b New York, NY, Jan 4, 50. *Study:* Yale Col, BA, 71; Yale Sch Music, studied comp with Robert Morris & Jacob Druckman, MM(comp), 73. *Works:* Afterlight (flute alone), Oxford Univ Press, 75; Or, 79; Piece in Gamelan Style, 80; Flames Must Not Encircle Sides, 81. *Rec Perf:* Flute Possibilities, CRI, 79; Whispers & Landings, Lumina Rec, 81; Blowing (Neil Rolnick), 1750 Arch Studio, 83. *Pos:* Creative assoc, fel comp & performer, Ctr Creative & Perf Arts, State Univ NY, Buffalo, 77-80; prin flute, Brooklyn Phil Orch, 83- *Teaching:* Private flute, 70-; adj instr contemp flute repertoire, Manhattan Sch Music, 83- *Awards:* Rena Greenwald Prize, Yale Sch Music, 73; Bicentennial Exemplary Grant, Conn Comn Arts, 76; Solo Recitalist Grant, Nat Endowment Arts, 83. *Mem:* Nat Flute Asn; BMI; New York Flute Club. *Publ:* Auth, The Other Flute: A Performance Manual of Contemporary Techniques, Oxford Univ Press, 75; Tone Development Through Extended Techniques, G Schirmer, 78. *Mailing Add:* 10 Leonard St New York NY 10013

DICKEY, LOUISE (PARKE)
FLUTE & PICCOLO
b Iowa City, Iowa, Feb 17, 42. *Study:* Univ Tulsa, with Max M Waits, BMus, 64; Eastman Sch Music, with Joseph Mariano, MMus, 66; Ecole Normale, Paris, with Gaston Crunelle, 67. *Pos:* Second flutist, Orquesta Sinfonica Maracaibo, 58-60 & Tulsa Phil Orch, 61-64; flutist, Georgia Chamber Consortium, 79- & Colo Wind Quintet, 80-81. *Teaching:* Instr flute, Lebanon Valley Col, 72-74; instr music appreciation, Univ Ga, 74-78. *Awards:* Fulbright Grant, US & French Govt, 66-67. *Mailing Add:* c/o LDP Artist Mgt 4610 Greenbriar Boulder CO 80303

DICKINSON, ALIS
WRITER, EDUCATOR
b Corpus Christi, Tex, Aug 25, 36. *Study:* Howard Payne Col, BA(hist), 57; Univ Tex, MM(organ), 62; studied organ perf with Finn Viderø, 63-65; NTex State Univ, PhD(musicol), 73. *Pos:* Co-ed, Doctoral Dissertations in Musicol, Int Musicol Soc & Am Musicol Soc, 74- *Teaching:* Adj prof musicol, NTex State Univ, 80- *Awards:* Fulbright Grant, 63-65. *Mem:* Int Musicol Soc; Am Musicol Soc; Mu Phi Epsilon. *Interests:* Early keyboard music. *Publ:* Auth, A Closer Look at the Copenhagen Tablature in the Royal Library, Copenhagen, Dansk Arbog Musikforskning VIII, 77; The Courante 'La Vignonne': In the Steps of a Popular Dance, Early Music Vol X, No 1; coauth, A Trumpet by Any Other Name: A History of the Trumpet Marine, Frits Knuf (in press). *Mailing Add:* 2227 Houston Pl Denton TX 76201

DICKOW, ROBERT HENRY
COMPOSER, EDUCATOR
b San Francisco, Calif, May 27, 49. *Study:* Univ Calif, Berkeley, with Andrew Imbrie, Edwin Dugger, Olly Wilson & Joachin Nin-Culmell, AB, 71, MA, 73, PhD, 79. *Works:* Sampler I, Santa Barbara Electronic Music Fest, 73; Movement for Strings, Orch St John's-Smith Sq, London, 74; Peace, Shawnee Press Inc, 78; Kentucky Portraits, comn by Transylvania Univ Bicentennial, 80; Contrasts, Pittsburgh New Music Ens, 80; Entrance Fanfare, 81 & Anagrams 82, Queen City Brass Publ, 82. *Teaching:* Actg instr harmony, Univ Calif, Berkeley, 76-78; asst prof music, Transylvania Univ, Lexington, Ky, 78- *Mem:* Col Music Soc; Soc Music Theory; Am Soc Univ Comp. *Publ:* Contribr, Sun Ra, In: New Grove Dict of Music & Musicians, Macmillan Press. *Mailing Add:* 2095 Rambler Rd Lexington KY 40503

DIDOMENICA, ROBERT
COMPOSER
b New York, NY, Mar 4, 27. *Study:* NY Univ, BS, 51; studied with Wallingford Riegger & Josef Schmid. *Works:* Symphony, 61; Concerto for Violin & Chamber Orchestra, 62; The Balcony (opera), 73; Black Poems (bar, piano & tape), 76; Sonata After Essays for Piano, 77; Piano Concerto No 2, 82. *Rec Perf:* On RCA, Columbia, Colpix, MGM, Atlantic & Deutsche Grammophon. *Pos:* Flutist, New York City Ctr Opera, New York Phil & Symph Air; soloist, Comp Forum & 20th Century Innovations. *Teaching:* Mem fac theory, New England Consv Music, 69-, assoc dean, 73-76, dean, 76- *Awards:* Rockefeller Found Grant, 65; Guggenheim Fel, 72-73. *Mem:* BMI. *Mailing Add:* New England Consv 290 Huntington Rd Boston MA 02115

DIEMENTE, EDWARD PHILIP
COMPOSER, EDUCATOR
b Cranston, RI, Feb, 27, 23. *Study:* Boston Univ, 41-43; Hartt Sch Music, BM, 48; Eastman Sch Music, MM, 49. *Works:* Quartet (1966), perf by Boston Symph Chamber Players, 69; Things Heard, comn by Am Music Ctr; Caritas, comn by Gary Karr; Orenda, Theodore Presser. *Pos:* Dir music, Cathedral St Joseph, Hartford, Conn, 63-76. *Teaching:* Prof comp, Hartt Sch Music, 49- *Mailing Add:* 72 Montclair Dr West Hartford CT 06107

DIEMER, EMMA LOU
COMPOSER, ORGAN
b Kansas City, Mo, Nov 24, 27. *Study:* Sch Music, Yale Univ, BM, 49, MM, 50; Eastman Sch Music, PhD, 60. *Works:* Toccata for Organ, Oxford Univ Press, 67; Anniversary Choruses, 70 & Seven Etudes for Piano, 72, Carl Fischer, Inc; Sextet for Piano & Woodwind Quintet, 76, Symphony No 2, 81, Seesaw Music Corp; Concerto for Flute, Southern Music Co, 83; Homage to Cowell, Cage, Crumb & Czerny for Two Pianos, Plymouth Music Co, 83. *Pos:* Comp-in-res, Arlington Sch, Va, 59-61. *Teaching:* Prof comp, Univ Md, College Park, 65-70; prof comp, theory & hist electronic music, Univ Calif, Santa Barbara, 71- *Awards:* Young Comp Grant, Ford Found, 59-61; Standard Music Award, ASCAP, 62-; comp fel, Nat Endowment for Arts, 80-81. *Bibliog:* Jane Weiner LePage (auth), Women Composers, Musicians & Conductors, Scarecrow Press, 80; Zaimont & Ferrera (auth), Contemporary Concert Music by Women, Greenwood Press, 82. *Mem:* Am Music Ctr; Mu Phi Epsilon; ASCAP; Am Guild Organists; Am Women Comp, Inc. *Interests:* Electronic & computer music; music for organ; art of composing. *Publ:* Auth, Rebel on the Organ Bench, 4/81 & Fantasies & Improvisations, 9/81, J Church Music; Loneliness of the Long Distance Organ Composer, Am Organist, 9/82; Writing for Mallet Instruments, Woodwind Brass & Perc, spring 83. *Rep:* 2249 Vista del Campo Santa Barbara CA 93101. *Mailing Add:* Dept Music Univ Calif Santa Barbara CA 93106

DIERCKS, JOHN HENRY
COMPOSER, EDUCATOR
b Montclair, NJ, Apr 19, 27. *Study:* Oberlin Col, BM, 49; Eastman Sch Music, with Bernard Rogers, MM, 50, with Alan Hovhaness & Howard Hanson, PhD, 60. *Works:* 12 Sonatinas, CSMP, Inc, 81; Suite for Strings, Shawnee Press, 81; Lyric Suite, Seesaw, 82; Suite No 2, 82 & Of Mountain & Valley,

82, CSMP; Mirror of Brass, Tenuto Press, 83. *Teaching:* Instr piano, Col Wooster, Ohio, 50-54; from instr to prof theory & comp, Hollins Col, Va, 54-, chmn dept music, 62- *Awards:* Serious Music Award, ASCAP, 68-72 & 82. *Mem:* ASCAP; Va Comp Guild. *Publ:* Contribr, Teaching Piano, Yorktown, 81. *Rep:* Crystal Spring Music Publ Inc Box 7472 Roanoke VA 24019. *Mailing Add:* Music Dept Hollins Col Hollins College VA 24020

DIETSCH, JAMES
BARITONE
Roles: Escamillo in Carmen, Ariz Opera, 83 & New York City Opera; Enrico in Lucia di Lammermoor, Am Opera Ctr, Juilliard Sch; Scarpia in Tosca. *Pos:* Performer, San Francisco Western Opera Theatre, New York Lyr Opera & Bel Canto Opera. *Mailing Add:* c/o Robert Lombardo Assoc 1 Harkness Plaza 61 W 62nd #6F New York NY 10023

DIETZ, HANNS-BERTOLD
EDUCATOR
b Dresden, Ger, Oct 12, 29; US citizen. *Study:* Musikhochschule Weimar, with H J Moser & R Muennich, BM, 48; Univ Notre Dame, MM, 54; Univ Innsbruck, Austria, with Wilhelm Fischer, PhD, 56. *Pos:* Dir music, Michaelis Kirche, Frankfurt am Main, Ger, 49-52. *Teaching:* Asst prof music hist & lit, St Mary's Col, Ind, 56-63; from assoc prof to prof musicol, Univ Tex, Austin, 63-; guest prof musicol, Univ Innsbruck, Austria, 68-70. *Awards:* Fulbright Grant, 68-69; Int Res & Exchanges Bd Sr Fel Grant, 78-79; Am Coun Learned Soc Travel Grant, 79. *Mem:* Gesellschaft Musikforschung; Am Musicol Soc; Am Soc 18th Century Studies. *Interests:* Music history from mid-17th through 19th centuries; 18th century Neapolitan opera and church music; 19th century instrumental music. *Publ:* Auth, Die Chorfuge bei G F Handel, Schneider, Tutzing, 61; Relation between Rhythm and Dynamics in Works of Beethoven, Cong Report Bonn, 70; Chron Maestri e Organisti Cappella Reale Naples 1745-1800, J Am Musicol Soc, 72; Varianten in Cimarosas Il matrimonio Segreto, Musikforschung, 78; numerous articles for New Grove Dict of Music & Musicians, 80. *Mailing Add:* 2305 Trail of Madrones Austin TX 78746

DI FRANCO, LORETTA ELIZABETH
COLORATURA SOPRANO
b New York, NY, Oct 28, 42. *Study:* With Maud Webber & Walter Taussig; Hunter Col; Juilliard Sch Music. *Roles:* Chloë in Pique Dame, Metropolitan Opera, 65; Zerlina in Don Giovanni; Lucia in Lucia di Lammermoor; Mimi & Musetta in La Boheme; Oscar in Un Ballo in maschera; Lauretta in Gianni Schicchi; and many others. *Pos:* Lyric coloratura soprano with major companies in New York; res mem, Metropolitan Opera, currently. *Awards:* Martha Baird Rockefeller Fund Grant, 63; First Prize, Metropolitan Opera Nat Coun Auditions, 65; Kathryn Long Course Scholar, Metropolitan Opera. *Mem:* Am Guild Musical Artists. *Mailing Add:* 170 West End Ave New York NY 10024

DIGIACOMO, SERAFINA
EDUCATOR, VOICE
Study: Col Notre Dame, Md, BA; Peabody Consv Music, MM. *Pos:* Recitalist, Aspen Music Fest & throughout East Coast. *Teaching:* Mem fac voice, Ital diction & opera wkshp, Peabody Consv Music, currently, chmn voice, Prep Dept, currently; adj instr, Goucher Col, currently. *Mailing Add:* Peabody Consv Music 1 E Mt Vernon Pl Baltimore MD 21202

DI JULIO, MAX (JOSEPH)
EDUCATOR, COMPOSER
b Philadelphia, Pa, Oct 10, 19. *Study:* Univ Denver, BM, MME; Univ Colo; Aspen Sch, with Darius Milhaud. *Works:* Portrait of Baby Doe (opera); Boom Town (musical); Ski Run (string orch); A Sacred Service (choir & electric guitar); Reflections on the City (overture); Little Children, Listen (film/TV song); Celebration (A Festive Overture). *Pos:* Trumpeter, US Air Force Band, formerly; staff arr, KOA Radio, Denver, formerly; guest cond & arr, Denver Symph, formerly; arr, NBC Radio, Denver; guest cond, Omaha Symph, Sioux City Symph, Iowa & others; musical dir & cond, Denver Post Operas, Bonfils Theatre. *Teaching:* Prof music & chmn, Div Fine Arts, Loretto Heights Col, currently. *Mailing Add:* Music Dept Loretto Heights Col 3001 S Federal Blvd Denver CO 80236

DI LELLO, EDWARD V
COMPOSER, EDUCATOR
b Astoria, NY, May 3, 52. *Study:* Sarah Lawrence Col, with Stanley Walden, Andre Singer & Chester Biscardi, AB, 74. *Works:* Purgatory (opera after Yeats), 74; The Cat and the Moon (opera after Yeats), 74; Short Study for Solo Clarinet, 74; Crazy Jane (three songs for sop & cello), 75; Eight Short People (woodwind quartet), 78. *Teaching:* Mem fac, Wesleyan Univ, currently. *Awards:* Sandtvoort Found Scholar, 72-73; Comp Assistance Award, Am Music Ctr, 78. *Mailing Add:* 54 E 4th St Apt B4 New York NY 10003

DILLON, ROBERT
COMPOSER, EDUCATOR
b Downs, Kans, Sept 29, 22. *Study:* Univ Okla, with Spencer Norton, BFA, 47, DME, 71; Univ Southern Calif, with Halsey Stevens, MM, 49; Univ Colo, with Charles Eakin, Cecil Effinger & Philip Batstone. *Works:* Southwestern Panorama (band); Quartz Mountain (band); The Far Country (band); Four Winds (band); Distant Hills (band); Brass Quintet; Allegro Festoso (four clarinets). *Teaching:* Pub sch, Bethany, Okla, 51-55; mem fac music, Cent State Univ, 66- *Awards:* First Prize, Harvey Gaul Compt, 50 & Okla Heritage Compt, 75. *Mailing Add:* 1300 East Dr Edmond OK 73034

DINES, BURTON
CONDUCTOR, CELLO
b Pittsburgh, Pa, Apr 2, 25. *Study:* Manhattan Sch Music, BM, 49; Am Symph Orch League Summer Workshops, cond with Richard Lert, 58-63; Duquesne Univ, MM, 61. *Pos:* Cellist, Pittsburgh Symph, 50-63; prin cello, Am Symph Orch League, 58-63; asst prin cello, Fla Phil, 70-82; music critic, The Village Post, Miami, Fla, 73-75; music dir, Miami Chamber Symph, 79- *Teaching:* Instr music, Ball State Univ, Ind, 63-65; asst prof music, Miami Dade Community Col, 65-71. *Mem:* Am Symph Orch League; Fla Asn Musical Excellence (mem bd, 82-). *Mailing Add:* 7820 SW 148th Ave Miami FL 33193

DI PASQUASIO, GARY PETER
CONDUCTOR, TEACHER
b Yonkers, NY, Nov 29, 52. *Study:* Manhattan Sch Music, BM, 74, MM, 76. *Pos:* Asst cond, Providence Opera Theater, 79-81, Iceland Symph Orch, 82-83 & Opera Metropolitana, Caracas, 83- *Mailing Add:* 306 W 75th St New York NY 10023

DIPIETRO, ALBERT S
TRUMPET, EDUCATOR
Study: New England Consv Music, BM, 68; Eastman Sch Music; studied trumpet with Edwin Betts, Daniel Patrylak, Roger Voisin, Andre Come & Armando Ghitalla, cond with Frederick Prausnitz & voice with Mark Pearson. *Pos:* Prin trumpet, Portland Symph & New England Chamber Opera Co; cond, Scholarship Brass Ens; founder & dir, Gabrieli Brass Ens. *Teaching:* Mem fac trumpet, Longy Sch Music, currently. *Mailing Add:* Longy Sch Music One Follen St Cambridge MA 02138

DI PIETRO, ROCCO
COMPOSER, PIANO
b Buffalo, NY, Sept 15, 49. *Study:* With Hans Hagen & Lukas Foss, 65-70, Bruno Maderna, 71-73. *Works:* Aria (piano), perf by comp at Darmstadt Fest, 78; Melodia della Terra (violin), perf by Christiane Edinger & Y Orch, New York, 80; Bagatelle, perf by Lukas Foss & Ojai Chamber Orch, 80; Melodia Nera, perf by Jan Williams on Danish Radio, 81; Etudes From the Youth's Magic Horn, perf by Lukas Foss & Brooklyn Phil, 83; Violin Concerto, perf by Christiane Edinger & Bavarian Radio Orch, 83; and others. *Teaching:* Comp in res, Acad Arts, 81-82. *Awards:* ASCAP Fel, 71. *Mailing Add:* 350 Campus Dr Snyder NY 14226

DIRKS, JEWEL DAWN
COMPOSER
b Lovell, Wyo, Nov 16, 51. *Study:* Eastman Sch Music, with Joseph Schwantner, MM, 75, with Warren Benson, DMA, 77; Colo State Univ, BM. *Works:* Ecliptic, 76 & Elegy for Kathy's Harp, 77, New Music Ens, Redlands Univ; My Sister's Recipes, comn by Radford Found, 82-83; Aus dem Handbuch, New Music Fest, Memphis State Univ, 82; Ear-Bird, New Music Fest, Bowling Green State Univ, 83. *Teaching:* Instr, Univ Okla, 77-78; asst prof, Radford Univ, 79- *Mailing Add:* Rte 1 Box 78 Christiansburg VA 24073

DISSELHORST, DELBERT DEAN
ORGAN
b Keokuk, Iowa, Nov 3, 40. *Study:* Univ Ill, BMus, 62, MMus, 65; Staatliche Hochschule Musik, Frankfurt, Germany; Union Theol Sem; Univ Mich, DMA, 70. *Rec Perf:* Tracker Organ at Iowa, Univ Iowa Press Rec, 73. *Teaching:* Asst prof music, Hastings Col, 65-68; vis asst prof, Univ Nebr, Lincoln, 69; prof, Univ Iowa, 70- *Awards:* Fulbright Grant, 62-64; Palmer Christian Award, Univ Mich, 82. *Mem:* Am Guild Organists; Am Asn Univ Prof. *Mailing Add:* 360 Samoa Pl Iowa City IA 52240

DITTMER, LUTHER ALBERT
EDUCATOR, PUBLISHER
b Brooklyn, NY, Apr 8, 27; US & Swiss citizen. *Study:* Columbia Univ, AB, 47, AM, 49; Univ Basel, PhD, 52. *Teaching:* Instr, Manhattan Sch Music, 55-57; from instr to assoc prof, Brooklyn Col, 56-76; dir, Inst mittelalterliche Musikforschung, 57-; prof titulaire & dir music dept, Univ Ottawa, 76-79. *Mem:* Am Musicol Soc (mem coun, 64-66); Deutsche Musikforschende Gesellschaft; Soc Suisse Musicol; Plainsong & Mediaeval Music Soc; Mediaeval Acad Am. *Interests:* Mediaeval music history. *Publ:* Auth, The Worcester Fragments, Am Inst Musicol, 57; Eine zentrale Quelle der Notre Dame-Musik, 59, Anonymous IV, 59, Robert de Handlo, 59 & Firenze pluteo 29,1, 67 & 71, Inst Mediaeval Music. *Mailing Add:* Melchtalstrasse 11 CH-4102 Binningen Switzerland

DI VIRGILIO, NICHOLAS
EDUCATOR, TENOR
b North Tonawanda, NY. *Study:* Eastman Sch Music, BM, 58; study voice with John Howell & opera with Boris Goldovsky. *Roles:* Hoffmann in Tales of Hoffmann, San Francisco Opera, 67; Mefistofele in Faust, New York City Opera, 69; Alfredo in La Traviata, Miami Opera, 68; Don Jose in Carmen, Belgium Opera, 68; Laca in Jenufa, Lyon Opera, France, 70; B F Pinkerton in Madama Butterfly, 71 & Edgardo in Lucia di Lammermoor, 72, Metropolitan Opera. *Teaching:* Prof voice, Univ Ill, Urbana, 76- *Mailing Add:* 310 W 47th St New York NY 10036

DIXON, DWIGHT MITCHELL
COMPOSER, PIANO
b Champaign, Ill, July 12, 49. *Study:* Univ Southern Calif, with Halsey Stevens, BA, 71. *Works:* Genese, Ballet-Theatre Joseph Russillo, Paris, 75; Bahia, Heidelberg Operahouse, 77; Romantics, Cologne Operahouse, 78;

Four Seasons, Seattle Arts Comn & Cornish Sch, 79; Strand, Merce Cunningham Studio, New York, 80; Industrial Suite I, New York Stock Exchange, 82. *Pos:* Membre adherent, Soc Auteurs & Comp Dramatiques Paris, France, 77-; co-dir, Electronic Music Ens, New York, 81- *Teaching:* Pianist, Mills Col, 73-74 & Univ Wash, 74-75; dir electronic music studio, Cornish Sch Allied Arts, 78-79. *Awards:* First Place, Wash State Comp Compt, 67; First Place, Calif Cello Club, 73. *Rep:* Akiva Artists Mgt 1755 Broadway New York NY. *Mailing Add:* 29 Tompkins Pl Brooklyn NY 11231

DIXON, JAMES ALLEN
CONDUCTOR & MUSIC DIRECTOR, EDUCATOR
b Estherville, Iowa, Apr 26, 28. *Study:* Univ Iowa, BM, 52, MM, 56; private study with Dimitri Mitropoulos, 48-60. *Rec Perf:* Royal Philharmonic, 68 & 69, American Composers Orchestra, 78 & Center for New Music, Univ Iowa, 79, CRI. *Pos:* Cond, Seventh Army Symph, WGer, 52-54, Univ Iowa, 54-59 & 62- & New England Consv, Boston, 59-61; assoc cond, Minneapolis Symph, 61-62; music dir, Tri City Symph, Davenport, Iowa, 65- *Teaching:* Prof orch, Univ Iowa, 54-59 & 62- & New England Consv Music, 59-61. *Awards:* Gustav Mahler Medal, Mahler Bruckner Soc, 63; Laurel Leaf, Am Comp Alliance, 78; Ditson Cond Award, Columbia Univ, 80. *Mailing Add:* c/o Tri City Symph PO Box 67 Davenport IA 52805

DJEDJE, JACQUELINE COGDELL
EDUCATOR
b Jesup, Ga, Nov 4, 48. *Study:* Fisk Univ, BA, 70; Univ Calif, Los Angeles, MA(ethnomusicol), 72, PhD(ethnomusicol), 78. *Teaching:* Asst prof music, Tuskegee Inst, 75-79 & Univ Calif, Los Angeles, 79- *Mem:* Soc Ethnomusicol (coun, 79-81); Int Coun Traditional Music. *Interests:* West African one string fiddle tradition; Afro-American religious music. *Publ:* Auth, American Black Spiritual and Gospel Songs from Southeast Georgia: A Comparative Study, Ctr Afro-Am Studies, Univ Calif, Los Angeles, 78; Black Religious Music from Southeast Georgia, Ala Ctr Higher Educ, 79; Distribution of the One String Fiddle in West Africa, Prog Ethnomusicol, Univ Calif, Los Angeles, 80; co-ed, Dagomba One String Fiddle Traditions, 82 & auth, The Concept of Patronage: An Examination of Hausa & Dagomba One String Fiddle Traditions, 82, J African Studies, African Studies Ctr, Univ Calif, Los Angeles. *Mailing Add:* Music Dept Univ Calif 405 Hilgard Ave Los Angeles CA 90024

DLUGOSZEWSKI, LUCIA
COMPOSER, PERCUSSION
b Detroit, Mich, June 16, 25. *Study:* Detroit Consv Music, 40; Wayne State Univ, 46-49; Mannes Col Music, 50-51; studied piano with Greta Suton & comp with Felix Salzer & Edgar Varese. *Works:* Lords of Persia III (chamber orch), 71; A Zen in Ryoko-In (invented perc orch), 71; Theater Flight Nagiere (new instrm), New York, 71; Angels of the Inmost Heaven (trumpets, trombone & horns), 72; Fire Fragile Flight, New York, 73; Densities (chamber ens), New York, 74; Abyss and Caress (concerto for trumpet & 17 instrm), New York, 75. *Pos:* Music dir & comp in res, Eric Hawkins Dance Co, New York, currently; inventor of over 100 perc instrm incl timbre piano. *Teaching:* Mem fac, NY Univ, formerly, New Sch Social Res, formerly & Found Mod Dance, 68- *Awards:* Nat Inst Arts & Lett Award, 66; BMI-Thorne Fel, 72; Nat Endowment Arts Grant, 78. *Bibliog:* John Gruen (auth), L D Surfacing, Vogue, 10/70; Allen Hughes (auth), And Miss D Experiments—a Lot, Time Mag, 3/7/71; Musician of the Month, Hi Fidelity-Musical Am, 6/75. *Publ:* Auth, Notes on New Music for the Dance, Dance Observer, 11/57; A New Folder (poetry), 69; coauth (with F S C Northrup), article on philosophical aesthetics, Main Currents, 70. *Mailing Add:* 107 W 10th St New York NY 10011

DOBBS, MATTIWILDA
SOPRANO, EDUCATOR
b Atlanta, Ga. *Study:* Spelman Col, BA, 46; studied voice with Lotte Leonard, 46-50; Teachers Col, Columbia Univ, MA, 48; Mannes Col Music, 48-49; Berkshire Music Ctr, 49; studied French music with Pierre Bernac, 50-52. *Works:* Italian Girl in Algiers, La Scala, 53. *Pos:* Appearances with maj opera co in US & Europe; conct tours throughout US, Europe, Australia, Israel & USSR. *Teaching:* Prof voice, Univ Tex, Austin, 73-74 & Howard Univ, currently; artist in res, Spelman Col, 74-75. *Awards:* Second Prize, Marian Anderson Awards, 47; John Hay Whitney Fel, Paris, 50; First Prize, Int Compt, Geneva, 51. *Rep:* Joanne Rile Mgt Box 27539 Philadelphia PA 19118. *Mailing Add:* Dept Music Howard Univ Washington DC 20059

DOBELLE, BEATRICE
SOPRANO, EDUCATOR
b Brooklyn, NY, Feb 4, 32. *Study:* Hartt Col Music; Curtis Inst Music; Manhattan Sch Music. *Rec Perf:* Hello, America, Tikva Rec, 61. *Roles:* Amahl and the Night Visitors, Ulm, Germany, 64; Aida in Aida, Riverside Opera, Calif, 69; Carmen in Carmen, Cavalleria Rusticana, I Pagliacci, Aida in Aida & Tosca in Tosca, Israel Nat Opera, 70-72; Rosalinde & Orlofsky in Die Fledermaus, Germany, Belgium, Holland & Schlate Agency, Salzburg, Austria, 82. *Pos:* Leading sop, Ulm Opera House, Germany, 54 & Israel Nat Opera, 70-72. *Teaching:* Prof voice, Boston Consv Music, 77-; lectr bel canto, Braun Univ, 83, Nat Asn Teachers Singing, 83 & Boston Consv Music, 83. *Awards:* Fuller Brush Award, Hartt Col Music, 49; Curtis Award, Curtis Inst Music, 50; Scholar, Univ Fla, Gainesville, 79. *Mem:* Am Guild Musical Artists; Actors Equity Asn; Nat Asn Teachers Singing; Int Asn Experimental Res Singing. *Publ:* Contribr, Trichordon—Use of Belting or Not, Boston Consv Music, 79. *Mailing Add:* 11 New Whitney St Boston MA 02115

DODD, KIT STANLEY
VIOLA, EDUCATOR
b Eugene, Ore, July 31, 55. *Study:* Univ Oregon, BM, 77; Wichita State Univ, MM, 79. *Pos:* Asst prin violist, Eugene Symph Orch, 73-77 & Wichita Symph Orch, 77-81; acting asst prin violist, Syracuse Symph Orch, 81-; prin violist & soloist, Syracuse Camerata, 82- *Teaching:* Instr viola, Wichita State Univ, 79-80. *Awards:* Cong Strings, Am Fedn Musicians, 73. *Mem:* Am Fedn Musicians; Syracuse Symph Orch Comt. *Mailing Add:* 400 Tyler Terr Liverpool NY 13088

DODGE, CHARLES M
COMPOSER, EDUCATOR
b Ames, Iowa, June 5, 42. *Study:* Univ Iowa, BA, 64; Columbia Univ, MA, 66, DMA, 70. *Works:* Earth's Magnetic Field, Nonesuch Rec Comn, 70; Speech Songs, 72 & In Celebration, 75, CRI; Palinode for Computer and Orchestra, Am Comp Orch Comn, 76; Cascando, CRI, 78; Any Resemblance Is Purely Coincidental, Folkways Rec, 80; He Met Her in the Park, Swedish Nat Radio Comn, 83. *Pos:* Res visitor, Bell Lab, 71-77. *Teaching:* Asst prof music, Columbia Univ, 70-77; vis res musician, Ctr Music Experiment, Univ Calif, San Diego, 74; assoc prof, Brooklyn Col, City Univ New York, 77-80, prof, 80-; vis comp in res comput music, Mass Inst Technol, summers, 79-82; comp in res, Bowdoin Summer Music Fest, 83. *Awards:* BMI Awards, 63, 64, 66 & 67; Bearns Prize, Columbia Univ, 64 & 67; Citation, Am Acad & Inst Arts & Lett, 75. *Bibliog:* Paul Griffiths (auth), A Guide to Electronic Music, Thames & Hudson, 79; Barry Shrader (auth), Introduction to Electro-Acoustic Music, Prentice-Hall, 82. *Mem:* Am Comp Alliance (pres, 71-75); Am Music Ctr (pres, 79-82). *Publ:* Coauth, Computer Music: Synthesis, Composition and Performance, Longman Inc (in prep); contribr, Computer Music, MIT Press (in prep). *Mailing Add:* 56 Garden Pl Brooklyn NY 11201

DODSON, GLENN
TROMBONE, EDUCATOR
b Berwick, Pa. *Study:* Curtis Inst Music, with Charles Gusikoff. *Pos:* Trombone soloist, US Marine Band, formerly; prin trombonist, New Orleans Symph, 56-65 & Philadelphia Orch, 68-; asst first trombonist, Chicago Symph Orch, 65-68. *Teaching:* Mem fac trombone, Curtis Inst Music, 69- *Mailing Add:* Curtis Inst Music 1726 Locust St Philadelphia PA 19103

DOHNANYI, CHRISTOPH VON
ADMINISTRATOR, CONDUCTOR & MUSIC DIRECTOR
b Berlin, Germany, Sept 8, 29. *Study:* Law Sch, Univ Munich, 47; Musikhochschule, Munich, 48; Fla State Univ, 51; Berkshire Music Ctr, 52. *Rec Perf:* Five Symphonies (Mendelssohn), Wozzeck & Lulu (Berg), Salome (Strauss), Erwartung, Six Songs & Op 8, (Schoenberg) & Petrouchka Suite (Stravinsky), London Rec. *Pos:* Coach & cond, Frankfurt Opera, Germany, 52-57; music dir & cond, Lübeck, 57-63 & Kassel, Germany, 63-66; prin cond, Cologne Radio, 64-69; music dir, Frankfurt Munic Theaters, 68-78; artistic dir & prin cond, Hamburg State Opera, 78-; music dir-designate, Cleveland Orch, 84-; guest cond, Chicago Symph, NY Phil, San Francisco Opera, Metropolitan Opera, Munich, Milan, Berlin, Vienna & Salzburg Fest. *Awards:* Richard Strauss Prize Comp & Cond. *Rep:* Colbert Artist Mgt Inc 111 W 57th St New York NY 10019. *Mailing Add:* Severance Hall 11001 Euclid Ave Cleveland OH 44106

DOKTOR, PAUL KARL
VIOLA, EDUCATOR
b Vienna, Austria, Mar 28, 19. *Study:* Vienna State Acad Music, dipl, 38; studied with Karl Doktor. *Rec Perf:* Sonatas & concertos by Brahms, Bach, Hindemith, Walton & others. *Pos:* Solo violist, Col Musicum Zuerich, 40-47; mem, Busch Chamber Orch; second viola, Busch Quintet; founder, New York String Sextet, Rococo Ens & Doktor String Trio. *Teaching:* Instr music, Univ Mich, 48-51, Mannes Col Music, 52-, NY Univ, 68- & Juilliard Sch, 71-; guest prof, Inst Hautes Etudes Musicals, Switzerland, 73. *Awards:* Unanimous First Prize, Geneva Int Music Compt, 42; Artist Teacher of Year, Am String Teachers Asn, 77. *Mem:* Am String Teachers Asn; Bohemians. *Mailing Add:* 215 W 88th St New York NY 10024

DOLLITZ, GRETE FRANKE
GUITAR, TEACHER
b Kalden Kirchen, Germany, June 12, 24; US citizen. *Study:* Hunter Col, City Univ New York, BA, 46; Univ NC, cert, 69. *Pos:* Producer, writer & announcer, An Hour with the Guitar, WRFK-FM, 77- *Teaching:* Instr, Va Commonwealth Univ, 70-75, St Gertrude's High Sch, Richmond, Va, 79-82, Va Union Univ, 79- & St Catherine's Sch, 80- *Mailing Add:* 2305 Norman Ave Richmond VA 23228

DOMBOURIAN-EBY, ZARTOUHI
FLUTE & PICCOLO
b New Orleans, La, May 28, 54. *Study:* La State Univ, Baton Rouge, BA, 75; La State Univ, MM, 77; studied with Albert Tipton, 77-78; Northwestern Univ, currently. *Pos:* Second flute, Baton Rouge Symph, 73-77; second flute & piccolo, New Orleans Pops Orch, 73-79; prin flute, Civic Orch Chicago, 78-81; prin piccolo & utility flute, Colo Phil, 80; substitute flute & piccolo, Chicago Symph Orch, 80-82; prin piccolo & third flute, Seattle Symph Orch, 82- *Teaching:* Instr music, La State Univ, Baton Rouge, 78; affil artist flute & woodwind quintet, Pacific Lutheran Univ, 82- *Awards:* Orch Audition Second Prize, Nat Flute Asn, 81. *Mem:* Nat Flute Asn; Nat Asn Col Wind & Perc Instr; Seattle Flute Soc. *Interests:* Piccolo in 19th century orchestration. *Publ:* Ed, Flute Talk, Instrumentalist, 81-82. *Mailing Add:* 3222 13th Ave W Seattle WA 98119

DOMBROWSKI, STANLEY
VIOLIN

b Greensburg, Pa, May 7, 32. *Study:* New England Consv Music, BM, 54; Paris Consv; Berkshire Music Ctr, 51-55; studied with R Burgin, W Kroll, R Possett, J Calvert & I Markevitch. *Pos:* Sonata recital & chamber music conct performer, Northeast US & France; mem, Pittsburgh Symph, 58- *Awards:* George Whitefield Chadwick Gold Medal, 54. *Mem:* Int Conf Symph & Opera Musicians; Pittsburgh Musical Soc; Pi Kappa Lambda. *Publ:* Contribr to Senza Sordino, Int Conf Symph & Opera Musicians. *Mailing Add:* RD 1 New Kensington PA 15608

DOMINGO, PLACIDO
TENOR

b Madrid, Spain, Jan 21, 41. *Study:* Royal Northern Col Music, England, hon doctorate, 80. *Rec Perf:* Trovatore, RCA, 69; Don Carlo, Angel, 70; Toscas, RCA & Angel, 72; Manon Lescaut, Angel, 72; Andrea Chenier, RCA, 76; Otello, RCA, 78; Luisa Miller, Deutsche Grammophon, 79. *Roles:* Otello in Otello, Hamburg Staatsoper, Metropolitan Opera, Covent Garden, La Scala & Vienna Staatsoper; Hoffmann in The Tales of Hoffmann, Covent Garden & Metropolitan Opera; Don Jose in Carmen, Covent Garden, Vienna Staatsoper & Metropolitan Opera; Riccardo in Masked Ball, Covent Garden & Metropolitan Opera; Des Grieux in Manon Lescaut, Metropolitan Opera, La Scala, Munich Staatsoper & Arena Verona; Werther in Werther, Metropolitan Opera & Munich Staatsoper; Calaf in Turandot, Arena Verona & Metropolitan Opera. *Awards:* Medaille Arts Et Lett, France, 81; Fel, Royal Col Music, London, 82. *Mailing Add:* c/o Eric Semon Assoc Inc 111 W 57th St New York NY 10019

DOMINICK, LISA ROBINSON
WRITER, EDUCATOR

b Pittsburg, Tex, Apr 22, 52. *Study:* Loyola Univ of South, BMus, 76, MMus, 77; La State Univ. *Teaching:* Instr music hist, piano & class piano, Loyola Univ of South, 78- *Mem:* Am Musicol Soc; Soc Ethnomusicol; Col Music Soc; Nat Guild Piano Teachers; Int Webern Soc. *Interests:* Twentieth century Dutch music; 20th century western composers influenced by the East. *Publ:* Auth, The Music of Tom deLeeuw, 1977-1983, Key Notes, 83; The Eighteenth Annual Festival-Conference of the American Society of University Composers: The Composer in the University Revisited, Perspectives of New Music, 83; The Music of Tom de Leeuw, Bohn, Scheltema & Holkema (in prep). *Mailing Add:* Col Music Loyola Univ 6363 St Charles Ave New Orleans LA 70118

DONAHUE, CHRISTINE (HELEN)
SOPRANO

b Dallas, Pa, Jan 2, 53. *Study:* Wilkes Col, BS(music educ), 74; Juilliard Sch Music, MM(voice & opera), 77; Univ Houston, 77-80. *Roles:* Rosina in Barber of Seville, 80 & Cio Cio San in Madame Butterfly, 80, Tex Opera Theater; Marguerite in Faust, Youngstown Ohio Symph Soc, 81; Countess in Marriage of Figaro, Hinsdale Opera Theater, 82; Lucia in Lucia di Lammermoor, Opera Del, 82; Violetta in La Traviata, Cleveland Opera, 82; Governess in Turn of the Screw, Asolo Opera Theater, Sarsota Fla, 83. *Pos:* Singer, Houston Opera Studio, 77-80. *Awards:* Second Pl, Metropolitan Opera Nat Auditions, 77 & Marcella Sembrich Vocal Compt, 77; Rockefeller Fund Music Grant, 81. *Mem:* Am Guild Musical Artists. *Rep:* Lew & Benson Moreau-Neret Inc 204 W 10th St New York NY 10014. *Mailing Add:* 111 W 68th St New York NY 10023

DONAKOWSKI, CONRAD LOUIS
EDUCATOR, WRITER

b Detroit, Mich, Mar 13, 36. *Study:* Palestrina Inst Music, dipl, 54; Xavier Univ, BA, 58; Columbia Univ, PhD, 69. *Pos:* Dir music, St Thomas Church, East Lansing, Mich, 78- *Teaching:* Prof musicol, Mich State Univ, 66-, asst dean, 79- *Awards:* Rockefeller Grant, 69; Nat Endowment for Humanities Grant, 73; Bicentennial Artist Prize, Ohio Hist Asn, 76. *Mem:* Am Musicol Soc; Am Guild Organists (bd dir, Lansing Chap, 78-80). *Interests:* Romanticism; relations between music, history and religion. *Publ:* Auth, A Muse for the Masses: Ritual and Music in an Age of Democratic Revolution, Univ Chicago Press, 77; fifteen articles in Program Notes, 77-80; coauth, Music in the Napoleonic Era, In: Dict of the Napoleonic Era, Greenwood. *Mailing Add:* 4573 Keweenaw Dr Okemos MI 48864

DONATH, HELEN
SOPRANO

b Corpus Christi, Tex, July 10, 40. *Study:* Del Mar Col, Tex; studied with Carl Duckwall, Paola Nevikova & Klaus Donath. *Rec Perf:* On Angel, Philips, London, Deutsche Grammophon, Nonesuch & Eurodisc. *Roles:* Inez in Il Trovatore, Cologne Opera, 62; Pamina in Die Zauberflöte; Zerlina in Don Giovanni; Eva in Die Meistersinger; Sophie in Der Rosenkavalier; Susanna in Le Nozze di Figaro; Micaëla in Carmen. *Pos:* Sop, Cologne Opera House, 62, Hanover Opera House, 63-68 & Bayerische Staatsoper, Munich, 68-72; guest singer, Vienna Staatsoper, La Scala, Milan, San Francisco Opera & others; conct soloist, Europe & US. *Awards:* Pope Paul Medal; Salzburg 50 Yr Anniversary Medal; Deutsche Schallplattenpreis. *Mailing Add:* c/o Colbert Artists Mgt 111 W 57th St New York NY 10019

DONATO, ANTHONY
COMPOSER, VIOLIN

b Prague, Nebr, Mar 8, 09. *Study:* Eastman Sch Music, BMus, 31, MMus, 37, PhD, 47; violin study with Gustave Tinlot, comp with Howard Hanson, Bernard Rogers & Edward Royce, cond with Eugene Goosens. *Works:* Quintet for Winds, New York Wind Quintet, Univ Iowa Quintet & others, 53;

Solitude in the City, comn by Thor Johnson, 54; Sinfonietta No 2, Chicago Symph, Nat Gallery Orch & Peninsula Fest Orch, 59; Centennial Ode, Chicago Symph, Omaha Symph & others, 67; String Quartet No 1, comn by Roth Quartet; String Quartet No 3, La Salle, Fine Arts, Eastman & other quartets; Quartet No 4, comn by Chicago Union League Club. *Pos:* Mem, Rochester Phil Orch, 27-31 & Hochstein Quartet, 29-31; solo appearances throughout east, midwest & southwest with various chamber orgn; cond, Northwestern Univ Chamber Orch, 47-58. *Teaching:* Head violin dept, Drake Univ, 31-37, Iowa State Teachers Col, 37-39 & Univ Tex, Austin, 39-46; prof theory & comp, Northwestern Univ, 47-76. *Awards:* Fulbright Award, 52-53; Huntington Hartford Found Fel, 61. *Publ:* Auth, Preparing Music Manuscript, Prentice-Hall, 63. *Mailing Add:* 6915 10th Ave W Bradenton FL 33529

DONOVAN, JACK P
EDUCATOR, ADMINISTRATOR

b Omaha, Nebr, July 5, 20. *Study:* Univ Nebr, BSc(educ), 42, MMus, 47; Teachers Col, Columbia Univ, 50-51; Univ Southern Miss, PhD, 67. *Teaching:* Music supvr & choral music teacher, York City Sch, Nebr, 49-52; choral music teacher, Cedar Rapids City Sch, Iowa, 52-53; prof & chmn music dept, Valley City State Col, 53-67; prof & coordr grad studies, Univ Southern Miss, 67- *Mem:* Music Educr Nat Conf; Am Choral Dir Asn. *Mailing Add:* Sch Music Univ Southern Miss Hattiesburg MS 39401

DONOVAN-JEFFRY, PEGGY (MARGARET)
EDUCATOR, DIRECTOR—OPERA

b San Francisco, Calif. *Study:* Univ Calif, Berkeley, BA, 55, MA(hist), 59, Royal Acad Music, London, LRAM(piano & piano accompaniment), 57; Stanford Univ, DMA(cond & opera), 64. *Pos:* Music & stage dir, San Francisco Talent Bank, 60-72; guest music dir & cond, West Bay Opera, 62-63 & 80-81; guest stage dir, Goldovsky Wrkshps, 63-78. *Teaching:* Music dir opera wrkshp, Univ Calif, Berkeley, 60-61; prof music & dir opera theatre, Sonoma State Univ, 64- *Mem:* Nat Opera Asn (reg dir, 66-68); Cent Opera Serv. *Publ:* Contribr, Bayreuth: The Early Years, Cambridge, 80. *Mailing Add:* 16 S Green Larkspur CA 94939

DOOLEY, WILLIAM EDWARD
BASS-BARITONE

b Modesto, Calif, Sept 9, 32. *Study:* Eastman Sch Music, BA, 54; Acad Music, Munich, 56-57; studied with Lucy Lee Call & Viktoria Vita Prestel. *Rec Perf:* For RCA Victor. *Roles:* Rodrigo in Don Carlo, Heidelberg Opera, 57-59; Krapp in Krapp's Last Tape, Bielefield Opera, 63; Apollo in Orestie, 63 & Cortez in Montezuma, 64, Deutsche Oper Berlin; Don Pizarro in Fidelio; Guglielmo & Don Alfonso in Cosi fan tutte; and many others. *Pos:* Bass-baritone, Heidelberg Opera, WGermany, 57-59; Bielefeld Opera, WGermany, 59-62, Deutsche Oper Berlin, WGermany, 59-62, Metropolitan Opera, 63-, Salzburg Fest, Austria, 64-, Santa Fe Opera, 69-, Vienna Staats Opera, 76- & Florence May Fest, 77. *Awards:* Best Singer Award, Theatre Nations, Paris, 61; Berlin Cult Award, 64; Kammersänger, Berlin Senate, 70. *Mailing Add:* c/o Columbia Artists Mgt W 57th St New York NY 10019

DOPPMANN, WILLIAM GEORGE
PIANO, COMPOSER

b Springfield, Mass, Oct 10, 34. *Study:* Cincinnati Consv Music, studied piano with Robert Goldsand, 41-51; Univ Mich, studied comp with Ross Lee Finney, BMus, 56, piano with Benning Dexter, MMus, 58. *Works:* Evensong (violin solo), Charles Treger, 63; Early Lightmusic, 76; Rikki (children's ballet), Ballet Tacoma, 82; Distances From a Remembered Ground, perf by comp at Tully Hall, New York, 82; Spring Songs (voice with instrm), 20th Century Consort, Washington, DC, 82; Dance Variations (solo clarinet), G Schirmer, 83. *Rec Perf:* Music of Weber (David Shifrin), Nonesuch Rec, 82. *Teaching:* Asst prof & pianist in res, Iowa State Univ, 60-61; assoc prof & pianist in res, Univ Iowa, 61-67; prof & pianist in res, Univ Tex, Austin, 67-73; vis prof, Col Consv Music, Univ Cincinnati, 79-80. *Awards:* Winner, Walter Naumburg Compt & Michaels Mem Award Compt, 54; Comp Hon Award, Wash State Arts Coun, 80. *Rep:* Traci Cozort Assoc 22307 Shoreland Dr S Seattle WA 98144. *Mailing Add:* 4511 Watauga NE Tacoma WA 98422

DORATI, ANTAL
CONDUCTOR & MUSIC DIRECTOR, COMPOSER

b Budapest, Hungary, April 9, 06; nat US. *Study:* Franz Liszt Acad Music, Budapest, dipl(comp & piano), 24; Univ Vienna, 23-25; Macalester Col, DMus, 57; George Washington Univ, Hon Dr, 75; Univ Md, Hon Dr, 76. *Pos:* Cond, Budapest Royal Opera House, 24-28, Dresden State Opera, 28-29, Munster State Opera, 29-32 & Ballet Russe Monte Carlo, 33-37; music dir, Ballet Russe, 38-40, Ballet Theatre, 40-44, Dallas Symph Orch, 45-49, Minneapolis Symph Orch, 49-60, Washington Nat Symph, 69-77 & Detroit Symph Orch, 77-; chief cond, BBC Symph Orch, 62-66 & Stockholm Phil, 66-74; sr cond, Royal Phil Orch, London, 74-78, cond laureate, 78; guest cond, major orchs in US & Europe. *Awards:* London-Decca Gold Rec, 75; Grand Prix Disque (20); Mahler Medal. *Mem:* Royal Acad Sweden; hon mem, Royal Acad Music London. *Mailing Add:* Detroit Symph Orch Ford Auditorium 20 E Jefferson Detroit MI 48226

DORDICK, JOHANNA
ADMINISTRATOR, SOPRANO

b Detroit, Mich, Aug 29, 35. *Study:* Univ Calif, Los Angeles; Calif State Univ, Los Angeles; Univ Miami; Limeston Col; studied opera with Martial Singher, Jan Popper & Fritz Zweig, 74; studied music & voice with Walter Golde, Norman Cordon & Bernhard Kwartin. *Roles:* Leonora in Il Trovatore; Aida in Aida; Tosca in Tosca, Karlsruhe Badisches Staatstheater, WGermany. *Pos:*

Perf leading roles with Coconut Grove Playhouse, Palm Beach Music Carnival & Deauville Summer Music Theater, 60-68; perf throughout US, Europe, Cent Am & South Am; founder & artistic dir, Los Angeles Opera Repty Theater. *Mem:* Opera Am; Nat Opera Asn. *Mailing Add:* 680 Wilshire Pl Suite 303 Los Angeles CA 90005

DORFMANN, ANIA
PIANO, EDUCATOR
b Odessa, Russia. *Study:* With Aisberg & Leschetizky; Paris Consv, with Isidor Philipp, dipl. *Rec Perf:* C Major Concerto, Beethoven, RCA, 45. *Pos:* Performer with leading orchs throughout Europe & US. *Teaching:* Mem fac piano, Juilliard Sch, 66- *Mailing Add:* Juilliard Sch Lincoln Ctr New York NY 10023

DORIAN, FREDERICK
WRITER, EDUCATOR
b Vienna, Austria, July 1, 02; US citizen. *Study:* Univ Vienna, PhD, 25; State Acad Music, Vienna, 26. *Pos:* Music ed & auth prog bk, Pittsburgh Symph Orch, 45-, coauth, 82-83. *Teaching:* Prof music & Andrew Mellon Lectr, Carnegie Mellon Univ, 36-75, lectr, 36-75; vis prof, Curtis Inst Music, 73-77, Hebrew Univ, Jerusalem, Israel, 78; fac mem, Marlboro Music Fest, 73-77. *Awards:* Andrew Mellon Res Grant, 58-59; Pittsburgh Found Res Grant, 66; Am Israel Cult Found Grant, 78. *Mem:* Am Musicol Soc; Int Musicol Soc. *Publ:* Auth, The Fugue in the Works of Beethoven, Denkmäler der Tonkunst, 27; The History of Music in Performance, W W Norton, 42; The Musical Workshop, Harper, 47; Committment to Culture, Univ Pittsburgh Press, 65; coauth (with Judith Meibach), Masters of the Violin, Carlo Tessarini-Johnson Reprint, 82. *Mailing Add:* 144 N Dithridge Pittsburgh PA 15213

DORNYA, MARYA D
SOPRANO
b Pulaski, Va, June 10. *Study:* Mary Washington Col, Univ Va, BA(music); studies with Ray McDermott; NY Univ; Hunter Col Opera Wkshp. *Roles:* Natalia in Natalia Petrovna, New York City Opera, 64, Leonore in Fidelio, Fiordiligi in Cosi fan tutte, Donna Anna in Don Giovanni, Musetta in La Boheme, Rosalinda in Die Fledermaus & Ariadne in Ariadne auf Nexos. *Pos:* Founder & gen dir, Jandora Int Opera Fest & Seminar; guest artist with Concert Opera Asn, Detroit Symph, Toledo Symph Orch, Miami Symph Orch, Rochester Symph, Kansas City Phil, Frysk Orch & Nat Orch Belgium; soprano with major opera companies in Europe & US. *Teaching:* Private piano instr. *Awards:* M B Rockefeller Fund Grant; Sullivan Found Grant; Winner, Nat Fedn Music Clubs. *Mem:* Mu Phi Epsilon. *Mailing Add:* c/o Ray McDermott 2109 Broadway New York NY 10025

DORSAM, PAUL JAMES
EDUCATOR, COMPOSER
b New York, NY, Jan 25, 41. *Study:* New England Consv Music, BM(trumpet), 62, BM(educ), 63, MM, 67; Boston Univ, DMA, 74. *Works:* Symphony 4, comn by Vt Phil Orch, 68; Toccatina Cononica, Int Trumpet Guild Conv, 78; Salem Rites, Univ Memphis, 78; Ave Maria, 79 & A Chameleon's Triumph, 79, comn by Va Commonwealth Univ; Sensuous Numerology, comn by Int Trumpet Guild Univ Mo, 79; Haec Dies, comn by The Alex Wilder Duo, 79. *Pos:* Cond, Vt Phil Orch, 68-70; ed & owner, Kleppinger-Pfaff Music Publ, 78- *Teaching:* Instr, St Michael's Col, Vt, 67-70; asst prof, Va Commonwealth Univ, 73-79; assoc prof, William Carey Col, Miss, 79-80; dir instrm music educ, Tuckahoe Pub Sch, NY, 81- *Mem:* Am Musicol Soc; Soc Music Theory; Music Educr Nat Conf; Int Trumpet Guild; Am Soc Univ Comp; Col Music Soc. *Interests:* Corelli; figured bass; palestrina; music pedagogy. *Mailing Add:* 142 Garth Rd Scarsdale NY 10583

DOSCHER, BARBARA M
EDUCATOR, MEZZO-SOPRANO
b Chicago, Ill. *Study:* Studied with Aksel Schiøtz, Werner Singer, Herman Reutter & Berton Coffin, 67-71; Univ Colo, Boulder, DMA, 71. *Roles:* The Elijah, Dallas Symph Orch & recitals in Ill, Tex, Colo & NC, 51. *Teaching:* Asst prof vocal pedagogy, studio voice & voice, Univ Colo, Boulder, 78-82, assoc prof, 82- *Awards:* Univ Colo Teaching Excellence Award, 82-83. *Mem:* Music Teachers Nat Asn (state voice chmn, 75-82); Nat Asn Teachers Singing (secy Colo-Wyo chap, 77-78); Col Music Soc. *Publ:* Auth, The Beginning Voice Class, Nat Asn Teachers Singing Bulletin, 75; The Singer: Stepchild of Competitions, Am Music Teacher, 80; coauth, A Mile High: The 1980 National Convention, Nat Asn Teachers Singing Bulletin, 80. *Mailing Add:* Campus Box 301 Col Music Univ Colo Boulder CO 80309

DOTY, EZRA WILLIAM
ADMINISTRATOR, ORGAN
Study: Univ Mich, AB, 27, BMus, 29, MA(phil), 29, PhD(aesthet), 36; Univ Leipzig; Leipzig Landeskonsv, 32-33. *Works:* Mist (organ), J Fisher, 36. *Pos:* Exec dir, New York Off Cult Affairs, 64-65. *Teaching:* Founding dean, Col Fine Arts, Univ Tex, Austin, 38-72, chmn, Dept Music, 38-64. *Mem:* Nat Asn Sch Music (pres, 55-58). *Publ:* Auth, The Analysis of Form in Music, Crofts, 44. *Mailing Add:* 206 Skyline Dr Austin TX 78746

DOUGLAS, JOHN THOMAS
TEACHER & COACH, MUSIC DIRECTOR
b Morgantown, WVa, June 3, 56. *Study:* Wittenburg Univ, BMus(piano & voice), 77; Bowling Green State Univ, MA(piano), 79; studied with John Moriarty, 80-81. *Pos:* Co-dir, Am Opera Theatre Boston, 83-; asst cond, Cent City Opera, Colo, 83- *Teaching:* Staff accmp, New England Consv, 79-81, instr & coach, 81-, coach opera dept, 82-; instr & coach, Boston Consv, 80-, prin coach opera dept, 82- *Mailing Add:* Boston Consv 8 The Fenway Boston MA 02115

DOUGLAS, SAMUEL OSLER
COMPOSER, EDUCATOR
b Mansfield, La, Mar 31, 43. *Study:* La State Univ, with Dinos Constandinides & Kenneth B Klaus, MM, 68, DMA, 72. *Works:* Prelude and Passacaglia (orch), 68; Sinfonia Ecclesiastica (chamber symph with chorus), 70; Disciples of Death (film score), 71; Selected Definitions from The Devil's Dictionary by Ambrose Bierce (sop, clarinet, double bass & piano), 72; The Devil's Hair (one act opera), Baton Rouge, 72; Sonata (reader, poem by Leo Stanford), 72; The Night Before Christmas (narrator), 73. *Teaching:* Assoc prof music, Univ SC, 73- *Mailing Add:* Music Dept Univ SC Columbia SC 29208

DOUGLASS, ROBERT SATTERFIELD
MUSICOLOGIST, EDUCATOR
b Senath, Mo, Apr 1, 19. *Study:* NTex State Univ, BMus, 48, MMus, 53, PhD(musicol), 63. *Pos:* Music critic, Ft Worth Star Telegram, 63-63; commentator, Pendulum, ABC Radio Network, 67- *Teaching:* Music, McKinney Pub Sch, Tex, 47-49 & Kingsville Pub Sch, 49-53; instr music hist, NTex State Univ, 53-54; prof musicol, Southwestern Baptist Theol Sem, 54- *Mem:* Am Musicol Soc; Music Critics Asn; Conf Southern Baptist Church Musicians. *Interests:* Music history; church music. *Publ:* Auth, Church Music Through the Ages, Conv, 67; Music in Academic Therapy, Southwestern Musician, 68; Mechanics of Research, Sem, 70. *Mailing Add:* Sch Church Music Southwestern Baptist Theol Sem Ft Worth TX 76122

DOUVAS, ELAINE
OBOE, EDUCATOR
Study: Cleveland Inst Music, studied oboe with John Mack & chamber music with Marcel Moyse. *Pos:* Prin oboe, Atlanta Symph, 73-77, Grand Teton Music Fest, summers 74-79, Marlboro Music Fest, 79-80 & Metropolitan Opera Orch, currently. *Teaching:* Mem fac oboe, Manhattan Sch Music, 78- & Mannes Col Music, 82- *Mailing Add:* 230 Central Park W New York NY 10024

DOVE, NEVILLE
CONDUCTOR, PIANO
b Johannesburg, SAfrica, Jan 29, 52. *Study:* Juilliard Sch, MFA, 75. *Rec Perf:* Piano Recital, EMI, 74. *Pos:* Cond & coach, Musikoramatiska Skolan, Stockholm, Sweden, 78-81; assoc cond, Opera Co Boston, 81- *Awards:* Bronz Medal, Int Piano Cont, Geneva, 76. *Mailing Add:* 539 Washington St Boston MA 02111

DOWD, CHARLES (ROBERT)
PERCUSSION, TIMPANI
b Syracuse, NY, Apr 8, 48. *Study:* San Jose State Univ, BA(perc perf), 70; Stanford Univ, MA(perc perf), 71; Juilliard Sch, with Saul Goodman, 74. *Works:* Eleven short works for solo vibraphone, three percussion quartets & one multiple percussion solo work. *Rec Perf:* Solo Vibes/Solo Drums: Charles Dowd, KM Rec, 82. *Pos:* Prin solo timpanist & head perc sect, Eugene Symph Orch, 75-; artist clinician, Ludwig/Musser Indust, 78- & Avedis Zildjian Corp, 83- *Teaching:* Assoc prof music, perc & jazz studies, Sch Music, Univ Ore, Eugene, 75- *Bibliog:* Fred Crafts (auth), Drumming Up Demand for Modern Music, Eugene Register Guard, 1/5/78; Karen M DuPriest (auth), Charles Dowd: Musicmaker, The Observer, Wilammette Valley, 10/29/81; Kim Carlson (auth), Ghetto Drummer Finds Fame, Ore Daily Emerald, 3/2/83. *Mem:* Percussive Arts Soc; Am Fedn Musicians; Nat Asn Col Wind & Perc Instr; Nat Asn Jazz Educr. *Interests:* Percussion materials written on snare drum, timpani, vibraphone, marimba and drum set. *Publ:* Auth, A Primer for the Rock Drummer, 71 & A Thesaurus for the Jazz/Rock Drummer, 74, Gwyn Warner Brothers; coauth, Master Technique Builders for Snare Drum, 82, auth, The Well-Tempered Timpanist, 82 & Velocity Warm-Ups for Jazz Vibraphone, 84, Belwin-Mills. *Rep:* Ludwig Indust 1728 N Damen Ave Chicago IL 60647. *Mailing Add:* Ore Artists Mgt 1804 Cal Young Rd Suite 45 Eugene OR 97401

DOWER, CATHERINE ANNE
EDUCATOR, LECTURER
b South Hadley, Mass, May 19, 24. *Study:* Hamline Univ, AB, 45; Smith Col, MA, 48; Catholic Univ Am, PhD, 68. *Rec Perf:* Westfield Sings, Gregorian Inst Am, 62. *Teaching:* Instr music & organist, St Rose Sch & Church, Meriden, Conn, 49-53; supvr music, Holyoke Pub Sch, 53-55; instr, Univ Mass, Amherst, 55-56; prof music, Westfield State Col, Mass, 56-; vis assoc prof music hist, Herbert Lehman Col, City Univ New York, 70-71. *Awards:* Distinguished Serv Award, Westfield State Col, 79, 81 & 83; Plaque, Springfield Symph Orch Asn, 82; Acad Arts & Sci PR Medal, 77. *Bibliog:* Donald Thompson (auth), Music Research in Puerto Rico, La Fortaleza, Gov PR, 82. *Mem:* Am Musicol Soc; Church Music Asn Am; Acad Arts & Sci PR; Acad Int PR; Irish Am Cult Inst (chmn, Holyoke chap, 80-). *Interests:* Puerto Rican music following the Spanish American War; Irish classical music. *Publ:* Auth, Aaron Copland: A World Wide Influence on the Contemporary Music Scene, 70 & Ulysses Kay, Distinguished American Composer, 72, Musart; Libraries With Music Collection in the Caribbean Area, Notes, 77; Ramon Morla, Composer-Organist, Sacred Music, 79; Puerto Rican Music Following the Spanish American War, Univ Press Am, 83. *Mailing Add:* 60 Madison Ave Holyoke MA 01040

DOWNES, EDWARD OLIN DAVENPORT
WRITER, EDUCATOR
b Boston, Mass, Aug 12, 11. *Study:* Columbia Col, 29-30; Manhattan Sch Music, 30-32; Univ Paris, France, 32-33; Univ Munich, Ger, 32, 34-36 & 38-39; Harvard Univ, PhD(music hist), 58. *Pos:* Music critic, Evening Transcript, Boston, 39-41 & Interstate Broadcasting Co, 68-; asst music critic, New York

Times, 55-58; quizmaster, Metropolitan Opera Broadcasts, 58-; musicol in res, Bayreuth Fest Master Classes, 59-65; prog annotator symphonic music, New York Phil, 60-74. *Teaching:* Lectr music hist, Wellesley Col, 48-49; instr, Longy Sch Music, 48-49; assoc prof music hist, Univ Minn, 50-55; guest lectr, Metropolitan Music Art, 60-66; prof music hist, Queens Col, City Univ New York, 67-81 & NY Univ, 81- *Bibliog:* William Dooley (auth), Return of a Critic, Boston Evening Transcript, 9/39; Gary Dietrichs (auth), The Quizmaster, Opera News, 12/8/73; D & B Rosenberg (auth), Edward Downes, Musical Man of Letters, Music Makers, Columbia Univ Press, 79. *Mem:* Am Musicol Soc (coun mem, 58-60 & 69-71); Int Musicol Soc; Music Libr Asn; Gesellschaft Musikforschung; Am Soc Theatre Res. *Interests:* Opera history, especially Richard Wagner and 18th-century classicism. *Publ:* Ed, Verdi, the Man in His Letters, L B Fischer, 42; auth, Secco Recitative in Early Classical Opera Seria 1720-1780, J Am Musicol Soc, 61; co-ed, Temistocle ... di J C Bach, Universal Ed, Vienna, 65; Perspectives in Musicology, Norton, 73; auth, Philharmonic Guide to the Symphony, 76, reprinted as Guide to Symphonic Music, 81, Walker Co. *Mailing Add:* 1 W 72 St New York NY 10023

DOWNEY, JAMES CECIL
EDUCATOR, WRITER
b Grandbay, Ala, Feb 13, 31. *Study:* William Carey Col, BA(music theory), 58; Univ Southern Miss, MM(music theory), 63; Tulane Univ, PhD(musicol), 68. *Teaching:* Assoc prof music, William Carey Col, 66-68, prof, 68-, admin dean, 82- *Awards:* Jaap Kunst Award, Soc Ethnomusicol, 64; Nat Endowment Humanities Fel, 71. *Mem:* Am Musicol Soc; Soc Ethnomusicol; Popular Cult Asn; Music Libr Asn; Phi Mu Alpha Sinfonia. *Publ:* Auth, Frontiers of Baptist Hymnody, Chuch Musician, 64; Revivalism, The Gospel Songs, and Social Reform, Ethnomusicol, 65; White Spiritual, In: New Grove Dict of Music & Musicians, 77; Recollections of a Jazz Funeral, Regist, 77; Mississippi Music—That Gospel Sound, In: Sense of Place: Mississippi, Univ Miss Press, 79. *Mailing Add:* 1856 Beach Dr Gulfport MS 39501

DOWNEY, JOHN WILHAM
COMPOSER, EDUCATOR
b Chicago, Ill, Oct 5, 27. *Study:* DePaul Univ, BM, 49; Chicago Musical Col, MM, 51; Consv Nat Musique, Paris, 56; Univ Paris, Sorbonne, PhD(Dr lett), 57. *Works:* Cello Sonata, 67 & Jingalodeon, 68, Ed Francaise Musique; Symphonic Modules Five, Theodore Presser Co, 72; Agort, Ed Francaise Musique, 73; What If, 73, A Dolphin, 74, String Quartet No 2, 76, The Edge of Space, 80, Lydian Suite, 81 & Silhouette, 82, Theodore Presser Co. *Rec Perf:* Cello Sonata, CRI; Agort, What If, A Dolphin, Adagio Lyrico & Octet for Winds, Orion; String Quartet No 2, Gasparo; The Edge of Space, Chandos & Musical Heritage Soc. *Teaching:* Assoc prof humanities, Chicago City Col, Amundsen, 58-64; prof theory & comp, Univ Wis, Milwaukee, 64- *Awards:* Fulbright Scholar, 52-54 & 78-79; Chevalier de l'Ordre des Arts et Lettres, French Govt, 80; Award, Nat Endowment Arts, 78 & 83. *Mem:* Am Soc Univ Comp; ASCAP; Wis Contemp Music Forum (chmn, 70-); Am Fedn Musicians; Delta Omicron. *Publ:* Auth, John J Becker—Midwest Composer, Focus Mag, 61; La Musique Populaire Dans l'Oeuvre de Bela Bartok, Centre Doc Univ, Paris, 66; Texture Ar Psycho-Rhythmics, Perspectives New Music, 83. *Mailing Add:* 4413 N Prospect Shorewood WI 53211

DRAGANSKI, DONALD CHARLES
LIBRARIAN, COMPOSER
b Chicago, Ill, Sept 22, 36. *Study:* Sch Music, DePaul Univ, with Alexander Tcherepnin, BMus, 58; Rosary Col, River Forest, Ill, MALS, 66. *Works:* Recitative and Scherzo for Woodwind Quintet, Crown Music; The Bestiary (song cycle), Galaxy Music. *Pos:* Music librn, Roosevelt Univ, Chicago, 73-; bassoonist, North Winds Woodwind Quintet, Evanston, Ill, 76- *Mem:* Music Libr Asn; Chicago Soc Comp. *Publ:* Auth, Back in the Stacks, Ill Libr, 67; The Art of Pogonology, 69 & Towelbearer to the Gods, 71, RQ Quart. *Mailing Add:* 2113 Forestview Rd Evanston IL 60201

DRAKE, ARCHIE
BASS-BARITONE
b Great Yarmouth, UK, Mar 12, 25; US citizen. *Study:* Music Acad West, with Lotte Lehmann; Opera Theatre, Univ Calif, Los Angeles; Univ Southern Calif, with William Eddy. *Rec Perf:* Charles Ives Songs, Columbia. *Roles:* Belcore in Elisir d'amore, Los Angeles Grand Opera, 60; Mephistopheles in Faust; Don Alfonso in Cosi fan tutte; Figaro in Le Nozze di Figaro; Candy in Of Mice and Men, 70 & Lazarus in Calvary, 71, Seattle Opera; Captain Muliken in Colonel Jonathan the Saint, Denver Opera, 71. *Pos:* Res artist, Seattle Opera, currently; appearance with Pac NW Wagner Fest, 75; perf with many opera co in US; conct appearances, 21 countries. *Awards:* Grammy Award for Charles Ives songs. *Mailing Add:* Seattle Opera PO Box 9248 Seattle WA 98109

DRAPER, DAVID ELLIOTT
EDUCATOR
b Greenville, Miss, Jan 29, 43. *Study:* Col Consv Music, Univ Cincinnati, BM 65, MM, 67; Tulane Univ, PhD, 73. *Teaching:* Prof ethnomusicol, Univ Calif, Los Angeles, 76- *Mem:* Pi Kappa Lambda; Phi Mu Alpha; Soc Ethnomusicol; Am Folklife Ctr, Libr Cong (trustee, 76-). *Interests:* Musical and anthropological aspects of Afro-American and American Indian societies. *Publ:* Auth, Occasions for Performance of Native Choctaw Music, Vol III, No 2 & Breath in Music: Concept, Practice Among Choctaw, Vol IV, 83, Selected Reports in Ethnomusicol; Christian Hymns of Mississippi Choctaw, Am Indian Cult & Res J, 83; Cognitive Models and Music (Mardi Gras Indians), Univ Calif, Los Angeles (in press); Choctaw Music, In: New Grove Dict of Music in US (in press). *Mailing Add:* Dept of Music Univ of Calif Col Fine Arts Los Angeles CA 90024

DRAPER, GLENN WRIGHT
CONDUCTOR, EDUCATOR
b Roanoke, Va, July 18, 28. *Study:* Ind Univ, BM, 51; Southern Methodist Univ, MM, 64; High Pt Col, Hon Dr Humanities, 76. *Pos:* Dir choral music, Pfeiffer Col, 56-60, Univ Mo, 60-68 & Univ Tenn, Chattanooga, 68- *Mem:* Tenn Musician; Am Choral Dir Asn; Music Educr Nat Conf; Am Guild Organists. *Mailing Add:* 810 Crown Pt Rd W Signal Mountain TN 37377

DRAPKIN, MICHAEL LEWIS
CLARINET, BASS CLARINET
b Van Nuys, Calif, Apr 14, 57. *Study:* Studied with Gary Gray, 73-75; Eastman Sch, with Stanley Hasty, BM, 79. *Pos:* Freelance perf, New York, 79-82 & 83-; prin clarinet, Nat Opera Touring Co, New York City Opera, 81-82; assoc prin bass clarinet, Honolulu Symph, 82-83. *Awards:* Margaret Boyes Fel, Berkshire Music Ctr, 78. *Publ:* Auth, Symphonic Repertoire for the Bass Clarinet, Roncorp, 79. *Rep:* Juan Motime & Assoc 8530 N Keystone Ave Skokie IL 60076. *Mailing Add:* 90 Pinehurst Ave Suite 2F New York NY 10033

DREILING, ALYZE LOGGIE
VIOLIN
b Detroit, Mich, July 20, 59. *Study:* Studied with Mischa Mischakoff, 72-77; Ind Univ, with Josef Gingold, BM, 81. *Pos:* Solo appearances with Detroit Symph, 76, Knoxville Symph, 82-, Austria Summer Fest with Philharmonia Hungarica, Fla Chamber Orch & Knoxville Chamber Orch, 83; asst concertmaster, Knoxville Symph, 82-83. *Mailing Add:* 30956 Dalhay Livonia MI 48150

DRENNAN, DOROTHY CARTER
WRITER, COMPOSER
b Hankinson, NDak, Mar 21, 29. *Study:* Barry Col, Miami, Fla, BMusEd, 69; Univ Miami, Coral Gables, MM, 71, PhD, 75. *Works:* The Word (cantata), Coral Gables First United Methodist Chancel Choir, 71; Here Is The Rose (conct for trombone & sprechchor), Dean Hey, 73; Songs of William Blake (song cycle), Curtis Rayam, 74; Turn, Atlanta New Music Ens, 79; Kyrie Eleison, La State Univ Conct Choir, 81. *Pos:* Bd mem, Fla Opera Repty, Miami, 75- *Mem:* Am Musicol Soc; Am Soc Univ Comp; Col Music Soc; ASCAP. *Publ:* Auth, Henry Brant's Choral Music, Am Choral Dir Asn J, 1/77; Henry Brant's Use of Ensemble Dispersion, Music Rev, 2/77. *Mailing Add:* 7880 SW 12 St Miami FL 33144

DRESHER, PAUL JOSEPH
COMPOSER, ELECTRONIC
b Los Angeles, Calif, Jan 8, 51. *Study:* Univ Calif, Berkeley, AB(music), 77; Univ Calif, San Diego, MA(comp), 79. *Works:* This Same Temple, perf by various piano duos, 77; Night Songs, comn by Nat Endowment Arts, 79-81; Liquid & Steller Music, private publ, 81; Study for Variations, comn by Nancy Karp & Dancers, 81-82; The Way of How, 81 & Are Are, 82-83, George Contes Performance Works; Casa Vecchia, comn by Kronos String Quartet, 82. *Teaching:* Fac comp & theory, Cornish Inst, 81-83. *Awards:* Comp fel, Nat Endowment Arts, 79; grant, Martha Baird Rockefeller III Fund, 82; Goddard Leiberson fel, Am Acad & Inst Arts & Lett, 82. *Mem:* Broadcast Music Inc. *Rep:* Robin Kirck & Assoc PO Box 9475 Berkeley CA 94709. *Mailing Add:* 1937 Carleton St Berkeley CA 94704

DRESSEN, DAN FREDRICK
TENOR, EDUCATOR
b Pipestone, Minn, Apr 10, 51. *Study:* Bemidji State Univ, BS(music educ), 73; Univ Minn, MFA, 82. *Rec Perf:* In A Winter Garden (Libby Larson), Pro Arte, 83. *Roles:* C C Pope in Black River, Minn Opera Co, 80; Count Almaviva in Barber of Seville, Midwest Opera Theater, 82; Rufus in Death in the Family, 83 & Arturo in Lucia di Lammermoor, 83, Minn Opera Co. *Pos:* Tenor soloist, Plymouth Congregational Church, Minneapolis, 78- *Teaching:* Asst prof voice, St Olaf Col, Northfield, Minn, 82- *Mailing Add:* Music Dept St Olaf Col Northfield MN 55057

DRESSLER, JOHN CLAY
FRENCH HORN, EDUCATOR
b Akron, Ohio, Aug 7, 49. *Study:* Baldwin-Wallace Col, BMusEd, 71; Ind Univ, MMus, 74. *Rec Perf:* Piano accmp on Crystal Rec, 75. *Pos:* Prin horn, Jacksonville Symph Orch, 74-76; co-prin & third horn, Savannah Symph Orch, 82; utility horn, Atlanta Symph Orch, 82- *Teaching:* Lectr music, Jacksonville Univ, 74-76; instr, Univ Pacific, 76-77; asst prof, Univ Ga, 80- *Mem:* Nat Asn Col Wind & Perc Instr; Int Horn Soc; Music Educr Nat Conf; Ga Music Educrs Asn; Music Teachers Nat Asn. *Publ:* Auth, Audition Materials for Horn, Instrumentalist, 82; Brass Reviews, 82 & The Use of Mutes and the Right Hand in Horn Playing, 83, Nat Asn Col Wind & Perc Instr J; Audition Materials: An Update, Horn Call, 83. *Mailing Add:* Sch Music Univ Ga Athens GA 30602

DREW, JAMES M
COMPOSER, CONDUCTOR & MUSIC DIRECTOR
b St Paul, Minn, Feb 9, 29. *Study:* Private study with Edgard Varese, 56, Wallingford Riegger, 56-59; Tulane Univ, MA, 64. *Works:* The Maze Maker, 71, West Indian Lights, 73, Lux Incognitus, 75, Orangethorpe Aria, 79, Five O'Clock Ladies, 80 & Open/Closed Forms, 83, Theodore Presser. *Rec Perf:* Open/Closed Forms, Maxus, 83. *Pos:* Dir, Am Music Theatre, Los Angeles, 76- & Mysterious Traveling Cabaret, 80-; co-dir, Teatro Mascara, Madrid, 78-80; dir music & experimental theater, Contemp Arts Ctr, New Orleans, 80- *Teaching:* Comp in res, Yale Univ, 67-73; vis comp, Calif State Univ, 76-77

& Univ Calif, Los Angeles, 77-78. *Awards:* Guggenheim Fel, 72-73; Panamericana Prize, Nuevo Musica, 74; grant, Meet the Comp, NY Arts Coun & Am Music Ctr, 75. *Bibliog:* Garry E Clarke (auth), Essays on American Music, Greenwood Press Inc, 77; Monica Dart (auth), An American Original, Arts Soho, London, 81. *Mem:* ASCAP; Nat Asn Am Comp & Cond. *Publ:* Auth, Information, Space and a New Time-Dialectic, Yale J Music Theory, 68; Composicion, nuevo direccion, Barcelona, 69; Ritmo Negre, Ethnica, 70. *Rep:* Theodore Presser Co Bryn Mawr PA 19010. *Mailing Add:* 2716 Whitney Pl #615 Metairie LA 70002

DREW, LUCAS
DOUBLE BASS, EDUCATOR
b Richmond, Va, June 10, 35. *Study:* Univ Miami, BM, 57; Univ Ill, MS, 58; Fla State Univ, EdD, 71; studied double bass with Allen Warner, Dmitri Shmuklovsky & Edward Krolick. *Rec Perf:* Music for Double Bass & Harpsichord from the Baroque Period, Music for Double Bass and Piano from the Classical Period & Music for Double Bass and Piano from the 19th & 20th Centuries, Coronet Rec Co. *Pos:* Prin double bass, Miami Phil Orch, 23 years & Miami Opera, 17 years; ed, Int Soc Bassists, 74-82; organizer, Miami Third Century USA Fest Am Music, 76; double bassist, Contemp Baroque Trio, 77-; artistic dir, Highlands Chamber Music Fest, NC, 82-; gen ed, Frederick Zimmermann Mem Series for Double Bass, Univ Miami Music Publ, currently. *Teaching:* Prof double bass & chmn dept applied music, Univ Miami, 59-; vis mem fac double bass, Ind Univ, Dartmouth Col, Brevard Music Ctr, Stetson Univ & other wkshps in US, Europe & Latin Am, 59-*Bibliog:* Samuel Applebaum (auth), The Way They Play, Vol II, Paganiniana Publ. *Mem:* Co-founder, Int Soc Bassists; Am String Teachers Asn (pres, 82-). *Publ:* With Belwin-Mills, G Schirmer, Carl Fischer & others. *Mailing Add:* Sch Music Univ Miami Coral Gables FL 33124

DREYER, LESLIE I
VIOLIN, WRITER
b Brooklyn, NY, Oct 1, 30. *Study:* Juilliard Sch Music, dipl(violin), 51; Columbia Univ, BS, 56. *Pos:* Concertmaster, Juilliard Opera Orch, 48-51; freelance violinist, 51-60; assoc prin violin, Metropolitan Opera Orch, 60- *Teaching:* Fac mem & piano trio, Aegina Arts Ctr, Greece, summer 72 & 73. *Publ:* Auth, Trailing the Met On Tour, Opera News, 4/8/78; Don't Mug Musicians, New York Times, 10/17/79; An Opera Buff's Guide to Etiquette, 3/80 & The Deaf Music Critic, 5/80, Ovation; The Pit & the Pendulum, Opera News, 3/14/81; The Saboteur Claquer, Ovation, 1/82. *Mailing Add:* 170 W End Ave Apt 7-E New York NY 10023

DRIEHUYS, LEONARDUS BASTIAAN
MUSIC DIRECTOR & CONDUCTOR
b The Hague, Netherlands, Mar 25, 32. *Study:* Royal Consv Music, The Hague, Netherlands, dipl(oboe & piano). *Pos:* Prin oboe, Netherlands Opera, Amsterdam, 52-59, cond, 59-65; cond, Nederlandse Omroepstichting, 65-; music dir, Het Gelders Orkest, Arnhem, 70-74 & Charlotte Symph Orch, 77-*Awards:* Fock Medal Oboe. *Rep:* Int Artist Mgt 111 W 57th St New York NY 10019. *Mailing Add:* Charlotte Symph Orch 111 E 7th St Charlotte NC 28202

DRIGGERS, ORIN SAMUEL
EDUCATOR, PIANO
b Moncks Corner, SC, Aug 7, 41. *Study:* NTex State Univ, with Robert Ottman, MM(theory), 67; La State Univ, with Jack Guerry, MM(piano), 73, DMA(piano), 75. *Teaching:* Instr music, NGreenville Col, 65-68 & Mars Hill Col, 68-71; prof, Univ Cent Ark, 75-80, chmn music dept, 80- *Awards:* Outstanding Col Music Teacher, Ark State Music Teachers Asn, 83. *Mem:* Ark State Music Teachers Asn (treas, 77-79, second vpres, 81-83, first vpres, 83-); Music Teachers Nat Asn; Music Educr Nat Conf; Phi Mu Alpha; Pi Kappa Lambda. *Publ:* Auth, Steps to Effective Memorization, 79 & Preparing Students for Auditions and Competition, 82, Ark State Music Teachers Asn Newslett; J K F Fischer's Ariadne Musica (in prep). *Mailing Add:* Dept Music Univ Cent Ark Conway AR 72032

DRINKALL, ROGER LEE
CELLO
b Cleveland, Ohio, May 10, 37. *Study:* Curtis Inst Music, BMus, 59; Univ Ill, MMus, 62. *Rec Perf:* Gordon Binkerd Cello Sonata, CRI, 74; Grieg & Chopin Cello Sonatas, 82, Schiffman Concerto & Solo Sonata, 82 & Solo Suite, Sonata, Duo (Kelly), 83, Orion Master Rec. *Teaching:* Artist in res, Queens Col, Charlotte, 62-68 & Univ Tenn, Chattanooga, 68-76; prof cello, Fla State Univ, Tallahassee, 76- *Awards:* Young Artist Award, Nat Fedn Music Clubs, 59; Grant, Kate Neal Kinley Award, 62; Award, Ford Found, 74. *Rep:* Albert Kay Assoc Conct Mgt 58 W 58th St New York NY 10019. *Mailing Add:* 2819 Pound Dr Tallahassee FL 32312

DRIVER, HOWARD (GLEN)
CRITIC-WRITER
Pos: Dance & music critic, Honolulu Advertiser, 72- & Honolulu Star Bulletin & Advertiser, 80-; regional contribr, Opera News, 76- *Mailing Add:* Honolulu Advertiser Honolulu HI 96802

DRIVER, ROBERT BAYLOR
ADMINISTRATOR, DIRECTOR-OPERA
b Sao Paulo, Brazil, Aug 26, 42. *US citizen. Study:* Univ Va, BA, 64; Middlebury Col, MA, 71; Johns Hopkins Univ. *Pos:* Asst stage dir, Die Bayerische Staatsoper, 66-68; asst dir, Ky Opera Asn, 68-71; assoc dir, Kansas City Lyr Opera, 74-75; artistic dir, Opera Theater Syracuse, 75- & Indianapolis Opera, 81- *Mem:* Opera Am Inc (secy, 81-). *Rep:* Opera Ctr 410 E Willow Syracuse NY 13203. *Mailing Add:* 708 E Michigan St Indianapolis IN 46202

DROSSIN, JULIUS
COMPOSER, EDUCATOR
b Philadelphia, Pa, May 17, 18. *Study:* Univ Pa, with Harl McDonald, BMus, 38; New Sch Music, with George Rochberg, 46-48; Western Res Univ, MM, 52, PhD, 56. *Works:* Friday Night Service, perf by Park Synagogue Choir, 56; Symphony No 1, perf by Cleveland Phil, 59; Symphony No 2, perf by Cleveland Conct Guild Orch, 60; String Quartet No 5, perf by Oberlin String Quartet, 61; Cello Sonata No 1, perf by comp & Arthur Loesser, 69; String Quartet No 6, Advent Rec, 70; Cello Sonata No 2, perf by comp & Eunice Podis, 72. *Pos:* Cellist, Cleveland Orch, 48-57; choir dir, Park Synagogue, 57-65. *Teaching:* Asst prof music, Villa Maria Col, 51-59; prof, Fenn Col, 56-65; chmn music dept & prof harmony, counterpoint & hist, Cleveland State Univ, 65- *Mem:* Cleveland Fedn Music; Am Soc Jewish Music; Cleveland Comp Guild (pres, 68-72); Cleveland Chamber Music Soc. *Publ:* Coauth, Music of the Twentieth Century, Prentice-Hall, 81. *Mailing Add:* 24051 S Woodland Rd Shaker Heights OH 44124

DRUCKER, ARNO PAUL
ADMINISTRATOR, EDUCATOR
b Philadelphia, Pa, Dec 25, 33. *Study:* Eastman Sch Music, BMus, 54, MMus, 55; Peabody Consv Music, DMA, 70. *Pos:* Pianist, Baltimore Symph Orch, 75- *Teaching:* Asst prof music, WVa Univ, 59-67; prof music, Essex Community Col, 68-; fac mem, Peabody Consv Music, 78- *Awards:* Fulbright Fel, 56; Outstanding Educr Am, Fuller & Dees, 75. *Mem:* Col Music Soc; Nat Asn Sch Music; Sonneck Soc; Am Liszt Soc; Am Asn Univ Prof (secy Essex chap, 82-). *Mailing Add:* 1 Glencliffe Circle Baltimore MD 21208

DRUCKER, EUGENE SAUL
VIOLIN
b Coral Gables, Fla, May 17, 52. *Study:* Juilliard Sch, studied violin with Oscar Shumsky, dipl, 72; Columbia Univ, BA, 73. *Pos:* Violinist, Speculum Musicae, 72-73; NY Chamber Soloists, 73-82 & Emerson Quartet, 76- *Teaching:* Chamber music, Hartt Col Music, 80- *Awards:* Bronze Medal, Queen Elisabeth Violin Compt, Brussels, 76. *Mailing Add:* 23 W 73rd St New York NY 10023

DRUCKER, RUTH
EDUCATOR, VOICE
Study: Eastman Sch Music, BM, MM, perf cert; Music Acad West, with Lotte Lehmann; Akad fur Music, Vienna; Mozarteum, Salzburg. *Pos:* Performer, Baltimore Symph, Nat Symph Orch, Harford Opera Theatre & Baltimore Chamber Opera; soloist, Goucher-Hopkins Choral Soc, Handel Choir, Towson Chamber Players, Peabody Contemp Music Ens & Smithsonian Inst. *Teaching:* Mem fac voice & art song, Peabody Consv Music, currently; prof voice, Towson State Univ, currently. *Awards:* Fulbright Grant. *Mailing Add:* Peabody Consv Music 1 E Mt Vernon Pl Baltimore MD 21202

DRUCKER, STANLEY
CLARINET, EDUCATOR
b Brooklyn, NY. *Study:* Curtis Inst Music, studied clarinet with Leon Russianoff; Nat Orch Asn. *Rec Perf:* On Columbia, Odyssey, Bartok, CRI, Westminster, Contemp, Music Minus One & New World. *Pos:* Mem, New York Phil, 48-, solo clarinetist, currently; solo clarinetist, Indianapolis Symph, formerly, Busch Chamber Players, formerly & Buffalo Phil, formerly; guest artist, Juilliard Quartet; ed clarinet music, Int Music Co & Consolidated Music Co, currently. *Teaching:* Mem fac clarinet, Juilliard Sch, 68- *Mailing Add:* New York Phil Avery Fisher Hall New York NY 10023

DRUCKMAN, JACOB
COMPOSER, CONDUCTOR
b Philadelphia, Pa, June 26, 28. *Study:* Juilliard Sch, with Vincent Persichetti, Bernard Wagenaar & Peter Mennin, BS, 52, MS, 54; studied with Aaron Copland & Tony Aubin. *Works:* Windows (orch), comn by Serge Koussevitsky Music Found, Libr Cong, 72; Animus IV (tenor, tape & six instrumentalists), comn by Inst Recherche Coord Acoustique/Musique, 77; Concerto for Viola and Orchestra, comn by New York Phil Soc, 78; Aureole (orch), comn by Leonard Bernstein & New York Phil Soc, 79; Bo (marimba, harp, bass clarinet & three accompanying female voices), perf by Daniel Druckman, Barbara Allen & Dennis Smiley, 80; Prism (orch), comn by Baltimore Symph Orch, 80; String Quartet #3, comn by Fromm Found, 81. *Pos:* Mem bd dir, Serge Koussevitsky Music Found, 73-, pres, currently; mem bd dir, ASCAP, 76 & 82-; mem, Am Acad Inst Arts & Lett; comp in res, New York Phil, 82-84. *Teaching:* Mem fac music, Juilliard Sch, 56-72; prof & dir electronic music studio, Brooklyn Col, 72-76 & Sch Music, Yale Univ, 76- *Awards:* Guggenheim Fel, 57 & 68; Am Acad & Inst Arts & Lett Award, 69; Pulitzer Prize in Music for Windows, 72. *Bibliog:* Caras & Gagne (auth), Soundpieces, Scarecrow Press, 82; Charles Moritz (ed), Current Biography, H W Wilson Co, 5/81. *Publ:* Auth, Stravinsky's Orchestral Style, Juilliard Rev, 57 & reprinted in Musik der Zeit; A New Romanticism?, Ovation Mag, 83. *Rep:* Boosey & Hawkes 24 W 57th St New York NY 10019. *Mailing Add:* 780 Riverside Dr New York NY 10032

DRUESEDOW, JOHN EDWARD, JR
LIBRARIAN, EDUCATOR
b Cambridge, Ohio, May 1, 39. *Study:* Miami Univ, Ohio, BM, 61; Ind Univ, Bloomington, MM, 63, MA, 66, PhD, 72 & piano with Alfonso Montecino & György Sebök; studied musicol with Willi Apel. *Pos:* Music librn, Miami Univ, Ohio, 66-74; dir consv libr, Consv Music, Oberlin Col, 74- *Teaching:* Lectr music hist, Consv Music, Oberlin Col, 76- *Mem:* Music Libr Asn; Am Musicol Soc; Int Asn Music Libr; Sonneck Soc. *Interests:* Music of the

Spanish Baroque; music in US before 1900; music bibliography. *Publ:* Auth, Cuatro Piezas de Mario Davidovsky, Rev Musical Chilena, Vol 20, 66; contribr, Dictionary of Contemporary Music, E P Dutton, 74; auth, Aspectos Teoricos Modales de un Libro Espanol ..., Vol 29, Rev Musical Chilena, 75; contribr, American Reference Books Annual, Libraries Unlimited, 76-; auth, Library Research Guide to Music, Pierian Press, 82. *Mailing Add:* 142 Cedar St Oberlin OH 44074

DRUIAN, JOSEPH
CELLO, EDUCATOR
b Vologda, USSR, Oct 27, 16. *Study:* Curtis Inst Music, dipl, 43. *Pos:* Conct cellist with Yvonne Druian, US; prin solo cellist, Dallas Symph Orch, four yrs & Philadelphia Orch, currently. *Teaching:* Instr, Princeton Univ, currently & Settlement Music Sch, currently. *Mailing Add:* Philadelphia Orch 1420 Locust St Philadelphia PA 19102

DRUMMOND, DEAN
COMPOSER
b Santa Monica, Calif, Jan 22, 49. *Study:* Univ Southern Calif; Calif Inst Arts, with Leonard Stein. *Works:* Zurrjir (flute, clarinet, piano & perc), 76; Dirty Ferdie (perc quartet), 76; Post Rigabop Mix (flute solo), 77; Copegoro (zoomoozophone & perc), 78; Invented Zoomoozophone, 78; Columbus (flute & 3 zoomoozophonists), 80; Mysteries (flute, violin, cello, zoomoozophonists & perc), 82. *Teaching:* Asst, Univ Calif, San Diego, formerly. *Awards:* Margaret Grant Mem Comp Prize, 76; Nat Endowment Arts Grant, 79. *Mailing Add:* 95 W 95th #34G New York NY 10025

DRUZINSKY, EDWARD
HARP
b St Louis, Mo, June 16, 24. *Study:* Curtis Inst Music, 40-42. *Pos:* First harpist, Pittsburgh Symph Orch, 48-52, Detroit Symph Orch, 52-57 & Chicago Symph Orch, 57- *Teaching:* Instr harp, Carnegie Inst, 48-52; lectr, Univ Mich, 54-57; prof, Northwestern Univ, 65-81. *Mailing Add:* 429 W Roslyn Pl Chicago IL 60614

DUARTE, JOHN WILLIAM
GUITAR, COMPOSER
b Sheffield, UK, Oct 2, 19. *Study:* Manchester Univ, BSc, AMCT. *Works:* Catalan Folksong Variations Op 25; English Suite Op 31; Sonatinette Op 34; Six Friendships (two guitars); Sans Cesse Op 34; Prelude Op 13; Suite Piemontese Op 46. *Awards:* First Prize, Int Comp Cont, 58. *Mem:* Hon fel, Soc Classic Guitar NY; hon mem, Guitar Soc Sweden; hon mem, Guitar Soc Wellington; Comp Guild. *Mailing Add:* 30 Rathcoole Gardens London N8 9NB England United Kingdom

DUBOSE, CHARLES BENJAMIN
MUSIC DIRECTOR
b Greenville, SC, Aug 20, 49. *Study:* Furman Univ, BMusEd, 71; Univ Ga, MFA, 74; Armed Forces Sch Music, 75-76. *Pos:* Dir, US Army Herald Trumpets, US Army Band, Ft Myer, Va, 76-80, dir US Army Orch, 80- *Mem:* Phi Mu Alpha Sinfonia; Pi Kappa Lambda; Int Trumpet Guild; Nat Band Asn. *Mailing Add:* US Army Band Ft Myer VA 22211

DUCKWORTH, WILLIAM ERVIN
COMPOSER, EDUCATOR
b Morganton, NC, Jan 13, 43. *Study:* ECarolina Univ, comp with Martin Mailman, BM, 65; Univ Ill, Urbana, comp with Ben Johnston, trombone with Robert Gray & music educ with Charles Leonhard, EdD, 72. *Works:* Gambit, 67 & Pitch City, 69, Media Press; When In Eternal Lines to Time Thou Growst, Fleisher Collection, Philadelphia, 70; A Whispering ..., Smith Publ, 72; Seven Shades of Blue, Bowdoin Col Music Press, 74; The Time Curve Preludes: Book I & II, C F Peters Corp, 77-78; Southern Harmony: Books I-IV, comn by Wesleyan Univ Singers, 80-81. *Pos:* Pres, Media Press, Champaign, Ill, 69-72; found & dir, Asn Independent Comp & Perf, 69-72. *Teaching:* Assoc prof theory & comp, Atlantic Christian Col, 66-73 & Bucknell Univ, 73- *Awards:* Nat Endowment Arts Comp Fel, 77; Nat Endowment Humanities Fel, 81. *Mem:* ASCAP; Col Music Soc; New Music Alliance. *Publ:* Coauth, Theoretical Found of Music, Wadsworth Publ Co, 78; auth, A Creative Approach to Music Fundamentals, Wadsworth Publ Co. *Mailing Add:* Dept Music Bucknell Univ Lewisburg PA 17837

DUCLOUX, WALTER ERNEST
EDUCATOR, MUSIC DIRECTOR
b Kriens, Switz, Apr 17, 13; US citizen. *Study:* Univ Munich, PhD, 35; State Acad Music, Vienna, studied cond with Weingartner, 37. *Rec Perf:* Interrupted Melody, Metro-Goldwyn-Mayer, 54; Die Liebe Der Danae (Strauss), 64, Mathis Der Maler (Hindemith), 66 & Friedenstag (Strauss), 67, Am Prem Univ Southern Calif, Los Angeles. *Pos:* Opera & conct cond, Switz & US, 37-43; opera & orch dir, Univ Southern Calif, 53-68, Univ Tex, Austin, 68- *Teaching:* Prof music, opera & cond, Sch Music, Univ Southern Calif, Los Angeles, 53-68; prof music, drama, opera & cond, Univ Tex, Austin, 68-, Ashbel Smith prof, 80- *Awards:* Centennial prof opera, Frank Erwin Jr, Austin, 83. *Mem:* ASCAP; Am Symph Orch League; Life & charter mem, Nat Opera Asn; Life mem, Am Fedn Musicians; Charter mem, Cent Opera Serv Metropolitan. *Publ:* Transl, opera into English, G Schirmer, 59-70. *Mailing Add:* 2 Wildwind Pt Austin TX 78746

DUDLEY, ANNA CAROL
SOPRANO, EDUCATOR
b Puunene, Maui, Hawaii, Jan 20, 31. *Study:* Oberlin Col, BA, 52; Consv Music, Oberlin Col, with Marion Sims, MA, 56. *Rec Perf:* Songs & Grounds (Henry Purcell), 78, Machado Songs & Divertimento in Quattro Esercizi (Dallapiccola), 79, 1750 Arch Rec; Great Praises, Songs by Richard Swift, CRI, 79. *Pos:* Soloist, Elizabethan Trio, San Francisco, 76- & San Francisco Contemp Music Players, 80-; soloist, numerous orch & chamber groups. *Teaching:* Instr singing, San Francisco State Univ, 76-; dir, Cazadero Baroque Wkshp, Calif; instr, Basically Baroque Symposium, Univ Calif, San Diego. *Mem:* San Francisco Early Music Soc (pres, 82-). *Mailing Add:* 1745 Capistrano Ave Berkeley CA 94707

DUDLEY, RAYMOND C
PIANO, EDUCATOR
b Bowmanville, Ont, June 20, 31. *Study:* Royal Consv, Univ Toronto, ARCT, LRCT, RCAD. *Rec Perf:* Complete Haydn Sonatas. *Pos:* Soloist, New York Phil, London Phil Orch, BBC Symph & CBC Symph & Detroit, Vancouver & Toronto orchs; ann conct tours, Europe, US & Can. *Awards:* Artist of Yr, Music Teachers Nat Asn, 78. *Mem:* Phi Mu Alpha; Music Teachers Nat Asn; SC Music Teachers Asn; Am Fedn Musicians; Col Music Soc. *Mailing Add:* 57 Olde Springs Rd Columbia SC 29204

DUEHLMEIER, SUSAN HUNTER
HARPSICHORD, EDUCATOR
b Salt Lake City, Utah. *Study:* Univ Utah, BMus, 70; MMus, 72; Boston Univ. *Teaching:* Fel, Univ Utah, 70-72, chmn, Summer Arts Piano Fest, 76-, adj assoc prof music, 76- *Awards:* John R Park Fac Award, Univ Utah, 83. *Mem:* Nat Fedn Music Clubs; Music Teachers Nat Asn; Mu Phi Epsilon; Am Musicol Soc; Nat Guild Piano Teachers. *Rep:* E Bates 1466 S 6th East Salt Lake City UT 84105. *Mailing Add:* 1926 Orchard Dr Salt Lake City UT 84106

DUER, SUSAN R
PIANO & FORTEPIANO
b Philadelphia, Pa. *Study:* Col Music, Temple Univ, MM, 68; Peabody Consv Music, DMA, 76; Inst Fortepiano Studies, Wellesley Col, 77; Baroque Perf Inst, Oberlin Col, 81; Sixth Aston Magna Acad. *Rec Perf:* Short Favorites by Mozart and Beethoven, Audio Motif Ltd, 83. *Teaching:* Lectr piano, Col Music, Temple Univ, 68-79. *Awards:* Fulbright-Hays Alternate Fel, 68-69; Individual Artist Grant, Nev State Coun Arts, Nat Endowment Arts, 82-83 & 83-84; Solo Recitalists Grant, Nat Endowment Arts, 83-84. *Bibliog:* Article, Temple Univ Alumni Rev, winter 79; Dimitri Drobatschewsky (auth), article, Ariz Repub, 7/1/82; Cynthia Gaffey (auth), article, Arts Alive, 1-2/83. *Mem:* Am Musicol Soc; Col Music Soc; Am Fedn Musicians. *Publ:* Auth, The Piano Music of Alexander Reinagle (1756-1809), Brockport Keyboard Fest, 77. *Mailing Add:* c/o Edward Lewis Assoc PO Box 26771 Las Vegas NV 89126

DUESENBERRY, JOHN F
COMPOSER, ELECTRONIC
b Boston, Mass, Oct 10, 50. *Study:* Boston Univ, studied comp with Joyce Mekeel, Allan Schindler & John Goodman, BMus(theory & comp), 74; Univ Mass, Amherst, studied comp with Robert Stern, MM(comp & theory), 78; Boston Sch Electronic Music; Mass Inst Technol, studied comput music with Barry Vercoe. *Works:* Incidental Music: The Sleep of Reason, comn by Theatre Dept, Boston Univ, 74; Songs from A Season in Hell, Marg Sego, 74; Etude, First Australian Electronic Music Fest, 79; Three Variations, Two Interludes, 80, Moduletude, 80, Phrase, 80 & Movements for Tape & Prepared Piano, 80, Opus One Rec. *Teaching:* Instr, Boston Sch Electronic Music, 74-76, dir, 78-79. *Awards:* Artists Found, Mass Coun Arts & Humanities Fel, 79. *Bibliog:* Martin Brody (auth), Rev of John Duesenberry, Opus One Rec #60, Comput Music J, winter 81. *Mem:* Am Soc Univ Comp; Am Music Ctr; Col Music Soc; Comput Music Asn. *Publ:* Auth, VCA Control—Linear & Exponential, Musicians Guide, 75; Rhythmic Control of Analog Sequencers, 78 & Prerecorded Timing Signals—Techniques & Applications, 79, Polyphony. *Mailing Add:* 514 Harvard St #3B Brookline MA 02146

DUESING, DALE L
BARITONE
b Milwaukee, Wis. *Study:* Lawrence Univ, BM, 67; Hochschule Musik, Munich, Ger, cert artist, 68. *Rec Perf:* Don Giovanni (Massetto), Deutsche Grammophon, 77; Zemlinsky Lyric Symphony, Polydor, Ger, 80. *Roles:* Olivier in Capriccio, Glyndebourne Fest Opera, 76; Papageno in Die Zauberflöte, Metropolitan Opera, 78; Billy Budd in Billy Budd, San Francisco Opera, 79; Harlekin, Salzburg Fest, 80; Belcore in L'elisir d'amore, Chicago Lyric Opera, 81; Guglielmo in Cosi fan tutte, Paris Opera, 82; Pelleas in Pelleas et Melisande, Metropolitan Opera, 83. *Rep:* Columbia Artists 165 W 57th St New York NY 10019. *Mailing Add:* 17765 Bonnie Lane Brookfield WI 53005

DUFALLO, RICHARD JOHN
CONDUCTOR, CLARINET
b East Chicago, Ind, Jan 30, 33. *Study:* Am Consv Music, Chicago, BMus, 53; Univ Calif, Los Angeles, BA, 56, MA, 58. *Rec Perf:* Festival Chamber Ensemble (Xenakis, Del Tredici, Takemitsu & Nono), Libr Cong, 70, 72, 73 & 76; Concerto for Two Pianos (Mozart), RCA London; Symphony No 2 (Escher), Composer's Voice, Amsterdam; St Thomas Wake (Davies) & Symphony No 5 (Antheil), Louisville First Ed. *Pos:* Asst cond, New York Phil, formerly; assoc cond, Univ Calif Los Angeles Symph, 59 & Buffalo Phil, 62-67; coordr, Ojai Fest, Calif, 61-63; cond, Ctr Creative & Perf Arts, Buffalo, NY, 64-67; artistic dir & cond, Conf Contemp Music, Aspen Music Fest, Colo, 70-; music dir & cond, 20th Century Music Series, Juilliard Theatre, Lincoln Ctr, New York, 72-79; prin cond & artistic adv, Metropolitan Opera's

Mini-Met, 72-74; guest cond with orch in NAm & Europe, formerly; artistic adv, Het Gelders Orkest, Arnhem, Holland, 80- Teaching: Lectr music, Univ Calif, Los Angeles, 59. Bibliog: To Be Modern, You Must Look Back, New York Times, 7/12/70; Artistic Profile, High Fidelity, 5/73; New Music Is My Nemesis, Louisville Courrier, 11/26/78. Mailing Add: c/o Herbert Barrett Mgt 1860 Broadway New York NY 10023

DUFFY, JOHN
COMPOSER, CONDUCTOR

Works: Concerto for Stan Getz and Concert Band & Concerto for the Paul Winter Consort, comn by Duke Univ; Freedom (choral), comn for Berkshire Bicentennial; scores for Broadway & Off-Broadway productions including, MacBird, Mother Courage, Playboy of the Western World & Horseman Pass By; scores for many award winning ABC, NBC, TV specials & for features & documentaries produced independently. Pos: Comp & music dir, Am Shakespeare Fest, Tyrone Guthrie, Vivian Beaumont, Long Wharf & McCarter Theatres, formerly; comp, cond & music dir, WNET-Channel 13 series, Civilization and the Jews, currently; dir, Meet The Composer, 74-; freelance comp, ABC, NBC, NET TV, films & theatre. Awards: Laurel Leaf Award, Am Comp Alliance, 80; Emmy Award for Original Music & Music Dir, A Talent for Life, 80; Int Doc Film Fest Award for Outstanding Score, A Talent for Life, 81. Mailing Add: 120 W 70th St New York NY 10023

DUFFY, THOMAS C
COMPOSER, CONDUCTOR & MUSIC DIRECTOR

b Brooklyn, NY, June 17, 55. Study: Univ Conn, BS(music ed), 77, MM(comp), 79; Cornell Univ, with Karel Husa, DMA(comp), 83. Works: Rage Against the Fading of the Light, Univ Conn Wind Ens, 76; Exploding Cinders, Univ Conn Jazz Ens, 79; Rage Against the Fading of the Light, Cornell Univ Wind Ens, 80; Ca Montre, 81; For Those Who Weep, 82 & To The Triptych's Piper, 82, Cayuga Chamber Orch; Somer's March, Yale Univ Conct Band, 83. Rec Perf: Exploding Cinders (Thomas Duffy), Amphion Rec, 79; Overture to Candide (Leonard Bernstein), 82, Report (Lubos Fiser), 83 & Rage Against the Fading of the Light (Thomas Duffy), 83, Cornell Univ Wind Ens Ser. Pos: Dir jazz ens, Univ Conn, 76-79 & Cornell Univ, 82; dir music, Nutmeg Summer Playhouse, Univ Conn, summers 80 & 81; dir bands, Yale Univ, 82- Teaching: Instr theory, comp, cond & ear training, Hartford, Consv, 79-80; instr jazz hist & music appreciation, Cayuga Community Col, 81-82; instr theory & cond, Yale Univ, 82- Mem: Am Comp Alliance; BMI; Am Soc Univ Comp; New England Col Band Asn; Col Band Dir Nat Asn. Interests: Linear motion in the counterpoint of Requiem by Georgi Ligeti. Rep: 10 D 123 York St New Haven CT 06511. Mailing Add: 3-A Yale Station New Haven CT 06520

DUGGER, EDWIN ELLSWORTH
COMPOSER, EDUCATOR

b Poplar Bluff, Mo, Mar 21, 40. Study: Consv Music, Oberlin Col, with Richard Hoffman, BM, 62; Princeton Univ, with Roger Sessions, Earl Kim & Milton Babbitt, MFA, 64. Works: Abwesenheiten und Wiedersehen (11 performers & tape), 71; Adieu (wind & perc ens & tape), 72; Matsukaze, 76; Fantasy (piano), 77; Duo (flute & viola), 79; Variations and Adagio (nine performers), 79; Septet, 80. Teaching: Lectr, Consv Music, Oberlin Col, 65-67; assoc prof music, Univ Calif, Berkeley, 67- Awards: Comns, Fromm Found, 69 & Koussevitzky Found, 73; Guggenheim Fel, 73. Mem: BMI. Mailing Add: 268 Columbia Ave Kensington CA 94708

DUMM, BRYAN JAMES
CELLO

b Rochester, NY, Aug 13, 62. Study: Eastman Sch Music, 80- Pos: Cellist, Rochester Phil Orch, 81- Mailing Add: 35 Holley Ridge Circle Rochester NY 14625

DUMM, THOMAS A
EDUCATOR, VIOLA

Study: Cleveland Inst Music, BM; Ohio State Univ; studied viola with Max Aronoff & Abraham Skernick. Rec Perf: On Vox. Pos: Prin viola, Baltimore Symph, formerly, Rochester Phil, formerly & St Louis Symph Orch, currently; mem, Cleveland Orch, formerly & St Louis String Quartet, currently; concerto, recital & chamber music perfs. Teaching: Vis lectr viola, Univ Md, College Park, formerly & Eastman Sch Music, formerly; mem fac viola & chamber music, St Louis Consv Music, currently. Mailing Add: St Louis Consv Music 560 Trinity Ave St Louis MO 36130

DUMONT, LILY
PIANO, TEACHER & COACH

b Berlin, Germany; US citizen. Study: Sternsche Consv, studied with Jenny Krause; Hochschule Musik, with Leonid Kreutzer; studied with George Bertram; theory & harmony with Jacob Dumont, Roosevelt Univ, Vienna, studied Schenker theory with Oswald Jonas. Rec Perf: Chopin, His Master's Voice; Chopin, Polydor; Haydn-Mozart, Conct Hall Soc. Teaching: Private instr, Dartmouth Col, Boston, New York & Washington, DC; instr advan coaching & master classes, Longy Sch Music, 52-; artist in res, Southeastern Mass Univ, 68, instr master classes, 72- Mem: Music Teachers Nat Asn; Mass Music Teachers Asn. Mailing Add: 263 Hawthorn St New Bedford MA 02740

DUNBAR, PAUL EDWARD
ADMINISTRATOR, ORGAN

b Gasville, Ark, Mar 31, 52. Study: Henderson State Univ, BM, 74; La State Univ, Baton Rouge, MM, 75, DMA, 80. Teaching: Head organ dept, Bob Jones Univ, 78-, univ organist, 78-, chmn div music, 81- Mem: Music Educr

Nat Conf (pres student group, 71-74); Am Guild Organists (dean Greenville chap, 79-81, sub-dean, 83). Publ: The Six Schübler Chorales for Organ: A Performing Edition, La State Univ, 81. Mailing Add: Music Dept Bob Jones Univ Greenville SC 29614

DUNCAN, CHARLES F, JR
WRITER, GUITAR & LUTE

b Savannah, Ga, Mar 23, 40. Rec Perf: Four Centuries of Music For Flute and Guitar, Golden Crest, 79. Pos: Guitar Forum Ed, Am String Teacher, 80- Teaching: Instr guitar, Emory Univ, 76- Mem: Music Teachers Nat Asn (pres Atlanta chap, 80-82); Am String Teachers Asn. Publ: Auth, various articles in Am String Teacher, Guitar Rev, Guitar Player, 76-80; The Art of Classical Guitar Playing, Summy-Birchard, 80; The Modern Approach to Classical Guitar, Hal Leonard, 81-83. Rep: Alkahest Agency PO Box 12403 Northside Sta Atlanta GA 30355. Mailing Add: 155 Balling Rd Atlanta GA 30305

DUNCAN, DAN J (DANNY JOE)
OBOE & ENGLISH HORN, EDUCATOR

b Manhattan, Kans, Apr 16, 40. Study: Northwestern Univ, BME, 62; Wichita State Univ, MME, 64; Ind Univ, DME, 79. Pos: Second oboe & solo English horn, Corpus Christi Symph Orch, 65-81. Teaching: Supvr music, Lamar Pub Sch, Mo, 64-65; assoc prof music, Tex A&I Univ, 65-81 & Eastern Ky Univ, 81- Mailing Add: 137 Frankie Dr Richmond KY 40475

DUNCAN, DOUGLAS JON
ADMINISTRATOR, EDUCATOR

b Osage, Iowa, Aug 2, 50. Study: Simpson Col, BM, 72; Philadelphia Musical Acad, MMus, 74; studied with Licia Albanese; studied voice with Richard Torigi. Roles: Ford in Falstaff, Philadelphia Musical Acad. Pos: Singer, Des Moines Metro Opera, formerly, managing dir, 74-; singer, Augusta Opera Co, formerly, Cedar Rapids Symph, formerly, Pa Opera Co, formerly, Philadelphia Musical Theatre, formerly, & Opera Co Philadelphia, formerly. Teaching: Mem fac, Philadelphia Musical Acad, formerly; asst prof music, Simpson Col, 75-80, adj instr voice, currently. Mailing Add: 411 W Ashland Indianola IA 50125

DUNHAM, BENJAMIN STARR
ADMINISTRATOR, RECORDER

b New York, NY, Sept 19, 44. Study: Deerfield Acad, dipl, 62; Harvard Col, BA, 66; studied recorder with Marrie Bremer, 67-70; Boston Univ, 70; Cath Univ, 71-74. Pos: Asst ed, Music Educr Jour, 67-70; ed, Symph News & dir publc relations & publ, Am Symph Orch League, 71-78, exec dir, 82-; exec dir & ed Am Ens, Chamber Music Am, 78-82; mem, The Washington Consort, early music ens, 73-78; prin rec, Handel Fest Orch, Kennedy Ctr, Washington, DC, 77-78. Teaching: Fac mem music, Trinity Col, Washington, DC, 73-75. Awards: Arts Adminr of Yr, Arts Mgt, Adelphi Univ Arts Mgt Prog. Bibliog: Harold Schonberg (auth), The Boom in Chamber Music, New York Times, 1/79. Mem: Chamber Music Am; Am Rec Soc (alt bd mem, 80-); Nat Guild Community Sch Arts (mem bd trustees, 82-84). Publ: Ed, The Education of Performing Musicians, Contemp Music Project, 73; Educating the Performing Musician, 73 & Symphony Orchestras Are Playing for Keeps, 77, Symph News; Chamber Music is Booming, Am Arts, 79; Chamber Music: Inclusive, Not Exclusive, Am Ens, 81. Mailing Add: 188 N Columbus Ave Mt Vernon NY 10553

DUNHAM, JAMES FRASER
VIOLA, TEACHER

b Washington, DC, Aug 27, 50. Study: Calif Inst Arts, BFA, 72, MFA, 74. Rec Perf: Ravel Quartet, Delos Rec, 77; Sapieyevski Concerto, Crystal Rec, 83; Mozart Early Quartets, Dvorak Quintet, Op 77, Schoenberg Quartet No 2, Boccherini Quintets & Weber Clarinet Quintet, Nonesuch Rec. Pos: Participant, Marlboro, Berkshire Music Ctr & Chestnut Hill Concerts, summers 68-; violist & founding mem, Sequoia String Quartet, 72-; prin viola, Calif Chamber Symph, 72-80; asst prin, Los Angeles Chamber Orch, 73-78. Teaching: Mem fac chamber music & viola, Calif Inst Arts, 74. Awards: Walter W Naumburg Found Chamber Music Award, 76. Mailing Add: c/o Artists Alliance 12615 Pacific Ave #1 Los Angeles CA 90066

DUNKEL, PAUL EUGENE
CONDUCTOR & MUSIC DIRECTOR, FLUTE

b New York, NY, July 22, 43. Study: Queens Col, City Univ New York, BA, 64; Teachers Col, Columbia Univ, MA, 67. Rec Perf: Music of Ravel, Nonesuch, 77; Music of Ruth Crawford Seeger, New World, 78; Early Music of Elliott Carter, CRI, 82. Pos: Assoc cond, Am Comp Orch, 77-; music dir, Orch New York, 77-80; music dir & prin cond, White Plains Symph Orch, 82- Teaching: Guest instr flute, Eastman Sch Music, 75-76 & New England Consv, 76-77. Awards: First Prize Woodwind Compt, Musicians Club of NY, 66; Second Prize Int Woodwind Compt, Birmingham, England, 66; Leopold Stokowski Prize, Am Symph Orch, 82. Mailing Add: 85 Mercer Ave Hartsdale NY 10530

DUNKEL, STUART
EDUCATOR, OBOE

Study: Boston Univ, BM; studied oboe with Ralph Gomberg, Harold Gomberg, John Mack, Robert Bloom & Harry Shulman. Pos: Performer, Hong Kong Phil, 81, Springfield Symph, RI Symph, Mozart Esplande Orch & Handel & Haydn Soc Orch; mem, New Boston Wind Quintet, currently; prin oboe, Pro Arte Chamber Orch Boston, currently & Boston Opera Co, currently; solo recitalist at New England univ, sch & churches. Teaching: Mem fac oboe, Longy Sch Music, currently. Mailing Add: Longy Sch Music 1 Follen St Cambridge MA 02138

DUNN, FRANK RICHARD
MUSIC DIRECTOR, FRENCH HORN
b Birmingham, Ala, Feb 27, 29. *Study:* State Acad, Vienna, dipl, 56; Univ Calif, Berkeley, MA, 62. *Rec Perf:* Wald und Nachtieder der Romantik, Amadeo Schallplattenges, 70; Baroque Music (horn & orch), MCA, Westminster, 81. *Pos:* Asst cond, Oakland Symph, 60-62 & dir, Conct Theater Asn, 60-67 & Pac Music Soc, 73- *Teaching:* Asst prof music, Ind Univ, 75-76. *Awards:* Alfred Hertz Scholar, 55-56. *Publ:* Auth, Mozarts Unvollendete Hornkonzerte, Mozart Jahrbuch, 61; coauth, Observations on French Horn Musicians, J Occup Medicine, 76. *Mailing Add:* 27 Skyline Circle Santa Barbara CA 93109

DUNN, LYNDA
ADMINISTRATOR
b Scarsdale, NY, Dec 27, 52. *Study:* Parsons Sch Design, 70; NY Univ, 72; Sch Gen Studies, Hunter Col, 73-77. *Pos:* Asst mgr, Am Comp Alliance, 77-83; orch mgr, Am Comp Orch, 82-83, gen mgr, 83- *Mem:* Am Symph Orch League; Am Fedn Musicians. *Mailing Add:* Am Comp Orch 170 W 74th St New York NY 10023

DUNN, MIGNON (MIGNON DUNN-KLIPPSTATTER)
MEZZO-SOPRANO
b Memphis, Tenn. *Study:* Studied with Karin Branzell; Southwestern Memphis, Hon Dr Music, 74. *Rec Perf:* Salome, Rigoletto, Louise & Mother of Us All, Deutsche Grammophon. *Roles:* Performed with major companies worldwide & performed all major roles of repertory with Metropolitan Opera, 59- *Pos:* Mezzo-soprano, Metropolitan Opera, 59- *Rep:* Toni Russo 165 W 57th New York NY 10019. *Mailing Add:* PO Box 431 East Granby CT 06026

DUNN, SUSAN REGENIA
SOPRANO
b Malvern, Ark, July 23, 54. *Study:* Hendrix Col, BA, 76; Ind Univ, Bloomington, MM, 80. *Roles:* Aida, 82 & Amelia in Un Ballo in maschera, 83, Peoria Opera Co; sop soloist in Requiem (Verdi), New York Choral Soc, 83. *Awards:* First Prize, WGN, Ill Opera Guild, 83; G B Dealey First Prize, Dallas Morning News & Dallas Opera, 83. *Mem:* Mu Phi Epsilon. *Rep:* Kazuko Hillyer Inc 250 W 57th St New York NY 10107. *Mailing Add:* 408 W Springfield Urbana IL 61801

DUNN, THOMAS BURT
CONDUCTOR & MUSIC DIRECTOR, ORGAN
b Aberdeen, SDak, Dec 21, 25. *Study:* Johns Hopkins Univ, BS, 46; Peabody Consv, teachers cert(organ), 46; Harvard Univ, MA, 48; Royal Consv Amsterdam, dipl(orch cond), 55. *Rec Perf:* Messiah (Handel), Sine Qua Non, 77; Arias (Handel), Walton-Facade, Suite No 1 (Bach) & Cantata No 51 (Bach), Decca; Hymns, RCA; King of Instruments, Aeolian Skinner. *Pos:* Cond, Cantata Singers, NY, 58-65; music dir & cond, Fest Orch & Chorus, NY, 58-68; artistic dir & cond, Handel & Haydn Soc, Mass, 67-; ed in chief, E C Schirmer Music Co, Mass, 69-76. *Teaching:* Instr, Peabody Consv, 47-49, Swarthmore Col, 49-51, Univ Pa, 55-60, Union Theol Sem, 61-69, State Univ NY, Buffalo, 71-72, Westminster Choir Col, 72-74, Aspen Music Sch, 73-75, Blossom Fest Sch, 73-76 & Ithaca Col, 76-77; dir choral activ, Boston Univ, 77- *Mailing Add:* 158 Newbury St Boston MA 02116

DU PAGE, FLORENCE ELIZABETH
COMPOSER, MUSIC DIRECTOR
b Vandergrift, Pa. *Study:* Studied piano with Ignace Hilsberg, 30-33, harmony with Rubin Goldmark, 33-35, comp & orch with Tibor Serly, 45-50 & organ with Dr Thomas Richner, 60-65. *Works:* Two Sketches for String Orchestra, Vogel, 46; Lost Valley, 46 & The Pond (symph orch), 48, Porter Press; Alice in Wonderland (ballet suite), Carl Fischer, 51; Trial Universelle (sacred chamber opera), Church Advent, 63; Whither (sacred drama), Chamber Orch Westbury; New World for Nellie (ballad opera), Rowland Emmet, 65. *Pos:* Organist & choral dir, Episcopal Church, NY, 54-66 & Atlanta Lutheran Church, 70-77. *Teaching:* Music supvr, Advent Tuller Day Sch, 54-62; Choral dir, Cathedral Sch St Mary, 63-66. *Awards:* Nat Award, Boston Women's Symph, 41. *Bibliog:* The Pond Symphony Award, New York Times, 41; Saratoga Festival, New York Times, 48; Ballet Suite, Rochester Symposium, 48. *Mem:* Am Guild Organists (subdean Chautauqua chap, 69-70); Am Women Comp; ASCAP. *Mailing Add:* 3760 Harts Mill Ln Atlanta GA 30319

DURE, ROBERT
COMPOSER, EDUCATOR
b Baltimore, Md, Nov 25, 34. *Study:* Peabody Consv Music, with Louis Cheslock & Robert Hall Lewis; Univ Md, with Lester Trimble & Morton Subotnick. *Works:* King Lear (orch & solo voice); Preludium (orch); Piece for Eight (orch); Analytic Melody (violin & piano); Canon for Winds (woodwind trio); Movement for String Quartet; String Quartet—1965. *Teaching:* Mem fac, Prince Georges Co Community Col, 65-67 & Ind Univ, 77- *Mailing Add:* 5336 W Johnson Rd La Porte IN 46350

DURHAM, LOWELL M
COMPOSER, EDUCATOR
b Boston, Mass, Mar 4, 17. *Study:* Univ Utah; Univ Iowa, with Philip Greeley Clapp & Addison Alspach; studied with Leroy Robertson. *Works:* Prelude and Scherzo (string orch), 44; New England Pastorale (string orch), 55; Variations for Strings, 60; This is My Country (double chorus), perf by Mormon Tabernacle Choir at Pres Johnson's Inauguration, 64 & at Pres Nixon's Inauguration, 68; Folkscape for Orchestra, 67; Calm as a Summer Morn (chorus & orch), 71; Choralise (a cappella chorus), 72. *Mailing Add:* Music Dept Univ Utah 204 Gardner Hall Salt Lake City UT 84112

DURHAM, THOMAS LEE
COMPOSER, EDUCATOR
b Salt Lake City, Utah, Aug 26, 50. *Study:* Univ Utah, BM, 74, MM, 75; Univ Iowa, PhD, 78. *Works:* Jesus the Savior Is Born, 79, God Be with You, 80, Whence Is That Goodly Fragrance, 82 & Anthem, 83, Deseret Music Publ; For the Strength of the Hills, Pioneer Music Press, 83. *Teaching:* Grad asst, Univ Utah, 74-75; grad instr, Univ Iowa, 75-78; asst prof theory & comp, Brigham Young Univ, 78-83, assoc prof, 83- *Mem:* Utah Acad Arts, Lett & Sci. *Interests:* Computer analysis of American orchestral repertoire. *Mailing Add:* 151 South 240 East Orem UT 84057

DUSCHAK, ALICE GERSTL
SOPRANO
Study: Hochschule Musik & darstellende Kunst, Vienna, dipl; Mozarteum, Salzburg; studied with Maestro Moratti & Elisabeth Schumann. *Rec Perf:* On Educo Rec. *Pos:* Leading sop, Opera House Muenster; guest appearances, opera houses in Austria & Germany; radio broadcasts, Vienna State Opera; concert & oratorio soloist, Europe & US. *Teaching:* Mem fac, MacPhail Col Music, 41-44, Cath Univ Am, 44, Washington Musical Inst, 44-45, Howard Univ, 52-53 & Peabody Consv, currently. *Mem:* Int Soc Contemp Music. *Publ:* Auth, numerous articles on vocal technique & interpretation. *Mailing Add:* Peabody Consv Music Baltimore MD 21202

DUTT, HENRY (ALLAN)
VIOLA
b Muscatine, Iowa, Nov 4, 52. *Study:* Ind Univ, with David Dawson, George Janzer & Abraham Sernick, BMus, MMus(viola perf), 77. *Pos:* Violist, Kronos String Quartet, 77- *Bibliog:* Paul Hertelendy (auth), The Kronos Quartet: Displaying a California Style, Musical Am, 10/80; Wolfgang Schreiber (auth), Die Entdeckerlust, Suddeutsche Zeitung, 3/13-14/83; Tom O'Connor (auth), String Fever, Focus Mag, 4/83. *Mailing Add:* Kronos Quartet 1238-Ninth Ave San Francisco CA 94122

DUTTON, BRENTON PRICE
COMPOSER, TUBA
b Saskatoon, Sask, Mar 20, 50. *Study:* Consv Music, Oberlin Col, BM, 75, MM, 76. *Works:* Symphony 2, 77, Symphony 3, 77, On Looking Back, 78, December Set, 79, Theme Varie, 80, Seesaw Music; Carnival of Venice, Touch of Brass, 82; Dialogues of the Sybarites, Seesaw Music, 83. *Pos:* Prin tuba, L'Orchestre Symphonique du Quebec, 71-74. *Teaching:* Assoc music, Consv Music, Oberlin Col, 75-76; asst prof music, Cent Mich Univ, 76-81; assoc prof music, San Diego State Univ, 82- *Mailing Add:* 7030 Keighley Ct San Diego CA 92120

DUTTON, JAMES N
CONDUCTOR & MUSIC DIRECTOR, ADMINISTRATOR
b Sioux City, Iowa, Mar 10, 21. *Study:* Morningside Col; Univ Nebr, Lincoln; Northwestern Univ, BM, MM; studied perc with Edward Metzenger, 41-43; studied comp with Albert Nolte, 42 & Robert Delaney, 47; studied cond with Leonard Bernstein, 48 & 49, Pierre Monteux, 53-55, 57 & 60 & Richard Lert, 57. *Pos:* Soloist with various groups & orchs incl Chicago Symph Orch, 46, Dutton-French Duo, 47-52, James Dutton Quartet, 61-70 & Jamz Dutton Perc Arts Orch, 70-; cond, Am Consv Chamber Players, 50-51, Abendmusik series & Music Fest, Beverly Hills, Ill, 50-60, Chicago Artists Chamber Music, 53-57, Chicago Artists Opera, 54-61, Am Consv Chorus, 56-57, STown Youth Conct, Chicago & Homewood, 57-63, Am Consv Lab Band, 66-70 & Jamz Dutton Perc Arts Orch, 70-; lectr TV series, WTTW, Chicago, 57-60 & Beverly Hills Forum, Chicago, 60; guest cond, Midwest Band Clinic & St Louis Phil, 59-; founder & dir, Perc Arts Studio, Chicago, 60- & Birch Creek Music Ctr, Egg Harbor, Wis, 76-; timpani & perc, Mr Kicks (Broadway musical), Chicago, 62, Bolshoi Ballet Orch, Chicago, 63 & Vienna Phil, 64. *Teaching:* Instr, appl perc & chamber music & dir chamber music prog, Am Consv Music. *Mem:* Phi Mu Alpha; Pi Kappa Lambda; Am Symph Orch League. *Mailing Add:* 505 N Lake Shore Dr Chicago IL 60611

DUTTON, LAWRENCE WILLARD
VIOLA
b New York, NY, May 9, 54. *Study:* Eastman Sch Music, with Francis Tursi; Juilliard Sch, with Lillian Fuchs, BM, 77, MM, 78. *Rec Perf:* Andrew Imbrie String Quartet No 4 & Gunther Schuller String Quartet No 2, New World Rec, 78; The Koussevitzky Legacy—Piston's Concerto for String Quartet Wind Instruments & Percussion, CRI, 78; The Twentieth Century Concert Vol II, Smithsonian Rec, 82. *Pos:* Violist, Emerson String Quartet, 77- & Lincoln Ctr Chamber Music Soc, 82- *Teaching:* Vis artist, Hartt Sch Music, 80- & Middlebury Col, 81- *Awards:* Naumberg Chamber Music Award, 78. *Mem:* Chamber Music Am. *Mailing Add:* 60 W 76th St New York NY 10023

DUTTON, MARY ANN ENLOE
EDUCATOR, MUSIC DIRECTOR
b Phoenix, Ariz, July 4, 31. *Study:* Ariz State Univ, MA, 54; Northwestern Univ, studied voice with Hermanus Baer & opera with Robert Gay; San Diego State Univ; San Francisco State Col; Univ Ariz, studied voice with Eugene Conley. *Rec Perf:* Masterworks Chorale Concert, Flagstaff Fest of Arts, 82; Glendale Community Col Artists Series Concert, Jack Miller Prod, 83. *Pos:* Dir, four overseas tours, YMCA Youth Chorus, 60-63 & Masterworks Chorale, 79-; music dir, Phoenix Grace Lutheran Church, 13 yrs; vpres bd dir, Ariz Opera Co, currently. *Teaching:* Prof music, Glendale Community Col, 64-; mem fac & co-dir opera, Summer Music Camp, Northern Ariz Univ, 70- *Mem:* Sigma Alpha Iota; Nat Asn Teachers Singing; Nat Soc Arts & Lett; Nat Opera Asn. *Mailing Add:* 4925 W Banff Lane Glendale AZ 85306

DVORAK, THOMAS L
CONDUCTOR, EDUCATOR
b Madison, Wis, Oct 14, 41. *Study:* Univ Wis, Platteville, BS, 63; Univ Wis, Madison, MM, 68. *Rec Perf:* Music Educr Nat Conf, Univ Wis Wind Ens, 81 & 22nd Ann Col Band Dir Nat Asn, Univ Wis Ens, 83, Crest Rec. *Teaching:* Dir music, McFarland Pub Sch, Wis, 68-75; asst prof, Univ Mich, 75-79; assoc prof & dir bands, Univ Milwaukee, 79- *Awards:* Outstanding Sec Educr Am. *Mem:* Col Band Dir Nat Asn; Wis Bandmasters Asn; Nat Band Asn. *Publ:* Coauth, Introducing the Trumpet, GIA Chicago, 77; auth, Good Music For Young Bands, 80 & The NBA Compositions: A Review of Pieces, 82, Instrumentalist. *Mailing Add:* Univ Wis PO Box 412 Milwaukee WI 53201

DVORINE, SHURA
COMPOSER, PIANO
b Baltimore, Md, June 22, 23. *Study:* Baltimore City Col; Peabody Consv Music, dipl, 43. *Works:* Pensive Nocturne (piano), 48; The Lovers' Concerto (ballet), 67; The Ballet School; Ballet No 3, 72; Ballet School II, 73; I Danced with an Angel (song); What Do I Keep (song). *Pos:* Soloist, Baltimore Symph, Nat Gallery Symphonette & Radio City Music Hall Symph Orch; solo & chamber music concerts throughout US. *Teaching:* Mem fac piano, Univ Ill, formerly, Westchester Consv Music, formerly & Prep Sch, Peabody Consv Music, 71- *Mem:* ASCAP; Am Guild Authors & Comp; Music Teachers Nat Asn. *Mailing Add:* Peabody Consv Music 1 E Mt Vernon Pl Baltimore MD 21202

DVORKIN, JUDITH
COMPOSER, PIANO
b New York, NY. *Study:* Barnard Col, BA; Columbia Univ, MA; studied with Roger Sessions. *Works:* Three Letter: John Keats to Fanny Brawne (baritone & orch), New Century Players, 60; Moments in Time (bass voice & chamber group), Raymond Michaelski, 61; Cyrano, Limelight Players, 65; The Crescent Eyebrow (conct opera), Conn Opera Asn, 79; Song Cycle for Mezzo-Soprano, Linda Eckard, 80; Four Women, Jacqueline Sharpe, 81; Six Zoological Considerations, Julia Lovett, 83. *Bibliog:* John Tasker Howard (auth), Our American Music, Crowell, 54; Miriam Stewart-Green (auth), Women Composers Works, Univ Kans Press, 80. *Mem:* Am Music Ctr. *Rep:* Claire Rosengarten 490 West End St New York NY 10024. *Mailing Add:* 19 E 80th St New York NY 10021

DWYER, DORIOT ANTHONY
FLUTE, EDUCATOR
b Ill. *Study:* Eastman Sch Music, with G Barrere, William Kincaid & Joseph Mariano, BMus, 43; studied with Edith Dwyer & Ernest Leigl; Harvard Univ, Hon Dr, 82; Simmons Col, Hon Dr, 82. *Pos:* Second flute, Nat Symph, 43 & Los Angeles Phil, 45-52; prin flute & soloist, Boston Symph Orch, 52- & Hollywood Bowl; flutist, Boston Symph Chamber Players, currently, Doriot Anthony Dwyer and Friends, currently & other chamber music groups; performer, Camel Back Fest, Berkshire Fest, Rocky Mountain Music Fest & others. *Teaching:* Mem fac, Pomona Col, formerly, New England Consv Music, formerly & Berkshire Music Ctr, currently; adj prof flute, Boston Univ, currently. *Awards:* Sanford Fel, Yale Sch Music, 75. *Bibliog:* Phyllis Lehmann (auth), Women in Orchestras: The Promise and the Problems, 12/82. *Mem:* Nat Coun Women. *Rep:* Am Int Artists 275 Madison Ave New York NY 10016. *Mailing Add:* 3 Cleveland Rd Brookline MA 02146

DYDO, JOHN STEPHEN
COMPOSER, GUITAR
b San Francisco, Calif, May 2, 48. *Study:* Columbia Col, BA, 70; Columbia Univ, DMA, 75. *Works:* Trio Sonata, 73, Winter Song, 75 & Capriccio (violin & seven players), 77, Asn Promotion New Music; Fandango (clarinet & guitar), Mobart Music Publ, 80; Short Mass, 80 & Cantata, 81, Am Comp Ed; Carmina Sacra, Am Comp Ed, 81. *Pos:* Dir, Comp Ens, New York, 76-79; asst ed, Contemp Music Newsletter, 77-80; res assoc, Inst Sonology, Utrecht, Netherlands, 81-83. *Awards:* Young Comp Award, BMI, 72; Bearns Prize, 72; Comp Assistance Fel, Nat Endowment Arts, 79. *Mem:* Am Comp Alliance; Asn Promotion New Music. *Publ:* Auth, Surface Relations Between Language and Music as Compositional Aids, Interface, 83. *Mailing Add:* 90 Morningside Dr New York NY 10027

DYER, JOSEPH
EDUCATOR
b Philadelphia, Pa, Mar 6, 38. *Study:* Boston Univ, AM, 65, PhD, 71. *Pos:* Musicol, Handel & Haydn Soc Boston, 68- *Teaching:* Assoc prof music, Boston State Col, 67-82 & Univ Mass, Boston, 82- *Interests:* Early Christian and medieval chant and liturgy. *Publ:* Auth, Singing with Proper Refinement ..., Early Music, 78; A Thirteenth Century Choirmaster ... Elias Salomon, Musical Quart, 80; Augustine and the Hymni Ante Oblationem ..., Revue des Etudes Augustiniennes, 81; The Offertory Chant of the Roman Liturgy ..., Studi Musicali, 82. *Mailing Add:* 73 Wade St Newton Highlands MA 02161

E

EAGLE, CHARLES THOMAS, JR
EDUCATOR, WRITER
Study: Univ Tex, Austin, BM, 55, MM, 56; Univ Kans, with E Thayer Gaston & William W Sears, PhD, 71. *Pos:* Staff researcher & music therapist, Vet Admin Hosp, Topeka, 66-68. *Teaching:* Instr music, pub sch, Midland, Tex,

56-58; asst prof music educ, Univ Miami, 69-72; prof music therapy, Southern Methodist Univ, 75-, prof music psychophysics, 81- *Bibliog:* Kate Herner Mueller (auth), Effects of Existing Mood ... on Responses to that Music, Coun Res Music Educ Bulletin, 73; Avery T Sharpe (auth), Music Therapy Index, 76 & Thomas A Regelski (auth), Music Psychology Index, Vol 2, 80, J Music Therapy. *Mem:* Brit Soc Music Therapy; Music Educr Nat Conf; Nat Asn Music Therapy (secy, 73-76, vpres, 76-78); Soc Res Psychology Music & Music Educ; Tex Music Educr Asn. *Interests:* Influence of music on behavior. *Publ:* Coauth, The Function of Music in LSD Therapy for Alcoholic Patients, J Music Therapy, 70; ed, Music Therapy Index, Vol 1, Nat Asn Music Therapy, 76; Music Psychology Index, Vol 2, Inst Therapeutics Res, 78; auth, Chapter 1: An Introductory Perspective of Music Psychology, Nat Asn Music Therapy, 80; coauth, Project MUSIC Series, Inst Therapeutics Res, 82. *Mailing Add:* 1817 Field Cove Plano TX 75023

EAGLE, DAVID WILLIAM
WRITER, EDUCATOR
b Crookston, Minn, Aug 13, 29. *Study:* Univ Minn, BS, 57, BA, 57, PhD, 77. *Pos:* Writer, Pickwick Int, Minneapolis, 80-82 & Intersound, Minneapolis, 82-; flutist, Take Five Woodwind Quintet, St Paul, 81- *Mem:* Am Musicol Soc; Col Music Soc; Nat Flute Asn. *Interests:* Social history of flute-playing in 19th century Great Britain. *Publ:* Auth, The Tower Bands, Showcase, 81. *Mailing Add:* 2904 W River Pkwy Minneapolis MN 55406

EAKIN, CHARLES
EDUCATOR, COMPOSER
b Pittsburgh, Pa, Feb 24, 27. *Study:* Manhattan Sch Music, with Vitorio Giannini; Carnegie-Mellon Univ, with Nikolai Lopatnikoff; Univ Minn, with Paul Fetler. *Works:* The Box (opera); Being of Sound Mind (opera); Symphony No 2, The Durango; Capriccio for Trombone and Tape; Violin Concerto; Paul's Piece (violin, piano & perc); Tonight I Am (sop & tape). *Teaching:* Fac mem, Baylor Univ, 60-64; prof music, Univ Colo, Boulder, 64- *Mailing Add:* Music Dept Univ Colo Boulder CO 80309

EARLE, EUGENIA
EDUCATOR, KEYBOARD
Study: Mannes Sch Music, dipl; Teachers Col, Columbia Univ, MA, EdD; Vienna Acad Music, harpsichord with Eta Harich-Schneider & Fernando Valenti; studied piano with Felix Salzer & Isabella Vengerova, theory analysis with William Mitchell & Felix Salzer & musicol with Paul Henry Lang & Christophe Wolff. *Rec Perf:* On Musical Heritage Soc. *Pos:* Solo recitals, chamber music concerts & wkshps throughout US. *Teaching:* Mem fac tech music, Mannes Col Music, 47-63, mem fac harpsichord, 77-; mem fac, Sch Sacred Music, Union Theol Sem, 63-73, Rutgers Univ, formerly & Teachers Col, Columbia Univ, 67-; mem fac organ, Manhattan Sch Music, 75-, mem fac harpsichord, 82- *Mem:* Col Music Soc; Am Musicol Soc; Int Musicol Soc; Music Teachers Nat Asn. *Publ:* Lee Roberts Publications. *Mailing Add:* Manhattan Sch Music 120 Claremont Ave New York NY 10027

EARLS, PAUL
COMPOSER
b Springfield, Mo, June 9, 34. *Study:* SW Mo State Col, 51-53; Eastman Sch Music, BM, 55, MM, 56, PhD, 59. *Works:* Trine, 71 & City Ring, 75, Ione Press; The Death of King Phillip, New England Chamber Opera, 76; A Grimm Duo, Boston Lyric Opera, 76; Doppelgänger, Nora Post, Buffalo, 77; Modulations (electronic), perf by Lasers, Mass Inst Technol, 82; Icarus, Ars Electronica, 82 & Munich Opera & Boston Musica Viva, 83. *Pos:* Fel, Ctr Advan Visual Studies, Mass Inst Technol, 70- *Teaching:* Assoc prof music, Duke Univ, 66-71 & Mass Inst Technol; vis prof, Univ Calif, Chico, 74-; comp-in-res, Univ Lowell, 77-78. *Awards:* Fel, Guggenheim Found, 70. *Bibliog:* Brian DuMaine (auth), Trapping the Light Fantastic, United Mainliner, 2/81; Freff (auth), Future, Music & Sound Output, 6/82. *Publ:* Auth, Harry Partch: Verses, In: Yearbook, Int-Am Inst Musical Res, 67; Szygy, by David del Tredic, Perspectives of New Music, 70; Sounding Space, Sound Sculpture, 75. *Mailing Add:* 40 Massachusetts Ave Cambridge MA 02139

EAST, JAMES EDWARD
CLARINET, EDUCATOR
b Hays, Kans, July 15, 41. *Study:* Consv Music, Oberlin Col, with George Waln, BM(clarinet perf), 63; Cleveland Inst Music, with Robert Marcellus, MM(clarinet perf), 69; Eastman Sch Music, with Stanley Hasty; studied with Leon Russianoff, 75. *Rec Perf:* Frieze (Frazeur), Grenadilla Rec, 76; Metamorphoses (Hartley), Advan Rec, 78. *Pos:* Asst solo clarientist, US Navy Band, Washington, DC, 65-69; prin clarinetist, Erie Phil Orch, Pa, 79- *Teaching:* Lectr, Prince George's Community Col, 65-; assoc prof, State Univ NY, Fredonia, 70- *Mem:* Int Clarinet Soc; ClariNetwork Int; Music Teachers Nat Asn. *Mailing Add:* 181 Temple St Fredonia NY 14063

EATON, JOHN C
COMPOSER, EDUCATOR
b Bryn Mawr, Pa, Mar 30, 35. *Study:* Princeton Univ, AB, 57, MFA, 59; studied comp with Roger Sessions, Milton Babbitt, Edward T Cone. *Works:* Concert Piece, 66, Mass, 70, Heracles (opera), 72, Myshkin (opera), 72 & The Lion and Androcles (children's opera), 73, Shawnee Press; Danton and Robespierre (opera), 78 & The Cry of Clytaemnestra (opera), 80, Schirmer. *Teaching:* Prof music, Ind Univ, Bloomington, 70- *Awards:* Prix de Rome, Am Acad, Rome, 59-62; citation, Nat Inst Arts & Letters, 72. *Bibliog:* Adventure in Sound, Time Mag, 5/24/68; Peter G Davis (auth), A Vivid Rendering of a Modern Opera, New York Times, 2/24/80; Andrew Porter (auth),

Eleleleleu!, New Yorker, 3/30/80. *Publ:* Auth, Song Cycleon Holy Sonnets of John Donne, 60 & Concert Music for Solo Clarinet, 71, Shawnee; The Exhilirating Adventures of New Music Since 1950, Music in Am Soc, Rutgers Univ, 79; Stories That Break Into Song, Kenyon Rev, 82; Duo, G Schirmer, 83. *Mailing Add:* Sch Music Ind Univ Bloomington IN 47401

EATON, ROY (FELIX)
PIANO, MUSIC DIRECTOR
b New York, NY, May 14, 30. *Study:* Manhattan Sch Music, study with Harold Bauer, 46, BM, 50, MM, 52; Lucerne Consv, study with Edwin Fisher, 49. *Pos:* Conct pianist, Europe, SAm & US, 49-; music dir, Benton & Bowles Advert, New York, 59-82; pres, Roy Eaton Music Inc, 82- *Teaching:* Instr comp, Manhattan Sch Music, 80- *Awards:* Chopin Award, Kosciuszko Found, 50. *Mem:* ASCAP; Soc Advert Musicians, Producers, Authors & Comp. *Rep:* Barberi Paull 15 W 72nd St New York NY 10023. *Mailing Add:* 595 Main St New York NY 10044

EBERHARD, DENNIS
COMPOSER
b Cleveland, Ohio, Dec 9, 43. *Study:* Cleveland Inst Music, with Marie Martin; Univ Ill, with Salvatore Martirano; studied with Wlodzimierz Kotonski. *Works:* Anamorphoses (wind ens), 67; Mariner (three brass, perc, cello, clavichord & tape), 69-70; Chamber music (perc), 71; Parody (sop, chamber ens & perc), 72; Morphos (wind orch), 73; Ikona (tape), 75; Visions of the Moon (sop & instrm ens with text by e e cummings), 78. *Teaching:* Lectr, Univ Ill, 72-73; fac mem, Western Ill Univ, 76-77. *Awards:* BMI Award, 68; Nat Endowment for Arts Grant, 77; Kate Neil Kinley Mem Fel, 78. *Mailing Add:* Am Acad Via Angelo Masina 5 Rome Italy

EBY, MARGARETTE FINK
ADMINISTRATOR, EDUCATOR
b Detroit, Mich. *Study:* Wheaton Col; Am Consv Music; Wayne State Univ, BA(music), 55, MA(music), 62; Univ Mich, PhD(musicol), 71; Detroit Inst Musical Arts; piano study with Lillian Powers & Margaret Mannebach, organ with Frank VanDusen & James Moeser. *Pos:* Artistic dir, Fair Lane Music Guild, 73-77; dean, Col Humanities & Fine Arts, Univ Northern Iowa, 77-81; provost & vchancellor, Univ Mich, Flint, 81-83; pres, Flint Community Cult Fest Inc & Basically Bach Fest-85, Flint, 83- *Teaching:* Private piano, 52-68; instr music, William Tyndale Col, 58-68; asst prof, humanities & music, Wayne State Univ, 71-72; assoc prof music hist, Univ Mich, Dearborn, 72-77; chairperson, Dept Humanities, 75-77; prof music, Univ Mich, Flint, 81- *Mem:* Am Musicol Soc; Int Coun Fine Arts Deans. *Interests:* Music of the early baroque with emphasis on central Germany. *Publ:* Auth, The Pedal Piano: Its Antecedents and Possibilities, Diapason, 61; Dilliger, In: New Grove Dict of Music & Musicians, Macmillan, 80. *Mailing Add:* 1400 E Kearsley Flint MI 48503

ECHOLS, PAUL
EDUCATOR, MUSIC DIRECTOR
Study: Duke Univ, BA; NY Univ, with Gustave Reese & James Haar. *Pos:* Contemp music ed, Peer Int; coord ed, Charles Tues Soc; dir early music wkshps. *Teaching:* Mem fac music, Brooklyn Col, NY Univ, formerly; mem fac early music, Mannes Col Music, currently, dir, Mannes Camerata, 81- *Mailing Add:* Mannes Col Music 157 E 74th St New York NY 10021

ECKERLING, LAWRENCE DAVID
CONDUCTOR & MUSIC DIRECTOR, PIANO
b Chicago, Ill, Oct 23, 56. *Study:* Ind Univ, BME(choral & instrm), 80, MM(instrm cond), 82. *Pos:* Music dir, Pro Musica Chamber Orch, Skokie, Ill, 81-82; asst cond, Omaha Symph, 82-; music dir & mgr, Omaha Area Youth Orch, 82- *Mem:* Am Symph Orch League; Cond Guild. *Mailing Add:* 801 N 48th St #1 Omaha NE 68132

ECKERT, MICHAEL SANDS
COMPOSER, EDUCATOR
b San Mateo, Calif, Oct 27, 50. *Study:* Antioch Col, BA, 72; Univ Chicago, studied comp with Ralph Shapey, MA, 75, PhD, 77. *Works:* Sea-Changes (mezzo & 12 players), 77, Duo for Flute (alto flute & piano), 78, Am Comp Ed; String Quart, Columbia Univ Music Press, 79; Three Poems of Emily Dickinson (sop & 8 players), 81 & Piano Variations, 82, Am Comp Ed; Songs from the Chinese (baritone & piano), comn by NC Music Teachers Asn, 83. *Teaching:* Vis instr music, Antioch Col, 75-76; asst prof, Tulane Univ, 77-81 & Univ NC, Chapel Hill, 81- *Awards:* Joseph H Bearns Prize, Columbia Univ, 75; Charles E Ives scholar, Am Acad Arts & Lett, 76; comp fel, Nat Endowment for Arts, 80. *Bibliog:* Bernard Holland (auth), Concert: Contemporary Music, New York Times, 1/12/81; Howard Carpenter (auth), Review of String Quartet, Am Music Teacher, 1/81. *Mem:* Am Comp Alliance; Am Musicol Soc. *Publ:* Auth, Text and Form in Dallapiccola's Goethe-Lieder, Perspectives of New Music, 79. *Mailing Add:* 407 Walnut St Chapel Hill NC 27514

ECKERT, THOR, JR
CRITIC
b New York, NY, Nov 14, 49. *Study:* Colgate Univ, BA, 71. *Pos:* Music & theatre critic, Christian Sci Monitor, 74-81, nat music critic, 81- *Awards:* Nat Headliner Award, Press Club Atlantic City, 83. *Mem:* Music Critics Asn. *Mailing Add:* 1 Lincoln Plaza New York NY 10023

ECKHART, JANIS GAIL
MEZZO-SOPRANO
b Long Beach, Calif. *Study:* Univ Calif, Los Angeles, BA; Acad Real Musica Madid, with Lloret; studied with Judith Oas-Natalucci, NY & Rome. *Roles:* Carmen in Carmen, Seattle Opera, Cincinnati Opera & Conn Opera; Fenena in Nabucco, New York City Opera, 81; Nicklausse in Les Contes d'Hoffmann, Opera Metropolitana, Caracas, Venezuela, 81; Maddalena in Rigoletto, Opera De Monte Carlo, Monaco, 83. *Awards:* Frank Sinatra Music Award, 71; Sullivan Grant, Nat Opera Inst, 76-; First Place Award, Nat Arts Club, 77. *Mem:* Am Guild Musical Artists; Screen Actors Guild; Actors Equity. *Rep:* Janina Burns Assoc 136 Kingsland St Nutley NJ 07110. *Mailing Add:* 25 W 64th St #2B New York NY 10023

EDDLEMAN, G DAVID
COMPOSER, EDITOR
b Winston-Salem, NC, Aug 20, 36. *Study:* Appalachian State Univ, BS, 58; Va Commonwealth Univ, MMus, 63; Boston Univ, DMA, 71. *Works:* Intimations, 69 & Dance of Alone, 73, perf by Ens MW2, Krakow, Poland; Piece for Adam Kaczynski, perf by Adam Kaczynski, 74; The Innkeeper's Carol (choral), Shawnee Press, 75; Sing, O Sing (choral), 76, Clap Your Hands (choral), 77 & David Danced Before the Lord (choral), 82, Carl Fischer. *Pos:* Choral dir, Grove's High Sch, Savannah, Ga, 59-60 & Lafayette Sch, Morristown, NJ, 63-68; dir, Third Army Chorus, Atlanta, Ga, 60-62; ed, Silver Burdett Co, 72- *Teaching:* Teaching assoc, Boston Univ, 68-72. *Awards:* Standard Panel Award, ASCAP, 82. *Mem:* Am Soc Univ Comp; Col Music Soc; Am Choral Dir Asn. *Publ:* Auth & ed, Reading Rhythm, 74, contribr, Silver Burdett Music, Vols 1-8, 74, 78 & 81, auth, Oh Your Own, Vol 5, 78, ed, Silver Burdett Music, Vols 2 & 8, 81 & 82 & Dick Thompson Choral System, 82, Silver Burdett. *Mailing Add:* 12 James Ct Rockaway NJ 07866

EDDLEMAN, (ROBERT) JACK
STAGE DIRECTOR—OPERA
b Millsap, Tex, Sept 7, 33. *Study:* Univ Tulsa; Univ Mo, Kansas City; Inst Advan Studies Theatre Arts. *Roles:* Yeomen of the Guard, Kansas City Lyr Opera, 72. *Pos:* Dir & prod, Kansas City Lyr Opera, Lake George Opera Co, New York City Opera & Opera St Paul; res stage dir, New York City Opera, currently. *Mailing Add:* 162 Ninth Ave New York NY 10011

EDDY, TIMOTHY
CELLO, EDUCATOR
Study: Manhattan Sch Music, BM, MM; studied cello with Bernard Greenhouse. *Rec Perf:* On Columbia, Vanguard, Nonesuch, CRI, Vox & Desto. *Pos:* Tours of US with Music from Marlboro ser, formerly; cellist, Bach Aria Group, currently, Galimir Quartet, currently & New York Phil Chamber Ens, currently; soloist, Dallas Symph, formerly, Denver Symph, formerly & NC Symph, formerly. *Teaching:* Artist in res, State Univ NY, Stony Brook, currently; mem fac violoncello, New England Consv Music, currently & Mannes Col Music, 80- *Awards:* Winner, Dealy Cont, Denver Symph Guild Compt & NC Symph Cont. *Mailing Add:* New England Consv Music 290 Huntingdon Rd Boston MA 02115

EDER, TERRY EDWARD
MUSIC DIRECTOR, EDUCATOR
b Austin, Tex, Aug 19, 46. *Study:* Tex Christian Univ, BME, 69, MME, 73; Univ Okla, DMA(choral cond), 79; study with B R Henson & Julius Herford. *Pos:* Choral dir, McAllen, Independent Sch District, Tex, 69-71 & 73-74. *Teaching:* Assoc prof music, Univ NDak, 78-; dir choral studies, Grand Forks, NDak, 78- *Mem:* Am Choral Dir Asn; Music Educr Nat Conf. *Mailing Add:* 921 32nd Ave S #18 Grand Forks ND 58201

EDLEFSEN, BLAINE ELLIS
EDUCATOR, OBOE & ENGLISH HORN
b Soda Springs, Idaho, Aug 24, 30. *Study:* Brigham Young Univ, BA, 52; Eastman Sch Music, MM, 53, Dr Musical Arts, 66. *Pos:* Oboist & English hornist, Utah Symph Orch, 53-59 & Eastman Wind Ensemble, 59-61; prin oboe, Champaign-Urbana Symph Orch, 61-; oboist, Ill Woodwind Quintet, 61- *Teaching:* Instr oboe, music theory & hist, Brigham Young Univ, 53-61; prof oboe & chamber music lit, Univ Ill, Urbana, 61- *Mem:* Int Double Reed Soc (treas & mem bd dirs, 72-74). *Interests:* Symbolization and articulation of oboe tones; phonetics of oboe playing. *Publ:* Coauth, The Oboe Student Method Book, Level I, 69, Level II, 70, Level III, 71, auth, Studies and Melodious Etudes for Oboe, Level I, 69, Level II, 70 & Level III, 71 & Tunes for Oboe Technic, Level I, 69, Level II, 70, Level III, 71, Belwin-Mills Publ; coauth (with James Hall), Making the American-Scrape Oboe Reed (film), Motion Picture Prod Ctr, Univ Ill, 69; Polymer Impregnation and Protection of Oboe Reeds, Instrumentalist, 81. *Mailing Add:* Music Dept Univ Ill 114 W Nevada St Urbana IL 61801

EDMONDSON, JOHN BALDWIN
COMPOSER, EDITOR
b Toledo, Ohio, Feb 3, 33. *Study:* Univ Fla, with Russell Danburg, BA, 55; Univ Ky, with Kenneth Wright & Bernard Fitzgerald, MMus(comp), 59. *Works:* Pageantry Overture (conct band); Hymn and Postlude (band); Flute Fever (band); Miss Kenucky (vocal); Fun-Way Band Method (with Paul Yoder), 2 vols, 73-74; Song for Winds (conct band); Let's Fly (vocal). *Pos:* Chief arr, Univ Ky Wildcat Marching Band & others, 63-70; educ ed, Hansen Publ, 70-79; dir conct band publ, Jenson, 79-80; free lance comp, arr & ed, 80- *Teaching:* Instrm music, cent Ky area pub sch, 60-70. *Awards:* ASCAP Popular Awards, 70- *Mem:* ASCAP. *Mailing Add:* 20502 NW 2nd Ct Miami FL 33169

EDMUNDS, JOHN FRANCIS
EDUCATOR, COMPOSER
b Cheraw, SC, Dec 12, 28. *Study:* Univ Fla, BA, 51; Fla State Univ, MME, 56. *Works:* Britannia, Carl Fischer, 65; Latin & Lace, MPH, 65; March of the Longhorns, Southern Music, 72; Embarcadero, Schmitt, Hall & McCreary, 73; March of the Centurions, Columbia Pictures, 77; Joie de Vivre (overture), perf by La State Univ Wind Ens, 83. *Pos:* Dir bands, Colonial High Sch, Orlando, Fla, 58-64; asst dir bands, Univ Tex, Austin, 64-67. *Teaching:* Prof music theory & staff arr, La State Univ, Baton Rouge, 67-, cond conct band, 78-80. *Awards:* Serious Music Award, ASCAP, 71. *Mem:* ASCAP. *Mailing Add:* 835 Colonial Dr Baton Rouge LA 70806

EDWARDS, ELAINE VIRGINIA
EDUCATOR, ADMINISTRATOR
b Burlington, Iowa. *Study:* Chicago Musical Col, BMus, 52, MMus, 53; studied with Beveridge Webster, Walter Robert, Menahem Pressler, Haruko Kataoka, Leon Fleisher & Mirecourt Trio. *Teaching:* Instr, Monmouth Col, 53-55 & 56-60; grad asst, Ind Univ, 60-62; lectr, Emporia State Univ, 65-66; asst prof, 66-74, assoc prof, 74-82, prof, 82- *Awards:* Young Artist's Award, Soc Am Musicians, 53. *Mem:* Suzuki Asn Am; Music Teachers Nat Asn. *Interests:* Collection, listing, annotation, evaluation and performance of selected 20th century piano trios. *Publ:* Auth, Rules for Successful Suzuki Teaching, Suzuki J, 3/83. *Mailing Add:* 1402 West St Emporia KS 66801

EDWARDS, GEORGE (HARRISON)
COMPOSER, EDUCATOR
b Boston, Mass, May 11, 43. *Study:* Oberlin Col, BA, 65; Princeton Univ, MFA, 67. *Works:* String Quartet, Comp Quartet, 70; Kreuz und Quer, Mobart Publ, 71; Monopoly, New England Consv Symph Orch, 73; Gyromancy, New York Phil Prospective Encounters, 78; Veined Variety, 78 & Northern Spy, 81, Mobart Publ; Moneta's Mourn, comn by Koussevitzky Music Found. *Teaching:* Fac mem theory, New England Consv, 68-76; asst prof music, Columbia Univ, 76- *Awards:* Am Acad Rome Fel, 73; Walter F Naumburg Found Rec Award, 74; John Simon Guggenheim Mem Found Fel, 80. *Mem:* Comp Rec Inc (secy, 80-); Am Comp Alliance. *Mailing Add:* 838 West End Ave New York NY 10025

EDWARDS, JOHN S
ADMINISTRATOR
b St Louis, Mo, July 23, 12. *Study:* Univ NC, AB, 32; Harvard Univ, MA, 34; Cleveland Inst Music, Hon DMA, 78; DePaul Univ, DHL, 79. *Pos:* Asst mgr, St Louis Symph, 35-38, mgr, 39-43; asst mgr, Nat Symph, 35-39, mgr, 48-57; bus mgr, Los Angeles Phil, 43-45; assoc mgr, Pittsburgh Symph, 45-48, mgr, 58-67; exec vpres & gen mgr, Chicago Symph, 67- *Awards:* Gold Baton Award, Am Symph Orch League, 68. *Mem:* Am Symph Orch League (pres, 54-68, exec coun mem, 64- & chmn, 68-73); Asn Class Music (mem exec comt, 82-); Int Soc Perf Art Admin (mem bd, 82-). *Mailing Add:* 400 E Randolf St #2410 Chicago IL 60601

EDWARDS, LEO D
EDUCATOR, COMPOSER
b Cincinnati, Ohio, Jan 31, 37. *Study:* Mannes Col Music, BS; Brooklyn Col, City Univ New York, MA; Col Consv Music, Univ Cincinnati; studied comp with Scott Huston, Norman Dello Joio & Robert Storer & theory & analysis with Carl Schachter, Felix Salzer & William Mitchell. *Works:* String Quartet, 68, rev ed, 70; Fantasy Overture, Lyndhurst, NY, 71; Etude for Brass, Brooklyn, 72; Psalm 150 (sop & orch), New York, 72. *Teaching:* Chmn theory, Bella Shumatcher Sch Music, Larchmont, NY, 65-76; fel, Brooklyn Col, City Univ New York, 66-68; Mem fac tech of music, Mannes Col Music, 67-71 & 75-, dir, Extension Div, 76-80. *Awards:* Joseph Dillon Mem Award in Pedagogy; Music Teachers Nat Asn Citation, 75; Nat Endowment Arts Grant, 76. *Mailing Add:* 677 West End Ave New York NY 10025

EDWARDS, RYAN (HAYES)
BARITONE, EDUCATOR
b Columbia, SC, Aug 5, 41. *Study:* Univ Tex, Austin, BMus, 64; Juilliard Sch, 68-71; Tex Christian Univ, MMus, 71. *Roles:* Enrico in Lucia di Lammermoor, Marcello in La Boheme, Rodrigo in Don Carlos & Don Carlo di Vargas in Forza del Destino, 76, Metropolitan Opera; Macbeth in Macbeth, Boston Opera, 76; Athaniel in Thais, Gtr Miami Opera, 79; Scarpia in Tosca, Cincinnati Opera, 81; major soloist with NY Phil, Chicago Symph, Pittsburgh Symph, London Symph & others. *Pos:* Baritone, Metropolitan Opera, 76- *Teaching:* Assoc prof voice & opera, Northwestern Univ, 81- *Rep:* Robert Lombardo Assoc 61 W 62 St #6F New York City NY 10023. *Mailing Add:* 2519 Orrington Ave Evanston IL 60201

EFFINGER, CECIL STANLEY
COMPOSER, EDUCATOR
b Colorado Springs, Colo, July 22, 14. *Study:* Colo Col, BA, 35; Am Consv, France, with Nadia Boulanger, 39; Colo Col, Hon DMus. *Works:* Little Symphony, No 1 Op 31, Carl Fischer, 45; Invisible Fire (oratorio), H W Gray, 57; Fifth Symphony, Op 62, Carl Fischer, 58; Four Pastorales (oboe & chorus), G Schirmer, 62 ; Fifth Quartet, Op 70, Hungarian Quartet, 63; Paul of Tarsus (oratorio), G Schirmer, 68; This We Believe (oratorio), Broadman, Nashville, 74. *Teaching:* Prof music, Univ Colo, Boulder, 48-81, comp in res, 81- *Awards:* Award, Walter Naumburg Found, 57; Gov Award Humanities, Colo Arts Coun, 75. *Bibliog:* David Music (auth), The Choral Music of Cecil Effinger, Choral J, 80; Wesley Blomster (auth), Colorado's Senior Composer, Colo Arts Coun Publ, 82. *Mem:* ASCAP; Bohemian Club. *Mailing Add:* 2620 Lafayette Dr Boulder CO 80303

EFFRON, DAVID LOUIS
CONDUCTOR & MUSIC DIRECTOR, EDUCATOR
b Cincinnati, Ohio, July 28, 38. *Study:* Univ Mich, BMus, 60; Ind Univ, MMus, 62; Cologne Hochschule, Germany, 63. *Rec Perf:* Prince Louis Ferdinand Rondo, Desmar Label, 80; Livre for Orch (Lutoslawski), 81, After Tones of Infinity (Schwanter), 81, Lincoln Portrait (Copland), 82, New Morning (Schwanter), 82 & Eastman Overture (Walker), 82, Mercury Golden Imports. *Pos:* Asst cond, Cologne Opera, 63-64; chorusmaster & cond, New York City Opera, 64-69; cond, Nat Ballet, Washington, DC, 70; artistic dir & music dir, Cent City Opera, Colo, 72-77; music dir, Merola Prog, San Francisco Opera, 78-79 & Heidelberg Castle Fest, 80- *Teaching:* Mem fac & cond, Symph & Opera Theatre, Curtis Inst Music, 70-77 & Philharmonia, Symph Orch & Opera Theatre, Eastman Sch Music, 77- *Awards:* Fulbright Grant, Germany, 63; Performance of Modern Music, ASCAP, 79. *Mailing Add:* 70 Kansas Rochester NY 14609

EGER, JOSEPH
CONDUCTOR, LECTURER
b Hartford, Conn, July 9, 25. *Study:* Curtis Inst Music; studied with Monteux, Stokowski & Steinberg. *Works:* Carolina (film), many transcripts & arr. *Rec Perf:* Stravinsky Album, Shostakovitch, Brahms, Haydn & Baroque; Around the Horn, RCA. *Pos:* Perf with and/or cond, New York Phil, Los Angeles Phil, Israel Phil, Pittsburgh Symph, Am Symph Orch, Orch Symph L'Etate, Greece, Haifa Symph, London Phil Orch, Royal Phil & others; music dir & cond, Symph United Nations, New York Orch Soc, currently. *Teaching:* Instr & coach, Aspen Inst & Peabody Consv. *Awards:* Two awards, New York City Mayor. *Mailing Add:* 40 W 67th St New York NY 10023

EGNER, RICHARD JOHN
PIANO, LECTURER
b St Louis, Mo, Jan 29, 24. *Study:* Univ Chicago, PhD, 56; studied piano with Rudolph Ganz, Robert Casadesus & Artur Schnabel; St Louis Inst Music, Hon Dr Music, 64. *Works:* Suite for Orch, New York Phil Symph Orch, 57; Symph No 4, St Louis Symph Orch, 68; Theme and Variations for Orchestra, Berlin Phil Orch, 83; Sonata No 3 for Piano. *Rec Perf:* Echoes of Carnegie Hall, Columbia Rec, 62; Contemporary Music in a New Key, RCA Victor, 67. *Pos:* Piano soloist, St Louis Symph Orch, Chicago Symph & Cleveland Symph; contribr, Music News Mag. *Awards:* Paderewski Gold Medal, Chicago Musical Col, 59. *Mem:* Am Musicol Soc. *Publ:* Auth, A Brief History of Musical Theory From Boethius to the Present, 80 & The Evolution of Polyphony from Antiquity to Bach, 83, Allen & Unwin Ltd. *Mailing Add:* 216 Crosman Terrace Rochester NY 14620

EHLE, ROBERT CANNON
COMPOSER, ELECTRONIC
b Lancaster, Pa, Nov 7, 39. *Study:* Eastman Sch Music, BMus, 61; NTex State Univ, MMus, 65, PhD, 70. *Works:* Lunar Landscape, Eastman-Rochester Symph, 61; Sound Piece, Carl Fischer Inc, 66; A Jayy Symphony, Univ NC Jayy Lab Band, 77; A Space Symphony, Luck Orch Libr, 80; The City is Beautiful, Ithaca Col Choral Fest, 81; A Whole Earth Symphony, Univ NC Wind Ens, 81; Forty-three compositions, Dorn Publ, 82-83. *Pos:* Rec engineer, Eastman Sch Music, 58-61. *Teaching:* Res asst instr, NTex State Univ, 64-70; instr, Denver Inst Technol, 70-71; prof & asst dir, Sch Music, Univ Northern Colo, 71- *Awards:* Dallas Symphony Rockefeller Found Award, 66. *Bibliog:* Hugh Davis (auth), International Electronic Music Catalog, MIT Press, 4-6/67; Maurice Hinson (auth), A Guide to the Pianists Repertoire Supplement, Ind Univ Press, 79; Allen Strange (auth), Electronic Music, William C Brown Co, 83. *Mem:* ASCAP. *Interests:* Sociology of Contemporary Music. *Mailing Add:* Sch Music Univ Northern Colo Greeley CO 80639

EHRHARDT, FRANKLYN WHITEMAN
BASS-PROFUNDO
b Richmond Hill, NY, Feb 6, 22. *Study:* Brooklyn Consv Music, grad, 50. *Rec Perf:* African Tour, Paris Studio, 66. *Roles:* Comdr Yamadori & Bonze in Madama Butterfly, Atlanta Wagner Opera Co & Newark Symph Hall, 60; Doctor in La Traviata, Brooklyn Acad Music, 66; Sparafucile & Ceprano in Rigoletto, Ital Lyr Asn; Marchese in La Traviata, RI Opera, 68; Frate in Don Carlos, Metropolitan Opera Asn, 71; Colline in La Boheme; Mephistopheles in Faust. *Pos:* Bass, Robert Shaw's Col Chorale, 47-50 & Leonard dePaur State Dept, 66; mgr, Ambassador Quarter, Bur Conct, Univ Wis, 54; bass soloist, Men Song Enterprises & Columbus Boys Choir. *Mailing Add:* 474 Prospect St South Orange NJ 07079

EHRLICH, CLARA SIEGEL
PIANO, EDUCATOR
b Chicago, Ill, May 11, 11. *Study:* Sherwood Music Sch, BM, 26; studied piano with Andre Skalski, 27-32, Sergei Tarnarvsky, 32-37. *Pos:* Founder & pianist, Siegel Chamber Music Players, 45-54; dir & perf, Univ Chicago, Downtown, 58-59, Cosmopolitan Sch Music, 62-63; dir chamber music wkshp, DePaul Univ; numerous appearances with Chicago Symph String Quartet, Fine Arts Quartet, Chicago Symph Woodwind Quartet, Berkshire Quartet; soloist, Minneapolis Symph, Milwaukee Symph, Rochester Symph, Portland Symph, Buffalo Symph & Chautauqua. *Teaching:* Dir chamber music, Univ Chicago, Downtown, 40-42 & Chautauqua Inst, New York, 73-; dir chamber music & instr piano, DePaul Univ, 76- *Mailing Add:* 30 E Huron #1204 Chicago IL 60611

EHRLICH, DAVID
VIOLIN

b Bielsko, Poland, Jan 7, 49. *Study:* Israel Consv; Tel Aviv Univ, artist dipl, 72; studied with Ilona Feher; Northern Ill Univ, BA, MMus. *Pos:* Concertmaster & soloist, Tel Aviv Chamber Orch, 68-72; soloist with Israeli orchs; performer, conct & recitals throughout US; radio & TV appearances in Israel & US; assoc concertmaster, Indianapolis Symph Orch, currently. *Awards:* Scholar, Am-Israel Cult Found, 69-72; Second Prize, Young Artists Compt, Springfield, Mo, 73; Nat Young Artists Winner, Nat Fedn Music Clubs, 75. *Rep:* Sound Rising Artistic Mgt Skokie IL. *Mailing Add:* 5054 Olympia Ct Indianapolis IN 46208

EHRLICH, DON A
VIOLA, TEACHER

b Buffalo, NY, Dec 18, 42. *Study:* Consv Music, Oberlin Col, with William Berman, BM, 64; Manhattan Sch Music, with William Lincer, MM, 66; Univ Mich, with Frank Bundra, DMA, 72. *Pos:* Asst prin viola, San Francisco Symph, 72-; violist, Aurora String Quartet, San Francisco, 79- *Teaching:* Inst viola, San Francisco Consv, 72- *Mailing Add:* 806 Shrader San Francisco CA 94102

EHRLING, SIXTEN E
CONDUCTOR & MUSIC DIRECTOR, TEACHER

b Malmö, Sweden, Apr 3, 18. *Study:* Royal Acad Music, Stockholm, 36; studied piano & cond, 40; several hon degrees. *Rec Perf:* All symphonies and other works of Sibelius, 52-55. *Pos:* Music dir, Royal Opera, Stockholm, 53-60 & Detroit Symph Orch, 63-73; found & music dir, Meadow Brook Music Fest, 64- *Teaching:* Orch & cond, Juilliard Sch, 73- *Awards:* Various orders, Sweden, Norway, Denmark, Holland & Finland. *Rep:* ICM Artists 40 W 57th St New York NY 10019. *Mailing Add:* 10 W 66th St New York NY 10023

EICHENBERGER, RODNEY (BRYCE)
CONDUCTOR, EDUCATOR

b Kimball, Nebr, July 8, 30. *Study:* St Olaf Col, Northfield, Minn, BA, 52; Univ Denver, MA, 58; Univ Wash; Univ Iowa. *Rec Perf:* Chamber Singers of USC, Protone Rec, 81; Musica Sacra et Profana, Op Music, 83. *Teaching:* Prof music, Univ Wash, 63-76 & Univ Southern Calif, 76- *Mem:* Am Choral Dir Asn; Music Educr Nat Conf; Phi Mu Alpha Sinfonia. *Mailing Add:* Univ Southern Calif Sch Music 840 W 34th St Los Angeles CA 90089

EICHHORN, ERICH A
VIOLIN

b Germany, Mar 1, 35. *Study:* Musik Hochschule, Stuttgart, studied violin with Odnoposoff & Kurt Stiehler, conct dipl, 61. *Pos:* Concertmaster, Orch State Acad, Stuttgart, 56-61; asst concertmaster, SGerman Radio Symph, Stuttgart, 62-66; prin second violin, Buffalo Phil, 66-67 & St Louis Symph, 76-68; solo perf, St Louis Symph, 68; first violin, Cleveland Orch, 68- & Fac String Quartet, Cleveland State Univ; founder & mem, Cleveland Octet, 77. *Teaching:* Lectr violin, Cleveland State Univ, 76- *Awards:* Asn German Indust Prize, 65. *Mailing Add:* 1510 Crest Rd Cleveland OH 44121

EIKUM, REX L
EDUCATOR, TENOR

b Moscow, Idaho, Aug 5, 32. *Study:* Univ Idaho, BA(music), 54, MA(music), 63; Columbia Univ, summer 59; Ind Univ, 64-67. *Rec Perf:* Song of the Earth, Bowling Green State Univ. *Roles:* Count Almaviva in The Barber of Seville, Mich Opera Theater; Dick Johnson in The Girl of the Golden West, Nemorino in L'elisir d'amore & Sam in Susannah, Colo Springs Opera; Italian tenor in Capriccio & One of Sons in The Golden Cockerel, Lake Erie Opera; Conrad Valenrod in I Lituani, Lithuanian Opera Asn Chicago. *Pos:* Specialist & supvr choral & vocal music, Clarkston Pub Sch, Wash, 54-64. *Teaching:* Grad asst, Ind Univ, Bloomington, 64-67; prof voice, Bowling Green State Univ, 67-, chmn perf studies dept, 75- *Mem:* Music Educr Nat Conf; Am Guild Musical Artists; Nat Asn Teachers Singing. *Mailing Add:* 64 Greenview Ct Howard OH 43028

EIVE, GLORIA
MUSICOLOGIST, WRITER

b Los Angeles, Calif, Dec 23, 36. *Study:* Univ Calif, Los Angeles, 54-55; Univ Calif, Santa Barbara, BA(music hist & lit), 57; Univ Calif, Berkeley, MA(music), 60 & 75-78 . *Teaching:* Private instr piano, harmony & musicianship, 63-; teacher music, F D Burke Sch Girls, San Francisco, 71-72 & French Am Bilingual Sch, San Francisco, 72-74; instr harmony & musicianship, Univ Calif Extension, 76-79; teaching asst music, Univ Calif, Berkeley, 77-78 & Music Bd, Univ Calif, Santa Cruz, 78-79; guest lectr, San Francisco State Univ, 80. *Awards:* Woodrow Wilson Traveling Fel, Faenza, Italy, 60-61. *Mem:* Am Musicol Soc; Am Soc Ethnomusicol; Studi Romagnoli. *Interests:* Italian music of the 18th century; Italian-Americans in the Western States—music, culture and the role of women. *Publ:* Auth, Paolo Alberghi, Gregorio Babbi, Cristoforo Babbi, Babbi Family & Faenza, In: New Grove Dict of Music & Musicians, 80; Virtuosi del Diciottesimo Secolo: La Famiglia Babbi, 78 & Giuseppe Sarti e le Attivita Musicali Faentine nel '700, 83, Studi Romagnoli; ed, Tartini's Improvised Ornamentation, as Illustrated by Manuscripts from the Berkeley Collection of Eighteenth Century Italian Instrumental Music, Accad Tartiniana (in prep); A Manuscript Collection of Eighteenth Century Italian Instrumental Music in the University of California, Berkeley Music Library, in Microfiche Reproduction, Annotated, N K Gregg (in prep). *Mailing Add:* 176 Jordan Ave San Francisco CA 94118

EKIZIAN, MICHELLE LYNNE
COMPOSER, TEACHER

b Bronxville, NY, Nov 21, 56. *Study:* Manhattan Sch Music, BM, 77, MM(comp), 78; studied comp with Chou Wen-chung, Vladimir Ussachevsky, Mario Davidovsky & Nicolas Flagello; Columbia Univ, currently. *Works:* The Illumination of Saint Gregory (orch), 78 & Three Armenian Poems (sop & orch), 78, comn by Armenian Diocese North Am; Hidden Crosses (nine instrm & two ms), 81; Akhtamar (two violins, piano & perc), perf at Columbia Univ, 81; Octoechos (double string quartet), perf by St Paul Chamber Orch, 83; The Exiled Heart (orch), G Schirmer Assoc Music Publ, Inc, 83. *Teaching:* Asst music, Columbia Univ, 81- *Awards:* First Prize, Devora Nadworney Awards, 80 & Victor Herbert-ASCAP Awards, 81, Nat Fedn Music Clubs; BMI Student Comp Award, 82; Comp Assistance Grant, Am Music Ctr, 83. *Mem:* Am Comp Alliance; Nat Asn Comp, USA (NY chap bd mem & secy, 80-); Am Music Ctr; BMI. *Rep:* BMI 320 W 57th St New York NY 10019; Am Comp Alliance 170 W 74th St New York NY 10023. *Mailing Add:* 8 Prince Willow Lane Mamaroneck NY 10543

ELAN, TERRY MICHAEL
DOUBLE BASS

b Kalamazoo, Mich, June 16, 49. *Study:* Univ Mich, studied bass with Lawrence Hunt, BM, 71; studied with Zvi Zohar, 71-75. *Pos:* Prin bass, Jerusalem Symph, Israel, 71-74 & Winnipeg Symph, Man, 76-79; section bass, Israel Phil Orch, Tel Aviv, 74-75 & 79-82; assoc prin double bass, Phoenix Symph Orch, currently. *Mem:* Am Fedn Musicians. *Mailing Add:* c/o Phoenix Symph Orch 6328 N Seventh St Phoenix AZ 85014

EL-DABH, HALIM
COMPOSER, EDUCATOR

b Cairo, Egypt, Mar 4, 21; US citizen. *Study:* Cairo Univ, grad; New England Consv Music, with Francis Judd Cooke, MM, 53; Tanglewood Inst, with Irving Fine & Aaron Copland; Brandeis Univ, MFA, 54; Columbia-Princeton Electronic Music Laboratory, New York. *Works:* Clytemnestra (dance epic for Martha Graham), New York, 58; Ballet of Lights, 60; Family Tree (Egyptian & Ethiopian string instrm); Lament of the Pharaohs (sound & light), perf daily at Great Pyramids, Giza, Egypt, 60-77; Opera Flies (orch, based on the shootings at Kent State Univ, 69), Washington, DC, 71; Of Gods and Men (drums & piano), 73; Unity at the Cross Roads (orch), Alexandria & Cairo, Egypt, 78. *Pos:* Field work & res in US, Europe & Africa. *Teaching:* Mem fac, Howard Univ, 66-69; prof ethnomusicol, Kent State Univ, 69- *Awards:* Fulbright Fel for US study; Guggenheim Fels, 59 & 61. *Mailing Add:* Music Dept Kent State Univ Kent OH 44242

ELDER, CHARLOTTE DE VOLT See de Volt, Charlotte

ELDREDGE, STEVEN
COACH, CONDUCTOR & MUSIC DIRECTOR

Study: Calif State Univ; Cleveland Inst Music. *Pos:* Asst cond & chorus master, West Bay Opera, Palo Alto, Calif, 77-79; musical staff, San Francisco Opera, 79, coach, Merola & Affil Artist Prog, music dir, Brown Bag Opera; asst cond, San Francisco String Opera & Am Opera; chorus master & musical asst, Sacramento Opera, currently. *Teaching:* Mem fac, San Francisco Consv Music, 77-79. *Mailing Add:* Sacramento Opera 5380 Elvas Sacramento CA 95819

ELHBA, MARIO (LEVEQUE)
VIOLIN, COMPOSER

b Gwadur, Baluchistan, Feb 2, 46; US citizen. *Study:* Consv Nat de Region de Marseille, cert, 59; Akad Musik & darstellenden Kunst, Graz, 63-65; studied violin with Maurice Hewitt, 66-71, Alois Haba, 70-71 & Wynn Earl Westover, 78- *Pos:* Stage asst & orch mem, Wurttembergishe Staatstheatre, Stuttgart, 65-66; orch mem violin, Orch Amici Musici, Rome, 72-77; soloist, Tex Renaissance Fest, 82, Westheimer Fest, 82, Tex Scarborough Faire, 83, Kind Richard Summer Tour, 83 & Houston Fest, 83; exponent of Diolon manner of violin performance. *Bibliog:* J Dyke (auth), On the Road with Mario Elhba, Travel Log, 7/83. *Mailing Add:* c/o W E Westover PO Box 895 Huntsville TX 77340

ELIAS, JOEL J
TROMBONE, LECTURER

b Brooklyn, NY, Apr 10, 52. *Study:* Ind Univ, with Lewis Van Haney & Thomas Beuersdorf, BME, 74; Juilliard Sch, with Edward Herman, Jr, MM(trombone), 76. *Pos:* Prin trombone, Sacramento Symph, 81- & Des Moines Metro Opera, 81, 82 & 83. *Teaching:* Lectr low brass, Univ of Pac, 82- & Calif State Univ, Chico, 83- *Mem:* Int Trombone Asn. *Publ:* Auth, Basics in Breathing, Brass Bulletin, 11/80; coauth, The Art of Trombone Section Playing, Instrumentalist (in prep). *Mailing Add:* 846 56th St Sacramento CA 95819

ELIAS, ROSALIND
MEZZO-SOPRANO

b Lowell, Mass, Mar 13, 31. *Study:* New England Consv Music; St Cecilia Acad, Rome; studied with Daniel Ferro; Merrimack Col, Hon Dr. *Rec Perf:* And David Wept (video), CBS. *Roles:* Grimgerde in Die Walküre, 54, Erika in Vanessa, 58 & Charmian in Antony and Cleopatra, 66, Metropolitan Opera; Fidalma in Il Matrimonio Segreto; Dorabella in Cosi fan tutte; Suzuki in Madama Butterfly. *Pos:* Ms with maj opera co in US, Europe & England; res mem, Metropolitan Opera. *Mem:* Sigma Alpha Iota. *Mailing Add:* c/o Columbia Artists 165 W 57th St New York NY 10019

ELIASEN, MIKAEL
COACH, PIANO
b Copenhagen, Denmark, Dec 3, 44; Can citizen. *Study:* McGill Univ, Montreal, LMus, 66; study in Vienna, 66-70. *Rec Perf:* Schumann Songs, London Rec, 68; French Songs, 76 & German Songs, 78, Musical Heritage. *Pos:* Freelance accmp; coach & accmp, Nat Opera Co, Can & Philadelphia Opera Co. *Teaching:* Coach, masterclasses in New York, Australia, Orient, Israel, Can & US, currently; guest artist vocal repertoire, Brigham Young Univ, 77-78, Univ Seoul, 80, Brisbane Univ, 81 & Rubin Acad, Israel, 82-83. *Mem:* Am Fedn Musicians. *Mailing Add:* 235 W 75th St New York NY 10023

ELIASON, ROBERT E
CRITIC-WRITER, TUBA
b Flint, Mich, Mar 28, 31. *Study:* Univ Mich, BM, 55; Manhattan Sch Music, studied tuba with William Bell, MM, 59; Univ Mo, Kansas City, DMA, 68. *Pos:* Prin tuba, Kansas City Phil, 61-69; res assoc, Smithsonian Inst, 70-71; cur musical instrm, Henry Ford Museum, 71- *Awards:* Scholar, Olds Band Instrm Co, 68. *Mem:* Galpin Soc; Int Coun Museums Comt Musical Instrm (mem adv bd, 80-83); Am Musical Instrm Soc (treas, 78-); Sonneck Soc; Tubists Univ Brotherhood Asn (int pres, 73-75). *Interests:* Nineteenth century American makers of woodwind & brass musical instruments. *Publ:* Auth, Graves & Co Musical Instrument Makers, Henry Ford Museum, 75; Early American Brass Makers, Brass Press, 79; 18 articles on Am wind instrm makers, New Grove Dict of Music & Musicians, Macmillan, 80; John Meacham, 81 & George Catlin, Hartford Musical Instrument Maker, 82 & 83, J Am Musical Instrm Soc. *Mailing Add:* 549 N Melborn Dearborn MI 48128

ELISHA, HAIM
COMPOSER, MUSIC DIRECTOR
b Jerusalem, Israel, Sept 27, 35; Israeli & US citizen. *Study:* Rubin Acad, Israel, piano dipl, 58; Juilliard Sch, BMus, 62; New England Consv Music, MMus, 68; Jewish Theol Sem, DSM, 80. *Works:* Ten Variations (cello & piano), Broude Brothers, 76; Brass Quintet, perf by Canterbury Brass Quintet, 76, 77 & 78; Dance Suite, perf by Hudson Valley Phil, 79; String Trio, 80 & Shir Aliz (voice & cello), 80, Israel Music Inst; Certain Quite Opera, comn by Theatre for the New City, 81. *Pos:* Music dir, Cape Ann Symph Orch, Mass, 67-74; organist, Temple Beth Sholom, Roslyn, NY, 81- *Teaching:* Prof comp, Rockland Community Col, 68- *Mem:* Am Music Ctr. *Mailing Add:* 120 W 86th St New York NY 10024

ELKUS, JONATHAN (BRITTON)
COMPOSER, WRITER
b San Francisco, Calif, Aug 8, 31. *Study:* Univ Calif, Berkeley, BA, 53; Stanford Univ, MA, 54; studied comp with Charles Cushing, Leonard Ratner, Ernst Bacon & Darius Milhaud. *Works:* Tom Sawyer, 53 & Treasure Island, 61, Novello; The Mandarin, Carl Fischer, 67. *Teaching:* Prof music, Lehigh Univ, 57-73; vis lectr, Univ Calif, Davis, 77 & Yale Col, 77; dir music, Cape Cod Acad, 79- *Awards:* Fel, Ford Found, 62. *Mem:* ASCAP. *Interests:* Music of Charles Ives. *Publ:* Auth, Charles Ives and the American Band Tradition, Am Arts Doc Ctr, Univ Exeter, UK, 74; An Encounter With The New Pirates, Yale Rev, 82. *Mailing Add:* Box 656 Osterville MA 02655

ELLEDGE, NANCY RUTH
SOPRANO, TEACHER
b NC. *Study:* Pfeiffer Col, BM, 69; Southern Methodist Univ, MM, 72; Okla City Univ. *Roles:* Annina in La Traviata, Adele in Die Fledermaus & Rita in Rita, Western Opera Theater, 80; Daphne in Meanwhile Back at Cinderella, New York City Opera, 81; Little Red Riding Hood, 83 & solo sop in Fascination Rhythms, 83, Tex Opera Theater. *Teaching:* Voice, Richland Col, 72-81 & Tex Christian Univ, 80-82. *Awards:* Scholar, Am Inst Musical Studies, 79. *Mem:* Actor's Equity Guild; Am Guild Musical Artists. *Mailing Add:* 7318 Dominique Dallas TX 75214

ELLERMAN, JENS
EDUCATOR, VIOLIN
b Hamburg, Ger, Mar 3, 38. *Study:* Hochschule Musik, Hamburg, with Eva Hauptmann; study in London & Rome with Alberto Lysy; Hochschule Musik, Berlin, MM, 65. *Teaching:* Assoc prof, Col Consv Music, Univ Cincinnati, 70-; fac mem, Aspen Music Fest, 75- & Juilliard Sch Music, 76- *Mem:* Am Asn Univ Prof. *Mailing Add:* 4070 Beechwood Ave Cincinnati OH 45229

ELLINGSON, LINDA JEANNE
COACH, SOPRANO
b Seattle, Wash, Aug 26, 47. *Study:* Univ Wash, BA(music educ), 69; Pac Lutheran Univ, MA(music educ), 83. *Roles:* Lauretta in Gianni Schicchi, Ft Lewis Light Opera Co, 74; Kathie in The Student Prince, Tacoma Opera Co, 75; Lucy in The Telephone, 76 & Monica in The Medium, 76, Ft Lewis Light Opera Co; Queen of the Night in The Magic Flute, 76 & Despina in Cosi fan tutte, 77, Highline Opera Studio; Ann in The Merry Wives of Windsor, Tacoma Opera Co, 77. *Pos:* Chorus mem, Portland Opera, 69-70 & Seattle Opera, 71-77; soloist, Tacoma Opera Co, 70-78 & Ft Lewis Light Opera Co, 73-77. *Teaching:* Instr vocal music, Puyallup pub sch, Wash, 70-81; instr voice, Highline Community Col, 76- *Mem:* Music Educr Nat Conf; Evergreen Orff Music Teachers; Nat Asn Teachers Singing. *Mailing Add:* 31012 39th Ave SW Federal Way WA 98003

ELLINWOOD, LEONARD WEBSTER
WRITER
b Thomaston, Conn, Feb 13, 05. *Study:* Aurora Col, BA, 26; Eastman Sch Music, MMus, 34, PhD, 36; Aurora Col, Hon Dr Music, 82. *Pos:* Head music cataloging, Music Div, Libr Cong, 40-43; subj cataloger, Subj Catalog Div, 43-60 & head humanities sect, 60-75. *Teaching:* Instr music, Mich State Univ, 36-39; lectr, Evergreen Sch Church Music, Colo, 46-52 & Col Church Musicians, Washington, DC, 62-69. *Mem:* Fel, Hymn Soc Am; Mediaeval Acad Am; Am Musicol Soc; Sonneck Soc; Organ Hist Soc. *Interests:* Mediaeval music; American music; hymnology. *Publ:* Co-ed, Works of Francesco Landini, Mediaeval Acad, 39; Hymnal 1940 Companion, Church Pension Found, 49; auth, History of American Church Music, Morehouse-Gorham, 53; co-ed, Dictionary of American Hymnology, Univ Music Ed, 83. *Mailing Add:* 3724 Van Ness St NW Washington DC 20016

ELLIOT, GLADYS CRISLER
OBOE, EDUCATOR
b Macon, Ga, Sept 5, 29. *Study:* NTex State Univ, BM, 51; private study with Clyde Roller, Arthur Krilov, Laurence Thorstenburg & Robert Bloom. *Pos:* Oboe sect, Dallas Symph Orch, 51-54; prin oboist, 55-64; prin oboist, Chicago Lyr Opera Orch, 64-; Contemp Chamber Players Univ Chicago, 64-81; Chicago Grant Park Summer Symph Orch, 66-; WGN Staff Orch, Chicago, 66-71 & Orch Ill, Chicago, 79-; oboist, Chicago Woodwind Quintet, 65-71. *Teaching:* Instr oboe, Southern Methodist Univ, Dallas, 59-63; instr oboe & woodwind repertoire classes, DePaul Univ, Chicago, 79- *Mem:* Int Double Reed Soc. *Mailing Add:* 300 N State St #4709 Chicago IL 60610

ELLIOT, WILLARD SOMERS
COMPOSER, BASSOON
b Ft Worth, Tex, July 18, 26. *Study:* NTex State Univ, BM; Eastman Sch Music, with Bernard Rogers, MM. *Works:* Bassoon Concerto, perf by Chicago Symph Orch at Ravinia Fest, 65; Hypnos and Psyche (tone poems); Quetzalcoatl (orch); The Snake Charmer (alto flute & orch); Trio (oboe, clarinet & bassoon); 2 Creole Songs (oboe, clarinet & bassoon); Poem (bassoon & string quartet). *Pos:* Bassoonist, Houston Symph, 46-49 & Dallas Symph, 51-64; solo & prin bassoonist, Chicago Symph, 69- *Teaching:* Fac mem, NTex State Univ, 49-51; DePaul Univ, 74- & Northwestern Univ, 74- *Awards:* Nat Fedn Music Club Prizes, 46 & 47; Koussevitzky Found Grant, 60. *Mailing Add:* Chicago Symph Orch 220 S Michigan Ave Chicago IL 60604

ELLIOTT, WILBER D
EDUCATOR, MUSIC DIRECTOR
b Portland, Ore, Oct 29, 31. *Study:* Univ Wash, BA(music educ), 54; Cent Wash Univ, ME(music educ), 61. *Teaching:* Choral dir, South Cent Sch District, Seattle, Wash, 56-58 & Clover Park High Sch, Tacoma, Wash, 58-60; dir music educ, Clover Park Sch District, Tacoma, Wash, 60-69; chmn, Dept Music, Boise State Univ, 69- *Mem:* Music Educr Nat Conf; Am Choral Dir Asn. *Mailing Add:* 1910 University Dr Boise ID 83725

ELLIS, BRENT E
BARITONE
b Kansas City, Mo, June 20, 46. *Study:* Juilliard Sch Music, 65-67 & 70-72; studied with Edna Forsythe, 62-65, Marian Freschl, 65-71, Daniel Ferro, 71- & Luigi Ricci. *Rec Perf:* Belcore in The Elixer of Love, Live From Lincoln Ctr, PBS. *Roles:* Maerbale in Bomarzo, Washington DC Opera Soc, 66; Rigoletto in Rigoletto, 83, Cortez in Montezuma & Prince Andrei in War & Peace, Opera Co Boston; Enrico in Lucia di Lammermoor, Scottish Opera; Renato in A Masked Ball, Houston Opera; Marcello in La Boheme, Glyndebourne Fest. *Pos:* Bar, Santa Fe Opera, 72-81, San Francisco Opera, 74-78, Boston Opera, 75-82, Vienna Staatsoper, 77-79, Metropolitan Opera, 79-81 & many other opera co in US, Can & Europe. *Awards:* Montreal Int Compt Winner, 73; Winner, WGN Ill Opera Guild Auditions of Air, 73; Young Artist of Year, Musical Am, 73. *Mailing Add:* c/o Columbia Artists 165 W 57th St New York NY 10019

ELLIS, MERRILL
COMPOSER, ELECTRONIC
b Cleburne, Tex, Dec 9, 16. *Study:* Univ Okla, BA, MM; Univ Mo; studied comp with Roy Harris, Spencer Norton & Charles Garland. *Works:* Nostalgia (60 strings, perc, tape, two films, carousel projection & theatrical events), Cong Strings, Cincinnati, 75; Kaleidoscope (orch, synthesizer, ms); Mutations (brass choir, tape, films & slides); A Dream Fantasy (solo clarinet, perc, tape, 16 mm film & slides); The Sorcerer (bar, tape, slides, visuals & theatrical setting); The Choice is Ours (tape, films, carousel projection, live laser displays & theatrical events); Celebration (flute, oboe, clarinet, bassoon, perc, tape, lasers & visual events), comn by Baylor Univ, Richard Shanley & Soc Commissioning New Music. *Pos:* Dir, Electronic Music Ctr & prof comp, Sch Music, NTex State Univ, 62-; perf electronic & intermedia comp, cent & SW US; lectr, various cols & univ. *Awards:* ASCAP Award, 79. *Mem:* ASCAP; Am Asn Univ Prof; Music Educr Nat Conf; Music Teachers Nat Asn. *Interests:* New compositional techniques; development of new instruments; new notation techniques. *Mailing Add:* 909 Ave E Denton TX 76201

ELLISON, GREER (GREER ELLISON WOLFSON)
FLUTE, TEACHER
b Charleston, WVa, Apr 11, 53. *Study:* Oberlin Consv Music, BMus, 74; Univ Mich, MMus, 75; Koninklijk Consv, study baroque flute with Bart Kuyken, solo dipl, 77. *Rec Perf:* Sonatas for Two Baroque Flutes, Op 2 (Telemann), Cambridge Rec, 82. *Pos:* Prin flute, Ars Musica Baroque Ens, Mich, 74-75, Haagse Begeleiding Orkest, Holland, 76-77 & Terre Haute Symph, Ind, 78-79; second flute, New York Chamber Soloists Inc, 80- *Teaching:* Instr flute, Ind State Univ, Terre Haute, 78-79, Vassar Col, Poughkeepsie, NY, 80-81 & State Univ NY, New Paltz, 79-82. *Awards:* Int Telephone & Telegraph Grant, 75-77. *Mailing Add:* 1153 Yorkshire Dr Cupertino CA 95014

ELLSWORTH, OLIVER BRYANT
EDUCATOR, WRITER
b Oakland, Calif, Apr 22, 40. *Study:* Univ Calif, BA, 61, MA, 63, PhD, 69. *Teaching:* Instr, Univ Colo, Boulder, 69-70, asst prof, 70-77, assoc prof, 77- *Bibliog:* Christopher Page (auth), Fourteenth-Century Instruments and Tunings: A Treatise by Jean Vaillan, Galpin Soc J, 3/80. *Mem:* Am Musicol Soc (coun rep Rocky Mountain chap, 82-). *Interests:* Medieval treatises on music theory. *Publ:* Auth, The Origin of the Coniuncta: A Reappraisal, J Music Theory, 73; A Fourteenth-Century Proposal for Equal Temperament, Viator, 74; An Unedited Source for Monastic Music Theory, Musicol Univ Colo, 77; Contrapunctus and Discantus in Late Medieval Terminology, Saints, Scholars & Heroes, 79. *Mailing Add:* Col Music Univ Colo Campus Box 301 Boulder CO 80309

ELMER, CEDRIC N(AGEL)
TEACHER, PIANO
b Reading, Pa, Jan 15, 39. *Study:* Combs Col, with Dr Romeo Cascarino & piano with Julia S Elmer, MusB, 61, MusM, 63; Philadelphia Musical Acad, with Allison Drake, MusBEd, 66. *Works:* Petite Pavane (piano), 63 & A Bit Mischievous (piano), 65, Comp Press; Liliputian Suite, perf by Reading Phil Orch, 67; Saraband (bs flute & harp), perf by Kathy Parker & Cedric Elmer, 79. *Pos:* Dir, Community Sch Music, Reading, Pa, 64-; Adjudicator piano, Am Col Musicians, 77- *Teaching:* Instr piano & comp, Community Sch Music, 63-; instr music, Reading Sch District, Pa, 66- *Mem:* ASCAP; Music Club Reading (pres, 72-74, corresp secy, 75-83); Berks Arts Coun (treas, 82-83); Phi Mu Alpha Sinfonia; Music Educr Nat Conf. *Publ:* Auth, Musical Remembrances, Berksiana Found, 76. *Mailing Add:* 413 Douglass St Reading PA 19601

ELMORE, CENIETH CATHERINE
EDUCATOR, PIANO
b Wilson, NC, July 4, 30. *Study:* Woman's Col Univ NC, BMus, 53; Univ NC, Chapel Hill, MMus, 62, MA, 63, PhD, 72. *Works:* Sonatina for Piano, 52, Five Pieces for Piano, 66 & North Carolina Suite (for piano), 79, perf by Cenieth Elmore. *Teaching:* Piano, Fuquay Springs Sch, 53-57, Mills Sch, 57-60 & Univ NC, Chapel Hill, 60-63; from asst to assoc prof, Campbell Univ, 63- *Mem:* Am Musicol Soc; NC Music Teachers Asn; Raleigh Piano Teachers Asn. *Mailing Add:* Rte 2 Box 186B Franklin NC 27525

ELMORE, ROBERT HALL
ORGAN, COMPOSER
b Ramaputnam, India, Jan 2, 13; US citizen. *Study:* Studied organ with Pietro Yon, 26-33; Royal Acad Music, London, England, lic(organ, conct piano & accmp), 33; Univ Pa, comp with Harl McDonald, BMus, 37; Alderson-Broaddus Col & Moravian Col, LLD & LHD, 58. *Works:* It Began at Breakfast (opera), 40; The Incarnate Word (cantata), 43 & The Cross (cantata), 47, J Fischer & Bro; Rhumba & Rhythmic Suite (organ), Gentry Press, 54; Psalm of Redemption (cantata), J Fischer, 58; Concerto (organ, brass & perc), H W Gray, 64; Sonata for Organ, Shawnee Press, 76. *Pos:* Organist & choir dir, Holy Trinity Episcopal Church, Philadelphia, Pa, 38-55, Cent Moravian Church, Bethlehem, Pa, 55-68 & Tenth Presby Church, Philadelphia, Pa, 69- *Teaching:* Vchmn music dept, Univ Pa, 37-50; instr organ, Philadelphia Col Perf Arts, 38- *Bibliog:* S R Lange (auth), An Analysis of Concerto for Brass, Organ & Percussion, Mich State Univ, 78; Alfred E Lunde (auth), A Conductor's Analysis of the Choral Works of Robert Elmore, Southwestern Baptist Theol Sem, Tex, 82. *Mem:* Am Guild Organists; life mem, Am Organ Players Club; Am Fedn Musicians. *Mailing Add:* 130 Walnut Ave Wayne PA 19087

ELSTER, REINHARDT
HARP
b Hammond, Ind, July 23, 14. *Study:* Curtis Inst Music, with Carlos Salzedo, 6 yrs. *Pos:* Prin harp, Metropolitan Opera Asn, 48- & Fest Casals, PR, 12 yrs. *Mailing Add:* c/o Metropolitan Opera Asn Lincoln Ctr New York NY 10023

ELVIRA, PABLO
BARITONE
b Santurce, PR, Sept 24, 38. *Study:* Casals Consv, with Pablo Casals. *Roles:* Rigoletto in Rigoletto, Ind Univ Opera Theater, Bloomington, 68; Tonio in I Puritani, 79, Lescaut in Manon, 80, Henry in Lucia di Lammermoor, 80 & 82, Figaro in The Barber of Seville, 81 & 82 & Les Mamelles de Tiresias, 82; Renato in Un Ballo in maschera, NJ State Opera, 82; and many others. *Pos:* Trumpeter & dir dance orch, formerly; leading bar, Metropolitan Opera, 79-; performed with major opera co & orchs in US & Mex. *Mailing Add:* c/o Eric Semon Assoc Inc 111 W 57th St New York NY 10019

ELYN, MARK ALVIN
BASS, TEACHER
b Seattle, Wash. *Study:* Univ Wash; Seattle Univ; private study with Robert Weede, 55-60. *Roles:* Ferrando in Il Trovatore, San Francisco Opera, 58; King Philip in Don Carlos, Basel, Cologne & Hamburg, 60-68; Fiesco in Simone Boccanegra, Cologne & Nürnberg, 61-68; Zaccaria in Nabucco, Cologne & Munich, 63-68; Don Giovanni in Don Giovanni, Cologne & Wiesbaden, 64-67; Rocco in Fidelio, Cologne & Barcelona, 64-69; Figaro in The Marriage of Figaro, St Louis Opera, 75. *Pos:* Mem, New York City Opera, 55-57 & San Francisco Opera, 58-60; lead bass, Stadtheater Basel, Switz, 60-61 & Opernhaus Köln, Ger, 61-69. *Teaching:* Prof voice, Univ Ill, Urbana-Champaign, 69- *Awards:* First Prize, Seattle Music & Art Found, 56; Martha Baird Rockefeller Aid Music Award, 60 & 61. *Mem:* Am Guild Musical Artists; Deutsche Bühnenangehörigen; Nat Asn Teachers Singing. *Mailing Add:* 2305 Burlison Dr Urbana IL 61801

EMERSON, GORDON CLYDE
CRITIC, MUSIC DIRECTOR
b Keene, NH, Sept 16, 31. *Study:* Univ NH, BA, 55; Amherst Col, with Alvin Etler, MA, 58; Yale Sch Music, with Quincy Porter & Mel Powell, MMus, 61. *Pos:* Tympanist, New Haven Symph Orch, 58-65; res comp & music dir, Long Wharf Theatre, New Haven, 64-73; chief music critic, New Haven Regist, 67-; music dir, New Haven Civic Orch, 68- *Mailing Add:* 198 Lawrence St New Haven CT 06511

EMERSON, STEPHEN HAROLD
CELLO, TEACHER
b Southgate, Calif, Dec 26, 48. *Study:* Calif State Univ, Long Beach, studied cello with Eileen Strang & Naoum Benditzky, BA, 71; Hartt Sch Music, studied cello with Paul Olefsky & Raya Garbousova, MM, 74. *Pos:* Sect cello, Hartford Symph Orch, 72-74; prin cello, Hartford Chamber Orch, 73-74; sect cello, Utah Symph, 74- & asst prin cello, 78-; cellist, Cantilena String Trio, Salt Lake City, 75-78. *Teaching:* Private instr cello, Long Beach, Calif, 68-72, Hartford, Conn, 72-74 & Salt Lake City, 74- *Mem:* Am Fedn Musicians; Int Conf Symph & Opera Musicians; Col Music Soc; Utah Fedn Music Clubs. *Mailing Add:* 9045 Cherbourg Pl Sandy UT 84092

EMIG, LOIS IRENE
COMPOSER
b Roseville, Ohio, Oct 12, 25. *Study:* Ohio State Univ, Columbus, BS, 46; Queens Col, City Univ New York; Peabody Consv Music. *Works:* Cantatas include: Come to Bethlehem, 54; Song of Bethlehem; Octavos include: Round for Christmas; Let Everything Praise the Lord; Pin a Star On a Twinkling Tree; Soft Is the Night; Candles, Candles. *Pos:* Librettist, adult & children's choirs; church organist. *Teaching:* Vocal & instrm music, pub sch, 46-65; private piano & theory, 54- *Mem:* ASCAP; Delta Omicron; Am Asn Univ Women. *Publ:* Auth, Let's Learn to Count, Bks I & II, 63; contribr, Choir Leader, Choir Herald. *Mailing Add:* 2149 Hampton Cir Winter Park FL 32792

EMMERICH, CONSTANCE M
PIANO, MUSIC DIRECTOR
b Stamford, Conn. *Study:* Juilliard Sch, with Rose Raymond, Johanna Harris & Bianca del Vecchio, cert; Smith Col, with Paul Doktor, Jean Goberman & Alvin Etler, BA; Yale Univ, with Paul Hindemith, MA. *Rec Perf:* Schumann Piano Quartet, 81 & Brahms C Minor Quartet, 81, Pelican Rec; Martinu Quartet, 81 & Mozart E Flat Piano Quartet, 83, Musical Heritage Soc. *Teaching:* Music dir, An die Musik, 76- *Awards:* First Prize Piano, Nat Fedn Music Clubs & Am Music Guild; Yaddo Fel. *Rep:* Byers Schwalbe & Assoc 1 Fifth Ave New York NY 10003. *Mailing Add:* 1060 Fifth Ave Suite 6A New York NY 10028

EMMONS, SHIRLEE (SHIRLEE EMMONS BALDWIN)
TEACHER, WRITER
b Stevens Point, Wis. *Study:* Lawrence Consv, BMus, 46; Curtis Inst Music, with Elisabeth Schumann, 48; Consv Giuseppe Verdi, Milan, with Mario Cordone, 53. *Roles:* Poppea, Am Opera Co, 55; Susan B Anthony, Phoenix Theater, 56; Ariadne in Ariadne auf Naxos, 57 & Fiordiligi in Cosi fan tutte, 57, Santa Fe Opera Co; Countess in The Marriage of Figaro, NBC Opera Co, 58-59; Maria Golovin, Spoleto Opera Fest, 59. *Pos:* Contrib ed, Nat Asn Teachers Singing Bulletin, 82. *Teaching:* Studio voice, Barnard Col, Columbia Univ, 64-67 & Princeton Univ, 67-82; assoc prof, Boston Univ, 82- *Awards:* Fulbright Award, 51; Marian Anderson Award, 53; Obie Award, Off-Broadway Theater Guild, 56. *Mem:* Nat Asn Teachers Singing (mem bd dir, New York chap, 80-); New York Singing Teachers Asn; Col Music Soc. *Publ:* Coauth, The Art of the Song Recital, Schirmer Bks, 79. *Mailing Add:* 12 W 96 St New York NY 10025

END, JACK
COMPOSER, EDUCATOR
b Rocherster, NY, Oct 31, 18. *Study:* Eastman Sch Music, BM, 40. *Works:* Three American Pastimes, Rochester Civic Orch, 52; Portrait by A Wind Ensemble, Eastman Wind Ens, 59; Three Salutations for Brass Exsemble, Eastman Brass Quintet, 62; Suite for Jazz Ensemble and Solo Percussion, Eastman Jazz Ens, 66; The Rocks and the Sea, Eastman Wind Ens, 71; The Strange Land, Glassboro Col Wind Ens, 83; Feast and Fantasy, Fredonia State Teachers Col Brass Ens. *Pos:* Woodwind performer, WHAM Radio Staff Orch, 40-50; second clarinet, Rochester Phil, 42-44. *Teaching:* Instr clarinet, Eastman Sch Music, 40-50, instr hist & theory jazz, 45-50. *Mailing Add:* 36 Potter Pl Fairport NY 14450

ENDO, AKIRA
CONDUCTOR & MUSIC DIRECTOR
b Japan, Oct 16, 38; US citizen. *Study:* Univ Southern Calif, BM, 62, MM, 64. *Rec Perf:* Lukas Foss: Oboe Concerto, Crystal Rec, 71; Duke Ellington: The River, 81, David Amram: Saxophone Concerto, 81, Fred Fox: Night Ceremonies, 82 & Gottchak: Cakewalk (complete), 82, First Ed Rec. *Pos:* Music dir & prin cond, Am Ballet Theatre, 69-79; res cond, Houston Symph, 74-76; music dir & cond, Austin Symph, 74-82 & Louisville Orch, 80- *Awards:* Third Prize, Dimitri Mitropoulos Int Music Compt Cond, 68 & 69. *Mailing Add:* 8853 Mountain Ridge Circle Austin TX 78759

ENENBACH, FREDRIC
COMPOSER, EDUCATOR
b Des Moines, Iowa, Dec 1, 45. *Study:* Northwestern Univ, BMus, 67; Yale Univ, MMus, 69. *Works:* Sinfonia, 75 & Symphony No 2, 78, Indianapolis Symph Orch; Crimson Bird (opera), Univ Cincinnati Opera Studio, 81; CAM

5, Camerata Woodwind Quintet, 81; Origins, Redwood Rec, 82; String Quartet No 2, Int String Quartet, 83. *Rec Perf:* Origins, Redwood Rec, 83. *Teaching:* Assoc prof music & chmn music dept, Wabash Col, 69- *Awards:* Greenwald Award, Yale Univ, 69; hon mention, League Comp & Int Soc Contemp Music, 80; John J Coss Fel, Wabash Col, 83. *Mem:* ASCAP; Am Soc Univ Comp; Am Musicol Soc. *Mailing Add:* 608 Thornwood Rd Crawfordsville IN 47933

ENGEL, LEHMAN
COMPOSER, CONDUCTOR
b Jackson, Miss, Sept 14, 10. *Study:* Col Consv Music, Univ Cincinnati; Juilliard Sch, with Rubin Goldmark, dipl, 34; studied with Roger Sessions, 34; Boguslawski Col, Hon MusD, 44; Millsaps Col, LHD, 71; Univ Cincinnati, Hon MusD, 71. *Works:* Pierrot of the Minuet (opera), Cincinnati, 28; Malady of Love (opera), 54; The Soldier (opera), 56; Overture (orch), 61; The Shoe Bird (ballet), Jackson, Miss, 68; incidental music for 50 plays; film scores. *Rec Perf:* On RCA Victor, Columbia, Decca, Brunswick & Atlantic. *Pos:* Cond & producer, theater, radio, TV & films, 34-; guest cond with maj US orchs. *Teaching:* Lectr, Col Consv Music, Univ Cincinnati, formerly; Wagner Col, formerly & Smithsonian Inst, formerly; adj prof, Sch Educ, NY Univ, formerly; adj mem fac comp & theater music, Int Col, currently. *Awards:* Antoinette Perry Cond Award, 50 & 53; Los Angeles Drama Critics Circle Award, 80; Northwood Inst Award, 81. *Publ:* Auth, Getting Started in the Theatre, 73; This Bright Day (autobiography), 75; Their Words are Music, 75; The Critics, 76; The Making of the Musical, 77. *Mailing Add:* Int Col 1019 Guyley Ave Los Angeles CA 90024

ENGELHARDT, DOUGLAS GUSTAV
EDUCATOR, MUSIC DIRECTOR
b Denver, Colo, Apr 27, 27. *Study:* Ill Wesleyan Univ, BMus, 49; Drake Univ, MMusEd, 60; Boston Univ, DMA, 74. *Pos:* Chorus dir, Honolulu Symph Chorus, 81- & Hawaii Opera Theatre Chorus, 81- *Teaching:* Orch dir, Mansfield State Col, 61-64; orch dir & assoc prof music, Morehead State Univ, 68-75; assoc prof, Univ Wyo, 75-79 & Univ Hawaii, 79- *Mem:* Am String Teachers Asn; Am Choral Dir Asn; Music Educr Nat Conf; Nat Sch Orch Asn; Col Music Soc. *Mailing Add:* 1624 Kanunu #1203 Honolulu HI 96814

ENGLANDER, LESTER
BARITONE, TEACHER-COACH
b Philadelphia, Pa, June 5, 11. *Study:* Univ Pa, AB, 30; Curtis Inst, BMus, 38. *Rec Perf:* Mozart Requiem, Baritone soloist with Philadelphia Orch, RCA Victor, 40. *Pos:* Baritone for 30 years, generally secondary roles—Silvio, Schaunard, Father in Hansel & Gretel, Goro, Monterone, in San Carlo, Chicago, Philadelphia & Los Angeles; conct soloist, New York Phil & Philadelphia Orch, currently. *Teaching:* Dir singing, Lester Englander Studio Singing, Philadelphia, 32-; instr French diction, Curtis Inst, 37-41; lectr diction & coaching, Col Music, Temple Univ, 68-82. *Mailing Add:* 1222 Spruce St Philadelphia PA 19107

ENGLISH MARIS, BARBARA (JANE)
EDUCATOR, PIANO
b Granite City, Ill, Oct 13, 37. *Study:* Univ Ill, Urbana, BM, 58, MM, 61; Ecole Normale Musique, Paris, France, sixieme degre, 59; Peabody Consv Music, DMA, 76. *Teaching:* Mem fac piano, Peabody Inst, 69-76; vis pianist, Smith Col, 76-77; asst prof music, Univ Wis, Parkside, 78-81; assoc prof, Cath Univ Am, 81- *Awards:* Fulbright Award, 58-59; Nat Endowment Humanities Grant, 77-78; Teaching Excellence Award, Univ Wis, Parkside, 80. *Mem:* Col Music Soc (pres, 81 & 82); Music Teachers Nat Asn; Am Musicol Soc; Am Liszt Soc; Sonneck Soc. *Publ:* Coauth, Why, When, How—and How Not to Prepare a Piano, Piano Quart, 80; auth, Foreword to Racial and Ethnic Directions in American Music, Col Music Soc, 82. *Mailing Add:* 5321 Tuscarawas Rd Bethesda MD 20816

ENRICO, EUGENE JOSEPH
MUSICOLOGIST, EDUCATOR
b Red Lodge, Mont, July 25, 44. *Study:* Univ Mich, PHD, 70; Smithsonian Inst, 73. *Pos:* Dir conct broadcast by Radio Smithsonian, formerly; cond & performer recorder with conct in Washington, DC & Louisville, Ky; dir, Early Baroque Perf Wkshp, Lake Tahoe, currently. *Teaching:* Prof musicol, Univ Okla, Norman, currently. *Awards:* Ford Found Rackham Prize Fel, 68-70. *Mem:* Am Musicol Soc; Am Musical Instrm Soc; Col Music Soc. *Publ:* Auth, The Orchestra at San Petronio, 76; The Trumpet Music of Giuseppe Torelli, 77; contribr, articles on music of wind instruments, Encyl Brittanica, 15th ed. *Mailing Add:* 1709 Stonewood Circle Norman OK 73071

ENTREMONT, PHILIPPE
PIANO, CONDUCTOR & MUSIC DIRECTOR
b Rheims, France, June 7, 34. *Study:* Consv Nat Superieur Musique, Paris, with Jean Doyen. *Rec Perf:* Works of Stravinsky, Bernstein, Milhaud & Jolivet for Epic, Conct Hall & Columbia. *Pos:* Performer with major orch worldwide, 53-; cond & music dir, Wiener Kammerorch, 76- & New Orleans Phil Symph, 81-; res artist, Minn Orch, 83; guest cond, Royal Phil, Orch Nat France, Montreal Symph, San Francisco Symph, Vienna Chamber Orch & others. *Awards:* Harriet Cohen Piano Medal, 53; Grand Prix Marguerite Long-Jacques Thibaud Compt, 53; Grand Prix Disque, 67, 68, 69 & 70. *Bibliog:* John Gruen (auth), article, New York Times, 1/3/82; Bernard Holland (auth), Concert: New Orleans Philharmonic, New York Times, 1/11/82. *Mem:* L'Acad Int Musique Ravel (pres, 73-). *Mailing Add:* c/o ICM Artists 40 W 57th St New York NY 10019

EPHROSS, ARTHUR J
FLUTE & PICCOLO
b Boston, Mass, Mar 26, 20. *Study:* New England Consv, 39-40; private flute study with George Laurent, 39-46; Berkshire Music Ctr, 46. *Pos:* Piccolo, Dallas Symph Orch, 46-53 & Boston Pops Orch, 52-53; flutist, Chamber Arts Ens San Antonio, 69-; dir publ, Southern Music Co, 67- *Teaching:* Lectr flute, San Antonio Col, 72-75, Incarnate Word Col, 75-79 & Univ Tex, San Antonio, 79- *Mem:* ASCAP; Mid-Tex Flute Club (pres, 79-83); Nat Flute Asn (pres indust coun, 80). *Mailing Add:* 9203 Regal Rd San Antonio TX 78216

EPLEY, (WILLIAM) ARNOLD
MUSIC DIRECTOR, BARITONE
b Gadsden, Ala, May 18, 39. *Study:* Samford Univ, BM(music educ), 62; Southern Baptist Theol Sem, with Richard Dales & Jay Wilkey, MCM, 65, DMA, 76; Univ Tex, Austin, with Elizabeth Mannion, 82. *Rec Perf:* Bach Cantatas (bar solos), Rivergate, 73. *Roles:* Guglielmo in Cosi fan tutte, 64 & Marcello in La Boheme, 65, Ky Opera Asn. *Pos:* Recitalist, Louisville Bach Soc, 65-83. *Teaching:* Instr voice, Hanover Col, 72-74; dir choral activ, Univ Louisville, 73-76; chmn, Dept Music, La Col, 76-82; prof voice & dir choral activ, William Jewell Col, 82- *Mem:* Nat Asn Teachers Singing; Am Choral Dir Asn; Col Music Soc; Music Educr Nat Conf; Am Choral Found Inc. *Mailing Add:* William Jewell Col Liberty MO 64068

EPPERSON, GORDON
CELLO, EDUCATOR
b Williston, Fla, Jan 18, 21. *Study:* Cincinnati Consv Music, with Bowen & Kirksmith, MusB, 41; Eastman Sch Music, with Luigi Silva, MusM, 49; Boston Univ, with Mayes, MusAD, 60; studied with Eisenberg, Heermann & Piatigorsky. *Rec Perf:* Sonata, Op 6 (cello & piano, by Barber), 68 & Sonata No 2 (cello & piano, by Martinu), 68, Golden Crest Rec; Sonata, Op 8 (unaccompanied cello, by Kodaly), 78 & Son (cello & piano, by Grant Fletcher), 78, Orion Master Rec; Concerto for Cello (G F McKay), Coronet, 78. *Pos:* Cellist with orch, Indianapolis, Cincinnnati, Seattle & Rochester, 41-49. *Teaching:* Assoc prof cello, La State Univ, 52-61; prof, Ohio State Univ, 61-67; prof cello & aesthetics of music, Univ Ariz, 67- *Awards:* Fulbright scholar to New Zealand, Coun Int Exchange Scholars, 81. *Mem:* Col Music Soc (coun mem, 70-72); Violoncello Soc; Am String Teachers Asn (Ariz pres, 72-73). *Publ:* Auth, A Manual of Essential Cello Techniques, Sam Fox, 63; The Musical Symbol (aesthetics of music), Iowa State Univ Press, 67; Art of Music, In: Encycl Britannica, 15th ed; ed, Yampolsky: Violoncello Technique, MCA, 68; auth, The Art of Cello Teaching, Am String Teachers Asn, Presser, 81. *Rep:* New York Artists Bureau 170 W End Ave Suite 3N New York NY 10023. *Mailing Add:* 3248 N Olsen Ave Tucson AZ 85719

EPPLE, CAROL
FLUTE & BAROQUE FLUTE
Study: Brown Univ, BA; New England Consv Music, MM; studied flute with James Pappoutsakis & Karlhenz Zoeller; studied baroque flute with Frans Bruggen, Hans-Martin Linde & Shelley Gruskin; master classes with Barthold Kuijken. *Rec Perf:* On Titanic Rec. *Pos:* Perf with Handel & Haydn Soc, Cambridge Soc Early Music, Monadnock & Castle Hill festivals, Rock Ridge Music Ctr & others. *Teaching:* Mem fac flute & baroque flute, Longy Sch Music, currently. *Mailing Add:* Longy Sch Music One Follen St Cambridge MA 02138

EPSTEIN, DAVID M
MUSIC DIRECTOR, COMPOSER
b New York, NY. *Study:* Antioch Col, AB, 52; Brandeis Univ, with Fine & Berger, MFA, 54; Princeton Univ, with Sessions & Babbitt, PhD, 68. *Works:* Four Songs for Horn, Soprano, String Orchestra, Theodore Presser Co, 64; Sonority—Variations for Orchestra, 68, String Trio, 69 & Fantasy Variations for Solo Violin, Viola, 71, MCA Music; String Quartet 71, Night Voices, 74 & Vent-ures, 74, Carl Fischer Inc. *Rec Perf:* Piano Concerto (Barber), Turnabout Rec, 77; Suite from the Incredible Flutist (Piston), 77 & Dance Symphony (Copland), 77, Vox Rec; Night Voices (Epstein), 79 & Facade (Walton), 79, Candide Rec; Der Silbersee (Kurt Weill), Turnabout Rec, 80; Piano Concertos (Ravel), EMI, 81. *Pos:* Music dir, Educ Broadcast Corp, 62-64 & Worcester Orch, Worcester Fest, 76-80. *Teaching:* Asst prof theory & comp, Antioch Col, Ohio, 57-62; prof music, Mass Inst Tech, 65- *Awards:* Rockefeller Found Award, 70; Ford Found Rec Award, 72 & 76; Mass Artists Found Fel, 77. *Bibliog:* Barker C Howland (auth), Harrisburg and the Professor from MIT, Musical Am, 10/76; Jonathan M Dunsby (auth), Beyond Orpheus, Arnold Schoenberg Inst J, 10/79; Abram Chipman (auth), In New England, the BSO is Not Alone, Musical Am, 10/80. *Mem:* Perf Artists Assoc (bd mem, 74-); Am Soc Univ Comp (bd mem, 68-70); Int Soc Study of Time (bd mem, 76-); Am Fed Musicians; Soc Music Theory. *Interests:* Study of time structure and process in music. *Publ:* Auth, Beyond Orpheus: Studies in Musical Structure, MIT Press, 79; On Musical Continuity, In: Vol IV, Study of Time, Vol IV, Springer, 81; On Schenker's Free Composition, J Music Theory, 81; Das Erlebnis der Zeit in der Musik, Oldenbourg, Munich, 83; Brahms and the Mechanisms of Motion, Libr Cong (in prep). *Rep:* Thea Dispeker Mgt 59 E 54th St New York NY 10022. *Mailing Add:* Dept Music Mass Inst Tech Cambridge MA 02139

EPSTEIN, DENA JULIA
LIBRARIAN, WRITER
b Milwaukee, Wis, Nov 30, 16. *Study:* Univ Chicago, BA, 37; Univ Ill, BSLA, 39, MA, 43. *Pos:* Cataloger art & music, Univ Ill, Urbana, 39-43; sr music librn, Newark Pub Libr, 43-45; music cataloger & reviser, Copyright Cataloging Div, Libr Cong, 46-48; asst music librn, Univ Chicago, 64- *Awards:* Grant, Nat Endowment for Humanities, 71 & 73; Chicago Folklore

Prize, Int Folklore Asn, 78; Francis Butler Simkins Prize, Southern Hist Asn, 79. *Mem:* Am Musicol Soc; Music Libr Asn (pres, 77-79); Int Asn Music Libr; Int Coun Traditional Music; Sonneck Soc. *Interests:* History of American music publishing; history of Black folk music in the US & West Indies. *Publ:* Auth, Slave Music in the United States Before 1860, Music Libr Asn, 63; Music Publishing in Chicago Before 1871, Info Coordr, 69; African Music in British & French America, Musical Quart, 73; Folk Banjo: A Documentary History, Ethnomusicol, 75; Sinful Tunes and Spirituals: Black Folk Music to the Civil War, Univ Ill Press, 77. *Mailing Add:* 5039 S Ellis Ave Chicago IL 60615

EPSTEIN, ELI K
FRENCH HORN
b Philadelphia, Pa, July 30, 58. *Study:* Univ Pa; Settlement Music Sch; studied with Anton Ryva, John Simonelli & Herbert Pierson. *Pos:* Soloist, Philadelphia Orch, formerly; mem, Woodwind Quintet, Settlement Music Sch, formerly; French horn, Rochester Phil, currently. *Awards:* Anton Horner Mem Scholar, 71 & 72. *Mem:* Int Horn Soc. *Mailing Add:* 333 Meigs St Rochester NY 14607

EPSTEIN, FRANK BENJAMIN
PERCUSSION, MUSIC DIRECTOR
b Amsterdam, Holland, May 7, 42. *Study:* Univ Southern Calif, with Robert Sowner & William Uraft, BM, 65; New England Consv, with Earl Hatch, MM, 69; Berkshire Music ctr. *Rec Perf:* Collage, Inner City, 76 & Comp Rec, Inc, 83; recordings with Los Angeles Phil & Boston Symph Orch. *Pos:* Asst timpani & perc, San Antonio Symph Orch, 65-67; perc, Boston Symph Orch, 69-; music dir & founder, Collage Contemp Music Ensemble of Boston, 71- *Teaching:* Instr & dir perc ensembles, New England Consv, 71- *Mailing Add:* c/o New England Consv 290 Huntington Rd Boston MA 02115

EPSTEIN, MATTHEW ALLEN
ADMINISTRATOR, ARTIST MANAGER
b New York, NY, Dec 23, 47. *Study:* Univ Calif, Berkeley, 65-66; Univ Pa, BA, 69; studied opera with Joseph Kerman. *Pos:* Vpres & spec consult, Columbia Artists Mgt Inc, 73-; artistic consult, Lyr Opera Chicago, 80- & Carnegie Hall, 82- *Mailing Add:* 165 W 57th St New York NY 10019

EPSTEIN, PAUL
COMPOSER, EDUCATOR
b Boston, Mass, Apr 23, 38. *Study:* Brandeis Univ, with Harold Shapero, AB, 59; Univ Calif, Berkeley, with Seymour Shifrin, MA, 64; studied with Luciano Berio, 62-63. *Works:* Changes 1 (mallet instrm), 76; Oedipus, Perf Group, NY, 77; Night Tales, 77; Changes 4 (six instrm), 78; Approximations: Prelude 2 for Piano, 80; Passages for Seven Instruments (flute, oboe, bass clarinet, violin, viola, violoncello & piano), 82; Palindromes 2 (string quartet), 83; Palindromes 2 (two sax & two perc), 83. *Pos:* Ed, Painted Bride Quart, 75-82; music dir, Zero Moving Dance Co, currently. *Teaching:* Mem fac, Tulane Univ, 63-69 & Temple Univ, 69- *Awards:* Fulbright Grant to Italy, 62-63. *Publ:* Auth, articles in Arts in Soc, Perf & Painted Bride Quart. *Mailing Add:* 379 Heathcliffe Rd Huntingdon Valley PA 19006

ERB, DONALD JAMES
COMPOSER, EDUCATOR
b Youngstown, Ohio, Jan 17, 27. *Study:* Kent State Univ, with Harold Miles & Kenneth Gaburo, BS, 50; Cleveland Inst Music, with Marcel Dick, MM, 53; Ind Univ, with Bernhard Heiden, DM, 64. *Works:* Diversion for Two Other than Sex (trumpet & perc), 66; Christmasmusic (orch), 67 & Reconnaissance (violin, bass, perc & tape), 67; Klangfarbenfunk I (rock band & electronic sounds), 70; The Purple-Roofed Ethical Suicide Parlor, 72 & Harold's Trip to the Sky (viola, perc & piano), 72; Treasures of the Snow (soloist on grand piano, electric piano & celesta), Akron, 81. *Pos:* Comp in res, Dallas Symph, 68-69; co-dir, Portfolio (contemp music series), Cleveland, 66-72; staff comp, Bennington Comp Conf, 69-73; comp & librettist panelist, Nat Endowment Arts, 69-73, chmn, 77-79; performer, Warsaw Autumn Fest, 71-73. *Teaching:* Instr, Cleveland Inst Music, 53-61, comp in res & Kulas prof, 66-81; grad asst, Ind Univ, 61-62, vis prof, 75-76; comp in res, sch syst, Bakersfield, 62-63; asst prof comp, Bowling Green State Univ, 64-65; asst prof res electronic music, Case Inst Technol, 65-67; vis prof, Calif State Univ, Los Angeles, 77; Meadows prof comp, Southern Methodist Univ, 81-; featured comp, lectr & cond, fest Univ Minn, Ashland Col, Albany State & others. *Awards:* Grant for Symph Overtures, Rockefeller Found, 65; Cleveland Arts Prize, 66; Naumberg Rec Award, 74. *Mem:* Am Music Ctr (pres elect, 81); Cleveland Comp Guild; BMI; Am Comp Alliance. *Mailing Add:* 6733 Leameadow Dallas TX 75248

ERB, JAMES BRYAN
EDUCATOR, MUSIC DIRECTOR
b La Junta, Colo, Jan 25, 26. *Study:* Colo Col, BA, 50; Ind Univ, MM, 54; Harvard Univ, Ma, 64, PhD, 78. *Works:* Shenandoah, Lawson-Gould Music Publ, 75. *Pos:* Chorusmaster, Richmond Symph Orch, Va, 71- *Teaching:* Prof music, Univ Richmond, 54- *Awards:* Danforth Teacher Study Grant, Danforth Found, 62-65; Martha Baird Rockefeller Fund for Music Grant, 68-69. *Mem:* Am Musicol Soc; Am Asn Univ Prof; Col Music Soc. *Interests:* Lasso magnificats; Italian madrigal; 16th century motet. *Publ:* Ed, Orlando Di Lasso Sämtliche Werke Neue Reihe, Vol 13: Magnificat 1-24, 80, Vol 14-17 (in prep), Bärenreiter. *Mailing Add:* 4703 Patterson Ave Richmond VA 23226

ERDODY, STEPHEN JOHN
CELLO, EDUCATOR
b Rahway, NJ, July 22, 53. *Study:* Juilliard Sch, BM, 75, MM, 77. *Rec Perf:* Quartet No 7 (Perle), CRI Rec, 77; All Schubert Recording, Sine Qua Non Rec, 78; String Quartet (Zwillich), Cambridge Rec, 82. *Pos:* Cellist, New York String Quartet, 76-82. *Teaching:* Fac mem & perf, Aspen Music Fest & Music Sch, 76-82; lectr & artist in res, Univ Calif, Irvine, 78- *Awards:* Morris Loeb Prize, Juilliard Sch, 77; Univ Calif Career Develop Awards, 80 & 83. *Mem:* Chamber Music Am. *Mailing Add:* Music Dept Univ Calif Irvine CA 92717

ERICKSEN, K EARL
EDUCATOR
b Manti, Utah, May 22, 24. *Study:* Snow Jr Col, AA, 46; Brigham Young Univ, BS, 49; Utah State Uiv, MS, 64, EdD, 73. *Teaching:* Prof, Weber State Col, 61-, dir bands, 61-64, chair music dept, 78- *Mem:* Music Educr Nat Conf; Nat Asn Jazz Educr; Utah Music Educ Asn (pres, 77-79). *Mailing Add:* Music Dept Weber State Col Ogden UT 84408

ERICKSON, GORDON MCVEY
PERCUSSION, MALLET INSTRUMENTS
b Bismarck, NDak, July 30, 17. *Study:* Univ NDak, Grand Forks, 35-42; Black Hills State Col, BS, 61. *Pos:* Timpanist, Grand Forks Symph, 32-42 & Fargo-Moorhead Opera Co, 67-70; perc, Fargo-Moorhead Symph, 61- *Teaching:* Drum, elem sch, Grand Forks & Grand Forks Cent High Sch, 32-42. *Mem:* Am Fedn Musicians. *Mailing Add:* 356 7th Ave S Fargo ND 58102

ERICKSON, KAAREN (HERR)
SOPRANO
b Seattle, Wash, Feb 9, 53. *Study:* Western Wash State Col, 70-74; Calif Inst of Arts, BFA, 78; Music Acad of West, with Martial Singher & Maurice Abravanel, summers 76, 77, 78 & 81. *Roles:* Gilda in Rigoletto, Seattle Opera, Munich Opera & Houston Opera, 82-83; Noemie in Cendrillon, San Francisco Opera, 82; Pamina in Die Zauberflöte, Duetsche Oper, WBerlin, 82; Rezia in Oberon, Piccola Scala; Ellen Orford in Peter Grimes, 83 & Susanna in Figaro, 83, Seattle Opera; Wanda in Gerolstein, San Francisco Opera, 83. *Awards:* Third Prize, Montreal Int Compt, 81; First Prize, Munich Int Compt, 82. *Mailing Add:* c/o Calif Artists 23 Liberty St San Francisco CA 94110

ERICKSON, RAYMOND
EDUCATOR, HARPSICHORD
b Minneapolis, Minn, Aug 2, 41. *Study:* Whittier Col, studied piano with Margaretha Lohmann, BA, 63; Yale Univ, studied harpsichord with Ralph Kirkpatrick, PhD(music hist), 70; studied harpsichord with Albert Fuller, 71-76; piano coaching with Nadia Reisenberg, 72-73. *Rec Perf:* The Erickson Tapes, Syntonic Res, 73; Brandenburg Concertos (Bach), Smithsonian Rec. *Pos:* Dir, Aston Magna Found Acad 17th & 18th Century Culture, 78. *Teaching:* Acting instr music hist, Yale Univ, 68-70; asst prof, Queens Col, City Univ New York, 71-74, assoc prof, 74-81, prof, 81-, founding dir & chmn, Aaron Copland Sch Music, 81- *Awards:* Res fel, IBM Systems Res Inst, 70-71 & Alexander von Humboldt Stiftung, Fed Repub Ger, 77-78 & 83. *Bibliog:* Elizabeth Heston (auth), Back to Bach, Humanities, 2/83. *Mem:* Am Musicol Soc; Medieval Acad Am. *Interests:* Computer applications in music analysis; medieval music theory; 17th and 18th century cultural history. *Publ:* Auth, Musical Analysis and the Computer, Comput & Humanities, 68; A General-Purpose System for Computer-Aided Musical Studies, J Music Theory, 69; DARMS: A Reference Manual, private publ, 76; Concerning Measured Music, J Music Theory, 82; coauth, The DARMS Project: Implementation of an Artificial Language for the Representation of Music, Current Trends Ling (in prep). *Mailing Add:* 76 Laight St #1 New York NY 10013

ERICKSON, ROBERT
COMPOSER, EDUCATOR
b Marquette, Mich, Mar 7, 17. *Study:* Chicago Consv, 37-38; studied with Wesley LaViolette, 38; Hamline Univ, with Ernst Krenek, BA, 43, MA, 47; studied with Roger Sessions, 50. *Works:* Introduction and Allegro (orch), 48; Two String Quartets, 50 & 56; Divertimento (flute, clarinet & strings), 53; Piece for Bells & Toy Pianos, 65; Ricercar a 3 (contrabass & tape), 67; Percussion Loops (solo perc & computer), 73; 9 1/2 for Henry (tape & chamber ens), 78. *Teaching:* Instr, San Francisco, 52-56; prof, Univ Calif, 67- *Awards:* Drew Prize, 43; Yaddo Fels, 52, 53 & 65; Marion Bauer Prize, 57. *Publ:* Auth, Sound Structure in Music, Univ Calif Press, Berkeley, 75; The Structure of Music: A Listener's Guide, Greenwood Press, 77. *Mailing Add:* Dept Music Univ Calif San Diego La Jolla CA 92093

ERICKSON, SUMNER PERRY
TUBA, EDUCATOR
b Austin, Tex, Apr 1, 62. *Study:* Curtis Inst Music, 80-81; tuba with Paul Krzywicki. *Rec Perf:* Sonata for Tuba & Piano (David Powell), Curtis Inst, 81; Divertimento for Tuba & Concert Band (David Powell), US Air Force Band, 83; Concerto for Bass Tuba (Ralph Vaughan Williams), Pittsburgh Symph, 83. *Pos:* Prin tuba, Pittsburgh Symph Orch, 81-; founding mem, Triangle Brass Quintet, Pittsburgh, 81- *Teaching:* Instr tuba, Carnegie Mellon Univ, 82- & Duquesne Univ, 83- *Mem:* Tubist Universal Brotherhood Asn. *Mailing Add:* 5527 Ellsworth #101 Pittsburgh PA 15232

ERICKSON, SUSAN
EDUCATOR, SOPRANO
Study: Cent Wash Univ, BA; Western Wash Univ, MM(perf). *Pos:* Sop soloist with churches, cols & symph orchs throughout West; participant, Summer

Perf Inst, Oberlin, Summer Inst, Salzburg & Song Symposium, Boulder, Colo. *Teaching:* Mem fac voice, Western Wash Univ, formerly, Mont State Univ, formerly & Cleveland Inst Music, 82-; teacher, privately. *Mailing Add:* Cleveland Inst Music 11021 E Boulevard Cleveland OH 44106

ERLINGS, BILLIE RAYE
MUSIC RESEARCH
b Shreveport, La. *Study:* La State Univ, BMus, 55, MMus, 57; Univ Ore, DMA, 70. *Pos:* Consult, 24-Karat Experience Inc, Tucson, currently. *Teaching:* Instr, Univ Kans, 57-58; actg asst prof, Calif State Univ, Los Angeles, 61-63; asst prof music, Southern Ore Col, 63-66; acting asst prof music, Univ Ore, 66-69; assoc prof music, Stephen F Austin State Univ, 69-74; prof, Univ Ariz, 74- *Bibliog:* Thomas H Carpenter (auth), Utilization of Instructional Television in Music Education, US Dept Health, Educ & Welfare, 6/69; E L Lancaster (auth), Selecting Materials for Piano Classes, Clavier, 3/77; Nancy Dreyer (auth), Learning Piano Teaching in an Assistantship Program, Nat Piano Pedagogy Symposium, fall 82. *Mem:* Int Soc Music Educ; Col Music Soc; Nat Consortium Comput-Based Music Instr; Asn Develop Comput Instr Syst; Soc Res Music Educ. *Publ:* Auth, ITV Piano for Adult Beginners, Univ Ore TV Broadcast Div, 66-67; contribr, Televised Piano Instruction, Televised Music Instruction, Music Educr Nat Conf, 72; auth, Comprehensive Keyboard Skills: Piano Text, Nuove Music Inc, 75-76; Keyboard Sight Reading & Selected Musical Aptitude Achievement Tests, Coun Res Music Educ, 77; Goals & Rewards; Developing Aesthetic Sensitivity & Independent Learning, Piano Quart, spring 78. *Mailing Add:* Sch Music Univ Ariz Tucson AZ 85721

ERNEST, DAVID JOHN
EDUCATOR, COMPOSER
b Chicago, Ill, May 16, 29. *Study:* Wright Jr Col, dipl, 49; Chicago Musical Col, BMEd, 51; Univ Ill, Urbana, MS, 56; Sorbonne Univ, Paris, France, 58-59; Univ Colo, Boulder, EdD, 61. *Pos:* With St Cloud, State Univ Baroque Trio, formerly; music consult, Houghton Mifflin Co, 73-74; prin oboe, St Cloud Civic Orch, 76-, mem gov bd, 77-; mem music comt, St Cloud Fine Arts Coun, 76-; perf with Cent Minn Woodwind Quintet, 78- *Teaching:* Instrm, Ill Pub Sch, 55-56; instr music, Univ Colo, Boulder, 56-58 & 59-61; chmn div fine & applied arts, Glenville State Col, 61-63; prof music & music educ, St Cloud State Univ, 63-64; dept chmn, 69-79. *Awards:* Scholar, Chicago Musical Col, 49-51 & Fulbright, 58-59; Danforth Assoc, 62. *Mem:* Phi Mu Alpha; Nat Asn Col Wind & Perc Instr; Int Soc Harpsichord Builders; Music Educr Nat Conf; Int Double-Reed Soc. *Publ:* Auth, Vacancies In Music Education, 4/77, An Increase In Music Vacancies, 4/78, The Changing Music Market, 4/79, A Developing Job Market: The Middle School, 4/80 & Ten Years of Placement in Music, 2/81, Gopher Music Notes; Sonatine (oboe & string orch), Medici Press, 82. *Mailing Add:* Crest Rd Rte 5 St Cloud MN 56301

ERNESTON, NICHOLAS
ADMINISTRATOR, VIOLIN
b Salisbury, NC, Apr 11, 22. *Study:* Shenandoah Consv Music, BM, 42; Col Consv Music, Cincinnati Univ, MM, 48; Fla State Univ, studied cond with E Dohnanyi, PhD, 61. *Pos:* Concertmaster, Roanoke Symph Orch, formerly. *Teaching:* Prof music, Appalachian State Univ, 48, dean, Col Fine Arts, 68- *Awards:* Danforth Found Scholar, 59-60. *Mem:* Int Asn Fine Arts Deans. *Publ:* Auth, The Collegium Musicum, Fac Publ Appalachian State Univ, 68-69. *Mailing Add:* Music Dept Appalachian State Univ Boone NC 28608

ERNST, DAVID GEORGE
COMPOSER, CRITIC
b Pittsburgh, Pa, Sept 6, 45. *Study:* Duquesne Univ, BSMusEd, 67; Rutgers Univ, MA(comp & theory), 69, PhD(comp & theory), 78. *Works:* Exit, Shawnee Press, 72; Ironica 4, 81, Coludes, 81, Piece for Six, 81, Four Preludes, 82, Mass, 82 & Shadow, 82, Dorn Publ. *Awards:* First Hon Mention, Fest Arts Comp Cont, Shenandoah Col & Consv Music, 75. *Mem:* BMI; Am Fedn Musicians; Am Soc Univ Composers. *Publ:* Auth, Musique Concrete, Crescendo, 72; Evolution of Electronic Music, Schirmer-Macmillan, 77; Compositional Method for Electronic Composers, Polyphony, 78; Electronic Insights: Percussion Interfaces, Modern Drummer, 80; QUA4: An Advanced STG Control System, Polyphony, 80. *Mailing Add:* 156-31 87th St Howard Beach NY 11414

EROS, PETER
CONDUCTOR & MUSIC DIRECTOR
b Budapest, Hungary, Sept 22, 32. *Study:* Franz Liszt Music Acad, Budapest, dipl(piano, comp & cond). *Pos:* Asst cond, Holland & Salzburg Fest, 58-61; assoc cond, Amsterdam Concertgebouw Orch, 60-65; guest cond, worldwide, 63-; chief cond, Malmö Symph, Sweden, 66-68; prin guest cond, Melbourne Symph, Australia, 69-70; music dir, San Diego Symph Orch, 72-80, cond laureate, 80-81; res cond, Peabody Symph, Baltimore, 82-; music dir, Aalborg Symph Orch, Denmark, 82- *Teaching:* Mem fac, Amsterdam Music Consv, 60-65. *Awards:* Headline of Yr, San Diego Press, 73. *Mailing Add:* 7019 Bobhird Dr San Diego CA 92119

ERRANTE, FRANK GERARD
CLARINET, EDUCATOR
Study: Queens Col, City Univ New York, BA, 63; Univ Wis, Madison, MM, 64; Univ Mich, AMusD, 70. *Works:* Souvenirs de Nice, Shall-u-mo Publ, 75; Musing, 81 & Chrysalis, 82, F Gerard Errante. *Rec Perf:* The Dissolution of the Serial, CRI, 72; Solo for Clarinet with Delay System, 83 & Souvenirs de Nice, 83, Mark Educ Rec. *Pos:* Prin clarinetist, Norfolk Symph Orch, 71-74 & Va Opera Asn, 75-77; co-dir, Norfolk Chamber Consort, 72- *Teaching:* Orch & instrm music, New York City Pub Sch System, 64-67; instr clarinet,

Eastern Mich Univ, 68-69; prof clarinet & music lit, Norfolk State Univ, 70- *Awards:* Teacher of Year, Norfolk State Univ, 73; Second Prize, Int Gaudeamus Compt Interpreters Contemp Music, 76; Bravissimo Award, Norfolk, 80. *Bibliog:* Phillip Rehfeldt (auth), New Directions for Clarinet, Univ Calif Press, 77; Gerald Farmer (auth), Multiphonics & Other Contemporary Clarinet Techniques, Shall-u-mo Publ, 82. *Mem:* Int Clarinet Soc (SE regional chmn, 72-); Nat Asn Col Wind & Perc Instr; Am Soc Univ Comp; Col Music Soc. *Publ:* Ed, A Selective Clarinet Bibliography, Swift-Dorr Publ, 73; auth, Clarinet Multiphonics: Some Practical Applications, Int Clarinet Soc, 76; Contemp Aspects of Clarinet Performance, Woodwind World, 77; The Great Clarinet Bazaar, Int Clarinet Soc, 80; The Contemporary Clarinet, Clarinetwork, 82. *Rep:* Norma B Runner Sch Arts & Lett Old Dominion Univ Norfolk VA 23508. *Mailing Add:* 4116 Gosnold Ave Norfolk VA 23508

ERVIN, THOMAS ROSS
TROMBONE, EDUCATOR
b Springfield, Mass, Jan 30, 42. *Study:* Eastman Sch Music, with Remington, 58; Juilliard Sch, with Roger Smith, 62; Univ Ariz, with Lloyd Weldy, BMusEd, 65; Univ Southern Calif, with Robert Marsteller, MM(trombone), 71. *Rec Perf:* Encounters IV: Duel for Trombone and Percussion (William Kraft), Crystal Rec, 70; Pacific Brass Quintet, Avant Rec, 70. *Pos:* Prin trombone, Tucson Symph, 72- & Ariz Opera Co, 72- *Teaching:* Dir jazz studies, Univ Ariz, 71-76, prof music, 71- *Mem:* Int Trombone Asn (bd mem, 76-, pres, 78-80). *Publ:* Auth, Trombone Specifications, Int Trombone J, 74; Run Out of Stuff to Practice?, Int Trombone Newsletter, 79. *Rep:* Yamaha Musical Instrm PO Box 7271 Grand Rapids MI 49510. *Mailing Add:* Sch Music Univ Ariz Tucson AZ 85721

ERWIN, EDWARD
TROMBONE, EDUCATOR
Study: Eastman Sch Music. *Pos:* Mem, New York City Opera, formerly, New York City Ballet Orch, formerly & New York Phil, currently; performer, Sauter-Finnegan Orch, formerly & Alvino Rey Orch, formerly. *Teaching:* Mem fac trombone, Kean Col, currently & Manhattan Sch Music, 76- *Mailing Add:* New York Phil Avery Fisher Hall New York NY 10023

ESCOT, POZZI
EDUCATOR, COMPOSER
b Oct 1, 33. *Study:* Juilliard Sch Music, 54-57; Staatliche Hochschule, Hamburg, Ger, 57-61. *Works:* Cristhos, Chicago Univ Chamber Players, 65; Three Poems of Rilke, perf by Hugo Weisgall with Claremont String Quartet, 66; Lamentus, perf by Bethany Beardslee, 67; Sands, New York Phil, 75; Fergus Are, perf by Martha Folts, 77; Eure Pax, Nancy Cirillo, 81; Piano Concerto, Int Fest, Nice, France, 83. *Pos:* Ed, Sonus, 80- *Teaching:* Mem fac theory & comp, New England Consv Music, 64-67, 80-81, summer 82-; assoc prof music, Wheaton Col, 72- *Bibliog:* Razapeti, Belgrade TV, 74; Pozzi Escot—A Portrait, Karl Kravetz, 76. *Publ:* Auth, Sonic Design (2 vols), Prentice-Hall, 76 & 81. *Mailing Add:* 24 Avon Hill Cambridge MA 02140

ESKEW, HARRY (LEE)
EDUCATOR
b Spartanburg, SC, July 2, 36. *Study:* Furman Univ, BA(music), 58; New Orleans Baptist Theol Sem, MSM, 60; Tulane, Univ, PhD, 66. *Pos:* Ed, The Hymn, Hymn Soc Am, 76- *Teaching:* Prof music hist & hymnology, New Orleans Baptist Theol Sem, 65- *Awards:* Fel, Asn Theol Sem. *Mem:* Hymn Soc Am; Am Musicol Soc; Hymn Soc Gt Brit & Ireland; Int Arbeitsgemeinschaft Hymnologie; Sonneck Soc. *Interests:* American popular hymnody. *Publ:* Auth, William Walker, 1809-1875: Popular Southern Hymnist, The Hymn, Vol XV, 5-13; coauth, Hymnody Kit, Conv Press, 76; Sing with Understanding, Broadman Press, 80; auth, Shape-Note Hymnody & Gospel Music: Hymnody, In: New Grove Dict of Music & Musicians, 80. *Mailing Add:* 3939 Gentilly Blvd New Orleans LA 70126

ESKIN, VIRGINIA
EDUCATOR, PIANO
b Jackson Heights, NY, Nov 13, 40. *Study:* Trinity Col, London, England, lic, 59. *Rec Perf:* Piano Muisc Mrs Beach, Genesis Rec, 72; Piano Music Women Composers, Musical Heritage Soc, 77; Five Women Composers, 81, Beach Song Rec, 82, Foote Chamber Music, 83, Loeffler Chamber Music, 83 & Fanny H Mendelssohn, 83, Northeastern Rec. *Pos:* Conct cellist, Birmingham Symph, 58-59; pianist, Columbia Artists Mgt, 76- *Teaching:* Fel, Brandeis Univ, 72-76; teacher piano, Northeastern Univ, 72-81 & New England Consv, 81- *Mem:* Hon life mem, Sigma Alpha Iota. *Mailing Add:* c/o Columbia Artists 165 W 57th St New York NY 10025

ESPINOSA, ALMA O
EDUCATOR, HARPSICHORD
b Washington, DC, May 17, 42. *Study:* Eastman Sch Music, BM, 63; Pius XII Inst, Florence, Italy, MM(piano), 64; NY Univ, PhD(musicol), 76. *Teaching:* Vis asst prof musicol & harpsichord, Univ Okla, 75-76; asst prof, Univ Lowell, 77-83 & assoc prof, 83- *Awards:* Fulbright Grant, 72-74. *Mem:* Am Musicol Soc. *Interests:* Keyboard music of 18th century Spain; performance practice of 17th and 18th centuries. *Publ:* Auth, More on the Figured-bass Accompaniment in Bach's Time: Friedrich Erhard Niedt and The Musical Guide, Bach, 1/81; ed, The Keyboard Works of Felix Maximo Lopez: An Anthology, Univ Press Am, 83. *Mailing Add:* Col Music Univ Lowell Lowell MA 08154

ESPINOSA, (SISTER) TERESITA
EDUCATOR, ADMINISTRATOR
Study: Mt St Mary's Col, BM(perf), 59; Univ Southern Calif, MM(music educ), 61, DMA(music educ), 69. *Pos:* Music coordr, House of Studies, Los Angeles, 61-66. *Teaching:* Instr music & student activ coordr, Mt St Mary's Col, Doheny, 61-68, asst prof, 69-, prof & chairperson, 79- *Mem:* Music Educr Nat Conf; Am Choral Dir Asn; Col Music Soc. *Mailing Add:* 12001 Chalon Rd Los Angeles CA 90049

ESSELSTROM, MICHAEL JOHN
CONDUCTOR & MUSIC DIRECTOR, EDUCATOR
b Chicago, Ill, July 9, 39. *Study:* Univ Ill, BA, 61, MA, 62; Columbia Univ, EdD, 68. *Pos:* Cond, Ind Univ, South Bend Phil, 67-; music dir & cond, Elkhart Symph, 79- & Kokomo Symph, 81- *Teaching:* Prof cond, Ind Univ, South Bend, 67- *Awards:* Lilly Found Award, 76; Ind Univ Fac Fel, 82. *Mem:* Am Symph Orch; Music Educr Nat Conf; Phi Mu Alpha. *Publ:* Auth, Listening Comes Alive, Music Educr J, 71; Instrumental Music, 72 & Conducting from Memory, 74, Instrumentalist; Conducting Tips, Ind Musicator, 74. *Mailing Add:* 1726 E Cedar St South Bend IN 46617

ESTEBAN, JULIO
EDUCATOR, COMPOSER
b Shanghai, China, Mar 18, 06. *Study:* Consv Music, Univ Philippines, BMus; Escuela Munic Musica, Barcelona, Spain, MMus; Univ Santo Tomas, Manila, Hon DMus, 82. *Works:* Official UN Hymn of Philippines; over 35 motion picture scores. *Teaching:* Instr music, San Juan Letran Col, Manila, 25-28; from instr to assoc prof, Consv Music, Univ Philippines, 25-47; head piano dept, Phillippine Women's Univ, 43-44; dir, Consv Music, Univ Santo Tomas, Manila, 47-57; fac mem piano, Peabody Consv Music, 55- *Awards:* Knight Order Queen Isabella, Spain, 53. *Mem:* Music Teachers Nat Asn; Col Music Soc; Am Musicol Soc; Md State Music Teachers Asn; Phi Mu Alpha. *Publ:* Contribr to Am Music Teacher & Clavier. *Mailing Add:* Peabody Consv 1 E Mt Vernon Pl Baltimore MD 21202

ESTES, CHARLES BYRON
COMPOSER, PIANO
b Denver, Colo, June 17, 46. *Study:* Fullerton Jr Col, AA, 66; Col Idaho, BA, 69; Calif State Univ, Fullerton, MA, 79. *Works:* Le Roi de Frommagerie, David Gray Porter, 77; VBA, Power Vac, 78; A Midsummer Night's Dream, 81, Romeo & Juliet, 81, Twelfth Night, 81, Macbeth, 81 & Two Gentlemen of Verona, 81, Grove Shakespeare Fest. *Pos:* Pianist & vocalist, Paul Zen Quintet, 71-, Penumbra, 79-; founder & dir, Direct Image Ens, 74-; comp in res, Grove Shakespeare Fest, 80- *Bibliog:* John Underwood, Something Other, KSUL-FM, 78; David Porter, Who is Chuck Estes?, KPFK-FM, 83. *Mailing Add:* 1207 N Concord Fullerton CA 92631

ESTES, RICHARD (ALAN)
TENOR
b Louisville, Ky. *Study:* Sch Music, Stetson Univ, BM, 70; Catholic Univ Am, MM, 73; Am Opera Ctr, Juilliard Sch, 80. *Roles:* John the Baptist in Herodiade, Opera Orch New York, 80; Don Jose in Carmen, Ky Opera, 81; Alfredo in La Traviata, Opera Theatre Rochester, 81; Vanja in Katia Kabanova, 81 & Andres in Wozzeck, 82, Houston Grand Opera; Alfred in Die Fledermaus, Baltimore Opera, 82; Hoffmann in Tales of Hoffmann, Lake George Opera Fest, 82. *Awards:* Metropolitan Opera Regional Auditions Studio Award, 69. *Mem:* Am Guild Musical Artists; Actors Equity Asn. *Mailing Add:* 158-18 Riverside Dr W New York NY 10032

ESTES, SIMON
BASS-BARITONE
b Centreville, Iowa, 1938. *Study:* Univ Iowa, with Charles Kellis, 56-63; Juilliard Sch, 64-65. *Roles:* Ramfis in Aida, Deutsche Oper, 65; Figaro in The Barber of Seville, Boston Opera, 68; Banquo in Macbeth, Chicago Lyr Opera, 69; Oroveso in Norma, Metropolitan Opera, 76; Dutchman in The Flying Dutchman, Zurich, 77, Bayreuth, 78, Vienna Staatsoper & Paris Opera; and others. *Awards:* Munich Compt Prize, 65; Silver Medalist, Tchaikovsky Compt, Moscow, 66. *Bibliog:* Theodore W Libbey Jr (auth), I've Been Ready for the Met Since 1974, New York Times, 1/3/82; article, New York Times, 1/17/83; Stephanie von Buchau (auth), Keeping the Faith, Opera News, 3/26/83. *Mailing Add:* c/o Columbia Artists Mgt 165 W 57th St New York NY 10019

ESTILL, ANN (H M)
EDUCATOR, COLORATURA SOPRANO
US citizen. *Study:* Western Mich Univ, BM; Teachers Col, Columbia Univ, MA & prof dipl; NY Univ, DA, 82. *Works:* Songs of Solomon, perf by Ritha Devi, 81-82; Cycle of Seasons. *Roles:* Queen of the Night in The Magic Flute, Rome Fest Orch, 83; Zerbinetta in Ariadne auf Naxos, Rosina in The Barber of Seville, Gilda in Rigoletto & Cecily in La Divina. *Teaching:* Assoc prof music, Jersey City State Col, currently. *Mem:* Am Guild Musical Artists; Int Symph Peace; Sigma Alpha Iota. *Interests:* African & Afro-American classical music. *Mailing Add:* 1153 Kennedy Blvd Apt 2C Bayonne NJ 07002

ESTRIN, MITCHELL S
CLARINET
b Bethpage, NY, Dec 23, 56. *Study:* Juilliard Sch, with Stanley Drucker, BMus, 78, MMus, 79. *Rec Perf:* With New York Phil, Columbia Masterworks. *Pos:* Regular extra incl prin, New York Phil, 79-; clarinet & prin clarinet, Brooklyn Phil, 79-; solo clarinet, Newport Music Fest, 79-80; prin clarinet, San Francisco Ballet, 80- *Awards:* Louis A Sudler Found award, Chicago Symph Orch, 74; Elsie & Walter W Naumburg Scholar Clarinet, 78. *Mem:* Rec Musicians Am; Am Fedn Musicians. *Mailing Add:* 515 W 59th St New York NY 10019

ESTRIN, MORTON
PIANO, TEACHER
b Burlington, Vt, Dec 29, 23. *Study:* Private study with Vera Maurina-Press, 41-49; Sch Educ, NY Univ, 42-44; Juilliard Sch Music, with Rosina Lhevinne, 45. *Rec Perf:* Works of Meyer Kupferman, Serenus Rec, 63; Scriabin-Etudes, Op 8, 68, Morton Estrin Plays Brahms, 72, Rachmaninoff Preludes, Op 32, 72, Great Hits for Piano, 74 & Palm Court Music, 75, Connoisseur Soc Rec; Symphonic Etudes (Schumann), Grenadilla Rec, 82. *Pos:* Int concert pianist, 49- *Teaching:* Private piano, Hicksville, NY, 42-; adj star prof piano & theory, Hofstra Univ, 58- *Mem:* Col Music Soc; Am Asn Univ Prof; Am Fedn Musicians; Pi Kappa Lambda. *Publ:* Auth, Rachmaninoff Preludes Op 32, Clavier Mag, 72. *Rep:* Dodie Lefebre 498 West End Ave New York NY 10024. *Mailing Add:* 9 Clotilde Ct Hicksville NY 11801

ETLINGER, H RICHARD
EDUCATOR, ADMINISTRATOR
b Brooklyn, NY, Oct 17, 28. *Study:* Univ Mich, Ann Arbor, BA, 50; Sch Law, Univ Miami, LLB, 53, JD, 83; Sch Law, NY Univ. *Pos:* Vpres business affairs, Rec Div, RCA Victor, 63-71; Playboy Rec, 71-72; Motown Rec Corp, 72-75 & Casablanca Rec & Filmworks, 75-80. *Teaching:* Instr music business, Univ Calif, Los Angeles, 75-80; assoc prof music mgt business, Univ Pac, 82- *Bibliog:* Music Man Turned Professor, Pacifican, 9/24/83. *Mem:* Music Industry Educr Asn. *Mailing Add:* Consv Music Univ of Pacific Stockton CA 95211

ETZEL, MARION
EDUCATOR, VIOLIN
b Milwaukee, Wis, June 21, 42. *Study:* Alverno Col, BMus, 66; Univ Ill, Urbana, MS(music educ), 70, EdD(music educ), 79. *Teaching:* Orch, Wis Pub Sch, 70-75; asst prof music educ, Manchester Col, 78-82; assoc prof, Chicago Musical Col, 82- *Mem:* Music Educr Nat Conf; Am String Teachers Asn; Suzuki Asn Am; Karl Orff Asn. *Mailing Add:* 430 S Michigan Ave Chicago IL 60605

EUBANKS, RACHEL AMELIA
COMPOSER, ADMINISTRATOR
b San Jose, Calif. *Study:* Univ Calif, Berkeley, BA, 45; Columbia Univ, MA, 47; Pacific Western Univ, DMA, 80. *Works:* Prelude, 42; Trio for Clarinet, Violin & Piano, Fontainebleau Ens, 80 & Consv Fac Ens, 82; Symphonic Requiem, Korean Phil, Eubanks Consv Orch, 82; also many choral & vocal works. *Pos:* Pres & found, Eubanks Consv Music, 51- *Teaching:* Assoc prof theory & comp & chmn music dept, Wilberforce Univ, 49-50; prof theory & comp, Eubanks Consv Music, 51- *Mem:* Music Teachers Nat Asn; Music Educr Nat Conf; Soc Ethnomusicol. *Publ:* Auth, Musicianship, Vol I & II, Eubanks Consv, 61. *Mailing Add:* 4928 Crenshaw Blvd Los Angeles CA 90043

EVANS, AUDREY FERRO
PIANO, TEACHER
b Chicago, Ill. *Study:* Ill Wesleyan Univ, BM, 50; Am Consv Music, MM, 73. *Teaching:* Instr piano, Am Consv Music, 72- *Mem:* Sigma Alpha Iota; Soc Am Musicians; Suzuzki Asn Am. *Mailing Add:* 116 S Michigan Chicago IL 60603

EVANS, BILLY G
COMPOSER, PIANO
b Big Spring, Tex, Oct 27, 38. *Study:* NTex State Univ, with Samuel Adler. *Works:* Concerto (piano & winds); Piano Sonata; Quartet (piano, violin, clarinet & cello); Caprice (flute & piano); Five Variations on an Old Englishe Ayre (woodwind trio & piano). *Teaching:* Instr piano, WTex State Univ, 61- *Mailing Add:* 2509 14th Ave Canyon TX 79015

EVANS, JOSEPH
TENOR
b Brookhaven, Miss, Aug 13, 45. *Study:* NTex State Univ, BMus, 67; MM(voice), 73. *Rec Perf:* The American Flag (Dvorak), Columbia Masterworks, 77; Persephone (Stravinsky), PBS, 83. *Roles:* Alfredo in La Traviata, San Diego Opera, 78; Rodolfo in La Boheme, 78 & Duke of Mantua in Rigoletto, 79, Opera Co Boston; Leicester in Maria Stuarda, 81, Nadir in Pearl Fishers, 82 & Pinkerton in Madama Butterfly, 82, New York City Opera; Faust in Faust, San Diego Opera, 82. *Mailing Add:* 79 Evelyn St Stratford CT 06497

EVANS, MARGARITA SAWATZKY
EDUCATOR, SOPRANO
b Sunnyslope, Alberta, Apr 16, 32. *Study:* Studied with Odette de Foras; Cascade Col, AB(voice), 57; Univ Portland, with Felice Wolmut, MMus, 59. *Roles:* Desdemona in Otello, 58 & Leonore in Fidelio, 59, Portland Univ; Sop, Messiah (Handel), Creation (Haydn) & Elijah (Mendelssohn), Oratorio Soc. *Pos:* Recitalist lieder & art songs. *Teaching:* Asst prof voice, Olivet Col, 61-70; assoc prof, Wheaton Col, 70- *Awards:* Nat Leadership Award, Phi Beta, 58. *Mem:* Nat Asn Teachers Singing (Ill state gov, 82-). *Interests:* Coordination of mental, emotional and physical aspects of singing. *Mailing Add:* 1183 Valley Rd Lombard IL 60148

EVANS, MARK
COMPOSER, CONDUCTOR
b St Louis, Mo. *Study:* Calif Inst Arts, BMus(comp); Claremont Grad Sch, MA, PhD; studied comp with M Castelnuovo-Tedesco, Roy Harris, Ernest Kanitz & Aurelio de la Vega, cond with Fritz Zweig & Joseph Wagner & piano with Helena Lewyn & Julia Bal de Zuniga. *Works:* Stage musicals, film & TV scores, choral & chamber music & works for guitar. *Pos:* Comp & cond,

musical theatre, films, TV & radio, currently; pianist, organist, host & producer, Mark My Words (radio show), currently; consultant to arts & communications archives, Brigham Young Univ. *Publ:* Auth, Soundtrack: The Music of the Movies, 75 & Scott Joplin & the Ragtime Years, 76; The Morality Gap, 78; coauth, Pepito, 79; auth, Straight Shooting, 80. *Rep:* Am Fedn Musicians Local No 47 817 Vine St Los Angeles CA 90038. *Mailing Add:* 7608 1/2 Eads Ave La Jolla CA 92037

EVANS, PETER (HOLLINGSHEAD)
GUITAR, COMPOSER
b Durham, NC, Jan 26, 42. *Study:* Madrid, Spain, 61; Juilliard Sch Music, 78-79. *Works:* Concert Solos for the Classical Guitar, G Schirmer, 82; The Hums of Edward Bear (orchestral suite), 83. *Pos:* Conct guitarist, US, South Am, Can, Europe & Japan, 63-; vpres, Carmel Classic Guitar Fest, 82- *Mem:* ASCAP. *Rep:* Tournay Mgt Inc 127 W 72nd St New York NY 10023. *Mailing Add:* Palo Colo Canyon Carmel CA 93923

EVANS, PHILLIP
PIANO, EDUCATOR
b Grand Rapids, Mich, May 16, 28. *Study:* Mich State Univ, BMus, 48; Juilliard Sch, with B Webster, BS, 50, MS, 52; Cherubini Consv, Florence, Italy, with Dallapiccola, 56-57. *Rec Perf:* Evans' Play Bartok (solo piano works), 81 & Evans' Play Bartok (violin & piano sonatas), 83, Gasparo Co. *Teaching:* Fac mem, Juilliard Sch, 58-67 & Manhattan Sch Music, 67- *Awards:* Loeb Award, Juilliard Sch, 51; fels, Fulbright, 56 & 57 & Martha Baird Rockefeller Found, 59 & 61. *Bibliog:* Harold C Schonberg (auth), The Great Pianists, Simon & Schuster, 63. *Mailing Add:* 7 Hartley Rd Great Neck NY 11023

EVANS, RICHARD VANCE
ADMINISTRATOR, TROMBONE
b Medford, Ore, May 16, 40. *Study:* Wheaton Col, BMusEd, 62; Univ Ore, MMus, 63, DMA, 70. *Teaching:* Instr music, Dallas pub sch, Ore, 63-67 & Skagit Valley Col, 70-72; chmn, Music Dept, Whitworth Col, 73- *Mem:* Wash Music Educr Asn; Col Music Soc; Am Asn Univ Prof; Nat Asn Sch Music. *Publ:* Auth, Music Administration: An Annotated Bibliography, Prestige, 81. *Mailing Add:* W 519 Barnes Rd Spokane WA 99218

EVANS, SALLY ROMER
LIBRARIAN
b Chicago, Ill, Jan 4, 28. *Study:* Oberlin Col, BA, 49; Simmons Col, MS, 57. *Pos:* Music librn, Princeton Univ, NJ, 57-58; cataloguer music, Oberlin Col, 60-64; cataloguer music & art, Amherst Col, 72-76, music librn, 76- *Mem:* Music Libr Asn. *Mailing Add:* Music Libr Amherst Col Amherst MA 01002

EVANS-MONTEFIORE, APRIL
SOPRANO
b Bronxville, NY, Apr 10, 49. *Study:* Eastman Sch Music, studied piano; Juilliard Sch Music; Aspen Inst; studied with Madame Olga Ryss. *Roles:* Rachel in La Juive, Am Opera Repertory Co, 75; Rosalinda in Die Fledermaus, English Nat Opera, 80; Suzel in L'Amico Fritz, Am Opera Repertory Co, 81; Susanna & Emma in Knovanschina, 81 & Irene in Rienzi, 82, Opera Orch New York. *Awards:* Opera scholar, Liederkranz Opera Found, 74; opera grant, William Matthew Sullivan Found, 81. *Mailing Add:* c/o Warden Assoc Ltd 45 W 60th St Suite 4K New York NY 10023

EVENSEN, ROBERT LLOYD
LIBRARIAN
b Chicago, Ill, Sept 29, 45. *Study:* Roosevelt Univ, BA, 67; Univ Chicago, MA, 74. *Pos:* Creative arts librn, Brandeis Univ, 74- *Interests:* Bibliography of contemporary music. *Publ:* Contribr, The Boston Composer's Project, Mass Inst Technol, 83. *Mailing Add:* 6 Blair Pl Cambridge MA 02140

EVERSOLE, JAMES A
COMPOSER, EDUCATOR
b Lexington, Ky, Aug 1, 29. *Study:* Univ Ky, BMus, 51; Col Consv Music, Univ Cincinnati, MMus, 54; Columbia Univ, EdD, 66. *Works:* Bessie, An American Opera, Montclair State Col, 76-78; Voices from Beyond (song cycle), many performances, 77-; Songs of the Grande Ronde (cantata), comn by Eastern Ore State Col, 79; Interchanges (wind ens), Univ Conn Wind Ens, 79 & Va Col Band Dir Nat Asn, 81; The Years and Hours (cantata), Univ Conn, 81; Three Masques (sop & piano), comn by Carol Ann O'Connor, 81-82; Athedra I (trumpet & wind symph), 83. *Teaching:* Assoc prof music, Univ Mont, 55-63 & Jersey City State Col, 64-67; prof comp & theory, Univ Conn, 67- *Awards:* Fel, Nat Endowment Arts, 79. *Mem:* Am Soc Univ Comp (mem nat bd & regional dir, 78-81); Conn Comp Inc (vpres, 81-). *Publ:* Coauth, The Art of Sound, 2nd ed, Prentice-Hall, 78. *Mailing Add:* Music Dept Box U-12 Univ Conn Storrs CT 06268

EWART, PHILLIP SMITH
EDUCATOR, BASS
b Cedar Rapids, Iowa, Feb 2, 38. *Study:* Univ Ariz, BMus, 62, MMusEd, 65, DMA(voice), 73. *Roles:* Sarastro in The Magic Flute, Ariz Opera Co, 73. *Pos:* Soloist, DeCormier Folk Singers, New York, 67, Camerata Singers, New York, 68, Roger Wagner Chorale, Los Angeles, 74 & Ft Wayne Phil, Ind, 80. *Teaching:* Instr voice & choral, Univ Ariz, 69-74; from asst to assoc prof voice & opera, Ball State Univ, 74-; artist in res opera, Bowling Green State Univ, 83. *Mem:* Phi Mu Alpha Sinfonia (prov gov, 72-75); Nat Asn Teachers Singing; Col Music Soc; Nat Opera Asn. *Mailing Add:* 624 W Harvard Muncie IN 47304

EWING, MARIA
MEZZO-SOPRANO
b Detroit, Mich. *Roles:* Cherubino in Le Nozze di Figaro, 76 & Blanche in The Dialogues of the Carmelites, 81, Metropolitan Opera; Cenerentola in La Cenerentola, Geneva Opera, 81; Genevieve in Pelleas et Melisande, La Scala; and others. *Pos:* Perf with major opera co & orchs in US & Europe. *Mailing Add:* c/o Columbia Artists Mgt 165 W 57th St New York NY 10019

EWING, MARYHELEN
VIOLA, EDUCATOR
b Tulsa, Okla, Oct 28, 46. *Study:* Juilliard Sch Music, BM(violin), 68; Manhattan Sch Music, MMus(viola), 71. *Pos:* Mem, NJ Symph, formerly & Brooklyn Philharmonia, 71-76; participant, Aspen Music Fest, summers 69-73; prin & solo violist, NY Pro Arte Chamber Orch, 71-; violist, Blue Hill String Quartet, 75-; prin viola, Opera Orch New York, currently. *Teaching:* Mem fac violin & viola, Prep Div, Manhattan Sch Music, 72- *Mem:* Am Fedn Musicians. *Mailing Add:* Opera Orch New York 170 W 74th St New York NY 10023

EXLINE, WENDELL L
FRENCH HORN, EDUCATOR
b Enid, Okla, Aug 15, 22. *Study:* Northwestern Univ, BME, 48, MM, 49; Okla State Univ; Univ Calif, Los Angeles. *Pos:* First horn, Spokane Symph, 49-61. *Teaching:* Prof horn & hist music, Eastern Wash Univ, 49-79. *Mem:* Am Fedn Musicians; Am Musicol Soc; Int Horn Soc; Music Educr Nat Conf. *Mailing Add:* Rte 1 Box 24C H Medical Lake WA 99022

EYSTER, JASON
ADMINISTRATOR
b Toledo, Ohio, Oct 19, 52. *Study:* Princeton Univ, AB, 74; Sch Law, Fordham Univ, LLD, 78. *Pos:* Exec dir, Ars Musica, Baroque Orch, Ann Arbor, Mich, 80- *Awards:* Fulbright Fel, 76. *Mem:* Am Symph Orch League; Chamber Music Am. *Publ:* Auth, Copyright Protection for Musical Arrangements, 78, Duties of Directors of Non-Profit Organizations, 78 & The Song Shark, 78, Art & Law; co-ed, Author's Manual, Poets and Writers, 79. *Mailing Add:* 1025 N Fletcher Chelsea MI 48118

F

FABRE, (ALFRED) RENE
COMPOSER, TEACHER
Study: Green River Community Col, with Pat Thompson & Jean Faris, 70-72; studied comp, piano & orch with Lockrem Johnson, 72-76; Cornish Inst, with Janice Giteck, Roger Nelson & David Mahler, BA, 81. *Works:* Ballet, Untitled, Atelier Dance Co, 80; The Enigmatic Dream of Ernie Swedenborg II, Cornish Group, 80; Untitled (firecrackers), 82 & Untitled (accordian), 82, KRAB FM; 6 x 9 + 7, Art in Form, 83; Power Plays (music for theater), Armistice Prod, 83. *Pos:* Dir, Soundwork Studio, Seattle, Wash, 81- *Teaching:* Fac comp & theory, Green River Community Col, 73-75; dir & cond, Symphonic Wind Ens, 73-73; fac comp & electronic music, Cornish Inst, 80-; staff electronic music, Soundwork Studio, 81- *Mailing Add:* 2305 S Brandon Seattle WA 98108

FADEN, BETSY B B (BETSY GALE BRUZZESE FADEN)
ADMINISTRATOR, PIANO
b New Rochelle, NY, Jan 5, 51. *Study:* NY Col Music; Oberlin Col, 69-70, 71 & 75; Diller-Quaile Music Sch, teachers cert, 80. *Pos:* Mgr, Brooklyn Heights Orch, 81- *Teaching:* Instr music for children, Adamant Chamber Music Sch, 74-, exec dir, 80-; instr piano & theory, Diller-Quaile Music Sch, New York, 76-; instr, Roosa Sch Music, Brooklyn, 78-, asst dir, 79-80. *Mem:* Westchester Musicians Guild; Behre Piano Assoc Inc (vpres, 77-); Leschetizky Asn; Nat Music Teachers Asn; Brooklyn Heights Music Soc (vpres, 83). *Mailing Add:* 194 Warren St Brooklyn NY 11201

FAHRNER, RAYMOND EUGENE
COMPOSER, EDUCATOR
b Philadelphia, Pa, Feb 26, 51. *Study:* Trinity Col, BA(math & music), 73; Col-Consv Music, Univ Cincinnati, MM(comp), 77, DMA(comp), 80. *Works:* Becoming Declamatory, perf by Roy Maki, 78; Circle: A Circus for Mime and Orch, 81 & The Legend of Sleepy Hollow, 81, perf by Peanut Butter Theater; Simpatica (tape), perf by Intuition Mime Co, 81; Tales from the Arabian Nights, 82 & Mirror-go-Round/Baloooooons, 83, perf by Collage Prod; Sonata No 1 (trumpet & piano), perf by Edwin & Rosemary Williams, 83. *Pos:* Comp & music dir, Peanut Butter Theater, Cincinnati, 80-82; prod & comp, Collage Prod, Cincinnati, 82- *Teaching:* Freelance tutor theory & comp, 74-82; fac mem theory, Col-Consv Music Prep Dept, 79-80; asst prof theory & comp, Ohio Northern Univ, 82- *Awards:* Comp Fel Grant, Nat Endowment Arts, 81. *Mem:* Am Soc Univ Comp; Cincinnati Comp Guild (vpres, 82). *Mailing Add:* 306 S Johnson St Ada OH 45810

FAIELLA, IDA M
ADMINISTRATOR, SOPRANO
b Portchester, NY. *Study:* Hartt Col Music, BMus, 63; State Univ NY, Stony Brook, MMus, 71; studied with Adele Addison, Dan Merriman & Jennie Tourel. *Roles:* Jenny in The Three-Penny Opera, Papagena in The Magic Flute & Musetta in La Boheme, formerly. *Pos:* Founder & dir, L'Ensemble, New York & Cambridge, NY, 70-; music dir, Friendship Ambassadors Found

(cult exchange), 74-78. *Teaching:* Voice & sight-singing, Hartt Sch Music, 63-65; chmn arts dept, Convent Sacred Heart, Greenwich, Conn, 65-69; dir music, Convent Sacred Heart, New York, 69-75; instr voice, State Univ NY, Stony Brook, 69-71 & Bloomingdale House Music, 71-73. *Awards:* Prize-Winning Cert, Am Guild Musical Artists, 63; Cert Appreciation, Cracow Consv Music, Poland, 77. *Mem:* Chamber Music Am. *Mailing Add:* Content Farm Rd Cambridge NY 12816

FAINI, PHILIP JAMES
PERCUSSION, COMPOSER
b Masontown, Pa, Oct 13, 31. *Study:* WVa Univ, BMus, MMus. *Works:* Creation; Paradiddle Dandy; Bravura; Fuga V; Little G Minor Fugue; American Frontiers of Hope. *Rec Perf:* Protest in Percussion; Percussion on the Rocks. *Pos:* Appearances with symph on radio & TV broadcasts & films. *Teaching:* Prof perc & African music, WVa Univ, currently. *Awards:* First Place, Third Ann Comp Symposium Solos & Ens. *Mem:* Phi Mu Alpha; Nat Asn Col Wind & Perc Instr; Percussive Arts Soc. *Mailing Add:* 1056 Windsor Ave Morgantown WV 26505

FAIRLEIGH, JAMES PARKINSON
ADMINISTRATOR, EDUCATOR
b St Joseph, Mo, Aug 24, 38. *Study:* Univ Mich, BMus, 60, PhD, 73; Univ Southern Calif, MMus, 65. *Teaching:* From instr to asst prof theory & piano, Hanover Col, Ind, 65-75; assoc prof, RI Col, 75-80; head dept music, Jacksonville State Univ, Ala, 80- *Mem:* Ala Music Teachers Asn (state treas, 82-); Am Musicol Soc; Col Music Soc; Music Educr Nat Conf; Soc Music Theory. *Publ:* Auth, Form in Music: Incidental or Fundamental?, Ind Musicator, 66; Neoclassicism in Brahms's Later Piano Works, 67 & Serialism in Barber's Solo Piano Works, 70, Piano Quart; Mozart and the Genesis of the Piano Duet, Am Music Teacher, 80; Pachelbel's Magnificat Fugues, Am Organist, 80. *Mailing Add:* 70 Fairway Dr Jacksonville AL 36265

FAITH, RICHARD BRUCE
COMPOSER, PIANO
b Evansville, Ind, Mar 20, 26. *Study:* Chicago Musical Col, with Mollie Mangolies, BM, 50, with Rudolph Ganz, MM, 52; Ind Univ, with Walter Robert, 54-56. *Works:* Movements for Horn and Piano, 68 & Sonata for Piano, 69, Shawnee Press; Music I Heard With You, G Schirmer, 70; Concerto for Two Pianos, Shawnee Press, 74; Elegy for Orchestra, G Schirmer, 75; Two Nocturnes for Piano, Shawnee Press, 80; Concerto for Oboe and Orchestra, perf by Warren Sutherland & Tucson Symph, 82. *Teaching:* Asst prof music, Morningside Col, Sioux City, 56-60; assoc prof music, Univ Ariz, 69-78, prof music, 78- *Awards:* Fulbright Fel, 60-61. *Bibliog:* Theodore Guerrant (auth), The Piano Works of Richard Faith, Univ Md, 7/1/83. *Mailing Add:* 4502 N Caminito Este Tucson AZ 85718

FAJARDO, RAOUL J
COMPOSER, FLUTE
b Santiago, Cuba, Feb 17, 19; nat US. *Study:* Stanford Univ, BA, 50, MA, 51; Univ Santa Clara, 58; Solfeggio Consv Provincial, Santiago, Cuba, studied flute & music theory with Riso; Calif State Univ, Fullerton, 71. *Works:* On the Mountains (flute & harpsichord), 74; Song of Light (voice & piano), 74; Images of Spring (flute & violin), 74; Voice of the Heart (solo flute), 77. *Awards:* Distinguished Serv Music Medal, 75. *Mem:* Nat Flute Asn. *Publ:* Auth, Romance of the Flute, 76; contribr, articles on flute acoustics, various journals. *Mailing Add:* PO Box 8711 San Marino CA 91108

FAKO, NANCY JORDAN
FRENCH HORN, TEACHER
b White Plains, NY, May 19, 42. *Study:* Coaching with Chicago Civic Orch, 59-60; Ind Univ, BMus, 63. *Pos:* Horn, Fla Symph, 62-63, Houston Symph, 63-64, Chicago Symph, 64-68 & Chicago Lyr Opera Orch, 68-70. *Teaching:* Horn, Nat Music Camp, Interlochen, Mich, 68-70. *Mem:* Int Horn Soc (secy-treas, 74-78). *Mailing Add:* 337 Ridge Ave Elmhurst IL 60126

FALARO, ANTHONY J
COMPOSER, GUITAR
b Stratford, Conn, *Study:* With Vincent Berdice; Berklee Col Music, 61-63; Boston Consv Music, with George Brambilla, BM(comp), 65, with Avram David, MM(comp), 67. *Works:* The Windhover (voice & 11 instrm), 65; Spaces (nine brass, seven perc instrm), 66; Cosmoi (string orch), 67 & Suite for String Quintet, 71, Carl Fischer Inc; Refraction (chamber orch), Int Soc Contemp Music Library, Holland, 73; Synergy (string trio, piano & perc), 74; Bias (amplified oboe, English horn & tape), comn & perf by Joseph Celli, 76. *Teaching:* Guitar, Conn & Boston, formerly; mem fac, New York Asn Blind, 69- & Young Men & Young Women's Hebrew Asn, Scarsdale, NY, 69-; artist comp in res, Long Island sch syst, 71. *Awards:* Second Prize for Cosmoi, Gaudeamus Found Compt, Netherlands, 68. *Bibliog:* Interview, WNYC-FM, New York, 70. *Publ:* Auth, Glossary of Music Terms for Classic Guitar, private publ, 77. *Mailing Add:* 66-05 110th St Apt 2A Forest Hills NY 11375

FALK, LEILA BIRNBAUM
EDUCATOR
b New York, NY. *Study:* Mills Col, BA, 65; Brandeis Univ, 69. *Teaching:* Assoc prof music, Reed Col, 69- *Awards:* Fulbright Fel, 71. *Mem:* Am Musicol Soc; Col Music Soc. *Interests:* Oral transmission of medieval repertories. *Mailing Add:* Dept Music Reed Col Portland OR 97202

FALLETTA, JOANN
CONDUCTOR & MUSIC DIRECTOR, GUITAR & LUTE
b New York, NY, Feb 27, 54. *Study:* Mannes Col Music, BM, 76; City Univ New York, MM, 78; Juilliard Sch Music, MM, 83. *Pos:* Music dir & cond, Queens Phil, 79- & Denver Chamber Orch, 83- *Mailing Add:* 20-28 27th St Astoria NY 11105

FARAGO, MARCEL
COMPOSER, CELLO
b Timisoara, Roumania, Apr 17, 24; US citizen. *Study:* Consv Timisoara, 40; Royal Acad Music, Bucharest, 45; Accad Chigiana, Siena, Italy, study cello with G Cassado, 48; study comp with Lavagnino & Frazzi, Siena, 49; Consv Musique, Paris, study cello with Fournier & comp with Milhaud, 50. *Works:* Two String Quartets, 40 & 60; Prayer for Cello (pianoforte), Elkan, 69; Rhythm & Color (perc group), M Cole, 69; Children's March, 75; Mazel & Shlimazel (opera), 80; Acoustilon for Orchestra, 81. *Rec Perf:* Variations on A Theme (Paganini), Pandora, 83. *Pos:* Cellist, Munic Orch, Cape Town, 52-54; prin cellist, Munic Orch, Porto Alegre, 54-55; cellist & keyboardist, Philadelphia Orch, 55- *Mem:* ASCAP. *Mailing Add:* 168 Uxbridge Cherry Hill NJ 08034

FARBERMAN, HAROLD
COMPOSER, CONDUCTOR
b New York, NY, Nov 2, 29. *Study:* Juilliard Sch, dipl, 51; New England Consv, MM. *Works:* Concerto (alto sax & string orch), 65; Elegy, Fanfare and March, 65; The Losers, New York Symph, 71; Reflected Realities (violin concerto with orch & tape), Oakland Symph, 74; War Cry on a Prayer Feather (dramatic cantata for two soloists & orch), 76; Variations (perc & piano); The Great American Cowboy (film score; orch, jazz quartet & guitar); and many others. *Pos:* Violist, Boston Symph Orch, 51-63; cond, New Arts Orch, 64-69 & Oakland Symph Orch, 70-79; dir, Cond Guild Summer Inst, 80- *Awards:* ASCAP Award, 72; Am Acad Arts & Lett Award, 72; Oscar, 74. *Mailing Add:* c/o Herbert Barrett Mgt 1860 Broadway New York NY 10023

FARESE, MARY ANNE WANGLER
ADMINISTRATOR, EDUCATOR
b Bayonne, NJ, Feb 5, 42. *Study:* Marymount Col, BA & BM, 63; Duquesne Univ, MM, 64; NY Univ, MPh, 80. *Teaching:* Prof music, Fairleigh Dickinson Univ, 66-, chmn fine arts, currently. *Interests:* First performances of Wagner's operas in the United States. *Mailing Add:* 940 Maple Ave Ridgefield NJ 07657

FARISH, STEPHEN THOMAS, JR
EDUCATOR, WRITER
b Columbia, Va, May 5, 36. *Study:* ECarolina Col, BS, 58; Univ Ill, MM, 59, DMA, 62. *Teaching:* Prof voice, French diction & vocal lit, NTex State Univ, 62- *Mem:* Nat Asn Teachers Singing (gov Texoma region, 82-83); Int Asn Res Singing. *Publ:* Auth, Monday, March 15, 1982, Lent, 82; Research in Vocal Literature: A Non-Traditional Approach, J Res Singing, 82; Singing as an Abstract Art, Inter Nos, 82. *Mailing Add:* 1900 Emerson Lane Denton TX 76201

FARKAS, PHILIP FRANCIS
FRENCH HORN
b Chicago, Ill, Mar 5, 14. *Study:* Chicago Symph Training Orch, Chicago Civic Orch; Eastern Mich Univ, Hon Dr Music, 78. *Rec Perf:* Chicago Symphony Woodwind Quintet, Audiophile Rec, 57; American Woodwind Quintet, Shawnee Press, 65; Philip Farkas Plays the Horn, Coronet Rec, 70. *Pos:* Prin horn, Kansas City Phil, 33-36, Chicago Symph Orch, 36-41 & 47-60, Cleveland Orch, 41-47 & Boston Symph Orch, 45-46. *Teaching:* Assoc horn, Northwestern Univ, 53-60; prof, Ind Univ, Bloomington, 60- *Awards:* Distinguished Prof Music Award, Ind Univ, 80; Salute to Phil Farkas, NY Brass Conf Scholar, 81. *Bibliog:* Kenneth Neidig (auth), Philip Farkas Master Teacher, Instrumentalist, 79. *Mem:* Int Horn Soc (adv coun, 69-72); Am Fedn Musicians; Int Horn Soc. *Publ:* Auth, The Art of French Horn Playing, Summy-Birchard, 56; The Art of Brass Playing, 62 & A Photographic Study of 40 Virtuoso Horn Players' Embouchures, 70, Wind Music Inc; The Art of Musicianship, Musical Publ, 76. *Mailing Add:* 5994 E State Rd 46 Bloomington IN 47401

FARLEY, CAROLE
SOPRANO
b Le Mars, Iowa, Nov 29, 46. *Study:* Ind Univ, Bloomington, BA, 78. *Rec Perf:* Beethoven, Symphony No 9, Deutsche Grammophon, 78; Carole Farley Sings Operetta Arias, CBS, 79; Carole Farley Sings Tschaikowsky Arias, RCA, 82; La Voix Humaine (Poulenc), RCA Digital, 83; The Vampire (Marschner), Fonit Cetra, 83. *Roles:* La Belle Helene in La Belle Helene, New York City Opera, 76; Mimi in La Boheme, 76 & Lulu in Lulu, 77, Metropolitan Opera Co; Salome in Salome, Opera Rhin, Dusseldorf, 80; Lulu in Lulu, Can Opera, 80; The Tales of Hoffman, Winnipeg, Can, 82; The Merry Widow, Chicago Lyric Opera, 82 & Chatelet, 82-83. *Mem:* Am Guild Musical Artists. *Publ:* Auth, About Salome, Irish Hist Soc, 79. *Rep:* Eric Semon Assocs 111 W 57 St New York NY 10019. *Mailing Add:* 270 Riverside Dr New York NY 10025

FARMER, NANCY LOUISE
OBOE & ENGLISH HORN, TEACHER
b Palmer, Alaska, Dec 7, 46. *Study:* Univ Louisville, BMusEd, 70; Univ Alaska, Anchorage, MPA, 82. *Pos:* Second oboe & English horn, Louisville Orch, Kentucky, 67-70; prin oboe & English horn, Anchorage Symph, 70- & Anchorage Civic Opera, 70- *Teaching:* Instr oboe, Anchorage Community Col, 75- *Mem:* Int Double Reed Soc; Am Fedn Musicians; Music Educr Nat Conf. *Mailing Add:* 2626 Galewood Anchorage AK 99504

FARMER, PETER RUSSELL
EDUCATOR, COMPOSER

b Boston, Mass, Oct 14, 41. *Study:* Boston Consv, BM, 68; Univ Mich, MM, 76, DMA, 82. *Works:* Three Places In New England, Bennington Comp Conf, Vt, 70; Sonata for Five Brass Instruments, Tanglewood Contemp Music Fest, 72; Taking Charge (film), Univ Mich students, 74; Trio, Comp Forum, Univ Mich, 75; Skyline High, perf by Univ Symph Orch, Univ Mich, 76; Fantasy for Cello and Piano, Comp Forum, Univ Mich, 78; Trio-Duo, perf by David Colson, Ann Arbor, Mich, 80 & 81. *Pos:* Assoc ed, Allyn & Bacon Inc, Boston, 68-70. *Teaching:* Fel, Univ Mich, Ann Arbor, 74-77; instr music, Berklee Col Music, Boston, 80- *Awards:* Fel, MacDowell Colony, 72 & 74; First Prize Comp, Brookline Libr, Mass, 72; Comn, Bozeman-Gibson & Co, NH, 78. *Mem:* Ann Arbor Fedn Musicians. *Mailing Add:* 939 Boylston St Boston MA 02115

FARMER, VIRGINIA
EDUCATOR, VIOLIN

b Brooklyn, NY, Feb 8, 22. *Study:* Eastman Sch Music, BMus(violin); Columbia Univ, MA(music); Univ Ill, DMA(violin). *Rec Perf:* With Minneapolis Symph & Marlboro Fest Orch. *Pos:* Mem, Buffalo Symph, Baltimore Symph Orch, Minneapolis Symph Orch, Am Florestan String Quartet, Trialdy String Quartet & Vi-Ro-Vi Trio; performer, Marlboro Music Fest, 57. *Teaching:* Asst prof string ens, violin & viola, Univ Ill, Urbana-Champaign, currently. *Mem:* Am String Teachers Asn; Pi Kappa Lambda (secy, formerly); Am Fedn Musicians. *Mailing Add:* 118 W Vermont Urbana IL 61801

FARR, DAVID DONALD
MUSIC DIRECTOR, ORGAN

b Coquille, Ore, Feb 28, 42. *Study:* Univ Ore, BA, 65, MMus, 66; Col Church Musicians, FCCM, 68. *Pos:* Organist & choirmaster, St Mark's Church, Berkeley, 68-72, All Saints Church, Pasadena, Calif, 72-78 & St Mary Magdalen Church, Berkeley, 80-; music dir, Jr Bach Fest Asn, Calif, 83- *Teaching:* Music master, Col Prep Sch, Oakland, 70-72; dir campus ministry music, St Mary's Col, Moraga, Calif, 81-83. *Mem:* Asn Anglican Musicians (pres, 76-77); Am Guild Organists (subdean San Francisco chap, 71-72). *Publ:* Auth, The Working Relationship Between Principal Priest and Chief Musician, Diocese Los Angeles, 76. *Mailing Add:* 1506 Chestnut St Berkeley CA 94702

FARRAND, NOEL
COMPOSER

b New York, NY, Dec 26, 28. *Study:* Eastman Sch Music, Univ Rochester, with Edward Royce, Wayne Barlow & Howard Hanson, 46-48; Berkshire Music Ctr, with Copland, Foss, cond with Bernstein & Morel; Manhattan Sch Music, with Vittorio Giannini, BM, 52; private study with William Flanagan, Israel Citkowitz & George Antheil. *Works:* The Pearl, 54 & Trio (strings), 63 & Time's Long Ago, 66, BMI; For Orchestra with Speaker, Omaha Symph, 71 & NMex Fest Symph, 79; Epitaph (orch), 72 & Sonata, Op 40, 78, BMI. *Pos:* Exec secy, Rachmaninoff Soc, New York, 49-53; dir artists & repty, New Ed Rec, New York, 51-53; pres, Friends Am Music Inc, Taos, 74-; exec dir, NMex Music Fest, Taos, 77- *Awards:* Edward McDowell Asn Fel, 53; Huntington Hartford Found Grant, 64; grant, Helene Wurlitzer Found NMex, 73-74 & 74-75. *Mem:* Am Comp Alliance; BMI. *Mailing Add:* PO Box 1387 Taos NM 87571

FARRAR, DAVID
DIRECTOR—OPERA, BASSOON

b New York, NY. *Study:* Antioch Col, BA, 66; Univ Calif, Santa Barbara, MA, 69; Univ Southern Calif, DMA, 71. *Pos:* Prin bassoonist, Santa Barbara Symph Orch, 68-72; stage & dir prod, Va Opera Asn, 75-; stage dir, San Francisco Opera, 79, New York City Opera, 81, Los Angeles Opera, 82 & Royal Opera, London, 82. *Teaching:* Music, Univ Calif, Santa Barbara, 71-72 & Herbert H Lehman Col, City Univ New York, 73-76. *Mem:* Opera Am. *Rep:* Columbia Artists Mgt 165 W 57th St New York NY 10019. *Mailing Add:* 150 W 92nd St Apt #1B New York NY 10025

FARRELL, EILEEN
SOPRANO

b Williamantic, Conn, Feb 13, 20. *Study:* Studied with Merle Alcock & Eleanor McLellan; Hon degrees from Univ RI, Loyola Univ, Univ Hartford, Notre Dame Col, NH, Wagner Col & Col Consv Music, Univ Cincinnati. *Rec Perf:* On ABC Dunhill, Columbia, RCA, London & Angel Rec. *Roles:* Santuzza in Cavalleria rusticana, San Carlo, Tampa, Fla, 56; Maddalena in Andrea Chenier; Ariadne in Ariadne auf Naxos; Leonora in Forza del destino; Leonora in Il Trovatore; Marie in Wozzeck; Elisabetta in Maria Stuarda. *Pos:* Singer, Columbia Broadcasting Co, 41 & own prog, CBS, 6 years; soloist with major symph orchs in US & South Am. *Teaching:* Vis prof, Hartford Univ, formerly; mem fac, Music Sch, Ind Univ, Bloomington, formerly. *Awards:* Grammy Award. *Mailing Add:* c/o ICM Artists Ltd 40 W 57th ST New York NY 10019

FARRELL, PETER SNOW
EDUCATOR, CELLO

b Greensboro, NC, Sept 13, 24. *Study:* Eastman Sch Music, MMus, artists dipl. *Rec Perf:* Numerous orch & chamber music. *Pos:* Prin cellist, Columbus Phil Orch, formerly & San Diego Symph Orch, formerly; solo & chamber music perf, US & Europe; appearances at maj festivals; cellist, SONOR, Univ Calif, San Diego, currently; viola da gamba, Univ Calif Baroque Trio, currently. *Teaching:* Mem fac, Eastman Sch Music, formerly & Nat Music Camp, Interlochen, formerly; prof music, Univ Ill, Urbana, formerly & Univ Calif, San Diego, currently. *Mem:* Viola da Gamba Soc Am. *Publ:* Contribr to Am String Teacher & J Viola da Gamba Soc Am. *Mailing Add:* Music Dept Univ Calif San Diego La Jolla CA 92037

FARRER, JOHN
MUSIC DIRECTOR

b Detroit, Mich, July 1, 41. *Study:* Univ Mich, BMus, 64, MMus, 66; studied with Tibor Serly, 66; Mozarteum, Salzburg, Austria, dipl, 69. *Pos:* Music dir, Roswell Symph Orch, 72- & Bakersfield Symph Orch, 75- *Mailing Add:* Bakersfield Symph 400 Truxton Ave Suite 201 Bakersfield CA 93301

FAULCONER, BRUCE LALAND
COMPOSER, EDUCATOR

b Dallas, Tex, Sept 10, 51. *Study:* Univ Tex, Austin, BMus, 72, MM, 74, DMA, 78; Ohio State Univ, 80-81. *Works:* Interface I, Perf by Gaudeamus String Quartet, 78; Interstices 11/5, 81, Interface IV, 81, Music for Chamber Orchestra, 81 & Music for Saxophone and Percussion, 82, Dorn Publ; Concerto for Trumpet and Orchestra, comn by Ohio Arts Coun, 82; Sonata for Flute and Piano, Dorn Publ, 83. *Teaching:* Asst prof theory & comp, Southern Methodist Univ, 77-79; fel, Ohio State Univ, 79-81; vis lectr music, Denison Univ, 82- *Awards:* First prize, Elkhart Symph Int Comp Cont, 79; Nat Endowment Arts Comp Fel, 81; Ohio Art Coun Individual Artist Fel, 82. *Mem:* BMI; Am Soc Univ Comp; Col Music Soc; Tex Manuscript Archives. *Mailing Add:* 3601 Hillside Dr Dallas TX 75214

FAULL, ELLEN
EDUCATOR, SOPRANO

b Pittsburgh, Pa. *Study:* Curtis Inst Music; Columbia Univ. *Rec Perf:* On Columbia, RCA & Desto. *Roles:* Donna Anna in Don Giovanni, New York City Opera, 47; Albert Herring; Lizzie Borden; Regina; Carrie Nation. *Pos:* Leading sop, New York City Opera, 47-; mem bd, Kaufmann-Rudd Fund; adjudicator, Kennedy-Rockefeller Found Vocal Compt, 79 & Metropolitan Opera Auditions; performer, San Francisco, Boston, Philadelphia, Chicago, Cincinnati, Pittsburgh & other opera co & orchs throughout US & Europe. *Teaching:* Sarah Lawrence Col, formerly; teacher master classes, Santa Fe Opera, Westminster Choir Col, Washington Univ, Northwestern Univ & others; mem fac voice, Manhattan Sch Music, 70-, Juilliard Sch, 81-, Aspen Fest Sch & Mannes Col Music; vis prof, Univ Mich, Ann Arbor, 80-81. *Mailing Add:* Juilliard Sch Lincoln Ctr Plaza New York NY 10023

FAUST, RANDALL EDWARD
COMPOSER, FRENCH HORN

b Vermillion, SDak, July 3, 47. *Study:* Interlochen Arts Acad, 66; Eastern Mich Univ, BS, 72; Mankato State Univ, MM(comp), 73; Univ Iowa, DMA, 80. *Works:* Soliloquies (tenor, trombone, bass trombone & trombone octet), Glen Dodson & David Summers, 76; Gallery Music for Brass Quintet, Washington Brass Quintet, 76; Sonata for Bass Trombone, David Summers, 77; Concerto for Brass Quintet, Percussion & Strings, comn by Richard Bales & Nat Gallery Art, 77; Horn Call for Horn & Electronic Media, Randall Faust, 79. *Pos:* Hornist, fac woodwind quintet, Mankato State Univ, 72-73 & Shenandoah Consv, 73-82; contribr, New Music Reviews, Horn Call, 80-83; hornist, Auburn Wind Quintet, Auburn Univ, 82- *Teaching:* Asst prof horn, theory & electronic music, Shenandoah Consv, 73-82; asst prof horn, Auburn Univ, 82- *Mem:* Int Horn Soc; ASCAP; Nat Asn Col Wind & Perc Instr; Phi Mu Alpha Sinfonia. *Interests:* Music for brass instruments and electronic media. *Mailing Add:* Goodwin Music Bldg Music Dept Auburn Univ Auburn AL 36849

FAVARIO, GIULIO
CONDUCTOR, TEACHER-COACH

b Chicago, Ill. *Study:* Sherwood Music Sch, BMus, MMus. *Pos:* Asst cond, Lyr Opera Chicago, 64-77, chorusmaster, 77-; orch cond, Sherwood Music Sch, 65- *Teaching:* Coach, Opera Sch, Lyr Opera, 73-78; teacher music, Sherwood Music Sch, currently. *Mailing Add:* Lyr Opera Chicago 20 N Wacker Dr Chicago IL 60606

FAWVER, DARLENE ELIZABETH
LIBRARIAN, EDUCATOR

b Arlington, Va, June 28, 52. *Study:* Col William & Mary, BA, 74; Westminister Choir Col, BMus, 76; Ind Univ, MMus, 83, MLS, 80. *Pos:* Music librn, Ky State Univ, 80-81, Wichita Pub Libr, Kans, 82-83 & Converse Col, 83- *Teaching:* Assoc instr, Sch Music, Univ Ind, Bloomington, 77-80; instr, Ky State Univ, 80-81. *Awards:* Third Place, Alexander McCurdy Organ Compt, Westminster Choir Col, 74. *Mem:* Am Musicol Soc; Music Libr Asn. *Mailing Add:* 1514 Fernwood Glendale Rd Spartanburg SC 29302

FAY, (EARL) WILLIAM
EDUCATOR, ADMINISTRATOR

b Columbus, Ohio, Apr 22, 46. *Study:* Ohio Univ, BFA, 68; Cleveland Inst Music, MM, 74; studied trombone with Robert Boyd, Edward Kleinhammer & Robert D Smith. *Pos:* Cond brass ens, Cleveland Inst Music & Col Wooster, 76- *Teaching:* Asst chmn brass div, Cleveland Inst Music, 82-, assoc admis officer, 82- & interim registr, 81-82; fac mem, Col Wooster, 76- *Mailing Add:* 3312 Meadowbrook Cleveland Heights OH 44118

FEARING, SCOTT M
FRENCH HORN, EDUCATOR

b Tampa, Fla, June 10, 57. *Study:* NTex State Univ, with Clyde E Miller, BM, 79, MM, 82; studied with James London. *Pos:* Co-prin horn, Omaha Symph Orch, 81-82; utility horn, Nat Symph Orch, 82- *Teaching:* Vis instr music, Univ Nebr, Omaha, 81-82. *Mailing Add:* 3500 S 8th St Arlington VA 22204

FEARS, EMERY LEWIS
EDUCATOR
b Tuskegee Inst, Ala, July 23, 25. *Study:* Howard Univ, BMusEd, 51; Univ Mich, MMus, 62. *Pos:* Dir bands, J S Clarke High Sch, New Orleans, 51-52 & I C Norcom High Sch, Portsmouth, Va, 52-72; dir bands & curric specialist, Manor High Sch, Portsmouth, Va, 72-74; cond, Symph Wind Ens, Norfolk State Univ, 74- *Teaching:* Dir bands & assoc prof music, Norfolk State Univ, 74- *Awards:* Citation of Excellence, Nat Band Asn, 70. *Bibliog:* Edgar B Gangware (auth), Making America Musical, Sch Musician. *Mem:* Charter mem, Nat Band Asn (mem bd dir, 70-75); Music Educr Nat Conf; Va Band & Orch Dir Asn; Col Band Dir Nat Asn (pres southern div, 81-83); Am Bandmasters Asn. *Publ:* Auth, Organizing the Band and Orchestra Festival, 11/71 & Personalize Your Band, 5/73, Instrumentalist; contribr, The Successful Band, Am School Band Dir Asn Curric Guide, 73; auth, Marching Band Trends, Nat Band Asn J, 5/75. *Mailing Add:* 2605 Cecilia Terr Chesapeake VA 23323

FEBBRAIO, SALVATORE MICHAEL TURLIZZO
COMPOSER, EDUCATOR
b Mt Vernon, NY, Apr 30, 35. *Study:* Juilliard Sch Music, Manhattan Sch Music, Fordham Univ, NY Univ Grad Sch, MusB, MusM, MusEdM, PhD; comp study with Vittorio Giannini & Bernard Waaganaar & Ludmila Ulehla; cond with Nicolas Flagello & Hugh Ross. *Works:* Numerous orchestral, chamber & instrm works. *Pos:* Founder & exec dir, Febbraio Consv Music, 54-; concert radio & TV appearances incl perfs with Paul Whiteman, Arthur Godfrey, Ted Steele & Fred Robbins; appearances, Carnegie Hall, Town Hall & others. *Publ:* Auth, Theory of Music, 57; Essentials of Music, 73; Jazz Improvisation, 75. *Mailing Add:* 49 Parkway E Mt Vernon NY 10522

FEDER, SUSAN E
ADMINISTRATOR, CRITIC-WRITER
b New York, NY, Feb 21, 55. *Study:* Princeton Univ, with Lewis Lockwood & Carl Schorske, BA, 76; Univ Calif, Berkeley, with Daniel Heartz & Bonnie Wade, MA, 79. *Pos:* Prog ed, San Francisco Symph, 79-81; ed coordr, New Grove Dict Music in US, 81-; prog annotator, Am Comp Orch, 81-; music critic, Musical Times & Musical Am, 82- *Mem:* Music Critic Asn; Am Musicol Soc; Sonneck Soc; Soc Ethnomusicol; Am Symph Orch League. *Interests:* All aspects of American music. *Publ:* Auth, Program Notes, San Francisco Symph, 80-83 & Am Comp Orch, 81-83; articles, Dallas Opera, 82-83; Study Guide to Orchestral Music, Music Performance Trust Fund, 83. *Mailing Add:* 708 Greenwich St #2A New York NY 10014

FEESE, GERALD
EDUCATOR
b Hutchinson, Kans, Dec 3, 20. *Study:* Univ Wichita, BMus, 42; Univ Minn, MA, 50; Univ Iowa, PhD, 59. *Teaching:* Instr music theory, Univ Minn, 47-50; asst prof music, NCent Col, 52-54; asst prof music, WLiberty State Col, 55-56, assoc prof & chmn, Div Fine Arts, 61-62; asst prof & chmn dept music, Washington & Jefferson Col, 56-61; prof music, Kearney State Col, 62- *Mem:* Am Musicol Soc; Am String Teachers Asn. *Interests:* Medieval music; string teaching procedures. *Mailing Add:* Dept Music Kearney State Col Kearney NE 68847

FEIN, DAVID N
EDUCATOR, PERCUSSION
b New York, NY, Nov 1, 53. *Study:* Juilliard Sch, BMus, MMus. *Pos:* Perc, NJ Symph, currently & Boston Symph, currently; appearances with maj orch in US; freelance perc, timpanist & cond, currently. *Teaching:* Instr timpani & perc, Pre-Col Div, Juilliard Sch, 73. *Publ:* Checklist & Glossary of Percussive Instruments & Terms in English, German, Italian & French, 75. *Mailing Add:* NJ Symph Orch Newark NJ 07101

FEINSMITH, MARVIN P
COMPOSER, BASSOON
b New York, NY, Dec 4, 32. *Study:* Juilliard Sch Music, bassoon with Simon Kovar & comp with Henry Brant, 54-56 & 60-62; Mozarteum, Salzburg, 59; Manhattan Sch Music, MM, 67; NY Univ; Univ Denver. *Works:* Ethics of the Fathers (orch with sop solo & Hebrew text), Denver Symph, 75; Molly Brown Wouldn't Recognize It Anymore (film score), Denver, 75; Isaiah (orch with bar solo, Hebrew text & 12-foot chimes), Kansas City Phil, 79; 2 Hebraic Studies (solo bassoon); Yiddish Keit (wind quintet); Hebrew Medley (string quartet); Sky Sailing (film score). *Pos:* First bassoon, Indianapolis Symph Orch, 56-59; bassoonist, Symph of Air, 59-63, Little Orch Soc, 59-68 & various Broadway musicals & studio rec; alt first bassoonist, Israel Phil Orch, 68-70; solo bassoonist, Bernstein Mass, 72; asst prin bassoonist, Denver Symph Orch, 72- *Teaching:* Mem fac, Teachers Col, Ball State Univ, 56-59, Henry St Settlement, NY, 61-66, Denver Free Univ, 73-74 & Hillel Acad, 75-76. *Mailing Add:* 1457 S Fairfax Denver CO 80222

FEIST, LEONARD
ADMINISTRATOR, PUBLISHER
b Pelham, NY, Dec 12, 10. *Study:* Yale Univ, BA, 32; Columbia Univ, 33-34; Peabody Inst Music, Hon Dr Music, 76. *Pos:* Secy, Leo Feist Inc, 32-35; pres, Century Music Publ Co & Mercury Music Corp, 36-56, & Assoc Music Publ Inc, 56-64; exec vpres, Nat Music Publ Asn, 65-76, pres, 76- *Mem:* Nat Music Coun (dir, 63-66, treas, 66-71, pres, 71-76, chmn bd, 76-79); Music Publ Asn US (pres, 52-54); Nat Acad Popular Music (vpres, 75-); Copyright Soc US (vpres, 74-78); Am Music Conf (dir, 78-). *Publ:* Books & articles on popular music publ. *Mailing Add:* 49 E 86th St New York NY 10028

FELCIANO, RICHARD
COMPOSER, EDUCATOR
b Santa Rosa, Calif, Dec 7, 30. *Study:* Mills Col, with Darius Milhaud, MA, 55; Paris Consv, with Darius Milhaud; study with Luigi Dallapiccola, 58-59; Univ Iowa, PhD, 59. *Works:* Spectra, 66, Lamentations for Jani Christou, 70, The Angels of Turtle Island, 72, Chöd, 75, In Celebration of Golden Rain, 77, The Seasons, 78 & Orchestra, 80, E C Schirmer. *Teaching:* Prof, Lone Mountain Col, 59-67 & Univ Calif, Berkeley, 67-; comp in res, Boston, 71-73. *Awards:* Ford Found Fel, 64-71; Guggenheim Found Fel, 68; Am Acad Arts & Lett Award, 74. *Bibliog:* Arthur Custer (auth), The Angels of Turtle Island, Musical Quart, 74; Sigurd Christensen (auth), The Sacred Choral Music of Richard Felciano, Univ Ill, 76. *Mailing Add:* Dept Music Univ Calif Berkeley CA 94720

FELDER, DAVID C
COMPOSER, CONDUCTOR
b Cleveland, Ohio, Nov 27, 53. *Study:* Miami Univ, BM, 75; Cleveland Inst Music, MM, 77; Univ Calif, San Diego, PhD, 83. *Works:* Rondage, 77, Passageways I and II, 80, Scenes from a Former Life, 82, Coleccion Nocturna, 83, Rocket Summer, 83, Alexander Broude. *Pos:* Co-ed, Comp Mag, 76-81. *Teaching:* Instr electronic music comp, Cleveland Inst Music, 77-79; instr electronic music & choral cond, Univ Calif, San Diego, 79-82; co-dir New Music Ens & comp adv, Calif State Univ, Long Beach, 82- *Awards:* Comp Grant, Ohio Arts Coun, 79; Nat Endowment for Arts Comp Fel, 79, 82 & 83; Comp in res, Am Dance Fest, 82. *Bibliog:* David Cope (auth), New Directions in Music, William C Brown, third ed, 81-82. *Mem:* Am Music Ctr; Comp Forum; Am Soc Univ Comp; Pi Kappa Lambda; Col Music Soc. *Publ:* Auth, An Interview with Luciano Berio, Comp Mag, 77; An Interview with Karlheinz Stockhausen, Perspectives New Music, 78. *Mailing Add:* 5993 EPCH #8 Long Beach CA 90803

FELDMAN, GRACE ANN
VIOLA DA GAMBA, TEACHER
b Brooklyn, NY, Mar 17, 40. *Study:* Brooklyn Col, BA(music), 60; Yale Sch Music, Yale Univ, MMus, 63. *Rec Perf:* Jacobean Music, 64 & The Kinges Musick, 72, Decca; Musick for Voyces and Viols, Titanic Rec, 78; Music of William Byrd, 80, Musick of Shakespeares Time, 81 & Music of Orlando Gibbons, 83, Musical Heritage Soc. *Pos:* Dir & mem, New England Consort, New England Consort of Viols, New York Consort of Viols, Pro Musica Viol Consort, Manhattan Consort, Acadia Baroque Ens, New York Trio da Camera & Yale Pro Musica Antiqua, 75- *Teaching:* Instr viola da gamba & recorder & head early music dept & ens dept, Neighborhood Music Sch, 64-; instr viola da gamba, Wellesley Col, 64-67, New England Consv, 64-67, Wesleyan Univ, 79-82 & Hartt Sch, 79-82. *Mem:* Viola da Gamba Soc Am (mem exec bd, 82-). *Mailing Add:* 100 York St Apt 14M New Haven CT 06511

FELDMAN, HERBERT BRYON
COMPOSER
b New York, NY, Oct 6, 31. *Study:* Juilliard Sch Music, 48-52. *Works:* Ecclesiates (cantata); Moon Mad (song cycle); Dark House (sop & string quartet); Duets (two violins); Trio (oboe, viola, bassoon). *Teaching:* Instr, Juilliard Sch Music, 55-56 & Henry Street Settlement Music Sch, 56-58. *Mailing Add:* 51 Bayview Ave Great Neck NY 11022

FELDMAN, JOANN E
COMPOSER, EDUCATOR
b New York, NY, Oct 19, 41. *Study:* Queens Col, City Univ New York, with Hugo Weisgall, BA; Univ Calif, Berkeley, with Arnold Elston, Seymour Shifrin & William Denny, MA, 66. *Works:* Variations for Viola and Piano, 63; Antiphonies, 65; Woodwind Quintet, 66; Variations, 73; Homage to Stravinsky, 74; Two Songs Without Words (violin & piano), 74; The Ill-Tempered Cavalier (rhapsody for two pianos), 74. *Teaching:* Asst, Univ Calif, 65-66; mem fac, Sonoma State Univ, 66-72, prof music, currently. *Awards:* Mechlis Comp Prize, Queens Col, City Univ New York, 62; Univ Redlands Comp Prize, 65. *Mailing Add:* Music Dept Sonoma State Univ Rohnert Park CA 94928

FELDMAN, MARION
EDUCATOR, CELLO
Study: Juilliard Sch, BS, MS; studied with Luigi Silva, Bernard Greenhouse & Zara Nelsova. *Rec Perf:* With New York Lyr Arts Trio, Musical Heritage Rec. *Pos:* Solo & sonata recitalist, Carnegie Recital Hall & Merkin Hall; mem, New York Lyr Arts Trio & New Manhattan Trio, currently. *Teaching:* Mem fac, Prep Div, Manhattan Sch Music, 73-, mem fac cello, 82-; adj asst prof music, Consv Music, Brooklyn Col, currently. *Mailing Add:* Manhattan Sch Music 120 Claremont Ave New York NY 10027

FELDMAN, MARY ANN (JANISCH)
CRITIC
b St Paul, Minn. *Study:* Columbia Univ, MA, 57; Univ Minn, DPhil, 83. *Pos:* Prog annotator & dir publ, Minn Orch, 66- *Mem:* Music Critics Asn (mem bd, 77-81); Am Musicol Soc. *Interests:* Works of Chicago music critic George P Upton (1843-1919). *Mailing Add:* 2906 E Minnehaha Pkwy Minneapolis MN 55406

FELDMAN, MORTON
COMPOSER, EDUCATOR
b New York, NY, Jan 12, 26. *Study:* With Wallingford Riegger & Stefan Wolpe. *Works:* Ixion (ballet); False Relationships and the Extended Ending (two chamber groups), 68; For Frank O'Hara (flute, clarinet & piano trio), 73

& Rothko Chapel (viola, perc & chorus), 74, New York; Voices & Instruments (five woodwinds, horn, timpani, contrabass & chorus), 76; Neither (opera for solo sop & full orch, text by Samuel Beckett), Rome, Berlin & New York, 78; Spring of Chosroes (violin & piano), 78; and many others. *Pos:* Dir, June in Buffalo New Music Fest, 68- *Teaching:* Edgard Varese prof music & dir, Ctr Creative & Perf Arts, State Univ NY, Buffalo, currently. *Awards:* Nat Inst & Am Acad Arts & Lett Award, 70; Koussevitzky Found Comn, 75. *Mailing Add:* Ctr Creative & Perf Arts State Univ NY Buffalo NY 14214

FELDSHER, HOWARD M
COMPOSER, EDUCATOR
b Middletown, NY, July 11, 36. *Study:* Ithaca Col, with Warren Benson, BMusEd; Columbia Univ, MA(music & music educ), dipl(col teaching & admin); Univ Utah, with Theodore Antoniou. *Works:* Adagio and Allegro (bass clarinet & piano); Two Fugues (clarinet quartet); Habanera (oboe & piano); Calypso Song (flute & piano); Excursion (trumpet & piano); Little Suite for Brass (brass quartet); The Lure of Latin (trombone & piano). *Pos:* Dir publ, Aulos Music Publ, currently. *Teaching:* Music educator, Valley Cent Sch. *Mem:* ASCAP; Phi Mu Alpha Sinfonia; Music Educr Nat Conf; United Teachers Asn; Orange Co Music Educr. *Publ:* Contribr, articles on music & music educ to maj music educ periodicals. *Mailing Add:* PO Box 54 Montgomery NY 12549

FELICE, JOHN
PIANO, COMPOSER
b St Catherines, Ont, June 5, 38. *Study:* Univ Toronto, with John Beckwith & John Weinzweig, BM; New England Consv, with Robert Cogan, MM, 68; studied with Pierre Souvarian. *Works:* Quartet 1968 (horn, violin, flute & piano); Night Spaces (harp), 72; Triatro (piano), 72; Vision, 73; Museum Piece (toy piano, string bass & speaker-singer), 73; From Quasimodo Sunday (double bass solo), 76; Interlude (piano), 79. *Pos:* Performs piano frequently in Boston area. *Teaching:* Fac mem, Univ Settlement House, Toronto, 61-63 & New England Consv, 66-; music dir, Nat Ballet Sch, 63-65. *Awards:* Sigma Alpha Iota Comp Prize, 68. *Mailing Add:* c/o New England Consv 290 Huntington Rd Boston MA 02115

FELLIN, EUGENE C
EDUCATOR
b Milwaukee, Wis, Dec 30, 42. *Study:* Univ Wis, Milwaukee, BFA, 64; Univ Mich, MA(music), 66; Univ Wis, Madison, PhD, 70. *Teaching:* Teaching asst, Univ Wis, Madison, 66-69; prof music, Radford Univ, 70-, chmn dept, 75- *Mem:* Am Musicol Soc; Soc Italiana Musicol; Int Musicol Soc; Col Music Soc; Music Libr Asn. *Interests:* Italian 14th century music. *Publ:* Auth, Le Relazioni tra i Manoscritti del Trecento, Rivista Italian Musicol, 73; Notation-Types of Treccento Music, L'Airs Nova Italiana Treccento, 78. *Mailing Add:* Dept Music Radford Univ Radford VA 24142

FELTY, JANICE
MEZZO-SOPRANO
b Tucson, Ariz, BM, 69. *Study:* Univ Ariz, BM, 69. *Roles:* Suzuki in Madama Butterfly, San Francisco Opera Co, 75; Dorabella in Cosi fan tutte, 75 & Isolier in Le Comte Ory, 78, Santa Fe Opera Co; Mercedes, Washington Opera Co, 82. *Pos:* Solo singer, San Francisco Opera Co, 73-76, Santa Fe Opera Co, 75-78, Nat Symph, 81-82 & Santa Fe Chamber Music Fest, 81. *Awards:* Martha Baird Rockefeller Grant, 74. *Mem:* Am Guild Musical Artists. *Mailing Add:* Rte 1 Box 304 Newfane VT 05345

FENNELL, MARY ANN FEE
VIOLIN, TEACHER
b Knoxville, Tenn, June 19, 48. *Study:* Muskingum Col, BMus, 70, Univ Tenn, MMus, 76. *Pos:* Prin second violin, Knoxville Symph, 75-77, prin first violin, 77- *Teaching:* Instr strings & music hist, Knoxville Col, 71-78; instr strings, Maryville Col, 78- *Mem:* Music Study Club Knoxville (pres, 81-83); Suzuki Asn Am. *Mailing Add:* Knoxville Symph Orch 618 Gay St Knoxville TN 37902

FENNELLY, BRIAN LEO
COMPOSER, EDUCATOR
b Kingston, NY, Aug 14, 37. *Study:* Union Col, BMechEng, 58, BA, 63; Yale Univ, with Mel Powell, Donald Martino, George Perle, Allen Forte & Gunther Schuller, MMus(comp), 65, PhD(theory), 68. *Works:* Evanescences (instrm & tape), Am Comp Alliance, 69; String Quartet in Two Movements, 71-74 & In Wildness is the Preservation of the World, 75 & Sonata Seria (piano), 76, Joshua Corp; Quintuplo (brass quintet & orch), Margun Music, 78; Scintilla Prisca (cello & orch), 80 & Tropes and Echoes (clarinet & orch), 81, Am Comp Alliance. *Rec Perf:* Scintilla Prisca (cello & piano), 80 & Structures (Ghezzo; cello & piano), 81, Orion Master Rec; Empirical Rag, Serenus Rec, 82. *Teaching:* Teaching assoc, Yale Univ, 65-67; prof music, NY Univ, 68- *Awards:* Comp Prog Grant, Martha Baird Rockefeller Fund Music, 75, 77 & 80; Comp Fel, Nat Endowment for Arts, 77 & 79; Guggenheim Fel, 80. *Mem:* Am Comp Alliance (treas, 73-79, vpres, 82-); League Comp, Int Soc Contemp Music (US vpres, 76-77, 79-, pres, 77-79); Comp Forum (mem bd dirs, 75-79, mem bd adv, 79-); Am Soc Univ Comp; Soc Music Theory. *Interests:* Music theory. *Publ:* Auth, Structure and Process in Webern's Op 22, J Music Theory, 66; A Descriptive Notation for the Analysis of Electronic Music, Perspectives New Music, 67; contribr, Electronic Music: Notation, 74 & 12-Tone Techniques, 74, In: Dict of Contemporary Music. *Mailing Add:* 100 Bleecker St Apt 23B New York NY 10012

FENNER, BURT L
COMPOSER, EDUCATOR
b New York, NY, Aug 12, 29. *Study:* Mannes Col Music, with Roy Travis & Peter Pindar Stearns, BS(comp), 59; Columbia Univ, with Otto Luening & Jack Beeson, MA(comp), 61. *Works:* Variations (string quartet & orch); Giald (orch); Music for Brass & Timpani; Prelude (brass & tape); Scherzo (wind band); Study for Timpani & Low Instruments; I Like a Look of Agony (bar, ens & tape), Pittsburgh, 79. *Teaching:* Instr, Turtle Bay Music Sch, NY, Young Men's Hebrew Asn Sch Music, NY, Mannes Col Music, 61-70 & Pa State Univ, 70- *Awards:* Nat Endowment for Arts Grant, 75. *Mailing Add:* 620 Elmwood St State College PA 16801

FENNIMORE, JOSEPH
COMPOSER, PIANO
b New York, NY, Apr 16, 40. *Study:* Eastman Sch Music, studied piano with Cecile Genhart, 58; Juilliard Sch, studied piano with Rosina Lhevinne & comp with Hugo Weisgall, BMus, 62, MS, 65; Aspen, studied piano with Jeaneane Dowis & comp with Darius Milhaud, 67; studied comp with Virgil Thomson, 72-74. *Works:* Eventide (one act opera), 75; A Musical Offering (nine songs), 79; Sextet for Woodwind Quintet and Piano, comn by San Antonio Chamber Players, 80; Crystal Stairs (tarantella), 80; Marriage of the Torah (violin, viola, cello, clarinet, oboe, English horn, piano & perc), comn by St Luke's Chamber Players, 81; Second Sonata for Cello and Piano, 82; Crystal Stairs (piano solo), 82. *Pos:* Perf nationally & abroad with many orch, incl Arthur Fiedler & Boston Pops, 67-; founder & dir, Hear Am First conct ser, 72; asst cond, No, No, Nanette, 73-75; dir rec project devoted to Am music, Spectrum Rec, 79. *Teaching:* Instr piano, Princeton Univ, 72; fac mem, Col St Rose, Albany, NY, 81. *Awards:* Fulbright Fel, 68; First Place, Barcelona Concours Maria Canals Int Piano Compt, 69; ASCAP Award, 76. *Mailing Add:* 463 West St #105D New York NY 10014

FENSKE, DAVID EDWARD
LIBRARIAN, MUSICOLOGIST
b Sheboygan, Wis, June 29, 43. *Study:* Univ Wis, BMus, 65, PhD(musicol), 73. *Pos:* Admin asst & asst music librn, Univ Wis, 67-71; from assoc music librn to music librn, Ind Univ, 71-; ed, Annotations, 78- *Mem:* Music Libr Asn; Ind Univ Librn Asn (treas, 72-73, pres, 73-74); Am Musicol Soc. *Publ:* Auth, Texture in the Chamber Music of Johannes Brahms, 73; Contrapuntal Textures in the String Quartets, Op 51, No 1 and Op 67 of Johannes Brahms, Pendragon Press, 80; ed, Kalliwoda Symphony, Garland, 83; auth, Bruckner Resource Manual, Garland, 7/84. *Mailing Add:* 1640 Maplecrest Dr Bloomington IN 47401

FEOFANOV, DMITRY N
PIANO, EDUCATOR
b Moscow, USSR, Jan 12, 57; stateless. *Study:* Moscow Consv, dipl, 76; Univ Ill, Urbana-Champaign, MM(applied piano), 82. *Teaching:* Prof music, Univ Ky, 82- *Interests:* Rare piano four-hand music; Russian music. *Publ:* Auth, How to Transcribe the Mephisto Waltz for Piano, Am Liszt Soc, 82; ed, The Legacy of Russian Music: Unknown Piano Treasures, Dover, 83. *Mailing Add:* Sch Music Univ Ky Lexington KY 40506

FERDEN, BRUCE
CONDUCTOR
b Minn. *Study:* Moorhead State Col; Univ Miami; Univ Southern Calif; Juilliard Sch; studied cond with Peter Herman Adler, Daniel Lewis, Fennell & Tjeknavornian. *Pos:* Asst cond, New York Phil; music dir, Nebraska Chamber Orch; cond, San Francisco Symph, Detroit Symph, St Paul Chamber Orch, Utrecht Symph Orch, Holland, Pasadena Symph, National Symph of SAfrica Broadcasting Corp, Brooklyn Phil, White Plains Symph, Scottish Chamber Orch, Dallas Symph, New York City Opera Co, Netherlands Opera, Anchorage Civic Opera, & opera companies of Santa Fe, Omaha, Pittsburgh, St Louis & Minn. *Mailing Add:* c/o Colbert Artists Mgt 111 W 57th St New York NY 10019

FERGUSON, EDWIN EARLE
COMPOSER, MUSIC DIRECTOR
b Brocket, NDak, Aug 4, 10. *Study:* Drake Univ, with Franz Kuschan, BS, 31, LLB, 34; Yale Univ, JSD, 37; studied comp with Meyer Kupferman. *Works:* Volcanos (filmscore), 69 & Glaciers (filmscore), 74, Smithsonian Inst; A Woman Unashamed (song cycle), Phillips Collection, Washington, DC, 76; The St Luke Canticles (cantata), perf by Chevy Chase United Methodist Sanctuary Choir, 80; A Celebration of Psalms, comn by Laurel Md Oratorio Soc, 81; Songs of Delight and Denial (song cycle), Renwick Gallery, Washington, DC, 83; over 80 choral octavos published by various music publishers. *Pos:* Prof pianist & arr, Des Moines, Iowa, 28-35; dir music, Chevy Chase United Methodist Church, Md, 60- *Awards:* ASCAP Standard Award, 76- *Mem:* ASCAP; Am Guild Organists; Rotary Int Music Fel (vpres new music, 78-); Friday Morning Music Club, Washington, DC (program dir, 77-79, found trustee, 80-). *Mailing Add:* 5821 Osceola Rd Bethesda MD 20816

FERGUSON, GENE
TENOR, EDUCATOR
b Windsor, Mo, June 4, 40. *Study:* With Helge Roswänge, Costanzo Gero & Robert Vernon. *Roles:* Pinkerton in Madama Butterfly, Teatro Nuovo, Milan, 61; Florestan in Fidelio; Don Jose in Carmen; Vladimir in Prince Igor; Riccardo in Anna Bolena; Dimitri in Boris Godunov; Gabriele in Simon Boccanegra; and many others. *Pos:* Ten with maj opera co in Austria, WGermany & Italy. *Teaching:* Prof opera & voice, Univ SC, currently. *Awards:* Winner, Am Opera Auditions & Metropolitan Opera Nat Coun Auditions. *Rep:* Eric Semon Assoc 111 W 57th St New York NY 10019. *Mailing Add:* Music Dept Univ SC Columbia SC 29208

FERGUSON, RAY PYLANT
ORGAN, HARPSICHORD

b Poplar Bluff, Mo. *Study:* Staatliche Hochschule Music, Frankfurt, Fed Repub Ger; Syracuse Univ, MMus, 57. *Pos:* Organist, Detroit Symph Orch, 70- *Teaching:* Instr organ, Consv Music, Oberlin Col, 58-61; prof organ & harpsichord, Wayne State Univ, 64- *Awards:* Fulbright Scholar, 54-56; Nat Organ-Playing Compt Winner, Am Guild Organists, 58. *Mem:* Am Guild Organists (nat counr, 68-71, dean Detroit chap, 80-83). *Mailing Add:* Music Dept Wayne State Univ Detroit MI 48202

FERGUSON, SUZANNE (CAROL)
RECORDER, EDUCATOR

b East Stroudsburg, Pa, Aug 13, 39. *Study:* Converse Col, BA, 60; Vanderbilt Univ, MA, 61; Stanford Univ, PhD, 66; studied recorder with Erich Katz, viola da gamba with Robert Wayne Moss; Oberlin Baroque Perf Inst, summers 80, 81 & 83; Aston Magna Acad, summer 82. *Pos:* Founder & mem, Columbus Baroque Ens & The Augustans, 78-; mem, Arcadian Trio, Columbus, Ohio, 82- *Teaching:* Assoc prof English, Ohio State Univ, 71-83; private teacher recorder, 71-; dir & teacher recorder workshops, Put-in-Bay, Ohio, Cincinnati, Ohio, Chicago, Ill, Dayton, Ohio & Bradenton, Fla, 75-; prof & chmn English, Wayne State Univ, 83- *Mem:* Am Recorder Soc (Columbus chap pres, 71-72, 78-79, mem nat bd dir, 80-84); Viola da Gamba Soc Am. *Publ:* Auth, An Interview with Edgar Hunt, 82 & Interviews with Bernard Krainis and Jean Hakes, 83, Am Recorder. *Mailing Add:* English Dept Wayne State Univ Detroit MI 48202

FERNANDEZ, WILHELMENIA
SOPRANO

Rec Perf: Diva (film), 82; Wilhelmenia Fernandez Sings Spirituals, 83. *Roles:* Musetta in La Boheme, Mich Opera Theatre, 79 & Paris Opera, 79; Donna Elvira in Don Giovanni, 80 & Bess in Porgy and Bess, 82, Mich Opera Theatre; Musetta in La Boheme, 82 & Carmen in Carmen, 83, New York City Opera; Violetta Valery in La Traviata, Paris Opera Comique, 83; Countess Almaviva in The Marriage of Figaro, Mich Opera Theatre, 83. *Pos:* Sop, Mich Opera Theatre, 79- *Mailing Add:* c/o Munro Artists Mgt 344 W 72nd St New York NY 10023

FERRAZANO, ANTHONY JOSEPH See   Zano,   Anthony

FERRE, SUSAN INGRID
ORGAN, HARPSICHORD

b Boston, Mass, Sept 5, 45. *Study:* Tex Christian Univ, BA, 68, BMus, 68; Schola Cantorum, Paris, with Jean Langlais, dipl(organ & improvisation), 69; Eastman Sch Music, MMus, 71; NTex State Univ, DMA, 79. *Works:* Various works for theater, Avant Quart, 69-79. *Rec Perf:* Hommage a Jean Langlais, Avant Quart, 69. *Pos:* Musical dir, Tex Baroque Ens, 80-; perf, Notre Dame Cathedral, Paris, Int Organ Fest, Lahti, Finland & tours in Europe & SAm. *Teaching:* Teaching asst organ & harpsichord, NTex State Univ, 74-76, adj prof, 80-82. *Awards:* Fulbright Scholar, 68-69. *Mem:* Am Guild Organists. *Publ:* Contribr, A Survey of Bibliographic Materials on Langlais, 75, The Development and Use of the Bibelregal, 77, Liszt's Prelude & Fugue on B-A-C-H: An Analysis, 78 & co-ed, Foreign Correspondent, 79-82, Diapason. *Rep:* Randall Swanson 10066 Marsh Lane Dallas TX 75229. *Mailing Add:* 1902 W Shore Dr Garland TX 75043

FERRIANO, FRANK, JR
EDUCATOR, TROMBONE

b Milwaukee, Wis, Feb 6, 26. *Study:* Juilliard Sch Music, BS, 50; Teachers Col, Columbia Univ, MA, 63, EdD, 74. *Works:* Suite for Four Trombones & Suite for Brass Quintet, 75; American Revolution Fantasy for Band, 76; Carsshyn, 79; Chick C, 80; Happy Feet, 81. *Pos:* Bass trombone, Sauter-Finecan Orch, 53; first trombone, Bergen Phil Orch, Teaneck, NJ, 60-68. *Teaching:* Prof music, Univ Wis, Whitewater, 68- *Mem:* Music Educr Nat Conf; Nat Asn Jazz Educr; Int Trombone Asn. *Mailing Add:* Music Dept Univ Wisconsin Whitewater WI 53190

FERRIS, KIRKLAND DAVID
BASSOON

b Hartford, Conn, Dec 30, 43. *Study:* Oberlin Col, BMus, 66; Berkshire Music Fest, 68. *Pos:* Second bassoon, New Orleans Symph, 66-69 & Detroit Symph, 82-; prin bassoon, Louisville Orch, Honolulu Symph & Nat Orch Mex, 69-81; actg assoc prin bassoon, Minn Orch, 81-82. *Teaching:* Mem fac, Univ Louisville, formerly & Univ Hawaii, formerly; adj instr music, St Olaf Col, 81- *Mailing Add:* 1071 Winthrop Troy MI 48084

FERRIS, WILLIAM
COMPOSER, MUSIC DIRECTOR

b Chicago, Ill, Feb 26, 37. *Study:* DePaul Univ, 54-56; Am Consv Music, 57-60; private study with Leo Sowerby, 57-62. *Works:* De Profundis, comn by Fordham Univ, 65; Concert Piece, perf by Boston Symph, 67; October November, perf by Rochester Phil, 69; Bristol Hills, perf by Rochester Chamber Orch, 70; A Song of Light, comn by Spertus Col Judaica, 78; Snowcarols, perf by William Ferris Chorale, 80; Acclamations, comn & perf by Chicago Symph Orch, 83. *Pos:* Organist, Holy Name Cathedral, Chicago, 55-59 & 62-64; music dir, Sacred Heart Cathedral, Rochester, 66-70 & William Ferris Chorale, Chicago, 71- *Teaching:* Prof comp, Am Consv Music, 73- *Mem:* ASCAP; Am Guild Organists; Consociatio Int Musicae Sacrae; Am Music Ctr; Pueri Cantores. *Mailing Add:* 750 N Dearborn #2203 Chicago IL 60610

FERRITTO, JOHN EDMUND
CONDUCTOR & MUSIC DIRECTOR, COMPOSER

b East Cleveland, Ohio, Jan 20, 37. *Study:* Cleveland Inst Music, BM, 58; Sch Music, Yale Univ, MM, 65. *Works:* Canzona for Solo Viola, Marcia Ferritto; Sogni (orch), Springfield Symph Orch, 73; Ommagio a Berio e Fellini for Orchestra, Ohio Univ Orch, 77; Concerto (cello & orch), perf by Ronald Crutcher with Springfield Symph Orch, 80; Addio C M (solo clarinet), various performers, 82. *Rec Perf:* Oggi (sop, clarinet & piano), CRI. *Pos:* Exec asst, Music Ctr North Shore, 65-67; assoc cond, New Haven Symph Orch, 67-70; music dir & cond, Springfield Symph Orch, Ohio, 71-; music dir, Am Fedn Musicians Cong Strings, 82- *Teaching:* Lectr music, Univ Chicago, 66-67; dir orch, Hiram Col, 70-71; vis prof music theory, Univ Tex, Austin, summer 70; adj prof music, Wittenberg Univ, 71-83; assoc prof & dir orchestral activ, Kent State Univ, 83- *Mem:* Am Symph Orch League; Am Fedn Musicians; Col Music Soc; Am Comp Alliance. *Mailing Add:* 300 S Broadmoor Blvd Springfield OH 45504

FERRO, DANIEL E
TEACHER

b New York, NY, Apr 10, 21. *Study:* Juilliard Sch Music, BS, 48; Columbia Univ, MA, 49; Accad Santa Cecilia, Rome, Italy, 50; Accad Chigiana, Siena, Italy, 50; Mozarteum, Salzburg, Austria, 51. *Teaching:* Chmn voice dept & voice repertoire, Jordan Col Music, Butler Univ, 56-59; chmn voice dept, Manhattan Sch Music, 69-77; instr voice, Juilliard Sch Music, 72-; instr master classes throughout USA, Europe & China, currently. *Mem:* Nat Asn Teachers Singing; NY Teachers Singing Asn; Int Compt Singing; Int Asn Res Singing. *Mailing Add:* 300 Central Park W New York NY 10024

FESPERMAN, JOHN, JR
EDUCATOR, DIRECTOR MUSIC

b Charlotte, NC, Jan 12, 25. *Study:* Davidson Col, BS, 48; Yale Univ, BMus, 51; New England Consv Music, MMus, 60. *Works:* Couperin, Messe pour les Paroisses, Cambridge Rec, 73; Organ Music of N de Grigny, Orion Master Rec, 76. *Pos:* Dir music, Old North Church, Boston, 60-65; cur div musical instruments, Smithsonian Inst, 66- *Teaching:* Dir music, Marquand Chapel, Yale Univ, 49-51; instr, Davidson Col, 54; assoc prof, Ala Col, 56-59; emer fac, New England Consv Music, 59-65. *Interests:* Keyboard instruments and repertoire, 1600-1750. *Publ:* Ed, Music at the Old North: Then and Now, Organ Inst Quart, 63; auth, Three Snetzler Organs in the United States, Vol II, 72 & coauth, New Light on North America's Oldest Instruments: Mexico, Vol II, 72, Organ Yearbk, Amsterdam; ed, William Boyce, Ten Voluntaries for Organ or Harpsichord, Schirmer, 73; auth, Two Essays on Organ Design, Sunbury Press, 75. *Mailing Add:* Div Musical Instruments Smithsonian Inst Washington DC 20560

FETLER, PAUL
EDUCATOR, COMPOSER

b Philadelphia, Pa, Feb 17, 20. *Study:* Northwestern Univ, BM, 43; Yale Univ, MM, 48; Univ Minn, PhD, 56. *Works:* Contrasts for Orchestra, Minneapolis Symph, 58; Three Poems by Walt Whitman, Minn Orch, 76; Celebration, Indianapolis Symph Orch, 77; Three Impressions for Guitar & Orch, St Paul Chamber Orch, 78; Violin Concerto No 2, Minn Orch, 81; Missa De Angelis, St John's Univ & Abbey, 81; The Garden of Love, Rochester Chamber Orch, 83; Serenade, Minneapolis Chamber Symph, 83. *Teaching:* From instr to prof, Univ Minn, 48- *Awards:* Guggenheim Award, 53 & 60; Annual ASCAP Award, 62- *Mem:* ASCAP. *Mailing Add:* 420 Mount Curve Blvd St Paul MN 55105

FETSCH, WOLFGANG
EDUCATOR, PIANO

b Mannheim, Ger; US citizen. *Study:* Univ Denver, BM(piano), 52, MM(theory), 53; Ind Univ, with Bela Boszormenyi-Nagy, MusD(piano lit & perf), 58. *Pos:* Piano soloist with NC Symph, Rochester Phil, Charlotte Symph, Tokyo Symph, Nippon Phil Orch & others. *Teaching:* Instr, US Army Educ Prog, 46-50; asst prof, ECarolina Col, 57-62; prof, Tex A&I Col, 62-67 & Univ of Pac, 67- *Mem:* Music Teachers Asn Calif. *Mailing Add:* 7557 Andrea Ave Stockton CA 95207

FETTER, DAVID J
TROMBONE

Study: Eastman Sch Music, BMEd; Am Univ, MA(musicol); studied trombone with Emory Remington, Lewis Van Haney, Robert Marstellar, Edward Kleinhammer & Horst Raasch. *Pos:* Mem, San Antonio Symph, formerly; NC Symph, formerly; Radio Telefis Eireann Symph, Dublin, Ireland, formerly & Nat Ballet Orch, formerly; prin trombone, Baltimore Symph Orch, 10 years; co-prin trombone, currently; asst trombonist, Cleveland Orch, two years; founder & dir, Baltimore Trombone choir, currently. *Teaching:* Mem prep fac, Cleveland Inst Music, formerly & Peabody Consv, currently. *Mailing Add:* 2819 St Paul St Baltimore MD 21218

FIALKOWSKA, JANINA
PIANO, EDUCATOR

b Montreal, Can, May 7, 51. *Study:* Ecole Musique Vincent d'Indy, Baccalaureat Maitrise, 68; studied with Yvonne Lefebure, 68-69; Juilliard Sch, 70-75. *Rec Perf:* Liszt Album, 76 & Chopin Album, 77, RCA. *Pos:* Conct pianist, 75- *Teaching:* Asst prof to Sascha Gorodnitzki, Juilliard Sch, 80- *Awards:* First Grand Prize, Can Broadcasting Corp Nat Talent Fest, 69; grants, Can Coun, 70-75; Silver Medal, First Arthur Rubinstein Int Piano Compt, 74. *Mailing Add:* c/o ICM Artists Ltd 40 W 57th St New York NY 10019

FIELD, RICHARD LAWRENCE
VIOLA, LECTURER
b Wilmington, Del, July 21, 47. *Study:* Amherst Col, 65-66; Eastman Sch Music, BMus, 69; Juilliard Sch Music, MS, 71. *Pos:* Assoc prin viola, Denver Symph, 71-74; prin viola & Buffalo Phil, 74-79 & Baltimore Symph, 79-. *Teaching:* Lectr viola, Am Univ, 79-81, Peabody Inst, Johns Hopkins Univ, 82-83 & Cath Univ, 83- *Mailing Add:* 6404 Old Harford Rd Baltimore MD 21214

FIELDS, RICHARD WALTER
PIANO, EDUCATOR
b Oakland, Calif. *Study:* Juilliard Sch, with Irwin Freundlich, BM, 72, MM, 74; Manhattan Sch Music, with Robert Goldsand. *Rec Perf:* Richard Fields Plays Piano Music of William Grant Still, Orion Master Rec, 82. *Teaching:* Artist in res & fac mem piano, West Chester State Col, 79- *Awards:* Fel, Ford Found, 72; Prizewinner, Viotti Int Piano Compt, 75; Career Award, Rockefeller Fund, 82. *Rep:* Maureen Hooper 729 Rhoads Dr Springfield PA 19064. *Mailing Add:* 500 Rosedale West Chester PA 19380

FIELDS, ROBERTA PETERS See Peters, Roberta

FIELDS, WARREN CARL
EDUCATOR, CONDUCTOR
b York, Ala, March 12, 36. *Study:* Stanford Univ, BME, 58; Baylor Univ, MM, 63; Univ Iowa, PhD, 73. *Teaching:* Assoc prof musicol, Georgia Southern Col, 66- *Mem:* Am Musicol Soc; Sonneck Soc; Music Libr Asn; Am Choral Dir Asn; Georgia Hist Soc. *Interests:* Music and publishing in Georgia in the 19th century. *Mailing Add:* 17 Carmel Dr Statesboro GA 30458

FIENEN, DAVID NORMAN
EDUCATOR, ORGAN
b Evansville, Ind, Mar 12, 46. *Study:* Ind Univ, Bloomington, BMus, 68; Concordia Sem, St Louis, MARel, 71; Univ Minn, Minneapolis, DMA, 77. *Rec Perf:* Christmas from Gustavus, Delta (in prep). *Teaching:* Instr music & organist, St John's Col, 72-73; assoc prof & organist, Gustavus Adolphus Col, 73-, chmn music dept, 83- *Mem:* Am Guild Organists (mem exec bd Twin Cities chap, 83-); Hymn Soc Am; Am Guild English Handbell Ringers. *Publ:* Auth, The Problem of History for the Performing Musician, Cresset, 81. *Mailing Add:* Music Dept Gustavus Adolphus Col St Peter MN 56082

FIGLER, BYRNELL WALTER
EDUCATOR, PIANO
b St Louis, Mo, May 9, 27. *Study:* St Louis Inst Music, studied with Leo Sirota, BM, 50, MM, 53; Bavarian State Music Acad, Munich, 53-55; Univ Ill, Urbana, studied with Webster Aitken, Stanley Fletcher & Jacques Abram, 58-63. *Rec Perf:* Concert and Contest Solos, Austin Rec, 65. *Teaching:* Instr piano & artistic dir, Spokane Consv, 55-57; instr piano, Univ Ala, 62-65; prof piano, Ft Hays State Univ, 67- *Awards:* Fulbright Grant, 53-55. *Mem:* Music Teachers Nat Asn; Sonneck Soc. *Mailing Add:* Music Dept Ft Hays State Univ Hays KS 67601

FILLER, SUSAN M
EDITOR, LECTURER
b Gary, Ind, July 18, 47. *Study:* Univ Ill, Chicago, BA, 69; Northwestern Univ, MM, 70, PhD, 77. *Pos:* Ed newsletter, Am Musicol Soc (midwest chap), 81- *Mem:* Am Musicol Soc; Col Music Soc; Int Musicol Soc; Int Gustav Mahler Soc. *Interests:* Romantic and postromantic music, with special emphasis on compositions of Gustav Mahler and Alma Mahler. *Publ:* Auth, Mahler and the Anthology of Des Knaben Wunderhorn, J Can Asn Univ Sch Music, 78; The Case for a Performing Version of Mahler's 10th Symphony, 81, Review of Music Forum, Vol 5, 82 & The Songs of Alma Mahler, 83, J Musicol Res; Mahler's Sketches for a Scherzo in C and a Presto in F, Col Music Symposium, (in prep). *Mailing Add:* 441 W Barry Apt 427 Chicago IL 60657

FINE, VIVIAN
COMPOSER, PIANO
b Chicago, Ill. *Study:* Comp study with Ruth Crawford-Seeger & Roger Sessions, piano study with Djane Lavoie-Herz & Abby Whiteside. *Works:* Paean, Eastman Brass Ens, 69; Two Neruda Poems, perf by Jan De Gaetani, 71; Romantic Ode, Chamber Music Conf East, 76; Meeting for Equal Rights 1866, perf by New York Oratorio Soc, 76; The Women in the Garden, perf by San Francisco Opera, 82; Drama for Orchestra, comn & perf by San Francisco Symph, 83. *Teaching:* Instr, NY Univ, 45-48 & Juilliard Sch Music, 48-; fac mem, Bennington Col, 64- *Awards:* Comp Awards, Nat Endowment Arts, 74, Am Acad & Inst Arts & Lett, 79 & Rockefeller Found Music, 81. *Mem:* ASCAP; Am Acad & Inst Arts & Lett. *Mailing Add:* RFD 2 Box 630 Hoosick Falls NY 12090

FINK, LORRAINE FRIEDRICHSEN
VIOLIN, ADMINISTRATOR
b Oakland, Calif, Sept 1, 31. *Study:* San Francisco State Univ, BA, 53; WVa Univ, MM, 67; studied with Frank Houser, Henri Temianka & Maurice Wilk. *Pos:* First violinist, Oklahoma City Symph Orch, 54-62; Suzuki specialist, Ithaca Talent Educ, 66-70; ed, Suzuki World Mag, 82- *Teaching:* Dir & clinician, Suzuki Asn Athens, 70- *Mem:* Am String Teachers Asn (Ohio pres, 79-81); Suzuki Asn Americas (bd mem & secy, 75-78); Am Fedn Musicians. *Publ:* Auth, A Parent's Guide to String Instrument Study, 77, ed, String Orchestra Arrangements with Solo Part of Standard Violin Pieces, 77-81 & coauth, Quick Steps to Note Reading, Vol 1-4, 78, Neil Kjos, Inc. *Mailing Add:* 7 Briarwood Dr Athens OH 45701

FINK, MICHAEL ARMAND
EDUCATOR, COMPOSER
b Long Beach, Calif, Mar 15, 39. *Study:* Univ Southern Calif, BM, 60, PhD, 77; New England Consv Music, MM, 62. *Works:* Te Deum, 66, What Sweeter Music, 70 & Jubilate Deo, 76, E C Schirmer Music Co; Full Fadom Five, Mark Foster Music Co, 77; Sonata for Guitar Solo, 82 & Monteverdiana, 82, Southern Music Co; Festival Magnificat, Mark Foster Music Co, 83. *Pos:* Music dir, Southwest Regional Lab Educ Res & Develop, 71-75. *Teaching:* Lectr theory & comp, Calif State Univ, Fullerton, 70; assoc prof musicol, guitar & music indust, Univ Tex, San Antonio, 75- *Mem:* Col Music Soc (coun mem 81-83); ASCAP; Am Musicol Soc; Am String Teachers Asn; Music Indust Educr Asn (treas, 83-85). *Interests:* Music industry, computers; Renaissance, Baroque, and 20th-century music. *Publ:* Auth, Pierre Boulez: A Selective Bibliography, Current Musicol, 72; ed, Three Motets (Rovigo, Gatto, Perini), Akad Druck, 79; coauth, Rovigo, Francesco, In: New Grove Dict of Music & Musicians, 80; Autobiography and Diary of Alfred Einstein, Musical Quart, 80; auth, article on San Antonio, Tex, In: New Grove Dict of Music in US, 83. *Mailing Add:* 4826 Bucknell San Antonio TX 78249

FINK, MYRON S
COMPOSER, EDUCATOR
b Chicago, Ill, Apr 19, 32. *Study:* Univ Ill, BMus, 54, MMus, 55. *Works:* Fifteen Songs (poems by W Bynner), perf by various singers in US & Europe, 61-; Jeremiah (opera in four acts), Tri-Cities Opera, Binghamton, NY, 62 & 83; Trio (piano, violin & cello), Am Chamber Trio, 75 & 82; Sextet (piano & winds), Quintet of the Am & Weston Wind Quintet, 80-81; String Quartet No 2, New England String Quartet, 80. *Teaching:* Prof comp & theory, Hunter Col, 66-; instr theory, Curtis Inst, 69-72; adj prof, State Univ NY, Purchase, 73- *Mailing Add:* 10 Park Ave Old Greenwich CT 06870

FINK, PHILIP H
EDUCATOR, COMPOSER
b York, Pa, Apr 18, 35. *Study:* Univ Miami, BM, 57, MM, 58, PhD, 73. *Teaching:* Chmn, SW Miami Sr High Sch, 59-67; chmn & assoc prof strings & cond, Miami Dade Community Col, 68-72; chmn & prof, Fla Int Univ, 72- *Awards:* Columbia Pictures Arr Hall of Fame, 80. *Mem:* Nat Sch Orch Asn (chair, Southern Div, 75-77); Am String Teachers Asn; Music Educr Nat Conf; Fla Orch Asn; Nat Asn Sch Music. *Publ:* Coauth, Head Start Solos for Strings, Columbia Pictures Publ, 74; auth, Think Guitar String Method Book I, 74 & Book II, 78, Columbia Pictures Publ; coauth, New Things for Strings, Book Series, 79 & Pop Solos and Ensembles, Book Series, 82, Columbia Pictures Publ. *Mailing Add:* 14700 SW 82nd Ave Miami FL 33158

FINK, ROBERT RUSSELL
ADMINISTRATOR, EDUCATOR
b Belding, Mich, Jan 31, 33. *Study:* Mich State Univ, BM, 55, MM, 56, PhD, 67; Eastman Sch Music, 56-57; private French horn study with Philip Farkas, 58-59. *Teaching:* Instr, State Univ NY, Fredonia, 56-57; from asst prof to prof, Western Mich Univ, 57-78; dean & prof, Col Music, Univ Colo, Boulder, 78- *Mem:* Col Music Soc; Soc Music Theory; Music Educr Nat Conf; Music Teachers Nat Asn; Nat Asn Sch Music . *Publ:* Coauth, The Language of 20th Century Music, Macmillan, 75. *Mailing Add:* 643 Furman Way Boulder CO 80303

FINK, SEYMOUR MELVIN
PIANO, EDUCATOR
b Baltimore, Md, July 9, 29. *Study:* Peabody Consv Music, artist dipl, 48; Yale Col, BA, 52; Sch Music, Yale Univ, MMus, 53. *Teaching:* From asst prof to assoc prof piano, Sch Music, Yale Univ, 60-67; from assoc prof to prof, State Univ NY, Buffalo, 67-71, actg assoc provost, Arts & Lett Fac, 69-71; prof, State Univ NY, Binghamton, 71-, chmn, Dept Music, 71-74. *Awards:* Fels, Fulbright, 55-56 & Morse, Yale Univ, 63-64. *Mem:* Col Music Soc. *Mailing Add:* Dept Music State Univ NY Binghamton NY 13901

FINNEY, ROSS LEE
COMPOSER
b Wells, Minn, Dec 23, 06. *Study:* Carleton Col, BA, 27; studied with Nadia Boulanger, 27, Alban Berg, 31 & Roger Sessions, 35. *Works:* Symphonies No 1, 2, 3 & 4, Earthrise, Still Are New Worlds, Landscapes Remembered, Summer in Valley City, Fantasy in Two Movements for Solo Violin & Concerto for Alto Sax & Winds, C F Peters Corp. *Teaching:* Prof music, Smith Col, 29-49; prof & comp in res, Univ Mich, 49-73 & emer prof, 74-; endowed prof comp, Univ Ala, 82-83. *Awards:* Guggenheim Fel, 37 & 47; Pulitzer Scholar, 37; Brandeis Gold Medal, 67. *Mem:* Am Acad & Inst Arts & Letters; Am Acad Arts & Sci; Am Musicol Soc. *Mailing Add:* Sch Music Univ Mich Ann Arbor MI 48109

FINSTER, ROBERT MILTON
MUSIC DIRECTOR, ORGAN
b Santa Ana, Calif, Mar 1, 39. *Study:* Occidental Col, studied organ with Clarence Mader & choral music with Howard Swan, AB, 61; Eastman Sch Music, studied organ with David Craighead, MMus, 63, AMD, 69. *Pos:* Organist & choirmaster, Grace Episcopal Church, Elmira, NY, 64-69 & St John's Cathedral, Denver, 70-76; founder & dir, Cathedral Singers, Denver, 70-76 & Tex Bach Choir, 76-; parish musician, St Luke's Episcopal Church, San Antonio, 76- *Awards:* Presiding Bishop's Award in Music & Liturgy, Episcopal Church, 69. *Mem:* Asn Anglican Musicians; Am Guild Organists; Am Choral Dir Asn; Royal Sch Church Music; Nat Asn Pastoral Musicians. *Mailing Add:* 11 St Luke's Lane San Antonio TX 78209

FIOL, STEPHEN FRANK
EDUCATOR, BARITONE

b St Louis, Mo, Aug 3, 44. *Study:* Bethel Col, BM, 70; Wichita State Univ, with Dr George Gibson, MM, 76. *Roles:* Dr Falke in Fledermaus, 76 & Emil in South Pacific, 78, Music Theatre Wichita; Sharpless in Madame Butterfly, Wichita Symph, 78; Olin Blitch in Susanna, Opera Theatre Ill, 80; Popoff in Merry Widow, 80, Ramphis in Aida, 82 & Dr Malatesta in Don Pasquale, 82, Peoria Civic Opera. *Pos:* Dir Lyric Theatre, Sch Music, Millikin Univ, 76-; res stage dir, Peoria Civic Opera, Peoria, Ill, 78-82. *Mem:* Actors Equity Asn; Nat Opera Asn; Am Guild Musical Artists. *Mailing Add:* 167 N Fairview Decatur IL 62522

FIORITO, JOHN
BASSO BUFFO

b New York, NY. *Study:* New England Consv; studied with George London & John Moriarty. *Roles:* Leporello in Don Giovanni; Sir John Falstaff in Falstaff; Mustafa in L'Italiana in Algeri; Don Alfonso in Cosi fan tutte; Gianni Schicchi; Sulpice in La Fille du Regiment; Bartolo in Le Nozze di Figaro; Faninal in Der Rosenkavalier. *Pos:* Bar, Metropolitan Opera Nat Co, New York City Opera, Vienna State Opera, Houston Opera & others. *Mailing Add:* c/o Lew & Benson Moreau-Neret Inc 204 W 10th St New York NY 10014

FIRESTONE, ADRIA (BELINDA)
MEZZO-SOPRANO

b Los Angeles, Calif. *Study:* Univ Miami; Fla Int Univ, BA, 74; Sara Sforni-Corti, Consv Giuseppe Verdi, 76-79. *Roles:* Dalila in Samson et Dalila, Gtr Miami Opera Asn, 79; Medium in The Medium, Gtr Miami Opera Asn, 80; Prince Orlovsky in Die Fledermaus, Conn Grand Opera, 82; Aldonza in La Mancha, 82 & Jenney in Threepenny Opera, 83, Stage Co; Carmen in Carmen, New York City Opera Nat Touring Co, 83. *Awards:* Contrib Italian Cult Award, Dante Alighieri Soc. *Mailing Add:* 3701 S Flagler Dr B-107 West Palm Beach FL 33405

FIRKINS, JAMES T
TROMBONE, TEACHER

b Albuquerque, NMex, Aug 31, 54. *Study:* Univ Nev, with William Booth, 73-78; Univ Ill, with Tom Senff, 74; NMex State Univ, with Ronald Thielman, BA, 77. *Rec Perf:* Las Vegas Brass Quintet Christmas Album, Ashland Rec, 82; New Music by the Las Vegas Brass Quintet (in prep). *Pos:* Musician, resort hotels, Las Vegas, 74-; trombonist, Las Vegas Chamber Players, 78-, Las Vegas Brass Quintet, 79- & Las Vegas Symph Orch, 82- *Teaching:* Instr low brass instrm, Nev Sch Arts, 79- *Mem:* Int Trombone Asn. *Rep:* Am Artists Mgt Inc 300 West End Ave Suite 13A New York NY 10023. *Mailing Add:* 5939 Vegas Dr Las Vegas NV 89108

FIRKUSNY, RUDOLF
PIANO, EDUCATOR

b Napajedla, Czechoslovakia, Feb 11, 12. *Study:* Consv Brno, Czechoslovakia, studied piano with Vilem Kurz & comp with Leos Janacek; studied with Karel, Josef Suk & Artur Schnabel. *Works:* Piano Concerto; piano pieces & songs. *Rec Perf:* On DGG, RCA Victor, Columbia, Decca & Vox. *Pos:* Conct tours, Europe, 30-39; appearances with New York Phil, Boston Phil, Philadelphia Orch, Chicago Symph, Nat Symph & many others; recitalist throughout US; performer, South Am, 43-, Europe, ann 50-, Australia & Far East, 59-67 & Japan, 78. *Teaching:* Mem fac piano, Juilliard Sch, 65- *Mem:* Bohemians. *Mailing Add:* c/o Columbia Artists 165 W 57th St New York NY 10019

FIRTH, VIC (EVERETT JOSEPH)
TIMPANI, PERCUSSION

b Winchester, Mass, June 2, 30. *Study:* Juilliard Sch Music, with Saul Goodman; New England Consv, BM, 52. *Pos:* Solo timpanist, Boston Symph Orch, 52-, Boston Pops Orch, 52-74 & Boston Symph Chamber Players, 60- *Teaching:* Prof timpani & perc, New England Consv Music, 51- *Mailing Add:* 3 Pine Wood Rd Dover MA 02030

FISCHBACH, GERALD F
EDUCATOR, VIOLIN

b Milwaukee, Wis, Oct 24, 42. *Study:* Univ Wis, Milwaukee, BFA, 64; Univ Ill, MM, 65; Univ Iowa, DMA, 70. *Rec Perf:* Five Sonorous Inventions (C Curtis-Smith), CRI, 75. *Pos:* Cond numerous all-state orch festivals, 70-; dir int string & piano wkshps, 72-; asst concertmaster & soloist, Capella Acad Wien, Vienna, 75-; violinist numerous concerts US & abroad. *Teaching:* Assoc prof violin & orch, Univ Evansville, 70-73; prof violin & chamber music, Western Mich Univ, 73-79; prof violin & string pedagogy, Univ Wis, Milwaukee, 79- *Mem:* Hon life mem, String Teachers & Players Asn, New Zealand; Pi Kappa Lambda; Am String Teachers Asn (Mich state pres, 77-79, pres, 82-84). *Publ:* Auth, C'mon, Do It! (Contemplate the Contemporary), 78 & Getting From There To Here With A Smile, 80-81, Am String Teachers Asn. *Mailing Add:* Music Dept Univ Wis PO Box 413 Milwaukee WI 53201

FISCHER, BILL (WILLIAM S)
COMPOSER, CONDUCTOR

b Shelby, Miss, Mar 5, 35. *Study:* Xavier Univ, BS(music ed), 56; Colo Col, Colo Springs, MA(theory & comp), 62; Akad Music, Vienna, with Von Einem, 65-66. *Works:* Jesse An Opera, 66 & Suite for Orch and Voices, 66, Ready; Quiet Movement for Orch, Bote & Bock, 66; Concerto in D, Blues, 68 & Experience for Orch, 70, Ready; The Gospel Spirit (chorus), Ready & Cimino, 74; Dong, an Opera, Ready, 77. *Rec Perf:* Omen, Electronic Music, Arcana Rec, 69; Experience in E, Capitol Rec, 69; Concerto Grosso in D, 69 & Circles, 70, Atlantic Rec; Quiet Movement, Desto Rec, 71; Experience and

Judgment, Atlantic Rec, 74; Heart, a Melody of Time, Teresa Rec, 83. *Pos:* Cellist, New Orleans Baroque Quartet, 63-66; woodwinds player & keyboards, New York Studio Music, 67-80; cond, Dial M for Music, CBS TV, New York, 68-; arr & dir, Atlantic Rec, New York, 68-70. *Teaching:* Asst prof comp & theory, Xavier Univ, New Orleans, 62-66; lectr modern jazz, Cardiff Col, Wales, Gt Brit, spring 66; lectr modern music, High Sch Music & Art, 69-75. *Awards:* Fulbright Award, 66. *Bibliog:* Peter Yates (auth), Modern Music, Arts & Architecture, 65; Irving Kolodin (auth), Music to My Ears, Saturday Rev, 4/24/65; Marilyn Tucker (auth), Oakland Youth Orch, San Francisco Chronicle, 5/18/70. *Mem:* ASCAP; Soc Black Comp; Am Fedn Musicians. *Rep:* ASCAP 1 Lincoln Pl New York NY. *Mailing Add:* 1365 St Nicholas New York NY 10033

FISCHER, EDITH STEINKRAUS
COMPOSER, SOPRANO

b Portland, Ore. *Study:* Univ Minn, BA, 42; Juilliard Grad Sch Music, artist dipl, 47. *Works:* Five Canonic Movements, Everywhere, Christmas Tonight (choral anthem) & O God, Our Help (choral anthem), Providence Music Press; Poem (violin & piano), Kowalski; String Quartet III, Local String Quartet; Secular & Sacred Songs, perf by Edith S Fischer; Anthems & Responses, Newman Congregational Church, Rumford, RI. *Pos:* Sop soloist, Newman Church, Rumford, RI, 65- *Teaching:* Adj prof voice, Brown Univ, 70- *Mem:* Nat Asn Teachers Singing. *Mailing Add:* 33 Euclid Ave Riverside RI 02915

FISCHER, ELIZABETH
EDUCATOR, MEZZO-SOPRANO

b Dubuque, Iowa. *Study:* Nat Music Camp, 53, 54 & 59; Univ Mich, BMus, 56; Villa Schifanoia Inst Fine Arts, Florence, Italy, MMus, 57; Music Acad West, 62. *Rec Perf:* Missa Solemnis, Wis Choral Union, 62; Operatic Concert, 79 & Sacred Concert, 81, Bel Canto Found; Requiem (Verdi), Niles Symph Orch, 81; Vocal Recital, Northwestern Univ, 83. *Roles:* Dinah in Trouble in Tahiti, 59 & The Medium, 59, Am Opera Wkshp, Interlochen, Mich; Suzuki in Madama Butterfly, Milwaukee Skylight Theatre, 60 & Am Opera Auditions, Florence & Milan, Italy, 62; Giovanna in Rigoletto, Chicago Lyr Opera Co, 62 & 64; Suzuki in Madama Butterfly, 63 & Bersi in Andrea Chenier, 63, Cincinnati Opera Co. *Pos:* Artist-singer, Chicago Lyr Opera Co, 62-70. *Teaching:* Instr voice, Univ Wis, Milwaukee, 60-66 & Nat Music Camp, Interlochen, Mich, 61-; assoc prof, Northwestern Univ, 73-; artist-teacher, Brescia Col, 79, Furman Univ, 81 & Eastern Ill Univ, 83. *Awards:* Operatic Debut Italian Award, Am Opera Auditions, 62; Euclid McBride Award, Metropolitan Opera Nat Coun, 62; Young Artist Award, Nat Fedn Music Clubs, 63. *Mem:* Nat Asn Teachers Singing; Nat Fedn Music Clubs; Soc Am Musicians; Bel Canto Italian Opera Found (artistic adv, 73-83); Sigma Alpha Iota. *Rep:* Salvatore Monastero 4740 W North Shore Lincolnwood IL 60646. *Mailing Add:* Sch Music Northwestern Univ Evanston IL 60201

FISCHER, KENNETH CHRISTIAN
ADMINISTRATOR, ARTIST MANAGER

b Washington, DC, Dec 28, 44. *Study:* Col Wooster, BA, 66; Univ Mich, MA, 67. *Pos:* Mem bd trustees, Interlochen Ctr Arts, 72-74 & Levine Sch Music, 77-; vpres, Music at Noon, 77-; consult, Capital Woodwind Quintet, 78, Concord String Quartet, 72-, Wondrous Machine, 83 & Washington Bach Consort, 83; independent producer, King's Singers, 82- *Publ:* Auth, Music at Noon, Am Ens, 6/78. *Mailing Add:* 6518 Columbia Pike Falls Church VA 22041

FISCHER, NORMAN CHARLES
CELLO

b Washington, DC, May 25, 49. *Study:* Oberlin Col, BM, 71. *Rec Perf:* Avant-Garde Quartet in the USA, Vox, 71; Quartet #3 (Rochberg), 72 & Quartets #1 & #2 (Ives), 75, Nonesuch; Quartet #1 & Ricordanza (Rochberg), CRI, 75; Quinten & Emperor Quartets (Haydn), 79, String Quartets (Dvorak & Borodin), 80, Turnabout; Quartets #4, #5 & #6 (Rochberg), RCA, 82. *Pos:* Cellist, Concord String Quartet, 71- *Teaching:* Artist in res & adj assoc prof cello, Dartmouth Col, 74- *Awards:* Walter W Naumburg Chamber Music Award, 71. *Rep:* Sheldon Soffer Mgt 130 W 56th St New York NY 10019. *Mailing Add:* RFD 192 Norwich VT 05055

FISCHTHAL, GLENN JAY
TRUMPET, TEACHER

b Shell Lake, Wis, Feb 22, 48. *Study:* Cleveland Inst Music, BMus, 70; Calif Inst Arts, 71. *Pos:* Prin trumpet, Israel Phil, Tel Aviv, 76-79, San Diego Symph, 79-80, San Francisco Symph, 80- & Santa Fe Opera Orch, summer 83. *Teaching:* Fac mem trumpet, San Francisco Consv Music, 80- *Mem:* Nat Acad Rec Arts & Sci; Int Trumpet Guild. *Mailing Add:* 166 Liberty St San Francisco CA 94110

FISHBEIN, MICHAEL ELLIS
COMPOSER

b Wheeling, WVa, Mar 6, 50. *Study:* Univ Southern Calif, BMus, 78; Eastman Sch Music, MA, 80. *Works:* Three Orchestral Moods, 76, Fables from Aesop, 81, Variations for Band, 83 & Brass Quintet, 83, Epigram Music. *Teaching:* Asst, Dept Music Theory, Eastman Sch Music, 79-80; asst instr, Univ Mich, 81-83. *Mem:* BMI. *Publ:* Auth, articles on microtonal comp, Interval Mag. *Mailing Add:* 384 Howe Ave Shelton CT 06484

FISHBEIN, ZENON
PIANO, EDUCATOR
Study: Acad Santa Cecilia, dipl; Mozarteum, dipl; Manhattan Sch Music, MMus; studied piano with Zecchi, Denza, Tagliaferro & Zaslavsky. *Pos:* Soloist in recital with orchs throughout Europe, North Am, South Am & The Orient; radio, chamber music & TV performances. *Teaching:* Mem piano fac, Manhattan Sch Music, 63- *Awards:* Chopin Compt Rome, Geneva Compt & Viotti Compt; Harold Bauer Award. *Mailing Add:* Manhattan Sch Music 120 Claremont Ave New York NY 10027

FISHER, DOUGLAS JOHN
BASSOON
b San Diego, Calif, Apr 18, 62. *Study:* Tanglewood Inst, Boston Univ, 80; Music Acad of West, 82; Eastman Sch Music, currently. *Pos:* Co-prin bassoon, Spoleto Fest Orch, 81, Eastman Phil, Rochester, NY, 82-; utility bassoon, Syracuse Symph, 81-; asst second bassoon, Rochester Phil, 82- *Mem:* Am Fedn Musicians. *Mailing Add:* 424 University Ave PO Box 102 Rochester NY 14607

FISHER, FRED(ERIC IRWIN)
WRITER, PIANO
b Chicago, Ill, Aug 27, 30. *Study:* Northwestern Univ, BMus, 52; Eastman Sch Music, MMus, 53, DMA & perf cert, 63. *Rec Perf:* The French Mystique, Uni-Pro/Spectrum, 81. *Teaching:* Asst prof piano, Okla State Univ, 59-63, assoc prof, 63-68; prof, NTex State Univ, 68-82. *Awards:* Fulbright Grant, 58-59. *Mem:* Chinese Music Soc North Am. *Interests:* Development of the musical-circle idea in history and prehistory; Ives. *Publ:* Auth, Erik Satie's Piano Music: A Centenary Survey, Clavier, 66; The Yellow Bell of China & the Endless Search, Music Educ J, 73; Ives' Concord Sonata, Piano Quarterly, 75; Mathematic Techniques in Music History, College Music Soc Symposium, 78; Kuttner's Great Frame: A New Hypothesis, Chinese Music, 81. *Mailing Add:* 1318 Ridgecrest Circle Denton TX 76201

FISHER, GILBERT BLAIN
MUSIC DIRECTOR
b Kansas City, Kans, May 23, 40. *Study:* Cent Mo State Univ, BME, 62; St Louis Univ, MA, 71; Vienna Symposium, with Nigel Rogers & Helmut Rilling. *Pos:* Asst to musical dir, Little Theatre on Square, Sullivan, Ill, summer 66. *Teaching:* Dir vocal music, Mo Sch for Blind, St Louis, 62-; instr, music lit & piano, Hampton Inst, Va, summer 65. *Mem:* Am Choral Dir Asn (St Louis City District dir, 80-83); Opera for Youth (bd mem, 82-); Nat Opera Asn; Mo State Teachers Asn (St Louis District exec bd, 75-77); Music Educr Nat Conf. *Mailing Add:* 3520 Laclede Apt 812E St Louis MO 63103

FISHER, JERROLD
CONDUCTOR & MUSIC DIRECTOR, COMPOSER
b Upper Darby, Pa, Jan 29, 39. *Study:* State Col, Westchester, Pa, BS(music educ), 60; Syracuse Univ, 63-68; Am Univ, 63-68; study with Karl Kritz. *Works:* Christmas Suite, Harold Flammer, 74; Fanfare for Brass, 76 & Simple Holiday Joys, 76, Shawnee Press; Hosannah! (A Mass for Today), Carl Fischer, Inc, 83. *Pos:* Actg music dir, Syracuse Symph Orch & Opera, 70; music dir, Pocono Choral Soc, Stroudsburg, Pa, 78- & Haddonfield Symph Chorus, NJ, 83-; dir choral publ, Carl Fischer, Inc, 80-; assoc cond, Haddonfield Symph Orch, NJ, 82- *Teaching:* Dir vocal music, high sch, East Syracuse, NY, 63-; dir, Women's Chorus, Col New Rochelle, 80-83. *Awards:* Fel Grant Comp, Nat Endowment Arts, 76; Martha Baird Rockefeller Grant, 77. *Mem:* ASCAP; Music Educr Nat Conf; Am Choral Dir Asn; NYSSMA; Am Symph Orch League. *Mailing Add:* 112 W 72 St #5-B New York NY 10023

FISHER, PAUL GOTTSHALL
EDUCATOR, CONDUCTOR
b Reading, Pa, June 30, 22. *Study:* Lebanon Valley Col, BS, 47; George Peabody Teachers Col, MA, 48; Univ Mich, MM, 51, EdD, 69. *Rec Perf:* Praise God, Hope Rec, 73. *Pos:* First horn, Harrisburg Symph Orch, 40-80, asst cond, 70-80; first horn, Nashville Symph Orch, 47-48 & Lancaster Symph Orch, 67-74; dir music, First United Methodist Church, Lancaster, Pa, 67- *Teaching:* Prof instrm music, Miss Col, Clinton, 48-50; instr instrm music, Derry Township Sch, Hershey, Pa, 51-66; prof & chmn music, Millersville Univ, 66- *Mem:* Col Band Dir Nat Asn (pres eastern region, 81-83); Pa Col Bandmasters Asn (pres, 73-74 & 79-80); Pa Col Choral Dir Asn (pres, 60-61); Pa Music Educr Asn (pres eastern district, 56-58); Music Educr Nat Conf. *Mailing Add:* 214 E Charlotte St Millersville PA 17551

FISHER, ZEAL ISAY
VIOLA, TEACHER
b New York, NY, Dec 2, 30. *Study:* Miami Univ, BS(music educ), 52; Ind Univ, studied cond with Ernst Hoffman & viola with David Dawson, MMus, 54 & 73. *Works:* Chantecler (operetta), 63 & The Far Princess (opera), 72, James Lewis Casaday Theatre; String Quartet No 1, South Bend String Quartet, 69; Woodwind Quintet, New Wind Quartet plus Oboe, 74; Three Surrealistic Song, Dennis Doverspike & Lou Gard, 78; Suite for Flute and Strings, South Bend Symph, 80. *Rec Perf:* South Bend Bicentennial Pageant, Tri-Fidelity Assoc, 76. *Pos:* Prin & solo viola, South Bend Symph Orch, 58- & asst cond, 75-; prin viola, Midwest Pops Orch, 78- *Teaching:* Teacher orch, Cent High Sch, 58-67 & LaSalle High Sch, 65-; instr music appreciation, Ind Univ, South Bend, 82-83. *Mem:* South Bend Symph Orch Asn; Michiana Arts & Sci Coun (vpres, 74-76); Music Educr Nat Conf; Nat Sch Orch Asn. *Mailing Add:* 2920 Kettering Dr South Bend IN 46635

FISHMAN, JACK ADAM
DOUBLE BASS
b Neptune, NJ, June 4, 57. *Study:* Juilliard Sch, BM, 79, MM, 80; studied bass with John Schaeffer. *Pos:* Prin bass, Greater Palm Beach Symph, 80-81, Knoxville Chamber Orch, 82- & Knoxville Symph Orch, 82-; sect double bass, PR Symph, 81-82. *Mailing Add:* 193 Cambridge Ave Fair Haven NJ 07701

FISK, ELIOT HAMILTON
GUITAR
b Philadelphia, Pa, Aug 10, 54. *Study:* Aspen Music Sch, with Oscar Ghiglia, 70-76; Yale Univ, with Ralph Kirkpatrick & Albert Fuller, BA, 72, MM, 77; Banff Sch Fine Arts, with Alirio Diaz, 73. *Rec Perf:* Latin American Guitar, 80; Baroque Music (Froberger, Scarlatti & Bach), Am Virtuoso, 81; Classical Guitar (Soler, Haydn, Mozart & Paganini), 81; Guitar & Flute (with Carol Winenc), 81-82; Eliot Fisk Guitar (Martin, Ponce, Scarlatti & Paganini), 82, (Scarlatti, Paganini, Beaser & Britten), 83; Villa-Lobos Etudes & various Latin Am pieces, 83. *Pos:* Co-ed, Guitar Rev, 82- *Teaching:* Fac mem, Aspen Music Sch, 73-82; lectr, Yale Sch Music, 77-82; instr, Mannes Col Music, 78-82; prof, Hochschule Music, Köln, WGermany, 82- *Awards:* First Prize, Int Guitar Compt, City Garenano, Italy, 80; grant, Nat Endowment Arts, 82. *Mailing Add:* c/o Agnes Bruneau 711 West End Ave New York NY 10025

FISKE, JUNE
SOPRANO
b Passaic, NJ. *Study:* Bergen Col, AA, 75; studied with Alberta Masiello, Otto Guth & Felix Popper. *Rec Perf:* La Traviata, KYW TV, Philadelphia, 76; Mass, Kennedy Ctr Tonight, 81. *Roles:* Musetta in La Boheme, Hartford Opera, 75; Rosalinde in Die Fledermaus, New York City Opera, 77; Micaela in Carmen, Opera Co Philadelphia, 78; Miss Havisham in Miss Havishams Fire, New York City Opera, 79; Lady Macbeth in Macbeth, Long Island Opera Soc, 81; Irene in Rienzi, Opera Orch New York, 82; Minnie in La Fanciulla Del West, Va Opera. *Mailing Add:* 363 Crescent Dr Franklin Lakes NJ 07441

FISSINGER, EDWIN RUSSELL
COMPOSER, MUSIC DIRECTOR
b Chicago, Ill, June 15, 20. *Study:* Am Consv Music, with Leo Sowerby, BMus(comp), 47, MMus(comp), 51; Univ Ill, Urbana, DMA(cond), 65. *Works:* Psalm 134, Summy-Birchard Publ Co, 58; Sing Noel, World Libr Publ, 65; By the Waters of Babylon, Walton Music Corp, 75; Love Came Down at Christmas, 78, To Everything There Is a Season, 79, Something Has Spoken to Me in the Night, 80 & Lux Aeterna, 83, Jenson. *Rec Perf:* Fourteen albums, NDak State Univ Conct Choir, Mark Rec, 68-83. *Teaching:* Instr, Univ Ill, Urbana, 54-57; assoc prof choral music, Univ Ill, Chicago, 57-67; prof, NDak State Univ, 67- *Mem:* Am Choral Dir Asn; Music Educr Nat Conf. *Mailing Add:* 57 15th Ave N Fargo ND 58102

FITCH, BENJAMIN ROBERT
OBOE & ENGLISH HORN
b New York, NY, Apr 5, 58. *Study:* Juilliard Sch Music, 74-76; Northwestern Univ, with Ray Still, BMus, 80. *Pos:* Prin oboist, Spokane Symph Orch, 81- *Mailing Add:* 1924 W Dean Spokane WA 99201

FITZGERALD, GERALD
WRITER, PIANO
b Atlanta, Ga, Oct 31, 32. *Study:* NY Univ, BA, 55. *Pos:* Ed, Opera News, 56- & Ballet News, 79-; head press off, Spoleto Fest, 60-64; script writer, Live from the Met, PBS, 77-; writer, NBC-TV, currently. *Publ:* Coauth, Callas: The Great Years, Holt, Rhinehart & Winston, 74; The Golden Horseshoe, Viking, 64; picture ed, books on Verdi, Puccini & Wagner, Dutton; Celebration: The Metropolitan Opera, Doubleday; The Met—100 Years of Grand Opera, Simon and Schuster, 83. *Rep:* Helen Merrill 337 W 22nd New York NY 10011. *Mailing Add:* 203 W 81st St Apt 8C New York NY 10024

FITZGERALD, ROBERT BERNARD
EDUCATOR, COMPOSER
b Martinsville, Ill, Apr 26, 11. *Study:* Oberlin Col, BMus, 32; Jordan Col Music, MMus, 35. *Works:* Rondo Capriccio (trumpet & piano), 37, Concerto in A Flat Minor for Trumpet, 39 & Modern Suite (trumpet & piano), 40, Carl Fischer Inc; Four Gaelic Miniatures (flute & piano), Theodore Presser Co, 63; Antiphonal Suite (brass choir), 75, Burlesca (trumpet & piano), 75 & Ballad (trumpet & piano), 76, Southern Music Co; Gaelic Suite (trumpet & piano), Theodore Presser Co, 78. *Teaching:* Head wind instrm dept, Jordan Col Music, Indianapolis, 33-36; dir instrm music, Emporia State Teachers Col, Kans, 36-37; prof music, Hendrix Col, Conway, Ark, 37-38; asst prof & dir bands, Univ Idaho, 38-40; prof music & dir symph band, Univ Tex, Austin, 40-56; prof music, Univ Ky, Lexington, 56-76. *Mem:* Am Bandmasters Asn; Music Educr Nat Conf; Southeastern Comp League; ASCAP. *Mailing Add:* 2087 Old Nassau Rd Lexington KY 40504

FITZPATRICK, ROBERT
CONDUCTOR & MUSIC DIRECTOR, EDUCATOR
b Philadelphia, Pa. *Study:* Curtis Inst Music, studied clarinet with Anthony Gigliotti, 66-68; Temple Univ, studied clarinet with Anthony Gigliotti & cond with Robert Page, Otto Werner Mueller, Margaret Hillis, Keith Brown, Henry C Smith & Milan Horvat, BMus, MMus. *Pos:* Music dir, Garden State Phil, 76-82; prin cond, Orch Soc Philadelphia, 80-82. *Teaching:* Music dir & chmn fine arts, St Joseph's Prep Sch, 69-80; Mem staff orch, Curtis Inst Music, 80-, dean students, currently. *Mailing Add:* Curtis Inst Music 1726 Locust St Philadelphia PA 19103

FLAGELLO, EZIO D
BASS

b New York, NY. *Study:* Manhattan Sch Music, BMus, 53; Univ Perugia, Italy, dipl, 57. *Rec Perf:* I Puritani, London Rec, 60; Cosi fan Tutte, 64 & Erani, 65, RCA Rec; Don Giovanni, Deutsche Grammophon, 67; Love of 3 Kings, Delphi, 68; Lucrezia Borgia & Lucia di Lammermoor, RCA. *Roles:* Falstaff in Falstaff, King Philip in Don Carlos, Schicchi in Gianni Schicchi & Guardiano in Force of Destiny, Metropolitan Opera; Leporello in Don Giovanni, Metropolitan Opera Asn & Vienna Staatsoper; Figaro in Marriage of Figaro, Vienna Staatsoper Co; Alfonso in Lucrezia Borgia, La Scala di Milano. *Pos:* Leading basso, Metropolitan Opera Asn, 57-80, La Scala di Milano, 70- & Vienna Staatsoper, Austria, 72-74. *Awards:* Fulbright Fel, 56. *Rep:* Herbert Barrett Mgt 1860 Broadway New York NY 10023. *Mailing Add:* 2005 Samontee Rd Jacksonville FL 32211

FLAGELLO, NICHOLAS ORESTE
COMPOSER, CONDUCTOR

b New York, NY, Mar 15, 28. *Study:* Manhattan Sch Music, BM, MM, 50; St Cecilia Acad, Rome, MusD, 56; Univ Rome, DrPsychol, studied comp with Vittorio Giannini & Ildebrando Pizzetti & cond with Dmitri Mitropoulos. *Works:* Declamation (violin & piano), 67; Two Pieces: Marionettes (harp solo), 68; Serenade (small orch), 68; Te Deum for Mankind (orch), New York, 69; The Piper of Hamelin (children's opera), 70; Symphony of Winds (orch), 70; Passion for Martin Luther King, Jr (solo & orch), Wash, 74. *Pos:* Cond, Chicago Lyr Theatre, 60-61 & New York State Theatre, 68; asst to Antonio Votto, La Scala, Milan, 60; founder & cond, Fest Salerno & Fest Costa del Sol, Spain; piano recitalist & accmp; violinist, violist & oboist with symph & opera orchs. *Teaching:* Mem fac, Manhattan Sch Music, formerly & Curtis Inst Music, 64-65. *Awards:* First prize creativity, St Cecilia Acad, Rome, 56; ASCAP Awards, 61-; NY Critic's Circle Award, 61. *Mem:* Am Artists Astra Found; ASCAP; Bohemians. *Mailing Add:* 120 Montgomery Circle New Rochelle NY 10804

FLAHERTY, GLORIA
CRITIC, LECTURER

b Kearny, NJ. *Study:* Douglass Col, Rutgers Univ, BA, 59; Johns Hopkins Univ, PhD, 65. *Teaching:* Asst prof, Northwestern Univ, 64-71; assoc prof & chmn, Bryn Mawr Col, 71-77. *Awards:* Fulbright Grant to WGermany, 81-82. *Mem:* Am Musicol Soc; Music Libr Asn (div chmn, 82-); New England Music Libr Asn (mem exec bd, 83-); Am Soc 18th Century Studies (mem exec bd, 81-). *Mailing Add:* 909 Montgomery B2 Bryn Mawr PA 19010

FLANAGAN, THOMAS J
COMPOSER, EDUCATOR

b New Haven, Conn, Nov 30, 27. *Study:* Columbia Univ, AB, 49, New England Consrv, MusB, 51, MMus, 55. *Works:* Four Songs of Unknown Poete, G Schirmer Inc, 65; Melodies Lost, Song Cycle, 69; Psalm 130, Boston Music Co, 72; I Rise in Flames Cried the Phoenix, perf by Golden Fleece Inc, 80; Better Times for Love (sop, clarinet & piano), perf by CSC Trio, 82; Statutes on a Lawn, perf by Golden Fleece Inc, 83; Invocation of the Night, perf by many artists. *Teaching:* Prof music & music theory, St John's Univ, 63-, dir music, music & opera hist, 65- *Awards:* Meet the Comp Grant, 83. *Mem:* BMI; Am Music Ctr; Am Soc Univ Comp. *Mailing Add:* 845 West End Ave #8C New York NY 10025

FLASCH, CHRISTINE ELIZABETH
SOPRANO

b Milwaukee, Wis, May 5, 51. *Study:* Milton Col, BME, 69; Syracuse Univ, masters perf, 73; with Helen Boatwright, Ellen Faull & Grace Hunter. *Roles:* Rosina in Barber of Seville, Toledo/Dayton Opera, 80; Blonda in Abduction, Opera Co Philadelphia, 82, Pittsburgh Opera, 82; Adele in Die Fledermaus, Charlotte Opera, 82; Baby Doe in Ballad of Baby Doe, Ariz Opera, 82; Despina in Cosi fan Tutte, St Petersburg Opera, 83. *Awards:* Minna Kaufmann Ruud Award for Excellence Perf, 71. *Mem:* Am Guild Musical Artists. *Rep:* Munro Artists Mgt 344 W 72nd St New York New York 10023. *Mailing Add:* 675 West End Ave 6A New York NY 10025

FLATT, TERRY LEE
DIRECTOR—OPERA, EDUCATOR

b Healdton, Okla, Sept 12, 39. *Study:* Phillips Univ, BME, 61; Okla Univ, MM, 64; Ind Univ, Bloomington, MS(opera stage direction), 78. *Pos:* Artistic stage dir, Mid-Mich Opera Asn, 74-77; opera dir & voice, Idaho State Univ, 77-79; opera stage dir, Univ Nebr, 79-80 & Col Consrv Music, Cincinnati Univ, 81-82; dir opera & music theater, Viterbo Col, 82- *Mem:* Nat Opera Asn (regional gov, 80-82); Nat Asn Teachers Singing. *Mailing Add:* 1509 Farnam La Crosse WI 54601

FLECK, WILLIAM SCOTT
BASS

b Tyrone, Pa, Aug 28, 37. *Study:* Eastman Sch Music, BM, 62. *Roles:* Magnifico in La Cenerentola, Hawaii, 71; Le Porello in Don Giovanni, Columbus, 74; Morosus in The Silent Woman, Chautauqua, 75; Colline in La Boheme, Boston, 77; Banquo in MacBeth, Ariz, 78; Sacristan in Tosca, Metropolitan, 82; Rocco in Fidelio, Mexico City, 83. *Pos:* Bass, Metropolitan Opera, 79- *Teaching:* Asst prof voice & opera, Calif State Univ, Sacramento, 73-77. *Rep:* Munro Artists Mgt 344 W 72nd St New York NY 10023. *Mailing Add:* 24 Riverside Dr Ridgefield CT 06877

FLEISCHMANN, ERNEST MARTIN
ADMINISTRATOR

b Frankfurt, Ger, Dec 7, 24; Brit citizen. *Study:* Univ Capetown, SAfrica, BCom, 50, BMus, 54; SAfrican Col Music, 54-56. *Pos:* Gen secy, London Symph Orch, 59-67; dir Europe, CBS Rec, 67-69; gen dir, Hollywood Bowl, 69-; exec dir, Los Angeles Phil Asn, 69- *Awards:* John Steinway Award, 79; Pres Spec Award, Asn Calif Symph Orch, 80. *Bibliog:* Martin Bernheimer (auth), Reflections from the Man at the Bowl, Los Angeles Times, 7/6/69; Edward Greenfield (auth), Flowing Bowl, Guardian, London, 10/15/73; Thomas Thompson (auth), Importance of Being Fleischmann, New York Times Mag, 4/11/76. *Mem:* Am Symph Orch League; Major Orch Mgrs US & Can; Nat Endowment Arts. *Mailing Add:* 135 N Grand Ave Los Angeles CA 90012

FLEISHER, LEON
CONDUCTOR & MUSIC DIRECTOR, PIANO

b San Francisco, Calif, July 23, 28. *Study:* Studied with Artur Schnabel. *Rec Perf:* For Columbia Rec. *Pos:* Music dir, Theatre Chamber Players, Washington, DC, 68; cond & music dir, Annapolis Symph, 70-; conct performer & guest cond, US, Europe, Can, Latin Am & others. *Teaching:* Prof piano, Peabody Consrv Music, 59- *Awards:* First Prize, Int Queen Elisabeth Concourse, Belgium, 52; One of Ten Am Leading Conct Artists, Ford Found, 59. *Mem:* Am Asn Univ Prof. *Mailing Add:* Peabody Consrv Music 1 E Mt Vernon Pl Baltimore MD 21202

FLEMING, MILLICENT CLOW
ADMINISTRATOR

b Chicago, Ill, Oct 15, 35. *Study:* Northwestern Univ Summer Inst, 53; Chicago Musical Col, 53-55; Art Inst Chicago. *Pos:* Admin dir, New Col Music Fest, Sarasota, Fla, 80- *Mem:* Sarasota Music Club. *Mailing Add:* New Col Music Fest 5700 Tamiami Trail Sarasota FL 33580

FLETCHER, (H) GRANT
COMPOSER, CONDUCTOR & MUSIC DIRECTOR

b Hartsburg, Ill, Oct 25, 13. *Study:* Ill Wesleyan Univ, BM, 35; Univ Mich, MM, 39; Eastman Sch Music, PhD, 51. *Works:* An American Overture, Mills Music Co, 48-54; Two Orchestral Pieces, comn by Peninsula Fest, Wis, 56; Glyphs, comn by Philadelphia Chamber Orch, 68; Diversion for Strings, III, comn by Zurcher Kammer Orch, 71; Seven Cities of Cibola, perf by Indianapolis Symph, 74; Cinco de Mayo, comn by Ariz State Univ, 74; A More Proper Burial Music, comn by Int Festliche Musiktage, Switz, 77. *Rec Perf:* Sonata (cello & piano), Orion Masterrecordings, 78. *Pos:* Music dir & cond, Akron Symph, 45-48; cond, Chicago Symphietta, 49-56. *Teaching:* Cond symph, Chicago Musical Col, 49-51; prof music, Ariz State Univ, 56- *Awards:* Int Earnest LeMay Award, Mills Music, 48; Nat Chamber Music Award, Ohio Music Teachers Asn, 73; Int Bicentennial Choral Orch Award, 76. *Bibliog:* Wolfgang Zuppan (auth), Article: Grant Fletcher, Lexikon Des Blasermusik, Graz, Austria, 76 & 78. *Mem:* Phi Mu Alpha Sinfonia; Am Fedn Musicians; Sigma Alpha Iota; Am Music Ctr; ASCAP. *Publ:* Ed, Symphonic Music Article, In: World Book Encycl, Marshall Field, 55; auth, Syllabus for Advanced Integrated Theory, Ed I-V, 62-76 & Rhythm—Notation and Production, 67, GAF & Assoc; Sacred Cantata No 1, Neil Kjos Co, 74. *Mailing Add:* c/o GAF & Assoc 1626 E Williams St Tempe AZ 85281

FLINT, MARK DAVID
CONDUCTOR & MUSIC DIRECTOR

b Bluefield, WVa, Mar 5, 54. *Study:* WVa Univ, BM, 76; Consrv Music, Cincinnati Col, MM, 77. *Pos:* Music dir & prin cond, Mich Opera Theatre, 77-83; prin cond, Lake George Opera Fest, 77-81; music dir, San Francisco Opera Western Opera Theater, 80-82; guest cond & music dir, San Francisco Opera Spring Opera Theatre, 80-82, Opera Theater of St Louis, 82, Dayton Opera Asn, 82-84, Augusta Opera Asn, 83-84, Chicago Opera Theatre, 83-84, Orlando Opera Co, 83-85, New York City Opera, 84 & others. *Teaching:* Dir, Young Artists' Prog, Lake George Opera Fest, Glens Falls, NY, 77-79; Matrix-Midland Fest Arts, Mich, 77-79; dir, Intern Artists' Prog, Mich Opera Theatre, 77-83; dir opera workshop, Oakland Univ, 78-79. *Rep:* Columbia Artists Mgt Inc Crittenden Div 165 W 57th New York NY 10019. *Mailing Add:* 159-00 Riverside Dr #2M-70 New York NY 10032

FLOR, SAMUEL
CONDUCTOR, VIOLIN

b Grahumora, Austria; US citizen. *Study:* Royal Roumanian Consrv, Carolina Univ, dipl; Music Consrv Vienna, dipl. *Works:* Violin Mastery, Schmitt Hall McCreary, 63; The Positions for Violin & Viola, Henri Elkan & Boston Music Co, 70; Intonation and Rhythm, Henri Elkan, 73; I Like to Play the Violin, Boston Music Co, 82. *Pos:* Asst mgr & concertmaster, Aspen Music Fest, 54-65; mgr, Chamber Symph Philadelphia, 65-67; leader, Flor Quartet; conct artist, Europe, Africa & Asia; mem, Minneapolis Symph, formerly. *Teaching:* Prof, Royal Roumanian Consrv, formerly & Macalester Col, 49-55; dir, Vt Music & Arts Ctr, Johnson Col, Vt, 70- *Mem:* Am Asn Univ Prof; Music Educr Nat Conf. *Mailing Add:* 1049 Holly Tree Rd Abington PA 19001

FLOWER, EDWARD JOHN FORDHAM
GUITAR & LUTE

b Stratford on Avon, Warwickshire, England, June 23, 48. *Study:* Winchester Col, England, 61-66; Inst Musical Oscar Espla, Alicante, Spain, 66-69; studied with Jose Thomas, 66-69. *Rec Perf:* Art of the Minstrel, Grosvenor, 72; Warwickshire Lad, 73 & Sense & Nonsense, 74, Argo; Renaissance & Baroque Duets, 80, Classical & Romantic Duets, 80 & Duets for Flute & Guitar, Vol 1 & 2, 82, MMO; Pressed Flower, Classic Ed, 82. *Teaching:* Instr guitar, Ithaca Col, 75-; vis lectr, Univ Conn, 77-82; symposium dir, Boston Univ, 81- *Rep:* Fordham Russell & Smith Box 1851 Stockbridge MA 01262. *Mailing Add:* Prospect Hill Stockbridge MA 01262

FLOWERMAN, MARTIN
DOUBLE BASS, TEACHER
b Brooklyn, NY, Apr 17, 47. *Study:* Juilliard Sch Music, studied double bass with Frederick Zimmermann, 65. *Works:* Arr, compiled & ed, Double Bass Quartets from the Renaissance and Baroque Era, Margun Music Inc, 83. *Pos:* Double bassist, Juilliard Double Bass Quartet, 64-65, Nat Orch Asn, 64-66, Am Symph Orch, 65-66, Detroit Symph Orch, 66-67, Cleveland Orch, 67- & numerous perf with chamber music groups. *Teaching:* Private instr double bass & coach chamber music groups, currently. *Awards:* Grant, New York Daily Mirror, 63 & Nat Orch Asn, 66. *Mem:* Int Soc Bassists; Nat Orch New York. *Mailing Add:* 12000 Fairhill Rd Cleveland OH 44120

FLOYD, CARLISLE
COMPOSER, EDUCATOR
b Latta, SC, June 11, 26. *Study:* Converse Col, 43-45; Syracuse Univ, BM, 46, MM, 49; piano studies with Rudolf Firkusny & Sidney Foster. *Works:* Susannah, 57, Wuthering Heights, 59, The Mystery, 60 & Markheim, 67, Boosey & Hawkes; Of Mice and Men, 71, Flower and Hawk, 75 & Willie Stark, 84, Belwin-Mills Publ Corp. *Teaching:* Prof music, Fla State Univ, 47-76; M D Anderson prof music, Univ Houston, 76- *Awards:* Guggenheim Fel, 56; NY Music Critics Circle Award, 57; Nat Opera Inst Award, 83. *Mem:* ASCAP; Am Guild Musical Artists. *Mailing Add:* 4491 Yoakum Blvd Houston TX 77006

FLOYD, J(AMES) ROBERT
COMPOSER, PIANO
b Tyler, Tex. *Study:* NTex State Univ, BM, 48, MM, 50; Ind Univ, DM, 60. *Works:* Song of Deborah (chorus & jazz ens), 65; Variations (piano), 78; Prince of Pentacles (piano & electronics), 79; Waves (piano), 82. *Rec Perf:* Piano Music of Henze & Larry Austin, Advance, 68; Suitable for Framing, Aesthetic Res Ctr Can, 74. *Teaching:* Chmn div fine arts, Corpus Christi State Univ, 50-61; head keyboard dept, Sam Houston State Univ, 61-62 & Northern Ill Univ, 62-81; dir keyboard dept, Univ Miami, 81- *Awards:* Fulbright Award, 68; Performer in Res Award, Ford Found, 70; Nat Endowment Arts Award, 72-76. *Mailing Add:* 4841 SW 64 Court Miami FL 33155

FLOYD, JOHN (MORRISON)
PERCUSSION, EDUCATOR
b Thomasville, NC, Nov 19, 50. *Study:* ECarolina Univ, BM, 73; Va Commonwealth Univ, MM, 74; Eastman Sch Music, perf cert & DMA, 80. *Works:* Entrance and Exit, Va Commonwealth Univ Perc Lab Ens, Richmond, Va, 75; Mobile for Percussion Ensemble, Eastman Perc Ens, Rochester, NY, 77; Theme and Variations for Four Timpani, Studio 4 Prod, Northridge Calif, 77 & 80; Three Miniatures for B-flat Clarinet and Marimba, Alice Hemphill & Chris Lamb, Rochester, NY, 80. *Pos:* Prin perc, Richmond Symph, 73-75 ; prin timpanist, Roanoke Symph Orch, 77-; perc, Rochester Phil Orch, 80; prin timpanist & prin perc, NH Music Fest, Plymouth, 81- *Teaching:* Instr perc, Clarion State Col, 75-77; from asst prof to assoc prof, Va Polytechnic Inst & State Univ, Blacksburg, 77-; grad asst & adj instr, Eastman Sch Music, 79-80. *Awards:* Second Place Award, Int Comp Cont, Percussive Arts Soc, 76. *Bibliog:* John Beck (auth), Review of Theme and Variations for Four Timpani, Percussive Notes, Percussive Arts Soc, Vol 19, No 3; Christopher Stevens (dir), Percussion at Virginia Tech (radio prog), WVTF-FM, Roanoke, Va, 7/82 & 1/83. *Mem:* Percussive Arts Soc (exec bd mem, Va-DC chap, 74-75, pres Pa chap, 75-77); Nat Asn Col Wind & Perc Instr; Col Music Soc; Am Fedn Musicians. *Publ:* Auth, A Musical Approach to Percussion Technique, 77, Triplet Approach to Percussion Technique, 78 & Tuning of the Marching Snare Drum, 78, Notes from Va Tech, Va Tech Dept Music; Triplet Approach to Percussion Technique, 79 & Percussion Reviews, 82-83, Nat Asn Col Wind & Perc Inst J. *Mailing Add:* Dept Music Va Polytechnic Inst & State Univ Blacksburg VA 24061

FLOYD, SAMUEL ALEXANDER
EDUCATOR, ADMINISTRATOR
b Tallahassee, Fla, Feb 1, 37. *Study:* Fla A&M Univ, BS, 57; Southern Ill Univ, MME, 64, PhD, 69. *Teaching:* Band dir, Smith-Brown High Sch, Arcadia, Fla, 57-62; asst band dir, Fla A&M Univ, 62-64; from asst prof to assoc prof, Southern Ill Univ, 68-78; prof & dir, Inst Res Black Am Music, Fisk Univ, 78-; prof music & dir black music ctr, Columbia Col. *Mem:* Col Music Soc; Sonneck Soc; Pi Kappa Lambda. *Publ:* Auth, 99 Street Beats, Exercises, Cadences, Hansen, 61; Music as a Creative Experience, Symposium, 76; The Musical Work of Art, Music J, 78; Black American Music and Aesthetic Communication, BMR J, 80; coauth, Black Music in the United States, Kraus, 83. *Mailing Add:* 7619 Sussex Creek Dr Apt 109 Darien IL 60559

FLUEGEL, NEAL LALON
PERCUSSION, EDUCATOR
b Freeport, Ill, March 21, 37. *Study:* Ariz State Univ, BA, 60; Southern Ill Univ, Carbondale, MM, 63; Univ Wis, Madison, 65-66. *Pos:* Prin perc, Phoenix Symph Orch, 64-65 & Madison Symph Orch, 65-66; chmn, Annual Contemp Music Fest, 71- & Indianapolis Symph—Ind State Univ Contemp Music Fest; appeared on About Music, TV series, Terre Haute, 71-72; timpanist, Terre Haute Symph, currently; ed, Perc J; asst ed, Percussive Notes. *Teaching:* Instr, Ill pub sch, 60-62; instr music, Ariz State Univ, 64-65; teaching fel, Univ Wis, Madison, 65-66; assoc prof, Ind State Univ, Terre Haute, 66- *Mem:* Percussive Arts Soc; Music Teachers Nat Asn (chmn brass, woodwind & perc div, 73-77); Nat Asn Col Wind & Perc Instr; Am Musicol Soc; Mid-East Instrm Music Conf. *Publ:* Contribr to Instrumentalist, Music J & Am Music Teacher. *Mailing Add:* 130 Carol Dr Terre Haute IN 47805

FLY, FENTON G
EDUCATOR, DOUBLE BASS
b Springfield, Mo, May 27, 34. *Study:* Wichita Univ, BMusEd, 56; Ind Univ, MMusEd, 57; Univ Mo, Kans City, DMA, 66. *Pos:* Cond, Ill Valley Symph Orch, 71-72. *Teaching:* Kans & Ill Pub Sch, 57-72; assoc prof music, Ala State Univ, Montgomery, 72- *Mem:* Col Music Soc; Phi Mu Alpha Sinfonia. *Mailing Add:* Box 93 Sch Music Ala State Univ Montgomery AL 36195

FLYNN, GEORGE WILLIAM
COMPOSER, PIANO
b Miles City, Mont, Jan 21, 37. *Study:* Columbia Univ, BS(music), 64; MA(music comp), 66, DMA(music comp), 72. *Works:* Drive, comn & perf by Kenneth Cooper, 73; American Festivals & Dreams, perf by Gramercy String Quartet, 76; Second Symph, 81 & Meditations, Praises, 81, comn & perf by Sinfonia Musicale; American Rest, perf by Chicago Soundings, 82; Fantasy-Etudes (solo violin), Am String Teachers Asn, 83. *Rec Perf:* Wound, 74, Winter Music (John Cage), 74 & Four Pieces (violin & piano), 83, Finnadar Rec, Atlantic Rec Corp. *Pos:* Chmn bd dirs, Chicago Soundings, 81- *Teaching:* Asst prof music theory, Columbia Univ, 66-73; asst prof lit, Herbert H Lehmann Col, City Univ New York, 73-76; prof music comp, DePaul Univ, 77- *Mem:* ASCAP; Col Music Soc. *Publ:* Auth, Listening to Berio's Music, Musical Quart, 75; Music & Ideology, Chicago Symph Prog Guide, 80. *Mailing Add:* c/o Mary Ann Hoxworth 718 Wrightwood Ave Chicago IL 60614

FOGLER, MICHAEL LANDY
EDUCATOR, GUITAR
b Durham, NC, Oct 6, 53. *Study:* Univ NC, BM, 76; Fla State Univ, MM, 78; NC Sch Arts. *Pos:* Instr guitar, Centre Col, 78-80, Transylvania Univ, 78- & Univ Ky, 79- *Mem:* Col Music Soc; Guitar Found Am; Guitar Soc Lexington; Pi Kappa Lambda; Am String Teachers Asn. *Publ:* Auth, International Guitar Meeting in France, 79, A Concert Review, 81 & The 1987 Guitar Foundation of America Seminar Guitar Competition, 82, Guitar Found Am; The 1982 Guitar Foundation of America Seminar-Denver, Guitar & Lute, 82. *Mailing Add:* 387 Bob-O-Link Dr #1 Lexington KY 40503

FOLDI, ANDREW HARRY
BASS, EDUCATOR
b Budapest, Hungary, July 20, 26; US citizen. *Study:* Univ Chicago, MA(musicol), 48. *Rec Perf:* Modern Psalm (Schönberg), Columbia Rec, 65; Barber of Seville, 71, Italiana in Algiers, 72, Cenerentola, 72, Concert Hall; La Pietra del Paragone, Vanguard, 73. *Roles:* Bartolo in Barber of Seville, Metropolitan Opera & Vienna Staatsoper,, 57-83; Leporello in Don Giovanni, Munich Staatsoper, 61-81; Goldhandler in Cardillac, La Scala, 64; Schigolch in Lulu, Metropolitan Opera, 64-; Sancho Panza in Dan Quichotte, Chicago Lyric, 66-76; Alberich in The Ring, 68-81 & Beckmesser in Meistersinger, 76, Metropolitan Opera. *Teaching:* Dir music prog, Dept Adult Educ, Univ Chicago, 49-61; prof voice & chmn opera dept, DePaul Univ, 52-57; chmn opera dept, Cleveland Inst Music, 81- *Bibliog:* Rob Cuscaden (auth), Living an Opera Life, Chicago Sun-Times, 12/3/74; Anne Millerman (auth), Singing Career Owed to Santa Fe, New Mexican, 7/25/76; Raymond Erickson (auth), Schigolch in Person, New York Times, 12/14/80. *Mem:* Nat Asn Teachers Singing; Am Musicol Soc. *Publ:* Auth, An Introduction to Music, Am Found Continuing Educ, 59; The Enigma of Schigolch, Alban Berg Soc Newsletter, 81. *Rep:* Thea Dispeker 59 E 54th St New York NY 10022. *Mailing Add:* 15830 Van Aken Blvd Shaker Heights OH 44120

FOLEY, DAVID FRANCIS
COMPOSER
b Oak Park, Ill, Aug 8, 45. *Study:* Univ Mich, Ann Arbor, BMus, 69, MMus, 70. *Works:* Te Deum Laudamus, 80, Psalm 150, 82 & Magnificat & Nunc Dimittis, 83, comn by Cathedral Arts Inc; Peter Quince at the Clavier, Am Guild Organists Midwest Regional Conv, 83; Cat Music I & II & Les Choses Passaient, Dorn Publ. *Teaching:* Asst prof music theory & comp, Ball State Univ. *Awards:* BMI Award, 67 & 69; MacDowell Colony Fel, 79, 80 & 81. *Mailing Add:* 701 E Washington St Muncie IN 47305

FOLKERS, CATHERINE EILEEN
FLUTE, INSTRUMENT MAKER
b San Antonio, Tex, Nov 25, 53. *Study:* New England Consv, BMus, 75. *Pos:* Instr maker, C Folkers Hist Flutes, 78-; mem Baroque flute, Musicke Sundrie Kindes, 79- & Banchetto Musicale, 82- *Teaching:* Hist flutes & flute playing, Boston Museum Fine Arts, 82-83. *Interests:* Historical flutes; performing techniques. *Mailing Add:* 64 Hovey St Watertown MA 02172

FOLTER, SIEGRUN H
LIBRARIAN
b Germany; US citizen. *Study:* Univ Rochester, BA, 61; Univ Kans, MA & PhD, 69; Univ Ill, MS, 72. *Pos:* Music cataloger, Univ Ill, Urbana, 73-77, head music cataloging, 77-78; music cataloger, Herbert H Lehman Col, City Univ New York, 81- *Mem:* Music Libr Asn (secy-treas NY chap, 83-); Int Asn Music Libr. *Interests:* Music classification; music bibliography; auction and dealer's catalogs; Paganini. *Publ:* Auth, Library Restrictions on the Use of Microfilm Copies, Fontes Artis Musicae, No 4, 77; ed, Library of Congress Classification Class M: Music and Books on Music, Libr Cong, 3rd ed, 78. *Mailing Add:* Herbert H Lehman Col Bronx NY 10468

FOMIN, ARKADY GERSON
VIOLIN, ARTISTIC DIRECTOR
b Riga Latvia, USSR, Jan 24, 46; US citizen. *Study:* Spec Sch Music, Riga, Latvia, USSR, 64; Latvian State Consv Music, USSR, artist dipl, 69. *Pos:* Prin

violinist, Latvian Phil Chamber Orch, 70-74; first violinist, Dallas Symph Orch, 75-; violinist, Dallas Piano Trio, 75-79. *Teaching:* Prof violin, Latvian Col Music, USSR, 70-74; artist in res, Univ Tex, 75-81; artistic dir & founder, Summer Consv, Southern Methodist Univ, 76- *Mem:* Am Fedn Musicians; Am String Teachers Asn; Music Teachers Nat Asn. *Mailing Add:* 7402 Arbor Oaks Dallas TX 75248

FOMINAYA, ELOY
EDUCATOR, ADMINISTRATOR
b New York, NY, June 10, 25. *Study:* Lawrence Univ, BMus, 50; NTex State Univ, MMus, 53; Mich State Univ, PhD, 63. *Works:* Divertimento (three orch), Dallas Sch District, 52; Concerto for Viola, J Kenneth Byler, 64; Gift of the Ouachita (film score), NE La Univ, 65; Epilogue for String Orchestra, SArk Symph & Augusta Symph, 66; Many Roads (orch), Rosell High Sch Orch Parents Group, 73; Five Profiles for Woodwind Quintet, Blair Acad Music, Nashville, Tenn, 78; The Marshes of Glynn (tenor song cycle), Ga Coun Arts & Humanities, 82. *Rec Perf:* Requiem (Faure), 78, Great Mass in C Minor (Mozart), 79, Christmas Oratorio (Bach), 80, Requiem (Brahms), 81 & Cantata de Noel (Honnegger), 82, Meloan Co. *Teaching:* Dir instrumental, Dallas Independent Sch District, 51-53; assoc prof music, NE La Univ, 53-66; chmn fine arts, Augusta Col, 66-79 & prof, 66- *Mem:* Violin Soc Am; Ga Music Teachers Asn (pres, 69-70); Ga String Teachers Asn (pres, 70); Music Teachers Nat Asn (vpres southern div, 72); Ga Comp Asn (pres, 67). *Mailing Add:* 2500 Walton Way Augusta GA 30910

FONTRIER, GABRIEL
COMPOSER, EDUCATOR
b Bucharest, Rumania, Nov 21, 18; US citizen. *Study:* Queens Col, City Univ New York, with J E Castellini & Karol Rathaus, BA, 42; Columbia Univ, with Otto Luening, MA, 49. *Works:* Lullaby (tenor & orch), 45 & 2 American Songs (tenor & orch), 64, perf by Nassau Co Bicentennial Orch; Sonata (two pianos), 65 & Sonata (piano & cello), 72, Karol Rathaus Hall, Queens Col, City Univ New York; Wind Quintet, perf by Lincoln Ctr Chamber Players, 73; Sextette (three woodwind & three strings), comn by Nassau Co, 75; Goblin Market (three woodwind, two strings coloratura), Carnegie Recital Hall, 77. *Pos:* Music ed, Long Island Press, 47-61 & music critic, 64-78. *Teaching:* Prof music, Queens Col, City Univ New York, 47- *Awards:* Queens Col Choral Soc Prize, 61; Ford Found Fel, 75-76. *Mem:* ASCAP; Am Music Ctr. *Interests:* Audio electronics; acoustics. *Publ:* Coauth, A New Approach to Sight Singing, W W Norton, 61 & 65; numerous articles for Long Island Press, 47-78. *Mailing Add:* 28 Chaffee Ave Albertson NY 11507

FOOTE, LONA
ADMINISTRATOR, ARTIST MANAGER
b July 19, 50. *Study:* Col City New York, BA, 76, MA, 82. *Pos:* Adminr, Experimental Intermedia Found, 81-; freelance arts consult, 81- *Mailing Add:* Experimental Intermedia Found 224 Centre St New York NY 10013

FORBES, ELLIOT
EDUCATOR, CONDUCTOR
b Cambridge, Mass, Aug 30, 17. *Study:* Harvard Univ, AB, 41, MA, 47. *Rec Perf:* Harvard in Song, 59, Songs of the World, 61 & Des Prez Missa Mater Patris et Filia, 61, Carillon Rec. *Pos:* Cond, Harvard Glee Club & Radcliffe Choral Soc, 58-70. *Teaching:* Asst prof, Princeton Univ, 47-54, assoc prof, 54-58; prof, Harvard Univ, 58-61, Fanny Peabody Prof, 61- *Awards:* Hon prof fel in music, Univ Col NWales, UK, 76. *Mem:* Am Musicol Soc; Col Music Soc; Am Acad Arts & Sci; Lili Boulanger Mem Fund (trustee, 72-). *Interests:* Beethoven biography; choral music. *Publ:* Ed, Thayer's Life of Beethoven, Princeton Univ Press, 64; auth, The Choral Music of Beethoven, 69 & The Choral Music of William Mathias, 79, Am Choral Rev; coauth, Randall Thompson: A Choral Legacy, E C Schirmer, 83. *Mailing Add:* 182 Brattle St Cambridge MA 02138

FORCUCCI, SAMUEL L
EDUCATOR, CLARINET
b Granville, NY, July 8, 22. *Study:* State Univ NY Col, Potsdam, BS(music), 47; Syracuse Univ, MMus(comp), 51; Columbia Univ, EdD(music educ), 69. *Works:* Panis Angelicus, 69 & Everbody Square Dance, 69, Boston Music Co; Child of Wonder (cantata), Assoc Music Publ, 71; Song of Benediction, 72 & Alleluia, 75, Pro Art Music; Eucharistic Prayer (oratorio), perf by Cortland Col, 76; Rock in Baroque, Heritage Music Press, 77. *Teaching:* Dir music, Cent Sch, Boonville, NY, 47-50; prof music theory & chmn dept, State Univ NY Col, Cortland, 51- *Mem:* Music Educr Nat Conf; NY State Sch Music Asn; Am Fedn Musicians. *Publ:* Auth, Let There Be Music, Allyn & Bacon, 67; Teaching Music in Today's Secondary Schools, Holt, Rinehart & Winston, 77; A Folk Song History of America, Prentice-Hall, 84. *Mailing Add:* 17 Stevenson St Cortland NY 13045

FORD, BARBARA
EDUCATOR, SOPRANO
Study: Univ Mich, BM & MM. *Pos:* Recitalist & soloist, Spoleto Fest Two Worlds, Carnegie Recital Hall, 74, Nat Gallery Art, Washington, DC, 80 & throughout US, Germany, Italy & USSR. *Teaching:* Assoc prof voice, Sch Music, Fla State Univ, 72- *Mailing Add:* Sch Music Fla State Univ Tallahassee FL 32306

FORD, FREDERIC HUGH
CONDUCTOR, EDUCATOR
b Woonsocket, RI, Feb 5, 39. *Study:* Harvard Univ, AB, 60, AMT, 62; State Univ NY, Buffalo, MA(music hist), 69. *Rec Perf:* Orff Carmina Burana, Hughes Rec, 76. *Pos:* Cond, Glee Club, State Univ NY, Buffalo, 67-68, &

Wabash Col Glee Club, 72-79, Rutgers Univ Choir, Collegium Musicum & Queen's Chorale, 79- & Rutgers Glee Club, 83- *Teaching:* Instr music, Univ Va, 66-67; asst prof, Wabash Col, 72-79 & Rutgers Univ, 79- *Mem:* Am Choral Dir Asn; Intercollegiate Musical Coun (mem bd dir, 75-78 & 83-86); Am Musicol Soc. *Interests:* Eighteenth-century vocal and choral music. *Mailing Add:* Dept Music Mason Gross Sch Arts Rutgers Univ New Brunswick NJ 08903

FORMAN, JOANNE
COMPOSER, WRITER
b Chicago, Ill, June 26, 34. *Study:* Los Angeles City Col; Univ Calif, Los Angeles; Merritt Col; Univ NMex. *Works:* The Blind Men (opera), 78 & Polly Baker (opera), 78, Downeast Chamber Opera; e e cummings songs (song cycle), 78 & Rilkelieder (song cycle), 79, Perf Arts Press; Walden Songs (song cycle), Univ NMex Comp Symposium, 81; Ikarus (opera), SW Chamber Opera, 81; Dragonsongs (song cycle), Constellation, Baltimore, 83. *Pos:* Dir community proj, Free Southern Theater, 65; res comp & playwright, Children's Theater, Maine, 77-78; dir, SW Chamber Opera, 78-; arts ed, Taos News, 81-; contrib ed, Artlines, currently & Theaterwork, currently. *Awards:* Nat Endowment Arts Fel; Meet the Comp Award; Int Women's Writing Guild Award. *Mailing Add:* Box 3181 Taos NM 87571

FORNUTO, DONATO DOMINIC
COMPOSER, EDUCATOR
b New York, NY, Sept 12, 31. *Study:* City Col, City Univ New York, BA, 53; Hunter Col, City Univ New York, MA, 56; Teachers Col, Columbia Univ, EdD, 70. *Works:* Three Pieces for Clarinet and Piano, 64, Four Choral Settings on Poems of William Blake, 71, Concerto for Piano and Concert Band, 72, Songs of Innocence and Experience (mezzo & piano), 73, Suite for Alto Saxophone and Piano, 76 & Four Songs on Poems of Emily Dickinson, 81, Accentuate Music; Songs of Christina (Rossetti) (voice & piano), 82. *Teaching:* Music, New York City Bd Educ, 53-58 & Midland Park Jr-Sr High Sch, NJ, 58-67; vis prof, Teachers Col, Columbia Univ, 64-; prof music, William Paterson Col, 67- *Awards:* Symposium IV Second Place Award for New Band Music, Va Col Band Dir Nat Asn & Southeastern Comp League, 79; Standard Award, ASCAP, 82 & 83. *Mem:* Am Music Ctr; NJ Comp Guild; ASCAP; NY Singing Teachers Asn; Am Fedn Musicians. *Publ:* Auth, Tricks with Triads, Harmonic Variations, Diatonic Triads, 70, Tricks with Triads II, Triad Inversions, 71, Tricks with Triads III, Modal Harmonizations, 72, The Block Chord Style, 74 & Improvising the Blues, Vol I, 74, G Shirmer. *Rep:* Accentuate Music Publ 42 Cornell Dr Plainview NY 11803. *Mailing Add:* 26 Duncan St Waldwick NJ 07463

FORREST, JIM
ADMINISTRATOR, EDUCATOR
b Peoria, Ill, Sept 7. *Study:* Calif Inst Arts, BMus, 69; Calif State Univ, Los Angeles, MA(music), 71. *Pos:* Gen mgr, Guitar Found Am, 77-; ed in chief, Soundboard, 80- *Teaching:* Instr guitar, El Camino Col, 71-79 & Long Beach City Col, 74-82. *Awards:* Cert of appreciation, Guitar Found Am, 81 & Guitar Div, Am String Teachers Asn, 81. *Mem:* Guitar Div, Am String Teachers Asn; Guitar Found Am. *Mailing Add:* Box 5311 Garden Grove CA 92645

FORREST, SIDNEY
CLARINET, EDUCATOR
b New York, NY. *Study:* Juilliard Sch Music, 37-39; Univ Miami, BA, 39; Columbia Univ, MA, 41. *Rec Perf:* Solo Clarinet Works and Chamber Music (Mozart, von Weber, Brahms, Berg, Hindemith & others). *Pos:* Clarinet soloist, US Marine Band, 41-45; prin clarinet, Nat Symph Orch, 46-47; clarinetist, Nat Capital Wind Quintet, 61-72. *Teaching:* Prof clarinet, Peabody Consv Music, 46-, dir placement, 69-; prof clarinet, Univ Mich, Interlochen, summers 59-; adj prof, Cath Univ Am, 54- *Mem:* Clarinetwork; Music Teachers Nat Asn. *Publ:* Auth, High Tones on the Clarinet, The Clarinet, 68; Clarinet in Chamber Music, Bandwagon, 70; Clarinet Tone, Clarinet World, 3/7/83. *Mailing Add:* 9611 Kingston Rd Kensington MD 20895

FORRESTER, MAUREEN KATHERINE STEWART
CONTRALTO
b Montreal, Que, July 25, 30. *Study:* With Sally Martin, Frank Rowe & Bernard Diamant; Hon Dr Music from ten Can univ. *Rec Perf:* On RCA, Victor, Decca, Westminster, Philips, Columbia, DGG & Vanguard. *Roles:* Orfeo in Orfeo, Toronto, 61; Madame de la Haltiere in Cendrillon, San Francisco Opera & New York City Opera, 82-83; Klytemnestra in Elektra, Can Opera Co, 82-83. *Pos:* Appearances with Nat Symph, Cleveland Orch, Boston Symph, New York Phil, Israel Phil, Atlanta Symph & Berlin Phil; contralto, Can Opera Co, Nat Arts Ctr Opera, Ottawa, Washington Opera & New York City Opera. *Awards:* Nat Award Music, Banff Sch Fine Arts, 67; Harriet Cohen Int Music Award, 68; Molson Prize, 71. *Mem:* Sigma Alpha Iota. *Mailing Add:* c/o Harold Shaw 1995 Broadway New York NY 10023

FORSBERG, CARL EARL
EDUCATOR, VIOLIN
b Rochelle, Ill, Apr 12, 20. *Study:* Univ Ill, BM & BS, 43; State Univ Iowa, MA, 44; Ind Univ, PhD, 64. *Pos:* First violin, Ark Symph, 49- *Teaching:* Instr instrm, Northwestern State Univ La, 44-46; asst prof, Midland Col, Nebr, 46-49; from asst prof to prof music hist & violin, Univ Cent Ark, 49- *Awards:* Pres Award, Univ Cent Ark, 73; Outstanding Music Teacher, Ark State Music Teachers Asn, 81. *Mem:* Am Musicol Soc; Am String Teachers Asn; Music Teachers Nat Asn; Music Educr Nat Conf; Ark State Music Teachers Asn (treas, 58-62). *Interests:* The violin sonata; the sonatas for violin and piano by W A Mozart. *Mailing Add:* 5 Salem Rd Conway AR 72032

FORTE, JAMES PETER
COMPOSER, ADMINISTRATOR
b Boston, Mass, Sept 19, 36. *Study:* State Univ NY, BA, 79. *Works:* Piano Sonata No 2, comn by Paul Caponigro, perf by Lee Colby Wilson, 71 & Merilyn Neher, 80; String Quartet No 3, Boston Consv String Ens, 73; Duo for Violin & Piano, comn by Theodore Leutz, 74; Piano Sonata No 3, perf by Lee Colby Wilson, 74 & Ray Herbert, 81; Sinfonia for Strings, perf by Nat Iranian Radio TV Chamber Orch, 78 & New England Symph Orch, 81; Angel Bells (cantata for chorus & orch), comn by Hartford Nat Bank, 75; Who Lives in Love (boy's choir), Boston Archdiocesan Choir, 81. *Pos:* Music dir, Robbins Libr Conct Ser, 74-80; artistic & managing dir, New England Symph Orch, 81- *Mem:* Music Teachers Nat Asn; Mass Music Teachers Asn. *Mailing Add:* 37 Cleveland St Arlington MA 02174

FORTNER, JACK RONALD
COMPOSER, CONDUCTOR & MUSIC DIRECTOR
Study: Aquinas Col, BMus, 59; Juilliard Sch Music, studied comp with Hall Overton, 60; Univ Mich, MMus, 65, DMA, 68; studied cond with Richard Lert, 75; studied with Ross Lee Finney. *Works:* Quadri (orch), 68; Burleske (two chamber orch), 65; Spring (voice & nine instrm), 66; June Dawns, July Moons, August Evenings (orch), Eastern Wash State Col, 73; Flow Chart 1—Apres Jonas 5:5 (chamber ens), 76; De Plus en Plus (piano, clarinet, tape, films, slides & lights), 72; 4 Pieces (string quartet). *Pos:* Cond, Contemp Directions, Ann Arbor, 67-69; music dir, Sinfonia Chamber Orch, Grand Rapids, 68-69; Merced Symph Orch, Calif, 71-76 & Orpheus Ens, Fresno, Calif, 78- *Teaching:* Mem fac comp, Univ Mich, 65-69; prof comp & theory, Calif State Univ, Fresno, 70- *Awards:* Int Comp Prize, Fondation Royaumont Paris, 66; Rome Prize, Am Acad Rome, 67; grants, Nat Found Arts & Humanities & Martha Baird Rockefeller Found; Nat Endowment for the Arts grant, 75. *Mailing Add:* 6358 N Benedict Fresno CA 93711

FORTUNATO, D'ANNA
MEZZO-SOPRANO, EDUCATOR
Study: New England Consv Music, BM, MM, artists dipl; studied voice with Frederick Jagel, Margaret Harshaw & Ellen Repp; studied with John Moriarty, Sean Jurinac & Phyllis Curtin. *Rec Perf:* On CRI, Nonesuch & Harmonia Mundi. *Pos:* Maj roles with Opera Co Boston, Rochester Opera Theater & Augusta Opera; soloist, Boston Symph Orch, Detroit Symph, Minn Orch & NH Symph; appearances with Cantata Singers, Washington, DC, Choral Arts Soc, Baltimore Choral Arts Soc, Clarion Music Soc & Bethlehem Bach Fest. *Teaching:* Mem fac voice, Longy Sch Music, currently. *Rep:* Thea Dispeker 59 E 54th St New York NY 10022; Howard Hart Mgt 114 Clinton St Suite 5D Brooklyn Heights NY 11201. *Mailing Add:* Longy Sch Music One Follen St Cambridge MA 02138

FOSS, LUKAS
COMPOSER, EDUCATOR
b Berlin, Ger, Aug 15, 22; US citizen. *Study:* Lycee Pasteur, Paris, 33-37; Curtis Inst Music, dipl(comp, piano & cond), 37-40; Sch Music, Yale Univ. *Works:* Time Cycle (sop & orch or chamber group), Carl Fischer, 60 & 61; Echoi (clarinet, cello, piano & perc), 63 & Baroque Variations (orch), 67, Carl Fischer & Schott; Orpheus (violin, viola, or cello & orch), Salabert & G Schirmer, 81; American Cantata (tenor, chorus & orch), Boosey & Hawkes, 76; Night Music for John Lennon (concertante brass & orch), 77-80 & Quintets (orch), 79, Carl Fischer; over 80 others. *Pos:* Music dir & cond, Buffalo Phil, 62-70; Brooklyn Phil, 71- & Milwaukee Symph, 81- *Teaching:* Prof music, Univ Calif, 51-62. *Awards:* Rec Award, Am Comp Alliance; Creative Arts Award, Brandeis Univ, 83; Lawne Leaf Award, Am Comp Alliance, 83. *Mem:* Inst Arts & Lett. *Mailing Add:* 17 E 96th St New York NY 10028

FOSTER, DONALD HERBERT
EDUCATOR, WRITER
b Detroit, Mich, Apr 30, 34. *Study:* Wayne State Univ, BS, 56; Univ Mich, MMus, 59, PhD, 67. *Teaching:* Asst prof music, Olivet Col, 60-67; prof musicol, Col Consv Music, Univ Cincinnati, 67- *Awards:* Fulbright Grant, 62-63. *Mem:* Int Musicol Soc; Am Musicol Soc; Soc d'etude du 18th siecle; Am Asn Univ Prof. *Interests:* Eighteenth century French music. *Publ:* Auth, Parodies on Clerambault Cantatas by N Grandval, Recherches Musique Francaise Classique, 64; The Oratorio in Paris in the 18th Century, Acta Musicol, 72; ed, L N Clerambault: Two Cantatas for Soprano, A-R Ed, 79; auth, Franz Beck's Compositions for the Theater in Bordeaux, Current Musicol, 82; ed, Three Symphonies by J B Davaux, In: The Symphony 1720-1840, Garland Publ (in prep). *Mailing Add:* 393 Amazon Ave Cincinnati OH 45220

FOSTER, RICHARD
COACH
b Bangor, Maine, Mar 30, 30. *Study:* New England Consv Music, MusB, 53, MusM, 57; studied with Nadia Boulanger. *Pos:* Vocal accompanist & coach on concerts with members of Metropolitan Opera & New York City Opera on national tours, 59-; asst cond, Central City Opera, 66 & St Paul Opera, 73-74. *Teaching:* Opera coach, Temple Univ, 69-70; vis lectr voice & opera, Univ Hartford, 70- *Mailing Add:* 600 W End Ave New York NY 10024

FOSTER, ROBERT ESTILL
MUSIC DIRECTOR, EDUCATOR
b Raymondville, Tex, Jan 21, 39. *Study:* Univ Tex, BMus, 61; Univ Houston, MM(music ed), 63. *Works:* Over 100 publications of compositions and arrangements for band and/or band instruments, including: Patriotic Finale, 71 & The Screamer, 72, Alfred Publ Co & Chop Busters March, Warner

Brothers, 80. *Rec Perf:* Music of J J Richards, 76, Music of Persichetti, 78 & Music of James Barnes, 82, Crest Rec. *Pos:* Band & orch dir, O Henry Jr High, Austin, 61-62 & Lamar High Sch, Houston, 62-64; assoc dir bands, Univ Fla, 64-71; dir bands, Univ Kans, 71- *Mem:* ASCAP; Am Bandmasters Asn (bd dir, 83-); Music Educr Nat Asn; Kans Music Educr Asn; Kans Bandmasters Asn. *Publ:* Auth, Multiple Option Marching Band Techniques, Alfred Publ, 72; coauth, Championship Auxilliary Units, Alfred Publ, 79; auth, Helpful Hints on Playing the Trumpet (Cornet), Beiwin Publ Co, 83. *Mailing Add:* Rt 6 Long Shadows Dr Lawrence KS 66044

FOUSE, DONALD MAHLON
EDUCATOR, CONDUCTOR & MUSIC DIRECTOR
b Cleveland, Ohio, May 26, 27. *Study:* Ohio State Univ, BA, 53; Univ NC, MA, 58, PhD, 60. *Pos:* Assoc cond, St Petersburg Symph, Fla, 78-81; Cond & music dir, Southwest Minn Orch, 81- *Teaching:* Assoc prof music, NMex State Univ, Las Cruces, 68-77 & Southwest State Univ, Minn, 81- *Mem:* Am Musicol Soc; Col Music Soc. *Interests:* History and analysis of the symphony. *Publ:* Auth, The Sacred Music fo Giammateo Asola, A-R Publ, 63; The Virtuoso Listener, NMex Musician, 71; Giammateo Asola & Agostiaa Corona, New Grove Dict of Music & Musicians, 78. *Mailing Add:* PO Box 64 Vesta MN 56292

FOUSE, SARAH BAIRD
FLUTE, EDUCATOR
b Gary, Ind, Oct 13, 35. *Study:* Univ Mich, with Nelson Hauenstein, BM(wind instrm), 58; Univ Ky, with Alfred Tenboque, MM(perf), 61; study with Robert Covally, Aurele Nicolet & Charles DeLaney. *Rec Perf:* Flute Contest Music, Vol I, 66 & Vol II, 68, Coronet Rec Co; Artist Recital Series, Pandean Rec, 80. *Teaching:* Instr flute, Brevard Music Ctr, NC, summers 56-59 & Sewanee Summer Music Ctr, Tenn, 77; lectr, Univ Ky, 61-67; prof music, Univ Fla, 67- *Mem:* Nat Flute Asn (mem bd dir, 74-76); Music Educr Nat Conf; founder, Fla Flute Club at Gainesville. *Publ:* Auth, Introduction to Class Lessons in Flute, Deford Dig, 12/74; So You Want to Start a Flute Club!, Nat Flute Asn Newsletter, 7/76; 1976 National Flute Association Highlights, Music Dir, 10/76; Breath Control Exercises, Instrumentalist, 1/80; Teaching the Beginning Flute Embouchure, Sch Musician, 10/80. *Mailing Add:* 12832 SW 14th Ave Gainesville FL 32607

FOWLER, CHARLES BRUNER
WRITER
b Peekskill, NY, May 12, 31. *Study:* Crane Sch Music, State Univ NY, Potsdam, BS(music ed), 52; Northwestern Univ, MM, 57; Boston Univ, DMA, 64. *Pos:* Ed, Music Educr J, Music Educr Nat Conf, 65-71; consult & writer, Walt Disney Prod & numerous orgn, 71-; educ ed, Musical Am & High Fidelity, 74- *Teaching:* Supvr vocal music, Irondequoit Sch, 52-56; asst prof music, Mansfield State Col, 57-62; assoc prof, Northern Ill Univ, 64-65. *Awards:* Teacher study grant, Danforth Found, 62-64; Excellence Educ Jour, Educ Press Asn Am, 70; Minerva Award, State Univ NY, Potsdam, 82. *Mem:* Life mem, Music Educr Nat Conf; Music Critics Asn. *Publ:* Coauth, The Search for Musical Understanding, Wadsworth, 73; ed, An Arts in Education Source Book, John D Rockefeller, III Fund, 80; author of more than 100 articles in mag. *Mailing Add:* 320 Second St SE Washington DC 20003

FOWLER, JOHN
TENOR
Roles: Edgardo in Lucia di Lammermoor, Mich Opera, 82; Alfredo in La Traviata, Western Opera Co; Rinuccio in Gianni Schicchi, Cincinnati Opera; Der Rosenkavalier, Dallas Opera; Rigoletto, Long Beach Grand Opera; Les Contes d'Hoffmann, Belgium, 83. *Pos:* Tenor with opera co in US & Europe. *Mailing Add:* c/o Robert Lombardo Assoc 1 Harkness Plaza 61 W 62nd #6F New York NY 10023

FOWLER, NANCY
OBOE, EDUCATOR
Study: Ohio State Univ, BS, MM, PhD; Amsterdam Consv, Netherlands. *Pos:* Oboist, Berkshire Music Fest, formerly & throughout Ohio & southeastern US; mem, Univ Chamber Orch, Fla State Univ, currently & Tallahassee Woodwind Quintet, currently. *Teaching:* Prof oboe, Sch Music, Fla State Univ, 55- *Awards:* Fulbright Scholar. *Mailing Add:* Sch Music Fla State Univ Tallahassee FL 32306

FOWLES, GLENYS RAE
SOPRANO
b Perth, Australia. *Study:* With Margarita Mayer, Kurt Adler & Jani Strasser; AMusA(piano performer's). *Roles:* Oscar in Un Ballo in maschera, Australian Opera, 69; Marzelline in Fidelio; Micaela in Carmen; Tytania in A Midsummer Night's Dream; Marguerite in Faust; Susanna in Le Nozze di Figaro; Mimi in La Boheme; & many others. *Pos:* Lyr sop, Australia Opera, Melbourne Season, 69 & with maj co in Sydney, Scottish Opera, Glyndeboure Fest, Covent Garden & English Nat Opera; res mem, New York City Opera. *Awards:* Winner, Australian Broadcast Comn Vocal Compt, 67 & Metropolitan Opera Nat Coun Auditions, 68. *Mailing Add:* c/o Kazuko Hillyer Int Inc 250 W 57th St New York NY 10107

FOX, ALAN HUGO
ADMINISTRATOR, INSTRUMENT MAKER
b Chicago, Ill, Apr 1, 34. *Study:* Purdue Univ, BS, 55. *Pos:* Vpres, Fox Prod Corp, 60-69, pres, 69-; designer of modern day Fox Bassoon. *Mem:* Co-founder, Int Double Reed Soc. *Mailing Add:* T#1 South Whitley IN 46787

FOX, BARBARA J
SOPRANO

b Alexander City, Ala, Feb 27, 53. *Study:* Oklahoma City Univ, BM(vocal perf), 76; Curtis Inst, Philadelphia, studied opera with Boris Goldovsky, 81-82. *Roles:* Donna Elvira in Don Giovanni, Goldovsky Opera Tour, 81; Mother in Amahl & The Night Visitors, 82 & Rosalinda in Die Fledermaus, 83, Cincinnati Opera, ECCO Tour; Fiordiligi in Cosi Fan Tutte, Cincinnati Opera, 83. *Pos:* Apprentice Prog, Des Moines Metro Opera, 81; Young Am Artist Prog, Cincinnati Opera, 82, mem Ens Co, 82-83. *Awards:* Wilson Voice Award & Strain Award for Women's Voices, Okla Symph Young Artist Compt, 78. *Mem:* Guild Musical Artists. *Mailing Add:* c/o Ralstin 27 W 96th #7F New York NY 10025

FOX, FREDERICK ALFRED
COMPOSER, EDUCATOR

b Detroit, Mich, Jan 17, 31. *Study:* Wayne State Univ, with Ruth Wylie, BMus, 53; Univ Mich, with Ross Lee Finney, 53-54; Ind Univ, with Bernhard Heiden, MMus, 57, DMus(comp), 59. *Works:* The Descent (piano & perc), 69; Variations (piano trio), 70; Ad Rem (guitar), 70; Matrix (cello, strings & perc), 72; Ternoin (oboe & orch), 72; Time Excursions (sop & chamber ens), 76; Beyond Winterlock, 77. *Teaching:* Fac mem, Franklin Col, 59-61, Sam Houston State Col, 61-62 & Calif State Univ, Hayward, 64-75; comp in res, Minneapolis Pub Sch, Young Comp Proj, 62-63; prof comp & dir new music ens, Ind Univ, 74- *Awards:* Fel, Dallas Comp Conf, 60; Ford Found Grant, 63; Nat Endowment Arts Grant, 75. *Mailing Add:* 711 S Clifton St Bloomington IN 47401

FOX, HERBERT O
ARTIST MANAGER

b New York, NY, May 22, 18. *Study:* Union Col, NY, AB, 39. *Pos:* Sr vpres, Columbia Artists Mgt Inc, 40-; chmn, Columbia Artists Fest Corp, currently. *Mailing Add:* c/o Columbia Artist Mgt 7060 Hollywood Blvd Hollywood CA 90028

FOX, LELAND STANFORD
EDUCATOR, CRITIC-WRITER

b Worcester, Mass, Jan 25, 31. *Study:* Baylor Univ, BM, 56, MM, 57; Fla State Univ, PhD, 62. *Pos:* Ed, Opera J, Nat Opera Asn, 68- *Teaching:* Assoc prof opera, Univ Okla, 63-66; prof opera & music hist, Univ Miss, 66-, assoc dean grad sch, 82- *Awards:* Award of Appreciation, Nat Opera Asn, 79. *Mem:* Nat Opera Asn; Royal Musical Asn; Cent Opera Serv; Royal Sch Church Music. *Interests:* Italian opera in the 20th century. *Publ:* Auth, Opera-Comique: A Vehicle for Classical Style, Recherches IV, 64; ed, The Chautauqua Opera Association, 74 & Touring Opera, 75, Nat Opera Asn; auth, Beffroy de Reigny, A B Bruni & four other biographies, In: New Grove Dict of Music & Musicians, 80. *Mailing Add:* 2206 Church St Oxford MS 38655

FRABIZIO, WILLIAM V
EDUCATOR, COMPOSER

b Stockton, NJ, Oct 10, 29. *Study:* Trenton Col; Rutgers Univ; Temple Univ, with Clifford Taylor. *Works:* Statement (trumpet & 18 players); Symphonic Paraphrase (band); Synesthesia (band); Comments Among 4 Players (piano, four hands, cello & perc); Psalm 150 (string quartet & voice); Dialogues (trombone & string quartet); Credo Americana (solo voice & band). *Teaching:* Private sch, 57-63; instr, Temple Univ, 65-68 & New England Consv Music, 68-69; from instr to chmn music dept, Beaver Col, 70- *Awards:* Lindback Award, 72-73; Outstanding Educr Am Award, 73. *Mailing Add:* Music Dept Beaver Col Glenside PA 19038

FRACKENPOHL, ARTHUR ROLAND
COMPOSER, EDUCATOR

b Irvington, NJ, Apr 23, 24. *Study:* Eastman Sch Music, BA, 47, MA, 49; McGill Univ, Mus Doc, 57. *Works:* Brass Quintet, Elkan-Vogel Music Co, 66; Concertino for Tuba & Strings, King Music Co, 67; Three Short Pieces for String Quartet, G Schirmer, 70; Dance Overture for Band, Marks Music Corp, 76; A Child This Day, Mark Foster Music Co, 80; Rise Up, My Love, Shawnee Press, 81; Sonata for Tuba & Piano, Kendor Music, 83. *Teaching:* Instr music, Crane Sch Music, State Univ NY Col, Potsdam, 49-54, asst prof, 54-57, assoc prof, 57-61, prof, 61- *Awards:* First Prize Comp, Fontainebleau, France, 50; Ford Found Grant, 59-60; ASCAP Awards, 64- *Mem:* NY Sch Music Asn; Music Educators Nat Conf; Phi Mu Alpha Sinfonia; ASCAP. *Publ:* Auth, Harmonization at the Piano, William Brown, 4th ed, 81. *Mailing Add:* 13 Hillcrest Dr Potsdam NY 13676

FRAGER, MALCOLM
PIANO, EDUCATOR

b St Louis, Mo, Jan 15, 35. *Study:* With Carl Madlinger, 42-49; Tutoring Sch NY, 49-55; Am Consv, Fontainebleu; Columbia Univ, BA; studied with Carl Friedburg. *Rec Perf:* Chopin piano works, Telarc Rec; over 25 rec. *Pos:* Soloist, Berkshire Music Fest, 63-66; tours, USSR, 63, Iceland, 64 & worldwide, 64- *Teaching:* Master classes, St Louis Consv Music, currently. *Awards:* Michaels Mem Music Award, Chicago, 56; First Prize, Edgar M Leventritt Int Compt, 59 & Queen Elizabeth Compt, Belgium, 60. *Mailing Add:* c/o Columbia Artists Mgt 165 W 57th St New York NY 10019

FRAME, PAMELA
CELLO, TEACHER

b Rochester, NY. *Study:* Eastman Sch Music, study with Alan Harris & Ronald Leonard, BM & perf cert, 75; Manhattan Sch Music, with Bernard Greenhouse, MM, 77; study with M Rostropovich & Uzi Wiesel. *Pos:* Cellist, Affil Artists Inc & Pro Musicis Found, New York, 81- *Teaching:* Cello

privately, New York, 77- *Mem:* Am Fedn Musicians; Chamber Music Am. *Rep:* Francis Crociata 15 Swan St Rochester NY 14604; Del Rosenfield 714 Ladd Rd Bronx NY 10471. *Mailing Add:* 801 West End Ave #4A New York NY 10025

FRANANO, FRANK SALVATORE
FRENCH HORN, ADMINISTRATOR

b Kansas City, Mo, Dec 7, 26. *Study:* Interlochen Music Camp, cert, 43; private study with Merle Smith, 42-44 & Alfred Brain, Los Angeles, 45. *Pos:* Prin horn, Kansas City Phil, Mo, 43-82, Am Ballet Theater, 44, Starlight Theater, Kansas City, Mo, 51-, Seventh Army Symph, Ger, 53-54, Lyr Opera Kansas City, 57-, World Symph Orch, New York, 71 & Filarmonica de las Americas, Mexico City, 76; owner, Franano Music Contracting, Kansas City, 76; prin horn & personnel mgr, Kansas City Symph Orch, 82- *Teaching:* Instr appl horn, Consv Music, Univ Mo, Kansas City, 65-73, Drake Univ, Des Moines, 69-70 & Stephens Col, Columbia, Mo, 70-71. *Mem:* Int Horn Soc. *Mailing Add:* 7311 Ward Pkwy Kansas City MO 64114

FRANCE, HAL
CONDUCTOR, PIANO

b Phillipsburg, NJ, Dec 13, 52. *Study:* Northwestern Univ, BM(piano), 75; Juilliard Sch; Univ Cincinnati, MM(cond), 80. *Pos:* Res cond, Houston Grand Opera, 80-; assoc cond, Tex Opera Theater, 81-82. *Mailing Add:* Houston Grand Opera 615 Louisiana Houston TX 77002

FRANCESCATTI, ZINO (RENE)
VIOLIN, COMPOSER

b Marseille, France, Aug 9, 02. *Works:* Piano Preludes; Aria (violin & piano) & Polka (violin & piano), Int Music Co. *Rec Perf:* Works of Beethoven, Brahmns, Paganini, Bach, Mozart, Tchaikovsky, Sibelius and others, CBS Rec. *Pos:* Conct violinist, worldwide, 20-75, Europe, 28-38, South Am tours, 38, 47 & 52, US tour, 39 & Israel, 49-56, 58, 63 & 66; ed, class violin repertoire, Int Music Co, currently. *Awards:* Commandeur, Legion d'Honneur, France, Arts et Lettres, France & Leopold, Belgium. *Rep:* Columbia Artists Mgt 165 W 57th St New York NY 10019. *Mailing Add:* La Ciotat 13600 France

FRANCESCHINI, ROMULUS
COMPOSER, WRITER

b Brooklyn, NY, Jan 5, 29. *Study:* Philadelphia Consv Music, studied comp with Vincent Persichetti, BMus(comp), 54; study with Stefan Wolpe, 64-65 & Morton Feldman, 65-66. *Works:* Two Studies on a Basic Shape (flute & viola), Yellow Springs Inst Arts, Chester Springs, Pa, 81; Reflections (flute, alto sax & clarinet), Art Mus Cage Memorial Conct, Philadelphia, 82; Omaggio a Satie (piano), Soundings Press, 82; White Spirituals, William Billings Inst Am Music, New London, Conn, 82; Benjamin Carr's Federal Overture, A Paraphrase, perf by Nat Gallery Orch, Washington, DC, 83; Seven Poems of Mao Tsetung, Callisto Rec, 83; Paintings for Orchestra, perf by Philadelphia Youth Orch, 83. *Pos:* Asst cur, Fleisher Music Collection, Philadelphia, 61-; dir, Electronic Music Prod, Moorestown, NJ, 68-71; secy, Philadelphia Comp Forum, 68-74; assoc dir, Relache Ens for Contemp Music, Philadelphia, 77-; coordr, New Music Lab, Yellow Springs Inst Arts, Chester Springs, Pa, 82- *Teaching:* Adj fac mem music, Glassboro State Col, 73-75 & 78 & Rutgers Univ, Camden, 76-77. *Bibliog:* Joseph Franklin (auth), Romulus Franceschini, Electronic Composer, Drummer, Philadelphia, 76; Tom Johnson (auth), Aimless Major & Other Keys, Village Voice, New York, 3/80. *Publ:* Auth, Furniture Music (Variations on Themes by Erik Satie), Soundings, Santa Fe, 82. *Mailing Add:* Pickwick Apts U-12 Maple Shade NJ 08052

FRANCHETTI, ARNOLD
COMPOSER

b Lucca, Italy, Aug 18, 09. US citizen. *Study:* Florence Consv, with Father Alberto, MA, 36; Akad Tonkunst, Munich; Mozarteum, Salzburg. *Works:* Three Italian Masques, Galaxy, 60; Italy Inventions, Bongiovanni; Saxophone Sonata, 79; Nocturnes (perc), 79; Ricamd (perc), Larosa, 83. *Teaching:* Prof theory & comp, Hartt Sch Music, Univ Hartford, 48-81, dept chmn, 63-78, emer prof, 83- *Awards:* Grant, Inst Arts & Lett, 57 & Libr Cong, 58; Guggenheim Fel, 60; Ditson Award, 63. *Mem:* ASCAP. *Mailing Add:* Pleasant Valley Old Lyme CT 06371

FRANCO, JOHAN
COMPOSER

b Zaandam, Netherlands, July 12, 08. US citizen. *Study:* First Col Hague, Univ Amsterdam; private study with Willem Pijper, 28-33. *Works:* Symphony I, 33, Concerto Lirico No 1 (violin), 37, Virgin Queen's Dream Monologue, 47-52, Fantasy (cello & orch), 51, Symphony, V, 58, Concerto Lirico No 4 (perc), 70 & Concerto Lirico No 5 (guitar), 71, Am Comp Alliance. *Bibliog:* William Hoskins (auth), Johan Franco The Music and The Man, Am Comp Alliance Bulletin, Vol VIII, No 3, 59. *Mem:* Guild Carillonneurs in North Am; Guild of Carillonneurs of France; Am Comp Alliance. *Interests:* Music of the Count de Saint-Germain. *Publ:* Auth, The Count of Saint-Germain, Musical Quart, Vol XXXVI, No 4, 10/50. *Mailing Add:* 403 Lake Dr Virginia Beach VA 23451

FRANK, ANDREW (DAVID)
COMPOSER, EDUCATOR

b Los Angeles, Calif, Nov 25, 46. *Study:* Bard Col, BA, 68; Univ Pa, MA, 70. *Works:* Notturno for Solo Flute, 82, String Quartet No 3, 82, Three Preludes for Piano, 82, Sonata for Violin and Piano, 82, Symphony for String Orchestra, 83, Variations for Chamber Orchestra, 83 & Rhapsody III for Solo

Violin, 83, Mobart Music Publ Inc. *Teaching:* Assoc prof comp & theory, Univ Calif, Davis, 72- *Awards:* First Prize, Int Trumpet Guild, 75; Am Comp Alliance Rec Award, 79. *Mem:* Am Comp Alliance; Am Music Ctr. *Rep:* 968 Overlook Rd Berkeley CA 94708. *Mailing Add:* Music Dept Univ Calif Davis CA 95616

FRANK, CLAUDE
PIANO
b Nuremberg, Germany, Dec 24, 25; US citizen. *Study:* Private study with Artur Schnabel, 41-51; Columbia Univ, 42-44 & 47-48. *Rec Perf:* Boston Symph Orch Chamber Players, RCA Red Seal, 65-66; Beethoven: Ordeal & Triumph, WABC-TV, 66; The Complete 32 Piano Sonatas (Beethoven), RCA Victrola, 70; Concerto No 26 (Mozart), Sonic Arts, 81; Archduke Trio (Beethoven), Sine Qua Non, 82. *Teaching:* Mem fac music, Bennington Col, 48-55; Mannes Col Mus, 63- & Aspen Music Sch, 70-; prof music, Yale Sch Music, 72- *Awards:* Beethoven Soc Award, 79. *Bibliog:* Beethoven: Ordeal & Triumph, WABC-TV, 66. *Publ:* Contribr to Keynote Mag, Clavier Mag & Piano Quart. *Mailing Add:* 825 West End Ave New York NY 10025

FRANK, GREGORY
BASS
b Seattle, Wash. *Roles:* Bartolo in Le Nozze di Figaro, 83 & Osmin in Die Entführung aus dem Serail, 83, Lyric Opera Ctr Am Artists; bass in Die Meistersinger von Nürnberg, Chicago Symph Orch, 83; bass in The Song of Norway, Man of La Mancha, Great Waltz & Kismet, Seattle Civic Light Opera; and others. *Pos:* Bass, Lyric Opera Ctr Am Artists, 83- *Mailing Add:* Lyric Opera Ctr Am Artists 20 N Wacker Dr Chicago IL 60606

FRANK, JEAN FORWARD
COMPOSER
b Pittsburgh, Pa, Aug, 13, 27. *Study:* Chatman Col, with Louis P Coyner & Russell Wichmann; studied with Roland Leich & Joseph Wilcox Jenkins. *Works:* Time Of Our Lives (operetta); Princess of a Thousand Moons (operetta); Scatterpunctus (string orch); The Christmas Story (chorus); Into the Woods My Master Went (chorus); Afternoon Street Noise (piano); Contemplation (piano). *Mailing Add:* Box 234C Ridge Dr Mars PA 16046

FRANK, JOSEPH
TENOR
b Pa. *Study:* Curtis Inst; Ind Univ. *Roles:* Tanzmeister in Ariadne auf Naxos, 79 & Der Rosenkavalier, 82, Metropolitan Opera; The Confidence Man, 82 & Orpheus in the Underworld, 83, Santa Fe Opera; Madama Butterfly, Tulsa, 83; Triquet in Eugene Onegin, 83 & Basilio in The Marriage of Figaro, Hawaii Opera. *Pos:* Performer, Cincinnati Opera, Houston Grand Opera, Opera-Omaha, Philadelphia Opera, Ft Worth Opera & others. *Mailing Add:* c/o Columbia Artists 165 W 57th St New York NY 10019

FRANKENBERGER, YOSHIKO TAKAGI
VOCALIST, TEACHER
b Tokyo, Japan, March, 15, 46. *Study:* Col-Consv Music, Univ Cincinnati, BMus, 69. *Rec Perf:* Over 250 (mostly educ), 52-70, including Chuchan-ga Dobutsuen ni itta Ohanashi & Tokyo no Uta; Red Carnations (film), 58. *Pos:* Voice & piano recitals, Dayton, Ohio & Tokyo, Japan; TV & radio appearances, US & Japan. *Teaching:* Voice instr, St Joseph's Col, Ind, 72; voice & piano instr privately, Alvin, Tex, 73. *Awards:* Distinguished Serv Award, King Rec Co Ltd, Tokyo, 63 & 71; Japanese Poet Asn Award, 68. *Mailing Add:* 110 E Wildwinn Alvin TX 77511

FRANKLIN, CARY JOHN
COMPOSER, CONDUCTOR
b Cedar Rapids, Iowa, Nov 26, 56. *Study:* Macalester Col, BA, 79; Aspen Music Fest, summer 79. *Works:* When Soft Voices Die, Jenson Publ, 80; Shattered Dreams, perf by Minn Bach Soc, 81; Overture, perf by St Paul Chamber Orch, 82; two Christmas arr, perf by Dale Wavland Singers, 82; Hold Fast to Dreams, Walton Music Corp, 83. *Pos:* Asst music dir, Plymouth Music Ser, Minneapolis, Minn, 80-; cond, Minn Comp Forum, 81- & Mankato State Univ Orch, 82-; chorus master, Minn Opera, 81- *Awards:* Presser Found Award, 79. *Mem:* Am Symph Orch League; Cond Guild; Am Choral Dir Asn; Am Choral Found; ASCAP. *Mailing Add:* 1973 Lincoln Ave St Paul MN 55105

FRANKLIN, JOSEPH J
ADMINISTRATOR, COMPOSER
b Philadelphia, Pa, July 26, 44. *Study:* Philadelphia Musical Acad, BM, 72; Col Music, Temple Univ, MM, 75. *Works:* Double-Wing 50 on 2, 80, Double-Wing 50 on 3, 81, Soliloquy from the Insanity of Mary Girard, 81, Everything Going Out, Again, 82 & Callisto, 83, Relache. *Pos:* Mem, Philadelphia New Music Group, 74-75; exec dir, Relache, Ens Contemp Music, 76- *Awards:* Artist's Fel, Pa Coun Arts, 81 & 83. *Mem:* BMI; New Music Alliance; Gtr Philadelphia Cult Alliance. *Mailing Add:* 5910 Wayne Ave Philadelphia PA 19144

FRASER, BARBARA
VIOLIN
b Milwaukee, Wis, Aug 12, 33. *Study:* Wis Consv Music, BMus; Eastman Sch Music, perf cert, 55, MMus. *Pos:* Violinist, Rochester Phil, formerly, Houston Symph, formerly, Santa Fe opera, formerly, Concertgebouwahest, Holland, formerly & Chicago Symph, currently; mem, De Camarata Soc, Chicago, currently. *Mailing Add:* Chicago Symph Orch 220 S Michigan Ave Chicago IL 60604

FRAZEE, JANE
EDUCATOR, LECTURER
b Cumberland, Wis, July 16, 36. *Study:* Univ Wis, BM, 58; Univ Minn, MA, 61. *Pos:* Dir, Orff Cert Prog, Hamline Univ, 71- & Univ Ill, 80- *Teaching:* Instr music, Northrop Col Sch, 62-72, Macalester Col, 68-73, & St Paul Acad, Summit Sch, 78-; asst prof, Hamline Univ, 72- *Awards:* Fulbright Fel, 81-82. *Mem:* Am Orff-Schulwerk Asn (pres, 77); Music Educr Nat Conf. *Interests:* Curriculum development in Orff-Schulwerk. *Publ:* Coauth, A Baker's Dozen; This is the Day, Schmitt, 74-75; auth, Strawberry Fair, Schmitt, 77; Ten Folk Carols for Christmas, Schott, 77; Singing in the Season, Magnamusic-Baton, 83; Sound Ideas, Musik Innovations, 83. *Mailing Add:* 24 S St Albans St Paul MN 55105

FRAZEUR, TED C (THEODORE C FRAZEUR)
PERCUSSION, COMPOSER
b Omaha, Nebr, Apr 20, 29. *Study:* Univ Omaha, 47-48; Eastman Sch Music, BM, 51, MM, 56. *Works:* Symphony No 1, Rochester Phil, 62; Uhuru (perc septet), Kendor Music Inc, 72; Poets in a Landscape, State Univ NY, Fredonia Col, 72; Sonata for Viola & Percussion, Music Perc Inc, 75; Sea Cycle, 76-81 & The Book of the Dun Cow (horn & chamber orch), 83, State Univ NY, Fredonia Col. *Rec Perf:* The Percussionist, Mark Rec, 70; Theodore Frazeur & Friends, Grenadilla, 79. *Pos:* Prin perc & tympanist, Omaha Symph, 47-79; perc, Rochester Phil, 51-55; perc & tympanist, Erie Phil, 57-80; tympanist, Erie Chamber Orch, 80- *Teaching:* Prof perc, State Univ NY, Fredonia, 56- *Awards:* Res Fel, State Univ NY, 76, 79 & 80; Comp Award, Erie Pa Arts Coun, 80. *Mem:* Percussive Arts Soc (mem bd dirs, 72-74). *Mailing Add:* 3 Westerly Dr Fredonia NY 14063

FREDRICKS, RICHARD
BARITONE
b Los Angeles, Calif, Aug 15, 33. *Study:* El Camino Jr Col, AS; Univ Denver, with Florence Lamont Hinman; studied with Carlos Noble & Beverley Johnson. *Rec Perf:* On Desto & Columbia. *Roles:* Schaunard in La Boheme, 60 & Capt Jason McFarland in Lizzie Borden, 65, New York City Opera; Nottingham in Roberto Devereux, 75; Germont in La Traviata, 76; Sir Richard in I Puritani; Escamillo in Carmen; Malatesta in Don Pasquale. *Pos:* Leading roles with maj opera co in US; conct performer with maj orchs in US, Can & Israel. *Teaching:* Private lessons voice & coach repertoire. *Mailing Add:* c/o Columbia Artist Mgt 165 W 57th St New York NY 10019

FREDRICKSON, (LAWRENCE) THOMAS
COMPOSER, EDUCATOR
b Kane, Pa, Sept 5, 28. *Study:* Ohio Wesleyan Univ, BM, 50; Univ Ill, MM, 52, DMA, 60. *Works:* Music for the Double Bass Alone, Theodore Presser Co, 69; Brass Quintet, M M Cole Co, 72; Sinfonia II (orch), Champaign/Urbana Symph Orch, 73; Impressions (chorus), European-Am Music, 74; Sketches, Univ Ill Contemp Chamber Players, 80; Cycles (clarinet & piano), Howard Klug, 83. *Teaching:* Instr, Univ Ill, Urbana/Champaign, 52-60, asst prof, 60-63, assoc prof, 63-67 & prof, 68- *Awards:* Standard Award, ASCAP, 81-83. *Mem:* ASCAP. *Mailing Add:* 1814 Robert Dr Champaign IL 61821

FREED, ARNOLD
COMPOSER, WRITER
b New York, NY, Sept 29, 26. *Study:* City Col, City Univ New York, with Mark Brunswick & Philip James, BA(music); Juilliard Sch Music, with Vittorio Giannini, BA (comp); studied cond with Hugh Ross & Dean Dixon; NY Univ, with Gustave Reese, MA(musicol); Berkshire Inst, with Luigi Dallapiccola; studied piano with Pietro Scarpini & Paul Wittgenstein. *Works:* Alleluia (orch); Win, Place or Show (overture for orch); Three Elizabethan Songs (sop & piano); Gloria; Four Seasonal Madrigals; From Out of a Wood; Heaven-Haven. *Pos:* Chief music ed, Boosey & Hawkes Publ, currently; ed consult & dir choral activ, Hansen Publ; writer scores, TV, doc & films. *Mailing Add:* 535 E 89th St Apt 4L New York NY 10028

FREEDMAN, ELLIS J
ARTIST REPRESENTATIVE, ADMINISTRATOR
b Albany, NY, May 3, 21. *Study:* Cornell Univ, BA, 41, Sch Law, LLB, 43. *Pos:* Dir, Am Comp Orch Inc & Third Street Music Sch Settlement; secy & dir, Am Music Rec Inst Inc & Charles Ives Soc Inc; adv coun, Comp Rec Inc; secy, Koussevitzky Music Found Inc & Serge Koussevitzky Music Found in Libr Cong. *Mem:* Tcherepnin Soc Inc; Stefan Wolpe Soc Inc. *Mailing Add:* 415 Madison Ave New York NY 10017

FREEMAN, CARROLL (BENTON), JR
TENOR
b Memphis, Tenn. *Study:* Univ Southern Miss, BM, 69; Oklahoma City Univ, with Inez Silberg, 73; studied voice with Norma Newton. *Roles:* Lurtha in The King & I, Wolf Trap Farm Park, 72; Alfredo in La Traviata, New York City Opera, 82; Leandro in Arlecchino, Houston Grand Opera, 82; Almaviva in The Barber of Seville, Lyr Opera Kansas City, 82; Fritz in La Grande Duchesse du Gerolstein, Miami Opera, 83; Alfred in Die Fledermaus, Portland Opera, 83; Katz in The Postman Always Rings Twice, St Louis Opera Theater, 83. *Pos:* Apprentice, Wolf Trap, 72-74 & Merola Pros, 77; asst art dir, Inspiration Point Fine Arts Colony, 76-78; artist, Houston Opera Studio, 78-80. *Awards:* Bernhardt N Poetz Mem Award, San Francisco Opera Merola Prog, 77; Nat Opera Inst Career Support Grant, 80-81; Sullivan Found Career Support Grant, 82-83. *Mem:* Affil Artists Inc. *Rep:* Thea Dispeker Artists Rep 59 E 54th St New York NY 10022. *Mailing Add:* 1 Vincent Rd #1C Bronxville NY 10708

FREEMAN, COLENTON
TENOR

b Atlanta, Ga, Dec 17, 55. *Study:* Consv Music, Oberlin Col, BMus, 79, MMus, 79; Ind Univ, 79-81. *Roles:* Arturo & Normanno in Lucia di Lammermoor, 81, Il Messagiero in Aida, 81 & Aegisthus in Clytemnestra, 81, San Francisco; Don Jose in Carmen, Hamburg Staatsoper, WGer, 82; Rodolfo in La Boheme, 83 & Linfea in La Calisto, 83, Wolf Trap Opera Co. *Pos:* Soloist, Atlanta Symph, 73, 74 & 77, Indianapolis Symph, 80, San Diego Symph, 81, New Orleans Symph, 81, San Francisco Opera Orch, 81 & Collegiate Chorale, 82. *Teaching:* Assoc instr voice, Sch Music, Ind Univ, 79-81. *Awards:* Study Grant, Metropolitan Opera Asn, 82; Career Grant, Nat Opera Inst, 83. *Mem:* Am Guild Musical Artists. *Rep:* Columbia Artists Mgt Inc 165 W 57th St New York NY 10019. *Mailing Add:* 446 W 58th St #5R New York NY 10019

FREEMAN, EDWIN ARMISTEAD
EDUCATOR, COMPOSER

b Spartanburg, SC, May 2, 28. *Study:* Clemson Univ, BS, 49; Columbia Univ, studied with Luening & Monteux, MA, 68; La State Univ, DMA, 76. *Works:* String Quartet No 1, perf by New Orleans String Quartet, 55; Fantasy on a Ground, Oneonta Symph Orch, 59; When I Met You, New Orleans Pops Orch, 61 & 62; Dr Donne Preaches on Death, comn & perf by Greenwich Choral Soc, 67; Two Pieces for Band, perf by Clemson Univ Symphonic Band, 81. *Teaching:* Dir high sch & chmn arts prog, Dalton Sch, New York, NY, 65-69; assoc prof music, Clemson Univ, 69- *Awards:* Student Comp Radio Award, BMI, 55. *Mem:* Am Soc Univ Comp; Phi Mu Alpha. *Mailing Add:* 148 Folger St Clemson SC 29631

FREEMAN, JOANN (JOANN FREEMAN SHWAYDER)
MUSIC DIRECTOR

b New York, NY. *Study:* Vassar Col, BA, 45; Columbia Univ, 45-48; Juilliard Grad Sch Music, MS, 48. *Rec Perf:* Das Lied (Richard Moryl), CRI, 78. *Pos:* Artistic dir, Am Artists Ser, Bloomfield Hills, Mich, 70- *Mem:* Chamber Music Am. *Mailing Add:* Hill House 435 Goodhue Road Bloomfield Hills MI 48013

FREEMAN, JOHN WHEELOCK
WRITER, COMPOSER

b Bronx, NY, June 30, 28. *Study:* Yale Col, BA, 50; private study. *Works:* Along the River, perf by Grayson Hirst, John Ostendorf & Bronx Arts Ens, 80; To Wrestle with the Angel, perf by Occasional Singers, 82; Somewhere I Have Never Travelled, Harpsichord Unlimited, 82; Elizabethan Love Songs, perf by Ariel Trio, 82; Suite for Winds, perf by Bronx Arts Ens Chamber Orch, 83. *Pos:* Assoc ed, Opera News, 60-; US corresp, Nuova Rivista Musicale Italiana, 70-80. *Mem:* Music Critics Asn; Am Music Ctr; New York Singing Teachers Asn; Am Inst Verdi Studies. *Publ:* Coauth, The Golden Horseshoe, Viking Press, 65; contribr, The New Music Lover's Handbook, Harvey House, 73. *Mailing Add:* Opera News 1865 Broadway New York NY 10023

FREEMAN, ROBERT NORMAN
MUSICOLOGIST

b Vancouver, BC, Aug 29, 39. *Study:* Univ Calif, Los Angeles, BA, MA, PhD; Akad Music & Darstellende Kunst, Vienna. *Teaching:* Assoc prof music, Univ Calif, Santa Barbara, currently. *Awards:* First Prize, Atwater-Kent Awards, 68; Fulbright Scholar, 68-70. *Mem:* Int Musicol Soc; Am Musicol Soc; Am Soc Eighteenth Century Studies; Int Albrechtsbergergesellschaft. *Interests:* Eighteenth century music. *Publ:* Contribr, Die Musikforschung, Opera J, New Grove Dict of Music & Musicians & Notes. *Mailing Add:* Santa Barbara CA

FREEMAN, ROBERT SCHOFIELD
ADMINISTRATOR, PIANO

b Rochester, NY, Aug 26, 35. *Study:* Harvard Col, AB, 57; Princeton Univ, MFA, 60, PhD, 67. *Rec Perf:* The Seasons (Epstein), Desto, 72; Andante and Variations, Op 46 (Schumann), Vox, 80. *Teaching:* From instr to asst prof, Princeton Univ, 63-68; from asst prof to assoc prof, Mass Inst Technol, 68-73; vis assoc prof, Harvard Univ, 72; dir & prof, Eastman Sch Music, 73- *Awards:* Fulbright Grant to Vienna, 60-62; Martha B Rockefeller Fel, 62-63; Nat Endowment Humanities Grant, 68. *Mem:* Am Musicol Soc (mem coun, 73-75); Col Music Soc (mem coun, 76-78); Neue Bach Gesellschaft (Am chmn, 77-82); Nat Asn Sch Music; Int Musicol Soc. *Interests:* 18th Century Italian opera; J S Bach; Mozart. *Publ:* Auth, La Verita Nella Ripetizione, Musical Quart, 68; contribr, Festschrift for Oliver Strunk, Princeton Univ Press, 68; J S Bach, Cantata 176, In: Neue Bach Ausgabe, 68, Bärenreiter; Festschrift for Arthur Mendel, Boonin, 74; auth, Opera Without Drama, UMI, 81. *Mailing Add:* 1316 East Ave Rochester NY 14610

FREITAS, BEEBE
ARTISTIC DIRECTOR

Study: Oberlin Col, BA; Boston Univ, MA; Juilliard Sch. *Pos:* Mem, Hawaii Opera Theatre, 66-, artistic dir, 82-; res keyboard specialist, Honolulu Symph, currently; organist, First Presby Church & Punahou Sch Chapel. *Teaching:* Mem staff music dept, Univ Hawaii, currently. *Awards:* Ford Found Scholar; Accmp Scholar, Boston Univ; Perf Artist Award, Boston Pops Symph. *Mailing Add:* Hawaii Opera Theatre 987 Waimanu St Honolulu HI 96814

FRENCH, CATHERINE
ADMINISTRATOR

b New Jersey. *Study:* Manhattanville Col, BA(music hist), 68. *Pos:* Mgr, Am Symph Orch League, 70-72, asst dir, vpres pub affairs & chief operating officer, 74-80, exec vpres & chief exec officer, 80-; mgr, NJ Symph Orch, 72-74; dir, New York Pops, 83- *Mem:* Nat Music Coun (dir, 81-); NY State Coun on Arts (mem music panel, 71-72). *Mailing Add:* c/o Am Symph Orch League 633 E St NW Washington DC 20004

FRENCH, RICHARD FREDERIC
MUSICOLOGIST, EDUCATOR

b Randolph, Mass, June 23, 15. *Study:* Harvard Univ, BS, 37, MA, 39. *Pos:* Dir publ & vpres, Assoc Music Publ, 51-59; pres, New York Pro Musica, 59-70, dir, 59- *Teaching:* Asst prof music, Harvard Univ, 47-51; Robert S Tangeman prof sacred music, Union Theol Sem, NY, 65-73; prof, Inst Sacred Music, Yale Univ, 73- *Mem:* Am Musicol Soc; Int Soc Contemp Music. *Interests:* Music and liturgy; Russian; graduate educational curricula. *Publ:* Coauth, Music and Criticism, A Symposium, Harvard Univ, 50; auth, Dilemma of Music Publishing Industry, In: 100 Years of Music in America, Grosset, 64; transl, Boris Asaf'ev's, A Book About Stravinsky, UMI. *Mailing Add:* 95 E Rock Rd New Haven CT 06511

FRENCH, ROBERT BRUCE
ADMINISTRATOR, COMPOSER

b Springfield, Ky, Oct 9, 24. *Study:* Sch Music, Univ Louisville, BM, 50; George Peabody Col for Teachers, MM, 51; study with Roy Harris, 51-53. *Works:* The Riddle, 49 & The Three Ravens, 49, perf by Madrigal Singers, Univ Louisville; Song for Soprano and String Quartet, perf by Charme Riesley, Univ Louisville, 50; Sonata (violin & piano), perf by Solie Fott & James Sherrill, 51; Green is the Water, George Peabody Col Choir, 51; Concert Overture, George Peabody Col Symph Band, 51. *Pos:* Co-founder & pres, Louisville Acad Music, 54-; co-founder & mgr, Louisville Youth Orch, 58-60; music ed, Louisville Gazette, 58-59; organist & choirmaster, St John's Evangel & Reformed, 60-67. *Bibliog:* Jean Howerton (auth), Man Copies Concerto for 14 Hours a Day, Louisville, Courier J, 53; Joan Kay (auth), Teaching Takes in More Than Music, 74 & Robert French: A History of Music, 79, Louisville Courier J. *Interests:* Musicians and organizations in Louisville area. *Mailing Add:* 2740 Frankfort Ave Louisville KY 40206

FRENCH, RUTH SCOTT
TEACHER, VIOLIN

b Louisville, Ky, Oct 25, 31. *Study:* Meadowmount Sch Music, studied violin with Ivan Galamian, 51; Cincinnati Col Music, with Valentin Blumberg, 51-52; Cincinnati Consv Music, with Henry Meyer, 53-59; Aspen Music Fest, with Syzmon Goldberg, 56, Eudice Shapiro, 57-58 & Isidore Cohen, 59. *Pos:* First violin, Louisville Orch, 49-69, Ky Opera Orch, 53-69 & Brevard Fest Orch, 55; second violin, Aspen Fest Orch, 56-60. *Teaching:* Violin, Louisville Acad Music, 56- *Bibliog:* Agnes Crume (auth), Music Still Has a Home in the Old Speed Mansion, 7/20/69, Joan Kay (auth), Teaching Takes in More Than Music, 4/14/74 & Joan Kay (auth), Violinist Finds Place in New York Philharmonic, 10/13/77, Louisville Courier-J. *Mailing Add:* 2740 Frankfort Ave Louisville KY 40206

FRENI, MIRELLA
SOPRANO

b Modena, Italy, Feb 27, 35. *Rec Perf:* Don Carlo, TV, 83, The Marriage of Figaro, PBS & Madame Butterfly, film. *Roles:* Micaela in Carmen, Modena, Italy, 55; Nanetta in Falstaff, Covent Garden, 61 & La Scala, 62; Mimi in La Boheme, La Scala, 63, Metropolitan Opera, 65 & Lyr Opera Co Philadelphia; Amelia in Simon Boccanegra, Opera Co Philadelphia, 83; Elisabetta de Valois in Don Carlo, Metropolitan Opera, 83; Violetta in La Traviata & Marguerite in Faust, Covent Garden. *Pos:* Sop with major US & Europ opera co. *Awards:* Grammy Award, 64. *Bibliog:* Article, Opera News, 3/26/83. *Mailing Add:* c/o Herbert H Breslin Inc 119 W 57th St New York NY 10019

FRERICHS, DORIS (COULSTON)
TEACHER-COACH, COMPOSER

b Edgewater, NJ, Apr 20, 11. *Study:* Juilliard Sch Music, dipl piano, 31, artist degree, 34; artist pupil of Carl M Roeder. *Works:* From My Jewel Box, 79, A Royal Suite, 79, The Land of Tempo Marks, 79 & An Oriental Fantasy, 79, Willis Music Co. *Pos:* Nat dir music & art prog, People-To-People Int, 77-; mem nat music coun, Rep Nat Guild Piano Teachers, 80- *Teaching:* Fac mem piano, Juilliard Sch Music, 34-48 & Barrington Sch Girls, 39-42; coop fac, Teacher's Col, Columbia Univ, 48-55. *Awards:* Piano Guild Hall of Fame, Nat Guild Piano Teachers, 73; Award for Outstanding Serv to the Cause of Int Understanding, People-To-People Int, 78. *Mem:* Nat Guild Piano Teachers (adjudicator, 32-, nat chairman, 57- & nat musician leader for travel abroad, 76-); Juilliard Alumni Asn; Mu Phi Epsilon (vice pres, 50-52, nat artist chairman, 58-61). *Mailing Add:* 227 Claremont Rd Ridgewood NJ 07450

FREUND, DON (DONALD WAYNE)
COMPOSER, PIANO

b Pittsburgh, Pa, Nov 15, 47. *Study:* Aspen Music Sch, study comp with Darius Milhaud & Charles Jones, summer 68; Duquesne Univ, study comp with Joseph Willcox Jenkins, BM, 69; Eastman Sch Music, study comp with Samuel Adler & Warren Benson, study piano with Jose Echaniz, Walter Hendl & Barry Snyder, DMA, 72. *Works:* Piano Concerto, 70 & Clamavi, 74, Seesaw; The Bishop's Ghost, Southern Opera Theatre, 74; Papillons: String Quartet after R Schumann, Nat Symph String Quartet, 76; Cello Concerto, Memphis State Orch, 79; Triomusic, Verdehr Trio, 80; Passion with Tropes, Memphis State Col Fine Arts Collab, 83. *Teaching:* Prof, Memphis State Univ, 72- *Awards:* Winner, Int Soc Contemp Music Compt, League of Comp, 76; winner, Washington Int String Quartet Compt, 79; grant, Nat Endowment Arts, 79 & 82. *Mailing Add:* 5295 Keatswood Circle Memphis TN 38119

FREUNDLICH, LILLIAN
PIANO, TEACHER

b Cleveland, Ohio. *Study:* Oberlin Consv Music, BMus, 33; Juilliard Grad Sch Music, with Alexander Siloti, Josef & Rosina Lhevinne & Edward

Steuermann, 33-35. *Pos:* Nat perf career throughout US, 41- *Teaching:* Fac piano, Oberlin Consv Music, 41-42, Peabody Consv Music, 70- & Juilliard Sch Music, 77; master classes, wkshps & sem at col & univ, in US & Europe, currently; adjudicator piano compt. *Mem:* Pi Kappa Lambda; Music Teachers Nat Asn; Piano Teachers Cong. *Mailing Add:* 311 W 105th St New York NY 10025

FRICKER, PETER RACINE
COMPOSER, EDUCATOR

b London, England, Sept 5, 20. *Study:* Royal Col Music, 37-41; Univ Leeds, England, Hon DMus, 58. *Works:* Third String Quartet, 76; Fifth Symphony (organ & orch), 76; Sinfonia for Wind Instruments, 77; Anniversary for Piano, 77; Sonata for Two Pianos, 77; Serenade No 4 for Three Clarinets and Bass Clarinet, 77; Laudi Cancertati for Organ and Orchestra, 79. *Pos:* Comp, cond & music adminr, London, 46-64. *Teaching:* Dir music, Morley Col, London, 53-64; prof music, Royal Col Music, 55-64; Univ Calif, Santa Barbara, 64- *Awards:* Clements Prize, 48; Koussevitzky Award, 49; Collard Fel, 55. *Mem:* Hon mem, Royal Acad Music; Am Soc Univ Comp; Am Guild Organists; Am Music Ctr; Comp Guild Gt Brit (chmn, 55). *Publ:* Contribr to Listener, Soundings & Sunday Times. *Mailing Add:* Music Dept Univ Calif Santa Barbara CA 93106

FRIED, GREGORY MARTIN
CONDUCTOR, VIOLIN

b Omaha, Nebr. *Study:* Sch Music, Ind Univ, with Franco Gulli, BM(violin perf), 78; Lamont Sch Music, Univ Denver, MA(cond & violin perf), 80; Aspen Sch Music, studied cond with Paul Vermel & violin with Stephen Clapp. *Pos:* Concertmaster, Lamont Symph Orch, 78-80; first violin, Lamont String Quartet, 78-80; cond, Idaho State Civic Symph, 80-83. *Teaching:* Grad asst violin, Univ Denver, 78-80; instr violin & cond, Idaho State Univ, 80-83; asst prof violin & cond, Trinity Univ, 83- *Awards:* Wurlitzer Col Artist Award, Music Teachers Nat Asn, 80. *Mem:* Col Music Soc; Am String Teachers Asn; Am Symph Orch League; Cond Guild Am Symph Orch League; Music Educr Nat Conf. *Mailing Add:* Music Dept Trinity Univ 715 Stadium Dr San Antonio TX 78284

FRIED, JOEL ETHAN
CONDUCTOR, TEACHER

b Berkeley, Calif, Apr 22, 54. *Study:* Univ Southern Calif, BM(piano), 73, MM(piano), 75, DMA(opera), 79. *Pos:* Asst cond, New York City Opera, 80-82, Heidelberg Castle Fest, WGer, 81-; studienleiter, Saarländisches Staatstheater, WGer, 83- *Awards:* Second Prize, Am Cond Compt, 78. *Mem:* Cent Opera Serv; Am Symph Orch League. *Mailing Add:* Saarländisches Staatstheater Postfach 410 6600 Saarbrücken 3 Germany, Federal Republic of

FRIEDBERG, RUTH CRANE
PIANO, WRITER

b Atlantic City, NJ, July 2, 28. *Study:* Studied piano with Frank Sheridan, 47-49 & Vladimir Sokoloff, 49-54; Barnard Col, BA, 49; Univ NC, MA, 61. *Rec Perf:* Art Song in America, Vol I, 66 & Vol II, 73, Duke Univ Press. *Pos:* Keyboard artist, San Antonio Symph, 76- *Teaching:* Instr music, Duke Univ, 61-68, asst prof, 72-75; asst prof, San Antonio Col, 68-71; lectr, Incarnate Word Col, 77- *Bibliog:* Richard Sjoersdma (auth), review, Bulletin Nat Asn Teachers Singing, spring 82. *Mem:* Am Musicol Soc; Col Music Soc; Nat Asn Teachers Singing; Ars Lyrica. *Interests:* American art song, its composers and poets; twentieth century songs and piano music. *Publ:* Auth, The Solo Piano Works of Arnold Schoenberg, Music Rev, 62; The Songs of John Duke, Bulletin Nat Asn Teachers Singing, 63; Articles on twentieth century composers, In: New Grove Dict of Music & Musicians, 80; American Art Song and American Poetry, Vol I, 81 & Vol II, 83, Scarecrow Press. *Mailing Add:* 105 Elm Spring Lane San Antonio TX 78231

FRIEDE, STEPHANIE
MEZZO-SOPRANO

Roles: Cenerentola in La Cenerentola, Tex Opera Theatre, 81; Marcella in The Madman of San Domingo, Pa Opera Theatre, 82; Marton in Ma Tante Aurore, 82 & Cupid in Orpheus in the Underworld, 83, Asolo Opera; Rosina in The Barber of Seville, Colo Opera Fest, 83; Nicklausse in The Tales of Hoffmann, 83 & Rosina in The Barber of Seville, 83, Houston Grand Opera. *Pos:* Ms with various opera co in US. *Mailing Add:* c/o Lew & Benson Moreau-Neret Inc 204 W 10th St New York NY 10014

FRIEDMAN, CAROLE G
PIANO, ADMINISTRATOR

b Philadelphia, Pa, Mar 23, 45. *Study:* Skidmore Col, BA, 74; Goddard Col, MA, 80; studied with David Sokoloff, Emil Danenberg, Vivian Fine & Edna Golandsky. *Pos:* Dir, Music by Women, 76-77, New Perf Conv, 76-79 & Concerted Effort Inc, 78- *Teaching:* Piano & arts mgt, Russell Sage Col, 79-82; lectr music hist, State Univ NY, Albany, 83- *Awards:* Nat Endowment for Humanities, 80-82. *Mem:* Music Teachers Nat Asn; Int Cong Women Musicians. *Mailing Add:* 666 Madison Ave Albany NY 12208

FRIEDMAN, ERICK
VIOLIN, EDUCATOR

Study: Violin with Galamian, Milstein & Heifetz. *Rec Perf:* On RCA. *Pos:* Soloist, New York Phil, Chicago Symph, Boston Symph, London Symph, Berlin Phil & others; performer, Hollywood Bowl, Robin Hood Dell & Blossom Fest. *Teaching:* Mem fac violin, Manhattan Sch Music, 75- *Mailing Add:* c/o Int Artist Mgt 111 W 57th St New York NY 10019

FRIEDMAN, JAY KENNETH
TROMBONE

b Chicago, Ill, Apr 11, 39. *Study:* Roosevelt Univ, 58-61; Yale Univ, 61. *Pos:* First trombone, Fla Symph Orch, 60-62 & Chicago Symph Orch, 62-; rep, First Int Brass Symposium, Switzerland, 76. *Teaching:* Prof trombone, Ind Univ, 70. *Mem:* Int Trombone Asn. *Mailing Add:* Triple J Farm 2122 Maple Rd Joliet IL 60432

FRIEDMAN, VIKTOR
PIANO, EDUCATOR

Moscow, USSR, Sept 23, 38; US citizen. *Study:* Cent Musical Sch, Moscow State Consv, USSR, BMus, 57, MMus, 62, PhD(piano), 65. *Rec Perf:* Solo recital, Phillips Collection Concert Hall, 75 & Nat Radio Broadcast, 75-76; Piano Sonatas (Beethoven, Liszt, Haydn & Prokofiev), Orion Master Rec, Inc, 77. *Pos:* Solo pianist, Moscow State Mgt, USSR, 62-74. *Teaching:* Prof piano, Moscow State Consv, USSR, 65-74; pianist in res, Bryn Mawr Col, 77-81; lectr, Temple Univ, 80-81. *Mailing Add:* 2101 Chestnut St Apt 622 Philadelphia PA 19103

FRIES, ROBERT MCMILLAN
EDUCATOR, FRENCH HORN

b Ann Arbor, Mich, Jan 11, 32. *Study:* Curtis Inst, studied with Mason Jones, BMus(perf), 57; Univ Mich, MMus(lit), 66. *Pos:* Horn, US Marine Band, 53-56; third horn, New Orleans Phil, 57-59; prin horn, Detroit Symph, 59-63; co-prin horn, Philadelphia Orch, 63-65. *Teaching:* Horn, Wayne State Univ, 61-63 & Temple Univ, 63-65; prof horn & chamber music, Oberlin Col, 65- *Mailing Add:* Music Dept Oberlin Col Oberlin OH 44074

FRIGON, CHRIS DARWIN
COMPOSER, EDUCATOR

b Barre, Vt, July 26, 49. *Study:* Adamant Music Sch, dipl, 71; Sch Arts, Boston Univ, BM, 71, MM, 77. *Works:* Five Preludes (free-bass accordion), 73 & Spectra (piano, four hands & accessories), 75, Richard Romiti; Dosolfitela (flute & piano), Matthew Marvuglio, 77; The Dawn (alto flute & harp), Matthew Marvuglio & Faye Seeman, 79; The Camellias (solo flute), Matthew Marvuglio, 81. *Pos:* Music consult, Mich Coun Arts, 79. *Teaching:* Instr theory & comp, Adamant Music Sch, 69-71, comp in res, 74-75; dept assoc theory & comp, Berklee Col Music, 74- *Awards:* First Prize, Int Comp Compt, Am Accordion Musicol Soc, 73. *Mem:* Leschetizky Asn; Behre Piano Assoc. *Publ:* Co-ed (with Camille Roman), The Beatles: A Musical Evolution, 83, Claude Debussy and Twentieth Century Music, 83, Sonny Rollins: The Journey of a Jazzman, 83, Black Women Composers: A Genesis, 83 & Carlos Chavez: Mexico's Modern-Day Orpheus, 83, Twayne Publ. *Mailing Add:* 316 Webster St Marshfield MA 02050

FRISCH, RICHARD S
BARITONE, EDUCATOR

b Brooklyn, NY, May 9, 33. *Study:* Juilliard Sch Music, with Marion Freschl, BA, 61, MS, 62; Marlboro Music Fest, with Martial Singher. *Rec Perf:* Abraham and Isaac (Stravinsky), Columbia Rec, 70; In Praise of Diplomacy (Trimble), Comp Rec Inc, 72; Psalm 39 (Wuorinen), Bridge Rec, 82. *Pos:* Baritone, Group Contemp Music, 70- & Theater Chamber Players Kennedy Ctr, 72-80; appearances with New York Phil, San Francisco Symph, Denver Symph, Speculum Musicae, Contemp Chamber Ens & New Music Consort, 72-82. *Teaching:* Prof voice, Bennington Col, 73-79; assoc prof, C W Post Col, 74-76. *Awards:* Teaching Fel, Brooklyn Col, 63. *Mailing Add:* 825 West End Ave New York NY 10025

FRISCH, WALTER MILLER
EDUCATOR, WRITER

b New York, NY, Feb 26, 51. *Study:* Yale Univ, BA, 73; Univ Calif, Berkeley, MA, 77, PhD, 81. *Teaching:* Asst prof music, Columbia Univ, 82- *Mem:* Am Musicol Soc. *Interests:* Music of the 19th and 20th centuries, especially Austrian tradition: Schubert, Brahms, Schoenberg. *Publ:* Auth, Schubert, Storia Universale Della Music, Mondadori, 82; Brahms, Developing Variation, and the Schoenberg Critical Tradition, 19th Century Music, 82; Brahms and the Principle of Developing Variation, Univ Calif Press, 83. *Mailing Add:* Dept Music Columbia Univ New York NY 10027

FRITSCHEL, JAMES ERWIN
COMPOSER, EDUCATOR

b Greeley, Colo, May 13, 29. *Study:* Wartburg Col, BME, 51; Colo State Univ, Greeley, MA, 54; State Univ Iowa, Iowa City, PhD, 60; Dana Col, DFA, 82. *Works:* Be Still, Walton, 76; Psalm 19, comn by SW Baptist Col, Bolivar, Mo, 80; Everyone Sang, comn by Paul Hill Chorale, Washington, DC, 80; The Heavenly Dance, Lawson-Gould, 81; Trumpets of Zion, comn & perf by Plymouth Congregational Church, Des Moines, 81; Earth Magician, Music 70, 83. *Teaching:* Instr, pub sch, Nebr & Wyo, 54-58; prof music & choral dir, Wartburg Col, 59- *Awards:* Winner Comp Cont, Women's Choir, Columbia Col, SC, 76; McCowen Award, Iowa Choral Dir, 77. *Mem:* Am Choral Dir Asn; Music Educr Nat Conf; Am Asn Univ Comp. *Mailing Add:* 915 Harlington Pl Waverly IA 50677

FRITTER, PRISCILLA
FLUTE

b Cleveland, Ohio, June 9, 46. *Study:* Consv Music, Oberlin Col, studied flute with Robert Willoughby, BMus, 68. *Pos:* Prin flutist, Nat Ballet Co Orch, 68-72; second flutist, Kennedy Ctr Opera House Orch, 72-79, prin flutist, 79-; prin flutist, Wolf Trap Farm Park, Vienna, Va, 79- & New World Players Chamber Orch, 81- *Mailing Add:* 2206 Richland Place Silver Spring MD 20910

FRITZE, GREGORY PAUL
COMPOSER, TUBA
b Allentown, Pa, Jan 14, 54. *Study:* Boston Consv Music, BMus, 76; Sch Music, Ind Univ, MMus, 79. *Works:* Quintet for Brass, Minuteman Music Co, 77; Vertigo, 81 & Pacman Gets Caught, 82, Musica Nova Publ; Octubafest Suite, Harvey Phillips, 82; Jupiter Effect, Musica Nova Publ, 83. *Pos:* Fest coordr, New England Tuba Fest, Boston, 80-; music dept consult, Brown Univ, 82- *Teaching:* Assoc instr, Ind Univ, Bloomington, 77-78; instr comp, Berklee Col Music, 79- *Awards:* Walt Disney Fel, 77; grant, Meet the Comp Inc, 83. *Mem:* Col Music Soc; Am Fedn Musicians; Tubists Universal Brotherhood Asn; Am Soc Univ Comp. *Publ:* Auth, The 2nd Annual New England Tuba Festival, 81 & The 3rd Annual New England Tuba Festival, 82, Tubists Universal Brotherhood Asn J. *Mailing Add:* Berklee Col Music 1140 Boylston St Boston MA 02215

FROCK, GEORGE ALBERT
PERCUSSION, EDUCATOR
b Danville, Ill, July 16, 38. *Study:* Univ Ill, BS(music), 60; Univ Kans, MMus, 63. *Works:* Three Asiatic Dances, 66, Concertino for Marimba, 66, Variations for Flute & Perc, 66, Fanfare for Double Trio, 69 & Seven Solo Dances (timpani), 76, Southern Music Co; Two Structures, 79. *Rec Perf:* Music of Karl Korte, 75 & Extended Saxophone, 81, CRI. *Pos:* Timpanist, Memphis Symph Orch, 63-66, Austin Symph Orch, 66-; perc & asst dir bands, Memphis State Univ, 63-66. *Teaching:* Prof perc, Univ Tex, Austin, 66- *Mem:* Percussive Arts Soc; Tex Music Educr; Int Musicians; Tex Bandmasters; Pi Kappa Lamda; Phi Mu Alpha. *Mailing Add:* 6609 Jamaica Ct Austin TX 18731

FROMM, HERBERT
COMPOSER, ORGAN
b Kitzingen, Germany, Feb 23, 05; US citizen. *Study:* State Acad Music, Munich, MMus, 30; Lesley Col, DLit. *Works:* Many works publ by Boosey and Hawkes, Carl Fischer, E C Schirmer & Transcontinental Music. *Pos:* Music dir & organist, Temple Beth Zion, Buffalo, NY, 37-41 & Temple Israel, Boston, 41-73. *Awards:* Award, Ernest Bloch Soc, 45. *Publ:* Auth, The Key of See, Travel Journals, Plowshare Press, 66; Seven Pockets, Dorrance, 77; On Jewish Music, Bloch, New York, 78. *Mailing Add:* 100 Marion St Brookline MA 02146

FROMM, PAUL
PATRON, ADMINISTRATOR
b Kitzingen, Germany, Sept 28, 06; nat US. *Study:* New England Consv Music, Hon DMus; Univ Cincinnati, Hon MusD. *Pos:* Founder & dir, Fromm Music Found, Harvard Univ, 52-; dir, Am Music Ctr; emer overseer, Boston Symph Orch, currently. *Awards:* Ill Gov Award Arts, 78. *Mailing Add:* 1028 W Van Buren St Chicago IL 60607

FROMME, ARNOLD
EDUCATOR, TROMBONE
b Brooklyn, NY, Dec 2, 25. *Study:* Juilliard Sch Music, dipl, 48; Fontainbleu Sch; Berkshire Music Ctr, 43-49; Paris Consv, Accecit, 50; Manhattan Sch Music, BM, 48, MM, 69; NY Univ, PhD, 80. *Works:* Three Studies for Brass Quintet, Gen Music Publ, 69. *Rec Perf:* Eight New York Pro Music Albums, Decca, 61-66; Eight American Brass Quintet, Nonesuch, Desto, CRI, SABA, WGermany, Folkways, Serenus & Mercury, 63-70; Music of M Feldman, CRI, 68. *Pos:* Prin trombonist, Ballet Russe, 48-49, Ballet Theatre, 48-51, New York City Ballet, 50-51, RCA Victor Symph, 50-66, Columbia Rec Symph, 50-66, San Antonio Symph, 52-57, Symph Air, 54-62, New York Phil, 58-69, Little Orch Soc & others; sackbut performer, New York Pro Musica, 59-71; trombonist & founder, Am Brass Quintet, New York, 59-70. *Teaching:* Adj mem fac low brass, Univ Tex, Austin, 54-57; adj mem fac trombone, Bronx Community Col, 68-; adj mem fac music, Fairleigh Dickinson Univ, 70-78; asst prof, Jersey City State Col, 70- *Awards:* Martha Baird Rockefeller Found Grant, 67. *Mem:* Int Trombone Asn; Am Fedn Musicians; founder, Am Musical Instrm Soc (vpres, 72-75); Col Music Soc; Am Musicol Soc. *Interests:* Posthumous polychoral music of Giovanni Gabrieli; historic performance techniques on brass instruments. *Publ:* Auth, Chamber Brass: Neglected in Education, Music J, 69; Performance Technique on Brass Instruments During the XVIIth Century, J Res Music Educ, 72; Evidence & Conjectures on Early Trombone Technique, Int Trombone Asn Newsletter, 73. *Mailing Add:* 4 Janet Ln Berkeley Heights NJ 07922

FROST, THOMAS
ADMINISTRATOR, WRITER
b Vienna, Austria, Mar 7, 25. *Study:* Sch Music, Yale Univ, studied comp & theory with Paul Hindemith, 48-52. *Works:* Little Suite for Orchestra (after Bach), 63, Sheep May Safely Graze (after Bach), 64, Art Thou With Me (after Bach), 66 & Little Suite No 2 for Orchestra (after Bach), 70, Broude Music Publ. *Rec Perf:* To a Wild Rose (McDowell), Vera (film), Canyon Productions, 82. *Pos:* Producer & exec producer, CBS Masterworks Rec, 59-72, dir artists & repertoire, 72-80; mem bd dir, Young Audiences, 79-, Meet the Comp, 79 & Busoni Found, 81-; pres, Thomas Frost Prod, New York, NY, 80-; mem, Mayor's Adv Coun on Music Indust, 81- *Awards:* Gold Record Award, Rec Indust Asn Am, 63; Grammys, Nat Acad Rec Arts & Sci, 62, 65, 71 & 77. *Publ:* Auth, Bruno Walter's Last Recording Sessions, 63, How To Record A Symphony and Keep Your Cool, 69 & Stravinsky—Steel and Irony, 71, Stereo; Prince Igor (Igor Stravinsky), Esquire, 72; Pablo Casals Remembered (So Beautiful—A Simple Little Flower), High Fidelity, 74. *Mailing Add:* 350 Central Park W New York NY 10025

FRÜHBECK DE BURGOS, RAFAEL
CONDUCTOR & MUSIC DIRECTOR
b Burgos, Spain, Sept 15, 33. *Study:* Bilbao & Madrid Consv, dipl(violin, piano & comp), 44-52; Hochschule Musik, Munich, dipl(cond), 57-58. *Rec Perf:* Complete Works of Manuel De Falla, EMI, Decca & Spanish Columbia; Carmina Burana (Orff), Carmen (Bizet), Elias (Mendelssohn), Paullis (Mendelssohn), Requiem (Mozart) & Creation (Haydn), EMI. *Pos:* Music dir, Bilbao Symph Orch, 58-62, Nat Symph Orch, Madrid, 62-77 & Montreal Symph Orch, 74-76; gen musik dir, Dusseldorfer Symph, 65-74; prin guest cond, Nat Symph, Washington, DC, 80-; prin cond, Yomiuri Symph Orch, currently. *Awards:* Richard Strauss Prize, Munich, 59. *Rep:* Shaw Concts 1995 Broadway New York NY 10023. *Mailing Add:* 13 Reyes Magos Madrid Spain

FRUMKIN, LYDIA
EDUCATOR, PIANOFORTE
Study: Leningrad Consv, dipl(piano & pedagogy), 71. *Pos:* Performer solo & chamber music, US & USSR. *Teaching:* Instr accmp & chamber music perf, Leningrad Consv, 71-73; assoc prof pianoforte, Consv Music, Oberlin Col, 75- *Mailing Add:* Consv Music Oberlin Col Oberlin OH 44074

FRY, STEPHEN MICHAEL
LIBRARIAN
b Boise, Idaho, Jan 5, 41. *Study:* Univ Calif, Riverside, BA(music), 64; Claremont Grad Sch, MA(music), 65; Univ Southern Calif, MSLS, 69. *Pos:* Music librn, Univ Calif, Riverside, 67-70 & Ind Univ Pa, 70-72; assoc music librn, Northwestern Univ, 72-75; head music librn, Univ Calif, Los Angeles, 75- *Teaching:* Music, Calif Inst Women, Frontera, 66-67; assoc prof music, Ind Univ Pa, 70-72. *Mem:* Music Libr Asn (mem bd dir, 79-81); Int Assoc Music Libr; Am Musicol Soc; Guild Carillonneurs NAm. *Interests:* Music periodicals, bibliography & philately. *Publ:* Ed, The Life and Times of Sadakichi Hartmann, Univ Libr, Univ Calif, Riverside, 70; auth, Directory of Special Music Collections in Southern California, Southern Calif Chap Music Libr Asn, 70; Manual for cataloging and classifying bell materials, Anton Brees Libr, 74; New Reference Books (column), Notes, 75-79; Music Literature & Reference Books, In: A Basic Music Library, Am Libr Asn & Music Libr Asn, 79. *Mailing Add:* 4249 Coolidge Ave Los Angeles CA 90066

FUCHS, JOSEPH
VIOLIN, EDUCATOR
b New York, NY. *Study:* Inst Musical Art, studied violin with Franz Kneisel, dipl; Univ Maine, Hon DFA, 72. *Pos:* Soloist, Prades Fest, 53 & 54; recitalist, US, Europe, South Am & Japan. *Teaching:* Mem fac violin, Juilliard Sch, 46- *Awards:* Ford Found Award, 57, 58 & 59; Distinguished Artist-Teacher Award, Am String Teachers Asn, 70. *Mailing Add:* c/o Beverly Wright Artists 400 E 52nd St New York NY 10022

FUCHS, LILLIAN F
VIOLA, COMPOSER
b New York, NY, Nov 18, 10. *Study:* Inst Musical Art, studied viola with Louis Svecenski & Franz Kneisel & comp with Percy Goetschius, dipl. *Works:* Twelve Caprices (viola); Sixteen Fantasy Etudes (viola); Fifteen Characteristic Studies (viola); Sonata Pastorale (viola solo); Three Pieces (violin solo); Jota (violin & piano). *Rec Perf:* Six Solo Suites (Bach), Duos for Viola & Violin (Mozart), & others, Decca & Columbia Rec. *Pos:* Co-founder & mem, Perole String Quartet; soloist with major orchs in US & Europe; mem, Budapest String Quartet. *Teaching:* Prof viola, Manhattan Sch Music, 62- & Juilliard Sch, 71-; soloist & instr, Aspen Music Fest & Banff Ctr, Can. *Awards:* Artist-Teacher Award, Am String Teachers Asn, 79; Isaac Newton Seligman Prizes; Morris Loeb Mem Prize. *Mailing Add:* 186 Pinehurst Ave New York NY 10033

FUCHS, PETER PAUL
CONDUCTOR & MUSIC DIRECTOR, COMPOSER
b Vienna, Austria, Oct 30, 16; US citizen. *Study:* Acad Music, Vienna, cond dipl, 36; private study with Karl Weigl, Leonie Gombrich. *Works:* Partita Ricercata, Baroque Ens Ind Univ, 74; Polyphony for Orchestra, Baton Rouge Symph, 76; Eight Inventions for Winds, Chamber Ens, Eastern Music Fest, 78; Fantasy for Violins & Piano, Fredell Lack & Albert Hirsch, 82; Concertino for Piano and Orchestra, perf by Constance Knox Carroll with Greensboro Symph, 83. *Pos:* Music staff mem, Metropolitan Opera, 40-50; dir opera symph, La State Univ, 50-76; music dir, Baton Rouge Symph, 60-76 & Greensboro Symph, 75- *Teaching:* Instr opera, orch & cond, La State Univ, 50-76 & Univ NC, Greensboro, 77- *Awards:* Ford Found Grant, 54-55. *Mem:* Nat Opera Asn; Cent Opera Serv ; Am Symph Orch League. *Publ:* Auth, The Psychology of Conducting, MCA Music, 69; The Music Theater of Walter Felsenstein, W W Norton, 75. *Mailing Add:* 720 Lipscomb Rd Greensboro NC 27410

FUENTEALBA, VICTOR W
ADMINISTRATOR
b Baltimore, Md, Sept 1, 22. *Study:* Sch Law, Univ Md, JD, 50. *Pos:* Mem, Int Exec Bd, Am Fedn Musicians, 67-70, vpres, 70-78, pres, 78-; pres, Nat Music Coun, New York, 81- *Mailing Add:* 32nd Floor 1500 Broadway New York NY 10036

FUJIWARA, HAMAO
VIOLIN, TEACHER-COACH
Kamakura, Kanagawa, Japan, July 12, 47. *Study:* Toho Gakuen Sch Music, dipl, 68; Juilliard Sch, postgrad dipl, 75. *Rec Perf:* Violin Concerto No 2 (Bartok), Deutsche Grammophon, 71; Stradivari Concert I, 71 & Concert II,

72, Japan Columbia; Beethoven #7 Faure #1 Sonata, 72 & Debussy, Ravel Sonata, 73, Musica Magna, Belgium. *Pos:* Soloist & concertmaster, Musica Aeterna Orch, New York, 70-; violinist, Sea Cliff Chamber Players, New York, 75- *Teaching:* Fac mem violin & chamber music, Univ Maine, summers 75-79, Alfled Univ, summers 80- & violin, Juilliard Sch, 78- *Awards:* Silver Medal, Paganin; Int Violin Compt, Italy, 68 & Queen Elizabeth Int Compt, Belgium, 71. *Rep:* Judd Concert Bureau 155 W 68th St New York NY 10023. *Mailing Add:* 171 W 57th St New York NY 10019

FULD, JAMES J
WRITER

b New York, NY, Feb 16, 16. *Study:* Harvard Col, AB, 37. *Pos:* Writer, currently. *Mem:* Int Musical Soc; Am Musical Soc; Music Libr Asn; Sonneck Soc. *Interests:* First printings of well-known classical, popular and folk music; original libretti, music programs and posters. *Publ:* Auth, First Editions of Stephen C Foster, Musical Am, 57; The Book of World-Famous Music, Crown, 66; coauth, 18th-Century American Secular Music Manuscripts, Music Libr Asn, 80; auth, The Book of World-Famous Libretti, Pendragon, 83. *Mailing Add:* Rm 2100 300 Park Ave New York NY 10022

FULKERSON, GREGORY (LOCKE)
VIOLIN, EDUCATOR

b Iowa City, Iowa, May 9, 50. *Study:* Oberlin Col, BA, 71; Consv Music, Oberlin Col, BMus, MM, 71; Juilliard Sch Music, MM, 77. *Rec Perf:* Cadenzas & Variations, New World Rec, 82. *Pos:* Violinist, Cleveland Orch, 71-74; first violin, Audubon Quartet, 74-75; violin & viola, New York New Music Ens, 76-79; concertmaster, Honolulu Symph, 79-81. *Teaching:* Vis assoc prof violin, Ind Univ, Bloomington, 81-82 & Oberlin Col, 82- *Awards:* First Prize, Int Am Music Compt, Rockefeller Found, 80. *Rep:* TRM Mgt Inc 527 Madison Ave New York NY 10022. *Mailing Add:* 37 Elmwood Oberlin OH 44074

FULKERSON, JAMES ORVILLE
COMPOSER, TROMBONE

b Streator, Ill, July 2, 45. *Study:* Ill Wesleyan Univ, BM, 66; Univ Ill, Urbana, MM, 68. *Works:* Behind Closed Doors, Ed Mod, 72; Suite for Solo Cello, Seesaw Music, 78; Concerto for Amplified Cello, Victorian Time Machine, 78; Stations, Regions and Clouds IV, Ed Mod, 79; String Quartet #3, Dartington Ens & Second Stride Co, 82; Put Your Foot Down, Charlie, Dartington Dance Alliance, 83; 40 works publ by Seesaw Music & Ed Mod. *Rec Perf:* Antiphonies IV (Poised), Nonesuch Rec, 69; Signals (Elliott Schwartz), Deutsche Grammophon, 71; Music for Brass Instruments II, 79 & Co-Ordinative Systems #10 (James Fulkerson), 79, Irida Rec; To Be Alone (Barry Conyngham), Move Rec, Australia, 79; Soundweb (John Rimmer), Kiwi Rec, 79 & 82; A Trombone Piece (Phill Niblock), India Navigation, 82. *Pos:* Comp & trombonist, Ctr Creative & Perf Arts, Buffalo, 69-72; comp in res, Berlin, Germany, 73 & Victorian Col Arts, Melbourne, 82- *Teaching:* Instr trombone & comp, Dartington Col, 82- *Mailing Add:* Pump Cottage Hillcroft Staverton, Totnes Devon TQ9 6AL England United Kingdom

FULLER, ALBERT
HARPSICHORD, EDUCATOR

b Washington, DC. *Study:* Georgetown Univ, studied organ with Paul Callaway; Peabody Consv Music, solfege with Renee Longy, hist & comp with Nicholas Nabokov & organ with Ernest White; Pius X Sch Liturgical Music; Johns Hopkins Univ, BS; Yale Univ, MM, 54: studied theory with Paul Hindemith & harpsichord with Ralph Kirkpatrick. *Rec Perf:* On Cambridge, Decca & Nonesuch. *Pos:* Founder & dir, Aston Magna Found Music, currently; recitalist chamber music throughout US & Europe. *Teaching:* Mem fac music, Cath Univ Am, 49-51; mem fac harpsichord & chamber music, Juilliard Sch, 64- *Mailing Add:* Juilliard Sch Lincoln Ctr New York NY 10023

FULLER, JEANNE WEAVER
COMPOSER, EDUCATOR

b Regina, Sask, Oct 23, 17. *Study:* Pomona Col, BA, 37; Calif State Univ MA, 64; Univ Southern Calif, with Halsey Stevens. *Works:* Fugue for Woodwinds; Exsultate Justi (Psalm 32)(chorus); Maggy and Milly and Molly and May (women's voices); Now Come Near Ourselves Than We)(chorus); The Praise of Christmas (chorus); When Young Hearts Break (song); Jeux Aux Douze Tons (piano, four hands). *Teaching:* From instr to assoc prof, El Camino Col, 65- *Mailing Add:* 7025 Hedgewood Dr Rancho Palos Verdes CA 90274

FULLER, STEPHAN B
LIBRARIAN

b Loup City, Nebr, Aug 29, 52. *Study:* Univ Nebr, Lincoln, BME, 70; Simmons Col, MS, 75. *Pos:* Music librn, Hilles Libr, Harvard Univ, 79- *Mailing Add:* Hilles Libr Morse Music Libr 59 Shepherd St Cambridge MA 02138

FULTON, LAURAN ANN
SOPRANO

b Canyon, Tex, Mar 20, 55. *Study:* Juilliard Sch, studied voice with Richard Torigi, 79-80; Univ Mich, voice with John McCollum, BM, 76, MM(voice), 79; Aspen Music Fest, voice with Adele Addison, 75-79. *Roles:* Rossignol in Le Rossignol, 79 & Lisette in La Rondine, 79, Am Opera Ctr; Olympia in The Tales of Hoffmann, Pittsburgh Opera, 81; Norina in Don Pasquale, Long Beach Grand Opera, 81; Blonda in The Abduction from the Seraglio, Lake George Opera Fest, 81. *Awards:* Nat Asn Teachers Singing Scholar, 76; Winner, Detroit Grand Opera Auditions, 78. *Mem:* Am Guild Musical Artists. *Mailing Add:* c/o Columbia Artists 165 W 57th St New York NY 10019

FULTON, WILLIAM KENNETH
MUSIC DIRECTOR, EDUCATOR

b Pampa, Tex, Dec 9, 41. *Study:* NTex State Univ, BME, 64; Tex Tech Univ, MM, 68, PhD(fine arts), 81. *Teaching:* Choral dir, Perryton High Sch, Tex, 66-68 & Coronado High Sch, Tex, 68-75; chmn undergrad choral music educ, Univ Ill, Champaign, 75-76; assoc prof cond & choral lit, SWTex State Univ, 76- *Mem:* Am Choral Dir Asn; Tex Choral Dir Asn (vpres, 71-73, pres, 73-75); Tex Music Educr Asn (mem state bd dir, 73-75). *Interests:* Choral music of William Walton: performance editions of Gesualdo sacred motets, Monteverdi madrigals. *Publ:* Auth, William Walton's Choral Style: A Birthday Offering, Am Choral Dir Asn J, 82; ed, Ave Maria dulcissima ... Don Carlo Gesualdo, Jenson Music Publ, 82. *Mailing Add:* 107 Chaparral San Marcos TX 78666

FUNK, ERIC DOUGLAS
COMPOSER, EDUCATOR

b Deer Lodge, Mont, Sept 28, 49. *Study:* Portland State Univ, BA(comp), 71, BA(arts & lett), 71, MST(comp), 78; study with Tomas Svoboda, Sandor Veress & K Penderecki. *Works:* Rhayader, comn by Portland Ballet Co & Ore Arts Comn, 78; Emily, comn by Ore Symph Orch, 79; Dance Concertare, comn by NW Repty Dance Co, 80; Sonata for Guitar & Piano, comn by Metropolitan Arts Comn-Comp Ens, 81; The Circle Within (trumpet), comn by Fred Sautter, 81; Sanctuary (opera), Meryle Press, 82. *Pos:* Performer, Comp Ens, currently. *Teaching:* Instr theory & comp, Portland State Univ, 78-80 & Portland Community Col, 79- *Awards:* Ruth Lorraine Close Fel, 73; Ore Arts Comn Individual Fel, 78; comp cont winner, NW Repty Dance Co, 79. *Bibliog:* Robert Lindstrom (auth), article, NW Mag, Oregonian, 6/24/79; Marilyn Tucker (auth), article, San Francisco Examiner-Chronicle, 2/17/80 & 2/25/80; Cliff Waits (auth), article, Multnomah Monthly Mag, 3/83. *Mem:* Comp Forum; ASCAP. *Rep:* Meryle Press PO Box 17575 Portland OR 97217. *Mailing Add:* 1529 N Simpson Portland OR 97217

FUNKHOUSER, FREDERICK A
VIOLA

b Dayton, Ohio, Apr 23, 05. *Study:* Studied with Andrie Touret, France & Otakar Sevcik, Czechoslovakia, 27-28; Oberlin Col, BA & BMus, 29. *Pos:* Violist, Cleveland Orch, 29-, asst prin viola, 43- *Mailing Add:* 4046 Silsby Rd Cleveland OH 44118

FURMAN, JAMES
COMPOSER, EDUCATOR

b Louisville, Ky, Jan 23, 37. *Study:* Univ Louisville, BMusEd, 58, MMus(theory & comp), 65; Brandeis Univ, studied comp with Irving Fine, Arthur Berger & Harold Shapero, 62-64; Harvard Univ, 66. *Works:* Four Little Foxes (SATB), Oxford Univ Press, 71; Hehlehlooyuh (SATB), Hinshaw Music Inc, 78; The Quiet Life (SATB), 79, Come, Thou Long Expected Jesus (SATB), 80, Glory to God in the Highest (SATB), 81 & Jupiter Shall Emerge (in prep), Music 70-80 Inc; I Have a Dream (symphonic oratorio), Dorn Publ (in prep). *Rec Perf:* College Choirs at Christmas, Classics Rec Libr, 77. *Pos:* Choral dir, British Broadcasting Co, 66 & Am Symph Orch, 74. *Teaching:* Prof music, Western Conn State Col, 65-83. *Awards:* Award of Merit Distinguished Service Music, Nat Fedn Music Clubs, 65-67. *Bibliog:* Effie Gardner (auth), An Analysis of the Technique and Style of Selected Black American Composers of Contemporary Music, Mich State Univ, 78. *Interests:* Black gospel music. *Mailing Add:* 512 S 22nd St Louisville KY 40211

FUSCHI, OLEGNA
PIANO, EDUCATOR

b New York, NY. *Study:* Juilliard Sch Music, studied with Rosina Lhevinne, dipl, 59; studied with Arthur Rubinstein & Giomar Novaes. *Pos:* Soloist with maj orchs in US, South Am, Europe & USSR. *Teaching:* Mem fac, NC Sch Arts, 65-68; teacher master classes, Siena, Italy, 67; Mem fac piano, Juilliard Sch, 72-73, adminr, Pre-Col Div, 75, dir, 76- *Awards:* Josef Lhevinne Mem Award; Prix de Jacques Durand, Paris; Winner, Conct Artists Guild, 59. *Mailing Add:* c/o Gurtman & Murtha Assoc 162 W 56th St New York NY 10019

FUSNER, HENRY SHIRLEY
EDUCATOR, ORGAN

b Parkersburg, WVa, June 16, 23. *Study:* Juilliard Sch, BS, 44, MS, 45; Sch Sacred Music, Union Theol Sem, NY, SMD, 51. *Works:* Several sacred choral works, H W Gray Co. *Pos:* Organist & choirmaster, Church of Covenant, Cleveland, Ohio, 56-70 & First Presby Church, Nashville, Tenn, 70- *Teaching:* Organ & harmony, Juilliard Sch, 43-48; head organ & church music dept, Cleveland Inst Music, 59-71; head theory dept, Blair Sch Music, Vanderbilt Univ, 73- *Publ:* Auth, Leo Sowerby—Forgotten or Forsaken, 82 & Brahms and the Vo Beckerath Family, 83, Am Organist. *Mailing Add:* 824 Nanearle Pl Nashville TN 37220

FYFE, PETER MCNEELY
ORGAN, MUSIC DIRECTOR

b Covington, Tenn, Aug 23, 23. *Study:* Am Consv Music, BM, 47, MM, 49; Union Theol Sem, MSM, 51. *Pos:* Organ & choirmaster, St Michael's Episcopal Church, New York, 51-57, Trinity Parish, NY, 57-59 & Christ Church Episcopal, Nashville, 59-; asst choirmaster, Gen Theol Sem, 51-59; organist for performances by Cantata Singers, New York, 52-55, 56 & 57. *Teaching:* Instr organ, Blair Sch Music, Vanderbilt Univ, 64- *Mem:* Am Guild Organists (state chmn, 75-81); Asn Anglican Musicians; Am Choral Found; Am Choral Dir Asn; Church Music Conf (dir prov IV, 78-79). *Mailing Add:* 2814 Blair Blvd Nashville TN 37212

G

GAAB, THOMAS ANTHONY
GUITAR, TEACHER
b Fresno, Calif, Jan 17, 53. *Study:* Calif State Univ, Fresno, BA, 75; Univ Southern Calif, studied class guitar with Jonathan Marcus & Pepe Romero, MMus, 77, DMA, 80. *Pos:* Conct guitarist, currently. *Teaching:* Asst guitar studies, 77-80; instr, El Camino Col, 77-83 & Calif State Univ, Dominguez Hills, 82-83; lectr class guitar, Univ Southern Calif, 78-82; lectr, Univ Tex, San Antonio, 83- *Rep:* Marianne Marshall 34-66th Pl Long Beach Calif, 90803. *Mailing Add:* 3500 Oakgate Dr San Antonio TX 78230

GABEL, GERALD L
COMPOSER, TEACHER
b Dodge City, Kans, Apr 5, 50. *Study:* Univ Northern Iowa, studied comp with Peter Michaelides, BM, 74; Univ Calif, San Diego, studied comp with Roger Reynolds, Pauline Oliveros & Robert Erickson, MA, 77, PhD, 83. *Works:* Nocturnes for Piano, 75, Three Songs, 75, The Wicked Walk on Every Side, 77 & The Labyrinth, 77, Seesaw Music Corp; Saraphs for Three Bassoons, perf by Dr Robert Olson, 79; Songs and Epitaphs of the Golden Sun, perf by Atomic Cafe Ens, 79; Flight: Fantasy for Woodwind Quintet, perf by Aulos Quintet, 80. *Pos:* Dir, La Jolla Civic-Univ Chorus, 80-81. *Teaching:* Assoc music & cond, Univ Calif, San Diego, 77-81; chmn theory, comp & hist depts, Music & Arts Inst San Francisco, 81-82. *Awards:* Comp grant, Nat Endowment Arts, 79. *Mem:* ASCAP; Am Soc Univ Comp; Col Music Soc; Gustav Mahler Soc. *Mailing Add:* 9262-B Regents Rd La Jolla CA 92037

GABER, GEORGE
PERCUSSION, EDUCATOR
b New York, NY, Feb 24, 16. *Study:* New Sch Social Res; Queens Col, City Univ New York; Juilliard Sch Music; Manhattan Sch Music; Escolo Imperio & Federacao Escolas, Sao Paulo, Brazil, Hon Dipl Merit. *Rec Perf:* On MGM, RCA, Columbia, Decca, Capitol, Crest, Laurel & Urania. *Pos:* Mem, Ballet Russe Monte Carlo Orch, Goldman Band, Pittsburgh Symph, Los Angeles Phil, NBC-TV, ABC-TV & Aspen, Baltimore & NY World's Fair festivals; performer, cond & judge, Australia, Can, Brazil, Japan, China & others. *Teaching:* Distinguished prof music, Ind Univ, Bloomington, currently. *Mem:* Am Fedn Musicians; Am Asn Univ Prof; Bohemians; Col Music Soc. *Mailing Add:* 1909 Arden Dr Bloomington IN 47401

GABLE, FREDERICK KENT
EDUCATOR, CONDUCTOR & MUSIC DIRECTOR
b Konnarock, Va, Oct 17, 38. *Study:* Carthage Col, Ill, BA(music), 60; Univ Iowa, MA(musicol), 63, PhD(musicol). *Teaching:* Asst prof, Ariz State Univ, 63-67 & Univ Wis, Milwaukee, 67-68; from asst to prof, Univ Calif, Riverside, 68- *Interests:* Vocal music of Hieronymus Praetorius; early baroque performance practice; Collegium Musicum. *Publ:* Ed, Hieronymus Praetorius, Polychoral Motets (two vol), A-R Ed, 74; auth, Two Songs in Shakespeare's Twelfth Night, Am Recorder, 78; Possibilities for Mean-Tone Temperament on Viols, J Viola da Gamba Soc, 79; Hieronymus Praetorius, Jacob I and Jacob II Praetorius, In: New Grove Dict of Music & Musicians, 80. *Mailing Add:* Music Dept Univ Calif Riverside CA 92521

GABORA, GAELYNE
SOPRANO, TEACHER
b Regina, Sask. *Study:* Vienna State Acad Music, MMus; studied with Helena Issep, London, Erik Werba, Vienna, Bernard Diamant, Montreal & Pierre Bernac, Paris. *Rec Perf:* Gaelyne Gabora Sings Lieder, Discophon Barcelona, 76; Music for Voice and Violin With Taras Gabora Violin, Can Broadcasting Corp; Gaelyne Gabora With Borodin String Quartet, Melodia, 78; Gaelyne Gabora Sings Bach, Melodia Moscow, 78; Mozart Arias, 79 & Gaelyne Gabora Sings Lieder by Schubert, Brahms, Wolf, Strauss, 79, Melodia; Gaelyne Gabora Sings Cantatas of Handel & Purcell with Le Group Baroque de Montreal, CBC Int Rec. *Teaching:* Prof voice & vocal chamber music, St Louis Consv, 81- *Rep:* Sheldon Soffer Mgt Inc 130 W 56th St New York NY 10019. *Mailing Add:* 4481 Westminister Pl St Louis MO 63108

GABORA, TERAS
EDUCATOR, VIOLIN
b Yellow Creek, Saskatchewan, Can, Apr 23, 32. *Study:* Vienna State Acad Music, MMus, 56; studied with Yuri Yankelevich, Szymon Goldberg & Henryk Szeryng. *Rec Perf:* Danzi-Trio Concertante in F with Barry Tuckwell, Horn, 76, Music for Voice and Violin with Gaelyne Gabora, Soprano, 77; Schumann-Britten, 77, Le Groupe Baroque de Montreal, 79 & Bartok-Brahms, Can Broadcasting Corp Rec. *Pos:* Found & dir, Gabora String Quartet, 62-68 & Groupe Baroque Montreal, 68-80. *Teaching:* Prof violin, McGill Univ, Montreal, 59-64 & Consv Musique, Montreal, 64-80; prof & head string dept, St Louis Consv Music, 80- *Awards:* Austrian State Prize, Ministry of Cult Affairs, Vienna, Austria, 56. *Mailing Add:* 4481 Westminister Pl St Louis MO 63108

GABRIEL, ARNOLD D
CONDUCTOR, EDUCATOR
b Cortland, NY, May 31, 25. *Study:* Ithaca Col, BS(music educ), 50, MS(music educ), 53. *Rec Perf:* Ann Am Bandmasters Conv Concts, Crest Rec, 71-83. *Pos:* Commander & cond, US Air Force Band, 64-; mem adv bd, Sch Musician, Dir & Teacher, 70-, Instrumentalist Mag, 80- & Music Dept, Ithaca Col, 80-; guest cond, US col & univ. *Awards:* Distinguished Serv Music Award, Kappa Kappa Psi, 77; Gill Robb Wilson Award, Air Force Asn, 81; Acad Wind & Perc Arts Fel, Nat Band Asn, 82. *Mem:* Am Bandmasters Asn (pres, 80-81); Nat Band Asn; Nat Asn Am Comp & Cond; Phi Mu Alpha Sinfonia. *Mailing Add:* US Air Force Band Bolling AFB Washington DC 20332

GABURO, KENNETH LOUIS
COMPOSER
b Somerville, NJ, July 5, 26. *Study:* Eastman Sch Music, with Bernard Rogers, BM, MM, 49; Consv Santa Cecilia, Rome, with Goffredo Petrassi; Univ Ill, with Burrill Philips, DMA, 62; studied with Hubert Kessler & Herbert Elwell. *Works:* Shapes and Sounds, 60; The Hydrogen Jukebox (electronic score), 63; Lingua I-IV (six hour theatre piece), 65-70; Antiphony IV: Poised (piccolo, trombone, double bass & electronics), 66; Inside (quartet for double bass), 69; Mouthpiece (sextet for solo trumpet & slides), 70; Antiphony VI: Cogito (string quartet, slides & tape), 71. *Pos:* Comp at large & dir, New Music Choral Ens IV, currently; ed & founder, Ligua Press, currently. *Teaching:* Mem fac, Kent State Univ, 49-50 & McNeese State Col, 50-54; prof music, Univ Ill, Urbana-Champaign, 56-68, assoc fel, Inst Advanced Study, formerly; prof, Univ Calif, San Diego, 68-75, artist in res, Ctr Music Experiment, 72-75. *Awards:* UNESCO Award, 62; Guggenheim Grant, 67; Thorne Found Grant, 68. *Mailing Add:* PO Box 481 Ramona CA 92065

GACH, JAY ANTHONY
COMPOSER
b New York, NY, Mar 9, 50. *Study:* State Univ NY, Stony Brook, PhD, 82. *Works:* Caged Bird Improvisations, 77; Street Music #1, 80, Pro Patria Mori, 81; Street Music #2, 82, Membra 1—Anthem for Doomed Youth, 82 & Membra 11—What Passing Bells ..., 82, Am Comp Alliance. *Awards:* Bruno Maderna Compt Fel, Berkshire Music Fest, 79; Comp Conf & Chamber Music Ctr Fel, 82; Rome Prize Comp Fel, Am Acad Rome, 83-84. *Mem:* Am Comp Alliance; BMI; Am Music Ctr; Col Music Soc. *Mailing Add:* 35 Vinton St Long Beach NY 11561

GADEHOLT, IRENE
VIOLIN
b Buffalo, NY, Aug 1, 58. *Study:* Violin study with Raphael Spiro, 79-; Portland State Univ, BA, 81. *Pos:* Concertmaster & soloist, Portland Youth Phil, 73-79; first violin, Ore Symph Orch, 79- & Orpheus String Quartet, 80- *Mailing Add:* 2340 SW Elmhurst Ave Beaverton OR 97005

GAEDDERT, WILLIAM KENNETH
EDUCATOR, BARITONE
b Colby, Kans, Nov 27, 38. *Study:* Bethany Col, Kans, BMus, 60; Ill Wesleyan Univ, MMus, 64; Univ Iowa, with Herald Stark, MFA, 73, PhD, 76. *Teaching:* Instr music, Lebanon Pub Sch, Kans, 60-62; dir choral music, United Township High Sch, East Moline, Ill, 64-66; instr voice, Northwestern State Univ, La, 66-70; assoc prof, Baker Univ, 74- *Mem:* Phi Mu Alpha Sinfonia (pres, Iowa City Alumni Chap, 72-74); Nat Asn Teachers Singing (pres, Kansas City area chap, 79-81); Col Music Soc; Pi Kappa Lambda. *Publ:* Coauth, Art Song in the United States: An Annotated Bibliography, 76 & 78, Nat Asn Teachers Singing. *Mailing Add:* RR No 3 Baldwin City KS 66006

GAINACOPULOS, KAY THOMAS
MUSIC DIRECTOR, CLARINET
b Fond Du Lae, Wis, July 24, 39. *Study:* Lawrence Col, BM(music educ), 61; Peabody Consv, MM, 62; Ind Univ, DM, 77. *Pos:* Prin clarinetist, Honolulu Symph, 66-68. *Teaching:* Chairperson, Dept Music, Whitman Col, 74-79 & Col St Teresa, 79-80; assoc prof music, Univ Wis, Eau Claire, 80-82; assoc prof & dir bands, Univ Wis, Oshkosh, 82- *Mem:* Asn Conct Bands; Col Music Soc; Am Fedn Musicians; Int Clarinet Soc. *Mailing Add:* Music Dept Univ Wis Oshkosh WI 54901

GALANTE, JANE HOHFELD
PIANO, EDUCATOR
b San Francisco, Calif, Feb 14, 24. *Study:* Vassar Col, BA, 44; Univ Calif, Berkeley, MA, 49; piano study with Mieczyslaw Horszowski & Alexander Libermann. *Pos:* Founder & dir, Comp Forum, San Francisco, 46-56; guest pianist, Budapest, Griller, Hollywood, San Francisco, Honolulu & Kronos String Quartets, 51-81; tours, Amerika Haus, Ger, 52 & 54; trustee, May T Morrison Chamber Music Ctr, San Francisco State Univ, 56-; leader, Repty Ens, 63-70; mem, Lyra Ens, currently. *Teaching:* Instr, Univ Calif, 49-52 & Mills Col, Oakland, Calif, 50-52. *Mem:* Womens Musicians Club San Francisco; Am Fedn Musicians. *Mailing Add:* 8 Sea Cliff Ave San Francisco CA 94121

GALARDI, SUSAN M
ADMINISTRATOR, EDITOR
b Pittsburgh, Pa. *Study:* Carnegie-Mellon Univ, BA, 78; Dalcroze Sch Music; Manhattan Sch Music, studied voice with Ellen Repp. *Pos:* Asst ed, Musical Am Mag, New York, 80-; managing ed, Musical Am Dir Perf Arts, 80- *Publ:* Auth, What Pittsburgh Thinks of Previn, 78 & Singers in Limbo, 78, Pittsburgh Mag; Training of the Voice, Carnegie Mag, 78. *Mailing Add:* 169 W 81 St New York NY 10024

GALAS, DIAMANDA ANGELIKI
COMPOSER, SOPRANO
b Aug 29, 55. *Study:* Studied voice with Frank Kelley; studied piano with Ilana Mysior. *Works:* Wild Women With Steak Knives (solo voice), 80-; Tragouthia apo to Aima Exoun Fonos (solo voice & tape), 80; Litanies of Satan (solo voice, live signal processing & tape), 81; Panoptikon (solo voice, live signal processing & quadrophonic tape), 82. *Rec Perf:* Litanies of Satan & Wild Women with Steak Knives, Rough Trade Rec, London, 81. *Roles:* Contralto soloist in N'Shima, Brooklyn Phil, 81; sop soloist, Djamila, Brooklyn Phil Meet Moderns Ser. *Pos:* Sop soloist, US & Cent Am. *Bibliog:* Gregory Sandow (auth), Songs from the Blood, Village Voice, 82; Merle Ginsberg (auth), Diamanda Galas, New Music Express, London, 82; John Howell (auth), Diamanda Galas, Art Forum, 83. *Publ:* Auth, Intravenal Song, Perspectives Music, 83. *Mailing Add:* 2425 1st Ave San Diego CA 92101

GALBRAITH, NANCY RIDDLE
COMPOSER, PIANO
b Pittsburgh, Pa, Jan 27, 51. *Study:* Ohio Univ, BMus(comp), 72; WVa Univ, MMus, 75; studied comp with Leonardo Balada & piano with Nelson Whitaker. *Works:* Fantasy for Piano, perf by Nancy Galbraith, 80-82; Dance, comn by Renaissance City Woodwind Quintet, 82; Nonet, Carnegie-Mellon Univ Contemp Ens, 83. *Pos:* Dir music, Christ Lutheran Church, Pittsburgh, Pa, 78- *Mem:* Pittsburgh Alliance Comp (secy & bd dir, 79-). *Mailing Add:* 830 Reserve St Pittsburgh PA 15209

GALBRAITH, ROBERT SINCLAIR
BARITONE
b St Cloud, Minn, Nov 10, 52. *Study:* Apprentice, Minn Opera & Houston Grand Opera; Univ Wis; studied vocal with Dr Hermanus Baer & Norma Newton. *Roles:* Valentine in Faust, Lake George Opera, 81; Papageno in Die Zauberflöte, 81, Falke in Die Fledermaus, 82 & Belcore in L'Elisir d'amore, 82, Houston Grand Opera; Figaro in Barber of Seville, Minn Opera, 82; Sharpless in Madame Butterfly, Spoleto Fest, 83; Schaunard, Chicago Lyric Opera, 83. *Awards:* Grant, Nat Opera Inst, 80; winner, Bruce Yarnell Compt for Baritones, 82 & Eleanor Steber Compt, 82. *Bibliog:* Jay Cocks & Anne Constable (auth), Have Arias, Will Travel, Time Mag, 2/16/81; Annalyn Swan (auth), Two Wandering Minstrals, Newsweek, 6/6/83. *Mem:* Am Guild Musical Artists. *Rep:* Columbia Artists Mgt 165 W 57th St New York NY 10019. *Mailing Add:* 536 Ft Washington Ave #3B New York NY 10033

GALIMIR, FELIX
VIOLIN, EDUCATOR
b Vienna, Austria, May 20, 10; nat US. *Study:* Vienna Consv Music, dipl, 28; studied with Carl Flesch, 29-30. *Rec Perf:* Ravel String Quartet; rec on Columbia, Decca, Period, Vox, RCA Victor, Marlboro Rec & Vanguard Rec. *Pos:* Founder, Galimir String Quartet, Vienna, 29, reorganized, NY, 38-; conct performer throughout Europe & Near East, 29-36 & US, 38-; mem, NBC Symph Orch, 39-53; concertmaster, Symph Air, formerly. *Teaching:* Mem fac, Marlboro Music Sch & Fest, summers 53-, City Col, City Univ New York, 54- & Curtis Inst Music, 72-; mem fac chamber music, Juilliard Sch, 62-; mem fac violin, Mannes Col Music, 76- *Awards:* Grand Prix Disque, Paris, 37. *Mailing Add:* Juilliard Sch Lincoln Ctr New York NY 10023

GALKIN, ELLIOTT WASHINGTON
ADMINISTRATOR, EDUCATOR
b Brooklyn, NY, Feb 22, 21. *Study:* Brooklyn Col, BA, 43; Conservatoire Nat Superieure Paris, Dipl, 49; L'Ecole Normale Musique Paris, cert, 49; Cornell Univ, MA, 55, PhD, 60. *Pos:* Music critic & editor, Baltimore Sun, 62-77; dir, Peabody Consv, John Hopkins Univ, 77-82. *Teaching:* From asst prof to prof & chmn, Goucher Col, 56-77; prof, Peabody Consv, Johns Hopkins Univ, 57-77 & 83- *Awards:* Fulbright Grant to Vienna, 55; Deems Taylor Award, ASCAP, 72 & 75; George Peabody Medal, Peabody Consv, John Hopkins Univ, 82. *Mem:* Musicians Asn Baltimore, 56-; Music Critics Asn (pres, 74-77). *Interests:* Hist of cond; history music in Am; criticism. *Publ:* Translr, Karl Stumpf, Schule fur Viola d'Amore, Oesterreichischer Bundesverlag, 56; contribr, New Grove Dict of Music & Musicians, 6th ed; articles in Am, English & French journals. *Rep:* Byers & Schwalbe 1 Fifth Ave New York NY 10003. *Mailing Add:* 2211 Midridge Rd Timonium MD 21093

GALLAHER, CHRISTOPHER S
COMPOSER, EDUCATOR
b Ashland, Ky, June 10, 40. *Study:* Ind Univ, with Bernhard Heiden & Juan Orrego-Salas, MM, PhD. *Works:* 4 Pieces for Clarinet and Cello, 71; Trio for Flute, Cello, Piano; Music for Brass Quartet; Music for Cello, 72; Saxophone Quartet, 73; 3 Fragments (contralto, flute & three clarinets), 73; Variations (orch), 73; and 40 other publ works. *Teaching:* Mem fac, Frostburg State Col, 66-70; prof music, Morehead State Univ, 72- *Mailing Add:* Hill N Dale Estates Morehead KY 40351

GALLO, PAUL ARTHUR
CLARINET, CONDUCTOR & MUSIC DIRECTOR
b Bronx, NY, July 27, 44. *Study:* Juilliard Sch, BM, 68, MM, 72. *Pos:* Clarinetist, Clarion Concts Orch, 72- & Mostly Mozart Orch, New York, 76-; music dir, Northeastern Arts Ens, 76-; cond, Hudson Valley Phil, 79-81. *Teaching:* Instr clarinet, Vassar Col, 73-83. *Bibliog:* Donal Henahan (auth), How About the Basset Horn, New York Times, 5/29/83. *Mem:* ClariNetwork Int Inc. *Rep:* Peggy Friedman 11 Worth St New York NY 10013. *Mailing Add:* 27 Schyler Dr Poughkeepsie NY 12603

GALTERIO, LOU
DIRECTOR—OPERA, TEACHER-COACH
b Nov 29, 42. *Study:* Marquette Univ, Milwaukee, Wis. *Pos:* Dir opera prod, Manhattan Sch Music, 77-; stage dir, New York City Opera, Santa Fe Opera, Opera Theatre St Louis, Washington Opera Co, Houston Grand Opera, Tulsa Opera Co & others. *Teaching:* Instr perf tech, Wolf Trap Opera, summers 75-77 & Santa Fe Opera, 78 & 79; private coach, currently. *Mailing Add:* 50 Commerce St New York NY 10014

GALVANY, MARISA
SOPRANO
b Paterson, NJ, June 19, 38. *Study:* Studied with Armen Boyajian. *Rec Perf:* Macbeth (film), CBC, 73. *Roles:* Tosca in Tosca, Seattle Opera, 69; sop in Maria Stuarda, New York City Opera, 72; Norma in Norma, Metropolitan Opera, 79; Giorgetta in Il Tabarro, 83; Santuzza in Cavalleria Rusticana; Fiordiligi in Cosi fan tutte; Donna Anna in Don Giovanni; and many others. *Pos:* Res mem, New York City Opera; sop with major opera co in US, Mex & Europe. *Mem:* Am Guild Musical Artists; Can Actors Equity. *Mailing Add:* c/o Herbert Barrett Mgt 1860 Broadway New York NY 10023

GALWAY, JAMES
FLUTE, CONDUCTOR
b Belfast, Northern Ireland, Dec 8, 39. *Study:* Royal Col Music; Guildhall Sch Music; Consv Nat Superieur de Musique, Paris; Open Univ, Hon MA, 79; Queen's Univ, Belfast, Hon MusD, 79; New England Consv Music, Hon MusD, 80. *Rec Perf:* Works by C P E Bach, J S Bach, Beethoven, Franck, Mozart, Prokofiev, Rodrigo, Reicha, Telemann & Vivaldi. *Pos:* Flute, Wind Band Royal Shakespeare Theatre, Stratford on Avon, Sadler's Wells Orch, Royal Opera House Orch & BBC Symph Orch; prin flute, London Symph Orch & Royal Phil Orch; prin solo flute, Berlin Phil Orch, 69-75; solo flute, US, 78-; cond & soloist, Tex Chamber Orch. *Awards:* Order Brit Empire, 78; Musician of Yr, Inc Soc Musicians, 79; Grand Prix du Disque. *Publ:* Auth, James Galway: An Autobiography, 78. *Mailing Add:* c/o ICM Artists 40 W 57th St New York NY 10019

GAMBERONI, KATHRYN (LYNNE)
SOPRANO
b Butler, Pa, June 11, 55. *Study:* Col Consv Music, Univ Cincinnati, BM, 77. *Roles:* Kathie in Student Prince, Lake George Opera Fest, 80; Gerda in Fennimore and Gerda, Opera Theatre of St Louis, 81; Barbarina in Nozze Di Figaro, 82 & Mascha in Pique Dame, 82, San Francisco Opera; Blonde in Abduction from the Seraglio, Washington Opera, 83; Kitty in Anna Karenina, 83 & Adina in Elixir of Love, 83, Los Angeles Opera Theatre, 83. *Awards:* Grant, Rockefeller Found, 82; First Place, San Francisco Opera Auditions, 82; Career Develop Award, Nat Opera Inst, 83. *Mailing Add:* c/o Columbia Artists 165 W 57 St New York NY 10019

GAMBULOS, ELENA (ELLEN GAMBULOS-CODY)
SOPRANO
b Oklahoma City, Okla, Oct 30, 53. *Study:* Consv Music, Oberlin Col, BM 75; Boston Consv, MM, 78. *Rec Perf:* Love Can Be Still, Northeastern Press, 81. *Roles:* Rosina in Il Barbiere di Siviglia, New Cleveland Opera, 75; Giulietta in I Capuleti e i Montecchi, Loeb Drama Ctr, 77; Princess in The Light Princess, Newport Opera Fest, 79; Mme Heartthrob in Impresario, Opera Co Boston, 79-80 & Greater Miami Opera Asn, 82; Sophie in Werther, Boston Lyr Opera, 81; Rosalinda in Die Fledermaus, Gold Coast Opera Co, 83. *Pos:* In-sch rep, Opera Co Boston, 79-81; White House perf, 79. *Awards:* First Place, Nat Virtuoso Compt, Fest Music Soc, Indianapolis, 75 & Young Artists Auditions, Okla Symph, 80. *Rep:* Joseph Rivera 251 W 98th St Suite 7B New York NY 10019. *Mailing Add:* 301 W 53rd St Apt 12-D New York NY 10019

GAMER, CARLTON E
COMPOSER, EDUCATOR
b Chicago, Ill, Feb 13, 29. *Study:* Northwestern Univ, BMus, 50; Boston Univ, MMus, 51; Princeton Univ, 59-60. *Works:* Fantasy for Orchestra, Colo Springs Symph, 55; Sonata (violin & piano), Sidney Harth & Max Lanner, 61; Sonata Breve, Max Lanner, 63; String Quartet, R & N Hudson, A Skernick & L Parnas, 64; Archaios, Colo Springs Symph, 68; Piano Raga Music, 74 & Quietly, with Feeling, 78, Perspectives New Music. *Teaching:* Prof music, Colo Col, 54-; vis lectr, Princeton Univ, 74, sr fel, 76, vis prof, 76 & 81. *Awards:* Fel, Asia Soc, 62-63; rec grant, Am Soc Univ Comp, 73. *Mem:* Am Soc Univ Comp (mem nat coun, 67-70); Perspectives New Music; Soc Music Theory (mem exec bd, 79-82); BMI; Am Musicol Soc. *Publ:* Auth, Some Combinational Resources of Equal Tempered Systems, J Music Theory, 67; Electronic Music, Encycl Britannica, 68; coauth, Fanfares for the Common Tone, Perspectives New Music, 76; auth, Sketch of a Foundation for Music Theory Today, Symposium, Col Music Soc, 77; ET Setera: Some Temperamental Speculations, Music Theory: Spec Topics, 81. *Mailing Add:* Dept Music Colo Col Colorado Springs CO 80903

GANSON, PAUL
BASSOON
b Detroit, Mich, Sept 18, 41. *Study:* Univ Mich, BA, 64, MA, 68. *Rec Perf:* Concerto No 1 in B flat (Mozart); Sonata for Bassoon and Cello. *Pos:* Bassoonist, City of Belfast Orch, Toledo Orch, Dallas Symph Orch & Detroit Symph Orch, currently; founding mem, Detroit Symph Youth Orch. *Teaching:* Dept Music, Univ Windsor, 74; vis lectr bassoon, Sch Music, Univ Mich, 75. *Mem:* Orch Hall Inc; charter mem, Int Double Reed Soc. *Publ:* Contribr to The Bulletin, Detroit Hist Soc. *Mailing Add:* Detroit Symph Orch Ford Auditorium Detroit MI 48226

GANSZ, GEORGE LEWIS
CONDUCTOR, COMPOSER
b Apr 5, 24; US citizen. *Study:* Temple Univ, BS, 48; Univ Pa, MS, 49; Trinity Col, London, licentiate & fel, 55; studied with Pierre Monteaux, Eugene Ormandy & E Power Biggs. *Works:* Music compositions publ by J Fischer & Shawnee Press. *Pos:* Music dir, Lehigh Univ, Rutgers Univ, Va Mil Inst, Armed Forces Radio Network, Europe; cond, CBS & NBC. *Teaching:* Music fac cond, comp & arr, Univ Pa, Rutgers Univ & Lehigh Univ. *Mem:* Am Symph Orch League; Col Band Dir Nat Asn; Am Guild Organists; Col Music Soc; Royal Can Col Organists. *Mailing Add:* One Ringneck Rd Lexington VA 24450

GANZ, ISABELLE MYRA
MEZZO-SOPRANO, TEACHER
b New York, NY. *Study:* Univ Rochester; Univ Chicago; Juilliard Sch Music, studied with Lotte Leonard; Univ Houston, BA, 64, MM, 68; Eastman Sch Music, studied with Jan De Gaetani, DMA, 80. *Rec Perf:* Judeo-Spanish Romanceros, Spectrum Rec, 82. *Roles:* The Wanderer in Siegfried, Houston Grand Opera, 70; Gloria, Midland-Odessa Symph & Choral, 72;

Scheherazade & Des Knaben Wunderhorn, NJ Symph, 74. *Teaching:* Instr music, Univ St Thomas, Tex, 71-78, Am Inst Musical Studies, Austria, 76-78, High Sch for Perf & Visual Arts, Tex, 78-81, Hebrew Arts Sch, NY, 81- & Manhattan Sch Music, NY, 82- *Awards:* Rockefeller Grant, 73. *Mem:* Am Guild Musical Artists; Nat Asn Teachers Singing; Am Fedn Musicians; Cambriata Soloists, Inc; Alhambra. *Interests:* Ethnomusicology—music of Sephardic Jews. *Mailing Add:* 777 West End Ave #12-B New York NY 10025

GARABEDIAN, ARMEN
VIOLIN, TEACHER
b Armenia, USSR, Jan 22, 49. *Study:* Tchaikowsky Music Sch, Armenia, USSR, dipl, 66; Yerevan State Consv, Armenia, USSR, dipl, 71. *Pos:* Accmp concertmaster, Honolulu Symph Orch, 74-; concertmaster, Hawaii Chamber Orch & Ballet Hawaii, 76- *Teaching:* Instr violin & chamber music, Punahou Music Sch, Hawaii, 78-82; lectr violin, Univ Hawaii, 80- *Awards:* First Prize, Allied Art Compt, Los Angeles, 74. *Mem:* Am Fedn Musicians. *Mailing Add:* 440 Lewers St #802 Honolulu HI 96815

GARABEDIAN, EDNA (EDNA MAE GARABEDIAN-DUGUIE)
MEZZO-SOPRANO, TEACHER-COACH
b Fresno, Calif, May 28, 39. *Study:* Lotte Lehmann Sch Music; Music Acad of West, 62; Fresno State Univ, BA(music), 79. *Roles:* Madelon in Andre Chenier, San Francisco Opera, 74; Olga in Eugene Onegin, Kassel Opera House, 79-83 & San Francisco Opera, 79-83; Eboli in Don Carlos, Nürnberg Opera House, 80; Amneris in Aida, Stuttgart Opera House, 80-83 & Frankfurt Opera House, 80-83; Carmen in Carmen, Hannover Opera House, 81; Santuzza in Caverlleria Rusticana, München Staats Theater, 81-83 & Stuttgart Opera House, 81-83; Azucena in Il Trovatore, Stuttgart Opera House, 83 & Kassel Opera House, 83. *Pos:* Solo artist in European opera houses. *Teaching:* Assoc prof voice & opera, Am Univ, 64-68, Bowling Green State Univ, Ill, 68-70 & Calif State Univ, San Francisco, 70-78. *Awards:* Weyerhauser Award, Metropolitan Opera, 61; Distinguished Artists Award, New York City, 69; Am Medalist, Fourth Int Tchaikovsky Compt, Moscow, 70. *Mailing Add:* 3338 Lowe Ave Fresno CA 93702

GARBOUSOVA, RAYA (RAYA GARBOUSOVA-BISS)
CELLO, EDUCATOR
Study: Tiflis Consv, grad. *Pos:* Soloist with maj symph orchs in Europe & US; duo performer with Mstislav Rostropovich. *Teaching:* Mem fac, Chicago Music Col, formerly, Aspen Music Fest, formerly, Temple Univ, formerly, State Univ NY, Stony Brook, formerly & Ind Univ, formerly; teacher master classes, Cleveland Inst Music; vis prof violoncello, Hartt Sch Music, 70-; lectr, Northern Ill Univ, currently. *Awards:* Am String Teachers Asn Artist Teaching Award, 78. *Mailing Add:* Hartt Sch Music 200 Bloomfield Ave West Hartford CT 06117

GARBUTT, MATTHEW
CONDUCTOR, TUBA
b Calif. *Study:* Calif State Univ Northridge; Calif Inst Arts, with Lawrence Christinsen; Music Acad West, with Maurice Abravanel, summers 68-72; Acad Music & Dramatic Arts, Vienna; Ind Univ. *Pos:* Prin tuba player, Israel Phil, formerly; mem, San Diego Symph, 77-, asst cond, 80-; mem, San Diego Opera Orch, 77- *Mailing Add:* PO Box 3175 San Diego CA 92103

GARDINER, ROBERT
ARTIST MANAGER
b Brooklyn, NY, June 18, 29. *Study:* Univ Miami, BA, 50. *Pos:* Advert mgr, Mills Music Publ, New York, 60-63; artist mgr, New York, 63-70 & 72-; sales rep, S Hurok, New York, 70-72. *Mailing Add:* 610 West End Ave New York NY 10024

GARDNER, KAY
COMPOSER, FLUTE & ALTO FLUTE
b Freeport, NY, Feb 8, 41. *Study:* Univ Mich, studied cond with Elizabeth Green & flute with Nelson Hauenstein, 58-61; State Univ NY, Stony Brook, studied flute with Samuel Baron, MMus, 74; studied cond with Antonia Brico, 77-79. *Works:* When We Made the Music, 77, Winter Night, Gibbous Moon (saga for 11 flutes), 80, Ladies Voices: A Short Opera (text by Gertrude Stein), 81, The Rising Sun, 81, The Rootwoman, 82 & The Seasons, 82, Sea Gnomes Music; Winter Night, Gibbous Moon (saga for 11 flutes), comn by Longy Sch, 80; Ladies Voices (opera; text by Gertrude Stein), comn by Southwest Chamber Opera, 81; The Rising Sun, comn by Blue Hill Chamber Ens, Maine, 81; The Rootwomen, comn by Kansas City Women's Chorus, 82; The Seasons, comn by Arcady Chamber Players, Blue Hill, Maine, 82; Mindful of You, comn by Eric & Carol Rosenblith, 83. *Rec Perf:* Mooncircles, 75 & Emerging, 78, Urana Rec; Women's Orchestral Works, Galaxia Rec, 81; Moods & Rituals: Meditations for Solo Flutes, Even Keel Rec, 81. *Pos:* Columnist, Colla Sinistra, Paid My Dues, J Women's Music, 75-80; music dir & producer, Urana Rec, 75-79; music dir & cond, Nat Women's Music Festivals, Champaign-Urbana, Ill & Bloomington Ind, 75-83; music dir & prin cond, New England Women's Symph, Boston, 78-80; producer, Women's Orch Works, Boston Galaxia Rec, 80. *Awards:* ASCAP Standard Awards, 80-83; Palestrina-Schoenberg Award, 82. *Bibliog:* Gayle Kimball (auth), Women's Form in Music, In: Women's Culture, Scarecrow Press, 80; Judith Zaimont (auth), Concert Music by Women, Greenwood Press, 82; Jane Weiner LePage (auth), Women Composers, Conductors & Musicians of the 20th Century, Vol II, Scarecrow Press, 83. *Mem:* ASCAP; Int League Women Comp; Nat Flute Asn; Nat Asn Comp. *Mailing Add:* PO Box 33 Stonington ME 04681

GARDNER, PATRICK G
CONDUCTOR, EDUCATOR
b Visalia, Calif, Jan 13, 53. *Study:* Calif State Univ, Hayward, BA, 76; Univ Tex, Austin, with Morris Beachy, MM, 79, DMA, 81. *Rec Perf:* Said the Cat (Katherine Shieve), 80 & Second Childhood Kevin Hanlon, 81, Folkways Rec. *Pos:* Asst prof, Sch Music, Univ Mich, Ann Arbor, 81-, dir Mens Glee Club & Univ Choir, 81- *Mem:* Intercollegiate Musical Coun Male Choral Singing (mem nat bd dir, currently); Am Choral Dir Asn. *Mailing Add:* Sch Music Univ Mich Ann Arbor MI 48109

GARDNER, RANDY CLYBURN
FRENCH HORN, TEACHER
b South Bend, Ind, June 2, 52. *Study:* Valparaiso Univ, 70-72; Ind Univ, BM, 74; studied with Christopher Leuba, summer 74. *Pos:* Second hornist, Miami Phil, Fla, 74-75 & Philadelphia, Orch, 75- *Teaching:* Instr horn, New Sch Music, 77- *Mem:* Pi Kappa Lambda; Int Horn Soc. *Mailing Add:* 138 E St Andrews Dr Mt Laurel NJ 08054

GARFIELD, BERNARD HOWARD
BASSOON, COMPOSER
b Brooklyn, NY, 1924. *Study:* NY Univ; Royal Col Music, London; Columbia Univ, MA(comp). *Works:* Woodwind trios, quartets, piano solos bassoon pieces & songs. *Rec Perf:* Recordings incl Mozart Bassoon Concerto, Weber Hungarian Rondo, Vivaldi La Notte Concerto, Hindemith Sonata & woodwind chamber music repertoire. *Pos:* Mem, New York Woodwind Quintet, 46-57; prin bassoon, Philadelphia Orch, currently; guest soloist, San Francisco Symph & Little Orch Soc New York, formerly; mem, Philadelphia Woodwind Quintet, currently. *Teaching:* Fac mem, Curtis Inst Music, 75-80; adj prof, Col Music, Temple Univ, currently. *Mailing Add:* 871 Wayside Lane Haddonfield NJ 08033

GARLAND, DONALD See MacInnis, M Donald

GARLAND, PETER ADAMS
COMPOSER, PUBLISHER
b Portland, Maine, Jan 27, 52. *Study:* Calif Inst Arts, BFA, 72. *Works:* The 3 Strange Angels, Soundings Press, 72-73; Hummingbird Songs, Pieces Mag, 74-76; Dreaming of Immortality in a Thatched Cottage, comn & perf by San Francisco Consv New Music Ens, 77; The Conquest of Mexico, comn by Betty Freeman, 78-80; Matachin Dances, Cold Blue Rec, 80-81. *Pos:* Ed & publ, Soundings Press, 71- *Bibliog:* Charles Amirkhanian (auth), New Music on the West Coast, Musical Am, 78. *Mem:* BMI. *Interests:* Am experimental music; Silvestre Revueltas; Paul Bowles, Conlon Nancarrow; regional Mexican musics. *Publ:* Ed, Conlon Nancarrow: Study No 37, 82, Americas, 82, Soundings 13, 82, Conlon Nancarrow: Study No 3, 83 & Paul Bowles: Selected Songs, 83, Soundings Press. *Mailing Add:* PO Box 8319 Santa Fe NM 87504

GARLICK, ANTONY
EDUCATOR, COMPOSER
b Sheffield, England, Dec 9, 27; US citizen. *Study:* Royal Col Music, London, 47-49; Santa Cecilia Consv Music, Rome, MM, 54; Univ Toronto, with Harvey Olnick & John Weinzweig, MM, 58; Univ Va, with Milos Velimirovic. *Works:* Canto (tone poem); Sinfonietta (brass choir); Sonata da Cahiesa (oboe & organ); Rhapsody (alto sax & piano); Pieces for Eight (clarinets); Masquerade (band); Mardi Gras (orch); and others. *Teaching:* Prof music, Wayne State Col, 60- *Awards:* Nat Endowment Humanities Award, 76. *Mem:* Col Music Soc; Am Musicol Soc; Nebr Educ Asn; Musical Heritage Soc. *Mailing Add:* 602 Main St Wayne NE 68787

GARLICK, NANCY BUCKINGHAM
CLARINET, EDUCATOR
b White Plains, NY, Feb 1, 46. *Study:* Crane Sch Music, State Univ NY, Potsdam, BS, 68; Manhattan Sch Music, MM, 70; Ecoles Americaines de Beaux Arts, Fontainebleu, France, 73. *Rec Perf:* Wooster Symphony Orchestra 1982, Olympus Music, 83. *Pos:* Assoc prin clarinet, Nat Orch Asn, New York, 69-70; prin clarinet, New Haven Symph Orch, Conn, 71-75; soloist, Boston Pops Orch, New Haven Coliseum, 73 & Wooster Trio, 81. *Teaching:* Assoc prof woodwinds & cond, Col Wooster, 75- *Awards:* Nat Orch Asn Accomplishment Award, 70. *Mem:* Am Fedn Musicians; Col Music Soc; Int Clarinet Soc; Nat Asn Col Wind & Perc Instr. *Mailing Add:* 1439 Jones Ave Wooster OH 44691

GARLINGTON, AUBREY S
EDUCATOR, WRITER
b Seymour, Tex, Mar 27, 31. *Study:* Baylor Univ, BM, 52; Univ Chicago, MA, 56; Univ Ill, PhD, 65. *Teaching:* Instr, Syracuse Univ, 61-65, asst prof 65-71 & assoc prof, 71-77; prof, Univ NC, Greensboro, 77- *Awards:* Summer Res Stipend, Nat Endowment Humanities, 80. *Mem:* Am Musicol Soc; Int Musicol Soc. *Interests:* Opera in Florence in the 19th-century; interdisciplinary studies in the humanities, 18th-19th centuries. *Publ:* Auth, Sources for Study of Italian Opera, 19th Century, Syracuse University Library, Syracuse Libr, 77; A W von Schlegel and the Creation of German Romantic Opera, J Am Musicol Soc, 77; German Romantic Opera and the Problem of Origins, 77, E T A Hoffman's Oper u Komponist, 79, MusQuart; Opera, MusQuart, 82 & In: New Grove Dict of Music in US (in prep). *Mailing Add:* Sch Music Univ NC Greensboro NC 27412

GAROFALO, ROBERT JOSEPH
EDUCATOR, CONDUCTOR

b Scranton, Pa, Jan 25, 39. *Study:* Eastman Sch Music, studied trombone with Emory Remington, 59-60; Mansfield State Col, BS(music ed), 60; Cath Univ Am, MM(applied music), PhD(musicol & theory), 69; studied cond with Lloyd Geisler & Dr Richard Lert. *Rec Perf:* Catholic University of America Wind Ensemble & US Army Herald Trumpets, 75, The Wind Band Music of Hindemith, Holst & Grainger, 76 & The Max Winkler Original Manuscript Compositions, 77, Golden Crest; Military Band Music of the Confederacy, Co Mil Historians, 79; Battle Cry of Freedom, 81. *Pos:* Founder & cond, Heritage Am, Inc, 78-; consult, Md State Dept Educ, Nat Coun Accreditation Teacher Educ, Music Educr Nat Conf & several cols & sch throughout East coast, currently. *Teaching:* Pallotti High Sch, Laurel, Md, 65-66, St Mark's Elem Sch, Hyattsville, Md, 68-, Campus Sch, Washington, DC, 69-74 & Bishop Ireton High Sch, Alexandria, Va, 73-76; instr music, Keene State Col, 66-67; vis prof, New England Consv Music, Syracuse Univ & Univ Lethbridge, Alberta, Can; prof music, Sch Music, Cath Univ Am, 67-, actg dean, 77. *Mem:* Music Educr Nat Conf; Col Band Dir Nat Asn; Nat Cath Bandmasters Asn; Coun Res Music Educ; Asn Concert Band Am, Inc. *Publ:* Auth, Blueprint For Band: A Guide To Teaching Comprehensive Musicianship Through Band Performance, J Weston Walch, 76; coauth (with Garwood Whaley & Michael Mark), Ensemble Sessions: A Unique Collection of Rounds, Canons & Catches for the Student Instrumentalist, 2 vols, 79 & (with Garwood Whaley), Creative Musicianship Band Series: Imaginative Arrangements for Young Musicians with Activities for Stimulating Creativity, 81, Heritage Music Press; auth, Heritage Americana: A Unique Collection of American Civil War Military Brass Band Music Edited for Modern Brass Ensemble, Kjos Music West, 81; The Art & Craft of Conducting: An Interview with Frederick Fennell, Music Educr J, 12/81; and many others. *Mailing Add:* 6306 Pontiac St College Park MD 20740

GARRETT, MARGO
PIANO, EDUCATOR

b Raleigh, NC, July 25, 49. *Study:* NC Sch Arts, BMus, 71; Juilliard Sch, 71-73; Manhattan Sch Music, MM, 74. *Rec Perf:* Chamber Music of Robert Ward, Musical Heritage Soc, 79; Fantasy Pieces for Clarinet & Piano (Niels Gade), 82 & Sonata for Clarinet & Piano (F Poulenc), 82, Orion; Vocal Music of Charles Griffes, Musical Heritage Soc, 83. *Pos:* Collaborative pianist & accmp to nat & int known instrumentalists & singers, 73- *Teaching:* Master classes at major cols & univ throughout US, 73-; vocal coach & teacher accmp, NC Sch Arts, 70-72, Manhattan Sch Music, 74- & Berkshire Music Ctr, summer 79-; lectr accmp & coaching, Westminster Choir Col, 83- *Mailing Add:* 140 W 58th St New York NY 10019

GARRIGUENC, PIERRE
COMPOSER, EDUCATOR

b Narbonne, France; US citizen. *Study:* Ithaca Col, BMus, 68; Eastman Sch Music, studied comp with Karel Husa & Samuel Adler, MMus, 71. *Works:* Reflections, Op 19, Music for Brass Ens, Stanford Univ, 79; Movement for Concert Band & Jazz Ensemble, Op 29, comn by SUCO Music, 79; Choral, Op 14 (symph), Oswego Col Orch, 81; Wedding Tryptych, Op 30, First United Methodist Church, Fulton, NY, 82; String Quartet, Op 31, New Times Quartet, La State Univ, 83; String Trio, Op 33, comn by Sheldon Trio, State Univ NY, 83; Quintet, Op 34 (wind instrm), comn by CSC, Stanford, Calif, 83. *Pos:* Comp & arr, CBS, Hollywood, 48-62. *Teaching:* Instr & perf, Col Beausejour, Narbonne, France, 62-65; prof theory & comp, State Univ NY, Oswego, 73- *Mem:* ASCAP; Am Soc Univ Comp. *Mailing Add:* 129 E 7th St Oswego NY 13126

GARRISS, PHYLLIS WEYER
EDUCATOR, VIOLIN

b Hastings, Nebr, Dec 25, 23. *Study:* Hastings Col, AB & BM, 45; Eastman Sch Music, MM, 48; Aspen Inst, with Roman Totenberg; studied with Andre de Ribaupierre, Switzerland. *Teaching:* Instr theory & violin, DePauw Univ, 48-51; vis prof violin, Ball State Univ, summer 51-53 & Cannon Music Camp, Appalachian State Univ, summer 71 & 78, Meadowmount; asst prof lit & violin, Meredith Col, 51- *Awards:* State Unit Award Distinguished Service, Am String Teachers Asn, 79. *Mem:* Am String Teachers Asn (secy, 50-54); Music Educr Nat Conf; Music Teachers Nat Asn; Int Viola Soc. *Mailing Add:* 3400 Merriman Ave Raleigh NC 27607

GARROTT, ALICE
MEZZO-SOPRANO

b Battle Ground, Ind, July 13, 48. *Study:* Ind Univ, Bloomington, BMus(voice), MMus(voice). *Rec Perf:* Christopher Columbus, Queen Isabella, 76. *Roles:* Princess Bolokonsky, Vera Boronnel in The Consul, 77 & Old Baroness in Vanessa, 77 & 78, PBS TV. *Pos:* Ms, PBS TV & Spoleto Fest, NC, 77 & 78. *Awards:* Metropolitan Opera NW Ind Regional Audition Winner, 71 & 72. *Mem:* Delta Omicron. *Mailing Add:* c/o Robert Lombardo Assoc 1 Harkness Plaza 61 W 62nd #6F New York NY 10023

GARSIDE, PATRICIA ANN
FLUTE, EDUCATOR

b Norfolk, Nebr, Feb 3, 34. *Study:* Los Angeles City Col, AA, 53; Calif State Univ, Los Angeles, BA(music), 72; studied flute with Roger Stevens, George Drexler & Julius Baker. *Rec Perf:* Pasadena Chamber Orchestra & Soloists, WIM Rec, 82. *Pos:* Prin flute, Pasadena Symph, 53-77 & Pasadena Chamber Orch, 77- *Teaching:* Lectr flute, Calif State Univ, Los Angeles, Univ Southern Calif, 75- & Calif State Univ, Fullerton, 78- *Mem:* Am Fedn Musicians. *Mailing Add:* 2147 Gardi St Bradbury CA 91010

GARVELMANN, DONALD M
WRITER, ADMINISTRATOR

Pos: Dir, Music Treasure Publ, New York, 68- *Mem:* Am Liszt Soc. *Interests:* Nineteenth-century piano music. *Publ:* Ed, Thirteen Transcriptions of Chopin's Minute Waltz, 69, Youthful and Early Works of Alexander and Julian Scriabin, 70 & Henry Herz: Variations on Non Piu Mesta from Rossini's La Cenerentola, 70, Music Treasure Publ; auth, Scriabin: Complete Piano Music, Vox Prod Inc, 74. *Mailing Add:* 620 Ft Washington Ave New York NY 10040

GARVEY, DAVID
PIANO, COACH

b Reading, Pa. *Study:* Juilliard Sch, dipl, grad dipl. *Rec Perf:* For RCA, Angel, Spectrum, Cambridge, Vox & others. *Pos:* Piano accmp, Itzhak Perlman, Jennie Tourel, Leontyne Price & others worldwide. *Teaching:* Pianist & coach, Ivan Galamian's Summer Sch Strings, Meadowmount, 52-; prof music, Univ Tex, Austin, 76-; instr master classes, Univ Ill, Drake Univ, NC Sch Arts & many others. *Awards:* Rosenberg Award; Damrosch Prize. *Mem:* Am Matthay Soc; New York Singing Teachers Asn. *Mailing Add:* 1800 Lavaca St Apt 610 Austin TX 78701

GARWOOD, MARGARET
COMPOSER, PIANO

b Haddonfield, NJ, Mar 22, 27. *Study:* Philadelphia Col Perf Arts, MM(comp), 75; studied comp with Miriam Gideon. *Works:* The Trojan Women (one act opera), 67; The Cliff's Edge (song cycle for voice & piano), perf in New York, Washington, DC, Munich & Toronto, 68; The Nightingale & the Rose (one act opera), Carl Fischer, 73; Rappaccini's Daughter (opera), perf by Pa Opera Theatre, 83; A Joyous Lament for a Gilly-Flower (clarinet & piano), Southern Music Co, 83; 6 Japanese Songs (song cycle for voice, clarinet & piano), Leonardo Rec, 83. *Teaching:* Lectr piano, Philadelphia Col Perf Arts, 53-69, Muhlenberg Col, 76 & 78 & Settlement Music Sch, 60-69. *Bibliog:* Cristine Ammer (auth), Unsung, Greenwood, 80. *Mem:* ASCAP; Am Music Ctr; Philadelphia Musical Soc. *Mailing Add:* 6056 N 10th St Philadelphia PA 19141

GAST, MICHAEL C
FRENCH HORN, EDUCATOR

b Inglewood, Calif, Dec 1, 57. *Study:* Curtis Inst Music, BM, 81; studied horn with Mason Jones, chamber music with John DeLancie, Glenn Dodson, Felix Galimer, Jorge Bolet, Oscar Schumsky & Anthony Gigliotti. *Pos:* Extra horn, Philadelphia Orch, 81; horn, Colo Phil, 81; prin horn, Jacksonville Symph Orch, 81-82, San Antonio Brass, 82 & Sun River Music Fest, 83; asst prin horn, Santa Fe Opera, 82 & San Antonio Symph, 82- *Teaching:* Adj prof horn, Jacksonville Univ, 81-82. *Mailing Add:* 343 E Kings Hwy #1 San Antonio TX 78212

GATELY, DAVID E
EDUCATOR, DIRECTOR—OPERA

b Portland, Ore, Jan 27, 53. *Study:* Oberlin Col, BA, 75. *Pos:* Stage dir, Conn Opera, 81, Hinsdale Opera Theater, Ill, 81, Memphis Opera, 82, Wichita Music Theater, 82, Tex Opera Theater, 82, Western Opera Theater, San Francisco, 82, Glimmerglass Opera, Cooperstown, 82, Houston Grand Opera, 83, Opera Comique, Paris, 83, Charlotte Opera, 83 & Dayton Opera, 83. *Teaching:* Dramatic coordr, Houston Opera Studio, 78-79; vis instr opera, Westminster Choir Col, Princeton, NJ, 81-83. *Rep:* Munro Artists Mgt 344 W 72nd #11M New York NY 10023. *Mailing Add:* 119 W 15th #6RE New York NY 10011

GATES, CRAWFORD
MUSIC DIRECTOR, COMPOSER

b San Francisco, Calif, Dec 29, 21. *Study:* San Jose State Col, BA, 44; Brigham Young Univ, MA, 48; Eastman Sch Music, PhD, 54. *Works:* Promised Valley (folk opera), comn by State Utah, 47; Symphony No 2 (dramatic choral symph), Covenant Rec, 60; Symphony No 3, perf by Chicago Symph & others; O My Father, Columbia Rec; Symphony No 4 (choral symph), comn by State Utah; Symphony No 5 (choral symph), comn by Beloit Symph Orch. *Pos:* Music dir, Brigham Young Univ Symph & Opera, 64-66, Beloit-Janesville Symph Orch, 66-, Quincy Symph Orch, 69-70 & Rockford Symph Orch, 70- *Teaching:* Chmn music dept & artist in res, Beloit Col, 82- *Awards:* Max Wald Competition of New York Award (for Symph No 1), 55; Standard Award, ASCAP, 65- *Mem:* ASCAP; Music Educr Nat Conf; Nat Asn Sch Music. *Rep:* Perrotta Mgt 211 W 56th St Suite 18M New York NY 10019. *Mailing Add:* 911 Park Ave Beloit WI 53511

GATES, J(AMES) TERRY
EDUCATOR, MUSIC DIRECTOR

b Naperville Ill, Oct 4, 36. *Study:* Doublebass with Radivoj Lah, 58-61; cond with Thor Johnson, 60-63; Northern Ill Univ, BS, 58, MMus, 64; Univ Ill, Urbana, EdD, 74. *Pos:* Music dir, Southeastern Ohio Symph Orch, 73-79 & Tuscaloosa Symph Orch, 82-; cond, Ala Youth Symph, 83- *Teaching:* Assoc prof music, Muskingum Col, 72-77; asst prof grad music educ & asst dir, Sch Music, Ohio State Univ, 77-79; assoc prof orch & music educ, orch cond & dir grad music educ, Univ Ala, 79- *Mem:* Music Educrs Nat Conf; Am Educ Res Asn; Int Soc Bassists; Nat Sch Orch Asn; Ala Music Educrs Asn (orch div pres, 80-82). *Mailing Add:* PO Box 212 Tuscaloosa AL 35402

GATES, W EVERETT
COMPOSER, EDUCATOR

b Des Moines, Iowa, June 6, 14. *Study:* Drake Univ, with Anthony Donato; Eastman Sch Music, with Bernard Rogers, Burrill Phillips & Samuel Belou

BM, 37, perf degree(viola), 41, MM, 48. *Works:* Varicolor Variations (orch); Mountain Scenario (band); Night Song (string bass & piano); Seasonal Sketches (clarinet choir); Declamation and Dance (sax quartet); Incantation and Ritual (solo flute & sax); Old Encounters (flute choir). *Pos:* Violist, Rochester Phil, 37-48; prin violist & asst cond, Okla City Symph, 48-58. *Teaching:* Fac mem, Okla City Univ, 48-58 & Eastman Sch Music, 58-79, chmn music ed, 65-75, emer prof, 79-; guest lectr, various univs & conv. *Awards:* Univ Rochester Alumni Citation for Excellence of Teaching, 69; first prize, Nat Compt for New Flute Choir Music, 81. *Mem:* Pi Kappa Lambda; Music Educr Nat Conf; Col Band Dirs Nat Asn; Phi Mu Alpha. *Mailing Add:* 354 Marsh Rd Pittsford NY 14534

GATLIN, HELEN STANLEY See Stanley, Helen Camille

GATWOOD, CAROLE GRACE
CELLO
b Richmond, Ky, Aug 30, 52. *Study:* Sch Music, Ind Univ, BM, 74, MM, 77. *Pos:* Asst prin cello, Birmingham Symph, 75-77; cello sect, Denver Symph, 77-80 & Detroit Symph, 81- *Mailing Add:* c/o Detroit Symph Ford Auditorium Detroit MI 48226

GATWOOD, DWIGHT D
EDUCATOR, COMPOSER
b Nashville, Tenn, Sept 26, 42. *Study:* Eastern Ky Univ, BA, 64; George Peabody Col Teachers, MM, 66, PhD, 70. *Works:* Spirits of the Dead, Alexander Broude, Inc, 77; Metamorphosis, comn by Freed-Hardeman Col, Tenn, 78; Aberrations (multimedia), Brass Press, 78; Ode to Fear, perf by Thomas Palmer, 80; Nuit d'etoiles, comn by L'Institut Haitiano-Americain, 80; Hassan, the Camel Driver, comn by Tenn Music Teachers Asn, 81; Lord, Make Me Thy Torch, comn by Dyersburg State Col, Tenn, 82. *Teaching:* Asst prof music theory, LaGrange Col, Ga, 65-66; asst prof choral, Defiance, Col, Ohio, 70-72; prof theory & comp, Univ Tenn, 72- *Awards:* Comp of Year, Tenn Music Teachers Asn, 81; Featured Comp of Month, Polish Nat Radio, 1/83. *Mem:* Music Educr Nat Conf (nat chmn electronic music, 80); Am Soc Univ Comp; Col Music Soc; Int Electronic Music Asn. *Publ:* Auth, Techniques for Including Musical Examples in Theses and Dissertations, Nashville Res Publ, 70; Digital Synthesizers: A Need for Standards in Terminology, SYNE, 79; Overview: Three Decades of Electronic Music Composition and Performance, Instrumentalist, 81; Staffing the University Electronic Music Studio: the Composer-Technician, SYNE, 82; coauth, (with D Piatokowski), Muzyka Jutra, NURT, 83. *Mailing Add:* Music Dept Univ Tennessee Martin TN 38238

GAUGER, RONALD RAYMOND
ORGAN, EDUCATOR
b Burlington, Wis, Mar 23, 39. *Study:* Univ Wis, Madison, MS, 61, MM, 69, DMA, 74. *Teaching:* Assoc prof music, Univ Minn, Duluth, 69- *Mem:* Am Guild Organists (chap dean, 70-83); Organ Hist Soc; Col Music Soc. *Mailing Add:* 23 W Kent Rd Duluth MN 55812

GAULDIN, ROBERT LUTHER
EDUCATOR
b Vernon, Tex, Oct 30, 31. *Study:* NTex State Univ, BM(comp), 53; Eastman Sch Music, MA(theory), 56; Univ Rochester, PhD(theory), 58. *Teaching:* Prof theory, William Carey Col, 58-63 & Eastman Sch Music, 63- *Awards:* First Prize, BMI Comp Awards, 53 & Berkshire String Quartet Contest, 64; Ford Found Grant, 66-68. *Mem:* Soc Music Theory; Col Music Soc; Music Theory Soc NY (vpres, 80-81). *Interests:* Renaissance counterpoint; tonal process in Wagner's operas; Beethoven symphonies. *Publ:* Auth, Pitch Structure in the Second Movement of Webern's Concerto Op 24, In Theory Only, 77; A Labyrinth of Fifths: The Last Movement of Beethoven's Eighth Symphony, Ind Theory Rev, 78; Wagner's Parody Techniques: Traume and the Tristan Love Duet, 79 & The Cycle-7 Complex: The Relation of Set Theory to the Evolution of Ancient Musical Systems, 83, Spectrum. *Mailing Add:* 379 Wellington Ave Rochester NY 14619

GAULT, JOYCE ALENE
EDUCATOR
b Crawfordsville, Iowa, Feb 23, 29. *Study:* Univ Northern Iowa, BA, 50; Northwestern Univ, MMus, 52, DMus, 63. *Teaching:* Instr piano, Northern Univ SDak, 53-56; prof, Univ Northern Iowa, 57- *Mem:* Music Teachers Asn; Soc Am Musicians. *Mailing Add:* 304 Clark Dr Cedar Falls IA 50613

GAUSE, THOMAS DAVID
TRUMPET, COMPOSER
b Newton, Iowa, July 3, 51. *Study:* With Vincent Chicowicz, 71; Univ Northern Iowa, BMus; NTex State Univ, MMusEd, 78. *Works:* Blue Note, Freefall, 82; Desert Dawn, 83 & Three Pieces for Brass Quintet, 83, Medici Music Press. *Rec Perf:* LAB '77, NTex State Univ; Ashley Alexander's Alumni Band, 79 & Ashley Alexander Plays Frank Mantooth, 81, Sound and Sage; Christmas Album, Martin Mobile Rec, 82; Freefall, LAW Studios, 82; Desert Dawn, Willett Mobile Rec, 83. *Pos:* Second trumpet, Ft Worth Symph & Tex Little Symph, 77-78 & Las Vegas Symph, 78-; first trumpet, Ft Worth Brass Quintet, 77-78; co-prin trumpet, Las Vegas Brass Quintet, 80- *Teaching:* Instr trumpet, NTex State Univ, 76-78 & Univ Nev, Las Vegas, 80- *Mem:* Phi Mu Alpha Sinfonia; Nat Asn Jazz Educr; Int Trumpet Guild. *Publ:* Auth, Rehearsal Techniques and Objectives of Las Vegas Brass Quintet, Chamber Music Quart, 83. *Mailing Add:* c/o Am Artists Mgt Inc 300 West End Ave Suite 13A New York NY 10023

GAY, PAUL E
EDUCATOR, COMPOSER
Study: New England Consv Music, with Francis Judd Cooke & William Tesson, BM; Boston Univ, with Hugo Norden, MMus; studied cond with Pierre Monteux & Denis Wick. *Works:* Fantasy (piano & orch); 3 Lyric Pieces (string orch); Elterephenie (woodwind quintet, brass quintet, three perc, & piano), Boston Univ, 78; 3 Movements (brass trio); Chorale (three trombones); Bacchanalian Alarum (trumpet trio); Profiles of North Atlantic Sea Birds (woodwind quintet). *Pos:* Cond, New Hampshire Phil, 73-77. *Teaching:* Mem fac, Univ Lowell & Boston Consv Music, formerly; cond wind ens, Boston Univ, 77-, teaching assoc, currently. *Mailing Add:* Music Dept Boston Univ 121 Bay State Rd Boston MA 02215

GAY, ROBERT
EDUCATOR, DIRECTOR—OPERA
Study: Curtis Inst Music, 38; Mannes Col Music, 47; Boston Univ, MFA, 58. *Teaching:* Prof emer opera & dir opera wkshp, Northwestern Univ. *Mem:* Pi Kappa Lambda; Am Guild Musical Artists; Nat Opera Asn. *Interests:* First edition of Verdi's La Traviata; current opera productions; performance practices. *Mailing Add:* 13100 Summer Pl NE Albuquerque NM 87112

GEARY, BARBARA ANN
PIANO
b Chicago, Ill, July 2, 35. *Study:* Ind Univ, Bloomington, with Frederick Baldwin, MM, 61; studied with Vlado Perlemuter, 66-67 & 69-70. *Pos:* Solo recitalist, US, Mex & WEurope, 70-; traveling lectr, Alliance Francaise, 71-72; occasional soloist with Tulsa Phil & Okla Symph, 74-; recitalist, aboard Queen Elizabeth II, Southampton, England, 78-; Resource Sharing Touring Prog, State Arts Coun, Okla, 82-, SC Arts Comn, Columbia, 82- & Ariz Arts Comn, Phoenix, 83-; artist in res, State Arts Coun Okla, 80- *Teaching:* Asst prof piano, Ohio Univ, 63-69; vis prof, Univ NC, Chapel Hill, 70- *Bibliog:* M Van Deventer (auth), Playing on the High C's, Okla Home & Garden, 5/83. *Mem:* Am Liszt Soc. *Mailing Add:* 2545 S Birmingham Pl Tulsa OK 74114

GEBAUER, VICTOR EARL
EDUCATOR, CRITIC-WRITER
b Christchurch, NZ, Oct 13, 38; US citizen. *Study:* Concordia Sem, St Louis, MDiv, 64; Musicol Inst, Free Univ Berlin, cert, 69-70; Univ Minn, PhD, 76. *Pos:* Ed, Response, Lutheran Soc Worship, Music & Arts, 76-79; mgr, Fest Worship & Witness, Lutheran Churches NAm, 81-83. *Teaching:* Fac mem, Concordia Col, St Paul, 66-, dean chapel, 72-82 & chmn, Div Music & Fine Arts, 78-81. *Mem:* Am Musicol Soc. *Mailing Add:* Hamline & Marshall St Paul MN 55104

GEBER, STEPHEN
EDUCATOR, CELLO
Study: Eastman Sch Music. *Pos:* Mem, Boston Symph, formerly & Eastman-Rochester Symph, formerly; soloist, Boston Pops, formerly; soloist & mem, Rochester Phil, formerly; soloist, prin cello & Louis D Beaumont chair, Cleveland Orch, currently. *Teaching:* Mem fac cello, Blossom Fest Sch, currently & Cleveland Inst Music, 74- *Mailing Add:* 3242 Warrington Rd Shaker Heights OH 44120

GEBUHR, ANN KAREN
EDUCATOR, COMPOSER
b Des Moines, Iowa, May 7, 45. *Study:* Ind Univ, BM, 68, MM, 71, PhD, 83. *Works:* Synthesis for Three Flutes, perf by Ind Univ, 76; A Prairie Sunset, perf by Am Asn Univ Comp, 77; Fanfare, Variations & Fugue, Indianapolis Symph, 80 & Symph NHouston, 80; Fløjtespil, Roberta Brokaw, 80; Helas for Tenor and Organ, Clyde Holloway, 80; Ichabod, Houston Civic Symph, 83; Alleluia: Angelus Domini, Music Teachers Nat Asn, 83. *Teaching:* Asst prof theory & piano, Northern State Col, 69-76; assoc instr theory, Ind Univ, Bloomington, 76-78; assoc prof theory & comp, Houston Baptist Univ, 78- *Mem:* Soc Music Theory; Am Soc Univ Comp; Music Teachers Nat Asn. *Interests:* Structuralism in music. *Publ:* Auth, Structure in Argento's From the Diary of Virginia Wolf, Ind Theory Rev, 77. *Mailing Add:* Sch Music Houston Baptist Univ Houston TX 77074

GEDDA, NICOLAI
TENOR
b Stockholm, Sweden, July 11, 25. *Study:* Musical Acad Stockholm; studied with Karl Martin Oehman & Paola Novikova. *Rec Perf:* On EMI & other rec co, 52- *Roles:* Chapelou in Le Postillon de Longjumeau, Royal Opera, Stockholm, 52; tenor in Trionfo di Afrodite, La Scala, 53; Faust in Faust, Paris Opera, 54; Pittsburgh Opera, 57 & Metropolitan Opera, 57; Duke of Mantua in Rigoletto, Covent Garden, 54; Dimitri in Boris Godunov; Rodolfo in La Boheme; Count Almaviva in Il Barbiere di Siviglia; and many others. *Pos:* Tenor with Salzburg Fest, 57-59, Metropolitan Opera, 57- & Edinburgh Fest, 58-59; performer with major opera co in US & Europe. *Awards:* Royal Ct Singer, Swed govt; Order Danneborg, Danish govt; Christine Nilson Award. *Mem:* Royal Acad Stockholm. *Mailing Add:* c/o Shaw Conct Inc 1995 Broadway New York NY 10023

GEE, HARRY RAGLAN
EDUCATOR, WRITER
b Minneapolis, Minn, Feb 20, 24. *Study:* Curtis Inst Music, dipl(clarinet), 49; Univ Northern Colo, BA(music ed), 53; Univ Denver, MM(woodwinds), 54. *Works:* Solo de Concours (solo clarinet & band arr), Southern Music Co, 60; Ballade (sax), 62, 12 Saxophone Trios, 70 & Fugue in Baroque Style (sax trio), 76, Belwin-Mills Corp; Second Ballade (flute & piano), Kendor Music Publ, 80; Progressive & Varied Etudes (sax), Southern Music Co, 76; Passacaglia

(clarinet choir), Columbia Pictures Publ, 83. *Pos:* Clarinetist, Denver Symph & Civic Opera Orch, 51-54; sax soloist, World Saxophone Cong, Bordeaux, France, 74. *Teaching:* Instr music, Ark State Univ, 54-57; asst prof clarinet & sax, Butler Univ, 57-60; assoc prof, Ind State Univ, Terre Haute, 60-; instr clarinet, Nat Music Camp, Interlochen, Mich, 64-67; vis prof, Woodwind Workshop, Twickenham, England, 78. *Bibliog:* Carl E Hane, Jr (auth), Quart J, Notes, Music Libr Asn, 9/82. *Mem:* Am Fedn Musicians; NAm Sax Alliance; Asn Sax France; Nat Asn Wind & Perc Instr (regional chmn, 64-68); Int Clarinet Soc. *Interests:* Musical literature of saxophone soloists from 1884-1984. *Publ:* Auth, Studio Saxophone Teaching, Clarinet & Sax Soc, Great Britain, 1/80; Clarinet Solo de Concours, 1897-1980, Ind Univ Press, 81; Discography of Paris Conservatory Clarinet Solos, Nat Asn Wind & Perc Instr J, spring 81; French Clarinetists in America, 3 parts, Clarinet, spring, summer & fall 81; A Clarinetist's View on Stravinsky, Chamber Music Quart, winter 82. *Mailing Add:* 419 S 32nd St Terre Haute IN 47803

GEIGER, LOREN DENNIS
TUBA
b Buffalo, NY, Jan 23, 46. *Study:* Eastman Sch Music, BM, 68, MM, 70. *Works:* Boss Windjammer, Allentown, Pa Band, 76; Harpist's Heritage, 80 & Heroic Evocations, 83, Orchard Park Symph Orch; composed over 250 arrangements recorded by mil bands in US, Britain, Sweden, Norway, Germany & Japan. *Pos:* Band dir, Orchard Park Cent Sch, 69-; prin tuba, Amherst Symph Orch, 70-, Orchard Park Symph Orch, 73- & Clarence Pops Orch, 73- *Mem:* Music Educr Nat Conf; Nat Band Asn; Tubists Universal Brotherhood Asn; Int Mil Music Soc. *Publ:* Auth, B G McFall, Sch Musician, 73; Boombah Herald, private publ, 73- *Mailing Add:* 15 Park Blvd Lancaster NY 14086

GEIGER, RUTH
PIANO, TEACHER
b Vienna, Austria, Jan 30, 23; US citizen. *Study:* Juilliard Grad Sch, with Josef Lhevinne, dipl, 44; studied with Ernst Rosenberg. *Rec Perf:* Ruth Geiger Plays Schubert, Critics Choice Rec, 78. *Pos:* Recitalist and conct soloist, US, currently. *Teaching:* Piano, privately, NY, 46- *Awards:* Naumburg Found Award, 43. *Mailing Add:* 160 W 73rd St New York NY 10023

GEIL, WILMA JEAN
LIBRARIAN
b Pittsburgh, Pa, May 24, 39. *Study:* Swarthmore Col, BA, 61; Univ Ill, MS, 64, MM(musicol), 67. *Pos:* Assoc music librn, Univ Ill, Urbana, 64- *Awards:* Book of Yr Award, Music Libr Asn, 83. *Mem:* Music Libr Asn (bd mem at large, 83-85); Sonneck Soc (secy 75-83); Am Musicol Soc; Int Asn Music Libr. *Interests:* Bibliographical research in American music. *Publ:* Auth, American Sheet Music in the Walter N H Harding Collection at the Bodleian Library, Oxford University, Notes, Vol 34, No 4; Indexes, Vol 36, No 4 & Vol 37, No 4, Notes; coauth, Resources of American Music History, by D W Krummel, J Geil, D Dyen, and D Root, Univ Ill Press, 81. *Mailing Add:* 1403 S Busey Ave Urbana IL 61801

GEIRINGER, KARL J
WRITER, EDUCATOR
b Vienna, Austria, Apr 26, 99; US citizen. *Study:* Univ Vienna & Berlin, PhD, 23. *Pos:* Cur, Soc Friends Music, Vienna, 30-38. *Teaching:* Vis prof hist musical instrm, Royal Col Music, London, 38-39; prof music hist, Boston Univ, 40-62 & Univ Calif, Santa Barbara, 62-71. *Awards:* Guggenheim Fel; Bollingen Fel. *Bibliog:* C R Landon & R Chapman (auth), Studies in 18th Century Music, a Tribute to Karl Geiringen on His 70th Birthday, Oxford Univ Press, 70. *Mem:* Hon mem, Am Musicol Soc; Am Philosophical Soc; hon mem, Am Chap New Bach Soc; fel, Am Acad Arts & Sci; Am Brahms Soc (mem bd dir, 83-). *Interests:* Seventeenth-nineteenth century musical instruments. *Publ:* Auth, J S Bach, 66 & Instruments in the History of Western Music, 78, Oxford Univ Press; The Bach Family, 81 & Brahms, His Life and Work, third ed, 81, Da Capo Press; Haydn, a Creative Life in Music, third ed, Univ Calif Press, 82. *Mailing Add:* 1823 Mira Vista Ave Santa Barbara CA 93103

GELBLOOM, GERALD
VIOLIN, EDUCATOR
b Toronto, May 3, 26. *Study:* Juilliard Sch Music, studied violin with Mischa Mischakoff; Univ Hartford, AA; studied violin with Ivan Galamian. *Pos:* Mem, Busch Chamber Players, 47, Cleveland Orch, 47-49, Casals Fest Orch, 59-61, Boston Symph Orch, 61-, Boston Fine Arts Quartet, 62 & Music Guild String Quartet, 68-72; asst concertmaster, Baltimore Symph, 49-53; concertmaster, Hartford Symph, 54-61. *Teaching:* Mem fac, Peabody Consv Music, 49-54, Hartt Col Music, 59-61, Longy Sch Music, Sch Music, Boston Univ, Harvard Univ & Radcliffe Col, currently; chmn string dept, Hartford Sch Music, 54-59; artist & teacher, Brandeis Univ, 66-69. *Awards:* First Prize Gold Medalist, Can Nat Exhib, 33. *Mailing Add:* 16 Furber Lane Newton Center MA 02159

GELLER, DONNA MEDOFF
PIANO, EDUCATOR
b Canton, Ohio, Feb 13, 38. *Study:* Brandeis Univ, BA, 59; Univ Akron, MM, 80. *Pos:* Prin keyboardist, Akron Symph Orch, 80- *Teaching:* Dir accompanying & lectr, Univ Akron, 77- *Mailing Add:* 1838 Breezewood Dr Akron OH 44313

GELLER, IAN
COMPOSER, CONDUCTOR
b Chicago, Ill, Mar 18, 43. *Study:* Roosevelt Univ, with Karel Jirak, Robert Lombardo & Ramon Zupko; Am Consv, with Stella Roberts; Juilliard Sch, with Stanley Wolfe & Vincent Persichetti. *Works:* Time (ballet with string quartet & bar); Poem (orch); Aria & Variation (orch); From One Who Stays (voice & orch); Violin Sonata; Piano Trio. *Pos:* Music dir, Temple Israel, Long Beach; cond, Am Jewish Choral Soc, Los Angeles, 71-72; cantor, Am Shalom, Chicago, 72- *Teaching:* Fac mem, Northeastern Ill Univ, 72-74. *Awards:* Ill Arts Coun Grant, 73. *Mailing Add:* 1949 W Estes Chicago IL 60626

GELT, ANDREW LLOYD
COMPOSER, WRITER
b Albuquerque, NMex, Feb 2, 51. *Works:* Concerto-Quintet for Five Clarinets Assorted, Op 19, 72, Pathos, Op 23 (clarinet & tape), 77, Brass Quintet, Op 30, The Russian, 78, Symph No 1, Op 34, The Art of Eclecticism, Frederick Fennell, 78, Lamento for Strings, Op 22, 78, Herald Fanfare No 2, Op 33, 82 & Homage to Gesualdo, Op 33, 83, Edwin A Fleisher Collection Orchestral Music. *Pos:* Solo E flat clarinet & sax, NMex Symph Orch, 69-70. *Teaching:* Lectr theory, Univ Miami, 76-78; asst prof theory, woodwinds & commercial music, Pembroke State Univ, NC, 78-79; instr gen music, Richmond Tech Col, NC, 79; asst prof grad music theory, comp & commercial music, Temple Univ, 79-80. *Awards:* Perf compt winner, Am Fedn Music Clubs, 70 & 72; Pa Comp Proj Perf Grant, 81. *Bibliog:* Eve Oakley (auth), Symphony Concert to Offer a First, Fayetteville Observer, 79; Local Musician to Perform in Miami, Overbrook Press, 81; Elaine Morano (auth), Face to Face with Dr Fabulous, Midnight Magic Entertainment Mag, 2/82. *Mem:* Am Music Ctr; Col Music Soc; Am Soc Univ Comp; Nat Asn Comp USA; Int Clarinet Soc. *Publ:* Auth, A Statement Concerning Eclecticism and the Gesamtstilwerk, Am Soc Univ Comp Newsletter, 80; Jazz Style Periods as Possible Historical Indicator for Intoxicant Preference, Grassroots US J Drug & Alcohol Dependence, 82; Corps Style: Will it Determine Our Future Instrumentation Availability?, Instrumentalist, 82; After Cage ... Environmental Ear Training, Soundings, 83. *Mailing Add:* 10919 Fairbanks Rd NE Albuquerque NM 87112

GEMIGNANI, CAROL ANN See Page, Carolann

GEMMELL, HELEN ARMSTRONG See Armstrong, Helen

GENA, PETER
COMPOSER, EDUCATOR
b Buffalo, NY, Apr 27, 47. *Study:* State Univ NY, Buffalo, BA, 69, MA, 72, PhD, 76. *Works:* Egerya, Alea Encuentros, Spain & Kitchen, NY, 71; Valse, C F Peters, 78; Beethoven in SoHo, Orch Hall, Chicago & New Music Am 81, San Francisco, 80; S-13, S-14, Hubbard St Gallery, Chicago & New Music Am 82, Chicago, 80; Unchained Melodies, Int Comput Music Conf, NTex State Univ, 81; McKinley, NAm New Music Fest, NY, 83. *Pos:* Dir, Am New Music Ens; co-dir, New Music Am '82, Chicago. *Teaching:* Dir electronic music studio, Brock Univ, St Catharines, Ont, 71-74; lectr music, Calif State Univ, Fresno, 74-76; asst prof, Sch Music, Northwestern Univ, 76-83; vis artist, Sch Art Inst Chicago, 83- *Awards:* Nat Endowment Arts Grants, 78 & 82; Ill Arts Coun Chmn Grants, 80 & 83 & Lit Award, 82. *Mem:* New Music Alliance (mem bd, 80-, co-pres, 82-83). *Publ:* Auth, Programming Balbastre's Romance, Musical Box Soc Int, Vol XX, No 5; Musicol: Musical Instruction Composition-Oriented Language, In: Computing in the Humanities, Waterloo Press, 77; Freedom in Experimental Music: The New York Revolution, TriQuart 52, Fall, 81; Foreword and After Antiquity: John Cage in Conservation with Peter Gena, Cat New Music Am 82 Fest, Chicago, 82; co-ed, John Cage Reader, TriQuart 54, spring 82 & C F Peters, 83. *Mailing Add:* 509 Hunter Rd Glenview IL 60025

GENIA, ROBINOR
PIANO, EDUCATOR
b Odessa, USSR; US citizen. *Study:* Imperial Consv Odessa, artist dipl, 20; Curtis Inst Music, BMus, 33. *Teaching:* Instr piano, Settlement Music Sch, 34-53; prof, Philadelphia Musical Acad, 53-73; head piano dept, Third St Music Sch, 53- *Mem:* Music Educr Asn NJ; Behre Piano Assoc; Leschetizky Asn (pres, 72); Bohemians. *Mailing Add:* 105 W 72nd St New York NY 10023

GENOVESE, ALFRED
OBOE
Study: Curtis Inst Music, dipl; studied oboe with Marcel Tabuteau. *Pos:* Prin oboe, Baltimore Symph Orch, St Louis Symph, Metropolitan Opera Orch & Cleveland Orch, formerly; participant in many festivals incl Marlboro Music Fest & Casals Fest, PR; oboist, Boston Symph Orch, currently. *Mailing Add:* Boston Symph Orch Symph Hall Boston MA 02115

GENTEMANN, M ELAINE
COMPOSER, EDUCATOR
b Fredericksburg, Tex, Oct 4, 09. *Study:* Our Lady of Lake Univ, BMus(piano), 35; Am Consv Music, MM(comp), 42, Juilliard Sch; Columbia Univ. *Works:* Over 100 compositions published by Belwin-Mills, G Shirmer, Carl Fisher & others. *Teaching:* Prof piano & organ, Our Lady of Lake Univ, currently. *Awards:* Piper Prof, 58; Citation & Appreciation Cert, Our Lady of Lake Univ, 83. *Mem:* Am Musicol Soc; Tex Music Teachers Asn; Nat Guild Piano Teachers; Music Teachers Nat Asn; Sigma Alpha Iota. *Mailing Add:* Music Dept Our Lady of Lake Univ San Antonio TX 78285

GENTILESCA, FRANCO JOSEPH
DIRECTOR—OPERA, EDUCATOR

b New York, NY, May 30, 43. *Study:* St John's Univ, BA, 64; Pace Univ, BA, 68; asst to Luchino Visconti & Roman Polanski, 74. *Pos:* Stage dir opera, 72- *Teaching:* Instr opera wkshp, Am Inst Musical Studies, Gratz, Austria, 83. *Mem:* Am Guild Musical Artists (mem bd gov, 72-); Actor's Equity. *Mailing Add:* 2109 Broadway #14-10 New York NY 10023

GEOGHEGAN, JAMES HUGH
GUITAR, TEACHER

b Charleston, WVa. *Study:* Harvard Univ, AB, 78; Fletcher Sch Law & Dipl, MALD, 80; study with Julian Bream in England. *Rec Perf:* Music of Sor & Giuliani, Orion Rec, 77; Premieres for Two Guitars, Sail Rec, 80. *Teaching:* Fac mem guitar, Longy Sch Music, 72- & Tufts Univ, 79- *Mailing Add:* c/o Longy Sch One Follen St Cambridge MA 02138

GEORGE, EARL
COMPOSER, EDUCATOR

b Milwaukee, Wis, May 1, 24. *Study:* Eastman Sch Music, with Howard Hanson & Bernard Rogers, BM, 46, MM, 47, PhD, 58; Berkshire Music Ctr, with Bohuskav Martinu, 47. *Works:* Introduction and Allegro, perf by New York Phil, 47; New York City Symph, 47 & Minneapolis Symph, 50; Violin Concerto, perf by Minneapolis Symph, 54; A Thanksgiving Overture, Minneapolis Symph, 56; Violin Concerto, Symph of the Air, 57; Concerto (piano & orch), Syracuse Symph, 66. *Pos:* Music critic, Syracuse Herald J, 61- *Teaching:* Instr theory & comp, Univ Minn, 48-56; Fulbright lectr 20th century music, Univ Oslo, Norway, 55-56; prof comp, Syracuse Univ, 59- *Awards:* Gershwin Mem Prize, Bnai Brith, 47; fel, Guggenheim Found, 57. *Mem:* ASCAP; Am Music Ctr. *Mailing Add:* 21 Sewickley Dr Jamesville NY 13078

GEORGE, LILA-GENE PLOWE
TEACHER, COMPOSER

b Sioux City, Iowa, Sept 25, 18. *Study:* Univ Okla, BA, 39, DMus, 40; Cornell Univ, with Egon Petri, 42; Northwestern Univ, 50; Mills Col, 50-53; Columbia Univ, with Otto Luening & Vladimir Ussachevsky, 62-65; studied with Nadia Boulanger, France, 71-78, Lila & Herbert Ricker, Silvio Scionti & Edward Steuermann. *Works:* Merry-go round for Christmas (madrigal), 66 & For Winter's Rains & Ruins are Over (madrigal), 67, Galaxy Music Corp; Preludes & Postlude for Organ, Patricia McAwley, 73; Preludes & Postludes #3, Bruce Eicher, 74; Sonata for Viola & Piano, 75 & Prelude & Invention (violin), 76, Newl Gittelman; Quest (flute & piano), Ignacio Yepes, 78. *Teaching:* Piano, privately, Oklahoma City, Houston, New York & Latin Am, 38- *Awards:* Sigma Alpha Iota Okla Alumnae Comp Award, 69. *Mem:* Am Women Comp; Am Music Ctr; Am Musicol Soc. *Mailing Add:* 2301 Reba Dr Houston TX 77019

GEORGE, THOM RITTER
COMPOSER, CONDUCTOR

b Detroit, Mich, June 23, 42. *Study:* Eastman Sch Music, BM, 64, MM, 68; Cath Univ Am, DMA, 70. *Works:* Concerto for Bass Trombone, Accura Music, Inc, 65; Proclamations, 66 & Western Overture, 67, Boosey & Hawkes, Inc; Aria & Dance, Southern Music Col, 76; Would I Might Go Far Over Sea, 79 & Brass Quintet No 2, 80, G Schirmer, Inc; Pastorale, Southern Music Co, 80. *Pos:* Comp & arr, US Navy Band, 66-70; music dir & cond, Quincy Symph Orch, 70- *Teaching:* Lectr orch, Cath Univ Am, 69-70; lectr music, John Wood Community Col, 80- *Awards:* Annual Awards for Serious Music, ASCAP, 65-; Citation for Meritorious Serv, Quincy Col, 73; Seventh Sigvald Thompson Award, Fargo-Moorhead Symph Orch, 75. *Mem:* Am Music Ctr; ASCAP; Nat Band Asn; Founding mem, Cond Guild Am Symph Orch League. *Mailing Add:* 2125 Prairie Ave Quincy IL 62301

GEORGE, WARREN EDWIN
EDUCATOR

b Abilene, Kans, Mar 20, 36. *Study:* Univ Kans, Lawrence, BMusEd, 58; Mich State Univ, MMus, 59; Univ Kans, PhD, 69. *Pos:* Ed, J Band Res, 74- *Teaching:* Dir instrm music, Olathe Pub Sch, Kans, 60-63; teaching asst, Univ Kans, Lawrence, 63-64, res asst, 64-67, admin asst to dept chmn, 66; asst prof music, Univ Tex, Austin, 67-69, music & educ, 69-71, dir student teaching & supvr instrm student teachers, 70-73, assoc prof, 71-73, coordr undergrad studies, Dept Music, 71-73; prof & head music educ, Pa State Univ, 73-77; prof music educ & head div music, Col Consv Music, Univ Cincinnati, currently, assoc dean, currently. *Awards:* Outstanding Musician Award, Midwestern Music & Art Camp, Univ Kans, 53. *Mem:* Pi Kappa Lambda; Phi Mu Alpha; life mem, Music Educr Nat Conf; Ohio Music Educr Asn; Tex Music Educr Asn (vpres, 70-72). *Publ:* Contribr to var music & educ jour. *Mailing Add:* 8818 Castleford Cincinnati OH 45242

GEPHART, WILLIAM (ABEL)
TEACHER, BARITONE

b Spokane, Wash, July 5, 13. *Study:* DePauw Univ, AB, 35; Juilliard Grad Sch, dipl, 40; Consv Nat, Paris, dipl, 50. *Teaching:* Fac mem, Dalcroze Sch Music, 49-, Vassar Col, 68-69 & 74-75, Sch Sacred Music, Union Theol Sem, New York, 61-73 & Hartford Consv, 75- *Awards:* Fulbright Fel, 49-50. *Mem:* New York Singing Teachers Asn (pres, 68-70); Nat Asn Teachers Singing; Int Asn for Res in Singing; Am Acad Teachers Singing (treas, 67-72, secy, 72-). *Mailing Add:* 75 Bank St New York NY 10014

GERBER, STEVEN R
COMPOSER, PIANO

b Washington, DC, Sept 28, 48. *Study:* Haverford Col, BA, 69; Princeton Univ, MFA, 71. *Works:* Woodwind Quartet, 67, Trio for Violin, Cello & Piano, 68, String Quartet $1, 73 & Voices (piano), 76, Mobart; 2 Lyrics of Gerard Manley Hopkins, APNM, 76; String Quartet #2, 81 & Songs from The Wild Swans at Coole, 82, Am Comp Alliance. *Awards:* Kindler Found Comn, 68; NY State Coun Arts Rec Grant, 80-81; compt winner (for String Quartet #2), New Music Consort, 82. *Mem:* Am Comp Alliance; Am Music Ctr; Am Soc Univ Comp; Guild of Comp (vpres, 82-). *Mailing Add:* 639 West End Ave New York NY 10025

GERBOTH, WALTER WILLIAM
EDUCATOR

b Flushing, NY, Feb 27, 25. *Study:* Queens Col, City Univ New York, BA, 50; Columbia Univ, MS, 53. *Teaching:* Prof, Brooklyn Col, 56- *Mem:* Music Libr Asn (pres, 69-71); Am Musicol Soc (mem coun, 71-73); Int Asn Music Libr; Soc Ethnomusicol; Soc Asian Music. *Interests:* Musical Festschriften; the comic elements in music. *Publ:* Auth, Music of East and Southeast Asia: A Selected Bibliography, NY State Educ Dept, 63; Acquisitions: College Library, Manual Music Librarianship, Music Libr Asn, 66; An Index to Musical Festschriften and Similar Publications, W W Norton, 69; The Publics of the Music Library, Fontes Artis Musicae, 71. *Mailing Add:* 1156 E 43rd St Brooklyn NY 11210

GERHART, MARTHA
COACH

b Rahway, NJ. *Study:* Middlebury Col, AB, 59; Univ Colo, MMus, 64. *Works:* Lily (vocal score), perf by New York City Opera, 77. *Pos:* Asst dir, Queens Col Opera Studio, 72-75; asst cond, New York City Opera, 75-80 & San Francisco Opera, 80-82; master coach, Merola Prog, San Francisco Opera, 79- *Teaching:* Vocal coach & accmp, New York, currerntly. *Mem:* Nat Asn Teachers Singing; Cent Opera Serv. *Mailing Add:* 50 W 67th St New York NY 10023

GERIG, REGINALD ROTH
EDUCATOR, WRITER

b Grabill, Ind, Apr 20, 19. *Study:* Wheaton Col, Ill, BMus(piano), 42; Juilliard Sch Music, studied piano with Sascha Gorodnitzky, Carl Friedberg & Josef Raieff, BS(piano), 48, MS(piano), 49. *Pos:* Organist, Col Church, Wheaton, Ill, 53- *Teaching:* Mem fac piano, Nyack Col, 46-50, Eastman Sch Music, 50-52 & Wheaton Col, Ill, 52- *Mem:* Music Teachers Nat Asn; Ill State Music Teachers Asn; Nat Guild Piano Teachers; Am Liszt Soc. *Publ:* Auth, Famous Pianists and Their Technique, Robert B Luce Inc, 74 & 76; The Role of the Arm in Historical Piano Technical Thought, Am Liszt Soc J, 12/77; The Great Otto Ortmann, Piano Quart, winter 80-81. *Mailing Add:* 1328 Naperville Rd Wheaton IL 60187

GERLE, ROBERT
CONDUCTOR, VIOLIN

b Abbazia, Italy, Apr 1, 24. *Study:* Franz Liszt Acad Music, Budapest, MMus; Nemzeti Zenede, Budapest, MMusEd. *Rec Perf:* Complete Hungarian Dances (Brahms), Violin Concerto (Barber), Violin Concerto (Weill), 2 Concertos (Vivaldi), Westminster. *Pos:* Soloist, Budapest Symph, 41, BBC, Berlin Phil, London Symph Orch, Concerts Lamoureux & others; cond, Fri Morning Music Club Orch, Washington, DC, 76- & Transylvania Symph, Brevard Music Center, NC, 82-; guest cond, orchs in US & Brazil; conct tours, Europe, South Am, South Africa & US. *Teaching:* Prof, Peabody Consv Music, 55-68, Mannes Col Music, 59-70 & Manhattan Sch Music, 67-70; prof, artist in res & cond orchs, Ohio State Univ, 68-72; prof, cond orch & head instrm prog, Univ Md, Baltimore Co, 72-; prof, Cath Univ Am, 73-, cond, 74-75. *Awards:* Best of Concertos, New York Times, 67; Emmy Awards, 70 & 71. *Publ:* Contribr, Music Teachers Nat J & Am String Teachers Asn Mag; The Art of Practising the Violin, Stainer & Bell, 83. *Rep:* Elliot Siegel Music Mgt 3003 Van Ness St NW Suite W832 Washington DC 20008. *Mailing Add:* 101 Birchwood Rd Catonsville MD 21228

GERSCHEFSKI, EDWIN
COMPOSER, EDUCATOR

b Meriden, Conn, June 19, 09. *Study:* Yale Univ, PhB & MusB, 31; Matthay Pianoforte Sch, London, 31-33; studied piano with Schnabel, 35 & comp with Schillinger, 36-38. *Works:* Classic Symphony, Op 4, 31, Saugatuck Suite, Op 6, 31, Piano Quintet, Op 16, 35, The Salutation of the Dawn, Op 37, 52, Prayer of Saint Francis of Assisi, Op 61, No 4 (sacred song), 76, Arrangements for Ann, Op 78 (six piano solos), 78 & Letter from BMI, Op 83 (mixed chorus & small orch), 81, Comp Facsimile Ed; and many others. *Rec Perf:* New Music for Piano, Op 23, New Music Quart Rec, 37; An Evening with Gerschefski—1976, Rite Rec Prod, 76. *Pos:* Pianist, appearing on major radio & educ TV networks, 37-76, Asn Am Cols Tours, 42-51 & Univ Ga Trio, 60-67; mem bd, New Music Rec, 38-41; dir, Spartanburg Music Fest, 45-59; piano music ed, Boosey & Hawkes, 48-50; regional ed, J Music Theory, 55-60. *Teaching:* Assoc prof music, Converse Col, 40-, dean music sch, 45-59; fac mem, Cummington Sch Arts, Mass, summer 43, Appalachian State Teachers Col, summer 56 & Young Harris Col, summer 76-80; head music dept, Univ NMex, 59-60; head music dept, Univ Ga, 60-72, prof music, 72-76, emer prof, 76-; comp-lectr at univ throughout US. *Awards:* Ford Found Fel, 52; Gold Medal, Arnold Bax Soc, 63; Gov Award Arts, 73. *Bibliog:* Chappell White (auth), The Choral Music of Edwin Gerschefski, Choral J, Vol XIV, No 1; Gail W Cowart (auth), Gerschefski is Still Top Teacher, Athens Observer, Ga, 8/23/79; Gertrude Sternberg (auth), Lunch with a Hall of Fame Composer, Rec-Jour, Meriden, Conn, 1/23/82. *Mem:* Southeastern

Comp League (mem founders bd, 52-); Nat Asn Sch Music (regional vpres, 53-55, chmn, 70-72, mem bd dir, 71-72); Music Teachers Nat Asn; Ga Comp (pres, 61-63); charter mem, Am Comp Alliance. *Publ:* Auth, Fighting the Famine of Strings, Etude, 11/49; For a Balanced Training in Music, 2/64 & Creative Music for Children, 2/65, Ga Music News; Anyone Can Compose, Comp Facsimile Ed, 66; The Schillinger System of Musical Composition, Part 1, 4/69, Part 2, 11/69 & Part 3, 9/70, Music at Ga. *Mailing Add:* PO Box 162 Hiawassee GA 30546

GERSCHEFSKI, MARTHA
CELLO, EDUCATOR
Study: Brevard Music Ctr, 53-58; Juilliard Sch Music, studied cello with Luigi Silva & chamber music with mem Juilliard String Quartet, dipl(perf), 62; studied cello with Andre Navarra & coached with Edward Mattos & Nadia Boulanger, 65-68; Accad Musicale Chigiana, Siena, dipl merit, 68. *Pos:* Assoc prin cello, Am Symph Orch, 63-65; recitalist, Europe, 67-70, with Betty Ann McCall, 69-73 & Ga State Univ Fac; concert soloist, eastern US, 68; performer, with Ga Acad Music ens incl Acad Piano Quartet, 73-; prin cellist, Atlanta Chamber Orch, 80- *Teaching:* Fac mem cello, Allen Stevenson Private Sch Boys, New York, 62-65 & Ga State Univ, 70-73 & 82-; cofounder, co-dir & teacher cello, Ga Acad Music, 73- *Awards:* Koussevitzky Prize, New York Musicians Club, 65; Martha Baird Rockefeller Grant, 69. *Mailing Add:* 1375 Peachtree Battle Ave NW Atlanta GA 30327

GERSHUNOFF, MAXIM
ARTIST MANAGER & REPRESENTATIVE, ADMINISTRATOR
b New York, NY, June 10, 24. *Study:* Curtis Inst Music, trumpet with Caston, cert, 43; pvt study with Harry Glantz. *Pos:* Trumpet, Pittsburgh Symph Orch, 43-44, NBC Symph Orch, 44-46; solo trumpet, Lux Radio & LuxVieo Theatres, 49-55; admin dir music, Greek Theatre, Los Angeles, 50-53; adminr, Los Angeles Music Fest, Univ Calif, 56-63; admin dir, Santa Catalina Fest Arts, 60; vpres, Hurok Conct Inc, 60-72; artists mgr, Columbia Artists Mgt, 72-74; impresario & artists mgr, Maxim Gershunoff Attractions, Inc, 76- *Mem:* Am Symph Orch League. *Mailing Add:* Maxim Gershunoff Attractions 502 Park Ave New York NY 10022

GERSTER, ROBERT GIBSON
COMPOSER, EDUCATOR
b Chicago, Ill, Oct 13, 45. *Study:* Ohio State Univ, BMus, 67, MMus, 68; Univ Wash, DMA, 76. *Works:* Cantata for Woodwind Quartet, comn & perf by Soni Ventorum Woodwind Quartet, Seattle, 77; Fantasy-Variations, comn & perf by Ena Bronstein, 78; The Temple of Fire and Ice, comn & perf by Lawrence Sutherland & Fresno State Univ Wind Ens, 78; The Silver Palace of Night, comn & perf by Philip Lorenz, 81; The Range of Light, comn & perf by Jack Fortner & Orpheus, 82; The Pavilion of Eternal Spring, perf by Fresno Phil Orch, 83. *Pos:* Organist & choir dir, Good Shepherd Lutheran Church, Fresno, 77-; exec dir, Orpheus, Fresno, 81-83. *Teaching:* Asst music, Univ Wash, 68 & 71-73; lectr, Calif State Univ, Fresno, 74- & Fresno City Col, 81. *Awards:* Charles Ives Scholar, Nat Inst Arts & Lett, 73; Comp Fel, Nat Endowment Arts, 79. *Mem:* Am Soc Univ Comp; life mem, Col Music Soc; Am Guild Organists (mem bd regional chap, currently); BMI; Pi Kappa Lambda. *Interests:* Entitation in perceiving musical structure. *Mailing Add:* 2850 E Santa Ana Fresno CA 93726

GERVERS, HILDA F
TEACHER, WRITER
b London, England. *Study:* Royal Col Music, London, ARCM & GRSM, 32; Sch Music, Converse Col, Spartanburg, SC, MM, 67; NY Univ, Washington Square, NY, PhD(musicol), 74. *Pos:* Libr cataloguer, Mannes Col Music, 66-68. *Teaching:* Fac piano, Hoff-Barthelson Music Sch, Scarsdale, 71-81; adj lectr, Brooklyn Col, City Univ New York, 74-75. *Awards:* Grant, Rockefeller Brothers' Fund, Am Asn Univ Women, 64. *Mem:* Am Musicol Asn; Music Libr Asn; Int Asn Music Libr; Int Repty Musical Iconography; Westchester Musicians Guild. *Interests:* Keyboard music of the early baroque in England. *Publ:* Auth, Bartok's Five Songs, Op 15, Music Rev, 11/69; Liszt as Pedagogue, J Res Music Educ, winter 70; A Manuscript of Dance Music from 17th-century England, New York Pub Libr Bulletin, 77; ed, English Court and Country Dances of the Early Baroque from Drexel 5612, Am Inst Musicol, 82. *Mailing Add:* 242 Ancon Ave Pelham NY 10803

GESIN, LEONID
VIOLA, EDUCATOR
b Leningrad, USSR, June 11, 34. *Study:* Leningrad State Consv, 59. *Pos:* Violist, Leningrad State Phil Orch, 61-77, Rome Opera Theater Symph Orch, Italy, 78 & San Francisco Symph, 79; mem, String Quartet Leningrad State Phil Orch, 70-77; soloist, Leningrad Chamber Ens Orch, 70-77. *Teaching:* Instr viola, Children's Music Sch N2, Leningrad, 75-77 & San Francisco Consv, 81- *Mailing Add:* 276 Kavanaugh Way Pacifica CA 94044

GETTEL, COURTLAND D
TEACHER, FLUTE
b Boston, Mass, Sept 21, 43. *Study:* Consv Music, Oberlin Col, MusB, 66; State Univ Iowa, MA, 68; MFA, 73. *Works:* I Heard a Fly, Lerka Singers, Luther Col, 72; Watercycle, Univ Iowa Ctr New Music, 73; Three Variations on an Unstated Theme, West High Sch Orch, 75 & 78. *Pos:* Prin flute, Vt Phil Orch, 78- *Teaching:* Instr flute & theory, Luther Col, 70-73 & Idaho State Univ, 73-74; dir music, Gettel Music Studio, 74-83; asst prof, Green Mountain Col, 75- *Mailing Add:* RFD 1 West Rutland VT 05777

GHENT, EMMANUEL
COMPOSER
b Montreal, Can, May 15, 25; US citizen. *Study:* McGill Univ, studied bassoon with R deH Tupper, BS, 46, MD, 50; studied comp with Ralph Shapey, 61-63 & piano with Samuel Blumenthal. *Works:* Entelechy (viola & piano), 63 & Dithyrambos (brass quintet), 65, Oxford Univ Press; Hex (trumpet, chamber ens & tape), 66, Helices (violin, piano & tape), 69, Phosphones (comput generated music), 71, Lustrum (electric string quartet, brass quintet & tape), 74 & Baobab (computer generated music & film), 79, Persimmon Press. *Teaching:* Lectured at univ throughout US. *Awards:* Guggenheim Found Fel, 67; Nat Endowment Arts Grant, 74-76 & 80; NY State Coun Arts Grant, 75. *Mem:* Am Music Ctr; Am Soc Univ Comp; Comput Music Asn. *Publ:* Auth, Signals to Performers—A New Compositional Resource, Perspectives New Music, 67; The Coordinome in Relation to Electronic Music, Electronic Music Rev, 67; coauth, A High Speed Digital Control System, Lighting Design & Appln, 74; Computer Assisted Composition and Performance Control, Bulletin Comput Arts Soc, 77; auth, Real Time Interactive Compositional Procedures, Proc Am Soc Univ Comp, 78. *Mailing Add:* 131 Prince St New York NY 10012

GHEZZO, DINU D
CONDUCTOR, COMPOSER
b Tuzla, Constanta, Romania, July 2, 41; US citizen. *Study:* Romanian Consv, Bucharest, MA(cond & theory), 64, MA(comp), 66; Univ Calif, Los Angeles, PhD(comp), 73. *Works:* Music for Flutes and Tape, 72, Kanones for Flute, Cello and Harpsichord, 72, Celebrations (chamber orch), 77, Aphorisms (clarinet & piano), 79 & rev 83, Sketches for Clarinet and Orchestra, 81, Letters to Walt Whitman, 82 & From Here To There, 83, Seesaw Music Corp. *Pos:* Dir, New Repty Ens NY Inc, 76-; cond & dir, NY Univ Symph Orch, 76- & Wash Square Chamber Orch, 77-; co-dir & cond, NY Univ Contemp Players, 77-; dir, Am New Music Consortium, 81- *Teaching:* Asst prof, Romanian Consv, Bucharest, 68-69, Univ Calif, Los Angeles, 72-74, Queens Col, City Univ New York, 74-76; assoc prof, NY Univ, 76- *Awards:* ASCAP Awards, 76-; CAPS, NY State Coun Arts, 76; MacDowell Colony Res, MacDowell Found, 82. *Bibliog:* Joseph Machlis (auth), Introduction to Comtemporary Music, Norton, 79. *Mem:* Am New Music Consortium (pres, nat coordr, 81-); Int Soc Contemp Music (bd dir, 75-78); Am Soc Univ Comp; Col Music Soc; Am Music Ctr. *Mailing Add:* New York Univ 35 W Fourth St Rm 777 New York NY 10003

GHIAUROV, NICOLAI
BASS
b Velingrad, Bulgaria, Sept 13, 29. *Study:* Acad Music, Sofia, Bulgaria; Moscow Consv. *Rec Perf:* Anna Bolena; rec on London, Angel, Decca, Columbia, Supraphon & Balkanton. *Roles:* Don Basilio in Il Barbiere di Siviglia, Sofia Opera, 55; Varlaam in Boris Godunov, La Scala, Milan, 59; Mephistopheles in Faust, 65, Padre Guardiano in La Forza del Destino & Fiesco in Simon Boccanegra, Metropolitan Opera; King Philip in Don Carlos, Lyr Opera Co Philadelphia, 66 & Metropolitan Opera; Ramfis in Aida. *Pos:* Bass, La Scala, Milan, Lyr Opera Chicago, Metropolitan Opera, Lyr Opera Co Philadelphia, London Royal Opera, Bolshoi Opera, Vienna Staatsoper, Hamburg Staatsoper, Paris Opera & others. *Awards:* First Prize, Int Singing Cont, Paris, 55. *Mailing Add:* c/o Columbia Artists Mgt Inc 165 W 57th St New York NY 10019

GHIGLIA, OSCAR ALBERTO
GUITAR, BASSOON
b Livorno, Italy, Aug 13, 38; Ital citizen. *Study:* Music Consv Santa Cecilia, Rome, dipl, 62. *Rec Perf:* Guitar Music of Four Centuries, The Guitar in Spain, The Spanish Guitar of Oscar Ghiglia & Oscar Ghiglia Plays Scarlatti and Other Baroque Masters, Angel Rec; Dark Angels (with Jan de Gaetani), Nonesuch Rec, 77. *Pos:* Asst to Andres Segovia, 64; conct guitarist, Europe, Asia & North Am, 66- *Teaching:* Aspen Music Fest, Banff Ctr Arts, Can & Acad Chigiana, Siena, Italy, summers 69-; artist in res classical guitar, Hartt Sch Music, 81- *Awards:* Winner, Int Guitar Compt, 63. *Mailing Add:* c/o Colbert Artists Mgt 111 W 57th St New York NY 10019

GIACOBASSI, JULIE ANN
OBOE & ENGLISH HORN
b Normal, Ill, Mar 30, 49. *Study:* Univ Mich, with Florian Mueller, BMus, 71; studied with Joseph Robinson, David Weiss & Richard White. *Pos:* Prin oboist, Shreveport Symph, 71-72; English hornist, Kennedy Ctr Opera House Orch, 72-81 & San Francisco Symph, 81- *Teaching:* Instr oboe, Centenary Col, La Tech Univ, 71-72. *Mailing Add:* Davies Symph Hall San Francisco CA 94102

GIBB, STANLEY GARTH
COMPOSER, EDUCATOR
b Chicago, Ill, June 22, 40. *Study:* San Francisco Univ, with Herbert Bielawa & Wayne Peterson, BMus & MMus; NTex State Univ, with Merrill Ellis, DMA. *Works:* Overture to the Second Coming (choir & tape), 71; Parity (trombone & tape), 72; Sonic Flight (tape), 72; Bird Dance (tape), 72; Woman (tape), 73; Sound Action (perc & tape), 75; Documents (chamber choir), 76. *Teaching:* Fac mem, Univ Okla, 71-72 & NTex State Univ, 72-73; instr, Calif State Polytechnic Univ, assoc prof theory, comp & perc, currently. *Awards:* First Place, Percussive Arts Soc Comp Cont, 75. *Mailing Add:* Music Dept Calif State Polytech Univ Pomona CA 91768

GIBBONS, JOHN
HARPSICHORD, EDUCATOR
b St Louis, Mo, 41. *Study:* New England Consv, BM; Cincinnati Consv. *Rec Perf:* For Musical Heritage Soc, Titanic, Cambridge & Harmonia Mundi. *Pos:* Harpsichordist, Leslie Lindsey Mason Collection Musical Instrm, Museum Fine Arts, Boston; soloist with Boston Symph Orch, Boston Camerata & Orch of the 18th Century, Amsterdam; mem, Boston Music Trio, currently. *Teaching:* Harpsichord instr, New England Consv, currently. *Awards:* Erwin Bodky Prize, 76; New England Consv Chadwick Medal, 67; Fulbright Scholar. *Mailing Add:* 21 Prescott St Charleston MA 02129

GIBBS, GEOFFREY DAVID
COMPOSER, EDUCATOR
b Copiague, NY, Mar 29, 40. *Study:* Eastman Sch Music, studied comp with Bernard Rogers & Howard Hanson & electronic comp with Wayne Barlow, BMus, 62, MMus, 63, DMA, 74; studied piano with Gladys M Gehrig, comp with Elie Siegmeister & voice with Julius Huehn & Yi-Kwei Sze. *Works:* Symposium (oratorio), 70; Icon: Igor Stravinsky, perf by Jacksonville Univ Orch, 72; Symphony No 2, perf by Univ RI Symph Orch, 72; The Bond of Peace (cantata), 73; Capers (two pianos), 74; String Quartet, 75; Pastorale (cello or bassoon & piano). *Pos:* Lectr & recitalist modern art song, New England, 70-71. *Teaching:* Asst prof music, Univ RI, Kingston, 65-82, assoc prof, 82-, dir, Electronic Music Studio. *Mem:* Am Soc Univ Comp; Am Music Ctr; Pi Kappa Lambda; Music Educr Nat Conf; RI Music Educr Asn. *Publ:* Contribr to Kinsman. *Mailing Add:* Dept Music Univ RI Kingston RI 02881

GIBBS, RAYMOND
TENOR, EDUCATOR
b Dec 3, 42. *Study:* San Francisco Opera Merola Prog, 65; San Diego State Univ, BA(voice), 66; Manhattan Sch Music, MMus, 68. *Roles:* Romeo in Romeo et Juliette, San Diego Opera, 73; Pinkerton in Madama Butterfly, Metropolitan Opera & New York Opera, 74; Rodolfo in La Boheme, Metropolitan Opera & Munich Opera, 77; Pelleas in Pelleas et Melisande, Metropolitan Opera & New York Opera, 78; Cavaradossi in Tosca, Florentine Opera, Milwaukee, 79; Alfredo in La Traviata, Edmonton, Can, 82; Don Jose in Carmen, Toledo Opera & Memphis Opera, 83. *Teaching:* Prof voice & opera, Memphis State Univ, 78-; master classes, San Diego State, currently. *Awards:* San Francisco Opera Regional Winner, 65; Grant, William M Sullivan Found, 66. *Mem:* Phi Mu Alpha; Am Guild Musical Artists. *Rep:* Louise Williams Mgt 3650 Los Feliz Blvd Los Angeles CA 90027. *Mailing Add:* 8600 Thorncliff Fairway Cordova TN 38018

GIBSON, DAVID R
COMPOSER, EDUCATOR
b Albany, NY, Sept 20, 43. *Study:* Juilliard Sch Music, with Stanley Wolfe; Yale Univ, with Jacob Druckman. *Works:* 13 Ways of Looking at a Blackbird (voice & instrm); Embellishments #1 (string quartet & tape); Lion's Head (amplified bass); Shadows (three perc); Three Fragments (cello & piano); Ligatures (woodwind quartet), 74; Embellishments #2 (string quartet). *Pos:* Cellist, US Army String Quartet, 67-70; comp & cellist, Ctr for Creative & Perf Arts, State Univ NY, Buffalo, 72-74. *Teaching:* Mem fac, State Univ NY, Albany, 76- *Awards:* Harriett Fox Gibbs Award; Nat Endowment for Arts Grant, 74. *Mailing Add:* 25 N Main Ave Albany NY 12203

GIBSON, JON CHARLES
COMPOSER, SAXOPHONE
b Los Angeles, Calif, Mar 11, 40. *Study:* Sacramento State Univ, with Frederick Westphal & Harvey Reddick, 59-61; San Francisco State Univ, with Wayne Peterson & Henry Onderdonk, BA(music), 64. *Works:* Visitations (solo performer & tape), 68, 30's (ens & open instrm), 70, Untitled (solo, duet or trio of mixed instrm), 75, Melody IV (small ens), 75, Equal Distribution #1 (solo instrm & electronics), 77, Extensions (solo instrm & tape), 80 & Relative Calm (ens & tape), 81, Undertow Music Co. *Rec Perf:* Visitations, 72, Untitled, 75 & Clcles, 74, Chatham Square Rec; Einstein on the Beach, Philip Glass Ens, Tomato Rec; Music With Changing Parts, Phillip Glass Ens, Chatha Sq Rec; Four Organs, Phase Patters, with Steve Reich, Shandar Rec. *Pos:* Founding mem, New Music Ens, 61-64; performer & collabr with Steve Reich, 62-72 & with Terry Riley, 63-65; mem, Philip Glass Ens, 67-; performer with LaMonte Young, 70. *Teaching:* Numerous lectr & wkshp. *Awards:* Grants, Creative Artist Pub Serv Prog, 74 & 81, Nat Endowment Arts, 75, 77, 82 & 83 & Rockefeller Found, 82. *Bibliog:* David Reck (auth), Music Whole Earth, Scribners, 77; Robert Palmer (auth), Science Inspires Soho Avant-Guarde Composers, New York Times, 7/31/77; Richard Teitelbaum (auth), Less & Less, Solo Weekly News, 3/26/80. *Mem:* BMI. *Mailing Add:* 17 Thompson St New York NY 10013

GIDDINGS, ROBERT POTTER
LIBRARIAN, ADMINISTRATOR
b Boston, Mass. *Study:* Univ Rochester, AB, 37; studied with Emil Frey, Zürich & Matthay, London, 37-38; New England Consv Music, BA(music); Simmons Col, MS(libr sci), 57. *Pos:* Cur music, Boston Pub Libr, 59-62; supvr music cataloging, New York Pub Libr, 63-71; asst to publ, Wiscasset Music Publ, 81- *Mailing Add:* 17 Follen St Boston MA 02116

GIDEON, MIRIAM
COMPOSER, EDUCATOR
b Greeley, Colo, Oct 23, 06. *Study:* Boston Univ, BA, 26; studied with Lazare Saminsky & Roger Sessions, 31-42; Columbia Univ, MA(musicol), 46; Jewish Theol Sem, DSM(comp), 70; Brooklyn Col, DHL, 83. *Works:* Thirteen cycles for solo voice and instrumental ens, 45-, Lyric Piece for String Orch, 41, Symphonia Brevis, 53, Fortunato (opera), 58, Songs of Youth and Madness,

77; Sonata for Piano, 77, Trio for Clarinet, Violoncello & Piano, 78, Spiritual Airs, 79 & Spirit Above the Dust, 80, Am Comp Alliance Bulletin; and many others. *Teaching:* Fac, Brooklyn Col, City Col New York, 44-76, emer prof, 76-; assoc prof, Cantors Inst, Jewish Theol Sem Am, 55-; mem fac, Manhattan Sch Music, 67- *Awards:* Ernest Bloch Choral Award, 47; Colleqium Distinguished Alumni, Boston Univ, 74; grant, Nat Endowment for Arts, 75. *Bibliog:* D & B Rosenberg (ed), The Music Makers, Am Comp Alliance Bulletin, Vol 7 No 4; D Ewen (auth), Composers in America, Putnam, 82; J W LePage (auth), Women Composers, Conductors, Musicians of the 20th Century, Vol 2, Scarecrow Press, 83. *Mem:* Am Acad & Inst Arts & Lett; Am Comp Alliance; Int Soc Contemp Music; fel, MacDowell Colony. *Mailing Add:* 410 Central Park West New York NY 10025

GIEBLER, ALBERT CORNELIUS
EDUCATOR, ADMINISTRATOR
b Hays, Kans, Aug 17, 21. *Study:* Ft Hays State Univ, BM(music educ), 46; Univ Mich, Ann Arbor, MM(music theory), 50, with Hans T David, PhD(musicol), 57. *Teaching:* Instr instrm music, Russell High Sch, Kans, summer 46; supvr & instr music, Quinter High Sch, Kans, 46-48; prof music, Univ RI, 57-, chmn music dept, 68-79, coordr grad studies, 80- *Mem:* Music Teachers Nat Asn (chmn winds & perc div, 68-70); RI Music Teachers Asn (pres, 65-69 & 72-74); Music Educr Nat Conf; Am Musicol Soc; Col Music Soc. *Interests:* Development of musical settings of the mass during the Baroque period. *Publ:* Auth, The Band Music of Paul Creston, RI Music Educr Rev, 58; Johann Caspar Kerll's Missa Superba, A-R Ed, 67; Johann Caspar Kerll, In: New Grove Dict of Music & Musicians, 80. *Mailing Add:* Pine Hill Road Rt 5 Wakefield RI 02879

GIELEN, MICHAEL ANDREAS
CONDUCTOR
b Dresden, Germany, July 20, 27. *Study:* Univ Dresden, 36; Univ Berlin, 37; Univ Vienna, 40; Univ Buenos Aires, 50. *Works:* 4 Gedichte von Stefan George, 58; Variations for 40 Instruments, 59; Un dia Sobresale, 63; die glocken sind auf falscher spur, 69; Mitbestimmunes Modell, 74. *Pos:* Coach, Testro Colon, Buenos Aires, 47-50; cond, Vienna State Opera, 50-60 & Stockholm Royal Opera, 60-65; freelance cond, Cologne, Germany, 65-68; music dir, Belgian Nat Orch, 69-73 & Cincinnati Symph Orch, 80-; chief commander, Netherlands Opera, 73-75; music dir & gen mgr, Frankfurt Opera House, Germany, 77-; prin guest cond, BBC Symph Orch, London; guest cond, Washington Nat Symph, Chicago Symph, Pittsburgh Symph, Minn Orch, Detroit Symph & others. *Mailing Add:* Cincinnati Symph Orch 1241 Elm St Cincinnati OH 45210

GIFFIN, GLENN
CRITIC-WRITER
b Denver, Colo, Feb 27, 43. *Study:* Univ Colo, BMus, 65; Univ Denver, MA, 67. *Pos:* Asst music librn, Univ Colo, Boulder, 68-70; music ed, Denver Post Inc, 70- *Awards:* Fels, Rockefeller Found, 66-68, Corbett Found, 71 & Nat Endowment Arts, 72. *Mailing Add:* c/o Denver Post Corp PO Box 1709 Denver CO 80201

GILAD, YEHUDA
CLARINET, CONDUCTOR
b Kibbutz Gan-Shmuell, Israel, Sept 5, 52. *Study:* Menashe Consv, Israel, dipl, 68-71; studied clarinet with Giora Feidman, 68-71; Robin Acad Sch Music, 73-75; Sch Music, Univ Southern Calif, studied clarinet with Mitchell Lurie, BM, 75-80; studied chamber music with J Lowenthal, Brooks Smith, Marcel Moyse & cond with William Schaefer, Herbert Zipper & Daniel Lewis. *Rec Perf:* Pastoral Varie (clarinet & strings), Kibbutz 1, 74; Introducing the Yoav Chamber Ensemble, Orion Rec, 80; Affects, Town Hall Rec, 83. *Pos:* Solo clarinetist & founder, Yoav Chamber Ens, 77-; music dir, Joyeux Woodwind Chamber Players, 78- & Santa-Monica Symph Orch, 82-; prin clarinetist, Am Woodwind Chamber Players, 81-; assoc music dir, Orch 81-83, Los Angeles, 81-83; solo clarinetist, Kibbutzim Chamber Orch, recitals in US, Europe & Israel; participant, Marlboro Fest, Chamber Music West, San Francisco & Israeli Fest. *Teaching:* Lectr clarinet & chamber music, Community Sch, 77-, Sch Music, Univ Southern Calif, 81- & Calif Inst Arts, 83-; fac mem, Idyllwild Chamber Music Prog, currently. *Awards:* Am-Israel Cultural Found Award, 68-75; Robert Simon Award Music, 77-80; Outstanding Teacher of Year, Univ Southern Calif Community Sch, 79. *Mem:* Young Musicians Found; Chamber Music Am; Am Symph League Asn; Clarinet Int Soc. *Mailing Add:* 3131 S Figueroa St Los Angeles CA 90007

GILB, TYRA ELLEN
FLUTE & PICCOLO, TEACHER-COACH
b Berkeley, Calif, Sept 27, 55. *Study:* Juilliard Sch, BM, 77, MM, 78; Yale Sch Music, MM, 81. *Pos:* Solo recitalist, Carnegie Recital Hall, 79; prin flute, Des Moines Metro Opera, 80-; piccolo & flute, NC Symph, 82- *Awards:* Conct Artists Guild Int Compt Award, 79; Young Artists Award, Music Club NY, 79. *Mem:* Col Music Soc; Nat Flute Asn. *Mailing Add:* 111 El Camino Real Berkeley CA 94705

GILBERT, DAVID BEATTY
CONDUCTOR & MUSIC DIRECTOR, COMPOSER
b Huntingdon, Pa, Aug 4, 36. *Study:* Eastman Sch Music, BM, 57, MM, 58; studied cond with Ionel Perlea, 66-70; studied with Pierre Boulez, 69. *Works:* Petit Concert, perf by Mozart Trio, Washington, DC, 60; Poem VI for Alto Flute and Percussion, perf by Contemp Chamber Players, Univ Ill, 66; Centering I, comn & perf by Aeolian Chamber Players, 69; Four Songs of Wind, perf by Richard Pittman & Boston Musica Viva, 70; Centering II,, comn & perf by Joel Thome & Philadelphia Comp Forum, 70. *Rec Perf:*

Variazioni (George Crumb) & Fresco (Sydney Hodkinson), Louisville, Ky, 81; Concerto No 2 in F Minor (Chopin), Desto Rec, Peking, China, 83. *Pos:* Asst cond, New York Phil, 70-79; cond, Am Ballet Theatre, 71-75; music dir, Greenwich Symph Orch, 75- *Awards:* First Prize, Dimitri Mitropoulos Int Compt Cond, 70. *Rep:* Herbert Barrett Mgt 1860 Broadway New York NY 10023. *Mailing Add:* 84-50 Austin St #5A Kew Gardens NY 11415

GILBERT, JANET MONTEITH
COMPOSER, EDUCATOR
b New York, NY, Aug 6, 46. *Study:* Douglass Col, AB, 69; Villa Schifanoia, Florence, Italy, MA, 72; Univ Ill, Champaign, DMA, 79. *Works:* Solo for Clarinet, 72, Oenone (tape), 77, ... out of the looking glass (tape), 77, Paisaje (sop & tape), 79, Circumflexions (solo sop), 79, Am Comp Ed; A Psalm of Penitence, Repertory Singers, St Olaf Col, 82; Fusions, Minn Independent Choreographers Studio X Comn, 82. *Teaching:* Vis asst prof, Middlebury Col, 79-80; asst prof, St Olaf Col, 80- *Mem:* Am Comp Alliance; Am Soc Univ Comp; Col Music Soc; Minn Comp Forum; BMI. *Mailing Add:* 216 College St Northfield MN 55057

GILBERT, MICHAEL WILLIAM
COMPOSER, ELECTRONIC
b New York, NY, Aug 17, 54. *Study:* Boston Sch Electronic Music, 75-76; Hamphshire Col, BA(music), 79. *Works:* Moving Pictures, 79 & The Call, 81, rec Gibex; In the Dreamtime, rec Palace of Lights, 82. *Pos:* Consultant, currently. *Teaching:* Tech dir, Electronic Music Studio, Univ Mass, Amherst, 79-82; lectr electronic music, Holyoke Community Col & Univ Mass, 81-82. *Mailing Add:* 73 Spaulding St Amherst MA 01002

GILBERT, PIA SOPHIA
COMPOSER, EDUCATOR
b Kippenheim, Ger, June 1, 21; US citizen. *Study:* New York Col Music, teaching dipl, 43, artist dipl, 45. *Works:* Interrupted Suite, Transmutations, 76, Spirals and Interpolations, 77, Vociano, 81 & Food, 81, C F Peters. *Teaching:* Prof music for dance & res comp, Univ Calif, Los Angeles, 48- *Awards:* Various research grants, Univ Calif, Los Angeles, 77, 80 & 81-82. *Publ:* Coauth, Music for the Modern Dance, Brown, 68; auth, The Composer and the Dance, C F Peter News, 81. *Mailing Add:* 11400 Berwich St Los Angeles CA 90049

GILBERT, RICHARD
CLARINET, WRITER
b Bronx, NY, May 21, 43. *Study:* Peabody Consv Music, 61-65; Hofstra Univ, BS, 68; Grad Sch, NY Univ. *Pos:* Pres & founder, Grenadilla Rec, 72-; exec dir, Guild Contemp Music Inc, 79- *Mem:* Nat Asn Rec Arts & Sci; Asn Class Music; Music & Perf Arts Lodge; Int Clarinet Soc. *Publ:* The Clarinetists Solo Repertory—A Discography, 72 & The Clarinetists Discography, Vol II, 75, Grenadilla. *Mailing Add:* Guild Contemp Music 142-25 Pershing Cres St E 2F Kew Gardens NY 11435

GILBERT, STEVEN E(DWARD)
EDUCATOR, WRITER
b Brooklyn, NY, Apr 20, 43. *Study:* Brooklyn Col, City Univ New York, BA, 64; Yale Univ, MM, 67, MPhil, 69 & PhD, 70. *Teaching:* From asst prof to prof music, Cal State Univ, Fresno, 70- *Awards:* Student Comp Awards, BMI, 64, 66 & 67. *Publ:* Auth, The Twelve Tone System of Carl Ruggles, J Music Theory, Vol XIV, No 1; Carl Ruggles (1876-1971): An Appreciation, Vol XI, No 1 & The Ultra-Modern Idiom: A Survey of New Music, Vol XII, Perspectives New Music; Introduction to Trichordal Analysis, J Music Theory, Vol XVIII, No 2; coauth, Introduction to Schenkerian Analysis, W W Norton & Co, 82. *Mailing Add:* 544 Circle Dr S Fresno CA 93704

GILELS, EMIL
PIANIST
b Odessa, USSR, Oct 19, 16. *Study:* Odessa Consv, dipl, 35; Sch Mastership, Moscow Consv, 38. *Rec Perf:* On DGG, EMI & RCA. *Pos:* Concert pianist, USSR, 33-, Europe, 45-, USA, 55-, Mex, 55, Japan, 57 & Can, 58- *Teaching:* Prof, Moscow Consv, 54- *Awards:* Lenin Prize, 62; Medaille de Vermeil de la Ville de Paris, 67; Gold Medal, Brussels, 72. *Mailing Add:* c/o Columbia Artists Mgt 165 W 57th St New York NY 10019

GILES, ANNE DIENER
FLUTE, EDUCATOR
Study: Juilliard Sch Music, with Julius Baker, Jacob Berg & Marcel Moyse, BM(flute), MS(flute). *Rec Perf:* Brandenburg Concerti, Deutsche Grammophon; Music for Flute and Piano (Allen Giles), Crystal Records. *Pos:* Flute, Music Aeterna Orch, formerly; solo flutist, Juilliard Ens, formerly; prin flute & soloist, Los Angeles Phil, 71-83. *Teaching:* Mem fac flute, Music Acad West, currently. *Mailing Add:* Los Angeles Phil Orch 135 N Grand Ave Los Angeles CA 90012

GILL, RICHARD THOMAS
BASS
b Long Branch, NJ, Nov 30, 27. *Study:* Harvard Col, AB, 48; Harvard Univ, PhD, 56; vocal study with Herbert Mayer, 67-80. *Roles:* Sir Giorgio in I Puritani, 73 & Enrico in Anna Bolena, 74, New York City Opera; Friar Laurence in Romeo et Juliette, 75 & Pimen in Boris Godunov, 76, Metropolitan Opera; Ramfis in Aida, Houston Grand Opera, 77; King in Love for Three Oranges, Chicago Lyric Opera, 79; Sarastro in Magic Flute, New York City Opera, 83. *Teaching:* Lectr voice, Univ Tex, Austin, 81. *Bibliog:* Charles Michener (auth), Economic Bass, Newsweek, 5/5/75; Sally E Moore (auth), Richard Gill Changes Careers in His 40s, People Mag, 6/21/75; Stan Huygens (auth), De Harvard-professor werd zanger, De Telegraaf, Amsterdam, 6/11/77. *Mem:* Am Guild Musical Artists (first vpres, 77-79). *Mailing Add:* 2800 NW 51st Pl Ft Lauderdale FL 33309

GILLESPIE, ALLAN E
EDUCATOR, CONDUCTOR
b Grafton, NDak, Apr 29, 26. *Study:* Univ NDak, BA, 51; Univ Wis, MM, 56; Univ Mich, 60. *Pos:* Asst dir bands, Univ NDak, 51-54 & Univ Wis, 54-56. *Teaching:* Prof cond & dir bands, Univ Conn, 56- *Mem:* Col Band Dir Nat Asn (Eastern div pres, 64-66, nat chmn cond symposium, 78-80); Music Educr Nat Asn; Phi Beta Mu (state pres, 78-80); Nat Band Asn. *Mailing Add:* 27 Storrs Heights Rd Storrs CT 02628

GILLESPIE, DON CHANCE
EDITOR, PIANO
b Metter, Ga, Aug 25, 36. *Study:* Univ Ga, Athens, BA(music), 58, MA(musicol), 67; Univ NC, Chapel Hlll, PhD(musicol), 77. *Pos:* Asst, Music Libr, Univ Ga, 65; res asst, Univ NC, 68-69; corresp ed, Current Musicology, 68-70; dir rights clearance & spec ed proj, C F Peters Corp, 70- *Teaching:* Private piano, Metter, Ga, 63-64; instr piano, Univ Ga, 65-66. *Awards:* Fulbright Grant to Vienna, 58-59. *Mem:* Int Percy Grainger Soc (vpres, 81-); Am Musicol Soc; Sonneck Soc; Delius Soc. *Interests:* Music and life of John J Becker, avant-garde American composer. *Publ:* Auth, John Becker, Musical Crusader of Saint Paul, Musical Quart, 4/76; John Becker's Correspondence with Ezra Pound: The Origins of a Musical Crusader, Bulletin of Research in Humanities, spring 80; John Becker's Correspondence with Ezra Pound: The Origins of a Musical Crusader, Bulletin Res Humanities, spring 80; William Albright, John Becker, Alan Stout, Roger Hannay & Dennis Riley, In: New Grove Dict of Music & Musicians, 80; co-ed, A John Cage Reader, C F Peters Corp, 83. *Mailing Add:* 260 Sixth Ave New York NY 10014

GILLESPIE, JAMES ERNEST
CLARINET, EDUCATOR
b Tazewell, Va, Nov 30, 40. *Study:* Concord Col, BSME, 62; Ind Univ, MM, 63, DM, 69. *Pos:* Ed, Clarinet Soc J, Clarinet, 78- *Teaching:* Inst woodwinds, Concord Col, Athens, WVa, 63-66; asst prof clarinet, Northeast La Univ, Monroe, 69-78; prof music, NTex State Univ, Denton, 78. *Mem:* Int Clarinet Soc. *Publ:* Auth, The Reed Trio: An Annotated Bibliography, 71 & Solos for Unaccompanied Clarinet: An Annotated Bibliography, 73, Info Coordr; numerous articles in Instrumentalist, Woodwind World, School Musician, Clarinet & Clarinet & Saxophone. *Mailing Add:* Sch Music NTex State Univ Denton TX

GILLESPIE, JOHN E
EDUCATOR, PIANO
b Terre Haute, Ind, Jan 2, 21. *Study:* Univ Southern Calif, studied harpsichord with A Ehlers, MM, 47, MA, 48, PhD, 51. *Teaching:* Prof music, Univ Calif, Santa Barbara, 51- *Awards:* G Schirmer Award, 42; Fulbright Grant, 49-50. *Mem:* Am Musicol Soc; Sonneck Soc. *Publ:* Auth, The Musical Experience, Wadsworth, 68; Five Centuries of Keyboard Music, 72, ed, Nineteenth Century European Piano Music, 77 & Nineteenth Century American Piano Music, 78, Dover; auth, Nineteenth Century American Piano Music: A Selective Annotated Bibliography, Greenwood Press (in prep). *Mailing Add:* 1201 Las Alturas Santa Barbara CA 93103

GILLETTE, JOHN CARRELL
EDUCATOR, BASSOON
b Girard, Kans, May 16, 41. *Study:* Kans State Col, BME, 63, MS(music), 64; Ind Univ, Bloomington, DM(woodwind), 77. *Pos:* First bassoon, 64-65. *Teaching:* Assoc prof bassoon & music theory, State Univ NY, Fredonia, 67- *Mem:* Nat Asn Col Wind & Perc Instr (chmn, 77-); Am Fedn Musicians; Int Double Reed Soc. *Mailing Add:* 56 Curtis Pl Fredonia NY 14603

GILLICK, LYN (EMELYN SAMUELS)
COMPOSER, WRITER
b Brooklyn, NY, Nov 13, 48. *Study:* Skidmore Col, BS, 70; NY Univ, MA, 76; Memphis State Univ, with Don Freund. *Works:* Caucasian Chalk Circle, 77 & Macbeth, 77, La Mama; Venus Ascending, 79, In the Bittersweet Silence, 79 & Cages, 81, Ballet South; Neon Ballads (piano), Kevin Grey, 82; Concertino for Saxophone and Chamber Orchestra, Memphis New Music Orch, 82. *Pos:* Music dir, Ballet South, 78-82 & Tenn Ballet, 82- *Awards:* Memphis Penwomen's Award, 81. *Mem:* Am Music Ctr. *Publ:* Auth, New Music in Memphis (ser), Dixie Flyer, 80-82. *Mailing Add:* 2533 Hale Ave Memphis TN 38112

GILLOCK, JON
ORGAN, EDUCATOR
b San Francisco, Calif. *Study:* Univ Ark, BM, MM(organ); studied with John Cowell; Col Church Musicians, Washington Cathedral, with Leo Sowerby, Paul Callaway & Preston Rockhold; Juilliard Sch, with Vernon de Tar & Gustave Reese, DMA(organ); Consv Nat Superieur Musique, Paris, with Olivier Messiaen. *Pos:* Dir Music, Church of Incarnation, New York, currently; recitalist throughout US, Can & Europe. *Teaching:* Mem organ fac, Montclair State Col, currently; mem fac, Pre-Col Div, Juilliard Sch, 71-; fac organ, 81- *Publ:* Auth, Messiaen ... Communicable Language, Music, 4-74; Dietrich Buxtehude: Samtliche Orgelwerke, Notes, 3-75; compiled & ed, Messiaen's Organ Works: The Composer's Aesthetaic and Analytical Notes, Music 12-78. *Rep:* Paula Romanuax Kalamazoo MI. *Mailing Add:* Juilliard Sch Lincoln Ctr New York NY 10023

GILMAN, IRVIN EDWARD
FLUTE, EDUCATOR
b Philadelphia, Pa, Mar 28, 26. *Study:* Studied with William Kincaid, 52; Consv Music, Oberlin Col, BMus, 53; Manhattan Sch Music, MMus, 54. *Pos:* Asst prin flute & second flute, Detroit Symph Orch, 56-68; prin flute, Albany

Symph Orch, 69-; flutist & vpres, Capitol Chamber Artists, 69- *Teaching:* Instr flute, Manhattan Sch Music, 53-56 & Wayne State Univ, 62-63; assoc prof music, State Univ NY, Albany, 68- *Bibliog:* I E Gilman (auth), The Piccolo, Woodwind Anthology, 60 & The Still Surface Breaks (poem), Sislin-Splane Publ Co, 63. *Mem:* Am Fedn Musicians; Nat Flute Asn; United Univ Prof. *Mailing Add:* State Univ NY Pac 215 1400 Washington Ave Albany NY 12222

GILMORE, BERNARD
COMPOSER, EDUCATOR

b Oakland, Calif, Nov 19, 37. *Study:* Univ Calif, Los Angeles, with John Vincent, Boris Kremenliev & Lukas Foss; studied with Josef Tal; Stamford Univ, DMA(cond), 66. *Works:* Symphonic Movement (orch); Five Folk Songs (sop & band); Music for Six Horns; Dover Beach (sop, clarinet & string trio); Duo for Flute and Viola; Three Poems of Love (chamber chorus & chamber orch); Five Pieces for Piano. *Pos:* Horn, Boston Pops Tour Orch, 57, Los Angeles Phil, 56-61 & Haifa Symph Orch, Israel, 72-73. *Teaching:* Mem fac, Cornell Univ, 61-64; assoc prof cond, Ore State Univ, 66- *Awards:* Winner, Eastern Div, Col Band Dir Comp Cont, 65; Ore State Univ Found Grant (two). *Mailing Add:* Music Dept Ore State Univ Corvallis OR 97331

GILMORE, EV (EVERETT M GILMORE), JR
TUBA

b Wheeling, WVa, Dec 13, 35. *Study:* George Williams Col, with Harmon H Bro, 53-55; Lebanon Valley Col, Pa, BA, 58; Univ Denver, MA, 67; studied with Charles Gusikoff, 59-62. *Pos:* Tubist, US Army Field Band, Washington, DC, 58-60 & Wichita Symph Orch, 63-65; tubist & trombonist, Dallas Symph Orch, 65-, Dallas Brass Quintet, 66- & Tex Tuba Quartet, 77- *Teaching:* Adj prof tuba, Southern Methodist Univ, 66- *Mem:* Am Fedn Musicians; Int Conf Symph & Opera Musicians; Tubists Univ Brotherhood Asn. *Mailing Add:* 723 Skillman St Dallas TX 75214

GILMORE, JOHN
TENOR

b Bradford, Pa, July 23, 50. *Study:* Study voice with Elizabeth Mannion & Margaret Harshaw, 69-; Sch Music, Ind Univ, BM(voice), 76, MM(voice), 77. *Rec Perf:* Les Noces, Radio Nat France, 81; Lucia di Lammermoor, 82 & Don Carlo, 83, Metropolitan Opera, PBS. *Roles:* Tenor solo in Habat Mater, Philadelpha Orch, 81; tenor solo in Les Noces, New York Phil, 82; tenor solo in Oedipus Rex, Boston Symph, 82; tenor solo in Songfest, Cleveland Orch, 82; Prince Shiusky in Boris Godunov, Metropolitan Opera, 82; title role in Orlando Palindino, Pa Opera Theater, 82. *Pos:* Soloist, Metropolitan Opera, 81- *Teaching:* Fac artist in res, Sch Music, Univ Wis, Madison, 78-80. *Awards:* Young Artist, Nat Endowment of Arts, 77. *Mailing Add:* c/o Thea Dispeker Artist Mgt 59 E 54th St New York NY 10022

GIMPEL, JAKOB
PIANO, EDUCATOR

Study: Lwow Consv; studied with Edward Steuermann & Alban Berg. *Rec Perf:* Beethoven Fourth & Fifth Piano Concertos, Fantasie in F (Chopin) & Fantasie in C (Schumann), Genesis Rec. *Pos:* Soloist, US, 38- & Europe, 54- *Teaching:* Distinguished prof in res, Calif State Univ, Northridge, 71-; instr master classes, US & Europe. *Awards:* Ben Gurion Award, Israel; Order Merit First Class, Fed Repub Germany. *Mailing Add:* Dept Music Calif State Univ Northridge CA 91330

GINDIN, EDWARD M
CONDUCTOR, TEACHER

b Moscow, USSR, Sept 25, 38; US citizen. *Pos:* Violist, Moscow Symph Orch, USSR, 62-63, Chamber Orch, Moscow, 62-66 & Syracuse Symph, 78-; asst prin violist, Stanislavsky Opera Theatre, Moscow, 66-76; music dir & cond, Moscow Univ Chamber Orch, 66-76 & Syracuse Camerata Chamber Orch, 81- *Teaching:* Violin & viola, Moscow Univ, USSR, 66-76. *Mem:* Cent NY Asn Music Teachers. *Mailing Add:* 38 Presidential Ct Syracuse NY 13202

GINGOLD, JOSEF
EDUCATOR, VIOLIN

b Russia. *Study:* Studied violin with Vladimir Graffman, Eugene Ysaye; Kent State Univ, with Baldwin Wallace, DHL; Ind Univ, Hon Dr Music; Cleveland Inst Music, Hon Dr Music. *Pos:* Violinist, NBC Symph Orch, 37-44; concertmaster, Detroit Symph, 44-47 & Cleveland Orch, 47-60; juror many int violin compt incl Queen Elizabeth compt, Brussels, Sibelius Compt, Helsinki, Paganini Compt, Genoa & Tchaikovsky Compt, Moscow. *Teaching:* Prof violin, Ind Univ, 60-, distinguished prof, 65-; head chamber music dept, Meadowmount Sch Music, summers for 25 yrs; instr master classes, Consv Nat Superieur Musique, Paris & Toho Sch Music, Tokyo. *Awards:* Teacher of Year, Am String Teachers Asn, 68; Frederic Bachman Lieber Award Distinguished Teaching, 71; hon chmn & pres jury, First Int Violin Compt, Indianapolis, 82. *Mem:* Phi Mu Alpha; Pi Kappa Lambda. *Mailing Add:* 2511 E Second St Bloomington IN 46401

GINGRICH, DANIEL J
FRENCH HORN

b Berwyn, Ill, Apr 20, 53. *Study:* Chicago Musical Col, 72 & 73. *Pos:* Third horn, Rochester Phil Orch, 73-74 & Nat Symph Orch, 74-75; fourth horn, Chicago Symph Orch, 75- *Mailing Add:* c/o Chicago Symph Orch 220 S Michigan Ave Chicago IL 60604

GINSBURG, GERALD M
COMPOSER, TEACHER

b Lincoln, Nebr. *Study:* Oberlin Consv, BMus, 54; Manhattan Sch Music, MM, 58. *Works:* 37 songs, Carnegie Recital Hall, 74; The World Is a Beautiful Place (theater piece), Alice Tully Hall, 77. *Teaching:* Fac, Third St Music Sch, 60-65; music chmn, Columbia Grammar & Prep Sch, 66-75. *Mem:* New York Singing Teachers Asn. *Mailing Add:* One Sheridan Sq New York NY 10014

GINTER, ANTHONY FRANCIS
EDUCATOR, VIOLIN

b Windsor, Ont, Aug 28, 32. *Study:* Royal Consv Music, Toronto, artist dipl, 54; Univ Toronto, BA, 63; Ind Univ, MME, 65; Ohio State Univ, PhD, 76. *Pos:* Violinist, Toronto Symph Orch, 57-64 & Columbus Symph Orch, Ohio, 65-76. *Teaching:* Asst prof violin & orch, Otterbein Col, Ohio, 65-71; assoc in perf, Kenyon Col, Ohio, 72-77; assoc prof orch & music hist, Univ Calif, Riverside, 77- *Mem:* Am Musicol Soc; Am String Teachers Asn; Col Music Soc; Southern Calif Sch Band & Orch Asn; Music Teachers Asn Calif, Inc. *Interests:* Sonatas of Pierre Gavinies. *Publ:* Auth, Pierre Gavinies (1728-1800), Founder of French School of Violin Plalying, 78 & Jan Kubelik, Wizard of the Violin, 81, Am String Teacher. *Mailing Add:* 219 Maravilla Dr Riverside CA 92507

GIOCONDA, CARMEN MANTECA See Carmen, Marina

GIORDANO, JOHN
CONDUCTOR & MUSIC DIRECTOR

b Dunkirk, NY, Dec 31, 37. *Study:* Tex Christian Univ, BM, 60, MM, 62; Royal Consv, Brussels, 65. *Works:* Composition for Jazz Ensemble and Symphony Orchestra, 74. *Pos:* Appeared as sax soloist & with orch throughout US & Europe, 65-72; music dir, Youth Orch Gtr Ft Worth, 69-; guest cond, Ft Worth Symph, 71; music dir & cond, 72-; founder & cond, Tex Little Symph, 76-; guest cond, Nat Symph Belgium, Nat Symph El Salvador, Amsterdam Phil, Nat Symph Port & others. *Teaching:* Mem fac music, NTex State Univ, 65-72; mem fac & cond univ symph, Tex Christian Univ, 72- *Awards:* Fulbright Scholar, 65; Premiere Prix, Royal Consv, Brussels, 65. *Bibliog:* Symphony (film), 78. *Mem:* Phi Mu Alpha Sinfonia; Pi Kappa Lambda. *Mailing Add:* c/o Perrotta Mgt Inc 211 W 56 St New York NY 10019

GIPPO, JAN EIRIK
FLUTE & PICCOLO

b Long Beach, Calif, June 20, 46. *Study:* Univ Pac, 64-66; New England Consv Music, BA, 68, MA, 71. *Pos:* Flute & piccolo, St Louis Symph Orch, 77- *Teaching:* Flute, St Louis Univ, 79-; artist in res flute & perf, Weluter Univ, 79- *Mailing Add:* St Louis Symph 718 N Grand Blvd St Louis MO 63103

GIRARD, SHARON E
EDUCATOR, PIANO

b Los Angeles, Calif. *Study:* Mozarteum, with Bernard Paumgartner, cert, 61; Univ Calif, Los Angeles, with Rubsamen, Marrocco, Reaney & Hood, PhD, 75; Univ Ill, with Nettl, 79. *Pos:* Co-ed, Latin Am Music Review, Univ Tex, Austin, 79. *Teaching:* Assoc prof musicol, San Francisco State, 79- *Awards:* Nat Defense Educ Act Award, 72; Coun Learned Soc Award, 75 & 82; Nat Endowment Humanities Award, 79 & 80-82. *Mem:* Int Musicol Soc; Am Musicol Soc (secy & treas NCalif chap, 80-); Col Music Soc; Latin Am Studies Asn. *Interests:* Chant; Shrewsbury Manuscript; V Aleotti; Latin America and world music. *Publ:* Auth, Funeral Music in Venezuela, Ariz State, 80; ed, Renaissance Dance Music of Guatemala, Music Sacra, 81. *Mailing Add:* 557 Arball Dr San Francisco CA 94132

GIULINI, CARLO MARIA
CONDUCTOR & MUSIC DIRECTOR

b Barletta, Italy, May 9, 14. *Study:* Accad Santa Cecilia, Rome; Chigiana Acad, Siena; studied with A Casella & B Molinari. *Pos:* Music dir, Ital Radio Orch, formerly; La Scala, 51-56 & Los Angeles Symph Orch, 78-; prin guest cond, Chicago Symph Orch, 68-; cond, Vienna Symph Orch, 73-76 & Philharmonia Orch, London, formerly; guest cond with major orch & opera co in US & Europe. *Awards:* Grammy Award, 71. *Mailing Add:* Los Angeles Philharmonic 135 N Grand Ave Los Angeles CA 90012

GLASER, VICTORIA MERRYLEES
EDUCATOR, COMPOSER

b Amherst, Mass, Sept 11, 18. *Study:* Harvard Univ, study with Walter Piston, Nadia Boulanger, Tillman Merritt, Otto Gombosi & Archibald Davison, BA, 40, MA, 43. *Works:* Homeric Hymn, Assoc Music Publ, 61; Two Movements (orch), perf by New England Consv Youth Orch, 62; Birthday Fugue, perf by Boston Symph Orch Pops, 65 & 67; Three Carols (SAB & instrm), Religious Arts Guild, 78; Sonata (pianoforte, three players), perf by New England Consv, 79; On Seven Winds (SSA & instrm), perf by Centennial Dana Hall Sch, 81; Epithalamion (violoncello & violin), perf by Boston Women Comp, New England Consv, 82. *Teaching:* Instr, Wellesley Col, 43-46; dir chorus, glee club & theory, Dana Hall Sch, 44-59; from instr to chair theory, Prep Dept, New England Consv, 57-; instr fugue & 16th-century counterpoint, Longy Sch Music, 79- *Awards:* First Prize, Brookline Libr Music Asn, Boston, 63. *Mem:* Am Guild Organists; ASCAP. *Publ:* Training for Musicianship, private publ, 72 & Taplinger, 78. *Mailing Add:* 37 Hawthorn St Cambridge MA 02138

GLASOW, GLENN L
EDUCATOR, MUSIC DIRECTOR
b Pine City, Minn, July 24, 24. *Study:* Hamline Univ, studied comp with Ernst Krenek, BA, 47, MA, 48; Nordwest Deutsche Akad Musik, studied comp with Wolfgang Fortner, 54-55; Univ Ill, DMA, 67. *Pos:* Dir music, Radio KPFA, Berkeley, 59-61; music critic, KQED-TV, San Francisco, 67. *Teaching:* Asst prof music, Col St Catherine, 52-59; prof music & Asian studies, Calif State Univ, Hayward, 61- *Awards:* Danforth Teacher Award, 57; Elizabeth J Freund Chamber Music Prize, 57; Distinguished Teacher Award, State Calif, 68. *Interests:* Essays of Toru Takemitsu. *Publ:* Ed & translr, Collected Essays by Toru Takemitsu. *Mailing Add:* 5582 Claremont Oakland CA 94618

GLASS, BEAUMONT
COACH, DIRECTOR—OPERA
b New York, NY, Oct 25, 25. *Study:* Phillips Exeter Acad, 44; US Naval Acad, Annapolis, Md, BS, 49; San Francisco State Col, 54-55; Univ Calif, Berkeley, 55. *Rec Perf:* Grace Bumbry Recital, Holland Fest, 65; Grace Bumbry Brahms Recital, Salzburg Fest, 65. *Pos:* Stage dir, NW Grand Opera, Seattle, Wash, 56-57; stage dir, San Francisco Musical Club, 56-57; coach, New York City Opera, 59 & Zurich Opera House, 61-80; concts in Germany, Austria, US, Can, Holland, France, Switzerland & Spain, 64-80; accmp, Salzburg Fest, 65; studienleiter Zurich Opera House, 78-80; dir, Opera Theatre, Univ Iowa, 80-; coach & accmp, Fest Aix-en-Provence, 74 & 76-78. *Teaching:* Asst to Lotte Lehmann & stage dir, Music Acad West, 57-59; studienleiter opera coaching & dir, Int Opera Ctr Opera House, Zurich, Switz, 61-65; instr opera & art song & opera dir, Univ Iowa, 80- *Mem:* Metropolitan Opera Guild; Cent Opera Serv; Nat Opera Asn. *Mailing Add:* 301 Richards St Iowa City IA 52240

GLASS, JEROME
CONDUCTOR, EDUCATOR
b Minersville, Pa, Nov 13, 20. *Study:* NY Univ, BS; Univ Southern Calif, MMus; studied comp with Mario Castelnuovo-Tedesco & Ingolf Dahl. *Pos:* Cond, Seattle Phil Orch, currently. *Teaching:* Assoc prof music, Western Wash Univ, currently. *Mem:* Am Symph Orch League. *Mailing Add:* Music Dept Western Wash Univ Bellingham WA 98225

GLASS, PHILIP
COMPOSER
b Baltimore, Md, Jan 31, 37. *Study:* Univ Chicago, BA, 56; Juilliard Sch, with Vincent Persichetti & William Bergsma, MM, 62; studied with Nadia Boulanger, 64-65. *Works:* Music with Changing Parts, 70; Music in 12 Parts, New York, 74; North Star (two voices & instrm), 75; Another Look at Harmony (amplified instrm & voices), New York, 75; Einstein on the Beach (opera), Avignon, France, 76; Lucinda's Dance, 78; Satyagraha (operatic voices in Sanskrit & conventional instrm), comn by Netherlands Opera Co, 80. *Pos:* Comp in res, Pittsburgh Pub Sch, 62-64; performer, Philip Glass Ens, 68- & US & Europ conct tours, 68-; founder, Chatham Sq Prod, New York, 72. *Awards:* Changes Inc Grant, 71-72; Menil Found Grant, 74; Nat Endowment Arts Grant, 74 & 75. *Mem:* ASCAP. *Mailing Add:* 231 2nd Ave New York NY 10003

GLASSMAN, ALLAN
BARITONE
b Brooklyn, NY. *Study:* Hartt Col Music; Juilliard Sch; studied with William Metcalf. *Roles:* Dandini in La Cenerentola, Washington Opera, 83; Ford in Falstaff, Cleveland Opera, 83; Student in The Student from Salamanca, New York City Opera, 83; Figaro in Il Barbiere di Siviglia; Belcore in L'Elisir d'Amore; Morales & Dancairo in Carmen; Enrico in Lucia di Lammermoor; and others. *Pos:* Bar, Mich Opera Theatre, 75- & Washington Opera, 79-; perf with Philadelphia Opera, Can Opera, Aspen Fest & others. *Mailing Add:* 1890 E 14th Brooklyn NY 11229

GLAZE, GARY
TENOR
b Pittsburgh, Pa. *Study:* Univ Mich, Ann Arbor, with Ralph Herbert, MM; studied with Cornelius Reid. *Roles:* Don Ottavio in Don Giovanni, Opera Orch New York, 69; Count Almaviva in Il barbiere di Siviglia, Netherlands Operas & Colo Opera Fest, 83; Tamino in The Magic Flute, Prague Nat Opera; Tom Rakewell in The Rake's Progress, Teatro Colon, Buenos Aires; Albert Herring & Peter Quint in The Turn of the Screw; Ernesto in Don Pasquale; Ferrando in Cosi fan tutte; and others. *Pos:* Res mem, New York City Opera; appearances with opera co of Sante Fe, Philadelphia, San Antonio, Hawaii, Milwaukee, Pittsburgh & Colo; guest artist with symph orchs of Dallas, Buffalo, Milwaukee, Indianapolis & Rochester; perf, Little Orch Soc, Mostly Mozart Fest, Caramoor Fest, Musica Aeterna & Mendelssohn Choir Philadelphia; chamber music perf at Marlboro Fest, Newport Fest, Libr Cong & Mohawk Trails Conct. *Teaching:* Lectr, State Univ NY, Stony Brook. *Awards:* Outstanding Young Artist, Musical Am, 69; Sullivan Found Award; Martha Baird Rockefeller Fund Grant (two). *Mailing Add:* c/o Thea Dispeker 59 E 54th St New York NY 10022

GLAZE, LORRIE PIERCE See Pierce, Lorrie

GLAZER, DAVID
CLARINET, EDUCATOR
b Milwaukee, Wis, May 7, 13. *Study:* Univ Wis, Milwaukee, BEd, 35; Berkshire Music Ctr, 41-43. *Rec Perf:* Clarinet Quintet (Brahms), EMI Rec; Concertino & Concerto No 1 (Weber), Sonatas No 1 & 2 (Brahms), Trio (clarinet, cello & piano; Beethoven), Concert in E Flat (Krommer), Quintet (clarinet & string quartet Weber) & Introduction, Theme & Variations (Rossini), Vox Rec. *Pos:* Clarinetist, Cleveland Symph, 46-51 & New York Woodwind Quintet, 51- *Teaching:* Instr clarinet, Longy Sch Music, Cambridge, Mass, 54; fac mem, Mannes Col Music, 54- & State Univ NY, Binghamton & Stony Brook, 67- *Mem:* Musicians Club of NY; Int Clarinet Soc; Clarinetwork Soc; Am Bandmasters Asn; Clarinet & Sax Soc of England. *Mailing Add:* 25 Central Park W New York NY 10023

GLAZER, ESTHER
VIOLIN, EDUCATOR
b Chicago, Ill, May 5, 26. *Study:* Juilliard Sch, artist's dipl, 49. *Pos:* Soloist with major orchestras in US, Canada, Europe, Central & South America; appeared with Chicago Symph, New Orleans, Vancouver, Royal Phil & other orchestras. *Teaching:* Prof violin, Univ BC, Can, 61-64 & Univ Tampa, 71-; vis prof, Univ Wis, Madison, 80. *Awards:* First Prize, Naumburg Compt, 50. *Mailing Add:* c/o Regency Artists Class Divi 9200 Sunset Blvd Los Angeles CA 90069

GLAZER, GILDA
PIANO, EDUCATOR
b New York, NY. *Study:* Columbia Univ, with Nadia Reisenberg, MA. *Pos:* Mem, keyboard sect, Chicago Symph Orch; pianist, St Louis Symph Orch & Glazer Duo. *Teaching:* Fac mem piano, Hartt Col Music. *Awards:* Nat Guild Piano Award. *Mem:* Col Music Soc. *Publ:* Co-ed, Album of Transcriptions for Viola and Piano, Bradt, 79; auth, The Pianist As Ensemble Player, Am Piano Teacher. *Rep:* Esther Prince Mgt 101 W 57th St New York NY 10019. *Mailing Add:* 14 Summit St Englewood NJ 07632

GLAZER, ROBERT
VIOLA, CONDUCTOR
b Anderson, Ind. *Study:* Chicago Musical Col, with William Primrose, MM. *Rec Perf:* Music of Hubay, Hussar Label. *Pos:* Mem, Chicago Symph Orch; co-prin violist, St Louis Symph; violist, Hartt String Quartet, Hartt Col Music. *Awards:* Tanglewood Award, Nat Fedn Music Clubs. *Mem:* Am Symph Orch League, Cond Guild; Col Music Soc. *Publ:* Auth, The Viola—New Horizons, 64, Metamorphosis, Violinist Becomes Violist, 65 & Training The Orchestral String Player, 67, Instrumentalist; The Importance of Chamber Music, Soundpost, 76. *Rep:* Esther Prince Mgt 101 W 57th St New York NY 10019. *Mailing Add:* 14 Summit St Englewood NJ 07632

GLAZIER, BEVERLY
COMPOSER, PIANO
b Syracuse, NY, May 8, 33. *Study:* Wayne State Univ, with Selden, BS, 55; Syracuse Univ, with Bette Kohler, George McGrath, Howard Boatright & Brian Israel, 78. *Works:* Screaming Eagle, perf by Cent New York Bicentennial Choir, 77; Woman of Valor, Women Arts Conv, 78; V'shomru, Temple Sinai, Sharon, Mass, 80; A New Song Unto the Lord, perf by State Fair Choir, NY, 81; Sing Out Hadassah, comn by Hadassah, 82; Akdamut, Temple Sinai Comp Cont, 82; Meduah Yehudi, Soc New Music, 82. *Awards:* Meet the Comp Grant, 82. *Mem:* Arthur V Wagonen Music Guild, NY (prog chmn, 75-80); Int League Women Comp; Pro Art-Eltinge Guild, NY (vpres, 81-); Syracuse Symph Guild (bd mem, 82-). *Mailing Add:* 5212 Winterton Dr Fayetteville NY 13066

GLEASON, CATHARINE C See Crozier, Catharine

GLENN, CARROLL
VIOLIN, EDUCATOR
Study: Inst Musical Art, Juilliard Sch, dipl; studied violin with Dethier & Galamian. *Teaching:* Artist in res, NTex Univ, 63-64; mem fac, Eastman Sch Music, 64-75, Interlochen, summers 64-66 & Temple Univ, 72-74; mem fac violin, Manhattan Sch Music, 75- *Awards:* Naumberg Prize, Nat Fedn Music Clubs. *Mailing Add:* 310 W 83rd St New York NY 10024

GLICK, JACOB
VIOLA, EDUCATOR
b Philadelpia, Pa, Jan 29, 26. *Study:* Peabody Consv, 47-49; New Sch Music, 55-56; private studies with Max Aranoff, Lillian Fuchs & Valentin Blumberg. *Rec Perf:* Hieroglyphics (Henry Brant), Variazioni sopra una melodia (Robert Moevs) & Soundscape for String Quartet (Lionel Nowak), 82, CRI; Aldebaran-Jean Eichelberger (Ivey), Folkways; Trois Chants sacres (Henri Pousseur), Candide; Focus (Eddie Sauter), Verve; Quintet for Piano & Strings (Alberto Ginastera), Orion. *Pos:* Violist, Contemp Chamber Ens, 61- & Contemp Quartet, 65-; dir, Chamber Music Ctr, Johnson, Vt, 76 & 77; musical dir, Chamber Music Conf & Comp Forum of East, 82. *Teaching:* Instr violin, viola & chamber music, Bennington Col, 69- *Mem:* Charter mem, Viola d'Amore Soc Am; Comp Forum. *Mailing Add:* Dept Music Bennington Col Bennington VT 05201

GLICKMAN, SYLVIA
PIANO, EDUCATOR
b New York, NY, Nov 8, 32. *Study:* Juilliard Sch Music, BS, 54, MS, 55; Royal Acad Music, London, England, LRAM, 56. *Works:* Suite (cello & piano), Royal Acad Music Musicians, 56; three Emily Dickinson songs, Cosmopolitan Club & Haverford Col, 79-80; Prayer Service (cantor, choir & flute), Main Line Ref Temple, 76. *Rec Perf:* Piano Sonata (A Swan), RCA, 73; Piano Quintet (Bartok), Leonarda Prod, 81; Four Sonatas (A Reinagle), Orion Master Rec, 82. *Pos:* Pianist-in-res & dir chamber music, Haverford Col, 69-; pianist, Pa Chamber Players, 83- *Teaching:* Fac piano, New England

Consv Music, 56-68 & Princeton Univ, 83-; prof, Rubin Acad Music, Jerusalem, 67-68; assoc prof music, Haverford Col, 75- *Awards:* Morris Loeb Award of Excellence, Juilliard Sch Music, 55; Edward Hecht Award for Comp, Royal Acad Music, 56; Solo Recitalist Award, Nat Endowment for Arts, 81-82. *Mem:* Sonneck Soc; Am Music Ctr; Delaware Valley Comp Forum; Philadelphia Comp Forum; Am Soc Univ Comp. *Publ:* Ed, Amy Beach: Virtuoso Piano Music, Da Capo Press, 82. *Rep:* Raymond Weiss Artist Mgt 300 W 55th St New York NY 10019. *Mailing Add:* 1210 W Wynnewood Rd Wynnewood PA 19096

GLIDDEN, ROBERT BURR
EDUCATOR, ADMINISTRATOR
b Green Co, Iowa, Nov 29, 36. *Study:* Univ Iowa, BA, 58, MA, 60, PhD, 66. *Pos:* Exec dir, Nat Asn Sch Music, Washington, DC, 72-75; dean, Col Musical Arts, Bowling Green State Univ, 75-79 & Sch Music, Fla State Univ, 79- *Teaching:* Asst prof music, Ind Univ, Bloomington, 67-69; assoc prof, Univ Okla, Norman, 69-72. *Mem:* Nat Asn Sch Music (treas, 77-82, vpres, 82-); Col Music Soc (mem coun, 75-77); Music Educr Nat Conf; Music Teachers Nat Asn. *Mailing Add:* Sch Music Fla State Univ Tallahassee FL 32306

GLINSKY, ALBERT VINCENT
COMPOSER
b New York, NY, Dec 9, 52. *Study:* Juilliard Sch Music, BMus, 76, MMus, 78. *Works:* Rhapsody for Solo Violin, Flute, Strings & Timpani, 74, Mass for Children's Voices, 78, Dream Concerto, 78, Masquerade-Three Tableaux After Beardsley, 82, Elegy for Piano, 82, Sunbow, 83 & Twilight Serenade, 83, Am Comp Ed Inc. *Teaching:* Fac mem, Montclair State Col, currently & Third St Music Sch, New York, currently. *Awards:* Nat Endowment Arts Fel, 80; Jerome Found Grant, 82; Creative Artists Pub Serv Prog Fel, 83. *Mem:* Am Comp Alliance; BMI; Int Symph World Peace; Am Music Ctr. *Mailing Add:* 2130 Broadway New York NY 10023

GLOVER, BETTY S
TROMBONE, EDUCATOR
b Hudson, Ill, Jan 24, 23. *Study:* Cincinnati Consv Music, BM, 44, MM, 48. *Pos:* Prin first trombone, Kansas City Phil Orch, 44-48 & Columbus Phil Orch, 48-49; Bass trombone & tenor tuba, Cincinnati Symph Orch, 52- *Teaching:* Adj assoc prof brass instrm & cond brass choir, Col-Consv Music, Univ Cincinnati, 52- *Mem:* Int Trombone Asn; Pi Kappa Lambda; Sigma Alpha Iota; l'Alliance Francaise. *Mailing Add:* 8791 Cottonwood Dr Cincinnati OH 45231

GLOVINSKY, BEN
COMPOSER, EDUCATOR
b St Louis, Mo, Oct 28, 42. *Study:* Wash Univ, with Harold Blumenfield & Robert Wykes; Stanford Univ, with Humphrey Searle; Ind Univ, with Bernhard Heiden. *Works:* Variation-Fantasy on a Pioneer Theme (orch); Sinfonietta (winds, brass & perc), 69; Ceremonial Music (band); Music for Bass Clarinet and Piano; Romanza (wind quintet); Oboe Sonatina; Four Songs on Poems of Robert Herrick (vocal). *Pos:* Prin oboist, Sacramento Symph Orch, 66- *Teaching:* Prof music, Calif State Univ, Sacramento, 65- *Mailing Add:* Dept Music Calif State Univ Sacramento CA 95819

GNAM, ADRIAN
CONDUCTOR, OBOE
b New York, NY, Sept 4, 40. *Study:* Col Consv Music, Univ Cincinnati, BMus, 61, BS, 62, MMus, 62, perf cert(oboe & English horn). *Pos:* Cond, prin oboe & mem bd dir, Eastern Music Fest, NC; oboist, Heritage Chamber Quartet & Chamber Arts Ens; oboe soloist, Tanglewood, Carnegie Hall, Town Hall & Kennedy Ctr; guest cond, ECent Regional Ohio All-State Orch, 71 & 73, SCent Regional Ohio All-State Orch, 72 & Ohio String Teachers Asn Orch; prin oboe, Am Symph Orch & Cleveland Orch, formerly. *Teaching:* Music dir & cond, Symph & Chamber Orch, Univ Ohio. *Mem:* Am Symph Orch League; Pi Kappa Lambda; Phi Mu Alpha Sinfonia; Am Fedn Musicians; Ohio Music Educr Asn. *Mailing Add:* c/o Joanne Rile Mgt Box 27539 Philadelphia PA 19118

GNAZZO, ANTHONY JOSEPH
COMPOSER, ELECTRONIC
b New Britain, Conn, Apr 21, 36. *Study:* Hartt Sch Music, BMus, 57; Univ Hartford, BA, 63; Brandeis Univ, MFA, 65, PhD, 70. *Works:* Music for Piano III, 71; Five Part Invention (mixed voices), 72; Music for Cello and Tape, 72; Stereo Radio Five: About Talking (tape), 72; Compound Skill Fracture (actor, tape & film), 74; Symphony (multimedia), 76; Untitled Piece in Four Movements, 76. *Pos:* Res assoc, Univ Toronto, 65-66; comput scientist, IBM Corp, 66-67; dir, Tape Music Ctr, Mills Col, 67-69; design consult & equipment technician, Calif State Univ, Hayward, 69-71 & 73-; electronic music consult, Univ Calif, Berkeley, 69-73. *Teaching:* Mem fac, Simon Fraser Univ, formerly, Mills Col, Calif, formerly, York Univ, Ont, formerly & Univ Calif, Davis, formerly. *Mailing Add:* 3005 Dana St Berkeley CA 94705

GNIEWEK, RAYMOND
VIOLIN
b East Meadow, NY, Nov 13, 31. *Study:* Eastman Sch Music, MusB, 54. *Pos:* Mem, Rochester Phil Orch, 49-53, concertmaster, 53-57; concertmaster, Metropolitan Opera Orch, 57- & Santa Fe Opera, 58; soloist with symph orch in Chicago, Detroit, San Diego, Tanglewood Recital Ser & others. *Awards:* Distinguished Alumni Award, Eastman Sch Music, 77. *Mailing Add:* 91 Cent Park W New York NY 10023

GOCKLEY, R DAVID
DIRECTOR—OPERA
b Philadelphia, Pa, July 13, 43. *Study:* New England Consv Music; Brown Univ; Columbia Univ. *Pos:* Box off & house mgr, Santa Fe Opera, 68; asst to managing dir, Lincoln Ctr for Perf Arts, New York, 70; bus mgr, Houston Grand Opera, 70-72, gen dir, 72-; gen dir, Tex Opera Theater, currently; mem music adv panel, Opera Sect, Nat Endowment Arts, currently. *Mem:* Opera Am (mem bd dir, currently). *Mailing Add:* 2019 Branard Houston TX 77098

GODEL, EDITH
LIBRARIAN
b Merano, Italy, Aug 17, 19; US citizen. *Study:* Univ Torimo, Italy, Dr, 45; Simmons Col, MS, 49. *Pos:* Librn, Charles Ives Music Libr Western Conn State Col, currently. *Mem:* Music Libr Asn. *Mailing Add:* c/o Charles Ives Music Libr Western Conn State Col Danbury CT 06810

GODFREY, DANIEL STRONG
EDUCATOR, COMPOSER
b Bryn Mawr, Pa, Nov 20, 49. *Study:* Yale Univ, with Robert Morris, BA, 73, Yale Sch Music, with Mario Davidovsky & Robert Moore, MM, 75; Univ Iowa, with Richard Hervig, Donald Jenni & Peter Lewis, PhD, 82. *Works:* Five Character Pieces (viola & piano), comn & perf by Emanuel Vardi & Paul Jones, 76; Celebration, perf by James Avery, 79; String Quartet, perf by Stradivari Quartet, 80; Trio (clarinet, viola & horn), Margun Music, 81; Rhapsody for Organ, perf by Robert S Lord, 82; Septet, perf by Pittsburgh New Music Ens, 82; Music for Marimba and Vibraphone, comn & perf by Steven Schick, 83. *Teaching:* Vis asst prof theory & comp, Univ Pittsburgh, 81-83; asst prof theory, Syracuse Univ, 83- *Mem:* Am Comp Alliance; Minn Comp Forum; Am Music Ctr; Soc Music Theory; Am Soc Univ Comp. *Mailing Add:* 616 Fellows Ave Syracuse NY 13210

GODIN, ROBERT
EDUCATOR, COMPOSER
b Springfield, Mass, Jan 14, 54. *Study:* Hartt Sch Music, with Stuart Smith; Univ Mass, with Philip Bezanson; studied with Harry Partch. *Works:* 24 Minutes for 4 Trios (voices & tape), 77; Trio for One (live performer, two films & two soundtracks), 77; Paper Music, 77; Soundcurrents (five players), 77. *Teaching:* Artist in res, Mass Col Art, 75- *Mailing Add:* Mass Col Art 364 Brookline Ave Boston MA 02215

GODWIN, JOSCELYN
MUSICOLOGIST, EDUCATOR
b Kelmscott, UK, Jan 16, 45. *Study:* Magdalene Col, Cambridge Univ, BA, 65, MusB, 66, MA, 70; Cornell Univ, PhD, 69; Royal Col Organists, FRCO, 66. *Teaching:* Instr, Cleveland State Univ, 69-71; assoc prof theory, musicol & harpsichord, Colgate Univ, 71- *Awards:* Abingdon Prize, Cambridge Univ, 66; Harding Prize, Royal Col Organists, 66. *Mem:* Am Musicol Soc; Royal Col Organists. *Publ:* Ed, Henry Cowell, New Musical Resources, 69; A Scarlatti, Marco Attilio Regolo, 75; Robert Fludd, Hermetic Philosopher, 78. *Mailing Add:* Dragon Acres Earlville NY 13332

GOEKE, LEO FRANCIS
TENOR
b Kirksville, Mo, Nov 6, 36. *Study:* Mo State Col, BS, 57; La State Univ, Baton Rouge, with Dallas Draper, MusM, 60; Iowa State Univ, with David Lloyd, MFA, 61; studied with Hans Heinz & Margaret Harshaw. *Rec Perf:* For Decca & RCA Rec. *Roles:* Capriccio, 75 & Tom Rakewell in The Rake's Progress, 80, Glyndebourne; Cosi fan tutte, The Barber of Seville & The Magic Flute, New York Opera & Metropolitan Opera; The Abduction from the Seraglio, Teatro Fenice, Italy; The Tales of Hoffmann, Western Mich Opera Theater; and others. *Pos:* Leading ten, Metropolitan Opera, 70- & NY State Opera, 72-; ten with major opera co in US & Europe. *Mailing Add:* Box 47 Rte 203 Chatham NY 12037

GOEMANNE, NOEL
COMPOSER, MUSIC DIRECTOR
b Poperinge, West Flanders, Belgium, Dec 10, 26; nat US. *Study:* Lemmens Inst Belgium, laureate dipl, 48; studied organ & improvisation at Consv Royal Musique, Liege, Belgium; studied with Flor Peeters, Staf Nees, Marinus DeJong & Jules Van Nuffel; St Joseph's Col, Ind, Hon Dr Music, 80. *Works:* Missa Internationalis, 72 & Fanfare for Festivals, 73, Hope Publ Co; Ode to St Cecilia, 76 & The Walk (multi-media choral drama), 78, Mark Foster Co; Canon in D (voice arr), 79, Partita (on a Shaker melody), 80 & Trilogy (organ), 82, Harold Flammer; Missa Brevis, Neil A Kjos, 82. *Pos:* Piano recitalist, Sta NAMUR, Belgian Nat Radio Broadcast, 50-51; organist, choral dir & lectr at univ, col & churches in US, Europe, Philippines & Can, 52- *Awards:* Award of Appreciation, Manila Inst Sacred Music, 74; ASCAP award, 74-; Pro Ecclesia Medal, Pope Paul VI, 77. *Bibliog:* Julien Van Remoortere (auth), Noel Goemanne: Componist-Orgelist, Vlaandren, 68; Mary Spaeth (auth), Noel Goemanne, International Composer, In: Composers, Choristers Guild Lett, 83. *Mem:* ASCAP; Am Guild Organists; Am Choral Dir Asn. *Publ:* Auth, The Piano: A Necessary Foundation for the Study of the Organ, 68, Liturgical Music in the Philippines, 71 & The Bernstein Mass—Another Point of View, 73, Sacred Music. *Mailing Add:* 3523 Woodleigh Dr Dallas TX 75229

GOEPFERT, ROBERT HAROLD
EDUCATOR, PIANO
b New York, NY, Oct 30, 35. *Study:* Cooper Union, BS, 57; New England Consv Music, MusM, 67; Boston Univ, MusAD, 81. *Pos:* Dir, Cent Mass Inst Music, 74- *Teaching:* Dept chair & prof music, Anna Maria Col, 68-; lectr

music, Tufts Univ, 69- *Awards:* Emil Schweinburg Award, 53; Frank Huntington Beebe Found Award, 67. *Bibliog:* Raymond Morin (auth), Pianist Against Forced Lessons, Worcester Telegram, 9/22/69. *Mailing Add:* 14 Judith Rd Newton Center MA 02159

GOFF, BRYAN
TRUMPET, EDUCATOR
 Study: Univ Colo, BMusEd, MMus. *Pos:* Soloist, Univ Colo Symph, Colo Springs Symph, Boulder Phil & Fac Brass Quintet, Univ Colo. *Teaching:* Colo pub sch & privately; assoc prof trumpet, Fla State Univ, 74- *Mailing Add:* Sch Music Fla State Univ Tallahassee FL 32306

GOLCZEWSKI, MAGDALENA
VIOLIN
b Lublin, Poland, May 27, 43; US citizen. *Study:* Royal Acad London, with Rosemary Rapapport, Max Rostal & David Oistrakh, dipl, 59; Consv Royale Bruxelles, with Arthur Grumiaux, dipl, 62; Juilliard Sch Music, with Paul Marano & Ivan Galamian, MA, 65. *Pos:* Violinist, Am Symph, 70-72 & Metropolitan Opera Orch, 72- *Awards:* Henry Wood Prize, 59; Premier Prix Violon & Musique Chambre, 59-60. *Mailing Add:* 44 W 69th St Am 3B New York NY 10023

GOLD, CECIL VINER
CLARINET, EDUCATOR
b New York, NY, Mar 30, 43. *Study:* Juilliard Sch; Univ Nebr, BM, 69; Univ Idaho, MM, 72; Cath Univ Am. *Rec Perf:* The Cambini Wind Quintet, Coronet Rec, 79. *Pos:* Prin clarinet, Greensboro Symph Orch, 81- *Teaching:* Asst prof music, Univ Idaho, 72-76 & Univ Akron, 76-79; asst prof clarinet, Univ NC, Greensboro, 80-; teacher, Anne Arundel Community Col, currently. *Bibliog:* Frederick Westphal (auth), Guide to Teaching Woodwinds, William C Brown, 75. *Mem:* Clarinetwork Int; founder, Int Clarinet Soc Res Libr. *Publ:* Auth, Clarinet Performance Practices in the USA, 79 & Contemporary Clarinet Technique, 79, Spectrum Music, 83. *Rep:* Spectrum Music Publ Co Greensboro NC. *Mailing Add:* 13316 Bayberry Dr Germantown MD 20874

GOLD, DIANE WEHNER
FLUTE, EDUCATOR
b Rochester, NY, May 20, 41. *Study:* Eastman Sch Music, Univ Rochester, BMus, 62; Teachers Col, Columbia Univ, MMus, 65. *Rec Perf:* Music for Flute and Strings, Leonarda Rec, 81; The Huntington Trio, CRI, 83. *Pos:* Prin flute, Nittany Valley Symph, State College, Pa, 65- & Altoona Symph, Pa, 82-; flute & piano, Huntingdon Trio, Philadelphia, 78-; flute, Pa Chamber Players, Philadelphia, 83- & Bach Fest Orch of Bethlehem. *Teaching:* Instr flute, Music Acad, State Col, Pa, 65- & Bucknell Univ, Lewisburg, Pa, 79-; instructional asst flute, Juniata Col, Huntingdon, Pa, 75- *Mem:* Sigma Alpha Iota; Nat Flute Asn; Int League Women Comp. *Mailing Add:* 1226 S Garner St State College PA 16801

GOLD, EDWARD (JAY)
PIANO, TEACHER
b Brooklyn, NY, July 25, 36. *Study:* City Col New York, BA, 57; Sch Music, Yale Univ, MMus, 60; Mannes Col Music, piano with Nadia Reisenberg, 63-64. *Works:* Phos hilaron, Music for Liturgy, 71; Mass of John the Baptist, St Mary the Virgin Church Choir, 72; Ten Canticles, Music for Liturgy, 72. *Rec Perf:* Romantic Cello Encores, 71, Gottschalk Piano Music, 73, Music of Israel, 73 & Dussek Piano Music, 74, Musical Heritage Soc. *Teaching:* Instr piano, Henry St Settlement, 61-66, Dalcroze Sch Music, 64- & Staten Island Jewish Community Ctr, 78- *Publ:* Contribr, Music for the Holy Eucharist and the Daily Office, Music for Liturgy, 71; ed, The Bicentennial Collection of Am Keyboard Music, 1790-1900, McAfee Music Corp, 75. *Mailing Add:* 205 W 79th St New York NY 10024

GOLD, ERNEST
COMPOSER, MUSIC DIRECTOR
b Vienna, Austria, July 13, 21. *Study:* State Acad, Vienna, 38; studied with George Antheil, 47-49. *Works:* Pan American Symphony, NBC Symph, 41; Piano Concerto #1, perf by Marisa Regules with Nat Orch Asn, 45; String Quartet #1, Hollywood String Quartet, 48; Songs of Love & Parting, G Schirmer Music, 63; Boston Pops March, Boston Pops, 66; Symphony for Five Instruments, Wimbledon Music, 80; Piano Sonata, Ronald Gianattosio, 82. *Rec Perf:* On the Beach, Roulette, 58; Exodus, RCA Victor, 60; Film Themes of Ernest Gold, London Rec, 64; It's A Mad, Mad, Mad, Mad, World, 65 & The Secret of Santa Vittoria, 68, United Artists; Cross of Iron, EMI, 76; Good Luck Miss Wyckoff, Polydor, Japan, 81. *Pos:* Music dir, Santa Barbara Symph, 57-59. *Awards:* First Prize (string quartet), Soc Publ Am Music, 57; Golden Globe (On the Beach), Hollywood Foreign Press Asn, 59; Acad Award (Exodus), Acad Motion Picture Arts & Sci, 60. *Mem:* Acad Motion Picture Arts & Sci (mem exec bd music branch, 81-84); Nat Asn Am Comp & Cond (pres, west coast chap, 65-66); Acad Rec Arts & Sci (bd mem, 68-71); Acad TV Arts & Sci. *Rep:* Robert Light Agency Artists Managers 8281 Melrose Ave Los Angeles CA 90046. *Mailing Add:* 500 Pased Miramar Pacific Palisades CA 90272

GOLD, MORTON
CONDUCTOR, COMPOSER
b New York, NY, June 10, 33. *Study:* Boston Univ, BMus, 53 & DMA, 60; Harvard Univ, MAT, 54; Berkshire Music Ctr, 54-55 & 58; Domaine Sch Cond, 56-58. *Works:* Rhapsody (orch), 54 & A Dedication Overture, 59, Boston Pops Orch; Haggadah: A Search for Freedom, comn by Temple Adath Jeshurun, Syracuse, NY, 74; Haudalah: A Sabbath Pagent of Farewell, comn

by Temple Tifereth Israel, Des Moines, Iowa, 76; Songs of Praise: An Oratorio of Thanksgiving, comn by Beth El Synagogue, Omaha, Nebr, 78; Proverbs of the Sages, 78 & Days of Joy, 80, comn by Beth Abraham Youth Chorale, Dayton, Ohio. *Pos:* Music critic, York County Coast Star, Maine, 77-82; dir music, Temple Israel, West Bloomfield, Mich, 82- *Teaching:* Prof music, Nasson Col, 64-82; teacher & cond, Amherst Summer Music Ctr, 69-74 & York County Community Col, 74-82. *Awards:* Award of Merit, Nat Fedn Music Clubs, 74 & 76. *Bibliog:* Alan Hoffman, Shop Talk, ASCAP, winter 82-83. *Mem:* Col Music Soc; Nat Band Asn. *Mailing Add:* 5387 Hammersmith Dr West Bloomfield MI 48033

GOLDBERG, BERNARD Z
FLUTE, EDUCATOR
b Belleville, Ill, Jan 27, 23. *Study:* Juilliard Sch, studied flute with Georges Barrere, dipl, 43; Marlboro Col, studied flute with Marcel Moyse; studied flute with John Kiburz & Lucien Lavaillotte; studied with Diran Alexanian & Pablo Casals. *Pos:* Flutist, Cleveland Orch, 43-44, prin flutist, 44-46; prin flute & soloist, Pittsburgh Symph, 47-; soloist, Casals, Prades, Mostly Mozart & Marlboro Fests; founder & cond, Three Rivers Training Orch, currently; assoc cond, Pittsburgh Youth Symph, currently. *Teaching:* Fac mem chamber groups & flute & orch cond, Duquesne Univ, currently. *Mailing Add:* 840 Chislett Pittsburgh PA 15206

GOLDBERG, JUDITH
SOPRANO
b Wilmington, Del. *Study:* Oberlin Consv Music, Oberlin Col, BA; Acad Vocal Arts, with Nicola Moscona. *Pos:* Chorister (sop), Metropolitan Opera, 81- *Mailing Add:* 2109 Broadway New York NY 10023

GOLDBERG, SZYMON
CONDUCTOR, VIOLIN
b Poland, 1909; US citizen. *Study:* With Carl Flesch. *Rec Perf:* 16 Sonatas (Mozart), Radu Lupu. *Pos:* Soloist, Berlin Phil Orch, formerly, concertmaster, 29-39; concertmaster, Dresden Phil, 25; soloist, tours of Europe, Japan, China, Palestine & Dutch Indies, 34-40 & world tours, 46 & 47; cond & soloist, Netherlands Chamber Orch, 55-; guest cond, BBC Symph Orch, Boston Symph Orch, London Symph, Chicago Symph, Philadelphia Orch & Cleveland Orch. *Teaching:* Mem fac violin, Juilliard Sch, 78-, Curtis Inst Music, 81- & Manhattan Sch Music, 81- *Mailing Add:* Curtis Inst Music 1726 Locust St Philadelphia PA 19103

GOLDBERGER, DAVID
EDUCATOR, PIANO
b Memphis, Tenn, July 25, 25. *Study:* Priv study with Artur Schnabel, Egon Petri, Karl Ulrich Schnabel & Leonard Shure, 44-57; Teachers Col, Columbia Univ, MA, MEd & EdD, 75-78. *Rec Perf:* Sonatinas of Beethoven & Clementi, 68, Piano Works of Mozart, 70, Beethoven Piano Works, 71 & Schubert Impromptus, 74, Opus Rec. *Teaching:* Fac mem, Mannes Col Music, 55-; adj fac mem, New Sch & Douglas Col, 79-81; assoc prof, Long Island Univ, 81- *Awards:* Hall Fame, Nat Guild Piano Teachers, 68; NY Found Arts Grant, 82. *Mem:* Music Teachers Nat Asn; Col Music Soc; Nat Guild Piano Teachers. *Interests:* Schubert's piano music. *Publ:* Co-ed, CMP Piano Library, 23 vol, Consolidated, 61-73; auth, Master Classes of Artur Schnabel, Piano Teacher, 63; co-ed, Russian Music for the Young Pianist, 6 Vol, MCA, 67-69; auth, An Unexpected New Source for Schubert's Sonata in A Minor, D 845, 19th Century Music, 82. *Mailing Add:* 375 Riverside Dr New York NY 10025

GOLDEN, EMILY
MEZZO-SOPRANO
 Study: Juilliard Sch; Manhattan Sch Music, BM. *Roles:* Secretary in The Consul, Atlanta Civic Opera, 80; Stephano in Romeo et Juliette, San Francisco Spring Opera, 80; Mallika in Lakme, Eve Queler's Opera Orch New York, 80; ms in L'Enfant et les Sortileges, PBS, 80; Second Lady in The Magic Flute, Kennedy Ctr, 83; Cenerentola in La Cenerentola, Atlanta Opera, 83; Prince Orlofsky in Die Fledermaus, Western Opera Theater & Ky Opera Asn. *Pos:* Ms with several opera co in US. *Awards:* G B Dealey Compt Award. *Mailing Add:* c/o Columbia Artists 165 W 57th St New York NY 10019

GOLDINA, ARIANNA (ARIANNA GOLDINA-LOUMBROZO)
PIANO, TEACHER
b Riga, Latvia; US citizen. *Study:* Juilliard Sch Music, with Martin Canin, dipl, 79, MM, 80; Int Summer Acad Mozarteum, with Carlo Zecchi, 79; NY Univ, with Herbert Stessin, currently. *Pos:* Solo & duo pianist, 77-; accmp, Juilliard Sch Music, 77- *Teaching:* Fel piano, Juilliard Sch Music, 79-83; Instr piano, NY Univ, 81- & Roosa Sch Music, 81- *Awards:* Ruth D Rosenman Award in Piano, Juilliard Sch Music, 79; second prize, Int Piano Rec Compt, 82; Bosendorfer Prize, Int Paris Chamber Music Compt, 83. *Rep:* Artist Promotional Bureau Inc 6072 A Glenway Brookpark OH 44142. *Mailing Add:* 120 Cabrini Blvd Apt 101 New York NY 10033

GOLDOVSKY, BORIS
PIANO, EDUCATOR
b Moscow, Russia, June 7, 08; nat US. *Study:* Consv Music, Moscow, 18-21; Acad Music, Berlin, 21-23; Franz Liszt Acad Music, Budapest, with E Dohnanyi, dipl, 30; Curtis Inst Music, with F Reiner, dipl(cond), 32; Bates Col, Hon MusD, 56; Cleveland Inst Music, Hon MusD, 69; Northwestern Univ, Hon DFA, 72; Southeastern Mass Univ, Hon MusD, 81. *Pos:* Intermission commentator, Metropolitan Opera Co broadcasts, 46- *Teaching:* Dir opera dept, New England Consv Music, 42-; head opera dept, Berkshire

Music Ctr, 46-61 & Curtis Inst Music, 77; artistic dir, Goldovsky Opera Inst, 63- *Mem:* Fel, Am Acad Arts & Sci. *Publ:* Auth, Accents on Opera, 53; Bringing Opera To Life, 68; coauth (with Arthur Schoep), Bringing Soprano Arias to Life, 73; (with Thomas Wolf), Manual of Operatic Touring, 75; (with Curtis Cate), My Road to Opera, 79. *Mailing Add:* 183 Clinton Rd Brookline MA 02146

GOLDSCHMIDT, BERNHARD
EDUCATOR, VIOLIN
Study: Western Reserve Univ, dipl; Philadelphia Consv; Peabody Inst Music; Berkshire Music Ctr. *Pos:* Prin second violin & Alfred M & Clara T Rankin chair, Cleveland Orch, currently, mem, String Quartet, currently. *Teaching:* Chmn, String Dept, Blossom Fest Sch, currently; mem fac violin, Cleveland Inst Music, 74- *Mailing Add:* 2640 Blanche Ave Cleveland Heights OH 44118

GOLDSMITH, KENNETH MARTIN
VIOLIN, EDUCATOR
b Sharon, Pa, July 18, 38. *Study:* Wayne State Univ, 56-58; Mannes Col Music, 60-62; George Peabody Col Teachers, BM, 66; Stanford Univ, MA, 68. *Rec Perf:* Romantic Piano Trios, Genesis, 75; Chihara/Cowell, CRI, 77; Piano Trios (Mendelssohn), MCA, 78; Trio in A Minor (Tschaikowsky), 79; Trio in F Minor, Op 65 (Dvorak), 81, Trio in A Major, Op Posthumous (Brahms), 81, Triple Concerto (Beethoven), 82, Double Concerto (Harrison) & Triple Concerto (Reale), 83, TR Rec. *Pos:* Violinist, Detroit Symph Orch, 58-60, Casals Fest Orch, 61-65, 69, 71, 73, 75 & 78, Am Symph Orch, 62-63, Lincoln Ctr Chamber Orch, summer, 68, San Francisco Opera Orch, 70, Los Angeles Chamber Orch, 71-73 & others; concertmaster, Nashville Symph Orch, 63-65, Bach Fest Orch, Carmel, 67-70, San Jose Symph Orch, 67-70, Cabrillo Fest Orch, 71-74 & others; mem, Mirecourt Trio, 73- *Teaching:* Instr, Blair Acad Music, 64-66 & Univ of South, summers 64 & 65; lectr, Stanford Univ, 68-71; assoc prof, Calif State Univ, Fullerton, 71-75; lectr & artist in res, Grinnell Col, 75-; vis assoc prof, Univ Iowa, 77. *Mailing Add:* 1415 Broad St Grinnell IA 50112

GOLDSMITH, RICHARD NEIL
CLARINET, CONDUCTOR
b Bronx, NY, Sept 27, 53. *Study:* Queens Col, BM, 75; Manhattan Sch Music, MM, 77; NY Univ. *Rec Perf:* Sketches for Clarinet & Orch, Grenadilla Rec, 80. *Pos:* Clarinetist & mgr, Dover Woodwind Quintet, 75-; solo clarinet, New Repty Ens, NY, 75-; prin clarinet, Haydn-Mozart Chamber Orch, 80- & Windmill Ens, 82- *Teaching:* Asst cond conct band, NY Univ, 81-; instr clarinet, Queens Col, 81- & Third St Music Ens, 82- *Mem:* Associated Musicians NY; Chamber Music Am; Col Music Soc; Queens Coun Arts. *Mailing Add:* 68-11 Burns St Forest Hills NY 11375

GOLDSTEIN, LAUREN
BASSOON
b Glendale, Calif, July 5, 48. *Study:* Temple Univ, with Bernard Garfield, 66-68; Juilliard Sch, with Harold Gohzer, BMus, 68, MMus, 71; studied with Loren Glickman. *Rec Perf:* NY Bassoon Quartet, Leonarda, 79; P D Q Bach, Vanguard, 80 & 83; Speculum Musicae, CRI, 83. *Pos:* Prin bassoonist, NJ Symph, 70-71, Am Ballet Theater, 80-81 & Paul Taylor Dance Co, 80-83; bassoonist & contrabassoonist, Am Comp Orch, 79-83. *Awards:* Meet the Comp Award, 80; Martha Baird Rockefeller Grant, 80; Am Music Ctr Award, 80. *Mem:* Am Comp Orch. *Mailing Add:* 45 Werner Pl Teaneck NJ 07666

GOLDSTEIN, LEE SCOTT
COMPOSER, MUSIC DIRECTOR
b Woodbury, NJ, Nov 16, 52. *Study:* Baldwin-Wallace Col, BMus(comp), 76; Queens Col, City Univ New York, with Hugo Weisgall, MFA(comp), 80. *Works:* An Idiot Dance (opera one act), Baldwin-Wallace Col, 76; An Imperial Message (parable for sop & chamber ens, based on text of Kafka), Am Soc for Jewish Music, 81; Music For A Dance (flute, viola, clarinet & cello), The Yard, 82; Musings (mixed chor), Baldwin-Wallace Col, 83. *Pos:* Screening Comt, Richard Rodgers Prod Award, Am Acad and Inst Arts and Lett, 80- *Teaching:* Adminr & coach, Queens Col Opera Studio, City Univ New York, 80-; lectr & coach, Jewish Theol Sem Am, 80- *Awards:* Charles Ives Fel, Am Acad and Inst Arts and Letters, 78. *Mailing Add:* 212 E|90th #5WF New York NY 10028

GOLDSTEIN, LOUIS R
PIANO, LECTURER
b Kenosha, Wis, Dec 20, 47. *Study:* Oberlin Consv, with Joseph Hungate, BM, 70; Calif Inst Arts, with Leonid Hambro, MFA, 72; Eastman Sch Music, with David Burge, perf cert, 78, DMA, 80; studied with Rudolf Ganz. *Works:* Chukchi (two pianos), Donna Coleman & Louis Goldstein, 80; Foundations Music, Susan Stone & 12 perc, 82. *Rec Perf:* Polonaise-Fantaisie (Chopin), 79, Bagatelles, (Beethoven), 79, Karinhall (Mosko), 80, Kreisleriana (Schumann), 81, Evocations (Ruggles), 81 & Sonata (Copland), 81, WFDD-FM Radio Rec Studio; Sonatas & Inerludes (Cage), Salem Col Rec Studio, 82. *Pos:* Co-founder & co-dir, Calif New Music Ens, 72-76; pianist, Newband, 77-79. *Teaching:* Asst prof applied piano & hist, Wake Forest Univ, 79; fac mem Am music, Am Foundations, Reynolda House Mus of Am Art, 82- *Awards:* Nat Fedn Music Clubs Double Award of Merit, 79; Int Piano Rec Compt Grand Prize, 82. *Mailing Add:* 1825 Mallard Lakes Dr Winston-Salem NC 27106

GOLDSTEIN, MALCOLM
COMPOSER, VIOLIN
b Brooklyn, NY, Mar 27, 36. *Study:* Columbia Col, BA, 56; Columbia Univ, MA(comp), 60. *Works:* Majority 1964, Soundings, 64; Illuminations From Fantastic Gardens, perf by Judson Dance Theater Ens, 64; Yusha's Morning Song, perf by New Music Ens Dartmouth Col, 77; On the First Day of Spring There Were Forty Pianos, Bosendorfer Conct Ser, 81; Marin's Song, Illuminated, perf by Experimental Intermedia Found Ens, 81; A Breaking of Vessels, Becoming Song, comn & perf by Macalester Col Orch, 81; The Seasons: Vermont, perf by Real Art Ways Ens, 83. *Rec Perf:* A Summoning of Focus, Organic Oboe Rec; Three Songs (Alison Knowles), Ed After Hard, Denmark, 78; Soundings for Solo Violin, MG Rec, 80; The Seasons: Vermont, Folkways Rec, 83. *Pos:* Cofounder & dir, Tone Roads, New York, formerly; comp & violinist, Judson Dance Theater, New York, formerly & Experimental Intermedia Found, New York, currently; dir, New Music Ens Dartmouth Col, 75-78. *Teaching:* Instr music, New England Consv Music, 65-67; artist in res, Goddard Col, 72-75; asst prof music, Bowdoin Col, 78-82. *Bibliog:* Cate Miodini (auth), The Evolution of Marin's Song, Illuminated, Downtown Rev, New York, 82. *Mem:* Am Music Ctr. *Publ:* Contribr, Sound Textures, Dict Contemp Music, 71; Auth, From Wheelock Mountain: Music & Writings of Malcolm Goldstein, Pieces-Anthology, 75; The Gesture of Improvisation, Percussive Art Soc Newsletter, 83; Improvisation: Towards a Whole Musician in a Fragmented Society, Inst Studies in Am Music, 83; The Politics of Improvisation, Perspectives of New Music, winter 83-84. *Mailing Add:* PO Box 134 Sheffield VT 05866

GOLER, HARRIETT
EDUCATOR, PIANO
Study: Sch Fine Arts, Syracuse Univ, 45-49; Cleveland Inst Music, BM, 63 & post grad studies; studied piano with Arthur Loesser, Beryl Rubenstein, Leonard Shure & Theodore Lettvin, theory with Marcel Dick, Verna Straub & Alvaretta West & advan piano pedagogy with Ruth Edwards. *Pos:* Pianist, Cleveland Chamber Players, currently. *Teaching:* Fac mem, Cleveland Inst Music, 68. *Mem:* Sigma Alpha Iota. *Mailing Add:* Cleveland Inst Music 11021 East Blvd Cleveland OH 44106

GÖLLNER, MARIE LOUISE (M L MARTINEZ)
EDUCATOR
b Ft Collins, Colo, June 27, 32. *Study:* Vassar Col, BA, 53; Eastman Sch Music, 53-54; Univ Heidelberg & Munich, PhD, 62. *Pos:* Res asst, Bavarian State Libr, Munich, 64-67. *Teaching:* From asst to assoc prof, Univ Calif, Los Angeles, 70-78, chmn dept music, 76-80, prof, 78- *Awards:* Nat Endowment Humanities Res Grant, 83. *Bibliog:* Kürschners Deutscher Gelehrten-Kalender, 76. *Mem:* Int Asn Music Libr; Am Musicol Soc; Int Musicol Soc. *Interests:* Polyphonic music of the late Middle Ages; Renaissance tablatures; Joseph Haydn. *Publ:* Auth, Die Music des früen Trecento, Hans Schneider, 63; Bayerische Staatsbibliothek: Katalog der Musikhandschriften 2: Tabulaturen, G Henle, 79; Haydn: Sinfonie No 94, Wilhelm Fink, 79; ed, Orlando di Lasso: Das Hymnarium, Bärenreiter, 80; Eine neue Quelle zur italienishen Orgelmusik des Cinquecento, Hans Schneider, 82. *Mailing Add:* Dept of Music Univ of Calif Los Angeles CA 90024

GOLTZER, ALBERT
OBOE, EDUCATOR
b Brooklyn, NY. *Study:* Inst Music Art, Juilliard Sch; Nat Orch Asn; studied oboe with Labate, Nazzi & Brenner. *Pos:* Solo oboe, St Louis Symph, 46-48, CBS Symph, 48-55 & WOR Symph, 50-51; assoc solo oboe, New York Phil, currently. *Teaching:* Instr, Hartt Sch & Aspen Music Fest, formerly & Manhattan Sch Music, currently; mem fac oboe, Juilliard Sch, 77- & Mannes Col Music, 78- *Mailing Add:* 165 W 66th New York NY 10023

GOLTZER, HAROLD
BASSOON, EDUCATOR
Study: Inst Musical Art; Nat Orch Asn. *Pos:* First bassoon, CBS Symph, 37-50; mem, New York Phil, 58-, asst prin bassoon, currently. *Teaching:* Mem fac bassoon, Mannes Col Music, 41-, Hartt Col Music, 50-58, Aspen Music Fest Sch, 55-64, Juilliard Sch, 56- & Manhattan Sch Music, 70-; instr, Nat Orch Asn, 58-70. *Mailing Add:* 165 West End Ave New York NY 10023

GOMBERT, KARL E
EDUCATOR, TRUMPET
Ft Wayne, Ind, Aug 14, 33. *Study:* Ball State Univ, BS, 55, DA, 77; Mich State Univ, MA, 66. *Teaching:* Band, Lancaster High Sch, Wells County, Ind, 57-62; teacher band & orch, Ft Wayne Community Sch, Ft Wayne, Ind, 62-66; musicologist, Edinboro State Col, 66- *Mem:* Am Musicol Soc; Music Educr Nat Conf; Col Music Soc; Inst Studies Am Music; Old Stoughton Musical Soc. *Interests:* American music for the stage; 19th century opera, operettas & musical shows. *Publ:* Auth, A Shortage of String Players: Why?, Instrumentalist, 67; coauth, Toward a Musical Classroom, Kendall-Hunt, 69; auth, The First Opera in America or Who's on First, Music J, 81. *Mailing Add:* PO Box 348 Edinboro PA 16412

GOMEZ, VICENTE
GUITAR, COMPOSER
b Madrid, Spain, July 8, 11; US citizen. *Study:* Real Consv Madrid, 27; studied classical guitar with Quintin Exquembre. *Works:* Romance de Amor, 40, Triste Santuario, 41, Granada Arabe, 41, Brasileira, 43 & Latigazos de Pasion, 43; Belwin Mills; music for Blood & Sand (film), 41, Captain From Castile (film), 46 and others. *Rec Perf:* Over 12 albums rec on Decca Rec, 39-64. *Pos:* Conct guitarist, Europe, US, SAm, Africa & Russia, 36-58; owner & perf, La Zambra, New York, 46-; founder, Acad Spanish Arts, Los Angeles, 53. *Teaching:* Private guitar, 58- *Awards:* Best Class Guitarist, Am Guild Banjoists, Mandolinists & Guitarists. 40-41. *Mem:* Hon mem, Class Guitar Soc NY; ASCAP; Am Fedn Musicians. *Mailing Add:* 3811 W Burbank Blvd Burbank CA 91505

GOMEZ, VICTOR E
TEACHER, VIOLIN
b Niagara Falls, NY, Nov 7, 30. *Study:* State Univ Col, Fredonia, NY, BS(music educ), 53; Syracuse Univ, MM(music), 69. *Pos:* Violinist, Erie Phil Orch, Pa, 51-53, Buffalo Civic Orch & Syracuse Symph Orch, 70- *Teaching:* Orch dir, music coordr & teacher, Central Sch, Holland Patent, NY, 54- *Mem:* Am Fedn Musicians; Int Conf Symph & Opera Musicians; Music Educr Nat Conf; NY State Music Asn. *Mailing Add:* 7221 Coleman Mills Rd Rome NY 13440

GONDEK, JULIANA (KATHLEEN)
SOPRANO, TEACHER
b Pasadena, Calif. *Study:* Univ Southern Calif, BM, 75, MM, 77; Britten-Pears Sch Adv Musical Studies, Aldeburgh, England, with Sir Peter Pears, 77. *Rec Perf:* Yoav Chamber Ens, Orion Rec, 80. *Roles:* Pamina in The Magic Flute, 82, Mary in Hugh the Drover, 82 & Marchesa in Un Giorno di Regno, 83, Bronx Opera; Gulnara in Il Corsaro, San Diego Opera, 82; Mimi in La Boheme, Goldovsky Grand Opera Touring Co, 82; Giovanna in Giovanna d'Arco, NY Grand Opera, 83. *Pos:* Artist, Yoav Chamber Ens, 78- & Affiliate Artists Inc, 82- *Teaching:* Instr private voice, Community Sch Perf Arts, Univ Southern Calif, 75-79 & private studio, Los Angeles & New York, 75- *Awards:* Grand prize, San Diego Opera Ctr, 79; Sullivan Found Grant, Nat Opera Inst, 80-; Rockefeller Found Grant, 80-81. *Bibliog:* Russell Kishi (producer), Two on the Town (film), CBS KNXT News, Los Angeles, 81. *Mem:* Am Guild Musical Artists. *Mailing Add:* 811 Ninth Ave 3C New York NY 10019

GONZALEZ, DALMACIO
TENOR
b Olot, Gerona, Spain, May 12, 46. *Study:* Voice & lang with Gilbert Price, operatic repertory with Arleen Augur & lieder & art songs with Anton Dermota. *Roles:* Ugo in Parisina, Barcelona & Nice; Nemorini in L'Elisir d'Amore; Count Almaviva in The Barber of Seville; Duke of Mantua in Rigoletto; Alfredo in La Traviata; Don Ottavio in Don Giovanni; Ernesto in Don Pasquale. *Pos:* Radio & TV appearances, Italy; recital & oratorio performances; ten, Metropolitan Opera & New York City Opera. *Teaching:* Voice, 10 yrs. *Rep:* Harrison Parrott Ltd 12 Penzance Pl London W11 4PA England United Kingdom. *Mailing Add:* c/o Columbia Artists Mgt 165 W 57th St New York NY 10019

GONZALEZ, LUIS JORGE
COMPOSER, EDUCATOR
b San Juan, Argentina, Jan 22, 36. *Study:* Nat Univ Cuyo, Arg; Peabody Consv Music, with Earle Brown & Robert Hall Lewis. *Works:* Hypallages (woodwind quartet, piano & perc), New York, 73; Tamaras, 78; Poltergeist Symphony; Voces I (clarinet & piano); Voces II (chamber ens); Oxymora (cello & piano); Stichomythias (violin & piano). *Teaching:* Instr piano, Prep Div, Peabody Consv Music, 72-77; asst prof theory & analysis & comp, Univ Colo, Boulder, currently. *Awards:* Winner, Viotti Int Compt, 71, 74 & 76; Percussive Arts Soc Award, 75; Arg Nat Endowment for Arts Award, 75 & 76. *Mailing Add:* Music Dept Univ Colo Boulder CO 80309

GONZALEZ, MANUEL BENJAMIN
COMPOSER, EDUCATOR
b Arecibo, PR, Jan 3, 30. *Study:* Empire State Col, State Univ NY, BS, 76; Lehman Col. *Works:* Nela, Park Theater, 74; A Puerto Rico Cantata, Bronx Botanical Gardens, 79; El Jibaro, Carnegie Recital Hall, 80; El Juramento (1976), 80, Los Jibaros Progresistas, 81 & Una Jibara, 82, Lincoln Ctr. *Teaching:* Instr music theory & music dir chorus, Puerto Rican Traveling Theatre, 78- *Awards:* Comp of the Year, Inst PR, 76; Meet the Comp Award, 79-83. *Mem:* ASCAP. *Mailing Add:* 2180 Bronx Park E Bronx NY 10462

GOODBERG, ROBERT EDWARD
FLUTE, EDUCATOR
b Hartford, Conn, Mar 29, 47. *Study:* Eastman Sch Music, BM, 69; Columbia Univ, MA, 72. *Rec Perf:* Music for Voice and Flute (with Yolanda Mareulesen), Orion. *Pos:* Flute, Woodwind Arts Quintet, 75-; soloist, Hartford Symph Orch, Eastman-Rochester Symph Orch & Nat Symph Korea. *Teaching:* Instr flute, Univ Wis, Stevens Point, 72-75; assoc prof music, Univ Wis, Milwaukee, 75-; prof flute & chamber music, Ewha Univ, Korea, 79-80. *Awards:* Sr Fulbright Lectureship, 79-80; Nat Endowment Arts. *Mem:* Nat Flute Asn; Nat Asn Col Wind & Perc Instr; Am Fedn Musicians. *Publ:* Auth, A Long Tone Exercise for Flutists, Instrumentalist, 77. *Mailing Add:* 4958 N Hollywood Ave Milwaukee WI 53217

GOODE, DANIEL
COMPOSER, CLARINET
b New York, NY, Jan 24, 36. *Study:* Oberlin Col, BA, 57; Columbia Univ, MA(music comp), 62; Univ Calif, San Diego, with Gaburo Oliveros, 68-70. *Works:* Orbits, Experimental Intermedia, 72; Circular Thoughts (solo clarinet), Theodore Presser, 74; Five Thrushes—Two Fiddles and Piano, Kitchen, 78; Phrases of the Hermit Thrush, perf by Phil Orch Cinn & Northern NJ Phil, 81; Faust Crosses the Raritan (live synthesizer), Scores: Anthology, 81; Fiddle Studies, Northern NJ Phil, 82; 40 random numbered clangs, perf by Gamelan Son of Lion, 82. *Rec Perf:* The Thrush From Upper Dunakyn, Opus One Rec, 81. *Pos:* Music dir gallery series, Walker Art Ctr, Minneapolis, Minn, 67-68; comp & perf, Gamelan Son of Lion (a gamelan ens), 75- *Teaching:* Instr music theory, Univ Minn, 64-67; assoc prof & dir electronic music studio, Rutgers Univ, 71- *Awards:* Comn for Sound Sculptures, NJ State Coun on Arts, 80; Comp Grant, Nat Endowment for Arts, 82. *Mem:* Am Soc Univ Comp. *Mailing Add:* Box 268A Main Rd Neshanic NJ 08853

GOODE, JACK C
COMPOSER, ORGAN
b Marlin, Tex, Jan 20, 21. *Study:* Baylor Univ, BMus, 38-42; Tulsa Univ, 46; Am Consv Music, MMus, 46-47; Berlin Hochschule, summer 57. *Works:* Born A King (cantata), Abingdon Press; Rondino (solo alto sax & band), Kjos; Fancy for the Trumpet Stop (organ), The Voice of the Lord (anthem) & God Has Gone Up (anthem), H W Gray; Seven Communion Meditations (organ), Flammer; The 7 Last Words of Christ, Second Presby Church, Chicago, 83; and others. *Pos:* Performer organ recitals, Germany, 60. *Teaching:* Prof music, Northwestern Univ, 49-50, Wheaton Col, 50-68 & Am Consv Music, 68- *Mem:* Phi Mu Alpha Sinfonia; Am Guild Organists (dean, 62); Hymn Soc Am. *Publ:* Auth, Pipe Organ Registration, Abingdon Press, 64, transl Japanese, Pax Enterprises, Osaka, 81. *Mailing Add:* 21 Hackberry Lane Glenview IL 60025

GOODE, RICHARD STEPHEN
PIANO, TEACHER
b Bronx, NY, June 1, 43. *Study:* Curtis Inst, study piano with Rudolf Serkin & Mieczyslaw Horszowski, dipl, 64; Mannes Col Music, study piano with Nadia Reisenberg, cond with Carl Bamberger & theory with Carl Schachter, BS, 69. *Rec Perf:* Sonata in A, op posthumous (Schubert), 79 & Sonata in B flat, op posthumous (Schubert), 80, Desmar; Sonatas, op 120 (Brahms), RCA Victor, 81; Sonatas, op 120 (Brahms), 81, Concerti in G, K 453 (Mozart), 82, Concerti in A, K 488 (Mozart), 82, Fantasy and Humoreske (Schumann) & Sonata in C minor, op posthumous (Schubert), 83, Nonesuch; 32 piano sonatas, variations & bagatelles (Beethoven), Bk of Month Club, 83-86. *Pos:* Mem, Boston Symph Chamber Players, 67-69; founding mem, Chamber Music Soc Lincoln Ctr, 69-79. *Teaching:* Mem piano fac, Mannes Col Music, New York, 69-; instr chamber music, Yale Univ, Norfolk Summer Sch, 82- *Awards:* Ford Found Prize, 71; First Prize, Clara Haskil Compt, 73; Avery Fisher Prize, 80. *Rep:* Byers and Schwalbe Mgt Inc #1 5th Ave New York NY 10003. *Mailing Add:* 12 E 87th St New York NY 10028

GOODFELLOW, JAMES RICHARD
ADMINISTRATOR
b Lincoln, Nebr, Dec 17, 50. *Study:* Lewis & Clark Col, BS, 72. *Pos:* Perf arts dir, Alaska State Coun on Arts, 74-77; dir coop projects, Arts Alaska Inc, 77-81; adminr dir, Sitka Summer Music Fest, 81- *Mem:* Chamber Music Am. *Publ:* Auth, A Festival of Music and Art, Alaska J, 79. *Mailing Add:* 1242 W 10th Ave Anchorage AK 99501

GOODFELLOW, SUSAN STUCKLEN
FLUTE, EDUCATOR
b Flushing, NY, July 3, 43. *Study:* Studied flute with William Kincaid, 59-61; Juilliard Sch Music, BA, 66; Univ Chicago, MA, 67. *Pos:* First flute, New York Symph, 63-65; flute, Chicago Chamber Orch, 68-69, Symph West, 78-80 & Carmel Bach Fest, 81. *Teaching:* Instr flute, Lehnhoff Sch Music, 70-73, Chicago State Univ, 72-73 & Brigham Young Univ, 77- *Mem:* Am Fedn Musicians; Nat Flute Asn; Music Teachers Nat Asn. *Publ:* Contribr, Britannica Book of Music, Doubleday, 80. *Mailing Add:* 1867 S 900 E Salt Lake City UT 84105

GOODKIND, ALICE ANDERSON
VIOLIN, ARTIST
b San Francisco, Calif. *Study:* San Francisco State Col; San Diego State Univ, BA, 67; violin studies with Frank Houser, Giorgio Ciompi, Rafael Druian & Herman Silberman. *Pos:* Violinist, Oakland Symph, 60-63; first violin sect, San Diego Symph Orch, 68-, San Diego Opera Orch, 70-, Sherwood Hall Orch & La Jolla Chamber Orch, 70- *Awards:* Bank of Am Fine Arts Award, San Francisco, 58; Cong Strings Award, Am Fedn Musicians, 62 & 63. *Publ:* Auth, In Rehearsal with Peter Erös, 80, A View From the Stands, 81 & Harpists Bizarre, 81, self publ; coauth, Concert de Cuisine, San Diego Symph Asn, 83; also cartoons in Senza Sordino, Sound Post & Am Soc Bassists J. *Mailing Add:* 1535 Forest Way Del Mar CA 92014

GOODLOE, ROBERT D
BARITONE
b St Petersburg, Fla, Oct 5, 36. *Study:* Northwestern Univ, BS, 58, MS, 59. *Roles:* Marcello in La Boheme, 75, Schaunard in La Boheme, 77-80, Mathisen in Le Prophete, 77-80 & Donald in Billy Budd, 77-80, Metropolitan Opera Gala; Eisenstein in Die Fledermaus, Artists Int Opera Co, 77-80 & Conn State Opera, 80-82; Germont in La Traviata, Orlando Opera, 80-82; appeared in 50 roles with Metropolitan Opera. *Pos:* Prin artist, Metropolitan Opera, 64- *Awards:* First Place Winner, Metropolitan Opera Nat Auditions, 64. *Rep:* Tony Hartmann Assoc 250 W 57th St Suite 1120 New York NY 10107. *Mailing Add:* 1 Lakeside Rd Mehopac NY 10541

GOODMAN, BERNARD MAURICE
CONDUCTOR & MUSIC DIRECTOR, VIOLIN
b Cleveland, Ohio, June 12, 14. *Study:* Cleveland Inst Music, 32-35; violin studies with Carlton Cooley & Joseph Fuchs, 32-35; Western Reserve Univ, BS, 35; cond studies with George Szell, 60. *Pos:* Mem, Walden String Quartet, 34-74; first violin, Cleveland Orch, 36-46; cond, Univ Ill Symph Orch, 47-74; cond & music dir, Champaign-Urbana Symph Orch, 60-74, Bloomington-Normal Symph Orch, 71-74 & Sun City Symph Orch, 81- *Teaching:* Prof violin & chamber music, Cornell Univ, 46-47; prof violin, chamber music & cond, Univ Ill, Urbana, 47-74. *Mailing Add:* Pemaquid Point Rte 2 Box 382 New Harbor ME 04554

GOODMAN, JEFFREY DAVID
GUITAR & LUTE, TEACHER

b San Diego, Calif. *Study:* Univ Calif, Berkeley, BA, 70; Occidental Col, MA, 74. *Rec Perf:* A 20th Century Recital, Brit Broadcasting Co, Oxford, 80; Frances (Film), EMI, 82. *Pos:* Music dir, Vienna Int Guitar Fest, 78 & 79 & Oxford Guitar Fest, 80. *Teaching:* Lectr music & guitar perf, Univ Calif, Los Angeles, 76- *Publ:* Auth, Beginner's Guide to the Classical Guitar, Rosewood Press, 82; Video Technology as an Aid in Teaching, 82 & The Guitarist's Guide, 83, Guitar & Lute. *Mailing Add:* 1039 B Pacific St Santa Monica CA 90405

GOODMAN, JOSEPH MAGNUS
COMPOSER, PIANO

b New York, NY, Nov 28, 18. *Study:* Johns Hopkins Univ, BA, 38; Yale Univ with Paul Hindemith, 45; Harvard Univ, MA, 48; study with Gian Francesco Malipiero in Venice, 50-51. *Works:* Fantasia on "Windsor", Pressers, 61; Concertante (wind quintet & orch), comn by Thor Johnson, 65; Quintet for Winds, A Broude, 66; Trio (flute, violin, piano), Assoc Music Publ, 67; Responds for Worshipbook, Westminster Press, 72; Jadis III (flute & bassoon), Gen Music Publ Co, 75; Four Songs on Poems of Juan R Jimenez (sop & wind quintet), comn by Soni Ventorum, 81. *Teaching:* Prof music, Queens Col, City Univ New York, 52-53 & 55-; instr music, Brooklyn Col, City Univ New York, 53-55; head comp dept, Union Theol Sem, Sch Sacred Music, 59-73. *Awards:* Fulbright Award, US Gov, 50. *Mem:* ASCAP. *Mailing Add:* 100 Sunnyside Ave Pleasantville NY 10570

GOODMAN, LUCILLE FIELD
EDUCATOR, SOPRANO

b New York, NY, Jan 3, 29. *Study:* Juilliard Sch, studied voice with Rose Walter & Szekely Freschel, 46-62; Brooklyn Col, City Univ New York, BA, 49, MS(music educ), 70. *Pos:* Conct soloist, Carnegie Recital Hall, 77 & 80. *Teaching:* Music specialist, New York City Pub Sch, 67-74; assoc prof voice & music educ, Brooklyn Col, 74- *Awards:* Young Am Artist, Brooklyn Acad Music, 52; Women in Music, First Nat Cong Women in Music, 80. *Mem:* Music Educr Nat Conf; Int Cong Women in Music; NY State Sch Music Asn; Women's Interart Ctr. *Publ:* Auth, Sexist Songs: Out of Tune with the Times, Teacher Mag, 10/80. *Rep:* 720 Greenwich St New York NY 10014. *Mailing Add:* Consv Music Brooklyn Col Brooklyn NY 11210

GOODMAN, ROGER
HARPSICHORD, TEACHER & COACH

b New York, NY, May 23, 46. *Study:* Consv Music, Oberlin Col, BMus, 68; Northwestern Univ, MMus, 72; Trinity Col Music, London, with Valda Aveling & Edgar Hunt. *Rec Perf:* The Richness of 17th Century France, 80 & Music From the Mature Baroque, 80, Sound Environment Rec Ser. *Pos:* Music dir, Jubal's Lyre, Chicago, 79- & Fireworks, NY, 82-; artist, Affil Artists Inc, New York, 81- *Teaching:* Private teacher, harpsichord, 72-; vocal coach, 76; fac mem music hist, New Sch Soc Res, New York, 81- *Bibliog:* Robert Moulthrop (dir), Roger Goodman at the Harpsichord (film), Art Studio; Telequest Inc, 82. *Mem:* Am Musicol Soc. *Interests:* Harpsichord works of Jacques Champion de Chambonnieres. *Rep:* Maxim Gershunoff Inc 502 Park Ave at 59th St New York NY 10022. *Mailing Add:* 201 E 12th St Apt 103 New York NY 10003

GOODWIN, GORDON
EDUCATOR, COMPOSER

b Cape Girardeau, Mo, Jan 22, 41. *Study:* Univ Tex, with Hunter Johnson, Kent Kennan & Clifton Williams, DMA, 69. *Works:* Sonata After the St Cecilia Society (1726) (baroque ens), Washington, DC, 75; Codes for Orchestra; Pufferbellies (band); Shuffle Chaconne (trombone & wind ens); Forks (brass choir); Concerns (woodwind quartet & trombone); Anonymous V (sax solo). *Teaching:* Fac mem, Univ Tex, 67-73; prof music, Univ SC, 73- *Mailing Add:* Music Dept Univ SC The Horseshoe Columbia SC 29208

GOOLKASIAN RAHBEE, DIANNE ZABELLE
COMPOSER, PIANO

b Somerville, Mass, Feb 9, 38. *Study:* Boston Consv, studied piano with Antoine Louis Moeldner; Juilliard Sch, with Joseph Bloch, Alton Jones, Hugo Weisgall, Robert Starer, Vittorio Giannini & Arnold Fish; Mozarteum, with Enrico Mainardi, Salzburg, Austria; also studied with David Saperton, piano with Lily Dumont, Russell Sherman & Veronica Jochum Von Moltke & comp with John Heiss. *Works:* Tarantella (duet), Carousel, Columbia Pictures, 72; Pictures, Op 3, Boston Music Co Publ, 79; Phantasie Variations, Op 12, 80, Preludes, Op 5, 80, Essays, Op 4, 80, Abstracts, Op 7 & Expressions, Op 8, 81, privately publ. *Teaching:* Piano, private instr, New York, NY & Boston, Mass, 58- *Mem:* New England Pianoforte Teachers Asn; Mass Music Teachers Asn; Nat Guild Piano Teachers; Int League Women Comp. *Mailing Add:* 45 Common St Belmont MA 02178

GOOSSEN, (JACOB) FREDERIC
COMPOSER, EDUCATOR

b St Cloud, Minn, July 30, 27. *Study:* Univ Minn, Minneapolis, with Donald Ferguson, BA, 49, with James Aliferis, MA, 50, PhD, 54. *Works:* Stanzas & Refrains, Albany Symph Orch, 73; Orpheus Singing, Nat Gallery Orch, 74; Let Us Now Praise Famous Men, Peer-Int Corp, Publ, 75; Trio for Violin, Cello, Piano, Am Chamber Trio, 78; Symphony No 2, Nat Gallery Orch, 78; Fantasy, Aria & Fugue, Bradford Gowen, 80; Clausulae, Peer-Int Corp, Publ, 80. *Teaching:* Prof theory, Berea Col, 55-58; prof comp & theory, Univ Ala, 58- *Mem:* Am Comp Alliance. *Rep:* Am Comp Alliance 170 W 74th St New York NY 10023. *Mailing Add:* 3125 Fourth Ct E Tuscaloosa AL 35405

GORDON, DAVID J
TENOR

b Philadelphia, Pa, Dec 7, 47. *Study:* Col Wooster, 65-68; McGill Univ, Can, 68-70. *Rec Perf:* Shakespeare's Music, Delos Rec, 81; 20th Century Consort, Smithsonian Collection of Rec, 81. *Roles:* Ernesto in Don Pasquale, 80 & Nemorino in L'Elisir d'amore, 81, Lyr Opera Chicago; David in Die Meistersinger von Nürnberg, San Francisco Opera, 81; Beppe in Pagliacci, Lyr Opera Chicago, 82; Almaviva in The Barber of Seville, Lyr Opera Chicago, 82; Pedrillo in The Abduction from the Seraglio, Washington Opera, 83; Mime in Das Rheingold, San Francisco Opera, 83. *Pos:* Artist & mem, 20th Century Consort, 79- *Rep:* Thea Dispeker 59 E 54th St New York NY 10025. *Mailing Add:* 251 W 97th #6C New York NY 10025

GORDON, JERRY LEE
TENOR, ADMINISTRATOR

b Greenville, Ohio, Sept 15, 38. *Study:* Col-Consv Music, Cincinnati Univ, BS(music educ), 60, MM(voice), 67, DMA(voice), 73. *Rec Perf:* The Light in the Wilderness (Dave Brubeck), Decca Rec, 67. *Roles:* Les Noces, Atlanta Symph, Ga, 68; Carmina Burana, Honolulu Symph, 79; La Cenerentola, Honolulu Opera Theatre, 72; King David, Ft Smith Symph, 75; Messiah, Tübingen Univ Orch, Jerusalem, 77. *Pos:* Dean acad, Am Inst Musical Studies, Graz, Austria, 81-; recitalist & oratorio performer, southwest & northeast US, currently. *Teaching:* Lectr, Wilmington Col, 69-70; adj asst prof, Univ Hawaii, 70-73; asst prof song lit, vocal pedagogy & opera lit, Baylor Univ, 73- *Mem:* Delta Omicron; Phi Mu Alpha Sinfonia. *Mailing Add:* 2601 Rockview Waco TX 76710

GORDON, MARJORIE
SOPRANO, ADMINISTRATOR

b New York, NY, July 28. *Study:* Hunter Col, BA; private study since age 2; studied voice with Samuel Margolis. *Rec Perf:* Shadows of the Heart, Orion, 77. *Roles:* Over 40 roles in Am opera co, 40-; Queen of the Night in Magic Flute, Lucia in Lucia di Lammermoor, Rosina in Barber of Seville, Constanza & Blonda in Abduction, Lauretta in Music Master, Despina & Fiordiligi in Cosi fan Tutte, Piccolo Opera Co; Olympia in Tales of Hoffmann, New York City Opera Co, 55; Gilda in Rigoletto, Chautauqua Opera Co; Micaela in Carmen, Pittsburgh Opera Co. *Pos:* Exec dir, Detroit Opera Theatre, 60-62 & Piccolo Opera Co, 62-; soloist with major orch in US & abroad, currently. *Teaching:* Asst prof voice, Duquesne Univ, 55-57; adj prof, Wayne State Univ, Univ Mich, Mich State Univ & Meadow Brook Sch Music, 61- *Mem:* Nat Opera Asn; Nat Asn Teachers Singing; Mich Music Teachers Asn (state voice chair, 70-76); Cent Opera Serv; Am Fedn TV & Radio Artists. *Publ:* Auth, Opera Study Guide, Mich Arts Coun, 68. *Mailing Add:* c/o Piccolo Opera Co 18662 Fairfield Ave Detroit MI 48221

GORDON, NATHAN
VIOLA, CONDUCTOR

b New York, NY. *Study:* Juilliard Sch Music, cert(violin) & cert(viola). *Pos:* International soloist; first viola, Symph of Air & NBC, Pittsburgh, Detroit & Chautauqua Symphonies; perf chamber music, Kroll Quartet, Budapest Quartet, NBC Quartet & others; founder, Gateway to Music, Pittsburgh & Excursions in Music, Detroit; cond, Detroit Women's Symph, formerly & Dearborn Orch; solo viola, Detroit Symph Orch, currently. *Teaching:* Mem fac, Univ Mich, currently, Wayne State Univ, currently, Dalcroze Sch Music, Univ Mich, Interlochen Arts Acad & Nat Music Camp, Meadowbrook Sch Music, Duquesne Univ & Ind Univ. *Mem:* Am Fedn Musicians; Mich Orch Asn; Music Teachers Asn. *Mailing Add:* c/o Lee Jon Assoc 18662 Fairfield Ave Detroit MI 48221

GORDON, RODERICK DEAN
EDUCATOR, OBOE & ENGLISH HORN

b Winfield, Kans, Nov 1, 15. *Study:* Univ Wis, Madison, BMus, 39, PhD, 53; Univ Iowa, MA, 41. *Pos:* Prin oboist, Wis Symph, 34-39 & Schenectady Symph Orch, 43-46; cond, Gen Electric Choir, Schenectady, 43-46; consult in architectural acoust; adv, Educ Testing Serv, Princeton, NJ. *Teaching:* Acoustics & instrm music, Nat Music Camp, Interlochen, summers 46-55; assoc prof music & chmn grad & undergrad prog in music educ, NTex State Univ, 49-62; prof music, Univ Mich, Ann Arbor, summers 61 & 65 & Univ Ill, Urbana, summers 56 & 57; prof music & chmn dept music, Sch Fine & Applied Arts, Boston Univ, 62-63; prof music & coordr music educ & grad studies, Southern Ill Univ, Carbondale, 63-, actg dept chmn, 65. *Mem:* Music Educr Nat Conf; Music Teachers Nat Asn; Sigma Xi. *Interests:* Investigating the uses of electronic instrumentation to the teaching of applied music. *Publ:* Contribr, Research in Music Education, In: Music Education in Action, 53; auth, The World of Musical Sound Acoustics, Kendall & Hunt Publ, 79, rev ed 83. *Mailing Add:* 1208 Chautauqua St Carbondale IL 62901

GORDON, SHERRY L
VIOLA, EDUCATOR

b Geneva, NY, Feb 14, 54. *Study:* Evangel Col, BME, 79; coached with Sam Minasian, 83. *Pos:* Mem, Springfield Symph Orch, Mo, 70-, prin violist, 81-; mem, Springfield Regional Opera Orch, 79-, prin violist, 81-; violist, Springfield Symph String Quartet, 80- *Teaching:* Instr violin & viola, Evangel Col, 83- *Mem:* Mu Phi Epsilon. *Mailing Add:* 836 W Sunset Springfield MO 65807

GORDON, STEWART LYNELL
EDUCATOR

b Olathe, Kans, Aug 28, 30. *Study:* Staatliches Konservatorium Saarlands, cert, 51; Univ Kans, BA, 53, MA, 54; Univ Rochester, DMA, 65. *Works:* Runaway (musical), 77 & Aunt Polly (musical), 81, Collegiate Players, New

York; Sweet Mississippi (musical), Oak Grove Players, Washington, DC, 82; Hello, I Love You (musical), Univ Md Creative & Perf Arts Bd Players, 82. *Rec Perf:* Sonata Op 143 (Schubert) & Sonata Op 11 (Schumann), 60, Preludes (Rachmaninoff), 61 & Dances (Schubert), 62, Washington Rec; Stewart Gordon Plays Piano Favorites, Refirmation Rec, 65; Preludes of Frietus Brunco, Educo Rec, 78. *Teaching:* Chmn music dept, Wilmington Col, Ohio, 57-60; chmn music dept, Univ Md, College Park, 65-78, prof piano & keyboard lit, 65-, dir, Int Piano Fest & Compt, 71- *Awards:* Teacher Study Grant, Danforth Found, 63; Distinguished Serv Music Award, Md State Teachers Asn, 79. *Publ:* Auth, Series 1973-1980 New Davidetes, Am Music Teachers. *Mailing Add:* Music Dept Univ Md College Park MD 20742

GORELKIN, PAULA RATH
PIANO, EDUCATOR

b San Antonio, Tex, July 31, 44. *Study:* Juilliard Sch Music, 62-63; Amsterdam Consv Music, Holland, solo dipl, 65; Cath Univ Am, MMus, 69; studied piano with Nadia Reisenberg, William Masselos, Irwin Freundlich & Jan Ode. *Pos:* Artistic co-dir, mgr & pianist, Musica Da Camera Inc, Atlanta, Ga, 80-83, artistic dir, mgr & pianist, Emory Univ, 75- *Teaching:* Mem fac piano, Peabody Consv Music, 70-75 & Dunbarton Col, 73-74; mem fac theory, Mercer Univ, 76-78; dir & co-founder, AJCC Sch Music, 76-79. *Mem:* Nat Guild Piano Teachers; Mu Phi Epsilon. *Publ:* Auth, Reaching the Problem Student Through Practice Sight Reading, Am Music Teacher, 77; coauth, Hand Gymnastics: An Overlooked Approach for Heightened Pianistic Success, Piano Quart (in press). *Mailing Add:* 1331 Breezy Lane NE Atlanta GA 30329

GORODNITZKI, SASCHA
PIANO, EDUCATOR

b Kiev, Russia. *Study:* Inst Musical Art, with Percy Goetschius; Juilliard Sch, studied piano with Josef Lhevinne & comp with Rubin Goldmark, 26-32. *Rec Perf:* On Capitol, Pickwick & Columbia Master Rec. *Pos:* Soloist with maj symphs US; tours, US, Can & Latin Am. *Teaching:* Mem fac, Juilliard Sch, summers 32-42, fac piano, 48-; teacher master classes, Music Fest & Inst, Temple Univ, 68, 69 & 70. *Awards:* Schubert Mem Prize, 30. *Mailing Add:* Juilliard Sch Lincoln Ctr New York NY 10023

GORSKI, PAUL
VIOLIN, EDUCATOR

b Chicago, Ill, Aug 9, 41. *Study:* Univ Ill, BA, 65, MM, 67. *Pos:* Assoc concertmaster, New Orleans Phil, 65-73; concertmaster, Santa Fe Opera, 63-78 & NC Symph, 73-; violin, New Old Quartet Found, 81- *Teaching:* Assoc prof violin, Meredith Col, 78- *Mem:* Am Fedn Musicians (mem exec bd, 81-). *Mailing Add:* Rte 8 Box 207 Raleigh NC 27612

GORTON, JAMES ALLEN
OBOE, EDUCATOR

b Corpus Christi, Tex, Feb 13, 47. *Study:* Eastman Sch Music, BMus, 69; studied oboe with Charles Morris, 58-64, Louis Rosenblatt, 64-65, John deLancie, 65 & Robert Sprenkle, 65-69. *Pos:* Second oboe, Rochester Phil Orch, 66-69; first oboe, Rochester Chamber Orch, 67-69, NH Music Fest Orch, 68-71, Pittsburgh Ballet Orch & Pittsburgh Opera Orch; mem orch, Bach Fest, Bethlehem, Pa, 67-69; assoc prin oboe, Pittsburgh Symph Orch, 71-81, co-prin oboe, 81-; oboist, New Pittsburgh Quintet, 72- *Teaching:* Oboist in res, Mid-Am Woodwind Quintet, Kans State Teachers Col, 69-71, lectr, 69-71; mem fac, Carlow Col, Pittsburgh, 71- & Carnegie-Mellon Univ, 73-76. *Mailing Add:* Pittsburgh Symph Orch 600 Penn Ave Pittsburgh PA 15222

GOSLEE, GEORGE
EDUCATOR, BASSOON

Study: Eastman Sch Music, BM & perf cert, 39; studied with Vincent Pezzi. *Pos:* Mem, Nat Orch Asn, New York, formerly, Indianapolis Symph, formerly & Philadelphia Orch, formerly; prin bassoon & Louise Harkness Ingalls chair, Cleveland Orch, 43 & 46- *Teaching:* Mem fac bassoon, Cleveland Inst Music, 62- *Mailing Add:* 21775 Edgecliff Dr Cleveland OH 44123

GOSMAN, LAZAR
CONDUCTOR, VIOLIN

b Kiev, USSR, May 27, 26; US citizen. *Study:* Cent Spec Music Sch, dipl, 44; Moscow Tchaikowsky Consv, 49. *Rec Perf:* Six Brandenburg Concerto (J S Bach), 68, Concerto-grosso (F Handel), 73, 14th Symphony (D Shostakovich), 74, Concerti (A Vivaldi), 75, Piano Concerto (W Mozart), 76 & Symphony (J Haydn), 76, Melodia. *Pos:* Music dir, Leningrad Chamber Orch, USSR, 61-79; Kammergrt of St Louis, Mo, 78- & Soviet Emigre Orch, 79- *Teaching:* Prof chamber music, Leningrad State Consv, 60-77; prof violin, St Louis Consv Music, 77-82; prof violin & chamber music, State Univ NY, Stony Brook, 82- *Bibliog:* Lawrence Van Gelder (auth), Making Music and New Life, NY Times, 12/19/82. *Mailing Add:* 3 E Gate Setauket NY 11733

GOSSARD, HELEN M
EDUCATOR, PIANO

b Ambridge, Pa, Nov 15, 22. *Study:* Carnegie Inst Technol, BFA, 46; Univ Southern Calif, MM, 52. *Teaching:* Instr piano, Cadek Consv, Univ Chattanooga, 47-55; assoc prof piano & piano pedagogy, Carnegie-Mellon Univ, 55- *Awards:* Ryan Teaching Award, Carnegie-Mellon Univ, 78. *Mem:* Am Guild Organists (mem exec comt, 78-80); Nat Guild Piano Teachers; Music Teachers Nat Asn. *Publ:* Auth, Charting the Scales & Arpeggio Fingerings, Clavier, 79. *Mailing Add:* Music Dept Carnegie-Mellon Univ Pittsburgh PA 15213

GOSSETT, PHILIP
EDUCATOR, WRITER

b New York, NY, Sept 27, 41. *Study:* Amherst Col, BA, 63; Columbia Univ; Princeton Univ, MFA, 65, PhD, 70. *Pos:* Gen ed, Opera Omnia Rossini, Pesaro, Italy, 73-; coord ed, Works Giuseppe Verdi, 77- *Teaching:* Prof music hist & theory, Univ Chicago, 68- *Awards:* Alfred Einstein Award, Am Musicol Soc, 68; Fels, Guggenheim Found, 72 & Nat Endowment Humanities, 82. *Mem:* Am Musicol Soc (mem coun, 70-72, dir, 74-76); Soc Italiana Musicol; Int Musicol Soc. *Interests:* Nineteenth century music; Italian opera; Beethoven sketches. *Publ:* Ed & transl, intro & notes to Jean-Philippe Rameau's Treatise on Harmony, Dover, 70; contribr, Beethoven's Sixth Symphony: Sketches for the First Movement, J Am Musicol Soc, 74; co-ed (with Charles Rosen), Early Romantic Opera, 44 vol, Garland, 77-83; auth, Le Sinfonie di Rossini, Fondazione Rossini, 79; Anna Bolena and the Maturity of G Donizetti, Oxford, 83. *Mailing Add:* Dept Music Univ Chicago 5845 S Ellis Ave Chicago IL 60637

GOTTFRIED, MARTIN
CRITIC-WRITER

b New York, NY, Oct 9, 33. *Study:* Columbia Univ, BA, 55. *Pos:* Music critic, Village Voice, New York, 60-63; drama critic, Women's Wear Daily, 63-74, New York Post, 74-77, Sat Rev, 77- & Cue, 78- *Awards:* George Jean Nathan Award, 68; Rockefeller Found Fel, 68. *Mem:* New York Drama Critics Circle; Dramatists Guild. *Publ:* Auth, A Theater Divided, 68; Opening Nights, 70; playwright, The Director, 72; auth, The Broadway Musical, 79. *Mailing Add:* 484 W 43rd St Apt 36A New York NY 10036

GOTTLIEB, JACK S
COMPOSER, WRITER

b New Rochelle, NY, Oct 12, 30. *Study:* Queens Col, BA, 53; Brandeis Univ, MFA, 55; Univ Ill, Urbana, DMA, 64. *Works:* String Quartet, 54, Tea Party (one act opera), 55, Twilight Crane (woodwind quintet), 62, Love Songs for Sabbath (sacred service), 65, Downtown Blues for Uptown Halls (three songs with clarinet & piano), 67, The Song of Songs, Which is Solomon's, 76 & Psalmistry (four singers, chorus & eleven players), 80, G Schirmer. *Pos:* Asst to Leonard Bernstein, New York Phil, 58-66; music dir, Temple Israel, St Louis, 70-73; vpres, Ambern Enterprises, Inc, New York, formerly, consult, 77- *Teaching:* Asst prof music, Hebrew Union Col, New York, 73-77. *Awards:* Nadworney Mem Award, Nat Fedn Music Clubs, 57; Brown Univ Choral Cont Award, 61; Nat Endowment Arts Grant, 76. *Mem:* ASCAP. *Mailing Add:* 150 W 79th St #12E New York NY 10024

GOTTLIEB, JAY MITCHELL
PIANO, COMPOSER

b New York, NY. *Study:* Dartmouth Col Summer Congregation Arts, with Walter Piston, Henry Cowell, Vincent Persichetti & Carlos Chavez, cert, 64; Juilliard Sch Music, with Robert Armstrong, 64-67; Hunter Col, City Univ New York, with Louise Talma & Ruth Anderson, BA, 70; Am Consv, Fontainebleau, France, with Nadia Boulanger & Robert Casadesus, cert, 71; Harvard Univ, with Lukas Foss, Leon Kirchner & Earl Kim, MA, 72; Berkshire Music Ctr, with Oliver Messiaen, Yvonne Loriod & Yehudi Wyner, cert, 75; private study with Nadia Boulanger in Paris, 75-76; Int Summer Course New Music, Darmstadt, Ger, with György Ligeti, Mauricio Kagel, Christobal Halffter & Aloys Kontarsky, 76. *Works:* Synchronisms for Two Percussionists and Tape, 71 & Sonata for Violin and Piano, 71, Seesaw Music Corp. *Rec Perf:* Trios Contes de l'Honorable Fleur (Maurice Ohana), Philips, 78; Medea Songs (Eugene Kurtz), Sappho, 78; Atavisme (Armande Altai), RCA, 79; Lys de Madriguax (Maurice Ohana), Erato, 79; Appello (Barbara Kolb), Hessicher Rundfunk, Frankfurt, Ger, 80; Concord (Charles Ives), Point d'Orgue, Paris, 82. *Pos:* Rehearsal pianist, Boston Symph Orch, 73-75 & Cantata Singers, 73-75. *Teaching:* Instr harmony, Hunter Col, City Univ New York, 70; res tutor music, Harvard Univ, 71-75. *Awards:* Lili Boulanger Mem Prize, 79; Nat Endowment for Arts Perf Grant, 80; Laureate, Yehundi Menuhin Found, 82. *Publ:* Ed, Appello, Boosey & Hawkes, 77. *Mailing Add:* 484 W 43rd St Apt 3M New York NY 10036

GOTTSCHALK, ARTHUR WILLIAM
COMPOSER, EDUCATOR

b San Diego, Calif, Mar 14, 52. *Study:* Univ Mich, with Ross Lee Finney, Leslie Bassett, George Balch Wilson & William Bolcom, BMus, 74, MA, 75, DMA, 78. *Works:* Children of the Night (woodwind quintet), Seesaw Music Corp, 76; Communique (orch), comn by Fargo-Moorehead Symph, 78; Concerto for Wind & Perc Orch, comn by Univ Conn Wind Ens, 80; Slide Show (solo bass trombone with trombone quartet), 80 & Night Play (double bass & perc), 82, Seesaw Music Corp; Stations (electronic tape & perc), comn by Columbia-Princeton Electronic Music Ctr, 82; Jeu du Chat (alto sax & piano), Dorn Publ, 83. *Pos:* Dir, Electronic Music Studio, Shepherd Sch Music, Rice Univ, 77-; comp in res, Columbia-Princeton Electronic Music Ctr, 82. *Teaching:* Fel comp & theory, Univ Mich, 75-77; asst prof, Shepherd Sch Music, Rice Univ, 77-83, assoc prof, 83- *Awards:* Charles Ives Prize, Am Acad & Nat Inst Arts & Lett, 78; Sigvald Thompson Orch Award, Fargo-Moorehead Symph Asn, 78. *Mem:* ASCAP; Am Asn Advan Sci. *Mailing Add:* Shepherd Sch Music Rice Univ Houston TX 77001

GOTWALS, VERNON D
ORGAN, EDUCATOR

b Conshohocken, Pa, Nov 12, 24. *Study:* Philadelphia Consv Music, 40-41; Drew Univ, 41-43; Amherst Col, AB, 47; Princeton Univ, MFA, 51. *Pos:* Staff reviewer rec, Am Organist, 67- *Teaching:* Prof music & organist, Smith Col, 52- *Mem:* Am Guild Organists; Am Asn Univ Prof; Music Libr Asn; New Bach Soc; Am Musicol Soc. *Interests:* Eighteenth century music; Brahms;

organ. *Publ:* Ed, Joseph Haydn: Eighteenth Century Gentleman & Genius, Univ Wis Press, 63; co-ed, Folk songs for Women's Voices Arranged by Johannes Brahams, Smith Col, 68; auth, Brahms and the Organ, 70, Music: The Am Guild Organist Mag; Haydn and the Organ, 83, Am Organist. *Mailing Add:* 45 Washington Ave Northampton MA 01060

GOULD, ELEANOR DIANE
VIOLA, MEZZO-SOPRANO
b Brooklyn, NY, Dec 16. *Study:* Mannes Col Music; Univ Ill, BMus; Carnegie-Mellon Univ, MFA; Univ Cincinnati. *Pos:* Solo & ens vocal recitals, Germany, 79-81; perf with Halifax & Atlanta Symphs, Cincinnati Symph Orch, Purlie & other Broadway shows; cond, Berea Col Orch & Berea Youth Orch. *Teaching:* Asst prof music, Northern Mich Univ & Berea Col. *Bibliog:* Previn (ed), Orchestra, Doubleday, 81. *Mem:* Am Fedn Musicians; Col Music Soc; Int Viola Soc; Amateur Chamber Music Players. *Mailing Add:* 135 W 106th St New York NY 10025

GOULD, ELIZABETH (ELIZABETH GOULD HOCHMAN)
COMPOSER, PIANO
b Toledo, Ohio, Mar 8, 04. *Study:* Oberlin Col & Consv; Music Sch & Fine Arts, Univ Mich, BA & BMus, 26; studied piano with Guy Maier & Artur Schnabel, dipl, 26. *Works:* Six Affinities, comn & perf by Philadelphia Brass Quintet, 62; Suite for Woodwinds, Brass & Percussion, comn & perf by Toledo Symph, 65; Ray and the Gospel Singer (comic opera), comn & perf by Music Under the Stars, 67; Mini-Symphony, comn & perf by Toledo Symph, 73; Hymn of the Ascension, comn & perf by Am Guild Organists, 75; Fantasy and Passacaglia, comn & perf by Bowling Green String Trio, 81; Ballad for an Indonesian Feast, comn & perf by Masterworks Chorale, 82. *Teaching:* Private piano, 26- *Awards:* Second Prize, Gedok, Mannheim Int Compt, 61; First Prize, Delta Omicron Int Compt, 65; Cert of Merit, Mu Phi Epsilon, 66, 67 & 69. *Mem:* ASCAP; Am Music Ctr; Mu Phi Epsilon; Nat Music Teachers Asn; Ohio Music Teachers Asn. *Mailing Add:* 3137 Kenwood Blvd Toledo OH 43606

GOULD, MARK
TRUMPET, EDUCATOR
b New York, NY, Sept 22, 47. *Study:* Boston Univ, BA, 70. *Pos:* Co-prin trumpet, Metropolitan Opera, 74- *Teaching:* Prof trumpet, Juilliard Sch, 82- *Mailing Add:* 420 Riverside Dr New York NY 10025

GOULD, MORTON
COMPOSER, CONDUCTOR
b Richmond Hill, NY, Dec 10, 13. *Works:* Spirituals for Orchestra, Latin American Symphonette, American Salute, Jekyll and Hyde Variations, Interplay & others. *Rec Perf:* With Columbia, RCA, Varese Saraband & others. *Pos:* Cond & pianist, NBC Mutual & CBS Networks, 30-45; guest cond, Am Symph, New York Phil, Chicago Orch, Philadelphia Orch, Cleveland Orch & others in US, Mex, SAm, Japan, Australia & Israel. *Awards:* Best Classical Rec, Grammy, 66. *Mem:* ASCAP; Am Symph Orch League. *Rep:* 866 Third Ave New York NY 10022. *Mailing Add:* 327 Melbourne Rd Great Neck NY 11021

GOULD, RONALD LEE
EDUCATOR, CONDUCTOR
b Joliet, Ill, Dec 25, 32. *Study:* NCent Col, Ill, BM, 54; Union Theol Sem, NY, SMM, 56 & SMD, 70. *Roles:* Dancairo in Carmen, 78 & Parpignol in La Boheme, 79, Youngstown Symph Soc. *Pos:* Asst organist & choirmaster, St James Episcopal Church, New York, NY, 54-56; organist & choirmaster, Church of Transfiguration, Providence, RI, 56-60 & St John's Episcopal Church, Youngstown, Ohio, 60- *Teaching:* Prof organ & music hist, Youngstown State Univ, 60- *Awards:* Danforth Teacher's Grant, Danforth Found, 66-67. *Mem:* Am Guild Organists; Am Musicol Soc; Music Libr Asn; Asn Anglican Musicians. *Interests:* Latin liturgical music in 16th century German Reformation. *Publ:* Auth, A University Organ Complex, Music, The American Organist, 4/78. *Mailing Add:* 2025 Guadalupe Ave Youngstown OH 44504

GOURDIN, JACQUELINE
EDUCATOR, KEYBOARDS
Study: Boston Consv Music, BM; Col Music, Univ Lowell, MM; L'Ecole Normale de Musique, Paris; studied piano with Georg Fior, Jules Gentil, Bela Nagy & Alfred Cortot. *Pos:* Solo & chamber ens appearances throughout US & Europe; founding mem, Orion Chamber Ens. *Teaching:* Mem fac music, Boston Consv Music, currently. *Awards:* Whitney Medal, Boston Consv Music. *Mailing Add:* 47 Larchmont Dorchester MA 02124

GOVICH, BRUCE MICHAEL
EDUCATOR, BASS
b Lorain, Ohio, Oct 15, 30. *Study:* Baldwin-Wallace Col, studied voice with Burton Farlinghouse, BME, 56; Univ Ill, studied voice with Bruce Foote, MMus, 58, DMus, 67. *Rec Perf:* Esther (Meyerowitz), 57 & Belltower (Krenek), 59, Univ Ill Custom Rec; St Matthew Passion (Bach), Century Rec Co, 60. *Roles:* Tshelio in Love of the 3 Oranges, Lake Erie Opera Theater, 65; Oratorio Works of Bach, Baldwin-Wallace, Chicago, Wheaton, Okla, Miss, & others, 48-; Jesus in Passion According to St John, 83. *Pos:* Soloist, Lima Symph, 64-68 & Lake Erie Opera Theater, 65; musical dir, Southwestern Repty Theater, 69-78 & Okla Theater Ctr, 72-78. *Teaching:* Asst prof voice, opera & chorus, Ill State Univ, 59-63; assoc prof, Findlay Col, 63-68; prof voice, Univ Okla, 68- *Mem:* Am Guild Musical Artists; Nat Asn Teachers Singing; Nat Opera Asn; Am Choral Dir Asn; Music Educ Nat Conf. *Mailing Add:* 410 E Keith Norman OK 73071

GOWEN, BRADFORD PAUL
PIANO, WRITER
b Bethesda, Md, Nov 11, 46. *Study:* Eastman Sch Music, BM, 68, MM, 69; studied with Leon Fleisher, 73. *Works:* In the Harmonies of Music (SATB), Assoc Music Publ, 78; Two Attitudes for Piano, self perf, 82. *Rec Perf:* Exultation: Debut Recording by Bradford Gowen, New World Rec, 79; Piano Quarterly Presents Bradford Gowen, Piano Quart, 82. *Teaching:* Instr, Lynchburg Col, 72-74; adj instr, Sweet Briar Col, 72-73; asst prof, Emporia State Univ, 74-77; artist in res, Univ Ala, 77-81; assoc prof, Univ Md, 81- *Awards:* First prize, Kennedy Ctr—Rockefeller Found Int Compt, 78. *Bibliog:* David Burge (auth), Competition Winner Bradford Gowen, Contemp Keyboard, 8/79; Joseph Banowetz (auth), Five Remarkable Talents, Piano Quart, 82. *Mem:* Music Teachers Nat Asn; Sonneck Soc; Am Liszt Soc. *Publ:* Auth, Samuel Adler's Piano Music, 1/76 & Neglected Repertoire: Some Contemporary Sonatinas, 11-12/79, Am Music Teacher; Typecasting: A Prizewinner's Dilemma, Piano Quart, Spring 80. *Rep:* ICM Artists Ltd 40 W 57th St New York NY 10019. *Mailing Add:* 8504 Paxton Ct College Park MD 20740

GOWER, ALBERT EDWARD
COMPOSER, EDUCATOR
b Weed, Calif, June 4, 35. *Study:* Calif State Univ, Sacramento, BA, 56; Univ Ore, MM, 62; NTex State Univ, PhD, 68. *Works:* Three Short Pieces for Baritone Horn, Tenuto Publ, 68; Sing His Praise, Troubadour Press, 72; Sonata for Tuba, Brass Press, 77; Villanele for Horn, comn by Univ Southern Miss Band, 82; Lighting Golden Autumn Days with Love (SATB), perf by Univ Southern Miss Chorus, 83; Excursion, perf by Loyala Univ Band; Symphony #1, perf by Univ Southern Miss Orch. *Teaching:* Prof music theory & comp, Univ Southern Miss, 68- *Mem:* ASCAP; Am Fedn Musicians. *Mailing Add:* 2910 Magnolia Pl Hattiesburg MS 39401

GRADOJEVICH, OLGA RADOSAVLJEVICH See Radosavljevich, Olga

GRADY, JOHN FRANCIS
MUSIC DIRECTOR, ORGAN
b Great Neck, NY, May 19, 34. *Study:* Fordham Univ, BA, 57; Columbia Univ, 58-59; Juilliard Sch Music, 59-60; State Michoagan, Mex, Dr Hon Causa, 74. *Works:* Responsorial Psalmody, St Patrick's Cathedral, 70-; Gloria, St Patrick's Cathedral Choir & Orch, 79. *Rec Perf:* The Organs of St Patrick's Cathedral, Mirrosonic Sound, 76; Renata Scotto & Christmas at St Patrick's Cathedral, 81 & Christmas With The Canadian Brass & John Grady at the Great Organ of St Patrick's Cathedral, 81, RCA Victor. *Pos:* Dir music, Holy Family Church, UN, 63-67 & St Patrick's Cathedral, 70-; off organist, Metropolitan Opera Asn, 65- *Awards:* Chevalier L'Ordre Arts & Lett, Dept Fine Arts, Govt France, 81. *Mem:* Founder, Nat Asn Cath Cathedral Organists & Choirmasters (pres, 71-73); Bohemians; Am Guild Organists (mem exec bd, New York chap, 78-80). *Publ:* Ed, Nisi Dominus, Assoc Music, 78. *Rep:* Roberta Bailey Artists Int 25 Walnut St Boston MA 01915. *Mailing Add:* c/o St Patrick's Cathedral 14 E 51st St New York NY 10022

GRAF, ENRIQUE G
PIANO, TEACHER
b Montevideo, Uruguay, July 18, 53. *Study:* Falleri-Balzo Consv, Montevideo, dipl, 70; Peabody Consv, studied piano with Leon Fleisher, BM, 78. *Pos:* Concert pianist. *Teaching:* Co-chmn piano dept, Peabody prep, 75- *Awards:* First Prize, Nat Ens Compt, 77 & Univ Md Int Compt, 78; Winner, East & West Artists Compt, 82. *Mem:* Md Music Teachers Asn. *Rep:* Pat Feuchtenberger Rte 2 Box 142 Bluefield VA 24605. *Mailing Add:* 10 S Calhous St Baltimore MD 21223

GRAF, ERICH LOUIS
FLUTE, EDUCATOR
b Ann Arbor, Mich, Apr 11, 48. *Study:* Univ Mich, 66-67; Summer Fest, Nice, France, 68-69; Juilliard Sch, BS, MMus, 74. *Rec Perf:* Voice of the Whale; Night of the Four Moons. *Pos:* Flautist, Aeolian Chamber Players, 69- & Graf-Whiteside Flute Duo; solo flautist, Erick Hawkins Dance Co, 74 & Stamford Symph Orch, formerly; prin flute, Utah Symph, currently. *Teaching:* Adj mem fac, Bowdoin Col, formerly; adj mem fac flute, Univ Utah, currently. *Mailing Add:* Utah Symph 123 W Temple S Salt Lake City UT 84101

GRAF, UTA
SINGER, EDUCATOR
Study: Dr Hoch's Consv, Frankfurt, teaching dipl; studied voice with Ginster, drama with Busch-Gadski & coaching with Popper & Ulanowsky. *Pos:* Mem, Duesseldorf, Aachen, Koeln, San Francisco, Nederlands, Dresden, Muenchen & Covent Garden Opera Co; concerts in US, Can, South Am & Europe. *Teaching:* Mem fac, Aspen Sch Music & New England Consv; mem fac voice, Manhattan Sch Music, 64- *Mailing Add:* Manhattan Sch Music 120 Claremont Ave New York NY 10027

GRAFFMAN, GARY
PIANO
b New York, NY, Oct 14, 28. *Study:* Curtis Inst Music, with Isabelle Vengerova, 36-46; Columbia Univ, 47-48; studied with Vladimir Horowitz & Rudolph Serkin. *Rec Perf:* Works of Tchaikovsky, Rachmaninoff, Brahms, Beethoven, Chopin, Prokofiev & others as soloist & with New York, Philadelphia, Boston, Cleveland, Chicago & San Francisco Orchs on Columbia Masterworks & RCA Victor. *Pos:* Pianist worldwide with major orchestras & as soloist. *Teaching:* Mem fac piano, Curtis Inst Music, 80- *Awards:* Rachmaninoff Fund Spec Award, 48; Leventritt Award, 49; Ford Found Fel, 62. *Publ:* Auth, I Really Should be Practicing, 81. *Mailing Add:* Curtis Inst Music 1726 Locust St Philadelphia PA 19103

GRAHAM, BRUCE A
VIOLA
b Virginia, Minn, Oct 1, 56. *Study:* Wheaton Col, BM, 79; Eastman Sch Music, MM, 81; studied with Francis Torsi. *Pos:* Sect viola, Knoxville Symph, 81-82 & prin viola, 82- *Mailing Add:* 1800 Liberty St #19 Knoxville TN 37921

GRAHAM, COLIN
DIRECTOR—OPERA
b Hove, Sussex, UK, Sept 22, 31. *Study:* Royal Acad Dramatic Arts, with Frederick Ranalow & Phyllis Bedells, dipl, 53. *Pos:* Asst stage dir, English Opera Group, 54-60, artistic dir, 63-75; artistic dir, Aldeburgh Fest, 69-; artistic dir & founding dir, English Music Theatre Co, 75-; dir prod, English Nat Opera, 78-; assoc artistic dir & dir prod, Opera Theater St Louis, 78-; dir prod, Metropolitan Opera, New York City Opera, Santa Fe Opera, Glyndebourne Opera, Royal Opera, Covent Garden & others. *Teaching:* Dramatic coach, several opera co; teacher, London Opera Ctr. *Awards:* Orpheus Award, 72; Churchill Fel, 75. *Mem:* Brit Actors Equity; Can Actors Equity; Am Guild Musical Artists. *Publ:* Contribr, Opera & Musical Times. *Mailing Add:* c/o Columbia Artists Mgt 165 W 57th St New York NY 10019

GRAHAM, JOHN
VIOLA, EDUCATOR
Study: Univ Calif; studied viola with Philip Burton, William Primrose, Benzo Sabatini & George Neikrug. *Pos:* Mem, Beaux Arts String Quartet, 65-70 & Galimir String Quartet, currently; perf, Marlboro & Santa Fe Fest, Guarneri & Juilliard String Quartets & Speculum Musicae. *Teaching:* Mem fac viola, Mannes Sch, 76- & State Univ NY, Purchase & Stony Brook. *Mailing Add:* c/o Hamlen/Landau Mgt 140 W 79th St Suite 2A New York NY 10024

GRAHN, ULF AKE WILHELM
COMPOSER, MUSIC DIRECTOR
b Solna, Sweden, Jan 17, 42. *Study:* Stockholm City Col; Stockholm's Music Pedagogiska Inst, violin pedagog degree, 68; Cath Univ Am, MM, 73. *Works:* Ancient Music (piano & orch), perf by Danish Radio Symph & Barbro Pahlman, 72; Concerto for Orchestra, perf by Cincinnatti Col Consv Phil Orch, 81; Images, comn by Duo Contempora, Holland, 81; Piano Quartet, comn by Micheal Stover, 82; Rondeau, comn by Swedish Broadcast Corp, 82; Summer Deviations, comn by Rikskonserter, Sweden, 82; Sonata (violin & piano), comn by Libr Cong, 83. *Pos:* Prog dir & founder, Contemp Music Forum, 73-83; artistic dir & founder, Aurora Players, 82. *Teaching:* Instr music, Stockholm & Lidingo Music Schs, 64-72; vis instr & teaching asst elem music comp, Cath Univ Am, 72-75; lectr, Northern Va Community Col, 75-80. *Mem:* Am Soc Univ Comp (regional co-chmn, 77-79); Am Music Ctr; Soc Swedish Comp; STIM (US rep, 81). *Publ:* Contribr, Svenska Musick Perspektiv, Royal Acad Music, 71; auth, Satsning Pa College Kultur och Elektronstudios i USA, Tonfallet, Rikskonserter, 72; Improvisation en Modenyck, Tonfallet, Sweden, 72; contribr, EC Delegation Sponsors Concert, Europe, 82; Svensk Tonsattare i USA, Musik Revy, Bengt Plejel, 83. *Mailing Add:* 7229 Deborah Dr Falls Church VA 22046

GRAMENZ, FRANCIS L
ADMINISTRATOR, LIBRARIAN
b Independence, Iowa, Dec 5, 44. *Study:* Drake Univ, BM, 69; Boston Univ, MA(musicol), 72; Simmons Col, MS, 77. *Pos:* Music bibliographer, Boston Univ, 73-78, head, Music Libr, 78-, cur, Boston Symph Orch Perf Tape Arch, 78- & Arthur Fieldler Reading Rm & Collection, 82- *Teaching:* Lectr music hist & piano, Emmanuel Col, Boston, 73-76. *Mem:* Am Musicol Soc; Music Libr Asn; Int Asn Music Libr; Boston Area Music Libr; Music Libr Asn (chmn, New England chap, 82-). *Mailing Add:* 1401 Walnut St Newton MA 02161

GRANAT, JUAN WOLFGANG
VIOLA
b Karlsruhe, Germany, Nov 29, 18. *Study:* With Rudolph Zwinkel; Master Sch Svecik & Marteau, Munich, with Herma Studeny, dipl. *Rec Perf:* With Philadelphia Orch. *Pos:* Prin violist, Swiss Italian Broadcasting Orch, formerly, maj Argentine Symph Orchs, 40-45, Havanna Phil Orch, formerly, Pro Arte Opera, Havana, Ballet Alicia Alonson, 46-53, Reading Symph & Lancaster Symph, 65-; violist, Quartetto Montecenari, 39-40, Minneapolis Symph, 54-56, Philadelphia Orch, 56- & Robin Hood Dell Orch, 58-; violist, Cuban Chamber Music Soc, Havana, 46-53, guest artist, 55, 57 & 58. *Teaching:* Prof violin, Consv Levy, Havana & Nat Consv Mantanzas, Cuba, 46-53. *Awards:* NY Madrigal Soc Ann Town Hall Debut Award, 57. *Mem:* Viola Res Soc; Am Fedn Musicians. *Mailing Add:* 4738 Osage Ave Philadelphia PA 19143

GRANEY, JOHN F, JR
ADMINISTRATOR, EDUCATOR
b Methuen, Mass, Oct 27, 31. *Study:* Holy Cross Col, BA, 53; Boston Univ, MEd, 57; Univ Notre Dame, MS, 60. *Pos:* Prog dir & founder, Music at Canterbury, 76-78 & Music in Deerfield, 79- *Mem:* Chamber Music Am; Green Mountain Consortium. *Mailing Add:* Wells St PO Box 214 Deerfield MA 01342

GRANGER, LAWRENCE GORDON
CELLO
b San Diego, Calif, Mar 1, 52. *Study:* Calif State Univ, Hayward, with Allen Gove, BA, 75; private study with Bonnie Hampton, Laszlo Varga & Gabor Rejto. *Pos:* Prin cello, Oakland Symph, 76-79; section cello, San Francisco Symph, 79- *Mailing Add:* 1771 Via Ventana San Lorenzo CA 94580

GRANGER, MILTON LEWIS
EDUCATOR, COMPOSER
b Kansas City, Mo, Nov 17, 47. *Study:* Univ Mo, Kansas City, BMus, 69; Northwestern Univ, DMus, 78. *Works:* Pigeons, Hollins Col Theater Arts Dept, 77; Give or Take a Million, BMI, 79; This Bright Day, Mill Mountain Playhouse, 82; Coal, Karen Hagerman, 82. *Rec Perf:* The American Saxophone, 71 & Music for Tenor Saxophone, 71, Brewster. *Pos:* Artistic dir, Southwest Va Opera Soc, 79- *Teaching:* Assoc prof music, Hollins Col, 71- *Awards:* Allied Arts Award, Soc Am Musicians, 71. *Mem:* Music Teachers Nat Asn; Nat Opera Asn. *Publ:* Auth, Understanding Memorization, Clavier, 77. *Mailing Add:* Box 9607 Hollins College VA 24020

GRANT, KERRY
ADMINISTRATOR, EDUCATOR
b Pasadena, Calif, Sept 30, 45. *Study:* Univ Calif, Irvine, BA, 69, MFA, 72; Univ Calif, Berkeley, PhD, 77. *Teaching:* Asst prof, McGill Univ, 77-80; chmn, Div Fine Arts, Trinity Western Col, 80-81; asst dir & assoc prof music, Univ Okla, 81- *Mem:* Am Musicol Soc; Music Libr Asn; Soc Ethnomusicol; Soc Eighteenth Century Studies. *Interests:* The life and work of Dr Charles Burney; history of wind music. *Publ:* Auth, Dr Charles Burney As Critic and Historian of Music, UMI Press, 83; co-ed, The Memoires of Dr Charles Burney, Univ Toronto (in prep). *Mailing Add:* 112 Brookwood Dr Noble OK 73068

GRANT, WILLIAM PARKS
COMPOSER, EDUCATOR
b Cleveland, Ohio, Jan 4, 10. *Study:* Capital Univ, BM, 32; Ohio State Univ, MA, 33; Eastman Sch Music, PhD, 48. *Works:* Symphony No 2, Eastman-Rochester Symph Orch, 48; Essay for Horn and Organ, E Power Biggs & Harold Meek, 49; Laconic Suite for Brass, Contemp Music Ctr Philadelphia, 49; String Quartet No 1, Degen String Quartet New York, 50; Rythmic Overture, Eastman-Rochester Symph Orch, 51; Instrumental Motet, Am Soc Ancient Instrm, 52; Suite No 2 for String Orchestra, Nat Gallery Orch, 54. *Teaching:* From asst to assoc prof music, Tarleton State Col, 37-43; asst prof, La State Univ, 44-47 & Temple Univ, 47-51; from assoc prof to prof, Univ Miss, 53-74. *Awards:* Fel, Yaddo, 49 & Huntington Hartford Found, 59 & 63; Delius Prize, Jacksonville Univ, 77. *Mem:* Int Gustav Mahler Soc; Am Comp Alliance; Am Music Ctr; Southeastern Comp League. *Interests:* Mahler's symphonies. *Publ:* Auth, ten articles on Mahler, Chord & Discord, 34-70; Music Which Has Proved Its Value—What Is It?, Musical Courier, 36; Music for Elementary Teachers, Appleton-Century-Crofts, 51-60; Handbook of Music Terms, Scarecrow Press, 67; Bruckner and Mahler—The Essential Difference of Their Styles, Music Rev, 2/71. *Mailing Add:* 1720 Garfield Ave Oxford MS 38655

GRANTHAM, DONALD
COMPOSER, EDUCATOR
b Duncan, Okla, Nov 9, 47. *Study:* Univ Okla, with Spencer Norton, BMus, 70; Am Consv, with Nadia Boulanger, 73-74; Univ Southern Calif, with Ramiro Cortes, Robert Linn & Halsey Stevens, MM, 74, DMA, 80. *Works:* Trio (violin, cello & piano), 77 & Cuatro Caprichos de Francisco Goya (solo violin), 77, Orion Rec; Three Choral Settings of Poems by William Butler Yeats, 77 & Seven Choral Settings of Poems by Emily Dickinson, 83, E C Schirmer; El Album de Los Duendecitos, perf by Indianapolis Symph Orch, 83; La Noche en la Isla (baritone, horn & piano), Comp Rec Inc, 83; From the Diaries of Adam and Eve (sop, baritone & string orch), comn by Kerrville Music Found, 83. *Teaching:* Lectr, Univ Southern Calif, 70-75; assoc prof, Univ Tex, Austin, 75- *Awards:* Prix Lili Boulanger, Harvard Univ, 76; citation music, Am Acad & Inst Arts & Lett, 81; Rudolph Nissim Award, ASCAP, 83. *Mem:* ASCAP. *Publ:* Auth, A Harmonic Leit-Motif System in Charles Ive's Psalm 90, In Theory Only, 80; coauth, The Technique of Orchestration, Prentice-Hall, 3rd ed, 83. *Mailing Add:* 2700 Clarkdale Lane Austin TX 78758

GRASS, WILLIAM
EDUCATOR, FLUTE
Study: DePauw Univ, BM; New England Consv, MM; Ind State Teachers Col; Berkshire Inst; Arthur Jordan Consv; studied with Tipton, Fitzgerald, Laurent, Pappoutsakis, Mazzeo, Gillet & Cook. *Pos:* Mem, Boston Ballet, Worcester Symph & Boston Pops Esplanade Orch; perf with Boston Symph Orch, RI Phil, Opera Co Boston, Pro Arte Woodwind Quintet & Four Arts Trio. *Teaching:* Mem fac, New England Consv, formerly, Smith Col, formerly, Dana Hall, formerly, Milton Acad, formerly, Univ Lowell, formerly & Boston Consv, currently. *Mailing Add:* Boston Consv 8 The Fenway Boston MA 02215

GRATOVICH, EUGENE
VIOLIN, EDUCATOR
b Ukraine, Sept 26, 41; US citizen. *Study:* Boston Univ, BMus, 63, DMA, 68; Univ Ill, Urbana, MusM, 65. *Rec Perf:* Sonatas (Arthur Foote & J A Carpenter), 76 & 20 Century Ukrainian Violin Music, 79, Orion Rec; Music of Cage, Messiaen, Flynn & Ives, Finnedar Rec, 83. *Pos:* Soloist, Philadelphia Orch, 56 & St Louis Symph, 73; first violin, Esterhazy String Quartet, 68-72; concertmaster, San Gabriel Symph Orch, Calif, 75-76; co-dir, Chicago Soundings Ens, 79-83, Gratovich-Golmon Duo, 81- *Teaching:* Assoc prof violin, Univ Mo, Columbia, 68-72; assoc prof chamber music, Univ Calif San Diego, La Jolla, 73-74; assoc prof & head string dept, DePaul Univ, 76-83; coordr grad violin studies, Cleveland Inst Music, 83- *Awards:* Fulbright Grant to Germany, 65-66. *Mem:* Music Teachers Nat Asn (chmn strings, 82-); Am Soc Musicians (bd mem, 82-84); Am String Teacher Asn (vpres Ill chap, 82). *Publ:* Auth, Case for an Electronic Violin, Instrumentalist, 73; Violin Sonatas

of Charles Ives, Music Educr, 74; Performing Hints for Sonatas of Ives, Am String Teacher Asn, 74; contrib, An Ives Celebration, Univ Ill Press, 77; ed, 16 Contemporary Violin Etudes, Am String Teacher Asn, Presser, 83. *Mailing Add:* 2639 N Burling St Chicago IL 60614

GRAUER, VICTOR A
COMPOSER, THEORETICIAN
b Poughkeepsie, NY, Oct 11, 37. *Study:* Syracuse Univ, with F Morris, BMus(comp), 59; Wesleyan Univ, with D P McAllester, MA(ethnomusicol), 61; State Univ NY, Buffalo, with H Pousseur & L Hiller, PhD(comp), 72. *Works:* Inferno, Folkways Rec, 67; Ezekiel I, Heinz Chapel Choir, Univ Pittsburgh, 71; North, 74 & Polyhyperchord, 77, Creative Assoc Buffalo; Passage, Pittsburgh String Consort, 83. *Pos:* Res assoc Cantometric Proj, Columbia Univ, 62-66. *Teaching:* Lectr music, Univ Pittsburgh, 81- & asst prof, 70-73. *Mem:* Col Music Soc. *Interests:* Creation of the Cantometrics method (1959-66) with Alan Lomax. *Publ:* Auth, Some Song Style Clusters, Ethnomusicol, 65; coauth, The Cantometrics Coding Book, Am Acad Arts & Sci, 68; auth, Modernism/Post-Modernism/Neomodernism, Downtown Rev, 81-82. *Mailing Add:* 1118 Portland St Pittsburgh PA 15206

GRAVE, FLOYD KERSEY
EDUCATOR, ADMINISTRATOR
b Yonkers, NY, Jan 20, 45. *Study:* Eastman Sch Music, BMus, 66; NY Univ, MA(musicol), 69, PhD(musicol), 73. *Teaching:* Asst prof theory & musicol, Univ Va, Charlottesville, 74-81, dir grad studies, 77-81; asst prof, Rutgers Univ, 81-83, fel Rutgers Col, 81-; dir admissions BMus prog, 82- *Awards:* German Acad Exchange Serv Fel, 79; Am Philosophical Soc Grant, 79; Sesquicentennial Assoc, Univ Va, 79. *Mem:* Am Musicol Soc; Soc Music Theory; Music Libr Asn; Col Music Soc; Alban Berg Soc. *Interests:* Music theory, criticism and aesthetics of the 18th and 19th centuries. *Publ:* Auth, Abbe Vogler's Revision of Pergolesi's Stabat Mater, J Am Musicol Soc, 77; Abbe Vogler and the Study of Fugue, Music Theory Spectrum, 79; Abbe Vogler and the Bach Legacy, 18th Century Studies, 80; Abbe Vogler's Theory of Reduction, Current Musicol, 80; Rhythmic Harmony in Mozart, Music Rev, 80. *Mailing Add:* 78-A Cedar Lane Highland Park NJ 08904

GRAVES, TERRY ALLEN
GUITAR, EDUCATOR
b South Bend, Ind, Aug 6, 53. *Study:* Ind Univ, South Bend, BMus, 76; Univ Southern Calif, MMus, 79. *Pos:* Class guitarist, Falla Guitar Trio, 79- *Teaching:* Lectr guitar, El Camino Col, 80-, Cypress Col, 81- & Univ Redlands, 81- *Rep:* Marianne Marshall 34 66th Pl Long Beach CA 90803. *Mailing Add:* 3704 Barham E-110 Los Angeles CA 90068

GRAVES, WILLIAM LESTER, JR
EDUCATOR, CONDUCTOR
b Terry, Miss, Aug 26, 15. *Study:* Northwest Mo State Col, BS, 45; Drake Univ, MMEd, 48; Univ Colo, EdD, 63. *Works:* Passacaglia & Fugue for Strings, Mills Music, Inc, 62; Hear Us, O Lord From Heav'n Thy Dwelling Place, Elkan-Vogel, 65; Prelude & Fugue for Orchestra, 65 & A Choral Suite, 68, comn by Miss Univ Women; Unto Thee Do We Cry, Southern Music Co, 69. *Pos:* Music consult, Tenn State Dept Educ, 61-64. *Teaching:* Instr music, Graceland Col, 46-53; head dept instrm music, Pub Sch, Clarksdale, Miss, 53-61; prof music, Miss Univ Women, 64- *Mem:* ASCAP; Music Educr Nat Conf; Miss Music Educr Asn (pres, 60-61 & 78-80). *Publ:* Auth, Improving Intonation, Instrumentalist, 63; ed, Mississippi Notes, State Music Educ J, Miss Music Educr, 66-74 & 80-81; auth, Music in the Schools-How Does Yours Measure Up?, Miss Advan, 67. *Mailing Add:* 1421 College St Columbus MS 39701

GRAY, DOROTHY LANDIS
EDUCATOR, MUSIC DIRECTOR
b Lebanon, Pa, Apr 23, 22. *Study:* Lebanon Valley Col, BS(music educ), 44; Westminster Choir Col, MM, 46. *Teaching:* Assoc prof voice & choral, Ark Col, 46- *Mem:* Nat Opera Asn; Nat Asn Teachers Singing; Am Choral Dir Asn; Music Teachers Nat Asn. *Mailing Add:* Music Dept Ark Col Batesville AR 72501

GRAY, SCOTTY WAYNE
ADMINISTRATOR, EDUCATOR
b Lytle, Tex, May 8, 34. *Study:* Baylor Univ, BM, 55; Southwestern Baptist Theol Sem, MCM, 59, DMA, 66. *Teaching:* Prof church music, Southwestern Baptist Theol Sem, 66-, asst dean acad div, 82- *Mem:* Hymn Soc Am; Southern Baptist Church Music Conf (exec coun, 68-70). *Mailing Add:* 3312 Westfield Ave Ft Worth TX 76133

GRAZIANO, JOHN
COMPOSER, EDUCATOR
b New York, NY, May 7, 38. *Study:* City Col, City Univ New York, studied comp with Mark Brunswick, BA, 64; Yale Univ, studied comp with Yehudi Wyner & theory with Allan Forte, MM, 70, PhD, 75. *Works:* Chamber Concerto, perf by Theatre Chamber Players, Washington, DC, 75; Chamber Music (six madrigal), perf by The Western Wind, 77; In Memoriam: Mark Brunswick, perf by Int Soc Contemp Music, 81. *Teaching:* Assoc prof, City Col, City Univ New York, 69- *Mem:* Sonneck Soc; Am Music Ctr; Am Musicol Soc. *Mailing Add:* 146-18 32nd Ave Flushing NY 11354

GREATBATCH, TIMOTHY ALAN
COMPOSER, EDUCATOR
b Indianapolis, Ind, Feb 12, 53. *Study:* New Sch Music, BM(piano), 76; Univ Pa, MA(comp), 79. *Works:* Quintet (clarinet, violin, viola, violoncello &

piano), Orpheus, 80, Contemp Directions Ens, Univ Mich, 81 & Meet the Comp Series, Phila Art Alliance, 81; Crystallum (chamber concerto), Nebr Sinfonia, 83. *Teaching:* Instr, New Sch Music, 77-82, asst prof 19th century harmony, comp & 20th century hist, Univ Pa, 78-79. *Awards:* David S Bates Award, Fresno Free Col Found, 80. *Mailing Add:* Music Dept New Sch Music 301 S 21st Philadelphia PA 19103

GREEN, ANDREW
EDUCATOR, FLUTE
b New York, NY, Nov 24, 51. *Study:* Johns Hopkins Univ, BA(music); Manhattan Sch Music, studied flute with Marcel Moyse, James Galway & Barthold Kuijken, MM; Aston Magna Acad; Res Ctr Musical Iconography; City Univ New York, currently. *Pos:* Solo flute performances. *Teaching:* Instr music hist, Mannes Col Music, 81- *Mem:* Am Musicol Soc. *Interests:* Music iconography. *Mailing Add:* 801 West End Ave Apt 4A New York NY 10025

GREEN, BARRY L
DOUBLE BASS, WRITER
b Newark, NJ, Apr 10, 45. *Study:* San Jose State Col, perf cert, 64; Ind Univ, with Murray Grudner & Janos Starker, BMus, 65; Univ Cincinnati, MMus, 66. *Rec Perf:* Baroquebass, 71, New Music for Bass, 73 & Romantic Music for Bass, 75, Piper Co; Heritage Chamber Quartet, 76, Bass Evolution, 80 & Sound of the Bass, 81, Redmark QCA Rec. *Pos:* Prin bass, Nashville Symph, 64-65 & Cincinnati Symph, 66-; mem, Cassals Fest Orch. *Teaching:* Adj prof music & bass, Col Consv Music, Univ Cincinnati, 66-; dir & founder, Int Summer Sch Bass, 76-81; music consult, Inner Game Corp, Los Angeles, Calif, 77- *Awards:* Corbett Award, Int Soc Bassists, 83. *Bibliog:* Appelbaum (auth), The Way They Play, Vol 7, Paganni Publ, 79. *Mem:* Int Soc Bassists (founder & exec dir, 78-82); Am String Teachers Asn. *Publ:* Auth, Fundamentals of Doublebass Playing, 71 & Advanced Techniques of Doublebass Playing, 76, Piper Co. *Mailing Add:* 3449 Lyleburn Pl Cincinnati OH 45220

GREEN, DOUGLASS MARSHALL
EDUCATOR, COMPOSER
b Rangoon, Burma, July 22, 26; US citizen. *Study:* Univ Redlands, BMus(organ & comp), 49, MMus(comp), 51; Boston Univ, PhD(musicol), 58. *Works:* Missa Brevis in Honorem & Six Preludes on Medieval Hymns for Organ, 60, Gregorian Inst; Four Conversations for Four Clarinets, Assoc Music Publ, 61; Chaconne for Violin and Harpsichord, 61 & Fantasy for Harpsichord, 62, comn & perf by Harold Chaney; Homage to Ives for Viola and Piano, comn & perf by Peter Mark, 68. *Teaching:* Assoc prof, Nanko Gakuen, Sendai, Japan, 51-54; asst & assoc prof, St Joseph Col, Conn, 58-66 & Univ Calif, Santa Barbara, 66-70; from assoc prof to prof, Eastman Sch Music, 70-77; prof, Univ Tex, Austin, 77- *Awards:* Fulbright Grant, 56-57; Deems Taylor Award, ASCAP, 78. *Mem:* Soc Music Theory (mem exec bd, 78-81, vpres, 81-); Col Music Soc (mem coun, 79-81, mem exec bd, 81-); Am Musicol Soc; Am Guild Organists. *Publ:* Auth, Form in Tonal Music, Holt, Rinehart & Winston, 65, rev ed, 79; Berg's De Profundis: Finale of Lyric Suite, Newsletter Int Alban Berg Soc, 77; Allegro Misterioso of Berg's Lyric Suite, J Am Musicol Soc, 78; coauth, Garland History of the Symphony, Vol 1: 18th Century Neapolitan Symphonies, Garland Publ Co, 83. *Mailing Add:* 5600 Ridge Oak Dr Austin TX 78731

GREEN, GENE MARIE
OBOE & ENGLISH HORN, TEACHER
Study: Oberlin Consv Music; Mozarteum, Salzburg, Austria; Yale Sch Music Summer Sch; studied oboe with Devere Moore; studied oboe d'amore & English horn with Thomas Stacy & Laurence Thorstenberg. *Pos:* Mem, Sommer-Akad Orch, formerly; oboist, Albany Symph Orch, currently; recitalist & mem chamber ens, Capital District. *Teaching:* Instr oboe & clarinet, privately & at Skidmore Col, currently. *Mailing Add:* Music Dept Skidmore Col Saratoga Springs NY 12866

GREEN, GEORGE CLARENCE
COMPOSER, VIOLIN
b Mt Kisco, NY, Aug 23, 30. *Study:* Eastman Sch Music, with Baris Koutzen & Bernard Rogers, MusB, 52, MusM, 52; Berkshire Music Ctr, with Aaron Copland; Cornell Univ, with Robert Palmer, DMA, 69. *Works:* String Quartet, 63; Proloque and Fugue (violin & cello); Fantasies Concertantes (violin & cello); Violin Sonata; Three Pieces for Violin and Piano; Triptych (trumpet solo); Perihelion (band), 73. *Pos:* First violin, Cincinnati Symph Orch, 59-61. *Teaching:* Mem fac, Univ Kans, 54-58, Ohio State Univ, 58-59 & Cornell Univ, 66-71; prof music, Skidmore Col, 71- *Awards:* Comp Prize, Cummington Sch Arts, 63. *Mem:* ASCAP; Am Soc Univ Comp; Music Theory Soc (NY state dir, 73-75); Col Music Soc; Am String Teachers Asn. *Mailing Add:* 6 Sunny Ln Ballston Spa NY 12020

GREEN, JOHN ELWYN
ADMINISTRATOR, EDUCATOR
b Cleveland, Ohio. *Study:* Univ Ill, BMus, 46, MMus, 48; Univ Southern Calif, EdD, 59. *Teaching:* Assoc prof music educ & dir bands, Calif State Univ, Long Beach, 59-64, chmn, Dept Music, 61-64; head, Dept Music, WTex State Univ, 64-69, prof, 64-78, dean, Sch Fine Arts, 69-78; prof music educ & dean, Col Fine Arts, Univ Southern Miss, 78- *Publ:* Coauth, Playing & Teaching Brass Instruments, 61 & Playing & Teaching Percussion Instruments, 62, Prentice-Hall, 62; Sound & Symbol: The Language of Music, Belwin, 65. *Mailing Add:* 1011 Oakleigh Dr Hattiesburg MS 39401

GREEN, JOHN W
COMPOSER, CONDUCTOR & MUSIC DIRECTOR
b New York, NY, Oct 10, 08. *Study:* Harvard Univ, AB, 28; studied piano with Herman Wasserman & Ignace Hilsberg; studied theory with Walter Raymond Spalding & Clair Leonard. *Works:* Night Club Suite, 32, Music for Elizabeth (fantasia for piano & orch), 42, Raintree County (three themes for symph orch), 66, Combo, 67 & Mine Eyes Have Seen (symph in one movement), 78, Boosey & Hawkes Inc. *Rec Perf:* Sousa Marches, 51 & Porgy & Bess, 51, Decca; An American in Paris, MGM Rec, 51; Raintree County (film score & three themes for symph orch), RCA Victor, 58, Columbia Rec, 63 & Entr'acte, 76; Cinderella (Rodgers & Hammerstein), Columbia Masterworks, 64. *Pos:* Comp, cond & arr, Paramount Studios, 30-33; staff music dir, cond & arr, CBS, 33-35; gen music dir, cond & comp, MGM Studios, 49-58; music dir & cond, Promenade Concts, 59-61 & Symph for Youth, Los Angeles, 59-61. *Teaching:* Artist in res, Harvard Univ, 79. *Awards:* Five Oscars, Acad Motion Picture Arts & Sci, 51-68; Nat Citation, Nat Fedn Music Clubs, 55. *Mem:* Am Guild Authors & Comp (mem nat coun, 69-81, vpres, 77-81); ASCAP (mem bd dir, 80-); Am Fedn Musicians. *Rep:* ICM Artists Ltd 40 W 57th St New York NY 10019. *Mailing Add:* 903 N Bedford Dr Beverly Hills CA 90210

GREEN, JONATHAN D
TENOR
b New York, NY, May 4, 45. *Study:* Middlebury Col, BA; Manhattan Sch Music; Yale Univ. *Pos:* Prin tenor, New York City Opera, currently; appearances, Central City Opera, Cincinnati Opera, St Paul Opera Asn & Milwaukee Under the Stars. *Awards:* Winner, NY Liederkranz Compt, 75. *Rep:* Munro Artist Mgt 344 W 72nd St New York NY 10023. *Mailing Add:* 34 W 75th St New York NY 10023

GREEN, MARIAN C
CRITIC-WRITER, EDUCATOR
b Morristown, NJ, June 16, 40. *Study:* Bryn Mawr Col, BA, 61, MA, 64; NY Univ, PhD, 78. *Pos:* Founding ed, J Musicol, Imp Printing Co, 82- *Teaching:* Lectr music hist, NY Univ, 69-71 & asst prof, 78-79. *Mem:* Am Musicol Soc; Music Libr Asn. *Interests:* Early Renaissance music; 15th-century sacred music in France, Italy and England. *Mailing Add:* 1226 Bates Ct Louisville KY 40204

GREEN, REBECCA MCMULLAN
VIOLIN
b Mobile, Ala, Sept 17, 53. *Study:* Memphis State Univ, BMus, 75; Col Consv Music, Univ Cincinnati, 76-78. *Pos:* Violinist, Mobile Symph Orch, 69-70; first violinist, Memphis Symph Orch, 71-75; assoc concertmaster, Cincinnati Symph Orch, 78-, mem first violin sect, currently. *Teaching:* Adj fac mem, Col Consv Music, Univ Cincinnati. *Mem:* Pi Kappa Lambda. *Mailing Add:* 607 McAlpin St #15 Cincinnati OH 45220

GREENAWALT, TERRENCE LEE
CONDUCTOR, PIANO
b Hamburg, Pa, Aug 5, 36. *Study:* West Chester State Col, Pa, BS(music educ), 58; Eastman Sch Music, MA(music theory), 62, PhD(music theory), 72; studied with Jose Echantz & Emory Remington. *Rec Perf:* Conn Music Educr Asn Western Region Fest, Univ Bridgeport, Vogt Recs, 83. *Pos:* Bandsman & arr, Fifth Army Band, Ft Sheridan, Ill, 58-60. *Teaching:* Band & choir dir, Belleville High Sch, NJ, 60-61 & Groton High Sch, NY, 62-63; coordr theoret studies, Univ Bridgeport, 63-, chmn music dept, formerly & dir grad studies, currently. *Awards:* Orpheus Award, Phi Mu Alpha, 78. *Mem:* Conn Music Educr Asn; Music Educr Nat Conf; Soc Music Theory; Col Music Soc. *Mailing Add:* Music Dept Univ Bridgeport Bridgeport CT 06601

GREENBAUM, MATTHEW JONATHAN
COMPOSER
b New York, NY, Feb 12, 50. *Study:* Studied with Stefan Wolpe, 69-71; City Col New York, with Mario Davidowsky, MA, 75; Grad Ctr, City Univ New York, currently. *Works:* Aria #1, Group Contemp Music, 77; Notker's Tale, Johnson Comp Conf, 81; Chamber Music for Flute, Piano & Cello, comn & perf by Contemp Trio, 82. *Awards:* Martha Baird Rockefeller Award, 82. *Mem:* BMI; Am Music Ctr. *Mailing Add:* 99 Perry St New York NY 10014

GREENBERG, MARVIN
EDUCATOR
b New York, NY, June 24, 36. *Study:* NY Univ, BS, 57; Columbia Univ, MA, 58, EdD, 61. *Teaching:* Music, New York City Sch System, 57-63; prof educ, Col Educ, Univ Hawaii, Honolulu, 63-82, prof music educ, 83- *Bibliog:* Vicki V Lott (auth), A Study of Musical Achievement of Culturally Disadvantaged Children Based on the Music for Preschool Curriculum of Marvin Greenberg, La State Univ, 78. *Mem:* Hawaii Music Educr Asn (mem exec bd, 64-69 & 75-78 & pres, 76-77); Music Educr Nat Conf (mem western div, exec bd, 76-77); Hawaii Asn for Educ Young Children (exec bd mem, 80-82); Soc Res Music Educ; Coun Res Music Educ. *Interests:* Musical development of infants. *Publ:* Auth, Musical Achievement & the Self Concept, J Res Music Educ, spring 70; Preschool Music Curriculum, Hawaii Educ Res & Develop Ctr, 70; coauth, Music Handbook for the Elementary School, Parker Publ Co, 72; auth, Your Children Need Music, Prentice-Hall Inc, 79; Teacher's Guide and Program Notes: Honolulu Symph Children's Concert, Hawaii Dept Educ, 80- *Mailing Add:* 2411 Dole St MB 203 Honolulu HI 96822

GREENBERG, MICHAEL E
CRITIC
b San Antonio, Tex, Mar 16, 47. *Study:* Macalester Col. *Pos:* Critic at large, San Antonio Express News, 79- *Mem:* Music Critics Asn. *Mailing Add:* PO Box 2171 San Antonio TX 78297

GREENBERG, NAT
ADMINISTRATOR
b Warsaw, Poland, May 25, 18; US citizen. *Study:* Study with Fred Zimmerman, 40-46; Col City New York, BS, 41. *Pos:* Mgr, Ft Wayne Phil, 59-66, Rochester Phil, 66-69, Columbus Symph, 69-76, San Antonio Symph Opera, 76-82 & Kansas City Symph, 82- *Teaching:* Instr string bass, Kansas City Consv, 53-59. *Mem:* Am Symph Orch League (mem bd, 72-74); Int Soc Perf Arts Adminr; Asn Col Univ & Community Arts Adminr; Metropolitan Orch Mgrs (pres, 71-74); Am Fedn Musicians. *Mailing Add:* c/o Kansas City Symph 1029 Central Kansas City MO 64105

GREENBERG, PHILIP
CONDUCTOR & MUSIC DIRECTOR
b Jan 26, 48. *Study:* Ind Univ, BM(appl violin perf), 71; Univ Mich, MMus(cond & appl violin perf), 72. *Pos:* Asst cond, Detroit Symph Orch, 74-78; music dir, WShore Symph, 76-81 & Youth Symph Detroit Civic Orch, formerly; res cond, Phoenix Symph Orch, 81-83; guest cond, Danish Radio Orch, formerly, Santa Cecila Orch, Rome, formerly, Ari Orch, Milan, formerly, Grand Rapids Civic Ballet, Mich & many others in US & Europe. *Teaching:* Prof music, Hope Col, 72-74 & Olivet Col, 71- *Awards:* First Prize & Orch Prize, Nicolai Malko Int Cond Compt, Copenhagen, 77. *Rep:* Herbert Barrett Mgt Inc 1860 Broadway New York NY 10023. *Mailing Add:* 221 John St Grand Rapids MI 49503

GREENBERG, ROGER D
SAXOPHONE, EDUCATOR
b Pottsville, Pa, Apr 7, 44. *Study:* Juilliard Sch, BMus, 70; Univ Southern Calif, MMus, 73. *Rec Perf:* Art of Fugue (Bach), Protone Rec, 72; Westwood Wind Quintet Plays Music by Revueltas ..., 74 & Harvey Pittel Saxophone Quartet, 80, Crystal Rec; Art of the Saxophone, WIM Rec, 80; Harvey Pittel Saxophone Quartet, Harojama Rec, 82. *Pos:* Soloist, band & orch recitals US & Europe, 70- & World Sax Cong, Bordeaux, France, 74; on call saxophonist, Los Angeles Phil Orch, 71-80 & Denver Symph Orch, 80-; mem, Harvey Pittel Sax Quartet, 78- *Teaching:* Asst prof sax, Univ Northern Colo, 80- *Mem:* World Sax Cong (regional coordr, 72-73); North Am Sax Alliance. *Publ:* Auth, Performance Analysis of William Schmidt Saxophone Concerto, Sax J, 82. *Mailing Add:* 5217 W 26th St Greeley CO 80634

GREENE, ARTHUR
PIANO
b New York, NY, Apr 26, 55. *Study:* Yale Univ, with Ward Davenny, BA, 76; Juilliard Sch, with Martin Canin, MM, 78; State Univ NY, Stony Brook, DMA. *Rec Perf:* Beethoven Sonatas, 82 & Chopin & Brahms, 82, Columbia. *Pos:* Three solo tours Japan, 80-83; Xerox pianist, Affiliate Artists, NY, 82- *Awards:* First Prize, Gina Bachauer Int Piano Compt, 78. *Mailing Add:* PO Box 201 East Setauket NY 11733

GREENE, DONALD EDGAR
EDUCATOR
b Scranton, Pa, Jan 23, 30. *Study:* Mansfield State Col, BS, 51; Eastman Sch Music, MM, 64; Univ Wis, Madison, 73-75. *Pos:* Cond, Cent Wis Symph Orch, 76-81. *Teaching:* Assoc prof music, Univ Wis, Stevens Point, 67-, chmn dept music, 68-76 & 83- *Mem:* Music Educr Nat Conf. *Mailing Add:* Music Dept Univ Wis Stevens Point WI 54481

GREENE, JOSHUA
MUSIC DIRECTOR, TEACHER
b New York, NY, Aug 2, 52. *Study:* Mannes Col Music, BM(orch cond), 74; Manhattan Sch Music, MM(orch cond), 76. *Pos:* Music dir, Theater Opera Music Inst, 80- & Adelphi Chamber Orch , 82- *Teaching:* Vocal coach opera & lieder, privately, 70-; instr theory, Mannes Col Music, 74-76; vocal coach opera, Manhatton Sch Music, 74-76. *Mailing Add:* 210 W 101 St #145 New York NY 10025

GREENE, MARGO LYNN
COMPOSER, WRITER
b Brooklyn, NY, June 10, 48. *Study:* Bennington Col, with Louis Calabror; Barnard Col, AB, 69; Columbia Univ, with Vladimir Ussachevsky, Mario Davidovsky, Charles Wuorinen, Jack Beeson & Bulent Arel, MA(comp), 72; Grad Sch & Univ Ctr, City Univ New York, with Mario Davidovsky, Joel Lester & George Perle. *Works:* Movement for String Quartet, Columbia Comp, 70; Study for Solo Clarinet, perf by Stephen Hartman, 71; Variations for Clarinet Solo, perf by Virgil Blackwell, 72; Five Songs for Mezzo Soprano and Orchestra, Columbia Comp, 72; Targets (electronic tape), Columbia-Princeton Electronic Music Ctr, 73; Letting Go (violin solo), perf by Dinos Constantinides, 78; Quintet (flute, oboe, clarinet, violin & cello), Am Soc Univ Comp & Hartt Sch Music, 78. *Rec Perf:* Shortcut (Margo Greene), Media Sound Studio, 75. *Pos:* Rec asst to Vladimir Ussachevsky, Columbia-Princeton Electronic Music Ctr, 72-74; exec secy to Julius Rudel, New York City Opera, 74-75; auditor, NY State Coun Arts, 76-83; staff reviewer, Rec Rev, Los Angeles, 77-81. *Teaching:* Asst music, humanities & piano lit, Columbia Univ, 71-72; instr piano, 92nd St Y Sch Music, 72-74. *Awards:* Nat Student Comp Compt Prize, Hartt Sch Music, 78. *Mem:* Am Soc Univ Comp (mem exec comt, 78-80); Am Music Ctr; Int League Women Comp; Col Music Soc; Alban Berg Soc. *Publ:* Auth, The Fragmentation of 20th Century Music, Catalyst Mag, 76; Musicians and Money, Keynote Mag, 77; Electronic Pioneers: Arel, Davidovsky, Gaburo, Ussachevsky, 77, Schoenberg: The Five String Quartets, 78 & Liszt: 12 Etudes d'Execution Transcendante, 78, Rec Rev Mag. *Mailing Add:* 210 W 90th St New York NY 10024

GREENFIELD, LUCILLE J
TEACHER, COMPOSER
b New York, NY, Feb 24, 38. *Study:* Columbia Univ, BS(music), 59. *Works:* Three Songs for Children, 72, Follow Your Fading Star, 72, Walk with Love, 72, Drifting on By, 72, Wrong Side of the Street, 72, Life's Rolling Sea, 72 & How Many Miles Must I Run, 73, Glad Tone Music Publ. *Teaching:* Comp piano & voice, Studio Gladyces de Jesus, 69- *Awards:* First Prize, for The Alienated Ones, Comp Auth & Artists Am Cont Chamber Orch Comp, 83. *Mailing Add:* 338 W 15th St New York NY 10011

GREENHOE, DAVID STANLEY
TRUMPET, EDUCATOR
b Flint, Mich, Jan 9, 42. *Study:* Studied trumpet with Clifford Lillya, 54-60 & with Gilbert Johnson, 66-68; Eastman Sch Music, 64; Ball State Univ, MM, 69. *Rec Perf:* Assortments (Knight), Now Rec, 75. *Pos:* Mem & soloist, US Marine Band, Washington, DC, 64-68; solo trumpet, Lake Placid Sinfonietta, NY, 75-; prin trumpet, Tri-City Symph, Davenport, Iowa, 79- *Teaching:* Prof trumpet & chmn brass dept, Ball State Univ, 68-79; prof trumpet, Univ Iowa, 79- *Awards:* Orpheus Award, Delta Lambda Chap, Phi Mu Alpha Sinfonia, 79. *Mem:* Int Trumpet Guild. *Rep:* Butler Mgt 638 S Governor Iowa City IA 52240. *Mailing Add:* Sch Music Univ Iowa Iowa City IA 52242

GREENHOUSE, BERNARD
EDUCATOR, CELLO
b Newark, NJ, Jan 3, 16. *Study:* Juilliard Sch, dipl, 38; study with Emanuel Feverman, 40-41; Pablo Casals, 46-47. *Rec Perf:* Concerto (Victor Herbert), 51, Concerto (Dvorak), 64, Concerto (Boccherini), 65 & Concerto (Haydn), 65, Conct Hall; Concerto III (Beethoven), Philips Rec, 78. *Pos:* Prin cellist, CBS Symph, New York, 38-42; mem, Dorian String Quartet, New York, 39-42, Bach Aria Group, New York, 46-76 & Beaux Arts Trio, 55- *Teaching:* Prof cello, Manhattan Sch Music, 50-, Juilliard Sch, 51-61 & State Univ NY, Stony Brook, 60- *Awards:* Best Rec 1980, Gramophone Mag, London; Artist Teacher of Yr, Am String Teachers Asn, 82; Grand Prix du Disque. *Mem:* Violoncello Soc (pres, 55-60); Bohemians; hon mem, Am String Teachers Asn. *Rep:* Columbia Artist Mgt Inc 113 W 57th St New York NY 10019. *Mailing Add:* 5 Tinker Lane East Setauket NY 11733

GREENLEAF, ROBERT BRUCE
EDUCATOR, CLARINET
b Auburn, Ala, Apr 28, 49. *Study:* Fla State Univ, with Harry Schmidt, Albert Tipton & John Boda, BM, 71; La State Univ, with Paul Dirksmeyer & John Patterson, MMA 72, DMA, 74. *Works:* Variations on an Original Theme, Winds & Ivories, 78. *Teaching:* Asst prof music, Auburn Univ, 74-80, assoc prof, 81- *Mem:* Music Teachers Nat Asn; Nat Asn Col Wind & Perc Instr. *Mailing Add:* 101 Goodwin Music Bldg Auburn Univ Auburn AL 36849

GREER, THOMAS HENRY
COMPOSER, CONDUCTOR
b Gustine, Tex, July 24, 16. *Study:* McMurry Col, BS, 38; Southern Methodist Univ, MM, 51; NTex State Univ, PhD(musicol), 68. *Works:* Andante and Allegro for Trumpet, 59; Three Songs for Soprano and String Quartet, Midwestern Univ Quartet, Ussachevsky Symposium, 65; Variations on Ragtime Annie, 66; Metamorpheses on a Country Theme, San Angelo Symph Orch, Tex, 73; many others. *Rec Perf:* Flying Fiddles, 49 & Adaptation of Romance (Wieniawski), 49, ABC. *Pos:* Bandleader, Sixth Army Group, US, Europe & Africa, 53-55; concertmaster, Wichita Falls Symph Orch, Tex, 61-66; cond, Midwestern Univ Chamber Orch, 61-68 & Pan Am Univ Valley Symph, 68-74. *Teaching:* Prof music lit, Henderson State Univ, 51-53; prof theory, Howard Payne Univ, 53-57; music coordr, San Angelo Sch, Tex, 57-61. *Awards:* Distinguished Alumnus, McMurry Col, 75. *Bibliog:* James Hoggard (auth), Midwestern University Teacher Fiddles With Rare Fiddles, Wichita Falls Rec News, 12/10/65; Project Researches Finish on Violins, Harlinger Valley Morning Star, 9/26/76; Vickie Stafford (auth), Violin Maker, Rebuilder (film), Cablevision, Austin, Tex, 10/82. *Mem:* Am Musicol Soc; Tex Music Educr Asn; Tex String Teachers Asn. *Publ:* Contribr, Musical Scandal in the 20th Century, Fac Papers Midwestern Univ, 64-65; auth, Music and Its Relation to Futurism, Cubism, Dadaism, Surrealism, 1905-1950, NTex State Univ Press, 68; Violin Varnish, 76 & Sources: Lute Tablatures, 77, Creative Guitar Int. *Mailing Add:* 7012 Mt Carrell Austin TX 78745

GREGG, CHANDLER
TEACHER, PIANO
b Boston, Mass, Jan 6, 33. *Study:* Harvard Col, AB, 55; Harvard Univ, AM, 58; studied piano with Albion Metcalf, Bruce Simonds & Denise Lassimonne, 49-70. *Works:* Acceptance, Religious Arts Guild, Boston, 65. *Pos:* Dir music, Unitarian Soc Wellesley Hills, Mass, 60-; ed, Am Matthay Asn, 68-74. *Teaching:* Private instr piano, Mass, 55-; instr, Conn Col, 67-68; fac mem, Boston Consv Music, 69- *Mem:* Am Matthay Asn (vpres 76-78 & pres, 78-82); Am Guild Organists. *Mailing Add:* East Long Pond Rd Plymouth MA 02360

GREGORIAN, HENRY
VIOLIN
b Tabriz, Iran, May 14, 24; US citizen. *Study:* Tehran Consv Music, dipl, 46; Longy Sch Music, dipl, 51; Boston Univ, MS, 53. *Pos:* First violinist, Minn Orch, 55 & 69-; concertmaster, St Paul Chamber Orch, 65. *Teaching:* Violin & music, private instr, 45-80, Tehran Consv, 46, Univ Minn, 66-70. *Mailing Add:* 1111 Nicollet Mall Minneapolis MN 55403

GREGORIAN, ROUBEN
CONDUCTOR, COMPOSER
b Tifliz, Russia, Sept 23, 15; nat US. *Study:* Armenian Cent Col, Iran; Tehran Consv Music, Iran; Ecole Normale de Musique, studied comp with Arthur Honneger; Nat Consv Music France, studied orch dir with Forestier & Fournier. *Works:* Iranian Suite (symph orch), Iran & US; Tatragoms Bride (symph poem), Easter Cantata (chorus), Nairy Symphonic Suite & Orch & Hega Orchestral Fantasie, US; Armenian Di Vine Liturgy for Soli, Chorus & Orchestra, 80-81; Second Suite for Orchestra, 81. *Rec Perf:* Oratorio de Noel, Op 12; Armenia Sings, Robert Mesrobian & Komitas String Quartet; Armenian Folk Songs, Komitas Choral Soc Boston. *Pos:* Dir, Tehran Consv, 48-51 & Komitas Choral Soc Boston, 55-; music dir & cond, Tehran Symph, 48-51, Portland Maine Symph, 59-62, Boston Women's Symph, 64-65, New England Symph Orch, 83-; head, Iranian Nat Comn, UN Educ Sci & Cult Orgn, 48-51; cond, Boston Consv Orch, 55-79; choral dir, Boston Consv Chorus, 52-79; founder & first violinist, Komitas String Quartet, 53-; guest cond, Boston Esplanade Conct, 62, Boston Pops Orch, 52-79, St Paul Chamber Orch, 67, Yerevan State Phil Orch, USSR, 67, Tehran Symph & Nat Iranian TV Orch, 76-78, New York Chamber Players, 80 & Pasadena Symph Orch, 81; assoc cond, Brotherhood Temple Ohavei Shalom Civic Symph Orch, 63-65; music dir & cond, New England Symph Orch, 83- *Teaching:* Instr violin, Tehran Consv, 46-51; instr violin, Boston Consv, 54-79, instr chamber music, 54-79. *Mem:* Int Folk Music Coun, England; Nat Asn Am Comp & Cond; Mass Fedn Music Clubs. *Publ:* Auth, Iranian Folk Songs (two vol), Iranian Ministry Educ; Iranian Folk Songs, Kjos Publ Co. *Mailing Add:* 67 Betts Rd Belmont MA 02178

GREITZER, SOL
EDUCATOR, VIOLA
Study: Juilliard Sch, studied violin with Louis Persinger & viola with Milton Katims, dipl. *Pos:* Worldwide performances with maj orchs & as soloist; prin violist & soloist, New York Phil, currently. *Teaching:* Adj mem fac music, Mannes Col Music, 81- & Queens Col, City Univ New York, currently; prof violin & viola, Sch Educ, NY Univ, currently. *Mailing Add:* New York Phil Avery Fisher Hall New York NY 10023

GREIVE, TYRONE DON
EDUCATOR, VIOLIN
b Sioux City, Iowa, July 30, 43. *Study:* Morningside Col, studied violin with Leo Kucinski, BM, 65; Carnegie-Mellon Univ, studied violin with Sidney Harth, MA, 70; Univ Mich, studied violin with Angel Reyes, DMA, 77. *Pos:* Concertmaster, Sioux Falls Symph, 64-75, Lakeside Summer Symph, 64-65, Black Hills Chamber Orch, 70-73 & Shreveport Music Fest, 78- *Teaching:* Asst prof violin, Augustana Col, Sioux Falls, SDak, 64-77 & Stephen F Austin State Univ, 77-79; asst prof, Univ Wis, Madison, 79-83, assoc prof, 83- *Mem:* Am Fedn Musicians; Am String Teachers Asn (vpres SDak chap, 71-74); Violin Soc Am. *Publ:* Auth, Szymanowski's Violin Sonata: An Introduction and Some Performance Suggestions, Strad, 82; String Tone and the Importance of the Sounding Point, Instrumentalist, 83; Tuning and the String Player, Sch Musician, 83; Karol Szymanowski's Works for Strings: An Introduction to Their Background, Style, and Performance Problems, Am String Teacher, 83. *Mailing Add:* 513 Rushmore Lane Madison WI 53711

GRENIER, VICTORIA R
FLUTE & PICCOLO, EDUCATOR
b Oregon City, Ore, Oct 24, 44. *Study:* Ind Univ, BM, 66; Northwestern Univ, MM, 74. *Teaching:* Coordr woodwinds, Sch Music, DePaul Univ, 78-82, asst prof flute & chair perf studies, 82- *Mem:* Nat Flute Asn. *Publ:* Auth, Human Factors—The Other Side of Teaching, 82 & The Flute:Common Ailments,|83, Instrumentalist; A Performance Guide to A Night Piece by A Foote, Flute Talk, Instrumentalist, 83. *Mailing Add:* 861 Greenwood Glencoe IL 60022

GRICE, GARRY B
TENOR, EDUCATOR
b Dayton, Ohio, Jan 25, 42. *Study:* Univ Dayton, BA, 64; study with Hubert Kockritz, Cincinnati, Ohio. *Roles:* Don Jose in Carmen, Milwaukee Florentine, 80; Don Jose in Carmen, 81-82, Bacchus in Ariadne auf Naxos, 82 & Avito, 82, New York City Opera; Manrico in Il Trovatore, Indianapolis Opera, 82; Otello in Otello, Des Moines Metro Opera, 82; Radames in Aida, Rochester Opera Theater, 83. *Teaching:* Instr voice & opera, Wash State Univ, Pullman, 82- *Awards:* Grant, William Matheus Sullivan Found, 81; Artist Award, McCoy Found, 82. *Mailing Add:* c/o Matthews/Napal Ltd 270 West End Ave New York NY 10023

GRIEBLING, KAREN JEAN
COMPOSER, VIOLA
b Akron, Ohio, Dec 31, 57. *Study:* Eastman Sch Music with Francis Tursi, Samuel Adler, Warren Benson & Joseph Schwantner, BM, 80; Univ Houston, with Lawrence Wheeler, Milton Katims & Michael Horvit, MM, 82; Univ Tex, Austin, currently. *Works:* Piano Sonata, Univ Houston, 82; Five Tzu-Yeh Songs, Ill State Univ, 82; String Quartet V, perf by Eudoxa Quartet, 82; Two Anthems for Church, perf by Church of the Good Shepherd, 82-83; Johnny Appleseed (ballet), Akron Ohio Ballet, 83; Three Sonnets, Univ Tex, 83. *Pos:* Violist, Dror String Quartet, Univ Houston, 80-82, Houston Ballet Orch, 80-82 & Orch of Tex, 83- *Teaching:* Piano, violin, viola & theory, privately, 72-; instr violin & viola, Suzuki Univ Houston, 80-82; teaching asst theory, Univ Tex, Austin, 82- *Awards:* Seven Year Comp Cont Award, Nat Fedn Music Clubs, 76; ASCAP Award, 82. *Mem:* Nat Fedn Music Clubs; Am Women Comp; Viola Soc; Am Fedn Musicians. *Mailing Add:* 4606 Ave H Austin TX 78751

GRIEBLING, LYNN (LYNN LOUISE GRIEBLING-MOORES)
SOPRANO, TEACHER
b Milwaukee, Wis, June 16, 45. *Study:* St Olaf Col, BMus, 67; Univ Wis, MMus, 69. *Roles:* Mahler Symphony #8, Cleveland Orch, 73; Les Musiciens du Ray, 73-79; Four Last Songs (Strauss), Houston Symph & Ballet, 80-81; Mama Stark in Willie Stark, Houston Opera, 81. *Teaching:* Lectr voice & vocal lit, Carleton Col, 70-73; artist teacher, Shepherd Sch, Rice Univ, 80- *Mem:* Am Guild Musical Art. *Mailing Add:* Shepherd Sch Music Rice Univ Houston TX 77251

GRIEBLING, MARGARET ANN
COMPOSER, OBOE
b Akron, Ohio, Nov 17, 60. *Study:* Eastman Sch Music, BM, 82; San Francisco Consv Music, currently; studied oboe with John Mack, Robert Sprenkle & Harvey McGuire. *Works:* Two Bagatelles for Bassoon & Oboe, 74; Goldsmith's Pasticcio, comn by Huntingdon Trio of Philadelphia, 79; Atlanta (orch tone poem). *Pos:* Prin Oboe, Heidelberg Opera Orch, 81 & Blossom Music Ctr Fest Band, 82-83. *Awards:* First & Second Prizes, Nat Fedn Music Clubs, 70-78; BMI Grant, 74; Young Adult Comp Orch Award, Nat Fedn Music Clubs, 78. *Mem:* Int Double Reed Soc; Mu Phi Epsilon (pres, vpres, secy & treas, 78-82); Am Fedn Musicians. *Mailing Add:* 753 Cliffside Dr Akron OH 44313

GRIEBLING, STEPHEN THOMAS
COMPOSER, PIANO
b Dec 10, 32. *Study:* Mt Union Col, BS, 54. *Works:* Sonata (viola), 70, Caprice (oboe), 72, Queensmere, 74, Intermezzo (orch), 76, Three Songs from Lamp & Bell, 78, Fugue (brass quintet), 81 & For Everything There is A Season, 82, Southern Music Co. *Awards:* First Place, Nat Sch Orch Asn, 76; winner, Ithaca Col Choral Compt, 82. *Mem:* Ohio Fedn Music Clubs. *Mailing Add:* 753 Cliffside Dr Akron OH 44313

GRIFFEL, L MICHAEL
EDUCATOR, CRITIC-WRITER
b New York, NY, Nov 12, 42. *Study:* Yale Col, BA, 63; Juilliard Sch Music, MS, 66; Columbia Univ, MA, 68, PhD, 75. *Pos:* Ed-in-chief, Current Musicol, Columbia Univ, 70-72. *Teaching:* Assoc prof music, Grad Sch, City Univ New York, 78- & Hunter Col, City Univ New York, 78-; chmn dept, 82-; teacher music hist, Mannes Col Music, 80- *Awards:* Nat Endowment Humanities Summer Stipend, 80. *Mem:* Am Musicol Soc (coun mem, 69-71); Col Music Soc; Int Musicol Soc. *Interests:* Nineteenth century music history, with specialization on Schubert symphonies, piano music & opera. *Publ:* Ed, Musicological Method in American Graduate Schools, Current Musicol, 67-68; coauth, The Strange Case of John Shmarb: An Aesthetic Puzzle, J Aesthetics & Art Criticism, 75; auth, A Reappraisal of Schubert's Methods of Composition, Musical Quart, 77; coauth, Scholars Who Teach, Nelson-Hall, 78; Schirmer History of Music, Schirmer Bks, 82. *Mailing Add:* Dept Music Hunter Col City Univ New York NY 10021

GRIFFEL, MARGARET ROSS
WRITER
b New York, NY, July 9, 43. *Study:* Barnard Col, AB, 65; Boston Univ, MA, 66; Columbia Univ, MA, 69, PhD, 75. *Pos:* Music reviewer & writer, Riverdale Press, NY, 67-72; co-ed in chief, Current Musicol, Columbia Univ, 72-73 & ed in chief, 73-74; reviewer & ed, Schirmer Books, 77-82; consult & ed, G Schirmer Inc, 78- *Mem:* Am Musicol Soc; Int Musicol Soc. *Interests:* Opera. *Publ:* Co-ed, Schirmer History of Music, Shirmer Bks, 82; auth, bibliog to chap #1 through #13, In: New Oxford History of Music, VIII, Oxford Univ Press, 82. *Mailing Add:* 3135 Johnson Ave #9E Bronx NY 10463

GRIFFIN, ELINOR REMICK WARREN See Warren, Elinor Remick

GRIFFIN, JUDSON T
VIOLA, EDUCATOR
b Lewes, Del, Sept 7, 51. *Study:* With Mischa Mischakoff, 68-69; Eastman Sch Music, with Francis Tursi, BM, 73; Juilliard Sch, with Lillian Fuchs, MM, 75, DMA, 77. *Pos:* Mem, Strawberry Banke Piano Quartet, Portsmouth, NH, 70 & 71, Rochester Phil Orch, 70-73; freelance musicians, New York, 73-; New York Chamber Soloists, Aston Magna, Conct Royal, Mozartean Ens, Ens for Early Music, New Repty Ens & many other groups; prin viola, Aspen Chamber Symph, summer 76-80, Aston Magna, Monadnock Music, Newport Fest, Vt Mozart Fest, Castle Hill Fest & Composers Conf; violist, Smithson String Quartet, Smithsonian Inst, 82- *Teaching:* Asst prof violin, viola & chamber music, Sch Music, Univ NC, Greensboro, 77-79; mem fac viola & chamber music, Aspen Music Sch, 79- *Awards:* William J Henderson Award, 75 & Viola Comp Winner, 76, Juilliard Sch; winner, Aspen Viola Compt, 77. *Mem:* Am Fedn Musicians; Am Viola Soc; Am Music Ctr. *Publ:* Contribr to Notes. *Mailing Add:* 170 Claremont Ave Apt #7 New York NY 10027

GRIGGS, PETER JOHNSON
COMPOSER, GUITAR & LUTE
b New York, NY, Apr 6, 52. *Study:* Juilliard Sch Music, 68-70; Bowdoin Col, BA, 70-74; Wesleyan Univ, 74-75. *Works:* Pavane, 81 & When the Sun Stands Still, 83, perf by Peter Griggs with Iris Brooks & Glen Velez; Spirals-Gamelan, comn by Nat Endowment Arts Consortium Comn Prog, 82; 100 Camels in the Courtyard, 82 & Forty-Fives, 83, Ear Mag East; Music from Past Lives, comn by Ellen Webb Dance Co, 83. *Pos:* Freelance comp & perf, 77-; music consult, East Ramapo Sch Dist, 79-81; music panelist, NJ State Coun Arts,

83. *Awards:* Grant, Meet the Comp, 77-82. *Bibliog:* Tom Johnson (auth), Composers in Collaboration, Village Voice, 6/1/82; Ed Rothstein (auth), Bargemusic: Peter Griggs, NY Times, 7/14/82. *Mailing Add:* 115 S Mountain Rd New City NY 10956

GRIGSBY, BEVERLY PINSKY
COMPOSER, EDUCATOR
b Chicago, Ill, Jan 11, 28. *Study:* Studied comp with Ernst Krenek, 48-51; Univ Southern Calif, 44-47 & currently; San Fernando Valley State Col, BA, 61; Calif State Univ, Northridge, MA, 63. *Works:* Fragments from Augustine, The Saint (dramatic cantata), perf by Larry Jarvis, 74; Love Songs (tenor & guitar), perf by Terry Bowers & Ronald Purcell, 74; Dithyrambos (violin & cello), NY New Music Ens, 80; Movements for Guitar, comn & perf by William J Davila, 82; Shakti (flute & tape), comn & perf by Gretel Shanley, 83; The Mask of Eleanor (chamber opera for sop & ens), comn & perf by Ann Gresham, 83. *Pos:* Co-founder & co-dir, Int Inst Study Women's Music, 82- *Teaching:* From asst prof to prof music & dir comput music comp, Calif State Univ, Northridge, 63-; co-chair, Consortium Comput Assisted Instr, Calif State Univ Syst, 79-; vis prof, Manuel Ponce Consv, Mex, 83. *Awards:* Nat Endowment Arts Grant, 78; Chancellor's Maxi-Grant Res, 78 & Distinguished Prof Award, 78, Calif State Univ Syst. *Mem:* Am Soc Univ Comp (chair region VIII, 77-81); Nat Asn Comp USA; Am Musicol Soc; Int Cong Women Music (assoc dir, 83). *Publ:* Auth, Report to the Chancellor—Project for Innovation in the Instructional Process—Computer Assisted Instruction in Music, Perf Arts Rev, Vol 8, No 3; Women Composers of Electronic & Computer Music, Part I USA, Musical, Vol I, 83; Women Composers ..., Part II Canada, Vol II, In: Woman: An Int Perspective, Greenwood Press (in prep). *Mailing Add:* Music Dept Calif State Univ Northridge CA 91330

GRIKA, LARRY A
VIOLIN, TEACHER
b Chicago, Ill, Oct 14, 32. *Study:* Chicago Musical Col, Roosevelt Univ, BM, 54, MM, 55. *Pos:* Violin, Lyr Opera Chicago, 54 & 55; first violin, Cincinnati Symph Orch, 61-64 & Philadelphia Orch, 64-; mem, Amerita Chamber Orch, 70-80; participant, Casals Fest, 82. *Teaching:* Fac mem, Antioch Col, 59-62; Glassboro State Col, 75-78 & Temple Univ, 82- *Awards:* Oliver Ditson Award Violin, Chicago Musical Col, 53-54. *Mailing Add:* 215 Phillellena Rd Cherry Hill NJ 08034

GRILLO, JOANN DANIELLE
MEZZO-SOPRANO
b New York, NY, May 14, 39. *Study:* Hunter Col, BS, 76; New York Col Music; Am Acad Dramatic Arts; studied with Lorenzo Anselmi, Daniel Ferro, Joan Dornemann, Samuel Margolis, Marinka Gurewich, Anton Guadagno & Kathryn Long. *Roles:* Amneris in Aida, New York Fest, 58 & Frankfort Opera, 67; Charlotte in Werther, Gran Teatro Liceo, Barcelona, 63 & 78; Jocasta in Oedipus Rex, Frankfort Opera, 67; Carmen in Carmen, Frankfort Opera, 67, Vienna Staatsoper, 78 & Paris Opera, 81; Suzuki in Madama Butterfly, NJ State Opera, 83; Santuzza in Cavalleria Rusticana; Rosina in Il Barbiere di Siviglia; and many others. *Pos:* Res artist, Metropolitan Opera, 63-; ms with major opera co in US & Europe. *Rep:* Joseph A Scuro Int Artists Mgt 111 W 57th St New York NY 10019. *Mailing Add:* Metropolitan Opera Lincoln Ctr New York NY 10023

GRIM, WILLIAM EDWARD
CLARINET, TEACHER
b Columbus, Ohio, Aug 29, 55. *Study:* Ohio Wesleyan Univ, BM(clarinet), 77; Univ Akron, MM(perf), 79; Kent State Univ. *Teaching:* Asst clarinet, Univ Akron, 78-79; asst music hist, Kent State Univ, 80-82; prof music hist, theory & woodwinds, St Andrews Presby Col, 82- *Mem:* Am Musicol Soc; Int Clarinet Soc; Col Music Soc; Nat Asn Col Wind & Perc Instr; Music Educr Nat Conf. *Interests:* Joseph Haydn; 18th and 19th century music history. *Mailing Add:* 2009 Lake Dr Laurinburg NC 28352

GRIMES, DOREEN
EDUCATOR, COMPOSER
b Weatherford, Tex, Feb 1, 32. *Study:* Southern Methodist Univ, BMus, 49, MMus, 50; NTex State Univ, PhD, 66. *Works:* Drugstore Panorama (opera), perf by Angelo State Univ students, 76; Mass of the Good Shepherd, perf by choir & congregation, Good Shepherd Church, 78; Sing a Joyful Song, perf by Abilene Boys Choir, 79; Come in Adoration, perf by Good Shepherd Choir, 80; The Face of a Pioneer Woman, perf by J Stovall, 81; A Day in the Country, Univ Wis, 81 & Univ Redlands, 81; Vermillion Red, Univ Wis, 82. *Pos:* Dir, Grimes Sch Music, 50-62. *Teaching:* Chmn music theory dept, Sch Music, Eastern NMex Univ, Portales, 62-71; prof music, Angelo State Univ, 71- *Awards:* Woman of the Year, Eastern NMex Univ, 65. *Mem:* Tex Soc Music Theory; Soc Music Theory; Tex Music Educr Asn; Music Teachers Nat Asn; Col Music Soc. *Publ:* Auth, Computer-Assisted Instruction Materials, 73; A Stylistic Approach to Diatonic Harmony, 77, Harmony & Form in the Music of Scott Joplin, 77, A Stylistic Approach to Chromatic Harmony, 78 & The Mass in the 20th Century, 80, Angelo State Univ Press. *Mailing Add:* 3202 Lindenwood San Angelo TX 76904

GRIMES, EV
EDUCATOR, RADIO PRODUCER
b Paterson, NJ, 47. *Study:* Susquehanna Univ, BS, 68; Univ Vt, MA(music), 72; Univ Kans. *Pos:* Class music dir, WRUV-FM, Burlington, Vt, 71-72; radio announcer & prod, WQCR-FM, South Burlington, Vt, 72-75; prod, KANV, Lawrence, Kans, 75-79; independent radio prod, 79- *Awards:* Best Cult Prog,

Nat Fedn Community Broadcasters, 78; Best Cult Doc, Corp Pub Broadcasting, 79; Prix Italia, Nat Pub Radio, 81. *Mem:* Int League Women Comp. *Interests:* Psychology & sociology of music; 20th century music in the United States. *Mailing Add:* PO Box 42 Grand Isle VT 05458

GRIMM, BETTY JANE
EDUCATOR, SOPRANO
b Huntington, WVa. *Study:* Marshall Univ, AB, 42; Univ Mich, MA, 47; Columbia Univ, perf cert, 50. *Roles:* Azucena in Il Trovatore, Mascagui Opera, 49 & Fla State Univ Opera Guild; Amneris in Aida & Maddalena in Rigoletto, Interlochen Opera Theatre; Bloody Mary, Nat Opera Co; Math Teacher in Help! Help! The Globolinks!, 72 & Medium in Ali Baba, 75, Fla State Univ Opera Guild. *Teaching:* Choral & band dir, Cerido Rivera High Sch, 45-47; instr, Nat Music Camp, Interlochen, 45-50; prof music, Fla State Univ, 50- *Mem:* Pi Kappa Lambda; Sigma Alpha Iota; Am Choral Div Asn; Nat Asn Teachers Singing. *Publ:* Auth, Technical & Artistic Elementary Singing, Kendall-Hunt, 78, rev ed, 81; Treble Voice Acoustics, Choral J, Am Choral Dir Asn, 82. *Mailing Add:* Sch Music Fla State Univ Tallahassee FL 32306

GRISCOM, RICHARD WILLIAM
LIBRARIAN
b Chattanooga, Tenn, Sept 14, 56. *Study:* Univ Tenn, Knoxville, BM, 78; Ind Univ, Bloomington, MM & MLS, 81. *Pos:* Prin perc, Knoxville Symph Orch, 76-78; announcer, WUOT-FM, 76-80; music cataloguer, Northwestern Univ, Evanston, Ill, 81- *Mem:* Music Libr Asn; Am Musicol Soc. *Interests:* Literature on Schubert; computer applications in libraries; international broadcasting. *Publ:* Auth, Periodical Use in a University Music Library, Serials Librn, 83. *Mailing Add:* 1935 Sheridan Rd Evanston IL 60202

GRIST, RERI
SOPRANO
b New York, NY. *Study:* Queens Col, City Univ New York, BA(music); studied voice with Claire Gelda. *Rec Perf:* Works by Mozart, Strauss, Verdi & others on EMI, RCA Victor, Columbia & other labels. *Roles:* Consuelo in West Side Story, 57; Blondchen in Entführung aus dem Serail, Santa Fe Opera, 59; Queen of the Night in The Magic Flute, Glyndebourne, 62; Despina in Cosi fan tutte, 63 & Zerbinetta in Ariadne auf Naxos, 63, Naples; Gilda in Rigoletto, Montreal Opera, 66; Rosina in The Barber of Seville, Metropolitan Opera, 66. *Pos:* Sop, Zürich Opera, 60-, Vienna Staatsoper, 63- & Salzburg Fest, 64- *Awards:* Marian Anderson Award; Blanche Thebom Opera Guild Award; Queens Col Orch Soc Award. *Mailing Add:* c/o Columbia Artists Mgt 165 W 57th St New York NY 10019

GROCOCK, ROBERT
TRUMPET, EDUCATOR
b New Haven, Conn, Nov 1, 25. *Study:* Eastman Sch Music, with Pattee Evenson, perf cert(trumpet), 48, BM, 48, MM, 50; studied with Harry Glantz, 48-50; Ind Univ, 73-76. *Pos:* Freelance trumpet, East & Midwest, 43-; trumpet, Rochester Phil, 43-48 & Chicago Symph, 51-52; prin trumpet, Interlochen Fac-Staff Orch, 52-60 & 63-70; founder & prin trumpet, DePauw Univ Fac Quintet, 52- *Teaching:* Instr trumpet, Eastman Sch Music & Syracuse Univ, 48-50; teacher trumpet, Nat Music Camp, Interlochen, Mich, 52-60 & 63-70; prof trumpet & theory, DePauw Univ, 52-, dir, Perf Arts Ser, 79- *Awards:* Ford Found Grant, 72; Lily Found Grant, 80. *Mem:* Nat Asn Col Wind & Perc Instrm (nat pres, 62-64); charter mem, Int Trumpet Guild. *Interests:* Musical acoustics; arts administration. *Publ:* Contribr, Instrumentalist, 55-65; ed, Slide and Valve (quart column), Nat Asn Col Wind & Perc Instrm Bulletin, 58-62; Advanced Method for Trumpet, 68. *Mailing Add:* 720 Terrace Lane Greencastle IN 46135

GRODNER, MURRAY
EDUCATOR, DOUBLE BASS
b New York, NY, Aug, 23, 22. *Study:* Double bass with Morris Tivin, 38-41 & Frederick Zimmermann, 41-42; Manhattan Sch Music, BM, 51, MM, 54. *Rec Perf:* Quintet (Dvorak), Vox Rec, 61; Baroque Chamber Players, Coronet Rec, 64; Quartet (Barati), CRI Rec, 65; Trio Sonata in G (Handel), Ind Univ, 73. *Pos:* Asst prin bassist, Pittsburgh Symph, 42-43 & 46-48; prin bassist, Houston Symph, 48-51; bassist, NBC Symph, 51-54, Baroque Chamber Players, 60-79 & Musica Sonora, 75-; guest bassist, Nat Radio Symph, Denmark, 63-64. *Teaching:* Prof double bass, Ind Univ, 55-79 & 82-; lectr, Calif State Univ, Sacramento, 79-82. *Bibliog:* Samuel Applebaum (auth), The Way They Play, Paganini Publ, 78. *Mem:* Am String Teachers Asn (state pres, 63); Int Soc Bassists, 83. *Interests:* Currently published music for double bass in form of solo literature and chamber music. *Publ:* Auth, Comprehensive Catalog of Available Literature for the Double Bass, Lemur Musical, 58, 64 & 74; Organized Method of String Playing, Bass Vol, Southern Music, 68; ed, Concepts of String Playing, Ind Univ Press, 79. *Mailing Add:* Sch Music Ind Univ Bloomington IN 47405

GRONQUIST, ROBERT E
CONDUCTOR, HARPSICHORD
b Aurora, Ill, Oct 15, 38. *Study:* Sch Music, Univ Ill, BA, 60; Univ Aix en Province, France; Univ Calif, Berkeley. *Works:* This Endris Night, E C Kerby, Toronto; Mass; Relavation; The Lord Zouche's Masque. *Pos:* Cond, various New England ens; dir musical activ, Simmons Col, Boston. *Teaching:* Instr harpsichord, music hist & cond, Smith Col, 64-67; asst prof, Trinity Col, Conn, 67-72; assoc prof, Simmons Col, 72- *Awards:* Rockefeller Grant, Aspen Music Fest. *Mem:* ASCAP; Am Musicol Soc; Col Music Soc. *Interests:* Editing Renaissance and baroque music, French early 20th century. *Publ:* Auth, Ravel's Trois Poemes de Stephane Mallarme, Musical Quart, 78. *Mailing Add:* Dept Music Simmons Col 300 The Fenway Boston MA 02115

GROOM, LESTER HERBERT
ORGAN, EDUCATOR
b Chicago, Ill, Jan 19, 29. *Study:* Wheaton Col, Ill, BMus, 51; Northwestern Univ, organ with Barrett Spach, MusM, 52; Am Consv Music, comp with Stella Roberts, 53-54. *Works:* 24 Psalm Voluntaries (organ), Hope Publ Co, 64; Grant to Us, Lord (SATB & organ), FitsSimons Publ Co, 75; An Easter Alleluia (SATB), Belwin-Mills, 79; Blessed be the Lord (SATB, string orch & oboe), comn by Seattle Pac Univ; O Lord, Our Lord, Psalm VIII (SATB, organ, three trumpets & timpani), comn & perf by Univ Presby Church, Seattle, 83; A Joyful Procession (organ), Basil Ramsey, England (in prep). *Pos:* Organist, First Presby Church, Seattle, Wash, 79- *Teaching:* Asst prof organ & church music, Blue Mountain Col, 57-62 & Baker Univ, 62-67; assoc prof organ, theory & comp, Seattle Pac Univ, 68- *Mem:* Am Guild Organists (Miss state chmn, 59-62); Music Teachers Nat Asn. *Publ:* Auth, Professional Attitudes for Organ Students, 62 & Parables for Practice, 64, Diapason; The Futility of Teaching Organ Literature, Am Music Teacher, 65; six articles, Organ Techniques, Music Ministry, 66-67; Improve Your Improv—Not How, But Why, Am Music Teacher, 81. *Mailing Add:* 10629 NE 26th St Bellevue WA 98004

GROSS, ALLEN ROBERT
CONDUCTOR, EDUCATOR
b New York, NY, Apr 2, 44. *Study:* Queens Col, BA, 65; Univ Calif, Berkeley, MA, 67; Stanford Univ, with Sandor Salgo, DMA, 78; Vienna Music Acad, with Hans Swarowsky, Monteux & Susskind. *Pos:* Staff cond, Munic Opera Houses, Friedburg & Aachen, WGer, 73-78; music dir, Heidelberg Castle Fest, WGer, 75-78; cond, Junges Kammerorchester Heidelberg, 76-78; guest cond, Chamber Orch Louisville Orch, Ky Opera Asn, Schwäbisches Sinfonie-Orch & others. *Teaching:* Asst prof, dir opera & orch cond, Univ Louisville, 78-; asst prof instrm activ, Occidental Col, currently. *Mem:* Nat Opera Asn; Am Symph Orch League; Col Music Soc. *Mailing Add:* Occidental Col 1600 Campus Rd Los Angeles CA 90041

GROSS, CHARLES HENRY
COMPOSER
b Cambridge, Mass, May 13, 34. *Study:* Harvard Col, AB, 55; Mills Col, with Darius Milhaud & Leon Kirchner, 57; New England Consv, with Judd Cooke. *Works:* The Great White Hope, Broadway show, 68; Robert Frost, doc, 69; Teacher, Teacher, film score, 70; Bicentennial Minutes, 75-76; The Dain Curse, CBS, 77; Heartland, film score, 80; Nurse, CBS. *Awards:* Emmy, Nat Acad TV Arts & Sci, 78-79; Wrangler Award, Western Heritage Ctr & Cowboy Hall of Fame, 81. *Mem:* ASCAP; Acad Motion Picture Arts & Sci; Nat Acad Rec Arts & Sci; Nat Acad TV Arts & Sci; Comp & Lyricists Guild Am. *Rep:* Gorfaine & Schwarz Agy 3815 W Olive St Burband CA 91505. *Mailing Add:* 186 Riverside Dr New York NY 10020

GROSS, DOROTHY (SUSAN)
ADMINISTRATOR, WRITER
b New York, NY, Nov 17, 46. *Study:* Brown Univ, AB, 67; Manhattan Sch Music, MM, 69; Ind Univ, PhD, 75. *Pos:* Secy, Comput Music Asn, 80- *Teaching:* Instr music, State Univ NY, Purchase, 72-74; lectr, Lehman Col, 74-76; Asst prof music theory, Univ Minn, 76- *Bibliog:* Rosalie Sward (auth), The Computer Assists in Attempting to Solve a Problem of Twentieth Century Music, Proc 1978 Int Comput Music Conf, 79. *Mem:* Minn Music Theory Consortium (pres, 82-83); Col Music Soc; Music Educr Nat Conf; Soc Music Theory; Nat Consortium Comput-Based Music Instr. *Interests:* Computer application to music theory, analysis and instruction. *Publ:* Coauth, Integration of CAI into a Music Program, J Comput-Based Instr, 80; Ideas on Implementation and Evaluation of a Music CAI Project, Col Music Symposium, 81; auth, A Computer-assisted Music Course, Comput in Humanities, 81; coauth, Implementation and Evaluation of a Computer-assisted Course in Musical Aural Skills, AEDS J, 82. *Mailing Add:* 911 22nd Ave S #181 Minneapolis MN 55404

GROSS, STEVEN LEE
FRENCH HORN
b Ann Arbor, Mich, Oct 19, 54. *Study:* With Louis Stout, 68-76; Albion Col, Mich, 72; Inst Advan Musical Studies, Switz, 73; Aspen Music Sch & Fest, 74 & 77; studied with Michael Hatfield, 74-78; Berkshire Music Ctr, 75 & 76; studied with Philip Farkas, 76-78; Sch Music, Univ Mich, BMus, 76; studied with Dale Clevenger, 77-; Sch Music, Ind Univ, MMus & perf cert, 78. *Pos:* Asst prin horn, Nat Symph Orch, 78-80 & Atlanta Symph Orch, 80-; assoc prin horn, Chautauqua Symph Orch, summer 81. *Teaching:* Instr horn, Univ Richmond, 78-79; private horn instr, 78- *Awards:* C D Jackson Prize, Berkshire Music Ctr, 75; First Prize, First Int Heldenleben Horn Compt, 76. *Mem:* Int Horn Soc. *Mailing Add:* 5061 Martin's Crossing Stone Mountain GA 30088

GROSSMAN, ARTHUR
BASSOON
b New York, NY, Sept 25, 34. *Study:* Curtis Inst Music, artists dipl, 55. *Rec Perf:* Arthur Grossman Plays Bassoon, Coronet; Galliard Sonatas, Selma y Salaverde Fantasies & Music for Bassoon and Strings, Musical Heritage Soc; The Virtuoso Bassoon, Ravenna; Bravura Bassoon, Pandora; Arthur Grossman Plays Solo Music for Bassoon and Contrabassoon, Crystal. *Pos:* Prin bassoon, Indianapolis Symph, 56-60, Cincinnati Symph, 60-61 & Israel Phil, 77-78; bassoon, Casals Fest, 61-69 & Soni Ventorum Wind Quintet, 61- *Teaching:* Prof bassoon, Univ Wash, 68- *Mailing Add:* Sch Music Univ Wash Seattle WA 98195

GROSSMAN, DEENA
COMPOSER

b Fairfield, Calif, Jan 31, 55. *Study:* Col Creative Studies, Univ Calif, Santa Barbara, BA(music comp), 77; Shepherd Sch Music, Rice Univ, comp with Paul Cooper, currently; studied comp with Thea Musgrave, Peter Fricker & Lou Harrison. *Works:* The World is Round (women's chorus & narrator), perf by Womens Chorus, Univ Calif, Santa Barbara, 77; So Clear a Puzzle (clarinet, cello & Am gamelan), comn by Wendy Rogers Dance Co, 78; Sea Cliff Hands Quartet (oboe, violin, banjo & double bass), comn by Sheila Kaminsky Dance Co, 79; The Story (flute & oboe), comn by Magic Theater Co, 81; Three Colors for Oboe, perf by Brenda Schuman-Post, 81; Music of Spaces (violin, clarinet, doubling bass clarinet & piano), comn & perf by Menage, 83; Leopard Flowers (sop & piano), comn & perf by Jodi Martin, 83. *Pos:* Co-chair, Conf Contemp String Quartets Women Comp, 80-81; music staff, KPFA Radio, 80-82. *Teaching:* Private flute, 73- *Awards:* Grad Fel, Shepherd Sch Music, Rice Univ, 82- *Mem:* Int League Women Comp. *Mailing Add:* 269 28th St San Francisco CA 94131

GROSSMAN, JERRY MICHAEL
CELLO, EDUCATOR

Cambridge, Mass, Dec 15, 50. *Study:* Curtis Inst Music, 69-71. *Rec Perf:* Weill & Dohnanyi Cello Sonatas, 81 & Prokofief, Janacek, Bartok Works for Cello, 82, Nonesuch Rec; Six Suites (solo cello; Bach), AAG Music Inc, 83. *Teaching:* Instr cello, Curtis Inst Music, Philadelphia, 79-, State Univ NY, Purchase, 81- & Quartet Prog, Troy, NY, 82- *Rep:* TRM Mgt 527 Madison Ave New York NY 10022. *Mailing Add:* 315 W 105th St New York NY 10025

GROSSMAN, NORMAN L
EDUCATOR, COMPOSER

b New York, NY. *Study:* Comp with Peter Mennin, 50-53; Berkshire Music Ctr, with Aaron Copland, 51 & 53; Juilliard Sch Music, BS, 52, MS, 53; studied comp with Vincent Persichetti, 54-55, fel, Princeton Univ Sem in Advan Musicol Studies, 59. *Teaching:* Fel, Juilliard Sch Music, 54-55; mem fac, Peabody Consv Music, 60-61; vis assoc prof, Univ Nebr, 62-63; mem fac lit & materials music, Juilliard Sch, 63- *Awards:* Fulbright Fel to Italy, 53-54. *Mailing Add:* Juilliard Sch Lincoln Ctr Plaza New York NY 10023

GROUT, DONALD JAY
EDUCATOR, HISTORIAN

b Grand Rapids, Iowa, Sept, 28, 02. *Study:* Syracuse Univ, AB, 23; Harvard Univ, AM(music), 32, PhD(music), 39; Eastman Sch Music, Hon DMus, 81; Dickinson Col, Hon DMus, 83. *Teaching:* Instr music, Harvard Univ & Radcliffe Col, 40-42; assoc prof music lit, Univ Tex, Austin, 42-45; prof music, Cornell Univ, 45-62, Given Found prof musicol, 62-70, emer prof, 70- *Awards:* One Guggenheim & three Fulbright Fels, 51-52, 59-60 & 65-66. *Mem:* Am Musicol Soc (pres, 52-54 & 60-62); Int Musicol Soc (pres, 62-64 & vpres, 65-67); British Acad; Royal Acad Belgium. *Interests:* History of music. *Publ:* Auth, A Short History of Opera, Columbia Univ Press, 47; A History of Western Music, W W Norton, 60; Alessandro Scarlatti, An Introduction to His Opera, Univ Calif Press, Berkeley, 79. *Mailing Add:* Cloudbank Bacher Rd Skaneateles NY 13152

GRUBB, THOMAS
TEACHER-COACH, PIANO

b Bridgehampton, NY, Jan 7, 40. *Study:* Eastman Sch Music, Univ Rochester, BA, 60; Yale Univ, MA, 62; Ecole de Piano, Paris, with Magda Tagliaferro, dipl, 64; Manhattan Sch Music, with Dora Zaslavsky & Artur Balsam, MM, 66. *Pos:* Judge, Metropolitan Opera Guild Auditions, 81-82 & Concours Int Chant Paris, 82; lit consult for music, Schirmer Books, 81-83; coach & pianist for Pierre Bernarc's master classes in French song in US & Can. *Teaching:* Artist-teacher vocal lit, French diction & vocal coaching, Manhattan Sch Music, 64-, Curtis Inst Music, 70-77, NY Univ, 78-82 & Acad Vocal Arts, Philadelphia, 78- *Mem:* Nat Asn Teachers Singing. *Interests:* Coach and pianist for Pierre Bernac's master classes in French song in United States and Canada. *Publ:* Auth, Singing in French, A Manual of French Diction and French Vocal Repertoire, Schirmer Bks, 79. *Rep:* Schirmer Bks 866 Third Ave New York NY 10022. *Mailing Add:* 160 W 73rd St New York NY 10023

GRUBB, WILLIAM
CELLO

b Greencastle, Ind, Mar 30, 51. *Study:* Juilliard Sch, studied cello with Harvey Shapiro, BM, 74, MM, 76, DMA, 82. *Rec Perf:* Hummel Quintet, Monitor Rec, 80. *Pos:* Perf, Aspen Soloists, New York, 76- *Teaching:* Instr cello, Aspen Music Fest, 76. *Awards:* Victor Herbert Award, 76 & Alumni Award, 80, Juilliard Sch. *Mem:* Violoncello Soc New York. *Publ:* Auth, A Survey of Cello Technique, PennDragon, 83. *Mailing Add:* 60 Riverside Dr #8A New York NY 10024

GRUBER, ALBION MATTHEW
EDUCATOR, COMPOSER

b Savannah, Ga, Oct 27, 32. *Study:* Univ Ala, BMus, 54, MMus, 55; Eastman Sch Music, PhD(music). 69. *Works:* Trichotomy for Strings, perf by Chatanooga Symph, 58; Charade for Orchestra, perf by Savannah Symph, 64; Woodforms, perf by Aeolian Chamber Players New York, 71. *Teaching:* Instr, Savannah Country Day Sch, Ga, 57-64; prof music theory, Nazareth Col, Rochester, NY, 64- *Mem:* Col Music Soc; NY State Theory Teachers Asn; Soc Music Theory. *Publ:* Auth, Mersenne & Evolving Tonal Theory, J Music Theory, 70; transl & ed, Treatise on Music, Inst Mediaeval Music, 72; auth, Understanding Rhythm in Brahms, Clavier, 74; transl & ed, Dictionary of Music, Inst Mediaeval Music, 82. *Mailing Add:* 973 Harvard St Rochester NY 14610

GRUBEROVA, EDITA
SOPRANO

b Bratislava, CSSR, Dec 23, 46; Austrian citizen. *Study:* Konsv Bratislava, dipl, 68; studied with Ruthilde Boesch, Vienna. *Roles:* Queen of the Night in Queen of the Night, 70, Zerbinetta in Ariadne auf Naxos, 76, Lucia in Lucia di Lammermoor, 78, Violetta in La Traviata, 81 & Gilda in Rigoletto, 83, Vienna Staatsoper; Konstanze, La Scala, Milano, 75; Zerbinetta in Ariadne auf Naxos, Metropolitan Opera, 79. *Pos:* Mem, Banska Bystrica, CSSR, 68-70 & Vienna Staatsoper, 70- *Mailing Add:* c/o Columbia Artists Mgt 165 W 57th St New York NY 10019

GUADAGNO, ANTON
CONDUCTOR, COMPOSER

b Castellammare de Golfo, Italy, May 2, 25; US citizen. *Study:* Consv Palermo; Consv Santa Cecilia, Rome, deg(comp & cond); Consv Vincenzo Bellini, grad; Akad Mozarteum, Salzburg, with Carlo Zecchi; studied with Franco Ferrare, H von Karajan & A Paumgartner. *Works:* Hymn for Holy Infancy, Vatican, 50. *Rec Perf:* For Angel Rec, RCA Victor, London Decca Rec & EMI. *Pos:* Musical adminr, Philadelphia Lyr Opera, 66-72; res cond, Staatsoper, Vienna; guest cond throughout US, Europe, Can & England. *Awards:* Gold Medal, Chile, 70; Grand Prix du Disc, Paris, 73. *Mailing Add:* c/o Eric Semon Assoc 111 W 57th St Suite 1209 New York NY 10019

GUARINO, ROBERT
TENOR

b RI. *Study:* Univ RI; Manhattan Sch Music. *Roles:* Il Corsaro, Long Island Opera Soc, 81; Cassio in Otello, 83 & Don Ottavio in Don Giovanni, 83, Des Moines Metro Opera. *Pos:* Tenor, Mich Opera Theatre, formerly, New York Opera Theatre, formerly, Northern Va Opera Theatre, formerly, Lake George Opera, formerly & Providence Opera, formerly; recitalist, Smithsonian Inst, formerly, Phillips Collection, formerly, Liederkranz Found, formerly & Benson & Hedges Music Fest, Snape, England, formerly; soloist, Boston Symph, formerly, Harrisburg Symph, formerly, Masterwork Chorus & Orch, formerly, New York Choral Soc, formerly, Long Island Choral Soc, formerly & Waterloo Music Fest, formerly. *Awards:* First Prize, Liederkranz Found Compt & Wash Int Compt Singers; C D Jackson Award, Tanglewood Music Fest. *Mailing Add:* c/o Sullivan & Lindsey Assoc 133 W 87th St New York NY 10024

GUARNERI, MARIO
TRUMPET

b Berkeley, Calif, Dec 5, 42. *Study:* Univ Southern Calif, BM, 64; Juilliard Sch Music, MM, 66. *Rec Perf:* Trumpet & Bassoon Concerto Album, Crystal Rec, 78; After the Butterfly, Nonesuch Rec, 80. *Pos:* Trumpet section, Los Angeles Phil, 67-81; prin trumpet, Los Angeles Chamber Orch, 81- *Teaching:* Instr trumpet & head brass dept, Calif Inst Arts, 70- *Mailing Add:* Brass Dept Calif Inst Arts Valencia CA 91355

GUARRERA, FRANK (FRANCESCO GUARRERA)
BARITONE, EDUCATOR

Philadelphia, Pa, Dec 3, 23. *Study:* Curtis Inst Music, cert, 48. *Roles:* Rigoletto in Rigoletto, Escamillo in Carmen, Figaro in Barber of Seville, Gianni Schicchi in Gianni Schicchi, Simon Boccanegra in Simon Boccanegra, Horace Tabor, Sir John Falstaff & 30 more leading bar roles, all major co throughout US & Can. *Pos:* Res mem, New York Metropolitan Opera, 48-78; leading bar, La Scala, Milan, Italy, 48-, all major co in US & Can, 48-78 & San Francisco Opera, 53-69. *Teaching:* Prof voice, Univ Wash, 79- *Awards:* Anniversary Award, Philadelphia Grand Opera, 68; Citation, Consul General of Italy, 68; Silver Cup Award for 25 Years, New York Metropolitan Opera, 73. *Mem:* Life mem, Am Guild Musical Arts (vpres, 60-74). *Mailing Add:* 4514 Latona Ave NE Seattle WA 98105

GUCK, MARION A
EDUCATOR

b Rochester, NY, May 17, 49. *Study:* State Univ NY Col, Geneseo, BA, 71; Univ Mich, MMus, 76, PhD, 81. *Pos:* Ed, In Theory Only, 75-78; assoc ed, Perspectives New Music, 81- *Teaching:* Lectr, Univ Mich, 78-79; vis asst prof, Univ Cincinnati, 81-82; asst prof, Univ Hawaii, 82-83 & Temple Univ, 83- *Mem:* Soc Music Theory; Col Music Soc. *Interests:* Analysis of chromatic-tonal and of 20th century music; study of the metaphoric foundations of musical thought. *Publ:* Auth, Analysis Symposium: Brahms, Der Tod das Ist die Kühle Nach, Op 96/1, 76, Symmetrical Structures in Schoenberg's Op 19/2, 77, The Functional Relations of Chords, 78 & Musical Images as Musical Thoughts, 81, In Theory Only. *Mailing Add:* Col Music Temple Univ Philadelphia PA 19122

GUDAUSKAS, GIEDRA NASVYTIS
COMPOSER

b Kaunas, Lithuania, July 10, 23; US citizen. *Study:* State Consv Kaunas, Lithuania, 33-40; Roosevelt Univ, Chicago, BMus, 52; Univ Calif, Los Angeles, 62-64. *Works:* Four Songs for Soprano, 69 & God's World, 73, Salesian Brothers; Los Angeles Sketches, Brentwood-Westwood Symph, 75; Variations on Lithuanian Folk Theme, 78 & Impressions on Three Lithuanian Proverbs, 80, Highland Music Co, Norwalk, Calif; Medley of Lithuanian Folk Songs, Univ Calif, Los Angeles, Women's Chorus, 80 & Loyola Women's Choral Fest, 80. *Pos:* Accmp modern dance, Dana Nasvytis Studio, Lithuania, 40-43, Jewish Ctr Chicago, 44-46 & Cities Jewish Ctr, Santa Monica, 61-63; dir music, Los Angeles Lithuanian Community Bilingual Sch, 64-69. *Awards:* Commendation, Los Angeles US Bicentennial Comt, 75. *Bibliog:* Draugas, Lithuanian Worldwide Daily Newspaper, Chicago, 73 & 82. *Mem:* ASCAP. *Rep:* Highland Music Co 14751 Carmenita Rd Norwalk Calif 90650. *Mailing Add:* 1030 Gretna Green Way Los Angeles CA 90049

GUENTHER, EILEEN MORRIS
ORGAN, EDUCATOR

b Leavenworth, Kans, Jan 20, 48. *Study:* Univ Kans, studied with Richard Gayhart & James Moeser, BA, BM(organ), 70; Cath Univ Am, studied with Robert Twyneham & Conrad Bernier, MA(musicol), 73, DMA(organ), 73. *Rec Perf:* Litanies, 78 & The Filene Organ at John F Kennedy Center, 79, Vista Rec, London, England. *Pos:* Minister music, Foundry United Methodist Church, Washington, DC, 76-; producer, The Royal Instrument, WGMS AM/FM, Washington, DC; reviewer, Am Organist, Am Guild Organists, 77-. *Teaching:* Instr piano & organ, Holton Arms Sch, Bethesda, Md, 74-79; studio instr organ, George Washington Univ, 77-. *Awards:* First Place, Nat Organ Compt, Ft Lauderdale, Fla, 73. *Mem:* Am Guild Organists (dean DC chap, 76-78, nat counr, 82-); Friday Morning Music Club; Am Fedn Musicians; Sigma Alpha Iota. *Publ:* Auth, French Keyboard Noel Variations of the 17th and 18th Centuries, Diapason, 12/73-2/74; contribr, New Grove Dict of Music & Musicians, 80 & Music Mag. *Mailing Add:* 412 Fellini Ct SE Vienna VA 22180

GUENTHER, RALPH R
COMPOSER, FLUTE

b Concordia, Mo, Nov 24, 14. *Study:* Cent Methodist Col, AB; Univ Rochester, MA; Eastman Sch Music, with Bernard Rogers, Edward Royce, Anthony Donato & Burrill Phillips, PhD. *Works:* Celebration (oratorio), comn by Tex Christian Univ, 73; Bells of Ireland (song cycle), Ft Worth, 76; Suite for Solo Flute, 78; How Fast the Moon (song cycle to texts by James Newcomer), 78; Variations (oboe & strings); Set of Four (a cappella chorus); Improvisations (flute & piano). *Rec Perf:* Celebration (for soloist, chorus, & orch), TCU Press. *Pos:* Prin flutist, Ft Worth Opera Orch, 49-83 & Ft Worth Symph, 56-80; cond, Tex Christian Univ Symph, 50-66; prin flutist, Ft Worth Symph, 56-80, assoc cond 63-76, cond, 69-70. *Teaching:* Prof, Tex Christian Univ, 48-80. *Mailing Add:* 4604 Barwick Ft Worth TX 76132

GUENTHER, ROY JAMES
EDUCATOR, TROMBONE

b Marion, Kans, June 8, 44. *Study:* Univ Kans, BMusEd, 66, BM, 68; Cath Univ Am, MA, 74, PhD, 79; trombone study with Arnold Jacobs, Frank Crisafuli, John Marcellus & John Hill. *Pos:* Bandsman, US Marine Band, Washington, DC, 68-72. *Teaching:* Instr low brass, Univ Kans, 66-68; asst prof music, George Washington Univ, 78-83, assoc prof, 83- *Mem:* Am Musicol Soc (coun mem, 81); Soc Music Theory; Int Trombone Asn; Nat Acad Rec Arts & Sci; Am Fedn Musicians. *Interests:* Nineteenth and early 20th century music of Russia; Russian music theory. *Publ:* Auth, numerous reviews of classical concerts, Washington Post, 82-; translr, Musorgsky's Days & Works: A Biography, 83 & contribr, Russian Theoretical Thought in Music, 83, UMI Res Press. *Mailing Add:* 412 Fellini Ct SE Vienna VA 22180

GUERRANT, MARY THORINGTON
TEACHER, COMPOSER

b Taft, Tex, May 7, 25. *Study:* Austin Col, BA, 46; Univ NC, Chapel Hill, with Jan Philipp Schinhan, 46-48; studied piano with Bomar Cramer, 52-61 & 63-68; studied with Rosalyn Tureck, London, 62; Tex Tech Univ, studied comp with Mary Jeanne van Appledorn & piano with Louis Catuogno, MM(piano), 71, PhD(fine arts), 76. *Works:* Pecos Ruins (woodwind ens), 23rd Annual Symposium Comtemp Music, Tex Tech Univ, 74; Passacaglia (solo piano), perf by Mary Guerrant, 76; The Shepherds, Tex Tech Univ, Music Theatre & Tex Tech Symph, 76. *Rec Perf:* The Shepherds, 76; Solo Piano Recital, Dorian Systems, 80. *Teaching:* Piano, privately, Sherman, Tex, 52-68 & Lubbock, Tex, 80-; instr piano, Austin Col, 57-58; assoc prof piano & comp, Tunghai Univ, Taiwan, 76-77. *Mem:* Music Teachers Nat Asn; Tex Music Teacher's Asn; Lubbock Music Teacher's Asn; Am Music Scholar Asn; Am Col Musicians. *Publ:* Auth, Who Says Your Hands are Too Small?, Clavier, 5-6/79; How Secure is Your Memory?, Piano Quart, summer 79; What Constitutes a Compelling Piano Performance?, 4-5/80 & Art and Reality: The Culmination of a Concept in Beethoven's Last Works, 4-5/81, Am Music Symposium; Three Aspects of Music in Ancient China & Greece, J Col Music Soc, fall 80. *Mailing Add:* 3301 24th St Lubbock TX 79410

GUGGENHEIM, JANET GOODMAN
ACCOMPANIST, PIANO

b Spokane, Wash, Aug 24, 38. *Study:* Univ Calif, Berkeley, BA, 61; Juilliard Sch, with Rosina Lhevinne, MS, 63; private study with Ilona Kabos & Myra Hess, London. *Pos:* Studio accmp, Juilliard Sch, 61-63; accmp, Casals Master Classes, Univ Calif, Nat Educ TV, 60 & 61 & int artists incl Itzhak Perlman, Pierre Fournier, Young Uck Kim & Oto Ughi; pianist, Chamber Soloists San Francisco, 79-83; perf with Michael Grebanier in Duo-Recital series, 80- & Chamber Music West, San Francisco Consv Music, 83. *Teaching:* Instr chamber music & piano, Dominican Col, 77-78. *Awards:* Fels, Hertz, Univ Calif, Berkeley, 60 & 61 & Martha Baird Rockefeller Found, 64. *Bibliog:* Marian C McKenna (auth), Myra Hess, Hamish Hamilton, London; Robert K Wallace (auth), A Century of Music Making, Ind Univ Press, 76; Paul Hertelendy (auth), Accompanists, San Jose Mercury News, 80. *Mem:* San Francisco Womens Musician Club. *Mailing Add:* 2325 Harvard El Cerrito CA 94530

GUIGUI, EFRAIN
CONDUCTOR & MUSIC DIRECTOR

b Buenos Aires, Arg, Sept 19, 35; US citizen. *Study:* Music Consv, Buenos Aires, 54; Boston Univ, BA, 59. *Rec Perf:* For CRI. *Pos:* Assoc cond, Am Ballet Theatre, 66-68; cond, Music in Our Time, Town Hall, New York, 66-68; cond & music dir, Comp Conf, Wellesley, Mass, 66-; prin guest cond, PR Symph, San Juan, 68-74; music dir, Vt Symph Orch, 74- & Dartmouth Col Symph Orch, 75- *Mem:* Vt Coun Arts; Am Symph League. *Mailing Add:* 161 Austin Dr RR Cond #21 Burlington VT 05401

GUINALDO, NORBERTO
COMPOSER, ORGAN

b Buenos Aires, Argentina, March 2, 37; US citizen. *Study:* Univ Calif, Riverside, MM(theory & comp), 78; Schola Cantorum, Paris, studied organ & improvisation with Jean Langlais, dipl superieure d'Orgue; studied improvisation with Jean Guillou, 73. *Works:* Toccata an Fugue (organ), 64 & Three Litanies (organ), 68, J Fischer & Brother; Five Spanish Carols (organ), Concordia Publ House, 68; Spanish Organ Carols, Ausburg Publ House, 76; Path to Peace (oratorio), comn by Am Guild Organists Pasadena chap & Salem Lutheran Church, 78; Credo (organ), perf by comp, 83. *Rec Perf:* The Organ on Mormon Temple Hill, Advent Rec, 73. *Pos:* Organist, United Methodist Church, Garden Grove, Calif, 65- *Teaching:* Lectr organ, Chapman Col, 69-72. *Mailing Add:* 12051 Orange St Norwalk CA 90650

GUINN, JOHN
CRITIC-WRITER

b Charleston, WVa, Mar 25, 36. *Study:* Univ Notre Dame, BMus, 57, MMus, 59. *Pos:* Music critic, Detroit Free Press, Mich, 75- *Teaching:* Asst prof music, Univ Detroit, 61-75. *Awards:* Distinguished Coverage of Fine Arts, Detroit Press Club Found, 81-83. *Mem:* Music Critics Asn; Mich Coun Arts. *Publ:* Auth of reviews & interviews, Musical Am, 75-; opera reviews, Opera Can, 82- *Mailing Add:* c/o Detroit Free Press 321 W Lafayette Blvd Detroit MI 48231

GUINN, LESLIE
BARITONE, EDUCATOR

b Conroe, Tex, Apr 29, 35. *Study:* Northwestern Univ, BMus. *Rec Perf:* Songs of Stephen Foster & Schumann Duets and Lieder, Nonesuch Rec. *Roles:* Carmina Burana, New York, 66; Wozzeck, Stuttgart, 83. *Pos:* Singer, Philadelphia Orch, Boston Symph, Chicago Symph, Nat Symph, Los Angeles Phil & many other orchs; appearances at Tanglewood, Marlboro, Saratoga, Caramoor, Chautauqua & Aspen Festivals; performer solo recitals, opera & chamber music. *Teaching:* Prof voice, Univ Mich, Ann Arbor, currently; fac mem, Aspen Music fest, currently. *Awards:* Three Martha Baird Rockefeller Grants; Am Opera Auditions Winner; Winner, Rockefeller Found—Kennedy Ctr Int Compt, 79. *Mem:* Nat Asn Teachers Singing. *Mailing Add:* c/o Melvin Kaplan Inc 1860 Broadway New York NY 10023

GULBRANDSEN, NORMAN R
TEACHER-COACH, MUSIC DIRECTOR

b Salt Lake, Utah, Oct 3, 18. *Study:* Univ Utah, BS, 42; Northwestern Univ, MM, 45; Univ Southern Calif, 48-49. *Pos:* Founder & cond, Missoula Mendelssohn Club, Mont, 46-51; dir music, Glenview Community Church, Ill, 67-74. *Teaching:* Dir choral activ, Mont State Univ, 45-51; choral dir, Brigham Young Univ, 52-61; prof voice, Northwestern Univ, 63- *Mem:* Nat Asn Teachers Singing. *Mailing Add:* Sch Music Northwestern Univ Evanston IL 60201

GULLI, FRANCO
VIOLIN, EDUCATOR

b Trieste, Italy, Sept 1, 26. *Rec Perf:* Complete Sonatas (Beethoven); Concerto No 5 (Paganini); Sonata in F (Mendelssohn); Double Concerto (Mendelssohn); F Major Concerto (Mendelssohn); rec on Musical Heritage, RCA, Decca, Angelicum & Audio Fidelity Rec. *Pos:* Appearances with maj orchs in US & Can & prin festivals in Europe; recitalist chamber music, Trio Italiano D'Archi. *Teaching:* Master classes, Accad Chiagina, Siena, 64-72; teacher, Consv Music, Lucerne, Switz, formerly; prof violin, Ind Univ, Bloomington, 72- *Rep:* Columbia Artists Mgt 165 W 57th St New York NY 10019. *Mailing Add:* 1000 S Ballantine Rd Bloomington IN 47401

GUMNER, MARION F See Burkat, Marion F

GUNDERSHEIMER, MURIEL (BLUMBERG)
HARP

b Chicago, Ill, Dec 5, 24. *Study:* Eastman Sch Music, 42-43; Northwestern Univ, BMus, 46. *Pos:* Harpist, Wankegan Ill Symph, 40-46, Chicago Civic Orch, 44-46, Tucson Symph, 46-47 & Columbus Symph Orch, 53- *Mem:* Womens Music Club. *Mailing Add:* 2671 Bryden Rd Columbus OH 43209

GUNTER-MCCOY, JANE HUTTON
WAGNERIAN SOPRANO, EDUCATOR

b Kingston, NY, Feb 9, 38. *Study:* Eastman Sch Music, BMus; Sch Music, Ind Univ, MMus; studied voice with Leonard Stine, Dorthee Manski, Robert K Evans, Frank St Leger, Wolfgang Vacano, Edwig McArthur, Fred Popper, Constance Peters & Antonia Lavanne & violin with Millard Taylor & Urico Rossi. *Rec Perf:* With Robert Shaw Chorale & Amor Artis Chorale & Orch; on Decca Rec. *Pos:* Soloist, tours of Can, Europe, North Am & South Am, Robert Shaw Chorale, Schola Cantorum, Amor Artis Chorale & Orch, New York, Musica Aeterna & Musica Sacra, NY; soloist, Am Ballet Theatre & Wagner & Beethoven Soc, Metropolitan Opera; opera tours, Boris Goldovsky Opera Co, Chamber Music Soc, Lincoln Ctr & Cantica Hebraica, NY; soprano soloist, Park Ave Christian Church, New York & Church of Our Savior, New York; guest soloist, Riverside Church, New York; opera, oratorio & recital performances. *Teaching:* Mem fac voice, Mannes Col Music, 66- *Mem:* Sigma Alpha Iota. *Mailing Add:* 334 W 86th St Apt 2B New York NY 10024

GUNTHER, WILLIAM (WILLIAM GUNTHER SPRECHER)
COMPOSER, MUSIC DIRECTOR

b Saarbruecken, Germany, Jan 20, 24; US citizen. *Study:* Studied in Germany, Israel & New York, with Georg Singer, Paul Ben-Haim & Madame

Vengerova. *Works:* Piano Sonata, Radio Jerusalem, Israel, 45; Si J'Fais Ca ..., Ed Int, 52; The Yinglish Song Book, Belwin-Mills, 64; Three Ghetto Songs, Bloch Publ Co, 64-67; Jerusalem Concerto, Wilsom Publ, 69; Great Is Thy Faith, WABC-TV, New York, 70; Five Musical Bridges in Ragtime, WMCA-AM Radio, New York, 81-82. *Pos:* Music dir, WEVD-FM Radio, New York, 69-; music dir & pres, Bronx Phil Symph Soc Inc, 71- *Awards:* Robert Stolz Medallion, 73 & Robert Stolz Dipl Honour, 81, Int Robert Stolz Soc; Sholem Aleichem Award, Queens Col, City Univ New York, 83. *Bibliog:* Victoria Secunda (auth), Bei Mir Bist Du Schön, Walker & Co, 82. *Mem:* Am Fedn Musicians; ASCAP. *Mailing Add:* 2235 Cruger Ave Bronx NY 10467

GUNZENHAUSER, STEPHEN CHARLES
MUSIC DIRECTOR & CONDUCTOR
b New York, NY, Apr 8, 42. *Study:* Mozarteum, Salzburg, dipl, 62; Oberlin Col, BMus, 63; New England Consv Music, MMus, 65; Hochschule Musik, Cologne, WGermany, artist dipl, 68. *Pos:* Guest cond, Rhenish Chamber Orch, Cologne, 67-69, City of Gelsenkirchen Orch, 72, Pro Musica, Del, 74-75, Nat Orch Costa Rica, 75 & Radio Orch Ireland, Dublin, 79 & 82; asst cond, Monte Carlo Nat Orch, 68-69 & Am Symph Orch, New York, 69-70; cond, Hessian State Broadcasting Network Orch, 69, RIAS Orch Berlin, 69, Knoxville Symph, 82 & Duluth-Superior Symph, Wis, 82; music dir, Brooklyn Ctr Chamber Orch, 70-72, Kennett Symph Orch, Pa, 74-78, Wilmington Chamber Orch, 76 & Del Symph Orch, 78-; exec dir, Wilmington Music Sch, 74-; trustee, Nat Guild Community Sch Arts, 77-; prin cond, Lancaster Symph, Pa, 78- *Awards:* Fulbright Grant, 65-68; First Prize, Santiago Compt, Spain, 67. *Mem:* Cond Guild; Am Symph Orch League; Music Teachers Nat Asn; Am Fedn Musicians. *Rep:* Maxim Gershunoff Attractions 502 Park Ave New York NY 10022. *Mailing Add:* Delaware Symph PO Box 1870 Wilmington DE 19899

GUSHEE, LAWRENCE A
MUSICOLOGIST, EDUCATOR
b Ridley Park, Pa, Feb 25, 31. *Study:* Yale Univ, BA, 52, PhD(hist music), 63. *Teaching:* From instr to asst prof hist music, Yale Univ, 60-67; from asst prof to assoc prof, Univ Wis, Madison, 67-76; prof musicol, Univ Ill, Urbana-Champaign, 76- *Awards:* Morse Fel, Yale Univ, 64-65; Guggenheim Fel, 70-71; Alfred Einstein Award, Am Musicol Soc, 70. *Mem:* Medieval Acad Am; Am Musicol Soc; Soc Ethnomusicol. *Interests:* Theory of medieval music; jazz. *Publ:* Auth, Musica Disciplina Aureliani Reomansis, Am Inst Musicol; New Sources for the Biography of Johannes de Muris, J Am Musicol Soc, 69; Music Theoretical Writings of the Middle Ages as Genre, In: Musikgeschichte in Gattungen, Francke Verlag, 73; Parisian Court and City Minstrels in the Fourteenth Century, Img Kongress-bericht Berlin 74, 78. *Mailing Add:* Sch Music Univ Ill Urbana IL 61801

GUSHEE, MARION SIBLEY
EDUCATOR, ADMINISTRATOR
b Portland, Maine, Apr 10, 33. *Study:* Oberlin Col, AB, 55; Oberlin Consv Music, MusB(piano), 55; Ecole Normale Musique, Paris; Yale Univ, PhD, 65. *Pos:* House ed & musicol consult, A-R Ed, 72-77. *Teaching:* From instr to asst prof hist music, Yale Col, 62-63, Boston Univ, 64-65 & Univ Wis, Madison, 67-76; asst prof musicol, Univ Ill, Urbana, 77- *Mem:* Am Musicol Soc; Music Libr Asn; Sonneck Soc. *Interests:* Paraliturgical music; baroque music, especially performance practice. *Publ:* Auth, A Polyphonic Ghost, J Am Musicol Soc, 63. *Mailing Add:* 202 W Vermont Ave Urbana IL 61801

GUSTAFSON, BRUCE
CRITIC, HARPSICHORD
b Brockton, Mass, Sept 30, 45. *Study:* Kalamazoo Col, BA, 67; Univ Okla, MMus, 69; Univ Mich, PhD, 77. *Pos:* Musicol ed, The Diapson, Des Plaines, Ill, 79- *Teaching:* Asst prof music, Eureka Col, 67-71; asst prof music, St Mary's Col, Ind, 76-81 & Franklin Marshall Col, 81- *Awards:* Surdna Res Grant, Franklin and Marshall Col, 82. *Mem:* Am Musicol Soc; Am Guild Organists. *Interests:* Bibliographic and stylistic studies of French harpsichord music. *Publ:* Auth, A Letter from Mr Lebegue, Recherches s la Musique fr classique, 77; French Harpsichord Music of the 17th Century, UMI Res Press, 79; Ornamentation According to Neumann, 79 & (The) Messiah: Baroque Oratorio, Rite, and Sacred Cow, 81, The Diapson. *Mailing Add:* 641 N Pine St Lancaster PA 17603

GUSTAFSON, DWIGHT LEONARD
ADMINISTRATOR, CONDUCTOR
b Seattle, Wash, Apr 20, 30. *Study:* Bob Jones Univ, BA(voice), 52, MA(sacred music), 54; Fla State Univ, DMus(comp & theory), 67. *Works:* The Jailer (one-act opera), 54 & The Hunted (one-act opera), 60, comn by Bob Jones Univ; various short choral selections, Shawnee Press, Lorenz Press & Broadman Press, 60-; Ring Out Ye Crystal Spheres, comn by Greenville County Chorus & Youth Orch, 72; To Thee Old Cause (mixed chorus & brass choir), comn by SC Music Educr Asn, 76 . *Teaching:* Instr music, Bob Jones Univ, 54-, actg dean sch fine arts, 54-56, dean sch fine arts, 56- *Mem:* Music Educr Nat Conf; Am Choral Dir Asn (state pres, 76-79); Southeastern Comp League; Pi Kappa Lambda. *Mailing Add:* 111 Stadium View Dr Greenville SC 29609

GUSTAFSON, LEE
TEACHER
b Moline, Ill. *Study:* Oberlin Col, MusB, 62; Ind Univ, MusM, 64; Am Consv Music, DMA, 71. *Teaching:* Asst prof voice, Eureka Col, 67-71; mem fac voice, Am Consv, 71- *Mem:* Nat Asn Teachers Singing; Chicago Singing Teachers Guild. *Mailing Add:* Am Consv Music 116 S Michigan Ave Chicago IL 60603

GUSTAFSON, NANCY J
SOPRANO, EDUCATOR
b Evanston, Ill, June 27, 56. *Study:* Mt Holyoke Col, BA, 78; Northwestern Univ, MM, 80. *Roles:* Helmwige in Die Walküre & Woglinde in Das Rheingold, San Francisco Opera, 83. *Awards:* First Prize, Union League Civic & Arts Found, 81; Gropper Mem Award, San Francisco Opera Ctr Nat Auditions, 82. *Mem:* Am Guild Musical Artists. *Mailing Add:* 2414 Lawndale Evanston IL 60201

GUSTIN, DANIEL ROBERT
ADMINISTRATOR
b Saginaw, Mich, Nov 30, 41. *Study:* Albion Col, BA, 63; Boston Univ. *Pos:* Asst mgr, Boston Symph Orch, currently; mgr, Boston Symph Chamber Players, currently; admin dir, Berkshire Music Ctr, currently. *Mailing Add:* Symph Hall Boston MA 02115

GUTBERG, INGRID
PIANO, ORGAN
b Riga, Latvia; US citizen. *Study:* Mozarteum, Salzburg, Austria, studied piano, organ & cond with Ledwinka, Luboshutz, Nemenoff & Geiringer, MM(piano, organ & cond), 48, Boston Univ, DMA(piano perf), 58. *Rec Perf:* Two Piano Music of Latvia and France, LHF, Vogt, Boston, 76. *Pos:* Duo-piano recitalist (with Karen Gutberg), Western Europe, US & Can, 52-; organist & choir dir, Church of Redeemer, Chestnut Hill, Mass, 58-72 & Covenant Congregational Church, Boston, 76- *Teaching:* Instr piano & organ, Mozarteum, 48-52; teaching assoc piano, organ & ens, Boston Univ, 56-63, wkshps piano teachers, 62-; lectr music & organist in res, Mass Inst Technol, 77-82. *Mem:* Col Music Soc; Am Musicol Soc; Am Guild Organists; Am Col Musicians; Sigma Alpha Iota. *Mailing Add:* 11 Dane St Boston MA 02130

GUTIERREZ, HORACIO TOMAS
PIANO
b Havana, Cuba, Aug 28, 48; US citizen. *Study:* Studied with Sergei Tarnowsky; Juilliard Sch, dipl, 70. *Rec Perf:* Solo Record (Liszt), Tschaikowsky-Liszt & Schumann-Grieg, EMI. *Pos:* Performer with major orchs world-wide, currently. *Awards:* Second Prize, Tschaikowsky Compt, 70; Avery Fisher Award, Lincoln Ctr & US Musicians, 82. *Rep:* Columbia Artists Mgt 165 W 57th St New York NY 10019. *Mailing Add:* 257 Central Park W New York NY 10024

GUTKNECHT, (EDYTHE) CAROL
SOPRANO
b Miami, Fla. *Study:* Randolph-Macon Woman's Col, Lynchburg, Va, BA(music), 67; Northwestern Univ, Evanston, Ill, MMus, 68; Music Acad of West, Santa Barbara, study with Martial Singher, 74. *Roles:* Title role in Madame Adare, New York City Opera, 80; Olympia, Antonia & Giulietta in The Tales of Hoffmann, Canadian Opera, Toronto, 81; Hanna in Haunted Castle, Mich Opera Theatre, 82; Rosalinda in Die Fledermaus, Chicago Lyr Opera, 82; Drolla in Die Feen, 82 & Curley's Wife in Of Mice and Men, 83, New York City Opera; Nedda in Pagliacci, Seattle Opera, 83. *Teaching:* Instr voice, Consv, Wis Col, Milwaukee, 74-77. *Awards:* Grant, Martha Baird Rockefeller Fund, 75. *Mem:* Am Guild Musical Artists; Nat Asn Teachers Singing; Music Educr Nat Conf. *Rep:* Kazuko-Hillyer Int 250 W 57th St New York NY 10107. *Mailing Add:* 2034 Ripley St Philadelphia PA 19152

GUTTER, ROBERT (HAROLD)
MUSIC DIRECTOR, EDUCATOR
b New York, NY, June 16, 38. *Study:* Yale Univ, BM, 59, MM, 60. *Rec Perf:* Contemporary American Music, Opus One, 73 & 74. *Pos:* Prin trombone, Nat Symph Orch, 60-64; music dir, Des Moines Symph, 67-69; Springfield Symph Orch, Ohio, 69-71 & Springfield Symph Orch, Mass, 70- *Teaching:* Assoc prof applied music, Univ Wis, Madison, 64-67; prof orch, Drake Univ, 67-69 & Wittenberg Univ, 69-70. *Mem:* Am Symph Orch League; Am Fedn Musicians. *Rep:* Sheldon Soffer Mgt 130 W 56th St New York NY 10019. *Mailing Add:* 67 Maple St Springfield MA 01105

GUY, F DEAN
EDUCATOR
b Spartanburg, SC, Oct 8, 37. *Study:* Converse Col, BMus, 60; Cleveland Inst Music, MA, 66. *Teaching:* Prof theory, Cleveland Inst Music, 66-82, chmn, 82- *Mailing Add:* 3323 Bradford Rd Cleveland Heights OH 44118

H

HAAN, RAYMOND HENRY
COMPOSER, MUSIC DIRECTOR
b Falmouth, Mich, Apr 26, 38. *Study:* Calvin Col, AB, 59; Univ Mich, MA, 72. *Works:* Over 200 compositions for chorus, organ & handbell, over 90 publ by 18 publ co, 74- *Pos:* Dir music, Cutlerville East Christian Reformed Church, Grand Rapids, 60- *Awards:* Comp Award, ASCAP, 80- *Mem:* ASCAP. *Mailing Add:* 49 Marcus SW Grand Rapids MI 49508

HAAR, JAMES
EDUCATOR, WRITER
b St Louis, Mo, July 4, 29. *Study:* Harvard Univ, BA, 50, PhD(music), 61; Univ NC, MA, 54. *Teaching:* From instr to asst prof music, Harvard Univ, 60-67; assoc prof, Univ Pa, 67-69; prof, NY Univ, 69-78; W R Kenan Jr prof,

Univ NC, 78- *Awards:* Fels, Villa I Tatti, 65 & Am Coun Learned Soc, 73. *Mem:* Am Musicol Soc (vpres, 72-74, pres, 76-78); Renaissance Soc Am. *Interests:* Italian madrigal; history of theory; humanism and music. *Publ:* Auth, Classicism and Mannerism in 16th Century Music, Int Rev Music Aesthet & Sociology, 70; Pythagorean Harmony of the Universe, In: Dict of the History of Ideas, 73; Some Remarks on the Missa la sol fa re mi, Josouin des Prez, 76; Chromaticism and False Relations in 16th Century Music, J Am Musicol Soc, 77; co-ed, The Duos of Gero, Broude Bros, 78. *Mailing Add:* Dept Music Univ NC Chapel Hill NC 27514

HAAS, JONATHAN LEE
TIMPANI, PERCUSSION
b Chicago, Ill, June 9, 54. *Study:* Washington Univ, St Louis, BA, 76; Juilliard Sch, studied with Saul Goodman, MM, 79. *Rec Perf:* New Music from London, 81 & The Music World, 82, Leonarda Prod; Beethoven's Sixth Symphony, Delos Rec, 82. *Pos:* Perc, St Louis Symph, 74-76; timpanist & perc, Am Symph, 79-; prin timpanist, Chamber Symph New York, 80- & Charlotte Symph, 81; founding mem, New York Quintet, 81- *Teaching:* Mem fac perc, Peabody Inst, 82- *Awards:* Saul Goodman-Roland Kohloff Scholar, Juilliard Sch, 78; Martha Baird Rockefeller Grant Individual Performers, 79. *Bibliog:* John Rockwell (auth), Timpanist's Debut in Carnegie Hall, 79 & Tim Page (auth), 6 Premieres, New York Times, 83. *Mem:* Percussive Arts Soc. *Mailing Add:* 142 West End 15M New York NY 10023

HABER, MICHAEL PRESS
CELLO
b Chicago, Ill, Jan 25, 42. *Study:* Brandeis Univ, BA, 63; Ind Univ, studied cello with Janos Starker, MM, 66; Univ Southern Calif, with Piatigorsky, 71-72. *Pos:* Cellist, Cleveland Symph Orch, 69-71, Casals Fest Orch, 73-75, Marlboro Music Fest, 74 & Comp String Quartet, Columbia Univ, 76-77. *Teaching:* Aspen Music Sch, 72-73 & Oberlin Col, 74; vis prof, Ind Univ, 79; assoc prof cello & chamber music, Univ Akron 83-; vis prof, Ind Univ, 79. *Mailing Add:* 165 W 66th St New York NY 10023

HABERLEN, JOHN B
EDUCATOR, MUSIC DIRECTOR
b Greensburg, Pa, Apr 27, 42. *Study:* Pa State Univ, BS, 62, MM, 63; Univ Ill, DMA, 73. *Pos:* Dir choral activ, Ga State Univ, 73- *Mem:* Am Choral Dir Asn (state pres, 82-85); Music Educr Nat Conf. *Publ:* Auth, Microrythms, 72 & coauth, Performance Practices of William Billings, 73, Choral J; auth, Mastering Conducting Techniques, 77 & coauth, Elizabethan Madrigal Dinners, 78, Mark Foster; auth, William Dawson and the Copyright Law, Choral J, 83. *Mailing Add:* Ga State Univ University Plaza Atlanta GA 30303

HABERMANN, MICHAEL ROBERT
PIANO
b Paris, France, Feb 23, 50; US citizen. *Study:* Nassau Community Col, AAS, 76; Long Island Univ, BA, 78, MA, 79; Peabody Inst, currently. *Rec Perf:* Sorabji: A Legend in His Own Time, Music Heritage Soc & Music Masters, 81; Sorabji: Le Jardin Parfume, Music Masters, 82; Piano Music by Alexandre Rey Colago, Educo, 82. *Pos:* Conct pianist, US & Mexico, 77- *Teaching:* Adj fac mem piano, Shippensburg State Col, 82- *Awards:* Long & Widmont Mem Found Award, 82. *Bibliog:* Robert Sherman (auth), Lifting the Veil from a Musical Enigma, NY Times, 5/20/77; Joseph Banowetz (auth), Five Remarkable Talents, Piano Quart, No 118, 82; Jose Antonio Alcaraz (auth), Esfie sin Secreto, Proceso, No 273-5, 82. *Mem:* Am Liszt Soc; Col Music Soc; Am Music Scholar Asn. *Publ:* Auth, Kaikhosru Shapurji Sorabji, Piano Quart, No 122, 83. *Rep:* Donald Garvelmann 620 Fort Washington Ave New York NY 10040. *Mailing Add:* 5 Rooney Ct Glen Cove NY 11542

HACHE, REGINALD W J
PIANO, EDUCATOR
b Waterville, Maine, Nov 26, 32. *Study:* New England Consv Music, BMus, MMus, DMA. *Works:* Kaleidoscope (ballet); Concerto (piano & orch); Fantasy 1984 (piano solo); Suite for Piano; Treasure Island (background music); Images of the Freedom Trail (two pianos & narration). *Rec Perf:* Contemporary Music for Gymnastic Competitions; Double Concertos, Poulenc, Mendelssohn, Bach, Mozart & Gershwin; Mussorgsky's 2 Piano Arrangement of Pictures at an Exhibition, Schwann. *Pos:* Soloist, Boston Pops, ten yrs; performer, Radio, Cambridge, Mass, formerly & TV, Boston, Cambridge & Philadelphia, formerly; soloist & ambassador, US 7th Army Symph, tours of US & Europe. *Teaching:* Assoc prof music, Northeastern Univ, currently. *Mem:* Musical Theaters Asn. *Publ:* Piano Class Methods for Laboratory, Books I-IV. *Mailing Add:* 68 Fordville Rd Duxbury MA 02332

HADCOCK, MARY G
VIOLA, TEACHER
b Long Branch, NJ, Nov 14, 39. *Study:* Eastman Sch Music, BMus, 61, MMus, 63; studied viola with Francis Tursi & Karen Tuttle. *Rec Perf:* Music for Quiet Listening, 59, Symphonic Marches, 61 & Eastman Phil Musical Diplomats USA, 62, Mercury; Messiah (Handel), Sine Qua Non, 77. *Pos:* Violist, Rochester Phil, 61-62, Buffalo Phil, 63-65, Boston Philharmonia, 65-73, Boston Pops Esplanade Orch, 65- & Boston Ballet, 65-; violist first desk, New England Chamber Orch, 68-78; violist, Handel & Haydn Soc, 68-78; violist first desk, 73, 75 & 76; violist, Opera Co Boston, 70-78, violist first desk, 74-76; violist, Opera New England, 76-78, prin violist, 78. *Teaching:* Private instr viola, 65-; instr viola & musicianship, Exten Div, New England Consv, 65-68, viola & chamber music, summer 78; instr viola, Longy Sch Music, 76- *Mailing Add:* 3 Fairview Ave Bedford MA 01730

HADCOCK, PETER
CLARINET, EDUCATOR
Study: Eastman Sch Music, BM; studied clarinet with Hasty. *Pos:* Prin clarinet, Buffalo Phil, formerly; mem, Boston Pops, currently; asst prin clarinet, Boston Symph Orch, currently. *Teaching:* Mem fac, State Univ NY, Buffalo, formerly & Community Sch, Buffalo, formerly; mem fac clarinet & chamber music, New England Consv Music, currently. *Mailing Add:* New England Consv Music 290 Huntington Rd Boston MA 02115

HADDAD, GEORGE RICHARD
EDUCATOR, PIANO
b Eastend, Sask, May 11, 18; US citizen. *Study:* Univ Toronto, LTCM, BMus, MA, 40; Juilliard Grad Sch, dipl, 42; Paris Consv, dipl, 49; Royal Acad, ARCTM, 50. *Works:* Piano Pieces, Yorktown Music Press, 77. *Pos:* Guest artist, Detroit, Toronto, Columbus, Montreal, Buffalo, Luxembourg, Cleveland, Vancouver, Victoria, Calgary & Regina Symphs. *Teaching:* Prof, Ohio State Univ, 52- *Awards:* Prix de Can, Canadian Govt, 53. *Mem:* Pi Kappa Lambda. *Mailing Add:* 2689 River Park Dr Columbus OH 43220

HAEFER, (JOHN) RICHARD
EDUCATOR
b Bucyrus, Ohio, Apr 7, 45. *Study:* Ohio State Univ, BM, 67; Univ Ariz, MM, 71; Univ Ill, PhD, 81. *Teaching:* Instr music & dir multicultural prog, Eastern NMex Univ, 75-76; asst prof music & dir, Collegium Musicum, Ariz State Univ, 76-82, assoc prof music hist, 82- *Awards:* Smithsonian Inst Vis Res Fel, 73; Nat Endowment Humanities Summer Stipend, 82; Fulbright Fel, 83. *Mem:* Soc Ethnomusicol; Int Coun Trad Music; Am Musicol Soc; Am Musical Instrm Soc; Sonneck Soc. *Interests:* North American Indian music; non-European organology; Medieval Iberian musical instruments. *Publ:* Auth, Papago Music & Dance, Navajo Community Col Press, 77; coauth, Song in Piman Curing, Ethnomusicol, 78; North America, Indian Music & Representative Tribes, In: New Grove Dict of Music & Musicians, 80; auth, Songs of Papago Celkona Cycle, Swallow Proc, 80; O'odlham Celkona (The Papago Skipping Dance), Univ NMex Press, 80. *Mailing Add:* Sch Music Ariz State Univ Tempe AZ 85287

HAEFLIGER, KATHLEEN ANN
LIBRARIAN, WRITER
b Kansas City, Mo, Apr 20, 47. *Study:* Col St Teresa, Minn, BA(piano); Univ Minn, studied musicol with Donna Cardamone, Johannes Riedel & Robert T Laudon & piano with Bernhard Weiser, MA(musicol), 77, Libr Sch, MA(libr sci), 78. *Pos:* Music libr asst, Music Libr, Univ Minn, Minneapolis, 72-79; music ref librn, Rita Benton Music Libr, Univ Iowa, 79-80, actg music librn, 80- *Awards:* Nat Endowment Humanities & Asn Col & Res Libr Grant, 83. *Mem:* Music Libr Asn; Am Musicol Soc; Sigma Alpha Iota; Pi Kappa Lambda. *Interests:* Early 19th century vocal and keyboard composers, especially Schubert; relationship between words, literature, and music in 19th and 20th centuries. *Publ:* William Carlos Williams & Edna St Vincent Millay, In: New Grove Dict of Music in US (in prep). *Mailing Add:* 1310 Marcy St Iowa City IA 52240

HAGEN, DENNIS BERT
ADMINISTRATOR, CONDUCTOR
b Spokane, Wash, Mar 4, 38. *Study:* Witworth Col, Wash, BA, 59; Ind Univ, Bloomington, MME, 63, PhD, 73. *Pos:* Cond, Chehalem Symph, 80-; dir, Champoeg Hist Pagent, Ore, 82- *Teaching:* Prof music, Geroge Fox Col, 64-, chmn fine arts, 65- *Mem:* Col Band Dir Nat Asn (northwest pres, 70-72); Ore Col Music Adminr. *Mailing Add:* Music Dept George Fox Col Newburg OR 97132

HAGENAH, ELIZABETH A(RTMAN)
PIANO, EDUCATOR
b Buffalo, NY. *Study:* Eastman Sch Music, with Cecile Genhart, BM, MM, 50; Curtis Inst Music, with Isabella Vengerova, 50-54; Hochschule Musik, 55-57; Sch Music, Boston Univ, 65. *Rec Perf:* Piano Concerto (Schumann), Eastman Sch Music; Solo Concerts, Sch Music, Boston Univ, 79-83; Works for Clarinet & Piano (in prep), Sonata for Piano (Louis Spohr) & Preludes Bk II (Debussy) (in prep). *Pos:* Co-founder & dir, Stockbridge Madrigal Soc, 65-70; founder, pres & art dir, Stockbridge Chamber Concts Inc, 65-70; organizer summer conct ser, Molkenkur, Heidelberg, WGermany, 83. *Teaching:* Fac mem prep dept, Eastman Sch Music, 53-55; prof piano, Sch Music, Boston Univ, 72- *Awards:* Fulbright Fel, 55-57. *Mem:* Nat Music Teachers Asn; Mass Music Teachers Asn. *Publ:* Auth, Organized Listening (in prep). *Mailing Add:* Prospect Hill Stockbridge MA 01262

HAGER, LAWSON J
EDUCATOR, FRENCH HORN
b Stamford, Tex, July 10, 44. *Study:* Hardin-Simmons Univ, BM, 67; NTex State Univ, MM, 71. *Pos:* Prin French horn, Abilene Phil Orch 74- *Teaching:* Asst prof brass & music lit, Hardin-Simmons Univ, 73- *Mem:* Phi Mu Alpha; Tex Music Educr Asn. *Mailing Add:* Drawer J/Music Dept Hardin-Simmons Univ Abilene TX 79698

HAGGH, RAYMOND HERBERT
EDUCATOR, ADMINISTRATOR
b Chicago, Ill, Sept 4, 20. *Study:* Northwestern Univ, BMus, 49, MMus, 50; Harvard Univ, 55-56; Ind Univ, PhD, 61; Univ Cologne, 68-69. *Works:* Choral, orch, instrm comp, perf in US sch & univ, 50-60. *Pos:* From instr to assoc prof, Dept Music, Memphis State Univ, 50-60; from asst prof to prof & dir, Sch Music, Univ Nebr, Lincoln, 60- *Awards:* Fel, Fund Advan Educ, Ford Found, 55-56; Teacher grant, Danforth Found, 57-58; Woods Found

Fel, 68-69. *Mem:* Am Musicol Soc; Music Teachers Nat Asn. *Publ:* Translr, commentary & notes to Hugo Riemann's History of Music Theory, Bks I & II, Univ Nebr Press, 62 & 66 & Da Capo Press, 74; translr, intro & notes to Daniel Gottlob Türk's School of Clavier Playing, Univ Nebr Press, 82. *Mailing Add:* 4708 Kirkwood Dr Lincoln NE 68516

HAGON, JOHN PETER
EDUCATOR, MUSIC DIRECTOR
b Milwaukee, Wis, Jan 19, 37. *Study:* Univ Wis, Madison, BMus, 58; Boston Univ, MMus, 70; studied opera cond with Boris Goldovsky, 74. *Pos:* Dir music, Wild Rose pub sch, Wis, 61-66 & Barnstable High Sch, Hyannis, Mass, 67-74. *Teaching:* Instr music, Dean Jr Col, Franklin, Mass, 74-78; chmn, Dept Music Educ, Berklee Col Music, 80- *Mem:* Music Educr Nat Conf; Nat Band Asn. *Mailing Add:* Berklee Col Music 1140 Boylston St Boston MA 02215

HAHN, MARIAN ELIZABETH
PIANO, TEACHER
b Greenwich, Conn. *Study:* Oberlin Col, with John Perry, BA, 71; Juilliard Sch, with Felix Galimir, Guido Agosti & Ilona Kabos, MM, 72; study with Leon Fleisher, 74-77 & Benjamin Kaplan, 77-80. *Pos:* Solo recitalist perf incl Carnegie Recital Hall, Metropolitan Museum Art, Dame Myra Hess Series & many others, 74-; soloist, with orch incl Cleveland Orch, NC Symph, New York Orch & others, 71-, European tour, 83; participant, Marlboro Music Fest & Grand Teton Music Fest, 82 & 83. *Teaching:* Private piano, New York, 71-80; mem fac piano & chamber music, NC Sch Arts, 80-, mem fac lit, 82- *Awards:* First prize, Kosciuszko Found, 69; Conct Artists Guild Winner, 73; Prizewinner, Leventritt Compt, 76. *Mem:* Col Music Soc; Music Teachers Nat Asn. *Mailing Add:* 1714 Lynwood Ave Winston-Salem NC 27104

HAHN, SANDRA LEA
COMPOSER, PIANO
b Spokane, Wash, Jan 5, 40. *Study:* Wash State Univ, with William Brandt; Univ Wis, with Robert Crane. *Works:* Music for The Cave Dwellers (theatre), comn by Speech & Drama Dept, Wash State Univ; Quartet (flute, clarinet, bassoon & piano); Sonorities (flute, harpsichord, & perc); Piano Trio; Variations (flute & piano); Five Miniatures (flute & piano); Sonata (cello). *Pos:* Pianist, Milwaukee Symph Orch, 66-67. *Teaching:* Instr piano, Univ Idaho, 70- *Awards:* Winner, Wis State Music Teachers Comp Cont. *Mailing Add:* 719 Mabelle Moscow ID 83843

HAIEFF, ALEXEI
COMPOSER
b Blagoveshchensk, USSR, Aug 25, 14. *Study:* Juilliard Sch, with Rubin Goldmark & Frederick Jacobi; studied with Nadia Boulanger, 38-39; Am Acad, Rome. *Works:* Ballet in E, 55; Piano Sonata, 55; Eclogue (harp & strings), 63; Cello Sonata, 65; Eloge (chamber orch), 67; Caligula (bar & orch), 71; Gifts and Semblances (piano), 76. *Teaching:* Fel, Am Acad, Rome, 47-48, comp in res, 52-53 & 58-59; prof, Univ Buffalo, 62-68; comp in res, Univ Utah, 68-71. *Awards:* Guggenheim Fel, 46 & 49; NY Music Critics Circle Award, 52; UNESCO Rec Award, 58. *Mailing Add:* 230 W 55th New York NY 10019

HAIGH, MORRIS
COMPOSER
b San Diego, Calif, Jan 26, 32. *Study:* Pomona Col, studied comp with Halsey Stevens & Carl Parrish, BA, 53; Eastman Sch Music, studied comp with Bernard Rogers, MA, 54, studied comp with Wayne Barlow & Samuel Adler, PhD, 73. *Works:* Serenade for Flute and Piano, T Presser, 55; Fantasia on a Lutheran Chorale for Horns and Organ, Shawnee Press, 63 & Robert King Music, 82. *Mailing Add:* 259 Barrington St Rochester NY 14607

HAIGH, SCOTT (RICHARD)
DOUBLE BASS
b Oak Park, Ill, Sept 2, 54. *Study:* Am Fedn Cong Strings, 71-72; Northwestern Univ, with Warren Benfield, 72-75; Aspen Music Fest, with Stuart Sankey, 74-75. *Pos:* Prin bass, Orquesta Sinfonica del Estado de Mexico, 75-76; bassist, Milwaukee Symph Orch, 77-78; bassist, Cleveland Orch, 78-81 & first asst prin bass, 82- *Bibliog:* Susan Saiter (auth), Musician Comes Home, Evanston Rev, Pioneer Press, 4/26/79; Musician's Career Influenced by AFM Congress of Strings, Int Musician, Am Fedn Musicians, July 79. *Mailing Add:* 16004 Nelacrest Rd #1 East Cleveland OH 44112

HAILSTORK, ADOLPHUS CUNNINGHAM
COMPOSER, CONDUCTOR
b Rochester, NY, Apr 17, 41. *Study:* Howard Univ, studied comp with Mark Fax, BM, 63; Am Inst Fountainebleau, with Nadia Boulanger, 63-; Manhattan Sch Music, with Ludmila Ulehla, Nicholas Flagello, Vittorio Giannini & David Diamond, BM(comp), 65, MM, 66; Mich State Univ, with H Owen Reed, PhD(comp), 71; Electronic Music Inst, NH, with John Appleton & Herbert Howe, 72. *Works:* Celebration (orch), J C Penney, 75; Suite (organ), Hinshaw Music, 76; Spiritual (brass octet), comn by Edward Tarr, 76;; Sonatina (flute & piano), 77 & Bagatelles for Brass, 77, Fema Publ; Cease Sorrows Now (chorus), Marks Music, 77; Duo (tuba & piano), 81 & Out of the Depths (band), 82, Fema Publ. *Rec Perf:* Celebration, Columbia Rec, 80; A Charm at Parting, Univ Mich Rec, 82. *Teaching:* Asst prof music, Youngstown State Univ, 71-77, assoc prof, 76; assoc prof & comp in res, Norfolk State Univ, 77- *Awards:* Co-winner, Ernest Bloch Award, 71; Max Winkler Award, Belwin Mills, 77; First Prize, Va Col Band Dir Symposium New Music for Band, 82. *Bibliog:* Alice Tischler (auth), 15 Black Composers, 80; Lucius R Wyatt, Composers Corner, Black Music Res Newslett, spring, 82. *Mem:* ASCAP. *Mailing Add:* 521 Berry Pick Lane Virginia Beach VA 23462

HAIMO, ETHAN TEPPER
COMPOSER, EDUCATOR
b St Louis, Mo, Mar 22, 50. *Study:* Univ Chicago, AB, 72; Princeton Univ, MFA, 74, PhD, 78. *Works:* Scene from Macbeth, perf by Contemp Chamber Players, Chicago, 70; String Quartet No 1, Comp Conf, 71; Convergence (synthesized tape), 74; String Quartet No 2, perf by Colden String Quartet, 75; Trio, perf by Notre Dame Trio, 78; Quartet (oboe & strings), perf by Kinhave Ens, 80; Contrasts (voice & piano), perf by Debbie & Michael Toth, 81. *Teaching:* Asst prof, Boston Univ, 75-76; asst prof, Univ Notre Dame, 76-82 & assoc prof, 82- *Awards:* Fel, Fromm Found, 71 & Mellon Found, 79 & 81. *Mem:* Soc Music Theory; Am Soc Univ Comp. *Interests:* Contemporary music theory, particularly 12-tone theory. *Publ:* Auth, Rhythmic Theory and Analysis, 78, Generated Collections and Interval Control, 79 & Inversional Invariants in Diatonic Music, 81, In Theory Only; Secondary and Disjunct Order Positions ... Perspectives (in press); coauth, Isomorphic Partitioning and Schoenberg's ... J Music Theory (in prep). *Mailing Add:* Dept Music Univ Notre Dame Notre Dame IN 46556

HAJDU, JOHN
MUSICOLOGIST, EDUCATOR
b Pa, Jan 4, 45. *Study:* DePauw Univ, BMus(comp), 66; Am Consv, Fontainebleau, summers 67 & 68; studied with Nadia Boulanger, Annette Dieudonne & Pierre Bernac, 69-70; Univ Colo, MMus(hist & lit), 70, PhD(musicol), 73. *Pos:* Admin asst, Rocky Ridge Music Ctr, 73-74, mem adv bd, 80-; mem, Lully Comt, Broude Brothers, 80- *Teaching:* Lectr music, Col Arts & Sci, Univ Colo, 71-72; asst prof music, Univ Calif, Santa Cruz, 73-79, assoc prof, 79-, chmn, Bd Studies Music, 80-; lectr, Carmel Bach Fest, 80- *Awards:* Noah Greenberg Award, 80; Nat Endowment for Humanities Grant, 82. *Mem:* Am Musicol Soc. *Interests:* French choral music from the time of Louis XIV. *Publ:* Auth, Jean Gilles (1668-1705): A Biography, In: Musicology at the University of Colorado, Univ Colo Regents, 78; Can the Computer Help to Humanize the Lecture Hall?, Teacher on the Hill, spring 79; seven biographical articles in New Grove Dict of Music & Musicians, Macmillan, London, 80; coauth (with J R Anthony), French Music of the XVIIth and XVIIIth Centuries, a Checklist of Research in Progress, Recherches Musique Francaise Classique, 82; Gille's Messe Des Morts, AR Ed, 83. *Mailing Add:* Porter Col Univ Calif Santa Cruz CA 95064

HALE, JAMES PIERCE
EDUCATOR, PERCUSSION
b Chicago, Ill, Dec 5, 28. *Study:* Am Consv Music, BME, 54; Univ Ill, MS, 56. *Teaching:* Prof perc, Univ Fla, 57- *Awards:* Univ Fla Res Grant, 68; Col Fine Arts Outstanding Serv Award, 82. *Mem:* Percussive Arts Soc. *Mailing Add:* Music Dept Univ Fla Gainesville FL 32611

HALE, (NATHAN) KELLY
EDUCATOR, CONDUCTOR
b Fairfax, Okla, Oct 13, 42. *Study:* Univ Okla, BME(piano & voice), 64; Univ Tex, Austin, MM(opera perf), 72, DMA(opera perf), 74. *Pos:* Asst cond, Santa Fe Opera Co, 63-65. *Teaching:* Opera & orchestral cond, Univ Tex, 73-76; opera coach & cond, Col Consv Music, Univ Cincinnati, 76- *Mem:* Nat Opera Asn; Cent Opera Serv; Am Guild Organists. *Mailing Add:* 1457 Aster Pl Cincinnati OH 45224

HALE, ROBERT
BASS-BARITONE
b Kerrville, Tex, Aug 22, 33. *Study:* Bethany Nazarene Col, BMusEd, 56; Univ Okla with Orcenith Smith, MMusEd, 63; New England Consv Music, with Gladys Miller, artist dipl, 67; Boston Univ, with Ludwig Bergmann; San Francisco State Univ; Northwestern Univ. *Rec Perf:* 15 albums on Phillips, Columbia & ABC. *Roles:* Julius Caesar in Julius Caesar; Don Giovanni in Don Giovanni; Escamillo in Carmen; Mephistopheles in Faust; Der Fliegende Holländer; Banquo in Macbeth; Mefistofele in Mefistofele. *Pos:* Leading bass-baritone, New York City Opera, 67-80; guest appearances, San Diego Opera Co, 74-84, Hamburg Staatsoper, 78-82, Frankfurt Stadtische Bühnen, 78-84, Teatro Colon, Buenos Aires, 80, Monte Carlo, 82, Marsielle, 82 & Stuttgart, 83; solo appearances with maj orchs in US & Can. *Awards:* Singer of Year, Nat Asn Teachers Singing, 63; Rockefeller Found Grant, 67-68; Sullivan Found Grant, 68. *Mem:* Am Guild Musical Artists; Nat Acad Rec Arts & Sci; Pi Kappa Lambda; Phi Mu Alpha Sinfonia; Mu Phi Epsilon. *Mailing Add:* c/o Herbert Barrett Mgt 1860 Broadway New York NY 10023

HALE, RUTH JUNE
CLARINET, TEACHER
b Abington, Pa. *Study:* Univ Colo, with Val Henrich, BM, 55, with Aaholm, MM, 81; Univ Tübingen, Germany, with Calgeer, 77; Musickhochschule, Frankfurt, Germany, with A K Hermann, 78. *Pos:* Guest clarinetist, Schreibner Quartet, Germany, 78, Wendel Trio, Munich, 83 & Blume String Ens, Switz, 83; clarinetist, Ars Artium, Denver, 79- *Awards:* Arts & Humanities Grant, City of Boulder, Colo, 82. *Mem:* Am Ens; Col Musicol Soc; The Clarinet. *Mailing Add:* 375 Seminole Dr Boulder CO 80303

HALEN, ERIC J
VIOLIN, EDUCATOR
b Bellevue, Ohio, Nov 6, 57. *Study:* Cent Mo State Univ, BMus, 77; Univ Ill, MMus, 79. *Pos:* Actg concertmaster, Tex Chamber Orch, 83; guest soloist, St Louis Symph, 83. *Teaching:* Instr violin & artist, Tex Christian Univ, 81-; fac mem, Univ Ill, 83. *Mem:* Am Fedn Musicians. *Mailing Add:* 4391 Berke Rd Ft Worth TX 76115

HALEN, WALTER JOHN
EDUCATOR, COMPOSER

b Hamilton, Ohio, Mar 17, 30. *Study:* Miami Univ, BMus, 52; Ohio Univ, studied comp with Karl Ahrendt, MFA, 53; Northwestern Univ, studied comp with Anthony Donato; Ohio State Univ, PhD, 69; studied comp with Mark Walker. *Works:* Sinfonia Sonore, perf by Columbus Symph Tri State Symposium, Ohio, 62; Meditation for Oboe, Piano, Percussion, Seesaw Music Co; Two Poems of Dance for Instrumental Ensemble and Voices, comn by Music Teachers Nat Asn, 76; A Free Americay (string orch), Kendor Music, 79; Promenade and Hoedown (string orch), 79 & Stick-Horse Parade for String Orch, 83, Shawnee Press, Inc. *Pos:* Violist & violinist, Toledo Symph, 56-58; concertmaster, Springfield Symph, Mo, 62-66; violist, Lakeside Symph, Ohio, summer 79. *Teaching:* Orch & strings, Bellevue Pub Sch, Ohio, 56-61; asst prof orch, strings & theory, Drury Col, 62-67; prof orch, strings & comp, Cent Mo State Univ, 67- *Awards:* Teacher Recognition Award, Mason-Hamlin Music Teachers Nat Asn, 74; Congratulatory Award, Wurlitzer Music Teachers Nat Asn, 78. *Mem:* Music Teachers Nat Asn (mem state exec bd, 78-, orch instrm chair, 78-82); Am String Teachers Asn; ASCAP; Music Educr Nat Conf; Am Symph Orch League. *Publ:* Auth, String Quartet Literature for High School, Instrumentalist, 5/70; 400 at Workshop, Orch News, 9/73. *Mailing Add:* Rte 5 Green Acres Warrensburg MO 64093

HALEY, ELIZABETH N See Norden, Betsy

HALEY, JOHNETTA R
EDUCATOR, PIANIST

b Alton, Ill, Mar 19, 23. *Study:* Lincoln Univ, BSME, 45; Univ Ill, 47; Washington Univ, St Louis, 58; Southern Ill Univ, MMus, 72; studied piano with Martha Ayres & Thomasina Green & voice with O Anderson Fuller. *Teaching:* Piano & voice, Lincoln High Sch, East St Louis, Ill, 45-48; music, Turner Elem Sch, Kirkwood, Mo, 50-55; Turner Jr High Sch, 50-55 & Niplier Jr High Sch, 55-72; assoc prof music, Southern Ill Univ, Edwardsville, 72-80, actg dir, East St Louis Campus, 72-, prof, 81- *Mem:* Col Music Soc; Nat Choral Dir Asn; Artist Presentation Soc; Mu Phi Epsilon; Mid-West Kodaly Music Educr. *Mailing Add:* Dept Music Southern Ill Univ Edwardsville IL 62026

HALGEDAHL, (EDWARD) HOWARD
CONDUCTOR, EDUCATOR

b Marengo, Wash, Feb 8, 17. *Study:* Univ Ariz, BM, 39; Eastman Sch Music, MM, 46; L'Ecole Monteux, 52. *Pos:* Solo bassoon & asst cond, Wichita Symph, 47-72; cond orch, band & choir, Winfield High Sch, Kans, 51-72; cond orch & asst to dir, Nat Music Camp, Interlochen, Mich, 53-80; cond orch, opera & oratorio, Emporia State Univ, 72- *Teaching:* Prof music theory & bassoon, Wichita State Univ, 47-51 & Emporia State Univ, 72- *Mem:* Am Fedn Musicians; Music Educr Nat Conf; Kans Music Educr Asn. *Publ:* Auth lyrics & script, Kanza, Kans Centennial Pageant, 61; auth, Ford Foundation Contemporary Music Project, Music Educr Nat Conf J Seattle Convention, 63; Poems for two LaPresto songs, Carl Fischer, 65. *Mailing Add:* 512 W 15th Ave Emporia KS 66801

HALL, CARL DAVID
FLUTE, TEACHER

b Mulberry, Fla, June 14, 51. *Study:* Univ SFla, Tampa, BA(music), 77; master classes with Rampal, Baker, Moyse & Larrieu; Blossom Fest Sch, Cleveland Orch; Inst Adv Musical Studies, Switz. *Pos:* Prin flutist, Fla Gulf Coast Symph, Tampa Bay Area, 70-; piccolo, New Orleans Phil, 81-82; piccolo & third flute, Santa Fe Opera Orch, summers 82- *Teaching:* Instr flute, Univ Tampa, 71-, Univ Cent Fla, Orlando, 77-81. *Mailing Add:* 7809 Alafia Dr Riverview FL 33569

HALL, CHARLES JOHN
COMPOSER, EDUCATOR

b Houston, Tex, Nov 17, 25. *Study:* Andrews Univ, BM(music theory), 52; Univ NMex, MM(comp), 60; Mich State Univ, with H Owen Reed & Paul Harder, PhD(comp), 70. *Works:* Five Microscopics, perf by Fargo-Moorhead Symph Orch, 70; Recitative (orch), Houston Symph Orch, 71 & Twin Cities Orch, Mich, 76; Babylon, A Suite for Band, Orion Music Press, 73; Ulalume, Southwestern Contemp Music Fest, 74; The Coming King (choir & brass), Orion Music Press, 76; Scherzo, Just for Fun, Indianapolis Symph Orch, 78; A Celebration Overture, comn & perf by South Bend Symph Orch, 83. *Teaching:* Instr music, High Sch, NMex, Mo & Mich, 56-67; prof music, Andrews Univ, 69-81 & chmn, 81- *Awards:* Sigvald Thompson Award, Fargo-Moorhead Orch, 70; Delius Award for Orch, Fla State Univ, 77. *Mem:* Am Soc Univ Comp; Am Music Ctr; ASCAP; Music Educr Nat Conf. *Publ:* Auth, Hall's Musical Years—The 20th Century, Op Music, 80. *Mailing Add:* Box 397B Route 1 Berrien Springs MI 49103

HALL, JANICE L
SOPRANO

b San Francisco, Calif, Sept 28, 53. *Study:* Colo Women's Col, BA, 75; Boston Consv Music, MMus, 77. *Roles:* Gilda in Rigoletto, San Diego Opera, 78; Oscar in Un Ballo in maschera, Washington Opera, 80; Zerlina in Don Giovanni, New York City Opera, 81; Perichole in La Perichole, Houston Grand Opera, 81; Rosina in Il Barbiere di Siviglia, Hamburg Staatsoper, 82; Anne in The Rake's Progress, Oper der Stadt Köln, 82; Norina in Don Pasquale, Santa Fe Opera, 83. *Rep:* Shaw Concts Inc 1995 Broadway New York NY 10023. *Mailing Add:* 25 Nagle Ave #44 New York NY 10040

HALL, MARION AUSTIN
ADMINISTRATOR, EDUCATOR

b Picayune, Miss, Sept 19, 31. *Study:* La State Univ, BME, 58, MM, 60; Univ Ill, DMA, 67. *Teaching:* Asst prof voice, Georgetown Col, Ky, 60-64; assoc prof, Drake Univ, 66-69, prof, 69-, music dept chmn, 82- *Mailing Add:* Music Dept Drake Univ Des Moines IA 50311

HALL, MARNIE L
ADMINISTRATOR

b Clay Center, Kans, June 5, 42. *Study:* Univ Kans, BM(violin), 66; Manhattan Sch Music, MM(violin), 68. *Pos:* Violinist, Am Symph Orch, 66-; pres & producer, Leonarda Prod, 77- *Mailing Add:* PO Box 124 Radio City Station New York NY 10101

HALL, THOMAS MUNROE
VIOLIN

b Tallahassee, Fla, Sept 1, 43. *Study:* Fla State Univ, BM, 64, MM, 66. *Pos:* Violinist, US Army Strings, 66-69, Meridian String Quartet, 67-, Cincinnati Symph Orch, 69-70, Chicago Symph Orch, 70-, Chicago Arts Quartet, 75- *Mem:* Chicago String Ens (bd dir, 76-); Int Conf Symph & Opera Musicians (ed, Senza Sordino, 82-). *Mailing Add:* 2800 Lake Shore Dr Chicago IL 60657

HALL, TOM
EDUCATOR

Study: Ithaca Col, BM; Boston Univ, MM. *Pos:* Founder & cond, Ithaca Art Ens, 78; music dir, Concord Chorus, currently; asst cond, Boston Univ, currently; mem staff, Old South Church, currently. *Teaching:* Asst cond, Tanglewood Inst, Boston Univ, 78; cond fel, Aspen Music Fest, 79; mem fac theory, Longy Sch Music, formerly. *Mem:* Handel & Haydn Soc. *Mailing Add:* Choral Dept Boston Univ Boston MA 02215

HALLMAN, LUDLOW B, III
EDUCATOR, MUSIC DIRECTOR & CONDUCTOR

b Dayton, Ohio, Aug 1, 41. *Study:* Consv Music, Oberlin Col, BMus, 63; Southern Ill Univ, MMus, 65; Mozarteum, Salzburg, Austria, Kapellmeister dipl, 70. *Pos:* Performer, Santa Fe Opera, St Louis Symph, Bangor Symph, Portland Symph, Maine, Salzburg Fest & Mozart Opera Salzburg; musical dir & cond, Salzburg Baroque Ens; asst cond, Bangor Symph Orch, currently. *Teaching:* Assoc prof orch & voice, Univ Maine, currently, musical dir & cond, Opera Theatre & Univ Orch. *Awards:* Winner, Young Artist Compt, St Louis Symph Orch, 65; John Haskall Fel, 66; Abgangs Prize, Austrian Govt, 67. *Mem:* Nat Asn Teachers Singing; Nat Opera Asn; Am Symph Orch League. *Mailing Add:* Dept Music Univ Maine Orono ME 04469

HALLMARK, RUFUS EUGENE, JR
EDUCATOR

b Nashville, Ark, Dec 24, 43. *Study:* Davidson Col, BA(music), 65; Boston Univ, MA(musicol), 67; Princeton Univ, PhD(musicol), 75. *Pos:* Tenor soloist, Boston Camerata, 73-77. *Teaching:* Asst prof, Brown Univ, 71-72, Mass Inst Technol, 72-77 & Col Holy Cross, 77-80; assoc prof, Aaron Copland Sch Music, Queens Col, City Univ New York, 81- *Awards:* Woodrow Wilson Found Fel, 65-66; Nat Endowment Humanities Fel, 81-82; Mellon Found Fel, 81-84. *Mem:* Am Musicol Soc (prog chmn, 78, mem coun, 78-81); Robert Schumann Gesellschaft, Dusseldorf; Music Libr Asn. *Interests:* German lieder, especially source-critical and analytical work on songs of Robert Schumann and Franz Schubert. *Publ:* Auth, The Sketches for Dichterliebe, 19th Century Music, 77; The Genesis of Schumann's Dichterliebe, UMI Res Press, 79; Schubert's Auf dem Strom, In: Schubert Studies, Cambridge, 82; ed, J S Bach, Cantata 114, Ach lieben Christen, seid getrost, In: Neue Bach Ausgabe, 82; coauth, Text and Music in Schubert's Pentameter Lieder, In: Text & Music, Broude, 83. *Mailing Add:* 134 Summit St Brooklyn NY 11231

HALSTED, MARGO ARMBRUSTER
CARILLON, WRITER

b Bakersfield, Calif, Apr 24, 38. *Study:* Stanford Univ, BA, 60, MA, 65; Univ Calif, Riverside, MA(music), 73. *Pos:* Concert performances, US & Europe, 67-; ed, Carillon News, 81-; chmn, Leuven Carillon Comt. *Teaching:* Assoc carillonneur, Stanford Univ, 67-77; carillonneur & lectr, Music Dept, Univ Calif, Riverside, 77- *Awards:* Medal of City, Bergues, France, 72; Medal, Univ Calif, Berkeley, 79. *Mem:* Guild Carillonneurs North Am (mem bd dir, 70-78, secy, 71-77); Am Guild Organists; Am Musicol Soc; Col Music Soc. *Interests:* Carillons; carillon music; organ music. *Publ:* Auth, The Toccatas of Girolamo Frescobaldi, Music, 75; Carillons in East & West Germany, 75, The Bells of Berkeley, 80 & A Look at Today's Belgian Carillon Art, 80 & compiler, Index (1940-1980), 82, Bulletin Guild Carillonneurs North Am; ed, The Leuven Carillon Book, Univ Calif, 83. *Mailing Add:* Music Dept Univ Calif Riverside CA 92521

HAMBRO, LEONID
PIANO, EDUCATOR

b Chicago, Ill, June 26, 20. *Study:* Juilliard Sch Music, dipl, 42. *Pos:* Off pianist, WQXR Radio Sta, 45-62 & New York Phil Orch, 47-62. *Teaching:* Instr piano lit & improvising, Juilliard Sch Music, 48-54; head piano dept, Calif Arts Music Sch, 70- *Awards:* Naumberg Piano Compt Winner, 46. *Bibliog:* Bill Irwin (auth), Leonid Hambro—An Unconventional Classical Career, Keyboard, 12/82. *Mem:* Am Fedn Musicians; Bohemians. *Mailing Add:* 909 S Serrano Ave Los Angeles CA 90006

HAMILTON, DAVID (PETER)
CRITIC
b New York, NY, Jan 18, 35. *Study:* Princeton Univ, AB, 56, MFA, 60; Harvard Univ, MA, 60. *Pos:* Music ed, W W Norton & Co, 68-74; music critic, Nation, 68-; guest music critic, New Yorker, 74. *Teaching:* Fac mem music criticism, Aspen Music Sch, 73 & music hist, Juilliard Sch, 80-81. *Awards:* Deems Taylor Award, ASCAP, 75. *Mem:* Music Critics Asn (vice pres, 81-83); Am Musicol Soc; Music Libr Asn; Asn Rec Sound Collections (bd mem, 83-). *Publ:* Auth, The Listener's Guide to Great Instrumentalists, Facts-on-File, 82. *Mailing Add:* 91 Central Park West New York NY 10023

HAMILTON, JERALD
EDUCATOR, ORGAN
b Wichita, Kans, Mar 19, 27. *Study:* Univ Kans, BM, 48, MM, 50; studied with Andre Marchal, Paris, France, 54-55; Royal Sch Church Music, Croydon, England, summer 55; Organ Inst, Methuen, Mass, with Catharine Crozier, summer 56; Sch Sacred Music, Union Theol Sem, with Gustav Leonhardt, summer 56. *Pos:* Organist & choirmaster, Trinity Episcopal Church, Lawrence, Kans, 45-49, Grace Cathedral, Topeka, Kans, 49-59, St David's Church, Austin, Tex, 60-63, Episcopal Church Found, Univ Ill, 63- *Teaching:* From instr to asst prof organ & theory, Washburn Univ Topeka, 49-59; asst prof organ, Ohio Univ, 59-60 & Univ Tex, Austin, 60-63; lectr church music, Episcopal Theol Sem of Southwest, 61-63; from assoc prof to prof organ & organ lit, Univ Ill, Urbana-Champaign, 63- *Mem:* Am Guild Organists; Asn Anglican Musicians; Phi Mu Alpha; Phi Kappa Lambda. *Publ:* Coauth, Four Centuries of Organ Music...An Annotated Discography, Detroit Studies in Music Bibliog (in prep). *Rep:* Phyllis Stringham Conct Mgt 425 Mountain Ave Waukesha WI 53186. *Mailing Add:* Route 1, Box 137 Sidney IL 61877

HAMILTON, ROBERT
PIANO, EDUCATOR
b South Bend, Ind, Apr 1, 37. *Study:* Ind Univ, BM, 59; Cath Univ Am, MM, 62; studied with Sidney Foster, Amos Allen & Dora Zaslavsky. *Rec Perf:* Solo piano rec of Bartok & Rachmaninoff, Philip Rec, 70, McLean, Orion Rec, 72 & Advance Rec, 73, Barber & Copland, BBC, 75 & Carl Nielsen, Orion Rec, 83. *Teaching:* Asst prof music, Ind Univ, 67-75; assoc prof & piano dept chmn, Wichita State Univ, 75-80; prof & keyboard chmn, Ariz State Univ, 80- *Awards:* Perf grants, Rockefeller Found, 62, 64 & 66 & US Dept State, 62-67; Prizes, Busoni, Montevideo, Casella & Rudolph Ganz Compt, 63-65. *Mem:* Bohemians; Am Liszt Soc. *Rep:* Wayne Wilbur Mgt PO Box 1378 Grand Cent Sta New York NY 10163. *Mailing Add:* 2439 E Del Rio Tempe AZ 85282

HAMM, CHARLES EDWARD
EDUCATOR, MUSICOLOGIST
b Charlottesville, Va, Apr 21, 25. *Study:* Univ Va, BA, 47; Princeton Univ, MFA, 50, PhD, 60. *Teaching:* Instr music theory & music hist, Cincinnati Consv, 50-57; assoc prof comp & musicol, Newcomb Col, Tulane Univ, 59-63; prof musicol, Univ Ill, Urbana, 73-76 & Dartmouth Col, 76- *Awards:* Ctr Int Comp Studies Grant, 66; Guggenheim Fel, 67-68; Fulbright Grant, 67-68. *Mem:* Am Musicol Soc; Int Musicol Soc; Ital Soc Musical. *Interests:* Fifteenth century sacred music; American music; opera. *Publ:* Auth, Manuscript Structure in the Dufay Era, Acta Musicol, 62; A Chronology of the Works of Dufay, Princeton Univ, 63; The Reson Mass, J Am Musicol Soc, 65; Opera, Allyn & Bacon, 66; Petrushka, Norton, 67; Anonymous English Music in Continental Manuscripts, Musica Disciplina, 68. *Mailing Add:* Bragg Hill Rd Norwich VT 05055

HAMME, ALBERT P
EDUCATOR, SAXOPHONE
b York, Pa, Jan 5, 39. *Study:* Ithaca Col, BS, 61; State Univ NY, Binghamton, MST, 67. *Teaching:* Instr teacher, Endicott Pub Sch, NY, 61-67; assoc prof jazz hist, orch & improvisation, State Univ NY, Binghamton, 64-81 & chmn music dept, 81- *Mem:* Music Educr Nat Conf; NY State Sch Music Asn; Am Fedn Musicians. *Mailing Add:* Music Dept State Univ NY Binghamton NY 13901

HAMMER, STEPHEN
EARLY WIND INSTRUMENTS, EDUCATOR
Study: Oberlin Col, BA; studied oboe with Robert Sprenkle, Wayne Rapier, James Caldwell & Fernand Gillet, baroque oboe with Michel Piguet & recorder with Scott-Martin Kosofsky. *Rec Perf:* On Nonesuch, Smithsonian Rec & Titanic. *Pos:* Builder hist instruments; mem, Aston Magna, Banchetto Musicale, Smithsonian Chamber Players, Conct Royal & Bach Ens; asst music dir, Castle Hill Fest; performer, Boston Pops, Boston Camerata, Boston Ballet, Bethlehem Bach Fest & Music for General Peace. *Teaching:* Mem fac early music & baroque flute, New England Consv Music, currently; mem fac baroque oboe, Longy Sch Music, currently; mem fac, Smith Col, currently, Mt Holyoke Col, currently, Orford Fest, Quebec, currently, Aston Magna Acad, currently & Castle Hill Fest, currently. *Mailing Add:* Longy Sch Music One Follen St Cambridge MA 02138

HAMMITT, JACKSON LEWIS, III
EDUCATOR, PIANO
b McKeesport, Pa, Feb 22, 38. *Study:* Ohio Wesleyan Univ, BMus, 59; Univ Mich, with Marilyn Mason, MMus, 61, with John McCollum, PhD, 70. *Pos:* Dir music, First Methodist Church, Pittsburgh, 61-62; organist, Grace Episcopal Church, Chadron, Nebr, 69-; cond, Platte Valley Oratorio Soc, Scottsbluff, Nebr, 71-76. *Teaching:* Fel music lit & choir, Univ Mich, 62-67; lectr music hist, Univ Mo, Columbia, summer 67; prof music hist & piano, Chadron State Col, 67- *Mem:* Am Guild Organists; Am Choral Dir Asn; Music Teachers Nat Asn; Am Musicol Soc; Music Educr Nat Conf. *Mailing Add:* 630 Pine Crest Dr Chadron NE 69337

HAMMOND, FREDERICK FISHER
HARPSICHORD, EDUCATOR
b Binghamton, NY, Aug 7, 37. *Study:* Yale Univ, BA, 58, PhD, 65. *Rec Perf:* On Nonesuch, Decca, CRI, Orion & ABC. *Pos:* Asst music dir, Castel-franco Veneto Fest, 75- & Clarion Music Soc, New York, 77- *Teaching:* Instr music, Univ Chicago, 62-65; fel, Am Acad Rome, 65-66 & Harvard Ctr Renaissance Studies, 73; asst prof, Queens Col, City Univ New York, 66-68; asst prof, Col Fine Arts, Univ Calif, Los Angeles, 68-73, assoc prof, 73-80, prof, 80-; instr harpsichord, Calif Inst Arts, currently. *Mem:* Am Musicol Soc; Conn Acad Arts & Sci; Elizabethan Club Yale Univ. *Publ:* Auth, articles on 17th century music. *Mailing Add:* Dept Music Col Fine Arts Univ Calif Los Angeles CA 90024

HAMMOND, IVAN FRED
EDUCATOR, TUBA
b Paoli, Ind, Feb 25, 41. *Study:* Ind Univ, perf cert, 61, BM, 63, MM, 65. *Pos:* Tubist, NC Symph, L'Orch Symph Quebec & Shenandoah Fest Orch, Am Symph Orch League, formerly & Bowling Green Brass Quintet, currently; mem, Great Lakes (Toledo Symph Orch) Brass Quintet, Toledo Tuba Trio & Badinage (trumpet, tuba & piano trio), currently; solo, brass quintet & orch performances throughout US, Can & Japan; opera tech dir, Bowling Green State Univ, formerly. *Teaching:* Fac mem, Inter-Provincial & Scarborough Music Camps, Ontario, currently; prof perf studies, Bowling Green State Univ, currently. *Mem:* Tubists Universal Brotherhood Asn. *Interests:* Tuba design. *Mailing Add:* Col Musical Arts Bowling Green State Univ Bowling Green OH 43403

HAMMOND, PAUL G
EDUCATOR, WRITER
b Cincinnati, Ohio, Sept 22, 45. *Study:* Morehead State Univ, AB, 67; Southern Baptist Theol Sem, MCM, 70, DMA, 74. *Teaching:* Assoc prof, Ouachita Baptist Univ, 73- *Mem:* Am Choral Dir Asn; Nat Asn Teachers Singing; Hymn Soc Am; Sonneck Soc. *Interests:* Nineteenth-century shape note and revival hymnody. *Publ:* Auth, The Hymnody of the Second Great Awakening, Hymn, 79; A New Source for the Tune Warrenton, Hymn (in prep); Jesse B Aikin & the Christian Minstrel, Am Music (in prep). *Mailing Add:* Ouachita Baptist Univ PO Box 710 Arkadelphia AR 71923

HAMPSON, (W) THOMAS
BARITONE
b Elkhart, Ind, June 28, 55. *Study:* Eastern Wash State Col, BA, 77; Ft Wright Col, BFA, 79. *Rec Perf:* Bach Cantatas, Telefunken (in prep). *Roles:* Harlequin in Ariadne auf Naxos, Los Angeles Opera Theater, 81; Guglielmo in Cosi fan tutte, Figaro in il Barbiere di Siviglia & Heerrufer in Lohengrine, Deutsche Oper Am Rhein, Düsseldorf, WGermany, 81-83; Guglielmo in Cosi fan tutte, St Louis Opera Theater, 82; Prinz in Prinz von Homburg, Darmstadt, Staatstheater, WGermany, 82; Jacobsleiter, Radio Symph Orch, Berlin, WGermany, 83; Dr Malatesta in Don Pasquale, Santa Fe Opera, 83. *Pos:* Lyric baritone, Deutsche Oper Am Rhein, Düsseldorf, WGermany, 81- *Awards:* Lotle Lehman Grand Award, Music Acad West, 78; Second Prize, s-Hertogenbosch Int Vocal Concours, 80; first place, Metropolitan Opera Nat Coun Award, 81. *Rep:* Columbia Artists Mgt 165 W 57th New York NY 10019. *Mailing Add:* Ostendorf Strasse 12 4000 Dusseldorf 1 Germany, Federal Republic of

HAMVAS, LEWIS T
EDUCATOR, COMPOSER
b Budapest, Hungary, Nov 10, 19; US citizen. *Study:* Juilliard Sch Music, BS, 48, MS, 49; studied with Egon Petri, Josef Raieff & Vincent Persichetti. *Works:* Psalm 66 (SAB & organ), 53 & Sonata (oboe & piano), 53, Harold Flammer; Sonata (violin & piano), perf by J L Weed & Lewis Hamvas, 58; Sonata (violoncello & piano), perf by Leona Marek & Lewis Hamvas, 63; I Have a Dream (Martin Luther King), comn & perf by SDak All State High Sch Orch & Chorus, 72; Three Piano Duets, comn by SDak Music Teachers Asn & Music Teachers Nat Asn, 82. *Teaching:* Instr music, Bard Col, 52-54; prof piano, Yankton Col, 54- *Mem:* SDak Music Teachers Asn (vpres, 75-79). *Publ:* Auth, Some Contemporary Teaching Pieces, 62 & If You Were the Judge, 80, Am Music Teacher. *Mailing Add:* 609 Douglas Yankton SD 57078

HAN, TONG-IL
PIANO, EDUCATOR
b Ham-Hung, Korea, Dec 4, 41; US citizen. *Study:* Juilliard Sch Music, BM, MM. *Rec Perf:* Chopin Piano Selections, 76, Chopin's 24 Preludes, Op 28, 78 & Piano Lessons with Tong-Il Han, 80, Philips, Korea. *Pos:* Conct pianist, New York Phil Orch, Chicago Phil Orch, London Phil Orch, Am Symph Orch, Cleveland Orch, Pittsburgh Symph Orch, Oslo Phil Orch and others. *Teaching:* Artist in res, Ind Univ, Bloomington, 69-71; prof music, Ill State Univ, 71-78 & NTex State Univ, 78- *Awards:* Biennial Michael's Found Award, 62; Int Leventritt Found Award, 65. *Mem:* Dallas Music Teachers Asn; Tex Music Teachers Asn; Music Teachers Nat Asn. *Rep:* Arthur Owen 142 Montague Mansions London W1H1LA England. *Mailing Add:* 7628 Mullrany Dr Dallas TX 75248

HANANI, YEHUDA
CELLO, EDUCATOR
Study: Juilliard Sch; Harvard Univ. *Pos:* Performer in North & South Am, Europe, Far East & Israel; participant in music festivals worldwide; mem, Seraphim Trio, currently; cond masterclasses & seminars at univs & conservatories worldwide. *Teaching:* Mem fac cello & chamber music, Peabody Consv Music, currently; adj lectr cello, Rutgers Univ, currently. *Awards:* Am-Israel Cult Found Scholar, 63; three Rockefeller Grants. *Mailing Add:* c/o Harold Shaw 1995 Broadway New York NY 10023

HANCOCK, EUGENE WILSON (WHITE)
EDUCATOR, ORGAN

b St Louis, Mo, Feb 17, 29. *Study:* Univ Detroit, BM, 51; Univ Mich, MM, 56, Sch Sacred Music, Union Theol Sem, SMD, 67. *Works:* A Palm Sunday Anthem, H W Gray, 71; Come Here, Lord, J Fischer & Brother, 73; A Babe Is Born, 75 & O Taste and See, 80, H W Gray; Jubilate (Psalm 100), Anglo-Am Music Publ, 82; Our Father, Augsburg Music Publ, 83; Psalm 23, Mar-Vel Publ, 83. *Rec Perf:* Music for Advent, Christmas and Epiphany, Rec Publ Co, 76; Favorite Hymns, William P Greenwood, 78; Praise the Lord, Alfred J Butler, 82. *Pos:* Asst organist & choirmaster, Cathedral St John the Divine, 63-66; organist & choirmaster, St Philip Episcopal Church, New York, 74-82. *Teaching:* Prof music, Bor Manhattan Community Col, 70- *Awards:* Advancement Musical Cult Award, David I Martin Br, Nat Asn Negro Musicians, 81. *Mem:* Am Guild Organists (nat counr, 77-82); Nat Asn Negro Musicians; Bohemians; ASCAP; Am Soc Univ Comp. *Mailing Add:* 257 Central Park W #10C New York NY 10024

HANCOCK, GERRE (EDWARD)
CONDUCTOR, ORGAN

b Lubbock, Tex, Feb 21, 34. *Study:* Univ Tex, Austin, BMus, 55; Univ Paris, France, dipl, 56; Sch Sacred Music, Union Theol Sem, New York, studied organ & improvisation with Boulanger, Langlais & Alain. *Works:* The Plumb Line and the City (cantata), Christ Church, Cincinnati, 67; Fantast on Divinum Mysterium for Organ, 74 & Go Ye Therefore (anthem), 75, Belwin-Mills Publ Corp; Organ Improvisations for Hymn Singing, Hinshaw Music, Inc, 75; Missa Resurrectionis, Oxford Univ Press, 75; Prelude and Fugue on Union Seminary, Belwin-Mills Publ Corp, 83. *Rec Perf:* The Plumb Line and the City (Hancock), 68 & Improvisation I (Hancock), 71, Audiocraft; Improvisation II (Hancock), Audiocraft, 75; Twentieth Century Anthems, 78, A Capella at Saint Thomas, 79, The Great Service (Byrd), 81 & Christmas at Saint Thomas, 82, Hessound. *Pos:* Asst organist, St Bartholomew's Church, New York, 60-62; organist & choirmaster, Christ Church, Cincinnati, 62-71; organist & master choristers, St Thomas Church, New York, 71- *Teaching:* Lectr organ & improvisation, Col Consv Music, Univ Cincinnati, 65-71; Juilliard Sch, 71-, Yale Univ, 74- *Awards:* Am Guild Organists Fel, 60; Royal Sch Church Music Fel, 82. *Bibliog:* Sing Joyfully (film), Peter Rosen, 75. *Mem:* Am Guild Organists (nat counr, 66-72); Founder, Asn Anglican Musicians (pres, 70-72). *Rep:* Murtagh McFarlane Artists Inc 3269 W 30th St Cleveland OH 44109. *Mailing Add:* 1 W 53rd St New York NY 10019

HANCOCK, JUDITH ECKERMAN
ORGAN, CONDUCTOR

b Milwaukee, Wis, Oct 18, 34. *Study:* Syracuse Univ, BMus, 56; Sch Sacred Music, Union Theol Sem, New York, 61. *Rec Perf:* Organs of New York, Vol I, 78, Twentieth Century Music, 78 & Christmas at St Thomas, 82, Hessound. *Pos:* Music dir, Watts St Baptist Church, Durham NC, 56-59; First Presby Church, Forest Hills, NY, 59-61, Church of the Redeemer, Cincinnati, 68-71 & St Thomas Church, New York, 71- *Mem:* Am Guild Organists. *Rep:* Murtagh McFarlane Artists Inc 3269 W 30th St Cleveland Ohio 44109. *Mailing Add:* 1 W 53rd St New York NY 10019

HAND, FREDERIC WARREN
GUITAR, COMPOSER

b Brooklyn, NY, Sept 15, 47. *Study:* Mannes Col Music, BM, 69; studied with Julian Bream, 71-72. *Works:* Homage (guitar), Franco Colombo-Belwin Mills, 71; Four Excursions for Guitar & Flute, Boosey & Hawkes, 71; Five Studies for Guitar, 79 & Baroque and On the Street, 81, G Schirmer; Trilogy (guitar), Theodore Presser Co, 83. *Rec Perf:* Miniatures for Flute and Guitar, Golden Crest Rec, 71; Jazzantiqua, Musical Heritage Soc & Music Masters Rec, 71; Baroque and On the Street, CBS Records, 82; Frederic Hand Plays the Music of Frederic Hand, Musical Heritage Soc & Music Masters Records, 83. *Pos:* Affil artist, State Arts Coun Ariz, Ala, Calif, Colo, NY & Wash, 74-82. *Teaching:* Guitar instr, Mannes Col Music, 72- *Awards:* Fulbright Scholar to England, 71-72. *Mem:* ASCAP. *Mailing Add:* 808 West End Ave New York NY 10025

HANDEL, DARRELL D
COMPOSER, EDUCATOR

b Lodi, Calif, Aug 23, 33. *Study:* Univ of Pac, BM, 56, MM, 57; Eastman Sch Music, PhD, 69. *Works:* Suzanne's Animal Music (harp), Ed Salabert, Paris, 73; Study of Two Pears (chorus), Lawson-Gould, 74; A Recitative for Guitar, Guitar Found Am, 76; The Candle a Saint (chorus), Gregg Smith Singers, 79; Chamber Concerto for Harp, Columbia Univ Press, 80; Acquainted with the Night (ms & orch), CCM Phil, 81. *Teaching:* Asst prof, Univ Kans, 66-71 & Univ SC, 71-76; assoc prof comp & theory, Univ Cincinnati, 76-; guest comp, Charles Ives Ctr Am Music, New Milford, Conn, 80. *Mem:* ASCAP; Am Soc Univ Comp; Am Music Ctr; Comp Forum. *Publ:* Auth, Britten's Use of the Passacaglia, Tempo, 70. *Mailing Add:* 198 Lafayette Circle Cincinnati OH 45220

HANGEN, BRUCE BOYER
CONDUCTOR & MUSIC DIRECTOR

b Pottstown, Pa, Feb 2, 47. *Study:* Eastman Sch Music, BMus, 70; Berkshire Music Ctr, 72 & 73. *Rec Perf:* Magic of Christmas, Bonnin Rec Studio, 81. *Pos:* Cond in res, Eastman Sch Music, 72-73; asst cond, Syracuse Symph Orch, 72-73; cond asst, Buffalo Phil Orch, 73; assoc cond, Denver Symph Orch, 73-79; music dir & cond, Portland Symph Orch, Maine, 76- *Awards:* Eleanor Crane Award, Berkshire Music Ctr, 72. *Rep:* Harold Shaw Conct Inc

1995 Broadway New York NY 10023. *Mailing Add:* 4 Catherine Dr Scarborough ME 04074

HANKLE, MARCIA GRIGLAK
FLUTE & PICCOLO

b Pittsburgh, Pa, Dec 10, 49. *Study:* Oberlin Consv, BM, 71; Duquesne Univ, MM, 72. *Pos:* Piccolo, Wheeling Symph, WVa, 72; second flute & piccolo, Nat Ballet Can Orch, 74-77; first flute, New York City Symph, 74; flutist, Galliard Quintet, 78- *Teaching:* Instr flute, Riverdale Sch Music, NY, 77-81. *Mem:* Am Fedn Musicians. *Mailing Add:* c/o Am Chamber Conct 890 West End Ave New York NY 10025

HANKS, THOMPSON W, JR
TUBA, EDUCATOR

b Beaumont, Tex, July 3, 41. *Study:* Lamar State Col Technol; Eastman Sch Music; studied tuba with Richard Burkhart, Donald Knaub & Arnold Jacobs. *Rec Perf:* Numerous with New York Brass Quintet. *Pos:* Solo tuba, San Antonio Symph, formerly, PR Symph, formerly, Minneapolis Symph, formerly, New York City Ballet, currently, Chautauqua Symph Orch, currently & New York Brass Quintet, currently; founding mem, New York Tuba Quartet; freelance tuba player. *Teaching:* Mem fac tuba, Manhattan Sch Music, 74-; mem fac tuba & chamber music, New England Consv Music, currently; instr brass, Yale Sch Music, currently. *Awards:* Donald Swann Award, Tanglewood, Mass, 64. *Mem:* Tubists Universal Brotherhood Asn. *Mailing Add:* New England Consv Music 290 Huntington Rd Boston MA 02115

HANLON, KENNETH M
EDUCATOR, COMPOSER

b Baltimore, Md, May 16, 41. *Study:* Univ Southern Calif, with Ramiro Cortes; Peabody Consv Music, with Louis Cheslock. *Works:* Suite for Doubles (woodwind soloist & jazz ens), perf by Ralph Gair & Stan Kenton Neophonic Orch, 70; Mourning Sound (baritone & piano), 71; Contemplations (clarinet & piano). *Teaching:* Fac mem, Peabody Prep Sch, 61-68; asst prof music & chmn dept, Univ Nev, 70- *Mailing Add:* Dept Music Univ Nev Las Vegas NV 89114

HANLON, KEVIN FRANCIS
COMPOSER

b South Bend, Ind, Jan 1, 53. *Study:* Ind Univ, South Bend, BMus(comp), 76; Eastman Sch Music, MMus(comp), 78; Univ Tex, DMA(comp), 83. *Works:* Symphony #1, Alexander Broude Inc, 82; String Trio, 82, Cumulus Nimbus, 82 & The Lullabye of My Sorrows (in prep), Adv Book Info. *Teaching:* Asst prof, Univ Ky, 82-83; vis lectr, Univ Ariz, 83- *Awards:* BMI Award, 78; ASCAP Award, 79; Koussevitzky Prize, Tanglewood Music Fest, 81. *Bibliog:* Lance Brunner (auth), Kevin Hanlon, New Grove Dict of Music & Musicians, 83. *Mem:* BMI; Am Comp Alliance; Am Soc Univ Comp. *Mailing Add:* 257 Lyndhurst Pl #8 Lexington KY 40508

HANLY, BRIAN VAUGHAN
VIOLIN, EDUCATOR

b Perth, Australia, Sept 3, 40. *Study:* Australian Music Examinations Bd, perf dipl, 60; Ind Univ, with Josef Gingold, 65-68. *Rec Perf:* Western Arts Trio, Vol I, 75 Vol 2, 77, Vol 3, 79, Vol 4, 81 & Vol 5, 83, Laurel Rec Co. *Pos:* Cond, Univ Wyo Chamber Orch, 73-; mem, Western Arts Trio, tours in US, Mex, South Am, Europe, Australia, 75- *Teaching:* Prof music, Univ Wyo, 73-; artist teacher violin, Interlochen Ctr Arts, Mich, 70-73. *Mailing Add:* Music Dept Univ Wyo Box 3037 Laramie WY 82071

HANNA, JAMES RAY
EDUCATOR, COMPOSER

b Siloam Springs, Ark, Oct 15, 22. *Study:* Northwestern Univ, with Karl Eschmann, BM, 48, with Robert Delaney & Anthony Donato, MM, 49; Ind Univ, with Willi Apel, Paul Nettl & Bernard Heiden. *Works:* Sostenuto for String Orch, Radio Luxembourg, 52; Song of the Redwood Tree, Robert King Music Co, 54; Trio for Flute, Clarinet & Bassoon, Jack Spratt Music Co, 56; Fugue & Chorale for Four Percussions, Music for Perc, 57; Elegy for Chamber Orchestra, Carl Fischer, 59; Symphony No 2, perf by La Coun Music & Perf Arts, 68. *Pos:* Sect violist, Lake Charles Symph, 58-65 & Baton Rouge Symph, 80-83. *Teaching:* Prof theory & comp, Univ Southwestern La, 49-83. *Mem:* Southeastern Comp League (secy, 56-58); Am Musicol Soc; Am Fedn Musicians; Int Viola-Forschungsgesellschaft; Col Music Soc. *Publ:* Auth, Arthur Honegger, In: Dict of Contemporary Music, E P Dutton, 74. *Mailing Add:* 523 W Taft St Lafayette LA 70503

HANNAY, ROGER DURHAM
COMPOSER

b Plattsburg, NY, Sept 22, 30. *Study:* Syracuse Univ, BMus, 52; Boston Univ, MMus, 53; Eastman Sch Music, PhD, 56. *Works:* Requiem, comn by Concordia Col, Moorhead, Minn, perf by Eastern Fest Phil, 73; Pied Piper (clarinet & tape), Seesaw Music Corp, 75; Symphony 3, comn by Nat Endowment Arts, 76; Symphony 4, comn by Kenan Found, 77; The Journey of Edith Wharton (opera), 82; Fantome (cello, viola & piano), C F Peters. *Teaching:* Assoc prof music, Concordia Col, Moorhead, Minn, 58-66; prof comp, Univ NC, Chapel Hill, 66- *Awards:* Nat Endowment Arts Comp Award, 76; Kenan Found Creative Res Award, 77; ASCAP Standard Music Awards, 80, 81 & 82. *Mem:* New York Comp Forum; Southeastern Comp League; Music Teachers Nat Asn; ASCAP. *Mailing Add:* 609 Morgan Creek Rd Chapel Hill NC 27514

HANNER, BARRY NEIL
BARITONE, EDUCATOR

b Stinesville, Ind, Feb 20, 36. *Study:* Curtis Inst Music, BM, 61. *Roles:* Almaviva in Il Barbiere di Siviglia, 64, Giorgio Germont in La Traviata, Jean Charles, Tony, Stolzius, Eisenstein in Die Fledermaus & Petrucchio in The Taming of the Shrew, Nürnberg Opera. *Pos:* Lyr bar, Badisches Staatstheater, 62-65 & Nürnberg Opera, 65- *Teaching:* Instr voice, Fach Akad Musik, 71- & dean, Opera Dept, 72- *Mailing Add:* Austrasse 16 8501 Burgthann Germany, Federal Republic of

HANNIGAN, BARRY T
PIANO

b Denver, Colo, Jan 11, 51. *Study:* Colo Col, BA, 73; Univ Colo, MMus, 75; Eastman Sch Music, DMA, 80. *Works:* Suite for Piano; Asagiri for Flute and Piano; Music for Organ; Sonata for Two Pianos; Meditations for Piano; Mojhcelevenhocc (large mixed chorus). *Rec Perf:* Sonata: By the Waters of Babylon, Opus One Rec, 82. *Teaching:* Adj prof music, Eastman Sch Music, Univ Colo, Colo Col & Nazareth Col, 73-78; asst prof, Bucknell Univ, 78- *Awards:* Ford Found Comp Grant, 72; Pa Coun Arts Grant, 81 & 82. *Mem:* Col Music Soc; Music Teachers Nat Asn; Pi Kappa Lambda. *Mailing Add:* 349 N 4th St Lewisburg PA 17837

HANNUM, HAROLD BYRON
EDUCATOR, ORGAN

b Cleveland, Ohio, Mar 23, 01. *Study:* Columbia Union Col, AB, 23; Peabody Consv, John Hopkins Univ, teachers cert, 26; Northwestern Univ, MMus, 35. *Teaching:* Instr music, Columbia Union Col, 24-29; prof music, Andrews Univ, 29-44; prof music & organist, Loma Linda Univ, 44-70. *Mem:* Hymn Soc Am; Am Soc Aesthet; Am Guild Organists. *Publ:* Auth, Music and Worship, 69 & Christian Search for Beauty, 75, Southern Publ Asn; Let the People Sing, Rev and Herald, 81. *Mailing Add:* 5073 Sierra Vista Riverside CA 92505

HANSELL, SVEN H
EDUCATOR, HARPSICHORD

b New York, NY. *Study:* Univ Pa, BA, 56; Harvard Univ, MA, 58; Univ Ill, Urbana, PhD, 66. *Teaching:* Instr, Univ Ill, Urbana, 63-68; asst prof, Univ Calif, Davis, 69-73; prof, Univ Iowa, 73- *Awards:* Martha Baird Rockefeller Grant, 65; Mellon Found Res Grant, 68; Penrose Grant, Am Philosophical Soc, 72. *Bibliog:* Interview, Tonfallet, Stockholm, 9/26/80. *Mem:* Am Musicol Soc (mem nat coun, 72-74); Int Musicol Soc; Sonneck Soc; Pi Kappa Lambda. *Interests:* Baroque music; 19th century American music. *Publ:* Auth, Works for Solo Voice of Johann Adolph Hane, Info Coordr, 68; several articles, In: New Grove Dict of Music & Musicians; Sacred Music at the Incurabili in Venice, J Am Musicol Soc, 70 & 72. *Mailing Add:* Sch Music Univ Iowa Iowa City IA 52242

HANSEN, EDWARD ALLEN
EDUCATOR, ORGAN

b Tacoma, Wash, Feb 21, 29. *Study:* Univ Wash, BA, 50, MA, 52, PhD, 65; Organ Inst, Mass, 51, 53, 57 & 58; Acad Ital Organ Music, Italy, 80; studied with Rene Saorgin, 78 & 80. *Pos:* Organist & choirmaster, Plymouth Congregational Church, Seattle, 57-; organist, Seattle Symph, 59-69. *Teaching:* Prof organ, music hist & cond, Univ Puget Sound, 69- *Mem:* Am Fedn Musicians; Am Asn Univ Prof; Am Guild Organists (nat pres, 81-). *Mailing Add:* Sch Music Univ Puget Sound Tacoma WA 98416

HANSEN, JAMES A
BASSOON, TEACHER

b Stafford Springs, Conn, Dec 7, 38. *Study:* Hartt Col Music, Univ Hartford, BA(music educ), 70; Butler Univ, MM(bassoon), 74. *Pos:* First bassoon, US Coast Guard Band, 59-63 & Halifax Symph Orch, 63-67; bassoon & clarinet, Charlottetown Summer Fest, Can, 65-78; second bassoon, Indianapolis Symph Orch, 67- *Teaching:* Instr bassoon & clarinet, Ind Cent Univ, 68- *Mailing Add:* Indianapolis Symph PO Box 88207 Indianapolis IN 46208

HANSEN, JAMES ROGER
VIOLIN

b Joliet, Ill, Sept 22, 08. *Study:* Cosmopolitan Sch Music, Chicago, BMus, 52; Chicago Consv Music, 55; Loyola Univ. *Pos:* Violinist, Kansas City Phil Orch, 35-42, Pittsburgh Symph Orch, 45-46 & Chicago Symph Orch, 46- *Teaching:* Mem fac, Chicago Consv Music. *Mem:* Chicago Fedn Musicians. *Mailing Add:* 2332 Bryant Ave Evanston IL 60201

HANSEN, PETER SIJER
EDUCATOR

b Hayward, Calif, Feb 5, 11. *Study:* Univ Calif, AB, 31; Univ Rochester, MMus, 35; Univ NC, PhD, 39. *Teaching:* Asst prof music hist & lit, Univ Tex, 40-42; chmn dept music, Stephens Col, 46-53; chmn dept music, Newcomb Col, Tulane Univ, 53-, prof in charge, Tulane-Newcomb Jr Yr Abroad, Paris, 62-63. *Awards:* Fulbright Fel, 51-52. *Mem:* Am Musicol Soc. *Interests:* Sixteenth century vocal forms; contemporary arts; 20th century opera. *Publ:* Auth, Introduction to Twentieth Century Music, 61, 2nd ed, 67, 3rd ed, 71, Allyn & Bacon. *Mailing Add:* 1331 Louisiana Ave New Orleans LA 70115

HANSEN, ROBERT HOWARD
STAGE DIRECTOR, BARITONE

b Lorain, Ohio, June 16, 51. *Study:* Northwestern Univ, BA, 73; Boston Univ, MMus, 76. *Roles:* Count Almaviva in Figaro, Boston Summer Opera Theatre,

78; Endymion in La Calisto, Boston Univ Opera Theatre, 78. *Pos:* Gen dir, Red River Lyric Theatre, 80- *Teaching:* Lectr voice, Keene State Col, 76-78; asst prof voice & music theatre, Midwestern State Univ, 78- *Mem:* Col Music Soc; Nat Asn Teachers Singing; Nat Opera Asn; Cent Opera Serv. *Mailing Add:* 2420 Fain St Wichita Falls TX 76308

HANSEN, TED (THEODORE C HANSEN)
COMPOSER, EDUCATOR

b Denver, Colo, Feb 5, 35. *Study:* Univ Colo, Boulder, BM, 64; Ariz State Univ, MM, 67; Univ Ariz, AMusD, 74. *Works:* Three Movements for Orch, 75, String Quartet #1, 75, Symphony #1, 76, Suite for Brass Quintet, 76, Montage for Violin and Piano, 77, Configuration for Piano, 80 & Contrasts for English Horn and Strings, 82, Seesaw Music Corp. *Teaching:* Asst prof music theory, Ariz State Univ, 67-74; assoc prof, Univ Tulsa, 75- *Mem:* ASCAP; Am Fedn Musicians. *Publ:* Auth, 20th Century Harmonic and Melodic Aural Perception, Univ Press Am, 82. *Mailing Add:* Pt Harbor Lake Keystone Box 132A Cleveland OK 74020

HANSHUMAKER, JAMES
WRITER, EDUCATOR

b Lima, Ohio, Apr 8, 31. *Study:* Ohio State Univ, BSc, 53, MA, 57, PhD, 61. *Pos:* Host & producer, The Lively Arts, PBS & CBS, formerly. *Teaching:* Prof music educ, Sch Music, Univ Southern Calif, 62-, assoc dir, 81- *Publ:* Auth, articles, monogr & text bks publ in US & abroad, Music Educr Nat Conf, Ind Musical Soc, Coun Res Music Educ & Alfred Publ Inc. *Mailing Add:* 521 N Mansfield Ave Los Angeles CA 90036

HANSLER, GEORGE EMIL
EDUCATOR, CONDUCTOR

b Minneapolis, Minn, Oct 27, 21. *Study:* Univ Wis, Milwaukee, BS, 43; Teachers Col, Columbia Univ, MA, 47; NY Univ, PhD, 57. *Teaching:* Head music dept, Dumont Pub Sch, NJ, 47-49; instr, Cent Conn State Col, 55-58; prof, Jersey City State Col, 58- *Mem:* Am Choral Dir Asn; Music Educr Nat Conf; Nat Asn Teachers Singing. *Mailing Add:* 2039 Kennedy Blvd Jersey City NJ 07305

HANSON, ERIC ALLEN
BARITONE

b Seattle, Wash, July 18, 54. *Study:* Univ Wash; study with Leon Lishner & Franco Iglesias. *Roles:* Melchior in Amahl and the Night Visitors, Seattle Opera Asn, 81; Dr Malatesta in Don Pasquale, Asolo Opera Co, 82; Figaro in Il Barbiere di Siviglia, Columbia Artists, 82 & Phil Maracay, 83. *Mailing Add:* c/o Warden Assoc Ltd 45 W 60th St #4K New York NY 10023

HANSON, JOHN R
EDUCATOR

b Jamestown, NY, Feb 14, 36. *Study:* Eastman Sch Music, BM, 58, MA, 60, PhD, 69. *Teaching:* Instr theory, Univ Kans, Lawrence, 60-64; asst prof, Carroll Col, 66-70 & Eastman Sch Music, 70-77; from asst to assoc prof, State Univ NY, Binghamton, 77- *Mem:* Founder, Music Theory Soc NY State (pres, currently); Col Music Soc; Soc Music Theory; Asn Develop Computer Based Instr Syst; Am Guild Organists. *Interests:* Dissonance in Palestrina. *Publ:* Auth, Music Fundamentals Workbook, Longman Inc, 79. *Mailing Add:* Music Dept State Univ NY Binghamton NY 13901

HANSON, RAYMOND
PIANO, EDUCATOR

Study: Northwestern Univ; DePaul Univ; studied with Walter Knupfer, Moshe Paranov & Harold Bauer. *Rec Perf:* On Telefunken-Decca, Heliodor & CRI. *Pos:* Soloist, Chicago Symph, Boston Pops, Hartford Symph & Berkshire Music Ctr; European tours; solo, duo-piano & chamber music perf in US, Can & Mex; mem, Hartt Trio. *Teaching:* Fac mem, Univ Conn, formerly; prof & chmn piano, Hartt Sch Music, 46- *Mailing Add:* Hartt Sch Music Univ Hartford West Hartford CT 06117

HARADA, KOICHIRO
EDUCATOR, VIOLIN

Study: Toho Sch Music, with Hideo Saito; Juilliard Sch, with Paul Mahanowizky, Ivan Galamian & Dorothy De Lay. *Pos:* First violinist & founder, Tokyo String Quartet, formerly; guest artist, Chamber Music Soc Lincoln Ctr, formerly; performer, Kennedy Ctr & Spoleto Fest, formerly; violinist, Kulas Choir, currently. *Teaching:* Fac mem, Aspen Sch Music; lectr violin, Yale Sch Music, currently; Kulas chair violin, Cleveland Inst Music, 81- *Mailing Add:* Cleveland Inst Music 11021 East Blvd Cleveland OH 44106

HARBISON, JOHN H
COMPOSER

b Orange, NJ, Dec 20, 38. *Study:* Harvard Col, BA, 60; Hochschüle Musik, Berlin; Princeton Univ, MFA, 63. *Works:* Elegiac Songs, 75, Diotima (orch), 77, Full Moon in March (opera), 79, Piano Concerto, 80 & Winter's Tale (opera), 80, Assoc Music Publ; Violin Concerto, Emmanuel Chamber Orch, 80; Mottetti di Montale (song cycle), Margun, 81. *Rec Perf:* Cantatas 100, 44 & 7 (Bach), 73 & Musikalische Exequien (Schütz), 73, Advent. *Pos:* Comp in res, Pittsburgh Symph Orch, 82-84; music dir, Cantata Singers, Cambridge, Mass, 69-74 & 79-82. *Teaching:* Comp in res, Reed Col, Portland, Ore, 68-69; prof music, Mass Inst Tech, Cambridge, 69-82. *Awards:* Am Inst Arts & Lett

Award, 71; Brandeis Univ Creative Arts Citation, 71; Kennedy Ctr-Friedheim Award, 80. *Bibliog:* Joan Peyser (auth), Harbison's Continuing Ascent, New York Times, 8/81; Michael Walsh (auth), Composer With a Hot Hand, Time, 8/81; Ellen Pfeiffer (auth), Musician of the Month, Musical Am, 3/82. *Rep:* Cooper-Grant 711 W End Ave 4DN New York NY. *Mailing Add:* 563 Franklin St Cambridge MA 02139

HARDER, PAUL
EDUCATOR, COMPOSER
b Indianapolis, Ind, Mar 10, 53. *Study:* Butler Univ, BM, 44; Eastman Sch Music, MM, 45; studied with Nadia Boulanger, 48; Royal Acad Music, Copenhagen, 51-52; Univ Iowa, with Philip Bezanson, PhD, 59. *Works:* Sinfonietta (orch), Univ Redlands, 59; Overture (orch), 62; A Wisp of Time (string orch), 64; The Pleasant Truth (orch), 72; Serenade (sop, clarinet, horn & strings); The Swallow (chorus); Serenade (orch). *Pos:* Mem, Rochester Phil Orch, 44-45 & Lansing Symph, 44-45. *Teaching:* Fac mem, Mich State Univ, 45-73; prof music & dean, Sch Arts & Humanities, Calif State Col, Stanislaus, 73-, acad dean, 76- *Publ:* Auth, Bridge to 20th Century Music, Boston, 73; Harmonic Materials in Tonal Music, 3rd ed, 76. *Mailing Add:* Dept Music Stanislaus State Col Turlock CA 95380

HARDIN, BURTON ERVIN
FRENCH HORN, COMPOSER
b Lincoln, Nebr, Aug 21, 36. *Study:* Univ Okla, BME, 56, DME, 68; Univ Wichita, MM, 64;. *Works:* Haunting Horns, Summy Birchard, 64; Old Main, Volkwein, 74; Rededication Overture, 76 & Fantiphonale, 79, comn by Eastern Ill Univ; Flights of Fancy (song cycle), 83 & Hornissimo (eight horns), 83, Israel Brass Publ. *Rec Perf:* Burt Hardin Plays It All, 76 & Horn with Voices, 79, Coronet. *Teaching:* Instrm, Wichita, Kans, 61-64; instr, Univ SC, 64-67; assoc prof, Clarion State Col, 68-69; prof horn, orch & rec technol, Eastern Ill Univ, 69- *Awards:* Comp Award, Sigma Alpha Iota, 68 & Am Sch Band Dirs Asn, 74. *Publ:* Auth, Brass Embouchure, Instrumentalist, 75; Unfinished Horn Compositions by Mozart, 79 & Komm, Süsser Tod, 79, Horn Call; Home-Built PZM Microphones, 82 & Build a Plate-Type Reverb, 82, Audio Amateur. *Mailing Add:* 824 Franklin Dr Charleston IL 61920

HARDISH, PATRICK MICHAEL
COMPOSER, LIBRARIAN
b Perth Amboy, NJ, Apr 6, 44. *Study:* Juilliard Sch, study orch with Jacob Druckman & comp with William Schimmel, 69-72; Pratt Inst, MS, 80; Columbia Univ, with Harvey Sollberger & Susan T Sommer, 78-81; private study with Otto Luening. *Works:* Accordioclusterville, comn & perf by William Schimmel, 77-78; Abstractions (chamber ens), comn by William Schimmel, 79; Do Not Go Gentle Into That Good Night (baritone voice & piano), perf by Richard Frisch & Max Lifchitz, 79; String Quartet No 1, North/South Ed, 80; Tremotrill (orch), comn by Queens Phil, 81; Duo Concertante (bassoon & piano), North/South Ed, 81; Entrance (chamber ens), perf by North/South Consonances, 82. *Pos:* Music libr asst, Columbia Univ, 82- *Awards:* Meet the Composer Award, NY State Coun Arts, 78, 82 & 83; fels, Bennington Col, 80 & Va Ctr Creative Arts, 81 & 82. *Mem:* Am Music Ctr; Music Libr Asn ; Nat Asn Comp; BMI; NJ Guild Comp. *Mailing Add:* 713 Lincoln Dr Perth Amboy NJ 08861

HARDISTY, DONALD MERTZ
EDUCATOR, COMPOSER
b Butte, Mont, Feb 24, 32. *Study:* Univ Mont, BME, 55, MME, 56; Eastman Sch Music, DMA, 69. *Works:* Six Graded Collections of Original and Transcribed Rounds Arranged for Bassoon Ensembles, Int Double Reed Soc, 76; Pisces of the Zodiac (woodwind quintet), 79 & Bassoon Episodes Fantastique (bassoon & piano), 80, Shawnee Press; Secrets of the Triple Crowing Bassoon Reed, Int Double Reed Soc, 80; A Trilogy of Songs for Clarinet, Bassoon and Piano, comn by NMex Music Teachers Asn, 82. *Pos:* Bassoonist, Univ Mont, 55, Tucson Symph, 58-61; Houston Symph, 63, Eastman Wind Ens, 67-69 & El Paso Symph, 73; prin bassoon, Las Cruces Symph Orch, 69- *Teaching:* Instr & assoc choral dir, Univ Ariz, 58-61; instr instrm music, Tucson pub sch, 62-63; assoc prof music, Houston Baptist Univ, 63-64; asst prof music & dir bands, Calif State Col, Chico, 64-67; grad asst ens & cond dept, Eastman Sch Music, 67-69; assoc prof, NMex State Univ, 69-78, grad adv music educ & chmn theory prog, 69-, prof & actg head music dept, 79- *Awards:* Comp of Year, NMex Music Teachers Asn, 82. *Mem:* Asn Conct Bands Am; ASCAP; NMex Music Educr Asn (pres, 79-83); Music Teachers Nat Asn; NMex Music Teachers Asn (vpres & pres elect, 82-). *Interests:* Construction of bassoon reeds; ear training. *Publ:* Auth, Global Mind Power for the American Music Teacher: An End to Musically Illiterate Musicians, Am Music Teachers J, 80; Be More Creative with Rounds, Sch Musician Dir & Teacher, 8-9/81 & 11/81; Make Your Bassoon Reeds Last Longer, Woodwind, Brass & Perc Mag, 1/82; Tuning Those Bassoons, Part 1, The Bocal, 2/82 & Part II, Tuning Individual Notes & Registers, 3/82, Instrumentalist Mag, ; Become a Better Musician: Use Global-Mind Power, Calif Music Educr Asn News, 2-3/82. *Mailing Add:* 3020 E Majestic Ridge Las Cruces NM 88001

HARDWICK, CHARLES T
VIOLIN, TEACHER & COACH
b Bellingham, Wash, Feb 3, 37. *Study:* Eastman Sch Music, perf cert, BM, 59, MM, 61; violin studies with Joseph Knitzer. *Pos:* Asst prin second & first, Rochester Phil, 59-61; first violin sect, Pittsburgh Symph Orch, 61-, Chautauqua Symph, 62-68 & Grand Teton Music Fest, Jackson, Wyo, 80-82.

Teaching: Instr & coach chamber music, Glassboro State Col Summer Music Camp, 74-77; instr violin, Carnegie Mellon Univ, 76-77. *Mem:* Am Fedn Musicians. *Mailing Add:* 1317 Denisonview St Pittsburgh PA 15205

HARE, ROBERT YATES
EDUCATOR, CONDUCTOR
b McGrann, Pa, June 14, 21. *Study:* Univ Detroit, MusB, 48; Wayne State Univ, MA, 50; Univ Iowa, PhD, 59. *Pos:* French hornist, Pittsburgh Symph Orch, 41-43 & 44-45, Buffalo Phil, 43-44, Cincinnati Summer Opera Co, 45 & Indianapolis Symph Orch, 45-46; French hornist, San Antonio Symph Orch, 47-49, orchestrator, 47-49; cond, San Jose Youth Symph, 57-59; trustee, Columbus Symph Orch, 75-79. *Teaching:* Instr, Marietta Col, Ohio, 49-51 & Del Mar Col, 51-55; prof & chmn grad studies, San Jose State Univ, 56-65, cond symph band, 56-63; prof & dean music, Eastern Ill Univ, 65-74, cond univ symph, 68-74; prof music, Ohio State Univ, 74-, dir, Sch Music, 74-78; coordr audio-rec engineering, 79-82, arts admin res officer, 82- *Awards:* Professional Promise Scholar, Carnegie Inst Tech, 39. *Mem:* Music Educr Nat Conf; Music Teachers Nat Asn; Am Musicol Soc; Col Music Soc; Phi Mu Alpha Sinfonia. *Publ:* Contribr, Connchord, Instrumentalist & Ill J Music. *Mailing Add:* 2494 Farleigh Rd Columbus OH 43221

HARGER, GARY
TENOR
b New Haven, Conn. *Study:* Ithaca Col, BA(drama & speech), 73. *Rec Perf:* Shenandoah, Columbia Red Seal, 75; Wozzeck, 81 & Lady Macbeth of Mtsensk, 81, nat broadcast San Francisco Opera. *Roles:* Corporal in Shenandoah, Broadway, 75; Village Drunk in Lady Macbeth of Mtsensk, 81 & Andres in Wozzeck, 81, San Francisco Opera; Nemorino in L'Elisir d'Amore, Western Opera Theater, 81; Almaviva in The Barber of Seville, Chautauqua Opera, 82 & Tex Opera Theater, 83; Robin Hood in The Adventures of Friar Tuck, Lake George Opera, 83. *Pos:* Singer, Shenandoah, 75-77, Chautauqua Opera, 79-82, San Francisco Opera, 81 & Lake George Opera. *Mem:* Actors Equity Asn; Am Guild Musical Artists. *Rep:* Sara Tomay Mgt 127 W 72nd St New York NY 10025. *Mailing Add:* 250 Old Tavern Rd Orange CT 06477

HARITUN, ROSALIE ANN
EDUCATOR, CLARINET
b Johnson City, NY, May 30, 38. *Study:* Baldwin-Wallace Consv Music, BME, 60; Univ Ill, Champaign-Urbana, studied with Charles Leonhard, MS, 61; Teachers Col, Columbia Univ, 66, studied with Gladys Tipton, EdD, 68, studied behavioral modification techn with Douglas Greer, 71. *Teaching:* Instrm music & band, Patchogue Elem Sch, 61-63; band dir, Patchogue Jr High Sch, 63-56; teaching asst music educ, Teachers Col, Columbia Univ, 66-68; instr, Sch Music, Temple Univ, 68-71; instr instrm music, New York bd educ, 71-72; assoc prof music educ & clarinet, Sch Music, ECarolina Univ, 72- *Mem:* Nat & Int Music Soc; Col Music Soc; Music Educr Nat Conf; NC Music Educr Asn; Pi Kappa Lambda. *Publ:* Coauth, Sequential Approach to Behavioral Objectives in Music, 74 & Television for Developing Teaching Skills, 75, NC Music Educr J; auth, Basic Teaching Skills for Beginning Music Teachers, 77 & Daily Teaching Routines: Red-Tape or Reality, 83, Sch Musicians. *Mailing Add:* 206 N Oak St Apt 8 Greenville NC 27834

HARKNESS, REBEKAH
COMPOSER, ADMINISTRATOR
b St Louis, Mo, Apr 17, 15. *Study:* Mannes Col Music, with Fred Werle; Fontainebleau, with Nadia Boulanger; Dalcroze Sch; studied orch with Lee Hoiby; Franklin Pierce Col, Hon DFA, 68; Lycoming Col, Hon DH, 70. *Works:* Mediteranean Suite (orch), 57; Journey to Love (ballet), 58; Musical Chairs (orch), 58; Gift to the Magi (orch), 59; Letters to Japan (orch), 61; Macumba (suite), 65; Elements (orch), 65. *Pos:* Founder & pres, Rebekah Harkness Found, 59-; founder & pres, Harkness Ballet Co, 64-, artistic dir, 70-; established Harkness House for Ballet Arts, 65. *Awards:* Handel Award, 67; Shield Award Am Indian & Eskimo Cult Found, 67; Ann Award Ballet Des Jeunes, 75. *Mem:* Trustee, John F Kennedy Ctr Perf Arts. *Mailing Add:* 4 E 75th St New York NY 10021

HARLAN, CHRISTOPH
EDUCATOR, GUITAR
b Dreilingen, WGermany, Mar 30, 52. *Study:* Akad Musik, Vienna, Austria, teaching cert, 72, perf dipl(class guitar), 73; studied with N Yepes, Oscar Ghiglia, A Diaz & L Brouwer. *Rec Perf:* Solo Works for Guitar, Hempfield Rec, 81; Classical Guitar Chamber Music, Vol I & II, Class Cutter Rec, 82. *Pos:* Solo guitarist, currently. *Teaching:* Dept chmn guitar, Cleveland Inst Music, 78-; asst prof guitar, Kent State Uinv, 78- *Mem:* Guitar Found Am; Am String Teachers Asn; Cleveland Baroque Soloists; Am Fedn Musicians. *Publ:* Auth, Training of the Mind, Am String Teacher, winter 78; Guitar Sings, Cleveland Inst Music Newslett, 2/81. *Mailing Add:* 2713 Lancashire Rd #8 Cleveland Heights OH 44106

HARLEY, J ROBERT
TRUMPET
b Jersey City, NJ, Feb 2, 45. *Study:* Juilliard Sch Music, trumpet with Edward Treutel, BS, 68; Manhattan Sch Music, MM, 71. *Pos:* Bandsman & soloist, Cities Serv World's Fair Band Am, 64-65; first trumpet, NJ Symph, 65-72 & NJ State Opera, 70- *Mem:* Am Fedn Musicians; Chamber Music Soc. *Mailing Add:* 26 E Hunter Ave Maywood NJ 07607

HARLING, JEAN M
FLUTE, EDUCATOR
b Detroit, Mich, July 27, 23. *Study:* Wayne State Univ, BS; studied with John Wummer. *Pos:* Flautist, Buffalo Phil, 46-48 & Honolulu Symph, 58- *Teaching:* Instr flute, Punahau Music Sch, 58-63; lectr, Univ Hawaii, 63- *Mem:* Nat Flute Asn; Ens Players Guild; Mu Phi Epsilon. *Mailing Add:* 11 Aimikana St Kailua HI 96734

HARLOW, RICHARD ERNEST
CELLO
b Detroit, Mich, Nov 11, 54. *Study:* Univ Mich, BMus, 76. *Pos:* Cellist, Flint Symph Orch, 72-73 & Philadelphia Orch, 76-; asst prin cellist, Toledo Symph Orch, 73-76. *Mailing Add:* Philadelphia Orch 1420 Locust St Philadelphia PA 19102

HARMAN, DAVID REX
CLARINET, CONDUCTOR
b Redding, Calif, Nov 9, 48. *Study:* Calif State Univ, Sacramento, BA, 70, MA, 71; studied with Ulysse Delecluse, 71-72; Eastman Sch Music, DMA(clarinet), 74. *Rec Perf:* Berg Kammerkonzert, Musical Heritage, 76; Solo Recitalist Series, Crystal Rec, 82. *Teaching:* Assoc prof music, Colo State Univ, 74-81 & Univ Conn, 81- *Awards:* French Govt Scholar, 71-72. *Mem:* Col Music Soc; Clarinetwork; Am Fedn Musicians. *Publ:* Auth, The Musical Language of Carl Ruggles, Am Music Teacher, 76; The Poetic Sources for Schubert's Der Hirt auf dem Felsen, Woodwind World, 78. *Mailing Add:* 353 Warrenville Rd Mansfield Center CT 06250

HARMON, ROGER DEAN
LUTE, EDUCATOR
b Stuttgart, West Germany, Apr 4, 53; US citizen. *Study:* State Univ NY, BM, 74 & MA, 75. *Pos:* Dir, Baltimore Consort, 77-82. *Teaching:* Instr lute, Peabody Inst, Johns Hopkins Univ, 78- *Interests:* Renaissance repertories for lute solo, lute ensemble and consort. *Publ:* Auth, The Repertories of the Lute, Vihuela, and Guitar, 1507-1780, 77 & Exercises and Graded Repertory in Italian, German and French Tablature, 78, Follett; coauth, A Medieval Songbook, Univ Va Press, 82. *Mailing Add:* 34 Elsmere Ave Delmar NY 12054

HARMON, THOMAS FREDRIC
ORGAN, EDUCATOR
b Springfield, Ill, Feb 28, 39. *Study:* Wash Univ, AB, 61, PhD, 71; Stanford Univ, MA, 63. *Rec Perf:* Festival of Early Latin American Music, Eldorado, 75; Three Centuries of American Organ Music, Orion, 76; Latin American Musical Treasures, Eldorado, 77; Harris Conducts Harris, Varese Sarabande, 79; Two American Contemporaries: Four Premieres, Protone, 79; Survey of Interpretation, Am Guild Organists Educ Materials, 80. *Pos:* Organist, First United Methodist Church, Santa Monica, 72- *Teaching:* Prof & organist, Univ Calif, Los Angeles, 68-, chmn, Dept Music, 83- *Mem:* Am Guild Organists (dean Los Angeles chap, 74-76); Organ Hist Soc; Am Musicol Soc. *Interests:* Organ music of J S Bach; performance practice of music of the 17th, 18th and 19th centuries. *Publ:* Auth, The Performance of Mozart's Church Sonatas, Music & Lett, 70; Performance and the Affektenlehre in Bach's Orgelbuechlein, Diapason, 72 & 73; The Muehlhausen Organ Revisited, Bach, 73; The Registration of J S Bach's Organ Works, Frits Knuf, 78; Gottfried Silbermann: the French Connection ..., McGill Univ, 81. *Mailing Add:* 15945 Miami Way Pacific Palisades CA 90272

HARNED, SHIRLEY (LEE)
MEZZO-SOPRANO
b West Point, Ky. *Study:* Studied with Josephine Cunningham, 63-66 & 69-73; Univ Wash, with Leon Lishner, 66-69. *Roles:* Wellgunde & Siegrune in Der Ring des Nibelungen, Pac Northwest Wagner Fest, 75-83; Nicklausse in The Tales of Hoffmann, Seattle Opera, 80; Lady Macbeth in Macbeth, Mexico City Opera, 82; Azucena in Il Trovatore, 82, Santuzza in Cavalleria rusticana, 83, Seattle Opera; Prince Orlovsky in Die Fledermaus, Portland Opera, 83. *Mem:* Am Guild Musical Artists; Actors Equity Asn; Nat Opera Asn. *Mailing Add:* 3807 12th St W #1 Seattle WA 98119

HARNESS, WILLIAM EDWARD
TENOR
b Pendleton, Ore, Nov 26, 40. *Study:* San Francisco Merola Opera, 72 & 73; Seattle Opera, one yr; studied voice with Mary Curtis Verna & opera coaching with Otto Guth, Luigi Ricci & Robert DeCeunynck. *Roles:* Communicant & tenor arias in St Matthew Passion, San Francisco Spring Opera, 73; Tonio in La Fille du regiment; Ferrando in Cosi fan tutte; Rodolfo in La Boheme; Rinuccio in Gianni Schicchi; Pinkerton in Madama Butterfly; Faust in Faust. *Pos:* Tenor, San Francisco Opera Co, 73, New York City Opera, 76, Metropolitan Opera, 77, Hamburg Opera, 78, Boston, Ft Worth, Houston, Memphis, Seattle & San Francisco Spring Operas; recitalist & performer, Vancouver Orch, BC, Seattle Orch, Los Angeles Phil, San Francisco Orch, Minn Symph Orch & Milwaukee Symph Orch; sacred conct artist, 78- *Awards:* Enrico Caruso Award, 73; Nat Opera Inst Fel, 73-74; Martha Baird Rockefeller Grant, 74-76. *Mem:* Am Guild Musical Artists; Can Actors Equity. *Rep:* Columbia Artists Mgt 165 W 57th St New York NY 10019. *Mailing Add:* 2132 W 235th Pl Torrance CA 90501

HARNISCH, LARRY (LAWRENCE MYRLAND)
CRITIC-WRITER
b Chicago, Ill, 51. *Study:* Univ Ariz, BMus, 71. *Pos:* Music critic & feature writer, Ariz Daily Star, Tucson, 81- *Mem:* Music Critics Asn. *Mailing Add:* PO Box 26807 Tucson AZ 85726

HARPER, ANDREW HENRY
ADMINISTRATOR, MUSIC DIRECTOR
b Charlotte, NC, June 12, 35. *Study:* Furman Univ, BA(music), 57; Fla State Univ, MM, 62; Ind Univ, PhD, 67. *Pos:* Musical dir, Ft Wayne Civic Theater, 72-77; chorusmaster, Ft Wayne Phil, 72-77. *Teaching:* Chmn & assoc prof, Dept Music, Tenn Wesleyan Col & Div Music, Ind Univ, Ft Wayne, 67-77; chmn & prof, Dept Music, Okla State Univ, 77-82 & Dept Music, Univ SAla, 82- *Awards:* Fel, Southern Fel Fund, 58-62; Fac Travel Grant to Hungary, Ind Univ, 68 & 73; Outstanding Teacher Award, Ind Univ, Ft Wayne, 70. *Mem:* Music Educr Nat Conf; Int Soc Music Educ. *Publ:* Auth, Education Through Music, Phi Delta Kappan, 73; Music in Film, Okla State Univ Filmathon Proc, 80; A New Facet in the Education of Professional Musicians, Sibelius Acad, Helsinki, 83. *Mailing Add:* 2908 Crown Colony Ct Mobile AL 36619

HARPER, HEATHER MARY
SOPRANO
b Belfast, Ireland, May 8, 30. *Study:* Trinity Col Music, London; studied with Frederic Husler, Helene Isepp & Frederic Jackson; Queen's Univ, Hon DMus. *Rec Perf:* Symphony No 8 (Mahler); Symphony No 9 (Beethoven); Requiem (Verdi); Don Giovanni (Mozart); Le Nozze de Figaro (Mozart); Missa Solemnis (Beethoven); Seven Early Songs (Berg); rec on EMI, Decca, Philips & CBS. *Roles:* Britten's War Requiem, Coventry Cathedral, 62; Ariadne in Ariadne auf Naxos; Chrysothemis in Elektra; Marschallin in Der Rosenkavalier; Ellen Orford in Peter Grimes; Arabella in Arabella; Kaiserin in Frau ohne Schatten. *Pos:* Toured with BBC Symph Orch, US, 65 & USSR, 67; recital tour, Australia, 65; ann concert & opera tours, US, 67- & worldwide; perf with maj opera co incl Covent Garden, Deutsche Oper, Teatro Colon, Metropolitan Opera, San Francisco Opera & La Scala. *Awards:* Edison Award, 71; Grammy, 79. *Mailing Add:* c/o ICM Artists 40 W 57th St New York NY 10019

HARPHAM, VIRGINIA RUTH
VIOLIN
b Huntington, Ind, Dec 10, 17. *Study:* Morehead State Univ, AB, 39. *Pos:* Violinist, Nat Symph Orch, Washington, 56-, prin second violin sect, 64-; mem, Lywen String Quartet, 60-69 & Nat Symph String Quartet, 73- *Mailing Add:* 3816 Military Rd NW Washington DC 20015

HARREL, (JOHN) RALPH
EDUCATOR, PIANO
b Pratt, Kans, March 16, 18. *Study:* Bethany Col, Kans, BMus, 39; Juilliard Sch Music, dipl, 48; Teachers Col, Columbia Univ, EdD, 60. *Pos:* Cond, Bethany Oratorio Soc, Kans, 48-51. *Teaching:* Prof piano & choir, Bethany Col, Kans, 48-51; prof piano & chmn music dept, Morningside Col, 60-68; prof piano, SW Tex State Univ, 68-, chmn music dept, 68-71, dean Sch Creative Arts, 71- *Mem:* Int Coun Fine Arts Deans; Tex Coun Arts Educ. *Mailing Add:* 216 W Mimosa Circle San Marcos TX 78666

HARRELL, LYNN
CELLO
b New York, NY, Jan 30, 44. *Study:* Juilliard Sch, with Leonard Rose & Lev Aronson; Curtis Inst, with Orlando Cole. *Rec Perf:* Tchaikovsky piano trio in A minor, op 50, Beethoven Archduke trio & trio no 7 in B flat & Haydn cello concertos no 1 in C major & no 2 in D major, EMI/Angel; Brahms double concerto for violin and cello, CBS Masterworks; Brahms Sonatas for cello and piano no 1 in E minor op 38, no 2 in F major, op 99, Elgar cello concerto Tchaikovsky Rococo Variations & Pezzo Capriccioso & Schumann cello concerto in A minor, op 129, Saint-Saens cello concerto no 1 in A minor, op 33, London/Decca. *Pos:* Cellist, with major orchestras including New York, Chicago, Philadelphia, Cleveland, Los Angeles, London, Berlin, Vienna, Paris & Israel; cellist, Cleveland Orch, 62-64, prin cellist, 64-71. *Teaching:* Prof cello, Juilliard Sch Music, 77- *Awards:* Grammy for Tchaikovsky Trio; Avery Fisher Prize; Merriweather Post Award. *Mailing Add:* c/o Columbia Artists 165 W 57th St New York NY 10019

HARRINGTON, DAVID
VIOLIN
b Portland, Ore, Sept 9, 49. *Study:* Univ Wash, with Emanuel Zetlin & Veda Reynolds. *Pos:* First violin, Kronos String Quartet, 73- *Bibliog:* Paul Hertelendy (auth), The Kronos Quartet: Displaying a California Style, Musical Am, 10/80; Wolfgang Schreiber (auth), Die Entdeckerlust, Suddeutsche Zeitung, 3/13-14/83; Tom O'Connor (auth), String Fever, Focus Mag, 4/83. *Mailing Add:* Kronos Quartet 1238-Ninth Ave San Francisco CA 94122

HARRIS, ALAN
EDUCATOR, CELLO
Study: Univ Kans, BM; Ind Univ, MM & perf cert. *Rec Perf:* On Vox. *Pos:* Mem, Heritage Quartet, currently; solo & chamber music performer. *Teaching:* Mem fac, Eastman Sch Music, formerly, Ohio Wesleyan Univ, formerly, Inter-Am Univ, PR, formerly & Aspen Music Fest, 74-; Mem fac string ens & cello, Cleveland Inst Music, 76- *Mailing Add:* Cleveland Inst Music 11021 East Blvd Cleveland OH 44106

HARRIS, C DAVID
HARPSICHORD, EDUCATOR
b Minneapolis, Minn, Jan 6, 39. *Study:* Northwestern Univ, BM, 60, MM, 61; Univ Mich, PhD, 67; Hochschule Musik Vienna, Univ Vienna. *Teaching:* Prof music hist & harpsichord, Drake Univ, 65- *Interests:* Baroque keyboard music and chamber music. *Publ:* Auth, Viennese Keyboard Music at Mid-Baroque, 69 & Fourth International Harpsichord Festival, Rome, 72, The Dispason;

Problems in Editing Harpsichord Music, In: Notations and Editions, William C Brown, 74; Fifth International Harpsichord Week, Music, 78; Sixth International Harpsichord Week, Am Organist, 80. *Mailing Add:* 3116 Vine St West Des Moines IA 50265

HARRIS, CARL GORDON, JR
EDUCATOR, MUSIC DIRECTOR
b Fayette, Mo, Jan 14, 35. *Study:* Philander Smith Col, AB, 56; Univ Mo, Columbia, AM 64; Consv Music, Univ Mo, Kansas City, DMA, 72. *Teaching:* Dir choirs, Philander Smith Col, 59-71; prof music, chmn dept & dir choirs, Va State Univ, 68- *Mem:* Phi Mu Alpha Sinfonia; Am Guild Organists (subdean southside Va chap, 80-84); Am Choral Dir Asn; Choristers Guild (mem bd dir, 81-84). *Publ:* Auth, The Negro Spiritual: Stylistic Development Through Performance Practices, 73; Three Schools of Black Choral Composers and Arrangers, 74 & The Unique World of Undine Smith Moore: Teacher-Composer-Arranger, 76, Choral J; Le Negro-Spiritual: Le Development de son Style par le Concert, Coeur Joie Chant Choral, 77. *Mailing Add:* 4530 W River Rd Ettrick VA 23803

HARRIS, DANIEL ALFRED
TEACHER, BARITONE
b Dayton, Ohio, May 19, 03. *Study:* Otterbein Col, BA & dipl(voice), 23; private study in New York, 25-27 & Italy, France & Belgium, 27-35. *Roles:* Ali in Marouf, Cincinnati Summer Opera, 36-39, St Louis Opera, 37, Chicago City Opera, 38 & Metropolitan Opera, 38; over 75 baritone roles in Italy, France, Belgium, Caracas, Chicago, St Louis & Cincinnati. *Pos:* Mem, Metropolitan Opera, 37-39; dir opera theater, Consv Music, Oberlin Col, 50-69; Am specialist vocal music, Int Educ Serv, Seoul, Korea, 58; mem, Nat Adv Comn, Nat Cult Ctr (later Kennedy Ctr), 59; soloist, with New York Phil, Boston Symph & Nat Orch Asn. *Teaching:* Instr voice & opera, La State Univ, 39-40; from asst prof to prof voice, Consv Music, Oberlin Col, 40-69; prof, Sch Music, Univ Miami, Fla, 69-76; teacher voice & repertoire, privately, Coral Gables, Fla, 76- *Mem:* Nat Opera Asn (first vpres, 55-56, pres, 57-58); Nat Asn Teachers Singing. *Publ:* Coauth, Word by Word Translations of Songs and Arias, Part II—Italian, Scarecrow Press Inc, 72. *Mailing Add:* 5840 SW 48th St Miami FL 33155

HARRIS, DONALD
COMPOSER, ADMINISTRATOR
b St Paul, Minn, Apr 7, 31. *Study:* Univ Mich, with Ross Lee Finney, BMus, 52, MMus, 54; studied with Max Deutsch, Nadia Boulanger & Andre Jolivet; Berkshire Music Ctr, with Boris Blacher & Lukas Foss. *Works:* Ludus II (flute, clarinet, violin, cello & piano), 73; On Variations (chamber orch), 76; Charmes (sop & orch), 77; For the Night to Wear (ms & seven instrm), 78; Balladen (solo piano), 79; Of Hartford in a Purple Light (sop & piano), 79; Prelude to Concert in Connecticut, 81. *Rec Perf:* On CRI, Delos & Golden Crest Rec. *Pos:* Music consult, Am Cult Ctr, US Info Serv, 65-67; asst to pres acad affairs, New England Consv Music, 67-71, vpres, 71-74, exec vpres, 74-77. *Teaching:* Lectr, Schoenberg Inst, 74; comp in res, Hartt Sch Music, 77-, chmn dept comp & theory, 77-80, dean, 80- *Awards:* Comn, Cleveland Orch, 76, Elizabeth Sprague Coolidge Found, 77 & Koussevitzky Music Found, 77. *Mem:* League Int Soc Contemp Music; ASCAP; Am Soc Univ Comp; Int Alban Berg Soc; Conn Comn Arts. *Interests:* Alban Berg; Berg-Schoenberg correspondence; musicology. *Mailing Add:* 20 Ironwood Rd West Hartford CT 06117

HARRIS, JOHANA
PIANO, TEACHER
b Ottawa, Can, Jan 1, 13. *Study:* Can Consv Music; Juilliard Grad Sch; Hochschule, Berlin. *Rec Perf:* Exotic & Dance Music (Debussy), 55, Water & Nature Music (Debussy), 55, Fantasy for Piano & Orchestra (Harris), 56, Abraham Lincoln Walks at Midnight (Harris), 56 & Quintet for Piano & Strings (Harris), 57, MGM; Concerto for Amplified Piano, Brass, String Basses & Percussion (Harris), 80 & Concerto for Piano & Strings, 81 (Harris), Varese-Serabande. *Teaching:* Fac mem, Juilliard Sch, 28-33, Univ of South Sewanee, 48-51 & Rolland Int Wkshp, 77-; prof piano, Calif Inst Arts, 64-69 & Cornell Univ; lectr, Univ Calif, Los Angeles, 69- *Bibliog:* Roy Harris: An American Voice (TV doc), BBC, 81. *Interests:* American folk songs in Library of Congress. *Publ:* Contribr, Music Round About Us, 56, Music Round the Clock, 56, Voices of America, 57 & Discovering Music Together, 58, Follett. *Mailing Add:* 1200 Tellem Dr Pacific Palisades CA 90272

HARRIS, ROBERT A
PIANO, EDUCATOR
b Rich Hill, Mo. *Study:* Pittsburg State Univ, BMus, 50, BSEd, 53; Aspen Music Sch, studied piano with Rosina Lhevinne, 58 & 65-70. *Pos:* Dir music, United Methodist Church, 65- *Teaching:* Prof choral music, Col Our Lady of the Ozarks, 49-58; prof piano, organ & music hist, Mo Southern State Col, 72- *Mem:* Am Music Scholar Asn; Music Teachers Nat Asn; Fel United Methodist Musicians; Nat Fedn Music Clubs; Nat Fedn Jr Music Clubs. *Mailing Add:* 1344 S Main Carthage MO 64836

HARRIS, ROBERT ALLEN
EDUCATOR, COMPOSER
b Detroit, Mich, Jan 9, 38. *Study:* Wayne State Univ, with Ruth Wylie, BS, 60, MA, 62; Eastman Sch Music, with Bernard Rogers, 63-65; Mich State Univ, with H Owen Reed, PhD, 71. *Works:* Adagio (string orch), 66; Five Bagatelles (flute, clarinet & bassoon), 68; Benedictus (womens voices), 68; Psalms (sop, horn & piano), 68; Moods, 69; Caligula (incidental music), 70; Requiem: A Canticle of Immortality (two soloists, chamber choir, chorus & orch), 70-71. *Pos:* Choirmaster & dir music, Trinity Church North Shore,

Wilmette, Ill, 77. *Teaching:* Music, Detroit pub sch, 60-64; asst prof, Wayne State Univ, 64-70; from assoc prof to prof, Mich State Univ, 70-77; prof cond & choral orgn, Northwestern Univ, 77- *Awards:* Rockefeller Found Grant, 71 & 72. *Mem:* Am Choral Cond Asn; Music Educr Nat Conf; ASCAP; Pi Kappa Lambda; Phi Mu Alpha. *Mailing Add:* Sch Music Northwestern Univ Evanston IL 60201

HARRIS, RUTH BERMAN See Berman, Ruth

HARRISON, E EARNEST
OBOE, EDUCATOR
b Moberly, Mo, July 13, 18. *Study:* Eastman Sch Music, BM(oboe perf) 42, MM(lit & perf), 46; private instr with John Minsker, 48-54. *Rec Perf:* Adventure in Music Series, RCA, 58-60. *Pos:* Oboist, Rochester Phil, 39-42 & 45-46; solo oboist, Houston Symph, 46-48, San Antonio Symph, 48-51, Nat Symph, 51-66. *Teaching:* Prof oboe perf, Univ Houston, 46-48, Trinity Univ, 48-51, Catholic Univ, Howard Univ, George Washington Univ, Am Univ & Peabody Consv Music, 51-66; prof music, Univ Ky, 61-62 & La State Univ, 66- *Mem:* Music Educr Nat Conf; Nat Asn Col Wind & Perc Instr; Int Double Reed Soc. *Publ:* Ed, Sonata in A Major, Southern Music, 71; auth, The Story of the Oboe and English Horn, 73 & contribr, Woodwind World: Brass and Percussion, Swift-Dorr. *Mailing Add:* 2053 Tamarix St Baton Rouge LA 70808

HARRISON, LOU
COMPOSER, EDUCATOR
b Portland, Ore, May 14, 17. *Study:* San Francisco State Univ, with Henry Cowell & Arnold Schoenberg. *Works:* Third Symphony, 37-82 & Double Music, 41; C F Peters; Elegiac Symphony, 41-75, Rapunzel, 54, At the Tomb of Charles Ives, 64, String Quartet Set, 78-79 & Solstice, Peer Int. *Pos:* Music critic, New York Herald Tribune, 43-47. *Teaching:* Prof comp & world music, Mills Col, 36-39 & 80-, Black Mountain Col, 48-49 & San Jose State Univ, 67-80. *Awards:* Guggenheim Fel, 52 & 54; Fromm Award, 55; grant, Rockefeller Found, 67-80. *Mem:* Am Acad Arts & Lett; BMI. *Mailing Add:* 7121 Viewpoint Rd Aptos CA 95003

HARRISS, ELAINE ATKINS
FLUTE, PIANO
b Springfield, Tenn, Oct 20, 45. *Study:* Sch Music, George Peabody Col Teachers, BME, 66, MME, 67, EdS, 68; Univ Mich, Ann Arbor, PhD, 81. *Pos:* Freelance accmp, Martin, Tenn, 68-; prin flutist, Jackson Symph, Tenn, 71-; flutist, Univ Trio, Univ Tenn, 73- *Teaching:* Private piano & flute, 68- *Mem:* Music Educr Nat Conf; Music Teachers Nat Asn (secy-treas WTenn, 78-79); Nat Flute Asn; Sigma Alpha Iota (vpres Rho province, 71-74 & 75-78); Nat Guild Piano Teachers. *Mailing Add:* Rte 4 Box 191 Martin TN 38237

HARRISS, ERNEST CHARLES
EDUCATOR, WRITER
b Sebring, Fla, Sept 14, 39. *Study:* George Peabody Col, Nashville, BA, 64, MM, 65, PhD, 69; Univ Mich, 74-75; Univ Hamburg, 79-80. *Teaching:* Assoc prof music hist & lit, Univ Tenn, 70-77, prof, 77-83. *Awards:* Res Grant, Alexander von Humboldt Stiftung, 79-80. *Mem:* Int Musicol Soc; Am Musicol Soc (chap officer, 82-83, mem coun, 83-); Music Libr Asn; Deutsche Gesellschaft Musikforschung. *Interests:* Eighteenth century subjects, especially literature on music and works of C P E Bach. *Publ:* Auth, J F Agricola's Anleitung zur Singkinst: A Rich Source by a pupil of J S Bach, 78; A Chronology of the Works of Johann Sebastian Bach, 80; Bach; rev transl, Johann Mattheson's Der volkommene Capellmeister, UMI Res Press, 81. *Mailing Add:* Rte 4 Box 191 Martin TN 38238

HARROD, WILLIAM V
OBOE & ENGLISH HORN
b Springfield, Ohio, July 8, 30. *Study:* Cincinnati Col Music, BM, 52; Eastman Sch Music, MM, 58. *Pos:* English horn & oboe, Cincinnati Symph Orch, 59- *Mailing Add:* 66 Hadley Rd Cincinnati OH 45218

HARROLD, JACK
TENOR, TEACHER
b Atlantic City, NJ, June 10, 20. *Study:* Acad Vocal Arts, with Giovanni Martinelli & Eleanor McClellan, cert, 42. *Rec Perf:* The Unsinkable Molly Brown (Willson) Capitol Rec, 60; Silverlake (Kurt Weill) Nonesuch Digital, 81. *Roles:* Prince Orlofsky in Die Fledermaus, Central City Opera 59 & 69; Baron Popoff in The Merry Widow, New York City Opera, 60, 64, 65 & 83; Baron Lauer in Silverlake, 81 & Baron Pasha in Candide, 82-83, New York City Opera; Orlando Paladino, 82 & Der Avocat in Des Esels Schatten, 83, Salzburg Fest. *Pos:* Leading tenor, New York City Opera, 45-, Salzburg, Austria Fest, 81-82 & Opera Colo, 83. *Teaching:* Vis distinguished prof voice & opera, Univ Okla, 66-70 & Univ Del, 76-80; prof musical comedy, Eugene O'Neill Theatre Inst, 79-80. *Bibliog:* Martin Sokol (auth), New York City Opera, Macmillan, 80. *Mem:* The Players, New York; Am Guild Musical Artists; Actors Equity; Am Fedn TV & Radio Artists. *Mailing Add:* Dorchester Towers 155 W 68 St New York NY 10023

HARROWER, PETER (STILLWELL)
BASS, EDUCATOR
b Atlanta, Ga, July 6, 23. *Study:* Ga Inst Tech, BS, 51; Accad Santa Cecilia, Rome, cert, 57. *Roles:* Sparafucile in Rigoletto, Volksoper, Vienna, 57; Samuele in Un Ballo in Maschera, Lyr Opera Chicago, 59; Bluebeard in Duke Bluebeard's Castle, San Francisco Opera, 63; LaRoche in Capriccio, 68 & Sarastro in The Magic Flute, 69, Santa Fe Opera; Count Waldner in Arabella,

Houston Grand Opera, 78; Doc West in A Quiet Place, Houston Grand Opera, 83. *Teaching:* Prof singing, Ga State Univ, 60- *Awards:* Fulbright Scholar, 55 & 56; Martha Baird Rockefeller Fund Music Grant, 63. *Mem:* Am Guild Musical Artists; Nat Asn Teachers Singing. *Mailing Add:* Ga State Univ Music Dept Univ Plaza Atlanta GA 30303

HARRY, DON
TUBA, EDUCATOR
b Anadarko, Okla. *Study:* Ind Univ, grad; studied with William Bell & Joseph Novotny. *Pos:* Mem, Oklahoma City Symph, 72; tuba, Buffalo Phil, 73- *Teaching:* Mem fac tuba, Juilliard Sch, 78- *Mailing Add:* Juilliard Sch Lincoln Ctr New York NY 10023

HARRY, WILLIAM (THOMAS)
CELLO, EDUCATOR
b Berkeley, Calif, Dec 29, 24. *Study:* David Mannes Music Sch, 44-48; Pablo Casals Master Class, Zermatt, Switz, 56. *Rec Perf:* The Gotham Trio, Orion, 82. *Pos:* Prin cellist, New Orleans Symph Orch, 48-52 & San Antonio Symph Orch, 55-59; cellist, Pac String Trio, 59-70 & Gotham Trio, 71- *Teaching:* Cello & chamber music, Mannes Col Music, 73-; adj asst prof cello, Queens Col, 74-76. *Awards:* Dipl d'Honneur, Fondation Eugene Ysaye, Bruxelles, 67. *Rep:* Albert Kay Assocs Inc 58 W 58th St New York NY 10019. *Mailing Add:* 817 West End Ave Apt 8D New York NY 10025

HARSANYI, JANICE
SOPRANO, EDUCATOR
b Arlington, Mass, July 15, 29. *Study:* Westminster Choir Col, BMus, 51; Philadelphia Acad Vocal Arts, 52-54. *Rec Perf:* On Columbia, Decca & CRI. *Pos:* Concert singer, 54-; performer concerts & recitals, major US & Europ cities. *Teaching:* Voice, Westminster Choir Col, 51-63, chmn dept, 63-65; cond voice master classes & choral clinics, various cols, 54-; lectr music, Princeton Theol Sem, 56-63; teacher voice, Univ Mich, summers 65-70 & NC Sch Arts, 71-78; artist in res, Interlochen Arts Acad, 67-70; mem fac music, Salem Col, 73-76; prof voice, Fla State Univ, 78-, chmn dept, 79- *Mem:* Nat Asn Teachers Singing; Music Teachers Nat Asn; Sigma Alpha Iota. *Mailing Add:* 725 Duparc Circle Tallahassee FL 32312

HART, KENNETH WAYNE
ADMINISTRATOR, ORGAN
b Ottumwa, Iowa, Dec 13, 39. *Study:* Grinnell Col, BA, 62; Sch Sacred Music, Union Theol Sem, MSM, 67; Col Consv Music, Univ Cincinnati, DMA, 72. *Pos:* Dir music, Westminister Presby Church, Nebr, 71-75. *Teaching:* Instr music, Berea Col, 67-69; chair music dept & assoc prof, Emporia State Univ, 75- *Awards:* Friend of Music, Sigma Alpha Iota, 83. *Mem:* Am Guild Organists (sub-dean, 72 & 83 & dean, 74); Am Choral Dir Asn; Presby Asn Musicians (state chair, 73-75); Kans Music Educr Asn; Music Educr Nat Conf. *Publ:* Auth, Organ Transcriptions (J S Bach), Music, Am Guild Organists, 72; Cincinnati Organ-Builders of the 19th Century, Cincinnati Hist Soc Bulletin, 73 & The Tracker, 76-77; co-ed, French Roccoco Flute Style (J B de Boismortier), 79 & Comparison of G P Telemann's Use of Recorder and Transverse Flute, 82, Emporia Res Studios, 82. *Mailing Add:* Music Dept Emporia State Univ Emporia KS 66801

HART, WILLIAM SEBASTIAN
CONDUCTOR
b Baltimore, Md, Oct 30, 20. *Study:* Peabody Consv Music, teacher's cert, 39; Johns Hopkins Univ, BA, 40; Golden State Univ, PhD, 56; Allen Univ, Hon Dr Music, 58; Mt St Mary's Col, LHD, 62; Univ Tex, LLD, 65. *Works:* Duet for Timpani, Music Perc, 58. *Rec Perf:* Piano Concerto No 1 (Mendelssohn), 62, Rienzi (Wagner), 62, Cinderella (E Coates), 62, Masquerade (Khatchatourian), 65, Vocal Arias, 65 & Piano Concerto No 1 (F Chopin), 76, Dominion Rec. *Pos:* Timpanist, Baltimore Symph Orch, 39-58; cond, Baltimore Bureau Music, 47-58; musical dir, Gettysburg Symph Orch, 58-; guest cond, Royal Phil Orch, 65, 69, 79 & 83, Nat Symph Orch, 69 & London Phil Orch, 83. *Teaching:* Fac mem, Peabody Consv Music Baltimore, 39-62, Baltimore Col Commerce, 58-75 & Morgan State Univ, 62-65. *Mailing Add:* 1800 Cromwell Bridge Rd Baltimore MD 21234

HARTER, NATALIA RAIGORODSKY See Raigorodsky, Natalia

HARTH, SIDNEY
CONDUCTOR & MUSIC DIRECTOR, VIOLIN
b Cleveland, Ohio, 29. *Study:* Cleveland Inst Music, BMus, 49. *Rec Perf:* String Quartet No 2 (Bloch), Vanguard, 63; Sonata No 1 & No 3 (Brahms), 73, Sonata 1 (Faure), 73 & Duo in A (Schubert), 73, Musical Heritage; Sometimes (Schubert), Conct Soc, 75; Tournaments (Lorghoano), 80 & Elegy (Lorghoano), 80, Louisville Symph. *Pos:* Concertmaster, Louisville Symph Orch, 54-60, Chicago Symph Orch, 61-64, Los Angeles Symph Orch, 73-79 & New York Phil, 80-81. *Teaching:* Mellon prof & head dept, Carnegie Mellon Univ, Pittsburgh, Pa, 63-73; music dir orch, Mannes Col, New York, 81-; prof violin, Yale Univ, 82- *Awards:* Naumberg Award, 49; Wrenkawski Compt, 59. *Mailing Add:* c/o Sheldon Soffer Mgt 130 W 56th St New York NY 10019

HARTLEY, GERALD S
COMPOSER
b Spokane, Wash, Sept 18, 21. *Study:* Univ Wash, Seattle, comp with George Frederick McKay, BA, 48, MA, 49. *Works:* Sketches for String Orchestra, 48 & Divertissement for Woodwind Quintet, 51, Assoc Music Publ; Plymouth Town: Sea Chantey Rhapsody (band), Carl Fischer, 64; Choral Fanfare for Christmas, Hal Leonard Music, Inc, 65; A Fuguing Tune (band), Shawnee Press, 67. *Mailing Add:* East 1011 Overbluff Rd Spokane WA 99203

HARTLEY, WALTER SINCLAIR
COMPOSER, EDUCATOR
b Washington, DC, Feb 21, 27. *Study:* Eastman Sch Music, BM, 50; Grad Sch, Univ Rochester, MM, 51, PhD, 53. *Works:* Concerto for 23 Winds, Accura Music, 57; Sinfonia No 3 for Brass, Theodore Presser Co, 63; Sinfonia No 4 for Winds, MCA Music, 65; Concerto for Alto Saxophone & Band, Theodore Presser Co, 66; Variations for Orchestra, FEMA Music Publ, 73; Concerto for Tuba & Percussion, Accura Music, 74; Symphony No 2 for Winds, Accura Music, 78; over 146 works composed. *Teaching:* Instr music, Nat Music Camp, Interlochen, Mich, 56-64; prof, Davis & Elkins Col, 58-69 & State Univ NY, Fredonia, 69- *Awards:* Comn, Koussevitzky Music Found, Libr Cong, 54; Conn Brass Award, GC Conn Co, 63; Phi Mu Alpha Orpheus Award, 83. *Bibliog:* Peter Popiel (auth), The Tuba Music of Walter Hartley, Instrumentalist, 4/70. *Mem:* ASCAP; Am Soc Univ Comp; Col Music Soc; Phi Mu Alpha Sinfonia. *Mailing Add:* 27 Lowell Pl Fredonia NY 14063

HARTLIEP, NIKKI LI
SOPRANO
b Naha, Okinawa, Sept 22, 55; US citizen. *Study:* Univ Alaska, 73-75; Am Consv Music, 75-77; San Francisco Consv Music, BM, 81. *Roles:* Countess in Marriage of Figaro & Mimi in La Boheme, Western Opera Theatre, 82; Mimi in La Boheme, San Francisco Opera Showcase, 82; Anna in Nabucco, San Francisco Opera Co, 82; The Female Chorus in Rape of Lucretia, San Francisco Opera Showcase, 83; Madama Butterfly in Madama Butterfly, Marin Opera, 83; Mimi in La Boheme, Opera Colo, 83. *Pos:* Artist, San Francisco Opera Co, 82-83. *Mem:* Am Guild Musical Artists. *Mailing Add:* 38 Broderick St San Francisco CA 94117

HARTMAN, VERNON
BARITONE
b Dallas, Tex, July 12, 52. *Study:* Southwest Tex State Univ; NTex State Univ; Acad Vocal Arts, Philadelphia, dipl. *Roles:* Silvio in I Pagliacci, Count Almaviva in The Marriage of Figaro & Marcello in La Boheme, New York City Opera; Guglielmo in Cosi fan tutte, Spoleto Fest, Italy, 77; Orsino in Twelfth Night, Pa Opera Theater, 83; Don Giovanni in Don Giovanni, Des Moines Metro Opera, 83; Figaro in The Barber of Seville, Metropolitan Opera, 83. *Pos:* Leading bar, New York City Opera; bar, Metropolitan Opera, currently; performer with US opera co & orchs; appearances on film, TV & radio. *Mailing Add:* c/o Lew & Benson, Moreau-Neret Inc 204 W 10th St New York NY 10014

HARTWAY, JAMES JOHN
COMPOSER, EDUCATOR
b Detroit, Mich, Apr 24, 44. *Study:* Wayne State Univ, with Ruth Shaw Wylie, BA, 66, MM, 69; Mich State Univ, with H Owen Reed, PhD, 72. *Works:* Couleurs (orch & perc solo), 69; Anagogia (piano), 70; 3 Ways of Looking at a Blackbird (sop, flute, piano & perc), 70; Sequence (chorus & perc), 70; 7 Ways of Looking at a Blackbird (orch & sop solo), 72; 2 Rube Goldbergs (band), 73; Waiting to Be Processed (women's voices, typewriters, perc & tape), 73. *Teaching:* Instr, Lansing Community Col, 70-71; assoc prof music, Wayne State Univ, 71- *Awards:* Second Place, Phi Mu Alpha Cont, 71; First Prize, Young Musicians Found Cont, 74; Mich Arts Award Music, 78. *Mailing Add:* Music Dept Wayne State Univ 20524 Shady Ln St Clair Shores MI 48080

HARTWELL, ROBERT WALLACE
ADMINISTRATOR, EDUCATOR
b Dayton, Ohio, Oct 21, 36. *Study:* Capital Univ, BMusEd, 58; Ohio State Univ, MA, 65; Col Consv Music, Univ Cincinnati, DMusEd, 79. *Teaching:* Dir bands, Worthington Pub Sch, Ohio, 58-67; instr cond & music appreciation & univ band, Eastern Ky Univ, 67- *Mem:* Col Band Dir Nat Asn; Music Educr Nat Conf; Ky Music Educr Asn (pres, 83-). *Mailing Add:* 118 Windsor Dr Richmond KY 40475

HARTZELL, KARL DREW, JR
EDUCATOR
b Atlanta, Ga, Mar 31, 39. *Study:* Wesleyan Univ, AB, 60; Eastman Sch Music, MA, 65, PhD, 71. *Teaching:* Instr music, State Univ NY, Albany, 67-74, asst prof, 74-81, assoc prof, 81- *Awards:* Fac fel, State Univ NY, 71, 72, 74, 77 & 80; res grant, Nat Endowment Humanities, 75. *Mem:* Am Musicol Soc; Henry Bradshaw Soc; Plainsong & Mediaeval Music Soc; Mediaeval Acad Am. *Interests:* History of music in England to the end of the 12th century. *Publ:* Auth, An Unknown English Benedictine Gradual of the Eleventh Century, Anglo-Saxon England, 75; A St Albans Miscellany in New York, Mittellateinisches Jahrbuch, 75; An English Antiphoner of the Ninth Century? Rev Benedictine, 80; The Early Provenance of the Harkness Gospels, Bulletin Res Humanities, 81. *Mailing Add:* 10 Glenwood St Albany NY 12203

HARTZELL, LAWRENCE WILLIAM
EDUCATOR, COMPOSER
b Mt Pleasant, Pa, July 1, 42. *Study:* Baldwin-Wallace Col, BM, 65; Univ Kans, MM, 66, PhD, 70. *Works:* Sonata (piano), perf by Penelope Hendel, 66; Introduction and Allegro (brass choir & perc), 70 & Toccata Concertata (organ & brass choir), 70, perf by Univ Wis, Eau Clai; Symphony for Band, perf by Univ Wis, Eau Claire, Symph Band, 73; Quintet (trumpet & strings), Toronto Symph, 74; Theme, Variations and Fugue (three trumpets), perf by Baldwin-Wallace Col students, 77; Two Birthday Dedications, perf by Baldwin-Wallace Col Choir, 83. *Pos:* Choirmaster, Christ Church Cathedral, Eau Claire, Wis, 69-71; music dir, First Congregational United Church Christ, Berea, Ohio, 74-77. *Teaching:* Asst prof music theory, Univ Wis, Eau Claire,

68-73 & chmn, 69-73; assoc prof music theory, hist & lit, Baldwin-Col, Berea, Ohio, 73- & chmn music theory, 74-80. *Awards:* Award, Shell Oil Co, 81; grant, Reeves Found, Dover, Ohio, 82. *Mem:* Mid-West Music Theory Soc (secy-treas, 74-75 & vpres, 75-76); Beethoven Haus, Bonn; Sonneck Soc; Moravian Music Found. *Publ:* Auth, Karel Husa: The Man and the Music, Musical Quart, 76; American Music, 1600-1750: I, The Spanish Colonies; II, The English Colonies, 76 & III, The German Colonies, 77, Bach; Early Organs in the American Southwest, Tracker, 78; Music and the Mystics of the Wissahickon, J Am Ger Inst, 79. *Mailing Add:* 423 Adrian Dr Berea OH 44017

HARTZELL, MARJORIE HELEN
HARP
b Plainfield, NJ, May 1, 38. *Study:* Eastman Sch Music, BM, 60; Acad Chigiana, with Nicanor Zabeleta, 61. *Pos:* First harpist, Buffalo Phil, 60-66, Albany Symph, 68- & Lake George Opera Fest, currently. *Awards:* Fulbright Grant, 66. *Mailing Add:* 10 Glenwood St Albany NY 12203

HARVEY, ARTHUR WALLACE
EDUCATOR, LECTURER
b Boston, Mass, May 20, 39. *Study:* Gordon Col, Wenham, Mass, BS, 59; Boston Univ, MM, 65; Temple Univ, Philadelphia, DMA, 74; Glassboro State Col; Univ Maine; Univ Miami; Univ Mich. *Pos:* Guest cond, Mt Allison Univ summer music camp, 63-74 & fest choruses & bands in many states; music dir, Camp Lebanon Music Camp, NJ, summer 68, Korean Christian Crusade, 77 & Les Chalets Francais, Maine, summer 81; dir music, Grace Chapel, Havertown, Pa; organist, Reflections of Love Conct Youth Choir, formerly & Living Praise Conct Youth Choir, formerly, Graded Choir Prog; minister music, Vineland Baptist Church, 67-68, Barrington Baptist Church, RI, 71-73, Lafayette Christian Church, Lexington, 74-76, First United Methodist Church, 67-68, Livermore Falls Baptist Church, Maine & Lewisville Baptist Church, NB, formerly & Lexington Ave Baptist Church, Danville, Ky, currently; guest tenor soloist, oratorios, cantatas & masses, formerly; dir, Madison Co Christian Youth Celebrate Life & Livermore Falls Community Band, formerly; dir & founder, Mechanic Falls Community Band & Livermore Falls Choral Soc, formerly. *Teaching:* Dean music, Atlantic Bible Col, NB, Can, 61-62; dir music, Livermore Falls Pub Sch, Maine, 63-65; instr, Philadelphia Col Bible, 65-66; dir bands, Vineland Sr High Sch, 66-71; asst prof, Barrington Col, 71-73; prof, Eastern Ky Univ, Richmond, 73- *Mem:* Music Educr Nat Conf; Am Orff Schulwerk Asn; Ky Music Educr Asn; Ky Alliance Arts Educ. *Interests:* Arts for handicapped (music emphasis); music therapy; creativity and creative teaching; music education pedagogy; aesthetic education; humanistic education; psychology of music; music ministry, psychology of worship; music and the brain. *Publ:* Auth, Therapeutic Uses of Music in Special Education, Nat Asn Creative Children & Adults J, 81; Maslow's Legacy: Conditions & Characteristics of Creative Educators, New Directions in Teaching, 82; Music and the Brain, New Dimensions in Educ, 82. *Mailing Add:* 234 Susan Dr Richmond KY 40475

HARVEY, MARION BRADLEY
EDUCATOR, SINGER
b Philadelphia, Pa, Sept 3, 16. *Study:* Juilliard Sch Music, dipl; Univ Pa, BMus, MA. *Roles:* Clarina in La Cambiale di Matrimonio, New York, 39; Madama Rosa in Il Campanelo di Notte, Gotham Opera Co; Esmerelda in The Bartered Bride, Wilmington Opera Soc. *Pos:* Mem, Philomel Trio; lieder recitalist. *Teaching:* Mem fac voice, Philadelphia Consv Music, 46-62, Philadelphia Col Perf Arts, 62 & Wilmington Music Sch, 62. *Mem:* Nat Asn Teachers Singing; Am Musicol Soc. *Mailing Add:* 2514 Knowles Rd Wilmington DE 19810

HARVEY, RAYMOND C
MUSIC DIRECTOR
b New York, NY, Dec 9, 50. *Study:* Oberlin Consv, BMus, 73, MMus, 73; Sch Music, Yale Univ, MMA, 78. *Pos:* Assoc cond, Des Moines Metro Opera, Iowa, 77-80; assoc cond, Tex Opera Theater, 78-79, music dir, 79-80; Exxon, Arts Endowment Cond, Indianapolis Symph Orch, 80-83; music dir, Marion Phil Orch, Ind, 82- *Rep:* Affiliate Artists Inc 155 W 68th St New York NY 10023. *Mailing Add:* 2078 Landmark Dr Indianapolis IN 46260

HARWOOD, C WILLIAM
CONDUCTOR & MUSIC DIRECTOR
Pos: Assoc cond, Houston Symph Orch, currently; cond, Houston Grand Opera, Opera-Omaha, Ky Opera, St Louis Opera Theatre & Ark Opera Theatre, formerly; music dir, Tex Opera Theatre, Yale Symph & Eastern Opera Theatre, formerly & Houston Symph summer season & Stokowski Legacy Series, currently; prin guest cond & music dir, Ark Symph Orch, 80-81, music adv, 82- *Awards:* Stokowski Mem Cond Award, Am Symph Orch, 81. *Mailing Add:* 1601 S Shepherd Dr Houston TX 77019

HARWOOD, DONALD
BASS TROMBONE, EDUCATOR
b Zion, Ill. *Study:* Sherwood Sch Music; Eastman Sch Music; Yale Univ; studied with Edward Kleinhammer, Donald Knaube, John Clark & John Swallow. *Pos:* Bass trombonist, Metropolitan Opera Orch, 69-75 & New York Phil, currently. *Teaching:* Mem fac bass trombone, Juilliard Sch, 75- & Mannes Col Music, 80- *Mailing Add:* New York Phil Avery Fisher Hall New York NY 10023

HARWOOD, JAMES C
CONDUCTOR, SAXOPHONE
b Springfield, Mass, Aug 26, 46. *Study:* Univ Mich, with William Stuffins & Larry Jeal, BME, 64-68; New England Consv, with Hadcock Schuller, MME, 70; Teachers Col, Columbia Univ, with John Wummer & Leon Russianoff, 78- *Pos:* Clarinet soloist, Harvard Band, 71; music dir, Byram Hills Armonk, NY, 76-78 & Concordia Col, 80-; tenor sax, Guggenheim Band, 81-; cond, Wind Ens; dir, Westchester Youth Jazz Ens. *Teaching:* Instr, Phillips Acad, 71-73 & Dalton Sch, 74-76. *Mem:* Music Educr Nat Conf; Nat Asn Jazz Educr; Am Fedn Musicians. *Mailing Add:* 100 Pelham Rd #50 New Rochelle NY 10805

HASHIMOTO, EIJI
EDUCATOR, HARPSICHORD
Tokyo, Japan, Aug 7, 31. *Study:* Tokyo Univ Fine Arts & Music, BM(organ), 54; Univ Chicago, MA(comp), 59; Sch Music, Yale Uiv, MM(harpsichord), 62. *Rec Perf:* Harpsichord Works (J F Dandrieu), 69, Eight Sonatas for Harpsichord (T Arne), 74 & Suites & Sonatas (J Kuhnau), 76, Musical Heritage Soc, Inc; 13 Sonatas (D Scarlatti), Fontec Rec Co, Tokyo, Japan, 82; J S Bach & Sons, Camerata Tokyo Rec Co, Tokyo, Japan, 83. *Pos:* Harpsichordist in res, Univ Cincinnati, 68- *Teaching:* Lectr, Toho Gakuen Sch Music, Tokyo, Japan, 66; asst prof harpsichord, Col Consv Music, Univ Cincinnati, 68-72, assoc prof, 72-77, prof & artist in res, 77- *Awards:* Res grant, French Govt, 67; Prize of Excellence, Japanese Govt, 78 & 81. *Publ:* Ed, D Scarlatti, 100 Sonatas in 3 volumes, 75, C P E Bach, Eighteen Sonatas (W 50, 51, 52) in 3 volummes, 83 & D Scarlatti, Complete Keyboard Works in 16 volumes (in prep), Zen On Music Co, Tokyo; Suites & Lessons for Harpsichord, Hengel & Cie, Paris, 83. *Rep:* Nat Artists Serv Bureau 2216 Bedford Terrace Cincinnati OH 45208. *Mailing Add:* 8966 Farmedge Lane Cincinnati OH 45231

HASKELL, HARRY OGREN
CRITIC-WRITER
b Kansas City, Mo, Oct 26, 54. *Study:* Brown Univ, BA, 76. *Pos:* Music ed, Kansas City Star, 77- *Mem:* Music Critics Asn. *Mailing Add:* 1729 Grand Ave Kansas City MO 64110

HASSELMAN, MARGARET PAINE
EDUCATOR, TEACHER
b New York, NY, Oct 15, 40. *Study:* Smith Col, BA(music), 62; Univ Calif, Berkeley, MA(music hist), 64; PhD(music hist), 70. *Rec Perf:* Music From the Age of Discovery (Jamestown), Asn Preservation Va Antiquities, 82. *Teaching:* Private lessons piano, music theory & harpsichord, Blacksburg, Va, 78-; adj asst prof music, Va Polytechnic Inst, 81- *Awards:* Fulbright Scholar, 66. *Mem:* Am Musicol Soc; Music Teachers Nat Asn (vpres, 79-83); Nat Guild Piano Teachers (adjudicator, 81-). *Interests:* Fourteenth century French chanson and performance practice. *Publ:* Contribr, A New Source for Medieval Music Theory, Acta Musicologica, 67; coauth, More Hidden Polyphony in a Machaut Manuscript, Musica Disciplina, 70; contribr, Performance Practice ... in France at the Close of the Middle Ages, Cambridge Univ Press (in press). *Mailing Add:* 601 Rainbow Ridge Blacksburg VA 24060

HASSELMANN, RONALD HENRY
TRUMPET, ADMINISTRATOR
b Chicago, Ill, Mar 3, 33. *Study:* Northwestern Univ, BMusEd, 54, MMusEd, 57; studied with Renold Schilke, Adolph Herseth & Arnold Jacobs. *Pos:* Prin trumpet, Lyric Opera, Chicago, Ill, 56-58; assoc prin trumpet, Minn Orch, 58-, assoc personnel mgr, 80- *Teaching:* Instr trumpet, St Olaf Col, 63-82 & Univ Minn, 70- *Mem:* Inst Trumpet Guild (pres, Minn chap, 77-). *Mailing Add:* 4928 Fifth Ave Minneapolis MN 55409

HASTINGS, BAIRD
CONDUCTOR, CRITIC-WRITER
b New York, NY, May 14, 19. *Study:* Paris Consv, with L Fourestier, dipl, 46; Berkshire Music Ctr, with B Goldovsky, dipl, 57; Salzburg Acad, with B Paumgartner, dipl, 61; Harvard, AB; Queens Col, MA; Sussex Col, PhD. *Rec Perf:* String Music, Vocarium, 61; Mozart and Haydn, Educo, 76. *Pos:* Cond, Mozart Fest Orch, 60-; critic, Hartford Times, 67-70; adminr & libr, Juilliard Sch, 73- *Teaching:* Lectr music hist, Trinity Col, 65-70. *Awards:* Fulbright Scholar, 49-50; Scholar, Tanglewood, 57. *Mem:* Am Musicol Asn; Boston Musician's Asn; Bohemians. *Interests:* Mozart; music and dance. *Publ:* Auth, Berard, Inst Cont Art, 50; Sonata Form in Classic Orchestra, Trinity Col, 65; ed, Nicolas Legat, 78 & Don Quixote (Minkus), 79, Horizon; auth, Choreographers and Composers, G K Hall, 83. *Mailing Add:* 33 Greenwich Ave New York NY 10014

HASTINGS, EMILY (CECILIA)
MEZZO-SOPRANO, CONTRALTO
b Morgantown, WVa. *Study:* Cleveland Inst Music, 73-77; London Opera Ctr, perf dipl, 78. *Roles:* Cinderella in La Cenerentola, Blossom Fest Opera, Ohio, 77; Elsbeth in Feuersnot, Chelsea Opera Group, 78; Lisetta in Il Mondo della Luna, Wexford Fest Opera, 78; Orlofsky in Die Fledermaus, Manhasset Bay Opera Co, 80; La Chatte in L'enfant et les Sortileges, Metropolitan Opera, 82-83; Cherubino in The Marriage of Figaro, Stamford State Opera, 83. *Pos:* Apprentice artist, Metropolitan Opera Co, 80- *Awards:* Grant, Martha Baird Rockefeller Fund for Music, 80. *Mem:* Mu Phi Epsilon; Am Guild Musical Artists. *Mailing Add:* c/o TRM Mgt Inc 527 Madison Ave New York NY 10022

HATCHER, PAULA BRANIFF
FLUTE & PICCOLO, RECORDER
b Santa Monica, Calif, Feb 10, 47. *Study:* Peabody Consv Music, BM, MM. *Rec Perf:* Trios for Flute, Cello and Piano, Vox; Charlie Byrd: A Direct Disc Recording, Crystal Clear; rec on Folkways. *Pos:* Performer worldwide, 68-; mem, Half & Half, 68-79, Baltimore Pro Musica Rara, 71-, New York Camerata, 71-76 & Charlie Byrd Trio, 76-; founder, Paula Hatcher Jazz Quartet, 71-; artist, Affiliate Artists, 71; soloist, Guadalajara Symph Orch & Baltimore Symph Orch; US radio & TV appearances. *Teaching:* Flute, privately, 68-; mem fac recorder, Peabody Consv Music, 72-; adj prof music, Brooklyn Consv, City Univ New York, 80-82; instr workshops & masterclasses throughout US. *Bibliog:* Two US Info Agency films, 76. *Mailing Add:* Peabody Consv Music 1 E Mt Vernon Pl Baltimore MD 21202

HATCHER, WILLIAM B
EDUCATOR, CONDUCTOR
b Shenandoah, Iowa, Sept 9, 35. *Study:* Univ Nebr, BME, 57, MMus, 60; Univ Southern Calif, 69-76; Oakland Univ, 68; Univ Ore, with Helmuth Rilling, 77 & 82. *Rec Perf:* Madrigal Singers European Tour, Williamson, 81; Chamber Singers, Pasadena City Col, Custom Fidelity, 72, 73 & 76; Sing We Merrily—Hollywood Presbyterian Church Tour of England, Capitol. *Pos:* Choral & perf arts chmn, Santa Barbara High Sch, 60-69. *Teaching:* Assoc prof choral, Pasadena City Col, 69-79; vis prof, Univ Wash, 76-77; asst prof choral & cond, Calif State Univ, Los Angeles, 79-81, lectr, 81-; lectr, Univ Calif, Los Angeles, 81- *Mem:* Calif Music Educr Asn; Col Music Soc; Southern Calif Vocal Asn (vpres, 73); Am Choral Dir Asn (state pres, 81-). *Publ:* Coauth, Choral Skills, Bock Publ Co, 82. *Mailing Add:* 23142 Dolorosa St Woodland Hills CA 91367

HATFIELD, LENORE SHERMAN
VIOLIN
b Garden City, Kans, June 26, 35. *Study:* Eastman Sch Music, BMus 57; Univ Mich, MMus, 58; Univ Southern Calif. *Pos:* Mem, Indianapolis Symph, Rochester Phil & Cincinnati Symph, formerly; asst concertmaster, Aspen Fest Orch, currently; recitalist, TV & radio. *Awards:* Coleman Chamber Music Award, 60; Sword of Honor, 60; Rose of Honor, 72. *Mem:* Sigma Alpha Iota (pres, formerly); MacDowell Soc. *Mailing Add:* c/o Alfred C Myers 3642 Heekin Ave Cincinnati OH 45226

HATFIELD, MICHAEL
FRENCH HORN, EDUCATOR
b Evansville, Ind, Oct 1, 36. *Study:* Ind Univ, BS & performers cert, 58. *Pos:* Mem, Cincinnati Woodwind Quintet, 61-76; princ French horn, Cincinnati Symph Orch, 61-; co-prin horn, Aspen Fest Orch, 74- *Teaching:* Adj prof horn, Consv Music, Univ Cincinnati, 61-; fac horn, Aspen Music Fest, 74-; vis prof horn, Ind Univ, Bloomington, 82-83. *Mailing Add:* 7368 Quail Hollow Rd Cincinnati OH 45243

HATFIELD, WARREN GATES
ADMINISTRATOR, EDUCATOR
b Chicago, Ill, Dec 10, 31. *Study:* Univ Northern Iowa, BA, 52; Univ Iowa, MA, 59, PhD, 62. *Teaching:* Dir bands instrm music, SDak State Univ, 61-73, head dept music, 67-, prof, 68- *Awards:* Outstanding Educr Am, 70; Distinguished Serv Award, Phi Beta Mu, 80. *Mem:* SDak Bandmasters Asn (pres, 71-73); SDak Arts Coun (vpres, 81-); Music Educr Nat Conf; Nat Asn Sch Music. *Publ:* Auth, Diagnostic Uses of the Musical Aptitude Profile, Instrumentalist, 9/68. *Mailing Add:* 320 19th Ave So Brookings SD 57006

HATHAWAY, DANIEL
ARTIST MANAGER, MUSIC DIRECTOR
b Topeka, Kans, Jan 15, 45. *Study:* Harvard Col, AB, 67; Princeton Univ, 67-68; Episcopal Divinity Sch, MDiv, 71. *Pos:* Dir music, Christ Church, Cambridge, Mass, 68-71; Sunset Hill, Pembroke Country Day Sch, Kansas City, Mo, 71-74; Grace & Holy Trinity Cathedral, Kansas City, Mo, 71-74; Groton Sch, Mass, 74-77, Trinity Cathedral, 77- & Great Lakes Shakespeare Fest, 82- *Teaching:* Lectr organ, Cleveland State Univ, 79- *Mem:* Am Anglican Musicians. *Publ:* Auth, The New Old Organs of Northeast Ohio, Gamut, Cleveland State Univ, 81. *Mailing Add:* 2021 E 22nd St Cleveland OH 44115

HATTEN, ROBERT SWANEY
EDUCATOR, PIANO
b Naha AFB, Okinawa, Sept 15, 52. *Study:* Baylor Univ, BM(piano), 73; Ind Univ, MM(piano), 75, PhD(music theory), 82; State Univ NY, Stony Brook, with Charles Rosen, 75-76. *Teaching:* Vis asst prof, State Univ NY, Buffalo, 78-80; asst prof, Houston Baptist Univ, 80-81 & Univ Mich, 81- *Interests:* Semiotics of music; theories of style; interdisciplinary studies; recent opera. *Publ:* Auth, Beyond Schenker: The Argument and the Alternative, 79 & An Approach to Ambiguity in the Opening of Beethoven's Op 59, No 3, 80, Ind Theory Rev; Myth in Music: Deep Structure or Surface Evocation?, 80 & Nattiez's Semiology of Music, 80, Semiotica; Explaining Style Growth and Change: A Richer Semiotic Model, Plenum Press, 82. *Mailing Add:* Sch Music Univ Mich Ann Arbor MI 48109

HATTON, GAYLEN A
EDUCATOR
b Red Mountain, Calif, Oct 4, 28. *Study:* Brigham Young Univ, with Leon Dallin & Crawford Gates, BA, 51, MA, 54; Univ Utah, with Leroy Robertson, PhD, 64. *Works:* Essay for Orchestra, 57; Diversion (band), 63; Music for Band, 66; Odette Baby (jazz ballet), 67; Opus Psychedelia (electronic ballet), 70; Prelusion (orch), 75; Three String Quartets. *Pos:* Horn, Utah Symph,

54-63. *Teaching:* Fac mem, Univ Utah, 57-63, Calif State Univ, Sacramento, 63-78, Sun Valley Music Camp, 63-72 & Sugar Mt Music Camp, 71-72; prof horn, Brigham Young Univ, 79- *Awards:* Rosenblatt Award, 67; Sacramento Symph Award, 67; Nat Endowment for Arts Grant, 70. *Mailing Add:* Brigham Young Univ 560 South 500 East Orem UT 84058

HATTON, HOWARD
EDUCATOR, SINGER
Study: Univ Colo, BM, 39, MM, 41; Univ Mich, MM, 47; studied singing with Alexander Grant, Arthur Hackett, Charles Panzera & Pierre Bernac. *Pos:* Performer, Cent City Opera Co, 40-41 & Robert Shaw Col Chorale, 41-42; recital, opera, radio appearances in US & Europe. *Teaching:* Instr voice, Allegheny Col, 47-49, Univ Mich, summers 48-50, Univ Wash, summer 63 & Univ Wis, summer 74; prof singing, Consv Music, Oberlin Col, 49-; instr fac wkshps, Nat Asn Teachers Singing, 62-63 & 72; teacher masterclass, Univ Manitoba, 76. *Mem:* Nat Asn Teachers Singing. *Mailing Add:* Consv Music Oberlin Col Oberlin OH 44074

HAUCK, BETTY VIRGINIA
VIOLA
b Annapolis, Md, Dec 4, 45. *Study:* Interlochen, 60; Longy Sch Music, jr dipl, 63; Cummington Sch Arts, summers 63 & 64; Manhattan Sch Music, with Yehudi Menuhin & Lillian Fuchs, 63-64; Brandeis Univ, with Robert Koff, BA, 68; New England Consv Music, with Burton Fine, MM, 71; studied viola with Louise Rood & chamber music coaching with Eugene Lehner, Rudolf Kolisch, Robert Mann & Raphael Hillyer. *Rec Perf:* Two Cantatas (Bach), Advent, 73; Music by John Harbison, CRI, 73; Musical Tales (Deak), Op One, 82. *Pos:* Soloist, Boston Pops, 67 & Monadnock Music, 79; viola, Aspen Fest Orch, 66, Boston Opera Co Orch, 70-75, Boston Ballet Orch, 70-75 & Apple Hill Chamber Players, 73-; prin viola & soloist, Emmanuel Music Orch, Boston, 71-75; prin viola, NH Symph, 75-80. *Teaching:* Coach, Kinhaven Music Camp, Weston, Vt, 66; private instr viola & violin, 67-; instr Suzuki violin, Title III Proj, Inst Arts & Sci, Manchester, NH, 69; private instr & coach chamber music, Apple Hill Ctr Chamber Music, summers 71-; private instr, Belmont Music Sch, Mass, 71-76 & Young Musicians Develop Prog, Keene, NH, 76-81; adj mem fac, Keene State Col, 78-82. *Awards:* Coffey Award Music, Brandeis Univ, 68. *Mailing Add:* Box 79 East Sullivan NH 03445

HAUFRECT, HERBERT
COMPOSER
b New York, NY, Nov 3, 09. *Study:* Cleveland Inst Music, with Quincy Porter, Arthur Loesser & Severin Eisenberger, 26-30; Juilliard Sch Music, with R Goldmark, 30-34. *Works:* The Story of Ferdinand, Leeds Music, 39 & Am Comp Ed, 74; Square Set for String Orchestra, Assoc Music Publ, 42; Etudes in Blues (piano), Assoc Music Publ, 54 & Am Comp Ed, 74; A Woodland Serenade (woodwind quintet), Rongwen Music, 54; Symphony for Brass and Timpani, Boosey & Hawkes, 67; Divertimento for Chamber Orchestra, perf by Woodstock Chamber Orch, 83; Variations on a Catskill Mountain Folksong, perf by Roxbury Arts Group, 83. *Pos:* Field Rep, Spec Skills Div, Resettlement Admin, WVa, 36-37; staff comp & arr, Fed Theatre Proj, WPA, 38-39; arr & ed, Mills Music, Assoc Music Publ & Belwin, 45-76; nat music dir, Young Audiences Inc, 50-80. *Bibliog:* Norman Cazden (auth), Haufrecht: Composer and the Man, Am Comp Alliance Bulletin, 11/4/59; Mary Ellen Murphy (auth), Herbert Haufrect, Keyboard Jr, Vol 19, No 6. *Mem:* Am Comp Alliance; Am Music Ctr; Am Fed Musicians; Juilliard Alumni Asn. *Publ:* Ed, Folk Sing, Berkley Medallion, 60; auth, Folk Songs in Settings by Master Composers, Funk & Wagnalls, 70 & Da Capo Press, 77; coauth, Folk Songs of the Catskills, State Univ NY Press, 82. *Mailing Add:* Box 14 Shady NY 12479

HAUG, LEONARD HAROLD
CONDUCTOR, EDUCATOR
b Eau Claire, Wis, Sept 18, 10. *Study:* Univ Wis, BM, 34, MA(music), 35. *Pos:* Asst band dir, Univ Wis, Madison, 35-38. *Teaching:* From instr to prof, Univ Okla, 38-77, asst dean col fine arts, 71-77, emer prof, 77- *Mem:* Am Bandmasters Asn (bd dir, 74-76); Col Band Dir Nat Asn; Int Mil Music Soc. *Mailing Add:* 1521 S Pickard Norman OK 73069

HAUGLAND, A OSCAR
COMPOSER, EDUCATOR
b Emmons, Minn, Jan 28, 22. *Study:* Eastman Sch Music, with Howard Hanson, Bernard Rogers & Herbert Elwell; Northwestern Univ, with Robert Delaney. *Works:* Incidental Music to Peer Gynt, 65; Restaurationen, 1825, Fargo-Morehead Symph Orch, 75; Magazine Madrigals, 76; Toccata (organ), 78; Maggie and Milly and Molly and May (sop & bassoon), 78; Natures Mysteries (piano), 79; Growing Up Madrigals, 79. *Teaching:* Fac mem, WVa Univ, 49-52 & 54-60 & Northwestern Ill Univ, 60- *Mailing Add:* 756 S 3rd St De Kalb IL 60115

HAUPT, CHARLES V
VIOLIN
b New York, NY, June 4, 39. *Study:* Juilliard Sch Music; Ecole Normale Musique; Mannes Col Music. *Pos:* Concertmaster, San Antonio Symph, 67-68, Buffalo Phil Orch, 71- & Mostly Mozart Fest, NY, 81-; creative assoc, Ctr Perf & Creative Arts, 68-72. *Awards:* Fulbright Grant, 61-62. *Mem:* Bohemians. *Mailing Add:* c/o Am Chamber Conct 890 West End Ave New York NY 10025

HAUPT-NOLEN, PAULETTE
ADMINISTRATOR, CONDUCTOR
b Denver, Colo, May 14, 44. *Pos:* Exxon-Arts Endowment Cond, San Francisco Opera, 76-77; artistic dir, Music Theater Conf, O'Neill Theater Ctr Opera, 78-; assoc cond & artistic adminr, Opera Co Philadelphia, 79-81; gen dir, Lake George Opera Fest, 81- *Awards:* Study grant for Metropolitan Opera, Rockfeller Found. *Mailing Add:* Sunset Trail Glens Falls NY 12801

HAUSE, JAMES B
EDUCATOR
b Waltz, Mich, Apr 5, 29. *Study:* Univ Mich, BMus, 51, MMus, 52, EdD, 69. *Teaching:* Dir & instr music, Quincy Pub Sch, Mich, 54-58; from asst prof to prof, Western Mich Univ, 58-71; prof & head dept music, Eastern Mich Univ, 71- *Mem:* Music Educr Nat Conf; Mich Sch Band & Orch Asn (hon vpres, 68-70); Mich Acad Sci Arts & Lett; Nat Asn Sch Music; Am Asn Univ Prof. *Publ:* Compiler & ed, A Handbook for Teachers of Band and Orchestra Instruments, Mich Sch Band & Orch Asn, 67; auth, The Beginnings of MSBOA, Mich Sch Band & Orch Asn, spring 70—fall 71; Planning the Year in Instrumental Music, 9/77 & The First Division Rating: A By-product of Good Teaching, 5/77, Notes. *Mailing Add:* 1049 Louise Ypsilanti MI 48197

HAUSE, ROBERT LUKE
CONDUCTOR & MUSIC DIRECTOR, EDUCATOR
b Shelby, NC, Dec 12, 35. *Study:* Univ Mich, BME, 58, MM, 60. *Works:* Sonatina for Violin and Piano, 79 & Toccata in G Major for Orchestra, 79, Shawnee Press. *Rec Perf:* 9th Symph (Beethoven), Crest Rec, 83. *Pos:* Asst cond, Jacksonville Symph Orch, 60-62; cond, Cent Fla Community Orch, 65-67. *Teaching:* Assoc prof & cond, Stetson Univ, 62-67; dir, cond & prof, ECarolina Univ, 67- *Awards:* Hon Award, Nat Sch Orch Asn, 67; Cert Excellence, Music Educr Nat Conf, 73 & 77. *Mem:* Music Educr Nat Conf; Phi Mu Alpha Sinfonia (prov gov, 76-). *Mailing Add:* 2208 Charles St Greenville NC 27834

HAUTZIG, WALTER
PIANO
b Vienna, Austria; US citizen. *Study:* State Acad Music, Vienna, 36-38; Consv Music, Jerusalem, 38-39; Curtis Inst Music, dipl, 43. *Rec Perf:* Schubert Sonata B-flat & Moments Musicaux, Beethoven Sonatas for Piano & Cello (with Paul Olefsky) & Brahms Sonatas for Piano & Cello (with Paul Olefsky), Monitor Rec; Schubert Valses & Dances, Turnabout Rec; Schubert Fantasies & The Peking Recital, Musical Heritage Rec; over 50 records with RCA Japan. *Pos:* Concert pianist with major orchestras in over 50 countries. *Teaching:* Prof piano, Peabody Consv, Johns Hopkins Univ, 60- *Mem:* Am Asn Univ Prof; Mieczyslaw Munz Scholarship Fund Inc (pres, 81-). *Publ:* Auth, An American in China, Hi Fidelity, Musical Am, 79. *Rep:* Conct Mgt Eric Semon Assoc 111 W 57 St New York NY 10019 *Mailing Add:* 505 West End Ave New York NY 10024

HAWLEY, WILLIAM
COMPOSER
b Bronxville, NY, 1950. *Study:* Sch Music, Ithaca Col; Calif Inst Arts, BFA, 74, MFA, 76; studied comp with Morton Subotnick, James Tenney, Harold Budd, Alan Chaplin & Earle Brown. *Works:* Lumina (electronic), 74; Zeno (orch), 74-75; Wave (electronic), 75; Cage (piano), 77; Receding Moment (violin & piano), 77; Music for Cello and Piano (chamber music), 78; Seven Steps (two pianos), 78; & others. *Mem:* ASCAP; founding mem, Independent Comp Asn, 77. *Mailing Add:* 345 E 56th New York NY 10022

HAWN, HAROLD GAGE
EDUCATOR, MUSIC DIRECTOR
b Huntingdon, Pa, Jan 8, 23. *Study:* Eastman Sch Music, BM, 49, MM, 50; Ind Univ, DMus, 66. *Pos:* Minister music, Norview Presby Church, Norfolk, Va, 53-59, Cent Baptist Church, Norfolk, 71-73 & Azalea Baptist Church, Norfolk, 73-; choirmaster, Miles Mem United Methodist Church, Norfolk, 59-71; ed, Nat Opera Asn, Newsletter, quart 79- *Teaching:* Instr voice, opera, TV & chorus, State Teachers Col, Fredonia, NY, 50-51; dir music voice, piano, chorus & opera, Griffiss Air Force Base, Rome, 51-53; prof music, Old Dominion Univ, Norfolk, Va, 53- *Awards:* Award of Appreciation, Nat Opera Asn, 79 & US Sch Music, Amphibious Base, Norfolk, 83. *Mem:* Nat Opera Asn Inc; Nat Asn Teachers Singing; Opera Youth Inc. *Interests:* Music theatre works in English for youth. *Mailing Add:* 8045 Carlton St Norfolk VA 23518

HAXTON, (RICHARD) KENNETH
COMPOSER, CELLO
b Greenville, Miss, Oct 20, 19. *Study:* Univ Miss, BA, 41. *Works:* Moses (dramatic oratorio), Miss Col Chorus & Greenville Symph, 72; Chorale Prelude & Fugue, 76 & 82, Fantasia on Two Folk Songs, 78 & 82, Piano Concerto No 1, 79 & The Sound and the Fury, 82, Greenville Symph Orch; Prelude, Passacaglia & Fugue, McNeese Orch, 78; Elegy for Orch, Univ Miss Orch & Monroe Symph, 80. *Pos:* Founder & business mgr, Greenville Symph Orch, 59-80. *Mailing Add:* 410 Wetherbee St Greenville MS 38701

HAYASHI, YASUKO
SOPRANO
b Kanagawa, Japan, July 19, 48. *Study:* Univ Arts, Tokyo, with Shibata & N Rucci; Consv Giuseppe Verdi, Milan, with Campogalliani; Scuola Perfez, Teatro alla Scala, Milan, with Lia Guarini. *Roles:* Madama Butterfly in Madama Butterfly, La Scala, 72 & NJ State Opera, 82; Maria Stuarda in Maria Stuarda, Fifth Fest della Valle D'Itria, Italy, 79; Carolina & Elisetta in Il Matrimonio segreto; Fiordiligi in Cosi fan tutte; Desdemona in Otello; Serpetta in La Finta giardiniera; Rachel in La Juive. *Pos:* Sop with Japanese, Europ & US opera co. *Awards:* Concours Voci Rossiniane, Italian TV, 72. *Mailing Add:* c/o Int Artist Mgt 111 W 57th St New York NY 10019

HAYASHI, YUKO
ORGAN, EDUCATOR
Japanese citizen. *Study:* Tokyo Univ Arts; New England Consv, BM, 56, MM, 58, artists dipl, 61. *Teaching:* Fac mem, New England Consv, 60-71, chmn organ dept, 71- *Mem:* Am Guild Organists; Organ Hist Soc. *Mailing Add:* 325 Tappan St Brookline MA 02146

HAYES, DEBORAH
EDUCATOR, WRITER
b Miami, Fla, Dec 13, 39. *Study:* Oberlin Col, AB, 60; Stanford Univ, AM, 61, PhD, 68. *Teaching:* From instr to asst prof, Col Music, Univ Colo, Boulder, 68-78, assoc prof music hist & lit, 78- *Mem:* Am Musicol Soc (local chap secy-treas, 69-70). *Interests:* J P Rameau (1687-1764); 18th century music theory; history of women composers and their music, especially 18th century. *Publ:* Auth, Rameau's Nouvelle Methode, J Am Musicol Soc, 74; Christian Huygens, the Science of Music, In: Musicology at Colorado, 78 & co-ed, Musicology at Colorado, 78, Univ Colo; auth, Women Composers of 18th-Century Classic Music, Am Women Comp News, 83; Ruth Shaw Wylie Collection, Sonneck Soc Newslett, 83. *Mailing Add:* 3290 Darley Ave Boulder CO 80303

HAYES, JOSEPH (C)
COMPOSER, EDUCATOR
b Marietta, Ohio, Dec 5, 20. *Study:* Boston Consv Music, 40-41; New England Consv Music, 46-49; Boston Univ, studied comp with Gardner Read, BMus, 50. *Works:* Sunday 3:00 PM (symph), Independent Music Publ, 56; Song of the Colours (a cappella), Grosse Pointe Chamber Singers, 64; Time Capsules (double women's chorus & woodwind quintet), comn & perf by Women's Chorus, Wayne State Univ, 68; Hornotations for Horn and Strings, Ernestine Barnes, 71; Episodes for Five Winds, comn & perf by Chamber Music Wkshp, 73; Two Soliloquies for Violoncello, Irene Sharp, 73; Ode for Flute and Harp, Carol Perkins & Mary MacNair, 77. *Teaching:* Instr band & theory, Claflin Col, 52-53; dir instrumental music & theory, Jarvis Christian Col, 53-56; instr comp, flute & sax, Detroit Community Music Sch, 62- *Mem:* Nat Asn Comp; Phi Mu Alpha Sinfonia. *Mailing Add:* 17120 Kentucky Detroit MI 48221

HAYMAN, RICHARD WARREN JOSEPH
CONDUCTOR, COMPOSER
b Cambridge, Mass, Mar 27, 20. *Study:* Private studies with Arthur Fiedler, Alfred Newman, Victor Young, George Stoll, Lionel Newman & Max Steiner; Detroit Col Bus, Hon Dr Humanities, 80. *Works:* No Strings Attached, 53, Skipping Along, 53, Dansero, 53, Serenade to a Lost Love, 53 & Carriage Trade, 53, Yorkville Music Co; Freddie the Football, Berdick-Hayway Music, 73; Olivia, Yorkville Music Co, 80. *Rec Perf:* On Mercury Rec, 50-65, Time Rec, 65-70, United Artists Rec, 70-72, ABC Rec, 72-74 & Audio Fidelity Rec, 82. *Pos:* Prin pops cond, Detroit Symph Orch, 70-, Ala Symph Orch, 75-, Hartford Symph, 75-, St Louis Symph Orch, 76- & Calgary Phil Orch, 77- *Awards:* Bill Randle Award for Best Rec-Instrm, WERE Radio, Cleveland, 53; Best TV Commercial Jingle, Nat Acad Rec Arts & Sci, 60. *Mem:* Nat Acad Rec Arts & Sci; ASCAP; Am Fedn Musicians. *Rep:* Sheldon Soffer Mgt 130 W 56th St New York NY 10028 *Mailing Add:* 1020 Park Ave New York NY 10028

HAYS, DORIS ERNESTINE
COMPOSER, PIANO
b Memphis, Tenn, Aug 6, 41. *Study:* Univ Chattanooga, BM, 63; Munich Hochschule Music, artist dipl, 66; Univ Wis, MM, 68. *Works:* Sunday Nights, Sunday Mornings, Tetra Music, 77; UNI (dance suite for string quartet, flute & chorus), A Broude, Inc, 78; Southern Voices for Orchestra, 82 & Southern Voices for Tape, 83, Henmar Press; Celebration of No (tape, violin & film), 83 & Flowing Quilt (tape & violin), 83, Tallapoosa Music; Tunings (string quartet), Tetra Music, 83. *Rec Perf:* Doris Hays Plays Henry Cowell, 77 & Adoration of the Clash, 79, Finnadar Rec; Voicings, Folkways, 83. *Pos:* Concert pianist, major European & US fest, 71-; consult, Silver Burdett, Inc, 72-79 & Nat Pub Radio, 80. *Teaching:* Asst prof, Queens Col, 75-76. *Awards:* Cert of Merit, Nat Asn Music Clubs, 77; Nat Endowment Arts Grant, 77, 79 & 82. *Bibliog:* Mary Campbell (auth), Artist With a Mission, Assoc Press, 10/77; Alan Kozinn (auth), Women Composers Get Piccolo Forum, News & Courier, Charleston, SC, 5/30/81; Jane Weiner LePage (auth), Women Composers, Conductors & Musicians of the Twentieth Century, Scarecrow Press, 83. *Mem:* Int League Women Comp (asst chair, 79-82); Frau & Musik, Germany; ASCAP. *Mailing Add:* 697 West End Ave Penthouse B New York NY 10025

HAYS, ELIZABETH L
EDUCATOR, HARPSICHORD
b Fresno, Calif, July 22, 37. *Study:* Univ Calif, Berkeley, BA, 60; Vienna Acad Music, with Eta Harich-Schneider, 61-63; Stanford Univ, with Putnam Aldrich, George Houle & Leonard Ratner, MA, 66, PhD, 77. *Pos:* Ed, harpsichordist & coach, Carmel Bach Fest, 65. *Teaching:* Asst prof music hist, Univ Tex, Austin, 70-71; from asst to assoc prof music, Grinnell Col, 77- *Awards:* Martha Baird Rockefeller Found Grant, 71-72. *Mem:* Am Musicol Soc; Col Music Soc; Riemenschneider Bach Inst; San Francisco Early Music Soc. *Interests:* F W Marpurg's keyboard treatises; 18th century French and German composition & performance styles; early keyboard fingerings. *Mailing Add:* Dept Music Grinnell Col Grinnell IA 50112

HAYS, ROBERT DENECKE
COMPOSER, EDUCATOR
b Boise, Idaho, Jan 31, 23. *Study:* Univ Ore, with Arnold Elston, BS, 47, MS, 49; Columbia Univ, 50-51; Ind Univ, studied comp with Bernard Heiden, DM,

65. *Works:* Design (band), Belwin Inc, 64; Dramatic Fanfares, 65, Southern to the Top, 65 & America's Jr Miss, 65, Berryman Publ; Interchanges (oboe & tape), perf & comn by Roger Rehm, 79. *Pos:* Dir bands, Univ Southern Miss, 56-60; creative dir, Audio Prod, Los Angeles, 69-72. *Teaching:* Prof comp & theory, Univ Southern Miss, 65-69 & Cent Mich Univ, 72-; prof & coordr, Cent Mich Univ, 77. *Awards:* Miss Educ TV Award, 69. *Mailing Add:* 5365 S Winn Rd Mt Pleasant MI 48858

HAYS, WILLIAM PAUL
EDUCATOR, ORGAN
b Westville, Okla, Feb 11, 29. *Study:* Univ Ark, BM, 50; Ind Univ, MM, 52; Union Theol Sem, SMD, 70. *Pos:* Organist & choirmaster, Pulaski Heights Methodist, Little Rock, 52-53 & United Presby, Garden City, NY, 66-68; Continuo Organist, Holy Trinity Bach Vesters, 70- *Teaching:* Asst prof organ, Hendrix Col, 52-53; assoc prof, Union Col, 54-66; assoc prof organ & musicol, Westminister Choir Col, 77- *Mem:* Music Teachers Nat Asn (pres, Eastern div, 79-82); Am Guild Organists; Am Musicol Soc; Am Asn Univ Prof. *Publ:* Ed, Twentieth-Century Views of Music Hist, Schribners, 72; contribr, New Grove Dict of Music & Musicians. *Mailing Add:* 443 W 50th St Apt 2W New York NY 10019

HAYWARD, THOMAS (TIBBETT)
TENOR, EDUCATOR
b Kansas City, Mo, Dec 1, 21. *Study:* Kansas City Consv Music, 38-40. *Rec Perf:* For RCA Victor, Decca Rec, Everest Rec & Cambridge Rec, 47-60. *Roles:* Rodolfo in La Boheme, Chicago Opera, 47; Cavaradossi in Tosca, Alfredo in La Traviata, Alfred in Die Fledermaus, Lt Pinkerton in Madama Butterfly, Rob Roles in Peter Grimes, Il Duka in Rigoletto & Der Sänger in Der Rosenkavalier, Metropolitan Opera, 45-59. *Pos:* Leading ten, New York City Opera, 43-45 & Metropolitan Opera Asn, 45-59; guest artist, Chicago Lyr Opera, New Orleans, Pro Arts, Havana & San Carlo Napoli, Italy. *Teaching:* Prof opera & voice, Southern Methodist Univ, 64- *Awards:* Winner, Metropolitan Opera Auditions, 45. *Bibliog:* Ronald Davis (auth), Biography of Thomas Hayward, Southern Methodist Univ, 83. *Mem:* Nat Asn Teachers Singing; Am Guild Musical Artists; Am Fedn TV & Radio Artists. *Mailing Add:* 7515 A Highmont Dallas TX 75230

HAYWOOD, CARL WHEATLEY
CONDUCTOR, EDUCATOR
b Portsmouth, Va, Sept 7, 49. *Study:* Norfolk State Univ, studied organ with Larry Palmer, BA, 71; Southern Methodist Univ, studied choral with Lloyd Pfautsch, organ with Robert Anderson, MM(choral cond), MSM(organ), 73; Univ Southern Calif, studied choral with Charles Hirt, comp with Halsey Stevens, MSM(choral cond), 73, DMA(choral music), 76. *Works:* Three Psalms, 76, As Toilsome I Wander'd Virginia's Woods, 76, Choral Benediction, 78, There is a Balm, 81, Done Made My Vow, 82 & Didn't My Lord Deliver Daniel, 83, I Sherman Greene Choral. *Rec Perf:* St Paul (Mendelssohn), 79, Requiem (Brahms), 80, The Creation (Haydn), 81, Ordering of Moses (Dett), 82, Mass in G (Schubert), 82 & Missa Brevis (Kodaly), 83, I Sherman Greene Choral Concts. *Pos:* Assoc cond, Chapel Choir, Southern Methodist Univ, 71-73; minister music, Second Baptist Church, Los Angeles, 73-75; cond, I Sherman Greene Chorale, 78- *Teaching:* Assoc prof choral music & organ, Norfolk State Univ, 75- *Mem:* Am Guild Organists; Am Choral Dir Asn; Nat Asn Negro Musicians; Col Music Soc; Music Educr Nat Conf. *Mailing Add:* 3553 Campion Arenne Virginia Beach VA 23462

HAYWOOD, CHARLES
EDUCATOR, TENOR
b Grodno, Russia, Dec 20, 04. *Study:* City Col New York, BS, 26; Inst Musical Art, artist dipl, 31; Juilliard Sch, with Schoen-Rene & Alfredo Valenti, dipl, 35; Columbia Univ, with Paul H Lang & James L Mursell, MA, 40, PhD, 49. *Pos:* Soloist, Little Church Around the Corner, New York, 29-35 & Free Synagogue, Carnegie Hall, 36-50. *Teaching:* Instr voice, Juilliard Sch Music, 39-46; prof musicol, Queens Col, City Univ New York, 39-73; vis prof folk music, Hunter Col, City Univ New York, 58-59; vis prof opera, Shakespeare & music, Univ Calif, Los Angeles, 61-62. *Awards:* Folger Shakespeare Fel, 51; Henry E Huntington Libr Res Fel, 52-53; Fulbright Res Fel, 67-68. *Mem:* Int Coun Traditional Music; Soc Ethnomusicol; Am Musicol Soc. *Interests:* Folksong; music in the Shakespearean theatre. *Publ:* Auth, James A Bland, E B Marks, 46; Cervantes and Music, Hispania, 5/48; Bibliography of North American Folklore and Folksong, Dover, 60; ed, Folksongs of the World, John Day, 66; auth, Charles Dickens and Shakespeare, Dickensian, 5/70. *Mailing Add:* 145 E 92nd St New York NY 10028

HAZZARD, PETER (PEABODY)
COMPOSER, CONDUCTOR
b Poughkeepsie, NY, Jan 31, 49. *Study:* Berklee Col Music, BM(comp), 71; studied comp with John Bavicchi & William Maloof & cond with Jeronimas Kascinskas. *Works:* Sonata No II for Clarinet & Marimba, Opus 23, Jacksonville State Univ Chamber Players, 71; Fantasia on a Theme of Brahms, Op 31 (piano), various perfs, 74; Fanfare for December 9, 1901, Op 32, Mass Inst Technology Concert Band, 75; Concerto for Clarinet & Band, Op 43, Jacksonville State Univ & others, 78; Landmark Suite, Op 49, Ludwig Music Co, 80; Elegy Written in a Country Churchyard, Op 47 (sop & band), Berklee Concert Band, 80; Silver Jubille Overture, Op 52, Concord Band, 83. *Pos:* Asst cond, Arlington Symph Orch, Mass, 71-78; cond, Berklee Concert Band, Berklee Col Music, 76-83; cond & music dir, Melrose Symph Orch, 83. *Teaching:* Instr music, Berklee Col Music, 71-, chmn traditional studies, 78-83; dir instrm music, Lawrence Acad, 83- *Bibliog:* Nat Segaloff (auth), So You Want to Be Beethoven!, Boston Herald Mag, 9/18/77; Caren Demoulas (auth), Music Always on His Mind, Woburn Daily Times, 1/14/83. *Mem:* ASCAP; Harvard Musical Asn. *Mailing Add:* Lawrence Acad Groton MA 01450

HEAD, EMERSON WILLIAMS
TRUMPET, EDUCATOR
b Wilmington, NC, Apr 9, 35. *Study:* Univ Mich, studied trumpet with Clifford Lillya, BM, 57, MM, 61; Cath Univ Am, studied with Lloyd Geisler, DMA, 80. *Rec Perf:* Music for Trumpet & Piano, 78, Music for Trumpet & Orchestra, 80 & Favorites for Trumpet & Band, 80, Trumpeter Rec. *Pos:* Prin trumpet, Brevard Music Fest, 56-66, Jacksonville Symph, 57-59 & Winston-Salem Symph, 59-62; cond, Wake Forest Univ Bands, 59-62, Univ Md Symph Orch, 62-67 & 78-79, Prince Georges Phil, 69-79 & Metro Washington Baha'i Chorale, 74-77; trumpet soloist, Theater Chamber Players, Kennedy Ctr, 80-; trumpet recitalist, clinician & soloist. *Teaching:* Instr instrm music, Duval Co Pub Sch, Jacksonville, Fla, 57-59 & Wake Forest Univ, 59-62; prof trumpet, Univ Md, College Park, 62- *Mem:* Int Trumpet Guild. *Mailing Add:* 23010 Howard Chapel Rd Brookeville MD 20833

HEALEY, DEREK EDWARD
COMPOSER, EDUCATOR
b Wargrave, Berkshire, England, May 2, 36. *Study:* Royal Col Music, London, ARCM, 57; Univ Durham, England, BMus, 61; Univ Toronto, Can, DMus, 74. *Works:* Organ Concerto, 65, Serenata for Strings, 68 & Butterflies, 70, Alexander Broude; Arctic Images, Recordi, 71; Six Canadian Folk Songs, G V Thompson, 73; Shape Note Symph, Alexander Broude, 75 & 79; Seabird Island, Guelph Fest Opera, 77. *Rec Perf:* Organ Concerto, Can Broadcasting Corp, 71. *Teaching:* Lectr, Univ Victoria, Can, 69-71; vis lectr, Univ Toronto, Can, 71-72; assoc prof, Univ Guelph, Can, 72-78 & Univ Ore, 79- *Awards:* Farrar Prize, Royal Col Music, 57; Second Int Comp Prize, Univ Louisville, Ky, 80; Delius Fest Comp Cont, 81. *Bibliog:* MacMillan & Beckwith (auth), Contemporary Canadian Composer, Oxford Univ Press, 75; Michael Schulman (auth), The Long Journey to Seabird Island, Perf Arts Can, 77; Rick MacMillan (auth), Derek Healey, PROC, Can, 80. *Mem:* Am Music Ctr; fel, Royal Col Organists; Am Soc Univ Comp; Can Music Ctr. *Rep:* PROC 41 Valleybrook Dr Toronto Ont Can M3B 2S6. *Mailing Add:* 2877 Timberline Dr Eugene OR 97405

HEARNE, JOSEPH FREDERIC
DOUBLE BASS
b Lorain, Ohio, Aug 20, 42. *Study:* Juilliard Sch Music, 60-62; New England Consv Music, 62-64. *Pos:* Mem, Oregon Symph Orch, 59-60, Aspen Fest Orch, 61 & Boston Symph Orch, 62-; asst prin, Boston Pops Orch, 65- *Mailing Add:* c/o Boston Symph 301 Massachusetts Ave Boston MA 02115

HEARTZ, DANIEL LEONARD
EDUCATOR
b Exeter, NH, Oct 5, 28. *Study:* Univ NH, AB, 50; Harvard Univ, AM, 51, PhD, 57. *Teaching:* Instr, Univ Chicago, 57-58, asst prof, 58-60; asst prof, Univ Calif, Berkeley, 60-65, assoc prof, 65-67, prof, 67-, chmn music dept, 69-73; res fel humanities, Princeton Univ, 63-64. *Awards:* Guggenheim Fel, 67-68 & 78-79; Dent Medal, Royal Music Asn, 70; Kinkeldy Award, Am Musicol Soc, 71. *Mem:* Am Musicol Soc (vpres, 74-76); Royal Music Asn; Soc Francaise Musicol. *Publ:* Ed, Preludes, Chansons and Dances for Lute, 64; Theorie und Kompositionsstudien bei Mozart, 64-69; auth, Pierre Attaingant, Royal Printer of Music, 69. *Mailing Add:* 1098 Keith Ave Berkeley CA 94708

HEATON, CHARLES HUDDLESTON
ORGAN, EDUCATOR
b Centralia, Ill, Nov 1, 28. *Study:* DePauw Univ, BMus, 50; Union Theol Sem, NY, MSacMus, 52, DSacMus, 57. *Works:* Where Is This Stupendous Stranger, 79 & See Us, Lord, About Thine Altar, 83, H W Gray Co. *Pos:* Minister music, Second Presby Church, St Louis, Mo, 56-72; organist & dir, Temple Israel, St Louis, 59-70 & East Liberty Presby Church, Pittsburgh, 72-; organ recitalist, currently. *Teaching:* Lectr sacred music, Eden Theol Sem, 68-71 & Pittsburgh Theol Sem, 73-76; private teacher organ, currently. *Mem:* Hymn Soc Am; Fel, Am Guild Organists (nat counr, 67-70). *Publ:* Auth, How to Build a Church Choir, 58 & A Guidebook to Worship Services of Sacred Music, 62, Bethany Press; ed, Hymnbook for Christian Worship, Bethany Judson Press, 70. *Mailing Add:* 5436 Plainfield St Pittsburgh PA 15217

HEBERT, BLISS
DIRECTOR—OPERA
b Faust, NY, Nov 30, 30. *Study:* Syracuse Univ, BA, 51, MMus, 52; studied piano with Robert Godsand, Simone Barrere, Lelia Gousseau & Pierre Bernac. *Rec Perf:* Igor Stravinsky's major operas, Columbia. *Pos:* Stage dir, Santa Fe Opera, 57-, Houston Opera, 63-, San Francisco Opera, 63-, Metropolitan Opera, 73, Baltimore Opera, 73-, Miami Opera, 75- & Dallas Opera, 77-; gen mgr, Washington Opera Soc, 60-63; dir, San Francisco Opera Co, 63, Houston Opera Co, 64; Cincinnati Opera Co, 68, Vancouver Opera Co, 69, New Orleans Opera Co, 70, Toronto Opera Co, 72, Dallas Opera Co, 77 & others; guest dir, Juilliard Sch, 75-76. *Teaching:* Mem fac, Boston Univ, 52-53 & Univ Wash, 69. *Mem:* Phi Mu Alpha. *Mailing Add:* c/o Robert Lombardo 30 W 60th St #3A New York NY 10023

HECK, THOMAS F
LIBRARIAN, GUITAR & LUTE
b Washington, DC, July 10, 43. *Study:* Univ Notre Dame, BA(music hist), 65; Yale Univ, PhD(music hist), 70. *Pos:* Head, Music-Dance Libr, Ohio State Univ, Columbus, 78- *Teaching:* Asst prof music, Case Western Reserve Univ, 71-74, John Carroll Univ, 74-75 & Chapman Col, 75-76; assoc prof music, Ohio State Univ, 82- *Awards:* Fulbright Grad Fel, 68-69. *Mem:* Am Musicol Soc; Music Libr Asn; Int Asn Music Libr; Guitar Found Am. *Interests:* History of the guitar; history of music printing and dating of undated printed

music; design of bibliographic data bases. *Publ:* Auth, Lute Music: Tablatures, Textures and Transcriptions, J Lute Soc Am, Vol VII, 19-30; contribr, articles on guitarists, In: New Grove Dict of Music & Musicians, 80; ed, Franz Schubert: Sixteen Songs With Guitar Accompaniment, Tecla Ed, 80; auth, Guitar Music in the Archive of the Guitar Foundation of America: A Computerized Catalog, Guitar Found Am, 81. *Mailing Add:* Music Libr Sullivant Hall Ohio State Univ Columbus OH 43210

HEDBERG, FLOYD CARL
EDUCATOR, CONDUCTOR
b Topeka, Kans, Aug 1, 26. *Study:* Washburn Univ, BMus, 49; Kans Univ, MMusEd, 54; Univ Northern Colo, DEd, 75. *Pos:* Cond, Topeka Symph Chorus, 62- *Teaching:* Dir choral activ, Washburn Univ, 61-, chmn dept music, 82- *Mailing Add:* Music Dept Washburn Univ Topeka KS 66621

HEDWIG, DOUGLAS FREDERICK
TRUMPET, EDUCATOR
b New York, NY, June 24, 51. *Study:* Manhattan Sch Music, BM, 73; Juilliard Sch, MM, 76. *Rec Perf:* Music of the Federal Era, New World Rec, 78; Cantata: She Is Thy Life (Bruce Adolphe), Orion Rec, 82. *Pos:* Trumpet extra, Metropolitan Opera Orch, 73-; trumpet, Piedmont Brass Quintet, 78; Metropolitan Brass Quartet, 76-; asst prin cornet, Guggenheim Concert Band, 77-; premiere perf of works for trumpet by Starer, Goedicke & Hovhaness. *Teaching:* Instr trumpet, Extension Div, Manhattan Sch Music, 77; artist in res, Western Carolina Univ, 78; instr, Dupont Music Studio, 81- *Awards:* Two new works written for & dedicated to Douglas Hedwig by Bruce Adolphe & Robert Starer. *Mem:* Int Trumpet Guild; Col Music Soc; Music Educr Nat Conf; Nat Asn Col Wind & Perc Instr. *Mailing Add:* 255 W 95th St 3A New York NY 10025

HEGENBART, ALEX FRANK
EDUCATOR, COMPOSER
b Amsterdam, Netherlands, Aug 2, 22; US citizen. *Study:* Amsterdam Consv, MM, 45. *Works:* Simeon's Prayer, Brodt Music Co, 60; Meditation, Abingden Press, 66; Sing, O Sing, perf by Charlotte Choral Soc, 68; Hear Ye! (A Christmas Cantata), Gaston Col Chorus & Orch, 73; folk song arr, Western Piedmont Symph Orch, 80; Meditations on The Lord's Prayer, Avondale Presby Church, 80. *Pos:* Minister music, various churches, 58-76. *Teaching:* Chmn music dept, Gaston Col, Dallas, 78- *Mailing Add:* 33 Paradise Cir Belmont NC 28012

HEGYI, JULIUS
CONDUCTOR, VIOLIN
b New York, NY, Feb 2, 23. *Study:* Juilliard Sch Music, BA, 43; studied violin with Sascha Jacobsen, Jacques Gordon & Eddy Brown; studied comp with Vittorio Giannini; studied cond with Dimitri Mitropoulos. *Pos:* Founder, Hegyi & Amati String quartets, 41 & Music in Round Ser, 51; cond, Wagner Col Symph, 41-43, San Antonio Little Symph, 48-51, Abilene Symph, 52-55, Southwestern Symph Ctr, 51-56, Chattanooga Symph, 55-65, Albany Symph, 66- & Berkshire Symph, 66-; assoc cond, San Antonio Symph, 48-51; founder & dir, Sewanee Summer Music Ctr, 58; founder & cond, Carlatti Orch, 64; solo recitals & chamber music concerts in US & Mex; mem, Gordon & Am String Quartets, New York Phil, City Ctr Ballet, RCA Victor Symph & Bershire Quartet, formerly; mem & dir chamber music activities, Williams Trio; spec consult, Nat Endowment Arts, 79- *Teaching:* Fac music, Williams Col, 65-, lectr, cond & violinist in res, 71- *Awards:* Alice Ditson Award, 57; Nat Cond Recognition Award, Am Symph League, 59; Award Artistic Excellence, Albany League Arts, 77. *Mem:* NY Little Orch Soc. *Mailing Add:* Northwest Hill Rd Williamstown MA 01267

HEIBERG, HAROLD WILLARD
PIANO, EDUCATOR
b Twin Valley, Minn, Feb 6, 22. *Study:* St Olaf Col, BM, 43; Teachers Col, Columbia Univ, MA, 49, private piano with K U Schnabel & Leonard Shure & voice with Gerhard Huesch & Cornelius Reid. *Pos:* Minister music, Trinity Lutheran Church, Brooklyn, NY, 56-71; choral dir, New York Theol Sem, 59-68. *Teaching:* Instr piano, Cleveland Music Sch Settlement, 52-56; coach & lectr German lieder, Summer Vocal Inst, Am Inst Musical Studies, Graz, Austria, 70-; prof music, NTex State Univ, Denton, 71- *Mem:* Lutheran Soc Worship, Music & Arts; Music Teachers Nat Asn; Tex Music Teachers Asn; Pi Kappa Lambda. *Mailing Add:* 2111 N Locust St Denton TX 76201

HEIDEN, BERNHARD
COMPOSER, MUSIC DIRECTOR
b Frankfurt, Ger, Aug 24, 10; US citizen. *Study:* Hochschule Musik, Berlin, grad 33; Cornell Univ, MA, 46. *Works:* Sonata (sax & piano), European Am, 37; Sonata (horns & piano), 39 & Quintet (horn & strings), 52, Assoc Music Publ; Sonata (cello & piano), Peer Int, 58; The Darkened City (opera), European Am, 68; Partita for Orchestra, Assoc Music Publ, 70. *Pos:* Staff arr, Radio Station WWJ, Detroit, 38-39; asst bandmaster, US Army, 43-45. *Teaching:* Fac mem, Art Ctr Music Sch, Detroit, 35-43; prof music, Ind Univ, Bloomington, 46-81. *Awards:* Mendelssohn Prize, 33; fel, Guggenheim Found, 66-67 & Nat Endowment Arts, 76. *Bibliog:* Ann Stimson Yama (auth), The Darkened City, Opera J, Vol XII, No 4. *Mailing Add:* 915 E Univ Bloomington IN 47401

HEIER, DOROTHY R
TRUMPET, EDUCATOR
b Factoryville, Pa, Oct 28, 27. *Study:* Nyack Col, BSM, 52; Manhattan Sch Music, MM, 55; Teachers Col, Columbia Univ, with William Vacchiano, EdD, 63. *Pos:* Solo trumpet, Suburban Symph, Rockland Co, NY, 56-65;

music rev, Nat Asn Col Wind & Perc Instr J, currently. *Teaching:* Instr, Toccoa Falls Col, 52-54; from instr music to assoc prof, Nyack Col, 55-65; prof, William Paterson Col, 65- *Mem:* Int Trumpet Guild; Nat Asn Col Wind & Perc Instr (state chmn, 70 & 83). *Publ:* Auth, Trumpet Variations, 63 & Trombome Variations, 63, Lillenas Publ; How to Cope with 20th Century Music, Brass-Woodwind, 70. *Mailing Add:* 680 Ramapo Valley Rd Oakland NJ 07436

HEIFETZ, DANIEL
VIOLIN, EDUCATOR
b Kansas City, Mo, Nov 20, 48. *Study:* Calif Inst Arts; Curtis Inst Music, with Efrem Zimbalist & Ivan Galamian. *Pos:* Conct violinist, US, Can, Europe & South Am; unaccompanied violin recital, CBS TV; performer, Can Broadcast Corp TV; mem bd govs, Inst for Humane Resource Develop, Philadelphia; mem bd adv, Nat Cathedral Choral Soc, Washington, DC. *Teaching:* Mem fac violin, Peabody Consv Music; lectr & instr masterclasses in univ throughout US. *Awards:* First Prize, Merriweather Post Compt, Washington, DC, 69; Fourth Prize, Int Tchaikovsky Compt, Moscow, 78. *Mem:* The Bohemians. *Mailing Add:* Baltimore MD

HEIFETZ, JASCHA
VIOLINIST
b Vilna, Russia, Feb 2, 01; US citizen. *Study:* Royal Sch Music, Vilna, dipl, 10; studied with Leopold Auer; Petrograd Consv Music; Northwestern Univ, MusD, 49. *Pos:* Concert perf in Russia, Germany, Austro-Hungary, Scandinavia & US, 17, Australia & New Zealand, 21, Far East, 23 & World Tour, 25-27. *Teaching:* Fac mem dept music, Univ Southern Calif, currently. *Awards:* Grammy Award; Commander, Legion of Honor, France. *Mem:* Am Guild Musical Artists; Asn des Anciens Eleves du Consv. *Mailing Add:* Music Dept Univ Southern Calif Los Angeles CA 90089

HEILBRON, VALERIE J
COMPOSER
b Meriden, Conn, Apr 25, 48. *Study:* San Francisco State Univ, with Dr Henry Onderdonk, MA(comp), 82. *Works:* Duet for Violin and Piano, On a Theme by T S Elliot, Oakland Symph, 81; Ladies' Voices, Veil of Isis, 81; Argument in E (brass quintet; also chamber ens), San Francisco Symph & Oakland Symph, 82; K B & Blue, Green and White, Publ Wadsworth, 83. *Awards:* Peter Frampton Award for Excellence Contemp Music, Frampton & San Francisco State Univ, 82. *Mem:* BMI; Int League Women Comp. *Mailing Add:* c/o TCLM Prod Box 356 Mill Valley CA 94941

HEILNER, IRWIN
COMPOSER, WRITER
b New York, NY. *Study:* Teachers Col, Columbia Univ, BS, MA, MS; private study with Rubin Goldmark, Nadia Boulanger & Roger Sessions. *Works:* Swing Symphony, Mav Szimfonikusok, Hungary, 44; Boogie Woogie Rhapsody, Paragon Music Publ, 48; Chinese Songs, CRI, 48; Songs for Voice and Piano, Mary Meyers & Doris Montville, 75; Concerto In Memory of Dvorak (violin), El Paso Youth Symph, 79 & Nutley Symph Orch, 81; Songs for Voice and Guitar, Walter Spalding & Bonnie Feather, 81. *Mem:* Am Comp Alliance; Am Music Ctr. *Publ:* Auth, Numerous Reviews of Music, Records and Books, Jewish Currents, 74-; Tenament Songs: The Popular Music of the Jewish Immigrants, WIN Mag, 82. *Mailing Add:* 101 Dawson Ave Clifton NJ 07012

HEIM, LEO EDWARD
TEACHER, PIANO
b Chandler, Ind, Sept 22, 13. *Study:* Sch Lib Arts, Northwestern Univ, 31-32; Am Consv Music, BM, 35, MM, 47. *Pos:* Organist, First Church Christ, Wilmette, Ill, 36- *Teaching:* Piano, Am Consv Music, 35-, dean, 56-71, pres, 71-81, emer pres, 81- *Mem:* Phi Mu Alpha Sinfonia; Soc Am Musicians. *Mailing Add:* 515 Vine Ave Park Ridge IL 60068

HEIM, NORMAN MICHAEL
CLARINET, COMPOSER
Study: Univ Evansville, BME, 51; Univ Rochester, MM, 52, DMA, 62. *Works:* Preludium and Canzone, Op 22, Kendor Music, Inc, 81; Four Episodes, Op 49, Dorn Publ, 81; Celebration Suite, Op 41, Kendor Music, Inc, 82; Symphonic Sketches, Op 46, 82, Invocation, Op 53, 82, Sonata da Chiesa, Op 48, 82 & Concerto da Camera, Op 36, 83, Dorn Publ. *Rec Perf:* Music for Clarinet Choir, Kendor Rec Studio, 78; Clarinet Ensemble Music, Peabody Inst Rec Studio, 82. *Teaching:* Instr music, Cent Mo Col, 52-53; asst prof, Univ Evansville, 53-60; prof, Univ Md, 60- *Bibliog:* Stephen Johnsten (auth), Music of Norman Heim, Clarinet, 83. *Mem:* Int Clarinet Soc; Nat Asn Col Wind & Perc Instr; Int Soc Prom Wind Music; Music Educr Nat Conf; Music Libr Asn. *Interests:* Research in clarinet literature pedagogy and performance practices. *Publ:* Auth, Aspects of Teaching Wind Instruments, Mit Teilungs Blatt, 81; Bass Clarinet Music Part VII Duos and Trios, Clarinet, 82; Wagner and the Clarinet, Alta Musik, 83; The Use of the Clarinet in Church, Nat Asn Col Wind Perc Instr J, 83; The Basset Horn, Woodwind, Brass & Perc, 83. *Mailing Add:* 7402 Wells Blvd Hyattsville MD 20783

HEIN, MARY ALICE
EUDCATOR
b Oakland, Calif, Feb 22, 24. *Study:* Holy Names Col, AB, 45, MA, 63; New England Consv, 45-46; Liszt Acad Music, Budapest, cert, 71. *Teaching:* Music supvr, Calif pub sch, 45-51 & Calif Sisters of Holy Names, 54-63; asst prof music, Holy Names Col, 63- *Awards:* Int Res & Exchanges Fel, 70-71; Ford Found & Hewlett Found Grants, 73-; Kodaly Centennial Award, Hungarian Govt, 83. *Bibliog:* Joyce Chopra (dir), Music Lessons (film), Ford Found, 80. *Mem:* Music Educr Nat Conf; Int Kodaly Soc (secy-treas, 75-79 & mem bd, 79-); Orgn Am Kodaly Educr (mem bd, 76-78). *Mailing Add:* Holy Names Col 3500 Mountain Blvd Oakland CA 94619

HEINRICH, ADEL VERNA
EDUCATOR, ORGAN

b Cleveland, Ohio, July 20, 26. *Study:* Flora Stone Mather Col, Case Western Reserve Univ, BA; Union Theol Sem, NY, MSM; Univ Wis, Madison, AMusD; studied organ with Hugh Porter, John Harvey, E Power Biggs, Andre Marchal & Jean Langlais, cond with Robert Shaw & Robert Fountain, harpsichord with Eugenia Eare, comp with Harold Friedel & analysis with Julius Herford. *Works:* A Carol Is Born (chorus); Alleluia-Alleluia (chorus); Four Choral Paraphrases on Hymns of Praise (organ). *Pos:* Asst orch cond, Colby Community Symph Orch, 64-74; recitalist organ & harpsichord, with instrm, soloists or choir, US recital halls, cols & univ, currently. *Teaching:* Mem fac, Colby Col, 64- & Colby Church Music Inst, summers 64- *Awards:* Mellon Grant, 78-79. *Mem:* Am Musicol Soc; Int League Women Comp; Am Guild Organists. *Publ:* Auth, A Collation of the Expositions in Die Kunst der Fuge of J S Bach, Bach, 4/81; Bach's Die Kunst der Fuge: A Living Compendium of Fugal Procedures, Univ Press Am, 82. *Mailing Add:* 1 Highland Ave Waterville ME 04901

HEINTZE, JAMES RUDOLPH
EDUCATOR, LIBRARIAN

b Washington, DC, Oct 10, 42. *Study:* Loyola Col, BS, 67; Am Univ, MA, 69; Univ Md, College Park, MLS, 72. *Pos:* Music librn, Am Univ, 69- *Teaching:* Lectr Am music & piano, Am Univ, 74- *Interests:* American music; colonial Maryland; librarianship: American music discographies, reference tools. *Publ:* Auth, Music of the Washington Family: A Little-Known Collection, Musical Quart, Vol 56, No 2; American Music Before 1865, Notes, Vol 34, No 3 & Vol 37, No 1; Alexander Malcolm: Musician, Clergyman and Schoolmaster, Md Hist Mag, Vol 73, No 3; Esther W Ballou & Alexander Malcolm, In: New Grove Dict of Music & Musicians, 80. *Mailing Add:* 4101 Denfeld Ave Kensington MD 20895

HEISS, DAVID HENRY
CELLO, TEACHER

b Binghamton, NY, May 3, 54. *Study:* State Univ NY, Binghamton, with Donald McCall, BA(music), 76; Juilliard Sch, with Leonard Rose, MM, 79. *Works:* The Elephant Man (Broadway score), Samuel French Inc, 80. *Pos:* Solo cellist & arranger, The Elephant Man, Broadway, 78-80; conct cellist, Joanne Rile Mgt, 80-; steady extra cellist, Metropolitan Opera Orch, 81- *Teaching:* Private cello, 70- *Awards:* New York Debut Award, Artists Int, Inc, 76. *Mem:* Am Fedn Musicians. *Rep:* Joanne Rile Mgt PO Box 27539 Philadelphia PA 19118. *Mailing Add:* 304 W 75th St Apt #10E New York NY 10023

HEISS, JOHN CARTER
COMPOSER, FLUTE & PICCOLO

b New York, NY, 1938. *Study:* Studied flute with Hosmer, Lora & Tipton, 54-62; Lehigh Univ, studied comp with Babbitt, Kim, Luening, Milhaud & Westergaard, 60-65; Aspen Music Sch, 62 & 63; Princeton Univ, MFA(music), 67. *Works:* Inventions, Contours & Colors, 77 & Songs of Nature, 78, Boosey & Hawkes; Capriccio for Flute, Clarinet & Perc, 77, Flute Concerto, 78, Chamber Concerto, 79, Eloquy, 79 & From Infinity Full Circle, 79, E C Schirmer. *Rec Perf:* Quartet for Flute, Clarinet, Cello & Piano, 72, Four Movements for Three Flutes, 77 & Inventions, Contours & Colors, 77, CRI; other rec by Nonesuch, Golden Crest, Turnabout & Arista. *Pos:* Prin flute, Boston Musica Viva, 69-74. *Teaching:* Fac, Barnard Col, Columbia Univ & Mass Inst Technol, formerly; fac music, New England Consv, currently. *Awards:* ASCAP Awards, 75-; grants, Martha Baird Rockefeller Found, 76 & 82 & Guggenheim Found, 78-79. *Mem:* ASCAP; Am Asn Univ Prof; Am Fedn Musicians; Am Music Ctr; Col Music Soc. *Publ:* Auth, articles on contemp perf tech & on Stravinsky, Perspectives of New Music, Instrumentalist, Winds Quart & other jour. *Mailing Add:* 61 Hancock St Auburndale MA 02166

HELD, DAVID PAUL
EDUCATOR, CONDUCTOR

b Sheboygan, Wis, Aug 24, 38. *Study:* Concordia Teachers Col, BS, 60; Univ Northern Iowa, MS, 65; Univ Southern Calif, DMA, 76. *Pos:* Dir music, Immanuel Luthern Church, Waterloo, Iowa, 60-66 & St John Luthern Church, Orange, Calif, 66-79. *Teaching:* Prof, Concordia Teachers Col, 79-, div chmn, 82- *Mem:* Am Choral Dir Assoc; Hymn Soc Am; Liturgical Conf; Am Guild Organists. *Publ:* Auth, Eighteenth Century Chorale Preludes for Organ and a Solo Instrument, Church Music, 78; The Joy of Children's Choral Sound, Choristers Guild, 80; The Role of Congregational Singing in the Church, Issues, 82. *Mailing Add:* 372 Shannon Rd Seward NE 68434

HELDRICH, CLAIRE
EDUCATOR

Study: Manhattan Sch Music, MM. *Rec Perf:* On CBS Masterworks, Vox, Nonesuch, CRI, New World & Op One. *Pos:* Dir, New Music Consort, formerly; performer, Group Contemp Music, formerly, Contemp Chamber Ens, formerly, Continuum, formerly, Speculum Musicae, formerly, Am Comp Orch, formerly & Orch 20th Century, formerly. *Teaching:* Dir, Summer Perc Prog, Reykjavik Col Music, Iceland, formerly; mem fac, Prep Div, Manhattan Sch Music, 76-, dir, Contemp Ens, 81-; distinguished vis prof, Middlebury Col, 81-82. *Mailing Add:* 545 W 111th St #10G New York NY 10025

HELLER, DUANE L
COMPOSER, EDUCATOR

b Douglas, Wyo, May 8, 51. *Study:* Univ Denver, with Normand Lockwood; Univ Southern Calif, with Halsey Stevens; Cornell Univ, with Karel Husa & Robert Palmer. *Works:* Vocalises (strings); Variations on a Theme of Paganini

(chamber ens); Adam and Eve (cantata for double chorus, soli, four celli, piano & perc); O Magnum Mysterium (double chorus, two flutes); Love Songs (bar & cello); Symphony: in memoriam (1976-80); Motet II: Tenebrae Factae Sunt. *Teaching:* Asst prof music, Ore State Univ, currently. *Awards:* Victor Herbert Citation, ASCAP, 77; grants, Nat Endowment Arts & Ore Arts Comn. *Mailing Add:* Dept Music Ore State Univ Corvallis OR 97331

HELLER, JACK JOSEPH
ADMINISTRATOR, CONDUCTOR & MUSIC DIRECTOR

b New Orleans, La, Nov 30, 32. *Study:* Juilliard Sch Music, dipl, 52; Univ Mich, MMus, 58; Univ Iowa, PhD, 62. *Pos:* Asst concertmaster, New Orleans Opera Asn, 47-49; violinist, New York, 50-55; concertmaster, Toledo Symph Orch, 55-58; music dir & cond, Manchester Symph Orch, 68- *Teaching:* Prof music, Univ Conn, Storrs, 60- & assoc dean fine arts, 82- *Awards:* Weekend with Music, Standard Oil NJ & New York Phil, 49. *Interests:* Communication process from performer to listener; musical perception. *Publ:* Coauth, Orientation for Considering Models of Musical Behavior, In: Handbook Music Psychol, 80; Psychomusicology & Psycholinguistics: Parallel Paths or Separate Ways? Psychomusicol, 81; Music & Language, Ann Arbor Symposium 1979, Music Educr Nat Conf, 81; Theoretical Model of Musical Perception & Talent, 81 & Music Cognition, 82, Coun Res Music Educ. *Mailing Add:* 60 Farmstead Rd Storrs CT 06268

HELLER, JOAN
SOPRANO, EDUCATOR

b Baltimore, Md. *Study:* Oberlin Col, with Ellen Repp, BMus, 66; New England Consv, MMus, 70; study with Phyllis Curtin, Tanglewood, Gerald Moore, Mozarteum & Cathy Berberian, Holland Fest. *Rec Perf:* Music of James Yannatos, Sonory Rec, 76; New England Conservatory Faculty Composers--Cogan, Golden Crest Rec, 77; Mother ....! Mother ....! A Jazz Symphony, Pablo Rec, 80; New Events: Boston Composers of the 70's, 80 & New Events: Boston Composers of the 70's, 82, Spectrum Rec; Music of Chinary Ung, CRI, 82; Solo Brothers—A Jazz Symphony, Rudy Van Gelder Studios, 83. *Roles:* Music for Voices, Mallate Instruments & Organ (Steve Reich), Boston Symph Orch, 73; Miss Donnithorne's Maggot (Peter Maxwell Davies), Collage, 79; Cantata della Fiaba Estrema (Hans Werner Henze), John Oliver Chorale, 79; Pierrot Lunaire (Schoenberg), Contemp Chamber Ens, 82; Solo Brothers (Charles Schwartz), Phil Virtuosi, 83; Canti Lunatici (Bernard Rands), Collage, 83. *Pos:* Conct soloist, contemp music, currently. *Teaching:* Asst prof voice, Sch Music, Yale Univ, 74-83. *Awards:* C D Jackson Prize, Berkshire Music Ctr, 70; High Fidelity, Musical Am Award, Berkshire Music Ctr, 72. *Mem:* Nat Asn Teachers Singing. *Rep:* Guy Freedman 37 Robins Crescent New Rochelle NY 10801. *Mailing Add:* 141 Spring Water Ln New Canaan CT 06840

HELLER, LESLEY
VIOLIN, TEACHER

b New York, NY. *Study:* Hartt Col Music, with Raphael Bronstein, BM, 72. *Rec Perf:* Heller-Burnham Violin Duo, Musical Heritage Soc, 81. *Pos:* Violinist, Metropolitan Opera, 76-; mem, Heller-Burnham Violin Duo, 73- *Teaching:* Violin & viola, Manhattan Sch Music, 78-; vis instr, violin, viola & chamber music, Wesleyan Univ, 80- *Mem:* Chamber Music Am. *Mailing Add:* 150 West End Ave Apt 9-C New York NY 10023

HELLER, MARIAN
CELLO

b New York, NY, Mar 26, 46. *Study:* Juilliard Sch, with Luigi Silva, Leonard Rose & Joseph Gingold, BS, 67. *Pos:* Cellist, Bangor String Quartet, Music in Maine, 67-69; asst prin cello, Nat Arts Ctr Orch, Can, 69-75 & Metropolitan Opera, 77- *Mailing Add:* 525 West End Ave New York NY 10024

HELLERMANN, WILLIAM DAVID
COMPOSER, GUITAR & LUTE

b Milwaukee, Wis, July 15, 39. *Study:* Studied with Stefan Wolpe, 62-65; Columbia Univ, MA, 69; Sch of Arts, Columbia Univ, DMA, 76. *Works:* Time and Again (symph orch), 68 & Passages 13: The Fire (trumpet & tape), 71, Theodore Presser; To the Last Drop, Schirmer Books, 73; But, the Moon ... (chamber concerto), 75, Anyway ... (symph orch), 76, Tremble (solo guitar), 77 & Three Weeks in Cincinnati in December (solo flute), 79, Theodore Presser. *Rec Perf:* On the Edge of a Node, CRI, 74; Patterns II (James Fulkerson), 75 & Patterns VII (James Fulkerson), 75, Folkways. *Pos:* Gen mgr, Comp Forum Inc, 68-81; ed, Calendar for New Music, 79-; cur music & sound, Proj Studios One, 80-; pres, Soundart Found Inc, 82- *Awards:* Prix de Rome, Am Acad Rome, 72-74; Creative Artists Pub Serv Award, 75 & 78; Nat Endowment Arts Comp Librettists Award, 76 & 79. *Bibliog:* Tom Johnson (auth), Getting into Tremble, Village Voice, 78; Pierre Job (auth), L'Art Vide, Le Monde de la Musique, Paris, 78; Amanda Smith (auth), William Hellermann: Maximal Composer, Soho Weekly News, 79. *Mem:* BMI; Am Comp Alliance. *Mailing Add:* 45 Greene St New York NY 10013

HELMERS, WILLIAM ALAN
CLARINET, TEACHER

b Wilmington, Del, Mar 1, 75. *Study:* Eastman Sch Music, BM, 79; Juilliard Sch Music, MM, 80; studied with Stanley Hasty, Joseph Allard, Ronald Reuben & Mitchell Lurie. *Pos:* Clarinet & bass clarinet, Milwaukee Symph, 80-; clarinet, Milwaukee Chamber Music Soc, 81- *Teaching:* Instr woodwind chamber music & clarinet, Wis Consv, 81- *Awards:* Bronz Medal, Int Clarinet Compt Music Fest Toulon, 79. *Mailing Add:* 2537 N Downer Ave #16 Milwaukee WI 53202

HELPS, ROBERT EUGENE
COMPOSER, PIANO

Passaic, NJ, Sept 23, 28. *Study:* Study comp with Roger Sessions & piano with Abby Whiteside. *Works:* Adagio for Orchestra, Symph of Air, 56; Gossamer Noons & Symphony No One, CRI; The Running Sun, comn by Thorne Music Fund, 73; Piano Concerto No Two, comn by Ford Found, 75; many piano pieces published by C F Peters. *Rec Perf:* Sonata No Three (Rofer), New World Rec; Sonata No One (Rofer), CRI Rec; Quartet (piano solo), Desto Rec. *Teaching:* Instr piano, San Francisco Consv, 68-70, New England Consv, 70-72, Manhattan Sch Music, 73-76 & Univ SFla, 78- *Awards:* Naumburg Award, 58; Guggenheim Award, 68. *Mem:* Nat Acad Arts & Lett. *Mailing Add:* 711 Desert Hills Way Sun City Center FL 33570

HELTON, SALLY CARR
LIBRARIAN, EDUCATOR

b Charlotte, NC, Feb 26, 53. *Study:* ECarolina Univ, study perc with Harold Jones, BME, 76; Ind Univ, with Alan P Merriam, Hans Tischler & Walter Kaufman, MA, 80, with David E Fenske & Frank Gillis, MLS, 81, with Ruth M Stone, Mantle Hood & James Koetting, 81- *Pos:* Rec technician, Arch Traditional Music, Bloomington, Ind, 78-80 & preserv & rec technician, Cylinder Proj, 83-; proj supv, Comput Arch Proj, Folklore Inst Arch, Bloomington, 82-83. *Teaching:* Lectr folklore & ethnomusicol, Ind Univ, Bloomington, 81- *Mem:* Am Musicol Soc; Soc Ethnomusicol; Music Libr Asn; Sigma Alpha Iota; Int Soc Study of Time. *Interests:* Concepts of time in music event; ethnomusicology and Western art music; music and sound archiving. *Publ:* Auth, Markers and Audience Behavior: Relationships Surrounding the Musical Event, 81, co-ed, Discourse in Ethnomusicology II: A Tribute to Alan P Merriam, 81 & Discourse in Ethnomusicology III: Social Interaction in Music Event (in press), Ethnomusicol Publ Group. *Mailing Add:* 908 S Mitchell Bloomington IN 47401

HEMKE, FREDERICK L
EDUCATOR, SAXOPHONE

b Milwaukee, Wis, July 11, 35. *Study:* Consv Nat Musique, Paris, 56; Univ Wis, Milwaukee, BS, 58; Eastman Sch Music, MM, 62; Univ Wis, Madison, DMA, 75. *Rec Perf:* The American Saxophone & Music for Tenor Saxophone, Brewster Rec; Contest Music for Saxophone, Lapider Rec; Quintet (sax & string quartet), Benson, CRI; Incantations (Ralph Shapey), Nonesuch. *Pos:* Saxophonist, Chicago Symph Orch, 62-81. *Teaching:* Prof music & chmn dept wind & perc, Sch Music, Northwestern Univ, 62- *Awards:* Hugo Anhalt Musicians Award. *Mem:* Phi Mu Alpha Sinfonia; Pi Kappa Lambda; Music Educr Nat Conf; Am Musicol Soc. *Publ:* Fred Hemke Saxophone, Southern Music Co; Teacher's Guide to the Saxophone, A Selected Bibliography of the Saxophone, A Comprehensive History of Saxophone Literature & The Orchestral Saxophone, Selmer Co. *Mailing Add:* 128 Lawndale Wilmette IL 60091

HENAHAN, DONAL J
CRITIC

b Cleveland, Ohio, Feb 28, 21. *Study:* Kent Univ, 39-40; Ohio Univ, 40-42; Northwestern Univ, BA, 48; Univ Chicago, 49; Chicago Sch Music, 50-57. *Pos:* Music critic, Chicago Daily News, 57-67 & New York Times, 67- *Mem:* Century. *Mailing Add:* c/o New York Times 229 W 43rd St New York NY 10036

HENDERSON, CLAYTON WILSON
ADMINISTRATOR, EDUCATOR

b Middletown, Conn, June 10, 36. *Study:* Ohio Univ, BFA, 58, MFA, 60; Washington Univ, study musicol with Paul Pisk, PhD, 69. *Teaching:* Instr music, Southern Ill Univ, 64-69; assoc prof music, Beloit Col, Wis, 69-74; prof & dean, Sch Music, Millikin Univ, Decatur, Ill, 74-80; prof & chmn, Dept Music, St Mary's Col, Notre Dame, Ind, 80- *Mem:* Am Musicol Soc; Col Music Soc; Int Musicol Soc; Oral Hist Asn. *Interests:* American music, especially the music of Charles Ives. *Publ:* Auth, Quotation in the Music of Ives, Reports of IMS Congress, Copenhagen, 72 & Music Educr J, 74; American Minstrelsy, In: New Grove Dict of Music & Musicians, Macmillan, 81. *Mailing Add:* 52635 Swanson Dr South Bend IN 46635

HENDERSON, DONALD GENE
MUSICOLOIST, EDUCATOR

b Indianapolis, Ind, Apr 11, 32. *Study:* Ind Univ, BME, 53; Univ Vienna, 57-58; Univ Mich, PhD, 61. *Teaching:* Prof musicol, Converse Col, SC, 61- *Awards:* Fulbright Scholar Vienna, 57-58; Nat Endowment Humanities Fel, 78-79. *Mem:* Am Musicol Soc; Music Libr Asn. *Interests:* Nineteenth century. *Publ:* Auth, H Pfitzner's Palestrina: A 20th Century Allegory, Music Rev, 70; Hans Pfitzner, In: Dict Contemp Music, Dutton, 74; auth & ed, Symphonic Works of Peter von Winter, Garland, 82; auth, The Magic Flute of Peter Winter, Music & Letters, 83. *Mailing Add:* Sch Music Converse Col Spartanburg SC 29301

HENDERSON, HUBERT PLATT
EDUCATOR, MUSIC DIRECTOR

b Milford, Conn, Aug 24, 18. *Study:* Univ NC, AB, 41, MA, 50, PhD, 62. *Pos:* Consult, Ky Arts Comn, 66- *Teaching:* Instr brass & asst dir bands, Univ NC, 46-51; instr music hist & dir bands, Mont State Univ, 54-55; assoc prof music & dir bands, Univ Md, 55-65; chmn dept music, Univ Ky, 65-67, dir, Sch Fine Arts, 66-71, dir, Off Fine Arts Exten, 71- *Mem:* Am Musicol Soc; Col Music Soc. *Interests:* Early 17th century English song; baroque wind music; Lowell Mason journals of European travel, 1837. *Publ:* Auth, University Music Schools and Programmed Public Performances, Southern Humanities Rev, summer 71. *Mailing Add:* 925 Albany Circle Lexington KY 40502

HENDERSON, IAN H
LECTURER, HARPSICHORD

b Hamilton, Scotland, Jan 28, 25; US citizen. *Study:* Oberlin Consv Music, AB, 46, EdMusB, 47 & EdMusM, 48; Syracuse Univ, PhD, 53. *Pos:* Clavichord & harpsichord, tours to cols, art groups, hist soc & museums, 79- *Teaching:* From instr to asst prof, State Univ NY, Col Brockport, 48-54, dean fine arts & prof music, 65-80, prof emer, 80-; prof, State Col, Ind State Col, 54-58; assoc prof, Syracuse Univ, 58-65. *Mailing Add:* 4039 N Lake Rd Brockport NY 14420

HENDERSON, JEANNE MARGARET
HARP, TEACHER

b Mandan, NDak, Oct 8, 22. *Study:* Wis Col Music, studied harp with Emma Osgood Moore; Juilliard Sch, studied harp with Marcel Grandjany; Univ Wis, Milwaukee, studied harp with Margaret Rupp Cooper, BS(music educ). *Teaching:* Instr harp, Milwaukee pub sch, 55-, Univ Wis, Milwaukee, 66-, Alverno Col, 71- & Univ Wis, Oshkosh, 72-76. *Awards:* Cert Appreciation, Am Harp Soc. *Mem:* Sigma Alpha Iota; Am Harp Soc (mem bd dir, 82-); MacDowell Club. *Publ:* Auth, The Harp Program in the Public Schools, Am Harp J, 77; coauth, Harp in Your School?, Salvi, 78. *Mailing Add:* 3941 N 71st St Milwaukee WI 53216

HENDERSON, ROBERT
CONDUCTOR & MUSIC DIRECTOR

Rec Perf: On Varese-Sarabande. *Pos:* Assoc cond, Utah Symph, 81-82; music dir, Ark Symph, 81-; guest cond, Los Angeles Phil, Redlands Bowl Symph, Idyllwild Fest Orch & Choir & Univ Southern Calif Contemp Music. *Mailing Add:* Ark Symph 319 W 2nd Little Rock AR 72201

HENDL, WALTER
CONDUCTOR & MUSIC DIRECTOR, PIANO

b West New York, NJ, Jan 12, 17. *Study:* Piano with David Saperton & Clarence Adler, 34-37; Curtis Inst Music, cond with Fritz Reiner, 37-41. *Works:* Dark of the Moon, 45; A Village Where They Ring No Bells; Loneliness. *Pos:* Asst cond & pianist, New York Phil, 45-49; music dir, Dallas Symph Orch, 49-58, Chautauqua Symph Orch, 53-72 & Ravinia Fest, 59-63; assoc cond, Chicago Symph Orch, 58-64; orch dir, Erie Phil, Pa, 76-; guest cond, Europe, USSR & South Am. *Teaching:* Mem fac, Sarah Lawrence Col, 31-41; dir, Eastman Sch Music, 64-72. *Awards:* Alice M Ditson Award, Columbia, 53. *Mailing Add:* Erie Phil 409 Baldwin Bldg Erie PA 16501

HENDRICKS, BARBARA
SOPRANO

b Stephens, Ark, Nov 20, 48. *Study:* With Jennie Tourel. *Roles:* Erisbe in Ormindo, San Francisco Spring Opera, 74; Jeanne in Verlobung in San Domingo; Amor in Orfeo ed Euridice; Vixen in The Cunning Little Vixen; Nannetta in Falstaff. *Pos:* Sop with US & Europ opera co & orchs; recitalist. *Awards:* Grand Prix du Disque, 76. *Mailing Add:* c/o Columbia Artists Mgt 165 W 57th St New York NY 10019

HENDRICKSON, STEVEN ERIC
TRUMPET, TEACHER

b Decorah, Iowa, Apr 2, 51. *Study:* Luther Col, BA, 73. *Pos:* Trumpet, Chicago Civic Orch, 73-76; second trumpet, London Symph, Canada, 76-78; asst prin trumpet, Nat Symph, 82- *Teaching:* Instr studio trumpet, Concordia Col, 79-82, Elmhurst Col, 79-82 & North Park Col, 79-82. *Mem:* Int Trumpet Guild. *Mailing Add:* 2409 Page Terrace Alexandria VA 22302

HENDRIX, RICHARD
VIOLIN

b Martinsville, Ind, May 15, 58. *Study:* Ind Univ; studied with James Buswell, Taduez Wronski, Franco Gulli & Daniel Gullet. *Pos:* Recitals & concts in US. *Awards:* Violin Award, Matinee Musical Perf, 76; Second Place, Int Compt Conct Artists Guild, 79. *Mem:* Am Fedn Musicians. *Mailing Add:* 824 W 54th St Indianapolis IN 46208

HENIGBAUM, JOHN
FRENCH HORN

b Bettendorf, Iowa, Sept 16, 22. *Study:* Studied horn with Philip Farkas, 45-49; Oglethorpe Univ, BA, 66. *Pos:* Third horn, Chicago Symph Orch, 49-51; prin horn, Atlanta Symph, 62-77, third horn, 77- *Mailing Add:* 1297 Singleton Valley Circle Norcross GA 30093

HENKE, HERBERT H
EDUCATOR

Study: Oberlin Col, BME, 53, BM, 54, MME, 54; Univ Southern Calif, EdD, 66; Univ Mich; Rotterdams Consv. *Teaching:* Cleveland pub sch, 54-56; supvr vocal music, Oberlin city sch, 56-58; asst prof music & music educ, Univ Md, 58-62; prof, Consv Music, Oberlin Col, 62-; choral dir & chmn music dept, Am Sch London, 81-82. *Mailing Add:* Consv Music Oberlin Col Oberlin OH 44074

HENKEN, MORRIS
EDITOR

b Philadelphia, Pa, Mar 11, 19. *Study:* Temple Univ, BS, 40; Army Music Sch, warrant, bandmaster, 43; Juilliard Sch, dipl choral cond, 51. *Pos:* Ed & publ, New Choral Music, 52-53 & Music Article Guide, 67-; ed, WFLN Philadelphia Guide to Events & Places, 61- *Teaching:* Head theory dept, Settlement Music Sch, Philadelphia, 57-75. *Publ:* Auth, Quotable Quotes, Music J, 76. *Mailing Add:* 6923 Sherman St Philadelphia PA 19119

HENNAGIN, MICHAEL
COMPOSER, EDUCATOR

b The Dalles, Ore, Sept 27, 36. *Study:* Los Angeles City Col, with Leonard Stein, 57-59; Aspen Music Sch, with Darius Milhaud, 60 & 61; Berkshire Music Ctr, with Aaron Copland, 63; Curtis Inst Music, BM, 63. *Works:* Walking on the Green Grass (SATB), Boosey & Hawkes, 62; The Unknown (mixed media), 68, The Family Man (mixed media), 71, Sonata for Piano, 77 & Three Emily Dickinson Songs (SA), 76, Walton Music Corp; Dance Scene (symphonic band), Jenson Publ Inc, 79; Sonata for Flute and Piano, Walton Music Corp, 82. *Pos:* Comp, TV & motion picture, NBC, ABC, CBS & others, 59-65. *Teaching:* Asst prof music, Emporia State Univ, 66-72; prof, Univ Okla, 72- *Awards:* Comp Fel, Music Educr Nat Conf & Ford Found, 65-66; Comp of Year, Music Teachers Nat Asn, 75-76; Nat Endowment Arts Grant, 76. *Mem:* ASCAP; Music Teachers Nat Asn; Okla Music Teachers Asn; Am Soc Univ Comp. *Mailing Add:* PO Box 2844 Norman OK 73070

HENRY, JAMES DONALD
MUSIC DIRECTOR, EDUCATOR

b Kingsport, Tenn, Aug 14, 33. *Study:* Western Ky Univ, BS(music), 56; Ind Univ, MM(woodwind), 60. *Rec Perf:* Twentieth Century Classics, Carolina Rec, 65. *Teaching:* Instr, Fourth Army Band Training, Ft Chaffee, Ark, 56-58; grad asst, Ind Univ, Bloomington, 59-60; from asst prof to prof woodwinds & dir marching band, Duke Univ, 60- *Mailing Add:* Col Sta Box 6695 Durham NC 27706

HENRY, JOSEPH
CONDUCTOR, COMPOSER

b Toledo, Ohio, Oct 10, 30. *Study:* Eastman Sch Music, BM, 52, MM, 53, AMD, 65. *Works:* Chromophon, perf by Buffalo Phil, 70; Suite for Orch, Eastman Rochester Symph; Taegrals, Manhattan Quartet. *Pos:* Music dir, Utica Symph, 62-66, Ohio Univ Orch, 79- & Bay View Fest Chamber Orch, 81-; guest cond, US & Europe. *Teaching:* Instr music, Wis State Univ, 55-57; cond orch & prof music theory, State Univ NY, Oswego, 67-79. *Awards:* Fulbright Grant, 57-59. *Mem:* Orgn Ohio Orch; Am Symph Orch League. *Mailing Add:* Sch Music Ohio Univ Athens OH 45701

HENRY, OTTO WALKER
COMPOSER, EDUCATOR

b Reno, Nev, May 8, 33. *Study:* Boston Univ, with Karl Geiringer, Hugo Norden & Gardner Read, MusB, 58, MA, 59; Tulane Univ, with Howard Smither & Gilbert Chase, PhD, 70. *Works:* Passacaglia (trombone & piano), Robert King Music Co, 61; Liberty Bell (perc), 71, Omnibus 1 & 2 (indeterminant instrm), 71, Do Not Pass Go (three timpani), 72 & The Sona of Martha (sop & perc), 72, Media Press; Sanctus (mixed chorus), Hinshaw Music, Inc, 77. *Teaching:* Chmn dept music, Washington & Jefferson Col, 61-66; assoc prof music & dir electronic music, East Carolina Univ, 68- *Awards:* Hilda Honigman Comp Cup, NC Fedn Music Clubs, 77. *Mem:* Soc Ethnomusicol; Am Musicol Soc; Int Alban Berg Soc; Am Asn Univ Prof; Southeastern Comp League. *Publ:* Auth, The Electrotechnology of Modern Music, 70 & Music and the New Technology, 72, Arts in Soc; Boulez in Music Today, Ethnomusicol, 5/72. *Mailing Add:* 407 S Student St Greenville NC 27834

HENRY, WILLIAM
VIOLIN

Study: Univ Southern Calif; Juilliard Sch Music; studied with Nathan Milstein & Franco Gulli. *Pos:* Soloist, Carnegie Hall, Tully Hall, Avery Fisher Hall, Town Hall, New York, Metropolitan Museum & MNYC TV, New York; performer, Casals Music Fest, Aspen Music Fest, Grand Teton Music Fest & Lincoln Ctr Prog Perf Arts, formerly; mem, New York Chamber Soloists, formerly & Orpheus Ens, New York, currently; founding mem, Raphael Trio, formerly; concertmaster, San Diego Symph, 83- & Opera Orch New York, currently; recitalist, Italy, Switzerland, France, Portugal, Azores, Austria, Germany, Repub China & US, currently. *Bibliog:* New Stars on the Horizon Ser & Listening Room, WQXR Radio, New York. *Mailing Add:* Opera Orch New York 211 W 56th St New York NY 10019

HENSCHEN, DOROTHY ADELE
HARP, EDUCATOR

b Cleveland, Ohio, Aug 25, 21. *Study:* Consv Music, Oberlin Col, BMus(piano & harp); Salzebo Harp Colony, Camden, Maine. *Pos:* First harpist, Canton Symph Orch, Ohio & Akron Symph Orch; harpist, Kenley Players, Warren & Dayton, Ohio, Front Row Theater, Cleveland & symph orchs incl Austin, Waco, San Antonio & Corpus Christi. *Teaching:* Asst prof harp, Univ Tex, 44-49; asst prof harp & piano, Mt Union Col, 49-; lectr harp, Univ Akron, currently. *Mem:* Am Harp Soc. *Mailing Add:* 1001 Overlook Dr Alliance OH 44601

HERBISON, JERALDINE SAUNDERS
COMPOSER, TEACHER

b Richmond, Va, Jan 9, 41. *Study:* Va State Col, BS, 63; Univ Mich, Interlochen, 73 & 79. *Works:* Six Duos for Violin & Cello, Herbison & Zaret, 76 & Herbison & Forester, 80; Sonata for Unaccompanied Cello, James Herbison, 78-80; Melancholy on the Advent of Departure (Quartet), Andersen, Andersen, Herbison & Anders, 80; Nine Art Songs (voice & piano), Janis Peri, 80 & Sarah King, 82; Variations for String Orchestra, Tidewater Comp Guild Fest Orch, 81; Promenade (chamber orch), Odessey Ens, 82; Sonata for Cello & Piano, James Herbison & Jan Kaplan, 82. *Pos:* Ed newsletter, Tidewater Comp Guild, 79- *Teaching:* Instr music, Prince Georges Co, 63-66, Goochland Co, 63-66 & Isle of Wight Pub Sch, 68-70; instr orch, Hampton pub sch, 70- & Newport News pub sch, 70- *Awards:* Nat Music Camp Hon Comp Award, 79. *Mem:* Music Educr Nat Conf; Va Music Educr Asn; Am String Teachers Asn; Nat String Orch Asn; Tidewater Comp Guild. *Mailing Add:* 114 O'Canoe Pl Hampton VA 23661

HERDER, RONALD
COMPOSER, WRITER

b Philadelphia, Pa, Dec 21, 30. *Study:* Univ Pa, BFA, 52; Miami Univ, Ohio, MA, 54; Fontainebleau Consv, with Nadia Boulanger, cert, 57. *Works:* Movements (orch), 63 & Requiem II: Games of Power, 69, Assoc Music Publ; Requiem for Jimmy Dean, comn by Harkness Ballet, 70; Requiem III: Birds at Golgotha, perf by Contemp Chamber Ens, 75; incidental music for As You Like It, perf by Purchase Contemp Ens, 83. *Pos:* Ed in chief, Assoc Music Publ, 65-73; dir spec proj, Educ Audio Visual, New York, 74-78; music ed, Oxford Univ Press, 82- *Teaching:* Fac mem comp, State Univ NY, Purchase, 74-; prof comp, Manhattanville Col, 78-, music dir, Musical Theater Wkshp, currently. *Awards:* Maurice Ravel Comp Prize, Fontainebleau Consv, 57; Concorso Int, Italian Govt, 63; grant, Nat Endowment Arts, 75. *Mem:* BMI. *Publ:* Auth, Tonal/Atonal, 71 & Spanish Montunos (performance method), 72, Continuo Music Press; coauth, How to Make Electronic Music, 76 & auth, Elements of Music: Rhythm, 77, Educ Audio Visual; Training your Musical Ear (cassette set), Shacor Inc, 83. *Mailing Add:* Music Dept Manhattanville Col Purchase NY 10577

HERFORTH, HARRY BEST
EDUCATOR, TRUMPET

b Sharpsburg, Pa, Sept 18, 16. *Study:* Pittsburgh Musical Inst, 35-37; New England Consv Music, orch dipl, 40, soloist dipl, 41, BM, 66; Berkshire Music Ctr, 40, 41 & 46; Army Music Sch, 42. *Works:* Five Pieces for Brass Quintet, Shawnee Press, 80. *Pos:* Asst first trumpet, Boston Symph, 46-51 & Cleveland Orch, 51-58; founder, first trumpet & dir, Cleveland Brass Quintet, 55- *Teaching:* Prof trumpet, Kent State Univ, 57- & Oberlin Col, 60-61 & 65-66. *Mailing Add:* 2940 Coleridge Rd Cleveland Heights OH 44118

HERMAN, EDWARD, JR
TROMBONE, EDUCATOR

b New York, NY. *Study:* Trombone with Ernest Clarke, Gorden Pulis & William Bell. *Pos:* First trombone, New Orleans Symph, formerly, Ballet Theater Orch, formerly & New York City Opera Orch, formerly; Mem, New York Phil, 52-, solo trombonist, 56-, prin trombone, currently. *Teaching:* Mem fac, Hofstra Univ, formerly & Manhattan Sch Music, 61-; mem fac trombone, Juilliard Sch, 70- *Mailing Add:* New York Phil Avery Fisher Hall New York NY 10023

HERNANDEZ, ALBERTO H
LIBRARIAN, ADMINISTRATOR

b Santurce, PR, Jan 21, 52. *Study:* Univ PR, BA, 74; State Univ NY Geneseo, MLS, 76; Columbia Univ, MA, 83. *Pos:* Asst dir, PR Arts & Cultural Ctr, Rochester, NY, 74-76; libr dir, Consv Music, PR, 82-; lectr, Music Lit Reviewer, 83. *Mem:* Music Libr Asn. *Interests:* Piano music of Latin America. *Mailing Add:* Calle 32 B53#7 Sta Rosa Bayamon PR 00619

HERR, BARBARA
OBOE, EDUCATOR

Study: Consv Music, Oberlin Col, BM; Temple Univ; studied oboe with James Caldwell & Louis Rosenblatt. *Pos:* Mem, Mostovoy Soloists, Tanglewood Fest Orch, formerly; prin oboe, Am Wind Symph, formerly; asst prin oboe, St Louis Symph Orch, currently; soloist, St Louis Symph Orch, Kammergild Chamber Orch, Rarely Perf Music Ens & Alton Symph. *Teaching:* Mem fac oboe, St Louis Consv Music, currently. *Mem:* Int Double Reed Soc. *Mailing Add:* St Louis Consv Music 560 Trinity Ave St Louis MO 63130

HERR, JOHN DAVID
ORGAN, EDUCATOR

b Lancaster, Pa, Jan 22, 31. *Study:* Eastman Sch Music, BM, 59, MM, 60; int organ master class with Flor Peeters, cert, 73; Organ Inst, Oberlin Col, with Harald Vogel, 75 & 83. *Works:* Elegy for Chamber Ensemble, Eastman Contemp Music Fest, 61; A Covenant of Peace, Fest Choir, United Church Christ, 82. *Rec Perf:* Choral and Organ Music, Century Advent, 71; Harp of Joy, Century Advent & Musical Heritage Soc, 76. *Pos:* Minister of music, Plymouth Church of Shaker Heights, 61- *Teaching:* Fac, Cleveland Inst Music, 81-; adj assoc prof organ, Kent State Univ, 81- *Mem:* Am Guild Organists (dean, 64-66); Music Teachers Nat Asn. *Mailing Add:* 3305 Chalfant Rd Shaker Heights OH 44120

HERREN, LLOYD K, SR
EDUCATOR, ADMINISTRATION

b Crescent, Okla, Jan 18, 22. *Study:* George Peabody Col, BS(music educ), 48, MM(choral), 49; Univ Tex, Austin, EdD, 55. *Teaching:* Supvr & asst prof music, Northeastern Okla State Univ, 49-51; choral dir & assoc prof music, Tex A&I Univ, 52-56; prof music & dept chair, Ft Hays Kans State Univ, 56-66; prof & chmn div humanities, Metro State Col, 66- *Mem:* Founding mem, Am Choral Dir Asn; Music Teachers Nat Asn; Nat Asn Teachers Singing. *Mailing Add:* 9873 W Hawaii Dr Lakewood CO 80226

HERRING, DAVID WELLS
TROMBONE

b Madison, Wis, Aug 21, 55. *Study:* Ind Univ, BMus, 78. *Pos:* Bass trombone, Minn Orch, 82- *Mailing Add:* 2430 Clinton Ave S Minneapolis MN 55404

HERRING, (CHARLES) HOWARD
ARTIST REPRESENTATIVE, PIANO

b Ponca City, Okla. *Study:* Southern Methodist Univ, BM, 71; Manhattan Sch Music, with Robert Goldsand, MM, 73. *Pos:* Co-dir, Ctr Music Sch, 79-83; founding dir & pianist, Marland Chamber Music Fest, 80-; artist rep, 83- *Teaching:* Piano, Ctr Music Sch, 79-83. *Awards:* Okla Arts Coun Grant, 80, 82 & 84; Nat Endowment Arts Grant, 83. *Mailing Add:* 309 W 104th #9C New York NY 10025

HERROLD, REBECCA MUNN
EDUCATOR, WRITER
b Warren, Pa. *Study:* Univ Miami, Fla, BMus, 60; San Jose State Univ, MA, 68; Stanford Univ, DMA, 74. *Teaching:* Asst prof music, Youngstown State Univ, 74-75 & Ore State Univ, 75-80; assoc prof, San Jose State Univ, 80-*Awards:* Grant, Apple Educ Found, 81-82. *Mem:* Col Music Soc; Nat Consortium Comput Based Music Instr; Calif State Coun Comput Based Music Instr (co-chair, 81-83). *Publ:* Auth, Computer-Assisted Instruction: A Study of the Stanford Ear-Training Program, 77 & An Introduction to Opera, 80, ERIC; New Approaches to Elementary Music Education, Prentice-Hall, 83. *Mailing Add:* Music Dept San Jose State Univ San Jose CA 85192

HERSH, ALAN B
EDUCATOR, PIANO
b Brooklyn, NY, Apr 6, 40. *Study:* Manhattan Sch Music, with Robert Goldsand, BM, 60, MM, 62; Univ, with Sidney Foster, DMus, 71. *Teaching:* Chmn, Dept Music & Div Fine & Perf Arts, Augustana Col, Ill, 76-, prof piano & theory, 76- *Awards:* Harold Bauer Award, Manhattan Sch Music, 60; John Edwards Fel, Ind Univ, 70; Univ Iowa House Fel, 82. *Mem:* Music Educr Nat Conf; Soc Am Musicians; Soc Music Theory. *Mailing Add:* Music Dept Augustana Col Rock Island IL 61201

HERVIG, RICHARD B
COMPOSER, EDUCATOR
b Story City, Iowa, Nov 24, 17. *Study:* Augustana Col, SDak, BA, 39; Univ Iowa, with Phillip Greeley Clapp, MA, 41, PhD, 47. *Works:* An Entertainment (clarinet, vibraphone & marimba), perf in Seattle, Chicago, Iowa City & New York, 78; Sonata No 2 for Clarinet & Piano, Galaxy, 79; Chamber Music for Six Players, Assoc Music Publ, 82; Airs & Roulades (clarinet & wind ens), perf in Washington, DC & Boston, 83; Sonata for Violin and Piano, Assoc Music Publ (in prep). *Teaching:* Instr, Luther Col, Iowa, 42; assoc prof, Long Beach State Col, 52-55; prof comp & theory, Univ Iowa, 55-, dir, Ctr New Music, 66- *Mem:* Am Soc Univ Comp (chairperson nat coun, 81-); BMI; Col Music Soc; Soc Music Theory. *Mailing Add:* 1822 Rochester Ave Iowa City IA 52240

HERZBERG, JEAN (M)
SOPRANO, EDUCATOR
b Iron Mountain, Mich. *Study:* Lawrence Univ, BME, 73; Sch Music, Ind Univ, MM(voice & opera), 80; studied with Eileen Farrell, Camilla Williams, Lorna Haywood & Eva Likova. *Rec Perf:* Psalm of Joy, Moravian Music Found, 76; Susannah, PBS Prod, 80. *Roles:* Britten War Requiem, Atlanta Symph, 80, Lincoln Symph, 81 & Knoxville Symph, 82; Handel Messiah, Knoxville Symph, 81-82 & Lansing Symph, 82; Beethoven 9th Symph, Nashville Symph, 82 & Atlanta Nat Symph, 82; Mozart Requiem, Grand Rapids Symph, 82; Wellgunde in Das Rhinegold, 83 & Ortlind in Die Walküre, 83, San Francisco Opera; Verdi Requiem, San Francisco Fest Masses, 83. *Pos:* Soloist with National, Atlanta, Pittsburgh and many other symphony orchestras. *Teaching:* Asst prof voice, Mich State Univ, 80-*Awards:* Henry Wenger Award, Detroit Metropolitan Opera Coun, 82; Leonardo da Vinci Award, San Francisco Opera Merola Prog, 82. *Mem:* Nat Asn Teachers Singing. *Mailing Add:* Music Dept Mich State Univ East Lansing MI 48824

HESKES, IRENE
WRITER, LECTURER
b New York, NY. *Study:* Wash Square Col; Juilliard Sch Music; Eastman Sch Music; Harvard Univ; Hebrew Union Col, Jewish Inst Religion; Cantors Inst, Jewish Theol Sem Am. *Pos:* Music educ specialist & choir leader, NY religious sch, 50-56; lectr-recitalist & vocal soloist, Northeastern area synagogues & orgn, 54-70; lectr-educr & staff music consult, Theodor Herzl Inst Jewish Agency, New York, 60-76; dir, Nat Jewish Music Coun, 68-80; founder & dir, Am Yiddish Theater Music Restoration & Revival Project, 80-; educr, lectr & consult to communal ctrs, music groups & religious orgn; speaker-participant at nat workshops & conf; adj lectr at seminaries & cols. *Awards:* William Mason Fel. *Mem:* Am Musicol Soc; Int Musicol Soc; Sonneck Soc; Music Libr Asn; Col Music Soc. *Publ:* Auth, The Cantorial Art, JWB, 66; Studies in Jewish Music, 71 & Jews in Music, 74, Bloch; Ernest Bloch: Creative Spirit, JWB, 76; The Resource Book of Jewish Music: An Annotated Bibliography, Greenwood Press (in prep). *Mailing Add:* 90-15 68th Ave Forest Hills NY 11375

HESS, ROBERT
COACH, EDUCATOR
b Brooklyn, NY, May 17, 30. *Study:* Carnegie-Mellon Univ, BFA, 52; New England Consv Music, MM, 54. *Pos:* Translr, operas & songs by Poulenc, Offenbach, Haydn & others, in particular, Puccini's La Rondine & Rimsky-Korsakov's Complete Songs. *Teaching:* Instr musical theatre styles, Am Musical & Dramatic Acad, New York, 68-79; vis lectr vocal coaching & musical theatre, Hartt Sch Music, 71- *Awards:* Librettests' & Translators' Grant, Nat Endowment Arts, 74. *Mem:* ASCAP; Am Fedn Musicians. *Mailing Add:* 115 W 73rd St New York NY 10023

HESTER, BYRON
FLUTE & PICCOLO, TEACHER
b Electra, Tex, Apr 16, 25. *Study:* Juilliard Sch, with Georges Barrere; Curtis Inst Music, with William Kincaid. *Pos:* Prin flutist, Indianapolis Symph Orch, 51-53 & Houston Symph Orch, 53- *Teaching:* Prof flute, Univ Houston, 54-*Mailing Add:* c/o Houston Symph Orch 615 Louisiana Houston TX 77002

HETTRICK, JANE SCHATKIN
EDUCATOR, ORGAN
Study: Queens Col, City Univ New York, AB; Univ Mich, MM, DMA. *Pos:* Organ recitalist, US & Europe, currently. *Teaching:* Asst prof music, Rider Col, 74-80, assoc prof, 80- *Awards:* Fulbright Hays Grant, Austrian Govt; Nat Endowment Humanities Fel; Rider Col Res Grants. *Mem:* Am Musicol Soc; Am Guild Organists. *Interests:* Music of Antonio Salieri; German organ and organ music of 1500 to 1800; J S Bach; Arnolt Schlick. *Publ:* Auth, The German Organ of the Early Renaissance, Diapason, 80; ed, Antonio Salieri: Concerto per l'organo, Doblinger, 81; G P Telemann: Parthie, Sweet Pipes, 81; auth, Haydn and the Organ, J Church Music, 82; ed, Antonio Salieri: Symphonies, Garland, 83. *Mailing Add:* 48-21 Glenwood St Little Neck NY 11362

HETTRICK, WILLIAM EUGENE
EDUCATOR, WRITER
b Toledo, Ohio, Nov 15, 39. *Study:* Univ Mich, BMus, 62, MA, 64, PhD, 68. *Pos:* Dir, Collegium Musicum, Hofstra Univ, 69-; ed, J Am Musical Instrm Soc, 79- & Musica Selecta, 79- *Teaching:* Asst prof, Hofstra Univ, 68-75, assoc prof, 75-81, prof, 81- *Awards:* Fulbright Comn Grant, 66-67; Nat Endowment Humanities Stipend, 71. *Mem:* Am Musical Instrm Soc; Am Musicol Soc; Am Recorder Soc; Gesellschaft bayerische Musikgeschichte. *Interests:* Renaissance and Baroque music of Germany; history of musical instruments. *Publ:* Auth, G Aichinger: Cantiones Ecclesiasticae (1607), 72 & B Klingenstein: Rosetum Marianum (1604), 77, A-R Ed; series of articles on Martin Agricola in Am Recorder, 80-83. *Mailing Add:* 48-21 Glenwood St Little Neck NY 11362

HEUSSENSTAMM, GEORGE
COMPOSER, EDUCATOR
b Los Angeles, Calif, July 24, 26. *Study:* Self-taught piano; Univ Calif, Los Angeles, 44-66; Los Angeles City Col, 47-48; Los Angeles State Col Appl Arts & Sci, 61-62; studied with Leonard Stein, 61-62. *Works:* Die Jugend (solo clarinet), 63; Callichoreo (woodwind quartet), 68; Tournament (four brass sextets & four perc), 71; Texture Variations (flute, violin, cello & harpsichord), 72; Monologue (clarinet), 73; Playphony (perc), 76; Brass Quintet No 3, 77; and many others. *Pos:* Mem, Comt Encounters, Pasadena; music critic, Pasadena Star-News; music copyist; mgr, Coleman Chamber Music Asn, 71-*Teaching:* Mem fac music theory, Calif State Col, Dominguez Hills, 76-81, Ambassador Col, 77-78, Calif State Univ, Los Angeles, 80- & Calif State Univ, Northridge, 82- *Awards:* ASCAP Awards, 74-83; Nat Endowment Arts Fel Grant, 76; Winner, Int Double Reed Soc, 77. *Mem:* ASCAP; Am Soc Univ Comp; Int Soc Contemp Music; Western Alliance Arts; Nat Asn Comp USA (nat vpres, currently). *Mailing Add:* 5013 Lowell Ave La Crescenta CA 91214

HEWITT, HARRY DONALD
COMPOSER, ADMINISTRATOR
b Detroit, Mich, Mar 4, 21. *Works:* Principal works include 29 symphonies, 22 string quartets & 18 piano sonatas (over 3000 pieces total), over 300 pieces performed publicly during the past fifty years. *Mem:* Del Valley Comp (pres, 75-); ASCAP. *Mailing Add:* 345 S 19th St Philadelphia PA 19103

HEYDE, NORMA L
EDUCATOR, SOPRANO
b Herrin, Ill, Dec 31, 27. *Study:* Sch Music, Univ Mich, BMus, 49, MMus, 50; Mozarteum Summer Acad, Salzburg, Austria, cert, 56; studied with Rosa Ponselle, 57-64. *Pos:* Soprano, US orch & choral soc; recitalist, art galleries & col conct series. *Teaching:* Instr voice, Sch Music, Univ Mich, 50-54 & Eastern Mich Univ, 54-57; dir of weekly "Hymns of Freedom" Broadcasting, Univ Mich Sta WUOM, 54-57; dir of music, 1st Presby Church, Milford, Del, 58-67; instr, Col of Pa, 69; priv teacher of voice, York, Pa, 67-71; assoc prof music, Salisbury State Col, Md, 75- *Mem:* Nat Asn Teachers Singing; Music Educr Nat Conf; Nat Music Teachers Asn; Col Music Soc; Pi Kappa Lambda. *Mailing Add:* 508 Kings Highway Milford DE 19963

HEYLER, MARY ELLEN
MEZZO-SOPRANO
b Santa Monica, Calif, Nov 11, 54. *Study:* Calif State Polytechnic Univ, BA(music), 77; Music Acad West; Univ Southern Calif. *Works:* Tisbe in La Cenerentola, Ariz Opera Co, 77; Queen of Hearts in Alice in Wonderland, Los Angeles Sch Independent Cinema Artists & Producers, 81; title role in La Cenerentola, Pac West Coast Opera, 81; Cherubino in Le nozze di Figaro, Nev Opera Co, 82; Siebel in Faust, Aachen Stadttheater, 83. *Rec Perf:* Liebeslieder Op 52 (Brahms), 80 & Sins of My Old Age (Rossini), 82, Nonesuch. *Pos:* Solo ms, Aachen Stadttheater, WGermany, 83- *Awards:* Second Place, Metropolitan Opera Western Region Finals, 77; Nicolai Gedda Award, Music Acad West, 78. *Mem:* Am Fedn TV & Rec Artists. *Mailing Add:* c/o William Felber & Assoc 2126 Cahuenga Blvd Hollywood CA 90068

HEYMONT, GEORGE A
CRITIC-WRITER, LECTURER
b Brooklyn, NY, July 8, 47. *Study:* Brooklyn Col, City Univ New York, BA, 69. *Pos:* Fine Arts ed, Bay Area Reporter, 76- *Teaching:* Lectr, The Young Artist and the Media, various apprentice prog & univ. *Awards:* Cable Car Award, Outstanding Music Critic, 79, Outstanding Feature Writing, 82 & 83. *Mem:* Music Critics Asn; Nat Opera Asn. *Publ:* Auth, Desert Aria, Westways, 81; Maureen Forrester: Singing Workaholic, 82, Signing Opera, Signing Opera, 82, Performing Arts; Thomas Stewart & Evelyn Lear, Dynamic Years, 82; Brother, Can You Spare $350,000, Skies West, 82. *Mailing Add:* 487-B Dolores St San Francisco CA 94110

HIBBARD, WILLIAM ALDEN
COMPOSER, EDUCATOR
b Newton, Mass, Aug 8, 39. *Study:* New England Consv Music, BMus(violin), 61, MMus(comp), 63; Univ Iowa, PhD(comp), 67; studied violin with Marguerite Estaver, Richard Burgin & Ruth Posselt; studied comp with Francis Judd Cooke, Donald Martino & Richard Hervig. *Works:* Fantasy (organ, trumpet, trombone & perc), comn by Boston Symph Orch, Am Guild Organists & Radio WCRB, 65; Menage (sop, trumpet & violin), comn by Soc Commissioning New Music, Baton Rouge, La, 74; Processionals (orch), comn by Am Comp Orch, NY, 80; Schickstück (vibraphone), written for Steven Schick, 81; P/M Variations—Revisited (four double basses), 82; Three Whitman Miniatures (mixed chorus & piano), 82; Sinfonia on Expanding Matrices (string orch), 83. *Rec Perf:* Chamber Music for Six Players (Richard Hervig), CRI. *Teaching:* Music dir, Ctr New Music, Univ Iowa, 66-, mem fac comp & theory, Sch Music, 66-77, dir, Ctr New Perf Arts, 69-76, prof, 77-. *Awards:* Philip Greeley Clapp Award, 67; Old Gold Summer Res Fel, 75 & 76. *Publ:* Auth, Some Aspects of Serial Improvisation, Am Guild Organists Quart, 10/66 & 1/67. *Mailing Add:* 725 E College St Iowa City IA 52240

HICKS, DAVID
DIRECTOR—OPERA, EDUCATOR
b Philadelphia, Pa, June 3, 37. *Study:* Temple Univ, BS(music), 59; studied with Martial Singher & Eleanor Stebor. *Pos:* Singer with opera co, formerly; conct artist, Community Concerts, 62-70; asst dir, New York City Opera, 67-73; freelance dir, 73-; artistic adv, Florentine Opera Co, Milwaukee, formerly, stage dir, 80- *Teaching:* Stage dir & instr operatic actg, Acad Vocal Arts, Pa, 73-77; actg mem fac, Am Opera Ctr, Juilliard Sch, 78- *Mem:* Am Guild Musical Artists (mem bd gov, 65-75). *Mailing Add:* c/o Robert Lombardo Assoc 61 W 62nd St Suite 6F New York NY 10023

HICKS, ROY EDWARD
MUSIC DIRECTOR, EDUCATOR
b McGregor, Tex, Jan 14, 31. *Study:* Paul Quinn Col, BA, 49; Prairie View A&M Univ, MA, 56; Univ Ala, University, currently. *Works:* Ready, 73, I Couldn't Hear Nobody Pray, 73 & The Hands of Time, 74, Somerset Press; Integer Vitae, Agape Press, 74; This Little Light of Mine, Tuskegee Inst Choir, 81. *Rec Perf:* The Tuskegee Institute Choir ... Live!, Brigadier Studios, 79. *Roles:* Joe in Show Boat, Dallas Summer Musicals, 69. *Teaching:* Head music dept, Palestine Independent Sch Dist, Tex, 49-58 & Dallas Independent Sch Dist, 50-70; chmn dept music & choir dir, Tuskegee Inst, 70- *Mem:* Music Educr Nat Conf; Ala Music Educr Asn; Am Choral Dir Asn; Nat Asn Negro Musicians. *Mailing Add:* Tuskegee Inst 437 Montgomery Rd Tuskegee AL 36088

HIGBEE, DALE STROHE
RECORDER, CRITIC-WRITER
b Proctor, Vt, June 14, 25. *Study:* Harvard Univ, AB, 49; Univ Tex, Austin, PhD, 54; studied flute with Georges Laurent, 45-47, Arthur Lora, 47 & Marcel Moyse, 70; studied recorder with Carl Dolmetsch, 57. *Pos:* Flute & piccolo, Vt State Symph, 42-43 & 45; first flute, Columbia Symph, SC, 54-55, Charlotte Oratorio Orch, NC, 65-72; flute & recorder, Charlotte Camerata, NC, 65-; first flute, Charlotte Symphonette, NC, 66-68; bk & rec rev ed, Am Recorder, 67-; first flute, Western Piedmont Symph, NC, 70-77; second flute & piccolo, Charlotte Opera Orch, NC, 70-72; recorder, Higbee Recorder Quartet, 83- *Mem:* Am Recorder Soc (bd dir, 63-65); Dolmetsch Found (gov, 63-); Am Musical Instrument Soc (bd dir, 72-74); Galpin Soc; Am Musicol Soc. *Interests:* Recorder; flute; musical instruments. *Publ:* Auth, A Plea for the Tenor Recorder by Thomas Stanesby, Jr, 62, Third-octave Fingerings in 18th Century Recorder Charts, 62 & Michel Corrette on the Piccolo and Speculations Regarding Vivaldi's Flautino, 64, Galpin Soc J; Notes on Hindemith's Trio for Recorders, Am Recorder, 69; coauth, A Survey of Musical Instrument Collections in the United States and Canada, Music Libr Asn, 74. *Mailing Add:* 412 S Ellis St Salisbury NC 28144

HIGBEE, DAVID JOHN
EDUCATOR, SAXOPHONE
b Scottsbluff, Nebr, July 31, 40. *Study:* Univ Colo, Boulder, BME, 62, MMus, 63, DMA, 79. *Works:* Trio Sonata, (in prep) & The Saxophone: Techniques and Information (in prep), Dorn Publ. *Teaching:* Instr music, Denver Pub Sch, 63-70 & Black Hills State Col, 70-71; Prof music hist, Bethany Col, 71- *Mem:* Phi Mu Alpha Sinfonia; Nat Asn Jazz Educr; Music Educr Nat Conf; North Am Sax Alliance; Nat Asn Col Wind & Perc Instr. *Publ:* Auth, The Saxophone: Techniques and Information, Dorn Publ (in prep). *Mailing Add:* Bethany Col Lindsborg KS 67456

HIGGINS, THOMAS
WRITER, EDUCATOR
b Milwaukee, Wis. *Study:* Ecole Normale Musique, Paris, studied piano with Jules Gentil, dipl, 51; Chicago Musical Col, studied piano with Rudolph Ganz, BM, 54; Roosevelt Univ, studied piano with Maurice Dumesnil, MM, 56; Univ Iowa, PhD, 66. *Teaching:* Prof music, NE Mo State Univ, 65-; vis prof music hist, Univ NC, Chapel Hill, 73 & Univ Louisville, 80. *Awards:* Danforth Found Grant, 60; Am Coun Learned Soc Fel, 68; Nat Endowment Humanities Fel, 80. *Interests:* Chopin performance practice, interpretation and biography. *Publ:* Auth, Tempo and Character in Chopin, Musical Quart, 73; ed, Chopin: Preludes, Op 28, Critical Score, W W Norton, 73; auth, Znak Luku u Chopina, Rocznik Chopinowski, 80; Delphine Potocka and Frederic Chopin, Am Liszt Soc J, 80 & 81; Whose Chopin?, In: 19th Century Music, Univ Calif Press, 81. *Mailing Add:* 4236 Cleveland Ave St Louis MO 63110

HIGGINSON, JOSEPH VINCENT See de Brant, Cyr

HIGHTOWER, GAIL
BASSOON, EDUCATOR
b Jamaica, NY, Mar 29, 46. *Study:* Manhattan Sch Music, BMus, 67, MMus, 69. *Pos:* Bassoonist, Symph New World, 68-78; artistic dir & founder, Univ Symph Inc, 78-; pres, Hightower Prod Inc, 83- *Teaching:* Lectr music, Aaron Copland Sch Music, Queens Col, 70- *Awards:* Scholar, Rockefeller Found, 65; grant, Nat Endowment Arts, 78. *Bibliog:* D Antoinette Handy (auth), Black Women in American Bands & Orchestras, Scarecrow Press Inc, 81. *Mailing Add:* 163-49 130th Ave Jamaica NY 11434

HILKEVITCH, JOYCE TURNER
ADMINISTRATOR, LECTURER
b New York, NY, Oct 19, 21. *Study:* Hunter Col, BA, 42; Univ Chicago, MA, 64. *Pos:* Founding exec dir, Grant Park Concerts Soc, 77-81; founder & pres, Mostly Music, Inc, 74- *Teaching:* Staff assoc, Music Dept, Northeastern Ill Univ, 79- *Mem:* Chamber Music Am. *Mailing Add:* 4948 S Kimbark Ave Chicago IL 60615

HILL, CAROLYN ANN
ADMINISTRATOR, CONDUCTOR & MUSIC DIRECTOR
b Oklahoma City, Okla, May 1, 38. *Study:* Univ Okla, BMus, 62, MMus, 63; Int Summer Acad Mozarteum, dipl cond, 68. *Pos:* Music dir & cond, New York Music Soc, 72- & Livingston Symph Orch, NJ, 73- *Teaching:* Instr music, Chapin Sch, 64-68; head, Columbia Prep Sch Music, 68-72; head, Music Dept, United Nations Int Sch, 72- *Bibliog:* Michael Redmond (auth), numerous articles, Newark Star Ledger, 70, 81 & 82; Joan Harvison (auth), Determined to Direct, Okla City Times, 10/1/72; Stefan Janis (auth), Children's Concerts, Newark Star Ledger, 83. *Mem:* Am Fedn Musicians; Music Educr Nat Conf; Am Symph Orch League. *Mailing Add:* 111 Barrow St New York NY 10014

HILL, GEORGE R
EDUCATOR, LIBRARIAN
Study: Stanford Univ, AB(music), 65; Grad Libr Sch, Univ Chicago, AM(libr sci), 66; Grad Sch Arts & Sci, NY Univ, PhD(musicol), 75. *Pos:* Librn I, Music Div, New York Pub Libr, 66-70; asst music librn, NY Univ, 71-72; fine arts librn, Univ Calif, Irvine, 72-73. *Teaching:* Assoc prof music hist, Baruch Col, City Univ New York, 73- *Awards:* Stipend, Deutscher Akad Austauschdienst, 70-71 & 77. *Mem:* Music Libr Asn (secy, 78-); Int Asn Music Libr; Am Musicol Soc; Col Music Soc. *Interests:* Descriptive and enumerative music bibliography; 18th century symphony; performance practice of early music. *Publ:* Auth, articles, In: New Grove Dict of Music & Musicians; A Thematic Catalog of the Instrumental Music of Florian Leopold Gassmann, Boonin, 76; coauth, Music Price Indexes, Notes, 78-; ed, F L Gassmann Seven Symphonies, Garland Publ, 81. *Mailing Add:* Box 838 Madison Sq Sta New York NY 10159

HILL, JACKSON
COMPOSER, EDUCATOR
b Birmingham, Ala, May 23, 41. *Study:* Univ NC, Chapel Hill, AB, 63, PhD(musicol), 70; studied comp with Iain Hamilton, 64-66 & Roger Hannay, 67-68; Chishaku-In, Kyoto, Japan, 77. *Works:* Three Mysteries, Hinshaw Music, 73; Missa Brevis (SATB), 74, Tantum Ergo (SATB), 76 & Three Motets for Holy Week (SATB), 77, C F Peters; Serenade (small ens), Seesaw Music Corp, 78; Sangraal (orch), Fleisher Collection, 78; English Mass, Worldwide Music Corp, 80. *Pos:* Perf as violinist, pianist & cond, formerly; choral asst, countertenor & cond, Exeter Col, Oxford Univ, 75. *Teaching:* Lectr, Duke Univ, 66-68; from asst prof to prof, Bucknell Univ, 68-, head, Dept Music, 80-; vis fel, Clare Hall, Cambridge Univ, England, 82-83. *Awards:* Annual ASCAP Awards, 78-; McCollin Prize, Musical Fund Soc Philadelphia, 79; Nat Flute Asn Award, 81. *Mem:* Am Soc Univ Comp; ASCAP; Am Musicol Soc; Soc Ethnomusicol; Soc Asian Music. *Interests:* Music and mysticism; Asian influences in contemporary music; Japanese traditional music. *Publ:* Auth, The Harold E Cook Collection of Musical Instruments, Bucknell Univ Press, 75; Music and Mysticism: A Summary Overview, Studia Mystica, 79; Ritual Music in Japanese Esoteric Buddhism, Ethnomusicol, 82. *Rep:* R M Young 72 Clark Rd Wolverhampton WV3 9PA England. *Mailing Add:* Dept of Music Bucknell Univ Lewisburg PA 17837

HILL, JOHN DAVID
EDUCATOR, TROMBONE
b Detroit, Mich, Oct 2, 28. *Study:* Wayne State Univ, BS, 50; Ind Univ, MM, 56; Univ Kans, PhD, 68. *Pos:* Trombonist, US Air Force Band & Symph Orch, Washington, DC, 52-55 & Baltimore Symph Orch, 56-57. *Teaching:* Instr, Univ Kans, 57-63; prof & assoc dir, Sch Music, Univ Iowa, 63- *Mem:* Int Trombone Asn; Music Educr Nat Conf; Nat Asn Sch Music. *Publ:* Auth, The Establishment of Orchestral Repertoire Sessions for the Low Brass Instruments, Nat Asn Col Wind & Perc Instr Bulletin, Vol XVI, No 1; A Study of the Achievement of Culturally Deprived and Advantaged Children, Studies in Psychology Music, Vol VI, 70; ed, Sonata a 3, No 1 by Antonio Bertali, 71 & co-ed, Six Sonatas for Brass Quintet by Antonio Bertali, Musica Rara, 72; Performance Practices of the 16th, 17th and 18th Centuries, J Int Trombone Asn, Vol IX, 80. *Mailing Add:* RR 2 Iowa City Iowa City IA 52240

HILL, JOHN WALTER
EDUCATOR
b Chicago, Ill, Dec 7, 42. *Study:* Univ Chicago, AB, 63; Harvard Univ, MA, 66, PhD, 72. *Teaching:* Instr, Univ Del, 70-71; asst prof, Univ Pa, 71-78; assoc prof, Univ Ill, 78- *Mem:* Am Musicol Soc; Int Musicol Soc; Soc Italiana Musicol; Col Music Soc. *Interests:* Italian theater and church music of the 16th, 17th and 18th centuries. *Publ:* Auth, Le relazioni di Antonio Cesti con

la corte e i teatri di Firenze, Riv Ital Musicol, 76; Vivaldi's Griselda, J Am Musicol Soc, 78; The Life & Works of F M Veracini, UMI Res Press, 79; Oratory Music in Florence, Acta Musicol, 79; Realized Continuo Accompaniments from Florence, ca 1600, Early Music, 83. *Mailing Add:* 407 W Pennsylvania Ave Urbana IL 61801

HILL, (WALTER) KENT
EDUCATOR, ORGAN
b Meigs, Ga, Sept 29, 34. *Study:* Consv Music, Oberlin Col, studied organ with Richard Hudson & Leo Holden, BM, 57; Royal Danish Consv, studied organ with Aksel Andersen, cert, 60; Eastman Sch Music, studied organ with David Craighead, MM, 61, DMA, 66. *Pos:* Dir music, First Methodist Church, Thomasville, Ga, 57-59; church musician, Grace Episcopal Church, Elmira, NY, 69- *Teaching:* Instr music, Tex Tech Univ, 63-67; prof & chmn dept, Mansfield Univ, 67- *Mem:* Am Guild Organists (dean Elmira Chap, 69-70); Music Educr Nat Conf; Music Teachers Nat Asn; Dalcroze Soc; Anglican Asn Musicians. *Mailing Add:* PO Box 1096 RD 3 Mansfield PA 16933

HILL, PAMELA JEAN
FLUTE & PICCOLO, TEACHER
b Detroit, Mich, Sept 15, 48. *Study:* Univ Mich, studied flute with Nelson Hauenstein, BMus, 70; Wayne State Univ, with Ervin Monroe, MM, 80. *Pos:* Flutist, Detroit Symph Orch, 77-; prin flute, Oakway Symphony, Farmington, Mich, 80- & Mich Opera Theatre, Detroit, 81- *Teaching:* Band dir, Franklin High Sch, Livonia, Mich, 71-73; orch dir, Greenhills Sch, Ann Arbor, Mich, 81- *Awards:* First Place, Int Woodwind Compt, Middlesbrough Eisteddfod, England, 66. *Mem:* Tuesday Musicale, Detroit. *Mailing Add:* 425 E Liberty Milford MI 48042

HILL, ROBERT JAMES
CLARINET, TEACHER
b Cleveland Heights, Ohio, July 10, 59. *Study:* Cleveland Inst Music, BMus, 81, artist dipl, 82. *Rec Perf:* Embarking for Cythera (O'Brien), CRI, 82; The Premiere Clarinet, Cleveland Inst Music Studios, 83. *Pos:* Prin clarinet, Reconaissance Contemp Music Ens, 78-83; solo clarinet, New Cleveland Chamber Players, 79-; prin clarinet, Cleveland Chamber Orch, 80-83; solo recitalist, Cleveland Chamber Arts Asn, 81- *Teaching:* Chmn clarinet dept, Cleveland Music Sch Settlement, 76-; instr chamber music, SEuclid-Lyndhurst Sch, Ohio, 82; clarinet, Case Western Reserve Univ, currently. *Awards:* Leonard Bernstein Soloist Award, 82; Lorin Maazel Int Lett Recognition, 82. *Rep:* Cleveland Chamber Arts Asn 11021 East Blvd Cleveland OH 44106. *Mailing Add:* 4369 Ardmore Rd South Euclid OH 44121

HILL, TERRY
CONDUCTOR
b Provo, Utah, Apr 13, 46. *Study:* Brigham Young Univ, BMus, 69, MA, 77; Univ Ariz. *Pos:* Cond, Utah Valley Youth Symph, 73-, Snowbird Arts Fest Orch & Nat Youth Symph, 76-79 & Brigham Young Univ Clinic Orch, summer 81; asst cond, Salt Lake Chamber Orch, 74-76; asst cond & rec dir, Mormon Youth Symph & Chorus, 75- *Teaching:* Cond orch, Timpview High Sch & Provo High Sch, 73-; teaching asst orch, Univ Ariz, 81-82. *Awards:* Outstanding Music Educ Student, Brigham Young Univ, 64. *Mem:* Am Symph Orch League; Music Educr Nat Conf; Am String Teachers Asn; Nat Sch Orch Asn; Pi Kappa Lambda. *Mailing Add:* 1495 N 300 W Provo UT 84604

HILL, WILLIAM RANDALL
PERCUSSION
b Burlington, NC, Jan 31, 54. *Study:* Sch Music, Ind Univ, with George Gaber, BM & perf cert, 77; Cleveland Inst Music, with Cloyd Duff, MM, 80. *Pos:* Prin timpanist & perc, Omaha Symph Orch, 78-80, Honolulu Symph Orch, 80- & Denver Symph Orch, 80- *Mailing Add:* 715 S Raritan Denver CO 80223

HILLER, LEJAREN ARTHUR, JR
COMPOSER, EDUCATOR
b New York, NY, Feb 23, 24. *Study:* Princeton Univ, BA, 44, MA, 46, PhD, 47; Univ Ill, MMus, 58. *Works:* Illiac Suite for String Quartet, 57, A Triptych for Hieronymus, 66, Machine Music for Piano, Percussion and Tape, 64 & A Preview of Coming Attractions for Orchestra, 75, Theodore Presser; Persiflage for Flute, Oboe and Percussion, Waterloo Music Publ, 77; String Quartet No 7, C F Peters, 79; Quadrilateral for Piano and Tape, perf by Yvar Mikhashoff, 81. *Pos:* Dir, Experimental Music Studio, Univ Ill, Urbana, 58-68. *Teaching:* Asst prof, Univ Ill, Urbana, 58-61, assoc prof, 61-64, prof, 64-68; Frederick B Slee prof comp, State Univ NY, Buffalo, 68-80, Birge-Cary prof comp, 80- *Awards:* Sr Fulbright lectr music, Warsaw, Poland, 73-74 & Salvador, Brazil, 80; Nat Endowment Arts Award, 76 & 79. *Bibliog:* Gagne & Caras (auth), Soundpieces, Interviews with 24 American Publishers, Scarecrow Press, 81. *Mem:* ASCAP; Am Soc Univ Comp; Computer Music Soc; Am Music Ctr. *Mailing Add:* 359 Berryman Dr Snyder NY 14226

HILLER, ROGER LEWIS
CLARINET, EDUCATOR
b New York, NY, Feb 26, 33. *Study:* Berkshire Music Ctr; Chautauqua Music Sch; Juilliard Sch Music, BMus, 54; studied with Daniel Bonade & Robert McGinnis. *Pos:* Prin clarinet, Houston Symph Orch, 56-59, Metropolitan Opera Orch, 59-, Chautauqua Symph Orch, summers 60-; chamber musician. *Teaching:* Assoc prof clarinet, NY Univ, currently; mem fac, Chautauqua Music Sch, formerly. *Mailing Add:* 73-24 194th St Flushing NY 11366

HILLHOUSE, WENDY CAROL
MEZZO-SOPRANO
b New Orleans, La. *Study:* Univ Calif, Berkeley, BA, 74; San Francisco Consv Music, BMus(voice), 80. *Rec Perf:* Le Testement de Villon, Fantasy Rec, 72. *Roles:* Orlovsky in Die Fledermaus, Merola Opera Prog, 81; Erminio in The Triumph of Honor, 82, Emily Dickinson in The Women In the Garden, 82 & Nerillo in L'Ormindo, 83, San Francisco Opera Ctr; Rosina in The Barber of Seville, Sacramento Opera, 83; Medea in Teseo, Pocket Opera, 83; Alto solos in St Matthew Passion, Fest Masses, San Francisco, 83. *Awards:* First Place, Metropolitan Opera Auditions, San Francisco District, 80; Kent Family Award, San Francisco Opera Auditions, 81; Winner, Eleanor Steber Music Found, 82. *Rep:* Robert Lombardo Assoc One Harkness Plaza Ste 6F 61 W 62nd New York NY 10023. *Mailing Add:* 155 Westgate St Redwood City CA 94062

HILLIARD, JOHN STANLEY
COMPOSER
b Hot Springs, Ark, Oct 29, 47. *Study:* Ouachita Univ, studied comp with W F McBeth, BMus, 69; Va Commonwealth Univ, MMus, 72; Cornell Univ, studied comp with Karel Husa, DMus, 83; Southern Methodist Univ, with Donald Erb. *Works:* The Grand Traverse, 75, Fantasy, 77, Three Trees, 79, Samadhi, 82, Poems of May Sarton, 82, Two Solos for Unaccompanied Flute, 82 & Menhir, 83, Am Comp Ed. *Teaching:* Teacher asst, Va Commonwealth Univ, 70-72 & Cornell Univ, 77-80; instr, Interlochen Ctr for Arts, Mich, 74-77; comp-in-res, Howard Payne Univ, 80- *Awards:* Comp grant, Finnish Ministry of Educ, 75. *Mem:* Am Comp Alliance; BMI. *Mailing Add:* Sch Music Howard Payne Univ Brownwood TX 76801

HILLIARD, TOM (THOMAS LEE)
COMPOSER, CONDUCTOR
b Detroit, Mich, Jan 20, 30. *Study:* Northeastern Ill State Univ, BA, 70; DePaul Univ, studied comp with Leon Stein & Philip Winsor, 74- *Works:* Stonehenge, 70 & Rondo, 70, Downbeat Wkshp Publ; Grand Junction's Functions, Opus Music Publ Inc, 75; Line Tracing, 76, Service Number One, 76, Air For Squared Circle, 77 & Service Number Two, 79, DePaul Univ Contemp Music Ens. *Rec Perf:* The Legend of Bix, Argo Rec, 59. *Pos:* Choral dir, Int Harvester, Ill, 74-77; woodwind, Mill Run Theatre Niles, Ill, 77-81. *Teaching:* Band dir, Glencoe sch syst, 64-65; instr music, DePaul Univ, 75-80. *Awards:* Nat Endowment Arts Comp Fel, 75. *Mem:* Am Fedn Musicians; BMI. *Mailing Add:* 372 Provident Ave Winnetka IL 60093

HILLIS, MARGARET (ELEANOR)
CONDUCTOR, EDUCATOR
b Kokomo, Ind, Oct 1, 21. *Study:* Ind Univ, BA, 47; Juilliard Sch Music, 47-49; numerous hon degrees from US univ, 67-80. *Rec Perf:* Les Noces (Stravinsky), Vox; Bartok Four Slovak Songs (1917) & Eight Songs from '27 Choruses' (1935), Bartok; Missa Brevis, (Wilhelm Killmayer) & Mass (Lou Harrison), Epic; Contemporary Christmas Carols (David Kraehenbuehl, Charles Jones, Manus Sasonkin, Arthur Harris & John Gruen), Contemporary Rec. *Pos:* Dir, Metropolitan Youth Chorale, 48-51; music dir & cond, Am Conct choir, 50-, Am Conct Orch, 50-, Kenosha Symph Orch, 61-68 & Elgin Symph Orch, Ill, 71-; cond, Union Theol Sem, 50-60, Juilliard Sch Music, 51-53 & Do-It Yourself Messiah, 76-; asst cond, Collegiate Chorale, New York, 52-53; choral cond, Am Opera Soc, New York, 52-68; dir choral dept, Third St Music Sch Settlement, 53-54; founder & music dir, Am Choral Found Inc, 54-; choral dir, New York Opera Co, 55-56, Chicago Symph Chorus, 57-, Santa Fe Opera Co, 58-59, Chicago Music Col, Roosevelt Univ, 61-62 & San Francisco Symph Orch, 82-83; dir music, New York Chamber Soloists, 56-60; music asst to dir, Chicago Symph Orch 66-68; res cond, Chicago Civic Orch, 67-; cond & choral dir, Cleveland Orch Chorus, 69-71 & Sch Music, Northwestern Univ, 70-77; guest cond, Chicago Symph, Cleveland Orch, Minn Orch, Nat Symph Orch and others. *Teaching:* Inst music, Union Theol Sem, 50-60; instr choral, Choral Inst, 68-70 & 75; prof cond, Sch Music, Northwestern Univ, 70-77; vis prof cond, Sch Music, Ind Univ, 78-82. *Awards:* Steinway Award, 69; Sigma Alpha Iota Found Award, 74; Grammy Award, 77, 78, 79, & 82. *Mem:* Nat Soc Lit & Arts; Am Symph Orch League; Asn Prof Vocal Ensembles; Am Music Ctr; Asn Choral Cond. *Mailing Add:* c/o Sheldon Soffer Mgt 130 W 56th St New York NY 10019

HILLMER, LEANN
EDUCATOR, MUSIC DIRECTOR
b Lincoln Co, Kans, Nov 10, 42. *Study:* Univ Kans, BMus, MMus; Mannes Col Music; studied with Roy H Johnson, John Goldmark, Evelyn Swarthout, Paul Berl, Robert Baustian, Luigi Ricci & Jan Strasser. *Pos:* Mem, Opera Theater of NVa, Wash Opera, Omaha Opera, Kansas City Lyr Theatre & Santa Fe Opera; asst chorusmaster, New York City Opera; assoc music dir, Metropolitan Opera Studio; music dir, Minn Opera Studio; asst music dir, Minn Opera Co. *Teaching:* Dir opera wkshp, Univ Kansas, formerly, assoc prof opera & accmp, currently; staff accmp, Am Univ, formerly; coach, Lieder Prog, Tanglewood Music Fest, formerly. *Awards:* Winston Churchill Traveling Fel, ESU, 74. *Mem:* Mu Phi Epsilon. *Mailing Add:* 408 Murphy Hall Univ Kans Lawrence KS 66045

HILLS, RICHARD L
EDUCATOR, CLARINET
b Iowa City, Iowa, Dec 25, 25. *Study:* Univ Iowa, studied with Himie Voxman, BA, MA, MFA, PhD, 72. *Teaching:* Dir bands, West Allis Pub Sch, Wis, 51-54; prof woodwinds, Univ Mo, Columbia, 55- *Mem:* Music Educr Nat Conf; Nat Asn Col Wind & Perc Instr; Int Clarinet Cong. *Mailing Add:* Music Dept Univ Mo Columbia MO 65211

HILLYER, KAZUKO TATSUMURA
ARTIST MANAGER
b Osaka, Japan. *Study:* Toho Acad Music; Boston Univ, BA; NY Univ, MA(musicol). *Pos:* Founder & mgr, Pacific World Artists Inc, 68-, Kazuko Hillyer Int, 72- & Conct Arts Soc, 76; arranged tours for Los Angeles Phil, Cleveland Orch, Noh Nat Theater, Black Theatre Prague & Budapest Phil; initiator, Beacon Theater Proj, 77. *Teaching:* Lectr, arts mgt. *Awards:* Smetana Medal. *Mem:* Founder, Concert Arts Soc. *Mailing Add:* 250 W 57th St New York NY 10107

HILLYER, RAPHAEL
VIOLA, EDUCATOR
Study: Curtis Inst; Dartmouth Col, grad; Harvard Univ, grad. *Pos:* Mem, Boston Symph Orch & NBC Symph; founding mem, Juilliard Quartet; soloist, Europe & North & South Am. *Teaching:* Mem fac, Juilliard Sch & Am Univ; mem fac & coordr string dept, Yale Sch Music, 75- *Mailing Add:* c/o Kazuko Hillyer Inc 250 W 57th St New York NY 10107

HILTON, RUTH B
LIBRARIAN, EDUCATOR
b Detroit, Mich, Oct 9, 26. *Study:* Cornell Univ, BA, 47; Syracuse Univ, MLS, 67. *Pos:* Asst music librn, Cornell Univ, 58-68; music librn, NY Univ, 68- *Mem:* Coun Music Librn Asn (treas & bd mem, 69-75); Nat Libr Asn (mem coun, 70-77, secy, treas & bd mem, 75-77); Int Asn Music Libr; Am Musicol Soc; Am Music Ctr. *Publ:* Auth, index to early music in selected anthologies, 78; contribr, Notes, New Grove Dict of Music & Musicians, New Grove Dict of Music in US & RILM Abstracts. *Mailing Add:* Music Libr NY Univ 70 Wash Sq S New York NY 10012

HIMES, DOUGLAS D
ADMINISTRATOR, LECTURER
b Wheeling, WVa, Apr 2, 52. *Study:* Univ Pittsburgh, BS, 74, MA(musicol), 78. *Pos:* Organist & dir music, Smithfield United Church, 73-78 & Parkwood United Presby Church, 78-81; dir perf arts div, Munson-Williams-Proctor Inst, 81- *Teaching:* Asst organist & teaching fel, Univ Pittsburgh, 75-79; instr music, Knaben-Volksschule, Salzburg, 80. *Mem:* Asn Col Univ & Community Arts Adminr; Am Musicol Soc; Int Stiftung Mozarteum; Deutsche Mozart-Gesellschaft; Am Guild Organists. *Interests:* W A Mozart keyboard music. *Publ:* Auth, A New Wedding Processional of Jean Langlais, Diapason, 78; coauth & ed, Derra de Moroda Dance Archives; The Dance Library: A Catalogue, Robert Wölfle, Munich, 82. *Mailing Add:* 310 Genessee St Utica NY 13502

HINDELL, LEONARD
BASSOON, EDUCATOR
Study: Manhattan Sch Music, with Stephen Maxym, BM, MM. *Rec Perf:* Solo bassoon recital, MACE Rec. *Pos:* Bassoon & contrabassoon, Metropolitan Opera, 64-72; recitalist & chamber music performer; participant, Newport Romantic Music Fest, formerly; bassoonist, New York Phil, currently; mem, Woodwind Quintet in Res, currently. *Teaching:* Mem fac, Consv Music, Brooklyn Col, formerly; mem fac ens, Manhattan Sch Music, 69-, mem fac bassoon, 74-; mem fac, Mannes Col Music, 80- *Awards:* Harold Bauer Award, 64. *Mailing Add:* 277 West End Ave New York NY 10023

HINES, JEROME
BASS
b Hollywood, Calif, Nov 8, 21. *Study:* Univ Calif, Los Angeles, BA, 43; studied with Gennaro Curci, Samuel Margolis & Rocco Pandiscio; Whitworth Col, Hon DMus, 64; Bloomfield Col, Hon DMus, 69; Taylor Univ, Hon DMus, 72; Kean Col, Hon DHL, 76; Stevens Inst Technol, Dr Eng, 82. *Works:* I Am the Way (opera). *Rec Perf:* Sutter in Golden Child, NBC TV, 60; Scenes from Attila, Mefistofele, Boris Godunov & Don Quichotte, CBC TV; Rec on London/Decca, EMI, Columbia, Victor, Word & RCA Rec. *Roles:* Monterone in Rigoletto, San Francisco Opera, 41; Mephistofeles in Faust, New Orleans Opera Asn, 44 & 67; Archibaldo in L'Amore dei Tre Re, Wash Opera, 81; Don Basilio In Il Barbiere di Siviglia, 82 & Gurnemanz in Parsifal, 82, Metropolitan Opera; Moses in Moses, 82; King Mark in Tristan und Isolde, New Orleans Opera Asn, 83; and others. *Pos:* Bass, Civic Light Opera Co Los Angeles, 40; San Francisco Opera Co, 41, Hollywood Bowl, 42 & 47, Opera Asn Golden West, 43, New Orleans Opera Co, 42, 46, 67 & 83 & with major opera co in Europe & North Am; leading bass, Metropolitan Opera, 46-; performer, Glyndebourne Fest, 63, Edinburg Fest, 53, Munich Opera Fest, 53 & 54 & Wagner Opera Fest, Bayreuth, Germany, 58-61 & 63. *Awards:* Caruso Award, 46; Cornelius N Bliss Award, 50. *Mem:* Am Guild Musical Artists. *Publ:* Auth, This is My Story, This is My Song, 68 & Tim Whosoever, 70, Fleming H Revell Co; Great Singers on Great Singing, Doubleday. *Rep:* Shaw Concerts Inc 1995 Broadway New York NY 10023. *Mailing Add:* 370 N Wyoming Ave South Orange NJ 07079

HINES, ROBERT STEPHAN
ADMINISTRATOR, CONDUCTOR
b Kingston, NY, Sept 30, 26. *Study:* Juilliard Sch, BS, 52; Univ Mich, MMus, 56. *Teaching:* Asst prof, Southern Ill Univ, 57-61; prof, Wichita State Univ, 61-71; prof, Univ Hawaii, Manoa, 72-, chmn, 80- *Mem:* Am Choral Dir Asn; Am Asn Univ Prof; Music Teachers Nat Asn; Am Fedn Musicians. *Interests:* Twentieth century Latin diction; ear training & sight singing. *Publ:* Ed, Composer's Point of Views: Essays on 20th Century Choral Music, Univ Okla, 63, Greenwood, 80; Composer's Point of View: Essays on Orchestra Music, Univ Okla, 70; auth, Singer's Manual of Latin Diction & Phonetics, 75 & coauth, Ear Training & Sight Singing, Vol 1 & 2, 79 & 80, Schirmer Bks. *Mailing Add:* Music Dept Univ Hawaii Honolulu HI 96822

HINGER, FRED DANIEL
PERCUSSION, EDUCATOR
b Cleveland, Ohio, Feb 9, 20. *Study:* Eastman Sch Music, BM, perf cert; studied perc with Tichy, Albright, Street & Podensky. *Pos:* Mem, Rochester Phil, 39-41; perc & xylophone soloist, US Navy Band, 42-48; prin perc, Philadelphia Orch, 48-51, prin timpanist, 51-67; prin timpanist, Metropolitan Opera Orch, currently; pres, Hinger Touch-Tone Corp, currently. *Teaching:* Mem fac, Curtis Inst Music, 'formerly & Yale Sch Music, 72-; mem fac perc, Manhattan Sch Music, 67-, chmn dept, 82- *Mailing Add:* Metropolitan Opera Asn Lincoln Ctr New York NY 10023

HINSHAW, DONALD GREY
ADMINISTRATOR, MUSIC DIRECTOR
b Yadkinville, NC, Aug 23, 34. *Study:* Davidson Col, BS, 55; New Orleans Baptist Theol Sem, MSM, 58. *Pos:* Minister music, First Baptist Church, Wilson, NC, 58-65; choral ed, Carl Fischer, 68-75; pres, Hinshaw Music Inc, 75- *Teaching:* Prof music, Atlantic Christian Col, 59-65. *Mem:* ASCAP; BMI; Music Publ Asn; Nat Music Publ Asn; Church Music Publ Asn (treas, 81-83). *Mailing Add:* Manns Chapel Rd Chapel Hill NC 27514

HINSON, (GRADY) MAURICE
EDUCATOR, PIANO
b Marianna, Fla, Dec 4, 30. *Study:* Juilliard Sch Music, 47 & 50; Univ Fla, BA, 52; Consv Nat, Univ Nancy, France, 53; Univ Mich, MM, 55, DMA, 58. *Rec Perf:* Music of Portugal, Educo Rec, 75. *Teaching:* Instr, Univ Mich, 54-57; prof music, Sch Church Music, Southern Baptist Theol Sem, 57-; guest prof, Drake Univ, summer 77, Univ Southern Calif, summer 81 & 82 & Univ Ga, summer 80. *Awards:* Deems Taylor Award, ASCAP, 80; Distinguished Mem Citation, Ky Music Teachers Asn, 81. *Bibliog:* Carola Grindea (auth), Two Scholars of the Piano Literature, Piano J, 2/83. *Mem:* Music Teachers Asn (pres, southern div, 64-66); Ky Music Teachers Asn (pres, 62-64); Am Liszt Soc; Am Guild of Organists (dean, L'ville chap, 60-62). *Interests:* Piano literature & bibliography, piano music in America. *Publ:* Auth, Guide to the Pianist's Repertoire, Ind Univ Press, 73 & suppl, 79; The Piano Teacher's Source Book, Belwin-Mills, 74 & 80; The Piano in Chamber Ensemble, 78, Music For Piano and Orchestra, 82 & Music For More Than One Piano, 83, Ind Univ Press. *Mailing Add:* 213 Choctaw Rd Louisville KY 40207

HINTON-BRAATEN, KATHLEEN
VIOLIN, WRITER
b Ventura, Calif, Sept 15, 41. *Study:* Consv Music, Oberlin Col; Calif State Univ, San Francisco; Calif State Univ, Northridge; Calif State Univ, Fullerton; Univ Md, College Park. *Rec Perf:* With Nat Symph Orch. *Pos:* Violinist, Nat Symph Orch, currently, asst personnel mgr, formerly; asst personnel mgr, Cincinnati Symph Orch, formerly & San Antonio Symph, formerly; co-founder, 20th Century Consort, Music in Maine String Quartet. *Publ:* Contribr, New York Times, Christian Science Monitor, Washington Post Mag, Accent Mag, NMex Mag & others. *Mailing Add:* 4813 S 28th St Arlington VA 22206

HIPP, JAMES WILLIAM
ADMINISTRATOR, EDUCATOR
b Guntersville, Ala, May 2, 34. *Study:* Univ Tex, Austin, BM, 56, MM, 63, DMA, 79. *Teaching:* Assoc chmn div music, Southern Methodist Univ, 71-73, chmn, 76-; dir sch music, Ill Wesleyan Univ, 73-76; dean sch music, Univ Miami, 83- *Mem:* Nat Asn Sch Music; Col Music Soc; Music Educr Nat Conf; Tex Asn Music Sch (pres, 81-82); Dallas Civic Music Asn (pres elect, 82-). *Publ:* Auth, Evaluating Music Faculty in Higher Education, Prestige, 83. *Mailing Add:* Sch Music Univ Miami Coral Gables FL 33124

HIRSH, ALBERT
EDUCATOR, PIANO
b Chicago, Ill, July 1, 15. *Study:* Chicago Musical Col, 24-27; private study in music & piano, 27-36. *Teaching:* Prof music & artist in res, Univ Houston, 50-; performer & teacher, Am Inst Musical Studies, Graz, Austria, 73-80. *Awards:* Teaching Excellence Award, Univ Houston, 81. *Mem:* Phi Mu Alpha Sinfonia; Chamber Music Soc Houston (dir, 80-); J S Bach Soc Houston (musical dir, 56-75). *Mailing Add:* 5711 Jackwood St Houston TX 77096

HIRST, GRAYSON
TENOR
b Ojai, Calif, Dec 27, 39. *Study:* Juilliard Sch Music, with Jennie Tourel, Christopher West & Tito Capobianco; Music Acad West, with Martial Singher; Opera Theater, Univ Calif, Los Angeles with Jan Popper; Aspen Music Fest Sch, with Jennie Tourel & Elmer Nagy. *Roles:* Young Conductor in Divina, Juilliard Opera Theater, 66; Guiscardo in Padrevia, 67 & Alfons in Scarlet Mill, 68, Brooklyn Col Opera; Ormindo, 69 & Orsino in Beatrix Cenci, 71, Opera Soc Washington, DC; Lord Byron, Am Opera Ctr, Juilliard Sch, 72; Pantagleize, Brooklyn Col Opera, 73. *Teaching:* Private lessons voice & coach repertoire. *Mailing Add:* c/o Thea Dispeker 59 E 54th St New York NY 10022

HIRSU, VALENTIN
CELLO, EDUCATOR
b Bucharest, Romania, July 7, 47; US citizen. *Study:* Ciprian Porumbescu Consv Music, Bucharest, Romania, MA, 71; study with Andre Navarro, 72. *Pos:* Solo cello perf with most major symph orchs in Romania, 60-73; prin cello, Bori Symph Orch, Italy, 74-75; cellist, New York Phil, 76- *Teaching:* Prof cello, G Enesco Sch Music, Bucharest, Romania, 71-73 & Consv Music, Tel-Aviv, 73-75; prof cello & chamber music, Hebrew Art Sch, NY, 77- *Mailing Add:* 140 West End Ave New York NY 10023

HISS, CLYDE S
EDUCATOR, BARITONE
b Cleveland, Ohio, Dec 27, 33. *Study:* Baldwin-Wallace Consv Music, BMus, 59; Univ Ill, MMus, 60, DMA, 67. *Rec Perf:* Abstrakte Oper #1 (Blacher), Studio Reihe Neuer Musik, 63. *Teaching:* Instr, Mercer Univ, Macon, 60-62; asst, Univ Ill, Urbana-Champaign, 62-65; prof mens glee, studio voice & opera theater, ECarolina Univ, 65- *Mem:* Nat Asn Teachers Singing; Nat Opera Asn; Am Inst Verdi Studies; Cent Opera Serv. *Mailing Add:* Sch Music ECarolina Univ Greenville NC 27834

HITCHCOCK, H(UGH) WILEY
EDUCATOR, WRITER
b Detroit, Mich, Sept 28, 23. *Study:* Dartmouth Col, AB, 44; Univ Mich, MMus, 48, PhD(musicol), 54. *Pos:* Consult, Nat Endowment Humanities, 67-, Naumburg Found, 72- & Rockefeller Found, 72-; co-ed, New Grove Dict of Music in US. *Teaching:* From instr to assoc prof musicol, Univ Mich, 49-61; prof, Hunter Col, City Univ New York, 61-71, chmn dept, 62-67; vis prof, NY Univ, 62-68; prof musicol & founding dir, Inst Studies Am Music, Brooklyn Col, City Univ New York, 71-; prof, Grad Ctr, City Univ New York, currently. *Awards:* Fulbright Res Scholar Italy, 54-55 & France, 68-69; Guggenheim Fel, 68-69; Nat Endowment Humanities Fel, 82-83. *Mem:* Am Musicol Soc; Music Libr Asn (pres, 66-67); Charles Ives Soc (pres, 73-). *Interests:* American music; French & Italian Baroque era music. *Publ:* Auth, Music in the United States, 69, 2nd ed, 74; Ives, Oxford Univ, 77; ed, An Ives Celebration, Univ Ill, 77; Giulio Caccini, Nuove Musiche (1614), A-R Ed, 78; The Works of Marc-Antoine Charpeutier, Picard, 82. *Mailing Add:* 1192 Park Ave New York NY 10028

HIXON, DON L
LIBRARIAN, WRITER
b Columbus, Ohio, Aug 9, 42. *Study:* Calif State Univ, Long Beach, BA(music), 65, MA(music), 67; Univ Calif, Los Angeles, MSLS, 67. *Pos:* Fine Arts Librn, Univ Calif, Irvine, 74- *Mem:* Music Libr Asn; Int Asn Music Libr; Am Musicol Soc; Int Musicol Soc; Music OCLC Users Group. *Interests:* Music bibliography. *Publ:* Auth, Music in Early America, 70, Women in Music, 75 & Nineteenth Century American Drama, 77, Scarecrow Press; Verdi in San Francisco, 1851-1899: A Preliminary Bibliography, Univ Calif, Irvine, 80. *Mailing Add:* 9392 Mayrene Dr Garden Grove CA 92641

HO, CORDELL
COMPOSER
b San Francisco, Calif, Aug 27, 48. *Study:* Univ Ore, 66-68; Univ Vienna, Austria, 68-69; Univ Calif, Berkeley, BA, 72, MA, 75. *Works:* Sketches of Vienna, String Quartet, Univ Calif, 74-75; Universe, Oakland Symph Orch, 74; Versification, Berkeley Contemp Chamber Players, 75; Grunt (electronic film score), 76 & Listen (film score), 77, Fifa Films; Doxology 2, Lawrence Moe, 80; Hui Jia (Returning Home), comn by Virginia Lum, 82. *Awards:* Rockefeller Found Grant, 82. *Mem:* Am Music Ctr. *Mailing Add:* 2838 Washington St San Francisco CA 94115

HO, TING
COMPOSER, EDUCATOR
b Chungking, China, Jan 12, 46; US citizen. *Study:* Bucknell Univ, BA, 67; Kent State Univ, MA, 70; Eastman Sch Music, studied comp with Samuel Adler, Warren Benson, Wayne Barlow & Joseph Schwantner, PhD, 74. *Works:* Sun Times, Montclair Harp Quartet, 75; Bo Music (orch), Montclair State Chamber Orch, 77; Songs of Wine (chorus), Montclair State Chamber Chorus, 78; Four Preludes for Piano, Edmund Battersby, 79 & 83; Give Me Brahms and Ravel ..., New Music Fest, Univ Del, 82; Medusa (orch), New Orleans Phil Symph Orch, 82; Lovelies (chorus), Montclair State Chamber Chorus, 82. *Pos:* Asst prof theory & comp, Montclair State Col, 74- *Awards:* Comp Grant, Nat Endowment Arts, 78; Fel, Nat Endowment Humanities, 80; Comp Grant, NJ Arts Coun, 82. *Mem:* BMI; Col Music Soc; Nat Asn Comp USA. *Mailing Add:* 6 South Shore Rd Denville NJ 07834

HOBART, MAX
VIOLIN, EDUCATOR
b Jan 30, 36. *Study:* Univ Southern Calif, violin with Vera Barstow, cond with Ingolf Dahl & chamber music with Gabor Rejto. *Rec Perf:* Dvorak Quintet, Op 77, Deutsche Grammophon; Brahms Viola Quintets & Schubert Octet, Nonesuch Rec; Beethoven 9th Symph. *Pos:* Performer, Virtuosi Roma, formerly; toured Europe; mem, Grad String Quartet, New England Consv Music, formerly, New Orleans Phil, formerly, Nat Symph, formerly & Cleveland Orch, formerly; Robert L Beal & Enid & Bruce A Beal Chair, Boston Symph Orch, 65-, mem, Chamber Players, currently; asst concertmaster, Boston Pops Orch, currently, guest cond, 83; cond, Boston Consv Music Symph Orch, currently; Civic Symph Orch Boston, currently & NShore Phil Orch, currently. *Teaching:* Mem fac, Berkshire Music Ctr, currently; mem fac violin & chamber music, New England Consv Music, currently; teacher orch, Boston Univ, currently. *Mailing Add:* Boston Symph Orch Symph Hall Boston MA 02115

HOBSON, ANN STEPHENS (ANN HOBSON-PILOT)
HARP
b Philadelphia, Pa, Nov 6, 43. *Study:* Philadelphia Musical Acad, 61-64; Cleveland Inst Music, BM, 66; Marlboro Music Fest, 66 & 67; studied harp with Marilyn Costello & Alice Chalifoux. *Rec Perf:* Trio (Debussy). *Pos:* Prin harp, Nat Symph, formerly, Boston Symph Orch, 65-, Boston Pops, currently & Boston Symph Chamber Players, currently; second harp, Pittsburg Symph, formerly; founding mem, New England Harp Trio; soloist, Boston Symph Orch, Boston Pops, Nat Symph Richmond Symph, Wichita Symph & others. *Teaching:* Mem fac, Ambler Music Fest, 68 & 69, Philadelphia Musical Acad, formerly & New England Consv Music, 71- *Mailing Add:* Symph Hall Boston MA 02115

HOBSON, (ROBERT) BRUCE
COMPOSER, TEACHER
b Hartford, Conn, Aug 16, 43. *Study:* Columbia Col, BA, 65; New England Consv Music, MMus, 67; Sch of Arts, Columbia Univ, 3 yr. *Works:* Three Portraits (bar voice & piano), 69, Quintet, 70, Sonata for Two Pianos, 71 & Three (two solo trumpets & orch), 76, APNM; Two Movements (solo piano), Mobart Music Publ, 77; Octet, 79 & Two Isorhythms (solo piano), 82, APNM. *Pos:* Treas & vpres, Guild Comp, New York, NY, Inc, 76-; treas & partner, Asn Prom New Music, 81- *Teaching:* Piano, privately, Manchester & Arlington, Vt, 66-; fel, Univ Mich, 67-68. *Awards:* Comp Forum, New York Pub Libr, 72; fel, Comp Conf, 81. *Mailing Add:* Church St Dorset VT 05251

HOBSON, CONSTANCE YVONNE TIBBS
EDUCATOR, PIANO
b Washington, DC, Sept 22, 26. *Study:* Sch Music, Howard Univ, studied piano with Hazel Harrison & theory with Madeline Coleman, BMus, 47; Cath Univ, studied piano with Emerson Meyers, MMus, 51. *Pos:* Mem adv bd, Ctr Ethnic Music, Howard Univ, 81-; nat consult, Ctr Study Southern Cult, Univ Miss, 81-; guest cond, Howard Univ Conct Band, 82-83. *Teaching:* From teaching asst to prof theory, Howard Univ, 46-83. *Mem:* Col Music Soc; Music Educr Nat Conf; life mem, Nat Asn Negro Musicians; Sigma Alpha Iota; Fri Morning Music Club Inc. *Interests:* Black musicians and the literature of Black composers; contemporary literature. *Publ:* Ed, Chronological Chart of 50 Black Composers—Past and Present, Howard Univ, 71; coauth (with Cazost), Hazel Harrison, Premiere Pianiste, Black Music Res Newsletter, Fisk Univ, 82; Born to Play: The Life and Career of Hazel Harrison, Greenwood Press, 83. *Mailing Add:* 1301 Delaware Ave SW #112 Washington DC 20024

HOCHER, BARBARA JEAN
SOPRANO
b Houston, Tex. *Study:* NTex State Univ, BM; New England Consv Music, MM. *Roles:* Mimi in La Boheme, Lake George Opera, 77; Birdie in Regina, Mich Opera, 77; Lady with the Cake Box in Postcard From Morocco, Washington Opera & Central City Opera, 81; Fiordiligi in Cosi fan tutte, 82 & Birdie in Regina, 82, Wolf Trap Opera Co; Mrs Grose in Turn of the Screw, Washington Opera, 82; Rosalinde in Die Fledermaus, Eugene Opera, 83; Constanze in Abduction From the Seraglio, Glimmerglass Opera Theater, 83. *Awards:* Sullivan Found Grant, 72-80; Metropolitan Opera Grant, 73-76; Martha Baird Rockefeller Found Grant, 74. *Mem:* Sigma Alpha Iota. *Mailing Add:* 315 W 86th Apt 2D New York NY 10024

HOCHHEIMER, LAURA
EDUCATOR, VIOLIN
b Worms, Ger, Apr 18, 33; US citizen. *Study:* Beaver Col, Jenkintown, Pa, studied violin with Veda Reynolds; Eastman Sch Music, BM(violin), 55; Ohio Univ, MFA(violin), 57; Ind Univ, PhD(music educ), 70. *Pos:* Mem, Hamilton Symph Orch, Chicago Chamber Orch & Springfield Symph Orch, Ohio, currently. *Teaching:* Instr strings & vocal music & cond orch, Bainbridge Elem & High Sch, NY, 57-58; instr music, Chicago Pub Sch, 58-64; grad asst violin, Ind Univ, Bloomington, 64-66, instr strings & orch, Lab Sch, 64-66; from instr to assoc prof, WLibery State Col, WVa, 68-70; vis asst prof music, Univ BC, Vancouver, Can, 70-71; fac mem, Towson State Col, 71-73; asst prof music, Col Consv Music, Cincinnati Univ, 73-76; assoc prof, James Madison Univ, 76-81 & Clemson Univ, 81- *Awards:* Fulbright Fel, 66-67. *Mem:* Music Educr Nat Conf; Am Orff-Schulwerk Asn; Va Music Educr Asn (mem, elem sect, exec bd, 78-81); SC Music Educr Asn; Am Fedn Musicians. *Publ:* Auth, Musical Drama Encourages Participation by Handicapped, Music Educr J, 9/64 & Chicago Sch J & Rehabilitation Lit, 65; New Courses In Special Education, Va Music Educr Asn, Notes, fall 77; A Sequential Sourcebook for Elementary School Music St Louis, Magnamusic-Baton, Inc, 2nd ed, 79. *Mailing Add:* Box 48, Strode Tower Clemson Univ Clemson SC 29631

HOCHMAN, ELIZABETH GOULD See Gould, Elizabeth

HODAM, HELEN
SOPRANO, EDUCATOR
Study: Ill Wesleyan Univ, BM; Hartt Col Music, MM; Manhattan Sch Music; Juilliard Sch Music; Univ Vienna; Mozarteum, Salzburg; Aspen Sch Music; Royal Acad Music, London; Goethe Inst, Munich; Alliance Francaise, New York & Paris; studied voice with Luigi Rossini, Paul Schilawsky, Paul Steinitz, Irene Aitoff, Olga Eisner, Grace Perry, Erik Werba, Eva Gauthier, Jennie Tourel & Ernst Wolff. *Pos:* Sop soloist, Christ Methodist Church, New York, Paper Mill Playhouse, formerly & Berkshire Players, formerly; opera appearances, New York, Philadelphia & Wash. *Teaching:* Asst prof singing, Mary Hardin-Baylor Col, 53-54; assoc prof, Muskingum Col, 54-63; mem fac, Am Inst Musical Studies, 73- & New England Consv Music, 78-; prof singing, Consv Music, Oberlin Col, 63- *Awards:* Winner, Young Singers Auditions & Conct Guild Award. *Mailing Add:* New England Consv Music 290 Huntington Rd Boston MA 02115

HODGKINS, CLAIRE (CLAIRE HODGKINS WRIGHT)
VIOLIN, EDUCATOR
b Portland, Ore, Mar 7, 29. *Study:* Lewis & Clark Col; Univ Southern Calif, with Jascha Heifetz, William Primrose, Henryk Szeryng & Boris Sirpo. *Pos:* Soloist with Europ & Am orchs; mem, TV, motion picture & rec orchs. *Teaching:* Asst, Univ Southern Calif, 62-77; prof violin & cond chamber orch, Loma Linda Univ, 72-82 & Univ Redlands, 81-83. *Mem:* Am String Teachers; Calif Music Teachers; Music Teachers Nat Asn. *Mailing Add:* Los Angeles CA 90027

HODGKINSON, RANDALL THOMAS
PIANO, TEACHER

b Lyndhurst, Ohio, May 4, 55. *Study:* New England Consv Music, BM, 76, MM, 80; Curtis Inst Music. *Rec Perf:* Music of Donald Martino and Roger Sessions, New World Rec, 83. *Teaching:* Mem fac piano, New England Consv Music, 83- *Awards:* Portland Young Artist Compt Prize Winner, 76; J S Bach Int Compt Prize Winner, 76; Am Music Compt First Prize, 81. *Rep:* Herbert Barrett Mgt 1860 Broadway New York NY 10023. *Mailing Add:* 64 Linnaean Cambridge MA 02138

HODGSON, PETER JOHN
EDUCATOR, WRITER

b Birmingham, England, Apr 6, 29; US citizen. *Study:* Royal Acad Music, LRAM, 51; Royal Col Music, ARCM, 51, MMus, 65; Royal Col Organists, ARCO, 57; Trinity Col, London, LTCL, 63; Univ London, BMus, 64; Univ Colo, Boulder, PhD(musicol), 70. *Pos:* Consult, Music Principia Col, Elsah, Ill, 77. *Teaching:* Res music master, Univ Sch, Victoria, BC, 52-55; instr music hist, theory & piano, Mt Royal Col, 55-65, dir fine arts, 62-65; from asst prof to assoc prof, Ball State Univ, 68-76, prof & chmn dept acad studies in music, 76-78; dean, New England Consv Music, 78-83; prof music & chmn dept, Tex Christian - Univ, 83- *Interests:* _ Historical developments of Renaissance musical structures; historical evolution of the sonata; 20th century British ecclesiastical music. *Publ:* Auth, various teaching monogr on topics of music hist, 68-; Toward an Understanding of Renaissance Musical Structure, Ball State Univ, 72; contribr, Advanced Music Questions, Educ Testing Serv, Princeton, 77; auth, Toward a Metaphysical Perception of Structure in Music: An Alternative View of Musical Form, In: Ten Years of Musicology at the University of Colorado, Univ Colo, Boulder, 1/78. *Mailing Add:* Ft Worth TX 76115

HODKINSON, SYDNEY PHILLIP
COMPOSER, CONDUCTOR

b Winnipeg, Manitoba, Can, Jan 17, 34. *Study:* Eastman Sch Music, BM, 56, MM, 58; Univ Mich, DMA, 68. *Works:* Vox Populous, 72, Edge of the Olde One, 76, Dance Variations, 79, Sinfonie Concertante, 80 & Chansons de Jadis, 81, Presser Publ; Bumberboom, AMP, 81; Neuvas Canciones Book II, comn by Espace Musique-Ottawa, 82. *Rec Perf:* Dissolution of the Serial & Valence, SD 292, 71, Megalith Triology, SD 363, 77 & Dance Variations, SD 432, 80, Comp Rec, Inc; Edge of the Olde One, Grenadilla GS 1048, 80. *Teaching:* From instr to asst prof, Univ Va, 58-63; from asst prof to assoc prof, Ohio Univ, 63-66; assoc prof, Univ Mich, 68-73; prof music, Eastman Sch Music, 73- *Awards:* Fel, Nat Inst Arts & Letters, Am Acad, 71, Nat Edowment for Arts, 75-76 & 77-78 & J S Guggenheim Found, 78-79. *Mem:* Broadcast Music Inc; Col Music Soc; Music Educ Nat Conf; Am Music Ctr; Am Fedn Musicians. *Mailing Add:* Eastman Sch Music 26 Gibbs St Rochester NY 14604

HOEKSTRA, GERALD RICHARD
EDUCATOR

b Blue Island, Ill, July 4, 47. *Study:* Calvin Col, BA, 69; Ohio State Univ, PhD, 75. *Teaching:* Asst prof music hist & choir, Trinity Christian Col, 75-79; asst prof music hist & collegium, Wichita State Univ, 79-81 & St Olaf Col, 81- *Mem:* Am Musicol Soc; Col Music Soc; Am Choral Dir Asn. *Interests:* Renaissance chanson. *Publ:* Auth, An 8-Voice Parody of Lassus: Pevernage's Bon jour mon coeur, Early Music, 79; Andre Pevernage: Sieben Chansons (Das Chorwerk, 131), Möseler Verlag, 82; Andre Pevernage: The Complete Chansons (four vol): Recent Researches in the Music of the Renaissance, A-R Ed Inc (in press). *Mailing Add:* Music Dept St Olaf Col Northfield MN 55057

HOFFMAN, ALLEN
COMPOSER

b Newark, NJ, Apr 12, 42. *Study:* Hartt Col, with Arnold Franchetti. *Works:* Idyll (orch); Mother Goose (wind ens with sop solo); Mass (chorus, a capella); Madrigals (chorus, a capella); Haiku (chorus, a capella); 3 Nonsense Songs (chorus, a capella); Recitative and aria (solo duoble bass). *Teaching:* Fac mem, Hartt Col, 67-75 & Hartford Consv Music, 71-77. *Awards:* Nat Found Arts & Humanities Award, 66; Nat Soc Arts & Lett Award, 68; MacDowell Fels, 68-72. *Mem:* ASCAP; Am Music Ctr; Am Asn Univ Prof; Music Educr Nat Conf; Conn Music Educr Nat Conf. *Mailing Add:* 366 Ridgewood Rd West Hartford CT 06107

HOFFMAN, CYNTHIA
EDUCATOR, VOICE

Study: Univ Redlands, BM; Columbia Univ, MA; studied voice with Browning-Henderson, Ferro, Brown, Harshaw & Schaper, acting with Meisner, Handman & Shepherd & Alexander technique with T Matthews. *Rec Perf:* On Vanguard Rec. *Pos:* Recitalist. *Teaching:* Mem fac & recitalist, Oren Brown Voice Sem, Amherst Col, formerly; master teacher & panelist, Symposia on Care Professional Voice, Juilliard Sch, formerly; mem fac voice, Manhattan Sch Music, 74- *Awards:* Am Guild Musical Artists Award. *Mailing Add:* Manhattan Sch Music 120 Claremont Ave New York NY 10027

HOFFMAN, GRACE
MEZZO-SOPRANO, EDUCATOR

b Cleveland, Ohio, Jan 14, 25. *Study:* Western Reserve Univ, with Lila Robeson; Manhattan Sch Music, with Friedrich Schorr; studied with Grant Garnell, Mario Wetzelsberger & Mario Basiola. *Rec Perf:* Salome (Strauss), London Rec; Das Lied von der Erde (Mahler), Vox. *Roles:* Mamma Lucia in Cavalleria rusticana, Wagner Opera Co, New York, 51; Fricka in Die Walküre, La Scala; Carmen in Carmen; Dorabella in Cosi fan tutte; Amneris

in Aida; Cassandra in Troyens; Elisabetta in Maria Stuarda. *Pos:* Mem, Zurich Munic Opera, 53-55 & Stuttgart Opera, 55-; guest appearances with maj opera co in US, South Am & Europe; oratorio & conct appearances throughout Europe. *Teaching:* Prof voice, Hochschule Music, Stuttgart, 78- *Awards:* Württembergerische Kammersängerin, 60; Outstanding Serv Medal, Baden-Wüttemberg, 78; Austrian Kammersängerin, 80. *Mailing Add:* c/o Staatsopre Postfach 982 7 Stuttgart Germany, Federal Republic of

HOFFMAN, IRWIN
CONDUCTOR & MUSIC DIRECTOR

b New York, NY, Nov 26, 24. *Study:* Juilliard Sch, 50. *Pos:* Music dir, Vancouver Symph, 52-64 & Fla Gulf Coast Symph, 68-; actg music dir & assoc cond, Chicago Symph, 64-70; chef permanent, Belgian Radio & TV Symph, 73-76. *Rep:* Judd Conct Bureau 155 W 57th St New York NY 10023. *Mailing Add:* 1901 Brightwaters Blvd St Petersburg FL 33704

HOFFMAN, JAMES
PERCUSSION, ADMINISTRATOR

Study: Brown Military Acad; studied with Myron Collins & Leo Hamilton. *Pos:* Prin perc & personnel mgr, San Diego Symph Orch, 59-; perc, San Diego Opera Orch, currently & Calif Ballet Orch, currently; studio musician. *Mailing Add:* San Diego Symph Orch PO Box 3175 San Diego CA 92103

HOFFMAN, JOEL H
COMPOSER, PIANO

b Vancouver, BC, Sept 27, 53; US citizen. *Study:* Univ Wales Cardiff, Great Britain, BM, 74; Juilliard Sch, with Carter, Babbitt & Persichetti, MM, 76, DMA, 78. *Works:* Variations for Violin, Cello and Harp, 78, September Music, 80, Lyra Music Co; Music From Chartres, Shawnee Press, 81; Concerto for Violin, Viola, Cello & Orchestra, 82, Suite, 82, Chamber Symphony, 82, Divertimento, 82 & Harp Sonata, 83, Galaxy Music Corp. *Teaching:* Fel, Juilliard Sch, 76-78; asst prof comp, Col-Consv Music, Univ Cincinnati, 78- *Awards:* Bearns Prize, Columbia Univ, 76; ASCAP Awards, 79-83. *Mem:* ASCAP; Am Music Ctr; Col Music Soc; Nat Asn Comp, USA. *Mailing Add:* Col-Consv Music Univ Cincinnati Cincinnati OH 45221

HOFFMAN, PAUL K
PIANO, EDUCATOR

b Buffalo, NY, Mar 2, 48. *Study:* Eastman Sch Music, with Cecile Genhart & Brooks Smith, BM, 70, MM, 72; Hochschule Musik, Salzburg, with Kurt Neumueller, 72-73; Hochschule Musik, Vienna, with Dieter Weber, 73-74; Peabody Consv, with Leon Fleisher, 75-80. *Rec Perf:* Rhapsodie on a Theme by Paganini (Rachmaninoff), Voice of Am, 70; They Knew What They Wanted (Ernst Krenek), Orion, 80; piano solos (Beugniot & Smith), Radio France, 81; piano solos (Cowell, Cage, Ives & Higgins), Radio Koeln, 83. *Teaching:* Instr, Univ Md, Baltimore, 74-80; asst prof, Rutgers Univ, New Brunswick, NJ, 80- *Awards:* Fulbright-Hays Grant, Int Inst Educ, 72-74; assoc teacher award, Am Music Scholar Asn, 82. *Mem:* Am Soc Univ Comp; NJ Music Teachers Nat Asn; Sonneck Soc; Am Music Ctr; Col Music Soc. *Rep:* Artists Mgt 84 Prospect Ave Douglaston NY 11363. *Mailing Add:* 402 S First Ave Highland Park NJ 08904

HOFFMAN, THEODORE B
COMPOSER, EDUCATOR

b Palo Alto, Calif, Oct 18, 25. *Study:* Stanford Univ, AB, 48; Mills Col, MA, 51; Univ of Pac, PhD, 59. *Works:* Variations on Jesu Meine Freunde, Univ SFla Wind Orch, 65; Variations on We Shall Overcome, Armin Watkins, 65, 66, 71 & 81; Suite from The Tempast, St Petersburg Symph, 66; Golden Goose, Early Music Studio Munich, 70 & 71; Nine Japanese Haiku, Brodt Music, 72; Santiago Pageant, Tampa Community Chorus & Woodwinds, 74 & 75; Mass, Univ SFla, 76. *Pos:* Music dir, San Benito Col, 59-62 & Perry Mansfield Sch Theatre & Dance, 61. *Teaching:* Instr, San Francisco State Col, 57-59; prof humanities, music hist, theory & comp, Univ SFla, 62- *Awards:* SE Band Dir Award, 64. *Mem:* Am Soc Univ Comp; ASCAP. *Publ:* Auth, 170 concert reviews, Tampa Tribune, 62-65; Variations on Jesu Meine Freude, J Band Res, 65; Western Influences in the Japanese Art Song, Monumenta Nipponica, 66. *Mailing Add:* 313 Lake Hobbs Rd Lutz FL 33549

HOFFMANN, JAMES
COMPOSER, MUSIC DIRECTOR

b Oct 2, 29. *Study:* New England Consv, BM; Yale Univ, BM, MM; Univ Ill, DMA; studied comp & theory with Carl McKinley, Francis Judd Cooke, Quincy Porter, Paul Hindemith, Burrill Phillips & Hubert Kessler; Hochschule Musik, Berlin, with Boris Bracher & Josef Rufer. *Works:* Depth Charge, Crest Rec, 78; Hot Potatoes (solo trombone), 80; Seesaw (clarinet & bass clarinet), 81; Machol (sop sax), 81; Windings (brass & winds), 81; Trio (trumpet, trombone & piano), 83. *Teaching:* Mem fac, Oberlin Col, formerly, San Jose State Univ, formerly; chmn, Dept Undergrad Theory, New England Consv Music, 68-80, mem fac theory, currently, co-dir, Enchanted Circle contemp music ser, currently. *Mailing Add:* New England Consv Music 290 Huntington Rd Boston MA 02115

HOFFMANN, RICHARD
COMPOSER, EDUCATOR

b Vienna, Austria, Apr 20, 25; US citizen. *Study:* Violin with Aurel Nemes, 30-35 & comp with Georg Tinter, 35; Univ New Zealand, MusB, 45; studied comp with Arnold Schoenberg, 47-51; Univ Calif, Los Angeles, 49-51. *Works:* Memento Mori, 66-69; Music for Strings, 70-71; String Quartet No 3, 72-74; Souffleur, 75-76; In Memoriam Patris (comput generated), 76; String Quartet No 4 (with comput generated sounds), 77; Intavolaturn, 80; publ by Heinrichshofen, Universal Ed & Bomart-Mobart. *Pos:* Guest lectr throughout

New Zealand, Europe, Can & US; co-ed, Schoenberg Gesamtausgabe, 61; artist in res, Huntington Hartford Found, Villa Montalvo Cult Col, 65-66. *Teaching:* Lectr music, Univ Calif, Los Angeles; fac mem, Consv Music, Oberlin Col, 54-; vis prof, Univ Calif, Berkeley, 65-66, Univ New Zealand, Wellington, Harvard Univ, Univ Iowa & Univ Vienna. *Awards:* Music Award, Nat Inst Arts & Lett, 66; Guggenheim Fel, 70 & 77; Nat Endowment Arts Grant, 76, 77 & 79; and many others. *Mem:* Founding mem, Am Soc Univ Comp. *Interests:* Schoenberg. *Mailing Add:* Music Dept Oberlin Col Oberlin OH 44074

HOFFREN, JAMES A
EDUCATOR, TRUMPET
b Cloquet, Minn, Dec 18, 30. *Study:* Univ Minn, Duluth, BS(music educ), 52; Eastman Sch Music, MM(trumpet), 53; Univ Ill, Urbana-Champaign, EdD(music educ), 63. *Pos:* Band dir, Buchanan High Sch, Mich, 54-58; prin trumpet, South Bend Symph Orch, 56-58, Wichita Symph Orch, 58-61, Jacksonville Symph Orch, Fla, 68-79;. *Teaching:* Prof music, Jacksonville Univ, 63- *Mem:* Fla Asn Schs Music (pres, 80-82); Fla Col Music Educr Asn (pres, 74-76); life mem, Music Educr Nat Conf. *Publ:* Auth, Stop, Look and Listen, Music Educ J, 1/68. *Mailing Add:* Music Dept Jacksonville Univ Jacksonville FL 32211

HOFMEISTER, GIANNINA LOMBARDO
TEACHER, PIANO
b Chicago, Ill, Oct 26, 42. *Study:* St Mary of Woods Col, BA(music), 60-64; Butler Univ, MMus, 65-70; study with Frank Cooper, 70-78; Ind Univ, special coaching with Gyorgy Sebok, 80. *Rec Perf:* Giannina Hofmeister, Hofmeister, 70. *Pos:* Asst cond & pianist, Miss Moffat, Indianapolis, 83. *Teaching:* Instr piano, Butler Univ, 64-68 & St Mary of Woods Col, 82-; artist in res, Purdue Univ, 68-70, Metropolitan Arts Coun, 75-79 & St Mary of Woods Col, 80-81; coordr, Women's External Prog Degree, St Mary of Woods Col, 83- *Awards:* Distinguished Music Award, Ind Piano Teachers Guild, 80; Award, Steinway & Wilking Music Co, 77. *Bibliog:* Judy Stein (auth), Giannina Hofmeister, Purdue Exponent, 69; Alpha Blackburn (dir), Giannina Hofmeister (film), Channel 6 TV, Indianapolis, 78. *Mem:* Ind Piano Teachers Guild (treas, 78-79 & pres, 79-81); Mu Phi Epsilon; Bösendorfer Piano Roster; Ind Arts Commission. *Rep:* Albert Kay Assoc Inc 58 W 58th St New York NY 10019. *Mailing Add:* 8181 Morningside Dr Indianapolis IN 46240

HOFSTETTER, FRED THOMAS
EDUCATOR, ADMINISTRATOR
b Columbus, Ohio, Apr 5, 40. *Study:* St Joseph's Col, with John Egan, BA(music educ), 70; Ohio State Univ, with Norman Phelps, MA(music theory), 71, with William Polland, PhD(music theory), 74. *Teaching:* Fel, Ohio State Univ, 70-74; prof music, Univ Del, 74-, dir, Off Computer-Based Instr, 75-, prof educ studies, 80- *Awards:* Teacher Training Grant, Nat Sci Found, 75-82; Home Music Learning Syst Grant, Atari Inc, 82; Music Videodisc Series Grant, Nat Endowment for Humanities, 82. *Mem:* Nat Consortium Comput-Based Music Instr (pres, 75-79); Soc Music Theory; Music Educr Nat Conf; Col Music Soc; Asn Comput in Humanities. *Interests:* Computer-based recognition of perceptual patterns and learning styles in student acquisition of aural skills. *Publ:* Auth, The Nationalistic Fingerprint in 19th-Century Romantic Chamber Music, Comput & Humanities, 79; Microelectronics and Music Education, Music Educr J, 79; Applications of the GUIDO System to Aural Skills Research, Col Music Symposium, 81; Computer-Based Recognition of Perceptual Patterns and Learning Styles in Rhythmic Dictation Exercises, J Res Music Educ, 82; Computers in Music Education: The GUIDO System, In: Computers in Curriculum & Instr, ACSD, 83. *Mailing Add:* Off Comput-Based Instr Univ Del Newark DE 19711

HOGENSON, ROBERT CHARLES
COMPOSER, PIANO
b Kirksville, Mo, Nov 22, 36. *Study:* Northeast Mo State Teachers Col, BS, 58; La State Univ, MMus, 60; Mich State Univ, PhD, 67. *Works:* Quartal Jaunt (band), 68-70; Sonata for Clarinet, 74-75; Moore's Creek Bridge (band), comn by Del Wind Ens, 77; Three Songs for Soprano, comn by Del Contemp Music Fest, 79-82; Suite for Woodwind Quintet, comn by Del Woodwind Quintet, 82; Sesquicentennial Fanfare, comn by Atlanta Symph Brass & Wilmington Symph, 83; Two Songs for Choir, comn by Del Chorale, 83. *Teaching:* Assoc prof music, Southwest Tex State Univ, 62-68, Univ Del, 68-78 & 79-83 & Univ Hawaii, Hilo, 78-79. *Mem:* Del Music Teachers Nat Asn (pres, 83). *Mailing Add:* Music Dept Univ Del Newark DE 19711

HOGG, MERLE E
EDUCATOR, COMPOSER
b Lincoln, Kans, Aug 25, 22. *Study:* Emporia State Univ, Kans, BS(music) & BS(educ), 48; Univ Iowa, MA, 51, MFA, 52, PhD, 54. *Works:* Concerto for Brass, Robert King Music, 57; Suite for Band, Shawnee Press, 69; Sonata for Brass Choir, G Schirmer, 71; Variations for Bassoon & Piano, Ens Publ, 73; Etude I for Tuba and Piano, 78, Three Studies for Euphonium & Piano, 78 & Interludes for Symphonic Brass, 78, Music Graphics Press. *Pos:* Trombone, ten tuba & bs trumpet, San Diego Symph Orch, 64-; trombone & bs trumpet, San Diego Opera Orch, 66- *Teaching:* Prof music, Eastern NMex Univ, 53-62, San Diego State Univ, 62- *Mem:* Col Music Soc; Am Soc Univ Comp; Music Educr Nat Conf; Am Asn Univ Prof; Nat Asn Jazz Educr. *Mailing Add:* Dept Music San Diego State Univ San Diego CA 92182

HOHSTADT, THOMAS DOWD
CONDUCTOR & MUSIC DIRECTOR
b Ryan, Okla, Sept 5, 33. *Study:* Eastman Sch Music, BMus, 55, MMus, 56, DMus Arts, 62; Vienna Akad Musik, 60. *Pos:* With US Army Band, 56-59, Rochester Symph & Houston Symph; asst cond, Honolulu Symph, 62-63; musical dir, Amarillo Symph, 63-74 & Midland-Odessa Symph, Tex, 74-; founder, Gtr SW Music Fest; consult, Nat Endowment Humanities; music adv, UN. *Teaching:* Mem cond staff, Eastman Sch Music, 60-62. *Mem:* Phi Mu Alpha; Am Symph Orch League; Tex Comn Humanities. *Publ:* Auth, Solo Literature for the Trumpet, 60; Composer Impetus Lineaus, 62; Modern Concepts in Music for Brass, 67. *Mailing Add:* 3522 Maple St Odessa TX 79762

HOIBY, LEE
COMPOSER, PIANO
b Madison, Wis, Feb 17, 26. *Study:* Univ Wis, BA, 47; Mills Col, MA, 52; Curtis Inst Music, cert, 52; Simpson Col, Hon Dr Fine Arts, 83. *Works:* The Scarf (opera), Belwin-Mills, 60; A Month in the Country (opera), Boosey & Hawkes, 64; After Eden (ballet), 67 & Summer and Smoke (opera), 71, Belwin Mills; Piano Concerto #2, 80; Something New for the Zoo (opera), 81; The Italian Lesson (musical monologue), 82. *Rec Perf:* Piano Concerto #1, CRI, 65; After Eden, 66 & Rachmaninoff Suites No 1 & 2, 67, Desto Rec. *Awards:* Fulbright Fel, 53; Arts & Lett Award, Am Acad Arts & Sci, 57; Guggenheim Fel, 58. *Mem:* ASCAP; Am Fedn Musicians; Am Guild Organists. *Mailing Add:* Box 71 Long Eddy NY 12760

HOLDEN, RANDALL LECONTE, JR
EDUCATOR, ADMINISTRATOR
b Bronxville, NY, Dec 4, 43. *Study:* Colby Col, AB, 65; Univ Conn, MA, 66; Univ Wash, MM, 68, DMA, 70. *Pos:* Prod mgr, Ky Opera Asn, 77- *Teaching:* Asst prof music hist, Ariz State Univ, 71-76; assoc prof, Univ Louisville, 76- *Mem:* Nat Opera Asn (mem bd dir, 80-); Sonneck Soc; Col Music Soc. *Interests:* Opera history & production; American music. *Publ:* Auth, University Louisville Opera Program, Opera Quart, 83. *Mailing Add:* 1391 S Third St Louisville KY 40208

HOLLAND, BERNARD P
CRITIC
b Norfolk, Va, Feb 26, 33. *Study:* Univ Va, BA; Vienna Acad Music, 58-62; Paris Consv, 63-64. *Pos:* Music critic, New York Times, 81- *Awards:* Deems Taylor Award, ASCAP, 79. *Mailing Add:* c/o New York Times Music Dept 229 W 43rd St New York NY 10036

HOLLAND, SAMUEL STINSON
ADMINISTRATOR, TEACHER
b Louisville, Ky, Sept 24, 52. *Study:* Univ Tex, Austin, with John Perry, BM, 75; New Sch Music Study, with Frances Clark, prof cert, 77; Univ Houston, with Abbey Simon, MM, 79. *Teaching:* Instr piano & piano pedagogy, New Sch Music Study, 79-, dir, 81-; adj instr piano pedagogy, Westminster Choir Col, 82- *Mem:* New Jersey Music Teachers Asn (pres, 82-); Music Educr Asn. *Publ:* Coauth, Musical Fingers I, II, III & IV, New Sch Music Study Press, 83; co-ed, Sounds of Jazz I & II, New Sch for Music Study Press, 83. *Mailing Add:* Box 217 Kingston NJ 08528

HOLLANDER, LORIN
PIANO, COMPOSER
b Queens, NY, July 19, 44. *Study:* Juilliard Sch, with Eduard Steurmann & Vittorio Giannini, 64; C W Post Col. *Works:* Up Against the Wall (piano); Lullaby. *Rec Perf:* On RCA Victor. *Pos:* Concerts, Bell Telephone Hour, Carnegie Hall & NBC Radio & TV, 57; conct tours with major US orchs, 59-, Europe, 65-; adv, Off Gifted & Talented, US Dept Health, Educ & Welfare, Am Symph Orch League, World Cong Gifted & Pres Scholars; mem, Rockefeller Panel Arts, two years; mem bd dir, Arts Connection & Int Art Jazz, currently. *Teaching:* Lectr, currently. *Bibliog:* Old Friends New Friends (doc), WNET-TV. *Mailing Add:* c/o ICM Artists 40 W 57th St New York NY 10019

HOLLIDAY, KENT ALFRED
TEACHER, COMPOSER
b St Paul, Minn, Mar 9, 40. *Study:* Hamline Univ, BA, 62; Univ Minn, MA, 64, PhD, 68. *Works:* Long's Peak Storm Profile, 74, The Big City Awakes, 74 & Wistful Duet, 74, Myklas Press; Fantasy & Toccata (clarinet & piano), 80 & Triptych (horn & piano), 81, Seesaw Music; Helix (solo piano), comn by Va Music Teachers Asn, 83. *Teaching:* Assoc prof music, Univ Southern Colo, 65-72, Colo State Univ, 72-74, Va Polytechnic Inst, 74- *Mem:* Phi Mu Alpha; Music Teachers Nat Asn. *Publ:* Auth, Performer's Corner, 75 & Refurbishing Your Old Upright, 76, Clavier; Chamber Music for Burgeoning Pianists, Am Music Teacher, 77; Getting the Most Out of Your Metronome, Clavier, 81; Evolution of the Sarabande, Divisions, 81. *Mailing Add:* 1102 Willard Dr Blacksburg VA 24060

HOLLINGSWORTH, SAMUEL H, JR
BASS
b Birmingham, Ala, June 29, 22. *Study:* Juilliard Sch, 40-42. *Pos:* Prin bassist, Nashville Symph, 46-82, Chamber Symph Philadelphia, 68, Dallas Symph, 68-70 & Pittsburgh Symph, 70-; Asst tour mgr, Chamber Symph Philadelphia, 67-68. *Teaching:* Instr bass, George Peabody Col for Teachers, 46-55 & New Sch Music, 66-68. *Mailing Add:* 4403 Centre Ave Apt C6 Pittsburgh PA 15213

HOLLINGSWORTH, STANLEY W
EDUCATOR, COMPOSER
b Berkeley, Calif, Aug 27, 24. *Study:* San Jose State Col; Mills Col, with Darius Milhaud; Curtis Inst Music, with Gian-Carlo Menotti; Am Acad, Rome. *Works:* The Mother (opera), 54; La Grande Breteche (TV opera), 57; Stabat Mater (chamber music with orch), 57; The Mother (opera); The Selfish Giant (opera); Harrison Loved His Umbrella (opera); La Grande Breteche (TV opera). *Teaching:* Fac mem, San Jose State Col, 61-63; assoc prof music, Oakland Univ, 76-80, prof, 80- *Awards:* Guggenheim Fel, 58-59; Nat Endowment for Arts Grants, 76 & 78. *Mailing Add:* Dept Music Oakland Univ Rochester MI 48063

HOLLISTER, DAVID MANSHIP
COMPOSER, EDUCATOR
b New York, NY, May 1, 29. *Study:* Harvard Col, AB, 51; Univ Iowa, MA, 65, MFA, 66, PhD, 68. *Works:* Corronach (string orch), New Orleans Symph, 67; String Quartet No 1, Evansville String Quartet, 78; Divertimento, perf by Arthur Goldstein & Morton Estrin, 81; The Girl Who Ate Chicken Bones, Soho Repty Theatre, New York, 82; Duo for Viola and Piano, perf by Veronica Salas & David Hollister, 83; Planh (oboe & cello), perf by Sara Schwartz & Jodi Beder, 83; Songs of Death, perf by Eric Benson & David Hollister, 83. *Teaching:* Asst prof music, Univ New Orleans, 68-70, York Col, City Univ New York, 70-73 & Hofstra Univ, 78-; adj assoc prof, Baruch Col, City Univ New York, 74- *Awards:* First Hon Mention, Harvey Gaul Compt, Pittsburgh, Pa, 79; fel, Comp & Librettist Prog, Nat Endowment Arts, 81; grant, Meet the Comp, 82 & 83. *Mem:* Col Music Soc; Am Music Ctr; BMI; Am Fedn Musicians; Am Guild Authors & Comp. *Mailing Add:* 10 E 16th St New York NY 10003

HOLLOWAY, CLYDE
EDUCATOR, ORGAN
b Clarksville, Tex, Sept 5, 36. *Study:* Univ Okla, BMus, 57, MMus, 59; Union Theol Sem, DSM, 74; Am Guild Organists, AAGO. *Teaching:* Prof music, Ind Univ, formerly; prof organ, Rice Univ, 77- *Awards:* Fulbright Scholar, 59-60; Winner, Nat Playing Compt, Am Guild Organists, 64. *Mem:* Am Guild Organists; Pi Kappa Lambda. *Mailing Add:* c/o Murtagh & McFarlane Artists Inc 3629 W 30th St Cleveland OH 44109

HOLLOWAY, DAVID
BARITONE
b Grandview, Mo, Nov 12, 42. *Study:* Univ Kans, with Robert Baustian, MusB(voice), 64, MusM(voice), 66; Santa Fe Opera Apprentice Prog, 66-67; Metropolitan Opera Studio, 70-71; studied with Luigi Ricci, 71-72. *Rec Perf:* The Taming of the Shrew, CRI; Songs (Frederick Rzewski), Desto; Songs (Vally Weigle). *Roles:* Belcore in L'Elisir d'amore, Kansas City Lyr Opera, 68; Doctor Malatesta in Don Pasquale; George Milton in Of Mice and Men; Guglielmo in Cosi fan tutte; Marcello in La Boheme; Figaro in Il Barbiere di Siviglia; Nick Shadow in The Rake's Progress. *Pos:* Mem, Deutsch Opera Rhein, Dusseldorf, 81-; appearances with maj opera co in US & Can. *Teaching:* Mem fac voice, Univ Kans, 66-69. *Awards:* Martha Baird Rockefeller Fund Grant, 70; Nat Opera Inst Grant, 71-72; Hi Fidelity Award, 71. *Mailing Add:* c/o Columbia Artista Mgt 165 W 57th St New York NY 10019

HOLLOWAY, JACK E
COMPOSER, CONDUCTOR
b Topeka, Kans. *Study:* Mills Col with Darius Milhaud, 46-47; Univ Calif, Berkeley, with Roger Sessions, BA, 51; Aspen Music Sch, with Darius Milhaud, summers, 57 & 58; studied cond with Hans Rosbaud, Zurich & Cologne, 58; Music Acad, Cologne, WGer, with B Zimmermann, 58-59. *Works:* Violin-Piano Sonata #1, Ronald Stoffel & B Abromowitsch, 56; Violin-Cello-Piano Trio, D Schneider, H Strauss & B Abramowitsch, 57; Violin-Piano Sonata #2, comn by Berkley Piano Club, 57; The Mystic Trumpeter, Aspen Music Ens, 57; Sonor, Aspen Music Fest Student Orch, 58; String Quartet No 1, Am Univ String Quartet, 58; Configuration (solo violin sonata), Ronald Stoffel, 59. *Rec Perf:* The Mystic Trumpeter, 57 & Sonor, 58, Aspen Music Fest. *Awards:* Fulbright Grant, 58-59; Comp Fel, Nat Endowment for Arts, 81-82. *Mem:* Int Soc Contemp Music (mem exec comt, 51-53); Am Music Ctr. *Mailing Add:* 2722 Kline Circle #1 Las Vegas NV 89121

HOLMBERG, MARK LEONARD
EDUCATOR, ORGAN
b St Paul, Minn, Mar 15, 38. *Study:* Augustana Col, BMus, 60; Sch Sacred Music, Union Theol Sem, MSM, 62; Northwestern Univ, PhD, 74. *Works:* Chorale-Preludes Carillon, perf by Albert Gerken & Mark Holmberg, 76-; Festive Anthems & Introits, Baptist Church Choir, Lawrence, Kans, 77- *Pos:* Minister music, Trinity Lutheran Church, 62-68. *Teaching:* Asst music theory & comp, Northwestern Univ, 68-71; acting asst prof, Univ Kans, 71-74, asst prof & carillonneur, 74- *Mem:* Midwest Music Theory Soc; Am Guild Carillonneurs; Am Guild Organists. *Publ:* Auth, Harmonic Reading: An Approach to Chord Singing, Univ Press Am, 83. *Mailing Add:* Murphy Hall 342 Univ Kans Lawrence KS 66045

HOLMES, RICHARD
TIMPANI, CONDUCTOR
Study: Juilliard Sch, BA, MA; San Francisco Consv; studied timpani with Peggy Cunningham, timpani & perc with Saul Goodman, Morris Goldenberg & Eldon Bailey & cond with Jean Morel, Jorge Mester, Walter Susskind & Alfred Wallenstein. *Pos:* Performer with Los Angeles Phil Orch, New York Phil, Metropolitan Opera, Boston Symph Orch & Aspen Fest; solo perf, Meet

the Artist, WCBS-TV, formerly; cond & music dir, Youth Symph Orch New York, formerly; cond, Kirkwood Symph, Mo, formerly; prin timpani, St Louis Symph, currently. *Teaching:* Mem fac cond, perc & chamber music, Aspen Music Fest; asst to Saul Goodman, Juilliard Sch, formerly, cond asst to Alfred Wallenstein, formerly; mem fac music, St Louis Consv Music, currently, music dir, Consv Orch, currently. *Mailing Add:* St Louis Consv Music 560 Trinity Ave St Louis MO 63130

HOLMES, ROBERT WILLIAM
ADMINISTRATOR, CRITIC-WRITER
b Somerville, Mass, Jan 9, 29. *Study:* Boston Univ, BMus(music hist) 53, MA(music hist), 55, PhD(musicol), 60. *Pos:* Prog annotator, Isabella Stewart Gardner Museum, 57-62, Detroit Symph Orch, 65-81 & Los Angeles Chamber Orch, 80-81; exec dir, Univ Southern Calif, Idyllwild, 80-82; dean, Col Arts & Architecture & dir, Univ Arts Serv, Pa State Univ, 82- *Teaching:* Asst prof music hist & lit, Oakland Univ, Mich, 60-62; adj assoc prof musicol, Wayne State Univ, Mich, 64-66; chmn music dept, Western Mich Univ, 66-72, found dean, Col Fine Arts, 72-80. *Publ:* Ed, The Future of the Arts in Michigan: A Ten Year Projection, Mich Coun Arts, 78; auth, Bela Bartok, Dayton-Hudson Found, 81. *Mailing Add:* 1206 Westerly Parkway State College PA 16801

HOLMES, WILLIAM C
EDUCATOR
b Orville, Ohio, Apr 26, 28. *Study:* Wooster Col, BA, 51; Columbia Univ, AM, 53, PhD, 68. *Teaching:* From asst to assoc prof, Univ Calif, 60-68; from assoc prof to prof, Univ Calif, Irvine, 68- *Mem:* Am Musicol Soc; Int Musicol Soc. *Mailing Add:* Dept Music Univ Calif Irvine CA 92717

HOLMQUIST, JOHN EDWARD
GUITAR, EDUCATOR
b Lander, Wyo, Feb 2, 55. *Study:* Summer Sch, Banff Int, with Alirio Diaz, 75; IV Recontres Int, with Alirio Diaz, 76; Univ Minn, with Jeffrey Van, BFA, 78; studied with Gilbert Biberian, London, 78-80. *Rec Perf:* Winners of the Guitar '78 International Competition, CBS TV, 78; Las Folias de Espana, Cavata Rec Co, 81. *Pos:* Chmn class guitar dept, Wis Consv Music, 80- *Awards:* First Prize, Guitar '78 Int Compt, 78. *Mem:* Guitar Found Am; Col Music Soc. *Mailing Add:* 1808 N 48th St Milwaukee WI 53208

HOLOMAN, DALLAS KERN
MUSICOLOGIST, CONDUCTOR
b Raleigh, NC, Sept 8, 47. *Study:* Duke Univ, BA, 69; Princeton Univ, MFA, 71, PhD, 74. *Teaching:* Vis instr music, Westminster Choir Col, 72; prof music, chmn dept, dir early music ens & cond symph orch, Univ Calif, Davis, 75- *Awards:* Woodrow Wilson Fel, 69-70; Fulbright Hays Fel, Paris, 72-73. *Mem:* Am Musicol Soc; Music Libr Asn; Asn Nat Hector Berlioz. *Publ:* Contribr, Acta Musicol, Col Music Symposium, Early Music, J Am Musicol Soc & others. *Mailing Add:* 203 Aurora Ave Davis CA 95616

HOLT, HENRY
CONDUCTOR & MUSIC DIRECTOR
b Vienna, Austria, Apr 11, 34. *US citizen. Study:* Los Angeles City Col, with Hugo Strelizer; Univ Southern Calif, with Ingolf Dahl; studied with Wolfgang Martin. *Pos:* Gen dir, Portland Opera, Ore, 64-66; music & educ dir, Seattle Opera, 66-; consult, Nat Endowment Arts, Ford Found & Rockefeller Found, formerly; artistic dir, Hidden Valley Opera, currently; cond ballet co, Kansas City, currently. *Teaching:* Private lessons, currently. *Mem:* Nat Opera Inst (mem bd, currently). *Mailing Add:* Seattle Opera PO Box 9248 Seattle WA 98109

HOLTZ, JOHN
EDUCATOR, MUSIC DIRECTOR
Study: WVa Univ, BMus; Univ Mich, MMus; studied with Claire Coci, Clyde English, Marilyn Mason & Robert Noehren. *Pos:* Music dir, Christ Episcopal Church, Fairmont, WVa, formerly; founder & chmn, Hartt Ann Int Contemp Organ Music Fest, 64-; recitalist & lectr throughout US, Europe, Japan, Nigeria & Australia. *Teaching:* Assoc prof & chmn organ, liturgical music & harpsichord depts, Hartt Sch Music, currently. *Mailing Add:* Hartt Sch Music Univ Hartford West Hartford CT 06117

HOLTZMAN, JULIE
PIANO
b Montreal, Can, July 13, 45. *Study:* McGill Univ; Consv Music & Dramatic Arts, Montreal, grad; Juilliard Sch Music; studied with Louis Bailly & Ernst Oster, piano with Rosina Lhevinne, Germaine Malepart & chamber music with Claus Adam. *Rec Perf:* For Radio-Can Int Serv. *Pos:* Conct pianist, US, Can, Mex, Europe & Far East; performer, CBC, BBC, Radiodiffusion-TV Belgium, WNYC radio & TV, WNCN, WBAI & WQXR; soloist, English Sinfonia Orch, 70 & Brooklyn Phil, 74. *Mailing Add:* 210 Central Park South New York NY 10019

HOLVIK, KARL MAGNUS
EDUCATOR, CONDUCTOR
b Minneapolis, Minn, July 24, 21. *Study:* Concordia Col, Minn, BA, 43; Eastman Sch Music, MA, 47; Univ Iowa, PhD, 53. *Pos:* Mem, Amateur Band Asn Austria, Norway, Sweden & Denmark, 74- *Teaching:* From instr to prof, Univ Northern Iowa, 47- *Awards:* Gold Medals, Concordia Col, 43 & Amateur Music Asn, Norway, Sweden & Denmark, 71. *Mem:* Iowa Bandmasters Asn (pres, 55-56); Col Band Dir Nat Asn (pres, 73-75); Am Bandmasters Asn. *Publ:* Numerous articles on music educ, clarinet perf, teaching & cond. *Mailing Add:* 2515 Iowa St Cedar Falls IA 50613

HOMAN, FREDERIC WARREN
EDUCATOR, ORGANIST

b St Joseph, Mo, Dec 25, 32. *Study:* Univ Nebr, Omaha, BFA, 54; Ind Univ, MMus, 58, PhD, 61. *Pos:* Organist & dir music, First Presby Church, Warrensburg, Mo, 63-74. *Teaching:* From instr to asst prof music theory, hist, organ & piano, Tex Lutheran Col, 59-62; from asst prof to prof music theory & organ, Central Mo State Univ, 62-, actg head, Music Dept, summers 80 & 82. *Mem:* Music Teachers Nat Asn Inc (west cent div vpres, 70-72); Am Musicol Soc; Soc Music Theory; Music Educr Nat Conf; Am Guild Organists. *Publ:* Auth, Final and Internal Cadence Patterns in Gregorian Chant, J Am Musicol Soc, 64; High School Activities—Theory, Am Music Teacher, 72, 74 & 75. *Mailing Add:* 429 Grover Warrensburg MO 64093

HOMBURG, AL(FRED JOHN)
EDUCATOR, TENOR

b Ellis, Kans, Mar 4, 37. *Study:* Oklahoma City Univ, BMus, 58; WVa Univ, MMus, 66; Univ Pittsburgh, 79. *Works:* Ladder of Love, perf by Al Homburg, 59; Choral of the Month No 2 (nine choral arr), Charles Hansen Publ Co, 65; Tomorrow Is Now, perf by Al Homburg, 67; Justification by Faith, perf by First Presby Church Choir, Johnson City, Tenn, 73; Christmas Doll, comn by Chic Lowe, 83; Gospel Album, perf by Homburgs, 83. *Rec Perf:* Magi Cat, 71, There's A Little Ol' Church, 71 & Still Waters, Woodland Sound; Teachers Lament, Varsity Studio, 71; Ladder of Love, 73, Tomorrow Is Now, 73 & Folk Songs of America, 75, Woodland Sound. *Roles:* Alfredo in Die Fledermaus, Little Rock State Opera, Ark, 60; Frederick in Pirates of Penzance, Twilight Time, Oklahoma City, 60; John Wesley in The Invisible Fire, Wesley Methodist, 60; Alfredo in Die Fledermaus, Frostburg State Col Summer Fest, Md, 69; tenor solos in The Messiah, Oglebay Park, Wheeling, WVa, 71; John Wesley in The Invisible Fire, First Preby, Johnson City, Tenn, 73; Paul Revere in Our Sacred Honor, Soldiers & Sailors Hall, Pittsburgh, Pa, 76. *Pos:* Dir music, St Paul's Lutheran Church, Cumberland, Md, 63-72 & 81- *Teaching:* Instr music, Oklahoma City Univ, 59-62, Allegany Community Col, Cumberland, Md, 63-66, Pittsburgh Pub Sch, 73- & Duquesne Univ, Pittsburgh, 73- *Mem:* Am Fedn Musicians; Phi Mu Alpha Soc. *Mailing Add:* 696 Fayette St Cumberland MD 21502

HOMER, PAUL ROBERT
EDUCATOR, ADMINISTRATOR

b New York, NY. *Study:* Columbia Col, Columbia Univ, BA, 48; Teachers Col, Columbia Univ, MA, 50; Univ Wis. *Pos:* Organist & choir dir, Cent Park United Methodist Church, 68- *Teaching:* Prof music, State Univ NY, Buffalo, 54-, dean of arts, 69-71, chmn music dept, 74-78. *Mem:* Music .Educr Nat Conf; Am Orff-Schulwerk Asn; Am Musicol Soc. *Mailing Add:* Perf Arts Dept State Univ Col, NY Buffalo NY 14222

HONG, SHERMAN
EDUCATOR, PERCUSSION

b Greenville, Miss, Apr 6, 41. *Study:* Univ Southern Miss, BME, 64; Northwestern Univ, MM, 65; Univ Southern Miss, DME, 74. *Pos:* Timpanist, Jackson Symph Orch, 68-80; clinician, Slingerland Drum Co, 81-83 & Ludwig Drum Co, 83- *Teaching:* Assoc prof music, Univ Southern Miss, 66- *Mem:* Percussive Arts Soc; Coun Res Music Educ; Sunbelt Judges Asn. *Interests:* Music pedagogy and music education. *Publ:* Coauth, Percussion Section: Developing the Corps Style, Band Shed, 78 & 80; auth, Common Sense in Marching Percussion, Percussive Notes, 80; Adjudicating the Marching Percussion Section, Instrumentalist, 81. *Mailing Add:* South Sta Box 5032 Hattiesburg MS 39401

HOOD, BOYDE WYATT
TRUMPET, COMPOSER

b Dallas, Tex, Aug 18, 39. *Study:* Eastman Sch Music, BM, 64; Ball State Univ, MM, 68. *Pos:* Prin trumpet, Dallas Symph Orch, 58-60 & Victoria Symph, 70-77; asst prin sect trumpet, Rochester Phil, 60-64; asst prin trumpet, Milwaukee Symph Orch, 64-67; first & second trumpet, Los Angeles Chamber Orch, 80-82; sect trumpet, Los Angeles Phil, 82- *Teaching:* Instr music, Ball State Univ, 67-70; assoc prof, Univ Victoria, 70-77; adj assoc prof, Univ Southern Calif, 79- *Mailing Add:* 6047 Laurelgrove Ave North Hollywood CA 91606

HOOD, BURREL SAMUEL
EDUCATOR, MUSIC DIRECTOR

b Hattiesburg, Miss, Dec 14, 43. *Study:* Miss State Univ, BS, 66, MME, 68, EdD, 73. *Pos:* Assoc band & choral dir, Philadelphia City Sch, Miss, 66-69 & dir bands & dept chmn, 69-71; music dir, First Baptist Church, Philadelphia, Miss, 67-71. *Teaching:* Prof music, Miss State Univ, 73- *Mem:* Music Educr Nat Conf; Miss Music Educr Asn (pres, 82-84); Alliance Arts Educ. *Interests:* Effect of daily musical instruction on personal and social adjustment and school attendance. *Publ:* Auth, Research in Music Education: The Forbidden Zone, 76 & ed, Research Notes (column), 79-82, Miss Music Educr. *Mailing Add:* 411 Myrtle St Starkville MS 39759

HOOGENAKKER, VIRGINIA RUTH
VIOLIN, EDUCATOR

b Des Moines, Iowa, Apr 8, 21. *Study:* Belhaven Col, BMus; Chicago Musical Col, MMus. *Pos:* Prin second violin, Jackson Symph Orch; musical dir, Ascension Lutheran Church. *Teaching:* Assoc prof violin & music theory, chmn dept music, Belhaven Col. *Mem:* Mu Phi Epsilon (nat vpres & prov gov, 62-68); Miss Music Teachers Asn (mem bd, 66-76, pres, 73-74). *Publ:* Contribr, J Church Music. *Mailing Add:* 2020 Plantation Blvd Jackson MS 39211

HOOGERWERF, FRANK WILLIAM
ADMINISTRATOR, EDUCATOR

b Rotterdam, Netherlands, June 24, 46; US citizen. *Study:* Calvin Col, Grand Rapids, BA, 69; Univ Mich, MM, 70, PhD, 74. *Teaching:* Asst prof Music, Emory Univ, 74-79, assoc prof & chmn dept, 79- *Awards:* Ford Found Grants, 70 & 73; Rackham Prize Fel, Univ Mich, 72; Nat Endowment Humanities Fel, 81. *Mem:* Am Musicol Soc; Col Music Soc; Sonneck Soc; Hymn Soc Am. *Interests:* Twentieth-century music and American music. *Publ:* Auth, Willem Pijper as Dutch Nationalist, Musical Quart, 76; The String Quartets of Willem Pijper, Music Rev, 77; John Hill Hewitt: Sources and Bibliography, Emory Univ, 82; Music in Georgia, Da Capo Press, 83; Confederate Sheet Music Imprints, Inst Studies Am Music, 84. *Mailing Add:* Dept Music Emory Univ Atlanta GA 30322

HOOK, WALTER (EUGENE)
BARITONE, TEACHER

b Kansas City, Mo. *Study:* Consv Music, Univ Mo, BMus, 63; City Col New York, 68; Juilliard Sch, studied voice with Orin Brown, 75. *Rec Perf:* Taming of the Shrew (Giannini), CRI, 69; Sweet Bye & Bye (Beeson), Desto, 73; Captain Jinks of the Horse Marines (Beeson), RCA, 75. *Roles:* Four villains in the Tales of Hoffmann, 69-70 & Gianni Schicchi in Gianni Schicchi, 70-72, Lyr Opera Kansas City; Falstaff in Salieri's Falstaff, Philadelphia Acad Music, 73; Horace Tabor in Baby Doe, 76, Giorgio Germont in La Traviata, 76 & 77 & Count Almaviva in The Marriage of Figaro, 77, Lyr Opera Kansas City; Dandini in La Cenerentola, Colo Opera Fest, 78. *Awards:* Grant, Nat Opera Inst, 72 & 73. *Mailing Add:* 312 W 20th New York NY 10011

HOOSE, ALFRED JULIUS
COMPOSER, EDUCATOR

b Wheeling. WVa, Sept 17, 18. *Study:* Eastman Sch Music, 47; Hartt Col Music, 50; New England Consv Music, MMus, 52; study with Antonio Modarelli, 45-46, F Judd Cooke, 53, Hugo Norden, 67-74 & Fred Lerdahl, 74-75. *Works:* Music for Viola, Clarinet & Pianoforte, perf by Annex Players, 75; The Lord Shall Build Up Sion (chorus, wind orch, piano, timpani & perc instrm), perf by Arlington Phil Orch, & Arlington-Belmont Chorus, Mass, 78; Wind Quintet No 2, perf by New Boston Wind Quintet, 79; Chaconne for Organ, perf by Kenneth Grinnell, 80; Trio (flute, viola & piano), perf by Michele Sahm, John Englund & Ann Taffel, 80; Diversion (viola, vibraphone, roto-toms & piano), perf by John Ziarko, Dean Anderson, Neil Grover & Randall Hodgkinson, 81. *Pos:* Organist choirmaster, St John's Episcopal Church, Newtonville, Mass, 56-61 & Christ Church, Waltham, Mass, 64-72. *Teaching:* From asst prof to assoc prof music & dir glee club & chorus, Boston State Col, 65-82. *Mem:* Am Guild Organists; Am Music Ctr; Am Soc Univ Comp. *Mailing Add:* Bldg # 1 1105 Lexington St Waltham MA 02154

HOOVER, CYNTHIA ADAMS
ADMINISTRATOR

b Lexington, Nebr, Dec 16, 34. *Study:* Wellesley Col, BA(music hist), 57; Harvard Univ, MAT(music), 58; Brandeis Univ, MFA(music hist), 61. *Pos:* Cur, Div Musical Instrm, Smithsonian Inst, 61- *Teaching:* Asst, Wellesley Col, 58-60. *Mem:* Am Musicol Soc (nat coun mem, 71-73 & 75-77, mem bd dir, 76-78); Am Musical Soc (mem bd gov, 72-, vpres, 77-81); Sonneck Soc (first vpres, 75-77); Comite Int Musees et Collections d'Instruments Musique Icom. *Interests:* Music in American life; musical instruments made and used in America. *Publ:* Auth, Harpsichords and Clavichords, Smithsonian Inst, 70; Music Machines—American Style, Smithsonian Inst, 71; The Phonograph and Museums, In: The Phonograph & Our Musical Life, Inst Studies Am Life, 80; The Steinways and Their Pianos in the Nineteenth Century, J Am Musical Instrm Soc, 81. *Mailing Add:* Div Musical Instruments Smithsonian Institution Washington DC 20560

HOOVER, ERIC JOHN
FLUTE, EDUCATOR

b Alexandria, La, Apr 1, 44. *Study:* Duquesne Univ, BS(music educ), 66; Peabody Consv; New England Consv Music; Cath Univ Am, MM(flute), 70. *Pos:* Flutist, US Army Band, Washington, DC, 67-70; prin flutist, San Antonio Symph Orch, 70-74 & Brevard Music Ctr, NC, 70- *Teaching:* Prof flute, Univ Ill, Urbana, 74-77 & Ariz State Univ, 77- *Mem:* Nat Flute Asn. *Publ:* Auth, Tips for Playing Auditions, Instrumentalist, 82-83. *Mailing Add:* Sch Music Ariz State Univ Tempe AZ 85287

HOOVER, KATHERINE L
COMPOSER, FLUTE

b Elkins, WVa, Dec 2, 37. *Study:* Eastman Sch Music, BM(music theory) & perf cert, 59; flute study with William Kincaid, 60-61; Manhattan Sch Music, MA(music theory), 74. *Works:* Songs of Joy, Carl Fischer Inc, 74; Divertimento (flute, violin, viola & cello), 76 & Trio (violin, cello & piano), 78, Leonarda Prod Inc; Psalm 23 (chorus & orch), comn by New York Episcopal Diocese, 81; The Medieval Suite (flute & piano), 82, Leonarda Prod Inc; From the Testament of Francois Villon (baritone, bassoon & string quartet), comn by Leonard Hindell, 82; New Trio, comn by Huntington Trio, 83. *Rec Perf:* London Diversions, Sonar, 76; For the Flute (flute & various instrm), Leonard Prod Inc, 80; Works by F Martin, N Chance, U Mamlok, Op One, 81; The Medieval Suite, Leonarda Prod Inc, 83. *Pos:* Found & dir, Festivals I-IV Women's Interart Ctr, New York, 78-81; various perf in New York with leading orgns, incl Stuttgart Ballet, Martha Graham Dance Co, Caramoor Fest Orch, Royal Ballet, New York Grand Opera, New York City Opera & Broadway shows. *Teaching:* Instr flute, Juilliard Prep, 63-71; fac mem music theory, Manhattan Sch Music, 71- *Awards:* Comp Grant, Nat Endowment Arts, 79; Standard Award, ASCAP, ann. *Mem:* Int League Women Comp (bd mem, 81-); Am Women Comp; ASCAP; Am Fedn Musicians. *Publ:* Auth, Fanny and Lili Who?, Keynote Mag, 9/78. *Mailing Add:* 160 W 95th St New York NY 10025

HOPE, SAMUEL HOWARD
ADMINISTRATOR, COMPOSER
b Owensboro, Ky, Nov 5, 46. *Study:* Eastman Sch Music, BM, 67; Yale Univ, MMA, 70. *Pos:* Dean & comp in res, Atlanta Boy Choir, 70-73; exec dir music alumni, Yale Univ, 74-75; exec dir, Nat Asn Sch Music, 75- *Mem:* Nat Music Coun; Am Soc Univ Comp (exec comt, 78-82); Am Music Ctr; Music Teachers Nat Asn; Music Educr Nat Conf. *Mailing Add:* 11250 Roger Bacon Dr Suite 5 Reston VA 22090

HOPKIN, JOHN ARDEN
EDUCATOR, BARITONE
b Laramie, Wyo, Feb 11, 47. *Study:* Brigham Young Univ, BMus, 71; NTex State Univ, MMus, 74; Eastman Sch Music, DMA, 78. *Rec Perf:* The Disappointment, Vox Turnabout, 76. *Roles:* Bob in The Old Maids and the Thief, Goldovsky Opera Co, 72; Sid in Albert Herring, 75 & Malatesta in Don Pasquale, 76, Chautauqua Opera Co. *Pos:* Dir opera, Bay View Music Fest, 83. *Teaching:* Assoc prof voice & opera & dir opera, Tex Christian Univ, 77- *Mem:* Nat Asn Teachers Singing; Pi Kappa Lambda. *Mailing Add:* 3545 Winifred Ft Worth TX 76133

HOPKINS, BARBARA AVIS
FLUTE, TEACHER
b Scranton, Pa, Dec 27, 59. *Study:* Hartt Sch Music, BMus, 82. *Pos:* Flutist, Northeastern Pa Phil, 82-, Scranton Singers Guild, 82- & Greater Hazelton Oratorio Soc, 82- *Teaching:* Lectr applied flute, Marywood Col, 83- *Awards:* First Prize Orch Audition Compt, Nat Flute Asn, 82; Winner, Young Artist Compt, New York Flute Club, 83. *Bibliog:* Lorraine Ryan (auth), Abington's Flutist Takes National Prize, Scranton Times, 9/5/82; Bill Savage (auth), A Unique Talent, Abington J, 1/5/83. *Mem:* Nat Flute Asn; New York Flute Club; Am Fedn Musicians. *Mailing Add:* RD 4 Box 274 Clarks Summit PA 18411

HOPKINS, DONALD ERIC
VIOLIN, EDUCATOR
b Schenectady, NY, June 7, 31. *Study:* Juilliard Sch Music, BS, 54; Univ Tex, MM, 58. *Rec Perf:* Quartets (Hindemith & Janacek), Golden Crest, 78; Works by Beach & Foote, 80, Quintet (Bartok), 81 & Quartets (Husa & Rainier), 83, Leonarda. *Pos:* Violinist, Alard String Quartet, 54- *Teaching:* Instr music theory & appreciation, Wilmington Col, Ohio, 56-62; assoc prof 20th century music & cond, Pa State Univ, 62-; vis lectr, Univ Canterbury, Christchurch, NZ, 63-64. *Awards:* Young Artists Award, Nat Fedn Music Clubs, 55. *Mem:* Am Fedn Musicians; Col Music Soc; Am String Teachers Asn. *Mailing Add:* 523 N Allen St State College PA 16801

HOPKINS, HARLOW EUGENE
ADMINISTRATOR, CONDUCTOR
b Flint, Mich, Jan 25, 31. *Study:* Olivet Nazarene Col, BS(music educ), 53; Am Consv Music, MMusEd, 56; Ind Univ, Bloomington, DMus, 74. *Teaching:* Fac mem, Olivet Nazarene Col, 54-, chmn div fine arts & dept music, 67- *Mem:* Col Band Dir Nat Asn; Nat Band Asn; Music Educr Nat Conf; Int Clarinet Soc; Christian Instrm Dir Asn (secy, 82-). *Mailing Add:* 697 Oak Run Bourbonnais IL 60914

HOPKINS, JAMES FREDRICK
COMPOSER, EDUCATOR
b Pasadena, Calif, Apr 8, 39. *Study:* Univ Southern Calif, with Halsey Stevens, BM, 60; Yale Univ, with Quincey Porter, MM, 62; Princeton Univ, with Edward T Cone, PhD, 69. *Works:* Three Pieces for Orchestra, Denver Symph, 68; Concert Music, Fine Arts Quartet, 74; Phantasms, Nat Symph, 75; Symphony #4, Visions of Hell, Ore Symph, 76; Symphony #2 for Wind Orchestra, Univ Southern Calif Wind Orch, 79; Voces Organi, Pasadena Choral Orch, 80; Brass Quintet #1, Chicago Brass Quintet, 81. *Teaching:* From instr to asst prof, Northwestern Univ, 62-71; from assoc prof to prof, Univ Southern Calif, 71- *Mailing Add:* Univ Southern Calif Sch Music 840 W 34th St Los Angeles CA 90089

HOPKINS, ROBERT ELLIOTT
PIANO, EDUCATOR
b Greensboro, NC, Oct 2, 31. *Study:* Eastman Sch Music, BM, 53, MM, 54, DMA, 59; Akad Musik, Vienna, Austria, 60. *Teaching:* Head music dept, Mars Hill Col, 60-63; prof piano, organ & harpsichord, Youngstown State Univ, 63-; vis lectr piano, Westminster Col, Pa, 68-81. *Awards:* S Lewis Elmer Award, Am Guild Organists, 62 & 66. *Mem:* Am Matthay Asn; Am Musicol Soc; Am Guild Organists (dean, Youngstown Chap, 68 & 73); Hist Organ Soc; Riemenschneider Bach Inst. *Publ:* Ed, Alexander Reinagle: The Philadelphia Sonatas, A-R Ed, 78; contribr, Alexander Reinagle (1756-1809), New Grove Dict Music & Musicians, 80. *Mailing Add:* 21 Audubon Lane Poland OH 44514

HOPSON, HAL HAROLD
COMPOSER, EDUCATOR
b Mound, Tex, June 12, 33. *Study:* Baylor Univ, BM, 54; Southern Sem, MA, 56. *Works:* God With Us, World Conv Christian Churches, Mexico City, 74; Festival Psalm, comn by WVa State Col Fest Music, 78; God of Our Fathers Whose Almighty Hand, 79; Praise the Lord of Heaven, comn by Presby Mens Conv, 82; The Singing Bishop, Montreat Music Conf, 82; Fugue Fantasy, 82; 487 publ works with 25 publ. *Pos:* Organist & choirmaster, First Presby Church, Ashland, Ky, 64-69; Vine St Christian Church, Nashville, 69-74 & Westminster Presby Church, Nashville, 74-83. *Teaching:* Ad fac comp, Scarritt Col, 76-83; assoc prof comp & church music & chmn dept church music, Westminster Choir Col, 83- *Awards:* ASCAP Standard Award, 77-;

winner compt cont, Am Guild English Handbell Ringers, 82. *Mem:* Am Guild Organists (dean, Huntington WVa chap, 67-69); Presby Asn Musicians (nat bd, 79-82); Choristers Guild (nat bd, 83-); Am Choral Dir Asn; Hymn Soc Am. *Mailing Add:* Westminister Choir Col Hamilton Ave Walnut Lane Princeton NJ 08540

HOPWOOD, JULIE ANN
VIOLIN
b Dearborn, Mich, June 26, 54. *Study:* Bowling Green State Univ, with Paul Makara & Emil Raab, BM(violin perf), 76; WVa Univ, 76-77. *Pos:* First violin, Toledo Symph, 74-76 & Savannah Symph, 77-79; asst concertmaster, Charleston Symph, WVa, 76-77; alt violin, Wheeling Symph, WVa, 76-77; asst prin second violin, Charlotte Symph Orch, 79- *Mem:* Am Fedn Musicians. *Mailing Add:* Charlotte Symph Orch 110 E 7th St Charlotte NC 28202

HORAKU See Burnett, Henry

HOREIN, KATHLEEN MARIE
OBOE, TEACHER
b Indianapolis, Ind, Jan 17, 52. *Study:* Brevard Music Ctr, with Eric Barr, 73; Ball State Univ, BS(music educ), 74; West Chester State Col, MA(music hist & lit), 83. *Pos:* Assoc prin oboist, Lancaster Symph Orch, 75-; prin oboist, Lancaster Opera Wkshp, 75-; second oboist, York Symph orch, 76- & Harrisburg Symph Orch, 78- *Teaching:* Instrm music, Cent Dauphin Sch Dist, Harrisburg, Pa, 80-83. *Mem:* Music Educr Nat Conf; Pa Music Educr Asn; Int Double Reed Soc; Pi Kappa Lambda. *Mailing Add:* RD #2 N View Dr Ephrata PA 17522

HORN, LOIS B(URLEY)
PIANO, TEACHER
b Syracuse, NY, Sept 8, 28. *Study:* Syracuse Univ, BM, 50; Mich State Univ, MM, 52; studied with Ernst Victor Wolff, Eugene List & Leon Fleisher. *Rec Perf:* Women In Music, Arnold Rec Studio, 78. *Pos:* Organist, First Methodist Church, Starkville, Miss, 54-55 & St Paul's Methodist Church, Syracuse, NY, 55-; adjudicator (piano), Nat Guild Piano Teachers, 70-, NY Fedn Music Clubs, 70-, NY State Sch Music Asn, 70-, private studios & festivals, 70-; partner & perf with Kathleen Freer, clarinetist), Two Musicians, Manlius, NY, 80-; solo performer & accmp throughout central NY. *Teaching:* Asst prof piano, Mich State Univ, 50-54; asst prof & music ed, Miss State Col & Miss State Col Women, 54-55; teacher, private studio, Manlius, NY, 56-; lectr & artist in res, Cazenovia Col, 65- *Awards:* Rose of Honor & Sword of Honor, Sigma Alpha Iota, 60; Outstanding Serv Award, Cent NY Asn Music Teachers, 62; Crouse Award for Keyboard Excellence, Civic Morning Musicals, 76. *Mem:* NY State Fedn Music Clubs (mem bd dir, 79-); Civic Morning Musicals (mem bd dir, 60-81); Cent NY Asn Music Teachers (pres, 73-75); Sigma Alpha Iota (alumnae pres, 60-62 & province vpres, 62-73); Eltinge Guild Pianists (pres, 62-64). *Publ:* Auth, Private Piano Teachers Value to Public School Music, NY Sch Music News, 81. *Mailing Add:* 3978 Pompey Ctr Rd Manlius NY 13104

HORNE, MARILYN
MEZZO-SOPRANO, SOPRANO
b Bradford, Pa, Jan 16, 34. *Study:* Univ Southern Calif, with William Vennard; studied with Lotte Lehman; five hon degrees. *Rec Perf:* Televised concerts, 79, 81 & 82; Presenting Marilyn Horne, Souvenirs of a Golden Era & many other rec on London, Columbia & RCA. *Roles:* Hata in The Bartered Bride, Los Angeles Guild Opera, 54; Marie in Wozzeck, San Francisco Opera, 60; Jocasta in Oedipus Rex, La Scala, 69; Adalgisa in Norma, Metropolitan Opera, 70 & Vancouver Opera; Carmen in Carmen, Metropolitan Opera, 72-73; Isabella in L'Italiana in Algeri, La Scala, 75; Rosina in Il barbiere di Siviglia, Vienna Opera, 78; and many others. *Pos:* Ms & sop with major opera co in US, Can & Europe. *Awards:* Handel Medallion, 81; Rossini Found Golden Plaque, 83; Grammy Awards. *Mailing Add:* c/o Columbia Artists Mgt 165 W 57th St New York NY 10019

HORNER, JERRY
VIOLA, EDUCATOR
b Los Angeles, Calif, Mar 28, 35. *Study:* Ind Univ, perf cert, 64, BM, 64, MM, 68. *Rec Perf:* Songs for Voice, Clarinet, Flute & Viola (Stravinsky), 80; Piano Quintet (Shostakovich), Chandos, London, 83. *Pos:* Prin violist, Dallas Symph, 68-69 & Pittsburgh Symph, 73-75; violist, Claremont Quartet, 69-73 & Fine Arts Quartet, 80- *Teaching:* Fac mem viola & chamber music, NC Sch Arts, 69-73; assoc prof, Ind Univ, 75-78; prof, Univ Wis, Milwaukee, 80- *Mailing Add:* Music Dept Univ Wis Milwaukee WI 53201

HOROWITZ, VLADIMIR
PIANO
b Kiev, Russia, Oct 1, 04; US citizen. *Study:* Kiev Consv; studied with Felix Blumenfeld & Sergei Tarnowski. *Pos:* Concert pianist with all major US orch, especially works of Liszt, Prokofiev, Scriabin, Rachmaninoff, Chopin & Schumann, 28- *Awards:* Eighteen Grammy Awards, 66-78; Prix Disque, 70 & 71; Prix Disque Montreuil, 71; Royal Phil Soc Gold Medal, 72. *Mailing Add:* c/o Columbia Artists Mgt 165 W 57th St New York NY 10019

HORSZOWKSI, MIECZSLAW
PIANO, EDUCATOR
b Poland. *Study:* Lwow Consv, with Mieczslaw Sotys & Henryk Melcer; studied with Leshetizky. *Pos:* Performer & recitalist throughout Europe; appearances with maj orchs. *Teaching:* Mem fac piano, Curtis Inst Music, 42- *Mailing Add:* Curtis Inst Music 1726 Locust St Philadelphia PA 19103

HORTON, WILLIAM LAMAR
EDUCATOR, BARITONE
b Rock Hill, SC, Aug 26, 35. *Study:* Furman Univ, Greenville, SC, BM, 56; Southern Baptist Theol Sem, Louisville, Ky, MSM, 58, DMA, 70; Univ Mich; Univ Southern Calif; L'Academie des Arts Musicaux, Paris, France. *Works:* Salvation to Our God, 58 & Song of the Lamb, 60, Schmidt, Hall & McCreary; Praise to the Lord, Broadman Press, 60; How Excellent Is Thy Name, Walton Music Corp, 62; Cindy, Southwestern Music Publ Co, 77. *Rec Perf:* Baritone soloist, The Messiah (Handel), Ark Symph Chorus, 67 & The Creation (Haydn) Okla Symph Chorus, 75; Mozart's Requiem, 79 & Brahm's Requiem, 81, Canterbury Choral Soc, Oklahoma City. *Teaching:* Assoc prof music, Ouachita Baptist Univ, Arkadelphia, 62-68; prof music, Okla Baptist Univ, Shawnee, 68- *Awards:* Okla Musician of Yr, Gov David Boren, 75; Orpheus Award, Phi Mu Alpha Sinfonia, 82. *Mem:* Phi Mu Alpha Sinfonia (prov gov, 65-75); Omicron Delta Kappa; Okla Music Teachers Asn (vpres, 70-74); Nat Asn Teachers Singing (pres, Okla Chap, 75-76). *Publ:* Auth, Introduction to Singing, 68 & Score Reading, 74, Conv Press. *Mailing Add:* PO Box 1603 Shawnee OK 74801

HORVATH, JANET
CELLO
b Toronto, Can, July 13, 52. *Study:* Univ Toronto, BMus; Ind Univ, MMus; studied with Vladimir Orloff & Janos Starker. *Pos:* Prin cellist, Aspen Chamber Symph, 77; assoc prin cellist, Indianapolis Symph Orch, 77-79 & Minn Orch, 79-80 & 83-; participating artist, Marlboro Music Fest, 79; mem, 79 Music from Marlboro Conct tour; soloist, Bayreuth Fest, Indianapolis Symph; recitalist, Can radio; mem, Prevcil Piano Trio. *Awards:* Can Govt Award. *Mailing Add:* Minn Orch 1111 Nicollet Mall Minneapolis MN 55403

HORVIT, MICHAEL MILLER
COMPOSER, EDUCATOR
b Brooklyn, NY, June 22, 32. *Study:* Yale Univ, BMus, 55, MMus, 56; Boston Univ, DMA, 59. *Works:* Moonscape, Houston Ballet, 75; The Gardens of Hieronymus, Shawnee Press, 77; Adventure in Space (opera), Piccolo Opera Co of Detroit, 81; Trio for Violin, Cello & Piano, Lyric Arts Ens, Houston, Tex, 82; Concerto for Guitar and Orchestra, Miguel Alcazar & Nat Phil of Mex, 83; Antiphon V for Viola & Tape, Int Viola Cong, 83. *Pos:* Music dir, Temple Emanu El, Houston, Tex, 67- *Teaching:* Assoc prof theory & lit, Southern Conn State Col, 59-66; prof, theory & comp, Univ Houston, 66- *Awards:* Martha Baird Rockefeller Grant, 68; Nat Endowment Arts Fel, 74; New Music Prize, Houston Symph Orch, 76. *Mem:* ASCAP; Am Soc Univ Comp; Am Music Ctr; Col Music Soc; Nat Opera Asn. *Publ:* Co-ed, Music for Analysis, 78, Techniques and Materials of Tonal Music, 2nd ed, 79 & Music for Sight Singing, 83, Houghton-Mifflin. *Mailing Add:* 8114 Braesdale Lane Houston TX 77071

HOSKINS, WILLIAM BARNES
COMPOSER, EDUCATOR
b Ft Pierce Farms, Fla, Oct 26, 17. *Study:* Oberlin Consv, BMus, 39, MMus, 41; Columbia Univ, with Normand Lockwood & Otto Luening, 47. *Works:* Israfel (choral & orch), perf by Oklahoma City Symph, Jacksonville Symph & others, 54-59; String Quartet No 1, Univ NC String Quartet & Atlanta Symph Quartet, 55-56; Concert Overture No 1, perf by Oklahoma City Symph, Jacksonville Symph & Tri-City Symph, 56-64; Variations on a Random Theme (piano), Gerson Yessin & William Leland, 60-76; Galactic Fantasy & Eastern Reflections, Spectrum Rec, 79. *Pos:* Freelance comp, synthesist & recordist, currently. *Teaching:* Instr piano & theory, WVa Univ, 40-42; dir comp & theory, Col Music, Jacksonville Univ, 48-54, pres, 54-58, dean, 58-61, prof music & comp in res, 60-82. *Mem:* Am Soc Univ Comp; Southeastern Comp League (pres, 56-57). *Interests:* Intensive listening project for Institute of General Semantics. *Publ:* Auth, On Music and General Semantics, Inst Gen Semantics Bulletin, 51; On General Semantics & Music, Music and Dance in the Southeastern United States, 52. *Mailing Add:* 5454 Arlington Rd Jacksonville FL 32211

HOSLER, MARY BELLAMY HAMILTON
ADMINISTRATOR, EDUCATOR
b Raleigh, NC, Nov 7, 40. *Study:* Oberlin Col & Consv, BA, 62, BMus, 63; Yale Univ; Carnegie Mellon Univ, MFA, 65; Univ Wis, Madison, PhD, 78. *Pos:* Dir, Wausau Consv Music, 81-83. *Teaching:* Assoc prof music hist, piano & piano pedagogy, Univ Wis, Marathon Ctr, Wausau, 72- *Mem:* Am Musicol Soc; Wis Music Teacher's Asn (district chmn, 78-80). *Interests:* Eighteenth-century music aesthetics & perfomance practice. *Publ:* Auth, Changing Views of Instrumental Music in Eighteenth-Century Germany, UMI Research Press, 81. *Mailing Add:* 1717 N 13th St Wausau WI 54401

HOSWELL, MARGARET
EDUCATOR, SINGER
Study: Univ Chicago; Juilliard Sch; studied voice with Althouse, Freschl, Schmidt-Walter & Hamlin; Staatliche Hochschule Musik, Munich. *Rec Perf:* On Vanguard Rec. *Pos:* Oratorio, concert & opera appearances, Fest Two Worlds & others. *Teaching:* Fac mem, New England Consv, 68-73; fac mem voice, Summer Vocal Inst, Graz & Manhattan Sch Music, 80- *Awards:* Two Fulbright Grants, Munich. *Mailing Add:* Manhattan Sch Music 120 Claremont Ave New York NY 10027

HOTOKE, SHIGERU
CONDUCTOR & MUSIC DIRECTOR, TENOR
b Eleele, Kauai, Hawaii, Jan 21, 27. *Study:* Univ Hawaii, BEd, 51, dipl, 52; Univ San Diego; Univ Southern Calif, with Robert Shaw, Julius Herford & Mac Harrel. *Rec Perf:* With Love From A Madrigal Island, Sounds of Hawaii;

Carmina Burana, Locations; Kalua. *Roles:* Ernesto in Don Pasquale, Univ Hawaii, 57; Goro in Madama Butterfly, 63 & 72 & Ottokar in Gypsy Baron, 67, Honolulu Symph; Beppe in I Pagliacci, 68, Emperor in Turandot, 69 & 77 & Eric in The Flying Dutchman, 71, Hawaii Opera Theatre. *Pos:* Singer, Robert Shaw Chorale, 53-54; soloist & cond, Cent Union Church, 54-74; founder & dir, Kailua Madrigal Singers, 63-; chorus master, Hawaii Opera Theatre, 64-73; artistic dir, Hawaii Music Fest. *Teaching:* Instr chorus, Nanakuli High Sch, 51-53; instr, Kailua High Sch, 53-82 & head music dept, 55-82; voice coach & asst cond, Idyllwild Sch Music Arts & Theatre Arts, 63-68. *Awards:* Bi-Centennial Award, Nat Endowment Arts; Teacher of Yr, Hawaii, 72; Award, Sertoma Club Hawaii, 77. *Mem:* Hawaii Music Educr Asn; Am Choral Dir Asn; Music Educr Nat Conf; Musicians Asn Hawaii; Asn Hawaiian Music. *Mailing Add:* 3279 Kaohinani Dr Honolulu HI 96817

HOUGH, CHARLES WAYNE
LYRIC BARITONE
b West Chester, Pa, Apr 28, 33. *Study:* Eastern Col, Pa, BA; Eastern Sem, Pa, MRE; Southwestern Baptist Sem, Tex, MCM. *Pos:* Soloist, oratorio & opera, US; mem, Southern Baptist Radio-TV Choir. *Teaching:* Mem fac, Univ SDak, five yrs; asst prof voice & madrigal group, Univ Eastern Wash, 71- *Awards:* Winner Men's Div Voice Cont, Bob Jones Univ, 52. *Mem:* Phi Mu Alpha Sinfonia. *Interests:* Psychology of music. *Mailing Add:* 522 Irene Pl Cheney WA 99004

HOUGHTON, EDWARD FRANCIS
EDUCATOR, MUSIC DIRECTOR
b New Brunswick, NJ, Oct 7, 38. *Study:* Rutgers Univ, BA(music), 62; Univ Nev, Reno, MA(music), 63; Univ Calif, Berkeley, PhD(music), 71. *Pos:* Music dir, Renaissance Singers, 82- *Teaching:* Prof music, Univ Calif, Santa Cruz, 70- *Awards:* Eisner Prize, Univ Calif, Berkeley, 66; Nat Endowment Humanities Fel, 80-81. *Mem:* Am Musicol Soc (pres northern Calif chap, 81-83); Accad Tartiniana, Padua, Italy. *Interests:* Study and performance of Renaissance polyphony. *Publ:* Auth, Rhythm and Meter in 15th Century Polyphony, J Music Theory, 73. *Mailing Add:* Dept Music Univ Calif Santa Cruz CA 95064

HOUSE, MARY ELAINE See Wallace, Mary Elaine

HOUSE, ROBERT WILLIAM
EDUCATOR, ADMINISTRATOR
b Bristow, Okla, Nov 28, 20. *Study:* Okla State Univ, BFA, 41; Eastman Sch Music, MMus, 42; Univ Ill, EdD, 54. *Pos:* Dir, Sch Music, Southern Ill Univ, 67-76. *Teaching:* Assoc prof music educ & chmn dept, Nebr State Col, 46-55; prof music educ & dept head, Univ Minn, Duluth, 55-67 & ETex State Univ, 76- *Mem:* Music Educr Nat Conf; Am String Teachers Asn; Tex Music Educr Asn; Nat Asn Sch Music. *Publ:* Coauth, Foundations and Principles of Music Education, McGraw-Hill, 59, rev ed, 72; auth, Instrumental Music for Today's Schools, 65 & Administration in Music Education, 73, Prentice-Hall; contribr, The Future of Music Education in Higher Education, Music Educ for Tomorrows Soc, 76; The Professional Preparation of Music Administrators, Symposium in Music Educ, 82. *Mailing Add:* RR 2 Box 93 Commerce TX 75428

HOUSE, SHARI TYLE
VIOLA
b Portland, Ore, Sept 7, 46. *Study:* Reed Col, BA, 68; Aspen Music Sch, with Rolf Persinger & Samuel Rhodes, 70-72. *Pos:* Violist, New Orleans Phil, 72-73, Omaha Symph, 82- & Nebr Sinfonia, 82-; asst prin viola, Miami Phil, 73-75 & Orquestra Sinfonica Paraiba, Brazil; prin viola, Lincoln Symph, Nebr, 82- *Mailing Add:* 4727 Meredith Ave Omaha NE 68104

HOUSEWRIGHT, WILEY LEE
EDUCATOR, ADMINISTRATOR
b Wylie, Tex, Oct 17, 13. *Study:* NTex State Univ, BS, 34; Columbia Univ, MA, 38; New York Univ, EdD, 43. *Teaching:* Dir music, Public Schs, Tex & NY, 34-41; asst prof music, Univ Tex, Austin, 46-47; prof music, Fla State Univ, 47-79, dean, Sch Music, Fla State, 66-79; vis prof music, Univ Mich, Ind Univ & New York Univ, 55-65. *Awards:* Fulbright Scholar to Japan, 56-57; Distinguished Prof, Fla State Univ, 61; Distinguished Alumni Citation, NTex State Univ, 67. *Mem:* Music Educr Nat Conf (pres, 68-70); Am Musicol Soc; Sonneck Soc; Music Libr Asn. *Interests:* American music research; early music of Florida. *Publ:* Coauth (with Carl Ernst & M Grentzer), Birchard Music Services, Vols I-VI, Birchard Co, 63. *Mailing Add:* 515 S Ride Tallahassee FL 32303

HOUTMANN, JACQUES
CONDUCTOR & MUSIC DIRECTOR
b Mirecourt, France, Mar 27, 35. *Study:* Ecole Normale Musique, Paris, conct lic, 62; Santa Cecilia, Rome, dipl, 63; Univ Richmond, Hon DFA, 76. *Rec Perf:* Three Symphonies, 72 & Grande Messe des Morts, Gossec; Panurge (opera), Gretry. *Pos:* Asst cond, New York Phil, 65-66; cond, Phil, Lyon, France, 67-71; music dir & cond, Richmond Symph & Richmond Sinfonia, 71-; guest cond with many orchs in Europe, US & South Am. *Awards:* First Prize, Compt Cond, Besancon, France, 60 & Dimitri Mitropoulos Compt, 64. *Mem:* Am Symph Orch League. *Mailing Add:* c/o Am Int Artists 275 Madison Ave New York NY 10016

HOVDA, ELEANOR
COMPOSER, EDUCATOR
b Duluth, Minn, Mar 27, 40. *Study:* Am Univ, BA(music), 63; Sch Music, Yale Univ; Univ Ill, Urbana; Kolner Kurse Neue Music, 66; Sarah Lawrence

Col, MFA(perf arts), 71. *Works:* Waveschart, comn by New Sound Comp Perf Group, 70; Air Moment (33 flutes), comn by NY Flute Club, 73; Spring Music with Wind & Embermusic (grand piano & friction mallets), 73 & 78; The Lion's Head, Chamber Music Soc Am Symph Orch, 75; Journeymusic, comn by Jerome Found & perf by Orch of Our Time, 81; Breathing (multiple flutes), Walker Art Ctr, 83; Trails III & Crossings (dancer, clarinet, doublebass & perc), Walker Art Ctr Perspectives, 83. *Pos:* Exec dir, Arrowhead Regional Arts Coun, 80- *Teaching:* Fac mem, Sarah Lawrence Col, 74-75; fac music & dance, Am Dance Fest, New London, Conn, summer 74-77; vis artist, Wesleyan Univ, Middletown, Conn, 75-77; vis artist dance, Col St Scholastica, 79- *Mem:* Am Music Ctr; New York Comp Forum; Minn Comp Forum; Col Music Soc; Int League Women Comp. *Mailing Add:* Arrowhead Reg Arts Coun 217 Old Main 2215 E 5th St Duluth MN 55812

HOVEY, SERGE
COMPOSER
b New York, NY, Mar 10, 20. *Study:* Private study harmony & counterpoint with Joseph Achron, 34-36; piano with Richard Buhlig, 36-38; comp with Arnold Schoenberg, 38-40; comp with Hanns Eisler, 46-47. *Works:* Tales From the Old Country, Decca, 48; Fable (ballet suite), Philadelphia Orch, 49; The World of Sholem Aleichem, music for the play, perf world-wide, 53-; Sholem Aleichem Suite, Cincinnati Symph, 58; A Scottish-American Fantasy, Berlin Radio Orch & Grand Chorus, 59; Hangman, doc film score, 64; The Songs of Robert Burns, Jean Redpath & Chamber Ens, 77-81. *Pos:* Music dir, Coronet Theater Prod, Bertolt Brecht's Galileo, 47; music ed, Film Sect, UNESCO; comp & arr, United Prod Am, 51. *Awards:* Silver Medal, San Francisco Int Film Fest, 70; Grant, Nat Endowment Arts, 81; Standard Award, ASCAP, 82-83. *Bibliog:* James J McCaffery (auth), The Robert Burns Songbook, Burns Chronicle, 80. *Mem:* ASCAP; Am Music Ctr. *Mailing Add:* 512 Arbramar Ave Pacific Palisades CA 90272

HOVHANESS, ALAN
COMPOSER
b Somerville, Mass, Mar 8, 11. *Study:* Univ Rochester, PhD(music), 58; Bates Col, PhD(music), 59. *Works:* Symphony No 1, Exile, C F Peters, 42; Arevakal, 53, Easter Cantata, 53, Prelude and Quadruple Fugue, 54 & Symphony No 2, Mysterious Mountain, 55, Assoc Music Publ; Magnificat, 59 & And God Created Great Whales, 69, C F Peters. *Mailing Add:* 17259 138th Ave SE Renton WA 98055

HOWARD, CLEVELAND L
MUSIC DIRECTOR, EDUCATOR
b Greenport, NY, May 2, 31. *Study:* Col Music, Boston Univ, MusB, 53, Sch Fine & Applied Arts, MMus, 54, DMA, 69. *Teaching:* Dir vocal music, Wareham Pub Sch, 54-55; music teacher, Schenectady Pub Sch, 55-60; clinician choral, Ithaca Col, summer 59 & New England Consv Music, summers 79 & 80; chmn music dept, Mont Pleasant High Sch, Schenectady, 60-69; assoc prof music, Univ NH, 69- & chmn music dept, 79- *Awards:* Award, Inst High Sch Music Teachers, Nat Coun Learned Soc & Ford Found, 62. *Mem:* NY State Sch Music Asn; Am Choral Dir Asn (NH pres, 73-75); Music Educr Nat Conf; Nat Asn Sch Music. *Mailing Add:* Music Dept Univ NH Durham NH 03824

HOWARD, DEAN CLINTON
COMPOSER, CLARINET
b Cleveland, Ohio, Nov 17, 18. *Study:* Baldwin Wallace Col, BSM, 41; Univ Mich, MMus, 42. *Works:* Divertimento for Orchestra, Belwin Inc, 66; An Illinois Symphony, perf by Peoria Symph, 67 & Chicago Symph, 70; Perspectives for Orchestra, comn by Peoria Symph Orch, 72; Three Improvizations for Clarinet and Piano, 79 & Wind Song for Flute and Piano, 79, Kendor Music Inc; Celebration for Orchestra, comn by Peoria Civic Ctr Authority, 82; Turnabout, Chamber Opera, 83. *Teaching:* Instr, Buena Vista Col, 46-47 & State Univ NY Col, Fredonia, 54-58; prof music, Bradley Univ, 48- *Awards:* Putnam Award, Bradley Univ, 62; Baldwin Wallace Col Achievement Award, 76. *Mem:* Phi Mu Alpha Sinfonia. *Mailing Add:* 1814 Bradley Ave Peoria IL 61606

HOWARD, (DANA) DOUGLAS
PERCUSSION, EDUCATOR
b Greeneville, Tenn, Apr 21, 48. *Study:* Univ Tenn, BS, 70; Cath Univ Am, MM, 73; studied with Alan Abel, Anthony Ames, Michael Combs & Charles Owen. *Pos:* Timpanist & perc, US Air Force Band, Washington, DC, 71-74; prin perc, Louisville Orch, 74-75; prin perc & asst timpanist, Dallas Symph Orch, 75- *Teaching:* Adj prof perc, Southern Methodist Univ, 77-; instr, Aspen Music Fest & Sch, 82- *Mem:* Percussive Arts Soc. *Mailing Add:* c/o Dallas Symph PO Box 26207 Dallas TX 75226

HOWARD, GEORGE SALLADE
CONDUCTOR & MUSIC DIRECTOR, COMPOSER
b Reamstown, Pa, Feb 24, 03. *Study:* Ohio Wesleyan Univ, AB, 29; NY Univ, MA, 36; Chicago Consv Music, BMus, MMus, MMus, MusD. *Works:* Numerous marches & songs, Southern Music Publ Co & Ludwig Music Publ Co, 43-70. *Pos:* Chief band & music, US Air Force, 42-63; cond, US Air Force Band & Symph, Washington, DC, 44-63; guest cond, US & abroad, 63-83. *Teaching:* Dir music, Mansfield State Col, 36-40; dir band, orch & chorus, Pa State Univ, 40-42. *Awards:* Sousa Found Gold Medal, 82; Distinguished Band Cond Hall Fame, Nat Band Asn, 82. *Mem:* Music Educr Nat Conf; ASCAP. *Mailing Add:* 4917 Ravenswood Dr San Antonio TX 78227

HOWARD, SAMUEL EUGENE
PIANO, TEACHER
b Birmingham, Ala, May 18, 37. *Study:* Birmingham-Southern Col, BM, 59; Juilliard Sch Music, artist dipl, 61; studied with Rosina Lhevinne, 59-63, Vronsky & Babin, 59-61 & Ilona Kabos, 63-66. *Rec Perf:* Music of Brahms & Stravinsky, WDR, Cologne, 66; Music of Ravel, RIAS, Berlin, 66; Music for Two Pianos, 72 & Encores for Two Pianos, 72, Mastercraft; Le Sacre du Printemps (Stravinsky), Concertgebouw, Amsterdam, 77. *Pos:* Duo-pianist, BBC, 65; Wilfrid Van Wyck Ltd, London, 65 & Columbia Artists Mgt Inc, 67. *Teaching:* Artist in res piano, Birmingham-Southern Col, 61-83 & Univ Ala, Birmingham, 83- *Awards:* Martha Baird Rockefeller Fund for Music Grant, 65-66. *Rep:* Columbia Artists Mgt Inc 165 W 57th St New York NY 10019. *Mailing Add:* 14 Cross Creek Park Mountain Brook AL 35213

HOWARD, WAYNE
WRITER, MUSICOLOGIST
b Grenada, Miss, Sept 7, 42. *Study:* Belhaven Col, BA & BM, 64; Ind Univ, MM, 67, PhD, 75. *Pos:* Regional dir, Independent Scholars of Asia, 82- *Teaching:* From instr to asst prof, Kent State Univ, 73-76; vis lectr, Univ Ga, summer, 79. *Mem:* Am Musicol Soc; Soc Ethnomusicol. *Interests:* Oriental music; vedic chant traditions of India. *Publ:* Auth, Samavedic Chant, Yale Univ Press, 77; A Yajurveda Festival in Kerala, Pendragon Press, 81; The Music of Nambudiri Unexpressed Chant, Asian Humanities Press, 82; Music and Accentuation in Vedic Literature, World Music, 82; Veda Recitation in Varanasi, Motilal Banarsidass (in prep). *Mailing Add:* 315 Shirley Ave Winona MS 38967

HOWAT, ROBERT V
EDUCATOR, PIANO
b Chicago, Ill, Mar 6, 33. *Study:* Univ Chicago, BA, 55 & MA, 57. *Rec Perf:* Piano Music of Alexander Tcherepnin, Orion Master Rec, 79. *Teaching:* Instr, Univ Chicago, 57-60; prof music, Wittenberg Univ, Ohio, 60- *Awards:* Premier Assoc, Fontainebleau Consv, 52; Piano Prize, Artist's Adv Coun, 58; Distinguished Teaching Award, Wittenberg Alumni Asn, 73. *Mailing Add:* 2421 Rebecca Dr Springfield OH 45503

HOWE, HUBERT S, JR
COMPOSER, EDUCATOR
b Portland, Ore, Dec 21, 42. *Study:* Princeton Univ, studied comp & theory with J K Randall, Milton Babbitt & Godfrey Windham, AB, 64, MFA, 67, PhD(musical comp), 72. *Works:* Computer Variations (electronic), 67-68; Kaleidscope (electronic), 69; Interchanges (electronic), 70-71; Three Studies in Timbre (electronic), 70-73; Macro-Structures (electronic), 71; Freeze (electronic), 72; Scherzo (orch), 75. *Pos:* Founder & ed, Proc Am Soc Univ Comp, formerly; assoc ed, Perspectives New Music, 69- *Teaching:* Electronic Music Inst, NY Univ, formerly, Southern Ill Univ, formerly, Univ NH, formerly & Dartmouth Col, formerly; mem fac, Juilliard Sch, 74-82; assoc prof & dir, Electronic Music Studio, Queens Col, City Univ New York, 67-78 & Grad Ctr, 78- *Mem:* League Comp—Int Soc Contemp Music (pres US sect, 71-76); Am Comp Alliance; Col Music Soc; Am Soc Univ Comp; Am Music Ctr. *Publ:* Auth, Electronic Music Synthesis, 75; contribr to BYTE & Interface. *Mailing Add:* 14 Lexington New York NY 10956

HOWE, RICHARD ESMOND, JR
ADMINISTRATOR, EDUCATOR
b Murray, Utah, Apr 30, 27. *Study:* Univ Utah, 46; Juilliard Sch, BS(music), 51, MS(music), 52; Univ Florence, Italy, 52-53; Eastman Sch Music, DMA, 56; studied piano with Katherine Bacon, Pietro Scarpini & Cecile Staub Genhart. *Teaching:* Mem fac, Grinnell Col, 56-73, chmn dept, 59-62, 65-67 & 70-72, prof music, 63-72, chmn div humanities, 71-72; dean & mem fac music hist, theory & practice, San Francisco Consv Music, 73- *Awards:* Fulbright Grants, Italy, 52-53 & 53-54. *Interests:* Keyboard music of Baldassare Gallupi. *Mailing Add:* 409 Countryview Dr Mill Valley CA 94941

HOWELL, ALMONTE CHARLES, JR
MUSICOLOGIST, EDUCATOR
b Richmond, Va, May 2, 25. *Study:* Univ NC, AB(music), 46, PhD(musicol), 53; Harvard Univ, MA, 47. *Teaching:* Asst prof music, Southwestern at Memphis, 54-56; from asst prof to prof musicol, Univ KY, 56-67; res prof musicol, Univ Ga, 67- *Awards:* Fulbright Student Grant, France, 50-51 & res grant, Spain, 62-63. *Mem:* Am Musicol Soc; Music Libr Asn; Col Music Soc; Pi Kappa Lambda; Phi Mu Alpha Sinfonia. *Interests:* French and Spanish Renaissance and baroque keyboard music; Spanish Renaissance and baroque music theory. *Publ:* Auth, Paired Imitation in 16th Century Spanish Keyboard Music, Musicol Quart, 7/67; contribr, Pablo Nassare's Escuela Musica: A Reappraisal, In: Studies in Musicology, Univ NC, 69; auth, Seventeenth-Century Music Theory: Spain, J Music Theory, 72. *Mailing Add:* Dept Music Univ Ga Athens GA 30602

HOY, HENDRICKS
COMPOSER, PIANO
b Jenkintown, Pa, Aug 27, 36. *Study:* Fontainebleau Consv Music, studied comp with Nadia Boulanger; Philadelphia Col Perf Arts, BMus, 62; Temple Univ, 65-68. *Works:* Three Sonatas for Violin, Op 40, 76; Whitman Cycle, Op 43 (tenor, violin & piano), Op 43, 77; Duo Sonata (violin & viola), Op 41, comn by Carol Stein, 76 & Duo Sonata (violin & cello), Op 42, comn by Cynthia W Cooke, 77; Chamber Concerto (two flutes, violin, viola, cello & piano), Op 45, 80; Hashkivaynu (tenor & piano), Op 46, No 1, 80; Missa Breve (chorus, soloists, orch & organ), comn by Morris Osborn for St Paul's Cathedral, Washington, DC, 82. *Rec Perf:* Hoy Plays Hoy, 72, Hoy Music for Voice, 74 & A Tribute to Violette De Mazia, 74, Encore Rec. *Pos:* Music

consult, WUHY-FM Prog Ser on Poetry & Arts, 73; artistic dir, Philadelphia Contemp Music Comt, 74 & 75 & Encore Rec, 76-; artistic consult to the Philadelphia Singers, 81- *Teaching:* Private instr piano & comp, 54-; fac mem, Philadelphia Col Perf Arts, 62-65 & Settlement Music Sch, 65-73. *Awards:* Esther Gowen Hood Mem Scholarship Award, 60-62; dipl merit; G B Viotti Int Comp Compt, Vercelli, Italy, 74. *Mem:* ASCAP; Am Music Ctr; Nat Asn Am Comp & Cond (bd dir, 75-77). *Mailing Add:* 7744 Albright Ave Elkins Park PA 19117

HOYLE, WILSON THEODORE
CELLO, EDUCATOR
b Huntville, Ala, Aug 17, 42. *Study:* Eastman Sch Music, BM, 64; Yale Univ, MMus, 67; Manhattan Sch Music, DMA, 81. *Rec Perf:* American String Quartets 1900-1950, 72 & Penderecki: A Portrait, 72, Vox; Four American Composers, Desto, 73; Amercan Society of University Composers, Advance Rec, 76; Hear America First, Spectrum, 80. *Pos:* Cellist, Am Symph Orch, 68-69, New York City Ballet Orch, 69-70 & Kohon Quartet, 69-80; co-dir, Hear Am First Conct Series, 77-81. *Teaching:* Prof music, cello & chamber music, Kean Col, 70- *Mem:* Violoncello Soc. *Mailing Add:* 276 Riverside Dr New York NY 10025

HRUBY, FRANK
CRITIC-WRITER, CONDUCTOR
b Emporia, Kans, June 29, 18. *Study:* Eastman Sch Music, with Howard Hanson, Bernard Rogers & Paul White, BM, 40, MM, 41. *Pos:* Founder & cond, Hattiesburg, Miss Little Symph, 46-48; music dir & cond, Cain Park Summer Theater, 46-56 & Singer's Club Cleveland, 56-65; Music critic & ed, Cleveland Press, 56-82. *Teaching:* Asst prof music & theory, Miss Southern Col, 46-48; head music & fine arts dept, Univ Sch, Cleveland, 48-75. *Mem:* Music Critics Asn (secy, 78-80). *Mailing Add:* 2350 Beachwood Blvd Cleveland OH 44122

HSU, DOLORES MENSTELL
EDUCATOR
b Portland, Ore, Nov 4, 30. *Study:* Lewis & Clark Col, BA; Mozarteum, Salzburg, Austria, piano dipl; Univ Vienna; Univ Southern Calif, PhD. *Teaching:* Prof music & chmn, Grad Studies Music, Univ Calif, Santa Barbara, currently. *Awards:* Am Asn Univ Women Fel, 57-58; Fulbright Res Fel, 73; Outstanding Educr of Am Award, 73. *Mem:* Am Musicol Soc; Col Music Soc; Am Soc Eastern Arts; Mu Phi Epsilon; Soc Ethnomusicol. *Publ:* Contribr to Music Rev, Musical Quart, Yale J Music Theory, Piano Teacher, Piano Quart, Festschriften & 19th Century Music. *Mailing Add:* Dept Music Univ Calif Santa Barbara CA 93106

HSU, JOHN (TSENG-HSIN)
EDUCATOR, VIOLA DA GAMBA
b Swatow, China, Apr 21, 31; US citizen. *Study:* New England Consv Music, BMus, 53, MMus, 55, Hon Dr Music, 71. *Rec Perf:* Pieces de viole (Louis de Caix d'Hervelois & Antone Forqueray), Disques Alpha, Belgium, 67; The three Viola da gamba Sonatas (J S Bach), Da Camera, Germany, 71; The five Viola da gamba Suites (Antone Forqueray), 72 & Pieces de viole (Martin Marais), 73-76; Concerto in A Minor (recorder, viola da gamba & orch; G P Teleman), Cambridge Rec, 77; Pieces de viole (Jacque Morel, Charles Dolle & Martin Marais), 78 & Baryton Trios, Vol I & II (Joseph Haydn), 81-82, Musical Heritage Soc. *Pos:* Founding mem, Amade Trio & Haydn Baryton Trio; recitals and radio broadcasts in Europe & Am. *Teaching:* Prof music, Cornell Univ, 55-; artist & mem fac, Aston Magna Found Music, 73-; artist in res, Univ Calif, Davis, winter 83. *Awards:* Cornell Soc Humanities Fel, 71-72. *Mem:* Riemenschneider Bach Inst, 71. *Publ:* Auth, The Use of the Bow in French Solo Viole Playing of the 17th and 18th Centuries, In: Early Music, Oxford Univ Press, Oct, 78; Handbook of French Baroque Viol Technique, Broude Brothers Ltd, 81. *Mailing Add:* 601 Highland Rd Ithaca NY 14850

HSU, MADELEINE
EDUCATOR, PIANO
b France; US citizen. *Study:* Ecole Normale Musique, Paris, artist dipl, 60; Juilliard Sch, BMus, 70, MS, 71; NY Univ, currently. *Pos:* Concert artist, Europe, South & North Am, Africa, 52-; co-ed chronicles, Opus, Boise State Univ, 82- *Teaching:* Prof piano, Boise State Univ, 71-; clinician, adjudicator & lectr, Music Teachers Nat Asn, 76- *Awards:* Josef Lhevinne Mem Award, Juilliard Sch, 70; Mu Phi Epsilon Mem Found Grant, 81. *Bibliog:* Madeleine Hsu in Concert (videotapes), KAID Pub TV, Boise State Univ, 71- *Mem:* Music Teachers Nat Asn; Piano Guild. *Publ:* Auth, Vacances Beethoveniennes, Musica, Paris, 63; Beethovenian Holidays: Wilhelm Kempff, Clavier, 70; The Naked Face of Talent: Rosina Lhevinne, Am Music Teacher, 81. *Mailing Add:* Dept of Music Boise State Univ Boise ID 83725

HSU, WEN-YING
COMPOSER
b Shanghai, China, May 2, 09; US citizen. *Study:* George Peabody Col, BS(comp), 55; New England Consv, MM(musicol), 59. *Works:* Trio for Violin, Cello & Piano, 56 & Fantasia for Two Pianos, 56, Taipei City Hall; Prelude to the Water Tune, 66 & Percussions East and West (14 instrm), 66, Univ Southern Calif; Violin Suite, perf by T K Wang with Los Angeles Phil, 66; Songs of Sung, perf by Edith Rath, 69; Sky Maidens Dance Suite, Hollywood Wilshire Symph Orch, 70; Vocal Series No I, No II, & No III, Piano Sonata, Scenes in a Chinese Village (piano), Sound of Autumn & others, Wen Ying Studio. *Teaching:* Piano, privately, 51-54; prof music, Nat Acad Fine Arts, Taiwan, 57-58 & 60-62 & Col Chinese Cult, Taiwan, 70-72. *Awards:* Parade of Am Music, Nat Fedn Music Clubs, 69; Award of Distinguished Serv Music, Nat League Am Pen Women, 80; Presidential

Achievement Award, President Ronald Reagan, 82. *Mem:* ASCAP; Sigma Alpha Iota; Nat Asn Comp, USA; Nat League Am Pen Women (chmn comp contest, 76-82); Am Musicol Soc. *Interests:* Chinese music; discovering music theory on an old stringed instrument, ku-ch'in previously unknown. *Publ:* Auth, Origin of Music in China, Chinese Culture, 72; The Ku-ch'in, Cent Bk Co, Taiwan, 76; The Cat and Translations of Chinese Poems, Wen Ying Studio. *Rep:* Wen Ying Studio PO Box 888 Plaza Sta Pasadena CA 91102. *Mailing Add:* 440 N Madison Ave #117 Pasadena CA 91101

HUBER, CALVIN RAYMOND
COMPOSER, EDUCATOR
b Buffalo, NY, July 12, 25. *Study:* Univ Wis, BA, MA, 49; NY Univ, with Curt Sachs & Gustave Reece, 50-51; Univ NC, Chapel Hill, with William S Newman, 56-59, PhD, 64. *Works:* Profunditties (woodwinds); Elegy (5 flutes); Baubolero (band); Fanfare for a Ceremony (band); Anecdotes (brass-bar & piano); and others. *Pos:* Trombonist & arr in jazz & big bands, Skitch Henderson Orch & others. *Teaching:* Instr, Carson-Newman Col, 51-56 & 59-62; instr & dept chmn, Wake Forest Univ, 62-74; prof orch, hist, lit & musicol & dir grad studies music, Univ Tenn, 74-; vis instr, Univ Wis & Univ NC, Greensboro. *Mailing Add:* Music Dept Univ Tenn Knoxville TN 37996

HUBER, JOHN ELWYN
EDUCATOR, ADMINISTRATOR
b Hays, Kans, Dec 15, 40. *Study:* Ft Hays State Univ, BM, 62; Univ Mich, MM, 67. *Teaching:* Instr piano, Colby Pub Sch, Kans, 62-65; instr music, Ft Hays State Univ, 67-70, asst prof, 70-74, assoc prof, 74-, chmn dept, 82- *Mem:* Music Educ Nat Conf; Kans Music Educr Asn; Music Teachers Nat Asn; Kans Music Teachers Asn (second vpres, 70-71 & 76-77, pres elect, 82-83). *Mailing Add:* 600 Park St Hays KS 67601

HÜBNER, CARLA (CARLA V HÜBNER-KRAEMER)
PIANO, TEACHER-COACH
b Santiago, Chile, May 1, 41. *Study:* Consv Nac Musica, Univ Chile, Lic Interpretacion Superior(piano), 64; Columbia Univ, MA(musical), 74; studied with Claudio Arrau. *Rec Perf:* Musica Argentina Contemporanea, Inst Torcuato di Tella, Buenos Aires, 69; Musica Chilena Contemporanea, Asoc Nac de Compositores & Inst de Estension Musical, Santiago, 70; Gaudeamus Prizewinners 1971, Gaudeamus Found, 72; New Music from South America, Mainstream, 72. *Pos:* Concert pianist & recitalist, Chile, Arg, Peru, PR, Europe & US. *Teaching:* Vocal coach art song, Nat Consv Music, Santiago, 61-64; teacher piano perf & vocal coach art song, privately, Washington, DC, 74-; lectr piano, Mt Vernon Col, Washington, DC, 79-; coordr music, 81- *Awards:* Prizewinner, Int Compt Interpreters Contemp Music, Gaudeamus Found, 71 & 73. *Rep:* Lois Fishman 2901 18th St NW #506 Washington DC 20009. *Mailing Add:* 1917 Biltmore St NW Washington DC 20009

HUDSON, BARTON
EDUCATOR, HARPSICHORD
b Memphis, Tenn, July 20, 36. *Study:* Midwestern Univ, BMus, 56; Ind Univ, MMus, 57, PhD, 61; Staatliche Hochschule Musik, Freiburg, 59-60. *Teaching:* Asst prof, Cent Mo State Univ, 61-64; from asst prof to prof, WVa Univ, 64- *Interests:* Renaissance music; baroque keyboard music. *Publ:* Auth, Notes on Gregorio Strozzi and His Capricci, J Am Musicol Soc, 67; ed, Antoine Brumel, Opera Omnia, 6 vol, 69-72 & Thomas Crecquillon, Opera Omnia, 4 vol, 74, Am Inst Musicol; auth, A Neglected Source of Renaissance Polyphony, Acta Musicologica, 76; auth & coauth, 46 articles, In: New Grove Dict of Music & Musicians, 81. *Mailing Add:* 473 Devon Rd Morgantown WV 26505

HUDSON, RICHARD ALBERT
EDUCATOR, WRITER
b Alma, Mich, Mar 19, 24. *Study:* Oberlin Consv Music, Oberlin Col, BMus, 49; Syracuse Univ, MMus, 51; Univ Calif, Los Angeles, PhD, 67. *Works:* Trios for Organ, Vol 1, 71 & Vol 2, 72, Suite of Organ Carols, 76 & Hymn Preludes and Free Accompaniments, Vol 12, 78, Augsburg Publ House. *Teaching:* Assoc prof organ & theory, Converse Col, Spartanburg, SC, 49-50; instr, Oberlin Col, Ohio, 53-55; prof music, Univ Calif, Los Angeles, 67- *Mem:* Am Musicol Soc; Int Musicol Soc; Am Guild Organists. *Interests:* Evolution of instrumental forms during Renaissance and Baroque period. *Publ:* Auth, The Ripresa, the Ritornello & the Passacaglia, J Am Musicol Soc, 71; The Folia, Fedele, and Falsobordone, Musical Quart, 72; 20 articles, In: New Grove Dict of Music & Musicians, Macmillan, 80; Passacaglio and Ciaccona, UMI Res Press, 81; The Folia, the Saraband, the Passacaglia, & The Chaconne, (4 vol), Haenssler-Verlag & Am Inst Musicol, 82. *Mailing Add:* 7036 Bevis Ave Van Nuys CA 91405

HUETTEMAN, ALBERT G
ADMINISTRATOR, EDUCATOR
b Elizabeth, NJ, Apr 25, 35. *Study:* New England Consv Music, Boston, BMus, 56; Ohio Univ, Athens, MFA, 57; Univ Ill, Urbana, 60-61; Univ Iowa, PhD, 68. *Teaching:* Instr, Hastings Col, Nebr, 57-60; vis instr, Univ Ill, Urbana, summer 61 & Univ Iowa, 65-66; asst prof & chmn piano dept, Ind State Univ, Terre Haute, 61-64 & Coe Col, 64-65; assoc prof & chmn music dept, Otterbein Col, Ohio, 67-72; prof & assoc dept head, Univ Mass, Amherst, 74-, grad prog dir, 75- & actg dept head, 76-77. *Mem:* Music Educr Nat Conf; Music Teachers Nat Asn; Mass Music Teachers Asn. *Publ:* Contrib ed, Instrumental Musician, Careers Guidance Serv, Inc, 74; auth, Social Security Affects the Music Teacher, Clavier, 1/74; Tax Deductions for the Private Music Teacher, 11-12/74 & The IRS Maze: Is There a Way Out?, 2-3/78, Am Music Teacher; Computer Programs in Music Theory & Ear-Training, Instant Software, Inc, 83. *Mailing Add:* 19 Arnold Rd Delham MA 01002

HUGHES, CHARLES WILLIAM
EDUCATOR, WRITER

b Portsmouth, RI, Feb 20, 1900. *Study:* Teachers Col, Columbia Univ, BS, 23, MA, 24; Columbia Univ, PhD, 33. *Teaching:* Adj instr, Teachers Col, Columbia Univ, 25-26; instr, Hunter Col, 27-35, asst prof, 35-48, assoc prof, 48-69; prof, Herbert H Lehman Col, 69-70. *Awards:* Grant, Chapelbrook Found, 58-59. *Mem:* Am Musicol Asn; Hymn Soc Am. *Interests:* Seventeenth century music; American music and hymnody; music of Percy Grainger. *Publ:* Auth, Chamber Music in American Schools, 33; contribr, Encycl of the Arts, 46 & The Human Side of Music, 48, Philosophical Libr; coauth, American Hymns Old and New, Vol I, auth, Vol II, Columbia Univ Press, 80; Percy Grainger: The Choral Music in the Band Music, Studies in Music, No 16, 82. *Mailing Add:* 28 Ralph Ave White Plains NY 10606

HUGHES, DAVID GRATTAN
EDUCATOR, WRITER

b Norwalk, Conn, June 14, 26. *Study:* Harvard Univ, AB, 49, AM, 54, PhD(music), 56. *Pos:* Ed in chief, J Am Musicol Soc, 60-63. *Teaching:* From instr to prof, Harvard Univ, 56-76, Fanny P Mason prof music, 76-; vis asst prof music hist, Yale Univ, 54-58; Brechemin distinguished prof musicol, Univ Wash, 78-79. *Mem:* Am Musicol Soc; Medieval Acad Am; Int Musicol Soc. *Interests:* Medieval liturgical music; plainsong. *Publ:* Auth, Liturgical Polyphony at Beauvais in the 13th Century, Speculum, 59; Further Notes on the Grouping of the Aquitanian Tropers, J Am Musicol Soc, 66; The Sources of Christus Manens, Aspects of Medieval & Renaissance Music, 66; coauth (with John Bryden), An Index of Gregorian Chant, Harvard Univ Press, 69; auth, A History of European Music, McGraw-Hill, 74. *Mailing Add:* Dept Music Harvard Univ Cambridge MA 02138

HUGHES, JOHN (GILLIAM)
EDUCATOR, ORGAN

b Clinton, Ky, July 7, 21. *Study:* Studied with Marcel Dupre, 44-45; Auditor Consv Nat Paris, 45; Southwestern at Memphis, with Thomas H Webber, AB, 47; Juilliard Sch Music, with Ernest White, MS, 49; NY Univ, 49-52; Fla State Univ, PhD, 61; Acad Musicale Chigiana, Siena, Italy, with Fernando Germani, 61; Eastman Sch Music, 65. *Works:* Isaiah's Vision (anthem), Bourne, 65. *Rec Perf:* Music at Union University, Rec Publ Co, Century Rec, 68; Sesquicentenial Music—1978, Sound Enterprises, 78. *Teaching:* Prof organ & music hist & chmn div fine arts, Union Univ, Tenn, 52-68; prof, dean col fine arts & chmn div fine arts, Univ Ark, Little Rock, 68- *Awards:* Fac Grant, Univ Ark, Little Rock, 79; vis scholar, Stanford Univ, 79. *Mem:* Am Musicol Asn; Soc Ethnomusicol; Am Guild Organists; Nat Music Teachers Asn. *Interests:* Organs on the eastern seaboard of the US, before 1800; correlative chart covering the arts, social history, religion and philosophy from 2500 BC to present. *Publ:* Auth, The Bamboo Organ of the Las Pinas, Am Organist, 4/65. *Mailing Add:* Eight Towne Park Court #13 Little Rock AR 72207

HUGHES, ROBERT GROVE
COMPOSER, CONDUCTOR & MUSIC DIRECTOR

b Buffalo, NY, Sept 16, 33. *Study:* Univ Buffalo, BA, 56; studied with Luigi Dallapiccola, 59-60; studied with Lou Harrison, 60-61. *Works:* Quadroquartet, 73 & Cones (orch), 75, Cabrillo Music Fest; HCE (multi-orch), San Francisco Symph, 77; Music for the Kama Sutra, Oakland Symph Orch, 81; Sonitudes (flute & cello), Carl Fischer Inc, 82; The True and False Occult, Margaret Fisher Dance Co, 83; Cadences (two orch), Tanz-Form Köln State Opera, Germany, 83. *Rec Perf:* Water Music (Ned Rorem), 66, Pacifika Rondo (Lou Harrison), 68 & Music by Black Composers, 69, Desto; Le Testament (Pound), Fantasy, 71; Cinque Canti/Esercizi (Luigi Dallapiccola), 78 & The Ship of Death (Peter Lopez), 83, 1750 Arch. *Pos:* Bassoon & contrabassoon, Oakland Symph, 64-; first bassoon, San Francisco Ballet, 63-70 & Cabrillo Music Fest, 63-80; cond & co-music dir, Arch Ens Experimental Music, Berkeley, 77- *Awards:* Comp Prize for Sonitudes, Calif Cello Club, 74; Award Adventuresome Prog Contemp Music, ASCAP, 80; res scholar, Fulbright-Hays, 81. *Publ:* Auth, Ezra Pound: Composer of the Opera Le Testament, Paideuma J, Univ Maine, 71. *Mailing Add:* Studio #16 1420 45th St Emeryville CA 94608

HUGO, JOHN WILLIAM
CONDUCTOR, TENOR

b Schenectady, NY, Apr 28, 56. *Study:* Houghton Col, BMus, 78; New England Consv, MM(choral cond); Berkshire Music Ctr; vocal studies with Phyllis Curtin, 80. *Pos:* Tenor soloist, Church Advent Choir, Boston, 78-82; assoc cond, New England Consv Chorus, 81- *Teaching:* Instr choral cond, New England Consv, 81- *Mailing Add:* 31 Burbank #304 Boston MA 02115

HUJSAK, (RUTH) JOY
HARP, EDUCATOR

b Buffalo, NY, May 13, 24. *Study:* Eastman Sch Music, organ with Catherine Crozier & Harold Gleason, BM, 45; Lamont Sch Music, Univ Colo, cert, 47; San Francisco State Col & Schmitz Sch Piano, piano with E Robert Schmitz, 48; studied harp with Marjorie Call, 61-74 & piano with Leo Smit, 61-65. *Works:* Short Harp Solos, Mina-Helwig Publ Co, 82. *Pos:* Piano accmp, Miss State Univ for Women, 46-47 & private studio & conct work, 47-68. *Teaching:* Instr piano, organ & theory, Marion Col, 45-46; lectr, Univ Calif, San Diego, 68- & Pt Loma Col, 77-; instr harp, Univ San Diego, 77- & San Diego State Univ, 78- *Mem:* Am Harp Soc. *Mailing Add:* 8732 Nottingham Pl La Jolla CA 92037

HULL, ROBERT LESLIE
CONDUCTOR, EDUCATOR

b New York, NY, Feb 11, 16. *Study:* Ashland Col, 33-37; Univ Rochester, MusB, 39, MusM, 41; Cornell Univ, PhD, 45. *Pos:* Dir, Elmira Civic Chorus, NY, formerly; music dir & cond, Ft Worth Symph & Ballet Soc, 57-63; cond, Ariz Chamber Orch, 67; guest cond, Pittsburgh Symph, Buffalo Phil, Rochester Phil, Phoenix Symph & Tuscon Symph. *Teaching:* Asst prof music, Duke Univ, 43-47; assoc prof & dir univ music, Cornell Univ, 47-56; dean, Sch Fine Arts, Tex Christian Univ, 56-59; vis prof, Univ Kans, 64; prof music & dean, Col Fine Arts, Univ Ariz, 64- *Awards:* Winner, NC Comp Cont, 47. *Mem:* Am Symph Orch League (mem exec bd, 55-57); Music Teachers Nat Asn; Am Musicol Soc; Tucson Arts Coun; Nat Coun Fine Arts Deans. *Mailing Add:* Dept Music Univ Ariz Tucson AZ 85721

HULTBERG, WARREN EARLE
EDUCATOR, PIANO

b Great Falls, Mont. *Study:* Univ Nev, Reno, BA, 57; Univ Southern Calif, MA, 59, PhD, 64. *Pos:* Prof musician, Great Falls, San Francisco, Reno & Los Angeles, 38-63; owner & operator music studio, Reno, Nev, 50-60. *Teaching:* Lectr music, Univ Southern Calif, 59-63; prof, State Univ NY, Potsdam, 63- *Mem:* Am Musicol Soc; Col Music Soc; Am Fedn Musicians; Music Educr Nat Conf; Asn Develop Computer-Based Instructional Systems. *Interests:* Sixteenth century Spanish music theory and performance practices; computers and musicology. *Publ:* Auth, Transcription of Tablature to Standard Notation, In: Computers & Music, Cornell, 70; Diego Pisador's Libro de Musica de Vihuela, In: Fest Essays, Brigham Young, 76. *Mailing Add:* 72 Leroy St Potsdam NY 13676

HUMEL, GERALD
COMPOSER, CONDUCTOR

b Cleveland, Ohio, Nov 7, 31. *Study:* Hofstra Univ, with Elie Siegmeister, BA, 54; Consv Music, Oberlin Col, MM, 58; Univ Mich, with Ross Lee Finney & Roberto Gerhard. *Works:* Flute Concerto, 64 & Herodias (ballet), 67, Bote & Bock; Die Folterunge der Beatrice Cenci, Schott, 72; Lilith (ballet), Staatstheater Darmstadt, 73; Othello und Desdemona (ballet suite), 78 & Lepini (large orch), 78, Schott; Zwei Giraffen Tanzen Tango (ballet), Stadtstheater Bremen, 80. *Pos:* Freelance comp, currently; cond, Gruppe Neue Musik, Berlin, currently. *Awards:* Guggenheim Fel, 66; German Critics Prize, 67; Berlin Arts Prize, 73. *Mem:* Akad Künste Berlin. *Mailing Add:* Claudiusstr 12 1000 Berlin 21 Germany, Federal Republic of

HUNKINS, ARTHUR B
COMPOSER, EDUCATOR

b New York, NY, Apr 12, 37. *Study:* Ohio Univ, with Karl Ahrendt; studied with Nadia Boulanger, Paris; Univ Mich, with Ross Lee Finney, DMA. *Works:* O Come, O Come, Emmanuel (chorus), 75; Five Pieces for Orchestra; Te Deum (ten, bar, male chorus & orch); Gloria (chorus); Libera nos (chorus); Five Short Songs of Gladness; Ecce Quam Bonum (organ). *Teaching:* Fac mem, Southern Ill Univ, 61-63 & North Tex State Univ, 63-65; assoc prof theory, comp & electronic, Univ NC, Greensboro, 65- *Awards:* Nat Fedn Music Club Awards; BMI Award; Joseph Bearns Prize. *Mailing Add:* Music Dept Univ NC Greensboro NC 27412

HUNSBERGER, DONALD
EDUCATOR, CONDUCTOR

b Souderton, Pa, 1932. *Study:* Trombone with Frederick Stoll; Eastman Sch Music, BMus, MMus, DMusA; Cath Univ; Peabody Consv Music; studied trombone with Emory Remington, orchestration with Bernard Rogers, cond with Frederick Fennell, Howard Mitchell & Ifor Jones & arr with Rayburn Wright. *Pos:* Bass trombonist & trombone soloist; guest cond, over 30 all-state band festivals & numerous univ ens; staff arr, US Marine Band, Washington, DC, formerly. *Teaching:* Theory, lower brass & ens, State Univ NY Col, Potsdam, formerly; co-chmn, Dept Cond & Ens, Eastman Sch Music, currently, cond, Wind Ens, Wind Orch & Eastman-Dryden Orch, 65-; lectr, US, Japan, Norway & England. *Awards:* Award of Merit, Nat Asn Local Historians, 77. *Mem:* Music Educr Nat Conf; ASCAP; Col Band Dir Nat Asn (pres elect, currently); NY State Band Dir Asn. *Publ:* Auth, The Art of Conducting, Alfred Knopf Inc, 83. *Mailing Add:* 160 Alpine Dr Rochester NY 14618

HUNT, ALEXANDRA
SOPRANO

US citizen. *Study:* Vassar Col, BA; Juilliard Sch Music, BS; Sorbonne Univ, France. *Rec Perf:* Songs by MacDowell, Griffes & Carpenter, Orion Master Rec, 77. *Roles:* Marie in Wozzeck, La Scala & Hamburg Staatsoper, 72-73; Katya in Katya Kabanova, Wexford Fest, Ireland, 72 & Janacek Fest, Czechoslovakia, 78; Passion According to St Luke (Penderecki), Philadelphia Orch, 73; Jenufa in Jenufa, Little Orch Soc, 74; Lulu in Lulu, Metropolitan Opera, 77; Lady Macbeth in Macbeth, Int Verdi Cong, 77; Wagner Conct, Bogota Phil, Colombia, 82; other appearances in Romania & Bulgaria. *Rep:* Am/Europ Artists Alliance 200 W 70th St Suite 3G New York NY 10023. *Mailing Add:* 170 W 74th St New York NY 10023

HUNT, CHARLES B, JR
EDUCATOR

b Nashville, Tenn, July 20, 16. *Study:* Peabody Col, BS & MA, 38; Eastman Sch Music & Northwestern Univ, summers 36 & 37; Univ Calif, Los Angeles, PhD, 49. *Pos:* Prin clarinet, Nashville Symph Orch, 34-54. *Teaching:* Dir, Sch Music, Peabody Col, 55-65, dean grad sch, 65-74; dean, Col Commun & Fine Arts, Southern Ill Univ, 74-83, prof music, 83- *Mem:* Nat Asns Sch Music (pres, 62-65). *Mailing Add:* Music Dept Southern Ill Univ Carbondale IL 62901

HUNT, KAREN
SOPRANO

b Cedar Rapids, Iowa. *Study:* Univ Iowa; NTex State Univ; Univ Mich. *Roles:* Pamina in Die Zauberflöte; Gilda in Rigoletto; Micaela in Carmen; Mimi in La Boheme; Baby Doe in The Ballad of Baby Doe; Juliette in Romeo et Juliette; Nannetta in Falstaff, Washington Opera, 82. *Pos:* Perf with Washington Opera, Opera Co Boston, Theatre Musicale Paris, Cincinnati Opera, Central City Opera, Opera de Lyon, Baltimore Opera, Tulsa Opera, Pittsburgh Opera & New York Phil. *Mailing Add:* c/o Dorothy Cone Inc 250 W 57th St New York NY 10019

HUNT, MICHAEL FRANCIS
COMPOSER, EDUCATOR

b New Castle, Ind, Nov 28, 45. *Study:* St Louis Inst Music, BM, 68; Wash Univ, PhD, 74. *Works:* Three Interval Studies, Art Publ Soc, 69; Asymptopia I & II, perf by Los Angeles Phil Orch, 72 & St Louis Symph Orch, 73; The Television Suite, Art Publ Soc, 76; Other Realities, Mid-Am Dance Co, 82. *Teaching:* Assoc prof theory & comp, Fontbonne Col, 77- *Awards:* ASCAP Standard Awards. *Mem:* Am Music Ctr; ASCAP; Am Soc Univ Comp; Col Music Soc; Nat Asn Comp USA. *Mailing Add:* 2019 Sidney St Louis MO 63104

HUNTER, LAURA ELLEN
SAXOPHONE, EDUCATOR

b Ann Arbor, Mich, June 13, 56. *Study:* Consv Musique, Bordeaux, France, with J M Londeix, 74; Univ Mich, with Don Sinta, BMusEd, 79, MM(sax), 80. *Pos:* Mem, Duo Vivo, Great Lakes Perf Artists Assocs, 79- *Teaching:* Instr woodwinds, Tex Southern Univ, 80-; instr sax, Rice Univ, 81- *Awards:* Conct Artist Guild Award, 80; Ima Hogg Nat Young Artists Award, 81; Solo Fel, Nat Endowment Arts, 83. *Mem:* Nat Sax Alliance; Pi Kappa Lambda. *Rep:* Great Lakes Perf Artists Assocs 301 E Washington Ann Arbor MI 48104. *Mailing Add:* 3485 High Eugene OR 97405

HUNTLEY, LAWRENCE DON
EDUCATOR, FRENCH HORN

b Warren, Pa, July 31, 44. *Study:* Mansfield State Col, BS(mus educ), 66; ECarolina Univ, MM(mus educ), 67; studied horn with Philip Farkas, Ind Univ, Bloomington, Mus D, 75. *Rec Perf:* Third Horn, Bedford Springs Fest Orch, Pa, 82. *Pos:* Prin horn, Ridgefield Orch, 74- *Teaching:* Instrm music teacher, NY State Pub Sch, 67-70; prof music, Western Conn State Univ, 72- *Mem:* Music Educr Nat Conf; Conn Music Educr Asn; Am Asn Univ Prof; Am Fedn Musicians. *Publ:* Auth, A Survey of Brass Techniques Classes in the Music Education Curriculum in Selected Colleges and Universities in the United States, Nat Asn Col Wind & Perc Instr J, Vol XXIV, winter 75-76. *Mailing Add:* 189 Middle River Rd Danbury CT 06810

HURD, PETER WYETH
HARPSICHORD, EDUCATOR

b Philadelphia, Pa, Mar 22, 30. *Study:* Syracuse Univ, with Ernst Bacon, John Edmunds & Lionel Nowak, 51; Manhattan Sch Music, MM(comp), 54; Stanford Univ, with Putnam Aldrich, DMA, 71. *Teaching:* Instr theory, Southern Methodist Univ, Dallas, 57-61; asst prof theory, NMex State Univ, 62-64 & Tex Tech Univ, Lubbock, 67-69; assoc prof hist & theory, Holy Names Col, Oakland, 71- *Mailing Add:* 94 Bayo Vista Ave Oakland CA 94611

HURLEY, SUSAN
COMPOSER, EDUCATOR

b Winchester, Mass, Mar 30, 46. *Study:* Univ Mass, Amherst, BMus, 77; Sch Music, Ind Univ, 79-; Eastman Sch Music, MMus, 82. *Works:* Nocturne (violin & sax), comn & perf by R Bingham & R Frascatti, 82; Prana (orch & winds), Univ Mass Wind Ens, Amherst, 83. *Teaching:* Assoc instr comp, Ind Univ, Bloomington, 80-; fac mem theory & comp, Nat Music Camp, Interlochen, Mich, 82- *Mem:* Col Music Soc; Am Soc Univ Comp; Int League Women Comp. *Mailing Add:* PO Box 155 Pownal VT 05261

HURNEY, KATE
SOPRANO

b Quincy, Mass, Sept 14, 40. *Study:* Jackson Col, Tufts Univ, BA; New England Consv; Dalcroze Sch; Acad Chigiana, Siena, Italy; Int Opera Studio, Zurich; spec studies at Juilliad Sch, Mannes Sch Music & Manhattan Sch Music. *Rec Perf:* Various recordings for Decca, Poseidon, Sudwest Funk & Music Minos One. *Roles:* Performances with Zurich Operhaus, Karlsruhe Staatstheatre, Opera Paris, London, Houston Grand Opera, Boston Opera, Dallas Civic Opera & many others. *Pos:* Soloist in Mother Of Us All, currently & with Miami, Houston, Buffalo, Stamford & Int Bach Orch. *Awards:* Grants, Martha Baird Rockefeller Found; fel, Avalon Found. *Mailing Add:* 235 W 76th St Apt 10B New York NY 10023

HURSH-MEAD, RITA VIRGINIA
WRITER, MUSICOLOGIST

b Mifflinburg, Pa, Aug 15, 26. *Study:* Conn Col, BA, 48; Western Reserve Univ, 66-67; Wayne State Univ; Hunter Col, with H Wiley Hitchcock, MA, 70; City Univ New York, PhD, 78. *Pos:* Asst to dir & prod ed, Inst Studies Am Music Monogr Ser, 75-76; actg dir, Inst Studies Am Music, 76-79. *Teaching:* Adj lectr music, Hunter Col, 71-72; res asst, Brooklyn Col, 72-79, adj lectr, 73; res assoc, 79-80. *Bibliog:* Marshall Bialosky (auth), Book Review, Composer USA, fall 82; David Hamilton (auth), Henry Cowell's New Music, Music Libr Asn Notes, Dec, 82; Dika Newlin (auth), Henry Cowell's New Music, Pan Pipes of Sigma Alpha Iota, winter 82. *Mem:* Am Musicol Soc; Music Libr Asn; Sonneck Soc. *Interests:* American music; contemporary music; Henry Cowell. *Publ:* Auth, Cowell, Ives and New Music, Musical Quart, 10/80; Latin American Accents in New Music, Latin Am Music Rev, fall/winter 82; Henry Cowell's New Music Society, J Musicol, 10/82; Tchaikovsky, Shakespeare and Related Music, Musical Heritage Rev, Vol 7, No 4; Today's Music: Three American Composers, In: Women Making Music, Univ Calif Press (in press). *Mailing Add:* 300 Mercer St Apt 6M New York NY 10003

HURT, CHARLES RICHARD
TROMBONE, EDUCATOR

b Bristol, Va, May 19, 47. *Study:* Univ Tenn, BS(music), 69; Northwestern Univ, with Frank Crisafulli, MMus, 72; Univ Tex, with Donald Knaub; private study with Carsten Svanberg. *Pos:* Prin trombonist, Austin Symph Orch, 78- *Teaching:* Instr trombone, Southwest Tex State Univ, 77- *Mem:* Int Trombone Asn; Col Music Soc; Tex Music Educr Asn; Nat Asn Col Wind and Perc Teachers. *Mailing Add:* c/o Austin Symph 1101 Red River Austin TX 78701

HURWITZ, ISAAC
VIOLIN, EDUCATOR

Study: Harvard Univ, BA; Juilliard Sch, MS; Royal Col Music, London; studied violin with Ivan Galamian & Dorothy DeLay, chamber music with Leonard Shure & the Juilliard Quartet & cond with Otto-Werner Mueller & Wolfgang von der Nahmer. *Pos:* Mem, Hartford Symph, Hartford Chamber Orch & Worcester String Quartet; recitalist, Wigmore Hall & Carnegie Recital Hall, in Cologne & Munich & at various Am cols & univ. *Teaching:* Fac mem, Juilliard Prep Div, 92nd St Y, Wesleyan Univ & Perf Arts Sch Worcester; asst dir, Merrywood Music Sch, 62-65; dir instrm music, Wesleyan Univ, 66-77; fac mem violin & chamber music, Longy Sch Music, currently. *Awards:* Fulbright Fel, 58-59. *Mailing Add:* Longy Sch Music One Follen St Cambridge MA 02138

HURWITZ, ROBERT IRVING
EDUCATOR, CONDUCTOR

b Bronx, NY, Nov 7, 39. *Study:* Brooklyn Col, AB, 61; Ind Univ, Bloomington, MM, 65, PhD, 70. *Pos:* Music dir & cond, Ore Mozart Players, 82- *Teaching:* Assoc prof theory, Univ Ore, 65-; exchange prof music, Kirkby Fields Col Educ, Liverpool, England, 69-70; vis assoc prof theory, Univ Ariz, 75-76. *Awards:* Fulbright Grant; Ersted Award Distinguished Teaching, Univ Ore. *Mem:* Am Musicol Soc (secy, 78-79); Soc Music Theory. *Mailing Add:* 2908 Washington St Eugene OR 97405

HUSA, KAREL
COMPOSER, CONDUCTOR

b Prague, Czechoslovakia, Aug 7, 21; US citizen. *Study:* Consv Music, Prague, BM & MM, 45; Acad Musical Arts, DMA, 47; Ecole Normale Musique, Paris, lic, 48; Consv Music, Paris, dipl, 49; studied privately with A Honegger & Nadia Boulanger. *Works:* Sonata for Violin and Piano, 72, Sonata for Piano No 2, 76, Monodrama (ballet), 76, Am American Te Deum (chorus, bar solo & orch), 77, The Trojan Woman (ballet), 81, Work for Orchestra (in prep) & Orchestral Work (in prep), AMP. *Rec Perf:* Miraculous Mandarin (suite by Bartok), 54 & Symphonie No I (Brahms), 55, Club Francais Disque; Fantasies for Orchestra, Cornell Rec, 61 & Grenadilla, 81; Mosaiques for Orchestra, 65 & Symphonie, Serenade, Nocturne, 71, CRI; Music for Prague 1968 and Appotheosis of this Earth, Golden Crest Rec, 72; Monodrama and Apotheosis of this Earth, Louisvle Rec, 83. *Pos:* Guest cond, Czechoslovak Radio, Prague, 45-46 & European radios, 46-54. *Teaching:* Mem jury comp, Consv Paris, France, 49-54 & Fontainebleau Sch Music & Arts, France, 51, 52-53; asst prof, Cornell Univ, 54-56, assoc prof, 56-62, prof, 62-72, Kappa Alpha Professorship, 72- *Awards:* Czechoslovak Acad Arts & Sci Award for Sinfonietta, 48; Guggenheim Found Fel, 64-65; Pulitzer Prize Music, 69. *Bibliog:* Elliott W Galkin (auth), Deserving Pulitzer Prize Winner, Baltimore Sun, 5/11/69; Shirley Fleming (auth), Musician of the Month, Musical Am, High Fidelity, 7-8/69; Dr Lawrence W Hartzell (auth), Karel Husa: The Man and the Music, Musical Quart, Vol LXII, No 1. *Mem:* Assoc mem, Belgian Acad Arts & Sci; assoc mem, Soc Auteurs, Comp & Ed Musique, Paris; assoc mem, BMI; assoc mem, Am Music Ctr; Am Symph Orch League. *Rep:* MAA 224 King St Englewood NJ 07631. *Mailing Add:* 1032 Hanshaw Rd Ithaca NY 14950

HUSTON, THOMAS SCOTT, JR
COMPOSER, EDUCATOR

b Tacoma, Wash, Oct 10, 16. *Study:* Eastman Sch Music, BMus, 41, MMus, 42, PhD, 52. *Works:* Symphony No 3 Four Phantasms, Chicago Symph Orch, 68; Phenomena, Heritage Quartet, 68; Sounds at Night (brass), Betty Glover, 75; Intensity No 11, Tufts Univ, 77; Shadowy Waters, Sonos III Trio, 77; Time-Reflections (cantata), comn by WGVC FM Radio, perf by Moorhead State Univ, 79; Symphony No VI, The Human Condition, Gerhard Samuel, 82. *Teaching:* Instr piano, Univ Redlands, 46-47; instr piano & theory, Kearney State Teachers Col, 47-50; teaching asst, Eastman Sch Music, 50-52; prof comp & theory, Univ Cincinnati, 52- *Awards:* Lyre Award, Olympiad of Arts, A B Young-Lundstrom, 72. *Mem:* Broadcast Music Inc; Am Music Ctr; New York Comp Forum; Cincinnati Comp Guild. *Mailing Add:* 370 Terrace Ave Cincinnati OH 45220

HUSZTI, JOSEPH BELA
CONDUCTOR & MUSIC DIRECTOR, EDUCATOR

b Lorain, Ohio, Sept 27, 36. *Study:* Northwestern Univ, MM, 59; Oberlin Col, Univ Calif, Los Angeles & Univ Southern Calif with Howard Swan, Todd Duncan & Helmuth Rilling. *Rec Perf:* Univ Del Conct Choir, RCA Victor Custom, Dir Rec, 76; Young Artists Program at Tanglewood, Boston Symph

Orch, 77; Int Koorfest, Mirasound, Holland, 79; Univ Calif, Irvine, Conct Choir, AEA, Pasadena, Calif, 79. *Pos:* Dir, Young Artists Prog, Tanglewood, Lennox, Mass, 72-77; cond & music dir, Calif Chamber Choral, 77- *Teaching:* Assoc prof music, Univ Del, 66-72 & Boston Univ, 72-77; prof music, Univ Calif, Irvine, 77- *Awards:* First prize (cond), Llangollen Eisteddfod, Wales, 65; Ecumenical Medal, Vatican, Pope Paul IV, 65; ACE Award, Nat Cablenetwork, 82. *Mem:* Am Choral Dir Asn (pres western division, 81-83); life mem, Col Music Soc; Southern Calif Vocal Asn. *Mailing Add:* 787 S Woodland Orange CA 92669

HUTCHESON, JERE TRENT
COMPOSER, EDUCATOR

b Marietta, Ga, Sept 16, 38. *Study:* Stetson Univ, BM, 60; La State Univ, MM, 63; Mich State Univ, PhD, 66. *Works:* Fantaisie-Impromptu (piano), 74 & Passing, Passing, Passing (chamber with sop), 75, Seesaw Music Corp; Earth Gods Symph (woodwind quintet & wind orch), Am Comp Alliance, 77; Chromophonic Images (symphonic band), Margun Music Inc, 78; The Song Book (tenor & flute), 79, Concerto for Piano and Wind Orchestra, 80 & Metaphors, Ballet for Orchestra, 81, Am Comp Alliance. *Teaching:* Prof theory & comp, Mich State Univ, 65-, chairperson comp, 75- *Awards:* Distinguished Comp of Year, Nat Music Teachers Asn, 76; grants, Nat Endowment for Arts, 78 & Guggenheim, 80. *Mem:* BMI; Am Comp Alliance. *Publ:* Coauth, Music for High School Chorus, Allyn & Bacon, 67; auth, Musical Form and Analysis, A Programmed Course (2 vols), Crescendo, 72. *Mailing Add:* 6064 Abbott Rd Lansing MI 48823

HUTCHINS, FARLEY KENNAN
COMPOSER, EDUCATOR

b Neenah, Wis, Jan 12, 21. *Study:* Lawrence Consv Music, MusB, 44; Sch Sacred Music, Union Theol Sem, with T Tertius Noble, Harold Friedell & Normand Lockwood, MSM, 46, SMD, 51. *Works:* Set of American Folk Songs (orch); Fantasia (organ & brass choir); Suite for Flute and Piano; Concert Piece (tuba & piano); Six Medieval Songs (bar & four instrm); Passacaglia (trumpet & organ); Trumpet Concerto. *Pos:* Dir music, Westminister Presby Church, Akron, 57-83 & First Congregational Church, Akron, 75-83; keyboard, Akron Symph, 63-83; music critic, Akron Beacon J, 66- *Teaching:* Assoc prof organ & music hist, Miss Southern Col, 46-50; assoc prof music, Baldwin-Wallace Col, 51-55, prof 56-57; prof, Univ Akron, 57-83. *Mem:* Asn Am Guild Organists; Music Educr Nat Conf; Col Music Soc; Music Teachers Nat Asn. *Interests:* Renaissance and baroque music; composition. *Publ:* Auth, Buxtehude Dietrich: The Man, His Music, His Era, Music Textbook Co. *Mailing Add:* Music Dept Univ Akron Akron OH 44320

HUTCHINSON, LUCIE MARY
ADMINISTRATOR, EDUCATOR

b Portland, Ore, Mar 24, 19. *Study:* Marylhurst Col, BMus(piano perf), 47; Univ Southern Calif, Los Angeles, studied with Gustav Reese, Carl Parish, Halsey Stevens, Paul Pisk & piano with Nadia Reisenberg & Muriel Kerr, MMus(hist, lit & criticism), 58; Ind Univ, Bloomington, with Willi Apel, Walter Kaufmann, John R White, Bela Nagy & Abby Simon, PhD(musicol), 69. *Teaching:* Instr & chmn, Dept Music, Ft Wright Col, 62-64; fac mem, Marylhurst Col, 67-76, chmn, Music Div, 76-; chmn, Ore Col Music Adminr, 78-82. *Mem:* Col Music Soc; Am Musicol Soc; Int Musicol Soc. *Mailing Add:* Fac House Marylhurst OR 97036

HUTCHINSON, WILLIAM ROBERT
ADMINISTRATOR, EDUCATOR

b Woodstock, Ill, Jan 12, 29. *Study:* Am Consv Music, BMus, 50, MMus, 52; Univ Chicago, PhD, 61. *Teaching:* Assoc dean acad affairs, Univ Calif, Los Angeles, 70-, prof music, 79- *Interests:* Systematic musicology; aesthetics and psychology of music. *Publ:* Auth, The Problems of Universals in Music, In: Music and Man, 78; coauth, The Significance of the Acoustic Component of Consonance in Western Triads, J Musicol Res, 78; The Acoustic Component of Consonance, Interface, 78; Information Theory for Musical Continua, J Music Theory, 81; An Index of Melodic Activity, Interface. *Mailing Add:* Univ Calif 405 Hilgard Ave Los Angeles CA 90024

HUTCHISON, (DAVID) WARNER (WALTER HUDSON)
COMPOSER, EDUCATOR

b Denver, Colo, Dec 15, 30. *Study:* Lamont Sch Music, Univ Denver, 48; Rockmont Col, 49-51; Sch Church Music, Southwestern Baptist Theol Sem, BS(music), 54; NTex State Univ, with George Morey, Samuel Adler, Merrill Ellis & William Latham, MM, 56, PhD, 71; Sch Music, Ind Univ, with Roy Harris, 58; Eastman Sch Music, with Wayne Barlow & Kent Kennan, 59; French horn with Thomas Holden, Morris Secon & Clyde Miller. *Works:* Hornpiece I (horn & tape), 71; The Sacrilege of Alan Kent (baritone, orch & tape), 71; I Shall Have Music (double choir), 72; Suite a-la-mode (piano), 72; Antigone (tape), 72; Homage to Jackson Pollock (narrator, perc & slides), 73; Monday Music (piano & synthesizer), MacDowell Colony, 73. *Pos:* Guest cond with various choirs & bands; adjudicator, high sch music fests in Tenn, NY, Tex & NMex; ed, Proc Am Soc Univ Comp. *Teaching:* Dir bands & instr music, Houghton Col, 56-58 & Union Univ, 59-66; prof music, head dept & dir electronic music lab, NMex State Univ, 67- *Awards:* Ford Found & Music Educr Nat Conf Grant, 67-68; MacDowell Colony Fel, 73 & 74; ASCAP Standard Award, 74. *Mem:* ASCAP; Am Soc Univ Comp (mem exec bd, 73-); Phi Mu Alpha; Pi Kappa Lambda. *Mailing Add:* PO Box 3174 Univ Park Branch Las Cruces NM 88003

HYDE, FREDERICK B(ILL)
EDUCATOR, HARPSICHORD

b Springfield, Mass, May 23, 08. *Study:* Harvard Col, BA, 30; Yale Univ, MA, 42, PhD, 54. *Teaching:* From asst prof to prof music hist, Univ Ala, 49-78. *Mem:* Am Musicol Soc (chmn Gulf States chap, 63-66). *Publ:* Auth, Review of Herbert Schneider, Die französische Kompositionslehre in der ersten Hälfte des 17 Jahrhunderts, J Am Musicol Soc, summer 74. *Mailing Add:* 59 Four Winds Northport AL 35476

HYLA, LEE
COMPOSER, PIANO

b Niagara Falls, NY, Aug 31, 52. *Study:* Berkshire Music Ctr, 74; New England Consv, BMus, 75; State Univ NY, Stony Brook, MA, 78. *Works:* Concerto for Piano and Chamber Orchestra, perf by Rebecca La Breque, 74; Bassius Ophelius (solo bass), 75, Also Norway (13 instrm), 77, Revisible Light (solo piano), 78, Pre-Amnesia (solo alto sax), 80, Amnesia (six instrm), 80 & String Trio, 81, APNM. *Rec Perf:* Revisible Light, Opus One, 82. *Teaching:* Adj asst prof, St John's Univ, 82- *Awards:* Comp Fel, NJ Coun Arts, 81; Fel, MacDowell, Yaddo & Ossabow Island Found, 79-82. *Mailing Add:* 43 Bond St New York NY 10012

HYNES, ELIZABETH
SINGER

b Flint, Mich, Apr 30, 47. *Study:* Ind Univ, Bloomington, BMus. *Pos:* Perf, New York City Opera, Opera Soc Washington, Ft Worth Opera Asn, Ambler Music Fest, Chautauqua Opera & Colo Springs Opera Fest; concert perf, Nat Symph, Pittsburgh Symph & St Louis Symph. *Awards:* William Matheus Sullivan Musical Found Award, 75; Nat Opera Asn Grant, 76. *Rep:* Columbia Artists Mgt 165 W 57th St New York NY 10019. *Mailing Add:* 160 W 71st St 11C New York NY 10023

HYSON, WINIFRED PRINCE
COMPOSER, TEACHER-COACH

b Schenectady, NY, Feb 21, 25. *Study:* Radcliffe Col, AB, 45; Am Univ, 61-65. *Works:* An Island of Content, Abendmusik Series, 75; Memories of New England, Mu Phi Epsilon Conct Series, 76; Song to the Soul of a Child, Southern Md Choral Soc, 78; Gestures, Tidewater Music Fest, 78; View from Sandburg, Phillips Collection Conct, Lydian Chamber Players, 79; Three Love Songs from the Bengali, perf by Huntington Trio, Bucknell Col, 81; Songs of Job's Daughter, Arsis Press, 83. *Teaching:* Piano, music theory & comp, private studio, Bethesda, Md, 65- *Awards:* First Place, Annapolis Fine Arts Fest Comp Cont, 71; Second Place, Mu Phi Epsilon Original Comp Cont, 71; Individual Merit Award, Nat Fedn Music Clubs, 78. *Mem:* Md State Music Teachers Asn (dir music theory prog, 74-80 & vpres, 75-79); Friday Morning Music Club (chmn comp group, 77-81); Int League Women Comp; Southeastern Comp League; ASCAP. *Publ:* Auth, A Music Theory Program for Maryland Students, Am Music Teacher, 80; The Keyboard Companion, Hansen House, 83. *Mailing Add:* 7407 Honeywell Ln Bethesda MD 20814

HYTREK, THEOPHANE
COMPOSER, EDUCATOR

b Stuart, Nebr, Feb 28, 15. *Study:* Alverno Col, BM(organ); Wis Consv, BM(comp), MM(organ); DePaul Univ, with Leon Stein, MM(comp); Eastman Sch Music, with A Irvine McHose, Wayne Barlow & Bernard Rogers, PhD(comp), studied comp with Bernard Dieter & Samuel Lieberson. *Works:* Sonata for Piano and Violin, 49; Chamber Concerto (solo winds & orch), 55; The Hound of Heaven (tone poem); Prelude and Allegro for Oboe and Piano, 55; Violin Sonata, 62; Postlude-Partita on the Old One Hundredth (organ), 67; Psalms (organ & instrm), comn by Am Guild Organists, 69. *Teaching:* Mem fac, Alverno Col, 41-, chairperson music dept, 56-68, prof, 68-74. *Awards:* Nat Asn Col Wind & Perc Instr Award, 59; Wis Fedn Music Clubs Award, 62; Am Guild Organists Award, 67. *Publ:* Auth, Aspects of Style in the Performance of Organ in Developing Teaching Skills in Music, Cath Univ Press, 60; Facing Reality in the Liturgical Music Apostulate Contained in the Crisis in Church Music, Liturgical Conf, Washington, DC, 67. *Mailing Add:* 3401 S 39th St Milwaukee WI 53215

I

IANNACCONE, ANTHONY
COMPOSER, CONDUCTOR

b Brooklyn, NY, Oct 14, 43. *Study:* Manhattan Sch Music, with Vittorio Giannini & David Diamond, BM, 66, MM, 68; Eastman Sch Music, with Samuel Adler, PhD, 73. *Works:* Lysistrata for Orchestra, Seesaw Music Corp, 68; Rituals for Violin and Piano, 73, Parodies for Woodwind Quintet, 74 & Bicinia for Flute and Sax, 75, Carl Fischer; Trio for Flute, Clarinet, Piano, Theodore Presser Inc, 79; Walt Whitman Song for Chorus, Soloists and Winds, E C Schirmer Music Co, 81; Images of Song and Dance, Neil A Kjos Music Co, 83. *Rec Perf:* Walt Whitman Song, Redwood Rec, 83; Images of Song and Dance No 1, Images of Song and Dance No 2, After a Gentle Rain & Plymouth Trilogy, Cornell Univ Rec, 83. *Teaching:* Instr music lit, cond & orch, Manhattan Sch Music, 68-70; prof, comp, orch & cond, Eastern Mich Univ, 71- *Awards:* Comp fel, Nat Endowment Arts, 74; Ravel Prize, Ravel Centenniary Comn, 76; Mo Public Radio Assoc Prize for Chamber Music, Univ Mo, 78. *Bibliog:* Joseph Machlis (auth), Anthony Iannaccone, In: Introduction to Contemporary Music, 79; Arthur Cohn (auth), Anthony Iannaccone, In: Recorded Classical Music, 81. *Mem:* ASCAP; Col Music Soc; Am Soc Univ Comp. *Mailing Add:* 521 Kewanee Ypsilanti MI 48197

IENNI, PHILIP CAMILLO
COMPOSER, EDUCATOR
b Newark, NJ, Sept, 23, 30. *Study:* Juilliard Sch Music, BS, 52, MS, 53. *Works:* The Passiaon According to St John, perf by San Francisco Symph & Univ Calif Chorus, 62. *Pos:* Asst ed & music critic, Musical Am Mag, 56-58. *Teaching:* Prof, San Francisco Consv, 58-60, Dominican Col San Rafael, 60-67 & Can Col, Calif, 69- *Mailing Add:* 739 Arlington Rd Redwood City CA 94062

IGELSRUD, DOUGLAS BENT
EDUCATOR, PERCUSSION
b Minneapolis, Minn, June 23, 41. *Study:* Univ Miami, BM, 63; Univ Iowa, MA, 65; Cleveland Inst Music, with Cloyd Duff, 68-69; studied with Saul Goodman, 75. *Works:* Soundings—Timpani Solo, Kendor Music, 79. *Rec Perf:* The Celestial Hawk (orch, perc & piano; Keith Jarrett), ECM, 80. *Pos:* Asst timpanist, San Antonio Symph Orch, 69-70; perc, Syracuse Symph Perc Ens, 71-; perc, Syracuse Symph Orch, 71-79, prin timpanist, 79- *Teaching:* Asst prof perc, Ithaca Col, 70-71. *Mem:* Percussive Arts Soc (pres, NY chap, 82-). *Mailing Add:* 45 Sherry Dr Syracuse NY 13219

IGESZ, BODO
DIRECTOR—OPERA
b Amsterdam, Netherlands, Feb 7, 35. *Study:* Amsterdam Univ, 52-57; Juilliard Sch Music, with Frederic Cohen, 57-60. *Pos:* Asst stage dir, Netherlands Opera, 60-63; stage dir, New York Metropolitan Opera, 63- & opera prod in US & Europe, 63-; translr opera libretti, currently. *Teaching:* Mem fac, Juilliard Sch Music, 59; instr lang, formerly; dramatic coach, currently. *Awards:* Holland-Am Found Grant, 58-60. *Mem:* Am Guild Musicians & Artists. *Mailing Add:* 55 W 76th St New York NY 10023

ILKU, ELYSE (ELIZABETH JEAN ILKU)
HARP, TEACHER
b Hartley, Iowa. *Study:* Iowa State Univ, 46-47; Iowa State Teacher's Col, 47-49; Curtis Inst Music, with Carlos Salzedo, dipl, 53. *Pos:* Mem, Columbia Mgt Tour Angelaires, 50-54; prin harp, New Orleans Symph, 54-57 & Detroit Symph, 58-83; staff harpist, CBC, Halifax, NS, 57-58. *Mem:* Sigma Alpha Iota. *Mailing Add:* 10785 Elgin Huntington Woods MI 48070

IMBRIE, ANDREW WELSH
COMPOSER, EDUCATOR
b New York, NY, Apr 6, 21. *Study:* Princeton Univ, AB, 42; Univ Calif, Berkeley, MA, 47; studied with Leo Ornstein & Roger Sessions. *Works:* Violin Concerto, 58, Fourth String Quartet, 69, Third Symphony, 71, Angle of Repose, 76 & Flute Concerto, 77, Shawnee Press; Short Story (piano), C F Peters, 82; Pilgrimage, perf by Collage Ens Boston, 83. *Pos:* Mem bd gov, San Francisco Symph Orch, currently. *Teaching:* Prof music, Univ Calif, Berkeley, 49-; mem fac, San Francisco Consv Music, currently. *Awards:* Am Acad & Inst Arts & Lett Award, 50; Walter W Naumburg Rec Award; Walter Hinrichsen Award for Comp. *Bibliog:* M Bogkan (auth), Andrew Imbrie: Third Quartet, Perspectives New Music, Vol 3, No 1. *Mem:* Koussevitzky Music Found Inc; Am Acad Arts & Sci; Am Acad & Inst Arts & Lett. *Publ:* Auth, Roger Sessions: In Honor of His Sixty-fifth Birthday, Perspectives New Music, 62; The Symphonies of Roger Sessions, Tempo, 72; Extra Measures and Metrical Ambiguity in Beethoven, Beethoven Studies, 73. *Rep:* BMI 40 W 57th St New York NY 10019. *Mailing Add:* 2625 Rose St Berkeley CA 94708

INGHAM, MICHAEL CURTIS
BARITONE
b Texhoma, Okla, July 16, 44. *Study:* Amarillo Col, AA, 64; Okla Univ, BM(singing), 67; Denver Univ, MA(singing), 70; Ind Univ, 70-72. *Rec Perf:* Spätlese/Drei Gesänge (Krenek), 77, Gesänge Des Späten Jahres (Krenek), 78 & The Dissembler (Krenek), 79, Orion; Spästlese (Krenek), 80, The Bell Tower (Krenek), 80 & Reisebuch Aus den Österreichischen Alpen (Krenek), 82, ORF. *Roles:* Scarpia in Tosca, Detroit Opera, 72; Escamillo in Carmen, Reno Opera, 72; Dandini in La Cenerentola, Bear Valley Fest, 76; Don Basilio in The Barber of Seville, Va Opera, 77; Don Quixote in El Retablo de Maese Pedro, Ojai Fest, 79; Bannadonna in The Bell Tower, Steirischer Herbst Fest, Graz, 80. *Teaching:* Assoc prof music, Univ Calif, Santa Barbara, 72- *Mailing Add:* 1129 San Pascual Santa Barbara CA 93101

INGLE, WILLIAM (BILLY EARL)
TENOR
b Tex, Dec 17, 34. *Study:* Westminster Choir Col, BM, 57; Acad Vocal Arts, cert, 63; Italy Opera House, with Luigi Ricci & Dr Piccozi, 63. *Rec Perf:* Scenes from Rigoletto, NBC, 61; Maschinist Hopkins, Austria Nat Symphonieorchester, Vienna, 73; Jahrmarkt, 78, Jeanne D'Arc, 81, The Prodigal Son, 81 & The Rake's Progress, 82, ORF-TV, Austria. *Roles:* Alfredo Germont in La Traviata, Städtische Buhnen Frankfurt am Main, Germany, 68; Don Ottavio in Don Giovanni, Landestheater Hannover, Germany, 68; Rosillon in The Merry Widow, Theater an der Wien, Vienna, 69; Duke in Rigoletto, Graz Vereinigte Bühnen, Austria, 72; Janek in Sache Macropolos, Deutsche Oper am Rhein, Düsseldorf, Germany, 75; Adorno in Simone Boccanegra, Bremen Opera House, Germany, 78; Lyonel in Martha, Braunschweig Staatstheater, Germany, 81. *Pos:* Solo opera tenor, Stadttheater Bremerhaven, Germany, 66-68; leading lyr tenor, Graz Opera House, Austria, 68-72 & Linz Opera House, Austria, 72- *Awards:* Fulbright Grant, 63. *Mailing Add:* Hauserstrasse 13 4040 Linz Austria

INGLEFIELD, RUTH KARIN
HARP, EDUCATOR
b Plainfield, NJ, Nov 30, 38. *Study:* Goucher Col, BA, 60; Paris Consv, Ire Prix Harp, 60; Col Consv Music, Univ Cincinnati, MM, 70, PhD, 73. *Works:* Songs/Solos for Sonja, Int Harp Inc, 75. *Rec Perf:* Ruth K Inglefield Plays Works of Roush, Bach & Debussey, 83. *Pos:* Conct harpist, Europe & US, 60- *Teaching:* Assoc prof harp & music hist, Bowling Green State Univ, 73- *Awards:* Outstanding Teacher Award, Bowling Green State Univ, 80; Outstanding Serv to Profession, Am Harp Soc, 82. *Mem:* Int Harp Asn; Am Harp Soc (regional dir, 81-83); Am Musicol Soc. *Interests:* The history and biography of the harp; harp notation. *Publ:* Auth, Marcel Grandjany: Biography, 77 & ed & contrib, Music in American Education and Society, 82, Univ Press; coauth, Writing for the Pedal Harp, Univ Calif Press, 83. *Rep:* Beaux Arts Concts Suite 1102 210 Fifth Ave New York NY 10010. *Mailing Add:* Col Musical Arts Bowling Green State Univ Bowling Green OH 43403

INGRAHAM, PAUL
FRENCH HORN, EDUCATOR
Study: Studied French horn with Gunther Schuller, John Barrows & Morris Secon; Ithaca Col, BS. *Pos:* Assoc first horn, Metropolitan Opera Orch, formerly; solo horn, Minneapolis Symph, formerly, Casals Fest Orch, formerly, Mostly Mozart Fest, currently & New York City Ballet, currently; mem, New York Brass Quintet, 63- *Teaching:* Mem fac French horn, Yale Sch Music, 65- & Manhattan Sch Music, 80-; vis lectr, Hartt Sch Music, 69- *Mailing Add:* Hartt Sch Music Univ Hartford West Hartford CT 06117

INSKO, WYATT (MARION), III
ORGAN, EDUCATOR
b Lexington, Ky, July 31, 29. *Study:* Ind Univ, BM, 50, PhD, 64; Univ Mich, MM, 51. *Pos:* Organist & choirmaster, Fourth Presby Church, 62-68; harpsichordist, Sinfonia Concertante, San Francisco, 81- *Teaching:* Chmn, Music Dept, San Francisco Col Women, 68-78; fac mem, San Francisco Consv Music, 69- *Mem:* Am Guild Organists (mem exec bd San Francisco chap, 83-); Va Chamber Music Soc (mem bd dir, 62-64). *Publ:* Contribr, Beethoven as Organist and Organ Composer, In: A Beethoven Dict, Philosophical Libr, 56; ed, The Cracow Organ Tablature (1548), Monumenta Musicae in Polonia (in prep). *Mailing Add:* 1201 Ortega St San Francisco CA 94122

INTILI, DOMINIC JOSEPH
EDUCATOR, PIANO
b Cleveland, Ohio, May 2, 26. *Study:* Consv Music, Oberlin Col, BMus, 50, MMus, 51; Case Western Reserve Univ, PhD, 77. *Teaching:* Instr piano, Cleveland Music Sch Settlement, 53-62; chmn music dept, Mercy Col Detroit, 62-65; prof music, Ind Univ, 65- *Awards:* Distinguished Teaching Award, Commonwealth Pa, 80 & 83. *Mem:* Pa Music Teachers Asn; Col Music Soc; Am Musicol Soc; Music Teachers Nat Asn. *Mailing Add:* 656 Grant St Indiana PA 15701

INWOOD, MARY B B
COMPOSER, TEACHER
b Boston, Mass, July 27, 28. *Study:* Yale Sch Music, 46-47; Queens Col, BA, 75, MA, 79; City Univ New York, currently. *Works:* Three Movements for Brass Sextet, 75, String Quartet #III, 76, Seesaw Music Corp; Cheerful and Tender Songs, L'Art Musique Corp, 80; Seven Bagatelles for Wind Trio, 81 & Trio for Oboe, Horn & Piano, 83, Seesaw Music Corp; Incidental Music for The Cenci (Shelly), comn by PM Club, City Univ New York, 82. *Pos:* Col asst, Music Libr, Brooklyn Col, 83. *Teaching:* Instr music theory, Roosa Sch Music, 81-83. *Mem:* ASCAP; Col Music Soc; Am Soc Univ Comp. *Mailing Add:* 166 Congress St Brooklyn NY 11201

IRBY, FRED, III
EDUCATOR, TRUMPET
b Mobile, Ala, July 20, 48. *Study:* Grambling State Univ, BS, 71; Southern Ill Univ, Edwardsville, MMus, 74; study with Susan Slaughter. *Pos:* Trumpet, St Louis Munic Opera, 72-74 & Kennedy Ctr Opera House Orch, 76- *Teaching:* Instr music, St Louis pub sch, 71-74; prof trumpet, Howard Univ, 74- *Mem:* Music Educr Nat Conf; Nat Asn Jazz Educr; Int Trumpet Guild. *Mailing Add:* 14829 Fireside Dr Silver Spring MD 20904

IRVIN, MARJORY RUTH
EDUCATOR, WRITER
b Brooklyn, Ill, July 31, 25. *Study:* Ill Wesleyan Univ, BM, 46, MM, 48; studied with Claudio Arrau, Joseph Battista, Jeanne-Marie Darre & Rudolph Reuter. *Teaching:* Assoc prof piano & theory, Milwaukee-Downer Col, 48-64; prof, Lawrence Univ, 64- *Mem:* Col Music Soc; Sigma Alpha Iota; Pi Kappa Lambda; Nat Consortium Computer-Based Music Instr. *Interests:* Life and music of Augusta Holmes (1847-1903) and Marcelle de Manziarly (1899-). *Publ:* Auth, Incompatibility—Diabolus Digitus, Piano Quart, 71; A New Look for New Sounds, Clavier, 73; It's George, Not Jazz, Am Music Teacher, 73; coauth, Music in Perspective, Harcourt Brace, 76; auth, Women's Work is Never Done, Touchstone, 80. *Mailing Add:* 1749 N Meade St Appleton WI 54911

IRVINE, DEMAR (BUEL)
EDUCATOR, COMPOSER
b Modesto, Calif, May 25, 08. *Study:* Univ Calif, Los Angeles, AA, 27; Univ Calif, Berkeley, BA, 29, MA(music), 31; George Ladd Prix de Paris, 31-33; Stern Consv, Berlin; Schola Cantorum, Paris; studied with J Müller-Herman and J Katay, Vienna; Harvard Univ, PhD, 37. *Works:* String Quartets No 1, 31, No 2, 34 & No 3, 45; Romantic Overture (orch), 32; Sonatina for Piano,

43; In the Garden (song cycle), 44; Symphonies No 1, 53 & No 2, 56; Reynard the Fox (fable for wind sinfonietta), 55. *Teaching:* Instr, Crane Music Dept, State Normal Sch, Potsdam, NY, 35-36; music dir, Am Int Col, 36-37; instr, Sch Music, Univ Wash, 37-38, asst prof, 38-47, assoc prof, 47-60, grad prog adv, 50-68, prof 60-78, dir sch music, 62-63, prof emer, 78- *Mem:* Am Musicol Soc. *Publ:* Auth, Methods of Research in Music, 45; Writing About Music, 56 & 68; Massenet: A Chronicle of His Life and Times, 74. *Mailing Add:* 4904 NE 60th St Seattle WA 98115

IRVING, JANET
EDUCATOR, SINGER
Study: Barnard Col; Columbia Univ, BS(music educ); studied voice with Frantz Proschowski, Cecille Gilly, Jacques Stuckgold & Toti dal Monte. *Pos:* Mem, Columbia Choir & Dessoff Choir; soloist, numerous broadcasts & symph concerts, US, Europe & SAfrica; recitalist, Gardner Museum & in Boston area. *Teaching:* Mem fac, New England Consv Music, 63-66; mem fac voice, Longy Sch Music, currently. *Mem:* Nat Asn Teachers Singing (vpres, currently). *Mailing Add:* Longy Sch Music One Follen St Cambridge MA 02138

IRVING, ROBERT AUGUSTINE
CONDUCTOR
b Winchester, Great Britain, Aug 28, 13. *Study:* New Col, Oxford Univ, BM, 35; Royal Col Music, ARCM, 36. *Works:* As You Like It, New York Theater, 49; music for Floodtide (film), 49. *Rec Perf:* Numerous rec with Phil Orch, Royal Phil Orch, Covent Garden Orch & Conct Arts Orch New York, 50- *Pos:* Assoc cond, BBC (Scottish Orch), 46-49; musical dir & adv, Royal Ballet, England, 49-58; musical dir & prin cond, New York City Ballet, 58-; guest cond with leading Am & English symph orchs. *Awards:* Capezio Award for Serv to World of Dance, 75. *Mailing Add:* 160 W End Ave #27T New York NY 10023

IRWIN, PHYLLIS ANN
ADMINISTRATOR, EDUCATOR
b Manhattan, Kans, Mar 24, 29. *Study:* San Diego State Univ; Vienna State Acad Music & Dramatic Art; Hofstra Col; Univ Houston, BS, 51, MEd, 57; Mozarteum, Salzburg; Columbia Univ, EdD, 65. *Teaching:* Instr music, Houston Independent Sch, 51-61; grad asst & instr music, Teachers Col, Columbia Univ, 61-63; from asst prof to prof, Calif State Univ, Fresno, 63- & chmn, Music Dept, 82- *Mem:* Calif Music Educr Asn; Music Educr Nat Conf; Col Music Soc. *Publ:* Auth, Music Fundamentals: A Performance Approach, Holt, Rinehart & Winston, 82; coauth, The Teacher, The Child and Music, Wadsworth Publ, 85. *Mailing Add:* 6012 N Harrison Fresno CA 93711

ISAAC, CECIL
CONDUCTOR, EDUCATOR
b Indianapolis, Ind, Oct 30, 30. *Study:* Oberlin Consv Music, BM, 54; Oberlin Col, BA, 54; Columbia Univ, study with Paul Henry Lang, MA, 59, study with Curt Sachs & Erich Hertzmann, MPhil, 73. *Pos:* Cond, Sherman Symph, 66- *Teaching:* Lectr, Columbia Univ, 59-62; from asst prof to prof, Austin Col, 62- *Awards:* Teacher Award, Danforth Found, 65; Grant, Nat Endowment Humanities, 78 & 81. *Mem:* Am Musicol Soc; Am Symph Orch League Cond Guild. *Interests:* Beethoven; orchestral music of late 18th-century; early German romanticism. *Mailing Add:* 428 Anita Dr Sherman TX 75090

ISAAC, GERALD SCOTT
TENOR
b Toronto, Ontario, Can, Feb 22, 54. *Roles:* Njegus, San Francisco Opera, 81; Chicago Lyric Opera, 81 & Can Opera Co, 81; Orlofsky in Die Fledermaus, Chicago Lyric Opera, 82 & Can Opera Co, 82; Orestes in La Belle Helene, Can Opera Co, 83; Njegus, New York City Opera, 83. *Pos:* Vocal coach, Stratford Fest, Can, 77. *Awards:* Maureen Forester Gutherie Award, Stratford Fest, Can, 77. *Mailing Add:* c/o Shaw Conct Inc 1995 Broadway New York NY 10023

ISAAK, DONALD J
PIANO, EDUCATOR
b SDak, Oct 23, 27. *Study:* Juilliard Sch Music, 47-50; Akad Musik Darstellende Kunst, Vienna, Austria; Northwestern Univ, MM, 57 & DMus, 63. *Rec Perf:* Violin and Piano Sonatas of Franck, Richard Strauss, Brahms and Szymanowski, with Vincent Skowronski, Ebsko Rec, 76-82. *Teaching:* Assoc prof music, Ariz State Univ, 62-72 & Northwestern Univ, 71- *Awards:* Ariz Soc Arts & Lett Distinguished Serv Award, 71. *Mailing Add:* Sch Music Northwestern Univ Evanston IL 60201

ISBIN, SHARON
GUITAR & LUTE, EDUCATOR
b Minneapolis, Minn, Aug 7, 56. *Study:* Aspen Music Fest, with Oscar Ghiglia, 71-75; Banff Music Fest, with Alirio Diaz, 72; Yale Univ, BA, 78, Yale Sch Music, MMus, 79; studied with Rosalyn Tureck. *Rec Perf:* Sharon Isbin (guitar), 76 & Sharon Isbin, Vol II, 79, Sound Environment & Sine Qua Non; Sharon Isbin Plays Spanish Works for Guitar, 80 & Sharon Isbin (guitar recital), 80, Denon/Digital; Sharon Isbin & Carol Winenc, Pro Arte Rec, 83. *Teaching:* Asst instr guitar, Aspen Music Fest, 73; col sem lectr, Yale Univ, 76-78; prof guitar, Manhattan Sch Music, 79- *Awards:* Guitar '75 Award, Toronto, 75; Munich Int, 76; Queen Sofia 1979, Madrid, 79. *Bibliog:* Beverly Maher (auth), Sharon Isbin—Young Poet of the Guitar, Music J, 3-4/80; D R Martin (auth), Sharon Isbin, Guitar Player, 5/80; Soe MacCreadie (auth), Rosalyn Tureck & Sharon Isbin, Guitar, London, fall 81. *Mem:* Sigma Alpha Iota. *Rep:* Columbia Artists Mgt Inc 165 W 57th St New York NY 10019. *Mailing Add:* 418 Central Park West New York NY 10025

ISRAEL, BRIAN M
EDUCATOR, COMPOSER
b New York, NY, Feb 5, 51. *Study:* Lehman Col, City Univ New York, with Ulysses Kay, BA, 71; Cornell Univ, with Robert Palmer & Burrill Phillips, MFA, 74; DMA, 75. *Works:* Dance Suite (baritone horn), Sonata No 1 (2 tubas), Serenda (3 trumpets), Sonata No 2 (2 tubas), Suite (solo tuba), Tower Music (3 tubas), Sonata da Chiesa (4 trumpets), Theo Presser. *Teaching:* Asst, Cornell Univ, 72-75; assoc prof, Syracuse Univ, 75- *Awards:* Cornell Fel, 71-72; first prize, Chautauqua Chamber Singers Choral Compt, 83. *Mailing Add:* 126 Wilson Syracuse NY 13203

ISRAELIEVITCH, GAIL BASS
HARP, EDUCATOR
b Chicago, Ill, Dec 26, 49. *Study:* Consv Nat France, 70; Ind Univ, BM, 71; Northwestern Univ. *Pos:* Second harp, Milwaukee Symph Orch, 74-76 & St Louis Symph Orch, 79- *Teaching:* Prof harp, Jeunesse Musicale, Mt Oxford, Can, 81 & Nat Music Camp, Interlochen, Mich, 82. *Bibliog:* Namar Pellegrini, Radio Shop, WFMT, Chicago, 75; Musician in the Kitchen, St Louis Globe Democrat, 82. *Mailing Add:* 6965 Pershing St Louis MO 63130

ISRAELIEVITCH, JACQUES
VIOLIN, EDUCATOR
b Cannes, France, May 6, 48; nat US. *Study:* Paris Consv, 64; Ind Univ, perf cert, 68. *Rec Perf:* Violin & iano Sonato (Thomas Beversdorf), Orion Rec, 74. *Pos:* Conct performer throughout Western Europe, Japan, Greece & North Am; harpist, Ind Univ, 67-72; asst concertmaster, Chicago Symph Orch, 72-78; founder, Chicago Pops Orch, 75; concertmaster, Eloise & Oscar Johnson Jr Chair, St Louis Symph Orch, 78-; artist in residence, Webster Univ, St Louis, 78- *Teaching:* Instr, Ind Univ Sch Music, 70-72; mem fac, Am Consv Music, 74-78. *Awards:* First Prize, Paris Consv Music, 64; winner, Paganini Int Compt, Genoa, Italy, 65. *Mem:* Am String Teachers Asn. *Mailing Add:* 6965 Pershing St Louis MO 63130

ISTOMIN, EUGENE
PIANO
b New York, NY, Nov 26, 25. *Study:* Studied with Kyriena Siloti; Mannes Sch Music, 35-38; Curtis Inst Music, with Rudolf Serkin & Mieczyslav Horszowski, 39-43. *Rec Perf:* Schumann Concerto & Rachmaninoff Second Concerto, Columbia Masterworks. *Pos:* Mem, Adolf Busch Chamber Players, 44-45 & Istomin, Stern, Rose Trio, 61-; performer, Casals Fest & PR Fest, 50- *Awards:* Philadelphia Youth Cont Winner, 43; Leventritt Award, 43. *Mailing Add:* c/o ICM Artists Ltd 40 W 57th St New York NY 10019

IVEY, JEAN EICHELBERGER
PIANO, COMPOSER
b Washington, DC, July 3, 23. *Study:* Trinity Col, AB, 44; Peabody Consv Music, MMus(piano), 46; Eastman Sch Music, studied comp with Wayne Barlow, Kent Kennan & Bernard Rogers, MMus(comp), 56; Univ Toronto, studied electronic music with Myron Schaeffer & Hugh Le Caine, DMus, 72. *Works:* O Come Bless the Lord (mixed chorus), 66 & Lord, Hear My Prayer (mixed chorus), 66, McLaughlin & Reilly; Terminus (ms & tape, text by R W Emerson), 72, Aldebaran (viola & tape), 73, Three Songs of Night (song cycle for sop, flute, clarinet, viola, cello, piano & tape), 73, Hera, Hung from the Sky (ms, 12 instrm & tape, text by C Kizer), 74, Music for Viola and Piano, 75 & Skaniadaryo (piano & tape), 75, C Fisher Publ; and many others. *Rec Perf:* Music by Jean Eichelberger Ivey; Pinball; Hera, Hung from the Sky; Cortege for Charles Kent; rec on Folkway Rec, CRI & Grenadilla. *Pos:* Ed, Am Soc Univ Comp Newslett, 68-70; piano recitalist throughout US, Mex & Europe; guest comp & judge comp contests. *Teaching:* Trinity Col, 45-55, Cath Univ Am, 52-55, Misericordia Col, 55-57 & Xavier Univ, La, 60-62; mem fac comp & founder & dir, Electronic Music Studio, Peabody Consv Music, 69- *Awards:* ASCAP Annual Awards, 72-; Grants, Martha Baird Rockefeller Fund, 73, Nat Endowment Arts, 78 & others. *Bibliog:* Article, Am Music Ctr Newslett, Vol 20, No 3; A Woman Is, NBC TV; interview, Yale Contemp Oral Hist Proj. *Mem:* Fel, MacDowell Colony; League Comp, Int Soc Contemp Music (dir US sect, 72-75 & 79-); ASCAP; Am Soc Univ Comp; Col Music Soc. *Publ:* Contribr, Electronic Music: A Listener's Guide, 73. *Mailing Add:* 320 W 90th St New York NY 10024

J

JABLONSKY, STEPHEN
EDUCATOR, COMPOSER
b New York, NY, Dec 5, 41. *Study:* City Col New York, BA, 62; NY Univ, MA & PhD, 73. *Works:* Wisconsin Death Trip, New York Phil, 76. *Pos:* Cond fel, Nat Orch Asn, 73-75. *Teaching:* Assoc prof theory & cond, City Col New York, 68- *Awards:* Comp grant, Nat Endowment Arts, 75. *Mailing Add:* 155 Staples Rd Easton CT 06612

JACKSON, ANITA LOUISE
EDUCATOR, PIANO
b Durant, Miss. *Study:* Jackson State Univ, BME, 59; Northwestern Univ, MMus, 64, PhD, 75. *Teaching:* Assoc prof music, Jackson State Univ, 66- *Mem:* Music Teachers Nat Conf; Music Educr Nat Asn; Col Music Soc; Soc Res Music Educ. *Interests:* Keyboard music. *Publ:* Auth, A Case for Mainstreaming, Am Music Teacher, 79; The Effect of Group Size on Individual Achievement in Beginning Piano Classes, J Res Music Educ, 80; Piano Lessons at Age 4.9, Am Music Teacher, 82; The Arts/The Sciences: A Student Research Profile, Coun Res Music Educ Bulletin, 83. *Mailing Add:* Box 17016 Jackson State Univ Jackson MS 39217

JACKSON, BARBARA ANN GARVEY
EDUCATOR

b Normal, Ill, Sept 27, 29. *Study:* Univ Ill, BM, 50; Eastman Sch Music, MM, 52; Stanford Univ, PhD, 59; Meadowmount Sch Music, summer 59; Baroque Perf Inst, Oberlin Col, summers 78 & 81-83. *Pos:* Mass (Isabella Leonarda), Leonarda Prod, 82. *Teaching:* Asst prof music Univ Ark, 54-56, assoc prof, 61-70, prof, 71-; spec music teacher, Los Angeles Pub Sch, 56-57; asst prof music, Ark Tech Univ, 57-61. *Mem:* Sigma Alpha Iota; Am String Teachers Asn; Am Musicol Soc; Viola da Gamba Soc Am; Col Music Soc. *Interests:* Seventeenth & 18th century music, especially violin music and playing; women composers. *Publ:* Coauth (with Benward), Practical Beginning Theory, William C Brown, 82. *Mailing Add:* 235 Baxter Lane Fayetteville AR 72701

JACKSON, BIL
CLARINET

b Fulton, Mo, June 13, 60. *Study:* Interlochen Arts Acad, with Frank Kowalsky, 74-78; Northwestern Univ, with Robert Marcellus, 78-80. *Rec Perf:* Premiere Rhapsodie, Golden Crest Rec, 78; Mozart Concerto, Hawaii Rec Inc, 81. *Pos:* Prin clarinet, Honolulu Symph, 80-82, Aspen Chamber Symph, 80- & Denver Symph, 82- *Teaching:* Fac mem clarinet & chamber music, Aspen Music Fest, 83- *Awards:* Winner, Int Clarinet Compt, Denver, Colo, 75 & 76; Alternate Third, Int Clarinet Compt, Prague, Czechoslovakia, 81. *Mem:* Int Clarinet Soc. *Rep:* 715 S Raritan Denver CO 80223. *Mailing Add:* 3 Staff Circle Fulton MO 65251

JACKSON, BRINTON
LIBRARIAN, ADMINISTRATOR

b Kalispell, Mont, May 19, 19. *Study:* Columbia Teachers Col, MA; Mont State Univ, BM, 43. *Pos:* Circulation librn, Juilliard Sch, 65-79, head librn, 79- *Mailing Add:* 45 Riverside Dr New York NY 10024

JACKSON, DENNIS CLARK
EDUCATOR, BARITONE

b Dallas, Tex, Dec 30, 37. *Study:* Tex Wesleyan Col, BA, 60; Wichita State Univ, MM, 63; Univ Mich, with Pierre Bernac, John McCollum & Eugene Bossart, DMA, 70. *Rec Perf:* Gasparo, KMGH, Denver, 77. *Roles:* Falke, 75 & Father in Childhood of Christ, 76, Denver Symph; Danilo, Denver Opera, 77; Sharpless in Madama Butterfly, Greeley Phil, 79; Horace Tabor, Nebr, 83. *Pos:* Opera dir, Univ Colo, Boulder, 81- *Teaching:* Asst prof music, Union Col, Ky, 63-70; assoc prof voice & chmn dept music, Nebr Wesleyan Univ, 69-70; prof voice, Univ Colo, Boulder, 72- *Mem:* Nat Asn Teachers Singing (chmn nat conv, 80); Nat Opera Asn. *Publ:* Auth, 1980 Convention—Denver, Nat Asn Teachers Singing Bulletin, 11-12/79. *Mailing Add:* 920 Waite Dr Boulder CO 80303

JACKSON, DONNA CARDAMONE
EDUCATOR

b Utica, NY, Nov 16, 37. *Study:* Wells Col, AB, 59; Harvard Univ, AM, 64, PhD, 72. *Teaching:* Prof musicol, Sch Music, Univ Minn, 69- *Awards:* Fulbright Grant, 66-67; fel, Am Asn Univ Women, 67-68 & Am Coun Learned Soc, 76-77. *Mem:* Am Musicol Soc; Soc Musicol Ital. *Interests:* Italian Renaissance music. *Publ:* Auth, The Debut of the Canzone Villanesca Alla Napolitana, Studi Musicali, 75; Forme Metriche e Musicali Della Canzone Villanesca e Della Villanella Alla Napolitana, Rivista Ital Musicol, 77; Adrian Willaert and His Circle, A-R Ed, 78; The Canzone Villanesca Alla Napolitana and Related Forms, 1537-1570, UMI Res, 81; Madrigali a Tre et Arie Napolitane: A Typographical and Repertorial Study, J Am Musicol Soc, 82. *Mailing Add:* 890 18th Ave SE Minneapolis MN 55414

JACKSON, DOUGLAS
EDUCATOR, PERCUSSION

Study: Wichita State Univ, BMusEd, MMusEd. *Pos:* Guest cond, Hartt Symph, Repertory Orch, Chamber Winds & Symphonic Wind Ens. *Teaching:* Mem fac, Boston Univ, formerly & Wichita State Univ, formerly; assoc prof perc, Hartt Sch Music, 71- *Mem:* Percussive Arts Soc; Nat Asn Col Wind & Perc Instr; Music Educr Nat Conf. *Mailing Add:* Hartt Sch Music Univ Hartford West Hartford CT 06117

JACKSON, HANLEY
COMPOSER, EDUCATOR

b Bryan, Tex, June 7, 39. *Study:* Calif State Univ, Northridge, BA, 63; Calif State Univ, Long Beach, MA, 66; studied comp with Gerald Strang & Aurelio de la Vega. *Works:* Tangents II (orch), MCA, 70; A Child's Ghetto, Walton, 72; Cradle Hymn and Hodie, 75 & Tangents IV (piano solo), 75, Shawnee Press; Birds of Ogden, Jensen Publ, 80. *Teaching:* Lectr, Calif State Univ, Long Beach, 67-68; assoc prof comp, Kans State Univ, 68- *Awards:* Comp Award, Southwest Music Fest, 67; Kans Comp Yr, Nat Asn Music Clubs. *Mem:* ASCAP; Music Teachers Nat Asn (theory & comp chmn, 79-81); Am Music Ctr; Am Soc Univ Comp. *Publ:* Auth, Synthesis: Analog and Digital, L & M Publ, 82. *Mailing Add:* Music Dept Kans State Univ Manhattan KS 66506

JACKSON, HELEN TUNTLAND
ADMINISTRATOR

b Sioux Falls, SDak, July 7, 44. *Study:* Drake Univ, BME, 66; Eastman Sch Music, with Russell Saunders, MM(perf & lit), 70. *Pos:* Exec dir, David Hochstein Mem Music Sch, Rochester, NY, 71-; panel mem, NY State Coun Arts, 77-81; comnr, Nat Asn Sch Music, 79- *Mem:* Nat Guild Community Sch Arts (mem bd dir, 78-81). *Mailing Add:* David Hochstein Mem Music Sch 50 N Plymouth Ave Rochester NY 14614

JACKSON, ISAIAH (ALLEN)
CONDUCTOR

b Richmond, Va, Jan 22, 45. *Study:* Harvard Col, BA, 66; Stanford Univ, MA, 67; Juilliard Sch Music, MS, 69, DMA, 73. *Pos:* Asst cond, Am Symph, 70-71 & Baltimore Symph, 71-73; assoc cond, Rochester Phil, 73-; music dir, Flint Symph, 82- *Rep:* Class Div Regency Artists 9200 Sunset Blvd Los Angeles CA 90069. *Mailing Add:* 324 Culver Rd Rochester NY 14607

JACKSON, JAMES LEONARD
MUSIC DIRECTOR, ADMINISTRATOR

b Farmersville, Tex, Oct 17, 32. *Study:* Abilene Christian Univ, BS, 54; NTex State Univ, MMusEd, 60; Univ Okla, DMusEd, 70. *Teaching:* Choral dir, Garland Tex pub sch, 57-62 & 76-78; dean & choral dir, Christian Col Southwest, 62-71; chmn dept music, David Lipscomb Col, 78- *Mem:* Am Choral Dir Asn. *Publ:* Auth, Church Music Handbook, Williams Printing, 83. *Mailing Add:* 3800 Belmont Blvd Nashville TN 37215

JACKSON, RAYMOND T
PIANO, EDUCATOR

b Providence, RI, Dec 11, 33. *Study:* New England Consv, BMus, 55; Juilliard Sch, BS, 57, MS, 59, DMA, 73; Am Consv, dipl, 61. *Rec Perf:* Raymond Jackson Performance Records: The Black Artists Series, Cespico Rec, 81. *Pos:* Recitalist & orchestral soloist, internationally. *Teaching:* Asst prof music, Univ RI, summers 68-79 & Concordia Col, 70-77; instr piano, Mannes Col, 70-77; prof, Howard Univ, 77- *Awards:* Marguerite Long Int Piano Compt Award, Paris, 65; award, 10th Int Piano Compt, Rio de Janeiro, 65; Ford Found Fel, 71 & 72. *Bibliog:* Raoul Abdul (auth), Blacks in Classical Music, Providence J Bulletin, 76; George Kehler (auth), The Piano in Concert, Vol I. *Mem:* Nat Asn Negro Musicians; Chopin Club; Fri Morning Music Club; Pi Kappa Lambda. *Rep:* Int Artists Mgt Ltd 10572 Jason Lanee Columbia MD 21044. *Mailing Add:* 9205 Harvey Rd Silver Spring MD 20910

JACKSON, RICHARD H
LIBRARIAN

b New Orleans, La, Feb 15, 36. *Study:* Loyola Univ, BM, 58; Tulane Univ, MA, 62; Pratt Inst, MSLS, 68. *Pos:* Music librn, Maxwell Music Libr, Tulane Univ, 59-62; libr clerk, New Sch Social Res, 62-65; head Americana Collection, New York Pub Libr, 65- *Mem:* Music Libr Asn; Am Musicol Soc; Int Asn Study Popular Music; Am Music Ctr; Sonneck Soc (mem bd, 81-). *Interests:* Nineteenth century classical & popular American music. *Publ:* Auth, United States Music: Sources of Bibliographic and Collective Biography, Inst Studies Am Music, 73; ed, Piano Music of Louis Moreau Gottschalk, 74 & The Stephen Foster Song Book, 74 & Popular Songs of 19th-century America, 76, Dover Publ; co-ed, The Little Book of Louis Moreau Gottschalk, New York Publ Libr, Continuo Music Press, 76. *Mailing Add:* 111 Amsterdam Ave New York NY 10023

JACOB, KAREN HITE
MUSIC DIRECTOR, HARPSICHORD

b Wilkensburg, Pa, Feb 14, 47. *Study:* Univ NC, Greensboro, with Kathryn Eskey & Gordon Wilson, BM, 69; Univ NC, Chapel Hill, with James Pruett, MAT, 70; studied with Malcolm Bilson, Max von Egmond & Andrew Pledge. *Pos:* Founder & coordr, Charlotte Chamber Music Wkshp, 73-81; artist dir, Carolina Pro Musica (formerly Carolina Consort), 77- *Teaching:* Theory & harpsichord, Community Sch Arts, 72- *Bibliog:* John Alexander (dir), Interest in the Medieval (TV show), WPCQ TV, Charlotte, 81. *Mem:* Am Guild Organists; Choristers Guild Am; founding mem, Southeastern Hist Keyboard Soc. *Interests:* Music from 1100 to 1780. *Mailing Add:* 2516 E 5th St Charlotte NC 28204

JACOBI, ROGER EDGAR
ADMINISTRATOR, EDUCATOR

b Saginaw, Mich, Apr 7, 24. *Study:* Univ Mich, BM, 48, MM, 51; Albion Col, Mich, Hon Dr Music, 80. *Pos:* Pres, Interlochen Ctr Arts, Mich, 71- *Teaching:* Music, Ann Arbor Pub Sch, Mich, 48-56, music coordr, 59-68; lectr, Univ Mich, 57-59, asst prof, 59-63, assoc prof, 63-66, prof, 66-, asst dean 68-71, assoc dean, 71-72. *Awards:* Nat Patron Award, Delta Omicron Music Fraternity, 80; pres citation, Nat Fedn Music Clubs, 81. *Mem:* Am Coun Arts; Col Music Soc; Int Soc Perf Arts Adminr; Music Educr Nat Conf (mem bd dir, 64-68); Nat Asn Sch Music. *Publ:* Coauth, Teaching Band Instruments to Beginners, Prentice Hall, 66; contrib, Source Book III, 66 & Scheduling Music Classes, 68, Music Educr Nat Conf; Long Range Planning Committee Report, Mich Coun Arts, 77. *Mailing Add:* Interlochen Ctr Arts Interlochen MI 49643

JACOBS, CHARLES GILBERT
EDUCATOR, ORGAN

b Weehawken, NJ, Mar 26, 34. *Study:* Peabody Consv Music, BS, 54; studied piano with E Steuermann, E Balogh & cond with I Jones & G Hurst; NY Univ, studied with C Sachs & G Reese, MA, 57, PhD, 62. *Teaching:* Actg asst prof, Univ Calif, Davis, spring 63; instr, Colby Col, Maine, 63-64; from instr to distinguished prof, City Univ New York, 65-; asst prof music, McGill Univ, 69-70. *Awards:* Grants from Am Philosophical Soc, Am Coun Learned Soc & Kosciuszco Found. *Mem:* Col Music Soc; Am Musicol Soc; Int Musicol Soc; Royal Musical Asn; Sociedad Espanola de Musicologia. *Interests:* Renaissance and early-Baroque composers and repertories; Hindemith. *Publ:* Auth & ed, L de Milan: El Maestro (Valencia, 1535), Penn State Univ Press, 71; A Valente: Intavolatura di Cimbalo (Naples, 1576), Clarendon Press, 73; auth, Francisco Correa de Arauxo, Martinus Nijhoff, 73; auth & ed, M de Fuenllana: Orphenica Lyra (Seville, 1554), Clarendon Press, 78; LeRoy et Ballard's 1572 Mellange de Chansons, Penn State Univ Press, 82. *Mailing Add:* 22-73rd St New Bergen NJ 07047

JACOBS, EVELYN POOLE
VIOLA, EDUCATOR
b Philadelphia, Pa, July 2, 39. *Study:* Temple Univ, BS, 61; Curtis Inst, studied with Max Aronoff, BM, 65. *Pos:* Violist, Amado String Quartet, 63-; prin violist, Bethlehem Bach Choir Orch & Opera Co Philadelphia, 77- *Teaching:* Instr viola, New Sch Music, Philadelphia, 65- *Mem:* Viola Soc Am; Viola d'Amore Soc Am. *Mailing Add:* 49 Northwestern Ave Philadelphia PA 19118

JACOBS, KENNETH A
COMPOSER, EDUCATOR
b Indianapolis, Ind, Sept 13, 48. *Study:* NMex State Univ, with Warner Hutchson, BA, MM; Univ Tex, Austin, with Karl Korte, Thomas Wells & Kent Kennan, DMA. *Works:* Children of the Hermit (tuba & tape); Drifter's Heart (viola & tape); Caravans (string orch & tape); Gestures in the Face of Time (sop & tape); Treasures of a Captured Sun (piano solo); Windows to Three (piano); Celestial Illusions, Silver Reflections (tape & synchronized artwork). *Teaching:* Lectr, NMex Western Univ, 71; assoc prof music & dir electronic music, Univ Tenn, 74- *Awards:* First Prize, Tex Music Educr Comp Cont, 74. *Mem:* Phi Kappa Phi; Pi Kappa Lambda. *Mailing Add:* Music Dept Univ Tenn Knoxville TN 37996

JACOBS, WESLEY D
TUBA, LECTURER
b Independence, Mo, Nov 30, 46. *Study:* Long Beach State Col, BM, 67; Juilliard Sch Music, MM, 68. *Rec Perf:* Wesley Jacobs Tuba, 83. *Pos:* Prin tuba, San Francisco Opera, 68-70 & Detroit Symph Orch, 70- *Mailing Add:* 2118 Babcock Troy MI 48084

JACOBSEN, EDMUND
VIOLIN
b Minneapolis, Minn, Feb 5, 36. *Study:* Univ Minn, BA, 58; Manhattan Sch Music, MM, 65. *Pos:* Served with Seventh Army Orch, 58-60; mem, Minneapolis Symph Orch, 60-62 & Milwaukee Symph Orch, 62-63; freelance musician, New York, 63-66; mem, Metropolitan Opera Orch, 67-71, assoc concertmaster, 71-; music dir, Aigina Arts Ctr, Greece, 71-72. *Mem:* Am Fedn Musicians. *Mailing Add:* Metropolitan Opera Asn Lincoln Ctr New York NY 10023

JACOBSON, GLENN ERLE
EDUCATOR, PIANO
b International Falls, Minn, June 2, 35. *Study:* Oberlin Consv Music, BMus, 57; Manhattan Sch Music, MMus, 59; studied with Leonard Shure & Ernst Oster. *Rec Perf:* Trio for Flute, Cello & Piano, Desto, 71; Music for Flute, Cello & Piano, Vox-Turnabout, 74; Duo for Viola & Piano, CRI, 75. *Pos:* Pianist, New York Camerata, 63-; affil artist, 69-73. *Teaching:* Instr piano, Manhattan Sch Music, 60-76; asst prof, C W Post Col, 71- *Awards:* Huntington Beebe Found, 65. *Mailing Add:* 135 W 79th St New York NY 10024

JACOBSON, JOSHUA R
CONDUCTOR, ADMINISTRATOR
b Boston Mass, Jan 9, 48. *Study:* Harvard Univ, BA, 69; New England Consv, MM, 71. *Pos:* Cond, Zamir Chorale Boston, 69- & Northeastern Univ Choral Soc, 72- *Teaching:* Assoc prof, Northeastern Univ, 72- *Mem:* Am Choral Dir Asn; Am Choral Found; Col Music Soc; Am Jewish Choral Fest; Am Musicol Soc. *Publ:* Auth, A Selective Bibliography of Jewish Choral Music, Choral J, 78; Spazziam, A Balletto by Salamone Rossi, Am Choral Review, 79; Before the Concert, Choral J, 81. *Mailing Add:* 35 Garland Rd Newton MA 02159

JACOBSON, ROBERT (MARSHALL)
WRITER, EDITOR
b Racine, Wis, July 28, 40. *Study:* Univ Wis, BA, 62; Columbia Univ, MA(musicol), 63. *Pos:* Managing ed, Lincoln Ctr Prog, 65-73; ed in chief, Opera News, 73- & Ballet News, 79-; contrib ed, Ovation, 80-; broadcaster intermission features, Metropolitan Opera Sat, currently. *Publ:* Auth, Articles in Opera News, Saturday Rev, Life, Los Angeles Times, Cue, New York Times, New York Post, Musical Am, New York & Ovation, 63-; Auth, Reverberations, William Morrow & Co, 74; Opera People, Vendome Press, 82. *Mailing Add:* 100 Hudson St New York NY 10013

JAEGER, INA CLAIRE
EDUCATOR, VIOLIN
b Ashtabula, Ohio, July 18, 29. *Study:* Eastman Sch Music, BM, 52, MM, 55. *Pos:* Second violinist, Rochester Phil Orch, 53-54; first violinist, Univ Symph Orch, Gainesville, Fla, 61-65 & 67-80; second violinist, Fla String Quartet, Univ Fla, 63-66 & 67-72 & New Orleans Phil Orch, 66-67. *Teaching:* Prof, Univ Fla, 67- *Mem:* Music Educr Nat Conf; Fla Music Educr Asn. *Publ:* Coauth, Fundamentals of Music Theory, 73, auth, Basic Elements in Music Theory: Workbook, 74 & Basic Elements in Music Theory: A Modular Program of Instruction, 76, Univ Fla. *Mailing Add:* 519 NW 19th St Gainesville FL 32603

JAFFE, DAVID AARON
COMPOSER, MANDOLIN
b Newark, NJ, Apr 29, 55. *Study:* Bennington Col, study with Henry Brant, BA(comp), 78; Stanford Univ, MA(comp), 83, DMA(comp), 83. *Works:* Marketplace, perf at New England Consv, 80; Dybbuk, comn by Chamber Music Conf & Comp Forum East, 80; Damp Nights in Drafty Motels, comn by Julie Feves, 81; May All Your Children Be Acrobats, comn by Purchase Guitar Ens, 81; A Little Kid Sees A Skyscraper, perf at Am Fest Microtonal Music, 82; Silicon Valley Breakdown, Venice Biennale, 82; Would You Just As Soon Sing ..., Mostly Modern Orch, 83. *Pos:* Comp in res, Chamber Music Conf & Comp Forum East, 80; res asst, Ctr Comput Res Music & Acoustics, Stanford Univ, 82- *Teaching:* Instr comput music, Stanford Univ Summer Wkshp, 82 & 83; guest lectr tour, Princeton Univ, Hartt Sch Music, Manhattan Sch Music & Bennington Col, 83. *Awards:* Presser Found Scholar, 78; Nat Endowment Arts Comp Grant, 83; Second Prize, for Silicon Valley Breakdown, NEWCOMP Cont. *Mem:* Computer Music Asn; Comp Forum Inc; Minn Comp Forum; BMI. *Publ:* Coauth (with Julius Smith), Extensions of the Karplus-Strong Plucked String Algorithm, Comput Music J, summer 83. *Mailing Add:* Box 4268 Stanford CA 94305

JAFFE, STEPHEN ABRAM
COMPOSER, PIANO
b Washington, DC, Dec 30, 54. *Study:* Consv Musique, Geneva, Switz, 71-72; Univ Pa, AB, 76, AM, 78. *Works:* Three Yiddish Songs (sop chamber orch), Pa Comp Guild, 78; Centering (violin duo), Mobart Inc, Quan Macomber; Arch (flute, clarinet, bass-clarinet, violin, viola, violoncello, piano & celesta), Fleisher Col, Am Acad, Rome, 81; Partita (violoncello, piano & perc), Da Capo Chamber Players, 81; Four Images (orch), Orch della RAI di Roma, 82-83; New Work, comn by Nonesuch, 83 & New York New Music Ens, 83. *Rec Perf:* Centering (78), CRI, 83. *Pos:* Dir conct ser, Painted Bride, 79-81 & Encounters with the Music of our Time, Duke Univ, 81- *Teaching:* Instr, Swarthmore Col, 80-81; asst prof, Duke Univ, Durham, NC, 81- *Awards:* Bearns Prize, Columbia Univ, 76; Rome Prize, Am Acad, Rome, 80-81; Nonesuch Comn Award, Warner Commun Inc, Am Music Ctr, 82. *Mem:* BMI; Col Music Soc. *Mailing Add:* Dept Music Duke Univ 6695 Col Station Durham NC 27708

JAFFEE, KAY
RECORDER, WRITER
b Lansing, Mich, Dec 31, 37. *Study:* Univ Mich, with Hans T David & Wiley Hitchcock, BA, 59; NY Univ, with Gustave Reese, Jan LaRue, Martin Bernstein, Victor Yellin & Martin Chusid; studied recorder with Bernard Kranis, 63-65. *Rec Perf:* Las Cantigas de Santa Maria, 72 & Douce Dame, 74, Vanguard Rec Soc; A Renaissance Christmas Celebration, 77, Welcome Sweet Pleasure, 78, Italia Mia, 79, Spanish Music in the Age of Exploration, 80 & The Christmas Story, 82, CBS. *Pos:* Lit ed, Columbia Masterworks, 63-64; co-founder & res dir, The Waverly Consort, 64- *Teaching:* Vis instr early music, NY Univ, summers 75-78 & Dartmouth Col, summer 76. *Bibliog:* Helen Epstein (auth), Let's Bring Back the Renaissance, New York Times, 1/12/75; Hubert Saal (auth), Strike up the Shawm, Newsweek, 1/2/78; Exploring a Lost Continent, Time, 2/18/80. *Mem:* Am Musicol Soc; Am Musicol Instrm Soc; Am Recorder Soc. *Interests:* Early music performance, 1100-1750; French lyric drama, 1675-1800. *Publ:* Auth, Divers Notes on Brass Instruments in English Periodicals, Brass Quart, summer 64; Conference Report: The Boston Early Music Festival and Exhibition, J Musicol, 1/82. *Mailing Add:* 305 Riverside Dr New York NY 10025

JAFFEE, MICHAEL
MUSIC DIRECTOR, LUTE & PLUCKED INSTRUMENTS
b New York, NY, Apr 21, 38. *Study:* NY Univ, BA, 59, MA, 63; study with Gustave Reese. *Works:* The Consort, Eliot Feld Ballet Co, 74. *Rec Perf:* Las Cantigas de Santa Maria, 72 & Douce Dame, 74, Vanguard Rec Soc; A Renaissance Christmas Celebration, 77, Welcome Sweet Pleasure, 78, Italia Mia, 79, Spanish Music in the Age of Exploration, 80 & The Christmas Story, 82, CBS Masterworks. *Pos:* Artistic dir, Waverly Consort, 64- *Teaching:* Instr instrm & vocal perf, NY Univ, summers 75-78 & Dartmouth Col, summer 76. *Bibliog:* Helen Epstein (auth), Let's Bring Back the Renaissance, New York Times, 1/12/75; Hubert Saal (auth), Strike Up the Shawm, Newsweek, 1/2/78; Exploring a Lost Continent, Time, 2/18/80. *Mem:* Am Musicol Soc; Chamber Music Am (pres, 77-83). *Publ:* Auth, Harmony in the Solo Guitar Music af Heitor Villa-Lobos, Guitar Review, 66; The Waverly Consort's Roman de Fauvel, Keynote, 79; column in Am Ens, Chamber Music Am, 79-83. *Mailing Add:* 305 Riverside Dr New York NY 10025

JAGER, ROBERT EDWARD
COMPOSER, MUSIC DIRECTOR
b Binghamton, NY, Aug 25, 39. *Study:* Univ Mich, BM, 67, MM, 68. *Works:* Diamond Variations, Columbia Pictures Music, 68; Concerto Grosso for Stage Band & Symphony Orch, Elkan-Vogel, 70; Variations on Theme of R Schumann, Columbia Pictures Music, 72; Symphony No 2 for Band, Kjos Music, 78; Concerto for Brass Tuba, 80, Concerto for Band, 81 & Tableau, 83, Edward B Marks. *Rec Perf:* Music of Robert Jager, Crest Rec, 79 & CBS, 83. *Teaching:* Staff arr & comp, Armed Forces Sch Music, 62-65; instr cond, Old Dominion Univ, 68-71; prof comp & music theory & dir theory & comp, Tenn Tech Univ, 71- *Awards:* Ostwald Award, Am Bandmasters Asn, 64, 68 & 72; Volkwein Award, Am Sch Band Dir Asn, 75; Roth Award, Nat Sch Orch Asn, 64 & 66. *Mem:* ASCAP; Am Bandmasters Asn; Nat Band Asn; Phi Mu Alpha Sinfonia. *Mailing Add:* Rte 9 Box 17 Cookeville TN 38501

JAHN, THEODORE LEE
CLARINET, EDUCATOR
b Spokane, Wash, June 12, 39. *Study:* Oberlin Col, with George Waln, BM(perf), 61; Ohio State Univ, with Donald McGinnis, MA(woodwinds), 64; Ind Univ, with Bernard Portnoy, DM(woodwinds), 75. *Rec Perf:* Pittsburgh Concerto (Badings), Am Wind Symph Orch, RCA, 64. *Pos:* Prin clarinetist, Am Wind Symph Orch, 64-66 & Augusta Symph Orch, 81-82. *Teaching:* Instr woodwinds, Bemidji State Col, 64-67; assoc prof clarinet, Univ Ga, 67- *Mem:* Int Clarinet Soc; Nat Asn Col Wind & Perc Instr; ClariNetwork. *Mailing Add:* 151 Ramblewood Pl Watkinsville GA 30677

JAKEY, LAUREN RAY
CONDUCTOR, VIOLIN

b Yakima, Wash, July 10, 37. *Study:* Consv Music, Oberlin Col, BM, 59; Peabody Consv Music, MM, 64; Ind Univ, DM, 72. *Rec Perf:* Suite for Gamelan and Violin (Lou Harrison & Richard Dee), Ocean Rec, 75. *Pos:* First violinist, Houston Symph, 59-60, Baltimore Symph Orch, 62-64 & San Jose String Quartet, 77-; concertmaster, San Jose Symph Orch, 72-76; cond, Nova Vista Symph Orch, 78-, Calif Youth Symph, 79- & San Jose State Univ Symph Orch, 82- *Teaching:* Asst prof, Morningside Col, Sioux City, Iowa, 64-67; prof music, San Jose State Univ, 69- *Mem:* Am String Teachers Asn; Calif Music Educr Asn. *Mailing Add:* Music Dept San Jose State Univ San Jose CA 95192

JAMERSON, THOMAS H
BARITONE, TEACHER

b New Orleans, La, July 3, 42. *Study:* La State Univ, with Loren Davidson, MusB, 65, MusM, 71; studied with Cornelius Reid. *Rec Perf:* La Traviata; The Merry Widow. *Roles:* Count Almaviva in Le Nozze di Figaro, Metropolitan Opera Nat Co, 67; Demetrius in A Midsummer Night's Dream; Dark Fiddler in A Village Romeo and Juliet; Marcello in La Boheme; Ottone in L'Incoronazione di Poppea; Valentin in Faust; Faninal in Der Rosenkavalier. *Pos:* Recitals & appearances with major US symphs & opera co. *Teaching:* Voice, currently. *Awards:* Martha Baird Rockefeller Found Grant, 76-77. *Mem:* Am Guild Musical Artists. *Mailing Add:* c/o Lustig & Florian Mgt 225 W 57th St New York NY 10019

JAMES, CAROLYNE FAYE
MEZZO-SOPRANO

b Wheatland, Wyo, Apr 27, 45. *Study:* Univ Wyo, BMus, 54; Ind Univ, Bloomington, MMus, 67; studied with Daniel Ferro, Margaret Harshaw & Michael Trimble. *Rec Perf:* The Sweet Bye and Bye (Jack Beeson); Captain Jinks (Jack Beeson). *Roles:* Madame Flora in The Medium, St Paul Opera, 71 Houston Grand Opera, 72, Opera Theatre St Louis, 76 & Augusta Opera Co, 76; Baroness in The Young Lord, New York City Opera, 73; Leocadia Begbick in Aufstieg un Fall der Stadt Mahagonny, Opera Co Boston, 73; Mother Rainey in The Sweet Bye and Bye, 73; Mrs G in Captain Jinks, 76; Mrs Cratchit in A Christmas Carol, 79; Filippyevna in Eugene Onegin, San Antonio Symph, 83. *Pos:* Ms with major opera cos in US & Europe. *Teaching:* Asst prof voice, Univ Iowa, Iowa City, 68-72. *Awards:* Lilliann Garabedian Award, Santa Fe Opera, 67; Corbett Found Grant, 68; Young Artist Award, Nat Fedn Music Clubs, 72. *Mailing Add:* c/o Columbia Artists Mgt 165 W 57th St New York NY 10019

JAMES, LAYTON BRAY
HARPSICHORD, PIANO

East Orange, NJ, Mar 2, 41. *Study:* Col Wooster, BA, 63; Cornell Univ, MA(musicol), 67; Stanford Univ, 68-69. *Rec Perf:* Sinfonias (J C Bach), Nonesuch, 77; Appalachian Spring (Copland), Sound 80, 78; Four Seasons (Vivaldi), 81 & Concertos for Two Violins (Bach), 82, Columbia Masterworks. *Pos:* Harpsichordist & pianist, St Paul Chamber Orch, 69-; choirmaster, Colonial Church Edina, Minn, currently. *Teaching:* Instr music hist, Univ Hawaii, 67-68; lectr Baroque perf & lit, Westminster Choir Col, summers, currently. *Mem:* Am Guild Organists; Am Fedn Musicians. *Mailing Add:* c/o St Paul Chamber Orch 315 Landmark Ctr St Paul MN 55102

JAMES, MARION VERSE
EDUCATOR, PIANO

b Brooklyn, NY, Oct 30, 19. *Study:* Douglass Col, Rutgers Univ, BA, 41; Col Arts & Sci, NY Univ, MA, 46, Sch Educ, cert adv study, 67. *Works:* Songs for sop; A Suite for Piano; Chorale Prelude for Chamber Orch (for two pianos). *Pos:* Duo pianist with Vittorio Verse, 41-61; prof accmp & coach, opera co, singers & instrumentalists; pianist in fac trio, Am Music Fest, New York, 70-78. *Teaching:* Prof music, Jersey City State Col, 59-, dir, Madrigal Singers, 70; substitute & private instr piano & theory, New Brunswick, 42-49 & Metuchen, NJ, 49-60. *Mem:* Sigma Alpha Iota (pres cent NJ chap, 70); Am Asn Univ Prof (JCSC chap secy, 79-81, vpres 81-83, pres 83-); Music Educr Nat Conf; Piano Teachers Cong NY; Soc Music Theory. *Publ:* Ed, Etude—A Guide for the Advancement of Music Education in New Jersey, NJ Music Educr Asn, 67; contribr, Lincoln Ctr Student Prog (an evaluation), Ctr Educ Res & Field Serv, NY Univ, 72. *Mailing Add:* Music Dept Jersey City State Col 2039 Kennedy Blvd Jersey City NJ 07305

JAMES, MARY ELLIOTT
VIOLA, EDUCATOR

b Jan 31, 27; US citizen. *Study:* San Francisco Consv; Univ Calif, Berkeley, BMus, 56; Univ Southern Calif; studied with William Primrose, Philip Burton & Lionel Tertis, 68. *Pos:* Violist, Portland Symph, 47-49, San Francisco Symph, 56-63 & Los Angeles Phil & studio orchs, 63-68; mem, Columbia Rec Orch; assoc prin viola, Aspen Fest Chamber Orch; soloist, Domaine Sch, Comp Conf & Sch Orpheus Music Fest. *Teaching:* Prof music & mem fac quartet, Pittsburg State Univ, 68-; coach chamber music, Bennington Col, 72- & Univ Southern Calif. *Awards:* Alfred Hertz Scholar, Univ Calif, Berkeley, 52-54. *Mem:* Am Viola Soc; Viola D'Amore Soc Am; Am String Teachers Asn; Kans Higher Educ Asn. *Interests:* Figured bass realization of six cantatas by J B Morin. *Mailing Add:* 1919 S Elm Pittsburg KS 66762

JAMESON, R PHILIP
EDUCATOR, TROMBONE

b Worster, Ohio, Dec 7, 41. *Study:* Juilliard Sch, BM, 64, MS, 65; Columbia Univ, EdD, 80. *Pos:* Trombonist, Radio City Music Hall, 60-67, Musica Aeterna Orch, 61-67, Am Symph Orch, 62-67 & Band of Am, 64-67. *Teaching:* Prof music, Univ Ga, 67-; instr trombone, Juilliard Sch, 74-75. *Awards:* Fromme Found fel, Boston Symph Orch, 61; Naumburg Prize, Juilliard Sch, 65; Fulbright Professorship, 78. *Mem:* Nat Acad Rec Arts & Sci; Nat Asn Col Wind & Perc Instr (state chmn, 70-80); Music Educr Nat Conf; Ga Music Educr Asn; Int Trombone Asn. *Mailing Add:* Dept Music Univ Ga Athens GA 30601

JANDER, OWEN HUGHES
EDUCATOR

b Mt Kisco, NY, June 4, 30. *Study:* Univ Va, BA, 51; Harvard Univ, PhD, 62. *Teaching:* Prof music hist, Wellesley Col, 60- *Awards:* Guggenheim Fel, 67; Nat Endowment for Humanities Grant, 70. *Interests:* Seventeenth century Italian vocal music; Beethoven. *Publ:* The Wellesley Edition Cantata Index Series, Wellesley Col, 61-73; auth, 80 articles, In: New Grove Dict Music; Form and Content in the Slow Movement of Beethoven's Violin Concerto, Musical Quart, spring 83. *Mailing Add:* 72 Denton Rd Wellesley MA 02181

JANIEC, HENRY
MUSIC DIRECTOR & CONDUCTOR, EDUCATOR

b Passaic, NJ, Nov 21, 29. *Study:* Consv Music, Oberlin Col, BMusEd, 52, MMusEd, 53; Wofford Col, Hon Dr. *Pos:* Music dir & cond, Spartanburg Symph, Charlotte Symph, Chautauqua Student Orch, Spartanburg City Sch Orch, Charlotte Opera Asn & Chautauqua Opera Co; artistic dir, Brevard Music Ctr; radio & TV commentator. *Teaching:* Dean & prof music, Converse Col, currently. *Awards:* SC Gov Award; Presidential Citation, Nat Fedn Music Clubs. *Mem:* SC Arts Found; Delta Omicron; Pi Kappa Lambda; Am Symph Orch League; Music Educr Nat Conf. *Publ:* Contribr to Musical Am, Sch Musician & various newspaper rev. *Mailing Add:* 113 Beechwood Dr Spartanburg SC 29302

JANIS, BYRON
PIANO

b Pa, Mar 24, 28. *Study:* With Adele Marcus & Vladimir Horowitz; Chatham Sq Music Sch. *Rec Perf:* Piano Concerti No 1 & 2 (Liszt); Piano Concerto No 3 (Rachmaninoff). *Pos:* Soloist, NBC Symph Orch, 44, US tours, 44-47, South Am tour, 48, Europ tour, 52 & USSR tours, 60 & 62; recitalist. *Awards:* Knight Arts & Lett, France, 65. *Mailing Add:* c/o ICM Artists 50 W 57th St New York NY 10019

JANKOWSKI, LORETTA PATRICIA
COMPOSER, EDUCATOR

b Newark, NJ, Oct 20, 50. *Study:* Eastman Sch Music, BM, 72, PhD, 79; Univ Mich, MM, 74. *Works:* Lustrations, 78, A Naughty Boy, 79, Praise the Lord (Psalm 148), 81, Homage to Chopin, 81, Reverie, 82 & Die Sehnsuchten, 82, Alexander Broude, Inc; Sonata for B Flat Trumpet and Piano, Dorn Publ, 82. *Teaching:* Instr theory & comp, Northern Ill Univ, 77-78; asst prof, Calif State Univ, Long Beach, 79-80; adj prof comp, Kean Col, 81- *Awards:* Winner, ABA-Ostwald Band Comp Cont, 76; Music Award, Womens Asn Symph Orch, 77. *Mem:* BMI; Am Music Ctr; Am Women Comp, Inc; Int League Women Comp; Am Comp Alliance. *Mailing Add:* 291 Ravens Wood Mountainside NJ 07092

JANKS, HAL
TROMBONE, EDUCATOR

Study: New England Consv Music, MM; Eastman Sch Music, BM. *Pos:* Bass trombonist, Metropolitan Opera Orch, currently & Chautauqua Symph Orch, currently. *Teaching:* Instr trombone, Temple Univ, currently, Chautauqua Music Fest, currently & Lowell Univ, currently; mem fac trombone, Manhattan Sch Music, 81- *Mailing Add:* Metropolitan Opera Asn Lincoln Ctr New York NY 10023

JANOWSKY, MAXIM DUBROW
EDUCATOR, DOUBLE BASS

b Hartford, Conn, Apr 17, 43. *Study:* Studied with Isador Janowsky, Fred Zimmerman, Georges Moleaux & Oscar Zimmerman. *Pos:* Double bass, Detroit Symph, currently. *Teaching:* Instr double bass, Wayne State Univ, currently, Univ Windsor, Ont, currently & Schoolcraft Col, currently. *Mem:* Am String Teachers Asn. *Mailing Add:* Detroit Symph Ford Auditorium Detroit MI 48226

JANSON, THOMAS
COMPOSER

b Racine, Wis, Oct 26, 47. *Study:* Valparaiso Univ, BMus, 69; Univ Mich, with Leslie Bassett & Ross Lee Finney, MMus, 70 & DMA, 75. *Works:* Celestial Autumn, 74, Eternal Voices, 75, Sparkler, 78, Organ Concerto, 76, The Harlequin, 81 & Variations for Orch, 82, Belwin-Mills Publ Corp. *Teaching:* Asst prof music comp, Univ Pittsburgh, 73-80; assoc prof, Kent State Univ, 80- *Awards:* Charles E Ives Award, Nat Inst Arts & Lett, 72; Nat Fedn Music Clubs Award of Merit, 73; winner, Marion Col Hymn Cont, 81. *Mem:* Cleveland Comp Guild; Col Music Soc; Int Alban Berg Soc; Soc Music Theory. *Mailing Add:* 3688 Fishcreek Rd Stow OH 44224

JANSONS, ANDREJS
CONDUCTOR, COMPOSER

b Riga, Latvia, Oct 2, 38; US citizen. *Study:* Juilliard Sch Music, BS(oboe), 60; Manhattan Sch Music, MM(cond), 73. *Works:* Suite of Old Lettish Dances, Southern Music Co, 76; Orpheus Songs (voice & orch), perf by Bronx Arts Ens, 80-81; A Brush with Magic (musical), Los Angeles, 81; Homo Novus (musical), Pabst Theatre, Milwaukee, 83; Spriditis (musical), Coach House Press, 83. *Rec Perf:* Latvian Folk Songs & Dances, 66 & Latvian Folk Songs & Dances II, 68, Monitor Rec; Ars Antiqua, 70, Latvian Folk Songs, 73 & Behold, a Bright Star, 74, Kaibala Rec. *Pos:* Oboist, Baltimore Symph,

60-62 & Pittsburgh Symph, 62-64; cond, NY Latvian Concert Choir & Orch, 76-; guest cond, Milwaukee Symph, 83. *Publ:* Auth, Koklesana (The Art of Playing the Kokle), ALA, 65; Koklesana II, Gen Goppers Found, 78. *Mailing Add:* 73 Glenwood Ave Leonia NJ 07605

JANZEN, ELDON A
EDUCATOR, MUSIC DIRECTOR
b Medford, Okla, Mar 21, 28. *Study:* Okla State Univ, BMusEd, 50; NTex State Univ, MMusEd, 53. *Pos:* Dir bands, New Boston Pub Sch, Tex, 54-58 & Greenville, Tex, 59-61; dir bands, Irving Pub Sch, 62-67, dir music activ, 68-70. *Teaching:* Prof music, Univ Ark, Fayetteville, 70-, dir bands, 70- *Mem:* Tex Bandmasters Asn (pres, 69); Ark Bandmaster Asn (pres, 70); Col Band Dir Nat Asn (pres SW div, 83-84). *Publ:* Auth, The Symphonic Band Sound, 72, Correcting Wind Problems in the Orchestra, 74 & Analyzing the Sound of Wind Groups, 76, Sch Musician. *Mailing Add:* Band Bldg Univ Ark Fayetteville AR 72701

JANZER, GEORGES
VIOLA, EDUCATOR
b Budapest, Hungary, Sept 15, 14. *Study:* Franz Liszt Acad, Budapest, studied violin with Oscar Studer. *Rec Perf:* On DGG, Decca, Columbia & Discophiles Francais, 43-55; Six Quartets (Bartok) & Quartets (Beethoven), Valois: Teldec, 71; 4 Flute Quartets (Mozart) & Trios (Haydn & Schubert), Philips. *Pos:* Solo concts & radio broadcasts, 34-; concertmaster, Budapest Symph Orch; founding mem & violist, Vegh Quartet, 40-; mem, Grumiaux Trio, 62- *Teaching:* Violin, Music Acad, Hannover, 60-63 & Music Acad, Dusseldorf, 63-; prof viola, Ind Univ, 72- *Awards:* Grand Prix du Disque for Mozart Quintet with Clarinet (with Vegh Quartet); Grand Prix for Mozart Divertimento (with Grumiaux Trio); Best Chamber Music Rec of Yr for 5 Beethoven String Trios (with Grumiaux Trio), US. *Mailing Add:* 1901 Ruby Lane Bloomington IN 47401

JARRETT, JACK MARIUS
COMPOSER, EDUCATOR
b Asheville, NC, Mar 17, 34. *Study:* Univ Fla; Eastman Sch Music, with Bernard Rogers; studied with Boris Blacher, Berlin; Ind Univ, with Bernard Heiden, DM. *Works:* Serenade (string orch), 57; Cyrano de Bergerac, 72; Choral Symphony on American Poems (chorus & orch or band); Holiday for Horns (four horns & band). *Pos:* Asst cond, Richmond Symph Orch, 80-83; cond, Richmond Opera Co & Richmond Ballet Co, currently. *Teaching:* Fac mem, Dickinson Col, 58-61, Univ Richmond, 62-64 & Univ NC, 67-75; prof, Va Commonwealth Univ, 75- *Awards:* Edward Benjamin Award, 57; Fulbright Grant, 61; Comp in Res Award, Ford Found, 65-67. *Mailing Add:* Dept Music Va Commonwealth Univ Richmond VA 23284

JARRETT, KEITH DANIEL
PIANO, COMPOSER
b Allentown, Pa, May 8, 45. *Study:* Berklee Sch Music; piano study with Eleanor Sokoloff. *Works:* Arbour Zena, perf by Radio Symph Orch, Stuttgart, 76; Sun Bear Concerts (piano), perf by Keith Jarrett, 76; Ritual For Piano, perf by Dennis Russell Davies, 77; My Song, perf by Keith Jarrett Quartet, 78; The Celestial Hawk (piano & orch), perf by Keith Jarrett & Syracuse Symph, 80; Invocations (organ & sop sax), perf by Keith Jarrett, 81; Concerts (piano), perf by Keith Jarrett, 82. *Rec Perf:* Solo Concerts, 73; The Köln Concert, 75, Sun Bear Concerts, 76, Staircase Hourglass Sundial Sand, 76 & Hymns, Spheres, 76, Econ Rec; Invocations—The Moth & the Flame, 81; Concerts (Bregenz & Munich), Econ Rec, 82. *Teaching:* Private lessons & workshops, currently. *Awards:* Record of the Year, New York Times, 75; Grosser Deutscher Schallplatten Preis, 79; Album of the Decade, Stereo Readers Poll, Germany, 80. *Bibliog:* Peter Rüedi (auth), The Magician and the Jugglers, Ecm Rec, 82; Edward Strickland (auth), Keith Jarrett and the Abyss, Fanfare Mag, 83; John Rockwell (auth), All American Music, Alfred A Knopf, 83. *Rep:* Vincent Ryan 135 W 16th St New York NY 10011. *Mailing Add:* PO Box 127 Oxford NJ 07863

JAY, STEPHEN
ADMINISTRATOR, EDUCATOR
Study: Manhattan Sch Music, BM, MM; Juilliard Sch; NY Univ; Teachers Col, Columbia Univ. *Pos:* Pres, St Louis Consv, formerly & Sch for Arts, formerly; mem, Expansion Arts Panel, Nat Endowment Arts; mem music comt, Mo Arts Coun; delegate, Second Int Kodaly Symposium, Hungary. *Teaching:* Mem fac, Wis Consv Music, formerly; dean & chmn theory & comp, Manhattan Sch Music, formerly; assoc prof & chmn music dept, NY Univ, formerly & Univ Col Arts & Sci, formerly; head theory dept & asst dir, Third St Music Sch, New York; introduced Kodaly principles of music educ to US; adj prof music, Case Western Reserve Univ, 82; dean & mem fac theory & analysis, Curtis Inst Music, currently. *Mem:* Nat Guild Community Sch for Arts (vpres, currently); Orgn Am Kodaly Educr; Int Kodaly Soc; Nat Black Colloquium. *Mailing Add:* Curtis Inst Music 1726 Locust St Philadelphia PA 19103

JAZWINSKI, BARBARA MARIA
EDUCATOR, COMPOSER
b Chorzow, Poland, May 14, 50; US citizen. *Study:* Nat Acad Music, Warsaw, Poland, BA, 71; Stanford Univ, MA, 72. *Works:* Music for Flute, Oboe, Clarinet, Viola, Piano & Percussion, 70 & Diachromia, 71, Acad Music, Warsaw; Spectri Sonori, 73 & Music for Chamber Orchestra, 74, Berkeley Chamber Orch; String Trio, League Comp, Int Soc Contemp Music Conct Ser, 78; The Seventh Night of the Seventh Moon, NY Univ Contemp Players, 82; Deep Green Lies the Grass Along the River, NY New Music Ens, 83. *Teaching:* Adj lectr theory & musicol, Brooklyn Col, 80-81; instr theory & ear

training, NY Univ, 81-; adj lectr theory, Col Staten Island, City Univ New York, 83- *Awards:* Prince Pierre of Monaco Musical Comp Award, 81. *Mem:* Am Comp Alliance; Int Soc Cont Music (treas, 80-). *Mailing Add:* 500 E 63rd St 13F New York NY 10021

JEAN, KENNETH
CONDUCTOR
b NY. *Study:* San Francisco State Univ; Juilliard Sch, 75-76. *Pos:* Cond, Youth Symph New York, formerly, music dir, formerly; prin cond, White Mountains Art & Music Fest, formerly; mem staff, Aspen Music Fest, formerly; cond asst, Cleveland Orch, 76-78; guest cond, Hong Kong Phil, Cleveland, Baltimore, Indianapolis & St Louis Orchs, Orch Swiss Radio & Int Fest Youth Orch, Aberdeen, Scotland, 80; asst cond, Detroit Symph Orch, 79-81, cond, 81- *Awards:* Winner, Baltimore Young Cond Compt. *Mailing Add:* Detroit Symph Orch Ford Auditorium Detroit MI 48226

JEANRENAUD, JOAN
CELLO
b Memphis, Tenn, Jan 25, 56. *Study:* Ind Univ, with Fritz Magg, BMus, 77. *Pos:* Cellist, Kronos String Quartet, 78- *Bibliog:* Paul Hertelendy (auth), The Kronos Quartet: Displaying a California Style, Musical Am, 10/80; Wolfgang Schreiber (auth), Die Entdeckerlust, Suddeutsche Zeitung, 3/13-14/83; Tom O'Connor (auth), String Fever, Focus Mag, 4/83. *Mailing Add:* Kronos Quartet 1238-Ninth Ave San Francisco CA 94122

JEFFERS, RONALD H
COMPOSER, EDUCATOR
b Springfield, Ill, Mar 25, 43. *Study:* Univ Mich, with George Wilson, Ross Lee Finney & Leslie Bassett, BM, 66, MA, 68; Univ Calif, San Diego, with Roger Reynolds, Pauline Oliveros & Robert Erickson. *Works:* Mass Confusion (men's voices), 66; In Time of War (chorus & instrm), 67; Now Conscience Wakes (soloists, handbells & orch), 68; Missa Concrete (triple chorus), 69, rev 73; In Memoriam (seven trumpets, four oboes, two flutes, piano & perc), 73; Tota Pulcra Es (four voices, cello, clarinet & two narrators), 74; Time Passes (female vocalist, tape, gongs, bells & dancer), 74. *Teaching:* Fac mem, Occidental Col, 69-70, Univ Calif, San Diego, 70-72, Univ Wis, Eau Claire, 72-73 & State Univ NY, Stony Brook, 73-74; assoc prof, Ore State Univ, 74- *Awards:* Ohio State Univ Choral Compt. *Mailing Add:* Dept Music Ore State Univ Corvallis OR 97331

JEFFERY, PETER GRANT
EDUCATOR, LIBRARIAN
b New York, NY, Oct 19, 53. *Study:* Brooklyn Col, BA, 75; Princeton Univ, MFA, 77, PhD, 80. *Pos:* Cataloguer ms & ed publ, Hill Monastic Ms Libr, St John's Univ, 80-82. *Teaching:* Instr music, Bergen Community Col, 80; instr Gregorian chant & medieval music, St John's Univ, 80-82; Mellon Fac Fel, Harvard Univ, 82- *Awards:* Lado Award, 75; Am Coun Learned Soc Grant, 77; Delmas Found Res Venice Fel, 79. *Mem:* Am Musicol Soc; Medieval Acad Am; NAm Acad Liturgy; Soc Liturgica; Soc Ethnomusicol. *Interests:* Liturgical chant of church and synagogue, 4th-16th centuries, AD. *Publ:* Auth, Notre Dame Polyphony in the Library of Boniface VIII, J Am Musicol Soc, 79; A Bibliography for Music Manuscript Research, St John's Univ, 80; Popular Culture and the Medieval Liturgy, Worship, 81; An Early Cantatorium Fragment, Scriptorium, 82; articles on chant, In: Harvard Dict Music, 3rd ed (in prep). *Mailing Add:* 345 E 16th St Brooklyn NY 11226

JEFFORD, RUTH MARTIN
VIOLIN
b Des Moines, Iowa. *Study:* Midland Col, 31-33; Am Consv Music, 34-40; Aspen Sch Music, 51 & 55; Mannes Col Music, 54-55; Ecole Normale de Musique, Paris, 57-58. *Pos:* Concertmaster, Anchorage Symph Orch, 46-54, 55-57 & 58- & Robert Shaw Chorale Touring Orch, 60. *Mailing Add:* N Shore Lake Wasilla Box 217 Wasilla AK 99687

JELINEK, JEROME
CELLO, EDUCATOR
b Detroit, Mich, Mar 23, 31. *Study:* Univ Mich, BMus, 52, MM, 53; Royal Acad Music, London, ARAM(Lon), 68. *Rec Perf:* Cello Works by Finney & Bassett, 73 & Piano Quartet (Bolcom) & Piano Trio (Finney), 83, CRI. *Pos:* Cellist, Detroit Symph Orch, 51-53, Univ Mich Stanley Quartet, 61-74, Jelinek-Gurt Duo, 72- & Am Trio, 76- *Teaching:* Asst prof, Univ Ore, 57-61; prof cello & chamber music & chmn string dept, Univ Mich, Ann Arbor, 61- *Awards:* Fulbright Award, London, 56-57; Harriet E Cohen Int Cello Award, London, 57. *Mem:* Col Music Soc; Violoncello Soc Inc New York. *Publ:* Auth, Fundamentals of Elementary Cello Technique, Univ Music Press, 64. *Mailing Add:* Sch Music Univ Mich Ann Arbor MI 48109

JENKINS, DONALD P
MUSIC DIRECTOR & CONDUCTOR, EDUCATOR
Study: Consv Music, Oberlin Col; Juilliard Sch Music. *Pos:* Chorus master, Juilliard Opera Theater, formerly; guest cond, Denver Classic Chorale, formerly; Univ Wis Summer Session, formerly, NMex All-State Girls' Chorus, formerly & Ark Intercol Choral Asn, formerly; judge, Colo-Wyo & WTex-NMex Dist Auditions, Metropolitan Opera, formerly & San Francisco Opera Regional Auditions, currently; cond, Colorado Springs Chorale, 67-; co-founder, cond & artistic leader, Colo Opera Fest, currently. *Teaching:* Prof choral groups & voice, Colo Col, currently, cond, Col Choir, currently. *Mailing Add:* 1220 N Tejon Colorado Springs CO 80903

JENKINS, JOHN ALLAN
ADMINISTRATOR, EDUCATOR
b Pittsburgh, Pa, Nov 21, 34. *Study:* Univ Mich, BM, 57, MM, 60, MA, 71 & PhD, 74. *Teaching:* Dir bands, Univ Mass, Amherst, 63-, prof chamber winds, 79-, dir fine arts ctr, 80- *Mem:* New England Col Band Asn; Col Band Dir Nat Asn (secy-treas Eastern div, 70-82); Asn Col, Univ & Community Arts Adminr. *Interests:* Early Scottish wind music. *Mailing Add:* 265 Northeast St Amherst MA 01002

JENKINS, JOSEPH WILLCOX
EDUCATOR, COMPOSER
b Philadelphia, Pa, Feb 15, 28. *Study:* Philadelphia Consv, with Vincent Persichetti; Eastman Sch Music, with Thomas Canning, Bernard Rogers & Howard Hanson, BM, MM; with Ralph Vaughan Williams. *Works:* Toccata for Winds, 78; 3 Bagatelles, 78; Pieces of 8 (band), 78; String Quartet; Sinfonia de la Frontera, New Mex Bicentennial; American Overture; Charles County (band). *Pos:* Affil, US Army Band & Chorus, 51-53 & 56-59; ed music publ firm, 61-62. *Teaching:* Prof theory, orch & comp, Duquesne Univ, currently. *Awards:* Ford Found Grant, 60-61; Ostwald Award, Am Bandmasters Asn, 61; ASCAP Awards, 65-73. *Mailing Add:* Music Dept Duquesne Univ Pittsburgh PA 15282

JENKINS, NEWELL
CONDUCTOR, MUSICOLOGIST
b New Haven, Conn, Feb 8, 15. *Study:* Orchesterschule Sächsische Staatskapelle; Freiburg Musiksem, Germany; studied with Carl Orff & Erich Doflein, Germany; Yale Univ, BMus, 41. *Rec Perf:* Over 50, mainly of Italian comp. *Pos:* Founder & dir, Piccola Accad Musicale, Italy, 52 & Clarion Music Soc, 67-; dir, Castelfrance Fest. *Teaching:* Prof, NY Univ, formerly; guest prof, Univ Calif, Irvine. *Awards:* Second Ann New York Handel Award, 59; Cavaliere Italian Repub, Order of Merit, 67. *Bibliog:* George Malko (auth), A Detective Armed with a Baton, 1/10/82 & Donal Henahan (auth), Opera: Agostino Steffani Premiere, 1/15/82, New York Times. *Mem:* Am Musicol Soc. *Interests:* Musical scores misplaced or abandoned; baroque music. *Publ:* Auth, Thematic Catalogue of the Works of G B Sammartini, 76. *Mailing Add:* Clarion Music Soc 1860 Broadway New York NY 10023

JENKINS, SPEIGHT
DIRECTOR—OPERA, CRITIC-WRITER
b Dallas, Tex. *Study:* Univ Tex, BA; Columbia Univ, LLB. *Pos:* Music critic, New York Post, formerly; contrib ed, Ovation Mag, currently; host, Live from the Met, PBS, currently; producer music prog, WQXR radio, New York, currently; gen dir, Seattle Opera Asn, 83- *Publ:* Auth, Opera Through the Eyes of Singers, Alfred Knopf (in prep). *Mailing Add:* Seattle Opera Asn PO Box 9248 Seattle WA 98109

JENKINS, SUSAN ELAINE
COMPOSER, EDUCATOR
b Lewis, Del, Apr 8, 53. *Study:* Univ Del, BS(music educ), 75; Ohio State Univ, with Thomas Wells, MM(comp), 79. *Works:* Music for Dancer & Tape, Dance Dept Conct, Univ Del, 74; String Quartet, Univ Del Res String Quartet, 75; Meditations I & II (chorus), Rehoboth Presbyterian Church, 79; Griqua (electronic tape), Electronic Music Fest, Univ Tenn, 80; The Ralley Rag (piano), Elizabeth Ralley, 82; For Lovers Parted and Lovers Never Joined (bass, piano & perc), Doug Anderson & Susan Jenkins, 83. *Teaching:* Cond, Sussex Cent Jr High, 75-77; grad res asst, comput assoc proj arts & humanities, Ohio State Univ, 78-82; programmer & analyst data processing, micros & sound, 82- *Awards:* Perf Award for Griqua, Nat Conf Women Music, Univ Calif, Santa Barbara, 79. *Mem:* Founder, Central Ohio Comp Alliance; Am Soc Univ Comp; Am Women Comp, Inc; Soc Music Theory; Col Music Soc. *Publ:* Auth, Sound Systems on Micros, ACM-SIGUCCS, 83. *Mailing Add:* 4825 Kingshill Dr #302 Columbus OH 43229

JENKINS, SYLVIA
PIANO, TEACHER
b San Jose, Calif. *Study:* Stanford Univ; Music Acad West; Accad Chigiana, Siena, Italy; San Francisco Consv Music, BMus, 63. *Rec Perf:* Seven Cello & Piano Sonatas (Beethoven & Brahms), Musicelli, 81. *Pos:* Music dir, Crown Chamber Players, Univ Calif, Santa Cruz, 71- *Teaching:* Instr music, San Francisco State Univ & Lone Mountain Col, 63-72; lectr, Univ Calif, Santa Cruz, 70-; music dir, 71- *Awards:* First Prize, Instrumental Conct Compt, San Francisco Critics Circle, 50; Piano Prize, Munich Int Compt, 61. *Mailing Add:* 775 26th Ave San Francisco CA 94121

JENNI, D(ONALD) MARTIN
COMPOSER, EDUCATOR
b Milwaukee, Wis, Oct 4, 37. *Study:* DePaul Univ, with L Stein & A Tcherepnin, BMus, 54; Univ Chicago, with G Cooper, AM, 62; Stanford Univ, with H Searle & L Ratner, DMA, 66. *Works:* Inventio super Nomen, Am Comp Alliance, 66; Mond/monde, Ill Sesquicentennial Comn, 68; Cucumber Music, Assoc Music Publ, 69; Eulalia's Rounds, Am Comp Alliance, 72; Musica dell'autunno, 75 & Cherry Valley, 76, Assoc Music Publ; Ballfall, Am Comp Alliance, 81. *Pos:* Comp in res, Secondary Sch Syst, Ann Arbor, Mich, 60-61; musical dir, Compgnie de Danse Jo Lechay, 75-82. *Teaching:* Chmn theory & comp, DePaul Univ, 66-68; vis prof, Stanford Univ, 68 & 77; prof, Univ Iowa, 68- *Awards:* Young Comp Award, BMI, 53, 55 & 56; Humanities Award, Stanford Univ, 65 & 66; Comp Award, Nat Endowment for Arts, 81. *Mem:* Am Comp Alliance; Int Soc Contemp Music (mem bd, 66-71); Am Music Ctr. *Interests:* Medieval languages, literature. *Publ:* Auth, Cum novo cantico: A Primer of Biblical and Medieval Latin, Eble Music Co, 83. *Mailing Add:* Sch Music Univ Iowa Iowa City IA 52242

JENNINGS, HARLAN FRANCIS
EDUCATOR, BARITONE
b Kansas City, Kans, May 24, 44. *Study:* Washburn Univ, BMus, 66; Univ Kans, MMus, 69; Col-Consv Music, Univ Cincinnati, DMA, 78. *Rec Perf:* Magelonelieder (Brahms), 79, Liederkreis, Op 39 (Schumann), 81 & Songs (Debussy & Mahler), 82, Young Artists Series, WKAR TV. *Roles:* Sharpless in Madama Butterfly, Opera Grand Rapids, 74; Don Giovanni in Don Giovanni, Opera Co Gtr Lansing, 77; Dr Falke, 77 & Sharpless in Madama Butterfly, 81, Northern Ind Opera Asn; Sharpless in Madama Butterfly, 82, Sgt Belcore in L'Elisir d'Amore, 83 & Count Almaviva in The Marriage of Figaro, 83, Lyric Opera Northern Mich. *Teaching:* Assoc prof voice, opera hist, German & French diction, Mich State Univ, 73- *Mem:* Sonneck Soc; Col Music Soc. *Interests:* History of grand opera in the American West. *Publ:* Auth, Grand Opera in Kansas in the 19th Century, Kans Hist, 80. *Mailing Add:* 787 Burcham 12 East Lansing MI 48823

JENNINGS, ROBERT LEE
EDUCATOR
b Whitehall, Mich, Feb 23, 28. *Study:* Augustana Col, BME, 53; Teachers Col, Columbia Univ, summers 55 & 56; Temple Univ, summer 56; Western Mich Univ, MA(music), 60; Mich State Univ, PhD(music), 69. *Pos:* Choir dir, Whitehall High Sch, Mich, 55-56 & Muskegon Sr High Sch, Mich, 56-60. *Teaching:* Instr voice, Western Mich Univ, 62-63; asst prof voice & choral music, Univ SDak, 63-66; prof music, Univ Wis, Whitewater, 66- *Mem:* Nat Asn Teachers Singing (pres state chap, 78-79, state gov, 80-81); Am Choral Dir Asn; Wis Choral Dir Asn; Music Educr Nat Conf; Wis Music Educr Conf. *Publ:* Auth, Music Education as a Therapy, Mich Music Educr, 4/61; High School Experiment: The Honors Chorale, Music Educr J, 2-3/65. *Mailing Add:* Dept Music Univ Wis Whitewater WI 52190

JENNINGS, THEODORE MCKINLEY, JR
ADMINISTRATOR, EDUCATOR
b Laurel, Miss, Oct 15, 29. *Study:* Fisk Univ, Tenn, BA(music), 52, MA(musicol), 54; Ind Univ, Bloomington, PhD(musicol), 67. *Pos:* Choir dir & minister music, New Rocky Valley Baptist Church, Grambling, La, 77-81; mem, NE La Arts Coun, 82- *Teaching:* Choir dir, Ark Baptist Col, 56-58; asst prof music, Grambling State Univ, 63-67, coordr humanities team, 68-69, head music dept, 68- *Awards:* Nat Endowment Humanities Fel, 76-77. *Mem:* Am Musicol Soc; Music Educr Nat Conf; La Music Educr Asn; Phi Mu Alpha Sinfonia (gov province 14, 77-78). *Mailing Add:* 305 Lewis St Grambling LA 71245

JENSEN, JAMES A
EDUCATOR, COMPOSER
b Dayton, Ohio, Dec 29, 44. *Study:* Kans State Col, with Donald Key & Markwood Holmes, BM, MM; Fla State Univ, with John Boda & Carlisle Floyd, DMus. *Works:* 3 Movements (brass quartet), 69; In Memoriam: Dr Martin Luther King, Jr (sop & seven instrm), 69; Orpheus Variations (chamber orch), 70; 4 Songs (sop & piano), 71; Viola Sonata, 72; Woodwind Quintet, 72; Primogenitur (song cycle for sop & chamber orch), 73. *Teaching:* Assoc prof music, Samford Univ, 68- *Mailing Add:* Dept Music Samford Univ Birmingham AL 35229

JENSEN, RICHARD MARSH
PERCUSSION, EDUCATOR
b Seattle, Wash, Mar 28, 52. *Study:* Univ Wash, 69-71; Manhattan Sch Music, 71-72; Col Consv Music, Univ Cincinnati, BMus. *Works:* Life, Change & Thought, comn by Contemp Dance Theatre, Cincinnati, 78. *Pos:* Prin perc, Colo Phil, Evergreen, 72; asst prin perc, Cincinnati Symph Orch, 72-; perc, Grand Teton Music Fest, 78-82. *Teaching:* Instr perc, Univ Cincinnati, 75-76. *Mem:* Percussive Arts Soc. *Publ:* Contribr, Master Technique Builders for Snare Drum, Belwin Mills, 82. *Mailing Add:* 729 Betula Ave Cincinnati OH 45229

JEPPESEN, LAURA
VIOLA DA GAMBA, EDUCATOR
Study: Wheaton Col, BA; Yale Univ, MA; studied with Nancy Cirillo & Broadus Erle; Hochschule Music, Hamburg, with Johannes Koch; Consv Royale Brussels, with Wieland Kuijken. *Rec Perf:* On Nonesuch, Desmar, Harmonia Mundi, Philips & Titanic. *Pos:* Mem, Boston Camerata, currently; Boston Museum Trio, currently & Orch 18th Century, currently; performer, Banchetto Musicale, Aston Magna La Petite Band & others. *Teaching:* Mem fac, Univ Mass, formerly; mem fac early music & viola da gamba, New England Consv Music, currently. *Awards:* Fulbright Scholar, 71-72; Belgian Govt Grant, 72-74; Bunting Fel, Radcliffe Col, 81. *Mailing Add:* New England Consv Music 290 Huntington Rd Boston MA 02115

JEPSON, WARNER
COMPOSER
b Sioux City, Iowa, Mar 24, 30. *Study:* Oberlin Consv, BM, 53. *Works:* San Francisco's Burning (ballad opera), San Francisco Playhouse, 60; Totentanz (ballet score), San Francisco Ballet Co, 67; The Bed (film score), James Broughton, 68; Peace (flute & tape), Owen James, 68; The Machine (electronic tape environment), San Francisco Museum Modern Art, 69; Luminous Procuress (film score), Stephen Arnold, 71; Irving Bridge, 73 & Lostine, 74, Nat Ctr Experiments TV, KQED. *Pos:* Comp in res, Nat Ctr Experiment TV, KQED, 72-75. *Teaching:* Instr comp, piano & theory, San Francisco Consv Music, 64-67; head theory dept, Family Light Music Sch, Sausalito, Calif, 70-75. *Awards:* Nat Endowment Humanitites Grant, 75; Emmy, 74. *Mailing Add:* 512 Diamond St San Francisco CA 94114

JERGENSON, DALE ROGER
COMPOSER, TENOR

b St Paul, Minn, Sept 28, 35. *Study:* San Diego State Col, BA, 61, MA, 63; Univ Calif, Los Angeles. *Works:* Symphony for Band, 65 & Tanka Pieces, 70, Seesaw Music; The Lament of Job, 70 & The Vision, 71, G Schirmer; King Henry, 78 & Gloria, 80, Jergenson Prod; Song of the Birds, comn by Richard Rath, 80. *Rec Perf:* Music of Arnold Schoenberg, 64 & Vespers (Monteverdi), 64, Columbia Masterworks; The Glory of Gabrieli, 65; Tanka Pieces, Requiem for a City & The Vision, Grenadilla Rec, 77. *Pos:* Touring soloist & chorister, Gregg Smith Singers & The Roger Wagner Chorale, 20 yrs. *Teaching:* Asst prof vocal music, WTex State Univ, 64-65; assoc prof music, Univ Calif, Los Angeles, 67-68. *Mem:* Am Fedn Musicians; Am Guild Musical Artists. *Mailing Add:* 15035 Wyandotte St Van Nuys CA 91405

JERNIGAN, MELVYN
TROMBONE, EDUCATOR

Study: Curtis Inst Music; studied trombone with William H Hill, Charles Gusikoff, Robert Harper & Arnold Jacobs. *Pos:* Mem, St Louis Symph Orch, currently; mgr, St Louis Quintet, currently; performer, Spoleto Fest, 77 & 78. *Teaching:* Mem fac trombone & low brass, St Louis Consv Music, currently & St Louis Univ, currently. *Mailing Add:* St Louis Consv Music 560 Trinity Ave St Louis MO 63130

JETER, JAMES YANDELL
BASSOON

b Paris, Tex. *Study:* Univ Tex, Austin, with James Dickie, BMus, 71; Juilliard Sch, with Harold Goltzer, MMus, 73; private study with Milan Turkovic, Vienna, 74-76. *Rec Perf:* A Christmas Carol (Thea Musgrave), Moss Rec Group, 79; Solo Bassoon Recording, Musical Heritage Soc, 83. *Pos:* Solo perf, Biel Symph Orch, Switzerland, 7/75, Carnegie Recital Hall Debut, 2/80 & Francaix Concerto for Bassoon and Piano, St Stephen's Church, New York, 11/82; prin bassoon, Goldovsky Opera Inst, 77; bassoon, Va Opera, 79-80, prin bassoon, 82-; bassoon, Metropolitan Opera Orch, 80- & Opera Orch New York, 82-; solo bassoonist, Virtuosi Quintet, New York, 83- *Mem:* Int Double Reed Soc; Am Fedn Musicians. *Publ:* Auth, The Composer Speaks, Int Double Reed Soc J, 81. *Rep:* Akiva Artists 1755 Broadway Suite 503 New York NY 10019. *Mailing Add:* 171 W 80th #8 New York NY 10024

JOBELMANN, HERMAN FREDERICK
DOUBLE BASS

b Portland, Ore. *Study:* Multnomah Col; extensive private study on piano, bs viol & music educ. *Pos:* Prin bs, Ore Symph Orch, 35-; mem, Portland Symph Orch, 25 yrs, prin bs, 12 yrs; prin bs & tour mgr, Clebanoff Strings, Roger Wagner Chorale, formerly; prin bs & orch manager, Metropolitan Opera Nat Co, 65-67; string bs & librn, Eastern Music, 65-; Opera Co of Boston, 67-68. *Teaching:* Music at Multnomah Col, Portland Univ, Portland State Col & Lewis & Clark Univ, formerly. *Mailing Add:* 17102 SW Eldorado Tigard OR 97223

JOCHSBERGER, TZIPORA HILDE
ADMINISTRATOR, COMPOSER

b Leutershausen, Ger, Dec 27, 20; US citizen. *Study:* Palestine Acad Music, 42; Sem Col Jewish Music, Jewish Theol Sem, SMM, 58, DSM, 72. *Works:* Hebrew Madrigals, perf by Western Winds, throughout US & Europe; Melodies of Israel, Shengold Publ, 61; Hebrew Folk Melodies, 78, Favorite Hassidic & Israeli Melodies, 78, A Harvest of Jewish Song, 80, Contrasts for Piano, 81 & Bekol Zimra, 81, Tara Publ. *Pos:* Founder, Rubin Acad Music, Jerusalem, 47-50; founder & dir, Hebrew Arts Sch, New York, 52- *Teaching:* Instr music, Arab Women's Training Col, Jerusalem, 42-47; instr music educ, Teachers Inst Women, Yeshiva Univ, 54-73 & Cantors Inst & Teachers Inst, Jewish Theol Sem, 56-73. *Mem:* ASCAP; Music Coun Nat Jewish Welfare Bd (vpres, 58); Am Soc Jewish Music (mem bd gov, 74). *Mailing Add:* 5 W 86th St New York NY 10024

JOCHUM, VERONICA
PIANO, EDUCATOR

b Berlin, Germany. *Study:* Staatliche Musikhochschule, Munich, Konzertreife Prüfung, 55, conct dipl, 57; studied with Eliza Hansen, Edwin Fischer & Josef Benvenuti, 58-59 & Rudolf Serkin, 59-61. *Rec Perf:* On Philips, Deutsche Grammophon & Golden Crest. *Pos:* Conct tours with maj orchs throughout North & South Am, Europe & Africa incl Berlin Phil, Boston Symph, Baltimore Symph, London Symph, London Phil, Vienna Symph, Concertgebouw Orch & Los Angeles Chamber Orch; radio & TV appearances; recitalist in more than 50 countries; participant, Marlboro Music Fest, 59-60; artist in res, Eastern Music Fest, 67-72 & 78, Tanglewood, 74, Montreux Fest, 79-81, Bregeur Fest, 80-81, Grant Park, 82 & others. *Teaching:* Mem fac music, Settlement Sch Music, Philadelphia, 59-61 & Berkshire Music Ctr, 74; mem fac piano, New England Consv Music, 65-; guest lectr, Radcliffe Sem Ser, 70. *Rep:* Jacques Leiser Artist Mgt Dorchester Towers 155 68th St New York NY 10023. *Mailing Add:* 14 Gray Gardens W Cambridge MA 02138

JOHANNESEN, GRANT
PIANO, EDUCATOR

b Salt Lake City, Utah, July 30, 21. *Study:* McCune Sch Music, BMus, 39; Princeton Univ, studied piano with Robert Casadesus & theory with Robert Sessions, 41-44; Fontainebleau Sch Arts, with Robert Casadesus & Nadia Boulanger, 47-49; Cleveland Inst Music, Hon Dr Music, 75; Univ Utah, HHD, 77; Gov State Univ, Hon Dr Music, 81. *Works:* Improvisation on a Mormon Hymn (piano), Oxford Univ Press. *Rec Perf:* Sixty for HMV, Capitol, Vox & Golden Crest. *Pos:* Debut, New York Phil, Carnegie Hall, 50;

adv & music dir, Cleveland Inst Music, 73-76, pres, 77-; panelist, Nat Endowment Arts, 81-; world tours incl Soviet Union, Australia, the Orient & SAfrica. *Teaching:* Performer, fac mem & admin bd, Aspen Fest, 60-66. *Awards:* Premier Prix, Reine Elisabeth Concours, 49; Harriet Cohen Int Piano Award, 51; Distinguished Contribution to Music World Award, East West Univ, 83. *Rep:* Thea Dispeker 59 E 54th St New York NY 10022. *Mailing Add:* Cleveland Inst Music 11021 East Blvd Cleveland OH 44106

JOHANOS, DONALD
MUSIC DIRECTOR & CONDUCTOR

b Cedar Rapids, Iowa, Feb 10, 28. *Study:* Eastman Sch Music, MusB, 50, MusM, 52; Coe Col, Hon DFA, 62. *Pos:* Music dir, Altoona Symph, Pa, 53-56, Johnstown Symph, Pa, 55-56 & Honolulu Symph Orch, 79-; assoc cond, Dallas Symph Orch, 57-61, res cond, 61-62, music dir, 62-70; assoc cond, Pittsburgh Symph, 70-79; artistic dir, Hawaii Opera Theater, 79-; guest cond, Mostly Mozart Fest, New York, Hong Kong Phil, Mexico City Orch, Pittsburgh Opera Co, Opera Co Philadelphia, Ambler Fest, Amsterdam Concertgebouw Orch, Rochester Phil, Vancouver Symph, Chicago Symph Orch, San Francisco Symph, Netherlands Radio Phil, Swiss Radio Orch & others. *Teaching:* Pa State Univ, 53-55, Southern Methodist Univ, 58-62 & Hockaday Sch, Dallas, Tex, 62-65. *Awards:* Grants, Am Symph Orch League & Rockefeller Found, 55-58. *Mem:* Am Fedn Musicians; Int Cong Strings. *Mailing Add:* Honolulu Symph Orch 1000 Bishop St Suite 901 Honolulu HI 96813

JOHANSON, BRYAN
COMPOSER, GUITAR

b Yakima, Wash, Dec 18, 51. *Study:* Portland State Univ, BS, 75; Aspen Sch Music, 78. *Works:* Fantasy, Op 17, David Tanenbaum, 79; Piano Trio No 1, Op 19, Florrstan Trio, 80; Duo No 2, Op 8, Comp Graphics, Ltd, 80; Duo No 5, Op 19, Walter Tanenbaum Duo, 80; Labyrinth, Op 39, David Tanenbaum, 81; Elizabethan Songs, Op 42, Composers Ens, 83; Quietude, Op 35, St Paul Chamber Orch, 83. *Teaching:* Asst prof, Portland State Univ, 79- *Awards:* Second Prize, Aspen Composition Cont, Aspen Music Fest, 78 & Univ Calif, Los Angeles Organ Comp Cont, 80; First Prize, St Paul Chamber Orch Cont, 83. *Mem:* ASCAP. *Mailing Add:* Music Dept Portland State Univ Portland OR 97207

JOHANSSON, ANNETTE
MEZZO-SOPRANO, EDUCATOR

Study: Eastman Sch Music, perf cert; Ind Univ; Univ Hawaii, MM. *Roles:* Madame Larina in Eugene Onegin, Hawaii Opera Theatre, 83. *Pos:* Recitalist & oratorio soloist in midwest US & Hawaii; appearances with Spring Quintet, formerly. *Teaching:* Mem fac, Cent Mich Univ, 76-79; lectr voice, Univ Hawaii, Honolulu, formerly, asst prof, 79- *Mailing Add:* 1002-A Prospect St #31 Honolulu HI 96822

JOHN, PATRICIA SPAULDING
HARP, COMPOSER

b Canton, Ill, July 16, 16. *Study:* Mills Col, 34-35; Curtis Inst Music, 36-37; William Marsh Rice Univ, BA, 37-41. *Works:* Sea Changes, Suite for Harp Alone, 68, Aprille (harp), 69, Mnemosyne (harp), 69, Tachystos (harp), 71, Henriette (harp), 74, Americana, Suite for Harp Alone, 78 & Serenata (harp), 81, Pantile Press. *Pos:* Solo harp, int recitalist, 42-; prin harpist, Springfield Civic Symph, 47-48 & Galveston Civic Symph, 52-55; assoc harpist, Houston Symph, 55-56. *Teaching:* Harp, private studios, 42-; prof, Houston Baptist Univ, 76-; vis prof, Stowe Summer Sch Music, England, 73. *Bibliog:* Marion Bannerman (auth), Review of New Music, Am Harp J, 68-; Susan McDonald (auth), Review of New Music, Notes, Quart J Music Libr Asn, 73; Associasione Lirica Concertistica Ambrosiana, La Donna Nella Creazione Musicale, Bibliot Germanica Milano, Italy, 79. *Mem:* Am Harp Soc (pres, San Jacinto chap, 75, vpres, 79); UK Harpists Asn; Asn Int Harpistes, France. *Interests:* Development of harp and harpists of the past. *Publ:* Auth, Javanese Tjelempung, 70, Conversation at Queekhoven, Holland, 73 & Madness of Sir Tristram, 76, Am Harp J; The Krumpholtz, UK Harpists Mag, 80; Chertsey Tiles, Sir Tristram, Folk Harp J, 81. *Mailing Add:* 1414 Milford Ave Houston TX 77006

JOHNSON, A PAUL
COMPOSER, MUSIC DIRECTOR

b Indianapolis, Ind, Jan 27, 55. *Study:* Studied comp with Thomas Briccetti & Russell J Peck & piano with William Eltzroth. *Works:* Musical Mirage Express (children's musical), Ind Rept Theatre & Syracuse Stage, 76; Dream Child (musical theatre), Palisades Theatre, 79; Autumn Trio (chamber music), Pinellas Co Arts Coun, 80; Suite After Charles of Orleans (chamber music), Fla Friends of Early Music, 80; Garcia Lorca's Bicycle Ride (theatre piece), Salvador Dali Museum, 82; Parchman Plays the Game (mime ballet), Midsummer Mime Theatre, 82; Anzollo & Valeria (opera), Asolo Opera, 83. *Pos:* Gen mgr, Contemp Music Found, 74-77; comp & music dir, Ind Repty Theatre, 76-77; comp in res, Palisades theatre, 78-79 & Pinellas Co Arts Coun, 79-82. *Awards:* Ind Arts Comn Fel, 79 & 82; Fla Arts Coun Fel, 80. *Mailing Add:* 554 63rd Ave S St Petersburg FL 33705

JOHNSON, ALVIN H
EDUCATOR, MUSICOLOGIST

b Virginia, Minn, Apr 18, 14. *Study:* Univ Minn, BA, 36; Yale Univ, PhD, 54; Univ Pa, Hon MA, 71. *Teaching:* From instr to asst prof music hist, Yale Univ, 50-60; lectr, Hartford Col, 57-58 & Swarthmore Col, 62-66; assoc prof, Ohio State Univ, 60-61; assoc prof lit, hist & musicol, Univ Pa, 61-82. *Awards:* Morse Fel, Yale Univ, 58-59; Fulbright Res Fel to Italy, 58-59. *Mem:* Am Musicol Soc (treas, 70- & exec dir, currently); Renaissance Soc Am. *Interests:* Music of the Renaissance, 16th century. *Publ:* Coauth, Art of Music, Crowell, 60. *Mailing Add:* Dept Music Univ Pa Philadelphia PA 19104

JOHNSON, BEVERLEY PECK
TEACHER, SOPRANO

b Walla Walla, Wash. *Study:* Ellison White Consv Music. *Teaching:* Voice, Juilliard Sch Music, 65-; adj prof, Brooklyn Col Music, 82- *Awards:* Tenth Anniversary Symposium & Voice Found Special Award. *Mem:* Bohemians. *Mailing Add:* Juilliard Sch Music Lincoln Ctr New York NY 10023

JOHNSON, CALVERT
ORGAN, EDUCATOR

b Takoma Park, Md, Nov 15, 49. *Study:* Kalamazoo Col, with Danford Byrens, BA(music), 71; Northwestern Univ, with Karel Paukert, MM(organ), 72, DM(organ), 75. *Pos:* Dir music, First United Methodist Church, 75-77; organist, Grace Episcopal Church, Muskogee, Okla, 79-82. *Teaching:* Asst prof, Northeastern Okla State Univ, 77- *Awards:* Grant, French Govt, 74-75; Nat Endowment Humanities Grant, 81. *Mem:* Am Guild Organists (sub-dean Tulsa chap, 79-81 & dean, 81-82); Am Musicol Soc; Am Recorder Soc; Am Asn Univ Prof (vpres Northeastern Okla State Univ chap, 80-81); Music Teachers Nat Asn. *Interests:* Performance practices and repertoire of early Spanish, Italian, and Portuguese keyboard music. *Publ:* Auth, Rhythmic Alteration in Renaissance Spain, 76, Felix-Alexandre Guilmant, 77 & Spanish Keyboard Ornamentation, 1535-1626, 78, Diapason; La Musique d'orgue espagnol, Orgues Meridionales, 78. *Mailing Add:* 317 W Morgan Tahlequah OK 74464

JOHNSON, CLYDE E
EDUCATOR, COMPOSER

b Fennimore, Wis, Feb 16, 30. *Study:* Univ Iowa, BM, 51, MA, 55, PhD, 57. *Works:* Prelude & Toccata (solo piano), Albert Singerman & others, 56; Sonata (clarinet & piano), perf by comp, 57; Iowa Flowering, Three Songs, Judy Johnson, 58; Sonata No 2 (clarinet & piano), comn by Parsons Col, 59; Etudes (band), comn by Glenwood High Sch, 67; North Star Seasons (band), Conct Band, Univ Minn, Morris, 81; Trombone Monologue, Jeff Johnson, 83. *Teaching:* Asst prof, Bowling Green State Univ, 58-59; from asst prof to assoc prof, Parsons Col, 59-61; from asst prof to prof, Univ Minn, Morris, 61- *Awards:* Fulbright Fel, 57. *Mailing Add:* 408 W 5th St Morris MN 56267

JOHNSON, DAVID NATHANIEL
COMPOSER, ORGAN

b San Antonio, Tex, June 28, 22. *Study:* Curtis Inst, 39-41; Trinity Univ, BM, 50; Syracuse Univ, MM, 51, PhD, 56. *Works:* Trumpet Tune in D Major for Organ, 62, The Lone Wild Bird (choral), 65, Lovely Child, Holy Child (choral), 66, Gloria Deo I & II (choral), 67, Service of Nine Lessons & Carols, 69, Wedding Music for Organ I-IV, 70-84, Carols of Many Lands I-III (choral), 79-82, and over 400 others, Augsburg Publ House. *Pos:* Organist, St Olaf Col, Northfield, Minn, 60-67. *Teaching:* Prof music, Alfred Univ, 56-60; prof organ & head music dept, St Olaf Col, 60-67; prof, Syracuse Univ, 67-69; prof & head organ dept, Ariz State Univ, 69-81. *Bibliog:* Robert P Wetzler (auth), Contemporary Composers: D N Johnson, J Church Music, 9/69. *Mem:* Am Guild Organists. *Publ:* Auth, A Hymn Tune Index, Hymn Soc Am, 4/60; Practice Habits, J Church Music, 5/65; What is Sacred Music?, Musart, 4/71; Instruction Book for Beginning Organists, 62, rev ed, 73 & Choral Arranging, 84, Augsburg Publ House. *Mailing Add:* 905 W Tulane Tempe AZ 85283

JOHNSON, ELLEN SCHULTZ
LIBRARIAN, EDUCATOR

b Beatrice, Nebr, Apr 11, 18. *Study:* Friends Univ, AB, 39; Univ Ill, Urbana-Champaigne, BS, 41; Univ Kans, 76-81, Western Ky Univ, 70-73. *Pos:* Librn, Wichita State Univ, 59-68, Western Ky Univ, 68-73 & Univ Kans, 73- *Teaching:* Asst prof music res, Wichita State Univ, 59-68 & Western Ky Univ, 68-73; librn, Univ Kans, 77- *Mem:* Sigma Alpha Iota; Sonneck Society; Mountain Plains Music Libr Asn; Asn Rec Sound Collections. *Interests:* Computerized cataloging; historical sound recording collections; music historians and educators; jazz; opera. *Publ:* Auth, Interview: Harold Gleason, Diapason, 11/82; Interview: Helmut Wunnenberg, Am Music Teacher, 9-10/82; Music Collections—University of Kansas, Mountain Plains Libr Asn, 83. *Mailing Add:* 3112 Longhorn Dr Lawrence KS 66044

JOHNSON, GORDON JAMES
CONDUCTOR & MUSIC DIRECTOR

b St Paul, Minn, Oct 25, 49. *Study:* Bemidji State Univ, BS, 71; Winona State Univ, MS, 76; Univ Ore, Eugene, DMA, 82. *Rec Perf:* Elijah (Mendelssohn), Sound Design, 82. *Pos:* Cond, Univ Ore Sinfonietta, 81; music dir & cond, Great Falls Symph Asn, 82-; music adv & cond, Glacier Symph Orch, Kalispell, Mont, 82- *Teaching:* Instr music, Col Great Falls, 82- *Awards:* Cond Fel, Women's Inst St Paul Chamber Orch, 70; Ruth Lorraine Close Music Award, Univ Ore, 81 & 82. *Mem:* Am Symph Orch League. *Publ:* Auth, Improving Your Concerts Through Research, Ore Music Educr J, winter 80-81. *Mailing Add:* 1608 4th Ave N Great Falls MT 59401

JOHNSON, GRACE GREY
EDUCATOR, PIANO

b Jacksonville, Fla. *Study:* Howard Univ, BMus(educ), 47; Columbia Univ, MA(music educ & piano), 52; Sch Fine Arts & Appl Arts, Boston Univ, DMA(music educ & hist), 64. *Rec Perf:* 25 Christian Hymns for conct perf, Jambe Rec Co, 80. *Teaching:* From instr to prof music, Fla A&M Univ, 47- *Mem:* Nat Music Soc; Am Musicol Soc; Nat Asn Teachers Educ; Music Educr Nat Conf; Fla Col Music Educr Asn. *Publ:* Auth, Consideration of Auditory and Visual Processes in Music, Fla A&M Univ Res Bulletin, 80. *Mailing Add:* 1601 Hernando Dr Tallahassee FL 32304

JOHNSON, GUY C
EDUCATOR, TEACHER

b Marinette, Wis, Nov 8, 33. *Study:* Univ Wis, Milwaukee, BFA, 55; Ind Univ, MM, 56. *Pos:* Solo appearances, with US orch incl Milwaukee Symph, Rochester Symph, Austin Symph, Jewish Symph, Santa Barbara Symph, Waukasha Symph & Lutheran Symphonic Band Milwaukee. *Teaching:* Asst prof piano, Drury Col, 56-57 & Luther Col, Iowa, 59-68; assoc prof, Friends Univ, 68- *Mem:* Wichita Area Piano Teachers League (pres, 80-81); Kans Music Teachers Asn (2nd vpres, 83); Wichita Art Asn; Nat Guild Piano Teachers. *Mailing Add:* Friends Univ 2100 Univ Wichita KS 67213

JOHNSON, JAMES (DAVID)
PIANO

b Greenville, SC, Aug 7, 48. *Study:* Univ Ariz, BM, 70, MM, 72, DMA, 76; study with Ozan Marsh, Patricia Benkman-Mark, Lee Luvisi, Robert Muczynski, Anjelica von Sauer, David Gibson & Louis Kentner. *Rec Perf:* 15 Etudes de Virtuosite (Moszkowski), VLR-LP, 73; Chaminade Concertstück, 77 & Five Pieces (Dohnanyi), 77, Orion; Mendelssohn Concerto in G minor, 77 & 80 & Beethoven Concerto No 1, 83, Musical Heritage Soc. *Pos:* Piano soloist, with orch incl Boston Pops, Royal Phil, Victoria Symph, Greenville Symph, Anchorage Symph & Fairbanks Symph; solo piano recitals, chamber music concts throughout US, Pianists Found Am. *Teaching:* Prof piano, Univ Alaska, Fairbanks, 74- *Awards:* Ten Best Rec List, Clavier Mag, 79; Record of Month, 9/80 & 4/83, Musical Heritage Soc. *Mem:* Music Teachers Nat Asn; charter mem, Alaska Music Teachers Asn. *Rep:* Pianists Found Am 210 Fifth Ave Suite 1102 New York NY 10010. *Mailing Add:* 58 F St Fairbanks AK 99701

JOHNSON, JOYCE LYNNE
EDUCATOR, TEACHER

b Evanston, Ill, Feb 1, 51. *Study:* Rosary Col, BA, 73; Univ Chicago, AM, 76, PhD, 83. *Teaching:* Lectr music hist & theory, Rosary Col, 76-81. *Awards:* Marion Talbot Fel, Am Asn Univ Women, 79. *Mem:* Am Musicol Soc; Am Guild Organists. *Interests:* Late 18th century oratorio; musical life in 18th century Rome. *Publ:* Auth, Giuseppe Riconsciuto: Un Oratorio di Jommelli ..., Archivum Scholarum Piarum, 81; ed, Symphonies of Pasquale Aufossi, In: The Symphony 1740-1820, Garland Publ, 83. *Mailing Add:* 7819 Kostner Skokie IL 60076

JOHNSON, JUNE DURKIN
EDUCATOR, SOPRANO

b Danbury Conn, June 22, 26. *Study:* Juilliard Sch Music, BS, 49; Univ Kans, MM, 50; Univ Ill, DMA, 67. *Teaching:* Instr, Eastern NMex Univ, 57-60; prof music, Eastern Ill Univ, 60- *Awards:* Fulbright Scholar, Berlin, Germany, 58-59; Nat Endowment Humanities Grant, 78; Distinguished Fac Award, Eastern Ill Univ, 78. *Mem:* Nat Opera Asn; Cent Opera Serv; Nat Asn Teachers Singing. *Mailing Add:* 2615 S Fifth Charleston IL 61920

JOHNSON, MARY JANE (ROSE)
SOPRANO

b Pampa, Tex, Mar 22, 50. *Study:* Tex Tech Univ, BME, 72; WTex State Univ, MM, 78. *Roles:* Agatha in Der Freischütz, New York Lyric Opera Co, 81; Musetta in La Boheme, 82 & Adina in L'Elisir d'Amore, 82, Opera Co Philadelphia; Rosalinda in Die Fledermaus, 82 & Zanthe in Die Liebe der Danae, 82, Santa Fe Opera Co; Musetta & Freia in Das Rheingold, San Francisco Opera Co, 83; Jenifer in The Midsummer Marriage, Tippett, 83. *Teaching:* Instr voice, McMurray Col, 74-76; head voice dept & opera wkshp, Amarillo Col, 77-80. *Awards:* Winner, First Pavarotti Int Vocal Compt, 81. *Mem:* Nat Asn Teachers Singing; Mu Phi Epsilon; Am Guild Musical Artists. *Mailing Add:* 1710 S Polk Amarillo TX 79102

JOHNSON, ROSE-MARIE
VIOLIN, TEACHER

b Seattle, Wash. *Study:* Juilliard Sch, with Galamian & Delay, artist dipl, 60; Univ Southern Calif, with Shapiro, DMA, 72. *Pos:* Violinist, Minneapolis Symph Orch, 60-67, St Paul Chamber Orch, 67-68, Univ Southern Calif Piano Trio, 70-72, Kennedy String Quartet, 72-73, Arctic Chamber Trio & Ens, 74-79 & Oriana Piano Trio, 83-; concertmaster & soloist, Arctic Chamber Orch, 74-79. *Teaching:* Asst prof violin, viola & chamber music, Univ Alaska, 74-79; artist in res, Kyung Hee Univ, Seoul, Korea, 78 & Montalvo Ctr Arts, Saratoga, Calif, 83. *Awards:* Fel, John D Rockefeller III Fund, Kennedy Found & Thailand Govt, 72-73. *Mem:* Am String Teachers Asn; Chamber Music Am; Int League Women Comp; Col Music Soc; Int Viola d'amore Soc. *Interests:* Music for violin and chamber ensembles using strings by women composers. *Publ:* Auth, Annotated Bibliography of Music for the Viola d'amore, Viola da Gamba Soc J, 70. *Mailing Add:* 175 Red Rock Way Apt K207 San Francisco CA 94131

JOHNSON, ROY HAMLIN
PIANO, COMPOSER

b Beckley, WVa, July 7, 29. *Study:* Eastman Sch Music, studied piano with Sandor Vas, BM(perf cert), 49, MM(artist's dipl), 51, DMA, 61; Paris Consv, studied piano with Yves Nat, 52. *Works:* A Carillon Book for the Liturgical Year, Summer Fanfares, Sonata for Carillon & Fantasy for Carillon, Guild of Carilloneurs; Second Carillon Sonata, comn by Univ Calif, Berkeley, 83. *Rec Perf:* Roy Hamlin Johnson, Pianista, Ed Discografic Univ Nac Rosario, Argentina, 65; Sonata Teutonica (John Powell), 77, Sonate Psychological (John Powell), 83 & Variations and Double Fugue (John Powell), 83, CRI. *Pos:* Pianist, Rochester Phil, 53- *Teaching:* From asst prof to assoc prof, Univ Kans, 54-65; from assoc prof to prof, Univ Md, College Park, 65- *Awards:* Fac Res Awards, Univ Md, College Park, 68, 75, 78 & 81; Nat Endowment for Arts Res Grant, 76. *Interests:* John Powell's piano music and Symphony in A. *Publ:* Auth, Performance Edition, Sonata Teutonica, Oxford Univ Press, 83. *Mailing Add:* 6804 Dartmouth Ave College Park MD 20740

JOHNSON, ROY HENRY
EDUCATOR, COMPOSER
b Moline, Ill, Feb 25, 33. *Study:* Eastman Sch Music, with Louis Mennini, Wayne Barlow & Bernard Rogers, BM, MM; Fla State Univ, with John Boda, DM(comp). *Works:* Canzona Liturgica (orch), 55; Missa Brevis (a cappella chorus), 61; Serenade (solo flute), 63; Three Pieces for Marimba, 68; Variations (two pianos), 72; Fantasy (trombone & piano), 73; Variations for Orchestra, 74. *Teaching:* Mem fac, Bethany Col, 56-68; prof theory & comp, Fla State Univ, 60- *Awards:* First prize, Fla Technol Univ Contemp Music Fest, 74. *Mailing Add:* Sch Music Fla State Univ Tallahassee FL 32306

JOHNSON, THEODORE OLIVER
EDUCATOR, VIOLA
b Elkhart, Ind, Oct 9, 29. *Study:* Univ Mich, BM, 51, MM, 52, DMA, 59. *Pos:* Concertmaster, Lansing Symph Orch, 67-69 & Grand Rapids Symph Orch, 72-73; prin viola, Lansing Symph Orch, 82- *Teaching:* From instr theory to asst prof, Univ Kan, 58-64; from asst prof to prof, Mich State Univ, 64- *Publ:* Auth, An Analytical Survey of the Fifteen Two-Part Inventions by J S Bach, Univ Press Am, 82. *Mailing Add:* 651 Hillcrest Ave East Lansing MI 48823

JOHNSON, TOM
COMPOSER, PIANO
b Colo, 39. *Study:* Yale Univ, BA, MMus; studied with Morton Feldman. *Works:* The Four Note Opera (five singers & piano), Failing (solo string bass), Risks for Unrehearsed Performers, An Hour for Piano, perf by Frederic Rzewski, Nine Bells, perf by Tom Johnson, Five Shaggy Dog Operas, Dragons in A (orch), and others, Assoc Music Publ & Two-Eighteen Press. *Pos:* Critic, Village Voice, 71- *Awards:* Grants, Nat Endowment Arts & Creative Artists Pub Serv; res, DAAD, Berlin, 83. *Mailing Add:* c/o Two Eighteen Press PO Box 218 Village Station New York NY 10014

JOHNSON-HAMILTON, JOYCE
CONDUCTOR, TRUMPET
b Lincoln, Nebr, July 7, 38. *Study:* Univ Nebr, with Dennis Schneider, BME, 60, MM, 63; Aspen Music Sch, studied trumpet with Robert Nagel, 61-68; studied trumpet with Bernard Adelstein, 65 & 67; Stanford Univ, 69-73, studied cond with Sandor Salgo, 71-73; studied cond with George Cleve, 72-74, Denis DeCoteau, 73-75 & Richard Lert, 74-76. *Rec Perf:* Music Makers: Brass, Standard Sch Broadcasts, 75. *Pos:* Prin trumpet, Ore Symph, 65-68, Oakland Symph, 72-76 & San Jose Symph, 76-80; asst prin trumpet, San Francisco Symph, 68-69; asst cond, Oakland Symph, 73-76; founder & cond, Sinfonia of Northern Calif, 74-79; cond, San Jose Dance Theatre, 76-, San Jose Symph Young Peoples' Conct, 77-82, San Jose State Univ Orch, 79-82, Napa Valley Symph, Napa, Calif, 80- & Diablo Symph, Walnut Creek, Calif, 80-; guest cond, Hidden Valley Chamber Orch, Carmel Valley, 79, Music in May, Pac Univ, 82, Nebr Chamber Orch, 83 & Seoul Phil Orch, 83. *Teaching:* Lectr trumpet, Stanford Univ, 75-80 & San Jose State Univ, 77-80. *Mem:* Int Trumpet Guild (mem bd dir, 79-83). *Mailing Add:* 2 Bassett Lane Atherton CA 94025

JOHNSTON, BENJAMIN BURWELL, JR
COMPOSER, EDUCATOR
b Macon, Ga, Mar 15, 26. *Study:* Cath Univ Am, 44-45; Col William & Mary, BA, 49; Col Consv Music, Univ Cincinnati, MM, 50; Univ Calif, Berkeley, 50; Mills Col, MA, 52; Univ Ill, Urbana-Champaign, 52-54; studied comp with Darius Milhaud, John Cage, Harry Partch, Robert Palmer & Burrill Phillips. *Works:* Gambit (ballet for dancers & orch), comn by Merce Cunningham, 59; Museum Piece (film score), orientation film, Museum Hist & Technol, Smithsonian Inst, 68; Auto Mobile (theatre), for Smithsonian Inst exhibit, 68-69; Carmilla (chamber opera), 70; String Quartet #4, 74 & Crossings (string quartet), 76, New York; Mass (chorus, eight trombones & rhythm section), 72; and many others. *Teaching:* Prof music, Univ Ill, Urbana-Champaign, 51-, assoc mem, Ctr Advan Studies, 66. *Awards:* Grants, Univ Ill Res Bd, 58- & Nat Found Arts & Humanities, 66; Guggenhiem Fel, 59-60. *Mem:* ASCAP; Am Soc Univ Comp; Soc Auteurs & Compositeurs Dramatiques; Pi Kappa Lambda. *Mailing Add:* Sch Music Univ Ill Urbana IL 61801

JOHNSTON, DONALD O
COMPOSER, EDUCATOR
b Tracy, Minn, Feb 6, 29. *Study:* Macalester Col, 47-49; Northwestern Univ, with Robert Mills Delaney & Philip Warner, BM, 51, MM, 54; Eastman Sch Music, with Howard Hanson & Bernard Rogers, DMA, 61. *Works:* The Eyes of the Lord, Elkan-Vogel, 61; Ritual for Band, Bourne, 62; Essay for Trumpet and Band, Witmark, 64; Songs of Praise, Harold Flammer, 71; Montage, G Schirmer, 75; Shout With Joy, Ludwig, 77; Symphonic Rondo, Marks, 79. *Teaching:* Prof music, Col Idaho, 54-55 & Univ Mont, 60-; asst prof music, Ripon Col, Wis, 55-58. *Mem:* ASCAP. *Mailing Add:* 91 Arrowhead Dr Missoula MT 59803

JOLAS, BETSY
COMPOSER, EDUCATOR
b Paris, France, Aug 5, 26. *Study:* Bennington Col, studied comp & theory with Paul Boepple, organ with Carl Weinrich & piano with Schnabel, BA, 46; Paris Consv, studied comp with Darius Milhaud, analysis with Olivier Messiaen & fugue with Simone Ple Caussade, 46. *Works:* Trois rencontres (string trio & orch), 72; Quatour III, 9 Etudes (string quartet), comn by Kindler Found, 73; Chansons d'approche (piano); Well Met (twelve instrm), 73; Opera; Le Pavillon au bord de la riviere (musical theatre for recitor, voices & instrm ens), 75; Caprice a une voix (voice), 76; and many others. *Pos:* Singer & accmp, Dessoff Choirs, NY, formerly; ed, Ecouter aujourd'hui, French Radio-TV Network, 55- *Teaching:* Substitute instr analysis, Paris Consv, currently; vis prof comp, Yale Sch Music, currently. *Awards:* Prix des Auteurs et Compositeurs de Langue Francais, Off Radiodiffusion TV Francaise, 61; awards, Am Acad Arts & Lett, 73 & Koussevitsky Found, 74. *Bibliog:* I Krasteva (auth), Betsy Jolas, Schweizerische Musikzeitung, Vol 6, 74; Biographical Sketch of Betsy Jolas, Mens en Melodie 30, 9/75; Esperanza Pulio (auth), Con Betsy Jolas en Paris, Heterofonia, Vol 11, No 6. *Publ:* Auth, Il Fallait Voter Seriel Meme Si, Preuves, Vol 178, 40-42. *Mailing Add:* Yale Sch Music 1303A Yale Sta New Haven CT 06520

JOLLES, SUSAN
HARP
b Scranton, Pa, Mar 24, 40. *Study:* Harpist, Y Chamber Symph, currently, Am Comp Orch, currently, Jubal Trio, currently & Contemp Chamber Ens, currently. *Awards:* Fromm Fel, 62; Naumberg Chamber Music Award, 77. *Mailing Add:* 100-49 67 Dr Forest Hills NY 11375

JOLLY, KIRBY REID
CONDUCTOR, TRUMPET
b Cleveland, Ohio, Aug 1, 30. *Study:* Syracuse Univ, BMus(educ), 52, MS(educ), 56; NY Univ, PhD, 71. *Rec Perf:* Old Bethpage Brass Concert, Crest Rec, 81. *Pos:* First trumpet, Syracuse Symph Orch, 50-56; soloist & guest cond, Goldman Band, 65-74; founder & music dir, Am Conct Band, 72-; dir, Old Bethpage Brass, 76- *Teaching:* Dir music, Patchogue-Medford Pub Sch, 75- *Awards:* Nat Band Asn Citation Excellence, 74; NY State Coun Arts Perf Grant, 74- *Mem:* Music Educr Nat Conf; NY State Coun Adminr Music Educ (pres, 81-82). *Mailing Add:* 29 21st St Jerico NY 11753

JOLLY, TUCKER
TUBA, TEACHER
b Houston, Miss, Dec 30, 46. *Study:* Fla State Univ; NTex State Univ, BMus, 70; Univ Conn, MA, 76. *Rec Perf:* Baroque Brass, 78, Classical Brass, 79 & Rass & Other American Things, 79, Klavier. *Pos:* Tubist, Eastern Brass Quintet, 70-80; prin tuba, US Coast Guard Band, 70-74, New Haven Symph, 74-80 & Ohio Chamber Orch, 82- *Teaching:* Adj fac music, Univ Conn, 77-80; asst prof, Univ Akron, 80- *Mem:* Tubist Universal Brotherhood Asn (district coordr, 79-80). *Mailing Add:* 652 Loomis Ave Cuyahoga Falls OH 44221

JONES, BARNARD RAY
COMPOSER, CONDUCTOR
b Istanbul, Turkey, Oct 30, 56; US citizen. *Study:* Sch Music, Northwestern Univ, BM(comp), 77; Mills Col, MFA(electronic music & rec), 83. *Works:* Motet, comn by Alfred Weisberg, 78; Disco String Quartet, 79 & Blind Date, 80, Newdance Consort; Album I, II, III, Kapture, 80; Trojan Women, Theater Dept, Loyola Univ, 81; Stardust Sketch, 82 & Around, 82, Kapture. *Pos:* Res cond, Tidewater Conct Asn, 77-80; music dir, Newdance Consort, 78-79. *Mailing Add:* Orchard Meadow Mills Col Oakland CA 94616

JONES, CHARLES
COMPOSER, EDUCATOR
b Tamworth, Ont, June 21, 10. *Study:* Violin with Sascha Jacobsen & Samuel Gardner; Inst Musical Art, dipl(violin), 32; Juilliard Sch, with Bernard Wagenaar, dipl(comp), 39. *Works:* Down with Drink (ballet), 43; Threnody (solo viola), 47; Piers the Plowman (ten, chorus & orch), 63; I Am a Mynstral (ten & four instrm), 67; Triptychon (violin, viola & piano), 75; Psalm (piano), 76; and many others. *Teaching:* Mem fac, Bryanston Music Sch, formerly, Mills Col, 39-44 & Music Acad West, formerly; instr comp, Aspen Music Sch, 51-; mem fac lit & materials music, Juilliard Sch, 54-; mem fac & chmn comp dept, Mannes Col Music, 72- *Awards:* Copley Award & Grant, Soc Publ Am Music. *Mem:* ASCAP. *Mailing Add:* Mannes Col Music 157 E 74th St New York NY 10021

JONES, GEORGE MORTON
CLARINET, MUSICOLOGIST
b Evergreen, Ala, Jan 8, 29. *Study:* Eastman Sch Music, BMus & perf cert(clarinet), 51, MMus, 53; NY Univ, PhD, 72. *Pos:* Clarinetist, Rochester Phil, Rochester Civic Orch & Rochester Pops Orch, 51-54, Berkshire Music Ctr & Yaddo Fest, 52, Princeton Symph, 54-65, Trenton Symph, 60-65, Princeton Collegium Musicum, 69-76 & Douglass Col Woodwind Quintet, 69-76; prin clarinet, Nat Opera Orch, 78. *Teaching:* Chmn & prof musicol, woodwinds & clarinet, Douglass Col, Rutgers Univ, 54-, dir, Clarinet Ens, currently. *Publ:* Contribr to Musik in Geschichte und Gegenwart & Clarinet. *Mailing Add:* 130 Shady Brook Lane Princeton NJ 08540

JONES, GEORGE THADDEUS
COMPOSER, EDUCATOR
b Asherville, NC, Nov 6, 17. *Study:* Univ NC, Chapel Hill, AB, 38; Eastman Sch Music, MA, 42, PhD, 50; studied with Nicholas Nabokov, Howard Hanson, Nadia Boulanger, Glen Haydon & Bernard Rogers. *Works:* Overture to an Imaginary Drama, Nat Symph Orch, 50; String Trio, Eighth Fest Am Music, Bales Nat Gallery, 50; The Cage (opera), NBC, 59; Break of the Day (opera), ABC, 61; Poem for Peace (orch), NC Symph Orch, 61; Sonata—1964, Phillips Collection, 64; The Deadly Garden, comn by Orgn Am States, 78. *Teaching:* Instr, US Navy Sch Music, Washington, DC, 42-48; prof theory & comp, Catholic Univ Am, 50- *Awards:* Fulbright Scholar, 52-53; grants, Dept Health Educ & Welfare, 64 & Dept State, 67-68. *Mem:* ASCAP; Am Musicol Soc; Am Soc Univ Comp. *Publ:* Auth, Music Composition, Summy-Birchard, 63; Symbols Used in Music Composition, Dept Health Educ & Welfare & Catholic Univ, 64; Music Theory, Barnes & Noble, 74. *Mailing Add:* Sch Music Catholic Univ Am Washington DC 20064

JONES, GWENDOLYN (K)
MEZZO-SOPRANO

b Tulsa, Okla, Apr 12, 48. *Study:* Oklahoma City Univ, BMus, 71. *Roles:* Carmen in Carmen, 75 & Cenerentola in La Cenerentola, 77, Ariz Opera; Siebel in Faust, 78 & Genevieve in Pelleas et Melisande, 79, San Francisco Opera; Cenerentola in La Cenerentola, Va Opera, 81; Carmen in Carmen, Sacramento Opera, 82; Octavian in Der Rosenkavalier, Tulsa Opera, 83. *Awards:* Second Place, Nat Metropolitan Opera Auditions, 68; Nat Opera Inst Grant, 73; William Mateus Sullivan Found Grant, 82. *Mailing Add:* c/o Warden Assoc Ltd 45 W 60th St New York NY 10023

JONES, JANE TROTH
EDUCATOR

b Centralia, Wash, Aug 7, 20. *Study:* Cent Wash Univ, BAEd(music), 42, MEd(music), 62; German Music Ctr, Univ Ore, 70-71; Orff Inst, Salzburg, Austria, 71; English Music Ctr, Univ Ore, 78-79. *Teaching:* Renton Pub Sch, 41-43, Seattle Pub Sch, 43-45; coordr elem sch music, Eugene Pub Sch, 59-72; prof music educ, Cent Wash Univ, 72- *Mem:* Wash Music Educr Asn; Music Educr Nat Conf; Mu Phi Epsilon. *Interests:* Influence of music in the lives and works of painters. *Publ:* Auth, Music and the Painter's Canvas (in prep). *Mailing Add:* Music Dept Cent Wash Univ Ellensburg WA 98926

JONES, JEANNE NANNETTE
VIOLIN

b Lake City, Fla, June 4, 48. *Study:* Jacksonville Univ, BM, BME; Col Consv Music, Univ Cincinnati, MMus; Brevard Music Ctr; Am String Teachers Asn Wkshp, Austria, 72; Kato Havas Summer Violin Sch, UK, 73; Rome Fest Orch Summer Inst, Italy, 74. *Pos:* Prin second violin, Jacksonville Symph Orch, currently. *Teaching:* Asst strings, Col Consv Music, Univ Cincinnati, 69-71; instr orch, Duval Co sch, Fla. *Mem:* Mu Phi Epsilon; Pi Kappa Lambda; Music Educr Nat Conf; Am String Teachers Asn; Fla Orch Asn. *Mailing Add:* 4770 Apache Ave Jacksonville FL 32210

JONES, JENNY LIND
VIOLIN

Study: Univ Ind, cert, BM, MM; Curtis Inst Music; studied violin with Josef Gingold, Ivan Galamian, Paul Mackanowitsky & Franco Gulli. *Rec Perf:* On Vox. *Pos:* Concertmaster, Univ Ind Concert Orch, formerly; soloist with Ind Univ Phil Orch & Chicago area orchs, formerly; mem, Giovanni String Quartet, formerly, St Louis String Quartet, currently & St Louis Symph Orch, currently. *Teaching:* Ind Univ Summer Clinics, formerly; mem fac violin, St Louis Consv, currently. *Awards:* First Place, Coleman Chamber Music Compt, Pasadena, Calif; Sr & Young Artists Awards, Farwell, Tuley & Soc Am Musicians. *Mem:* Pi Kappa Lambda. *Mailing Add:* St Louis Consv Music 560 Trinity Ave St Louis MO 63130

JONES, JOYCE
ORGAN, COMPOSER

b Taylor, Tex, Feb 13, 33. *Study:* Univ Tex, BMus, 52, MMus, 53, DMA, 70; Southwestern Baptist Theol Sem, MSM, 57. *Works:* Joyce Jones Collection, Bks I & II, Bradley Publ, 78. *Pos:* Conct organist, Community Concerts, 59- *Teaching:* Organist in res, Baylor Univ, 69- *Awards:* G B Dealey Award, Dallas Morning News, 58. *Mem:* Fel, Am Guild Organists. *Publ:* Auth, Organ Pedal Mastery, 79, Organ Improvisation, 81 & Church Service Playing, 81, Bradley Publ. *Rep:* Roberta Bailey Artists Int 25 Walnut St Boston MA 02108. *Mailing Add:* 3525 Carondolet Waco TX 76710

JONES, LINDA
COACH, PIANO

Study: Univ Iowa, BM, MA, MFA; studied with John Simms, David Saperton, Robert Goldsand & Martin Canin. *Rec Perf:* Ode to Akhmatova (Ivana Themmen). *Pos:* Music staff & asst conductor, Washington Opera Soc, 72-74, Dallas Civic Opera, 73-74, Opera Co of Boston, 73-76, Santa Fe Opera Co, 76-81, Opera Theatre of St Louis, 79- *Teaching:* Opera coach, Manhattan Sch Music, 81- *Awards:* Nat Opera Inst Grant. *Mailing Add:* Manhattan Sch Music 120 Claremont Ave New York NY 10027

JONES, MARK RAYMOND
TUBA

b Buffalo, NY, Sept 1, 57. *Study:* Univ Buffalo, 75-79; Juilliard Sch, with Don Harry, 76-80; studied tuba with Warren Deck, 82. *Pos:* Adj performer, Buffalo Phil, 77; tubist, Juilliard Brass Quintet, 81- *Mem:* Tubists Universal Brotherhood Asn. *Mailing Add:* 104 Briarcliffe Rd Cheektowaga NY 14225

JONES, MASON
FRENCH HORN, EDUCATOR

b Hamilton, NY, June 16, 19. *Study:* Curtis Inst Music, 36-38; Colgate Univ, Hon MusD, 70; studied French horn with Anton Horner, Fritz Reiner & Marcel Tabuteau. *Rec Perf:* Works by Chabrier, Telemann, Mozart, Richard Strauss & Saint-Saens. *Pos:* Mem, Philadelphia Orch, 38-78, first hornist, 40-78, personnel mgr, 63-, cond sch concerts, 72-; founder & mem, Philadelphia Woodwind Quintet, 50-; co-founder, Philadelphia Brass Ens, 57-; cond, Episcopal Acad Orch, 58-60; asst cond, Philadelphia Chamber Orch, 61-64. *Teaching:* Horn & brass ens, Curtis Inst Music, 46-; mem fac, Col Music, Temple Univ, 76- *Awards:* C Hartman Kuhn Award, Philadelphia Orch, 53, 56 & 68. *Mem:* Philadelphia Art Alliance. *Mailing Add:* Curtis Inst Music 1726 Locust St Philadelphia PA 19103

JONES, NANCY THOMPSON
SOPRANO, TEACHER-COACH

b Humansville, Mo, Oct 31, 38. *Study:* Col-Consv Music, Univ Cincinnati, with Hubert Kockritz, Scott Huston & Sonia Essin, BMus, 60; Pittsburg State Univ, Kans, with Margaret Thuenemann, MMus, 62; Am Inst Musical Studies, Austria, with Heinrich Schmidt & Harold Heiberg, 76. *Rec Perf:* The Sweet Bye and Bye, Desto, 73; Captain Jinks and the Horse Marines, RCA, 75; Then There Will Be Singing, Soundtrek, 81. *Roles:* High Priestess in Aida, 72 & 77, First Lady in Magic Flute, 74, Mary in Captain Jinks, 75, Echo in Ariadne auf Naxos, 78, Donna Elvira in Don Giovanni, 79 & Zulma in Italian Girl, 81, Kansas City Lyr Opera. *Pos:* Artist, Kansas City Lyr Opera & Am Guild Musical Artists, 67; soloist, Kansas City Phil, Kansas City Symph, Liberty Symph & Mo River Fest Arts, 75-; conct artist, Kans Comn Arts, 82. *Teaching:* Instr voice, William Jewell Col, Mo, 75- *Awards:* Sterling Achievement Award, Mu Phi Epsilon Int, 60. *Bibliog:* Terry Teachout (auth), Priestess Goes High, Kansas City Star, 77. *Mem:* Mu Phi Epsilon Int; Actors Equity; Am Guild Musical Artists; Nat Asn Teachers Singing. *Mailing Add:* 2301 Strader Terrace St Joseph MO 64503

JONES, PATRICIA COLLINS
MUSICOLOGIST, PIANO

b Lebanon, Pa, July 27, 43. *Study:* New England Consv Music, 61-64; Juilliard Sch Music, BMus(piano), 66; Ohio Univ, MFA(theory), 68; Rutgers Univ, PhD(musicol), 77. *Pos:* Recital, chamber music & solo performances with orchs. *Teaching:* Instr music theory & piano, Univ NC, Greensboro, 70-72; instr music theory, piano & res asst, Rutgers Univ, 73-75; lectr music theory, Univ Wis, Milwaukee; lectr hist & lit, Wis Consv Music, formerly, acad dean; lectr fine arts, Marquette Univ, currently. *Mem:* Int Musicol Soc; New Bach Soc; Col Music Soc; Pi Kappa Lambda; Soc Music Theory. *Publ:* Auth, An Introduction to the Fundamentals of Music, 75. *Mailing Add:* Wis Consv Music 1584 N Prospect Ave Milwaukee WI 53202

JONES, PERRY OTIS
EDUCATOR, CONDUCTOR

b Winfield, Kans, Mar 30, 36. *Study:* Univ Iowa, BA, MA, PhD, 57-68; studied with Robert Shaw, Eric Ericson, Dan Moe & Frank Pooler. *Rec Perf:* Cavalcade of Christman Music, CBS, 79-82. *Teaching:* Dir choral activ, SDak State Univ, 67-77; chmn & dir choral activities, Univ Nev, 68-, prof choral, 79- *Mem:* Music Educr Nat Conf; Am Choral Dir Asn (pres SDak chap, 68-74 & Nev chap, 83-). *Publ:* Auth, Reactions to Brock McElheran's Patterns in Sound, 9/70 & The History of Women's Liberation in Choral Music, 2/76, Am Choral Dir Asn; Choral Ensemble Drill, self publ, 75. *Mailing Add:* 2275 Hunter LaRe Dr Reno NV 89507

JONES, ROBERT M
LIBRARIAN, EDUCATOR

b Dallas, Tex, Feb 5, 44. *Study:* Tex Christian Univ, BMusEd, 67; NTex State Univ, MLS, 70. *Pos:* Head music acquisitions div, Music Libr, Univ Ill, Urbana, 71-78, head music bibliog res unit, Univ Libr, 78-82, spec proj coordr, 82- *Teaching:* Instr libr admin, Univ Ill, Urbana, 71-78, asst prof, 79- *Mem:* Int Asn Music Libr (secy, libr music teaching inst div, 80-); Am Libr Asn; Music Libr Asn; Am Musicol Soc; Soc Ethnomusicol. *Interests:* Popular music, 60-; music bibliographic research to 1700; 19th century American sheet music. *Publ:* Ed, Popular Music: A Survey of Books, Folios and Periodicals with an Index to Recently Reviewed Recordings, 72-78, auth, Study Scores and Performing Editions of Wind Chamber Music, 74 & Study Scores and Performing Editions of Percussion Music, 74, Music Libr Asn Notes. *Mailing Add:* 902 W Nevada Urbana IL 61801

JONES, ROBERT WILLIAM
COMPOSER, EDUCATOR

b Oak Park, Ill, Dec 16, 32. *Study:* Chicago Consv Music, 49-50; Univ Redlands, BM, 59, MM, 60. *Works:* Toccata Concertante, 67 & Hist Whist, 68, Shawnee Press; Revelations, AGO, 71; Pilgrimage, Episcopal Diocese Mich, 76; Burning Tree, Plymouth Symph League, 76; Passion, 80 & A Plymouth Symphony, 82, Mich Coun Arts. *Pos:* Comp in res, Music Educr Nat Conf, Ford Found Contemp Music Proj, West Hartford, Conn, 65-69 & Livonia, Mich, 69-72. *Teaching:* Instr theory & hist, Schoolcraft Col, 72- *Mem:* ASCAP. *Mailing Add:* 9247 W Outer Dr Detroit MI 48219

JONES, ROGER PARKS
COMPOSER, EDUCATOR

b Coral Gables, Fla, Aug 7, 44. *Study:* Univ Miami, BM, 66, MM, 68, PhD, 72. *Works:* 21 Distinctive Duets (tuba duets), UMMP, 72; Symphonic Variations (band), Wingert-Jones Publ Co, 74; I'm Nobody (mixed chorus), Walton Music Corp, 75; Design No 2 (solo clarinet), Shall-u-mo Publ, 76; Sea Fever (mixed chorus), Walton Music Corp, 77; Dialogue (euphonium & piano), Laissez-Faire Music, 81; Symphony No 2, comn by Monroe Symph Orch, 81. *Teaching:* Comp in res, Kans Coop Col Comp Proj, Emporia, Kans, 71-74; assoc prof, Northeast La Univ, 74- *Mem:* Tubists Universal Brotherhood Asn. *Mailing Add:* Rt 1 Box 207A Pace Rd West Monroe LA

JONES, ROLAND LEO
VIOLIN, TEACHER

b Ann Arbor, Mich, Dec 16, 32. *Study:* Univ Mich, BMus; Columbia Univ, 5 yrs; Interlochen Music Camp; Meadowmount Music Sch; Berkshire Music Ctr; studied with Nat Orch Asn Training Orch. *Rec Perf:* Concerto No 2 (Chopin); Milena (Alberto Ginastera). *Pos:* Soloist, Ann Arbor Civic Symph, 51 & 53; violinist, Denver Symph Orch, 60-74, Fine Arts Fest, Jackson Hole, Wyo, 64-65 & Highland Chamber Players, 78-79; founder & first violinist,

Highland String Quartet, 79-; tours throughout US & Can. *Teaching:* Violin & viola, privately, 50- *Awards:* Scholar, Interlochen Nat Music Camp & Berkshire Music Ctr. *Mem:* Musicians Soc Denver Inc; Music Teachers Nat Asn. *Mailing Add:* 3004 S Kearney Denver CO 80222

JONES, SAMUEL
COMPOSER, EDUCATOR

b Inverness, Miss, June 2, 35. *Study:* Millsaps Col, BA, 57; Eastman Sch Music, Univ Rochester, MA, 58, PhD, 60; cond study with Richard Lert & William Steinberg; comp study with Howard Hanson, Wayne Barlow & Bernard Rogers. *Works:* In Retrospect, 59, Symphony No 1, 60, Elegy (string orch), 63, Overture for a City, 64, Let Us Now Praise Famous Men, 72, Fanfare and Celebration, 80 & A Symphonic Requiem, 83, Carl Fischer. *Rec Perf:* Symphony No 4 (Paul Cooper), 76, Elegy, 76 & Let Us Now Praise Famous Men, 76, CRI. *Pos:* Dir instrm music, Alma Col, Mich, 60-62; music dir, Saginaw Symph, 62-65; from asst cond to cond, Rochester Phil, NY, 65-72; assoc dir cond, Am Symph Orch League Cond Wkshp, Orkney Springs, Va, 68-76. *Teaching:* Founding dean, Shepherd Sch Music, Rice Univ, 73-79, prof cond & comp, 73- *Awards:* Res Award, Martha Baird Rockefeller Music Fund, 72; grant, Ford Found, 75; ASCAP Award, 82. *Bibliog:* Howard Hanson (auth), Jones Has Unusual Opportunity As Head of Rice University Music School, Rochester Times-Union, 7/2/73; Jay Carr (auth), Jones Impresses in Symphony Debut, Detroit News, 10/5/73; Arthur Cohn (auth), Samuel Jones, Rec Class Music, Schirmer Books, 81. *Mem:* Cond Guild; Am Symph Orch League (vpres, 75-76); ASCAP; Am Music Ctr; Am Fedn Musicians; Col Music Soc. *Publ:* Auth, The Symphony Orchestra: Dinosaur in a Dynamic World?, 72 & Toward a Philosophy of Music Criticism, 75, Symph News; Holons and Cubbyholes: Toward Integration of the Music Curriculum, Music J, 76; A Master Class with Richard Lert: Pacing and Tempo in Don Juan, 82 & A Master Class with Richard Lert: Orchestral Balance in Don Juan, 82, J Cond Guild. *Rep:* Robert Gewald Mgt 58 W 58 New York NY 10019. *Mailing Add:* 2235 Southgate Blvd Houston TX 77251

JONES, STEPHEN GRAF
EDUCATOR, TRUMPET

b Columbus, Ohio, Oct 17, 47. *Study:* Ohio State Univ, BS(music educ), 70; Wichita State Univ, MM, 72; Univ Mich, DMA, 78. *Rec Perf:* Rose Variations (RR Bennett), Century Rec, 70; Landscapes (Karel Husa), 78 & Masques (Ramon Zupko), 79, CRI. *Pos:* Prin trumpet, Kalamazoo Symph Orch, 72-; trumpet, Western Brass Quintet, 72- *Teaching:* Prof trumpet, Western Mich Univ, 72- *Mem:* Int Trumpet Guild (secy, 81-85). *Mailing Add:* 1507 Winters Dr Kalamazoo MI 49002

JONES, WARREN
TEACHER

b Washington, DC, Dec 11, 51. *Study:* New England Consv Music, BM, 73; San Francisco Consv Music, MM, 77. *Pos:* Asst cond, San Francisco Opera, 75-77; asst cond & vocal coach, Metropolitan Opera, 78- *Teaching:* Fac mem, San Francisco Consv Music, 74-75 & Newton Col, 73-74. *Mailing Add:* 711 West End Ave #6JN New York NY 10025

JONES, WENDAL S
BASSOON, EDUCATOR

b Erie, Colo, Aug 7, 32. *Study:* Univ Northern Colo, BA, MA; Univ Iowa, with Philip Bezanson, Richard Hervig & Charles Garland, PhD. *Works:* Violin Sonata (chamber music), 78; Overture (orch); The Kid's New Bag (orch); Three Fantasies (horn & piano) Woodwind Quintet (chamber music); Three Diverse Songs (ten & woodwind quintet); Praise! (orch, chorus & soloist). *Pos:* Prin bassoonist, Spokane Symph Orch, currently. *Teaching:* Mem fac, Univ Ariz, 61-67; prof music, Eastern Wash Univ, currently. *Awards:* First Prize, Nat Asn Col Wind & Perc Instr Cont; Am Music Ctr Award. *Mailing Add:* Spokane Symph Orch Flourmill Suite #203 Spokane WA 99201

JONES, WILLIAM JOHN
EDUCATOR, FLUTE & PICCOLO

b Pontiac, Mich, Nov 30, 26. *Study:* Taylor Univ, BA, 47; Wayne Univ, BSEd, 48, MA, 49; Northwestern Univ, PhD, 52. *Teaching:* Flute, privately, 51-; instr, Appalachian State Teachers Col, 54-61; fac mem & dept chmn, Ferrum Jr Col, 61-63; assoc prof music & dept chmn, Olivet Col, 63-65; prof, Univ SAla, 65- *Awards:* Grant, Nat Endowment Humanities, 78 & 82. *Mem:* Col Music Soc (mem southern chap bd, 82-); Am Musicol Soc; Sonneck Soc; Nat Asn Col Wind & Perc Instr; Music Educr Nat Asn. *Publ:* Auth, The Wind Band Story—A History, Sch Musician, 74; Music Materials ..., Ethnic Slide Library of USA, Symposium, 77; Inaugurating a Successful Bagpipe Program, Sch Musician, 78; The Alto Flute, Instrumentalist, 79. *Mailing Add:* 1100 Goldsboro Ct Mobile AL 36608

JORDAHL, ROBERT A
COMPOSER, EDUCATOR

b Ottumwa, Iowa, Sept 19, 26. *Study:* Univ Tex, Austin, comp with Kent Kennan, BM, 50, MMEd, 51; Eastman Sch Music, comp with Wayne Barlow, PhD, 65. *Works:* The Prospector (ballet), perf by Anchorage Civic Ballet, 67; Evangeline (ballet), perf by Lake Charles Civic Ballet, 76; Dances For a New Land, perf by Lake Charles Symph Orch, 82; Images, perf by McNeese State Univ Orch, 83; also many others. *Teaching:* Asst prof music, Keuka Col, 62-65; assoc prof, Alaska Methodist Univ, 65-68; prof, McNeese State Univ, 68- *Mem:* Sonneck Soc. *Mailing Add:* 4706 Ponderosa Rd Lake Charles LA 70601

JORDAN, PAUL
CONDUCTOR, ORGAN

b New York, NY, Mar 12, 39. *Study:* State Inst Music, Frankfurt, degree, 63; Sch Music, Yale Univ, MMus, 67; studied cond with Gustav Meier, 66, Irwin Fischer, 76 & Jerome Laszloffy, 81. *Works:* Anthem for Chorus, Soloist, Winds, Cello, Organ & Tympani, Trinity Church Choir, New Haven, Conn, 73; Trio for Oboe, Viola & Piano, Catawba Soloists, 75; To Martin Luther King, Edith Ho, 75; Sonata for Recorder & Oboe, Larry Zukof & Geoffrey Barron, 77; Cantata for Christmas, Endwell Community Chorus, 78; Rhapsody and Waltz for Tenor Saxophone & Piano, Al Hamme & Paul Jordan, 79; Seventeen Comments on Jeremy's Idea, Univ Symph Orch, State Univ NY, Binghamton, 82. *Rec Perf:* From Amsterdam to Leipzig, 80 & Orgelbuechlein (J S Bach), 81, Spectrum Rec. *Pos:* Dir music, United Church on Green, New Haven, Conn, 64-74; founder, New York Trio Da Camera, 65-73. *Teaching:* Instr organ & musicianship, Yale Sch Music, 68-69; assoc prof orch, organ & harpsichord, State Univ NY, Binghamton, 73- *Bibliog:* An Interview with Paul Jordan, Am Recorder, 77. *Mem:* Cond Guild; Am Symph Orch League; Am Guild Organists; Col Music Soc. *Publ:* Auth, An Organ City in Connecticut, 73, An Organist; coauth, Organ-Playing (trans of H Hesse's Poem), Am Organist, 73; auth, Helmut Walcha: Artist-Teacher, Col Music Symposium, 82. *Mailing Add:* 39 Lake Ave Binghamton NY 13905

JORDAN, ROBERT
PIANO

b Chattanooga, Tenn, May 2, 40. *Study:* Eastman Sch Music, BM, 62; Juilliard Sch Music, MS, 65; Sorbonne, Paris, France, cert, 69. *Rec Perf:* Robert Jordan, Pianist, Orion, 83. *Pos:* Soloist, Buffalo Orch, Baltimore Orch, Prague Orch, Bavarian Radio Orch, Chattanooga Orch, Del Orch & others; mem bd dir, Triad Presentations Inc, 72-74, adv coun, 74-; pres & mem bd gov, Paris Inst Music, NY, 73- *Teaching:* Asst prof music, Bronx Community Col, 72-77; artist in res, Morgan State Univ, 76-79 & Univ Del, 79; assoc prof, State Univ NY, Fredonia, 80- *Awards:* Gold Medal, Nat Piano Guild Rec Compt, 59 & 62; First Prize (piano), Young Instrumentalists Compt, 63; Chancellor's Award for Excellence in Teaching, State Univ NY, 83. *Mailing Add:* 52 E Main St Fredonia NY 14063

JORGENSEN, JERILYN
VIOLIN

b Oakland, Calif, Nov 20, 54. *Study:* Eastman Sch Music, BM, 76; Juilliard Sch, BM, MM, 76-80. *Rec Perf:* Prayer for String Quartet (Israel Kremen), Orion Rec, 83. *Pos:* First violinist, Da Vinci Quartet, 80- *Mailing Add:* 68 Maryland Pl Colorado Springs CO 80906

JORGENSON, DALE ALFRED
ADMINISTRATOR, CONDUCTOR

b Litchfield, Nebr, Mar 20, 26. *Study:* Harding Col, BMus, 48; George Peabody Col, MMus, 50; Ind Univ, PhD, 57. *Teaching:* Asst prof voice, Tex Woman's Univ, 58-59; prof & head dept music, Bethany Col, WVa, 59-62; prof & dir fine arts, Milligan Col, 62-63; prof music & head fine arts, Northeast Mo State Univ, 63- *Mem:* Nat Asn Sch Music (mem bd, 78-81); Music Educr Nat Conf; Am Soc Aesthetics; Am Musicol Soc. *Interests:* Harmonic dualism; related arts; values theory in aesthetics. *Publ:* Auth, A Resume of Harmonic Dualism, Music & Lett, 61; Arts on the Campus, Nat Asn Sch Music, 70 & 71; Axiological Schizophrenia, Christianity Today, 83; Humanistic Traditions and the Christian Faith, Col Press, 83. *Mailing Add:* 1512 S Cottage Grove Kirksville MO 63501

JORY, MARGARET FAIRBANK
ADMINISTRATOR

b Chicago, Ill, Sept 11, 36. *Study:* Radcliffe Col, AB, 58; Bedford Col, Univ London, 58-59. *Pos:* Freelance opera dir & stage mgr, San Francisco Opera, Honolulu Opera, Cincinnati Summer Opera & others, formerly; stage mgr & asst stage dir, Metropolitan Opera Nat Co, 65-66; programmer, Arts Prog, Inst Int Educ, New York, 67-69; artistic dir, Midem Classique, Paris & Cannes, 69-70; dir, Lincoln Ctr Student Prog, Juilliard Sch, 72-74 & Hunter Col Conct Bur, 74-77; exec dir, Am Music Ctr, New York, 77-83; dir, Symph & Conct Dept, ASCAP, New York, 83- *Mailing Add:* ASCAP 1 Lincoln Plaza New York NY 10023

JOSEPHSON, DAVID S
EDUCATOR, WRITER

b Montreal, Can, Apr 15, 42. *Study:* Columbia Univ, BA, 63, MA, 65, PhD, 72; private study piano with Yvonne Hubert & Robers Goldsand. *Teaching:* Instr, Music Dept, Columbia Univ, 70-72; asst prof, Brown Univ, 72-79, chmn & assoc prof 79- *Mem:* Am Musicol Soc; Royal Musical Asn; Int Musicol Soc; Music Libr Asn. *Interests:* Tudor music; John Taverner; Percy Grainger; English folk music; Mozart. *Publ:* Auth, In Search of the Historical Taverner, Tempo, 72; Percy Grainger: Country Gardens and Other Curses, Current Musicol, 73; John Taverner: Tudor Composer, UMI Res Press, 79; Percy Aldridge Grainger, In: New Grove Dict of Music & Musicians, 80; Grainger, Folksong, Music Hall: A Centenary Essay, Lang Festschrift, Norton (in prep). *Mailing Add:* Box 1924 Music Dept Brown Univ Providence RI 02912

JOSEPHSON, KENNETH GEORGE
COMPOSER, CELLO

b Holyoke, Mass, Feb 22, 26. *Study:* Columbia Univ, BA, 50; Eastman Sch Music, MA, 55. *Works:* String Quintet, perf by Univ Tenn Chamber Players, 77; View From Lookout Mountain, perf by Tri City Orch & Chattanooga Symph Orch, 81; Tunes of Chichamauga, Chattanooga Symph Orch, Rome Symph & Atlanta Symph, 82-83; Concerto (cello & orch), Rome Symph Orch,

83; 50th Anniversary March, 83 & Some Songs of Stephen Foster, 83, perf by Chattanooga Symph Orch. *Pos:* Asst prin cello, Chattanooga Symph Orch, 65- *Teaching:* Fac mem, Lycoming Col, Williamsport, Pa, 59-61 & Bucknell Univ, Lewisburg, Pa, 61-63; assoc prof, Shorter Col, Rome, Ga, 63- *Mailing Add:* Shorter Col Rome GA 30161

JUHOS, JOSEPH FRANK
FLUTE, EDUCATOR
b Cluj, Romania; US citizen. *Study:* Franz Liszt Acad Music, Budapest, artist & prof flute dipl, 61. *Pos:* Prin flute, Hungarian State Opera Budapest & Budapest Phil Soc Orch; mem, Woodwind Quintet Hungarian Opera, Budapester Nonet & Cleveland Baroque Soloists; soloist, WCLV & WNYC radio, TV & concerts. *Teaching:* Mem fac, Franz Liszt Acad, Budapest, formerly; mem fac, Consv State Music Sch, Hamburg, Germany, 67-68; chmn prep orch instrm, Cleveland Inst Music, 69-; instr, Cuyahoga Community Col; instr masterclasses flute, US & Europe. *Mailing Add:* 13531 Detroit Ave 9-A Cleveland OH 44107

JUNG, MANFRED
TENOR
Roles: Siegmund in Die Walküre & Parsifal in Parsifal, Metropolitan Opera, 83; Siegfried in Siegfried, Florestan in Fidelio & Siegmund in Die Walküre, Düsseldorf, 83; Max in Der Freischütz, Deutsche Oper, 83; Siegfried in Der Ring des Nibelungen, Bayreuth Opera. *Pos:* Ten with major opera co in US & Europe. *Mailing Add:* c/o Columbia Artists 165 W 57th St New York NY 10019

JUSTUS, WILLIAM
BARITONE
b Kansas City, Mo, Nov 12, 36. *Rec Perf:* Light in the Wilderness, Decca, 68. *Roles:* Ford in Falstaff, Boston Opera, 75; Germont in La Traviata, Cincinnati Opera, 77; Amanasro in Aida, Houston Opera, 79; Tabor in Baby Doe, Central City Opera, 81; Ezio in Attila, New York City Opera, 81; Gerard in Andrea Chenier, San Diego Opera, 81; Rigoletto in Rigoletto, Cincinnati Opera, 82. *Mailing Add:* c/o Kazuko Hillyer Inc 250 W 57th St New York NY 10107

K

KABAT, JULIE PHYLLIS
COMPOSER
b Washington, DC, Apr 17, 47. *Study:* Brandeis Univ, AB, 70; studied with Jacob Druckman & Hall Overton. *Works:* In Return, Concord String Quartet, 74; Invocation in Centrifugal Form, Circle Repertory Theater Co, 77; Five Poems by H D, Julie Kabat & Ben Hudson, 82; The Queen of Hearts, Julie Kabat & David Moss, 82; The Night Fisherman, Newband, 83; On Edge, Julie Kabat. *Awards:* Nat Endowment Humanities Award, 80-82; Beard's Fund Rec Grant, 82; Creative Artists Pub Serv, NY State Coun Arts, 83. *Mem:* Concerted Effort Inc (pres & secy, 79-); Am Music Ctr; Int League Women Comp. *Mailing Add:* 104 Homestead Ave Albany NY 12203

KACH, CLAIRE
LIBRARIAN
b Mannheim, Germany, Dec 11, 25; US citizen. *Study:* Queens Col, City Univ New York, BA(music), 70; Sch Libr Serv, Columbia Univ, studied music librarianship with Susan T Sommer, MS, 73; studied violin with Ernst Rosenberg, Jackson Heights, NY. *Pos:* Music specialist, Queens Borough Pub Libr, Jamaica, NY, currently & asst head art & music div, currently. *Mem:* Music Libr Asn. *Mailing Add:* Art & Music Dept Queens Borough Pub Libr 89-11 Merrick Blvd Jamaica NY 11432

KACINSKAS, JERONIMAS
COMPOSER, CONDUCTOR & MUSIC DIRECTOR
b Vidukle, Lithuania, Apr 17, 07; US citizen. *Study:* State Music Sch, Klaipeda, Lithuania, BA, 28; State Consv Prague, Czechoslovakia, DMA, 31. *Works:* String Quartet No 1, Ondrichkof Quartet, Prague, 30; Nonet, Chech Nonet, London, 38; Last Supper, NBC, 52; Symphonic Fantasy No 2, Cambridge Symph Orch, 60; Mass, Belmont Choral Soc, 63; Triptic (sop & orch), New York Symph Orch, 68; Blak Ship (opera), Lithuanian Opera Co & Chicago Lyr Opera Orch, 78. *Pos:* Dir, Lithuania Radio Orch, State Phil & State Opera, 38-44 & Melrose Symph US, Mass, 58-67. *Teaching:* Cond & fac mem, State Music Sch Klaipeda, 32-38; fac mem cond, State Consv Vilnius, 40-43; fac mem cond & comp, Berklee Col Music, Boston, 68- *Awards:* Music Prize, Lithuanian Am Community Cult Coun, 83. *Mailing Add:* Berklee Col Music 1140 Boylston St Boston MA 02215

KADERAVEK, KAREN BETH
CELLO, TEACHER
b Des Moines, Iowa, Dec 26, 55. *Study:* Drake Univ, BM, 77 & Univ Mich, MM, 79; studied with Leslie Parnas & Samuel Mayes. *Pos:* Mem, Vaener String Trio, 78-; prin cello, Vt Symph, 81-; mem, Handel & Haydn Soc, 82- & Worchester String Quartet, 83- *Teaching:* Instr cello, chamber music & theory, S Shore Consv, 82- *Mem:* Boston Musicians Asn. *Rep:* Perf Artist Asn New England 161 Harvard Ave Rm 11 Allston MA 02134. *Mailing Add:* 177 St Botolph St #8 Boston MA 02115

KADERAVEK, MILAN
EDUCATOR, COMPOSER
b Oak Park, Ill, Aug 5, 24. *Study:* Am Consv Music, with Leo Sowerby, BM(comp), 50, MM(comp), 58; Univ Ill, Urbana-Champaign, with Gordon Binkerd, DMA(comp), 70. *Works:* String Quartet No 1, Curtis String Quartet, 56-57; Sinfonietta, Albuquerque Civic Symph, 60; Introduction and Allegro for Saxophone Quartet, Theodore Presser, 76; Music for Orchestra, Univ Ill Symph, 70; Rhapsody (cello & strings), Roehampton Music Fest, London, England, 76; Music For A Celebration, comn by Drake Univ, 80; Fantasia (flute, oboe & clarinet), Dorn Publ, 81. *Pos:* Freelance musician & arr, Chicago, 40-42 & 46-53; prin clarinet, Des Moines Symph, 54-60. *Teaching:* Asst prof woodwinds, Drake Univ, 54-60 & prof & head theory & hist dept, 72-; instr music theory, Univ Ill, Urbana-Champaign, 60-65; from asst to assoc prof & head music dept, Univ Ill, Chicago Circle, 65-72. *Awards:* Tamiment Inst Award, 56; Albuquerque Civic Symph Award, 60. *Mem:* Col Music Soc; Soc Music Theory; Cent Midwest Theory Soc; ASCAP. *Mailing Add:* 5617 Waterbury Circle Des Moines IA 50312

KAGAN, HILEL
VIOLIN, TEACHER
b Riga, Latvia, Mar 12, 39. *Study:* Riga Consv Music, Latvia, 61; Leningrad Consv Music, USSR, 65-70. *Pos:* Concertmaster, Chicago Opera Theatre, 76 & Am Chamber Symph, 78-; prin II violin, Lyric Opera Chicago, 82. *Mem:* Chicago Fedn Musicians; Soc Am Musicians. *Mailing Add:* 1626 C Central Evanston IL 60201

KAGAN, MARTIN I
ADMINISTRATOR
b Ft William, Ont, Can, Dec 30, 46. *Study:* Waterloo Lutheran Univ, BA, 69; York Univ, MES, 72. *Pos:* Gen mgr, Cantaur Theatre Co, Montreal, Que, 76-77, Dennis Wayne's Dancers, Ltd, New York, NY, 77-78 & Jacob's Pillow Dance Fest, Lee, Mass, 78-80; exec dir, Opera Am, 80- *Mailing Add:* c/o Opera Am 633 E St NW Washington DC 20004

KAHANE, JEFFREY (ALAN)
PIANO
b Los Angeles, Calif, Sept 9, 56. *Study:* San Francisco Consv Music, BMus, 77; Juilliard Sch. *Pos:* Conct pianist & recitalist, 77- *Awards:* Second Prize, Clara Haskil Int Piano Compt, 77; Fourth Prize, Van Cliburn Int Piano Compt, 81; First Prize, Arthur Rubinstein Piano Master Compt, 83. *Mailing Add:* c/o Hamlen-Landau Mgt Inc 140 W 79th St Suite 2A New York NY 10024

KAISER, AMY
CHORAL CONDUCTOR, EDUCATOR
Study: Smith Col, AB; Columbia Univ, MA(musicol); studied cond with Iva Dee Hiatt, John Nelson, Otto Werner Muller & George Schick & voice with Anna Hamlin & Margaret Hoswell; Aspen Choral Inst, studied piano with Lucy Greene, 72-75. *Pos:* Cond, Marwick Opera, Opera on the Sound, Long Island & Fest Lirico Int, Barga, Italy, 74-78; cond chorale & orch, YM-YWHA, New York, 78. *Teaching:* Dir choirs, Smith Col, 71-74; dir choral music, State Univ NY, Stony Brook, 74-78; fac mem chorus & choral cond, Mannes Col Music, 77- *Awards:* Fulbright Fel; Woodrow Wilson Fel. *Mailing Add:* c/o Ira Lieberman Artist Rep 11 Riverside Dr New York NY 10023

KAISER, CARL WILLIAM
TENOR, EDUCATOR
b Mishawaka, Ind, June 28, 33. *Study:* Ind Univ, Bloomington, with Eugene Bayless, BMusEd, 56; Catholic Univ Am, with Themy Gedrgz, MMus, 61; Hochschule Musik, Hamburg, Ger, with Helmut Melchert, 62. *Rec Perf:* Third Japanese Ambassador in Le Rossignol, Columbia Rec, 60; Live from Copenhagen Cathedral, Orpheus Rec, 72. *Roles:* Rodolpho in La Boheme, Bremerhaven, Hannover, Osnabrück & Cologne, 64, 68, 70 & 73; Nemorino in L'elisir d'amore, Bremerhaven & Hannover, 65 & 70-72; Pinkerton in Madame Butterfly, Bremerhaven, Hannover, Krefeld & Stuttgart, 65-77; Don Ottavio in Don Giovanni, Hannover & Nürnberg, 70-73; Tamino in Magic Flute, Hannover, Wuppertal & Bremerhaven, 72, 74 & 75; Rinuccio in Gianni Schicchi, Hannover, Braunschweig & Berlin, 74-77; Fra Diavolo in Fra Diavolo, Hannover & Bremerhaven, 75-77. *Pos:* Res first lyric ten, Stadttheater Lübeck, 62-63, Stadttheater Bremerhaven, 63-66, Stadttheater Krefeld-Mönchengladbach, 66-68 & Niedersächsische Staatstheater Hannover, 68-77. *Teaching:* Assoc prof music, Calvin Col, 77- *Mem:* Nat Asn Teachers Singing; Metropolitan Opera Guild; Nat Opera Asn (Mich state gov, 83). *Mailing Add:* 3049 Claystone SE Grand Rapids MI 49506

KAISERMAN, DAVID NORMAN
PIANO, EDUCATOR
b Cleveland, Ohio, July 15, 37. *Study:* Juilliard Sch, studied piano with Sascha Gorodnitzki, theory with Vincent Persichetti, BS, 59, MS, 60; Univ Iowa, studied perf pract with Robert Donington, DMA, 77. *Teaching:* Asst prof piano, Iowa State Univ, 63-68; from assoc prof to prof, Univ Puget Sound, 68-77; prof, Univ Okla, 77-80; prof, Univ Louisville, 80- *Awards:* Josephine Fry Bi-Annual Award, Piano Teachers' Cong New York, 63; First Prize Teacher Div, Nat Guild Piano Teachers Int Piano Rec Compt, 73 & 83; Master Teacher Cert, Musics Teachers Nat Asn, 83. *Mem:* Am Fedn Musicians; Music Teachers Nat Asn; Col Music Soc; Am Liszt Soc; Nat Guild Piano Teachers. *Interests:* Solo piano music of S M Liapunov, 1859-1924. *Publ:* Auth, Edward MacDowell—The Keltic & Eroica Piano Sonatas, Music J, 66; Baroque Music—For Specialists Only?, Am Music Teacher, 67; The Solo Piano Music of S M Liapunov, J Am Liszt Soc, 78. *Mailing Add:* Sch Music Univ Louisville Louisville KY 40292

KALAJIAN, BERGE
COMPOSER

b West New York, NJ, Jan 29, 24. *Study:* New York Trade Sch, dipl, 49; studied music harmony, counterpoint & comp with Josef Schmid, 50-59; Manhattan Sch Music, BM, 62. *Works:* Sonata for Flute & Piano, Woodwind Quintet, Trio for Flute, Viola & Piano, Suite for Piano, String Quartet & Four Pieces for Piano, H Branch Publ. *Pos:* Tuner & technician, Sohmer Piano Co, 49-51. *Teaching:* Fac mem, Manhattan Sch Music, 70-77 & Mannes Col Music, 71-76; adj prof, Queens Col, 75- *Mem:* Piano Technicians Guild; ASCAP; Nat Asn Comp & Cond; Am Music Ctr; Master Piano Technicians Guild Am. *Mailing Add:* 3417 Cannon Pl Bronx NY 10463

KALICHSTEIN, JOSEPH
PIANO, EDUCATOR

b Tel Aviv, Israel, Jan 15, 46. *Study:* Juilliard Sch, BS, MS; studied piano with Edward Steuermann & Ilona Kabos. *Rec Perf:* Works by Mendelssohn, RCA; works by Bartok & Prokofiev, Vanguard; works by Chopin & Brahms, Erato. *Pos:* Solo & conct pianist with maj orchs throughout Cent & North Am, Korea, Japan, Europe, Australia & Hong Kong, 67-; mem, Kalichstein Laredo Robinson Trio, currently; performer, CBS TV, formerly, French & German TV, formerly & Mostly Mozart Fest, summers 80- *Teaching:* Margie W May chair piano & mem fac piano & chamber music, St Louis Consv Music, currently. *Awards:* Winner, Young Conct Artist's Audition, 67; First Prize, Leventritt Int Compt, 69; Edward Steuermann Mem Prize, 69. *Rep:* Harold Shaw Concerts 1995 Broadway New York NY 10023; Frank Saloman Assoc Suite 4C 201 W 54 St New York NY 10019. *Mailing Add:* St Louis Consv Music 560 Trinity St Louis MO 63130

KALISKY, RONIT
SOPRANO

b Tel-Aviv, Israel. *Study:* Northern Ill Univ, BM, MM 79; Juilliard Music Sch. *Roles:* Sop, Elijah, 78 & Messiah, 79, Mormon Tabernacle, Salt Lake City; Queen of the Night in Die Zauberflöte, Philadelphia Opera Co, 80 & Avery Fisher Hall; Rossignol in Nightingale, 80 & Lucia in Lucia di Lammermoor, 81, Am Opera Ctr; Konstanze in Abduction From the Seraglio, Seattle Opera Co, 82. *Rep:* Thea Dispeker 59 E 54 St New York NY 10022. *Mailing Add:* 26 W 87 St New York NY 10024

KALLIR, LILLIAN
PIANO, EDUCATOR

b Prague, Czechoslavakia; US citizen. *Study:* Mannes Col Music; Berkshire Inst; studied with Herman de Grab & Isabelle Vengerova. *Rec Perf:* Complete Works of Chopin, RCA Victor. *Pos:* Recitalist; conct tours with major orchs in US, Europe, South Am & others. *Teaching:* Mem fac piano, Mannes Col Music, 75- *Awards:* Winner, Nat Music League Awards; Am Artists Award. *Mem:* Sigma Alpha Iota. *Rep:* Columbia Artist Mgt 167 W 57th St New York NY 10019. *Mailing Add:* 825 West End Ave New York NY 10025

KALMANOFF, MARTIN
COMPOSER

b Brooklyn, NY, May 24, 20. *Study:* Harvard Univ, studied comp with Walter Piston, BA, 41, MA, 42. *Works:* Victory at Masada, 68; Photograph 1920 (libretto by Gertrude Stein), 72; Kaddish for a Warring World (soloist & orch), Toronto, 72; The Way of Life (cantata), perf by Bronx Arts Ens, 78; The Harmfulness of Tobacco (one act opera), New York, 79; The Joy of Prayer (sacred serv), Moss Music Group, 83; Opera, Opera (libretto by William Saroyan). *Pos:* Head, Operation Opera, 50- *Awards:* Winner, Robert Merrill Best Opera Cont, 50; Richard Rodgers Grant, 68; NY State Coun Arts Grant, 78. *Mem:* ASCAP; Nat Opera Asn; Cent Opera Serv. *Publ:* Articles on music, Opera News. *Mailing Add:* 392 Central Park W 14P New York NY 10025

KALT, PAMELA C
SOPRANO

b Mt Vernon, NY, Dec 17, 46. *Study:* State Univ Col NY, Fredonia, BA, 68; Mannes Col Music, 70; Mozarteum Hochschule, Salzburg, Austria, dipl, 71. *Roles:* Carrie in Carousel, 83 & Cio Cio San in Madame Butterfly, 83, Cincinnati Opera. *Pos:* Mem, Cincinnati Opera, 82-83. *Mailing Add:* 336 W 77th St New York NY 10024

KALT, PERCY GERMAN
VIOLIN, CONDUCTOR

b Salt Lake City, Utah, Jan 28, 31. *Study:* Univ Utah, BS, 57, MM, 68; Staatliche Hochschule Musik, Stuttgart, dipl(violin), 63; Univ Mich, DMA(violin), 73. *Works:* Solo Sonata for Violin, private publ, 79. *Rec Perf:* Cantatas & Oratorios (Bach), Erato, 63-66; Nymphenburger Schlosskonzert, Parnass-Eurodisc, 65; Ten Violin Sonatas (Beethoven), Brigham Young Univ, 71; Violin Concerto (Berg), 74 & Piano Quartets (Brahms), 74, Univ Mich; violin solos, Mormon Tabernacle Choir (violin solos), CBS, 78 & 83; Suzuki Violin System, Vol 1-5, Bonneville Int Corp, 79. *Pos:* Concertmaster, SW German Chamber Orch, 63-66, Utah Valley Symph Orch, 67-69, Columbia Symph Orch, 78 & 83, Symph West, 81 & Mexico City Phil Orch, 82. *Teaching:* Prof music & violin, Brigham Young Univ, 66-72 & 75-; asst prof violin & chamber music, Univ Mich, 73-75. *Awards:* Fulbright Scholar, 61; Title IV Grant, Nat Def Educ Act, 72. *Mem:* Am Fedn Musicians; Am String Teachers Asn. *Interests:* Violin and piano sonatas of Beethoven; Paganini mastery of technical problems; devotional solos. *Mailing Add:* 4089 Devonshire Circle Provo UT 84604

KAM, DENNIS KOON MING
COMPOSER, EDUCATOR

b Honolulu, Hawaii, May 8, 42. *Study:* Oberlin Consv Music, Oberlin Col, BM, 64; Univ Hawaii, MFA, 66; Univ Ill, DMA, 74. *Works:* Five Phases for Solo Flute, Media Press, 69; Two Moves and the Slow Seat, Belwin-Mills, 73; Go, Smith/Sonic Arts Publ, 74; Big Blue (choir), 76 & Continuum (choir), 80, Belwin-Mills; Antiphonal Fanfares, 82 & Rendezvous II (trombone & piano), 82, Needham Publ. *Pos:* Comp in res, Contemp Music Proj Ford Found, Music Educr Nat Conf, 70-72. *Teaching:* Assoc prof & chmn theory & comp dept, Sch Music, Univ Miami, 74- *Awards:* BMI Awards, 63 & 67. *Mem:* Am Soc Univ Comp (region IV co-chmn, 77-80 & 83-); Soc Music Theory; Col Music Soc; BMI. *Mailing Add:* 11471 SW 80 Terr Miami FL 33173

KAMIEN, ANNA
CONDUCTOR, COMPOSER

b New York, NY Jan 29, 12. *Study:* Studied piano & harmony with August Walther; Ecole Normale Musique, Paris, with Vuilliard & Di Gueraldi, piano with Alfred Cortot & counterpoint with Nadia Boulanger, 30-35; studied form with Annette Dieudonne & piano with Lazar Levy. *Works:* Ruth (opera), 54; Chinese Odes (chorus & orch); Chinese Odes (flute, Oboe, 2 violins, viola & piano); Piano Quintet, 58; Sonatina for Violin and Piano, 57; String Quartet, 60; Memories (mezzo-sop & piano), 64. *Pos:* Cond, Hadassah Chorus, 45-75. *Teaching:* Private piano, 35-45. *Mailing Add:* 185 West End Ave New York NY 10023

KAMINSKY, AKIVA
ARTIST REPRESENTATIVE

b New York, NY, Sept 20, 45. *Study:* City Univ New York, PhD, 82; New England Consv. *Pos:* Pres, Akiva Artists, New York, 80- *Mailing Add:* 1755 Broadway Suite 503 New York NY 10019

KAMSLER, BRUCE H
DIRECTOR—OPERA, PIANO

b Chicago, Ill, Nov 12, 52. *Study:* Chicago Musical Col, Roosevelt Univ, BM, 74. *Pos:* Artistic dir, Chicago Opera Repty Theatre, 76- *Mailing Add:* PO Box 921 Chicago IL 60690

KANG, DONG-SUK
VIOLIN

b Seoul, Korea, Apr 28, 54; US citizen. *Study:* Juilliard Sch, with Ivan Galamian & Sally Thomas; Curtis Inst Music; studied with Zino Francescatti & Leonid Kogan. *Pos:* Performer on four continents with Philadelphia Orch, Royal Phil, London Phil, Munich Phil, BBC Orch, San Francisco Symph Orch, Nat Symph, Montreal Symph, St Louis Symph Orch, Belgium Orch, Luxembourg Orch, Lamoureux Orch & others; guest artist, Chamber Music Soc Lincoln Ctr, New York, formerly & Brooklyn Acad Music, formerly; participant, Spoleto Fest, Italy & Charleston, Santa Fe Fest & Seattle Chamber Music Fest. *Awards:* Winner, San Francisco Symph Compt, 71 & Merriweather Post Compt, Washington, DC, 71. *Mailing Add:* Hamlen Landau Mgt Inc 140 West 79th St Suite 2A New York NY 10024

KANG, HYO
VIOLIN, EDUCATOR

b Seoul, Korea. *Study:* Juilliard Sch, dipl & post grad dipl; studied violin with Dorothy DeLay. *Pos:* Mem, Theater Chamber Players, Kennedy Ctr, currently; performer throughout US & Far East. *Teaching:* Mem fac violin, Philadelphia Col Perf Arts, formerly, New England Consv Music, currently & Aspen Music Sch, currently; mem fac pre-col div, Juilliard Sch, 78-, violin asst to Dorothy DeLay, 80- *Mailing Add:* New England Consv Music 290 Huntington Rd Boston MA 02115

KANOUSE, MONROE
CONDUCTOR, PIANO

b Berkeley, Calif, July 11, 36. *Study:* Univ Calif, Berkeley, BA, 57, MA(music theory), 64. *Pos:* Coach & assoc music dir, Western Opera Theater, 67-72; asst cond, San Francisco Opera, 70-72; free lance cond, Lake George Fest, Florentine Opera, Milwaukee, San Diego Opera & others, 73-80; permanent cond, Oakland Opera, 81- & Sacramento Opera, 81- *Awards:* Martha Baird Rockefeller Fund Grant, 68; Kurt Herbert Adler Fund Award, 70. *Mem:* Am Fedn Musicians. *Mailing Add:* 581 Capp St San Francisco CA 94110

KANTER, RICHARD S
OBOE

b Chicago, Ill, July 7, 35. *Study:* Curtis Inst Music, dipl. *Pos:* With Lyric Opera, Chicago & Grant Park Symph Orch, Chicago; mem oboe sect, Chicago Symph Orch, 61- *Mailing Add:* 2743 N Pine Grove Chicago IL 60614

KANTOR, PAUL M
VIOLIN, TEACHER-COACH

b Staten Island, NY, Nov 29, 55. *Study:* Aspen Music Sch, 71-78; Juilliard Sch, BM, 77, MM, 78. *Pos:* Concertmaster, New Haven Symph Orch, Conn, 78- & Aspen Chamber Symph, Colo, 80-; first violinist, Lenox Quartet, 81-; mem, Nat Musical Arts, Washington, DC & Wall Street Chamber Players, New Haven, Conn. *Teaching:* Fac mem, Aspen Music Fest, Colo, 78-; asst prof, Yale Sch Music, 81- *Mem:* Chamber Music Am; Am Fedn Musicians. *Mailing Add:* c/o Yale Sch Music PO Box 2104A Yale Station New Haven CT 06520

KANWISCHER, ALFRED O
COMPOSER, PIANO

b Rochester, NY. *Study:* Heidelberg Col, with Egon Petri, BM, 54; Mich State Univ, MM, 56; Aspen Fest, with Rosina Lhevinne & Darius Milhaud, 60; Boston Univ, with Bela Nagy, DMA, 67. *Works:* Piece for Two Pianos & Percussion, Young Artists Inc, 67; Four Impressions, Fest Arts Trio Compt, Baton Rouge, La, 76; Sonata in One Movement No 2, comn by Nat Music Teachers Asn, 79; Woodwind Quartet, Piano Sonata & Solo Clarinet, private comn. *Pos:* Soloist & duo-pianist, Europe & US, 67-72; artistic dir & performer, John Ringling Fest Concerts, Sarasota, Fla, 72-76. *Teaching:* From teaching assoc to asst prof, Boston Univ, 62-72; artistic dir & performer, Peabody Piano Sem, Peabody Inst Music, 76-79 & Berkshire Music Ctr, formerly; assoc prof piano, San Jose Univ, 79-80; freelance lectr, 80- *Mem:* Col Music Soc. *Publ:* Auth, The Keyboard, Nat Student Musician, 65; Why Auditions, Music Teachers Asn Mag, Tenn, 76; regular contribr to Music Teachers Asn Calif Mag. *Mailing Add:* Community Servs Monterey Peninsula Col 980 Fremont Blvd Monterey CA 93940

KAPLAN, BARBARA CONNALLY
EDUCATOR, SOPRANO

b LaGrange, Ga, Aug 19, 23. *Study:* Agnes Scott Col, with Evan Evans, AB(voice), 44; Eastman Sch Music, with Arthur Kraft & Herman Gerhart, MA(music lit & voice), 46; Fla State Univ, with Walter James & Richard Collins, PhD(music educ), 66; Univ SFla, MA(libr sci), 76; Liszt Acad Music, Budapest, with Laszlo Vikar, Katalin Forrai & Erzsebet Szönyi, 74 & 77. *Roles:* Siebel in Faust, Tampa Phil; Kate in Kiss Me Kate, 62 & Natalie in The Merry Widow, 62, Tampa Lyr Theatre. *Pos:* Mem chorus, Chautauqua Opera Co, 43-44; soloist, Tampa Phil, 56-62; dir youth choirs, First Presby Church, Tallahassee, 62-63. *Teaching:* Asst prof music, Ga State Col Women, 46-48; music specialist, Hillsborough Co Sch, Tampa, Fla, 56-62; assoc prof music, Univ Tex, Austin, 63-68; prof, St Leo Col, 68-77; guest prof, Univ Wash, 67 & Tel-Aviv Univ, 79; assoc prof music educ, Auburn Univ, 78- *Awards:* PEO Fel, 62; Berneta Minkwitz Int Fel, Delta Kappa Gamma, 67; Res Grant, Int Res & Exchanges Bd, 77. *Mem:* Music Educr Nat Conf; Orgn Am Kodaly Educr; Ala Music Educr Asn (exec bd, 83-); Ala Elem Music Educr Asn (pres, 83-); Int Kodaly Soc. *Interests:* Music literature for children; music aptitude studies; folk music analysis (southeastern United States). *Publ:* Coauth, Sound Beat and Feeling & Sound Shape & Symbol, In: New Dimensions in Music Series, Am Bk Co, 72, 76 & 80; Harp Album: Repertoire Primer, Studio P/R Publ; auth, Censorship and the Performing Arts, In: An Intellectual Freedom Primer, Libr Unlimited; On Education, Musical Am, 75; Music Education for the Children of the Dream, Parts I & II, Kodaly Envoy, 82. *Mailing Add:* Rte 3 Box 81A Summit Ln Auburn AL 36830

KAPLAN, BURTON
EDUCATOR, CONDUCTOR & MUSIC DIRECTOR

b New York, NY, Dec 28, 36. *Study:* Columbia Col, BA, 57; Juilliard Sch Music, with Dorothy Delay & Ivan Galamian; Fontainebleau Sch Music, with Yehudi Menuhin & Nadia Boulanger, 62. *Rec Perf:* NY State All-State String Orch, Crest Rec, 79. *Pos:* Dir Educ, Downeast Chamber Music Ctr, Castine, Maine, 77-; music dir & cond, Downeast Chamber Orch, 77- & Empire State Youth Orch, 79-82. *Teaching:* Chmn string dept, Third Street Music Sch, 69-77 & assoc dir educ, 75-77; prof violin, Consv Music, Brooklyn Col, City Univ New York, 79- & Manhattan Sch Music, 82- *Awards:* Winner, Youth Div, Am Symph Orch League Compt, Downeast Chamber Orch, 79. *Mem:* Am String Teachers Asn; Music Educr Nat Conf. *Publ:* Auth, A Point of View of Violin Teaching: Toward the Creation of a Method of Methods, 67, A Rhythm Sight-Reader, Books 1 & 2, 77, A Basic Skills Pitch Sight-Reader, Book 1, 81 & The Musicians Practice Log, 83, G Schirmer. *Mailing Add:* 817 West End Ave New York NY 10025

KAPLAN, LEWIS
VIOLIN, TEACHER

b Passaic, NJ, Nov, 10, 33. *Study:* Juilliard Sch, BS, 58, MS, 60; studied violin with Ivan Galamian; studied cond with Jean Morel. *Rec Perf:* Contra Mortem Et Tempus (Rochberg), 67 & Eleven Echoes of Autumn 1965 (Crumb), 68, CRI; Whisper Moon (Bolcom), Folkways, 70; Dream Sequence (Crumb), Odyssey, 77. *Pos:* Founder & violinist, Aeolian Chamber Players, 61-; co-founder & music dir, Bowdoin Summer Music Fest, 64. *Teaching:* Fac mem violin & chamber music, Juilliard Sch, 64- *Bibliog:* Edward Rothstein (auth), New York Times, 2/7/82; Valerie O'Brien (auth), Cover Story, Musical Am, 8/82. *Mailing Add:* Consv Music Brooklyn Col Brooklyn NY 11210

KAPLAN, LOIS JAY
COMPOSER, CONDUCTOR & MUSIC DIRECTOR

b Chicago, Ill, Feb 6, 32. *Study:* De Paul Univ, BMus, 58; Univ Wis, Madison, MS, 63; Jacksonville Univ, MA, 78; studied comp with Alexander Tcherepnin & cond with Paul Stassevitch. *Works:* La Salle Street Sketches, perf by Wurttemburg Kammersymphonie & Bavarian Chamber Orch, 70; Pallas Athena, Southern Music, 73; Salute to the Citizen Soldier, 79 & This Indeed We'll Defend, 80, perf by US Army bands, 80; Phantasy I (electronic music), Electronic Music Studio, Fla State Univ, 81. *Pos:* Cond, DePaul Univ Stadium Band, 54-58; music dir, Univ Chicago, Settlement House, 56-59 & 61-63 & Univ Theatre, 57-59; cond & dir, numerous Ger & US civilian & mil orch, bands & choirs in Europe, 59-61 & 68-70; cond, Ft McClellan Players & Anniston Little Theatre Orch, Ala, 74-77. *Teaching:* Trombone, privately, 50-63; instrm supvr, Chicago Pub Sch, 57-59. *Mem:* Fel, Int Acad Poets, Cambridge, England; fel, Centro Studi Scambi Int Accad Leonardo Da Vinci, Rome, Italy; Ala Coun Arts & Humanities (chmn steering commt, 75-). *Mailing Add:* 616 Lenwood Dr Anniston AL 36201

KAPLAN, MELVIN IRA
OBOE, ARTIST MANAGER

b Aug 29, 29; US citizen. *Study:* Juilliard Sch, BS, 50, MS, 51. *Rec Perf:* Two Prayer Settings (M Powell), 65-81, End of Summer (Weisgall) & Cantatas 1, 3 & 4 (H Aitken), CRI; Telemann Cantatas & Die Serenaden (Hindemith), Nonesuch; Anna Magdelena Note Book (J S Bach) & 13 Wind Divertimento (Mozart), Decca. *Pos:* Oboist, Fest Winds, 51-, New York Chamber Soloists, 57-; prin oboe & mgr, Musica Aeterna Orch, 57-; mgr, Melvin Kaplan Inc, 60- *Teaching:* Woodwind ens, Juilliard Sch, 53-81, oboe, 54-81. *Mailing Add:* RR1 Box 277 Charlotte VT 05445

KAPLAN, ROBERT BARNET
COMPOSER, PIANO

b Brookline, Mass, July 26, 24. *Study:* New England Consv, with Lucy Dean, 36-39; studied orch & comp with Paul Allen, 40-42, piano with Jules Wolffers, 45; Settlement Music Sch, Philadelphia, studied comp with Willson Osborne, 45-46. *Works:* Andante con variazioni (one piano, four hands), Opus 33, 72, Notturno for Flute, Opus 35, 73 & Duo da Camera for Viola, Opus 36, 74, Branden Press; Impromptu for Piano, Opus 39, Willis Music, 78; Tempo di Ballo, Opus 1, 80 & Fantasy-Variations for Piano, Opus 40, 82, Am Comp Soc. *Pos:* Dir music, Salon of Allied Arts, Boston, Mass, 48-52; founder, music dir & cond, South Shore Phil Orch, 83- *Teaching:* Pianoforte, organ, harmony & theory, privately, 38- *Mem:* New England Piano Teachers Asn; founder, Am Comp Soc Propagation, Publ & Perf of 20th Century Masterpieces (pres, 79-). *Mailing Add:* 196 Old Ocean St Marshfield MA 02050

KAPLAN, WILLIAM MEYER
EDUCATOR

b Madison, Wis, Nov 3, 29. *Study:* Juilliard Sch Music, BS, 51; Univ Chicago, MA, 57; Univ Mich, DMA, 67. *Pos:* Bassoonist, Denver Symph Orch, 56-62 & Detroit Symph, 64-66. *Teaching:* Assoc prof, Univ Ill, Chicago, 66-, dept head, 81- *Mem:* Col Music Soc; Int Double Reed Soc. *Publ:* Auth, W Hans Moennig: A Tribute, Double Reed, 80. *Mailing Add:* Dept of Music Univ Ill Chicago IL 60680

KAPUSCINSKI, RICHARD
CELLO, EDUCATOR

Study: Curtis Inst Music; studied violoncello with Leonard Rose & Felix Salmond. *Pos:* Asst prin cellist, Cleveland Orch, formerly; prin cellist, Baltimore Symph; mem, Boston Symph Orch, formerly; first cellist, Japan Phil; cellist, La Salle String Quartet, Boston Fine Arts Quartet & Gabrielle Trio; musical dir, Lorain Co Youth Orch, 77-78. *Teaching:* Fac mem, Cincinnati Col Music, Peabody Consv Music, Boston Univ, New England Consv Music & The Quartet Prog, Troy, NY, summer 79; prof violoncello, Consv Music, Oberlin Col, 67-; prog dir, Merrywood Music Sch, Lenox, Mass, 69-71; mem string fac, Univ Ill, Urbana, summers 73, 75 & 76; guest fac mem, Inst Higher Educ, Montreaux, Switzerland, summer 74. *Mailing Add:* Consv Music Oberlin Col Oberlin OH 44074

KARAYANIS, PLATO
DIRECTOR—OPERA

b Pittsburgh, Pa, Dec 26, 28. *Study:* Carnegie-Mellon Univ, BFA(music), 52; Curtis Inst Music, dipl(voice & opera), 56. *Pos:* Adminr, San Francisco Opera, 64; adminr & asst stage dir, Metropolitan Opera Nat Co, 65-67; baritone & dir opera, Germany & Switzerland; adminr, exec vpres & treas, Affil Artists Inc, 67-77; gen dir, Dallas Opera, 77- & Affil Artists, Opera Am; co-developer, Affil Artist Opera Prog, San Francisco; grantee, Martha Baird Rockefeller Fund Music. *Mailing Add:* Dallas Opera 3000 Turtle Creek Plaza Dallas TX 75219

KARCHIN, LOUIS (SAMUEL)
COMPOSER

b Philadelphia, Pa, Sept 8, 51. *Study:* Eastman Sch Music, BMus, 73; Harvard Univ, with Earl Kim, Fred Lerdahl & Arthur Berger, MA, 75, PhD, 78. *Works:* Chamber Concerto for Bassoon, perf by New York New Music Ens, 80; Viola Variations, perf by Lois Martin, 81; Duo for Violin & Voice, perf by Rolf Schulte & Fred Sherry, 82; Orchestral Variations, comn & perf by Portland Maine Symph, 82; Canonic Mosaics, comn & perf by Parnassus Contemp Music Ens, 83. *Teaching:* Asst prof music, NY Univ, 79- *Awards:* Koussevitsky-Tanglewood Award, Berkshire Music Ctr, 71; Bearns Prize, Columbia Univ, 72; comp award, Nat Endowment Arts, 82. *Mem:* Am Comp Alliance; Int Soc Comtemp Music (pres, 82-). *Mailing Add:* 100 Bleecker St New York NY 10012

KAREL, CHARLES
BARITONE

b Newark, NJ, Apr 22, 35. *Study:* Studied with John Charles Thomas, 50-53, Robert Weede, 61-62 & Sam Sakarian, 81-83. *Roles:* Simon Boccanegra in Simon Boccanegra, Bel Canto Opera Co, 82; Rigoletto in Rigoletto, Lyric Opera Kansas City, 82. *Pos:* Perf in Broadway prod of Hello Dolly & Milk & Honey, stage & film versions of The Music Man. *Mem:* Am Guild Musical Artists; Am Fedn Tv & Radio Artists; Screen Actors Guild; Actors Equity Asn. *Rep:* Tornay Mgt 127 W 72nd St New York NY 10023. *Mailing Add:* 1 Nevada Plaza 26-J New York NY 10023

KARLINS, M(ARTIN) WILLIAM
COMPOSER, EDUCATOR

b New York, NY, Feb 25, 32. *Study:* Manhattan Sch Music, with Vittorio Giannini, BM(comp), 61, MM(comp), 61; Univ Iowa, with Philip Bezanson & Richard Hervig, PhD(comp), 65; private study with Frederick Piket, 54-57 & Stefan Wolpe, 60-61. *Works:* Concerto Grosso No 1, Carl Fischer, 60;

Reflux (concerto for double bass & wind ens), 72 & Concert Music No 5, 73, Seesaw Music Corp; Concert Music No 4, Carl Fischer, 78; And All Our World is Dew—Woodwind Quintet No 2, comn & perf by Camerata Quintet, 78; Symph No 1, comn & perf by Am Chamber Symph, 80; Concerto (alto sax & orch), comn by Robert Black perf by Black & Nürnberger Symphoniker. *Rec Perf:* Variations on Obiter Dictum, CRI; Solo Piece With Passacaglia, Advan Rec; Music for Tenor Saxophone & Piano, Brewster Rec & Golden Crest. *Pos:* Co-dir, New Music Chamber Ens, New York, 59-61 & private ens, New York, 60-62; dir, Western Ill Univ Comtemp Music Ens, 65-67; dir, Northwestern Univ Contemp Music Ens, 67-81. *Teaching:* Asst prof theory & comp, Western Ill Univ, 65-67; assoc prof, Northwestern Univ, 67-73 & prof, 73- Awards: Rec grant, Am Comp Alliance & CRI, 73; fel, MacDowell Colony, 77; comp grant, Nat Endowment Arts, 79. *Mem:* Am Comp Alliance; Am Music Ctr; Chicago Soc Comp (pres, 76-81); New Music Chicago. *Mailing Add:* 1809 Sunnyside Circle Northbrook IL 60062

KARLSRUD, EDMOND
BASS, ARTIST REPRESENTATIVE
b Scobey, Mont, June 10, 27. *Study:* Univ Minn, ALA, 46; Juilliard Sch Music, BSM, 49. *Roles:* Fasolt in Das Reingold, Seattle Opera; Landgrave Hermann in Tannhäuser, New Orleans Opera; Doctor in La Traviata, Atlanta Opera; over 400 performances with Metropolitan Opera. *Pos:* Conct soloist, over 1600 performances, 48-; pres, Karlsrud Conct Inc, Mamaroneck, NY, 53-; soloist, Metropolitan Opera, 68-79. *Mailing Add:* Karlsrud Conct 948 The Parkway Mamaroneck NY 10543

KARMAZYN, DENNIS
CELLO
b Los Angeles, Calif, Oct 10, 50. *Study:* Paris Consv France, with Paul Tortelier, 68-69; Univ Southern Calif, with Gregor Piatigorsky, 70-73. *Pos:* Conct artist, Columbia Artists Mgt, 81-; cello soloist, perf with many leading orch in Am & Europe. *Awards:* First Prize, Denver Symph Nat Compt, 70. *Mailing Add:* 56 Cedar Lake W Denville NJ 07834

KARNS, DEAN MEREDITH
EDUCATOR, ADMINISTRATOR
b Anita, Iowa. *Teaching:* Asst prof, Coe Col, 60-77, assoc prof, 77-, chmn music dept, 79- Mem: Soc Music Theory. *Mailing Add:* Music Dept Coe Col Cedar Rapids IA 52402

KARNSTADT, CYNTHIA
SOPRANO, TEACHER
b Luling, Tex, May 19, 50. *Study:* Univ Tex, Austin, with Martha Deatherage, BM(applied voice), 72, MM(applied voice), 75, 76; studied with David Garvey, Gustava Weiss & Steve Blier, 77-82. *Pos:* Sop, opera houses throughout Western Europe. *Teaching:* Private voice asst, Univ Tex, 73-76. *Awards:* First Place, Nat Asn Teachers Singing Artist Award, 74; fels, Martha B Rockefeller Found, 78-79 & 81-82; first prize, Wagnerian Compt, Liederkranz Found, 80. *Mem:* Pi Kappa Lambda. *Rep:* European Am Artists 27 Pine New Canaan CT 06840. *Mailing Add:* 449 W 56th #6A New York NY 10019

KARP, THEODORE CYRUS
MUSICOLOGIST, WRITER
b New York NY, July 17, 26. *Study:* Juilliard Sch Music, with James Friskin, piano dipl, 45; Queens Col, with Karol Ratheus & Curt Sachs, BA, 47; NY Univ with Gustave Reese & Curt Sachs, PhD, 60. *Teaching:* Prof music hist, Univ Calif, Davis, 63-73 & Northwestern Univ, 73- Awards: Nat Endowment Humanities Fel, 67-68; fel, Inst Res Humanities Univ Wis, 78-79. *Mem:* Am Musicol Soc (chmn midwest chap, 80-82); Int Musicol Soc. *Publ:* Auth, A Lost Medieval Chansonnier, Musical Quart, 62; contribr, Aspects of Medieval and Renaissance Music, W W Norton, 66; auth, Towards a Critical Edition of Notre Dame Organa Dupla, Musical Quart, 67; Dictionary of Music, Dell, 73; contribr, A Musical Offering, Pendragon, 76. *Mailing Add:* 806 Chilton Lane Wilmette IL 60091

KARR, GARY MICHAEL
DOUBLE BASS, EDUCATOR
b Los Angeles, Calif, Nov 20, 41. *Study:* Juilliard Sch, BMus, 65; studied with Herman Reinshagen, Gabor Rejto, Jennie Tourel, Leonard Shure, Alfred Antonini, Raphael Bronstein & Leonard Rose. *Pos:* Recitalist, Can, US, Mex & Europe; co-founder, Karr-Lewis Duo with Harmon Lewis, 71-; performances & wkshps, Switz & UK; soloist, New York Phil, Chicago Symph, Toronto Symph, Oslo Symph, English Chamber Orch, BBC, CBS, NBC & New York Chamber Music Soc. *Teaching:* Mem fac, NC Sch Arts, formerly, Univ Wis, formerly, Juilliard Sch, formerly, Yale Univ, formerly, New England Consv Music, formerly, Ind Univ, formerly, Univ Southern Calif, formerly, NY Univ, formerly, Northern Ariz Univ, formerly & others; vis prof double bass, Hartt Sch Music, 76- Mem: Phi Mu Alpha Sinfonia; founder, Int Inst String Bass (pres, 67-74). *Mailing Add:* Hartt Sch Music Univ Hartford West Hartford CT 06117

KARSON, BURTON LEWIS
EDUCATOR, CONDUCTOR
b Los Angeles, Calif, Nov 10, 34. *Study:* Univ Southern Calif, BA, 56, MA, 59, DMA, 64. *Pos:* Founder, Orange Co Music Ctr; writer & critic, Los Angeles Times, 66-71; pianist & harpsichordist; organist & musician, St Joachim's Church, Costa Mesa, Calif; choral cond, Lutheran Chorale of Los Angeles, 79-; artistic dir, Baroque Music Fest, Corona Del Mar, Calif. *Teaching:* Instr music, Univ Col, Univ Southern Calif, 58-59, univ organist, 60-61; instr, Glendale Community Col, Calif, 60-65; asst prof, Calif State

Univ, Fullerton, 65-69, assoc prof, 69-74, prof, 74-; lectr, Los Angeles Phil Symph Orch. *Mem:* Am Musicol Soc; Am Guild Organists; Phi Mu Alpha Sinfonia; Pi Kappa Lambda. *Interests:* Music history and criticism in early California; 17th-18th century music in Darmstadt, Germany. *Publ:* Ed, Festival Essays for Pauline Alderman, 76; contribr to Musical Quart & Perf Arts. *Mailing Add:* 404 De Sola Terr Corona Del Mar CA 92625

KARTMAN, MYRON
VIOLIN, CONDUCTOR & MUSIC DIRECTOR
Study: Juilliard Sch Music, BS, 56; Eastman Sch Music, MM, 57; Boston Univ, DMA, 70. *Rec Perf:* On CRI Pleides & Gold Crest Rec. *Pos:* Soloist, New York Phil, formerly, Boston Civic Orch, formerly, Tampa Phil, formerly & Birmingham Symph, formerly; founding mem & first violinist, Antioch String Quartet; first violinist, Ill String Quartet, Southern Ill Univ & Cadek Quartet, Univ Ala; violinist, Steinerius Duo, 69- & Regenstein Trio, Northwestern Univ, currently; music dir & cond, Cent Ky Youth Orch, 79; cond, Northwestern Univ Chamber Orch, currently. *Teaching:* Prof music & chmn string dept, Univ Ala, formerly; prof violin & chmn string dept, Northwestern Univ, 77- Mailing Add: 2536 Hurd Ave Evanston IL 60201

KASHKASHIAN, KIM
VIOLA, TEACHER
b Detroit, Mich, Aug, 31, 52. *Study:* Peabody Consv, with Walter Trampler & Karen Tuttle, BM, 73; Philadelphia Musical Acad, with Karen Tuttle, MM, 74. *Pos:* Soloist, English Chamber Orch, Berlin Radio Orch, New York Phil, Bavarian Radio, Stuttgart Radio & Zurich Chamber Orch; recitalist, New York, Washington DC, Boston, Los Angeles, San Francisco, Hamburg & Munich; performer chamber music, Marlboro Fest, Spoleto Fest, Chamber Music West & Lockenhaus Fest. *Teaching:* Viola, New Sch Music & Mannes Col Music. *Awards:* Pro Musica Found Award, 79; Martha Baird Rockefeller Grant, 81. *Mailing Add:* 210 W 70th St New York NY 10023

KASICA, JOHN
EDUCATOR, PERCUSSION
Study: Juilliard Sch, BM; studied perc with Saul Goodman & Elden Bailey. *Pos:* Performer, New York Phil, Metropolitan Opera, New York City Opera, New York City Ballet, Erick Hawkins Mod Dance Co, Musica Aeterna, Juilliard Ens, Young Audiences Perc Quartet, Aspen Music Fest, Spoleto Fest Two Worlds, Italy & Kerkrade Music Fest, Netherlands; solo mallet player & perc, St Louis Symph Orch, currently, mem, Perc Quartet, currently. *Teaching:* Mem fac, Univ Mo, St Louis, formerly & St Louis Community Col, Florissant Valley, formerly; adj mem fac perc, Webster Col, currently; mem fac perc, chamber music & ens, St Louis Consv Music, currently. *Mailing Add:* St Louis Consv Music 560 Trinity Ave St Louis MO 63130

KASLOW, DAVID MARTIN
FRENCH HORN, EDUCATOR
b Brooklyn, NY, May 12, 43. *Study:* Manhattan Sch Music, BM(perf), 63, MM(perf), 69. *Works:* Incidental Music-Coriolanns, perf by Univ Denver, 70. *Pos:* Solo horn, Nat Ballet Can, 62-65 & Aspen Fest Chamber Orch, summer 69; second horn, Central City Opera Orch, 69-74. *Teaching:* Prof horn, Univ Denver, 69- Mem: Int Horn Soc. *Mailing Add:* 365 S Williams Denver CO 80209

KATAHN, ENID
PIANO, EDUCATOR
b Pittsburgh, Pa, Apr 10, 32. *Study:* Juilliard Sch, 49-52; Hartt Sch Music, BM, 55; George Peabody Col Teachers, MM, 70; coaching with Leon Fleisher. *Rec Perf:* Keys, 72, Moving Up, 75 & Enid Katahn Plays, 78, Peacetree Rec. *Teaching:* Instr, Hartt Sch Music, 52-55 & Univ NC, Chapel Hill, spring 62; artist & teacher, Blair Sch Music, Vanderbilt Univ, 69-; asst prof, George Peabody Col, 72-77. *Awards:* Teacher of Yr, Nashville Area Music Teachers Asn, 82. *Mem:* Music Teachers Nat Asn. *Mailing Add:* Blair Sch Music Vanderbilt Univ 2400 Blakemore Ave Nashville TN 37212

KATES, STEPHEN EDWARD
CELLO, EDUCATOR
b New York, NY, May 7, 43. *Study:* Juilliard Sch, dipl, 69; Univ Southern Calif, with Gregor Piatigorsky, 64-67; studied with Claus Adam, Marie Rosanoff & Leonard Rose. *Rec Perf:* On RCA, Melodya, Denon, First Ed Rec, Orion, First Ed Sonic Arts & CRI. *Pos:* Soloist with major orchs in US, Europe, Asia & Far East; recitalist, Hong Kong, Tokyo, Taiwan, Italy, Austria, Hungary, Can & Moscow; participant, Spoleto Fest, 79-80 & SBank Summer Music Fest, London, 80; guest artist, Chamber Soc Lincoln Ctr & Op One Conct Soc, Baltimore. *Teaching:* Prof cello, Ohio State Univ, 69-72; instr cello & chamber ens, Peabody Consv Music, 74- Awards: Silver Medal, Third Int Tchaikovsky Cello Compt Moscow, 66; Ford Found Grant, 71; San Francisco Symph Found Award. *Mailing Add:* 838 West End Ave New York NY 10025

KATIMS, MILTON
CONDUCTOR, VIOLA
b New York, NY. *Study:* Columbia Univ, BA(music); three hon doctorates. *Rec Perf:* Cond with Seattle Symph, RCA, Columbia & Vox Rec; violist with Casals, Stern, NY Quartet, Columbia & Mercury; viola quintets with Budapest String Quartet, Columbia; Bach Six Solo Suites, Pantheon. *Pos:* First desk violist, Toscanini NBC Symph, 43-54; cond, NBC, 47-54; music dir & cond, Seattle Symph, 54-76; artistic dir, Univ Houston Sch Music, currently. *Teaching:* Fac mem, Juilliard Sch Music, 46-54. *Awards:* Alice M Ditson Award, 67. *Publ:* Twenty-five transcriptions & editions for Viola, Int Music Co, 40-70. *Rep:* Maxim Gershunoff 502 Park Ave New York NY 10022. *Mailing Add:* Sch Music Univ Houston Houston TX 77004

KATZ, GEORGE LEON
EDUCATOR, PIANO
b New York, NY. *Study:* Juilliard Sch, studied piano with Josef Raieff, BS(music), 54, MS(music), 56; studied piano with Marguerite Long & Alfred Cortot, 56-58. *Teaching:* Prof piano, Ohio Univ, 59-73; head piano fac, Drake Univ, 73- *Awards:* Walter Naumburg Award, 56. *Mem:* Music Teachers Nat Asn. *Mailing Add:* 1016 Woodland Pk Dr West Des Moines IA 50265

KATZ, HELEN-URSULA
KEYBOARD, EDUCATOR
b New York, NY. *Study:* Juilliard Sch, with Albert Fuller, BM, MM, DMA(harpsichord); Mannes Col Music, piano with Edith Oppens, dipl(piano); Amsterdam Consv, studied harpsichord with Gustav Leonhardt. *Rec Perf:* On Desto and Roxelle. *Pos:* Performer as sololist with chamber groups and orchestras in concert and TV; conductor; pres, Roxelle Publ & Rec. *Teaching:* Mem fac, Mass Inst Technol, Mannes Col Music & Aspen Music Fest, formerly; mem fac lit & materials music, Juilliard Sch, 77- *Awards:* Double Fulbright Award for recorder with Frans Bruggen at Amsterdam Muzieklyceum & harpsichord with Gustav Leonhardt at Amsterdam Consv; Edward M Steuermann Mem Prize. *Mailing Add:* Juilliard Sch Lincoln Ctr New York NY 10023

KATZ, ISRAEL J
EDUCATOR
b New York, NY, July 21, 30. *Study:* Univ Calif, Los Angeles, BA, 56, PhD, 67. *Teaching:* Asst prof music, McGill Univ, Montreal, Can, 68-69; assoc prof, Columbia Univ, 68-75 & York Col, City Univ New York, 77 & Grad Ctr. *Awards:* John Simon Guggenheim Mem Found Fel, 75-76; Nat Endowment for Humanities Grant, 81-82. *Mem:* Soc Ethnomusicology (treas, 71-75); Int Folk Music Coun (mem ed & exec bd, 77-79); Am Musicol Soc; Am Soc Jewish Music (chmn bd, 74-). *Interests:* European & Middle Eastern folk music. *Publ:* Auth, Judeo Spanish Traditional Ballads from Jerusalem, Inst Mediaeval Music, 72-75; The Traditional Folk Music of Spain: Explorations and Perspectives, Yearbk Int Folk Music Coun, 74; co-ed, Proceedings of the International Symposium on the Cantigas de Santa Maria, Hispanic Sem Medieval Studies (in prep); coauth, Folk Literature of the Sephardic Jews, Univ Calif (in prep). *Mailing Add:* 461 Ft Washington Ave New York NY 10033

KATZ, MARTHA STRONGIN
VIOLA, EDUCATOR
b New York, NY, Mar 10, 43. *Study:* Curtis Inst Music; Juilliard Sch; Manhattan Sch Music; Univ Southern Calif; studied with Raphael Bronstein, Ivan Galamian, Lillian Fuchs & William Primrose & chamber music with Gabor Rejto, Raphael Hillyer, Gregor Piatigorsky & Jascha Heifetz. *Rec Perf:* Adagio and Fugue in C Minor (Mozart), RCA; Complete String Quartets of Brahms; Quartet No 14 in D Minor (Schubert). *Pos:* Mem, Univ Southern Calif String Quartet, 64-66 & Toledo String Quartet, 66-69; violist & founding mem, Cleveland String Quartet, 69-80; soloist with Orch Suisse Romande, various orchs at Berkshire Music Ctr, Mozarteum, Salzburg & Buffalo Phil Orch tour. *Teaching:* Mem fac, Univ Toledo, 65-69, Interlochen, 69-70, Curtis Inst Music, 69-71, State Univ NY Col, Buffalo, 71-76 & Aspen Music Fest, 72-; adj prof chamber groups & viola, Eastman Sch Music, currently. *Awards:* Int Prize Winner, Munich Compt, 65; Highest Award, Geneva Int Viola Compt, 68; Max Reger Award, 68. *Mailing Add:* Eastman Sch Music 26 Gibbs St Rochester NY 14604

KATZ, PAUL
CELLO, EDUCATOR
b Los Angeles, Calif, Nov 16, 41. *Study:* Univ Southern Calif, BMus; Manhattan Sch Music, MMus, 64; studied with Gregor Piatigorsky, Leonard Rose, Gabor Rejto, Bernard Greenhouse & Janos Starker & chamber music with Lillian Fuchs, Daniel Guilet, Raphael Hillyer & William Primrose. *Rec Perf:* Adagio and Fugue in C Minor (Mozart), RCA; Complete String Quartets of Brahms; Quartet No 14 in D Minor (Schubert); Haydn Quartets, Op 64, No 5 & Op 76, No 2. *Pos:* Perf for Violoncello Soc NY, 64; soloist, Marlboro Music Fest, 68-69, Los Angeles, New York & Toronto; cellist & founding mem, Cleveland String Quartet, 69- *Teaching:* Mem fac, Univ Toledo, 65-59, Interlochen, 69-70, Curtis Inst Music, 69-71 & State Univ NY Col, Buffalo, 71-76; prof chamber groups & cello, Eastman Sch Music, currently. *Awards:* Prize Winner, Int String Quartet Compt, Munich, 65 & with Toledo Quartet, Geneva Compt, 66; Group of Month Award, High Fidelity & Musical Am, 73. *Mailing Add:* Eastman Sch Music 26 Gibbs St Rochester NY 14604

KATZEN, DANIEL
FRENCH HORN, EDUCATOR
Study: Eastman Sch Music, dipl; Ind Univ; Mozarteum, Salzburg, studied French horn with Milan Yancich, Morris Secon & Dale Clavenger. *Pos:* Prin horn, Salzburger Kammerorchester, formerly; alt prin horn, Camerata Acad Salzburg, formerly; extra horn, Munich Phil, formerly; mem, Israel Chamber Orch, formerly & Rochester Phil, formerly; mem horn sect, Boston Symph Orch, 79-; performer, Phoenix Symph, San Diego Symph & Grant Park Symph, Chicago. *Teaching:* Mem fac French horn, New England Consv Music, currently. *Mailing Add:* New England Consv Music 290 Huntington Rd Boston MA 02115

KAUFMAN, CHARLES
ADMINISTRATOR, EDUCATOR
Study: Columbia Univ, BS; NY Univ, MA, Grad Sch Arts & Sci, PhD; studied with Jan LaRue, Gustave Reese, James Haar, Martin Bernstein & Victor

Yelin. *Pos:* Writer music articles, NY Times; pres, Mannes Col Music, 79- *Teaching:* Mem fac, NY Univ, formerly, Wash Sq Col, formerly & Hunter Col, City Univ New York, formerly; mem fac music hist, Mannes Col Music, 75- *Interests:* American music; organology; the baroque era. *Publ:* Contribr to NY Folklore Quart, Current Musicol, J Am Instrm Soc, Notes, Musiklexicon & New Grove Dict of Music & Musicians, 6th ed. *Mailing Add:* Mannes Col Music 157 E 74th St New York NY 10021

KAUFMAN, FREDRICK
COMPOSER, ADMINISTRATOR
b Brooklyn, NY, Mar 24, 36. *Study:* Manhattan Sch Music, BM, 58, MM, 60; studied comp with Vittorio Giannini, Karlheinz Stockhausen & Vincent Persichetti. *Works:* Violin Concerto, Pittsburgh Symph, 69 & Boulder Symph Orch, 78; Nothing Ballet, Israel Phil & Royal Swedish Ballet, 73-82; Percussion Trio, Darmstadt Fest for New Music, 74; Mobile String Quartet, Philadelphia String Quartet, 82; When the Twain Meet, London Chamber Orch & Philadelphia Col Perf Arts Symph Orch, 82-83; Fragrances, Cleveland Inst Music & Philadelphia Col Perf Arts, 82-83. *Teaching:* Asst prof music, Univ Wis, 69-71; asst prof cond & comp, Rubin Acad Music, Israel, 72-76; assoc prof comp & chmn music dept, Eastern Mont Col, 77-82; prof comp & dean, Philadelphia Col Perf Arts, 82- *Awards:* Darius Milhaud Comp Award, Aspen Music Fest, 71; Fulbright Lectr Award, 77; Cert Outstanding Serv to Jazz Educ, Nat Asn Jazz Educr, 78. *Publ:* Coauth, African Roots of Jazz, Alred Publ, 80. *Mailing Add:* 329 S 13th St Philadelphia PA 19107

KAUFMAN, MINDY F
FLUTE & PICCOLO, EDUCATOR
b White Plains, NY, Nov 4, 56. *Study:* Eastman Sch Music, BM & perf cert, 78. *Pos:* Second flutist, Rochester Phil Orch, 76-79, piccolo, 78-79; prin piccolo player, NY Phil, 79- *Teaching:* Mem fac, Westchester Consv Music; instr flute, Mercy Col, currently. *Mailing Add:* New York Phil Avery Fisher Hall New York NY 10023

KAUFMANN, HENRY WILLIAM
EDUCATOR, WRITER
b Cambridge, Mass, Oct 23, 13. *Study:* Yale Univ, BMus, 45, MMus, 46; Harvard Univ, PhD(music hist & theory), 60. *Pos:* Ed, Symposium, Col Music Soc, 64-67; consult panelist, Nat Endowment Humanities, 75- *Teaching:* Instr music, Milton Acad, Mass, 46-48; asst prof, Univ Wis, Madison, 48-50; lectr, Longy Sch Music, 50-58; asst prof music theory, Boston Univ, 50-56; from asst prof to assoc prof music hist, Ohio State Univ, 58-62; assoc prof, Rutgers Univ, New Brunswick, 62-64, chmn dept music, 64-73, prof, 64-, jr dir dept music yr in Italy, 73-74. *Awards:* Weil Fel, 64. *Mem:* Am Musicol Soc; Col Music Soc; Renaissance Soc Am; Medieval Soc. *Interests:* Art history; Italian literature; music of the Renaissance. *Publ:* Auth, The Life and Works of Giulio Fiesco, In: Aspects of Medieval and Renaissance Music, Norton, 66; More on the Tuning of the Archicembalo, J Am Musicol Soc, 70; Art for the Wedding of Cosemo de Medici and Eleanora of Toledo (1539), Paragone, 5/70; contribr, Music for a Noble Florentino Wedding (1539), In: Words and Music, The Scholar's View, Harvard Univ Cambridge, 72; Music for a Favola Pastorale, In: A Musical Offering: Essays in Honor of Martin Berstein, Pendragon, 77. *Mailing Add:* Music Dept Rutgers Univ New Brunswick NJ 08903

KAUFMANN, WALTER
COMPOSER, WRITER
b Carlsbad, Czechoslovakia, Apr 1, 07; US citizen. *Study:* Univ Prague, Berlin; Spokane Consv Music, DMus, 55. *Works:* Six symphonies, 30-56; seven operas, 34-66; Madras Express (fantasy for orch), 48; Rubaiyat (voice & orch), 52; Passacaglia and Capriccio (brass); and many others. *Pos:* Dir, Bombay Radio, 35-46; cond, Brittish Brodacasting Corp, 46-47; cond & music dir, Winnipeg Symph Orch, 48-57. *Teaching:* Instr & head dept piano, Halifax Consv Music, 47-48; from lectr to prof, 57-77, Ind Univ, Bloomington, emer prof musicol, 77- *Mem:* Int Soc Musical Res; Soc Ethnomusicol. *Publ:* Auth, Rasa, Raga-Mala and Performance Times in North Indian Ragas, 65 & The Mudras in Samavedic Chant and Their Realtionship to the go-on Hakase of the Shomyo in Japan, 67, Ethnomusicol; Musical Notations of the Orient, 67 & The Ragas of North India, 68, In: Essays in Musicol; Tibetan Buddhist Chant, 75, The Ragas of Sougth India, 76 & Musical References in the Chinese Classics, 76. *Mailing Add:* Sch Music Ind Univ Bloomington IN 47401

KAVAFIAN, ANI
VIOLIN, EDUCATOR
b Istanbul, Turkey, May 10, 48. *Study:* Juilliard Sch Music, BM, MS. *Rec Perf:* Brandenburg Concerto (Bach). *Pos:* Soloist, Detroit Symph, Nat Symph, Boston Pops & others; solo recitalist, New York; appearances, Mostly Mozart Fest, Great Performers Ser, Lincoln Ctr, Spoleto Fest, Italy, Marlboro Music Fest & Aldeburgh Fest, UK. *Teaching:* Adj mem fac strings, Mannes Col Music, currently. *Awards:* Prize winner, Naumburg Compt, 75; Avery Fisher Prize, 76; Pro Musicis Sponsorship Award, 83. *Rep:* Herbert Barrett Mgt Inc 1860 Broadway New York NY 10023. *Mailing Add:* Mannes Col Music 157 E 74th St New York NY 10021

KAVASCH, DEBORAH HELENE
COMPOSER, SOPRANO
b Washington, DC. *Study:* Mozarteum, Univ Salzburg, 69-70; Bowling Green State Univ, BA, 71, BM, 72, MM, 73; Univ Calif, San Diego, with Robert Erickson, Pauline Oliveros & Bernard Rands, PhD, 78. *Works:* Requiem, perf by Extended Vocal Techniques Ens, 78; The Owl and the Pussycat (vocal

ens), Ed Reimers, 80; Soliloquy (solo voice), perf by Deborah Kavasch, 81; Nocturne (solo clarinet), comn & perf by William Powell, 82; Abelard (soprano & viola), Rarities for Strings (in press). *Roles:* Armide in Armide, Alan Curtis & Berkeley Symph, 83. *Pos:* Found mem, Extended Vocal Techniques Ens La Jolla, Calif, 76- *Teaching:* Lectr theory, Bowling Green State Univ, 73; assoc music, Univ Calif, San Diego, 76-79; asst prof theory & voice, Calif State Col, Stanislaus, 79-83. *Mem:* Am Soc Univ Comp; Col Music Soc. *Interests:* Extended vocal techniques. *Publ:* Auth, An Introduction to Extended Vocal Techniques: Some Compositional Aspects and Performance Problems, Univ Calif, 80. *Mailing Add:* 6666 Beadnell #26 San Diego CA 92117

KAY, ULYSSES
COMPOSER, EDUCATOR
b Tucson, Ariz, Jan 07, 17. *Study:* Univ Ariz, BMus, 38; Eastman Sch Music, MMus, 40; further study at Berkshire Ctr, Tanglewood, Yale Univ & Columbia Univ. *Works:* The Quiet One (film), Film Doc Inc, 48; Serenade for Orchestra, The Louisville Orch, 53; Markings (orch), Detroit Symph, 66; Quintet Concerto, Juilliard Sch, 74; Jubilee (three-act opera), Opera/South, 76; Chariots (orch), perf by Philadelphia Orch, 79; Frederick Douglass (three-act opera), Nat Endowment Arts, 83. *Pos:* Music Consult, BMI, 53- *Teaching:* Vis prof music, Univ Calif, Los Angeles, 66-67; prof music, Herbert H Lehman Col, City Univ New York, 68- *Awards:* Julius Rosenwald Fel, 47-48; Prix de Rome, Am Acad in Rome, 49-52; Guggenheim Fel, 64-65. *Mem:* Am Music Ctr; BMI. *Mailing Add:* 1271 Alicia Ave Teaneck NJ 07666

KAYE, BERNARD L
FLUTE & PICCOLO, CLARINET
b New Haven, Conn, Sept 12, 27. *Study:* Yale Univ, BA, 49; Sch Dental Med, Harvard Univ, DMD, 53 & Med Sch, MD, 55; studied with Joyce Bailey Kaye. *Rec Perf:* Numerous rec with Jacksonville Symph, Fla. *Pos:* With, Yale Univ Symph, Yale Univ Marching & Conct Bands, New Haven Symph & Univ Kans Symph, formerly; prin saxophonist, Jacksonville Symph Orch, Fla, 62-, soloist, 76; prin woodwind, Jacksonville Starlight Symphonette, Fla, 62-; mem bd dir & chmn artist & prog comt, Jackson Symph Asn, Fla, 79-; mem bd dir, WJCT Radio, currently. *Mem:* Jacksonville Musicians Asn. *Mailing Add:* 820 Prudential Dr Suite 702 Jacksonville FL 32207

KEARNEY, LINDA (YVONNE)
EDUCATOR, FLUTE & PICCOLO
b Baton Rouge, La, Jan 25, 52. *Study:* Cleveland Inst Music, BA(music), 74, MA(music), 75, dipl, 77. *Rec Perf:* The Life and Adventures of Nicholas Nickleby, Audio Rec Studios, 82. *Pos:* Flute & piccolo, Nat Training Orch, Australian Broadcasting Comn, Sydney, 70-72; Sydney Symph Orch, 72 & Canton Symph Orch, Ohio, 79-82. *Teaching:* Flute, Cleveland Inst Music, 73-, Ursuline Col, 74- & Cleveland State Univ, 78- *Mem:* Pi Kappa Lambda. *Mailing Add:* 1126 E 77th St Cleveland OH 44103

KEARNS, WILLIAM KAY
EDUCATOR, FRENCH HORN
b Wilmington, Ohio, Jan 17, 28. *Study:* Ohio State Univ, BMus, 52, MA, 54; Univ Ill, PhD, 65. *Pos:* French horn, Wichita Symph, 52-53, Ohio Symph, Springfield, 53-62, Columbus Symph, 53-65 & WVa Symph, Wheeling, 54-58; music critic, Camera, Boulder, Colo. *Teaching:* Music hist, lit & French horn, Columbus pub sch, Ohio, 52-53, Ohio State Univ, 53-65, Friends Univ, 52-53, Bemidji State Col, Minn, 65 & Univ Colo, 65- *Mem:* Am Musicol Soc; Col Music Soc; Music Educr Nat Conf; Am Folklore Soc. *Publ:* Coauth, A Resource Book for Music Appreciation, 69; auth, Folk Music of Colorado and the United States, 77; contribr, numerous professional journals. *Mailing Add:* 2065 King Ave Boulder CO 80302

KEATS, DONALD H(OWARD)
COMPOSER, EDUCATOR
b New York, NY, May 27, 29. *Study:* Yale Univ, MusB, 49; Columbia Univ, MA, 51; Staatlich Hochschule Musik, Hamburg, Germany, 54-56; Univ Minn, PhD, 62. *Works:* Symphony #1, Galaxy Music, 59; An Elegiac Symphony, 64, Piano Sonata, 67, String Quartet #1 & String Quartet #2, 69, Boosey & Hawkes; A Love Triptych (three song cycles for sop & piano), 70; Polarities (violin & piano), 71. *Rec Perf:* String Quartet No 2, CRI Rec. *Teaching:* From asst to prof & chmn music, Antioch Col, 57-75; vis prof, Univ Wash, 69-70; prof, Sch Music, Univ Denver, 75-, Lawrence C Phipps prof, 82- *Awards:* Fulbright Scholar, 54-55 & 55-56; Guggenheim Fel, 64-65 & 72-73; Nat Endowment Arts & Humanities Grant, 75. *Mem:* ASCAP; Am Music Ctr; Am Soc Univ Comp; Col Music Soc. *Mailing Add:* 9261 E Berry Ave Englewood CO 80111

KECHLEY, DAVID STEVENSON
COMPOSER, EDUCATOR
b Seattle, Wash, Mar 16, 47. *Study:* Univ Wash, BA & BMus, 70, MMus(comp), 74; Cleveland Inst Music, DMA(comp), 79. *Works:* Second Composition for Large Orchestra, perf by Seattle Symph, 68; Sonata for Flute and Harp, perf at Am Harp Soc Nat Conf, 74; Five Ancient Lyrics on Poems by Sappho, perf by Northwest Chamber Orch, 76 & Shreveport Symph, 83; Dance Music III (Streams of Hoofed Wings), comn & perf by Footpath Dance Co, Cleveland, Ohio, 80; The Funky Chicken for String Orchestra, Pine Valley Press, 81; Pathways: A Symphony in Four Movements, comn & perf by Winston-Salem Symph, 81; Sonata for Viola and Piano, Sonatine Music, 83. *Teaching:* Asst prof, Univ NC, Wilmington, 79- *Awards:* Nat Endowment for Arts Grant, 76 & 79; Guggenheim Fel, 78; First Prize, Comp Compt, Shreveport Symph, 81. *Mem:* ASCAP; Col Music Soc; Am Soc Univ Comp. *Mailing Add:* 1509 Grace St Wilmington NC 28401

KECHLEY, GERALD
COMPOSER, MUSIC DIRECTOR
b Seattle, Wash, Mar 18, 19. *Study:* Univ Wash, with George F McKay, BA, 46, MA, 50; Berkshire Music Ctr, with Aaron Copland. *Works:* Piano Trio, 64; Deadalus and the Minotaur (chorus & orch); The Golden Lion (opera); Drop Slow Tears (chorus & chamber ens); Prologue, Enactment, Epilogue (orch); The Beckoning Fair One (opera); Antiphony for Winds (band); Pleasure it is; and many others. *Pos:* Asst dir, Collegium Musicum & Madrigal Singers, 77-79, dir, 79- *Teaching:* Music dir, Centralia Jr Col, 53; fac mem music, Univ Mich; fac mem sch music, Univ Wash, 53-67, prof theory & comp, 67- *Awards:* First prize, Nat Fedn Music Clubs Cont, 45; Guggenheim Fel, 49 & 51. *Mem:* ASCAP. *Mailing Add:* 5230 12th Ave NE Seattle WA 98105

KECK, GEORGE R
EDUCATOR, PIANO
b Rogers, Ark, Aug 15, 42. *Study:* Univ Ark, Fayetteville, BM(perf), 60-65, MM(perf), 65-68; Univ Iowa, with Albert T Luper, PhD(musicol), 82. *Teaching:* Assoc prof piano & musicol, Ouachita Univ, Arkadelphia, 69- *Mem:* Am Musicol Soc; Col Music Soc; Sonneck Soc; Music Teachers Nat Asn; Music Libr Asn. *Interests:* Nineteenth-century American sheet music. *Mailing Add:* Box 711 OBU Arkadelphia AR 71923

KEENE, CHRISTOPHER
CONDUCTOR, WRITER
b Berkeley, Calif, Dec 21, 46. *Study:* Univ Calif, Berkeley. *Works:* The Consort (ballet), 70. *Pos:* With Spoleto Fest, 68, 69, 71, gen dir, 73, music dir, 76; music dir, Am Ballet Co, 69-70, Artpark, 75-, Syracuse Symph Orch, 75-, Long Island Phil, 79- & New York City Opera, 83-; cond, Sante Fe Opera, 71, Metropolitan Opera, 71, Covent Garden, 73, Chicago Symph, 76 & Berlin Opera, 76; guest cond, New York Phil, 83, Edinburgh Fest, 83 & others. *Mailing Add:* 650 West End Ave New York NY 10024

KEENE, CONSTANCE
PIANO, EDUCATOR
Pos: Soloist, Boston Symph, Philadelphia Phil, Chicago Symph, New York Phil, Halle Phil & Berlin Phil; performer, Gstaad Fest, Switz. *Teaching:* Mem fac piano, Manhattan Sch Music, 67-, chmn dept, 82- *Awards:* Winner, Naumburg Award. *Mailing Add:* Manhattan Sch Music 120 Claremont Ave New York NY 10027

KEENE, JAMES A
EDUCATOR, WRITER
b Detroit, Mich, Dec 27, 32. *Study:* Eastman Sch Music, BM, 54; Wayne State Univ, MMEd, 59; Univ Mich, PhD, 69. *Teaching:* Prof music & chmn dept, Mansfield State Col, 75-80 & Western Ill Univ, 80- *Interests:* Music education in America. *Publ:* Auth, Some Physiological Aspects of Instrument Playing, Instrumentalist, 69; Music Education in the Private Schools of Vermont, J Res Music Educ, 71; Instrumental Instruction and Kinesthetic Learning, Instrumentalist, 73; Samuel Read Hall—Early Associate of Music Education, Music J, 74; History of Music Education in the United States, Univ Press New England, 82. *Mailing Add:* 1303 W Adams St Macomb IL 61455

KEEZER, RONALD
COMPOSER, EDUCATOR
b Eau Claire, Wis, June 4, 40. *Works:* Eloszo (orch); 4 Brass Structures (wind ens); 3 Movements for Percussion; Transformations (piano trio); Introspections (five players, narrator & perc); Doth Not Wisdom Cry (chorus); Impetus (film score). *Teaching:* Instr music, Univ Wis, Eau Claire, currently. *Mailing Add:* 121 E Palk Ave Eau Claire WI 54701

KEHLE, ROBERT GORDON
EDUCATOR, TROMBONE
b Tacoma, Wash, May 21, 51. *Study:* Wash State Univ, BA & BM, 75; Ind Univ, MM(music), 77. *Pos:* Casual trombone, Spokane Symph, 71-75; prin trombone, Springfield Symph, 79-; trombone, Central Plains Brass Quintet, 80- *Teaching:* Asst prof trombone & jazz, Pittsburg State Univ, Kans, 78. *Mem:* Int Trombone Asn; Tuba Universal Brotherhood Asn; Nat Asn Jazz Educr. *Publ:* Ed, Regional Jazz Calendar, Pittsburg State Univ, 78- *Mailing Add:* 2104 W Broadway C-5 Pittsburg KS 66762

KEHLER, GEORGE BELA
PIANO, EDUCATOR
b Szöd-Szödliget, Hungary, July 11, 19. *Study:* Jr Col Vac, Hungary, 37, BA; Ferenc Liszt Royal Hungarian State Consv Music, Budapest, BMus, 41, MMus, 44; Univ Budapest, PhD, 41; studied with Edwin Fisher, Carl Martienssen, Zoltan Horusitzky, Franz Ledwinka, Erno Daniel, Bela Böszörmenyi-Nagy & Wilhelm Kempff. *Rec Perf:* Beethoven Sonatas, Works of Liszt, Schumann & Chopin, Works of Franck & Horusitzky, Works of Mozart & Schubert, Dombay Rec. *Pos:* Soloist, Budapest Symph Orch, Mozarteum Orch & Marshall Symph Orch, Tex; solo recitals in Budapest, Vienna, London, Berlin, Mexico City, Salzburg, New York, Kans, Ill, Tex & Tenn, yearly for over 20 years. *Teaching:* Privately, Austria & Germany; guest instr, Bethany Col, Ill Wesleyan Univ, Kilgore Col & Lutheran Col; prof music, ETenn State Univ, currently. *Publ:* Auth, The Piano in Concert (two vol), Scarecrow Press, 82. *Mailing Add:* 1408 Ridgecrest Rd Johnson City TN 37601

KEISER, MARILYN JEAN
ORGAN, EDUCATOR
b Alton, Ill, July 12, 41. *Study:* Wesleyan Univ, BSM, 63; Union Theol Sem, SMM, 65, SMD, 77. *Pos:* Assoc organist, St John the Divine, New York, 66-70; music dir, All Souls Church, Asheville, 70-83; dir, Community Chorus, Univ NC, Asheville, 80-83. *Teaching:* Assoc prof, Ind Univ, Bloomington, 83- *Mem:* Am Guild Organists (nat counr, 73-81); Standing Comn Church Music (consult, 73-79, 82-). *Publ:* Auth, Teaching Music in Small Churches, Church Hymnal Corp, 83. *Rep:* Karen Holtkamp 3269 W 30th Cleveland OH 44109. *Mailing Add:* 1101 Carnaby East Bloomington IN 47401

KELLA, JOHN JAKE
VIOLA, TEACHER
b Hilo, Hawaii, Oct 14, 48. *Study:* Chamber music with Hungarian String Quartet, 70 & Juilliard String Quartet, 73-76; Juilliard Sch, BM, 74, MM, 75; NY Univ, PhD, 83; studied viola with William Lincer, Oscar Shumsky, Dorothy Delay & Walter Trampler. *Pos:* Violist, Riverside String Quartet, 74-76, Parnassus String Quartet, 79 & Metropolitan Opera Orch, 81-; asst prin violist, Am Ballet Theater, 76-82; prin violist, Bolshoi Ballet, Nat Ballet Can, Berlin Opera Ballet, D'Oyly Carte Opera Co London & Joffrey Ballet, 78-79. *Teaching:* Instr viola & chamber music, NY Univ, 81-; teaching fel, Juilliard Sch, 82- *Mem:* Chamber Music Am; Music Nobilis Inc (pres, 76-); Orthopaedic Ctr Arts (music adv, 83-). *Publ:* Auth, William Lincer as a Teacher, Strad, 81; William Lincer: 50 Years of String Teaching, Music Educ J, 82; Profile: William Lincer, Int Musician, 82; coauth, Psychological Profile of Musicians, J Psychology (in press); Occupational Hand Disorders of String Players, J Hand Surgery (in press). *Mailing Add:* 150 West End Ave 9G New York NY 10023

KELLER, HOMER (TODD)
COMPOSER, EDUCATOR
b Oxnard, Calif, Feb 17, 15. *Study:* Eastman Sch Music, studied comp with Howard Hanson, BM(comp), 37, MM(comp), 38; studied comp with Arthur Honegger & Nadia Boulanger, 50-51. *Works:* Piano Concerto, Carl Fischer Rental Libr, 49; Symphony No 3, 58, Interplay for Flute, Horn & Percussion, 69 & Sonorities for Orchestra, 71, Am Comp Alliance; Serenade for Clarinet & Strings, Carl Fischer Inc, 74; Salutation of the Dawn (SATB), Ludwig Music Publ, 74. *Teaching:* Instr piano & theory, Ind Univ, Bloomington, 41-42; asst prof music, Univ Mich, 47-54; instr comp, Nat Music Camp, Interlochen, Mich, 48-76; guest lectr, Univ Hawaii, Honolulu, 56-58; prof comp, Univ Ore Sch Music, 58-77. *Awards:* Henry Hadley Found Award (for Symph No 1), 39; Fulbright grant, 50-51. *Mem:* Am Comp Alliance; Am Soc Univ Comp (mem nat coun, 68-73); Am Music Ctr; Music Teachers Nat Asn; Soc Ore Comp. *Mailing Add:* Sch Music Univ Ore Eugene OR 97403

KELLER, MICHAEL ALAN
LIBRARIAN, EDUCATOR
b Sterling, Colo, Apr 5, 45. *Study:* Hamilton Col, BA, 67; State Univ NY, Buffalo, MA, 70; State Univ NY, Col Geneseo, MLS, 72. *Pos:* Music librn, Cornell Univ, 73-81, actg undergrad librn, 76; head music libr, Univ Calif, Berkeley, 81- *Teaching:* Sr lectr musicol & bibliog, Cornell Univ, 73-81. *Mem:* Am Libr Asn; Music Libr Asn (mem bd dirs, 76-78); Int Asn Mus Libr; Am Musicol Soc; Res Libr Group. *Interests:* Late Renaissance and Baroque Italian instrumental music; music bibliography. *Publ:* Auth, Bibliography of Blake Texts Set to Music, Blake Soc Newslett, spring 72; Music Serials in Microfilm and Reprint Editions, Notes, Vol 29, 73; Where Does Policy Come From? A Dialogue, Cornell Univ Libr Bulletin, 1-2/74; contribr, Senaillie, Guenin & Dauvergne, In: New Grove Dict of Music & Musicians, Macmillan, London, 80; auth, Music, In: Selection Sources & Strategies: A Guideline for Librarians in Larger Libraries, 83. *Mailing Add:* 240 Morrison Hall Univ Calif Berkeley CA 94720

KELLIS, LEO ALAN
COMPOSER, TEACHER
b Los Angeles, Calif, Aug 17, 27. *Study:* Univ Calif, Los Angeles; studied piano with Niel McKie & Herman Wasserman & comp with Julius Gold. *Works:* Suite en Valse (two pianos); Four Nocturnes; Fantasy (2 pianos); Two Concert Etudes (piano); Rhapsody on a Children's Tune (piano); Hello From the Zoo (piano suite); Rhapsody Aravelian (piano); and others. *Pos:* Conct pianist. *Teaching:* Instr piano, privately, currently. *Mailing Add:* 771 Norumbega Dr Monrovia CA 91016

KELLOCK, JAMES ROBERT
ADMINISTRATOR, FRENCH HORN
b Trenton, NJ, Aug 12, 47. *Study:* New England Consv Music, BMus, 70. *Works:* Music for Horn Quintets, Hornseth Music, 82. *Pos:* Dir & french horn, Takoma Brass Quintet, 76-; chamber music prod, Div Perf Arts, Smithsonian Inst, 80-82; pres, Takoma Prod Inc, 82-; exec dir, Soc Educ Perf Arts, 83- *Mem:* Chamber Music Am; Cult Alliance Washington; Am Fedn Musicians. *Publ:* Ed, 19th Century American Band Music in Print, Smithsonian Travelling Exhibition Serv, 76; Maryland Band Director's Graded Solo/ Ensemble Guide, Md Band Dir Asn, 76-80; Music Educators National Conference Graded Solo/Ensemble Directory, 78. *Mailing Add:* 4808 44th St NW Washington DC 20016

KELLOCK, JUDITH GRAHAM
SOPRANO
b Trenton, NJ. *Study:* Sch Arts, Boston Univ, BM, 73; Aspen Music Fest, vocal study with Jan De Gaetani, 76-80; private study with Jan De Gaetani. *Rec Perf:* Music of Stephen Foster and Paul Dresser, Sine Qua Non. *Roles:* Pamina in Die Zauberflöte & Tytania in Midsummer Nights Dream, Harvard

Univ; Hin und Zuruck (Hindemith), Alea III; David Del Tredici & Final Alice, St Louis Symph, 79; sop roles in Impresano (Mozart), Opera New England Orch, 80. *Pos:* Solo appearances with St Louis Symph, Minn Orch, Aspen Fest Orch, Pro Arte Chamber Orch, Commonwealth Orch & Alea III. *Teaching:* Instr voice, Longy Sch Music, 78- & chmn, 81- *Awards:* Fel, Aspen Music Fest, 76-79; Travel Grant, Inst Int Educ, 79. *Mailing Add:* 75 Aldrich St Boston MA 02131

KELLOGG, CAL STEWART
CONDUCTOR, COMPOSER
b Long Beach, Calif, July 26, 47. *Study:* Consv Musica Santa Cecilia, Rome, dipl(bassoon), 67, dipl(comp), 72, dipl(cond), 73. *Rec Perf:* The Saint of Bleecker Street (Menotti), PBS, 78. *Pos:* Guest cond, Accad Nat Santa Cecilia, Rome, 75-77, Maggio Fiorentino, Florence, 75-77, RAI Orch Rome, 76-78, Teatro Dell'Opera, Rome, 76-80, New York City Opera, 76-79, Spoleto Fest, SC, 78-82 & Washington Opera, 80- *Awards:* First Prize, Gino Marinuzzi Cond Compt, Italy, 75; Second Prize, Guido Cantelli Cond Compt, Italy, 75. *Mailing Add:* c/o Columbia Artists Mgt 165 W 57th St New York NY 10019

KELLY, DANIS GRACE
HARP, TEACHER
b Temple, Tex, May 17, 46. *Study:* Interlochen Arts Acad, 64; Curtis Inst Music, 64-66; Cleveland Inst, BM, 68. *Pos:* Prin harpist, Chicago Little Symph, 66-68, Fla Symph, 68-69, Milwaukee Symph, 69- & Santa Fe Opera, 73- *Teaching:* Instr harp, Interlochen Arts Acad, 67, Wis Consv, 69- & Univ Wis, Madison, 77- *Awards:* First Prize, Am Harp Soc Cont, 63. *Mem:* Pi Kappa Lambda; Am Harp Soc. *Mailing Add:* 5650 N River Forest Dr Milwaukee WI 53209

KELLY, MICHAEL THOMAS
CLARINET
b Baltimore, Md, Sept 21, 37. *Study:* Peabody Consv Music, BMus, 60; Cath Univ Am, MMus, 66. *Pos:* Extra woodwind player, Baltimore Symph, 66- & Nat Symph, 81-; bass clarinet utility woodwind, Am Camarata New Music, 73- *Mailing Add:* 16701 New Hampshire Ave Spencerville MD 20868

KELLY, PAUL ROBERT
EDUCATOR, LECTURER
b Madison, Wis, Sept 21, 47. *Study:* Concord Col, BA, 70; Univ Iowa. *Pos:* Dir, Music Business Prog, Elmhurst Col, 79-; secy & newsletter ed, Music Industry Educr Asn Notes, 82-83; ed, Exchange Mag, Music Events Inc, 83-; pres, Music Bus Publ. *Mem:* Midwest Music Exchange (co-founder & secy-treas, 81-); Music Indust Educr Asn; Col Music Soc (founder & pres Great Lakes chap, 82-); Am Musicol Soc. *Publ:* Contribr, Col Music Soc Symposium: The Undergraduate Music Business Program, Col Music Soc, 81. *Mailing Add:* 226 Larch Ave Elmhurst IL 60126

KELLY, (J) ROBERT
COMPOSER, VIOLA
b Clarksburg, WVa, Sept 26, 16. *Study:* Juilliard Sch Music, studied violin with Samuel Gardner, 35-36; Salem Col, studied comp with Matthew N Lundquist, 37-38; Cincinnati Col Music, studied violin with Emil Heermann, 38-39; Curtis Inst Music, studied comp with Rosario Scalero, BMus, 42; Eastman Sch Music, studied comp with Herbert Elwell, MMus, 52. *Works:* Symphony No 2, Galaxy Music Corp, 62; The White Gods, 63 & Emancipation Symph, 63, Am Comp Alliance; Concerto for Violin & Orchestra, Galaxy Music Corp, 68; Concerto for Viola & Orchestra, 78, Concerto for Violin, Viola & Orchestra, 82 & Compositions for Cello, 83, Am Comp Alliance. *Teaching:* Prof music, Sch Music, Univ Ill, Urbana, 46-76, assoc mem, Ctr Advan Study, 63-65. *Bibliog:* Music of Robert Kelly, BMI, 67. *Mem:* BMI; Am Comp Alliance; Am Music Ctr; Am Viola Soc. *Publ:* Auth, Theme and Variations, A Study of Linear Twelve Tone Composition, 70 & Aural and Visual Recognition, A Musical Eartraining Series, 70, Univ Ill. *Rep:* Am Comp Alliance 170 W 74th St New York NY 10023. *Mailing Add:* 807 S Urbana Ave Urbana IL 61801

KELLY, SHERRY HILL
SOPRANO, TEACHER
b Utica, NY, Sept 29, 34. *Study:* Westminster Choir Col, BM, 56; Univ NC, Greensboro, MM, 71; studied with John Finley Williamson, Erno Balogh, Norman Farrow & Janice Harsanyi. *Roles:* Sop soloist, Passion According to St John, Winston-Salem Symph, 72; Mass in C (Schubert), Salisbury Symph, 75; L'Accademia Musicale Chiqiana recital, 71 & Elijah, Glorieta, NMex, 77; sop, What Is Man (Nelson), First Presby Church, Ft Lauderdale, 83. *Pos:* Founder & cond, Belmont Consort Singers, 75- *Teaching:* Voice, Wingate Col, 58-59; asst prof, Piedmont Bible Col, 64-69 & Livingstone Col, 72-75; assoc prof vocal pedagogy, Belmont Col, 75-, vocal coordr, 78-, distinguished prof, 83- *Mem:* Am Choral Dir Asn; Nat Asn Teachers Singing (pres Nashville chap, 82-); Pi Kappa Lambda; Music Teachers Nat Asn. *Mailing Add:* 5013 Meadow Lake Rd Brentwood TN 37027

KELM, LINDA
SOPRANO
b Salt Lake City, Utah, Dec 11, 44. *Study:* Private study with Elizabeth Hayes Simpson, 63-74; Aspen Music Sch, with Jennie Tourel, 68; study with Judith Oas, 75- *Roles:* Third Norn in Götterdämmerung & Helmvige in Die Walküre, Seattle Opera Asn, Pac Northwest Fest, 77-82; Dirce in Demophoon, Sagra Umbra Musicale, Perugia, Italy, 82; Turandot, San Francisco Opera, 82; Brünhilde in Siegfried, Milwaukee Symph, 83. *Awards:* Career Grants, Nat Opera Inst, 80-81. *Mailing Add:* 375 Riverside Dr New York NY 10025

KEMNER, GERALD E
COMPOSER, EDUCATOR
b Kansas City, Mo, Sept 28, 32. *Study:* Yale Univ, with Quincy Porter, MM(comp), 55; Eastman Sch Music, with Howard Hanson, Henry Cowell & Bernard Rogers, DMA(comp), 62. *Works:* Ezekial (chorus); Variations on the Easter Sequence; First Light and the Quiet Voice. *Teaching:* Fac mem, Augustana Col, 62-66 & Univ Mo, Kansas City, 66- *Awards:* Howard Hanson Prize, 62. *Mailing Add:* Univ Mo 4949 Cherry Kansas City MO 64110

KEMP, KATHLEEN MURPHY
CELLO
b Auburn, NY, Nov 12, 52. *Study:* Eastman Sch Music, BMus, MMus(perf). *Pos:* Cello, Rochester Phil, 74-, Aspen Fest Orch, 75 & 76 & Aspen Chamber Orch, 77. *Teaching:* Chamber music asst, Eastman Sch Music, 75-78. *Awards:* Winner, Eastman Concerto Compt, 74; Winner, Music Acad Concerto Compt, 74. *Mem:* NY Cello Soc. *Mailing Add:* Rochester Phil 108 East Ave Rochester NY 14604

KENDALL, CHRISTOPHER WOLFF
CONDUCTOR, LUTE
b Zanesville, Ohio, Sept 8, 49. *Study:* Antioch Col, BA(music), 72; Univ Cincinnati with Lane & Schippers, MM(cond), 74. *Rec Perf:* Folger Consort, Shakespeare's Music, 81 & Folger Consort, A Distant Mirror, 81, Delos; 20th Century Consort Vol I, 81, Vol II, 82 & Vol III, 83, Smithsonian Collection Rec. *Pos:* Artistic dir & cond, 20th Century Consort, Washington, DC, 76-; founder & lutenist, The Folger Consort, Washington, DC, 77-; artistic dir, Millennium Ensemble Inc, Washington, DC, 80- *Bibliog:* Kenneth W Fain (auth), Christopher Kendall, Washington's Champion of Chamber Music, Washington Star, 3/80; Carson Connor (auth), Christopher Kendall, Washington Post, 12/81; Pat Waring (auth), The Millennium—1,000 Years of Music, Cape Arts, 12/81. *Mailing Add:* 221 Constitution Ave NE #23 Washington DC 20002

KENDALL, GARY KEITH
BASS-BARITONE, EDUCATOR
b Springfield, Mo. *Study:* Univ Mo, BS & MM, 67; Ind Univ; Curtis Inst, opera dipl, 73. *Roles:* Colline in La Boheme & Count Des Grieux in Manon Lescault, Milwaukee Florentine, 74, 76 & 79; Sarastro in Die Zauberflöte, Vienne Volksoper, 76; Mayor in Hero, Philadelphia Opera Co, 76, 77; Colline in La Boheme, Cent City Opera, 76 & Miami Opera, 79, 81 & 82; Mephisto in Faust, Rochester Opera, 80; Raimondo in Lucia di Lammermoor, Greensboro, 82; Don Giovanni in Don Giovanni, Miss Opera, 82. *Teaching:* Asst prof voice, Col Consv, Cincinnati Univ, 82- *Awards:* Second Prize, Nat Arts Club, 73; First Place, Nat Fedn Music Clubs, 73 & Geneva Int Comp, 74. *Mem:* Nat Asn Teachers Singing. *Rep:* Herbert Barrett Mgt 1860 Broadway New York NY 10023. *Mailing Add:* 2348 Ohio Ave Cincinnati OH 45219

KENDRICK, VIRGINIA BACHMAN
COMPOSER
b Minneapolis, Minn, Apr 8, 10. *Study:* Univ Minn, 28-33. *Works:* April Whimsy, Music is Beauty & In This Soft Velvet Night, Fema; From My Window, Sam Fox; White Sky, Pop; Little Miss Whuffit, Belwin. *Pos:* Organ consult, Schmitt Music Co, formerly; pianist, Audahazy Sch Class Ballet, currently. *Mem:* Mu Phi Epsilon. *Mailing Add:* 5800 Echo Rd Shorewood MN 55331

KENNAN, KENT WHEELER
COMPOSER, EDUCATOR
b Milwaukee, Wis, Apr 18, 13. *Study:* Univ Mich, 30-32; Eastman Sch Music, BM, 34, MM, 36. *Works:* Night Soliloquy, Carl Fischer, 36; Three Pieces For Orchestra, Mercury Rec, 39; Three Preludes (piano), G Schirmer, 39; Scherzo, Aria & Fugato, Southern Music, 48; Sonata For Trumpet & Piano, Remick Music Corp, 56; Two Preludes (piano), Lawson-Gould, 63. *Teaching:* Instr theory & piano, Kent State Univ, 39-40; from instr to prof theory & comp, Univ Tex, Austin, 40-47 & 49-83; prof theory, Ohio State Univ, 47-49; instr orch & comp, Eastman Sch Music, summers 54 & 56. *Awards:* Prix de Rome Music Comp, Am Acad in Rome, 36. *Mem:* Phi Mu Alpha Sinfonia; ASCAP; Nat Asn Comp USA. *Publ:* Auth, The Technique of Orchestration, 1st ed, 52 & 2nd ed, 70, Counterpoint, 1st ed, 59 & 2nd ed, 72 & coauth, The Technique of Orchestration, 3rd ed, 83, Prentice-Hall. *Mailing Add:* 1513 Westover Rd Austin TX 78703

KENNEDY, (CHARLES) BRYAN
FRENCH HORN, TEACHER
b Detroit, Mich, Mar 25, 55. *Study:* Univ Mich, BM(horn), 79. *Pos:* Solo horn, Nat Symph Orch, Costa Rica, 75-77; second horn, Mich Opera Theatre, Detroit, 77-79, Richmond Sinfonia, Va, 79-82 & Detroit Symph Orch, 82-; third horn, Richmond Symph, 79-82; mem, Detroit Chamber Winds, currently. *Teaching:* Instr horn, private study, 72- & Nat Consv Costa Rica, 75-77. *Awards:* Fourth Prize, 77 & Second Prize, 78, Heldenleben Int Horn Compt. *Mailing Add:* 605 N Denwood Dearborn MI 48128

KENNEDY, DALE EDWIN
MUSIC DIRECTOR, EDUCATOR
b Chickasha, Okla, June 6, 37. *Study:* Univ Okla, BME, 59, PhD, 79; Univ NMex, MME, 65. *Works:* Easter Anthem (with George Collaer), Del Norte High Sch Band & Choir, Albuquerque, NMex, 66; Melange, Jazz Ens, Oklahoma City Univ, 71. *Pos:* Dir band, choir & orch, Albuquerque Pub Sch, 60-69; instrumentalist with Albuquerque Symph, Okla Symph, Dallas Pops Orch, Dallas Symph, Dallas Woodwind Trio, Wichita Symph, Santa Fe opera,

Oberlin Teachers Perf Inst, Albuquerque Wind Ens & others. *Teaching:* Prof music educ & band dir, Oklahoma City Univ, 69-72; dir bands, Richland Col, 72-80, Wichita State Univ, 80-82 & Univ Mo, Columbia, 82- *Mem:* Col Band Dir Nat Asn (state chmn, 80-82); Music Educr Nat Conf; Pi Kappa Lambda. *Publ:* Auth, The Art of Picking the Right Music, Sch Musician, 70; Seating the Band for Maximum Sound, Instrumentalist, 70; contribr, Music in US Junior Colleges, Music Educr Nat Conf, 78. *Mailing Add:* 1301 Woodhill Rd Columbia MO 65201

KENNEDY, JOSEPHA (MARIE)
EDUCATOR, WRITER
b Elmira, NY, Mar 21, 28. *Study:* Nazareth Col Rochester, studied voice with Arthur Kraft, BA, 50, MS, 58; Columbia Univ, studied with P H Lang, PhD(musicol), 69. *Rec Perf:* Four Shakespeare Songs, Fine Arts Rec, 64. *Pos:* Choir dir, St Louis Roman Cath Church, 71- *Teaching:* From asst prof to prof, Nazareth Col Rochester, 49-42; *Interests:* Seventeenth century Italian paraliturgical music; Dufay; women in early opera. *Publ:* Auth, Flannery O'Connor: Poet to the Outcast, Renascence, 64; Dufay & Don Pedro the Cruel, Musical Quart, 75; Giovanni Battista Beria, in: New Grove Dict of Music & Musicians, 81; The Look That Bestows Goodness, Sisters Today, 83. *Mailing Add:* Nazareth Col Rochester 4245 East Ave Rochester NY 14610

KENNEDY, MATTHEW W
EDUCATOR, PIANO
b Americus, Ga, Mar 10, 21. *Study:* Fisk Univ, AB, 46; Juilliard Sch Music, MS, 50. *Pos:* Dir, Fisk Jubilee Singers, 57-67, 71-73 & 75-; solo recitals, Carnegie Hall, Nat Gallery Art & Town Hall, Philadelphia, 58-60; prog chmn, Nashville Fine Arts Club, 67-69; bd mem, John W Work Mem Found, 73- & Nashville Symph Asn, 75-78. *Teaching:* Assoc prof, Fisk Univ, 47-48 & 54-, actg chmn, Music Dept, 75-78. *Awards:* United Negro Col Fund Fel, 69; Omega Man of Yr, 74. *Mem:* Music Teachers Nat Asn; Nashville Fine Arts Club; Tenn Arts Comn. *Publ:* Spirituals, Abingdon Press, 74. *Mailing Add:* 2417 Gardner Lane Nashville TN 37207

KENNEDY, RAYMOND F
EDUCATOR, ETHNOMUSICOLOGIST
b Brooklyn, NY. *Study:* Juilliard Sch Music, dipl, 59, BS, 62; Queens Col, City Univ New York, studied ethnomusicol with Mieczyslaw Kolinski & Willard Rhodes & comp with Hugo Weisgall, MA(comp), 68. *Pos:* Staff critic, Am Rec Guide, 68- *Teaching:* Assoc prof music, John Jay Col Criminal Justice, 71-; lectr ethnomusicol & jazz hist, Mannes Col Music, 71-; vis lectr, Univ Hawaii, NY Univ & Columbia Univ. *Mem:* Soc Asian Music (vpres, 79-81); Soc Ethnomusicol; Col Music Soc; Nat Asn Jazz Educr. *Publ:* Auth, Pop Music in the Twentieth Century (6-part sound film strip), EAV, 73; Music in Oceania, Music Educr J, 10/74; Calypso Music, In: Collier's Encycl, 74; Music of Ponape & Chamorro Music, In: New Grove Dict of Music & Musicans, 6th ed. *Mailing Add:* 582 Washington Ave Pleasantville NY 10570

KENNELL, RICHARD PAUL
TEACHER, COMPOSER
b Dansville, NY, Apr 17, 49. *Study:* Northwestern Univ, with William Karlins & Stephen Syverud. *Works:* Solo for Clarinet and Reverberation Unit, 72; Wiesenhuttenplatz 29 (tape), 72; Metamorphose (tape), 72; Elestroax II (alto sax & tape), 72; Fantasia & Fugue (tape), 73. *Teaching:* Instr, pub sch, 73-74; instr, William Rainey Harper Col; asst dean, Col Musical Arts, Bowling Green State Univ, currently. *Awards:* Prize winner, First Int Cont Electronic Music, Bourges, France, 73. *Mailing Add:* Bowling Green State Univ Bowling Green OH 43403

KENT, RICHARD LAYTON
EDUCATOR, COMPOSER
b Harris, Mo, Jan 23, 16. *Study:* Drake Univ, BME, 40; New England Consv, MM, 47; Boston Univ, DMA, 61. *Works:* Lord is My Shepherd (SATB, a cappella), 71, Three Spring Songs (SSA, a cappella), 71 & Five Carol Preludes (organ), 71, World Libr Publ; Alleluia (SATB, a capella), 78, Four Housman Songs (SATB, a cappella), 78, Remember Now Thy Creator (SATB, a cappella), 80 & Magnificat (SSA & woodwind quintet), 81, Lawson-Gould. *Teaching:* Music, Larrabee Consolidated Sch, Iowa, 40-42; prof, Fitchburg State Col, 47-82, chmn fine arts dept, 15 yr. *Awards:* Sibelius Medal, Helsinki Univ, 63; Lowell Mason Award, Mass Music Educr Asn, 78; Fac Mem of Yr, Fitchburg State Col Student Govt, 81. *Mem:* Am Musicol Soc; Col Music Soc; Am Choral Dir Asn; Int Musicol Soc; Music Educr Nat Conf. *Publ:* Auth, Popular Music, Music Educr J, 10/57; ed & contribr, Windows of Song, Westwood Press, 68. *Mailing Add:* 1171 Main Leominster MA 01453

KER, ANN STEELE
COMPOSER, EDUCATOR
b Warsaw, Ind, Nov 10, 37. *Study:* Ind Univ, BME, 74; Univ Notre Dame. *Works:* Hear This!, Neil A Kjos Publ Co, 73; Triptych, Ind Music Co, 80; Three Men on Camelback, Harold Flammer Inc, 82; One Glorious God, 82 & For Me, O Lord, 83, Richmond Music Press; Softly, 82 & Ways to Praise, 83, Neil A Kjos Publ Co. *Pos:* Organist, First Presby Church, Warsaw, Ind, 69-79; co-founder & bd mem, Northern Ind Opera Asn, 78-; dir music, Cent Christian Church, Huntington, Ind, 79-80 & Redeemer Lutheran Church, 80-; cond, Lutheran Circuit Fest Chorus, 81- *Teaching:* Instr organ & theory, Huntington Col, Ind, 73- *Mem:* League Women Comp; Am Guild Organists (bd mem, 78-81); Am Choral Dir Asn; Nat Guild Piano Teachers; Women in Music. *Mailing Add:* 1607 N Springhill Rd Warsaw IN 46580

KERMAN, JOSEPH WILFRED
MUSICOLOGIST, CRITIC-WRITER
b London, England, Apr 3, 24. *Study:* NY Univ, BA; Princeton Univ, PhD, 51; Fairfield Univ, DHL. *Pos:* Co-ed, 19th-Century Music, currently; ed, Calif Studies in 19th Century Music, currently. *Teaching:* Dir grad studies, Westminster Choir Col, 49-51; mem fac music, Univ Calif, Berkeley, 51-71, chmn music dept, 60-63, prof, 74-; vis fel, All Souls Col, Oxford Univ, 66, Heather prof, 72-74. *Awards:* ASCAP Deems Taylor Award; Am Musicol Soc Kinkeldey Award; Fulbright Grant. *Mem:* Fel, Am Asn Advan Sci; Am Musicol Soc; Col Music Soc. *Publ:* Auth, Opera as Drama, 56; The Elizabethan Madrigal, 62; The Beethoven Quartets, 67; Ludwig van Beethoven Autograph Miscellany, 1786-1799: the Kafka Sketchbook, 70; Listen, 72; The Masses and Motets of William Byrd, 80. *Mailing Add:* Music Dept Univ Calif Berkeley CA 94720

KERMANI, PETER RUSTAM
PATRON
b Albany, NY, May 21, 40. *Study:* St Lawrence Univ, BA, 62. *Pos:* Pres, Albany Symph Orch, 77-; mem bd dir, Am Symph Orch League, 79-, pres, 82-; mem bd dir, Am Comp Orch, 82-; mem adv coun, CRI, 82- *Mailing Add:* PO Box 5031 Albany NY 12205

KERRIGAN, WILLIAM PAUL
PERCUSSION, EDUCATOR
b Cleveland, Ohio, June 16, 53. *Study:* Temple Univ, with Alan Abel, Jack Moore & Charles Owen, BM, 75, MM, 77. *Rec Perf:* Atmos Percussion Quartet, Drexel Univ, 79; Peter Nero and The Philly Pops July 4, Nat Pub TV, 80; Opera Co Philadelphia, Nat Pub TV, 82; Concerto for Nine Players, Swarthmore Col, 83; Atmos Percussion Quartet, Am Cable Vision, 83; Atmos Percussion Quartet II, Drexel Univ, 83. *Pos:* Perc, Opera Co Philadelphia, 75- & Peter Nero & The Philly Pops, 80-; founder & mem, Atmos Perc Quartet, 77-; prin timpani & perc, Pa Ballet Orch, 81-82. *Teaching:* Mem fac perc, Settlement Music Sch Philadelphia, 74- & Community Col Philadelphia, 77-; artist in res perc, Drexel Univ, 77- *Awards:* First Place, Ohio Music Educr Asn, 71; Distinguished Adjudicator, Atmos Perc Quartet, Drexel Univ & Percussive Arts Soc, 81; Governors Award, Commmonwealth of Pa, 81. *Bibliog:* Daniel Webster (auth), Atmos Percussion Quartet, Philadelphia Inquirer, 10/81; Atmos Percussion Quartet, Del Co Community Col, 11/81; Dorothy Storck (auth), Atmos Percussion Quartet, Philadelphia Inquirer, 6/83. *Mem:* Percussive Arts Soc; Am Fedn Musicians; Orch Soc Philadelphia. *Mailing Add:* 1209 W Wynnewood Rd #108 Wynnewood PA 19096

KESHNER, JOYCE GROVE
CONDUCTOR & MUSIC DIRECTOR, COMPOSER
b New Haven, Conn, May 24, 27. *Study:* Southern Conn State Col, BS, 48; Juilliard Sch Music; Mannes Col Music; City Univ New York, MA, 72; Westminster Choir Col, 74; Acad Aston Magna, 82; studied piano with Joseph Raiff, Martin Canin, John Goldmark & Francis Dillon, cond with Abraham Kaplan, Rudolph Thomas, Harold Aks, Carl Bamberger & Edward Murray, comp with Fredric Werle & Mario Davidovsky & voice with Ruth Hand & James McClure. *Works:* String Quartet, 71; Piece for Solo Bassoon; Waiting Born (flute, voice & piano); Monophonic Piece for Bassoon; Lord What is Man (bar, chorus & small orch). *Rec Perf:* Joshua (Handel); I Know I Love You; A Joyful Noise; Alexander's Feast (Handel), 83. *Pos:* Cond, Music Prog, Temple B'nai Jacob, New Haven, 46-48; Chorus, Jewish Community Ctr, Paramus, 57-60 & Paramus Chorale, 63-66; cond & music dir, Ars Music Chorale & Orch, 66- & Ars Musica Camerata, 66-; guest cond, Brockport Symph Orch, NY & Summit Chorale, 77. *Teaching:* Piano, voice, theory & cond, privately, 60-; affil artist, Ramapo Col, NJ, 73-76. *Awards:* Lofts Found Award, City Col New York, 71. *Interests:* Musicology; bel canto. *Mailing Add:* 794 Wynetta Pl Paramus NJ 07652

KESSLER, JEROME
CONDUCTOR, CELLO
b Ithaca, NY. *Study:* Columbia Col, AB, 63; Sch Law, Univ Calif, Los Angeles, JD, 66. *Works:* Kol Nidrei, Elkan-Vogel, 81. *Rec Perf:* Introducing I Cellisti, 70, Sonatas of Saint Saens & Faure, 73 & Music of Nicholas Slonimsky, 74, Orion Master Rec. *Pos:* Music dir, Hollywood Chamber Orch, 74-, I Cellisti, 65- & Topanga Symph Orch, 82- *Mem:* Col Music Soc; Am Soc Music Arrangers; Los Angeles Copyright Soc. *Mailing Add:* 1717 N Highland Ave Los Angeles CA 90028

KESSLER, MINUETTA
COMPOSER, PIANO
b Gomel, Russia; US citizen & nat Can citizen. *Study:* Juilliard Sch Music, 32-36; private study with Ernest Hutcheson. *Works:* Alberta Concerto, perf by CBC Orch, Montreal, 47; Sonata Concertante, Wheelock Auditorium, 56; Sonata for Cello & Piano, Brookline Libr Music Asn, Mass, 61; String Quartet No 1, comn by Mass Music Teachers Asn, 81; New York Suite (piano & orch), perf by Belmont Symph Orch, 82. *Rec Perf:* Music for Solo Instruments, 79 & Childhood Cameos, 81, AFKA. *Teaching:* Primary musical educ, Longy Sch Music, 80-; private teaching on all levels. *Awards:* Award for Serious Music, ASCAP, 45 & 46; Comp Prize, Brookline Libr Music Asn, Mass, 57-58; three comp awards, Nat League Am Pen Women, 82. *Bibliog:* Richard Dyer (auth), Jordan Hall Concert Music Critic, Boston Globe, 9/68; Richard Louv (auth), Unleashing Creativity, Family Weekly, 1/80; Eva Jacob (auth), Musical Prodigies and How They Grow, Boston Sunday Globe, 2/78. *Mem:* New England Piano Teachers Asn (pres, 65-67); Music Teachers Nat Asn (pres, 79-81, pres Boston chap, 81-); Comp, Authors & Publ Can; European Piano Teachers Asn; Nat League Am Pen Women (music ed, 82-).

Publ: Auth, Liturgical Music, Transcontinental; Staftonia and Piano is My Name, Musical Resources; Teaching Books for Piano, Boston Music; Piano Music for Grades 1-3, Willis Music Co. *Mailing Add:* 30 Hurley St Belmont MA 02178

KESSNER, DANIEL AARON
COMPOSER, EDUCATOR
b Los Angeles, Calif, June 3, 46. *Study:* Univ Calif, Los Angeles, AB, 67, MA, 68, PhD, 71. *Works:* Strata (1971), 71 & Wind Sculptures, Alexander Broude; The Telltale Heart, 82, perf by Netherlands Opera Co & Utrecht Symph; Array, Trio (violin, guitar & vocal) & Six Aphorisms, Belwin Mills; Equali I, perf by Netherlands Radio Chamber Orch. *Teaching:* Prof comp & theory, Calif State Univ, Northridge, 70- *Awards:* BMI Award, 70 & 71; Queen Marie-Jose Int Comp Prize, 72. *Mem:* Nat Asn Comp; Am Music Ctr. *Mailing Add:* 10955 Cozycroft Ave Chatsworth CA 91311

KESTENBAUM, MYRA
VIOLA, EDUCATOR
b Los Angeles, Calif. *Study:* Juilliard Sch Music, with Ivan Galamian & William Primrose; Mannes Col Music, with Paul Doktor. *Rec Perf:* On Columbia, RCA & Sheffield Town Hall Rec. *Pos:* Prin violist & soloist, Los Angeles Chamber Orch, 72-79; soloist & chamber musician, Aspen Music Fest, Marlboro Music Fest, Ojai Music Fest, Claremont Music Fest, Carmel Music Fest, Cape Fest, Cape Cod, Islands Fest, Cape Cod & throughout US, Can, Europe, Australia & NZ; founding mem, Ko-Kela (piano quartet). *Teaching:* Master classes around US; mem fac, San Francisco Consv Music, formerly; Calif State Univ, Northridge, formerly & Calif State Univ, Fullerton, formerly; vis lectr viola, Univ Calif, Los Angeles, currently. *Mailing Add:* c/o Robert Levin Assoc Inc 250 W 57th St Suite 1332 New York NY 10107

KETCHAM, CHARLES
MUSIC DIRECTOR & CONDUCTOR
b San Diego, Calif, Oct 31, 42. *Study:* San Diego State Col; Eastman Sch Music; Vienna Acad Music. *Pos:* Music dir, Am Opera Wkshp, Vienna, 69-70; San Diego Ballet, formerly & San Diego Master Chorale, formerly; asst cond, Gulbenkian Orch, Lisbon, Portugal, 70-73 & San Diego Symph Orch, 73-82; guest cond, ORTF Radio Orch, France, formerly, Seville Phil, Spain, formerly, Radio Orch, Holland, formerly & Rochester Phil, formerly; cond, Exxon Affiliate Artists, 73; assoc cond, Utah Symph Orch, formerly, cond, currently. *Awards:* Fulbright Scholar, 69-70. *Mailing Add:* 93 E 4800 S Murray UT 84107

KEYES, NELSON
COMPOSER, EDUCATOR
b Tulsa, Okla, Aug 26, 28. *Study:* Univ Tex, with Kent Kennan & Wilbur Ogdon; Univ Southern Calif, with Ingolf Dahl & Halsey Stevens. *Works:* Music for Monday Evenings (orch), 59; Abysses, Bridges, Chasms (orch), 71; Bandances (band); Bassooneries (four bassoon duets); two ballets; vocal solos; musical plays. *Teaching:* Mem fac, Long Beach City Col, 55-59, Univ Southern Calif, 60-61 & Kans State Teachers Col, 65-69; prof theory, Univ Louisville, 69- *Awards:* Huntington Hartford Found Grant, 51; Friends of Music Prize, Univ Calif, 57; Ford Found Res Grant, 61-65. *Mailing Add:* Sch Music Univ Louisville Louisville KY 40292

KHAN, ALI AKBAR
SAROD, COMPOSER
b Shivpur, Bengal, India, Apr 14, 22. *Study:* Studied with Allauddin Khan; Rabindra Bharati Univ, Calcutta, LittD, 74. *Works:* Misra Shivranjani, 57; Chandranandan, 60; Gauri Manjari, Hindol-Hem, 61; several new ragas. *Pos:* Music dir, All India Radio, Lucknow, 46-48 & Bombay Film Indust, 54-55; founder, pres & head master, Ali Akbar Col Music, Calcutta, 56-, San Raphael, Calif, 68-; conct artist, Lincoln Ctr, 79, Albert Hall, 81, Kennedy Ctr, 82, Carnegie Hall, 83 & others in India, Europe, USA, Japan & Australia. *Teaching:* Fac mem, McGill Univ, 59-61; head music dept, Am Soc Eastern Arts, 65-67; instr class vocal & instrm music, Ali Akbar Col Music, Calif, 68-; fac mem, McGill Univ 59-61. *Mailing Add:* Ali Akbar Col Music 215 West End Ave San Rafael CA 94901

KHANER, JEFFREY M
FLUTE
b Montreal, Can, Dec 22, 58. *Study:* Juilliard Sch, BMus, 80. *Pos:* Prin flutist, Atlantic Symph, Halifax, Can, 80-81 & Mostly Mozart Fest, New York, 81 & 82; co-prin flutist, Pittsburgh Symph, 81-82; prin flutist, Cleveland Orch, 82- *Teaching:* Instr flute, Cleveland Inst Music, 82- *Mailing Add:* c/o Cleveland Orch Severance Hall Cleveland OH 44106

KHANZADIAN, VAHAN
TENOR, TEACHER-COACH
b Syracuse, NY, Jan 23, 39. *Study:* Univ Buffalo, NY, BS, 61; Curtis Inst Music, with Martial Singher, cert, 61-63. *Roles:* Ruggero in La Rondine, San Francisco Spring Opera, 68; Pinkerton in Madama Butterfly, San Francisco Opera, 68; Rodolfo in La Boheme, Vancouver Opera Asn, 70; Turiddu in Cavalleria Rusticana, Portland Opera Asn, 70; Alfredo in La Traviata, New Orleans Opera Asn, 71; Chenier in Andrea Chenier, Baltimore Opera Asn, 73; Duke in Rigoletto, New York City Opera, 73. *Teaching:* Fac mem voice, Acad Vocal Arts, Philadelphia, 80- *Awards:* Grants, Martha Baird Rockefeller Found, 71 & 73 & William M Sullivan Found, 71 & 74. *Mailing Add:* c/o The Acad Vocal Arts 1920 Spruce St Philadelphia PA 19103

KIBBIE, JAMES WARREN
ORGAN, EDUCATOR
b Vinton, Iowa, Mar 13, 49. *Study:* New England Consv, 67-78; NTex State Univ, BMus, 68, MMus, 72; Univ Mich, with Marilyn Mason, DMA, 81. *Rec Perf:* Mozart, Goemanne Works, with Tex Boys Choir, Treble, 74; Unicorn, with Tex Boys Choir, Vox, 76; The World Rejoices, Vox/Turnabout, 77; Jehan Alain, Works, Solstice, 80; Charles Tournemire, Works, Spectrum, 82. *Teaching:* Instr organ, NTex State Univ, 71-72; instr organ & piano, Tarrant Co Jr Col, Hurst, Tex, 76-78; asst prof organ, Univ Mich, Ann Arbor, 81- *Awards:* First Prize, Univ Presbyterian Church Compt, San Antonio, Tex, 71 & Int Organ Compt, Prague, Czechoslovakia, 79; Grand Prix, Int Organ Compt, Chartres, France, 80. *Mem:* Am Guild Organists; Col Music Soc; Organ Hist Soc; Asn Artistide Cavaille-Coll. *Interests:* Continuing research in tonal and mechanical design of historic organs. *Mailing Add:* 2055 Pontiac Trail Ann Arbor MI 48105

KIBLER, KEITH E
BASS-BARITONE
b Amsterdam, NY, Oct 28, 51. *Study:* Union Col, BA(English & music), 73; New England Consv Music, MA(voice), 76. *Roles:* Supt Budd in Albert Herring, St Louis Opera Co, 76; Marquis in La Traviata, Wolf Trap Co, 76; Father in Die Kluge, Boston Lyr Opera Co, 77; Hortensius in Daughter of the Regiment, Opera New England, 78; Baron Kelbar in Un Giorno di Regno, Boston Lyr Opera Co, 80; Sciarrone & Jailer in Tosca, Boston Symph Orch, 80; Ieporello in Don Giovanni, NH Symph, 80. *Pos:* Soloist with Boston Pops Orch, Boston Symph Orch, New England Consv Symph Orch, Portland Symph Orch, Rochester Phil Orch & others, 75- *Awards:* William Matheus Sullivan Found Grant, 76; Fel, Berkshire Music Ctr, 78 & 79; Beebe Traveling Fel, 83. *Mailing Add:* RD 2 Gloversville NY 12078

KIDD, RONALD R
EDUCATOR
b Stockton, Calif, July 29, 29. *Study:* Univ Ill, BMus, 51; Univ Tex, MMus, 53; Yale Univ, PhD, 67. *Teaching:* Instr piano, chamber music & hist, Lawrence Univ, 55-59 & Purdue Univ, 64-; vis prof hist, Univ Va, 76. *Publ:* Auth, The Emergence of Chamber Music with Obligato KB, Acta Musicol, 72; 21 entries, In: New Grove Dict of Music & Musicians, 81; articles in Notes, J Am Musicol Soc & Clavier. *Mailing Add:* SC 35 Purdue Univ Lafayette IN 47907

KIERIG, BARBARA ELAINE
SOPRANO, EDUCATOR
b St Louis, Mo. *Study:* Fontbonne Col, St Louis, 55-57; Univ Ill, BMus, 61, MMus, 63; Mozarteum, Salzburg, work with Dr B Paumgartner, 63-65. *Pos:* Lyr sop, Salzburg Chamber Opera, Vienna Chamber Opera, Salzburg Landestheater, Mozart-Opera-Salzburg, Salzburg Fest & Nat Opera (incl Europe, SAfrica & US tours), 65-74; district judge, Metropolitan Opera Auditions, Spokane, 80 & 83, Portland, 82 & Seattle, 83. *Awards:* Fulbright Grant; Rockefeller Grant. *Mailing Add:* NW 1055 Clifford Pullman WA 99163

KIESLER, KENNETH
CONDUCTOR & MUSIC DIRECTOR
b New York, NY, Aug 18, 53. *Study:* Univ NH, BMus, 75; Aspen Music Sch, with John Nelson & Erich Leinsdorf, summers 76 & 78; Ind Univ, with Fiora Contino, summer 77; private study with James Wimer; Peabody Consv Music, MMus, 80. *Pos:* Cond, Peabody Prep Orch, 79-80; music dir, Prince Georges Phil, 79-80 & Springfield Symph Orch, Ill, 80-; asst cond, Indianapolis Symph Orch, 80- *Teaching:* Aspen Music Sch & Johns Hopkins Univ. *Bibliog:* Susan Mogerman (auth), New Maestro, Ill Times, 3/81; John Ryan (auth), Kenneth Kiesler on Key, State J Regist, 4/1/82. *Mem:* Am Symph Orch League; Cond Guild. *Mailing Add:* 2228 Rome Dr Indianapolis IN 46208

KIEVMAN, CARSON
COMPOSER, MUSIC DIRECTOR
b Los Angeles, Calif, Dec 27, 49. *Study:* Stage dir with James R Rawley, 65-70; Inst Ferienkurse Neue Musik, Darmstadt, 74; Berkshire Music Ctr, studied comp with Messiaen, 75; Calif Inst Arts, studied comp with Brown, Subotnick & Tenney, BFA(music comp), 75, MFA(music comp), 76. *Works:* The Earth Only Endures, 75, The Temporary & Tentative Extended Piano, 77, Wake Up, It's Time to Go to Bed, 78, Multinationals & The Heavens, 79 & Music for Percussion, Piano & Orchestra, 83, Assoc Music Publ; Intelligent Systems, comn by Südwestfunk, 84. *Pos:* Founding co-dir, Independent Comp Asn, 76-77; comp in res, New York Shakespeare Fest, 78-79; comp & stage dir, Berkshire Music Ctr, summer 78 & Südwestfunk/Donaueschinger Musiktage, 81-84. *Awards:* Excellence in Music Comp, BMI, 74-75; Jury's Prize/Publ Fourth Int Comp Fest, Boswil, Switz, 76; fel, Nat Endowment Arts, 80. *Bibliog:* Heuwell Tircuit (auth), A Composer With A New Trend, San Francisco Chronicle, 77; Brian Kellman (dir), Farm for the Arts, Arts in Am, Macdowell Colony (film), US Int Arts Films, 78; Richard Dyer (auth), Soundrama Causes Stir, Boston Globe, 78. *Mem:* BMI; Am Music Ctr; Dramatists Guild. *Publ:* Auth, Soundtheater—Musical Notes, Vision Mag, 81. *Mailing Add:* c/o Intelligent Co 15 Jones St 6H New York NY 10014

KIHSLINGER, MARY RUTH
FRENCH HORN, EDUCATOR
b Milwaukee, Wis, June 7, 42. *Study:* Alverno Col, BM, 64; Univ Wis, MM, 67. *Pos:* First horn, Toledo Opera Orch, 67- *Teaching:* Instr music, Muskago-Norway pub sch, 64-65; assoc prof, Univ Toledo, 67- *Mem:* Int Horn Soc; Music Educr Nat Conf; Mu Phi Epsilon. *Mailing Add:* Dept Music Univ Toledo Toledo OH 43606

KILENYI, EDWARD
EDUCATOR, PIANO
b Philadelphia, Pa. *Study:* Franz Liszt Acad, Budapest, with Ernst von Dohnanyi, artist dipl. *Rec Perf:* Over 100 works on Columbia, Pathe & Remington Rec. *Pos:* Recitalist, BBC, formerly & Libr Cong, formerly; conct performer throughout sixteen countries with maj US & Europ orchs. *Teaching:* Prof piano, Sch Music, Fla State Univ, 53- *Awards:* Grand Prix du Disque, Paris. *Mailing Add:* 2206 Ellicott Dr Tallahassee FL 32312

KIM, BYONG-KON
COMPOSER, EDUCATOR
b Taegu, Korea, May 28, 29; US citizen. *Study:* Ind Univ, Bloomington, MMus, 64, DMus, 68; studied with B Heiden, W Kaufmann, W Apel & T Kozma. *Works:* String Quartet, La Salle String Quartet, 66; Nak-Dong-Kang (symph poem), Seoul Phil Orch, 70; Violin Sonata, Eudice Shapiro, 74; Sori for Marimba, 76 & Concertino for Percussion, 76, M Peter; Symphony, Ind Univ Orch, 78; Sori for Orchestra, Osaka Phil Orch & Seoul Phil Orch, 78, 80 & 82. *Rec Perf:* Korean Music Series, No 1, Falcon, Kyoto, Japan, 81. *Pos:* Dir & cond, New Music Ens, Cal State Univ, Los Angeles, 71- & Los Angeles Seoul Chorale, 78-80. *Teaching:* Dir theory & comp, Villa Maria Inst Music, Buffalo, NY, 66-68; prof theory & comp, Calif State Univ, Los Angeles, 68- *Mem:* Nat Asn Comp USA (Los Angeles chap pres, 70-76); Contemp Music Proj (eastern region prog head, 67-68). *Mailing Add:* 30458 Via Victoria Rancho Palos Verdes CA 90274

KIM, EARL
COMPOSER, EDUCATOR
b Dinuba, Calif, Jan 6, 20. *Study:* Univ Calif, Los Angeles, 40-41; Univ Calif, Berkeley, with Roger Sessions, MA, 52; studied with Arnold Schoenberg. *Works:* Dialogues (piano & orch), 59; They Are Far Out (sop, violin, cello & perc), 66; Gooseberries, She Said (sop, five instrm & perc), 68; Earthlight (violin, sop, piano & lights), 73; Eh, Joe (TV play), 74; Monologues (piano trio), 76; Violin Concerto, 79. *Pos:* Guest comp in res, Princeton Univ, 60, Hartt Col, 63, Brandeis Univ, 66, Marlboro Music Fest, 66, Dartmouth Fest Arts, 71 & Berkshire Music Ctr, 72; cond, Ariel Chamber Ens, Cambridge, Mass, 77- *Teaching:* Assoc prof music, Princeton Univ, 52-67; prof, Harvard Univ, 67-71, James Edward Ditson prof, 71- *Awards:* Nat Inst Arts & Lett Award, 65; Brandeis Univ Creative Arts Award, 71; Nat Endowment Arts Fel, 75, 77 & 79. *Mailing Add:* Music Dept Harvard Univ Cambridge MA 02138

KIM, JUNG-JA
PIANO, EDUCATOR
Study: Juilliard Sch, dipl & post grad dipl; studied piano with Jinwoo Chung, Kyusun Choi, Irwin Freundlich & Ilona Kabos & chamber music with Walter Trampler & Felix Galimir. *Pos:* Recitalist, US, France, Switz, Korea, England, Holland, Norway & Germany; concerto appearances with Baltimore Symph, St Louis Chamber Symph, Frysk Orch, Holland, Spokane Symph & New York Phil. *Teaching:* Mem fac piano & coordr piano dept, Boston Consv, currently. *Mailing Add:* Boston Consv 8 The Fenway Boston MA 02215

KIM, YOUNG MI
SOPRANO
b Seoul, Korea, Nov 6, 54. *Study:* Consv Santa Cecilia, Rome, with Giorgio Favaretto, Jolanda Magnoni & Joan Dornemann, BA, 79; Acad Santa Cecilia, Rome, MA, 80. *Roles:* Sop in Messiah, Minn Orch Co, 82; Adina in L'Elisir D'Amore, Philadelphia Opera Co, 82; Madama Butterfly, Houston Grand Opera Co, 83. *Awards:* First Prize, Puccini Int Compt, Lucca, Italy, 79; Winner, Maria Callas Sop Compt, RAI TV Broadcasting Co, Milan, Italy, 80. *Rep:* Thea Dispeker 59 E 54th St New York NY 10022. *Mailing Add:* 149 Pl 24 Flushing NY 11354

KIM, YOUNG-UCK
VIOLIN, EDUCATOR
Study: Curtis Inst Music; studied violin with Ivan Galamian. *Rec Perf:* On DGG-Polydor Rec. *Pos:* Conct tours & recitals with prominent cond in US & abroad. *Teaching:* Mem fac violin, Mannes Col Music, 76- *Mailing Add:* c/o Columbia Artists 165 W 57th St New York NY 10019

KIMES, JANICE LOUISE
MUSIC DIRECTOR, COACH
b Cheboygan, Mich. *Study:* Hamline Univ, BA, 75. *Works:* Old Irish Blessing, perf by Bel Canto Voices & Cargill Chorale, 77; What Is Christmas, Epoch Universal Publ, 81. *Rec Perf:* Bel Canto Voices, 82. *Pos:* Choral dir, Hamline Methodist Church Youth & Children's Choirs, Minn, 70-73, St Odilia Church Adult Choir, Minn, 77- & Minn Orch Children's Chorus, 82; founder & dir, Bel Canto Voices, Minn, 76- & Cargill Chorale, Minn, 76-; producer, specials for KMSP-TV, 77-; accmp, Minn Opera Co, 77-, choral dir, 81-, mem artistic staff, 82-; accmp, Opera St Paul, 80-81, choral ens dir, 81; accmp, Midwest Opera Theatre Co, 80- *Teaching:* Coach & accmp, Opera Wkshp, Col St Catherine, 76- *Mem:* Am Choral Dir Asn; Am Guild Organists; Twin Cities Choirmasters Asn; Am Guild Musical Artists. *Mailing Add:* 1740 Millwood Roseville MN 55113

KIMMEL, CORLISS ANN
PERCUSSION
b Washington, DC, June 10, 53. *Study:* Anchorage Community Col, AA & AAS, 80; Univ Alaska, Anchorage, BS, 82. *Pos:* Prin perc, Anchorage Symph Orch, 70-, Anchorage Civic Opera, 75-, Anchorage Community Theater, 82-; sect perc, Alaska Fest Music, 71-80. *Mem:* Anchorage Musicians Asn. *Mailing Add:* PO Box 546 Chugiak AK 99567

KIN, VLADIMIR
CONDUCTOR, EDUCATOR
Study: Moscow Consv; Leningrad Consv. *Pos:* Cond, Moscow State Phil, formerly & Leningrad Phil Orch, formerly. *Teaching:* Mem fac cond, Manhattan Sch Music, 81- *Mailing Add:* c/o Int Artist Mgt 58 W 72nd St New York NY 10023

KING, ALVIN JAY
COMPOSER, EDUCATOR
b Orrville, Ohio, Aug 24, 17. *Study:* Ohio State Univ, BA, 41; Yale Univ, BMus, 48; Univ Colo, MMus, 50, DMA, 66. *Works:* Metaphor Ten Winds, comn by Minn Comp Forum for Harmoni Mundi, 81; Temptation in the Wilderness, perf by St Paul Chamber Orch & Univ Ark Chamber Orch, 81-83; Three Goethe Songs for Soprano & Winds, 82 & Magnificat (sop, clarinet & horn), 82, perf by Janis Hardy & Harmoni Mundi; Four Sketches for Orch, perf by Minneapolis Civic Symph, 82; Suite for Guitar, comn by Gary Carner for Alan Johnston, 83. *Pos:* Cond, Grand Junction Civic Symph, Colo, 64-67. *Teaching:* Asst prof music theory & comp, Univ Ark, Fayetteville, 57-60; chmn music dept & asst prof, Midland Col, 60-63; prof, Macalester Col, 67-83. *Awards:* Paris Consv Grant, 45; Wooley Fel, Inst Int Educ, 50; McClesky Comp Award, Univ Tex, 55. *Mem:* Minn Comp Forum. *Mailing Add:* 722 E 5th St St Paul MN 55106

KING, CARLTON W, III
EDUCATOR, MUSIC DIRECTOR
b Milford, Del, Dec 28, 47. *Study:* ECarolina Univ, BMus(theory & comp); Univ Md, MMus(musicol). *Pos:* Mem, A Newe Jewell & Smith/King Duo; French horn & organ, US Army, three yrs; dir, Kynge's Consort; music critic, Patuxent Publ Co, Columbia, Md. *Teaching:* Co-founder & music dir, Collegium Musicum, ECarolina Univ, formerly; mem fac, Selma M Levine Sch Music, Washington, DC; instr recorder, Georgetown Univ, George Washington Univ & Univ Md. *Mem:* Am Fedn Musicians; Am Recorder Soc; Viola da Gamba Soc; Am Musicol Soc. *Rep:* Am Chamber Concerts 890 West End Ave New York NY 10025 *Mailing Add:* 413 Montgomery St Laurel MD 20707

KING, JAMES AMBROS
TENOR
b Dodge City, Kans, May 22, 25. *Study:* La State Univ, Baton Rouge, with Dallas Draper, MusB, 50; Univ Kansas City, Mo, MA, 52; studied with Martial Singher, Ralph Errolle, Max Lorenz, Oren Brown & William Hughes. *Roles:* Don Jose in Carmen, San Francisco Opera, 61; Turiddv in Cavalleria rusticana; Rodolfo in La Boheme; Apollo in Daphne; Radames in Aida; Macbeth in Otello; Siegmund in Die Walküre; and many others. *Pos:* Tenor, Metropolitan Opera, Deutsche Oper, Vienna Staatsoper, San Francisco Opera, La Scala & others. *Teaching:* Prof music, Univ Ky, Lexington, 52-61. *Awards:* Kammersänger, Ger govt; Grammy Award; Grand Prix Disque. *Mem:* Phi Mu Alpha Sinfonia. *Mailing Add:* c/o Harold Shaw 1995 Broadway New York NY 10023

KING, TERRY BOWER
CELLO, CONDUCTOR
b Santa Monica, Calif, Aug 20, 47. *Study:* Mt St Mary's Col, BM, 72; Claremont Grad Sch, cello with Gregor Piatigorsky, 68-75; Univ Southern Calif, studied cond with Hans Swarowsky, 74. *Rec Perf:* Mendelssohn Trios, ABC/MCA, 76; Haydn Cello Concertos, 78 & Brahms Trios for Violin, Cello & Piano, 79, TR Rec; Cowell Cello Music, CRI, 79; Tchaikovsky Trio, Grand Prix Rec, 80; Beethoven Triple Concerto, 81 & L Harrison Double Concerto, 82, TR Rec. *Pos:* Mem, Mirecourt Trio. *Teaching:* Instr cello, San Francisco Consv Music, 72; lectr, Calif State Univ, Fullerton, 72-75; lectr & artist-in-res, Grinnell Col, 75-, cond & music dir, Community Orch, 75-; guest lectr violoncello, Univ Iowa, 81-82. *Mem:* Am Symph Orch League; Am String Teachers Asn; Col Music Soc. *Interests:* Unknown works by known composers. *Rep:* Raymond Stuhle 1515 Univ Lawrence KS; Tornay Mgt Inc 127 W 72nd St New York NY 10023. *Mailing Add:* 1410 Elm St Grinnell IA 50112

KINGMAN, DANIEL C
COMPOSER, EDUCATOR
b Los Angeles, Calif, Aug 16, 24. *Study:* Eastman Sch Music, with Bernard Rogers; Mich State Univ, with H Owen Reed, PhD, 64. *Works:* The Indian Summer of Dry Valley Johnson (opera), 65; Symphony in One Movement, 65; Earthscapes with Birds (sop & orch), 73; Canonic Etudes (brass), 73; Hammersmith (string quartet), 78; Four Miniatures (brass quartet); Rhapsody (two flutes & viola). *Teaching:* Prof music, Calif State Univ, Sacramento, 56- *Awards:* Huntington Hartford Fel; MacDowell Colony Fel, 78. *Mailing Add:* Calif State Univ 600 Jay St Sacramento CA 95819

KINGSLEY, GERSHON
COMPOSER, TEACHER
b Oct 28, 25. *Study:* Los Angeles State Col; Los Angeles Consv, BM, 52; Juilliard Sch; Columbia Univ. *Works:* Concerto Moogo, 72, What is Man, 72 & Confrontations, 72, Bourne Music. *Pos:* Founder, First Moog Quartet, 70-73. *Teaching:* Instr electronic music, New Sch Social Res, 71-73. *Awards:* ASCAP Award, 73. *Mem:* ASCAP; Gesellschaft fuer Musikalische Auffuhrung. *Mailing Add:* 150 W 55th St New York NY 10010

KIORPES, GEORGE ANTHONY
EDUCATOR, PIANO
b Yonkers, NY, Sept 24, 31. *Study:* Peabody Consv Music, with Austin Conrad, Henry Cowell & Clarence Snyder, BMus, 54, artist dipl, 55, MMus,

56; Boston Univ, DMA, 75. *Pos:* Organist & choir dir, First Moravian Church, Greensboro, NC, 62- *Teaching:* Instr, Peabody Consv Music, 53-55; asst prof, Greensboro Col, 55-56 & 58-65; prof, Univ NC, 65- *Mem:* Music Teachers Nat Asn; Nat Fedn Music Clubs; NC Music Teachers Asn; Am Liszt Soc; Am Guild Organists. *Publ:* Auth, The Intricacies of Chopin's Trills, Clavier, 79; Arpeggiation in Chopin, Piano Quart, 81; Chopin's Short Trills and Snaps: An Insoluble Enigma?, Am Liszt Soc, 83. *Mailing Add:* 3917 Madison Ave Greensboro NC 27410

KIPNIS, IGOR
HARPSICHORD, WRITER
b Berlin, Ger, Sept 27, 30; US citizen. *Study:* Westport Sch Music,, Conn, dipl, 48; Harvard Univ, AB, 52. *Rec Perf:* Sixty-two LP's (40 solo) for CBS, Angel, Nonesuch, Intercord, Vanguard, Grenadilla, Golden Crest & London. *Pos:* Contrib ed, Am Rec Guide, 55-61 & Stereo Rev, 61-; music critic, Music Courier, 61, Notes, 61, New York Herald Tribune, 61-62 & New York Post, 62; solo recital, New York Hist Soc, 62, New York Phil Orch, 75 & Chicago Symph, 75; tours throughout Europe, South Am, Israel & Australia, 67-; fortepianist, Fest Music Soc, Indianapolis, 81; host weekly radio prog, Age of Baroque, WQXR, New York, 66-68. *Teaching:* Chmn baroque dept, Berkshire Music Ctr, 64-67; assoc prof, Fairfield Univ, Conn, 71-77; vis tutor harpsichord & baroque music, Royal Northern Col Music, Manchester, England, 82- *Awards:* Grant, Martha Baird Rockefeller Fund for Music Inc, 66 & 68; Best Harpsichordist Award, 78, 79 & 80 & Best Class Keyboardist Award, 82, Keyboard Mag. *Bibliog:* Ingo Harden (auth), Selfmademan am Cembalo, Fono Form, 5/71; Dorothy Packard (auth), The Harpsichord Is In Very Good Shape, Clavier, 11/75; Owen Goldsmith (auth), Igor Kipnis, Contemp Keyboard, 1/78. *Mem:* Am Fedn Musicians; ASCAP; Am Musicol Soc; Am Music Instrm Soc; hon mem, Riemenschneider Bach Inst. *Publ:* Auth, Music of the Baroque, In: New York Times Guide to Listening Pleasure, 68; ed, A First Harpsichord Book (music anthology), Oxford Univ Press, 70; Dussek: The Sufferings of the Queen of France, Alfred Music, 75; Telemann: Overture in E flat Major, 78 & Krebs: 6 Preludes (in prep), Oxford Univ Press. *Rep:* Am Int Artists 275 Madison Ave New York NY 10016. *Mailing Add:* 20 Drummer Ln West Redding CT 06896

KIRBY, F(RANK) E(UGENE)
MUSICOLOGIST, WRITER
b New York, NY, Apr 6, 28. *Study:* Colo Col, BA, 50; Yale Univ, PhD, 57. *Pos:* Contrib ed, Piano Quart, 68-, spec proj ed, 79-; consult, Younger Humanist Fel Prog, Nat Endowment Humanities, 72. *Teaching:* Instr music, Williams Col, 57-58; vis asst prof, Univ Va, 58-59; guest asst prof, Univ Tex, 59-60; asst prof, WVa Univ, 61-63; from asst prof to assoc prof, Lake Forest Col, 63-77, prof, 77-; lectr, DePaul Univ, 72 & 75; vis assoc prof musicol, Washington Univ, 73-74. *Mem:* Int Musicol Soc; German Musicol Soc; Am Asn Univ Prof; Am Musicol Soc; Col Music Soc. *Interests:* History of keyboard music; history of the symphony; 18th and 19th century music. *Publ:* Auth, Beethoven's Pastoral Symphony as a Sinfonia Characteristica, Musical Quart, Vol LVI, 605-623 & In: The Creative World of Beethoven, Norton, 71; coauth (with D E Lee), Die Rolle der Musik bei der Entstehung von Goethes West-östlichen Divan, In: Interpretationen zum West-östlichen Divan Goethes, Wiss Buchges, Darmstadt, 73; auth, Beethoven's Gebrauch von Charakteristichen Stilen: Ein Beitrag zum Problem der Einheit in der Mehrsätzigkeit, In: Beriche über den Internationalen Musikwissenschaftlichen Kongress Bonn 1970, Bäenreiter, Kassel, 73; Musical Form, In: Encycl Britannica, 74; ed, Music of the Classic Period: An Anthology with Commentary, Schirmer Bks, 78; contribr to Musical Quart, Music & Lett, J Am Musicol Soc & Notes. *Mailing Add:* 2000 Greenbriar Lane Riverwoods IL 60015

KIRCHNER, LEON
COMPOSER, EDUCATOR
b Brooklyn, NY, Jan 24, 19. *Study:* Univ Calif, Berkeley, AB, 40; studied with Ernest Bloch & Roger Sessions. *Works:* The Times are Nightfall (sop & piano), 43; String Quartets, 49, 58 & 66; Toccata (strings, winds & perc), 55; Words from Wordsworth (chorus), 66; Music for Orchestra, 69; Lily (opera), perf by New York City Opera, 77; Flute Concerto, 78. *Teaching:* Fac mem, San Francisco Consv, 46-48 & Univ Southern Calif, 50-54; Luther B Marchant prof music, Mills Col, 54-61; prof, Harvard Univ, 61-66, Walter B Rosen prof, 66- *Awards:* New York Music Critics Circle Award, 50 & 60; Naumburg Award, 54; Pulitzer Prize, 67. *Mem:* ASCAP; Soc Contemp Music; League Am Comp; Nat Inst Arts & Lett; Am Acad Arts & Lett. *Mailing Add:* Music Dept Harvard Univ 8 Hilliard St Cambridge MA 02138

KIREILIS, RAMON J
CLARINET, EDUCATOR
b Urbana, Ill, June 25, 40. *Study:* NTex State Univ, BM(music educ) & MM(clarinet), 64; Univ Mich, Ann Arbor, DMA, 67. *Rec Perf:* Learning Unlimited, Hal Leonard Publ Corp, 75; Two British Quintets, Spectrum, 80. *Pos:* Prin clarinetist, Colo Springs Symph Orch, 72-83; admin dir, Int Clarinet Cong, 73-83. *Teaching:* Assoc prof music, Univ Denver, 76-81 & prof, 82; fac acad, Int E'Ete Wallonie, Belgium, 80. *Awards:* Senate Res Grant, Univ Denver, 79 & 83; Nat Endowment Arts Rec Grant, 83. *Mem:* Founder, Int Clarinet Soc (pres, 73-78); Colo Music Educr Asn; Phi Mu Alpha. *Publ:* Auth, The Practice of Practicing, Instrumentalist, 76; Prague International Clarinet Competition, Clarinet, 81; Woodwind Solos and Studies, Instrumentalist, 81. *Mailing Add:* Music Dept Univ Denver Denver CO 80208

KIRK, COLLEEN JEAN
MUSIC DIRECTOR, EDUCATOR
b Champaign, Ill, Sept 7, 18. *Study:* Sch Music, Univ Ill, Urbana, BS, 40, MS, 45; Teachers Col, Columbia Univ, EdD, 53. *Teaching:* Instr music, Danvers pub schs, 40-44, Watseka pub schs, 44-45 & Univ High Sch, Urbana, 45-49; Asst prof educ music, Univ Ill, Urbana, 49-58, assoc prof, 58-64, prof, 64-70; prof, Fla State Univ, 70- *Awards:* President's Teaching Award, Fla State Univ, 79; Harold A Decker Choral Award, Ill chap, Am Choral Dir Asn, 81. *Mem:* Am Choral Dir Asn (pres Southern div, 71-75, nat pres, 81-83); Am Choral Found Inc; Music Educr Nat Conf; Fla Music Educr Asn; Asn Prof Vocal Ens. *Publ:* Coauth, Modern Methods in Elementary Education, Henry Holt & Co, 59; A Selected Bibliography of Music Education Materials, Music Educr Nat Conf, 59; auth, Preparing the Next Generation of Choral Conductors, 10/78 & Presidents Comments, 81-83, Choral J. *Mailing Add:* 2028 Wildridge Dr Tallahassee FL 32303

KIRK, ELISE KUHL
MUSICOLOGIST, EDUCATOR
b Chicago, Ill, Feb 14, 32. *Study:* Aspen Inst Music, studied piano with Claudio Arrau, 53; Univ Mich, BMus, 53, MMus, 54; Univ Zurich, studied musicol with Kurt von Fischer, 61-63; Cath Univ Am, PhD, 77. *Pos:* Ed, Dallas Civic Opera Mag, 78- *Teaching:* Adj lectr, Baruch Col, City Univ New York, 72-77; vis prof, Cath Univ Am, summers 76 & 77; adj prof music, Univ Dallas, 78-; adj mem fac hist & lit, Sch Arts, Southern Methodist Univ, currently. *Awards:* Fel, Smithsonian Inst & Am Coun Learned Soc. *Mem:* Am Musicol Soc; Int Musicol Soc; Col Music Soc; Sigma Alpha Iota; Gifted Students Inst. *Publ:* Contribr, Am Music Teacher, Notes, Musical Quart, Current Musicol, Symposium, New Grove Dict of Music & Musicians, 6th ed, Opera News & Dallas Civic Opera Mag. *Mailing Add:* 6516 Forest Creek Dr Dallas TX 75230

KIRK, THERON WILFORD
COMPOSER, CONDUCTOR
b Alamo, Tex, Sept 28, 19. *Study:* Baylor Univ, BM; Eastman Sch Music; Chicago Musical Col, Roosevelt Univ, MM. *Works:* Vignettes (orch), Mills, 63; Five Shakespearean Songs (SATB), 63 & Night of Wonder (SATB), 65, Shawnee Press; Intrada (orch), 65, Hemisdance (string orch), 69 & The Lib: 393 BC, 72, C Fischer Inc; Prayers from the Ark (STB), MCA Music, 76. *Pos:* Cond chorale & chamber orch, San Antonio Col, 65- *Teaching:* Chmn music dept, San Antonio Col, 75- *Awards:* ASCAP Comp Award, 70-; Orpheus Award, Phi Mu Alpha Sinfonia, 75; Piper Prof, Mimmie Piper Stevens Found, 76. *Mem:* Am Choral Dir Asn (pres, 68-70). *Mailing Add:* 2502 Old Brook San Antonio TX 78230

KIRKENDALE, WARREN
MUSICOLOGIST
b Toronto, Can, Aug 14, 32; US citizen. *Study:* Univ Toronto, BA, 55; Univ Vienna, DPhil, 61. *Teaching:* Asst prof musicol, Univ Southern Calif, 63-67; assoc prof, Duke Univ, 67-75, prof, 75-82; chmn musicol, Univ Regensburg, 83- *Awards:* Fels, Nat Endowment Humanities, 70 & 83 & Am Coun Learned Soc, 74. *Mem:* Int Musicol Soc; Am Musicol Soc; Soc Ital Musicol; Gesellschaft Musikforschung; Gesellschaft Herausgabe von Denkmälern Tonkunst Österreich. *Interests:* Eighteenth century Austria; 16th-17th century Italy; relationships between music and literature, rhetoric, visual arts and liturgy. *Publ:* Auth, New Roads to Old Ideas in Beethoven's Missa Solemnis, Musical Quart, 70; Franceschina, Girometta, and Their Companions ..., Acta Musicol, 72; L'Aria di Fiorenza, id est Il Ballo del Gran Duca, Leo S Olschki, 72; Fugue and Fugato in Rococo and Classical Chamber Music, Duke Univ Press, 79; Ciceronians versus Aristotelians on the Ricercar ..., J Am Musicol Soc, 79; Circulatio-Tradition ... and Josquin ..., Acta Musicol (in press). *Mailing Add:* Musikwissenschaftliches Inst Univ Regensburg Regensburg D-8400 Germany, Federal Republic of

KIRKPATRICK, GARY HUGH
PIANO, EDUCATOR
b Manhattan, Kans, Aug 10, 41. *Study:* Eastman Sch Music, BM, 62; Acad Music & Dramatic Arts, Vienna, artists dipl, 67. *Rec Perf:* Sonata for Three Hands, MHS, 66; Piano Fantasy, CRI, 76; Trio (Thomas Christian David), Crystal Rec, 83. *Pos:* Concert pianist, Europe, Near East, Cent Am, Russia, US & Can; perf with numerous chamber music groups, US & abroad; staff pianist, Interlochen Music Acad, 62-63. *Teaching:* Vis instr, Univ Kans, 67-69; artist instr, Interlochen Ctr for Arts, 69-73; prof music, William Paterson Col NJ, 73- *Awards:* First Prize, Stepanov Piano Compt, Vienna, 64; Second Prize, Int Piano Compt, Spain, 66. *Rep:* Grapa Concts USA 1995 Broadway Suite 204 New York NY 10023. *Mailing Add:* Box 598 Hewitt NJ 07421

KIRKPATRICK, RALPH
HARPSICHORD, EDUCATOR
b Leominster, Mass, June 10, 11. *Study:* Harvard Univ, BA, 31; Oberlin Consv, Hon DMus, 57; Univ Rochester, Hon DMus, 73. *Rec Perf:* Scarlatti Sixty Sonatas, Columbia, 55; Complete Keyboard Works of Bach, 58-67 & Scarlatti 18 Sonatas, 70, Deutsche Grammophon. *Pos:* Concert performances principally on harpsichord throughout US & Europe, 33- *Teaching:* Instr, Salzburg Mozarteum Acad, summers 33-34; fac mem, Yale Univ, 40-76 & emer prof music, 76-; Ernest Bloch prof, Univ Calif, Berkeley, 64. *Awards:* Fels, John Knowles Paine, 31-32 & John Simon Guggenheim, 36; Italian Legion Merit, 55. *Mem:* Am Musicol Soc; Music Libr Asn; Neue Bach Soc. *Publ:* Ed, J S Bach Goldberg Variations, 38 & Domenico Scarlatti Sixty Sonatas, 53, G Schirmer; auth, Domenico Scarlatti, Princeton Univ Press, 53; ed, J S Bach, Clavier-Buechlein Vor Wilhelm Friedemann, Yale Univ Press, 59; Domenico Scarlatti, Complete Keyboard Works in Facsimile, Johnson, NY, 72. *Mailing Add:* Old Quarry Guilford CT 06437

KIRKWOOD, LINDA WALTON
VIOLA, EDUCATOR
b New Rochelle, NY, Jan 29, 53. *Study:* New England Consv Music, studied with Burton Fine & George Neikrug, BM, 71. *Pos:* Violist, Tremont String Quartet, Geneseo, NY, 77- *Teaching:* Asst prof viola, State Univ NY, Geneseo, 77- *Mailing Add:* Music Dept State Univ NY Geneseo NY 14454

KIRSCHEN, JEFFRY M
FRENCH HORN
b Philadelphia, Pa, Dec 25, 52. *Study:* Temple Univ, studied horn with Nolan Miller & Kendall Betts, BM, 75; Curtis Inst Music, studied horn with Mason Jones, BM, 77. *Pos:* Prin horn, Nat Ballet Can, 77; actg prin horn, Seattle Symph Orch, 78-80; co-prin horn, Utah Symph Orch, 80- *Awards:* Second Place, Am Horn Competition, 81. *Mem:* Int Horn Soc. *Publ:* Ed, Hansel and Gretel Choral, Hornists Nest, 80. *Mailing Add:* 272 S 1000 E Salt Lake City UT 84102

KIRSHBAUM, BERNARD
EDUCATOR, WRITER
b San Diego, Calif, Oct 2, 11. *Study:* Juilliard Sch, teacher dipl, 33, artist dipl, 35; Teachers Col, Columbia Univ, BS, 43, MA(music educ), 45. *Rec Perf:* Faculty Duo Piano Recital, Lirs Classic, 61; Faculty Duo Piano Recitals, Long Island Inst Music, 62-64; Artist in Recital, Lirs Classic, 70. *Teaching:* Dir piano & harmony, Kirshbaum Piano Studio, 55-; prof piano & theory, Long Island Inst Music, 60-68. *Mem:* Hon mem, Piano Teachers Cong New York; Asn Piano Teachers Long Island (pres, 76-78 & prog chmn, 80-83); Leschetizky Asn, Inc (exec bd mem, 78-83); Nat Guild Piano Teachers; Nat & NY State Music Teachers Asns. *Publ:* Auth, Building a Concert Career, Clavier, 12/73; Rapport with Students, Piano Guild Notes, 5/79; Want to Be a Piano Teacher—Care First, Piano Guild Notes, 9/80; So You Want to Be a Concert Artist, Piano Guild Notes, 11/80; The Art of Duo-Piano Performance, Am Music Teacher, 2/81. *Rep:* Camerica Publ 489 Fifth Ave New York NY 10017. *Mailing Add:* 78-18 165th St Flushing NY 11366

KIRSTEN, DOROTHY
SOPRANO
b Montclair, NJ, July 6, 19. *Study:* With Ludwig Fabri, Jose Ruben, Ruth Moltke & Antoinetta Stabile; Ithaca Col, Hon DMus; Santa Clara Univ, Hon DFA. *Rec Perf:* On Columbia. *Roles:* Musetta in La Boheme, Chicago Opera Co, 40; Mimi in La Boheme, Metropolitan Opera, 45; Minnie in La Fanciulla del West; Cio-Cio-San in Madama Butterfly; Tosca in Tosca; Violetta in La Traviata; Cressida in Troilus and Cressida. *Pos:* Mem, Metropolitan Opera, formerly & San Francisco Opera, formerly; singer with maj opera co in Can, Mex, USSR, Sweden & US, formerly. *Awards:* Handel Medal. *Mailing Add:* Met Opera Asn Lincoln Ctr Plaza New York NY 10023

KITE-POWELL, JEFFERY THOMAS
EDUCATOR, RENAISSANCE WOODWINDS
b Miami, Fla, June 24, 41. *Study:* Col-Consv Music, Univ Cincinnati, BM(music), 63, BS(music educ), 64; Univ NMex, MA(musicol), 69; Univ Hamburg, Germany, PhD(musicol), 76. *Pos:* Managing dir, Miami Choral Soc Inc, 77-80. *Teaching:* Assoc prof music hist, Miami-Dade Community Col, 80- *Awards:* Phi Mu Alpha Sinfonia Orpheus Award, 81. *Mem:* Phi Mu Alpha Sinfonia (pres, 80-81, corresp secy, 79-80); Am Musicol Soc; Col Music Soc. *Interests:* The music of the Renaissance and early Baroque periods, instrumental and vocal, sacred and secular. *Publ:* Auth, Hymnen für Orgel aus der Visby (Petri) Orgeltabulatur, 78 & The Visby (Petri) Organ Tablature—Investigation, 79, Heinrichshofen; Johann Barr, In: New Grove Dict of Music & Musicians, 80; ed, Hamburgische Kirchenmusik im Reformationszeitalter, K D Wagner Verlag, 82; translr, Introduction to Acoustics, Heinrichshofen (in prep). *Mailing Add:* 8600 SW 126 Terr Miami FL 33156

KITZKE, JEROME PETER
COMPOSER, PIANO
b Milwaukee, Wis, Feb 6, 55. *Study:* Univ Wis, Milwaukee, with John Downey, BFA, 78. *Works:* Haecceity-Hesse (sop, flute, clarinet, violin, cello, piano, vibes & perc), 75, The Rime of the Ancient Mariner (SATB), 76, A Day of Dappled Seaborne Clouds (sop, cello, bassoon, perc & narrator), 78, The Snow Crazy Copybook (orch), 80, A Thousand Names to Come (melodrama), 81, Present Music (flute, clarinet, violin, cello, piano, vibes, xylophone & drums), 82 & In the Throat of River Mornings (sop, baritone, flute, piccolo, clarinet, horn en Fa, violin, cello, double bass, harp, piano & perc), 83, Burgher Music Publ. *Pos:* Asst dir, Music from Almost Yesterday, Milwaukee, Wis, 77-79; comp in res, Alverno Col, 79-82. *Awards:* BMI Award Student Comp, 81; ASCAP Grants Young Comp, 81. *Mem:* BMI. *Mailing Add:* 3038 N Frederick Milwaukee WI 53211

KITZMAN, JOHN ANTHONY
TROMBONE, EDUCATOR
b Whitewater, Wis, Apr 27, 45. *Study:* Univ Mich, BMus, 67. *Pos:* Second trombone, Dallas Symph, 72-74, prin trombone, 74-; mem, Dallas Brass Quintet; mem bd dir, Gtr Dallas Youth Orch. *Teaching:* Adj prof trombone, Southern Methodist Univ, 75- *Mem:* Int Trombone Asn. *Mailing Add:* 8215 Meadow Rd Apt 1121 Dallas TX 75231

KIVY, PETER NATHAN
CRITIC-WRITER, EDUCATOR
b New York, NY, Oct 22, 34. *Study:* Univ Mich, BA, 56; Yale Uniiv, MA(musicol), 60; Columbia Univ, PhD, 66. *Teaching:* Prof philosophy, Rutgers Univ, 68- *Awards:* Deems Taylor Award, ASCAP, 80. *Mem:* Am

Musicol Soc. *Interests:* Aesthetics and philosophy of music. *Publ:* Auth, Charles Darwin on Music, J Am Musicol Soc, 59; Herbert Spencer and a Musical Dispute, Music Rev, 64; Child Mozart as an Aesthetic Symbol, J Hist Ideas, 67; What Mattheson Said, Music Rev, 73; The Corded Shell: Reflections on Musical Expression, Princeton Univ Press, 80. *Mailing Add:* 37 W 12 St New York NY 10011

KLAVITER, JANE BAKKEN
PIANO, COACH
b Chicago, Ill, Jan 26, 48. *Study:* Univ Ill, studied coaching with Paul Ulanowsky & John Wustman & piano with Malcom Bilson, Soulima Stravinsky & Stanley Fletcher, BA(piano perf), 69, MA(piano perf), 71; studied with Luigi Ricci. *Pos:* Asst cond, Int Music Fest, Venezuela, 73; asst cond, Dallas Civic Opera, 73-80, asst chorus master, 74-75; prompter, Lyr Opera Chicago, 81-83 & Los Angeles Phil, 82. *Teaching:* Fac mem, Manhattan Sch Music, 84-; private coach opera & song lit. *Awards:* Am Inst Musical Studies Grant, 70; Sterling Staff, Mu Phi Epsilon Int Compt, 70; Nat Opera Inst Grant, 75 & 76. *Bibliog:* Peter Gorner (auth), Lyric's Unsung Heroine, Chicago Tribune, 10/22/81. *Mailing Add:* 210 W 70th St Apt 1107 New York NY 10023

KLEEN, LESLIE
COMPOSER
b Minden, Nebr, Nov 27, 42. *Study:* Univ Denver, BM, 65; Cornell Univ, MA, 68; State Univ NY, Buffalo, PhD, 74. *Works:* Dance 1975, Electronic Music Plus Fest, 76; Concerto for Wind Ensemble, comn by Ohio Univ Wind Ens, 79; Starfall, Ohio Univ Sch Theatre, 79; Seed, Song, Flower, Music Teachers Nat Asn Conv, 80; Woolen Mill, Athen Int Film Fest, 81; Violin Designs, Int Comput Music Conf, 82; Chromasone, Ohio Univ, 83. *Pos:* Dir electronic music studio, Athens, Ohio. *Teaching:* Asst prof music comp & theory, Ohio Univ, 74- *Mem:* Col Music Soc; Am Soc Univ Comp; Comput Arts Soc; Nat Consortium Comput-Based Music Instr; Pi Kappa Lambda. *Publ:* Auth, Automatic Music Notation, Interface, 72; Two Research Projects in Musical Applications of Electronic Digital Comput, Nat Sci Found, 75; Music Notation Produced by Programmable Character Generator, Asn Develop Comput Based Instr Syst, 80; A Generalized Orchestra Compiler for 280 Microprocessors, Int Comput Music Conf, 83. *Mailing Add:* 66 Columbia Ave Athens OH 45701

KLEIN, DAVID E
ADMINISTRATOR
b Detroit, Mich, Oct 6, 31. *Study:* Univ Mich, AB, 53; Sch Medicine, Western Reserve Univ, MD, 57. *Pos:* Bd mem, Interlochen Ctr Arts, 68-70; pres, Cleveland Opera, 76-82; chmn bd, Chamber Music Am, 82- *Mailing Add:* 2711 Colchester Rd Cleveland OH 44106

KLEIN, JERRY (GERALD LOUIS)
CRITIC
b Peoria, Ill, Dec 19, 26. *Study:* Bradley Univ, BMus, 50; Univ Ill, 51-52. *Pos:* Critic, Peoria Journal Star, 60- *Teaching:* Critical writing, Bradley Univ, 73-76. *Mailing Add:* Peoria Journal Star 1 News Plaza Peoria IL 61643

KLEIN, KENNETH
CONDUCTOR & MUSIC DIRECTOR
b Los Angeles, Calif, Sept 5, 39. *Study:* Univ Southern Calif, BMus; studied cond with Fritz Zweig, eight yrs; studied with Richard Lert; Aspen Fest, with Isler Solomon, 61; Bayreuth Fest Master Classes, 66; studied with Nadia Boulanger, 66. *Rec Perf:* Mexican Contemporary Music; Symph No 1 (Chavez), 79. *Pos:* Music dir, Guadalajara Symph, 61-; founder & cond, Westside Symph Orch, Los Angeles, 63-68; guest cond, USSR, Rumania, Sweden, Fed Repub Germany, Buenos Aires, Mexico City & with Houston Symph, Ore Symph, PR Symph & Stuttgart Ballet; artistic dir, Homage to Pablo Casals, Guadalajara, 75. *Teaching:* Vis lectr orch & woodwind ens, Univ Calif, Santa Cruz, currently. *Awards:* Coleman Chamber Music Award (String Quartet), 62 & String Dept Award, 62, Univ Southern Calif. *Mem:* Pi Kappa Lambda. *Rep:* Harold Shaw Mgt 1995 Broadway New York NY 10023. *Mailing Add:* Dept Music Univ Calif Santa Cruz CA 95064

KLEIN, KRISTINE J
LIBRARIAN
b Rochester, NY, Mar 14, 56. *Study:* State Univ NY, Brockport, BA, 79; State Univ NY, Geneseo, study with Ruth Watanabe & John Kucaba, MLS, 80. *Pos:* Librn music specialist, Memphis Pub Libr, 80-83; asst dept head, Fine Arts Dept, Tampa Pub Libr, 83- *Mem:* Music Libr Asn; SE Music Libr Asn; Recorder Soc Am. *Interests:* Black musicians before 1875. *Mailing Add:* 2001 Dekle Ave Apt F Tampa FL 33606

KLEIN, LEONARD
COMPOSER, PIANO
b Clarkdale, Ariz, Feb 19, 29. *Study:* Univ Ariz, BMus, 50; Mills Col, MA, 55; Univ Iowa, PhD, 61. *Works:* Concerto (piano), Oklahoma City Symph, 62; Invention Fantasy, George Gaber Ind Univ Perc Ens, 64; Fantasy (violin & piano), Mills Perf Group, 65; Concert Piece No 1 (cello), Mills Perf Group & Bonnie Hampton, 66; Trio for Violin, Cello & Piano, Gotham Trio, 74; Sonata (piano, four hands), Rezits & comp, 77; Sonata for Violin & Piano, Amado & comp, 83. *Rec Perf:* Trio for Violin, Piano & Cello (Leonard Klein),

Orion Rec, 83. *Teaching:* Music, Univ Okla, 61-63 & Ind Univ, 63-65; asst prof, Mills Col, 65-71; prof, Stockton State Col, 71- *Mem:* NJ Guild Comp; Am Fedn Musicians. *Rep:* Albert Kay Assoc Inc 58 W 58 St New York NY 10019. *Mailing Add:* 2104 Grove Northfield NJ 08225

KLEIN, LUTHAR
COMPOSER, EDUCATOR
b Hannover, Germany, Jan 27, 32; US citizen. *Study:* Free Univ Berlin; Hochschule Musik, Berlin, with Boris Blacher; Univ Minn, PhD, 60. *Works:* Musique a Go-Go, 67, Symmetries for Orchestra, 68 & Design for Orchestra, 72, Theodore Presser; Paganini Collage (violin & orch), N German Radio Orch, 74; Masque of Orianna, 75 & Symphony No 3, 77, Theodore Presser; Musiqua Antiqua, Toronto Symph Orch, 77. *Teaching:* Asst prof & chmn grad studies music, Univ Tex, 62-68 & Univ Toronto, 68-; vis prof, Hochschule Musik, formerly. *Awards:* Rockefeller Grants, 64, 65 & 67; Rockefeller Found New Music Prize, 67; Fulbright Fel, 69. *Mem:* ASCAP. *Mailing Add:* 44 Wallingford Toronto ON M3A 2V2 Canada

KLEIN, MITCHELL SARDOU
CONDUCTOR
b New York, NY, Aug 13, 47. *Study:* Brandeis Univ, BA, 68; Col Notre Dame, BA, 72; Calif State Univ, Hayward. *Rec Perf:* Flagstaff Fest, 82. *Pos:* Assoc cond, Kansas City Phil, 80-82; cond, Calif Music Ctr Orch, 83-; guest cond, Seattle Symph, Richmond Symph, Flagstaff Fest, Kansas City Ballet & Oakland Ballet. *Teaching:* Lectr music, Col Notre Dame, Belmont, Calif, 73-80 & Calif Music Ctr, 76, 77, 79, 81 & 82. *Rep:* Cond Int Mgt 95 Cedar Rd Ringwood NJ 07456. *Mailing Add:* 266 Lenox Ave Oakland CA 94610

KLEIN, STEPHEN TAVEL
TUBA, TEACHER
b Buffalo, NY, Mar 3, 29, 50. *Study:* Univ Calif, Berkeley, AB, 71; Eastman Sch Music, MA, 74. *Pos:* Prin tuba & chief arr, Air Force Band Golden West, March AFB, 74-77; freelance musician, movies & TV shows, Los Angeles, 77-; prin tuba, Orange Co Pac Symph, Calif, 80- *Teaching:* Instr tuba & euphonium, Calif State Univ, Long Beach, Calif State Univ, Fullerton, Biola Col & Pomona Col, 77- *Mem:* Tubists Universal Brotherhood Asn; Am Musicol Soc; Col Music Soc; Nat Asn Col Wind & Perc Instr. *Mailing Add:* 10748 Ashworth Cir Cerritos CA 90701

KLEINSASSER, JEROME S
ADMINISTRATOR, EDUCATOR
Study: Univ Minn, PhD, 72. *Teaching:* Chmn, Dept Fine Arts, Calif State Col, Bakersfield, 81- *Interests:* Historical musicology. *Publ:* Ed, Magnificat, Augsburg Publ, 74. *Mailing Add:* Dept Fine Arts Calif State Col Bakersfield CA 93309

KLEMPERER, REGINA MUSHABAC See Mushabac, Regina

KLENZ, WILLIAM
EDUCATOR, COMPOSER
b La Connor, Wash, May 24, 15. *Study:* Curtis Inst Music, BM, 38; Univ NC, BA, 40, MA, 48, PhD, 55; Yale Sch Music, with Paul Hindemith, 46. *Works:* Te Deum, BBC & Radiodiffusion Francaise, 45; Pacem in Terris, Am Univ, 65; String Quartet, 1967, 69. *Teaching:* Assoc prof hist, Duke Univ, 66; prof aesthetics, State Univ NY, Binghamton, 68-81; vis prof, Yale Univ, 71-73. *Publ:* Auth, Giovanni Maria Bononcini, Duke Univ Press, 62; Per Aspera ad Astra, The Stairway to Jupiter, 69 & Brahms, Op 38, Piracy, Pillage ..., 71, Music Rev; Musical Experience in Contemporary Life, Col Music Symposium, 77. *Mailing Add:* 29 Vincent St Binghamton NY 13905

KLETZSCH, CHARLES FREDERICK
COMPOSER
b Milwaukee, Wis, Apr 4, 26. *Study:* Harvard Univ, with Walter Piston & Archibald Davison, BA, 51, MA, 53. *Works:* Chamber Works, Dunster House Music Soc, 52- *Teaching:* Comp in res, Dunster House, Harvard Univ, 52- *Mailing Add:* Dunster House Libr Harvard Univ Cambridge MA 02138

KLICK, SUSAN MARIE
FLUTE, EDUCATOR
b Washington, DC. *Study:* Univ Wis, BM, Northwestern Univ, MM; studied with Donald Peck & Walfrid Kujala. *Pos:* Prin flute, Colo Phil, 79 & 81 & Civic Orch Chicago, 82; prin guest concerto soloist, Heidelberg Chamber Orch, 79-80; extra flute, Chicago Symph Orch, summer 82. *Teaching:* Asst prof flute & music hist, Pa State Univ, 81- *Awards:* First Prize, Int Young Artist Compt, Nat Flute Asn, 79 & Soc Am Musicians Nat Flute Compt, 80. *Mem:* Nat Flute Asn. *Mailing Add:* 225 S Buckhout St #3-A State College PA 16801

KLIEWER, DARLEEN CAROL
EDUCATOR, SOPRANO
b Redfield, SDak. *Study:* Bethany Col, BME, 61; Wichita State Univ, MM, 68. *Rec Perf:* Harmonium (Vincent Persichetti), 80. *Roles:* Pamina in Magic Flute, Mimi in La Boheme, Antonia in The Tales of Hoffman, Marie in Bartered Bride, Martha in Martha, Micaëla in Carmen & Leonora in Il Trovatore, 72-73, Städtisches Bühne Flensburg. *Teaching:* Instr voice,

Friends Univ, 68-69 & Oberlin Consv, 71-72; assoc prof, Ariz State Univ, 75- *Mem:* Sigma Alpha Iota; Nat Asn Teachers Singing (vpres, 78-79); Music Teachers Nat Asn. *Mailing Add:* Sch Music Ariz State Univ Tempe AZ 85287

KLIMKO, RONALD JAMES
EDUCATOR, BASSOON

b Lena Wis, Dec 13, 36. *Study:* Milton Col, BMusEd, 59; Univ Wis, MM, 66, PhD, 68; study comp with Hilmar Luckhardt, Robert Crane & Irwin Sonenfield; study bassoon with Otto Eifert, 61, Richard Lottridge, 63-66, William Waterhouse, 77, Cecil James, 77 & Maurice Allard, 83- *Works:* Woodwind Quintet, perf by Northwest Wind Quintet, 67; Violin Sonata, perf by Jackie Melvin & Steven Folks, 69; The Highway (ballet), perf by Indianapolis Symph, 68 & Spokane Symph, 72. *Pos:* Bassoonist, Spokane Symph, 77-; prin bassoon, Summer Fest Orch, Univ Ind, 80; co-ed, The Double Reed, 82- & Journal of the International Double Reed Society, 82-, Int Double Reed Soc. *Teaching:* Asst prof theory & bassoon, Moorhead State Col, 66-67 & Ind State Univ, Terre Haute, 67-68; prof, Univ Idaho, 68-; vis prof bassoon, Ind Univ, Bloomington, 80- *Mem:* Am Fedn Musicians; Am Fedn Teachers; Int Double Reed Soc (secy, 78-81). *Publ:* Auth, Bassoon Performance Practices and Teaching in the United States and Canada, Sch Music Publ, 74; The C Kruspe Bassoon and the World's Columbian Exposition of Chicago, 1893, Int Double Reed Soc, 79; contribr, Impressions of Edinburgh, 1980, Les Amis du Bassoon, Francais, Paris, 80. *Mailing Add:* Sch Music Univ Idaho Moscow ID 83843

KLIPPSTATTER, KURT L
EDUCATOR, MUSIC DIRECTOR

b Graz, Austria, Dec 17, 34. *Study:* Consv Graz, dipl. *Pos:* Artistic dir, Memphis Opera Theatre, 72-76; music dir, Ark Symph, 73-80. *Teaching:* Fac mem cond & coaching, Memphis State Univ, 73-76 & Hartt Sch Music, 76- *Awards:* Musician of Yr Citation, Fedn Music Clubs, 76. *Mem:* Am Symph Orch League; Cent Opera League. *Mailing Add:* 20 Coppergate Rd PO Box 431 East Granby CT 06026

KLOBUCAR, BERISLAV
CONDUCTOR & MUSIC DIRECTOR

b Zagreb, Yugoslavia, Aug 28, 24; Austrian citizen. *Study:* Studied with Lovro v Matacic & Clemens Krauss. *Rec Perf:* Die Frau ohne Schatten & Die Meistersinger, TV films. *Pos:* Asst cond, Opera House, Zagreb, Yugoslavia, 43-51; cond, Vienna State Opera, 53-; gen music dif, Graz Opera, 60-71; mem dir, Graz Phil, Austria, 62-72; music dir & res cond, Royal Opera, Stockholm, 72-; guest cond, opera co & orchs in North & South Am & Europe. *Mem:* Hon mem, Royal Swedish Acad Music. *Mailing Add:* c/o Thea Dispeker 59 E 544th St New York NY 10022

KLOTH, TIMOTHY TOM
COMPOSER, EDUCATOR

b Cleveland, Ohio, May 4, 54. *Study:* Capital Univ, BM, 76; Eastman Sch Music, MM, 78; NTex State Univ. *Works:* The Southern Quintet, NTex State Univ & ETex State Univ, 78; The Radiant Tower, Va Commonwealth Univ & NTex State Univ, 78; Harper's Inquiry, NTex State Univ, 80; Non-Inconsequenza, perf by Tom Everett, 80; Cavatina, Va Commonwealth Univ & Iowa State Univ, 81; CELL05, perf by Olov Franzen, 82; Ionospheres, perf by Richard Von Grabow, 82. *Teaching:* Teaching asst, Eastman Sch, 76-78; instr theory, Iowa State Univ, 81-82; asst prof comput & electronic music & hist, Va Commonwealth Univ, 82- *Mem:* Am Soc Composers, Authors & Publishers; Am Soc Univ Composers; Phi Mu Alpha. *Mailing Add:* 2100 Grove Ave Apt 1 Richmond VA 23220

KLOTMAN, ROBERT HOWARD
EDUCATOR, VIOLIN

b Cleveland, Ohio, Nov 22, 18. *Study:* Ohio Northern Uiv, BS, 40; Case Western Res, MA, 51; Teachers Col, Columbia Univ, EdD, 56. *Works:* Herald Quartet, 58, Carnaval Da Camera, 65, Belwin-Mills Music Co; Suite for Strings, Alfred Publ Co, 82. *Teaching:* Teacher & coordr music, Cleveland Heights Pub Sch, Ohio, 46-59; dir music educ, Akron Pub Sch, Ohio, 59-63; div dir music, Detroit Pub Sch, 63-69; prof music, Ind Univ, Bloomington, 63-, chmn music educ dept, 69-; scholar in res, Fairfax County Sch, 73. *Awards:* Recognition Merit, Children's Concert Soc Akron, 63. *Mem:* Music Educr Nat Conf (pres, 76-78); Am String Teachers Asn (pres, 62-64); ASCAP; Sinfonia Soc Am. *Interests:* Music & string education. *Publ:* Auth, Action with Strings, Southern Music Co, 62; Music Education: The Training of Teachers, Encycl Educ, 71; The School Music Administrator & Supervisor: Catalysts for Change in Music Education, Prentice-Hall, 73; coauth, Learning to Teach Through Playing: String Techniques & Pedagogy, Addison Wesley, 2nd ed, 77; Foundations of Music Education, Schirmer Bks, 83. *Mailing Add:* 2740 Spicewood Lane Bloomington IN 47401

KLOTZMAN, DOROTHY ANN HILL
EDUCATOR, CONDUCTOR

b Seattle, Wash, Mar 24, 37. *Study:* Juilliard Sch, studied comp with William Bergsma, Vincent Persichetti & Darius Milhaud, BS, 58, MS, 60. *Works:* Sonata for Trumpet and Two Trombones; Nothing Heavy and Nothing at Rest (symphonic band); Good Day Sir Christmas (sop solo, chorus & instrm ens); Divertimento (chamber orch); Concerto (sax & orch); Chimera (ballet); Variations (orch). *Pos:* Cond, Goldman Band, 73; guest cond, Guggenheim Concerts Band, 80 & 81. *Teaching:* Cond, Symphonic Band, Brooklyn Col, 70-, prof & chairperson dept music, 71-, cond, Symph Orch, 80- *Awards:*

Benjamin Award Comp, 55 & 58; Fromm Prize Comp, Aspen Music Sch, 60; E Harris Harbison Award, Danforth Found, 72. *Mem:* Am Music Ctr; Am Musicol Soc; Col Music Soc; Music Libr Asn; Am Soc Comp & Perf. *Mailing Add:* Consv Music Brooklyn Col Brooklyn NY 11210

KLUGER, JOSEPH H
ADMINISTRATOR

b Paterson, NJ, Feb 9, 55. *Study:* Trinity Col, Conn, BA(music), 77; NY Univ, MA(arts admin), 79. *Pos:* Asst mgr, New York Phil, 81-82, orch mgr, 82- *Mailing Add:* 315 W 70th St Apt 9B New York NY 100?3

KNAACK, DONALD (FRANK)
COMPOSER, PERCUSSION

b Louisville, Ky, July 4, 47. *Study:* Sch Music, Univ Louisville, BMusEd, 69; Manhattan Sch Music, MM, 73. *Works:* Eclipse, 79, ... for John Cage, 79, Dance Music I and II, 80, Confines, 81, I-VI for solo piano, 82, Inside the Plastic Lotus, 83 & Between Day and the Darkness, 83, Menil Music. *Rec Perf:* Erratum Musicale, Atlantic-Finnadar Rec, 77; Eclipse, Bayerischer Rundfunk, Nuremberg, 80; ... for John Cage, 80, Dance Music I and II, 80 & Inside the Plastic Lotus, 83, Belgium TV; Inside the Plastic Lotus, Hat Hut Rec, 83. *Pos:* Co-prin perc, Louisville Orch, 67-69; comp & perc, Ctr Creative & Perf Arts, State Univ NY, Buffalo, 74-77; comp, soloist & lectr, conct halls, univ & museums, 78- *Teaching:* Assoc prof perc, State Univ NY, Buffalo, 74-77. *Awards:* Grants, Creative Artists Pub Serv Award, 77, Try Found, Los Angeles, 80 & Calif Arts Coun, 81. *Mem:* Phi Mu Alpha Sinfonia; ASCAP. *Rep:* Serv to Arts PO Box 186 Shokan NY 12481; Davor and Partners 225-227 Rue De La Croix Nivert 75015 Paris France. *Mailing Add:* PO Box 186 Shokan NY 12481

KNAPP, JOHN MERRILL
EDUCATOR

b New York, NY, May 9, 14. *Study:* Yale Univ, AB, 36; Columbia Univ, MA, 41. *Teaching:* Prof music hist, Princeton Univ, 46-82. *Mem:* Int Musicol Soc; Am Musicol Soc; Col Music Soc. *Interests:* Handel; Music of 18th Century England; Wagner. *Publ:* Auth, Selected List of Music for Men's Voices, Princeton, 52; The Magic of Opera, Harper & Row, 72; Instrumentation Draft of Wagner's Rheingold, J Am Musicol Soc; ed, Handel's Amadigi, 74 & Handel's Flavio, 83, Barenreiter Verlag. *Mailing Add:* 108 Rosedale Lane Princeton NJ 08540

KNAUB, DONALD
TROMBONE, EDUCATOR

Study: Eastman Sch Music, BM, MM. *Rec Perf:* On Golden Crest Rec. *Pos:* Trombone, Rochester Phil, formerly & Chautauqua Symph, formerly. *Teaching:* Mem fac, Ohio State Univ, formerly, Univ Southern Calif, formerly & Music Acad West, currently; prof trombone, Univ Tex, 77- *Mailing Add:* Dept Music Univ Tex Austin TX 78712

KNESS, RICHARD MAYNARD (RICHARD M KNEISS)
TENOR

b Rockford, Ill, July 23, 37. *Study:* San Diego State Univ, BA, 58; studied with Clemens Kaiser-Breme, Martial Singher, Frederick Wilkerson & Marinka Gurewich. *Roles:* Duca di Mantova in Rigoletto, St Louis Opera, 66; Florestan in Fidelio; Faust in Damnation de Faust; Don Jose in Carmen; Sam Polk in Susannah; Paul in Tote Stadt; Canio in Pagliacci. *Pos:* Appearances with maj opera co in Europe & US, 67-78 & maj symph in US, 67-; leading dramatic tenor, Metropolitan Opera Asn, 77- *Awards:* Grammy Award for Best Classical Rec, 67. *Rep:* Columbia Artists Mgt 165 W 57th St New York NY 10019. *Mailing Add:* 240 Central Park S Suite 3N New York NY 10019

KNIEBUSCH, CAROL LEE
FLUTE, EDUCATOR

b Woodstock Ill, Aug 15, 38. *Study:* Ill Wesleyan Univ, BMusEd, 60; Ind Univ, MMus, 62; studied flute with Marcel Moyse, Samuel Baron, James Pellerite, John Krell, Harry Houdeshel, James Galway, William Bennett & Geoffrey Gilbert. *Pos:* Flautist, Vancouver Symph Orch, 64-66 & Baltimore Symph Orch, 66-69; prin flute, Roanoke Symph, currently; flute ed, Sch Musician, currently. *Teaching:* Instr, Univ BC, 62-66; asst prof theory, analysis & flute, James Madison Univ, currently. *Mem:* Nat Flute Asn; Am Fedn Musicians; Delta Omicron; Music Teachers Nat Asn; Nat Theory Soc. *Publ:* Contribr to Nat Flute Asn Newslett, Woodwind World & Notes. *Mailing Add:* Music Dept James Madison Univ Harrisonburg VA 22807

KNIETER, GERARD L
ADMINISTRATOR, EDUCATOR

b Brooklyn, NY, June 2, 31. *Study:* NY Univ, BS, 53, MA, 54; Columbia Univ, EdD, 61. *Teaching:* Asst prof music & educ, San Jose State Univ, 62-65; actg dean & assoc prof music, Duquesne Univ, 65-67; head doctoral prog, prof & chmn dept music educ, Temple Univ, 67-78; prof music & dean, Col Fine & Applied Arts, Univ Akron, 78- *Mem:* Int Coun Fine Arts Deans; Coun Arts & Sci Deans; Soc Ethnomusicol; Col Music Soc; Am Asn Higher Educ. *Interests:* Psychological aspects of teaching. *Publ:* Auth, Humanistic Dimensions of Aesthetic Education, Music Educ Tomorrow's Soc, 76; Music as Aesthetic Education, Nat Asn Sec Sch Prin, 79; co-ed, The Teaching Process & Arts and Aesthetics, Cemrel, Inc, 79; auth, Current Issues & Future Directions in Music Ed, McGill Symposium, 79; Cognition & Musical Development, Ann Arbor Symposium, 81. *Mailing Add:* 1248 Country Club Rd Akron OH 44313

KNIGHT, ERIC W
CONDUCTOR, COMPOSER
Study: Study comp with Mark Brunswick, 54; City Col New York, BA(music), 54; Columbia Univ, MA(comp), 60. *Works:* Americana Overture, 76, Symphony in Four American Idioms, 76, Three Elements for Orchestra, 79 & Canadian Tribute, 80, G Schirmer; The Reel Chaplin, Bourne Co, 82; The Great American Bicycle Race, comn by WMAR-TV, Baltimore, 83. *Pos:* Arr & orch, Boston Pops, 70-78; prin cond, Baltimore Symph Orch, 80-83 & NC Symph Orch, 80-83; cond, New York City Opera, 83- *Awards:* Gold Award, 20th Int Film & TV Fest New York, 77. *Mem:* ASCAP. *Mailing Add:* 317 W 89 St New York NY 10024

KNIGHT, MORRIS H
COMPOSER, EDUCATOR
b Charleston, SC, Dec 25, 33. *Study:* Univ Ga, BFA, 56; Ball State Univ, MM, 66. *Works:* Symphony No 3, Ind Univ Phil, 66; Piano Concerto, Nat Symph, 69; Four Brass Quintets, New York Brass Quintet, 70; Entity One: Music for the Global Village Conation, 73 & Message from Tralfamadore, 83, perf by Morris Knight. *Pos:* Prog dir, WRFC, Athens, Ga, 55-63 & KSFR, San Francisco, Calif, 63-64. *Teaching:* Prof comp, Ball State Univ, 66- ; dir, Fac Acoustic Res, 75- *Awards:* Publ & Rec Award, Ford Found, 72; Standard Awards, ASCAP, 73-; fel, Lilly Endowment, 79-80. *Bibliog:* Edward Tatnall Canby (auth), Audio, etc, Audio Mag, 75; Robert Taylor (auth), A Message From Another Planet, Boston Globe, 79; Pamela Denny (auth), Knight Music—A New Art Form, Arts Insight, 80. *Publ:* Coauth, Aural Comprehensive (two vol), McGraw-Hill, 70. *Mailing Add:* 2424 Petty Rd Muncie IN 47304

KNOPT, TINKA
PIANO, ADMINISTRATOR
Study: Peabody Consv Music, BM, MM, DMA; Santiago Compostela, Spain, dipl. *Pos:* Performances in US & Spain. *Teaching:* Co-chmn, Prep Dept, Peabody Consv Music, 68-78, mem fac piano & piano pedagogy & assoc dean, currently. *Awards:* Nat Endowment Humanities Grant to Spain. *Mem:* Md State Music Teachers Asn (mem bd, formerly); Music Teachers Nat Asn (pres eastern div, formerly & vpres, currently); Baltimore Music Teachers Asn (pres, formerly). *Mailing Add:* Peabody Consv Music 1 E Mt Vernon Pl Baltimore MD 21202

KNOX, CHARLES
COMPOSER, EDUCATOR
b Atlanta, Ga, Apr 19, 29. *Study:* Univ Ga, BFA, 51; Ind Univ, with Bernhard Heiden, MM, 55, PhD, 62. *Works:* Solo for Trumpet with Brass Trio, Philharmusica Corp, 68; Solo for Tuba with Brass Trio, Tenuto Publ, 69; Festival Procession, Choristers Guild, 72; Symphony for Brass and Percussion, Philharmusica Corp, 74; Voluntary on Hyfrydol, 80 & A Gloria, 81, Neil A Kjos Music Co. *Pos:* Prin trombone, Atlanta Symph Orch, 47-51 & Third Army Band, 51-54. *Teaching:* Assoc prof, Miss Col, 55-65; prof, Ga State Univ, 65- *Mem:* Am Music Ctr; ASCAP; Southeastern Comp League; Col Music Soc; Nat Consortium Comput Based Music Instr. *Mailing Add:* Ga State Univ Univ Plaza Atlanta GA 30303

KOBER, DIETER
CONDUCTOR & MUSIC DIRECTOR, EDUCATOR
b Germany; US citizen. *Study:* Univ Nebr, BME, 47; Chicago Musical Col, MM, 48; Chicago Musical Col & Univ Chicago, DFA, 50; Mozarteum, Salzburg, cond cert, 52. *Rec Perf:* Serenade (Heiden-Mozart), CBS, 61; Salute to Copenhagen, Voice Am, 62; Water Music (Handel), Vox Turnabout, 76; Concerto di Aranjuez, 76 & Flute Concert (Carl Nielsen), 77, CBS; On Michigan Avenue (Mozart), Universal, 79; Siegfried Idyll (Wagner), CBS, 82. *Pos:* Music dir, Chicago Chamber Orch, 54- & Art Inst Can, 58-62; guest cond, Europe & US orchs, 70- *Teaching:* Music, pub sch, Cook, Nebr, 46-47; instr, Chicago Musical Col, 48-49; prof music, City Col Chicago, 50- *Bibliog:* John von Rhein (auth), Chicago Chamber Orchestra: Have Music, Will Travel, Chicago Tribune, 5/82. *Mem:* Am Symph Orch League; Am Fedn Teachers; Am Fedn Musicians; Phi Mu Alpha Sinfonia. *Publ:* Co-ed, Handbook of Music History, Follett, 48; Wedding Music, Music News, 70; Music of the Chamber Orchestra—Monthly, WNIB, 70-; Music in the Cathedral, Chicago Symphonic Perspective, FM Radio Mag, 75. *Mailing Add:* 410 S Michigan Ave Chicago IL 60605

KOBERSTEIN, FREEMAN G
PIANO, EDUCATOR
Study: Univ Minn, studied piano with Imald Ferguson & Dmitri Mitropoulos, BA, 39, MA, 53; Juilliard Sch, studied piano with Olga Samaroff Stokowski; studied with Harold Craxton. *Pos:* Soloist, Minneapolis Symph & orchs in Belgium & Germany. *Teaching:* Prof pianoforte, Consv Music, Oberlin Col, 46- *Awards:* Winner, Helen Swan Prize & Oberhoffer Award. *Mailing Add:* Consv Music Oberlin Col Oberlin OH 44074

KOBLER, LINDA
HARPSICHORD, PIANO
b New York, NY. *Study:* Peabody Consv Music, with Lillian Freundlich, Leon Fleisher & Shirley Mathews, BM(piano), 75, BM(harpsichord), 75; Juilliard Sch, studied piano with Irwin Freundlich & harpsichord with Albert Fuller, MM, 77. *Pos:* Mem, Tafelmusik, New York, 83- *Teaching:* Mem fac piano, Peabody Consv Music, 72-75 & Third St Music Sch, New York, 83-; mem fac music hist, Juilliard Sch, 76-78. *Awards:* Aber T Unger Award, Peabody Consv Music, 75; Concert Artist Guild Award, 83. *Mailing Add:* 2130 Broadway #811 New York NY 10023

KOBLITZ, DAVID
COMPOSER, EDUCATOR
b Cleveland, Ohio, Oct 5, 48. *Study:* Univ Pa, BA, 70; Univ Mich, MM, 72. *Works:* Trism, 71 & Gris-Gris, 73, Margun Music Inc; Harmonica Monday, perf by Gageego Players, 75; Eight Three-Part Inventions, 76 & Le Cru Et Le Cuit, 79, Marqun Music Inc; Tokens on the Dream Exchange, comn & perf by Speculum Musicae, 81; Delayed Departures, comn & perf by Collage. *Teaching:* Adj instr comp & music theory, Rutgers Univ, 76-81; adj instr Am music, Pace Univ, NY, 77- *Awards:* Guggenheim Fel, 79; Nat Endowment Arts Comp Fel, 75-80. *Rep:* Margun Music Inc 167 Dudley Rd Newton Centre MA. *Mailing Add:* 241 E 76th St #7C New York NY 10021

KOCH, FREDERICK (CHARLES)
COMPOSER, PIANO
b Cleveland, Ohio, Apr 4, 28. *Study:* Cleveland Inst Music, BM(piano), 49; Case Western Reserve Univ, MA(music), 50; Eastman Sch Music, DMA(comp), 70. *Works:* Feed my Lambs/Be not Afraid, Boosey & Hawkes, 63; Three Songs (childrens set), Galaxy Music, 68; String Quartet, No 2, Seesaw Music, 72; Composites for Band, Southern Music, 73; Five Memories, Carl Fischer, 76; O Clap your Hands (SATB), G Schirmer, 78; Barometric readings for percussion quartet, Seesaw Music, 77. *Pos:* Dir, The Studio, Rocky River, Ohio, 52-68 & Koch Sch Music, Inc, 68- *Teaching:* Instr piano & theory, Baldwin Wallace Col, 64-66; lectr music appreciation, Cuyahoga Community Col, 69-70; pianist & comp, Koch Sch Music, 71- *Awards:* Standard Awards, ASCAP, 73-; Cleveland Fine Arts Prize, Women's City Club, 77; Nat Endowment for Arts grant, Nat Found Arts, 78. *Mem:* Am Music Ctr; Am Soc Univ Comp; Cleveland Comp Guild; Ohio Music Teachers Asn; Mus Teachers Nat Asn (comp chmn, 72-74). *Publ:* Auth, Herbert Elwell and his music, Nat Asn Teachers Singing Bulletin, 70; Reflection on Composing, Carnegie Mellon Univ (in prep). *Mailing Add:* 2249 Valleyview Dr Cleveland OH 44116

KOCHANSKI, WLADIMIR JAN
PIANO
US citizen. *Study:* Juilliard Sch Music, with Rosina Lhevinne, 53-56, Eduard Steueremann, 56-59, BS, 59. *Rec Perf:* Wladimir Kochanski, Pharoah Prod, 62; Wladimir Kochanski in Concert, 78, Wladimir Kochanski Favorite Encores, 78, Wladimir Kochanski Great Romantic Piano Favorites, 80, & Kochanski Plays for the Children, 80, Studio West; Christmas with Kochanski, 82 & Wladimir Jan Kochanski, Tribute to Poland, 82, Peters Productions. *Pos:* Pres & founder, Della Moser Pennington Found, Calif, 68-82. *Awards:* Knighted by Polish Government in Exile, London, England, Order of Polonia Restituta, 82; Special commendation from Pope John Paul II for contribution to music and humanitarian, 82. *Bibliog:* Robert Summers (producer), Backstage with Kochanski (film), 81. *Mem:* Am Fedn Musicians. *Publ:* Auth, The People's Pianist, Crown-Summit, 82. *Mailing Add:* c/o Komar Mgt 1122 West St Oceanside CA 92054

KOCMIEROSKI, MATTHEW
PERCUSSION, EDUCATOR
b Roslyn, NY, Aug 18, 53. *Study:* Nassau Community Col, with Ronald Gould, 71-73; Mannes Col Music, with Walter Rosenberger & Howard Van Hyning, 74-77. *Pos:* Prin perc, Queens Symph Orch, 75-78; perc, Martha Graham Dance Co, 80, New Perf Group, Seattle, 80- & Comp Improvisors Orch, Seattle, 81- *Teaching:* Asst dir perc ens, Mannes Col Music, 77-80; instr perc, Cornish Inst Allied Arts, Seattle, 81- *Mem:* Percussive Arts Soc. *Mailing Add:* 11719 36th Ave NE Seattle WA 98125

KOFSKY, ALLEN
TROMBONE, EUPHONIUM
b Cleveland, Ohio, Mar 25, 26. *Study:* Cleveland Inst Music, 46-48. *Pos:* Prin trombone, Kansas City Phil Orch, 48-55; second trombone, euphonium & bass trumpet, Cleveland Orch, 61- *Teaching:* Lectr trombone, Baldwin-Wallace Col, 60- *Mailing Add:* 23914 Edgehill Dr Cleveland OH 44122

KOGAN, ROBERT COLVER
COMPOSER, CONDUCTOR
b New York, NY, Sept 2, 40. *Study:* Juilliard Sch Music, studied cello with Claus Adam, dipl, 65; studied cond with Bruno Maderna, Salzburg & M Gielen, Cologne, 66-68; Brooklyn Col, studied music comp with Jacob Druckman & R Starer, MA, 74. *Works:* Sonata No 2 (flute, marimba & viola), Lang Perc Publ Co, 75; Trio No 1 (piano, violin & violoncello), Staten Island Chamber Music Players, 79; Gemini (marimba, vibraphone & orch), Staten Island Symph, 80; Pianorama (piano solo), Mimi Stern-Wolfe, WBAI-FM NY, 83; Sonata #3 Flutes & Harpsichord, Andrew Bolotowsky, 83. *Pos:* Guest cond, Mozarteum, Salzburg, Am Symph, Brooklyn Phil, Albany Symph & Nat Symph, Ecuador; music dir, Staten Island Symph, 80- *Teaching:* Adj prof cello & orch, Wagner Col, 76- *Awards:* Nat Endowment Arts Comp Fel, 76; Criterion Found Comp Grant, 79. *Mailing Add:* 400 Argyle Rd Brooklyn NY 11218

KOHLOFF, ROLAND
PERCUSSION, EDUCATOR
b Mamaroneck, NY. *Study:* Juilliard Sch, with Saul Goodman, dipl, 56. *Pos:* Prin timpanist, San Francisco Symph, 56-72, San Francisco Opera Orch, 56-72 & New York Phil, 72- *Teaching:* Mem fac perc, Juilliard Sch, 78- *Mailing Add:* New York Phil Avery Fisher Hall New York NY 10023

KOHN, JAMES DONALD
EDUCATOR, PIANO
b Chicago, Ill, Mar 7, 28. *Study:* Chicago Musical Col, BM, 50, MM, 51; Univ Iowa, PhD, 67. *Teaching:* Instr piano, Culver Mil Acad, 52-57; instr piano & organ, Luther Col, 57-61; prof piano, Univ Wis, Oshkosh, 63- *Mem:* Col Music Soc; Music Teachers Nat Asn. *Mailing Add:* Dept Music Univ Wis Oshkosh WI 54901

KOHN, KARL (GEORGE)
COMPOSER, PIANO
b Vienna, Austria, Aug 1, 26; US citizen. *Study:* NY Col Music, studied piano with Carl Werschinger & cond with Prüwer, artists cert, 44; Harvard Col, with Walter Piston, Irving Fine & Randall Thompson, BA, 50; Harvard Univ, MA, 55. *Works:* Three Scenes for Orchestra, 58, Interludes for Orchestra, 64, Episodes for Piano & Orchestra, 66, Centone per Orchestra, 73, The Prophet Bird for Chamber Orchestra, 76 & Innocent Psaltery for Wind Orchestra, 76, Carl Fischer Inc; Prophet Bird II for Piano & Chamber Orchestra, PTM Press, 80; and others. *Pos:* Mem bd dir, Monday Evening Conct, Los Angeles, 60- *Teaching:* Thatcher prof music, Pomona Col & Claremont Grad Sch Music, 50-; fac mem, Berkshire Music Ctr, 52-58. *Awards:* Fulbright Res Grant, 55; Guggenheim Mem Fel, 61; Nat Endowment Arts Fel, 76, 79 & 80. *Bibliog:* Lawrence Morton (auth), Current Chronicle, Musical Quart, 63; Pauline Oliveras (auth), Kohn's Concerto Mutabile, Perspectives New Music, 64. *Publ:* Auth, Music in American Life, Rand McNally, 67; The Renotation of Polyphonic Music, G Schirmer, 81. *Mailing Add:* 674 W Tenth St Claremont CA 91711

KOHNO, TOSHIKO
FLUTE & PICCOLO
b Tokyo, Japan, May 28, 54. *Study:* Eastman Sch Music, BM & perf cert, 76; private study with Doriot Anthony Dwyer. *Pos:* Second flute, Buffalo Phil, 73-76; assoc prin flute, Montreal Symph, 76-78; prin flute, Nat Symph, 78- *Teaching:* Instr flute, McGill Univ, 76-78 & Catholic Univ, 82- *Awards:* First prize, Geneva Int Compt, 73 & San Francisco Symph Found Compt, 73. *Mailing Add:* c/o Nat Symph Orch Kennedy Ctr Washington DC 20566

KOHS, ELLIS BONOFF
COMPOSER, EDUCATOR
b Chicago, Ill, May 12, 16. *Study:* Univ Chicago, MA, 38; Juilliard Graduate Sch, 38-39; Harvard Univ, 39-41. *Works:* Passacaglia for Organ and Strings, CBS, 46; Symphony No 1, San Francisco Symph, 51; Chamber Concerto for Viola and Strings, Columbia Rec, 53; Lord of the Ascendant, comn by Thor Johnson, 54; Symphony No 2, Univ Ill Symph, 57; String Quartet No Two, CRI, 63; Amerika, Western Opera Theater, 70. *Teaching:* Asst prof, Wesleyan Univ, 46-48; assoc prof, Col of the Pacific, Stockton, Calif, 48-50; prof, Univ Southern Calif, 50- *Awards:* BMI Publication Award, 46; Ditson Award, Columbia Univ, 46; Cert of Merit, Nat Asn Comp, 79. *Mem:* Music Libr Asn; Nat Asn Comp; Am Comp Alliance; BMI; Am Music Ctr. *Publ:* Auth, Music Theory (two vols), Oxford Univ Press, 61; Musical Form: Studies in Analysis and Synthesis, Houghton Mifflin, 76; Musical Composition: Projects in Ways and Means, Scarecrow Press, 80. *Mailing Add:* 8025 Highland Trail Los Angeles CA 90046

KOJIAN, MIRAN HAIG
VIOLIN, EDUCATOR
b Beirut, Lebanon, June 3, 40. *Study:* Paris Nat Consv, dipl, 56; Curtis Inst Music, MusB, 63; Cath Univ Am, with Henryk Szeryng, MusM, 64; studied with Ivan Galamian, five yrs, Lynn Talluel, two yrs & Jascha Heifetz, one yr. *Pos:* Mem, Cleveland Orch, 65-67; concertmaster, Kansas City Phil, 67-69; co-concertmaster, Nat Symph Orch, 69-; founder & first violinist, Nat Symph String Quartet. *Teaching:* Mem fac violin, Am Univ, 69-71 & currently; prof, Cath Univ Am, 69- *Awards:* First Prize, Paris Nat Consv, 56. *Mailing Add:* Nat Symph Orch Kennedy Ctr Washington DC 20566

KOJIAN, VARUJAN (HAIG)
CONDUCTOR & MUSIC DIRECTOR
b Beirut, Lebanon, Mar 12, 45; US citizen. *Study:* Paris Nat Conv, 53-56; Curtis Inst Music, dipl, 59; Univ Southern Calif, with Heifetz, 60-64. *Rec Perf:* Symphony No 2 & Armenian Suite (Yardumian), 81, Dante Symphony (Liszt), 81, Symphonie Fantastique (Berlioz), 82, Symphony No 3 & Tragic Overture (Brahms), 82 & Film Scores (Korngold & John Williams), 83, Varese-Sarabande. *Pos:* Asst concertmaster & asst cond, Los Angeles Phil, 65-71; prin guest cond, Royal Opera, Stockholm, 73-80; music dir, Utah Symph, 80-83 & Chautauqua Symph, 81- *Rep:* Colbert Artists Mgt 111 W 57th St New York NY 10019. *Mailing Add:* 241 N Vine St #1204E Salt Lake City UT 84103

KOLAR, HENRY
VIOLIN, CONDUCTOR
b Chicago, Ill, Dec 1, 23. *Study:* DePaul Univ, with Leon Stein, BMus, 48; Northwestern Univ, MMus, 49; Univ Colo, DMA, 70; Acad Music, Vienna, 61-62; studied with Robert Kurka & Alfred Uhl; Univ Southern Calif, with Ingolf Dahl. *Works:* Memorialis, comn by San Diego Symph, 58; Music for Brass, comn by Young Audiences Am, San Diego chap, 68; Divertimento (violin, horn & double bass); Rhapsody (cello & piano); Little Suite (two violins); Aphorisms (strings); String Quartet. *Pos:* Cond, Mesa Col Orch, formerly, San Diego Youth Symph, formerly, La Jolla Civic Orch, formerly & Univ San Diego Symph, currently; concertmaster, San Diego Symph, Sherwood Hall Orch, El Paso Symphonette & La Jolla Chamber Orch; mem, Mod Arts Quartet; violinist, Alcala Trio; guest cond, various music fests in southwest US. *Teaching:* Fac mem, San Diego Mesa Col, 66-70; prof music & chmn dept fine arts, Univ San Diego, 70- *Mem:* Am String Teachers Asn; Music Educr Nat Conf; ASCAP. *Mailing Add:* 4715 Glacier Ave San Diego CA 92120

KOLB, BARBARA
COMPOSER, EDUCATOR
b Hartford, Conn, Feb 10, 39. *Study:* Hartt Sch Music, BM, 61, MM, 64, with Arnold Franchetti, 57-64; Berkshire Music Ctr, with Gunther Schuller, 60, 64 & 68. *Works:* Solitaire (for piano & tape), 72, 1st version 75, 2nd version, 78, Homage to Keith Jarrett and Gary Burton, 76, Appello, 76, Songs Before An Adieu (for sop, flute, alto fl & guitar), 77-79, Grisaille (for orch), 79, The Point That Divides the Wind (for organ), 82, Boosey & Hawkes. *Pos:* Clarinetist, Hartford Symph Orch, 60-65. *Teaching:* Mem fac, Brooklyn Col, City Univ New York, 73-75; guest prof, Temple Univ, 78. *Awards:* Prix de Rome, 69-71; fels, Guggenheim Found, 72 & 76. *Mailing Add:* 41 W 72nd St New York NY 10023

KOLDOFSKY, GWENDOLYN
EDUCATOR, PIANO
Study: Studied with Viggo Kihl, Tobias Matthay, Harold Craxton & Marguerita Hasselmans. *Pos:* Accompanist. *Teaching:* Guest lectr, Univ BC, formerly, Univ Ore, formerly & Banff Ctr Fine Arts, formerly; mem fac, Music Acad West, currently; prof voice & accmp, Univ Southern Calif, currently. *Awards:* Simon Ramo Award, Friends of Music Award & Associates Award, 80, Univ Southern Calif. *Mailing Add:* 5268 Los Feliz Blvd Los Angeles CA 90027

KOLKER, PHILLIP A M
EDUCATOR, BASSOON
Study: Univ Rochester, AB; Eastman Sch Music, studied bassoon with K David Van Hoesen, perf cert, MM. *Pos:* Assoc prin bassoonist, Minn Orch, formerly, soloist, formerly; soloist, Baltimore Symph, formerly, Eastman-Rochester Orch, formerly & Orch Piccola, formerly; prin bassoonist, Milwaukee Symph Orch, formerly, Santa Fe Opera Orch, formerly, St Paul Opera Orch, formerly, Eastman Chamber Orch, formerly & Baltimore Symph Orch, 72-; baroque bassoon & renaissance winds performer, Pro Musica Rara, Baltimore, currently; mem, Mt Gretna Chamber Players, summers 75- *Teaching:* Mem fac bassoon, Eastman Sch Music, formerly, Univ Wis, Milwaukee, formerly, Univ Minn, formerly & Peabody Consv Music, 72- *Mailing Add:* 3505 Taney Rd Baltimore MD 21215

KOLODIN, IRVING
CRITIC-WRITER
b New York, NY, Feb 22, 08. *Study:* Inst Musical Art, 27-31. *Pos:* Mem staff, New York Sun, 32-50, assoc music critic, New Rec Column, 36-50, music ed & critic, 45-50; prog annotator, New York Phil Orch, 53-58; ed rec suppl, Saturday Rev, 47-, music ed, 50-52, assoc ed, 52-; contribr, Sunday ed, Newsday, Garden City, NY, 78-; vpres & ed, Nat Arts Group Ltd, New York. *Teaching:* Instr harmony & theory, Inst Musical Art, 30-31; lectr music criticism, Juilliard Summer Sch, 38 & 39; mem fac, Juilliard Sch, 68- *Publ:* Auth, Metropolitan Opera 1883-1966, 66; The Continuity of Music, 69; Interior Beethoven: A Biography of the Music, 74; The Opera Omnibus: Four Centuries of Critical Give and Take, 76; In Quest of Music, 80. *Mailing Add:* Saturday Rev 150 E 58th St New York NY 10155

KOMMEL, A MARGRET
EDUCATOR, SOPRANO
b Pittsburgh, Pa, Jan 19, 20. *Study:* Wittenberg Col, BME, 41, BM(voice), 43; Juilliard Grad Sch Music, dipl, 46; Ohio State Univ, MA(vocal pedagogy), 63. *Roles:* Contessa in The Marriage of Figaro, 62, Santuzza in Cavalleria rusticana, 63, Rosalinda in Die Fledermaus, 63, Mimi in La Boheme, 63, Cio-Cio-San in Madame Butterfly, 64, Nedda in Pagliacci, 64 & Violetta in La Traviata, 65, Springfield Civic Opera Co. *Pos:* Prod coordr, Ohio Lyr Theater Inc, Springfield, 83- *Teaching:* Prof music, Penn Hall Jr Col, 46-51; Muskingum Col, 51-53; Susquehanna Univ, 53-56 & Wittenberg Univ, 56-; prof voice, Chautauqua Sch Music, summers 46-55. *Mem:* Life mem, Sigma Alpha Iota; Am Asn Univ Women; Pi Kappa Lambda; Nat Asn Teachers Singing (nat secy, 70-79). *Mailing Add:* 3352 Flowerdale Rd Springfield OH 45504

KONDOROSSY, LESLIE
COMPOSER, CONDUCTOR & MUSIC DIRECTOR
b Pozsony (Bratislava), CSSR, June 25, 15; US citizen. *Study:* Franz Liszt Acad Music, Budapest, Hungary, comp & cond, 40; Western Reserve Univ, 59-64; Sophia Univ, Tokyo, Japan, summer 74. *Works:* The Voice (one act opera), Am New Opera Theater, 54; Son of Jesse (oratorio), comn by Oratorio Found, 67; Shizuka's Dance (children's opera), WBOE Radio Sta, Cleveland, 69; Kalamona and the Four Winds, 71, Meditation for Organ, 72 & Ammophila Arundinace (piano), 73, Hermes Music Publ; Ruth and Naomi (church opera), Church of Master, Cleveland, 74. *Pos:* Found & cond, New Am Opera Theater, Cleveland, 53-56; found & pres, Little Chamber Music Soc, 54-66; rep abroad, Radio WCLV Fine Art Sta, 66-70. *Teaching:* Music, 16 instrm, Cult Arts Bureau, Cleveland, 54-71; private instr piano, violin & clarinet, 71- *Awards:* Cult Decoration Medal, Hungarian World Fedn, Budapest, 68; Award, Martha Holden Jennings Found, Cleveland, 71. *Bibliog:* Rose Wilder (auth), Listener Always Knows It Is Kondorossy, Musical Courier, 3/58; Conrad H Rawski (auth), Brief Report on L Kondorossy, Musical Leader, 5/62. *Mem:* ASCAP; Am Music Ctr; Cent Opera Serv; Cleveland Fedn Musicians; Bibliot Int Musique Contemp, Paris. *Publ:* Contribr, Great Musicians and Little Stories, Calif Hungarian Life, 8/3/58; Was Haydn a Hungarian?, Fine Music, 11/8/58; Zoltan Kodaly, Hungarian Daily News, 3/19/67; Leslie Kondorossy Defends Modern Music, 12/1/72 & The Father of German Music, 2/2/73, Fine Arts, Cleveland. *Mailing Add:* 14443 E Carroll Blvd University Heights OH 44118

KONIKOW, ZALMAN
PATRON, ADMINISTRATOR
b Detroit, Mich, Feb 19, 24. *Study:* Wayne State Univ; Sch Dentistry, Univ Mich, DDS; Horace Rackum Sch Graduate Studies, MS. *Pos:* Pres, Chamber Music Soc Detroit, 67- *Awards:* Michiganian of Year, Detroit News, 83. *Mem:* Chamber Music Am. *Mailing Add:* 26635 Woodward Ave Huntington Woods MI 48070

KONO, TOSHIHIKO
CELLO
b Ashiya, Japan. *Study:* Kyoto Univ, Japan, LLB; Mannes Col Music; Stanford Univ; Berkshire Music Ctr; Kneisel Hall Sch; studied with Gaspar Cassado & Zara Nelsova. *Pos:* Co-prin cellist, New Orleans Phil, 67-68; cellist, Am Symph Orch, 68-; res artist, Acadia String Quartet, Bar Harbor, Maine Fest, 71-; prin cellist, Westchester Phil, 71-73; leader, Kono Trio, 77-; artistic dir, Mid-Summer Fest Chamber Music, Osaka, Japan, 81; perf with Kyoto Symph, Am Symph Orch In-Sch Concts, Little Orch Soc, Dr's Orch Soc NY, New York Ballet Orch, Manhattan Plaza Chamber Orch, Arcady Chamber Players, Oratorio Soc NY, St Cecilia Chorus & Orch & Naumburg Messiah Orch. *Teaching:* Fac mem music, Sch for Strings, New York, currently. *Awards:* Fromm Fel, Fest Contemp Music, Berkshire, 71. *Mem:* Assoc Musicians Gtr NY; Am Fedn Musicians; Violoncello Soc; Int Platform Asn. *Publ:* Coauth, Excitement of the New York Music World, Yomiuri News, Japan, 81. *Mailing Add:* 400 W 43rd St New York NY 10036

KONTOS, LYDIA G
ADMINISTRATOR
b New York, NY, May 21, 51. *Study:* Cath Univ Milan, Rome, cert, 67; Merton Col, Univ Oxford, cert, 68; Hunter Col, City Univ New York, BA, 72. *Pos:* Asst adminr, Hunter Col Conct Bureau, 68-73; independent consult pub relations, New York, 75-79; dir, Merkin Conct Hall, Hebrew Arts Sch, New York, 79- *Mailing Add:* 536 Main St Roosevelt Island NY 10044

KOOPER, KEES
VIOLIN, EDUCATOR
b Amsterdam, Netherlands. *Study:* Northwestern Univ, MMus, 52; Amsterdam Consv, dipl. *Rec Perf:* Profile Spain, Dot, 58; Intrada, 20th Century Fox, 59; Pixis Double Concerto, Vox-Turnabout, 74; Enesco-Bloch Sonatas, Golden Crest, 79; Violin Concerto (Mozart), 79, Violin Concerto (Tchaikowsky), 81 & Violin Concerto (Barber), 82, NOS. *Pos:* Concertmaster, Nashville Symph, 53-57 & Amsterdam Phil Orch, 76-; artist in res, Wesleyan Col, 57-60; violinist, New York String Sextet, 60-74 & Cremona Trio, 60-68. *Teaching:* Prof music, Peabody Consv, 53-57; lectr, New Sch Soc Res, New York, 63-76; assoc prof, Pace Univ, 67-76. *Awards:* Laureat, Queen Elizabeth Concours, 51. *Mem:* Am Fedn Musicians; Violin Soc Am. *Mailing Add:* 210 Riverside Dr New York NY 10025

KOPEC, PATINKA
VIOLA, VIOLIN
b Bratislava, Czeckoslovakia, May 14, 47; US citizen. *Study:* Juilliard Sch, BM, 69, MM, 71. *Pos:* Violinist, Jack Paar Show, 73-74; violist & violinist, solo & chamber music perf, currently; freelance commercials, rec & studio work. *Teaching:* Mem fac, Juilliard Sch, 71-73; Aspen Music Fest, 71-73; Philadelphia Musical Acad, 73-79 & NY Univ, 77-79; adj asst prof music, Queens Col, 73- & State Univ NY, Purchase, 75- *Mailing Add:* 131 Riverside Dr #4A New York NY 10024

KOPLEFF, FLORENCE
SINGER, EDUCATOR
b New York, NY, May 2, 24. *Rec Perf:* L'enfance du Christ (Berlioz); Ninth Symphony (Beethoven); Second Symphony (Mahler) & Pacem in Terris (Milhaud); rec with Robert Shaw Chorale. *Pos:* Soloist, Robert Shaw Chorale & leading US orchs; performer, recitals & oratorios; participant, maj music festivals. *Teaching:* Artist in res voice, Ga State Univ, currently. *Mem:* Life mem, Am Guild Musical Artists. *Mailing Add:* 1935 Ardmore Rd NW Atlanta GA 30309

KOPP, FREDERICK EDWARD
COMPOSER, CONDUCTOR
b Hamilton, Ill, Mar 21, 14. *Study:* Carthage Col, BA, 36; Univ Iowa, MA, 41; Eastman Sch Music, PhD, 57; studied with Pierre Monteux, Gustan Strube & Louis Hasselsmanns. *Works:* Terror Suite (wood wind, brass & perc), 69, Portrait of a Woman (flute & piano), 69 & October '55 (clarinet & string quartet), 70, Seesaw Music; Symphony No 1 in One Movement, 77, Symphony No 2 in A (young orch), 77, The Denial of St Peter, 77 & Dance Mass in Latin American Rythmns, 78, Pine Forest Music. *Rec Perf:* The Smile of Recife, Family Theatre, 63; The Creeping Terror, Metro Int Pictures, 65; Air Freight Specialist, Flying Tiger Airlines; Pepito, Pine Forest Music, 72; That Woman's Gotta Hang!!, Theatre Am, 71; It Came from Hollywood, Am Contemp Entertainment, Paramount Pictures, 80. *Pos:* Cond, Baton Rouge Symph, 46-48, Univ Ga Symph, 50-52 & Univ Symph, Calif State Univ, Los Angeles, 59-62; comp & cond, film studios, Hollywood, Calif, 62- *Teaching:* Assoc prof orch, theory & comp, Univ Ga, 50-52; Asst prof orch & theory, Calif State Univ, Los Angeles, 59-62; vis prof theory & comp, Southwestern La Col, 40-41, State Univ NY Col, Fredonia, 48-49 & Moorpark Col, 70-74. *Bibliog:* Stackhouse (auth), Styllistic Use of Folk Songs, Eastman Sch Music, 56. *Mem:* ASCAP; Am Fed Musicians. *Publ:* Auth, Something Like This Happens Every War, Great Western Publ, 81. *Mailing Add:* 102 N Garfield Pl #D Monrovia CA 91016

KOPP, JAMES B
LIBRARIAN, ADMINISTRATOR
b Macon, Ga, June 18, 53. *Study:* Duke Univ, AB, 75; Univ Pa, MA, 79, PhD, 82. *Pos:* Librn, Sch Music, Ga State Univ, 80- *Mem:* Int Asn for Study of Popular Music; Southeast Am Soc for Eighteenth-Century Studies. *Interests:* Eighteenth-century opera; 18th-century instrumental music; 20th-century popular American music. *Publ:* Auth, Theatrical Politics and the Drame Lyrique, Studies in Eighteenth-Century Culture, Univ Wis Press, 83. *Mailing Add:* Dept Music Ga State Univ Univ Plaza Atlanta GA 30303

KOPP, LEO LASZLO
CONDUCTOR & MUSIC DIRECTOR, EDUCATOR
b Budapest, Hungary, Oct 7, 06; US citizen. *Study:* With Leo Winer, Vincent d'Indy & Paul Gräner; Univ Pac, Hon MusD, 67. *Pos:* Cond opera & symph, Oldenburg Opera, 26, Königsberger Rundfunk, 28 & maj co in US incl Chicago, Milwaukee Florentine & St Paul; music dir, Lincoln Symph, Nebr. *Teaching:* Asst prof opera, Am Consv Music, currently. *Mem:* Hon mem, Lincoln Music Asn. *Mailing Add:* Am Consv Music 116 S Michigan Ave Chicago IL 60603

KORAS-BAIN, AGLAIA
PIANO
b San Francisco, Calif, Aug 13, 56. *Study:* Curtis Inst Music, study with Rudolf Serkin & M Horszowski, BMus, 79; Temple Univ, MMus, 81. *Pos:* Concert pianist, 81- *Teaching:* Fac mem piano & chamber music, Temple Univ, 78-80; fac mem piano, Philadelphia Col Perf Arts, 80. *Awards:* First Prize, Int Chopin Young Pianists Compt, 73 & Int Am Music Scholarship Asn Compt, 77; Fine Artistry & Musical Excellence, Conct Artists Guild, 82. *Mem:* Curtis Inst Music Alumni Asn. *Mailing Add:* c/o Robert McKutcheon 445 W 45th St New York NY 10036

KORDE, SHIRISH K
COMPOSER, EDUCATOR
b Kampala, Ugonda, June 18, 45. *Study:* Berklee Col Music, BM, 69; New England Consv, study with Robert Cogan & Ernest Oster, MM, 71; Brown Univ, PhD(cond), 76. *Works:* Spectra, 73, Constellations for Saxophone Quartet, 74 & Chamber Concerto, 80, Dorn Publ; String Quartet, comn by Groton Ctr Arts, 80; Spiral, comn by Kenneth Radnofsky, 82. *Teaching:* Instr, Berklee Col Music, 73-76; assoc prof, Col Holy Cross, 76-; vis prof, New England Consv, 79-81. *Awards:* Artist Fel, Mass Coun Arts, 79; Artist in Res, Mass Coun Arts, 80; Res Grant, Col Holy Cross, 82. *Mem:* Am Musicol Soc; Col Music Soc; Am Music Ctr. *Publ:* Auth, North Indian Alap—An Analytical Model, Sonus, spring 82. *Mailing Add:* 71 Maple St Acton MA 01720

KORET, ARTHUR (SOLOMON)
EDUCATOR, TENOR
b Hartford, Conn, Feb 20, 16. *Study:* Trinity Col, 34-36; studied with Wyllys Waterman, Oscar Seagle, Edward Gehrman & Adolph Katchko. *Roles:* Canio in I Pagliacci & Faust in Faust, 46, Colony Opera Guild. *Pos:* Soloist, Hartford Symph, Cleveland Orch & NBC Symph, 46-; cantor, Emanuel Synagogue, 48- *Teaching:* Vis prof voice, Hartt Sch Music, 54- *Awards:* Kavod Award, Cantors Assembly Am, 76. *Mailing Add:* Hartt Sch Music Univ Hartford West Hartford CT 06117

KORF, ANTHONY
COMPOSER, CONDUCTOR
b New York, NY, Dec 14, 51. *Study:* Manhattan Sch Music, BA, 73, MA, 75. *Works:* Symphonia, perf by New Amsterdam Symph Orch, 78; Double Take, perf by Parnassus, 80; A Farewell, perf by Group for Contemp Music, 80; Symph, comn by Am Comp Orch, Jerome Found, 82; Brass Quintet, Carl Fischer, 82; Oriole, comn by An Die Musik, 82. *Rec Perf:* Chamber Piece No 2 (Wolpe), 79, Pennplay (Davidovsky), 79, The Winds (Wuorinen), 79, Soundsoup (Lundborg), 79 & Octet (Olan), 79, RCA; Sextet (Mamlok), 80 & Paraphrases (Babbitt), 81, CRI. *Pos:* Dir, Parnassus, 74-; vpres bd, New Phil Orch, Riverside, currently. *Awards:* Grant, Am Music Ctr, 78 & 80; ASCAP Award, 79. *Mem:* Am Composers Alliance; Chamber Music Am; BMI. *Mailing Add:* 258 Riverside Dr New York NY 10025

KORMAN, JOAN
VIOLA, EDUCATOR
Study: Los Angeles Consv; Univ Calif, Los Angeles; studied violin with Lester Druckenmiller & Joachim Chassman. *Pos:* Mem, Giovanni String Quartet, formerly, Boston Ballet, formerly, Boston Opera, formerly, Univ Calif, Los Angeles Orch, formerly, Ojai Orch, Japan, formerly & Korman Duo, currently; soloist, Boston Pops, formerly, mem, formerly; soloist, St Louis Symph Orch, formerly, asst prin viola, currently. *Mailing Add:* St Louis Consv Music 560 Trinity Ave St Louis MO 63130

KORMAN, JOHN
VIOLIN, EDUCATOR
Study: Univ Calif, Los Angeles, violin with Jascha Heifetz, BSEE; Univ Southern Calif; studied violin with Eudice Shapiro. *Rec Perf:* On Vox. *Pos:* Mem, Giovanni String Quartet, formerly, Boston Symph Orch, formerly, Boston Sinfonietta, formerly, Los Angeles Phil Orch, formerly, Calif Chamber Symph, formerly & Korman Duo, currently; soloist, Aspen Fest Orch; soloist & mem, Boston Pops, formerly; soloist, St Louis Symph Orch, formerly, assoc concertmaster & Louis D Beaumont chair, currently. *Mailing Add:* St Louis Consv Music 560 Trinity Ave St Louis MO 63130

KORN, MITCHELL
COMPOSER, 12-STRING GUITAR
b New York, NY, Jan 3, 52. *Study:* Calif Inst Arts, BA, 71; Bard Col, BA, 73. *Works:* Minerals & Gems, 77, Ebflo, 80 & Episodic Footfalls, 81, M Koon Ens. *Rec Perf:* The Natural Sciences, OBM Network Rec, 83. *Pos:* Artistic dir & comp in res, New York, 80- *Awards:* Conct Artist of Yr, Netherland Conct Asn, 79; Hadassah Myrtle Wreath in Arts, 81. *Mem:* ASCAP; Affil Artists. *Mailing Add:* 88 University Pl New York NY 10003

KORN, PETER JONA
COMPOSER, MUSIC DIRECTOR
b Berlin, Germany, Mar 30, 22; US & German citizen. *Study:* Jerusalem Consv, with Stefan Wolpe, 36-38; Univ Calif, Los Angeles, with Arnold Schönberg, 41-42; Univ Southern Calif, with Ernst Toch & Hanns Eisler, 46-47. *Works:* Beggars Opera Variations, 55 & Third Symphony, 57, Simrock; Exorcism of a Liszt Fragment, 72, Eine kleine Popmusik, 74, Heidi in Frankfurt (opera), 78 & Beckmesser Variations, 79, Schuberth; Trumpet Concerto, Nymphenburg, 80. *Pos:* Dir, Richard-Strauss Consv, Munich, 67- *Teaching:* Instr comp, Trapp Consv, Munich, 60-61; vis lectr, Univ Calif, Los Angeles, 64 & 65. *Awards:* F H Beebe Fund Award, 56 & 57; Hartford Found Fel, 56, 57 & 61; Munich Music Award, 68. *Mem:* Deutscher Komponistenverband (vpres, 82-); Gesellschaft Musikalische Auffuhrung (mem bd, 77-); Richard-Strauss-Gesellschaft Munich (vchmn, 78-); Orff-Schulwerk-Gesellschaft Munich (vchmn, 76-); ASCAP. *Publ:* Auth, The Changing of the (Avant-) Garde, Saturday Rev, 59; Diary of a Young Man of Fashion, High Fidelity, 66; coauth, The Symphony, In: Symphony in America, Penguin, 67; auth, Musikalische Umweltverschmutzung, Breitkopf & Härtel, 75; Wenn die Ohren Trauer tragen, Playboy, Germany, 80. *Mailing Add:* Gabriel-Max-Str 9 D-8000 Munich 90 Germany, Federal Republic of

KOROMZAY, DENES KORNEL
VIOLA, EDUCATOR
b Budapest, Hungary, May 18, 13; US citizen. *Study:* Royal Franz Liszt Acad Music, Budapest, MA, 30; Hochschule Musik, Berlin, with Carl Flesch, MA, 34. *Rec Perf:* Six Quartets (Bartok), DGG, 62; 16 String Quartets (Beethoven), 65 & Late Quartets (Schubert), 68, EMI; Six Quartets (Bartok), Vox, 76. *Pos:* Violist, Hungarian String Quartet, 35-72 & New Hungarian String Quartet, 72-79. *Teaching:* Prof viola & chamber music, Consv Music, Oberlin Col, 72-79; adj prof viola & chamber music, Univ Colo, Boulder, 79-; lectr viola & chamber music, Banff Ctr, Alta, 79- *Awards:* Bartok Centennial Plaque & Dipl, 82; Kodaly Centennial Plaque & Dipl, 83. *Mailing Add:* 711 Lincoln Pl Boulder CO 80302

KORTE, KARL RICHARD
COMPOSER, EDUCATOR
b Ossining, NY, Aug 25, 28. *Study:* Juilliard Sch, with Peter Mennin, BS, 53, with Vincent Persichetti, MS, 56; study comp with Otto Luening & Aaron Copland. *Works:* Matrix (woodwind quintet, piano & perc), comn by New York Woodwind Quintet, 68; Remembrances (flute & tape), 71 & Pale is This Good Prince (oratorio), 73, Elkan-Vogel Co; Concerto for Piano & Winds, E C Schirmer Co, 76; Trio (piano, violin & vocal), Voices of Change, 82; Double Concerto (flute, double bass & comput tape), B Turtezky, 83. *Teaching:* Asst prof, Ariz State Univ, 63-64; assoc prof music, State Univ NY, Binghamton, 64-71; prof comp, Univ Tex, Austin, 71- *Awards:* Fels, Guggenheim Found, 60 & 70 & Nat Endowment Arts, 75 & 78; Gold Medal, Queen Elizabeth Int, 70. *Mem:* Meet the Comp (Tex pres, 81-). *Mailing Add:* Music Dept Univ Tex Austin TX 78712

KORTH, THOMAS A
TEACHER, COMPOSER
b Philadelphia, Pa, Aug 13, 43. *Study:* Howard Univ, MusB, 66, MM, 68; Univ Md, DMA, 75. *Works:* Disparities II (sax & tape), Miller Signom, Bordeaux, France, 74; These, Howard Univ Women's Choir, 77; Five Pieces for Bass Clarinet & Piano, Lawrence Bocaner, 83. *Teaching:* Assoc prof theory & comp, Howard Univ, Wash DC, 71- *Mem:* Am Fedn Musicians; Am Asn Univ Comp; Col Music Soc. *Mailing Add:* 11418 Pitsea Dr Beltsville MD 20705

KOSCIELNY, ANNE
PIANO
b Tallahassee, Fla, May 12, 36. *Study:* Eastman Sch Music, BM, 58; Vienna Acad Music, 58-60; Manhattan Sch Music, MM, 65. *Teaching:* Assoc prof piano, Hartt Col Music, Univ Hartford, 64-; artist fac, Taos Sch Music, 69-81. *Awards:* First Prize, Rec Compt, Nat Guild Piano Teachers, 54; Kosciuszko Chopin First Prize, New York, 57; Fulbright Scholar, Int Inst Educ, 58. *Mailing Add:* 200 Bloomfield Ave West Hartford CT 06117

KOSLOFF, DORIS LANG
MUSIC DIRECTOR, COACH
b Brooklyn, NY. *Study:* Queens Col, City Univ New York, BA, 67; Sch Fine & Applied Arts, Boston Univ, MM, 69. *Pos:* Prin coach, Wolf Trap Farm Park Perf Arts, 70-72; music dir, Opera Express, Hartford, Conn, 76-; music adminr, Conn Opera, Hartford, 80-82, music dir, 82- *Teaching:* Instr opera, Hartt Col Music, Univ Hartford, 74-76. *Mem:* Am Guild Musical Artists. *Publ:* Auth, The American Woman Conductor—A Personal Perspective, In: American Women in Music, Greenwood Press, 83. *Mailing Add:* 7 Hampshire Lane Simsbury CT 06070

KOSOWICZ, FRANCIS JOHN
ORGAN, CLAVICHORD
b Lowell, Mass, July 20, 46. *Study:* Pius X Sch Liturgical Music; Manhattanville Col; Iona Col; Univ Mass; Amherst Col; studied with Charles A McGrail, E Power Biggs, Edgar Hilliar, Richard Casper, Walter Ehret & Vincent Perischetti. *Works:* Wedding, 67 & 70; Carillon Snow Piece, Alastair Beattie, 73; Imperial Suite (organ, flute, electronic gear & oriental dancer), F J Kosowicz, Deborah Ortlip & Marietta Cheng, 74. *Rec Perf:* Bermuda Cathedral Thanksgiving Day Service, ZBM & ZFB Studios, Hamilton, Bermuda, 67. *Pos:* Organist, St Catherine's Church, Graniteville, Mass, 59-64, Chapel of Peace, King's Pt, Bermuda, 65-66 & Holy Trinity Chapel, Gia Le, Vietnam, 67-68; artist in res, Abbey of the Holy Ghost, Conyers, Ga, 65; founder, Roane Arts & Humanities Coun Inc, Spencer, WVa, 77; consult, US Dept Defense, Washington, DC, 72-74; solo organist, La Sonora Tecolutla, Veracruz, Mex, 75-76. *Awards:* Performer of Yr, Conciertos Guadalajara, Mex, 80. *Bibliog:* David Greenburg (auth), State Page, Charleston Newspapers, 78. *Mem:* Am Guild Organists (state chmn, 80-); Am Musicol Soc; Organ Hist Soc. *Publ:* Co-ed, Book of Worship for the US Forces, US Govt Printing Off, 74; auth, Bruce Shull Organ, Op 1, WVa Arts News, 79; Pipings, Recitals, 80 & The Clavichord, 83, Am Organist. *Mailing Add:* 13C Harmony Rte Spencer WV 25276

KOTIK, PETR
COMPOSER, FLUTE
b Prague, Czechoslovakia, Jan 27, 42; US citizen. *Study:* Prague Consv Music, BA(flute), 61; Music Acad, Vienna, MA(flute, comp), 66; Music Acad, Prague, MA(flute), 69. *Works:* Music For Three, Universal Ed, Vienna, 64; John Mary, perf by SEM Ens, 74-78; Many Many Women, Labor Rec, 76-; Explorations, 78-81 & Solos and Incidental Harmonies, 83, SEM Ens. *Rec Perf:* Solo Flute Music by P Kotik, Cramps Rec, 76; Many Many Women, Labor Rec, 81. *Pos:* Creative assoc, Ctr Creative & Perf Arts, State Univ NY, Buffalo, 69-74; artistic dir, SEM Ens, 70- *Teaching:* Instr flute & comp, State Univ NY, Buffalo, 73-77; instr comp, York Univ, Toronto, 75-76. *Awards:* Spec Prize, Gaudeamus Compt, Holland, 65; Nat Endowment Arts Comp Grant, 75. *Mailing Add:* 230 14th St Brooklyn NY 11215

KOTTICK, EDWARD LEON
EDUCATOR, INSTRUMENT MAKER
b Jersey City, NJ, June 16, 30. *Study:* NY Univ, with Martin Bernstein & Gustave Reese, BA, 53; Tulane Univ, with Gwynn McPeek, MA, 59; Univ NC, with Glen Haydon, PhD, 62. *Teaching:* Asst prof, Alma Col, 62-65; vis prof, Univ Kans, 65-66; assoc prof, Univ Mo, St Louis, 66-68; Univ Iowa, 68- *Publ:* Auth, The Chansonnier Cordiforme, J Am Music Soc, 67; The Unica in the Chansonnier Cordiform, Am Inst Musicol Rome, 67; Flats, Modality & Musica Ficta, J Music Theory, 68; Tone & Intonation on the Recorder, McGinnis & Marx, 74; The Collegium: A Handbook, Oct House, 77. *Mailing Add:* 2001 Muscatine Iowa City IA 52240

KOUT, TRIX
FLUTE, RECORDER
Study: San Jose State Col, BA, New England Consv, MM, artists dipl; Boston Univ; studied flute with Katherine Sorensen, Wayne Sorensen & James Pappoutsakis. *Rec Perf:* On CRI. *Pos:* Perf with Cabrillo Music Fest & Am Wind Symph Orch; concerts throughout New England. *Awards:* Fac mem flute & recorder, Longy Sch Music, currently. *Awards:* Fel, Berkshire Music Ctr & Yale Music, Norfolk; Radcliffe Inst Grant. *Mailing Add:* Longy Sch Music One Follen St Cambridge MA 02138

KOVALENKO, OLEG IVANOVITCH
CONDUCTOR
b Kiev, Ukraine, USSR, July 7, 36. *Study:* Univ Calif, BA, 59; Stanford Univ, MA, 60. *Pos:* Asst cond, St Louis Symph, 63-66 & Indianapolis Symph, 72-75; guest cond, Chicago Symph, Dallas Symph & Baltimore Symph. *Awards:* Ella Lyman Cabot Trust Fel, Boston, 62. *Mailing Add:* c/o Calif Artists Mgt 23 Liberty St San Francisco CA 94110

KOWALKE, KIM H
MUSICOLOGIST, CONDUCTOR & MUSIC DIRECTOR
b Monticello, Minn, June 25, 48. *Study:* Macalester Col, BA, 70; Dept Music, Yale Univ, with Allen Forte, Robert Bailey & Leon Plantinga, MA, 71, MPh, 74, PhD, 77. *Pos:* Pres, Kurt Weill Found Music, 81- *Teaching:* Asst prof music, Occidental Col, 77-82, assoc prof, 82- *Mem:* Am Musicol Soc; Col Music Soc; Sonneck Soc. *Interests:* Kurt Weill; 19th and 20th century opera; American musical theater. *Publ:* Auth, Kurt Weill in Europe, UMI Res Press, 79; Kurt Weill: Composer Without a Category, Opera, 80; Reflections on the Silver Lake, 80 & Recollections of Forgotten Songs, 81, Nonesuch; Reviews in Notes, Am Music & Musical Quart. *Mailing Add:* Dept Music Occidental Col Los Angeles CA 90042

KRABER, KARL
FLUTE, EDUCATOR
b New York, NY. *Study:* Harvard Col, AB(music), 58; Consv Santa Cecilia, Rome, Italy, 59-61; studied flute with Pappoutsakis, Gazzelloni, Rampal & Moyse. *Rec Perf:* Works by Starer, Gaber, Moss, Stearn, Davidovsky & Fennelly, CRI Rec, 72; French Woodwind Music, Vox Turnabout, 72; Avant-Garde Woodwind Music, Vox Box, 74. *Pos:* Flutist, Dorian Wind Quintet, 65-, Aeolian Chamber Players, 65-68 & 74-76 & New York Chamber Soloists, 70-75. *Teaching:* Prof flute, Brooklyn Col, 68-; instr flute & chamber music, Mannes Col Music, 72-; vis prof flute, Ind Univ, Bloomington, 80-81 & Oberlin Consv, 83; vis assoc prof, Univ Tex, Austin, currently. *Awards:* Fulbright Grant to Italy, 59-61; Nat Endowment Arts Solo Recitalist Fel, 83. *Mem:* New York Flute Club (bd mem, 73-75); Nat Flute Asn (bd mem, 77-79); Am Fedn Musicians. *Mailing Add:* 160 W 87th St New York NY 10024

KRACHMALNICK, SAMUEL
CONDUCTOR

b St Louis, Mo, Sept 1, 28. *Study:* Juilliard Sch Music, with Jean Morel. *Pos:* French horn, Nat Symph Orch, formerly; cond, maj orch in Can, Italy, Mex, Switz, US & SAm. *Teaching:* Sr lectr & dir orch & opera, Univ Calif, Los Angeles, currently. *Awards:* Koussevitzky Mem Prize; Mann Prize. *Mailing Add:* Music Dept Univ Calif Los Angeles CA 90024

KRAFT, LEO ABRAHAM
COMPOSER, EDUCATOR

b New York, NY, July 24, 22. *Study:* Queens Col, BA, 45; Princeton Univ, MFA, 47. *Works:* Partita #4, perf by New England Consv, 75; Dialectica (four instrm), Da Capo Chamber Players, Baltimore, 78. *Rec Perf:* Concerto #3 for Cello, Wind Quintet & Percussion, Partita #3 for Wind Quintet & Trios and Interludes, Flute, Viola, Piano ..., Serenus; Spring in the Arbor, Chamber Cycle for Soprano, Flute, Cello, Piano & Dialogues for Flute and Tape, CRI; Line Drawings, Flute & Percussion, Opus One Rec. *Teaching:* Prof harmony & counterpoint, Aaron Copland Sch Music, 47- *Awards:* Fulbright Fel, 54; ASCAP Awards, 61- *Mem:* League Comp, Int Soc Contemp Music; Am Music Ctr (pres, 76-79); Soc Music Theory (mem bd, 78-79); Col Music Soc. *Publ:* Auth, A New Approach to Ear Training, 67 & 71, Gradus, An Integrated Approach to Harmony, Counterpoint & Analysis, 76, coauth, A New Approach to Sight Singing, rev ed, 76 & ed, A New Approach to Keyboard Harmony, 78, Norton. *Mailing Add:* 9 Dunster Rd Great Neck NY 11021

KRAFT, WILLIAM
COMPOSER, EDUCATOR

b Chicago, Ill, Sept 6, 23. *Study:* Columbia Univ, BS(music), 51, MA(comp), 54; private perc study with Morris Goldenberg & timpani with Saul Goodman. *Works:* Concerto (4 perc soloists & orch), 64 & Contextures: Riots-Decade 860, 67, Piano Concerto, 72 & Tuba Concerto, 75, Los Angeles Phil; The Sublime and the Beautiful, perf by Collage, 79; Triple Play, Los Angeles Phil, 82; Double Play, St Paul Chamber Orch, 82. *Pos:* Perc, Los Angeles Phil, 55-63, prin timpanist & perc, 63-81; musical dir, Los Angeles Perc Ens & Chamber Players, 56- & Young Musicians Found & Debut Orch, 70-72; comp in res & dir, Los Angeles Phil, 81-84 & New Music Group, Meet The Comp, 82-84. *Teaching:* Lectr comp, Calif Inst Arts, 71-72 ; vis prof comp, Univ Southern Calif, 77-78. *Awards:* Fel, Huntington Hartford, 64 & Guggenheim, 67 & 72; Res Scholar, Rockefeller Found, Bellagio, Italy, 73. *Bibliog:* A Cohn (auth), The True Essence of Percussion, Am Rec Guide, 7/69; D W M (auth), Rather Delightfully Wild-The Music of William Kraft, Am Rec Guide, 5/71; C Eisner (auth), Percussion is Music to his Ears, Wis State J, 2/18/78. *Mem:* Am Music Ctr (bd dir, 77); Int Soc Contemp Comp (chmn bd, 73-); ASCAP (bd rev, 82-). *Publ:* Auth, Don't Call My Moneymakers Noisemakers, Los Angeles Times, 59; The Complete Percussionist, Ludwig Drummer, 64; Article, KPFK Folio, 71; Three Places in Old Europe, Los Angeles Times, 72. *Rep:* New Music West Publishers PO Box 7434 Van Nuys CA 91409. *Mailing Add:* c/o Los Angeles Phil Asn 135 N Grand Ave Los Angeles CA 90012

KRAJEWSKI, MICHAEL
CONDUCTOR & MUSIC DIRECTOR

b Detroit, Mich, July 7, 50. *Study:* Wayne State Univ, BS(music ed), 72; Col Consv Music, Univ Cincinnati, MM(cond), 77. *Pos:* Dorati fel cond, Detroit Symph Orch, 79-80, asst cond, 82-; artist intern, Mich Opera Theatre, 81; music dir, St Clair Shores Symph Orch, 82- *Mem:* Cond Guild of the Am Symph Orch League. *Mailing Add:* 614 Chrysler Dr Apt 204 Detroit MI 48207

KRAKAUER, DAVID
CLARINET

b New York, NY, Sept 22, 56. *Study:* Sarah Lawrence Col, BA, 78; Paris Consv, 76-77; Juilliard Sch, with Leon Russianoff, MM, 80. *Rec Perf:* From Here on Farther (Stefan Wolpe), Nonesuch Rec, 82; Clarinet Trio (Richard Wilson), Opus One Rec, 83. *Pos:* Participant, Marlboro Music Fest, 78-79 & Music from Marlboro Tours, 80-81; prin clarinet, New Haven Symph, 79-; mem, Aspen Wind Quintet, 81-; clarinetist, Continuum, 81- & S E M Ens, 82-; guest mem, New York Philomusica, 82- *Teaching:* Lectr clarinet, Vassar Col, 83; coach chamber music, Aspen Music Fest, 83. *Awards:* Second Prize, Nat Clarinet Compt, Denver, 74. *Mailing Add:* 225 W 80th New York NY 10024

KRAMER, BRUCE
BASS

b San Francisco. *Study:* Univ Calif, Berkeley, BA, 75; Eastman Sch Music, MM, 77. *Roles:* Figaro in The Marriage of Figaro, Midwest Opera Theater, 80 & Wolf Trap, 81; Colline in La Boheme, Annapolis Opera Co, 82; Ferrando in Il Trovatore, Opera Theater Rochester, 83; Sparafucile in Rigoletto, Glimmerglass Opera Theater, 83. *Pos:* Apprentice artist, Central City Opera, 77 & Lake George Opera, 78; mem, Minn Opera Studio, 79-80. *Awards:* Winner, Am Opera Auditions, 80. *Rep:* Kazuko Hillyer Int 250 W 57 New York NY 10107. *Mailing Add:* 207 W 106 New York NY 10025

KRAMER, GREGORY PAUL
COMPOSER, ELECTRONIC

b Los Angeles, Calif, Oct 14, 52. *Study:* Calif Inst Arts, BFA(comp), 72; NY Univ, MA(comp), 77. *Works:* Role, Views Prod, 72; Monologue, private publ, 77; Lullabye for Gregory in Canada, Border Music, 79; Veils of Transformation, Horton Music, 80; Blue Wave, Kazuko Oshima, 81; Pointed Moment, Electronic Arts Ens, 82. *Rec Perf:* Inquietude, Inquietude II, Cauldron, Hudson, Three Beasts Set Out & Sentenced (with interruptions), GK Studio, 81-82. *Pos:* Dir, Electronic Arts Ens, 75-83; co-founder, Pub

Access Synthesizer Studio, 77. *Teaching:* Adj asst prof comput & synthesizer tech, NY Univ, 75-79. *Awards:* Comp Fel, Nat Endowment for Arts, 80; Golden Circuit, World Electronic Music Soc, 83. *Mem:* Harvestworks Inc (mem bd, currently). *Mailing Add:* Nelson Ln Garrison NY 10524

KRAMER, JONATHAN D(ONALD)
COMPOSER, WRITER

b Hartford, Conn, Dec 7, 42. *Study:* Harvard Univ, BA, 65; Univ Calif, Berkeley, MA, 67, PhD, 69; Stanford Univ, 68. *Works:* Canons of Blackearth, Opus One Rec, 73; Renascence for Clarinet & Tape, G Schirmer, 74; Moving Music for 13 Clarinets, perf by Phillip Rehfeldt, Melvin Warner, L McDonald & K Wilson, 76; Five Studies on Six Notes, Opus One Rec, 80; Music for Piano, No 5, Orion, 80; No Beginning, No End, perf by Cincinnati Chamber Orch & Chorus, 83; Moments In and Out of Time, G Schirmer, 83. *Pos:* Program annotator, Cincinnati Symph Orch, 80- *Teaching:* Asst prof theory, Oberlin Consv, 70-71 & Yale Univ, 71-78; prof comp & theory, Col Consv Music, Univ Cincinnati, 78- *Awards:* Int Rostrum comp, Nat Pub Radio—UN Educ Sci & Cult Orgn, 83; grants, Nat Endowment Arts, Nat Endowment Humanities, Martha Baird Rockefeller Fund & others. *Bibliog:* Judy Lochhead (auth), When Are Ends Beginnings, In Theory Only, 82. *Mem:* Cincinnati Comp Guild (chmn adv bd, 80-); Nat Asn Comp USA (mem nat coun, 78-); Soc Music Theory; Am Soc Univ Comp; Int Soc Study Time. *Publ:* Auth, Multiple and Nonlinear Time in Beethoven's Opus 135, Perspectives New Music, 73; The Fibonacci Series in 20th Century Music, J Music Theory, 73; Moment Form in Twentieth Century Music, Musical Quart, 78; New Temporalities in Music, Critical Inquiry, 81; Beginnings and Endings in Western Art Music, Can Music Rev, 82. *Mailing Add:* Col Consv Music Univ Cincinnati Cincinnati OH 45221

KRANZ, MARIA HINRICHS
EDUCATOR, PIANO

b Melrose Park, Ill. *Study:* Am Consv Music, MMus, 52. *Teaching:* Chmn sec piano, Am Consv Music, 76- *Mailing Add:* Am Consv Music 116 S Michigan Ave Chicago IL 60603

KRAPF, GERHARD W
ORGAN, COMPOSER

Meissenheim, Ger, Dec 12, 24; US citizen. *Study:* Musikhochschule, Karlsruhe, Ger, dipl, 50; Univ Redlands, Calif, MMus, 51. *Works:* Easter Antiphon (SATB & brass), 64 & Partita Mit Freuden Zart (organ), 65, Concordia Publ House; Little Organ Psalter, Carl Fischer, 71; Easter Salutation (SATB, brass & organ), Belwin Mills, 80; A New Song (organ), SMP, 81; Psalm 90 (SATB a cappella), Augsburg Publ House, 81; Psalm 148 (SATB, brass & organ), Heritage Press, 83. *Rec Perf:* The Tracker Organ at Iowa (disc), Univ Iowa Press, 73; A Sound Story (video tape), Univ Alberta Dept Radio & TV, 79. *Pos:* Regional church music supvr, Synod of Baden Protestant Church, Ger, 51-53. *Teaching:* Asst prof organ & theory, Univ Wyo, Laramie, 55-61; prof organ, Univ Iowa, 61-77; prof organ & church music, Univ Alberta, Can, 77- *Bibliog:* Donald Johns (auth), Composers for the Church: Gerhard Krapf, Church Music, 74. *Mem:* Int Heinrich Schütz Soc; Joh Nep David Soc; Music Libr Asn; Royal Can Col Organists; Am Hymn Soc. *Interests:* Organ; church music; performance practice. *Publ:* Auth, Organ Improvisation: A Practical Approach to Chorale Elaborations for the Service, Augsburg Publ House, 67; transl, H Klotz, The Organ Handbook, Concordia Publ House, 69; Werckmeister's ... Orgelprobe of 1698, Sunburg Press, 76; contribr, The Reformation Tradition, Church Music History, In: Key Words in Church Music, Condordia Publ House, 78; auth, Bach: Improvised Ornamentation and Keyboard Cadenzas, SMP, 83. *Mailing Add:* 11704 43rd Ave Edmonton AB T6J 0Y7 Canada

KRASNER, LOUIS
CONDUCTOR, EDUCATOR

b USSR. *Study:* New England Consv Music, with Eugene Gruenberg, teacher dipl & soloist dipl; studied with Carl Flesch, Lucien Capet & Sevcik, Europe; New England Consv Music, Hon Dr Music, 81. *Rec Perf:* Berg & Schoenberg Concertos, Columbia LP. *Pos:* Concertmaster, Minneapolis Orch, 44-49 & Syracuse Symph Orch, 60-68; cond, Syracuse Univ Orch, 60- *Teaching:* Prof violin & chamber music, Syracuse Univ, 49-71, emer prof, 71-; summer fac, Am Fedn Music Inst Cong Strings, PR & Mich State Univ, 60-65 & 71; Regent's lectr, Univ Calif, La Jolla, 71; fac, Cong Strings, Univ Southern Calif, Los Angeles, summer 72; lectr, Harvard Univ, Princeton Univ, Hartt Col, Johns Hopkins Univ, Yale Univ & Univ Minn, 78-79; mem fac, Berkshire Music Ctr, currently. *Awards:* Gov Award for Excellence in Arts, State of RI, 68; Distinguished Serv Award, Am String Teachers Asn, 83; Samuel Simons Sanford Award, Yale Univ, 83. *Mem:* Hon mem, Acad Filarmonica, Bologna, Italy; Col Music Soc; Int Alban Berg Soc (vpres, 83). *Publ:* Ed, String Problems, Players and Paucity, Berkshire Music Ctr, 65; auth, In Consideration of the Creative Arts: Aesthetics Without Art, Music J, 2/66; Cross-Fertilization of Conservatory and College on the American Campus: A Point of View, Col Music Symposium, fall 67; A Performance History of Schoenberg's Violin Concerto, J Arnold Schoenberg Inst, 2/78; The Vienna Premiere of the Alban Berg Violin Concerto, Int Alban Berg Soc Newsletter, fall 80. *Mailing Add:* New England Consv 290 Huntington Rd Boston MA 02115

KRATZER, DENNIS LEON
CONDUCTOR, EDUCATOR

b Bowling Green, Ohio, Sept 21, 48. *Study:* Bowling Green State Univ, BM, 71, MM, 73; Ohio State Univ, currently. *Rec Perf:* 1964 All Ohio Youth Choir, Coronet Rec Co, 64; 1966 All Ohio Youth Choir, Hi Fidelity Rec, 66; Collegiate Chorale & Orchestra, Century Rec Corp, 68; Faure

Requiem—King David Choir, Rec Publ Co, 71; Musical Portraits, Toledo Museum Art, 73; Otterbein Col Conct Choir, Coronet Rec Studio, 77; Christmastide, WMC Prod, 78. *Pos:* Dir music, Worthington United Presby Church, Ohio, 75-; cond & musical dir, Kenely Players, 80- & Cantari Prof Choir, 82- *Teaching:* Dir choral activ, Ohio Northern Univ, 73-75 & 79- & Otterbein Col, 75-79. *Mem:* Music Educ Nat Conf; Nat Asn Teachers Singing; Am Choral Dir Asn; Am Fedn Musicians; Phi Mu Alpha Sinfonia (vpres, 70 & pres, 71). *Mailing Add:* 5247 Valley Lane East Columbus OH 43229

KRAUS, LILI (LILI KRAUS MANDL)
PIANO, TEACHER
b Budapest, Hungary, Mar 4, 08; New Zealand citizen. *Study:* Royal Acad Music, Budapest, dipl, 25; Vienna Consv Music, 27; studied with Bela Bartok, Zoltan Kodaly & Arthur Schnabel; Chicago Musical Col, Hon Dr; Tex Christian Univ, LHD; Williams Col, Hon MusD. *Rec Perf:* Grazer Fantasie (Schubert), 69 & The Complete Piano Concerti (Mozart), 73, CBS Masterworks; Lili Kraus Plays Fantasies & Sonatas (Schubert), Vanguard Rec; Sonatas (Mozart), Odyssey Rec. *Pos:* Concert pianist & partner, Kraus-Goldberg Duo, appearing in recitals & with major orchestras throughout the world, 25- *Teaching:* Artist in res, Tex Christian Univ, 67-83; conduct piano master classes in universities throughout the world. *Awards:* Cross of Honor for Sci & Art, Fed Repub Austria. *Mem:* Music Teachers Asn Calif; Sigma Alpha Theta. *Publ:* Ed, The Complete Original Cadenzas by W A Mozart, 71. *Mailing Add:* c/o Alix B Williamson 1860 Broadway New York NY 10023

KRAUS, PHILIP ARTHUR
DIRECTOR—OPERA, BARITONE
b New York, NY, Nov 17, 50. *Study:* Northwestern Univ, BME, 72, MM, 74. *Rec Perf:* Fidelio (Beethoven), Decca, London. *Roles:* Gianni Schicchi in Gianni Schicchi, Light Opera Works, 82 & Hinsdale Opera Theater; Vicar in Albert Herring, Taddeo in Italian Girl in Algiers & Don Alfonso in Cosi fan tutte, Chicago Opera Theater; The Witch in Hansel & Gretel, WTTW TV; Prisoner in Fidelio & Nachtigal in Die Meistersinger, Chicago Symph Orch. *Pos:* Artistic dir, Light Opera Works, Evanston, Ill, 79-; staged, HMS Pinafore, 81, Orpheus in the Underworld, 81, Die Schöne Galathee, 82, Gianni Schicchi, 82, Candide, 82, Pirates of Penzance 83 & Ariadne auf Naxos, 83. *Teaching:* Prof opera, Sch Music, DePaul Univ, 82- *Awards:* Louis Sudler Award for Excellence in Oratorio; Cramer Award for Excellence in Opera. *Mailing Add:* 9418 Kedvale Ave Skokie IL 60076

KRAUSE, ROBERT JAMES
EDUCATOR, OBOE & ENGLISH HORN
b Milwaukee, Wis, July 1, 43. *Study:* Univ Miami, with Julien Balogh, BMus, 65, MMus, 67, DMA, 81. *Pos:* English hornist, Ft Lauderdale Symph & Miami Phil, 66-67; prin oboist, Roswell Symph, Roswell, NMex, 67-68, Natchitoches-Northwestern Symph, Natchitoches, La, 68-73 & Amarillo Symph, Amarillo, Tex, 73- *Teaching:* Assoc prof oboe & theory, WTex State Univ, 73-; instr oboe, Nat Music Camp, Interlochen, Mich, 78- *Awards:* Am Guild Musical Artists Award, 65. *Mem:* Phi Mu Alpha (fac adv, 75-); Nat Asn Col Wind & Perc Instr; Int Double Reed Soc. *Mailing Add:* 522 12th Ave Canyon TX 79015

KRAUSS, ANNE McCLENNY
PIANO, EDUCATOR
b Suffolk, Va, Mar 26, 21. *Study:* Hollins Col, AB, 43; Teachers Col, Columbia Univ, MA, 47; Harvard Univ Summer Sch, studied music hist with Donald Grout, 55. *Rec Perf:* Instrumental Music in Early America, Soc Preserv Am Musical Heritage, 66. *Pos:* Pres & founder, Blue Ridge Chamber Music Players, 60-62. *Teaching:* Assoc prof music hist & piano, Hollins Col, 47-71. *Mem:* Va Music Teachers Asn (vpres, 70-71, pres Highlands chap, 81-83); Sonneck Soc. *Interests:* Life of Alexander Reinagle and early American keyboard music. *Publ:* Auth, Reinagle, Alexander—His Teaching in Glasgow, Am Music Teacher, 69; co-ed, Collection of Early American Keyboard Music, Willis, 71; Scots Tunes & Variations by A Reinale, Hinshaw, 75; auth, Reinagle, Alexander—Teaching Pieces He Wrote in America, Clavier, 76; co-ed, Dances of the Young Republic, Hinshaw, 77. *Mailing Add:* 1014 Highland Circle Blacksburg VA 24060

KRAUT, HARRY JOHN
ARTIST MANAGER & REPRESENTATIVE
b Brooklyn, NY, Apr 11, 33. *Study:* Harvard Col, AB, 54. *Pos:* Assoc mgr, Boston Symph Orch, 58-71; adminr, Berkshire Music Ctr, 63-71; exec vpres, Amberson Enterprises Inc, 71 & Jalni Music, Video Music Prod, 76; exec prod, Bernstein-Beethoven, 80 & Brahms by Bernstein, 83 and others. *Awards:* Emmy Award, Nat Acad TV Arts & Sci. *Mem:* Harvard Glee Club Found (pres 67-74); Peabody Inst (trustee, 79-); Asn Class Music (treas, 82-); Harvard Musical Asn. *Mailing Add:* 1 Lincoln Plaza 16R New York NY 10023

KREGER, JAMES
CELLO, EDUCATOR
b Nashville, Tenn. *Study:* Juilliard Sch, with Leonard Rose & Harvey Shapiro, BM, MS; studied with Pablo Casals; Accad, Chigiana, Siena. *Pos:* Soloist at festivals throughout world; tours with Music from Marlboro throughout US; recitalist chamber music throughout North & South Am, Europe & Far East. *Teaching:* Mem fac violoncello, Juilliard Sch, 81-; guest teacher master classes, Europe, Japan & US. *Awards:* Winner, Int Tchaikovsky Compt, Moscow; Morris Loeb Award; Felix Salmond Prize. *Mailing Add:* c/o Beverly Wright Artists 400 E 52nd St New York NY 10022

KREHBIEL, ARTHUR DAVID
FRENCH HORN, EDUCATOR
b Reedley, Calif. *Study:* Fresno State Col; Northwestern Univ, BA; studied French horn with Phil Farkas, W Hoss & James Winter. *Pos:* Asst first horn, Chicago Symph, formerly; prin hornist, Detroit Symph, formerly & San Francisco Opera Orch, currently; performer, Bach Fest, formerly, Marin Symph, formerly & San Jose Symph, formerly; soloist, New & Unusual Music ser & Mostly Mozart Fest; soloist, San Francisco Symph, formerly, prin French hornist, currently. *Teaching:* Mem fac, DePaul Univ, formerly; instr horn & dir brass choir, Wayne State Univ, formerly; teacher, Int Horn Wkshp, Brussels, 82; mem fac French horn & chamber music, San Francisco Consv Music, currently. *Mailing Add:* San Francisco Consv Music 1201 Ortega St San Francisco CA 94122

KREHBIEL, CLAYTON
EDUCATOR, TENOR
Study: Univ Kans, BMusEd; Teachers Col, Columbia Univ, MMusEd. *Pos:* Mem chorus, major TV & radio prog, New York, formerly; mem, Fred Waring Glee Club, formerly; perf with Boston Symph Orch, NBC Symph & CBS Symph, formerly; tenor soloist & asst cond, Robert Shaw Chorale, formerly; cond chorus, Cleveland Orch, formerly. *Teaching:* Coordr choral activities, Univ Kans, 17 yrs & Kent State Univ, formerly; prof choral music & music educ, Fla State Univ, 71- *Mailing Add:* 2812 Cavan Dr Tallahassee FL 32308

KREIGER, ARTHUR V
COMPOSER, ELECTRONIC
b New Haven, Conn, May 8, 45. *Study:* Univ Conn, BA, 67, MA(music), 70; Columbia Univ, DMA(comp), 77. *Works:* Fanfare for Alto Flute, Mobart Music Publ, 77; Trio (flute, cello & piano), 77 & Four Settings of W C Williams, 78, Asn Prom New Music; Tapestry (perc quartet), Am Comp Alliance, 78; Fantasy for Piano and Electronic Tape, 79 & Passacaglia on Spring and All, 81, Asn Prom New Music; Remnants (orch), Am Comp Alliance, 83. *Pos:* Technician, Columbia-Princeton Electronic Music Ctr, 76-78. *Teaching:* Lectr music, Columbia Univ, 81-83; co-adj instr music, Rutgers Univ, 78- *Awards:* Rome Prize, Am Acad Rome, 79-80; fel, John Simon Guggenheim Mem Found, 80-81; Nat Endowment Arts Grant, 82. *Mem:* Am Comp Alliance; BMI. *Mailing Add:* 313 W 88th St 1B New York NY 10024

KRELL, JOHN
FLUTE & PICCOLO, EDUCATOR
Study: Univ Mich, dipl; Curtis Inst Music, with William Kincaid. *Pos:* Solo piccoloist & mem flute sect, Philadelphia Orch, 52-82. *Teaching:* Mem fac, Settlement Music Sch, formerly, Temple Univ, formerly & Philadelphia Col Perf Arts, formerly; mem fac flute, Curtis Inst Music, 80- *Mailing Add:* Curtis Inst Music 1726 Locust St Philadelphia PA 19103

KREMENLIEV, BORIS A
COMPOSER, CRITIC & WRITER
b Razlog, Bulgaria, May 23, 11; US citizen. *Study:* DePaul Univ, Chicago, BMus, 35, MMus, 37; Eastman Sch Music, PhD, 42. *Works:* Pravo Horo, first perf by Rochester Civic Orch, 40, Symphony No. 1, 41; Balkan Rhapsody, perf by Sofia Phil & Stuttgart Phil, 68; Second String Quartet, perf by Roth String Quartet, 66, Aldo Bruzzichelli, Florence, 70; Sonata for String Bass, perf by Burtrum Turetzki & Keith Humble, 72; Crucifiction, perf by Sydney Symph Orch, 81; Elegy, perf by Melbourne Symph Orch, 82. *Pos:* Music dir, SGer Network, 45-46; foreign corresp critic, Melos, Ger, 67-71. *Teaching:* Prof comp & ethnomusicol, Univ Calif, Los Angeles, 45-78. *Awards:* Ford Found Grant, 62; Distinguished Contrib Am Music Award, ASCAP, 69-73; Comp Award, Inst Creative Arts, 66-67. *Bibliog:* A Brashovanow (auth), Boris Kremenliev, In: Die Music in Geschichte und Gegenwart, Bärenreiter Kassel-Basel-Tours, London, 58; K Stoichev, I (auth), Boris Kremenliev as Composer, 69 & Sia Atanasova, II (auth), Boris Kremenliev as Professor, Bulgarska Narodna Muzika V Kaliforniiskia Univ, 73, Slaviana, Bulgaria. *Mem:* Soc Ethnomusicol (pres Southern Calif chap, 61-72 & nat first vpres, 62-64); ASCAP; Am Fedn Musicians; Screen Comp Asn US. *Interests:* Historical and analytical study of Slavic peoples music. *Publ:* Auth, Bulgarian-Macedonian Folk Music, Univ Calif Press, 52; contribr, Types of Bulgarian Folksongs, Slavic & East European Rev, Univ London, 56; The Influence of Folklore on the Modern Czech School of Composition, Czechoslovak Acad Sci, Mouton Publ, 70; Multidisciplinary Approach to Ethnomusicology, Bulgarian Acad Sci, 82; Mnogoglasie: A Compositional Concept in Rural Bulgaria, Univ Calif Press, 83. *Mailing Add:* 10507 Troon Ave Los Angeles CA 90064

KREMER, GIDON
VIOLIN
b Riga, Latvia, 1947. *Study:* Studied with Sturestep; Moscow Consv, with David Oistrakh. *Pos:* Piano recitalist & soloist with orchs in more than 30 countries. *Awards:* First Prize Latvian Repub, 63; Prize, Queen Elizabeth Compt Brussels; First Prize, Fourth Int Tchaikovsky Compt, 70. *Mailing Add:* c/o ICM Artists Ltd 40 W 57th St New York NY 10019

KRENEK, GLADYS NORDENSTROM See Nordenstrom, Gladys

KRESKY, JEFFREY JAY
WRITER, EDUCATOR
b Passaic, NJ, May 14, 48. *Study:* Columbia Univ, with Charles Wuorinen & Otto Luening, BA, 69; Princeton Univ, with Milton Babbitt, MFA, 71, PhD, 74. *Works:* Night Music, Paul Price Publ, 80. *Teaching:* Assoc prof, William

Paterson Col, currently; mem fac, Manhattan Sch Music, currently. *Awards:* Student Comp Award, BMI, 70; Comp comn, Nat Endowment Arts, 76; ASCAP Comp Award, currently & yearly. *Mem:* Am Music Ctr; Soc Music Theory; ASCAP. *Publ:* Auth, Tonal Music: Twelve Analytic Studies, Ind Univ Press, 78. *Mailing Add:* 325 Stilwell Pl Ridgewood NJ 07450

KRIEGER, JEFFREY STEPHEN
CELLO
b Joliet, Ill, Sept 7, 57. *Study:* Hartt Sch Music, with David Wells, 75-81; Juilliard Sch, with Channing Robbins, 82- *Pos:* Prin cellist, Hartford Symph Orch, 79- *Mailing Add:* 293 New Park Ave Hartford CT 06106

KRIESBERG, MATTHIAS
COMPOSER, EDUCATOR
b Queens, NY, Mar 21, 53. *Study:* Columbia Univ, with Harvey Sollberger, Charles Wuorinen, Vladimir Ussachevsky, & Jack Beeson, BA, 73, MA, 76; Juilliard Sch, with Milton Babbitt, DMA, 79. *Works:* Three Untitled Pieces for Piano (chamber music), 70-72; Scalene (string trio), 72; Esja (piano chamber concerto), New York, 74; Not From This Anger (ten & chamber ens), 75; Computer Piece on the Hexachord B F Sharp G E Flat A Flat E, 76; Short Symphony (orch), 78; State of Siege (perc ens). *Pos:* Founder, New Structures Ens, 74, dir, currently. *Teaching:* Mem fac, Juilliard Sch, 76- *Awards:* First Prize, Suffolk Symph Concerto Cont, 69; BMI Award, 72; grant, Alice M Ditson Fund, 73-74. *Mailing Add:* 300 Riverside Dr New York NY 10025

KRIEWALL, JUDY (JUDITH WASHBURN KRIEWALL)
FLUTE
b Lake Forest, Ill, Oct 26, 56. *Study:* With Walfrid Kujala, 74-79 & Donald Peck, 77-79; Sch Music, Northwestern Univ, BM, 78, MM, 79. *Pos:* Extra, Chicago Symph Orch, 78-79; second flute, Seattle Symph Orch, 79- *Mailing Add:* 742 N 92nd St Seattle WA 98103

KRIGBAUM, CHARLES RUSSELL
EDUCATOR, ORGAN
b Seattle, Wash, Mar 31, 29. *Study:* Organ Inst, Andover, Mass, 50; Princeton Univ, BA, 50, MFA, 52; studied with Weinrich & Andre Marchal; Berkshire Music Ctr, 51 & 52; Hochschule für Musik, Frankfurt am Main, with Helmut Walcha, two yrs. *Rec Perf:* Antiphon & Chorale for Organ Solo (R Donovan); Magnificat & Mass (Donovan); Messiaen, Organ Works (four rec); The Art of Fugue (J S Bach, two rec). *Pos:* Recitalist throughout US & Europe. *Teaching:* Univ organist & prof music, Yale Sch Music, 70- *Awards:* Fulbright Grant. *Mem:* Am Guild Organists. *Mailing Add:* 50 Elihu Hamden CT 06514

KRIMSKY, KATRINA (MARGARET KRIMSKY SIEGMANN)
COMPOSER, PIANO
b St Simon's Island, Ga, Mar 5, 38. *Study:* Eastman Sch Music, BM, 59. *Works:* Stella Malu, 81 & Song for Hans, 81, Katrina Krimsky; Duogeny, 81, Crystal Morning, 81, Villa in Brazil, 81, Moonbeams, 81 & Mial, 81, Katrina Krimsky & Trevor Watts. *Rec Perf:* In C (Terry Riley), Columbia Rec, 68; Katrina Krimsky, Transonic Rec, 75; Stella Malu, ECM, 81; The Baby's Family, (Villa-Lobos), 1750, Arch Rec, 83. *Teaching:* Instr piano, Mills Col, 73-79. *Mem:* BMI, Switzerland. *Mailing Add:* Kurbergstr 24 8049 Zurich Switzerland

KROEGER, KARL
COMPOSER, MUSICOLOGIST
b Louisville, Ky, Apr 13, 32. *Study:* Univ Louisville, BM, 54, MM, 59; Univ Ill, MS, 61; Brown Univ, PhD, 76. *Works:* String Quartets No 1 & No 2, 60 & 66, Concerto for Oboe & Strings, 61, Sinfonietta for Strings, 66 & Suite for Orchestra, 66, Comp Facsimile Ed; Divertimento for Band, Boosey & Hawkes, 72; Pax Vobis (Cantata), 76 & Concerto for Alto Saxophone, 82, Comp Facsimile Ed. *Pos:* Head, Am Collection, Music Div, New York Pub Libr, 62-64; comp in res, Eugene Pub Sch, Ore, 64-67; dir, Moravian Music Found, Winston-Salem, NC, 72-80; music librn, Univ Colo, Boulder, 82- *Teaching:* Asst prof comp, Ohio Univ, 67-68; asst prof music hist, Moorhead State Univ, 71-72; vis lectr Am music, Univ Keele, England, 80-81; assoc prof, Univ Colo, Boulder, 82- *Awards:* Ford Found Fel, 64-66; overseas vis fel, Leverhulme Trust, London, England, 80; sr res fel, Nat Endowment Humanities, 81. *Mem:* Sonneck Soc (mem bd trustees, 79-82); Am Musicol Soc; ASCAP; Hymn Soc Am; Music Libr Asn. *Interests:* Eighteenth century American music, particularly the music of William Billings. *Publ:* Ed, Moramus Edition of Moravian Choral Music, Boosey & Hawkes, 73-; A Moravian Music Sampler, Moravian Music Found, 74; auth, Isaiah Thomas as a Music Publisher, Am Antiquarian Soc Proc, 76; ed, The Complete Works of William Billings, Vol 1, Am Musicol Soc, 81; auth, William Billings' Music in Manuscript Copy, Notes, 82. *Mailing Add:* Col Music Univ Colo Boulder CO 80309

KROLICK, EDWARD (JOHN)
DOUBLE BASS, EDUCATOR
b Rochester, NY, Aug 1, 23. *Study:* Eastman Sch Music, BMus, 48, MMus, 51; Univ Ill, BS(music educ), 56. *Pos:* Double bass, Rochester Phil, 46-48, San Antonio Symph Orch, 48-50; prin double bass, Champaign-Urbana Symph Orch, 59-, Memphis Symph Orch, 64-69. *Teaching:* Prof double bass & strings, Univ Ill, 51- *Mem:* Am String Teachers Asn; Int Soc Bassists. *Publ:* Auth, Basic Principles of Double Bass Playing, Music Educr Nat Conf, 57; Bassists, Please Stand, Instrumentalist, 10/65; coauth, Prelude to String Playing (Bass Book), Boosey and Hawkes, 72; auth, Improve the Bass Section of Your Orchestra, Nat Sch Orch Asn, 10/73; auth & ed, Fundamentals of Double Bass Playing (film), Univ Ill, 78. *Mailing Add:* 602 Ventura Rd Champaign IL 61820

KROSNICK, AARON BURTON
VIOLIN, EDUCATOR
b New Haven, Conn, June 28, 37. *Study:* Yale Col, studied violin with Joseph Fuchs, BA, 59; Meadowmount Sch, with Ivan Galamian; Kneisel Hall Summer Sch; Juilliard Sch Music, MS, 61; Royal Consv Music, Brussels, Belgium, studied violin with Arthur Grumlaux. *Rec Perf:* Music of Frederick Delius, Musical Heritage Soc. *Pos:* Concertmaster, Springfield Symph Orch, 62-67, Jacksonville Symph Orch, 69-80, Sewanee Fest Orch, 70-76, 78-80 & 82 & Fla Bicentennial Chamber Orch, 76. *Teaching:* Instr music, Wittenberg Univ, 62-67; mem fac, Syracuse Univ, summer 65, Kneisel Hall Summmer Sch Ens Playing, 66-69, Sewanee Summer Music Ctr, 70-76, 78-80 & 82 & Rome Fest, 77; prof, Jacksonville Univ, 67- *Awards:* Fulbright Scholar, 61-62. *Mem:* Music Teachers Nat Asn; Fla State Music Teachers Asn; Gainesville Music Teachers Asn. *Mailing Add:* 6816 Lenczyk Dr Jacksonville FL 32211

KROSNICK, JOEL
CELLO, EDUCATOR
b New Haven, Conn, Apr 3, 41. *Study:* Columbia Col, BA, 63; studied with William D'Amato, Luigi Silva, Claus Adam & Jens Nygard. *Rec Perf:* On Columbia, CRI, Orion & Nonesuch. *Pos:* Co-founder & dir, Group Contemp Music, 62-63; cellist, Iowa Quartet, 63-66 & Juilliard String Quartet, 74-; soloist, US & Europe, 70- *Teaching:* Asst prof music, Univ Iowa, 63-66 & Univ Mass, 66-70; artist in res, Calif Inst Arts, 70-74, Mich State Univ, formerly & Libr Cong, formerly; mem fac chamber music, Juilliard Sch, 74- *Mailing Add:* c/o Juilliard Quartet Colbert Artists 111 W 57th St New York NY 10019

KROSNICK, MARY LOU WESLEY
PIANO, COMPOSER
b Bayonne, NJ, June 11, 34. *Study:* Juilliard Sch, with Rosina Lhevinne, BS(piano), 57; Univ Wis, with Gunnar Johansen, MA, 58; Sch Music, Yale Univ, with Quincy Porter, MM(theory & comp), 61. *Works:* The Rain Comes, perf by New York Phil Symph, 49; Fantasy (solo violin, winds & perc), perf at Fest Am Music, Univ Redlands, Calif, 60; Piano Sonata, perf at Yale Univ, 61, CW Post Ctr, Long Island Univ, 61 & Wittenberg, 64; Fugue in Romantic Style, perf at Rome Fest, Italy, 78. *Rec Perf:* Konzertstück (Weber), Jacksonville Symph, 61; Music People, Stereo 90, 74; Piano Preludes (Frederick Delius), Musical Heritage Soc, 77; Piano Sonata (Gail Kubik), Sound 80, 80. *Teaching:* Fac mem, Wittenberg Univ, Springfield, Ohio, 62-67; piano fac, Kneisel Hall, Blue Hill, Maine, summer 66-67; piano fac & chmn, Sewannee Summer Music Ctr, Tenn, 72-82; asst prof music, Jacksonville Univ, Fla, 78-; private piano lessons, 62-74. *Awards:* First Prize, Young Comp Cont, New York Phil, 49; First Prize, Int Rec Fest, 57 & Teachers Div, Int Rec Compt, 72, Am Col Musicians. *Mem:* Sigma Alpha Iota; Jacksonville Music Teachers Asn; Fla State Music Teachers Asn; Music Teachers Nat Asn; life mem, Friday Musicale Jacksonville. *Mailing Add:* 6816 Lenczyk Dr Jacksonville FL 32211

KRUGER, RUDOLF
ADMINISTRATOR, MUSIC DIRECTOR
b Berlin, Germany; US citizen. *Study:* Staatsakademie Music & Darstellende Kunst, Vienna, Austria, studied cond with Felix von Weingartner & Josef Krips, dipl, 38; Tex Wesleyan Col, Hon DFA, 83. *Pos:* Asst cond, Southern Symph & Columbia Choral Soc, SC, 39-42, New Orleans Symph, 42-45 & New Orleans Opera House Asn, 42-45; cond, Young People's Conct, 42-45, Light Opera Div New Orleans Opera, 43, Chicago Light Opera, 69 & Crescent City Conct Asn, New Orleans, 54-55; music dir, Jackson Miss Opera Guild, 48-51, Mobil Ala Opera Guild, 49-55, New Orleans Light Opera Co, 49-50 & Ft Worth Symph Asn, 63-65; music dir & cond, Ft Worth Opera Asn, 55-58, gen mgr & musical dir, 58-; guest cond, Shreveport La Opera, 62, 63 & 75-80, New Orleans Opera, 69, Cincinnati Opera, 69, Dallas Ballet Asn, 71, PR Opera, 72, State Opera Hannover, Ger, 74 & Teheran Opera, Iran, 76; musical dir & cond, Ft Worth Ballet Asn, 65-66. *Teaching:* Dir opera wkshp, Tex Christian Univ, 55-58. *Awards:* Cert recognition, Tex Fedn Music Clubs, 67. *Mem:* Am Fedn Musicians. *Mailing Add:* 5732 Wessex Ave Ft Worth TX 76133

KRUMMEL, D(ONALD) W(ILLIAM)
EDUCATOR, LIBRARIAN
b Sioux City, Iowa, July 12, 29. *Study:* Univ Mich, BMus, MMus, AMLS & PhD, 51-58. *Pos:* Ref librn music, Libr Cong, Washington, DC, 56-61; assoc librn, Newberry Libr, Chicago, 62-69. *Teaching:* Instr music, Univ Mich, Ann Arbor, 52-56; prof libr sci & music, Univ Ill, Urbana, 70- *Awards:* Scholar in res, Aspen Inst Humanistic Studies, 69; Guggenheim Found Fel, 76. *Mem:* Music Libr Asn (pres, 81-83); Int Asn Music Libr (pres comn bibliog res, 67-77); Am Musicol Soc (coun, 68-71 & 76-79); Am Libr Asn (coun, 64-68). *Interests:* Music bibliography and librarianship; American music. *Publ:* Auth, Guide for Dating Early Published Music, Boonin, Bärenreiter, 74; English Music Printing, 1553-1700, Oxford, 75; ed, Bibliographical Inventory to the Early Music in the Newberry Library, G K Hall, 77; coauth, Resources of American Music History, Univ Ill Press, 81; ed, Physiology of the Opera by Scrici, Inst Studies in Am Music, 81. *Mailing Add:* 702 W Delaware Ave Urbana IL 61801

KRZYWICKI, JAN
COMPOSER, PIANO
b Philadelphia, Pa, Apr 15, 48. *Study:* Juilliard Sch, with Vincent Persichetti & Elliot Carter, 66-68; Aspen Music Fest, with Darius Milhaud; Fontainebleau, with Nadia Boulanger, summer 67; Univ Kans, BMus, 71; Philadelphia Musical Acad, with Theodore Antoniou & Joseph Castaldo, MMus, 75. *Works:* Motet Passionale (chorus & orch); Continuum (ballet),

comn by Pa Ballet Co, 75; Sonata for Double Bass & Piano; Pastorale (bar horn & wind ens); Convocare (two trumpets & three horns), comn by Amherst Music Ctr, 77; Snow Night (marimba & piano), 77; Poem (unaccmp boys' & men's voices), 77. *Pos:* Cond, New Music Ensemble & Early Music Ensemble. *Teaching:* Instr theory & comp, Philadelphia Col Perf Arts, 72- *Mailing Add:* Sch Music Philadelphia Col Perf Arts Philadelphia PA 19102

KRZYWICKI, PAUL
TUBA, EDUCATOR
b Philadelphia, Pa. *Study:* Ind Univ, with William Bell, BMus, MMus; studied with Joseph Novotny & Abe Torchinsky. *Pos:* Mem, New York Brass Sextet, formerly, Cambridge Brass Quintet, formerly, Boston Opera & Ballet Orch, formerly, Portland Symph, Maine, formerly & Buffalo Phil Orch, formerly; performer, Aspen Fest Orch, formerly; mem tuba sect, Philadelphia Orch, 72- *Teaching:* Mem fac tuba, Curtis Inst Music, 72- *Mailing Add:* Curtis Inst Music 1726 Locust St Philadelphia PA 19103

KUBEY, ARTHUR M
BASSOON, LECTURER
b Paterson, NJ, Feb 27, 18. *Study:* Ernest Williams Sch, 35-36; studied bassoon with Simon Kovar. *Pos:* Prin bassoon, Chautauqua Symph, 41-76; prin bassoon, Pittsburgh Symph, 43-76, co-prin bassoon, 76- *Teaching:* Sr lectr bassoon, Carnegie Mellon Univ, 44- *Mailing Add:* 5283 Forbes Ave Pittsburgh PA 15217

KUBIAK, TERESA JANINA See Wojtaszek, Teresa (Janina) Kubiak

KUBIK, GAIL
COMPOSER, CONDUCTOR
b South Coffeyville, Okla, Sept 5, 14. *Study:* Eastman Sch Music, Univ Rochester, MusB, 34; Am Consv Music, MusM, 35; Harvard Univ, with Walter Piston, 37-38; Monmouth Col, Hon MusD, 55. *Works:* A Mirror for the Sky (folk opera), perf on Broadway, 46; Piano Sonata, Southern Music Corp, 47; A Record of Our Time: Cantata for Chorus & Orchestra, perf by Los Angeles Phil, 50-57; Symphony Concertante (viola, piano, trumpet & orch), rec by Orch y French Radio, 52-53; Violin Concerto, perf by Ruggiero Ricci, 52; Symphony No 2, comn by Rockefeller Found, 55; Symphony No 3, perf by New York Phil, 56. *Pos:* Staff comp & musical prog adv, NBC, 40-41; Dir music, Bur Motion Pictures, US Off War Info, 42-43; guest symph cond, Rome, Paris, Palermo, London, New York and others, 52- *Teaching:* Prof violin & comp, Monmouth Col, Ill, 34-37 & Dakota Wesleyan Univ, 34-37; prof comp, Teachers Col, Columbia Univ, 38-40; prof & comp in res, Scripps Col, 70-80. *Awards:* Prix de Rome, Am Acad Rome, 50; Guggenheim Found Fels, 44 & 65; Pulitzer Prize, Columbia Univ, 52. *Mem:* ASCAP; Phi Mu Alpha Sinfonia; Fel, MacDowell Colony; Century Asn. *Mailing Add:* PO Box 192 Claremont CA 91711

KUCHLER, KENNETH GRANT
VIOLIN, RECORDER
b Ogden, Utah. *Study:* Univ Utah, BS, 43, MS, 51; Univ Calif, Berkeley, 43-44; Westminster Col, hon DM, 79. *Pos:* Assoc concertmaster, Utah Symph Orch, currently. *Publ:* Auth, Recorder Program in a Small College, Instrumentalist, 57. *Mailing Add:* 304 S 12th E St Salt Lake City UT 84102

KUCHMENT, VALERIA M See Vilker-Kuchment, Valeria M

KUEHN, DAVID LAURANCE
EDUCATOR, ADMINISTRATOR
b San Marcos, Tex, Oct 26, 40. *Study:* NTex State Univ, BMus, 62; Univ Ill, MS(music educ), 64; Eastman Sch Music, DMA, 74. *Teaching:* Asst dir bands, Univ Wis, Eau Claire, 65-67; asst prof music, NTex State Univ, 67-75, assoc prof & asst dean, 75-80; prof & chmn music dept, Calif State Univ, Long Beach, 80- *Mem:* Nat Asn Col Wind & Perc Instr (nat pres, 76-78); Tubists Universal Brotherhood Asn; Nat Asn Sch Music; Calif Music Exec Asn (pres, 83). *Mailing Add:* Dept Music Calif State Univ Long Beach CA 90840

KUETHER, JOHN WARD
BASS
b Milwaukee, Wis, Oct 3, 57. *Study:* Univ Wis, Milwaukee, with Yolanda Marculescu, BA, 82. *Roles:* Don Magnifico in La Cenerentola, Wis Opera Theater, 82; Seneca in Coronation of Poppea, Skylight Comic Opera, 82; Masetto in Don Giovanni, Des Moines Metro Opera, 82; Bonze in Madame Butterfly, Music Under the Stars, 83; Falstaff in The Merry Wives of Windsor, Univ Wis, Milwaukee, 83. *Pos:* Res artists, Skylight Comic Opera Ltd, Milwaukee, Wis, 82- *Mailing Add:* Skylight Comic Opera 813 N Jefferson Milwaukee WI 53202

KUHN, LAURA DIANE (SHIPCOTT)
CRITIC, MUSIC DIRECTOR
b San Francisco, Calif, Jan 19, 53. *Study:* Col Marin, AA, 78; studied piano with Robert Hagopian & voice with John Hudnall, 80-82; Dominican Col, BA, 81; Univ Calif, Los Angeles, currently. *Pos:* Dir & founder, Marin Contemporary Vocal Ens, 81-82; music critic, Independent J, 81-82; asst to pres bd dir, Marin Opera Co, 81-82; music critic books & rec, Los Angeles Times, 82-; res asst to Nicolas Slonimsky, 83- *Mem:* Am Musicol Soc; Music Critics Asn. *Publ:* Contribr prog annotations, Marin Symph, Dominican Col & Winifred Baker Chorale, 80-82; contribr, Perspectives New Music, 83. *Mailing Add:* 410 3/4 Landfair Ave Los Angeles CA 90024

KUHN, TERRY LEE
EDUCATOR, RECORDER
b Hubbard, Ore, Sept 9, 41. *Study:* Univ Ore, BS, 63, MM, 67; Fla State Univ, PhD, 72. *Teaching:* Asst prof music educ, Univ Md, 72-77; prof, Kent State Univ, 77- *Mem:* Music Educr Nat Conf; Ohio Music Educr Asn. *Publ:* Coauth, Contemporary Music Educator, AHM, 78; Fundamental Classroom Music Skills, Holt, 79; Modern Folk Guitar, Knopf, (in prog). *Mailing Add:* Sch Music Kent State Univ Kent OH 44242

KUJALA, WALFRID EUGENE
FLUTE & PICCOLO, EDUCATOR
b Warren, Ohio, Feb 19, 25. *Study:* Eastman Sch Music, BM, 48, MM, 50; studied flute with Joseph Mariano. *Pos:* Second flute & piccolo, Rochester Phil, 48-54; prin piccolo, Chicago Symph, 54-; prin flute, Grant Park Symph, Chicago, 55-60. *Teaching:* Instr flute, Eastman Sch Music, 50-54; prof flute, Sch Music, Northwestern Univ, 62- *Mem:* Nat Flute Asn (secy, 72-74, vpres, 74-75). *Publ:* Auth, The Flutist's Progress, Progress Press, 70. *Mailing Add:* 1261 Ash St Winnetka IL 60093

KUMER, DENNIS MICHAEL
EDUCATOR, ADMINISTRATOR
b Pittsburgh, Pa, Dec 23, 47. *Study:* Carnegie-Mellon Univ, BFA, 70; Duquesne Univ, MME, 81. *Teaching:* Asst prof music educ & actg dean, Sch Music, Duquesne Univ, 82- *Mem:* Music Educr Nat Conf; Percussive Arts Soc; Int Fedn Musicians. *Mailing Add:* Sch Music Duquesne Univ Pittsburgh PA 15282

KUNITZ, SHARON LOHSE
TEACHER, COMPOSER
b Williston, NDak, May 3, 43. *Study:* Augsburg Col, 61-63; Univ Colo, Boulder, BMus, 65; Univ Wash, 65-66; Univ Denver, MA, 67. *Works:* Hallelujah, Sing Your Praise!, Reformation Sunday, 76; Scenes of the Southwest, 78, The Crickets Came to Dance, 78, Pretzel Prance, 80 & Camp Hook, 82, Myklas Music Press; Concerto for Friends, NMex Music Teachers Asn, 79; My Flesh Shall Rest in Hope, perf by James Whitlow, 83. *Teaching:* Fac mem piano & theory, NMex Jr Col, 73-75; fac mem music hist, NMex State Univ, 77- *Mem:* NMex Alliance Arts; NMex Women Comp Guild; NMex Music Educr Asn; Music Teachers Nat Asn (chmn jr piano, 83-); NMex Music Teachers Asn (pres, 80-82). *Publ:* Auth, Maestroscope, C A I Music Theory, Maestro Music, 83. *Mailing Add:* 412 W Roosevelt Grants NM 87020

KUNZEL, ERICH
CONDUCTOR & MUSIC DIRECTOR
b New York, NY, Mar 21, 35. *Study:* Dartmouth Col, AB, 58; Harvard Univ; Brown Univ, AM, 60; study with Pierre Monteux, 56-64; hon DLit, Univ Northern Ky, 75. *Rec Perf:* Numerous recordings on Decca Gold, Atlantic, Vox/Turnabout, MMG, Telarc & Caedmon. *Pos:* Cond, Santa Fe Opera, 57, 64 & 65, Cincinnati Pops Orch, 77-, Toronto Symph Orch Promenades, 78-, Can Opera Co, 81- & Winnipeg Symph Orch Pops, 81-; res cond, Cincinnati Symph Orch, 65-75; music dir, New Haven Symph Orch, 74-77 & San Francisco Symph Orch Pops, 81-; prin pops cond, Indianapolis Symph Orch, 82- & Rochester Phil Orch, 83- *Teaching:* Dir choral music, Brown Univ, 58-65; music dir, Phil Orch & chmn opera, orch & grad cond depts, Consv Music, Univ Cincinnati, 65-71. *Mem:* Am Symph Orch League; Metropolitan Opera Guild; Phi Mu Alpha Sinfonia; Am Fedn Musicians; Pierre Monteux Mem Found. *Publ:* Ed, Various Choral Works, Boosey & Hawkes, 63. *Rep:* Tica Roberts Mitchell Mgmt 527 Madison Ave New York NY 10022. *Mailing Add:* Swans Island ME 04685

KUPFERMAN, MEYER
COMPOSER, EDUCATOR
b Manhattan, NY, July 3, 26. *Study:* Queens Col; self-taught in music comp. *Works:* Little Symphony, Weintraub Music Co, 51; Sonata on Jazz Elements, Gen Music Publ Co, 58; Infinities Thirteen, Bodowin Music Press, 65; Fantasy Sonata, 70, Three Non-Objectives, 82, Sound Phantoms #7, 82 & Symphony No 10: FDR, 82, Gen Music Publ Co. *Teaching:* Prof comp & chamber music, Sarah Lawrence Col, 51- *Awards:* Guggenheim Fel, 75; grant, Nat Endowment Arts, 76; Acad & Inst Arts & Lett Music Award, 82. *Mem:* ASCAP; Am Fedn Musicians. *Mailing Add:* 86 Livingston St Rhinebeck NY 12572

KURAU, W(ARREN) PETER
EDUCATOR, FRENCH HORN
b Torrington, Conn, Aug 16, 52. *Study:* Eastman Sch Music, BM(music educ) & perf cert(horn), 74; Guildhall Sch Music & Drama, cert, 75; Royal Col Music, ARCM, 75; Univ Conn, MA, 77; Fla State Univ, with Verne Reynolds, David Cripps, Paul Ingraham & William Capps. *Pos:* Asst prin horn, Rochester Phil Orch, 83- *Teaching:* Asst prof music, Univ Mo, Columbia, 77-83, assoc prof, 83- *Awards:* Int Telephone & Telegraph Int Fel, 74; Fac Quality Improvement Award, 79; Third Place, Heldenleben Int Horn Compt, 79. *Mem:* Music Educr Nat Conf; Col Music Soc; Int Horn Soc (area rep, 81-83); Nat Asn Col Wind & Perc Instr. *Publ:* Contribr, Brass Music Reviews, Nat Asn Col Wind & Perc Instr J, 82-83. *Mailing Add:* 141 S Fitzhugh #4 Rochester NY 14608

KURLAND, SHELLY (SHELDON)
VIOLIN, EDUCATOR
b New York, NY, June 9, 28. *Study:* Juilliard Sch, BS, 55; Tulsa Univ, MS, 56. *Rec Perf:* With Shelly Kurland Strings, solo & background music for 6000 rec sessions. *Pos:* Violin, Cornell Univ Trio & Cumberland Trio, 56-;

Organizer, owner & contractor, Shelly Kurland Strings, 70- & A Strings of Nashville, 81- *Teaching:* Asst prof music, Cornell Univ, 56-64; assoc prof, Peabody-Vanderbilt Univ, 64-70. *Mailing Add:* 1805 Kingsbury Dr Nashville TN 37215

KURTZ, ARTHUR DIGBY
COMPOSER, PIANO
b Chicago, Ill, May 7, 29. *Study:* St Louis Inst Music, MA, 58; studied with Nadia Boulanger, 59-61; Sorbonne, 61-63. *Works:* 3 Preludes for Piano, Op XIII, comn by New Music Circle & perf by Jack Hurte, 65; String Quartet No 1, Op XI, perf by Lincoln String Quartet, 68; Songs for High Voice, Op X & XV, perf by Mary Newander, 68; Variations for Brass, Op XXV, comn by music dept, Ft Hays, Kans, 70; Sonatina for Unaccompanied Flute, Op XXIX, comn & perf by Frand Bowen, 72; Isaiah VI, Op XXXI, comn by Ken Dorn, 72; 5 short concert pieces for guitar, Op XXXXIV, comn by Larry Bowlles, 81. *Bibliog:* de Marie-Jean Londeix (auth), 125 Ans de Musique Pour Saxophone, Ed Alphonse Leduc, Paris, France, 75; Ingeborg Dobeinski (auth), Unaccompanied Flute Solo Literature of the 20th Century, Univ Cologne, Germany, 77. *Mem:* Am Music Ctr. *Mailing Add:* 685 Oakwood Webster Groves MO 63119

KURTZ, EUGENE ALLEN
COMPOSER
b Atlanta, Ga, Dec 27, 23. *Study:* Eastman Sch Music, with Bernard Rogers, MA, 49; Ecole Normale Musique, Paris, with Arthur Honegger & Darius Milhaud, 49-51; study with Max Deutsch, 53-57. *Works:* The Solitary Walker (monologue for orch), 64, Conversations for 12 Players, 66, Ca ..., Diagramme Pour Orchestre, 72, The Last Contrabass in Las Vegas, 74, Five-Sixteen (piano), 82 & Flashback (orch), 82-83, Ed Jobert, Paris. *Pos:* Consult, Ed Jobert, Paris, 72- *Teaching:* Guest prof comp, Univ Mich, Ann Arbor, 67-68, 70-71, 73-74 & 80-81, Eastman Sch Music, 75, Univ Ill, Urbana, 76 & Univ Tex, Austin, 77-78. *Awards:* Nat Endowment Arts Comp Fel Grant, 82-83. *Mem:* Soc Auteurs, Comp & Ed Musique. *Mailing Add:* 6 Rue Boulitte Paris 75014 France

KURTZ, S JAMES
EDUCATOR, COMPOSER
b Newark, NJ. *Study:* New York Univ, BA, 55, MA, 60; Univ Iowa, PhD, 71; studied clarinet with Simeon Bellison. *Works:* Fantasy for Unaccompanied Clarinet, 66, Suite, 66, Three Impressions, 66 & Notturno for Clarinet or Flute & Piano, 69, Omega Music Co; also publ by Sam Fox & Lyric Arts Publ. *Rec Perf:* Septet for Winds (Hindemith), Golden Crest, 71; Goethe-Lieder for Three Clarinet & Soprano (L Dallapiccola), Epic Rec. *Pos:* Prof clarinetist, New York, NY, 53-65. *Teaching:* Prof music, James Madison Univ, 65- *Awards:* James Madison Univ res grant on early wind music, 72; Marion Bauer Comp Award. *Mem:* Nat Asn Col Wind; Int Clarinet Soc. *Publ:* Ed, Stamitz, Quartet for Clarinet & Strings, Op 19/3, Musica Rara, 70. *Mailing Add:* Music Dept James Madison Univ Harrisonburg VA 22807

KURTZMAN, JEFFREY GORDON
EDUCATOR
b Detroit, Mich, Mar 23, 40. *Study:* Univ Colo, studied piano with Paul Parmelee, BM, 63; Aspen Music Sch, studied piano with Rosina Lhevinne, 63; Univ Ill, MM, 67, PhD, 72. *Teaching:* Vis lectr, Cornell Univ, 68-69; instr, Middlebury Col, 69-72, asst prof, 72-75; from asst prof to prof, Shepherd Sch Music, Rice Univ, 75- *Mem:* Int Musicol Soc; Col Music Soc; Music Libr Asn; Am Musicol Soc (nat prog chmn, 81). *Publ:* Auth, Some Historical Perspectives on the Monteverdi Vespers, Analecta Musicologica, 75; Giovanni Francesco Capello, An Avant-Gardist of the Early Seventeenth Century, Musical Disciplina, 77; Essays on the Monteverdi Mass and Vespers of 1610, Rice Univ Studies, 78; An Early Seventeenth-Century Manuscript of Canzonette e Madrigaletti Spirituali, Studi Musicali, 79. *Mailing Add:* Sheperd Sch Music Rice Univ Box 1892 Houston TX 77251

KURZBAUER, HEATHER RAQUEL
VIOLIN
b Cleveland, Ohio, Mar 28, 55. *Study:* Yale Univ, BA, 77, with Szymon Goldberg, MM, 81. *Pos:* Concertmaster, Spoleto Fest, Charleston, SC, summers 77-79, Colo Music Fest, Boulder, summers 81-83, Grand Teton Music Fest, 83, Netherlands Chamber Orch, 82 & Amsterdam Phil Orch, 82-; prin violin, NJ Symph, summer 79. *Teaching:* Instr violin, Yale Univ, 79-81. *Mailing Add:* 15100 Shaker Blvd Shaker Heights OH 44120

KUSHNER, DAVID ZAKERI
EDUCATOR, ADMINSTRATOR
b Ellenville, NY, Dec 22, 35. *Study:* Boston Univ, BMus, 57; Univ Cincinnati, MMus, 58; Univ Mich, PhD, 67. *Teaching:* Asst prof music, Miss Univ Women, 64-66; from assoc prof to prof, Radford Univ, 66-69; prof music, coordr grad studies & musicol studies, Univ Fla, 69-; vis prof, Florence Study Ctr, Fla State Univ, 75. *Bibliog:* Ylda Novik (auth), David Kushner, Piano Guild Notes, 5-6/71. *Mem:* Charter life mem, Am Liszt Soc (mem bd dir, 67-); Am Musicol Soc (chmn southern chap, 71-75); life mem, Music Teachers Nat Asn; Music Educr Nat Conf; assoc mem, Sigma Alpha Iota. *Interests:* Music of Ernest Bloch; 19th century American music education; music criticism. *Publ:* Auth, Ernest Bloch and His Music, William Maclellan, 73; Ernest Bloch: A Retrospective on the Centenary of His Birth, Col Music Soc Symposium, fall 80; Ernest Bloch, In: New Grove Dict of Music & Musicians, 82; Ernest Bloch, Refardt Lexikon, 82; The Masonic Influence on 19th-century American Musical Education, J Musicol Res, spring 83. *Mailing Add:* 356 Music Bldg Univ Fla Gainesville FL 32611

KUSS, MALENA
MUSICOLOGIST, EDUCATOR
b Cordoba, Arg, Aug 11, 40; US citizen. *Study:* Southern Methodist Univ, MM(perf), 64; Univ Calif, Los Angeles, PhD(musicol), 76; studied comp with Alberto Ginastera, piano with Rosina Lhevinne & Gyorgy Sandor & musicology with Gilbert Reaney, Leonard Stein & Robert Stevenson. *Pos:* Dir, Ctr Latin Am Music Bibliography, NTex State Univ, 82-; rev ed, Latin Am Music Rev, 82- *Teaching:* Assoc prof music, NTex State Univ, 76- *Awards:* Fulbright-Hays Fel, Inst Int Educ, 73-74; Nat Endowment Humanities Fel, 82; Am Philosophical Soc, 83. *Mem:* Int Musicol Soc; Int Asn Music Libr, Archives & Documentation Ctr; Am Musicol Soc; Music Libr Asn; Soc Ethnomusicol. *Interests:* Latin American nativism in 19th and 20th century opera; contemporary music theater, Germany; Latin American music bibliography. *Publ:* Auth, Huemac by Pascual de Rogatis: Native Identity in Argentine Lyric Theater, Yearbook Inter-Am Musical Res, 74; Latin American Music in Contemporary Reference Sources, Acad Printing, 76; Charles Seeger's Leitmotifs on Latin America, Yearbk Int Folk Music Coun, 79; Type, Derivation, and Use of Native Idioms in Ginastera's Don Rodrigo (1964), Latin Am Music Rev, 80; contribr numerous articles in New Grove Dict of Music & Musicians, Handbuch des Musiktheaters & other ref sources. *Mailing Add:* Sch Music NTex State Univ Denton TX 76203

KUZELL, CHRISTOPHER
EDUCATOR, VIOLIN
b San Bernardino, Calif, July 22, 27. *Study:* Calif State Univ, Los Angeles, BA, 50, MA, 57; Univ Southern Calif, DMA, 80. *Works:* Six Little Pieces for Marimba, 71 & Sonata for Marimba, 79, Mitchell Peters; Symphony No 1, San Luis Obispo Co Symph Orch, 82. *Pos:* Concertmaster, Pac Consv Perf Arts Rec Orch, 71- & San Luis Obispo Co Symph Orch, 74- *Teaching:* Prof music theory & jazz ens, Allan Hancock Col, 62- *Mem:* Music Asn Calif Community Col; Southern Calif Sch Band & Orch Asn; Am Soc Univ Comp. *Mailing Add:* 907 E El Camino Santa Maria CA 93454

KUZMA, JOHN JOSEPH
CONDUCTOR & MUSIC DIRECTOR
b Cincinnati, Ohio, Mar 16, 46. *Study:* Eastman Sch Music, BMus(organ), 68; Univ Copenhagen, 69; Univ Ill, with Harold Decker, MMus(choral cond), 71; studied organ with Robert Noehren. *Rec Perf:* Ceremony of Carols (Britten), Missa Brevis (Britten), Three Two-Part Songs (Britten), 83 & America the Beautiful, 83, Pro Arte Rec. *Pos:* Music dir St Paul's Church, San Diego, 71-75 & Am Boychoir Sch, Princeton, 82-; univ organist, Univ Calif, Santa Barbara, 75-77; boychoir dir, Crystal Cathedral, 76-79; founder & cond, San Diego Chamber Orch, 79-82. *Teaching:* Asst prof music, Univ Calif, Santa Barbara, 75-77. *Awards:* Fulbright Grant, 69. *Mem:* Am Guild Organists (dean San Diego chap, 74 & 81). *Mailing Add:* 19 Lambert Dr Princeton NJ 08540

KUZMYCH, CHRISTINA
COMPOSER, EDUCATOR
b Perth, Australia; US citizen. *Study:* Ind Univ, BMus, 76, MMus, 77, 77-83. *Works:* Shapes and Sounds I, Ind Univ Ens, 76; Fragments for Solo Cello, Paul Finklestein, 77; When the Distant Guns of Autumn Lease, David Martin & Hanna Brickman, 77; String Quartet, Thouvenel String Quartet, 77; Archipian, perf by Ind Univ Symph Orch, 78; Shapes and Sounds II, Ind Univ Ens, 79; Shapes and Sounds IV, Jean Lansing, 83. *Teaching:* Assoc instr comp, instrumentation & notation, Ind Univ, 79-81. *Mem:* Am Soc Univ Comp; Int League Women Comp; Nat Asn Comp; Pi Kappa Lambda. *Mailing Add:* 1415 E 3rd #124 Bloomington IN 47401

KWAK, SUNG
CONDUCTOR
b Seoul, Korea, Dec 11, 43; US citizen. *Study:* Mannes Col Music, BS, 70. *Pos:* Cond, Joffrey Ballet Co, 71-76; Exxon Arts Endowment cond, Atlanta Symph, 77-80; asst cond, Cleveland Orch, 80-; music dir & cond, Austin Symph, 82- *Rep:* Herbert Barrett 1680 Broadway New York NY 10019. *Mailing Add:* 2585 Kemper Rd #32-B Shaker Heights OH 44120

KWALWASSER, HELEN
EDUCATOR, VIOLIN
b Syracuse, NY, Oct 11, 27. *Study:* Curtis Inst Music, with Efrem Zimbalist, 39-41; Juilliard Sch Music, with Ivan Galamian, 45-47. *Rec Perf:* Janadek Quartet (Galimir), Vanguard, 55; Mozart Haffner Serenade, Westminster, 56; Vivaldi Seasons, 60 & Bach Brandenburgs, 62, Odyssey; Schubert Sonatinas, Classical Cassette Club, 71; Trios (Riegger, Persichetti, Piston, Arensky & Ravel), Golden Crest, 72; Aitken Cantata, Desto, 76. *Pos:* Soloist & concertmaster, Mozart Chamber Orch, Am Chamber Orch, 55-58 & Princeton Chamber Orch, 64-70; violinist, Galimir Quartet, 56-58 & New York Chamber Soloists, 72-; concertmaster, Toledo Orch, 61-63 & Pa Ballet, 65-72; violinist & founding mem, Temple Trio, 70- *Teaching:* Lectr violin, Bowling Green State Univ, 61-64; prof & chmn dept strings, Temple Univ, 70- *Awards:* Winner, World Youth Fest Compt, Praque, Czechoslovakia, 47 & Musical Fund Soc, 48. *Mailing Add:* 424 Owen Rd Wynnewood PA 19096

KYR, ROBERT HARRY
COMPOSER, EDUCATOR
b Cleveland, Ohio, Apr 20, 52. *Study:* Yale Univ, BA, 74; Univ Pa, MA, 78; Harvard Univ, 78-81. *Works:* Crystal Liturgies (ten soloists, perc & string orch), 75; Surfacing (piano solo), 79; The Aleph (orch), 80; Maelstrom (sop & chamber ens), 81; Sunlight Parables (ten, string quartet & piano), 82; How Bright the Star (cello & piano), 83; Book of the Hours (sop, countertenor & orch), 83. *Teaching:* Lectr, Dept Music, Yale Univ, 82-83; vis prof, Univ Giessen, WGermany, 83-84. *Mailing Add:* 22289 Blossom Dr Rocky River OH 44116

L

LA BARBARA, JOAN (JOAN LA BARBARA SUBOTNICK)
COMPOSER, SOPRANO
b Philadelphia, Pa, June 8, 47. *Study:* Syracuse Univ; NY Univ, BS, 70; Berkshire Music Ctr. *Works:* Tapesongs, Chiaroscuro Rec, 77; Reluctant Gypsy, Wizard Rec, 79; Klee Alee, 79 & Shadow Song, 79, comn by Radio in Am Sector, West Berlin; Erin, comn by VPRO Radio, Holland, 80; As Lightning Comes, in Flashes, Wizard Rec, 83; The Solar Wind, comn by Nat Endowment Arts Comp Prog, 83. *Rec Perf:* Drumming (Steve Reich), 74 & Music for Mallet Instruments, Voices and Organ (Steve Reich), 74, Deutsche Grammophon; The Rape of El Morro (Don Sebesky), CTI, 75; Commitment (Jim Hall), A & M/Horizon, 75; North Star (Philip Glass), Virgin, 77 & CBS, 77; May Rain (Lou Harrison), Musical Heritage Soc, 79; The Last Dream of the Beast (Morton Subotnick), Nonesuch (in prep). *Roles:* Premier perf of comn works incl Music in 12 Parts (Philip Glass), 74, Another Look at Harmony (Philip Glass), 75, Einstein on the Beach (Philip Glass), 76, Solo for Voice 45 from Songbooks (John Cage), 76, Windsor Jambs (Earle Brown), 82 & Three Voices (Morton Feldman), 83. *Pos:* Mem, Steve Reich & Musicians, 71-74, Philip Glass Ens, 73-76; vis Slee comp, Ctr Creative & Perf Arts, State Univ NY, Buffalo, 77; contrib new music ed, Musical Am/High Fidelity, 77-; comp in res, Deutscher Akademischer Austauschdienst Künstler Prog, 79. *Teaching:* Fac mem extended vocal tech & experimental music, Musik Hochschule, Hochschule der Kunst, West Berlin, 79 & Calif Inst Arts, 80-; residencies incl Musik Akad Stadt Basel & Univ Ill, Urbana-Champaign. *Awards:* Multi-Media Grant, CAPS & NYSCA, 78-79; grant, Nat Endowment Arts Visual Arts Prog, 79-80 & Nat Endowment Arts Music Comp Prog, 80-81. *Mem:* ASCAP; Am Music Ctr; Am Fedn TV, Radio & Rec Artists; Screen Actors Guild; Actors Equity Asn. *Interests:* New music, specifically the experimental music tradition and extended vocal techniques. *Rep:* Beverly Wright Artists' Rep 400 E 52nd St Suite 51 New York NY 10022. *Mailing Add:* PO Box ii Old Chelsea Station New York NY 10113

LABOUNTY, EDWIN MURRAY
COMPOSER, EDUCATOR
b Garretson, SDak, Feb 19, 27. *Study:* Ind Univ, with Bernhard Heiden, BM, 49, MM, 53, DM, 62. *Works:* Fatal Interview (song cycle), 52; Horn Sonata (chamber music), 53; Blue and Blue Green (two pianos), 60-73; Sea Afternoon (choir, harp, oboe, cello & glockenspiel), 61; Excursus (piano & orch), 62; Excursus #2 (orch), 72; Now Is the Time for All Good Men (tape), 73; and others. *Teaching:* Music supvr, NCountry Sch, Lake Placid, 54-59; mem fac, Memphis State Univ, 62-68; assoc prof music, Western Wash State Univ, currently. *Mailing Add:* 433 16th St Bellingham WA 98225

LACHERT, HANNA KATARZYNA
VIOLIN
b Podkowa, Warsaw, Nov 25, 44. *Study:* Lyceum Music, Warsaw, 63; Acad Music, MA, 67; Hochschule Musik, Hannover, Germany, 67-68; Consv Royal Musique, Brussels, 68-69; Univ Conn, MA, 71. *Rec Perf:* Works of Szymanowski & Bartok, Telarc Rec. *Pos:* Recitalist & soloist with orchs, radio & TV broadcasting, Poland, Finland, Yugoslavia, Germany, England, Italy & Belgium, 70 & US & Mex, 70-; violinist, New York Phil, 72- *Awards:* Premier Prix, Consv Royal Musique, Brussels, 68-69. *Mailing Add:* New York Phil Avery Fisher Hall New York NY 10023

LACK, FREDELL (MRS RALPH EICHHORN)
VIOLIN, TEACHER
b Tulsa, Okla. *Study:* Juilliard Sch Music, dipl, 45; studied with Tosca Berger, Josephine Boudreaux, Louis Persinger, Ivan Galamian & George Enesco. *Teaching:* Artist in res & prof violin & chamber music, Univ Houston, 59- *Awards:* Prize of Liege, Queen Elizabeth of Belgium Int Compt, 51; Outstanding Perf Artist, Arts Coun & Mayor of Houston, 82; Farfel Award, Univ Houston, 83. *Bibliog:* Sam Applebaum (auth), The Way They Play, Bk VII, Paganiniana Press, 80. *Mem:* Am String Teachers Asn; Young Audiences Inc; Nat Music Teachers Am. *Rep:* Albert Kay Assoc 58 W 58th St New York NY 10019. *Mailing Add:* 4202 S MacGregor Houston TX 77021

LACKMAN, SUSAN COHN
COMPOSER, EDUCATOR
b Tsingtao, China, July 1, 48; US citizen. *Study:* Temple Univ, studied piano with N Hinderas, BMusEd, 70; Am Univ, MA, 71; Rutgers Univ, studied comp with R Moevs, PhD, 81. *Works:* String Quartet No 1, perf by Rutgers String Quartet, 76; Dinner Music for Brass Trio, perf by C Gottschalk, M Fischer & W Gallo, 83; Chamber Symph, comn by Fla Symph (in prep). *Teaching:* Instr, Am Univ, 70-71 & Rutgers Univ, 76-78; asst prof theory & comp, Rollins Col, 81- *Awards:* Sword of Honor, Sigma Alpha Iota, 70. *Bibliog:* Sumner Rand (auth), Composers of Note, Orlando Sentinel, 2/14/82. *Mem:* Int League Women Comp (mem bd dir, 81-, secy, 82-); Sigma Alpha Iota (Orlando area pres, 83-); Col Music Soc; Music Educr Nat Conf. *Publ:* Auth, Musicians Are So Insular, Music J, 74; Premiere Reactions to Carmen, Opera J, 81. *Mailing Add:* Rollins Col Box 2650 Winter Park FL 32789

LACY, EDWIN V
EDUCATOR, BASSOON
b Hopkinsville, Ky, Aug 1, 37. *Study:* Murray State Univ, BMusEd, 60; Ind Univ, Bloomington, studied bassoon with Leonard Sharrow & William Waterhouse, MMus, 66, DMus, 79. *Pos:* Prin bassoonist, Evansville Phil Orch, Ind, 59- & Owensboro Symph Orch, Ky, 67- *Teaching:* Prof & head, Music Dept, Univ Evansville, 67-, founder & dir jazz prog, 68- *Awards:* Orpheus Award, Phi Mu Alpha Sinfonia, Epsilon Upsilon Chap, 82; Friend

of Arts, Sigma Alpha Iota, Beta Epsilon Chap, 83. *Mem:* Int Double Reed Soc; Nat Asn Jazz Educr; Phi Mu Alpha Sinfonia; Am Fedn Musicians; Music Educr Nat Conf. *Mailing Add:* Music Dept Univ Evansville Evansville IN 47702

LADEWIG, JAMES LESLIE
EDUCATOR
b Waukesha, Wis, Dec 19, 48. *Study:* Northwestern Univ, BM, 71; Univ Calif, Berkeley, PhD, 78. *Teaching:* Vis asst prof music hist, Vassar Col, 78-79; asst prof, Wellesley Col, 79- *Awards:* Am Coun Learned Soc Fel, 82. *Mem:* Am Musicol Soc. *Interests:* Music of Girolamo Frescobaldi. *Publ:* Auth, Luzzaschi as Frescobaldi's Teacher: A Little-Known Ricercare, Studi Musicali, 81; The Origins of Frescobaldi's Variation Canzonas Reappraised, Frescobaldi Studies, (in prep). *Mailing Add:* Wellesley Col Wellesley MA 02181

LAFAVE, KENNETH JOHN
CRITIC & WRITER, COMPOSER
b Tucson, Ariz, Dec 4, 51. *Study:* Sch Music, Univ Ariz, BA(theory), 73, MA(comp), 80. *Works:* Fantasy for Clarinet and Chamber Orchestra, perf by Laslo Veres & Phil Orch Tucson, 81; Three Songs, perf by Helena Scribner, 82. *Pos:* Music critic, Ariz Daily Star, Tucson, 75-81 & gen arts reporter, currently; ed asst, Edward B Marks Music Corp, New York, 81-82. *Publ:* Auth, An Interview with John Lanchbery, Ballet News, 81; George Rochberg: Odyssey to Opera, Opera News, 82; The Crisis in Music Publishing, Keynote, 82; Words or Music? Stagebilt, Carnegie Hall, 82; George Balanchine: Musician, Ballet News, 6/83. *Mailing Add:* 3437 E Elida Tucson AZ 85716

LAFFORD, LINDSAY ARTHUR
EDUCATOR, ORGAN
b Gloucester, England, Oct 27, 12; US citizen. *Study:* Royal Col Music, London, ARCM, 34; Royal Acad Music, London, LRAM, 34; Fel Royal Col of Organists, 35; Trinity Col Music, London, FTCL, 47. *Works:* Alleluia! The Lord is Risen, 66, 3 Fancies for 2 Trumpets & Organ, 67, He Shall Come Down Like Rain, 68 & The Liturgy of the Lord's Supper, 70, J Fischer & Brothers; I Love to Think that Jesus Saw, Ludwig, 79. *Pos:* Organist & choirmaster, St John's Cathedral, Hong Kong, 35-39; univ organist, Princeton, NJ, 39-40; dir chorus & orch, Washington Univ, St Louis, 46-48. *Teaching:* Instr music hist & theory & dir, Haverford Col & Swarthmore Col, 39-43; asst prof music hist & organ, Middlebury Col, Vt & Washington Univ, St Louis, 45-48; prof & chmn, Music Dept, Hobart & William Smith Cols, 48-79. *Mem:* ASCAP; Am Guild Organists (sub-dean Miami chap, 83-). *Mailing Add:* St Philip's Church 1142 Coral Way Coral Gables FL 33134

LAING, FONTAINE LOUISE
PIANO, TEACHER
b Chicago, Ill, Feb 24, 33. *Study:* Aspen Music Sch, with Vronsky & Babin, 52; Univ Tex, with Dalies Frantz, BM(piano), 55; Univ Mich, with Benning Dexter, MM(piano), 57, MM(chamber music), 79; Oakland Univ, with Flavio Varani, 76-81; Ind Summer Chamber Music Inst, with Menachim Pressler, 82; Int Inst Chamber Music, with Jorge Demus, 82. *Rec Perf:* Salon Music (flute), Golden Crest, 75; Flute Fantasy, Little Piper, 77; Zonjic-Monroe International Chamber Orch, Danzon, Can, 80; The 20th Century Flute, Little Piper, 82. *Pos:* Soloist, Pontiac-Oakland Symph, 77 & Oakways Symph, 78; also chamber music appearances, Ohio & Mich; pianist, Int Flute Conv, 80 & 81; dir, Novi Chamber Music Soc, 81- *Teaching:* Instr piano, Detroit Consv, 59-61, Grosse Pointe Consv, 61-77 & Detroit Community Music Sch, 78- *Mem:* Detroit Musicians League; Tuesday Musicale of Detroit; Mu Phi Epsilon. *Mailing Add:* 22753 Cortes Novi MI 48050

LAIRES, FERNANDO
PIANO
b Lisbon, Portugal, Jan 3, 25; US citizen. *Study:* Nat Consv Music, Lisbon, dipl, 45. *Rec Perf:* Piano works by various comp on several rec, 68-69, Piano Sonatas (Beethoven), 73, various Portuguese works for piano, 74 & Pictures at an Exhibition (Mussorgsky), 75, Educo Rec; Concerto for Two Pianos and Orchestra, Advan Rec, 77. *Pos:* Dir, Univ Md Int Piano Fest & Compt, 78-81. *Teaching:* Prof piano, Nat Consv Music, Lisbon, 49-56, Interlochen Arts Acad, 68-72 & Peabody Consv Music, 72- *Awards:* Beethoven Medal, Harriet Cohen Int Music Awards, London, 56. *Bibliog:* Tschaikowsky Compt, ABC Cable TV (film), Moscow, 82. *Mem:* Am Liszt Soc Inc (pres, 76-); Bohemians. *Mailing Add:* 9000 Gettysburg Lane College Park MD 20740

LAITMAN, LORI (LORI LAITMAN ROSENBLUM)
COMPOSER
Jan 12, 55. *Study:* Yale Univ, BA, 75, MM, 76; studied flute with John Wummer & Thomas Nyfenger, comp with Jonathan Kramer & Frank Lewin. *Works:* Catabasis, Drew Univ Consort, 74; Cong Sycle, Aviva Chamber Players, New York, NY, 80; The Taming of the Shrew, Folger Theater Group, Washington, DC, spring 83; And They Dance Real Slow in Jackson, New Playwrights Theatre, spring 83. *Pos:* Flutist, Vt Symph, spring 77; comp, various films & theatres, New York, NY & Washington, DC, 78- *Teaching:* Flute, Hebrew Arts Sch, Turtle Bay Music Sch, New York, NY, 78-80, Jewish Community Ctr Gtr Washington, 81- & Int Consv Music, Washington, DC, 83- *Mem:* Friday Morning Music Club; Int League Women Comp; Nat Asn Comp, USA; Nat Flute Asn; Flute Soc Washington, Inc (chairperson Va student recitals, 83). *Mailing Add:* 8602 Bunnell Dr Potomac MD 20854

LAKE, BONNIE (JOSEPHINE)
FLUTE, EDUCATOR
b Cleveland, Ohio. *Study:* Consv Music, Oberlin Col, with Robert Willoughby, BM, 52, BMus, 52, MM, 55; Somer Akademie Mozarteum, with

Kurt Redel, Salzburg, cert(flute), 58; Acad Int, with J P Rampal, Nice, cert(chamber music), 61; study with William Kincaid, 54-62. *Pos:* Third flute & piccolo, Indianapolis Symph Orch, 55-57; asst first flute, Baltimore Symph, 57-; performer solo & chamber music throughout US & Europe. *Teaching:* Adj prof flute & chamber music, Oberlin Consv, 52-54, grad asst, 54-56; adj instr flute, Jordan Col of Music, Butler Univ, 55-57; instr flute & chamber music, Peabody Inst Music 58-; adj prof flute, Goucher Col, 62- *Mem:* Music Teachers Nat Asn; Nat Flute Asn. *Mailing Add:* 1101 N Calvert St Baltimore MD 21202

LAKE, OLIVER EUGENE
COMPOSER, SAXOPHONE
b Marianna, Ark, Sept 14, 42. *Study:* Lincoln Univ, BA(music educ), 68; Washington Univ, studied arr & comp with Oliver Nelson & Ron Carter, 70. *Works:* Alto Violin, comn by Brooklyn Phil, 80; Eraser of Day, 81; Urban Art, comn by Brooklyn Phil, 83. *Rec Perf:* NTU: Point from Which Creation Begins, 71 & Heavy Spirits, 75, Freedom; Holding Together, Black Saint, 76; Life Dance of Is, 78 & Shine!, 78, Artista-Novus; Prophet, 80 & Sun-Raise, 80, Black Saint. *Pos:* Music dir & organizer, Black Artist Group, St Louis, 68-72; musician in res, Am Ctr Artists & Students, Paris, 73; solo accmp, Jane Honor Dance Co, Paris, 74; saxophonist, solo & with Black Artists Trio & Quartet, 74-81 & Oliver Lake Quartet, 81; accmp with Anthony Braxton, Merce Cunningham Dance Co, 75; co-founder & perf, World Saxophone Quartet, 77-81; founder, Jump Up, 80, performer, 82; numerous tours of US, Can, Europe & Africa. *Awards:* Grants, Nat Endowment Arts, 76 & 81 & Creative Arts Pub Serv Prog, 81. *Mem:* Am Fedn Musicians. *Publ:* Auth, Life Dance, Africa, 79. *Rep:* Marty Cann 611 Broadway New York NY. *Mailing Add:* PO Box 653 Cooper Station New York NY 10003

LALLERSTEDT, FORD MYLIUS
EDUCATOR, ORGAN
b Atlanta, Ga. *Study:* DeKalb Col, 68-70; Juilliard Sch Music, BM, 72, MM, 73, DMA, 76; studied with Vernon de Tar & Gustave Reese. *Pos:* Organist & dir music, Presby Church, New Rochelle, NY, 71- *Teaching:* Mem fac theory & hist music, Curtis Inst Music, 73-; teaching asst solfege & ear training, Juilliard Sch Music, 74-76; is asst prof music, State Univ NY Col, Purchase, formerly, instr organ, 75-76; mem fac tech music, Mannes Col Music, 77-, organ & chamber music coach, 80- *Awards:* Prizes in Organ, Juilliard Sch Music, 73; Second Prize, NY-Am Guild Organists Young Artists Compt; Third Prize, Nat Organ Playing Compt, Ft Wayne, Ind. *Mailing Add:* Curtis Inst Music 1726 Locust St Philadelphia PA 19103

LAMARCHINA, ROBERT A
CONDUCTOR & MUSIC DIRECTOR
b New York, NY, Sept 3, 28. *Study:* Paris Consv Musique; Curtis Inst Music, with Feuermann & Piatigorsky; Peabody Consv Music. *Pos:* Solo cellist, St Louis Symph, Los Angeles Phil & Chicago Symph, formerly; mem, NBC Symph Orch, formerly; cond, Spoleto Fest Two Worlds, Fujiwara Opera Japan, Moscow Radio Orch, Metropolitan Opera, New York City Ctr Opera, New York Phil, Chicago Symph, St Louis Symph, Zurich Symph, Honolulu Symph & other maj orchs & opera co; cond & music dir, Hawaii Opera Theater, currently. *Rep:* Sardis Artists Mgt Corp 180 West End Ave New York NY 10023. *Mailing Add:* Hawaii Opera Theatre 9874 Wajmany St Honolulu HI 96814

LAMB, GORDON HOWARD
CONDUCTOR & MUSIC DIRECTOR, EDUCATOR
b Eldora, Iowa, Nov 6, 34. *Study:* Simpson Col, BME, 56; Univ Nebr, MM, 62; Univ Iowa, PhD, 73. *Works:* Three Choral Vignettes, E B Marks; Hodie Christus Natus Est, G Schirmer; and other arr & ed. *Pos:* Choral cond, Iowa Pub Sch, 57-68 . *Teaching:* Choral cond, Univ Tex, Austin, 70-74; prof music, Univ Tex, San Antonio, 74-, choral cond & div dir music, 74-78, vpres, Acad Affairs, 79- *Awards:* Robert McCowen Award, Am Choral Dir Asn Iowa, 82. *Mem:* Am Choral Dir Asn. *Publ:* Auth, Guide For the Beginning Choral Conductor, 73 & coauth, Selection of Repertoire, 73, Am Choral Dir Asn; auth, Psalm Tone Technique of Palestrina in His Magnificats, Choral Rev, 73; Charles Ives: 1874-1954, Choral J, 74; Choral Techniques, William C Brown, 2nd ed, 79. *Mailing Add:* Vpres Acad Affairs Univ Tex San Antonio TX 78285

LAMB, JOHN DAVID
COMPOSER
b Portland, Ore, Mar 11, 35. *Study:* San Francisco State Univ, BA, 56; studied comp with Volfgangs Darzins, 56-60; Univ Wash, MA, 58. *Works:* Night Music, perf by Sigurd Rascher, 56; Concerto (horn), E Holtzel & Swabian Symph Orch, 58; Idyll, Cutsforth, Aushalomov & Portland Jr Symph, 62; King Midas, Dir Studio, Seattle, 66; Scherzo & Chaconne, 73 & St George, 75, Northwest Chamber Orch; Högbo Midsommar, Högbo Music Fest, Sweden, 76. *Awards:* Comp in res, Music Educr Nat Conf, 65. *Mailing Add:* 1907 E Blaine Seattle WA 98112

LAMB, MARVIN LEE
COMPOSER, ADMINISTRATOR
b Jacksonville, Tex, July 12, 46. *Study:* Sam Houston State Univ, studied with John Butler & Newton Strandberg, BM, 68; NTex State Univ, studied with William P Latham & Merrill Ellis, MM, 72; Univ Ill, studied with Paul Zonn & Ben Johnston, DMA, 77. *Works:* Prarie Suite (brass quintet), Shawnee Press Inc, 71; In Memoriam, Benjy (sax quartet), Media Press, 74; Ballad of Roland, Dorn Publ, 80; Music for Julius Baker, 81 & Solowalk for Flute, 81, Wimbledon Music Inc; Prism, 82 & Vision of Basque, 83, Medici Press Inc. *Teaching:* Fac mem, Atlantic Christian Col, 73-77; asst prof & dir electronic

music, George Peabody Col, Vanderbilt, 77-79; assoc prof & head theory & comp, Southern Methodist Univ, 79-83; chmn music dept, Tenn Tech Univ, 83- *Awards:* ASCAP Standard Awards, 77-; Charles Ives Ctr Am Music Res Fel, 82. *Mem:* ASCAP; Am Music Ctr; Col Music Soc. *Mailing Add:* Box 5045 Tenn Tech Univ Cookeville TN 38503

LAMB, NORMA JEAN
LIBRARIAN, SOPRANO
b Plattsburgh, NY, June 18, 29. *Study:* State Univ NY, Col Potsdam, BS, 51; Northwestern Univ, MM, 55; Case Western Reserve Univ, MSLS, 59. *Pos:* Head music dept, Buffalo & Erie County Pub Libr, 59-; sop soloist, Cent Presby Church, Buffalo, NY, 65- *Mem:* Music Libr Asn (chair pub libr comt, 83-). *Mailing Add:* 29 Seattle St Buffalo NY 14216

LAMBRO, PHILLIP
COMPOSER, PIANO
b Wellesley, Mass, Sept 2, 35. *Study:* Univ Miami, 53-55; Music Acad West, studied piano with Gyorgy Sandor & comp with Donald Pond, cert, 55. *Works:* Miraflores (string orch), 55, Dance Barbaro (perc), 58-60, Two Pictures (solo perc & orch), 65-66, Toccata (piano), 65, Four Songs, 67, Music for Wind, Brass & Percussion, 69 & Structures (string orch), 70, Wimbledon Music Inc. *Rec Perf:* Meditation (string orch), 73, Structures (string orch), 73 & Music for Wind, Brass & Percussion, 73, Cortes-Lambro Crystal. *Awards:* Best Music for Doc Film, Nat Bd Rev Award, 71; grant, Nat Endowment for Arts, 76. *Bibliog:* Who Speaks for the Contemporary Composer, Los Angeles Times Calendar, 6/1/75. *Mem:* ASCAP. *Mailing Add:* c/o Wimbledon Music Inc 1888 Century Park E #10 Century City CA 90067

LAMMERS, MARK (EDWARD)
EDUCATOR, TROMBONE
b Sibley Co, Minn, Oct 14, 31. *Study:* Markato State Univ, Minn, BS, 53, MS, 58; Univ Minn, PhD, 83. *Pos:* Trombonist, Minneapolis-St Paul Orch, 54-70, Civie Orch Minneapolis, 55-69 & NH Music Fest Orch, summer 72. *Teaching:* Instr music, St Clair Pub Sch, 53-54; band dir, Roseville Pub Sch, Minn, 54-70; assoc prof & chmn, Dept Music, Gustavus Adolphus Col, St Peters, Minn, 70- *Mem:* Am Fedn Musicians; Music Educr Nat Conf; Int Trombone Asn; Nat Asn Jazz Educr. *Mailing Add:* Music Dept Gustavus Adolphus Col St Peter MN 56082

LAMNECK, ESTHER EVANGELINE
CLARINET
b Marion, Ind. *Study:* Juilliard Sch Music, with Stanley Drucker, BM, 72, MM, 73, DMA, 80. *Rec Perf:* New American Trio, 73 & Heritage Wind Quintet, 76, Musical Heritage Soc; Letters to Cunegonde (clarinet & cello), 83 & Sonata Concerta (clarinet & piano), 83, Capriccio Rec. *Pos:* Clarinet soloist, Pro Musicis Found, 75-; mem, New Am Trio, 72-, Virtuosi Quintet, 76-78 & Lamneck Steigerwalt Duo, 76-; guest soloist, Juilliard Orch, Houston Symph & others, currently. *Awards:* Naumburg Found Scholar, 77. *Mailing Add:* 62 Saratoga Ave Yonkers NY 10705

LA MONTAINE, JOHN
COMPOSER, PIANO
Study: Studied comp with Stella Roberts, Howard Hanson, Bernard Rogers, Bernard Wagenaar & Nadia Boulanger. *Works:* Novellis, Novellis, Op 38 (opera), The Shephardes Playe, Op 38 (opera) & Symphonic Variations for Piano and Orchestra, Op 50, Fredonia Press; Birds of Paradise, Op 34, Joffrey Ballet; Concerto for Piano and Orchestra, Op 9, comn by Ford Found; Wilderness Journal (symph for bass-baritone, organ & orch), comn by Jouett Shouse; Be Glad Then America (bicentennial opera), Op 43, Fredonia Press. *Rec Perf:* Conversations for Violin and Piano, The Nine Lessons of Christmas for Chorus, Harp & Percussion & others, Fredonia Discs. *Pos:* Founder & publ, Fredonia Press, 75- *Teaching:* Comp-in-res, Am Acad, Rome, 62, Eastman Sch Music, Univ Utah, NTex Univ & Whittier Col. *Awards:* Rheta Sosland Prize for Chamber Music; Pulitzer Prize, 59; Guggenheim Fel; Am Acad Arts & Lett Award. *Mailing Add:* c/o Fredonia Press 3947 Fredonia Dr Hollywood CA 90068

LAMOUTTE, SYLVIA MARIA
PIANO, ADMINISTRATOR
b San Juan, PR, Nov 29, 35. *Study:* Univ PR, 54; New England Consv Music, BM, 58, MM, 60; study piano with Elisa Tavarez & Miklos Schwalb, duo piano with Luboschutz & Nemenoff, early music with Daniel Pinkham & ens with Francis J Cooke. *Pos:* Bd mem, Pro Arte Musical Inc, 76-77; panelist & music critic, TV prog, Mirador Puertorriqueno, currently; exec dir, Corp of PR Symph Orch, 81-; soloist, PR, US & Dominican Repub. *Teaching:* Fac piano, New England Consv Music, 59-60; private music lessons, PR, 60-80. *Awards:* Walter W Naumburg Scholar, 59-60. *Mem:* Soc Musical PR (bd mem, 76-77); Asociacion Pro Orquesta Sinfonica PR (vpres, 78 & pres, 78-81); Am Musicol Soc; Nat Guild Piano Teachers; Am Music Scholar Asn. *Publ:* Compilations, adaptions and arrangements of Puertorican folk music and traditional music for piano from preparatory level to grade 4, private publ; auth, Adaptation for Chord Organs of Puertorican Folk Music (seven vols) & Biografias Cortas de Compositores Puertorriquenos, Charles Hansen Music Publ Inc. *Mailing Add:* 267 San Jorge St Apt 12-C Santurce PR 00912

LAMPROPULOS, ATHENA
SOPRANO
b Klamath Falls, Ore. *Study:* Univ Wash, BA; Teatro Dell'Opera, with Luigi Ricci, two years; La Scala Milan, with Ettore Campogalliani. *Roles:* Margherita in Mefistofele; Maddalena in Andrea Chenier; Santuzza in Cavalleria rusticana; Donna Anna in Don Giovanni; Minnie in La Fanciulla

del West; Tosca in Tosca; Aida in Aida; and many others. *Pos:* Soprano, with major companies in Italy, France, Israel & US. *Awards:* Fulbright Grant to Italy, two years; Gold Medal, Reggio Emilia, Italy, 62. *Mailing Add:* 302 W 79th New York NY 10024

LAMY, CATHERINE
SOPRANO
b Boston, Mass. *Study:* Curtis Inst Music; Boston Consv. *Rec Perf:* Violetta in La Traviata, PBS. *Roles:* I Pagliacci, Italy, 77; Olympia, Antonia & Stella in The Tales of Hoffmann, Ky Opera Asn, 80-81, Augusta Opera Asn, 80-81 & Piedmont Opera Theater, Winston-Salem, NC, 80-81; Mimi in La Boheme, New York City Opera, 82; The Magic Flute, Va Opera, 83; La Traviata, Opera Theatre Rochester, 83; Faust, Cleveland Opera, 83; Desdemona in Otello, Des Moines Metro Opera, 83. *Pos:* Sop, Santa Fe Opera, Dallas Opera Co, Tex Opera Theater & Opera Co Boston. *Rep:* Munro Artists Mgt 344 W 72nd St New York NY 10023. *Mailing Add:* 215 W 83rd St New York NY 10024

LANCASTER, EMANUEL LEO
EDUCATOR, PIANO
b Murray, Ky, Aug 9, 48. *Study:* Murray State Univ, BME, 70; Univ Ill, Champaign-Urbana, MS, 71; Northwestern Univ, PhD, 78. *Teaching:* Asst prof group piano, William Rainey Harper Col, 71-79; instr, Nat Music Camp, 73-75; assoc prof piano pedagogy, Univ Okla, Norman, 79- *Mem:* Nat Piano Found; Music Teachers Nat Asn; Music Educr Nat Conf; Col Music Soc; Tex Group Piano Asn. *Publ:* Coauth, Keyboard Strategies (Master Text, Solo 1A, Solo 1 B, Ensemble 1A & Ensemble 1B), G Schirmer, Inc, 80. *Mailing Add:* 3923 Pine Tree Circle Norman OK 73069

LANCASTER, THOMAS SCOTT
CONDUCTOR, EDUCATOR
Jeffersonville, Ind, Sept 12, 39. *Study:* Ind Univ, BMus, 61, MMus, 63, DMus, 71. *Rec Perf:* Music From House of Hope Presbyterian Church, 82 & Minn Comp, 83, privately recorded. *Pos:* Music dir, Minn Chorale, 77-83; choir dir, House of Hope Presbyterian Church, 78-; cond, Bach Chamber Players, 80- *Teaching:* Instr & dir chor, Eastern Ky Univ, 65-67; prof music, Univ Minn, 69- *Mem:* Int Bach Soc; Am Musicol Soc; Am Choral Found. *Mailing Add:* Sch Music Scott Hall Univ Minn Minneapolis MN 55455

LANDAU, SIEGFRIED
COMPOSER, MUSIC DIRECTOR
b Berlin, Germany, Sept 4, 21; US citizen. *Study:* Stern Consv, Berlin; Klindworth-Scharwenka Consv, Berlin; Guildhall Sch Music & Drama, London, LGSM(comp), 40; Mannes Col Music, studied cond with Pierre Monteux, dipl(cond), 42 . *Works:* Longing for Jerusalem (sop & orch), 41; Chassidic Suite (viola & piano), 41; The Golem (ballet), 46; The Sons of Aaron (opera), 59; Friday Evening Service (chamber music); The Dybbuk (ballet); Choruses. *Rec Perf:* On Vox-Candide & Turnabout. *Pos:* Cond, Kinor Symphonietta, 45-54, Brooklyn Phil, 55-71 & Westchester Symph, 62-; music dir & cond, Chattanooga Opera Asn, 59-73 & Westphalia Symph Orch, WGermany, 73-75. *Teaching:* Mem fac, NY Col Music, 44-60 & Cantors Inst, Jewish Theol Sem, 49-69. *Awards:* Outstanding Contrib Music Educ Award, Music Teachers Asn, 63; fel, Jewish Acad Arts & Sci, 71; Arts Award, Westchester Arts Coun, 76. *Mem:* Soc Mici Della Music Jesi; Nat Jewish Music Coun; ASCAP; Am Musicol Soc; Asn Am Cond & Comp. *Mailing Add:* Westchester Symph Box 35 Gedney Sta White Plains NY 10605

LANDSMAN, JEROME LEONARD
EDUCATOR, VIOLIN
b Chicago, Ill, Dec 23, 23. *Study:* Eastman Sch Music, studied violin with Eudice Shapiro, Jascha Heifetz & Jacques Gordon, BS, 48; Univ Southern Calif, studied cond with Richard Burgin & orch with Ingolf Dahl, MS, 49, studied chamber music with Felix Salmond, Gabor Rejto & Luigi Silva, DMA, 66. *Pos:* Mem, res string quartet, Univ Wash, 49-50. *Teaching:* Prof violin, Ind Univ Pa, 51-57; prof music, Univ Hawaii, 60-65, Univ Tex, El Paso, 66-67, Southern Methodist Univ, 67-69 & Montclair State Col, 71-; prof & chmn, Music Dept, Allegheny Col, 69-71. *Awards:* Award, Danforth Found, 57. *Mem:* Music Educr Nat Conf; Am String Teachers Asn. *Publ:* Auth, An Annotated Catalog of American Violin Sonatas and Similar Works from 1947-1961, B-Asta; Let us Have Professional String Teachers, Instrumentalist, 68; coauth, Freedom to Play, Alex Broude Inc, 81. *Mailing Add:* 16 Stonehenge Rd Upper Montclair NJ 07043

LANDSMAN, JULIE
FRENCH HORN, EDUCATOR
b Brooklyn, NY, Apr 3, 53. *Study:* Juilliard Sch Music, BM, 75. *Works:* Trio, Peters Publ, 82. *Pos:* First horn, Houston Symph, 82- *Teaching:* Prof horn, Shepherd Sch Music, Rice Univ, 83- *Awards:* Naumberg Award, Juilliard Sch Music, 75. *Mem:* Am Fedn Musicians; Int Horn Soc. *Mailing Add:* Houston Symph Orch 615 Louisiana Houston TX 77002

LANE, LOUIS
CONDUCTOR
b Eagle Pass, Tex, Dec 25, 23. *Study:* Univ Tex, BMus, 43, Eastman Sch Music, MusM, 47; Akron Univ, Hon MusD, 73, Cleveland State Univ, Hon MusD, 74. *Pos:* Mem, Cleveland Orch, 47-73, assoc cond, 60-70, res cond, 70-73; cond, Akron Symph Orch, Ohio, 59-; music dir, Lake Erie Opera Theatre, Cleveland, 64-72; co-dir, Blossom Fest Sch, 69-73; prin guest cond, Dallas Symph Orch, 73-78; co-cond, Atlanta Symph Orch, 77-; guest cond, major US & Europ orchs. *Teaching:* Mahler Medal, 71; Ditson Award, Columbia Univ, 72. *Awards:* Chevalier L'Ordre Arts & Lett, France. *Mem:* Phi Mu Alpha; Pi Kappa Lambda. *Mailing Add:* Thomas Hall Hill & Ctr Sts Akron OH 44325

LANE, RICHARD BAMFORD
COMPOSER, TEACHER
b Paterson, NJ, Dec 11, 33. *Study:* Eastman Sch Music, BM, 55, MM, 56. *Works:* Four Songs (ms & orch), 56, The Penguin (piano), Sonata for Flute & Piano #1, Cradle Song (SSA) & String Song, C Fischer; Suite for Alto Saxophone & Piano, Boosey & Hawkes, 56; A Hymn to the Night (SATB), Mills Music, 56. *Teaching:* Comp in res, Rochester Sch, NY, 54-60, Lexington Sch, Ky, 60-61; piano & comp, privately, 61- *Awards:* Eastman Sch Rec & Publ Prize, 56; Young Comp Proj Grant, Ford Found, 59 & 60. *Mem:* ASCAP; Am Music Ctr; Bohemians; Comp Guild NJ; Music Educr Asn NJ. *Mailing Add:* 173 Lexington Ave Paterson NJ 07502

LANEY, MAURICE I
EDUCATOR, TROMBONE
b Terre Haute, Ind, Sept 8, 21. *Study:* Albion Col, BA, 43; Eastman Sch Music, MM, 48; Ind Univ, PhD, 64. *Teaching:* Asst prof theory, Univ Louisville, 48-64; asst head, Dept Music, Carnegie-Mellon Univ, 64-68; prof & head theory & lit area, Eastern Mich Univ, 68- *Mem:* Phi Mu Alpha Sinfonia (nat pres, 82); Sinfonia Found (pres, 79-82); Col Music Soc; Soc Music Theory. *Mailing Add:* Music Dept Eastern Mich Univ Ypsilanti MI 48197

LANG, MORRIS ARNOLD
PERCUSSION, EDUCATOR
b New York, NY, Feb 2, 31. *Study:* Juilliard Sch Music, BA, 53. *Rec Perf:* Eight Pieces for Kettledrums (Elliot Carter), Columbia, 75. *Pos:* Assoc timpani & perc, New York Phil, 55-; perc, New York City Ballet, 53-55. *Teaching:* Instr music, Manhattan Sch Music, 71-75; prof, Brooklyn Col, 73- *Awards:* George Wedge Award, Juilliard Sch, 52. *Mem:* Percussive Arts Soc (mem bd dir, 79-); Col Music Soc. *Publ:* Auth, New Conception, 65 & Fourteen Contemporary Etudes, 67, Belwin; Three Puerto Rican Songs, Lang Perc, 76; co-ed, Dictionary of Percussion Terms, Lang Perc, 78; auth, Timpani Tuning, Lang Perc, 82. *Mailing Add:* 200 Mercer St New York NY 10012

LANG, ROSEMARY RITA
EDUCATOR, CLARINET
b Weisburg, Ind, Apr 29, 20. *Study:* Arthur Jordan Consv Music, BMEd, 47; Jordan Col Music, Butler Univ, MA, 52. *Works:* Four Pieces for Woodwind Quintet, Lang Music Publ, 76. *Teaching:* Mem fac, Jordan Col Music, 47-51; assoc prof woodwinds, theory & ens, Jordan Col Fine Arts, Butler Univ, 47- *Mem:* Am Fedn Musicians; Mu Phi Epsilon. *Publ:* Auth, Saxophone: Beginning Studies in the Altissimo Register, 72, Woodwind Class Method, 78 & Clarinet: Short Cuts to Virtuoso Technique, 80, Lang Music Publ. *Mailing Add:* 821 N Temple Ave Indianapolis IN 46201

LANGAN, KEVIN JAMES
BASS
b New York, NY, Apr 1, 55. *Study:* New England Consv Music; Ind Univ, with Margaret Harshaw, BM(voice), 77, MM(voice), 80. *Rec Perf:* Samson et Dalilah, 80 & Aida, 81, PBS. *Roles:* Sarastro in Magic Flute, St Louis Opera Theatre, 80 & Opera Omaha, 82; Timur in Turandot, 82 & Bartolo in Nozze di Figaro, San Francisco Opera, 82; Osmin in Entführung aus dem Serail, Opera de Lyon, France, 82; Seneca in L'Incoronazione di Poppea, Can Opera Co, 83; Colline in La Boheme, San Francisco Opera, 83. *Awards:* Grant, Metropolitan Opera Nat Coun, 80; Florence Bruce Award, San Francisco Opera, 80. *Mailing Add:* c/o Columbia Artists Mgt Inc 165 W 57th St New York NY 10019

LANGLEY, KENNETH JOHN
VIOLIN
b Bayonne, NJ, Sept 26, 48. *Study:* Manhattan Sch Music, BMus, 70. *Pos:* Violinist, NJ Symph Orch, 70-73 & New Orleans Phil, currently; mem & soloist, Berlin String Quartet, formerly & Berlin Chamber Orch, formerly; mem, Springfield Symph Orch, formerly; recitalist, WNYC radio, New York. *Teaching:* Violin, Perf Arts Sch, NJ, 72-74 & Wittenberg Univ, formerly. *Mailing Add:* New Orleans Phil 203 Carondelet St Ste 903 New Orleans LA 70130

LANGLEY, LEANNE
EDUCATOR
b Coral Gables, Fla, Jan 29, 53. *Study:* Baylor Univ, BM, 75; Univ NC, Chapel Hill, PhD, 83. *Works:* A Most Unusual Champion, 75, It Is Well With My Soul, 77, Wonderful Surprises, 77 & And Like A River Glorious, 79, Word, Inc; Forth in Thy Name, Purifoy Publ, 83. *Teaching:* Adj asst prof music London Prog, Univ Notre Dame, 83- *Awards:* Am Fel, Am Asn Univ Women, 80-81. *Mem:* Am Musicol Soc; Royal Musical Asn; ASCAP. *Interests:* History of musical journalism; social history of British music. *Publ:* Auth, Our Thing Called Opera, Musical Times, 82; Use of Manuscripts & Archives in Music Periodicals Research, Periodica Musica, 83. *Mailing Add:* 477 Holloway Rd London N7 England United Kingdom

LANGLITZ, DAVID CARL
TROMBONE
b Rochester, NY, Feb 8, 53. *Study:* Juilliard Sch Music, BMus, 75, MMus, 76. *Pos:* Trombonist, Spoleto Fest, summer 72, Aspen Music Fest, summers 73-74 & Lincoln Ctr Chamber Music Soc, New York, 78; prin trombonist, Metropolitan Opera Orch, 74- *Teaching:* Instr, Montclair State Col. *Mem:* Am Fedn Musicians. *Mailing Add:* 210 W 70th St Apt 614 New York NY 10023

LANGTON, SUNNY JOY
SOPRANO
b Los Angeles, Calif. *Roles:* Lisa in La Sonnambula, Spoleto Fest, 80; Gilda in Rigoletto, New Cleveland Opera; Ariadne auf Naxos & Adele in Die Fledermaus, 82, Lyr Opera, Chicago; The Abduction from the Seraglio, New Orleans Opera. *Pos:* Prin artist, Oper der Staats Cologne, 82- *Awards:* Third Place, Metropolitan Opera Nat Auditions, 76; Young Singer Award, Nat Opera Inst, 78. *Mailing Add:* c/o Columbia Artist Mgt 165 W 57th st New York NY 10019

LANKESTER, MICHAEL JOHN
CONDUCTOR, COMPOSER
b London, England, Nov 12, 44. *Study:* Royal Col Music, London, with Adrian Boult, ARCM, 66. *Works:* Play of the Year (TV series), 76-78. *Rec Perf:* Ariadne (Gordon Crosse), Areo Rec, 76; Purgatory, Decca Rec, 77. *Pos:* Music dir, Nat Theatre Great Britain, 68-73; assoc cond, Pittsburgh Symph Orch, 80- *Teaching:* Prof cond, Royal Col Music, London, 73-80, head, Opera Dept, 76-80. *Mailing Add:* c/o Dido Senger The Garden 103 Randolph Ave London W 9 England United Kingdom

LANKSTON, JOHN
TENOR
b Lawrenceville, Ill. *Study:* Vincennes Univ, AA; Col-Consv Music Cincinnati, BM; vocal study with Annette Havens. *Roles:* Eisenstein in Die Fledermaus, New York City Opera, Florentine Opera, Milwaukee, Wis, Artpark, Lewiston, NY & others, 70-; Florestan in Fidelio, Harford Opera, Baltimore, Md, 72; Ashmedai in Ashmedai, 76-77 & Peter Quint in Turn of the Screw, 76-79, New York City Opera; Tamino in The Magic Flute, Florentine Opera, Milwaukee, Wis, 78; Olim in Silverlake, 80 & Dr Pangloss & Governor in Candide, 82-, New York City Opera. *Pos:* Soloist, New York City Opera, 66-, Caramour Fest, Katonah, NY, 68-72, Nat Educ TV Opera, New York, 69-70 & Wolf Trap Fest, Washington, DC, 76-81. *Mailing Add:* 155 W 81st St New York NY 10024

LANSKY, PAUL
COMPOSER, EDUCATOR
b New York, NY, June 18, 44. *Study:* Queens Col, City Univ New York, with George Perle & Hugo Weisgall; Princeton Univ, with Milton Babbitt, Edward T Cone & James K Randall. *Works:* Modal Fantasy (piano), CRI, 69; Mild und Leise (comput), Columbia Odyssey, 73-74; Crossworks (chamber ens), Nonesuch & Boelke Bomart, 74-75; Dance Suite (piano), Boelke Bomart, 77; Six Fantasies on a Poem by Thomas Campion (comput), CRI, 78-79; Folk-Images (comput), 80-81; As If (comput & string trio), 81-82. *Pos:* Horn, Dorian Quintet; assoc ed, Perspectives New Music. *Teaching:* Assoc prof music, Princeton Univ, currently. *Awards:* Bearns Prize; Am Acad & Inst Arts & Lett Award. *Mailing Add:* Dept Music Princeton Univ Princeton NJ 08644

LANZILLOTTI, LEONORE
MEZZO-SOPRANO
b NY. *Study:* Studied with Karin Branzell, Marienka Michna & Carlo Moresco. *Roles:* Prinz Orlovsky in Die Fledermaus, Honolulu Opera, 64; Carmen in Carmen; Siebel in Faust; Beppe in Amico Fritz; Suzuki in Madama Butterfly; Amneris in Aida; Ulrica in Ballo in maschera. *Pos:* Mezzo-soprano with maj opera co in US. *Awards:* Maria de Varady Scholar, New York City Opera, 68; Karin Branzell Scholar, 69 & 70; Sullivan Found Grant, 69 & 71. *Mailing Add:* c/o Ira Lieberman Artist Rep 11 Riverside Dr New York NY 10023

LAPIN, GEOFFREY
CELLO
b Baltimore, Md, Oct 14, 49. *Study:* Peabody Consv Music, dipl; Ind Cent Univ, BS; Butler Univ, MM. *Pos:* Cellist, Esch Piano Trio, formerly & Indianapolis Symph Orch, currently; prin cellist, Lafayette Symph Orch, 80-'. *Awards:* Raub Music Perf Scholar, 69. *Mem:* Am Fedn Musicians; Phi Mu Alpha Sinfonia. *Mailing Add:* 618 E 46th St Indianapolis IN 46295

LA PORTA, JOHN DANIEL
COMPOSER, EDUCATOR
b Philadelphia, Pa, Apr 13, 20. *Study:* Manhattan Sch Music, BM, 56; MME, 57; studied clarinet with Herman Pade, William Dietrich, Joseph Gigliotti & Leon Russiannoff, flute with Robert Morris, comp with Dr Ernst Toch & Alexiis Haieff & jazz improvisation with Lennie Tristano. *Works:* Mid-Century Event, comn by Oyster Bay High Sch, 59; The Most Miner, perf by John La Porta Quartet, 58; Spanish Rhapsody (sax quartet), Berklee Press, 74; Essay for Clarinet Alone, Kendor Music Inc, 79. *Rec Perf:* Metronome All Stars, 51; Anthropology, Spotlight Rec, 52; The John La Porta Quintet, Debut Rec, 56; The Clarinet Artistry of John La Porta, Fantasy Rec, 59; Ebony Concerto & The Woody Herman Orchestra, 59, Everest Rec; Fusion, Carnegie Hall, 60. *Pos:* Musical dir, Jazz Comp Wkshp, NY, 52-54; performer & comp, Music in the Making, Cooper Union, NY, 54-59; music dir, Jazz Found Am, 56-61. *Teaching:* Music, Parkway Music Inst, 48-51 & Oyster Bay High Sch, 54-58; jazz wkshp, Manhattan Sch Music, formerly; mem fac, Nat Stage Band Clinics, formerly; reed consult & asst music dir, Newport Youth Band & Newport Int Youth Band; head band, Berklee Col Music, 62-, lectr music, 76- *Awards:* ASCAP Awards, 68-83. *Mem:* Nat Asn Jazz Educr; Am Fedn Musicians. *Publ:* Auth, Developing the School Jazz Ensemble (22 vol), 63, Developing Sight Reading Skills in the Jazz Idiom, 64, A Guide to Jazz Improvisation, 66 & Ear Training, Phase I, 67, Berklee Press; Tonal Organization of Improvisational Techniques, Kendor Music Inc, 77. *Mailing Add:* Berklee Col Music 1140 Boylston St Boston MA 02215

LAREDO, JAIME
VIOLIN, CONDUCTOR
b Cochabamba, Bolivia, June 7, 41. *Study:* Curtis Inst Music; studied with Ivan Galamian & Josef Gingold. *Rec Perf:* Complete Bach Sonatas; Schubert Trout Quintet; Mendelssohn, Bruch, Mozart & Bach Concertos. *Pos:* Mem, Kalichstein-Laredo-Robinson Trio, currently; cond, Scottish Chamber Orch, currently; appearances with major orchs in US & Europe. *Teaching:* Violin, Curtis Inst Music, currently. *Awards:* Winner, Queen Elizabeth Int Music Compt, Belgium, 59; Handel Medal, New York, 60. *Bibliog:* Tim Page (auth), article, New York Times, 1/23/83. *Mailing Add:* Curtis Inst Music 1726 Locust St Philadelphia PA 19103

LAREDO, RUTH
PIANO, TEACHER
b Detroit, Mich. *Study:* Curtis Inst Music, BMus, 60. *Rec Perf:* Complete Sonatas for Piano 1-10 (Scriabin), Etudes Op 42 & other short works, Connoisseur Soc, 70; Ravel Trio, 73, Complete Solo Piano Music, Vol I thru VII (Rachmaninoff), 80, Miroirs (Ravel), 81, Sonatine (Ravel), 81 & LaValse (Ravel), 81, Columbia Rec; Sonata, Op 26 (Barber) & Souvenirs, Nonesuch Rec, 82. *Teaching:* Fac mem piano, Curtis Inst Music, 60; fac mem piano & chamber music, Blossom Fest, 70-71; asst prof piano, Yale Sch Music, 74-76; fac mem piano & chamber music, Aspen Sch Music, 75. *Awards:* Best Classical Artist of Year, Rec World Mag, 80; Best Chamber Music Perf, 80 & Best Classical Perf, 82, Nat Acad Rec Arts & Sci. *Mailing Add:* c/o Gurtman & Murtha 162 W 56th St New York NY 10019

LARGE, JOHN W
EDUCATOR
Study: Univ NMex, BFA & MMus, 50-54; Ind Univ, DMus, 62; Ecole Normale de Musique, Paris, studied vocal lit with Pierre Bernac, lic conct, 63; Stanford Univ, PhD, 71. *Pos:* Mem, Tanglewood Opera Theater, 60; concert performer in France, Germany & US, 62-; dir, Santa Fe Inst Vocal Studies, 81-; gen dir, Manuel Garcia Int Compt Singing, 83. *Teaching:* Assoc prof music, State Univ NY, Potsdam, 65-66, San Francisco State Univ, 66-69, Univ Southern Calif, 69-72, Santa Clara Univ, 73-74 & NTex State Univ, 78-; prof & head dept, Int Sch Geneva, Switzerland, 72-73; asst prof, Univ Calif, San Diego, 74-78. *Awards:* Fulbright Scholar, France, 62-63; Winner, New York City Conct Artists Guild, 64; Regents Fac Fel, Univ Calif, San Diego, 76. *Mem:* Int Asn Experimental Res Singing (gen secy, 73-). *Mailing Add:* Music Sch NTex State Univ Denton TX 76203

LARGENT, EDWARD J, JR
EDUCATOR, COMPOSER
b Waukegan, Ill, Feb 8, 36. *Study:* Ohio State Univ, with Marshall Barnes & Mark Walker, BS, 60, BM, 63, PhD, 72; Univ Ill, with Salvatore Martirano & Thomas Frederickson, MM, 64. *Works:* Symphony for Brass, 66; Cantata for Easter, 66; Trio (violin, horn & piano), 67; Sextet for Winds, 69; Song (sop, flute & piano), 69; Horn Sonata, 70; Experimental Tapes #2, Sirens, 73. *Teaching:* Fac mem, Western Ky Univ, 66-70; assoc prof music, Youngstown State Univ, 70- *Awards:* Second Prize, Phi Mu Alpha Cont, Ohio State Univ, 63 & 66. *Mailing Add:* Sch Music Youngstown State Univ Youngstown OH 44555

LARIMER, FRANCES H
EDUCATOR, PIANO
b Tavares, Fla. *Study:* Northwestern Univ, BM, 52, MM, 54. *Teaching:* Assoc prof piano, pedagogy & group piano, Northwestern Univ, 67-; guest prof, Rubin Acad Music, Jerusalem, summers 71, 73 & 76. *Awards:* Fac Fel, Ctr Teaching Professions, Northwestern Univ, 71-74; grant, Spencer Found, 74. *Mem:* Music Teachers Nat Asn; Music Educr Nat Conf; Col Music Soc; Int Soc Music Educr. *Publ:* Ed, Contemporary Collection for Piano Students, Summy-Birchard Publ, 74; Auth, Teaching with Tape, Clavier Mag, 75; contribr, piano music rev, Notes, 79. *Rep:* 2760 Crawford Ave Evanston IL 60201. *Mailing Add:* Sch Music Northwestern Univ Evanston IL 60201

LARIMER, MELVIN SHERLOCK
CONDUCTOR, EDUCATOR
b Bronson, Mich, Nov 17, 30. *Study:* Albion Col, AB, 53; Univ Mich, MA, 63; Mich State Univ, MME, 80. *Rec Perf:* High sch choral & operetta rec, Nat Music Camp, annually. *Teaching:* Choral dir, Alma, Pontiac & Traverse City Pub Sch, Mich, 53-70 & Nat Music Camp, 62-; choral dir & dept chmn, Olivet Col, 70-75 & Albion Col, 76- *Awards:* Teacher of Year, Mich Sch Vocal Asn, 65. *Mailing Add:* Music Dept Albion Col Albion MI 49224

LARKIN, BRUCE DAVID
PERCUSSION, RECORDER
b Grand Rapids, Sept 2, 48. *Study:* Univ Mich, BMus, 76; Sarah Lawrence Col, MFA, 78. *Pos:* Prin perc, Grand Rapids Symph, 69-70; music dir, New York Recorder Guild, 82- *Mem:* Am Musicol Soc; Am Recorder Soc. *Mailing Add:* 240 W 98th St Apt 5A New York NY 10025

LARSEN, HENRY
CLARINET, COMPOSER
b Port Reading, NJ. *Study:* New England Consv, with Carolillo, 48-50; Hartt Sch Music, with Bellison, BMus, 52, MMus, 61; New England Consv, with Mazzeo, 55-56. *Works:* Concerto for Clarinet and Jazz Band, 82. *Pos:* Asst prin clarinet, Hartford Symph, 50-74. *Teaching:* Assoc prof clarinet, saxophone & chamber music, Hartt Col Music, 50- *Mem:* Am Fedn Musicians (mem exec bd, 59-68); Pi Kappa Lambda. *Publ:* Auth, The Young Clarinetists Friend, Larsen Prod, 82. *Rep:* Woodwind Ed PO Box 457 Sta K Toronto Ont Can M4P 2G4. *Mailing Add:* 192 N Main St West Hartford CT 06107

LARSEN, LIBBY (ELIZABETH BROWN)
COMPOSER

b Wilmington, Del, Dec 24, 50. *Study:* Univ Minn, BA, 71, MA, 75, PhD, 78. *Works:* Bronze Veils, comn & perf by William McGlaughlin, 79; Ulloa's Ring, comn by Schubert Club St Paul, 80; Pinions, comn & perf by St Paul Chamber Orch, 81; In A Winter Garden, comn & perf by Plymouth Music Series, 82; Overture, comn by Am Comp Orch, 83; Travelling in Every Season, comn by Schubert Club St Paul, 83; Deep Summer Music, comn & perf by Minn Orch, 83. *Pos:* Co-founder & managing comp, Minn Comp Forum, St Paul, 73-; comp in res, Minn Orch, Minneapolis, 83- *Awards:* Grants, Nat Endowment Arts, 83 & Exxon/Rockefeller Found & Meet the Comp, 83-85. *Bibliog:* Minnesota Artists: Libby Larsen (film), KTCA TV, 81; Charles Ward (auth), Libby Larsen: Making Music on the Prairie, Houston Chronicle, 10/24/81; Bruce Morrow (auth), Orchestrating Life and Music, Minn Daily, 3/15/82. *Mem:* Minn Comp Forum Inc; Am Music Ctr; Meet the Comp. *Rep:* E C Schirmer Music Co 112 South St Boston MA 02111. *Mailing Add:* 2028 Dayton Ave St Paul MN 55104

LARSEN, ROBERT L
EDUCATOR, CONDUCTOR

b Walnut, Iowa, Nov 28, 34. *Study:* Simpson Col, BM, 56; Univ Mich, MM(piano perf), 58; Ind Univ, MusD(opera & cond), 71; studied piano with Sven Lekberg, Joseph Brinkman, Rudolph Ganz, Walter Bricht, cond with Wolfgang Vacano, Tibor Kozma & operatic stage dir with Boris Goldovsky. *Pos:* Artistic dir, Des Moines Civic Opera, 64-65 & Des Moines Metro Opera Co, currently; conct pianist & accmp, currently; cond, Madrigal Singers, currently; stage dir, Carmel Bach Fest, Calif, 82. *Teaching:* Prof & chmn, Div Fine Arts, Simpson Col, currently; coach, Berkshire Music Ctr, formerly, Oglebay Park, WVa, formerly, Chicago, formerly & New York, formerly. *Awards:* Gov Award Music, Iowa Arts Coun, 74. *Mem:* Phi Mu Alpha; Pi Kappa Lambda. *Mailing Add:* 713 W Ashland Indianola IA 50125

LARSON, ANDRE PIERRE
ADMINISTRATOR, EDUCATOR

b Little Fork, Minn, Nov 10, 42. *Study:* Univ SDak, BFA, 64, MM, 67; WVa Univ, PhD, 74. *Pos:* Ed, Newsletter of the Shrine to Music Museum, 73- & Catalog of the Collections, Shrine to Music Museum, 80 & 82, Shrine to Music Museum Found; ed newsletter, Am Musical Instrm Soc, 76- *Teaching:* Prof musicol & dir, Shrine to Music Museum & Ctr for Study Hist Musical Instrm, Univ SDak, 72- *Mem:* Am Musical Instrm Soc (pres, 81-); Int Comt Musical Instrm Museums & Collections Int Coun Museums; Sonneck Soc. *Interests:* History of musical instruments. *Mailing Add:* 325 Linden Vermillion SD 57069

LARSON, ANNA (BARBARA)
COMPOSER, LECTURER

b Knoxville, Tenn, Nov 9, 40. *Study:* Sarah Lawrence Col, studied comp with Andre Singer, BA(music), 62; studied piano with Florence Robertson, 70-77 & Tamara Dmitrieff, 78-79; Va Commonwealth Univ, studied comp with Jack Jarrett, MMus, 78; Duke Univ, studied comp with Robert Ward & cond with Allen Bone, 79-80; Univ Md, comp study with Mark Wilson, cond with William Hudson & theory with Thomas Delio, currently. *Works:* Dirge Without Music (collage of poetry accmp by synthesized sounds), 75, Impromptu (piano), 77 & Song for Piano, 77, perf by comp; Dance for Orchestra (full orch & piano), perf by Va Commonwealth Univ Orch, 78; The Picnic (children's musical play), perf at Spring Hill Elem Sch, 81; Nora! Nora! (tenor aria), perf by John Hanks & Lee Ann Cheeves, 81; The Listeners (bar voice & piano, on poem by Walter de la Mare), Arsis Press (in press). *Teaching:* Music, Milton Acad, Mass, 62-63, Jack & Jill Sch, Richmond, Va, 66-68 & Col Sch, Richmond, Va, 68-70; adj lectr, George Washington Univ, spring 78; guest lectr, Lynchberg Col, 79 & 83. *Awards:* Va Ctr Creative Arts Fel, 79 & 83. *Mem:* Pi Kappa Lambda; Int League Women Comp; Am Women Comp; SEastern Comp League. *Mailing Add:* 8014 Falstaff Rd McLean VA 22102

LARSON, DAVID DYNES
CONDUCTOR, EDUCATOR

b Evanston, Ill, Nov 25, 26. *Study:* Univ Mich, BM, 49, MM, 50; Sch Sacred Music, Union Theol Sem, SMD, 61. *Pos:* Music dir, NShore Choral Soc, 73-; guest cond, Shanghai Phil Orch & Chorus, China, 82. *Teaching:* Asst prof music, Wilmington Col, Ohio, 50-54; prof, Kobe Col, Nishinomiya, Japan, 54-66 & 81-82; prof cond, Chicago Musical Col, Roosevelt Univ, 66- *Awards:* Res fel, Roosevelt Univ, 74. *Mem:* Am Choral Dir Asn; Am Musicol Soc; Col Music Soc; Hymn Soc Am. *Interests:* Choral music for women's voices written for the 18th-century Venetian Ospedali. *Publ:* Ed, Hymns of the Church, United Church of Christ, Japan, 63; auth, Women and Song in Eighteenth Century-Venice, Choral J, 10/77. *Mailing Add:* 2743 Broadway Evanston IL 60201

LARSON, LENNOX ADAMSON
TEACHER, PIANO

b Carey, Idaho, Nov 18, 26. *Study:* Univ Utah, BS, 47; Worcester Col, Oxford, England, cert, 81. *Teaching:* Assoc prof piano, Univ Utah, 60- *Mem:* Nat Music Teachers Asn; Fedn Music Clubs. *Mailing Add:* 1334 Chandler Dr Salt Lake City UT 84103

LARSON, SUSAN
SOPRANO

b New Rochelle, NY, Feb 13, 44. *Study:* Ind Univ, BA; New England Consv, MA. *Roles:* Melisande in Pelleas et Melisande; Fiordiligi in Cose fan tutte; Pamina in Die Zauberflöte; Marchesa in Un Giorno di Regno; Nero in The Coronation of Poppea; Donna Elvira in Don Giovanni; Dorinda in Orlando, Am Repertory. *Pos:* Prin sop, Emmanuel Music; soloist, Boston Symph Orch, Lyr Opera Chicago, Santa Fe Chamber Music Fest, Basel Stadtheater, Banchetto Musicale & Monadnock Music Fest; founding mem, Liederkreis Ens. *Mailing Add:* c/o Howard Hart Mgt 114 Clinton St Suite 5D Brooklyn NY 11201

LARUE, ADRIAN JAN PIETERS
EDUCATOR, WRITER

b Sumatra, Indonesia, July 31, 18; US citizen. *Study:* Harvard Univ, BS, 40, PhD(musicol), 52; Princeton Univ, MFA, 42. *Pos:* Res consult, Moravian Music Arch, 62-; coun mem, Smithsonian Inst, 67-73; mem, Fulbright selection panels, 59-62 & 67-70; chmn liaison comt, Am Musicol Soc, Kennedy Ctr, Mozart & Haydn Fest, 73-76. *Teaching:* Instr music, Wellesley Col, 42-43 & 46-47, asst prof, 47-49, assoc prof, 49-57, chmn dept music, 49-57 & 70-73, exec dean, 62-63; Fulbright res prof, Austria, 54-56; prof, Grad Sch Arts & Sci, NY Univ, 57- *Awards:* Fels, Ford Found, 54-55 & Guggenheim & Am Coun Learned Soc, 64-65. *Publ:* Ed, Report Int Musicol Cong, 61-62; Festschrift Otto Erich Deutsch, 63; coauth & ed, Aspects of Medieval and Renaissance Music: A Birthday Offering for Gustave Reese, 66 & auth, Guidelines for Style Analysis, 70, Norton; The Okinawan Court-Song Tradition, Harvard Univ (in prep). *Mailing Add:* 15 Edgehill Dr Darien CT 06820

LASOCKI, DAVID RONALD GRAHAM
WRITER, FLUTE

b London, England, Jan 8, 47. *Study:* Univ Iowa, MA, 72, PhD, 83. *Teaching:* Instr musicol, Lake Forest Col, 73-74 & Univ Iowa, 81. *Mem:* Am Musicol Soc. *Interests:* History, music and performance practices of woodwind instruments; editions of 18th century woodwind music. *Publ:* Ed, Hotteterre, Principles of the Flute, Recorder and Oboe, Praeger, 68; Coauth, Free Ornamentation for Woodwind Instruments, 1700-1775, 76 & The Classical Woodwind Cadenza: A Workbook, 78, McGinnis & Marx; auth, New Light on Handel's Woodwind Sonatas, Am Recorder, 81; coauth, The Art of Preluding, 1700-1830, for Flutists, Etc, McGinnis & Marx, 83. *Mailing Add:* 1614 Morningside Dr Iowa City IA 52240

LASZLOFFY, JEROME
CONDUCTOR, EDUCATOR

b New York, NY, Aug 23, 30. *Study:* Study with Pierre Monteux, 60-64; Manhattan Sch Music, MEd, 61; study with Pierre Boultz, 69. *Pos:* Cond, Cent Fla Ballet Orch, 62, Queens Fest Orch, 63-66, Univ Conn Orch, 66-80, New Britain Symph, Conn, 67. *Teaching:* Prof cond, Univ Conn, 66- *Mailing Add:* 444 Middle Turnpike Mansfield Depot CT 06251

LATEINER, JACOB
EDUCATOR, PIANO

b Havana, Cuba, May 31, 28. *Study:* Curtis Inst Music, piano with Isabelle Vengerova, chamber music with William Primrose & Marcel Tabuteau & theory with Constant Vauclain & Gian Carlo Menotti, 40-47; studied comp with Felix Greissle & Arnold Schönberg. *Rec Perf:* On Westminster, RCA & Columbia Masterworks. *Pos:* Recitalist touring US, Europe & Australia, 47-; soloist, New York Phil, Los Angeles Phil, Berlin Phil, Boston Orch, Cleveland Orch, Chicago Symph, Minneapolis Symph & BBC-London Symph Orch; chamber music concts with Jascha Heifetz & Gregor Piatigorsky, 62-68. *Teaching:* Mem fac piano, Mannes Col Music, 63-70 & Juilliard Sch Music, 66-; fac mem & perf artist, Aspen Music Fest & Sch, 65, 66 & 71; prof piano, New York Sch Educ, currently. *Awards:* Ford Found Fel Perf Artist, 59 & 67. *Rep:* Tornay Mgt 1995 Broadway New York NY 10023. *Mailing Add:* Juilliard Sch Music Lincoln Ctr New York NY 10023

LATHAM, WILLIAM P
COMPOSER, EDUCATOR

b Shreveport, La, July 4, 17. *Study:* Cincinnati Consv Music, BSc(music educ), 38; Col Music Cincinnati, BMus, 40, MMus(comp), 41; Eastman Sch Music, Univ Rochester, PhD(comp), 51. *Works:* Suite for Trumpet and String Orchestra, perf by Eastman-Rochester Orch, 51; Symphony No 2 (sinfonietta), perf by Peninsula Fest Orch, 54; Concerto Grosso (2 sax & orch), Dorn Publ, 62; Sysiphus 1971 (sax & piano), comn by Francois Daneels, 71; Fusion, Symphonic Wind Ensemble, comn by Loyola Univ, 75; Gaudeamus Academe (chr), comn by NTex State Univ, 81; Te Deum Tejas (sop, flutes & perc), Dorn Publ, 81. *Teaching:* Prof music, Univ Northern Iowa, 46-65; prof music, NTex State Univ, 65, dir grad studies music, 69, distinguished prof, 78- *Awards:* First Prize, grad div, Nat Comp Cont, Phi Mu Alpha Sinfonia, 51; ann ASCAP Awards, 62- *Mem:* Am Soc Univ Comp; ASCAP; Phi Mu Alpha Sinfonia; Col Music Soc; Pi Kappa Lambda. *Mailing Add:* 1815 Southridge Dr Denton TX 76201

LATHOM, WANDA B
EDUCATOR, MUSIC THERAPIST

b Sheridan, Wyo, July 11, 36. *Study:* Univ Kans, BME, 58, MME, 61, PhD, 70. *Pos:* Dir music therapy, Parsons State Hospital, Kans, 61-66. *Teaching:* Music, Clay Center, Kans Pub Sch, 58-59; asst prof & dir music therapy, Montclair State Col, NJ, 69-72; prof music & dir music therapy, Univ Mo, Kansas City, 72- *Awards:* President's Award, Nat Asn Music Therapy, 83. *Mem:* Nat Asn Music Therapy; Midwest Regional Asn Music Therapy; Music Educr Nat Conf; Mo Music Educr. *Interests:* Music therapy. *Publ:* Auth, Role of Music Therapy in Education of Handicapped Children and Youth, Hawkins & Assoc, 80; Survey of Current Functions of a Music Therapist, J Music Therapy, spring 82; coauth, Music for the Severely Handicapped, Music Educr J, 4/82; Musical Preferences of Older People Attending Nutrition Sites, Educ Gerontology, 82; co-ed, Music Therapy for Handicapped Children, Inst Therapeutic Res, 83. *Mailing Add:* 489 E 55th St Kansas City MO 64110

LATHROP, GAYLE POSSELT
EDUCATOR, COMPOSER

b Chicago, Ill, Feb 7, 42. *Study:* Ind Univ, with Thomas Beversdorf & Bernhard Heiden; Humboldt State Univ, with Leon Wagner; studied with John Gibson & Robert Muczynski, 76-78. *Works:* State of the Union, (band), 68; Anaphora #1 (solo guitar), 77; Meditation #1 (guitar & viola), 77; Duologue (flute & tape), 77; Cues (prepared flutes & perc), 78; Towhit (women's speech chorus), 78; Tenebrae Service (chorus), Tucson, 79. *Teaching:* Music dir, Hoopa Pub Sch, Calif, 68-70; instr guitar, Humboldt State Univ, 72 & Col of Redwoods, 73-76; instr music, Susquehanna Univ, 78- *Mailing Add:* Music Dept Susquehanna Univ Selinsgrove PA 17870

LATIMER, JAMES H
COMPOSER, PERCUSSION

b Tulsa, Okla, June 27, 34. *Study:* Ind Univ, Bloomington, BM, 56; Boston Univ, MM, 64; Berkshire Music Ctr, 63. *Works:* Variations on the Westminster Clock Theme (four solo timpani), 55; Blood on the Moon (perc), 58; Movement (band), 57; MEH (orch), 59; Coquette (perc), 67; Woman in Red (perc), 68; Motif for Percussion, 69. *Pos:* Music dir, Wis Youth Symph Orchs, 72-78 & Capitol City Band Asn, currently; mem, New Boston Perc Ens; timpanist, Madison Symph Orch; founding mem, Madison Marimba Quartet; ed, Who's Who in the World of Percussion, currently. *Teaching:* Mem fac, Fla A&M Univ, 57-62; head perc dept, Univ Wis, Madison, 68- *Awards:* John Hay Whitney Fel, 62. *Rep:* Frothingham Mgt 384 Washington St Wellesley Hills MA 02181. *Mailing Add:* 3922 Hillcrest Dr Madison WI 53705

LATIOLAIS, DESIREE JAYNE
COMPOSER, PIANO

b Natchitoches, La, Oct 20, 28. *Study:* Southwestern La Inst, BA(music), 48; La State Univ, MM(music), 50; Univ Mich; Ohio State Univ. *Works:* Passacaglia & Double Fugue (orch), perf by Northwestern La Symph, 51; Introduction & Allegro, perf by La State Univ Symph Orch, 51; Sonata for Clarinet and Piano, perf by Burdette Green & Jane Hamborsky, 71 & 72; Suite for Piano, perf by comp, 73-74 & 80-81; Passacaglia & Double Fugue (two pianos), perf by Harriet Green & comp, 74-76; Duo for Cello & Violin, perf by Marya Giesy & Karl Kornacker, 74; Salome (voice, cello, flute & piano), 80 & 81. *Teaching:* Guest lectr, Ohio State Univ, Columbus, 69-73; instr, Denison Univ, 73-76. *Awards:* First Place Award Comp, Nat Fedn Music Clubs, 72. *Mem:* Ohio Music Teachers Asn; Ohio Fedn Music Clubs. *Publ:* Auth, Study Guide for Ohio Music Teachers Association Certification, Ohio Music Teachers Asn, 80. *Mailing Add:* 3100 Raccoon Valley Rd Granville OH 43023

LAUFER, BEATRICE
COMPOSER, LECTURER

b New York, NY. *Study:* Juilliard Sch Music, studied comp with Roger Sessions & Marion Bauer, studied orch with Vittorio Giannini, 43-45; studied with Marion Bauer, 46-50. *Works:* Song of the Fountain (choral), Leeds Music Publ, 52; Ile, based on a play by Eugene O'Neill (one-act opera), perf by Royal Opera Co, Stockholm, Sweden, 58 & rec Yale Sch Music, 80; Symphony No 2, perf by Oklahoma City Symph Orch, 62; And Thomas Jefferson Said, 75, Cry (orch trilogy), 77, Symphony No 1, 82 & The Great God Brown, based on a play by Eugene O'Neill (ballet), Belwin-Mills Publ. *Pos:* Cond radio prog, Young Am Artists, 62-78 & The Cond Speaks, 67-69, WNYC. *Awards:* Am Asn for UN Award, 52; Bicentennial Grant, Conn Comn Arts, 75; ASCAP Award, 77- *Mem:* ASCAP; Am Music Ctr; Am Symph Orch League; Delta Omicron. *Publ:* Auth, Problems on Writing an Opera and Some Afterthoughts, Am Comp Alliance Bulletin, 56; A Woman Composer Speaks Out, 6/67 & Bernstein and Ginastera Premiers Featured as Kennedy Center Opens, 6/72, ASCAP Today. *Mailing Add:* PO Box 3 Lenox Hill Station New York NY 10021

LAUGHTON, JOHN CHARLES
EDUCATOR, CLARINET

b Sioux City, Iowa, Oct 9, 46. *Study:* Univ Iowa, BMus, 68, DMA, 80; Cath Univ Am, MMus, 72. *Pos:* Clarinet soloist, Apple Hill Chamber Players, East Sullivan, NH, 74-; dir, Tidewater Music Fest, St Mary's City, Md, 82- *Teaching:* Assoc prof music, St Mary's Col, Md, 74- *Awards:* Fulbright Fel, 83. *Publ:* Auth, The Wind Chamber Music of Darius Milhaud, Chamber Music Quart, Medici Music Press, 83. *Rep:* Chamber Artists Mgt Apple Hill East Sullivan NH 03445. *Mailing Add:* PO Box 83 St Mary's City MD 20686

LAURIDSEN, MORTEN JOHANNES
COMPOSER, EDUCATOR

b Colfax, Wash, Feb 27, 43. *Study:* Whitman Col; Univ Southern Calif, DMA, 74; studied comp with Halsey Stevens, Ingolf Dahl, Robert Linn & Harold Owen. *Works:* Mid-Winter Songs (for chorus & piano or orch); Four Madrigals on Renaissance Texts; Sonato for Trumpet and Piano; Be Still, My Soul, Be Still; Cuatro Canciones sobre Poesias de Federico Garcia Lorca; Four Psalms (for chorus); and other choral & chamber works. *Rec Perf:* On Orion, Protone & Opus Rec. *Teaching:* Assoc prof music theory & comp, Univ Southern Calif, 67- *Awards:* Sam & Harriette Stark Fel; Alchin Fel; ASCAP Award. *Mailing Add:* Music Dept Univ Southern Calif 840 W 34th St Los Angeles CA 90089

LAUT, EDWARD ALLEN
EDUCATOR, CELLO

b Oct 16, 44. *Study:* Ind Univ, with Janos Starker, BMus, 66; Catholic Univ Am, MMus, 72. *Pos:* Prin, Manila Symph, Philippines, 66-68; US Air Force Band, Bolling AFB, Washington, DC, 69-73 & Atlantic Symph, Halifax, NS, 73-74; assoc prin, Montreal Symph, Quebec, 68-69; asst prin pro-tem, Cleveland Orch, 74-77. *Teaching:* Prof violoncello, Univ Kans, Lawrence, 77- *Mailing Add:* Dept Music Univ Kans Lawrence KS 66045

LAWERGREN, BO T
COMPOSER, EDUCATOR

b Sweden, Jan 4, 37. *Study:* Univ Uppsala, Sweden, Fil Kand, 59; Australian Nat Univ, Canberra, PhD, 64. *Works:* Captain Cook (mini opera), perf by Contemp Chamber Players, Univ Chicago, 75; Marche Funebre (trombone & piano), perf by Per Brevig & Adolovni Acosta, 76; Concerto (piano & orch), perf by East & West Artist Orch, 77; Farfar (solo piano), perf by Adolovni Acosta, 78; Arietta (mixed choir), comn by Gregg Smith Singers, 78; Semi-zoo (opera), perf by East & West Artists Orch, 79. *Teaching:* Assoc prof, Hunter Col, 70-82, prof, 82- *Awards:* Grant, Nat Endowment Arts, 76; fels, Martha Baird Rockefeller Fund, 76 & Yaddo, Saratoga, NY, 77. *Mem:* ASCAP; Catgut Soc; Galpin Soc; Am Musicol Soc; Int Coun Traditional Music. *Interests:* Acoustics of musical instruments; archaeology of musical instruments. *Publ:* Auth, On the Motion of Bowed Violin Strings, Acustica, Vol 44, 194-206; Acoustics and Evolution of Arched Harps, Galpin Soc J, Vol 34: 110-129; Acoustics of Musical Bows, Acustica, Vol 51: 63-65; Harmonics of S-Motion of Bowed Violin Strings, J Acoustical Soc Am, Vol 73: 2174-2179; The Cylinder Kithara in Etruria, Greece, Anatolia, Imago Musicae I, 83. *Mailing Add:* Hunter Col 695 Park Ave New York NY 10021

LAWLESS, LYNDON KENT
MUSIC DIRECTOR, BAROQUE VIOLIN

b Tulsa, Okla, July 10, 45. *Rec Perf:* Brandenburg Concertos, Timegate, 82. *Pos:* Music dir & founder, Ars Musica, Ann Arbor, Mich, 70- *Publ:* Auth, Why Original Instruments?, Continuo Mag, 82. *Mailing Add:* 528 Second St Ann Arbor MI 48103

LAWRENCE, ARTHUR PETER
WRITER, EDUCATOR

b Durham, NC, July 15, 37. *Study:* Davidson Col, AB, 59; Fla State Univ, MMus, 61; Stanford Univ, DMA, 68. *Pos:* Ed & publ, Diapason, Chicago, Ill, 76-82; assoc ed, Am Organist, 82- *Teaching:* Instr organ & choral, Centre Col, Danville, Ky, 68-69; asst prof, Univ Notre Dame, 69-71; from asst to assoc prof & dept chmn, St Mary's Col, Notre Dame, Ind, 69-80. *Mem:* Am Guild Organists (sub-dean & dean, 70-73); Am Musicol Soc; Am Musical Instrm Soc; Organ Hist Soc; Int Musicol Soc. *Interests:* Eighteenth century French harpsichord repertoire; 19th & 20th century American organ building. *Publ:* Coauth, Organ-Harpsichord Duo Repertoire, Diapason, 74; Rev in Notes, Tracker, Diapason, Music, Am Organist & J Am Musical Instrm Soc. *Mailing Add:* 122 E 27th St 4C New York NY 10016

LAWRENCE, DOUGLAS HOWARD
BARITONE

b Los Angeles, Calif, Sept 26, 42. *Study:* Univ Southern Calif, BMus, 66, MMus, 73; studied voice with William Vennard & song lit with Koldofsky. *Rec Perf:* War Requiem (Britten), Klavier, 73; Sacred Service (Bloch), Angel, 76. *Roles:* Germont in La traviata, San Francisco Opera, 73; Ottone & Coronation of Poppea, Washington DC Opera Soc, 74; Lescaut in Manon Lescaut, San Diego Opera, 74; appearances with Los Angeles Phil, Boston Symph, Hollywood Bowl, San Francisco Symph, Milwaukee Symph, Carmel Bach Fest, Phil Orch, Ore Bach Fest & Bethlehem Bach Fest. *Teaching:* Instr, El Camino Col, 67-73; lectr, Univ Southern Calif, 73-76; artist in res, Occidental Col, 81-82. *Awards:* Opera Inst Am Grant, 73. *Mem:* Nat Asn Teachers Singing; Am Guild Musical Artists. *Rep:* Hamlen Landau Mgt Inc 140 W 79th St Suite 2A New York NY 10024. *Mailing Add:* 740 S Euclid Pasadena CA 91106

LAWRENCE, JOY ELIZABETH
EDUCATOR, ORGAN

b Cleveland, Ohio, Feb 13, 26. *Study:* Mt Union Col, BM, 48; Union Theol Sem, SMM, 51; Case Western Reserve Univ, PhD, 74. *Pos:* Organist & dir music, Rocky River Methodist Church, 51-55. *Teaching:* Choral & gen music, Elem Sch, Strongsville, Ohio, 55-56, Elem Sch, Rocky River, Ohio, 56-61, Horace Mann Jr High Sch, Lakewood, Ohio, 61-63, Monticello Jr High Sch & Roxboro Jr High Sch, Cleveland Heights, Ohio, 63-74; assoc prof music educ, Kent State Univ, 74- *Mem:* Music Educr Nat Conf; Am Choral Dir Asn; Am Guild Organists; Ohio Music Educr Asn; Soc Gen Music. *Interests:* Related arts; history and philosophy of music education. *Publ:* Coauth, Music and Related Arts for the Classroom, Kendall Hunt, 78; A Musician's Guide to Church Music, Pilgrim Press, 81; Approaches to Allied Arts, 9/82 & Plug Into a Computer to Plan Your Repertory, 12/78, Music Educr J; auth, We Are America's Children—We Celebrate Ourselves, Triad, Ohio Music Educr Asn, 4/83. *Mailing Add:* 3565 Cedarbrook University Heights OH 44118

LAWRENCE, KEVIN JOHN
EDUCATOR, VIOLIN

b Boston, Mass, Aug 16, 57. *Study:* Juilliard Sch, BM, 79, MM, 80. *Teaching:* Fac mem, Meadowmount Sch, Westport, NY, 80-; artist in res, Univ Va, 80-, cond string orch, 82- *Mem:* Col Music Soc. *Mailing Add:* 1160 Stonefield Lane Charlottesville VA 22901

LAWRENCE, LUCILLE
HARP, EDUCATOR

Study: Harp with Carlos Salzedo. *Pos:* Recitalist, radio symph & orchs; judge, Int Harp Cont, Israel, 62, 65, 73 & 76. *Teaching:* Mem fac harp, Mannes Col Music, 42-, Manhattan Sch Music, 67- & Berkshire Music Ctr, 69- *Mem:* Music Educr Nat Conf. *Mailing Add:* Mannes Col Music 157 E 74th St New York NY 10021

LAWRENCE, MARK HOWARD
TROMBONE, EDUCATOR
b Ames, Iowa, Oct 6, 48. *Study:* Univ Mich, 67-68; Curtis Inst Music, BM, 68-72. *Pos:* Prin trombone, Nat Symph Colombia, 72, Denver Symph, 73-74 & San Francisco Symph, 74-; trombone, Empire Brass Quintet, 81-82. *Teaching:* Prof trombone, San Francisco Consv, 78- & Boston Univ, 81-82. *Mem:* Int Trombone Asn. *Mailing Add:* 20 Tilden Circle San Rafael CA 94901

LAWRENCE, VERA BRODSKY
WRITER, PIANO
b Norfolk, Va, July 1, 09. *Study:* Piano with Josef & Rosina Lhevinne & theory with Rubin Goldmark; Juilliard Sch. *Pos:* Admin publ, Contemp Music Proj. *Teaching:* Instr, Curtis Inst & Juilliard Sch, formerly. *Awards:* Grants, Rockefeller Found, 70 & 71 & Nat Endowment Humanities, 78-84; fel, Guggenheim Found, 76. *Mem:* Music Libr Asn; Sonneck Soc. *Interests:* Nineteenth century American music history, specifically New York. *Publ:* Ed, The Wa-Wan Press (five vols), Arno/NY Times, 70; auth, Music for Patriots, Politicians, and Presidents, Macmillan, 75. *Mailing Add:* 425 E 58th St New York NY 10022

LAWSON, ALICE (ALICE LAWSON ABER)
HARP
b St Paul, Minn, Nov 19, 16. *Study:* Univ Minn, BA, 42, Dominican Col San Rafael, MA, 76; Western Colo Univ. *Pos:* Harpist, Minn & Calif, 35-62; hist musicol, 70-; publ & owner, Harp Publ, 70- *Teaching:* Harp, Girls Schools, Dominican Col & privately, 60-76. *Mem:* Am Harp Soc; Am Musicol Soc. *Interests:* Harps and history and music of harps. *Publ:* Ed, Two Catalogues: Music for Harp, Voice, Oboe, Piano and Cello with Notes, Harp Publ, 70 & 75; auth, Johann Baptist Krumpholtz, 73 & Jean Baptist Cardon, 74, Am Harp J; articles in New Grove Dict of Music & Musicians, 80. *Mailing Add:* 3437 Tice Creek Dr No 2 Walnut Creek CA 94595

LAYCOCK, RALPH GEORGE
MUSIC DIRECTOR, EDUCATOR
b Raymond, Alta, Feb 11, 20. *Study:* Brigham Young Univ, with Leroy Robertson, with John Halliday, BA(music), 41; Juilliard Sch Music, with Thor Johnson, Edgar Schenkmann, Arthur Christman & Vittorio Gianini, MS(cond), 48; Univ Southern Calif, with Walter Ducloux & Halsey Stevens, DMA(cond), 70. *Pos:* Woodwinds & Bass, Utah Symph, 48-49; cond, Utah Valley Symph, 78- *Teaching:* Asst prof woodwinds, Drake Univ, 49-53; prof music, Brigham Young Univ, 53- *Mem:* Music Educr Nat Conf; Am Fedn Musicians. *Publ:* Auth, Conductor's Corner (column), Instrumentalist, 64-72; coauth, And It Came to Pass, Trimedia, 64; auth, Simplified Accompaniments for LDS Hymns, Deseret Bk, 75; Music for the Home, Sonos, 75. *Mailing Add:* E 464 HFAC Brigham Young Univ Provo UT 84602

LAYTON, BILLY JIM
COMPOSER, EDUCATOR
b Corsicana, Tex, Nov 14, 24. *Study:* New England Consv Music, with Carl McKinley & Francis Judd Cooke, BMus, 48; Yale Sch Music, with Quincy Parker, MMus, 50; Univ Calif, Berkeley, 54; Harvard Univ, with Walter Piston, PhD, 60; studied musicol with Otto Gombosi & Nino Pirrotta. *Works:* Five Studies for Violin and Piano, 52; An American Portrait (symphonic overture), 53; Three Dylan Thomas Poems (mixed chorus & brass sextets), 54-56; String Quartet in Two Movements, 56; Three Studies for Piano, 57; Divertimento (chamber orch), 58-60; Dance Fantasy for Orchestra, 64. *Teaching:* Mem fac, New England Consv Music, 59-60 & Harvard Univ, 60-66; prof, State Univ NY, Stony Brook, 66-, chmn music dept, 66-72, 82- *Awards:* Creative Arts Award, Brandeis Univ, 61; Guggenheim Fel, 63; Rome Prize, 54-57. *Mem:* Am Music Ctr (dir, 72-74); founding mem, Am Soc Univ Comp; ASCAP; Am Musicol Soc; Int Soc Contemp Music (dir US sect, 68-70). *Publ:* Contribr to Perspectives of New Music. *Mailing Add:* 4 Johns Rd Setauket NY 11733

LAZAR, JOEL
CONDUCTOR & MUSIC DIRECTOR
b New York, NY, Mar 19, 41. *Study:* Harvard Univ, with Walter Piston, Randall Thompson & Pierre Boulez, AB, 61, AM, 63; private cond study with Jascha Horenstein, 70-73. *Rec Perf:* Saul and David (Carl Nielsen), Unicorn Rec, 76. *Pos:* Res cond, Tulsa Phil Orch, 78-80 & music dir, 80-83. *Teaching:* Instr music, NY Univ, 66-69; asst prof, Univ Va, Charlottesville, 69-71. *Awards:* Fel, Frank Huntington Beebe Fund, 71-73. *Mem:* Hon mem, Bruckner Soc Am. *Rep:* Shaw Concts Inc 1995 Broadway New York NY 10023. *Mailing Add:* 9100 Friars Rd Bethesda MD 20817

LAZAROF, HENRI
COMPOSER, EDUCATOR
b Sofia, Bulgaria, Apr 12, 32. *Study:* Sofia Acad Music; studied with Paul Ben-Haim; Ste Cecilia Acad, Rome, with Goffredo Petrassi, 55-57; Brandeis Univ, with Harold Shapero, MFA, 59. *Works:* Spectrum (trumpet, orch & tape), 73; Duo for Cello and Piano, 73; Concertazioni (trumpet, six instrm & tape), 73; Flute Concerto, 73; Adieu (clarinet & piano), 74; Third Chamber Concerto (12 soloists), 74; Viol: Canti da requiem (solo viola & two string ens), 77. *Teaching:* Mem fac, Univ Calif, Los Angeles, 65- *Awards:* La Scala Award, Milan, 66; Koussevitzky Int Rec Award, 69; Nat Endowment Arts Grant, 73. *Mailing Add:* 718 N Maple Dr Beverly Hills CA 90210

LAZARUS, ROY
EDUCATOR, STAGE DIRECTOR
b New York, NY. *Study:* Juilliard Sch Music, 54-55; Syracuse Univ, BM & MM, 67. *Works:* The Impressario (Mozart), New English Version, comn & perf by Ky Opera Asn, 78. *Rec Perf:* The Most Happy Fella, Columbia Rec, 56. *Roles:* Ramfis in Aida, Baltimore Opera, 55; Zuniga, 58 & William Jennings Bryant in Ballad of Baby Doe, 58, New York City Opera; Don Basilio in Il Barbiere di Siviglia, 59 & Horace in Regina, 59, Santa Fe Opera. *Pos:* Dir & gen mgr, Oberlin Music Theatre, 69-72; dir opera theatre, Juilliard Sch Music, 67-68; stage dir, San Francisco Opera, Detroit Opera, Ky Opera & Kansas City Opera, 74- *Teaching:* Voice, Ind Univ, 65-66; assoc prof, musical theatre, Consv Music, Oberlin Col, 68-72; dir opera, Col Musical Arts, Bowling Green State Univ, currently. *Awards:* Distinguished Alumnus Award, Syracuse Univ, 72. *Bibliog:* Maestro, doc film, PBS, Louisville, Ky, 77. *Mailing Add:* Rte 1 Box 155 North Edgecomb ME 04556

LEAR, EVELYN
SOPRANO
b Brooklyn, NY, Jan 8, 30. *Study:* NY Univ; Hunter Col; Juilliard Sch, with Sergius Kagen; studied with Maria Ivogün, Irma Beilke & Daniel Ferro. *Rec Perf:* Buffalo Bill (film), 76; Evelyn Lear Sings Sondheim and Bernstein; Magic Flute; Wozzeck; Rosenkavalier; Boris Godunov; Strauss Lieder; rec on Angel & Deutsche Grammophon. *Roles:* Komponist in Ariadne auf Naxos, Deutsche Oper, 57; sop, Four Last Songs, London Symph Orch, 57; Lulu in Lulu, Vienna Fest, 62; Contessa & Cherubino in Le Nozze di Figaro, Salzburg Fest, 62; Lavinia in Mourning Becomes Elektra, Metropolitan Opera, 67; Marie in Wozzeck, La Scala, 71; Marschallin in Der Rosenkavalier, Metropolitan Opera, La Scala, Buenos Aires, Brussels, Berlin & Budapest, 71-; and many others. *Pos:* Mem, Juilliard Opera Wkshp, formerly, Deutsche Oper, 59 & Metropolitan Opera, 67-; soloist, US & Europe, 60- *Awards:* Conct Artists Guild Award, 55; Max Reinhardt Award; Kammersängerin, Deutsche Oper. *Mailing Add:* 420 Bonaventure Blvd Ft Lauderdale FL 33326

LEAVITT, DONALD LEE
LIBRARIAN
b Annapolis, Md, Sept 2, 29. *Study:* Am Univ, BA; Ind Univ. *Pos:* Chief, Music Div, Libr Cong, currently. *Mem:* Rec Libr Comn; Int Asn Music Libr; Int Asn Sound Archives; Music Libr Asn; Am Musicol Soc. *Publ:* Contribr, Notes, Fontes Artis Musicae, Libr Trends & Phonographic Bulletin. *Mailing Add:* 12602 Crimson Ct Bowie MD 20715

LEAVITT, JOSEPH
ADMINISTRATOR, EDUCATOR
b Chelsea, Mass. *Study:* New England Consv Music, dipl, 40; Am Univ, BMus, 54; Manhatan Sch Music; Boston Univ; Harvard Univ. *Rec Perf:* Adventures in Music (10 albums), RCA Victor, 54; Golden Age Suite (Shostakovich), Westminster Rec. *Pos:* Prin musician, Nat Symph Orch, 49-67, asst mgr, 67-69; gen mgr, NJ Symph, 69-71; exec dir & exec prod, Wolf Trap First Nat Park Perf Arts, 70-73; exec dir, Baltimore Symph Orch, 73- *Teaching:* Chief instr arts mgt, Univ Md, summer 74-76; adj prof mgt, Goucher Col, 77- *Mem:* Int Soc Perf Art Adminr (mem bd dir, 78-82); Am Symph Orch League; Boston Musicians Asn. *Publ:* Auth, Reading by Recognition, 60 & The Rhythms of Contemporary Music, 63, Belwin. *Mailing Add:* 1110 Hampton Garth Towson MD 21204

LEAVITT, MICHAEL P
ADMINISTRATOR, ARTIST MANAGER
b New York, NY, Dec 9, 44. *Study:* Kans Wesleyan Univ, BA, 65; Queens Col, City Univ New York, MA, 67; Grad Ctr, City Univ New York, MPh, 79. *Pos:* Exec dir, Horizon Concerts, 78-79; managing dir, Gregg Smith Singers, 78-79; pres, Allied Artist Bur, 79- & MPL Advert, 81- *Mem:* Nat Asn Perf Arts Mgrs & Agts; Sonneck Soc; Music Libr Asn; Am Musicol Soc. *Mailing Add:* 195 Steamboat Rd Great Neck NY 11024

LEBARON, ANNE
COMPOSER, HARP
b Baton Rouge, La, May 30, 53. *Study:* Univ Ala, with Fred Goosen, BA, 74; State Univ NY, Stony Brook, with Bülent Arel, MA, 76; Columbia Univ, with Chou Wen-chung; Hamburg Hochschule, with György Ligeti. *Works:* Memnon, Lyra Music Co Inc, 79; Metamorphosis, APR Publ Inc, 80; Rite of the Black Sun, perf by New Music Consort, 80; Metamorphosis, perf by Quintet of Am, 81; After a Dammit to Hell, comn & perf by Jay Barksdale, 81; The Sea and the Honeycomb, perf by Mannheim Music Viva, 82; Rite of the Black Sun, Assoc Music Publ Inc, 82; Orpheus Lives, Soho Repty Theatre, 83. *Rec Perf:* Concerto for Active Frogs, Say Day-Bew, 78; Jewels, Trans Museq, 80; Doggone Catact, Op One Rec Inc, 83; The Travels of Dog and Cat, Arch 1750, 83. *Teaching:* Instr theory & comp, State Univ NY, Stony Brook, 76-77 & 81, asst to dir electronic music studio, 77-78. *Awards:* Grant, Fulbright Comn, 80-81; Comp/Librettist Grant, Nat Endowment Arts, 81-82; CAPS Award, NY State Coun Arts, 83-84. *Mem:* Am Music Ctr; Am Comp Alliance; BMI; Am Harp Soc; Am Women Comp (treas, 78-83). *Publ:* Coauth, Darmstadt 1980, Perspectives of New Music, 81. *Mailing Add:* 63 W 8th St Rm B New York NY 10011

LEBHERZ, LOUIS P
BASS
b Bethesda, Md, Apr 14, 48. *Study:* Chapman Col, BA(music), 71; Ind Univ, Bloomington, 73-74. *Rec Perf:* Aroldo (Verdi), CBS, 79; Jone (Petrella), Bongiovanni, Italy, 81. *Roles:* King Marke in Tristan Und Isolde, Opera Orch NY, 78; Baldassare in La Favorita (Donizetti), 81, Sparafucile in Rigoletto (Verdi), 81 & Burbo in Jone (Patrella), 81, Fundacion Teresa Carreno,

Caracas, Venezuela; Zaccaria in Nabucco (Verdi), Int Athens Fest, France 81; Fiesco in Simon Boccanegra (Verdi), 82 & Capelio in Icaduleti E Imontecchi (Bellini), 52, Teatro Massimo, Caracas, Venezuela. *Pos:* Dramatische Bass, Staatstheater, Karlsruhe, Ger, 84- *Rep:* Lombardo Assoc 61 W 62nd St #6F New York NY 10023. *Mailing Add:* PO Box 5221 Carmel CA 93921

LEBLANC, ALBERT HENRY
EDUCATOR
b Baton Rouge, La, Sept 18, 42. *Study:* La State Univ, BMusEd, 65; Univ Ill, MS(music educ), 69, PhD(music educ), 75. *Pos:* Eval specialist, Aesthetic Educ Prog, Cent Midwest Regional Educ Lab, Inc, St Louis, Mo, 73-76. *Teaching:* Assoc prof, Dept Music, Mich State Univ, 76- *Mem:* Music Educr Nat Conf; Col Music Soc; Music Educ Res Coun (mem exec comt, 80-). *Interests:* Factors which influence music listening preference. *Publ:* Auth, Organizing the Instrumental Music Library, Instrumentalist, 74; A Graduate Level Listening Test in Music History Analysis, 76, Generic Style Music Preferences of Fifth Grade Students, 79 & Effects of Style, Tempo and Performing Medium on Children's Music Preference, 81, J Res Music Educ; An Interactive Theory of Music Preference, J Music Therapy, 82. *Mailing Add:* Dept Music Mich State Univ East Lansing MI 48824

LEBOW, LEONARD S
COMPOSER, TRUMPET
b Chicago, Ill. *Study:* Roosevelt Univ, studied trumpet with Renold Schilke, BMus, 52; Chicago Musical Col, studied comp with K Jirak, MMus, 59. *Works:* Suite for Brass, Summy-Birchard Publ, 56; Midwest Landscape, 56 & Western Suite, 57, Chicago Symph Brass Quintet; Popular Suite for Brass, Leblanc Publ, 62; Ride the Matterhorn, Disneyland Park Prod, 72; Four Movie Scenes for Brass. *Pos:* Trumpet player & arr, Hotel Sahara, 52-54; freelance trumpet, Chicago, 54-64 & Los Angeles, 64- *Teaching:* Music, Chicago Pub Sch, 54-62, Cook Co Sch, Ill, 62-64 & Los Angeles Co & City Sch, 64- *Awards:* ASCAP Popular Awards, 66-82. *Mem:* ASCAP. *Mailing Add:* 15020 Moorpark St Sherman Oaks CA 91403

LECLAIR, JUDITH
BASSOON, EDUCATOR
Study: Eastman Sch Music, BM. *Pos:* Prin bassoon, San Diego Symph, formerly & New York Phil, 79- *Teaching:* Mem fac bassoon, Univ Calif, La Jolla, formerly, Mannes Col Music, 81- & Manhattan Sch Music, 82- & Univ Calif, San Diego, 82- *Mailing Add:* Manhattan Sch Music 120 Claremont Ave New York NY 10027

LECLAIRE, DENNIS JAMES
COMPOSER, EDUCATOR
b Providence, RI, Dec 19, 50. *Study:* Boston Univ, BM(musicol), 73; NY Univ, MA(musicol), 77. *Works:* Divertimento for 2 Oboes & English Horn, comn & perf by George Hughes, 82; Fantasy for Woodwind Quintet, perf by Corey Hill Chamber Players, 82; Nocturne for Horn & Piano, perf by Marshall Sealy, 82; 3 Preludes for Piano, perf by Linda Papatopoli, 82; The Sun Has Set, 82 & The Sweet Kingdom Within, 82, perf by Gertraude Marshall; Nocturnes for Piano, perf by Linda Papatopoli, 83. *Pos:* Musicol adv, Opera Co Boston, 79-81; prin horn, Sinfonie by Sea, 81-; horn, Cape Cod Symph, 82- & Cape Ann Symph, 82- *Teaching:* Dept assoc traditional music, Berklee Col Music, 80- *Mem:* Am Musicol Soc; Col Music Soc. *Mailing Add:* 134 B Fuller St Brookline MA 02146

LEDBETTER, STEVEN JOHN
WRITER, EDUCATOR
b Minneapolis, Minn, Dec 13, 42. *Study:* Pomona Col, BA(music), 64; NY Univ, with Gustave Reese, MA(musicol), 68, PhD(musicol), 71. *Pos:* Dir publ, Boston Symph Orch, 79- *Teaching:* From instr to asst prof music, NY Univ, 69-72; asst prof, Dartmouth Col, 72-79. *Mem:* Am Musicol Soc (mem coun, 79-82); Sonneck Soc (mem bd trustees, 82-). *Interests:* Italian madrigal and Luca Marenzio; Gilbert and Sullivan operetta; American music, especially Boston school & George W Chadwick. *Publ:* Ed, Luca Marenzio: Madrigali a 4, 5, e 6 voci (1588), Broude Brothers, 78; auth, Marenzio's Early Career, J Am Musicol Soc, 79; Managed by a Job?, Musical Times 79; ed, Songs to Poems by Arlo Bates, Da Capo, 79; Gilbert and Sullivan: Trial by Jury, Broude Brothers (in prep). *Mailing Add:* Symph Hall Boston MA 02115

LEDEEN, LYDIA R HAILPARN
EDUCATOR, PIANO
b New York, NY, Apr 6, 38. *Study:* Juilliard Sch Music, with Edward Steuermann, BS, 53, MS, 54; Consv de Musisque Paris, with Nadia Boulanger, dipl licence de concert, 53 & 55; Columbia Univ, with Robert Casadeseus, MA, 57, PhD, 59, EdD, 60. *Works:* Songs My Children Love, 65 & Five Diversions for Three Winds, 68, Horn Realm; Sonata (cello), comn & perf by Edward Szabo, 70; Fantasie (recorder & piano), comn & perf by Norman Lowrey, 80. *Pos:* Pianist, Soc for Second Perf Contemp Music, 50-53; mem, Hailparn & Sternklar piano team, 70-80, Nova Crwth Baroque Ensemble, 77- & Drew Chamber Players, 80-, Drew Univ. *Teaching:* Prof music, Drew Univ, 66-, chmn music dept, 66-79. *Awards:* Prix d'excellence, Comtemp French Music Competition, 54; First Place Medal, Int Recording Compt, 55; grant, Nat Endowment for Humanities, 77. *Bibliog:* Julius Hijman (auth), Een Amerikaans Proefschriftover Nederlandse Pianomuziek, Mens en Melodie, 2/59. *Mem:* Col Music Soc; Am Musicol Soc; Int Musicol Soc. *Publ:* Auth, Variation Form from 1525 to 1750, Music Rev, Vol 22, 14; Songs That Sound of Conflict, Music J Anthology, 68; ed, Dissonance: A Journal of Diverse Musical Ideas, Drew Music Dept, 69-76; auth, Haydn: The Seven Last Words, A New Look At An Old Masterpiece, Music Rev, Vol 34, 1; Sources and recources, Cadenzas to the Beethoven Piano Concerti Symposium, Col Music Soc, Vol 21, 1. *Mailing Add:* Music Dept Drew Univ Madison NJ 07940

LEE, ALFRED E
PIANO, HARPSICHORD
Study: New England Consv, BM; Sch Music, Yale Univ, MM; studied piano with Lucille Monaghan, Ellsworth Grumman & Paul Sander, ens with Joseph Fuchs, harpsichord with Ralph Kirkpatrick & solfege with Gaston Dufresne. *Pos:* Soloist, Buffalo Phil Orch, Reading Symph Orch, Salem Phil Orch & Robbins Libr Conct Ser; solo & ens appearances throughout US & Europe. *Teaching:* Instr piano, harpsichord & ear training, Boston Consv, currently. *Mailing Add:* 39 Fuller Brookline MA 02146

LEE, BYONG WON
EDUCATOR
b Yangp'yong, Korea, Dec 20, 41; US citizen. *Study:* Seoul Nat Univ Col Music, Korea, BM, 64; Univ Wash, MA, 71, PhD, 74. *Teaching:* Asst prof ethnomusicol, Univ Hawaii, Honolulu, 74-82, assoc prof, 82-; Fulbright Prof ethnomusicol, Seoul Nat Univ, Korea, 80-81. *Awards:* Res fel, Soc Sci Res Coun, 77; Fulbright Lectr & Res Grant, Int Inst Exchange Scholars, 80-81. *Mem:* Soc Ethnomusicol; Int Coun Traditional Music (26th conf adminr, 81); Korean Musicol Soc; Ctr Korean Studies, Univ Hawaii (res comt mem, 78-). *Interests:* Music acculturation; relationship between the merchant class and arts. *Publ:* Auth, Structural Formulae of Melodies in the Two Sacred Buddhist Chant Styles of Korea, Korean Studies I, 77; Evolution of the Role and Status of Korean Female Entertainers, In: World of Music, 79; Korea, In: New Grove Dict of Music & Musicians, 80; La musique d'interpretation traditionnelle de Coree, Revue de Coree, vol 13, 3, 81; Micro- and Macro-Structure of Korean Buddhist Chant, Korea J, vol 22, 3, 82. *Mailing Add:* Univ Hawaii Music Dept 2411 Dole St Honolulu HI 96822

LEE, DAI-KEONG
COMPOSER
b Honolulu, Hawaii, Sept 2, 15. *Study:* Univ Hawaii; Princeton Univ; studied with Roger Sessions, New York; Juilliard Sch, studied comp with Frederick Jacobi; Berkshire Music Ctr, studied comp with Aaron Copland; Columbia Univ, studied comp with Otto Leuning, MA, 51. *Works:* Introduction and Allegro for Strings, comn by CBS, 41; Introduction and Scherzo (strings), 41; Prelude and Hula (orch), perf by Chautauqua Orch, 41, New York Phil, 41 & Nat Symph, 42; Hawaiian Festival Overture (orch), perf by New York Phil, 42, Minneapolis Symph, 42-43 & major orch US; Golden Gate Overture, CBS British Am Music Fest, 42; Pacific Prayer (orch), New York City Symph & ABC Symph Orch, 44. *Pos:* French horn, Honolulu Symph Orch, formerly; guest cond, Sydney ABC Symph, Australia, formerly. *Awards:* Guggenheim Fels, 45 & 51. *Mem:* League Comp; Am Music Ctr. *Mailing Add:* 245 W 104th St New York NY 10025

LEE, DOUGLAS ALLEN
LECTURER, EDUCATOR
b Carmel, Ind, Nov 3, 32. *Study:* DePauw Univ, BMus, 54; Univ Mich, Ann Arbor, MMus, 58, studied piano with Theodore Lettvin, Gyorgy Sandor, 60-63, PhD, 68. *Teaching:* Fel, Univ Mich, 61-63; instr, Mount Union Col, 59-61 & Nat Music Camp, Interlochen, Mich, 59-62; prof music, Wichita State Univ, 64- *Awards:* Res travel grant, Am Philosophical Soc, 80; res fel, Nat Endowment for Humanities, 80-81. *Mem:* Am Musicol Soc; Col Music Soc; Music Teachers Nat Asn (chmn hist instrm, 69-71). *Interests:* Eighteenth century instrumental music; musical Americana. *Publ:* Auth, The Works of Christoph Nichelmann: A Thematic Index, Info Coordr, 71; ed, Christoph Nichelmann: Two Concertos, A-R Ed, 77; contribr, New Grove Dict of Music & Musicians, 80 & in prep; ed, Six Sonatas for Solo Violin and Continuo—Franz Benda, A-R Ed, 81; auth, Franz Benda: A Thematic Catalogue of His Works, Pendragon Press (in prep). *Mailing Add:* Box 53 Wichita State Univ Wichita KS 67206

LEE, JACK KENNETH
COMPOSER, CONDUCTOR
b Akron, Ohio, Feb 11, 21. *Study:* Kent State Univ, 39-40; Ohio State Univ, BS, 43, MA, 46; Southern Col Fine Arts, Hon Dr Music, 63. *Works:* The American Dream, Sam Fox Publ Co; 100 Years of College Football, Oz Publ Co; Crown of Glory, New Kjos Publ Co; Civil War Rhapsody, A Dance from a Dream & Bear Down Arizona, Hal Leonard Music Publ Inc; and many others. *Pos:* Supvr music, Worthington Ohio Pub Sch, 47-49. *Teaching:* Drillmaster band, Univ Mich, 48-52; dir bands, Univ Ariz, 52- *Awards:* Distinguished Service to Music Medal, Kappa Kappa Psi, 71; Sudler Trophy, Sousa Found, 83. *Mem:* Am Fedn Musicians; Sousa Found. *Publ:* Auth, Modern Marching Band Techniques, 54 & Modern Conducting Techniques, 70, Hal Leonard Publ. *Mailing Add:* Dept Music Univ Ariz Tucson AZ 85721

LEE, KI JOO
EDUCATOR, VIOLIN
b Oct 10, 33; US citizen. *Study:* Am Consv Music, MM, 66. *Works:* Rec on New World Rec Co, Korea; Cantata, perf by Yegreen Orch & Chorus, Seoul, Korea. *Pos:* First violin, Seoul Phil Orch, 55-64; founder & dir, New World Sch Music, Elmhurst, Ill, 82- *Teaching:* Instr violin, Am Consv Music, 65-; instr violin & cond orch, NCent Col, 68-70. *Mailing Add:* 2447 S 6th Ave North Riverside IL 60546

LEE, NOÉL
PIANO, COMPOSER
b Nanking, China, Dec 25, 24; US citizen. *Study:* Harvard Univ, BA, 48; New England Consv Music, artist dipl, 48; private study with Nadia Boulanger in Paris, 48-53. *Works:* Five Songs on Lorca (sop, flute & guitar), CRI, 55; Dialogues (violin & piano), Theodore Presser, 58; Convergences (flute & harpsichord), Billaudot, Paris, 72; Caprices on the Name Schönberg (piano &

orch), 72 & Songs of Calamus (voice & instruments), 76, comn by French Nat Radio. *Rec Perf:* Approx 115 rec for Telefunken, Valois, Boite a Musique, Lumen, His Masters Voice, Philips-Phonogram, Arion, Erayo, Ricordi, Fona, Musical Heritage, CRI & Nonesuch, 56- *Teaching:* Vis prof piano, Cornell Univ, 67 & 72. *Awards:* Nat Inst Arts Lett Award, 59. *Rep:* Bureau Int de Concts Kiesgen 252 rue du Fbg St Honore Paris France. *Mailing Add:* 4 Villa Laugier Paris 75017 France

LEE, PATRICIA TAYLOR
EDUCATOR, PIANO

b Portland, Ore, Aug 22, 36. *Study:* Mills Col, studied with D Milhaud, L Kirchner & A Libermann, BA, 57; Yale Univ, with Leo Schrade, MA, 59; Temple Univ, with Adele Marcus, DMA, 79. *Rec Perf:* Trio for Clarinet, Violin & Piano (Weiner), Duchesne Rec, Belgium, 74. *Pos:* Off pianist, Sacramento Symph, 63-75; publ dir, Nat Piano Found, 78- *Teaching:* Instr piano, Univ Calif, Davis, 69-75; prof piano & piano pedagogy & chmn keyboard dept, West Chester Univ Pa, 78- *Mem:* Col Music Soc; Music Teachers Nat Asn; Pa Music Teachers Asn; Am Fedn Musicians; Nat Piano Found. *Publ:* Auth, Between Parents and Piano, 79, So You've Always Wanted to Play the Piano!, 79, A Business Manual for the Independent Music Teacher, 80, Why Not Teach or Play Something New Today?, 81 & Preparing Your Piano Students for College Admission, 83, Nat Piano Found. *Mailing Add:* 624 Mulford Rd Wyncote PA 19095

LEE, SOO CHUL
VIOLIN, EDUCATOR

b Seoul, Korea, Sept 29, 44. *Study:* Col Music, Seoul Nat Univ, BM, 68; Am Consv Music, with Adia Ghertorici & Albert Igolnikov, MM, 79. *Pos:* Concertmaster, Seoul Baroque Ens, 64-75; first violin, Seoul Phil Orch, 68-75. *Teaching:* Fac mem violin, Chung Joo Teachers Col, Chung Joo Univ, 73-75, Sun Wha Fine Arts Sch, 73-75 & Am Consv Music, 81- *Mem:* Am Fedn Musicians; Am String Teachers Asn. *Mailing Add:* 4457 W Ainslie St #3 Chicago IL 60630

LEE, SUNG-SOOK
SOPRANO

b Korea. *Study:* Sook Myuug Women's Univ, BA; Juilliard Sch Music. *Rec Perf:* Stabat Mater (Rossini), Vox. *Roles:* Leading role in Tamu Tamu, Chicago, 73; Sheherazade, La Scala, 75; Madama Butterfly in Madama Butterfly, London Royal Opera & New York City Opera; Turandot & La Boheme, New York City Opera; Don Giovanni, Korean Opera, 78; Mimi in La Boheme, Florentine Opera, 83. *Pos:* Soloist & recitalist with symph orchs. *Awards:* Silver Medal, Int Madam Butterfly Compt, Japan, 73. *Mem:* Am Guild Musical Artists. *Mailing Add:* c/o Herbert Barrett Mgt 1860 Broadway New York NY 10023

LEE, SYLVIA OLDEN
TEACHER-COACH

b Meridian, Miss, June 29, 17. *Study:* Sch Music, Howard Univ; Oberlin Consv Music, BMus, 38; St Cecilia Acad, Rome, 53; Hochschule Musik, Munich, Ger, 56-59. *Teaching:* Asst prof organ, Talladega Col, Ala, 38-39; asst prof piano, Dillard Univ, New Orleans, 42-43; opera coach, Columbia Univ, 51 & Metropolitan Opera, 54-55; coach voice interpretation, Univ Cincinnati, 67-69 & Curtis Inst Music, 70- *Mem:* Pi Kappa Lambda. *Mailing Add:* 229 W Upsal Philadelphia PA 19119

LEE, THOMAS OBOE
COMPOSER, LECTURER

b Beijing (Peking), China, Sept 5, 45; US citizen. *Study:* Berkshire Music Ctr, with Betsy Jolas, summer 76; New England Consv, with W T McKinley, MM, 76; Harvard Univ, with Earl Kim, PhD, 81. *Works:* Phantasia for Elvira-Shatayev, 81, The Mad Frog, 81 & Octopus Wrecks, 81, Margun Music Inc; The Cockscomb, comn by Fromm Music Found, 81; The MacGuffin, Needham Publ Corp, 82; Third String Quartet, Margun Music, 82; The Gainsborough Five, 83 & Phantasia for Elvira-Shatayev, 83, Margun Music Inc. *Teaching:* Instr theory & comp, Berklee Col Music, 73-79; asst prof, Swarthmore Col, 79-80; fac mem music theory, New England Consv, 83- *Awards:* Fel, Mass Coun Artists Found Inc, 77 & 83 & John Simon Guggenheim Mem Found, 83; First prize, Int Comp Compt Stroud Fest, England, 81; grant, Martha Baird Rockefeller Fund for Music, 82. *Mem:* Comp in Red Sneakers, Inc; BMI; Am Comp Alliance; Am Music Ctr; Col Music Soc. *Mailing Add:* 24 Francesca Ave Somerville MA 02144

LEE, WILLIAM FRANKLIN, III
ADMINISTRATOR, COMPOSER

b Galveston, Tex, Feb 20, 29. *Study:* NTex State Univ, BM, 49, MS, 50; Univ Tex, MM & PhD, 56; Consv Nac Musica, Lima, Peru, MusD, 68; studied with Nadia Boulanger, Fountainebleu & Paris; Eastman Sch Music, 62. *Works:* Earth Genesis, Collier-Dexter Ltd, 67; Concerto Grosso for Brass Quintet and Orchestra, 77; Eight Vingettes for a Festive Occasion, 77, Woodwind Quintet No I, 78 & Woodwind Quintet No II, 78, Peer-Southern Music Co; Veri, 82 & Three Cryptics, 83, Universal Ed. *Teaching:* Theory & comp, St Mary's Univ, 52-55; asst to dean, Fine Arts & dir, Jr String Proj, Univ Tex, 55-56; dir, Dept Music, Sam Houston State Univ, 56-64; dean, Sch Music, Univ Miami, Coral Gables, 64-82; provost & exec vpres, 82- *Awards:* Serious Comp Awards, ASCAP, 68-83; Deems Taylor Award, ASCAP, 81. *Mem:* ASCAP; Nat Asn Jazz Educr (nat pres, 72-74); Nat Acad Rec Arts & Sci; Am Music Ctr. *Publ:* Auth, Music Theory Dict, 66 & The Nature of Music, 66, Charles Hansen; 1002 All American Jazz Book, Sihouette Music Corp, 76; Bill Lee's Jazz Dict, Shattinger Int Music Corp, 79; Stan Kenton—Artistry in Rhythm, Creative Press, 81. *Mailing Add:* 240 Ashe Bldg Univ of Miami Coral Gables FL 33124

LEECH, ALAN BRUCE
BASSOON, EDUCATOR

b Lima, Ohio, Oct 19, 44. *Study:* Col Consv Music, Univ Cincinnati, BM, 66, MM, 68, studied bassoon with Otto Eifert & cond with Max Rudolf & Erich Kunzel. *Works:* Little Leaves, Bozeman Chamber Quartet, 75; Achromatic Occurrance, Karen & Alan Leech Duo, 79; Sands, Mont Consort, 81; Galadriel's Mirror, Collage, 81; To Carl, Mont Consort, 82. *Pos:* Prin bassoonist, Am Wind Symph Orch, Pittsburgh, summers 66-67, Lexington Phil, Ky, 67-68, Knoxville Symph Orch, Tenn, 68-71 & Bozeman Symph, Mont, 72- *Teaching:* Instr bassoon, theory & lit, Univ Tenn, Knoxville, 68-72; assoc prof music, Mont State Univ, 72- *Mem:* Am Fedn Musicians (local vpres, 82-); Music Educr Nat Conf; Int Double Reed Soc; Nat Asn Col Wind & Perc Instr (Mont chmn, 80-). *Publ:* Contribr, Bassoon Performance Practices & Teaching in the United States & Canada, Univ Idaho Press, 74. *Mailing Add:* 12 N Western Dr Bozeman MT 59715

LEECH, KAREN DAVIDSON
FLUTE, EDUCATOR

b Cleveland, Ohio, Dec 17, 45. *Study:* Smith Col, BA, 67; Col Consv Music, Univ Cincinnati, MM, 70; studied flute with George Hambrecht, William Herbert, Julius Baker, William Bennett & Marcel Moyse. *Rec Perf:* The Montana Consort (two TV specials), Mont State Univ TV Ctr, 81. *Pos:* Prin flute, Bozeman Symph, 72-; flutist, Gallatin Woodwind Quintet & Mont Consort, 80- *Teaching:* Instr music hist, Univ Tenn, 70-72; asst prof flute, ens & music hist, Mont State Univ, 72- *Mem:* Col Music Soc; Nat Asn Col Wind & Perc Instr; Am Fedn Musicians; Nat Flute Asn. *Publ:* Auth, Flute Embouchure Problems, J Mont Music Educr Asn, 76; Recital Attendance Course Produces Critical Listeners and Student Credit Hours, Nat Asn Col Wind & Perc Instr J, 80. *Mailing Add:* 12 N Western Dr Bozeman MT 59715

LEEDY, DOUGLAS
COMPOSER, CONDUCTOR & MUSIC DIRECTOR

b Portland, Ore, Mar 3, 38. *Study:* Pomona Col, BA, 59; Univ Calif, Berkeley, MA, 62; studied Karnatic vocal music with K V Narayanaswamy. *Works:* Usable Music I for Very Small Instruments With Holes, Source III, 68; Entropical Paradise: Six Sonic Environments (electronic), Seraphim Rec, 69; The Twenty-Fourth Psalm, perf by Pomona Col Choir Orch, 72; Canti: Music for Contrabass and Contrabass Choir Ens, perf by Bertram Turetzky, 75; Harpsichord Book III, Flotsam Music Co, 82; Chorale-Fantasy on Wie Schoen Leuchtet, E C Schirmer (in prog). *Teaching:* Lectr & head electronic music studio, Univ Calif, Los Angeles, 67-70; prof electronic music, Estudio de Fonologia, Centro Simon Bolivar, Caracas, 72; asst prof music, Reed Col, Portland, Ore, 73-78. *Awards:* Grant, US & Polish Govt, 65-66; Fromm Found Comn, 66; Sr Res Grant, Am Inst Indian Studies, 79-80. *Bibliog:* Valerie Samson (auth), Interview with Douglas Leedy, Ear (West), Vol 4, No 4. *Mem:* Int Heinrich Schütz Soc; Music Libr Asn. *Interests:* History, theory and practice of tuning and intonation; performance practice of early Western music. *Publ:* Auth, In Praise of Other Intervals, Cum Notis Variorum No 59, 82; New Music for an Old Temperament?, Interval, 82-83; A Personal View of Meantone Temperament, The Courant, 83; ed, Chansons from Petrucci in Original Notation ..., Musica Sacra et Profana, 83. *Mailing Add:* 121 SW Salmon St Ste 1000 Portland OR 97204

LEES, BENJAMIN
COMPOSER

b Harbin, China, Jan 8, 24. US citizen. *Study:* Univ Southern Calif, 46-48; studied with George Antheil, 49-54. *Works:* Visions of Poets (cantata), 62, Violin Concerto, 63, Concerto for String Quartet and Orchestra, 64, Symphony #3, 69, Variations for Piano & Orchestra, 76, Passacaglia for Orchestra, 76 & Concerto for Brass Choir and Orchestra, 83, Boosey & Hawkes, Inc. *Teaching:* W Alton Jones Chair, Peabody Consv, 62-64 & 66-68; asst prof, Queens Col, 64-66; guest prof, Manhattan Sch Music, 70-72. *Awards:* Guggenheim Fel, 54 & 66; UN Educ, Scientific & Cult Orgn Award, Paris, 58; Sir Arnold Bax Medal, London, 58. *Bibliog:* Deryck Cooke (auth), The Music of Benjamin Lees, 59 & Benjamin Lees' Visions of Poets, 64 & Nicolas Slonimsky (auth), Benjamin Lees In Excelsis, 75, Tempo Mag, London. *Mem:* ASCAP. *Mailing Add:* 28 Cambridge Rd Great Neck NY 10023

LEFEVER, MAXINE LANE
PERCUSSION, EDUCATOR

b Elmhurst, Ill, May 30, 31. *Study:* Ill Wesleyan Univ, 59-51; Western State Col Colo, BA, 55-58; Purdue Univ, MS, 62-64. *Works:* Series perc ens, Kendor Music, 60-83; marimba ens, Ludwig Music Publ Co, 82. *Pos:* Ed, Nat Band Asn J, 68-78; Pres, Am Bands Abroad, Inc, 72- *Teaching:* Instr, elem sch, Ill & Colo, 54-60; prof bands, Purdue Univ, 62- *Awards:* Hon mem, US Navy Band, 71; Citation Excellence, Nat Band Asn, 77; Medal of Order, John Philip Sousa Found. *Mem:* Nat Band Asn (exec secy, 68-78); John Philip Sousa Found (exec secy, 78-); Col Band Dir Nat Asn. *Publ:* Contribr to Instrumentalist, 62- & Sch Musician, 68- *Mailing Add:* Box 2454 West Lafayette IN 47906

LEFFERTS, PETER MARTIN
EDUCATOR, LECTURER

b Boston, Mass, Mar 12, 51. *Study:* Columbia Univ, BA, 73, MA, 76, MPhil, 78, PhD, 83. *Teaching:* Asst prof music hist, Univ Chicago, 81- *Mem:* Am Musicol Soc; Col Music Soc. *Interests:* Polyphonic music of late medieval England. *Publ:* Auth, Polyphonic Music of the Fourteenth Century, XV, In: Motets of English Provenance, L'Oiseau Lyre, 80; Two English Motets on Simon de Montfort, 81 & coauth, New Sources of English 13th and 14th Century Polyphony, 82, Cambridge Univ Press; co-ed, Polyphonic Music of the Fourteenth Century, XVI-XVII, In: English Music for Mass and Offices, L'Oiseau Lyre, 83. *Mailing Add:* Univ Chicago Dept Music 5845 S Ellis Ave Chicago IL 60637

LEFKOFF, GERALD
WRITER, COMPOSER
b Brooklyn, NY, June 13, 30. *Study:* Juilliard Sch Music, BS, 52; Catholic Univ Am, MM, 54, PhD, 60. *Works:* Soundscape (orch & tape), WVa Symphonette, 72; Soundscape for 24 Trios, 75 & Strands, 78, Pittsburgh Symph Orch; Sonata for Viola, 83 & String Quartet 1983, 83, Glyphic Press. *Pos:* Violist, Nat Symph Orch, 56-58. *Teaching:* Instr, Bowling Green State Univ, 58-60; prof, WVa Univ, 61- *Mem:* Am Soc Univ Comp; Soc Music Theory. *Interests:* New tunings; 12 pitch class theory; tonal harmony; computer analysis; invented ratioglyphic-field notation. *Publ:* Ed, Computer Applications in Music, WVa Univ, 67; coauth, Programed Ear Training, Harcourt Brace World, 70; auth, Analyzed Examples of Four-Part Harmony, 80 & Reading and Writing Intervals, 80, Glyphic Press. *Mailing Add:* 665 Killarney Dr Morgantown WV 26505

LEFKOWITZ, MISCHA
VIOLIN
b Riga, USSR, Aug 17, 55; US citizen. *Study:* Spec Sch Music, Riga, USSR, dipl, 71; Wayne State Univ, BM, 75, MM, 76; studied with Mischa Mischakoff, Nathan Milstein, Henri Temianka & Roman Totenberg. *Pos:* First violinist, Los Angeles Phil, 77-; concertmaster, Am Chamber Symph, 80- *Teaching:* Lectr violin, Calif State Univ, Dominques Hills, 81- *Awards:* First Prize, Rep Cont Young Soloists, USSR, 71 & Int Rotary Awards, Calif, 82; Prizewinner, Int Am Music Compt, NY, 83. *Mem:* Chamber Music Am. *Rep:* Robert Lombardo Assoc 61 W 62 Suite 6F New York NY 10023. *Mailing Add:* 11302 Summertime Lane Culver City CA 90230

LEHMAN, PAUL ROBERT
ADMINISTRATOR, EDUCATOR
b Athens, Ohio, Apr 20, 31. *Study:* Ohio Univ, BSEd, 53; Univ Mich, MMus, 59, PhD, 62. *Pos:* Music spec, US Off Educ, Washington, DC, 67-68. *Teaching:* From instr to asst prof, Col Music, Univ Colo, 62-65; from assoc prof to prof, Music Dept, Univ Ky, 65-70; prof music, Eastman Sch Music, 70-75; prof, Sch Music, Univ Mich, 75-, assoc dean, 77- *Mem:* Music Educr Nat Conf (pres, 84-86); Col Music Soc (mem exec bd, 81-83). *Publ:* Author of approx 50 articles, books and reviews. *Mailing Add:* Sch Music Univ Mich Ann Arbor MI 48109

LEHMAN, RICHARD
TRUMPET, EDUCATOR
Study: Ohio State Univ, BME; Univ Louisville, MM. *Pos:* Prin trumpet, New Louisville Brass Quintet, formerly, Springfield Symph Orch, currently & Bloomington Normal Symph, currently; mem, Louisville Orch, formerly. *Teaching:* Prof trumpet, Ill State Univ, currently. *Awards:* Winner, Nat Fedn Music Clubs Solo Compt, 79; Winner, Int Trumpet Guild Solo Compt, 79 & 80. *Mailing Add:* 1444 E College Ave Normal IL 61761

LEHNER, EUGENE
VIOLA, EDUCATOR
b Pozsony, Hungary, July 5, 06; US citizen. *Study:* Franz Liszt Consv, Budapest, artist dipl, 26; New England Consv Music, Hon Dr Music, 83. *Pos:* Violist, Kolisch Quartet, 26-39, Boston Symph Orch, 38-82 & Stradivarius Quartet, 41-60. *Teaching:* Assoc instr chamber music, Boston Univ, 65- & New England Consv Music, 68-; assoc instr viola, Wellesley Col. *Mem:* Fel, Acad Arts & Sci. *Mailing Add:* New England Consv 290 Huntington Rd Boston MA 02115

LEHNERTS, (MARY) FRANCES
EDUCATOR, MEZZO-SOPRANO
b Minneapolis, Minn. *Study:* Univ Minn, BS; Teachers Col, Columbia Univ, MA; Juilliard Sch Music, artist dipl, 45; studied with Florence Kimball, Povla Frijsh, Conrad Bos, Maggie Teyte, Goldowsky & Sachse. *Roles:* Mrs Sedley in Peter Grimes, Berkshire Music Fest; Aldagisa in Norma, New Opera Co, 48; Amneris in Aida, Jacksonville Opera Co, Fla; Azucena in Trovatore, Chautauqua Opera & St Paul Opera Co; Carmen in Carmen, Gainesville Opera; Dalila in Samson & Dalila, Univ Ala; Valkuri in Die Valkuri, Opera Nat, Mexico City; Mother in Hansel & Gretel, NBC Opera Co. *Pos:* Instr singing, Bronx House Music Sch, 50-, Cath Univ Am, 52-54 & Teachers Col, Columbia Univ, 55-; adj asst prof, NY Univ, 68- *Mem:* Mu Phi Epsilon. *Mailing Add:* 440 Riverside Dr New York NY 10027

LEHR, CATHERINE (CATHERINE LEHR RAMOS)
CELLO
b Cleveland, Ohio. *Study:* Eastman Sch Music, studied with Ronald Leonard, BMus, 71; Ind Univ, studies with Janos Starkar & Fritz Magg, MMus, 74. *Rec Perf:* El Gato Triste, Land of Make Believe (Chuck Mangione), 73. *Pos:* Asst prin cello, St Louis Symph, 75-; cellist, Trio Cassatt, 80- *Mailing Add:* 6000 Waterman 2E St Louis MO 63112

LEHRER, PHYLLIS ALPERT
PIANO, EDUCATOR
b Bronx, NY. *Study:* Univ Rochester, with Frugoni & Basile, AB, 61; Juilliard Sch Music, with Adele Marcus, MS, 63; studied with Paula Kessler Hondins, Lily Dumont & Harold Zubruck. *Rec Perf:* Phantasie Variations, Op 12, Merkin Hall, 80; Phantasie in C, Op 17 (Schumann), Educo Rec, 83. *Teaching:* Fac ear training & teaching fel, Juilliard Sch Music, 64-65; fac piano, Longy Sch Music, 69-71; asst prof music & chmn piano dept, Westminster Choir Col, 72- *Mem:* Music Teachers Nat Asn; NJ Music Educr Asn; Int Soc Study Tension perf (Am rep, 81-). *Mailing Add:* Westminster Choir Col Hamilton Ave & Walnut Lane Princeton NJ 08540

LEHRMAN, LEONARD J(ORDAN)
COMPOSER, CONDUCTOR & MUSIC DIRECTOR
b Ft Riley, Kans, Aug 20, 49. *Study:* Harvard Col, with Earl Kim, Leon Kirchner, Lukas Foss & David Del Tredici, BA(music), 71; Ind Univ, with Tibor Kozma, Wolfgang Vacano, John Eaton & Donald Erb, BM(piano) & MM(cond), 75; Cornell Univ, with Robert Palmer, Karel Husa, Thomas Sokol & Malcom Bilson, MFA(comp), 75, DMA(comp), 77; studied with Olga Heifetz, 60-67, Elie Siegmeister, 60-67, Nadia Boulanger, 69 & 71-72 & Leonard Bernstein, 74. *Works:* Sonata for Piano & Tape, perf by Robert Miller, 70; Tales of Malamud: Idiots First, 74 & Karla, 74, Theodore Presser Co; Sima (two-act opera), Carl Fischer Inc, 76; How Do I Love You? (text by Karl Shapiro), perf by Thomas Sokol Chorale, 77; Hannah (three-act opera), perf by Seventh Army Soldiers' Chorus, Germany, 80; Let's Change the World (musical), perf by soloists of Hamburg Staatsoper & Staattheater Bremerhaven, 82. *Rec Perf:* Tales of Malamud, WBAI TV, 78. *Pos:* Chief prod, WHRB Radio, 68-69; asst cond & asst chorus master, Metropolitan Opera, 77-80 & Heidelberg Fest, Augsburg, 77-80; cond & comp, Basler Theater Schauspielhaus Wien, Stadttheater Bremerhausen, 80-83; chief coach & kapellmeister, Theater des Westens, Berlin, 83- *Teaching:* Lectr music theory, Cornell Univ, 73; tutor music theater, Empire State Col, 76-77; asst prof music theater, theory & piano, State Univ NY, Geneseo, Metropolitan Music Sch & Univ Md, 77-79. *Awards:* Comp Second Prize Am Music Award, Nat Fedn Music Clubs, 68 & 77; Fulbright-Hays Grant, 71-72; Off-Broadway Opera Away, Village Voice, 78. *Bibliog:* B R Dumbek (auth), Hochachtung vor den Wort, Heidelberger Tageblatt, 5/16/80; Hannelore Ahorn (auth), Bald Schwingt er die Taktstock in Berlin, Nodesee Zeitung, Bremerhaven, 5/6/83. *Mem:* Col Music Soc; ASCAP; Am Symph Orch League Cond Guild; Octagon. *Publ:* Contribr, Interviews With Claude Helffer, Boston After Dark, 68; auth, Two Recent American Premieres, Int Brecht Soc Newsletter, 74; Hannah: A Maccabean Anti-War Feminist Opera at an American Military Theater in Heidelberg, Jewish Currents, 81. *Mailing Add:* Nassauische Strasse 25 D-1000 Berlin 31 Germany, Federal Republic of

LEHRMAN, PAUL DAVID
WRITER, ELECTRONIC
b New York, NY, Oct 29, 52. *Study:* Columbia Univ, with Vladimir Ussachevsky, Mario Davidovsky & Charles Dodge, 70-73; State Univ NY, Purchase, BFA, 75. *Works:* Son of Five (perc quartet & tape), perf by Purchase Perc Ens, 76. *Rec Perf:* Threepenny Opera, Triton Prod, 78; Method Acting (Jim Gelfand), Normandy Sound/Calf Rec, 79. *Pos:* Music dir, Caravan Theatre, Cambridge, Mass, 78 & Suffolk Theater Co, Boston, 80; music dir & producer, Sharc Studios, Port-of-Spain, Trinidad, 78-79; admin dir, Class Acts, Boston, 81- *Publ:* Auth, The Boston Phoenix Guides to Boston Bands, 80-83, Serkin & the BSO: Beethoven by the Numbers, 81, Boston Phoenix; Michael Kamen: Classical Oboist Turned Rock Producer, Music & Sound Output, 81; Will Ackermann: Audiophile Production on a Budget, Musician Player & Listener, 82; Composing with the Apple Computer, High Fidelity, 83. *Mailing Add:* 31 Maple Ave #1 Cambridge MA 02139

LEIBUNDGUTH, BARBARA
FLUTE & PICCOLO, EDUCATOR
b Chicago, Ill, Mar 6, 55. *Study:* Northwestern Univ, with Walfrid Kujala, BMus, 76; Blossom Fest Sch Cleveland Orch, with Maurice Sharp, 77; studied with Marcel Moyse, 79-82. *Pos:* Prin flute, Civic Orch Chicago, 75-76, Omaha Symph, 76- & Nebr Sinfonia, Midlands Woodwind Quintet, 76-; prin piccolo, Grand Teton Fest Orch, 79-83; participant, Marlboro Fest, 83; asst prin flute, San Francisco Symph, 83- *Teaching:* Instr flute, Univ Nebr, Omaha, 77- *Mem:* Nat Flute Asn. *Mailing Add:* 208 N 37th St #500 Omaha NE 68131

LEINSDORF, ERICH
CONDUCTOR & MUSIC DIRECTOR
b Vienna, Austria, Feb 4, 12; nat US. *Study:* Vienna State Acad Music, with Paul Pisk; Univ Vienna; Mozarteum, Salzburg; studied piano with Paul Emerich & cello with Lilly Kosz; hon degrees from Baldwin-Wallace Col, 45, Rutgers Univ, 52; Williams Col, 66 & Columbia Univ, 67. *Rec Perf:* Over 100 incl 19 full length operas & all Mozart, Beethoven & Brahms symph; rec on RCA Victor, Westminster, Columbia, Decca, London, & EMI. *Pos:* Asst cond, Salzburg Fest, 34-37; cond, Metropolitan Opera, 37-43; music dir & cond, Cleveland Orch, 43; music dir, Rochester Phil, 47-56 & Boston Symph Orch, 62-69; dir, New York City Ctr Opera, 56, Metropolitan Opera, 57-62 & Berkshire Music Ctr Fest, 63-69; guest cond, maj orchs in US & Europe. *Mem:* Am Arts Alliance; Nat Coun Arts; fel, Am Acad Arts & Sci. *Publ:* Auth, Cadenza (autobiography), 76; The Composer's Advocate, 81; contribr to Atlantic Monthly, Sat Rev, New York Times & High Fidelity. *Rep:* Harrison Parrott Ltd 12 Penzance Pl London W11 4PA England. *Mailing Add:* c/o Dodds 209 E 56th St New York NY 10022

LEISNER, DAVID
GUITAR, COMPOSER
b Los Angeles, Calif, Dec 22, 53. *Study:* Wesleyan Univ, Middletown, Conn, BA, 76; study comp with Richard Winslow, guitar with David Starobin & John Duarte & interpretation with Karen Tuttle & John Kirkpatrick. *Works:* Love is the Crooked Thing, Op 2 (voice & guitar), perf by Sanford Sylvan & David Leisner, 80; Night Scenes, Op 5 (guitar), perf by David Leisner, 82; Simple Songs, Op 4 (voice & guitar), Assoc Music Publ, 82; Dances in the Madhouse, Op 6 (violin & guitar), comn by Pac Strings, Los Angeles, 82. *Rec Perf:* The Viennese Guitar, Titanic Rec, 80. *Pos:* Guitarist, Affil Artists, New York, 81- *Teaching:* Instr guitar, Amherst Col, 76-78 & New England Consv, Boston, 80- *Awards:* Second Prize, Int Guitar Compt, Toronto, 75; Silver

Medal, Int Guitar Compt, Geneva, 81; Alice M Ditson Fund Grant, 82. *Bibliog:* John Wager-Schneider (auth), A Conversation with David Leisner, Soundboard Mag, 5/81. *Publ:* Auth, Perspectives on Henze's Drei Tentos, 77 & Breathing Life Into Music, 78, Soundboard & Gendai, 78; numerous reviews, Soundboard, 83- *Rep:* Aaron & Gorden Conct Mgt 25 Huntington Ave Boston MA 02116. *Mailing Add:* 90 Pinehurst Ave #6F New York NY 10033

LEKHTER, RUDOLF
VIOLIN
b Odessa, Soviet Union. *Study:* Solyarsky Music Sch, with Boris Brant; Odessa Consv; Leningrad Cosnv, studied violin with Michail Wyman, doctorate. *Pos:* Mem, Leningrad Phil, 74-78, Minn Orch, 79- & Nordic String Quartet, currently. *Teaching:* St Olaf Col, currently. *Mailing Add:* 8454 W 35th St St Louis Park MN 55426

LELCHUK, NINA (SIMON)
PIANO, EDUCATOR
b Leningrad, USSR, Feb 22, 39; US citizen. *Study:* Moscow State Consv, USSR, MA, 62, PhD, 65; studied with Sviatoslav Richter & Henry Neuhaus. *Pos:* Recitals, Acad Fil, Romano, Italy, 79, Carnegie Hall, 80, 81 & 82, Chicago Symph Hall, 81 & 82 & with St Louis Symph, 82, Vancouver Symph, 83, Pittsburgh Symph, 83 & Cleveland Orch, 83. *Teaching:* Assoc prof piano, Moscow Consv, 62-78; affil prof, State Univ NY, Purchase, 79- & Manhattan Sch Music. *Awards:* Spec talent prize, Charles Munch, Paris, 57; dipl, Van Cliburn Int Piano Compt. *Publ:* Auth, The Way to Get Perfection in Piano Art, 66, Art of Piano Playing, 68 & About My Teacher, 72, Music, Moscow, USSR. *Mailing Add:* 220 Cabrini Blvd #3H New York NY 10033

LE MIEUX, RAYMOND WILLIAM
EDUCATOR, CONDUCTOR
b Marquette, Mich. *Study:* Univ Mich, Marquette, BA, 27; Eastman Sch Music, BM(viola & comp), 34; Columbia Univ, MA(musicol), 45, Teachers Col, EdD, 66. *Pos:* Viola, Rochester Phil Orch, 32-34; cond, New York City All-City High Sch Orch, 42-45 & All-City Orch, New York City Bd Educ, 46-65; TV host educ prog, CBS, NBC & NYE, 50-65. *Teaching:* Instr, Montclair State Col, 36-39; chmn, Dept Music, Manhattan Sch Music, 50- *Awards:* Outstanding Achievement Award, Nat Black Music Caucus, 80. *Mem:* NY State Coun Music Teacher Educ Prog (pres, 73); Music Educr Nat Conf. *Publ:* Coauth, Music: Grades 7, 8 & 9, 51, auth, Problems & Practices in New York City Schools, 53 & ed, Teaching Music in the Elementary Grades, 59, NY Bd Educ; auth, Teachers' Guides to 16mm Films, McGraw Hill, 60 & 70; 11 musicians, In: Dict of American Negro Biography, W W Norton, 83. *Mailing Add:* 120 Claremont Ave New York NY 10027

LEMMON, ALFRED EMMETTE
WRITER, ORGAN
b Lafayette, La, Dec 8, 49. *Study:* Loyola Univ, BM, 71; Tulane Univ, MA, 74, PhD, 81. *Pos:* Cataloger ms div, Hist New Orleans Collection, 81- *Teaching:* Vis lectr hist Mex music, Inst Nac Bellas Artes, Mexico City, 81. *Bibliog:* Andres Ruiz Tarazona (auth), El Musicologo Norteamericano Alfred Lemmon, El Pais, Madrid, 81; Fernando Ita (auth), La Musica, Elemento Basico, Uno Mas Uno, Mexico City, 82. *Mem:* New Orleans Friends of Music (vpres, 80-). *Interests:* Colonial Latin American music; Spanish music. *Publ:* Auth, Jesuits and Music in the Provincia de Nueva Granada, Arch Hist Soc Jesu, 79; Manuscrito Teorico Musical de Santa Eulaia, Rev Musical Chilena, 80; Toward an Inventory of Music Books in Colonial Mexico, Annario Musical, 81; Indian Hasks of Central America, World Music, 82; A Seventeenth Century Nahuatl Hymn, Tlalocan, 82. *Mailing Add:* 533 Royal St New Orleans LA 70130

LEMMON, GALEN
PERCUSSION, EDUCATOR
Pos: Soloist, Palo Alto Chamber Orch, Ohlone Jr Col Wind Ens & other groups; performer, San Francisco Concerto Orch, San Jose Opera Wkshp, Midsummer Mozart Fest, Santa Clara Chorale, New Sounds San Jose, San Jose Civic Light Opera & San Francisco Symph; prin perc, San Jose Symph, 75- *Teaching:* Lectr perc, Col Notre Dame, Calif, currently. *Mailing Add:* Dept Music Col Notre Dame Belmont CA 94002

LENGEFELD, WILLIAM CHRIS
EDUCATOR, CONDUCTOR
b Hamilton, Tex, July 24, 37. *Study:* Baylor Univ, BM, 59, MM, 62; Univ Iowa, PhD, 69. *Teaching:* Band dir, Midway Sch, Waco, Tex, 60-63; grad asst musicol & theory, Univ Iowa, 63-66; assoc prof, Scripps Col, Claremont, Calif, 66-; instr, Claremont Grad Sch, summer 70 & 71, Webb Sch, Claremont, 79 & Univ LaVerne, summer 83; lectr, Univ Calif, Riverside, 79. *Mem:* Am Musicol Soc; Col Music Soc; Musicians Club Pomona Valley. *Interests:* Music and motets of Pierre Colin (1539-1565) of Auton. *Publ:* Auth, Pierre Colin, In: New Grove Dict of Music & Musicians, 80. *Mailing Add:* 218 E Villanova Dr Claremont CA 91711

LENIADO-CHIRA, JOSEPH
CONDUCTOR & MUSIC DIRECTOR, COMPOSER
b Brooklyn, NY, Feb 24, 34. *Study:* Juilliard Sch, with Jean Morel & Vincent Perschetti, 52-55; Aspen Sch, with Izler Solomon & Hans Schweiger, 55-56; Univ Miami, with Joel Belou, BMus, 61. *Works:* Adagio for Orchestra, Miami Phil Orch, 61; A Distant Place, Chira Chamber Orch, 65 & 66; Pavanne for Strings, Hartford Symph Orch, 68; Romanza (solo piano), perf by Joseph Leniado-Chira, 82; A Distant Place, 83, Night Music, 83 & Pavanne for Strings, 83, Symph on the Sound; The Legend of Kincret, Bronx Art Ens, 83.

Pos: Guest cond, Aspen Sch, 55, Miami Phil, 61, Tanglewood, 63 & Hartford Symph, 68; cond, Joffrey Ballet Orch, 64; music dir & cond, Chira & Am Chamber Orch, 64-66 & Symph on the Sound, 71- *Teaching:* Trumpet & brass, Third Street Settlement Sch, New York, 62-65 & piano & trumpet, North Shore Consv, New York, 63-64; vis prof, solfege, Juilliard Sch, 65-66. *Awards:* Nineteen Medals in Music, Fla Music Educr Asn & Orgn 51-52. *Mem:* Am Symph Orch League; Bohemians Club; Cond Guild; Ernest Bloch Soc; ASCAP. *Mailing Add:* 18 Zygmont Lane Greenwich CT 06830

LENNEBERG, HANS
EDUCATOR, WRITER
b Olpe, Germany, May 16, 24; US citizen. *Study:* Brooklyn Col, BA, 56; NY Univ, MA, 60; Pratt Inst, MLS, 61. *Pos:* Asst chief art & music div, Brooklyn Pub Libr, 61-63; music librn, Univ Chicago, 63- *Teaching:* Instr, Brooklyn Col, 58-60; lectr, Univ Chicago, 63-67, assoc prof music, 68- *Mem:* Am Musicol Soc; Music Libr Asn; Int Asn Music Libr. *Interests:* Biography; social history of music; music publishing. *Publ:* Auth, The Myth of the Unappreciated (Musical) Genius, Musical Quart, 81; Early Circulating Libraries and the Dissemination of Music, Libr Quart, 82; Bach, Handel and Comparative Success, Bach, 82-83; The First Unappreciated Genius, J Musicol Res, 83. *Mailing Add:* 5531 S Harper Ave Chicago IL 60637

LENNON, JOHN ANTHONY
COMPOSER
b Greensboro, NC, Jan 14, 50. *Study:* Univ San Francisco, BA, 72; Univ Mich, MMus, 75, DMA, 78. *Works:* Distances Within Me, Dorn Publ Co, 79; Metapictures, RAI Orch, Rome, Italy, 81; Another's Fandango, Michael Lorimer Publ, 82; Death Angel, Columbia Univ Press, 82; Ghostfires, comn by J F Kennedy Ctr Theatre Chamber Players, 82. *Teaching:* Assoc prof comp, counterpoint & harmony, Univ Tenn, 77- *Awards:* Charles Ives Prize, Nat Inst Arts & Lett, 77; Prix de Rome, Am Acad, 80-81; Guggenheim Fel, 81-82. *Mem:* Am Comp Alliance; Am Soc Univ Comp; BMI; Am Music Ctr. *Mailing Add:* Dept Music Univ Tenn Knoxville TN 37996

LENO, HAROLD LLOYD
EDUCATOR, CONDUCTOR
b Burt, NDak, Nov 14, 25. *Study:* Walla Walla Col, BA, 48; Teachers Col, Columbia Univ, MA, 54; Univ Ariz, AMusD, 70. *Teaching:* Instr music, Portland Union Acad, Ore, 48-49 & 51-53 & Walla Walla Valley Acad, 50-51; asst prof, Union Col, Nebr, 53-60; prof, Walla Walla Col, 60- *Bibliog:* Donald Hall (auth), The Brass Family, In: Musical Acoustics, Wadsworth, 80. *Mem:* Music Educr Nat Conf; Int Trombone Asn; Int Trumpet Guild; Western Alliance Arts Adminr; Tubists Universal Brotherhood Asn. *Publ:* Auth, Lip Vibration Characteristics of the Trombone Embouchure, Instrumentalist, 71 & Brass Bulletin, 74; Music, How it Affects the Whole Man, Ministry Mag, 73; Music, Its Far-Reaching Effects, Rev & Herald, 76; Lip Vibration of Trombone Performers, private publ, 79. *Mailing Add:* 1303 Barleen Dr Walla Walla WA 99362

LENTCZNER, BENNETT
CONDUCTOR & MUSIC DIRECTOR, ADMINISTRATOR
b Brooklyn, NY, Mar 9, 38. *Study:* Juilliard Sch Music, BS, 60; Teachers Col, Columbia Univ, MA, 62; Ball State Univ, Dr Arts, 76. *Pos:* Cond & music dir, Roanoke Youth Symph, 82-; artistic dir, SW Va Opera Soc, 82- *Teaching:* Assoc prof trumpet & cond, Radford Univ, 74-, dir instrm ens, 74-82, acting dean, Sch Fine Arts, 82- *Awards:* Citation Excellence, Nat Band Asn, 80. *Mem:* Col Band Dir Nat Asn (Va state chmn, 79-81, secy-treas southern div, 81-82); Nat Band Asn (Va state chmn, 79-); Music Educr Nat Conf. *Mailing Add:* 524 Woods Ave SW Roanoke VA 24016

LENZ, VIRGINIA BLAKEMAN See Blakeman, Virginia

LEON, TANIA J
CONDUCTOR, COMPOSER
b La Habana, Cuba, May 14, 44; US citizen. *Study:* Nat Consv, La Habana, Cuba, MA(music educ), 65; NY Univ, BA(music educ), 73, BS(comp), 75. *Works:* Spiritual Suite, comn by 41st Eucharistic Cong Philadelphia, 76; Latin Lights, Brooklyn Phil Orch, 79; I Got Ovah, Third St Music Sch, 80; Pets Suite, Syracuse Univ Orch, 80; Concerto Criollo, Brooklyn Phil Orch, 80; Four Pieces for Cello, Interart Fest, 80; De-Orishas, Western Wind Ens, 82. *Pos:* Cond, Dance Theatre Harlem, 69-81, Brooklyn Phil Community Conct Serv, 77- & New York Opera, 80-; guest cond, Juilliard Orch, Fest Two Worlds, Spoleto, Italy, 71, Genova Symph Orch, Nervi Fest, 72, Buffalo Phil Orch, 75, Conct Orch Long Island, 76 & 80, Sadler's Wells Orch, London, 77, 79 & 80, Lincoln Ctr Outdoors Fest, 80, Orch of Our Time, New York, NY, 80, Universal Symph, 81, Brooklyn Col Symph Orch, 81, John F Kennedy Ctr Opera House Orch, 81, Radio City Music Hall, 82, Colonne Orch, Paris, France, 82 & Mich Opera, 82; music dir, Wiz, 78, Godspell, 78, Death, Destruction and Detroit, 79, Beggars Soap Opera, 79, Edison, 80, Rice & Beans, 80, Maggie Magalita, 81 & Golden Windows, 82. *Awards:* Achievement Award, Nat Coun Women of US, 80; Byrd Hoffman Found Award, 81; Western Wind Comn, 82. *Mem:* ASCAP; Am Music Ctr Inc; Ctr New Music; Int Artists Alliance. *Rep:* Perrotta Mgt 211 W 56th St Suite 18M New York NY 10019. *Mailing Add:* 35-20 Leverich St B430 Jackson Heights New York NY 11372

LEONARD, NELS, JR
EDUCATOR, OBOE
b Ashland, Ky, Feb 16, 31. *Study:* Marhsall Univ, AB, 52; Col Consv Music, Univ Cincinnati, 52-53; Univ SDak, MM, 57; WVa Univ, PhD, 68; Trinity Col

Music, London, 74; studied in Montevideo, Uruguay with Abel Carlevaro, 80-81. *Teaching:* Instr music, woodwinds & band, Univ SDak, 55-57; asst dir music, NC State Univ, Raleigh, 57-59; prof music, WLiberty State Col, 59- *Bibliog:* Ruth & Jerry Mock (auth), Guitarist Leonard, Veteran Teacher, Professor, Creative Guitar Int, 79; Lars Svenssen (auth), Nels Leonard, Jr: en av USA: u frümsta pa Klassisk Gitarr, Falkoping Daily News, Sweden, 7/81. *Mem:* WVa Music Educr (pres elect, 67-69, pres, 69-71); Music Educr Nat Conf; WVa Col Music Educr; Am String Teachers Asn. *Publ:* Auth, Harmonic Fingerings for Oboe, 60 & Literature for the Oboe, 61, Instrumentalist; ed, Notes & Tempo, WVa Music Educr, 61-67; auth, A Scraping Procedure for Making Oboe Reeds, Woodwind World, 66; contribr, Woodwind Anthology, Instrumentalist. *Mailing Add:* 15 Crestview Dr Wheeling WV 26003

LEONARD, PETER
CONDUCTOR & MUSIC DIRECTOR, FRENCH HORN
b Boston, Mass, July 18, 52. *Study:* Berkshire Music Ctr, 71; Juilliard Sch, BM, MM, 74; study with Jean Morel at Aspen & Juilliard. *Rec Perf:* Works by Thomas & Widdoes, Op One Rec, 75; Miss Julie (Ned Rorem), Painted Smiles Rec, 79; Air Music (Rorem), 81, Gradus ad Parnassum, 81 & Orchestral Music (R Sessions), 82, First Ed Rec. *Pos:* Assoc cond, Greenwich Phil, 70-74 & Long Island Symph, 76-79; music dir, New York Lyr Opera, 79-80, Bergen Phil, NJ, 79- & Youngstown Symph, Ohio, 81-; cond in res, Louisville Orch, Ky, 79-81. *Awards:* Fel, Fromm Found, 71; Juilliard Sch Fel, 72-74; Nat Arts Asn Award, 83. *Rep:* Shaw Concerts Inc 1995 Broadway New York NY 10023. *Mailing Add:* PO Box 337 Meredith NH 03253

LEONARD, RONALD
CELLO
b Rhode Island. *Study:* Curtis Inst Music. *Pos:* Mem, Cleveland Orch, formerly & Rochester Phil, formerly; prin cellist, Los Angeles Phil Orch, currently; chamber music perf & soloist with leading orchs. *Teaching:* Prof cello, Eastman Sch Music, formerly. *Rep:* Regency Artists 9200 Sunset Blvd Suite 23 Los Angeles CA 90069. *Mailing Add:* Los Angeles Phil Orch 135 N Grand Ave Los Angeles CA 90012

LEONARD, STANLEY SPRENGER
PERCUSSION, COMPOSER
b Philadelphia, Pa, Sept 26, 31. *Study:* Northwestern Univ; Eastman Sch Music, BM & perf cert, 54. *Works:* Symphony for Percussion; Bachiana for Percussion; Fanfare and Allegro; Prelude for Four Marimbas; Solo Dialogue; Antiphonies; Suite of Psalms. *Rec Perf:* 35 for Mercury, Capitol, Everest, Columbia, Command, Angel & Philips. *Pos:* Prin timpanist, Pittsburgh Symph Orch, 56-; performer & soloist worldwide, currently. *Teaching:* Sr lectr perc, Carnegie-Mellon Univ, 58-78 & Duquesne Univ, 83. *Mem:* Am Fedn Musicians; Percussive Arts Soc; ASCAP. *Publ:* Contribr to Percussive Notes. *Mailing Add:* 551 Sandrae Dr Pittsburgh PA 15243

LEPAGE, JANE WEINER
CRITIC-WRITER, EDUCATOR
b Montague, Mass, May 7, 31. *Study:* Boston Univ, BMus, 56; Univ Mass, MS, 57; Bennington Col, with Henry Brant, 60. *Teaching:* Chmn & assoc prof music, North Adams State Col, 67- *Awards:* Prof grants, Mass Music Educr, 75 & Commonwealth Mass, 81 & 83. *Bibliog:* Dika Newlin (auth), Libr J, 80. *Mem:* Int League Women Comp; Am Women Comp; Nat Music Educr; Mass Music Educr; Am Asn Univ Women. *Publ:* Auth, Reach Out and Create, Mass Music Educ News, 75; Women Composers, Conductors, and Musicians of the 20th Century: Selected Biographies, Scarecrow Press, 80 & 83. *Mailing Add:* Stratton Hills #F6 Williamstown MA 01267

LEPAK, ALEXANDER
EDUCATOR, PERCUSSION
Study: Hartt Sch Music, with Alfred Friese & Henry Adler, BMus. *Pos:* Solo timpanist & prin perc, Hartford Symph, currently; dir, Hartt Conct Jazz Band, currently. *Teaching:* Prof perc & theory, Hartt Sch Music, 47-; mem fac, Henry Adler Studios, formerly, Nat Youth Orch Can, currently. *Mem:* Nat Asn Col Brass & Perc Teachers. *Mailing Add:* Hartt Sch Music Univ Hartford West Hartford CT 06117

LEPKE, CHARMA DAVIES
COMPOSER, EDUCATOR
b Delavan, Wis, Oct 1, 19. *Study:* Wellesley Col, studied organ with Carl Weinrich & theory with Nadia Boulanger, BA, 41, MA, 42; Am Consv Music, studied piano with Rudolph Reuter, MMus, 46. *Works:* Egoli—In Johannesburg (piano), Lovedale Press, 56; Call to Remembrance (SATB), Mercury Music Corp, 66; Canzona (piano), perf by Mary Louise Boehm, 68; Great & Marvelous (song for high voice), Coburn Press, 76; Parade & Four for Five (piano), Hal Leonard Corp, 83. *Pos:* Church organist, 72- *Teaching:* Instr piano & organ, Fairfax Hall Jr Col, Waynesboro, Va, 42-44; instr piano, Univ Nebr, Lincoln, 46-50 & privately, 77- *Mem:* Am Guild Organists; Music Teachers Nat Asn. *Publ:* Ed music, Amagama Okuhlabelela, Am Bd Mission Natal South Africa, 56. *Mailing Add:* 223 W Geneva St Delavan WI 53115

LERDAHL, FRED (ALFRED WHITFORD)
COMPOSER, WRITER
b Madison, Wis, Mar 10, 43. *Study:* Berkshire Music Ctr, studied with Arthur Berger & Roger Sessions, 64 & 66; Lawrence Univ, with James Ming, BMus, 65; Princeton Univ, with Earl Kim, E T Cone, Milton Babbitt, MFA, 67. *Works:* Wake (sop & choral ens), 68, Aftermath (three singers & choral ens), 73, Chords (orch), 74, rev ed, 83, Eros (ms & choral ens), 75, First String Quartet, 78 & Second String Quartet, 80-82, Mobart Music Publ; Waltzes (violin, viola, cello & bass), Spoleto Fest, US, 81. *Pos:* Comp in res, Marlboro

Music Fest, 67-68 & Int Res & Coord Acoustics Music, Paris, 81-82. *Teaching:* Actg asst prof music, Univ Calif, Berkeley, 69-71; from asst prof to assoc prof, Harvard Univ, 71-79; assoc prof, Columbia Univ, 79- *Awards:* Fel, Guggenheim Found, 74-75; Rec Awards, Walter W Naumburg Found, 77 & Martha Baird Rockefeller Found, 82. *Mem:* Am Music Rec Inst (pres, 83-); Koussevitzky Music Found (mem bd dir, 79-, vpres, 82-); Am Music Ctr; Soc Music Theory. *Interests:* Music theory and music psychology. *Publ:* Coauth, Toward a Formal Theory of Tonal Music, 77 & Generative Music Theory and Its Relation to Psychology, 81, J Music Theory; On the Theory of Grouping and Meter, Musical Quart; A Grammatical Parallel Between Music and Language, In: Music, Mind & Brain, Plenum Press, 82; A Generative Theory of Tonal Music, MIT Press, 83. *Rep:* Mobart Music Publ Jerona Music 81 Trinity Pl Hackensack NJ 07601. *Mailing Add:* 419 W 115th St Apt #21 New York NY 10025

LERMAN, RICHARD M
COMPOSER, ELECTRONIC
Study: Brandeis Univ, BA(music), 66, MFA(film), 70. *Works:* Travelon Gamelon, Folkways Rec, 82; Plaza Music, 3 Rivers Arts Fest, 81; Incident at Three Mile Island, World Music Days, 81; Transduction System I, Merce Cunningham Co, 82; Second Mesa, Inst Contemp Art, 83; Approaching Ground Zero, Sound-Image-Events, 83. *Pos:* Dir & perf, Sound-Image-Events, Newton, Mass, 81- *Awards:* Artist's Fel Music Comp, Mass Artist's Found, 78. *Bibliog:* Skip Blumberg (dir), Music for Bicycle Orchestra (videotape), Walker Art Ctr, 80; Randall Conrad (auth), Media Arts in Boston, Film & Video Monthly Independent, 5/83. *Mem:* BMI; Am Music Ctr; New Music Alliance; Am Soc Univ Comp. *Mailing Add:* 52 Channing Rd Newton MA 02159

LERNER, BENNETT LAWRENCE
PIANO, TEACHER-COACH
b Cambridge, Mass, Mar 21, 44. *Study:* Manhattan Sch Music, with Robert Helps, BMus, MMus, 75; studied with Claudio Arrau, Rafael de Silva & German Diez. *Pos:* Performer, Group for Contemp Music, New Music Consort, Newband, Nat Pub Radio & Voice Am; soloist, Arthur Fiedler & Boston Pops, Miami Beach Symph & Fla Gulf Coast Symph; recitalist, Charles Ives Centennial Fest, 75, Phillips Collection, Washington, DC, Gala Conct NY Radio Sta WNCN, 82 & tours US & Europe. *Teaching:* Mem fac, Greenwich House Music Sch, 79- & Sarah Lawrence Col, 83-84. *Awards:* Martha Baird Rockefeller Fund Music Award, 79. *Mailing Add:* 160 W 95th St Apt 3A New York NY 10025

LERNER, MIMI
MEZZO-SOPRANO
b Poland. *Study:* Queens Col, City Univ New York, BA; Carnegie-Mellon Univ, MFA(voice). *Roles:* Sesto in La Clemenza di Tito (debut), Anna Bolena & Julius Caesar, New York City Opera; Rosina in The Barber of Seville, Brussels; The Tales of Hoffmann, Otello & Susannah, Pittsburgh Opera. *Pos:* Appearances with San Diego, Cincinnati & Ky opera co; orchestral soloist, currently. *Awards:* Nat Opera Inst Grant. *Mailing Add:* 5625 Beacon St Pittsburgh PA 15217

LE ROUX, JEAN-LOUIS
CONDUCTOR & MUSIC DIRECTOR, OBOE
b Le Mans, France, Apr 15, 27; US citizen. *Study:* Lycee de Rennes, France, BA, 44; Ecole Superieure Commerce Paris, dipl, 46; Consv Nat Musique Paris, 49. *Rec Perf:* String Quartet (Loren Rush), 77 & Intermezzi (Edwin Dugger), 78, CRI; Music for the Tempest (Paul Chihara), MMG, 82 & Ref Rec, 82; The San Francisco Contemp Music Players, Grenadilla, 83; Music for Warriors (Charles Fox), PBS, 83. *Pos:* Prin oboe, San Francisco Symph, 60-80; music dir, San Francisco Contemp Music Players, 75- & Chamber Symph San Francisco, 83-; cond, San Francisco Ballet, 77- *Teaching:* Instr perf, Mills Col, Oakland, Calif, 63-73; instr cond, San Francisco Consv Music, 66-72. *Awards:* Chevalier l'Ordre Arts Lett, 81. *Rep:* Jonathan Kleid 880 Franklin St #705 San Francisco CA 94102. *Mailing Add:* 2874 Washington St San Francisco CA 94115

LEROY, EDMUND
EDUCATOR, BARITONE
b Washington, Ga. *Study:* Furman Univ, BA, 66; Union Theol Sem, MSM, 68; Juilliard Sch, MM & DMA, 70-78. *Roles:* Bass soloist, Bethlehem Bach Fest, 73; soloist, Aspen Fest Orch, 73; recitalist, Alice Tully Hall, Lincoln Ctr, New York, 73; soloist, St Louis Symph, 81. *Teaching:* Lectr, Temple Univ, Philadelphia, 70-73; asst prof music, Washington Univ, St Louis, 76-82; fac mem voice, St Louis Consv Music, 82-83; assoc prof music, Rollins Col, Winter Park, Fla, 83- *Awards:* First Prize, Naumburg Int Compt, Lieder, 73; Caruso Mem Prize, Juilliard Sch, 73-75. *Mem:* Nat Asn Teachers Singing (vpres St Louis chap, 80); Am Guild Organists. *Publ:* Auth, Point Counterpoint: Placement, Nat Asn Teachers Singing Bulletin, 82. *Mailing Add:* Music Dept Rollins Col Winter Park FL 32789

LESEMANN, FREDERICK
COMPOSER, EDUCATOR
b Los Angeles, Calif, Oct 12, 36. *Study:* Consv Music, Oberlin Col, with Joseph Wood & Richard Hoffmann, BM, 58; Univ Southern Calif, with Ingolf Dahl, MM, 61, DMA, 72; Comput Music Wkshp, Stanford Univ, 77. *Works:* Paradiso XXI (five visions from Dante); Symphony in Three Movements, 74; Caoine, Music for Brass, 74; Nataraja (prepared piano), 75; Orchestra Music, 76; Fantasy (piano solo), Washington, DC, 76; Legends (suite), 77. *Pos:* Mgr, Ojai Fest, 63-66. *Teaching:* Lectr music theory & comp, Univ Southern Calif, 66-71; asst prof, 71-76, dir, Electronic Music Studio, 74-, assoc prof music theory & comp, 76- *Awards:* Martha Baird Rockefeller Fund Grant, 73; ASCAP Award, 75; Nat Endowment Arts Comp Grant, 76. *Mailing Add:* Sch Music Univ Southern Calif Los Angeles CA 90089

LESSARD, JOHN AYRES
COMPOSER, EDUCATOR
b San Francisco, Calif, July 3, 20. *Study:* Ecole Normale Musique Paris, dipl(harmonie & contrepoint), 39; studied with Nadia Boulanger, 37-41; Longy Sch Music dipl(comp), 40. *Works:* Toccatain Four Movements (harpsichord), 51, Sinfonietta Concertante, 61, Trio in Sei Parti (violin, cello & piano), 66, Quodlibets (trumpet & trombone), 67, Fragments from the Cantos of Ezra Pound, 69, Woodwind Quintet II, 70 & Threads of Sound Recalled (piano), 82, Joshua Music Inc. *Teaching:* Prof comp, State Univ NY, Stony Brook, 62- *Awards:* Alice Ditson Award, Columbia Univ, 46; Guggenheim Found Fel, 46-53; Nat Acad Arts & Lett Award, 52. *Mem:* Am Comp Alliance (bd mem, 56-58, 63-65, 74-76 & 81-83); Am Music Ctr; Comp Rec Inc (bd mem, 74-83). *Rep:* Am Comp Alliance 170 W 74th St New York NY 10023. *Mailing Add:* 15 Scotts Cove Lane East Setauket NY 11733

LESSER, LAURENCE
CELLO, EDUCATOR
b Los Angeles, Calif, Oct 28, 38. *Study:* Harvard Univ, 61, BA; Univ Southern Calif, studied with Gregor Piatigorsky; studied with Gaspar Cassado. *Rec Perf:* Monn Concerto (Schoenberg); Concerto (Lazarof); Chamber Music in Heifetz-Piatigorsky Series; rec on Columbia, RCA, Melodiya & Desto. *Pos:* Soloist with maj orchs of Europe, North & South Am & Japan; pres, New England Consv, currently. *Teaching:* Asst to Piatigorsky, Univ Southern Calif, formerly; teacher, Peabody Consv Music, formerly; mem fac violoncello & chamber music, New England Consv Music, currently; vis prof, Toho Sch Music, Tokyo. *Awards:* Cassado Prize, Siena, Italy, 62; Fourth Prize, Tchaikovsky Compt, Moscow, 66; Ford Found Conct Artist Award. *Mailing Add:* New England Consv Music 290 Huntingdon Ave Boston MA 02138

LETTVIN, THEODORE
PIANO
b Chicago, Ill, Oct 29, 26. *Study:* Curtis Inst Music, with Rudolf Serkin & Mieczlaw Horszowski, BM, 49. *Rec Perf:* The Carnival of Marriage, Columbia Rec; Beethoven Triple Concerto, Univ Mich. *Teaching:* Artist in res, Univ Colo, 56-57; head piano dept, Cleveland Music Sch Settlement, 57-68; prof piano, New England Consv Music, 68-77 & Univ Mich, 77- *Mem:* Nat Inst Arts & Lett; Nat Music Teachers Asn; Am Asn Univ Prof; Am Fedn Musicians. *Rep:* Am Int Artists 275 Madison Ave New York NY 10016. *Mailing Add:* 716 W Huron St Ann Arbor MI 48103

LETZLER, DENNIS CHARLES
ARTIST MANAGER & REPRESENTATIVE
b Cincinnati, Ohio, Oct 29, 38. *Study:* Cincinnati Consv Music, 56-59. *Pos:* Sales, promotion & producer, Capitol/Angel Records, Los Angeles, Calif & NY, 57-70; sales rep, Columbia Artists Mgt, NY, 70-73 & Hurok Concerts, NY, 74-77; exec dir, Unity Concerts, Montclair, NY, 78-80; mgr & sales, Kazuko Hillyer Int, NY, 80- *Mailing Add:* 11 Riverside Dr New York NY 10023

LEUBA, (JULIAN) CHRISTOPHER
FRENCH HORN, EDUCATOR
b Pittsburgh, Pa, Sept 28, 29. *Study:* Roosevelt Col, BMus, 51; studied French horn with Aubrey Brain, London, England, 52 & cond with Pierre Monteux & Richard Lert, 63-66. *Rec Perf:* Horn Quartet Omnibus, Everest Rec, 60; Mozart Duos & Beethoven Sextet, Audiophile Rec, 60; Bernhard Heiden Quintet, Olympic, 70; Three American Sonatas, Crystal Rec, 77; Dauprat Six Sextets, Coronet Rec, 77; The Lyric Horn, Prospect Rec, 79. *Pos:* Prin horn, Minneapolis Symph, 56-60, Phil Hungarica, Vienna, Austria, 58 & Chicago Symph, 60-62. *Teaching:* Prof brass, Univ Wash, 68-79; affiliate, Western Wash Univ, 79-; vis prof horn, Royal Flemish Consv, Antwerp, Belgium, 78 & 79. *Mem:* Int Horn Soc; Galpin Soc; Nat Band Asn; Am Symph Orch League. *Publ:* Auth, The Descant Horn, Instrumentalist, 60; A Study of Musical Intonation, Prospect, 62, French & German transl, Brass Bulletin, Switz, 81; A New Look at Breath Support, Instrumentalist, 80. *Mailing Add:* 4800 NE 70th St Seattle WA 98115

LEVARIE, SIEGMUND
EDUCATOR
b Austria, July 24, 14; US citizen. *Study:* New Vienna Consv, cond dipl, 35; Univ Vienna, PhD, 38. *Pos:* Dir & founder, Collegicum Musicum, Univ Chicago, 38-52; exec dir, Fromm Music Found, 52-56. *Teaching:* Fac mem, Univ Chicago, 38-52; dean, Chicago Musical Col, 52-54; prof, City Univ New York, 54- *Mem:* Am Musicol Soc. *Publ:* Auth, Guillaume de Machaut, In: Great Religious Composers Series, Sheed & Ward, 54 & Da Capo Press, 70; Musical Italy Revisited, Macmillan, 63 & Greenwood Press, 73; coauth (with Ernst Levy), Tone: A Study in Musical Acoustics, Kent State Univ Press, 68 & rev 80; ed (with introd), Lucy Van-Jung Page (1892-1972): Recollections of Pupils and Friends, Holywell Press, 77; coauth (with Ernst Levy), Musical Morphology: A Discourse and a Dictionary, Kent State Univ Press, 83. *Mailing Add:* 624 Third St Brooklyn NY 11215

LEVI, NANNETTE
VIOLIN
b San Francisco, Calif. *Study:* Juilliard Grad Sch, with Louis Persinger, 44-48; Pablo Casals Master Class, Zermatt, Switz, 56. *Rec Perf:* The Gotham Trio, Orion, 82. *Pos:* Concertmaster & soloist, Bach Fest, Carmel, Calif, 47-57; concertmaster, San Antonio Symph Orch, 57-59; violinist, Pac String Trio, 59-70 & Gotham Trio, 71- *Teaching:* Violin & chamber music, Mannes Col Music, 70- *Awards:* Dipl d'Honneur, Fond Eugene Ysaye, Bruxelles, 67. *Rep:* Albert Kay Assocs Inc 58 W 58th St New York NY 10019. *Mailing Add:* 817 West End Ave New York NY 10025

LEVI, PAUL ALAN
COMPOSER, PIANO
b New York, NY, June 30, 41. *Study:* Oberlin Col, BA(music), 63; Juilliard Sch, with Hall Overton & Vincent Persichetti, MMus(comp), 72, DMA(comp), 78. *Works:* Five Progressions for 3 Instruments, perf by New York New Music Ens & others, 71; PBS Signature Tune, PBS, 72; The Truth, comn by Chamber Music Northwest, 75; Thanksgiving (one-act opera), Juilliard Opera Training Dept, 77; Elegy and Recreations, comn by Chamber Music Soc Lincoln Ctr, 80; Spring Sestina, comn by Music Today Ser, 82; Mark Twain Suite, comn by New York Choral Soc, 83. *Pos:* Music panelist, NY State Coun Arts, 81-84, chmn, 83-84; comp in res, Chamber Music Northwest, 75 & Wolf Trap Farm Park, 76. *Teaching:* Mem fac theory & comp, NY Univ, 79-; mem fac theory, Queens Col, 79; mem fac music lit, Lehman Col, 81-82. *Awards:* German Acad Exchange Serv Grant Munich, 73-74; Nat Endowment Arts Fel Grants, 76 & 80; Guggenheim Found Fel, 83-84. *Bibliog:* Judith Martin (auth), The Composer Vs Blank Paper, Washington Post, 8/76. *Mem:* League Comp—Int Soc Contemp Music (vpres, 78-79, pres, 79-82, co-pres, 82-83); Am Comp Alliance (mem bd gov, 81-83); Am Music Ctr; BMI; Am Fedn Musicians. *Publ:* Auth, The New Orchestra: Inaugural Concert, Contemp Music Newslett, 75; The 1982 World Music Days in Belgium, Am Music Ctr Newslett, 83. *Mailing Add:* 105 W 73rd St New York NY 10023

LEVIN, GREGORY JOHN
COMPOSER, EDUCATOR
b Washington, DC, Mar 8, 43. *Study:* Harvard Univ, with Leon Kirchner & Billy Jim Layton, BA, 67; Brandeis Univ, with Arthur Berger & Seymour Shifrin, MFA, 69; studied with Luciano Berio & Pierre Boulez. *Works:* Suite for Flute, Oboe and Piano (chamber music), 63; Improvisation on Levin #1 (chamber music), 66; Improvisation on Levin #2, 67; Five Picasso Portraits (brass quintet), 72; The White Goddess (tape, audio & visual feedback, film, string bass, voice & piano), 72; Black-Point Cut-Off (film, string bass, piano & tape), 73; Feedback (color TV, piano & tape), 73; and others. *Pos:* Asst cond, Brandeis Choral Union, 68-70; writer liner notes, Acoustics Res Inc & Deutsche Grammophon, 69; musical dir & cond, Syracuse New Music Ens, 70-72 & Levin Ens, 72-; cond, Syracuse Univ Orch & Symph Orch, 71; dir, Calgary Chamber Players, 74- *Teaching:* Asst prof music theory & comp, Sch Music, Univ Syracuse, 70-72 & Univ Calgary, 73-; middle sch & high sch teaching specialist, RI Coun Arts, 72-; vis asst prof, Univ RI, 72-73; comp in res, Ind Univ, South Bend, 72. *Awards:* Scholar, Harvard Univ, 61-67; Woodrow Wilson Fel, 67-68; Brandeis Univ Fel, 68-70. *Mailing Add:* Music Dept Univ Calgary Calgary AB T2N 1N4 Canada

LEVIN, RAMI YONA
COMPOSER, OBOE
b Brooklyn, NY, Feb 27, 54. *Study:* Yale Univ, studied with Yehundi Wyner & Robert Morris, BA, 75; Univ Calif, San Diego, MA, 78; Aspen Sch Music; studied with Miriam Gideon & Kenneth Gaburo. *Works:* Now We Are Six (song cycle), Yale Univ, 75, Univ Calif, 77 & Trinity Church, Berkeley, Calif, 79; becummings, Aspen Music Sch, 77; Ambages for Solo Guitar, George Sakellariou, 78; Unfoldings, Morley Wind Group, London, 80; Dialogue for Flute & Oboe, Purcell Room, London, 80; Movements for String Quartet, Locrian String Quartet, 81; Blues Toccata for Piano, Nat Asn Comp, 83. *Pos:* Oboist, Yale Univ Conct Band, 71-75, Yale Repty Theatre, 71 & 75 & Morley Wind Group, London, England, 79-80. *Mem:* Int League Women Comp; Nat Asn Comp; Am Women Comp. *Mailing Add:* 5631 S Dorchester Ave Chicago IL 60637

LEVINE, JAMES LAWRENCE
CONDUCTOR & MUSIC DIRECTOR
b Cincinnati, Ohio, June 23, 43. *Study:* Aspen Fest Sch, with Wolfgang Vacana; Juilliard Sch, with Jean Morel, studied piano with Rosina Lhevinne; studied cond with Fausto Cleva, Max Rudolf & George Szell; Marlboro Fest, studied piano with Rudolf Serkin; studied voice with Jennie Tourel, Adel Addison, Mack Harrell & Hans Hotter; Cincinnati Univ, Hon DM. *Rec Perf:* Giovanna d'Arco (Verdi); I Vespri Siciliani (Verdi); Il Barbiere di Siviglia (Rossini); Norma (Bellini); La Forza del destino (Verdi); Symphonies 1, 3, 4, 5, 6 & 10 (Mahler); and others. *Pos:* Asst cond, Cleveland Orch, 64-70; music dir, Ravinia Fest, 73- & Cincinnati May Fest, 74-78; prin cond, Metropolitan Opera, 73-76, music dir, 76-; guest cond, maj US & Europ orchs. *Bibliog:* Bernard Holland (auth), James Levine's Upbeat Libretto for the Met's Future, New York Times, 1/17/82. *Rep:* Columbia Artists Mgt 165 W 57th St New York NY 10019. *Mailing Add:* Metropolitan Opera Lincoln Ctr New York NY 10023

LEVINE, JEFFREY LEON
COMPOSER, EDUCATOR
b Brooklyn, NY, Sept 15, 42. *Study:* Brown Univ, BA; Yale Univ, with Mel Powell, MM; Accad Chigiana, Siena, Italy, dipl; studied with Gunther Schuller & Franco Donatoni. *Works:* Piano Concerto, 71; Divertimento (ten solo instrm), 73; Crystals (ballet), comn by Oakland Ballet, 75; Form (two pianos); Piano Trio, 77; Tapestry (double string quartet), 83; Clarinoodle (clarinet sextet), 71. *Pos:* String bassist, Europe & US; mem, Perf Arts Orch; cond, Concordia Chamber Orch. *Teaching:* Lectr, Rutgers Univ, 65-68 & Univ Calif, Berkeley, 72-74; mem fac, Bennington Col, currently. *Awards:* Fulbright Grant, 68; Nat Endowment for the Arts Grant, 78. *Mem:* ASCAP. *Mailing Add:* Music Dept Bennington Col Bennington VT 05201

LEVINE, JOSEPH
MUSIC DIRECTOR & CONDUCTOR

b Philadelphia, Pa, Aug 14, 12. *Study:* Curtis Inst Music, BMus(cond & piano), studied cond with Fritz Reiner & Artur Rodzinski, piano with Josef Hofmann, harpsichord with Wanda Landowska & opera with Hans Wohlmuth & Ernst Lert. *Rec Perf:* Ballet scores, Capitol Rec, 52-57. *Pos:* Asst cond, Philadelphia Grand Opera Co, 38-40; founder & cond, New Ctr Music Orch, Philadelphia, 40-43 & Chamber Opera Soc, 46-50; pianist, Philadelphia Orch, 40-43 & 46-50; cond, USAF Tactical Air Ctr Symphonette, 43-45; piano accmp with Joseph Szigeti, 46-50; music dir & cond, Co-Opera Co, Philadelphia, 47-50, Am Ballet Theatre, New York, 50-58, Omaha Symph Orch, 58-69 & Bremerton Symph, 79-; mem, foreign tours with State Dept cult exchange prog, 50-58 & Cornish Trio, 69-73; music dir, Omaha Civic Opera Soc, 61-69 & Omaha Starlight Theatre, 61; Am cond, Royal Ballet England, 63-65; assoc cond, Seattle Symph Orch, 69-73 & Hawaii Opera Theatre & Honolulu Symph Orch, 73-76; guest cond, US, Europe, Can, Cent & South Am & Asia. *Teaching:* Mem fac, Curtis Inst Music, 33-40 & Cornish Sch Allied Arts, Seattle, 69-73 & 76-79. *Awards:* Achievement Recognition Inst, Libr Cong. *Mailing Add:* 2917 W Eaton St Seattle WA 98199

LEVINE, JULIUS
DOUBLE BASS

Study: Brooklyn Col, BA; Juilliard Sch Music, studied bass with Frederick Zimmermann, BS. *Rec Perf:* Numerous on Columbia & Marlboro Rec Soc. *Pos:* Mem, New York Chamber Soloists, 58-; soloist double bass, Fest Casals & Musica Aeterna Orch; appearances with Budapest, Juilliard, Galimir, Guaneri & Curtis Quartets & other chamber music groups. *Teaching:* Mem fac double bass, Mannes Col Music, 67-, Queens Col & Brooklyn Col, City Univ New York, currently, Columbia Univ, currently, State Univ NY, Stony Brook, currently & Peabody Consv Music, currently. *Mailing Add:* Peabody Consv Music Johns Hopkins Univ Baltimore MD 21202

LEVINSON, GERALD
COMPOSER, EDUCATOR

b Mineola, NY, June 22, 51. *Study:* Univ Pa, with George Crumb, Richard Wernick & George Rochberg; Berkshire Music Ctr, with Bruno Maderna; Univ Chicago, with Ralph Shapey, MA, 74, PhD, 77; studied with Olivier Messiaen. *Works:* Winds of Light (violin & piano), 73; Oddyssey (solo flute), 73; Skryzbka (violin solo), 73; Sky Music (13 instrm), 74-75; Two Poems, 76; Trio for Clarinet, Cello & Piano, 76; Chant des Rochers (chamber orch), Pittsburgh, 76. *Teaching:* Asst prof music, Swarthmore Col, 77- *Awards:* Georges Lurcy Found Fel, 74-75; Prem Prix Comp, Paris, 76; Goddard Lieberson Fel, Am Acad & Inst Arts & Lett, 79. *Mailing Add:* Music Dept Swarthmore Col Swarthmore PA 19081

LE VITA, DAVID NAHON
PIANO, CONDUCTOR

b New York, NY, June 2, 06. *Study:* Leipzig Consv, 29; Leipzig Univ, PhD, 31; study with Ralph Leopold, Paolo Gallico, Percy Grainger, Robert Teichmuller & Harold Bauer. *Pos:* Dir, Prospect Plaza Music Ctr, 36-38; musicologist, Brooklyn Museum, 37-72; cond, Brooklyn Museum Symph Orch, 47-72. *Teaching:* Fac mem piano & music hist, Henry St Settlement, 40-43; dir piano dept, Music Sch Settlement, 45-48. *Awards:* Award of Merit, Nat Fedn Music Clubs, 58; New York City Citation Distinguished & Exceptional Service Music. *Bibliog:* Music & Its Parallels in Visual Arts, Mag Art, 44; Allen Hughes (auth), Musical Life in New York, Musical Am, 52; Gladys Mathew (auth), An Impressario Grows in Brooklyn, Music J, 63. *Mem:* Int Musicol Soc; Am Musicol Soc; Soc Ethnomusicol; Nat Asn Comp & Cond; The Bohemians. *Publ:* Auth, Fiddles of the Master Craftsmen, Brooklyn Museum Press, 45. *Mailing Add:* Rocky Hill Rd PO Box K6 Greenwood Lake NY 10925

LEVITIN, SUSAN
FLUTE

b Chicago, Ill, Apr 16, 41. *Study:* Eastman Sch Music, with Joseph Marian, BM & perf cert, 62; studied with William Kincaid, Ralph Johnson & Pierre Monteux. *Rec Perf:* Night Soliloquy (Kent Kennan), Mercury, 62. *Pos:* First flute, Eastman Wind Ens, 59-62 & Eastman Phil, 61-62; second flute, Rochester Phil, 61-62; flute soloist, Chicago Ens, 76- *Mailing Add:* 1465 E Park Pl Chicago IL 60637

LEVY, DAVID BENJAMIN
EDUCATOR, ADMINISTRATOR

b New York, NY, Mar 29, 48. *Study:* Eastman Sch Music, BM, 69, MA, 71; Univ Rochester, PhD, 80. *Teaching:* Asst prof music, Wake Forest Univ, 76-, dir concts, 82- *Awards:* Fel, Deutsche Akad Austauschdienst, 71-72. *Mem:* Am Musicol Soc; Col Music Soc; Music Critics Asn. *Interests:* Beethoven; 19th century London; Joseph Martin Kraus; history of criticism. *Publ:* Auth, W R Griepenkerl and Beethoven's Ninth Symphony, Eastman Press, 79. *Mailing Add:* Box 7345 Winston-Salem NC 27109

LEVY, FRANK E
COMPOSER, CELLO

b Paris, France, Oct 15, 30; US citizen. *Study:* Juilliard Sch Music, BS, 51; Univ Chicago, MA, 54. *Works:* Lament (narrator, oboe, strings & perc), 75; Adagio & Scherzo for Four Saxophones, 76, Go Down, Death (narrator, trumpet, harp & solo dancer), 76, Seven Bagatelles for Oboe, Cello & Harp, 77, Symphony #3, 77 & Sonata for Violin & Piano, 77, Seesaw Music Corp; other publ by Seesaw & Cor Publ Co. *Mem:* ASCAP. *Mailing Add:* 19 Virginia St Tenafly NJ 07670

LEVY, GERARDO
FLUTE, CONDUCTOR

b Berlin, Germany, Oct 23, 24; US citizen. *Study:* Colleqium Musicum Buenos Aires, Argentina; Boston Univ, BM, 60. *Rec Perf:* Four Sonate Da Camera, Dischi Ricordi, Italy, 65; Master Virtuosi of New York, Master Virtuoso Rec Soc, 66; In Dulci Jubilo (Stokowski), Bach Guild, Vanguard Soc, 67; Leo Kraft, 73 & M Davidovsky, 74, CRI; Leo Kraft, No 1, Serenus Rec Ed, 74; La Pietra Del Paragone, Vanguard Soc, 78. *Pos:* Cond, Caecilian Chamber Ens, 65; prin flutist, Clarion Conct Soc, 68; solo flutist, Laurentian Chamber Players, 71; co-prin flutist, New York City Opera Orch, currently. *Teaching:* Fac mem flute & chamber music, Sarah Lawrence Col, 71, NY Univ, 77, & Sessioni Senesi Per La Musica E L'Arte, 78. *Mem:* New York Flute Club; Am Fedn Musicians. *Mailing Add:* 171 W 79th St Apt 152 New York NY 10024

LEVY, JANET M
WRITER, EDUCATOR

b Troy, NY, Oct 18, 38. *Study:* Vassar Col, AB, 60; Stanford Univ, AM, 61, PhD, 71. *Teaching:* Instr, Cornell Univ, 65-66; actg asst prof, Univ Va, 66-67; lectr & asst prof, City Col, City Univ New York, 67-78; adj grad fac, New Sch Social Res, 82- *Awards:* Fulbright Scholar, 62-63; Younger Humanist Award, Nat Endowment Humanities, 72-73. *Mem:* Am Musicol Soc; Col Music Soc; Soc Music Theory. *Interests:* Analysis, criticism and theory, primarily in 18th and 19th century music. *Publ:* Auth, Quatuor Concertant, In: New Grove Dict Music & Musicians, 80; Gesture, Form and Syntax in Haydn's Music, In: Haydn Studies, Norton, 81; Texture as a Sign in Classic and Early Romantic Music, J Am Musicol Soc, fall 82; Beethoven's Compositional Choices: The Two Versions of Opus 18, No 1, First Movement, Univ Pa Press, 82. *Mailing Add:* 165 West End Ave #23M New York NY 10023

LEVY, JOANNA
MEZZO-SOPRANO

b New York, NY. *Study:* Ithaca Col, BM; Hofstra Univ, MA. *Roles:* Herodias in Salome; Suzuki in Madama Butterfly; Erda in Das Rheingold; Mother in The Consul; Witch & Mother in Hänsel und Gretel; Baba the Turk in The Rake's Progress; Cornelia in Giulio Cesare. *Pos:* Appearances with New York City Opera, Atlanta Civic Opera, Opera Theater Rochester & others. *Mailing Add:* c/o Salmon & Stokes 280 Riverside Dr Suite 3B New York NY 10025

LEVY, KENNETH
EDUCATOR, WRITER

b New York, NY, Feb 26, 27. *Study:* Queens Col, AB, 47; Princeton Univ, MFA, 49, PhD(music), 55. *Teaching:* Instr, Princeton Univ, 52-54, prof music, 66-; from asst prof to assoc prof, Brandeis Univ, 54-64, Frederick R Mann prof, 64-66. *Awards:* Guggenheim Fel, 55-56. *Mem:* Am Musicol Soc; Fr Musicol Soc. *Interests:* Medieval and Renaissance music; 19th century. *Publ:* Assoc ed, Antologie de la Chanson Parisienne au Seizeme Siecle; auth, New Material of the Early Motet in England, Am Musicol Soc J; Chansonin the Last Half of the 16th Century, Die Musik in Geschichte und Gegenwart. *Mailing Add:* Dept Music Princeton Univ Princeton NJ 08540

LEVY, MARVIN DAVID
COMPOSER

b Passaic, NJ, Aug 2, 32. *Study:* NY Univ, with Philip James, BA, 54; Columbia Univ, with Otto Luening, MA, 56. *Works:* Kyros (dance poem), 61; Mourning Becomes Electra (libretto after O'Neill), Metropolitan Opera, 67; Piano Concerto, Chicago, 70; Trialogues, Chicago, 72; Masada (oratorio), comn by Nat Symph, 73; In Memoriam W H Auden, New York, 74; Canto de los Marranos (sop & orch), San Francisco, 77. *Pos:* Music critic, 52-58. *Teaching:* Mem fac, Brooklyn Col, City Univ New York, 74-76. *Awards:* Prix de Rome, 62 & 63; Ford Found Grant, 65; Nat Endowment Arts Grant, 74. *Rep:* Sheldon Soffer Mgt Inc 130 W 56th St New York NY 10019. *Mailing Add:* 41 W 82nd St New York NY 10024

LEWANDO, OLGA WOLF
EDITOR, TEACHER-COACH

b Chicago, Ill. *Study:* Consv Music, Univ Mo, Kansas City; Juilliard Sch Music. *Pos:* Ed, Music & Artists Mag, New York; writer for various publications, formerly; ed, Music Insider Mag, New York and founder, Harbinger Found, currently. *Teaching:* Instr music, Kansas City Pub Sch, Mo, formerly; dir piano & theory dept, Rudolph Wurlitzer Sch Music, New York, formerly; private piano, comp & coaching, New York, currently. *Mem:* ASCAP; Music Critics Asn; Int Soc Perf Arts Adminr; Music Teachers Nat Asn; Cent Opera Serv. *Publ:* Auth, Nine volumes on music education published by Boston Music Co; many art songs, short works in various forms, and arrangements published by Belwin-Mills, BMI and Bourne, Inc. *Mailing Add:* 303 W 66 St New York NY 10023

LEWANDOWSKI, LYNNE
HARP MAKER, LECTURER

b Pa, May 14, 53. *Study:* Sarah Lawrence Col, BA, 75; studied baroque oboe with Nora Post. *Pos:* Founder, Lewandowski Harps, 75- *Awards:* Nat Endowment Arts & Arts Coun Windham City Grant, 82. *Bibliog:* Nora Post (auth), Lynne Lewandowski: Harpmaker, Folk Harp J, 80. *Mem:* Am Musical Instrm Soc; Am Craft Coun. *Interests:* Lutherie (historical harps). *Mailing Add:* 67 Main St Brattleboro VT 05301

LEWENTHAL, RAYMOND
PIANO, EDUCATOR

b San Antonio, Tex, 1926. *Study:* Juilliard Sch Music; Chigiana Acad, Siena; studied with Lydia Cherkassey, Olga Samaroff Stowkowski, Alfred Cortot &

Guido Agosti. *Rec Perf:* On RCA, Columbia, Angel & Westminster. *Pos:* Recitalist & soloist with orchs in US, Europe, South Am, Australia & Africa. *Teaching:* Mem fac, Berkshire Music Ctr, 74; mem fac piano, Manhattan Sch Music, 74- *Awards:* Chevalier L'Ordre Artes & Lett, France, 70; Gainsborough Award; Winner, Young Artists Cont, Univ Calif, Los Angeles. *Interests:* Nineteenth century music. *Mailing Add:* 51 E 78th St New York NY 10021

LEWIN, FRANK
COMPOSER, EDUCATOR
b Breslau, Germany, Mar 27, 25; US citizen. *Study:* Baldwin Consv Music, with Felix Deyo, cert, 48; Southern Methodist Univ with Hans David; Utah State Agr Col, with Roy Harris; Sch Music, Yale Univ, with Richard Donovan & Paul Hindemith, BMus, 51. *Works:* Innocence and Experience, Am Comp Alliance, 61; The Defenders, Demeter Music Inc, 63-65; Music for the White House, Parga Music, 65; Requiem for Robert F Kennedy, Demeter Music, 69; Gulliver (opera), 75, Beyond the Sundown, 75 & Variations of Greek Themes, 77, Parga Music. *Teaching:* Freelance comp, 51- Teaching: Prof film comp, Sch Music, Yale Univ, 71-; prof modern media music, Sch Arts, Columbia Univ, 75- *Awards:* Nat Endowment Arts Fel, 77 & 82; NJ State Coun Arts Fel, 83. *Bibliog:* Mark Evans (auth), Soundtrack, Hopkins & Blake, 75; Zeitgenössische Schlesische Komponisten, Laumann, Ger, 80. *Mem:* BMI; Am Music Ctr; Am Comp Alliance. *Publ:* Auth, The Soundtrack in Nontheatrical Motion Pictures, 58 & Man and His Sound—Expo '67, 68, Soc Motion Picture & TV Engineers. *Mailing Add:* 113 Magnolia Lane Princeton NJ 08540

LEWIS, ARTHUR
VIOLA, EDUCATOR
b Philadelphia, Pa, Oct 30, 35. *Study:* Col of Pac, BA & BM, 58; New England Consv, MM, 59; Ind Univ, DM, 66. *Pos:* Asst prin viola, Aspen Fest Orch, 63-79; violist, Philadelphia Orch, 67-68; prin viola, Baltimore Symph, 68-72 & Santa Fe Opera, 80-81. *Teaching:* Prof music lit & viola, Int Cong of Strings, 70 & Ill State Univ, 72- *Awards:* Fulbright Scholar, 59. *Publ:* Ed, Notes on Music Idea & History, Aspen Fest. *Mailing Add:* Rte 1 Bloomington IL 61701

LEWIS, BARBARA CONNOLLY
CONDUCTOR, COACH
b Beverly, Mass, Oct 16, 27. *Study:* Radcliffe Col, BA, 49; Harvard Univ, choral cond with G Wallace Woodworth, MAT, 51. *Pos:* Co-founder & cond, Princeton Madrigal Singers, NJ, 59-70; founder & cond, Open Readings, Belmont, Mass, 71- *Teaching:* Assoc, Sch Arts, Boston Univ, 70-74; founder, chmn & coach, Vocal Dept, Belmont Music Sch, 76- *Awards:* Wyman Fel, Harvard Univ, 49. *Mem:* Am Musicol Soc; Asn Am Choral Cond. *Mailing Add:* 35 Clover St Belmont MA 02178

LEWIS, (JOHN) CARY
PIANO, EDUCATOR
b Uvalde, Tex, Nov 23, 42. *Study:* NTex State Univ, BMus, 64, MMus, 65; Eastman Sch Music, with Eugene List, Brooks Smith, DMA & perf cert, 72; Acad Music, Vienna, Austria, with Dieter Weber. *Rec Perf:* A Gottschalk Festival, Vox-Turnabout, 72; Gottschalk Piano Duets, Vanguard, 76; Brahms Chamber Music, Orion, 78; Music by Portuguese Composers, Educo, 78; Chamber Music (Carl Vollrath), Coronet, 79; Violin Sonatas of Robert Schumann, Crystal, 81; Chamber Music of Carl Czerny, Musical Heritage Soc, 83. *Teaching:* Asst prof music, Nebr Wesleyan Univ, 71-76; assoc prof, Ga State Univ, 76-; instr piano, various summer fest incl, Nat Music Camp, Interlochen, Mich, 73- & Red Lodge, Mont, 81- *Awards:* Fulbright Award, 69-71. *Bibliog:* Various reviews of recitals & rec in newspapers & mag. *Mem:* Phi Mu Alpha; Music Teachers Nat Asn; Am Fedn Musicians; Col Music Soc; Am Liszt Soc. *Mailing Add:* 1284 Vista Leaf Dr Decatur GA 30033

LEWIS, DAVID S
EDUCATOR, CLARINET
b Baltimore, Md, Dec 10, 29. *Study:* Concord Col, BS, 52; Univ Mich, MM, 57; WVa Univ, PhD, 68. *Pos:* Prin clarinet, Roanoke Symph Orch, 59-63 & Singapore Symph Orch, 84; rec rev, Clarinet, 74-; co-prin clarinet, Singapore Symph Orch, 79-80. *Teaching:* Asst prof woodwinds & theory, Concord Col, 57-63 & Frostburg State Col, 64-66; prof clarinet & theory, Ohio Univ, 66- *Awards:* Fulbright Grant, 79 & 84; Baker Award, Ohio Univ, 83. *Mem:* Col Music Soc; Int Clarinet Soc; Clarinetwork. *Publ:* Auth, An Analytical Review of George Perle's Three Unaccompanied Clarinet Sonatas, In: Gillespie's Solos for Unaccompanied Clarinet, Detroit Studies Music Bibliog, 73; Nielsen's Concerto for Clarinet: Discrepancies between Part and Score, Clarinet, 74; coauth, Harmonic Dictation: A Programmed Course, private publ. *Mailing Add:* Sch Music Ohio Univ Athens OH 45701

LEWIS, ELISABETH PARMELEE
EDUCATOR, VIOLIN
b Urbana, Ill, June 26, 20. *Study:* Univ Mich, BMus(violin), 45, MMus(violin), 48; studied with Hugo Kortschak & Gilbert Ross. *Teaching:* Instr music, Sullins Col, Va, 45-47; assoc prof violin, Wesley Col, NDak, 49-53; assoc prof music, Univ NDak, Grand Forks, 53- *Mem:* Music Teachers Nat Asn (secy east cent div, 60-62); Am String Teachers Asn; Music Educr Nat Conf; Soc Music Theory; Col Music Soc. *Mailing Add:* 301 N 7th St Grand Forks ND 58201

LEWIS, GERALD DAVID
EDUCATOR, CONDUCTOR
b Elkhart, Ind, Dec 14, 22. *Study:* Chicago Consv Music, studied violin with Ludwig Becker, 40-42; Juilliard Sch Music, studied violin with Joseph Fuchs,

BS, 50; Univ Southern Calif, studied violin with Sascha Jacobsen, MM(violin), 54. *Pos:* Violinist, St Louis Symph & St Louis Sinfonette, 50-53, Los Angeles Phil, 53-57; first violin, Res String Quartet, Ind Univ, 65-70. *Teaching:* Orch dir, South Bend Community Sch, 60-70, Ind Univ, South Bend, 64-70; assoc prof orch, violin & theory, Gustavus Adolphus Col, 70- *Awards:* Gold Merit Award, Am String Teachers Asn, 64. *Mem:* Minn String Task Force (secy, 79-81); Am String Teachers Asn; Minn Music Educr Asn. *Mailing Add:* Music Dept Gustavus Adolphus Col St Peter MN 56082

LEWIS, HARMON
HARPSICHORD, ORGAN
Study: Millsaps Col, BA; Indiana Univ, MMus, DMus; studied organ with Donald Kilmer & Oswald Ragatz, harpsichord with Marie Zorn & Renaissance & Baroque ornamentation with Austin Caswell & Flora Contino. *Pos:* Recitalist, US & Can; mem, Karr-Lewis Duo, 71-; mem trio with Eugenia Zukerman & Gary Karr. *Teaching:* Fac mem, Centre Col, Ky & Dalhousie Univ, formerly; vis lectr harpsichord & organ, Hartt Sch Music, 77- *Mailing Add:* Hartt Sch Music Univ Hartford West Hartford CT 06117

LEWIS, HENRY
CONDUCTOR & MUSIC DIRECTOR, DOUBLE BASS
b Los Angeles, Calif, Oct 16, 32. *Study:* Univ Southern Calif. *Rec Perf:* On Decca. *Pos:* Mem & cond, Seventh Army Symph Orch, 55-57; founder, Los Angeles Chamber Orch, 58; double bassist, Los Angeles Phil, formerly, cond, 61-65; music dir, Los Angeles Opera Co, 65-68 & NJ Symph, 68-76; cond, Am Symph Orch, 67 & Metropolitan Opera, 72; guest cond, maj world orchs. *Mailing Add:* c/o Int Artist Mgt 111 W 57th St New York NY 10019

LEWIS, JUNGSHIN LIM
CELLO, EDUCATOR
b Seoul, Korea; US citizen. *Study:* Peabody Consv Music, BM, 73; studied with Laurence Lesser & Stephen Kates, MM, 67-77. *Pos:* Conct cellist with maj symph orch in North Am & Far East, 68-; first cellist, Calgary Phil Orch, Alberta, 73-75, Richmond Symph Orch, 76-78 & Dallas Ballet Orch, 81-; cellist, Koryo Piano Trio, 78- *Teaching:* Prof cello, Longwood Col, 75-78 & Tex Women's Univ, 81- *Mailing Add:* 17703 Bent Oaks Dallas TX 75252

LEWIS, L RHODES
CONDUCTOR, EDUCATOR
b Emporia, Kans, Dec 27, 19. *Study:* Baker Univ, BMus, 41; Kans State Univ, MS(music educ), 49; Univ Iowa, PhD, 56. *Pos:* Cond & musical dir, Am Community Symph Orch, 61- *Teaching:* Supvr music, Swink Colo Pub Sch, 48; prof band, orch & choir cond, Eastern Ore State Col, 49-63; prof cond & teacher supvr, Univ Wis, Eau Claire, 63-, chmn, 63-73. *Awards:* Croix de Commandeur, French Legion of Honor, Paris, 61. *Mem:* Am Symph Orch League (mem bd dirs, 56-58); Wis Symph Orch Asn; Music Educr Nat Conf; Am Asn Comp & Cond; Am Fedn Musicians. *Mailing Add:* 471 Roosevelt Eau Claire WI 54701

LEWIS, LUCINDA
FRENCH HORN
b Kansas City, Mo, May 8, 53. *Study:* Manhattan Sch Music, BM & MM. *Pos:* Prin horn, NJ Symph Orch, 77- *Mailing Add:* 4 W 31st St New York NY 10001

LEWIS, MALCOLM WALLACE, JR
COMPOSER, EDUCATOR
b Cuba, NY, Nov 14, 25. *Study:* Ithaca Col, BS, 48, BM, 50, MM, 53; Cornell Univ, studied comp with Robert Palmer, 51-53. *Works:* Poem for Soprano Saxophone and Piano, 80, Elegy for a Hallow Man (sax solo), 80, Clarinet Concerto, 80, Three Etudes for Piano, 82, Seven Olde French Songs, 83 & Reflections & Dance (flute solo), 83, Dorn Publ. *Teaching:* Private teacher music, Cody, Wyo & Billings, Mont, 53-61; teacher art, Bozeman Cent Sch, 61-62; assoc prof music, Ithaca Col, 62- *Mem:* BMI; Phi Mu Alpha. *Interests:* Musical techniques. *Mailing Add:* 630 W Dryden Rd Freeville NY 13068

LEWIS, MARCIA ANN
MEZZO-SOPRANO, EDUCATOR
b Dodgeville, Wis, Feb 27, 41. *Study:* Univ Wis, Madison, BM(vocal educ), 63, MM(appl voice), 65; Northwestern Univ, DMA(vocal perf), 78. *Roles:* Florence Pike in Albert Herring, Northwestern Univ Opera Theatre, 69; alto soloist in Messiah, Apollo Music Club Chicago, 76; ms in Stabat Mater, Civic Symph Oak Park-River Forest, 77; Princess in Suor Angelica, Hinsdale Opera Theater, 78; performer, Alto Rhapsody (Brahms) & Requiem (Mozart), Park Forest Singers, 79 & 80; alto soloist in Mass in C (Beethoven), DuPage Chorale, 83; performer, Song Cycle (Richard Wienhorst), Lutheran Sch Theology, 83. *Pos:* Soloist, First Church of Christ, Des Plaines, Ill, 76- *Teaching:* Instr voice & opera, Augustana Col, 65-68; asst prof voice & dir choral & opera dept, Northeastern Ill Univ, 71-74; assoc prof voice, Valparaiso Univ, 78- *Awards:* Fac Growth Award, Am Lutheran Church & Augustana Col, 67; Upper Midwest Winner, Metropolitan Opera District Cont, 68. *Mem:* Nat Asn Teachers Singing (bd mem Chicago chap, 74-75, treas, 75-77, rec secy, 77-79, vpres, 79-80, pres, 80-82). *Mailing Add:* 9630 W Higgins Rd #2C Rosemont IL 60018

LEWIS, PETER TOD
COMPOSER, EDUCATOR
b Charlottesville, Va, Nov 6, 32. *Study:* Univ Calif, Santa Barbara, with Roger Chapman; Univ Calif, Los Angeles, with Lukas Foss & John Vincent; Berkshire Music Ctr, with Wolfgang Fortner; Brandeis Univ, with Arthur Berger & Irving Fine. *Works:* Capriccio Concertato (two pianos), 60;

Evolution (orch), 61; Contrasts (wind quintet), 62; We Stood on the Wall (chorus), 65; ... and Bells ... and Time (dialogue for violin & piano), 67; Signs and Circuits (string quartet & tape), 70; Innerkip (piano & tape), 72; and many others. *Teaching:* Instr, Philadelphia Musical Acad, 65-68; res comp, Southern Ill Univ, 68-69; prof music, Univ Iowa, 69- *Awards:* Scholar, Berkshire Music Ctr, 60; Huntington Hartford Found Grant, 60; MacDowell Fel, 61 & 80. *Mailing Add:* 510 Grant St Iowa City IA 52240

LEWIS, PHILIP JAMES
VIOLIN, EDUCATOR
b Glendale, Calif, Dec 12, 47. *Study:* Peabody Consv Music, with Berl Senofaky, BM, MM, 68-72; studied with Ivan Galamian, 64-66. *Rec Perf:* Solo recitals, string quartets & piano trios, CBC, BBC & MBC, 73- *Pos:* Concertmaster, Calgary Phil Orch, Alberta, 73-75; violinist, Koryo Trio, Ft Worth Opera & Richardson Symph & with symph in North Am, Europe & Far East. *Teaching:* Artist in res, Va Commonwealth Univ, 75-78; artist violinist, NTex State Univ, 78- *Awards:* Career Grant, Young Musicians Found Los Angeles, 72; Young Artist of Year, Fine Arts Pasadena, 75. *Mailing Add:* 17703 Bent Oaks Dallas TX 75252

LEWIS, ROBERT HALL
COMPOSER, CONDUCTOR
b Portland, Ore, Apr 22, 26. *Study:* Eastman Sch Music, BM, 49, MM, 51, PhD, 53; Vienna Acad Music, dipl(theory & comp), 57; Paris Consv, dipl(cond), 64. *Works:* Serenades for Piano Solo, C F Peters, 71; Symphony No 2, 71, Three Prayers of Jane Austen, 76, Nuances II for Orchestra, 77, Duetto da Camera (violin & pianoforte), 77 & Osservazioni II for Winds, 78, Theodore Presser Co; String Quartet No 3, perf by Concord String Quartet, 81. *Rec Perf:* Symphony No 2, 74, Nuances II for Orchestra, 77, & Concerto for Chamber Orchestra, 80, CRI; Osservazioni II for Winds, 82, Moto, 83, with Philharmonia Orch. *Pos:* Prin trumpet, Oklahoma City Symph, 51-52. *Teaching:* Prof theory & comp, Goucher Col, 57-; prof comp & orch, Peabody Inst, 58-; prof theory, Johns Hopkins Univ, 69. *Awards:* Guggenheim Fel, 66 & 80; Walter Hinrichsen Award Comp, Columbia Univ, 73; Am Acad Arts & Lett Award, 76. *Bibliog:* Luis Gonzalez (auth), The Symphonies of Robert Hall Lewis, 77 & Robert Martin (auth), The Music of Robert Hall Lewis, in prep, Univ Microfilms. *Mem:* Col Music Soc; Am Soc Univ Comp. *Mailing Add:* 328 Broadmoor Rd Baltimore MD 21212

LEWIS, WILLIAM
TENOR, TEACHER-COACH
b Tulsa, Okla. *Study:* Colo Univ; Tex Christian Univ, BM, 53; NY Univ. *Works:* Revelation (libretto), 62, Cornucopia (song cycle), 67 & Flatboatman (lyric), 69, Menorca Publ. *Rec Perf:* Threni (Stravinsky), Columbia Rec, 59; Samuel Barber Collection, Vanguard Rec, 59; Treasury of Operettas, RCA Custom Rec, 62; Alceste (Lully), Vanguard Rec, 75; Mother of Us All, Santa Fe Opera Fest Rec, 76; Das Lied von der Erde, 80 & Guntram (Strauss), 81, BBC Broadcasting, 81. *Roles:* Aeneas in Trojans, Metropolitan Opera, 74; Erik in The Flying Dutchman, San Francisco Opera, 75; Aron in Moses und Aron, Teatro La Scala, Milano, 77; Don Jose in Carmen, Vienna State Opera, 78; Alwa in Lulu, Hamburg State Opera, 78; Oedipus in Oedipus Rex, Paris Opera, 79; Hoffmann in Tales of Hoffmann, Royal Opera, Covent Garden, London, 82. *Pos:* Leading tenor, Metropolitan Opera, 57-, San Francisco Opera, 75-, Teatro Alla Scala, Milano, 77-80 & Royal Opera, Covent Garden, London, 81-82. *Teaching:* Assoc prof voice & opera, Pa State Univ, 66-69 & State Univ NY, Binghamton, 69-71; dir opera, NY Univ Opera Sem, Belgium, 70-72. *Awards:* Metropolitan Opera Nat Auditions Winner, 55. *Mailing Add:* c/o Robert Lombardo 61 W 62nd New York NY 10023

LEYDEN, NORMAN
CONDUCTOR
b Springfield, Mass, Oct 17, 17. *Study:* Yale Univ, BA, 38, MusB, 39; Teachers Col, Columbia Univ, MA, 65, EdD, 68. *Works:* Concerto for Trombones, 59; Serenade for String Orchestra, 65; The Secret River (ballet). *Pos:* Founding cond, Westchester Youth Symph, White Plains, NY, 57-68; cond, Ore Symph Pops, 71- & Seattle Symph Pops, 73-; assoc cond, Ore Symph, 74-; guest cond, Minn Orch, 75-, Spokane Symph, 75-, San Francisco Symph, 77-, Chicago Grant Park Symph, 79- & Baltimore Symph, 80- *Teaching:* Asst prof music, Portland State Univ, 70-75. *Mem:* Am Fedn Musicians; Am Symph Orch League. *Mailing Add:* Oregon Symph 813 Southwest Alder Portland OR 97205

LIAN, CAROL
PIANO
b Brooklyn, NY, Oct 4, 46. *Study:* Queens Col, studied piano with Gertrude Kramer, David Hollander, Volya Cossack & Constance Keene, BA, 69. *Rec Perf:* Carol Lian Plays, 78 & Chopin, 83, Carousel Rec. *Pos:* Artist in res, Molde, Norway, 71-72; mem, Am Embassy Sponsored Tour, Norway, 78; solo pianist in US & Europe, currently. *Bibliog:* Allen Hughes (auth), Carol Lian Makes Debut as Pianist, 5/17/76 & Robert Sherman (auth), Young Performers in the Spotlight, 4/4/82, New York Times; Phillis Riffel (auth), Pianist to Perform at King's College, Gannett Westchester Newspapers, 11/14/82. *Mailing Add:* c/o Shirley Altman Mgt Foster Ct Croton-on-Hudson NY 10520

LIAUBA, DANUTE
EDUCATOR, PIANO
b Amsterdam, NY, Aug 19, 55. *Study:* Nazareth Col Rochester, NY, BS(music), 76; Ind Univ, Bloomington, MM(musicol), 82; Eastman Sch Music. *Pos:* Music librn, Bucknell Univ, 81- *Teaching:* Assoc instr, Sch Music, Ind Univ, Bloomington, 77-79; instr piano, Taylor Music Ctr, 80-81; lectr

music, Bucknell Univ, 81- *Mem:* Am Musicol Soc; Soc Ethnomusicol; Nat Guild Piano Teachers. *Interests:* Life and music of M K Ciurlionis; Baltic musicology; Lithuanian folk music. *Mailing Add:* 371 McCall Rd Rochester NY 14616

LIBERMAN, BARBARA (LEE)
PIANO, HARPSICHORD
b St Louis, Mo, Aug 9, 36. *Study:* Northwestern Univ, 54-55; Chicago Musical Col, Roosevelt Univ, with Frederick Schauwecker, Rudolf Ganz & Mollie Margoleis, 55-56; Juilliard Sch Music, with James Friskin, BS, 59; Wash Univ, MM, 61. *Rec Perf:* Catfish Row (George Gershwin), Vox, 76. *Pos:* Florence G & Morton J May Keyboard, St Louis Symph, 75- *Mailing Add:* c/o St Louis Symph 718 N Grand Blvd St Louis MO 63103

LIBIN, LAURENCE ELLIOT
CURATOR, EDUCATOR
b Chicago, Ill, Sept 19, 44. *Study:* Northwestern Univ, BMus, 66; Univ Chicago, with Howard Brown & Edward Lowinsky, 66-71; Kings Col, Univ London, with Thurston Dart, MMus, 68. *Pos:* Cur, Metropolitan Museum Art, New York, 73- *Teaching:* Asst prof, Ramapo Col, Mahwah, NJ, 72-73; lectr, Columbia Univ, currently, City Col New York, currently & NY Univ, currently. *Mem:* Fel, Royal Soc Arts; Am Musical Instrm Soc; Am Musicol Soc. *Interests:* History, construction, iconography, and collection of musical instruments of all cultures. *Publ:* Coauth, Unknown Handel Sources in Chicago, J Am Musicol Soc, 69; contribr, Symphony, In: Encycl Britannica, 74; auth, A Dutch Harpsichord in Chicago, Galpin Soc J, 75; contribr, An 18th-Century View of the Harpsichord, Early Music, 76; Collections of Musical Instruments, In: New Grove Dict of Music & Musicians, Vol VI, 80. *Mailing Add:* c/o Metropolitan Museum of Art Fifth Ave at 82 St New York NY 10028

LIBOVE, CHARLES
VIOLIN, EDUCATOR
Study: Curtis Inst Music; Juilliard Sch Music; studied with Ivan Galamian, Demetrius Dounis, Fritz Reiner. *Pos:* Soloist with New York Little Orch, St Louis Symph & Nat Orch Asn; performer with int festivals incl Spoleto, Osaka, du Marais, Stratford, Ont, Lincoln Ctr Mozart & Casals Fest; Mem, Paganini Quartet, formerly & Beaux Arts String Quartet, currently; founder & mem, Philharmonia Trio, currently. *Teaching:* Mem fac violin & chamber music, Peabody Consv Music, currently. *Mailing Add:* Peabody Consv Music 1 E Mt Vernon Pl Baltimore MD 21202

LICAD, CECILE (BUENCAMINO)
PIANO
b Manila, Philippines, May 11, 61. *Study:* Curtis Inst Music, with Rudolf Serkin, Miezyslaw Horzowski & Seymour Lipkin, 73-78; Inst Young Perf Musicians, with Rudolf Serkin, 78-81; Marlboro Fest, 77-81. *Pos:* Conct pianist & soloist with maj orch in US, London, Japan, Philippines, Can & Hong Kong, 81- *Awards:* Gold Medal Award, Leventritt Found, 81. *Bibliog:* Solti and the Chicago Spectaculars (TV film), Amsterdam Co Chicago, 5/1/82. *Rep:* Columbia Artist Mgt Inc 165 W 57th St New York NY 10019. *Mailing Add:* 711 West End Ave New York NY 10025

LICHTMANN, MARGARET S
FLUTE & PICCOLO, EDUCATOR
b Gilmer, Tex, Aug 7, 45. *Study:* Univ Tex, Austin, BMus, 67; Univ Denver, MMus(flute), 72; Boston Univ. *Pos:* Prin flautist, Boston Fest Orch, formerly; substitute, Denver Symph Orch, 71-74; freelance, Denver area, 71-74; solo recital tour, West Europe, 76; organizer & founder, Denver Philo-musica. *Teaching:* Instr flute, Rivier Col, formerly, Univ Iowa, formerly & Arapahoe Col, formerly; asst prof music, Univ Miss, currently. *Mem:* Nat Flute Asn; Am Musicol Soc; Am Fedn Musicians; Mu Phi Epsilon (vpres, Univ Tex chap, 64, pres, Boston Univ chap, 76). *Mailing Add:* Music Dept Univ Miss University MS 38677

LICHTMANN, THEODOR DAVID
PIANO, EDUCATOR
b Bern, Switz, Dec 25, 38. *Study:* Univ Zurich, teachers dipl; Akad Musik, Vienna; Hochschule Musik, Munich; Univ Tex, MMus; studied piano with Irma Schaichet & Leonard Shure. *Rec Perf:* On Decca & London. *Pos:* Recitalist, Europe & US; performer radio & TV, Switz & Denver. *Teaching:* Assoc prof piano & accmp, Univ Denver, currently. *Mem:* Am Asn Univ Prof; Col Music Soc. *Publ:* Contribr to ARBA & Libr Unlimited. *Mailing Add:* 1015 Monaco Parkway Denver CO 80220

LIDRAL, FRANK WAYNE
EDUCATOR, ADMINISTRATOR
b Algoma, Wis, Apr 11, 20. *Study:* Univ Wis, Milwaukee, BS, 41; Northwestern Univ, studied clarinet with Domenico DeCaprio, MMus, 47; Eastman Sch Music, DPhil, 56. *Teaching:* Assoc prof music, Cent Mo State Univ, 47-56; prof, Ind State Univ, Terre Haute, 56-60; prof, Univ Vt, 60-82, chmn, Music Dept, 60-73. *Mem:* Music Educr Nat Conf (mem nat bd, 57-59); Music Teachers Nat Asn (mem Eastern div bd, 69-71); Nat Asn Col Wind & Perc Instr (pres, 57-59); Nat Asn Sch Music (chmn region six & mem nat bd, 70-72). *Mailing Add:* 10 Country Club Dr South Burlington VT 05401

LIEBER, EDVARD
COMPOSER, PIANO
b Rockville Centre, NY, Apr 11, 48. *Study:* Manhattan Sch Music, 66-68; coaching in piano with Artur Rubinstein, 69-71; coaching in comp with Iannis Xenakis, 72. *Works:* Berlinerstück, comn for 1976 Berlin Fest, WGer, 76; 24

Dekooning Preludes, perf by Edvard Lieber, 78; Homage to Franz Kline, 78 & Montauk, 79, perf by Edvard Lieber; Neither Arakawa Nor Jasper Johns Are Each Other, perf by New York Arts Chorus & Soloists, 79; Abandoned Resemblances, perf by Edvard Lieber, 81. *Rec Perf:* 24 De Kooning Preludes, 78, Prelude to Jackson Pollock's Autumn Rhythm, 78, Homage to Franz Kline, 78, 15 Interludes to the Mechanism of Meaning, 79 & Swan Dive, 80, White Rec; Revolvo, Cologne TV, 81; Variations On A Theme Of John Cage, White Rec, 82. *Teaching:* Instr music, Sch Visual Arts, New York, 78- *Awards:* Perf Grants, Meet The Comp, 79-83; Solo Recitalist Award, Nat Endowment Arts, 81. *Bibliog:* Helen A Harrison (auth), DeKooning's Art Inspires Composer, New York Times, 3/18/79; Mary Rawson (prod), Portrait of an Artist (film), WQED-TV, Pittsburgh, 1/2/80; Shirley Romaine (prod), Focus on Edvard Lieber (film), Cox Cable, 1/18/83. *Rep:* Esther Brown 1199 Park Ave New York NY 10028. *Mailing Add:* 114 Buchanan St Centerport NY 11721

LIEBERMAN, FREDRIC
EDUCATOR, COMPOSER
b New York, NY, Mar 1, 40. *Study:* Eastman Sch Music, BMus, 62; Univ Hawaii, Honolulu, MA, 65; Univ Calif, Los Angeles, PhD, 77. *Works:* Suite for Piano, 64, Sonatina for Piano, 64 & Two Short String Quartets, 66, E C Schirmer; Leaves of Brass (brass quartet), Franco Colombo, 67; Psalm 137: By the Rivers of Babylon (chorus SATB), E C Schirmer, 71. *Pos:* Ed, Ethnomusicology, 77-80. *Teaching:* Asst prof music, Brown Univ, 68-75; assoc prof, Univ Wash, 75-, dir Sch Music, 81- *Mem:* Soc Ethnomusicol; Soc Asian Music; Col Music Soc (mem exec bd, 74-77); Conf Chinese Oral & Perf Lit (mem exec bd, 71-74 & 78-80). *Interests:* Ethnomusicology, especially musics of China and the Himalayas; theoretical organology. *Publ:* Auth, Computer-Aided Analysis of Javanese Music, Cornell Univ Press, 70; Working with Cents: A Survey, Ethnomusicol, 71; Should Ethnomusicology Be Abolished?, Col Music Symposium, 77; Chinese Music: An Annotated Bibliography, Garland Publ, 2nd ed, 79; A Chinese Zither Tutor: The Mei-an Ch'in-p'u, Univ Wash Press, 83. *Mailing Add:* Sch of Music Univ of Wash Seattle WA 98195

LIEBERMAN, GLENN
COMPOSER
b Brooklyn, NY, May 29, 47. *Study:* Manhattan Sch Music, BM, 71, MM, 72. *Works:* Termini, perf by Parnassus, 75; Metalwork, perf by Group Contemp Music, 77; Dialectic, comn & perf by New Music Consort, 78; Beards of a Father, comn & perf by NJ Phil, 78; Music for Ten Stringed Instruments, comn & perf by NY String Ens, 78; Passaglia, comn & perf by Odyssey Chamber Players, 79; Concerto for Piano & String Orchestra, comn & perf by Am Chamber Orch, 83. *Pos:* Dir rec, Manhattan Sch Music, 75- *Awards:* Grants, Comp Assistance Program, Am Music Ctr, 78, Creative Artists Pub Serv, 79-80 & Martha Baird Rockefeller Fund for Music, 81. *Mem:* Am Comp Alliance; BMI; Am Music Ctr. *Mailing Add:* 302 W 79th St New York NY 10024

LIEBERSON, PETER GODDARD
COMPOSER, CONDUCTOR
b New York, NY, Oct 25, 46. *Study:* NY Univ, BA, 70; Columbia Univ, study comp with Milton Babbitt & cond with Charles Wuorinen, MA, 73; Brandeis Univ, study comp with Donald Martino. *Works:* Concerto (4 groups instrm), 73, Concerto for Violoncello (with accmp trios), 74, Piano Fantasy, 74-75, Accordance, 75-76, Tashi Quartet, 78-79, Three Songs (sop & chamber orch), 81 & Piano Concerto, 80-83, G Schirmer. *Rec Perf:* Concerto (4 groups instrm), CRI, 75. *Awards:* Charles Ives Fel, Nat Inst Arts & Lett, 74. *Mem:* BMI; Am Comp Alliance. *Mailing Add:* 1542 Centre St Newton MA 02161

LIEBMAN, JOYCE ANN
PIANO, TEACHER
b New York, NY, Apr 25, 31. *Study:* Mannes Col Music, teachers dipl, 53; Adelphi Univ, BA(humanities), 80; studied piano with Isabelle Vengerova, Olga Stroumillo & Helen Schafranek. *Works:* The Story of America, 76, From Mars to Oz, 77, Queen Tut's Egyptian Follies, 78 & The HMS Pinafore Cantata, 79, Joyce Music Co. *Pos:* Founder, music dir & pianist, Connoisseur Chamber Ens, Roslyn Harbor, NY, 73-; perf, assembly prog, elementary sch, Long Island, New York, NJ & Conn, 80-; dir, children's music wkshps, Museum of Fine Art, Roslyn, NY, 80-; music consult & wkshp leader, NY State Educ Dept, Albany, 80-; chamber music coordr, Nassau Co Forum, Celebration Arts, 82 & 83. *Teaching:* Music dir, instr music & musical theatre, Human Resources Sch, Albertson, NY, 64-80. *Mem:* Music Educr Nat Conf; Nassau Music Educr Asn. *Publ:* Auth, Joyce Ann Liebman, On Stage, Everybody, Music Educr J, 73. *Mailing Add:* 18 Meadow Lane Roslyn Heights NY 11577

LIFCHITZ, MAX
EDUCATOR, COMPOSER
b Mexico City, Mex, Nov 11, 48. *Study:* Juilliard Sch Music, BM, 70 & MS, 71; Berkshire Music Ctr, 72; Harvard Univ, MM, 73. *Works:* Solo, Juilliard Ensemble, 68; Consorte, Karen Phillips & Walter Trampler, 71; Kaddish, Cabrillo Music Fest, Calif, 73; Intervencion (1976), St Paul Chamber Orch, 76; Yellow Ribbons No 5, Naomi & Stanley Drucker, 81; Yellow Ribbons No 12, Bronx Arts Ensemble, 82; I Got Up, Mex Forum Contemp Music, 82. *Rec Perf:* Little Cosmic Dust (Ann McMillan), 82 & Sonatas No 1 & 2 (David Maves), 83, Op One Rec. *Pos:* Pianist, Juilliard Ens, 68-74; mgr & cond, Columbia Univ Chamber Music Readings, 77-; exec vpres & cond, North-South Consonance, Inc, 80- *Teaching:* Jr fel music, Univ Mich, Ann Arbor, 74-77; guest lectr comp, Interlochen, Mich, summer 75; instr theory, Manhattan Sch Music, 76-77; asst prof comp, Columbia Univ, 77- *Awards:*

Fels, Nat Endowment for Arts, 75 & J S Guggenheim Mem Found, 82-83; First Prize, Gaudeamus Found, Holland, 76. *Bibliog:* Esperanza Pulido (auth), Heterofonia, 78. *Mem:* Nat Asn Comp, USA (prog comt chmn, 80-); Am Symph Orch League; Am Fedn Musicians; BMI; Col Music Soc. *Mailing Add:* 862 W End Ave New York NY 10025

LIFSON, LUDMILLA V
EDUCATOR
b Leningrad, Russia, June 27, 45. *Study:* Leningrad State Consv Music, USSR, BM, MM, artist dipl, 63-68. *Pos:* Conct pianist, Russia & US, 66- *Teaching:* Coach & accmp, Leningrad State Consv Music, USSR, 68-76, & teacher piano & chamber music, 76-78; instr piano, Longy Sch Music, 79- & Providence Col, 82- *Awards:* First Prize, Soviet Compt Student's Chamber Ens, 67. *Mem:* Music Teachers Nat Asn Inc; Am Fedn Musicians. *Mailing Add:* 89 Scenic Dr Cranston RI 02920

LIGHTFOOT, PETER WILLIAM
BARITONE
b New York, NY, Apr 12, 50. *Study:* Tufts Univ, BA, 72; Juilliard Sch Music, prof dipl, 79. *Rec Perf:* El Cid, Columbia Broadcasting, 76. *Roles:* Ford in Falstaff, Wolftrap Opera, 80; Leonce in A Bayou Legend, Opera/South, 80; Cardenio in The Madman of Santa Domingo, Pa Opera Theater, 82 ; Guglielmo in Cosi fan Tutte, Wolf Trap Opera, 82; Cardenio in the Madman of Santa Domingo, Opera Del, 83; Porgy in Porgy & Bess, Swedish Nat Radio Symph, Stockholm, 83; Guglielmo in Cosi fan Tutte, Greater Miami, 84. *Awards:* Grants, Sullivan Found, 79 & Nat Opera Inst, 83; Career Bronze Medal, Nat Opera Inst, 83. *Mailing Add:* c/o Tony Hartmann Assoc 250 W 57th St New York NY 10107

LIGHTNER, HELEN LUCILLE
EDUCATOR
b Baker, Ore. *Study:* Teachers Col, Columbia Univ, MA & EdD, 76; voice study with George Fergusson, Sergius Kagen, Arpad Sandor & Estelle Liebling. *Teaching:* Assoc prof music, NY Univ, 61- *Mem:* New York Singing Teachers Asn (pres, 82-84); Nat Asn Teachers Singing (New York gov, 78-82); Am Asn Univ Prof; Music Educr Nat Conf. *Mailing Add:* 175 W 76 St Apt 12C New York NY 10023

LIGOTTI, ALBERT F
CONDUCTOR, TRUMPET
b New York, NY, Feb 26, 27. *Study:* Queens Col, BA, 49; Columbia Univ, MA, 50; studied with William Vacchiano, 50-57. *Works:* Daily Exercises for Trumpet, 81 & Little Fugue in G Minor (J S Bach for wind ens), 82, Jeffco Music Publ; Five Mystical Songs (Ralph Vaughan Williams for wind ens), Galaxy Music Co, 82. *Pos:* Extra trumpet, New York Phil Symph, 57-68 & Metropolitan Opera Co, 57-68; music dir & cond, Athens Symph, 78- *Teaching:* Instr trumpet, Manhattan Sch Music, 63-68; assoc prof cond & trumpet, Univ Ga, 68- *Awards:* John E Castellini Award, Div Fine Arts, Queens Col, 80. *Mem:* Col Band Dir Nat Asn (chmn wind ens, southern div, 79-); Music Educr Nat Conf. *Publ:* Coauth (with E Voth), An Aid for Young Trumpet Players Undergoing Orthodontic Treatment, Instrumentalist, 74. *Mailing Add:* 220 Greencrest Dr Athens GA 30605

LILJESTRAND, PAUL F
COMPOSER, PIANO
b Montclair, NJ, May 15, 31. *Study:* Juilliard Sch Music, BS, 52, MS, 53; Union Theol Sem, SMM, 58. *Works:* Three Canticles, Hope Puts Co, 70; If Ye Be Merry, G Schirmer, 70; Christmas Triad, Galaxy, 80; Reflections, Shawnee, 80. *Pos:* Minister music, Brookdale Baptist Church, 56-66 & Calvary Baptist Church, New York, 66- *Teaching:* Chmn dept music, Northeastern Bible Col, 58-69 & Nyack Col, 70- *Mem:* ASCAP. *Mailing Add:* Music Dept Nyack Col Nyack NY 10960

LIMA, LUIS
TENOR
b Cordoba, Arg, Sept 12, 48. *Study:* Voice with Carlos Guichandut & Gina Cigna. *Roles:* Pinkerton in Madama Butterfly, Lisbon; Gemma di Vergy, Carnegie Hall, 76; Faust, La Scala, 77; Alfredo in La Traviata, Metropolitan Opera, 78-79; La Boheme, 79 & Rigoletto, 79, New York City Opera. *Pos:* Tenor, maj opera houses incl Munich, Vienna, Milan, Paris, Zurich, Strasbourg, Barcelona & Liege. *Mailing Add:* c/o Columbia Artist Mgt 165 W 57th St New York NY 10019

LINCER, WILLIAM
VIOLA, EDUCATOR
b New York, NY. *Study:* Juilliard Inst Music. *Pos:* Mem, Gordon String Quartet; perf, Libr Cong & Casals Fest, Prades; solo violist, Cleveland Orch & New York Phil, 43- *Teaching:* Mem fac viola & chamber music, Juilliard Sch Music, 69-; prof viola, New York Sch Educ, currently. *Awards:* Elizabeth Sprague Coolidge Chamber Music Award. *Mailing Add:* 147 W 79th St New York NY 10024

LINCOLN, HARRY B
EDUCATOR
b Fergus Falls, Minn, Mar 6, 22. *Study:* Macalester Col, BA, 40; Northwestern Univ, MM, 46, PhD, 51; Univ Rome, cert, 50. *Teaching:* From instr to prof, State Univ NY, Binghamton, 51- *Awards:* Distinguished Serv Prof, State Univ NY, Binghamton; grants, Nat Endowment Humanities, 78-80. *Mem:* Am Musicol Soc (mem coun, 68-70); Col Music Soc (pres, 68-70). *Publ:* Ed, Directory of Music Faculties in USA, Col Music Soc, 67-74; The Madrigal Collection L'Amorosa Ero (1588), State Univ NY Press; Seventeenth Century Keyboard Music in the Chigi Manuscripts of the Vatican Library, Am Inst Musicol, 68. *Mailing Add:* 20 Dellwood Rd Binghamton NY 13903

LINCOLN, ROBERT DIX
ADMINISTRATOR, EDUCATOR
b Woodstock, Ohio, Dec 3, 24. Study: Consv Music, Univ Cincinnati, BM, 49, MM, 50; Ecoles Art Am, Fontainebleau, France, cert, 52; Consv Nat, Paris, with Nadia Boulanger, 54-55. Works: Ariosa for String Orchestra, perf & comn by Knoxville Chamber Orch, 57; Twelve Piano Pieces, Scribners Music Libr, 63; Sonatina for String Orchestra, Am String Teachers Asn, 68. Pos: Dir music, Riverview Neighbors House, Cincinnati, 48-50; pianist, solo & orchestra concerts in France, England & US. Teaching: Assoc prof music, ETenn State Univ, 50-57; prof, Rutgers Univ, 57-, chmn dept music, 75- Awards: French Govt Fel, 54; Fulbright Award, 54-55. Interests: Ecole Louis Niedemeyer; French contribution to chant accompaniment. Mailing Add: 251 Lawrence Ave Highland Park NJ 08904

LINDAHL, CHARLES E
LIBRARIAN, EDUCATOR
Study: Hope Col, BA; Eastman Sch Music, MM; Columbia Univ, MLS; studied clarinet with Jerome Stowell, Walter Wollwage, Gino Ciofi & Stanley Hasty; Chicago Musical Col; Berkshire Music Ctr. Pos: Assoc librn, Eastman Sch Music, 75-; contrib ed, Music Libr Asn Notes, currently, compiler & ed, Music Periodicals (column), 75-82. Teaching: Dir instrm music, Chicago Pub Sch, 60-65; asst prof music bibliog, Eastman Sch Music, currently. Mem: Music Libr Asn; Int Asn Music Libr; Am Musicol Soc; Sonneck Soc. Publ: Auth, Galpin's Copy of His Textbook, Galpin Soc J, Vol 29; compiler & ed, Directory of Music Research Libraries (USA Section), Bärenreiter, rev ed, 83. Mailing Add: Sibley Music Libr Eastman Sch Music 26 Gibbs St Rochester NY 14604

LINDBERG, WILLIAM EDWARD
EDUCATOR, ORGAN
b McKeesport, Pa, Feb 3, 23. Study: Carnegie Mellon Univ, BFA(music & music ed), 51, MFA, 52; Univ Pittsburgh, PhD(musicol), 76. Pos: Minister of music, Brentwood Presby Church, Pittsburgh, 52-67; organist & choirmaster, Church of Ascension, Pittsburgh, 67- Teaching: Versailles Boro & Lincoln Twp Sch, McKeesport, Pa, 54-58; asst prof, Univ Pittsburgh, 72- Mem: Am Guild Organists (dean Pittsburgh chap, 59-61); Organ Hist Soc; Asn Anglican Musicians; Col Music Soc; Am Musicol Soc. Interests: Pipe organs of A B Felgemaker. Mailing Add: 229 Constitution Dr Pittsburgh PA 15236

LINDEMAN, CAROLYNN A
EDUCATOR, WRITER
b Kane, Pa, June 5, 40. Study: Consv Music, Oberlin Col, BMus, 62; Mozarteum Acad Music, Salzburg, Austria, 60-61; San Francisco State Univ, MA, 72; Stanford Univ, DMA, 79. Teaching: Music consult, Commack Unified Sch District, 62-67; assoc prof music, San Francisco State Univ, 73- Mem: Calif Coun Music Teacher Educ (secy & mem bd, 83); Music Educr Nat Conf; Int Cong Women Music (mem adv bd, 81-); Col Music Soc; Sonneck Soc. Publ: Coauth, The Musical Classroom: Models, Skills and Backgrounds for Elementary Teaching, Prentice-Hall, 79; auth, Meet the Women Composers of Rags, In: Heresies 10, Heresies Collective, 80; contribr, Resource Guide on Women in Music, Kikimora Publ Co, 81; auth, Pianolab: An Introduction to Class Piano, Wadsworth Publ, 83. Mailing Add: 260 Via Lerida Greenbrae CA 94904

LINDENFELD, HARRIS NELSON
COMPOSER
b Benton Harbor,Mich, May 15, 45. Study: Univ Va, BA, 69, MA, 71; Cornell Univ, DMA, 75. Works: Reflexion sur la paysage, comn & perf by Jan Tavalin Schwartz, 78; Three Dickinson Songs, comn & perf by Trio Dolce, 78; The Duchess, perf by Syracuse Soc New Music, 79; Brass Quintet, comn & perf by Catskill Brass Quintet, 81; Two Songs (The Cow & Dolor), Highgate Music, 82; Three Songs After Rilke, comn & perf by Syracuse Soc New Music, 82; Symphony, comn by Utica, NY Symph Orch, 83. Awards: Comp Assistance Prog Award, Am Music Ctr, 80; Nat Endowment Arts Comp Award, 80; Camargo Found Fel, France, 81. Mem: Am Comp Alliance; Syracuse Soc New Music (pres, 80-81); Am Soc Univ Comp (regional co-chmn, 80-82); BMI. Mailing Add: 24 Mulberry St Clinton NY 13323

LINDGREN, LOWELL EDWIN
EDUCATOR, WRITER
b Willmar, Minn, Sept 6, 42. Study: Univ Minn, BA, 63, MFA, 65; Harvard Univ, PhD, 72. Teaching: Assoc prof, Harvard Univ, 75-79 & Mass Inst Technol, 79-; vis assoc prof, Eastman Sch Music, 83- Awards: Fels, Berkshire Music Ctr, 64, Martha Baird Rockefeller Found, 71 & Am Coun Learned Soc, 77. Mem: Am Musicol Soc (coun mem, 81-83); Soc Eighteenth Century Studies. Interests: Baroque music and musicians, especially in Italy and England. Publ: Auth, The Three Great Noises, Musical Quart, 75; contribr, New Grove Dict of Music & Musicians, 80; auth, Camilla and the Beggar's Opera, Philological Quart, 80; auth, Ariosti's London Years, Music & Lett, 81; coauth, The Schirmer History of Music, Schirmer, 82. Mailing Add: 287 Harvard St #62 Cambridge MA 02139

LING, JAHJA WANG-CHIEH
CONDUCTOR, PIANO
b Jakarta, Indonesia, Oct 25, 51; US citizen. Study: Juilliard Sch, BM, 74, MM, 75; Sch Music, Yale Univ, MMA, 80, studied with Leonard Bernstein, Seiji Ozawa, Colin Davis, Andre Previn, Otto-Werner Mueller & John Nelson. Pos: Exxon-Arts Endowment asst cond, San Francisco Symph, 81-83, assoc cond, 83-; music dir, San Francisco Symph Youth Orch, 81- & San Francisco Consv Music Orch, 82-; Exxon-Arts Endowment Cond, 81- Awards: Bronze Medal, Second Rubinstein Int Piano Master Compt, Israel, 77; Cert Honor, Sixth Tchaikovsky Int Piano Compt, Moscow, 78; Leonard Bernstein Fel, Boston Symph, 80. Mem: Am Symph Orch League. Rep: Columbia Artists Mgt Inc 165 W 57th St New York NY 10019. Mailing Add: c/o San Francisco Symph Davies Symph Hall San Francisco CA 94102

LING, STUART JAMES
EDUCATOR
b Youngstown, Ohio, Mar 17, 18. Study: Syracuse Univ, BMus, 40, MMus, 47, PhD, 54. Teaching: Supvr music, Manlius Pub Sch, NY, 40-42; grad asst music educ, Syracuse Univ, 46-49; prof music educ, Col Wooster, 49- Mem: Music Educr Nat Conf; Ohio Music Educ Asn (secy, 73-75, pres, 80-82, vpres, 82-); Am Fedn Musicians; Col Band Dir Nat Asn; Nat Band Asn. Publ: Auth of many articles publ over past 30 years in Music Educr J, Instrumentalist & Triad. Mailing Add: 839 N Bever St Wooster OH 44691

LINK, KURT
BASS
Study: Consv Music, Lawrence Univ, BM(vocal perf); studied with Evelyn Lear, Margaret Hillis & Richard Stillwell. Roles: Sarastro in The Magic Flute; Figaro in The Marriage of Figaro; Ramfis in Aida; Colline in La Boheme. Pos: Soloist with Univ Mo, Downers Grove Oratorio Soc & Chicago Symph Orch. Awards: Winner, Nat Asn Teachers Singing Compt, 77; Metropolitan Opera Regional Auditions Award, 81. Mailing Add: Lew & Benson Moreau-Neret Inc 204 W 10th St New York NY 10014

LINN, ROBERT T
COMPOSER, EDUCATOR
b San Francisco, Calif, Aug 11, 25. Study: Mills Col, 47-49; Univ Southern Calif, BM, 50, MM, 51; studied comp with Darius Milhaud, Halsey Stevens, Roger Sessions & Ingolf Dahl. Works: Concertino for Oboe, Horn, Percussion & String Orchestra, comn by Pasadena Symph Asn, 72; Fantasia for Cello & String Orch, comn by Neville Marriner & Los Angeles Chamber Orch, 76; Twelve, Monday Evening Concts, 77; Diversions for Six Bassoons, comn by Double Reed Soc, 79; Concertino for Flute & Wind Orchestra, comn by Univ Southern Calif, 80; Songs of William Blake, comn by Victor Valley Col, 82; Concertino for Woodwind Quartet & String Orchestra, comn by Pasadena Chamber Orch, 82. Teaching: Fac mem, Univ Southern Calif, 58-, prof & chmn music theory & comp dept, 73- Awards: Numerous grants & awards from orgns such as ASCAP, MacDowell Asn, Huntington Hartford Found & others. Mem: Nat Asn Am Comp & Cond. Mailing Add: 3275 DeWitt Dr Los Angeles CA 90068

LINSCOME, SANFORD ABEL
EDUCATOR, SINGER
b Houston, Tex, Jan 2, 31. Study: McNeese State Col, BME, 54; Univ Ill, MM, 59; Univ Tex, Austin, DMA, 70. Pos: Singer, Robert Shaw Chorale, 54-55; performer, recitals & oratorios, midwestern & southern US, 55-65. Teaching: Instr singing & choral dir, Univ Ala, 58-60; res ten & prof music, Univ Northern Colo, 65- Awards: First Place, Southern USA Young Artist Cont, 53. Publ: Auth, A History of Musical Development in Denver, Colorado: 1858-1908, 70; contribr to Colo Mag & New Grove Dict of Music & Musicians. Mailing Add: 2659 16th Ave Greeley CO 80631

LINTON, STANLEY STEWART
EDUCATOR
b Hale, Mo, Jan 20, 19. Study: Cent Mo State Univ, BS, 40; Northwestern Univ, MM, 42; Teachers Col, Columbia Univ, EdD, 52. Teaching: Dir choral music, Univ Wis, Oshkosh, 52-64, coordr music educ, 60-76, prof cond & music psychology, 76- Awards: Coop Research Grant, US Off Educ, 67-68. Interests: Basic musicianship in choral rehearsal. Publ: Auth, Teaching Musicianship in the Choral Class, Coun Res Music Educ, 67; Audio-Tutorial Music Modules, Personalized Instr in Educ Today, 77; Newer Systems of Individualized Learning, Col Music Symposium, 78; Conducting Fundamentals, 82 & Music Fundamentals, 83, Prentice-Hall. Mailing Add: 1679 Maricopa Dr Oshkosh WI 54901

LIPKIN, SEYMOUR
PIANO, CONDUCTOR & MUSIC DIRECTOR
b Detroit, Mich, May 14, 27. Study: Curtis Inst, studied piano with Rudolf Serkin, David Saperton & Miecio Hornszowski, BMus, 47; Berkshire Music Ctr, studied cond with S Koussevitzky, 46, 48 & 49. Rec Perf: Stravinsky Piano Concerto, Columbia, 59. Pos: Asst cond, New York Phil, 59; music dir, Long Island Symph, 63-79; music dir, Joffrey Ballet, 66-68 & 72-79, prin guest cond, 68-72. Teaching: Piano, Curtis Inst Music, 69- & Manhattan Sch Music, 72- Awards: First prize, Rachmaninoff Compt, 48; Ford Found Comn, 59. Rep: TRM Mgt 527 Madison Ave New York NY 10022. Mailing Add: 666 West End Ave New York NY 10025

LIPKIS, LARRY (LAURENCE ALAN)
COMPOSER, EDUCATOR
b Los Angeles, Calif, July 27, 51. Study: Univ Calif, Los Angeles, BA, 73; Univ Pa, AM, 75. Works: Pierrot in Love, perf by Lehigh Valley Youth Symph Orch, 78; Beauty and the Beast, perf by People's Theatre Co, 79; The Prince

of Cacao, Kaleidoscope Ser, 81; Waltz-Fantasy, perf by Dimitri Toufexis, 82; Capriccio, perf by Lehigh Valley Chamber Orch, 83; Be Thou Faithful, G Schirmer, 83. *Teaching:* Asst prof music theory & comp, Moravian Col, 75-, comp in res, 79- *Awards:* Fel, Pa State Coun on Arts, 82. *Mem:* Am Music Ctr; Am Musicol Soc; Am Soc Univ Comp; Nat Asn Comp. *Mailing Add:* Dept Music Moravian Col Bethlehem PA 18018

LIPMAN, MICHAEL (AVRAM)
CELLO
b Meriden, Conn, Mar 15, 54. *Study:* Hartt Col Music, with Paul Olefsky, 72-74; Blossom Music Ctr, with Leonard Rose, 75; Estman Sch Music, with Ronald Leonard, BMus & perf cert cello, 76, with Paul Katz, MMus, 78. *Pos:* Assoc prin cello, New Haven Symph, 78-79; prin cello, Aspen Chamber Symph, 78-80; cello, Pittsburgh Symph Orch, 79- *Teaching:* Asst prof cello, Eastman Sch Music, 77-78. *Awards:* First Place, Aspen Music Fest Concerto Compt, 78. *Mailing Add:* 5841 Walnut St Apt #31 Pittsburgh PA 15232

LIPOVETSKY, LEONIDAS
PIANO, EDUCATOR
b Montevideo, Uruguay. *Study:* Juilliard Sch Music, BM, MM. *Pos:* Recital tours in US, Europe & South Am. *Teaching:* Assoc prof piano, Fla State Univ, 69- *Awards:* Van Cliburn Scholar; Pan Am Union Fel; Martha Baird Rockefeller Fund Grant. *Mailing Add:* 1802 Atapha Nene Tallahassee FL 32301

LIPP, CHARLES HERBERT
COMPOSER, BASSOON
b Indianapolis, Ind, Feb 16, 45. *Study:* Univ Ill, DMA(comp), 82. *Works:* Glass Key, comn by Krakow Experimental Music Studio, 79; Expectations' Refutations, comn by Warsaw Experimental Music Studio, 80. *Teaching:* Instr, Northern Ill Univ, 72-74, Univ Saskatchewan, Canada, 74-75, Univ Nev, Las Vegas, 76-78. *Awards:* Fulbright Fel to Poland, 78-79. *Mem:* Am Comp Alliance; BMI; Am Music Ctr; Int Double Reed Soc. *Publ:* Auth, Meet the Composer: Interview with Donald Erb, The Instrumentalist, 79; Interview with Milan Turkovic, The Double Reed J, 83. *Mailing Add:* 306 W Hill St Champaign IL 61820

LIPPMAN, EDWARD A
EDUCATOR, MUSICOLOGIST
b New York, NY, May 24, 20. *Study:* City Col, City Univ New York, BS, 42; NY Univ, MA, 45; Columbia Univ, PhD(musicol), 52. *Teaching:* From instr to assoc prof music, Columbia Univ, 54-69, prof, 69-; lectr, Bryn Mawr Col, 72-73. *Awards:* Harriet Cohen Int Music Award, 54; Am Coun Learned Soc Fel, 67-68. *Mem:* Am Musicol Soc. *Interests:* Philosophy and aesthetics in music; 19th century history of music; ancient Greek conceptions of music. *Publ:* Auth, Musical Thought in Ancient Greece, Columbia Univ, 64; Theory and Practice in Schumann's Aesthetics, J Am Musicol Soc, fall 64; Stil, In: Die Musik in Geschichte und Gegenwart, Barenreiter, 65; The Problem of Musical Hermeneutics, Art & Philosophy, 66 & A Humanistic Philosophy of Music, 77, NY Univ. *Mailing Add:* Dept Music Columbia Univ New York NY 10027

LIPTON, DANIEL B
CONDUCTOR
b Paris, France; French & US citizen. *Study:* Manhattan Sch Music, MA, 57; Juilliard Sch, studied oboe with Harold Gomberg, comp with V Giannini, piano with L Epstein, choral cond with Abe Kaplan & orch cond with Jean Morel, 57-63; Mannes Col, 63-65; Ecole Normale Superieure, with Nadia Boulanger, 65-67. *Pos:* Asst cond, Mannes Col Music, 65; Denver Symph Orch, 69-70; cond, Am Ballet Theatre, 68; kapellmeister, Opera House, Zürich, 73-75; prin cond & artistic dir, Orquesta Sinfonica Nac & Opera de Colombia, 75-; guest appearances in Amsterdam, Barcelona, Bilbao, Bologna, Caracas, Dijon, Florence, Hilversum, London, Madrid, Nice, Paris, Rouen, Santiago, Venice & Zurich. *Teaching:* Teacher ear training, Mannes Col Music, 65. *Awards:* Fulbright Grant, 65-67; Ital Govt Grant, Accad Chigiana, Siena, 65-67; Cruz de Boyaca, Pres Repub Colombia, 78. *Mailing Add:* 200 Central Park S New York NY 10019

LISTER, JOHN RODNEY
COMPOSER
b Ft Payne, Ala, May 31, 51. *Study:* Blair Sch Music, 64-69; New England Consv, BMus, 73; Brandeis Univ, MFA, 77; studied with Peter Maxwell Davies & Virgil Thomson. *Works:* Alex (berceuse du chat), London, 78; Though the Night Is Gone (A Certain World, Bk II), perf by Keith Kibler & Co, Goethe Inst, Boston, Mass, 80; A Little Cowboy Music Too, comn & perf by Fires of London, 81; A True Account of Talking to the Sun at Fire Island (Frank O'Hara), comn by Mrs Gardner Cox, perf by Dinosaur Annex, 82; Mass (Wondrous Love), comn by Church of Advent, Boston, Mass, 82-83; Warble, comn by Fromm Found, 83. *Pos:* Co-dir, Music Prod Co, 82- *Teaching:* Instr, Prep Div, New England Consv, 77-78 & 82-; instr, Emerson Col, 79-82. *Awards:* Bernstein Fel, Berkshire Music Ctr, 7 3; grant, Martha Baird Rockefeller Fund for Music, 81. *Mem:* BMI. *Mailing Add:* c/o Mary K Sego 356 Somerville Ave Somerville MA 02143

LISTOKIN, ROBERT
CLARINET, EDUCATOR
Study: Juilliard Sch, BS(music), 56; studied with Daniel Bonade & Leon Russianoff. *Rec Perf:* Concerto for Six (Donovan), Columbia; Auric Trio, Duo (Poulenc; clarinet & bassoon), Quintet (Bernard Heiden), Quintet (David

Amram), Concerto (William Bergsma), Solos for Clarinet & others, Golden Crest Rec. *Pos:* Prin clarinet, Symph of Air, 59-65 & Columbia Rec, 59-65; clarinet, Aeolian Chamber Players & Winston Salem Symph; prin clarinet, Chautauqua Symph, 81, NY Fest Winds & Clarion Quintet; rec soloist, Piedmont Chamber Orch & Claremont Quartet. *Teaching:* Clarinet & chamber music, Queens Col, 60-65, NC Sch Arts, 65-83, Duke Univ, Wake Forest Univ & Salem Col. *Awards:* George Wedge Prize, 65 & Outstanding Teacher, 72, Juilliard Sch. *Publ:* Auth, Clarinet Practise Techniques, Instrumentalist, 70; coauth, The Wind Quintet, Instrumentalist, 72. *Mailing Add:* NC Sch Arts PO Box 4657 Winston-Salem NC 27104

LITTLE, FRANK (FRANCIS E)
TENOR, EDUCATOR
b Greeneville, Tenn, Apr 22, 36. *Study:* ETenn State Univ, with Lillian Rhea Hunter, BS; Col Consv Music, Univ Cincinnati, with Robert Powell, MMus; Northwestern Univ, with Walter Carringer, DMus; studied with Clemens Glettenberg. *Roles:* Normanno in Lucia di Lammermoor, Chicago Lyr Opera, 70; Tambourmajor in Wozzeck; Leicester in Maria Stuarda; Luigi in Il Tabarro; Alfredo in La Traviata; Macduff in Macbeth; Narraboth in Salome. *Pos:* Leading ten, Chicago Lyr Opera, 70-76, Wash Opera, 73-74, Philadelphia Lyr Opera, 73-75, Chicago Symph Orch, Cincinnati Symph Orch, Milwaukee Symph Orch & maj Am summer festivals; conct artist & recitalist. *Teaching:* Mem fac, DePaul Univ, formerly; chmn & prof opera & voice, Furman Univ, currently. *Awards:* Nat Opera Inst Grant, 72; Hon Citation Wash Col Acad; Metropolitan Opera Nat Coun Auditions Regional Winner. *Mem:* Pi Kappa Lambda. *Publ:* Contribr to Music J. *Rep:* Colbert Artists Mgt 111 W 57th St New York NY 10019. *Mailing Add:* 150 Thackery Lane Northfield LA 60093

LITTLE, GWENDOLYN
SOPRANO
Can citizen. *Study:* Royal Consv Music, with George Lambert & Louis Quilico; studied with Boris Goldovsky & Otto Guth. *Rec Perf:* Serva Padrona (video/film), Can Broadcast Corp. *Roles:* Hero in Beatrice et Benedict; Laetitia in The Old Maid and the Thief; Despina in Cosi fan tutte; Zerlina in Don Giovanni; Lauretta in Maestro di Musica; Musetta in La Boheme; Gilda in Rigoletto. *Pos:* Sop with maj opera co in US & Can incl New York City Opera, Portland, Washington, DC, Montreal, Quebec, Ottawa, Toronto & Vancouver. *Awards:* Can Coun Grants (four); Sir Tyrone Guthrie Award, Stratford Fest, Ont. *Mailing Add:* c/o Maxim Gershunoff Inc 502 Park Ave New York NY 10022

LITTLE, MEREDITH ELLIS
WRITER, HARPSICHORD
b Stockton, Calif, Mar 10, 34. *Study:* Stanford Univ, BA, 56, MA, 57, PhD, 67; harpsichord study with Putnam Aldrich. *Teaching:* Asst prof, Oakland Univ, Rochester, Mich, 67-69; vis lectr, Am Univ, 69-70 & Univ Md, College Park, 70-72; lectr early music, Stanford Univ, 72-76. *Awards:* Fulbright Fel, 63. *Mem:* Am Musicol Soc. *Interests:* History of baroque music & dance. *Publ:* Auth, What Questions Should a Performer Ask a, Current Musicol, 72; The Contribution of Dance Steps to, J Am Musicol Soc, 75; Dance Under Louis XIV and XV, Early Music, 75; 20 articles, In: New Grove Dict of Music & Musicians, 80. *Mailing Add:* 1514 E Kleindale Rd Tucson AZ 85719

LITTLE, WM A(LFRED)
EDUCATOR, ORGAN
b Boston, Mass, July 28, 29. *Study:* Tufts Col, BA, 51; Trinity Col, London, LTCL, 52; Harvard Univ, MA, 53; Univ Mich, PhD, 61. *Works:* Communion Service-D, 68, Ave Verum, 71 & Be Ye Perfect, 75, St Paul's Church. *Pos:* Organist & choirmaster, Tufts Univ, 47-52 & St Paul's Church, Ivy, Va, 67-; asst organist & choirmaster, St Paul's Cathedral & Church Advent, Boston, Mass, 48-57; ed, German Quart, 70-78 & Organ Works of F Mendelssohn, 77. *Teaching:* Asst prof German, Williams Col, 57-63; assoc prof & chmn, Tufts Univ, 63-66; prof & chmn, Univ Va, 66- *Mem:* Am Asn Teachers German (mem nat exec coun, 66-77); Am Guild Organists (dean, 77-78). *Interests:* German organ music of the 18th and 19th centuries. *Publ:* Auth, Gottfried A Bürger, Twayne, 74; F Mendelssohn Bartholdy, VEB Deutscher Verlag Musik, 77. *Mailing Add:* Kirklea Ivy VA 22945

LITTON, JAMES HOWARD
MUSIC DIRECTOR, ORGAN
b Charleston, WVa, Dec 31, 34. *Study:* Westminster Choir Col, BMus, 56, MMus, 58; Canterbury Cathedral, England, 62; Royal Sch Church Music, England, FRSCM, 83. *Rec Perf:* Epitaph for This World and Time (Hamilton), CRI Rec, 71; Mass (Bernstein), Columbia Rec, 71; various liturgical cassettes, Episcopal Radio TV, 71-83; 20th Century American Choral Music, Gamut Rec, 80. *Pos:* Organist & choirmaster, Trinity Church, Southport, Conn, 58-64 & Christ Church Cathedral, Indianapolis, Ind, 64-68; organist & dir music, Trinity Church, Princeton, NJ, 68-82 & St Bartholomew's Church, New York, 82- *Teaching:* Instr music, Berkeley Divinity Sch, New Haven, Conn, 62-64 & Butler Univ, 64-68; asst prof, Westminster Choir Col, 68-74, head, Church Music Dept, 70-72; dir music, Princeton Theol Sem, 74-82. *Mem:* Am Guild Organists; Royal Col Organists; Church Music Soc; Am Choral Dir Asn; Col Music Soc. *Publ:* Ed, Canticle Series—Music, Hinshaw, 76-83; co-ed, Book of Common Prayer—Altar Book, 78; co-ed, Manual for Clergy & Church Musicians, 80, co-ed, Congregational Music for Eucharist, 81 & Service Music, In: The Episcopal Hymnal 1982 (in prep), Church Hymnal Corp. *Mailing Add:* 8 Carnation Pl Lawrenceville NJ 08648

LIVINGS, GEORGE
TENOR
b Dallas, Tex, July 21, 45. *Study:* Austin Col, with Bruce Lunkley; Juilliard Sch, with Hans Heinz. *Roles:* Belfiore in Finta giardiniera (debut), Opera Co Boston, 71; Alfredo in La Traviata, Glimmerglass, 76; Don Ottavio in Don Giovanni; Rodolfo in La Boheme; Almaviva in Il Barbiere di Siviglia; La Traviata & Dialogue of the Carmelites, Metropolitan Opera. *Pos:* Soloist, Metropolitan Opera, currently. *Awards:* Lucrezia Bori Award, Metropolitan Opera. *Mailing Add:* c/o Courtenay Artists Inc 411 E 53rd St Suite 6F New York NY 10022

LIVINGSTON, DAVID
EDUCATOR, COMPOSER
b Corbin, Ky, Jan 10, 25. *Study:* Western Ky Univ, with Weldon Hart & Roy Harris; Univ Ky, with Kenneth Wright; Ohio State Univ, with Marshall Barnes, PhD(comp & theory). *Works:* Theme and Variations (orch); Adagio (four trombones); Pastorale for Winds (wind ens); Prelude and Fugue (wind ens); Mirage (wind ens); Killarney Holiday (wind ens); Symphony #1, perf by Owensboro Symph & Columbus Ohio Symph. *Teaching:* Instr pub sch, Frankfort, Ky, 52-63; prof music, Western Ky Univ, 65- *Awards:* Phi Mu Alpha Award. *Mailing Add:* 2325 Bellevue Dr Bowling Green KY 42101

LIVINGSTON, HERBERT
EDUCATOR
b Syracuse, NY, May 3, 16. *Study:* Syracuse Univ, BMus, 37; Univ NC, AB, 42, AM, 47, PhD(music), 52. *Teaching:* From instr to assoc prof music, Mich State Univ, 50-56, actg chmn, Dept Lit & Fine Arts, 53-56, assoc prof, 56-57; prof, Ohio State Univ, 57-, chmn, Dept Music Hist, 62- *Mem:* Am Musicol Soc; Music Libr Asn; Col Music Soc Res. *Interests:* Music bibliography; 18th century music; keyboard literature. *Mailing Add:* Sch Music Ohio State Univ Columbus OH 43210

LIVINGSTON, JAMES FRANCIS
CLARINET, CONDUCTOR
b Monmouth, Ill. *Study:* Knox Col, BA, 58; Ind Univ Sch Music, Bloomington, MM & perf cert, 60; studied clarinet with Henry Gulick & cond with Tibor Kozma. *Rec Perf:* Pastorale Variee (Ben-Haim), 62, Concerto for Woodwind Quintet (Etler), 63, 11 Studies for 11 Players (Rorem), 65, Museum Pieces (Rhodes), 73, Ilinx (Tauriello), 75, Louisville Orch First Ed; Concertino (Seiber), Louisville Orch First Ed, 75 & RCA Gold Seal. *Teaching:* Assoc prof music, Sch Music, Univ Louisville, 60- *Mailing Add:* Sch Music Univ Louisville Belknap Campus Louisville KY 40292

LIVINGSTON, JULIAN RICHARD
COMPOSER, MUSIC DIRECTOR
b Spencer, Ind, Aug 25, 32. *Study:* Ind Univ, with Bernard Heiden, BMusic, 55. *Works:* Paleophony (symph orch), NJ State Symph, 74; Rondo Brilliante (two pianos), perf by Lillian Livingston & Clarefield, 76; Ann Rutledge, Monmouth Consv Women's Chorus, 76; Twist of Treason (opera), comn by Battleground Arts Ctr, 77; Richard Cory, Elysium Chorale, 82; Molly (opera buffa), comn by Battleground Arts Ctr, 83. *Pos:* Dir, Elysium Chorale, Freehold, NJ, 76- *Mem:* Comp Guild NJ; Battleground Arts Ctr (trustee, 77-); Phi Mu Alpha Sinfonia. *Mailing Add:* PO Box 124 Tennent NJ 07763

LIVINGSTONE, ERNEST FELIX
EDUCATOR, MUSICOLOGIST
b Berlin, Germany, Sept 9, 15; US citizen. *Study:* Univ Berlin, 35; Univ Rochester, EdM, 48, BMus, 49, MA, 52, PhD(musicol), 62. *Pos:* Lectr & recitalist, German Literary Soc, NY. *Teaching:* Instr English, Eastman Sch Music, 49-53, admin asst to dean sch lib & app studies, 50-54, vis prof musicol, 62-80, prof musicol, 80-; instr music, hist & lang, Milwaukee Country Day Sch, 54-60; fac mem, Univ Wis, 57-60; prof mod lang, Rensselaer Polytech Inst, 60-80, chmn dept arts, 73-80; guest lectr, Univ Copenhagen & Univ Gottingen. *Awards:* Res Grant, Eastman Sch Music, 63; Distinguished Fac Award, Rensselaer Polytech Inst, 74. *Mem:* Am Musicol Soc; Soc Music Theory; Int Musicol Soc; Am Asn Univ Prof. *Interests:* Modern foreign languages, especially German, French and Spanish; analysis of musical compositions. *Publ:* Auth, The Place of Music in German Education from the Beginnings Through the 16th Century, J Res Music Educ, winter 67; Das Formproblem des 4.Satzes der 4.Symphonie Beethovens, Bericht Int Musikwiss Kongress, Bonn 1970, 9/70; The Place of Music in German Education Around 1600, J Res Music Educ, summer 71; The Final Coda in Beethoven's String Quartet in F Minor, Opus 95, In: Essays on Music for Charles Wamen Fox, Eastman Sch Music Press, 79; Unifying Elements in Haydn's Symphony No 104, In: Haydn Studies, Norton, 81. *Mailing Add:* Eastman Sch Music 26 Gibbs St Rochester NY 14604

LIZOTTE, ANDRE
CLARINET, EDUCATOR
Pos: Clarinetist, New England Opera Theater, formerly, Goldovsky Opera Theater, formerly, Metropolitan Opera Co, formerly, Am Ballet Theater, formerly, Boston Ballet, formerly & others; mem, New England Wind Sinfonia, currently; prin clarinet, Opera Co Boston, currently. *Teaching:* Instr, Mt St Charles Acad, formerly; mem fac clarinet, Berklee Col Music, currently. *Mailing Add:* Berklee Col Music 1140 Boylston St Boston MA 02215

LLISO, JOSEPH M
MUSIC DIRECTOR, PIANO
b Manhattan, NY, Oct 12, 43. *Study:* Tex Christian Univ, BM, 65; Hunter Col, City Univ New York, MA, 69. *Pos:* Music dir, Pan Am Symph Orch, 73-

Teaching: Dir music, Fordham Univ, Lincoln Ctr, 70-74. *Awards:* Musician of Yr Award, Cult Inst PR, 74. *Mem:* Am Symph Orch League. *Mailing Add:* 112 Hendrix St Brooklyn NY 11207

LLOYD, GERALD J
COMPOSER, EDUCATOR
b Lebanon, Ohio, Sept 6, 38. *Study:* Col Consv Music, Univ Cincinnati, with Scott Huston & Jeno Takacs, BM, 60, MM, 62; Eastman Sch Music, with Bernard Rogers, PhD, 67; Electronic Music Studios, Amherst, with Everett Hafner. *Works:* Associations I (orch); Concertino (piano & orch); L'Evenement (trumpet & piano); Three Sketches (tuba & piano). *Teaching:* Mem fac, Western Mich Univ, 66-69, Sch Perf Arts, San Diego, 69-71, Drake Univ, 71-75 & Capital Univ, 76-82; prof music, Ohio Univ, currently. *Awards:* Perf grants, Rockefeller Found. *Mailing Add:* Music Dept Ohio Univ Columbus OH 43210

LOACH, DONALD GLENN
EDUCATOR, CONDUCTOR
b Denver, Colo, Jan 6, 27. *Study:* Univ Denver, BA, 49; Yale Sch Music, study cond with Antonia Brico, study theory with Paul Hindemith, BMus, 53, MMus, 54; Univ Calif, Berkeley, with Ed Lowinsky, Joseph Kerman, Daniel Heartz & Richard Crocker, PhD(musicol). *Pos:* Cond, Oratorio Soc Charlottesville, 70-82. *Teaching:* Asst instr, Yale Sch Music, 54-55 & instr, 55-59; assoc instr, Univ Calif, Berkeley, 59-63; asst prof music, glee club & univ singers, Univ Va, 64-70, assoc prof, 70-, chmn, McIntire Dept Music, 82- *Bibliog:* Dika Newlin (auth), The Mass as Concert-Piece, Chord & Discord II, No 9; John Haskins (auth), Virginia University Glee Club Sings With Taste, Evening Star, Washington, DC, 12/14/64; Kay Peaslee (auth), Oratorio's Bach Mass "Stunning", Charlottesville Observer, 4/3/80. *Mem:* Int Musicol Soc; Am Musicol Soc; Col Music Soc (pres Va chap, 72-73). *Interests:* Renaissance music. *Publ:* Auth, A Stylistic Approach to Species Counterpoint, J Music Theory I, 57; Tschudi, In: New Grove Dict of Music & Musicians, 80. *Mailing Add:* 112 Old Cabell Hall Univ Va Charlottesville VA 22903

LOBINGIER, CHRISTOPHER CRUMAY
COMPOSER, LIBRARIAN
b Mahoning Township, Pa, Feb 5, 44. *Study:* Carnegie-Mellon Univ, BFA(music comp), 68; studied comp with Nadia Boulanger, 68 & 69; Peabody Consv Music, with Robert Hall Lewis, 73-75. *Works:* Cinq Dissonances pour Olivier Goret d'apres Satie (piano), perf by C Lobingier, Paris, France, 69; Nuptial Colors (organ), perf by Colin Stiff, London, England, 69; Five Galactic Dances (piano), perf by Michael Coonrod, Baltimore, Md, 75; Desperate Living (film score with B Allen Yarus), perf by John Waters, Baltimore, Md, 77; Marimba Happy Music Birthday (marimba solo), perf by Donna Di Stefano, Los Angeles, Calif, 78; Introduction and Golden Apparition (clarinet & piano), perf by Patricia Shands, Baltimore, Md, 81. *Pos:* Rec librn, Peabody Inst Music, 78- *Mem:* Music Libr Asn. *Mailing Add:* Apt 1-R 2745 N Calvert St Baltimore MD 21218

LOCK, WILLIAM ROWLAND
EDUCATOR, CONDUCTOR
b Toronto, Can, Feb 27, 32. *Study:* Royal Consv Music, Toronto, ARCT, 54; MacPhail Col Music, Minneapolis, BM, 58, MM, 59; Univ Southern Calif, DMA, 72. *Works:* The Huron Carol, 72 & She's Like the Swallow, 72, Shawnee Press; Two Indian Songs of Canada, Frederick Harris Music Co, 77. *Pos:* Ed choral rev, Worship & Arts, 71-; contrib ed, J Church Music, 80-; ed bk rev, In Tune, 82- *Teaching:* Instr music, St Paul Bible Col, 58-62 & Pasadena Col, 63-64; prof, Biola Univ, 63-, dir grad studies church music, currently. *Mem:* Los Angeles Choral Cond Guild (pres, 72-74); Nat Oratorio Soc (vpres, 81-); Am Choral Dir Asn; Hymn Soc Am; William Lock Singers & Players. *Mailing Add:* 13967 Whiterock Dr La Mirada CA 90638

LOCKE, RALPH P
EDUCATOR, CRITIC-WRITER
b Boston, Mass, Mar 9, 49. *Study:* Harvard Univ, BA, 66; Univ Chicago, MA(music hist & theory), 74, PhD(music hist & theory), 80. *Pos:* Writer, music concert reviews, interviews & feature articles, Boston After Dark & Boston Phoenix, 68-72. *Teaching:* Instr music hist, Univ Chicago, summer 74; instr musicol, Eastman Sch Music, 75-80, asst prof, 80- *Awards:* Best biblio article, Music Libr Asn, 82; grant, Am Coun Learned Soc, 83. *Mem:* Am Musicol Soc; Soc Francaise Musicol; Int Musicol Soc. *Interests:* Late 18th and 19th century music. *Publ:* Auth, New Berlioz Letters, 19th Century Music, 77; coauth, New Schumann Materials in Upstate New York, Fontes Artis Musicae, 80; auth, Liszt's Saint-Simonian Adventure, 19th Century Music, 80-81; Hymns for the Temple of Peace: Music, Musicians, and the Saint-Simonians, Univ Chicago Press (in prep). *Mailing Add:* Eastman Sch Music 26 Gibbs St Rochester NY 14604

LOCKINGTON, DAVID KIRKMAN
CONDUCTOR & MUSIC DIRECTOR, CELLO
b Dartford, Kent, England, Oct 11, 56. *Study:* Cambridge Univ, England, BA(music), 78; Yale Univ, MA(music), 81; study cello & cond with Aldo Parisot & Otto Werner-Mueller. *Works:* Lobosianas Brasileras, 80 & Magnificat & NuncDimitis (voice & three cellos), 80, perf by Int Cello Quartet; Idec Fixe, perf by Acad in Wilderness Chamber Orch, 82; Neomotion, perf by Arvada Chamber Orch, 83. *Pos:* Asst prin cellist & asst cond, Denver Symph, 81-; music dir, Acad in Wilderness, Denver, 81- *Awards:* Henry & Lily Davis Fund, 78; Royal Soc for Arts, 78; Woolsey Hall

Concerto Compt, Yale Univ, 80. *Mailing Add:* Denver Symph Orch 1245 Champa Denver CO 80204

LOCKLAIR, DAN STEVEN
COMPOSER, ORGAN
b Charlotte, NC, Aug 7, 49. *Study:* Mars Hill Col, BM, 71; Sch Sacred Music, Union Theol Sem, SMM, 73; Eastman Sch Music, DMA, 81. *Works:* Good Tidings from the Holy Beast (opera), Seesaw, 78; Inventions (organ), 82 & Prism of Life (orch), 82, E C Kerby Ltd, Toronto; Grace (motet), Music 70, 82; Lairs of Soundings (sop & strings), 82, Constellations (organ & perc), 83 & Flutes, 83, E C Kerby Ltd. *Pos:* Church musician, First Presby Church, Binghamton, NY, 73-82. *Teaching:* Lectr music, Hartwick Col, 73-82; asst prof, Wake Forest Univ, 82- *Awards:* ASCAP Award, 81-83; Friend of Arts, Sigma Alpha Iota, 82. *Mem:* ASCAP; Am Guild Organists; Col Music Soc; Am Music Ctr. *Mailing Add:* 921 S Main St Winston-Salem NC 27101

LOCKLAIR, WRISTON
ADMINISTRATOR, WRITER
b Charlotte, NC. *Study:* Belmont Abbey Col, AA; Univ NC, Chapel Hill, BA. *Pos:* Arts ed, Charlotte Observer, CBS TV & radio, formerly; critic, Herald Tribune, formerly; account exec & asst to pres, Rober S Taplinger Assoc, New York, currently; asst to pres & dir pub relations, Juilliard Sch, 70- *Publ:* Contrib to New York Times, New York Herald Tribune, New York Mag, Opera News, Musical Am & City Ctr Publ. *Mailing Add:* Juilliard Sch Lincoln Ctr New York NY 10023

LOCKSHIN, FLORENCE LEVIN
COMPOSER, PIANO
b Columbus, Ohio, Mar 24, 10. *Study:* Piano with Frank R Murphy, 20-35; Ohio State Univ, studied orch with Morris Wilson, BS, 31; Smith Col, studied orch with Alvin Etler, 53. *Works:* The Cycle (ballet for orch), comn & perf by Smith Col Orch, 56; Annie Bradley's Tune (orch), perf by Brooklyn Phil Orch, 59; Paean (orch), perf by Stockton Symph Orch, 62; Introduction Lament and Protest (orch), perf by Columbus Phil Orch, 67; Scavarr (orch), Indianapolis Symph Orch, 69; Cumbia (orch), Nat Orch Panama, 77; Trilogy—Poems of Prospice (chorus & orch), Nat Orch Venezuela, 80. *Pos:* Solo pianist, Columbus Music Bureau, 25-35 & Radio, Columbus, Ohio, 25-35; comp & perf, Piano Quartette, Mansfield, Ohio, 46-51; conct pianist, Mid-West, currently. *Teaching:* Private piano instr, Columbus, Ohio, 25-35. *Mem:* Am Women Comp; Am Music Ctr; hon mem, Am Fedn Musician, 51. *Mailing Add:* Baker Hill Northampton MA 01060

LOCKWOOD, ANNEA FERGUSON
COMPOSER
b Christchurch, New Zealand, July 29, 39. *Study:* Univ Canterbury, New Zealand, BM, 61; Royal Col Music, London, studied comp with Peter Racine Fricker & piano with E Kendall Taylor, LARM, ARCM; Darmstadt Ferienkürs Neue Musik, 61-62; Musikhochschule, Cologne, Germany, 63-64; Electronic Music Ctr, Bilthoven, Holland, 63-64. *Works:* Glass Concert (glass, amplification), 69 & Tiger Balm (tape), 71, Source Mag; Malaman (voice), 74; Spirit Catchers (voices amplified), Schirmer Bks, 81; Delta Run (tape, slide, movement), 81; Sound Map of the Hudson River (tapes, installation), 83. *Rec Perf:* The Glass World of Anna Lockwood, Tangent Rec, 69; World Rhythms, 1750 Arch Rec, 78; Tiger Balm, Opus One Rec, 81. *Pos:* Res psychoacoustics,, Inst Sound & Vibration Res, Southampton Univ, England, in collaboration with Peter Grogono, 69-72; creator ser prog trance music, BBC Radio, England, formerly. *Teaching:* Lectr, England, 71-73 & Vassar Col, currently; instr, Hunter Col, City Univ New York, 73-; wkshps, Cambridge Univ, Glasgow Univ, Rutgers Univ, State Univ NY, Bedford Hills Correctional Facility & Modern Art Gallery, Vienna. *Awards:* Fels, Gulbenkian Found, 72, Creative Artists Prog Serv, 77 & Nat Endowment Arts, 79. *Mailing Add:* Baron de Hirsch Rd Crompond NY 10517

LOCKWOOD, CAROLYN
EDUCATOR, DIRECTOR—OPERA
Study: NTex State Univ, BA; Ind Univ, MA; Univ Vienna. *Pos:* Prod stage mgr, Santa Fe Opera, formerly; co mgr, Opera Theatre St Louis, formerly; tech consult, Lincoln Ctr Proj, Sydney Opera House, Berlin State Opera & US Inst Theatre Technicians. *Teaching:* Chmn col opera dept, Hunter Col, formerly; stage dir, Ind Univ, formerly; mem fac opera, Manhattan Sch Music, currently. *Mailing Add:* 21 W 86th St New York NY 10024

LOCKWOOD, LARRY PAUL
COMPOSER, CONDUCTOR
b Duluth, Minn, June 18, 43. *Study:* Manhattan Sch Music, with David Diamond & Mario Davidovsky, BM(comp), 67, MM(comp), 69; Cornell Univ, with Robert Palmer, DMA(comp), 75. *Works:* Trio Variations, Parnassus, 77; Duets for 2 Percussionists, Paul Price Publ, 77; Quartet for Strings, Riverside Quartet, 80; Cantata for the Fest of Lights, 80, Concerto for Viola, 81 & Concerto for Two Violins, 82, New York String Ens. *Rec Perf:* Suite for Band, Cornell Univ, 75. *Pos:* Perf librn, Manhattan Sch Music, 73-; artistic dir, New York String Ens, 77- *Awards:* Ludwig Vogelstein Found Grant, 74; Nat Endowment Arts Fel, 76; Zorn Found Grant, 80. *Mem:* ASCAP; Nat Asn Comp (pres, 77-78). *Publ:* Coauth, Interview with Charles Wuorinen, NY Arts J, 78. *Mailing Add:* 172 W 79th St Apt 14G New York NY 10024

LOCKWOOD, LEWIS HENRY
EDUCATOR, MUSICOLOGIST
b New York, NY, Dec 16, 30. *Study:* Queens Col, BA 52; Princeton Univ, with Oliver Strunk & Arthur Mendel, MFA, 55, PhD, 60. *Pos:* Series ed, Studies in Musical Genesis and Structure, Oxford Univ Press (in prep). *Teaching:* Instr, Princeton Univ, 58-59, asst prof, 59-65, assoc prof, 65-68, prof, 68-80; prof, Harvard Univ, 80- *Awards:* Alfred Einstein Award, Am Musicol Soc, 70. *Mem:* Am Musicol Soc, (vpres, 70-72); Int Musicol Soc; Soc Ital Musicol. *Interests:* Music of Italian Renaissance; studies of style and of composition processes of Beethoven through sketches and autograph manuscripts. *Publ:* Auth, The Counter-Reformation and the Masses of Vincenzo Ruffo, Cini Found, Venice, 70; The Autograph of the First Movement of Beethoven's Sonata for Cello & Piano, Op, 69, Music Forum, Columbia Univ Press, 70; On Beethoven's Sketches and Autographs: Some Problems of Definition and Interpretation, Acta Musicologica, 70; Music in Renaissance Ferrara, Oxford Univ Press (in prep). *Mailing Add:* Music Dept Harvard Univ Cambridge MA 02138

LOCKWOOD, NORMAND
COMPOSER, EDUCATOR
b New York, NY, Mar 19, 06. *Study:* Sch Music, Univ Mich; studied with Ottorino Respighi & Nadia Boulanger. *Works:* Concerto (organ & brasses), Assoc Music Publ, 50; Prairie (chorus & orch), Broude Bros Ltd, 52; Requiem for a Rich Young Man (opera), 64, Piano Concerto, 74, To Margarita Debayle (voice & piano), 77 & Symphony for Large Orchestra, 79, Am Comp Alliance; Eight Preludes for Organ, Augsburg Publ House, 80. *Teaching:* Asst prof comp & theory, Oberlin Col, 32-42; lectr comp, Columbia Univ, 45-52; prof music & comp-in-res, Univ Denver, 61-75. *Awards:* Fel, Am Acad, Rome, 29-32 & John Simon Guggenheim Mem Found, 42-44; Marjorie Peabody Waite Award, Am Acad Arts & Lett, 81. *Mailing Add:* Univ Park Sta Box 10053 Denver CO 80210

LOEB, DAVID
COMPOSER, THEORIST
b New York, NY, 1939. *Study:* Mannes Col Music, studied comp with Peter Stearns & theory & analysis with Carl Schachter & William Mitchell, BS, 62; Sch Music, Yale Univ, MMus, 64; Columbia Univ. *Works:* Fantasia e due Scherzi, August Wenzinger & Hannelore Mueller, 70; Concerto for Eight Winds and String Orchestra, perf by Buffalo Phil, 71; Sonata for Viola da Gamba, August Wenzinger, 72; String Quartet #4, 72, String Quartet #8, 74, Primavera Quartet; Symphony for an Orchestra of Japanese Instruments, comn & perf by Pro Musica Japonica, 76; Nachttaenze (viola da gamba & string orch), perf by August Wenzinger & Hamburg Chamber Orch, 77. *Teaching:* Instr comp & theory & co-chmn tech of musics, Mannes Col Music, 64-; instr comp & theory, Curtis Inst Music, 73- *Awards:* Annual Award, ASCAP, 65-; Contemp Comp Award, Viola da Gamba Soc, London, 66; Chinese Class Music Asn Award, 71 & 74. *Bibliog:* Yasushi Togashi & Motoko Shimojima (auth), Focus on David Loeb, Hogaku-no-tomo, 75. *Interests:* Application of Schenkerian (linear) analysis to Japanese music. *Publ:* Auth, Mathematical Aspects of Music, Vol II, 70 & Analytic Aspects of Japanese Koto Music, Vol IV, 77, Music Forum, Columbia Univ Press; several short articles & reviews in Japanese music periodicals, Hogaku-no-tomo & Gaku-do. *Mailing Add:* c/o Curtis Inst Music 1726 Locust St Philadelphia PA 19103

LOEBEL, DAVID
CONDUCTOR & MUSIC DIRECTOR
b Cleveland, Ohio, Mar 7, 50. *Study:* Northwestern Univ, BS, 72, MM, 74. *Pos:* Asst cond, Syracuse Symph Orch, 74-76 & Cincinnati Symph Orch, 82-; music dir & cond, Binghamton Symph Orch, 77-82 ; music adv, Anchorage Symph Orch, 83- *Awards:* Third Prize, 76 & co-winner, 78, Baltimore Symph Orch Young Cond Compt; Urban Orch Award for Adventuresome Prog, ASCAP, 81. *Mailing Add:* c/o Cincinnati Symph Orch 1241 Elm St Cincinnati OH 45210

LOEBEL, KURT
VIOLIN, EDUCATOR
b Vienna, Austria, Dec 19, 21; US citizen. *Study:* State Acad Music, Vienna, 36-38; Juilliard Sch Music, dipl, 43; studied with Louis Persinger, 45-46; Cleveland Inst Music with Joseph Knitzer, BM, 50, MM, 52. *Rec Perf:* Glenn Gould String Quartet, Symphonia Quartet, Columbia Rec, 60. *Pos:* First violinist, Cleveland Orch, 47- *Teaching:* Fac mem violin, Cleveland Inst Music, 52-; fac mem chamber music, Blossom Fest Sch, 68- *Bibliog:* Deena & Bernard Rosenberg (auth), Music Makers, Columbia Univ Press, 79. *Mem:* Pi Kappa Lambda. *Publ:* Auth, A Symphony Player Looks at Conductors, Instrumentalist, 75; Classical Music Instrumentalist, Music Educr J, 77. *Mailing Add:* Cleveland Inst Music 11021 E Boulevard Cleveland OH 44106

LOEW, HENRY
DOUBLE BASS, EDUCATOR
Study: Studied double bass with Anselme Fortier. *Pos:* Mem, St Louis Munic Opera Orch, Indianapolis Symph Orch, Nat Symph Orch & Seattle Symph Orch, formerly; founder, Gateway Fest Orch, St Louis; prin double bass, St Louis Symph Orch, currently. *Teaching:* Fac mem, Wash Univ, formerly & St Louis Consv Music, currently. *Awards:* New York Phil Scholar Winner. *Mailing Add:* St Louis Consv Music 560 Trinity Ave St Louis MO 63130

LOFT, ABRAM
EDUCATOR, VIOLIN
b New York, NY, Jan 7, 22. *Study:* Columbia Col, BA, 42; Columbia Univ, MA, 44, PhD(musicol), 50. *Rec Perf:* Many recordings as mem of Fine Arts

Quartet incl Bartok cycle, Beethoven cycle, Haydn cycle & others for Everest, Columbia, Vox, Decca & Gasparo, 57-80. *Pos:* Mem, Fine Arts Quartet, 54-79. *Teaching:* Instr, Columbia Col, Columbia Univ, 46-50, asst prof, 50-54; prof & distinguished prof, Univ Wis, Milwaukee, 63-79; prof chamber music & chair string dept, Eastman Sch Music, 79- *Awards:* Perf Award, Wis Arts Coun, 66; Teaching Award, Am String Teachers Asn, 67; Perf Arts Award, Lincoln Acad Ill, 67. *Mem:* Am Musicol Soc; Col Mus Soc. *Interests:* Musicians guilds, unions; history of chamber music. *Publ:* Auth, Violin & Keyboard: The Duo Repertoire, Grossman/Viking, 73; Unions, Musicians, In: New Grove Dict of Music in US (in prep); transl, rev & articles in Musical Quart, Music Libr Asn Notes & Am Mus Soc J. *Mailing Add:* Eastman Sch of Music 26 Gibbs St Rochester NY 14604

LOGAN, WENDALL
COMPOSER, EDUCATOR
b Thomson, Ga, Nov 29, 40. *Study:* Fla A&M Univ, BS, 62; Am Consv; Southern Ill Univ, with Will Bottje, MA, 64; Univ Iowa, with Richard Hervig & Robert Shallenberg, PhD, 68. *Works:* Songs of Our Times (chorus & chamber orch), 69; From Hell to Breakfast (actors, dancers, musicians & electronic sounds), 75; Electric Time (perc ens), Boston, 76; Polyphony I (orch); Ice and Fire (song cycle); Song of the Witchdoktor (voice); Proportions (nine players & cond). *Rec Perf:* On Orion & Golden Crest Rec. *Teaching:* Mem fac, Fla A&M Univ, 63, Ball State Univ, 67-69 & Western Ill Univ, 70-73; prof music, Oberlin Col, 73- *Awards:* Grants, Nat Endowment Arts & Martha Baird Rockefeller Found. *Mailing Add:* 167 S Pleasant St Oberlin OH 44704

LOHMANN, RICHARD BRENT
VIOLIN, TEACHER
b Milwaukee, Wis, July 9, 55. *Study:* Oberlin Consv, with Andor Toth, BM, 77; Univ Wis, Madison, with Thomas Moore, MM, 79. *Pos:* Violin, Fla Phil, 79-80, Peninsula Fest Orch, Fish Creek, Wis, 79-82 & Colo Fest Orch, 83; asst concertmaster, Omaha Symph Orch, 80- *Teaching:* Asst violin, Pa State Univ, 77-78; asst music hist, Univ Wis, Madison, 78-79. *Mailing Add:* 513 S 38th Ave Omaha NE 68105

LOHUIS, ARDYTH J
ORGAN, EDUCATOR
b Melrose Park, Ill. *Study:* Ill Wesleyan Univ, BSM, 60; Northwestern Univ, MM, 62; studied organ with Vernon De Tar, 62; Univ Cincinnati, DMA, 70. *Teaching:* Assoc prof organ & church music, Va Commonwealth Univ, 69-, asst chair dept music, 74-80. *Mem:* Am Guild Organists (dean West Jersey chap, 68-69 & Richmond Va chap, 78-80); Music Teachers Nat Asn; Delta Omicron. *Mailing Add:* 9409 Redington Dr Richmond VA 23235

LOINAZ, YVONNE DALIS (IRENE DALIS)
MEZZO-SOPRANO, ADMINISTRATOR
b San Jose, Calif, Oct 8, 25. *Study:* San Jose State Univ, AB, 46; Columbia Univ, Ma, 47; studied with Otto Mueller, 51-53. *Rec Perf:* Parsifal (Wagner), Philips, 62. *Roles:* Princess Eboli in Don Carlo, Metropolitan Opera, 57-73 & San Francisco Opera, 58; Amneris in Aida, Metropolitan Opera, 57, San Francisco Opera, 59 & Covent Garden, 60; Amme in Die Frau Ohne Schatten, San Francisco Opera, 59 & Metropolitan Opera, 66; Ortrud in Lohengrin, San Francisco Opera, 60, Metropolitan Opera, 61 & Bayreuth Fest, 62; Kundry in Parsifal, Metropolitan Opera, 61-68, Bayreuth Fest, 65; Lady Macbeth in Macbeth, Metropolitan Opera, 64; Isolde in Tristan and Isolde, San Francisco Opera, 67. *Pos:* Prin artist, Oldenburgisches Stattstheater, Germany, 53-55, Berlin Opera, 55-66, Metropolitan Opera, 57-77, San Francisco Opera, 57-77 & Hamburg Opera, 57-77; dir, San Jose State Auditions, Metropolitan Opera, currently; gen dir, San Jose Opera Theater, 78- *Teaching:* Prof opera, San Jose State Univ, 76- *Awards:* Fulbright Award, Inst Int Educ, 51; Distinguished Serv Medal, Columbia Univ, 61. *Mem:* Am Guild Musical Artists; Cent Opera Serv; Nat Opera Asn. *Publ:* Contribr, Opera Quart, 83. *Mailing Add:* 1635 Mulberry Lane San Jose CA 95125

LOLYA, ANDREW
FLUTE, EDUCATOR
Study: Juilliard Sch Music, with Arthur Lora. *Rec Perf:* Solo perf & chamber music on various rec labels. *Pos:* First flute, Mozart Fest Orch, 76, Symph of Air, formerly, Little Orch Soc, formerly, New York City Ballet, currently & Joffrey Ballet Orch, currently; mem, New Art Wind Quintet. *Teaching:* Mem fac flute, Manhattan Sch Music, 73-, Dalcroze Sch Music, currently & Mannes Col Music, 74- *Mailing Add:* Mannes Col Music 157 E 74th St New York NY 10021

LOMBARDI, EUGENE PATSY
CONDUCTOR & MUSIC DIRECTOR, EDUCATOR
b North Braddock, Pa, July 7, 23. *Study:* Westminster Col, BA(pub sch music), 48, DMus, 81; Columbia Univ, MA, 48; George Peabody Col, dipl(educ specialist), 72. *Pos:* Concertmaster, Louisville Civic Symph Orch, 49-50; asst concertmaster, Phoenix Symph Orch, 50-62, concertmaster, 62-69, asst cond, 67-69; cond, Phoenix Symphonette, 54-61, Phoenix Symph Youth Orch, 56-66, Univ Symph Orch, Ariz State Univ, 57- & Phoenix Pops Orch, 72-83; violinist, New Art String Quartet, 65-; concertmaster, Flagstaff Fest Symph, 67-81 & Flagstaff Fest Chamber Orch, 67-81; cond & music dir, Sun Cities Symph Orch, 83- *Teaching:* Band & orch cond, Lincoln High Sch, Midland, Pa, 48-49; orch cond, Male High Sch & DuPont Manual High Sch, Louisville, Ky, 49-50 & Phoenix Union High Sch, 50-57; prof music, Ariz State Univ, 57- *Awards:* Gold Medal Award, Nat Soc Arts & Lett, 73. *Mem:* Am Fedn Musicians; Ariz Music Educr Asn; Am String Teachers Asn. *Mailing Add:* 920 E Manhatton Dr Tempe AZ 85282

LOMBARDO, ROBERT MICHAEL
COMPOSER, EDUCATOR
b Hartford, Conn, Mar 5, 32. *Study:* Hartt Col Music, with Arnold Franchetti & Isadore Freed, BMus, 54, MMus, 55; Hochschule Musik, with Boris Blacher, 58-59; Univ Iowa, with Philip Bezanson, PhD, 61. *Works:* Quintet for Winds, comn by Fromm Found, perf by Boston Symph, 57; Aria & Allegretto (orch), Hilversum Radio Kamerorkest, Holland, 59; Threnody for Strings, Cincinnati Symph Orch, 65 & Chicago Symph Orch, 72; Serge Koussevitzky Music Dialogues of Lovers, comn by Serge Koussevitzky Music Found, Libr Cong, perf by Contemp Chamber Players, Univ Chicago, 66; String Quartet No 2, comn by Mr & Mrs Lee A Freeman, perf by Fine Arts Quartet, 75; Fanfare for WFMT, comn by WFMT Fine Arts Station, 82. *Teaching:* Comp-in-res theory & comp, Chicago Musical Col, Roosevelt Univ, 65- *Awards:* Fels, John Simon Guggenheim Found, 65, Nat Endowment for Arts, 76 & 81 & Ill Arts Coun, 81 & 83. *Mem:* Am Comp Alliance; Chicago Soc Comp; Am Soc Univ Comp; BMI. *Mailing Add:* 1040 W Wellington St Chicago IL 60657

LOMON, RUTH
COMPOSER, PIANO
b Montreal, Can, Nov 7, 30; US citizen. *Study:* McGill Univ; New England Consv; Darmstadt summer courses; study comp with Witold Lutoslawski. *Works:* Songs from a Requiem, perf by Jane Bryden & Paul Suits, 82; Dust Devils, 82, Five Ceremonial Masks, 83 & Soundings, 83, Arsis Press; Seven Portals of Vision, perf by Joanne Vollendorf, 83; Diptych (woodwind quintet), perf by Lyricum Wind Ens, 83. *Pos:* Pianist, Lomon-Wenglin Duo, 74. *Awards:* Yaddo Fel, 77; Meet the Comp Award, 81; Norlin/MacDowell Fel, 82. *Mem:* Am Soc Univ Comp; Am Women Comp; Am Music Ctr; BMI; Int League Women Comp. *Mailing Add:* 2-A Forest St Cambridge MA 02140

LONDON, EDWIN WOLF
COMPOSER, CONDUCTOR
b Philadelphia, Pa, Mar 16, 29. *Study:* Consv Music, Oberlin Col, BMus, 52; Univ Iowa, PhD, 61; studied comp with Luigi Dallapiccola & Darius Milhaud; studied French horn with Gunther Schuller & Martin Morris. *Works:* Osanna, 65, Brass Quintet, 65, Portraits of Three Ladies (American), 67, Poe Bells, 72, Day of Desolation, 72, Psalm of These Days I, II, III, IV, V, 76-80 & Moon Sound Zone, 82, C F Peters Corp. *Rec Perf:* Concatenations (George Balch Wilson), CRI, 70; Portraits of Three Ladies (American), Acoustic Research—DGG, 70; Dream Thing On Biblical Episodes, Urbes, 75; Mass (Salvatore Martirano), New World Rec, 77; Nocturnes (Morgan Powell), Crystal Rec, 79; Concerto for Clarinet & Chamber Orch (Elliott Schwarts), Orion Rec, 79; Psalm of These Days III, CRI, 79. *Teaching:* From instr to assoc prof, Smith Col, 60-68; prof & chmn comp & theory, Sch Music, Univ Ill, 68-78; vis prof, Univ Calif, San Diego, 72; prof & chmn music, Cleveland State Univ, 78- *Awards:* John Simon Guggenheim Found Fel, 69; Nat Endowment Arts Grants, 73, 75 & 80; Cleveland Arts Prize, Womens City Club, 82. *Bibliog:* Christopher McGahan (auth), E London's Women's Choral Music, Univ Ill, 83. *Mem:* Am Soc Univ Comp (chmn nat coun, 77-81); Am Music Ctr; Col Music Soc; Meet the Comp Inc; Comp Forum. *Mailing Add:* 3304 Warrington Rd Shaker Heights OH 44120

LONDON, GEORGE
DIRECTOR—OPERA, BASS-BARITONE
b Montreal, Can, May 30, 20; US citizen. *Study:* Los Angeles City Col, with Hugo Strelitzer & Nathan Stewart; studied with Enrico Rosati & Paola Novikova. *Rec Perf:* For Columbia, Angel, London & RCA. *Roles:* Boris Godunov in Boris Godunov, Bolshoi Theatre, Moscow, 60; Golaud in Pelleas et Melisande; Don Giovanni in Don Giovanni; Count Almaviva & Figaro in Le Nozze di Figaro; Amonasro in Aida; Wanderer in Siegfried; Wolfram in Tannhäuser. *Pos:* Bass-baritone, Edinburgh Fest, 50, Metropolitan Opera, 51-66, Bayreuth Fest, 51-64 & Salzburg Fest, 52; guest appearances, Buenos Aires, Venice, Zagreb, Belgrade & Moscow; stage dir, Seattle Opera, 73; mem, Opera Adv Panel, Nat Endowment for Arts; bd dir, New York City Ctr Music & Drama; art adminr, J F Kennedy Ctr, Washington, DC, formerly; gen dir, Opera Soc, Washington, DC, 75-; exec dir, Nat Opera Inst, Washington, DC. *Awards:* Kammersänger, Vienna Staatsoper, 54; Mozart Medal, Vienna, 71. *Mem:* Am Guild Musical Artists. *Mailing Add:* 7 Slade Ave Baltimore MD 21208

LONDON, LAWRENCE BERNARD
COMPOSER, CLARINET
b Oakland, Calif, May 29, 49. *Study:* Harvard Col, BA, 71. *Works:* String Quartet, Telluride Fest, 79; Starry Nights, Cabrillo Music Fest, 80; Suite for Gamelan & Harp, New Music Am, 80; Wayang Bill, Gamelan Si Darius, 81; Doggy Days, Aspen Music Fest, 82; Yolla Bolly Skies, San Francisco Contemp Players, 83. *Rec Perf:* Water Music, Desto, 69; Dallapiccola, Arch, 80. *Teaching:* Instr counterpoint, Mills Col, 83- *Mailing Add:* 1034 Channing Way Berkeley CA 94710

LONDON, S(OL) J
WRITER, LECTURER
b New York, NY, Oct 15, 17. *Study:* Univ Louisville, BA, 37, MD, 41. *Pos:* Writer, currently. *Mem:* Am Musicol Soc; Am Inst Verdi Studies. *Interests:* Medical musicology: neurobiology of music; joint history of music & medicine; clinical histories of musicians; doctors in music. *Publ:* Auth, Beethoven: A Titan's Last Crisis, Arch Int Med, 63; Aging in Musicians, Gerontology, 64; Vox Humana (The Physiology of the Human Voice & Music), J Am Med Asn, 65; Louis Berlioz, MD, New England J Med, 69; Devil in Paris (Paganini's Clinical History), High Fidelity, 79. *Mailing Add:* 85-28 215th St Hollis Hills NY 11427

LONG, CHARLES (PATRICK)
BARITONE
b Pittsburgh, Pa, Feb 1, 48. *Study:* Carnegie-Mellon Inst, voice & piano, 66-68; private voice lessons with Aldo Ditullio, 69- *Roles:* Jack Rance in Fanciulla Del West, New York City Opera, 77-78; Cardenio in Il Furioso, Spoleto Fest USA, Washington Opera, 78-79; Valentin in Faust, Seattle/Portland Opera, 79; Rigoletto in Rigoletto, Mich Opera Theatre, 80; Manfredo in L'Amore Dei tre Re, Washington DC Opera, 81; Eugene Onegin in Onegin, Lyric Opera Philadelphia, 81; Escamillo in Carmen, New York Opera, 82, & Ft Worth Opera, 82; Scarpia in Tosca, Washington DC Opera, 82 & New York Opera, 83. *Awards:* Rockefeller Grant, 74; Bruce Yarnell Mem Award, 75. *Mem:* Am Guild Musical Artists. *Rep:* Louise Williams Mgmt 3650 Los Feliz Blvd Los Angeles CA 90027. *Mailing Add:* 708 W 171st St New York NY 10032

LONGAZO, GEORGE
EDUCATOR, BASSOON
b Gary, Ind, June 15, 25. *Study:* Northwestern Univ, BM, 50; Ind Univ, comp with Bernard Heiden, MM, 54; Univ Southern Calif, DMA, 69. *Pos:* Contrabassoonist, Nat Symph Orch, 55-62; first bassoon, Monterey Co Symph, 64-65 & San Jose Symph, 65-66. *Teaching:* Instr music, Monterey Peninsula Col, 64-65; asst prof, San Jose State Univ, 65-66; prof, Calif State Univ, Chico, 69- *Mem:* Int Double Reed Soc; Soc Music Theory. *Publ:* Auth, Our Colleagues in the People's Republic of China, Double Reed, 82. *Mailing Add:* 1161 Filbert Ave Chico CA 95926

LONGWITH, DEBORAH
SOPRANO
b Indianapolis, Ind, Sept 5, 49. *Study:* Col Consv Music, Univ Cincinnati, BM, 71, MM, 73; coaching with Carolina Segrera, 78-82. *Roles:* Clorinda in La Cenerentola, Milwaukee Florentine Opera, 76; Mimi in La Boheme, Whitewater Opera, Richmond, Ind, 77; Cio-cio-san in Madama Butterfly, 78, Gretel in Hansel & Gretel, 78 & Susanna in Nozze di Figaro, 79, Cincinnati Opera; Fiordiligi in Cosi fan tutte, New York Lyric Opera, 79; Juliette in Romeo et Juliette, San Francisco Spring Opera, 81. *Awards:* Sullivan Award, 78. *Mem:* Am Guild Musical Artists. *Mailing Add:* c/o Robert Lombardo Assoc 1 Harkness Plaza 61 W 62 Suite 6F New York NY 10023

LONGYEAR, REY MORGAN
WRITER, EDUCATOR
b Boston, Mass, Dec 10, 30. *Study:* Los Angeles State Col, BA, 51; Univ NC, MA, 54; Cornell Univ, PhD, 57. *Works:* Saturnalia, 61 & Percussion Quartet, 62, Univ Southern Miss Perc Ens. *Teaching:* From asst prof to assoc prof, Univ Southern Miss, 58-63; assoc prof, Univ Tenn, 63-64; from assoc prof to prof, Univ Ky, 64- *Awards:* Fel, J S Guggenheim Memorial Found, 71. *Mem:* Int Musicol Soc; Am Musicol Soc (chap pres 61-63 & 74-75); Col Music Soc; Soc Italiana Musicologia. *Interests:* Classic and romantic music. *Publ:* Auth, Schiller and Music, Univ NC Press, 66; Nineteenth Century Romanticism in Music, Prentice-Hall 69 & 73; The Minor Mode in 18th Century Sonata Form, J Music Theory, 71; ed, Mattei, Zingarelli: Selected Symphonies, 80 & The Northern Italian Symphony, 1800-1840, 82, Garland Press. *Mailing Add:* Sch Music Univ Ky Lexington KY 40506

LOOMIS, JAMES PHILLIP
TEACHER, CLARINET
b Bowling Green, Ohio, Dec 28, 29. *Study:* Bowling Green State Univ, BMus, 51; Univ Michigan, MM(perf clarinet), 63, DMA(perf clarinet), 71. *Rec Perf:* University Michigan Band on Tour, Vanguard Rec, 63. *Pos:* Solo clarinetist, US Air Force Band of the West, formerly; clarinetist, Toledo Symph & Northwest Symph, formerly. *Teaching:* Prof woodwinds, Wheaton Col Consv, 69-72; instr clarinet, Bowling Green State Univ 64- *Mem:* Int Clarinet Soc; NAm Fedn Musicians. *Publ:* Co-ed, Bibliography of Woodwind Teaching Material, G Munson, 63; auth, Towson Chamber Players; Compositions by Theldon Myers, 82 & Kammermusik für Bläser: Donzi; Spohr, Vol 9, #2, The Clarinet. *Mailing Add:* 7327 Kern Valley Dr Ft Wayne IN 46815

LOPEZ, PETER DICKSON
COMPOSER, ELECTRONIC
b Berkeley, Calif, July 8, 50. *Study:* Calif State Univ, Hayward, BA, 72; Univ Calif, Berkeley, with Wilson & Nin-Culmell, MA, 74, with Dugger, PhD, 78. *Works:* Intrections (3 pianos & tape), perf by Berkeley Contemp Chamber Players, 75; Seven Pieces (violin & piano), perf by Henryk Wieniawski Fest Players, 80; IFASIA (octet), perf by San Francisco Contemp Music Players, 80; CHominge (violin, tape & electronic), perf by Jeff Cox & comp, 81; The Ship of Death (male voice & chamber orch), 1750 Arc Rec Co, 83. *Pos:* Assoc dir, Electronic Music Studio, Univ Calif, Davis, 82- *Teaching:* Vis lectr comp & electronic music, Univ Calif, Davis, 82- *Awards:* George Ladd Paris Prize, 76-78; Lili Boulanger Prize, 81; First Prize, East & West Artists' 7th Ann Int Comp Compt, 82. *Mem:* Col Music Soc; BMI; Am Music Ctr; Am Soc Univ Comp. *Mailing Add:* 2215 Santa Clara St Richmond CA 94804

LOPEZ-COBOS, JESUS
CONDUCTOR
b Toro, Spain, Feb 25, 40. *Study:* Madrid Univ, PhD(phil), 64; Madrid Consv, dipl(comp), 66; Vienna Acad, with Swarowsky, dipl(cond), 69. *Rec Perf:* Lucia di Lammermoor (Donizetti), Otello (Rossini) & Jose Carreras (operatic & recital), Philips Rec; Dante Symphony (Liszt), Te Deum (Bizet), Alona (Poulenc), Philar Lorengar (operatic recital), Ancient Airs & Dances (Respighi), 3-Cornered Hat (Falla), Capriccio Espagnole (Rimsky-Korsakov), Espana (Chabrier) & Rustic Wedding Symphony (Goldmark), Decca Rec.

Pos: Guest cond, major US & Europ opera houses, 69-; General music dir, Deutsche Oper, Berlin, 81-; prin guest cond, London Phil Orch, 81- *Awards:* First Prize, Besancon Int Cond Compt, 69; Prince Asturias Award, Spain, 81. *Mailing Add:* c/o ICM Artists 40 W 57th St New York NY 10019

LOPEZ-SOBA, ELIAS
PIANO, EDUCATOR
b Ponce, PR, April 17, 27. *Study:* Longy Sch Music, sr dipl & soloist dipl, 53; Bennington Col; Akad Musik, Vienna, reifeprufung, 56. *Pos:* Concert tours, US, UK, Austria, Italy, Spain, Cent Am & Caribbean; chamber music concerts, Austrian Radio Network, Radio TV Espana, RAI, Italy, Can Broadcasting Corp & radio & TV, PR; exec dir, Fest Casals Inc, 73-74, exec vpres, 74-75, pres, 75-77. *Teaching:* Assoc prof, Univ PR, 61-65, head dept music, 63-64, dir dept cult activ, 64-65 & 67-71, mem fac, 78. *Awards:* Fulbright Scholar, 53, 54 & 55; Gold Medal, Concours Int d'Interpretation Musicale Geneva. *Mem:* Inst Puerto Rican Cult; Am Musicol Soc. *Mailing Add:* Calle Del Parque 352 Penthouse San Juan PR 00912

LOPRESTI, RONALD B
COMPOSER, EDUCATOR
b Williamstown, Mass, Oct 28, 33. *Study:* Eastman Sch Music, BMus, 55, MMus, 56. *Works:* The Masks, Carl Fischer Inc, 56; Pageant Overture, Theodore Presser Co, 58; Suite for Five Trumpets, Shawnee Press Inc, 61; Elegy for a Young American, Theodore Presser Co, 64; Ode to Independence, Carl Fischer Inc, 77; Introduction, Chorale, Jubilee, 79 & Tundra, 82, Shawnee Press Inc. *Teaching:* Instr theory, Tex Tech Col, 59-60; Ford Found comp, Winfield Pub Sch, Kans, 60-62; asst prof music, Ind State Col, Pa, 62-64; prof comp & theory, Ariz State Univ, 64- *Awards:* Serge Koussevitsky Award, 55; Col Band Dir Comp Award, 57; Writer's Award, ASCAP, 63-82. *Mem:* ASCAP. *Mailing Add:* 200 E Geneva Dr Tempe AZ 85282

LORANGO, THOMAS (VINCENT)
PIANO
b Buffalo, NY, June 8, 59. *Study:* Curtis Inst Music, BM, 79. *Pos:* Conct pianist & recitalist, 79- *Awards:* Leventritt Found Award, 79; Julius Katchen Mem Scholar Found Award, 79-83; Young Recitalist Award, Nat Endowment Arts, 82. *Rep:* Columbia Artists Mgt 165 W 57th New York NY 10019. *Mailing Add:* 241 W 97th #13M New York NY 10025

LORD, ROBERT SUTHERLAND
EDUCATOR, ORGAN
b Marblehead, Mass, June 4, 30. *Study:* Dartmouth Col, AB, 51; Yale Univ, MA, 54, PhD, 60; studied organ & improvisation with Jean Langlais. *Teaching:* Asst prof music & col organist, Davidson Col, 59-62; assoc prof musicol & univ organist, Univ Pittsburgh, 62- *Mem:* Am Musicol Soc (mem nat coun, 81-83); Am Guild Organists (WPa regional chair, 69-73); Organ Hist Soc (mem nat coun, 70-72); Int Musicol Soc. *Interests:* French organ music of 19th-20th centuries; Charles Tournemire and Ste Clotilde tradition in Paris. *Publ:* Auth, The Sainte-Clotilde Traditions—Franck, Tournemire, and Langlais, Diapason, 75; The First Pipe Organ Andrew Carnegie Ever Gave, Bicentennial Tracker, Organ Hist Soc, 76; Charles Tournemire et les Sept Chorals-Poemes d'Orgue, L'Orgue, Paris Les Amis Orgue, 79; The Sainte-Clotilde Tradition—Toward a Definition, Am Organist, Am Guild Organist, 82; Liturgy and Gregorian Chant in L'Orgue Mystique of Charles Tournemire, Organ Yearbook (in prep). *Mailing Add:* 204 Music Bldg Univ Pittsburgh Pittsburgh PA 15260

LORD, STEPHEN H
COACH, ADMINISTRATOR
b Concord, Mass, Apr 8, 49. *Study:* Oberlin Col, BM, 72; Longy Sch. *Pos:* Coach, Houston Grand Opera, 77-80; head music staff & artistic consult, Opera Theatre St Louis, 80-; head coach, Can Opera Co Ens, Toronto, 83- *Teaching:* Guest instr, Blossom Fest Sch, Kent, Ohio, 79- & Westminster Choir Col, 81-; instr, St Louis Consv, 83- *Mailing Add:* Annie Moore Rd Bolton MA 01740

LORENZ, ELLEN JANE (ELLEN JANE LORENZ PORTER)
COMPOSER, WRITER
b Dayton, Ohio, May 3, 07. *Study:* Wellesley Col, with Hamilton Macdougall & Randall Thompson, BA, 29; studied with Nadia Boulanger, 31; Wittenberg Univ, MSM, 71; Union Grad Sch, PhD, 78; Lebanon Valley Col, Hon DMus, 46. *Works:* Christmas/Folk Style (cantata), Lorenz Publ Co, 66; The Grab Bag (suite), perf by Dayton Phil Orch, 55; Five Micro-Studies for Piano, perf by Ludolph Vander Hoeven, 70; Japanes Suite (flute & piano), perf by Takuo Yuasa, 71; Folk Hymns for Bells, Sacred Music Press, 82; Five Flourishes for Brass, perf by Dayton Phil Brass Quintet, 83. *Pos:* Ed in chief, Lorenz Publ Co, Dayton, 32-68; dir, several church choirs, Dayton, Ohio, 32-74 & Dayton Madrigal Group, 45-69; ed, Organ Portfolio, Lorenz Publ Co, 38-65; narrator & music annotator, Children's Concts, Dayton Phil Orch, 50-65. *Teaching:* Instr advan comp, Univ Dayton, 80 ; instr sacred music, United Theol Sem, Dayton, Ohio, 72- & Seattle Pac Univ, 82. *Bibliog:* Howard Zettervall (auth), Meet the Composer, Choristers Guild Lett, 82. *Mem:* ASCAP; Mu Phi Epsilon (pres Dayton Alumni, 82-84); Dayton Chamber Music Soc (pres, 60-62); Hymn Soc Am; hon life mem, Am Guild English Handbell Ringers (chmn Dayton area, 71-72). *Interests:* American folk hymns, particularly camp meeting spirituals. *Publ:* Auth, The Incredible Story of the Sunday School Song, Choristers Guild Lett, 78; Glory Hallelujah: The Story of the Camp Meeting Spiritual, Abingdon Press, 80; A Manual of Handbell Ringing in Church, Lorenz Publ Co, 81; A Hymn-Tune Detective Stalks Lowell Mason, J Church Music, 82; William B Bradbury, The Camp Meeting Spiritual and the Gospel Song, Hymn, 82. *Mailing Add:* 324 Oak Forest Dayton OH 45419

LORIMER, MICHAEL
GUITAR
b Chicago, Ill, Jan 13, 46. *Study:* With Andres Segovia. *Pos:* Guitarist, worldwide tour incl USSR. *Publ:* Contribr, Guitar Player. *Mailing Add:* c/o Shaw Concerts Inc 1995 Broadway New York NY 10023

LOTZENHISER, GEORGE WILLIAM
ADMINISTRATOR, CONDUCTOR
b Spokane, Wash, May 16, 23. *Study:* Eastern Wash Univ, BA(music) & BEd, 47; Univ Mich, MMus, 48; Univ Ore, EdD, 56. *Works:* Seventeen pieces for various solo instruments, 20 for various brass ensembles & one for orchestra, published by Belwin, Carl Fischer & Rubank Music Companies. *Pos:* First trombone, US Navy Band, 42-43 & Spokane Phil, 46-47; dir, US Naval Band, Saipan & Tinian, 45 & ROTC Band, Univ Ariz, 48-55; cond, Massed Bands & Orch All State Ore, Ariz, NMex, Wash, Idaho, Mont & Can, 46-, Univ Symph Orch, Univ Ariz, 49-50 & Symph Brass Choir, Univ Ariz, 52-60; first trombone & prin brass, Tucson Symph Orch, 48-60 & Spokane Symph, 60-62; trombonist, Tucson Symphonietta, 50-60; assoc cond, Tucson Symph Orch, 57-60. *Teaching:* Instr brass, Univ Ariz, 48-49, asst prof music, 49-56, assoc prof, 56-60; prof music, Eastern Wash Univ, 60-, head div music, 60-61, dir div creative arts & chmn dept music, 61-69, dean sch fine arts, 72-83, emer prof, 83- *Awards:* Music Educr Nat Asn; Eastern Wash Music Educr (pres, 65-67). *Publ:* Coauth, Music, A Programmed Music Theory Text, 200, Am Bk Co. *Mailing Add:* Rt 2 Box 146 Cheney WA 99004

LOUCKS, RICHARD NEWCOMB
EDUCATOR, WRITER
b Pomona, Calif, Aug 24, 19. *Study:* Pomona Col, BA, 42; Eastman Sch Music, MA, 48, PhD, 60. *Teaching:* Prof music theory & music hist, Pomona Col, 48- *Mem:* Am Musicol Soc; Col Music Soc. *Interests:* Keyboard organology, specifically the construction, history and use of clavichords. *Publ:* Auth, Arthur Shepherd, American Composer, Brigham Young Univ Pres, 80. *Mailing Add:* 176 W Oak Park Dr Claremont CA 91711

LOUKAS, BILLIE (BILLIE LOUKAS POULOS)
SOPRANO
b Salt Lake City, Utah, Mar 20, 33. *Study:* Univ Southern Calif, with Walter Ducloux, 54; Univ Münster, Germany, 55-56. *Rec Perf:* Mimi in La Boheme, Rosalinda in Die Fledermaus, Amelia in Un Ballo in Maschera, Lauretta in Gianni Schicchi, Monica in The Medium & Magda in The Consul, Utah Opera Co. *Pos:* Soloist, Salt Lake Phil Orch, 54- & Lawrence Welk TV Show, 58; lead sop & soloist, Fred Waring's Pennsylvanians, 64-67; sop & public relations dir, Utah Opera Co, 77- *Rep:* Utah Opera Co 50 W Second S Salt Lake City Utah 84101. *Mailing Add:* 2526 Valley View Ave Salt Lake City UT 84117

LOVE, SHIRLEY
MEZZO-SOPRANO
b Detroit, Mich, Jan 6, 40. *Study:* With Avery Crew, Marinka Gurewich & Margaret Harshaw. *Roles:* Zweite Dame in Die Zauberflöte, Metropolitan Opera, 64; Dinah in Trouble in Tahiti; Hermia & Hippolita in Midsummer Night; Dorabella in Cosi fan tutte; Cherubino in Le Nozze di Figaro; Rosina in Il Barbiere di Siviglia; Jocasta in Oedipus Rex. *Pos:* Ms, Teatro Communale, Bologna & Florence, Lyric Opera Chicago, Cincinnati Opera Asn, Lake George Opera Fest, Opera Co Philadelphia & others; res mem, Metropolitan Opera, currently. *Mailing Add:* c/o Thea Dispeker 59 W 54th St New York NY 10022

LOVELL, WILLIAM JAMES
COMPOSER
b Brooklyn, NY, Oct 26, 39. *Study:* Cleveland State Univ, comp with J D Bain Murray & Rudolph Bubalo, BA, 72; Cleveland State Univ, MM, 75. *Works:* String Quartet, perf by Cleveland Orch, 72; Yerma (play music), comn by Drama Dept, Case Western Reserve Univ, 72; Elegy, comn by Cleveland State Univ Chorale, 73; Overture for Band, perf by Cleveland State Univ Conct Band, 74; East of Olduvai, 74; Intextimbregation, 75; A Journey Through the Percussive Forest (tape & perc), perf by Gregory Geisert, 75. *Teaching:* Instr, Cleveland Music Sch Settlement, 71-73; asst chmn, Music Dept, Cleveland State Univ, 74- *Mem:* Cleveland Comp Guild (prog chmn, 73-77). *Publ:* Auth, Theory and Fundamentals of Music Composition, Am Corresp Inst, 80. *Mailing Add:* 5603 E Pleasant Valley Independence OH 44131

LOWE, DONALD ROBERT
EDUCATOR
b Pittsburg, Kans, Aug 30, 36. *Study:* Wichita State Univ, BME, 58, MME, 64; Univ Mo, Kansas City, DMA, 72. *Teaching:* Instrm music, Kansas City Pub Sch, Mo, 58-73; assoc prof music educ & dir grad music studies, Univ Ga, 73- *Mem:* Col Music Soc; Music Educr Nat Conf; Ga Music Educr Asn. *Interests:* Life and work of Carl Busch, a Danish-American musician. *Publ:* Auth, Carl Busch & The First Goldman Band Composition Contest: A Pivotal Point in the Historical Evolution of the Modern Wind Band Repertoire, J Band Res, 78; Suzuki and the Beginning Wind Class, Instrumentalist, 78; Carl Busch: Danish-American Music Educator, J Res Music Educ, 83. *Mailing Add:* Sch Music Univ Ga Athens GA 30602

LOWE, JEANNE CATHERINE
ADMINISTRATOR, PIANO
b Jersey City, NJ, Apr 12, 42. *Study:* Montclair State Col, BA, 63; Sch Sacred Music, Union Theol Sem, New York, SMM, 70; Concordia Sem, 66; instrumental studies with Michael Santeramo, Louis E Zerbe, Russell Hayton,

George Powers, Edward Clark, Jan Bender, Dorothy Priesing, Anthony La Magra, Murray Present & Carol Anievas. *Pos:* Dir, Sunset Sch Music, 80-; exec dir, Roosa Sch Music, 81- *Teaching:* Asst prof music, Concordia Col, 70-75; instr piano, Brooklyn Col, 78-81 & Roosa Sch Music, 78-81. *Mailing Add:* 816 43rd St Brooklyn NY 11232

LOWE, SHERMAN
BASS
b NC. *Study:* NC Sch Arts, dipl; Acad Chigiana, Siena; Hochschule Mozarteum, Salzburg, Austria. *Roles:* Padre Guardiano in La Forza del Destino, 77; Zuniga in Carmen, Atlanta Lyric Opera, 78; Curtis in The Taming of the Shrew, Wolf Trap Fest, 79; The Consul, 80 & Ariadne auf Naxos, 80, Atlanta Civic Opera; Samson and Delila, Atlanta Choral Guild, 80; Mozart Requiem, Rhode Island Civic Chorale and Orch, 81. *Pos:* Soloist & recitalist throughout Italy, formerly. *Awards:* Int Voice Compt Winner, 77; Am Opera Auditions Southeastern Regional Winner, 81. *Mailing Add:* c/o Sullivan & Lindsey Assocs 133 W 87th St New York NY 10024

LOWENS, IRVING
CRITIC, MUSIC HISTORIAN
b New York, NY, Aug 19, 16. *Study:* Columbia Univ, with Edwin John Stringham, Howard A Murphy & Quinto Maganini, BS, 39; Univ Md, MA, 57, 57-59. *Works:* Variations on a Peruvian Theme (orch); Fantasy (string orch, string quartet & flute); The Miller O'Fyfe (flute & piano); Laudate (women's voices); Old Christmas Returned (song); Peasants (song); Clarinet Concertino. *Pos:* Contrib music critic, Washington Evening Star, 53-60, chief music critic, 61-78; ref librn sound rec, Music Div, Libr Cong, 60-61, asst head ref sect, 61-66. *Teaching:* Sr res fel & vis prof, Inst Studies Am Music, Brooklyn Col, City Univ New York, 75-76; fac mem, Peabody Inst, 77-, dean & assoc dir, 78- *Awards:* Grants, Nat Endowment Arts, 69 & Nat Endowment Humanities, 76; ASCAP Deems Taylor Award, 73 & 77. *Mem:* Fel, Am Antiquarian Soc; Inter-Am Asn Music Critics (vpres, 73-); Sonneck Soc (chmn pro tem, 74-75, pres, 75-81); Music Critics Asn (pres, 71-75); Music Libr Asn (pres, 65-66). *Publ:* Auth, Music and Musicians in Early America, 64; A Bibliography of Songsters Printed in America Before 1821, 76; Music in America and American Music, 78; Haydn in America, 79; numerous articles on music history & bibliography. *Mailing Add:* 5511 N Charles St Baltimore MD 21210

LOWENS, MARGERY MORGAN
EDUCATOR, WRITER
b Scranton, Pa, Dec 2, 30. *Study:* Syracuse Univ, BMus(piano & piano pedagogy), 52, MMus(piano), 53; Union Theol Sem, MSM(organ), 55; Univ Mich, PhD(musicol), 71. *Pos:* Minister music, First Presby Church, Wilkes-Barre, Pa, 55-60; assoc ed, Symph News, Am Symph Orch League, 66-68. *Teaching:* Instr piano & organ, Wilkes Col, 57-59; dir choral activ, Wyo Sem, Pa, 57-59; teaching fel theory, Univ Mich, Ann Arbor, 65-66; fac mem, Peabody Consv, 76- *Awards:* Nat Grad Scholar, Sigma Alpha Iota, 53; MacDowell Colony Fel, 71 & 80; Nat Endowment Humanities Res Grant, 80. *Mem:* Sonneck Soc (vpres, 83-); Am Musicol Soc; Int Musicol Soc; Col Music Soc; Am Guild Organists. *Interests:* Late 19th and early 20th century American music, especially the life and works of Edward MacDowell. *Publ:* Contribr, Edward MacDowell, Da Capo, 69; coauth, A Selective Bibliography of the Published Writings and Music of Irving Lowens, Music in Am & American Music, 78; auth, articles, In: New Grove Dict of Music & Musicians, 80. *Mailing Add:* 5511 N Charles St Baltimore MD 21210

LOWENTHAL, JEROME
PIANO, EDUCATOR
b Philadelphia, Pa. *Study:* With William Kapell, Eduard Steuermann & Alfred Cortot. *Rec Perf:* On Vanguard, Columbia & RCA. *Pos:* Soloist, Philadelphia, Pittsburgh, Baltimore, Cincinnati, Houston & Suisse Romande Orchs & others; performer recitals & chamber music in over 40 countries in North & South Am, Europe & Asia. *Teaching:* Mem fac piano, Music Acad West, currently. *Mailing Add:* c/o Columbia Artists 165 W 57th St New York NY 10019

LOWREY, NORMAN EUGENE
COMPOSER, EDUCATOR
b Midland, Mich, Jan 13, 44. *Study:* With Samuel Jones; Tex Christian Univ, with Ralph Guenther; Eastman Sch Music, with Samuel Adler, Warren Benson, Wayne Barlow & Joseph Schwantner. *Works:* Sculpture (cello & orch), 63; Celebration Overture (orch), 67; Perspectives (double woodwind trio & perc), 71; Solitary Gestures (trumpet & narrator), 72; A Child's Christmas in Wales (Dylan Thomas poem with narrator), 74; Fragments and Overlays (bassoon & tape), 75; Trumantra (five trumpets, tape & audience), 78. *Teaching:* Instr, San Diego State Univ, 71-72; mem fac humanities, Stephens Col, 72-76; assoc prof music, Drew Univ, 77- *Awards:* Louis Lane Award Comp, Eastman Sch Music. *Mailing Add:* 26 Main Madison NJ 07940

LOWY, JAY STANTON
ADMINISTRATOR
b Chicago, Ill, Nov 22, 35. *Study:* Univ Calif, Los Angeles. *Pos:* Gen prof mgr, Famous Music Corp, 67-69; vpres, Artists & Repertoire, Dot & Paramount Rec Co, 69-71; pres & chief operating officer, Capitol-EMI Music Co, 72-74; vpres & gen mgr, Jobete Music Co Inc, 76- *Awards:* One of Top Two Hundred Music Exec, Billboard Mag, 76. *Bibliog:* Paul Baraatta (auth), Lyric Writing, Am Song Fest Inc, 82. *Mem:* Nat Acad Rec Arts & Sci (nat secy-treas, 77-79, nat pres, 79-81, nat trustee, 81-); Calif Copyright Conf (dir, 75-77, vpres, 76-77, pres, 77-78). *Mailing Add:* 4823 Atoll Ave Sherman Oaks CA 91423

LUBET, ALEX J
COMPOSER, EDUCATOR
b Harvey, Ill, June 9, 54. *Study:* Roosevelt Univ, BMus, 75; Univ Iowa, MA, 77, PhD, 79. *Works:* Shabbat Shalom, Minn Comp Forum, 81; For Four Trombones, Des Moines Symph Trombone Quartet, 82; Two Octave Etudes, Nat Asn Comp, USA, 82; The Song of the Jain Temples, Comp Comn Prog, 82; Three Short Pieces After Webern, 82 & Jaltarang, 83, comn by McKnight Found; Masada, St Paul Chamber Orch, 83. *Teaching:* Asst prof theory & comp, Univ Iowa, 75-79; asst prof, Univ Minn, Minneapolis,, 79- *Awards:* Young Comp Award, Nat Asn Comp, USA, 81; fel, McKnight Found, 82; Standard Award, ASCAP, 82-83. *Mem:* ASCAP; Am Soc Univ Comp; Nat Asn Comp, USA; Am Music Ctr; Minn Comp Forum. *Mailing Add:* 72 Pleasant St SE Minneapolis MN 55455

LUBIN, ABRAHAM
BARITONE, LECTURER
b London, England, Nov 25, 37; US citizen. *Study:* Jews Col, London, hazzan, 57; London Col Music, ALCM, 57; Univ Cincinnati, BM, 66; DePaul Univ, MM, 72; Univ Chicago. *Pos:* Cantor, Beth Abraham Synagogue, Dayton, 59-68 & Congregation Rodfei Zedek, Chicago, 68-; ed, J Synagogue Music, 79- *Awards:* Yuval Award, 72 & Citation, 75, Cantors Assembly Am. *Mem:* Hon fel, Cantors Inst; Cantors Assembly (mem exec coun, 79-81); Am Musicol Soc; Am Soc Jewish Music; Pi Kappa Lambda. *Publ:* Auth, The Hazzan, Jewish Spectator, 73; Minhag Ashkenaz: A Millenium in Song, J Synagogue Music, 78; The Influence of Jewish Music and Thought in Certain Works of Leonard Bernstein, Tatzlil, Israel, 80. *Mailing Add:* 5121 S Cornell Ave Chicago IL 60615

LUBIN, STEVEN
PIANO
b Brooklyn, NY, Feb 22, 42. *Study:* Harvard Col, AB, 63; Juilliard Sch Music, MA(piano), 65; NY Univ, PhD(musicol), 74; piano studies with Rosina Lhevinne, Nadia Reisenberg, Seymour Lipkin & Beveridge Webster. *Rec Perf:* Sonatas K332, 333 (Mozart), Spectrum, 80; Two-Fortepiano Works (Mozart), Arabesque, 81; Concertos Fortepiano & Period Orchestra (Mozart & Haydn), Arabesque Digital, 82. *Pos:* Musical dir, fortepianist & pianist, Mozartean Players, New York, 78- *Teaching:* Instr piano, Vassar Col, 70-71; asst prof theory & coordr grad theory prog, Cornell Univ, 71-75; asst prof theory & music hist, State Univ NY, Purchase, 75- *Awards:* Martha Baird Rockfeller Fund Music Grant, 68; Nat Endowment Arts Grant, 83. *Mem:* Am Musicol Soc; Soc Friends Mozart. *Interests:* Analysis of Beethoven's sonata forms; nature of Mozart's Viennese concerto performances. *Publ:* Auth, Trazom's Visit, Music J, 78. *Rep:* Am Int Artists 275 Madison Ave New York NY 10016. *Mailing Add:* 500 Kappock St Bronx NY 10463

LUCARELLI, BERT (HUMBERT J)
OBOE & ENGLISH HORN, TEACHER
b Chicago, Ill, July 20, 38. *Study:* Chicago Musical Col, Roosevelt Univ, BMus, 59; studied with Robert Bloom & Ray Still. *Rec Perf:* John Corigliano, Concerto for Oboe, RCA; Telemann Partitas, Bax-Bliss Quintets (oboe & strings) & Mozart Serenade #10 (winds), Musical Heritage Soc; Sensual Sound of the Soulful Oboe, Jonella Rec; Benjamin Britten, Six Metamorphoses After Ovid, Op 49 & Sonata Album (Hindemith, Poulenc & Saint-Saëns), Lyrichord. *Pos:* Prin oboe, Chicago Lyr Opera, formerly, Chicago Grant Park Symph, formerly, Fla Symph Orch, formerly, Chicago Symph Orch, Ballet Russe Monte Carlo, Royal Ballet London & Aspen Festival Orch; mem, New York Baroque Ens, formerly, Lark Woodwind Quintet, currently, & New York Bach Soloists, currently; asst prin oboe, Chicago Symph Orch; soloist, Victoria Int Fest, Vancouver & Romantic Music Fest, Newport, RI, currently; soloist & recitalist worldwide. *Teaching:* Oboe, Henry St Settlement Music Sch, 63-68; vis lectr, Hartt Sch Music, 68-77, assoc prof & chmn winds, perc & ens, 77-; mem fac, Aspen Music Fest. *Awards:* Rockefeller Grant; Oliver Ditson Scholar; NY State Coun Arts Grant. *Mem:* Am Fedn Musicians; Bohemians. *Mailing Add:* 160 W 73rd St New York NY 10023

LUCAS, CAROL A
PIANO, MUSIC DIRECTOR
b Brooklyn, NY. *Study:* Eastman Sch Music, piano with Maria Faini & Brooks Smith, BMus, 68, MMus, 71. *Pos:* Asst music dir, Eastern Opera, 81- & Manhattan Savoyards, 81-; chorus mistress, Brooklyn Opera Soc, 81-82; cond, Columbia Community Concerts Nat Tour, 82. *Teaching:* Vocal coach, New York, 79- & Des Moines Metro Opera, 82- *Rep:* Eastern Opera 530 E 89th St New York NY 10028. *Mailing Add:* 46 W 88th New York NY 10024

LUCAS, JAMES
DIRECTOR—OPERA
b San Antonio, Tex. *Study:* Hiram Col, BA; Stanford Univ, Juilliard Sch Music; studied with Boris Goldovsky. *Roles:* Directed 118 different operas and conducted over 40. *Pos:* Freelance dir & prod, Metropolitan Opera, New York Opera, San Francisco Opera, Opera Co Philadelphia, Miami Opera, Seattle Opera, Ft Worth Opera, Baltimore Opera, New Orleans Opera, Can Opera Co, Vancouver Opera, Manitoba Opera Co, Opera de PR, Opera de Santiago. *Teaching:* Fac mem, Mannes Col Music, 65-69 & Temple Univ, 65-69; stage dir opera, Manhattan Sch Music, 69-79. *Mem:* Am Guild Musical Artists; Am Fedn Musicians. *Mailing Add:* 201 W 85th St New York NY 10024

LUCAS, THEODORE D
ADMINISTRATOR, COMPOSER
b San Diego, Calif. *Study:* San Diego State Univ, AB, 63, MA, 64; Univ Ill, DMA, 70. *Teaching:* Chair music dept, Beloit Col, 69-76; dean sch fine arts, Southwestern Univ, Tex, 76- *Mailing Add:* Music Dept Southwestern Univ Georgetown TX 78626

LUCCHESI, PEGGY (MARGARET C LUCCHESI)
PERCUSSION, EDUCATOR
b Oakland, Calif, June 12, 28. *Study:* Univ Calif, Berkeley, AB(music), 49; Royal Acad Music, London, LRAM(orch & cond), 52; San Francisco State Col, MA(music educ), 57. *Rec Perf:* Rec perf with San Francisco Symph. *Pos:* Perc, San Francisco Symph, 55-80 & San Francisco Opera, 61- *Teaching:* Instr perc, San Francisco Consv Music, 55-62 & 72- & Univ Calif, Berkeley, 68- *Mem:* Percussive Arts Soc; San Francisco Women's Musician's Club. *Mailing Add:* 31 Yorkshire Dr Oakland CA 94618

LUCHSINGER, RONALD
DIRECTOR—OPERA, EDUCATOR
Study: Univ Dubuque, BA; Wayne State Univ, Hartt Sch Music, MMus. *Pos:* Resident stage dir, Conn Opera Asn, Hartford, Conn & Troupers Light Opera, Darien, Conn; dir, New York Opera-Drama Studio & Opera Wkshp, Nat Asn Teachers Singing; artistic dir, New Lyric Theater. *Teaching:* Mem fac, Oakland Univ, formerly; teaching assoc opera, Hartt Sch Music, 71- *Mailing Add:* 2 Treat St #13A West Haven CT 06516

LUCIER, ALVIN AUGUSTUS
EDUCATOR, COMPOSER
b Nashua, NH, May 14, 31. *Study:* Yale Univ, BA, 54; Brandeis Univ, MFA, 60. *Works:* Bird and Person Dyning, Cramps Rec, Italy, 76; Music on a Long Thin Wire, 80, I Am Sitting in a Room, 81, Music for Solo Performer, 82 & Still and Moving Lines of Silence in Families of Hyperbolas, 83, Lovely Music Rec; Music for Small Orchestra and Pure Wave Oscillator (Crossings), perf by Chicago Symph Orch, 83. *Teaching:* Prof music, Brandeis Univ, 62-70 & Wesleyan Univ, 70- *Awards:* Fulbright Scholar to Rome, 60-62; Nat Endowment Arts Fel, 76 & 81. *Bibliog:* Gordon Mumma (auth), Alvin Lucier's Music for Solo Performer, Source #2, 72; Thomas de Lio (auth), Music of Alvin Lucier, Interface, Vol 10, 81. *Mem:* Comp Forum. *Publ:* Ed, Source Mag #10, CPE, 72; contribr, Individuals: Post-Movement Art, E P Dutton, 76; Three Points of View, Musical Quart, Vol LXV, No 2; The Tools of My Trade, Sonus, Vol 1, No 1; auth, Chambers, Wesleyan Univ Press, 80. *Rep:* Performing Artservices Rm 347 325 Spring St New York NY 10013. *Mailing Add:* 7 Miles Ave Middletown CT 06457

LUCKMAN, PHYLLIS
COMPOSER, TEACHER-COACH
b New York, NY, Sept 3, 27. *Study:* Hunter Col, BA, 47; Calif State Univ, Hayward, with Fred Fox; Mill Col, with Darius Milhaud, MA, 73. *Works:* Severity (cello & piano), 76; Symphony for Massed Cellos (orch); Fantasia (two flutes); Five Puzzles (solo clarinet); Hart Crane/Proem (solo perc); Spirals (harpsichord); Songs from Underground (tape & string quartet). *Teaching:* Private cello, currently. *Mailing Add:* 668 Fairmont Ave Oakland CA 94611

LUDEWIG-VERDEHR, ELSA
CLARINET, EDUCATOR
b Charlottesville, Va, Apr 14, 36. *Study:* Oberlin Consv Music, BMus, 57, BMusEd, 59; Eastman Sch Music, MMus, 58, DMA, 64. *Rec Perf:* Elsa Ludewig-Verdehr (Tedesco, Carter & Frohne), Grenadilla, 78; Three Wind Quintets of J P Mueller, Crystal, 78; Reicha Wind Quintets, Musical Heritage, 79; Unaccompanied Solos for Clarinet, Vol IV (Bassett & Desportes), Mark Rec, 83. *Pos:* Second clarinet, Rochester Phil, 59-62; mem, Richards Wind Quintet, 62-; mem, Verdehr Trio, 72- *Teaching:* Instr clarinet, Ithaca Col, 59-62; asst prof clarinet, Mich State Univ, East Lansing, 62-68, assoc prof music, 69-77 & prof, 77- *Awards:* Distinguished Prof Award, Mich State Univ, 79. *Bibliog:* Mary Jungerman (auth), Elsa Ludewig-Verdehr, Clarinet Mag, Vol V, No 3. *Mem:* Int Clarinet Soc; Clarinetwork Int; Nat Asn Col Wind & Perc Instrm. *Publ:* Auth, Numerous articles in Clarinet Mag, Nat Asn Col Wind & Perc Instrm J & Instrumentalist, 64-83. *Mailing Add:* 1635 Roseland East Lansing MI 48822

LUDGIN, CHESTER HALL
BARITONE
b New York, NY, May 20, 25. *Study:* Lafayette Col; Am Theater Wing Prof Training Prog; vocal studies with William S Brady & Armen Boyajian. *Rec Perf:* The Tenor (Weisgall), Westminster, 58; The Ballad of Baby Doe (Moore), MGM, 60; The Crucible (Ward), CRI, 62. *Roles:* Lead bar roles with, San Francisco Opera Co, New York City Opera, Houston Opera, Seattle Opera, Canadian Opera & many others. *Pos:* Leading bar, Netherlands Opera & with many major opera co & symph orch in NAm. *Awards:* Chalmers Cup for Outstanding Perf, Central City Opera Asn, 66. *Rep:* Thea Dispeker Artists Rep 59 E 54 St New York NY 10022. *Mailing Add:* 205 West End Ave New York NY 10023

LUDWIG, JOHN MCKAY
ADMINISTRATOR
b New Orleans, Aug 14, 35. *Study:* Univ NC, AB, 57; Yale Univ, MFA, 63. *Pos:* Coordr perf arts, Walker Art Ctr, Minneapolis, 64-69; gen mgr, Minn Opera Co, 64-73; mem bd dir, Firehouse Theatre Inc, Minneapolis, 66-69, Minn Dance Theater & Sch, 71 & Opera Am, 71-76; consult, Nat Endowment Arts, 71-; gen dir, Wolf Trap Found, Vienna, Va, 73-75; artistic adminr, San Francisco Opera Asn, 75-77; exec dir, Nat Opera Inst, Washington, 77- *Mailing Add:* c/o Wolf Trap Found 1624 Trap Rd Vienna VA 22180

LUENING, OTTO
COMPOSER, MUSIC DIRECTOR
b Milwaukee, Wis, June 15, 1900. *Study:* State Acad Music, Munich, 15-17; Munic Consv Music, Zurich, with Volkmar Andreae, 17-20; Univ Zurich, 19-

20; studied with Philipp Jarnach & Ferruccio Busoni; hon degrees from several Am univ. *Works:* Evangeline (opera), 32; Fantasy in Space (tape), 52; Rhapsodic Variations for Tape & Orchestra (with Ussachevsky), 54; Gargoyles (violin & tape), 60; Synthesis (tape & orch), 62; Short Symphony (orch), rev 79; Fantasia for Piano Trio, 82. *Rec Perf:* For CRI. *Pos:* Cond, Rochester Am Opera Co, 25-28; music dir, Brander Matthews Theatre, Columbia, NY, 47-59; co-dir, Columbia-Princeton Electronic Music Ctr, 59-; co-founder & pres, Am Music Ctr, 39-59 & CRI, 68-70. *Teaching:* Coach & exec dir opera dept, Eastman Sch Music, 25-28; assoc prof, Univ Ariz, 32-34; chmn music dept, Bennington Col, 34-44, music dir, Sch Arts, 40-41; assoc prof & chmn music dept, Barnard Col, 44-47; prof, Columbia Univ, 49-68, music chmn, Sch Arts, 66-70, prof emer, 68- *Awards:* Guggenheim Fel, 30-32 & 74-75; Thorne Music Fund Found Award, 72; Creative Arts Award, Brandeis Univ, 81. *Mem:* Life mem, Nat Inst Arts & Lett (vpres, 53); co-founder, Am Music Ctr (chmn, 40-60); co-founder, Am Comp Alliance (pres, 45-51); League Comp (mem exec bd, 43); Int Soc Contemp Music (mem bd dir, 74-81). *Publ:* Coauth, The Development and Practice of Electronic Music, 75; auth, The Odyssey of an American Composer: Autobiography, 80. *Mailing Add:* 460 Riverside Dr New York NY 10027

LUKASHUK, VLADIMIR
VIOLIN, VIOLA
b Hamtramck, Mich, July 24, 19. *Study:* Berkshire Music Ctr, summer 40; Univ Mich, Ann Arbor, with Vassily Besekirsky, BM(violin), 42; Univ Southern Calif, with Sanford Schoenbach, MM(viola), 53. *Pos:* Viola, Hollywood Bowl Orch, summer 46-47, Los Angeles Phil, 46-47 & Universal Int Movie, 47-50; first violin, Cincinnati Symph Orch, 52-, mandolin, currently. *Teaching:* Head viola dept, instr viola, chamber music & prin viola, Transylvania Music Camp, summers 53-57; instr strings, Northern Ky Univ, 74- & privately, currently. *Bibliog:* Bill Straub (auth), Man of Music, Ky Post, 8/28/82; Loura Tesseneer (auth), Establishing a Musical Heritage, Communique, winter 82; Sherrie O'Rear (auth), Lukashuks—Performing and Teaching Classical Music, Kenton Co Recorder, 2/2/83. *Mailing Add:* 3882 Turkeyfoot Rd Erlanger KY 41018

LUKE, RAY E
CONDUCTOR, COMPOSER
b Ft Worth, Tex, May 30, 28. *Study:* Tex Christian Univ, BMus, 49, MMus, 50; Eastman Sch Music, PhD, 60. *Works:* Dialogues for Organ and Percussion; Prelude and March; Rondo; Sonics and Metrics for Concert Band. *Pos:* Assoc cond, Oklahoma City Symph Orch, 68-73, music dir & cond, 73-74. *Teaching:* Prof music, Oklahoma City Univ, currently. *Awards:* Gold Medal, Queen Elizabeth Comp Compt, Belgium, 70; ASCAP Award, 12 consecutive yrs. *Mem:* ASCAP; Am Music Ctr. *Mailing Add:* 6017 Glencove Pl Oklahoma City OK 73132

LUM, RICHARD S
CONDUCTOR, EDUCATOR
b Honolulu, Hawaii, Jan 17, 26. *Study:* Univ Hawaii, BMusEd, 51, 5th yr dipl, 52; Northwestern Univ, MMusEd, 53. *Pos:* First trumpeter, Honolulu Symph Orch, 53-62. *Teaching:* Band dir, McKinley High Sch, Honolulu, 53-60; dir bands, Univ Hawaii, Honolulu, 60- *Mem:* Am Bandmasters Asn (mem bd dir, 79-81); Col Band Dir Nat Asn (state chmn, 83); Nat Band Asn (Hawaii state chmn, 83); Hawaii Music Educr Asn (pres, 59); Oahu Band Dir Asn (pres, 66). *Mailing Add:* 3375 Halelani Dr Honolulu HI 96822

LUND, FLOICE RHODES
MUSIC DIRECTOR, WRITER
b Atlanta, Ga, July 1, 38. *Study:* Univ Tenn, BMus, 58; Northwestern Univ, MMus, 61; Kodaly Musical Training Inst, 75. *Works:* I'm Going Home On A Cloud, 78 & Come, All You Children, Come, 78, Kodaly Ctr Am; The Lord's Prayer, Lundmark Publ, 81. *Pos:* Founder & dir, Broadmoor Chamber Singers, Natick, Mass, 79-83 & Support Serv, Natick, 80-83; ed, KCA Choral Series, Kodaly Ctr Am, West Newton, Mass, 78- *Teaching:* Mem adj fac musical materials & recorder, Kodaly Ctr Am, 77- *Mem:* Orgn Am Kodaly Educr (vpres, 78); Int Kodaly Soc; Am Choral Dir Asn; Music Educr Nat Conf; Am Orff Schulwerk Asn. *Interests:* Folk song—locating authentic folk material for music teachers to use. *Publ:* Ed, 185 Unison Pentatonic Exercises, 78, You Can Sing, Too!, 79 & auth, Research and Retrieval, 81, Kodaly Ctr Am; ed, 50 Easy Two-Part Exercises, European Am, 77; auth, What Is Kodaly Music Education?, Lundmark Publ, 81. *Mailing Add:* 10110 N Coleman Rd Roswell GA 30075

LUNDBERG, HARRIET A
PIANO, EDUCATOR
b Brooklyn, NY, Feb 28, 44. *Study:* Ind Univ, BME; Boston Consv Music, studied comp & theory with Avram David & Hugo Norden, MM; studied piano with Bronja Foster, Daniel Fletcher, Vincenzo Vitale & Maria Bono. *Works:* Woodwind Quintet, 72; Journals (five songs for high voice), 77; Music for a Threesome (woodwind trio); Enigmas (piano); Monologues (three pieces for harp); String Suite; White in the Moon (three songs for high voice). *Pos:* Co-founder, North Shore Piano Studios, 77. *Teaching:* Mem fac piano, Boston Consv Music, 70- *Awards:* Second Place, Delta Omicron Compt. *Mailing Add:* 103-A Summit Ave Winthrop MA 02152

LUNDBORG, (CHARLES) ERIK
COMPOSER, PIANO
b Helena, Mont, Jan 31, 48. *Study:* Univ Mont; New England Consv, BM, 70; Columbia Univ, MA, 74. *Works:* Music Forever No 2, NJ Perc Ens, 73; Passacaglia, Light Fantastic Players, 74; Butte Chord, Group for Contemp Music, 75-76; Combone, Speculum Musicae, 75-78; Soundsoup, Parnassus,

76, 77 & 80; Piano Conct, Am Comp Orch, 80; Ghost Sonatine, New Music Consort, 83. *Pos:* Cond & pianist, Comp Ens, 72-78. *Teaching:* Adj instr music, Baruch Col, City Univ New York, 78- & Univ Pittsburgh, 83- *Awards:* Nat Endowment Arts Grant, 75, 81 & 83; Guggenheim Fel, 76. *Bibliog:* Gunther Schuller (auth), Recent American Music, Austrian Music Jour, 78. *Mem:* Int Soc Contemp Music (mem bd, 75-78); BMI; Am Comp Alliance (mem bd, 80-82). *Mailing Add:* 403 W 115th St New York NY 10025

LUNDE, IVAR
CONDUCTOR, COMPOSER
b Tønsberg, Norway, Jan 15, 44. *Study:* Tønsberg Høyere Almenskole, AA, 64; Consv Music, Oslo, studied oboe with KeesLahnstein; Mozarteum, Salzburg, Austria, studied oboe with Andre Lardrot, MM, 65. *Works:* Une Petite Suite Pour Cinq, Shawnee Press Inc, 65; Nuances (clarinet choir), Kendor Music Inc, 75; Concerto for Harpsichord & Woodwind Quartet, Southern Music Co; Symphony No 1, 77 & Symphony No 2, 80, Norwegian Music Info Ctr; Capricious Suite (band), Shawnee Press, 80; Akvareller (piano), Norsk Musikforlag, Oslo, 80. *Pos:* Prin oboist, Norwegian Opera, 64-66; oboist, Nat Gallery Orch, Washington DC, 66-68; music dir & cond, Chippewa Valley Symph, Eau Claire, Wis, 78- & Chippewa Valley Youth Symph, 81- *Teaching:* Instr oboe & theory, Univ Md, College Park, 66-68; asst prof oboe & theory, Univ Wis, Eau Claire, 68- *Awards:* First Prize, Kendor Music & Univ Md, 76, Oslo Conct Hall, 78 & Int Double Reed Soc, 80. *Mem:* Soc Norwegian Comp; Am Fedn Musicians; Col Music Soc; Nat Asn Wind & Perc Instr; Southeastern Hist Keyboard Soc. *Publ:* Auth, The Oboe Reed: Construction and Adjustment, Wis Sch Musician, 69; Solving the Double Reed Dilemma, Prog Publ, 78; Corrections to the Paumgartner Edition of the Oboe Concerto in C Major by W A Mozart, 78 & How to Prevent Your Oboe from Cracking (Up!), 79, Nat Asn Wind & Perc Instr J. *Mailing Add:* 3432 Cummings Eau Claire WI 54701

LUNDE, NANETTE GOMORY
HARPSICHORD, EDUCATOR
b Darby, Pa, Feb 3, 43. *Study:* Oberlin Consv Music, BMus, 65; Sch Music, Northwestern Univ, MMus, 66; Akad Mozarteum, Salzburg, Austria, two dipl, 65. *Teaching:* Asst prof harpsichord, piano & baroque perf pract, Univ Wis, Eau Claire, 69- *Mem:* Southeastern Hist Keyboard Soc; Col Music Soc; Am Fedn Musicians. *Publ:* Auth, Harpsichord of Note, Harpsichord, 71-72; Music of the Baroque in Norway, Clavier, 78; Partia in G Minor (Transcription of Bach d minor Partia), Musica Sacra et Profana, 78; I G Wernicke: The Contrapuntist of Scandinavia, Early Keyboard J, 82. *Mailing Add:* 3432 Cummings St Eau Claire WI 54701

LURIE, BERNARD
VIOLIN, EDUCATOR
Study: Hartt Sch Music, BMus, MMus; Settlement Music Sch; Berkshire Music Ctr; studied with Samuel Feldman, Lillian Cinberg, Irwin Eisenberg, Bela Urban & Raphael Bronstein; studied chamber music with Nathan Gottschalk, William Kroll & Ruth Poselt. *Pos:* Concertmaster, Hartford Fest Orch, Hartford Symph & Conn Opera Orch; cond, Gtr Hartford Youth Orch; dir, Inter-Provincial Music Camp, Ont. *Teaching:* Vis prof & founder orch, Univ Mass, Amherst, formerly; assoc prof violin & ens, Hartt Sch Music, 55- *Mailing Add:* Hartt Sch Music Univ Hartford West Hartford CT 06117

LURIE, MITCHELL
CLARINET, EDUCATOR
Study: Curtis Inst, dipl. *Pos:* Prin clarinet, Pittsburgh & Chicago Symph Orchs, formerly; performer, Libr Cong, Casals Fests & others. *Teaching:* Fac mem, Music Acad West, currently; prof clarinet & woodwind chamber music, Univ Southern Calif, currently; instr master classes woodwind chamber music, Jerusalem Music Centre. *Mailing Add:* Sch Music 840 W 34th St Univ Southern Calif Los Angeles CA 90089

LUSK, BEN TERRY
COACH
b Chicago, Ill, Dec 30, 38. *Study:* Northwestern Univ, BMEd, 60, MM(piano), 62. *Pos:* Vocal coach, Santa Fe Opera, 64-73, chorus master, 74-78; coach, San Francisco Opera, 69-83. *Teaching:* Opera coach & chorus master, Juilliard Sch, 70-72. *Mailing Add:* 50 Elsie St San Francisco CA 94110

LUSMANN, STEPHEN (ARTHUR)
BARITONE
b Cherokee, Iowa, July 15, 54. *Study:* State Univ NY, Fredonia, BMusEd, 77; Col Consv Music, Univ Cincinnati, MMus, 80, artist dipl, 82; study with Andrew White & Italo Tajo. *Roles:* Marullo, Cincinnati Opera & Pittsburgh Opera, 82; Marcello in La Boheme, 82, Marco in Gianni Schicchi, 82, The King in Die Kluge, 82, Dr Falke, 83, Belcore in Elixir of Love, 83 & Guglielmo in Cosi fan tutte, 83, Cincinnati Opera. *Mailing Add:* 137 Warner St #11 Cincinnati OH 45219

LUSTIG, LEILA SARAH
COMPOSER, MUSIC BROADCASTER
b Louisville, Ky, Apr 30, 44. *Study:* Univ Calif, Los Angeles, studied comp & theory with Roy Harris, John Vincent & Roy Travis, BA, 66, MA, 68; Univ Wis, Madison, with Bert Levy & Robert Crane, PhD, 72. *Works:* Six Significant Landscapes, John Aielli, 79 & Michael Deluca, 82; Ossipee: November, comp & Elda Tate, 80; Opposites, Natoma Noble & Robert Culbertson, 80; Vocalissimus, Camenae String Quartet & Gary Burgess, 83; Buffalo Prints, Norwood Brass Quintet, 83. *Pos:* Sr prod, cult affairs, KUT-FM, Austin, 75-79; prod & dir music, WNMU-FM, Marquette, Mich, 79-80; prog dir, WQED-FM, Pittsburgh, 80-81; prod, WNED-FM, Buffalo, 80- *Awards:* Meet the Comp Award, 83. *Mem:* BMI. *Mailing Add:* 311 Wellington Rd Buffalo NY 14216

LUTTRELL, NANCY KAY
VIOLIN, EDUCATOR
b Kansas City, Kans, Nov 29, 46. *Study:* Wichita State Univ, BM, 68, studied with Jame Ceasar, MM, 73; Aspen Music Sch, with Eudice Shaperio, 68 & 69; Consv Music, Univ Mo, Kansas City, with Tiberius Klausner, 68 & 70. *Pos:* Concertmaster, Vienna Symposium Orch, summer 76; assoc concertmaster, Wichita Symph, 79- *Teaching:* Instr violin, Bethel Col, 74-77 & Wichita State Univ, 80- *Awards:* Naftzger Young Artist, 67; Musicanza Award, Mu Phi Epsilon, 67. *Mem:* Kans Music Teachers Asn; Am String Teachers Asn. *Mailing Add:* 1832 Faulders Lane Wichita KS 67218

LUTYENS, SALLY SPEARE
COMPOSER, EDUCATOR
b Syracuse, NY. *Study:* Univ Southern Calif, 47; Bennington Col, 49; piano studies with Claude Frank. *Works:* The Minister's Black Veil, 76 & The Burning Babe, 79, Chorus Pro Musica; The Light Princess, Newport Opera Fest, 79; From the Poems of Alfred Starr Hamilton, Soc New Music, 82; Missa Brevis, Chorus Pro Musica, 82. *Teaching:* Comp & piano, Cambridge Sch, 67-71, head dept music, 71-74; head dept music, Col Atlantic, 77-80. *Mailing Add:* 60 John St Newport RI 02840

LUVISI, LEE
PIANO, TEACHER
b Louisville, Ky, Dec 12, 37. *Study:* Curtis Inst Music, with Rudolf Serkin & Mieczyslaw Horszowski, dipl, 57. *Rec Perf:* Polonaise, Op 89, Sonata, Op 101 & Sonata, Op 109 (Beethoven), Six Moments Musicaux (Schubert) & Carnaval (Schumann), Rivergate Rec; Kammermusik No 2 (Hindemith), Louisville Orch First Ed. *Pos:* Artist-mem, Chamber Music Soc Lincoln Ctr, 83. *Teaching:* Fac piano, Curtis Inst, 57-62; artist-in-res & head piano dept, Univ Louisville Sch Music, 63-; fac & artist, Aspen Music Fest, 72- *Rep:* Herbert Barrett Mgt 1860 Broadway New York NY 10023. *Mailing Add:* 1703 Trevillian Way Louisville KY 40205

LUXNER, MICHAEL DAVID
CONDUCTOR & MUSIC DIRECTOR, EDUCATOR
b Brooklyn, NY, Oct 13, 50. *Study:* Eastman Sch Music, BM, 72, MA, 72, PhD, 78; studied with Charles Bruck, 72-75. *Pos:* Asst cond, Pierre Monteux Fest, 77-81, Colo Phil Orch, 82 & Savannah Symph Orch, 82-; music dir, Northern Ohio Youth Orch, 80-82. *Teaching:* Asst prof theory & lit, Consv Music, Oberlin Col, 76-82. *Mailing Add:* Savannah Symph Orch PO Box 9505 Savannah GA 31412

LYALL, MAX DAIL
EDUCATOR, PIANO
b Okla, Feb 14, 39. *Study:* Okla Baptist Univ, BMus, 61; Univ Okla, MMus, 63; Peabody Consv Music, studied piano with Leon Fleisher, DMA, 80. *Works:* Music from Way Back When, Broadman Press, 74; A Symphony of Song, Triune Music Inc, 78; Klassics for Kids, Broadman Press, 82. *Rec Perf:* Authentic Original (Max Lyall), Triangle Rec, 77; Max, Rhythm, and Song, JP Prod, 80; Heavenly Concert, Southern Baptist Conv Calif, 81. *Teaching:* Asst prof piano & music, Belmont Col, 66-74; assoc prof, Golden Gate Baptist Theol Sem, 74- *Mem:* ASCAP; Southern Baptist Church Music Conf; Am Asn Univ Prof. *Mailing Add:* Dept Music Golden Gate Baptist Theol Sem Mill Valley CA 94941

LYNCH, WILLIAM FRANK
OBOE
b Biloxi, Miss, Nov 14, 50. *Study:* Univ Ala, BMus, 73; Sch Music, Yale Univ, with Robert Bloom & Ronald Roseman, MMus, 75. *Pos:* Oboist, Orch Santa Fe, 75-76 & Santa Fe Opera Asn, summer 76; Prin oboist, Jackson Symph Orch, 78- *Teaching:* Artist in res, St John's Col, NMex, 75-76; instr oboe, Metropolitan Sch Arts, 77-78. *Awards:* Harriet Hale Woolley Scholar, 76. *Mailing Add:* 944 Harding St E Jackson MS 39202

LYNE, GREGORY KENT
CONDUCTOR & MUSIC DIRECTOR, EDUCATOR
b Wichita, Kans, Sept 22, 46. *Study:* Washburn Univ Topeka, BME, 68; Kans State Univ, MS(comp), 71; Univ Northern Colo, DA(cond), 76. *Teaching:* Asst prof, Univ Wash, 74-76 & Eastern NMex Univ, 76-80; assoc prof, DePaul Univ, 80-, dir choral activ & coordr voice prog, currently. *Mem:* Am Choral Dir Asn; Col Music Soc; Music Educr Nat Conf. *Publ:* Auth, Effective Bodily Communication: A Key to Expressive Conducting, Choral J, 79. *Mailing Add:* Dir Choral Activ DePaul Univ 804 W Belden Ave Chicago IL 60614

LYNN, GEORGE
COMPOSER, EDUCATOR
b Edwardsville, Pa, Oct 5, 15. *Study:* Westminster Choir Col, studied comp with Roy Harris, organ with Carl Weinrich & cond with J F Williamson & Paul Boepple, BMus, 38; Princeton Univ, MFA, 47, studied comp with Randall Thompson; Harding Univ, LLD, 59. *Works:* Two operas; Gettysburg Address (bar, chorus & orch); Greek Folksong Rhapsody (contralto, chorus & orch); three string quartets; Organ Trio Sonata; three sacred symphonies (a cappella chorus); Song of Gratitude (chorus & orch); and many songs & piano & organ works. *Teaching:* Mem fac, Westminster Choir Col, 47-50 & 63-69; comp in res, Univ NMex, 70; adj prof choral groups, voice & church music, Loretto Heights, 71-; adj prof, Colo Sch Mines, 71-80; teacher choral wkshps throughout US. *Awards:* Martha Baird Rockefeller Award; Loretto Heights Col Fac Res Grant; ASCAP Awards, 60- *Mailing Add:* 314 Lake Ave Colorado Springs CO 80906

M

MA, YO-YO
CELLO, EDUCATOR
b Paris, France, 55. *Study:* Juilliard Sch, studied cello with Leonard Rose; Harvard Univ, BA; studied cello with Janos Scholz. *Rec Perf:* Beethoven Triple Concerto, Deutsche Grammophon; Cello Concerto (Saint-Saens), Cello Concerto (Lalo), Two Concertos (Haydn) & others on Deutsche Grammophon & CBS Masterworks. *Pos:* Soloist & performer with major orchs worldwide. *Teaching:* Mem fac cello, Mannes Col Music, 81-; artist in res, Harvard Univ. *Awards:* Avery Fisher Prize, 78. *Mailing Add:* c/o ICM Artists 40 W 57th St New York NY 10019

MAAG, JACQUELINE
EDUCATOR
b Omaha, Nebr, Feb 27, 22. *Study:* Northwestern Univ, BMus, 45, MMus, 48. *Teaching:* Dir music, Sunset Hill Sch, Kansas City, Mo, 45-47; from instr to assoc prof voice & music hist, Albion Col, 48-63, prof music, 63-, chmn div fine & appl arts, 64-67. *Mem:* Medieval Acad Am; Nat Asn Teachers Singing; Am Musicol Soc; Music Educr Nat Conf; Music Teachers Nat Asn. *Interests:* Musicology; medieval and Renaissance music; vocal pedagogy; contemporary Swiss vocal literature. *Mailing Add:* Dept Music Albion Col Albion MI 49224

MAAS, MARTHA C
EDUCATOR, WRITER
b Louisville, Ky, Aug 6, 34. *Study:* DePauw Univ, BMus, 56; Univ Mich, MMus, 59; Yale Univ, PhD(music hist), 68. *Teaching:* Asst prof music hist & lit, hist musicol & collegium, Ohio State Univ, 68-74, assoc prof, 74- *Mem:* Am Musicol Soc; Am Musical Instrm Soc; Viola da Gamba Soc Am. *Interests:* History of musical instruments; history of performance practices; women composers. *Publ:* Ed, English Pastime Music, 1630-1660: An Anthology of Keyboard Pieces, Yale Collegium Musicum, ser II, Vol 4, A-R Ed Inc, 74; auth, On the Shape of the Ancient Greek Lyre, Galpin Soc J, 74; The Phorminx in Classical Greece, J Am Musical Instrm Soc, 76. *Mailing Add:* Sch Music Ohio State Univ Columbus OH 43210

MAAZEL, LORIN
CONDUCTOR & MUSIC DIRECTOR
b Paris, France, Mar 6, 30; US citizen. *Study:* Studied in Italy, 51; Berkshire Music Ctr, summers 51 & 52; cond & violin with Vladimir Bakaleinikoff; Univ Pittsburgh, Hon MusD, 68; Beaver Col, HHD, 73. *Rec Perf:* With Cleveland Orch & Vienna Phil, London Rec, Deutsche Grammophon & with Berliner Philharmonie, Angel Rec, New Philharmonia & CBS. *Pos:* Cond, fest in Edinburgh, Scotland, Bayreuth, Germany & Salzburg, Austria, 60-70, Metropolitan Opera, 62, world tours in Far East, Asia, Europe, Latin Am & USSR, 65-71, Vienna Opera, 66 & La Scala, Milan, 66 & 67; music dir, Berlin Radio Symph Orch & West Berlin Opera, 65-71 & Vienna State Opera, 82; assoc prin cond, Philharmonia Orch London, 70-72, prin guest cond, 76-; music dir, Cleveland Orch, 72-, cond emer, 82-; prin guest cond, French Nat Opera, 77- *Mailing Add:* Cleveland Orch Severance Hall Cleveland OH 14106

MABREY, CHARLOTTE NEWTON
EDUCATOR, PERCUSSION
b Tuscaloosa, Ala, May 9, 52. *Study:* La State Univ; Univ Ill, BM, 75, MM, 77. *Pos:* Prin perc, Jacksonville Symph, 77- *Teaching:* Instr perc, Fla Jr Col, 78-80; asst prof music, Univ NFla, 81- *Mem:* Percussive Arts Soc. *Mailing Add:* Jacksonville Symph Orch Plaza 2 Ste 9009 580 W 8 St Jacksonville FL 32209

MABRY, RAYMOND EDWARD
LIBRARIAN, WRITER
b Little River, Kans, Jan 23, 38. *Study:* Curtis Inst Music, studied organ with Alexander McCurdy, BM, 62; Ind Univ, studied organ with Clyde Holloway, MM, 69, MLS, 71. *Pos:* Organist & choirmaster, Second Presby Church, Richmond, Va, 62-67; asst head, Fine Arts Dept, Atlanta Pub Libr, 71-73; librn, Art & Music Dept, Richmond Pub Libr, Va, 75- *Bibliog:* John Schneider, article in Musical America, 4-20. *Publ:* Auth, A Chronological Survey of Organ Compositions from the 14th Century to J S Bach, Am Guild Organists Quart, 7/65; program notes for phonograph recording, The Woolsey Hall Organ at Yale University, Lyrichord, 70; When All Else Fails, Read the Instructions, 5/72, transl, Norbert Dufourcq's The Milieu, Work and Art of Cesar Frank, 5/72 & Hans Klotz's Organ Works, 8/72, Diapason. *Mailing Add:* Art & Music Dept Richmond Pub Libr 101 E Franklin St Richmond VA 23219

MABRY, SHARON CODY
EDUCATOR, MEZZO-SOPRANO
b Newport, Tenn, July 16, 45. *Study:* Fla State Univ, BME, 67; George Peabody Col Teachers, MME, 70, DMA, 77. *Rec Perf:* New Music for Mezzo, Owl Rec, 83. *Roles:* Pierrot Lunaire, Nashville Chamber Players, 76; Witch in Hansel and Gretel, Univ Tenn Opera, Chattanooga, 82; Kate Pinkerton in Madama Butterfly, Nashville Symph, 82; Elegy (Kenton Coe), Johnson City Symph & Kingsport Symph, 82; Ancient Voices of Children, Nashville Inst Arts, 83. *Teaching:* Instr music, Austin Peay State Univ, 70-74, asst prof, 74-77, assoc prof, 77-80, prof, 80- *Awards:* Fel, Nat Endowment Arts, 68; Richard Hawkins Award, Austin Peay State Univ, 79. *Mem:* Nat Asn Teachers Singing (gov mid-south region, 81-83). *Interests:* Music by women composers. *Publ:* Auth, Vocal Problems in the Performance of Pierrot Lunaire, Nat Asn Teachers Singing Bulletin, 80; New Music: Who Cares if You Like It?, Internos, Nat Asn Teachers Singing, 83. *Mailing Add:* 1988 Norwood Trail Clarksville TN 37040

MCANANEY, HAROLD
COMPOSER

b Dublin, Ireland, Oct 28, 48. *Study:* Sch Museum of Fine Arts; studied with Tibor Pusztai, Oliver Knussen & Lawrence Scripp. *Works:* Braille Music, 70; Card Piece, 71; Sentientevents, 73; Myxomycete, comn by Carpenter Ctr for Visual Arts, Harvard Univ, 73. *Pos:* Comp in res, Movement Lab, Boston Ctr for Arts, 70-73; founder, Annex Players, 72. *Awards:* Ford Found Fel; Louis Comfort Tiffany Fel; Boston Museum Fine Arts Fel. *Mailing Add:* PO Box 605 Stinson Beach CA 94970

MCANDREW, JOSEPHINE K
VIOLIN, TEACHER

b Canton, Ohio. *Study:* Cleveland Inst Music; Juilliard Grad Sch, dipl, 46. *Pos:* Violinist, Pocono Manor Quartet, summers 42-43; conct violinist, USO Camp Shows, 43-45; concertmaster, Amarillo Symph, 50-67; first violinist, Chicago Little Symph, 65-68, Dallas Symph, 67-68, Chicago Chamber Orch, 69-70, Chicago Lyr Opera Orch, 69-70, Grant Park Symph, Chicago, 69-71 & Houston Symph, 71- *Teaching:* Private teacher violin, 50-; artist & teacher violin, Amarillo Col, 50-67 & WTex State Col, 50-56; mem fac, Nat Music Camp, Interlochen, Mich, 62-67. *Awards:* Joseph Fuchs Scholar; Louis Persuirer Scholar; Louis Persuirer Fel. *Mailing Add:* c/o Houston Symph Orch 615 Louisiana Houston TX 77002

MCBAINE, ARIEL BYBEE See Bybee, Ariel

MCBETH, WILLIAM FRANCIS
COMPOSER, CONDUCTOR

b Ropesville, Tex, Mar 9, 33. *Study:* Hardin-Simmons Univ, BM, 54, DMus, 73; Univ Tex, MMus, 57; Eastman Sch Music, studied with Howard Hanson & Bernard Rogers, 59-64. *Works:* Masque, 68, Divergents, 69, Seventh Seal, 72, To Be Fed by Ravens, 75, Capriccio Concertant, 76, Kaddish, 77 & Feast of Trumpets, 82, Southern Music Co. *Rec Perf:* McBeth Conducts McBeth (Vol I), 72 & McBeth Conducts McBeth (Vol II), 75, Golden Crest; Seventh Seal, 78 & Caccia, 79, CBS Sony; Four Frescos, Crystal Rec, 80. *Pos:* Cond & musical dir, Ark Symph Orch, 69-73. *Teaching:* Res comp & prof music, Ouachita Univ, 57- *Awards:* Howard Hanson Prize, Eastman Sch Music, 63; Standard Award, ASCAP, 65-; Comp Laureate, State Ark, 75. *Bibliog:* Dana Davis (auth), Musical Dynamo, Instrumentalist, 2/78; Martha Gwin (auth), Music Man, Arkansan, 12/79; Mark Childress (auth), Many Lives of Francis McBeth, Southern Living, 12/80. *Mem:* Am Bandmasters Asn (mem bd dir, 80-82); ASCAP; Phi Mu Alpha. *Publ:* Auth, Effective Performance of Band Music, Southern Music Co, 72, Japanese ed, Piper Group, 75; New Theories of Theory, Southern Music Co, 79. *Mailing Add:* Dept Music Ouachita Univ Arkadelphia AR 71923

MACBRIDE, DAVID HUSTON
COMPOSER

b Oakland, Calif, Oct 3, 51. *Study:* Hartt Col Music, BM, 73; Columbia Univ, MA, 76, DMA, 80. *Works:* Gageego, 81, My Last Duchess (dance), 82, Elegies (harp & orch), 82, The Pond in a Bowl, 83, Twin, 83 & Parallax for Electric Guitar & Orchestra, 83, Am Comp Alliance. *Mem:* BMI; Am Comp Alliance; Col Music Soc; Comp Forum. *Mailing Add:* 509 W 110th St New York NY 10025

MCBRIDE, ROBERT GUYN
COMPOSER, EDUCATOR

b Tucson, Ariz, Feb 20, 11. *Study:* Univ Ariz, MusB, 33, MusM, 35. *Works:* Symphonic Melody, 68; Folk Song Fantasy, 70; 1776 Overture, 75; Improvisation, 76; Brooms of Mexico (ballet), 77; Sportmusic, 77; numerous works for solo instrm & piano accmp, bands & instrm groups. *Pos:* Oboist, Tucson Symph Orch, formerly; solo oboist, Bennington Col, Pioneer Valley, Greenfield, Mass, Vt Symph, Boston Pops Orch & Gordon String Quartet, formerly; clarinetist, League Comp Wind Quintet, 41. *Teaching:* Theory & wind instrm, Bennington Co, 35-46; assoc prof music, Univ Ariz, 57-60, prof, 60- *Awards:* Guggenheim Fel, 37; Award, Am Acad Arts & Lett, 42; Comp Press Award, 43. *Mem:* Am Comp Alliance. *Mailing Add:* 3236 E Waverly St Tucson AZ 85716

MCCABE, ROBIN L
PIANO

b Puyallup, Wash. *Study:* Univ Wash, with Bela Siki, BMus, 71; Juilliard Sch Music, with Ilona Kabos & Rudolf Firkusnj, MMus, 73, DMA, 76. *Rec Perf:* Robin McCabe: Stravinsky & Mussorgsky, Vanguard Rec, 78; Robin McCabe Plays Liszt & Robin McCabe Plays Bartok, 81 & French Flute and Piano Music, 81, Grammafön BIS. *Teaching:* Victoria Int Fest, summers, 76-; fac mem piano, Juilliard Sch Music, 77-; teacher master classes, Europe & the Orient, 81. *Awards:* Conct Artist's Guild Prize, Int Conct Artist's Guild, 75; grant, Martha Baird Rockefeller Fund Music, 78. *Bibliog:* Helen Drees Ruttencutter (auth), Pianist's Progress, New Yorker Mag, 77 & Harper & Row, 79. *Mem:* Mu Phi Epsilon; Liszt Soc. *Publ:* Auth, Far East Tour: A Musical Feast, NW Arts Mag, 82; Confessions of a Pianophile, 82 & Pianist's Palate, 83, Piano Quart. *Rep:* Herbert Barrett Concert Mgt 1860 Broadway New York NY 10023. *Mailing Add:* 160 West 73rd St New York NY 10023

MCCAFFREY, PATRICEA (PATRICIA ANNE MCCAFFREY)
MEZZO-SOPRANO

b Chicago, Ill, Aug 26, 48. *Study:* NC Sch Arts, 67; Univ Miami, BMus, 74; Zurich Int Opera Studio, 76-77. *Roles:* Carmen in Carmen, 77, Brangane in Tristan und Isolde, 78, Eboli in Don Carlos, 78 & Octavian in Der Rosenkavalier, 78-79, Opernhaus Kiel, Germany; Jane Seymour, New York City Opera, 81; Dorabella in Cosi fan tutte, St Louis Opera Co, 82; Charlotte

in Werther, Miami Opera Co, 82. *Awards:* Grants, Bagby Found, 76, Opernstudio of Zürich, 76, Santa Fe Opera, 76, James McCracken. *Mem:* Am Guild Musical Artists Equity; Actors Equity; Am Fedn TV & Radio Artists. *Mailing Add:* c/o Columbia Artists Mgt 165 W 57 St New York NY 10019

MCCANN, WILLIAM JOHN
CONDUCTOR, FRENCH HORN

b Joliet, Ill, Apr 20, 41. *Study:* Univ Mich, studied with Louis Stout, BMusEduc, 63, MMus(perf), 65; Cath Univ Am, studied with Paul Ingraham, DMA, 74. *Rec Perf:* Three albums, Symphonic Band, State Univ NY, New Paltz, 70-73. *Pos:* Recitalist, 65-; horn soloist, Wis, 68, Univ Del, 72 & Cath Univ Am Orch, 73; horn soloist, Hudson Valley Phil Orch, NY, 69, 78 & 80, prin horn, 70-, asst to cond, 80-; cond, Hudson Valley Phil Wind Symph, 77- & Hudson Valley Youth Orch, 81-; prin horn, Albany Symph Orch, 82-83; guest cond high sch bands in Mass, Utah, Mich, NJ, Ohio, Wis & NY & co music festivals in Ulster, Suffolk, Greene, Sullivan, Broome & Orange Co, formerly. *Teaching:* Instr bands & horn, Kent State Univ, 65-67; asst prof, Univ Wis, Milwaukee, 67-68; assoc prof, State Univ NY, New Paltz, 68-; lectr horn, Vassar Col, 74- *Mem:* Col Band Dirs Nat Asn; Int Horn Soc; Nat Asn Col Wind & Perc Instr; Phi Kappa Lambda. *Publ:* Auth, Articulation of the Soprano Brass, Nat Asn Col Wind & Perc Instr J, 70 & Mo Sch Music Mag, 72; Trumpet & Horn: Correcting Problems Early, Sch Musician, 73; 12 articles in Joliet Herald News & four articles in Sch Musician. *Mailing Add:* RD 1 Box 211 Rosendale NY 12472

MCCARTHY, KEVIN JOSEPH
PIANO, LECTURER

b Philadelphia, Pa, Sept 4, 52. *Study:* Philadelphia Musical Acad, artists dipl, 74; Swarthmore Col, 74-76; Juilliard Sch, BM, 79, MM, 81; Moscow Consv, dipl, 83. *Teaching:* Prof music & piano perf, Univ Pa, 72-76; chmn piano dept, Sch Music, Swarthmore Col, 76-78; artist in res piano, Whitby Sch, 78-82 & Brunswick Sch, 78-82. *Rep:* James P Colias Field Point Park Greenwich CT 06830. *Mailing Add:* 144 Mason St Greenwich CT 06830

MCCARTHY, PETER JOSEPH
MUSIC DIRECTOR, EDUCATOR

b Albany, NY, Feb 24, 38. *Study:* Crane Sch Music, State Univ NY, Potsdam, BS, 63; Sch Music, Cath Univ Am, PhD(musicol), 72. *Pos:* Choral dir, Fordham Univ, 67-68; music dir, Del Choral Soc, 72-; founder & music dir, Alumni Choir Inc, Newark, Del, 73-81, Salesianum Alumni Theater & Community Chorus, 82-; music dir, Salesianum Alumni Theater & Community Chorus, 82- *Teaching:* Chairperson music & choral, Col New Rochelle, 66-68 & Trinity Col, 68-72; assoc prof, Univ Del, 72- *Mem:* Am Choral Dir Asn (pres, Washington, DC, 68-72 & Del, 72-79 & 81-83); Am Choral Found; Am Musicol Soc; Music Educr Nat Conf; Am Symph Orch League. *Mailing Add:* 15 Lovett Ave Newark DE 19711

MCCARTY, FRANK LEE
COMPOSER, EDUCATOR

b Pomona, Calif, Nov 10, 41. *Study:* San Diego State Univ, studied comp with David Ward-Steinman, AB, 64; Univ Southern Calif, studied comp with Ingolf Dahl & David Raksin, MM, 66; Univ Calif San Diego, studied comp with Robert Erickson & Pauline Oliveros, PhD, 75. *Works:* A Song for Gar (children's opera), comn by San Diego Opera, 70; Introduction to Percussion, Orch Venezuela, 72; Scratch, New York Comp Forum, 74; Exitus for Band, Joseph Boonin, 75; Soundpieces from Scratch, New England Consv Contemp Ens, 78; Variation Duos, Tokyo, Japan, 81; Takeoff (orch), French Nat Orch & Radio, 81. *Pos:* Perc, San Diego Symph, 61-71; timpanist & prin perc, Orange County Symph, 67-70. *Teaching:* From instr to asst prof music, Calif State Univ, Fullerton, 66-71; asst prof, Univ Pittsburgh, 71-76; assoc prof & head comp, Sch Music, Univ NC, Greensboro, 76- *Awards:* Comp Cont Winner, Nat Fedn Music Clubs, 63, 65 & 66 & BMI, 66; grant, Pa Arts Coun, 75. *Mem:* Percussive Arts Soc (notation comt chair, 75-80); BMI; Am Soc Univ Comp; Sonneck Soc. *Interests:* Percussion notation; electronic music; avant garde. *Publ:* Auth, Entropy as Value-Theory in the Arts, J Aesthetics, 73; Woodwinds: Extensions of Conventions, Instrumentalist, 74; Electronic Music Systems, Perspectives New Music, 75; Symbols for Percussion Notation, Perc, 80; Am Composers' Theatre, Theatre Southwest, 82. *Mailing Add:* 1347 New Garden Rd Greensboro NC 27410

MCCARTY, PATRICK
COMPOSER, EDUCATOR

b Zanesville, Ohio, Jan 23, 28. *Study:* WVa Univ, with A Oscar Hoagland & Weldon Hart; Eastman Sch Music, with Bernard Rogers, Alan Hovhaness & Howard Hanson, PhD. *Works:* At a Solemn Music (sop & orch); Ballata (band); Benedictus (chorus with winds); & other works for orch, band & chamber groups. *Teaching:* Fac mem, ECarolina Col, 54-56 & Newark State Col, 57-60; prof & assoc dean, Loyola Univ, 61- *Mailing Add:* 1043 Anthony New Orleans LA 70123

MCCATHREN, DON (DONALD E)
CONDUCTOR & MUSIC DIRECTOR, EDUCATOR

b Gary, Ind, July 6, 24. *Study:* Ind State Univ, BSMusEd, 47; Chicago Musical Col, Roosevelt Univ, MM, 49; Ind Univ, 50; Huron Col, Hon DMus, 71. *Rec Perf:* Duquesne University Symphony Band, 60-70, American Youth Symphony Recording, 65-75 & Contest Soloist for the Clarinet Family, 70, Mark Educ Rec. *Pos:* Dir educ serv, G Leblanc Corp, Kenosha, Wis, 53-58; pres, Am Youth Symph, Band & Chorus, 64- *Teaching:* Instr woodwind, Chicago Musical Col, 48-50; instr clarinet, Ind Univ, Bloomington, 50-51; prof music, Duquesne Univ, 58- *Awards:* Contribution to Music Award, Sch Musician. *Bibliog:* They are Making America Musical, Sch Musician, 71.

Mem: Duquesne Univ Mid-East Instrm Music Conf (chmn, 59-). *Interests:* Band, orchestra and woodwind instruments. *Publ:* Auth, Playing and Teaching the Clarinet Family, 60 & Organizing the School Stage Band, 61, Southern Music; Teachers Guide to Alto, Bass & Contrabass Clarinet, Selmer Co, 74; Woodwind Notebooks for Clarinet, Saxophone, Oboe, Bassoon & Flute, 76 & Fingering Charts for Clarinet, Saxophone, Oboe, Flute & Bassoon, 76, private publ. *Mailing Add:* Sch Music Duquesne Univ Pittsburgh PA 15281

MCCAULEY, BARRY
TENOR

b Altoona, Pa, June 25, 50. *Study:* Eastern Ky Univ, BME, 73; Ariz State Univ. *Roles:* Don Jose in Carmen, San Francisco Spring Opera Theatre; Faust in Faust, San Francisco Opera Co, 78 & New York City Opera; Lensky in Eugene Onegin, San Antonio Symph, 83. *Pos:* Affiliate artist, San Francisco Opera Co, 77-79; opera singer in US & France. *Awards:* Richard Tucker Award, 80. *Bibliog:* Am Guild Music. *Mailing Add:* c/o Columbia Artists Mgt 165 W 57th St New York NY 10019

MCCAULEY, JOHN JOSEPH
CONDUCTOR, PIANO

b Des Moines, Iowa. *Study:* Univ Ill, Urbana, BS, BMus; Juilliard Sch Music, MS; Mozarteum Summer Acad, Salzburg, Austria, dipl(piano & cond). *Rec Perf:* Night of the Murdered Poets, Grenadilla, 80. *Pos:* Music dir & cond, Encompass Music Theater, 79-80, Bel Canto Opera, New York, 80- & Eastern Opera Theater, New York, 82- *Teaching:* Adj prof music, Herbert Lehman Col, City Univ New York, 72- *Mem:* Am Inst Verdi Studies. *Mailing Add:* Music Dept, Herbert Lehman Col City Univ New York New York NY 10468

MCCAULEY, WILLIAM ERWIN
TENOR, EDUCATOR

b Tennessee Ridge, Tenn, Dec 19, 39. *Study:* Bob Jones Univ, BS, 63, MFA, 65, MA, 69; Col Consv Music, Univ Cincinnati, DMA, 79. *Roles:* Nemorino in L'Elisir d'Amore, Bob Jones Univ Opera Asn, 70; tenor in Messiah, 74 & 81, The Creation, 75 & 82 & Elijah, 80, Bob Jones Univ Oratorio Soc. *Teaching:* Prof voice & speech, Tenn Temple Univ, 65-68; prof voice, Bob Jones Univ, 69-; grad asst, Col Consv Music, Univ Cincinnati, 71-74. *Awards:* Fel, Nat Endowment Humanities, 80. *Mem:* Am Choral Dir Asn. *Interests:* The concert arias of W A Mozart; the operas of Verdi. *Mailing Add:* 108 Oxford St Greenville SC 29607

MCCLAIN, FLOYD AUSTIN
COMPOSER, EDUCATOR

b Alva, Okla, Apr 30, 17. *Study:* Northwestern State Col, BS, 40; New England Consv Music, BM(comp), 51; Am Consv Music, BM(clarinet), 56, MM(comp), 56. *Works:* Symphony in C, Yale Symposium, 51; Dakota, Dakota, Dakota, Yankton Col, 61; Jerry's Blues, perf by SDak All State Orch & Chorus, 73; Woodwind Trio, SDak Music Teachers Asn Conv, 74; Hangin', Lewis and Clark Playhouse, Yankton, SDak, 76; A Little Joke, Southern Music, 78; Variations and Theme, Yankton Col, 83. *Pos:* Concertmaster, Sioux City Munic Band, 74-76. *Teaching:* Prof theory & woodwinds, Yankton Col, 51- *Mem:* SDak Band Masters Asn. *Mailing Add:* 604 E 15th St Yankton SD 57078

MCCLELLAN, WILLIAM MONSON
LIBRARIAN, EDUCATOR

b Groton, Mass, Jan 7, 34. *Study:* Colo Col, with Albert Seay, BA, 56, MA(music hist), 61; Univ Mich, MA(libr sci), 59. *Pos:* Music librn, Univ Colo, Boulder, 59-65 & Univ Ill, Urbana-Champaign, 65-; ed, Notes, Music Libr Asn, 77-82. *Teaching:* Instr music, Univ Colo, Boulder, 59-65; prof libr admin, Univ Ill, Urbana-Champaign, 65- *Mem:* Music Libr Asn (vpres, 70-71, pres, 71-73, past-pres, 73-74); Am Musicol Soc; Int Asn Music Libr, Arch & Doc Ctr. *Interests:* Guidelines for developing academic music collections and services; music information and reference tools. *Publ:* Auth, A Checklist of Music Serials in Nine Libraries of the Rocky Mountain Region, Univ Colo, 63; Guidelines for Surveying Music Library Resources and Services, In: Proc 52nd Ann Meeting, Nat Asn Sch Music, 77; Judging Music Libraries, Col & Res Libr, 7/78; Bibliography of Works by Albert Seay, In: A Festschrift for Albert Seay: Essays by His Friends and Colleagues, Colo Col, 82. *Mailing Add:* 1020 W Hill Champaign IL 61821

MACCLINTOCK, CAROL C
WRITER, EDUCATOR

b St Joseph, Mo, Nov 19, 10. *Study:* Univ Chicago, 28-30; Univ Ill, BMus, 32; Univ Kans, 34-35; Ind Univ, PhD, 55. *Teaching:* Assoc prof, Colo Women's Col, 35-40, Stephens Col, 40-41; prof voice, Univ Ill, 41-44; instr, Ind Univ, 44-46; prof musicol, Southern Ill Univ, 59-64 & Univ Cincinnati, 64-76. *Publ:* Ed, Complete Works of Giaches de Wert, Rome & Dallas, 61-77; transcriber & ed, The Bottegari Lutebook, Wellesley Col, 65; Giaches de Wert (1535-1595): Life and Works, 66 & Le Balet comique de la Royne, 71, Am Inst Musicol; auth, The Solo Song 1580-1730: A Norton Music Anthology, W W Norton & Co, Inc, 73; Readings in the History of Music in Performance, Ind Univ Press, 79. *Mailing Add:* 3374 Eden Dr Bloomington IN 47401

MCCLOSKY, DAVID BLAIR
TEACHER, BARITONE

b Oswego, NY, Sept 27, 02. *Study:* New England Consv Music, 25; studied with Ernst Victor Wolff, Berlin & with Fernando Tanara, Milan, 35. *Pos:* Soloist, all major symph orch in US; radio announcer, WNAC Boston, 23-24; singer, Chicago Opera Co, 35 & Manhattan Opera Co, 37; voice therapist, Syracuse, NY, 46; founder & dir, Plymouth Rock Ctr Music & Drama, 46-55; clinical voice therapist & consult, Col Medicine, NY State Univ, Syracuse; clinical voice therapist & consult, Mass Eye & Ear Infirmary, 51-, clinical assoc otolaryngology, currently. *Teaching:* Teacher, New England Consv, Vassar Col, Univ Mich, Syracuse Univ, Boston Univ & Boston Consv Music, currently. *Mem:* Mass Coun Arts & Humanities. *Publ:* Your Voice at Its Best, Little, Brown & Co, 59, Spanish Publ, Argentina, 60, Japanese Publ, 75, Boston Music Co, 78. *Mailing Add:* 26 Bay Ridge Lane Duxbury MA 02332

MCCLYMONDS, MARITA PETZOLDT
EDUCATOR, WRITER & EDITOR

b St Louis, Mo, Dec 4, 35. *Study:* Culver-Stockton Col, BA, 56; Univ Calif, Berkeley, MA, 71, PhD, 78. *Teaching:* Asst prof, Univ Va, 81- *Bibliog:* Dennis Libby (auth), Opera Seria, Musical Times, 7/82; Nicholas Kenyon (auth), Jommelli's La Schiava Liberata: A Composer Scorned by Mozart Offers Wit and Beauty, Musical Am, 4/83. *Mem:* Am Musicol Soc; Am Soc 18th Century Studies; Soc Italian Hist Studies. *Interests:* Baroque and classical music with emphasis on opera, Mozart and Haydn. *Publ:* Auth, The Evolution of Jommelli's Operatic Style, J Am Musicol Soc, 80; Niccolo Jommelli, In: New Grove Dict of Music & Musicians, 80; Niccolo Jommelli: The Last Years, 1769-1774, UMI Res Press, 80; Jommelli Lijkt op Mozart Maar is Toch Anders, Volkskrant, Amsterdam, 9/17/82. *Mailing Add:* McIntire Dept Music Univ Va Charlottesville VA 22903

MCCOLL, WILLIAM D
CLARINET, EDUCATOR

b Port Huron, Mich, May 18, 33. *Study:* Oberlin Consv, with Waln; Manhattan Sch Music, with Blayman; Vienna Acad, with Wlach, Reifezeugnis, 55. *Rec Perf:* Works by Mozart & Villa-Lobos, 65 & works by Goodman, Piston & Krenek, 66, Lyrichord; works by Danzi, Crystal, 77; Soni Ventorum Plays Villa-Lobos, Ravenna, 78; Soni Ventorum Plays Poulenc & Villa-Lobos, Musical Heritage Soc, 79; works by Francaix, Arrieu, Ketting & Gerster, Crystal, 80; works by Mozart & Beethoven, Musical Heritage Soc, 82. *Pos:* First clarinet, Phil Hungarica, 59-60 & PR Symph Orch, 60-68; clarinet, Casals Fest, 60-68 & Soni Ventorum Quintet, 60- *Teaching:* Prof clarinet, PR Consv, 60-68 & Univ Wash, 68- *Mailing Add:* Music Dept Univ Wash Seattle WA 98195

MCCOLLUM, JOHN (MORRIS)
TENOR, EDUCATOR

b Coalinga, Calif, Feb 21, 22. *Study:* Univ Calif, Berkeley, BA, 47; Am Theatre Wing, 51-53; private voice studies with Mynard Jones & Edgar Schofield. *Rec Perf:* Israel in Egypt (Handel), L'Allegro ed Il Pensieroso (Handel) & The Creation (Haydn), Decca; Ode for St Cecilia's Day (Handel), Columbia; Judas Maccabaeus (Handel), Westminster; Symphony No 9 (Beethoven) & Amahl and the Night Visitors (Menotti), RCA Victor. *Roles:* Belmonte in Die Entfuhrung aus dem Serail & Ottavio in Don Giovanni, New York City Opera; Almaviva in Il barbieri di Siviglia, Can Opera Co; Ferrando in Cosi fan tutte, Santa Fe Opera; Pelleas in Pelleas et Melisande, Goldovsky Opera Co; Des Grieux in Manon, Ft Worth Opera; mem, Male Chorus in The Rape of Lucretia, Wash Opera Soc. *Pos:* Conct, oratorio & opera singer, 51- *Teaching:* Prof music, Sch Music, Univ Mich, 62-; artist & teacher perf & voice, Aspen Music Fest & Sch, Colo, 64-76; give recitals & master classes in universities & colleges throughout the US, 70- *Awards:* Singing Award, Atwater Kent Auditions, Los Angeles, 50; grant, Martha Baird Rockefeller Found, 60. *Mem:* Nat Asn Teachers Singing; Am Acad Teachers Singing. *Mailing Add:* 2117 Brockman Blvd Ann Arbor MI 48104

MACCOMBIE, BRUCE FRANKLIN
ADMINISTRATOR, COMPOSER

b Providence, RI, Dec 5, 43. *Study:* Univ Mass, BA, 67, MM, 68; Univ Iowa, PhD, 71. *Works:* Three Designs, Assoc Music Publ, 76; Parkside Music, comn by Univ Wis, 78; Gerberau Musics, 78 & Nightshade Rounds, 82, Assoc Music Publ. *Pos:* Dir publ, G Schirmer Inc & Assoc Music Publ, 80- *Teaching:* Assoc prof, Yale Sch Music, New Haven, 75-80. *Awards:* Fels, Sutherland Dows, Univ Iowa, 70 & Goddard Lieberson, Am Acad & Inst Arts & Lett, 79. *Mem:* Comp Forum, Inc (vpres, 82-); Am Comp Alliance, (mem bd gov, 81-). *Mailing Add:* c/o G Schirmer Inc 866 Third Ave New York NY 10022

MCCORMICK, DAVID CLEMENT
EDUCATOR, TUBA

b Destrehan, La, Aug 17, 30. *Study:* Southeastern La Univ, BMusEd, 51; Northwestern Univ, MMus, 52, PhD, 70. *Pos:* Tuba player, US Army Band, Washington, DC, 52-55. *Teaching:* Fac mem & dir bands, Manchester Col, 55-59 & 67-70; dir bands, J Sterling Morton High Sch, 59-67; prof music, Southeastern La Univ, 70- *Mem:* La Music Educr Asn. *Mailing Add:* Box 798 Southeastern La Univ Hammond LA 70402

MAC COURT, DONALD VINCENT
BASSOON, EDUCATOR

b Ross, Calif, May 6, 34. *Study:* Bassoon with Raymond Ojeda, Simon Kovar & Eli Carmen, 52-58; San Francisco State Col, BA, 56; Manhattan Sch Music, MM, 58. *Rec Perf:* Brandenburg #1 (Bach), Columbia, 65; Branches (Chihara), CRI, 70; Octandre (Varese), 72 & Trio Sonatas (Handel), 77 & 79, Nonesuch; Bassoon Variations (Wuorinen), New World, 77; Trio and Sextet (Poulenc), Nonesuch, 83. *Pos:* Prin bassoon, New York City Ballet Orch, 65-; bassoonist, Contemp Chamber Ens, 65- & New York Woodwind Quintet, 72- *Teaching:* Assoc prof music, State Univ NY, Purchase, 72- *Mailing Add:* 63 Wellington Pl Westwood NJ 07675

MCCOY, WESLEY LAWRENCE
EDUCATOR, FRENCH HORN

b Memphis, Tenn, June 27, 35. *Study:* La State Univ, BMusEd, 57, PhD, 70; Univ Louisville, MMusEd, 58; Southern Baptist Theol Sem, MSM, 60. *Pos:* Horn, Knoxville Symph, 62-67, Columbia Symph, 69-72, Ark Symph, 72-80 & Enid-Phillips Symph, 80- *Teaching:* Asst prof music, Carson-Newman Col, 62-67 & Univ SC, 69-72; from assoc prof to prof, Univ Ark, Little Rock, 72-80; chmn, Fine Arts, Phillips Univ, 80- *Mem:* Asn Conct Bands (dir, 79-80); Col Band Dir Nat Asn (state chmn, 78); Music Educr Nat Conf; Phi Mu Alpha Sinfunra (prov gov, 83-). *Mailing Add:* 1904 Blue Jay Ct Edmond OK 73034

MCCRACKEN, CHARLES, JR
BASSOON, TEACHER

b New York, NY, May 12, 54. *Study:* NC Sch Arts, with Mark Popkin, 72-75; State Univ NY, Purchase, with Donald MacCourt, 75-76; studied with Loren Glickman, 76-77. *Rec Perf:* Summersong (David Chaitken), CRI, 83. *Pos:* Perf with New York Phil, NJ Symph, Contemp Chamber Ens, Am Ballet Theatre, New York City Opera, Baltimore Symph, Musica Sacra, Group Contemp Music & other ens; mem, Laureate Ens; founding mem, Sylvan Wind Quintet; mem, Am Symph Orch, currently. *Teaching:* Instr bassoon & chamber music, Bennington Col, 82- *Mem:* Am Fedn Musicians; Int Double Reed Soc. *Mailing Add:* 810 W 183rd St 4E New York NY 10033

MCCRACKEN, CHARLES P
CELLO, EDUCATOR

b Jonesboro, Ark, Apr 11, 26. *Study:* Univ Colo, Boulder, 43-44; Denver Univ, 46-48; Juilliard Sch Music, with Felix Salmond & Leonard Rose, 48-52. *Rec Perf:* Cello Sonata (Hall Overton), EMS, 61; Concerto for Cello and Chamber Orchestra (Ramiro Cortes), 61, & String Quartet (Elie Siegmeister), 70, CRI; Pierrot Lunaire (Arnold Schoenberg), Columbia, 69; Vitebsk Trio (Aaron Copland), CRI, 70; String Quartet No 4 (Ilhan Mimaroglu), 81 & Sonatas for Cello & Piano (Beethoven & Barber), 82, Finnandar. *Pos:* Solo cellist, New York City Opera Co, 50-52 & Metropolitan Opera Co, 53-55; cellist, Galimir String Quartet, 59-54, Marlboro Trio, 68- & Beaux Arts String Quartet, 70- *Teaching:* Vis prof & artist in res cello, State Univ NY, Potsdam, 70-74; adj prof chamber music & cello, State Univ NY, Purchase, 75-79. *Awards:* Most Valuable Player Cello, Nat Acad Rec Arts & Sci, 81. *Mailing Add:* 205 W 54th St 7E New York NY 10019

MCCRACKEN, JAMES E
TENOR

b Gary, Ind, Dec 16, 26. *Study:* Columbia Univ; study with Marcello Conati, Italy, Elsa Seyfert, Ger & Joyce McLean, USA; Ind Univ, Hon DMus. *Rec Perf:* Florestan in Fidelio, 64, Duets Love and Passion, 65 & Pagliacci, 69, London; Otello, Angel EMI, 70; Carmen, Deutsche Grammophon, 72; Le Prophete, Columbia Masterwork, 76; Gurre Lieder, Phillips, 80. *Roles:* Performed in Otello, Fidelio, Samson & Delilah, Le Prophete, Il Trovatore, Aida, Carmen, Turandot & Pagliacci with Vienna State Opera, Zurich Opera, Royal Opera Covent Garden, Metropolitan Opera, San Francisco Opera Co, Berlin State Opera & Munich Opera, 60-; tenor in Otello, Canio in Pagliacci, Munich Opera, 80- *Publ:* Coauth, A Star In The Family, 71. *Rep:* Columbia Artists Mgt 165 W 57th St New York NY 10019. *Mailing Add:* Postfach 14 Flugfeld Dubendorf 8600 Switzerland

MCCRAY, JAMES JOSEPH
HELDENTENOR, EDUCATOR

b Warren, Ohio, Feb 21, 39. *Roles:* Jim Mahoney in Aufstieg und Fall der Stadt Mahagonny, Stratford Fest, Can, 65; Don Jose in Carmen; Vladimir in Prince Igor; Canio in Pagliacci; Dick Johnson in La Fanciulla del West; Cavaradossi in Tosca; Manrico in Der Fliegende Holländer and many others. *Pos:* Heldentenor with New York City Opera, San Francisco Opera, Kansas City Lyr Theater & other co in Hawaii, Miami, Newark, Omaha, St Paul, Seattle & Tel Aviv. *Teaching:* Chmn & prof cond, comp & choral groups, Colo State Univ, Ft Collins, currently. *Awards:* Nat Coun Aud Winner & Schoen-Rene Award, Metropolitan Opera. *Rep:* Ludwig Lustig Inc 41 W 72nd St New York NY 10023. *Mailing Add:* Music Dept Colo State Univ Ft Collins CO 80523

MCCREERY, RONALD D
ADMINISTRATOR, CONDUCTOR

b Chicago, Ill, Nov 8, 41. *Study:* Bowling Green State Univ, BS, 65; Kent State Univ, MMus, 72. *Pos:* Cond, Youth orch, Columbus, Ga, 67-70. *Teaching:* Instr orch, Sylvania pub sch, Ohio, 65-67; asst prof music, Univ Wis, Oshkosh, 72-78; dir, Sch Music, Univ Southern Miss, 78-, cond, Symph Orch, 78- *Mem:* Pi Kappa Lambda; Pi Mu Alpha Sinfonia; Am Fedn Musicians; Miss Music Teachers Asn; Miss Teachers Nat Asn. *Mailing Add:* 900 Sioux Lane Hattiesburg MS 39401

MCCRORY, MARTHA
EDUCATOR, CELLO

b Quincy, Ill. *Study:* Univ Mich, BMus, 41; Eastman Sch Music, MMus, 44, artist dipl(violoncello) 45; Univ London. *Pos:* Cellist, All-Am Youth Orch, summer 40 & Rochester Phil, 42-46; asst prin cello, San Antonio Symph, 47-53 & Chattanooga Symph, 55-62; dir, Sewanee Summer Music Ctr, 62-; freelance rec & TV studio work, Nashville, 64- *Teaching:* Asst prof, Drake Univ, 44-47; assoc prof, Univ South, 62- *Mem:* Am String Teachers Asn (pres, 71-72, vpres, 72-83); Nat Fedn Music Clubs; Am Fedn Musicians; Music Educr Nat Asn. *Mailing Add:* Mississippi Ave Sewanee TN 37375

MCCULLOH, BYRON B
COMPOSER, TROMBONE

b Oklahoma City, Okla, Mar 1, 27. *Study:* Eastman Sch Music, BM, 49, perf cert, 50, MM, 51. *Works:* Symphony Concertante (timpani), 73, Concertino #1 (trombone), 74, Symphony #1, 76, Monographs (wind ens), 79 & Spectra, 80, Carl Fischer; Concertino #2 (trombone), 80 & Brass Quintet #1, 82, Accura Music. *Pos:* Bass trombonist, Oklahoma City Symph, 51-52, St Louis Symph, 52-56, Pittsburgh Symph, 56- & Chautauqua Symph, 58-68. *Teaching:* Artist lectr trombone, Carnegie-Mellon Univ, 69-; assoc prof, Eastman Sch Music, 77-78. *Mem:* Am Fedn Musicians; Int Cong Symph & Opera Musicians; ASCAP; Am Music Ctr; Col Music Soc. *Mailing Add:* 1306 Penn Ave Pittsburgh PA 15221

MCCULLOH, JUDITH MARIE
EDITOR, SCHOLAR

b Spring Valley, Ill, Aug 16, 35. *Study:* Ohio Wesleyan Univ, BA, 56; Ohio State Univ, MA, 57; Ind Univ, PhD, 70. *Pos:* Asst to dir, Archives Traditional Music, Ind Univ, Bloomington, 64-65; asst ed, Univ Ill Press, Champaign, 72-77, assoc ed, 77-82, sr ed, 82- *Mem:* John Edwards Mem Found; Sonneck Soc; Soc Ethnomusicol (coun mem, 76-79, treas, 82-). *Interests:* Transcription and analysis of traditional and popular American music. *Publ:* Contribr, Wake Up Dead Man, Harvard Univ Press, 72; co-ed, Stars of Country Music, Univ Ill Press, 75; auth, Uncle Absie Morrison's Historical Tunes, Mid-South Folklore, 76; ed, Ethnic Recordings in America, Am Folklife Ctr, Libr Cong, 82; contribr, The Ballad Image, Comparative Folklore & Mythology, 83. *Mailing Add:* 403 W Oregon Urbana IL 61801

MCDERMOTT, VINCENT
COMPOSER, EDUCATOR

b Atlantic City, NJ, Sept 5, 33. *Study:* Univ Pa, studies with Vanclain, G Rochberg & K Stockhausen, BFA, 59, PhD, 66; Univ Calif, Berkeley, MA, 61; Inst Ethnomusicol, Univ Amsterdam, Holland, 65-66; Akad Perf Arts Surakarta Cent Java, Indonesia, 71 & 78. *Works:* Pictures at an Exhibition (electronic tape & slides), Milwaukee Art Ctr, 75; Siftings upon Siftings (orch), perf by Indianapolis Symph Orch, 79; Kagoklaras (piano & gamelan), perf by Gamelan Pacifica, 82; Rain of Hollow Reeds (electronic tape), perf by Ore Symph Orch, 82; A Perpetual Dream (chamber opera), Zagreb Music Biennial, Yugoslavia, 83; Swift Wind (voice & double bass), Dorn Publ (in prep); Magic Grounds (piano solo). *Pos:* Dir & assoc dir, Pro Musica Nova, formerly; dir, Venerable Showers of Beauty Gamelan, currently. *Teaching:* Mem fac, Hampton Inst, 66-67, Wis Conv Music, 67-77 & Lewis & Clark Col, 77- *Awards:* Fulbright-Hays Fel, 78; Creative Arts Fel, Ore, 79. *Bibliog:* Thomas Everett (auth), Five Questions, 75 Answers, Composer 15, 75. *Mem:* BMI; Soc Asian Music; Comp Forum NY; Nat Asn Comp USA; Am Soc Univ Comp. *Publ:* Auth, Current Chronicle, Musical Quart, 66, 68 & 74; A Conceptual Musical Space, J Aesthetics & Art Criticism, 72; coauth, Central Javanese Music, Ethnomusicol, 75. *Mailing Add:* 1501 SE Holly Portland OR 97214

MCDONALD, ARLYS LORRAINE
LIBRARIAN

b Edison, Nebr, Jan 6, 32. *Study:* St Mary of Plains Col, BMus, 63; Univ Ill, Champaign-Urbana, MMus, 65; NTex State Univ, Inst Music Librn, 69. *Pos:* Music librn, Ariz State Univ, 68-71, head, Music Libr, 71- *Teaching:* Asst prof voice & music hist, St Mary of Plains Col, 65-68. *Awards:* Grant, Higher Educ Act, 69. *Mem:* Music Libr Asn; Int Asn Music Libr. *Publ:* Contribr, Phoenix, In: New Grove Dict of Music in US, 83. *Mailing Add:* 2700 E Allred D-47 Mesa AZ 85204

MACDONALD, JOHN ALEXANDER
CONDUCTOR, EDUCATOR

b Durant, Okla, Jan 1, 29. *Study:* Consv Music, Oberlin Col, BMus, 51; Univ Mich, MA(musicol), 57, PhD(music), 64. *Works:* Pat-a-Pan, 71, O Come Emmanuel, 74, The Holly & the Ivy, 74, O Tannenbaum, 74, March of the Kings, 75, Cantique de Noel, 80 & Variant on a Spanish Carol, 81, Akron Symph Orch & Chorus. *Pos:* Choral cond, Akron Symph Orch, 62-82; asst dir, Blossom Fest Chorus, Cleveland Orch, 68-74. *Teaching:* Instr music, Bd Educ, Grand Rapids, Mich, 55-58; prof music, Univ Akron, 59- *Mem:* Am Musicol Soc; Am Fedn Musicians. *Interests:* Sacred vocal music of the Baroque, particularly of Giovanni Legrenzi (1626-1690). *Publ:* Auth, Franz Schubert Neue Ausgabe: String Quintets, Notes: Am Libr Asn, 72; Rhythm: Where it all Begins, 82, Preparing for a Successful Rehearsal, 83 & On Matters of Vocal Health and of Pitch, 83, Byzantine Echo. *Mailing Add:* 1721 Deepwood Dr Akron OH 44313

MCDONALD, LAWRENCE
CLARINET, EDUCATOR

Study: Northwestern Univ, BME, 64, MM, 66; Univ Mich, PhD, 75; studied with Robert Marcellus, Clark Brody & Jerome Stowell. *Rec Perf:* On Gasparo, Orion & Advance. *Pos:* Co-prin clarinet, Honolulu Symph Orch, formerly; prin clarinet, Toledo Symph, currently & Peninsula Fest Orch, currently; mem, Oberlin Woodwind Quintet, currently. *Teaching:* Mem fac, Univ Mich, formerly & Eastern Mich Univ, formerly; prof clarinet, Consv Music, Oberlin Col, 70- *Mailing Add:* Consv Music Oberlin Col Oberlin OH 44074

MCDONALD, SUSANN HACKETT
HARP, EDUCATOR

b Rock Island, Ill, May 26, 35. *Study:* Ecole Normale Superieur Musique, Paris; Paris Consv, dipl, 55; studied with Marie Ludwig, Lily Laskine, Henriette Renie & Julius Herford. *Rec Perf:* Dussek sonatas; Rosetti sonatas; Sonata for Violin & Harp (Spohr); 20th century harp music; Mediterranean

Reflections; The Romantic Harp; The Virtuoso Harp. *Pos:* Conct harpist, US, South Am, Europe & Orient tours, 60-76 & 79 Columbia Artists, 76-79; leader, Int Harp Week, Holland, 76, 77 & 79; dir & founder, Calif Summer Harp Wkshp. *Teaching:* Head harp dept, Univ Southern Calif, formerly, Univ Ariz, formerly, Calif State Univ, Los Angeles, formerly & Ind Univ, 81; mem fac, Juilliard Sch, 75- *Awards:* Premier Prix, Paris Consv, 55. *Mem:* Sigma Alpha Iota. *Mailing Add:* Harp Dept Juilliard Sch New York NY 10023

MCELFISH, DIANE ELIZABETH
VIOLIN, EDUCATOR
b Pittsburgh, Pa, May 25, 56. *Study:* Col Consv Music, Univ Cincinnati, BA, 78; Sch Music, Ind Univ, MM, 80; Xian Music Inst, China, er-hu study, summer 82. *Pos:* Violinist, Aspen Fest Orch, 79; violinist in res, Grand Rapids Symph Orch, 80-; second violin, Dorian String Quartet, 81- *Teaching:* Adj instr violin, Calvin Col, Grand Rapids, Mich, 80- *Mailing Add:* 321 Lafayette NE #3 Grand Rapids MI 49503

MCELHERAN, (N) BROCK
CONDUCTOR, EDUCATOR
b Winnipeg, Manitoba, Can, Jan, 6, 18. *Study:* Univ Toronto, BA, 39 & MusB, 47. *Works:* Patterns in Sound, Funeral March for the Deaths of Heroes & Here Comes the Avant-Garde, Oxford Univ Press; A Bilogy, Carl Fischer. *Rec Perf:* Saul (Handel), Handel Soc, 52. *Pos:* Dir, Saratoga-Potsdam Choral Inst, 70- *Teaching:* Prof cond & coordr choral activities, Crane Sch Music, State Univ NY Col, Potsdam, 47- *Mem:* Am Choral Dir Asn; Music Educr Nat Conf; Am Music Teachers Asn. *Publ:* Auth, Conducting Technique, Oxford Univ Press, 65. *Mailing Add:* Dept Music State Univ NY Col Potsdam NY 13676

MCFARLAND, J PATRICK
OBOE & ENGLISH HORN
b Rio de Janeiro, Brazil, Feb 13, 39. *Study:* San Jose State Col, BA. *Pos:* Prin English horn, Atlanta Symph Orch; owner, McFarland Oboe Shop, currently. *Mailing Add:* 1079 Lindridge Dr NE Atlanta GA 30324

MCFARLAND, ROBERT
BARITONE
Study: Sch Music, Ind Univ. *Roles:* Die Feen, Der Frieschutz, La Boheme, Madama Butterfly & Escamillo in Carmen, New York City Opera, 80-81; Enrico in Lucia di Lammermoor, Rigoletto in Rigoletto & Count DiLuna in Il Trovatore, 82, Opera Theatre Syracuse; Iago in Otello, Des Moines Metro Fest, 82; Belcore in The Elixir of Love, Des Moines Metro Fest, 82 & Los Angeles Opera Repty, 83. *Awards:* Winner, Metropolitan Opera Auditions. *Mailing Add:* Kazuko Hillyer Inc 250 W 57th St New York NY 10107

MCGARY, THOMAS JOSEPH
EDUCATOR, CONDUCTOR
b Louisville, Ky, Aug 9, 42. *Study:* Sch Music, Univ Louisville, BMus, 64, MMus, 68; Consv Music, Univ Cincinnati, PhD, 73. *Works:* He Loved Us First, Brock Univ Choir, 77. *Teaching:* Asst prof & chmn, Spalding Col, 70-71; assoc prof & chmn, Brock Univ, 74-82 & Nazareth Col, NY, 82. *Publ:* Auth, The Bach Cantatas, Where on Earth Did They Come from, I, 82, II, 83, Continuo, Toronto; Partial Signature Implication in Codex Escorial V.III.24, Music Rev, London, 79; The Missae Brevis of J S Bach, Diapason, 72. *Mailing Add:* 9 Little Briggins Circle Fairport NY 14450

MCGEE, WILLIAM JAMES
COMPOSER, EDUCATOR
b Great Falls, Mont, June 8, 36. *Study:* Ind Univ, with Bernard Heiden & Thomas Beversdorf. *Works:* Miniature for Orchestra; Variations (woodwind trio); Rhapsody (violin & piano); Jesus Was a Baby (double chorus, flute, piano & perc); 2 Philosophical Observations (piano); A Joyful Procession (Homage to Beethoven)(organ); Carol Variations on Nous voici dans la ville (organ). *Teaching:* Fac mem, Southern Missionary Col, 66-75; assoc prof music & chmn music dept, Pac Union Col, 76- *Mailing Add:* Music Dept Pac Union Col Angwin CA 94508

MCGINTY, DORIS EVANS
EDUCATOR
b Washington, DC, Aug 2, 25. *Study:* Howard Univ, BMusEd, 45, BA, 46; Radcliffe Col, MA, 47; Oxford Univ, LMH, DPhil, 54. *Teaching:* From instr to prof musicol, Howard Univ, 47- *Awards:* Fulbright Fel, 50-52; General Educ Fel, 51-52. *Mem:* Am Musicol Soc; Col Music Soc (coun mem, 81-83); Sonneck Soc. *Interests:* Music in the black community & prominent black musicians in Washington, DC; music at Howard University. *Publ:* Auth, John Lovell, J Negro Educ, 75; Two Aspects of Afro-American Song: Spiritual and Gospel, Schulfunk Westdeutscher Rundfunk, 76; Conversations with Camille Nickerson, 79 & The Washington Conservatory of Music and School of Expression, 79, Black Perspective Music; Gifted Minds and Pure Hearts, J Negro Educ, 82. *Rep:* Dept Music Col Fine Arts Howard Univ 6th & Fairmont St NW Washington DC 20012. *Mailing Add:* 1735 N Portal Dr NW Washington DC 20012

MCGLAUGHLIN, WILLIAM
MUSIC DIRECTOR & CONDUCTOR, TROMBONE
b Philadelphia, Pa, Oct 3, 43. *Study:* Temple Univ, BMus, 67, MMus, 69. *Pos:* Assoc prin trombone, Pittsburgh Symph, formerly, cond, 75; asst prin trombone, Philadelphia Orch, formerly; founder & cond, Pittsburgh Symph Players & Pittsburgh Camerata, 73; asst cond, Pittsburgh Chamber Orch, 75; assoc cond, St Paul Chamber Orch, formerly, prin cond, formerly; music dir & cond, Tucson Symph, 83- *Rep:* Am Int Artists 275 Madison Ave Suite 1618 New York NY 10016. *Mailing Add:* Tucson Symph 443 S Stone Ave Tucson AZ 85701

MCGRAW, CAMERON
WRITER, COMPOSER
b Cortland, NY, Apr 28, 19. *Study:* Middlebury Col, BA, 40; Cornell Univ, with Egon Petri, John Kirkpatrick, Donald J Grout & Robert Palmer. *Works:* Dance Suite, NC Symph, 65. *Pos:* Comp & accmp, Halprin-Lathrop Dance Group, 49-50; contrib ed, Music Libr Asn Notes, 66-73. *Teaching:* Instr, State Univ NY, Potsdam, 48-49 & Cornell Univ, 52-53; co-dir & co-founder, Jenkintown Music Sch, 54- *Mem:* Music Libr Asn. *Interests:* History, development and repertoire of music originally written for one piano four-hands. *Publ:* Ed, Four Centuries of Keyboard Music Anthology (four vols), Boston Music Co, 66-68; auth, Piano Duet Repertoire, Ind Univ Press, 81. *Mailing Add:* 439 Greenwood Ave Wyncote PA 19095

MACH, ELYSE JANET
EDUCATOR, WRITER
b Chicago, Ill. *Study:* Valparaiso Univ, Ind, BM, 61; Northwestern Univ, Evanston, Ill, MM(piano), 62, PhD(music), 65. *Teaching:* Prof piano (appl & class), theory & music hist, Northeastern Ill Univ, Chicago, 64- *Bibliog:* Harvey Sachs (auth), Virtuosos of Our Time, Thames and Hudson, 82; Glen Plaskin (auth), Vladimir Horowitz, Morrow, 83. *Mem:* Am Liszt Soc (secy, 70-76); Int Liszt Ctr, London; English Liszt Soc; Music Educr Nat Conf; Ill Music Teachers Asn. *Interests:* Pianists, piano pedagogy and keyboard music. *Publ:* Ed, The Liszt Studies, Assoc Music Publ, 73; auth, Contemporary Class Piano, Harcourt Brace Jovanovich, 76 & 82; Great Pianists Speak for Themselves, Dodd, Mead & Co, 80 & Robson Publ, London, 81; ed, Franz Liszt, Rare and Familiar—28 Pieces for Piano, Assoc Music Publ, 82. *Mailing Add:* 6551 N Wauesha Ave Chicago IL 60646

MACHLIN, PAUL STUART
EDUCATOR, CONDUCTOR
b Mineola, NY, Apr 22, 46. *Study:* Yale Univ, BA, 68; Univ Calif, Berkeley, MA, 69, PhD, 75. *Teaching:* Assoc prof music & dir choral activ, Colby Col, 74- *Awards:* Nat Endowment for Humanities Fel for Col Teachers, 82-83; Deutscher Akad Austauschdienst Fel, 70-71. *Mem:* Am Musicol Soc; Col Music Soc; Sonneck Soc. *Interests:* Jazz history, Thomas "Fats" Waller, stride piano music; Richard Wagner's The Flying Dutchman; prose writings of Sir Donald Francis Tovey. *Publ:* Auth, Wagner, Durand and The Flying Dutchman: The 1852 Revisions of the Overture, Music & Lett, 74; A Sketch for the Dutchman, Musical Times, 76. *Mailing Add:* Dept Music Colby Col Waterville ME 04901

MACHLIS, JOSEPH
EDUCATOR, WRITER
b Riga, Latvia. *Study:* City Col, City Univ New York; Columbia Univ; Juilliard Sch. *Pos:* Translr operas, currently. *Teaching:* Emer prof music, Queens Col, City Univ New York, currently; mem fac grad seminars, Juilliard Sch, 77- *Publ:* Auth, American Composers of Our Time, Crowell, 63; Enjoyment of Music, 4th ed, 77, Introduction to Contemporary Music, 2nd ed, 79 & Lisa's Boy (novel), 82, Norton. *Mailing Add:* Juilliard Sch Lincoln Ctr New York NY 10023

MACHOVER, TOD
COMPOSER, CELLO
b Mt Vernon, NY, Nov 24, 53. *Study:* Univ Calif, Santa Cruz, 71-73; Columbia Univ, 73-75; Juilliard Sch, BM, 75, MM, 77. *Works:* Light (chamber orch & comput), 79, Soft Morning, City!, (sop, double bass & comput), 80, Winter Variations (chamber ens), 81, String Quartet No 1, 81, Chansons d'Amour (piano), 82, Fusione Fugace (live comput), 82 & Electric Etudes (cello & electronics), 83, Ricordi. *Pos:* Solo cello, Can Opera Co, 75-76. *Teaching:* Prof, Third St Music Sch, New York, 74-75; comp in res, Inst Recherche & Coordination Acoustique Musique, 78-79, dir music research, 80- *Awards:* Charles Ives Fel, Nat Inst Arts & Lett, 76; Conct Grant, Martha Baird Rockefeller Fund, 79; Koussevitzky Prize, 83. *Bibliog:* Flora Lewis (auth), IRCAM, Computers & Music, New York Times, 1/80; Dominique Jameux (auth), Recherche en Musique, Art Press, Paris, 4/83; Joan Logue (auth), Video Portrait—T Machover, Centre Georges Pompidou, spring 83. *Mem:* Comp Forum; New England Comput Music Asn; Int Comput Music Asn; BMI. *Publ:* Ed, Le Compositeur et l'Ordinateur, 81 & Porte Ouverte a l'IRCAM, 83, Inst Recherche & Coordination Acoustique Musique; auth, Some Thoughts on Computer Music, MIT Press, 83. *Rep:* Judith Finell Music Serv 155 W 68th St New York NY 10023. *Mailing Add:* IRCAM 31 rue St Merri Paris 75004 France

MCHUGH, CHARLES RUSSELL
COMPOSER, PIANO
b Minneapolis, Minn, Aug 5, 40. *Study:* Univ Minn, BA, 63, MA, 67, PhD, 70. *Works:* Theme and Variation 1965, Minn Orch & Ore Symph, 73; Requiem, Minn Orch, 76; Confluence Symphony No 3, Minn Civic Orch, 77; Beloved Let Us Love One Another, Dale Warland Singers, 81; Nocturne for Strings, St Paul Chamber Orch, 83. *Teaching:* Instr music, Univ Minn, 65-70; asst prof comp, Carleton Col, 73-74. *Bibliog:* D R Martin (auth), So You Want to be a Composer, Minn Monthly, 7/79. *Mem:* Am Fedn Musicians. *Mailing Add:* 1924 Colfax S No 5 Minneapolis MN 55403

MCINNES, DONALD
VIOLA, EDUCATOR
b Mar 7, 39. *Study:* Univ Southern Calif, with William Primrose, MM; Univ Calif, Santa Barbara, with Stefan Krayk, AB. *Rec Perf:* On Deutsche Grammophon, Columbia, Musical Heritage Soc, Consortium & Angel Rec. *Pos:* Soloist & recitalist, US, Europe, Australia & Can. *Teaching:* Prof music, Univ Wash, formerly; mem fac, Banff Sch Fine Arts, formerly, Menuhin Sch, formerly, Music Acad West, summer 83 & Univ Mich, 83-; prof viola & artist in res, Col Consv Music, Univ Cincinnati, formerly. *Mailing Add:* 2331 Delaware Dr Ann Arbor MI 48103

MACINNIS, M DONALD
COMPOSER, EDUCATOR

b New York, NY, Apr 4, 23. *Study:* Princeton Univ, studied with Milton Babbitt, Bohuslav Martinu, Roger Sessions & Randall Thompson, BA, 48, MFA, 50; Berkshire Music Ctr, studied cond with Leonard Bernstein; Columbia Univ, studied electronic music with Vladmimir Ussachevsky. *Works:* Dialogues (orch), 60; Intersections (orch & tape recorder), 63; Variations (brass & perc), 64; Collide-a-Scope (12 brass instrm & tape), 71; Toccata (piano & tape), 71; Variations (cello & tape), Bowdoin Col, 73; In Memoriam John Fitzgerald Kennedy (chamber orch), Washington, DC, 75. *Pos:* Cond pres, Southeastern Comp League, 64-66; comp in res, Atlanta Symph, 68-69. *Teaching:* Cond conct band & Freshman Glee Club, Princeton Univ, 48-50; mem fac theory & comp, Music Dept, Univ Va, 50-, cond, Univ Singers, 56-67, res in electro-acoustic music, 65-, dir, Electronic Music Studio, 70- *Awards:* Comp Prize, Princeton Univ, 49, Ga State Univ, 68 & Bowdoin Col, 73. *Mem:* Am Soc Univ Comp (mem nat coun, 66-69 & 71-76); Va Music Teachers Asn; Kindler Found. *Mailing Add:* 316 Kent Rd Charlottesville VA 22903

MCINTOSH, KATHLEEN ANN
HARPSICHORD, EDUCATOR

b Portland, Ore, Nov 29, 44. *Study:* Univ Ore, BMus, 66; King's Col, Univ London, CAMS, 67; Univ Wash, MMus, 68. *Pos:* Co-dir, Arianna Ens, Los Angeles, 77. *Teaching:* Assoc prof harmony & chamber music, Los Angeles Valley Col, 74-; instr harpsichord, Occidental Col, 74- & Calif State Univ, Long Beach, 80-; mem fac, Cazader Baroque Wkshp, 78-81; artist in res, Claremont Grad Sch, 82. *Mem:* Am Musicol Soc; Southern Calif Early Music Soc. *Mailing Add:* 261 S Bonnie Ave Pasadena CA 91106

MACISAK, JANICE
VIOLIN, TEACHER

b Milwaukee, Wis. *Study:* Eastman Sch Music, with Joseph Knitzer & Carroll Glenn, BM, 64, perf cert, 66; Meadowmount, with Ivan Galamian, 65; Liszt Acad Franz Fest, Hungary, with Andre Gertler, cert, 77. *Pos:* Soloist & mem first violin sect, Rochester Phil Orch, 63-; first violinist, Aspen Fest Orch, summers 63 & 64; soloist & mem first violin sect, Rochester Chamber Orch, 63- *Teaching:* Instr violin, Prep Dept, Eastman Sch Music, formerly & State Univ NY, Brockport, formerly. *Mem:* Rochester Musicians Asn. *Mailing Add:* 480 Beach Ave Rochester NY 14612

MACK, GERALD
CONDUCTOR, EDUCATOR

Study: State Univ NY, Fredonia, BS; Teachers Col, Columbia Univ, MS. *Pos:* Dir vocal music, South Congregational Church, Hartford, Conn, formerly; cond, radio & TV choirs, formerly & Hartford Symph & Rochester Civic Phil, formerly; clinician, Carl Fischer Publ; perf with Balt Symph Orch & Am Symph Orch, formerly; dir, Gtr Hartford Youth Choral. *Teaching:* Dir vocal music, Greenwich High Sch, formerly; mem fac, Southern Conn State Col, formerly; prof Kodaly music educ, sr choral cond & artistic dir choruses, Hartt Sch Music, 66- *Publ:* Ed, Choral series, Lawson-Gould. *Mailing Add:* Hartt Sch Music Univ Hartford West Hartford CT 06117

MACK, JOHN
EDUCATOR, OBOE

Study: Juilliard Sch, with Bruno Labate & Harold Gomberg, 48; Curtis Inst Music, with Marcel Tabuteau, 51. *Pos:* First oboe, New Orleans Symph, 50-53, Nat Symph, 50-53, Casals Festivals, 50-53, Prades & Perpignam, 50-53 & Marlboro Fest, 63-68; mem US & Can tour, Sadler's Wells Ballet, 51-52; prin oboe & Edith T Taplin chair, Cleveland Orch, 65- *Teaching:* Chmn winds, Blossom Fest Sch, currently; mem fac oboe, Cleveland Inst Music, 65- *Mailing Add:* 36 Mornington Lane Cleveland Heights OH 44118

MACKAY, MARGERY (MARGERY MACKAY ANWYL)
MEZZO-SOPRANO, TEACHER

b Keene, NH, Sept 30, 25. *Study:* Syracuse Univ, 43-46; Univ Southern Calif, with William Vennard, BA, 48, MM, 71; Music Academy of West, with Lotte Lehmann, 52-53. *Rec Perf:* Three Songs (Schoenberg), 57, Le Marteau san Maitre (Boulez), 58 & The Sound of Music (film), 63, Columbia; In the Beginning (Copland), Everest, 69. *Roles:* Musetta in La Boheme, San Diego Opera; Preziosilla in La forze del destino, Suzuki in Madama Butterfly & Siebel in Faust, Seattle Opera; Mrs Page in Merry Wives of Windsor, Marcellina in Marriage of Figaro, Lola in Cavalleria rusticana & Maddalena in Rigoletto, New York City Opera, 54 & 55. *Teaching:* Vis lectr opera, applied voice & chamber music, Univ Calif, Santa Barbara, 69-; instr French diction & applied voice, Univ Tex, Austin, 71-72. *Mem:* Nat Asn Teachers Singing (Los Angeles chap pres, 68-69, southern Calif state gov, 82-); Am Guild Musical Artists (exec bd mem, 60-70); Pi Kappa Lambda. *Mailing Add:* 5071 Rhoads Ave #D Santa Barbara CA 93111

MCKAY, NEIL
COMPOSER, EDUCATOR

b Ashcroft, BC, Can, June 16, 24; US citizen. *Study:* Univ Western Ontario, BA, 53; Eastman Sch Music, MA, 55, PhD, 56. *Works:* Symphony No 1, E F Kalmus, 65; Kaleidoscope (chamber ens), 74 & Fantasy on a Quiet Theme (chamber orch), 74, Shawnee Press; A Dream Within a Dream (SATB), Music 70 Inc, 75; Kubla Khan (sop & chamber ens), Shawnee Press, 79; Soundprints (clarinet & koto or harp), Roncorp Inc, 83. *Teaching:* Prof comp & orch, Univ Wis, Superior, 57-65 & Univ Hawaii, Honolulu, 65- *Awards:* ASCAP Standard Awards, 65-; MacDowell Colony Fels, 61, 63 & 78. *Bibliog:* Ben Hyams (auth), Composers in Academia, Honolulu Mag, 3/83. *Mem:* ASCAP; Am Soc Univ Comp. *Mailing Add:* 3310 Keahi St Honolulu HI 96822

MCKEE, RICHARD DONALD, II
BASS

b Hagerstown, Md. *Study:* Yale Univ, BA, 64; Peabody Consv, 65; Univ Ill, MM, 69. *Roles:* Don Gregorio in L'Aio nell Imbarazzo, Wexford Fest, Ireland, 73; Dr Bartolo in Il Barbiere di Siviglia, Theatre Nat, Paris, 75 & New York Opera, 75; Falstaff in Falstaff, Lake George Opera Fest, 76; Hunding in Die Walküre, Portland Opera, 81; King of Clubs in Love for Three Oranges, San Diego Opera, 81; Don Pasquale in Don Pasquale, Glimmerglass Opera, 82. *Teaching:* Instr singing, Yale Univ, 69-72. *Mem:* Am Guild Musical Artists (mem bd gov, 79-). *Rep:* Tornay Mgt Inc 127 W 72nd St New York NY 10023. *Mailing Add:* 240 Oak St #21 Bridgeport CT 06606

MCKEE, ROSS R
EDUCATOR, ADMINISTRATOR

b Seattle, Wash, Aug 2, 14. *Study:* Manning Sch Music, dipl, 32; Col William & Mary; studied piano with Paul Pierre McNeely, John Crogan Manning, Rosalyn Tureck, Alexander Tcherepnin, Wager Swayne & Ernst von Dohnanyi. *Teaching:* Asst to dir, Manning Sch Music, San Francisco, 32-34; dir, Music & Arts Inst, San Francisco, 34-, chmn piano dept, 34- *Mem:* Calif Music Exec; Calif Music Teachers Asn; San Francisco Music Teachers Asn; Am Guild Organists. *Mailing Add:* Music & Arts Inst 2622 Jackson St San Francisco CA 94115

MCKENNEY, WILLIAM THOMAS
COMPOSER, EDUCATOR

b Falmouth, Ky, June 24, 38. *Study:* Col Consv Music, Univ Cincinnati, with Scott Huston; Eastman Sch Music, with Bernard Rogers, PhD. *Works:* Clarinet Concertino (with orch); 3 Miniatures (piano); Dialogue (woodwind quartet); The Lake (tape). *Teaching:* Assoc prof theory & analysis, comp & electronic studio, Univ Mo, Columbia, 67- *Awards:* Martin G Dumler Award, 63; Comp of Yr, Music Teachers Nat Asn, 71. *Mailing Add:* 1224 Jake Lane Columbia MO 65201

MCKENZIE, JACK H
EDUCATOR, ADMINISTRATOR

b Springfield, Mo, Nov 11, 30. *Study:* Southwest Mo State Univ, 48-50; Univ Ill, 54; Ariz State Univ, 56; China Acad, Taiwan, Hon PhD, 81. *Works:* Nonet, 54, Introduction & Allegro, 54 & Three Dances, 56, Golden Crest; Pastorale for Flute and Percussion, Music for Perc, 58; Suite for Side Man & Handclappers, 69 & Paths I for Solo Percussion, 70, Media Press; Song for Percussion & Trombone, Music for Perc, 79. *Rec Perf:* Breaking the Sound Barrier, Urania, 56; The Bewitched, 57 & US Highball, 60, Gate Five Rec; Canto, 67 & Computer Cantata, 67, MGM Rec. *Teaching:* Perc, Nat Music Camp, summers 54-65; prof music, Univ Ill, 56-69, assoc dean, Fine Arts Acad, 69-71, dean, 71-; vis instr perc, Interlochen Arts Acad, 62-65. *Mem:* Int Coun Fine Arts Dean (vchmn, 75-76, chmn, 76-77); Fine Arts Comn, Nat Asn State Univ & Land Grand Cols; founding mem, Percussive Arts Soc. *Publ:* Auth, Concert Snare Drum, Book I, Colin, 62; coauth, Music Educators Guide to Percussion, Belwin, 70; Percussion in the School Music Program, Payson, 76. *Mailing Add:* 27 Sherwin Circle RR 3 Urbana IL 61801

MACKENZIE, MELISSA TAYLOR
TEACHER, SOPRANO

b Brownsville, Tenn, Sept 23, 25. *Study:* George Peabody Col, BA, 46; Memphis State Univ, 69 & 70; Univ Tenn, Martin, 78; Freed-Hardeman Col, 80; studied piano with Myron Myers, voice with Mrs R L Jordan, Hans J Heinz & Alfred Cherrington Evans, French diction with Simone France & speech with Julia Duncan & Victor Morley. *Pos:* Soprano, Memphis Open Air Theatre, 48; concert soloist, NY & the South, 48-82; soprano soloist, Episcopal Actors Guild NY, 49-51 & Am Theatre Wing NY, 49-51; soprano soloist & dir music Rosh Hashannah & Yom Kippur, Temple Adas Israel, Brownsville, Tenn, 52-82; dir music, Gay Valley Camp, Brevard, NC, summers 59-62. *Teaching:* Piano, voice & organ, privately, Brownsville, Tenn, 53-; teacher music educ, Haywood Co Bd Educ, Brownsville, Tenn, 53- *Awards:* Hall of Fame, Am Col Musicians, 69. *Mem:* Nat Guild Piano Teachers; Am Col Musicians; Music Teachers Nat Asn; Nat Fedn Music Clubs. *Mailing Add:* 647 W Main St Brownsville TN 38012

MCKENZIE, WALLACE C
EDUCATOR, COMPOSER

b Alexandria, La, June 16, 28. *Study:* Univ Iowa, with Philip Greeley Clapp; NTex State Univ, with George S Morey; La State Univ, with Kenneth B Klaus. *Works:* Tagelied (orch); Sonatina (clarinet, viola & cello), 54; Trumpet Sonata, 57; Introduction and Allegro (brass), 58; Music (violin & tape), 72; 3 Danses Anachronistiques (recorders, cornemuse, viola da gamba & natural trumpet), 73; Music (harp & tape), 74. *Teaching:* New Orleans Baptist Theol Sem, 55-64 & Wayland Baptist Col, 64-68; prof musicol, La State Univ, 68- *Mailing Add:* Music Sch La State Univ Baton Rouge LA 70803

MACKEY, ELIZABETH JOCELYN
EDUCATOR, MUSICOLOGIST

b Corbin, Ky, Oct 30, 27. *Study:* Peabody Col, BS, 48; Greensboro Col, BM, 53; Univ Mich, MM, 56, PhD, 68. *Teaching:* Assoc prof, Minot State Col, 64-67; assoc prof, Ball State Univ, 69-74, asst prof, 74-80, prof, 80- *Awards:* Sword of Honor, 61 & Rose of Honor, 74, Sigma Alpha Iota. *Mem:* Sigma Alpha Iota (nat prog counr, 68-78); Int Am Musicol Soc; Am Choral Dir Asn; Sonneck Soc. *Publ:* Contribr, Widmann & Theile, In: New Grove Dict of Music & Musicians, Macmillan. *Mailing Add:* 1205 W Riverside Muncie IN 47303

MACKEY, RICHARD
FRENCH HORN, EDUCATOR
Study: New England Consv Music; studied horn with Willem Valkenier & solfege with Gaston Dufresne. *Pos:* Mem, Cleveland Orch, Detroit Symph & Japan Phil, Tokyo, formerly; performer, Marlboro Music Fest & Hollywood studios; mem horn sect, Boston Symph Orch. *Teaching:* Mem fac French horn, New England Consv Music, currently. *Mailing Add:* New England Consv 290 Huntington Rd Boston MA 02115

MACKIE, SHIRLEY M(ARIE)
COMPOSER
b Rockdale, Tex, Oct 25, 29. *Study:* La State Univ, BM, 49, MM, 50, 51-53; Aspen Inst, with Darius Milhaud, 53; Consv Musique, France, with Nadia Boulanger, 59 & 68. *Works:* Requiem, comn by L C Stivers, 67; Three Movements for Solo Clarinet, 68 & Five Dialogues for Flute & Clarinet, 68, private publ; Concertino for Solo Clarinet & Band, Univ Redlands Band, Calif, 69; Dance in the Brazos Brakes, 73 & Symphony for the Bicentennial, 76, comn by Tex Fedn Music Clubs; Comments 1976, comn by Univ Okla, 76. *Pos:* Prin clarinetist, Waco Symph Orch, 62-64; cond, Chamber Orch Waco, 63-69. *Teaching:* Assoc prof winds, theory & orch, Univ Mary Hardin-Baylor, 54-57; coordr vocal & instrm music, McLennan County, Dept Educ, Waco, Tex, 59-70, dir instrm music, 70-78. *Bibliog:* Karl Zelenka (auth), Komponierende Frauen, Ellenberg, Cologne, Germany, 80. *Mem:* Tex Comp Guild. *Publ:* Auth, Coming of Age, Clarinet, 55; Early American Clarinetists, Woodwind World, 57; contribr, The Forgotten Madrigal, 57 & The Unappreciated Eric Satie, 58, Music J; auth, Secular Music in America, Am Music Teacher, 64. *Mailing Add:* 100 Wilderness Rd Waco TX 76710

MCKINLEY, ANN W
EDUCATOR
b Pontiac, Mich, June 11, 29. *Study:* Univ Mich, BM, 50, MM, 53, PhD(musicol), 63. *Teaching:* Asst keyboard harmony, Univ Mich, 55-58; asst prof piano, Eastern Mich Univ, 59-63; lectr music, St Procopius Col, 65-67; lectr, George Williams Col, 67-68; asst prof theory, music hist & piano, NCent Col, 68-71, chmn creative arts div, 71-75, chmn music dept, 71-77, assoc prof, 71-75, prof music, 75-, chmn music dept, 83- *Mem:* Am Musicol Soc; Sonneck Soc. *Publ:* Auth, A New Concept in the Teaching of Opera, Col Music Symposium, spring 77; John Wustman (Master Accompanist for Pavarotti & Other Opera Greats) Keyboard, 6/82. *Mailing Add:* Dept Music NCent Col Naperville IL 60540

MCKINLEY, WILLIAM THOMAS
COMPOSER, PIANO
b New Kensington, Pa, Dec 9, 38. *Study:* Carnegie Mellon Univ, BA, 60; Yale Univ, MM, MMA. *Works:* Triple Concerto, MMC, 73; Symphony No 1, 79 & Paintings No 6, 81, Margun Music; Concerto for B Flat Clarinet, Margun Music, 81; The Mountain, 82 & Six Movements for String Quartet, 82, MMC; Paintings No 7, Margun Music, 82; over 200 jazz comp. *Rec Perf:* 1750 Arch, Golden Crest, Northeastern, GM, Delos & CRI. *Pos:* Ed, Master Musicians Collecting, currently. *Teaching:* Fac mem comp, Univ Chicago, 69-73; fac mem comp & jazz, New England Consv Music, 73- & Berkshire Music Ctr, 79 & 82. *Awards:* Fromm Found Comn, 76; Nat Endowment for Arts Fel, 81; Music Award, Am Acad & Inst Arts & Lett, 83. *Mailing Add:* 240 West St Reading MA 01867

MCKINNEY, ELIZABETH RICHMOND
EDUCATOR, PIANO
b Oakdale, La, Dec 8, 27. *Study:* La State Univ, BMus, 49, MMus, 50; Tex Woman's Univ, MA, 80. *Teaching:* Res piano, Southwestern Baptist Theol Sem, 50-79, asst prof, 79-81, chmn, Piano Dept, 79-, assoc prof, 82-; guest prof, Hong Kong Baptist Col, 71-72 & Hong Kong Baptist Sem, 71-72. *Mem:* Music Teachers Nat Asn; Southern Baptist Music Conf; Delta Omicron; Nat Guild Piano Teachers; Ft Worth Piano Teacher's Forum. *Mailing Add:* PO Box 22000 Ft Worth TX 76122

MCKINNEY, JAMES CARROLL
EDUCATOR, CONDUCTOR
b Minden, La, Jan 11, 21. *Study:* La State Univ, BMus, 49, MMus, 50; Univ Southern Calif, DMA, 69. *Teaching:* Asst prof music theory, Southwestern Baptist Theol Sem, 50-54, chmn, Theory Dept, 54-56, dean, Sch Church Music, 56-, prof voice pedagogy, 56-; vis prof, Univ Southern Calif, 58. *Mem:* Am Choral Dir Asn; Nat Asn Teachers Singing; Music Educr Nat Conf; Music Teachers Nat Asn; Southern Baptist Church Music Conf (pres, 78). *Interests:* Vocal music of Bach; theory and voice pedagogy; voice therapy. *Publ:* Auth, The Advanced Music Reader, 61, Vocal Fundamentals Kit, 76, Vocal Development Kit, 77 & Five Practical Lessons in Singing, 82, Convention Press; The Diagnosis and Correction of Vocal Faults, Broadman, 82. *Mailing Add:* PO Box 22000 Ft Worth TX 76122

MCKINNEY, ROGER WILLIAM
EDUCATOR, CLARINET
b Plattsburgh, NY, Mar 9, 31. *Study:* State Univ NY, Col Potsdam, BSME, 53; Juilliard Sch Music, BS(clarinet), 56, MS(clarinet), 57. *Pos:* Prin clarinet, Trenton Symph Orch, 60-, Princeton Chamber Orch, 65-67 & Pro Musica New Hope, 72-75. *Teaching:* Instr clarinet, State Univ NY, Col Potsdam, 53-54; prof music, Trenton State Col, 57. *Mem:* Am Fedn Musicians; Am Musicol Soc; Int Clarinet Soc. *Mailing Add:* Dept Music Trenton State Col Trenton NJ 08625

MCKINNON, JAMES WILLIAM
EDUCATOR, ORGAN
b Niagara Falls, NY, Apr 7, 32. *Study:* Niagara Univ, BA, 55; Columbia Univ, studied organ with Thomas Richner & Fred Swann & musicol with Paul Henry Lang, Eric Hertzaman & Edward Lippman, MA, 60, PhD, 65. *Pos:* Organist & choirmaster, St John's Grace Episcopal Church, 66-81. *Teaching:* Lectr music hist, Columbia Univ, 65-66; assoc prof, State Univ NY, Buffalo, 68-81, chmn dept, 68-70 & 80-81, prof, 81- *Bibliog:* William M Green (auth), The Church Fathers and Musical Instruments, Restoration Quart, 66. *Mem:* Am Musicol Soc; Royal Musical Asn; Music Libr Asn. *Interests:* Iconography of early music; Ancient Greek music instruments; early Christian music. *Publ:* Auth, Musical Instruments in Medieval Psalm Commentaries, J Musicol Soc, 68; The Tenth Century Organ at Winchester, Organ Yearbk, 74; Jubal vol Pythagoras, Musical Quart, 78; Exclusion of Instruments from Ancient Synagogue, Proc Royal Musical Asn, 79; 40 articles in New Grove Dict of Music & Musicians, 80. *Mailing Add:* 202 Morris Ave Buffalo NY 14214

MCLAIN, ROBERT MALCOLM
DOUBLE BASS, EDUCATOR
b Sweetwater, Tex, Dec 9, 31. *Study:* NTex State Univ, BA, 52, MA, 53; Univ Tex, Austin; study with Joseph Guastafeste. *Pos:* Asst prin bs, Dallas Symph Orch, 58-65; bs, Casa Manana Musicals, Ft Worth, 58-; prin bs, Ft Worth Opera Orch, 65-79 & Ft Worth Symph Orch, 65- *Teaching:* Instr double bs, Tex Christian Univ, 67- *Mailing Add:* 2313 Benbrook Dr Ft Worth TX 76110

MACLANE, ARMAND RALPH
EDUCATOR, BARITONE
US citizen. *Study:* Hunter Col, City Univ New York, BA(music & drama), 64; Boston Univ, MEd, 73. *Roles:* Scarpia in Tosca, Opera Rhin; Four Demonic Roles in The Tales of Hoffmann, Basel & Braunschweig, 68; Jochanaan in Salome, Opera Rhin Strasbourg, 76; Tonio in I Pagliacci, Opera Rhin & Oper Hause Düsseldorf, 77; Nabucco in Nabucco, Miami Opera, 81; Alberich in The Ring of the Nibelung, Staattheater Freiburg, 82; Telramund in Lohengrin, Freiburg, Hannover, Saarbrucken & Dortmund, 82. *Pos:* Baritone, Stadtische Buhne Nürnberg, 64-65, Staattheater Basel, 65-68, Opera Rhin Strasbourg, 73-78 & Staatheater Freiburg, 78- *Teaching:* Prof voice, Staatliche Hochschule Musik, Karlsruhe, 77- *Mailing Add:* Lotissement Les Cerisiers 3 Kesseldorf/Beinheim F-67930 France

MCLAUGHLIN, MARIAN
COMPOSER, CLARINET
b Evanston, Ill, Nov 26, 23. *Study:* Northwestern Univ, BME; New England Consv, studied with Francis Judd Cooke & Carl McKinley, MM(comp); studied with Walter Piston & clarinet with Robert Lindeman. *Works:* Lullaby to a Seafarer's Son (women's voices), 41; Nocturne & Scherzo (chamber music & solo flute), 54; Autumn Fires (women's choir), 60; Divertimento (viola & cello), 65; Five Archaic Studies (piano four hands), 73; Descants for Handbells, 74; One I Love (wind chimes). *Pos:* First clarinet, Evansville Phil Orch, formerly. *Teaching:* Instr theory & woodwinds, Univ Evansville, 44-46; teaching fel theoret subj, New England Consv, 47-48. *Awards:* Winner, Am Guild Organists Cont; First Prize, Fri Morning Music Club Comp Group Compt, 67. *Mailing Add:* 102 Duncannon Rd Bel Air MD 21014

MCLEAN, BARTON
COMPOSER, PIANO
b Poughkeepsie, NY, Apr 8, 38. *Study:* State Univ NY, Potsdam, BS, 60; Eastman Sch Music, MA, 65; Ind Univ, Bloomington, MusD, 72. *Works:* Dimensions II (piano & tape), 73 & Metamorphoses for Orchestra, 75, Broude; Dimensions III & IV (sax & tape), Dorn, 80; Ritual of Dawn (chamber ens), CRI, 82; The Electric Sinfonia, Dimensions VIII for Piano and Tape, Opus One Rec, 83. *Rec Perf:* Electronic Music from the Outside In & Music of a Timeless Earth, Folkways Rec; McLean: Electro-Symphonic Landscapes, Opus One Rec. *Teaching:* Asst prof comp, Ind Univ, South Bend, 69-76; prof comp & electronic music & dir, Electronic Music Ctr, Univ Tex, Austin, 76- *Awards:* Nat Endowment Arts Comp Fel, 76 & 82; Int Music Coun—Rostrum Award, UN Educ Sci & Cult Orgn, 81; Norlin-MacDowell Fel, 82. *Mem:* Am Soc Univ Comp (mem exec comt, 74-80); Col Music Soc; ASCAP; Comp Forum. *Mailing Add:* 6 Matador Circle Austin TX 78746

MCLEAN, EDWIN W
COMPOSER, PIANO
b Bastrop, La, Apr 3, 51. *Study:* Univ Colo, BMus(piano), 72, MMus(comp), 74; Yale Sch Music, comp with Krzysztof Penderecki & Jacob Druckman, MMus, 79. *Works:* Improvisation for the Pianist, 76 & Sonatine (piano), 77, Myklas Music Press; Duet Repertoire-Primer, Book I, Book II, Assoc Music Publ, 80; You Can Play Jazz, Belwin-Mills, 81; Box-Car Bertha, 83 & Winter, Psalm and Fire, 83, Assoc Music Publ. *Pos:* Free-lance comp & arr, 79- *Awards:* John Work Award, 78; Woods Chandler Prize, Yale Univ, 79; MacDowell Colony Fel, 79 & 80. *Mem:* Am Comp Alliance; BMI. *Mailing Add:* 3577 Loquat Ave Coconut Grove FL 33133

MAC LEAN, JOHN TORRY
COMPOSER, EDUCATOR
b Jersey City, NJ, Apr 12, 33. *Study:* Drew Univ, AB, 55; Fla State Univ, MA, 57, MM, 61; Columbia Univ, 58; Ind Univ, DMus, 68; Calif Inst Arts, 73. *Works:* Portrait for Oboe and Strings, Oklahoma City Symph, Brevard Music Ctr Orch & Mobile Symph, 65 & 68; Meditation for Viola and Piano, perf by viola students of David Dawson, Ind Univ, 66-75; Suite for Seven Wind Instruments, Oklahoma City Symph & Atlanta Chamber Orch, 66 & 70; Symphony, In Memoriam, Atlanta Symph, Baltimore Symph & Ind Univ Symph, 68 & 69; Symphonic Dance (orch), Oklahoma City Symph, Brevard

Music Ctr Orch & Spartanburg Symph, 68, 69 & 78; Serenades for Chamber Orchestra, Brevard Music Ctr Orch, 76; Three Songs for Soprano, Milly Bullock & Janice Janiec, 79. *Teaching:* Orch, Jacksonville Pub Sch, Fla, 61-63; instr, NC Wesleyan Col, 66-67; asst prof, WGa Col, 67-75; assoc prof, Converse Col, 75- *Mem:* Am String Teachers Asn; Southeastern Comp League (vpres, 83-); Am Fedn Musicians; Am Soc Univ Comp. *Rep:* BMI New York NY. *Mailing Add:* 146 Woodhaven St Spartanburg SC 29302

MCLEAN, PRISCILLA TAYLOR
COMPOSER, WRITER
b Fitchburg, Mass, May 27, 42. *Study:* Lowell Univ, studied comp with Dr Hugo Norden, BMusEd, 65; Ind Univ, studied comp with Bernhard Heiden & Thomas Beversdorf, MMus, 69. *Works:* Dance of Dawn (quad electronic), perf by McLean Mix, 74; Variations & Mozaics on a Theme of Stravinsky, Alexander Broude, Co, 75; Invisible Chariots (quad-stereo electronic), perf by McLean Mix, 75-77; Beneath the Horizon (tuba(s) & whale ens (tape)), perf by Melvyn Poore, 77-78; Fantasies for Adults & Other Children (eight pieces for sop, piano & two performers), Am Comp Alliance Publ, 78; The Inner Universe (eight pieces for piano, tape & slides), 79-82 & A Magic Dwells (orch & tape), 83, MLC Publ. *Rec Perf:* Variations & Mozaics on a Theme of Stravinsky, Louisville Orch Rec, 67; Dance of Dawn (quad electronic), CRI Rec, 74; Invisible Chariots (quad-stereo electronic), Folkways Rec, 75; Interplanes (two pianos), Advan Rec. *Pos:* Perf & comp, McLean Mix (New Am Music radio series), 74- *Teaching:* Assoc lectr, St Mary's Col, Ind, 73-76. *Awards:* Nat Endowment for Arts Comp Grant, 79-80 & 81-82; Martha Baird Rockefeller Fund for Music Inc Travel Grant, 81. *Bibliog:* David Ernst (auth), A Composer Profile, Polyphony Mag, 78; Steve Mamula (auth), Selected American Composers: A Profile and Analysis, Am Rec Guide, 82; Joseph Machlis (auth), Introduction to Contemporary Musics, W W Norton & Co, 2nd ed, 83. *Mem:* Am Soc Univ Comp (mem exec comt, 74-81); Am Music Ctr; Am Women Comp, Inc; BMI; Am Comp Alliance. *Interests:* Contemporary music. *Publ:* Auth, Fire and Ice: A Query, Perspectives New Music, 78; Vladimir Ussachevsky and Otto Luening, 1952, Music Libr Asn Notes Mag, 78; Zagreb's Music Biennale No 11, Musical Am Mag, 81; The McLean Mix: The Inner Tension of the Surrealistic, Am Women Comp News, 82. *Mailing Add:* 6 Matador Circle Austin TX 78746

MCLELLAN, JOSEPH DUNCAN
CRITIC
b Quincy, Mass, Mar 27, 29. *Study:* Boston Col, AB, 51, MA, 53. *Pos:* Music critic, Pilot, weekly newspaper, Boston Mass, 59-67 & Manhattan East, weekly newspaper, New York, 67-70; reviewer, concts & rec, Washington Post, 72-82; music critic, 82- *Mem:* Music Critics Asn. *Mailing Add:* 1224 Fairmont St NW Washington DC 20009

MCLENNAN, JOHN STEWART
COMPOSER
b Tyringham, Mass, Nov 26, 15. *Study:* Peabody Consv, 30; private comp & piano study with Carl Thorp & Aurelio Giorni, 28-31 & comp with Karol Rathaus & Erik Itor Kahn, 35-37. *Works:* Night Music, comn & perf by Hartford String Symph, 50's; Ballet: Proscenium, comn & perf by Nana Gollner, 51; Ballet: Lazarus, comn & perf by Nina Fonaroff, 53; Celebration, Tryptich & Night Music, perf by Barzin & Nat Orch Asn, 60's; Magnificat & Nunc Dimittis, Margun Music Inc, 78; Essay for String Quartet and Piano, comn by Frank E Taplin, 81. *Rec Perf:* Three Songs From James Joyce, 83, Three Songs From Edith Sitwell, 83, Ceremonial Music for Organ, 83 & Triptych for Organ, 83, Gun Mar Rec. *Mem:* Am Comp Alliance; BMI. *Mailing Add:* Ashintully Tyringham MA 01264

MCMAHAN, ROBERT YOUNG
COMPOSER, ACCORDION
b Washington, DC, July 12, 44. *Study:* Peabody Inst, studied with Stefan Grove & Robert Hall Lewis, BM(theory), 69, MM(comp), 72 & currently; St John's Col, Santa Fe, NMex, MA, 78. *Works:* Portrait of a Virgo (piano), Claire Wachter, 72; Whispers of Heavenly Death (mixed ens, electronic tape & sop), Ann Mathews, 72; Three Etudes for Piano, Nancy Roldan, 81; Sonata da Chiesa (oboe & accordion), comn by Res Musica Baltimore, 82. *Rec Perf:* Toccata for Accordion (Krenek), Orion, 75. *Teaching:* Instr & chmn theory dept & accordion dept, Peabody Inst, 73-; instr theory, Morgan State Univ, 76-79; instr theory & music lit, Towson State Univ, Baltimore Co, 80-; instr serious accordion, Univ Md, 80- *Awards:* First Place Virtuoso Div, Am Accordionists Asn Nat Compt, 64, 65, 67 & 70; Maria K Thatcher Mem Award, 72; First Prize, Annapolis Fine Arts Fest Comp Compt, 72. *Bibliog:* Carl Schoettler (auth), Low Instrument Esteem Irks Accordion Virtuoso, Baltimore Sunpapers, 4/17/75; Robert P Morgan (auth), Krenek: Various Works, High Fidelity, 6/76; Jerry De Muth, Avant-garde Accordion, Contemp Keyboard, 11/77. *Mem:* Am Soc Univ Comp; Music Teachers Nat Asn; Am Accordionists Asn; Res Musica Baltimore (mem bd dir, 80). *Mailing Add:* 3706 Diane Ave Hampstead MD 21074

MCMILLAN, ANN ENDICOTT
COMPOSER, WRITER
b New York, NY, Mar 23, 23. *Study:* Bennington Col, studied comp with Otto Luening, BA, 45; Berkshire Music Ctr, 48. *Works:* Gateway Summer Sound, 69 & Amber '75, Folkways Rec; April-Episode (harpsichord & tape), perf by Joseph Payne, 78; Gong Song, Folkways Rec, 79; A Little Cosmic Dust (piano & tape), 82, Whale I & II, 82 & Strings (violin & tape), 83, Am Comp Alliance. *Pos:* LP music ed, RCA Victor Rec Co, 49-55; prog dir, RTF, French radio, New York, 58-62; music dir, WBAI-FM, New York, 64-68; comp & writer, currently. *Awards:* Grants for comp, Guggenheim Found, 72 & Rockefeller Found, 79; Birthday Tribute, WGBH, Boston, annually. *Bibliog:* A Tribute to

Women in Music, Many Worlds of Music, BMI, 77; Greta Wehmeyer (auth), Edgard Varese, Gustave Bosse Verlag, Germany, 79; Tom Johnson (auth), Record Time, Village Voice, 80. *Mem:* MacDowell Colony; Am Comp Alliance; BMI; Am Music Ctr. *Publ:* Auth, La Bande Magnetique, un Moyen Nouveau d'Expression Artistique, J Musical, Paris, 77; The Listening Eye, Craft Horizons Mag, fall 70; Edgard Varese in Retrospect, Virtuoso Mag, 81; The Shape of Music—An Evening with Edgard Varese (in Swedish), Nutida Musik, Stockholm, 61-62 & (in Spanish) Tono Mag, Mexico City, 82. *Rep:* C/o Am Comp Alliance 170 W 74th St New York NY 10023. *Mailing Add:* 273 W 10th St 170 W 74th St New York NY 10014

MCMILLAN, THEODORA MANTZ
VIOLIN, EDUCATOR
b Minneapolis, Minn, Jan 12, 23. *Study:* Univ Minn, studied violin with A Koltan & Louis Krasner, BA, 45; Manhattan Sch Music, with Hugo Kortschak, 46-47; Aspen Musc Sch, with Szmon Goldberg. *Rec Perf:* Sextet for Horns and String Quartet (Beethoven), Audiophile Rec, 60; Arthur Berger String Quartet, CRI, 62; String Quartets, Op 18, No 1 & Op 59, No 3 (Beethoven), Dover Rec, 64. *Pos:* Concertmaster, NC Symph, 47-50; first violin, sixth chair, St Louis Symph, 55-57; first violin, tenth chair, Pittsburgh Symph, 57-61; second violin, Lenox String Quartet, 58-65. *Teaching:* Fromm Fel Player, Berkshire Music Ctr, 58-61; lectr chamber music, Grinnell Col, 62-65; coach, Aspen Music Sch, 63; prof violin & chamber music, Univ Ariz, 70- *Mem:* Am String Teachers Asn; Music Teachers Nat Asn. *Mailing Add:* Sch Music Univ Ariz Tucson AZ 85721

MCMILLIAN, GERALDINE
SOPRANO
b Welch, WVa, Apr 15, 53. *Study:* Southern Conn State Col, 73; Juilliard Sch, with Eleanor Steber, 74-79. *Roles:* Arminda in La Finta giardiniera, Juilliard Opera Dept, 78; Cecily in The Importance of Being Earnest, Pittsburgh Opera Wkshp, 79; Countess in Le Nozze di Figaro, Opera Ens New York, 80 & Henry St Settlement, 83; Fiordiligi in Cosi fan tutte, Henry St Settlement, 83. *Mailing Add:* 42-42 Colden St Flushing NY 11355

MCMULLEN, PATRICK T
ADMINISTRATOR, EDUCATOR
b Saginaw, Mich, Mar 11, 39. *Study:* Loras Col, BA, 61; Univ Iowa, MA, 64, PhD, 73. *Works:* Three Tunes for Two Trumpets, Shawnee Press, 80; Circles (voice & piano), 81. *Teaching:* Asst prof music, State Univ NY, Fredonia, 72-76, assoc prof, 76-82, prof & actg chair, 82-, chmn dept music, 83- *Awards:* Grant in Aid Res, State Univ NY, Fredonia, 73. *Mem:* Soc Res Music Educ; Coun Res Music Educ; Am Educ Res Asn; Music Educr Nat Conf. *Publ:* Coauth, Preference and Interest as Functions of Distributional Redundancy in Rhythmic Sequences, J Res Music Educ, 76; auth, Influence of Distributional Redundancy in Rhythmic Sequences on Judged Complex Ratings, Coun Res Music Educ, 76; The Process of Identifying Competencies for Music Teachers, Am Music Teacher, 2-3/77; coauth, Music Teaching, Research and You, New York Sch Music News, 11/80; auth, Music as a Perceived Stimulus Object and Affective Responses: An Alternative Theoretical Framework, Handbk Music Psychology, 80. *Mailing Add:* Music Dept State Univ Col Fredonia NY 14063

MCMURTRY, BARBARA H See Noel, Barbara H

MACNEIL, CORNELL HILL
BARITONE
b Minneapolis, Minn, Sept 24, 22. *Study:* Hartt Sch Music, Univ Hartford, studied with Friedrich Schorr, 44-45; studied with Virgilio Lazzari, Otto Guth, Dick Marzollo & Luigi Ricci. *Rec Perf:* Rigoletto (Verdi), London & Angel Rec; Un Ballo in Maschera (Verdi), Aida (Verdi), I Pagliacci (Leoncavallo), Cavalleria rusticana (Mascagni) & La Fanciulla del West (Puccini), London; Luisa Miller (Verdi), RCA. *Roles:* Rigoletto in Rigoletto, Metropolitan Opera, Vienna Staatsoper, Covent Garden & Paris Opera; Simon Boccanegra in Simon Boccanegra, Metropolitan Opera, Miami, Buenos Aires, Genova & Palermo; Macbeth in Macbeth, Metropolitan Opera, Covent Garden & Maggio Musicale, Florence; Nabucco in Nabucco, Metropolitan Opera, Buenos Aires & Arena Verona; Falstaff in Falstaff, Metropolitan Opera & Barcelona; Iago in Otello, Metropolitan Opera, Vienna Staatsoper & Naples; Scarpia in Tosca, Metropolitan Opera, San Francisco Opera & Chicago Lyr Opera. *Pos:* Bar with major opera co in Europe, North Am & South Am. *Awards:* Alumnus of Year, Hartt Sch Music, Univ Hartford, 76. *Mem:* Am Guild Musical Artists (pres, 71-77). *Mailing Add:* c/o Robert Lombardo Assocs 61 W 62nd St New York NY 10023

MCNEIL, JAN PFISCHNER (JANET LOUISE PFISCHNER)
COMPOSER, EDUCATOR
b Pittsburgh, Pa, Mar 20, 45. *Study:* Baldwin Wallace Col Consv, Berea, Ohio, BMus, 67; Univ Colo, Boulder, with David Burge, MMus, 70; Univ Ill, Champaign-Urbana, with Ben Johnston & Edwin London, 73-76. *Works:* Asphodel, comn by Fischer Found, Ames, Iowa, 71; In Soundless Grasses, Nat Endowment Arts, 71; Aureate Earth, Joseph Boonin, 72; Three Preludes to the Aureate Earth, 75, Opus 10: Songs of Commitment, Oplo, 75, Antiphons II, 75 & Sermon in Stone, 75, Carl Fischer Inc. *Pos:* Studio piano accomp, Univ Colo, boulder, 71; asst dir, Fine Arts Ctr, Clinton, Ill, 73-74. *Teaching:* Instr theory & comp, Univ SDak, Vermillion, 71-73; assoc instr theory, Univ Ill, Champaign-Urbana, 73-76; asst prof comp & theory, Wells Col, Aurora, NY, 76-78. *Awards:* Four First Prizes, Mu Phi Epsilon Int Music Soc, 67-75; MacDowell Colony Fel, 70. *Bibliog:* Mu Phi Epsilon Composition Contests, Mu Phi Epsilon Triangle, 67-78; Roger Scanlan (auth), Spotlight on Contemporary Composers, Nat Asn Teachers Singing Bulletin, 76. *Mem:* ASCAP; Am Soc Univ Comp; Col Music Soc. *Mailing Add:* 4590 Darley Ave Boulder CO 80303

MCNEIL-MORALES, ALBERT JOHN
EDUCATOR, CONDUCTOR

b Los Angeles, Calif, Feb 14, 24. *Study:* Univ Calif, Los Angeles, BA, 42, MM, 44; Univ Southern Calif, MS, 52; Westminster Choir Col, Univ Lausanne, with Howard Swan, Raymond Moreman, Roger Wagner & J Finley Williamson. *Pos:* Founder & dir, Albert McNeil Jubilee Singers, 64-; cond, Sacramento Chorale, 71- & Masterworks Chorus, 80-83. *Teaching:* Coordr sec music educ, choral & gen music, Los Angeles Unified Sch District, 54-69; prof music, choral & ethnomusicol, Univ Calif, Davis, 69- *Awards:* Choral Excellence, Musical Ambassadors, Nat Asn Negro Musicians Inc, 76; Gold Medallion, Choral Excellence, Int Canto Coral, Barcelona, 77 & Iowa Choral Dir Asn, 82. *Mem:* Life mem, Am Choral Dir Asn, Western Div (minority awareness comn, 82); Music Educr Nat Conf; Nat Asn Negro Musicians Inc; Phi Mu Alpha Sinfonia. *Publ:* Coauth, Silver Burdett Music, Books VII & VIII, Silver Burdett Co, 75, rev ed, 82. *Rep:* Int Concts Exchange Inc 1124 Summit Dr Beverly Hills CA 90210. *Mailing Add:* 447 Herondo St #210 Hermosa Beach CA 90254

MCPEEK, GWYNN SPENCER
EDUCATOR, WRITER

b Cardington, Ohio, Feb 5, 16. *Study:* Ohio State Univ, BS, 38; Ind Univ, MMus, 42; Univ NC, PhD, 49. *Teaching:* Bandmaster, high sch, Ala, 38-40; dir instrumental music, Birmingham-Southern Col, 40-41; asst prof & head dept music, Transylvania Col, 42-45; instr, Univ NC, 45-59; from assoc prof to prof, Newcomb Col, Tulane Univ, 49-63; dir choral music, prof music hist, Univ Wis, Madison, 63-68; prof musicol, Univ Mich, Ann Arbor, 68- *Awards:* Grants, Fulbright, 54-55 & Soc Sci Res Coun, Italy, 60-61. *Mem:* Am Musicol Soc; Music Teachers Nat Asn; Music Libr Asn. *Interests:* French secular music of the 15th century; English music, 1380-1450; poetry and music of the troubadors. *Publ:* Auth, Codex 697 of the Padua Monastery Library, In: Birthday Offering to Willi Apel, Ind Univ, 67; Musicology in America: Current Problems, In: Memorial Offering to Glen Haydon, Univ NC, 68; coauth, The Laborde Chansonnier, Brooklyn Medieval Inst, 68. *Mailing Add:* Sch Music Univ Mich Ann Arbor MI 48104

MCQUERE, GORDON DANIEL
EDUCATOR

b Hammond, Ind, Aug 20, 46. *Study:* Univ Tulsa, BM, 71; Univ Iowa, MA, 73, PhD, 78. *Teaching:* Assoc prof music theory, Baylor Univ, 75- *Mem:* Am Musicol Soc; Soc Music Theory. *Publ:* Auth, Concepts of Analysis in the Theories of B L Yavorsky, Music Rev, 80; ed, Russian Theoretical Thought in Music, 83, contrib, The Theories of Boleslav Yavorsky, 83 & Boris Asafiev & Musical Form as a Process, 83, In: Russian Theoretical Thought in Music, UMI Res Press. *Mailing Add:* Sch Music Baylor Univ Waco TX 76798

MCRAE, LEE
ARTIST MANAGER

b Beatrice, Nebr, June 23, 24. *Pos:* Treas, Pac Artists Rep Consortium, 81-83; bd dir, Phil Baroque Orch of West, 81- *Mem:* Viola da Gamba Soc; Am Recorder Soc; Early Music Soc. *Mailing Add:* 2130 Carleton St Berkeley CA 94704

MACURDY, JOHN
BASS

b Detroit, Mich, Mar 18, 29. *Study:* With Avery Crew, 47- *Rec Perf:* Symphony No 9 (Beethoven), Columbia; Don Giovanni (Mozart), Deutsche Grammophon & CBS; Beatrice et Benedict (Berlioz), Deutsche Grammophon; The Crucible (Ward), CRI. *Roles:* Gurnemanz in Parsifal, Ring Cycle, Boris Godunov & Pimen in Boris Godunov, Fiesco in Simon Boccanegra & Mephistopheles in Faust, Metropolitan Opera; Rocco in Fidelio, Metropolitan Opera, La Scala Opera & Chicago Lyr Opera; Arkel in Pelleas et Melisande, Paris Opera & San Francisco Opera. *Pos:* Leading basso, New York City Opera, 59-62, Metropolitan Opera, 62-, San Francisco Opera, 62- & Paris Opera, 76- *Awards:* Medal Artistic Merit, City of Detroit. *Mailing Add:* Tall Oaks Ct Stamford CT 06903

MCVOY, JAMES EARL
COMPOSER, EDUCATOR

b Syracuse, NY, Mar 4, 46. *Study:* Syracuse Univ, with Earl George, BMus, 68; Eastman Sch Music, with Wayne Barlow, MM, 70, with Samuel Adler & Warren Benson, PhD, 77. *Works:* Reflections for Orchestra, perf by Harrisburg Symph Orch, 73; Four Puns for Piano & Tape, comn by Pa Music Teachers Asn, 74 & 75; Magic Child (flute & tape), perf by Joyce Catalfano, Carl Adams & many others, 79; Cygnus (piano & violoncello), perf by Lloyd & Rheta Smith, 81 & 82; Triple Stars (flute, oboe & violoncello), perf by Huntingdon Trio, 81 & 82; Orion, perf by Susquehanna Symph, 82. *Teaching:* Asst prof theory & piano, Elizabethtown Col, 70-79; asst prof theory, West Chester State Col, 79-83, assoc prof, 83- *Mem:* Am Soc Univ Comp (co-chmn region III, 80-83); ASCAP. *Mailing Add:* 1322 Hall Rd West Chester PA 19380

MADDEN, RONALD
BARITONE

Study: Colgate Univ, grad. *Rec Perf:* Miss Julie. *Roles:* Count Almaviva in Le Nozze di Figaro, 81 & Tarquinius in The Rape of Lucretia, 81, Wolf Trap Summer Fest; Figaro in Il Barbiere di Siviglia, Dandini in La Cenerentola & Hermann in Les Contes D'Hoffmann, 82, Chicago Lyr Opera; Frank in Die Fledermaus, 82 & Schaunard in La Boheme, 83, Baltimore Opera Co. *Pos:* Mem, High Noon Ens, Dallas Civic Opera, formerly; appearances with San Francisco Spring Opera Theatre, Western Opera Theatre, Chautauqua Opera & Annapolis Opera. *Awards:* First Prize, Metropolitan Opera Nat Coun Auditions, 82. *Mailing Add:* 210 W 101st St New York NY 10025

MADDOX, ROBERT LEE
CONDUCTOR & MUSIC DIRECTOR, EDUCATOR

b Ranger, Tex, Jan 22, 35. *Study:* NTex State Univ, BA, 56, MME, 57; NY Univ, PhD, 72; studied cond with Pierre Deveaux, 72-73. *Pos:* Music dir & cond, Youth Symph of Carolinas, Charlotte, NC, 72-78 & Charlotte Pops Orch, 77- *Publ:* Auth, Ludwig Van Who?, Instrumentalist, 68; Does Your City Need a String Farm Program? NC Music Educr, 72. *Mailing Add:* 4508 Carriage Dr Charlotte NC 28205

MADDOX, WALTER ALLEN
VIOLIN

b Portland, Ore, Jan 17, 35. *Study:* Juilliard Sch Music, with Joseph Fuchs & Oscar Shumsky, dipl(violin). *Rec Perf:* With Pittsburgh Symph & Detroit Symph. *Pos:* Mem, Juilliard Orch, 58 & Pittsburgh Symph Orch, 60-62; second violin, Detroit Symph, currently. *Mailing Add:* Detroit Symph Ford Auditorium Detroit MI 48226

MADSEN, CLIFFORD K
EDUCATOR

b Price, Utah, May 3, 37. *Study:* Brigham Young Univ, BA, 59, MA, 60; Fla State Univ, PhD, 63. *Teaching:* Prof music educ, Fla State Univ, 60- *Mem:* Music Educr Nat Conf; Nat Asn Music Therapy. *Publ:* Coauth, Experimental Research in Music, Prentice-Hall, 70; Teaching Discipline: A Positive Approach for Educational Development, Allyn & Bacon, 70; co-ed, Research in Music Behavior, Teachers Col Press, 75; coauth, Contemporary Music Education, AHM, 78; Competency Based Music Education, Prentice-Hall, 80. *Mailing Add:* Music Educ Dept Fla State Univ Tallahassee FL 32306

MADSEN, NORMA LEE (NORMA LEE MADSEN BELNAP)
VIOLIN, EDUCATOR

b Tremonton, Utah, Dec 2, 27. *Study:* Brigham Young Univ, summer 47; San Francisco Consv Music, with Griller Quartet, summer 49; Univ Utah, BS, 51; Aspen Inst Music, 53; Music Acad West, 62. *Pos:* Asst concertmaster, Utah Symph, 44-; concertmaster, Univ Utah Symph, 48-59; second violin, Utah String Quartet, Young Audiences, Treasure Mountain & Am String Teachers Asn Quartet, 58-82; exec dir, Am String Teachers Asn Nat String Conf, Univ Utah, 70-75 & 79 & Snowbird, 76-78. *Teaching:* From lectr to prof music, Univ Utah, 51-; private instr, 51-; fac mem & registr, Treasure Mountain Fest Arts, 64-66. *Awards:* Teacher Recognition Award, Music Teachers Nat Asn, 70-72; 30 Yr Silver Bowl Serv Award, Utah Symph, 74; Musician of Yr Award, Salt Lake City Chap, Mu Phi Epsilon, 82. *Bibliog:* Harold Lundstrom (auth), Mu Phi Honors Norma Lee in Dallas, Deseret News, Salt Lake City, 8/21/68; Sara Nelson (auth), Totally Involved: A Lady of Music, Utah Chronicle, 1/6/75. *Mem:* Founder Univ Utah chap, Mu Phi Epsilon (first pres, 50, co-chmn, 54, mem nat coun & nat second vpres, 54-58); Nat Fedn Musicians (state first vpres, 78-82 & state bd, 82-); Utah String Teachers Asn (chmn Utah mem, 69-73); Music Teachers Nat Asn; Utah Music Teachers Asn. *Interests:* Composers, particularly members of Mu Phi Epsilon. *Publ:* Auth, Mu Phi Epsilon Composers and Their Works, Univ Utah Press, 56-58; ed, American Composer Listing for Strings and Harp, 68-74 & contribr, Scored for Traveling: Join the Utah Symphony and See the World, spring 72, The Triangle; contribr, American String Teachers Association Summer String Conference, Strad Mag, 11/71; University of Utah American String Teachers Association National String Conference Hosted 99, Am String Teacher, fall 72. *Mailing Add:* 1333 Chandler Dr Salt Lake City UT 84103

MADURA, ROBERT HAYES
CELLO

b Bismark, NDak, Aug 16, 55. *Study:* NC Sch of Arts, BM, 77; Mich State Univ, 79; study with Joel Krosnick, 79-80. *Pos:* Cellist, Arioso String Quartet, 77-79 & DeVos String Quartet, 79-; prin cellist, Grand Rapids Symph, 79- *Mailing Add:* 1939 Collins SE Grand Rapids MI 49507

MAGAD, SAMUEL
VIOLIN, CONDUCTOR

b Chicago, Ill, May 14, 32. *Study:* DePaul Univ, BMus, 55; studied with Paul Stassevitch. *Pos:* Violin soloist, 44-; mem, US Army Orch, 55-58; mem, Chicago Symph Orch, 58-, asst concertmaster, 66-72, co-concertmaster, 72-; concertmaster, Grant Park Symph Orch, 70-71; dir & first violinist, Chicago Symph Chamber Players, currently; founder, Chicago Symph Trio; first violinist, Eckstein Quartet, currently; music dir & cond, Northbrook Symph Orch, 80- *Mailing Add:* 1015 Edgebrook Glencoe IL 60022

MAGEAU, MARY
COMPOSER, EDUCATOR

b Milwaukee, Wis, Sept 4, 34. *Study:* DePaul Univ, studied comp with Leon Stein, BMus, 63; Univ Mich, with Ross Lee Finney & Leslie Bassett, MMus(comp), 69; Berkshire Music Ctr, with George Crumb, 70. *Works:* Celebration Music (conct band); Indian Summer (youth orch); Pacific Portfolio (student orch); Concerto Grosso (orch); Variegations (orch), 70; Montage (orch). *Rec Perf:* A New Lacrimae, Sound 80 Rec; Contrasts, Sonate Concertate & Scarborough Fair Variations, Grevillea Rec. *Pos:* Harpsichordist, Univ Mich Collegium, formerly & Brisbane Baroque Trio; pianist, chamber music perf in North Am & Australia. *Teaching:* Asst prof, Scholastica Col, 69-73; instr, Univ Wis, 71-72; guest lectr, Kelvin Grove Col, Brisbane, 74-83. *Awards:* Second Prize, Gottschalk Int Compt, 70; Comp Grant, Australian Coun, Sydney, 80; ASCAP Standard Award, 81- *Mem:* ASCAP; Int League Women Comp; Fel Australian Comp. *Mailing Add:* 57 Ironside St St Lucia Queensland 4067 Australia

MAGERS, WILLIAM DEAN
VIOLA, VIOLIN

b Horton, Kans, Feb 13, 34. *Study:* Univ Calif, BA, 55; Univ Southern Calif, MM, 58, DMA, 79. *Rec Perf:* Four String Quartet (Vincent Persichetti), ARA, 76; Piano Quintet (Vincent Persichetti), JM, 79. *Pos:* Violist, St Louis Symph, 58-63. *Teaching:* Asst prof, New Col, Sarasota, Fla, 67-70; vis instr, Univ Ill, 70-71; prof, Ariz State Univ, 71-; mem fac, Paul Rolland Int String Workshops, 73- *Mem:* Am String Teachers Asn (pres Ariz unit, 80-82). *Mailing Add:* Sch Music Ariz State Univ Tempe AZ 85287

MAGG, FRITZ
CELLO, EDUCATOR

b Vienna, Austria, Apr 18, 14; US citizen. *Study:* Hochschule für Musik, Cologne & Berlin, 32-34; Ecole Norwale de Musique, Paris, with Diran Alexanian, 36. *Rec Perf:* Latin American Music, Columbia, 39; Piano Trio (Mozart), Musicraft, 39; with Gordon String Quartet, Jerome Kern Tunes, Decca, 41 & Prokofiev, Schuman, Stravinsky Quartets, Concert Hall, 42; Chamber Music (Dvorak), Vox, 59. *Pos:* Prin cellist, Vienna Symph Orch, 34-36 & Metrop Opera Orch, New York, NY, 47-48. *Teaching:* Prof music & chmn string dept, Ind Univ, Bloomington, 48- *Publ:* Auth, Cello Exercises, G Schirmer, 68; Cello Exercises, Hobart Music Publ, 78; coauth, Concepts in String Playing, Ind Univ Press, 80. *Mailing Add:* 1320 E University St Bloomington IN 47401

MAGG, KYRIL
FLUTE & PICCOLO, EDUCATOR

b New York, NY, Mar 26, 45. *Study:* Berkshire Music Ctr, 64-65; Sch Music, Ind Univ, BM, 66, MM, 67; Acad Int d'ete, France, dipl, 71; study with Jean-Pierre Rampal, Julius Baker, James Pellerite & Doriot Anthony Dwyer. *Works:* Mendelssohn: A Midsummer Night's Dream Overture (transcribed four flutes), 76, European Am Music Corp, 80. *Pos:* Flute & piccolo soloist, US Army Band, Washington, DC, 67-70; asst prin flutist, Cincinnati Symph Orch, 72-73 & 74-; second flutist, Baltimore Symph Orch, 73-74. *Teaching:* Vis artist flute, Univ Brasilia, Brazil, 65; fac flutist, Ohio State Univ, Columbus, 70-72; adj prof flute, Col-Consv Music, Univ Cincinnati, 74- *Mem:* Nat Flute Asn (vpres, 81-82, pres 82-83 & chmn bd, 83-84). *Publ:* Auth, Teaching Chamber Music Aesthetics to Flute Students, Nat Flute Asn Newsletter, 82. *Mailing Add:* 2706 Morningridge Dr Cincinnati OH 45211

MAGYAR, GABRIEL
EDUCATOR, CELLO

b Budapest, Hungary, Dec 5, 14, US Citizen. *Study:* Madach Imre Gymnazium, Budapest, BA, 32; Royal Hungarian Franz Liszt Consv, MA, 36. *Pos:* Concert cellist, Europe, South Am & US, 32-49; cellist, Hungarian String Quartet, 56-72. *Teaching:* Prof cello & chamber music, Univ Okla, 49-56; Colby Col summers 62-72, Banff Art Ctr, summer 72, Univ Ill, Urbana-Champaign, 72-80. *Mem:* Phi Mu Alpha Sinfonia. *Mailing Add:* 708 Dover Pl Champaign IL 61820

MAHAN, KATHERINE HINES
EDUCATOR, WRITER

b Memphis, Tenn, June 16, 28. *Study:* Okla Baptist Univ, with Warren Angell, BM, 50; Peabody Col, MM, 56; Fla State Univ, with Wiley Houseright, PhD, 67. *Works:* Six Songs for Children's Choirs, Church Musician, Broadman Press, 51-52; A Child's Prayer of Thanks, In: How Great Is God, Mommie?, Publ Collections, 67; Columbus College Alma Mater, comn by Columbus Col Gov Asn, 70. *Teaching:* From asst prof to prof music, Columbus Col, Ga, 58- *Awards:* Fulbright Fel, 74; grant, Nat Endowment Humanities, 75 & 81 & Am Inst Pakistan Studies, 77. *Bibliog:* Mary M Byrne (auth), Women in India, Columbus Sunday Ledger, 10/74. *Mem:* Nat League Am Pen Women (hist & music chair, 78-84); Nat Fedn Music Clubs (nat chmn, Am music in armed forces, 80-); Soc Ethnomusicol (regional chmn, 80-); Sonneck Soc; Nat Asn Teachers Singing (regional chmn, 67-76). *Interests:* Music of Black Americans in the South; relationship of American Indians to the people of India; Pakistan in music. *Publ:* Auth, Showboats to Softshoes, 100 Years of Music, Cosco Press, 68; Maintaining Sanity in the Bicentennial, Ga Parent Teachers Asn J, 1/76; Hopkinson and Reinagle, J Music Educ, 4/76; coauth, History of Public Schools in Muscogee County, Cosco Press, 78; auth, Black Musicians in Georgia ... Were Teachers, Columbus Times Mag, 83. *Mailing Add:* 2339 Burton St Columbus GA 31904

MAHAR, WILLIAM J
EDUCATOR, LECTURER

b Syracuse, NY, Nov 30, 38. *Study:* St Bernard's Sem, AB, 60; Syracuse Univ, MA(musical), 66, PhD, 72. *Teaching:* Lectr, Herbert H Lehman Col, City Univ New York, 67-71; from asst prof to assoc prof, Capitol Campus, Pa State Univ, 71- *Mem:* Am Musicol Soc; Sonneck Soc. *Interests:* Blackface minstrelsy in American culture; vocal and instrumental music of the Civil War. *Publ:* Auth, Music in Pennsylvania, In: Pennsylvania 1776, 76; Williams vs Washington: The Relationship Between the Libretto and History, In: The First President, William Carlos Williams Rev, 81; rec, music & bk rev, Civil War Times Illustrated & Am Hist Illustrated, 81- *Mailing Add:* 301 St Marks Rd Mechanicsburg PA 17055

MAHLER, DAVID CHARLES
COMPOSER, PIANO

b Westfield, NJ, Aug 13, 44. *Study:* Concordia Col, study theory with Richard Hillert, BA, 67; Vandercook Col; Calif Inst Arts, study comp with Harold Budd & Morton Subotnick, 72. *Works:* Wind Peace (mag tape), Wind-Up Press, 72; Illinois Sleep (organ), 74 & Early Winters (two pianos), 74, Pieces; The King of Angels (mag tape), 78, Fantastic Slides (string duo), 79 & Voice

of the Poet (mag tape), 82, Wind-Up Press; Coast, comn by Gamelan Pacifica, 83. *Pos:* Music dir, and/or Service, Seattle, 75-82. *Awards:* Fel, Nat Endowment Arts, 78 & 79. *Publ:* Auth, I Didn't Want to Talk, 78 & Scorecard, 79, Wind-Up Press; Aviva, Prolog Mag, 79; Nobody Knows Who We Are, Spar Mag, 81. *Mailing Add:* 906 E Highland Dr Seattle WA 98102

MAHRT, WILLIAM PETER
MUSICOLOGIST, MUSIC DIRECTOR

b Spokane, Wash, Mar 9, 39. *Study:* Gonzaga Univ, 57-60; Univ Wash, BA, 61, MA, 63; Stanford Univ, with Putnam Aldrich & George Houle, PhD, 69. *Pos:* Choirmaster, St Ann Chapel, Palo Alto, Calif, 64-69 & 73- *Teaching:* Asst prof music, Case Western Reserve Univ, 69-71; asst prof music hist, Eastman Sch Music, 71-72; from asst prof to assoc prof, Stanford Univ, 72- *Awards:* Jr Fac Fel, Mellon Found; Newberry Libr Fel, Nat Endowment Humanities, 76. *Mem:* Am Musicol Soc; Church Music Asn Am (mem bd dir, 77-); Renaissance Conf Northern Calif (pres, 80-81); Medieval Asn of Pac; Int Musicol Soc. *Interests:* Theory and performance practice of Medieval and Renaissance music; music of the Roman liturgy. *Publ:* Auth, The Missae ad Organum of Heinrich Isaac, Univ Mich, 69; Gregorian Chant as a Fundamentum of Western Music Culture, Sixth Int Church Music Cong, 74; The Musical Shape of the Liturgy, 75-77 & Antonio Vivaldi and His Sacred Music, 78, Sacred Music; Guillaume Dufay's Chansons in the Phyrigian Mode, Studies in Music, UWO, 80. *Mailing Add:* Dept Music Stanford Univ Stanford CA 94305

MAHY, DAUNE SHARON
SOPRANO

b Woodland, Calif. *Study:* Westminster Choir Col, BM, 60, MM, 61; Ind Univ, Bloomington, DM, 78. *Roles:* Frasquita in Carmen, Ky Opera Asn, 70; Lucia in Where's Charley, Steamboat Cabin Theatre, 73-74; Laetitia in The Old Maid and the Thief, 77-78, Fanny in Cambiale di Matrimonia, 79 & Vespetta in Pimpinone, 79-80, Nebr Opera Ens; First Lady in Magic Flute & Despina in Cosi fan tutte, Rome Fest Orch, Italy, 83. *Pos:* Guest soloist, Omaha Symph, Rome Fest Orch, Louisville Bach Soc, Cleveland Opus One Orch, Nebr Sinfonia, Mansfield Symph, Lansing, Grand Rapids, Kenley Players & St Louis Municipal Opera. *Teaching:* From instr to asst prof, Univ Nebr, Omaha, 74-80; assoc prof singing, Consv Music, Oberlin Col, 80- *Mem:* Actors Equity; Nat Asn Teachers Singing. *Rep:* Great Lakes Perf Artists 310 E Washington St Ann Arbor MI 48104. *Mailing Add:* 319 N Prospect St Oberlin OH 44074

MAIA, CAROLYN (CAROLYN MAJA BURTON)
MEZZO-SOPRANO, TEACHER

b London, England, Apr 6, 39; US citizen. *Study:* Guildhall Sch Music & Drama, London, England, perf dipl, 60; studied with Hans Karg Bebenburg, Vienna, 63, Vera Rozsa, London, & William Eddy, currently. *Rec Perf:* Aspects of Flight (Richard Stoker), Gaudeamus, 80. *Roles:* Baba in The Medium, Focus Opera Group, London, 68; Prince Orlofsky in Die Fledermaus, Welsh Nat Opera Co, 71-75; Madame Popova in The Bear, 70 & Hermia in A Midsummer Night's Dream, 73, English Opera Group; Olga in Eugene Onegin, 75 & Cenerentola in La Cenerentola, 77, Seattle Opera; Rosina in Barber of Seville, Portland Opera, 76. *Pos:* Due Voci (vocal duo), 75-; soloist, Glyndebourne Fest Opera, English Opera Group, Welsh Nat Opera, Seattle Opera, Vancouver Opera Asn & San Diego Opera. *Teaching:* Private instr voice, Cornish Inst Allied Arts, Seattle, Wash, 76- *Mem:* Am Guild Musical Artists; Am Fedn TV & Radio Artists. *Mailing Add:* 10519 Exeter Ave NE Seattle WA 98125

MAIBEN, WILLIAM
COMPOSER, PIANO

b Salt Lake City, Utah, June, 15, 53. *Study:* Oberlin Consv, BMus, 75; Univ Wash, 76; Univ Utah, MMus, 78. *Works:* Quartet in E Minor, perf by Cincinnati Consv New Music, 75; Sonata (oboe & two violas), Educ Music Press, 76; Seven Songs of Bilitis, perf by Jordan Tang & New Music Ens, 78; Snowbird (comic opera), 79, Concerto for 2 Violins, 81, Quartet No 2, A Minor, 82 & Strangers in a Strange Land (orch), 83, Educ Music Press. *Rec Perf:* Quartet in E Minor, Crest Rec Co, 75; Street Music from San Francisco, 77, Seven Songs of Bilitis, 78 & Chamber Music of Debussy, 78, Univ Utah; Bach Goldberg Variations, Columbia Univ, 79; Piano Music of Debussy, Carnegie Recital Hall, 81; The Threepenny Opera, Pioneer Mem Theatre, 83. *Pos:* Music calligraphy & arr, Educ Music Press, 70-; staff accmp, Univ Utah, 81-; trustee, Magic Theatre Unlimited, 81-; composer, Clear Light of Void, 81-; cellist, Univ Utah Symph Orch, 76-78 & 81-; pianist, Salt Lake Symph, 82- & Theatre 138, Salt Lake City, 82-; guest cond & oboist, City Lights Orch, 83- *Teaching:* Asst music theory, Univ Wash, 75-76. *Awards:* Nat Comp Cont Award, Music Teachers Nat Asn, 75; BMI Award Comp, 76; Charles Ives Scholar, Am Acad & Inst Arts & Lett, 80. *Publ:* Ed, The Use of Hallucinogenic Drugs in Interpersonal Relations, Magic Theatre, 77; auth, Perspectives (Music from New York City #2), 80 & Lennon Extract (The Martyrdom of St John), 82, Perspectives New Music; coauth, The Mathematical Foundations of Mormon Theology, 82 & A Legal Defense of Our Erotic Relationship and the Theory of Context Creation, 83, Magic Theatre. *Rep:* Educ Music Press PO Box 17572 Salt Lake City UT 84117. *Mailing Add:* 2774 Wardway Dr Salt Lake City UT 84117

MAIHART-TRACK, MICAELA
PIANO

b Amstetten, Austria; US citizen. *Study:* Acad Music & Perf Arts, Vienna, Austria, conct dipl, 57. *Rec Perf:* Contemporary Austrian Works for Piano, Austrian State Radio, Vienna, 57, 74 & 77; Soiree de Vienne (Strauss), Rubin Rec, 70; Sonata for Violin and Piano (Gerhard Track), GIA Rec, 78;

Compositions by Ernst Track (violin & piano), Austrian State Radio, Vienna, 79. *Pos:* Int conct pianist, US, SAm, Europe & Asia, 55- *Teaching:* Piano, privately, 49-; master class piano, Univ Windsor, Can, 65, Neuberg Cult Days & Symposium, 77-80 & Int Fest Arts, Taiwan, 81. *Awards:* New World Cult Award, Assembly Baha, 81. *Bibliog:* Major Interest Shared with Family & Concert Pianist Lives Musical Life, In: Vocational Biographies, Sauk Centre, Minn, 73. *Mailing Add:* c/o PMI Artists Bureau 130 Baylor Pueblo CO 81005

MAILMAN, MARTIN
COMPOSER, EDUCATOR
b New York, NY, June 30, 32. *Study:* Eastman Sch Music, BM, 54, MM, 55, PhD, 60. *Works:* Liturgical Music, 66 & Symphony No 1, 69, Belwin Mills Publ Corp; Decorations, Boosey and Hawkes Inc, 74; Requiem, Requiem, Belwin Mills Publ Corp, 75; Symphony No 2, 80, Exaltations for Band, 82 & Concerto for Violin & Orchestra, 83, Boosey & Hawkes Inc. *Pos:* Comp in res, Ford Found, 59-61. *Teaching:* Comp in res & prof music, East Carolina Univ, 61-66; prof music & coord comp, NTex State Univ, 66- *Awards:* Comp Fel Grant, Nat Endowment Arts, 82; Queen Marie-Jose Prize, Geneva, Switzerland, 83; Award, Am Bandmasters Asn, 83. *Mem:* ASCAP; Music Educr Nat Conf; Tex Music Educr Asn. *Mailing Add:* Sch Music NTex State Univ Denton TX 76203

MAIMONE, RENATA
ADMINISTRATOR, EDUCATOR
b Berlin, Ger, June 11, 17; US citizen. *Study:* Voice training with Maria Hoover-Elsberg in Berlin & Boston; private piano, music theory & music hist study in Berlin; New England Consv, study choral cond. *Pos:* Freelance conct singer, New England, 41-50; sop soloist, St Paul's Cathedral & Old South Church, Boston, formerly; adminr, Long Island Youth Orch, 65-75; founder & exec dir, Long Island Baroque Ens, 69- *Teaching:* Adj prof music hist, Adelphi Univ, Garden City, NY, 79- *Mailing Add:* 55 Spruce St Roslyn Harbor NY 11576

MAIN, ALEXANDER
EDUCATOR, WRITER
b New Rochelle, NY, Oct 28, 25. *Study:* Yale Univ, BMus, 49; Columbia Univ, MA, 51; NY Univ, PhD(musicol), 60. *Teaching:* From asst prof to assoc prof music, Univ Ga, 52-61; assoc prof, Ohio State Univ, 61-65, prof, 65- *Mem:* Am Musicol Soc. *Interests:* Music, particularly Liszt, Hindemith, opera and the 18th to 20th centuries. *Publ:* Auth, Costanzo Fest: Opera Omnia, Am Inst Musicol, Vols I & II, 62 & 68; Maximilian's Second-Hand Funeral Motet, Musical Quart, 62; Lorenzo Masini's Deer Hunt, Commonwealth Music, 65. *Mailing Add:* Sch Music Ohio State Univ Columbus OH 43210

MAIORESCU, DORELLA TEODORA
HARP, EDUCATOR
b Bucharest, Romania. *Study:* Bucharest Acad Music, BMus, 68; Juilliard Sch Music, MS, 72; studied with Liana Pasquali, Marcel Grandjany & Nicanor Zabaleta, 80. *Rec Perf:* With New York Harp Ens. *Pos:* Solo harp recitalist, Romanian Broadcasting Co, 67-69, Romanian Athenaeum, Bucharest, 69, Alice Tully Hall, New York, 72, Malaga Symph Orch, 81 & Valladolid Symph Orch, 81; harpist, Am Symph Orch, 70-72 & New York Harp Ens; Arch & Stella Rowan Found Chair harp, Fort Worth Symph, currently. *Teaching:* Asst prof harp, NTex State Univ, currently. *Awards:* Bronze Medal, First Int Harp Compt, Hartford, Conn, 69; Spanish Govt Scholar, 80. *Mem:* Am Harp Soc; Am Fedn Musicians; Col Music Soc. *Mailing Add:* Dept Music NTex State Univ Denton TX 76203

MAJESKE, DANIEL H
EDUCATOR, VIOLIN
Study: Curtis Inst Music, with Ivan Galamian. *Rec Perf:* 24 Caprices for Solo Violin (Paganini), Advent, 76; Ein Heldenleben (Strauss) & Scheherazade (Rimsky-Korsakov), London. *Pos:* Concertmaster, Casals Fest Orch, formerly; mem, Cleveland Symph Orch, 55-, soloist, 57-, concertmaster & Blossom-Lee chair, 69-, first violin, String Quartet, currently. *Teaching:* Mem fac violin, Cleveland Music Sch Settlement, currently & Cleveland Inst Music, 81- *Mailing Add:* 1834 E 223rd St Euclid OH 44117

MAJOROS, DAVID JOHN
BARITONE, EDUCATOR
b Charleroi, Pa, Mar 22, 51. *Study:* Calif State Col, BS, 72; WVa Univ, MM(vocal perf), 76; Aspen Music Fest, vocal study with Daniel Ferro, summer 76; San Francisco Opera Merola Prog, vocal coaching with Margaret Singer, Susanne Webb, Warren Jones & W Anthony Waters, summer 80; Univ Ariz, AMusD(vocal perf), 80; vocal study with Eugene Conley, Daniel Ferro, Rose Crain & Joseph Golz; vocal coaching with James Benner, Rex Woods & Dr Paula Fan. *Works:* Vicar Gedge in Albert Herring, San Francisco Opera Merola Prog, 80; Franke in Die Fledermaus, 80, Figaro in The Barber of Seville, 80, Marcello in La Boheme, 81, Silvio in I Pagliacci, 82, Pantalon in Love For Three Oranges, 82 & Belcore in L'Elisir D'Amore, 83, Ariz Opera Co, 83. *Pos:* Artist in res, Ariz Opera Co, 79-80 & 82- *Teaching:* Instr voice, Univ Ariz, 81-82 & Ruisseau Consv, Tucson, 82- *Awards:* Gropper Award, San Francisco Opera Merola Prog, 80. *Mem:* Col Music Soc. *Rep:* Sullivan & Lindsey Assoc 133 W 87th St New York NY 10024. *Mailing Add:* c/o Ariz Opera 3501 N Mountain Ave Tucson AZ 85719

MAKI, PAUL-MARTIN
ORGAN, EDUCATOR
Study: Schola Cantorum, dipl; Eastman Sch Music, perf cert, BM, DMA; Syracuse Univ, MM; studied organ with Ocock, Craighead, Poister, Marchal & Langlais. *Pos:* Organist, Temple Sinai, Mt Vernon, NY; recitalist throughout US, Can, Europe & Australia. *Teaching:* Mem fac organ, Manhattan Sch Music, 75- *Mailing Add:* Manhattan Sch Music 120 Claremont Ave New York NY 10027

MAKRIS, ANDREAS
COMPOSER
b Salonica, Greece, Mar 7, 30; US citizen. *Study:* Nat Consv, Salonica, 50; Phillips Univ, 50; Consv, Mannes Col Music, 56; private study with Nadia Boulanger, 56. *Works:* Anamnesis, perf by Nat Symph Orch, 71; Fantasy and Dance (saxophone), 74; Sirens, 76; In Memory, 79; Variations and Song (orch), 79; Fanfare Alexander, perf by Nat Symph Orch, 80; Chromatokinesis, comn by Nat Symph Orch, 80; and others. *Pos:* First violin, Nat Symph Orch, 61-, comp in res, 79- *Awards:* Grants, Damrosh Found, 58, Nat Endowment Arts, 67 & Martha Baird Rockefeller Fund, 70; ASCAP Award, 80. *Mem:* ASCAP. *Mailing Add:* 11204 Oakleaf Dr Silver Spring MD 20901

MALAS, MARLENA KLEINMAN
EDUCATOR, SINGER
Study: Curtis Inst Music, BM; Juilliard Sch. *Rec Perf:* On Vanguard & Columbia. *Pos:* Perf with Metropolitan Opera Studio; affil, opera co of New York City, Santa Fe, Boston, Miami, Washington, DC, Baltimore, San Diego & Milwaukee; soloist, New York Phil, Philadelphia Orch, Marlboro Fest, Casals Fest & others; recitalist, worldwide. *Teaching:* Mem fac voice, Manhattan Sch Music, 82- *Mailing Add:* 245 W 104th St New York NY 10025

MALAS, SPIRO
BASS
b Baltimore, Md, Jan 28, 35. *Study:* Towson State, BS, 60. *Roles:* Figaro in Marriage of Figaro, 68-78 & Leporello in Don Giovanni, 68-78, New York City Opera; Dr Dulcamara in L'elisir d'amore, Covent Garden, 70; Don Pasquale in Don Pasquale, San Carlo & Naples, 73; Podesta, Rome, 73; Assur, Chicago, 75; Sergeant, Metropolitan Opera, 83. *Pos:* Lead bass, New York City Opera, 61-83, Chicago Opera, 71-83 & Metropolitan Opera, 81- *Mailing Add:* 245 W 104th St New York NY 10025

MALFITANO, JOSEPH JOHN
VIOLIN
b Newark, NJ, July 25, 20. *Study:* Violin with Raphael Bronstein, Valentin Blumberg & Louis Parsinger. *Pos:* Mem, Malfitano Duo; conct violinist, US & Can; mem violin sect, Metropolitan Opera Orch, currently. *Mem:* Bohemians. *Mailing Add:* Metropolitan Opera Asn Lincoln Ctr New York NY 10023

MALKOVICH, MARK PAUL
ADMINISTRATOR, LECTURER
b Eveleth, Minn, July 10, 30. *Study:* Columbia Univ, studied piano with William Beller, BS & MS, 53; Chicago Musical Col, studied piano with Dorothy Crost Bourgin; Juilliard Sch, studied piano with Adele Marcus. *Pos:* Artistic & gen dir, Newport Music Fest, 75-; guest lectr, TV & radio appearances & adjudicator at music compt. *Mem:* Harvard Musical Asn. *Mailing Add:* 50 Washington Sq Newport RI 02840

MALLETT, LAWRENCE ROGER
MUSIC DIRECTOR, EDUCATOR
b Centerville, Iowa, Aug 27, 47. *Study:* Univ Iowa, BM, BMEd, 69, DMA, 81; Ohio State Univ, MMus, 71. *Teaching:* Instr woodwind & asst dir band, Luther Col, Iowa, 71-73 & Purdue Univ, 73-76; asst prof & dir bands, Bemidji State Univ, 76-79 & Wright State Univ, 80-82; assoc prof, Gustavus Adolphus Col, 82- *Mem:* Col Band Dir Nat Asn; Music Educr Nat Conf; Minn Music Educr Asn; Am Fedn Musicians; Nat Band Asn (nat state chmn coordr & asst ed jour, 73-76). *Mailing Add:* 1477 Leonard St St Peter MN 56082

MALLORY, (WALTER) HAMPTON
CELLO
b Hong Kong, BCC, Apr 30, 50; US citizen. *Study:* Harvard Col, BA(music), 72; study with Maurice Gendron in Paris, 72-73; Curtis Inst Music, study with David Soyer, cert, 76. *Pos:* Cellist, Pittsburgh Symph Orch, 78- *Mem:* Am Fedn Musicians; Int Conf Symph Opera Musicians. *Mailing Add:* 218 Chapel Ridge Dr Glenshaw PA 15116

MALLORY, LAUREN SCOTT
CELLO
b Johnson City, Tenn, Sept 6, 47. *Study:* Ind Univ, Bloomington, with Janos Starker, BM(cello), 69. *Pos:* Section cellist, Pittsburgh Symph, 69-79, asst prin cellist, 79- *Mailing Add:* 218 Chapel Ridge Dr Glenshaw PA 15116

MALM, WILLIAM PAUL
EDUCATOR, LECTURER
b La Grange, Ill, Mar 6, 28. *Study:* Northwestern Univ, MB, 49 & MM(comp), 50; Univ Calif, Los Angeles, PhD(ethnomusicology), 59. *Teaching:* Instr, Univ Ill, Urbana, 50 & Navy Sch Music, 51-53; lectr, Univ Calif, Los Angeles, 58-60; prof music, Univ Mich, 60- *Awards:* Henry Russel Award for Teaching, Univ Mich, 66; Res Scholar, Villa Serbelloni, Rockefeller Found, 75; Ernst Block Prof, Univ Calif, Berkeley, 80. *Mem:* Soc Ethnomusicol (pres, 78-80); Am Musicol Soc (bd mem, 79-81); Asn Asian Studies. *Publ:* Auth, Japanese Music and Musical Instruments, 59 & Nagauta: The Heart of Kabuki Music, 63, Tuttle; Music Cultures of the Pacific, the Near East, and Asia, 67 & 77 & Six Hidden Views of Japanese Music, 83, Prentice-Hall. *Mailing Add:* Burton Tower Univ Mich Ann Arbor MI 48109

MALMIN, OLAF GERHARDT
EDUCATOR, MUSIC DIRECTOR
b Tacoma, Wash, Nov 26, 39. *Study:* Pacific Lutheran Univ, BMus, 62; Univ Iowa, choral cond with Daniel Moe, MA, 64, orch cond with James Dixon, voice with Albert Gammon & Charles Kellis, PhD, 73. *Rec Perf:* Augustana Choir, Marks Custom Rec, 72, 74, 77, 79 & 82. *Teaching:* Instr music, Clarion State Col, 65-66; asst prof, Buffalo State Univ Col, 66-70; from asst to assoc prof, Augustana Col, 70- *Mem:* Am Choral Dirs Asn; Nat Asn Teachers Singing. *Mailing Add:* Music Dept Augustana Col Sioux Falls SD 57197

MALONE, (MARY) EILEEN
HARP, EDUCATOR
b Victor, NY. *Study:* Eastman Sch Music, BM & perf cert, 31; Paris Consv, with Marcel Tournier; studied with Lucile Johnson & Marcel Grandjany; Nazareth Col, LHD, 82. *Rec Perf:* With Rochester Phil for Victor, Columbia & Mercury. *Pos:* Featured soloist, NBC Radio & TV, 36-60; solo harpist, Rochester Phil, 36-79; harp adv, Nat Fedn Music Clubs, 73-74; toured with New York Phil; solo appearances, Buffalo Symph, Okla Symph & others. *Teaching:* Prof harp, Eastman Sch Music, 30-; lectr, harp wkshps. *Awards:* Musician of Yr, Mu Phi Epsilon, 70. *Mem:* Founding mem, Am Nat Harp Soc (mem bd dir, currently); Int Harp Soc; NY State Music Asn; Mu Phi Epsilon; Am Asn Univ Prof. *Mailing Add:* Eastman Sch Music 26 Gibbs St Rochester NY 14604

MALOOF, WILLIAM J
COMPOSER, EDUCATOR
b Boston, Mass, May 19, 33. *Study:* Boston Univ, BM. *Works:* The Centurion (opera); Sinfonietta Concertante (orch); Two Antique Dances (flute & strings); Essay for Band; Homage to Bali (perc); Fantasy (flute & piano); Music for Piano and Percussion Quartet (chamber music); and others. *Pos:* Guest cond, Boston Pub Sch Symph Band & Orch; cond, US Naval Training Dance Band & Conct Orch. *Teaching:* Chmn comp dept & mem fac theory & comp, Berklee Col Music, 61- *Awards:* First Prize Contemp Comp, Ind State Univ & Indianapolis Symph Sixth Annual Music Fest. *Mailing Add:* 33 Pratt St Brighton MA 02134

MALTI, JOSEPHINE (JACKSON)
PIANO
b Corpus Christi, Tex. *Study:* Aspen Music Sch, with Alexander, Uninsky, Vronsky & Babin, 55-57; Bennett Col, with Marjorie Yates, AAS, 60; Mills Col, with Alexander Libermann, BA, 62. *Pos:* Pianist, Greenwich Piano Trio, 82- *Mem:* Chamber Music Am. *Mailing Add:* 2164 Hyde St San Francisco CA 94109

MAMLOK, URSULA
EDUCATOR, COMPOSER
b Berlin, Germany; US citizen. *Study:* Mannes Col; Manhattan Sch Music, BM & MM, 58. *Works:* Polyphony for Solo Clarinet, comn & perf by Jack Kreiselman, 68; Five Capriccios for Oboe, Piano, 73 & Variations & Interludes (four perc) & Sextet, 78, C F Peters; When Summer Sang, comn & perf by Da Capo Chamber Players, 80 & Panta Rhei—Trio for Violin, Violoncello & Piano, 81. *Teaching:* Fac comp, NY Univ, 67-76; asst prof, City Univ New York, 71-74; prof comp, Manhattan Sch Music, 74- *Awards:* Fels, Nat Endowment for Arts, 74 & 82 & Am Acad & Inst Arts & Lett, 81. *Mem:* Am Comp Alliance (mem bd dir, 68-74, 77-83); Am Music Ctr; Am Women Comp; Int League Women Comp. *Mailing Add:* 305 E 86th St New York NY 10028

MANAHAN, GEORGE
CONDUCTOR, EDUCATOR
Study: Manhattan Sch Music, MM; studied cond with George Schick & Peter Herman Adler. *Pos:* Dir, Contemp Music Ens, Mannes Col Music, formerly; cond, Erick Hawkins Dance Co, formerly; music dir & cond, New Amsterdam Symph; cond, Santa Fe Opera, New Music Consort, Washington Square Fest & Great Neck Symph; assoc cond, NJ Symph, currently. *Teaching:* Assoc cond orch, Manhattan Sch Music, 76-77, mem staff orch cond, 77- *Mailing Add:* Manhattan Sch Music 120 Claremont Ave New York NY 10027

MANCINELLI, ALDO L
EDUCATOR, PIANO
b Steubenville, Ohio. *Study:* Consv Music, Oberlin Col, BM, 52; Accad Santa Cecilia, Rome, with Carlo Zecchi, artist dipl, 55; studied with Claudio Arrau & Rudolf Firkusny. *Rec Perf:* Numerous on RAI-Radiotelevisione Ital, 55-60; Emperor Concerto (Beethoven), Regal Rec, 57; Music of Charles Griffes, Musical Heritage Soc, 78. *Pos:* Conct pianist, US, Europe, Asia & throughout North Africa. *Teaching:* Artist in res, Consv Nat Musique, Beirut, Lebanon, 55-57; prof music & artist in res, Univ Tulsa, 63-80 & Millikin Univ, 80- *Awards:* Winner, Ferruccio Busoni, Int Piano Compt, Italy, 54. *Mem:* Col Music Soc; Music Teachers Nat Asn; Am Liszt Soc; Ill Music Teachers Asn. *Mailing Add:* Sch Music Millikin Univ Decatur IL 62522

MANCINI, HENRY
COMPOSER, CONDUCTOR
b Cleveland, Ohio, Apr 16, 24. *Study:* Study cond & arr with Max Adkins; Juilliard Sch Music, 42-43; private comp study with Ernst Krenek, Mario Castlenuoveo-Tedesco & Dr Alfred Sendry; Duquesne Univ, Hon DMus, 76; Mt St Mary's Col, Md, Hon DHL, 80; Washington & Jefferson Col, Hon Dr Humanities, 81. *Works:* Complete musical scores for numerous motion pictures; TV film scores; TV themes. *Rec Perf:* Henry Conducts the London Symphony, Debut! Henry Mancini Conducting the Philadelphia Orchestra Pops, The Best of Mancini, Symphonic Soul, Brass, Ivory & Strings, Mancini Concert & others, RCA. *Pos:* Guest cond, Philadelphia Symph Orch, 69 & orchestras all over the world for the past 20 years; pianist & arr, Glenn Miller-Tex Beneke Orch, 45; mem music dept, Universal-Int Studios, 52-62. *Awards:* Oscars, Best Song: Moon River & Best Music Score: Breakfast at Tiffany's, 61, Best Song: Days of Wine and Roses, 62 & Best Song Score & Adaptation: Victor/Victoria, 82; 20 Grammy Awards, 58-70; Golden Globe Award, 71. *Mem:* ASCAP; Nat Music Publ Asn; Am Guild Authors & Comp; Comp & Lyricists Guild of Am. *Publ:* Auth, Sounds and Scores, Northridge Music, 73. *Mailing Add:* 9229 Sunset Blvd Suite 304 Los Angeles CA 90069

MANDAC, EVELYN LORENZANA
SOPRANO
b Malaybalay, Philippines, Aug 16, 45. *Study:* Univ Philippines, BA, 63; Juilliard Sch Music, MA, 67; studied with Aurelio Estanislao, Hans Heinz & Daniel Ferro. *Rec Perf:* Carmina Burana (Orff) & Symphony No 2 (Mahler), Philips Rec. *Roles:* Mimi in La Boheme, Wash Opera, 69; Despina in Cosi fan tutte; Zerlina in Don Giovanni; Norina in Don Pasquale; Gilda in Rigoletto; Pamina in The Magic Flute; Micaela in Carmen; and many others. *Pos:* Res mem, Metropolitan Opera; sop, San Francisco Opera, Houston Opera, Seattle Opera, Netherlands Opera Co, Glyndebourne Fest & many others in US & Europe; soloist, numerous US orchs incl Cleveland Phil, Philadelphia Orch, Los Angeles Phil & Chicago Phil. *Awards:* Rockefeller Fel, 64-67; Winner, Queen Elizabeth Voice Compt, Brussels, 66 & Metropolitan Opera Auditions, 66. *Mem:* Am Guild Musicians & Actors. *Mailing Add:* c/o Columbia Artists 165 W 57th St New York NY 10019

MANDEL, ALAN ROGER
PIANO, EDUCATOR
b New York, NY, July 17, 35. *Study:* Juilliard Sch Music, BS, 56, MS, 57; Akad Mozarteum, Salzburg, Austria, Ausgesichnet dipl, 63; study with Rosina Lhevinne, Leonard Shure, Rudolf Serkin & Hans Werner Henze. *Rec Perf:* The Complete Piano Works of Charles Ives, An Anthology of American Piano Music: 1790-1970 & Louis Moreau Gottschalk: Forty Works for Piano, Desto Rec; American Piano Music, Three Sides of George Rochberg and Elie Siegmeister: Sonata No 1 & Sonata No 5 for Violin and Piano, Grenadilla Rec; New Music of Elie Seigmeister: Sonata No 4 for Violin and Piano, Orion Master Rec; and many others. *Pos:* Artistic dir & pianist, Washington Music Ens, 81-; solo pianist with major orchs in the US & worldwide. *Teaching:* Instr music, Pa State Univ, 63-66; instr, Am Univ, Washington, DC, 66-67, from asst prof to prof & chmn piano div, 67- *Awards:* Fulbright Fel, 61-63. *Mailing Add:* 3113 Northampton St NW Washington DC 20015

MANDELBAUM, GAYNA FAYE
VIOLIN
b Detroit, Mich, Apr 11, 53. *Study:* Curtis Inst Music, with Ivan Galamian, BMus, 74; Sch Music, Ind Univ, with Josef Gingold, MMus, 76. *Pos:* First violin, Cincinnati Symph Orch, 76- *Mailing Add:* 2540 Vera Ave Cincinnati OH 45237

MANDELBAUM, M JOEL
COMPOSER, EDUCATOR
b New York, NY, Oct 12, 32. *Study:* Harvard Univ, AB, 53; Brandeis Univ, MFA, 57; Ind Univ, PhD, 61. *Works:* Three Dream Songs, Fanning Verlag, 78; Opera: The Dybbule, Queens Col Opera Studio, 79; Xerophony No 2, New Repty Ens, 79; Rainbows of Darkness, Branche, 80; Sea Surface Full of Clouds, Queens Col Orch Soc, 82. *Teaching:* From lectr to prof, Queens Col, City Univ New York, 61- *Mem:* Am Soc Jewish Music (mem gov bd, 77-). *Interests:* Microtonal music. *Mailing Add:* 39-49 46 St Sunnyside NY 11104

MANDL, LILI KRAUS See Kraus, Lili

MANERI, JOSEPH GABRIEL
COMPOSER, EDUCATOR
b New York, NY, Feb 9, 27. *Study:* With Josef Schmid, 47-58. *Works:* Piano Sonata, String Quartet & Trio (piano, bass & perc), 60, H Branch; Maranatha, 68 & Ephatha, 72, Margun; Piano Concerto, H Branch, 75; And Death Shall Have No Dominion, Margun, 77. *Teaching:* Instr comp & theory, Brooklyn Consv Music, 58-65 & New England Consv, 70- *Mailing Add:* New England Consv 290 Huntington Ave Boston MA 02115

MANES, STEPHEN GABRIEL
PIANO, EDUCATOR
b Bennington, Vt, Apr 11, 40. *Study:* Juilliard Sch Music, BS, 61, MS, 63; Acad Music, Vienna, 63-64. *Rec Perf:* Sonata in G Major, Op 37 (Tchaikovsky), Indianisches Tagebuch (Busoni) & others, Orion Master Rec, 74- *Pos:* Performer radio, Brit Broadcasting Corp, 75, WQXR, New York, 76 & others; soloist, major orchs US & abroad; participant, music fests & chamber music concts; appearances with Cleveland, Rowe & Tokyo String Quartets. *Teaching:* Vis instr music, Consv Music, Oberlin Col, 66-67; asst prof, Ball State Univ, 67-68; prof, State Univ NY, Buffalo, 68- *Awards:* Chopin Prize, Kosciuszko Found, 60; Town Hall Award, Conct Artists Guild, 62; Harriet Cohen Int Beethoven Prize, 64. *Mem:* Music Teachers Nat Asn; NY State Music Teachers Asn; Col Music Soc; Am Fedn Musicians; Am Asn Univ Prof. *Mailing Add:* 384 Voorhees Ave Buffalo NY 14126

MANFORD, BARBARA ANN
CONTRALTO, EDUCATOR
b St Augustine, Fla, Nov 13, 29. *Study:* Fla State Univ, BM, 51, MM, 70. *Rec Perf:* Seven German Songs (Spohr), 77, Two Songs (Brahms), 77 & Gypsy Songs, 82, Coronet. *Roles:* Mother in Fugitives (world premiere), Fla State Univ, 50; Berta in Barber of Seville, Teatro Nuovo, Milan, Italy, 62; Cornelia

in Julius Cesare, major opera houses in Italy, 64; Franchetta in Li Tre Amanti Ridicoli, Teatro Angelicum, Milan, Italy, 64; Amphissia in The Leper (world premiere), Tallahassee, Fla, 69; and many others. *Teaching:* Instr voice & Ital diction, Fla State Univ, 68-70; assoc prof, Ball State Univ, 70- *Awards:* Winner, Longio Vocal Contest, 64. *Mem:* Chicago Artists Asn; Nat Asn Teachers Singing; Music Teachers Nat Asn; Pi Kappa Lambda; Sigma Alpha Iota. *Mailing Add:* Colonial Crest Apt #104 405 S Morrison Muncie IN 47304

MANGIN, NOEL
BASS

b New Zealand. *Rec Perf:* Die Winterreise (Schubert); Selected Arias from Wagner, EMI; rec on Decca, Deutsche Grammophon & RCA. *Roles:* Don Basilio in Le Nozze di Figaro, 60; Sarastro in The Magic Flute, New York City Opera, 66; Pope Leo in Attila & Charon in Orfeo, English Nat Opera; Falstaff in Die Lustigen Weiber von Windsor & King Dodon in Le Coq d'Or, Hamburg State Opera. *Pos:* Mem, English Nat Opera, 63-66 & Hamburg State Opera, 67-76; perf with leading opera co incl La Scala, Covent Garden, Paris Opera, Deutsche Oper, Seattle Opera & Vienna Staatsoper. *Mailing Add:* c/o Herbert Barrett Mgt 1860 Broadway New York NY 10023

MANN, ALFRED
EDUCATOR

b Hamburg, Germany, Apr 28, 17; US citizen. *Study:* State Acad Music, Berlin, dipl, 37; Consv, Milan, 38-39; Curtis Inst Music, dipl, 42; Columbia Univ, AM, 50, PhD, 55; Spokane Consv Music, HonMusD, 47; Baldwin Wallace Col, HonMusD, 81. *Rec Perf:* On numerous Am & European labels. *Pos:* Cond, Cantata Singers, NY, 52-59 & Bach Choir Bethlehem, 69-81; dir publ, Am Choral Found, Inc, 61-; ed, Am Choral Rev, 61-; mem bd dir, Georg Friedrich Handel Ges, Halle, 67- & Gottinger Handelges, 67-; guest appearances in New York, Philadelphia, Boston, Gottingen, Leipzig & Berlin. *Teaching:* Instr, State Acad, Berlin, 37; instr & res asst, Scuola Musicale, Milan, 83 & Curtis Inst Music, 39-41; from asst prof to assoc prof, Rutgers Univ, 47-56, prof, 56-79 & emer prof, 80-; prof musicol, Eastman Sch Music, 80- *Mem:* Am Musicol Soc; Int Musicol Soc; Neue Bachgesellschaft (secy Am chap, 72-). *Interests:* History of music theory and choral music. *Publ:* Coauth, Thomas Attwoods Theorie—und Kompositionsstudien bei Mozart, 65 & auth, J J Fux, Gradus ad Parnassum, 67, Barenreiter; coauth, The Present State of Handel Research, Acta Musicologica, 69; auth, Beethoven's Contrapuntal Studies with Haydn, Musical Quart, 70; Haydn's Elementarbuch, Music Forum, 73; Hanuel's Composition Lessons, 79 & G F Handee, Composition Lessons, 79, Barenreiter. *Rep:* Am Choral Found 130 W 56th New York NY 10019. *Mailing Add:* Eastman Sch Music Univ Rochester Rochester NY 14604

MANN, BRIAN RICHARD
WRITER, EDUCATOR

b San Francisco, Calif, Oct 18, 49. *Study:* Univ Edinburgh, Scotland, BMus, 72; Univ Calif, Berkeley, MA, 73, PhD, 81. *Teaching:* Vis asst prof, Vassar Col, Poughkeepsie, NY, 82-83; assoc prof, Univ Nebr, Lincoln, 83- *Mem:* Am Musicol Soc. *Publ:* Auth, The Secular Madrigals of Filippo di Monte, UMI Res Press, 83. *Mailing Add:* Sch Music Univ Nebr Lincoln NE 68588

MANN, ROBERT
VIOLIN, COMPOSER

b Portland, Ore, July 19, 20. *Study:* Juilliard Sch, with Bernard Wagenaar, dipl; studied with Stefan Wolpe, Edouard Hurlimann & Edouard Dethier. *Works:* Five Movements (string quartet), 52; Duo for Violin and Piano, 75; Fantasy for Orchestra; Suite for Strings; Piano Sonata; Duo for Violin and Viola; eighteen Lyric Trios (narrator, violin & piano). *Pos:* Founder & first violinist, Juilliard Quartet, 48- *Teaching:* Fac mem chamber music, Juilliard Sch, 46-; mem fac & artist in res, Mich State Univ, 77- *Awards:* Naumburg Award, 41; Nat Endowment Arts Grant, 75. *Mem:* Am Comp Alliance. *Mailing Add:* Juilliard Sch Lincoln Ctr New York NY 10023

MANNING, ROBERT
DOUBLE BASS, EDUCATOR

b Creskill, NJ, Aug 14, 29. *Study:* Drake Univ, BMusEd, 51; Univ Southern Calif, MMus, 58; Long Beach State Univ; Fresno State Univ. *Pos:* Prin double bass, Kern Co Phil Orch, 53-68 & San Jose Symph Orch, 69-; cond summer music camp orchs, Gunnison, Colo, 54-58; Idyllwild Sch Perf Arts, Univ Southern Calif, 59-62 & 66, Univ Mont, 70 & Hayward, Calif, 73; adjudicator music festivals, 60-; cond hon fest orchs, Calif, 63- *Teaching:* Music, pub sch, McFarland, Calif, 53-55, Wasco, Calif, 55-60 & East Bakersfield, 60-68; mem fac, Bakersfield Col, 67-68; asst prof, San Jose State Univ, 68-73, assoc prof, 73-79, prof, 79- *Mem:* Life mem, Music Educr Nat Conf; Calif Music Educr Asn (treas cent sect, 60-61, mem state bd, 70-72). *Mailing Add:* 2880 Kring Dr San Jose CA 95125

MANNING, WILLIAM MEREDITH
EDUCATOR, CLARINET

b Flushing, NY, Apr 28, 33. *Study:* Drake Univ, BME, 54, MM, 57. *Teaching:* Dir instr music, pub sch, Sigourney, Iowa, 54-56; from instr to prof clarinet & theory, Univ Mont, 57-, actg chmn dept music, 69-70 & 71-72. *Mem:* Int Clarinet Soc; Nat Asn Col Wind & Perc Instr. *Mailing Add:* 2309 Valley View Dr Missoula MT 59803

MANNION, ELIZABETH (BELLE)
MEZZO-SOPRANO, EDUCATOR

b Seattle, Wash, July 19, 28. *Study:* Univ Wash, BS(music), 50; Cornish Sch Music, Seattle, performer's cert, 52; Hochschule Musik, Köln, Germany, 54-

55; Ind Univ, 65; studied with Arpad Sandor, George Schick, Otto Guth & many others. *Roles:* Appearances with Anchorage Opera, Bonn Opera, WGermany, Chicago Lyr Opera, Ind Opera Theater, NBC-TV Opera, New York & many others. *Pos:* Solo recitalist & instr master classes incl Town Hall, NY, command perf, White House, Carnegie Hall, Eastman Sch Music, Nat Gallery Art, Nat Arts Found, New York & others; oratorio & solo appearances with symph orch & soc in US incl Atlanta Symph, Baltimore Symph, Boston Symph, Dallas Symph, New Orleans Symph, Pittsburgh Symph & many others. *Teaching:* Instr voice, Cornish Sch Music & Drama, Seattle, 50-53; instr, Bowling Green State Univ, 65-66, Interlochen Summer Music Camp, Mich, 66, 67 & 68, private studio, Munich, WGermany, 74-75 & Aspen Music Fest, Colo, 80, 81 & 82; asst prof, Univ Mich, Ann Arbor, 66-68; assoc prof, Ind Univ, Bloomington, 68-73, prof, 73-77; prof, Fla State Univ, 77-78; Doty distinguished prof, Univ Tex, Austin, 78- *Awards:* Martha Baird Rockefeller Grants, 63 & 65; Teaching Excellence Award, Nat Fedn Music Clubs, 73; Teaching Excellence Award, Univ Tex, Austin, 80. *Mem:* Am Guild Musical Artists; Am Fedn TV & Radio Artists; Nat Asn Teachers Singing; Nat Fedn Music Clubs; Pi Kappa Lambda. *Mailing Add:* 3921 Knollwood Dr Austin TX 78731

MANNO, ROBERT
COMPOSER, BARITONE

b Bryn Mawr, Pa, July 27, 44. *Study:* Manhattan Sch Music, BS, 68; New York Univ, MA, 74. *Works:* Five Thematic Etudes (string quartet), 73; Landscapes (voice, wind quartet & double bass), 73; Three Quiet Pieces (harp solo), 74; Dreams and Riffs (horn & piano or chamber orch), 74-75; Amen, 74; A Woman's Love (sop & string orch), 75; Next to of Course God, 76. *Pos:* Jazz pianist, 62-65; mem chorus, New York City Opera, 68-77 & Metropolitan Opera, 77- *Awards:* Ernest Block Award, 71; First Prize, Delius Fest, Jacksonville, Fla, 75. *Mem:* Am Guild Musical Artists (mem bd gov, 81-82); Am Fedn TV & Radio Artists; Am Music Center. *Mailing Add:* 44 W 69th St #3B New York NY 10023

MANSFIELD, KENNETH ZOELLIN
ORGAN, EDUCATOR

b King City, Calif, Aug 21, 32. *Study:* Harvard Col, BA(music), 54; Harvard Univ, MA(music), 55. *Works:* Six Variations on Old Hundredth, Peer Int, 80. *Pos:* Organist & choir dir, St Luke's Episcopal Church, San Francisco, Calif, 64-66; organist, Lafayette-Orinda Presby Church, Lafayette, Calif, 68- *Teaching:* Prof music, Calif State Univ, Hayward, 68- *Mem:* Am Guild Organists (dean San Francisco chap, 75-77). *Mailing Add:* Music Dept Calif State Univ Hayward CA 94542

MANSON, EDDY LAWRENCE
COMPOSER, HARMONICA

b New York, NY, May 9, 22. *Study:* Juilliard Sch Music, dipl, 42; Sch Radio & TV, NY Univ, cert, 53; studied clarinet with Jan Williams, comp with Vittorio Giannini, Howard Brockway & Rudy Schramm, orch with Adolf Schmid & cond with Albert Stoessel & Louis Bostelman. *Works:* Fugue for Woodwinds, Assoc Publ, 55; Symph #1, Fla Symph Orch, 60; Nigun & Variations on Kol Nidrei, Synagogue of Perf Arts, 73; Bachiana Americana, Calif Chamber Symph Orch, 75; Analogues (string quartet & solo harmonica), 79 & Encounters (woodwind quintet), 80, Manson Ens; and many others. *Rec Perf:* Harmonica Impressions, 48-49 & Joey's Theme & Coney Island (Little Fugitive), 53, Columbia Rec; Suite From Little Fugitive, Folkways, 55; Harmonica Holiday, Mercury, 57; The Fi is Hi, RCA Victor, 57; The Great Eddy Manson Plays the Great Harmonica Favorites, 20th Century Fox, 62; Peg O' My Heart & Other Favorites, RCA, 63. *Pos:* Harmonica virtuoso, perf int, 45-; pres & creative dir, Eddy Manson Prod Inc, 60-; columnist, Overture Mag, 75-; founder, Am Soc Music Arr Comp Arr Wkshp, Los Angeles, 78; founder & dir, Manson Chamber Ens, 80-; music dir, Temple Sholom Aleichem, 80- *Teaching:* Numerous seminars & master classes, Univ Calif, Los Angeles; sr instr film scoring, orch & arr, Univ Calif, Los Angeles, 75-81; private instr comp, arr & harmonica, currently. *Awards:* Elizabeth Sprague Coolidge Award Chamber Music Comp, 42; Five Venice Film Fest Awards, 53, 56, 58, 61 & 62; 18 ASCAP Panel Awards; and others. *Bibliog:* Alex Fogel (auth), articles, Harmonica Happenings, summer 73; David Chagall (auth), How Music Soothes You, Family Weekly, 1/30/83. *Mem:* Am Guild Authors & Comp; Comp & Lyricists Guild Am; ASCAP; Am Fedn Musicians; Am Soc Music Arrangers (pres, 56-59 & 77-81). *Publ:* Coauth (with Tom Backer), In the Key of Feeling, Human Behavior Mag, 2/78; auth, Murder in the Music School, Allegro, 2/78; Napoleon; Pit Power, 7/26/81 & We Just Don't Play the Blues, 8/30/81, Los Angeles Times Calendar. *Rep:* Sheri Mann Agency 11601 Dunstan Way #309 Los Angeles CA 90049. *Mailing Add:* 7245 Hillside Ave #216 Los Angeles CA 90046

MANSOURI, LOTFOLLAH (LOTFI)
DIRECTOR—OPERA

b Tehran, Iran, June 15, 29. *Study:* Univ Calif, Los Angeles, AB, 53. *Pos:* Res stage dir, Zurich Opera, 60-65; chief stage dir, Geneva Opera, 65-75; artistic adv, Tehran Opera, 73-75; gen dir, Can Opera Co, 76-; opera adv, Nat Arts Ctr, Ont, 77; operatic consult & dir, Yes, Giorgio, MGM, 81; guest dir, many opera co incl Metropolitan Opera, San Francisco Opera, La Scala, Vienna Staatsoper, Vienna Volksoper, Salzburg Fest, Amsterdam Opera & Holland Fest. *Teaching:* Asst prof, Univ Calif, Los Angeles, 57-60; dramatic coach, Music Acad West, 59. *Mem:* Am Guild Musical Artists; Can Actors Equity Asn; Opera Am (vpres, 79-83). *Publ:* Coauth, An Operatic Life, 82. *Mailing Add:* Can Opera Co 417 Queens Quay W Toronto ON #M5V 1A2 Canada

MANSUR, PAUL MAX
EDUCATOR, FRENCH HORN
b Hammon, Okla, July 19, 26. *Study:* Univ Okla, BMus, 51, EdD, 65; Ariz State Univ, MAEd, 53. *Pos:* Prin horn, Sherman Symph Orch, 66-; ed, The Horn Call, J Int Horn Soc, 76- *Teaching:* Chmn dept music, Southeastern Okla State Univ, 65- *Mem:* Music Educr Nat Conf; life mem, Int Horn Soc. *Mailing Add:* 2227 Gershwin Dr Durant OK 74701

MANWELL, PHILIP
ORGAN, CONDUCTOR & MUSIC DIRECTOR
b Marysville, Calif, June 9, 46. *Study:* With Marcel Dupre, Paris, 64-65; Juilliard Sch, 65-72. *Works:* Mass, South Bergan Oratorio Soc, NJ, 69; Requiem, Christ's Church Choir, Baltimore, 81. *Rec Perf:* On Orion Master Rec. *Pos:* Asst cond, St Andrew Music Soc, NY, 66-68; cond, South Bergen Oratorio Soc, NJ, 68-70 & Wed Morning Choral, Calif, 82-; organist & choirmaster, Church of the Holy Trinity, New York, 76-80; dir music, Christ's Church, Baltimore, 80-82 & First Presby Church, Oakland, Calif, 82. *Teaching:* Chmn dept music, Nightingale-Bamford Sch, New York, 70-78. *Awards:* Valentine Prize in Organ, Juilliard Sch Music, 71. *Mem:* Am Guild Organists. *Publ:* Coauth, The Black and White of Music, Panonia Press, 68. *Rep:* Edith Mugdon Artist's Mgt 84 Prospect Ave Douglaston NY 11363. *Mailing Add:* 2619 Broadway Oakland CA 94612

MARCELLUS, JOHN ROBERT, III
EDUCATOR, MUSIC DIRECTOR
b Overton, Tex, Sept 17, 39. *Study:* Univ Md, BS, 64; Cath Univ Am, MMusic, 70, DMA, 73. *Rec Perf:* The Contemporary Music Forum, Opus One Rec, 76; Our Musical Past—19th Century Instrument Music, Libr Cong, 76; 19th Century Ballroom Music, Nonesuch Rec, 76; Am Brass Band Journal, Sine Qua Non, 77. *Pos:* Assoc prin trombone, Baltimore Symph Orch, 64-65; prin trombone, Nat Symph Orch, 65-78; music dir, Brighton Symph Orch, 80- *Teaching:* Instr trombone, NC Sch Arts, 65-69; adj prof appl music, Cath Univ Am, 66-78; lectr music, Am Univ, 68-78; prof trombone, Eastman Sch Music, 78-, Kibourn prof, 82- *Awards:* Elmer Fudpucker Award, Int Trombone Asn, 80. *Mem:* Founder, Int Trombone Asn; Music Educr Nat Conf; Nat Asn Wind & Perc Instr; Phi Mu Alpha Sinfonia. *Publ:* Contribr, Getting Down to Brass Facts: A Round Table, Music Educr J, 9/69; auth, The Alto Trombone & The Concerto Literature, Int Trombone Asn J, 73; Master Class, Accent, 78; contribr, Trombone Issue, Instrumentalist, 78; co-auth, Trombone Personnel of North American Orchestras, Int Trombone Asn J, 1/82. *Mailing Add:* 26 Gibbs St Rochester NY 14625

MARCELLUS, ROBERT
CONDUCTOR & MUSIC DIRECTOR, EDUCATOR
Study: Studied with Earl Handlon & Daniel Bonade. *Rec Perf:* Clarinet Concerto (Mozart), Columbia. *Pos:* Mem, Nat Symph, 45 & 49-53, prin clarinetist, 50-53; mem, US Air Force Band, 46-59; prin clarinetist, Cleveland Orch, 53-73; music dir & cond, Cleveland Phil Orch, 71-77; musical adv, Canton Symph, Ohio, 75 & 76; guest cond, Minn Orch, Detroit Symph, St Louis Little Symph, Nat Arts Ctr, Ottawa, Atlantic Symph, Halifax & World Youth Orch; music dir, Scotia Chamber Players, Halifax, currently & Interlochen Arts Acad Symph Orch, 77- *Teaching:* Head, Dept Clarinet Studies, Cleveland Inst Music, 59-73 & Wind Chamber Music Studies, Blossom Fest Sch, 68-73; prof clarinet & music dir, Univ Symph Orch, Northwestern Univ, 74- *Mem:* Pi Kappa Lambda; Delta Omicron. *Mailing Add:* 2025 Sherman Ave Evanston IL 60201

MARCO, GUY ANTHONY
WRITER, LIBRARIAN
b New York, NY, Oct 4, 27. *Study:* Am Consv Music, BMus, 51; Univ Chicago, MA(music), 54, MA(libr sci), 55, PhD(musicol), 56. *Pos:* Dir libr, Chicago Musical Col, 53-54; asst classics librn, Univ Chicago, 54; asst librn, Wright Jr Col, Chicago, 54-56; ref librn, Chicago Teachers Col, 57; librn, Amundsen Jr Col, 57-60; chief gen ref & bibliog div, Libr Cong, 77-78; dir, NAm, Libr Develop Consultants Int. *Teaching:* Instr musicol, Chicago Musical Col, 53-54; instr music, Wright Jr Col, Chicago, 54-56; vis lectr libr sci, Univ Wis, 55; instr music & humanities, Chicago City Jr Col, 56-60; instr music, Amundsen Jr Col, 57-60; assoc prof libr sci & chmn dept, Kent State Univ, 60-66; prof & dean sch libr sci, 66-77; prof & dir div libr sci, San Jose State Univ, 81- *Mem:* Am Musicol Soc; Music Libr Asn; Int Asn Music Libr; Asn Am Libr Sch; Am Libr Asn. *Interests:* Music bibliography; 16th century theory; form and structure; music printing. *Publ:* Auth, Syllabus for Music Bibliography, Univ Chicago, 53; The Earliest Music Printers of Continental Europe, Bibliog Soc Univ Va, 62; coauth, The Art of Counterpoint, Yale Univ Press, 68; Information on Music, Libr Unlimited, Vol 1, 75, Vol 2, 77, Vol 3, 83; also 100 articles & reviews. *Mailing Add:* 998 Meridian Ave Apt 39 San Jose CA 95126

MARCUS, ADA BELLE (GROSS)
COMPOSER, PIANO
b Chicago, Ill, July 8, 29. *Study:* DePaul Univ, studied piano with Sergei Tarnowsky, 41-46, comp with Alexander Tcherepnin, 61-62, MMus, 78; Am Consv, Chicago, studied comp with Leo Sowerby, 54-55; Chicago Col Music, Roosevelt Univ, studied comp with Karel B Jirak, 59-60. *Works:* Am Song Cycle, WTTW-TV, Chicago, 63; Song for Flute, Tempo Music Publ Inc, 70; Three Piano Works, WNYC-Radio, 78; Four Piano Works, 83, perf by Ada Belle Marcus; Textures (chamber work), 83 & Song Cycle, 83, perf by Chicago Chamber Orch; Song Cycle, Am Soc Univ Comp Nat Conf. *Mem:* Am Soc Univ Comp; Musicians Club Women (comp chmn, 81-); League Women Comp; Am Women Comp; Am Music Ctr. *Mailing Add:* 9734 Landings Lane Apt 502 Des Plaines IL 60016

MARCUS, ADELE
PIANO, EDUCATOR
b Kansas City, Mo. *Study:* Juilliard Sch, with Josef Lhevinne; studied with Artur Schnabel. *Pos:* Soloist & recitalist with maj orchs throughout US, Can, Europe & Israel. *Teaching:* Asst to Josef Lhevinne, Juilliard Sch, seven yrs, mem fac piano, 54-; mem fac, Aspen Sch Music, 64-70 & Fest & Inst, Temple Univ, 71- *Awards:* Naumberg Prize Winner. *Mailing Add:* Juilliard Sch Lincoln Ctr New York NY 10023

MARCUS, HERMAN
BASS
b Brooklyn, NY, July 14, 31. *Study:* Berkshire Music Ctr, 63; Aspen Fest, studied voice with Jennie Tourel, 64; studied with Eleanor Steber, 68-71. *Roles:* Supt Budd in Albert Herring, Aspen Fest, 64; Dr Grenvil in Traviata, 66-67, Benoit & Alcindoro in Boheme, 66-67 & Bartolo in Marriage of Figaro, 66-67, Metropolitan Opera Nat Co. *Pos:* With Camerata Singers, 65-68; with Roger Wagner Chorale, 67; bass, Metropolitan Opera Chorus, 68-69 & currently. *Mailing Add:* 170 W 73rd St New York NY 10023

MARCUS, LEONARD MARSHALL
ADMINISTRATOR, WRITER
b New York, NY, Aug 2, 30. *Study:* Harvard Col, AB, 51; Harvard Univ, MA, 53. *Pos:* Mgr, Columbia Rec Info Serv, 61-62; ed, Carnegie Hall Prog, 63-65; ed in chief, High Fidelity, Musical Am, 68-80; cond, Stockbridge Chamber Orch, 75- *Teaching:* Cond orch, Dalton Sch, 82- *Mem:* Independent Broadcasting Assoc (mem bd, 79-); Asn Classical Music (mem bd, 82-). *Publ:* Auth, numerous articles in High Fidelity, Musical Am, Juilliard Review, Keynote & others. *Mailing Add:* 299 Under Mountain Rd Lenox MA 01240

MARDEROSIAN, ARDASH
TROMBONE, TEACHER
b Highland Park, Mich, July 10, 30. *Study:* Univ Ill, Urbana, BM(perf), 57. *Pos:* Prin trombone, Lyr Opera Chicago, 63-, Grant Park Symph, 63- & Orch Ill, 78- *Teaching:* Lectr trombone, Chicago Musical Col, Roosevelt Univ, 72-83. *Mem:* Int Trombone Asn. *Mailing Add:* Lyr Opera Chicago 20 N Wacker Dr Chicago IL 60606

MAREK, DAN
VOICE, EDUCATOR
Study: Manhattan Sch Music, BM, MM; studied voice with Cornelius Reid, opera & coaching with George Schick & acting with Rose Lanver. *Pos:* Singer, Metropolitan Opera, New York City Opera & others; soloist, numerous recitals, oratorios & with leading orchs. *Teaching:* Mem fac voice, Mannes Col Music, 74- *Publ:* Contribr to Music J. *Mailing Add:* c/o Liegner Mgt 1860 Broadway Suite 1610 New York NY 10023

MARESCA, ROSALIA
SOPRANO, ADMINISTRATOR
b New York, NY, Aug 16, 23. *Study:* Studied in Italy & USA. *Roles:* Tosca in Tosca, cities throughout Italy, 58-59; sop in Cavalleria Rusticana & I Pagliacci, NY Opera Fest, 61-62; Musetta in La Boheme, Cincinnati Summer Opera & Philadelphia Opera; Aida in Aida, Hartford, Conn, Long Island & Chautauqua; sop in Il Trovatore, Washington DC, Brooklyn & Philadelphia; Butterfly in Madame Butterfly, Japan, Brooklyn & Tampa; also many others. *Pos:* Exec dir, San Carlo Opera of Fla, 73-78; general mgr, Fla Lyr Opera, 79- & Matinee Opera Theatre, 80- *Mailing Add:* 1055 Stephen Foster Dr Largo FL 33541

MARET, STANLEY
BASSOON, EDUCATOR
b Joplin, Mo, July 25, 26. *Study:* Eastman Sch Music, Rochester Univ, BM(comp & theory), 48; Univ Colo, MA(comp), 56; Univ Ill, Urbana, with Barrill Phillips. *Pos:* Contrabassoonist, Cleveland Orch, 62- *Teaching:* Theory & bassoon, Oberlin Col Consv, 59-61. *Mailing Add:* Severance Hall Univ Circle Cleveland OH 44121

MARGALIT, ISRAELA
PIANO, WRITER
b Haifa, Israel. *Study:* Israel Acad Music, Tel Aviv, artist degree; Hochschule Musik Munich; Mozarteum, Salzburg; Case Western Reserve Univ; Lake Erie Col, Hon DHL. *Rec Perf:* Piano Concerto No 3 (Prokofiev), Piano Concerto No 1 (Chopin) & Piano Sonata in B-flat Minor (Chopin), London Rec; Concerto (Chausson), Telarc Rec; Pictures at an Exhibition (Moussorgsky), Gilde des Disques Rec; First Piano Concerto (Brahms), TV Second Channel, Germany; Davidsbündlertänze (Schumann), TV First Channel, France. *Pos:* Piano soloist with Boston Symph, NY Phil, Hamburg Phil, Vienna Symph, Munich Phil, London Phil & others; judge, Int Music Compt. *Mem:* Sigma Alpha Iota. *Publ:* Auth, two scripts on life of Beethoven, ABC Cable TV. *Rep:* Columbia Artists Mgt Inc 165 W 57th St New York NY 10019. *Mailing Add:* 555 Park Ave New York NY 10021

MARGULIS, JOHN LAWRENCE
DIRECTOR—OPERA
b New York, NY, June 9, 48. *Study:* Ill Wesleyan Univ, BFA, 80. *Pos:* Dir, Miss Julie, New York Lyr Opera, 79, Tosca, Northern Ireland Opera, 80, Saint of Bleecker Street, Providence Opera, 81 & Birdbath, Quaigh Theatre, 82. *Mailing Add:* 243 Riverside Dr 302 New York NY 10025

MARINO, AMERIGO ANGELO
CONDUCTOR & MUSIC DIRECTOR
b Chicago, Ill, Feb 5, 25. *Study:* Chicago Musical Col; Sherwood Music Sch; Chicago Consv; studied with Nicolai Maklo, George Szell, Fritz Zweig, Alfred Wallenstein & Max Rudolph. *Pos:* Violinist, Los Angeles Phil, 47-49, Hollywood Bowl Orch, 47-49 & Paramount Pictures, 52-54; cond & comp, CBS Radio & TV, 53-56 & Liberty, Capitol & RCA Rec, 59-63; music dir, Glendale Symph, 58-63, St Louis Little Symph, 64-76, Birmingham Symph Orch, 64- & Ala Symph Orch, currently; guest cond, New York Phil & Chicago, Nat, St Louis & Houston Symphonies. *Awards:* Ford Fel, 63; Silver Bowl Award, Birmingham Fest Arts, 66; Obelisk Award, Birmingham Children's Fest, 76. *Mem:* Cond Guild; Am Symph Orch League. *Rep:* Maxim Gershunoff Attractions Inc 502 Park Ave New York NY 10022. *Mailing Add:* Ala Symph Orch PO Box 2125 Birmingham AL 35201

MARK, PETER
CONDUCTOR, VIOLA
b New York, NY, Oct 31, 40. *Study:* Juilliard Prep Sch, 53-57; Columbia Univ, BA(musicol), 61; Juilliard Sch Music, with Jean Morel, Joseph Fuchs & Walter Trampler, MS, 63. *Rec Perf:* Mary, Queen of Scots, 79 & A Christmas Carol, 80, Moss Music Group Rec. *Roles:* Shepherd boy in Tosca, Metropolitan Opera, 55-56. *Pos:* Boy sop soloist, Children's Chorus, New York City Opera & Metropolitan Opera, 53-55; prin freelance & string quartet violist, Juilliard Orch, Princeton Symph, Trenton Symph, Tiemann String Quartet, Beaux Arts & Los Angeles String Quartet, Santa Barbara Symph & Lyric Opera Chicago, 60-68; asst prin violist, Los Angeles Phil Orch, 68-69; solo violist, Europe, SAm & US, 65-77; gen dir & cond, Va Opera Asn, 75-; cond, Chamber Players, Santa Barbara Chamber Orch, 76-77; guest cond, Wolf Trap Orch, 79, New York City Opera, 81, Los Angeles Opera Repty Theater, 81 & Royal Opera House, London, 82. *Teaching:* Prof music & dramatic art, Univ Calif, Santa Barbara, 65- *Awards:* Woodrow Wilson fel, 61-62; Elias Lifchey Viola Award, 62-63; Creative Inst Award, Univ Calif, 68-69 & 71-72. *Mailing Add:* 639 Surf View Dr Santa Barbara CA 93109

MARKEY, GEORGE B
EDUCATOR, ORGAN
b Worthington, Minn, Aug 18, 25. *Study:* Comp with Theodore Bergman, Joanna Graudon, Dmitri Mitropoulos, Rudolf Serkin, Rupert Sircom, Leo Sowerby, Alexander McCurdy & Norman Coke-Jephcott; MacPhail Col Music, Univ Minn, BMus 43, MMus, 55; Curtis Inst Music, artists dipl, 49; Am Guild Organists, AAGO, 56, FAGO, 57. *Rec Perf:* Works of Bach, Bruhns, Buxtehude, Reubke, Mozart, Widor, Vierne, Dupre, Durufle, Reger Hindemith, Bach, Kellner, Lidon, Felton, Roger-Ducasse & Tournemire, Psallite, Germany; Works of Mendelssohn, Schumann & Durufle, Wicks Golden Label; recordings for Cologne West Deutsche Rundfunk. *Pos:* Minister music, Old First Church, Newark, 52-61; soloist, Int Fest Organ, 61 & 63 & Am Broadcasting Co; founder & dir, St Andrew's Music Soc, 61-70; organist & dir music, Madison Ave Presby Church, 61-70 & All Souls Unitarian Church, New York, 70-77; conct artist organ, tours throughout US, Can, Europe & Mex, 77; organist & choirmaster, St Paul's Protestant Episcopal Church, Chatham, NJ, 78-80 & Church of St Andrew & Holy Communion & Congregation Oheb Shalom, South Orange, NJ, currently; organist, Nat Broadcasting Co; recitalist, Regional & Nat Conv of Am Guild Organists. *Teaching:* Prof organ, Peabody Inst Music, 50-55 & Westminster Choir Col, 51-; dir, Guilmant Organ Sch, New York, 63-74; master classes & sem throughout US. *Mem:* Am Guild Organists; Bohemians; Am Asn Univ Prof. *Mailing Add:* 42 Maplewood Ave Maplewood NJ 07040

MARKOV, ALBERT
VIOLIN, EDUCATOR
Study: Kharkov & Moscow Consv, with Leschinsky & YankeLevich. *Works:* Violin sonatas, rhapsodies & vocal & piano comp. *Rec Perf:* With Melodiya Rec & Musical Heritage Soc Rec. *Pos:* Mem, Concordia Trio; performer, Carnegie Hall, Kennedy Ctr & throughout US, Can & Mexico; Soloist, Moscow Phil. *Teaching:* Mem fac violin, Manhattan Sch Music, 81- *Rep:* Harold Shaw 1995 Broadway New York NY 10023. *Mailing Add:* Manhattan Sch Music 120 Claremont Ave New York NY 10027

MARKOWSKI, VICTORIA
PIANO, EDUCATOR
b Nanticoke, Pa, July 4, 30. *Study:* Wyoming Sem, dipl, 48; Boston Consv Music, BM, 52; study with David Saperton, 71-79. *Pos:* Recitalist, Carnegie Recital Hall & Conct Artists Guild, 57-58. *Teaching:* Artist in res piano, Univ Southern Colo, 69- *Mem:* Music Teachers Nat Asn; Colo State Music Teachers Asn; Nat Guild Piano Teachers; Assoc Musicians Greater NY. *Publ:* Auth, So You Want to Improve Your Sightreading, Univ Soc Inc, 74; How to Read Music and Prove It on the Recorder, 83. *Mailing Add:* 2109 North Dr Pueblo CO 81008

MARKS, ALAN
PIANO
b Chicago, Ill. *Study:* Juilliard Sch, BM, 71; studied with Leon Fleisher, 72. *Rec Perf:* Solo Works of Boulez, Chavez & Sessions, CRI, 77; Piano Quintet (Rochberg), Nonesuch Rec, 80; Two Piano Sonatas (Schubert), Nimbus Rec, 83. *Pos:* Conct pianist & recitalist, 72- *Teaching:* Mem fac music, Lincoln Ctr Inst, 78-80. *Awards:* Rockefeller Grant, 71 & 76; Second Prize, Univ Md Int Piano Compt, 73 & Geza Anda Int Piano Compt, 79. *Mem:* Affil Artists Inc (mem bd, 76-78). *Mailing Add:* c/o Sheldon Soffer Mgt 130 W 56th St New York NY 10019

MARKS, VIRGINIA PANCOAST
EDUCATOR, PIANO
b Philadelphia, Pa, Feb 2, 40. *Study:* Temple Univ, BS(music), 61; studied with Leon Fleisher, 65-67; Am Univ, MA(music), 75. *Pos:* Conct pianist throughout US & Italy, 64- *Teaching:* Instr piano, Cornell Univ, 66-67; instr, Temple Univ, 68-69, opera coach, 69-71; prof piano, Bowling Green State Univ, 73- *Awards:* First Prize, Mu Phi Epsilon Int Compt, 64 & Conct Artists Guild, New York, 65; Distinguished Teaching Award, Bowling Green State Univ, 82. *Mem:* Music Teachers Nat Asn (mem exec bd, 81-); Friday Morning Music Club, Washington, DC. *Mailing Add:* Col Musical Arts Bowling Green State Univ Bowling Green OH 43403

MARKSON, HADUSSAH B
ADMINISTRATOR
b New York, NY, Aug 9, 27. *Study:* Queens Col, BA, 49; Hunter Col & Grad Ctr, City Univ New York. *Pos:* Dir, 92nd St Y Sch Music, 69-, artistic dir, Jewish Opera, 78-; producer, Lyrics & Lyricist Ser, 70-; bus mgr, Musico Judaico J, 77- *Mem:* Am Soc Jewish Music (secy, 77-); Nat Guild Community Sch Arts (secy, 80-, pres metropolitan chap, 82-); Am Musicol Soc. *Mailing Add:* 315 E 68th St New York NY 10021

MARKUSON, STEPHEN
BASS-BARITONE
b New York, NY. *Study:* State Univ NY, Fredonia, BA; Univ Ill, Champaign-Urbana, MA(perf). *Roles:* Don Pasquale in Don Pasquale; Don Magnifico in La Cenerentola, Atlanta Civic Opera, 81; Friar Lawrence in Romeo & Juliet, Aspen, Colo, 81; Composer in Prima la Musica, Poi le Parole, New York Chamber Opera, 81; Don Bartolo in Il Barbiere di Siviglia, 81 & Le Nozze di Figaro, 81, Florentine Opera, Milwaukee. *Pos:* Apprenticeship, Lake George Opera; bass & baritone with maj opera co in US & Can, currently. *Awards:* Grants, William Mathews Sullivan Found. *Mailing Add:* c/o Salmon & Stokes 280 Riverside Dr Suite #3B New York NY 10025

MARRINER, NEVILLE
CONDUCTOR & MUSIC DIRECTOR, VIOLIN
b Lincoln, England, Apr 15, 24. *Study:* Royal Col Music, ARCM; Paris Consv; Royale Acad Music, Hon LRAM. *Rec Perf:* Dvorak's Eighth Symphony, EMI; Amadeus (film score), 83. *Pos:* Violinist, Martin String Quartet, 46-53, Virtuoso String Trio, 50, Jacobean Ens, 52, London Phil, 52-56 & London Symph Orch, 56-; mem bd dir & founder, Acad St Martin in the Fields, 59-; cond, Los Angeles Chamber Orch, 69-77, London Symph, Orch Nat Paris & Dresden State Orch; music dir & cond, Minn Orch, 79-; guest cond, Gulbenkien Orch, Spain, Israel Chamber Orch, Australian Chamber Orch, New York Chamber Orch, New York Phil Orch, Strasbourg Phil Orch & others; dir, South Bank Fest Music, 75-78, Meadowbrook Fest, Detroit, 79- *Teaching:* Prof, Eton Col, 47 & Royal Col Music, 52. *Awards:* Grand Prix du Disque; Edison Award; Mozart Gemeinde Prize. *Rep:* Columbia Artists Mgt 165 W 57th St New York NY 10019. *Mailing Add:* Minn Orch 1111 Nicolet Mall Minneapolis MN 55403

MARSEE, SUSANNE I
MEZZO-SOPRANO
b San Diego, Calif, Nov 26, 41. *Study:* Univ Calif, Los Angeles, BA, 63; Juilliard Sch, 69-70. *Roles:* Seymour, in Anna Bolena, 73-80 & Octavian in Rosenkavalier, 75, New York City Opera; Dulcinne in Don Quichotte, Bellas Artes, 75; Preziosilla in Forza Del Destino, San Francisco Opera, 76; Dorabella in Cosi Fan Tutte, Spoleto Fest, Italy, 77; Sara in Roberto Devereux, Aix en Provence, 77; Carmen in Carmen, New York City Opera, 82; over 40 roles performed. *Pos:* Mem, New York City Opera, 70-; mem nat bd gov, Am Guild Musical Artists, New York, NY, 82- *Awards:* Grant, Corbett Found, 68-72 & Martha Baird Rockefellar Found, 70 & 73. *Mailing Add:* c/o Shaw Concerts 1995 Broadway New York NY 10023

MARSH, JACK ODELL
BASSOON, EDUCATOR
b Oklahoma City, Okla, Oct 31, 17. *Study:* Studied privately. *Pos:* First bassoon, Kans City Phil, 39-40, major motion picture studios, 40-, Phonia-Cal Chambers Symph, 55-75 & Roger Wagner Choral & Symph, 60-75. *Teaching:* Teacher bassoon, Univ Calif, Santa Barbara, 69-73 & Calif State Univ, Northridge, 82- *Bibliog:* Tony Joseph (auth), Bassoonist Seldom Seen, Often Heard, Ventura Free Press, 7/23/82. *Mailing Add:* Dept Music Calif State Univ Northridge CA 91330

MARSH, MILTON R
COMPOSER, EDUCATOR
b Hamilton, Bermuda, Sept 29, 45. *Study:* London Univ, cert educ, 64; Berklee Col Music, BM, 69; New England Consv Music, MMus, 71; Univ Mass. *Works:* Monism, 75, Poems for Saxophone Quartet, 80, Ode to Nzinga, 81 & Metamorphosis, 81, Milton Marsh Publ Co. *Pos:* Music consult, Nat Ctr Afro-Am Artists, Boston Mass, 71-72; comp & music consult, Marsh Publ, Boston, Mass, 77- *Teaching:* Vis prof music, State Univ NY, Oneonta, 72-73; prof & dir Afro-Am Music, State Univ NY, Buffalo, 73-77. *Mailing Add:* PO Box 635 Astor Sta Boston MA 02123

MARSH, OZAN F
EDUCATOR, PIANO
b Pasadena, Calif. *Study:* Coaching with Egon Petri, Emil Sauer & Robert Casadesus; advan coaching with Rachmaninoff, Horowitz, Bachaus & Godowsky. *Pos:* Conct pianist, US & abroad, currently; pianist in res, Ind Univ, Bloomington, 52-56 & Univ Ariz, 67- *Teaching:* Prof music, St Lawrence Univ, New York, 40-43 & Univ Ariz, Tucson, 67-; chmn piano

dept, Choate Sch, Manhattan Sch Music & Lebanon Valley Consv, 46-49; head piano dept, Jordan Col Music, Butler Univ, Indianapolis, 49-52 & Chautauqua Inst, NY, 57-; music consult, Converse Col, San Francisco State Univ & Linderwood Col, Mo, 56-67. *Awards:* Ariz Found Creative Teaching Award, Univ Ariz, 75. *Mem:* Pianists Found Am (pres & founder, 75-); Hon Mem Nat Fedn Music Clubs; Am Liszt Soc; Nat Guild Piano Teachers. *Interests:* Liszt manuscripts. *Publ:* Auth, Worlds Apart, Piano Quart, 80. *Mailing Add:* c/o Pianists Found Am 4001 E Blacklidge Dr #1 Tucson AZ 85712

MARSH, ROBERT C
CRITIC
b Columbus, Ohio, Aug 5, 24. *Study:* Cornell Univ, with Robert Palmer, 46-47; Harvard Univ, with Paul Hindemith, EdD, 51; Cambridge Univ, Thurston Dart, 53-56. *Pos:* Music critic, Chicago Sun Times, 56-; dir, Chicago Opera Proj, 83-*Awards:* Shared Peabody Award Educ Broadcasting Music, 76. *Publ:* Auth, Toscanini and the Art of Orchestral Performance, 56; The Cleveland Orchestra, 67. *Mailing Add:* 401 N Wabash Ave Chicago IL 60611

MARSHALL, ELIZABETH
PIANO
b Philadelphia, Pa, Mar 31, 37. *Study:* Vienna Acad Music, dipl(perf), 58; Manhattan Sch Music, BMus, MMus. *Rec Perf:* Complete piano works of Nicolas Flagello; Sonata for Piano (Vittorio Rieti); Musica in Quatro Tiempos (Leonardo Balada). *Pos:* Ed piano scores, Gen Music Publ Co, New York; solo recitalist, New York, Boston, Washington, DC & Newark; performer, Am cols & univ & Europ tours; guest artist, Manhattan Perc Ens. *Awards:* Martha Baird Rockefeller Award, 62. *Mailing Add:* c/o Janina K Burns Assoc 136 Kingsland St Autley NJ 07110

MARSHALL, HOWARD LOWEN
EDUCATOR, ADMINISTRATOR
b Prince William Co, Va, July 21, 31. *Study:* Shenandoah Consv Music, BMEd, 52; Col Consv Music, Univ Cincinnati, MMus, 58; Eastman Sch Music, PhD, 68. *Teaching:* Dir vocal music, Sycamore Sch Dist, Cincinnati, Ohio, 58-60 & Cheltenham High Sch, Wyncote, Pa, 60-63; asst prof music, Lake Forest Col, 66-73; prof music & chmn dept, Mercer Univ, 74- *Mem:* Am Musicol Soc. *Interests:* Renaissance vocal music; Romantic music. *Publ:* Auth, The Four-Voice Motets of Thomas Crecquillon, Inst Mediaeval Music, 71; Symbolism in Schubert's Winterreise, Studies in Romanticism, 73. *Mailing Add:* 1324 Maplewood Dr Macon GA 31210

MARSHALL, INGRAM DOUGLASS
COMPOSER, EDUCATOR
b Mt Vernon, NY, May 10, 42. *Study:* Lake Forest Col, BA, 64; Columbia Univ, 64-66; Calif Inst Arts, MFA, 71. *Works:* Fragility Cycles, rec on IBU, 78; Non Confundar, perf by Steve Reich Ens, 79 & Arch Ens, 79; Spiritus, perf by Oakland Symph, Calif, 81; Woodstone, perf by Berkeley Gamelan Ens, 82; Gradual Requiem, 83 & Fog Tropes, 83, New Albion. *Teaching:* Instr comp & electronic music, Calif Inst Arts, 71-74 & San Francisco Consv Music, 76. *Awards:* Fulbright Grant Sweden, 75; Nat Endowment Arts Comp Fel, 78 & 81; Creative Fel, Rockefeller Found, 82. *Mailing Add:* 500 Cole St San Francisco CA 94117

MARSHALL, JAMES THOMAS
COMPOSER, EDUCATOR
b Seattle, Wash, Oct 12, 41. *Study:* Whitman Col, BA, 63; Univ Wash, MA, 66; Univ Cincinnati, DMA, 77. *Works:* Later, Perhaps (film), comn by NJ Dept Educ, 70; Multisone, Union Polish Comp, Warsaw, 76; Rondellus, Ohio State Univ, 77; Elevation of Imagery, Carnegie Recital Hall, 79; Consone (solo guitar), Rio de Janeiro, 80; Symphony No 1, Suburban Symph Orch, Cleveland, 81. *Teaching:* Instr, Drake Univ, 66-68 & Montclair State Univ, 68-71; asst prof, Cleveland State Univ, 74-81 & Whitman Col, 81- *Mem:* Am Soc Univ Comp; Col Music Soc; Am Fedn Musicians; Nat Asn Col Woodwind & Perc Instr. *Mailing Add:* 611 E Isaacs Walla Walla WA 99362

MARSHALL, PAMELA JOY
COMPOSER
b Beverly, Mass, May 31, 54. *Study:* Eastman Sch Music, BM, 76; Comput Music Wkshp, Mass Inst Technol, 79; Yale Sch Music, MM, 80. *Works:* Miniatures for Unaccompanied Horn, 76 & Dances for the Morning (harp), 76, Seesaw Music Corp; Torrsong, Delius Fest, 78; Meadowlarks & Shawms, Experimental Music Studio, Mass Inst Technol, 79; A Chill Wind in Autumn (eight songs), New England Women's Symph, 79; Toccata Armonica, Yale Contemp Ens, 80; Macbeth, As You Like It & Richard III (incidental music), Shakespeare Ens, Mass Inst Technol, 82. *Pos:* Mem, Plymouth Phil, 76-78, Harvard-Radcliffe Orch, 77-78, Yale Symph Orch, 78-80, Wall Street Brass Quintet, 78-80 & Wellesley Symph Orch, 82-; comp & music dir, Shakespeare Ens, Mass Inst Technol, 81-82; software engineer, Digital Music Systems, 81- *Teaching:* Asst, Yale Sch Music, 78-80; prog for gifted pub sch children, Milton Acad, Mass, 81. *Awards:* MacDowell Colony Fel, 81. *Mem:* BMI. *Mailing Add:* 44 Quint Ave Allston MA 02134

MARSHALL, ROBERT LEWIS
EDUCATOR
b New York, NY, Oct 12, 39. *Study:* Columbia Univ, BA, 60; Princeton Univ, MFA, 62, PhD, 68. *Teaching:* Instr music, Univ Chicago, 66-68, asst prof, 68-71, assoc prof, 72-77, chmn dept, 72-78, prof, 77-83; prof, Brandeis Univ, 83-*Awards:* Otto Kinkeldey Prize, Am Musicol Soc, 74. *Mem:* Am Musicol Soc (mem bd dirs, 74-75); New Bach Soc (Am chap chmn, 74-77). *Interests:* Music of J S Bach and Mozart. *Publ:* Auth, The Compositional Process of J S Bach,

Princeton Univ Press, 72; ed, Studies in Renaissance and Baroque Music..., Bärenreiter, Boonin, 74; auth, Bach the Progressive: Observations on his Later Works, Musical Quart, 76; J S Bach's Compositions for Solo Flute, J Am Musicol Soc, 79; ed, Neue Bach-Ausgabe, Series I, Vol 19: Cantatas, Bärenreiter (in prep). *Mailing Add:* Brandeis Univ Waltham MA 02254

MARSON, LAUREL ROSE
COMPOSER
b Akron, Ohio, June 27, 52. *Study:* Univ Akron, with David Bernstein, BM, 74, MM, 76. *Works:* Für Ubermorgen (wind ens), 74; Three Movements for Percussion, 74; Three Movements (piano), 74; Three Movements (clarinet & horn), 74; Oedipus Rex (wind ens), 75; Chrysanthemums (voice & woodwind quintet), 75; I Have a Terrible Cold (voice & woodwind quintet), 75. *Awards:* John Phillip Sousa Band Award, 70. *Mailing Add:* 1667 Glenmount Ave Akron OH 44301

MARTEL, FERNAND
BARITONE, ORGAN
b Quebec, Que, Aug 11, 19. *Study:* Laval Univ, Que, dipl, 41; Juilliard Sch Music, dipl, 48; Sorbonne, Paris, dipl, 51. *Rec Perf:* Four Songs by Fernand Martel, 59 & Presenting Fernand Martel, 75, London Rec. *Roles:* Pelleas in Pelleas et Melisande, New York City Opera Co, 48; De Brettigny in Manon, Miami Opera Co, 51; Figaro in The Barber of Seville, CBC, Montreal, 54; Escamillo in Carmen, Opera du Quebec Co, 55; many others. *Pos:* Soloist with Toronto Orch, CBC, 53. *Mem:* Am Fedn Musicians; Am Guild Musical Artists; Am Guild Variety Artists; Am Fedn TV & Radio Actors; Actors Guild. *Mailing Add:* 439 W 9th St Long Beach CA 90813

MARTIN, BARBARA (ANN SULAHIAN-MARTIN)
MEZZO-SOPRANO
b Astoria, NY, July 20, 51. *Study:* Juilliard Sch, BS(music), MM; Metropolitan Opera Studios, 70-74. *Rec Perf:* Mohori (Chinary Ung), 76 & Six Elizabethan Songs (Dominick Argento), 78, CRI; In Time Past & Time Remembered (Jeffrey Kaufman), Grenadilla, 79; Vuci Siculani (Marc-Antonio Consoli), CRI, 81; Have You Heard? Do You Know? (Louise Talma), Musical Heritage (in prep). *Roles:* Rosina in The Barber of Seville, Dorabella in Cosi fan tutte, Suzuki in Madama Butterfly & Siebel in Faust, Metropolitan Opera Studios, 70-74; Cherubino in Le Nozze di Figaro, Central City Opera Asn, 72; German Mother & Voice Apollo in Death in Venice, Metropolitan Opera, 74; Ancient Voices of Children, NY Phil, 81 & Berlin Phil, 83. *Pos:* Guest artist, Contemp Chamber Ens, NY, 73-83; artist in res, Affil Artists, New York, 78-83; recitalist, Conct Artists Guild, New York, 82-83. *Awards:* Winner, Conct Artists Guild Award, 82. *Mem:* Am Fedn TV & Radio Artists. *Rep:* Columbia Artists 165 W 57th St New York NY 10019. *Mailing Add:* 72-12 Juno St Forest Hills NY 11375

MARTIN, CAROLANN FRANCES
CELLO, CONDUCTOR
b Woodward, Okla, Nov 20, 35. *Study:* Oklahoma City Univ, BMusEd, 57; Ohio State Univ, MA, 64; Univ Ariz, DMA, 79. *Pos:* Dir opera & cellist, Oklahoma City Symph, 57-58 & 67-69, Norfolk Symph, 58-61 & Columbus Symph, Ohio, 61-64; prin cellist, Sioux City Symph, formerly, Chicago Chamber Orch, 64-67 & Chicago Civic Symph, 64-67; cond, Siouxland Youth Symph, formerly, SE Kans Symph, formerly, Opera Theater, Pittsburg State Univ, formerly & Mid-Am Youth Symph, 77- *Teaching:* Music, pub sch, Okla, 57-58; asst prof, Wilson Br, Chicago City Col, 64-67; assoc prof, Morningside Col, 69-76; mem fac, Pittsburg State Univ, Kans, 77- *Awards:* Winner, Nat Cond Compt, 80. *Mem:* Am String Teachers Asn; Music Educr Nat Conf; Nat Sch Orch Asn; Cond Guild; Sigma Alpha Iota. *Mailing Add:* c/o Cond Int Mgt 95 Cedar Rd Ringwood NJ 07456

MARTIN, CHARLOTTE
PIANO, EDUCATOR
b Mexico City, Mex, Feb 8, 23. *Study:* Santa Barbara Jr Col, AA; Mex Nat Consv Music; Ecole Normale de Musique, Paris, with Alfred Cortot & Nadia Boulanger, teachers dipl, 39; Longy Sch Music, studied piano with Nadia Boulanger & Boris Goldovsky, soloist dipl(piano), 42; Nat Univ Mex, Hon Dr. *Rec Perf:* Numerous recordings as soloist & accmp, Educo Rec, 58- *Pos:* Concerts, recitals, lectures & orch perfs, 42-69. *Teaching:* Coach & accmp, Music Acad West, Santa Barbara, 54-64; titular prof, Sch Music, Univ Mex, formerly; artist in res, Okla Baptist Univ, currently. *Mem:* Okla Music Teachers Asn; Sigma Alpha Iota; Calif Music Teachers Asn. *Rep:* Van Wyck London UK. *Mailing Add:* 2126 N Beard St Shawnee OK 74801

MARTIN, DENNIS ROY
EDUCATOR, WRITER
b Decatur, Ill, July 29, 51. *Study:* Ill Weslyan Univ, BMus & BMusEd, 73; Univ Iowa, Iowa City, MA(musicol), 75, PhD(musicol), 79. *Teaching:* Prof music & chmn music dept, Minn Bible Col, 76- *Awards:* Grant, Sinfonia Found, 82. *Mem:* Am Musicol Soc; Sonneck Soc; Phi Mu Alpha Sinfonia. *Interests:* Eighteenth century British opera, vocal music and scenography; 19th century American cantata, opera and vocal music. *Publ:* Contribr, Elizabethan Madrigal Dinners, Mark Foster, 78; auth, Eine Collection curieuser Vorstellunge (1730) and Thomas Lediard ... Early Eighteenth-Century Operatic Scenography, 78 & Germany's First Major Opera House, A Reassessment ..., 81, Current Musicol; ed, The Haymakers, An Operatic Cantata (two vol), A-R Ed, 83. *Mailing Add:* 703 20th St SW Rochester MN 55901

MARTIN, DONALD R
DOUBLE BASS
b Buffalo, NY, Mar 16, 35. *Study:* Purdue Univ, BS, 56. *Pos:* Bassist, St Louis Symph, 62-; double bassist & organizer, Rarely Perf Music Ens, 67- *Mailing Add:* St Louis Symph 718 N Grand Blvd St Louis MO 63103

MARTIN, GERALDINE
EDUCATOR, VOICE

Study: Univ Calif, Los Angeles, BM; New England Consv Music, MM; Peabody Consv Music; Staatliche Hochscule Musik. *Roles:* TV & radio appearances incl The Stronger (Weisgall); Trouble in Tahiti. *Pos:* Performer, Opera New England, Cambridge Opera, Next Move Theater, Suffolk Theater & others; soloist, Baltimore Symph, Ford Cond Proj Symph Orch & Mass Inst Tech Symph Orch. *Teaching:* Mem fac third stream music & voice, New England Consv Music, currently & Exten Div, currently. *Mailing Add:* New England Consv Music 290 Huntington Rd Boston MA 02115

MARTIN, JUDITH LYNN
COMPOSER, ELECTRONIC

b St Paul, Minn. *Study:* Ind Univ, BA, 73, Sch Music, MA(comp), 80; studied with John Eaton & Iannis Xenakis. *Works:* Hoop, Art Park, 75; Inner Dialogue, Bertram Turetzky, 76; Celebration Song, Brooklyn Phil, 78; Ocean Side in the Well-Tempered Being, Sonora Ens, 81; Love Brings Good Fortune, Netherlands Radio Chamber Orch, 81; Secret Circuit, Brooklyn Acad Music, 82; Kites of the Moon, Orch Our Time, 83. *Teaching:* Free agt instr electronic music, NY Univ, 80-; artist in res, New York Found for Arts, 81-; curric designer lang arts, Manhattan Plaza Children's Ctr, 82- *Awards:* Int Gaudeamus Comp Compt Award, 81; Martha Baird Rockefeller Fund for Music, 81. *Bibliog:* Cynthia Bell (auth), Microtones via Sonora, Ear Mag, 82. *Mem:* Founder, Sonora House, Inc (dir, 76-); Minn Comp Forum. *Publ:* Auth, Sunbirds and Black Waterfall, Talbot, 82; The Importance of the Arts in an After-School Program, Ear Mag, 83. *Mailing Add:* Rockefeller Ctr Sta Box 2145 New York NY 10185

MARTIN, (SHEILA) KATHLEEN
PIANO, CONDUCTOR

b Sioux City, Iowa, Dec 9, 49. *Study:* Univ Iowa, piano with John Simms, BMus, 72, MA, 76; studied cond with Antonia Brico, 80; studied piano with Seymour Lipkin, 82- *Pos:* Cond & accmp, Phil Chamber Players, Boulder, Colo, 79-80; solo pianist, NY, 80-; artistic dir & pianist, Brava Chamber Ens, NY, 80- *Teaching:* Piano, Univ Calgary, 76-77; piano & theory, Calgary Consv Music, 76-77; piano, Univ Colo, 78-79; private vocal coaching & piano teaching, New York, 80- *Mem:* Chamber Music Am; Assoc Musicians Greater NY; Sigma Alpha Iota. *Interests:* Women composers. *Mailing Add:* 21 W 86th St New York NY 10024

MARTIN, LESLIE
BASS, EDUCATOR

Study: Cornish Sch Music, Seattle; Univ Wash; Am Consv Music; Berkshire Music Ctr, 50; studied double bass with John Tepley & George Moleux. *Pos:* Mem, Seattle Symph Orch, Gene Krupa, Jan Garber, Skinnay Ennis & Ted Weems Orch, formerly; mem bass sect, Boston Symph Orch, 57- *Teaching:* Fac mem, Univ Wash, formerly; mem fac double bass, New England Consv Music, currently. *Mailing Add:* New England Consv Music 290 Huntington Rd Boston MA 02115

MARTIN, LINDY S
ARTIST MANAGER

b NJ. *Mailing Add:* Personal Mgt Pinehurst NC 28374

MARTIN, PETER JOHN
CONDUCTOR, EDUCATOR

b Evanston, Ill, Aug 22, 49. *Study:* Northern Ill Univ, BSEd, 71; Wichita State Univ, MME, 73; Northwestern Univ, PhD, 83. *Rec Perf:* Central Kentucky Concert Band, USC Sound Enterprises, 78. *Teaching:* Asst dir bands, SE Mo State Univ, 73-74; dir band orgn, Transylvania Univ, 74-80 & Univ Southern Maine, 80- *Awards:* Northwestern Univ Res Grant, 83. *Mem:* Col Band Dir Nat Asn; Music Educr Nat Conf; Phi Mu Alpha Sinfonia; Nat Band Asn. *Publ:* Auth, Setting Musical Goals for Your Band, Instrumentalist, 80. *Mailing Add:* 180 South St Apt 8 Gorham ME 04038

MARTIN, RAVONNA G
COMPOSER, PIANO

b Jasper, Tex, Oct 18, 54. *Study:* Univ Alaska, Fairbanks, BA(music educ), 80, MA(music hist), 83. *Works:* Christmas Psalm (SATB, flute, oboe, organ & perc), comn by Fairbanks Choral Soc, 82; Alaska Animal Miniatures, Robert McCoy, 83; Tis You that Are the Music (ms & piano), perf at Carnegie Recital Hall, 83; Beauty Art Thou (SATB & piano), Lawson-Gould Publ, 83; Swashbuckler I and II, Fairbanks Youth Theater, 83; Five Meditations from Anne Bradstreet (ms & piano), Univ Alaska Found, 83; Christmas Liturgy (SATB, sop soloist, chamber orch & narrator), comn by Fest Fairbanks, 84. *Teaching:* Lectr, Univ Alaska, Fairbanks, currently. *Mailing Add:* 1815 Carr Ave Fairbanks AK 99701

MARTIN, ROBERT EDWARD
COMPOSER

b Hagerstown, Md, July 22, 52. *Study:* Dartmouth Col, summer 72; Peabody Consv Music, with Stefan Grove, Richard Rodney Bennett, Jean Ivey & Robert Hall Lewis, BM, 74; Electronic Music Inst; Univ NH. *Works:* Fugue (woodwind quintet), 71; 2 Ancient Pieces (piano), 72; Chanson (tenor, viola & perc), 73; Couplet (four trombones), 73; Antique Forms of Lost Friends (flute & viola), 73; Flute Piece (solo flute); & electronic pieces. *Awards:* Marie K Thatcher Prize, 71; James Skyes Prize Electronic Music, 72; Ives Scholar, Nat Inst Arts & Lett, 76. *Mailing Add:* 44 McKee Ave Hagerstown MD 21740

MARTIN, THOMAS PHILIPP
CONDUCTOR & MUSIC DIRECTOR, TRANSLATOR

b Vienna, Austria; US citizen. *Study:* Vienna Consv, dipl; studied piano with Bruno Eisner & theory with Egon Lustgarten & Eugen Zador. *Rec Perf:* A Night in Venice (Johann Strauss), Everest, 58; Dr Heidegger's Fountain of Youth (Jack Beeson), CRI, 79. *Pos:* Cond & chorus master, New York City Ctr, 44-56; assoc chorus master, Metropolitan Opera, 58-66; dir musical studies & opera theater, New York City Opera, 67-80. *Teaching:* Adj prof music & music educ & dir, Reimann Opera Studio, NY Univ, 81- *Awards:* Arturo Toscanini Award, JFK Libr, 74; Honor Cross, First Class Arts & Sci, Austria, 82. *Mem:* ASCAP; Nat Opera Asn. *Publ:* Co-translr, 45 opera & operetta libretti, G Schirmer, Ricordi, Boosey & Hawkes, Belwin Mills & others. *Mailing Add:* 219 W 13th St New York NY 10011

MARTIN, VERNON
LIBRARIAN, COMPOSER

b Guthrie, Okla, Dec 15, 29. *Study:* Univ Okla, BM, 56; Columbia Univ, MA, 59, MS(libr), 65. *Works:* Ladies Voices (chamber opera), Carl Fischer Inc, 79. *Pos:* Actg sr librn, New York Pub Libr, Lincoln Ctr, 64-66; music librn, NTex State Univ, Denton, 66-70; libr dir, Morningside Col, Sioux City, Iowa, 70-74; head art & music dept, Hartford Pub Libr, 74- *Teaching:* Instr libr & music, NTex State Univ, Denton, 66-70; assoc prof, Morningside Col, Sioux City, Iowa, 70-74. *Awards:* Standard Award, ASCAP, 68-72; res grant, Asn Col & Univ Int Intercult Studies, 71. *Mem:* ASCAP. *Interests:* Electronic music. *Publ:* Auth, Bibliography of writings on electronic music, Columbia/Princeton Electronic Music Ctr, 64. *Mailing Add:* 500 Main St Hartford CT 06103

MARTIN, WALTER (CALLAHAN), JR
EDUCATOR, BARITONE

b Artesia, NMex, May 29, 30. *Study:* Univ Ore, BM, 52, MM, 64; State Sch Music, Stuttgart, West Germany, with Hermann Reutter, 54-56; Univ Southern Calif, DMA, 76. *Roles:* Michele in Il Tabarro, Stuttgart State Opera, West Germany, 55; Count in The Marriage of Figaro, Mannheim, 57 & Koblenz, 59; Gerard in Andrea Chenier, 57 & Posa in Don Carlos, 58, Koblenz Munic Opera; Malatesta in Don Pasquale, Nat Theater Mannheim, West Germany, 58; Ford in The Merry Wives of Windsor, Heidelberg Munic Opera, 59; Marcello in La Boheme, Portland Opera, 64. *Pos:* Concert & oratorio singer in Germany, Can, Ireland & US, 53-; opera singer, Stuttgart, Mannheim, Heidelberg & Koblenz opera co, West Germany, 54-63; assoc ed music rev, Nat Asn Teachers Singing Bulletin, 74-79, 81- *Teaching:* Prof voice, Univ Redlands, 65- *Awards:* Int Res & Exchanges Bd Study Grant Poland, 79 & 80. *Mem:* Nat Asn Teachers Singing; Col Music Soc; Friends Polish Music. *Interests:* Polish art songs. *Publ:* Auth, The Vocal Works of William Walton, 77 & Karol Szymanowski: The Unknown Song Composer, 82, Nat Asn Teachers Singing Bulletin. *Mailing Add:* 429 Lotus Ct Redlands CA 92373

MARTINEZ, M L See Gollner, Marie Louise

MARTINO, DONALD JAMES
COMPOSER, EDUCATOR

b Plainfield, NJ, May 16, 31. *Study:* Syracuse Univ, BM, 52; Princeton Univ, MFA, 54; studied with L Dallapicola, Italy, 54-56. *Works:* Piano Concerto, Ione Press, 65; Cello Concerto, Dantalian, Inc, 72; Notturno, Ione Press, 74; Paradiso Choruses, 75, Triple Concerto, 79, Fantasies and Impromptus, 80 & String Quartet, 83, Dantalian, 83. *Teaching:* Assoc prof, Yale Univ, 59-69; chmn comp dept, New England Consv, 69-79; Irving Fine Prof, Brandeis Univ, 79-83; prof music, Harvard Univ, 83- *Awards:* Am Acad & Inst Award, 68; Brandeis Creative Arts Citation, Brandeis Univ, 68; Pulitzer Prize, 74. *Bibliog:* Henry Weinberg (auth), Trio, Perspectives of New Music; William Rothstein (auth), Pianississimo, J Music Theory. *Mem:* Col Music Soc; Am Soc Univ Prof; Am Music Ctr; BMI. *Publ:* Auth, The Source Set and its Aggregate Formations, J Music Theory, 61. *Mailing Add:* 11 Pembroke St Newton MA 02158

MARTINO, LAURENCE
BASS

b Conn. *Study:* Southern Conn State Col, dipl. *Roles:* Maurllo in Rigoletto, 81 & Frank in Die Fledermaus, 81, Conn Gran Opera; Ramfis in Aida, New York Grand Opera, 81; Bonze in Madama Butterfly, Dayton Opera, 81 & Glimmerglass Opera, 82; Ferrando in Il Trovatore, Stamford Opera, 82; Daniele in Il Duca d'Alba, Opera Orch New York, 82. *Pos:* Soloist, New Haven Symph & Yale Symph, formerly; bass, with major opera co & orch, currently. *Awards:* First Pl, Metropolitan Opera District Auditions, 81 & Nat Fedn Music Clubs State Auditions. *Mailing Add:* c/o Liegner Mgt 1860 Broadway Suite 1610 New York NY 10023

MARTIRANO, SALVATORE
COMPOSER, EDUCATOR

b Yonkers, NY, Jan 12, 27. *Study:* Consv Music, Oberlin Col, BM, 51; Eastman Sch Music, with Bernard Rogers, MM, 52; studied with Luigi Dallapiccola, 52-54; Am Acad, Rome, 56-59. *Works:* O, O, O, O, That Shakespearian Rag (vocal & instrm chamber ens), 59; Octet, 63; Underworld (four actors, two double bass, tenor sax & tape), 65; Ballad (amplified nightclub singer & instrm), 66; L's GA (politico with gas mask, helium bomb, three movie projectors & tape), 68; Action Analysis (12 people, bunny & controller), 68; Selections (alto flute, bass clarinet, viola & cello), 70. *Pos:* Introduced new instrm, Mar-Vil construction, New York, 71. *Teaching:* Mem fac, Univ Ill, Urbana-Champaign, 68- *Awards:* Guggenheim Fel, 60; Am Acad Arts & Lett Award, 60; Nat Endowment Arts Grant, 78. *Mailing Add:* Music Dept Univ Ill Urbana IL 61801

MARTON, EVA
SOPRANO
b Budapest, Hungary, June 18, 43. *Study:* Franz Liszt Music Acad, Budapest, Hungary. *Roles:* Reine de Schemakan in Le Coq d'or, Budapest Opera, 68; Eva in Die Meistersinger, Metropolitan Opera, 76; Venus & Elizabeth in Tannhauser, Bayreuth Opera, 77 & 78; Tosca in Tosca, Marseilles, 77 & Munich, 77; Leonora in Il Trovatore, La Scala, Milan, 78; Chrysothemis in Elektra, 78-79 & Empress in Die Frau ohne Schatten, 81, Metropolitan Opera; and others. *Pos:* Mem, Budapest Radio Chorus, two yrs; sop, Frankfurt Opera, 72-77 & opera houses worldwide; res sop, Metropolitan Opera, currently. *Bibliog:* Thomas P Lanier (auth), Having it All, Opera News, 2/12/83. *Rep:* Eric Semon Assoc 111 W 57th St New York NY 10019. *Mailing Add:* Metropolitan Opera Lincoln Ctr New York NY 10023

MARVIN, FREDERICK
PIANO, MUSICOLOGIST
b Los Angeles, Calif, June 11, 23. *Study:* Los Angeles City Col; Curtis Inst Music; studied piano with Maurice Zam, Arthur Schnabel & Claudio Arrau. *Rec Perf:* All Liszt Program; Sonatas by I Moscheles & L Berger; Sonatas (Padre Soler), Decca, Erato & Musical Heritage. *Pos:* Conct pianist & performer TV & radio, US, Europe & India. *Teaching:* Prof piano & artist in res, Syracuse Univ, currently. *Awards:* Knight Commander, Order Merito Civil, Spain, 69; Medaille Vermeil, Soc Acad Arts, Sci & Lett, France, 74; Beethoven Medal. *Mailing Add:* 246 Houston Ave Syracuse NY 13224

MARVIN, MARAJEAN B
EDUCATOR, SOPRANO
b Terry, Mont. *Study:* Univ Md, Col Park, BM, 71, MM, 73. *Roles:* Manon Lescaut, 67, Agathe in Der Freischütz, 67-68 & Constanze in Die Entführung aus dem Serail, 69, Städtisches Theater, Mainz, Ger; Mimi in La Boheme, Glimmerglass Opera Co, Cooperstown, NY, 75; Donna Anna in Don Giovanni, Prince Georges Opera Co, 75. *Pos:* Leading lyr sop, Städtisches Theater, Mainz, Ger, 66-69; assoc dir opera, Marjorie Lawrence Opera Theatre, Carbondale, Ill, 73-77; dir, Univ NC Opera Theatre, Chapel Hill, 77-83. *Teaching:* Instr music, Southern Ill Univ, Carbondale, 73-77; asst prof music, Univ NC, Chapel Hill, 77-83; assoc prof music, Ohio State Univ, 83- *Mem:* Nat Opera Asn (vpres, 79-82 & pres, 82-84); Nat Asn Teachers Singing; Nat Music Teachers Asn. *Publ:* Transl, J Offenbach, L'Isle de Tulipatan, Belwin-Mills, 82. *Mailing Add:* 1657 Moravian St Columbus OH 43220

MASARIE, JACK F
EDUCATOR, FRENCH HORN
b San Francisco, Calif, Nov 25, 42. *Study:* Juilliard Sch, BMus, 66; Bowling Green State Univ, MMus, 73. *Pos:* Asst prin horn, Detroit Symph Orch, 66-68; co-prin horn, Toledo Symph & Toledo Opera, 68-72; hornist, Bowling Green Woodwind Quintet, 70-71 & E Wind Quintet & Brass Art Quintet, currently; prin horn, Greensboro Symph. *Teaching:* Instr brass, Mary Manse Col, 68-72; asst prof music, Univ NC, Greensboro, currently. *Mem:* Int Horn Soc. *Mailing Add:* Dept Music Univ NC Greensboro NC 27412

MASCARO, ARNOLD JOHN, JR
FRENCH HORN, TEACHER
b Baton Rouge, La, Nov 29, 37. *Study:* La State Univ, BMus, 61, MMus, 62. *Pos:* Solo French horn, Contemp Brass Quintet, Philadelphia, 66-78; prin French horn, Fla Symph Orch, 68- & Marlboro Fest Orch, summer 70. *Teaching:* Instr French horn, US Naval Sch Music, 62-66 & Univ Cent Fla, Orlando, 78- *Mem:* Am Fedn Musicians. *Mailing Add:* 715 Florida Blvd Altamonte Springs FL 32701

MASCARO, JANET PERSONS
OBOE
b New Haven, Conn, Nov 26, 44. *Study:* Oberlin Consv Music, BM, 66; studied with Robert Bloom, 67. *Pos:* Prin oboe, Fla Symph Orch, 66-; second oboe, Marlboro Fest Orch, 70. *Teaching:* Instr oboe, Univ Cent Fla, 82- *Mailing Add:* Florida Symphony Orch PO Box 782 Orlando FL 32802

MASLANKA, DAVID HENRY
COMPOSER, EDUCATOR
b New Bedford, Mass, Aug 30, 43. *Study:* Mozarteum, Salzburg, cert, 64; Consv Music, Oberlin Col, BM, 65; Mich State Univ, MM, 68, PhD, 70. *Works:* Death and the Maiden (opera), 74; Three Pieces for Clarinet & Piano, 74 & Concerto for Piano, Winds & Percussion, 76, Carl Fischer; Variations on Lost Love, Marimba Prod, 77; music for Dr Who, 80; A Child's Garden of Dreams, Kjos Music, 81; Heaven to Clear When Day Did Close, Sonoton Musik Verlag, Munich, 82. *Teaching:* Prof, State Univ NY, Geneseo, 70-74, Sarah Lawrence Col, 74-80 & City Univ New York, 82- *Awards:* Nat Endowment Arts Fels, 74 & 75; Martha Baird Rockefeller Found Grant, 78; NY State Arts Coun Fel, 82. *Mem:* ASCAP; Am Music Ctr. *Rep:* Barberi Paull 15 W 72nd St New York NY 10023. *Mailing Add:* 30 Seaman Ave 4M New York NY 10034

MASON, ANNE C
VIOLA, EDUCATOR
b Hattiesburg, Miss, Jan 18, 36. *Study:* Univ Ala; Miss Col, BMus, MMusEd. *Rec Perf:* On Malaco & NARC Rec. *Pos:* Prin viola, Opera—South; first violin, Tupelo Symph & Greenville Symph; co-prin viola, Jackson Symph Orch, currently; mem viola sect, Miss Opera Orch, currently. *Teaching:* String ens, strings & piano, Hinds Jr Col, currently. *Mem:* Miss Music Educr Asn; Delta Omicron. *Mailing Add:* 1131 Annalisa Lane Jackson MS 39204

MASON, ANTHONY HALSTEAD
ADMINISTRATOR, PATRON
b New York, NY, Dec 23, 38. *Study:* Univ Denver, BA, 61, JD, 65. *Pos:* Bd dir, Phoenix Symph Assoc, Ariz, 77-, pres bd dir, 81- *Mailing Add:* 100 W Washington Phoenix AZ 85003

MASON, LUCAS (ROGER)
COMPOSER, FLUTE
b Beloit, Wis, July 28, 31. *Study:* Univ Wis, with Cecil Burleigh, Hilmer Luckhardt & Robert Crane, BM, 53, MM, 57. *Works:* Quilt of Love, Composers Theatre, 69; Melodrama, Nat Gallery Music Fest, 75; Manusia, perf by Gil Evans Orch, 75; Symphony No 1, German Radio Orch, 75; Night Air, perf by Rebecca Kelly Dance Co, 82; Kinetic Celebrations, Bryn Mawr Col, 82; Symphony No 2, Am Phil, 83. *Rec Perf:* Children of One, Real Rec, 69; Windfall, Sokolow Prod & Lobel Prod, 78. *Pos:* Staff mem, Alwin Nikolais Dance Theatre, 59-60, Noble Path Mime Theatre, 63-68 & Children of One, 68-73; dir, Composers Circle, 70-; music dir, Heritage Found, 79- & Dance Action, 82- *Teaching:* Instr, New Sch for Social Res, 72- *Mem:* Am Fedn Musicians. *Publ:* Auth, The New Tuning, Vittachi Publ, 83. *Mailing Add:* 234 W 13th Street New York NY 10011

MASON, MARILYN
ORGAN, EDUCATOR
Study: With Palmer Christian, Nadia Boulanger & Maurice Durufle. *Pos:* Organist, North Am, South Am, Europe, Africa & Australia; adjudicator, maj competitions worldwide. *Teaching:* Mem fac, Univ Mich, Ann Arbor, 54-, univ organist & chmn organ dept, currently. *Mailing Add:* c/o Murtagh-McFarlane Inc 3269 W 30th St Cleveland OH 44109

MASON, NEALE BAGLEY
EDUCATOR, CELLO
b Keene, NH, Sept 30, 19. *Study:* Yale Univ, BMus, 48; Teachers Col, Columbia Univ, MA(music & music educ), 49; Univ Ill, 63. *Pos:* Prin cellist, Jackson Symph Orch, Tenn, 60-; cond & musical dir, Owensboro Symph Orch, Ky, 67-72; prin cellist & asst cond, Paducah Symph Orch, Ky, 79- *Teaching:* Prof music, Murray State Univ, Ky, 49-82. *Awards:* Orpheus Award, Phi Mu Alpha Sinfonia, 83. *Mem:* Phi Mu Alpha Sinfonia; Am String Teachers Asn; Am Symph Orch League; Cond Guild; Col Music Soc. *Publ:* Auth, Essentials of Eighteenth Century Counterpoint, William C Brown Publ, 68. *Mailing Add:* 1505 Henry St Murray KY 42071

MASON, ROBERT M
WRITER
b Toledo, Ohio, May 27, 28. *Study:* Univ Toledo, BEd, 50, MA, 51. *Mem:* Am Musicol Soc Inc. *Interests:* Application of computational mathematics to the study of music theory, especially kinetic basis of tonality. *Publ:* Auth, A Formula, Nomogram, and Tables for Determining Musical Interval Relationships, 67 & An Encoding Algorithm and Tables for the Digital Analysis of Harmony, Parts I & II, 69, J Res Music Educ; Enumeration of Synthetic Musical Scales by Matrix Algebra, and a Catalog of Busoni Scales, J Music Theory, 70; coauth, Applied Matrix and Tensor Analysis, Wiley Intersci, 70; auth, Modern Methods of Music Analysis, Sch House Press (in prep). *Mailing Add:* 46 Mountain View Dr Peterborough NH 03458

MASSELOS, WILLIAM
PIANO, EDUCATOR
b Niagara Falls, NY. *Study:* Inst Musical Art, Juilliard Grad Sch, studied piano with Carl Friedberg, 39-44; studied with David Saperton, D Dounis & Nelly Reuschel; Hamilton Col, hon degree; New Sch Music, Philadelphia, hon degree, 82. *Rec Perf:* On Columbia Masterworks, RCA, MGM & Epic Labels. *Pos:* Recitalist, Aspen Music Fest & Dubrovnik Fest, Yugoslavia; soloist with New York Phil, Philadelphia Orch, Montreal Symph, London Phil & Am Symph. *Teaching:* Mem fac music, Ga State Univ, 72-75; vis lectr, Mt Holyoke Col, formerly; mem fac piano, Cath Univ Am, 76- & Juilliard Sch, 76- *Awards:* Elizabeth Sprague Coolidge Mem Medal; Harriet Cohen Int Music Award; Award of Merit, Nat Asn Am Comp & Cond. *Mailing Add:* 685 West End Ave New York NY 10025

MASSENA, MARTHA
EDUCATOR, PIANO
Study: Inst Musical Art, 26; Curtis Inst Music, with Josef Hofmann, BMus, 34. *Pos:* Appearances, Philadelphia Orch, Curtis Orch, New Chamber Orch, Curtis Quartet & Silver Jubilee Recital Am Music. *Teaching:* Mem fac suppl piano & vocal repertoire, Curtis Inst Music, 27-; head piano dept, New Sch Music, 42-59; vocal coach, Marlboro Col, 58-60; opera coach, Temple Univ, 67-69; instr, Music Acad West, summer 70-, head coach apprentice vocal dept, 74-77. *Mailing Add:* Curtis Inst Music 1726 Locust St Philadelphia PA 19103

MASSEY, ANDREW JOHN
CONDUCTOR
b Nottingham, UK, May 1, 46. *Study:* Merton Col, Oxford, BA, 68; Nottingham Univ, MA(analysis contemp cond tech), 69. *Pos:* Asst cond, Cleveland Orch, 78-83; founder & cond, Apollo Symph Orch; assoc cond, New Orleans Phil, 83- *Mem:* Am Fedn Musicians. *Rep:* Sheldon Soffer Mgt Inc 130 W 56th St New York NY 10019. *Mailing Add:* New Orleans Phil 203 Corondelet St Suite 903 New Orleans LA 70130

MASSEY, GEORGE
BARITONE, LECTURER
b Jacksonville, Fla, Sept 3, 47. *Study:* Jacksonville Univ, BME, 69; Col-Consv Music, Univ Cincinnati, with Andrew White & Italo Tajo, MM, 73. *Roles:* Marcello in La Boheme, San Francisco Opera, 79 & Florentine Opera, 82; Mercutio in Romeo et Juliette, Dallas Opera, 81; Belcore in L'Elisir d'amore, Houston Grand Opera, 82; Silvio in Pagliacci, Stanford State Opera, 83; Germont in La traviata, Central City Opera, 83. *Pos:* Artist in sch, Cincinnati Opera, 75-77; artist, Affil Artists, 80-; artist in res, Dallas Opera, 82. *Mem:* Am Guild Musical Artists; Actors Equity; Pi Kappa Lambda. *Mailing Add:* Ten Flower Rd Valley Stream NY 11581

MAST, PAUL
EDUCATOR
b Feb 6, 46. *Study:* Tex Tech Univ, BM, 68; Eastman Sch Music, MA, 71, PhD, 74; studied with Carl Schachter, 79 & 82. *Teaching:* Mem fac, Consv Music, Oberlin Col, 72-78, assoc prof music theory, 78-, chmn dept, 81- *Mem:* Soc Music Theory; Am Brahms Soc; Phi Kappa Phi; Phi Beta Kappa; Phi Mu Alpha. *Mailing Add:* Consv Music Oberlin Col Oberlin OH 44074

MASTROIANNI, THOMAS OWEN
EDUCATOR, PIANO
b Pittsburgh, Pa, Sept 1, 34. *Study:* Juilliard Sch, BS, 57, MS, 58; Ind Univ, DMus, 69. *Rec Perf:* Sonata For Piano by Freitas, Educo, 83. *Pos:* Conc pianist, US, Europe, Mexico, Caribbean & Nat China, 61- *Teaching:* Prof piano, Tex Tech Univ, 61-72; dean, Sch Music, Catholic Univ of Am, 72-81, prof & chmn piano, 81- *Mem:* Am Liszt Soc (exec secy, 78-); Music Teacher Nat Asn. *Mailing Add:* Catholic Univ Sch Music Washington DC 20064

MATA, EDUARDO
CONDUCTOR & MUSIC DIRECTOR
b Mex City. *Study:* Comp with Carlos Chevaz & Juliam Orbon; Berkshire Music Ctr, 64. *Pos:* Mus dir, Guadalajara Symph Orch, Int Music Fest & Nat Symph Orch Mex, formerly, Phil Orch, Univ Mex, 66-75, Phoenix Symph Orch, 74-78, Mex Casals Fest, 76 & Dallas Symph Orch, 77-; cond, extensively in Europe & US, formerly; artistic dir, Nat Opera Mexico City, 83- *Awards:* Sourasky Prize, 75. *Mailing Add:* PO Box 26207 Dallas TX 75226

MATESKY, ELISABETH ANNE
VIOLIN, TEACHER
b Los Angeles, Calif, Oct 1, 46. *Study:* Univ Southern Calif, BM(music), 64; Inst Special Music Studies, with Heifetz, dipl(perf), 64; Royal Col Music, London, 65-66. *Works:* Bradshaw Violin Concerto, Brigham Young Univ, 81. *Rec Perf:* Glazunov Violin Concerto, 68 & Violin Concerto (Brahms), 71, BBC Welsh Orch; Concerto (Brahms), Chaconne (Bach) & D Major Sonata (Prokofiev), 71 BBC TV; Violin Concerto #1 (Shostakovich), Bamberg Symph, 79. *Pos:* Concertmaster, Univ Southern Calif Symph, 63-64, Syracuse Symph Orch, 71-72 & Rockford Symph Orch, 81; concertmaster & violinist, Chicago Symph Orch, 72-73. *Teaching:* Artist in res violin & viola, Syracuse Univ, 71-72; artist in res violin, Beloit Col, 82- *Awards:* Fulbright Grant, 64-65. *Bibliog:* Grace Under Pressure, BBC TV, London, 70; Chester Lane (auth), Life of Elisabeth Matesky—Concert Artist & The Rebirth of a Career, Am Symph News, 7/81. *Mem:* Am Fedn Musicians; Mu Phi Epsilon. *Mailing Add:* 215 E Chestnut Chicago IL 60611

MATHER, BETTY BANG (BETTY LOUISE MATHER)
EDUCATOR, FLUTE
b Emporia, Kans, Aug 7, 27. *Study:* Oberlin Consv, BMus, 49; Columbia Teachers Col, with William Kincaid, MA, 51; Juilliard Sch, with Arthur Lora; Paris Consv, with Gaston Crunelle; private study with Jean-Pierre Rampal, Paris; Freiburg Musikhochsch, with Gustav Scheck. *Teaching:* Prof flute, Univ Iowa, 52-, baroque perf pract, 81- *Mem:* Nat Flute Asn (bd mem, 75-77 & 80-82); Nat Asn Col Wind and Perc Instr; Am Rec Soc (bd ed, 81-); Am Asn Univ Prof. *Publ:* Auth, Interpretation of French Music from 1675-1775, McGinnis & Marx, 73; coauth, Free Ornamentation in Woodwind Music, 1700-1750, 76 & The Classical Woodwind Cadenza, 78, McGinnis & Marx; auth, Make Up Your Own Baroque Ornamentation, Woodwind World, 80, Tibia, 82, Am Rec, 82 & Nat Flute Asn Newsletter, 83; coauth, The Art of Preluding, McGinnis & Marx, 83. *Mailing Add:* 308 Fourth Ave Iowa City IA 52240

MATHER, ROGER FREDERICK
FLUTE, EDUCATOR
b London, England, May 27, 17; US citizen. *Study:* Cambridge Univ, England, BA, 38, MA, 41; Mass Inst Technol, MSc, 40. *Teaching:* Instr flute, Village Fine Arts Soc, Bay Village, Ohio, 68-70; adj prof flute, Univ Iowa, 73- *Bibliog:* Betty Bang (auth), Mather's System of Flute Playing, Woodwind World, 6/72. *Mem:* Nat Flute Asn; Nat Asn Col Wind & Perc Instr; Am Rec Soc; Catgut Acoustical Soc. *Interests:* Flutes and flute playing; breath control and chest, throat, and head resonances for all wind instruments and speaking and singing voice. *Publ:* Auth, Care and Repair of the Flute, Instrumentalist, 72 & 73; The Choice of Flute Tube Material and Thickness, 74 & Is Your Flute Vibrating Properly?, 74, Woodwind World; The Art of Playing the Flute, Vol I—Breath Control, 80 & Vol II—Embouchure, 81, Romney Press. *Mailing Add:* 304 4th Ave Iowa City IA 52240

MATHES, RACHEL CLARKE
SOPRANO, EDUCATOR
b Atlanta, Ga, Mar 14, 41. *Study:* Birmingham-Southern Col, studied with Andrew Gainey, BA, 62; Akad Musik & Darstellende Kunst, Vienna, Austria,

62-63; with Edith Boroschek, Düsseldorf, Germany. *Roles:* Aida in Aida, Stadttheater Basel, 65; Die Frau in Märchen von der schönen Lilie, Schwetzingen, Germany, 69; Agave in Pentheus, Bonn Opera, Germany, 71; Medea in Medea; Santuzza in Cavalleria rusticana; Madama Butterfly in Madama Butterfly; Gutrune in Götterdämmerung. *Pos:* Leading sop, Stadttheater, Basel, Switzerland, 65-66, Deutsche Opera Am Rhein, Dusseldorf, WGermany, 66-67, Stadttheater, Bonn, WGermany, 71-72; appeared in opera houses in US & Europe, 72-74; res mem, Metropolitan Opera, formerly; mem bd dir, Birmingham Civic Opera, formerly. *Teaching:* Prof music, Birmingham-Southern Col, 77- *Awards:* Fulbright Scholarship Vienna, Austria, 62; Winner, Metropolitan Opera Regional Auditions, 62; First Prize, Friday Morning Music Club, 62 & Baltimore Opera Auditions, 65. *Mem:* Am Guild Musical Artists; Am Music Teachers Asn; Nat Asn Teachers Singing; Col Music Soc; Music Teachers Nat Asn. *Mailing Add:* Box A-33 Birmingham-Southern Col Birmingham AL 35204

MATHEW, DAVID (WYLIE), III
COMPOSER, MUSIC DIRECTOR
b Rochelle, Ill, Dec 18, 45. *Study:* Knox Col, BA, 67; Northern Ill Univ, MM, 71; NTex State Univ, DMA, 73. *Works:* Identity, Oxford Univ Press, 73; I Carry Your Heart, E B Marks, 74; Private Mirrors, 75 & 6 for 27, 75, Seesaw Music Corp. *Pos:* Dir, Savannah Symph Chorale, currently. *Teaching:* Assoc prof comp & choral cond, Ga Southern Col, 73- *Bibliog:* David Cope (auth), New Directions in Music, William C Brown, 75. *Mem:* ASCAP; Am Soc Univ Comp; Am Music Ctr; Am Choral Dir Asn; Music Educr Nat Conf. *Mailing Add:* Music Dept LB8052 Ga Southern Col Statesboro GA 30460

MATHEWS, JOHN FENTON
DOUBLE BASS, VIOLA DA GAMBA
b Pontiac, Mich, Mar 27, 26. *Study:* Wayne State Univ; Detroit Inst Musical Art; studied double bass with Gaston Brohan & chamber music with William Kroll; Peabody Consv Music. *Pos:* Double Bass, recitals, US & Europe, 56-; prin double bass, Baltimore Symph Orch, 59; solo viola da gamba, State Dept Tour Europe, 69; founder & music dir, Fest, Inc, currently. *Teaching:* Mem fac double bass, Kneisel Hall Chamber Music Sch, Cath Univ & Peabody Consv Music, currently. *Mailing Add:* 1410 Bolton St Baltimore MD 21217

MATHEWS, SHIRLEY
HARPSICHORD
Study: Goucher Col, AB; Univ Mich, studied piano with Benning Dexter; studied harpsichord with John Challis; Mannes Col Music, studied with Sylvia Marlowe. *Pos:* Harpsichordist, Baltimore Symph Orch, 59-; conct tours in US & Europe, formerly; soloist with orch; pianist & harpsichordist, chamber music recitals; pres, Musicians Co, Inc, 74-78; mem, Pro Musica Rara. *Teaching:* Dir, Music Baroque series, Goucher Col, 64-72. *Publ:* Auth, Two manuals on instr soundboard painting. *Mailing Add:* c/o Int Artists Mgt 58 W 72nd St New York NY 10023

MATHIESEN, THOMAS JAMES
EDUCATOR, WRITER
b Roslyn Heights, NY, Apr 30, 47. *Study:* Willamette Univ, BM, 68; Univ Southern Calif, MM, 70, DMA, 71. *Teaching:* Lectr musicol, Univ Southern Calif, 71-72; prof, Brigham Young Univ, 72- *Awards:* Am Counc Learned Soc Grant, 77. *Mem:* Am Musicol Soc (co-chmn, Rocky Mountain Chap, 79-80, Nat Coun Chap Rep, 79-81); Int Musicol Soc; Music Libr Asn. *Interests:* Ancient Greek music and music theory; history of music theory. *Publ:* Auth, A Bibliography of Sources for the Study of Ancient Greek Music, J Boonin, 74; Towards a Corpus of Ancient Greek Music Theory, Fontes Artis Musicae, 78; New Fragments of Ancient Greek Music, Acta Musicol, 81; Feast of Corpus Christi and the Regimen Animarum at Brigham Young University, J Musicol, 83; Aristides Quintilianus on Music, Yale Univ Press, 83. *Mailing Add:* Rte 2 Box 172 Hobble Creek Canyon Springville UT 84663

MATHIS, (GEORGE) RUSSELL
MUSIC DIRECTOR, EDUCATOR
b Streator, Ill, July 22, 26. *Study:* Ill Wesleyan Univ, BM, 47; Univ Ill, MS(music educ), 52, EdD, 62. *Pos:* Asst dir, Choral Activ, Sch Music, Univ Ill, 57-62; dir, Choral Activ, Sch Music, Univ Okla, 62-69; reviewer & columnist, Am Choral J, 69- *Teaching:* Asst provost, Spec Acad Prog, Sch Music, Univ Okla, 69-76, chairperson, vocal div, 76- *Awards:* Citation for Distinguished Serv, Nat Bd Music Educr, 76 & 78; Outstanding Choral Musician in Okla, Okla Chap, Am Choral Dir Asn, 78; Citation for Distinguished Serv to Choral Music, Southwest Div, Am Choral Dir Asn, 80. *Mem:* Am Choral Dir Asn (SW div pres, 69-72 & nat pres, 76-79); Music Teachers Nat Asn; Music Educ Nat Conf (mem nat bd, 76-79); Inter-Am Choral Asn; Phi Mu Alpha Sinfonia. *Publ:* Auth, Perspectives in Education, Music Educr Nat Conf Source Bk, 66. *Mailing Add:* Okla Univ Sch Music 560 Parrington Oval Norman OK 73019

MATHIS, WILLIAM ERVIN
ADMINISTRATOR, EDUCATOR
b Price, Utah, Aug 2, 31. *Study:* Carbon Col, Utah, AS, 55; Brigham Young Univ, BS(music educ), 57, MS, 61; Univ Mich, PhD(music), 69. *Pos:* Cond, Wichita Symph Youth Orch, 77- *Teaching:* Instr instrm music, Utah & Mich pub sch, 57-62; from instr to asst prof music educ, Brigham Young Univ, 62-66; teaching fel, Univ Mich, 66-67; coordr grad studies & assoc prof, Wichita State Univ, 69-81, chmn dept music perf & prof, 81- *Mem:* Music Educr Nat Conf; Kans Music Educr Asn; Col Music Soc. *Publ:* Auth, Evaluating Music Aptitude, Instrumentalist, 67; The Emergence of Simple Instrument Experiences in Early Kindergartens, 72 & Teaching and Experimentation with Simple Instruments in School Music Programs, 1900-1960, 73, J Res Music Educ; Where the Jobs Are—And What They Are, Music Educr J, 78; Peck Horns and Other Castoffs, Instrumentalist, 81. *Mailing Add:* 2343 Hathway Cr Wichita KS 67226

MATSON, SIGFRED CHRISTIAN
EDUCATOR, ADMINISTRATOR

b Chicago, Ill, Feb 17, 17. *Study:* Am Consv Music, BMus(piano), 37, MMus(piano), 38, MMus(comp), 39; Ohio Wesleyan Univ, BA, 43; Eastman Sch Music, DPhil, 47. *Pos:* Instr, Sioux Falls Col, 39-41; instr piano & theory, Ohio Wesleyan Univ, 41-44; prof, Monmouth Col, 47-49; head dept, Miss Univ Women, 49-78, prof, 49-80. *Awards:* Musician of Year, Miss Fedn Music Clubs, 73. *Mem:* Miss Music Educr Asn (pres, 61-62); Nat Asn Sch Music (chmn region 8, 62-64); Miss Music Teachers Asn (pres, 66-70); Music Teachers Nat Asn (pres, 76-78, rec secy, 79-83 & pres elect, 83-). *Mailing Add:* Star Rte Box 220-2 Columbus MS 39701

MATSUDA, KENICHIRO
VIOLA

b Sapporo, Japan, Mar 13, 54. *Study:* Northern Ill Univ, BM, 79, MM, 81. *Pos:* Asst prin viola, Grant Park Symph, Chicago, 81- & Grand Rapids Symph, 82- *Mailing Add:* c/o Grand Rapids Symph Orch Exhibitors Hall 220 Lyon St Grand Rapids MI 49503

MATSUMOTO, SHIGEMI (SHIGEMI MATSUMOTO STARK)
SOPRANO

b Denver, Colo. *Study:* Calif State Univ, Northridge, BMus, 68. *Roles:* Michaëla in Carmen, San Francisco Opera, 72; Despina in Cosi fan tutte, Portland Opera Co, 73; Mimi in La Boheme, 74 & Adina in Elixir of Love, 75, San Francisco Opera; Suzanna in Marriage of Figaro, Belgium Nat Opera Co, 78; Nanetta in Falstaff, San Antonio Opera, 79; Yolanda in The Freelance, Philadelphia Opera & Kansas City Lyr Opera, 81. *Awards:* First Prize, Metropolitan Opera Nat Auditions, 67; Grand Prize Winner, San Francisco Opera Nat Auditions, 68; Opera Inst Am Grant, 72. *Mem:* Am Guild Musical Artists. *Mailing Add:* 60 Riverside Dr Apt 1D New York NY 10024

MATTFELD, VICTOR HENRY
EDUCATOR, WRITER

b Bunceton, Mo, Sept 1, 17. *Study:* Univ Chicago, BA, 42; Am Consv Music, BMus, 44, MMus, 46; Yale Univ, PhD(music hist), 60. *Pos:* Ed in chief, E C Schirmer Music Co, Ione Press, 56-66; mem bd dir, Snug Harbor Cult Ctr, 76- *Teaching:* Instr organ & theory, Am Consv Music, 45-47; instr music, Yale Univ, 52-55; from instr to asst prof music & inst organist, Mass Inst Technol, 57-65; assoc prof, Col Staten Island, City Univ New York, 67-73, prof, 73-, chmn, Visual & Perf Arts, 75-77. *Awards:* Old Dom Found Fel, 65; Am Philosophical Soc Grant, 66. *Mem:* Am Guild Organists; Am Musicol Soc; Renaissance Soc Am; Am Musical Instrm Soc; Viola de Gambe Soc Am. *Interests:* Music publishing and editing; music of Renaissance. *Publ:* Auth, George Rhaw's Publications for Vespers; A Study of Liturgical Practices of the Early Reformation, Inst Medieval Music, 66. *Mailing Add:* Col Staten Island City Univ New York Staten Island NY 10301

MATTHEN, PAUL SEYMOUR
EDUCATOR, BARITONE

b Pawling, NY, May 5, 14. *Study:* Bard-St Stephen's Col, Columbia Univ, BA, 37, grad work, 37-39. *Pos:* Soloist, Radio City Music Hall, 40-43; performer, concerts with maj symph orchs & recitals throughout US, Can & Europe; dir, Am Bach Soc, NY, 49-51; leading bar, Stuttgart State Opera, Germany, 55-57. *Teaching:* Prof voice, Ind Univ, 58- *Mem:* Am Musicol Soc; Int Musicol Soc; Music Libr Asn. *Publ:* Contribr to Notes. *Rep:* Albert Kaye Assoc Inc 58 W 58 St New York NY 10019. *Mailing Add:* 1333 E Davis St Bloomington IN 47401

MATTHEWS, JUSTUS FREDERICK
COMPOSER, EDUCATOR

b Peoria, Ill, Jan 13, 45. *Study:* Calif State Univ, Northridge, BA, 67, MA, 68; State Univ NY, Buffalo, PhD, 73. *Works:* Bionic Music, Electrocentric Music, Inc, 77; Thoughts, Calif State Univ, Long Beach New Music Ens, 81-83; Like Leaves, Like Ashes, Calif State Univ, Long Beach Wind Symph, 83; All the dead voices ..., Calif State Univ, Long Beach Symph Orch, 83. *Teaching:* Assoc prof music comp, Calif State Univ, Long Beach, 71- *Mem:* Int Soc Contemp Music; writer affil, Soc European Stage Authors & Comp. *Publ:* Auth, Music 3150—A Fortran Program for Composing Music for Conventional Instruments, Northwestern Univ Press, 79. *Mailing Add:* 245 Harvard Ln Seal Beach CA 90740

MATTHEWS, WILLIAM
COMPOSER, EDUCATOR

b Toledo, Ohio, Apr 1, 50. *Study:* Consv Music, Oberlin Col, with Randolph Coleman & Walter Aschaffenberg; Univ Iowa, with Richard Hervig & Peter Lewis; Inst Sonology, Utrecht, with G M Koenig; Yale Univ, with Jacob Druckman, Robert Moore & K Penderecki. *Works:* Larchwood, 75; Letters from Home (11 instrm); Sumer is Icumen in & Lhude Sing (bassoon & tape); Ferns (piano); Political Pieces (brass quintet). *Teaching:* Asst prof music, Bates Col, currently. *Awards:* BMI Award (three); ASCAP Award; Charles Ives Prize; Nat Endowment for the Arts Individual Composer Fel; Am Composers Asn Award. *Mailing Add:* Dept Music Bates Col Lewiston ME 04240

MATTILA, EDWARD CHARLES
COMPOSER, EDUCATOR

b Duluth, Minn, Nov 30, 27. *Study:* Univ Minn, Duluth, BA(music), 50; New England Consv, MM, 56; Univ Minn, Minneapolis, PhD(comp), 63. *Works:* On Teaching (chorus, orch & soloists), Univ Kans Symph Orch & Chorus, 66; Partitions for String Orchestra, Comp Autograph Publ, 69; Six Arrays for Piano, perf by Carole Ross, 71; Symphony No 1, Univ Kans Symph Orch, 74; Thirteen Ways of Looking at a Blackbird, Univ Miami Chamber Choir, 78; Repercussions for Tape, Univ Memphis, Am Soc Univ Comp Nat Conf, 80; Movements for Computer and Dancers, Univ Kans Dance Co, 83. *Teaching:* Instr music, Concordia Col, 58-62; asst prof, Bishop Col, Tex, 62-64; asst prof, Univ Kans, Lawrence, 64-69, assoc prof, 69-75, prof, 75- *Bibliog:* John Pozdro (auth); Edward Mattila: Kansas Composer, Comp Mag, Vol 1, No 4; Tim Crouch (auth), Ten Years on the Contemporary Side with Dr Ed Mattila, Radio Mag, Univ Kans, 1/82; Chuch Twardy (auth), Creative Computers, Lawrence J-World, Kans, 10/31/82. *Mem:* Am Soc Univ Comp (mem nat coun, 76-81); Am Music Ctr; Col Music Soc. *Mailing Add:* Sch Fine Arts Univ Kans Lawrence KS 66045

MATTIS, KATHLEEN
VIOLA

Study: Univ Southern Calif; studied with Eudice Shapiro, George Kast, Charles Castleman, Heidi Castleman & Milton Thomas. *Rec Perf:* On Vox. *Pos:* Mem, Pasadena Symph Orch & Univ Southern Calif String Quartet, formerly & Trio Cassatt, currently; prin viola, NY String Orch, formerly; assoc prin viola, St Louis Symph Orch, currently. *Teaching:* Asst, Univ Southern Calif, formerly; fac mem, St Louis Consv, currently. *Mailing Add:* St Louis Symph 127 Jefferson Rd St Louis MO 63119

MATTRAN, DONALD ALBERT
ADMINISTRATOR, CONDUCTOR

b Chicago, Ill, July 8, 34. *Study:* Univ Mich, BMus, 57, MMus, 60. *Rec Perf:* Concerto for Cello and Jazz Band, Serenus, 70. *Pos:* Consult, Music Div, Kaman Corp, 80-; dir, Sch Music, Syracuse Univ, 82- *Teaching:* Asst prof, Univ NH, 61-65 & Boston Univ, 65-66; assoc prof cond & music educ, Hartt Sch Music, 66-71, dean, 71-80. *Mem:* Nat Asn Sch Music (secy, 78-81, mem exec comt, 78-81 & consult & evaluator, 71-); Col Music Soc; Music Educr Nat Conf. *Publ:* Coauth (with Mary Rasmussen), A Teacher's Guide to the Literature of Woodwind Instruments, Brass & Woodwind Quart, 66. *Mailing Add:* Dir Sch Music Syracuse Univ Syracuse NY 13210

MAUCER, JOHN FRANCIS
CONDUCTOR, COMPOSER

b New York, NY, Sept 12, 45. *Study:* Yale Univ, with Gustav Meier, BA, 67, MPhil, 71; Berkshire Music Ctr, with B Maderna, C Davis, S Ozawa & Leonard Bernstein. *Rec Perf:* Candide (Bernstein). *Pos:* Prod & art dir, Spec Yale Opera Co, 66-75; music dir, Yale Symph, 68-75; asst to Bernstein, Metropolitan Opera, 74; cond with major orchs in US, Europe, Can, Cent & South Am. *Mem:* Elizabethan Club. *Publ:* Contribr, Yale Alumni Mag. *Mailing Add:* Columbia Artists 165 W 57th St New York NY 10019

MAUK, FREDERICK HENRY, JR
EDUCATOR

b Ogdensburg, NY, Nov 13, 47. *Study:* Calif State Univ, Long Beach, AB, 69; Harvard Univ, AM, 74, PhD, 82. *Teaching:* Fel music, Harvard Univ, 74-80, asst prof, 83; instr, Mass Inst Technol, 80-82; asst prof & chmn, Dept Music, Goucher Col, 83- *Mem:* Am Musicol Soc; Col Music Soc; Am Soc Aesthet; Semiotic Soc Am. *Interests:* Music history; aesthetics; semiotics. *Mailing Add:* Dept Music Goucher Col Towson MD 21204

MAUK, STEVEN GLENN
SAXOPHONE, EDUCATOR

b Greeneville, Tenn, Nov 29, 49. *Study:* Univ Tenn, BS(music educ), 71; Univ Mich, MM(woodwinds), 72, DMA(perf), 76. *Rec Perf:* Horizon (Samuel Pellman), Cornell Wind Ens Rec, 79; Concertante (Clare Grundman), Susquehanna Sound Rec, 82; Divertimento (Akira Yuyama), MAI Rec, 82; Poem (Malcolm Lewis), Open Loop Rec, 83; Concertino (Jerry Bilik), 83 & Concert Piece (Samuel Pellman), 84, Cornell Wind Ens Rec. *Pos:* Freelance sax soloist, 75-; clinician & soloist, Selmer Co, Elkhart, Ind, 78- *Teaching:* Lectr music, Eastern Mich Univ, Ypsilanti, 72-75; assoc prof music, Ithaca Col, 75- *Awards:* Solo Winner, East & West Artists Int Compt, 80; Dana Teaching Fel, Ithaca Col, 81-82. *Mem:* North Am Sax Alliance (pres, 80-83); Am Fedn Musicians; Music Educr Nat Conf; Col Music Soc; NY State Sch Music Asn. *Publ:* Contribr, Sax Symposium, 77-83, Notes, Music Libr Asn, 79-83 & Chamber Music Quarterly, 83; coauth, A Class Method for Saxophone, private publ, 78-83; auth, A Practical Approach to the Saxophone, Medici Music Press (in prep). *Mailing Add:* 147 Pine Tree Rd Ithaca NY 14850

MAUL, ERIC (WILLIAM)
BASSOON

b Philadelphia, Pa, Feb 5, 52. *Study:* Curtis Inst Music, with Sol Schoenbach. *Pos:* Prin bassoon, Pa Ballet Orch, 73-82; utility bassoon, New Orleans Phil, 82- *Awards:* Winner soloist div, Philadephia Orch, 66 & 68. *Mailing Add:* 2304 Litchwood Lane Harvey LA 70058

MAULDIN, MICHAEL
COMPOSER, ADMINISTRATOR

b Port Arthur, Tex, June 14, 47. *Study:* Washburn Univ, with James Rivers, BM; Univ NMex, with William Wood, MM. *Works:* Variations on a Huron Carol (small orch), 73; Tombeau for Strings and Timpani, Albuquerque Youth Symph, 74; Celebration of the Sun: 3 Conservations (piano & small orch), 74; 3 New Mexico Landscapes (clarinet & piano), 75; 3 Jemez Landscapes, 76; Fiesta de Fe (choirs, handbells, brass, piano, organ & dancers), comn by United Presby Church, Synod of SW, 77; Petroglyph for Strings (orch), Chamber Orch Albuquerque, 78. *Pos:* Dir, Mauldin Sch Music, 72- *Awards:* First Place Piano & First Place Large Ens, NMex Comp Guild Bicentennial Cont; First Place, Ann Cont Chamber Orch Albuquerque, 78. *Mailing Add:* 12713 Summer Ave NE Albuquerque NM 87112

MAUNEY, MILES H
EDUCATOR
Study: Oberlin Col, BM, 47; Teachers Col, Columbia Univ, MA, 61; studied piano with Rosina Lhevinne, Isabella Vengerova & Olga Stroumilld. *Rec Perf:* On Zodiac Rec. *Pos:* Concerts & duo piano recitals for six years, Columbia Artists Mgt. *Teaching:* Piano, Univ Minn & Univ Ill; assoc prof pianoforte, Oberlin Col, 63- *Mailing Add:* Music Dept Oberlin Col Oberlin OH 44074

MAURER, JAMES CARL
VIOLIN, EDUCATOR
b Shreveport, La, Nov 9, 43. *Study:* Curtis Inst Music, BM, 64; Univ Southern Calif, MM, 66; studied with Ivan Galamian, Josef Gingold, Eudice Shapiro & Gabor Rejto. *Rec Perf:* Bach Brandenburg Concerto #2, Clarino Rec, 73; Night Music (Diamond) & Concertino (Pino), Crystal Rec, 79; Quintets for Clarinet & Strings (Bliss & Coleridge-Taylor), Uni-Pro Rec, 80. *Pos:* Dir, Denver Suzuki Inst, 66- & Denver Talent Educ, 81- *Teaching:* Instr violin, Univ Colo, 67-68; prof violin, Univ Denver, 71- *Awards:* Prize Winner, Dealy Award, 63; Munich Int String Quartet Compt, 65 & Coleman Chamber Music Compt, 65. *Mem:* Am String Teachers Asn; Suzuki Asn Am; Music Teachers Nat Asn; Suzuki Asn Colo; Denver Asn Musicians. *Mailing Add:* Music Dept Univ Denver Denver CO 80208

MAURO, ERMANNO
TENOR
b Trieste, Italy; Can citizen. *Study:* Univ Toronto, 64-67; Royal Consv Music, Toronto, 64-67; studied with Dr Herman Geiger-Torel. *Roles:* Il Trovatore, Vienna Staatsoper, 74; La Boheme, Covent Garden, 76; Manon Lescaut, La Scala, 78; Tosca, Hamburg Opera, 80; Simon Boccanegra, Paris Opera, 80; Forza del Destino, Metropolitan Opera, 82; Norma, San Francisco Opera, 82. *Rep:* Columbia Artists Mgt 165 W 57th New York NY 10019. *Mailing Add:* 1135 Talka Court Mississauga ON L5C 1B1 Canada

MAVES, DAVID W
COMPOSER, EDUCATOR
b Salem, Ore, Apr 3, 37. *Study:* Univ Ore, BMus(comp), 61; Univ Mich, MMus(comp), 63, AMusD, 73. *Works:* Oktoechos (instrm trio for horn, clarinet & perc), 74 & A Bestiary (chorus & perc), 78, C F Peters; Petite Sonatine Pour Deux Pianistes Pitoyable (piano duet), Bradley Publ, 81; Piano Sonata No I, C F Peters, 83; Piano Sonata No II, Bradley Publ, 83. *Teaching:* Ford Found comp in res, Raleigh, NC, 63-65; music coordr, Shaw Univ, 66-69; asst prof, Duke Univ, 73-76; chmn fine arts dept, Col Charleston, 77-82, comp in res, 82- *Awards:* Inter Am Music Award, Sigma Alpha Iota, 74 & 78; Comn, Spoleto USA Fest, 82; New Music Award, Bowling Green State Univ, 83. *Mem:* Col Music Soc (mem coun, 81-); Am Music Ctr. *Rep:* 31 Society St Charleston SC 29401. *Mailing Add:* Fine Arts Dept Col Charleston Charleston SC 29424

MAXIN, JACOB
EDUCATOR, PIANO
Study: Juilliard Sch Music, BS, MS; studied piano with Irma Wolpe, Edward Steuermann & Ilona Kabos & comp with Stefan Wolpe, Robert Ward, Vincent Persichetti & Roger Sessions. *Pos:* Performer, Young Artist's Series, 63; soloist, Philadelphia Orch; mem, Aeolian Chamber Players, formerly. *Teaching:* Mem fac, Juilliard Sch Music, formerly & Brandeis Univ, Univ Colo, Pomona Col & Bowdoin Col, summers, formerly; mem fac piano, New England Consv Music, currently. *Mailing Add:* New England Consv Music 290 Huntington Rd Boston MA 02115

MAXWELL, BARBARA
LIBRARIAN
b Colo, 1941. *Study:* Pomona Col, BA(music), 62; Univ Calif, Berkeley, MA(musicol), 65, MLS, 67. *Works:* Prelude and Toccata for Piano, perf by Sandra Green, 62. *Pos:* Ref libr, Univ Calif, Berkeley, 66-69; ref libr, State Univ NY, Binghamton, 69-70, music libr, 70-73; music cataloger, Libr Cong, 73-75; ref libr, George Washington Univ, 75-, chief ref libr, 75-80. *Teaching:* Instr musicol, State Univ NY, Binghamton, 71-72. *Mem:* Music Libr Asn; Medieval Acad Am. *Interests:* Monastic culture. *Publ:* Auth, Art Songs, Antiphony, 74. *Mailing Add:* 20 Pontiac Way Gaithersburg MD 20878

MAXWELL, DONALD EDWARD
ADMINISTRATOR, EDUCATOR
b Greenwich, Conn, June 10, 41. *Study:* Colgate Univ, BA; Friends Univ, BM, 66; Univ Okla, MM, 68, DME, 75. *Teaching:* Prof & coordr music, Midwestern State Univ, Wichita Falls, Tex, 71- *Mem:* Nat Asn Teachers Singing; Nat Asn Sch Music; Tex Asn Sch Music. *Interests:* The effect of white noise masking on trained singers. *Mailing Add:* 3101 Milby Wichita Falls TX 76308

MAXYM, STEPHEN
EDUCATOR, BASSOON
Study: Juilliard Sch Music; Int Sch Music, St Augustine's Abbey, England. *Pos:* Solo & first bassoon, Metropolitan Opera Orch, 39-76; mem, Pittsburgh Symph, formerly. *Teaching:* Mem fac, Juilliard Sch Music, Manhattan Sch Music & New England Consv, currently; vis artist, Hartt Sch Music, 79- *Publ:* Auth, several articles on instrm tech. *Mailing Add:* Juilliard Sch Music Lincoln Ctr New York NY 10023

MAY, ERNEST DEWEY
EDUCATOR, ORGAN
b Jersey City, NJ, May 8, 42. *Study:* Harvard Univ, AB, 64; studied with Nadia Boulanger & Andre Marchal, Paris, 64-66; Princeton Univ, with Arthur Mendel, MFA & PhD, 75. *Pos:* Organist & choirmaster, St James Church, Greenfield, Mass, 78- *Teaching:* Asst prof, Amherst Col, 69-75; assoc prof organ & musicol, Univ Mass, Amherst, 76- *Mem:* Am Musicol Soc; Am Guild Organists; Asn Anglican Musicians; New Bach Soc; Col Music Soc. *Interests:* Bach organ music; the publishing house of Breitkopf. *Publ:* Auth, J G Walther and the Lost Weimar Autographs, FS Mendel, 74; Eine neue Quelle für Bachs einzeln überlieferte Orgelchorale, Bach Jahrbuch, 74; Breitkopf's Role in the Transmission of Bach's Organ Chorales, Princeton, 74; co-ed, Neue Bach Ausgabe, Vol I/20, Bärenreiter, 83. *Mailing Add:* 44 Amherst Rd Pelham MA 01002

MAY, JULIA
EDUCATOR, MEZZO-SOPRANO
b Kansas City, Kans. *Study:* Northwestern Univ; studied with Coenraad V Bos, William Tarrasch, Karl Kritz, George Schick, Hermann Reutter & Alberta Masiello, BM, 46, MM, 56. *Roles:* Gertrude in Hansel and Gretel, Pittsburgh Opera Co; Giullietta in The Tales of Hoffmann; Suzuki in Madama Butterfly; Mary in Der Fliegende Holländer; Rebecca Nurse in The Crucible; Marthe in Faust; Emilia in Otello. *Pos:* Soloist with Chicago Symph, Pittsburgh Symph & Wheeling Symph Orch. *Teaching:* Instr voice & piano, Lab Sch Music, Chatham Col, 56-59; prof voice, Duquesne Univ, 59-, chmn, Voice Dept, 62- & Perf Dept, 83- *Awards:* Winner, Soc Am Musicians Cont, 51 & Ill Opera Guild & WGN Cont, 52; Fulbright Scholar Stuttgart, Germany, 53. *Mem:* Am Guild Musical Artists; Pi Kappa Lambda. *Mailing Add:* 1543 Beechwood Blvd Pittsburgh PA 15217

MAY, WALTER BRUCE
COMPOSER, EDUCATOR
b Springfield, Mo, Sept 28, 31. *Study:* SW Mo State Univ, BS, BSEd & dipl(organ), 51; Consv Nat, Paris, with Milhaud & G Dandelot, deuxieme medaille d'harmonie, 52; Univ Toronto, DMus, 66. *Works:* Service of Holy Communion, Christ Church Cathedral, Eau Claire, Wis, 58; Symphony No 1, Univ Symph, Am Fedn Music Clubs Mtg, Rice Labe, Wis, 62; Cantate Domino, First Lutheran Church, Eau Claire, Wis, 65; Symphony No 2, Greece Symph, New York, 73; Concerto 1 for Viola & Orchestra, 80, Concerto 3 for Viola & Orchestra, 82 & Suite 1 for Viola and Piano, 82, comn & perf by Emanuel Vardi. *Rec Perf:* Concerto No 1 for Viola & Strings, Zoe Rec, 82. *Teaching:* From instr to assoc prof music, Univ Wis, Eau Claire, 55-67; assoc prof & dept chmn, State Univ NY, Cortland, 67-69; prof & dept chmn, Eisenhower Col, 69-75 & Augustana Col, 75- *Awards:* Award of Merit, Am Fedn Music Clubs, 62. *Mem:* Col Music Soc. *Publ:* Auth, The Last Days (Cantata), Greenwood Press, 68; The Influence of Magic in Worship, Anglican Theol Rev, 69; ed, The Liturgical Music of Arthur Einstein, Temple Emanuel Providence, RI, 72. *Mailing Add:* 1520 S Summit Sioux Falls SD 57105

MAYER, FREDERICK DAVID
TENOR, EDUCATOR
b Lincoln, Nebr. *Study:* Midland Col, Fremont, Nebr, BA, 52; Columbia Univ, MA, 57, EdD, 59; vocal study with Luigi Contoni, La Scala & Hans Hopf, Munich. *Roles:* Ferrando in Cosi Fan Tutte, Ulm, Ger, 64; Graf in Almaviva, Berlin, Vienna, Munich & Stuttgart, 68-83; Tamino in Die Zauberflöte, Munich Gärtnerplatz, 73-; Ernesto in Don Pasquale, Basel, Switz, 76; Alfredo in La Traviata, Salzburg; Eisenstein in Die Fledermaus & Fra Diavolo in Fra Diavolo, Munich. *Pos:* Leading tenor, Staatstheater Am Gärtnerplatz, 68-; guest perf, leading opera houses Europe, 68- *Teaching:* Prof music & music educ, Columbia Univ, 59-68. *Awards:* Bayerische Kammersänger, Bavarian Govt, 74. *Publ:* Coauth, The Changing Voice, Prentice Hall, 65. *Mailing Add:* Tirschenreuther 19 Munich Germany, Federal Republic of

MAYER, GEORGE LOUIS
ADMINISTRATOR, LIBRARIAN
b Somerville, NJ, Sept 17, 29. *Study:* NY Univ, BA, 52; Columbia Univ, MS in LS, 54; Univ Cologne, Germany, 60-61. *Pos:* Librn, New York Public Libr, 53-55, sr librn music libr, 55-65; supv music librn, Gen Libr Perf Arts Lincoln Ctr, 65-74, prin librn & coordr, 74- *Awards:* Fulbright Found Grant, 60-61. *Mem:* Music Libr Asn; Music Asn; Int Asn Music Libr. *Interests:* Opera and vocal works. *Publ:* Auth, Annals of The New York City Opera 1944-1979, In: The New York City Opera, Macmillan, 81; contribr, Funk & Wagnalls New Encycl, 73; articles, reviews & discographies for Am Rec Guide, Saturday Rev, Libr J, Previews, Am Ref Books Ann, Opera Rev & others. *Mailing Add:* Libr & Museum Perf Arts Lincoln Ctr 111 Amsterdam Ave New York NY 10023

MAYER, LUTZ LEO
COMPOSER, EDUCATOR
b Hamburg, Germany, Dec 14, 34; US citizen. *Study:* Univ NC, Chapel Hill, AB(music), 56; Univ Ill, Champaign-Urbana, MM, 59. *Works:* The Boy with a Cart (suite), perf by Dallas Symph, 63; Refuge (opera), 65 & The Paranoid Parakeet (opera), 68, State Univ NY, Cortland. *Pos:* Music dir, Ithaca Opera Asn, 73-75. *Teaching:* Asst prof violin & theory, Tex Wesleyan Col, 60-63; asst prof music, State Univ NY, Cortland, 63-67, assoc prof, 67- *Awards:* Summer Res Fel, State Univ NY, 63, 66 & 74. *Mem:* Col Music Soc; Music Theory Soc New York; Soc Music Theory; Ft Worth League Comp. *Mailing Add:* Star Rte 1 Box 50 Preble NY 13141

MAYER, STEVEN ALAN
PIANO, TEACHER
Study: Juilliard Sch, with Stessin & Gorodritski, MM, 75; Peabody Inst, with Fleisher, 75-78; Manhattan Sch Music, with Keene. *Rec Perf:* Piano Concerto

(Reger), Leonarda Prod, 82. *Pos:* Piano soloist with Am Symph, Dallas Symph, Baltimore Symph, Utah Symph, Amsterdam Phil, Hague Phil, Netherlands Chamber Orch, Slovak Phil & recitals in Am & Europe. *Teaching:* Instr piano, Manhattan Sch Music, 82- *Awards:* Prize, Busoni Int Compt, 74; Univ Md Int Compt, 76 & Bachaver Int Compt, 78. *Mailing Add:* 333 W 86th St New York NY 10024

MAYER, WILLIAM ROBERT
COMPOSER, CRITIC-WRITER
b New York, NY, Nov 18, 25. *Study:* Juilliard Sch Music, 49; Yale Univ, BA, 49; Mannes Col Music, dipl(comp), 52. *Works:* A Death in the Family (three act opera), Belwin-Mills; One Christmas Long Ago (opera), Galaxy Music, 64; Snow Queen (ballet), Theodore Presser, 70; Octagon (piano & orch), MCA Music, 71; The Eve of St Agnes (chorus, soloists & orch), Theodore Presser, 72; Spring Came On Forever (chorus, soloists & orch), comn & perf by New York Choral Soc, 75; Dream's End (six players), perf by St Paul Chamber Orch, 78. *Pos:* Spec writer contemp music, US Info Agency, 74-76; treas, CRI, 74-76, chmn bd, 77-81. *Teaching:* Vis prof, Boston Univ, 66- *Awards:* Guggenheim Fel, 66; Ford Found Grant, 71; Comp-Librettist Grant, Nat Endowment Arts, 76. *Bibliog:* Elie Siegmeister (auth), Music Lovers Handbook, William Morrow & Co, 73; Joseph Machlis (auth), Introduction to Contemporary Music, W W Norton, 80. *Mem:* ASCAP; fel, MacDowell Colony (secy, 78-80, treas, 80-81); Youth Symph Orch NY (vpres, 68); Am Music Ctr. *Publ:* Auth, An Historic Meeting: Aram Khachaturian and Aaron Copland, America, US Info Agency, 64; Contemp Am Opera, US Info Agency, 66; Live Composers, Dead Audiences, New York Times Mag, 75; Modern American Music Notes a Breakthrough, Horizon, 77; Instilling the Living Breath of Theatre into an Opera Score, New York Times, 81. *Mailing Add:* 15 Grammercy Park S New York NY 10003

MAYES, SAMUEL H
CELLO, EDUCATOR
b St Louis, Mo. *Study:* Curtis Inst Music, artists dipl, 37. *Rec Perf:* Symphonie Concerto (Prokofiev), 63 & Don Quixote (Strauss), 71, RCA Victor. *Pos:* Prin cello, Philadelphia Orch, 39-48 & 64-73, Boston Symph, 48-64 & Los Angeles Phil, 74-75. *Teaching:* Prof cello, Univ Mich, 75- *Publ:* Ed, Brahms Symphonies & Overtures for Cello, 69, Tchaikovsky Symphonies for Cello, 70 & Beethoven Symphonies for Cello, 71, Henri Elkan. *Mailing Add:* Sch Music Univ Mich Ann Arbor MI 48109

MAYEUR, ROBERT GORDON
TEACHER, COMPOSER
b Houston, Tex. *Study:* NTex State Univ, BA, 54; Univ Calif Los Angeles, MA, 65; study with Ronald C Purcell, Tal Farlowe, Boris Kremenliev & Lucas Foss. *Works:* Overture for Orchestra, Santa Clara Phil, 64; Rock City, Los Angeles Neophonic Orch, 66. *Pos:* Columnist, Soundboard Mag, 81- *Teaching:* Instr, guitar & jazz hist, Santa Monica Col, 72-79, guitar, Los Angeles Valley Col, 79- *Mem:* ASCAP; Guitar Found Am; Am Guitar Soc; Am Fedn Musicians. *Publ:* Auth, Christmas Book for Classical Guitar, 70, The Guitar and Jazz, 75, The Guitar through the Ages, 76, Young Christian (guitar solo), 76 & Sonata XX--D Scarlatti, 82, self-published. *Mailing Add:* Los Angeles Valley Col 5800 Fulton Ave Van Nuys CA 91401

MAYFIELD, LYNETTE
FLUTE
b Alexandria, Va, Aug 11, 47. *Study:* Baldwin Wallace Col, BM, 69; Ind Univ, MM, 71; study with Julius Baker, 71-72. *Pos:* Assoc prin flute, Houston Symph Orch, 73- *Mailing Add:* 4057 Nenana Dr Houston TX 77025

MAZER, HENRY
CONDUCTOR & MUSIC DIRECTOR
b Pittsburgh, Pa, July 21, 21. *Study:* Carnegie-Mellon Univ; Duquesne Univ, 35-39; Carnegie Inst Technol, 39-40; Univ Pittsburgh, 45-46; studied with Georges Enesco. *Pos:* Pianist, personnel mgr & first apprentice cond, Pittsburgh Symph, formerly; cond, Wheeling Symph Orch, WVa, 47-59 & Fla Symph Orch, 59-66; assoc cond, Pittsburgh Symph Orch, 66-70, Chicago Symph Orch, 70-; music dir, Mendelssohn Choir & Cong of Strings, Cincinnati, Ohio, 71 & 72; music dir & cond, DePaul Univ Symph Orch, 78- *Mailing Add:* Chicago Symph Orch 220 S Michigan Ave Chicago IL 60604

MAZO-SHLYAM, EDA
PIANO, TEACHER
b USSR, 41; US citizen. *Study:* Spec Music Sch, Riga, Latvia, dipl, 59; Leningrad State Consv, USSR, MM, 65, artist dipl, 70. *Teaching:* Asst prof & accmp, Leningrad Consv, USSR, 60-70; assoc prof & soloist, Sverdlovsk Consv, USSR, 72-78; mem fac piano, Longy Sch Music, 80- *Awards:* Laureat, Latvian Repub Compt, 56; Best Accmp, All-Union Compt, USSR, 63; Second Place, Int Piano Compt, Grand Rapids, Mich, 83. *Mem:* Mass Music Teachers Asn. *Mailing Add:* 381 Lovell St Worcester MA 01602

MAZZOLA, JOHN WILLIAM
ADMINISTRATOR
b Bayonne, NJ, Jan 20, 28. *Study:* Tufts Univ, AB, 49; Fordham Law Sch, JD, 52. *Pos:* Attorney, Milbank, Tweed, Hadlem & McCloy, 52-65; secy, gen counsel & exec vpres, Lincoln Ctr Perf Arts, 65-68, pres & chief exec officer, 68-; consult, 83- *Awards:* Benjamin Franklin Fel, Royal Soc Arts, Great Britain; Chevalier des Artes & Lett, France; Commandatore, Ordre de Merite, Italy. *Mem:* Van Cliburn Found; Ravel Acad, France. *Mailing Add:* Lincoln Ctr for Perf Arts 132 W 65th St New York NY 10023

MECHEM, KIRKE LEWIS
COMPOSER, CONDUCTOR
b Wichita, Kans . *Study:* Stanford Univ, BA, 51; Harvard Univ, comp with Walter Piston & Randall Thompson, MA, 53. *Works:* Trio for Piano, Violin & Cello, Carl Fischer, 57; Symphony No 1, Boosey & Hawkes, 65; Piano Sonata, E C Schirmer, Boston, 66; Symphony No 2, Boosey & Hawkes, 69; Singing Is So Good a Thing: An Elizabethan Recreation, C F Peters, 72; American Madrigals, Carl Fischer, 76; Tartuffe: Comic Opera in 3 Acts, G Schirmer, 80. *Awards:* Boott Prize, Harvard Univ, 52; Am Music Award, Sigma Alpha Iota, 59. *Bibliog:* Donald B Miller (auth), Choral Music of Kirke Mechems, Am Choral Review, 70. *Mem:* ASCAP; Nat Opera Asn; Am Choral Dir Asn. *Mailing Add:* 49 Marcela Ave San Francisco CA 94116

MECKEL, PETER TIMOTHY
ADMINISTRATOR, EDUCATOR
b Yankton, SDak, Nov 28, 41. *Study:* Rockford Col; Occidental Col; Chapman Col. *Pos:* Gen dir & founder, Hidden Valley Music Sem, Am Inst Arts, Carmel Valley, Calif, 63- *Bibliog:* Martin Bernheimer (auth), Opera is Alive and Well in Carmel Valley, Los Angeles Times, 82. *Mem:* Music Educr Nat Conf; Calif Music Educr Asn. *Mailing Add:* PO Box 116 Carmel Valley CA 93924

MECKNA, MICHAEL
EDUCATOR, CRITIC-WRITER
b Long Beach, Calif, Feb 13, 45. *Study:* Calif State Univ, Long Beach, BA, 67; Boston Univ, 68-70; Univ Calif, Santa Barbara, PhD, 83. *Pos:* Prog host, KCSB-fm, Santa Barbara, 78-80; prog annotator, Santa Barbara Symph Orch, 79-; corresp ed, Current Musicol, 80-; contrib ed, Am Rec Guide, 81- *Teaching:* Instr folkmusic, Folklife Ctr, Calif State Univ, Long Beach, 75-77; instr guitar, Orange Coast Col, Costa Mesa, Calif, 77-78; instr music hist, Univ Calif, Santa Barbara, 79-82. *Awards:* Young Artist Award, Long Beach Symph Orch, 65; Aspen Fel, Music Critics Asn, 80. *Mem:* Am Musicol Soc; Sonneck Soc; Music Critics Asn; Int Horn Soc. *Interests:* History of aesthetics, criticism, and American music. *Publ:* Auth, Folkguitar for Class or Individual Instruction, Manuscript, 77; contribr, The Music of Peter Racine Fricker, Schott, 80; co-ed, Austrian Cloister Symphonists, Garland, 82; contribr, Copland, Sessions, and Modern Music, Am Music, 83; 20 articles, In: New Grove Dict of Music in US, Macmillan, 84. *Rep:* Dept Music Univ Calif Santa Barbara CA 93106. *Mailing Add:* 730 Elkus Walk #202 Goleta CA 93117

MEHTA, ZUBIN
CONDUCTOR & MUSIC DIRECTOR
b Bombay, India, Apr 29, 36. *Study:* St Xavier's Col, Bombay, 51-53; State Acad Music, Vienna, with Hans Swarowsky, 54-60; Sir George Willimas Univ, Montreal, LLD, 65; Occidental Col, Hon DMus. *Rec Perf:* On Decca Rec. *Pos:* Music dir, Montreal Symph Orch, 61-67, Los Angeles Phil Orch, 62-78, Israel Phil, 69- & New York Phil, 78-; guest cond, Metropolitan Opera, Salzburg Fest, Vienna Phil, Berlin Phil & La Scala. *Awards:* First Prize, Liverpool Cond Compt, 58; Order Lotus, India, 67; Commendatore, Italy. *Bibliog:* David K Shipler (auth), World-Class Violinists Adorn Festival in Israel, New York Times, 12/15/82; John Rockwell (auth), Zubin Mehta Will Appear in a Film about Zoroaster, New York Times, 4/10/83. *Mailing Add:* New York Phil Avery Fisher Hall New York NY 10023

MEIBACH, JUDITH KAREN (JUDITH KAREN MEIBACH SCHILONI)
WRITER, PIANO
b New York, NY, Aug 29, 37. *Study:* Barnard Col, Columbia Univ, BA, 58; Univ Pittsburgh, MA(music hist), 80. *Pos:* Assoc music ed, Prog Book Pittsburgh Symph Orch, currently; prog annotator, New Pittsburgh Chamber Orch, currently. *Teaching:* Fel, Dept Music, Univ Pittsburgh, 80-82 & Am Musicol Soc, 80- *Awards:* Mellon Fel, Univ Pittsburgh, 82. *Publ:* Coauth, Masters of the Violin, Vol IV, Johnson, 82. *Mailing Add:* 144 N Dithridge St Pittsburgh PA 15213

MEIDT, JOSEPH ALEXIS
EDUCATOR, CLARINET
b Grand Forks, NDak, Dec 5, 32. *Study:* Univ NDak, BA, 54, MEd, 55; Univ Southern Calif, 57-58; Univ Iowa, MFA(woodwinds), 65, PhD, 66; studied cello with Johan Lingeman. *Pos:* Numerous engagements with combos & big bands on sax, clarinet, flute & piano, 48-; prin clarinet, Grand Forks Symph Orch, 49-56, Univ NDak Conct Band, 51-54, Cedar Rapids Symph Orch, 65-66, Univ Iowa Symph Band, 65-66 & Duluth-Superior Symph Orch, 67-; choir dir, Sharon Lutheran Church, Grand Forks, NDak, 50-54, Zion Lutheran Church, Lake Bronson, Minn, 55-56, St Paul's Lutheran Church, Monrovia, Calif, 59-60, Messiah Lutheran Church, Pasadena, Calif, 60-61 & Pilgrim Lutheran Church, Superior, Wis, 68-70; first chair alto sax, Univ Southern Calif Symph Band, 57-58; tenor soloist, St Paul's Episcopal Church, Los Angeles, 57-59 & Iowa City Presby Church, 64-66; co-founder & dir, Head of Lakes Music Camp, 67-78; numerous university ensemble performances. *Teaching:* Band & choir, Lake Bronson, Minn, 54-56; teacher band & orch, Pasadena, Calif, 57-61; teacher choir, Needles, Calif, 61-62; teacher band, Nicollet, Minn, 62-64; instr music, Univ Wis, Superior, 66-, chmn dept, 76-81; staff mem, Symph Sch Am, currently. *Mem:* Nat Asn Col Wind & Perc Teachers; Int Clarinet Soc. *Mailing Add:* 44 Billings Dr Superior WI 54880

MEIER, GUSTAV
CONDUCTOR, EDUCATOR
b Wettingen, Switz, Aug 13, 29; US & Swiss citizen. *Study:* Zurich Consv Music, dipl, 48 & 53; Accad Chigiana Siena, with Paul van Kempen, 52-53;

Berkshire Music Ctr, with Eleazar de Carvalho, 57-58. *Works:* Numerous rec with Epic & Westminster. *Pos:* Musical dir & cond, Imperial Symph Orch, Addis-Ababa, Ethiopia, 54-56; Greater Bridgeport Symph Orch, Conn, 72- & Eastman Phil & Eastman Opera Theater, 73-76; guest cond, New York City Opera, Santa Fe Opera, San Francisco Opera & Zurich Opera; musical dir & cond, Lansing Symph Orch, 80- *Teaching:* Asst prof, Sch Music, Yale Univ, 60-63, assoc prof, 64-70, prof, 70-73; prof cond, Eastman Sch Music, 73-76; prof cond & dir orch & opera, Sch Music, Univ Mich, 76-; mem fac, Berkshire Music Ctr, summers 80- *Awards:* Distinguished Achievement Award, Univ Mich. *Mem:* Collection Music Soc; Am Swiss Fedn Musicians. *Mailing Add:* 2023 Seneca Ann Arbor MI 48104

MEIER, JOHANNA
SOPRANO
b Chicago, Ill. *Study:* Univ Miami, with Arturo di Filippi; Manhattan Sch Music, with John Brownlee. *Rec Perf:* Questions of Abraham (video/film), CRI; Arias (Wagner), Bavarian Radio Symph Orch, 82; Lieder Rec, Belaphone Rec. *Roles:* Countess in Capriccio, New York City Opera, 69; Sieglinde in Walkure, 77 & Senta in Flying Dutchman, 79, New Orleans; Ariadne in Ariadne auf Naxos, New York City Opera, 69; Marschallin in Der Rosenkavalier; Isolde in Tristan und Isolde, Mexico City, Can Opera Co, Seattle Opera, Welsh Nat Opera, Fenice Theatre, Venice, & Bayreuth Fest, 81; Governess in Turn of the Screw; Marguerite in Faust. *Pos:* Res mem, New York City Opera. *Awards:* Scholar, Pan Am Music Fest; Young Artist Award, Nat Fedn Music Club. *Mailing Add:* Columbia Artists 165 W 57th St New York NY 10019

MEINE, EVELYN DEVIVO
ADMINISTRATOR
b New Castle, Pa. *Study:* Oakton Community Col, AA, 73; DePaul Univ, BA, 75. *Pos:* Mgr spec serv, Chicago Symph Orch, 73- *Mem:* Am Symph Orch League; Music Educr Nat Conf. *Mailing Add:* 220 S Michigan Ave Chicago IL 60604

MEISTER, BARBARA L
PIANO, WRITER
b New York, NY, Jan 25, 32. *Study:* Barnard Col, BA, 53; Am Consv, Fontainebleau, France, 64. *Pos:* Pianist, Ariel Ens, Gaghiano Trio, Manhattan Chamber Ens & Meister-Schnitzer Duo. *Teaching:* Horace Mann Sch, NY, 75-80 & 92nd St YMCA, NY, 79- *Mem:* Bohemians. *Publ:* Auth, Nineteenth Century French Song, Univ Ind, 80; An Introduction to the Art Song, Taplinger, 80; The Comic Muse, Keynote Mag, 81; ed, 25 Humorous Art Songs, Schirmer (in prep); coauth, Songs of the Holocaust, Harper & Row (in prep). *Rep:* Julian S Bach 474 3rd Ave New York NY. *Mailing Add:* 200 E 84 St New York NY 10028

MEISTER, SCOTT ROBERT
COMPOSER, EDUCATOR
b Elyria, Ohio, Mar 19, 50. *Study:* Ashland Col, BM, 72; Univ Miami, MM, 74, DMA, 80. *Works:* Five Pieces for Percussion and Wind Orchestra, Appalachian State Univ, 75; Gypsy Fest, Ludwig Music Publ, 76; Trophys of War, Appalachian State Univ Symph Band, 76; Seven Short Pieces for Solo Vibraphone, Ludwig Music Publ, 76; Colors of Glass, Appalachian State Univ Symph Orch, 80; Gravitons, Indianapolis Symph Orch, 82; Voice Music, NC High Sch Choral Wkshp, 83. *Pos:* Dir, Cannon Music Camp, Boone, NC, 81- & Electronic Comput Music Ctr, 83-; ed, Music Now, J Southeastern Comp League, 82- *Teaching:* Assoc prof music, Appalachian State Univ, 74- *Awards:* Orch Comp Award, Ind State Univ & Indianapolis Symph Orch, 82. *Mem:* ASCAP; Percussive Arts Soc; Music Educr Nat Conf; Southeastern Comp League; Am Soc Univ Comp. *Publ:* Auth, Laminated Timpani Mallets, Sch Musician, 78; contribr, Micro Computers in Music, Oryx Press, 83. *Mailing Add:* Rte 3 Box 335G Boone NC 28607

MEKEEL, JOYCE HAVILAND
EDUCATOR, COMPOSER
b New Haven, Conn, July 6, 31. *Study:* Consv Nat Paris, with Nadia Boulanger, 55-57; Yale Sch Music, BM, 59, MM, 60; studied with Earl Kim. *Works:* Corridors of Dream, comn by Boston Musica Viva, 72; Hommage, Empire Brass Quintet, 73; Serena, Fromm Music Found, 75; Planh, comn by Nancy Cirillo, 75; Vigil, Louisville Orch, 77; Rune, 77 & Alarums & Excursions, 78, Northeastern Rec; The Shape of Silence (solo flute), C F Peters, 82. *Teaching:* Assoc prof, New England Consv, 64-70 & Boston Univ, 70- *Awards:* First Prize, Inter-Am Music Award, 65; fel, Radcliffe Inst, 68-70; comp asst grant, Nat Endowment for Arts, 75. *Mem:* Col Music Soc. *Publ:* Auth, Harmonic Theories of Marpurg & Kirnberger, J Music Theory, 60. *Mailing Add:* 119 Pembroke St Boston MA 02118

MELANO, FABRIZIO
DIRECTOR—OPERA
b New York, NY, Apr 3, 38. *Study:* New York Circle, Square Actor & Director's Wkshp, with William Ball. *Pos:* Exec stage dir, Santa Fe Opera, 67; res stage dir, Metropolitan Opera, formerly; stage dir, Lyric Opera Chicago, 78-, New York City Opera, 80, Houston Grand Opera, Miami Opera Asn, Dallas Civic Opera, San Diego Opera, Cincinnati Opera, currently & others. *Awards:* Austin Olbrini Travelling Fel, Columbia Univ, 61. *Mailing Add:* c/o Columbia Artists Mgt 165 W 57th St New York NY 10019

MELBY, JOHN (B), JR
COMPOSER
b Whitehall, Wis, Oct 3, 41. *Study:* Curtis Inst Music, BMus, 66; Univ Pa, with Henry Weinberg & George Crumb, MA, 67; Princeton Univ, with Peter

Westergaard, Milton Babbitt & J K Randall, MFA, 71, PhD, 72. *Works:* Two Stevens Songs, 75, Concerto (violin & tape), 79 & Concerto (cello & tape), 83, Margun Music Inc; Accelerazioni, 79, Chor der Steine (tape), 79 & Concerto (viola & tape), 82; Wind, Sand and Stars, ACA, 83; and others. *Pos:* Prog Dir, WUHY-FM Philadelphia, 67-68. *Teaching:* Asst prof music, West Chester State Col, 71-72, assoc prof, 72-73; asst prof, Univ Ill, Urbana, 73-79, assoc prof, Southern Ill Univ, Edwardsville, 64-70, assoc prof, 71-79, prof, 80- *Awards:* Martha Baird Rockefeller Comp Grant, 76; First Prize, Int Electroacoustic Music Awards, 79; Fel, John Simon Guggenheim Mem Found, 83. *Bibliog:* Charles Dodge (auth), Longman Inc (in prep). *Mem:* Am Comp Alliance; Am Music Ctr; Am Soc Univ Comp; BMI; Computer Music Asn. *Mailing Add:* 1910 C Melrose Dr Champaign IL 61820

MELLOTT, GEORGE KENNETH
CLARINET, EDUCATOR
b Cleveland, Ohio, Aug 18, 32. *Study:* Eastern Ill Univ, BS, 53, MS, 54; Univ Iowa, MFA, 62, PhD, 64. *Pos:* Prin clarinetist, St Louis Phil Orch, 64- & Orch & Chorus St Louis, 82- *Teaching:* Asst prof music, Cumberland Col, 63-64; asst prof, Southern Ill Univ, Edwardsville, 64-70, assoc prof, 71-79, prof, 80- *Mem:* Int Clarinet Soc; Clarinetwork Int; Nat Asn Col Wind & Perc Instr (nat secy-treas, 78-80). *Publ:* Auth, A Balanced Clarinet Embouchure, 74, An Approach to the Initial Attack on the Clarinet, 75, Keys to Correct Breathing for the Woodwind Player, 75-76, Resonance Fingerings for the Throat Tones, 76 & Preparing and Adjusting Single Reeds, 76-77, J Nat Asn Col Wind & Perc Instr. *Mailing Add:* RR 1 Box 330 Edwardsville IL 62025

MELNIK, BERTHA
EDUCATOR, PIANO
b Hartford, Conn. *Study:* Juilliard Sch, with Alexander Siloti, grad; Fontainebleau Sch Music, France, with Robert Casadesus & Camille Decreus, 38. *Pos:* Mem, Phil Piano Quartet, 47-52; asst cond, New York City Opera Co, 54-56; accmp, NBC-TV Opera Co, 56-57. *Teaching:* Mem fac, Opera Training Dept, Juilliard Sch, 58-, mem fac piano, Prep Div, 67-69; musical dir, Newark State Col Opera Wkshp, 62-64; mem fac piano, Prep Div, Manhattan Sch Music, 69-71. *Mailing Add:* Juilliard Sch Lincoln Ctr New York NY 10023

MELONE, ROGER (LEWIS)
CONDUCTOR
b Tulsa, Okla, July 3, 43. *Study:* Del Mar Col, Corpus Christi, Tex, 61-64; Tex Christian Univ, Ft Worth, 64-66; private comd studies with Victor Alessandro, 67-71. *Rec Perf:* Mastersinger of San Antonio Symph, Telarc Rec, 77. *Pos:* Choral dir, San Antonio Symph Orch & Grand Opera, 67-71, asst cond, 71-75 & assoc cond, 75-79; guest cond, Orch of Austin, Canton, Ohio, Chattanooga, Dallas, Sacramento, Savanah, Eglevsky & Houston Ballet Co, Opera Co of Detroit, Memphis & Mexico City, 71-; assoc cond, New Mex Symph Orch, 83- *Teaching:* Lectr cond, Incarnate Word Col, San Antonio, Tex, 70-74. *Mem:* Am Symph Orch League; Am Orch Dir Asn; Am Fedn Musicians. *Rep:* Albert Kay Assoc Inc Conct Artists Mgt 58 W 58th St New York NY 10019. *Mailing Add:* 9806 La Rue San Antonio TX 78217

MELTZER, ANDREW (HENRY)
CONDUCTOR
b New York NY, Aug 26, 47. *Study:* Consv Music, Oberlin Col, BM(music), 69, MM(orch & cond), 70. *Pos:* Musical adv & res cond, San Francisco Opera, 82. *Mailing Add:* 8 Cottage Row San Francisco CA 94115

MENARD, PIERRE JULES
EDUCATOR, VIOLIN
b Quebec, Can. *Study:* Meadowmount Sch Music, with Galamian, 57-62; Quebec Consv, 59; Juilliard Sch Music, perf cert, 65; Aspen Sch Music, perf cert, 65. *Rec Perf:* Clarinet Quintet (Brahms), Orfeo, 82; Death and the Maiden (Schubert), Teldec, 83. *Pos:* Concertmaster, Nashville Symph Orch, 65-70; mem, Vermeer Quartet, 70- *Teaching:* Assoc prof violin & chamber music, Northern Ill Univ, 70- *Awards:* First prize, Nat Compt, Can, 59; Prix d'Europe, Quebec Govt, 61. *Mailing Add:* 330 W Diversey Chicago IL 60657

MENDENHALL, JUDITH
FLUTE & PICCOLO
Study: New England Consv, with James Pappoutsakis, BMus, 72, with Paula Robison, 73-74; Curtis Inst Music, studied chamber music with Marcel Moyse & Sol Shoenbach, 74-75. *Rec Perf:* Madecasses (Chanson), Marlboro Rec Soc, 76. *Pos:* Mem, Aulos Wind Quartet, 75-80; concert flutist, currently. *Teaching:* Artist in res, NTex State Univ, 80-81; vis fac artist, San Diego State Univ, 81-82. *Awards:* Winner, Naumburg Int Chamber Music Compt, 78. *Mailing Add:* c/o Robert Levin Assoc 250 W 57th St Suite 1332 New York NY 10107

MENDRO, DONNA C
LIBRARIAN
b Dixon, Ill, July 24, 31. *Study:* Northern Ill Univ, BA, 67; Univ Denver, MA, 70. *Pos:* Recordings librn, Univ Colo, Boulder, 68-70 & Dallas Pub Libr, 72-; music cataloger, Univ Ill, Urbana, 70-72. *Mem:* Music Libr Asn; Music Libr Asn (chmn Tex chap, 79-80). *Publ:* Co-ed, Union List of Music Periodicals, Austin, Tex Music Libr Asn, 78; Checklist of Texas Composers, Dallas, Tex Music Libr Asn, 80. *Mailing Add:* 1515 Young St Dallas TX 75201

MENG, MEI-MEI
EDUCATOR, PIANO
Study: State Univ NY Col, Purchase, BFA, 75; Mannes Col Music, with Jeannette Haien, MA, 77; Queens Col, City Univ New York, 80; Curtis Inst Music, with Eleanor Sokoloff; Juilliard Prep Sch, studied piano with Adele

Marcus; studied with Herbert Stessin, Carl Schacter & Edward Aldwwell. *Pos:* Soloist, Hudson Valley Symph Orch, Music for Westchester Orch, Univ Wis Orch & State Univ NY Col, Purchase Orch. *Teaching:* Fac mem, Hunter Col, formerly; Queens Col, City Univ New York, formerly; Mannes Col Music, 76- & Westchester Consv Music, currently; fac mem theory, Curtis Inst Music, 82- *Awards:* Winner, Ida Schraeder Compt, Milwaukee & Nat Piano Playing Auditions; Bergen Phil Compt. *Mailing Add:* Curtis Inst Music 1726 Locust St Philadelphia PA 19103

MENNINI, LOUIS ALFRED
COMPOSER, EDUCATOR

b Erie, Pa, Nov 18, 20. *Study:* Oberlin Col, 39-42; Eastman Sch Music, with Bernard Rogers & Howard Hanson, BM, 47, MM, 49, PhD, 61. *Works:* Andante and Allegro, perf by Rochester Symph, 48; Arioso For Strings, perf by Phildelphia Orch, 48; Symphony No 1 da Chiesa, perf by Duke Univ Orch, 60; Sobatina for Cello, numerous solo performances, 52-; The Rope (opera), perf at Berkshire Music Fest, 55; The Well (opera), perf by Eastman Opera Co, 51; Symphone No 2 Da Festa, perf by Erie Phil, 63. *Teaching:* Prof comp, Univ Tex 48-49 & Eastman Sch Music, 49-65; prof & dean, Sch Music, NC Sch Arts, 65-71. *Awards:* Comp Award, Am Inst Arts & Lett, 49; two comns, Koussevitzky Found, 50; Nat Endowment for Arts Grant, 79. *Bibliog:* Francis Perkins (auth), article, NY Herald Tribune, 55. *Mem:* ASCAP; Phi Mu Alpha. *Mailing Add:* 5994 Sterrettania Rd Fairview PA 16415

MENOTTI, GIAN CARLO
COMPOSER, DIRECTOR—OPERA

b Cadegliano, Italy, July 7, 11. *Study:* Milan Consv; Curtis Inst Music, with Rosario Scalero, dipl, 33, Hon BM, 45. *Works:* Amelia Goes to the Ball (opera), perf by Philadelphia Musical Acad, 36, Metropolitan Opera & others; The Old Maid and the Thief (opera), perf by Philadelphia Opera Co, 37 & many others; Amahl and the Night Visitors (opera), comn by & perf on NBC-TV, 51; The Saint of Bleecker Street, perf by Broadway Theatre, New York, 54; The Halcyon, Symphony #1 (orch), Saratoga, NY, 76; Landscapes & Remembrances (cantata on impressions of Am), Milwaukee, 76; La Loca (The Mad Woman), perf by San Diego Opera, 79; and many other operatic, orch, choral & chamber works. *Pos:* Dir, Washington Opera, Spoleto Fest, Paris Opera, Hamburg State Opera, Munich Opera & Metropolitan Opera; producer, The Medium (film), 46; librettist; founder & pres, Fest Two Worlds, Spoleto, Italy, 58. *Teaching:* Mem fac, Curtis Inst Music, 41-45. *Awards:* Guggenheim Awards, 46 & 47; Pulitzer Prizes, for The Consul, 50 & for The Saint of Bleecker Street, 54; NY Drama Critics Circle Award, 54. *Mem:* Hon assoc, Nat Inst Arts & Lett; ASCAP. *Publ:* Auth, The Leper (play), 70. *Rep:* Thea Dispeker Artists' Rep 59 E 54th St New York NY 10022. *Mailing Add:* 27 E 62nd Apt 68 New York NY 10021

MENSCH, HOMER
DOUBLE BASS, EDUCATOR

b New Brunswick, NJ. *Study:* Manhattan Sch Music, with Anselme Fortier; Jacques Dalcroze Sch Music; Nat Orch Asn. *Rec Perf:* Rec with CBS & NBC, Young Audiences. *Pos:* Mem, Pittsburgh Symph, CBS Symph & New York Phil. *Teaching:* Mem fac double bass, Yale Univ, Douglass Col, Dalcroze Sch Music, Juilliard Sch Music, 70-, Mannes Col Music, 76- & Manhattan Sch Music, 80-; master teacher, Am String Teachers Asn; clinician, Music Educr Nat Conf. *Publ:* With Int Publ. *Mailing Add:* Manhattan Sch Music 120 Claremont Ave New York NY 10027

MENTSCHUKOFF, ANDREJ
GUITAR

b Treysa, WGermany, Apr 28, 46; British citizen. *Study:* Cambridge Univ, 69-71; studied guitar with Julian Bream, 69 & Andres Segovia, 72; Univ EAnglia, BA, 71. *Works:* Anamnesis, perf by Jeffery Meyerriecks, 80; Prelude No 5, perf by comp, 82. *Rec Perf:* Spanish Dreams, Ace Rec, 72; The Lord is my Song, ACS Rec, 82; The Intimate Guitar, AMI Rec, 82. *Teaching:* Instr, Cleveland Inst Music, 71-; head, Dept Guitar, Wooster Col, 81- *Bibliog:* Jim Marino (auth), article, Cleveland Press, 1/18/72. *Rep:* Davis Concts PO Box 18005 Cleveland OH 44118. *Mailing Add:* 3491 Northcliffe Rd Cleveland OH 44118

MENUHIN, YEHUDI
VIOLIN, CONDUCTOR

b New York, NY, Apr 22, 16. *Study:* Studied with Sigmund Anker, Louis Persinger, Georges Enesco & Adolf Busch; numerous hon degrees. *Rec Perf:* Violin Concerti (Beethoven, Brahms, Mendelssohn, Mozart, Elgar, Bartok & Vivaldi), Violin Sonatas (Bach, Bartok, Beethoven, Brahms, Corelli, Delius, Elgar & Vaughan Williams), Organ Concerti (Handel), Oboe Concerti (Handel), Suites (Handel), Concerti Grossi (Handel), Cantatas (Bach), Brandenburg Concerti (Bach), Orchestral Suites (Bach), Harpsichord Concerti (Bach), Piano Concerto No 3 (Beethoven), Symphonies (Boyce) and others. *Pos:* Founder, Yehudi Menuhin Sch, Surrey, England, 63-, Live Music Now, 77- & Int Menuhin Music Acad, Gstaad, Switz, 77-; dir, Bath Fest, England, 58-68; cond, Am Symph Orch, 66; pres, Trinity Col Music, 71; guest soloist in concerts worldwide. *Awards:* Gold Medal, 62 & Mozart Medal, 65, Royal Phil Soc; Handel Medal, New York, 76; Nat Music Coun USA Award, 82. *Bibliog:* Robin Daniels (auth), Conversations With Menuhin. *Mem:* Hon mem, Royal Acad Music; fel, Royal Col Music; sr fel, Royal Col Art; fel, Royal Soc Arts; fel, World Acad Art & Sci. *Interests:* Indian music; jazz violin. *Publ:* Auth, Theme and Variations, Heinemann, London, 72; coauth (with William Primrose), Violin and Viola, Macdonald Futura, 76; auth, Unfinished Journey, 77 & coauth, The Music of Man, 80, Macdonald & Jane's; The King, the Cat and the Fiddle, Holt Rhinehart, 83. *Mailing Add:* c/o Columbia Artists Mgt Inc 165 W 57th St New York NY 10019

MERCHANT, WALTER M
ADMINISTRATOR, PIANO

b Haskell, Tex, Feb 1, 27. *Study:* Southwestern Univ, 44-47; Univ Tex, Austin, BA, 49. *Pos:* Vpres, Am Col Musicians, 47- *Awards:* Hall of Fame, Am Col Musicians, 68. *Mailing Add:* PO Box 1807 Austin TX 78767

MERCURIO, PETER AMEDEO
DOUBLE BASS, EDUCATOR

b Rochester, NY, Sept 9, 13. *Study:* Eastman Sch Music, MA, 39; Los Angeles Valley Col, 60-61; Univ Calif, Los Angeles, 62. *Rec Perf:* Heifetz, Piatigorsky & Primrose, Chamber Music Rec, 50-70; Roger Wagner Choral, Capitol Rec, 60-70; Pre-Columbian Music, Gold Coast Rec, 60-70. *Pos:* Prin bass & soloist, motion picture & TV rec orch, 46-, Variociones Concertantes, 50-78, Glendale Symph Orch, 50-78 & Univ Calif, Los Angeles, Chamber Orch, 60-78. *Teaching:* Lectr string bass, Univ Calif, Los Angeles, 60-78, Santa Barbara, 68-78 & Univ Southern Calif, Los Angeles, 79-81; prof string bass, Music Acad West, Santa Barbara, 60- *Awards:* Outstanding Contrib String Bassist, Am String Teachers Asn, 67; Outstanding Contrib String Bass, Int String Bass Conf, 69; Outstanding World Contrib String Bass, Foreign Study League, Salzburg, Austria, 69. *Bibliog:* Los Angeles Music Ctr Prog, Pavilion Conct Artists, Vol I, No 2; Henri Temianka (auth), Face the Music, 70; James A Rives (auth), Famous Bass Players, Col Santa Fe, 72. *Mem:* Int String Bass (mem bd, 60-). *Mailing Add:* PO Box 2255 Van Nuys CA 91404

MERKER, K ETHEL
FRENCH HORN, EDUCATOR

b Chicago Heights, Ill, July 20, 23. *Study:* Northwestern Univ, BMusEd, MMus. *Rec Perf:* Super Fly (film soundtrack). *Pos:* First horn, NBC Symph Orch, 43-49; Boston Pops Tour, 65, Chicago Pops Orch, 70-; extra horn, Chicago Symph Orch, 50-69, asst first horn, Chicago Symph, 69-71; third horn, Chicago Lyr Opera Co, 56; mem, Univ Chicago Chamber Players, 68-69; TV broadcasts, Artists Show Case, WGN, 68-72. *Teaching:* Prof French horn, Ind Univ, formerly; lectr, DePaul Univ, currently. *Mailing Add:* Dept Music DePaul Univ 804 W Belden Chicago IL 60614

MERLE, MONTGOMERY
LECTURER, EDUCATOR

b Davidson, Okla, May 15, 04. *Study:* Univ Okla, Norman, BFA, 24; Fontainebleau Am Consv, dipl, 29; private study with Nadia Boulanger & I Philipp, Paris, 29-31; Eastman Sch Music, Univ Rochester, MM, 38, PhD, 48. *Works:* They Dared to Lead, perf by Eastman Sch Orch, 46; Three Piano Pieces, 56-60, Carl Fischer Inc; Five Piano Pieces, New Scriber Music Libr, 72; Leisure, H W Gray, 76. *Pos:* Vpres pub relations, Carl Fischer Inc, 67-71; pres, Nat Fedn Music Clubs, 71-75 & Nat Music Coun US, 75-81. *Teaching:* Instr theory, Univ Okla, 31-33; prof, Southwestern State Inst, Weatherford, Okla, 38-41; instr theory & piano, Eastman Sch Music, 43-45. *Awards:* Woman of Yr Award, Soroptomist Int Okla, 55; Appreciation Award, People to People, 71; Pres Citation, Nat Fedn Music Clubs, 81. *Bibliog:* Merle Montgomery (dir), Let's Go to Musicland (set of 13 films), Univ Okla, 56. *Mem:* Music Teachers Nat Asn; Nat Music Coun (vpres, 71-75, pres, 75-79 & chmn bd, 75-77); Nat Fedn Music Clubs (pres, 71-75); Mu Phi Epsilon Mem Found (chmn bd, 77-83). *Publ:* Auth, Music Theory Papers, 54 & Music Composition Papers, 57, Carl Fischer. *Mailing Add:* 4334 Carl's Ct Chantilly VA 22021

MERRILL, LINDSEY
ADMINISTRATOR, COMPOSER

b Madisonville, Ky, Jan 10, 25. *Study:* Univ Louisville, MusB(violin), 49; Yale Univ, MusM(violin & music hist), 50; Univ Rochester, PhD(music theory & comp), 63. *Works:* Gonga Din for Tape, 71; Brasserie Pittsbourgh for Brass Percussion & Tape, 71; Recitative & Aria (trumpet & piano), Ratio 4:5:6 (string quartet), Mother Goose Revisited (four pieces) & Charles Ives: New England Suite, 72, Ms Publ; London Bridge is Falling Down, Galaxy Music, 73; The Lord is in His Holy Temple, United Church Christ Hymnal, 74. *Teaching:* Instr violin & theory, Queens Col, 50-53; instr violin, theory & chamber music, Smith Col, 53-56; instr music, Bucknell Univ, 56-57, chmn dept, 66-67; dir, Sch Music, Kent State Univ, 67-75 & Blossom Fest Sch, Cleveland Orch & Kent State Univ, 67-75; dean, Consv Music, Univ Mo, Kansas City, 75- *Publ:* Music ed, Merriam-Webster Third Int Dict, 60. *Mailing Add:* 4949 Cherry Kansas City MO 64110

MERRILL, ROBERT
BARITONE

b Brooklyn, NY, June 4, 19. *Study:* Private vocal study with Samuel Margolis, 36-82; Gustavus Adolphus Col, Hon Dr Music, 70. *Rec Perf:* Sacred Service & Yankee Doodle Dandies, CBS Rec; Carmen, Aida, Rigoletto & La Traviata, RCA Rec; Fiddler on the Roof, London Rec. *Roles:* La Traviata, Toscanini, Metropolitan Opera, Covent Garden & Venice, 45-76; Carmen, Metropolitan Opera, Havana & Buenos Aires, 46-83; Il Trovatore, Metropolitan Opera, 47-73; Aida, Metropolitan Opera, Israel, Mexico City & Toledo, 47-82; Rigoletto, Metropolitan Opera, NJ & Mex, 49-75; Don Carlo, Metropolitan Opera, 50-73; Un Ballo in Maschera, Metropolitan Opera & Toscanini, 54-76. *Pos:* Bar, Metropolitan Opera Asn, 45-76. *Awards:* Harriet Cohen Int Music Award, 61; Handel Medallion, New York, 70. *Publ:* Auth, Once More from the Beginning, Macmillan, 65; Between Acts, McGraw-Hill, 76; The Divas, Simon & Schuster, 78. *Mailing Add:* c/o Columbia Artists Mgt Inc 165 W 57th St New York NY 10019

MERRIMAN, LYLE CLINTON
ADMINISTRATOR, EDUCATOR
b Tescott, Kans, Aug 7, 35. *Study:* Univ Kans, BME, 60; Univ Iowa, MA, 61, PhD, 63. *Pos:* Dean, Sch Music, La State Univ, Baton Rouge, 80- *Teaching:* Prof clarinet, Univ Iowa, 63-80. *Mem:* Music Educr Nat Conf. *Publ:* Auth, Woodwind Research Guide, Instrumentalist, 78; coauth, Woodwind Music Guide—Ensemble Music, Instrumentalist, 82. *Mailing Add:* 5295 Glenburnie Baton Rouge LA 70808

MERRIMAN, MARGARITA LEONOR
EDUCATOR, COMPOSER
b Barcelona, Spain, Nov 29, 27; US Cit. *Study:* Univ Tenn, Chattanooga, BMus, 48; Eastman Sch Music, MM, 53, PhD, 60. *Works:* Symphony No 1, Rochester Phil, 58; Millennium (oratorio), Thayer Consv Orch & Chorus, 73; Sonata for Cello and Piano, Mark Churchill, 73; Tunnels and Sidewalks (song cycle), Betti McDonald & Robert Malin, 74; Piano Sonata, Jon Robertson, 74; Concertante for Horn and Orchestra, 76 & Symphony No 2, 81, Thayer Consv Orch. *Teaching:* Dir music, Shenandoah Valley Acad, Va, 48-51; asst prof, Andrews Univ, 51-56 & Southern Col SDA, Collegedale, Tenn, 56-58; from assoc prof to prof & chmn music dept, Atlantic Union Col, 59- *Bibliog:* Raymond Morin (auth), Millennium Offered at Atlantic Union, Worcester Telegram, 4/22/74; Curtis Hammar (auth), Composing: Complex and Competitive, Worcester Sunday Telegram, 7/16/78; Richard J Schuler (auth), Review: Books, Sacred Music, Vol 109, No 2. *Mem:* Col Music Soc; Soc Music Theory; Am Soc Univ Comp; Nat Asn Sacred Music. *Publ:* Auth, A New Look at 16th Century Counterpoint, Univ Press Am, 82. *Mailing Add:* Box 704 South Lancaster MA 01561

MERRITT, CHRIS ALLAN
TENOR
b Oklahoma City, Okla, Sept 27, 52. *Study:* Vocal study with Inez Lunsford Silberg, 70-78; Oklahoma City Univ; Am Inst Musical Studies, Graz, Austria, summers 77 & 78. *Rec Perf:* Requiem (M Haydn), 80, Requiem (Addgasse), 81 & Lauritanische Litinni (L Mozart), 81, Schwann Verlag Düsseldorf, WGer. *Roles:* Faust in Faust, 80-81 & Nemorino in L'Elisir d'amore, 80-81, Landestheater Salzburg, Austria; Leopold in La Juive, Wiener Staats Oper, Austria, 81; Arturo in I Puritani, New York City Opera, 81-82; Tamino in Die Zauberflöte, Städtische Bühne Augsburg, WGer, 82-83; Argirio in Tancredi, Carnegie Hall Rossini Fest, 83; Rodolfo in La Boheme, Städtische Bühne Augsburg, WGer, 83-84. *Pos:* Lyric ten soloist, Landestheater Salzburg, Austria, 78-81 & Städtische Bühne Augsburg, WGer, 81-84. *Awards:* Second Place, Music Teachers Nat Asn Auditions, 77. *Bibliog:* Peter G Davis (auth), All in the Family, New York Mag, 81; Isaac Rehert (auth), Big Man With a Big Voice Gets Ready to Sing Opera in the Big Apple, Baltimore Sun, 9/5/81; Inge Michel (auth), A Beautiful Voice—A Then to Be a Person, Too, Neve Presse, Augsburg, WGer, 9/24/82. *Mem:* Am Guild Musical Artists. *Rep:* Columbia Artists Mgt Inc 165 W 57th St New York NY 10019. *Mailing Add:* Lilienthal Strasse 7 Augsburg D-8900 Germany, Federal Republic of

MERRYMAN, MARJORIE
COMPOSER
b Oakland, Calif, June 9, 51. *Study:* Scripps Col, with Gail Kubik, BA, 72; Brandeis Univ, with Seymour Shifrin, MFA, 76, PhD, 81. *Works:* Laments for Hektor, 77, Ariel, 78, Three Pieces for Piano, 74, The River Song (orch), 81 & Three Songs from Antigone, 82, APNM; The Garland (SATB), Lawson-Gould, 81. *Teaching:* Asst prof theory & comp, Boston Univ, 79- *Mem:* Asn Prom New Music; BMI. *Mailing Add:* 78 School St Belmont MA 02178

MESKE, EUNICE BOARDMAN
EDUCATOR, ADMINISTRATOR
Study: Cornell Col, Iowa, BME, 47; Teachers Col, Columbia Univ, MME, 51; Univ Ill, EdD, 63. *Teaching:* Prof music educ, Wichita State Univ, 57-72; vis prof, Ill State Univ, 72-74 & Chicago Musical Col, 74-75; dir sch music, Univ Wis, Madison, 75- *Awards:* Grants, Contemp Music Proj, 61 & 63 & Univ Wis, 78. *Mem:* Music Educr Nat Conf; Nat Asn Sch Music; Col Music Soc; Asn Supv & Curric Dev; Am Educ Res Asn. *Publ:* Coauth, Musical Growth in the Elementary Schools, 63, 70, 75 & 79 & (with Beth Landis), Exploring Music, 66, 71 & 75, Holt, Rinehart & Winston; Individualization in the Music Classroom, Music Educr Nat Conf, 74; auth, Music is Basic: The Evidence is Available, Music Power, 77; coauth (with Barbara Andress), The Music Book, Holt, Rinehart & Winston, 80. *Mailing Add:* 314 Lake Shore Dr Lake Mills WI 53551

MESSIER, LISE M
SOPRANO, TEACHER
b Barre, Vt, June 5, 55. *Study:* New England Consv Music, 73-75; State Univ NY, Purchase, BFA, 79-81; Berkshire Inst, 81. *Pos:* Solo recitalist, Vt Symph, Brooklyn Museum & others, 76- *Teaching:* Voice, Brattleboro Music Ctr, Vt, 81- *Mailing Add:* 600 W 218 Apt 1J New York NY 10034

MESTER, JORGE
CONDUCTOR & MUSIC DIRECTOR, EDUCATOR
b Mexico City, Mex, Apr 10, 35; US citizen. *Study:* Juilliard Sch, studied cond with Jean Morel, BS, 57, MS, 58; study with Albert Wolff in Holland. *Rec Perf:* The Medium (Menotti), Columbia Rec; 72 premier rec, Louisville First Ed Rec; Rite of Spring (Stravinsky), Bravo TV Network, 80. *Pos:* Music dir, Louisville Orch, 67-79, Aspen Music Fest, 69-, Kansas City Phil, 72-75 & Fest Casals, 79-; prin guest cond, St Paul Chamber Orch, 78-79; guest cond, Europe, SAm, Australia, Far East & New York City Opera; violist, Beaux Arts Trio, formerly; guest commentator & artist, Nat Pub Radio. *Teaching:* Cond & instr cond, Juilliard Sch, 56-68 & 80- *Awards:* Naumburg Award Cond, 68. *Bibliog:* Allan Kozinn (auth), Music and Mester Thrive in Aspen, New York Times, 6/18/78. *Rep:* Shaw Conots Inc 1995 Broadway New York NY 10023. *Mailing Add:* 320 Cent Park W New York NY 10023

METCALF, WILLIAM
BARITONE
b New Bedford, Mass, Jan 12, 34. *Study:* New England Consv, BMus; Juilliard Sch Music; studied with Marie Sundelius, Marion Freschl, Emmy Joseph & Winifred Cecil. *Rec Perf:* On Columbia, Vanguard, Kapp & CRI. *Roles:* Escamillo in Carmen; Ferryman & Traveller in Curlew River; Dott Malatesta in Don Pasquale; Marcello in La Boheme; Sharpless in Madama Butterfly; Robert Storch in Intermezzo; Figaro in Il Barbiere di Siviglia. *Pos:* Recitalist with New York City Opera, Am Opera Soc, New York Phil, Boston Symph & other major orch in US & Can. *Teaching:* Vocal, Acad Vocal Arts, Philadelphia, formerly; Hartt Sch Music, 70-; Manhattan Sch Music, 80- *Rep:* Thea Dispeker 59 E 54th St New York NY 10022. *Mailing Add:* Manhattan Sch Music 120 Claremont Ave New York NY 10027

METCALFE, WILLIAM
CONDUCTOR, RECORDER
b Toronto, Ont, July 17, 35. *Study:* Univ Toronto, BA, 58; Univ Minn, MA, 59, PhD, 67. *Pos:* Dir & founder, Univ Vt Baroque Ens, 65-; cond & found, Oriana Singers Vt, 80- *Teaching:* Chmn dept music, Univ Vt, 73-78; prof & chmn dept hist, Univ Vt, 74 & 80- *Mem:* Am Musicol Soc; Am Recorder Soc; Am Musical Instrm Soc. *Interests:* Relationship of English Renaissance & Baroque music to English social & political history. *Publ:* Auth, Dolce or Traverso: The Flauto Problem in Vivaldi, Am Rec, 65; Concert Programming for the Small Ensemble, Rec & Music Mag, 66; Recorder Cantatas of Telemann, Am Rec, 67. *Mailing Add:* Dept Hist Univ Vt Burlington VT 05405

METZ, JERYL (JERYL METZ WOITACH)
SOPRANO
b Bronx, NY, Oct 1, 48. *Study:* Los Angeles Valley Col, 67; Univ Southern Calif, BM(opera), 71. *Rec Perf:* Nat commercials, Eue-Screen Gems, 75. *Roles:* Queen of Night in Magic Flute, Cleveland Opera, 79 & Santa Fe Opera, 80; Violetta in La Traviata, Ariz Opera, 80 & Seattle Opera, 80; Madame Butterfly in Madame Butterfly, Eugene Opera, 82; Roxanna in King Roger-Szymanowski, Wolf Trap Meadow Ctr, 82; Abigaille in Nabucco, Conn Opera, 82; Lady Macbeth in Macbeth, Reno, Nev Opera, Cleveland Opera & Flagstaff, 82-83. *Bibliog:* Louise Kincaid (auth), Fast Start, J Am, 5/13/80; Allan Pearson (auth), This Time, Mozart Got Respect, Santa Fe Reporter, 7/10/80. *Mem:* Am Guild Musical Artists; Am Fedn TV Radio Artists; Screen Actors Guild. *Rep:* Tony Hartmann Assoc 250 W 57th St New York NY 10107. *Mailing Add:* 697 West End Ave #13A New York NY 10025

MEYER, LEONARD B
EDUCATOR, WRITER
b New York, NY, Jan 12, 18. *Study:* Columbia Univ, BA, 40, MA(music comp), 48; Univ Chicago, PhD, 55; Grinnell Col, DHL, 67; Loyola Univ, DHL, 70; Bard Col, DHL, 76. *Teaching:* From instr to asst prof, Univ Chicago, 46-56, assoc prof, 56-60, prof, 61-75; Benjamin Franklin Prof, Univ Pa, 75- *Awards:* Guggenheim Found Fel, 60-61; Ernest Bloch Prof, Univ Calif, Berkeley, 70. *Mem:* Am Musicol Soc (mem bd dir, 81-83); Soc Music Theory (mem bd dir, 81-83); fel, Am Acad Arts & Sci. *Interests:* Aethetics and psychology of music; relation between music history and cultural history. *Publ:* Auth, Emotion and Meaning in Music, 56, coauth, The Rhythmic Structure of Music, 60 & auth, Music, the Arts and Ideas, 67, Univ Chicago Press; Explaining Music: Essays and Explorations, Univ Calif Press, 73; Toward a Theory of Style, In: Concept of Style, Univ Pa Press, 80. *Mailing Add:* 201 S 34th St Philadelphia PA 19104

MEYEROWITZ, JAN
COMPOSER, LECTURER
b Breslau, Apr 23, 13; US citizen. *Study:* Hochschule Musik, Berlin, 33; Accad Santa Cecilia, Rome, 33. *Works:* The Barrier (opera), Sonsogno, Milano & Belwin Mills, 50; Eastward in Eden (opera), 51; Music for Christmas, 53, The Glory Around His Head (cantata), 55 & Symphony Midrash Esther, 57, Broude Brothers; Esther (opera), Assoc Publ, 57; Six Pieces for Orchestra, Sonsogno, Milano & Belwin Mills, 67. *Teaching:* Instr opera, Berkshire Music Ctr, 48-51 & 60; lectr, City Univ New York, 54-81. *Awards:* Guggenheim Fel, 56 & 58; Nat Endowment Arts Grant, 77. *Bibliog:* Felix Freissle (auth), Chronicle, Musical Quart, 57. *Mailing Add:* 27 Morningside Ave Cresskill NJ 07626

MEYERS, (HERMAN) EMERSON
COMPOSER, PIANO
b Washington, DC, Oct 27, 10. *Study:* Peabody Consv Music, artist dipl(piano), 31. *Works:* Suite for Strings & Clarinet, Nat Fedn Music Clubs, 43; Concertino (piano & orch), Nat Symph Orch, 49; Symphony No 1, Nat Gallery Orch & Liege Symph Orch, Belgium, 53-54; Alarna Variation (two pianos), comn by Washington Music Teachers Asn, 56; Dolcedo (opera), comn by Nat Coun Cath Men, 59; Moonflight Sound Pictures (electronic music), comn by Nat Gallery Art, 69; Rhapsody Fantastique (piano), comn by Kindler Fedn, 75. *Teaching:* Assoc prof, Am Univ, 49-51; from assoc prof to prof piano, Cath Univ Am, 51-59, prof electronic music, 61-76; prof lectr, George Washington Univ, 82-83. *Awards:* Fulbright Res Grants, Belgium, 56 & 67. *Mem:* Washington Music Teachers Asn (pres, 42 & 44); Md Music Teachers Asn (pres, 63); Eastern Div Music Teachers Asn (pres, 64); ASCAP; Am Soc Univ Comp. *Mailing Add:* #3006 29th Ave Hyattsville MD 20782

MEYERS, KLARA BOLGAR
EDUCATOR, SOPRANO
b Nyiregyhaza, Hungary, Jan 24, 24. *Study:* Acad Music Debrecen, Budapest; Philadelphia Musical Acad; Pa State Univ; Temple Univ; studied with Marion

Freschl, Martin Rich, Joseph Turnau, Otto Janowitz, Rose Landver & Ralph Berkowitz. *Roles:* Ann recitals lieder & vocal chamber music, Temple Univ, Philadelphia Museum Art, Wesley Col, Del, Bucks Co Community Col, radio & TV. *Teaching:* Instr voice, Col Music, Temple Univ, 61-63, asst prof, 64-77, assoc prof, 73-78, prof, 79- *Awards:* Lindbach Distinguished Teaching Award, 82. *Mem:* Nat Asn Teachers Singing (Pa gov, 80-83). *Publ:* Auth, Resonance & Choral Singing, 82, Nat Asn Teachers Singing Bulletin. *Mailing Add:* 8224 Westminster Rd Elkins Park PA 19117

MEYERSON, JANICE
MEZZO-SOPRANO
b Omaha, Nebr, Mar 12, 51. *Study:* Wash Univ, St Louis, BA, 72; New England Consv Music, MM, 75; Berkshire Music Ctr, 76 & 77. *Roles:* Brangaene in Tristan und Isolde, Philadelphia Orch, 77; Carmen in Carmen, Theatre Royal de la Monnaie, Brussels, 79; Judith in Bluebeard's Castle, New York Phil & Palacio de Bellas Artes, Mex City, 81; Baba the Turk in The Rake's Progress, Washington Opera, 81; soloist in Jeremiah Symphony, New York Phil, 83; soloist in Mahler's 3rd Symphony, Am Symph, 83; Amneris in Aida, Teatro Colon, Buenos Aires, 83. *Awards:* Grants, William Matheus Sullivan Found, 77 & Martha Baird Rockefeller Fund, 78-79. *Mem:* Affil Artists Inc; Am Guild Musical Artists. *Rep:* ICM Artists Ltd 40 W 57th St New York NY 10019. *Mailing Add:* 711 West End Ave New York NY 10025

MICEK, ISABELLE HELEN
TEACHER, PIANO
b Shelby, Nebr, July 28, 22. *Study:* St Louis Inst Music, BMus, 43, MMus, 72; Peabody Consv Music, studied piano with Gottfried Galston & Miklos Ivanich. *Teaching:* Instrm & vocal dir, Hull pub sch, Ill, 43-45 & Oakland pub sch, Iowa, 45-46; private instr piano, theory & voice, Columbus, Nebr, 46- *Awards:* Medallion of Merit Award, Art Pub Soc, 57. *Mem:* Music Teachers Nat Asn; Nebr Music Teachers Asn (pres NE dist, 73-78); Nebr Summer Music Olympics; emer mem, Columbus Community Concerts (pub chmn, 52-72, pres, 66-68). *Mailing Add:* 2115 18th St Columbus NE 68601

MICHAELIDES, PETER
EDUCATOR, COMPOSER
b Athens, Greece, May 29, 30. *Study:* Consv Music, Oberlin Col, with Joseph Wood; Univ Southern Calif, with Halsey Stevens, DMA. *Works:* Perspectives (song cycle for sop), 67; Forces I (chamber wind & perc ens), 69; Forces II (band), 70; Forces III, Psalm 130 (72-voice chorus, a cappella); Forces IV (chamber orch), 72; Lamentations (double chorus, double band, vocal soloists & speaking chorus); Magnification of the Nativity (two Eastern Orthodox hymns for Christmas). *Teaching:* Fac mem, Univ Calif, Santa Barbara, 62-64 & Lewis & Clark Col, 64-65; prof theory & analysis, orch & comp, Univ Northern Iowa, 65- *Mailing Add:* Music Dept Univ Northern Iowa Cedar Falls IA 50614

MICHALAK, THOMAS
CONDUCTOR & MUSIC DIRECTOR, VIOLIN
b Krakow, Poland. *Study:* With Irene Dubiska. *Pos:* Violin soloist, Warsaw Phil; cond, Ballet Russe, Monte Carlo, 64 & Pittsburgh Symph Orch, 74; asst cond, Chamber Soc Philadelphia, 64 & Marlborough Music Fest, 65-66; music dir, Phil Soc Northeastern Pa, 73, Canton, Ohio Symph Orch, 76 & NJ Symph Orch, 77-83, Cathedral Concert Ser, Newark, NJ. *Teaching:* Head orch, Ithaca Col, 67. *Awards:* Silver Medal, Moscow Int Compt; Koussevitzky Prize, 72. *Rep:* Herbert Barrett 1860 Broadway New York NY 10023. *Mailing Add:* NJ Symph Orch 213 Washington St Newark NJ 07101

MICHAUD, ARMAND HERVE
VIOLIN, COMPOSER
b Warwick, RI, Aug 13, 10. *Study:* New England Consv, BA; Providence Col; RI Col. *Works:* Fantasie (orch & string orch); Mass in A Minor; several short pieces for orch; Mass to St Therese, 81; Lord: Prayer, 80. *Pos:* Violinist, appearances with Providence Symph Orch, Nat Opera Co, RI Phil Orch, Boston Peoples Symph Orch & Pro Quartet. *Teaching:* Music, pub & private sch. *Mem:* Music Union; Chopin Club; Providence Symph Soc. *Mailing Add:* New London Turnpike Wyoming RI 02898

MICHII, MAKOTO
TEACHER, DOUBLE BASS
b Hokkaido, Japan, Nov 10, 35. *Study:* Musashino Acad Musicae, Tokyo, BMus, BA. *Pos:* String bassist, Japanese Phil Orch, Tokyo, 60-62 & Buffalo Phil Orch, 67-; prin string bassist, Yomiuri Nippon Symph Orch, Tokyo, 62-66; solo recitalist, Buffalo, 67. *Teaching:* Instr, Ctr Creative & Perf Arts, State Univ NY, Buffalo, 66-68. *Awards:* Fels, Fulbright Found, 66-68 & Koussevitzky, 67; Henry B Cabot Award, 67. *Publ:* Auth, Harmonics of String Bass, 63. *Mailing Add:* 116 Getzville Rd Snyder NY 14226

MICULS, MELITA LUIZE
MEZZO-SOPRANO
b Latvia, Aug 1, 45. *Study:* Col Consv Music, Univ Cincinnati; Acad Vocal Arts. *Roles:* Principessa in Suor Angelica, Teatro del Liceo, Barcelona, 72; Carmen in Carmen; Hippolita in Midsummer Night's Dream; Suzuki in Madama Butterfly; Zita in Gianni Schichi; Madelon in Andrea Chenier; Giulietta in Contes d'Hoffmann. *Pos:* Res mem, Israel Nat Opera; perf with opera co in Tel Aviv, Barcelona & Philadelphia. *Mailing Add:* 1453 Balfour Grosse Pointe MI 48230

MIDDAUGH, BENJAMIN
EDUCATOR, BARITONE
b Aquila, Tex, Feb 23, 34. *Study:* NTex State Univ, BMus, 56; Mich State Univ, MMus, 62; Fla State Univ, DMus, 68. *Roles:* Renato in Un Ballo in maschera, Birmingham Civic Opera, 66; Valentine in Faust, Fla State Opera & Birmingham Civic Opera, 66 & 69; Sharpless in Madame Butterfly, Miami Opera & Birmingham Opera, 67 & 79; John Sorel in The Consul, Birmingham Civic Opera, 69; Tony Esposito in Most Happy Fella, Jenny Wiley Summer Music Theater, 75; Henry Higgins in My Fair Lady, 81 & Don Quixote in Man of La Mancha, 83, Music Theater North. *Teaching:* Asst prof, Northwestern State Univ La, 62-63; asst prof voice, Univ Montevallo, 63-68, opera dir, 63-, assoc prof, 68-78, prof music, 78- *Awards:* Am Guild Musical Artists Award, 62; Birmingham Symph Award, 64; Nat Fedn Music Clubs Young Artist Award, 69. *Mem:* Nat Asn Teachers Singing (regional gov & dir, 77-79); Am Fedn Musicians; Pi Kappa Lambda (chap pres, 80-). *Publ:* Auth, The Songs of Ned Rorem—Aspects of Musical Style, 68, Telle Jour Telle Nuit by Francis Poulenc ..., 68, Modest Mussorgsky's Songs and Dances of Death, 69, The Lieder of Yjrö Kilpinen, 70 & The Operas of Lully and Rameau, 73, Nat Asn Teachers Singing Bulletin. *Mailing Add:* PO Box 66 Montevallo AL 35115

MIDDLETON, JAYNNE CLAIRE
SOPRANO, EDUCATOR
b Memphis, Tenn, Nov 14, 47. *Study:* Fla State Univ, with Elena Nikolaidi, BM, 69, MM, 72; NTex State Univ, with Virginia Botkin, DMA, 83. *Teaching:* Asst prof & dir opera, Hardin-Simmons Univ, 74- *Awards:* Grad Perf Award, Sigma Alpha Iota, 78. *Mem:* Sigma Alpha Iota; Nat Asn Teachers of Singing. *Mailing Add:* Sch Music Hardin-Simmons Univ Abilene TX 79698

MIDDLETON, ROBERT (EARL)
EDUCATOR, COMPOSER
b Diamond, Ohio, Nov 18, 20. *Study:* Harvard Col, BA, 48, MA, 54; studied comp with Nadia Boulanger & Walter Piston, piano with Beveridge Webster & Karl Ulrich Schnabel. *Works:* Command Performance (four act opera), Boston Opera Group, 61; Concerto di Quattro Duetti, Hudson Valley Phil, 63; Portraits of the Night (flute & piano), Claude Monteux, 67; Sinfonia Filofonica, Hudson Valley Phil, 69; Notebooks of Designs (piano), Ruslana Antonowicz, 69; Two Duologues (violin & piano), Matthew Raimondi, 75; Four Nocturnes (clarinet & piano), Paul Gallo, 80. *Teaching:* Instr, Harvard Univ, 50-53; fac mem, Vassar Col, 53-, George Sherman Dickinson prof, 74- *Awards:* Fel, John Knowles Paine, Harvard, 48-50 & Guggenheim, 65. *Publ:* Auth, Harmony in Modern Counterpoint, Allyn and Bacon, 67; Approximations for Viola and Piano, E B Marks, 70; On the Nature of Beasts, E C Schirmer, 71; Four Organ Preludes, E B Marks, 79. *Mailing Add:* Great Brook Rd Lebanon NH 03766

MIKHASHOFF, YVAR EMILIAN
PIANO, EDUCATOR
b Troy, NY, Mar 8, 44. *Study:* Eastman Sch Music; Juilliard Sch Music; Univ Houston, BMus, 67, MMus, 68; Univ Tex, Austin, DMA(comp), 73; studied with Betty Ganance, Armand Basile, Stanley Hummel, Adele Marcus, Beveridge Webster, Albert Hirsh & William Doppmann; studied comp & piano with Nadia Boulanger. *Works:* Dances for Davia, Southern Music Co, 80; The Pipes of Colchis, 83, Tiento & The Long Eyes of Earth, Quadrivium Music Press; and many others. *Rec Perf:* Concord Sonata, 80 & Sixty Years of Piano Music: Virgil Thomson, Vol I, 81 & Vol II, 83, Spectrum Rec; Waltz Project, Nonesuch Rec, 81; American Sonatas, CRI, 82; New Danish Piano Music, Paula Rec, Denmark, 83; Recitatives and Arias (Rudors) & Piano Concert (Sellars), CRI (in prep). *Roles:* Monsieur Fred in Le Racine, La Scala, 80 & Zagreb Biennale, 81. *Pos:* Conct pianist in US & Europe, 73-; proj dir, Am Music Proj Holland Fest, 82; co-dir, North Am New Music Fest; fest organizer & prod concts. *Teaching:* Assoc prof 20th century music, State Univ NY, Buffalo, 73-; instr sem, contemp music, Royal Consv, Copenhagen, Swedish Acad Music, Stockholm & Inst Contemp Arts, London; fac mem, Tanglewood Inst, Boston Univ, 81. *Awards:* Fulbright-Hays Grant; Am-Scandinavian Found Grant, 82; Arts Coun Gr Brit Comp Perf Award, 83. *Interests:* Liszt, Debussy and Ives. *Mailing Add:* 100 N Pearl St Buffalo NY 14202

MIKOWSKY, SOLOMON GADLES
EDUCATOR, PIANO
b Havana, Cuba, Mar 10, 36; US citizen. *Study:* Juilliard Sch, studied piano with Sascha Gorodnitzki, BS(piano), 60, MS(piano), 61; City Univ New York, summers 58 & 60; Columbia Univ, EdDoc(music), 73. *Teaching:* Mem fac piano, Pre Col Div, Juilliard Sch, 62-69; Manhattan Sch Music, 69- & Philadelphia Col Perf Arts, 71-75; adj asst prof music, NY Univ, 69-79. *Awards:* Scholar Piano Studies Abroad, Govt Cuba, 55-60; Piano Scholar, Juilliard Sch, 57-63; Cintas Fel, Inst Int Educ, 66. *Bibliog:* Robert Stevenson (auth), Nuevos Recursos para el Estudio de la Musica Latinoamericana, Heterofonia, Mex, 12/76 & 1-2/77; Jose I Lasaga (auth), El Nacionalismo Musical Llega a America, Ideal; Peter Kraus & Mark Bird (auth), The Music of Ignacio Cervantes, Latin Int, 78. *Mem:* Music Teachers Nat Asn; Assoc Music Teachers League; NY Fedn Music Clubs; NY State Music Teachers Asn. *Publ:* Auth, The XIX Century Cuban Danza, Columbia Univ, 73; auth, Ignacio Cervantes and the Cuban Danza, OAS Am, 74. *Mailing Add:* 390 Riverside Dr New York NY 10025

MILBURN, ELLSWORTH
COMPOSER, EDUCATOR
b Greensburg, Pa, Feb 6, 38. *Study:* Univ Calif, Los Angeles, with Henry Lazorof, BA; Mills Col, with Darius Milhaud, MA; Col Consv Music, Cincinnati Univ, with Scott Huston & Paul Cooper, DMA. *Works:* Soli III (clarinet, cello & piano), 71; Soli IV (four instrm), 72; Violin Sonata, 72; Lament (harp), 72; Gesualdo, 72-73; String Quartet, 74; Spiritus Mundi (sop & five instrm), 74. *Pos:* Music dir, Committee Theater, San Francisco, 63-68; writer, Imagination Inc, San Francisco, formerly. *Teaching:* Assoc prof, Col Consv Music, Cincinnati Univ, 70-75, dir, Contemp Music Ser, formerly; assoc prof, Rice Univ, 75- *Awards:* Merritt Prize; Morse Fel; Nat Endowment Arts Grant, 74. *Mailing Add:* Shepherd Sch Music Rice Univ Houston TX 77251

MILLER, ANNE WINSOR
OBOE, EDUCATOR
b Ann Arbor, Mich, July 5, 52. *Study:* Univ Mich, with Florian Mueller, BM, 73, MM, 75; Univ Ill. *Rec Perf:* Songs of Our Past, Krimm Rec, 73. *Pos:* Prin oboe, Lawrence Chamber Players, Kans, 79-; oboist, Kans Woodwind Quintet, 79-82, Wellington Trio, Lawrence, Kans, 82- & Consv Baroque Ens, Kansas City, Mo, 82- *Teaching:* Asst prof oboe, Univ Kans, 79-82; adj asst prof, Univ Mo, 82- *Awards:* Van der Heuvel Award, Univ Mich, 74. *Mem:* Int Double Reed Soc; Music Educr Nat Conf; Mo Music Educr Asn; Chamber Music Am; Nat Asn Col Wind & Perc Instr. *Publ:* Contribr, A Profile of Florian Mueller, Double Reed, 81. *Mailing Add:* 2101 Vermont St Lawrence KS 66044

MILLER, CLEMENT A
MUSICOLOGIST, EDUCATOR
b Cleveland, Ohio, Jan 29, 15. *Study:* Cleveland Inst Music, with Beryl Rubinstein, BM, 36, MM, 37; Western Reserve Univ, with Manfred Bukofzer, MA, 42; Univ Mich, with Curt Sachs, Alfred Einstein & Louise Cuyler, PhD, 51. *Teaching:* Dean fac & head musicol dept, Cleveland Inst Music, 52-65; prof music, John Carroll Univ, 66- *Awards:* Guggenheim Fel, 74-75. *Mem:* Am Musicol Soc; Renaissance Soc Am; Dolmatsch Soc. *Interests:* Musicology, especially of the Medieval and Renaissance periods. *Publ:* Ed, Heinrich Glarean, Dodecachordon, 65 & Johannes Cochleus, Tetrachordum Musices, 72, Am Inst Musicol; auth, Franchinus Gaffurius, Musical Quart, 75; Erasmus on Music, Musik Geschichte, 78; Heinrich Glarean, In: New Grove Dict of Music & Musicians, 80. *Mailing Add:* 18975 Van Aken Blvd Apt 411 Shaker Heights OH 44122

MILLER, CLYDE ELMER
EDUCATOR, FRENCH HORN
b Downers Grove, Ill, Sept 29, 17. *Study:* Northwestern Univ, BMusEd; Teachers Col, Columbia Univ, MA; studied with Louis Dufrasne, Josef Franzl, Barry Tuckwell, Philip Farkas, William Robinson, John Barrows, Froydis Hauge, Charles Kavaloski & James Winter. *Pos:* Solo prin horn, Dallas Symph Orch, 16 yrs, Metropolitan Opera Orch, NY Ballet Soc Orch, Chicago Grant Park Summer Orch, Dallas Civic Opera Orch & others; performer, New York Phil Orch, Chicago NBC Orch & others; horn, Ft Worth Symph, 65- & Ft Worth Ballet Orch, 65-; mem, Audraud Woodwind Quintet, NTex Univ, currently. *Teaching:* Private horn, 34-; assoc prof orch & French horn, NTex State Univ, currently. *Mailing Add:* 2907 Wilsonwood Dr Denton TX 76201

MILLER, DAVID
VIOLA
b Richmond, Va, Oct 22, 48. *Study:* Oberlin Col, BA, 70; Juilliard Sch, MM, 75. *Rec Perf:* Quartet in D, K.285 (Mozart), 76 & The Six Brandenburg Concerti (J S Bach), 78, Aston Magna; Baryton Trios Vol I (J Haydn), Musical Heritage Soc, 81; Serenade, Op 25 (Beethoven), Metropolitan Museum Art, Pleides, 81; Cantata 210, (J S Bach), 81 & Mass in B Minor, 82, Nonesuch Rec; Baryton Trios Vol II (J Haydn), Musical Heritage Soc, 82. *Pos:* Prin violist, Aston Magna, New York, 74- & Concert Royal, New York, 74-; violist, Classical Quartet, New York, 79- & Haydn Baryton Trio, 79- *Mem:* Music Before 1800 (mem bd dir, 81-). *Mailing Add:* 115 W 73rd St 7A New York NY 10023

MILLER, DEAN HAROLD
FLUTE, EDUCATOR
b Fremont, Ohio, Mar 25, 40. *Study:* Studied with Robert Willoughby, 56-58; Curtis Inst Music, with William Kincaid, BMus, 63; Acad Music, Vienna, Austria, artists dipl, 65. *Pos:* Prin flutist, Quebec Symph Orch, 66-68 & New Orleans Phil Symph Orch, 69-; asst first flutist, Minn Orch, 68-69. *Teaching:* Instr flute, Ball State Univ, 65-66; adj instr, Loyola Univ 71- *Mailing Add:* 1300 Pleasant St New Orleans LA 70115

MILLER, DONALD CHARLES
CONDUCTOR & MUSIC DIRECTOR, EDUCATOR
b Walton, NY, July 2, 31. *Study:* Eastman Sch Music, BM, 55; Kent State Univ, MA, 58; Ind Univ, 61-65. *Pos:* Music dir & cond, Montgomery Col Opera Theater, 66- *Teaching:* Prof music, Montgomery Col, 66- *Mem:* Am Guild Organists (exec bd mem, 81-82, sub-dean, 68-69). *Publ:* Auth, Harmony Outline with Partwriting Exercises, Harris Music Co, 76. *Mailing Add:* 7225 Mill Run Dr Derwood MD 20855

MILLER, EDWARD J
COMPOSER, EDUCATOR
b Miami, Fla, Aug 4, 30. *Study:* Hartt Col Music, with Isadore Freed & Arnold Franchetti; Berkshire Music Ctr, with Carlos Chavez & Boris Blacher, 55 & 58; studied with Blacher & Josef Rufer, 56-58. *Works:* Reflections—At the Bronx Zoo; Orchestral Changes; Anti-Heroic Amalgam; Orchestral Fantasies; La mi la sol—Isaac and Interpolations (soloists); The Folly Stone (brass quintet), 66; Quartet Variations (any four players & slides), 72. *Teaching:* Mem fac, Hartt Col Music, 59-71; prof music, Consv Music, Oberlin Col, 71- *Awards:* Koussevitzky Prize, 55; Fulbright Grant, 56-58; E C Schirmer Handel & Haydn Soc Award, 71. *Mailing Add:* Consv Music Oberlin Col Oberlin OH 44074

MILLER, IRA STEVEN
COMPOSER
b New York, NY, June 17, 51. *Study:* Harpur Col, with Karl Korte & William Klenz; State Univ NY Col, Binghamton, with Ezra Laderman; Univ Pittsburgh, with A Wayne Slawson, Frank McCarty, Thomas Janson & Robert Morris. *Works:* Space Plots (ballet), 72; Phaetomes II (film & tape), 74; Creation Music (chorus with narrator, chamber ens, perc & tape), 75; String Quartet, 76; Collage (flute & harpsichord), 76; Das Atem (woodwind quintet), 77; The Smile (a cappella), 77. *Awards:* Andrew W Mellon Fel, Univ Pittsburgh. *Mailing Add:* 812 Johns Rd Cherry Hill NJ 08034

MILLER, JOHN WILLIAM, JR
BASSOON, EDUCATOR
b Baltimore, Md, Mar 11, 42. *Study:* Mass Inst Technol, SB, 64; New England Consv Music, MusM, 67, artist's dipl, 69. *Rec Perf:* On Cambridge & Musical Heritage Soc. *Pos:* Dir, Boston Baroque Ens, 63-71; mem, Am Reed Trio, formerly; prin bassoonist & founding mem, Boston Philharmonia Chamber Orch, 68-71; prin bassoonist, Minn Orch, 71- *Teaching:* Instr bassoon, Boston Univ, 67-71 & Univ Minn, 71- *Awards:* Fulbright Award, 64-65; Irwin Bodky Award, Cambridge Soc Early Music, 68. *Mem:* Int Double Reed Soc. *Mailing Add:* 706 Lincoln Ave St Paul MN 55105

MILLER, JONATHAN DAVID
CELLO
b Dec 23, 43. *Study:* Juilliard Sch, 65-67; Hartt Col, BM, 67-70; Univ Calif, Berkeley. *Pos:* Prin cello, Hartford Symph, 67-71; cello, New York String Sextet, 69-71 & Boston Symph, 76-; cellist & dir, Boston Artists Ens, 79- *Teaching:* Cello, New England Consv, 75-77; Boston Consv, 76-78 & Tanglewood Inst, Boston Univ, 79- *Mailing Add:* Boston Symph Symph Hall 301 Massachusetts Ave Boston MA 02115

MILLER, KARL FREDERICK
EDUCATOR, COMPOSER
b New Rochelle, NY, Dec 27, 47. *Study:* Univ Okla, with Spencer Norton, BM, 69; NTex State Univ, with Dika Newlin, Merrill Ellis & Robert Ottman, MM, 74, DMA, 78. *Works:* Requiem for Strings, Univ Okla Symph Orch, 68; Short Sonata No 3 for Harpsichord, Dale Peters, 72; Concerto for Oboe, Harpsichord & Strings, Univ Microfilms, 73; Miniatures for Brass Choir and Percussion, NTex State Univ Brass Choir, 76; Variations on a theme by Shostakovich for Orchestra, Univ Microfilms, 77; Meditation III (comput music), Am Soc Univ Comp, 80; Fanfare, Aria & Toccata (organ), Kathryn Baker, 81. *Mem:* ASCAP; Am Soc Univ Comp; Ariz Conf Music Theory (secy, 79-80); Asn Rec Sound Collections; Roy Harris Archives. *Publ:* Auth, The Joyful Music of Mathias, Am Rec Guide, 78; If It Was Broadcast ..., Kastlemusik, 78; contribr, American Music Recordings, A Discography ..., ISAM, 82. *Mailing Add:* Sch of Music Univ of Ariz Tucson AZ 85721

MILLER, KENNETH EUGENE
EDUCATOR
b NManchester, Ind, Nov 9, 26. *Study:* Manchester Col, BS, 51; Am Consv Music, MMEd, 52, MM, 58; Northwestern Univ, PhD, 63. *Teaching:* Asst prof, Cottey Col, 52-58; from assoc prof to prof, Northeast Mo State Univ, 63-65 & Univ Mo, St Louis, 65- *Mem:* Am Asn Univ Prof; life mem, Col Music Soc; life mem, Am Choral Dir Asn; New Music Circle St Louis. *Interests:* Performance practices in vocal music; textbooks for vocal performance; vocal music education. *Publ:* Auth, A Study of Selected German Baroque Oratorios, Bärenreiter Verlag, 68; transl, P Spitta, The Passion Music of Sebastian Bach & Heinrich Schütz, Choral J, 75; auth, Passion Settings of the German Baroque, Am Choral Rev, 75; Handbook of Choral Music Selection, Score Preparation and Writing, Parker Publ Co, 79; Principles of Singing, Prentice-Hall, 83. *Mailing Add:* Dept Music, Univ Mo 8001 Natural Bridge Rd St Louis MO 63121

MILLER, LEWIS MARTIN
EDUCATOR, COMPOSER
b Brooklyn, Sept 4, 33. *Study:* Queens Col, City Univ New York, BA, 54; Manhattan Sch Music, MM, 61; NTex State Univ, PhD, 65. *Works:* January Thaw (SATB), Carl Fischer Inc, 64; The Faucet (TTBB & piano), G Schirmer Inc, 73; Here on the Mountain (SATB), Shawnee Press Inc, 74; Just Desserts (flute & bassoon), Southern Music Co, 75; Overture to Tartuffe (orch), 80 & Rondo giocoso (cello & piano), 81, Ludwig Music Publ Co; Capriccio for Two Pianos, Shawnee Press Inc, 81. *Pos:* Res comp, Ford Found Proj, Elkhart, Ind, 61-62 & El Paso, Tex, 62-63. *Teaching:* Prof theory & comp, Ft Hays State Univ, 66-83. *Awards:* ASCAP Standard Award, 79-83; Winner, Nat Sch Orch Asn, Scherl & Roth Compt for Overture to Tartuffe, 79. *Mem:* ASCAP; Col Music Soc; Music Teachers Nat Asn; Kans Comp Forum (chmn, 73). *Mailing Add:* 208 E 32nd St Hays KS 67601

MILLER, LUCILLE
SOPRANO
b Evansville, Ind. *Study:* Juilliard Sch Music, studied with Hans Heinz, perf dipl, 61; studied voice with Cesare Bardelli, 77-79 & Dick Marzollo, 70-80.

Roles: Tosca in Tosca, Nat Orch Asn, 61; Madama Butterfly in Madama Butterfly, Conn Opera Sch, 69; Leonora in Il Trovatore, 77 & Donna Anna in Don Giovanni, 78, Artists Int; Santuzza, Nac de la Opera de Venezuela, 79. *Awards:* Liederkranz Showcase Award, 63. *Mem:* Am Guild Musical Artists; Actors Equity. *Mailing Add:* 166-77 22nd Ave Flushing NY 11357

MILLER, MAYNE
PIANO
b Evanston, Ill. *Study:* Chicago Musical Col, BMus, 53; Cleveland Inst Music, MMus, 54. *Works:* Several chamber music works. *Rec Perf:* Fischer-Hungarian Set, CRI. *Pos:* Pianist, NAm & Europe. *Awards:* First Prize, Artists Adv Coun; Prizewinner, Ferruccio Busoni Piano Compt & Marguerite Long-Jacques Thibaud Compt. *Mailing Add:* c/o Wayne Wilbur Mgt PO Box 1378 Grand Cent Sta New York NY 10163

MILLER, PATRICIA A
MEZZO-SOPRANO, TEACHER
b Washington, DC. *Study:* Boston Univ, BM, 72; New England Consv, MM, 74; study with Luigi Ricci, Rome, Italy, 75-77; Accad Santa Cecilia, Rome, Italy, artist dipl, 76; studied with Eleanor Steber, Mary Davenport, Allan Rogers, Gladys Miller & Ernest Metz; study with Carolina Segrera, currently; Univ Beverly Hills, hon doctorate, 79. *Rec Perf:* Carmen in Carmen, RTI, SAm TV, 79; Dejanira in Ercole Amante, RCA, 81; L'Orfeo, Lisbon, Portugal, 82. *Roles:* Isabella in L'Italiana in Algeri, Basel Opera, Switzerland, 77; Annina in Der Rosenkavalier, San Francisco Opera, 79; Carmen in Carmen, Asarte Opera, 79; Dejanira in Ercole Amante, Lyon Opera, France, 81; Carmen in Carmen, New York City Opera, 81, Victoria State Opera, Melbourne, 82 & Ft Worth Opera, Tex, 82. *Pos:* Perf mem & artist, Affil Artists Inc, New York, 81-; artist in res, City of Jacksonville, Fla, 81 & Lafayette Col, Easton, Pa, 82. *Teaching:* Instr music, Arlington High Sch, Belmont, Mass, 72-73; instr voice, New England Consv, 73-74; assoc prof & artist in res, Univ Mo, 83- *Awards:* Palco de Honor, RTI, SAm TV, 79; Fulbright Grant, 76; first place, Metropolitan Opera Audition. *Bibliog:* Gerard Conde (auth), Ercole Amanta au TMP, Le Monde, 5/11/81; John Bridges (auth), Samson and Delilah Performance Triumphant, Asheville Citizen Times, 7/19/81; Au Victoria Hall, Requiem de Durufle et Stabat Mater de Poulenc, Tribune de Geneva, 3/23/82. *Rep:* Thea Dispeker 59 E 54th St New York NY 10022. *Mailing Add:* 121 E 31st St New York NY 10016

MILLER, PHILIP LIESON
LIBRARIAN, CRITIC
b Woodland, NY, Apr 23, 06. *Study:* Manhattan Sch Music; Juilliard Sch Music. *Pos:* Ref asst music div, NY Publ Libr, 27-45, asst chief, 46-59, chief, 59-66. *Awards:* Citation Award, Music Libr Asn, 66. *Mem:* Music Libr Asn (pres, 62-63); Asn for Rec Sound Col (pres, 65-71); Bohemians. *Publ:* Auth, Vocal Music, Vol 2, Knopf, 55; The Ring of Words, Doubleday, 63 & Norton, 73. *Mailing Add:* 129th E Tenth St New York NY 10003

MILLER, RALPH DALE
EDUCATOR, COMPOSER
b Whitehall, Ill, Mar 17, 09. *Study:* Ill State Univ, BEd, 36; Univ Iowa, MA, 39, MFA, 41, PhD, 42. *Works:* Suite Miniature, 42, Quartets No 1 and 2, 42, Quartet No 3, 44, Sinfonietta, 46 & Prelude and Scherzo, 46, Belwin, Inc; Three American Dances, Carl Fischer, Inc, 48; Night Poem, perf by Stockholm Symph Orch, Sweden, 50. *Teaching:* Pontiac & Normal, Ill, 36-41; assoc prof music, Duluth State Teachers Col, 42-47; assoc prof & chair fine arts div, Univ Minn, Duluth, 47-50, prof & chair div humanities, 50-70, prof, Sch Fine Arts, 70-82, prof emer, 82- *Mailing Add:* 2030 Lakeview Dr Duluth MN 55803

MILLER, RICHARD D
EDUCATOR, TENOR
b Canton, Ohio, Apr 9, 26. *Study:* Univ Mich, BM, MM; L'Accad de Santa Cecilia, Rome, dipl di canto. *Pos:* Leading lyr tenor, Stadttheater, Zurich, formerly & San Francisco Opera, formerly; performer with civic opera co & orchs in US; vocal consult, Am Music Teachers J, 60-72. *Teaching:* Lectr voice & dir, Univ Choir, Southern Ill Univ, 57; mem fac, Nat Music Camp, Interlochen, 57-62, Blossom Music Fest, 68-71 & Mozarteum, Salzburg, 72 & 78; assoc prof, Univ Mich, 57-62 & Baldwin-Wallace Consv, 62-64; prof, Consv Music, Oberlin Col, 64- *Awards:* Fulbright Award, Rome, 51; Silver Medal, Geneva Int Contests, 52. *Mem:* Nat Asn Teachers Singing; Music Teachers Nat Asn; Pi Kappa Lambda. *Publ:* Auth, English, French, German & Italian Techniques of Singing, 77. *Mailing Add:* 221 Forest St Oberlin OH 44074

MILLER, TERRY ELLIS
EDUCATOR, WRITER
b Dover, Ohio, Feb 19, 45. *Study:* Col Wooster, BM(organ), 67; Ind Univ, Bloomington, MM(musicol), 71, PhD(musicol), 77. *Pos:* Assoc dir, Ctr Study World Musics, Kent State Univ, 79- *Teaching:* Assoc prof, Sch Music, Kent State Univ, 75-; adj instr, Case-Western Res Univ, 80-81. *Awards:* Foreign area fel, Social Sci Res Coun, Ford Found, 72-74. *Mem:* Am Musicol Soc; Soc Ethnomusicol (chmn, Niagara Chap, 81-82); Sonneck Soc; Siam Soc. *Interests:* Black & white oral tradition hymnody & its roots in British Isles; shape-note music. *Publ:* Auth, Voices From the Past: Singing and Preaching at Otter Creek Church (Indiana), J Am Folklore, 75; Alexander Auld 1816-1898: Early Ohio Musician, Bulletin Cincinnati Hist Soc, 75; Otter Creek Church, Indiana: Lonely Bastion of ..., Found, 75; Old Time Shape-Note Singing Schools in E Kentucky, Southern Quart, 81. *Mailing Add:* 717 Avondale Kent OH 44240

MILLER, THOMAS WILLIAMS
ADMINISTRATOR, TEACHER
b Pottstown, Pa, July 2, 30. *Study:* West Chester State Col, BS(music educ), 52; ECarolina Univ, MA, 57; Boston Univ, MusAD, 64. *Teaching:* Dir instrm music, Susquenita High Sch, Pa, 55-56; instr trumpet, ECarolina Univ, 57-61, asst dean, 62-68 & dean, Sch Music, 69-71; dean, Sch Music, Northwestern Univ, 71- *Awards:* Distinguished Alumnus, West Chester State Col, 75. *Mem:* Pi Kappa Lambda (nat pres, 76-79); Nat Asn Sch Music (pres, 83-); Phi Mu Alpha Sinfonia. *Mailing Add:* Sch Music Northwestern Univ Evanston IL 60201

MILLEY, JANE E
ADMINISTRATOR
b Everett, Mass, May 20, 40. *Study:* Boston Univ, BMus, 61, studied piano & musicol, 68-74; studied with Claude Frank, Martin Canin & Maria Clodes, 63-75; Columbia Univ, MA, 66; Syracuse Univ, PhD, 77; Claremont Grad Sch & Univ Ctr, 78. *Pos:* Solo pianist & chamber musician; bd mem, Elmira Symph & Choral Soc, 70-72 & Long Beach Grand Opera, 80; external prog evaluator, Gordon Col Fac Develop Prog, 76-77; charter mem & founder, Sacramento Experimental Theatre, 78-; music dir search comt, Sacramento Symph Asn, 78-79; dir & coordr, Fine Arts Cult Ser, Sacramento City Col, 78-80; prog evaluator, Higher Educ Learning Package, 79-80; evaluator, Learning in New Dimensions, San Francisco & Boston, 80-; mem, Arts Policy Develop Task Force, Long Beach, 81- *Teaching:* Instr music, Foxhollow Sch, Lenox, Mass, 66; instr, Elmira Col, 67-70, coordr, founder & pianist, Fine Arts Trio, 67-75, dir, Early Instrm Consort, 69-75, asst prof, 70-75 & dir, Arts & Sci Prog, 74-75; vis lectr music hist, Corning Community Col, 72; admin asst, Col Arts & Sci, Syracuse Univ, 76-77; asst dean, Dept Humanities & Fine Arts, Sacramento City Col, 77-80; assoc dean, Sch Fine Arts, Calif State Univ, Long Beach, 80-81, interim dean, 81, prof music, 81- & dean, 82- *Awards:* Grants, Calif Arts Coun, Co Bd Supvrs, Sacramento & State of Calif, 79, Chevron, US Govt, TRW, Safeco & Regional Arts Found, 82. *Mem:* Calif Arts Coun; Am Asn Univ Prof (vpres Elmira Col chap, 73); Col Music Soc. *Publ:* Auth, Freshman Arts & Sci, Elmira Col Alumni Bulletin, 75; coauth, (with J Stark & J Leahy), Research and Planning for Higher Education, In: Association for Institutional Research, 9/78; auth, Case Study and Faculty Development Program Evaluation, Fac Develop & Eval in Higher Educ Newslett, fall 78; Program Evaluation and Research, In: Professional Development Through Growth Contracts Handbook, Gordon Col, 79, 3rd ed, 80; An Investigation of Case Study as an Approach to Program Evaluation, ERIC Clearinghouse of Higher Educ Collection, 79. *Mailing Add:* Sch Fine Arts Calif State Univ 1250 Bellflower Blvd Long Beach CA 90804

MILLIGAN, STUART CHARLES
LIBRARIAN, EDUCATOR
b Rochester, NY, Aug 8, 40. *Study:* Eastman Sch Music, Univ Rochester, BM, 64, MA, 66; State Univ NY, Geneseo, MLS, 79. *Works:* Three Songs for Bass, Voice & Piano, perf by Robert Bernard & Stuart Milligan, 68; Five Episodes for Two Pianos, perf by Stuart Milligan & Anne Taylor, 69; Piece for French Horn & Piano, perf by Daniel & Janice Nimitz, 70. *Pos:* Circulation librn, Sibley Music Libr, Eastman Sch Music, Univ Rochester, 70- *Teaching:* Asst prof music theory, Milligan Col, Tenn, 66-70. *Mem:* Music Libr Asn. *Interests:* Copyright issues relating to music and music-related materials; music microform publishing. *Publ:* Coauth, Index to Audio Equipment Reviews, Technical Reports No 6 Music Libr Asn, 6/79, No 8, 80, No 10, 81 & No 12, 82; auth, Music and Other Performing Arts Serials Available In Microform and Reprint Editions, Notes, Quart J Music Libr Asn, 12/80. *Mailing Add:* 35 Devonshire Ct Rochester NY 14619

MILLIGAN, THOMAS BRADEN, JR
WRITER, EDUCATOR
b Kingsport, Tenn, May 31, 47. *Study:* Carson-Newman Col, BA & BM, 69; Eastman Sch Music, MA, 74, PhD, 78; Univ Vienna; Acad Music, Vienna; studied piano with Frank Glazer. *Teaching:* Asst prof music hist, theory & piano, Carson-Newman Col, 78- *Awards:* Fulbright Scholar, 71-72. *Mem:* Am Musicol Soc; Col Music Soc; Nat Guild Piano Teachers. *Interests:* Music in London in the late 18th century, particularly the solo instrumental concerto. *Publ:* Auth, Zu einer frühen französischen Ausgabe Mozarts Klavierwerke, Int Gesellschaft Mozarteum, 81; The Harp Concerto in London in the Late 18th Century, Am Harp J, 81; Muzio Clementi and the Piano Concerto, Am Musicol Soc S-Cent, 82; The Concerto and London's Musical Culture in the Late 18th Century, UMI Res Press, 83. *Mailing Add:* 220 W Ellis St Jefferson City TN 37760

MILNES, SHERRILL
BARITONE
b Hinsdale, Ill, Jan 10, 35. *Study:* Coe Col, BA; Drake Univ, MA, 58; Northwestern Univ, 58-61; studied with Boris Goldovsky, Rosa Ponselle, Andrew White & Hermanes Baer; two hon degrees. *Rec Perf:* 27 albums for RCA Victor, London Decca, EMI Angel, Philips & Deutsche Grammophon, 67- *Roles:* Carlo Gerard in Andrea Chenier, Baltimore Civic Opera, 61; Escamillo in Carmen, Baltimore Civic Opera, 64; Valentin in Faust, Metropolitan Opera, 65; Henry VIII in Henry VIII, San Diego Opera, 83; Count di Luna in Il Trovatore; Iago in Otello; Don Carlo in La Forza Del Destino. *Pos:* Bar, Goldovsky Opera Co, 60-65, New York City Opera Co, 64-67 & Chicago Lyric Opera, 73-75; performer with major Am opera co & orchs, 62-; leading bar, Metropolitan Opera, 65- *Awards:* Ford Found Award, 62. *Mem:* Am Guild Musical Artists (mem bd gov, 69-); Affil Artists Inc; Phi Mu Alpha Sinfonia. *Mailing Add:* c/o Herbert Barrett Mgt 1860 Broadway New York NY 10023

MILOJKOVIC-DJURIC, JELENA
WRITER
b Beograd, Yugoslavia, Dec 2, 31; US citizen. *Study:* Univ Stockholm, Sweden, Fil Kand, 57; Univ Belgrade, Yugoslavia, MA, 63, PhD, 81. *Teaching:* Asst prof, Acad Theater, Univ Belgrade, 63-65; res assoc, Musicol Inst, Belgrade, 64-; lectr, Univ Colo, Boulder, 68 & Tex A&M Univ, 72-74. *Mem:* Union Comp & Music Authors, Yugoslavia; Am Musicol Soc; Rocky Mountain Asn Slavic Studies; Am Asn Advan Slavic Studies; Gesellschaft Musikforschung, Germany. *Interests:* Trends in music and arts of the 20th Century. *Publ:* Auth, The Yugoslav Children's Game Most ..., Southern Folklore Quartet, 60; Some Aspect of Byzantine Origine ..., Byzantinoslavica Acad Sci, 62; Papadike from Skopje, Oxford Univ Press, 66; The Music Eastern Europe, Am Asn Advan Slavic Studies, 78; Microtonal Theories of Alois Haba, Univ Mich, 82. *Mailing Add:* 1018 Holt St College Station TX 77840

MILSTEIN, NATHAN
VIOLIN
b Odessa, Russia, Dec 31, 04; nat US. *Study:* Consv Music St Petersburg, with Leopold Auer; studied with P Stoliarsky & Eugene Ysaye. *Pos:* Violinist on tour, Russia, 20-26, US, Europe & Can, 29- *Awards:* Grammy Award, 75; Cross Hon, Austria; Chevalier Legion Hon, France. *Mem:* Acad Santa Cecilia, Italy. *Mailing Add:* c/o Shaw Conct 1995 Broadway New York NY 10023

MILTENBERGER, JAMES E
PIANO, EDUCATOR
b Sidney, Ohio, Jan 22, 38. *Rec Perf:* Protest in Percussion, featured soloist with WVa Univ Perc Ens, Century, 70; Jazz Perspectives: Renaissance/Rock, Century, 71; Percussion on the Rocks, featured soloist with WVa Perc Ens, 73, Percussion 70, 77, Century. *Pos:* Miami Univ, Ohio, BM, 59; Eastman Sch Music, MM, 61, DMA, 65. *Teaching:* Prof piano & piano repertoire, WVa Univ, 62- *Mem:* Music Teachers Nat Asn. *Publ:* Contribr, Improvisation Section of Piano Course, Music Teachers Nat Asn, 77. *Mailing Add:* Creative Arts Ctr WVa Univ Morgantown WV 26506

MINDE, STEFAN P
CONDUCTOR & MUSIC DIRECTOR
b Germany, Apr 12, 36. *Study:* Mozarteum Salzburg, studied cond with Paumgartner, Staatsexamen, 58. *Pos:* Mem, Thomaner Chorus, Leipzig, 47-54; repetitor, Städtische Bühnen, Frankfurt on Main, 59-60; solo repetitor & asst cond, Staatstheater Wiesbaden, 60-63; first cond, Städtische Bühnen, Trier on Mosel, 63-67; asst cond, Berkshire Music Ctr, 67; asst cond & chorus master, San Francisco Opera, 67-70; gen dir & cond, Portland Oper Asn, 70- *Awards:* C D Jackson Price Award, Berkshire Music Ctr, 67; Nat Opera Asn Award, 82. *Mem:* Opera Am. *Mailing Add:* 1640 SE Holly Portland OR 97213

MING, JAMES W
EDUCATOR, COMPOSER
b Brownwood, Tex, May 21, 18. *Study:* Eastman Sch Music, studied comp with Bernard Rogers, Howard Hanson, Darius Milhaud & Nadia Boulanger, BM, 39, MM, 40. *Works:* Music for a Film, perf by Rochester Civic Orch, 39; Suite for Chamber Orchestra, perf by Orch de la Radiodiffusion Francaise, 50; Pastorale for Oboe & Strings, perf by orchs throughout US, 51; Missa Brevis (choir & brass), perf by choral groups throughout US, 57; Music for Fontainebleau, perf by chamber music ens in France & US, 60-; Three Poems of A MacLeish, perf by choral groups throughout US, 62-; Sonatina for Piano, perf by pianists thoughout US, 65- *Teaching:* Instr music, DePauw Univ, 42-44; T A Chapman prof, Lawrence Univ, 44-82; vis prof, Cornell Univ, 55-56. *Mem:* Am Soc Univ Comp; Col Music Soc. *Mailing Add:* 1110 E North St Appleton WI 54911

MINKLER, PETER JOHN
VIOLA
b Buffalo, NY, Apr 4, 60. *Study:* Cleveland Inst Music, with Robert Vernon, 78-80; Eastman Sch Music, with Francis Tursi, BM, 82. *Pos:* Section viola, Erie Phil, 79-80; substitute viola, Rochester Phil, 81-82; substitute viola, Buffalo Phil, summer 81, assoc prin viola, 82- *Awards:* First Award, Kiwanas Club Int Compt, Toronto, Can, 78; winner concerto compt, Greater Buffalo Youth Orch, 78 & Chautauqua Inst, 81. *Mailing Add:* 312 Pennsylvania St Buffalo NY 14201

MINOR, ANDREW COLLIER
EDUCATOR, CONDUCTOR
b Atlanta, Ga, Aug 17, 18. *Study:* Emory Univ, BA, 40; Univ Mich, MMus, 47, PhD, 51. *Rec Perf:* Missa Pro Defunctis (M Haydn), 65 & Missa Sancti Hieronymi (M Haydn), 67, Univ Mo Press & Music Heritage Soc; Te Deum (Hofer), 67, Joshua (Handel), 68 & Messe des Morts (Gossec), 77, Univ Mo Press. *Teaching:* Asst prof, Univ Mo, Columbia, 50-55, assoc prof, 55-58, prof, 58- & assoc dean grad sch, 68- *Mem:* Am Musicol Soc (secy Midwest chap, 64-65, chmn, 67-69, mem nat coun, 79-81). *Interests:* French Renaissance music; late 18th-century, French music; music of French revolution. *Publ:* Auth, Music in Medieval and Renaissance Life, 64 & coauth, A Renaissance Entertainment, 68, Univ Mo Press; ed, Opera Omnia of Jean Mouton (1460-1522), Am Inst Musicol, 67-74; contribr, Music of the French Revolution, In: Encycl of French Revolution, Greenwood Press, 83; Corteccia, Briant & Rampollini, In: New Grove Dict of Music & Musicians, Vol VI, Macmillan. *Mailing Add:* 203 Jesse Hall Columbia MO 65202

MINTON, YVONNE FAY
MEZZO-SOPRANO
b Sydney, Australia. *Study:* Sydney Consv Music, 60-61. *Rec Perf:* On Decca, EMI, RCA & Phillips. *Roles:* Maggie in One Man Show, London Co Coun, 64; Genevieve in Pelleas et Melisande; Dorabella in Cosi fan tutte; Octavian in Der Rosenkavalier; Thea in The Knot Garden; Brangäne in Tristan und Isolde; Marina in Boris Godunov; and others. *Pos:* Ms with all maj orchs in Australia, 58-61 & Royal Opera House, Covent Garden, 65-70; sings regularly with maj symph, 68-; guest artist with Cologne Opera, WGermany, 69-; performer with Chicago Lyr Opera, 70, Metropolitan Opera, 73, San Francisco Opera, 74 & Paris Opera. *Mailing Add:* Ingpen & Williams 14 Kensington Ct London England United Kingdom

MINTZ, DONALD M
EDUCATOR, ADMINISTRATOR
b Bronx, NY, May 9, 29. *Study:* Cornell Univ, with Donald Grout & Robert Palmer, BA, 49, with Donald Grout & William Austin, PhD, 60; Princeton Univ, with Oliver Strunk & Alfred Einstein, MFA, 51 . *Pos:* From contrib critic to staff writer, Washington Star, 60-69; exec dir, Md Arts Coun, 69-72. *Teaching:* Vis asst prof musicol, Cornell Univ, 59-60; grad fac mem, Peabody Consv, 68-72; dean, Sch Fine & Perf Arts & prof music, Montclair State Col, 72- *Awards:* Fulbright Grant, 55-56. *Mem:* Am Musicol Soc; Int Musicol Soc; Col Music Soc; Music Libr Asn. *Interests:* Music of Mendelsohn with particlar attention to manuscript studies. *Publ:* Auth, Melusina: A Mendelssohn Draft, Musical Quart, 10/57; Schumann as an Interpreter of Goethe's Faust, J Am Musicol Soc, summer 61; Mendelssohn and Romanticism, Studies in Romanticism, summer 64; Can a Musicologist Find Happiness as an Administrator?, Col Music Soc Symposium, fall 77. *Mailing Add:* 117 Cedar Rd Ringwood NJ 07456

MINTZ, SHLOMO
VIOLIN
b Moscow, USSR, Oct 30, 57. *Study:* Juilliard Sch, dipl. *Pos:* Concert violinist, with major orchestras on four continents. *Mailing Add:* c/o ICM Artists 40 W 57th St New York NY 10019

MIRANTE, THOMAS ANTHONY
COMPOSER, ADMINISTRATOR
b Utica, NY, Oct 11, 31. *Study:* State Univ NY, BS(music), 54; Ithaca Col, MS(music), 55; studied musical comp with David Diamond & Earl George. *Works:* The House on the Hill (choral), 68 & I Am (choral), 69, Assoc Music Publ; Eight Recital Encores (piano), Peer-Southern, 72; War Poems of Walt Whitman, comn by Oneida Area Civic Choral, 76; The Stream of Life, Lawson-Gould, 79; Silent Snow (choral), 79 & A Carol (choral), 81, Music 70. *Pos:* Band mem & piano soloist, Sixth Infantry Division Band, Ft Ord, Calif, 55-56; organist & choir dir, Post Chapel, Ft Riley, Kans, 56-57. *Teaching:* Dir music, Oneida Sch, NY, 79- *Awards:* Grant, Martha Baird Rockefeller Fund Music, 76; Meet the Comp Grant, Nat Endowment Arts & NY State Coun Arts, 76. *Mem:* BMI. *Mailing Add:* 208 N Main St Canastota NY 13032

MIRKIN, KENNETH PAUL
VIOLA
b Brooklyn, NY, May 27, 58. *Study:* Juilliard Sch, studied viola with Lillian Fuchs & William Lincer, BM, 79, MM, 80. *Pos:* Violist, San Francisco Symph, 81-82 & New York Phil, 82- *Mailing Add:* 33 Brighton Second Pl Brooklyn NY 11235

MISCHAKOFF, ANNE
EDUCATOR, VIOLA
b New York, NY, May 12, 42. *Study:* Smith Col, AB, 64; Univ Iowa, MA, 66; Univ Ill, DMA, 78. *Rec Perf:* On CRI & Motown. *Pos:* Violist, Contemp Chamber Players, formerly, Lexington String Quartet, Chicago, 66-68, Detroit Symph, Mischakoff String Quartet, 68-72 & Sierra String Quartet, 75-80; mem, Chautauqua Symph, 81; recitalist, Northwestern Chamber Music Soc, 82- *Teaching:* Viola & chamber music, Chautauqua Sch Music, formerly; lectr viola, Univ Evansville, 65-66; asst prof viola & music hist, Univ Pac, 75-80; assoc prof viola, Northwestern Univ, 80-; violist & mem fac, Int String Wkshps, Innsbruck, Austria, 82-83 & Bolzano, Italy, 83-84. *Mem:* Am String Teachers Asn (vpres Calif chap, 77-79, pres, 79-80, pres Ill chap, 83-); Am Viola Soc. *Publ:* Auth, Khandoshkin and the Beginning of Russian String Music, UMI, 83. *Mailing Add:* 47 Williamsburg Rd Evanston IL 60203

MISHKIND, ABRAHAM
EDUCATOR, CONDUCTOR
Study: Juilliard Sch Music, BS; Columbia Univ, MA; studied with Hans Letz, Eduard Dethier, Felix Salmond & Raphael Bronstein. *Pos:* Violinist, Pittsburgh Symph, 50-56, Detroit Symph, 59-63, Boston Pops Esplanade Orch, 60- & Hartford Symph, currently; first violinist, Heritage String Quartet, Univ Ky; solo violin, Pro Mozart Soc, Detroit; solo & chamber music recitals in US & Europe; numerous duo-violin recitals with Elaine Pinkerton Mishkind; leader of All in the String Family Quartet, 66- *Teaching:* Dir strings & cond, Univ Vt Summer Music Session, 58-70; asst prof & cond univ orch, Univ Ky, 63-65 & Hartt Sch Music, 66- *Mem:* Am String Teachers Asn. *Mailing Add:* 7 Sycamore Rd Bloomfield CT 06002

MISKELL, (WILLIAM) AUSTIN
TENOR, EDUCATOR
b Shawnee, Okla, Oct 14, 25. *Study:* Hochschule Music, Zurich, 50-60; Mozarteum, Salzburg, Austria, various dipl, 55-65; Royal Acad Music,

London, England, LRAM, 72. *Rec Perf:* Pergolesi's Salve Regina, PYE Studios, London, 65; Ballades, Rondeau and Virelais, Odyssey, 67; Adieu M'Amour, HMS, 69; I Sing America, EMI Columbia, 69; Elizabethan Top Twenty, EMI Studios, 70; Radha Krishna (John Mayer), Columbia, 71; Pergolesi Requiem, Resonor, Zurich, 72. *Pos:* Tenor soloist, Arte Antica & Ricecare Ens, Zurich, Switz, 55-75 & Elizabethan Consort, London, England, 58-75; artistic adv, R Rec Ltd, London, England, 70-75. *Teaching:* Vocal technique, Anglian Inst, London, England, 70-75; asst prof, Nat Univ, Bogota, Colombia, 76-82; dir vocal dept, Consv Music Tolima, Ibague, Colombia, 78-82; teacher, Italian Opera, Colombian Nat Opera, Bogota, 79-81; lectr voice, Univ NMex, 82-83; prof, Col Santa Fe, 82-83. *Awards:* Gold Medal, Pergolesi Soc, 59. *Mem:* Hon mem, Arte Antica (artistic adv, 50-72); VIA Soc Advancement Young Artists (artistic adv, 65-); fel, English Elizabethan Soc; Nat Asn Teachers Singing. *Interests:* J Maynard 1577; Thomas Weelkes, 1575-1623. *Publ:* Auth, The Salt Cathedral Book of Free Verse in English and Spanish, Armadillo, Bogota, Colombia, 81; Modern Music and the Singer, 82 & Romanticism and the Singer, 83, Note Bk Mag. *Mailing Add:* 221 Dartmouth SE Albuquerque NM 87106

MISSAL, JOSHUA M
COMPOSER
b Hartford, Conn, Apr 12, 15. *Study:* Eastman Sch Music, with Howard Hanson & Bernard Rogers, BM, 37, MM, 38; studied with Roy Harris. *Works:* America 200 (narrator, two choruses, four brass choirs, full orch), Wichita, 76; Improvisations (trumpet & piano), 78; Overture for Band; Cantata City of the Sun (chorus, orch & soloists), comn by Wichita State Univ; Concertante (five solo perc); Fanfare, Chorale, and Procession (brass choir); Jericho Suite (brass choir & perc). *Pos:* Violist, Rochester Phil, 34-40, Wichita Symph, 52-70, Olympia String Quartet, Wichita String Quartet & others; cond, Albuquerque Phil, 40-42, Miss Southern Civic Orch, 50-52, Scottsdale Civic Orch, Ariz, 79- *Teaching:* Fac mem, Univ NMex, 46-50, Southern Miss Univ, 50-52 & Wichita State Univ, 52-70; fac assoc, Ariz State Univ. *Mem:* ASCAP; Music Educators Nat Conf; Music Teachers Nat Asn. *Mailing Add:* 8308 E Meadowbrook Ave Scottsdale AZ 85251

MISTERLY, EUGENE WILLIAM
COMPOSER, TEACHER
b Los Angeles, Calif, Sept 25, 26. *Study:* Private comp study with Mary Carr Moore, 48-50 & Mario Castelnuovo-Tedesco, 63-67; Univ Southern Calif, 51-53; Occidental Col, 68. *Works:* Quintet (woodwinds), Los Angeles Wind Quintet, 49; Bettina (three act opera), Highland Park Symph, 64; Tell-tale Heart (cantata), CAP, 68; Henry V (three act opera), Highland Park Symph, 69; Testimony (cantata), NELA Opera Co, 72; Symphony Bali, 74 & Invention for Orchestra, 80, perf by Highland Park Symph. *Teaching:* Private instr piano, 47-, comp, 68- & orch, 75- *Awards:* MacDowell Club Award, Mary Carr Moore Ms Club, 48; Celia Buck Grant, Nat Asn Am Comp & Cond, 63 & 64. *Mailing Add:* 1363 Brampton Rd Los Angeles CA 90041

MITCHELL, (MARY) EMILY
HARP & IRISH HARP, SOPRANO
b Ft Worth, Tex, May 4, 53. *Study:* Eastman Sch Music, with Eileen Malone, BM & cert, 75; Royal Col Music, London, with Marisa Robles, ARCM, 78. *Rec Perf:* Emily Mitchell, 1st Prize Winner 7th Israel Harp Contest, Argo Rec. *Pos:* Conct harpist & recitalist, 81- *Awards:* First Prize, Seventh Int Harp Cont, Jerusalem, 79; Alpha Delta Kappa Grant, 79. *Mem:* Am Harp Soc (pres metropolitan New York chap, 82-84); Mu Phi Epsilon. *Rep:* Columbia Artists Mgt 165 W 57th St New York NY 10019. *Mailing Add:* 311 E 52nd St #1B New York NY 10022

MITCHELL, LEE
EDUCATOR
Study: Peabody Consv, BM; Univ Bern, Switz, PhD(ethnomusicol); studied piano with Elmer Burgess, Donald Carter, Guiomar Novaes & Rudolf Serkin & comp with Stefans Grove, Louis Cheslock, Sandor Veress, Ernst Krenek & Aaron Copland. *Works:* Comp perf by Baltimore Symph Orch, Bern Chamber Orch, Bern String Quartet & various other chamber groups. *Pos:* Conct perf, US, Holland, Germany, Switz, Hungary & Greece, formerly; TV perf, Baltimore, formerly; radio broadcasts, SAm, Switz & Hungary, formerly. *Teaching:* Guest lectr Medieval & Renaissance music, US & Europe; prof theoret studies, Konsv Musik, Biel, Switz, 71-76; instr music, Peabody Consv, currently. *Awards:* Piano Award, Univ Del; Ada Arens Morawetz Mem Award Comp, Peabody Consv; Rockefeller Found Award. *Mailing Add:* 8007 York Road Towson MD 21204

MITCHELL, MICHAEL KENNETH
WRITER, CONDUCTOR & MUSIC DIRECTOR
b China Lake, Calif, July 10, 46. *Study:* Univ Calif, Berkeley, AB, 69; Univ Calif, Santa Barbara, MA, 71. *Pos:* Assoc cond, chorusmaster & music dir, Singer's Training Prog, Seattle Opera, 77- *Teaching:* Coach opera perf, Seattle Opera, 78-82. *Mem:* Am Musicol Soc; Col Music Soc. *Interests:* Opera history and aesthetics; criticism. *Publ:* Auth, Study Guide for Understanding (30 prod), Seattle Opera Guild, 78-; Shattered Spear, TBA, (in prog). *Mailing Add:* 1023 Summit E #2 Seattle WA 98102

MITCHELL, SANDRA DARLING See Darling, Sandra

MITTELMANN, NORMAN
BARITONE
b Winnipeg, Manitoba, May 25, 32. *Study:* Curtis Inst Music, with Martial Singher & Ernzo Mascherini, dipl, 59. *Roles:* Amonasro in Aida, Zurich, 67;

William Tell, May Fest, Florence, 69; Rigoletto in Rigoletto, Chicago Opera Theatre, 77; Scarpia in Tosca, Venice, 79; John Falstaff in Falstaff, Hamburg, Berlin, 79; Nelusko in L'Africaine, San Francisco Opera; Mandryka in Arabella, La Scala. *Awards:* Fel, Rockefeller Found; Award, Fischer Found, 59. *Rep:* Robert Lombardo Assoc 61 W 62nd St Ste F New York NY 10023. *Mailing Add:* 610 Deer Springs Rd San Marcos CA 92069

MITZELFELT, H(AROLD) VINCENT
CONDUCTOR & MUSIC DIRECTOR, CELLO
b Chicago, Ill, Jan 13, 34. *Study:* Madison Col, 51-53; Union Col, BA, 53-55; Loma Linda Univ, MD, 55-60; studied with Antonio Movelli & Zolton Roszynai. *Rec Perf:* Music of Faith & Inspiration, Reader's Digest Rec Club, 62; Vesperae de Dominica (Mozart), 73 & American Contemporary Music (Stravinsky, Beach & Kantor), 76, Crystal Rec; Ode to Joy (Beethoven), M & K Real Time Rec, 78; Mass in C (Schubert), 78, Harp & Flute Concerto (Mozart), 80 & Choral Triptych (Ulysses Kay), 83, Grand Prix Rec. *Pos:* Dir & cond, Mitzelfelt Chorale, Los Angeles, 58-73; minister music, White Mem Univ Church, Los Angeles, 61-64; dir, Bach Fest, First Cong Church, Los Angeles, 61-64; founder & cond, Camerata Los Angeles Orch, 73- *Teaching:* Instr music, Union Col, 54-55; instr cond & orch, Immaculate Heart Col, 75-78. *Awards:* Grant, Ford Found, 75; Commendation Award, Los Angeles Co Bd Supvrs, 78; Nat Endowment Arts Rec Grant, 82-83. *Rep:* Conciertos Daniel 14 Los Madrazos St Madrid Spain. *Mailing Add:* 23203 Yvette Lane Valencia CA 91355

MIXTER, KEITH EUGENE
EDUCATOR, WRITER
b Lansing, Mich, May 22, 22. *Study:* Mich State Univ, BMus, 47; Univ Chicago, MA, 51; Univ NC, Chapel Hill, PhD, 61. *Pos:* Music librn, Univ NC, Chapel Hill, 53-61. *Teaching:* Asst prof music, Ohio State Univ, 61-65, assoc prof, 65-74, prof, 74-; vis fac musicol, Univ Colo, Boulder, summer 66 & Univ Wis, Madison, summer 69. *Awards:* Smith Fund Grant, Univ NC, Chapel Hill, 59. *Mem:* Am Musicol Soc (coun, 78-81); Music Libr Asn (mem exec bd, 61-63); Int Musicol Soc; Int Asn Music Libr. *Interests:* Bibliography; 15th century music. *Publ:* Ed, Sechs Motetten, Akad Druck Verlagsanstalt, 60; auth, General Bibliography for Music Research, Info Coordr, 62, 75; An Introduction to Library Resources for Music Research, Ohio State Univ, 63; Johannes Brassart: A Biographical and Bibliographical Study, Musica Disciplina, 64-65; ed, Opera Omnia (2 vols), Am Inst Musicol, 63. *Mailing Add:* 4455 Shields Pl Columbus OH 43214

MIZUNO, IKUKO
VIOLIN, WRITER
b Tokyo, Japan. *Study:* Toho-Gakuen Sch Music, Tokyo, BA, 65; Accad Musicale Chigiana, Siena, Italy, with Franco Gulli, 68; Geneva Consv Music, with Henryk Szeryng, 68; Sch Fine & Applied Arts, Boston Univ, MMus, 69. *Rec Perf:* Recital by Ikuko Mizuno, NHK, Tokyo, 68-83. *Pos:* Soloist, Boston Pops, 66-83; mem, first violin sect, Boston Symph Orch, 69- *Teaching:* Fac mem violin, Tanglewood Inst, Boston Univ, 69- & Longy Sch Music, 79-80. *Awards:* Award, Sch Fine & Applied Arts fac, Boston Univ, 66. *Mem:* Am Fedn Musicians. *Publ:* Auth, Life With the Boston Symphony, 70 & European Tour with the Boston Symphony, Nippon Keizai Newspaper, 76; Letters to Home, Shufu no Tomo, 76; Introduction to the Members of the Boston Symphony, Boston Symph Orch Prog, 81; Music Life in Boston, Kodansha, 83. *Mailing Add:* Boston Symph Orch Symph Hall Boston MA 02115

MOE, DANIEL T
EDUCATOR, COMPOSER
b Minot, NDak, Nov 2, 26. *Study:* Concordia Col, with Paul Christiansen, BA, 49; Hamline Univ, with Russell Harris; Univ Wash, with George McKay & John Verrall; Aspen Sch, with Darius Milhaud; Univ Iowa, with Phillip Bezanson, PhD, 61; Gustavus Adolphus Col, Hon DM, 76. *Works:* Exhortation from Proverbs (chorus with brass sextet); Cantata of Peace (chorus with trumpet, narrator & organ); Psalm Concertato (chorus with brass quartet & string bass); Te Deum (chorus with wind ens); Worship for Today (chorus with congregation & organ); Prelude and Hodie; The Greatest of These Is Love (solo voice & piano). *Teaching:* Choral dir, Univ Denver, 53-59; prof music & dir choral activ, Univ Iowa, 61-72; vis prof music, Univ Southern Calif, summer 63; prof choral cond, Consv Music, Oberlin Col, 72- *Awards:* First Prize, Seattle Centennial Comp Cont; Danforth Found Grant; Canticum Novum Award, Wittenberg Univ, 74. *Mailing Add:* Consv Music Oberlin Col Oberlin OH 44074

MOE, LAWRENCE HENRY
ORGAN, EDUCATOR
b Chicago, Ill, May 9, 17. *Study:* Northwestern Univ, BMusEd, 39, MM, 40; Harvard Univ, MA, 52, PhD, 56. *Rec Perf:* Music of Buxtehude, 70, Music of Frescobaldi, 72, English Voluntaries, 73, Preludes & Fugues (Bach), 74, Clavierübung III (Bach), 75, Music of R Felciano, 79 & Seventeenth Century Baroque Music, 82, Cambridge Rec. *Pos:* Organist & choirmaster, St Paul's Episcopal Cathedral, Boston, 54-57; organist, St Paul's Episcopal Church, Rome, Italy, 64-65. *Teaching:* From instr to assoc prof music theory, hist & organ, Cent Wash Col, 41-50; prof music hist, Univ Calif, Berkeley, 57- *Mem:* Am Guild Organists (dean, 62-63 & 74-76); Int Soc Musicol; Am Soc Musicol; Hist Organ Soc. *Mailing Add:* 1120 Miller Ave Berkeley CA 94704

MOE, ORIN
WRITER, EDUCATOR
b Grosse Pointe, Mich, May 11, 43. *Study:* Mt St Mary's Col, BM, 65; Univ Calif, Santa Barbara, PhD, 70. *Pos:* Assoc ed, Inst Res Black Am Music, Fisk Univ, 78- *Teaching:* Lectr music, Calif State Univ, Fresno, 70-71; asst prof,

Ga State Univ, Atlanta, 71-78 & Vanderbilt Univ, 78-80. *Mem:* Col Music Soc; Am Musicol Soc; Int Musicol Soc. *Interests:* Music of the classical period; 20th century American music; Black American music. *Publ:* Auth, Texture in Haydn's Early Quartets, Music Rev, 74; Structure in Haydn's The Seasons, Haydn Yearbk, 75; William Grant Still: Song of Separation, 80 & The Songs of Howard Swanson, 81-82, Black Music Res J; The Music of Eliott Carter, Symposium, 82. *Mailing Add:* 300 54th Ave N Nashville TN 37209

MOECKEL, RAINIER
VIOLA, EDUCATOR
Study: Acad Music, Detmold. *Pos:* Prin violist, Tronheim Symph, Norway, 70-74, Bamberg Symph Orch, formerly & Nuremberg Orch, formerly; mem, Mannheim Chamber Orch, 74-76. *Teaching:* Asst prof viola, Fla State Univ, 80- *Mailing Add:* Sch Music Fla State Univ Tallahassee FL 32306

MOESER, JAMES CHARLES
ORGAN, EDUCATOR
b Colorado City, Tex, Apr 3, 39. *Study:* Univ Tex, studied organ with William Doty & John Boe, BM, 61, MM, 64; Hochschule Musik, WBerlin, studied organ with Michael Schneider; Univ Mich, studied organ with Marilyn Mason, DMA, 67. *Rec Perf:* James Moeser at University of Kansas, Reuter, 69; The Art of the Organist, Century, 71. *Pos:* Organist & choirmaster, Plymouth Congregational Church, 67- *Teaching:* Prof organ, Univ Kans, 66-, dean, Sch Fine Arts, 75- *Awards:* Palmer Christian Award, Univ Mich, 82. *Mem:* Am Guild Organists. *Rep:* Murtagh-McFarlane Artists Mgt 3269 W 30th St Cleveland OH 44109. *Mailing Add:* 446 Murphy Hall Univ Kans Lawrence KS 66045

MOEVS, ROBERT WALTER
COMPOSER, EDUCATOR
b La Crosse, Wis, Dec 2, 20. *Study:* Harvard Col, with Piston, BA, 42; Consv Nat Musique, Paris, with Boulanger, 47-51; Harvard Univ, MA, 52. *Works:* Fourteen Variations for Orchestra, Koussevitzky Found & Boston Orch, 52; Three Symphonic Pieces, comn & perf by Cleveland Orch, 55; Attis (chorus & orch), comn & perf by Boston Orch, 58; Concerto Grosso (piano, perc & orch), Orch 20th Century, 60-68; Et Occidentem Illustra, comn by Rutgers Univ & perf by Boston Orch, 64; Musica da Camera, comn & perf by Contemp Chamber Ens, 65; Main-Travelled Roads, comn & perf by Milwaukee Symph Orch, 74. *Pos:* Mem adv comt, WNCN Class Radio, NY, 76- *Teaching:* Asst prof, Harvard Univ, 55-63; comp in res, Am Acad Rome, 60-61; prof music, Rutgers Univ, 64- *Awards:* Nat Inst Arts & Sci Award, 56; Guggenheim Fel, 63-64; ASCAP Award, 67- *Bibliog:* Bruce Archibald (auth), Composers of Importance, Musical Newsletter, 71; N Slonimsky (auth), Music Since 1900, Scribner's, 71. *Mem:* Int Soc Contemp Music (mem Am sect exec comt, 65-68); Am Soc Univ Comp; Am Music Ctr; ASCAP. *Publ:* Auth, Music and the Liturgy, Liturgical Arts 38, 69; Intervallic Procedures in Debussy, 69 & Mannerism and Stylistic Consistency in Stravinsaky, 71, Perspectives New Music; Penderecki and Utrenja, 72 & The Third Quartet of Eliott Carter, 75, Musical Quart. *Mailing Add:* Blackwell's Mills Belle Mead NJ 08502

MOFFO, ANNA
SOPRANO
b Wayne, Pa, June 27, 35. *Study:* Curtis Inst Music; studied with Euphemia Giannini-Gregory. *Rec Perf:* Marriage of Figaro & Flastaff, EMI; Lucia di Lammermoor, Carmen, Hansel & Gretel, Ariola; La Boheme & Giovanni, Angel; La Traviata, Madama Butterfly, Rigoletto & La Rondine, RCA Victor; Christmas Carols, Columbia; Die Fledermaus & Guiditta, Teldec. *Roles:* Violetta in La Traviata; Lucia in Lucia di Lammermoor; Manon in Manon-Massenet; Tosca in Tosca; Marie in La Fille du Regiment; Cio-Cio-San in Madama Butterfly; Gilda in Rigoletto; Mimi in La Boheme. *Pos:* Res mem, Metropolitan Opera, New York; sop, Chicago Lyric Opera, San Francisco Opera & opera houses Paris, London, Salzburg, Vienna, La Scala-Milan, Berlin, Tokyo, Aix-en-Provence & Edinburgh; recitalist throughout US, Europe, Australia, Asia & North & South Am; appearances on TV & films in US & abroad. *Awards:* Commendatore, Order of Merit, Repub Italy; Young Artist Award, Philadelphia Orch; Michelangelo Award; Orfee d'or. *Mailing Add:* Columbia Artists Mgt 165 W 57th St New York NY 10019

MOLAVA, PAMELA MAY
COMPOSER, LECTURER
Study: Royal Acad Music, London, LRAM, 48; NY Univ, BS, 56, MA, 58; The New Sch, 60-61. *Works:* Crumar-Om Prelude (electronic music), perf at the Hartford Pub Libr Auditorium, 81; EEN (electronic music), comn by the Gtr Hartford Arts Coun, 82; Cosmic Patterns (electronic music), comn by Truda Kaschmann Dance Ens, 83. *Pos:* Artistic dir, Studio of Electronic Music Inc, 80- *Teaching:* Instr electronic music, Hartford Consv Music & Dance, 83- *Mem:* Conn Comp Asn; New England Comput Music Asn (mem bd dir, 81-). *Mailing Add:* 25 Carver Circle Simsbury CT 06070

MOLDENHAUER, HANS
WRITER, ADMINISTRATOR
b Mainz, Ger, Dec 13, 06. *Study:* Munic Col Music, Mainz, Ger, with Hans Rosbaud; Whitworth Col, Wash, BS, 45; Chicago Musical Col, Roosevelt Univ, DFA(musicol), 51; Boguslawski Col Music, Chicago, Hon DMus, 45. *Pos:* Founder & dir, Spokane Consv, 42-, pres, 46-; organizer, Int Webern Fest, 62-78; founder & dir, Moldenhauer Arch, currently. *Teaching:* Lectr, Univ Wash, 61-64 & many other universities in US & Europe. *Awards:* Officer's Cross Order Merit, Fed Repub Ger, 80; Deems Taylor Award, ASCAP, 80; Goldenes Verdienstzeichen Landes Wien, 81. *Bibliog:* Paul Nettl (auth), Hans Moldenhauer, Pionier der Musikwissenschaft, Seine Sammlung in Spokane, Washington, Festschrift Alfred Orel, Austria, 60; Don L Roberts

(auth), Music History from Primary Sources—The Moldenhauer Archive, Bärenreiter, 73; Cecilia K Van de Kamp (auth), Moldenhauer Archives, Current Musicol, No 17, 74. *Mem:* Am Musicol Soc (chmn NW chap, 58-60); Int Webern Soc (pres, 62-). *Publ:* Auth, The Death of Anton Webern—A Drama in Documents, Philosophical Libr, 61; Anton von Webern: Perspectives, Univ Wash Press, 66; compiler & forward to Anton von Webern: Sketches, Carl Fischer Inc, 68; auth, Anton von Webern: A Chronicle of his Life and Work, Victor Gollancs, London, 78; Catalogue of the Moldenhauer Archives (in prep); and many articles in English & German. *Mailing Add:* 1011 Comstock Ct Spokane WA 99203

MOLESE, MICHELE
TENOR
b NY, Aug 29, 36. *Study:* Consv Milan, with Emilio Piccoli & Francesco Merli; Scuolo Perfezionamento La Scala, Milan. *Rec Perf:* On Columbia, Decca & Conct Hall. *Roles:* Fritz in Amico Fritz, Piccola Scala, Milan, 56; Kodanda in Dernier Sauvage, Paris Opera Comique, 63; Pollione in Norma; Faust in Damnation de Faust; Don Jose in Carmen; Nadir in Pecheurs de perles; Gerald in Lakme. *Pos:* Tenor, maj opera co in Europe & US. *Mailing Add:* c/o Tony Hartmann Assoc 250 W 57th St Suite 1120 New York NY 10107

MOLL, KURT
BASS
b Buir, Germany, Apr 11, 38. *Study:* Musik Hochschule, Cologne; studied with Emmy Muller. *Rec Perf:* On EMI & Deutsche Grammophon. *Roles:* Lodovico in Otello, Aachen Opera, 61; Rocco in Fidelio; Mephistopheles in Faust; Van Bett in Zar und Zimmermann; Don Alfonso in Cosi fan tutte; Sarastro in Die Zauberflöte; Colline in La Boheme. *Pos:* Mem, Staatsoper Hamburg & Bayerische Staatsoper, Munich; performer, Metropolitan Opera, currently; sang with maj opera co incl Vienna Staatsoper, Berlin Staatsoper, Milan La Scala, Moscow Bolshoi, San Francisco Opera, Chicago Opera & Miami Opera. *Bibliog:* Gary D Lipton (auth), Having Fun, Opera News, 3/12/83. *Mailing Add:* c/o Mariedi Anders Artists 535 El Camino Del Mar San Francisco CA 94121

MOLLICONE, HENRY
COMPOSER, CONDUCTOR
b Providence, RI, Mar 20, 46. *Study:* New England Consv Music, BM, 68, MM, 71; studied comp with Daniel Pinkham, Gunther Schuller, Donald Martino, Seymour Shifrin & Ron Nelson. *Works:* Te Deum, New England Consv Music, 66; The Face on the Bar Room Floor (one act opera), 78, CRI; Starbird (one act opera), Belwin-Mills, 80; Mass, comn by Cath Archdiocese Los Angeles, 80; Emperor Norton (one act opera), 81 & Mask of Evil (one act opera), 82, Belwin-Mills; incidental music for shows at Guthrie Theater, 72 & 74 & Old Globe Theater, San Diego, 83. *Rec Perf:* The Face on the Bar Room Floor, CRI, 81. *Pos:* Asst cond, New York City Opera Co, 72-76; freelance opera cond, Lake George Opera, Chamber Opera Theater of NY, Central City Opera & Long Beach Grand Opera, 79- *Awards:* Nat Endowment Arts Comp Grant, 80; Nat Opera Inst Masters Study Grant, 83. *Mem:* Am Fedn Musicians; Am Comp Alliance; BMI. *Rep:* Belwin-Mills Publ Corp 1776 Broadway New York NY 10019. *Mailing Add:* 14400 Addison St Sherman Oaks CA 91423

MONACO, RICHARD A
COMPOSER, EDUCATOR
b Richmond Hill, NY, Jan 10, 30. *Study:* NY Univ, 48-50; Cornell Univ, BA, 52, MA, 54, DMA, 60; Berkshire Music Ctr, with Aaron Copland & Roberto Gerhard, 63. *Works:* Sonata (trombone & piano), Phil Corp, 60; Lord, Thou Hast Been Our Dwelling Place, G Schirmer, 63; I Never Saw a Moor, Belwin-Mills, 69; Magnificat (chorus), Columbus Symph Orch Choir, 69; Blessed Be The Lord, J Fischer, 70; Three Miniatures (woodwind quintet), 77 & Live Short Pieces (flute & clarinet), 78, Shawnee Press. *Pos:* Cond, Oxford Chamber Orch, 65-69. *Teaching:* Prof music, Western Col for Women, 59-74; prof, Univ Ill, Chicago, 74- & dir choral activ, 82- *Awards:* Award for Composition, ASCAP, 70-72 & 78-82. *Mem:* Col Music Soc; ASCAP. *Mailing Add:* Dept Music Univ Ill Chicago IL 60680

MONK, MEREDITH J
COMPOSER
b Lima, Peru, Nov 20, 42; US citizen. *Study:* Sarah Lawrence Col, comp with Ruth Lloyd, Glen Mack & Meyer Kupferman, BA, 64; studied voice with Paul Ukena, William Horn & Vicki Starr. *Works:* Key, Lovely Music Ltd, 71; Vessel: An Opera Epic, House Found, 71; Our Lady of Late, Minona Rec, 74; Songs from the Hill, 79 & Tablet, 79, Wergo-Spectrum Rec; Dolmen Music, 81 & Turtle Dreams, 83, ECM Rec. *Pos:* Founder & artistic dir, The House Found for Arts, 68-; comp, choreographer & dir, over 40 works. *Teaching:* Mem fac, Goddard Col & Sarah Lawrence Col; lectr, NY Univ, 70-72. *Awards:* Creative Artists Pub Serv Fel, 76 & 82; John Simon Guggenheim Found Fel, 82; Outstanding Comp, Villager, 83. *Bibliog:* David Sterritt (auth), Meredith Monk, Christian Sci Monitor, 6/2/81; Neil Watkins (auth), Meredith Monk's Music, Modern Music & Rec, 12/81; Peter Greenaway (dir), Meredith Monk: American Composer (film), London, 9/82. *Mem:* ASCAP; Am Women Comp Asn; Am Music Ctr. *Mailing Add:* Barbara Dufty 228 W Broadway New York NY 10013

MONK, PATRICIA
EDUCATOR, PIANO
Study: Consv Music, Oberlin Col, BM; New England Consv Music, MM; Hochschule Musik, Berlin, Abschluss Prufung; Acad Music & Dramatic Art, Vienna; studied with Pablo Casals, piano with John Elvin, Bruce Simonds,

Nadia Reisenberg, Denise Lasimonne, Helmut Roloff, Howard Goding & Grete Hinterhofer & chamber music with Artur Balsam, Michel Scwalbe & Richard Klemm. *Rec Perf:* On RIAS, Berlin. *Teaching:* Mem fac, Smith Col, 67-69; mem fac piano, Longy Sch Music, currently. *Awards:* German Govt Grant, Berlin; Coun Arts & Sci Scholar, Berlin. *Mailing Add:* Longy Sch Music One Follen St Cambridge MA 02138

MONOD, JACQUES-LOUIS
COMPOSER, CONDUCTOR
b Paris, France, Feb 25, 27. *Study:* Juilliard Sch, with Olivier Messiaen & Rene Leibowitz; Columbia Univ, DMA; Berlin Consv. *Works:* Cantus Contra Cantum I (sop & chamber orch), 72; Chamber Aria (sop & chamber orch), Boston, 73; Cantus Contra Cantum II (violin & cello), 74 & Boston, 76; Cantus Contra Cantum III (double chorus, a cappella), 76. *Pos:* Voice & piano duo with Bethany Beardslee, 50-55; pianist, 56; performer, orch concerts & broadcasts in Europe, Scand & North & Cent Am, 56-; cond, BBC Third Prog, London, 60- & major orch & chamber ensembles; participant, Chamber Ens Conct Series, Australian & Italian Insts & London, 62-66; dir publ, Boelke-Bomart Mobart Inc, Hillsdale, NY. *Teaching:* Mem fac, New England Consv Music, Princeton Univ, Harvard Univ, Queens Col, City Univ New York & Columbia Univ, 72-78. *Awards:* Martha Baird Rockfeller Grant; Dorothy Spivak Grant; Nat Inst Arts & Lett Citation. *Mem:* Comp Guild for Performers; Asn Rene Leibowitz. *Mailing Add:* 395 Riverside Dr New York NY 10025

MONOSOFF, SONYA (SONYA MONOSOFF PANCALDO)
VIOLIN, EDUCATOR
b Cleveland, Ohio, June 11, 27. *Study:* Juilliard Sch, artists dipl, 48. *Rec Perf:* Fifteen Mystery Sonatas (Biber), 63; Eight Sonatas, 1681 (Biber), 63 & 82; Sonatas for Violin & Harpsichord (Bach), 70; Twelve Sonatas, Op 5 (Corelli), 76; Sonatas (Mozart), 76. *Teaching:* Instr, Smith Col, 64 & Mass Inst Technol, 65-66; prof, Cornell Univ, 72-; lectr baroque violin, Oberlin Perf Inst, summer 75 & 76, Bar-Ilan Univ, Tel Aviv, Israel, 82 & Fondazione Cini, Venice, Italy, summer 83. *Awards:* Best Record of Year Award, Stereo Rev, 70. *Mem:* Am Musicol Soc; Am Musical Instrm Soc; Chamber Music Am; Violin Soc Am. *Publ:* Auth, Bingio Marini, Baricht über den Int Kongress ..., Universal, 75; Viva the Early Violin, J Violin Soc Am, 77; String Fingering, Multiple Stopping, and others, In: New Grove Dict of Music & Musicians, 6th ed, 80. *Rep:* Joanne Rile Box 27539 Philadelphia PA 19118. *Mailing Add:* Lincoln Hall Cornell Univ Ithaca NY 14853

MONSEN, RONALD PETER
CLARINET, EDUCATOR
b Milwaukee, Wis, Sept 20, 40. *Study:* Univ Wis, Milwaukee, BSc, 63; Northwestern Univ, MMus, 67; London Royal Acad Music, perf dipl, 72; Univ Wis, Madison, DMA, 76; studied with Glenn Bowen, Jack Snavely, Jack Brymer, Jerome Stowell & Alan Hacker. *Pos:* Solo clarinet, Fulham Munic Orch, London, 71-72; clarinet, Ky Wind Quintet, 80- & Lexington Phil, 80- *Teaching:* Asst prof music, Univ Wis, Waukesha, 76-80; assoc prof clarinet, Univ Ky, 80-; vis prof, Royal Mil Sch Music, Kneller Hall, England, 82; fac mem clarinet & chamber music, 10th ann British Woodwind Wkshp, London, 82; recitalist & fac mem, Int Clarinet Cong, Univ Denver, 83. *Mem:* Pi Kappa Lambda; Phi Mu Alpha. *Publ:* Auth, Norwegian Music for Clarinet, Woodwind World, 74; Swedish Music for Clarinet, 76 & Clarinet Music of Jørgen Bentzon, 79, Clarinet; co-ed, Concert Piece-Clarinet-Rimsky Korsakov, Shall-U-Mo, 81. *Mailing Add:* 168 Bonnie Brae Dr Lexington KY 40508

MONSEUR, GEORGE
CONDUCTOR, EDUCATOR
Study: Ariz State Univ, BM; New England Consv Music, MM; studied cond with Leopold Stokowski, Leonard Bernstein, Leon Barzin & Attilio Poto. *Pos:* Music dir, Nat Symph Orch Ecuador, formerly; guest cond, Tanglewood Fest Orch, Nat Radio-TV Orch Athens, Nat Symph Costa Rica & Int Musical Fest Caracas. *Teaching:* Instr cond, Boston Consv Music, formerly; mem fac choral & solfege, Berklee Col Music, currently. *Mailing Add:* Berklee Col Music 1140 Boylston St Boston MA 02215

MONSON, DALE E
EDUCATOR
b Monterrey, Calif, Nov 26, 51. *Study:* Brigham Young Univ, BA, 75, MA, 76; Columbia Univ, PhD, 83. *Pos:* Ed in chief, Current Musicol, 78-80. *Teaching:* Asst prof, Sch Music, Univ Mich, 82- *Interests:* Opera of the 18th century, especially Halian opera seria circa 1740. *Publ:* Auth, Franz Grillporzer, Beethoven & the Classic/Romantic Dichotomy, IRASM, 82; ed, Adriano in Siria, An Opera Seria by Pergolesi, Garland, 83. *Mailing Add:* Sch Music Univ Mich Ann Arbor MI 48109

MONSON, KAREN ANN
CRITIC & WRITER, LECTURER
b New Haven, Conn, Mar 25, 45. *Study:* Radcliffe Col, Harvard Univ, BA, 66; Hochschule Musik, WBerlin, Germany, 66-67; Univ Southern Calif, 67-69. *Pos:* Music & dance critic, Los Angeles Herald-Examiner, 69-73; music critic, Chicago Daily News, 73-78. *Teaching:* Lectr music, Univ Chicago, 74-78. *Awards:* Deems Taylor Award for Music Criticism, ASCAP, 76; Peabody Award, 76; Armstrong Award, 80. *Publ:* Auth, Alban Berg, 78 & Alma, A Biography of Alma Mahler-Werfel, 83, Houghton Mifflin; regular contribr to High Fidelity, Musical Am & others. *Rep:* Robert Cornfield Literary Agency 145 W 79th St New York NY 10024. *Mailing Add:* 6634 Majorca Way E Phoenix AZ 85016

MONTAGUE, STEPHEN (ROWLEY)
COMPOSER, PIANO
b Syracuse, NY, Mar 10, 43. *Study:* St Petersburg Jr Col, AA(music), 63; Fla State Univ, with Carlisle Floyd, BM, 65, MM, 67; Ohio State Univ, with Herbert Brün & David Behrman, DMA(comp), 72. *Works:* Eyes of Ambush (chamber Ens), 73, Into the Sun (ballet), 77 & Paramell II: Entity (six perc), 77, Ed Modern; Varshavian Spring (orch & chorus), Warsaw Autumn Fest, Nat Endowment Arts, 80; Scythia (electronic tape), comn by Belgian Radio, Ghent, 81; Tigida Pipa (four voices & tape), comn by Singcircle, London, 83; At the White Edge of Phrygia (orch), comn by Acad London Orch, 83. *Pos:* Comp in res, Strider Dance Co, London, 74-75; freelance comp, London, 75- *Teaching:* Instr, Butler Univ, 67-69. *Awards:* Fulbright Fel to Warsaw, 72-74; Comp Bursary Award, Arts Coun Gt Brit, 80; MacDowell Colony Fel, 81 & 83. *Bibliog:* Keith Potter (auth), A Romantic Minimalist, Classical Music, 11/6/82; Olivia Maxwell (auth), Rhythm Crazy, Time Out, London, 2/18/83. *Mem:* Electro-Acoust Music Asn Gt Brit (mem exec comt, 82-83); Soc Prom New Music, England; Am Music Ctr; Am Soc Univ Comp; Gesellschaft Musikalische Aufführungs & Mechanische Vervielfältigungsrechte. *Publ:* Auth, Interview with Zygmunt Krauze, 78 & The MacDowell Colony for Creative Artists, 81, Contact; John Cage, Habla del Tiempo, Azar Politica, el Silencio Pauta, Mex, 83; JSignificant Silences of a Musical Anarchist, Class Music Mag, 82; John Cage at 70, Am Music J, 83. *Mailing Add:* 27 Southside, Dalmeny Ave London N7 OQH England United Kingdom

MONTANARO, DONALD
CLARINET, EDUCATOR
Study: Curtis Inst Music. *Pos:* Mem, New Orleans Symph, formerly; mem clarinet sect, Philadelphia Orch, 57-; performer, Marlboro & Casals Fest; soloist & chamber ens, Europe & Far East. *Teaching:* Mem fac clarinet, Curtis Inst Music, 80- *Mailing Add:* Curtis Inst Music 1726 Locust St Philadelphia PA 19103

MONTANARO, MARGARITA C See Csonka, Margarita

MONTANE, CARLOS (CARLOS HEVIA-MONTANE)
TENOR
b La Habana, Cuba, Dec 1, 41. *Study:* New England Consv, 63. *Rec Perf:* Messa di Requiem (Donizetti), 72 & Oberto Conte di San Bonifacio (G Verdi), 76, Raritas, WGermany; Messa di Requiem (Bottesini), Fonitcetra, Milan, 80. *Roles:* Riccardo in Masked Ball, Hamburg Staatsoper, WGermany, 78; Roberto Devereux, Liege Opera, Belgium, 81; Duke of Mantua, Metropolitan Opera, 81; Manrico in Il Trovatore, NJ State Opera, 83; Riccardo in Masked Ball, Deutsche Oper, Berlin, WGermany, 83; Don Alvaro in La Forzo del Destino, 83-84 & Ernani in Ernani, 83-84, Metropolitan Opera. *Pos:* Leading tenor, Metropolitan Opera, 73-; Deutsche Oper, Berlin, 73-83, Deutsche Oper, Duesseldorf, WGermany, 73-77, Frankfurt Opera, WGermany, 75-78 . *Rep:* Robert Lombardo Assoc 61 W 62nd St New York NY 10023. *Mailing Add:* c/o Metropolitan Opera Lincoln Ctr Plaza New York NY 10023

MONTEMURRO, PAUL A
EDUCATOR, TEACHER
b Chicago, Ill, Apr 20, 33. *Study:* Cent Methodist Col, BME, 58; Univ Mo, Columbia, MA, 61. *Pos:* Dir bands, HLV Pub Sch, Victor, Iowa, 61-62, Pilot Grove Pub Sch, 64-65 & Fulton Pub Sch, 65-67; brass specialist, Suburban Chicago area sch, 62-64. *Teaching:* Grad asst, Marching Bands & Brass, Univ Mo, 58-61; assoc prof music, Central Methodist Col, 67-72 & Okla State Univ, 72- *Mem:* Col Band Dir Asn; Nat Asn Jazz Educ; Phi Mu Alpha Sinfonia; Okla Bandmasters Asn. *Publ:* Auth, Marching Band ... Reflections, Stanbury Corp, 79. *Mailing Add:* Music Dept Okla State Univ 121 Seretean Ctr Stillwater OK 74078

MONTEUX, CLAUDE
FLUTE, EDUCATOR
Study: Black Mountain Col; studied flute with Georges Laurent & piano with Nin-Culmell & Heinrich Gebhardt. *Pos:* Recitalist, US & Europe; performer, London Symph, Royal Phil, Acad St Martin in the Fields & several chamber ens; prin flute, Kansas City Phil; flutist & asst cond, Ballet Russe de Monte Carlo; cond, Columbus Symph & Hudson Valley Phil; soloist & guest cond, Royal Phil Orch, French Radio Orch, RIIS, Brussels Radio & Pittsburgh Symph; music dir, Haydn Fest Asn. currently. *Teaching:* Mem fac, Ohio State Univ, formerly & Peabody Consv Music, formerly; instr flute, New England Consv Music, currently. *Rep:* Albert Kay Assoc Inc 58 W 58th St New York NY 10019. *Mailing Add:* New England Consv Music 290 Huntington Rd Boston MA 02115

MONTGOMERY, WILLIAM LAYTON
FLUTE & PICCOLO, EDUCATOR
b Waco, Tex, Mar 28, 34. *Study:* Marlboro Sch Music, with Marcel Moyse, 51-53; Cornell Col, BME, 53; Curtis Inst Music, with William Kincaid, 53-54; Catholic Univ Am, MM, 56, PhD, 75. *Pos:* Prin flutist, US Marine Band, 54-63, Nat Gallery Art Orch, 65-, Theater Chamber Players Kennedy Ctr, 68- & Washington Chamber Orch, 75-; flute ed, Instrm Mag, Evanston, Ill, 82- *Teaching:* Lectr flute, Catholic Univ Am, 57-65; lectr music hist, George Washington Univ, 63-65; prof, flute & chamber music & chmn instrm music div, Univ Md, College Park, 65- *Mem:* Nat Flute Asn (pres, 76-77); Flute Soc Washington (pres, 78-80 & 82-). *Interests:* Life and works of Francois Devienne. *Publ:* Contribr, New Grove Dict of Music & Musicians. *Mailing Add:* 3923 Commander Dr Hyattsville MD 20782

MOODY, WILLIAM JOSEPH
EDUCATOR, ADMINISTRATOR
b Duluth, Minn, Dec 27, 31. *Study:* Univ Minn, Duluth, BS, 52, PhD, 65; Jordan Col Music, Butler Univ, MM, 53. *Rec Perf:* Educ Rec Ref Libr, Belwin-Mills, 66-73; Univ Tex Symph Band, Crest Rec & Austin Custom Rec, 66-73. *Pos:* Dir bands, Univ Southern Miss, 61-66 & Univ Tex, Austin, 66-73. *Teaching:* Instrm music, Rossville High Sch, Ind & Duluth Cent High Sch, Minn, 53-61; vchmn, Univ Tex, Austin, 66-73; chmn music dept, Univ SC, Columbia, 73- *Awards:* Intern & fel, Am Coun Educ Acad Internship, 70. *Mem:* Nat Band Asn (pres, 68-70); Nat Asn Sch Music; Music Educr Nat Conf; Am Bandmasters Asn. *Publ:* Auth, Improving Band Sound, Instrumentalist, 60; It is the Rehearsal that Counts, Sch Musician, 61; Can the Band Director also be a Conductor? Instrumentalist, 70; New Directions for Marching Bands, Big 3 Music Corp, 70; Must Band Music be Bland Music?, Sch Musician, 72. *Mailing Add:* 6223 Westshore Rd Columbia SC 29206

MOON, PEGGY MACDONALD
DIRECTOR—OPERA
b Jackson, Minn. *Study:* Univ Minn, BS(theatre arts), 68. *Pos:* Staging dir & choreographer, Fairbanks Light Opera Theatre, Alaska, 74-80, producing dir, 82-83; staging dir, Anchorage Civic Opera, Alaska, 82-; adminr, Anchorage Conct Asn, currently. *Mailing Add:* SR 2 Box 4510 Hilltop Dr Chugiak AK 99567

MOORE, BARBARA (PATRICIA) HILL
SOPRANO, TEACHER
b St Louis, Mo, Dec 28, 42. *Study:* Lincoln Univ, Mo, BS(music educ), 65; Univ Ill, Champaign-Urbana, MS(music educ), 69. *Rec Perf:* Le Diable Amoureux (Robert Rodriguez), PBS, 79. *Roles:* Carmen in Carmen, St Louis Opera Theatre, 66; Carmela in La Vida Breve, Dallas Symph, 76; Dido in Dido and Aeneas, Dallas Chamber Opera, 78; Bess in Porgy & Bess, Miss, 82. *Teaching:* Music supvr, Kinloch Sch Dist, Mo, 65-66; teacher music, St Louis Cath Archdiocese, 66-67; instr voice, Millikin Univ, 69-74; chair dept voice & assoc prof, Southern Methodist Univ, 74- *Awards:* Excellence in Music, Friends of Music, 60; Ill Artist Award, Nat Asn Teachers Singing. *Bibliog:* Patsy Swank (dir), The Artist Teacher, Educ TV, 79; Robert Rodriguez, Opera: Le Diable Amoureux, PBS, Dallas, 79 & 80. *Mem:* Nat Asn Teachers Singing (treas Dallas chap, 76-78); Pi Kappa Lambda; Mu Phi Epsilon. *Mailing Add:* 1821 Carmel Cove Plano TX 75075

MOORE, CARMAN LEROY
COMPOSER, CRITIC
b Lorain, Ohio, Oct 8, 36. *Study:* Ohio State Univ, BS, 58; Juilliard Sch Music, MS, 67; studied with Hall Overton, Vincent Persichetti & Luciano Berio. *Works:* Wildfires and Field Songs, 75, Gospel Fuse, 75 & Hit: A Concerto for Percussion & Orchestra, 78, Peer/Southern; Fixed Do: Movable Sol, 80; Blue Cubes, Carman Moore & Ens, 82; Wild Gardens of the Loup Garou (four singing actors, five instrm & slides), 82; The Sorrow of Love (double choir & piano), Gregg Smith Singers, 83. *Pos:* Music critic, Village Voice, 66-78 & NY Times, 66-78; staff mem, NY State Coun Arts, 82- *Teaching:* Asst prof, Manhattanville Col, 69-74, Queens Col, City Univ New York, 69-74, Brooklyn Col, City Univ New York, 69-74 & Yale Sch Music, 70-71. *Awards:* Creative Artists Pub Serv Award, 74 & 76; Nat Endowment Arts Comp Grant, 75; Beards Found Award, 80. *Bibliog:* Donal Henahan (auth), This Week's Most Wanted Composer, New York Sunday Times, 2/19/75; Eileen Southern (auth), The Music of Black Americans, Norton. *Mem:* Am Music Ctr (mem bd dir, currently); Meet the Comp; founder, Experimental Intermedia Found; ASCAP. *Mailing Add:* 148 Columbus Ave New York NY 10023

MOORE, DALE (KIMBERLY)
BARITONE, CONDUCTOR
b Olathe, Kans, May 22, 32. *Study:* Univ Kans, BMus, 54, MMus, 56; Mozarteum, Salzburg, 54-55; Hon Dr Music, Lincoln Mem Univ, 64. *Rec Perf:* On the Road to Mandaly and Other Favorite American Concert Songs, Cambridge Rec, 73. *Roles:* Nick Shadow in The Rake's Progress, Lake Erie Opera Theatre, 64; the Vicar in Albert Herring, Opera Theatre of St Louis, 76 & 78 & British Broadcasting Corp-WNET TV Prod, 78. *Pos:* Bass soloist, Lord Nelson Mass, Cleveland Orch, 63; Bethany Col Messiah Week Fest, 64, 66 & 71 & Baldwin-Wallace Bach Fest, 65; soloist with St Louis Symphony & Minneapolis Orch, 69 & 72. *Teaching:* Dir, Consv Music, Denison Univ, 58-64; artist in res, Washington Univ, St Louis, Mo, 75-76; prof music, Col Wooster, 77- *Awards:* First Place, Nat Fedn Music Clubs Auditions, 63; Fulbright Scholar, 54-55. *Mem:* Nat Asn Teachers Singing (regional gov, 72-74). *Mailing Add:* 2915 Taylor Wooster OH 44691

MOORE, DAVID WILLARD
CELLO, WRITER
b Ithaca, NY, Mar, 13, 38. *Study:* Juilliard Sch, studied cello with Leonard Rose, BS, 60, MS, 61; NY Univ. *Rec Perf:* Quartets (Schoenberg), 65 & Early String Quartet in Am, 67, Vox; Contemporary Am Music for Solo Cello, 67 & Songs and Dances (cello, perc & keyboard; F Thorne), 68, Opus #1; Good Friends Duo (clarinet & cello; M Kupferman), Serenus, 78; Songs Newly Seen in the Dusk (ms & cello; Weigl), 80 & Scintilla Phisca (cello & piano; B Fennelly), 81, Orion. *Pos:* Cellist, Radio City Music Hall Orch, 61-76 & Kohon Quartet, 64-67; reviewer, Am Rec Guide, 68- *Teaching:* Asst prof, York Col, 73-76. *Mem:* Am Musicol Soc. *Mailing Add:* 68-19 Dartmouth St Forest Hills NY 11375

MOORE, DONALD I
EDUCATOR, CONDUCTOR
b Apr 11, 10; US citizen. *Study:* Carleton Col, AB(music), 32; Univ Northern Colo, AM, 40; Univ Mich, 47. *Works:* Requiem (band), 40 & Saul of Tarsus (band), 42, perf by many col & univ; Marcho Poco for Band, 49 & America (chorus, band & orch), 54, Mills Music; Patriotic Oratory for Horn & Band/ Orch, perf by many col & univ bands, 58; Domino Variations (band), perf by Univ Mich, Univ Colo & Baylor Univ, 59. *Teaching:* Dir band & orch, Dallas Pub Sch, 37-40; dir band, Univ Northern Colo, 40-42 & Juilliard Sch Music, 47-48; dir band & prof music, Baylor, 48-79. *Awards:* Distinguished Service Music Award, Kappa Kappa Psi, 68. *Mem:* Am Bandmasters Asn; Col Band Dir Nat Asn; Am Fedn Musicians. *Mailing Add:* 3300 N 29th Waco TX 76708

MOORE, DOROTHY RUDD
COMPOSER, SOPRANO
b New Castle, Del, June 4, 40. *Study:* Sch Music, Howard Univ, studied comp with Mark Fax, BM(theory & comp), 63; Am Consv, Fontainebleau, France, studied comp with Nadia Boulanger, summer 63; studied comp with Chon wen Chung, 67. *Works:* Symphony No 1, Nat Symph Orch, 63; Modes for String Quartet, Clarmoor String Quartet, 68; From the Dark Tower, Hilda Harris & Symph New World, 72; Dirge and Deliverance, perf by Kermit Moore & Zita Carno, 72; Weary Blues, perf by Rawn Spearman, Kermit Moore & Kelley Wyatt, 72; Dream & Variations, perf by Zita Carno, 75; Sonnets on Love, Rosebuds & Death, perf by Miriam Burton, Sanford Allen & Kelley Wyatt, 76. *Teaching:* Instr music, NY Univ, 69 & Bronx Community Col, 71. *Bibliog:* Dr Ora Williams (auth), American Black Women, Scarecrow Press, 73; Raoul Abdul (auth), Blacks in Classical Music, Dodd, Mead & Co, 77; Alice Tischler (auth), 15 Black American Composers, Univ Ill Press, 81. *Mem:* Am Comp Alliance; BMI; Am Women Comp; New York Singing Teachers Asn; Am Music Ctr. *Rep:* Am Comp Alliance 170 W 74th St New York NY 10023. *Mailing Add:* 33 Riverside Dr New York NY 10023

MOORE, DOUGLAS BRYANT
EDUCATOR, CELLO
b Cedar Rapids, Iowa, Jan 6, 46. *Study:* Ind Univ, BMus, 67; Cath Univ, MMus, 70, DMA, 77. *Rec Perf:* Cello/Piano Music of Arthur Foote, 79, Cello/Piano Music of Arthur Farwell & Charles W Cadman, 81 & Piano Trios of Arthur Foote, 83, Musical Heritage Soc Rec. *Pos:* Prin cellist, Albany Symph, 70-79; cellist, Williams Trio, 70- *Teaching:* Asst prof music, Williams Col, 71-77, assoc prof, 77-83, chmn dept music, 79-, prof, 83- *Mem:* Col Music Soc (vpres, Northeast chap, 81-); Sonneck Soc; Am Guild English Handbell Ringers. *Mailing Add:* Dept Music Williams Col Williamstown MA 01267

MOORE, F RICHARD
COMPOSER, EDUCATOR
b Uniontown, Pa, Sept 4, 44. *Study:* Carnegie Mellon Univ, BFA(comp & perf), 66; Univ Ill, 67; Stanford Univ, MS, 75, PhD, 77. *Pos:* Dir, Comput Audio Res Lab, Univ Calif San Diego, La Jolla, 79- & Ctr Music Experiment, 82- *Teaching:* Prof music, Univ Calif San Diego, La Jolla, 79- *Publ:* Coauth (with Mathews, Miller, Pierce & Risset), The Technology of Computer Music, MIT Press, 69; coauth, GROOVE: A Program to Compose, Store & Edit Functions of Time, 70; auth, The Futures of Music, Perspectives of New Music, 80; The Computer Audio Res Lab at Univ Calif San Diego, Comp Mus J, 82. *Mailing Add:* Comput Music Educ Q-037 Univ Calif San Diego La Jolla CA 92093

MOORE, JAMES, III
GUITAR & LUTE, EDUCATOR
b Richmond, Va, Sept 27, 40. *Study:* Studied with Frederick Neumann, Frank Wendt, Helen Travis Crawford, John Runge, Philip Lewis & Jesus Silva. *Pos:* Organizer & dir, James Moore Broken Consortia, Moore-Raff Guitar & Lute Duo & Baroque Trio. *Teaching:* Instr guitar & lute, Univ Richmond & Va Commonwealth Univ, currently. *Mem:* Lute Soc London; co-founder, Soc Class Guitar. *Publ:* Co-ed (with John Rung) Lute Songs & Folk Songs, 3 vols, 65-71. *Mailing Add:* 1709 Grove Ave Richmond VA 23220

MOORE, JOHN PARKER, JR
PIANO, EDUCATOR
b Okmulgee, Okla, Dec 4, 42. *Study:* Phillips Univ, Enid, Okla, BMus, 64; Tulsa Univ, MMus, 66; studied piano with Aldo Mancinelli, 54. *Works:* American Rhapsody, perf by Phillips Univ Band & Fourth Army Band, 64 & 69; Christ is Born, perf by Americal Div Band, Vietnam, 67. *Pos:* Army bandsman, Fourth US Army Band & Americal Div, 66-69; prin pianist, San Antonio Symph Mastersingers, 67-75; accmp & asst cond, Tex Bach Choir, San Antonio, 77-; prin keyboard, San Antonio Symph Orch, 82-83. *Teaching:* Instr music, San Antonio Col, 70-74; assoc prof, St Mary's Univ, 75- & chmn, 77- *Mem:* San Antonio Music Teachers Asn; Tex Music Teachers Asn; Music Teachers Nat Asn; Tex Music Educr Asn; Am Fedn Musicians. *Mailing Add:* One Camino Santa Maria San Antonio TX 78284

MOORE, KENNETH
EDUCATOR
Study: Univ Ill, BMus & BS(music ed); Juilliard Sch Music, MS. *Rec Perf:* On CRI, CP2, Columbia, Coronet, Desto, Epic, Gasparo & Grenadilla Rec. *Pos:* Perf with Cleveland Orch, New Orleans Phil, Berkshire Music Fest, Marlboro Music Fest & Shawnee Music Fest. *Teaching:* Fac mem, Davidson Col & Univ Wis; prof bassoon & cond ens, Oberlin Col, 55- *Mailing Add:* Music Dept Oberlin Col Oberlin OH 44074

MOORE, MARVELENE CLARISA
EDUCATOR, LECTURER

b Franklin, Tenn, Sept 13, 44. *Study:* Talladega Col, AB, 66; George Peabody Col, MME, 70, EdS, 71; Univ Mich, PhD, 77; Orff Schulwerk Inst, Salzburg, Austria, cert, summer 78; Dalcroze Inst, Geneva, Switzerland, cert, summer 81. *Pos:* Southern rep, Multi-Cult Awareness Comn, 81-; minister music, Lennon-Seney United Methodist Church, 82- *Teaching:* Assoc prof music educ, Univ Tenn, 78- *Awards:* Presser Music Found Award, Talladega Col, 65. *Mem:* Pi Kappa Lambda (pres, 81-83); Music Educr Nat Conf (treas, Nat Black Music Caucus, 81-); Am Orff-Schulwerk Asn. *Publ:* Auth, Authenticity in Music Education, Tenn Musician, 81; Multicultural Music Teacher Education, Ga Music News, 2/82. *Mailing Add:* 1814 Scarlett Oak Pl Knoxville TN 37919

MOORE, THOMAS
VIOLIN

b Fairfield, Ala, Jan 24, 33. *Study:* Drew Univ, with Dika Newlin; Columbia Univ, with Jack Beeson & Otto Luening, MA. *Works:* Fantasy (violin & orch); A Quality of Spring (piano & orch); Piping Songs (flute); Metamorphosis (piano). *Pos:* Violinist, Kansas City Phil, 70-71, Indianapolis Symph Orch, 71-73 & Fla Symph Orch, 73-; concertmaster, Miami Phil Orch, currently. *Teaching:* Fac mem, Miss State Col, 61-63, Mid Tenn State, 63-64, C W Post Col, 64-70 & Univ Miami, currently. *Mailing Add:* Sch Music Univ Miami Coral Gables FL 33124

MOORE, UNDINE SMITH
EDUCATOR, COMPOSER

b Jarratt, Va, Aug 25, 04. *Study:* Fisk Univ, AB, 26, Sch Music, dipl, 26; Teachers Col, Columbia Univ, MA & prof dipl, 31; Va State Univ, Hon DMus, 72; Ind Univ, Hon DMus, 76. *Works:* Daniel, Daniel Servant of the Lord, 52 & Mother to Son, 55, Warner Bros; Afro-American Suite (flute, cello & piano), Trio Pro Viva, 69; Lord, We Give Thanks to Thee (centennial), Warner Bros, 71; On Imagination, 80 & I, Too, 80, comn by Winston-Salem Univ, NC; Scenes from the Life of a Martyr, Carl Fischer Mus Co, 81; Three Centennial Pieces comn by Va State Univ, 82. *Pos:* Supvr music, Goldsboro, NC, 26-27. *Teaching:* Assoc prof music, Va State Univ, 27-72; adj prof, Va Union Univ, Richmond, 72-76; vis prof black man in Am music, Carleton Col, 72; intersemester wkshps black music, Col St Benedict, St Joseph, Minn, 73-75. *Awards:* Seventh Annual Humanitarian Award in Arts, Fisk Univ, 73; Music Laureate Medal, Commonwealth Va, 77; Distinguished Achievement Award, Tufts Univ, 81. *Bibliog:* Baker, Bett & Hudson (authors), The Black Composer Speaks, Scarecrow Press, 78; James Edward Moore (auth), The Choral Music of Unidine Smith Moore, Univ Cincinnati, 79; John R D Jones (auth), Choral Works of Undine Moore—Her Life and Work, NY Univ, 80. *Mem:* ASCAP; Am Choral Dir Asn; Black Caucus Music Educr Nat Conf; Va Comp Guild. *Publ:* Coauth, Audio Tapes, Video Tapes & Films, InterLibr Loan, Va State Univ, 71-72; contribr, Reflections on Afro-American Music, Kent State Univ Press, 73. *Mailing Add:* 4538 W River Rd Ettrick VA 23803

MOORMAN, JOYCE ELAINE See Solomon, Joyce Elaine

MORALES, ABRAM
TENOR

b Corpus Christi, Tex, Nov 30, 39. *Study:* Southern Methodist Univ, BME, MMus. *Roles:* Count Almaviva in The Barber of Seville, Des Moines Metro Fest, 76 & Seattle Opera, 83; Tonio in The Daughter of the Regiment, Houston Grand Opera & Opera Theatre Hawaii; Edgardo in Lucia di Lammermoor, San Francisco Opera, 81; Nemorino in The Elixir of Love, Des Moines Metro Fest, 82; Astrologer in Le Coq d'Or, New York City Opera & Kennedy Ctr, Washington, DC; Rudolfo in La Boheme; Essex in Roberto Devereux. *Mailing Add:* c/o Columbia Artists 165 W 57th St New York NY 10019

MORE, MICHAEL
ADMINISTRATOR, TENOR

b Kodiak, Alaska. *Study:* Ind Univ, BA(voice), 70; Univ Southern Calif, MA(vocal perf). *Roles:* Tenor in Cosi fan tutte, A Midsummer Night's Dream, Madama Butterfly, I Pagliacci, Il Barbiere di Siviglia, The Tales of Hoffman & Die Fledermaus. *Pos:* Soloist, Soldier's Chorus & US Army Field Band; performer, Ind Univ Opera Theatre, Anchorage Civic Opera, Univ Southern Calif Opera & Orange Co Opera; adminr & exec dir, Anchorage Civic Opera; mem, Mayor's Citizen's Adv Comt for Perf Arts Facil for Proj 80's; mem bd, Alaska Arts Alliance. *Teaching:* Mem fac, Univ Alaska, Anchorage, 73-76. *Mailing Add:* Anchorage Civic Opera Box 3316 Anchorage AK 99510

MOREAU, LORRAINE MARIE
SOPRANO, PATRON

b Springfield, Mass, Oct 18, 27. *Study:* Springfield Consv Music, dipl, 46; Hartford Sch Music, 47-48; Columbia Univ, 49-51. *Roles:* Marguerite in Faust, Nedda in Pagliacci, Butterfly in Madama Butterfly, Mimi & Musetta in La Boheme, Manon in Manon & Susanna in The Marriage of Figaro, Amato Opera Co, New York, 53-55; Musetta in La Boheme, NJ Symph Orch, 61. *Pos:* Sop, Four Star Conct Group, 55-58 & Christopher Lynch Conct Group, 56-57, Whalens Entreprises Inc, New York. *Awards:* Minnie W Scott Scholarship, Music Club of Springfield, Mass, 49. *Mem:* Nat Opera Asn. *Rep:* C Boyd 9459 E Jenon Dr Scottsdale AZ 85260. *Mailing Add:* 248 S 74th Way Mesa AZ 85208

MOREHEAD, DONALD KEITH
PERCUSSION, TEACHER

b Wheeling, WVa, Sept 9, 39. *Study:* WVa Univ, BA(music educ), 65; Cath Univ Am, MM(perc), 68; studied with Stanley Leonard & Fred Begun. *Pos:* Timpanist, Fla Symph, 59-62 & Lake George Opera Co, NY, 65; prin perc & asst timpanist, Indianapolis Symph, 70-80; perc, Indianapolis Symph, 81- *Teaching:* Instr perc, Navy Sch Music, Va, 66, Ind Central Univ, 76- & Ind State Univ, 82. *Mem:* Percussive Arts Soc. *Publ:* Contribr, PASIC '81 Mock Symphony Auditions, Perc Arts Soc, 82. *Mailing Add:* 3534 Sherbarne Lane Indianapolis IN 46222

MOREHEAD, PHILIP DAVID
CONDUCTOR & MUSIC DIRECTOR, TEACHER

b New York, NY, Mar 20, 42. *Study:* Private study with Nadia Boulanger, Paris & Fontainebleau, 62-63 & 64-65; Swarthmore Col, BA(French), 64; New England Consv, MM(piano), 71; Harvard Univ, MA(musicol), 76. *Pos:* Vocal coach & pianist, Boston Symph, Berkshire Music Ctr, 71-78; musical dir, New England Chamber Opera Group, Boston, 72-77, Boston Lyr Opera, 77-78 & Bach-Elgar Choir, Hamilton, Ont, 78-80; coordr, Orch Training Prog, Royal Consv Music, Toronto 80-82; asst cond, Lyr Opera Chicago, 80- *Teaching:* Asst prof, Holy Cross Col, Worcester, 71-73; instr, New England Consv, 74-75. *Mem:* Am Symph Orch League; Cent Opera Serv; Am Fedn Musicians; Am Verdi Soc; Donizetti Soc. *Publ:* Ed, New American Roget's College Thesaurus, rev ed, 78, New American Webster Handy College Dictionary, rev ed, 81 & Hoyle's Rules of Games, rev ed, in prep, New Am Libr. *Mailing Add:* 40 E Oak St Chicago IL 60611

MOREHOUSE, DALE W
CONDUCTOR & MUSIC DIRECTOR, BARITONE

b Orlando, Fla, Mar 2, 56. *Study:* Univ Cent Fla, BA(music educ), 77, BA(vocal perf), 78; Vienna Int Music Ctr, 77-78. *Pos:* Organist & dir music, St John Lutheran Church, Winter Park, Fla, 79-; chorus master & asst cond, Orlando Opera Co, 81-; musical dir, Encore Opera, Orlando, 81- & Fla Stages Repty Co, 82- *Teaching:* Vocal coach, Univ Cent Fla, 78-79; dir choral activ, Lake-Sumter Community Col, 78-80; adj prof voice, Valencia Community Col, 83- *Mem:* Am Guild Organists; Am Choral Dir Asn. *Mailing Add:* 234 E Miller St Orlando FL 32806

MORGAN, BEVERLY
SOPRANO

b Hanover, NH, Mar 17, 52. *Study:* Mt Holyoke Col, 69-71; New England Consv Music, coaching with Rudolf Kolisch & vocal study with Gladys Miller, BM, 73, MM, 75; Berkshire Music Ctr, with Phyllis Curtin, 74 & 75; private study with Phyllis Curtin, 75- *Rec Perf:* In the Beginning (Copland), DGG, 76; Three Songs (Ruth Seeger), New World, 77; Vox Clamans in Deserto (Carl Ruggles), Columbia, 77; Three Songs (Eduard Steuermann), CP2, 80; Six Songs (John McLennon), Margun, 81; Op 27 Songs (Alexander Zemlinsky), Northeastern, 82. *Roles:* Miss Julie in Miss Julie, New York Lyric Opera, 79; Kasturbai in Satyagraha, Netherlands Opera, 80; Siegrune in Walküre, San Francisco Opera, 81; Charlotte in Die Soldaten, Opera Co Boston, 82; Marzelline in Fidelio, Lansing Opera, 82; Micaela in Carmen, Peter Brook Theatre Co, 83; Countess in Marriage of Figaro, Monadnock Music Fest, 83. *Pos:* Soloist, with Boston Pops Orch, 75, Chamber Soc Lincoln Ctr, 76 & Boston Symph Orch, 76 & 77; artist in res, Marlboro Music, 80 & 82; recitalist, community concts throughout US, 82- *Awards:* Grand Prize, Financial Fed Miami Musical Showcase, 76; Concert Artists Guild Award, 77; grant, Martha Baird Rockefeller Fund, 79. *Mem:* Am Guild Musical Artists. *Rep:* Columbia Artist Mgt Inc 165 W 57th St New York NY 10019. *Mailing Add:* 404 Sixth Ave Brooklyn NY 11215

MORGAN, MAC (R)
BARITONE

b Texarkana, Tex, June 25, 17. *Study:* Eastman Sch Music, BM, 40, perf cert, 41, artist dipl, 42. *Rec Perf:* Seven Last Words of Christ, Cook Rec, 50; Threni (Stravinsky), Columbia Rec, 58; Mozart Requiem, RCA Victor, 64. *Roles:* Pantelone in Love for Three Oranges, 51, Silvio in Pagliacci, 51-52 & Sharpless in Madame Butterfly, 51, New York City Opera; Germont in La Traviata, 56-57, Figaro in Marriage of Figaro, 56-57, Guglielmo in Cosi Fan Tutte, 58-60 & Brice in Deseret, 58-60, NBC-Opera. *Teaching:* Instr voice, New England Consv Music, 58-62; prof music, Sch Arts, Boston Univ, 62-82. *Mem:* Nat Asn Teachers Singing (vpres Boston chap, 79-80); Am Acad Teachers Singing. *Mailing Add:* 4519 Lashley Ct Marietta GA 30067

MORGAN, PAULA MARGARET
LIBRARIAN

b Modesto, Calif, Aug 11, 35. *Study:* Mills Col, with Darius Milhaud, BA, 57; Columbia Univ, with Paul Henry Lang, MA, 59; Univ Calif, Berkeley, with Edward Lowinsky, Joseph Kerman, David Boyden, MLS, 64. *Pos:* Music librn, Princeton Univ, 64-; ed, Notes, Quart J Music Libr Asn, 82- *Mem:* Music Libr Asn. *Publ:* Author of articles on Am musicologists, New Grove's Dict Music & Musicians, 80. *Mailing Add:* C Floor Firestone Libr Princeton Univ Princeton NJ 08544

MORGANSTERN, DANIEL ROBERT
CELLO

b Brooklyn, NY, Dec 27, 40. *Study:* Juilliard Sch Music, BS, 63; studied with Leonard Rose, Luigi Silva & Channing Robbins. *Pos:* Prin cello, Am Ballet Theater, 63-, Lyr Opera Chicago, 68-; cellist, Am Chamber Trio, 74- *Teaching:* Instr cello & chamber music, Dartmouth Congregation Arts, 66; Northern Va Music School, 69-70. *Mailing Add:* c/o Am Chamber Concerts 890 West End Ave New York NY 10025

MORGANSTERN, MARVIN
VIOLIN, EDUCATOR
b New York, NY, Jan 6, 30. *Study:* Curtis Inst Music, grad, 54; Juilliard Sch Music, 60. *Pos:* Concertmaster, Curtis Symph Orch, 47-50; violinist chamber music with William Primrose, 47-50; mem, Scherman Little Orch, 50, City Ctr Opera, 56-58, Galimir String Quartet, 59-, Bach Aria Group, 59-62 & Cambia Chamber Players, 75-; participant, Casals Fest, San Juan, PR, 57; founding mem, Symph of Air, 58; organizer, Am String Trio, 65 & Haydn String Quartet, 73; performer, Haydn Quartet, pub TV ser, 74-75, 77 & 78. *Teaching:* Mem fac violin, Curtis Inst Music, 48-50, adj mem fac, 75-82; artist in res, State Univ NY, Albany, formerly; vis prof, State Univ NY, Buffalo, formerly. *Mailing Add:* 168 W 86th St New York NY 10024

MORGENSTERN, GIL
VIOLIN
b Edison, NJ, Apr 18, 54. *Study:* Juilliard Sch, with Ivan Galamian,, BM, 75. *Rec Perf:* Beethoven's First and Third Violin Sonatas, 82. *Pos:* Solo violinist with orch of Baltimore, St Louis, Indianapolis, Denver, Milwaukee, NJ & Santa Barbara; European tour, 80-81 & 81-82; Asian tour, 82; featured perf, New World Fest, Miami, 82. *Awards:* First Prize, Washington Int Compt, Nat Soc Arts & Letters Compt & Music Educr Asn Compt. *Mailing Add:* c/o Columbia Artists Mgt 165 W 57th St New York NY 10019

MORIARTY, JOHN
ADMINISTRATOR, EDUCATOR
b Fall River, Mass, Sept 30, 30. *Study:* New England Consv, BM, 52; Mills Col, with Egon Petri, summers 49, 50 & 52; Brandeis Univ, 54-55. *Rec Perf:* Tamerlano (Handel), 70, 6 rec as cond of Chamber Orch Copenhagen & 3 rec piano accmp, Cambridge Rec. *Pos:* Cond & stage dir, Opera Theater St Louis, Lake George Opera Fest & Oklahoma City Opera, formerly; artistic adminr, Opera Soc Washington, DC, 60-62 & Santa Fe Opera, 62-65; dir, Wolf Trap Co, Vienna, Va, 73-77; mem bd trustees, Boston Conct Opera Orch, 81-; artistic dir, Central City Opera, Colo, 82- *Teaching:* Chmn opera dept, Boston Consv, 73- *Awards:* Distinguished Alumni Award, New England Consv Alumni Asn, 82. *Mem:* Sigma Alpha Iota; Nat Opera Asn; Am Fedn Musicians. *Publ:* Auth, Diction, E C Schirmer, 73. *Mailing Add:* 109 Hemenway St Boston MA 02115

MORINI, ERICA
VIOLIN
b Vienna, Austria, Jan 5, 08; US citizen. *Study:* Master Class, Vienna Consv; private tutors; Hon Dr Music, New England Consv Music, Sigma Alpha Iota, 24, Smith Col, 55. *Rec Perf:* Brahms Concerto, 50 & Tschaikovsky Concerto, 50, London Phil; Bruckner G Minor & Glazunov, Deutsche Gramophone, 70; Beethoven Sonatos, 70, Mozart, 70 & Cesar Franck, 70, Decca. *Pos:* Violinist, currently. *Teaching:* Instr master classes, Manhattan Sch Music, formerly; private tutoring, formerly. *Awards:* Peer of the Greatest Gold Medal, New York, NY, 76. *Bibliog:* Harold C Schonberg (auth), She Plays Tchaikovsky Violin Concerto with Szell & New York Philharmonic, New York Times, 3/23/63; Robert Kimball (auth), Magnificent Morini In Majestic Recital, New York Post, 2/9/76. *Mailing Add:* c/o Harry Beall Mgt 119 W 57th St New York NY 10019

MORRELL, BARBARA JANE
VIOLA, VIOLIN
b Brooklyn, NY. *Study:* New England Consv, BM. *Pos:* Asst prin viola, Fla Symph Orch, 76-, actg prin viola, 79-80, co-prin viola, 80-82; violist, Univ Cent Fla String Quartet, 76- *Teaching:* Private instr viola & violin, 75-; violist & string consult, Orange Co pub sch, Fla, 76-80 & Volusia Co pub sch, Fla, 76- *Mem:* Am Fedn Musicians; Int Conf Symph & Opera Musicians. *Mailing Add:* Fla Symph Orch PO Box 782 Orlando FL 32802

MORRILL, DEXTER G
COMPOSER, EDUCATOR
b North Adams, Mass, June 17, 38. *Study:* Colgate Univ, BM, 60; Stanford Univ, with Leonard Ratner, BA, 62; Cornell Univ, with Robert Palmer, DMA, 70. *Works:* 3 Pieces for Solo Clarinet, 64; Concerto (trumpet & strings), 66; 3 Lyric Pieces (violin & piano), 69; No (chorus & tape), 73; Studies for Trumpet and Computer, 75; Ragtime (piano), 77; Fantasy Quintet (piano & computer), 78. *Teaching:* Res comp, Kans State Teachers Col, 64; fac mem, St John's Univ, NY, 66-68; prof comp, hist & lit, Colgate Univ, 69- *Awards:* Ford Found Fel, 62-64; Nat Endowment for Arts Grant, 77. *Mailing Add:* Music Dept Colgate Univ Hamilton NY 13346

MORRIS, JAMES PEPPLER
BASS-BARITONE
b Baltimore, Md, Jan 10, 47. *Study:* Univ Md, 65-66; Peabody Consv Music, with Rosa Ponselle, 66-68; Acad Vocal Arts, 68-70. *Rec Perf:* Banquo in Macbeth (video); rec on RCA & London/Decca. *Roles:* Crespel in Les Contes d'Hoffmann, Baltimore Civic Opera, 67; Don Basilio in Il Barbiere di Siviglia; Colline in La Boheme; Villain in Les Contes d'Hoffmann, 80-81 & Fiesco in Simon Boccanegra, Philadelphia Opera Co; Mephistopheles in Faust, Toronto Symph; Guglielmo in Cosi fan tutte, Salzburg Fest, 82-83. *Pos:* Opera & conct singer, US, Can, South Am, Europe & Australia, 70- *Mem:* Actors Equity; Am Guild Musical Artists. *Mailing Add:* c/o Colbert Artists Mgt 111 W 57th St New York NY 10019

MORRIS, R WINSTON
TUBA, EDUCATOR
b Barnwell, SC, Jan 19, 41. *Study:* ECarolina Univ, BS; Ind Univ, studied tuba with William J Bell, MM. *Rec Perf:* Four, Tenn Tech Tuba Ens; Concerto for Tuba (Robert Jager), Kosai Ens, 83. *Pos:* Founder, Tenn Tech Tuba Ens, 67; assoc ed, Brass Press & Instrumentalist, currently; tubist, Tech Fac Brass Quintet, currently; mem, Matteson-Phillips Tubajazz Consort, currently; guest soloist, Tokyo Kosai Wind Orch, 83. *Teaching:* Master classes, Japan, 83; prof tuba & euphonium, coordr brass div & dir, Brass Choir & Tuba Ens, Tenn Tech Univ, currently. *Mem:* Nat Asn Col Wind & Perc Instr ; Tubists Universal Brotherhood Asn; Music Educr Nat Conf; Phi Mu Alpha Sinfonia. *Publ:* Auth, articles on tuba performance, Instrumentalist, Brass World, Nat Asn Col Wind & Perc Instr J, Music Now, Getzen Gazette, Tubists Universal Brotherhood Asn, Accent & Brass Bulletin; Tuba Music Guide, 73. *Mailing Add:* Rt 10 Box 223 Cookeville TN 38501

MORRIS, RICHARD
PIANO, EDUCATOR
Study: Ind Univ, BM, MM, perf cert; studied with Adolph Weiser, Walter Robert, Bruno Eisner & Sidney Foster. *Pos:* Soloist, Ind Univ Phil, formerly; recitalist throughout US. *Teaching:* Head fac piano, Univ Mo, Columbia, 60-76; prof & chmn piano, Col Consv Music, Univ Cincinnati, 76-; teacher master classes & wkshps throughout US. *Mem:* Music Teachers Nat Asn. *Mailing Add:* Col Consv Music Univ Cincinnati Cincinnati OH 45221

MORRIS, ROBERT DANIEL
COMPOSER, MUSIC THEORIST
b Cheltonham, England, Oct 19, 43; US citizen. *Study:* Eastman Sch Music, with John La Montaign, BM, 65; Univ Mich, with Ross Lee Finney & Leslie Bassett, MM, 66, DMA, 67. *Works:* Phases (two pianos & electronics), Univ Mich CD Conct, 71; Streams and Willows (flute concerto), Pittsburgh Chamber Symph, 73; Thunders of Spring Over Distant Voices (electronic), Int Soc Contemp Music Paris Fest, 75; Strata (twelve instrm), Yale Summer Sch Norfolk, 74; In Different Voices, Yale Band, 76; Passim (seven instrm), Pittsburgh New Music Ens, 81; Inter Alia (trio), Huntingdon Trio, 82. *Teaching:* Instr, Univ Hawaii, 68-69; from asst prof to assoc prof, dir electronic music studio & chmn comp dept, Yale Univ, 69-76; assoc prof & dir grad studies, Univ Pittsburgh, 76-80; assoc prof, Eastman Sch Music, 80- *Awards:* Comp Asst Grant, Nat Endowment Arts, 78; First Prize, Harvey Gaul, 82; Am Coun Learned Soc Grant, 83. *Bibliog:* Gary C Clarke (auth), Essays in American Music, Greenwood Press, 79. *Mem:* Pittsburgh Alliance Comp (vpres, 79-80); Soc Music Theory. *Interests:* Computer assisted research in pitch-relations in contemporary music. *Publ:* Coauth, A General Theory of Combinatoriality and the Aggregate, Perspectives New Music, 78-79; auth, Set-Groups, Complementation and Mappings ..., J Music Theory, 81; Review of Rahn's Basic Atonal Theory, Spectrum, 82; Combinatoriality without the Aggregate, Perspectives New Music, 82. *Mailing Add:* 63 Belmont St Rochester NY 14620

MORRIS, STEPHEN MACKAY
COMPOSER, LECTURER
b Hartford, Conn, Oct 18, 44. *Study:* Hochschule Musik, WBerlin, with Boris Blacher, 64-65; Harvard Univ, with Luciano Berio, BA, 68. *Works:* Victimae Paschali Laudes, perf by Mid-Am Chorale, 68; Toward Brutus Creator I & V, perf by New York musicians in Comp Forum Ser, 72; Victimae Paschali Laudes II, perf by New York musicians at Cathedral Church of St John the Divine, 73; Oil Change, perf by Hartford Symph Orch, 75; Song IV-b, 76 & Check, 78, perf in Vt. *Mailing Add:* Westbrook CT 06498

MORRISON, FLORENCE
SOPRANO
b Philadelphia, Pa. *Study:* Voice with Raymond Buckingham, 76-82 & Tom Schilling, 77-83. *Roles:* Sister Genvieve in Suor Angelica, Stuyvesant Opera, 79; Despina in Cosi fan tutte, Interstate Opera, 80; Mimi in La Boheme, Repub Artists Opera, 80-82; The First Lady in The Magic Flute, 81 & Frasquita in Carmen, 82, Amato Opera; Gilda in Rigoletto, Interstate Opera, 82; Madama Butterfly in Madama Butterfly, Repub Artists Opera, 82 & 83. *Mailing Add:* c/o Michael Podoli Mgt 484 W 43rd St Apt #15E New York NY 10036

MORRISON, HARRY S
EDUCATOR
b Douds, Iowa, Oct 6, 27. *Teaching:* Dir opera & music theatre & prof music, Univ Idaho, 55-59 & Univ Mo, 60- *Mem:* Nat Asn Teachers Singing; Am Choral Dir Asn. *Mailing Add:* Music Dept Mo Univ Columbia MO 65211

MORRISON, JULIA (MARIA)
COMPOSER, WRITER
b Minneapolis, Minn. *Study:* Univ Iowa, Iowa City, BA, MFA; Univ Minn, Minneapolis, MA; NTex State Univ; res, Yaddo, Saratoga Springs, NY, 65-67. *Works:* Smile Right to the Bone (opera libretto), comn by Dika Newlin, 66; Love's Greeting on Your Day, Robert Miller & Valarie Lamoree, 70; The Man Nextdoor, NTex State Univ Perc Ens, 71; City River (piano, perc, tape & narrator), Dika Newlin, NTex State Univ, 72; Sestina for Orion, Wesdeutschen Rundfunk, Cologne, 73; Traveling After Dark, Perc Ens, Univ SDak, 81; Cold Turkey (lyr only), perf by Dika Newlin, 82. *Rec Perf:* Selected Poems, Harvard Ser Mod Poets on Rec, 67. *Pos:* Res fel, Comput Doc Study, Univ Minn, Minneapolis; res vis, Bell Lab Inc, NJ; copy ed, Consumer Electronics Monthly. *Awards:* Playwriting Award Merit, Samuel French, 65. *Bibliog:* Dika Newlin (auth), Mahler's Opera, Opera News, 3/18/72; David E Wallace (auth), Multimedia Works, Ore Col Educ, 72. *Mem:* ASCAP; hon mem, NY Mahlerites; Poets & Writers Inc. *Interests:* Contemporary Catholic liturgical music; religious significance of Mahler's Tenth Symphony; popular music and lyrics. *Publ:* Auth, Literary Journals in Minnesota, Minn Hist, 61; A Weathervane & Other Poems, Orion, 68; individual poems in various journals. *Rep:* Dika Newlin 1728 Floyd Ave Richmond VA 23220. *Mailing Add:* 41 W 86th St 14-D New York NY 10024

MORRISON, MAMON L
PIANO, TEACHER

b Coffeyville, Kans. *Study:* Univ Kans, Lawrence; Coffeyville Col, AA(piano), 53; Univ Colo, Boulder, BME, 57, BMus(piano), 57; Case Western Reserve Univ, MA(musicol & piano), 58; piano studies, Athens, Greece, 67, Vienna, Austria, 69 & Cath Univ, 70-72; studied piano with Jan Chiapusso, Theodore Lettvin, Howard Waltz, Storm Bull, Emerson Meyers & Bruno Eisner. *Pos:* Pianist with Univ Colo Summer Orch, Hochstein Symph Orch, Va Symph Orch, Va Commonwealth Univ Summer Orch & Va State Univ Orch; concert pianist in Europe & at cols & univ throughout US. *Teaching:* Instr piano, Cleveland Music Sch Settlement, 57-59 & Philadelphia Settlement Music Sch, 60-61; asst prof & chmn piano dept, Fla A&M Univ, 59-60; assoc prof & chmn piano dept, Va State Univ, 61- *Mem:* Phi Mu Alpha Sinfonia. *Mailing Add:* 2510 E Franklin Richmond VA 23223

MORRISON, RAY
BASS, TEACHER

b Asheville, NC, Oct 19, 46. *Study:* Mars Hill Col, AA, BA; Ind Univ, MMus; Univ Cincinnati; Mannes Col Music. *Roles:* Sang Am or world premiere of König Hirsch (Henze), Boulevard Solitude (Henze), The Duel (Al Carmines), The System (Jan Bach) & The Nose (Shostokovitch). *Pos:* Bass singer, Santa Fe Opera, Cincinnati Opera, Washington Opera, Metropolitan Opera Studio, New York City Opera, Artpark Opera, New York Lyr Opera, Opera Verismo, Opera Orch New York & Opera Classics NJ. *Teaching:* Instr voice, Univ Northern Iowa, Heidelberg Col, NY Univ & privately, New York, 68- *Mem:* Am Guild Musical Artists; Nat Asn Teachers Singing. *Mailing Add:* 304 W 14 St #5D New York NY 10014

MORROW, RUTH ELIZABETH
VIOLA, TEACHER

b Nashville, Tenn, May 7, 45. *Study:* Juilliard Sch, BM, 67, MM, 69; Nordwestdeutsche Musikakad, Detmold, Germany, 69-72; Accad Musicale Chigiana, Siena, Italy, dipl(viola), 70, dipl(chamber music), 71. *Rec Perf:* The Mannheimer Schule, Tonstudio H Scherer, Germany, 71 & RBM Musikproduktion, Mannheim, Germany, 73. *Pos:* Recitalist in US & Germany, 59-76; prin violist, Brevard Music Ctr Fest Orch, 58-59, Abiline Phil, 59-63, Juilliard Conct Orch, 68-69, Tibor Varga Kammerorchester, 69-70 & Kurpfalzisches Kammerorchester, 70-73; violist, Chanticleer String Quartet. *Teaching:* Private viola, Abilene, New York, West Caldwell, NJ & Boulder, formerly; instr, West Caldwell pub sch, NJ, 67-69; asst prof viola, violin & chamber music, Univ Colo, Boulder, 73-77, Colo Sch String Perf, 75-80 & Univ Southern Miss, 81-; artist & instr viola, Sewanee Summer Music Ctr, Univ of South, Tenn, 78-82. *Awards:* Young Artists of Nashville Award, 59; Perini Perf Award, Abilene Phil Orch, 63; Elsie & Walter Naumberg Scholarships, 64 & 66. *Bibliog:* Morrison-Reeves Libr & TV staff, You Are Music (film), WFYI-TV, Indianapolis, 8/3/82. *Mem:* Am Viola Soc; Int Viola Soc; Miss Music Teachers Asn; Music Teachers Nat Asn; Music Educr Nat Conf. *Interests:* Viola literature of the 19th century; 18th century performance and publication. *Publ:* Auth, The Romanticist's Viola, Viola Res Soc Newslett, 11/77; Mississippi Music Teachers Association Stringed Instrument Literature Syllabus, Miss Music Teachers Press, 83. *Mailing Add:* 1305 Adeline St Hattiesburg MS 39401

MORYL, RICHARD HENRY
COMPOSER, MUSIC DIRECTOR

b Newark, NJ, Feb, 23, 29. *Study:* Montclair State Col, BA, 57; Columbia Univ, MA, 59; Hochschule Musik, Berlin, 64. *Works:* Salvos, 68 & Soundings 69, Gen Music Publ; Multiples, 70, Serenade, 71 & Illuminations, 73, Music in Our Times Series, Gen Music Publ; Dragons, 72, Das Lied, 75, The Untuning of the Sky, 80 & The Flight of the Phoenix, 82, Gen Music Publ. *Pos:* Music dir, New England Contemp Ens, 70- & Charles Ives Ctr Am Music, 79- *Teaching:* Prof comp, WConn State Univ, 60-, Smith Col, 72-73. *Awards:* Fulbright Fel, Berlin, Germany, 63; Comp Grant, Nat Endowment Arts, 73, 75; Recording Award, Martha Baird Rockefeller Found, 77. *Bibliog:* Charles Whittenberg (auth), Younger Au Composer, Perspectives New Music, fall-winter, 69; Arthur Custer (auth), New England Touring Pro, The Musical Quarterly, 1/75; David Cope (auth), New Directions in Music, 70. *Mem:* Am Comp Alliance; Col Music Soc. *Mailing Add:* Rt 67 Roxbury CT 06783

MOSES, DON V
MUSIC DIRECTOR, EDUCATOR

b Garden City, Kans, Dec 21, 36. *Study:* Ft Hays Kans State Col, BME, 59; Ind Univ, MM, 61, DMA, 68. *Pos:* Music dir, Class Music Seminar, Eisenstadt, Austria, 76- *Teaching:* Music, Hays High Sch, Kans, 59-61; asst prof, Ind Univ, Bloomington, 63-73; prof, Univ Iowa, Iowa City, 73- *Mem:* Am Choral Dir Asn; Music Educr Nat Conf; Am Choral Found. *Interests:* Esterhazy archives in Eisenstadt, Austria; classical music performance practices. *Publ:* Coauth, Choral Conductors Approach to Orchestra Rehearsals, Prentice Hall (in prep). *Mailing Add:* 15 Forest Glen Iowa City IA 52240

MOSHER, ELIZABETH (ELIZABETH MOSHER-KRAUS)
EDUCATOR, SOPRANO

b San Francisco, Calif, Aug 7, 35. *Study:* Pomona Col, 53-55; Univ Southern Calif, BM, 57, MM, 58; Hamburg Hochschule Musik, Ger, 58-60. *Roles:* Eighteen leading roles, Biel-Solothurn Opera, Switzerland, 61-63; Agathe in Freischutz, San Francisco Opera, 65; Marguerite in Faust, Cincinatti Opera, 66; Suzel in L'Amico Fritz, Teatro Nuovo, Italy, 67; Phoebe in Castor et Pollux, Conct Opera Asn, 67; First lady in Magic Flute, Houston Grand Opera, 68; Liu in Turandot, Philadelphia Grand Opera, 68. *Teaching:* Assoc prof voice, Univ Mich, 70-78; assoc prof voice & song lit, Nat Music Camp, 70-82; prof voice & song lit, Univ Ariz, 78-; voice fac, Am Inst Music Studies, Austria, 81 & 83. *Awards:* Fulbright Scholar, 58; grant, Martha Baird Rockefeller Found, 63 & 65; Walter Naumburg Award for Conct Artists, 64. *Mem:* Nat Asn Teachers Singing (local pres, 81-); Music Teachers Nat Asn; Mu Phi Epsilon. *Mailing Add:* 5742 N Camino de las Estrellas Tucson AZ 85718

MOSLEY, ROBERT
BARITONE

b Coulder, Pa, June 22, 35. *Study:* With William Bretz, Giuseppe Danise & Pasquale Rescignio. *Roles:* Valentin in Faust, New York City Opera, 66; Leonce in Bayou Legend, Opera South, Jackson, Miss, 74; Father in Treemonisha; Solo in Carmina Burana; Scarpia in Tosca; Iago in Otello; Amonasro in Aida. *Pos:* Baritone with maj opera co in US. *Teaching:* Private lessons voice & coach repertoire. *Awards:* Marian Anderson Award; Weyerhaeuser Award, Metropolitan Opera Nat Coun Auditions; John Hay Whitney Award. *Mailing Add:* c/o Ira Lieberman Artist Rep 11 Riverside Dr New York NY 10023

MOSS, DAVID MICHAEL
COMPOSER, PERCUSSION

b New York, NY, Jan 21, 49. *Study:* Trinity Col, Conn, studied Indian Mrdangam drumming with T Ranganathan, BA, 70. *Works:* Drumsong, perf by Drumsong Ens, 79; Soundspots, Nat Pub Radio, 80-81; Terrain, 81-82 & New Vocal Music, 82, perf by David Moss; music for Light #18, perf by Kei Takei's Moving Earth Co, 83; music for King Lear, Marlboro Col, 83; New Solo Percussion, Vt Pub Radio, 83. *Rec Perf:* Terrain, 80 & Meltable Snaps It, 82, Cornpride; Cargo Cult Revival, Rift, 82; In the Dream Time, Palace of Lights, 82; Basslines, Elektra-Musician, 82; Archery, Parachute, 82; The Golden Palominos, OAO-Celluloid, 83. *Pos:* First perc, Bill Dixon Ens, Bennington, Vt, 70-73; founder & dir, Collab Ens, 72-75; dir, Perc Now, Marlboro, Vt, 77-; leader, Drumsong Ens, New York, 78- *Awards:* Nat Endowment Arts Grants, 81 & 82; Satellite Program Develop Fund Grant, 82. *Mem:* Comp Forum. *Rep:* Comp Forum 1 Fifth Ave New York NY 10003. *Mailing Add:* Moss Hollow Rd Marlboro VT 05344

MOSS, LAWRENCE KENNETH
COMPOSER, EDUCATOR

b Los Angeles, Calif, Nov 18, 27. *Study:* Pomona Col, Univ Calif, Los Angeles, BA, 49; Eastman Sch Music, MA, 50; Univ Southern Calif, with Kirchner & Dahl, PhD, 57. *Works:* Scenes for Small Orchestra, Fromm Comn, 61; Ariel (sop & orch), comn by New Haven Symph, 67; Paths, comn by Univ Chicago Symph, 70; String Quartet No 2, comn by Chamber Music Soc Baltimore, 74; String Quartet No 3, comn by Kindler Found, 81; Somewhere Inside Me ..., Phyllis Bryn-Julson, Kennedy Ctr, 82; Loves, comn by Nat Endowment Arts Consortium, 82. *Teaching:* Instr, Mills Col, 56-58; from asst to assoc prof, Yale Univ, 59-68; prof comp, Univ Md, College Park, 69- *Awards:* Fulbright Scholar, 53-54; Guggenheim Fels, 59-60 & 68-69; Morse Fel, Yale Univ, 64-65. *Mem:* Contemp Music Forum; Chamber Music Soc Baltimore. *Mailing Add:* 220 Mowbray Rd Silver Spring MD 20904

MOSSAFER-RIND, BERNICE
HARP, COMPOSER

b Seattle, Wash, Jan 19, 25. *Study:* Univ Wash, BA; Univ Calif, Los Angeles; Univ Southern Calif; Cornish Sch. *Works:* Catena de Terle (harp); Rhapsody in F Minor; Serena Sonata (harp); Rishon Le Lion. *Pos:* Soloist, Southern Calif Symph Orch, formerly; first harpist, Seattle Phil Orch, formerly & Seattle Youth Symph, formerly. *Mem:* Cond Club Seattle Symph Orch; Nat Asn Comp; Am Harp Soc; Am Symph Orch League. *Mailing Add:* 7935 Overlake Dr W Bellevue WA 98004

MOSTOVOY, MARC SANDERS
CONDUCTOR & MUSIC DIRECTOR

b Philadelphia, Pa, July 1, 42. *Study:* Temple Univ, BMus, 63; Acad Music, studied with Hans Swarowsky & Marcel Tabuteau, Nice, France, dipl, 63-66; Univ Pa; Combs Col Music, Hon Dr, 80. *Pos:* Music dir & cond, Concerto Soloists Philadelphia, 64-; music adv, Walnut St Theatre, Philadelphia, 70-; cult adv to Gov Pa, 71-77; music dir, Mozart on the Square, Philadelphia, 79- *Awards:* Distinguished Artist Award, Commonwealth Pa, 77. *Mem:* Am Symph Orch League; Musical Fund Soc Philadelphia; Philadelphia Music Soc; Philadelphia Art Alliance. *Mailing Add:* 1732 Spruce St Philadelphia PA 19103

MOTT, JONATHAN
VIOLIN

b Washington, DC, May 31, 47. *Study:* Consv Music, Oberlin Col; Duquesne Univ. *Pos:* Violinist, Nat Symph Orch, 69-73; concertmaster, Richmond Symph & Richmond Sinfonia, 74- *Teaching:* Vis prof violin, Col Consv Music; Cincinnati Univ, 77- *Mailing Add:* 803 W 30th St Richmond VA 23225

MOULDER, EARLINE
COMPOSER, ORGAN

b Buffalo, Mo, Oct 11. *Study:* Drury Col, BMus, 56; Ind Univ, studied organ with Oswald Ragatz, MMus, 63; Univ Mo, Kansas City; studied with Piet Kee & Andre Marchal. *Works:* Psalm 150 (organ), comn & perf by Air Force Acad Summer Conct, 71; Crucifixion (organ), perf by Jon Spong, 73; Prisms (organ), perf at St Patrick's Cathedral, NY, 83. *Pos:* Organist, Linwood Methodist Church, Kansas City, 56-60 & St Paul Methodist Church, Springfield, Mo, 61-81; exec ed, Drury Mirror, 75-77; music ed & journalist, US Navy Reserve, Treasure Island Masthead, 75-77. *Teaching:* Head organ dept, Drury Col, Springfield, Mo, 68- *Mailing Add:* Box 522 Buffalo MO 65622

MOULTON, SUZANNE LEROY
LIBRARIAN, ARTIST MANAGER
b Exeter, NH, Feb 26, 50. *Study:* James Madison Univ, BME, 74; Kent State Univ, with John Drusedow & Bennett Ludden, MLS, 79, with W Richard Shindle, Terry Miller & Halim El-Dabh, MA(musicol), 82. *Pos:* Music librn, Wallace Libr, Fitchburgh, Mass, 82- & perf arts dir, 82- *Teaching:* Fac asst music hist, Kent State Univ, 80-82. *Mem:* Am Musicol Sic; Music Libr Asn; Am Harp Soc (chap vpres, 81); Am Fedn Musicians. *Interests:* Solo harp works of Jan Ladislav Dussek; harp compositions of Carlos Salzedo. *Rep:* Wallace Libr 610 Main St Fitchburg MA 01420. *Mailing Add:* 520 Main St Apt 301 Fitchburg MA 01420

MOUNT, JOHN WALLACE
BASS-BARITONE, EDUCATOR
b Sioux City, Iowa, Nov 20, 46. *Study:* Univ Colo, Boulder, BM, 69, MM, 72. *Roles:* Coline in La Boheme, Santa Fe Opera, 74; Ferando in Il Trovatore, Houston Grand Opera, 74; Zurga in Pearl Fishers, 77, High Priest in Samson & Delilah, 78, Music Master & Harlequin in Ariadne auf Naxos, 78, Maesetto in Don Giovanni, 79 & Geronte in Manon Lescaut, 82, Hawaii Opera Theater. *Teaching:* Instr voice & opera, Univ Mont, 73-75; assoc prof, Univ Hawaii, Honolulu, 75- *Awards:* First Place, Regional Metropolitan Opera, 75, San Francisco Opera, 76 & Nat Opera Asn, 82. *Mem:* Nat Asn Teachers Singing (pres, 79-82, state gov, 82-); Nat Opera Asn (state gov, 75-); Am Guild Musical Artists; Pi Kappa Lambda; Am Asn Univ Prof. *Mailing Add:* 44-164-8 Hako Kaneohe HI 96744

MOUNT, LORNA BODUM STERLING See Sterling, Lorna

MOURANT, WALTER BYRON
COMPOSER
b Chicago, Ill, Aug 29, 10. *Study:* Eastman Sch Music, with Howard Hanson, BM, 35, MM, 36; Juilliard Sch, with Bernard Wagenaar. *Works:* Overture, NBC Symph, 40; Preamble to Constitution, CBS Orch & Chorus, 41; Valley of the Moon, 54, Air & Scherzo (oboe & strings), 54, Sleepy Hollow Suite (strings), 54 & Ecstasy (strings & harp), 55, Asn Music Publ; Aria for Orchestra, perf by Hamburg Symph, 60. *Mem:* Am Comp Alliance; BMI. *Mailing Add:* 11357A Los Osos Valley Rd San Luis Obispo CA 93401

MOYER, JOHN HAROLD
COMPOSER, EDUCATOR
b Newton, Kans, May 6, 27. *Study:* Bethel Col, AB, 49; George Peabody Col, MA, 51; Univ Iowa, PhD, 58. *Works:* Song of Kansas, Topeka Symph, 54; Symphony No 1, Iowa Univ Orch, 58 & Wichita Symph, 63; Psalm 95 (choral), Golden Music Publ, 63; Job (cantata), Newton Civic Chorus & Orch, Kans, 68; Trilogy, Tri-Col Choir, 74 & 76 & Wichita Symph, 74; Chaconne (trombones), Int Trombone Asn, Nashville, 82. *Teaching:* Instr music, Freeman Jr Col, 51-55 & Goshen Col, 57-59; prof, Bethel Col, 59- *Awards:* Comp of Yr, Kans Fedn Music Clubs, 71. *Mem:* ASCAP; Kans Music Teachers Asn (vchmn, 78-79); Wichita Area Piano Teachers League. *Publ:* Coauth, Handbook to the Mennonite Hymnary, Faith & Life Press, 83. *Mailing Add:* Box 146 North Newton KS 67117

MOYER, KARL EBY
LECTURER, ORGAN
b Hershey, Pa, June 13, 37. *Study:* Lebanon Valley Col, BS(music educ), 59; Sch Sacred Music, Union Theol Sem, SMM, 61; Temple Univ, MS(music hist), 74; Eastman Sch Music, DMA(organ & church music), 80. *Pos:* Organist & choirmaster, Messiah Lutheran Church, Williamsport, Pa, 72-74 & Lutheran Church of Good Shepherd, Lancaster, Pa, 75- *Teaching:* Instr organ, Susquehanna Univ, 72-74; prof music, Millersville State Univ, 72- *Mem:* Organ Hist Soc; Am Guild Organ; Hymn Soc Am; Pa Music Educr Asn; Music Educr Nat Conf. *Interests:* Music and musical activities of Dr E Oram Lyte, school song composer. *Publ:* Auth, What Shall We Do with the Wedding March?, J Church Music, 4/65; Christmas Hymns: Are They Christian?, J Church Music, 12/70. *Mailing Add:* 1309 Passey Lane Lancaster PA 17603

MOYERS, EMMETT EDWIN
VIOLIN, EDUCATOR
b Combs, WVa, Dec 4, 20. *Study:* Cincinnati Consv Music, BMus, 46, MMus, 47; Juilliard Sch Music, with Joseph Fuchs, 49; Univ Iowa, 64-65. *Pos:* First violinist, Dayton Phil Orch, 46-47 & Corpus Christi Symph Orch, 49-55; cond, Hays Symph, Kans, 58-64, concertmaster, 66- *Teaching:* Instr music, Cent Col, Mo, 47-49; asst prof music, Tex Col Arts & Indust, 49-55; supvr strings, Kingsville Pub Sch, Tex, 55-58; asst prof strings, Ft Hays State Univ, Kans, 58-65, assoc prof strings, 65- *Mem:* Am String Teachers Asn; Kans Music Educr Asn; Kans Music Teachers Asn; Music Educr Nat Conf; Pi Kappa Lambda. *Mailing Add:* Music Dept Ft Hays State Univ Hays KS 67601

MOYLAN, WILLIAM DAVID
COMPOSER, RECORDING ENGINEER & PRODUCER
b Virginia, Minn, Apr 23, 56. *Study:* Peabody Consv Music, with Jean Eichelberger Ivey, BM, 79; Univ Toronto, with Lothar Klein, MM, 80; Ball State Univ, with Ernesto Pellegrini & Cleve L Scott, DA, 83. *Works:* On Time-On Age (sop, flute, trumpet, piano & tape), 78, Wind Quintet, 80, Brass Quintet (with tape), 80, Concerto for Bass Trombone & Orchestra, 80, Trio (in Twenty Miniatures) for Flute, Horn & Piano, 81, Sonata for Horn, 82 & Solo and Duo for Tuba & Piano, 82, Seesaw Music Corp; 15 other publ works. *Rec Perf:* Trio (in Twenty Miniatures) for Flute, Horn & Piano, Opus One Rec, Inc, 83. *Teaching:* Assoc fac, Aspen Audio Rec Inst Aspen Music Fest,

79 & 80; asst prof, Col Music, Univ Lowell, 83- *Mem:* ASCAP; Am Soc Univ Comp; Nat Asn Comp; Col Music Soc; Minn Comp Forum. *Publ:* Auth, Henry Brant's An American Requiem, Winds Quart, 81; 1778: W A Mozart's Works for Flute and Orchestra, Flute J, 82. *Rep:* Seesaw Music Corp 2067 Broadway New York NY 10023. *Mailing Add:* Col Music Univ Lowell Lowell MA 01854

MRACEK, JAROSLAV JOHN STEPHEN
MUSICOLOGIST, EDUCATOR
b Montreal, Can, June 5, 28. *Study:* Royal Consv Music, studied with A Guerrero, ARCT, 48; Univ Toronto, BM, 51; Ind Univ, Bloomington, studied with Willi Apel, MA, 62, PhD, 65. *Teaching:* Instr, Ind Univ, Bloomington, 60-64; lecturer, Univ Ill, Urbana, 64-65; from asst prof to prof, San Diego State Univ, 65- *Awards:* Scholar, Can Coun, 59-60; Grant, Am Coun Learned Soc, 70; Research Grant, Statens Humanistiska Forskningsrad, Stockholm, 76. *Bibliog:* Miloslav Rechcigl (auth), Educators with Czech Roots, Czechoslovak Soc Arts & Sci, 80. *Mem:* Am Musicol Soc (chair southwest chap, 72-74, mem nat coun, 74-77); Int Musicol Soc; Czechoslovak Soc Arts & Sci (mem nat coun, 76-78); Music Libr Asn; Renaissance Soc. *Interests:* Seventeenth century music; G Animuccia; Czechoslovak music: Rorate chants, Smetana, Janacek, Martinu and Husa. *Publ:* Auth, Seventeenth Century Instrumental Dance Music in Uppsala, Reimers, 76; Sources of Rorate Chants in Bohemia, Hudebni veda XIV/3, 77; contribr, New Grove Dict of Music & Musicians, 80; Encyclopedia of Music in Canada, Univ Toronto Press, 81. *Rep:* 5307 West Falls View Dr San Diego CA 92115. *Mailing Add:* Dept Music San Diego State Univ San Diego CA 92182

MUCZYNSKI, ROBERT
EDUCATOR, COMPOSER
b Chicago, Ill, Mar 19, 29. *Study:* DePaul Univ, BMus, 50, MMus, 52; Acad Music, Nice, France, 61. *Works:* First Piano Concerto, perf by Chicago Symph Orch, 58; Dance Movements, 64 & Symphonic Dialogues, 65, perf by Nat Symph; Third Piano Sonata, Wigmore Hall, London, 77; Cavalcade: Suite for Orchestra, comn by Tucson Symph, 79; Concerto for Alto Saxophone/Orchestra, Theodore Presser Co, 81-82; forty published works. *Rec Perf:* Dance Movements & A Serenade for Summer, 78, Muczynski Plays Muczynski (solo piano), vol one, 82 & vol two, 83, Laurel Rec. *Teaching:* Prof music, comp in res & chmn comp area, Univ Ariz, 65- *Awards:* Fel grant, Ford Found, 59 & 61. *Mem:* ASCAP; Am Fedn Musicians. *Mailing Add:* 344 N Houghton Rd Tucson AZ 85748

MUELLER, ERWIN CARL
PERCUSSION, EDUCATOR
b Ft Wayne, Ind, June 24, 30. *Study:* Teacher's Col, Ball State Univ, BA(music educ), 54; Northwestern Univ, MM, 55; Ball State Univ, DA, 76. *Pos:* Timpanist, Chattanooga Symph & Opera Asn, 55-57; solo timpanist, Indianapolis Symph Orch, 57-65; perc, Indianapolis Perc Ens, 60-65. *Teaching:* Instr perc, Ind Cent Col, 57-69; prof, Ball State Univ, 58- *Mem:* Percussive Arts Soc (Ind chap pres, currently); Music Teachers Nat Asn. *Mailing Add:* Sch Music Ball State Univ Muncie IN 47306

MUELLER, FREDERICK A
BASSOON, COMPOSER
b Berlin, Ger, Mar 3, 21. US citizen. *Study:* Univ Houston, BM(comp), 57; Eastman Sch Music, Univ Rochester, MM(comp), 59; Fla State Univ, DM(comp), 62. *Works:* Piano & Winds Sextet, comn by Music Teachers Nat Asn & Ky Music Teachers Asn, 68; Dance Suite for Sax & Danseuse, Dorn Publ, 73; New Piano Studies for Youths, comn by Am Music Scholar Asn, Cincinnati, 83. *Rec Perf:* Numerous works rec by Soundmark, Ltd., Denver, 67- *Pos:* Professional bassoonist & record player with numerous chamber & symphonic ensembles, 47- *Teaching:* Dir music & assoc prof, Spring Hill Col, Mobile, Ala, 61-67; prof music, Morehead State Univ, 67- *Awards:* Music of Kentucky's Heritage Award, Popular Cult Asn of South, 79; Music Educr Nat Conf Res Award, Ky-Ohio Music Teachers Nat Conf, 80 & 82. *Mem:* Am Musicol Soc; Am Col Music Soc; Ky Music Teachers Asn (comp chmn, 68-); SE Comp League (treas, 65); Am Music Ctr, New York. *Interests:* Athanasius Kircher, S J Polymath; Kentucky's musical cultured heritage, 19th-century. *Mailing Add:* Music Dept Morehead State Univ Morehead KY 40351

MUELLER, HAROLD
CONDUCTOR & MUSIC DIRECTOR, EDUCATOR
b Austin, Tex, Jan 28, 20. *Study:* Sch Music, Univ Mich, Ann Arbor, BMus, 41, MMus, 46; Eastman Sch Music, perf cert(flute), 55, PhD(musicol), 56; L'Ecole Monteux, Hancock, Maine, summers 48-51. *Works:* Rondo for Woodwind Quintet, Ludwig Music Publ (in prep). *Pos:* Flutist, Columbus Phil Orch, 46-48, New Orleans Symph, 48-53, New Orleans Opera Orch, 48-53 & Rochester Phil Civic Orch, 55-56; flutist & bandleader, US Army Air Forces, 41-45; musical dir, Parkersburg Choral Soc, WVa, 77-79; musical dir, Parkersburg WVa Actors' Guild, 81 & 84. *Teaching:* Asst prof music hist, Univ Minn, Minneapolis, 56-57; from assoc prof to prof music hist & flute & adminr, Austin Col, 58-67; prof music, cond & radio commentator, Marietta Col, 67-, chair music dept, 67-75. *Awards:* Merit Award, Nat Fedn Music Clubs, 73 & 75. *Mem:* Am Musicol Soc (chair Tex chap, 63-65); Music Libr Asn; Col Music Soc; Am Asn Univ Prof; Cond Guild Am Symph Orch League. *Interests:* German sacred music; American music. *Publ:* Ed, Ten comp for Hammerschmidt, Concordia Publ House. *Mailing Add:* 518 Fourth St Marietta OH 45750

MUELLER, JOHN STORM
EDUCATOR, ORGAN
b East Liverpool, Ohio, Aug 4, 27. *Study:* Consv Music, Oberlin Col, BMus, 50; Univ Mich, MMus, 52; Boston Univ, DMA, 69. *Teaching:* Asst prof, Flora MacDonald Col, 54-55; prof organ, Salem Col, 55-; instr, NC Sch Arts, 67-; guest instr, Longy Sch Music, summer 65. *Awards:* Fulbright Fel, German Govt, 59-60. *Mem:* Am Guild Organists; NC Music Teachers Asn; Southeastern Hist Keyboard Soc. *Mailing Add:* 1524 Sharon Rd Winston-Salem NC 27103

MUELLER, OTTO WERNER
CONDUCTOR, EDUCATOR
b Bensheim, Germany, July 23, 26. *Study:* Musisches Gymnasium, Frankfurt. *Pos:* Dir, Chamber Music Dept, Radio Stuttgart, 45; founder & cond, Radio Stuttgart Kammerchor; cond, opera, operetta, ballet & symphonic concerts; comp & arr, Can Broadcast Corp, 51; guest cond, major orch in Europe, USSR & North & South Am incl symph orch in Moscow, Leningrad, Riga, Atlanta, Detroit, Montreal, Quebec & Vancouver, 68-73. *Teaching:* Consv de Musique & d'Art Dramatique, Montreal, 58; founder & dean, Victoria Sch Music, BC, 63; prof music, Unv Wis, 67; prof cond, Yale Univ Sch Music, 73- *Awards:* Emmy, US Acad TV Arts & Sci, 65. *Mailing Add:* Yale Sch Music 1303A Yale Sta New Haven CT 06520

MUELLER, ROBERT E
EDUCATOR, WRITER
b Tomah, Wis, July 27, 20. *Study:* Univ Wis, Milwaukee, BS(music educ), 42; Northwestern Univ, MM(theory & comp), 48; Ind Univ, Bloomington, PhD, 54. *Works:* Themes for Orch, Terre Haute Symph, 53; Three Etudes for Piano, Fontainebleau, France, 56; Concerto Movement, Southern Ill Univ Fine Arts Fest, 60; Make Her Wilderness Like Eden (overture & incidental music), Southern Ill Univ Theatre Dept, 67; Music and Poetry (piano & poetry reading), perf by Herbert Marshall, 73; Original Music for Diana, Southern Ill Univ Theatre Dept, 80; Sonata for Piano, 82. *Pos:* Fac recitals, St Louis, 48- *Teaching:* Music dir, Melrose & Jefferson Pub Sch, Wis, 45-48; prof theory & piano, Southern Ill Univ, Carbondale, 48-, chmn sch music, 61-66 & coordr grad studies, 77- *Mem:* Southern Ill Conct (mem bd, 48-82); Am Musicol Asn; Music Teachers Nat Asn; Midwest Music Theory; Soc Music Theory. *Publ:* Auth, Tonality in Berg's Wozzeck, Ill State Teachers Asn J, 58; History of Music Since 1938, Degrees in Music & Music in Higher Education, Thomson Cyclopedia of Music & Musicians, 75; Prokofieff's Third Piano Concerto & Chicago, Ill State Music Teacher's Anthology, 79. *Mailing Add:* 929 W Walnut Carbondale IL 62901

MUENZER, EDGAR C
VIOLIN, EDUCATOR
b Chicago, Ill, Oct 17, 27. *Pos:* Violin, US Air Force Symph, 46-55, Chicago Symph Orch, 56-; Chicago Strings, 60-65, Chicago Symph String Quartet, 65-, Melrose Duo, 78, Chadamin Trio, 80- & Chicago Symph Chamber Players, 82- *Teaching:* Prof violin, Northwestern Univ, 71-, second violin, Eckstein String Quartet, 73-83. *Mailing Add:* Chicago Symph Orch 220 S Michigan Ave Chicago IL 60604

MULFINGER, GEORGE LEONIDAS, JR
EDUCATOR, CELLO
b Syracuse, NY, June 21, 32. *Study:* New Sch Music, 46; Syracuse Univ, AB, 53, MS, 62; studied with Elizabeth Mann, Orlando Cole, Analee Camp Bacon & Alfreds Ozolins. *Rec Perf:* Symphony of Praise, Unusual Rec, 82. *Pos:* Cellist, Krasner Quartet, Syracuse, 61-64; prin cellist, Syracuse Symph, 62-65 & Bob Jones Univ Orch, 65- *Teaching:* Prof cello, cellist, Univ Quartet & prin cellist, Univ Orch, Bob Jones Univ, 65- *Mailing Add:* 25 Springdale Dr Greenville SC 29609

MULFINGER, JOAN WADE
VIOLIN, EDUCATOR
b New Milford, Pa, July 20, 33. *Study:* Eastman Sch Music, with Francis Tursi, BM, 55; Syracuse Univ, with Louis Krasner, 55-65. *Rec Perf:* Symphony of Praise, Unusual Rec, 82. *Pos:* Violist, Krasner String Quartet, 61-62; prin violist, Syracuse Symph, 61-62. *Teaching:* Strings, Rochester pub schs, New York, 54-55; instr strings, vocal & winds, Liverpool cent schs, New York, 55-58; instr, head string dept, 68-75 & violinist, Univ Piano Trio, Bob Jones Univ, 65-, concertmistress, Univ Symph Orch, 68-71 & 83. *Mem:* SC Music Teachers Asn; Am String Teachers Asn. *Mailing Add:* 25 Springdale Dr Greenville SC 29609

MULFORD, RUTH STOMNE
EDUCATOR, VIOLIN
b Chicago, Ill. *Study:* Vassar Col, studied violin with Boris Koutzen, BA, 48; Yale Sch Music, studied violin with Hugo Kortschak, MA, 51; Yale Grad Sch; Oslo Univ; Columbia Univ; City Col New York; State Univ NY, Fredonia; Keane Col; Westminster Choir Col; Univ Del. *Pos:* Lectr & performer throughout Del, NJ & NY, currently. *Teaching:* Lectr music hist & theory, Univ Del, 67-; private instr violin, Del Music Sch & Seaford, Del, currently. *Mem:* Am Musicol Soc; Col Music Soc; Asn String Teachers Am; Suzuki Am. *Interests:* Music for violin in 17th century Italy; music for Hardingfele; music by women composers. *Mailing Add:* 1910 Concord Rd Seaford DE 19973

MULLER, GERALD F
COMPOSER, MUSIC DIRECTOR
b Clifton, NJ, July 25, 32. *Study:* Juilliard Sch Music, with Irwin Freundlich & Vincent Persichetti, 49-52; Niagara Univ, AB, 59; Sch Music, Cath Univ,

with G Thaddeus Jones, MM, 65, DMA, 80. *Works:* Divine Paratrooper (cantata), 72 & Joshua (bicentennial folk opera), 76, Montgomery Col; Chronicles (opera), Montgomery Light Opera Asn, 78; Mary Surratt (opera), Montgomery Col, 81. *Pos:* Music dir, Cathedral of St Matthew, Washington, DC, 80- *Teaching:* Prof & artistic dir music wkshp, Montgomery Col, 65-, chmn, Music Dept, 68-80. *Awards:* Outstanding Educr Am, Outstanding Educr Am Orgn, 72. *Mem:* Music Educr Nat Conf; Am Asn Choral Dir; Am Guild Organists; Music Teachers Nat Asn. *Mailing Add:* Music Dept Montgomery Col Rockville MD 20850

MULLINS, HUGH E
COMPOSER, EDUCATOR
b Danville, Ill, June 25, 22. *Study:* Univ Southern Calif, with Ernest Kanitz, PhD, 50; Berkshire Music Ctr, with Bohuslav Martinu, Nicolai Lopatnikoff & Aaron Copland; Juilliard Sch, with Bernard Wagenaar. *Works:* Recital Music No 3 (oboe & xylophone), 75; Recital Music No 4 (clarinet & marimba), 75; Casanova Junction (concerto for trumpet, wind ens & perc), 77; Small-Room Music No 1 (two trombones), 77; Small-Room Music No 2 (two tubas), 77; Statistics (three pianos), 77; Tlamimilolpa (piano & three perc), 78. *Teaching:* Mem fac, James Millikin Univ, 45-47; prof music, Calif State Univ, Los Angles, 50- *Mailing Add:* 1322 Walnut Ave West Covina CA 91790

MUMFORD, JEFFREY CARLTON
COMPOSER
b Washington, DC, June 22, 55. *Study:* Univ Calif, Irvine, BA, 77, San Diego, MA, 81; private study with Elliott Carter & Lawrence Moss, 78- *Works:* Quartet No 3 (for strings) perf by NY String Quartet, 78; Linear Cycles VII (cambiamen II), Kurt Nikkanen, 79; Barbaglio dal Manca (solo piano), Barbro Dahlman, 81; A Wind of Suspended Prominences (clarinet & piano) comn & perf by William Powell & Zita Carno, 81; Violin Concerto No 1, perf by Am Composers Orch & Colonado Phil Orch, 81; duo concerto (violin cello solo & chamber ens) comn & perf by Fred Sherry, 82-83; notturno (flute, oboe, violin cello & harpsichord) comn & perf by Tafelmusik, 83. *Awards:* Martha Baird Rockefeller Fund for Music Inc Recording Grant, 79; ASCAP Found Grants, 79; Aaron Copland Scholar, Am Soc Composers, Authors & Publishers, 81. *Mem:* Am Soc Composers Authors & Publishers. *Mailing Add:* 2790 Broadway Apt 6A New York NY 10025

MUMMA, GORDON
COMPOSER, ELECTRONIC
b Framingham, Mass, Mar 30, 35. *Works:* Mographs, Berandol Canada Ltd, 66; Mesa, CBS Odyssey, 69; Hornpipe, Mainstream Rec, 70; Cybersonic Cantilevers, Folkways Rec, 75; Dresden Interleaf, 80 & Pointpoint, 83, Lovely Commun Ltd. *Rec Perf:* Casseopiea (Cacioppo), Advance, 65; The Wolfman (Ashley), Source Five, 66; Solo for Voice (Cage), 68 & Improvisation Ajoutee (Kagel), 68, CBS Odyssey; Burdocks (Wolff), Wergo, 72. *Pos:* Comp & performer, Cunningham Dance Co, New York, 66-74 & Sonic Arts Union, 66-75. *Teaching:* Prof 20th century music, electronic music & musical analysis, Univ Calif, Santa Cruz, 75-; Darius Milhaud prof, Mills Col, Oakland, Calif, 81. *Mem:* BMI; Soc Ethnomusicol. *Interests:* Twentieth century arts technology. *Publ:* Auth, Witchcraft, Cybersonics, Folkloric Virtuosity, Darmstater Beitrage, 74; Live Electronic Music, In: Develop & Practice of Electronic Music, Prentice-Hall, 75; From Where the Circus Went, In: Merce Cunningham, Dutton, 75; Roger Reynolds Portrait, C F Peters, 82. *Rep:* Artservices 325 Spring St New York NY 10013. *Mailing Add:* Porter Col Univ Calif Santa Cruz CA 95064

MUNAR, ALFREDO
CONDUCTOR & MUSIC DIRECTOR, ADMINISTRATOR
b Havana, Cuba, Feb 8, 30; US citizen. *Study:* Havana Consv Music, studied with Erich Kleiber. *Works:* Composed several ballets, three symphonies & several piano concerts. *Pos:* Conct pianist, US, Mex & Cent Am, formerly; guest cond, Philadelphia Orch, San Francisco Symph, Fla Phil & Sinfonica, Madrid, formerly; cond, Spanish Ballet, Cuban Ballet & Havana Phil Orch, formerly; assoc cond, Miami Beach Symph, 80, cond, 81-; music dir, Ballet Concerto, currently. *Awards:* Arturo Toscanini Musical Award, John F Kennedy Libr, 72. *Mailing Add:* Miami Beach Symph 420 Lincoln Rd Mall Miami Beach FL 33139

MUND, FREDERICK ALLEN
ADMINISTRATOR, EDUCATOR
b St Louis, Mo, Mar 5, 41. *Study:* Olivet Nazarene Col, Kankakee, Ill, BS, 62; Butler Univ, Indianapolis, MS, 65; George Peabody Col, Nashville. *Pos:* Music specialist, Sch Dist Riverview Gardens, St Louis, 65-68. *Teaching:* Prof music, Trevecca Nazarene Col, Nashville, 68- & dept chmn, 80- *Mem:* Nat Asn Teachers Singing; Music Consortiem Nashville; Tenn Asn Music Exec; Tenn Col Choral Fest (treas, 82-83). *Publ:* Auth, Keep the Music Ringing, Lillenas Publ Co, 79; Nazarene Hymnody, Hymn, 80; What Nazarenes Sang, Preachers Mag, 83. *Mailing Add:* Trevecca Nazarene Col 333 Murfreesboro Rd Nashville TN 37210

MUNDAY, KENNETH EDWARD
BASSOON, EDUCATOR
b Glendale, Calif, Jan 20, 53. *Study:* Calif Inst Arts, fine arts cert, 75; Marlboro Sch Music, 77, 79 & 80. *Rec Perf:* Arnold Schonberg Centennial, 79, Strauss & Honegger, 81, Telemann 300th Birthday Celebration, 81 & Idyll (Janacek-Mladi), 82, Nonesuch; Water Music, Delos, 82. *Pos:* Prin bassoon, Los Angeles Chamber Orch, 76- *Teaching:* Lectr music, Univ Redlands, 76-78, Calif State Univ, San Diego, 80-82 & Univ Calif, Los Angeles, 83- *Mem:* Nat Acad Rec Arts & Sci. *Mailing Add:* Los Angeles Chamber Orch 285 W Green St Pasadena CA 91150

MUNDT, RICHARD
BASS

b Chicago, Ill, Sept 8, 36. *Study:* Columbia Univ, BS; Acad Music, Vienna, with Hitz; studied with Alfredo Gandolfi, New York. *Roles:* Figaro in Le Nozze di Figaro; Don Basilio in Il Barbiere di Siviglia; Ramfis in Aida; Fasolt in Das Rheingold; Don Giovanni in Don Giovanni; Landgraf in Tannhäuser; Rocco in Fidelio. *Pos:* Bass, numerous opera houses in Am, Europe & Can; exec producer, Tappan Zee Playhouse & Tarry Town Music Hall, NY. *Awards:* Fulbright Award; Rockefeller Found Award. *Mem:* Actors Equity Asn; Am Guild Musical Artists. *Mailing Add:* PO Box 280 Nyack NY 10960

MUNFORD, GORDON
CONDUCTOR & MUSIC DIRECTOR, ARRANGER

Study: Studied with Darius Milhaud; Univ Southern Calif, with Halsey Stevens, Ingold Dahl & Mikos Rozsa; NY Univ, with Rudolf Schramm. *Rec Perf:* 1776, Columbia Rec; Little Mary Sunshine, Capitol Rec; I'm Just Wild About Vaudeville, ATCO. *Pos:* Cond & musical dir, Kenley Players, 64-75; Starlight Theatre, Municipal Theatre, Melodyland, Highland Park, Music Circus, Meadowbrook, NJ & Colonie, NY, 75-; dir & arr, Trojan Football Band, Univ Southern Calif; cond & arr for Jane Powell & Gordon MacRae, 79-; guest pops cond for over 40 symph orch incl Pittsburgh, Cleveland, St Louis & Dallas. *Mailing Add:* 8130 W Norton Ave Los Angeles CA 90046

MUNGER, DOROTHY M
PIANO, EDUCATOR

b Fostoria, Ohio, Apr 16, 15. *Study:* BMus(piano), 40; studied piano with Karin Dayas, Harold Triggs, Guy Maier, Rosina & Josef Lhevinne. *Rec Perf:* With Indianapolis Symph Orch. *Pos:* Soloist & pianist, Indianapolis Symph Orch, 38-44, pianist, harpsichordist & celeste player, 60-, prin keyboard chair, currently; conct appearances with orchs & chamber music ensembles; accmp & solo recitalist. *Teaching:* Piano & theory, Arthur Jordan Consv Music, 37-51; mem fac piano, theory & appreciation, Ind Cent Univ, 60-72; mem fac piano, Jordan Col Fine Arts, formerly & Butler Univ, 77- *Awards:* Steinway Artist, 52. *Mailing Add:* 5753 N College Ave Indianapolis IN 46220

MUNGER, SHIRLEY (ANNETTE)
EDUCATOR, COMPOSER

b Everett, Wash. *Study:* Univ Wash, BA(music), 46, MA(music), 51; Consv Nat Musique, Paris, dipl, 53; Univ Southern Calif, DMA(comp), 63. *Works:* Prelude Pastorale (organ), 57 & Four for Six (piano for six hands), 60, Galaxy Music Corp; Sonata for Violin & Piano, 59; Partita for Cello Quartet, Univ Southern Calif Cellists, 62; Concerto Grosso for Trumpet Trio and Wind Ensemble, West Chester Univ, 70; Songs of the American Revolution (chorus & band or piano), 75 & Clementi and Friends (elementary band), 77, Shawnee Press. *Teaching:* From instr to asst prof piano & theory, Univ Calif, Santa Barbara, 54-60; from asst prof to assoc prof, Univ Minn, Duluth, 63-68; prof theory, West Chester Univ Pa, 68- *Awards:* Fulbright Grant to France, 52-53; BMI Fel, 60-62; Helen S Anstead Award Music Comp, Univ Southern Calif, 63. *Mem:* Music Educr Nat Conf; Nat Band Asn; ASCAP. *Publ:* Contribr, Gigue Types in Keyboard Music from John Bull to J S Bach, Triangle, Mu Phi Epsilon, 51; Wagner's American Centennial March, J Band Res, 75; Composing and Arranging for the Marching Band, Marching Band Contemp Music Educ, 76. *Mailing Add:* 519 Sharpless St West Chester PA 19380

MURACO, THOMAS
PIANO, EDUCATOR

b Providence, RI, Dec 11, 49. *Study:* Aspen Music Fest, 69-74; Eastman Sch Music, studied piano, accmp & chamber music with Brooks Smith & Jeaneane Dowis, BM, 72. *Rec Perf:* Time to the Old (William Schuman), CRI, 80; Griffes Songs, Musical Heritage Soc, 83. *Teaching:* Fac mem, Aspen Music Fest, 74-79 & Banff Centre, Alta, summers 81 & 82; head accmp, Cleveland Inst Music, 80- *Mailing Add:* 175 W 72nd St New York NY 10023

MURADIAN, VAZGEN
COMPOSER, VIOLA D'AMORE

b Ashtarak, Armenia, Oct 17, 21; US citizen. *Study:* Spendiarian Prof Music Sch, Yerevan, Armenia, 39; Consv, with Benedetto Marcello, Venice, Italy, prof di musica, 48. *Works:* Concerto, Op 23 (viola d'amore & orch), Comp Hall, 63; Concerto, Op 25 (oboe & orch), 72, Concerto, Op 55 (bassoon & orch), 78 & Symphony, Op 56, 78, Alice Tully Hall; Concerto, Op 57 (oud & orch), Utah Symph, 82; thirty concertos for class instrm, three symphonies, six sonatas for solo violin, six sonatas for violion & piano, two sonatas for piano, four moto perpetuos for violin or piano & orch, 56 songs with orch, eight songs for chorus & orch on works of Shakespeare, Goethe, Dante, Hugo, and others. *Rec Perf:* Ararat (Isahakian), Guizak Rec, 68; Loves Eye (Shakespeare), Golden Age Rec, 79. *Teaching:* Music, Col Armeno, Venice, Italy, 45-50; pvt lessons violin & viola, New York, NY, 50- *Awards:* Tekeyau Prize, Beyrut, Lebanon, 62. *Mem:* ASCAP; Viola D'Amore Soc Am. *Mailing Add:* 269 W 72nd St New York NY 10023

MURAKAMI, SARAH THERESA YOSHIKO
EDUCATOR, PIANO

b Tokyo, Japan, Aug 8; US citizen. *Study:* Tokyo Univ Arts, 62-64; Cleveland Inst Music, BM, 68, MM, 69, AD, 74. *Pos:* Pianist, Murakami Trio, 78-; chmn piano, Sewanee Summer Music Ctr, 80. *Teaching:* Instr piano & theory, Hiram Col, 69-70; instr piano, Cleveland Inst Music, 70- *Mailing Add:* PO Box 479 Gates Mills OH 44040

MURATA, MARGARET KIMIKO
EDUCATOR, WRITER

b Chicago, Ill, July 29, 46. *Study:* Univ Chicago, AB, 67, AM, 71, PhD, 75. *Teaching:* Assoc prof music, Univ Calif, Irvine, 79- *Mem:* Am Musicol Soc; Int Musicol Soc; Soc Ital di Musicol. *Interests:* Baroque music in Rome, especially opera and cantata. *Publ:* Auth, Carnevale a Roma sotto Clemente IX, Rivista Italiana di Musicol, 77; The Recitative Soliloquy, Am Musicol Soc, 79; Further Remarks on Pasqualini, Analecta Musicol, 79; Opera for the Papal Court, 1631-1668, UMI Res, 81. *Mailing Add:* Sch Fine Arts Univ Calif Irvine CA 92717

MURCELL, RAYMOND
BASS-BARITONE

b Malden, Mass. *Study:* Univ Houston, BMus; Juilliard Sch Music, with Sergius Kagen, MMus. *Rec Perf:* Pietra del Paragone (Rossini), Vanguard; Angels' Visits, World Rec. *Roles:* Tassilone (Cavalli), Clarion Concerts, 79. *Pos:* Violinist, Atlanta Symph, formerly; soloist with maj symph orchs incl Cleveland Orch & Cincinnati Symph; soloist, with Robert Shaw Chorale, touring North Am, Europe & USSR, with Clarion Opera New York, four fest in Italy & with New York Chamber Soloists, throughout North & South Am; performer with Clarion Concerts, Musica Aeterna, Musica Sacra, Little Orch Soc, Amor Artis, Continuum & Collegiate Chorale; appeared at Casals Fest, Caramoor Fest, Alaska Music Fest, Mostly Mozart Fest, Lincoln Ctr & Vt Mozart Fest. *Mailing Add:* c/o Wayne Wilbur Mgt PO Box 1378 Grand Cent Sta New York NY 10163

MURDOCK, KATHERINE
VIOLA, EDUCATOR

Study: Boston Univ, BM; Oberlin Col Consv; Yale Univ; studied viola with Joseph Silverstein, Karen Tuttle & William Primrose. *Rec Perf:* On Columbia, Decca & CRI. *Pos:* Mem, Sonos Chamber Ens, formerly; prin violist, Harvard Chamber Orch, currently; asst prin violist, Boston Ballet & Boston Pops Orch, currently; recitals & chamber music, US & Europe. *Teaching:* Artist in res, MacPhail Ctr Arts, Univ Minn, formerly; instr viola & chamber music, Boston Consv, currently. *Mem:* Boston Musica Viva. *Mailing Add:* Boston Consv 8 The Fenway Boston MA 02215

MURRAY, ALEXANDER DOUGLASS
EDUCATOR, FLUTE

b South Shields, England, May 13, 29. *Study:* Royal Col London, with Robert Murchie, ARCM, 46; Paris Consv, with Gaston Crunelle, prem prix, 52. *Rec Perf:* Britten-Nocturne, Decca, 66; Baroque Sonatas on Historical Instruments, 72 & The Murray Flute, 74, Pandora; The World of the Flute, Decca, 75; J S Bach for Solo Traverso, 76 & Paris Conservatory Pieces, 77, Pandora. *Pos:* Solo flute, Royal Air Force No 1 Regional Band, 47-49; prin flute, Royal Opera London, 52-55 & London Symph, 55-66. *Teaching:* Prof flute, Mich State Univ, 67-74, Royal Dutch Consv, 74-77 & Univ Ill, Urbana, 77- *Awards:* Prizewinner, Prague Spring Fest, 59. *Bibliog:* Walfrid Kujala (auth), The Murray Flute, Instrumentalist, 72; Philip Bate (auth), The Alex Murray Flute, Galpin Soc J, 73; J L Voorhees (auth), Flute Systems of 19th or 20th Century, Frits Knuf, 80. *Mem:* Nat Flute Asn (dir, 73-74 & 78-80, prog chmn, 81); Soc Teachers Alexander Technique. *Publ:* Auth, The Murray Flute, Am Musical Instrm Soc, 72; The Murray Flute An Improvement, Music J, 73; John Dewey & F M Alexander, Soc Teachers Alexander Technique, 83. *Mailing Add:* 508 W Washington Urbana IL 61801

MURRAY, BAIN
COMPOSER, EDUCATOR

b Evanston, Ill, Dec 26, 26. *Study:* Oberlin Col, with Herbert Elwell, AB, 51; Harvard Univ, with Randall Thompson & Walter Piston, AM, 52; Univ Liege, studied musicol with Suzanne Clerx; studied with Nadia Boulanger. *Works:* Ballad (orch), 50; Peter Pan (ballet), 52; Safe in Their Alabaster Chambers (English horn & cello), 62; On the Divide (four woodwinds); A Fence (song cycle on e e cummings poems); Innisfree Isle (songs for voice & string quartet); Flame and Shadow (cycle on Teasdale poems for sop), Washington, DC, 78. *Pos:* Music critic, Cleveland Plain Dealer, 57-58 & Sun Newspapers, 59. *Teaching:* Asst, Harvard Univ, 54-55; instr, Consv Music, Oberlin Col, 55-57; assoc head theory dept, Cleveland Music Sch Settlement, 58-69; from instr to prof music, Cleveland State Univ, 66- *Awards:* Distinguished Serv Medal, Union Polish Comp; Kosciuszko Found Award, 78; ASCAP Awards, 78 & 79. *Mem:* ASCAP; Am Soc Univ Comp; Cleveland Comp Guild. *Publ:* Music ed, Our Musical Heritage, 64. *Mailing Add:* 1331 Cleveland Heights Blvd Cleveland Heights OH 44121

MURRAY, GEORGE
TENOR

Study: Peabody Consv Music, with Joan Karvellas & William Yannuzzi, 70-73. *Roles:* Ernesto in Don Pasquale, Hartford Opera Theatre, 80; Parpignol in La Boheme, Baltimore Opera, 83. *Pos:* Mem, Baltimore Opera Chorus, 79-; sr perf mem, Baltimore Music Club, currently; soloist, Grace Methodist Church, currently. *Mailing Add:* Baltimore Opera 40 W Chase St Baltimore MD 21201

MURRAY, ROBERT (J)
ADMINISTRATOR, STAGE DIRECTOR

b Hennessey, Okla, Jan 30, 33. *Study:* Phillips Univ, with Morris Poaster, BME, 54; Eastman Sch Music, with Julius Huehn & Leonard Treash, MM, 58. *Works:* Prayer Responses, perf by various churches, 64. *Roles:* Hortensio in Taming of the Shrew, New York City Opera, Boston Arts Fest, 60; Sharpless in Madame Butterfly, Opera Under the Stars, Rochester, NY, 61; Bomarzo, Nat Symph World Premiere, 65. *Pos:* Artistic dir, Greater Utica

Opera, NY, 64-67 & Opera Under the Stars, Rochester, NY, 67-74; dir, Fla State Opera, Tallahassee, 74-80; gen dir, Shreveport Opera, La, 80-; stage dir, 67 original opera prod; asst dir or prod mgr, 56 prod, 165 opera scenes for three prof opera companies & seven univ. *Teaching:* Opera, Wis State Univ, 60-63, Eastman Sch Music, 63-74 & Fla State Univ, 74-80; fac mem, Chatham Col Opera Workshop, Pittsburgh, Pa, 64-67. *Awards:* Distinguished Alumnus Award, Phillips Univ, 72. *Mem:* Opera Am; Nat Opera Asn (bd mem, 73-80, vpres, 79-80); Southern Opera Conf (secy, 80-). *Publ:* Coauth & ed, Nat Opera Asn Guidelines, Nat Opera Asn, 80. *Mailing Add:* c/o Shreveport Opera 515 Spring St Shreveport LA 71101

MURRAY, ROBERT P
VIOLIN, EDUCATOR
b South Bend, Ind, Oct 24, 36. *Study:* Am Consv Music, BMus, 59, MMus, 60; Ind Univ, Bloomington, DMus, 76. *Rec Perf:* Complete Violin Sonatas (A Rubinstein); Violin Sonatas (C Saint-Saens). *Pos:* Concertmaster & soloist, Chicago Chamber Orch, Amici Della Musica Chamber Orch, Bach Fest Orch, Calif & other orchs. *Teaching:* Artist in res, Univ Santa Clara, formerly; assoc prof music, Univ Northern Colo, 72-76, Baylor Univ, 76-78 & Va Commonwealth Univ, 78- *Awards:* First Prize, Am Consv, 57. *Mem:* Pi Kappa Lambda; Phi Mu Alpha Sinfonia; Am String Teachers Asn. *Mailing Add:* Dept Music Va Commonwealth Univ Richmond VA 23284

MURRAY, STERLING ELLIS
EDUCATOR
b Baltimore, Md, May 19, 44. *Study:* Univ Md, BMus, 67; Univ Mich, MA, 69, PhD, 73. *Teaching:* Prof music hist, West Chester Univ, 72-; guest lectr, Temple Univ, 73 & 75. *Mem:* Am Musicol Soc (Mid-Atlantic chap secy-treas, 75-77, coun rep, 81-); Sonneck Soc; Am Soc Eighteenth Century Studies; Col Music Soc. *Interests:* Eighteenth century instrumental music, both American and European; Bohemian contribution to classical style; symphony; divertimento. *Publ:* Auth, Timothy Swan and Yankee Psalmody, Musical Quart, 75; Performance Practices in Early American Psalmody, Am Choral Rev, 76; Weeping & Mourning: Funeral Dirges in Honor of General George Washington, J Am Musicol Soc, 78; A Checklist of Funeral Dirges in Honor of General Washington, Notes Music Libr Asn, 79. *Mailing Add:* 344 W Union St West Chester PA 19380

MURRAY, THOMAS
ORGAN, EDUCATOR
b Los Angeles, Calif, Oct 6, 43. *Study:* Occidental Col, BA, 65; studied organ with Clarence Mader. *Rec Perf:* Major Works of Mendelssohn, Gade, Durufle, Elgar, Saint Saëns & Cesar Franck on Historic American Organs. *Pos:* Organist & choirmaster, Cathedral Church of St Paul, Boston, Mass; recitalist, Denver, New York, Boston, Atlanta & other maj US cities; Europ tour, 70. *Teaching:* Asst prof organ & choral music, Yale Sch Music, currently. *Awards:* First Place, Am Guild Organists Nat Compt, 66. *Mem:* Am Guild Organists; Harvard Musical Asn. *Mailing Add:* Yale Univ Sch Music Stoeckel Hall 96 Wall St New Haven CT 06520

MUSGRAVE, THEA
COMPOSER, CONDUCTOR
Study: Smith Col, Hon Dr. *Works:* Concerto for Orchestra, 67 & Clarinet Concerto, 68, J & W Chester, London; Space Play, 74, Orfed II (flute & strings), 75, Mary, Queen of Scots (opera), 77, A Christmas Carol (opera), 79 & An Occurrence At Owl Creek Bridge (radio opera), 81, Novello Co, London. *Rec Perf:* Concerto for Horn & Orchestra, Decca Head. *Awards:* Koussevitzky Award, 74; two fels, Guggenheim Found, 74-75 & 82-83. *Rep:* Theodor Presser Inc Bryn Mawr PA 19010. *Mailing Add:* c/o Va Opera Asn 261 W Bute St Norfolk VA 23510

MUSHABAC, REGINA (REGINA MUSHUBAC KLEMPERER)
CELLO, EDUCATOR
b New York, NY, Sept 10, 49. *Study:* Prep Div, Juilliard Sch, with Leonard Rose, 61-67; Ind Univ, BMus, 71, MMus & perf cert, 73; studied cello & chamber music with Janos Starker. *Pos:* Prin cellist, Ind Univ Phil, 71-73, Lexington Phil, 73-75, Ohio Chamber Players, currently & others; soloist with orchs, 73-; mem, Concord Trio, 73-75, Elysian Trio, currently; chamber music recitalist, TV performances, Sao Paulo, Brazil, 73 & others. *Teaching:* Asst to Janos Starker, Ind Univ, 71-73; asst prof, Univ Ky, 73-75; head dept string instrm & assoc prof cello, Baldwin-Wallace Col, 75- *Awards:* Winner, Abraham & Strauss Compt, 67; Schiffer Award, Ind Univ, 73. *Mailing Add:* 19 Fourth Ave Berea OH 44107

MUSSER, BETTY JEAN
CELLO
b Toledo, Ohio, June 29, 56. *Study:* Bowling Green State Univ, with Sachiya Isomura, Itaho Babini, Winifred Mayes & David Saltzman, BM(perf), 78. *Pos:* Substitute cellist, Detroit Symph Orch, 80-; prin cellist, Toledo Symph Orch, Ohio, 80-82 & Mich Chamber Orch, 82-; solo & prin cellist, Mich Opera Theatre, 82- *Mailing Add:* c/o David R Saltzman 28686 Spring Arbor Southfield MI 48076

MUSSER, WILLARD I
EDUCATOR, MUSIC DIRECTOR
b Mohnton, Pa, Feb 2, 13. *Study:* Ithaca Col, BS(music), 33, MS(music), 46; Albright Col; Temple Univ. *Pos:* Lead trumpet, Reading Symph & Ringgold Band, 34-46; band dir, Schenectady, NY Sch District, 46-53. *Teaching:* Prof music, Hartwick Col, 53-56; prof music, State Univ New York, Potsdam, 56-72, emer prof, 75- *Mem:* New York State Music Asn (pres, 66-67); Music Educr Conf Eastern Division (pres, 78-79); Asn Conct Bands (pres, 80-81). *Publ:* General Music (six vol), Belwin/Mills, 54; Revised Arban, Alfred, 73. *Mailing Add:* PO Box 71 Greentown PA 18426

MUSSULMAN, JOSEPH AGEE
EDUCATOR
b East St Louis, Ill, Nov 20, 28. *Study:* Northwestern Univ, BM, 50, MM, 51; Syracuse Univ, PhD(humanities), 66. *Teaching:* Instr voice, St Cloud State Teachers Col, 51-52; asst to dean, Sch Music, Northwestern Univ, 52-54; asst prof music, Ripon Col, 54-57; from asst prof to assoc prof, 57-71, Univ Mont, prof, 71- *Awards:* Danforth Study Grant, 61-62 & 64-65; Nat Endowment Humanities Res Grant, 67-68. *Interests:* Social history of American music; music criticism; music in literature. *Publ:* Auth, A Descriptive System of Musical Prosody, Centennial Rev, summer 65; Mendelssohnism in America, Musical Quart, 7/67; Music in the Cultured Generation: A Social History of Music in America, 1860-1900, Northwestern Univ, 71; The Uses of Music: An Introduction to Music in Contemporary American Life, Prentice-Hall, 74; Dear People ... Robert Shaw, Ind Univ, 79. *Mailing Add:* Dept Music Univ Mont Missoula MT 59812

MUTI, RICCARDO
CONDUCTOR & MUSIC DIRECTOR
b Naples, Italy, July 28, 41. *Study:* Consv Naples, dipl(piano); Consv Milan, dipl(comp & cond). *Rec Perf:* Symphonies No 6 & 7 (Beethoven), Pictures at an Exhibition (Mussorgsky), The Firebird Suite (Ravel), The Rite of Spring (Stravinsky) & others. *Pos:* Prin cond, Orch Maggio Musicale Fiorentino, Florence, 69- & Phil Orch, London, 73-; prin guest cond, Philadelphia Orch, 77-80, music dir, 80-; guest cond operas & orchs in US & Europe. *Awards:* First Prize, Guido Cantelli Int Cont, 67; Andre Messager Prize, 77; Deutsche Schallplatten Prize, 77. *Bibliog:* Donal Henahan (auth), Concert: Philadelphians, With Arrau, Pianist, New York Times, 2/10/83. *Mailing Add:* Philadelphia Orch 1420 Locust St Philadelphia PA 19102

MYERS, KURTZ
LIBRARIAN
b Columbus Grove, Ohio, Feb 16, 13. *Study:* Hillsdale Col, AB, 34; Univ Mich, ABLS, 36, MA, 36; Columbia Univ, 46. *Pos:* Head, Audio Visual Div, Detroit Pub Libr, 46-54, chief, Music & Perf Arts Dept, 54-69; auth, Index to record rev, Notes, J Music Libr Asn, 48-; head, Music Dept, Buffalo & Erie Co Libr, 69-71; head, Arts & Recreation Dept, Denver Pub Libr, 71-76. *Awards:* Citation, Mich Arts Coun, 69; Distinguished Serv Citation, 72 & 33 1/3 Award, 81, Music Libr Asn. *Mem:* Music Libr Asn. *Publ:* Coauth (with Richard S Hill), Record Ratings, Crown, 56; auth, Index to Record Reviews (five vol), 78 & Supplementary Vol, Index Record Reviews (in prep), G K Hall & Co. *Mailing Add:* Belden Stratford Apt 910 2300 Lincoln Park W Chicago IL 60614

MYERS, MARCEAU CHEVALIER
ADMINISTRATOR, EDUCATOR
b Ottawa, Ill, Oct, 9, 29. *Study:* Mansfield State Col, BS, 54; Pa State Univ, MMEd, 57; Ind Univ, Bloomington; Columbia Univ, EdD, 72. *Rec Perf:* Choralis (Richard Moryl), Desto, 70. *Pos:* Mem, Nat Endowment Arts Jazz Awards Panel, 82- & ASCAP Standard Awards Panel, 83- *Teaching:* Asst prof music, Western Conn State Col, 60-65, chmn music dept, 65-70; dean consv music, Capital Univ, Ohio, 70-74; dean sch music, NTex State Univ, 74- *Awards:* Sinfonia Award, Capital Univ, 74; One O'Clock Lab Band Award, NTex State Univ Jazz Lab Bands, 76. *Mem:* Nat Asn Sch Music; Tex Asn Music Sch; Music Teachers Nat Asn. *Publ:* Auth, Improved Conducting Improves Performance, 2/62 & A Study of Earle Brown's December 1952, 8/75, Instrumentalist; Research Degrees in Music: Reflections and New Directions, Pro: 52nd Ann Meeting Nat Asn Sch Music, 11/77; Jazz and the Music Curriculum, Jazz Educr J, 3-4/83. *Mailing Add:* Sch Music NTex State Univ Denton TX 76203

MYERS, PAMELA
SOPRANO
b Baltimore, Md. *Roles:* Countess in The Marriage of Figaro, San Francisco Western Opera, 77; Mefistofele & La Boheme, New York City Opera, 79-80; Liu in Turandot, Baltimore Opera, 80; Lucia in Lucia di Lammermoor, Scottish Opera, 80-81; La Loca, WGermany, 80-81; Luisa Miller in Luisa Miller, Nancy, France, 81; Mimi in La Boheme, Baltimore Opera, 82. *Pos:* Sop with major opera co in US, Can & Europe, currently. *Mailing Add:* c/o Shaw Conct Inc 1995 Broadway New York NY 10023

MYERS, THELDON
COMPOSER, EDUCATOR
b Ill, Feb 4, 27. *Study:* Northern Ill Univ, BS(music educ), 51; Calif State Univ, Fresno, MA(theory & comp), 61; Peabody Consv, Johns Hopkins Univ, DMA(comp), 70; comp study with Arthur Bryon, Nadia Boulanger, Stefan Grove & Sandor Veress. *Works:* I Will Lift Up Mine Eyes, Transcontinental, 78; Compositions for Woodwinds, Golden Crest Rec, 79; Sonata for Clarinet, 81 & Sonatine for Saxophone, 81, Lake State Publ; Cadenza and Lament, Shall-U-Mo Publ, 81; The Joy of Christmas, Lake State Publ, 82; Compositions for Chorus, Golden Crest Rec (in prep). *Teaching:* Instr music, Ill Pub Sch, 51-57 & Calif Pub Sch, 57-63; prof music, Towson State Univ, 63- *Awards:* Grant, Towson State Univ, 79 & 83. *Mem:* ASCAP; Music Educr Nat Conf. *Publ:* Auth, The Reforms of Gluck, Opera News, 73; Henry Cowell, Composer, 75. *Mailing Add:* 1205 Wakeford Circle Baltimore MD 21239

MYOVER, MAX LLOYD
COMPOSER, MUSIC DIRECTOR
b Independence, Kans, July 6, 24. *Study:* Northwestern Univ, BMus, 46, MMus, 48. *Works:* Vocalise, perf by Eastman-Rochester Symph Orch, 48, St Louis Little Symph, 48 & Sioux City Symph, 49; Sinfonietta, perf by St Louis

Little Symph, 51; The Door, perf by Hawthorne Players, Ferguson, Mo, 71; Declaration for Bass, Baritone & Orch, Music Soc, St Louis, 72; USAM & Co, St Louis Community Col, Florissant Valley, 75 & 76. *Teaching:* Assoc prof music, Dakota Wesleyan Univ, 48-52. *Mem:* Nat Asn Comp. *Mailing Add:* 8624 Morningaire Circle Hazelwood MO 63042

N

NACHMAN, MYRNA S
PIANO, EDUCATOR
b New York, NY, June 22, 48. *Study:* Brooklyn Col, BA, 69; Sch Music, Yale Univ, MMA, 72, DMA, 79. *Pos:* Pianist, Yale Players for New Music, Cecilia Trio, Brooklyn Col Contemp Ens, Whitman Ens, Duree & Catskill Chamber Players; solo & chamber perf at Carnegie Recital Hall, Lincoln Ctr, Brooklyn Museum, NY Hist Soc, New Col Summer Fest, Candlelight Concert Series, Windfall Concert Series, Blue Mountain Lake Fest & various univ; field rep, NY State Coun Arts, 81-82. *Teaching:* Adj asst prof, Brooklyn Col, 72-77 & 78-81; vis asst prof, Williams Col, Mass, 77-78; artist-teacher in res, Nassau Community Col, NY, 81- *Mem:* Am Musicol Soc; Col Music Soc; Music Libr Asn; Nassau Music Educr Asn. *Publ:* Auth, record liner notes, Musical Heritage Soc, 81-; Mozart and the Piano Concerto, Musical Heritage Rev, 82; Joan Tower, Florence Price, Marc-Antonio Consoli, Preston Trombly, Lewis Spratlan & Doris Hays, In: New Grove Dict of Music in US (in prep). *Mailing Add:* 298 Garfield Pl Brooklyn NY 11215

NADLER, SHEILA
CONTRALTO
b New York, NY. *Study:* Manhattan Sch Music, 68; Juilliard Sch Music, with Maria Callas, 71-72. *Roles:* Waltraute in Götterdämmerung, Opera Nat, Brussels, 80; Fricka & Waltraute in Der Ring des Nibelungen, Opera de Lyon, 81; Anna in Les Troyens, La Scala, Milano, 82; Witch in Hansel and Gretel, Metropolitan Opera, 83; La Cieca in La Gioconda, 83 & Sosostris in The Midsummer Marriage, 83, San Francisco Opera. *Awards:* Rockefeller Grant, 70 & 73. *Mailing Add:* c/o Int Artists Mgt 111 W 57th St New York NY 10019

NAGEL, LOUIS B
PIANO, EDUCATOR
b Louisville, Ky, Jan 7, 43. *Study:* Juilliard Sch, studied piano with Josef Raieff, piano lit with Joseph Bloch, theory with Hugh Aitken, BS, 64, MS, 66, DMA, 73; studied with Vladmir Ashkenazy. *Pos:* Conct pianist, US & England, currently. *Teaching:* From mem fac to assoc prof piano, Univ Mich, Ann Arbor, 69-; mem fac, Nat Music Camp, Interlochen, Mich, currently. *Awards:* First Prize, Nat Fedn Music Clubs Compt, 67 & Geneva Int Perf Compt, 68. *Bibliog:* Articles & reviews, J Am Liszt Soc, 81- *Mem:* Am Liszt Soc; Nat Music Teachers Asn. *Mailing Add:* 1135 Kim St Ann Arbor MI 48103

NAGEL, ROBERT E, JR
TRUMPET, COMPOSER
b Freeland, Pa, Sept 29, 24. *Study:* Juilliard Sch Music, BS, 48, MS, 50. *Works:* Divertimento for 10 Winds, 51, Concerto for Trumpet and Strings, 51, Suite for Brass & Piano, 59, Trumpet Processional, 61 & Brass Trio No 2, 66, Mentor Music Inc; Sound of Trumpets, Lillenas. *Pos:* First trumpet, Little Orch Soc NY, 47-60; freelance first trumpeter, New York, 47-69; dir & first trumpet, New York Brass Quintet, 54- *Teaching:* Assoc prof trumpet, Sch Music, Yale Univ, 56-; instr, Univ Hartford, 69-80 & New England Consv, 76-; chmn brass dept, Manhattan Sch Music, 80- *Mem:* Co-founder, Int Trumpet Guild. *Mailing Add:* 18 Broadview Dr Brookfield CT 06804

NAGY, ROBERT D
TENOR
b Lorain, Ohio, March 3, 29. *Study:* Cleveland Inst Music. *Roles:* Guiseppe in La Traviata, Metropolitan Opera, 57; Florestan in Fidelio; Don Jose in Carmen; Canio in Pagliacci; Pinkerton in Madama Butterfly; Cavaradossi in Tosca; Alfred in Die Fledermaus. *Pos:* Tenor, Metropolitan Opera, currently; singer with maj opera co in Can & US. *Awards:* Weyerhaeuser Award, Metropolitan Opera Nat Coun Auditions, 56. *Mailing Add:* Metropolitan Opera Lincoln Ctr New York NY 10023

NAISTADT, FLORENCE
VIOLIN
b Syracuse, NY, Mar 31, 25. *Study:* With Conrad Becker & Andre Polah; Syracuse Univ, BM(violin), 48; studied with Louis Krasner. *Pos:* Violinist, Krasner Chamber Ens, 56 & Syracuse Baroque Ens, 56-58; asst concertmaster, Syracuse Symph, 69- *Mailing Add:* Syracuse Symph 411 Montgomery St Syracuse NY 13202

NAJAR, LEO MICHAEL
MUSIC DIRECTOR, VIOLA
b Grand Rapids, Mich, Jan 29, 53. *Study:* Univ Mich, with Francis Bundra, BMus(viola), 76, MMus(viola), 77. *Pos:* Asst prin viola, Toledo Orch, Ohio, 73-74; dir educ, Flint Inst Music, Mich, 78-80; music dir, Saginaw Symph Orch, Mich, 80- *Teaching:* Instr viola & chamber music, Univ Mich, Flint, 74-80; instr orch, Wayne State Univ, 83- *Awards:* Helen M Thompson Award, Am Symph Orch League, 82. *Mem:* Mich Orch Asn (mem bd, 82-); Cond Guild; Am Symph Orch Asn. *Mailing Add:* 4500 Brockway Saginaw MI 48603

NAJERA, EDMUND L
COMPOSER, EDUCATOR
b Ariz, Apr 13, 36. *Study:* Univ Calif, Berkeley, studied comp with Andrew Imbrie, AA; Univ Calif, Los Angeles, studied comp with Lucas Foss; Univ Va, MA. *Works:* Secundum Lucam, Grenadilla; In Dulci Jubilo, Vox & G Schirmer; Ad Flumina Babylonis, G Schirmer; Requiem Pro Amici, comn by Wesleyan Univ Ill; Plaudite, comn by Roger Wagner Chorale; Symphony #2, The Scarlet Letter, comn by Charlottesville Univ & Community Symph Orch; California Landscape, perf by Lake Placid Sinfonietta. *Rec Perf:* Solo Quartets (Brahms), Everest; Mass (Stravinsky), Columbia; Wait, To Mourn, Vox-Box. *Pos:* Soloist & arranger, Roger Wagner Chorale & Gregg Smith Singers, 56-80; cond, Piedmont-Va Community Col, 80-83. *Teaching:* Instr voice & theory, Univ Va, 80-83; prof theory & comp, Silliman Univ, Philippines, 83- *Awards:* Hubbell Award, ASCAP, 80; Meet the Comp Award. *Mem:* ASCAP; Am Fedn TV & Radio Artists; Screen Actors Guild; Am Guild Musical Artists. *Mailing Add:* 20925 Madrona Ave Torrance CA 90503

NALDINI, VASCO
PROMPTER, EDUCATOR
Pos: Prompter, La Scala Theatre, Milan, 51-74, Dallas Opera Co, 58- & frequent appearances with maj opera co in Salzburg, Vienna, Paris & London. *Teaching:* Instr prompting, Acad Int, Ozzima, currently. *Mailing Add:* Dallas Opera Majestic Theatre 1925 Elm Dallas TX 75201

NANNEY, HERBERT (BOSWELL)
EDUCATOR, ORGAN
b Whittier, Calif, Aug 1, 18. *Study:* Whittier Col, AB, 40; studied organ with Alexander Schreiner, 40; organ study with Marcel Dupre, 45; Curtis Inst Music, with Alexander McCurdy, artist dipl, 47; Stanford Univ, MA, 51. *Works:* Sonata in E Minor (Organ), perf by Warren Martin, 41, Dora Potect, 46, William Teague, 50-80, Robert Bennett, 75-82, John Walker, 78-81 & James Welch, 80 & 81; Trio for Oboe, Viola and Piano, perf by George Houle, Inez Lynch & Herbert Nanney, 50. *Rec Perf:* 1959 Summer Choir, Stanford Univ, Audio Assoc, 59; Christmas Music at Stanford, Music Libr Rec, 60; Choral and Organ Music, Stanford Mem Church, Beverly Music Libr Rec, 62; Am Guild Organists Convention Recital, Location Rec Service, 63. *Pos:* Organist, First Methodist Church, Pasadena, Calif, 37-40; organist & choirmaster, Am Cathedral, Paris, France, 45; minister music, Ninth Presby Church, Philadelphia, 46-47. *Teaching:* Instr music appreciation, Episcopal Acad, Overbrook, Pa, 41-42; prof organ, music theory & music lit, Stanford Univ, 47- *Mem:* Am Guild Organists (regional chmn, 75-81); Col Music Soc; Am Musicol Soc; Calif Music Teachers Asn. *Publ:* Auth, Mozart, 78-79 & Oratorio, 79-80, Encycl Americana. *Mailing Add:* 1963 Rock St #26 Mountain View CA 94043

NASH, PAUL
COMPOSER, WRITER
b New York, NY, Feb 19, 48. *Study:* Berklee Col Music, BM(comp), 72; New England Consv Music, grad work; Mills Col, MA(comp), 76; Univ Calif, Berkeley, grad work. *Works:* Movement for Saxophone Quartet, 74, Trio for Flute, Clarinet & Bassoon, 75, Nine for Nine (sop, voice & chamber ens), 76, Thought Before A Crossing, 78, Inner Struck Accord (string quartet), 81 & Sostenuto (sop, saxophone, 2 marimbas, 2 vibes), 82, Am Comp Ed; Interchanges (orch & jazz quartet), Found Music, 83. *Rec Perf:* A Jazz Composers Ensemble, Revelation Rec, 79. Performs own comp on custom made instruments of own design-seven string guitars tuned in an innovative fashion and a guitar in "just intonation" with 16 notes to the octave. *Pos:* Comp in res, San Francisco Sch District, 77-78 & San Francisco Music Wkshp, summer 78. *Teaching:* Instr guitar & arr, Berklee Col Music, 71-72 & ens comp, Lone Mountain Col, 77-79; head music prog theory comp, Urban Sch San Francisco, 79-80; adj instr comp, New Col Calif, 80-82. *Awards:* Fels, Cummington Community Arts, 73, Montalvo Ctr Arts, 80-81, MacDowell Colony, 82 & Briarcombe Found, 83. *Bibliog:* Max Harrison (auth), Paul Nash, Jazz J, London, 1/80; Tom Schnabel (auth), Paul Nash, Downbeat Mag, 6/80; M Camier (auth), Paul Nash, Jazz Mag, Paris, 4/81. *Mem:* Am Music Ctr; BMI; Am Comp Alliance. *Publ:* Auth, For Art's Sake, City Arts, 6/79; contribr, Antiphonal Voices for Flute Duet, Ear Mag, 1/78; auth, A Practical Guide To Polyrhythms, Nasci Publ, 81; contribr, No Longer on a String, City Arts, 9/82; Jazz Gets it's Due, San Francisco Bay Guardian, 11/82. *Mailing Add:* c/o Am Comp Alliance 170 W 74th St New York NY 10023

NATHAN, HANS
EDUCATOR
b Aug 5, 10; US citizen. *Study:* Friedrich Wilhhelms Univ, Berlin, PhD, 34; Harvard Univ, 36-38. *Teaching:* Prof musicol, Mich State Univ, 46-81; mem, Inst Advanced Study, Princeton, 57-58, vis, summer 79; vis prof, Tulane Univ, 66. *Awards:* Guggenheim Fel, 57-58; Fulbright Grant, Univ Rome, Italy, 52-53; Nat Endowment Humanities Grant, 70. *Bibliog:* F L Harrison & M Hood (auth), Musicology, Prentice Hall, 63. *Mem:* Am Musicol Soc. *Interests:* American music of the 18th and early 19th centuries; European 20th century music; Baroque music. *Publ:* Auth, The Sense of History in Musical Interpretation, Mus Rev, 52; Dan Emmett & the Rise of Early Negro Minstrelsy, Univ Okla Press, 62 & 77; William Billings: Data & Documents, Info Coordr, 76; co-ed, The Complete Works of William Billings, Vol II, Am Musicol Soc, 77; auth, On Dallapiccola's Working Methods, Perspectives New Music, 77. *Mailing Add:* 1112 Blue Spring Rd Princeton NJ 08540

NATOCHENNY, LEV N
PIANO, TEACHER
b Moscow, USSR; US citizen. *Study:* Moscow Music Col, BMus, 69; Moscow State Consv & Moscow Musical-Pedagogical Inst, MA, 71, DMA, 75. *Rec Perf:* Recitals, Carnegie Recital Hall, 79 & Merkin Conct Hall, 80; Recitals, Van Cliburn Series, Ft Worth, 81; First Tour of Italy, Bolzano, Merano & Amalfi, 81; Second Tour of Italy, Bolzano, Merano & Amalfi, 82; Recitals in Germany, Munich & Frankfurt, 83; soloist with Baltimore Symphony, 83 & Indianapolis Symph, 83; Indianapolis Symphony, 83. *Pos:* Conct piano soloist with Baltimore Symph & Indianapolis Symph & recitals at Carnegie Recital Hall, Merkin Concert Hall, Van Cliburn Series in Ft Worth, Tex and in Ger & Italy, 79- & Carnegie Hall, 81. *Teaching:* Sr instr, Moscow Musical-Pedagogical Inst, 69-70, asst prof, 70-72, assoc prof, 72-78; fac mem, Hebrew Arts Sch, New York, 80-; substitute prof piano, Sch Music, Ind Univ, Bloomington, 82. *Awards:* Gina Bachauer Mem Found Award, 79; first prize, Young Artists Int Piano Compt, Teachers Cong, 79; gold medal, Busoni Int Piano Compt, 81. *Rep:* Shaw Conct Inc 1995 Broadway New York NY 10023. *Mailing Add:* 33-52 85 St #601 Jackson Heights NY 11372

NAYLOR, TOM LYLE
EDUCATOR
b Wolbach, Nebr, May 10, 38. *Study:* Bob Jones Univ, BS, 61; Appalachian State Teachers Col, MA, 62; Ind Univ, MM, 69, DMus, 74. *Teaching:* Assoc prof, Cedarville Col, 66-67; assoc prof, Middle Tenn State Univ, 67-77, chmn dept music, 77- *Publ:* Auth, The Trumpet and Trombone in Graphic Arts: 1500-1800, Brass Press, 69. *Mailing Add:* 1606 Lakeshore Dr Murfreesboro TN 37130

NEAL, LENORA FORD
PIANO, EDUCATOR
b Ogden, Utah, Jan 6, 47. *Study:* Univ Utah, BM. *Pos:* Soloist, Utah Symph & Ballet West, 75; guest pianist, Snowbird Music Fest, 75; USO tour to Alaska & Far East; guest performer, Muhlfield Trio. *Teaching:* Mem fac piano, Univ Utah, currently; private instr piano. *Awards:* First Place, Utah State Fair Adv Piano Compt. *Mem:* Music Teachers Nat Asn; Mu Phi Epsilon; Nat Fedn Musicians. *Mailing Add:* 362 W 3300 S Bountiful UT 84010

NEE, THOMAS BACUS
CONDUCTOR, EDUCATOR
b Evanston, Ill, Oct 25, 20. *Study:* Univ Minn, BS, 43; Hamline Univ, MA, 47; Austrian State Acad, Univ Vienna, 51-52. *Rec Perf:* Men and Mountains, NH Music Fest Orch, 77. *Pos:* Music dir, NH Music Fest, 60- *Teaching:* Asst prof, Hamline Univ, 46-56 & Macalester, Col; prof, Univ Calif San Diego, La Jolla, 67- *Awards:* Musician of Year, Sigma Alpha Iota, 66; Granite State Award, Univ NH, 80. *Mem:* Am Symph Orch League. *Mailing Add:* 605 Normandy Rd Leucadia CA 92024

NEELY, JAMES BERT
DIRECTOR—OPERA, BARITONE
b Wichita Falls, Tex, Nov 19, 43. *Study:* Univ Tex, Austin, BM, 67, MM, 69; Ind Univ, Bloomington, DMus, 76. *Pos:* Stage dir, Western New York Opera, Buffalo, 80-83, artistic dir, 83- *Teaching:* Assoc prof voice & opera, State Univ NY, Fredonia, 77-81 & Southwest Tex State Univ, 81- *Mem:* Nat Asn Teachers Singing (pres STex chap, 83-); Phi Mu Alpha Sinfonia; Pi Kappa Lambda. *Mailing Add:* Rte 1 Box 18 Village West San Marcos TX 78666

NEGYESY, JANOS
VIOLIN, EDUCATOR
b Budapest, Hungary. *Study:* Franz Liszt Musicakademy, state exam, 61. *Rec Perf:* Violin Sonatas with Cornelius Carden (Charles Ives), 75 & Dedications to Janos Negyesy, 78, Thorofon. *Pos:* Concertmaster, Berlin Radio Orch, WGer, 70-74. *Teaching:* Prof violin, Univ Calif, San Diego, 79- *Publ:* Auth, New Violin-Technique, Music Acad, Basel, 78. *Mailing Add:* 344 Prospect St La Jolla CA 92037

NEILL, DIXIE ROSS
TEACHER-COACH, MUSIC DIRECTOR
b Lincolnton, NC. *Study:* Univ NC, Greensboro, BM(piano); Univ Tex, Austin, MM(music lit & accmp). *Rec Perf:* Carolyn Heafner Sings American Songs, CRI, 82. *Pos:* Rehearsal pianist & coach, Metropolitan Opera Asn, 74-76; musical preparer & guest vocal coach, Can Opera Co, formerly; musical preparer, Opera Co Boston, Chicago Lyr Opera Studio, Houston Grand Opera, Opera Soc Washington, DC & others, formerly; Music Dir, Opera Studio, Nederlandse Operastichting, Netherlands, formerly, music coordr, currently. *Teaching:* Private vocal coaching & teaching, 71- *Mailing Add:* c/o De Nederlandse Operastichting Korte Leideswarsstraat 12 N-1017 RC Amsterdam Netherlands

NEILL, (JOHN) WILLIAM
TENOR
b McAllen, Tex, Mar 17. *Study:* Univ Tex, Austin, BM(voice), MM(voice). *Rec Perf:* Silverlake (Severin), Elektra-Asylum, 80. *Roles:* Herodes in Salome, New York City Opera, 75; Siegmund in Die Walküre, Cincinnati Opera, 78; Lohengrin in Lohengrin, San Francisco Opera, 78; Peter Grimes in Peter Grimes, Can Opera Co, 80; Laca in Jenufa, Baltimore Opera, 81; Lennie in Of Mice and Men, Opera Co Gtr Miami, 82; Erik in Holländer, De Nederlandse Operastichting, 83; also many others. *Awards:* Merola Award, San Francisco Opera Auditions; Regional Winner, Metropolitan Opera Auditions; Martha Baird Rockefeller Found Grant, 68 & 69. *Rep:* Shaw Conct Inc 1995 Broadway New York NY 10023. *Mailing Add:* 780 Riverside Dr 5-F New York NY 10032

NELSON, BRADLEY R
COMPOSER, EDUCATOR
b San Diego, Calif, July 24, 50. *Study:* Univ Redlands, with Wayne Bohrnstedt; San Diego State Univ, with David Ward-Steinman; Eastman Sch Music, with Samuel Adler, Warren Benson & Joseph Schwantner. *Works:* The Lighting of Candles, 73; Music for Winds (with perc), 74; Aurora for Brass (quintet), 74; Three Songs for Tenor, Oboe and Bassoon, 74; Recantation (baritone solo & perc), 75; Starcraft, 76; Brass Music XI (ten brass & timpani), 78. *Teaching:* Mem fac, Jordan Col, Butler Univ, 76- *Awards:* Comp Award, Sigma Alpha Iota, Phi Mu Alpha Sinfonia & Mars Hill Col. *Mailing Add:* 3861 E 56th St Indianapolis IN 46220

NELSON, JOHN WILTON
CONDUCTOR & MUSIC DIRECTOR
b San Jose, Costa Rica, Dec 6, 41. *Study:* Wheaton Col, BMus, 63; Juilliard Sch, MM, 65, postgrad dipl, 67. *Pos:* Music dir, Pro Arte Chorale, Ridgewood, NJ, 65-75 & Greenwich Phil Orch, 66-74; cond, NY Mozart Fest, 67; Juilliard Opera Theatre, 68, New York City Opera, 73-75, Santa Fe Opera, 73, Geneva Grand Theatre, 74 & Metropolitan Opera, 74; cond & music dir, Indianapolis Symph Orch, 77-; music adv, Nashville Symph, 75; guest cond, Chicago Symph, New York Phil, Boston Symph, Philadelphia Orch, Cincinnati Orch, London Royal Phil, Suiss Romade and others. *Teaching:* Mem fac cond, Juilliard Sch, 68-72; dir, Aspen Choral Inst, 68-73. *Awards:* Irving Berlin Cond Award, 67. *Mailing Add:* Indianapolis Symph Orch PO Box 88207 Indianapolis IN 46208

NELSON, JON
EDUCATOR, PIANO
b Okmulgee, Okla, Aug 24, 36. *Study:* Univ Tulsa, BMus, 55, MMus, 56; Hochschule Musik, Munich, Ger, 58-59; private study with Rafael de Silva, New York, 59-60; Univ Wash, Seattle, PhD(musicol), 78. *Rec Perf:* Piano Concerto No 2 (Rachmaninov), Century Rec, 62. *Pos:* Annotator, Enid-Phillips Symph Orch, 73- *Teaching:* Prof musicol, Phillips Univ, Enid, Okla, 60- *Mem:* Col Music Soc; Music Teachers Nat Asn; Music Educr Nat Conf. *Interests:* Era 1875-1935. *Publ:* Auth, America's Music, 76 & Greek Music, 77, Phillips Press. *Mailing Add:* PO Box 2162 Univ Station Enid OK 73702

NELSON, JUDITH
SOPRANO
b Chicago, Ill, Sept 10, 39. *Study:* St Olaf Col, BA, 61. *Rec Perf:* Luigi Rossi Cantatas, 79 & Schubertiade, 79, Harmonia Mundi; Haydn Music for England, 80 & Handel Cantatas, 81, Decca; Fairy Queen (Purcell), Archive, 81; Dido & Aeneas (Purcell), Chandos, 81; Cantata 210 (Bach), Nonesuch, 81; and many others. *Roles:* Drusilla, Brussels, 78; Sant Alessio, Teatro Valle, Rome, 81; Falsirena, Basel, 82; Marzia, Innsbruck, 83. *Rep:* Lee McRae 2130 Carleton St Berkeley CA 84704. *Mailing Add:* 2600 Buena Vista Way Berkeley CA 94708

NELSON, LARRY A
COMPOSER, EDUCATOR
b Broken Brow, Nebr, Jan 27, 44. *Study:* Univ Denver, with Normand Lockwood; Southern Ill Univ, with Will Bottje; Mich State Univ, with H Owen Reed. *Works:* Duo for Cello and Piano (chamber music), 72; Variations for Orch, 73; Music for Clarinet & Tape (electronic), 73; Consequences of ... (performers, tapes, slides & lights), 73; Poem of Soft Music (flute, cello & piano), 76; Music II for Clarinet and Tape (electronic), Philadelphia, 76; Cadenzas and Interludes (clarinet & perc), West Chester, 77. *Pos:* Organizer & dir, New Music Ens, 72. *Teaching:* Mem fac, Mich State Univ, 70-71; assoc prof theory & comp, West Chester State Col, 71- *Awards:* Winner, Philadelphia Orch Soc Cont, 74. *Mailing Add:* Music Dept West Chester State Col West Chester PA 19380

NELSON, LORNA C
OBOE, ORGAN
b Grand Forks, NDak. *Study:* Univ Mont, BMusEd, 63; studied organ with Grethe Krogh & oboe with Jørgen Hammergaard, 79-80. *Pos:* Mem, Bozeman Symph, currently & Gallatin Woodwind Quintet, currently. *Teaching:* Instrm specialist, Great Falls pub sch, Mont, 63-65; private instr oboe, piano & organ, Mont, 65-; adj asst prof, Mont State Univ, 69- *Mem:* Int Double Reed Soc. *Interests:* Music for oboe and organ. *Mailing Add:* 503 N 20th Bozeman MT 59715

NELSON, PAUL
TRUMPET, COMPOSER
b Phoenix, Ariz, Jan 26, 29. *Study:* Phoenix Col; Ariz State Col; Teachers Col, Columbia Univ, BS; Harvard Univ, with Walter Piston & Randall Thompson, MA; Univ Vienna; studied with Paul Creston, Paul Hindemith & Lukas Foss. *Works:* Theme and Passacaglia; 53; Narrative (for orch), 56; Three Songs for Soprano & Eight Horns, 54; Sinfonietta, 60; Songs of Life (chorus & strings), 61; Vox Aeterna Amoris (mz & orch), 78; Aria & Scherzo (string quartet), 82. *Pos:* First trumpeter, Phoenix Symph, 49-50 & Monterey Co Symph, 50-51; staff comp & arr, US Mil Acad Band, West Point, 51-53, cond, Post Chapel Choir, 51-53. *Teaching:* Instr trumpet & music fundamentals, US Army Band Training Unit, Ft Ord, Calif, 50-51; instr comp & theory, Univ Louisville, 55-56; asst prof, Brown Univ, 64-83. *Awards:* Louisville Orch Student Award, 53; Rome Prize, Am Acad Rome, 60-63; Ariz Ann Music Proj Award, 62. *Mailing Add:* Music Dept Brown Univ Providence RI 02912

NELSON, PHILLIP FRANCIS
EDUCATOR, ADMINISTRATOR
b Waseca, Minn, Feb 17, 28. *Study:* Grinnell Col, BA, 50; Consv Nat Paris, 56-57; Univ NC, MA, 56, PhD, 58; Univ Paris, dipl, 57; Yale Univ, Hon MA, 71; Grinnell Col, LHD, 81. *Pos:* Music critic, Phoenix Gazette, 59-62; music consult, Taliesen West, 59-63; dir music, Ascension Lutheran Church, Scottsdale, Ariz, 59-63; chmn, Nat Screening Comt Fulbright Awards Musicol, 66 & 68; gen ed, Symposium, Col Music Soc J, 66-69; trustee, Curtis Inst Music, 80- *Teaching:* Asst prof, Ariz State Univ, 58-62, assoc prof, 62-63; prof & chmn dept music, Harpur Col, State Univ NY, Binghamton, 63-70; prof & dean, Yale Sch Music, 70-80; prof, dean & provost, Porter Col Dir Arts, Univ Calif, Santa Cruz, 80- *Awards:* Fulbright Fel, 56-57. *Mem:* Int Musicol Soc; Col Music Soc; Soc Francaise Musicol; Soc Ethnomusicol; Am Musicol Soc. *Publ:* Contrib ed, College and Adult Reading List, 62; Nicolas Bernier, A Resume of his Work, 60; Nicolas Bernier, Principles of Composition, Paris, 60, transl, New York, 64; contribr, New Grove Dict of Music & Musicians in US. *Mailing Add:* Porter Col Dir Arts Univ Calif Santa Cruz CA 95064

NELSON, ROGER WILLIAM
CONDUCTOR & MUSIC DIRECTOR, EDUCATOR
b Santa Cruz, Calif, Aug 24, 47. *Study:* Studied piano with Adolph Baller, 62-65; Pomona Col, BA 69; State Univ NY, Stony Brook, MMus, 74. *Rec Perf:* Songs for the Dawn of Peace (with Leon Lishner), Pan Rec, 81. *Pos:* Music coordr, Port Cost Players, Oakland, Calif, 74-77; fest dir, Assoc De L'est Varois Montauroux, France, summer 77 & 78. *Teaching:* Instr theory, hist & cond, Cornish Inst, Wash, 79-81; music dept head, 81- *Mailing Add:* 14538 20th Ave NE Seattle WA 98155

NELSON, RON
COMPOSER, CONDUCTOR
Not to be confused with Ronald A Nelson, an arranger-composer. b Joliet, Ill, Dec 14, 29. *Study:* Eastman Sch Music, BM, 52, MM, 53, DMA, 56. *Works:* The Christmas Story, 59, Oratorio: What is Man?, 64, Jubilee, 68, Rocky Point Holiday, 69, Three Nocturnal Pieces, 82, Mass of St La Salle, 82 & Five Pieces for Orch After Paintings by Andrew Wyeth, 83, Boosey & Hawkes. *Teaching:* Prof comp, theory & chmn music dept, Brown Univ, 56- *Awards:* ASCAP Awards, 62-; Howard Found Grant, 66; Nat Endowment Arts Grants, 73, 76 & 79. *Mem:* ASCAP; Music Educr Nat Conf. *Mailing Add:* 27 W Wood Rd Lincoln RI 02865

NELSON, SALLY FOSTER
TRUMPET
b West Chester, Pa, Oct 19, 52. *Study:* Ithaca Col, 70; New Sch Music, BA(perf), 74; Northwestern Univ, MM(perf), 81. *Pos:* Assoc trumpet, Chicago Civic Orch, 74-75; asst first & third trumpet, Ft Wayne Phil, 75-78; mem, Ind Chamber Orch, 75-78; assoc prin trumpet, Ore Symph Orch, 78-; prin trumpet, Peter Britt Music Fest, 82-; extensive freelancing with orchestras with small seasons & chamber orchestras. *Teaching:* Trumpet, Warner Pacific Col, currently. *Awards:* Pa State Award, 71-72; Leonard Bernstein Fel, Berkshire Music Ctr, 75; Am Brass Chamber Music Award, 76. *Mem:* Am Symph Orch League; Int Trumpet Guild; Portland Brass Soc; Int Conf Symph & Opera Musicians; Am Fedn Musicians. *Mailing Add:* 2920 SW 120th Ave Beaverton OR 97005

NELSON, WAYNE
CONDUCTOR, TENOR
b Cokato, Minn, Nov 29, 30. *Study:* Manhattan Sch Music, BMus, 58, MMus, 59; studied with Joseph Di Luigi, Samuel Margolis & Lillian Strongin. *Roles:* Renuccio in Schichi, Fifth Ave Opera, 60; Roderico in Othello, Harlem Opera, 60; Tamino in Magic Flute, Indianola, Iowa, 64. *Pos:* Managing dir & founder, Minot Community Opera Asn, 76-; soloist, Fred Warings Pennsylvanians, 60-61. *Teaching:* Assoc prof voice & opera, Minot State Col, 69- *Mem:* Nat Asn Teachers Singing (state gov, 76-80); Nat Opera Asn; Phi Mu Alpha Sinfonia. *Publ:* Auth, Repertory List for High School Solo Contests, NDak Educ Asn, 70; co-translr (with Gimi Beni), Bartered Bride (opera), Cent Opera Serv, 74. *Mailing Add:* 208 Seventh Ave Minot ND 58701

NELSON, WENDELL A
EDUCATOR, PIANO
b Riverside, Calif, Oct 17, 25. *Study:* Pomona Col, BA, 50; Univ Mich, MMus, 51; Northwestern Univ, DMus, 60. *Teaching:* Prof piano & music lit, Luther Col, 52-55 & Univ Calif, Santa Barbara, 57- *Awards:* Silver Medallion Merit, Associazione Cult Studio Italo-Am, Italy, 79. *Publ:* Auth, The Concerto, William C Brown Co, 69. *Mailing Add:* 3318 Calle Fresno Santa Barbara CA 93105

NELSOVA, ZARA
CELLO
b Winnipeg, Manitoba; US citizen. *Study:* Studied in London; studied with Pablo Casals & Emanuel Feureman. *Pos:* Cellist, tour USSR, 66; recitalist & soloist with maj orch in Europe, Israel, NAm & SAm, formerly; perf with Chicago Symph, Berlin Phil, Houston Symph, Syracuse Symph, Buffalo Phil & Los Angeles Chamber Orch, 81-82. *Teaching:* Artist in res, Col-Consv Music, Univ Cincinnati, 76-; fac mem, Music Acad West, currently. *Awards:* Centennial Medal Confedn & Silver Anniversary Jubilee Medal, Can. *Mailing Add:* Col-Consv Music Univ Cincinnati Cincinnati OH 45221

NERO, BERNARD DAVID
TRUMPET, TEACHER
b McKeesport, Pa, Jan 8, 54. *Study:* WVa Univ, with Roger Sherman, John Hall & Jack McKie, BMus, 74. *Pos:* Second & fourth trumpet, NC Symph, 74-75; prin trumpet, San Antonio Symph, 75-79 & Austin Symph Orch, 80- *Teaching:* Instr trumpet, Trinity Univ, San Antonio, 76-79 & St Mary's Univ, San Antonio, 79-81. *Mem:* Am Fedn Musicians. *Mailing Add:* Austin Symph 1101 Red River Austin TX 78701

NERO, BEVERLY
EDUCATOR, PIANO
b Pittsburgh, Pa, Oct 13, 52. *Study:* Duquesne Univ, BM & MM, 75; Kneisel Hall, Blue Hill, Maine, with Louis Pollak, 76; Int Music Inst, Spain, with Artur Balsam, 77. *Rec Perf:* Beethoven Sonatas for Cello & Piano, Modal Music, 82. *Pos:* Keyboard player, Pittsburgh New Music Ens, currently. *Teaching:* Instr, Glassboro Summer Music, NJ, 72-76; Duquesne Univ, 75- & Carnegie-Mellon Univ, 78-81. *Mem:* Pittsburgh Musical Soc; Pittsburgh Music Teachers Nat Asn; Music Teachers Nat Asn; Piano Guild. *Mailing Add:* 829 S Braddock Pittsburgh PA 15221

NERO, PETER (BERNARD)
PIANO, CONDUCTOR & MUSIC DIRECTOR
b New York, NY, May 22, 34. *Study:* Brooklyn Col, BA(music), 56; private study with Abram Chasins & Constance Keene, 51-57. *Works:* Sunday in New York (movie score), Hastings Music, 64; Fantasy & Improvisations, 65, His World, 70 & Suite in 4 Movements, 73, Bermar Publ Co. *Rec Perf:* Pianoforte, 61, Nero Piano in Town, 61, Nero Goes Pops, 63 & Reflections, 64, RCA Rec; Summer of '42, Columbia Rec, 72; Peter Nero Now, Concord Rec, 77; Peter Goes Pop, Applause Rec, 82. *Pos:* Music dir & cond, Philly Pops Orch, 79-; pops music dir & pops cond, Tulsa Phil, 83- *Awards:* Grammys, Nat Acad Rec Arts & Sci, 61 & 62; Best Pop Pianist, Contemp Keyboard Mag, 80. *Bibliog:* John Wilson (auth), Article, New York Times, 9/82. *Mem:* Am Symph Orch League, Cond Guild. *Mailing Add:* c/o Roy Gerber 9200 Sunset Blvd Los Angeles CA 90069

NETTL, BRUNO
EDUCATOR
b Prague, Czechoslovakia, Mar 14, 30. US citizen. *Study:* Ind Univ, AB, 50, PhD, 53; Univ Mich, MALS, 60. *Teaching:* From instr to asst prof, Wayne State Univ, 53-64; prof music & anthropology, Univ Ill, 64-, chmn, Div Musicol, 67- *Awards:* Fulbright Award, 56-58 & 68-69; Nat Endowment Humanities Fel, 81-82. *Mem:* Soc Ethnomusicol (pres, 69-71); Int Folk Music Coun; Am Musicol Soc (mem bd, 80-82). *Interests:* Ethnomusicology; American Indian music; music of Middle East and India. *Publ:* Auth, Music in Primitive Culture, Harvard Univ Press, 56; Theory and Method in Ethnomusicology, Free Press, 64; Folk and Traditional Music of the Western Continents, Prentice-Hall, 65; Folk Music in the US, Wayne State Univ Press, 3rd ed, 76; The Study of Ethnomusicology, Univ Ill Press, 83. *Mailing Add:* 1423 Cambridge Champaign IL 61821

NEUBERT, BERNARD DAVID
DOUBLE BASS, EDUCATOR
b Ft Benning, Ga, Aug 19, 53. *Study:* San Jose State Univ, BA, 74; Eastman Sch Music, MMus, 75; Univ Tex, Austin, DMus, 82. *Works:* Moby Bass, 81, Concert for Double Bass, 81, Peacock Feathers, 81 & Sound Design, 81, Silver Crest Rec. *Pos:* Prin bass, Springfield Symph, 75-78 & Wichita Symph, 78- *Teaching:* Asst prof, Univ Mass, Amherst, 75-78 & Wichita State Univ, 78- *Awards:* Fel, Nat Endowment Humanities, 80. *Mem:* Int Soc Bassists; Am String Teacher's Asn. *Publ:* Auth, Four Basic Concepts in Teaching String Instruments, 79 & Marking String Parts, 80, Kans Music Educ Asn; Electronic Bowed String Works: Some Obervations on Trends and Developments in the Instrumental/Electronic Medium, Perspectives of New Music, 83. *Rep:* Wichita Symph Orch 225 W Douglas Wichita KS 67202. *Mailing Add:* 5102 Crestview Wichita KS 67208

NEUBERT, HENRY GRIM, JR
EDUCATOR, DOUBLE BASS
b Philadelphia, Pa, Mar 5, 43. *Study:* Northwestern Univ, BME, 65, MM, 66. *Teaching:* Instr music, UFSD #4, Northport NY, 66-72; assoc prof studio double bass, Sch Music, Ithaca Col, 72- & cond symph band, 76- *Mem:* Int Soc Bassists; NY State Sch Music Asn. *Mailing Add:* 15 Stone Haven Dr Ithaca NY 14850

NEUHAUS, MAX
COMPOSER
b Beaumont, Tex, Aug 9, 39. *Study:* Manhattan Sch Music, BM, MM. *Works:* Numerous comp which include permanent & temp sound installations, sound objects & sound events utilizing radio & telephone networks, transportation syst, hydro-acoustics & architectural structures; Water Whistle I-XVII (17 hydraulic works), perf in 13 NAm cities, 71-75; Underwater Music I-IV (4 hydroelectronic works), perf in Bremen, Ger, New York, West Berlin & Amsterdam, 76-78. *Rec Perf:* Electronics and Percussion: Five Realizations by Max Heuhaus, Columbia Masterworks. *Pos:* Tours NAm & Europe, Contemp Chamber Ens, as perc soloist with Karlheinz Stockhausen & as solo recitalist, formerly; artist in res, Univ Chicago, Bell Telephone Lab & Walker Art Ctr Minneapolis; res fel, DAAD Kunstler Prog, Berlin. *Awards:* Fel, Nat Endowment Arts, 73; grants & awards, Nat Endowment Arts, Martha Baird Rockefeller Fund Music, Creative Artists Pub Serv Prog, Meet the Comp & NY State Coun Arts. *Bibliog:* Articles & reviews in publ incl Chicago Tribune, Nat Observer, Village Voice, Musical Am, New Yorker & New York Times. *Mailing Add:* 210 Fifth Ave New York NY 10010

NEULS-BATES, CAROL
MUSICOLOGIST, CRITIC-WRITER
b New York, NY, Dec 1, 39. *Study:* Wellesley Col, BA(music & hist), 61; Yale Univ, PhD(musicol), 70; NY Univ, 79; Am Symph Orch League Mgt Sem, 82. *Pos:* Managing ed, RILM Abstracts of Music Lit, Grad Ctr, City Univ New York, 71-75; asst to cur, Toscanini Mem Archives, New York Pub Libr, 75-76; asst ed, Col Music Symposium, 75-78; dir & prin investr, Women Am Music Proj, Grad Ctr, City Univ New York, 76-79; account exec, John O'Donnell Co, 82- *Teaching:* Lectr music, Univ Conn, 67-68; instr, Yale Univ, 68-70; asst prof, Hunter Col, City Univ New York, 73-75 & Brooklyn Col, City Univ New York, 78-82. *Awards:* Fel, Radcliffe Inst, 68-70; Nat Endowment Humanities Res Grant & Ford Found Res Grant, 76-79. *Mem:* Am Musicol Soc; Col Music Soc; Sonneck Soc; Nat Women's Studies Asn; Music Libr Asn. *Interests:* Nineteenth century; opera; American music; women's studies. *Publ:* Co-ed (with Adrienne Fried Block), Women in American Music: A Bibliography of Music and Literature, Greenwood Press, 79; ed, Women in Music: An Anthology of Sources Readings from the Middle Ages to the Present, Harper & Row, 82; auth, Designing a College Curriculum for the Study of Women in Music, In: Musical Woman: An International Perspective I (in prep); numerous articles, In: New Grove Dict of Music in US (in prep); Elizabeth Sprague Coolidge: 20th-century Benefactoress of Chamber Music, In: The Musical Woman: An International Perspective II (in prep). *Mailing Add:* 145 E 16th St New York NY 10003

NEUMAN, DANIEL MOSES
EDUCATOR
b Lausanne, Switz, Jan 18, 44; US citizen. *Study:* Univ Ill, PhD, 74. *Teaching:* Asst prof, Dartmouth Col, Hanover, NH, 71-80; assoc prof, Music Sch, Univ Wash, 80- *Mem:* Soc for Ethnomusicol; Soc for Asian Music. *Interests:* Social organization of musicians and cultural context of performance in India. *Publ:* Auth, Towards an Ethnomusicology of Culture Change in Asia, Asian Music, 76; The Social Organization of Hindustani Music, Ethnomusicol, 77; contrib, Gharanas: The Rise of Musical Houses in Delhi and Neighboring Cities, Univ Ill Press, 78; auth, The Life of Music in North India, Wayne State Univ Press, 80; Country Musicians and Their City Cousins: The Kinship of Folk and Classical Music Culture in N India, Barenreiter-Verlag Kassel, Philadelphia, 82. *Mailing Add:* Sch Music Univ Wash Seattle WA 98195

NEUMANN, FREDERICK C
WRITER, VIOLIN
b Bilsko, Poland, Dec 15, 07; US citizen. *Study:* Univ Berlin, PhD, 34; Columbia Univ, PhD, 52. *Teaching:* Prof music, Univ Richmond, 55-78; vis prof, Princeton Univ, 70-71, Yale Univ, 76-77 & Ind Univ, 78-79. *Awards:* Fels, Guggenheim Mem Found, 67 & 75 & Nat Endowment Humanities, 77. *Mem:* Am Musicol Soc; Int Musicol Soc; Soc Francaise Musicol; Neue Bach Gesellschaft; Am String Teachers Asn. *Interests:* Historical performance. *Publ:* Auth, Baroque and Post Baroque Ornamentation, Princeton Univ, 78; Essays in Performance Practice, UMI Res Press, 82; Ornamentation and Improvisation in Mozart, Princeton Univ (in prep). *Mailing Add:* 4102 W Franklin St Richmond VA 23221

NEUMANN, PHILIP WARREN
EDUCATOR, COMPOSER
b Salem, Ore, Sept 11, 54. *Study:* Univ Ore, studied comp with Homer Keller, 73; study Renaissance perf with George Houle, 74; Southern Ore State Col, BS(music), 77. *Works:* Soliloquy for Tuba, comn by Michael Knox, 76; Fantasy on Holly & Ivy, Terrace Publ, 76; Theme and Variations, 81 & Quintet in F, 82, perf by Metropolitan Brass Co; Variations on a Chinese Folksong, comn by Portland Horn Club, 82. *Pos:* Renaissance musician, Ore Shakespearean Fest, 73-77; dir, De Organographia, 77-; bass trombone, Salem Symph, 78-82 & Peter Britt Fest Orch, 81-83; instrm maker, early woodwinds, currently. *Teaching:* Adj prof recorder, Linfield Col, 79-; instr early music, Portland Community Col, 80-; instr Renaissance reeds, Seattle Wkshp, 83. *Awards:* First Prize Comp, San Francisco Recorder Soc Compt, 82. *Bibliog:* Charlotte Graydon (auth), Early Music Enthralls Young Couple, Oregonian, 79; Ron Cowan (auth) Renaissance Music Enjoys a Revival, Ore Statesman, 79; Tarna Lange, Early Woodwinds, Northwest Illustrated, KOIN-TV, Portland, 80. *Mem:* Early Music Guild Ore; Soc Ore Comp. *Interests:* Design and construction of Medieval and Renaissance reed instruments. *Publ:* Ed, Crumhornn Consort Music, Musica Sacra et Profana, Vol 4, 83. *Mailing Add:* 417 W 13th St McMinnville OR 97128

NEUMANN, RICHARD JACOB
COMPOSER, CONDUCTOR
b Vienna, Austria, June 21, 15; US citizen. *Study:* Prague Ger Consv Music, MA(comp), 37; Vienna Acad Music, MA(music educ), 37; Columbia Univ, 46-47. *Works:* Liturgical Music in Great Volume, Transcontinental Music Publ, 58-; Timpani & Piano Concerto, comn by Univ Ind, 78; 20 Ladino Songs, Transcontinental Music Publ, 79-; Nico Castel Book of Ladino Songs, 80 & Double Concerto for Oboe, Clarinet & String, 82, Tara Publ; Sephardic Service, Transcontinental (in prep). *Rec Perf:* Nileh Service, 60, Songs of the Bal Shem, 62 & Ladino folk Songs, 63, Collectors Guild; Sefarad, 79 & Centennial of Jewish Music, 79, Tambour Rec. *Pos:* Music dir, Hawthorne Sch, NY, 37-38; organist & choir leader, Temple Israel, New Rochelle, 38-39; choir leader, Yiddish Choral Soc New England, 39-42; music coordr, US Army, Vienna, 44-45; music dir, Educ Alliance, 46-50; dir music educ, Bd Jewish Educ, 72- *Teaching:* Music dir Jewish music, Salanter Yeshiva, Schechter Sch & Yeshiva Univ High Sch 52-73; asst prof Jewish chorus, Queens Col, City Univ New York, 72-80. *Awards:* Solomon Schechter Award, United Synagogue Am, 65 & 67; KAVOD Award, Cantors Assembly Am, 82; Meet the Composer Award, 82. *Mem:* Jewish Music Coun JWB

(vpres, 68-); Am Asn Jewish Music. *Interests:* Jewish liturgical especially sephardic music; school music. *Publ:* Coauth, Israel in Song, Bd Jewish Educ Press & Tara Publ, 73; auth, Music Guide for Jewish Teachers, Bd Jewish Music Educ Press, 75; coauth, Great Songs of Israel, Bd Jewish Educ Press, 76; auth, The Roots of Biblical Chant, 82 & Israel Sings, 83, Bd Jewish Educ Press. *Rep:* Bd Jewish Educ Greater NY 426 W 58th St New York NY 10019. *Mailing Add:* 3931 47th St New York NY 11104

NEVINS, DAVID HOWARD
ADMINISTRATOR
b New York, NY, Oct 13, 54. *Study:* Towson State Univ, BS, 75; Johns Hopkins Univ, MS, 77; Univ Md. *Pos:* Dir mkt & pub relations, Baltimore Symph Orch, 82- *Mem:* Am Symph Orch League. *Mailing Add:* Joseph Meyerhoff Symph Hall 1212 Cathedral St Baltimore MD 21201

NEVISON, HOWARD S
BARITONE, TEACHER
b Philadelphia, Pa, Feb 13, 41. *Study:* Settlement Music Sch, with Tilly Barmach, Pa; Curtis Inst Music, with Eufemia Gregory; studied with Martial Singher, Nicola Moscona & Giulio Gari. *Roles:* Germont in La Traviata, Israel Nat Opera, Tel-Aviv, 69; Dott Malatesta in Don Pasquale; Carlo Gerard in Andrea Chenier; Tonio in Pagliacci; Rabbi David in Amica Fritz; Lescaut in Manon; Guglielmo & Don Alfonso in Cosi fan tutte. *Pos:* Cantor & musical dir, Congregation Emanu-El, New York, 78-; singer with major opera co in Israel & US. *Teaching:* Private voice, currently. *Awards:* First Prize, Welsch Fest Eisteddfod Compt, UK. *Mailing Add:* 1 Sherman Sq New York NY 10023

NEWALL, ROBERT H
CRITIC
b Philadelphia, Pa. *Study:* Philadelphia Consv Music, 39-49; Univ Pa, BA, 45, MA, 48, 59-64. *Pos:* Critic, Bangor Daily News, 65- *Mailing Add:* c/o Magazine Bangor Daily News 491 Main St Bangor ME 04401

NEWELL, DOUGLAS MYERS
EDUCATOR, CONDUCTOR
b Charlotte, NC, Apr 27, 51. *Study:* NC Sch Arts, BMus, 74; New England Consv Music, MMus, 78; cond studies with Laszlo Halasz, Jean Morel & Richard Pittman. *Pos:* Music dir, Boston Summer Opera Theatre, 78-79; asst cond, Knoxville Symph Orch, 80-82; guest cond, Baylor Univ Symph & Opera Theater, 83; music dir, Enid-Phillips Symph Orch, 83. *Teaching:* Instr music hist, Walters State Community Col, 80-82; guest lectr orch, Sch Music, Baylor Univ, 83; asst prof cond, Phillips Univ, currently. *Awards:* Theodore Presser Achievement Award, 70. *Mem:* Am Symph Orch League. *Mailing Add:* 5710 Will Rogers Dr Enid OK 73701

NEWELL, ROBERT MAX
COMPOSER, EDUCATOR
b Blandersville, Ill, May 18, 40. *Study:* Ill Wesleyan Univ, BMus, 61; Paris Consv, with Olivier Messiaen, 65-66; Univ Ill, with Salvatore Martirano & Kenneth Gaburo, MM, DMA, 70; Berkshire Music Ctr, with Lukas Foss. *Works:* Edifice in Memoriam, 69; Ryonen (chorus, flute & tape), 71; Spirals (ms, ten & perc), 72; New London Street Cries (chorus & instrm). *Pos:* Touring musician, Inelectable Modality & Univ Ill Chamber Players, 72-75. *Teaching:* Comp, Univ Ill, Urbana-Champaign, 66-75 & Calif State Univ, Long Beach, 75-79; vis fac curric consult, Maharishi Int Univ, 73-74; assoc prof music, Chapman Col, currently. *Awards:* Fulbright Grant, 65; First Prize, Denver Symph Compt, 69 & Mars Hill Col Compt, 75. *Mem:* Am Soc Univ Comp; Col Music Soc; Am Comp Alliance. *Mailing Add:* Music Dept Chapman Col Orange CA 92666

NEWELL, THOMAS E, JR
FRENCH HORN, EDUCATOR
Study: Cincinnati Consv, BM, MM; studied with Gustave Albrecht & French horn with Mason Jones; Berkshire Music Ctr. *Rec Perf:* Solo rec, German Radio, Cologne. *Pos:* French horn, Boston Symph Orch & New England Wind Quintet, 63-72; mem, St Louis Symph, US Air Force Band, Washington Chamber Players, Houston Woodwind Quintet, Santa Fe Opera Orch & Cincinnati Fine Arts Quintet, formerly. *Teaching:* Mem fac, Cincinnati Consv, Sam Houston State Teachers Col, Tex Southern Univ & Concord Acad, formerly; mem fac French horn & chamber music, New England Consv Music, currently & Boston Consv, currently. *Mailing Add:* Boston Consv 8 The Fenway Boston MA 02215

NEWLAND, LARRY
CONDUCTOR & MUSIC DIRECTOR
b Winfield, Kans, Jan 24, 35. *Study:* Music Consv, Oberlin Col, BM, 55; Manhattan Sch Music, MM, 57; studied cond with Pierre Monteux & Jonel Perlea. *Pos:* Violist, New York Phil, 60-73, asst cond, 74-; music dir, Diabolus Musicus, New York, 74- & Harrisburg Symph, Pa, 78- *Teaching:* Instr orch cond, Cond Guild Inst, summer 83. *Awards:* Harold Bauer Mem, Manhattan Sch Music, 57; Koussevitzky Cond Prize, 63 & Bernstein Cond Fel, 64, Berkshire Music Ctr. *Rep:* Am Artists Mgt Inc 300 West End Ave New York NY 10023. *Mailing Add:* New York Phil Broadway & 65th New York NY 10023

NEWLIN, DIKA
COMPOSER, CRITIC-WRITER
b Portland, Ore, Nov 22, 23. *Study:* Mich State Univ, BA, 39; Univ Calif, Los Angeles, MA, 41; Columbia Univ, PhD, 45. *Works:* Cradle Song, perf by Cincinnati Symph Orch, 35; Chamber Symph (12 solo instrm), perf by

Darmstadt Fest Orch, WGer, 49; Piano Trio, perf by Chamber Ens Wiener Symph, Salzburg, 52; Fantasy on a Row, perf by comp, 58; Study in 12 Tones (viola d'amore & piano), perf by Karl Stumpf & comp, 59; Five Nativity Songs, perf by Gail Farrell & others, 81; Rock Songs, perf by comp, 82. *Rec Perf:* Piece In Seven Movements (Artur Schnabel), SPA Rec, 40's; Sonata for Viola and Piano (Honegger), 52 & Quatre Visages (viola & piano; Milhaud), Deutsche Grammophon Gesellschaft. *Pos:* Res vis acoustic researcher, Bell Lab, Murray Hill, NJ, 73-76; music critic, Richmond Times Dispatch, 80-; *Teaching:* Prof & chmn, Dept Music, Drew Univ, 52-65; prof, NTex State Univ, 65-73; prof, Va Commonwealth Univ, 78- *Awards:* Fulbright Award, 51-52; Mahler Medal Hon, Bruckner Soc Am, 57; fel, Yaddo Found, 60-66. *Bibliog:* Konrad Wolff (auth), Dika Newlin, Am Comp Alliance Bulletin, 12/62; Christine Ammer (auth), American Composers in European Idioms, Unsung, Greenwood Press, 80; Robert Craft (auth), Schoenberg and Dika, New York Rev, 12/80. *Mem:* BMI; Am Comp Alliance (mem bd gov, 41-); Am Musicol Soc (pres Southwest chap, 71-73). *Interests:* Current trends in American popular song. *Publ:* Auth, Bruckner Mahler Schoenberg, Kings Crown Press, 47, W W Norton, 2nd ed, 78; ed, Schoenberg and His School, 49 & Style and Idea, 50, Philosophical Libr; auth, The Mahler's Brother Syndrome, Musical Quart, 4/80; Schoenberg Remembered, Pendragon Press, 80. *Rep:* Am Comp Alliance 170 W 74th St New York NY 10023. *Mailing Add:* Dept Music Va Commonwealth Univ 922 Park Ave Richmond VA 23284

NEWMAN, ANTHONY
COMPOSER, EDUCATOR
b Los Angeles, Calif, May 12, 41. *Study:* Mannes Col Music, BS(organ); Harvard Univ, MA(comp); Boston Univ, DMA(organ); studied with Leonard Stein, Leon Kirchner & Luciano Berio. *Works:* Violin Sonata; Cello Sonata; Variations and Grand Contrapunctus (guitar); Piano Cycle No 1; Chimaeras I and II (harpsichord); Habitat (organ); Barricades (organ). *Pos:* Conct performer, US & Europe, 69- *Teaching:* Mem fac, Juilliard Sch, 67-78, State Univ NY Col, Purchase, 71- & Ind Univ, 78-82. *Mailing Add:* Dept Music State Univ NY Col Purchase NY 10577

NEWMAN, GRANT H
EDUCATOR
b Grand Forks, NDak. *Study:* Univ SDak, BFA, 54; Univ Ill, MS(music educ), 59, EdD(music educ), 66. *Teaching:* Asst prof, Eastern Ill Univ, 67-69; assoc prof, Univ Maine, Portland, 69-70; prof music, Southern Ill Univ, Edwardsville, 70-81 & Univ Maine, Orono, 81- *Mem:* Music Educr Nat Conf; Midwest Kodaly Music Educr Asn; Am Orgn Kodaly Educr; Col Music Soc. *Publ:* Doublethink and Music Education, Music Educr Nat Conf, 71; Teaching Children Music, William C Brown Co, 79 & 84. *Mailing Add:* 212 Lord Hall Univ Maine Orono ME 04473

NEWMAN, MICHAEL ALLAN
GUITAR
b New York, NY, Dec 21, 57. *Study:* Aspen Music Fest, with Oscar Ghiglia, 75-77; Accad Musicale Chigiana, Siena, Italy, with Ghiglia, dipl merito, 77; Mannes Col Music, with Albert Valdes Blain, BMus, 79. *Rec Perf:* Michael Newman: Classical Guitarist, 78 & Italian Pleasures, 81, Sheffield Lab. *Pos:* Soloist, Seattle Symph, Atlanta Symph, Honolulu Symph & Rochester Chamber Orch. *Teaching:* Inst guitar, Mannes Col Music, 79-; master classes, col & univ throughout US. *Awards:* Young Artists Award, Conct Masters Inc, 73; Prizewinner, Toronto Int Guitar Compt, 78. *Rep:* Sheldon Soffer Mgt Inc 130 W 56th St New York NY 10019. *Mailing Add:* RD #3 Box 210 Lebanon NJ 08833

NEWMAN, WILLIAM STEIN
MUSICOLOGIST, WRITER
b Cleveland, Ohio, Apr 6, 12. *Study:* Cleveland Inst Music, BS, 33; Western Reserve Univ, with Arthur Shepherd, Herbert Elwell, Carl Riemenschneider & Arthur Loesser, BS, 33, AM, 35, PhD, 39; Columbia Univ, with Eric Hertzmann & Paul H Lang, 40. *Pos:* Piano soloist with numerous orchestras & chamber music groups throughout US; contrib ed, Piano Quart. *Teaching:* Asst choral instr, Western Reserve Univ, 34-36; teacher, Cleveland Pub Sch, 35-40 & 41-42; instr, Cleveland Music Sch Settlement, 37-38; lectr, Bennington Col, Columbia Univ, Juilliard Sch, State Univ NY, Binghamton, Northwestern Univ & others, formerly; from asst prof to prof music, Univ NC, Chapel Hill, 46-62, alumni distinguished prof, 62-77, prof emer, 77- *Awards:* Am Coun Learned Soc Grant, 60-62; Nat Endowment Humanities Sr Fel, 72-73, 75 & 77-78; Nat Humanities Ctr Grant, 83-84. *Mem:* Music Teachers Nat Asn; hon mem, Am Musicol Soc (nat pres, 69-70); Int Musicol Soc; Music Educr Nat Conf; Col Music Soc. *Interests:* The instrumental sonata; problems of performance practices in the instrumental music of Bach, Mozart and Beethoven. *Publ:* Auth, A History of the Sonata Idea—The Sonata in the Baroque Era, The Sonata in the Classic Era & The Sonata Since Beethoven, Univ NC Press & W W Norton & Co; The Pianist's Problems, Harper & Row, 50, 2nd ed, 56, 3rd ed, 74, Da Capo Press, 4th ed, 83; Understanding Music, Harper & Row, 53, 2nd ed, 61; Performance Practices in Beethoven's Sonatas, W W Norton & Co, 71; over 200 articles & reviews in professional music publications. *Mailing Add:* 808 Old Mill Rd Chapel Hill NC 27514

NEWTON, CLIFFORD HAMMOND
TRUMPET
b Orlando, Fla, Oct 28, 49. *Study:* Univ SFla, BA, 71; Univ Northern Colo, MM, 76. *Pos:* Prin trumpet, Jacksonville Symph Orch, Fla, 78- *Mailing Add:* 4527 Hercules Ave Jacksonville FL 32205

NEWTON, NORMA
TEACHER-COACH, EDUCATOR
b Dolgeville, NY, May 20, 36. *Study:* Syracuse Univ, BM, 58; Paris Opera, 60; Univ Tex, MM, 62. *Roles:* Donna Elvira in Don Giovanni, 64 & 66 & Countess in The Marriage of Figaro, 64 & 66, New York City Opera; Countess in The Marriage of Figaro, Grant Park Chicago, 65; Euridice in Euridice, Hamburg, WGer, 69; Marie in Wozzeck, Wuppethal, WGer, 71; Butterfly in Madame Butterfly, Welsh Nat Opera, 73; Pamina in The Magic Flute, Graz, Austria, 73. *Teaching:* Vocal instr, Houston Opera Studio, 80-; lectr voice, Univ Tex, Austin, 80-81; artist-teacher, Rice Univ, Houston, 82- & private studio, New York, 83- *Awards:* Fulbright Scholar, 60; Martha Baird Rockefeller Award, 65 & 72; Nat Opera Inst Award, 75. *Mem:* Nat Asn Teachers Singing; Cent Opera Serv. *Mailing Add:* 7619 Streamside Dr Houston TX 77088

NIBLOCK, JAMES F
COMPOSER, EDUCATOR
b Scappoose, Ore, Nov 1, 17. *Study:* Wash State Univ, BA, 42; Colo Col, MA, 48; Univ Iowa, PhD, 52. *Works:* Soliloquy and Dance (band), Summy-Birchard Co, 57; Triptych for Brass and Percussion, Fema Music Publ, 60; Trigon for String Orchestra, Boosey & Hawkes Inc, 63; Twenty-six published works. *Teaching:* Prof theory, comp & music lit, Mich State Univ, 48- *Awards:* MacDowell Colony Fel, 60; Nat Endowment Arts, 78; All Univ Res Grant, Mich State Univ, 82. *Mem:* Pi Kappa Lambda; Phi Mu Alpha. *Interests:* Pre-Cortesizn musical instruments in Mexico. *Publ:* Coauth, Music for the High School Chorus, Allyn & Bacon Inc, 70. *Mailing Add:* 215 Elizabeth St East Lansing MI 48823

NIBLOCK, PHILL
ADMINISTRATOR, COMPOSER
b Anderson, Ind, Oct 3, 33. *Works:* Nothin' to Look At, Just a Record, India Navigation Rec, 82; Celli Plays Niblock, Real Art Ways Rec, 83; Newnewband Work, comn & perf by Newband, 83; Fall and Winterbloom (bass flute), perf by Eberhard Blum; Ear Piece (bassoon), perf by Arthur Stidfole; Summing I-III & IV (cello), perf by David Gibson; A Trombone Piece, perf by James Fulkerson. *Pos:* Dir, Music & Intermedia Prog, Experimental Intermedia Found, 69- *Teaching:* Prof, Col Staten Island, 73- *Awards:* Fels, Guggenheim Found, 80 & Nat Endowment Arts, 81; grants, New York State Coun Arts & Creative Artists Pub Serv Prog; Music & Films Installations Award, NY State Coun Arts, 82. *Bibliog:* Composers View, EMAS Newsletter, 7/81; Keith Potter (auth), Exploring a Minimal Exteme, Classical Music, London, 7/82; Robert Palmer (auth), Modern Twists on the Ancient Drone, New York Times, 8/8/82. *Publ:* Auth, articles in New York Times, Village Voice, Soho News, Arts & Cinema, Sight Lines & Ear Mag. *Mailing Add:* Experimental Intermedia Found 224 Centre St New York NY 10013

NICE, CARTER
MUSIC DIRECTOR & CONDUCTOR, VIOLIN
b Jacksonville, Fla, Apr 5, 40. *Study:* Eastman Sch Music, BMus, 62; Manhattan Sch Music, MMus, 64. *Rec Perf:* With New Orleans Symph. *Pos:* Asst cond & concertmaster, Fla Symph, 65-66 & New Orleans Phil, 67-79; music dir, Ind Fest Music Soc, 71 & Ballet Hysell, New Orleans, 74-79; music dir & cond, Sacramento Symph, 79-; guest cond, Tulsa Phil, Jacksonville Symph Orch & Okla Symph, formerly. *Teaching:* Chmn string dept & asst prof violin, Univ Okla, 66-67; dir, New Orleans Symph String Training Prog, 68-73; instr violin & cond, Univ Orch, Loyola Univ, 70-74. *Rep:* Maxim Gershunoff 502 Park Ave New York NY 10022. *Mailing Add:* Sacramento Symph Suite 11 451 Parkfair Dr Sacramento CA 95825

NICHOLAS, LOUIS THURSTON
EDUCATOR, CRITIC
b Trimble, Tenn, Oct 2, 10. *Study:* Southwestern Memphis, AB, 34; Univ Mich, MM, 39; Teachers Col, Columbia Univ, dipl, 52. *Pos:* Music dir & tenor, Temple, Congregation Ohavai Shalom, 46-77, West End Methodist Church, 46-57 & Vine St Christian Church, 58-69; music ed & critic, Nashville Tennessean, 51-75; recitalist & oratorio soloist. *Teaching:* Instr voice & diction, NTex State Teachers Col, 41-44; prof voice & vocal lit, George Peabody Col Teachers, 44-80; assoc diction, Belmont Col, 79-82. *Mem:* Nat Asn Teachers Singing (pres, 62-63); Am Acad Teachers Singing; Phi Mu Alpha Sinfonia; Music Teachers Nat Asn; fel, Am Inst Vocal Pedagogy. *Publ:* Contribr, Choral Dir Guide, Parker Publ Co, 67; auth, Thor Johnson—American Conductor, Peninsula Arts Asn, 82. *Mailing Add:* 207 Craighead Ave Nashville TN 37205

NICHOLS, CLINTON COLGATE
TENOR, EDUCATOR
b Pittsburgh, Pa, Jan 24, 35. *Study:* Okla Baptist Univ, BMusEd, 57; New Orleans Baptist Theol Sem, MSM, 59; Fla State Univ, DMus, 71. *Roles:* Canio in Pagliacci, Knoxville Opera, 64 & New York City Opera Co, 68-69; Ricardo in Masked Ball, Birmingham Opera Asn, 66; Oedipus Rex in Oedipus Rex, New York City Opera Co, 68; Messiah & Carmina Burana, New Orleans Phil Orch, 73 & 76-79; Rudolfo in La Boheme, Fla State Opera Asn, 77-78. *Pos:* Tenor soloist, Riverside Church, New York, 66-68; leading tenor, New York City Opera Co, 67-69. *Teaching:* Assoc prof church music & voice, New Orleans Baptist Theol Sem, currently. *Mem:* Nat Asn Teachers Singing; Am Choral Dir Asn; Southern Baptist Church Music Conf. *Mailing Add:* Music Dept New Orleans Baptist Theol Sem New Orleans LA 70126

NICHOLS, DAVID CLIFFORD
EDUCATOR, CLARINET

b Eau Claire, Wis, May 9, 40. *Study:* Univ Wis, River Falls, BS, 62; Ind Univ, MMus, 65, PhD(musicol), 73. *Pos:* Ed, Mo Sch Music Mag, 68-70. *Teaching:* Prof music, NE Mo State Univ, 66- *Mem:* Music Educr Nat Conf; Mo Music Educr Asn; Am Musicol Soc. *Interests:* Latin American music; colonial periods; Missouri music. *Publ:* Auth, A Mexican Tribute to Haydn, 82 & The Influence of Haydn Upon Music of Mexico (in press), Haydn Yearbook; Classicism and the Mexican Aesthetic, Latin Am Music Rev (in press). *Mailing Add:* 1401 E Highland Kirksville MO 63501

NICHOLSON, DAVID
MUSIC DIRECTOR, WRITER

b Regina, Sask, Can, Nov 28, 19; US citizen. *Study:* Studied pipe organ with Oscar Baker; Toronto Royal Consv Music; Sem Christ King, BC, BA, 45; studied plainsong with Dom Joseph Gajard, 55 & 65; Northwestern Univ, MM, 68; Harvard Univ; Edinburgh Univ; Cambridge Univ; Oxford Univ. *Rec Perf:* Requiem Mass (Thomas Luis de Victoria), Portland Symph Choir, 60; numerous rec, Educo Rec, GIA & RCA. *Pos:* In charge, Mt Angel Sem Choir, 60-64; choirmaster, Mt Angel Abbey, 68-74 & 76-80; guest choirmaster, St Mary's Cathedral, San Francisco, Calif, 73. *Mem:* Am Musicol Soc. *Publ:* Ed, Dict of Plainsong, Inst Mediaeval Music. *Mailing Add:* c/o Mt Angel Abbey St Benedict OR 97373

NICHOLSON, JOSEPH MILFORD
EDUCATOR, TROMBONE

b Penoke, Kans, Aug 15, 35. *Study:* Tex Wesleyan Col, BMus, 57; NTex State Univ, Denton, MME, 61; Univ Mo, Kansas City, DMA, 67. *Pos:* Prin trombonist, Springfield Symph, 67-78, Springfield Brass Quintet, 68-78. *Teaching:* Chmn music, Southwestern Assemblies Col, 56-60 & Evangel Col, 60- *Mem:* Int Trombone Asn; Phi Mu Alpha Sinfonia; Pi Kappa Lambda. *Publ:* Auth, History and Evolution of the Trombone, Music J, 67; The Christian and the Arts, CAM Mag, 1/68; The Trombone and Its Solo Literature, Brass & Perc Mag, 1/76; Perfomance Considerations of Early Music, Int Trombone Asn J, 1/76; Introduction to Church Music, Int Corresp Inst, 82. *Mailing Add:* Evangel Col Springfield MO 65802

NIEDT, DOUGLAS ASHTON
EDUCATOR, GUITAR

b St Louis, Mo, Oct 8, 52. *Study:* Juilliard Sch, 73; Univ Mo, BM, 74. *Rec Perf:* Douglas Niedt, Classic Guitar Artistry, 76 & Virtuoso Visions, Douglas Niedt Guitar, 81, Antigua Rec. *Teaching:* Asst prof guitar, Consv Music, Univ Mo, 75- *Mailing Add:* 1428 W 73rd St Kansas City MO 64114

NIELUBOWSKI, NORBERT JOHN
BASSON & CONTRABASSOON, TEACHER

b Chicago, Ill, Sept 4, 58. *Study:* private study with Willard Elliot & David Carroll. *Pos:* Bassoon & contrabassoon, Lyr Opera Chicago, 77-; bassoon, Grant Park Symph, 80- *Teaching:* Instr bassoon, Music Ctr of North Shore, Winnetka, Ill, 76- & DePaul Univ, 80- *Mailing Add:* 1212 Cleveland Evanston IL 60202

NIERENBERG, ROGER
MUSIC DIRECTOR

b New York, NY, June 14, 47. *Study:* Princeton Univ, BA, 69; Mannes Col Music, dipl, 71; Juilliard Sch Music, MM, 79. *Works:* Fire, Flood & Olive Tree, Shawnee Press, 67. *Pos:* Music dir, Pro Arte Chorale, Ridgewood, NJ, 76-, Juilliard Pre Col Orch, 79- & Stamford Symph, 80- *Awards:* Winner, Baltimore Symph Cond Compt, 78. *Mailing Add:* 27 W 96 St New York NY 10025

NIEWEG, CLINTON F
HARP, LIBRARIAN

b West Chester, Pa, Aug 11, 37. *Study:* West Chester Univ, BS(music educ), 59. *Pos:* Asst librn, Philadelphia Orch, 75-79, prin librn, 79- *Teaching:* Strings, Coatesville, Pa Sch, 59-62; orch dir, Wilmington, Del high sch, 62-64. *Mem:* Symph Orch Librn Orgn; Am Harp Soc; Soc Folk Harpers & Craftsmen. *Interests:* Errata in orchestra scores and parts. *Mailing Add:* 334 Willow Grove Ave Glenside PA 19038

NIGHTINGALE, DANIEL
LIBRARIAN, MUSIC COPYIST

b Illinois, 1950. *Study:* Am Consv Music, with Stella Roberts, BMus(comp & piano), 76. *Pos:* Music copyist, Nightingale Music Prep, 76- & a variety of artists & comp incl Laurindo Almeida & Lawrence Moss; music librn, CLC-Conejo Symph, Thousand Oaks, Calif, 80- & Calif Chamber Symph, Los Angeles, 82- *Mem:* Music Libr Asn; Am Fedn Musicians. *Interests:* Accuracy of printed editions of orchestral music with emphasis on reprints of standard works and 20th century music. *Mailing Add:* 952 1/2 W Glenoaks Glendale CA 91202

NIKKA, DAVID W
TROMBONE, ADMINISTRATOR

b Astoria, Ore, Aug 6, 54. *Study:* Boston Univ, BMus, 78. *Pos:* Pres & trombonist, Beacon Brass Quintet, 78-; prin trombonist, Pro Arte Chamber Orch, 81- & Boston Lyr Opera, 83- *Awards:* Ann Audition Award, Conct Artists Guild. *Mem:* Chamber Music Am; Am Fedn Musicians. *Rep:* Robin Wheeler 295 Huntington Ave Suite 208 Boston MA 02115. *Mailing Add:* 13 Tabor Pl # 3 Brookline MA 02146

NILSSON, RAYMOND
TENOR, EDUCATOR

b Sydney, New SWales, Australia, May 26, 20. *Study:* Brighton Col, England; Univ London; Univ Sydney, Australia, BA, New SWales State Consv Music, Australia, dipl. *Rec Perf:* Peter Grimes, Britten, HMV, London, 59; Psalmus Hungaricus, Kodaly, Everest, 62. *Roles:* Don Jose in Carmen, 48 & Alfredo in La Traviata, Carl Rosa Opera, Royal Opera House & Australia; Faust in Faust, Carl Rosa Opera; Edgardo in Lucia di Lammermoor, Royal Opera House; Peter Grimes in Peter Grimes, Australia; Camille in The Merry Widow, Sadler's Wells, London, Australia; leading roles in Jenufa, The Bartered Bride & The Saint of Bleecker Street in various opera houses in Europe, SAfrica & Australia, 78. *Pos:* Prin tenor, Royal Opera House, London, 53-61, San Francisco Opera, 63- & opera houses in Europe, SAfrica & Australia, 78. *Teaching:* Prof voice & opera, San Jose State Univ, 70-; coach opera, New Sydney Opera House, Australia, 77. *Mailing Add:* 1285 Middle Ave Menlo Park CA 94025

NIN-CULMELL, JOAQUIN M
COMPOSER, PIANO

b Berlin, Germany, Sept 5, 08; US citizen. *Study:* Schola Cantorum, 30; study with Manuel de Falla, 30-34; Paris Consv, 35. *Works:* Orchestral Compositions & Compositions (voice & piano), Max Eschig; Sonata Breve, Piano Tonadas & Choral Compositions, Broude Brothers; Piano Quintet, Boileau. *Teaching:* Prof music, Williams Col, 40-50; from prof to emer prof, Univ Calif, Berkeley, 50- *Awards:* Creative Arts Inst Fel, Univ Calif, 65. *Bibliog:* Gilbert Chase (auth), Music of Spain, Dover, 59. *Mem:* Corresp mem, Royal Acad Fine Arts San Fernando, Madrid. *Publ:* Auth, Prefaces to the Early Diaries of Anaïs Nin, Vol I, II & III. *Mailing Add:* 165 Hillcrest Rd Berkeley CA 94705

NISBET, MEREDITH WOOTTON
COMPOSER, VIOLIN

b Siloam Springs, Ark, Nov 14, 45. *Study:* Howard Payne Univ, BM & BME, 69; Univ Ark, MM(theory & comp), 72; studied violin with Richard Fuchs, 74-80; Quachita Baptist Univ, studied comp with Francis McBeth, 80-81; Univ Okla, studied comp with Michael Hennagin, currently. *Works:* Scherzo in Phrygian Mode (flute & piano), Univ Ky Prog Women's Music, 78; Intervallic IV (flute duet), Comp Lab, Univ Ark, 78; Exultation (organ), First Presby Church, Arkadelphia, 80; Sing, O Heavens, 81 & Alleluia (SSA), 83, Quachita Bapt Univ Chamber Singers; Prelude & Scherzo (piano trio), Nat Fedn Music Clubs, 81; Pastel Suite (violin & cello), Art Show of Debra Smith Barnes, 81. *Pos:* Prin second violin, North Ark Symph, 78-80; prin second violin & viola, South Ark Symph, 80- *Teaching:* Instr music, Howard Payne Univ, 69-70; grad asst, Univ Ark, 70-72; instr beginning strings, Joint Educ Consortium, 80- *Mem:* Am Women Composers. *Mailing Add:* 1908 Sylvia Arkadelphia AR 71923

NISKA, MARALIN FAE
SOPRANO

b San Pedro, Calif. *Study:* Univ Southern Calif, with Walter Ducloux, 58-59; Music Acad West, 58-60; Univ Calif, Los Angeles, with Jan Popper, BA, 60. *Roles:* Manon in Manon, Los Angeles Opera Co, 59; Minnie in Faniculla del West, NY State Theatre; Emilia Marty in The Makropoulos Affair, New York City Opera, 70; Musetta in La Boheme, Metropolitan Opera, 77; Cassandre in Troyens; Governess in The Turn of the Screw; Cleopatra in Giulio Cesare. *Pos:* Res mem, New York City Opera, formerly; sop, Metropolitan Nat Co, 65-67, Metropolitan Opera, formerly & many others; recitalist, US, Can, Mex & Netherlands. *Awards:* Woman of Yr, Los Angeles Times, 67. *Mem:* Am Guild Musical Artists; Screen Actors Guild. *Mailing Add:* c/o Tony Hartmann Assoc 250 W 57th St Suite 1120 New York NY 10107

NIXON, MARNI
TEACHER, SINGER

b Altadena, Calif. *Study:* Los Angeles City Col; Univ Calif, Los Angeles; Univ Southern Calif; Berkshire Music Ctr. *Rec Perf:* On Columbia, Capitol, RCA Victor & educ rec; Cabaret Songs and Early Songs by Arnold Schoenberg. *Roles:* My Fair Lady, Broadway, 64; Sound of Music (film), 64. *Pos:* Actress, Pasadena Playhouse, 40-45 & numerous TV shows & night clubs; soloist, Roger Wagner Chorale, 47-53; singer, appeared with New England Opera Co, formerly, Los Angeles Opera Co, formerly, Ford Found TV Opera, 48-63, San Francisco Spring Opera, 66 & Seattle Opera, 71-72. *Teaching:* Dir fac voice, Calif Inst Arts, 70-72; head apprentice div, Music Acad West, 80; dir opera wkshp, Cornish Inst Arts, formerly; private instr music. *Awards:* 19 Emmy Awards; two Action Children's TV Awards, 77. *Rep:* Maxim Gershunoff Attractions 502 Park Ave New York NY 10022. *Mailing Add:* 7323 Mercer Terr Dr Mercer Island WA 98040

NIXON, ROGER
COMPOSER, EDUCATOR

b Tulare, Calif, Aug 8, 21. *Study:* Univ Calif, Berkeley, with Arthur Bliss, Ernest Bloch & Roger Sessions, BA, 42, MA, 49; PhD, 52; studied with Arnold Schoenberg. *Works:* Elegiac Rhapsody (viola & orch), 67; The Bride Comes to Yellow Sky (opera), Eastern Ill Univ, 68; Viola Concerto (orch), San Francisco, 70; Ceremonial Fanfare No 1 (brass), 76; Ceremonial Fanfare No 2 (woodwinds, brass & perc), 76; Pacific Celebration Suite (band), 76; Pacific Pageant (band), 76. *Teaching:* Instr music, Modesto Jr Col, 51-59; prof music, San Francisco State Univ, 59- *Awards:* ASCAP Awards, 69-73; Ostwald Award, 73; Nat Endowment Arts Grant, 75. *Mailing Add:* 2090 New Brunswick Dr San Mateo CA 94402

NKETIA, J H KWABENA
EDUCATOR
b Mampong-Ashanti, Ghana, June 22, 21. *Study:* Birkbeck Col & Trinity Col Music, Univ London, BA, 49; Columbia Univ, studied comp with Henry Cowell & organology with Curt Sachs, 58; Juilliard Sch Music, 58; Northwestern Univ, 59. *Works:* Suite for Flute & Piano, 79, Volta Fantasy (piano), 79 & Antubam (cello & piano), 79, Brockport Col, State Univ NY Keyboard Fest. *Teaching:* Res fel, Univ Ghana, 52-61, prof music & drama, 61-80; prof music, Univ Calif, Los Angeles, 68-83; Andrew Mellon prof music, Univ Pittsburgh, 83- *Awards:* ASCAP Deems Taylor Award, 75; Prize, Int Music Coun, United Nations Educ, Sci & Cult Orgn, 81. *Mem:* Int Folk Music Coun (mem exec bd, 58-67); Int Soc Music Educ (mem bd dir & second vpres, 69-74); Int Musicol Soc; Int Music Coun (mem exec bd, 66-74); Soc Ethnomusicol. *Publ:* Auth, Funeral Dirges of the Akan People, Univ Ghana, 55; African Music in Ghana, Northwestern Univ Press, 62; Drumming in Akan Communities of Ghana, Thomas Nelson, 63; Folk Songs of Ghana, Oxford Univ Press, 63; The Music of Africa, W W Norton, 74. *Mailing Add:* Music Dept Univ Pittsburgh Pittsburgh PA 15260

NOBEL, (VIRGINIA) ANN
COMPOSER, FLUTE
b Oakland, Calif, Sept 24, 55. *Study:* Univ Redlands, with Barney Childs, BMus(comp & flute); Mills Col, with Terry Riley & Robert Ashley, MA(comp). *Works:* The Piano Tinkled Like Someone Breaking Glass in a Tin Box (clarinet & harpsichord), 77; Juniper Tree (chamber opera), 77; One of My Other Pieces (violin & cello), 78; This is the Passing of All Shining Things (violin & bassoon), 78; My Last True Love (double-reed quartet), 79; This is the Celebration of the Changing of the Light (horn, violin & piano), 79; The Raindrops on the Windowpane Sparkled (tape), 79. *Rec Perf:* With Improviser's Orch. *Pos:* Mem, Improviser's Orch, 74-79 & Independent Comp Asn, Los Angeles, currently. *Awards:* Sigma Alpha Iota Comp Award, 79. *Mem:* League Women Comp; Am Women Comp Inc. *Mailing Add:* 1023 Myra Ave Los Angeles CA 90020

NOBLE, WESTON HENRY
CONDUCTOR, EDUCATOR
b Nov 30, 22. *Study:* Luther Col, BA, 43; Univ Mich, Ann Arbor, MM, 53; Augustana Col, Hon Dr, 71. *Pos:* Cond, Luther Col Nordic Choir, Luther Col Conct Band & fest groups in major conct halls of Chicago, New York, Washington, DC, Los Angeles & Minneapolis; conct tours of Europe from Norway to Rumania; guest dir, music festivals in 42 states, Can & Europe. *Teaching:* Prof music, Luther Col, currently; guest fac mem, 27 cols & univ. *Mem:* Music Educr Nat Conf; Iowa Music Educr; Music Teachers Nat Asn; Col Music Soc; Am Bandmasters Asn. *Mailing Add:* 602 Mound Docorah IA 52101

NOBLEMAN, MAURICE
MUSIC DIRECTOR
b New York, NY, Nov 29, 27. *Study:* New York City Col, 50; Dartmouth Col, with Zoltan Kodaly, 66; studied with Dimitri Mitropoulos. *Rec Perf:* Pan-Am Prog, Voice of Am, 62. *Pos:* Asst cond, Am Symph Orch, NY, 52-54, assoc cond, 54-66, music dir, 66-76; music dir, Valley Symph Orch, NJ, 78- *Mem:* Assoc Musicians Greater NY. *Rep:* Michael Durkas Teaneck NJ. *Mailing Add:* 110 Beacon St Dunmont NJ 07628

NOEL, BARBARA H (BARBARA H MCMURTRY)
ADMINISTRATOR, EDUCATOR
b Mt Vernon, Wash, Feb 27, 29. *Study:* Oberlin Consv Music; Univ Ky, BM, 51, MM, 52; Univ Ill, PhD(musicol), 72. *Pos:* Dean, Col Humanities & Fine Arts, Tex Woman's Univ, 78-81; dean, Col Visual & Perf Arts, Southeastern Mass Univ, 81- *Teaching:* Chmn, Dept Music, Univ Richmond, 71-76 & Mankato State Univ, 76-78. *Mem:* Col Music Soc (vpres, 80-82, treas, 83-); Nat Asn Sch Music. *Interests:* Music of Prince Louis Ferdinand. *Publ:* Auth, Louis Ferdinand, In: New Grove Dict Music & Musicians, 80. *Mailing Add:* 73 Tucker Lane North Dartmouth MA 02747

NOH, JOYCE HIEW
VIOLIN
b Taekoo City, Korea, Oct 25, 52; US citizen. *Study:* New Sch Music, 68-72; Juilliard Sch Music, dipl, 73-77. *Pos:* Violinist, Baltimore Symph Orch, 77-79 & Chicago Symph Orch, 79- *Mailing Add:* 3533 Walnut Wilmette IL 60091

NOLD, DONAL CHARLES
EDUCATOR, TEACHER
b Irvington, NJ. *Study:* Juilliard Sch, BS, 51, MS, 52; studied with Marguerite Long & Pierre Bernac, Paris, 53-54. *Pos:* Asst cond, Santa Fe Opera Co, 64 & Central City Opera, 65-66. *Teaching:* Mem staff & chmn accmp dept, Manhattan Sch Music, 64-; instr vocal studies, Philadelphia Musical Acad, 67-71. *Mailing Add:* 124 W 71 St New York NY 10023

NOLEN, TIMOTHY
BARITONE
b Rotan, Tex, July 9, 41. *Study:* Trenton State Col, BM, 67; Manhattan Sch Music, MM, 69. *Roles:* Dandini in La Cenerentola, Chicago Lyr Opera, 76-83; Figaro in The Barber of Seville, San Francisco Opera, 76; Marcello in La Boheme, Seattle Opera, 79; Don Quixote in Man of La Mancha, Lake George Opera Fest, 81 & 83; Willie Stark in Willie Stark, Houston Grand Opera, 82; Junior in A Quiet Place, Houston Grand Opera, Kennedy Ctr, 83 & La Scala, 83-84; and many others. *Pos:* Artistic dir, Am Lyr Theater, 81- *Mailing Add:* 210 Riverside Dr 8E New York NY 10025

NOON, DAVID
COMPOSER, EDUCATOR
b Johnstown, Pa. July 23, 46. *Study:* Pomona Col, studied comp with Karl Kohn, BA, 68; NY Univ, studied musicol with Gustave Reese, MA, 70; Yale Univ, studied comp with Mario Davidowsky, MMA, 72, DMA, 77. *Works:* Berceuse Seche, Colo Phil, 74; String Quartet #1, Concord String Quartet, 75; String Quartet #2, Arriaga String Quartet, 78; Star-Captains, Houston Symph Orch, 81; Broken Blossoms, Symph Wind Ens, Northwestern Univ, 81; Art Deco, Pro Musica Chamber Orch, 82; Six Chansons, Musica Nova, Eastman Sch Music, 83. *Rec Perf:* Motets & Monodies, Crystal Rec; Six Chansons, Pro Viva Rec; Three Etudes, Protone Rec. *Teaching:* Instr comp, Northwestern Univ, 73-76; comp in res, Wurlitzer Found, Taos, NMex, 76-77; chmn music hist, Manhattan Sch Music, 81- *Awards:* Fulbright Fel, 72-73; comp award, ASCAP, 73- & BMI, 67 & 70. *Mem:* ASCAP; Am Musicol Soc; Col Music Soc; Music Libr Asn. *Mailing Add:* MSM 120 Claremont Ave New York NY 10027

NOONE, LANA MAE
FLUTE, EDUCATOR
b New York, NY, Dec 30, 46. *Study:* Mannes Col Music, with John Wummer, Carl Bamberger & Alexander Williams, BS, 68. *Rec Perf:* Dance with Rivka, Carrol Studios, 68. *Pos:* Soloist, Int Folk Fest, New York, NY, 65-69, Orch Am, New York, NY, 65, L'Amore Musica, West Hempstead, NY, 70-80, Am Concert Band, Jericho, NY, 72-79 & Edinburgh Music Fest, Scotland, 72; section flutist, Cosmopolitan Symph Orch, New York, NY, 65-68, Int Jugendorchester, WBerlin, Germany, 65, Long Island Symph Orch, 70-80 & Merrick Symph Orch, 80- *Teaching:* Adj prof flute, Nassau Community Col, 75- *Awards:* Winner Flute Soloist, LFNA Compt, New York, NY, 65. *Mem:* Am Fedn Musicians. *Publ:* Auth, Suffer the Little Children, Open Door Soc, 77. *Mailing Add:* Music Dept Nassau Community Col Garden City NY 11530

NORD, EDWARD ALLAN
CONDUCTOR & MUSIC DIRECTOR, PIANO
b Detroit, Mich, June 13, 48. *Study:* Consv Am, Fountainebleau, France, summer 65, 66, 68, 69 & 71; Univ Southern Calif, BM, 71, MM, 73; Berkshire Music Ctr, 72, 73 & 75. *Rec Perf:* L'Incoronazione di Poppea-Concert Suite (Monteverdi-Rodriguez), 74 & L'Orfeo-Concert Suite (Monteverdi-Rodriguez), 74, Canto (Robert Xavier Rodriguez), 74, Lyric Variations (Robert Xavier Rodriguez), 74 & Concerto II (Robert Xavier Rodriguez), 74, Orion Master Rec. *Pos:* Music dir & cond, Orion Chamber Orch, Los Angeles, 73-78; Tulare Co Symph Orch, Calif, 75-78; assoc cond, Ala Symph Orch, 78-; music dir, Educ Div, Ala Symph Orch, 81- *Teaching:* Lectr piano, Talladega Col, Ala, 82- *Awards:* Fels, Berkshire Music Ctr, 72 & 75; Obelisk Award, Greater Birmingham Arts Alliance, 81. *Publ:* Auth, Building Audiences of the Future—What About The Present?, Symph Mag, 82. *Mailing Add:* 3825 Buckingham Ln Birmingham AL 35243

NORDEN, BETSY (ELIZABETH N HALEY)
SOPRANO
b Cincinnati, Ohio. *Roles:* Zerlina in Don Giovanni, Metropolitan Opera, 74; Despina in Cose fan tutte, Spoleto Fest, Italy, 77-78; Sister Constance, Metropolitan Opera, 77 & 79, San Francisco Opera, 81-83; Sophie in Werther, Metropolitan Opera, 78; Vixen in Cunning Little Vixen, Philadelphia Lyric, 81; Vespina, Mostly Mozart, 82; Gretel in Hansel and Gretel, Metropolitan Opera, 83. *Pos:* Solo artist, Metropolitan Opera, 72-, Philadelphia Opera, 80-84, San Francisco Opera, 82 & Mostly Mozart Fest NY, 82. *Mailing Add:* Lew & Benson Moreau-Neret Inc 204 W 10th St New York NY 10014

NORDEN, HUGO
EDUCATOR, COMPOSER
b Providence, RI, Dec 31, 09. *Study:* Univ Toronto, BMus, 43, DMus, 48. *Works:* Passacaglia on Two Themes, perf by Boston Consv Orch, 81-82; Divertimento for Brass Quintet, perf by Am Soc Univ Comp, 83; Concerto in A Minor for Oboe & String Orchestra, comn by Baroque Players, Austin, 83. *Teaching:* Prof music theory, Boston Univ, 45-75, emer prof, 75-; fac mem, Boston Consv Music, 75- & Boston Col, 75- *Mem:* Am Soc Univ Comp; Fibonacci Asn. *Publ:* Auth, The Technique of Canon, Branden Press, 69; Foundation Studies in Fugue, 77 & Project Studies in Fugue, 77, Taplinger. *Mailing Add:* 11 Mendelssohn St Roslindale MA 02131

NORDENSTROM, GLADYS (GLADYS NORDENSTROM KRENEK)
COMPOSER
b Pokegama Township, Minn, May 23, 24. *Study:* Univ Minn, BA, 46; Hamline Univ, MA, 47. *Works:* El Greco Phantasy (string orch), 66, Elegy for Robert F Kennedy (orch), 69, Work for Orchestra #3, 75 & Wind Quintet, 76, Bärenreiter-Verlag, Kassel, Fed Repub Ger; Zeit XXIV (song), perf by Neva Pilgrim, 77; Signals from Nowhere (organ & electric tape), perf by M Haselboeck, 81; Parabola of Light (women's chorus), Univ Calif, Santa Barbara, 81. *Mem:* BMI. *Mailing Add:* PO Box 2085 Palm Springs CA 92263

NORDGREN, QUENTIN RICHARDS
EDUCATOR, ADMINISTRATOR
b Monroe, Utah, July 4, 20. *Study:* Brigham Young Univ, BA, 42, MA, 50; Ind Univ, PhD, 55. *Works:* String Quartet, perf by Brigham Young Univ Fac Quartet, 68; The Kingdom of God, Richnor Co, 81. *Teaching:* Instr music, Dixie Col, 52-55; from instr to prof, Brigham Young Univ, 55- *Mem:* Soc Music Theory. *Publ:* Auth, A Measure of Textural Patterns and Strengths, J Music Theory, 60; coauth, First Year Music Theory, Appleton Century Crofts, 62; auth, A Study in Chromatic Harmony, Parts I & II, 66 & 71 & Trends in Music Theory Textbooks, 67, Am Music Teacher; ed, Graduate Handbook, Dept Music, Brigham Young Univ, 74, 78 & 81; and others. *Mailing Add:* C-550 HFAC Brigham Young Univ Provo UT 84602

NORDSTROM, CRAIG KYLE
CLARINET, TEACHER

b Denver, Colo, June 17, 49. *Study:* Northwestern Univ, BME, 71; Catholic Univ Am, MM, 74. *Pos:* Bass clarinet, US Marine Band, 71-75, Vancouver Symph Orch, 75-77, Cincinnati Symph Orch, 77-79, Boston Symph Orch, 79- *Teaching:* Instr clarinet, Boston Univ, 79- & New England Consv Music, 79- *Mailing Add:* c/o Boston Symphony Hall 301 Mass Ave Boston MA 02115

NORELL, JUDITH REGINA
HARPSICHORD, TEACHER

b New York, NY. *Study:* Rubin Acad Music, Jerusalem, Israel, BM, 67; Royal Col Music, London, 68; Juilliard Sch Music, studied harpsichord with Albert Fuller, MM, 71. *Rec Perf:* Harpsichord Sonatas & Partitas (Allessandro & Domenico Scarlatti), Sine Qua Non, 78; Harpsichord Sonatas (Benedetto Marcello), Musical Heritage, 80; Greatest Hits of 1720, 80 & Greatest Hits of 1721, 81, Columbia; Mozart Sonatas (flute & harpsichord), Vox, 81. *Pos:* Dir, Baroque Music Masters, New York, 73-79; harpsichordist, Opera Soc, Washington, 72-75, Lucarelli-Norell-Siebert Trio, 79- & Bach Chamber Soloists, 82- *Publ:* Auth, Elizabeth Jacquet de la Guerre, Helicon 9, 79. *Rep:* Hamlen/Landau Mgt 140 W 79 St New York NY 10024. *Mailing Add:* 915 West End Ave New York NY 10025

NORMAN, JESSYE
SOPRANO

b Augusta, Ga, Sept 15, 45. *Study:* Howard Univ, with C V Grant, BM, 67; Peabody Consv Music, with Alice Duschak, Univ Mich, MMus, 68; studied with Pierre Bernac, Elizabeth Mannion & Carolyn Grant. *Rec Perf:* Songs from Des Knaben Wunderhorn (Mahler), Philips Rec; Song of the Wood Dove (Schoenberg), CBS Masterworks; and other rec for Columbia, EMI & Philips. *Roles:* Elizabeth in Tannhäuser, Deutsche Oper, 69; Jocasta in Oedipus Rex & Queen Dido in Dido & Aeneas, Opera Co Philadelphia, 82; Countess in Le Nozze di Figaro; Cassandra in Les Troyens; Selika in L'Africaine; Arminda in La Finta giardiniera. *Pos:* Sop with major opera co & orchs worldwide. *Awards:* First Prize, Bavarian Radio Corp Int Music Compt, 68; Grand Prix Disque, 73, 76 & 77; Deutsche Schallplatten Preis, 75. *Mem:* Sigma Alpha Iota; Pi Kappa Lambda. *Mailing Add:* c/o Harry Beall Mgt 119 W 57th St New York NY 10019

NORMAN, THEODORE
GUITAR, COMPOSER

b Montreal, Can, Mar 14, 12; US citizen. *Study:* Music study in Germany, France & Spain. *Rec Perf:* Le Marteau San Maitre (Boulez) & Schoenberg Serenade, Columbia LP; Metamorphosis of Kafka, perf by Monday evening conct, Los Angeles. *Pos:* First violinist, Los Angeles Phil, 35-42. *Teaching:* Head class guitar dept & lectr, Univ Calif, Los Angeles, 67- *Mem:* ASCAP. *Publ:* Transcribed, Josef Mathias Hauer 4 Pieces, Doblinger, 80; 12 Scriabine Preludes, Theodore Presser, 81; 24 Caprices of Paganini, 82 & Music by Soulima Stravinsky, Peters Ed; Music for the Guitar Soloist & Music by Haydn (3 guitars), Vivaldi (3 guitars) & Mozart (2 guitars), Schirmer; Music by Igor Stravinsky, Chester Ed. *Mailing Add:* 451 Westmount Dr Los Angeles CA 90048

NORRIS, KEVIN EDWARD
COMPOSER, ORGAN

b New York, NY, Apr 12, 39. *Study:* Am Consv Music, Chicago, with Leo Sowerby, BM, 62. *Works:* Penseroso, H W Gray, 79; Lenten Verses, Augsburg Publ House, 80; O Little One Sweet, Epoch Universal, 81; Psalm 23, GIA, 81; Celebration, H W Gray, 82; Toccatinas and Tidbits, 82 & Babe Lied in the Cradle, 82, Sacred Music Press. *Pos:* Minister music, Assumption Church, Morristown, NJ, 73- *Mailing Add:* 91 Maple Ave Morristown NJ 07960

NORTH, ALEX
COMPOSER, MUSIC DIRECTOR

b Chester, Pa, Dec 4, 10. *Study:* Juilliard Sch Music, 29-32, Moscow Consv, 33-35; studied with Ernst Toch, 36; studied with Aaron Copland, 38; studied with Sylvestre Revueltas, 39. *Works:* Hither and Thither of Danny Dither (musical), Marks Music Corp, 41; Revue (clarinet & orch), Belwin-Mills Publ Corp, 47; Holiday Set, New York Phil, 48; Little Indian Drum, Shapiro Bernstein Publ, 50; A Streetcar Named Desire, Witmark & Sons, 54; Cleopatra Suite, Robbins Music Corp, 63; Africa (symph #3), Graunke Symph Orch, Munich, Germany, 67. *Awards:* Guggenheim Fel, 47; Golden Globe Award for Shoes of the Fisherman, Foreign Press Asn, 69; Emmy Award for Rich Man, Poor Man, Nat Acad TV Arts & Sci, 75. *Bibliog:* Elie Siegmeister (auth), A World of Music, In: The Music Lovers Handbook, Wm Morrow & Co, 43; Irwin Bazelon (auth), Knowing the Score, Arco Publ Inc, 75; Page Cook (auth) The Sound Track, Film in Rev, 80. *Mem:* Am Fedn Musicians; Comp & Lyricists Guild Am; ASCAP; Am Youth Symph; Screen Comp Guild. *Mailing Add:* 630 Resoland Dr Pacific Palisades CA 90272

NORTON, LEW
BASS, EDUCATOR

Study: Univ Tulsa, BA, BM; Ind Univ. *Pos:* Solo bass, Tulsa Orch, Chautauqua Orch, Goldovsky Opera & Fromm Players, formerly; mem, St Louis & Houston Orch; mem bass sect, New York Phil, currently. *Teaching:* Mem fac, Tulsa Univ, Chautauqua, formerly & St Louis Consv Music, formerly; mem fac double bass, Manhattan Sch Music, 76- *Awards:* Fromm Found Award; Hi Fidelity Award; Henry B Cabot Award. *Mailing Add:* Manhattan Sch Music 120 Claremont Ave New York NY 10027

NORTON, PAULINE ELIZABETH
LIBRARIAN, LECTURER

b Grosse Pointe, Mich. *Study:* Univ Mich, AB, MA, PhD, 83. *Pos:* Supvr, Nat Endowment Humanities Sheet Music Cataloging Proj, William L Clements Libr, Univ Mich, music cur, 82- *Teaching:* Lectr hist Am music, New Col, 72; lectr jazz styles, Am Cult Prog, Univ Mich, 79- *Awards:* Fred Harris Daniels Fel, Am Antiquarian Soc, 76; Newberry Libr Res Fel, 76. *Mem:* Am Studies Asn; Am Musicol Soc; Sonneck Soc. *Interests:* History of American march and dance music, the American band, and American dance. *Publ:* Auth, Nineteenth-Century American March Music and John Philip Sousa, In: Perspectives on John Philip Sousa, Libr Cong, 83; articles on hist Am dance & Am dance forms, In: New Grove Dict of Music in US (in prep). *Mailing Add:* 1731 Broadview Lane Ann Arbor MI 48105

NOSSE, CARL E
ADMINISTRATOR, COMPOSER

b N Irwin, Pa, Jan 8, 33. *Study:* Tarkio Col, BA, 54; Duquesne Univ, MMus, 61; Fla State Univ, DMus, 73. *Works:* Shepherd's Meditation (mixed voices), Volkwein Publ, 63; And Am I Born To Die? (mixed voices), Sam Fox Publ, 66; Antiphon of Praise (mixed voices), Volkwein Publ, 67; Sonata Da Camera (cello & piano), 78; Sonnet/Dialogue (alto sax & guitar), Dorn Publ, 79; Incantation (trombone ens), Int Trombone Soc, 80; Valley of the Tulares, Stockton Symph Orch, 81. *Rec Perf:* Deep River, Broadman Press, 73. *Teaching:* Assoc prof comp, Fla State Univ, 72-80; dean & prof admin, Consv Music, Univ Pacific, 80- *Awards:* Second Prize Comp Award, Fla Contemp Music Fest, 74. *Mem:* ASCAP; Calif Music Exec (recorder, 83-). *Publ:* Contribr, What is a Fine Art, Fla State Univ. *Mailing Add:* Consv Music Univ Pacific Stockton CA 95211

NOTT, DOUGLAS DUANE
COMPOSER, EDUCATOR

b Yakima, Wash, Feb 27, 44. *Study:* Cent Wash Univ, with Robert Panerio, BA(music educ), 66, with Paul Creston, MA(comp), 70; Univ Ariz, with Robert Musynsky, DMA(comp), 78. *Works:* Rhapsodic Song for Alto, 70 & Son and Piano/Band, Shawnee Press; Adagio and Fugue, Yakima Symph Orch, 74-75; Cascade for Band, Carl Fischer, 75; String Quartet No 1, Univ Ariz, 77; Symphony No 1, Places, Yakima Symph Orch, 81 & Nat Endowment Humanities, 82; String Quartet No 1, Nat Endowment Humanities, 82. *Pos:* Dir music, Rochester Sch District, Wash, 66-69; chmn music dept, Yakima Valley Col, 73-75, humanities, 77-80. *Teaching:* Instr theory, Yakima Valley Col, 70- *Mem:* ASCAP; Music Educr Nat Conf . *Mailing Add:* 410 N 56th Ave Yakima WA 98908

NOVACK, SAUL
EDUCATOR, ADMINISTRATOR

b New York, NY, July 19, 18. *Study:* Col City New York, 39; Columbia Univ, MA, 41. *Teaching:* Lectr, Hunter Col, 46-52; prof & dean, Queens Col, City Univ New York, 52-; fac mem, Mannes Col Music, 56-57; prof, Grad Sch, City Univ New York, 71- *Awards:* Vis fel, Humanities Res Ctr, Australian Nat Univ, 75. *Mem:* Am Musicol Soc. *Interests:* History of tonality, especially before 1600; Schenkerian analysis. *Publ:* Auth, Some Thoughts on the Nature of the Musical Composition, Current Musicol, 68; Fusion of Design and Tonal Order: Josquin and Isaac, Music Forum II, 70; Tonal Tendencies in Josquin's Use of Harmony, Josquin des Prez, Oxford, 76; The Significance of the Phrygian Mode in the History of Tonality, Miscellanea Musicol, 77; The Analysis of Pre-Baroque Music, Aspects of Schenkerian Analysis, Yale Univ Press, 83. *Mailing Add:* 232 Beach 132 St Belle Harbor NY 11694

NOVAK-TSOGLIN, SOFIA
VIOLIN

b Kiev, USSR, June 19, 50. *Study:* Moscow State Consv, USSR, MA, 73. *Pos:* Violinist, Bolshoi Theatre, Moscow, USSR, 74-77 & Detroit Symph Orch, 81- *Mailing Add:* 273000 Franklin Rd Apt 716 Southfield MI 48034

NOVICH, MIJA
EDUCATOR, SOPRANO

b Chicago, Ill. *Study:* Northwestern Univ, with William Phillips, BME, 49; Aspen Sch Music, with Martial Singher & Darius Milhaud, summer 53; Mannes Col Music, vocal studies with Martial Singher & opera wkshp with Carl Bamberger & Otto Guth; studied with Arvilla Clark Andelin & Lili Wexberg. *Roles:* Donna Anna in Don Giovanni, Montreal Arts Fest, 56; Aida in Aida, New Orleans Opera Co, 58; Tosca in Tosca, Pittsburgh Opera Co, 58; Norma in Norma, Teatro Colon, Buenos Aires, 59; Donna Leonora in La forza del destino, Teatro Santiago Chile, 59; Manon in Manon Lescaut, Cincinnati Opera Co, 59; Amelia in Simon Boccanegra, Stadttheater Aachen, WGermany, 66. *Pos:* Opera & solo performer, US, Mex, Can, South Am & WGermany. *Teaching:* Instr voice, Duquesne Univ, 74-, dir opera wkshp, 77- *Awards:* First Prize, Women's Clubs Ill, 54; fel, Martha Baird Rockefeller Found, 56. *Mem:* Nat Asn Teachers Singing; Nat Music Teachers Asn; Music Teachers Asn. *Mailing Add:* 500 Hoodridge Dr Pittsburgh PA 15234

NOVICK, MELVYN JOSEPH
ADMINISTRATOR, TENOR

b Brooklyn, NY, Aug 7, 46. *Study:* High Sch Music & Art, dipl, 64; Manhattan Sch Music, with Conrad Thibault, BMus, 68, MMus, 70. *Roles:* Various comprimario roles in Goro, Art Park Fest, 75-82; comprimario, New York City Opera, 75-82; Gustone in La Traviata, Spoleto Fest, US, 77; Pong & Remendado, Syracuse Symph, 80 & 82; Spoletta in Tosca, Opera Metropolitana, 82. *Pos:* Tenor soloist, Alvin Ailey Dance Co, 71 & 72; cantor, Progressive Synagogue, 79-; registr & dir student serv, Aspen Music Sch & Fest, 82- *Teaching:* Assoc prof music, Wagner Col, 71-78. *Mem:* Am Guild Musical Artists; Am Fedn TV & Radio Artists. *Rep:* Helene Blue 205 West End Ave New York NY 10023. *Mailing Add:* 63 W Edsall Blvd Palisades Park NJ 07650

NOWAK, LIONEL
PIANO, COMPOSER
b Cleveland, Ohio, Sept 25, 11. *Study:* Cleveland Inst Music, with Quincy Porter, Roger Sessions, Herbert Elwell & Beryl Rubinstein. *Works:* Sonata for Solo Violin, 50; Quartet for Oboe and Strings, 52; Piano Trio, 54; Concert-piece for Kettledrums and Strings, 61. *Rec Perf:* Concert Piece for Kettledrums and Strings, Soundscape for Piano & Soundscape for String Quartet, CRI; Soundscape for Three Woodwinds & Soundscape for Bassoon and Piano, Golden Crest. *Pos:* Music dir, Humphrey-Weidman Dance Co, 38-42; cond, Spartanburg Symph Orch, 42-45; touring recitalist, Arts Prog, Asn Am Col, 45-63. *Teaching:* Mem fac, Fenn Col, 32-36; prof, Converse Col, 42-46 & Syracuse Univ, 46-48; mem fac piano, Bennington Col, 48- *Awards:* Citation, Vt Coun Arts, 81. *Mem:* Am Comp Alliance; fel, Vt Acad Arts & Sci. *Mailing Add:* Music Dept Bennington Col Bennington VT 05201

NUERNBERGER, LOUIS D
COMPOSER, EDUCATOR
b Wakefield, Nebr, Jan 5, 24. *Study:* Univ Mich, with Homer Keller & Ross Lee Finney, BM, 50, MM, 51, PhD, 63; Mozarteum, Salzburg, with Cesar Bresgen, 54-56; Ind Univ, with Bernhard Heiden; studied with Nadia Boulanger. *Works:* Magnificat (chorus with solo quartet, a cappella); Time Present—Die Erde Bleibt—Lux Perpetua (chorus with solo trio & chanters, double motet, a cappella); Koheleth (chorus with solo sextet & narrator, a cappella); Falcons of Arcos de la Frontera (chorus with three solo sop & narrator, a cappella); De profundis (chorus a cappella); Slouthe: A Portraite (chorus a cappella). *Teaching:* Asst prof theory, Berea Col, 59-64; vis prof music hist, Univ Mo, summer 64; prof music theory & dir, Collegium Musicum, Consv Music, Oberlin Col, 64- *Awards:* Fulbright Fel, Austria, 54-56. *Mailing Add:* 27 Colony Dr Oberlin OH 44074

NUNEMAKER, RICHARD EARL
CLARINET, SAXOPHONE
b Buffalo, NY, Nov 30, 42. *Study:* State Univ NY, Fredonia, BMus & perf cert, 64; Univ Louisville, MMus, 66; studied with Clark Brody, Jerry Stowell, Alan Sigel & William Willett. *Pos:* Bass clarinet, clarinet & sax, Louisville Orch, 64-66 & Houston Symph Orch, 67-; clarinet & sax, Houston Pops Orch, 70- & Cambiata Soloists, 71- *Teaching:* Band dir & instr woodwinds, Hobart Independent Sch, Ind, 66-67; fac mem & artist in res, clarinet, theory & chamber music, Sewanee Summer Music Ctr, Tenn, 66; instr clarinet, sax & chamber music, Univ St Thomas, 70- *Mem:* Int Clarinet Congress; Clarinetwork Inc. *Publ:* Auth, If the Shoe Fits, private publ, 79. *Mailing Add:* 2807 Linkwood Houston TX 77025

NUNLIST, JULI (ELIZABETH MOORA)
COMPOSER, EDUCATOR
b Montclair, NJ, Dec 6, 16. *Study:* Randolph-Macon Woman's Col, Barnard Col, BA, 40; Manhattan Sch Music, BM(comp), 61, MM(comp), 64. *Works:* Lento and Presto (piano), perf by Arthur Loesser & Ralph Votapek, 64; Spells (choral cycle), Univ Kans Conct Choir, 64; Platero and I (symph tone suite), Cleveland Suburban Symph, 72; Trois Chansons, Carolyn Dixon & Chamber Group, 74; Suite for Flute and Piano, comn by Fortnightly Musical Club, Cleveland, 78; String Quartet, perf by Koch Quartet, 64 & Worcester String Quartet, 79; Sieben Gedichte (Rilke), Ann Zibelman & Monica Jakuc, 82. *Pos:* Music dir, Craft Choreography Conf, Nat Regional Ballet Asn, 61-70. *Teaching:* Instr, Akron Univ, 70-73; chmn, Fine Arts Dept, Hathaway Brown Sch, 72-76; mem fac comp, Perf Arts Sch, Worcester, Mass, 76- *Mem:* Am Music Ctr; Am Women Comp Inc; Boston Women Comp Group. *Publ:* Contribr, Music, Your Silent Partner, Dance Mag, 8/64. *Mailing Add:* 288 Mirick Rd Princeton MA 01541

NURMELA, KARI KULLERVO
BARITONE
b Viipuri, Finland. *Study:* Akad Music & darstellende Kunst, Vienna, 55-58; study with Arturo Merlini, Milan, 70- *Rec Perf:* Tonio in I Pagliacci, EMI, 80. *Roles:* Tonio in I Pagliacci, Seattle Opera, 74; Iago in Otello, Washington Opera Asn, 76; Nabucco in Nabucco, Verdi Fest, San Diego, 81; Macbeth in Macbeth, Theatre Musical Paris, 82; Boris Ismailor, Spoleto Fest, 82 & Lyric Opera Chicago, 83; Baron Scarpia in Tosca, Royal Opera House, London, 83; Enrico in Lucia di Lammermoor, Vienna State Opera, Austria, 83. *Awards:* First Prize & Mozart Prize, Concours Int Chant Belgique, Brussels, 62; Verdi d'Oro, Parma, Italy, 81. *Rep:* S A Gorlinsky Ltd 35 Dover St London Gt Brit W1. *Mailing Add:* Rigistr 52 Zurich 8006 Switzerland

NUROCK, KIRK
COMPOSER, PIANO
b Camden, NJ, Feb 28, 48. *Study:* Eastman Sch Music, with Rayburn Wright, summer 65 & 66; Juilliard Sch, with Vincent Persichetti, Roger Sessions & Luciano Berio, BM, 70, MM(comp), 72. *Works:* Rhythm Chant, 71, Audience Oratorio, 75, Track, 76, Git Gon, 78, Maximal Textures, 78 & Sonata for Piano & Dog, 83, B Schött's Sohne, Mainz, Germany. *Pos:* Music dir, Ens Studio Theatre, 70-; cond, Broadway prod of Hair, Shelter, Two Gentlemen, Salvation & others, 71-80; mem bd dir, Ctr New Music, 71-75 & Meet The Comp, 73-; comp in res, Vt Summer Theatre Fest, 73; founder & artistic dir, Nat Sound Ctr Inc, 74- *Publ:* Auth, Natural Sound, Scores, 80; Music and Healing, Ear Mag, 81. *Rep:* Sheldon Soffer Mgt 130 W 56th St New York NY 10019. *Mailing Add:* 246 Eighth Ave New York NY 10011

NYFENGER, THOMAS
FLUTE, EDUCATOR
Pos: Flutist, New York Woodwing Quintet, formerly; soloist orch & chamber music. *Teaching:* Mem fac flute, Yale Sch Music, 57-, coordr wind dept, currently; coach chamber music currently. *Mailing Add:* Yale Sch Music Yale Univ PO Box 2104A New Haven CT 06520

NYQUIST, ROGER THOMAS
EDUCATOR, ORGAN
b Rockford, Ill, July 11, 34. *Study:* Augustana Col, Rock Island, Ill, with Philip McDermott, BM, 57; Syracuse Univ, with Arthur Poister, MM, 58; Ind Univ, Bloomington, with Oswald Ragatz, DM, 68. *Works:* Adagio (organ), H W Gray, 65. *Rec Perf:* Organ Masterpieces, Vol I, 73, Vol II, 75 & Roger Nyquist Plays Bach, Franck and Haydn, 74, Bridge Rec; Roger Nyquist Plays the Mission Organ, Univ Santa Clara, Chapel, 76; The Art of Roger Nyquist, 78, Poulenc and Franck, 79 & Bach, Reger, Bull, Johnson and Tournemire, 81, Orion Rec. *Teaching:* Instr, Southwestern Col, Winfield, Kans, 58-59; asst prof, Univ Calif, Santa Barbara, 62-67; prof & organist, Univ Santa Clara, 68- *Mem:* Am Guild Organists. *Mailing Add:* Music Dept Univ Santa Clara Santa Clara CA 95053

O

OAKES, RODNEY HARLAND
COMPOSER, ELECTRONIC
b Rome, NY, Apr 15, 37. *Study:* San Diego State Univ, with David Ward-Steinman, BA, 60; MA, 66; Univ Ariz, with Robert McBride; Univ Southern Calif, with Anthony Vazzana, DMA, 73. *Works:* Song for Two Voices (sop, alto & piano); Variations on an 18th Century Hymn Tune (organ & brass); Mass (strings), 65; You are the God (sop, basses & organ), 70; Synergy (ballet), comn by Nat Endowment Arts, 75; Grab the Ring (musical with Larry Heimgartner), 76; Abadada (children's musical with Heimgartner), 77. *Pos:* Dir, Electronic Music Studio, Los Angeles Harbor Col, 72-; performer, Chant Chance, PBS-TV, Los Angeles, Steps to Learning, CBS & throughout US. *Awards:* Celia Buck Grant, 66; Nat Endowment Arts Grant, 75. *Mem:* Music Educr Nat Conf; Am Soc Univ Comp; Audio Engineering Soc. *Publ:* Contribr to Composer & Synapse. *Mailing Add:* 500 Prospect Blvd Pasadena CA 91103

OBENSHAIN, KATHRYN GARLAND
EDUCATOR, WRITER
b Glen Alum, WVa, Nov 18, 31. *Study:* Mary Washington Col, BA, 53; Radford Col, MS, 67; Va Polytechnic Inst & State Univ, EdD, 74. *Works:* Lift Your Voices, Harold Flammer, 70; Holiday Songbag, 72 & Food, Fun & Festivals, 74, Shawnee Press; single songs for children publ in Humpty Dumpty, Jack & Jill & others. *Teaching:* Piano & church musician, Christiansburg Presby Church, Va, 53-71; from instr to prof music, Radford Univ, 68- *Awards:* Cert for Excellence in Res, Va Asn Res Educ, 74; Donald N Dedmon Award, Radford Univ Found, 81; Outstanding Alumnus Award, Mary Washington Col, 82. *Mem:* Radford Soc Am; Music Teachers Nat Asn; Va Music Teachers Asn (founder & pres Highlands chap, 70-74). *Publ:* Auth, Training Tomorrow's Teachers, Counterpoint, 74; Robert Schumann: Songwriter, 74; Schumann as Symphonist, 74 & Opera in America, 76, Am Music Teacher; Practice Problems? Try a Contract, Clavier, 81. *Mailing Add:* Music Dept Radford Univ Radford VA 24142

OBER, CAROL JEAN
CLARINET, TEACHER
b Muskegon, Mich, Nov 28, 40. *Study:* Univ Mich, BMus, 63, MMus, 65, teaching cert, 68. *Pos:* First clarinet, NC Symph, 65-66 & Can Opera Co, 68-73; asst prin clarinet, Detroit Conct Band, 66-; clarinettist & leader, Toronto Woodwind Quintet, 70-77; clarinet & bass clarinet, Mich Opera Theatre, 78-, prin clarinet, currently; recitalist throughout Mich & Can. *Teaching:* Private instr & lectr. *Awards:* Arion Award, 58. *Publ:* Auth, Clarinet Mouthpiece Designs & Acoustics, 65. *Mailing Add:* 1418 Morton St Ann Arbor MI 48104

OBERBRUNNER, JOHN
EDUCATOR, FLUTE
b New York, NY, Mar 1, 30. *Study:* Mannes Sch Music, 43-47; Syracuse Univ, BMus(music ed), 50. *Rec Perf:* Concerto (Ibert), 77 & Poem (Griffes), 82, Syracuse Symph. *Pos:* Prin flute, Syracuse Symph, 61- *Teaching:* Instrm music, Syracuse Publ Sch, 50-; prof flute, Syracuse Univ, 52- *Mem:* Music Educ Nat Conf; Nat Flute Asn. *Mailing Add:* 736 Ackerman Ave Syracuse NY 13210

OBERLE, FREYA ELLEN
CELLO
b Denver, Colo, May 8, 54. *Study:* New England Consv Music, BMus, 75; studied with David Soyer, Stefan Popov & Ben Zander; Berkshire Music Ctr, 76-77. *Pos:* Sect cellist, Atlantic Symph, 77-79; asst prin cellist, Opera Co Boston, 79; solo cellist, Alea III Contemp Ens, 79; cellist, New England Ragtime Ens, 79; prin cellist, Des Moines Metropolitan Opera, 81- *Teaching:* Cello, All-Newton Music Sch, 79. *Awards:* C D Jackson Master Award, Berkshire Music Ctr, 77. *Mem:* Boston Musicians Asn. *Mailing Add:* 115 Gibbs St Newton MA 02159

OBERLIN, RUSSELL
COUNTERTENOR, EDUCATOR
b Akron, Ohio, Oct 11, 28. *Study:* Juilliard Sch Music, dipl voice, 51. *Rec Perf:* Messiah (Handel) & Magnificat (Bach), Columbia Rec; Russell Oberlin Sings Handel Arias, Baroque Cantatas & A Russell Oberlin Recital, Decca & MCA Rec; 9 Vol Medieval Series, EA & Lyrichord Rec; 19 Pro Musica Albums, Columbia, Decca, Esoteric, Period & MCA Rec. *Roles:* Oberon in Midsummer Nights Dream, Royal Opera House, Covent Garden, San

Francisco Opera Co & Vancouver Int Fest Opera Co. *Pos:* Soloist & founding mem, New York Pro Musica, formerly. *Teaching:* Prof music, Hunter Col, City Univ New York, 66-; vis prof, Cambridge Univ, England, 77-78. *Awards:* Sr Res Award, Fulbright Fel, 68-69. *Mem:* Nat Asn Teachers Singing. *Interests:* High male singing: castrato, male alto and countertenor in United States, England and Australia. *Mailing Add:* Dept Music Hunter Col City Univ New York 695 Park Ave New York NY 10021

OBETZ, JOHN WESLEY
ORGAN, EDUCATOR
b Ashland, Pa, June 29, 33. *Study:* Northwestern Univ, BME, 54, MM, 55; Union Theol Sem, New York, SMD, 62. *Rec Perf:* Wachet Auf Ruft Uns Die Stimme (Max Reger), Op 52/2, Benedictus (Max Reger), Op 59/5, Toccata in D Minor (Max Reger), Op 59/5, Incantation Pour Un Jour Saint (Jean Langlais), Trois Paraphrases Gregoriennes (Jean Langlais), Ave Marie, Vae Maris Stells (Jean Langlais), Mores et Ressurectio (Jean Langlais) & Hymne d'Action de Grace "Te Deum", 81, Lyrichord; Views from the Oldest House (Ned Rorem), Paris in the 30s (Ned Rorem), Victimae Paschali (Tournemire), Le Jardin Suspendu (Alain) & Dieu Parmi Nous (Messiaen), Celebre Rec, 83. *Pos:* Auditorium organist, Reorganized Church Jesus Christ Latter Day Saints, 67- *Teaching:* Organist, Albion Col, Mich, 62-67; prof organ, Consv Music, Univ Mo, Kansas City, 70- *Bibliog:* Thomas Brown (auth), The Auditorium Organ with John Obetz, Am Organist, 6/83. *Mem:* Am Guild Organists (regional chmn, 72-78 & nat exec comt, 82-); Pi Kappa Lambda. *Rep:* Conct Mgt 13408 Flagstone Lane Dallas TX 75420. *Mailing Add:* RLDS Auditorium-Worship Comn PO Box 1059 Independence MO 64051

OBRECHT, ELDON ROSS
COMPOSER, DOUBLE BASS
b June 9, 20. *Study:* State Univ Iowa, BA, 40, MA, 42, PhD, 50. *Works:* Symphony in G, Univ Iowa Symph, 56; Sonata (French horn & piano), Paul Anderson & Margaret Pendleton, 57; Canzona (organ), Gerhard Drapf, 69; Diversions I & II, Seesaw-Okra, 72; Symphony #3, Univ Iowa Symph, 72; Sonata Movements (double bass & piano), Eldon Obrecht & Carole Thomas, 79. *Pos:* Mem, Nat Symph, 46-47. *Teaching:* Prof music, Univ Iowa, 47- *Mem:* Int Soc Bassists. *Mailing Add:* 1000 River St Iowa City IA 52240

O'BRIEN, EUGENE JOSEPH
COMPOSER
b Paterson, NJ, Apr 24, 45. *Study:* Univ Nebr, BMus, 67, MMus, 69; Staatliche Hochschule Musik, Cologne, Ger, with Bernd Alois Zimmermann, 69-70; Ind Univ, with Iannis Xenakis & John Eaton; Case Western Reserve Univ, studied comp with Donald Erb, DMA, 83. *Works:* Dedales, comn by Koussevitzky Found, 74; Ambages, G Schirmer, 75; Tristan's Lament, Sonitron Musikverlag, Munich, 79; Allures, Blackearth Perc Group, 79; Embarking for Cythera, Boosey & Hawkes, 78; Black Fugatos, Cleveland Orch Chamber Players, 83. *Teaching:* Assoc instr, Ind Univ, Bloomington, 70-71; instr comp, Cleveland Inst Music, 73-81 & comp in res & chmn comp dept, 81- *Awards:* Prix De Rome, Am Acad, Rome, 71-73; Music Award, Nat Inst Am Acad Arts & Lett, 80. *Mem:* ASCAP; Cleveland Comp Guild (pres, 77-79); Reconnaissance New Music Ens (dir, 78-). *Mailing Add:* 1681 Cumberland Rd Cleveland Heights OH 44118

O'BRIEN, JAMES PATRICK
EDUCATOR
b Torrance, Calif, Mar 6, 39. *Study:* Portland State Univ, BS, 61; Cent Wash State Univ, MEd, 66; Univ Colo, PhD, 69. *Teaching:* From asst prof to assoc prof, Ore Col of Educ, 68-73; lectr, Torrance Col of Advanced Educ, Adelaide, Australia, 73-75; from assoc prof to prof, Univ Ariz, 75- *Publ:* Auth, Non-Western Music, Kendall-Hunt, 77; A Guide to Successful Student Teaching, 4/80, Integrating World Musics, 9/80 & A Plea for Pop, 3/82, Music Educr J; Teaching Music, Holt, 83. *Mailing Add:* 8019 E Coronado Tucson AZ 85215

O'BRIEN, JOHN THOMAS
EDUCATOR, PIANO
b Waco, Tex, Aug 28, 31. *Study:* Baylor Univ, BMus, 52, MMus, 53; Acad Music & Dramatic Arts, Vienna, 55-56; New Sch Music Study, Princeton, dipl piano pedagogy, 63. *Pos:* Consult, Frances Clark Libr for Piano Students, 68-82. *Teaching:* Dir teaching training & piano pedagogy, New Sch Music Study, 68-70; assoc prof piano pedagogy, Goshen Col, 70-78 & Columbus Col, 78- *Mem:* Music Teachers Nat Asn. *Mailing Add:* Dept Music Columbus Col Columbus GA 31993

O'BRIEN, ORIN
EDUCATOR, BASS
Study: Juilliard Sch Music; Univ Calif, Los Angeles; studied double bass with Kestenbaum, Reinshagen & Zimmerman. *Pos:* Mem, City Ballet Orch & Saidenberg Little Symph, formerly; mem bass sect, New York Phil, 66- *Teaching:* Mem fac, Young Men's Hebrew Asn Sch Music, 67-71; mem fac double bass, Manhattan Sch Music, 69- *Mailing Add:* Manhattan Sch Music 120 Claremont Ave New York NY 10027

O'BRIEN, ROBERT FELIX
EDUCATOR, MUSIC DIRECTOR
b Breese, Ill, June 24, 21. *Study:* Navy Sch Music, 42-43; Southern Ill Univ, BS(music educ), 47; State Univ Iowa, MA(orch & cond), 49; Univ Colo, Boulder, 51-52. *Works:* Damsha Bua (victory clog), 69 & Lullaby, Oz Music Publ; Angst (brass choir), Nat Cath Bandmasters Asn; The Spirit of America, TV Music. *Pos:* Band dir, Iowa pub sch, 47-51. *Teaching:* Assoc prof & band dir, Univ Notre Dame, 52-55 & 55- & St Johns Univ, 54-55. *Awards:* Unseren

Freuden, Dachorganisation, Wiesbadener Karnel 1950 EV, Wiesbaden, Germany, 72; Adam P Lesinsky Award, Nat Cath Bandmasters Asn, 76. *Mem:* Founding mem, Nat Cath Bandmasters Asn (hon life pres, 52-); ASCAP; Am Bandmasters Asn; Col Band Dir Nat Asn. *Mailing Add:* 1452 Glenlake Dr South Bend IN 46614

O'BRIEN, VALERIE ELIZABETH
WRITER
b Glens Falls, NY, Mar 26, 54. *Study:* Oberlin Col, BA(English & music), 77; Columbia Univ, MS, 83. *Pos:* Freelance writer, Ovation, Musical Am, Symph Mag & Greenwood Press Publ, 79-; assoc ed, Ovation Mag, 79-80; ed, Int League Women Comp Newsletter, 81-82. *Mem:* Sonneck Soc; Music Libr Asn; affil mem, Int League Women Comp (mem bd dir, 82-); Int Alban Berg Soc. *Mailing Add:* 315 W 106th St New York NY 10025

O'CARROLL, CATHLEEN (CATHLEEN DALSCHAERT)
VIOLIN, TEACHER-COACH
b Auckland, New Zealand; US citizen. *Study:* New South Wales Consv, Australia, dipl, 48; Royal Acad Music, London, with Frederick Glinke, 54; Royal Consv Music, Belgium, 55; studied with Artur Grumiaux & Pablo Casals, 58. *Pos:* Soloist, Australian Broadcasting Comn, 49-51 & Musica Viva Chamber Orch, 56-68; first violin, Cleveland Orch, 60-67 & Philadelphia Orch, 67-; recitalist & soloist, US, Australia & Europe. *Teaching:* Asst prof violin, Royal Acad Music, London, 53-55; private lessons, currently. *Awards:* Violin Award, Royal Acad Music, London, 55; Premier Prix, Royal Consv Music, Brussels, 56; Second Prize, Int Violin Compt Prix d'Arche, Brussels, 57. *Mailing Add:* 1230 Forge Rd Cherry Hill NJ 08034

OCHS, MICHAEL
LECTURER, EDUCATOR
b Cologne, Ger, Feb 1, 37; US citizen. *Study:* City Col New York, BA, 58; Columbia Univ, MS, 63; NY Univ, MA, 64; Simmons Col, DA, 75. *Pos:* Music Libr fel, City Col, City Univ New York, 62-63, cataloger, 63-65; music librn, Brandeis Univ, 65-68, creative arts librn, 68-74; librn, Eda Kuhn Loeb Music Libr, Harvard Univ, 78- *Teaching:* Lectr music, City Col, City Univ New York, 64; asst prof libr sci, Simmons Col, 74-78; lectr music bibliog, Harvard Univ, 78-81; sr lectr, 81-; vis lectr music librarianship, Simmons Col, 80-81. *Mem:* Music Libr Asn (chmn, New England chap, 68-69, Comt Bibliog Description, 71-73, Music Libr Admin Comt, 75-76 & Finance Comt, 76-78, mem bd dir, 76-78); Int Asn Music Libr (chmn, Prog Comt, 79-81); Boston Camerata (mem bd dir, 79-); Asn Rec Sound Collections; Sonneck Soc. *Publ:* Auth, An Alphabetical Index to Robert Schumann: Werke, 67 & An Index to Das Chorwerk (vol 1-110), 70, Music Libr Asn; A Taxonomy of Qualifications for Music Librarianship: The Cognitive Domain, Notes, 33:27-44; Qualifications for Music Librarianship in the USA, Fontes Artis Musicae, 25:64-69; Truth, Beauty, Love, and Music Librarianship, Columbia Univ, 80. *Mailing Add:* Music Libr Harvard Univ Cambridge MA 02138

OCHSE, ORPHA CAROLINE
EDUCATOR, COMPOSER
b St Joseph, Mo, May 6, 25. *Study:* Cent Methodist Col, BM, 47; Rochester Univ, MM, 48; Univ Mo, PhD(music educ), 53. *Works:* Chaconne (organ); Prelude and fugue (flute & organ). *Pos:* Dir music, First Congregational Church, Pasadena, 58-70. *Teaching:* Instr music, Cent Methodist Col, 48-50, Western Ill State Col, 50-51 & Phoenix Col, 52-57; lectr music, Calif Inst Tech, 60-76; assoc prof, Whittier Col, 70-77, prof music, 77- *Mem:* Am Guild Organists; Organ Hist Soc. *Interests:* Comparative studies in early European organ design; performance practices in baroque organ music; history of the organ in the United States. *Publ:* Auth, A History of the Organ in the United States, Ind Univ, 74. *Mailing Add:* PO Box 675 Whittier CA 90608

OCKWELL, FREDERICK
CONDUCTOR & MUSIC DIRECTOR, EDUCATOR
Study: New England Consv, BM, 65; Univ Wash, MA, 67; Staatliche Hochschule Music, Cologne, Germany, 67-69. *Pos:* Mem, Seattle Symph, formerly, Gurzenich Orch Cologne, formerly, Hamburg State Phil, formerly & Hamburg Symph, formerly; asst cond, Cologne Opera Studio, 67-69 & Hamburg State Opera, 69-71; music dir, Fox River Valley Symph Orch, Aurora, Ill, 74- & Opera Ill, summer 78. *Teaching:* Assoc prof cond & perf orgn & cond, Univ Symph Orch, Northwestern Univ, 71- *Awards:* Fulbright Scholar, 67-69. *Mailing Add:* 813 Hamlin Evanston IL 60201

O'CONNOR, THOMAS E
ADMINISTRATOR, OBOE & ENGLISH HORN
b Boston, Mass, Apr 20, 47. *Study:* Univ NMex, BM, 70; Univ Mo, Kansas City, 71; Inst Adv Musical Studies, Montreux, Switz, 74. *Pos:* Prin oboe, NMex Symph Orch, 72-76 & Orch Santa Fe, 75-; English horn & oboe, Santa Fe Opera, 78-; artistic dir, Ens Santa Fe, 78- *Mailing Add:* PO Box 2091 Santa Fe NM 87501

ODE, JAMES AUSTIN
EDUCATOR, TRUMPET
b Brandon, SDak, Dec 9, 34. *Study:* Augustana Col, BA, 57; Eastman Sch Music, MM, 61, DMA & perf cert(trumpet), 65; studied trumpet with Will Vacchiano & Carmine Caruso. *Rec Perf:* The Ithaca Brass Quintet, 71 & Recital Solos for Trumpet, 72, Mark Rec; The Ithaca Brass Quintet, Golden Crest, 73. *Pos:* Prin trumpet, Ninth Div Band, Ft Carson, Colo, 57-59. *Teaching:* Asst band dir & instr brass, Augustana Col, 61-63; prof trumpet & music lit, Sch Music, Ithaca Col, 65-81; chmn, Music Dept, Trinity Univ, 81- *Awards:* Fel, Danforth Found, 57-65; Grant Music Librarianship, US Dept Health, Educ & Welfare, 69. *Mem:* Am Fedn Musicians; Music Educr Nat

Conf; Music Teachers Nat Asn; Phi Mu Alpha Sinfonia. *Publ:* Auth, Army Band Opportunities, Int Musicians, 60; Brass Instruments in Church Services, 68 & Hymns and How to Sing Them, 69, Augsburg. *Mailing Add:* 611 Serenade Dr San Antonio TX 78216

O'DETTE, PAUL RAYMOND
LUTE
b Pittsburgh, Pa, Feb 2, 54. *Study:* Schola Cantorum Basilieusis; studied with Eugen Dombois, Thomas Binkley, Christopher Parkening & Michael Lorimer. *Rec Perf:* Italian Lute Duets, Seraphim, 78; The English Lute, Nonesuch, 79; Early Venetian Lute Music, Arabesque, 81; My True Love Hath My Heart, Pantheon, 82; Popular Elizabethan Music, Focus, 82; Tabulatures de Leut, 82 & Lute Music (John Dowland), 83, Astree. *Pos:* Co-dir, Musicians Swanne Alley, 76. *Teaching:* Dir early music, Eastman Sch Music, 76- *Mem:* Lute Soc Am (mem bd dir, 79-81 & 83-); Lute Soc Gr Brit. *Interests:* Historical lute techniques; 16th century performance practices. *Publ:* Auth, Some Observations on Dalza's Dance Music, Luth & Musique II, Cent Nat Recherche Sci, 83. *Rep:* Aaron & Gorden Conct Mgt 25 Huntington Ave Boston MA 02116. *Mailing Add:* 13 S Goodman Rochester NY 14607

O'DONNELL, RICHARD
COMPOSER, PERCUSSION
b St Louis, Mo, Feb 13, 37. *Study:* St Louis Inst Music, with Samuel Alder; NTex State Univ. *Works:* Microtimbre I (amplified tam-tam), 69; Microtimbre II (seven things that ring & tape recorder); Polytimbre I (large group instrm); Polytimbre II (three minute cadenza on tape); Polytimbre III (perc quartet); Duo for Vibraphone & Synthesizer in C. *Pos:* Prin perc, St Louis Symph Orch, 59- *Teaching:* Adj instr perc & electronic studio, Washington Univ, currently. *Awards:* Gold Placque, Chicago Int Film Fest. *Mailing Add:* St Louis Symph 718 N Grand Blvd St Louis MO 63103

ODUM-VERNON, ALISON P (ALISON PAIGE ODUM)
SOPRANO, EDUCATOR
b Norfolk, Va. *Study:* Converse Col, studied with Perry Daniels, BME(voice perf); Fla State Univ, with Eugene Talley-Schmidt, MM(voice); study with Genevieve McGiffert, currently. *Roles:* Queen of the Night in The Magic Flute, Columbia, Mo, 79; Despina in Cosi fan tutte, Chattanooga Opera Asn, 79; Der Gesan in Die Weihe de Hauses, Fest Hellbrunn, 79; Clorinda in Cinderella, Va Opera Asn, 81; sop soloist in The Messiah, 81 & Carmina Burana, 82, Va Phil; Papagena in The Magic Flute, Va Opera Asn, 82. *Pos:* Asst prof music, Cent Methodist Col, 78-79 & artist in res, 79-80. *Mem:* Nat Asn Teachers Singing; Nat Opera Asn; Metropolitan Opera Guild. *Mailing Add:* 924 Park Ave Collingswood NJ 08108

OGASAPIAN, JOHN KEN
EDUCATOR, ORGAN
b Worcester, Mass, Oct 1, 40. *Study:* Boston Univ, BMus, 62, MMus, 64, PhD, 77. *Teaching:* Instr, Lowell State Col, 65-69, asst prof, 69-76; assoc prof, Univ Lowell, 76-79, prof, 79- *Mem:* Am Musicol Soc; Sonneck Soc; Organ Hist Soc; Am Guild Organists. *Interests:* History of American organs and organ building; American church music. *Publ:* Auth, Organ Building in New York City, 1700-1900, 77 & Henry Erben: Portrait of a 19th Century American Organ Builder, 80; Organ Lit Found; Church Organs, Baker Book House, 83. *Mailing Add:* 14 Park St PO Box 204 Pepperell MA 01463

OGDON, WILL (WILBUR LEE OGDON)
COMPOSER, EDUCATOR
b Redlands, Calif, Apr 19, 21. *Study:* Univ Wis, BM, 42; Hamline Univ, MA, 47; Univ Calif, Berkeley; Ecole Normale Musique; Ind Univ, PhD, 55. *Works:* Un Tombeau de Cocteau II, perf by Keith Humble & B Ogdon with Univ Calif San Diego Ens, 72; Un Tombeau de Cocteau III, perf by Nora Post, State Univ NY, Buffalo, 75; Sappho (chamber opera), perf by Phil Larson & B Ogdon, 75-79; Five Comments and Cappriccio for Orchestra, La Jolla Civic Univ Orch, 79; Images, A Winter's Calendar, APNM & Sonor, 80; Six Small Trios (marimba, trumpet & piano), Int Chamber Consort, Sonor & Seattle New Music Group, 81-82; Five Pieces for Violin and Piano, perf by Janos Neayesy & Keith Humble, 82- *Pos:* Music dir, KPFA, Berkeley, Calif, 62-64; dir music prog, Univ Ill, Champaign-Urbana, 65-66; mem, San Diego Opera Asn, 68-, mem bd dirs, 68-70; mem, Ctr Music Experiment & Related Res, 75-, publ dir, 75-77, chmn adv bd, 78-81; mem bd dirs, La Jolla Symph Asn, 80-; mem, Arnold Schoenberg Inst, currently. *Teaching:* Asst prof, Univ Tex, Austin, 47-50; assoc prof, Ill Wesleyan Univ, 56-65; prof, Univ Calif San Diego, La Jolla, 66-, chmn dept music, 66-71. *Awards:* Fulbright Award in Comp, 52-53; Creative Arts Fel, Univ Calif, 72; Nat Endowment for Arts Award in Comp, 75. *Mem:* Charter mem, Anton Webern Soc. *Interests:* Theoretical studies on music related to the music of Schoenberg, Webern, Krenek, Leibowitz (20th century). *Publ:* Auth, Series and Structure, Univ Mich, 55; A Webern Analysis, J Music Theory, 62; coauth (with Ernst Krenele & John Stewart), Horizons Circled, Univ Calif Press, 74; auth, On Rene Leibowitz Traite de la Comp avec Douze Sons, 77 & Tonality in Early Atonal Music: Schoenbergs Op 11, 1, 80, J A Schoenberg Inst. *Mailing Add:* Music Dept Univ Calif San Diego La Jolla CA 92093

O'GRADY, TERENCE JOHN
EDUCATOR, WRITER
b Chicago, Ill, Oct 13, 46. *Study:* Univ Wis, Madison, BS, 68, MS, 72, PhD, 75. *Teaching:* Asst prof commun & arts, Univ Wis, Green Bay, 75-81, assoc prof, 81- *Mem:* Am Musicol Soc; Soc Ethnomusicol; Col Music Soc; Int Asn Study Popular Music; Sonneck Soc. *Interests:* Aesthetics of contemporary music; popular music. *Publ:* Auth, Rubber Soul and the Social Dance

Tradition, Ethnomusicol, Vol 23, No 1; The Ballad Style in the Early Music of the Beatles, Col Music Symposium, Vol 19, No 1; Interpretive Freedom and the Composer-Performer Relationship, J Aesthetic Educ, 4/81; Aesthetic Value in Indeterminate Music, Musical Quart, 7/81; The Beatles: A Musical Evolution, Twayne Publ, 5/83. *Mailing Add:* 326 Bellevue Green Bay WI 54302

OHL, FERRIS E
CONDUCTOR, EDUCATOR
b Crawford County, Ohio, Sept 10, 14. *Study:* Heidelberg Col, BM, 36; Cincinnati Consv, MM, 46; Teachers Col, Columbia Univ, MA, 50, prof dipl, 52, EdD, 55; study with Robert Weede, Conrad Bos, John Smallman & Viola Peters. *Works:* Ferris Ohl, Choral Series, Plymouth Music Co, 60-65. *Rec Perf:* Choral Music, Heidelberg Col Conct Choir, 76-82. *Pos:* Cond, Heidelberg Conct Choir, 46-82 & Tiffinian Male Chorus, 50-65. *Teaching:* Prof music, voice & cond, Heidelberg Col, 46-; vis prof voice & cond, Columbia Univ, 64-65. *Awards:* Int Inst Arts & Letters Fel, 61; Univ Heidelberg Ger Medal, 78. *Mem:* Inst Arts & Letters; Nat Asn Teachers Singing; Am Choral Dir Asn; Choral Cond Guild; Music Educr Nat Conf. *Mailing Add:* 98 W Woodmere Tiffin OH 44883

OHL, JOHN FRANKLIN
EDUCATOR, MUSIC DIRECTOR
b Chicago, Ill, June 14, 08. *Study:* Northwestern Univ, BS, 31; Harvard Univ, AM(music), 39, PhD(music), 45. *Pos:* Dir, Fisk Univ Choir, 44-51 & Univ Collegium Musicum, Northwestern Univ, 53-59; choirmaster, Church of the Holy Comforter, Kenilworth, Ill, 55-72. *Teaching:* Prof & chmn dept music, Fisk Univ, 44-51; prof & chmn dept music hist & lit, Northwestern Univ Sch Music, 51-73; musicol in res, Shenandoah Col Consv Music, 73- *Mem:* Am Musicol Soc (mem coun, 58-61); Soc Music Liberal Arts Col (treas, 54-55); Music Libr Asn. *Interests:* Bach, Handel and Mozart. *Publ:* Coauth, Masterpieces of Music Before 1750, W W Norton, 51; auth, Beethoven: Missa Solemnis, Choral J, 2/81. *Mailing Add:* Rte 1 Box 133A Winchester VA 22601

OHLSSON, GARRICK OLOF
PIANO
b Bronxville, NY, Apr 3, 48. *Study:* Westchester Consv Music; Juilliard Sch, with Sascha Gorodnitski & Rhosina Lhevinne. *Rec Perf:* Several recordings of Chopin & Liszt for EMI. *Pos:* Conct pianist with major US & Can symph orch, incl San Francisco, Memphis, Buffalo, Houston, Toronto, Winnipeg & Chicago; tours to London, Berlin, Vienna, Rome, Milan, Dusseldorf & Baden-Baden; col & univ conct series, 69- *Awards:* First Prize, Busoni Piano Compt, Italy, 66, Montreal Piano Compt, 68 & Warsaw Int Chopin Compt, 70. *Mailing Add:* 1 Hubbard Dr White Plains NY 10605

OHYAMA, HELLCHIRO
VIOLA, EDUCATOR
b Kyoto, Japan, July 31, 47. *Study:* Guildhall Sch Music & Drama, with Y Neaman, AGSM, 70; Toho Music Sch, with T Eto; Indian Univ, with W Primrose. *Rec Perf:* Music from Marlboro, String Quintets (Mendelssohn), Columbia Rec, 74; Vivaldi, Sonic Arts Rec, 77; Santa Fe Chamber Music Festival (Schöne), Nonesuch Rec, 81. *Pos:* Prin violist, Los Angeles Phil, 79-; dir, Santa Fe Chamber Music Fest, 77- & Crossroads Sch Chamber Orch, 80- *Teaching:* Prof music, Univ Calif, Santa Barbara, 73- *Awards:* Carl Flesch Compt Prize, 70; Ind Univ Music Compt Award, 72. *Mem:* Chamber Music Am; Young Musicians Found. *Mailing Add:* c/o Los Angeles Phil 135 N Grand Ave Los Angeles CA 90012

OJA, CAROL J
WRITER
b Hibbing, Minn. *Study:* St Olaf Col, BA, 74; Univ Iowa, MA, 76; Grad Sch, City Univ New York, MPhil, 80. *Pos:* Res asst, Inst Studies in Am Music, Brooklyn Col, 80- *Mem:* Am Musicol Soc; Music Libr Asn; Sonneck Soc. *Interests:* Twentieth century American music, with a concentration on 1920's and 1930's. *Publ:* Auth, The Still-Life Paintings of William Michael Harnett and Their Reflections Upon 19th-Century American Musical Culture, 77 & The Copland-Sessions Concerts, 4/79, Musical Quart; Trollopiana: David Claypoole Johnston Counters Mrs Trollope's Views on American Music, Col Music Symposium, 81; ed, Stravinsky in Modern Music, Da Capo, 82; American Music Recordings: A Discography of 20th-Century US Composers, Inst Studies Am Music, 82. *Mailing Add:* 245 Smith St Brooklyn NY 11231

OKA, HIRONO
VIOLIN
b Tokyo, Japan, June 9, 57. *Study:* San Francisco Consv Music, 77-78; Curtis Inst Music, dipl, 81, cert, 82. *Pos:* Second violinist, Philadelphia Orch, 81- & New Philadelphia Quartet, 81-82. *Awards:* Japanese Music Award, Japan Cult Broadcasting Station, 76. *Mailing Add:* 42 S 19th St Philadelphia PA 19103

OLCOTT, JAMES LOUIS
TRUMPET, EDUCATOR
b Berkeley, Calif, Feb 27, 44. *Study:* San Francisco State Univ, with Victor Kress, BA(music educ), 66; Manhattan Sch Music, studied trumpet with William Vacchiano & Cecil Collins, MM(trumpet perf), 68; Teachers Perf Inst, Oberlin Col, with Gene Young, summers 69-71; Eastman Sch Music, with Edwin Betts, summer 62; studied trumpet with Philip Collins, 80 & 81. *Pos:* Prin trumpet, Ft Hays Civic Symph, 66-77; Peter Britt Music & Art Fest Orch, Jacksonville, Ore, 66 & 69-83; Brattleboro Fest Orch, Vt, 66-67; Ft Hays Brass Fac Quintet, 68-75; Tex Fest Chamber, summer 77, Richmond

Symph Orch, Ind, 78-82, Oxford Brass Quintet, Ohio, 79-, Hamilton Symph Orch, 79-, Blue Lake Orch, 79-, Cincinnati Chamber Orch, 79-, Cincinnati Ballet Orch, 81- & Cincinnati Brasswinds, 81-; mem, Metropolitan Opera Co, 66-68 & Nat Orch Asn, New York, 66-68; co-prin trumpet, Tidewater Brass Quintet, St Mary's City, Md, summer 73; trumpet, Contemp Arts Quartet, Oxford, 79-82. *Teaching:* Instr music, Ft Hays State Univ, 68-72, asst prof music, 72-76, assoc prof music, 76-77, dir jazz ens, formerly; instr, cond brass choir & dir jazz ens, Univ Wis, Eau Claire, 77-78; asst prof, Miami Univ, Oxford, 78-82, assoc prof music & dir jazz ens & trumpet ens, 82- *Mem:* Int Trumpet Guild; Nat Asn Jazz Educr; Music Educr Nat Conf; Ohio Music Educr Asn. *Mailing Add:* Music Dept Miami Univ Oxford OH 45056

OLDANI, ROBERT WILLIAM
WRITER, EDUCATOR
b Herrin, Ill, Sept 16, 47. *Study:* Univ Mich, Ann Arbor, MA, 75, PhD, 78; studied with Glenn Watkins, Gwynn McPeek & Roland John Wiley. *Teaching:* Asst prof music, Southern Ill Univ, Edwardsville, 79-82 & Ariz State Univ, 82- *Mem:* Am Musicol Soc. *Interests:* Russian music, principally 19th century. *Publ:* Auth, Boris Godunov and the Censor, 19th Century Music, 79; Was Boris Godunov Really Rejected Twice?, Opera J, 80; contribr, Mussorgsky: In Memoriam, 1881-1981, UMI Res Press, 82; The English National Opera's Guide to Modest Mussorgsky's Boris Godunov, John Calder Ltd, 82; auth, Mussorgsky and Diaghilev, Liberal & Fine Arts Rev, 82. *Mailing Add:* Sch Music Ariz State Univ Tempe AZ 85287

OLDS, PATRICIA HUNT
ADMINISTRATOR, EDUCATOR
b Cincinnati, Ohio, Oct 29, 31. *Study:* Col Consv Music, Cincinnati Univ, studied with La Salle Quartet, MMus(cello), 51; Ind Univ, MA, 62. *Pos:* First cellist, Columbus Little Symph, 52-54; cellist, Wright State Univ String Quartet, 68-72. *Teaching:* From instr to asst prof music hist & lit, Wright State Univ, 70-80, assoc prof, 80-; dir, founder & instr ens & viol, Early Music Ctr, Yellow Springs, Ohio, 79- *Mem:* Royal Musical Asn; Col Music Soc; Viola da Gamba Soc England; Viola da Gamba Soc Am (rep midwest reg, 80-82). *Publ:* Auth, The Decline of the Viol in 17th Century England, Viola da Gamba Soc Am J, 80. *Mailing Add:* 242 Northwood Dr Yellow Springs OH 45387

OLEVSKY, JULIAN
VIOLIN, EDUCATOR
b Berlin, Germany, May 7, 26; nat US. *Study:* Violin with Alexander Petschnikoff. *Rec Perf:* All Bach Sonatas & Partitas for Solo Violin; 12 Vivaldi Concerti; 15 Handel Sonatas; complete violin & piano works by Mozart; A Violin Recital; rec on Westminster Rec. *Pos:* World wide conct violin tours, 36- *Teaching:* Prof violin, Univ Mass, Amherst, currently. *Mailing Add:* 68 Blue Hills Rd Amherst MA 01002

OLIVEIRA, ELMAR
VIOLIN
b Waterbury, Conn, June 28, 50. *Study:* Hartt Sch Music; Manhattan Sch Music. *Rec Perf:* Numerous for CBS Masterworks, RCA, Delos, Melodiya, Vox Cum Laude & Grenadilla Rec. *Pos:* Conct violinist, 78- *Awards:* First Prize, Naumburg Compt; Gold Medal, Tchaikovsky Int Compt, Russia, 78; Avery Fisher Prize, 83. *Mailing Add:* c/o Robert Levin Assoc Inc 250 W 57th St Ste 1332 New York NY 10107

OLIVER, LISI
ADMINISTRATOR
b Frankfurt, Germany, Dec 13, 51, US citizen. *Study:* Univ Wis, Madison, with Gil Hemsley, 1975; Smith Col, BA. *Pos:* Prod stage mgr, Opera Co Boston & Opera New England, 76-78, assoc dir, 80-; asst dir, Komische Opera, Berlin, East Germany, 78-79; dep dir, Opera Co Philippines, 82- *Awards:* Director's Grant, Nat Opera Inst, 78. *Mailing Add:* 539 Washington St Boston MA 02111

OLIVER, NILS
CELLO, EDUCATOR
b Burbank, Calif, Apr 24, 52. *Study:* Univ Southern Calif, BM, 73; Manhattan Sch Music, MM, 75. *Rec Perf:* Music of William Henderson, Orion Rec, 81. *Pos:* Mem, Los Angeles Chamber Orch, 79- *Teaching:* Vis lectr violoncello, Univ Calif, Los Angeles, 79- *Awards:* Koussevitzky Award, Musicians Club New York, 74; Nat Cello Prize, Fri Morning Music Club, Washington, DC, 76; Nat String Award, Music Teachers Nat Asn, 76. *Mailing Add:* Dept Music Col Fine Arts Univ Calif Los Angeles CA 90024

OLIVEROS, PAULINE
COMPOSER, ACCORDION
b Houston, Tex, May 30, 32. *Study:* Univ Houston, studied accordion with Willard Palmer, 52; San Francisco State Col, studied comp with Robert Erickson, BA, 57. *Works:* Tashi Gomang, Cabrillo Fest Orch, 81; The Well, 82-83 & Traveling Companions (perc & dance), 83, Deborah Hay Dance Co, Austin, Tex; Gathering Together (piano, eight hands), Kitchen Benefit, New York, 83; The Wanderer, Springfield Accordion Orch, 83; The Wheel of Time, Smith, 83; Pieces of Eight, Harmonium Mundi, St Paul, Minn, 83. *Rec Perf:* I of IV, Odyssey Rec, 66; Bye Bye Butterfly, Arch Rec, 79; Horse Sings from Cloud, 83 & Rattlesnake Mountain, 83, Lovely Music. *Pos:* Dir, Tape Music Ctr, Mills Col, 66-67 & Ctr Music Experiment, Univ Calif, San Diego, 76-79. *Teaching:* Prof comp & experimental studies, Univ Calif, San Diego, 67-81. *Awards:* Best Foreign Work, Gaudeamus Found, Holland, 62; Guggenheim Fel, 73; First Prize (Stadtmusik), City of Bonn, Ger, 77. *Bibliog:* Morton Subotnik (auth), Trio for Flute, Piano & Page Turner, Perspectives New Music, 63; Robert Ashley (auth), Music with Roots in the Aether, Art

Serv, 76; Heidi Von Gunden (auth), The Music of Pauline Oliveros, Scarecrow Press, 83. *Mem:* Am Music Ctr; Comp Forum; Meet the Comp; New Music Alliance; Experimental Intermedia Found. *Publ:* Auth, Some Sound Observations, Source, 68; On Sonic Meditation, Painted Bride Quart, 74; Pauline's Proverbs, Printed Ed, 76; Software for People, New Wilderness Lett, 79; Initiation Dream, Astro Artz, 82. *Mailing Add:* Box 164 Mt Tremper NY 12457

OLMSTEAD, ANDREA LOUISE
WRITER, EDUCATOR
b Dayton, Ohio, Sept 5, 48. *Study:* NY Univ, MA, 74; Hartt Col Music, BM, 72. *Teaching:* Instr music lit, Aspen Music Sch, 72-76; prof music hist, Juilliard Sch, 72-80 & Boston Consv, 81- *Awards:* Sinfonia Found Grant Am Music, 80. *Mem:* Sonneck Soc; Am Musicol Soc. *Interests:* American 20th century composers, particularly Roger Sessions. *Publ:* Contribr, Current Musicol, 74-75; auth, Roger Sessions: A Personal Portrait, Tempo, 78; Review of Roger Sessions: Collected Essays, Perspectives New Music, 81; The Rome Prize, High Fidelity, Musical Am, 83; Roger Sessions and His Music, Toccata Press (in prep). *Mailing Add:* 255 Massachusetts Ave Apt 305 Boston MA 02115

OLMSTEAD, GARY JAMES
EDUCATOR, PERCUSSION
b Portland, Mich, Feb 4, 41. *Study:* Univ Mich, BM, 63; Ohio Univ, MFA, 66; Cleveland Inst Music, DMA, 75. *Teaching:* Prof perc, Indiana Univ Pa, 66- *Mem:* Percussive Arts Soc (vpres, 71-72 & pres, 73-77); Music Teachers Nat Asn. *Publ:* Auth, Bourree, Studio 4 Prod, 77; The Snare Drum Roll, Permus Publ. *Mailing Add:* 1245 Oak St Indiana PA 15701

OLSEN, A LORAN
COMPOSER, EDUCATOR
b Minneapolis, Minn, Oct 7, 30. *Study:* Grinnell Col, BA, 51; studied with Gaetani Comelli, 52, Blanche Bascourret, 54 & Nadia Boulanger, 54; Drake Univ, with Francis Pyle, MM, 55; Univ Iowa, with John Simms & Philip Bezanson, PhD, 60. *Works:* Song of Joy (choir & French horn); Study for Piano and Tape Recorder; Piano Concertino; Setting for Chamber Orchestra and Tape Recorder; Woodwind Trio; Quintet for Brass and Piano; Two Love Poems (sop, string quartet, vibraphone & tape). *Teaching:* Mem fac, Luther Col, 55-57, Wis State Univ, 58-60 & Hastings Col, 60-65; prof music, Wash State Univ, 65- *Awards:* Steiner Award, 51; First Prize, Iowa Young Comp Cont, 56; First Prize, Wis State Fair Comp Cont, 60. *Publ:* The Nez Perce Flute, Northwest Anthropology Res Notes, Vol 13, No 1. *Mailing Add:* Dept Music Wash State Univ Pullman WA 99164

OLSEN, DALE ALAN
EDUCATOR, SHAKUHACHI
b Albert Lea, Minn, July 10, 41. *Study:* Univ Minn, BA, 64, MA, 66; Univ Calif, Los Angeles, PhD, 73. *Teaching:* Prof, Fla State Univ, 73- *Awards:* Fulbright Fel, 79; artist in res, Japan Found, 79-81. *Mem:* Soc Ethnomusicol; Soc Asian Music; Soc Ethnomusicol, Southeast Caribbean Chap. *Interests:* Native music of Venezuela; folk music of Peru; music of Japanese immigrants in South America. *Publ:* Auth, Doce Conferencias in Ethnomusicologia ... Atlas Musical, Peru, 79; contribr, Symbol and Function in South American Indian Music & Folk Music of South American, In: Musics of Many Cult, Calif, 80; auth, The Social Determinants of Japanese Musical Life ..., Soc Ethnomusicol, 83; Japanese Music in Brazil, J Soc Asian Music, 83. *Rep:* Sch Music Fla State Univ Tallahassee FL 32306. *Mailing Add:* 2405 Willamette Circle Tallahassee FL 32303

OLSON, PHYLLIS EDWARD
ADMINISTRATOR, DOUBLE BASS
b Medford, Wis, Oct 15, 24. *Study:* Eastman Sch Music, BM, 46, MM(music lit), 48; studied string bass with Oscar Zimmerman. *Pos:* Bass sec mem, Rochester Phil, Denver Symph, 43-48; mem, Univ Ill Sinfonietta, 49-52; co-dir, Early Music Ens, Towson State Univ, 79- *Teaching:* Instr string bass & piano, Univ Ill, Urbana, 49-52; asst prof bass & music lit, Towson State Univ, 69-73, lectr, 79- *Mem:* Viola da Gamba Soc Am (pres, 80-); Am Musicol Soc; Am String Teachers' Asn; Int Soc Bassists. *Mailing Add:* 806 W University Pkwy Baltimore MD 21210

OLTMAN, C DWIGHT
CONDUCTOR & MUSIC DIRECTOR, EDUCATOR
b Imperial, Nebr. *Study:* McPherson Col, BS; Wichita State Univ, MM; study comp with Nadia Boulanger, France; study cond with Pierre Monteux & Max Rudolf. *Rec Perf:* St Matthew Passion by J S Bach, WVIZ, nat PBS telecast, 83. *Pos:* Music dir & cond, Ohio Chamber Orch, 72-; music dir & prin cond, Cleveland Ballet, 76-; music dir, Baldwin-Wallace Bach Fest, 76- *Bibliog:* Frank Hruby (auth), Conductor Comes from the West, Cleveland Press, 11/18/77; Wilma Salisbury (auth), Oltman Finds Happiness in all Directions, Plain Dealer, 11/8/81. *Mem:* Am Symph Orch League; Am Fedn Musicians; Cond Guild; Orgn Ohio Orch (bd dir, 82-). *Mailing Add:* 395 Cranston Dr Berea OH 44017

ONDREJKA, RONALD
CONDUCTOR & MUSIC DIRECTOR
b New York, NY, Oct 12, 32. *Study:* Eastman Sch Music, BM, 53, MM, 54. *Pos:* Cond, Radio City Music Hall Orch, 57-60, Monterey Co Symph, Calif, 60-61, Buffalo Phil Orch, 61-63, Cincinnati Symph, 63-65 & Pittsburgh Symph, 65-67; music dir, Santa Barbara Symph, 67-78 & Ft Wayne Phil, 78- *Mailing Add:* Ft Wayne Phil 1107 S Harrison St Ft Wayne IN 46802

O'NEAL, BARRY
COMPOSER, MUSIC PUBLISHER
b New York, NY, June 9, 42. *Study:* Boston Univ, BA, 64. *Works:* God's Grandeur (chorus & band), perf by Angelo State Univ Conct Choir & Wind Ens, 79; Dr Jekyll & Mr Hyde (opera), excerpts perf by Tom Hageman, Kathy Kelly & Eric Milnes, 81; Anniversary Suite (sop & piano), perf by Jane Bryden & Eric Milnes, 81; Psalm 70, Music 70, 81; Look, See the Star (chorus), 82 & Let Us Also (chorus & organ), 82, perf by Lafayette Ave Presby Church Choir; Meditation (mixed chorus), Music 70/80, 82. *Pos:* Rental librn, Assoc Music Publ Inc, 64-66, sales rep, 66-73, mgr, 79-; sales rep, G Schirmer Inc, 73-74, educ rep, 74-79. *Mailing Add:* 220 W 98th St New York NY 10025

O'NEAL, MICHAEL M
CONDUCTOR & MUSIC DIRECTOR, TENOR
b Bowling Green, Ky, Nov 28, 48. *Study:* Murray State Univ, Ky, BME, 70, MME, 71; Univ Ga, EdD, 83. *Roles:* Tenor in Messiah (Handel), 73, Cantata No 131 (Bach), 78 & Cantata No 78 (Bach), 82, Atlanta Symph Orch. *Teaching:* Asst prof choral & vocal & chmn music dept, NGa Col, 71-79; assoc prof choral & church music & chmn fine arts div, Mercer Univ, Atlanta, Ga, 79- *Mem:* Am Choral Dir Asn; Music Educr Nat Conf. *Mailing Add:* 3001 Mercer University Dr Atlanta GA 30341

ONISHI, AIKO
EDUCATOR, PIANO
b Tokyo, Japan; US citizen. *Study:* Eastman Sch Music, BM & perf cert, 53, artists dipl, 56; studied with Frank Mannheimer, 56 & 64-72 & with Myra Hess, 64-65. *Rec Perf:* Solo recital, Int Piano Fest, Univ Md, 65 & 72, Conv Music Teachers Asn Calif, 65 & 77 & Am Matthay Piano Fest, 77 & 82; solo, San Jose Symph, 74. *Teaching:* Assoc prof, Toho Sch Music, 56-66; prof piano, San Jose State Univ, 66- *Awards:* Pres Ann Scholar, San Jose State Univ. *Mem:* Music Teachers Asn Calif; Am Matthay Piano Asn (mem bd dirs, 81-); Mu Phi Epsilon. *Mailing Add:* Music Dept San Jose State Univ San Jose CA 95192

OOM-PAH MAN See Young, Frederick John

OPALACH, JAN
BASS-BARITONE
b Hackensack, NJ, Sept 2, 50. *Study:* Ind Univ, BMus, 73. *Rec Perf:* Mass in B minor (J S Bach), Nonesuch; Griffes Collected Songs, Musical Heritage Soc. *Roles:* Colline in La Boheme, Va Opera Asn, 79; Schaunard in La Boheme, New York City Opera, 80; Figaro in Le Nozze di Figaro, Ky Opera Asn, 81; Dulcamara in L'Elisir d'amore, 82 & Leporello in Don Giovanni, 82, Des Moines Metropolitan Opera; Nanni in L'Infedelta Delusa, Mostly Mozart Fest, 82; Dandini in La Cenerentola, Grand Rapids Opera, 83. *Awards:* First Prize, Metropolitan Opera Nat Coun, 79, W M Naumburg Compt Vocalists, 80 & Int Vocal Compt, s'Hertogenbosch, Holland, 81. *Rep:* John Gingrich Mgt Box 1515 New York NY 10023. *Mailing Add:* 209 W 97 #7A New York NY 10025

OPHEIM, VERNON HOLMAN
CONDUCTOR & MUSIC DIRECTOR, EDUCATOR
b Sedelia, Alta, Dec 29, 31; US citizen. *Study:* Concordia Col, BA(music), 54; MacPhail Sch Music, MM(music educ), 66; Univ Ill, Urbana, DMA(choral music), 71. *Works:* Why Weeps, Alas, My Lady Love, 75, Sing We, 75 & Agnus Del, 75, Schmitt-Hall McCreary; Vox Clamantis in Deserto, 83 & Omnis Qui se Exultat, 83, Broude Brothers Publ Co. *Teaching:* Supvr music, Moorhead pub sch, 55-66; instr, Univ Ill, 66-69; asst prof, Univ Maine, Orono, 69-72; prof, Univ Minn, Duluth, 72- *Awards:* Award for Distinguished Contrib to City of Gdansk, Poland, Gdansk Dept Cult & Art, 82. *Mem:* Am Choral Dir Asn (mem bd dir Minn chap, 76-81); Music Educr Nat Conf; Minn Music Educr Asn (vpres, 61-63); Am Musicol Soc; Col Music Soc. *Interests:* Johann Wanning (1537-1603). *Mailing Add:* 1826 Vermilion Rd Duluth MN 55803

OPPENS, URSULA
PIANO
b New York, NY, Feb 2, 44. *Study:* Radcliffe Col, BA, 65; Juilliard Sch Music, MS, 67. *Rec Perf:* Music for Two Pianos & Piano Four Hands (Stravinsky), Nonesuch, 77; The People United Will Never Be Defeated (Frederic Rzewski), Vanguard, 79; Petrouchka (Stravinsky), Nonesuch, 82. *Pos:* Mem, Speculum Musicae, 71-81, Am Comp Orch, 75-; perf world premieres of works by Elliot Carter, Charles Wuorinen, Frederic Rzewski, Christian Wolff, Tobias Picker, Peter Lieberson, Anthony Braxton, Donald Martino, John Harbison & Leo Smith. *Awards:* Gold Medal, Busoni Piano Compt, 69; Avery Fisher Prize, 76. *Bibliog:* Pamela Margles (auth), Music Mag, Toronto, 8/82; Glenn Plaskin (auth), New York Times, 1/2/83. *Mem:* Am Music Ctr; Comp Forum. *Mailing Add:* c/o Colbert Artists Mgt 111 W 57th New York NY 10025

OPPER, JACOB
EDUCATOR, CONDUCTOR
b Lodz, Poland, Nov 4, 35. *Study:* Fla State Univ, BM, 58, MM, 65, PhD, 70. *Teaching:* Assoc prof, Frostburg State Col, 70- *Awards:* Nat Endowment Humanities Award, 75 & 83. *Mem:* Am Musicol Soc; Am Soc 18th Century Studies. *Interests:* Relationship between music and philosophical consequences of natural science. *Publ:* Auth, Science and the Arts: A Study in Relationships from 1600-1900, Fairleigh Dickinson Univ Press, 73. *Rep:* Assoc Univ Presses Cranbury NJ 08512. *Mailing Add:* 126 Center St Frostburg MD 21532

ORBON, JULIAN
COMPOSER, EDUCATOR
b Aviles, Asturias, Spain, Aug 7, 25. *Study:* Oviedo Consv Music, Spain, 40; Berkshire Music Ctr, study comp with Aaron Copland, 46. *Works:* Himnus ad Galli Cantun, Broude Brothers, 55; String Quartet No 1, Southern Music Co, 59; Concerto Grosso, Boosey & Hawkes, 61; Three Symphonic Versions, Southern Music Co, 66; Tres Cantigas del Rey, Belwin Mills, 67; Mount Gelboe, Southern Music Publ, 67; Partita No 3, Boosey & Hawkes, 78. *Teaching:* Dir, Havana Consv Music, 44-60; assoc prof comp, Mex Nat Consv, 60-63; vis prof, Washington Univ, Mo, 63. *Awards:* Juan Landaeta Award, Latinamerican Fest, Caracas, Venezuela, 54; Guggenheim Fel, 59 & 68; Award, Am Acad Arts & Lett, 67. *Bibliog:* A Carpentier (auth), La Musica en Cuba, Fondo Cult, Mex, 72; Gerard Behague (auth), Music in Latin America, Prentice Hall Inc, 79. *Mem:* ASCAP. *Mailing Add:* 1245 Park Ave New York NY 10028

ORDANSKY, JEROLD ALAN
ADMINISTRATOR, COMPOSER
b Brooklyn, NY, Feb 18, 47. *Study:* Pa State Univ, BA, 68; Long Island Univ, MA, 77; Columbia Univ, with Charles Dodge, Bulent Arel & Chou Wen-Chung. *Works:* Songs of Wallace Stevens, North/South Consonance, 81; Psalm 148, 81 & Songs of Tagore, 81, New York Motet Choir; Paradise Lost, 82, Sonata for Clarinet, 82, Rounds for Three, 83 & Variations, 83, North/South Ed. *Pos:* Asst Mgr, G Schirmer, 80-; mgr, North/South Ed, 82-; supvr, Belwin Mills, 83- *Awards:* Meet the Comp Grant, 78, 82 & 83. *Mem:* Am Fedn Musicians; Comp Forum Inc; Am Music Ctr; Nat Asn Comp; BMI. *Mailing Add:* 567 7th St Brooklyn NY 11215

O'REILLY, F(RANK) WARREN
CRITIC-WRITER, EDUCATOR
b Ft Worth, Tex, Sept 14, 21. *Study:* Tex Wesleyan Col, BS, 46; Tex Christian Univ, MA, 47; Univ London, PhD, 52. *Pos:* Music ed, Miami News, 72-74; Adminr & exec dir, Charles Ives Centennial Fest & Symph, Miami, 74-75; pres & exec dir, Chopin Found US, Miami, 77-82; music ed & sr critic, Washington Times, Washington DC, 82- *Teaching:* Adj prof musicol, Univ Miami, Fla, 73- *Awards:* Plaque, for Charles Ives Centennial Fest Third Cent Honor, 74; Presidential Citation, Nat Fedn Music Clubs, 75; Bertramka Medal, Mozart Soc Prague, 80. *Mem:* Music Critics Asn; Nat Press Club; Washington Press Club. *Publ:* Contribr to many periodicals & jour in US & Europe, incl Musical Am, Opera & Wiener Chopin-Blatter. *Mailing Add:* 2475 Virginia Ave NW Washington DC 20037

O'REILLY, SALLY
VIOLIN, EDUCATOR
b Dallas, Tex, Oct 23, 40. *Study:* Tex Women's Univ, BS, 63; Ind Univ, MMus & perf cert, 65; Royal Consv Music, Brussels; NTex State Univ; Curtis Inst Music; studied with Marjorie Fulton, Jack Roberts, Ivan Galamian, Josef Gingold & Carlo Van Neste. *Rec Perf:* Works by Ravel, Lalo, Faure & others. *Pos:* Soloist, Dallas Symph, 57; concertmaster & soloist, Int String Quartet, PR, 60; founding mem, Caecilian Trio, 76. *Teaching:* Mem fac, Manhattan Sch Music, 72-81; assoc prof violin, La State Univ, 81-; sr Fulbright lectr, Nat Consv, Montevideo, Uruguay, 82. *Awards:* Hendl Award, 57 & Katwijk Cond Award, 58, Dallas Symph; Dealy Award, Merriweather Post. *Mem:* Sigma Alpha Iota; Pi Kappa Lambda. *Mailing Add:* Music Dept La State Univ Baton Rouge LA 70803

ORGEL, SETH HENRY
FRENCH HORN, TEACHER
b Syracuse, NY, Nov 7, 59. *Study:* Studied with Richard Oldberg, 77-80 & Dale Clevenger, 80-82. *Pos:* Rotating sect, Civic Orch Chicago, 79-81; asst & utility, Filarmonica Caracas, Venezuela, 81-82 & Syracuse Symph Orch, 82- *Publ:* Coauth, Auditioning for a Horn Position in the United States, The Horn Call, 83. *Mailing Add:* 530 Clarendon St Syracuse NY 13210

ORGILL, ROXANE
CRITIC
b Mount Vernon, NY, June 18, 53. *Study:* Univ Ill, Urbana-Chmpaign, BA, 75; King's Col, Univ London, MMus, 77. *Pos:* Music critic, Milwaukee J, 80-83 & The Record, Bergen Co, NJ, 83- *Mem:* Music Critic Asn. *Mailing Add:* 230 Riverside Dr 9-G New York NY 10025

O'RILEY, CHRISTOPHER (JAMES)
PIANO
b Chicago, Ill, Apr 17, 56. *Study:* New England Consv Music, artist dipl, 81. *Rec Perf:* Berg Kammerkonzert, Cantabile Rec, 80. *Pos:* Participant, Marlboro Music Fest, 82. *Teaching:* Boston Consv Music, 83- *Awards:* Fifth Prize, Van Cliburn Int Piano Compt, 80 & Leeds Int Piano Compt, 81; Avery Fisher Career Grant Award, Lincoln Ctr, 83. *Rep:* Thea Dispeker 248 E 79th New York NY 10021. *Mailing Add:* 404 Sixth Ave Brooklyn NY 10215

ORLAND, HENRY
COMPOSER, EDUCATOR
b Saarbruecken, Ger, Apr 23, 18. *Study:* Univ Strasbourg, France, Cert Etudes, 47; Northwestern Univ, BM, 49, MM, 50, PhD, 59. *Works:* Bassoon Concerto, Seesaw, 61; Double Concerto (flute & English horn), MCA, 62; A Christmas Candle Light Procession 64 & A Christmas Legend, 65, Seesaw; Symphony No 3, MCA, 67; Symphony No 4, Seesaw, 70; Initial, SW Ger Radio Orch, 72. *Pos:* Music dir & cond, Brentwood Symph, 64; Midwest Chamber Ens & Eden Singing Soc, 74-; music critic, St Louis Post-Dispatch, 64-69; lit & music critic, St Louis Globe-Democrat, 68- *Teaching:* Prof music, chmn & actg dean, St Louis Inst Music, 59-63; prof & chairperson, St Louis

Community Col, Florissant Valley, 63- *Awards:* Chicago Music Critics Award for Comp, 51; fel, Fromm Found, 57 & MacDowell Found, 72; Delius Prize (comp), Delius Asn, Fla, 74. *Mem:* ASCAP; Am Musicol Soc; Am Fedn Musicians; Music Critics Asn; Am Soc Univ Comp. *Mailing Add:* 21 Bon Price Terr St Louis MO 63132

ORLOVSKY, ARKADY
CELLO, EDUCATOR
b Russia. *Study:* Leningrad State Consv, studied with Mstislav Rostropovich, dipl. 66. *Pos:* Mem, Leningrad Phil, formerly; first cellist, Kirov Theatre Opera & Ballet, 64-67 & Rome Opera Theatre, formerly; prin cellist, Ind Symph Orch, 78- *Teaching:* Mem fac, Leningrad Consv, formerly; instr cello, Jordan Col Fine Artrs, Butler Univ, currently. *Awards:* Hon Dipl, All-Union Compt, Moscow, 66. *Mailing Add:* Jordan Col Fine Arts Butler Univ 46 St & Clarendon Rd Indianapolis IN 46208

ORMANDY, EUGENE
CONDUCTOR & MUSIC DIRECTOR
b Budapest, Hungary, Nov 18, 1899; nat US. *Study:* Royal State Acad Music, Hungary, BA, 13, state dipl(violin & prof), 15; numerous hon degrees from various Am univ. *Pos:* Violinist, cinema orch, formerly; cond cinema orch, Capitol Theater, New York, formerly & Minneapolis Symph Orch, 31-36; music dir & cond, Philadelphia Orch, 36-80, cond laureate, 80- *Teaching:* Head master classes, State Consv Music, Budapest, 19. *Awards:* Alice M Ditson Cond Award, 77; Gold Baton Award, Am Symph Orch League, 79; Broadcast Pioneer Award, 79; and many others. *Mem:* Mahler Soc; Bruckner Soc; hon life mem, Musical Fund Soc Philadelphia. *Mailing Add:* Philadelphia Orch Asn 1420 Locust St Philadelphia PA 19102

ORNSTEIN, DORIS
EDUCATOR, HARPSICHORD
b New York, NY. *Study:* Juilliard Sch Music; Bennington Col AB, 51; Univ London, harpsichord study with Christopher Wood; Mannes Col Music, studied with Sylvia Marlowe. *Rec Perf:* The Three Bach Sonatas for Viola da Gamba and Harpsichord, 80, Cleveland Baroque Soloists, 81 & Cleveland Baroque Soloists Play Marais and Forqueray, 83, Gasparo. *Pos:* Dir, Cleveland Baroque Soloists, 72-; harpsichord soloist, Aspen Music Fest, 72- *Teaching:* Artist in res, Case Western Reserve Univ, 68-; dir early music studies, Cleveland Inst Music, 68-; vis teacher harpsichord, Oberlin Consv Music, 70-72. *Awards:* Perf Support Award, Harpsichord Music Soc, 81-82. *Bibliog:* Robert Ornstein (dir), Harpsichord Building in America (film), Nat Endowment for Humanities, 75. *Publ:* Auth, On Preparing a Performing Edition of Handel's Cantata Mi Palpita il Cor, Bach, 79. *Mailing Add:* 3122 Woodbury Rd Shaker Heights OH

ORR, NATHANIEL LEON
EDUCATOR, ORGAN
b West Palm Beach, Fla, Nov 18, 49. *Study:* Fla State Univ, BM, 72; Univ NC, MM, 74, Chapel Hill, PhD, 79. *Teaching:* Asst prof, Tift Col, 76-78; asst prof, Ga State Univ, 78-83, assoc prof, 83- *Mem:* Col Music Soc; Am Musicol Soc (pres southern chap, 82); Am Liszt Soc. *Publ:* Coauth, The AGO in Atlanta, Am Organ, 80; auth, George Sand & Liszt, George Sand Newslett, 80; Liszt, Christus and the Transformation of the Oratorio, Am Liszt Soc J, 82; Effect of Scoring on Mozart's Sonata Form, Symposium, 83; Alfredo Barili: Atlanta Musician at the Turn of the Century, Am Music (in prep). *Mailing Add:* Box 124 Ga State Univ Atlanta GA 30303

ORR, WENDELL EUGENE
EDUCATOR, BASS
b Gilman, Ill, July 23, 30. *Study:* Lawrence Univ, BS, 52, BMus, 55; Univ Mich, MMus, 57; private study with Giovanni Manurita, Rome, 61-62. *Teaching:* Instr voice, chorus & opera, Univ Wis, Stevens Point, 58-63; instr voice & opera, Kans Emporia State Col, 63-64; asst prof voice, opera & men's chorus, Univ NH, 64-69; assoc prof voice & men's chorus, Youngstown State Univ, 69- *Mailing Add:* 7197 Elmland Poland OH 44514

ORREGO-SALAS, JUAN ANTONIO
COMPOSER, CRITIC–WRITER
b Santiago, Chile, Jan 18, 19. *Study:* Univ Chile, BA, 38, MA, 42 PhD, 53; Columbia Univ; Princeton Univ; Berkshire Music Ctr; studied with Randall Thompson & Aaron Copland, 44-46; Catholic Univ, Chile, Hon Dr Causa, 71. *Works:* Sextet, op 38, Peer Publ, 54; Serenata Concertante, op 40, comn by Louisville Orch, 55; Symphony No 3, op 50, comn by InterAm Music Fest, 61; Concerto a Tre, op 52, comn by Koussevitzky Found, 65; America, op 57 (cantata), comn by Cornell Univ, 66; The Days of God, op 73 (oratorio), comn by Nat Symph, 76; Tangos, op 82, comn by Miami Univ, 82. *Pos:* Music critic, El Mercurio, Santiago, 49-60. *Teaching:* Prof music comp, Univ Chile, 42-60; music comp & coral cond, Catholic Univ, Santiago, 56-60 & chmn music dept, 56-60; prof & dir music comp & musicol, Latin Am Music Ctr, Univ Ind, Bloomington, 60- *Awards:* Rockefeller Found Grant, 44; Chilean Music Fest Award, 48, 52 & 54; Guggenheim Fel, 45 & 54. *Bibliog:* Luis Merino (auth), Orrego-Salas, The Composer, Univ Chile, 79; G Behage (auth), Music in Latin America, Prentice-Hall, 79. *Mem:* Am Asn Univ Comp; Latin Am Studies Asn; Acad Bellas Artes, Chile. *Publ:* Auth, articles publ in Revista Musical Chilena, InterAm Music Bulletin, Musical Quart. *Rep:* Peer Int 1740 Broadway New York NY 10019. *Mailing Add:* 490 S Serena Lane Bloomington IN 47401

ORTIZ, WILLIAM
COMPOSER, EDUCATOR
b Salinas, PR, Mar 30, 47. *Study:* PR Consv Music, BMEd, 76; State Univ NY, Stony Brook, MA(comp), 78; State Univ NY, Buffalo, PhD(comp), 83. *Works:* 124 E 107th St, Opus One Rec, 79; Amor, Cristal y Piedra, 80 & Street Music, 80, Am Comp Ed; Piezas Tipicas Puertorriquenas, Dauphin Music Co, 81; Bembe, 81, Antillas, 81 & Resonancia Esferica, 82, Am Comp Ed. *Pos:* Music coordr, Black Mountain Col II, Buffalo, NY, 82-; dir, New Rican Experimental Ens, 83- *Teaching:* Instr music theory, Black Mountain Col II, Buffalo, NY, 82- *Awards:* Felipe Gutierrez Espinosa Int Comp Award, PR Soc Contemp Music, 80. *Mem:* Am Comp Alliance; Comp Forum; Asoc Nac Comp Puertorriquenos; Am Music Ctr; Guitar Found Am. *Mailing Add:* 124 W Northrup Pl Buffalo NY 14214

OSBORNE, CHARLES EUGENE
FLUTE, EDUCATOR
b Grand Rapids, Mich, Dec 24, 28. *Study:* Mich State Univ, BM, 51, MM, 53, PhD, 63. *Teaching:* Prof flute & theory, Mont State Univ, 54-57; prof flute, Western Mich Univ, 57- *Mem:* Am Fedn Musicians; Nat Asn Col Wind & Perc Instr; Nat Flute Asn; Nat Asn Music Therapists. *Publ:* Auth, Music for Flute and Percussion, 79, Music for Flute and Organ, 81 & The Compact Tuner, 81, Nat Asn Col Wind & Perc Instr J. *Mailing Add:* 2908 Winchell Kalamazoo MI 49008

OSBORNE, DONALD E(UGENE)
ARTIST MANAGER, ADMINISTRATOR
b San Francisco, Calif, Feb 28, 50. *Study:* San Francisco State Univ, BM(music), 72, MA(music), 74. *Pos:* Vpres, Mariedi Anders Artists Mgt, 79-81; dir, Calif Artists Mgt, 82- *Teaching:* Lectr, San Francisco State Univ, 74-76 & Calif State Univ, Sacramento, 78-79. *Mem:* Am Symph Orch League; Cent Opera Serv; Asn Col, Univ & Community Arts Adminr; Western Alliance of Arts Adminr; Chamber Music Am. *Mailing Add:* 23 Liberty St San Francisco CA 94110

OSBORNE, GEORGE D
ADMINISTRATOR
b Ft Worth, Tex, Aug 25, 38. *Study:* Oklahoma City Univ, BM, 60; studied with Fernando Cavaniglia Riccardo Picizzi, Rome, Italy, 61; Ind Univ, MM, 64. *Pos:* Gen dir, Opera Memphis, 71-76, Conn Opera, 79- & Hartford Ballet, 82-; gen mgr, Hartford Chamber Orch, 78- *Teaching:* Assoc prof opera & voice, Memphis State Univ, 66-76 & WVa Univ, 76-78. *Mem:* Comn Cult Affairs, City of Hartford (chmn, 80-); Cent Opera Serv (regional dir, 74-76); Opera Am; Hartford Symph Orch (mem bd dirs, 83-); Tenn Arts Comn (mem opera panel, 74-76). *Mailing Add:* 15 Lewis St Hartford CT 06103

OSSENKOP, DAVID CHARLES
LIBRARIAN, EDUCATOR
b Pasadena, Calif, Jan 2, 37. *Study:* Drew Univ, BA, 58; Columbia Univ, MA, 60, PhD, 68, MS, 70. *Pos:* Assoc librn music, State Univ NY, Potsdam, 70- *Teaching:* Lectr music hist & theory, Drew Univ, 64-65. *Mem:* Am Musicol Soc (treas, greater NY chap, 66-67); Music Libr Asn (prog chmn NY-Ontario chap, 81-82); Int Musicol Soc. *Interests:* German Lieder, 1750-1830. *Publ:* Auth, Editions of Beethoven's Easy Piano Pieces, Piano Quart, 61-62 & 70; Eidenbenz, Eschstruth, Reineck, Sack, Schubart & Weiss, In: New Grove Dict of Music & Musicians, 80; The Writings of Paul Henry Lang: A Selective Bibliography, Music & Civilization (in press). *Mailing Add:* 23 Pierrepont Ave Potsdam NY 13676

OSTERGREN, EDUARDO AUGUSTO
CONDUCTOR & MUSIC DIRECTOR, EDUCATOR
b Sao Paulo, Brazil, Apr 24, 43; US citizen. *Study:* Consv Sao Paulo, BMus, 62; Southern Methodist Univ, MMus, 68; Ind Univ, DMus, 80. *Works:* Sonata In Three Centuries (cello), Fema Music Publ, 71; Benedicamus Domino (organ), perf by Frances Van de Putte, Sao Paulo, 76; Little Red Riding Hood (string quartet), perf by Lafayette Symph String Quartet, 78. *Pos:* Violist, Duke Univ Symph Orch, 71-76 & prin violist, 73-74; music dir & cond, NC State Univ Orch & Chorus, 70-76 & Lafayette Symph Orch, 78- *Teaching:* Asst prof, NC State Univ, 70-76; prof, Purdue Univ, 78-; vis lectr music hist, Fed Univ Rio Grande, Sul, Brazil, 81. *Bibliog:* John Dibble (dir), The Making of a Concert (TV doc), 81. *Mem:* Am Symph Orch League. *Mailing Add:* 2616 Cayuga Trail Lafayette IN 47905

OSTRANDER, ARTHUR E
EDUCATOR, ADMINISTRATOR
b Plainfield, NJ, Oct 8, 42. *Study:* Bowdoin Col, AB, 64; Ind Univ, MM, 68, PhD, 71. *Pos:* Assoc prof & chair grad prog music, Ithaca Col, 71- *Publ:* Coauth, Music Sources, Prentice-Hall, 79. *Mailing Add:* 107 Campbell Ave Ithaca NY 14850

OSTRANDER, LINDA WOODAMAN
COMPOSER, ADMINISTRATOR
b New York, NY, Feb 17, 37. *Study:* Oberlin Consv, BMus, 58; Smith Col, MA, 60; Boston Univ, DMA, 72. *Works:* Concerto Grosso No 2, perf by Portland Maine Symph, 69; Time Studies, Boston Univ Ens, 70; Duet, perf by Lily Dwyang & Rita Simo, Boston Univ, 70; Game of Chance, perf by Music in Maine & Cantabrigia Brass, 70-; Time Out for Tuba, comn & perf by Barton Cummings, 79; Outside In, perf by Elma Lewis Children's Theatre, 81. *Teaching:* Lectr, Adelphi Suffolk Col, 61-63; adj asst prof, Southampton Col, 63-64; dept chmn, Bunker Hill Community Col, 73-78 & 79- *Awards:* Gilchrist-Potter Prize, Oberlin Col, 65-66; Comp/Librettist Award, Nat Endowment Arts, 69; grant, Nat Endowment Arts, 77. *Mem:* Am Music Ctr; Int League Women Comp. *Publ:* Coauth, Creative Piano, Houghton Mifflin, 78. *Mailing Add:* 48 Atwood Rd Southborough MA 01772

OSTROVE, GERALDINE E
LIBRARIAN, EDUCATOR
b Astoria, NY, July 22, 38. *Study:* Goucher Col, AB; Sch Libr & Info Serv, Univ Md, MLS; Peabody Consv, MMus. *Pos:* Dir libr, New England Consv, currently. *Teaching:* Lectr, Grad Sch Libr & Info Sci, Simmons Col, 81- & New England Consv, 83- *Mem:* Music Libr Asn (rec secy, 72-78); Int Asn Music Libr (chair US branch, 81-84); Sonneck Soc; Am Libr Asn; Asn Col & Res Libr. *Publ:* Co-ed, Boston Composers Project, MIT Press, 83; contrib to Notes, Fontes Artis Musicae & Musical Am. *Mailing Add:* Spaulding Libr New England Consv 33 Gainsborough St Boston MA 02115

OSTROVSKY, ARTHUR (ARTHUR WILLIAM AUSTIN)
VIOLIN, COMPOSER
b New York, NY, Jan 2, 12. *Study:* New York Consv Musical Art, BM, MM, DM, 27; studied with Arthur Lichstein & Ivan Simonovitz. *Works:* New York Suite; Quartette in C Major; Quartette in C Minor; Concerto in C Major. *Rec Perf:* Bach Suite; Double Concerto (Bach); Concerto (Sarn); G Minor Concerto (Bruch). *Pos:* Perf violin with Serge Koussevitsky, Berkshire Music Ctr, Leopold Stokowski, Robin Hood Dell, Pa & Frederica Stock Sr, Grant Park, Ill. *Awards:* Griffith Award. *Mem:* Bohemians. *Publ:* Contribr, Music Age. *Mailing Add:* 151 E 80th St New York NY 10021

OSTRYNIEC, JAMES PAUL
OBOE, COMPOSER
b Erie, Pa, Sept 27, 43. *Study:* Univ Loiusville, BMus, 65; Univ Hawaii, MFA, 67; Univ Mich, DMA, 72. *Works:* Movements for Orchestra, 67. *Pos:* Oboist, Baltimore Symph, 70-, asst prin oboist, currently. *Teaching:* Mem fac, Peabody Consv Music, 71; artist in res, Towson State Col, 72-; adj instr music, Western Md Col, currently. *Interests:* Contemporary oboe techniques in the United States. *Mailing Add:* Music Dept Western Md Col Westminster MD 21157

OTA, DIANE O
LIBRARIAN
b Grand Island, Nebr, Jan 8, 38. *Study:* Univ New Hampshire, BA(music hist), 70; Smith Col, MA(music hist), 72; Simmons Col, MS(libr sci), 74. *Pos:* Reference librn, Music Dept, Boston Pub Libr, 74-, first asst, 76- *Mem:* Music Libr Asn; Am Musicol Soc. *Mailing Add:* 34 W Woodbridge Rd North Andover MA 01845

OTEY, ORLANDO
PIANO, TEACHER
b Mexico City, Mex, Feb 1, 25. *Study:* Univ Mex, DMus, 45; Curtis Inst Music, 45-48; studied with Luis Moctezuma, Vladimir Sokoloff, Walter Gieseking, Manuel M Ponce & Gian-Carlo Menotti. *Works:* Piano Sonata, 48; Arbesque, 50; Sinfonia Breve, 56; Suite for Strings, 57; Tzintzuntzan (strings), 58; Poetica (solo trumpet & orch), 70; Piano Sonata, 82. *Pos:* Pianist, recitals & with orch, 29-; organist & choirmaster, St John's Episcopal Church, Bala Cynwyd, Pa, 62-64, Christ Episcopal Church, Media, Pa, 65-67 & Mt Salem United Methodist Church, Wilmington, Del, 73-; musical dir, Brandywine Pops Orch, 69-74 & Jewish Community Ctr Orch, 74-78; dir, Otey Music Sch, 70- *Teaching:* Fac mem, Nat Sch Music, Univ Mex, 41-45, Jenkintown Music Sch & Wilmington Mus Sch, Del, 65-70. *Mem:* Nat Asn Comp USA (pres Philadelphia chap, 59-61); life mem, Am String Teachers Asn; Am Symph Orch League; Music Educr Nat Conf. *Publ:* Auth, Otey Music Teaching Method, 73; Discover Natural, Exotic and Non-septonic Musical Keys, 78. *Mailing Add:* 2391 Limestone Rd Wilmington DE 19808

OTT, JOSEPH HENRY
CONDUCTOR, WRITER
b Atlantic, NJ, July 7, 29. *Study:* Private study in Philadelphia & Munich, Ger, 48-53; Sch Dance, Conn Col, dipl, 58; Univ Conn, BA, 60; Univ Calif, Los Angeles, MA, 65. *Works:* Viola Sonate, George Grossman, Pittsburgh, 68; Matrix III, St Paul Chamber Orch, 69; Extensions for Orchestra, Beloit Symph Orch, Wis, 74; Palo Duro, WTex State Univ Band, 78; Locus 1977, Nat Gallery Art, Washington, DC, 79; Warrensburg Suite, Central Mo State Univ, 80; Africotta II, UnivMich Band, 83. *Pos:* Exec asst, Bennington Comp Conf, Vt, 70-71. *Teaching:* Instr, George Washington Univ, 62-63; asst prof music, Milton Col, 65-71; comp in res, St Paul Inst Adv Study, 68; assoc prof music, Emporia State Univ, 71- *Awards:* First Prize, Citta di Trieste, Int Comp Symph Compt, 65, Univ Calif Atwater Kent Comp Cont, 65 & Wis Comp Compt, 68; ASCAP Standard Awards, 78- *Publ:* Auth, A New Approach to Orchestration, Instrumentalist, 68. *Mailing Add:* c/o Claude Benny Press 1401 State St Emporia KS 66801

OTTE, ALLEN CARL
PERCUSSION
b Sheboygan, Wis, Jan 17, 50. *Study:* Consv Music, Oberlin Col, BM, 72; Univ Ill with Herbert Brün; Northern Ill Univ, MM, 77; studied perc with Richard Weiner & Michael Rosen. *Works:* Hit or Miss (two perc), 75; Song (sop & six instrm), 76; Correlations (three keyboards), 77. *Rec Perf:* Blackearth Perc Group, Op One; The Perc Group Cincinnati, Op One, 80 & 81, CRI & CCG. *Pos:* Founding mem, Blackearth Perc Group, 72-79; founder & dir, The Perc Group Cincinnati, 79- *Teaching:* Lectr, Sask Summer Sch Arts, formerly; asst prof perc, Northern Ill Univ, 73-77 & Col Consv, Univ Cincinnati, 77- *Awards:* Rec Spec Merit, Stereo Rev, 75 & 82. *Bibliog:* Joan Conway (auth), Blackearth—The Early Years, New Perf II, 81; Eric Salzman (auth), New Music: Percussion, Stereo Rev, 8/82. *Mem:* Percussive Arts Soc (mem bd dir, 79-82). *Publ:* Coauth, Harry Partch: Genesis of a Music, Nu Mus West, 74; auth, References and Connections in Percussion Literature, private publ, 81; contrib, Literature for Percussion, Percussive Arts Soc, 82; ed & coauth, The Percussion Group Cincinnati, Op One Rec, 82. *Mailing Add:* Col Consv Music Univ Cincinnati Cincinnati OH 45221

OTTLEY, JOANN
SOPRANO, TEACHER-COACH
b Woodruff, Utah. *Study:* Univ Utah; Brigham Young Univ; Staatliche Hochschule Music, Cologne, WGer, with Josef Metternich. *Roles:* Carmina Burana, Utah Symph, Ballet West, Marin Symph & Modesto Symph, 75-83; Violetta in La Traviata, 80 & Lucia in Lucia di Lammermoor, 81, Utah Opera Co; Queen of Night in Magic Flute, Carmel Bach Fest, 82; Mimi in La Boheme, Utah Opera Co, 83. *Pos:* Orch soloist, currently. *Teaching:* Instr voice, Univ Utah, 71-73; vocal coach, Salt Lake Mormon Tabernacle Choir, 76- *Mem:* Nat Asn Teachers Singing. *Rep:* Iain B McKay 130 Social Hall Ave Salt Lake City UT 84111. *Mailing Add:* 2682 Verona Circle Salt Lake City UT 84117

OURADA, ANN ALICIA
VIOLIN, PIANO
b Duluth, Minn, Oct 13, 52. *Study:* New England Consv Music with Eric Rosenblith, BMus, 75; Boston Univ with Joseph Silverstein, MMus, 77. *Works:* Games, perf by Michael Duncan, 75. *Rec Perf:* On the Road From Rags to Jazz, New England Consv Ragtime Ensemble, 74. *Pos:* Prin second violin, Interlochen Arts Acad, 70-71; concertmistress, New England Consv Music, 72-75; first violinist, Res String Quartet, Battle Creek Symph, 77-78; first & second violin, Detroit Symph Orch, 80- *Teaching:* Violin, Detroit Community Music Sch, 81- *Awards:* Joseph Silverstein Award, 75 & C D Jackson Award, 78, Berkshire Music Ctr; Red Lion Inn Fel, 75. *Mem:* Am Fedn Musicians. *Mailing Add:* 421 Cloverly Rd Grosse Pointe MI 48236

OUZOUNIAN, MICHAEL VAHRAM
VIOLA
b Detroit, Mich, Apr 3, 51. *Study:* Cleveland Inst Music, 68-72. *Pos:* Prin viola, Metropolitan Opera Orch, 72- *Mailing Add:* 23 W 73rd New York NY 10023

OWEN, ANGELA MARIA
CRITIC-WRITER, TEACHER
b Berlin, Ger; US citizen. *Study:* Boston Consv Music, studied comp with Daniel Pinkham, BM, 52; Boston Univ Col Music, studied comp & theory with Gardner Read, MM, 53; L'Ecole Monteux, studied cond with Pierre Monteux, 53; Boston Univ, studied musicol with Karl Geiringer, PhD, 57; Stanford Univ, 68. *Works:* Assorted Songs (sop & voice with flute or clarinet obligato), comn & perf by Edith Zitelli, 63; Theme & Variations for Three Recorders, Univ Miami Music Publ, 72; L'apres midi d'une flutiste, Palo Alto Telemann Soc, 76; Conversations for Four Recorders, San Francisco Bay Area Chap, Am Recorder Soc, 79. *Pos:* Dir band & instrument music, Oxford City Sch, NC, 53-54; music supvr, Pub Sch, Weymouth, Mass, 56-59; Music dir, Mid-Peninsula Recorder Orch, Palo Alto, Calif, 67-; music reviewer, Peninsula Times Tribune, Palo Alto, Calif, 77- *Teaching:* Dir band & instr music, Oxford City Sch, NC, 53-54; music supvr, Pub Sch, Weymouth, Mass, 56-59; instr, Palo Alto Adult Sch, Calif, 62-82, Community Sch Music & Arts, Mountain View, Calif, 68-74, Foothill Col, Los Altos Hills, Calif, 74-76; recorder, privately, 77-81. *Awards:* First prize (for comp), Miami Chap, Am Recorder Soc, 72 & San Francisco Bay Area Chap, Am Recorder Soc, 79. *Mem:* Nat Music Critics Asn; Am Recorder Soc; Phi Kappa Lambda Music Honor Soc. *Publ:* Auth, The Authorship of J S Bach's Cantata No 15, Music & Lett, Vol 41, No 1; coauth, Prelude to Musicianship, Holt, Rinehart & Winston, 79. *Mailing Add:* 246 Walter Hays Dr Palo Alto CA 94303

OWEN, BARBARA
ORGAN, LECTURER
b Utica, NY, Jan 25, 33. *Study:* Westminster Choir Col, with Dr Alexander McCurdy, MusB, 55; Boston Univ, with Dr Karl Geiringer, MusM, 62; NGerman Organ Acad, with Harald Vogel. *Pos:* Dir church music, First Religious Soc, Newburyport, Mass, 63- *Awards:* Nat Endowment Humanities Fel, 74. *Mem:* Organ Hist Soc (pres, 56-60); Am Guild Organists (dean Boston chap, 73-75, regional chmn, 77-); Am Musicol Soc; Sonneck Soc; Brit Inst Organ Studies. *Interests:* History and music of the organ. *Publ:* Contrib, Harvard Dict of Music, 2nd ed, 69 & 3rd ed, 83; ed, A Century of American Organ Music, McAfee Music Corp, 75, 76 & 83; auth, The Organ in New England, Sunbury Press, 79; contrib, New Grove Dict of Music & Musicians, 80; ed, The Candlelight Carol Book, Mcafee Music Corp, 82. *Mailing Add:* 28 Jefferson St Newburyport MA 01950

OWEN, BLYTHE
COMPOSER, PIANO
b Bruce, Minn, Dec 26, 1898. *Study:* Chicago Musical Col, BMus, 41; Northwestern Univ, MMus, 42; Eastman Sch Music, PhD(comp), 53. *Works:* Concerto Grosso, Op 29, Chicago Chamber Orch, 61; Elizabethan Suit, Op 32, Walla Walla Symph Orch, 64; Serially Serious, Op 46, Nos 1-3 (piano), Orion, 71; Peace Hymn of the Republic, Op 50, No 2, Andrews Univ Chorale, 76; Trio for Clarinet, Cello & Piano, Op 59, Mich Music Teachers Asn, 80; Sonata Fantaisic for Cello & Piano, Spoleto Fest, 82; Praise the Lord, Op 67, No 2 (organ), comn by Erna Mae Koch, 83. *Rec Perf:* Festal Prelude (organ), Audio Servs, 66; How Lovely Are Thy Dwellings, Chapel Rec, 75; Festival Te Deum (choir & organ), Ark Rec, 78. *Teaching:* Instr, Northwestern Univ, 42-50 & Roosevelt Univ, 50-61; prof, Walla Walla Col, 61-65 & Andrews Univ, 65-75. *Awards:* Awards, Mu Phi Epsilon, 40-61, Delta Omicron, 44 & Univ Md, 57. *Bibliog:* Alfondi Bontor Maniora (auth), Dissertation on Choral Works of Blythe Owen, NY Univ. *Mem:* Music Teachers Nat Asn; Am Asn Univ Comp; Am Women Comp; Nat Guild Piano Teachers; Am Music Ctr. *Mailing Add:* 115 Kephart Lane Berrien Springs MI 49103

OWEN, CHARLES E
EDUCATOR, PERCUSSION

b Kinsman, Ohio, Sept 1, 12. *Study:* Studied with Malcolm Gerlach, 30-32 & Saul Goodman, 35-36; Cath Univ, BMus, 44. *Rec Perf:* Concerto for Marimba (Paul Creston), Columbia Rec, 63. *Pos:* Timpanist & marimba soloist, US Marine Band, 34-54; first perc, Philadelphia Orch, 54-72, Aspen Music Fest, 78-83 & Casals Fest, PR. *Teaching:* Instr perc, Temple Univ, 62-72; prof, Music Sch, Univ Mich, 72-, prof emer, 83- *Awards:* Harold Haugh Award, Univ Mich, 81; Hall of Fame, Percussive Arts Soc, 81. *Mem:* Percussive Arts Soc Mich (pres, 72-73); Percussive Arts Soc (bd mem, 73-82). *Mailing Add:* 1125 Elmwood Dr Ann Arbor MI 48104

OWEN, HAROLD J
COMPOSER, EDUCATOR

b 1931. *Study:* Univ Southern Calif, with Halsey Stevens, DMA. *Works:* Twelve Concert Etudes (clarinet); Fantasies on Mexican Tunes (three trumpets & piano); Chamber Music (four clarinets); Metropolitan Bus (cantata; piano, four hands); Overture dans le Style Francais (organ). *Teaching:* Prof orch, theory & comp, Univ Ore, currently. *Mailing Add:* Music Dept Univ Ore Eugene OR 97403

OWEN, RICHARD
COMPOSER

b New York, NY, Dec 11, 22. *Study:* Dartmouth Col, AB, 47; Harvard Law Sch, LLB, 50; Manhattan Sch Music, 60-63. *Works:* A Moment of War, Buenos Aires, 62; A Fisherman Called Peter, 65; Patterns (sop & orch), Gen Music, 70; Mary Dyer, Eastern Opera, 76; The Death of the Virgin, New York Lyr Opera Co, 83. *Mem:* ASCAP. *Mailing Add:* 21 Claremont Ave New York NY 10027

OWEN, STEPHEN
BASS-BARITONE

b Kunming, China. *Study:* Princeton Theological Seminary, dipl; study with Armen Boyajian, currently. *Roles:* Don Magnifico in La Cenerentola, Tex Opera Theater; Pistol in Falstaff, Wolf Trap Opera Co; Don Pasquale in Don Pasquale, Va Opera Theater; Prine Yamadori in Madama Butterfly, Opera Co Philadelphia; Colline in La Boheme, Wilmington Opera Co, 81-82 & Orlando Opera Co, 83; Ferrando in Il Trovatore, Opera Theater Syracuse, 83; Figaro in The Marriage of Figaro, Pa Opera Theater, 83. *Pos:* Performer with major Am opera co. *Mailing Add:* c/o Dorothy Cone Inc 250 W 57th St New York NY 10019

OWENS, DAVID
WRITER, COMPOSER

b Harlingen, Tex, Oct 16, 50. *Study:* Eastman Sch Music, BAMus, 72; Manhattan Sch Music, 73. *Works:* Quartet for Strings & Encounter (orch), Eastman-Rochester Orch; Five Phonemes (piano quartet), Fine Arts Quartet; Psalm (string orch), Mich Sinfonietta. *Pos:* Asst ed & columnist, Christian Science Monitor, 79- *Mem:* Am Music Ctr. *Interests:* Bringing common sense and fresh viewpoints to bridging the gap between audience, performer and modern composer. *Publ:* Auth, Is Classical Music Living in the Past?, Ovation, 1/82; Join the Avant-Garde and Be Safe, Piano Quart, Fall 80; article on orchestras & modern music, ASCAP in Action, Spring 83. *Mailing Add:* 1815 Beacon St Brookline MA 02146

OWINGS, JOHN C
PIANO, EDUCATOR

b San Antonio, Tex, Feb 5, 43. *Study:* Univ Tex, with Dalies Frantz, BMus, 65; Juilliard Sch, with Rosina Lhevinne & Martin Canin, MS(music), 70; studied with Wilhelm Kempff, 73 & 77. *Teaching:* Asst prof piano, Consv Music, Obelin Col, 70-76; prof music, Ind Univ, South Bend, 76- *Awards:* First Prize, Liszt Soc Compt, 68, Robert Casadesus Int Compt, 75 & Musical Arts Compt, 80. *Mem:* Col Music Soc; Music Teachers Nat Asn; Soc Am Musicians. *Publ:* Auth, The Piano Sonatas of Robert Casadesus, Piano Quart, 82. *Mailing Add:* 1822 Southern View Dr South Bend IN 46614

OZAWA, SEIJI
CONDUCTOR & MUSIC DIRECTOR

b Shenyang, China, Sept 1, 35; Japanese citizen. *Study:* Toho Sch Music, Tokyo. *Rec Perf:* Symphony of a Thousand (Mahler), The Planets (Holst) & Le Sacre du printemps (Stravinsky), Philips; Violin Concerto (Stravinsky); Violin Concerto (Berg); Gurrelieder (Schoenberg); Romeo et Juliette (Berlioz). *Pos:* Music dir, Ravinia Fest, Chicago, 64-68 & Toronto Symph Orch, Canada, 65-69; cond & music dir, San Francisco Symph Orch, 70-76; music dir, Boston Symph Orch, 73- *Teaching:* Artistic dir, Berkshire Music Ctr, 70- *Awards:* Emmy for Boston Symph Orch perf of Evening at Symphony; First Prize, Int Comp Orch Cond, 59; Koussevitzky Prize, Berkshire Music Ctr, 60. *Mailing Add:* Symphony Hall Boston MA 02115

P

PACHIOS, HAROLD CHRISTY
PATRON

New Haven, Conn, July 12, 36. *Study:* Princeton Univ, AB, 59; Georgetown Univ, JD, 65. *Pos:* Pres, Portland Symph Orch, 76-78, chmn adv bd, 78-; pres, Nat Coun Symph Orch, 78-; vchmn, Am Symph Orch League, 81. *Mailing Add:* c/o Preti/Flaherty/Beliveau 443 Congress St Portland ME 04101

PACINI, RENATO
CONDUCTOR & MUSIC DIRECTOR

b Utica, NY. *Study:* Acad Santa Cecilia, Rome; New England Consv Music, dipl, 32; Marian Col, Ind, LHD, 76. *Pos:* Concertmaster, State Symphony Orch, Boston, 32-36; asst concertmaster, Indianapolis Symph Orch, 38-77, asst cond, 50-55 & 55-68; music dir & cond, Lafayette Symph Orch, Ind, 57-76. *Teaching:* Violin, Jordan Col Music, 40-45 & private studio, 45-57. *Mem:* Hon mem, Ind Chap Nat Soc Arts & Lett. *Mailing Add:* Indianapolis Symph Orch POB 88207 Indianapolis IN 46208

PACKER, JANET SUSAN
VIOLIN, EDUCATOR

b New York, NY, Aug 14, 49. *Study:* Wellesley Col, BA, 70; Brandeis Univ, MA, 72. *Rec Perf:* String Trio (Lee Hyla), CRI, 83; All Done from Memory, Two for One Sextet (Ezra Sims), Northeastern, 83; Epistles (Haag Boyajiah), CRI, 83. *Pos:* Violinist, Dinosaur Annex, Opera Co of Boston, Mass, 77- & Boston Pops Esplanade Orch, 79- *Teaching:* Mem fac violin, All-Newton Music Sch, 78- & Longy Sch Music, 79- *Awards:* Winner, Young Artists Compt, Rochester, NY, 66; Billings Perf Award, Wellesley Col, 70. *Mailing Add:* 39 Sherman St Cambridge MA 02138

PACKER, RANDALL MARTIN
COMPOSER, TEACHER

b San Jose, Calif, Jan 23, 53. *Study:* Univ Ore, BS, 75; Calif Inst Arts, MFA(music), 81. *Works:* Phrases, 80, Le Bateau Ivre, 81 & Ariel Settings, 81, Am Comp Alliance. *Teaching:* Music, Windward Sch, Los Angeles, Calif, 82-83. *Awards:* ASCAP Comp Award, 80; Calif Inst Arts Scholar Award, 80. *Mem:* Am Comp Alliance; BMI. *Mailing Add:* 417 S Barrington #102 Los Angeles CA 90049

PAGE, CAROLANN (CAROL ANN GEMIGNANI)
SOPRANO

b Odessa, Tex. *Study:* Curtis Inst Music, BM; studied with Judith Raskin & Martin Katz. *Roles:* Cunegonde in Candide, The Broadway Theatre, New York, 75; Valencienne in The Merry Widow, Cincinnati Opera Co, 82 & Pittsburgh Opera Co, 82; Julie in Carousel, Cincinnati Opera Co, 83. *Pos:* Soloist, Philadelphia Orch, 83, Cleveland Orch, 83, Denver Symph, 83 & Okla Symph, 83; Solo artist, Marlboro Music Fest, Ambler Music Fest & Chautauqua Music Fest. *Mem:* Am Guild Musical Artists; Actors Equity; Am Fedn Musicians. *Rep:* Regency Artists, Ltd 9200 Sunset Blvd Los Angeles CA 90069. *Mailing Add:* 15 Laurel Ave Tenafly NJ 07670

PAGE, ROBERT (ELZA)
CONDUCTOR & MUSIC DIRECTOR, EDUCATOR

b Abilene, Tex, Apr 27, 27. *Study:* Abilene Christian Col, BA, 48; Ind Univ, MMus, 51; NY Univ, 55-59; Beaver Col, Hon Dr Music, 75. *Works:* Choral Compositions & Three Christmas Motets, G Schirmer. *Rec Perf:* Shostakovich Symphony #13, 70; Daphnis and Chloe (Ravel), 76; Porgy and Bess (Gershwin), 76; Requiem (Berloiz), 78. *Pos:* Bolton Dir Choruses, Cleveland Orch, 71-; dir, Blossom Fest Chorus, 73-; asst cond, Cleveland Orch, 79-; music dir & cond, Mendelssohn Choir Pittsburgh, 79-; cond & chorus master, Cleveland Opera, 80- *Teaching:* Dir choruses, Odessa High Sch, 48-50; music fac, Odessa Col, 50-51; dir choral activ, Eastern NMex Univ, 51-55; dir choral activ & prof music, Temple Univ, 56-75; dir Temple Univ Fest & Inst, 68-71; head dept music, Carnegie Mellon Univ, 75-80. *Awards:* Grammy Award, 67; Prix Mondial de Montreux for Shostakovich Symphony #13, 70; Grammy for Carmina Burana, 75; Grand Prix du Disque for Porgy and Bess, 76. *Mem:* Nat Endowment Arts; charter mem, Asn Prof Vocal Ens (vpres, currently); Am Choral Dir Asn; Am Choral Found; Nat Asn Teachers Singing. *Mailing Add:* 2283 Beechwood Blvd Pittsburgh PA 15217

PAGE, WILLIS
CONDUCTOR & MUSIC DIRECTOR

b Rochester, NY. *Study:* Eastman Sch Music, dipl. *Pos:* Mem, Boston Symph Orch, formerly; prin bass, Boston Pops, formerly; cond, Cecilia Soc Boston, formerly, Yomiuri Nippon Symph, Tokyo, 62-63, Des Moines Symph, 69-71, Jacksonville Symph Orch, 71- & all-state orchs NY, Iowa, Ky, Tenn & Fla; organizer & cond, New Orch Soc Boston; music dir & cond, Nashville Symph Orch, 73-; assoc cond, Buffalo Phil; guest cond with many North Am orchs, incl Boston Pops, Toronto, Rochester, Denver, Colorado Springs & Memphis. *Teaching:* Prof cond, Eastman Sch Music, 67-69; prof cond & dir musical activities, Drake Univ, 69-71. *Awards:* European Travel Award, Ford Found, 67. *Mailing Add:* Jacksonville Symph Orch Plaza 2 Suite #9009 580 W St Jacksonville FL 32209

PAGET, DANIEL
EDUCATOR, MUSIC DIRECTOR

b New York, NY, May 24, 43. *Study:* Columbia Univ, BA, 64, MA, 66. *Works:* Hadleyburg (musical play), Columbia Univ, 63 & 72; Rags (various ens), Ani Kavafian & comp, 70-; Romania!, perf by Carol Wincenc & Kenneth Cooper, 79- *Rec Perf:* Sing Me a Song of Song My (Mimaroglu), Atlantic, 71; Rituals and Reactions (Tanenbaum), CRI, 76; Voices for Today (Britten), Hessound, 77; Voyage (Roussakis), CRI, 83. *Pos:* Cond, Apollo Chamber Orch, currently & Paget Chorale, currently. *Teaching:* Choral dir & fac mem, Columbia Univ, 67-73; choral dir, Manhattan Sch Music, 73-; assoc prof music, John Jay Col Criminal Justice, City Univ New York, 70-83, prof, 83- *Mem:* Am Choral Dir Asn; Am Fedn Musicians; Am Symph Orch League; Col Music Soc. *Publ:* Auth, From the Saloon to the Salon, High Fidelity, 80; contribr to Rec in Rev, 81. *Mailing Add:* 601 W 115th St New York NY 10025

PAGLIALUNGA, AUGUSTO
TENOR, EDUCATOR
Study: New England Consv Music, studied voice with Frederick Jagel & opera with Boris Goldovsky, MM. *Roles:* Don Jose in Carmen, Baltimore Symph, Pittsburgh Symph & New York City Opera; Faust in Faust; Radames in Aida; Pinkerton in Madama Butterfly, 81; Canio in I, Pagliacci, Ariz State Opera, 81; Turiddu in Cavalleria rusticana, Los Angeles Opera, 81; Edgardo in Lucia di Lammermoor, 81 & Rodolfo in La Boheme, 82, Utah Opera Co. *Pos:* Leading ten, opera houses in Austria & Germany, formerly & US Opera Co, currently. *Teaching:* Distinguished mem fac, Consv Music, Freiburg, formerly; assoc prof voice, Univ Wash, currently. *Mailing Add:* Dept Music Univ Wash Seattle WA 98195

PAIGE, NORMAN
EDUCATOR, TENOR
b New York, NY. *Study:* Am Theatre Wing Prof Training Prog, 56; Juilliard Sch Music; NY Univ. *Pos:* Tenor, Chicago Opera Theatre, New York City Opera, San Francisco Opera, Portland Opera Asn, Opera Co Boston, Seattle Opera Co, Pittsburgh Opera Co, Cincinnati Opera Asn, Teatro Liceo, Barcelona, Civic Opera, Cologne & Vienna State Opera. *Teaching:* Assoc prof fine arts, Univ Kans, 69-76, prof 76- *Awards:* Fulbright Grant, 68. *Mem:* Am Guild Musical Artists; Asn Am Univ Prof; Pi Kappa Lambda; Guild German Stage Artists. *Publ:* Auth, Caruso: The Legend Lives, Opera Quart, 6/83. *Rep:* Jim Scovotti Asn 185 West End Ave New York NY 10023. *Mailing Add:* Sch Fine Arts Univ Kans Lawrence KS 66045

PALISCA, CLAUDE V
EDUCATOR, WRITER
b Fiume (Rijeka), Yugoslavia, Nov 24, 21; US citizen. *Study:* Queens Col, City Univ New York, BA, 43; Harvard Univ, MA, 48, PhD, 54; Yale Univ, Hon MA, 64. *Pos:* Dir res, Yale Music Curriculum Proj, 64-68; consult, US Off Educ, Nat Endowment for Humanities, J D Rockefeller, 3rd Fund, Martha Baird Rockefeller Fund for Music, Can Res Coun & Australia Arts Coun, 64-; ed, Yale Music Theory Translation Series, 66-; chmn, Adv Placement Comt Music, Col Entrance Exam Bd, 70-72. *Teaching:* Instr music, Univ Ill, Urbana, 53-54, asst prof, 54-59; assoc prof hist music, Yale Univ, 59-64, prof 64-80, dir grad studies dept music, 67-70, chmn dept music, 69-75, chmn & dir grad studies Renaissance Studies prog, 77-80, Henry L & Lucy G Moses prof, 80-, dir grad studies dept music, 82-83. *Awards:* Fels, Yale Sr Fac, 66-67, Nat Endowment for Humanities, 72-73 & John Simon Guggenheim, 60-61 & 81-82. *Mem:* Am Musicol Soc (vpres, 65-67, pres, 70-72); Am Coun Arts Educ (pres, 67-69); Int Musicol Soc (mem bd dirs, 72-77, vpres, 77-82); Renaissance Soc Am (mem coun, 72-74, mem exec comt, 79-); Arts Coun Greater New Haven (vpres, 74-75). *Publ:* Auth, Music in Our Schools: A Search For Improvement, Dept Health, Educ & Welfare, 64; co-translr, G Zarlino's The Art of Counterpoint, Yale Univ Press, 68; Baroque Music, Prentice-Hall, 68, Japanese transl, 75, Hungarian transl, 76 & Spanish transl, 78; ed, Hucbald, Guido & John on Music: Three Medieval Treatises, Yale Univ Press, 77; Norton Anthology of Western Music, 2 vols, W W Norton & Co, 80. *Mailing Add:* 68 Spring Rock Rd Pine Orchard Branford CT 06405

PALMER, ANTHONY JOHN
COMPOSER, EDUCATOR
b Youngstown, Ohio, Oct 9, 31. *Study:* Los Angeles City Col, with Leonard Stein, 54-56; Calif State Univ, Los Angeles, with Esther Andreas, Hugh Mullins & Francis Baxter, BA, 58, MA, 60; Univ Calif, Los Angeles, with Abraham A Schwadron, Gustav Reese, Walter Rubsamen, Mantle Hood, Thomas Marocco, Robert Stevenson & Edwin Hanley, PhD, 75. *Works:* Fusion I—Ryo No Ha (Gagaku West), 79 & Fusion II—West Meets East, 80, comn by Pac Asian Cult Museum, Pasadena; A Carol of Hope (SATB, piano), Gentry Music; See the Star (SATB, piano, perc), Highland Music; Your Hands Lie Open (TTBB) & The Hound's Serenade (SSATBB), Plymouth Music. *Teaching:* Instr choral & music appreciation, Calif Pub Sch, 59-75; assoc prof, Los Angeles Valley Col, 75-80 & Univ Tenn, 80- *Awards:* Creative Artist Fel Japan, Japan-US Friendship Comn, 83. *Mem:* ASCAP; Soc Ethnomusicol; Col Music Soc; Am Choral Dir Asn; Southern Calif Vocal Asn (pres, 63-65). *Interests:* World musics in music education and vocal/choral music. *Publ:* Auth, commentary and news articles, Calif Music Educr Asn News, 68-70; ed, Festival List of Required Music, High School, Southern Calif Vocal Asn, 73; coauth, A Choral Conductor's Manual, PM Press, Univ Tenn Music Dept, 81; auth, Treating the Choral Singer as a Person, Choral J, 81. *Mailing Add:* 11701 Bunting Dr Knoxville TN 37922

PALMER, LARRY GARLAND
EDUCATOR, HARPSICHORD
b Warren, Ohio, Nov 13, 38. *Study:* Harpsichord with Isolde Ahlgrimm, 58-59; Consv Music, Oberlin Col, BMus, 60; Eastman Sch Music, MM, 61, DMA, 63; studied harpsichord with Gustav Leonhardt, summers 64 & 67. *Works:* 'Twas in the Year That King Uzziah Died (anthem), Calvary Press, 76 & 83. *Rec Perf:* The Harpsichord Now and Then, 74 & Organ Works (Hugo Distler), 78, Musical Heritage Soc. *Pos:* Ed harpsichord, The Diapason, 69- *Teaching:* Asst prof music, St Paul's Col, 63-65; prof, Norfolk State Col, 65-70; prof harpsichord & organ, Meadows Sch Arts, Southern Methodist Univ, 70- *Mem:* Am Guild Organists (dean Norfolk chap, 68-70, dean Dallas chap, 77-79); Southeastern Hist Keyboard Soc. *Interests:* The 20th century harpsichord revival. *Publ:* Auth, Hugo Distler and His Church Music, Concordia, 67. *Mailing Add:* 10125 Cromwell Dr Dallas TX 75229

PALMER, MICHAEL
MUSIC DIRECTOR & CONDUCTOR, PIANO
b Indianapolis, Ind. *Study:* Ind Univ, grad; studied cond with Wolfgang Vacano, piano with Alfonso Montecino & Martin Marks & score studies with Julius Herford. *Pos:* Assoc cond, Atlanta Symph Orch, formerly; founder, Atlanta Youth Symph, formerly; music dir & cond, Wichita Symph Orch, 77-; guest cond, Denver Symph Orch, 77, co-prin guest cond, 78-81; guest cond, Houston Symph, 76-79, artistic dir & adv, summer concert ser, 77-80; music dir, Basically Bach Fest, Anchorage, currently; artistic dir & cond, Lake City Chamber Music Fest, Col, 79-; guest cond, Nat Symph, San Diego Symph, Oakland Symph, Indianapolis Symph, Kansas City Phil & many others. *Mailing Add:* Wichita Symph Orch 225 W Douglas Wichita KS 67202

PALMER, ROBERT M
COMPOSER, EDUCATOR
b Syracuse, NY, June 2, 15. *Study:* Eastman Sch Music, with Howard Hanson, BM, 38, MM, 39; studied with Roy Harris, 39; Berkshire Music Ctr, with Aaron Copland, 40. *Works:* Poem (violin & orch), 38; Three Epigrams (string quartet), 57; Nabochodonosor (brass ens & chorus), 64; Transitions (piano), 76; Organon I (flute, clarinet, violin & cello), 77; Carmina Amoris (sop, clarinet, violin & piano), 78; First Quartet for Piano & Strings; and others. *Teaching:* Fac mem theory, Univ Kans, 40-43; fac mem, Cornell Univ, 43-53& 56- Given Found prof music, currently; vis comp, Ill Wesleyan Univ, 54 & Univ Mich, 56; prof, Univ Ill, George E Miller, 55-56. *Awards:* Guggenheim Fel, 52; MacDowell Fel, 54; Fulbright Sr Res Grant, 60. *Mailing Add:* 108 Valley Rd Ithaca NY 14850

PALMER, WILLARD A
EDITOR, LECTURER
b McComb, Miss, Jan 31, 17. *Study:* Millsaps Col, BS, 39; Univ Houston, 46-50; Whitworth Col, Dr Humanities, 79; Millsaps Col, DMus, 83. *Works:* O Wondrous Child (choral), 69, Quodlibet on Praise to the Lord, 69, Now Thank We, 69, Carol of the Shepherd Boy, 69, Baroque Folk (piano), 69, A Contemporary Album for the Young (18 piano solos), 77, Blues & Fugue in D Minor, 77-80 & 16 Solos for Young Pianists, 82, Alfred Publ Co. *Pos:* Keyboard ed-in-chief, Alfred Publ Co, Sherman Oaks, Calif, 46-; choral dir, Mem Lutheran Church, Houston, Tex, 50-68; concert keyboard artist, currently. *Teaching:* Instr keyboard, Univ Houston, 48-64; lectr, Eastman Sch Music, Oberlin Sch Music, Riemenschneider Bach Inst, Gina Bachhauer Fest, Brigham Young Univ, Univ Wis, Royal Consv Toronto, Manhattan Sch Music & other inst, formerly. *Awards:* Award of Achievement, Am Guild Music, 63. *Mem:* Riemenschneider Bach Inst; Houston Harpsichord Soc. *Interests:* Baroque performance; practices in European & American libraries. *Publ:* Contribr, Creating Music at the Piano, 16 vol, 61-66, Alfred's Basic Piano Library, 16 vol, 81-83, ed, J S Bach Well Tempered Clavier, Vol I, 81 & Seven Centuries of Keyboard Music, 81, Alfred Publ Co; ed & auth of over 350 books. *Mailing Add:* 9602 Winsome Lane Houston TX 77063

PALMIERI, ROBERT MICHAEL
PIANO, EDUCATOR
b Milwaukee, Wis, Oct 30, 30. *Study:* Wis Consv Music, BM, 53; Eastman Sch Music, MM, 54. *Works:* Twenty Piano Exercises, Oxford Univ Press, 71. *Teaching:* Prof & coordr div keyboard instrm, Sch Music, Kent State Univ, 56- *Awards:* Kent State Univ Summer Res Fel, 69 & 83. *Mem:* Am Liszt Soc; Am Asn Univ Prof. *Publ:* Auth, Artist and Artisan, Am Music Teacher, 63; Rakhmaninov Resource Guide, Garland Publ (in prep). *Mailing Add:* 516 Beryl Dr Kent OH 44240

PALOMBO, PAUL MARTIN
COMPOSER, EDUCATOR
b Pittsburgh, Pa, Sept 10, 37. *Study:* Ind Univ of Pa, with Charles E Hoag, BS; Peabody Consv Music, with Robert Hall Lewis; Eastman Sch Music, with Bernard Rogers & Howard Hanson, PhD, 69. *Works:* Proteus (orch & tape), 69; Miniatures (organ & tape), 69; Metatheses (flute, oboe, harpsichord & double bass), 71; Rittatti anticamente (viola & piano), 72; Montage (violin & piano), 72; Sono No 1 (tape & harpsichord), 72, No 2 (harp & tape), 72, No 3 (double bass & tape), 73 & No 4 (string trio & tape), 74; Stogowsgenvolkssaurus (electronic music for a sculpture), 73-74. *Teaching:* Instr, Baltimore Co pub sch, 62-69; assoc dean acad affairs & dir grad studies, Col Consv Music, Univ Cincinnati, 69-78; prof & dir, Sch Music, Univ Wash, 78-81; prof comp, assoc dean acad affairs & dir grad studies & electronic music studio, Col Consv Music, Univ Cincinnati, formerly; dean, Col Fine Arts, Univ Wis, Stevens Pt, currently. *Awards:* Rockefeller Award, 65; Am Fest Music Awards, 67 & 78; Howard Hanson Prize, 69. *Mem:* Am Soc Univ Comp; Col Music Soc. *Mailing Add:* Music Dept Univ Wis Stevens Point WI 54481

PANCALDO, SONYA MONOSOFF See Monosoff, Sonya

PANDOLFI, ROLAND
FRENCH HORN, EDUCATOR
Study: New England Consv Music; Am Sch Fountainbleau; studied horn with William Valkener & chamber music with Nadia Boulanger. *Rec Perf:* Mozart Horn Quintet & other chamber music, Vox Rec. *Pos:* Soloist & clinician, Tenth Ann Wkshp Int Horn Soc, 78; prin horn, Milwaukee Symph Orch, formerly; prin horn & soloist, St Louis Symph Orch, currently; mem, St Louis Symph Woodwind Quintet, currently. *Teaching:* Mem fac French horn & chamber music, St Louis Consv Music, currently. *Mailing Add:* St Louis Consv Music 560 Trinity Ave St Louis MO 63130

PANERIO, ROBERT MAJOR
COMPOSER, EDUCATOR
b Roslyn, Wash, June 28, 29. *Study:* Cent Wash Univ, BA, 53, MA, 58; Eastman Sch Music, 63. *Works:* Marauders, 67 & Ensenada, 68, Carl Fischer Publ; Jubiloso, 75 & Preludio e Danza, 76, Southern Music Co; Romulus, comn by Hal Sherman, 76; Bellicoso, Southern Music Co, 83; Symphony No 1, perf by various artists. *Pos:* Prof arr & cond, 49- *Teaching:* Supvr instr music, Moses Lake Pub Sch, Wash, 53-62; dean humanities & prof comp, theory & trumpet, Big Bend Community Col, 62-63; prof comp, theory & trumpet, Cent Wash Univ, 63- *Awards:* Band Comp Award, Am Bandmasters Ostwald, 75. *Mem:* ASCAP; Am Fedn Musicians; Music Educr Nat Conf. *Mailing Add:* Music Dept Cent Wash Univ Ellensburg WA 98926

PANETTI, JOAN
COMPOSER, EDUCATOR
Study: Peabody Consv Music; Consv Musique Paris; Smith Col; Yale Sch Music. *Works:* Piano Concerto; Small Pieces for Gregory (four pieces, cello & strings); Cavatina (piano); Songs for Medium Voice. *Pos:* Pianist, tours of Europe & US; soloist with chamber music ens. *Teaching:* Mem fac, Princeton Univ, formerly & Swarthmore Col, formerly; Mem fac, Yale Sch Music, formerly, adj prof theory & analysis, 79-; music dir, Norfolk Summer Sch, 82- *Mailing Add:* Yale Sch Music Box 2104A Yale Station New Haven CT 06520

PANGBORN, ROBERT C
PERCUSSION, EDUCATOR
b Painesville, Ohio, Dec 31, 34. *Study:* Eastman Sch Music; Western Reserve Univ; Juilliard Sch Music; Oakland Univ. *Rec Perf:* With Cleveland Orch, Epic Rec; Symphonic Metamorphosis, London Rec; with Detroit Symph, Columbia Rec. *Pos:* Mallet perc, Cleveland Orch, 57-63; prin perc, Detroit Symph, 64- *Teaching:* Head, Perc Dept, Cleveland Inst Music, 58-63 & Detroit Community Music Sch; instr perc & appl music, Oakland Univ, currently. *Mem:* Percussive Arts Soc. *Mailing Add:* Dept Music Oakland Univ Rochester MI 48063

PANITZ, MURRAY W
FLUTE
b New York, NY, Aug 30, 25. *Study:* Eastman Sch Music, BM, 45; Manhattan Sch Music, MM, 50. *Pos:* Prin flute, Philadelphia Orch, 61- *Teaching:* Prof flute, Temple Univ, 77- *Mailing Add:* Philadelphia Orch 1420 Locust St Philadelphia PA 19102

PAPASTEFAN, JOHN JAMES
EDUCATOR, PERCUSSION
b Milwaukee, Wis, July 28, 42. *Study:* Univ Wis, Whitewater, BEd, 66; Appalachian State Univ, MA, 67; Walden Univ, PhD, 78. *Pos:* Timpanist & prin perc, Mobile Symph, 68-70; prin perc, Mobile Opera Orch, 74- *Teaching:* Grad asst, Appalachian State Univ, 66-67; assoc prof music, Univ South Ala, 67- *Mem:* Col Music Soc; Perc Arts Soc; Nat Asn Col Wind & Perc Instr; Music Educ Nat Conf; Am Fedn Musicians. *Publ:* Auth, Contemporary Timpani Techniques, 80 & Timpani Roll Notation: Observations & Clarifications, 81, Perc; Temple Blocks & Woodblocks, Woodwind, Brass & Perc, 1/83; coauth, Guide to Teaching Percussion, William C Brown Co, 83. *Mailing Add:* 209 Vanderbilt Dr Mobile AL 36608

PAPAVASILION, ERNEST JOHN
VIOLIN
b Lancaster, Pa, May 1, 37. *Study:* Eastman Sch Music, perf cert, 58, BMus, 59; Manhattan Sch Music, MMus, 61; studied with Joseph Knitzer, Raphael Bronstein, Ivan Galamian, Oscar Shumski & Mischa Mischakoff. *Pos:* Violinist, soloist, Eastman-Rochester Symph, 58; concertmaster, Broadway Theaters, 66-68; violinist, Metropolitan Opera, 68- *Awards:* Nat Honor, Nat Fedn Music Clubs, 55. *Mailing Add:* 242 W 76th St New York NY 10023

PAPERNO, DMITRY A
PIANO, EDUCATOR
b Kiev, USSR, Feb 18, 29; US citizen. *Study:* Cent Sch Music, dipl, 46; Moscow Tchaikovsky State Consv, MA, 51; Moscow Consv, aspirant dipl, 55. *Rec Perf:* Chopin, 55, Bach, Medtner, Debussy, 58, Chopin, Schumann, Liszt, 68 & Mendelssohn, Liszt, Brahms, Grieg, 74, Melodiya, Moscow, USSR; Scriabin, 79 & Tchaikovsky, The Seasons, 82, Musical Heritage Soc. *Pos:* Concert pianist, Mosconcert, 55-76. *Teaching:* Gnesin Moscow State Inst, USSR, 67-74; assoc prof piano, DePaul Univ, 77- *Awards:* Laureate, Fifth Int Chopin Compt, Warsaw, Poland, 55 & First Int Enescu Compt, Bucharest, Rumania, 58. *Mem:* Soc Am Musicians. *Publ:* Author of three articles, Soviet Music, 72 & 73; Rimsky-Korsakov and Tchaikovsky, Heirs of Glinka & Glimpses of D Shostakovich and S Prokofiev, 80, Chicago Symph Orch Prog; Notes of a Moscow Pianist, Hermitage, 83. *Rep:* Great Lakes Performing Artist Assoc 310 E Washington St Ann Arbor MI 48104. *Mailing Add:* 2821 W Jerome Chicago IL 60645

PARADISE, TIMOTHY JAMES
CLARINET
b Monte Vista, Colo, Sept 2, 47. *Study:* Pomona Col, BA, 69; Yale Sch Music, MM, 71; Staatliche Hochschule Musik, Munich, 72. *Pos:* Prin clarinetist, New Haven Symph, 70-71, Symph Orch Graunke, Munich, 71-72, Victoria Symph, BC, 72-77 & St Paul Chamber Orch, 77-; numerous solo recitals. *Awards:* Fulbright Fel, 71. *Bibliog:* Tim Page (auth), Belgian Chamber Group and 5 Soloists Perform, New York Times, 3/13/83. *Mailing Add:* c/o Franklin Agency 224 Franklin Ave W Minneapolis MN 55404

PARATORE, ANTHONY
PIANO
b Boston, Mass. *Study:* Boston Univ, studied piano with Bela Nagy, BA(music); Juilliard Sch, studied piano with Rosina Lhevinne, MS. *Rec Perf:* Concerto in E-flat for Two Pianos (Mozart), 74, 77 & 83, D'un espace deploye (Gilbert Amy), 74, Concerto for Two Pianos (Bartok), 82 & La Folia for Two Pianos (Manfred Trojahn), 82, New World Rec & Schwann Musica Mundi; Games of the Past for Two Pianos (Robert Moevs), 76. *Awards:* First Prize (piano duo), Munich Int Music Compt, 74. *Bibliog:* Helge Grünewald (auth), interview, Fono Forum, Munich, WGermany, 11/82; Jean Oelrich (auth), interview, Clavier Mag, 83. *Mailing Add:* 142 Chilton St Belmont MA 02178

PARATORE, JOSEPH
PIANO
b Boston, Mass. *Study:* Boston Univ, studied piano with Bela Nagy, BA(music), 70; Juilliard Sch, studied piano with Rosina Lhevinne, MS, 72. *Rec Perf:* Concerto in E-flat for Two Pianos (Mozart), 74, 77 & 83, D'un espace deploye (Gilbert Amy), 74, Concerto for Two Pianos (Bartok), 82 & La Folia for Two Pianos (Manfred Trojahn), 82, New World Rec & Schwann Musica Mundi; Games of the Past for Two Pianos (Robert Moevs), 76. *Awards:* First Prize (piano duo), Munich Int Music Compt, 74. *Bibliog:* Helge Grünewald (auth), interview, Fono Forum, Munich, WGermany, 11/82; Jean Oelrich (auth), interview, Clavier Mag, 83. *Mailing Add:* 142 Chilton St Belmont MA 02178

PARCELLS, RAMON EVERETT
TRUMPET, EDUCATOR
b Chicago, Ill, Oct 10, 44. *Study:* New England Consv Music, with Roger Voisin, BMus, 65; studied with Vincent Cichowicz, 70-76. *Pos:* Substitute mem, Boston Symph Orch, 65; prin trumpet, Winnipeg Symph Orch, 65-66; Canadian Broadcasting Corp, 70-82; soloist & dir brass ens, Strategic Air Command Band, US Air Force, 66-70; prin trumpet, Detroit Symph Orch, 82- *Teaching:* Prof trumpet, Nat Youth Orch Can, 74-79; adj prof, Univ Mich, 82- *Mailing Add:* c/o Detroit Symph Orch Ford Auditorium Detroit MI 48226

PARCHMAN, GEN LOUIS
COMPOSER, DOUBLE BASS
b Cincinnati, Ohio, May 2, 29. *Study:* Consv Music, Univ Cincinnati, BA(music), 56, MA(music), 58. *Works:* Symphony for Strings, 62, Winsel Overture, 64, Sonata for Reduced Orchestra, 64, Concerto for Percussion, 65, Marimba Concerto, 67 & Elegy for Orchestra, 68, Seesaw; Symphonies for Percussion, George Gabor, 70. *Pos:* Double-bassist, Cincinnati Symph Orch, 58-65. *Teaching:* Lectr, Univ Cincinnati, 72-76. *Awards:* ASCAP Awards, 60- *Mem:* ASCAP. *Mailing Add:* 1502 Clovernoll Dr Cincinnati OH 45231

PARDEE, MARGARET (MARGARET PARDEE BUTTERLY)
EDUCATOR, VIOLIN
b Valdosta, Ga, May 10, 20. *Study:* Juilliard Sch Music, dipl, 40, post grad dipl, 42 & 45; studied with Sascha Jacobsen, Albert Spalding, Louis Persinger & Ivan Galamian. *Pos:* Concert master, Great Neck Symph, 60- *Teaching:* Fac mem violin & viola, Juilliard Sch Music, 42-; fac mem, Meadowmount Sch Music, 56-, dir, 80- *Mem:* Violin Teachers Guild (treas, 40-); Soc Strings (dir, 56-). *Mailing Add:* Juilliard Sch Lincoln Ctr Plaza New York NY 10023

PARISOT, ALDO SIMOES
CELLO, EDUCATOR
b Natal, Brazil, Sept 30, 20; US citizen. *Study:* Yale Univ, MA. *Rec Perf:* Numerous recordings on Counterpoint/Esoteric Rec, Musical Masterpiece Soc, Guilde Internationale du Disque, Music Guild Rec, Epic Rec, Columbia Rec & others. *Pos:* Solo cellist, major tours in USA, Europe, Asia, Africa, SAm, 48-; compt judge in several int cello compt, incl Munich, Cassado (Florence, Italy), Chile, Brazil (Villa-Lobos Compt) & Evian, France; musical dir, Aldo Parisot Int Cello Course & Compt, 77- *Teaching:* Prof, Peabody Consv, 56-58, Sch Music, Yale Univ, 58-, Mannes Sch Music, 62-66 & New England Consv, 66-70. *Awards:* Peace Medal, UN, 82; Artist Teacher of Yr Award, Am String Teachers Asn, 83; numerous awards & honors. *Mailing Add:* 205 Moose Hill Rd Guilford CT 06437

PARK, RAYMOND ROY
EDUCATOR, PIANO
b Victor, Iowa, Aug 28, 31. *Study:* Cornell Col, BM & BME, 53; Aspen Inst Music, studied piano with Joanna Graudan, 52; Univ Mich, Ann Arbor, MM, 57, PhD, 67. *Teaching:* Prof music, Cent Mo State Univ, 64- *Mem:* Am Musicol Soc; Music Libr Asn. *Interests:* Essig Collection of Musical Instruments. *Publ:* Auth, article on Essig Collection of Musical Instruments, Triangle, Sigma Alpha Iota. *Mailing Add:* Rte 5 Green Acres Warrensburg MO 64093

PARKENING, CHRISTOPER W
EDUCATOR, GUITAR
b Los Angeles, Calif, Dec 14, 47. *Study:* Univ Southern Calif; Mont State Univ, Hon Dr Music, 83. *Rec Perf:* Parkening Plays Bach, The Christopher Parkening Album, Parkening and the Guitar, Christopher Parkening in the Classic Styles, Chistopher Parkening in the Spanish Style, Christopher Parkening Romanza & Christopher Parkening Sacred Music for the Guitar, Angel Rec. *Pos:* Conct guitarist, 71- *Teaching:* Head guitar dept, Univ Southern Calif, 71-75 & Mont State Univ, 76-83. *Publ:* Auth, Virtuoso Music for Guitar, Vol I & II & Christopher Parkening Method Book, Vol I, Sherry-Brener Ltd. *Mailing Add:* c/o Columbia Artists 165 W 57th St New York NY 10019

PARKER, ALAN
MUSIC DIRECTOR, CELLO

b Pasadena, Calif, Sept 9, 46. *Study:* Consv PR, 67; Occidental Col, AB, 68; Univ Denver, MA, 73. *Pos:* Broadcast prod specialist, Armed Forces Radio & TV Serv, US Air Force, 69-73; programmer & librn, KUSC-FM, Los Angeles, 75-78; music dir, Seal Beach Chamber Music Fest, 75- & Haydn Orch, 75- *Teaching:* Instr cello, privately. *Mem:* Music Teachers Asn Calif (treas Long Beach branch, 80-82); Am Symph Orch League; Chamber Music Am; Am Fedn Musicians. *Mailing Add:* 119 8th St Seal Beach CA 90740

PARKER, ALICE
COMPOSER, CONDUCTOR

b Boston, Mass, Dec 16, 25. *Study:* Smith Col, BA, 47; Juilliard Sch Music, MS, 49; Hamilton Col, Hon Dr, 79. *Works:* The Martyrs' Mirror, E C Schirmer, 71; The Family Reunion, Carl Fischer, 75; Songs for Eve, Hinshaw, 75; Gaudete, E C Schirmer, 77; Singers Glen, 78 & Echoes from the Hills, 79, Hinshaw; The Ponder Heart, Belwin-Mills, 82. *Pos:* Arranger, Robert Shaw Chorale, 49-67; comp & cond, 55- *Teaching:* Mem fac comp, Westminster Choir Col, summers 73- *Awards:* ASCAP Comp Awards, 68-; Nat Endowment for Arts Grant, 75. *Mem:* Asn Prof Vocal Ens; Am Choral Dir Asn; Am Symph Orch League; Hymn Soc Am; Int League Women Comp. *Publ:* Auth, Music Pocket Crammer, Doubleday, 64; Creative Hymn Singing, Hinshaw, 76. *Mailing Add:* 801 West End Ave New York NY 10025

PARKER, CRAIG BURWELL
TRUMPET, EDUCATOR

b Leavenworth, Kans, Feb 11, 51. *Study:* Univ Ga, BM, 73; Univ Calif, Los Angeles, MA, 76, PhD, 81. *Works:* Fugue in A Minor for Piano, Craig B Parker, 70; The Grass Menagerie, Kitty Blisset & John Cawthon, 72; Nocturne, Craig B Parker & Dera Goodner, 73; Sonata for Bassoon and Piano, Kenneth Deans & Craig B Parker, 73; Three Miniatures for Clarinet and Piano, Michelle Parker & Valerie Sucher, 75; Suite for Two Trumpets, Craig B Parker & Philip Clark, 83. *Pos:* Trumpeter, Long Beach Symph, 76-82 & Comp Brass Quintet, 77-82; hornblower, Santa Anita & Hollywood Park Racetracks, 81-82. *Teaching:* Asst music hist & theory, Univ Calif, Los Angeles, 74-79; asst prof music hist, theory & trumpet, Kans State Univ, 82- *Awards:* Edwin Sparks Fel,Phi Kappa Phi, 73-74. *Bibliog:* America's High School Soloist Hall of Fame: Craig Parker, Sch Musician, 1/69. *Mem:* Col Music Soc; Int Trumpet Guild; Nat Asn Col Wind & Perc Instr; Sonneck Soc. *Interests:* John Vincent; Olivier Messiaen; trumpet music of all epochs. *Publ:* Auth, John Vincent: A List of Compositions, Composer, 77. *Mailing Add:* Manhattan KS 66502

PARKER, JESSE
EDUCATOR, PIANO

b New York, NY, Oct 13, 31. *Study:* NY Univ, AB, 52; Stanford Univ, AM, 59, PhD, 74. *Rec Perf:* The Romantic Keyboard, Bridge Rec, 75. *Teaching:* Asst prof music, Univ Santa Clara, 70-73 & Univ Tex, Dallas, 75-79; prof, Cornish Inst, 79- *Mailing Add:* 1504 167th SE Bellevue WA 98008

PARKER, OLIN GRIFFITH
EDUCATOR, ADMINISTRATOR

b Plains, Kans, Feb 28, 22. *Study:* Bethany Col, BMus, 47; Univ Kans, MMusEd, 49, DEd, 61. *Pos:* Dir, Kans All-State Band, Audio House, Lawrence, 62. *Teaching:* Instr music, Macksville pub sch, Kans, 47-48; dir instrm music, Leavenworth city pub sch, Kans, 49-51; coordr music, Salina pub sch, Kans, 53-64; prof & assoc head, Sch Music, Univ Ga, 64- *Awards:* Orpheus Award, Phi Mu Alpha Sinfonia, 77; Distinguished Serv Award, Ga Music Educr Asn, 77. *Bibliog:* Cady & Scheider (auth), Cooperative Research Project E-016, Dept Health, Educ & Welfare, 62; A Schwadron (auth), Aesthetics: Dimensions for Music Education, Music Educr Nat Conf, 67; R Shuter-Dyson (auth), The Psychology of Music, Methuen, 78. *Mem:* Int Soc Music Educ; Music Educr Nat Conf; Coun Res Music Educ; Nat Music Therapy Asn; Col Music Soc. *Interests:* Development and perception, psychoacoustic and instrumental music. *Publ:* Coauth, An Information Retrieval System for Music Therapy, J Music Therapy, 72; auth, The Relationship of Musical Ability, Intelligence, and Socioeconomic Status to Aesthetic Sensitivity, Psychology Music, 78; The Concert Band: Its Real Core, Sch Musician, 82; The Recognition of Trumpets by Perception of Timbre, Proc Res Symposium, 82; Quantitative Differences in Frequency Perceptions, Bulletin of Coun Res Music Educ, 83. *Mailing Add:* 212 Fortson Dr Athens GA 30606

PARKER, R CLINTON
ADMINISTRATOR, EDUCATOR

b Hickory, NC, May 12, 41. *Study:* Appalachian State Univ, BS, 64; Univ NC, Chapel Hill, MM, 70; Univ Miami, PhD, 79. *Teaching:* Dir choral music, R J Reynolds High Sch, Winston-Salem, NC, 64-65 & Concord Sr High School, NC, 65-68; asst prof, Pikeville Col, 70-72; prof, Appalachian State Univ, 72-, asst dean, Fine & Applied Arts, 72-80, assoc vchancellor, Acad Affairs, 80- *Mem:* Am Choral Dir Asn (state pres, 72-75, div chair, 68-70); Music Educr Nat Conf; Phi Mu Alpha. *Mailing Add:* PO Box 2073 Boone NC 28607

PARKER, RICHARD ALLAN
EDUCATOR

b Springfield, Ohio, Dec 19, 44. *Study:* Wittenberg Univ, BSEduc, 66; Ohio State Univ, MA, 70, PhD, 74. *Pos:* Dir music, Grace United Methodist Church, Hartford City, Ind, 75- *Teaching:* Instr music, Northwestern Community Sch, Springfield, Ohio, 67-69; sr band dir & coord music, Delaware City Sch, Ohio, 71-74; prof music, Taylor Univ, 74- *Mem:* Am Orff Schulwerk Asn; Music Educr Nat Conf; Ind Music Educ Asn; Am Guild English Handbell Ringers. *Publ:* Auth, The Related Arts: Theory and Practice, Triad, 67; Rapport in the Conducting Process, Instrumentalist, 70. *Mailing Add:* 24 S Shamrock Rd Hartford City IN 47348

PARKER, WILLIAM KENT
BARITONE

b Butler, Pa, Aug 5, 43. *Study:* Princeton Univ, AB, 65; studied with Frederick Wilkerson, John Bullock & Rosa Ponselle. *Rec Perf:* On EMI & New World Rec. *Roles:* Fiorello in Il Barbiere di Siviglia, NVa Opera, Arlington, 68; Dott Malatesta in Don Pasquale; Albert in Werther; Guglielmo in Cosi fan tutti; Count Almaviva in Le Nozze di Figaro; Marcello & Sharpless in Madama Butterfly; Papageno in Die Zauberflöte. *Pos:* Bar, US Army Chorus, 66-70 & Vienna Volks Opera, 71-73; performer, recitals & concts in US & Europe. *Awards:* First Prize, Int Compt, Munich, Toulouse, Barcelona & Paris, 70; Winner, Joy in Singing Compt, 76; First Place, Kennedy Ctr & Rockefeller Found Compt, 79. *Mem:* Am Guild Musical Artists. *Mailing Add:* c/o Harry Beall Mgt 119 W 57th St New York NY 10019

PARKS, DAVID WAYNE
TENOR, LECTURER

b Danville, Pa, July 24, 55. *Study:* Westminster Choir Col, BMusEd, 77; Univ Mich, MMus, 81; Univ Ariz, vocal study with Jerold Siena, DMA, 83. *Rec Perf:* Mozart Requiem, Mark Rec, 79; Maria Elena (Thomas Pasatieri), Univ Ariz, 83. *Roles:* Bill in Hand of Bridge, Mich Opera Theatre, 80; Beppe in I Pagliacci, 82, Desk Clerk & Priest in Baby Doe, Remendado in Carmen, 83 & Nemorino in Elixer, 83, Ariz Opera Co. *Pos:* Singer & actor, Mich Opera Theatre, 80-81 & Ariz Opera Co, 82-83. *Teaching:* Vocal instr, Col of William & Mary, Williamsburg, Va, 83- *Mailing Add:* c/o Ariz Opera 3501 N Mountain Ave Tucson AZ 85719

PARLOFF, MICHAEL (LEON)
FLUTE & PICCOLO

b Baltimore, Md, Oct 14, 52. *Study:* Juilliard Sch, with Arthur Lora, Thomas Nyfenger & Geoffrey Gilbert, BM, 74. *Pos:* Prin flute, Metropolitan Opera Orch, 77- *Mailing Add:* 245 W 104th New York NY 10025

PARLY, TICHO (TICHO PARLY FREDERIK CHRISTIANSEN)
TENOR

b Copenhagen, Denmark, July 16, 28; US citizen. *Study:* With Hertha Bjoervig, Gabrielle Dauly, William Herman & Charles Paddock. *Rec Perf:* On DG. *Roles:* Graf in Nacht in Venedig, New Orleans Opera, 58; Leonardo in Re Cervo, Staatsoper, Kassel, 63; Florestan in Fidelio; Alwa in Lulu; Don Jose in Carmen; Mephisto in Doktor Faust; Bürgermeister in Besuch der alten Dame. *Pos:* Tenor with maj opera co in Arg, Europe, Mex & US. *Awards:* Commen Medal, Wagner Fest, Bayreuth, WGermany. *Mailing Add:* c/o Robert M Gewald Mgt 58 W 58th St New York NY 10019

PARMENTIER, FRANCIS GORDON
COMPOSER, LECTURER

b Green Bay, Wis, Apr 24, 23. *Study:* Bethany Col, BA, 45; Consv Nat Musique, Paris, cert, 52; studied comp with Henri Busser. *Works:* Four Sonnets from the Portugese, Little Symph San Francisco, 68; Vision (tenor & string quartet), comn by KQUED, San Francisco, 69; Double Entendre, San Francisco Symph, 70; Northern Diary (chorus & orch), Green Bay Symph, 71; Symphony #3, Wis Youth Symph, 76; Mirrors (piano & orch), comn by Green Bay Symph, 81; several other chamber works, song cycles & instrumental works. *Teaching:* Instr music theory, Mills Col, 54, Univ Wis, Green Bay, 69- *Mem:* Am Comp Alliance. *Mailing Add:* 3473 Nicolet Dr Green Bay WI 54301

PARNAS, LESLIE
CELLO, EDUCATOR

b St Louis, Mo, Nov 22, 32. *Study:* Curtis Inst Music, studied cello with Gregor Piatigorsky, artists dipl; studied cello with Pablo Casals. *Rec Perf:* On CBS, Sine Qua Non, Vanguard, Book of the Month & Pathe-Marconi. *Pos:* Artistic dir, Kneisel Hall Summer Sch String & Ens Music; soloist, US, South Am, Europe, SAfrica & USSR. *Teaching:* May Dept Stores chair cello & artist in res, St Louis Consv Music, 83-; assoc prof cello, Boston Univ; prof chamber groups & cello, Hartt Sch Music. *Awards:* Winner, Prix Pablo Casals, Paris, 57; Primavera Trophy, Rome, 59; Int Tchaikovsky Compt Prize, Moscow, 62. *Mem:* Charter mem, Chamber Music Soc Lincoln Ctr. *Mailing Add:* St Louis Consv 560 Trinity St Louis MO 63130

PARRIGIN, PERRY GOGGIN
ORGAN, EDUCATOR

b Paintsville, Ky. *Study:* Univ Ky, with Lela W Cullis, AB, 47; Ind Univ, with Oswald Ragatz, MM, 49, 52-53; Union Theol Sem, with Robert Baker, 49-50; Univ Colo, With Everett J Hilty, summer 61. *Pos:* Organist & choir dir, Mo United Methodist Church, Columbia, 53-63 & Calvary Episcopal Church, Columbia, 70-77; vis organist, Wilshire Methodist Church, Los Angeles, summer 60; vis organist & choir dir, St John the Baptist, London, England, summer 65; numerous recitals throughout the Midwest, East and South; organist, Mo United Methodist Church. *Teaching:* From instr to assoc prof, Univ Mo, 53-; vis instr, Ind Univ, Bloomington, summer 55. *Mem:* Am Guild Organists (dean Cent Mo chap, 81-82). *Mailing Add:* Dept Music Fine Arts Bldg Univ Mo Columbia MO 65211

PARRIS, ARTHUR
LECTURER, CRITIC

b Philadelphia, Pa, Mar 3, 24. *Study:* Juilliard Sch Music, with Beveridge Webster, BS, 48; Nat Consv Music, Paris, with Ple Causade, dipl, 50; Bryn Mawr Col, with Sylvia Kenney, MA, 58, PhD, 65. *Pos:* Music critic, Ann Arbor News, 70-72. *Teaching:* Mem fac piano, Settlement Music Sch Philadelphia, 53-63; from assoc prof to prof, West Chester State Col, 64-70; prof, Eastern Mich Univ, 70- *Mem:* Am Musicol Soc; Col Music Soc; Soc Ethnomusicol; Soc Music Theory; Am Asn Univ Prof. *Mailing Add:* Music Dept Eastern Mich Univ Ypsilanti MI 48197

PARRIS, ROBERT
COMPOSER, PIANO
b Philadelphia, Pa, May 21, 24. *Study:* Univ Pa, BS(music educ), 45, MS, 46; Juilliard Sch, with Peter Mennin, BS, 48; Berkshire Music Ctr, with Aaron Copland, 50; Ecole Normale Musique, Paris, with Arthur Honneger, 52-53. *Works:* Violin Concerto, 59; The Raids: 1940 (sop, violin & piano), 60; Lamentations and Praises (chamber ens & perc), 62; Walking Around (cantata for men's voices, clarinet, violin & piano), 73; The Messengers (orch), comn by Nat Endowment Arts, 74; Rite of Passage (chamber ens), 78; Two String Quartets; and others. *Rec Perf:* Concerto for Trombone and Orchestra (Parris); The Book of Imaginary Beginnings (Parris). *Pos:* Recitalist, piano, organ & chamber music. *Teaching:* Mem fac, Juilliard Summer Sch, 48 & Wash State Col, 48-49; private instr, 49-63; prof music, George Washington Univ, 63- *Awards:* Fulbright Grant, 52-53; NY State Coun Arts Grant, 74; Nat Endowment Arts Grants, 75 & 78. *Mem:* BMI. *Publ:* Contribr, Wash Evening Star, Kenyon Rev & Juilliard Rev. *Mailing Add:* 3307 Cummings Lane Chevy Chase MD 20015

PARSONS, DAVID
BARITONE
b Traverse City, Mich, 1952. *Study:* Univ Mich, BMus & MMus. *Roles:* Count Almaviva in The Barber of Seville; Eisenstein in Die Fledermaus; Macheath in The Beggar's Opera; Silvio in I Pagliacci, Mich Opera Theater, 78-79; Germont in La Traviata, Opera New England, 82; Frank in The Postman Always Rings Twice, Opera Theatre St Louis, 82 & 83; Enrico in Lucia di Lammermoor, Minn Opera, 83. *Pos:* Apprentice artist, Santa Fe Opera, 76 & 79; bar, Houston Grand Opera, Minn Opera, Opera New England, Tex Opera Theater, Opera Midwest & Aspen Music Fest. *Mailing Add:* c/o Colbert Artists Mgt 111 W 57th St New York NY 10019

PARSONS, JAMES BOYD
WRITER
b Gadsden, Ala, Mar 11, 56. *Study:* Fla State Univ, BA, 77; NTex State Univ, MA, 83; Princeton Univ, 81-82; Univ Pa, currently. *Pos:* Asst dept music, Pierpont Morgan Libr, New York, 82-83. *Awards:* Hewitt-Oberdoerffer Award, Am Musicol Soc, 80. *Mem:* Am Musicol Soc; Int Musicol Soc. *Interests:* Eighteenth and nineteenth century German music; relations between text and music and social context; music criticism; opera. *Publ:* Auth, A Vivaldi Opera in the New World, Opera J, 81; The Opera: 1598-1978, Dover, 83. *Mailing Add:* Dept Music Univ Pa 201 S 34th St Philadelphia PA 19104

PARSONS, MEREDITH WREN
MEZZO-SOPRANO
b Traverse City, Mich. *Study:* Middlebury Col, BA, 75; Cantica Sch Voice, London, cert, 80; study with Marlena Malas, 81- *Roles:* Maurya in Riders to the Sea, Opera Ens New York, 82; Diana in La Calisto, 83, L'Enfant in L'Enfant et les Sortileges, 83 & Widow in Kurt Weil After Dark, 83, Wolf Trap Opera; Mother in Amahl the Night Visitors, Lyr Opera Northern, Mich, 83. *Pos:* Apprentice artist, Santa Fe Opera, 77 & 80; res co ms, Mich Opera Theater, 78-79. *Awards:* Fel, T J Watson Found, 75; Third Prize, Liederkranz Found, 83. *Mailing Add:* 353 W 57th St New York NY 10019

PARTY, LIONEL
HARPSICHORD, EDUCATOR
b Santiago, Chile, Nov 17, 44; Chilean & French citizen. *Study:* Escuela Moderna Musica, Chile, with Elena Waiss, lic, 65; Musikhochschule, with Rosl Schmid; Juilliard Sch, with Albert Fuller, MS, 72, DMA, 76. *Teaching:* Mem fac harpsichord, Juilliard Sch, 77- *Awards:* Fulbright Grant, 70; First Prize, Fourth Int J S Bach Compt, 72. *Mailing Add:* 500 E 63rd St New York NY 10021

PARWEZ, AKMAL M
COMPOSER, BASS-BARITONE
b Rawalpindi, Punjab, Pakistan, Dec 25, 48; US citizen. *Study:* Univ Electro-Commun, Tokyo, BE, 67, ME, 69; Queens Col, City Univ New York, MA(comp), 74; Eastman Sch Music, PhD(comp), 81. *Works:* Elegy for A Khyber Rebel, 82, Traveler on Paths Unknown, 82 & Three Night Songs, 82, perf by Crane Chamber Ens; Second String Quartet, Southern Arts String Quartet, 83; fpp (flute, perc & piano), comn by NY Univ Contemp Players, 83. *Pos:* Choir dir, First Baptist Church, Rochester, NY, 75-77; music dir & cond, Penang Youth Orch, Malaysia, 78-80. *Teaching:* Adj lectr music, Queens Col, City Univ New York, 73-74; instr, Univ Rochester, 75-77; asst prof & dir choir, Malaysian Sci Univ, Penang, 77-80; asst prof, Crane Sch Music, State Univ NY, Potsdam, 81-82 & Brooklyn Consv Music, 83- *Bibliog:* Anwar Iqbal (auth), Eastern & Western Music—The Twain No More Divergent, Muslim, Rawalbindi, Pakistan, 2/21/81; Lisa Cania (auth), Mystic Moods: Faculty Recital by Composer-Singer Akmal Parwez, Racquette, Vol 5, No 3; Ekramul Haque (auth), Parwez: A Punjabi Exponent of Western Music, Asian Monitor, 5/20/83. *Mem:* Am Music Ctr; Am Soc Univ Comp; ASCAP; Col Music Soc; Nat Asn Comp USA. *Publ:* Auth, Dabus—Ecstasy in Penitence: Muslim Mystic Music in Malaysia, Univ Sains Malaysia, 79; Naushad: Composer-Laureate of Indian Film Music, 81 & Indian Influence on the Music of Messiaen & Holst, 81, Daily Jang, Pakistan; Transcendental Music, Col Music Symposium, 83; coauth, Ban Phulwari (Flowers in the Wild): Folk Songs & Dances of Northern Punjab, Pakistan Nat Coun Arts, 73, rev ed, 83. *Rep:* Comp Forum 1 5th Ave New York NY 10003. *Mailing Add:* 163-07 Crocheron Ave #1-B Flushing NY 11358

PASATIERI, THOMAS
COMPOSER, ARTISTIC DIRECTOR
b New York, NY, Oct 20, 45. *Study:* Juilliard Sch, with Vittorio Giannini & Vincent Persichetti, BMus, 65, MS, 67, DMA, 69; studied with Darius Milhaud. *Works:* Heloise and Abelard (sop, bar & piano), 71; The Trial of Mary Todd Lincoln, Net-TV, Boston, 72; The Seagull, 73; Ines de Castro, Baltimore, 76; Washington Square, Detroit, 76; Before Breakfast, 76; Far From Love (sop & four instrm); over 600 other songs & cycles. *Pos:* Artistic dir, Atlanta Civic Opera, 80- *Teaching:* Mem fac, NC Sch Arts, Siena, Italy, 67, Juilliard Sch, 67-69 & Manhattan Sch Music, 69-71; distinguished vis prof, Cincinnati Col Consv, 80-; instr master classes throughout US. *Awards:* Marion Freschi Prize; Brevard Fest Prize Orch Music; Aspen Fest Prize; and others. *Mem:* ASCAP. *Mailing Add:* 500 West End Ave New York NY 10024

PASCHKE, DONALD VERNON
EDUCATOR, BARITONE
b Menominee, Mich, Oct 22, 29. *Study:* Univ Ill, BS(music ed) & BMus(voice), 57, MMus(voice), 58; Univ Colo, DMA(vocal perf & pedagogy), 72. *Teaching:* Instr voice, Berea Col, 58-62; asst prof, Eastern NMex Univ, 62-71, assoc prof, 71-76, prof, 76- *Publ:* Ed & translr, Manuel Garcia, A Complete Treatise on the Art of Singing, 1847 & 1872, Part II, 75 & Part I, 83, Da Capo Press. *Mailing Add:* 228 Kansas Dr Portales NM 88130

PASLER, JANN CORINNE
WRITER, EDUCATOR
b Milwaukee, Wis, July 6, 51. *Study:* Vanderbilt Univ, BA, 73; Univ Chicago, MA, 74, PhD, 81. *Teaching:* Asst prof, Univ Va, 78-80, Col Consv Music, Univ Cincinnati, 81 & Univ Calif, San Diego, 81- *Mem:* Am Musicol Soc. *Interests:* Stravinsky; early 20th century Paris music, cultural history and the related arts. *Publ:* Auth, The Rite of Spring: Stravinsky's Visualization of Music, Dance Mag, 4/81; Stravinsky and the Apaches, Musical Times, 6/82; Debussy's Jeux: Playing with Time and Form, 19th Century Music, summer 82; Trends in Stravinsky Criticism and Research, Musical Times, 10/83; ed, Stravinsky Centennial Essays, Univ Calif Press (in prep). *Mailing Add:* 618 Solana Circle Solana Beach CA 92075

PASMANICK, KENNETH
EDUCATOR, BASSOON
b Rochester, NY, Aug 23, 24. *Study:* Eastman Sch Music, with Vincent Pezzi, 40-43; Juilliard Sch, with Simon Kovar, 46-47; Am Univ, BA, 62. *Pos:* Solo bassoonist, Martha Graham Ballet, 46, Nat Symph Orch, 47 & 83, Wash Opera Soc & Chamber Orch Nat Gallery Art, 47-65; founding mem, Nat Symph Wind Soloists, 80- *Teaching:* Lectr bassoon, Am Univ, 68-; asst prof bassoon & mem res woodwind quartet, Univ Md, 78- *Awards:* Gold Medal, El Salvador, 66 & gov Costa Rica, 67. *Mailing Add:* Nat Symph Orch JFK Ctr Perf Arts Washington DC 20566

PASTINE, GIANFRANCO
LYRIC TENOR
b Santa Margherita Ligure, Italy, Feb 1, 37. *Study:* Consv Giuseppe Verdi, Milan. *Roles:* Silvano in Mascagni, Teatro Nuovo, Milan, 63; The Tales of Hoffmann, Teatro Bellini, Catania, 82; Pinkerton in Madama Butterfly, Metropolitan Opera; Ernesto in Don Pasquale; Rodolfo in La Boheme; Cavaradossi in Tosca; Count Almaviva in Il Barbiere di Siviglia. *Pos:* Ten, La Scala, Vienna Opera, Metropolitan Opera & others. *Awards:* Winner, Nat Concours Asn Lirico Compagnia. *Mailing Add:* c/o Int Artist Mgt 111 W 57th St New York NY 10019

PASTOR, FREDA
EDUCATOR, PIANO
b Newark, NJ. *Study:* Piano with Elise Conrad & Sigismond Stojowski; Curtis Inst Music, with David Saperton, BMus(piano & accmp), 34; studied accmp with Harry Kaufman & sec piano with Abram Chasins. *Teaching:* Mem fac, Rutgers Univ, Camden; mem fac suppl piano, Curtis Inst Music, 36- *Mailing Add:* Curtis Inst Music 1726 Locust St Philadelphia PA 19103

PASTORE, PATRICE EVELYN
EDUCATOR, SOPRANO
b Newark, NJ, Nov 16, 46. *Study:* Bryn Mawr Col, BA, 68; New England Consv, with Jan de Gaetani & Eleanor Steber, MM(voice), 81, MM(musicol), 82. *Rec Perf:* The Owl & the Pussycat, 82; Whirlwinds II—Robert Cogan, Spectrum Rec, 83. *Pos:* Soloist & sect leader, First Parish, Weston, Mass, 74-82. *Teaching:* Instr 20th century music hist, New England Consv, 82; instr voice & dictation, Ithaca Col, 82- *Mailing Add:* 123 King Rd E Ithaca NY 14850

PASTREICH, PETER
ADMINISTRATOR
b Brooklyn, NY, 38. *Study:* Yale Univ, BA, 59; Am Symph Orch League, orch mgt, 60. *Pos:* Exec dir, St Louis Symph Orch, 66-78 & San Francisco Symph Orch, 78-; asst mgr, Denver Symph & Baltimore Symph, formerly; mgr, Kans City Phil, Nashville Symph & Greenwich Village Symph, formerly; bd mem, Calif Confederation Arts, currently; recommendation bd, Avery Fisher Artists Prog, currently; bd gov, Stern Grove Fest, currently; mem orch panel, Nat Endowment Arts. *Awards:* CLIO Award, Am TV & Radio Commercials Fest, 69; Distinguished Alumnus Award, Yale Univ Band, 77; grant, Avalon Found & Symph League. *Mem:* Am Symph Orch League. *Mailing Add:* c/o San Francisco Symphony Davies Symph Hall San Francisco CA 94102

PASZTOR, STEPHEN
CLARINET
b East Chicago, Ind, Nov 11, 28. *Study:* Am Consv Music, BA(music educ), 53, MA(music theory), 54. *Pos:* Clarinetist, Denver Symph Orch, 55-, Denver Woodwind Quintet, 67-77 & Central City Opera, 71-76. *Mem:* Int Clarinet Soc. *Mailing Add:* 5990 S Elati Littleton CO 80120

PATANE, GIUSEPPE
CONDUCTOR & MUSIC DIRECTOR
b Naples, Italy, Jan 1, 32. *Study:* Consv San Pietro a Majella, Naples, Italy, grad; studied with F Cilea, A Savasta, A Longo & T Gargiulo. *Rec Perf:* Arlecchino (video); Turandot (video); Adriana Lecouvreur (video); Tosca (video); Il Tabarro (video); Otello (video); La Traviata (film); rec on Decca, EMI, Eurodisc & Deutsche Grammophon. *Pos:* Asst cond, San Carlo Opera, 51; prin cond Italian repertoire, Berlin Opera, 63; gen music dir, Copenhagen Opera, formerly; cond Italian repertoire, San Francisco Opera, 67; prin guest cond, Vienna State Opera, currently; guest cond, Ravinia Fest, Chicago Symph Orch, 71, Metropolitan Opera, 75-, Cleveland Orch, 77 & 79-81, Paris Opera, currently, La Scala, Milan, currently, Royal Opera House, Covent Garden, currently & many maj orchs throughout Europe & US; prin cond, Am Symph, currently. *Mailing Add:* c/o Kazuko Hillyer Inc 250 W 57th St New York NY 10107

PATE, DENISE COFFEY See Coffey, Denise

PATE, JOSEPH MARTIN
BASS
b Nashville, Tenn, Aug 7, 54. *Study:* Acad Vocal Art, Philadelphia, dipl, 81. *Roles:* Leone in Attila, Opera Co Philadelphia, 77; Pistola in Falstaff & Trufaldino in Ariadne, Chautauqua Inst, 79; King in Aida, Cincinnati Opera, 81; Don Alfonson in Cosi fan tutte, 82 & Horace in Regina, 82, Wolf Trap Opera. *Mailing Add:* 546 Boulevard Westfield NJ 07090

PATENAUDE-YARNELL, JOAN
SOPRANO
b Ottawa, Ont, Sept 12, 44; nat US. *Study:* Ecole Vincint D'Indy, Montreal, 68-70; Kathryn Turney Long Sch, Metropolitan Opera Asn, licia Albanese, 73; Music Acad West, MMus, 76; studied with Bernard Diamant. *Rec Perf:* Songs of the Great Opera Composers, Vol 1-3; Corintha. *Roles:* Micaëla in Carmen, New York City Opera, 66; Laetita in The Old Maid and the Thief; Contessa, Susanna & Cherubino in Le Nozze di Figaro; Suor Angelica & Giorgetta in Il Tabarro; Marie in Child, Lake George Opera Fest, 74; Violetta in La Traviata; Cry of Clytaemnestra, San Francisco Opera, 81; and others. *Pos:* Affil artist, West Point Mil Acad, 70-72; State Dept artist, Poland, 77 & 78, Far East, 79 & 80, Australia, 81 & Japan, 82; sop, Can Opera Co, Toronto, Fort Worth Opera, Lyr Opera Kansas City, Lake George Opera Fest, New York City Opera, Pittsburgh Opera Co, Portland Opera Asn, San Francisco Opera & San Francisco Spring Opera. *Awards:* Can Coun Grants (four); winner, Metropolitan Opera Nat Coun Auditions; nat winner, CBC Talent Fest. *Mem:* Actors' Equity; Screen Actors Guild. *Publ:* Contribr to Opera Can. *Mailing Add:* c/o Shaw Concerts 1995 Broadway New York NY 10023

PATEY, EDWARD R
VIOLIN
b Jersey City, NJ, June 23, 40. *Study:* Manhattan Sch Music, BM(violin), 63, MM(violin), 65. *Pos:* Second violinist, Baltimore Symph Orch, 68- *Mailing Add:* 4012 Deepwood Rd Baltimore MD 21218

PATON, JOHN GLENN
TENOR, TEACHER
b New Castle, Pa, Feb 21, 34. *Study:* Cincinnati Consv Music, with Sonia Essin, BM, 55; Eastman Sch Music, with Julius Huehn, MM, 59. *Rec Perf:* Lohengrin, RCA Victor, 65. *Roles:* Belmonte in Abduction, Chautauqua Opera, 66. *Teaching:* Asst prof, Univ Wis, Madison, 61-68; prof, Univ Colo, Boulder, 68- *Mem:* Nat Asn Teachers Singing; Music Libr Asn. *Publ:* Auth, three articles on Hermann Reutter, Benjamin Britten & the aria Caro mio ben, NATS Bulletin, 70-82; ed, Vaccai's Practical Method of Italian Singing, G Schirmer, 75; auth, two articles on Italian cantata manusripts in Rome, Music Libr Ans, 79 & 80. *Mailing Add:* 2855 Heidelberg Dr Boulder CO 80303

PATRICK, JULIAN
BARITONE
b Meridian, Miss, Oct 26, 27. *Study:* Col Consv Music, Univ Cincinnati, dipl; studied with Cornelius Reid. *Rec Perf:* Trouble in Tahiti, Columbia Rec. *Roles:* Germont in La Traviata, Mobile Opera Co, Ala, 50; Eugene Onegin in Eugene Onegin, 83; Escamillo in Carmen; Belcore in L'Elisir d'Amore; Alfio in Cavalleria rusticana; Guglielmo in Cosi fan tutte; Marcello in La Boheme; and many others. *Pos:* Bar, Goldovsky Opera Theatre, formerly & major opera houses throughout the US. *Mailing Add:* c/o Thea Dispeker 59 E 54th St New York NY 10022

PATTENGALE, ROBERT RICHARD
ADMINISTRATOR, HARPSICHORD
b Buchanan, Mich, Aug 10, 36. *Study:* Western Mich Univ, BM, 58; Univ Mich, MM, 65, PhD, 73. *Pos:* Prog annotator, Fargo-Moorhead Symph, 75-, harpsichordist, 76- *Teaching:* Prof musicol, Moorhead State Univ, 68-, chmn music, 78- *Interests:* Eighteenth century vocal music; performance practice of baroque music. *Mailing Add:* 2303 19 1/2 St Moorhead MN 56560

PATTERSON, ANDY J
COMPOSER, EDUCATOR
b Gordon, Tex, Feb 20, 29. *Study:* Private comp study with Arnold Schoenberg, 45-46; Tex Christian Univ, BA(music), 48, MMus(comp), 51; Fla State Univ, DMus(comp), 69. *Works:* Hardin-Simmons University Anthem, Winneton Music Corp, 63; Hail to Thee, Hardin-Simmons Univ Press, 66; Symphony No 1, perf by Univ Houston Orch, 70; Canto Deciso, Crest Rec, 80; Easter Cantata, comn by Loyd Hawthorne & Hardin-Simmons Univ Choir, 81; Concerto for Trumpet, comn by Stacy Blair, 83. *Teaching:* Prof & head dept music theory & comp, Hardin-Simmons Univ, 59-, chmn grad studies music, 69-, dean sch music, 81. *Awards:* Nat Orpheus Award, Phi Mu Alpha, 79; Cullen Outstanding Teacher Award, 80. *Mem:* Am Soc Music Theory; Am Soc Univ Comp; Nat Asn Comp USA; Am Music Ctr Inc; Tex Music Educr Asn. *Publ:* Auth, Musical Form and Analysis, 60, Music Theory Text, 60, priv publ; A Place for Theory in Choral Programs? Tex Choirmaster Mag, 61; 147 comp in 30 vols, Sigma Alpha Iota, 71- *Mailing Add:* 1642 Swenson Abilene TX 79603

PATTERSON, DAVID NOLTE
COMPOSER, EDUCATOR
b St Louis, Mo, Jan 22, 41. *Study:* Washington Univ, with Robert Wykes; Harvard Univ, with Leon Kirchner & Luise Vosgerchian; studied with Olivier Messiaen & Nadia Boulanger, Paris. *Works:* Differences (six performers & tuba), 62; Shard (solo flute), 67; Chantier (violin & piano), 70; The Celery Flute Player (set of piano pieces), 72; Piece for 9 Instruments, 73; Pied Beauty (five performers & tape), 73; Winter Birds (three trumpets); The Fise Degrees (piano), 82. *Teaching:* Fac mem, Wellesley Col, 70-72 & Univ Mass, 72- *Awards:* Bohemians Prize, 70. *Mailing Add:* 25 Sacramento St Cambridge MA 02138

PATTERSON, RUSSELL
CONDUCTOR, ADMINISTRATOR
b Greenville, Miss, Aug 31, 28. *Study:* Southeastern La Univ, BA, BM, 49; New England Consv; Kansas City Consv Music, MM, 51. *Rec Perf:* Rigoletto, 59 & Barber of Seville, 59, RCA; Taming of the Shrew, CRI, 69; Sweet Bye and Bye, Desto, 73; Capt Jinks of the Horse Marines, RCA, 75. *Pos:* Gen dir, Lyric Opera Kansas City, 58-; musical dir, Point Lookout Fest, Mo, 68-69; artistic dir, Mo River Fest, 76- & Kansas City Symph Orch, 82- *Awards:* Cond Award, Ditson Fund, Columbia Univ, 82. *Mem:* Opera Am; Cent Opera Serv; Kans City Arts Coun; Soc Fel; Am Fedn Musicians. *Rep:* 3658 Madison Kansas City Mo 64111. *Mailing Add:* c/o Lyric Opera Kansas City Symph Orch 1029 Central Kansas City MO 64105

PATTERSON, T RICHARD
EDUCATOR, PIANO
b South Bend, Ind. *Study:* Oberlin Col, BM, 42, MM, 48. *Teaching:* Dir keyboard & prof piano, State Univ NY, Fredonia, 47- *Awards:* Citation, NY State Music Teachers Asn, 71. *Mailing Add:* 404 Lake Shore Dr West Dunkirk NY 14048

PATTERSON, WILLIAM G
PERCUSSION, EDUCATOR
b Kingsville, Tex, Aug 29, 49. *Study:* Del Mar Col, perf cert, 69; Univ Houston, BA(music perf), 71; Cath Univ, MM, 74; studied with Tony Ames, Fred Begun, Alan Abel & Buster Bailey. *Pos:* Perc, US Marine Band, 71-75 & San Antonio Symph, 78- *Teaching:* Instr perc, Lanier High Sch, Austin, Tex, 75-78 & St Mary's Univ, Tex, 78- *Mem:* Percussive Arts Soc; Am Fedn Musicians. *Mailing Add:* 4734 El Vedado San Antonio TX 78233

PATTON, JASPER WILLIAM
EDUCATOR, PIANO
b Nashville, Tenn, Feb 11, 28. *Study:* Univ Minn, MusB, 48, MusM, 50; Juilliard Sch Music; Ind Univ; study with Ozan Marsh, 55-56. *Teaching:* Instr music, Tenn State Univ, 48-58; asst prof music hist & appreciation, Tex Methodist Col, 58-64; assoc prof music, Southern Univ, Baton Rouge, 64-73 & Norfolk State Univ, 73- *Mem:* Phi Mu Alpha Sinfonia; Int Lizst Soc; Col Music Soc. *Publ:* Auth, Music, Burgess Publ Co, 81. *Mailing Add:* 708 Emerald Lake Dr Virginia Beach VA 23455

PATTY, JAMES LECIL
EDUCATOR, PIANO
b Griffithville, Ark, Oct 18, 21. *Study:* Hendrix Col, BM, 42, AB, 43; Univ Mich, theory with Hans David, MM, 53; Univ Ill, musicology with Otto Kinkeldy, 53-54; Northwestern Univ, PhD, 63. *Teaching:* Assoc prof theory & hist, Culver-Stockton Col, 58-60; prof theory & piano, Ark State Univ, Jonesboro, 65- *Mem:* Music Teachers Nat Asn; Nat Asn Jazz Educr; Ark State Music Teachers Asn; Phi Mu Alpha Sinfonia. *Mailing Add:* Music Dept Ark State Univ State University AR 72467

PAUKERT, KAREL
ORGAN, ADMINISTRATOR
b Skutec, Czechoslovakia, Jan 1, 35; US citizen. *Study:* State Consv Music, Prague, dipl, 56; Royal Consv Music, Ghent, Belgium, first prize(organ perf), 63, high dipl(organ perf), 64; studied organ with Jan Bedrich Krajs & Gabriel Verschraegen; studied oboe with Frantisek Hantak. *Rec Perf:* Praise the Lord, Agape Rec, 77; Organ Music from the Cleveland Museum of Art, Jaro-Halcyon, 79; The Organ in Japan, Vol 2, KML Rec, Tokyo, 80. *Pos:* Oboist, Theatre Jiri Wolker, 53-61; prin oboist, Nat Orch Iceland, 61-62; dep organist, St Bavon Cathedral, Ghent, Belgium, 62-64; organist & choirmaster, St Luke's Episcopal Church, Evanston, Ill, 66-73 & St Paul's Episcopal Church, Cleveland Heights, Ohio, currently; cur musical arts, Cleveland Mus Arts,

74-; artistic dir, AKI Music Fest, 77- *Teaching:* Instr, Washington Univ, 65-66; assoc prof organ & church music, Northwestern Univ, 66-73; chmn organ dept, Cleveland Inst Music, 74- *Bibliog:* Paul Hume (auth), Paukert: Volcanic Fun, Washington Post, 11/27/76; Voll Energie und Spannung, Südkurier, 8/18/79; Paukert Organ Recital in Long Beach, Los Angeles Times, 1/10/80. *Publ:* Ed, Two Centuries of Czech Organ Music, H T FitzSimons Co, 64. *Rep:* Dept Musical Arts Cleveland Mus Arts 11150 East Blvd Cleveland OH 44106. *Mailing Add:* 2404 Lalemant Rd University Heights OH 44118

PAUL, JAMES
CONDUCTOR, TENOR
b Forest Grove, Ore, Oct 17, 40. *Study:* Oberlin Consv Music, 59-65; Salzburg Mozarteum, Austria, with Max Lorenz & Julius Patzak, 63-64; St Louis Symph, with Walter Susskind, 70-71. *Pos:* Assoc cond, Kansas City Phil, 73-76 & Milwaukee Symph Orch, 76-80; res cond, Milwaukee Symph Orch, 80-81; prin guest cond, Baton Rouge Symph Orch, 81-82; music dir, 82- *Awards:* Serge Koussevitsky Mem Cond Prize, 67. *Rep:* Shaw Concerts Inc 1995 Broadway New York NY 10023. *Mailing Add:* PO Box #103 Baton Rouge LA 70806

PAUL, PAMELA MIA
PIANO
b New York, NY. *Study:* Juilliard Sch, BM, 70, MM, 72, DMA, 76. *Rec Perf:* Mozart Trio (piano, clarinet & viola), Turnabout, 82. *Pos:* Solo pianist with Vienna Symph, Hamburg Symph, New York Phil, Detroit Symph, Pittsburgh Symph, St Louis Symph, Minn Orch, Caramoor Fest Orch & other US & European symph orch; guest artist, chamber music fests Bregenz & Salzburg, Austria & For the Love of Music; perf & instr, People's Repub China. *Teaching:* Chairperson piano dept, St Louis Consv Music, 77- *Awards:* Outstanding Young Musician, Musical Am Mag, 80; Solo Recitalist Award, Nat Endowment Arts, 82. *Rep:* Artists Int 25 Walnut St Boston MA 02108. *Mailing Add:* 7541 Parkdale St Louis MO 63105

PAUL, THOMAS W
BASS
b Chicago, Ill, Feb 22, 34. *Study:* Occidental Col, BA, 56; Juilliard Sch Music, 57. *Rec Perf:* Messiah (Handel), RCA Victor, 66; Symphony No 9 (Beethoven), Sine Qua Non, 67; St John Passion (J S Bach), CBS, 68; Damnation of Faust (Berlioz), Deutsche Grammophon, 73; Ecuatorial (Varese), Nonesuch Rec, 75; Mass, Coronation (Mozart), Vox Rec, 76; Syringa (Carter), CRI, 82. *Roles:* Mephistopheles in Faust, 62, Ramfis in Aida, 63, Figaro in Marriage of Figaro & Pimen in Boris Godounov, 64, New York City Opera Co; Sparafucile in Rigoletto, San Francisco Spring Opera Co, 64; Oroveso in Norma, Rochester Opera Theater, 80; Tiresias in Oedipus Rex, Philadelphia Opera Co, 82. *Pos:* Leading basso, New York City Opera Co, 62-71; Guest soloist, New York Phil, Boston Symph, Chicago Symph, Cleveland Orch & Los Angeles Phil, 62-; Philadelphia Orch, Toronto Symph & Montreal Symph, currently. *Teaching:* Artist & fac mem voice, Aspen Sch Music, 71-; prof, Eastman Sch Music, 73-; artist & fac mem Bach perf, Bach Aria Inst, Stony Brook, NY, 81- *Awards:* First Prize, Liederkranz Found Singers, 62; Grant Operatic Study, Ford Found, 62. *Mem:* Phi Mu Alpha Sinfonia. *Mailing Add:* 790 Herman Rd Webster NY 14580

PAULL, BARBERI P
COMPOSER, WRITER
b New York, NY, July 27, 46. *Study:* Dalcroze Sch Eurhythmics, 72; Juilliard Sch Music, studied comp with Hall Overton, Jacob Druckman, Charles Wuorinen & Billy Taylor, dipl, 73; Berkshire Music Ctr, with Bruno Maderna, 72 & BMI Muisc Theatre Workshop, with Lehman Engle, 74-76; NY Univ, BA, MA. *Works:* America, 75 & Peace, 76, ABI; Welcome to the World, Bradley, 77; My Song to Sing, Belwin Mills, 78; Let it Shine on You, Silver-Burdett, 81. *Pos:* Dir & founder, Barberi Paull Music Theatre, Inc & Celebration Theatre, 72-75, Guideposts, 73- & CAVU Music Assoc, 75-; practicing psychotherapist adult & children music therapy. *Awards:* Delius Award for Antifon, 75 & award for Close to the Sky, Strong Found, 81; award for Baritone Songs, Soc Arts, 81. *Bibliog:* Eli Svengaard (auth), Art and Life, Dagbladet, Oslo, Norway, 72; Marsha Stewart (auth), My Song to Sing, Philadelphia Inquirer, 72; Lee Andrews (auth), A Woman Today, Serendipity Times, 75. *Mem:* ASCAP; Am Music Ctr; Am Women Comp; Int League Women Comp (mem bd dir, 78-80); Am Guild Authors & Comp. *Rep:* Glenn M Feit 488 Madison Ave New York NY 10022. *Mailing Add:* 15 W 72nd St New York NY 10023

PAULSON, STEPHEN JON
BASSOON, EDUCATOR
b Brooklyn, NY, July 13, 46. *Study:* Eastman Sch Music, BMus & perf cert, 68. *Works:* Concerto for Bassoon and Orchestra, 67. *Pos:* Second bassoonist, Rochester Phil Orch, 66-68, prin bassoonist, 68-70; co-prin bassoonist, Pittsburgh Symph Orch, 70-77; founder & dir, Upper Partials (chamber music series), Pittsburgh, 72-76; prin bassoonist, San Francisco Symph Orch, 77-; mem, Caselli Ens (wind quintet), 80- *Teaching:* Mem fac, San Francisco Consv Music; mem fac exten div, Univ Calif, Berkeley. *Mailing Add:* 333 Caselli Ave San Francisco CA 94114

PAULUS, STEPHEN HARRISON
COMPOSER, ADMINISTRATOR
b Summit, NJ, Aug 24, 49. *Study:* Univ Minn, Minneapolis, BA(piano), 71, MA(comp), 74, PhD(comp), 78. *Works:* The Village Singer, Opera Theatre of St Louis, 79; So Hallow'd Is The Time, Greenwich Choral Soc, Conn, 80; Letters for the Times, Tanglewood Fest, 80; Spectra for Small Orchestra,

Houston Symph, 80 & Am Symph Orch, 81; The Postman Always Rings Twice, Opera Theatre of St Louis, 82 & Edinburgh Fest, 83; Concerto for Orchestra, Minn Orch, 83. *Pos:* Managing comp & co-founder, Minn Comp Forum, 73-; Exxon/Rockefeller comp in res, Minn Orch, 83- *Awards:* Nat Endowment Arts Fel, 78; ASCAP Award, 78-; Guggenheim Fel, 82-83. *Mem:* ASCAP; Minn Comp Forum; Am Music Ctr. *Mailing Add:* 1710 Jefferson Ave St Paul MN 55105

PAULY, REINHARD G
WRITER, MUSICOLOGIST
b Breslau, Ger, Aug 9, 20; US citizen. *Study:* Columbia Univ, BA, 42, MA, 46; Yale Univ, MM, 48, PhD, 56. *Pos:* Violinist & violist, Oregon Symph Orch, 55-65; violist, Portland Opera, 55- *Teaching:* Prof music hist, Lewis & Clark Col, 48-; vis prof, Reed Col, 57-61. *Awards:* Guggenheim Fel, 60. *Mem:* Am Musicol Soc (mem nat coun, 72-75). *Interests:* French baroque music; violin; opera; 18th century choral music. *Publ:* Ed, Michael Haydn Choral Series, G Schirmer, 56-; auth, The Reforms of Church Music ..., Musical Quart, 56; Music in the Classic Period, 65 & 73 & Music and the Theater, 70, Prentice-Hall; Michael Haydn, In: New Grove Dict of Music & Musicians, Macmillan, 80. *Mailing Add:* Sch Music Lewis & Clark Col Portland OR 97219

PAVAROTTI, LUCIANO
TENOR
b Modena, Italy, Oct 12, 35. *Study:* Istituto Magistrale Carlo Sigonio, dipl magistrale, 55; studied with Arrigo Pola & Ettore Campogalliana. *Rec Perf:* Over 30, 64- *Roles:* Rodolpho in La Boheme, Reggio Emilia, Italy, 61, Covent Garden, 63, Metropolitan Opera, 68 & Chicago Opera, 73; Edgardo in Lucia di Lammermoor, Amsterdam, 63; Tonio in The Daughter of the Regiment, 71 & Nemorino in L'Elisir d'Amore, 73, Metropolitan Opera; Fernand in La Favorita, 73 & Manrico in Il Trovatore, 75, San Francisco Opera; Lord Arthur in I Puritani, Metropolitan Opera, 76; and many others. *Pos:* Ten, major Am & Europ opera co. *Awards:* Medaglia d'Oro Club Opera, Mexico City, 69; Dipl, Lyr Soc Fine Arts, NY & NJ, 72; Medaglia d'Oro Centenario Enrico Caruso, Naples, 73; and many others. *Mailing Add:* c/o Herbert H Breslin 119 W 57th St New York NY 10019

PAVLAKIS, CHRISTOPHER
ADMINISTRATOR, CRITIC-WRITER
b Haverhill, Mass. *Study:* Chicago Musical Col, BM(comp), 54; DePaul Univ, MM(comp), 56; Univ Ill; Roosevelt Univ; studied with Rudolf Ganz, Vittorio Rieti, John J Becker, Alexander Tcherepnin, Leon Stein & Ernest Levy. *Pos:* Ed & advert mgr, Instrumentalist, 63-64; pres, Kultura, New York, 64-71; co-founder & publ, Univ Music Ed, 67-; co-founder & vpres, High Density Syst Inc, 69- *Teaching:* Music, various private Chicago sch, 57-64; lectr, Northeastern Ill Univ, 63-64. *Awards:* Distinguished Alumni Award, DePaul Univ, 74. *Mem:* Am Musicol Soc; Music Libr Asn; Sonneck Soc; Am Music Ctr. *Interests:* American musical affairs, past and present. *Publ:* Auth, The American Music Handbook, Free Press, Macmillan, 74; numerous reviews of books, music & concerts, Music J, Notes & others, 75-78. *Mailing Add:* PO Box 52 Inwood Sta New York NY 10034

PAYMER, MARVIN E
ADMINISTRATOR, COMPOSER
b New York, NY, May 23, 21. *Study:* Hartt Col Music, BM, 51; Queens Col, City Univ New York, MA, 67; Grad Sch, City Univ New York, PhD, 77. *Works:* Piano Sonata, Aurora Mauro-Cottone, 47; Caprice for Strings, Theodore Presser, 51; Holiday Overture, Babylon Symph, 54; Prelude and Variations for String Orchestra, Hartt Symph, 62. *Pos:* Assoc dir, Pergolesi Res Ctr, 77- *Teaching:* Lectr music theory, York Col, NY, 73; asst prof music hist, Hunter Col, NY, 78-79. *Awards:* Fel, Andrew Mellon Found, 77-78 & Nat Endowment Humanities, 80. *Mem:* ASCAP; Am Musicol Soc; Col Music Soc; Int Musicol Soc. *Interests:* Works of Giovanni Battista Pergolesi. *Publ:* Auth, Giovanni Battista Pergolesi: A Thematic Catalogue of the Opera Omnia, Pendragon Press, 77; The Old Spuriosity Shop Revisited: New Light on Counterfeit Pergolesi, Musical Heritage Rev, Vol 11, No 15; Pergolesi, In: New Grove Dict of Music & Musicians, Macmillan, 79; City University of New York: The New Pergolesi Edition, Current Musicol, No 27, 79; coauth (with Barry Brook), The Pergolesi Hand: A Calligraphic Study, Notes, Vol 38, No 3. *Mailing Add:* 26 Strawberry Hill Ave Stamford CT 06902

PAYN, WILLIAM AUSTIN
MUSIC DIRECTOR, COMPOSER
b Ashtabula, Ohio, Feb 18, 46. *Study:* Westminster Choir Col, BM, 68; WVa Univ, MM, 78, DMA, 80. *Works:* Prisms, 75, Genesis, 75, Celebration, 76 & Spectrum, 80, Harold Flammer, Inc; Cymbalum, Hope Publ Co, 81; O God, Beneath Your Guiding Hand, Nat Music Publ, 81; Antiphonal Flourish, Am Guild English Handbell Ringers, 83. *Pos:* Dir music, Presby Church, Newark, Ohio, 68-71; Morristown, NJ, 71-78 & Sharon Community Church, Coraopolis, Pa, 78-82. *Teaching:* Prof, Bucknell Univ, Pa, 82- *Mem:* Am Choral Dir Asn; Am Guild Organists; Am Guild English Handbell Ringers. *Mailing Add:* 233 Market St Lewisburg PA 17837

PAYNE, FRANK LYNN
EDUCATOR, COMPOSER
b Asheville, NC, Nov 29, 36. *Study:* Univ Ark, BM, 59; NTex State Univ, comp with Samuel Adler & William Latham, MM, 61. *Works:* Images I and II for Oboe and Piano, 70, Quartet for Tubas, 71, Concerto for Brass Quintet and Wind Ensemble, 72, Toccata for Three Flutes, 72 & Sonata for Tuba and Piano, 77, Shawnee Press; Concert Suite for Trumpet and Trombone, Brass Press, 72; Miniatures for Clarinet Choir, Seesaw Music, 77. *Teaching:* Assoc prof music, Oklahoma City Univ, 67- *Mailing Add:* PO Box 60806 Oklahoma City OK 73146

PAYNE, MAGGI
COMPOSER, EDUCATOR
b Temple, Tex, Dec 23, 45. *Study:* Northwestern Univ, study flute with Walfrid Kujala, contemp music with Alan Stout & William Karlins, BMus, 68; Univ Ill, study contemp music with Ben Johnston, Ed London, Sal Martirano & Gordon Mumma, MMus, 70; Mills Col, study electronic music & media with Bob Ashley, MFA, 72. *Works:* Lunar Dusk & Lunar Earthrise, Lovely Music Rec, 79; Blue Metallics (electronic music & slides), 80, Ling (electronic music & slides), 81, Circular Motions (electronic tape with video), 81, Io (electronic tape with video), 82, Crystal (electronic tape with video), 82 & Solar Wind (electronic tape with video), 83, private publ. *Pos:* Juror, Ill Arts Coun, 83. *Teaching:* Instr acoustics, Mills Col, Oakland, 72-74, rec engineering, 80-; instr comp & rec engineering, San Francisco Art Inst, 82-83. *Awards:* Grant, Nat Endowment Arts, 79-80; Second Prize, Third Concorso Int for young electronic music comp, Italy, 81; Mellon Grant, 83. *Bibliog:* Bob Davis (auth), Maggi Payne at Mills Col, Synapse Mag, 77; Jim Horton (auth), Electronic/Computer Music News, Ear West Mag, 80. *Mem:* Am Fedn Musicians; Comp Forum. *Mailing Add:* Mills College Box 9830 Oakland CA 94613

PAYNTER, JOHN P
EDUCATOR, CONDUCTOR
b Dodgeville, Wis, May 29, 28. *Study:* Northwestern Univ, BM, 50, MM, 51. *Works:* Fanfaronade, Kjos, 50; Break, Break, Break, Summy-Birchard, 55; One Nation Indivisible, Schmitt, Hall McCreary, 70. *Pos:* Founder & cond, Northshore Conct Band Wilmette, 51-; cond & speaker, US, Can, Europe, Africa, Asia, Israel, Greece & Scandinavia; ed, New Music column, Instrumentalist, 59- *Teaching:* Mem fac, Sch Music, Northwestern Univ, 51-, dir bands, 53, prof cond, 74-, chmn, Dept Cond & Perf Orgn, currently. *Awards:* Acad Wind & Perc Arts Award, Nat Band Asn. *Mem:* Am Band Masters Asn; co-founder, Nat Band Asn; life mem, Phi Mu Alpha Sinfonia; Pi Kappa Lambda; Music Educr Nat Conf. *Mailing Add:* 1437 Hollywood Ave Glenview IL 60025

PAYSOUR, LAFLEUR (NADINE)
CRITIC-WRITER, LECTURER
b Mar 3, 51; US citizen. *Study:* Vassar Col, BA, 72; Columbia Univ, MS, 74. *Pos:* Music critic, Charlotte Observer, 74- *Awards:* Presser Scholar Award, Theodore Presser Found, 70. *Mailing Add:* Charlotte Observer PO Box 32188 Charlotte NC 28232

PEACOCK, CURTIS CUNIFFE
CONDUCTOR & MUSIC DIRECTOR, TEACHER
b Tela, Honduras, July 28, 45; US citizen. *Study:* Univ Tex, El Paso, 63-66; Univ Colo, Boulder, BM, 67, BMEd, 69, MM, 71; cond studies with Dr Lert, Orkney Springs, Va, 78. *Pos:* Music dir & cond, Casper Symph Orch, 72- *Teaching:* Prof strings, Casper Col, 71-; vis instr violin, Univ Colo, Boulder, summer 72. *Mailing Add:* 1225 E 24th St Casper WY 82601

PEAKE, LUISE EITEL
EDUCATOR, WRITER
b Königsberg, Germany, Jan 11, 25; US citizen. *Study:* Univ Tenn, BA, 50; Chicago Musical Col, MM, 53; Columbia Univ, PhD, 68. *Teaching:* Assoc prof musicol, Univ SC, 68- *Mem:* Am Musicol Soc (SE chap chmn, 72-75); Col Music Soc (Mid-Atlantic chap musicol chmn, 81-83); Music Libr Asn. *Interests:* Song cycle. *Publ:* Auth, The Other Winterreise, Musical Quart, 79; contribr, Song Cycle, New Grove Dict of Music & Musicians, 81; auth, The Antecedents of Beethoven's Liederkreis, Music & Lett, 83. *Rep:* 516 Santee Ave Columbia SC 29205. *Mailing Add:* Music Dept Univ SC Columbia SC 29208

PEARLMAN, LEONARD ALEXANDER
EDUCATOR, MUSIC DIRECTOR & CONDUCTOR
b Winnipeg, Can, Jan 12, 28. *Study:* Univ Man, BA, 49, MD, 53; State Univ NY, Buffalo, MM; Vienna State Acad Music, dipl, 56. *Pos:* Cond, St Catharines Symph Orch, Ont, 58-64. *Teaching:* Vis prof, Univ Md, 65; prof, Peabody Inst, 66-73 & 74-77; chmn, Dept Orch Activ, Consv Music, Univ Mo, Kansas City, 73-74; prof music, dir orch & cond univ opera, Sch Music, Univ Ariz, 77- *Mem:* Am Symph Orch League; Am Musicol Soc. *Publ:* Contribr, New Grove Dict of Music & Musicians, 6th ed. *Mailing Add:* 225 E Calle Turquesa Tucson AZ 85704

PEARLMAN, MARTIN
HARPSICHORD, MUSIC DIRECTOR
Study: Cornell Univ, BA; Yale Univ, MM(comp); studied harpsichord with Ralph Kirkpatrick & Gustav Leonhardt. *Pos:* Founder, dir & continuo, harpsichord & piano soloist, Banchetto Musicale; solo harpsichord recitalist, US & Europe. *Teaching:* Mem fac harpsichord, Longy Sch Music, currently. *Awards:* Erwin Bodky Award, Cambridge, 72; prize winner, Harpsichord Compt, Bruges, Belgium, 74; Fulbright Fel. *Mailing Add:* 144 Trapelo Rd Belmont MA 02178

PEARLMAN, RICHARD LOUIS
STAGE DIRECTOR, EDUCATOR
b Norwalk, Conn. *Study:* Columbia Col, AB, 54. *Pos:* Stage dir, Metropolitan Opera, 64-68; gen dir, Wash Opera, 68-70; dir, Opera Theatre, Eastman Sch Music, 76- & Aspen Music Fest, 76- *Teaching:* Assoc prof opera, Eastman Sch Music, 76- *Mem:* Am Guild Musical Artists. *Mailing Add:* 163 W 10th St New York NY 10014

PEARSON, BARBARA (ANN)
SOPRANO
b Chicago, Ill. *Study:* North Park Col. *Roles:* Mahler Eighth Symphony, 72 & Mahler IV Symphony, 73, Chicago Symph Orch; Donna Anna in Don Giovanni, Ghent Opera, Belgium, 74; Israel in Egypt, Chicago Symph, 82; Messiah Nat Symph. *Pos:* Solo singer, Cologne Opera, Ger, 72-75, Chicago's Grant Park Conct Series, formerly & Music of Baroque, 80- *Awards:* Metropolitan Opera Auditions Winner, 71. *Mailing Add:* c/o Sheldon Soffer Mgt 130 W 56th St New York NY 10019

PEARSON, FRANK COGSWELL, JR
EDUCATOR, ADMINISTRATOR
b Dayton, Ohio, June 20, 21. *Study:* Albion Col, BA, 43, MA, 47; Univ Mich, MMus, 48, with Einstein, Sachs, Haydon & Cuyler, PhD, 61. *Teaching:* Asst prof music, Albion Col, 50-63; prof & chmn dept, Dickinson State Col, 63-, head, Sch Arts & Sci, 80- *Mem:* Music Teachers Nat Asn (mem nat exec bd, 68-72 & 74-78, west cent div pres, 74-78); NDak Music Teachers Asn (pres, 64-66); Am Musicol Soc; Music Educr Nat Conf; Am Asn Univ Prof. *Interests:* Madrigals of English composer, Peter Philips. *Mailing Add:* Sch Arts & Sci Dickinson State Col Dickinson ND 58601

PEARSON, MARK
BASS-BARITONE, EDUCATOR
Study: Consv Music, Oberlin Col, BA; Stanford Univ, MA. *Rec Perf:* With Music Guild, Cambridge & Turnabout. *Pos:* Soloist, Boston Symph Orch, New York Pro Musica, Civic Symph Orch, Cecilia Soc & Chorus Pro Music. *Teaching:* Instr master classes & vocal wkshps, Westminster Choir Col; chmn voice dept, New England Consv Music, currently. *Mailing Add:* New England Consv Music 290 Huntington Rd Boston MA 02115

PEARSON, WILLARD B
TRUMPET
Study: Univ Mich, BME, 69, MM, 76; studied with Clifford Lillya & Gilbert Johnson. *Rec Perf:* On Crystal, Vanguard & Vox. *Pos:* Soloist, US Marine Band; assoc first trumpet, New Orleans Phil & Baltimore Symph Orch; substitute, Baltimore & St Louis Symph Orchs, currently; mem, New Orleans Symph Brass Quintet; recitalist & soloist throughout US. *Teaching:* Assoc prof trumpet, Oberlin Col, 79- *Mailing Add:* Music Dept Oberlin Col Oberlin OH 44074

PEASE, EDWARD JOSEPH
EDUCATOR, WRITER
b Gilman, Ill, May 29, 30. *Study:* Ind Univ, PhD, 60; Univ Freiburg, Ger. *Teaching:* Prof music, Western Ky Univ, 64- *Awards:* Fel, Am Coun Learned Soc, 64. *Mem:* Am Musicol Soc; Cong Res Dance; Int Horn Soc. *Interests:* Renaissance music; ballet history; horn literature and pedagogy; opera discography. *Publ:* Auth, Pixerecoort Handschrift, In: Die Music in Geschichte und Gegentnart, Vol 10, 62; A Report on Bologna, Codex Q16, In: Musica Disciplina, 66; A Jussi Bjoerling Discography, Bulletin Nat Asn Teachers Singing, 78; Researching the Music of Dance, 81 & Researching Theatrical Dance, 82, ERIC. *Mailing Add:* 823 Merideth Dr Bowling Green KY 42101

PEASLEE, RICHARD C
COMPOSER
b New York, NY, June 13, 30. *Study:* Yale Univ, BA, 52; Juilliard Sch Music, dipl, 56, MS, 58. *Works:* Marat/Sade Music, Highgate, 64-65; Stonehenge, Margun Music, 64; A Midsummer Night's Dream, 66-70 & October Piece, 71, Highgate; Nightsongs, 74 & The Devil's Herald, 75, Margun Music; The Children's Crusade, perf by The First All Children's Theatre, 81-83. *Teaching:* Artist music, Lincoln Ctr Inst, 78-81. *Awards:* Grant, Nat Endowment Arts, 82. *Mem:* BMI; Am Fedn Musicians. *Mailing Add:* 90 Riverside Dr New York NY 10024

PECK, DONALD OWEN
BASS
b Attleboro, Mass, Apr 13, 45. *Study:* Muhlenberg Col, BA, 68. *Rec Perf:* Commissioner in La Traviata, Live From the Met, 81. *Roles:* Fisherman in Peter Grimes, 77, Major Domo in Adriana Le Couvreur, 78 & 83, Fourth Lackey in Der Rosenkavalier, 79-80 & Customs Officer in La Boheme, 83, Metropolitan Opera. *Pos:* Chorister, New York City Opera, 68-69, Metropolitan Opera, 73- *Mem:* Am Guild Music; Am Fedn TV and Radio Artists. *Mailing Add:* 333 West End Ave New York NY 10023

PECK, DONALD VINCENT
FLUTE, EDUCATOR
b Yakima, Wash, Jan 26, 36. *Study:* Seattle Univ, 48-49; Curtis Inst Music, dipl, 51. *Works:* Composed original cadenzas to Mozart flute concertos. *Pos:* Mem, Seattle Symph Orch, 47-49 & Nat Symph Orch, 51-52; prin flutist, Kansas City Phil Orch, 55-57 & Chicago Symph Orch, 57-; guest soloist, recitalist & clinician with numerous orchs. *Teaching:* Instr flute & woodwind ens, DePaul Univ. *Mailing Add:* 220 S Michigan Ave Chicago IL 60604

PEDERSON, ILONNA ANN
OBOE & ENGLISH HORN, MUSIC DIRECTOR
b Minot, NDak, Dec 23, 40. *Study:* Oberlin Col; Univ Minn; New England Consv, BA; Manhattan Sch Music, MA. *Pos:* Dir, found & performer, New York Kammermusiker, 69-; oboe, oboe d'amore & English horn, Karl Richter's Munich Bach Orch, WGermany, 74-78; solo oboist, Can Opera Co. *Mem:* Chamber Music Am; Double Reed Soc. *Mailing Add:* 736 West End Ave Apt 9B New York NY 10025

PEEK, RICHARD MAURICE
ORGAN, COMPOSER
b Mason, Mich, May 17, 27. *Study:* Mich State Univ, BMus, 50; Union Theol Sem, New York, MSM, 52, DSM, 58. *Works:* Righteous Joseph (anthem), Canyon Press, 52; St Stephen (cantata), Brodt Music Co, 57; Hymn Preludes for the Church Year (organ), Carl Fischer Inc, 64; Blessed Is He (violin, harp & organ), 68 & Chaconne on O Filii et Filiae (organ, brass & perc), 71, Brodt Music Co; Aria (organ), H W Gray, Belwin-Mills, 79; Come Faithful People, Come Away (anthem), Hope Publ House, 82. *Pos:* Organist & choir dir, First Methodist Church, Mason, Mich, 46-48, Trinity Episcopal Church, Grand Ledge, Mich, 48-50 & Grace Episcopal Church, Plainfield, NJ, 50-52; minister music, Covenant Presby Church, Charlotte, NC, 52- *Awards:* NC Comp of Year, NC Fedn Music Clubs, 75. *Mem:* Am Guild Organists (dean Charlotte chap, 81-83); Presby Asn Musicians (mem exec comt, 72-74). *Interests:* Baroque church music. *Mailing Add:* 1621 Biltmore Dr Charlotte NC 28207

PEELLE, DAVID
COMPOSER, EDUCATOR
b Dayton, Ohio, June 1, 50. *Study:* Case Western Reserve Univ, BA, 73; studied comp with David Cope & Donald Erb. *Pos:* Audio engineer, Cleveland Inst Music, 78. *Teaching:* Teacher comp, Cleveland Inst Music, 75. *Mailing Add:* 2439 Overlook #12 Cleveland Heights OH 44106

PEETE, JERRY LAWRENCE
TENOR, COACH
b Memphis, Tenn, Dec 31, 32. *Study:* Sherwood Music Sch, with Maria Hussa-Greve, 61-64; private study with Orita Bruce Wilson, 58-60; master classes with Pierre Bernac, 65. *Rec Perf:* Jerry Peete Sings Songs of Schubert, Lassen, Ives, and Others, Golden Crest/Silver Crest, 80. *Roles:* Rodolfo in La Boheme, Pinkerton in Madama Butterfly & Radames in Aida, Sherwood Opera Theater, 63-64; El Remendado in Carmen & Count Gastone & Giuseppe in La Traviata, Goldovsky Opera Theater, 68-69. *Pos:* Over one hundred recitals. *Teaching:* Private voice coaching, 75- *Awards:* Cert Commendation, Metropolitan Nat Coun, 63. *Mem:* Am Guild Musical Artists. *Mailing Add:* c/o Gilbert-LaRoche Assoc PO Box 441 New York NY 10108

PEGRAM, WAYNE FRANK
CONDUCTOR, COMPOSER
b Nashville, Tenn, Mar 7, 39. *Study:* Tenn Tech Univ, BMus, 59; Univ Tenn, MMus, 65; Univ Northern Colo, DMA(comp), 75. *Works:* Short Suite for Brass Quintet, 70 & Blues for Jass Past, 82, Manuscript; Big Band Boogie, 76 & Processional Entrance, 78, Hal Leonard Publ; Coming on Strong, CL Barnhouse Publ, 82. *Teaching:* Dir band, Franklin High Sch, Tenn, 60-64, Knoxville S High Sch, Tenn, 66-67, Murfreesboro Cent High Sch, Tenn, 67-68 & Tenn Tech Univ, 68-; band asst, Univ Tenn Band, 64-65; jazz asst, Univ Northern Colo, 74-75. *Mem:* ASCAP; Music Educr Nat Conf; Tenn Bandmasters Asn (pres, 74-76); Phi Mu Alpha. *Interests:* Essence of musical style. *Publ:* Auth, Guideline for Developing the School Band Program, Parker, 70. *Mailing Add:* Box 5045 Tenn Tech Univ Cookeville TN 38505

PELAYO, HERNAN VICTOR
BARITONE, TEACHER-COACH
b Santiago, Chile, Feb 19; US citizen. *Study:* Nat Consv Music, Santiago, Chile, 38-42; Santa Cecilia Consv, Rome, Italy, 44; studied with Beniamino Gigli, Buenos Aires, Arg, 44. *Rec Perf:* The Merry Widow (La Viuda Alegre), RCA Victor, 53; Hernan Pelayo Canta, 53 & Selections of Zarzuelas, 54, Panart; Hernan Pelayo Sings International Favorites, Spanish Music Ctr & Pro-Arte, 54; Hernan Pelayo Sings Arias from Spanish Zarzuelas, 58 & Te Quiero, 76, RCA Victor; Hernan Pelayo Sings Opera & International Favorites, Orion, 80. *Roles:* Rigoletto in Rigoletto, New York City Opera Co Touring, 57; Escamillo in Carmen, New York City Opera Co, 57 & San Francisco Opera Co, 61; Marcello in La Boheme, San Francisco Opera Co, 61; Germont in La Traviata, Los Angeles Opera Co, 62 & La Scala Opera Co Touring, 76; Scarpia in Tosca, Sacramento Opera Co, 83. *Pos:* Gen mgr, Los Angeles Metropolitan Opera Co, 65-71 & Serapis Music & Arts Found, Los Angeles, 73-75; dir, Opera Wkshp, KFAC, Los Angeles, 70-71. *Teaching:* Vocal coach, Serapis Music & Arts Found, Los Angeles, 73-75, Univ Hong Kong, 80, Univ Taipei, Taiwan, 82 & privately, NHollywood, currently. *Awards:* Caruso Compt South Am Award, 44; Inspiration to Young in Music Trophy, State Calif, 72. *Mem:* Music Teachers Asn Calif; Nat Asn Teachers Singing. *Mailing Add:* 13046 Ebell St North Hollywood CA 91605

PELLE, NADIA
SOPRANO
b Queens, NY. *Study:* Eastman Sch Music, BM, 75, perf cert; voice with John Maloy, Irra Petina & Elisabeth Carron. *Roles:* Goldenstripe in The Cunning Little Vixen, 81 & 83, Cherubino in The Marriage of Figaro, 82 & Oberto in Alcina, 83, New York City Opera; Monica in The Medium, Wash Opera, 83; Euridice in Orfeo ed Euridice, Asolo Opera, 83. *Mailing Add:* c/o Columbia Artists 165 W 57th St New York NY 10019

PELLEGRINO, JOHN
EDUCATOR, TRUMPET
b Providence, RI, Mar 23, 30. *Study:* Boston Consv Music, BMusEd, 58; Univ Miami, MMus, 59; Yale Univ; Boston Univ. *Rec Perf:* Peloquin Chorale, 65, 67, 72 & 74; The Music of Arthur Custer, 75. *Pos:* Mem, Miami Symph Orch; prin trumpet, Portland Symph, RI Civic Choral & Orch, Peloquin Chorale & Orch & Westerly Community Chorus & Orch; prin trumpet, RI Phil Orch, currently, leader, Brass Quintet; recitalist throughout

New England area. *Teaching:* Assoc prof music, RI Col, 64- *Mem:* Music Educr Nat Conf; RI Music Educr Asn; Int Trumpet Guild; Warwick Arts Found (first vpres, currently). *Publ:* Contribr to RI Music Educr Rev. *Mailing Add:* 39 Natwick Ave Warwick RI 02886

PELLERITE, JAMES JOHN
FLUTE, EDUCATOR
b Clearfield, Pa, Sept 30, 26. *Study:* Juilliard Sch, flute with Frederick Wilkins, 46-48; New Music Sch, with William Kincaid, 48-49. *Pos:* Solo flutist, Indianapolis Symph Orch, 49-51, Detroit Symph Orch, 51-56 & Philadelphia Orch, 59-60. *Teaching:* Instr flute, Wayne State Univ, 49-55 & Bowling Green State Univ, Bowling Green, 50-54; prof, Ind Univ, Bloomington, 57- *Mem:* Music Teacher's Nat Asn; Nat Flute Asn. *Interests:* Flute literature and flute design. *Publ:* Auth, Handbook of Literature for the Flute, 63, 66 & 79, Modern Guide to Fingerings for the Flute, 68 & 77, Notebook of Techniques for the Flutist, 68 & Performance Methods for Flutists, 69, Zalo, Inc. *Mailing Add:* 109 N Glenwood Ave W Bloomington IN 47401

PELLETIER, SHO-MEI
VIOLIN, TEACHER
b Tucson, Ariz, July 25, 52. *Study:* Ariz State Univ, studied violin pedagogue with Frank Spinosa, 65-70; Meadowmount Sch Violin, studied violin pedagogue with Ivan Galamian; Univ Southern Calif, studied chamber music with Gregor Piatigorsky, 72; Sch Music, Ind Univ, studied chamber music with James Starker & violin pedagogue with Josef Gingold, BM, 74. *Works:* Children's Duos (violin duos for children), perf by Frank Spinosa & Sho-mei Pelletier, 68. *Rec Perf:* Santa Fe Opera, BBC, 76; recordings with Dallas Symph on RCA, Red Seal & Vox, 78- *Pos:* Soloist, Phoenix Symph Youth Orch, 66-69, Colo Phil, 72 & Mesa Symph, 81; mem, Arensky Trio, 70-74; assoc prin II violin, Santa Fe Orch, 74-79 & 82- & Dallas Opera Asn, 78-; mem, Dallas Symph String Quintet, 77; assoc prin II violin, Dallas Symph Orch, 78-80 & 82-, first violin sect, 80-82; prin violin, Santa Fe Opera Orch, 79-81; mem, Ravel & Kodaly Ens, 80- *Teaching:* Assoc instr violin, Ind Univ, 74-75; artist in res violin & chamber music, Dallas Arts Magnet High Sch, 78- *Mem:* Am Fedn Musicians; Music Educ Nat Conf; Int Conf Symph & Opera Musicians. *Mailing Add:* 4738 Ashbrook Rd Dallas TX 75227

PELLMAN, SAMUEL FRANK
COMPOSER, EDUCATOR
b Sidney, Ohio, Sept 16, 53. *Study:* Miami Univ, studied with David Cope, BMus, 75; Cornell Univ, studied with Robert Palmer & Karel Husa, MFA, 78, DMA, 79. *Works:* Silent Night, ABI, 78; Intermezzo (two flutes), 82 & Trump-it (solo), 82, ABI; ... in that hour when whirlwinds ..., Music Graphics Press, 83; Pentacle! (alto sax & tape), Dorn, 83. *Teaching:* Asst prof music, Hamilton Col, NY, 79- *Awards:* Second Prize, Am Soc Univ Comp, 77; Composer & Librettist Fel, Nat Endowment for Arts, 79. *Bibliog:* Peter Rabinowitz (auth), Tape Music: Making It Accessible, Musical Am, 82. *Mem:* Am Soc Univ Comp; Syracuse Soc for New Music (vpres, 82-); Am Music Ctr; BMI; Am Guild Organists. *Mailing Add:* Music Dept Hamilton Col Clinton NY 13323

PENA, ANGEL MATIAS
COMPOSER, DOUBLE BASS
b Laoag, Ilocos Norte, Philippines, Apr 22, 21. *Study:* Royal Sch Music, LRSM, 68; studied with Gary Hickling, 67. *Works:* Prelude & Fugue for Brass Quartet, Peer Int, 68; Concerto for double bass, perf by Manila Symph Orch, 69; Sonata for Double Bass & Piano, comn by Gary Hickling, 71; Un Petit Recueil (three double basses), Yorke Ed, 81; Three Pieces for String Quartet, Honolulu Symph String Quartet, 81; Concerto for Jazz Quartet and Orch, perf by Honolulu Symph, 82; Four Sketches for Chamber Orch, perf by Philippine Phil Orch, 82. *Pos:* Bass, Manila Symph Orch, 56-57; bass player & arr, Manila Broadcasting Co Orch, 58-63 & Honolulu Symph Orch, 69- *Awards:* Boy Scouts of Philippines Nat Hymn Cont Award, 51; Nat Pharmaceutical Asn, 53; Nat Symphonic Poem Comp Cont Award, 60. *Bibliog:* Pierre Bowman (auth), Angel Pena—Man Behind the Music, Honolulu Advertiser, 81; Exequiel S Molina (auth), From Jazz to Classics, Business Day, 82; Rosalinda Orosa (auth), Ultimate Recognition for Pena, Sunday Express, 83. *Mem:* Perf Right Soc Ltd, London; Songwriters Guild of Gr Brit; Musicians Asn Hawaii; Am String Teachers Asn; Int Soc Bassists. *Publ:* Contribr, A Jivy Musician in Tokyo, Manila Chronicle, 55; auth, Our Musical Backwords, Evening News, 60. *Mailing Add:* 802 Prospect St Apt 606 Honolulu HI 96813

PENDERECKI, KRZYSZTOF
COMPOSER, EDUCATOR
b Debica, Cracow, Poland, Nov 23, 33. *Study:* Univ Jagiellonski, Cracow; studied comp with Franciszek Skolyszewski, Arthur Malawski & Stanislaw Wiechowicz; State Higher Music Sch, Cracow, dipl, 58; Univ Rochester, Hon Dr. *Works:* Anaklasis (strings & perc), 60; Threnody for the Victims of Hiroshima (52 strings), 60; Dies irae (sop, ten, bass, chorus & large orch), 67; The Devils of Loudun (opera), 68; Partita (harpsichord, guitars, harp, double bass & chamber orch), 72; When Jacob Awoke (orch), 74; Violin Concerto, 77. *Pos:* Musical adv, Vienna Radio, 70-71; guest cond, London Symph Orch & Polish Radio Orch. *Teaching:* Lectr comp, State Higher Music Sch, Cracow, 58-66, prof extraordinary, 72-75, rector, 72-, prof, 75-; prof, Folkwang Hochschule Music, Essen, 66-72 & Yale Univ, 73- *Awards:* Fitelberg Prize, 60; Gottfried von Herder Prize, 77; Arthur Honegger Mem Award, 78. *Mem:* Royal Acad Music, London; Arts Acad German Dem Repub; Arts Acad WBerlin; Royal Acad Music, Stockholm. *Mailing Add:* c/o Jacques Leiser Mgt Dorchester Towers 155 W 68 St New York NY 10023

PENDLE, KARIN
EDUCATOR, MUSICOLOGIST
b Minneapolis, Minn, Oct 1, 39. *Study:* Univ Minn, BA, 61, MM, 64, PhD, 70. *Teaching:* Instr, Oberlin Col, 65-69; assoc prof, Univ Western Ontario, 70-76 & Univ Cincinnati, 76- *Awards:* Fel, Nat Endowment Humanities, 80. *Mem:* Am Musicol Soc; Col Music Soc; Nat Asn Teachers Singing. *Interests:* Opera librettos, history and literary qualities; women in music. *Publ:* Auth, Scribe, Auber and The Count of Monte Cristo, Music Rev, 73; The Operas Comiques of Gretry and Marmontel, Musical Quart, 76; Les Philosophes and Opera Comique: The Case of Gretry's Lucile, Music Rev, 77; Eugene Scribe and French Opera of the 19th Century, UMI, 79; A Working Friendship: Marsollier and Dalayrac, Music & Lett, 83. *Mailing Add:* 2308 Moerlein Ave Cincinnati OH 45219

PENHORWOOD, CONSTANCE JEAN See Cuccaro, Costanza

PENHORWOOD, EDWIN LEROY
COMPOSER, PIANO
b Toledo, Ohio, Aug 22, 39. *Study:* Univ Toledo, BEd, 62; Univ Iowa, studied piano with John Simms & perf practice with Robert Donington, MFA, 66; Consv Santa Cecilia, with Guido Agosti, 68-69. *Works:* Hosanna to the Son of David, Carl Fischer, 75; Christ the Lord is Risen, Abingdon Press, 76; The Greatest of These is Love, 76, Mother Goose on the Loose, 79, A Psalm Folksong, 81 & Psalm 150, 81, Hinshaw Music Publ. *Pos:* Minister music, Int Protestant Church, Switz, 69-72. *Teaching:* Instr voice, Berliner Kirchen Musikschule, 74-78. *Mem:* ASCAP. *Publ:* Auth, H W Zimmerman: Missa Profana, Der Kirchenmusiker, 81 & J Am Choral Music, 81. *Mailing Add:* 745 Austin Dr Lumberton NC 28358

PENINGER, JAMES DAVID
COMPOSER, TEACHER
b Orangeburg, SC, Dec 27, 29. *Study:* Col Charleston, BS, 51; Sch Music, Converse Col, BMus, 57, MMus, 59. *Works:* Over 400 comp, publ by 27 publ houses, 54- *Pos:* Minister music, Fernwood Baptist Church, 66-82 & Morningside Baptist Church, 82- *Teaching:* Instr, Spartanburg Co sch syst, 58- *Awards:* ASCAP Awards, 77- *Mem:* ASCAP; Am Choral Dir Asn; Music Educr Nat Conf; SC Music Educr Asn. *Mailing Add:* 829 Thackston Dr Spartanburg SC 29302

PENLAND, ARNOLD CLIFFORD, JR
ADMINISTRATOR, EDUCATOR
b Asheville, NC, Oct 8, 33. *Study:* Western Carolina Univ, BS, 56; George Peabody Col, MA, 59; Duke Univ, MEd, 66; Fla State Univ, PhD, 82; studied voice with Elda Vittori & Robert Malone, 48-56. *Roles:* Duke in Rigoletto, Ferrando in Cosi fan tutte, Camille in The Merry Widow, Brack in Down in the Valley & others. *Pos:* Supvr music, Raleigh Pub Sch, 60-67; dir, Raleigh Cult Ctr, 62-67. *Teaching:* State supvr music, Columbia, SC, 69-70; prof music, Col Fine Arts, Univ Fla, 70-81, asst dean, 81- *Mem:* Col Music Soc; Music Educr Nat Conf; Found Music Inc (vpres), Fla Music Educr Asn; Fla Col Educr Music Asn (secy & treas, 80-82). *Interests:* Aesthetic education; organization and administration of music schools in higher education. *Publ:* Auth, Composer in Residence: Three Influences, In: Public School Systems Yearbook, Teachers Col, Columbia Univ Press, 64; ed, Confrontation with the Arts: The Arts in Education, Western Carolina Univ, 70; auth, Music Model for Middle Schools, Fla Music Dir, Fla Music Educr Asn, 79. *Mailing Add:* 2809 S W 81 St Gainesville FL 32607

PENNARIO, LEONARD
COMPOSER, PIANO
b Buffalo, NY, July 9, 24. *Study:* Univ Southern Calif, 42; studied piano with Olga Steeb, Guy Maier & Isabelle Vengerova, comp with Ernst Toch & orch with Lucien Caillet. *Works:* Piano Concerto; Midnight on the Newport Cliffs; March of the Lunatics; Variations on the Kerry Dance. *Rec Perf:* On Capitol Rec & RCA Victor. *Pos:* Soloist with all maj US orchs; recitalist throughout US & Europe. *Mem:* Ephebian Soc; ASCAP. *Mailing Add:* c/o Columbia Artists Mgt 165 W 57th St New York NY 10019

PENNEYS, REBECCA A
PIANO, TEACHER
b Los Angeles, Calif, Oct 2, 47. *Study:* Study with Aube Tzerko & Leonard Stein, 57-64; Aspen, with Rosinna Lhevinne, 60; Ind Univ, with Menahem Pressler & Gyorgy Sebok, artist dipl, 72. *Pos:* Mem, New Arts Trio. *Teaching:* Mem fac, NC Sch Arts, 72-74 & Chautauqua Inst, summers currently; chmn piano dept, Wis Consv Music, 74-80; prof piano, Eastman Sch Music, 80- *Awards:* Spec Critics Award, Seventh Int Chopin Piano Compt, 65; Most Outstanding Musician, Vianna Da Motta Int Piano Compt, 71; Top Prize, Second Paloma O'Shea Int Piano Compt, 76. *Mailing Add:* 2680 Highland Ave Rochester NY 14610

PERAHIA, MURRAY
PIANO, CONDUCTOR
b New York, NY, 47. *Study:* Mannes Col Music, dipl(comp & cond); studied piano with Jeanette Haien, Mieczyslaw Horszowski & Artur Balsam. *Rec Perf:* Works of Chopin, Schumann & others on CBS Rec. *Pos:* Pianist, solo & with Chicago Symph Orch, Philadelphia Orch, New York Phil, Galimir Quartet, Marlboro Fest, Aldeburgh Fest & many others in US, Europe, Israel & Japan, 72- *Awards:* Leeds Int Piano Compt Winner, England, 72; Avery Fisher Prize, 75; Kosciusko Chopin Prize. *Bibliog:* Peter Mose (auth), A Conversation with Murray Perahia, 83. *Mailing Add:* c/o Frank E Saloman Mgt 201 W 54th St Suite 4C New York NY 10019

PERERA, RONALD CHRISTOPHER
COMPOSER, EDUCATOR
b Boston, Mass, Dec 25, 41. *Study:* Harvard Col, BA, 63; Harvard Univ, MA(music), 67; Inst Sonology, Univ Utrecht, 68. *Works:* Bright Angels, Three Poems of Günter Grass, Chanteys & Apollo Circling, E C Schirmer; Tolling, perf by Kenneth Fearn & Monica Jakuc, 80; The White Whale (bar & orch), 82; Crossing the Meridian, perf by Boston Musica Viva, 82. *Teaching:* Lectr, res asst & instr, Syracuse Univ, 68-70; vis asst prof, Dartmouth Col, 70-71; from asst prof to prof, Smith Col, 71- *Awards:* ASCAP Comp Award, 72-; Nat Endowment Arts Fel Grant, 76; Mass Arts & Humanities Found Fel, 78. *Mem:* ASCAP; Col Music Soc; Am Soc Univ Comp. *Publ:* Co-ed, The Development and Practice of Electronic Music, Prentice-Hall, 75. *Mailing Add:* 30 Lyman Rd Northampton MA 01060

PERESS, MAURICE
CONDUCTOR, ORCHESTRATOR
b New York, NY, Mar 18, 30. *Study:* Washington Sq Col, NY Univ, BA(music), 52; Mannes Sch Music. *Rec Perf:* Central Park in the Dark (Ives), 60, Music for Organ & Brass, 72, Mass (Bernstein), 72 & Rheinberger Concertos for Organ, 73, Columbia; Corigliano: Poem in October, RCA, 73; 12th Smart Rag, Kansas City Phil, 80. *Pos:* Asst cond, New York Phil, 60-61; music dir, Corpus Christi Symph, 61-74, Austin Symph, 70-72 & Kansas City Phil, 74-80; dir, World Premiere Bernstein Mass, 71 & Bureau Indian Affairs, Pilot Proj. *Teaching:* Prof cond, orch & opera, Aaron Copland Sch Music, City Univ New York, 83- *Awards:* Millicent James Scholar, New York Univ, 53. *Mem:* ASCAP; Am Symph Orch League (pres Cond Guild, 81-83). *Publ:* Contribr, A Baroque Trumpet Found in Greenwich Villiage, Brass Quart, 56; coauth, Some Music Lessons for Indian American Children, Bureau Indian Affairs, Ballard, 68. *Rep:* Maxime Gershunoff 502 Park Ave New York NY 10022. *Mailing Add:* 240 E 55th St New York NY 10022

PERETZ, MARC HARLAN
ADMINISTRATOR, EDUCATOR
b Quakertown, Pa, May 9, 47. *Study:* New England Consv Music, BM, 69; Col Music, Temple Univ, MM, 71, DMA, 78. *Teaching:* Instr & fel, Dept Music Educ, Col Music, Temple Univ, 69-74; asst prof & dir spec progs, Westminster Choir Col, 74-81; assoc prof & dir Cadek Consv Music, Univ Tenn, Chattanooga, 81- *Mem:* Am Asn Univ Prof; Am Musicol Soc; Music Educr Nat Conf; Nat Band Asn. *Interests:* The application of curriculum theory to music education. *Publ:* Auth, Program Preservation: Some Preliminary Thoughts, Tempe, 77 & Nysma News, 77. *Mailing Add:* Cadek Consv Music Univ Tenn Chattanooga TN 37402

PERICH, GUILLERMO
VIOLA, EDUCATOR
b Havana, Cuba, Oct 22, 24; US citizen. *Study:* Havana Consv, MM, 47; Sch Music, Boston Univ, 56-57. *Pos:* Prin viola, Havana Phil Orch, 56-59, Baltimore Symph Orch, 60-68 & St Louis Symph Orch, 68-71; assoc prin viola, Aspen Fest Orch, 67-69. *Teaching:* Prof violin, Havana Consv Music, 48-59; prof viola, Peabody Consv, 64-68; prof viola & chamber music, Univ Ill, 71- *Awards:* Gold Medal, Havana Phil Orch, 47. *Mem:* Am Fedn Musicians; Am Viola Soc; Am String Teachers Asn. *Interests:* Music for viola by Latin American and Spanish composers. *Mailing Add:* 2136 Music Bldg 1114 W Nevada St Urbana IL 61801

PERKINS, LEEMAN LLOYD
EDUCATOR
b Salina, Utah, Mar 27, 32. *Study:* Univ Utah, BFA, 54; Yale Univ, PhD, 65. *Pos:* Gen ed, Masters and Monuments of the Renaissance, Broude Brothers Ltd, currently. *Teaching:* Instr & asst prof, Yale Univ, 64-71; assoc prof, Univ Tex, Austin, 71-76; prof music, Columbia Univ, 76- *Awards:* Am Coun Learned Soc Fel, 73-74; Nat Endowment Humanities Grant, 79; Otto Kinkeldey Award, Am Musicol Soc, 80. *Mem:* Am Musicol Soc (mem bd dir, 80-81); Int Musicol Soc; Renaissance Soc Am; Amici Thomae Mori. *Interests:* Music of the Renaissance, expecially late 15th and early 16th centuries. *Publ:* Auth, Johannis Lheritier Opera Omnia, Am Inst Musicol, 69; Mode and Structure in the Masses of Josquin, Am Musicol Soc J, 73; Toward a Rational Approach to Text Placement, Dufay Fifth-Century Conf, 76; coauth, The Mellon Chansonnier, Yale Univ Press, 79; auth, Motet (1420-1600), In: New Grove Dict of Music & Musicians, 80. *Mailing Add:* Dept Music Columbia Univ New York NY 10027

PERKINS, MARION (LOUISE)
PIANO, EDUCATOR
b Minneapolis, Minn, Mar 21, 27. *Study:* Piano with Karl Ulrich Schnabel 47- & Artur Schnabel, 50-51; Univ Minn, BA, 48, MA, 55; Univ Southern Calif, PhD(musicol), 61. *Pos:* Pianist, conct tours in Europe, Mex & US, 51-; soloist at Town Hall, NY, Nat Gallery, Washington, DC & with US orchs. *Teaching:* Instr piano, Univ Mo, 58-60; assoc prof piano & music hist, Colo Woman's Col, 63-68; prof music, James Madison Univ, 68- *Awards:* Honors Music Hist Lit in Recogniton Prof Serv, Univ Southern Calif, 61. *Mem:* Music Teachers Nat Asn. *Interests:* Changing concepts of rhythm in the romantic era. *Mailing Add:* 66 Hope St Harrisonburg VA 22801

PERKINSON, COLERIDGE-TAYLOR
COMPOSER, CONDUCTOR & MUSIC DIRECTOR
Study: NY Univ, 49-51; Manhattan Sch Music, studied comp with Vittorio Giannini, Charles Mills & Earl Kim, BA(comp), 53, MA(comp), 54; Berkshire Music Ctr, 54; Mozarteum, 60. *Works:* Attitudes (solo cantata for tenor, violin, cello & piano), comn by Ford Found, 62; Commentary (solo cello & orch), comn by Nat Asn Negro Musicians, 64; Statements—Second

Sonata for Piano, Bicentennial Comn, 75; Bearden on Bearden (film score), Third World Cinema Inc, 80. *Rec Perf:* Belafonte '77, CBS Rec, 77; Belafonte Canadian TV Special, 77; D J Rogers—Trust Me, 79; Music Minus One; I Want You (Marvin Gaye), Motown; Jimmy Owens & Headin Home (Jimmy Owens), Horizon Rec. *Pos:* Cond, Brooklyn Community Symph Orch, 59-62; pianist, Max Roach Jazz Quartet, 64-65; co-founder & assoc cond, Symph New World, 65-70, actg music dir, 72-73; music dir, Alvin Ailey Am Dance Theatre, 68-69 & 78; guest cond, Dallas Symph Orch,, 77, Orch Filarmonica de Bogota, 78 & NC Symph Orch, 79, 80 & 81; composed, conducted & directed music for numerous films, TV programs & theatre shows. *Teaching:* Fac mem, Manhattan Sch Music, 54-59 & Brooklyn Col, 59-62. *Mailing Add:* 755 West End Ave New York NY 10025

PERLE, GEORGE
COMPOSER, WRITER
b Bayonne, NJ, May 6, 15. *Study:* NY Univ, PhD, 56. *Works:* Three Movements for Orchestra, Presser, 60; Songs of Praise and Lamentation, Boelke-Bomart, 74; Six Etudes for Piano, 76 & 13 Dickinson Songs, 78, Margun; Concertino for Piano, Winds & Timpani, 79 & A Short Symphony, 80, Boelke-Bomart; Ballade for Piano, Peters, 81. *Teaching:* Instr, Univ Louisville, 49-57; assoc prof, Univ Calif, Davis, 57-61; prof, Queens Col, City Univ New York, 61- *Awards:* Guggenheim Fel, 66-67 & 74-75; Award, Am Acad & Inst Arts & Lett, 77. *Bibliog:* Leo Kraft (auth), The Music of George Perle, Musical Quart, 7/71; Oliver Knussen (auth), George Perle, Composer, Tempo, 6/81. *Mem:* ASCAP; Am Musicol Soc; Am Acad & Inst Arts & Lett. *Publ:* Auth of numerous articles publ in US, England, SAm, Germany & Austria, 41-; Serial Composition & Atonality, 62-81, Twelve-Tone Tonality, 78, The Operas of Alban Berg, Vol I, Wozzeck, 80 & Vol II, Lulu (in prep), Univ Calif Press. *Rep:* Music Assoc Am 224 King St Englewood NJ 07631. *Mailing Add:* 333 Central Park W New York NY 10025

PERLIS, VIVIAN
WRITER, EDUCATOR
b Brooklyn, NY, Apr 26, 28. *Study:* Univ Mich, BM, 49, MM, 52; additional study Columbia Univ & Philadelphia Acad Music. *Pos:* Harpist, New Haven Symph, 60-71; ref librn, Yale Music Libr, 67-72; dir Charles Ives oral hist proj, 67-72; dir oral hist Am music proj, Yale Sch Music, 71- *Teaching:* Instr harp, Westport Sch Music, 57-68; instr music hist, Norwalk Community Col, 64-66; lectr Am music, Am Studies Prog, Yale Univ, 72-76 & Sch Music, Yale Univ, 76-78. *Awards:* Charles Ives Award, Am Acad Inst Arts & Lett, 71; Best book 1974, Conn Book Publ, 75; Kinkeldey Award, best book of 1974, Am Musicol Soc, 75. *Mem:* Am Musicol Soc (bd dir, 81-83); Sonneck Soc (vpres, 75-76); Charles Ives Soc (vpres, 74-); Oral Hist Asn; Am Studies Asn. *Publ:* Auth, Various articles in New Grove Dict, Musical Am, New York Times & Keynote; Ives and Oral History, Notes, 6/72; Charles Ives Remembered, Yale Press, 74; The Futurist Music of Leo Ornstein, Notes, 6/75; co-ed, An Ives Celebration, Univ Ill Press, 77. *Mailing Add:* 139 Goodhill Rd Weston CT 06883

PERLMAN, ITZHAK
VIOLIN, EDUCATOR
b Tel Aviv, Israel, Aug 31, 45. *Study:* Tel Aviv Acad Music; Juilliard Sch; Meadowmount Sch Music; studied with Ivan Galamian & Dorothy De Lay. *Rec Perf:* Works of Paganini, Bach, Bartok, Dvorak, Brahms & others for Angel, London, RCA Victor, DG & CBS Rec. *Pos:* Violinist with major Am & Europ orchs & at numerous music fest, 64-; recitalist worldwide. *Teaching:* Prof violin, Consv Music, Brooklyn Col, City Univ New York, currently. *Awards:* Leventritt Award, 64; Grand Prix Disque, 79; Grammy Award. *Bibliog:* Irvin Molotsky (auth), Reagans Hear Perlman and Protege, 11/8/82; Edward Rothstein (auth), Recital: Itzhak Perlman's Violin, 12/7/82 & David K Shipler (auth), World-Class Violinists Adorn Festival in Israel, 12/15/82, New York Times. *Mailing Add:* c/o ICM Artists Ltd 40 W 57th St New York NY 10019

PERLMUTTER, DONNA
CRITIC, LECTURER
b Philadelphia, Pa. *Study:* Pa State Univ, BA, 58; Yeshiva Univ, MS, 59; studied with Jakob Gimpel, 70-79. *Pos:* Music critic, Los Angeles Herald Examiner, 75-; Corresp, Opera News, 80-, Dance Mag, 80- & Ovation, 83. *Mem:* Music Critics Asn. *Mailing Add:* Los Angeles Herald Examiner 1111 S Broadway Los Angeles CA 90015

PERLONGO, DANIEL JAMES
COMPOSER, EDUCATOR
b Gaastra, Mich, Sept 23, 42. *Study:* Univ Mich, BMus, 64, MMus, 66; Acad St Cecilia, cert, 68. *Works:* Myriad (orch), St Cecilia Orch, 68; Ephemeron (orch), Italian Radio Orch Rome, 72; Variations (orch), 73 & Voyage (orch), 75, Pittsburgh Symph Chamber Orch, 73; Voyage (orch), Pittsburgh Symph Chamber Orch, 75; Concertino (orch), Nebr Sinfonia, 80; Aureole (sax quartet), Shawnee Press Inc, 82; Variations (orch), Am Comp Orch, 82. *Teaching:* Assoc prof, Indiana Univ Pa, 68- *Awards:* Rome Prize, Am Acad Rome, 70-72; Am Acad Arts & Lett Award, 75; Guggenheim Found Fel, 82-83. *Mem:* BMI; Am Comp Alliance; Pittsburgh Alliance Comp; Am Music Ctr. *Mailing Add:* R D 1 Box 344 Home PA 15747

PERLOW, MILDRED STERN
MUSIC DIRECTOR, VIOLA
b Newark, NJ, Mar 11, 22. *Study:* Univ Mich, BM, 43. *Pos:* Prin violist, Nat Orch Asn, 43-44; Columbus Phil, 44-45; Long Island Symph, 79-82 & Opera on the Sound, 81-; dir & violist, L'Amore di Musica Chamber Ens, 74- *Teaching:* Instr violin & viola, Adelphi Univ, 78- *Mem:* Chamber Music Am. *Mailing Add:* 58 Fairway Hempstead NY 11550

PERRET, PETER J
CONDUCTOR, EDUCATOR
b Rochester, Minn, Mar 25, 41; US & Swiss citizen. *Study:* Accad Musicale Chigiana, Italy, dipl, 62 & 66; Consv Royal Bruxelles, Belgium, premier prix, 64, dipl superieure, 66. *Rec Perf:* Works of Mozart, Roussel, Henze & others, Orch Suisse Romande, 66-72; works of Schubert, Bloch, Bruckner & others, Hessischer Rundfunk Orch. *Pos:* Coun Musicale & TV Suisse-Romandes, Geneva, Switz, 66-73; prin cond, Capetown Symph Orch, SAfrica, 73-74; Exxon Arts Endowment Cond, Buffalo Phil, 76-79; music dir, Winston-Salem Symph, 79- *Teaching:* Prof oboe & chamber music, Consv Populaire Musique Geneve, 68-73; vis prof cond, Capetown Univ, SAfrica, 73-74; prof cond, NC Sch Arts, 80- *Awards:* Deuxieme Prix, Concours Int Jeunes Chefs J'Orch, Besancon, France, 64; Premio Firenze, Aidem Int Cond Compt, Italy, 70. *Mailing Add:* 644 Spring St NW Winston-Salem NC 27101

PERRIN, PETER A
MUSIC DIRECTOR, COMPOSER
b Utica, NY, June 21, 34. *Study:* Comp with Henry Cowell, Darius Milhaud & Roger Sessions. *Works:* Four Songs with Viola, perf by Diana Hoagland, John Graham & Cheryl Seltzer, 69; Three on One Rhythm, perf by Speculum Musicae, 73; The Composer (for Stefan Wolpe), 75 & The Flight into Egypt, 77, perf by Western Wind Vocal Sextet. *Pos:* Cofounder & co-dir, Perf Comt Twentieth-Century Music, 66-69; founder & dir, Alliance for Am Song, 77- *Awards:* Winner, First Comp Cont, East & West Artists, 75; grant, Nat Endowment Arts, 80. *Mem:* Sonneck Soc; Am Music Ctr. *Interests:* American vocal music, primarily 20th century. *Mailing Add:* Box 497 Cooper Sta New York NY 10003

PERRIS, ARNOLD B
EDUCATOR, WRITER
b Cleveland, Ohio. *Study:* Case Western Reserve Univ, BA, MA; Northwestern Univ, PhD. *Pos:* Ed & educ dir, Summy-Birchard Co, 52-62; auth & narrator radio ser on music, Cleveland & St Louis, 71-; pres, St Louis Chamber Orch & Chorus, 74- *Teaching:* Fac mem music, Ohio Univ, Mich State Univ & Case Western Reserve Univ; vis lectr music, Univ Singapore, 75-76; minister educ, Repub Singapore, 75-76; assoc prof, Univ Mo, St Louis, currently. *Mem:* Music Educr Nat Conf; Am Musicol Soc. *Publ:* Auth, An Introduction to Symphonic Music, 75; contribr to Soc Ethnomusicol J & Musical Am. *Mailing Add:* 757 Wiggins Ferry St Louis MO 63141

PERRY, ALCESTIS BISHOP
VIOLIN, EDUCATOR
b Chicago, Ill, July 27, 34. *Study:* Eastman Sch Music, studied violin with Andre de Ribaupierre, BM, 55; Univ Ill, studied violin with Paul Rolland, MM, 56. *Pos:* Concertmaster, Ohio Chamber Orch, 79-, Akron Symph, 79-80 & Cleveland Opera Orch, 80- *Teaching:* Instr violin, Ithaca Col, 60-66 & private studio, 68-; instr violin & chamber music, Nat Music Camp, Interlochen, Mich, 72-; assoc prof, Univ Akron, 79-80. *Mailing Add:* 2812 Corydon Rd Cleveland Heights OH 44118

PERRY, DOUGLAS R
TENOR
b Buffalo, NY, Jan 19, 45. *Study:* Wittenberg Univ, BM, 66; Ball State Univ, MA, 68. *Rec Perf:* The Mother Of Us All, New World Rec; America Sings, Vox; Music of Franz Schubert, Grenadilla. *Roles:* Alfred in Fledermaus, Augusta Opera, 77; Simpleton in Boris Godunov, San Antonio Opera, 78; Bardolph in Falstaff, Opera Co Boston, 78; Guillot in Manon, New York City Opera, 79; Mahatma Gandhi in Satyagraha, Netherlands Opera, 80; Pong in Turandot, Houston Grand Opera, 82; Incredible in Andrea Chenier, Greater Miami Opera, 83. *Rep:* Columbia Artists Mgmt Inc 165 W 57th St New York NY 10019. *Mailing Add:* 170 West End Ave New York NY 10023

PERRY, EDSON CLIFTON
VIOLIN, VIOLA
b New London, Conn, Nov 30, 29. *Study:* Stetson Univ, BM, 52; La State Univ, MM, 54; studied with Otto Meyer, Irene Stafford, George Heck, Louis Ferraro, Frances Buxton, George Guile & Emile Cooper. *Pos:* Recitalist & soloist, US symph orch, 52-; prin viola, Jackson Symph Orch, 56-60; concertmaster, Huron Symph Orch, 66-69; prin violin, Ark Symph Orchs, 75-83. *Teaching:* Instr strings, orch & theory, Eastern Ky State Univ, 54-55; instr strings & orch, Univ SMiss, 56-59; prof music, Middle Tenn State Univ, 60-62; prof music hist & pedagogy, Huron Col, 66-69. *Mem:* Am Symph Orch League; Music Educr Nat Conf (secy, treas & vpres Miss, 66-69); Am String Teachers Asn (pres Miss, 66-69). *Publ:* Auth, Mississippi String Program, Miss Music Educr Mag, 58. *Mailing Add:* 11103 Beverly Hills Dr Little Rock AR 72211

PERRY, MARVIN CHAPMAN, II
TRUMPET, EDUCATOR
b Birmingham, Ala, Dec 12, 48. *Study:* Eastman Sch Music, BM, 70; Cath Univ Am, 73; Univ Montevallo, MMusEd, 75. *Pos:* Spec bandsman, US Army Band, 70-73; trumpet player, Birmingham Symph Orch, 73-75; prin trumpet, Indianapolis Symph Orch, 75- *Teaching:* Instr trumpet, Butler Univ, 76-; vis lectr appl trumpet, Ind Univ, Bloomington, 78-79. *Mem:* Int Trumpet Guild. *Mailing Add:* 3377 E 62nd St Indianapolis IN 46220

PERRY, STEPHEN BRUCE
TUBA
b Bristol, Conn, Nov 29, 53. *Study:* Cent Conn State Univ, BS, 76; Yale Sch Music, MM, 81. *Pos:* Prin tubist, Springfield Symph Orch, 80-; freelance tubist, 81- *Teaching:* Instr Tuba, Hartt Sch Music, 81- *Mailing Add:* Hartt Sch Music Univ Hartford West Hartford CT 06117

PERRY-CAMP, JANE (SCHIFFMAN)
EDUCATOR, PIANO

b Durham, NC, Oct 5, 36. *Study:* Duke Univ, AB, 58; Fla State Univ, studied piano with Edward Kilenyi & repertoire with Ernst von Dohnanyi, MM, 60, PhD(music theory), 68. *Pos:* Adv ed musicol, Eighteenth-Century Studies, 82-85. *Teaching:* Asst prof music, Brevard Community Col, Fla, 68-69; prof, St Petersburg Jr Col, Fla, 69-74; from asst to assoc prof, Sweet Briar Col, Va, 74-80; assoc prof music theory, Fla State Univ, 80- *Mem:* Am Soc Eighteenth Century Studies (mem exec bd southeast region, 81-84); Int Soc Study of Time; Am Musicol Soc; Col Music Soc. *Interests:* Textual investigation of Mozart autograph manuscripts; musical time and temporal proportion. *Publ:* Auth, The Golden Section Metaphor in Mozart, Music, and History, J Musicol Res, 79; A Laugh a Minuet: Humor in Late Eighteenth-Century Music, Col Music Symposium, 79. *Mailing Add:* 2304 Don Andres Ave Tallahassee FL 32304

PERSICHETTI, VINCENT
COMPOSER, EDUCATOR

b June 6, 15; US citizen. *Study:* Combs Consv, with Russell King Miller, BM, 34; Curtis Inst, with Fritz Reiner, dipl, 38; Philadelphia Consv, with Olga Samaroff, DM, 45. *Works:* Twelve piano sonatas, nine symphonies, six cantatas, four string quartets, twelve band works & seven harpsichord sonatas, Elkan-Vogel Inc, 52- *Teaching:* Head comp dept, Combs Col, 38-41 & Philadelphia Consv, 41-55; fac mem comp, Juilliard Sch, 47- *Awards:* Guggenheim Fel, 59, 69 & 73; First Kennedy Ctr Friedheim Award, 77; Medal of Honor, Italian Govt, 58. *Mem:* ASCAP; Nat Inst Arts & Letters. *Publ:* Auth, Twentieth Century Harmony (Creative Aspects & Practice), W W Norton, 61. *Mailing Add:* Hillhouse Wise Mill Rd Philadelphia PA 19128

PERYER, FREDERICK WILLIAM
ADMINISTRATOR, TUBA

b Flint, Mich, Aug 22, 32. *Study:* Western Mich Univ, BMus, 56; Univ Mich, Flint, 57-59. *Pos:* Freelance tubist, 56-; producer musical enrichment prog, Charles Stewart Mott Found, 56-; orch cond, 56-64; personnel mgr, Flint Symph Orch, 70-73, managing dir, 73-; asst to managing dir, Flint Inst Music, 72-73, managing dir, 73-81, exec dir, 81-83; fest & pub relations comt, Flint Bicentennial Comn, 75-76; dir, Conct Theater, CW Post Ctr, 83-; musical arr, Gen Motors Corp & TV prod. *Teaching:* Instr music, Flint pub sch, 56-69 & Carman Sch District, 69-73; instr tuba, Charles Stewart Mott Community Col & Univ Mich, Flint. *Mem:* Asn Col Univ & Community Arts Adminr; Am Symph Orch League; Mich Orch Asn; Am Fedn Musicians; Metropolitan Orch Managers Asn. *Mailing Add:* 1025 E Kearsley St Flint MI 48503

PESKANOV, ALEXANDER E
PIANO, COMPOSER

b Odessa, USSR; US citizen. *Study:* Music Sch Stoliarsky, 61-72; Juilliard Sch, BA, 73, MA, 80. *Works:* He Knows You Are Alone (soundtrack), MGM & United Artists, 80; Still Remember, Chappell Music Co, 80; Clairvoyance (soundtrack), Landsbery Prod, 82. *Awards:* Fel, Upis Bros Found, 74-75; Winner, Young Artists Recital Piano Compt, Piano Teachers Cong New York, 75. *Rep:* Columbia Artists 165 W 57 St New York NY 10019. *Mailing Add:* 835 Weber Ave W Babylon NY 11704

PESTALOZZI, MARTHA
EDUCATOR, PIANO

Study: Manhattan Sch Music, MM; Wells Col; studied piano with Hertenstein, Scoville & Goldsand. *Pos:* Accmp for singers & choral groups. *Teaching:* Fac mem, Westport Music Sch & Third Street Music Sch, formerly; mem fac piano minor, Manhattan Sch Music, 56- *Mailing Add:* Manhattan Sch Music 120 Claremont Ave New York NY 10027

PETERS, GEORGE DAVID
EDUCATOR, ADMINISTRATOR

b Evansville, Ind, Aug 30, 42. *Study:* Univ Evansville, BME, 64; Univ Ill, MS(music educ), 65, EdD, 73. *Works:* Neumes Treibend, 69, Dactylsung, 70, Formula 315, 73 & Reflectus #4, 75, M M Cole; 14 Concert Etudes, 76 & Newburgh Interludes, 76, Boonin. *Rec Perf:* Trombone Quartets, Grad Trombone Quartet, 70. *Teaching:* Prof music, Univ Ill, Urbana, 69-, asst dean fine arts, 72-79. *Publ:* Coauth, Music Teaching and Learning, Longman, 82. *Mailing Add:* Sch Music Univ Ill Urbana IL

PETERS, GORDON BENES
CONDUCTOR & MUSIC DIRECTOR, PERCUSSION

b Oak Park, Ill, Jan 4, 31. *Study:* Northwestern Univ, 49-50; Juilliard Sch Music, with Saul Goodman & Morris Goldenberg; Pierre Monteux Sch Cond, summers 52-63; Eastman Sch Music, 53-59. *Works:* Swords of Moda-Ling, 64 & The Drummer: Man, 78, Kemper-Peters Publ. *Pos:* Prin perc, US Mil Acad West Point Band, 50-53, Grant Park Symph, Chicago, 55-58 & Chicago Symph Orch, 59-; leader & founder, Marimba Masters, 54-59; perc, Rochester Phil, 55-59; cond, Elmhurst Symph Orch, 62-67; cond & adminr, Civic Orch Chicago, Truing Orch & Chicago Symph, 67- *Teaching:* Instr perc, Northwestern Univ, 63-68. *Awards:* ASCAP Award, 83. *Mem:* Cond Guild (treas, 79-81); Am Symph Orch League; Int Conf Symph & Opera Musicians. *Publ:* Articles, Instrumentalist Mag, Percussionist, Percussive Notes, Cond Guild J & Ludwig Drummer, 60- *Mailing Add:* 824 Hinman Ave Evanston IL 60202

PETERS, MITCHELL
PERCUSSION, EDUCATOR

b Red Wing, Minn, Aug 17, 35. *Study:* Eastman Sch Music, BMus & perf cert, 57, MMus, 58. *Works:* Sonata allegro (marimba & piano), 68; Yellow After the Rain (marimba), 71. *Pos:* Perc, Dallas Summer Musicals, 62-69; co-prin timpanist & perc, Los Angeles Phil Orch, formerly, prin timpanist & perc, currently. *Teaching:* Instr, Calif State Univ, Los Angeles, formerly & Univ Calif, Los Angeles, currently. *Mem:* ASCAP. *Mailing Add:* Dept Music Univ Calif Los Angeles CA 90024

PETERS, ROBERTA (ROBERTA PETERS FIELDS)
SOPRANO, LECTURER

b New York, NY, May 4, 30. *Study:* With William Hermann; Lehigh Univ, LHD, 77; Colby Col, Hon Dr Music, 81; St John's Univ, Hon Dr Music, 82. *Rec Perf:* Marriage of Figaro, Roberta Peters—Famous Operatic Arias, Ariadne auf Naxos, A Masked Ball, Lucia di Lammermoor, Orfeo and Euridice & Roberta Peters in Recital, RCA Victor & many others for Audio Fidelity, London, Cetra, Command Rec, Columbia Rec, Deutsche Grammophon & MPS-Saba. *Roles:* Lucia in Lucia di Lammermoor, Gilda in Rigoletto, Rosina in Il Barbiere di Siviglia, Amina in Sonnambula, Queen of the Night in Die Zauberflöte, Sophie in Der Rosenkavalier & Norina in Don Pasquale, Metropolitan Opera, 50- *Pos:* Lead soprano, Metropolitan Opera, 50-; soprano with major companies, incl Salzburg Fest, Vienna Staatsoper & Volksoper, Berlin Deutsche Opera, Munich Staatsoper & Gärtnerplatz, London Royal Opera, Leningrad Kirov, Moscow Bolshoi, Baltimore Opera, Cincinnati Opera, Conn Opera, Hawaii Opera, NJ State Opera, Philadelphia Grand Opera, Pittsburgh Opera Co, San Antonio Opera & Seattle Opera. *Publ:* Coauth, A Debut at the Met, Meredith Press, 67. *Rep:* ICM Artists Ltd 40 W 57th St New York NY 10019. *Mailing Add:* 64 Garden Rd Scarsdale NY 10583

PETERSEN, BARBARA A
ADMINISTRATOR, WRITER

b Evansville, Ind, June 14, 45. *Study:* Carleton Col, BA(music), 67; NY Univ, MA(musicol), 69, PhD(musicol), 77. *Pos:* Music ed, Broude Brothers Ltd, 73-77; coord concert music, BMI, 77-; activ mgr, Concert Res, currently. *Teaching:* Instr music, NY Univ, 71-73. *Mem:* New Music Young Ensembles (sec, 81-); Int Richard Strauss Gesellschaft; Music Libr Asn; Wagner Soc NY; Int League Women Comp. *Interests:* Vocal music of Wagner and Strauss; 19-20th century German lieder; performing rights societies; contemporary vocal chamber music and song. *Publ:* Auth, Richard Strauss and the Performance of His Lieder, 74 & An Unusual Strauss Manuscript in the BMI Archives, 78, Richard Strauss-Blätter, Vienna; Ton und Wort: The Lieder of Richard Strauss, UMI Res Press, 80; brochures on Miriam Gideon, Bernard Rands & Elliott Schwartz, BMI, 80-82; The Vocal Chamber Music of Miriam Gideon, Greenwood Press (in prep). *Mailing Add:* 260 W 72nd St Apt 4A New York NY 10023

PETERSEN, MARIAN F
EDUCATOR

b Salt Lake City, Utah. *Study:* San Francisco State Col, AB, 57; Univ Utah, MM, 61, PhD, 64. *Teaching:* Prof & chmn theory div, Consv Music, Univ Mo, Kansas City, 75- *Mem:* Soc Music Theory; Mu Phi Epsilon. *Interests:* Leroy J Robertson, American composer. *Mailing Add:* L11 Route #1 Lake Lotawana MO 64063

PETERSEN, PATRICIA H
RECORDER, TEACHER

b St Joseph, Mo, July 14, 45. *Study:* Carleton Col, BA, 67; Chicago Musical Col, 74; Sarah Lawrence Col, MFA, 76. *Pos:* Mem & bd dir, Music Before 1800, New York, 78-82 & Am Rec Soc, 80- *Teaching:* Instr theory & sightsinging, Columbia Col, 69-74; instr recorder, Am Rec Soc Summer Wkshps, 76- & Greensboro Col, NC State Univ, 82-; musician in res, NC State Univ, 82-83. *Mem:* Cappella Nova (vpres, 75-82); Rossignol (dir, 80-); Chamber Music Am. *Mailing Add:* 1001 N Gregson St Durham NC 27701

PETERSEN, PATRICIA JEANNETTE
VIOLA, TEACHER

b Bay City, Mich, Oct 7, 40. *Study:* Univ RI, MMus, 83. *Pos:* Violist, RI Phil Orch, 71-, New Music Ens, 72-73 & Artists Int Opera, 77-80. *Teaching:* Violin, viola & piano, privately, 77- *Mem:* Chamber Music Soc RI; Am Fedn Musicians; String Quartet Soc RI (mem bd, 80-); RI String Teachers Asn (vpres, 82-83). *Mailing Add:* 610 Tower Hill Rd North Kingstown RI 02852

PETERSON, HAL (HAROLD VAUGHAN)
COMPOSER, FRENCH HORN

b Oak Park, Ill, June 23, 48. *Study:* San Jose State Univ, BA, 69; Stanford Univ, MA, 71, DMA, 73. *Works:* Symphony (synthesizer & orch), Blixt Publ, 78; The Charismatic Bassist for Gary Karr, Hal Peterson Music Serv, 83. *Pos:* Prin horn, San Jose Civic Light Opera, 73-; asst prin & third horn, Monterey Symph Orch, 76- *Teaching:* Instr theory & piano, DeAnza Col, 75-79; lectr theory & comp, Stanford Univ, 76-78; instr theory & piano, Foothill Col, 83- *Mem:* ASCAP; Am Fedn Musicians. *Mailing Add:* 413 Rutland Ave San Jose CA 91528

PETERSON, LARRY W
ADMINISTRATOR, EDUCATOR

b Wichita, Kans, Dec 10, 41. *Study:* Tex Christian Univ, with Emmet Smith, BMus, 64, with Michael Winesanker, MMus, 69; Nat Consv, Paris, with Olivier Messiaen, 71; Univ NC, Chapel Hill, with William Newman & Howard Smither, PhD, 73. *Teaching:* Instr, Jersey City State Col, 73-75; asst prof, Peabody Sch Music, Nashville, 75-77 & dir & assoc prof, 77-80; chmn, Dept Music, Univ Del, Newark, 80- *Awards:* Fel, Nat Defense Educ Act, 69, Woodrow Wilson, 71 & Nat Endowment Humanities, 82. *Mem:* Music Educr Nat Conf; Am Musicol Soc; Music Teachers Nat. *Publ:* Auth, Complete Organ Works of Simon Lohet, Am Inst Musicol, 76. *Mailing Add:* 243 W Main St Newark DE 19711

PETERSON, LEROY H
VIOLIN, CONDUCTOR
b Regina, Sask, Sept 2, 37; US citizen. *Study:* Geneva Consv, Switz; Columbia Union Col, BA, 61; Peabody Consv Music, MMus, 63, artist dipl, 64; study with Ruggiero Ricci, Henryk Szeryng, Michel Schwalbe, Roman Totenberg, Berl Senofsky & Robert Gerle. *Rec Perf:* Four Strings and a Soul, 61, Evening Song, 68, Devotional Moments, 68, Moods and Reflections, 70, Vesper Hour of Music, 70, Music for Organ & Strings, 78 & Adagio, 82, Chapel Rec. *Pos:* Concertmaster, Worcester Symph Orch, 67-68. *Teaching:* Instr violin, John Nevans Andrews Sch, Takoma Park, Md, 63-64, Columbia Union Col, 64-65; Peabody Consv Music, 64-65 & Pioneer Valley Acad, 65-68; instr & cond, Atlantic Union Col, 67-78; asst prof music, Andrews Univ, 68-82; assoc prof, Pac Union Col, 83- *Awards:* Melissa Tiller Mem Prize, Peabody Consv Music, 64. *Bibliog:* W K Faber (auth), In Pursuit of Total Excellence, Focus, 77. *Mem:* Music Educr Nat Conf; Nat String Asn. *Mailing Add:* 170 Edgewood Pl Angwin CA 94508

PETERSON, MAX D
EDUCATOR, CONDUCTOR & MUSIC DIRECTOR
b Oskaloosa, Iowa, June 2, 42. *Study:* Univ Iowa, BM(music & voice), 64, MA(cond & choral lit), 66; Col-Consv Music Cincinnati, currently. *Pos:* Dir choral activ, WGa Col, 68-76; music dir & cond, Bach Choir Pittsburgh, 81- *Teaching:* Assoc prof music & dir choral activ, Carnegie Mellon Univ, 76- *Mem:* Am Choral Dir Asn (pres Ga chap, 71-73, chmn Pa Col & Univ chap, 80-); Am Choral Found; Riemenschneider Bach Inst; Neue Bach Gesellschaft; Asn Prof Vocal Ens. *Mailing Add:* Dept Music Carnegie Mellon Univ Pittsburgh PA 15213

PETERSON, WAYNE TURNER
COMPOSER, PIANO
b Albert Lea, Minn, Sept 3, 27. *Study:* Univ Minn, BA, 51, MA, 53, PhD, 60; Royal Acad Music, London, 53-54. *Works:* Free Variations, Boosey & Hawkes, 58; Metamorphoses (woodwind quintet), 67, Phantasmagoria (flute, clarinet & bass), 69 & Capriccio (flute & pianoforte), 73, Seesaw Music; Encounters (ens), perf by San Francisco Contemp Players, 76; An Interrupted Serenade (flute, harp & violoncello), Grenadilla, 79; Sextet (flute, clarinet, perc, harp, violin & violoncello), Speculum Musicae, 82. *Teaching:* Instr, Univ Minn, Minneapolis, 55-59; asst prof, Chico State Univ, Calif, 59-60; prof music, San Francisco State Univ, 60- *Awards:* Fulbright Scholar, 53-54; Nat Endowment Arts Comn, 76; Norman Fromm Comp Award, 82. *Mailing Add:* 810 Gonzalez Dr Apt 11A San Francisco CA 94132

PETHEL, JAMES L
COMPOSER, ORGAN
b Gainesville, Ga, Dec 24, 36. *Study:* Carson-Newman Col, BA, 59; George Peabody Col, MA, 60; studied with Phillip Slates & Arnold Salop. *Works:* Via Crucis, Intrada (organ), World Libr Publ, 72; Choral & Variations (organ), 74 & Morning Hymn (organ), 75, Lorenz Indust; We Look To Thee (choral anthem), Hinshaw Music, 78; Yours Is the Ship Lord, In My Fathers House (vocal solo), 79, Jesus, Priceless Treasure (organ collection), 80, M, Jesus, I Love Thee (piano collection), 81 & Of the Father's Love Begotton (organ collection), 82, Broadman Press; Sonata No 1 for Piano, 83. *Teaching:* Assoc prof music, Carson-Newman Col, 62- *Mem:* Am Guild Organists; ASCAP. *Mailing Add:* Rte 2 Box 255 Jefferson City TN 37760

PETHEL, STAN (STANLEY ROBERT)
COMPOSER, TROMBONE
b Gainesville, Ga, Feb 3, 50. *Study:* Univ Ga, BM, 72, MFA, 73; Univ Ky, DMA, 81. *Works:* Give Me Liberty, Damar Press, 76; Christ is Born, 80, Lift Up Your Voice, 82 & At the Name of Jesus, 82, Broadman Press; Simply Trusting, Hope Publ, 82; In the Eyes of Jesus, Alexander Broude Inc, 82; Jesus Came, Word Publ, 83. *Pos:* Band dir, Clark County Sch, 72-73. *Teaching:* Assoc prof theory & comp, Berry Col, 73. *Awards:* Nat Fedn Music Clubs Merit Award, 75-80. *Mem:* ASCAP; Music Educr Nat Conf; Ga Music Educr; Int Trombone Asn. *Mailing Add:* Box 91 Mt Berry GA 30149

PETIT, ANNIE
EDUCATOR, PIANO
Study: Ind Univ, with Gyorgy Sebok; studied with Benvenuti. *Pos:* Orch soloist & recitalist, Europe; founder & mem, Caecilian Trio, 75. *Teaching:* Artist in res, Univ Wis, Parkside, formerly; mem fac suppl piano, Curtis Inst Music, 74- *Awards:* First Prize Piano & Chamber Music, Nat Consv Music, 54; Interpretation Prize, Franz Liszt Compt, Budapest. *Mailing Add:* Curtis Inst Music 1726 Locust St Philadelphia PA 19103

PETROS, EVELYN
SOPRANO
b Washington, DC. *Study:* Am Univ, BA, 68; Bowling Green State Univ, BM(voice perf), 71. *Roles:* Dorabella in Cosi fan tutte, Santa Fe Opera, 77; Nina in The Seagull, Washington Opera, 78; Celia in La Fedelta Premiara, Glyndebourne Fest, England, 80; Cherubino in The Marriage of Figaro, Opera Theater St Louis, 81; Rosina in The Barber of Seville, Opera Co Boston, 81; L'Enfant in L'Enfant et les Sortileges, Metropolitan Opera, 81 & 83; Norina in Don Pasquale, Opera Omaha, 82. *Pos:* Sop soloist & recitalist, currently. *Awards:* First Place, Western Regional Auditions, Metropolitan Opera, 73; grants, Nat Opera Inst, 75 & Sullivan Musical Found, 83. *Mailing Add:* c/o Columbia Artists Mgt Inc 165 W 57th St New York NY 10019

PETTA, ROBERT MICHAEL
PERCUSSION, TEACHER
b Syracuse, NY, June 16, 49. *Study:* Onondaga Community Col, AA, 72; Manhattan Sch Music, BM, 74; studied with Morris Lang & Paul Price. *Pos:* Prin perc, Florida Symph, 74- *Teaching:* Instr perc, Valencia Community Col, 74-, Seminole Community Col, 74- & Univ Cent Fla, 79- *Mem:* Percussive Arts Soc. *Mailing Add:* 817 Carvell Dr Winter Park FL 32792

PEYTON, MALCOLM CAMERON
COMPOSER, EDUCATOR
b New York, NY, Jan 12, 32. *Study:* Princeton Univ, studied comp with Roger Sessions, BA, 54, MFA, 56; Nordwest Deutsche Hochschule Music, 56-57. *Works:* Sonnets from John Donne, Keith Kibbler, 68; Cello Piece 75, Choruses from e e cummings, 76 & The Blessed Virgin Compared to the Air We Breathe, 78, Mobart Music Publ; Songs from Walt Whitman, APNM, 81; Songs from Shakespeare, Mobart Music Publ, 82; Fantasies for Winds, Brass, Percussion, Stockholm Wind Symph Orch, 82. *Teaching:* Instr, Princeton Univ, 60-61; instr theory & comp, New England Consv, 65-79, chmn comp dept, 80- *Awards:* Fulbright Grant, 56; Nat Endowment Arts Grant, 76; Am Acad & Inst Arts Award, 80. *Mem:* BMI. *Mailing Add:* New England Consv 290 Huntington Rd Boston MA 02115

PFAUTSCH, LLOYD ALVIN
EDUCATOR, CONDUCTOR
b Washington, Mo, Sept 14, 21. *Study:* Elmhurst Col, BA, 43; Union Theol Sem, MDiv, 46, MSM, 48; Elmhurst Col, Hon DMus, 59; Ill Wesleyan Univ, LHD, 77. *Works:* God With Us, Lawson-Gould Music Publ, 62 & 78; Seven Words of Love, Hope Publ, 64 & 83; A Day For Dancing, 69, Gloria, 71 & Befana, 77, Lawson-Gould Music Publ; also over 200 choral comp & arr. *Teaching:* Prof, Ill Wesleyan Univ, 48-58; vis prof, Univ Ill, Champaign, 56-57; prof music & dir choral activ, Southern Methodist Univ, 58- *Awards:* ASCAP Awards, 59- *Mem:* Am Choral Dir Asn; Phi Mu Alpha; Pi Kappa Lambda; ASCAP. *Publ:* Auth, Mental Warm Ups For the Choral Conductor, 69 & English Diction For the Singer, 71, Lawson-Gould Music Publ; Choral Conducting: A Symposium, 73. *Mailing Add:* 3710 Euclid Ave Dallas TX 75205

PFEUFFER, ROBERT JOHN
BASSOON & CONTRABASSOON
b Cleveland, Ohio, Dec 25, 25. *Study:* Univ Mich, BMus, 51, MMus, 52. *Pos:* Bassoon & contrabassoon, Detroit Symph Orch, 52-62 & Philadelphia Orch, 62- *Teaching:* Instr bassoon, Wayne State Univ, Mich, 56-62; instr bassoon & wind ens, New Sch Music, Pa, 65-81. *Mailing Add:* 29 Mountwell Ave Haddonfield NJ 08033

PHELPS, NORMAN F
EDUCATOR, COMPOSER
b Beaver Dam, Wis, Apr 27, 11. *Study:* Univ Wis, with Cecil Burleigh; Univ Iowa, with Philip Greeley Clapp. *Works:* Dramatic Overture (orch), 46; Horn Sonata, 47; Noel, Phantasy (orch), 48; Oboe Sonata, 51; 2 Pieces (band), 60; Univ Story (film score), Ohio State Univ; The Ostrack Story, for NASA. *Teaching:* Fac mem, Jordan Consv, Ind, 35-49 & Ohio State Univ, 49- *Mailing Add:* 363 Triumph Way Columbus OH 43230

PHELPS, ROGER PAUL
ADMINISTRATOR, EDUCATOR
b Batavia, NY, Sept 6, 20. *Study:* Eastman Sch Music, BMus, 41; Northwestern Univ, 47; Univ Iowa, PhD, 51. *Teaching:* Coordr grad music, Univ Southern Miss, 51-59; prof music educ, NY Univ, 70-, chmn dept music & music educ, 82- *Awards:* US Off Educr Res Grant, 65 & 66. *Mem:* Miss Music Teachers Asn (pres, 56-58); Music Teachers Nat Asn (cert chmn, 60-63); Jour Res Music Educ; Music Educr Nat Conf (Chair music ed res coun, 64-66); NY State Sch Music Asn (chmn higher educ, 82-). *Publ:* Auth, The Psychology of Music and Its Literature, 75 & The Doctoral Dissertation: Boon or Bane?, 78, Col Music Symposium; A Guide to Research in Music Education, 2nd ed, Scarecrow Press, 80; The First Earned Doctorate in Music Education, Bulletin of Historical Res Music Ed, 83. *Mailing Add:* Room 777 Educ Bldg NY Univ 35 W Fourth St New York NY 10003

PHILIPS, JOHN (DOUGLASS)
PIANO, EDUCATOR
b Stanton, Tenn, Dec 20, 32. *Study:* Rollins Col, BM, 54; Ecole Normale Musique Paris, conct licence, 56; Peabody Consv Music, DMA, 77; private study with Alfred Cortot & Nadia Boulanger. *Teaching:* Assoc prof music, Fontbonne Col, currently. *Mem:* Am Musicol Soc; Col Music Soc; Music Teachers Nat Asn. *Interests:* Model language of Oliver Messiaen. *Publ:* Auth, Cortot Remembered, Clavier, 77. *Rep:* Byers Schwalbe One Fifth Ave New York NY 10003. *Mailing Add:* 4441 Arco Ave St Louis MO 63110

PHILIPS, MARY KATHRYN
EDUCATOR, PIANO
b Fallon, Nev, Nov 9, 25. *Study:* George Pepperdine Col, BA, 46; Claremont Grad Sch, MA, 48; Univ Calif, Los Angeles, PhD, 65. *Pos:* Ed, The Triangle of Mu Phi Epsilon, Mu Phi Epsilon, 75-80. *Teaching:* Instr & asst prof music, Pepperdine Col, 48-58; from asst prof to assoc prof, Calif Western Univ, 59-70, chmn dept music, 66-70; asst prof, Sch Perf Visual Arts, US Int Univ, 70-, actg head music div, 71-72. *Mem:* Am Musicol Soc; Col Music Soc; Int Musicol Soc; Music Libr Asn; Mu Phi Epsilon. *Interests:* Arioso recitative, emphasis on contemporary opera. *Mailing Add:* 4523 Orchard Ave San Diego CA 92107

PHILLIPS, BURRILL
COMPOSER, EDUCATOR
b Omaha, Nebr, Nov 9, 07. *Study:* Denver Col Music; Eastman Sch Music, BMus, 32, MM, 33. *Works:* Scherzo (orch), League Comp & City Symph New York, 44; Tom Paine (orch), Koussevitsky Found, Wallenstein & Columbia Univ, 46; Return of Odysseus (chorus & orch), Fromm Found, Robert Shaw, & Univ Ill Choir & Orch, 57; Second String Quartet, Elizabeth Coolidge Found, Paganini Quartet & Libr Cong, 59; Quartet for Oboe & Strings, Netherlands Oboe Quartet, Hilversum, Holland, 66-; Canzona V (chorus & piano), Claire Richards & Collegiate Chorale, Univ Ill, 71; The Unforgiven (opera), Nat Endowment Arts, 82. *Teaching:* Theory & comp, Eastman Sch Music, 33-49; prof music, Univ Ill, Urbana-Champaign, 49-64; vis prof, Juilliard Sch Music, 68-69 & Cornell Univ, 72-73. *Awards:* Guggenheim Found Music Compt Award, 42-43 & 61-62; Fulbright Grant, Spain, 60-61. *Mem:* ASCAP. *Mailing Add:* RD #1 Italy Hill Turnpike Branchport NY 14418

PHILLIPS, EUGENE WALTER
COMPOSER, VIOLIN
b Pittsburgh, Pa, July 28, 19. *Study:* Carnegie-Mellon Univ, studied violin with Hugo Kolberg & comp with Nicolai Lopatnikoff, 48-50; spec study with John Cage, 48. *Works:* Duo Concertante (violin & piano), perf by Eugene & Natalie Phillips with Chatham Col Contemp Music Fest, 53; Two Songs from Sonnets, Pittsburgh New Music Ensemble, 78; Fantasy (solo violin), perf by Daniel Phillips, 76; Portrait (solo viola), perf by Geraldine Walther in Munich & Steven Ansell in Pittsburgh, 78; Little Match Girl Cantata, perf by Eugene, Natalie, Daniel, Todd & Amy Phillips, 78; Interlude & Caprice (solo harp), perf by Gretchen Van Hoesen, 79 & Prelude, Toccata & Adagio, perf by Andre Previn with Pittsburgh Symph, 81. *Pos:* First violin, Pittsburgh Symph Orch, 48-54 & 65-; first violin & founder, Phillips String Quartet, 48- *Teaching:* Private teaching, 54; artist & lectr violin, viola & chamber music, Carnegie-Mellon Univ, 76- *Mem:* ASCAP; Pittsburgh Alliance Comp. *Mailing Add:* 5829 Northumberland St Pittsburgh PA 15217

PHILLIPS, HARVEY GENE
TUBA, EDUCATOR
b Aurora, Mo, Dec, 2, 29. *Study:* Univ Mo, 47-78; Juilliard Sch Music, 50-54; Manhattan Sch Music, 56-58; New England Consv Music, Hon MusD, 71. *Rec Perf:* Rec artist, Crest Rec, 58- *Pos:* Tubist, King Brothers Circus Band, 47, Ringling Brothers & Barnum & Bailey Circus Band, 48-50, New York City Ballet Orch, 51-71, Voice of Firestone Orch, 51-53, Sauter-Finegan Orch, 52-53, Band of Am, 52-54, NBC Opera Orch, 56-65, Bell Telephone Hour Orch, 56-66, Goodman Band, 57-62 & Fest Casal Orch, San Juan, PR, 64-76; founding mem & tubist, NY Brass Quintet, 54-67; exec vpres, personnel mgr & tubist, Symph of Air, New York, 57-66; vpres, Mentor Music Inc, NY, 58-79, Wilder Music Inc, 64-77 & Magellen Music Inc, 71-; cond & co-producer, Burke-Phillips All Star Conct Band, 60-62; exec vpres, Orch USA, New York, 62-65; vpres, Brass Artists Inc, NY, 64-; dir, First Int Tuba Symposium Workshop, 73; co-founder & producer, Matteson-Phillips Tubajazz Consort, 76-; originator, Octubafest. *Teaching:* Mem fac, Aspen Sch Music, summer 62, Univ Wis, summer 63, Hartt Sch Music, Univ Hartford, 62-64 & Mannes Sch Music, 64-65; admin asst to Julius Bloom, Rutgers Univ, 66-67; asst to pres financial affairs, New England Consv Music, 67-71; mem fac dept music, Ind Univ, Bloomington, 71-, distinguished prof, 79- *Awards:* Harvey Phillips Day Celebration, New England Consv Music, 71; Community Serv Award, Bloomington, Ind, 78. *Mem:* Am Fedn Musicians; Tubists Universal Brotherhood Asn (pres, 84-); Phi Mu Alpha Sinfonia; Mid-Am Fest Arts (bd mem, 82-); Bloomington Area Arts Coun. *Mailing Add:* Tubaranch 4769 S Harrell Rd Bloomington IN 47405

PHILO, GARY BRUCE
COMPOSER, ELECTRONIC BASS
b Jersey City, NJ, Apr 8, 53. *Study:* Berklee Col Music, BM(comp), 76; New England Consv Music, MM(comp), 79. *Works:* Outbursts & Reflections for Orchestra, Vt Phil, 81; Two Pieces for Solo Piano, Comp in Red Sneakers, 81; Three Pieces for Orchestra, New England Consv Youth Orch, 82; Sonata (two violins), Comp in Red Sneakers, 82; Trio (violin, clarinet & piano), Collage, 83; A New Work for Chamber Orchestra, comn by Pro Arte Chamber Orch, Boston, 83; Dreamtinge (tape & dancers), Peg Hill & Bicycle Shop Dancers, 83. *Pos:* Co-founder, Comp in Red Sneakers, Boston, Mass, 81-82. *Teaching:* Instr music, Regis Col, 80- *Mailing Add:* 20 Bigelow St Brighton MA 02135

PHILPOTT, LARRY LAFAYETTE
FRENCH HORN, EDUCATOR
b Alma, Ark, Apr 5, 37. *Pos:* Second horn, NC Symph, 59-60; prin horn, Savannah Symph, 60-62, Indianapolis Symph Orch, 64- & Flagstaff Fest, 67-; third horn, L'Orch Symph Quebec, 62-64. *Teaching:* Prof horn, DePauw Univ, 71- & Butler Univ, 72-; artist-in-res, Ind Univ, Indianapolis & Purdue Univ, 79- *Mem:* Int Horn Soc; Int Conf Symph & Opera Musicians; Am Fedn Musicians; Col Music Soc. *Mailing Add:* 740 Spring Mill Ln Indianapolis IN 46240

PICK, RICHARD SAMUEL BURNS
GUITAR, TEACHER
b St Paul, Minn, Oct 20, 15. *Study:* Univ Ill; Chicago Univ; DePaul Univ, BS. *Rec Perf:* Richard Pick Guitar, MLR; Americana & Guitarra Expanola, Bally; Above & Beyond, IRC. *Teaching:* Prof guitar, DePaul Univ, 70-, Richard Pick Sch Guitar, 73- & Sherwood Music Sch, 80- *Mem:* Am Fedn Musicians; founder, Chicago Guitar Soc (pres & chmn, 50-75); ASCAP. *Publ:* Auth, First Lessons for Classic Guitar, Book I, 52, 59 & 71, Fundamental Fingerboard Harmony, 53 & 66, Lessons for Classic Guitar, Book II, 55, Introduction to Guitar, 59 & Introduction to Effective Accompaniment for Guitar, 66, Forster Music Publ Inc. *Mailing Add:* 9136 Sheridan Ave Brookfield IL 60513

PICKER, MARTIN
EDUCATOR, WRITER
b Chicago, Ill, Apr 3, 29. *Study:* Univ Chicago, PhB, 47, MA, 51; Univ Calif, Berkeley, PhD, 60. *Teaching:* Instr, Univ Ill, Urbana-Champaign, 59-61; asst prof, Rutgers Univ, 61-65, assoc prof, 65-68, prof, 68- *Awards:* I Tatti Fel, Harvard Univ, 66; Nat Endowment Humanities Sr Fel, 72. *Mem:* Am Musicol Soc; Int Musicol Soc; Italian Musicol Soc; Dutch Musicol Soc; Renaissance Soc Am. *Interests:* History of music, primarily Renaissance music. *Publ:* Auth, The Chanson Albums of Marguerite of Austria, Univ Calif Press, 65; A Letter of Charles VIII of France, Aspects Medieval & Renaissance Music, 66; coauth (with M Bernstein), An Introductin to Music, Prentice-Hall, 66 & 72; auth, Josquiniana in Some Manuscripts at Piacenza, Josquin Prez, 77; ed, Fors Seulement: 30 Compositions, A-R Ed, 81. *Mailing Add:* 16 Barker Rd Somerset NJ 08873

PICKER, TOBIAS
COMPOSER
b New York, NY, 1954. *Study:* Juilliard Sch; Manhattan Sch Music; Princeton Univ, with Milton Babbitt, Elliott Carter & Charles Wuorinen. *Works:* Nova (violin, viola, cello, contrabass, piano), 79, Concerto No 1 (piano & orch), 81, The Blue Hula (flute, clarinet, perc, violin, cello, piano), 82, Violin Concerto (violin & orch), 82, Symph No 1, 83, Keys to the City (Piano Concerto No 2), 83 & The Encantadas (symph orch), 83, Helicon Music Corp/European Am. *Rec Perf:* Rhapsody, When Soft Voices Die, Sextet 3, Romance, 80 & Violin Concerto, 82, CRI. *Awards:* Nat Endowment Arts Comp Fel, 79 & 81; Charles Ives Scholar, 79; Guggenheim Fel, 81. *Mem:* Am Comp Alliance; BMI. *Mailing Add:* 255 W 108th St New York NY 10025

PIERCE, ALEXANDRA
COMPOSER, WRITER
b Philadelphia, Pa, Feb 21, 34. *Study:* Univ Michigan, BMus, 55; New England Consv Music, MMus, 58; Radcliffe Col, MA(music); Brandeis Univ, PhD(theory & comp), 68. *Works:* Behemoth (orch), Seesaw Music, 76; The Great Horned Owl (kelon marimba), Music Perc, 77; Buffalo Bill (clarinet, voice & tape), comn & perf by Clarinet & Friend, 77; Quartet, Music Dance (for clarinet, horn, marimba, prep piano), comn & perf by Eyes Wide Open Dance Repty, Los Angeles, 78; Job 22:28 (two clarinets), Seesaw Music, 78; Resurrection (SATB, flute & piano), Arsis Press, 79. *Pos:* Movement consult, Heller Method Training Prog, San Francisco, 78-80. *Teaching:* Danforth assoc humanities, Antioch Col, Ohio, 66-67; prof music & movement, Univ Redlands, 68-; movement teacher, Movement Enhancement Prof Training, Redlands, 81- *Awards:* First Prize, Mu Phi Epsilon Nat Comp Cont, 77 & 79; Standard Awards, ASCAP, 79- *Mem:* Am Women Comp (nat vpres, 78-83); Int League Women Comp; Soc Music Theory; Am Soc Univ Comp; ASCAP. *Publ:* Auth, Metric Structure, Parts I and II, Piano Quart, 77; Structure and Phrase, Parts I, II, III, In Theory Only, 80-83; coauth, Pain and Healing: For Pianists, Piano Quart, 82-; auth, Action and Reaction in Prepared Piano, Am Soc Univ Comp Article Ser, 83; Spanning: Essays in Music Theory, Performance and Movement, Univ Redlands, 83. *Mailing Add:* 126 E Fern Ave Redlands CA 92373

PIERCE, LORRIE (LORRIE PIERCE GLAZE)
EDUCATOR, PIANO
b LaCrosse, Wis, Dec 26, 39. *Study:* Southern Methodist Univ, studied with Gyorgy Sandor, BM, 61; Univ Mich, MM, 63; Columbia Univ Teachers Col; Aspen Sch Music, studied piano with Alexander Uninsky & Rosina Lhevinne; Music Acad West. *Pos:* Pianist, Dallas Opera, 58-61; coach & pianist, Santa Fe Opera, 66; asst musical dir, Metropolitan Opera Studio, 67-70; staff accmp, Martha Baird Rockefeller Fund Music, 75-81. *Teaching:* Instr masterclasses, Wesleyan Col, Ga, Stetson Univ, Fla & Stevens Col, Mo; guest instr, Fla Southern Col, Jersey City State Col & Colo Col; instr piano, Manhattan Sch Music, 70-, pianist & coach, Opera Wkshp, 70-78; instr piano, St Thomas Choir Sch, 78-; instr music, Interlochen Nat Music Camp, 81. *Mailing Add:* 107 W 86th St #12A New York NY 10024

PIERCE, ROBERT
FRENCH HORN, ADMINISTRATOR
Study: New England Consv, BM, MM; Berkshire Music Ctr. *Pos:* Prin horn, Baltimore Symph Orch, 58-81, assoc prin horn, 80-; freelance perf, Boston Symph Orch, Hartford Symph Orch & RI Symph Orch, formerly; mem, Baltimore Symph Orch Woodwind Quintet, currently; founding mem, Baltimore Chamber Players, currently. *Teaching:* Mem fac, New England Consv, formerly & Philips-Andover Acad, formerly; assoc dir, acting dean, French horn & brass ens, Peabody Consv, currently. *Mem:* Baltimore Chamber Music Soc (mem bd dir, currently). *Mailing Add:* Peabody Consv Music Baltimore MD 21202

PIERSON, EDWARD
BARITONE, EDUCATOR
b Chicago, Ill. *Study:* Roosevelt Univ, BA. *Rec Perf:* Carry Nation, Desto Rec, 70; Treemonisha, Deutsche Grammophon, 76; Edward Pierson Sings Hymns & Spirituals, KEM Rec, 79. *Roles:* Prince Igor in Prince Igor, 69, Boris Ismailov, 70, Scarpia in Tosca, 72, Jochanaan in Salome, 76, The Flying Dutchman, 77, Alfio in Cavalleria Rusticana, 77 & Don Basilio in The Marriage of Figaro, 78, New York City Opera. *Pos:* Soloist, New York City Opera, 66-77. *Teaching:* Assoc prof voice, Montclair State Col, 83- *Awards:* Grants, Martha Baird Rockefeller, 68 & 69. *Mem:* Am Guild Musical Artists (bd mem, 68-76); Actor's Equity Asn; Affil Artists. *Mailing Add:* 72 Summit Rd Elizabeth NJ 07208

PIERSON, THOMAS CLAUDE
EDUCATOR, WRITER

b Houston, Tex, May 13, 22. *Study:* Univ Nebr, BM, 43; Northwestern Univ, MM, 47; Eastman Sch Music, Univ Rochester, PhD, 52. *Teaching:* Assoc prof music, dept chmn & orch cond, Univ Houston, 54-62; assoc prof orch & cond, Mt St Mary's Col, Los Angeles, 62-66; prof & dept chmn, Tex A&I Univ, 66- *Awards:* Grant, Tex A&I Univ, 69 & 76; Nat Endowment Humanities Fel, 81-82. *Mem:* Tex Music Educr Conf; Music Educr Nat Conf; Col Music Soc; Int Soc Music Ed; Am Asn Univ Prof (chap treas, 81-82). *Publ:* Auth, The Songs of John Alden Carpenter, 62 & Teaching Basic Principles, 62, Tex Music Teachers; Integrate Comprehension and Performance, Clavier Mag, 63. *Mailing Add:* 5909 Fenway Dr Corpus Christi TX 78413

PIKLER, CHARLES ROBERT
VIOLIN

b Monrovia, Calif, Sept 5, 51. *Study:* Univ Minn, BA; Univ Conn, with Bronislaw Gimpel; Berkshire Music Ctr, with Roman Totenberg; studied with Ben Ornstein. *Pos:* Violinist, Minneapolis Symph, formerly, Cleveland Orch, formerly & Rotterdam Phil Orch, 76-78; mem first violin sect, Chicago Symph Orch, currently. *Mailing Add:* Chicago Symph Orch 220 S Michigan Ave Chicago IL 60604

PILAND, JEANNE SMITH
MEZZO-SOPRANO

b Raleigh, NC, Dec 3, 45. *Study:* ECarolina Univ, BMus, MMus. *Roles:* Cherubino in Le Nozze di Figaro, La Scala, Milan, 81; Count Rofrano in Der Rosenkavalier, 82. *Pos:* Ms with opera co, festivals & TV sta throughout US & Europe. *Awards:* Prize Winner, Baltimore Opera Auditions, 72-73; Grants, Martha Baird Rockefeller Found, 75, Nat Opera Inst, 76 & others. *Mem:* Pi Kappa Lambda; Sigma Alpha Iota. *Mailing Add:* c/o Spectrum Concertbureau 205 E 63rd St New York NY 10021

PILGRIM, NEVA STEVENS
SOPRANO

b Cottonwood Co, Minn. *Study:* Hamline Univ, with Robert Holliday, BA, 60; Yale Univ, with Blake Stern, MM, 62; Vienna Acad Music, with Kolo & Werba, 63. *Rec Perf:* Carissimi & Stradella Cantatas, Spectrum Rec, 83; George Rochberg, Songs in Praise of Krishna & Moonsongs & Haiku of Basho, CRI; Ernst Krenek, Songs with Piano & Instruments, Orion; Songs of Ecstasy, Desto; Cantatas (Stradella) & Cantatas (Scarlatti), Musical Heritage; Six Dark Questions, Redwood. *Roles:* Gilda in Rigoletto, Vienna Volksoper, 64; Mrs Popov in Brute, Chicago Contemp Chamber Players & CBS TV, 66; Juliette in Romeo et Juliette, Pamina in Die Zauberflöte, Mimi in La Boheme & Marguerite in Faust, Tri Cities Opera, 71-75; La Voix Humaine, perf across the US & Can. *Awards:* Ditson Fel, Yale Univ, 62; Martha Baird Rockefeller Grant, 67; Cert Merit, Sch Music, Yale Univ, 78. *Mem:* Am Music Ctr (bd mem, 80-); Nat Endowment Arts; NY State Coun Arts; Nat Asn Teachers Singing. *Mailing Add:* c/o Liegner Mgt 1860 Broadway Suite 1610 New York NY 10023

PILLIN, BORIS WILLIAM
COMPOSER

b Chicago, Ill, May 31, 40. *Study:* Univ Calif, Los Angeles, BA, 64; Univ Southern Calif, MA, 67. *Works:* Sonata for Clarinet & Piano, 68, Duo for Piano & Percussion, 71, Three Pieces for Double-Reed Septet, 72, Sonata for Cello & Piano, 76, Serenade for Piano & Woodwind Quintet, 76, Four Scenes for Three Trumpets & Piano, 79 & Concerto for Strings & Percussion, 81, Western Int Music. *Pos:* Music engraver for photo-offset, 67-; exec vpres, Western Int Music, 69-83. *Awards:* Woodrow Wilson Found Fel, 64-65; ASCAP Suppl Panel Award, 71-74. *Mem:* ASCAP; Nat Asn Comp; Am Soc Univ Comp. *Publ:* Auth, Some Aspects of Counterpoint in Selected Works of Arnold Schoenberg, Western Int Music, 70. *Mailing Add:* 4913 Melrose Ave Los Angeles CA 90029

PING-ROBBINS, NANCY R(EGAN)
WRITER, HARPSICHORD

b Nashville, Tenn, Dec 19, 39. *Study:* Sch Music, Ind Univ, Bloomington, BMus, 64; Univ Northern Colo, MA, 72; Univ Colo, Boulder, PhD, 79. *Rec Perf:* Early Popluar Music on the Virginal, 83 & Early Popular Music on the Piano, 83, Robbins Rec, 83. *Pos:* Music critic, Raleigh News & Observer, 81- *Teaching:* From instr to asst prof music, Univ NC, Wilmington, 74-79; assoc prof & coordr music dept, Shaw Univ, 79- *Awards:* Grant, United Negro Col Fund, Mellon Found, 82. *Mem:* Sonneck Soc; Am Musicol Soc (secy-treas regional chap, 81-83); Soc Ethnomusicol (secy-treas regional chap, 82-83 & chmn, 83-); Country Music Found. *Interests:* Bibliography of 20th century piano trios; black gospel groups in central North Carolina; music teachers & composers in the Antebellum South. *Publ:* Auth, New Music and Audiences, 2/1/76 & Minstrel Shows: How Stereotypes Developed, 4/10/77, Wilmington Star News, NC; Black Musical Activities in Antebellum Wilmington, NC, Black Perspective Music, fall 80; A Bibliography of Twentieth Century Piano Trios, Regan Press, 83; Music in North Carolina, In: New Grove Dict of Music in US (in prep). *Rep:* William E Robbins Jr 4600 Paisley Ct Raleigh NC 27604. *Mailing Add:* Box 58265 Raleigh NC 27658

PINK, HOWARD NORMAN
FRENCH HORN

b Los Angeles, Calif, May 10, 43. *Study:* Ariz State Univ, BM(French horn), 66. *Pos:* French hornist, Aspen Fest Orch, 64-; founder & mem, Original Aspen Horn Quartet, 72-; prin second French horn, New Orleans Phil, 73- *Mem:* Phi Mu Alpha Sinfonia (secy, 64, pres, 66). *Mailing Add:* 841 Fairfield Ave Gretna LA 70053

PINKHAM, DANIEL
COMPOSER, EDUCATOR

b Lynn, Mass, June 5, 23. *Study:* Harvard Col, AB, 43; Harvard Univ, MA 44. *Works:* Christmas Cantata, Robert King Music Co, 58; Organ Concerto, C F Peters Corp, 70; To Troubled Friends, 72, Masks (harpsichord concerto), 74, The Passion of Judas, 76, Brass Quintet, 83 & The Dreadful Dining Car (opera), 83, E C Schirmer Music Co. *Pos:* Music dir, King's Chapel, Boston, 57- *Teaching:* Vis lectr, Harvard Univ, 57-58; chmn, Early Music Dept, New England Consv, 58- *Awards:* Fulbright Award, 57; fel, Ford Found, 65; St Botolph Club Award, 81. *Mem:* Am Guild Organists; Am Acad Arts & Sci; Am Comp Alliance. *Mailing Add:* 150 Chilton St Cambridge MA 02138

PINKOW, DAVID J
FRENCH HORN, EDUCATOR

b Buffalo, NY, Nov 25, 44. *Study:* Eastman Sch Music, studied with Verne Reynolds, perf cert & BM, 66; Carnegie Mellon Univ, MFA, 68; Univ Md, currently. *Pos:* Asst prin horn, Rochester Phil Orch, 64-66; second horn, Pittsburgh Symph Orch, 66-68; third horn, Atlanta Symph Orch, 78-79. *Teaching:* Instr horn, Univ Ga, 74-80; asst prof, Univ Colo, 80- *Mem:* Int Horn Soc (Colo area rep, currently); Chamber Music Am; Music Educr Nat Conf; Music Teachers Nat Asn; Colo Music Educr Asn. *Mailing Add:* c/o LDP Artist Mgt 4610 Greenbriar Boulder CO 80303

PINNELL, RICHARD TILDEN
EDUCATOR, GUITAR & LUTE

b Whittier, Calif, Jan 9, 42. *Study:* Univ Utah; Brigham Young Univ, BA, 67, MA, 69; Univ Calif, Los Angeles, DPhil, 73, PhD, 76. *Teaching:* Fel, Univ Calif, Los Angeles, 70-75; instr, Santa Monica Col, 72-73, Los Angeles City Col, 72-77, Los Angeles Valley Col, 74-77 & Mt San Antonio Col, 76-77; asst prof, Univ Wis, Stevens Pt, 77- *Awards:* Scholar of Yr, Univ Wis, Stevens Pt, 81. *Mem:* Am Musicol Soc; Am Fedn Musicians; Guitar Found Am; Univ Wis Ctr Latin Am; Lute Soc Am. *Interests:* History of the guitar; history of jazz. *Publ:* Auth, Alternate Sources for ... Francesco Corbetta, J Lute Soc Am, 76; The Theorboed Guitar ... In: Books of Granata & Gallot, Early Music, 7/79; Francesco Corbetta and the Baroque Guitar, UMI Res Press, Ann Arbor, 80; F Corbetta: Chitarrista Barocco alla corte d'Ing, Fronimo, 10/81; La Guitarre Royalle: A Symposium ... at Fullerton, Soundboard, spring 82. *Mailing Add:* 712 Leonard St Stevens Point WI 54481

PINNELL, RUTH
EDUCATOR

b Kansas, Ill, Aug 30, 17. *Study:* La State Univ, BMus, 39; Univ Ill, MMus, 41; studied with Maggie Teyte, London, England, 64. *Teaching:* Instr voice, Yankton Col, 42-44 & Stephens Col, 44-47; asst prof, Univ Ky, 47-49; prof voice & vocal lit, Syracuse Univ, 49-83. *Awards:* Sword of Honor, 62 & Rose of Honor, 69, Sigma Alpha Iota. *Mem:* Nat Asn Teachers Singing; Music Teachers Nat Asn; Pi Kappa Lambda; Sigma Alpha Iota (Eta province pres, 63-68). *Rep:* 311 Arnold Ave Syracuse NY 13210. *Mailing Add:* PO Box 304 Kansas IL 61933

PINNER, JAY-MARTIN
VIOLA, EDUCATOR

b Montgomery Co, Md, Dec 4, 53. *Study:* With Ellis Chasens; Bob Jones Univ, with Dwight Gustafson & Joan Mulfinger, BA(sacred music), 76, MA(violin), 77; Univ NH, with Hans Nebel, cert(string instrm repair), 81. *Pos:* Concertmaster, Bob Jones Univ Symph, 73-75; prin viola, 78-80; prin viola, Greenville Symph, 81-; violist, Fac String Quartet, Bob Jones Univ, 82- *Teaching:* Instr private string & sch orch, Bob Jones Univ, 75-, head string dept, 82- *Mem:* Music Educr Nat Conf; Nat Sch Orch Asn; Am Viola Soc; Am String Teachers Asn (vpres SC Chap, 78-82 & pres, 82-). *Publ:* Auth, Cello Choir in South Carolina, Am String Teachers Asn Mag, 83. *Mailing Add:* 8 Faculty Row Greenville SC 29609

PISK, PAUL A(MADEUS)
COMPOSER, EDUCATOR

b Vienna, Austria, May 16, 1893; US citizen. *Study:* Vienna Consv, dipl, 16; Vienna Univ, PhD, 18; Univ Vienna, Hon Dr, 69. *Works:* Partitta (orch), Int Soc Contemp Music U E Music Fest, 25; Passacaglia (orch), perf by Zurich Symph, 53; Three Ceremonial Rites (orch), St Louis Symph, 66; numerous chamber, choral & solo works published by Universal Editions, Vienna, Schirmer, Carl Fischer Assoc Publ & others. *Pos:* Dir, Sch Music, Univ Redlands, 37-50. *Teaching:* Prof, Univ Tex, 50-63 & Wash Univ, 63-72; various summer teaching positions from 39-74. *Bibliog:* Essays In Honor of Paul A Pisk, Univ Tex Press, 65. *Mem:* Am Musicol Soc; Music Libr Asn; Pi Kappa Lambda Sinfonia; Am Comp Alliance; hon mem, Musical Theatres Asn. *Mailing Add:* 2724 Westshire Dr Los Angeles CA 90068

PITTMAN, RICHARD
CONDUCTOR

b Baltimore, Md, June 3, 35. *Study:* Peabody Consv, BMus, 57; Accad Musicale Chigiana, Siena, Italy, 61; Staatliche Hochschule Musik, Hamburg, 63-65; studied with Laszlo Halasz, Sergiu Celibidache & Pierre Boulez. *Rec Perf:* Premiere Performances by Boston Musica Viva, 71 & Boston Musica Viva Plays, 71, Delos; Microtonal Music (Ezra Sims, CRI, 77; New American Music, Nonesuch, 78; American Contemporary Music, CRI, 80; Music of Ellen Taaffe Zwilich, Cambridge, 81; Alarums & Excursions, Northeastern, 82. *Pos:* Music dir, Boston Musica Viva, 69-; cond, Concord Orch, 69-; guest cond, BBC Symph, London, England, BBC Jones Sinfonietta, BBC Phil, Manchester, England, BBC Welsh Symph, Cardiff, Frankfurt Radio Symph, Germany, Nat Symph, Washington, DC & Va Phil. *Teaching:* Instr cond & opera, Eastman Sch Music, 65-68; teacher orch cond, New England Consv, 68- *Mailing Add:* 41 Bothfeld Rd Newton Center MA 02159

PIZER, ELIZABETH FAW HAYDEN
COMPOSER, PIANO
b Watertown, NY, Sept 1, 54. *Study:* Boston Consv Music, Drama & Dance. *Works:* Fanfare Overture, San Jose State Univ Symphonic Band, 79; Five Haiku (sop & chamber ens) Am Soc Univ Comp Nat Conf, Memphis, Tenn, 80; Interfuguelude, Honolulu Symph Orch String Quartet, 80; Expressions Intime, Max Lifchitz, 81; Madrigals Anon, San Francisco Chamber Singers, 82; Sunken Flutes (electronic-tape), Inst Sonology, Utrecht, Holland, 82; When to the Sessions of Sweet, Silent Thought, Marla Kensey, 83. *Pos:* Broadcast coordr & producer, KCSM-FM, San Mateo, Calif, 81- *Teaching:* Coach & accompanist, San Jose State Univ, 78-80. *Awards:* Delius Prize for Best of Category, 82; Nat League Am Pen Women Prize for Vocal Solo Category, 82; Nat Assoc Comp, USA Cert Merit, 83. *Mem:* Int League Women Comp (chairperson, 82-); Am Music Ctr; Nat League Am Pen Women; Nat Asn Comp, USA; Am Soc Univ Comp. *Mailing Add:* PO Box 42 Three Mile Bay NY 13693

PIZZARO, DAVID ALFRED
ORGAN, MUSIC DIRECTOR
b Mt Vernon, NY, May 15, 31. *Study:* Sch Music, Yale Univ, MusB, 52, MusM, 53; Staatliche MusiK Akad, Detmold, Ger, 53-55; studied with Michael Schneider, Marcel Dupre, Kurt Thomas & Wolfgang Fortner. *Rec Perf:* David Pizarro Plays the Organ of Bradford Cathedral, Grosvenor, 70; Music of Holy Russia, Cambridge Russian Chorus, 71; Christmas Eve at the Cathedral, Vanguard, 75; 75 Years of Cathedral Music, Cathedral St John Divine, 76. *Pos:* Organist, St Philip's Protestant Episcopal Church, Durham, NC, 58-64, First Church, Congregational, Cambridge, Mass, 69-71 & St Stephen's Protestant Episcopal Church, Providence, RI, 72-74; organist & master choristers, Cathedral Church St John Divine, New York, 74-77; titular organist, 77- *Teaching:* Instr, Cent NC Univ, 59-65, Univ NC, Chapel Hill, 60-61 & Longy Sch Music, 65-71. *Awards:* Sherman Organ Prize, Yale Univ, 53; Fulbright Grant, 53; Deutscher Akad Austauschdienst Stipend, 54. *Mem:* Royal Col Organist; Am Guild Organists (dean & founder Durham chap, 60-63, dean Westchester chap, 80-82). *Publ:* Contribr, The Burial Office, 71 & Musica de Adventu Domini, 79, Anglican Soc. *Mailing Add:* 29 Pearl St Mt Vernon NY 10550

PLANTAMURA, CAROL LYNN
SOPRANO, EDUCATOR
b Los Angeles, Calif, Feb 8, 41. *Study:* Occidental Col, BA, 64; State Univ NY, with Heinz Rehfuss, MFA, 78. *Rec Perf:* Accord (Vinko Globokan), Wergo, 68; Rara Requiem (Sylvano Bussotti), DGG, 71; Madrigali a uno, due e tre voci di Luzzasco Luzzaschi, 78, Mottetti e Madrigali di Claudio Monteverdi, 80 & Arie di Girolamo Frescobaldi, 82, Italia; Academic Grafitti, Gramavision, 82; The Idea of Order at Key West, CRI, 83. *Pos:* Freelance musician in Europe, Australia, New Zealand & Japan, 66- *Teaching:* Prof voice & music lit, Univ Calif, San Diego, 78- *Awards:* Premio alla Scala, Int Soc Contemp Music, 73. *Interests:* Development of dialogue in 17th century opera; women musicians. *Mailing Add:* 9670 Caminito del Vida San Diego CA 92121

PLANTINGA, LEON BROOKS
MUSICOLOGIST, EDUCATOR
b Ann Arbor, Mich, Mar 25, 35. *Study:* Calvin Col, BA, 57; Mich State Univ, MMus, 59; Yale Univ, PhD(music hist), 64. *Teaching:* From instr to assoc prof, Yale Univ, 63-74, prof music hist, 74- *Awards:* Am Coun Learned Soc Grant, 68; Guggenheim Fel, 71-72; Nat Endowment Humanities Fel, 79-80. *Mem:* Am Musicol Soc (mem bd dir, 72-74); Int Musicol Soc; Soc Music Theory. *Interests:* Musical style and music criticism in the early 19th century; history of pianoforte music. *Publ:* Auth, Philippe De Vitry's Nova: A Translation, J Music Theory, 11/61; Berlioz' Use of Shakespearian Themes, Yale French Studies, 64; Schumann's View of Romantic, Musical Quart, 4/66; Schumann as Critic, Yale Univ, 67; Clementi: His Life and Music, Oxford Univ, 77. *Mailing Add:* Music Dept 143 Elm St Yale Univ New Haven CT 06520

PLATTE, JAY DANIEL
EDUCATOR, CONDUCTOR
b Peoria, Ill, Jan 27, 45. *Study:* Ft Wayne Bible Col, BMusEd, 69; Ball State Univ, MA, 71, DA, 81. *Teaching:* Instr music educ & cond, Ft Wayne Bible Col, 68-73, asst prof, 73-79, assoc prof, 79- *Mem:* Music Educr Nat Conf; Am Choral Dir Asn; Am Musicol Soc; Asn Develop Comput Instructional Syst. *Mailing Add:* 811 W Rudisill Blvd Ft Wayne IN 46807

PLATTHY, JENO
COMPOSER, CRITIC-WRITER
b Dunapataj, Hungary, Aug 13, 20. *Study:* Studied with Bela Bartok & Zoltan Kodaly; Peter Pazmany Univ, teacher's dipl, 42; Ferenc Liszt Consv, 43; Ferenez J Univ, PhD, 44; Cath Univ Am, MS, 65; Yangmingshan Univ, Hon PhD, 75. *Works:* String Quartet, Op 5, Royal Consv Music, Bruxelles, 39; Bamboo (bicentennial comn of US), Prince George Civic Opera Co, 76; Christmas String Quartet, Op 80, 80; Composition in the Mixolydian Mode, Op 81, 83. *Pos:* Music reviewer, Info, Tokyo & Nouvelle Europe, 57-82; exec dir, Fedn Int Poetry Asn UNESCO, 76-; pres, Third Int Cong Poets, 76. *Awards:* Laureate, Second World Cong Poets, 73 & United Poets Int, 76. *Mem:* ASCAP. *Publ:* Auth, Summer Flowers, 60; Autumn Dances, 63; Soures on the Earliest Greek Libraries, 68; Collected Poems, 81; Poems of Jesus and Other Poems, 82. *Mailing Add:* PO Box 39072 Washington DC 20016

PLESKOW, RAOUL
COMPOSER, EDUCATOR
b Vienna, Austria, Oct 12, 31; US citizen. *Study:* Queens Col, BA, 54; Columbia Univ, MA, 58. *Works:* Movement for Nine Players, Two Movements for Orchestra, 69, Three Songs, 72, Motet & Madrigal, 73, Cantata, 76 & Bagatelles for Piano & Six Instruments, 77, Am Comp Alliance; String Quartet, McG & Marx, 80. *Teaching:* Prof comp, C W Post Ctr, Long Island Univ, 70- *Awards:* Am Acad Arts & Lett Award, 74; Guggenheim Fel, 77. *Bibliog:* Maurice Hinson (auth), Piano in Chamber Music, Ind Univ Press, 78; Josef Machlis, Introduction to Contemporary Music, W W Norton & Co, 79. *Mem:* Am Comp Alliance; Am Music Ctr. *Rep:* Am Comp Alliance 170 W 74th St New York NY 10023. *Mailing Add:* 43-25 Douglaston Pkwy Douglaston NY 11363

PLISHKA, PAUL
BASS
b Old Forge, Pa, Aug 28, 41. *Study:* With Armen Boyajian; Montclair State Col. *Roles:* Colline in La Boheme, Metropolitan Opera Nat Co, 66; Oroveso in Norma; Sir George in I Puritani; Leporello in Don Giovanni; Figaro in Le Nozze di Figaro; Piman in Boris Godunov; Ramfis in Aida. *Pos:* Mem, Metropolitan Opera, currently; bass with maj opera co in US, Can & Italy. *Awards:* Winner, Baltimore Opera Auditions. *Mailing Add:* c/o Columbia Artists Mgt 165 W 57th St New York NY 10019

PLOG, ANTHONY (CLIFTON)
TRUMPET, COMPOSER
b Glendale, Calif, Nov 13, 47. *Study:* Univ Calif, Los Angeles, BA, 69. *Works:* Four Sierra Scenes, Brightstar Music, 72; Two Scenes, Brass Press, 74; Animal Ditties (trumpet, piano & narrator), 76 & Fanfare for Two Trumpets, 76, Wimbledon Music; Music for Brass Octet, Edward Tarr Brass Ensemble, 81; Ten Concert Duets (2 trumpets), Textures for Wind Ensemble, 82, Western Int Music. *Pos:* Assoc prin trumpet, Utah Symph, 74-76; trumpet soloist, recitals & concerti throughout Europe & US, 76- *Teaching:* Asst prof trumpet, Calif State Univ, Northridge, 76-78; lectr, Univ Southern Calif, 78-, Music Acad West, 79- & Calif State Univ, Long Beach, 83- *Mem:* Phi Mu Alpha. *Mailing Add:* 12615 Pacific Ave #1 Los Angeles CA 90066

PLSEK, STEPHANY KING
EDUCATOR, PIANO
b Brighton, Mass, June 18, 49. *Study:* Piano with Margaret Stedman Chaloff, 72-77; Berklee Col Music, BM, 74; New England Consv, MM, 78. *Works:* Piano Sonata, perf by comp, 75; String Quartet, New England Consv Quartet, 76; Verbum, perf by Greg Hopkins & comp, 77; Transformations I-VI , perf by comp, 78; Stereophonic Suite, perf by Thomas Plsek, 79. *Teaching:* Instr piano & theory, Berklee Col Music, 75- *Mailing Add:* 29 Trowbridge St Newton Center MA 02159

PLSEK, THOMAS JOSEPH
EDUCATOR, COMPOSER
b West, Tex, Oct 8, 47. *Study:* Tex Christian Univ, BM(theory), 70; Univ Houston, MM(theory), 72; studied trombone with Al Lube. *Works:* Logic Variations, Corey Hill Chamber Players, 82; Through the Sounding Glass, 82, Transduction System, 82-83, Improvisation System #1, 83 & Meditations on the Life & Death of Jumbo, 83, Sound, Image, Events. *Rec Perf:* New Events 2 (Shirish Korde), Spectra, 82. *Pos:* Organizer, Boston Sackbut Week, 73- *Teaching:* Instr music hist & acoustics & chmn trombone & low brass dept, Berklee Col Music, Boston, 72- *Mem:* Int Trombone Asn; New England Comput Music Asn (bd dir, 82-). *Mailing Add:* 29 Trowbridge St Newton MA 02159

PLUCKER, JOHN P
DOUBLE BASS
b Neenah, Wis, June 1, 53. *Study:* Univ Tulsa. *Pos:* Prin double bass, Jackson Symph Orch, 78-; sect double bass, Tulsa Phil, 73-75. *Teaching:* Instr double bass, Symph Sch Am, La Crosse, Wis, 78- *Publ:* Auth, Bertram Turetzky in Concert, Int Soc Bassists, 75. *Mailing Add:* 1129 Woodville Dr Jackson MS 39212

PLUCKER, MARGARET L
VIOLIN
b Racine, Wis, Nov 27, 57. *Study:* Wheaton Col; DePaul Univ, with Victor Aitay, BA, 79. *Pos:* Concertmaster, Mo Symph Soc, Columbia, summers 79-81; first violin sect, Ala Symph, 79-81; asst concertmaster, Jackson Symph, 81-, second violin, Symph Quartet, 81- *Mailing Add:* 1129 Woodville Dr Jackson MS 39212

PLUMB, BRUCE WILLIAM
VIOLA, EDUCATOR
b Toronto, Ont, Aug 30, 51. *Study:* Curtis Inst, with Max Aronoff, BM, 74. *Pos:* Artist assoc, Duke Univ, 75-79; mem Duo da Salo (with Barbara Lister-Sink), 76; violist, Pittsburgh Symph, 79-80; asst prin viola, Rochester Phil Orch, 80-83 & prin viola, 83- *Teaching:* Lectr, Carnegie Mellon Univ, 79-80; fac mem orch repertoire, Eastman Sch Music, 83. *Mailing Add:* 137 West Ave Fairport NY 14450

PODIS, EUNICE
PIANO, TEACHER
b Cleveland, Ohio, Jan 14, 22. *Study:* Western Reserve Univ, 38-40; private study with Arthur Rubinstein, 42 & Rudolf Serkin, 47. *Rec Perf:* Two Rhapsodies (Loeffler), Advent, 75; Beethoven Sonatas, Op 109 & 110, 77 & Album with John Mack, Oboe, 77, Telarc. *Pos:* Trustee, Cleveland Opera &

Musical Arts Asn, currently. *Teaching:* Artist in res piano, Cleveland Inst Music, 67- *Awards:* Nat Young Artists Award, 45 & Vera Wardner Dougan Award, 70, Nat Fedn Music Clubs. *Mem:* Fortnightly Music Club; Mu Phi Epsilon. *Publ:* Contribr, The Pianist Has More Fun Than Anybody, Fine Arts, 68; How Do You Get to Carnegie Hall?, Cleveland Inst Music Newsletter, 75; A Visit with Misse, Inst Chimes, 82; Recollections of Rubinstein, Cleveland Inst Music Newsletter, 83. *Mailing Add:* 2653 Ramsay Rd Cleveland OH 44122

PODNOS, THEODOR
VIOLIN, LECTURER

b Boston, Mass, Feb 27, 18. *Study:* Peabody Consv, Curtis Inst Music; Boston Univ, with Richard Burgin. *Pos:* First violin sect, New York Phil, 70- *Mem:* Am Fedn Musicians. *Interests:* Tunings in musical performances. *Publ:* Auth, And Where is Your A Today?, 48 & Woodwind Intonation, 49, Woodwind Mag; Bagpipes and Tunings, Info Coordr, 74; Intonation for Strings, Winds & Singers, Scarecrow Press, 81. *Mailing Add:* 915 Lincoln Pl Teaneck NJ 07666

PODOLSKY, LEO S
PIANO, EDUCATOR

b Odessa, Russia, May 25, 91. *Study:* Imperial Consv Branch, Odessa, Russia; Consv Music, Cracow, Poland, grad 12; State Acad, Vienna, Austria, 14; studied with George Lalewicz. *Works:* Over 100 piano works publ by Boosey & Hawkes, Belwin-Mills, Carl Fischer, Shawnee Press, Volkwein Brothers & Summy-Birchard. *Pos:* Concert pianist, tours throughout the world, incl two round the world tours. *Teaching:* Mem artist fac, Sherwood Music Ctr, 26-; vis prof, St Mary's Col, Ind, 18 years; guest fac, Mozarteum, Salzburg, Austria; cond various workshops & master classes. *Awards:* Anton Rubinstein Prize & Liszt Prize, State Acad Vienna. *Mailing Add:* 7424 Merrill Ave Chicago IL 60649

POE, GERALD DEAN
MUSIC DIRECTOR, EDUCATOR

b Grandby, Colo, Sept 18, 42. *Study:* Western State Col, Colo, BA, 64; Fla State Univ, Tallahassee, MMusEd, 65; Univ Colo, Boulder, DMA, 73. *Pos:* Dir bands, Univ Fla, Gainesville, 82- *Teaching:* Asst prof music, Minot Stte Col, 69-72; teaching fel, Univ Colo, Boulder, 72-73; asst prof music, Univ Portland, 73-75 & Univ Ore, Eugene, 75-82. *Mem:* Col Band Dir Nat Asn (mem bd dir, 80-82, secy, NW Div, 76-80, vpres, 78-80, pres, 80-82); Int Trumpet Guild; Music Educr Nat Conf. *Publ:* Auth, An Examination of Four Selected Solos Recorded by Louis Armstrong, Nat Asn Col Wind & Perc J, fall 75; Jo VanDen Booren's Game III for Trumpet and Organ, Woodwind, Brass & Perc World, 76; An Examination of Barney Childs' Duo for Trumpet, Nat Asn Col Wind & Perc Instr J, fall 76; The Marching Band ... More Than Just Music, 5/78 & Basic Intonation Tendencies on the Trumpet-Cornet, 5/78, Sch Musician. *Mailing Add:* 1716 NW 21st St Gainesville FL 32605

POGUE, SAMUEL FRANKLIN
EDUCATOR

b Cincinnati, Ohio, Apr 11, 19. *Study:* Princeton Univ, BA, 41, MFA, 63, PhD, 68; studied with Roger Sessions, Oliver Strunk, Roy Welch, Edward Cone & Lewis Lockwood. *Pos:* Staff assoc, Martha Baird Rockefeller Fund Music, 65-68. *Teaching:* Asst prof musicol, Col Consv Music, Univ Cincinnati, 68-72, assoc prof, 72-77, prof, 77- *Mem:* Am Musicol Soc (mem coun, 72-75); Int Musicol Soc; New Bach Soc. *Interests:* Sixteenth century music printing. *Publ:* Auth, Jacques Moderne, Lyons Music Printer, Droz, Geneva, 69; Cincinnati, MGG Suppl, 71; Further Notes on Jacques Moderne, Bibliog Hum et Renaissance, 75; A Sixteenth Century Editor at Work, J Musicol, 82; 17 articles, In: New Grove Dict of Music & Musicians. *Mailing Add:* Col Consv Music Univ Cincinnati Cincinnati OH 45221

POKORNY, GENE (JOHN EUGENE)
TUBA

b Los Angeles, Calif, May 15, 53. *Study:* Univ Redlands; Univ Southern Calif, with Tommy Johnson, BMus, 75. *Pos:* Prin tubist, Colo Phil Orch, 75, Israel Phil Orch, 75-78, Utah Symph Orch, 78-83 & St Louis Symph Orch, 83- *Mem:* Am Fedn Musicians; Tubists Universal Brotherhood Asn. *Publ:* Contribr, The Tuba and Brass Pedagogy in Israel, Tubists Universal Brotherhood Asn J, 81. *Mailing Add:* St Louis Symph Orch 718 N Grand Blvd St Louis MO

POLANSKY, LARRY C
COMPOSER, WRITER

b New York, NY, Oct 16, 54. *Study:* New Col; Univ Calif, Santa Cruz, BA, 76; Univ Ill, Champaign-Urbana, MA(comp), 78. *Works:* Quartet in F, perf by Array Ens, 76-; Four Violin Studies (what to do when the night comes...), perf by Mary Oliver, 82-; Shm'a: Fuging Tune in G, Soundings Press, 82; Three Monk Tunes (tap dancer & perc), perf by Anita Feldman, 83- *Pos:* Dir, founder & perf, New Kanon New Music Ens, 78-80; dir, Mill Contemp Music Ens, 81-; mem, Berkeley Mandolin Ens. *Teaching:* Asst theory & ear training, Univ Ill, Champaign-Urbana, 77 & 78; lectr orch & electronic music, Mills Col, Oakland, 82- & guitar instr, 82- *Awards:* Young Comp Award, BMI, 78; Am Music Ctr Award, 79; fel, Mellon Found, 82. *Bibliog:* Dan Junas (auth), Interview with Larry Polansky, Op Mag, P Issue, 83. *Mem:* Sonneck Soc Am Music. *Publ:* Coauth, Hierarchical Gestalt Perception in Music, J Music Theory, 82; auth, The Early Works of James Tenney, Soundings Press, 83; many articles on all aspects at Am Music, OP Mag, 83- *Mailing Add:* Music Dept Mills Col Oakland CA 94613

POLAY, BRUCE
CONDUCTOR & MUSIC DIRECTOR, EDUCATOR

b Brooklyn, NY, Mar 22, 49. *Study:* Univ Southern Calif, with Ellis Kohs, Ramiro Cortes & Hans Beer, BM, 71; Ariz State Univ, with Ronald Lo Presti, Robert Hamilton & Eugene Lombardi, currently. *Pos:* Cond & music dir, Southern Calif Philharmonia, 71-81 & Knox-Galesburg Symph, currently; asst cond, Ariz State Univ Symph Orch, 81-83; cond, Phoenix Symph Guild Youth Orch, 81-83. *Teaching:* Grad asst music hist, theory & orch, Ariz State Univ, 81-83; instr music, Knox Col, currently. *Mem:* Cond Guild; Am Symph Orch League; Music Educr Nat Conf; Southern Calif Sch Band & Orch Asn. *Rep:* Marianne Marshall 34-66th Pl Long Beach CA 90803. *Mailing Add:* Knox-Galesburg Symph Orch Box 31 Knox Col Galesburg IL 61401

POLIN, CLAIRE
COMPOSER, EDUCATOR

b Philadelphia, Pa. *Study:* Philadelphia Consv Music, BMus, 48, MMus, 50, DMus, 55; Juilliard Sch Music; Temple Univ; Berkshire Music Ctr; Dropsie Univ; Gratz Col. *Works:* Owain Madoc (brass quintet & perc), 72, Infinito (alto sax, sop, narrator, dancer, SATB choir), 78 & O Aderyn Pur (flute, sax & bird tape), 82, Seesaw; Cader Iris (brass quintet), Schirmer, 82; Res Naturae (woodwind quintet), Dorn, 82; Kuequenaku-Cambriola (piano & perc), comn by Philadelphia Tricentennial, 83; Mythos (harp & string orch), comn by Zabaleta, 83. *Teaching:* Prof flute, musicol & comp, Philadelphia Consv/Musical Acad, formerly; prof comp, music hist & contemp music, Rutgers Univ, 58- *Awards:* Leverhulme Fel, 68-69; Comn, Ga State Univ, 70-71; Spec Comp Award, Gedok, Mannheim, Ger, 72 & 76. *Bibliog:* The Work of Claire Polin, Composer, London, summer 69; Gwaith Claire Polin, Y Cymro, Wales, July 69; International Exchange Concerts, Music J, 74. *Mem:* ASCAP; Am Music Ctr; Am Asn Univ Comp; Am Musicol Soc; Guild for Prom Welsh Music. *Interests:* Biblical instruments; earliest Welsh musical tablatures and folk materials for harp. *Publ:* Auth, Music of The Ancient Near East, Vantage, 54 & Greenwood, 75; coauth, Art & Practice of Modern Flute Technique, (three vol), MCA Music, 67-74; The Bach Sonatas, 69 & Advanced Flutist (two vol), 77 & 80, Elkan-Vogel; auth, The AP Huw Manuscript, Inst Medieval Music Ltd, 82. *Mailing Add:* 374 Baird Rd Merion Station PA 19066

POLISI, JOSEPH WILLIAM
ADMINISTRATOR, BASSOON

b Flushing, NY, Dec 30, 47. *Study:* Univ Conn, BA, 69; Fletcher Sch Law & Diplomacy, Tufts Univ, MA, 70; Sch Music, Yale Univ, MM, 73, MMA, 75, DMA, 80; studied bassoon with William Polisi, Eli Carmen & Arthur Weisberg; Paris Consv, studied basson with Maurice Allard. *Rec Perf:* A Harvest of 20th Century Bassoon Music, Crystal Rec, 80. *Teaching:* Instr, Univ Nev, Las Vegas, 75-76; exec officer, Sch Music, Yale Univ, 76-80; dean fac, Manhattan Sch Music, 80- *Awards:* Cert of Merit, Yale Sch Music Alumni Asn, 82. *Publ:* Auth, The Bassoon Master Class at the Paris Conservatory, 75 & The Bassoon Ensemble: Past, Present, and Future, 79, Woodwind World; Teaching Bassoon Vibrato, Instrumentalist, 76; Towards the 21st Century: Thoughts on Musical Training in America, 82 & The Academy and the Marketplace: Cooperation or Conflict, 82, Proc of Ann Meeting, Nat Asn Sch Music. *Mailing Add:* Manhattan Sch Music 120 Claremont Ave New York NY 10027

POLISI, WILLIAM
EDUCATOR, BASSOON

b Philadelphia, Pa. *Study:* Curtis Inst Music, dipl, 35. *Pos:* First bassoon, New York Phil, formerly; bassoonist, Cleveland Symh & NBC Symph; mfr, Polisi bassoon. *Teaching:* Fac mem bassoon, Juilliard Sch, 51-; clinician, various cols in US. *Publ:* Publ, Polisi bassoon chart. *Mailing Add:* 54-20 Kissena Blvd Flushing NY 11355

POLIVNICK, PAUL HENRY
CONDUCTOR, VIOLA

b Atlantic City, NJ, July 7, 47. *Study:* Juilliard Sch Music, BM, 69. *Rec Perf:* Strauss Piano Quartet, 74 & Hadyn & Schoenberg String Trios, 74, Desmar Rec. *Pos:* Cond, Debut Orch Young Musicians Found Los Angeles, 69-73; assoc cond, Indianapolis Symph Orch, 77-80 & Milwaukee Symph Orch, 81. *Teaching:* Fac mem viola, Univ Calif, Los Angeles, 73-75. *Mem:* Am Symph Orch League. *Mailing Add:* c/o Maxim Gershunoff Attractions 502 Park Ave New York NY 10022

POLL, MELVYN
LYRIC TENOR

b Seattle, Wash, July 15, 41. *Study:* Univ Wash, BA, JD; studied with Marinka Gurewich, Elsa Seyfert, Martin Rich & Gustave Stern. *Roles:* Rodolfo in La Boheme, Pfalztheater, Kaiserslautern, Fed Repub Germany, 71; Edgardo in Lucia di Lammermoor; Faust in Faust; Pinkerton in Madama Butterfly; Alfredo in La traviata. *Pos:* Lyr ten, Israel Nat Opera, Tel Aviv & New York City Opera; recitalist. *Mailing Add:* c/o Thea Dispeker 59 E 54th New York NY 10022

POLLACK, DANIEL
PIANO, EDUCATOR

b Los Angeles, Calif, Jan 23, 35. *Study:* Juilliard Sch, BS(music), 55; Acad Musik, Vienna, Austria, MS, 57. *Rec Perf:* Daniel Pollack Recital, Artia-MK (Russia), 58 & 61 & Columbia Spec Prod, 73; The Competition (Prokofiev), MCA, 81. *Teaching:* Asst prof, Hartt Col Music, Univ Hartford, 66-70; from assoc prof to prof piano, Univ Southern Calif, 71- *Awards:* Fulbright Grant, 57-58; Winner, Tschaikovsky Compt, 58; Martha Baird Rockefeller Grant, 63. *Mem:* Am Fedn Musicians; Kosciuszko Found; Music Teachers Nat Asn; Young Musicians Found. *Mailing Add:* 1323 Sierra Alta Way Los Angeles CA 90069

POLLACK, HOWARD JOEL
CRITIC, EDUCATOR
b Brooklyn, NY, Mar 17, 52. *Study:* Univ Mich, BM, 73; Cornell Univ, musicol with William Austin, MA, PhD, 81. *Pos:* Music critic, Rochester Democrat & Chronicle, 83- *Teaching:* Instr, Rochester Inst Technol, 78-81. *Mem:* Am Musicol Soc; Sonneck Soc. *Interests:* American music in the 20th century. *Mailing Add:* 185 Rutgers Rochester NY 14607

POLLACK, JILL M
EDUCATOR
b Freeport, NY, Aug 6, 40. *Study:* Juilliard Sch Music, 58-61; Manhattan Sch Music, BM & MM, 67. *Pos:* Coord & asst dir, various music fest, formerly; music coord, Women's Interest Ctr, New York, NY, 80-82. *Teaching:* Mem fac theory dept, Manhattan Sch Music, 70- *Mem:* Music Theory Soc NY (vpres, 80-); Theory & Practice; Soc Music Theory; Col Music Society. *Mailing Add:* Manhattan Sch of Music 120 Claremont Ave New York NY 10027

POLLAK, CAROLYN SUE
OBOE & ENGLISH HORN
b Boston, Mass, Jan 20, 48. *Study:* Ind Univ, Bloomington, studied with Jerry Sirucek, BM, 70; with Ray Still, 70-74; Univ Wis, Madison, MM, 73; Yale Univ, with Robert Bloom, 74. *Pos:* English horn & asst first oboe, San Antonio Symph, 70-71; mem, Wingra Woodwind Quintet, Univ Wis, Madison, 71-73; prin oboe, Fla Gulf Coast Symph, 73-74, Hudson Valley Phil, 77-78, NJ Symph, 78- *Bibliog:* Bruce Jones (auth), Symphony Best of Season, Tampa Tribune, 4/20/74; Peter Davis (auth), Chamber Concert with a Mix, New York Times, 4/8/79; Joseph Bertolozzi (auth), Ensemble Plays Good Music, Poughkeepsie J, 10/20/82. *Mem:* Int Double Reed Soc. *Mailing Add:* NJ Symph Orch 213 Washington St Newark NJ 07101

POLLARD, ELIZABETH BLITCH
LIBRARIAN, EDUCATOR
b Valdosta, Ga, June 16, 39. *Study:* Emory Univ, BA, 61, MLn, 70; Univ NC, 61-63; studied piano with Michael McDowell & Enid Katahn. *Teaching:* Instr music, Univ Ala, Huntsville, 70-77, asst prof, 77-81, assoc prof, 81-, head acquisitions, 82- *Mem:* Am Musicol Soc; Music Libr Asn. *Publ:* Auth, State of the Art: Reference Sources in the Fine Arts & Crafts, 77 & 78 & Current Survey of Reference Sources in Fine Arts & Crafts, 79 & 81, Reference Services Review. *Mailing Add:* 3903 Gardenside Dr Huntsville AL 35810

POLLOCK, ROBERT EMIL
COMPOSER, PIANO
b New York, NY, July 8, 46. *Study:* Swarthmore Col, with Claudio Spies, BA; Princeton Univ, with Edward T Cone, Peter Westergaard, Jacques-Louis Monod, J K Randall, Milton Babbitt & Robert Helps, MFA. *Works:* The Nose (chamber opera after Gogol); Flute Sonatina, 72; Trio (violin, clarinet & cello), 74 & Song Cycle (on Stephen Crane poems), 74, New York; 7 Preludes (piano), 75; The Descent (sop, flute & piano), 76; Metaphor II (clarinet & piano), 77; and many others. *Pos:* Conct pianist. *Awards:* Comp String Quartet Award, 70; MacDowell Fels, 72 & 76; State Arts Coun Grant, 75. *Mem:* Am Music Ctr; Guild Comp. *Mailing Add:* 2002 Central Ave Ship Bottom NJ 08008

POLOCHICK, EDWARD
CONDUCTOR, ADMINISTRATOR
Study: Swarthmore Col, BA, MM(piano); Peabody Consv, MM(cond); studied piano with Leon Fleisher, Anne Vanko-Liva & Clement Petrillo; cond with Michael Korn, William Smith & Theodore Morrison. *Pos:* Musical asst, Philadelphia Singers, 72-76; assoc cond, Baltimore Choral Arts Soc, 77-79; artistic dir, Montgomery Co Masterworks Chorus, 78-; dir chorus, Baltimore Sumph Orch, 79-; asst cond, Chautauqua Symph Orch, 80-; solo perf, Philadelphia Orch, Los Angeles Chamber Orch & Baltimore Choral Arts Soc, currently; guest cond, Philadelphia Orch, Swarthmore Col Orch, Peabody Chamber Chorus, Baltimore Choral Arts Soc, Chautauqua Symph Orch & Baltimore Symph Orch. *Teaching:* Coach & asst cond opera, Curtis Inst, 74-76; dir choral activ, Peabody Consv, asst cond, Peabody Orch, adv & cond, Opera Musica, currently. *Awards:* Winner, Leopold Stokowski Cond Award Philadelphia Orch, 78. *Mailing Add:* 1711 Bolton St Baltimore MD 21217

POLOGE, STEVEN
CELLO
b New York, NY, Jan 10, 52. *Study:* Eastman Sch Music, BMus, 74; Juilliard Sch Music, MMus, 78; studied with Ronald Leonard, Lorne Munroe, Leonard Rose, Channing Robbins & Avron Twerdowsky. *Pos:* Cello sect, Rochester Phil Orch, 73-75, Am Ballet Theater Orch, 74-76 & Buffalo Phil Orch, 75-76; prin cellist, Honolulu Symph Orch, 80- *Awards:* Erin & Douglas Way Young Artists Award, Nat Arts Club, 79. *Mailing Add:* 2206 McKinley Honolulu HI 96822

POMMERS, LEON
PIANO, EDUCATOR
b Pruzana, Poland, Oct 12, 14. *Study:* State Consv Music, Warsaw, 39; Queens Col, City Univ New York, BA, 65, MA, 68. *Rec Perf:* Sonatas for Cello & Piano (Hindemith & Debussy), Period; Sonatas for Violin & Piano (Brahms), Westminster; Sonatas for Violin & Piano (Mozart), Capitol. *Teaching:* Prof music, Queens Col, City Univ New York, 68- *Mem:* Bohemians; Am Asn Univ Prof. *Mailing Add:* Aaron Copland Sch Music Queens Col Flushing NY 11367

PONCE, WALTER
PIANO
b Cochahamba, Bolivia, July 4, 44; US citizen. *Study:* Mannes Col, studied piano with Nadia Reisenberg, BMus; Juilliard Sch, studied piano with Sasha Gorodnitzki, MM & DM, 69-71. *Pos:* Conct pianist, 71-; artist in res, State Univ NY, Binghamton, 72- *Awards:* Fulbright Grant, 62-66; Orgn Am States Award, 66-68. *Mailing Add:* c/o Robert Levin Assoc 250 W 57th St Suite 1332 New York NY 10107

PONÉ, GUNDARIS
CONDUCTOR, COMPOSER
b Oct 17, 32. *Study:* Univ Minn, BA, 54, MA, 56, PhD, 62. *Works:* Vivos Voco, Mortuos Plago (orch), 72, Diletti Dialettici, 73, Avanti! (orch), 75, Five American Songs (orch), 75, Concerto for Horn & Orch, 76, Eisleriana, 78 & La Serenissima (orch), 82, Alexander Broude, Inc. *Pos:* Artistic dir, Pone Ensemble for New Music, Inc, 74-, pres, 82; music dir, Music in the Mountains, Am Music Fest, 82- *Teaching:* Prof comp, State Univ New York, New Paltz, 63- *Awards:* First Prize, XX Trieste Int Compt for Symphonic Comp, 81; First Prize for Best Am Work, Kennedy Ctr Friedheim Awards Compt, 82; Creative Artists Pub Serv Award, NY State Comn, 82. *Bibliog:* Numerous articles in various journals in England, Soviet Union, Italy, West Germany & US. *Mem:* Am Comp Alliance; BMI. *Publ:* Auth, Action-Reaction, Music Rev, 66; Jaunas Muzikas Forma un Doma, 67 & Maksla un Politika, 71, Jauna Gaita; Webern and Luigi Nono, Perspectives of New Music, 72. *Rep:* Music Enterprises PO Box 101 New Paltz NY 12561. *Mailing Add:* 24 Woodland Dr New Paltz NY 12561

POOLE, JANE L
CRITIC-WRITER
b Seattle, Wash. *Study:* Univ Wash, BA, 69; Villa Schifanoia, Rosary Col, with Tito Gobbi, 74. *Pos:* Coordr artist relations, Angel & EMI Rec, 71-77; assoc ed, Opera News, 80- *Mailing Add:* Opera News 1865 Broadway New York NY 10022

POPE, BETTY FRANCES
LIBRARIAN, TEACHER
Brookhaven, Miss, Mar 9, 27. *Study:* William Carey Col, BA, 49; New Orleans Baptist Theol Sem, MRE, 56; Northeast La State Col, MMusEd, 63; NTex State Univ, MLS, 70. *Pos:* Asst cataloger, Libr, NTex St Univ, 69- *Teaching:* Music, Bruce Consolidated Sch, Miss, 49-52; instr piano, Kosciusko High Sch, Miss, 52-54; instr music, Baptist Childrens Home, Monroe, La, 54-56 & Truett McConnell Jr Col, 63-66; music librn, New Orleans Baptist Theol Sem, 66-68. *Mem:* Music Libr Asn. *Publ:* Auth, A Day in Egypt, Christian Single, 83. *Mailing Add:* 724 Bolivar Denton TX 76201

POPE, CONRAD
EDUCATOR
b Corona, Calif, Nov 21, 51. *Study:* New England Consv, with Malcolm Peyton & Donald Martino, BM, 75; Berkshire Music Ctr, with Gunther Schuller. *Works:* String Trio, 70; Joys (bar & 13 instrm), 71; Symphony, 73; Sonata for Solo Cello, 73; Two Songs (sop & piano), 78. *Pos:* Co-dir, Music: Here and Now, Boston Museum Fine Arts, 71-73. *Teaching:* Asst prof theory, hist & lit, Brandeis Univ, 78- *Awards:* Bernstein Fel, 71; George W Chadwick Medal, 73; Fulbright-Hays Grant, 73. *Mailing Add:* Brandeis Univ Waltham MA 02254

POPKIN, MARK ANTHONY
EDUCATOR, BASSOON
b New York, NY, July 25, 29. *Study:* Brooklyn Col, AB, 50; Stevens Inst Technol, MS, 55. *Rec Perf:* Several recordings with Clarion Wind Quintet, Golden Crest Rec. *Pos:* Bassoonist, Houston Symph, 50; freelance bassoonist, Mostly Mozart Fest, Chamber Soc Lincoln Ctr, Clarion Wind Quintet & Y Chamber Orch, currently. *Teaching:* Fac mem bassoon & chamber music, NC Sch Arts, 65- *Publ:* Coauth, Bassoon Reed Making, Instrumentalist Co, 69; auth, Course of Study for Private Bassoon Instruction, Music Teachers Nat Asn, 78. *Mailing Add:* 740 Arbor Rd Winston-Salem NC 27104

POPPER, FELIX
CONDUCTOR, COACH
b Vienna, Austria, Dec 12, 08; US citizen. *Study:* Acad Music, Vienna; Univ Vienna, PhD, 32. *Pos:* Music adminr & cond, New York City Opera, 58-81; opera coach, Mannes Sch Music, 60-65; Curtis Inst Music, 72-78 & Acad Vocal Arts, 79- *Mailing Add:* Acad Vocal Arts 1920 Spruce St Philadelphia PA 19103

POPPER, FREDRIC
CONDUCTOR, EDUCATOR
Study: Cleveland Inst Music, BM; New England Consv Music, MM; Acad Music, Vienna; Mozarteum, Salzburg; Paris Consv. *Pos:* Assoc cond, Metropolitan Opera Nat Co, formerly, NBC-TV Opera, formerly & Goldovsky Opera Theatre, currently; dir, Goldovsky Opera Inst, 65-; soloist & accmp, European & Am conct tours. *Teaching:* Mem fac, New England Consv Music, formerly, Hiram Col, formerly, Cleveland Inst Music, formerly, Hunter Opera Dept, formerly, Chatham Square Music Sch, 61-68; mem fac music & dir, Opera Wkshp, Mannes Col Music, currently; coach & asst to head, Opera Dept, Curtis Inst Music, 77- *Mailing Add:* Curtis Inst Music 1726 Locust St Philadelphia PA 19103

PORTER, ANDREW (BRIAN)
CRITIC-WRITER
b Cape Town, SAfrica, Aug 26, 28. *Study:* Univ Col, Oxford, MA, 52. *Pos:* Music critic, Financial Times, London, 52-72 & New Yorker, 72-; ed, Musical Times, London, 60-67. *Teaching:* Bloch prof music hist, Univ Calif, Berkeley. *Awards:* Deems Taylor Award, ASCAP, 73, 75 & 82. *Bibliog:* Patrick Smith (auth), Am Criticism: The Porter Experience, 19th Century Music, Vol II, No 3. *Mem:* Royal Musical Asn (mem coun, 60-70); Am Musicol Asn; Am Inst Verdi Studies (exec bd, 76-); ASCAP; Am Music Ctr (dir bd, 76-77). *Publ:* Auth, A Musical Season, Viking, 74; The Ring of the Nibelung, an English Translation, W W Norton, 76; Music of Three Seasons, Farrar Straus Giroux, 78; Music of Three More Seasons, Knopf, 81; co-ed, Verdi's Macbeth: A Sourcebook, W W Norton, 83. *Rep:* E Snapp 87 Robinson Ave Glen Cove NY 11542. *Mailing Add:* New Yorker 25 W 43rd St New York NY 10036

PORTER, DAVID GRAY
COMPOSER, PIANO
b Los Angeles, Calif, June 10, 53. *Study:* Comp with Donal Michalsky, Lloyd Rodgers, Gail Kubik & Nicolas Slonimsky, 73-78; Calif State Univ, Fullerton, BM, 75, MM, 80. *Works:* Events (two pianos), perf by comp & Chuck Estes, 74; Music for Charles Simmons (woodwinds & strings), 75 & Quartet (four mallet instrm), 76, perf by Direct Image Ens; Music for Piano or Harp, perf by comp, 80; comps for chamber ens & magnetic tape, 74-82. *Pos:* Co-founder & assoc dir, Direct Image Ens, 74-; performer, New Music Co, Calif State Univ, Fullerton, Pac Symph Orch, 74-83 & Cartesian Reunion Mem Orch, spring 80; programmer, KPFK FM, Los Angeles, 81-; prog host, Genesis of a Music, currently; musicologist, transcriber & ed, various southern Calif comps & Charles Ives Soc, currently; librn, Pac Symph Asn, currently. *Mailing Add:* 880 Arc Way Anaheim CA 92804

PORTER, ELLEN JANE LORENZ See Lorenz, Ellen Jane

PORTER, JAMES WHYTE
EDUCATOR, COMPOSER
b Paisley, Scotland. *Study:* Univ St Andrews, Scotland, MA, 58; Univ Edinburgh, Scotland, with Hans Redlich & Hans Gal, BMus, 61; Janacek Acad Music, Czechoslovakia, 64-65; Acad Music, Prague; Accad Chigiana, Italy, with H Scherchen. *Works:* A Midsummer Night's Dream (incidental music), comn by Glasgow Citizens' Theatre, Scotland, 65; The Birds (incidental music), comn by Edinburgh Fest Soc, 66. *Teaching:* Lectr music, Univ Edinburgh, 66-68; asst prof, Univ Calif, Los Angeles, 68-75, assoc prof, 75-81, prof, 81- *Awards:* Sawyer Prize for Music, Univ St Andrews, Scotland, 58. *Mem:* Soc Ethnomusicol; Int Folk Music Coun; Am Folklore Soc; Calif Folklore Soc (vpres, 78-82). *Interests:* East and West European folk music. *Publ:* Auth, Prolegomena to a Comparative Study of European Folk Music, Ethnomusicol, 77; ed, Folk Music, Selected Reports in Ethnomusicology, Dept Music, Univ Calif, Los Angeles, Vol III, No 1; auth, Europe: Folk Music, North and West & Europe: Prehistory, In: New Grove Dict Music & Musicians, 80; ed, The Ballad Image: Essays Presented to B H Bronson, Folklore & Mythology Ctr, Univ Calif, Los Angeles, 83. *Mailing Add:* Dept Music Col Fine Arts Univ Calif Los Angeles CA 90024

PORTER, SUSAN LORAINE
EDUCATOR
b Okmulgee, Okla, Aug 20, 41. *Study:* Southwestern Col, BMus, 64; Univ Denver, MA, 72; Univ Colo, Boulder, PhD, 77. *Teaching:* Instr music hist, Univ Colo, 73-75 & 76-77; instr, Univ Wis, Whitewater, 75-76; assoc prof, Ohio State Univ, Lima, 77- *Mem:* Am Musicol Soc; Sonneck Soc; Col Music Soc. *Interests:* Early American musical theatre (before 1825); American and English folk music; Normand Lockwood. *Publ:* Auth, Children in the Wood—The Rich Musical Tradition of an Anglo-American Ballad, Colo Music Educr, 75; The Actor-Singer in American Theatre at the Turn of the 19th Century, Musicol Univ Colo, 78; Eighteenth Century Opera: What's in a Name?, Sonneck Soc Newsletter, 80; contribr, Folk Instruments in the Elementary Classroom, Univ Press Am, 82; Normand Lockwood, In: New Grove Dict of Music in US (in prep). *Mailing Add:* 2300 Wellesley Dr Lima OH 45804

PORTNOI, HENRY
BASS
Study: Curtis Inst Music, double bass with Anton Torello. *Pos:* Prin bass, Boston Symph Orch; mem, Boston Symph Orch Chamber Players, Zimbler Sinfonietta, Pittsburgh Symph & Indianapolis Symph, formerly. *Teaching:* Instr double bass, New England Consv Music, currently. *Publ:* Auth, Creative Bass Teschnique. *Mailing Add:* New England Consv Music 290 Huntington Rd Boston MA 02115

PORTNOY, DONALD CHARLES
CONDUCTOR & MUSIC DIRECTOR, VIOLIN
b Philadelphia, Pa, Apr 5, 33. *Study:* Juilliard Sch Music, BS, 55; Cath Univ Am, MA, 59; Peabody Consv Music, DMA, 72. *Pos:* Cond & music dir, WVa Symphonette, 69-; Prof music, WVa Univ, 59- *Awards:* Contemp Music Prog Award, ASCAP, 75 & 79. *Mem:* Am Symph Orch League (mem bd dir, 79-); Cond Guild (pres, 83); WVa String Teachers Asn (past pres, 75); Music Educr Nat Conf. *Mailing Add:* PO Box 71 Morgantown WV 26505

PORTONE, FRANK ANTHONY, JR
FRENCH HORN, EDUCATOR
b Philadelphia, Pa, Feb 14, 52. *Study:* Col Music, Temple Univ, BM, 75. *Pos:* Prin French horn, Hong Kong Phil, 77-80 & Charlotte Symph, 80- *Teaching:* Instr French horn, Davidson Col, 82- *Mem:* Am Fedn Musicians; Int Horn Soc. *Mailing Add:* 1240 Worcester Pl Charlotte NC 28211

POST, NORA
OBOE & ENGLISH HORN, EDUCATOR
b Bayshore, NY, Dec 18, 49. *Study:* Univ Calif, San Diego, BA, 73; NY Univ, PhD, 79; studied with Ray Still, Heinz Molliger & Michel Piguet. *Rec Perf:* At the Corner of the Sky (Leo Smit), CRI, 76; Royal Fireworks Music (Handel), Erato, EMI, 76; In Woods (Leo Smit), Orion, 78; Concerto in D Major (Haydn), Arabesque, 82. *Teaching:* Asst prof, State Univ NY, Buffalo, 75-78; assoc prof, Rider Col, 81- *Awards:* Walter Anderson Fel, NY Univ, 73-75; Alice M Ditson Fund, Columbia Univ, 80; Am Philosophical Soc Award, 83. *Mem:* Am Musical Instrm Soc; Int Double Reed Soc; Stefan Wolpe Soc. *Interests:* Oboe's development during the 20th century and the Baroque era. *Publ:* Auth, Varese, Wolpe, and the Oboe, Perspectives New Music, Vol 20, No 1 & 2; The Twentieth Century Oboe in France and England: Makers and Players, Int Double Reed Soc, 82; The Seventeenth Century Oboe Reed, Galpin Soc J, 3/82; Schoenberg, Berlioz and the Oboe: Redesign for the Twentieth Century?, Darmstädter Beiträge Neuer Musik, Vol 18, 83; New Music is Dead—Long Live New Music, Symposium: J Col Music Soc, Vol 23, No 1. *Mailing Add:* 44 Davison Lane E West Islip NY 11795

POSTL, JACOBETH
EDUCATOR, LECTURER
b Chicago, Ill. *Study:* Chicago Musical Col, BM & MM, 42; Orff Inst Salzburg, summers 62 & 63; Univ Toronto, summers 64 & 65; DePaul Univ, Orff cert, 76. *Pos:* Ed & auth, Guideposts column, Orff Echo, Am Orff Schulwerk Asn, 79- *Teaching:* Dir, Music for Children Classes, Skokie, Ill, 50-62 & Ctr Musically Gifted, 65-73; lectr, DePaul Univ, 67- *Mem:* Am Orff Schulwerk Asn (treas, 70-74, vpres, 74-75 & pres, 75-76). *Mailing Add:* 1700 Seward St Evanston IL 60202

POSTLEWATE, CHARLES WILLARD
GUITAR, EDUCATION
b San Antonio, Tex, Jan 8, 41. *Study:* Wayne State Univ, BM & MM, 73; private & masterclass study with Michael Lorimer, studied with Joseph Fava. *Rec Perf:* Dual Image, Prism Studios, 81. *Pos:* Auth & ed, Jazz column, Soundboard Mag, Guitar Found Am, 82- *Teaching:* Instr guitar, Eastern Mich Univ, 72-75; asst prof guitar & chamber music, Wayne State Univ, 75-78; assoc prof guitar, Univ Tex, Arlington, 78- *Mem:* Am String Teachers Asn; Guitar Found Am; Col Music Soc. *Publ:* Auth, A Most Unusual Pair, Am String Teacher, 78; contribr, Guitar Masterclass, Belwin Mills, 80; auth, Andres Segovia—A Living Legend, Am String Teacher, 81. *Mailing Add:* Univ Tex Music Dept PO Box 19105 Arlington TX 76019

POTO, ATTILIO
EDUCATOR, CLARINET
Study: Nat Orch Asn, New York; studied clarinet with Tito Allega, John Rossi, Augusto Vannini & Emil Arcieri & cond with Leon Barzin & Serge Koussevitsky. *Pos:* Mem, Boston Symph Orch, formerly; cond, Mass State Symph Orch, formerly & Army Air Forces Sinfonietta, formerly; solo clarinet, Metropolitan Opera Co, formerly. *Teaching:* Cond orch & symphonic band, Boston Consv, formerly, coordr woodwinds & instr clarinet, cond & ens, currently. *Mailing Add:* Boston Consv 8 The Fenway Boston MA 02215

POTTEBAUM, WILLIAM G
COMPOSER, EDUCATOR
b Teutopolis, Ill, Dec 30, 30. *Study:* Quincy Col, BS(music educ), 53; Eastman Sch Music, with Wayne Barlow, Howard Hanson & Bernard Rogers, MMus(comp & theory), 60, PhD(music comp), 74; Stuttgart Musika Hochschule, studied comp with Hermann Reutter, 54-55; Electronic Music Sem, Univ Toronto, with Myron Schaeffer, 66. *Works:* Concerto for Orchestra, Buffalo, 66; Toccata (orch); Insignia (variations on related motives for orch); 2 Masses (chorus); Theatre Piece (clarinet & tape); Beauty and the Beast (electronic); How the Animals Got Their Names (electronic film score). *Teaching:* Instr pub sch, 55-61; assoc prof music, State Univ NY Col, Brockport, 63-, assoc chmn, Dept Music, 69-70. *Awards:* First Place, Am Music in the Univ Cont, 66. *Mem:* Music Educr Nat Conf; Col Music Soc; Nat Endowment Arts. *Publ:* Coauth, Listening in Depth, 65; Music in Europe, 65; Music in Assisted Instruction Teacher & Student Manuals, 67. *Mailing Add:* 333 St Andrews Dr Rochester NY 14626

POTTENGER, HAROLD PAUL
EDUCATOR, COMPOSER
b Aurora, Mo, Nov 21, 32. *Study:* Univ Mo, BS(music educ), 54; Univ Wichita, MMusEd, 58; Ind Univ, DMusEd, 69. *Works:* Various instrm & choral comp, arr & transcriptions, Broadman Press, Lillenas Publ Co, G Schirmer Inc & Word Music, Inc, 53-83; Suite for Band, Summy-Birchard Co, 65. *Teaching:* Head dept music, dir bands & assoc prof music, Southwest Baptist Univ, 65-68, dean, Sch Music & Fine Arts, 78-82; assoc prof, US Int Univ, Calif, 68-70; dir bands & assoc prof, Bradley Univ, 70-80. *Mem:* Col Band Dir Nat Asn; Music Educr Nat Conf; Col Music Soc. *Interests:* An analysis of rhythm reading skill. *Publ:* Auth, Instrumental Handbook, Beacon Hill Press, 71. *Mailing Add:* 1101 Highland Terrace Bolivar MO 65613

POTTER, DAVID KINSMAN
DOUBLE BASS, EDUCATOR
b Malden, Mass, Jan 7, 32. *Rec Perf:* The Secret Life of an Orchestra (short TV doc); Milena; Cantata for Soprano & Orchestra (Alberto Ginastera), 73. *Pos:* Mem double bass sect, Denver Symph Orch, currently. *Teaching:* Instr double bass, Colo State Univ, formerly; adj mem fac, Univ Colo, Denver. *Mailing Add:* Denver Symph Orch 1245 Champa Denver CO 80204

POTTER, JOHN MATTHEW
WRITER, EDUCATOR

b Milwaukee, Wis, Sept 22, 39. *Study:* Univ Wis, Madison, BA, 61; Harvard Univ, MA, 62; Univ Mich, PhD, 67. *Teaching:* Assoc prof, Hunter Col, City Univ New York, 68- *Interests:* Relations of literature and music. *Publ:* Coauth, Electra, 80 & Mozart's Die Entfuhrung aus dem Serail, 82, Opera News; auth, Wagner: Myth and Music, 81, Cosima Wagner: Nineteenth Century Heroine, 82 & Brünnhilde's Choice, 83, Opera News. *Mailing Add:* 6 Fay Lane South Salem NY 10590

POULOS, BILLIE LOUKAS See Loukas, Billie

POWELL, ARLENE KARR
PIANO, EDUCATOR

b Chicago, Ill. *Study:* Studied with Rudolph Ganz & Rosina Lhevinne; Juilliard Sch Music, dipl; Chicago Musical Col, BMus, MMus; Consv Am, Fontainebleau, cert. *Pos:* Conct pianist, Estelle Lutz Conct Bur, Chicago & Stuart MacClellan Theatrical Enterprises, Chicago, currently. *Teaching:* Prof music, Orange Coast Col, 76- *Mem:* Calif Group Piano Asn (pres & mem bd dir, currently); Compton Civic Symph Orch Asn; Music Asn Calif Community Cols; Calif Music Educr Asn; Music Educr Nat Conf. *Mailing Add:* 9255 Caldium Ave Fountain Valley CA 92708

POWELL, KEITH DOM
FRENCH HORN, COMPOSER

b Downey, Calif, Dec 10, 55. *Study:* State Univ NY, Albany, with Paul Ingraham, State Univ NY, Stony Brook, with Paul Ingraham, BA, 78; Univ Wis, Milwaukee. *Works:* Two Christmas Tunes, Wayte Wind Quintet & Renaissance City Woodwind Quintet, 78; Four Place Settings, Renaissance City Woodwind Quintet, 83. *Pos:* Prin horn, Racine Symph, 78-80 & Milwaukee Civic Conct Band, 80-82; hornist, Wayte Wind Quintet, Wis, 78-82 & Renaissance City Woodwind Quintet, Pa, 82- *Mem:* Chamber Music Am; Int Horn Soc. *Mailing Add:* 824 Kennebec St Pittsburgh PA 15217

POWELL, MEL
COMPOSER

b New York, NY, Feb 12, 23. *Study:* Studied piano with Sara Barg & Nadia Reisenberg, 28-40, comp with Ernst Toch, 46-47; Yale Univ, with Paul Hindemith, MusB, 52. *Works:* Filigree Setting, 59 & Haiku Settings, 60, G Schirmer; Settings for Soprano & Chamber Group, 79, Little Companion Pieces, 80 & String Quartet, 82, MKS Music Co. *Pos:* Prin horn, Am Music Ctr, 47-50. *Teaching:* Prof music, Yale Univ, 58-69; dean sch music, Calif Inst Arts, 69-72, provost, 72-76 & prof musical comp, 76- *Awards:* Nat Inst Arts & Lett Grant, 58; Guggenheim Found Fel, 60. *Bibliog:* L Thimmig (auth), Music of Mel Powell, Music Quart, 61. *Mem:* ASCAP. *Publ:* Auth, Webern's Influence in Am, New York Times, 5/59; A Note on Rigor, Perspectives New Music, Fall 62; Electronic Music & Musical Newness, Am Scholar, 63. *Rep:* MKS Music Co 14054 Chandler Blvd Van Nuys CA 91401. *Mailing Add:* Calif Inst Arts McBean Pkwy Valencia CA 91355

POWELL, MORGAN EDWARD
COMPOSER, TROMBONE

b Graham, Tex, Jan 7, 38. *Study:* NTex State Univ, studied comp with Samuel Adler, BM, 59, MM, 61; Univ Ill, Urbana-Champaign, studied comp with Kenneth Gaburo, 65-67. *Works:* Darkness II (brass quintet & perc); Midnight Realities (solo tuba); Blueberry Blue (piano); Inacabado (solo trombone); Alone (solo trumpet); Light and Shadows (orch & jazz ens); Loneliness (chorus & instrm). *Rec Perf:* On Advance Rec, Crystal Rec & Univ Brass Rec Co. *Pos:* Performer, Contemp Chamber Players, 75; trombonist & cond, Univ Ill Jazz Band. *Teaching:* Instr jazz comp, NTex State Univ, 61-63 & Berklee Sch Music, 63-64; prof theory & comp, Univ Ill, Urbana-Champaign, 66- *Awards:* Best Comp Award, Intercol Jazz Fest, Notre Dame Univ, 61; ASCAP Awards, 70-78; Nat Endowment Arts Grant, 74. *Mem:* ASCAP. *Mailing Add:* Music Dept Univ Ill Urbana IL 61801

POWELL, NEWMAN WILSON
WRITER, EDUCATOR

b David, Panama, Sept 27, 19; US citizen. *Study:* Ohio Univ, BFA, 42; Am Consv Music, MusM, 44; Stanford Univ, MA, 54, PhD, 59. *Teaching:* From instr to assoc prof, Valparaiso Univ, 43-61, prof, 61- *Mem:* Music Librr Asn; Am Musicol Soc; Int Musicol Soc. *Publ:* Ed, Function of the Tactus in the Performance of Renaissance Music, In: Musical Heritage of the Church, Vol 6, Concordia, 63; Festschrift Theodore Hoelty-Nickel: A Collection of Essays on Church Music, Valparaiso Univ, 67. *Mailing Add:* Dept Music Valparaiso Univ Valparaiso IN 46383

POWELL, ROBERT JENNINGS
MUSIC DIRECTOR, COMPOSER

b Benoit, Miss, July 22, 32. *Study:* La State Univ, BM(organ & comp); Sch Sacred Music, Union Theol Sem, New York, MSM, 58. *Works:* Communion Service, Church Hymnal Corp, 75; Yuletide Carols for Brass & Organ, Art Masters Studios, 80; Apperception, Sacred Music Press, 81; Behold, the Tabernacle of God, Augsburg Publ House, 82. *Pos:* Asst organist & choirmaster, Cathedral St John Divine, New York, 57-59; organist & choirmaster, St Paul's Church, Meridian, Miss, 59-65; dir music, St Paul's Sch, Concord, NH, 65-68; organist & choir dir, Christ Church, Greenville, SC, 68- *Awards:* ASCAP Standard Music Award, 68- *Mem:* Am Guild Organists (dean, 81-); Asn Anglican Musicians. *Mailing Add:* 10 N Church St Greenville SC 29601

POWELL, THOMAS ROBERTS
BARITONE

b Philadelphia, Pa, Sept 26, 19. *Study:* Univ Pa, BS, 42; Juilliard Extension Sch, BM, 49. *Rec Perf:* La Boheme, RCA, 55. *Roles:* Police Commissioner in Rosenkavalier, New York City Opera, 53; Mityuk in Boris Godunov, Metropolitan Opera Co, 60. *Pos:* Chorister & comprimario, New York City Opera Co, 49-56; chorister, Metropolitan Opera Co New York, 57- *Mem:* Am Guild Musical Artists (bd mem, 60-66); Am Fedn Radio & TV Artists. *Mailing Add:* Metropolitan Opera Asn Lincoln Ctr New York NY 10023

POWERS, JEFFREY STEVEN
FRENCH HORN, TEACHER-COACH

b Buffalo, NY, Apr 18, 54. *Study:* Austin Col, Sherman, Tex, BA, 75; Blossom Fest Sch of Cleveland Orch, with Albert Schmitter, Myron Bloom, James London & Roy Waas, 76; Cleveland Inst Music, MM(horn), 77. *Pos:* French horn, Hong Kong Phil Orch, 77-78, NJ Symph Orch, Newark, 78-79, Filarmonica Caracas, Venezuela, 79 & Cleveland Orch, 80- *Teaching:* Instr horn & ens coach, Hong Kong Govt Music Adminr Off, 78; instr horn & chamber music coach, Summer Music Experience, Hudson, Ohio, 80- *Mem:* Am Fedn Musicians. *Mailing Add:* 2374 Euclid Heights Blvd Apt 101 Cleveland OH 44106

POWERS, WILLIAM
BASS-BARITONE

b Chicago, Ill, Sept 22, 41. *Study:* Ill Wesleyan Univ, with Lewis E Whikehart, dipl; Am Consv Music, with David Austin; studied with Frederick D Wilkerson; study with John Bullock, currently. *Rec Perf:* Ein Deutsches Requiem (Brahms) & The Taming of the Shrew (Giannini), CRI. *Roles:* Leporello in Don Giovanni, New York City Opera, 72; Jokanaan in Salome, Conn Opera, 82; Escamillo in Carmen, East Lansing, 82; Four Villains in The Tales of Hoffmann, Lake George Fest, 82; Falstaff in Falstaff, 83 & Mephistopheles in Faust, Cleveland Opera; Scarpia in Tosca, Charlotte, 83; and others. *Pos:* Performer with major Am opera co. *Awards:* Baltimore Opera Audition Winner; Sullivan Found Fel; Rockefeller Grants. *Mailing Add:* c/o Courtenay Artists Inc 411 E 53rd St Suite 6F New York NY 10022

POWLEY, E HARRISON, III
EDUCATOR, PERCUSSION

b Orange, NJ, Jan 10, 43. *Study:* Eastman Sch Music, with William G Street, Michael Collins, Erich Schwandt, Charles W Fox & Hendrik van der Werf, BM(perc & music educ), 65, MA(musicol), 68, PhD(musicol), 74. *Pos:* Perc, Rochester Phil Orch, 63-65 & 66-69. *Teaching:* Instr perc, Eastman Sch Music, 66-69; asst prof music, Brigham Young Univ, 69-75, assoc prof, 75-82, prof, 82- *Awards:* Fulbright Fel, 65-66; NDEA Title IV Grant, 66-69; res award, Col Fine Arts & Communications, Brigham Young Univ, 81-83. *Mem:* Int Musicol Soc; Am Musicol Soc (chap chmn, 79-80); Music Librr Asn; Col Music Soc; Percussive Arts Soc. *Interests:* Italian madrigal of late 16th century; history of timpani and percussion; symphonies of Druschetzky. *Publ:* Auth, Bonini & Florio, In: New Grove Dict of Music & Musicians, Macmillan, 80; co-ed, Complete Percussion Music of William G Street, Eastman Sch Music, 83; ed, Editions of Symphonies by Druschetzky, Hertel, Molter & Fischer, Garland Press, 84; auth, Il Trionfo di Dori: Performing Edition, Galaxy Music (in prep). *Mailing Add:* E-221 HFAC Brigham Young Univ Provo UT 84602

POZDRO, JOHN WALTER
COMPOSER, EDUCATOR

b Chicago, Ill, Aug 14, 23. *Study:* Am Consv Music, with Edward Collins, 41-42; Northwestern Univ, with Robert Mills Delaney, BMus, 43, MMus, 49; Eastman Sch Music, with Howard Hanson, Bernard Rogers & Alan Hovhaness, PhD, 58. *Works:* All Pleasant Things; They That Go Down to the Sea; Landscapes I & II, 64 & 70; Preludes for Piano, 74 & 77; Bagatelle (clarinet & piano), 78; three symphonies & six sonatas for piano. *Rec Perf:* Third Symph; Piano Sonatas No 2 & 3; They That Go Down to the Sea. *Pos:* Dir, Annual Symph Contemp Am Music, Univ Kans, 58-69. *Teaching:* Instr, Iowa State Univ, 49-50; vis prof, Northwestern Univ; prof, Univ Kans, 50-, dir div music theory & comp, 61- *Awards:* Delius Found Award, 74; Nat Endowment Arts Grant, 76; ASCAP Award, 78-79. *Mem:* ASCAP; Pi Kappa Lambda; Kans Music Teacher Asn. *Mailing Add:* Dept Music Univ Kans Lawrence KS 66094

PRANSCHKE, JANET
SOPRANO

b Steubenville, Ohio. *Study:* Ithaca Col, BA; Juilliard Am Opera Ctr; Mannes Col Music. *Roles:* Hanna Glawari in The Merry Widow, Washington, DC Civic Opera, 81; Mimi in La Boheme, 82 & Julie in Ma Tante Aurore (Boieldieu), 82, Asolo Opera; Adina in The Elixir of Love, Des Moines Metro Fest, 82. *Pos:* Apprentice aritist, Santa Fe Opera & Chautauqua Opera; soprano, Va Opera, New York City Opera Theatre, Annapolis Opera, Glimmerglass Opera, Washington, DC Civic Opera & Goldovsky Opera Theatre. *Awards:* Sullivan Found Award; First Prize, Liederkrantz Found; Winner, Int Vocal Compt, Munich, Germany. *Mailing Add:* c/o Sullivan & Lindsey Assoc 133 W 87th St New York NY 10024

PRATER, JEFFREY L
COMPOSER, EDUCATOR

b Endicott, NY, Oct 4, 47. *Study:* Iowa State Univ, with Gary White, BS, 69; Mich State Univ, with H Owen Reed, MM, 73; Univ Wash, with William Bergsma. *Works:* Two Movements (brass sextet), 69; Two Soliloquies (solo violin), 71; Kinetics, 73; Hexalogues (woodwind quintet & marimba), 75; Eulogy for the Wilderness, 76; Three Reflexives (trumpet, trombone & perc),

78. *Teaching:* Fac mem, Univ Wis, Marinette, 72-76; asst prof theory, analysis & comp, Iowa State Univ, 77- *Awards:* Winner, Comp Cont, Contemp Music Fest, Ind State Univ, 74 & Iowa Choral Dir Asn Cont, 78. *Mailing Add:* Iowa St Univ Ames IA 50011

PRAUSNITZ, FREDERIK W
MUSIC DIRECTOR, EDUCATOR
b Cologne, Germany, Aug 26, 20; nat US. *Study:* Grad Sch, Juilliard Sch, studied cond with Albert Stoessel & Edgar Schenkman, piano with Carl Friedberg, comp with Karl Weigl, Bernard Wagenaar & Wallingford Riegger & opera with Erich Kleiber & Wilfred Pelletier. *Rec Perf:* Time-Life doc film, 59; rec on Angel, Argo, Columbia, EMI, Philips & Epic. *Pos:* Cond, Martha Graham Dance Co, 52-61, Jose Limon Dance Co, 52-61, Doris Humphrey Dance Co, 52-61, Jeunesses Musicales Orch, summers 59-61 & New England Consv Music Orch, 61-69; guest cond, BBC Orch, London Symph Orch & others throughout Europe & Cent & North Am, 57-; consult, Dimitri Metropoulos Compt Cond, 61, Lincoln Ctr Perf Arts, 63 & Oakland Univ, 69-71; music dir, Syracuse Symph, 71-75. *Teaching:* Mem fac chamber music & opera, Juilliard Sch Music, 46-61, assoc dir pub activ, 47-49, assoc dean, 49-61, dir, Juilliard Chorus, 56-61, assoc cond, Juilliard Orch, 56-61; instr cond sem, BBC Training Orch, England, 62-67 & Dartington Hall, England, summers 64, 66 & 67; lectr, Harvard Univ, 66-67; hon fel, Sussex Univ, England, 70; spec asst to provost perf arts, Oakland Univ, 71-; music dir, Peabody opera theatre & orch, 76-80, music dir emer, 80-, dir cond prog, Contemp Music Ens, 80- *Awards:* First prize, Young Cond Compt, Detroit Symph Orch, 44; Rockefeller Found Grant, 66; Gustav Mahler Medal Hon, Am Bruckner Soc, 74. *Mem:* Int Soc Contemp Music (dir, 60-62); Am Symph Orch League; Savage Club, London. *Publ:* Auth, Score and Podium, W W Norton, 80. *Mailing Add:* Peabody Consv Music 1 E Mt Vernon Pl Baltimore MD 21202

PREATE, SALLY EDWARDS
ADMINISTRATOR
b Washington, DC, Apr 9, 40. *Study:* Sarah Lawrence Col, BA, 62; Grad Faculties, Columbia Univ, 62-64. *Pos:* Gen mgr, Northeastern Pa Phil & Metropolitan Orch Mgrs Asn, 76-; vpres, Am Symph Orch League, 80-82. *Mailing Add:* Box 71 Avoca PA 18641

PREISS, JAMES
EDUCATOR, PERCUSSION
Study: Eastman Sch Music, BM; Manhattan Sch Music, MM; studied with Street, Beck, Hinger, Lang & Price. *Pos:* Mem, Eastman Wind Ens & Philharmonia & Rochester Phil; timpanist & marimba soloist, US Marine Band; participant, Brooklyn Philharmonia, Music for Westchester Symph, Opera Orch NY, Steve Reich & Musicians, Parnassus & 20th Century Ens. *Teaching:* Mem fac perc, Manhattan Sch Music, 70- *Mailing Add:* 32-33 35th St Astoria NY 11106

PRELL, DONALD D
DOUBLE BASS
b Santa Monica, Calif. *Study:* String bass, Utah Symph, 56, San Francisco Opera, 64-80 & San Francisco Symph, 64- *Mailing Add:* 485 Pennsylvania San Francisco CA 94107

PRESSER, WILLIAM HENRY
COMPOSER
b Saginaw, Mich, Apr 19, 16. *Study:* Alma Col, BA, 38; Univ Mich, MMus, 40; Eastman Sch Music, Rochester Univ, PhD, 47. *Works:* The Devil's Footprints (band); Rhapsody on a Peaceful Theme (violin, horn & piano); Sonatina (trombone or bassoon & piano); Second Sonatina (tuba & piano); Second Brass Quintet; Symphony No 2 (band). *Pos:* Violin & viola, Rochester Phil, 44-46. *Teaching:* Assoc prof music, Fla State Col for Women, 46-47; dept head, Florence State Col, Ala, 47-50 & WTex State Col, 50-51; instr, San Francisco Inst Music, 51-53; prof, Univ Southern Miss, 53-81. *Awards:* Eleven First Awards, Nat Comp Compt. *Mem:* ASCAP. *Mailing Add:* 211 Hillendale Dr Hattiesburg MS 39401

PRESSLAFF, HILARY TANN
COMPOSER, EDUCATOR
b Llwynypia, Wales, UK, 47. *Study:* Univ Wales, Cardiff, BMus, 68; Princeton Univ, with Milton Babbitt & B A Boretz, MFA, 75 & with Carlton Gamer & J K Randall, PhD, 81. *Works:* Templum (comput-synthesized tape), McMillan Theatre, NY & Kresge Hall, Boston, 76; As Ferns (string orch), Princeton Univ & La State Univ Orch, 78; A Sad Pavan Forbidding Mourning (guitar solo) perf by Ron Letteron, 82 & David Wolff, 83; Duo (oboe & viola), perf Susan St Armour & Gene Marie Green, 83. *Pos:* Assoc ed, Perspectives New Music, 79-; ed, Newsletter, Int League Women Comp. *Teaching:* Asst prof music, Bard Col, 77-80 & Union Col, 80- *Awards:* Union Col Pew Mem Trust Award, 83. *Mem:* Am Soc Univ Comp; Int League Women Comp. *Publ:* Auth, The Investigation, Perspectives New Music, Vol XX, 81; Review of American Society of University Composers 18th Annual Conference, Int League Women Comp Newsletter, Spring 83. *Mailing Add:* 128 N College St Schenectady NY 12305

PRESSLER, MENAHEM
PIANO, EDUCATOR
b Magdeburg, Germany; US citizen. *Study:* Tel Aviv, Israel, 39-46; studied with Egon Petri, Stenerman & Robert Casadesus. *Rec Perf:* Complete trios of Haydn, Beethoven, Brahms, Schumann, Mendelssohn, Schubert, Dvorak, Ravel, Ives, Tchaikovsky & Smetana, Philips, 83-; Two Concerti (Mozart), Musical Heritage. *Pos:* Mem, Beaux Arts Trio, currently. *Teaching:*

Distinguished prof piano, Ind Univ, 55, Banff Sch Arts, 55 & Univ Kans, 55. *Awards:* Grand Prix Disques, Acad Charles Cross, 64; Best Rec of Yr, England Phono Gramophone Mag, 81; Prix Honor, Montreux Fest, Switz, 83. *Mailing Add:* 1214 Pickwick Bloomington IN 47401

PRESTON, (MARY) JEAN
EDUCATOR, VOICE
b Montpelier, Idaho, Sept 3, 25. *Rec Perf:* Mass of St Cecilia (Scarlatti); King David (Honegger); Samson (Handel); Book of Mormon Oratorio (Robertson). *Pos:* Conct performer, Utah Symph, Houston Symph, Houston Grand Opera, Corpus Christi Symph, Houston Chamber Orch & Bach Soc; soloist. *Teaching:* Assoc prof voice, Univ Houston, currently. *Mailing Add:* Dept Music Univ Houston Houston TX 77004

PREVES, MILTON
VIOLA, LECTURER
b Cleveland, Ohio. *Pos:* Head viola sect, Chicago Little Symph, formerly; mem, Chicago Symph Orch, 34-, prin violist, 39-; mem, Mischakoff String Quartet & Chicago Symph String Quartet, currently; cond, NSide Symph, Chicago, currently & Wheaton Summer Symph, currently; soloist, summer conct, Ravinia Fest. *Teaching:* Lectr viola, DePaul Univ, currently. *Mailing Add:* 721 Raleigh Rd Glenview IL 60025

PREVIN, ANDRE
MUSIC DIRECTOR, COMPOSER
b Berlin, Germany, Apr 6, 29; US citizen. *Works:* Cello Concerto, 68 & Guitar Concerto, 74, Schirmer; Every Good Boy Deserves Favour, 77, Six Songs, 80, Principals, 81, Reflections, 82 & Piano Concerto (in prep), Chester Music. *Rec Perf:* Over 150 titles, EMI, Phillips, Decca & RCA. *Pos:* Music dir, Houston Symph, 67-69, London Symph, 68-79, Pittsburgh Symph, 76- & Royal Phil, 82- *Awards:* Acad Award, 59, 60, 62 & 63; Rec of Year, Gramophone Mag, 80; Six Grammy Awards Phonograph Rec. *Bibliog:* E Greenfield (auth), Andre Previn, Gramophone, 74; M Bookspan (auth), Andre Previn, Random House, 81; H Ruttencutter (auth), Andre Previn, New Yorker Mag, 83. *Publ:* Coauth, Music Face to Face, H Hamilton, 72; ed, Orchestra, McDonald & Jane, 81. *Rep:* Columbia Artists 165 W 57th New York NY 10019. *Mailing Add:* Pittsburgh Symph 600 Penn Ave Heinz Hall Pittsburgh PA 15222

PRICE, HENRY PASCHAL, III
TENOR
b Oakland, Calif, Oct 18, 45. *Study:* NTex State Univ, with Eugene Conley, BA, 69; studied with Oren Brown & Boris Goldovsky. *Roles:* Alfredo in La Traviata, Goldovsky Grand Opera Theater, 70; Count Almaviva in Il Barbiere di Siviglia; Alfred in Die Fledermaus; Duke of Mantua in Rigoletto; Tamino in The Magic Flute; Des Grieux in Manon; Camille in The Merry Widow. *Pos:* Lyr ten, Metropolitan Opera Studio, 70-74, Lake George Fest, 73-77, Am Opera Ctr, 73-74 & with many US opera co & symph orchs. *Awards:* Young Singer Grant, Nat Opera Inst, 72-73. *Rep:* Herbert Barrett Mgt 1860 Broadway New York NY 10023. *Mailing Add:* 54 W 71 St New York NY 10019

PRICE, JOHN ELWOOD
COMPOSER, EDUCATOR
b Tulsa, Okla, June 21, 35. *Study:* Lincoln Univ, studied comp with O A Fuller & piano with Gwendolyn Belchoir, BMus, 57; Univ Tulsa, studied comp with Bela Rozsa, MMus, 63; Wash Univ, St Louis, studied comp with Robert Wykes & Harold Blumenfeld, 67-68. *Works:* Scherzo I (clarinet & piano), perf by Oakland Youth Symph, 71; Sienfhoni (clarinet & choir), comn by Univ Ill Bands Clarinet Choir, 79; Spirituals for the Young Pianist, Belwin-Mills, 79; Louie Alexander (ballet), Tuskegee Dance Theatre, 83; Prayer: Martin Luther King (SSAATTBB), 83, Impulse and Deviation I (cello), 83 & ... And So Faustus Lost His Soul (small orch), 83, Anthology Black Music, Vol III. *Teaching:* Chmn music & fine arts, Fla Mem Col, 64-74, comp in res, 69-74; prof theory, lit & black music, Eastern Ill Univ, 74-80; Portia-Washington Pittman Fel, Tuskegee Inst, 81- *Awards:* Distinguished Fac Award, Eastern Ill Univ, Charleston, 79-80; Mayor's Comn Cult Affairs Award, City of Tuskegee, 83. *Bibliog:* Alice Tischler (auth), Fifteen Black American Composers, Info Coord, 81; Hildred Roach (auth), Black American Music: Past & Present, 2nd Ed, Krieger Publ Co, 83. *Mem:* ASCAP; life mem, Phi Mu Alpha Sinfonia; Nat Black Music Caucus; Nat Asn Comp USA; Soc Black Comp. *Publ:* Auth, The Black Musician as Artist and Entrepreneur, Phelps-Stokes Fund, 73-74; Joseph B Saint Georges: Genius of Guadeloupe, Mich State Univ Student Asn, 79. *Mailing Add:* 309 Gregory Pl Tuskegee AL 36088

PRICE, LEONTYNE
SOPRANO
b Laurel, Miss, Feb 10, 27. *Study:* Cent State Col, Ohio, BA, 49, DMus, 68; Juilliard Sch Music, 49-52; studied with Florence Page Kimball; numerous hon degrees. *Rec Perf:* For RCA Victor, 58- *Roles:* Sop in Four Saints in Three Acts, Broadway, 51; Bess in Porgy and Bess, Vienna, Berlin, Paris, London & New York, 52-54; Mme Lidoine in Dialogues des Carmelites, San Francisco Opera, 57; Aida in Aida, Paris Opera, 68; Fiordiligi in Cosi fan tutte; Donna Elvira in Ernani; Cleopatra in Antony & Cleopatra. *Pos:* Soloist with symph in US, Can, Europe & Australia, 54- & Hollywood Bowl, 55-59; sop, NBC-TV, 55-58, 60, 62 & 64, San Francisco Opera Co, 57-59, 60-61, 63, 65, 67, 68 & 71, Vienna Staatsoper, 58, 59-60 & 61, Berlin Opera, 64, Rome Opera, 66 & Paris Opera, 68; res mem, Metropolitan Opera, currently. *Awards:* Musician of Year, Musical Am Mag, 61; Schwann Catalog Award, 68; Grammy Awards (20). *Mem:* Am Fedn TV & Radio Artists; Am Guild Musical Artists; Actors Equity Asn; Sigma Alpha Iota. *Mailing Add:* c/o Columbia Artists Mgt 165 W 57th St New York NY 10019

PRICE, MARGARET
SOPRANO

b Apr 13, 41, Blackwood, Wales. *Study:* Trinity Col Music, London. *Rec Perf:* Tristan und Isolde & Un Ballo in Maschera, EMI; works by Beethoven, Elgar, Handel, Mahler, Puccini & Vaughn Williams. *Roles:* Cherubino in Marriage of Figaro, Welsh Nat Opera, 62 & Royal Opera House, 63; Pamina in Die Zauberflote & Marzellina in Fidelio, Royal Opera House; Aida in Aida, San Franciso Opera, 82; Mimi in La Boheme; Desdemona in Otello. *Pos:* Guest artist, Chicago Lyric Opera, Hamburg Staatsoper, La Scala, Munich Staatsoper, Paris Opera, Opernhaus Zurich, Vienna Staatsoper & others. *Awards:* Silver Melal, Worshipful Co Musicians; Elisabeth Schumann Prize for Lieder; Ricordi Opera Prize. *Mailing Add:* c/o Columbia Artists 165 W 57th St New York NY 10019

PRICE, PAUL (WILLIAM)
PERCUSSION

b Fitchburg, Mass, May 15, 21. *Study:* New England Consv, dipl; Cincinnati Consv, MM; studied perc with George Carey & Fred Noak. *Works:* Inventions (four percussionists), 47; 12 Solos for Timpani, 51; Exibitions (snare drum); Six Bass Drum Solos. *Pos:* Cond, Manhattan Perc Ens, 67-68; pres & ed, Music for Perc Inc; mem, Am Symph Orch, formerly; owner, Paul Price Publ. *Teaching:* Fac mem, Univ Ill, Boston Univ, Ithaca Col, Newark State Col & Manhattan Sch Music, 57- *Awards:* Outstanding Contrib to Am Music Award, Asn Am Comp Cond; Percussive Arts Soc Hall of Fame. *Mailing Add:* Manhattan Sch Music 120 Claremont Ave New York NY 10027

PRICE, RICHARD GALEN
FRENCH HORN, ARRANGER

b Ann Arbor, Mich, Jan 31, 56. *Study:* Univ Mich, with Louis Stout, BMus, 77; Aspen Music Fest, with John Cerminaro & Philip Farkas, 75-77; Juilliard Sch Music, with James Chambers, 77-79. *Rec Perf:* Rec with Musical Heritage Soc, Golden Crest & Music Masters. *Pos:* Hornist & founding mem, Borealis Wind Quintet, NY, 77-; freelance hornist, various NY groups, 77-; solo horn, Chamber Orch NY, 80- & Fairfield, Conn Chamber Orch, 80- *Mailing Add:* 4523 Broadway New York NY 10040

PRICE, ROBERT BATES
EDUCATOR, VIOLIN

b Greenwood, La, June 6, 34. *Study:* Berkshire Music Ctr, summers 55 & 56; Centenary Col La, BM, 57; Peabody Consv Music, violin study with William Kroll, 60; Univ Ark, MM, 65; Cath Univ, DMA, 77. *Pos:* Violinist, US Air Force Symph Orch, 57-61 & 65-69; concertmaster, Northwestern Symph Orch, Natchitoches, 70- & Rapides Symph Orch, Alexandria, La, 75- *Teaching:* Prof violin & viola, Northwestern State Univ, 70- *Mailing Add:* 340 Keegan Dr Natchitoches LA 71457

PRICE, SHELBY MILBURN, JR
EDUCATOR, MUSIC DIRECTOR

b Electric Mills, Miss, Apr 9, 38. *Study:* Univ Miss, BMus, 60; Baylor Univ, MMus, 63; Univ Southern Calif, DMA, 67. *Teaching:* Lectr church music, Univ Southern Calif, Los Angeles, 66-67; from asst prof to prof music, Furman Univ, 67-81; prof & dean sch church music, Southern Baptist Theol Sem, Ky, 81- *Mem:* Am Choral Dir Asn; Hymn Soc Am; Nat Asn Teachers Singing; Southern Baptist Church Music Conf. *Publ:* Coauth, A Joyful Sound: Christian Hymnody, Holt, Rinehart & Winston, 78. *Mailing Add:* 4126 Brentler Rd Louisville KY 40222

PRIDONOFF, ELIZABETH ANNA
PIANO, EDUCATOR

b Baton Rouge, La, July 19, 52. *Study:* George Peabody Col for Teachers, BM, 72; Juilliard Sch Music, MM, 75; Acad Musicale Chigiana, artist dipl, 75. *Teaching:* Asst prof piano, Col Consv Music, Univ Cincinnati, 82- *Awards:* First Place, Int Southwest Piano Compt, 77 & Nat Duo Piano Comp, 78. *Mem:* Matinee Musicale Club; Clifton Music Club; Woman's Music Club. *Rep:* Am Int Artist 275 Madison Ave New York NY 10016. *Mailing Add:* 1025 Marion Ave Cincinnati OH 45229

PRIDONOFF, EUGENE ALEXANDER
PIANO, EDUCATOR

b Los Angeles, Calif, Sept 15, 42. *Study:* Univ Southern Calif, with Lillian Steuber, 55-61; Curtis Inst Music, with Rudolf Serkin & Mieczyslaw Horszowski, BM, 66; Temple Univ, MM, 66. *Teaching:* From asst prof to assoc prof piano & chmn, Iowa State Univ, 68-71; from assoc to prof, Sch Music, Ariz State Univ, 71-80, chmn piano, 72-75, chmn perf div, 77-80; prof, Col Consv Music, Univ Cincinnati, 80-, head perf studied div, 82- *Mem:* Music Teachers Nat Asn; Am Music Scholar Asn. *Rep:* Am Int Artists 275 Madison Ave New York NY 10016. *Mailing Add:* 1025 Marion Ave Cincinnati OH 45229

PRIEST-STEVENS, MAXINE (MAXINE STEVENS)
EDUCATOR

Study: Oberlin Col, BA, BM; Ind Univ, MM; studied with Victor Babin, Bela Borszomenyi Nagy, Menachem Pressler & Vitja Vronksy. *Pos:* Performer solo & chamber music, currently. *Teaching:* Mem fac, Cleveland Inst Music, 63- *Mailing Add:* Cleveland Inst Music 11021 E Boulevard Cleveland OH 44106

PRIMUS, CONSTANCE MERRILL
TEACHER, RECORDER

b Denver, Colo, Aug 26, 31. *Study:* Univ Colo, Boulder, studied thesis with Alan Luhring & counterpoint & analysis with Cecil Effinger, BMus(hist & lit),

78. *Teaching:* Private flute & recorder, 64-; instr recorder, YWCA, Denver, 69-73 & Arvada Ctr Arts & Humanities, Colo, 78-; mem fac, Orff-Schulwerk, Univ Denver, summer, 76; dir, Am Recorder Soc Wkshp, Colorado Springs, 80- *Mem:* Am Rec Soc (vpres & dir educ, 80-, music dir, Denver chap, 75-77); Rocky Mountain Flute Asn. *Interests:* Canassi's Fontegara (1535). *Publ:* Coauth, American Recorder Society Education Program, Am Recorder Soc, 81. *Mailing Add:* 13607 W Mississippi Ct Lakewood CO 80228

PRINDLE, ROMA HOWARD
TEACHER, SOPRANO

b Harlan, Ky, Dec 15, 51. *Study:* Transylvania Univ, AB, 73; Hartt Col Music, MM, 79; studied with Brenda Lewis, 76-79. *Pos:* Dir, Opera Wkshp, 80- *Teaching:* Instr voice, Westfield State Col, 74-79 & Clarion State Col, 79-80; instr voice & opera, Augustana Col, 80- *Awards:* Second Place, Metropolitan Opera Nat Coun, 83. *Mem:* Nat Fedn Music Clubs (vpres, 82-83 & pres, 83-); Nat Asn Teachers Singing; Am Choral Dir Asn. *Mailing Add:* Music Dept Augustana Col Sioux Falls SD 57197

PRITCHARD, ROBERT STARLING
COMPOSER, PIANO

b Winston-Salem, NC, June 13, 29. *Study:* Sch Music, Syracuse Univ, BS, 48, MM, 50; studied with Kirk Ridge, Carl Friedberg, Robert Goldsand, Hans Neumann & Arturo Benedetti Michelangeli. *Works:* Choreographic Suite in Seven, 56; Isle of Springs Cantata, comn by Jamaica Progressive League, New York, 62; Ti Jacques Suite, Belwin-Mills, 65; Eulogy & Elegy for Clyde Kennard (text by John Howard Griffin), Tougaloo Col, Miss, 65; Mass on Peace & Reconciliation, comn by Grace Episcopal Church, Syracuse, NY, 66. *Rec Perf:* Robert Pritchard, Pianist, Spoken Arts, 62; Composers Recital, Powertree Rec, 65; Louis Moreau Gottschalk Centennial Concert, Vox Turnabout, 71. *Pos:* Founder & chmn, Panamerican/Panafrican Asn Inc, Baldwinsville, NY, 67-; chmn music adv bd, Corcoran Gallery Art, Washington, DC, 68-70; chmn bd gov, Kahre-Richardes Family Found, 72- *Teaching:* Artist in res, Repub Haiti, 58-59 & Repub Liberia, 59-60; mem fac music, Consv Port-au-Prince, Haiti, 58-59; chmn music dept, Univ Liberia, Monrovia, 59-60. *Awards:* Distinguished Serv to Music Citation, Orgn Am States, 69. *Interests:* Life and piano works of Louis Moreau Gottschalk; works of ecclesiastical guilds of Brazilian black composers of baroque and pre-classical period. *Publ:* Auth, Proposal for World Festival of Black Arts, Coun Ministers Mali Fedn, 60; Monograph on Multi-Culturalism, 74 & Anatomy of Transnational Cultural & Leisure Arts Embargo, 78, Panamerican/Panafrican Asn. *Mailing Add:* c/o New World Fest Concerts PO Box 143 Baldwinsville NY 13027

PRITCHETT, THEODORE M
ADMINISTRATOR, EDUCATOR

b Birmingham, Ala, July 27, 35. *Study:* Birmingham-Southern Col, AB, 57; Fla State Univ, MME, 60, PhD, 70. *Pos:* Dir, Univ Montevallo Chamber Choir, 70-; musical dir, Cent Players, Birmingham, 72-81; prod, Univ Montevallo Lyr Theatre, 78- *Teaching:* Choral dir, Hueytown High Sch, Ala, 56-59 & Bay Co High Sch, Panama City, Fla, 60-63; prof, Univ Montevallo, 63-, chmn music dept, 78- *Mem:* Ala Music Educr Asn; Asn Ala Col Music Adminr (pres, 80-83); Music Educr Nat Conf. *Mailing Add:* Music Dept Univ Montevallo Montevallo AL 35115

PRITTS, ROY A
COMPOSER, EDUCATOR

b Denver, Colo, Dec 17, 36. *Study:* Univ Denver, BMEd, 66, MA, 75; Univ Miami, currently. *Works:* Burnt Orange Kickor, Polyton Music & ASCAP, 75; The Last Question, 77 & Vision Beyond Time, 77, Gates Planetarium; UFO's: Strangers?, Columbia Pictures & Gates Planetarium, 77; Whirlpools of Darkness, Walt Disney Prod & Gates Planetarium, 80; Ringmodulation Two, 81 & Ringmodulation Three, 83, Denver Symph Orch. *Pos:* Arr, Stan Kenton Orch, 58-59; music dir, J Prod Inc, 63-66; pres, Polyton Prod Inc, 70-72. *Teaching:* Instr band & choir, Adams Co District #12, Thornton, Colo, 66-69; asst prof music technol, Univ Colo, Denver, 71-77, assoc prof, 77- *Awards:* Outstanding Comp, Nat Collegiate Jazz Fest, 63; Centennial Award, Bd Regents, Univ Colo, 76. *Mem:* Am Fedn Musicians; ASCAP; Audio Engineering Soc; Colo Asn Jazz Educr (pres, 76-78). *Publ:* Coauth, Power Amplifiers & Loudspeakers for Electronic Music, 74 & Live Electronic Music in Large Auditoriums, 75, Audio Engineering Soc J; auth, Creation of Psycho-acoustics for Synthetic Music, Inst Electrical & Electronic Engineers Proc, 77; coauth, Loudspeakers for Electronic Church Organs, ASA Proc, 79; auth, Sound Processing, Downbeat, 80. *Mailing Add:* 601 W 11th Ave #122 Denver CO 80204

PROCTER, CAROL ANN
CELLO, VIOLA DA GAMBA

b Oklahoma City, Okla, June 26, 41. *Study:* Eastman Sch Music, 58-60; New England Consv Music, BM, 63, MM, 65. *Pos:* Cello, Springfield Symph Orch, 61-65, Boston Symph Orch, 65- & Boston Pops Orch, 65-; asst prin, Japan Phil, Tokyo, 69-70; cello, New England Harp Trio, 71-, Curtisville Consortium, 74- & Berkshire String Trio, 80. *Awards:* Fulbright Award, 65; Fromm Fel, Berkshire Music Ctr, 65. *Mailing Add:* c/o Boston Symph 301 Massachusetts Ave Boston MA 02115

PROCTER, LELAND (HERRICK)
COMPOSER, EDUCATOR

b Newton, Mass, Mar 24, 14. *Study:* Eastman Sch Music, BM, 38; Univ Okla, MM, 40; Harvard Univ, 51-52. *Works:* Symphony No 1, perf by Oklahoma City Symph, 51; Quintet for Piano & Strings, perf by New England Consv

Music, 51; Five Easy Pieces (piano), Am Music Co, 52; Vikings (piano), Scribner Music Libr, 64; Symphony No 1, Polish Nat Radio Orch, 67; Seascape for Orchestra, comn & perf by Cape Cod Symph Orch, 76. *Teaching:* Head music dept theory & hist music, Southwestern State Col, 39-44; fac mem theory & comp, New England Consv Music, 46-58; vis lectr, Wellesley Col, 53-54 & Newton High Sch, 64-65. *Awards:* Second Place, Chamber Music Contest, for String Quartet No 1, Nat Fedn Music Clubs, 43; grant, Fund for Advan Educ, 51. *Mem:* Am Comp Alliance. *Publ:* Auth, Tonal Counterpoint, William C Brown & Co, 57. *Mailing Add:* 1 South Rd Hampden MA 01036

PRODAN, JAMES CHRISTIAN
EDUCATOR, OBOE & ENGLISH HORN
b Columbus, Ohio, Jan 4, 47. *Study:* Ohio State Univ, BS(music educ), 69, DMA, 76; Cath Univ, MM, 72. *Rec Perf:* Cambini Wind Quintet, Coronet Rec, 79. *Pos:* Prin oboe, Greensboro Symph, NC, 79-; solo English horn, Winston-Salem Symph, NC, 80- *Teaching:* Asst prof music, Univ Akron, 75-79 & Univ NC, Greensboro, 79- *Mem:* Int Double Reed Soc; Am Fedn Musicians; Am Symph Orch League; Music Educr Nat Conf; Nat Asn Col Wind & Perc Instr. *Interests:* Unpublished old and new music for double reeds. *Publ:* Auth, The Effect of Intonation of the Crow of the Reed on Oboe Tone Quality, Int Double Reed Soc, 77; Oboe Performance Practices in US and Canada, Inst Woodwind Res, 79; ed, Woodwind Notes, 79 & auth, Oboe Intonation Solutions, 80, NC Music Educr; coauth, Oboe Discography, Int Double Reed Soc, 82. *Mailing Add:* 1814 Dunleith Way Greensboro NC 27408

PROTO, FRANK
COMPOSER, DOUBLE BASS
b Brooklyn, NY, July 18, 41. *Study:* Manhattan Sch Music, with David Walter, MMus, 66. *Works:* Concerto in One Movement (violin, double bs & orch), 72, 3 Pieces for Percussion & Orchestra, 76, String Quartet No 1, 77, Concerto for Cello and Orchestra, 78, The Four Seasons (tuba, perc, strings & tape), 79, Concerto No 2 (double bs & orch), 81 & Concerto No 3 (double bs & orch), 83, Liben Music Publ. *Rec Perf:* The Sound of the Bass Vol 1, 77, Carmen: Symphony Jazz Ensemble, 77, The Sound of the Bass Vol 2, 78 & East Side Corridor: Symphony Jazz Ensemble, 77, QCA Red Mark; A Potrait of George, VOX, 80; Reflections: Music for Viola and Double Bass, 82, QCA Red Mark/ Liben. *Pos:* Double bassist, Cincinnati Symph Orch, 66- & comp in res, 70- *Teaching:* Artist in res double bs & comp in res comp, Univ Cincinnati, 67-78, instr double bs, 82. *Awards:* Int Rostrum Comp Award, Nat Public Radio/Am Music Ctr, 82. *Mem:* Am Music Ctr; Cincinnati Comp Guild; ASCAP. *Mailing Add:* 6265 Dawes Lane Cincinnati OH 45230

PROVENZANO, ALDO
COMPOSER
b Philadelphia, Pa, May 3, 30. *Study:* Juilliard Sch, with Peter Mennin, BS, 56, MS, 57. *Works:* The Cask of Amontillado (opera), 68; Malacchio (ballet); Essay (string quartet); Recitation (violin & piano); Jacktown (jazz score); and others. *Pos:* Comp, arr & cond for rec, films, TV & dance groups. *Teaching:* Instr, pub sch, 57-64, Eastman Sch Music, 64-69, Juilliard Sch, 69-70 & City Col New York, 71-75; dir, Exten Div, Philadelphia Col Perf Arts, 74-78. *Mailing Add:* 429 Burning Tree Rd Cherry Hill NJ 08034

PROVOST, RICHARD (CHARLES)
EDUCATOR, GUITAR & LUTE
b Holyoke, Mass, Feb 27, 38. *Study:* Hartt Sch Music, BMus, 56; studied with Andres Segovia, 68 & Julian Bream & Oscar Ghiglia, 69. *Rec Perf:* Guitar Old World/New World, Ars Nova & Ars Antiqua Rec, 68. *Teaching:* Chmn guitar, Hartt Sch Music, 64-; vis instr, Northern Col Music, Manchester, England, 71-72. *Mem:* Am String Teachers Asn (chmn, 79-80, symph dir, 80-82); Guitar Found Am; Lute Soc Am. *Interests:* Baroque guitar music printed between 1600 & 1650. *Publ:* Auth, The Guitar Music of Stephen Dodgson, Gendai Guitar, Japan, 78; Francesco Corbetta: A Historical Perspective, Soundboard, 81; ed, Compendium of Am String Teachers Asn Guitar Symposium, Am String Teachers Asn, 81; auth, Visualization: An Aid to Memorization, Guitar & Lute, 81; ed, Critical Edition of J S Bach's Fourth Lute Suite, Guitar Found, 82. *Mailing Add:* 34 Oak Dr Hebron CT 06248

PRUETT, JAMES WORRELL
EDUCATOR, LIBRARIAN
b Mt Airy, NC, Dec 23, 32. *Study:* Univ NC, Chapel Hill, BA, 55, MA, 57, PhD, 62. *Teaching:* Prof music & music librn, Univ NC, Chapel Hill, 61-76, prof music & chmn, 76- *Mem:* Music Libr Asn (pres, 73-75 & ed, Notes, 74-77); Am Musicol Soc (bd dir, 83-84). *Interests:* Renaissance and early baroque music; Laborde chansonnier. *Publ:* Auth, Charles Butler, In: Musical Quart, G Schirmer, 63; Requiem Mass, In: Musik in Geschichte & Gegenwart, Bärenreiter, 63; Studies In Musicology, Univ NC Press, 69; Arthur Bedford: English Polemicist of the Restoration, Colo Col, 82; Research Guide to Music, Am Libr Asn, in prep. *Mailing Add:* 343 Wesley Dr Chapel Hill NC 27514

PRUETT, LILIAN PIBERNIK
EDUCATOR, HARPSICHORD
b Zagreb, Yugoslavia, Oct 15, 30; US citizen. *Study:* Mozarteum, Salzburg; Vassar Col, AB, 52; Univ NC, Chapel Hill, MA, 57, PhD, 60. *Teaching:* Instr, Univ NC, Chapel Hill, 60-63; prof music, NC Cent Univ, 65-; dir keyboards, Int Music Workshops, Salzburg, Austria, 80- *Mem:* Am Musicol Soc (chap off, 56-60 & 75-77); Southeastern Historical Keyboard Soc. *Interests:* Sacred music of the Italian Renaissance; spread of mainstream historical developements into peripheral East European areas. *Publ:* Auth, Parody Techniques in Masses of Costanzo Porta, Studies in Musicol, Univ NC Press,

69; Liturgical Incunabula of La Giunta in Kotor, Zvuk, Sarajevo, 78; Music Research in Yugoslavia, Notes Music Libr Asn, 79; articles, In: The New Grove Dict of Music & Musicians, Macmillan, 80; contribr & ed, Directory of Music Research Libraries, Eastern Europe, RISM, Barenreiter (in prep). *Mailing Add:* 343 Wesley Dr Chapel Hill NC 27514

PTASZYNSKA, MARTA
COMPOSER, PERCUSSION
b Warszawa, Poland, July 29, 43. *Study:* Warsaw Acad Music, MA, 68; L'Ortf, Paris, 70; studied with Nadia Boulanger, France, 70; Cleveland Inst Music, artist dipl, 74. *Works:* Siderals, 74 & Spectri Sonori, 74, Polish Music Publ & E Marks Music Co; Epigrams, E Marks Music Co, 77; Quodlibet, Polish Music Publ, 79; Two Sonnets to Orpheus, 80-81 & Dream Lands-Magic Spaces, 81, E Marks Music Co; A Great Dark Sleep, Polish Music Publ, 81. *Teaching:* Asst prof, Warsaw Acad Music, 70-72; lectr, Bennington Col, Vt, 74-77 & Univ Calif, Berkeley, 77-79; artist comp in res, Univ Calif, Santa Barbara, 80-82. *Mem:* Percussive Arts Soc (mem bd dir, 81-); ASCAP; ZAIKS, Poland; Union Polish Comp. *Mailing Add:* 6 Evergreen Dr Bethel CT 06801

PUGH, DARRYL L
DOUBLE BASS
b Utica, NY, June 13, 55. *Study:* Berklee Col Music, BM, 73-77; studied with William Curtis & James Van Denmark. *Pos:* Bass expanded orch, Syracuse Symph Orch, 77-79, mem bass sect, 81-; mem sect & prin bass, Spoleto Music Fest, summer 82; bass, Concerti Mezzogiorno, summer 82. *Mailing Add:* 2815 E Genesee St Syracuse NY 13224

PUGH, RUSSELL ORIS
EDUCATOR, BASSOON
b DeKalb, Ill, Aug 10, 27. *Study:* Berkshire Music Ctr, summers 49, 51 & 52; Univ Ill, BS, 50, MS, 52; Univ Ark, EdD, 66. *Pos:* Prin bassoon, US Acad Band, 54-56, Savannah Symph, Ga, 56 & Memphis Symph, Tenn, 67- *Teaching:* Asst prof music, Kans State Col Pittsburg, 55-66; assoc prof music, Western Ky Univ, 66-69; prof, Memphis State Univ, 69- *Bibliog:* Bassoon Reeds, Univ Ill, 69; Bassoon Sonatas, Memphis State Univ, 82. *Mem:* Memphis Fedn Musicians; Asn Conct Bands Am; Music Educr Nat Asn. *Mailing Add:* 2464 MacKinnon Dr Memphis TN 38119

PULK, BRUCE HARRY
PERCUSSION
b Detroit, Mich, Dec 16, 50. *Study:* private instr with Salvatore Rabbio, 65-73; Univ Mich, with Theo Alcantara, Charles Owen & William D Revelli, BM, 73. *Pos:* Timpanist & head perc sect, Flint Symph Orch, 69-74; timpanist, Colo Phil, 74-75; timpanist & artist in res, Grand Rapids Symph Orch, 74-82; prin timpanist, Phoenix Symph Orch, 82- *Teaching:* Fac perc, Grand Valley State Col, Allendale, Mich, 77-82 & Calvin Col, Grand Rapids, 77-82. *Mem:* Percussive Arts Soc; Nat Acad Rec Arts & Sci; Grand Salon Orch. *Mailing Add:* c/o Phoenix Symph Orch 6328 N 7th St Phoenix AZ 85014

PURCELL, RON (RONALD CHARLES)
EDUCATOR, GUITAR & LUTE
b San Jose, Calif, Oct 5, 32. *Study:* Los Angeles Consv Music, BM, 60; Calif State Univ, Northridge, MA, 70; private studies with Andres Segovia, Emilio Pujol, Alirio Diaz. *Rec Perf:* Blanco y Negro (Music of the Old & New Worlds-Renaissance), 76 & Guitar Music of Mario Castelnuovo-Tedesco, 82, Klavier Rec. *Teaching:* Prof music & chmn guitar dept, Calif State Univ, Northridge, 67-; prof vihuela, lute & guitar, Lisbon Consv Music, summer 70-73. *Awards:* Vahdah Olcott-Bickford Achievement Award, Am Guitar Soc, 68. *Mem:* Am String Teachers Asn (guitar ed ASTA J, 74-); Guitar Found Am (pres & bd mem, 73-); Am Guitar Soc (vpres & pres, 76-); Am Musicol Soc. *Interests:* Vihuela, lute and guitar from the Renaissance to the present. *Publ:* Auth, Andres Segovia: Contributions to the World of Guitar, 75 & Classical Guitar, Lute and Vihuela—Discography, 76, Belwin-Mills; coauth, Solo Plus, Mel Bay, 81; auth, numerous articles in guitar journals. *Mailing Add:* 15035 Greenleaf St Sherman Oaks CA 91403

PURSELL, BILL (WILLIAM WHITNEY)
EDUCATOR, COMPOSER
b Oakland, Calif, June 9, 26. *Study:* Peabody Inst Music, studied comp with Nicholas Nabokov & Franz Bornschein, solfeggio with Renee Longy Miquelle & piano with Alexander Sklarevski, 44-46; Eastman Sch Music, studied comp with Wayne Barlow, Bernard Rogers & Howard Hanson, BM, 52, MM, 53, 52-56. *Rec Perf:* Our Winter Love, 63, Chasing a Dream, 64 & A Remembered Love, 66, Columbia Rec; Barbershop Days, 77, An American Christmas, 77 & On Parade (John Philip Sousa), 78, Nat Geographic. *Pos:* Comp & arr, Air Force Orch broadcasts, 46-49; conct & piano artist & prod, comp & arr in every major music ctr, incl London, 60-83; mem bd gov, Nat Acad Rec Arts & Sci, 79- *Teaching:* Assoc prof & comp in res, Belmont Col, currently. *Awards:* First Prize, Nat Scholastic Mag Comp Cont, 43; Otis B Boise Scholarship Comp, 44; First Winner, Edward B Benjamin Award Comp, Eastman Sch Music, 53. *Mem:* Savage Club of London; Phi Mu Alpha Sinfonia; Pi Kappa Lamda; app fel, Elizabethan Soc London; Am Fedn Musicians (mem exec bd Nashville chap, currently). *Mailing Add:* 895 S Curtiswood Lane Nashville TN 37204

PURVIS, WILLIAM WARREN
HORN
b Pittsburgh, Pa, July 10, 48. *Study:* Juilliard Sch Music, 66-68; Haverford Col, BA, 71; Hunter Col, studied comp with Jacques L Monod & Ruth Anderson & music hist with John Reeves White, 75-77; studied horn with

Forest Standley, James Chambers, A Robert Johnson & Adrian van Wordenberg. *Rec Perf:* Mozart Divertimenti, Vox-Candide, 73; Mozart Sinfonia Concertante, 80 & Poulenc Sextet, 83, Nonesuch Digital. *Pos:* Hornist, New York Woodwind Quintet, 74-, Orpheus Chamber Ens, 76-, Speculum Musicae, 79- & St Luke's Chamber Ens, 81- *Teaching:* Perf fac horn & chamber music, State Univ NY, Stony Brook, 79- & Columbia Univ, 81- *Rep:* John Gingrich Mgt Inc 2248 Broadway New York NY 10024e. *Mailing Add:* 675 West End Ave #8A New York NY 10025

PUTSCHE, THOMAS REESE
COMPOSER, EDUCATOR
b Scarsdale, NY, June 29, 29. *Study:* Univ Chicago, BA, 50; Juilliard Sch, 51-52; Hartt Sch Music, BMus, 54, MMus, 55. *Works:* The Cat and the Moon, Seesaw, 58; Fantasy Pieces (nine instrm), perf by Fromm Players, 59; Six Preludes (piano), 61 & Three Bugs (piano & orch), 65, Seesaw; Versions for Orchestra, perf by Hartt Symph, 69; Theme Song for Six Saxophones, Seesaw, 73; Rhapsody for Piano, Fest Conn Comp, 82. *Teaching:* Instr theory & comp, Hartt Col, 55-58; chmn, Hartford Consv, 59-60; prof theory & comp, Hartt Sch Music, 60- *Mem:* Int Soc Contemp Music (chmn Hartford chap, 64-66); Inst Contemp Am Music (chmn, 64-83); ASCAP; Am Soc Univ Comp; Soc Music Theory. *Mailing Add:* Hartt Sch Music Univ Hartford West Hartford CT 06117

PYNE, JAMES
CLARINET, EDUCATOR
Study: Univ Buffalo, dipl; Eastman Sch Music, MA. *Rec Perf:* With Buffalo Phil Orch. *Pos:* Mem, Lake Placid Summer Chamber Orch, formerly & Grand Teton Music Fest, formerly; craftsman clarinet, US, Can & Europe; prin clarinet, Buffalo Phil Orch, currently. *Teaching:* Mem fac, State Univ NY Col, Fredonia, formerly, Buffalo, currently & Cleveland Inst Music, 82- *Interests:* Clarinet mouthpiece design. *Mailing Add:* Cleveland Inst Music 11021 E Boulevard Cleveland OH 44106

Q

QUELER, EVE
CONDUCTOR & MUSIC DIRECTOR
b New York, NY. *Study:* Int Inst Cond, 72; Mannes Col Music, City Univ New York; private study with Joseph Rosenstock & Isabella Vengerova; Russell Sage Col, Hon Dr, 78; Colby Col, Hon Dr, 83. *Rec Perf:* Le Cid (Massenet), 74, Gamma di Vergy (Donizetti), 74, Edgar (Puccini), 76 & Arnoldo (Verdi), 78, CBS Rec, Columbia Masterworks; Nerone (Boito), Hungaroton Rec, 83. *Pos:* Founder & music dir, Opera Orch New York, 68-; assoc cond, Ft Wayne Phil, 70-71; guest cond, Montreal Symph, 75, San Antonio Symph, 75, Philadelphia Orch, 76, Cleveland Orch, 77, Hartford Symph, Kansas City Symph, 78 & numerous other fest & symph, formerly. *Teaching:* Dir, Nat Opera Orch Wkshp, Univ Md, College Park, July 78; instr, Hartt Col Music, 82 & State Univ NY, Potsdam, 83. *Awards:* Musician of Month, Musical Am Mag, 71; grant, Martha Baird Rockefeller Fund for Music, 68; Manhattan Cable TV Community Outreach Arts & Cult Award, 83. *Bibliog:* Raymond Ericson & Donal Henahan (auth), New York Times, numerous; Harriett Johnson (auth), New York Post, numerous; Andrew Porter (auth), New Yorker Mag, numerous. *Mem:* Am Inst Verdi Studies (mem adv bd, 79-83); Cent Opera Serv; Am Symph Orch League, Cond Guild. *Interests:* Donizetti operas; Parisina d'Este; Il Duca d'Alba; Dom Sebastien. *Publ:* Auth, National Opera Orchestra Workshop, Musical Am; My Views As A Woman Conductor, Opera News. *Mailing Add:* c/o Robert J Lombardo 61 W 62 St New York NY 10023

QUILICO, LOUIS
BARITONE, EDUCATOR
b Montreal, Can, Jan 14, 30. *Study:* Santa Cecilia Consv, 51; Quebec Consv, Rome, 53; Mannes Col Music, 54. *Roles:* 204 roles, incl Rigoletto in Rigoletto, Iago in Otello, Macbeth in Macbeth, Tonio in Pagliacci, Germont in La Traviata & Golaud in Pelleas et Melisande with Metropolitan Opera, 72- *Pos:* Bar, New York City Opera, 57-71, Convent Garden, London, 60-62, Paris Opera, 62-68, Metropolitan Opera, 72- *Teaching:* Prof voice, Univ Toronto, Can, 68- *Awards:* Compagnon de l'Ordre du Can, 74. *Rep:* Bob Lombarda Assoc 61 W 62nd St New York NY 10023. *Mailing Add:* 160 W 73rd St New York NY 10023

QUILLING, HOWARD LEE
COMPOSER, EDUCATOR
b Enid, Okla, Dec 16, 35. *Study:* Univ Southern Calif, with Ernst Kanitz & Ingolf Dahl, BM, 59, MM, 70; Calif State Univ, Los Angeles, MA, 66; Univ Calif, Santa Barbara, with Peter Racine Fricker & Emma Lou Diemer. *Works:* Concerto in One Movement for Piano and Orchestra, perf by James Cook, 69; Suite for Alto Saxophone and Wind Orchestra, Artisan Press, 70; Sonata #2: In Memory of Ingolf Dahl (piano), North-South Ed, 70; Sonata #2 for Violin and Piano, Eudice Shapiro, 71; Symphony for Wind & Percussion, comn by Bakersfield Col, perf by Univ Southern Calif Wind Orch, Bakersfield Col, Univ Calif, Santa Barbara, Symposium IV & Univ Richmond, 73; Trio for Violin, Cello & Piano, comn by Willamette Trio, perf by Willamette Trio & Oregon Trio, 74; Four Pieces for Five Brass, Annapolis Brass, 76. *Teaching:* Comp in res & prof music, Bakersfield Col, 71- *Awards:* BMI Music Theater Award, 68-69. *Mem:* Nat Asn Comp; Am Guild Organists. *Mailing Add:* 3001 Harmony Dr Bakersfield CA 93306

QUINN, JAMES JOSEPH
COMPOSER, EDUCATOR
b Chicago, Ill, Apr 30, 36. *Study:* De Paul Univ, BM(comp), 58, MM(theory), 63; Northwestern Univ, PhD, 71. *Works:* Portrait of the Land, 58 & Chorale of the Winds, 61, Kjos Publ; Requiem for a Slave, 66 & Ritual-D, 70, WTTW TV; Do Black Patent Leather Shoes Really Reflect Up?, Chicago, Philadelphia, Detroit & NY Co, 78-82; Rhapsody for Piano & Orch (in prep) & Black Patent Leather Shoes (in prep), Chicago Symph Orch. *Teaching:* Prof humanities & music, City Col Chicago, 65- *Awards:* Ostwald Am Bandmasters Asn Award, 59; Blue Ribbon Citation, TV Arts & Sci, 67. *Mailing Add:* Loop Col City Col Chicago Chicago IL 60601

QUINTIERE, JUDE
COMPOSER, ADMINISTRATOR
b Paterson, NJ, Sept 10, 39. *Study:* New York Col Music, NY Univ, comp with W T Pollak, 63; Columbia Univ, MA, 66. *Works:* Mountain Stream (electronic music), France Musique; Music for Clarinet & Tape, perf by Gerard Errante, New South Wales State Consv Music; Mover By Quintiere, perf by Bob Mover, John Hancock Hall, Boston, 78; Fur Goethe, perf by R Fisher, Museum Modern Art, 79; Music for Recorder & Tape, 79 & Roseland, 80, perf by Peter Rose. *Pos:* Dir music, Kathryn Posin Dance Co, 79-80. *Teaching:* Asst prof music, Tombrock Col, 67-74; lectr music, Fairleigh Dickinson Univ, 74-76. *Awards:* Am Music Ctr Grant, 75; ZBS Found Award, 77; Creative Artists Pub Serv Prog Fel, 78. *Mem:* Media for Arts (secy, 82-); Comp Forum (assoc dir, 79-81); Soundworks Inc (secy, 82-). *Mailing Add:* 47-49 Greene St New York NY 10013

QUIST, EDWIN ARNOLD
LIBRARIAN, ADMINISTRATOR
b Bennington, Vt, Feb 14, 51. *Study:* Colgate Univ, AB, 73; Peabody Consv Music, MM, 76; Catholic Univ Am, MSLS, 79. *Pos:* Librn, Peabody Consv Music, 76- *Mem:* Music Libr Asn; Am Musicol Soc; Sonneck Soc; Int Asn Music Libr. *Interests:* Musical life in New Sweden; John Cole. *Mailing Add:* 1911 Greenberry Rd Baltimore MD 21209

QUIST, PAMELA LAYMAN
COMPOSER, EDUCATOR
b RI, Apr 3, 49. *Study:* Peabody Consv Music, with Julio Esteban, Jean E Ivey & Robert Hall Lewis, BM(piano), MM(comp). *Works:* Sette Canzone d'Amore (ten, perc & guitar), 73; Three Poems (bassoon & clarinet), 74; Gravitation I (solo violin), 75; Lazaros (orch), 76; Meditations (solo trumpet), 77; Mosaic (cello & piano), 78; Syllogisms (piano), 79. *Rec Perf:* On Grenadilla Rec. *Teaching:* Vpres, Walden Sch Ltd, 73-; mem fac, State Univ NY Col, Geneseo, 74-75; mem fac theory musicianship, comp & piano & chmn musicianship dept, Peabody Inst, 75- *Awards:* Scholar, Vt Comp Conf, 73; Comp Award, Fri Morning Music Club, 75; Comp Prize, Annapolis Fine Arts Found, 75. *Mailing Add:* 1911 Greenberry Rd Baltimore MD 21209

QUITTMEYER, SUSAN
MEZZO-SOPRANO
Study: Ill Wesleyan Univ; Manhattan Sch Music. *Roles:* Dorabella in Cosi fan tutte, 79, Cherubino in The Marriage of Figaro, 79 & Pauline in Pique Dame, 82, San Francisco Opera; Cherubino in Marriage of Figaro, 83 & Olga in Eugene Onegin, 83, Hawaii Opera Theatre Fest; Carmen in Carmen, Mobile Opera Co, 83; Composer in Ariadne auf Naxos, San Francisco Opera, 83. *Pos:* Affiliate artist, San Francisco Opera, 79. *Mailing Add:* c/o ICM Artists Ltd 40 W 57th St New York NY 10019

QUIVAR, FLORENCE
MEZZO-SOPRANO
b Philadelphia, Pa. *Study:* Philadelphia Acad Music. *Roles:* Orfeo in Orfeo ed Euridice, Berlin Staatsoper, 82. *Pos:* Mem, Metropolitan Opera & Juilliard Opera Theatre, currently; ms, Los Angeles & New York Phil, Cleveland & Philadelphia Orch, Boston, Chicago & Cincinnati Symph; recitalist, US, England & Europe; soloist, Israel Phil European tour, 83. *Awards:* Nat Opera Inst Award; Baltimore Lyr Opera Compt Award; Marian Anderson Vocal Compt Award. *Mailing Add:* c/o Columbia Artists 165 W 57th St New York NY 10019

R

RAAD, VIRGINIA
PIANO, MUSICOLOGIST
b Salem, WVa, Aug 13, 25. *Study:* Wellesley Col, BA, 47; New England Consv, studied piano with David Barnett; Ecole Normale Musique, Paris, with Alfret Cortot, Berthe Bert, Jeanne Blancard & Emile Damais, dipl, 50; Univ Paris, with Jacques Chailley, PhD, 55. *Pos:* Conct pianist, US cols & univ, 65-; adjudicator, Nat Endowment Arts, Nat Endowment Humanities & others, currently. *Teaching:* Artist in res, Salem Col, 57-70; lectr & teacher masterclasses, US cols & univ, 65-; musician in res, NC Community Cols & Arts Coun, 71-72. *Awards:* Grants, French Govt, 50-55; Am Coun Learned Soc Grant, 62; Am rep, Debussy Centennial Celebration in Paris, 62. *Mem:* Am Musicol Soc (secy-treas Allegheny chap, 60-65); Music Teachers Nat Asn (chmn musicol prog, 83-85); Col Music Soc; Int Musicol Soc; Soc Francaise Musicol. *Interests:* Interdisciplinary studies in French art. *Publ:* Contribr, Debussy et l'evolution de la musique au XXe siecle In: L'Influence de Debussy: Amierique (Etats-Unis), Paris, 65; Notes of a Musician-in-

Residence, Piano Guild Notes, 3-4/73; Claude Debussy's Use of Piano Sonority, Am Music Teacher, 9-10/76, 1/77 & 4-5/77; Debussy and the Magic of Spain, Clavier, 3/79; Claude Debussy's Sarabande, Am Music Teacher, 6-7/81. *Mailing Add:* 60 Terrace Ave Salem WV 26426

RABBAI, JOSEPH
CLARINET, TEACHER
b Bridgeton, NJ, Aug 23, 38. *Study:* Temple Univ, BSEd(music), 60; Juilliard Sch Music, BM(clarinet), 62, MM(clarinet), 64. *Rec Perf:* Music of Leo Kraft, #1, Serenus Rec, 70; Four American Composers, 70, Concerto-a-tre (Robert Starer), 71 & Music for Winds (Saint Saens), 72, Desto Rec; Quartet for End of Time (O Messiaen), Candide-Vox, 72; Ariel (Ned Rorem), Desto Rec, 73; Wind Serenades (Mozart), Vox-Box, 80. *Pos:* Prin clarinet, Israel Phil Orch, 64-66, Am Symph Orch, 67- & Metropolitan Opera Orch, 82-; clarinet, New York City Opera, 69-81. *Mailing Add:* 300 W 109th St Apt 9-G New York NY 10025

RABSON, CAROLYN R
CELLO, LIBRARIAN
b Denver, Colo, Apr 13, 30. *Study:* Antioch Col, BA, 53; Crane Sch Music, State Univ NY, Potsdam, MA, 73; Univ Ill, Urbana, MS, 80. *Pos:* Proj dir, Nat Tune Index—Sonneck Soc, 77-79; staff asst, Resources Am Music Hist, 79-80; music cataloger, State Univ NY, Potsdam, 80-82; ref librn, Oberlin Consv Music, 82- *Interests:* Eighteenth century theatre music; thematic indexes; 17th century bowed string instruments. *Publ:* Auth, Songbook of the American Revolution, NEO Press, 74; coauth, National Tune Index and User's Guide, Univ Music Ed, 80; National Tune Index: A Systems Overview, Comput and the Humanities, 81; auth, Disappointment Revisited: Unweaving the Tangled Web, Am Music, 83; ed, Songs of Oberlin: Sesquicentennial Edition, Oberlin Consv Libr, 83. *Mailing Add:* Consv Libr Oberlin Col Oberlin OH 44074

RACKLEY, LAWRENCE (LAWRENCE RACKLEY SMITH)
EDUCATOR, COMPOSER
b Media, Ill, Sept 10, 32. *Study:* Northwestern Univ, MusB, 54, MM, 55; Eastman Sch Music, Univ Rochester, PhD, 58. *Works:* Confluences (orch), comn by Kalamazoo Symph Orch, 70; Convergence (organ & band), comn by Manatee Jr Col, 73; Rhapsodic Dialogues (violin & piano), comn by Mich Music Teachers Asn, 74; Sarasota Sailor Circus (band), comn by Sarasota High Sch, 75; River Raisin (band), comn by Monroe Co Arts Coun, 75; They/You/I/We (violin concerto), comn by Western Mich Univ & Kalamazoo Col, 78; Chaconne (2 harpsichords), comn by Bruce Gustafson & Arthur Lawrence, 80. *Teaching:* Asst prof music, Cent Mich Univ, Mt Pleasant, 57-63; prof, Kalamazoo Col, 63- *Mem:* ASCAP; Am Music Ctr; Col Music Soc; Am Soc Univ Comp; Catgut Acoustical Soc. *Interests:* Braille transcription. *Mailing Add:* 440 N Arlington Kalamazoo MI 49007

RADITZ, EDWARD
EDUCATOR, VIOLIN
b Philadelphia, Pa, June 21, 36. *Study:* Temple Univ, BSME, 57; Tulsa Univ, MM, 58; Ind Univ, 58-61; NY Univ, PhD, 75. *Pos:* Violinist, Tulsa Phil, 56-58; string specialist, Westfield pub sch, NJ, 61-64; violinist, NY & NJ, 64- *Teaching:* Prof, Jersey City State Col, 64- *Mem:* Music Educr Nat Conf; Am String Teachers Asn; Am Fedn Musicians. *Publ:* Coauth, The Basic Elements of Four-Part Harmony, Collegium, 80. *Mailing Add:* Music Dept Jersey City State Col Jersey City NJ 07305

RADNOFSKY, KENNETH
SAXOPHONE, EDUCATOR
Study: Univ Houston, BM; New England Consv, MM; studied with Joseph Allard & Jeffrey Lerner. *Rec Perf:* On Deutsche Grammophon, BBC, Spectrum & Golden Crest. *Pos:* Sax, Boston Symph, Philadelphia Orch, Santa Fe Orch & Opera Co Boston; soloist, Am Soc Univ Comp Nat Conf, Fest Tex Comp, Portland Symph & Brookline Acad Music. *Teaching:* Lectr sax, Yale Univ, currently; fac mem, Longy Sch Music & Boston Consv, currently. *Publ:* Various articles in Sax Sheet. *Mailing Add:* Yale Sch Music Box 2104A Yale Sta New Haven CT 06520

RADNOFSKY, NANCY
CLARINET, EDUCATOR
Study: Univ Houston, BM, MM; studied clarinet with Richard Pickar, Jeffrey Lerner & Pasquale Cardillo. *Pos:* Performer, Santa Fe Opera & Houston Educ TV; clarinet, Opera Co of Boston Orch. *Teaching:* Grad teaching fel clarinet, Univ Houston, formerly; mem fac, Longy Sch Music, currently. *Awards:* Winner, Houston Music Teachers Asn Chamber Music Compt & Nat Asn Col Woodwind, Brass & Perc Instr Compt. *Publ:* Coauth, mag articles on early musical life in Boston. *Mailing Add:* Longy Sch Music One Follen St Cambridge MA 02138

RADOSAVLJEVICH, OLGA (OLGA R GRADOJEVICH)
EDUCATOR, PIANO
b Belgrade, Yugoslavia, Dec 19, 37; US citizen. *Study:* Acad Music, Belgrade Yugoslavia, dipl, 54; Cleveland Inst Music, BM, 59, MM, 61 & artist dipl, 69. *Teaching:* Piano fac, Cleveland Inst Music, 60-, chmn sec piano dept, 79- *Mailing Add:* 10401 Brighton Rd Cleveland OH 44108

RADU, VALENTIN
ORGAN, CONDUCTOR & MUSIC DIRECTOR
b Bucharest, Romania, Oct 27, 56; US citizen. *Study:* Ciprian Porumbescu, Consv Music, Bucharest, Romania, BA, 79; Juilliard Sch, MA, 80, DMA, 83; studied with Franz Xaver Dressler, Lidia Sumnevia, Vernon De Tar & Andre

Isoire. *Pos:* Assoc organist, St Joseph Cathedral, Bucharest, Romania, 74-79; res organist, Bucharest Phil, 76-79; music dir & organist, Holy Cross Church, New York, 79-; founder, cond & music dir, Bach Players Orch, New York, 80- *Teaching:* Asst prof Bach music, Juilliard Sch, 81-83. *Awards:* First Prize, Acad Santa Cecilia, Rome, 73 & Romanian Comp Asn & Bucharest Consv Music, 76; Fourth Prize, Saarbrucker Int Orgelwettbewerb, 79; Dipl, Sixth Int J S Bach Compt, Leipzig, 80. *Bibliog:* Andrea Dittgen (auth), Listener in the Church Bewitched, Saarbrucker Zeitung, 6/13/81; Edgar Elian (auth), Un Recital Aparte, Muzica, Bucharest, 1-2/82; Viorel Cosma (auth), Un Recital Eveniment, Scinteia, Bucharest, 6/29/83. *Mem:* Am Guild Organists. *Rep:* Winfried Dritter Warndstrasse 125 Klarenthal Saar 6601 West Germany. *Mailing Add:* 11 Riverside Dr, 10-0-W New York NY 10023

RAFFERTY, J PATRICK
VIOLIN, TEACHER
b Toledo, Ohio, June 1, 47. *Study:* Bowling Green State Univ, BMus, 70; studied violin with Dr Paul Makara. *Pos:* Violinist, St Louis Symph Orch, 71-72, Cleveland Orch, 72-74 & Cincinnati Symph Orch, 74-78; concertmaster, St Louis String Orch, 71-72, Cincinnati Chamber Orch, 74-78, Brevard Music Ctr Orch, 81 & Dallas Bach Orch, 81-; assoc concertmaster, Dallas Symph, 78-; acting concertmaster, Seattle Symph Orch, 80 & 82 & San Diego Symph Orch, 81; soloist, St Louis Symph Orch, Cincinnai Symph Orch, Dallas Symph Orch, Highland Park Chamber Orch, Dallas Chamber Orch & Dallas Bach Orch. *Teaching:* Private teacher orch repertoire, 78- *Mem:* Violin Soc Am. *Mailing Add:* Dallas Symph Northpark Ctr Dallas TX 75225

RAFFMAN, RELLY
EDUCATOR, COMPOSER
b New Bedford, Mass, Sept 4, 21. *Study:* Dartmouth Col, BA(music), 47; Columbia Univ, MA(music educ), 49; Ind Univ, 50-51. *Works:* Come Be My Love, Broude Brothers, 59; The Passionate Pilgrim, Assoc Music Publ, 62; Midas (opera), comn by After-Dinner Opera Co, 63; Jubilate Deo, E C Schirmer, 66; Psalm IV, comn by Ill Wesleyan Contemp Symp, 70; The Three Ravens, Broude Brothers, 75; Fur Eliot, comn by Eliot Fisk, 82. *Teaching:* Jeppson prof music, Clark Univ, 54- *Awards:* Ernest Bloch Award, United Temple Chorus, 58; Ella Lyman Cabot Found Award, 64. *Publ:* Auth, New Approach to Analysis: Scalar Control, Col Music Soc Symposium, Vol XV, spring 75. *Mailing Add:* Music Dept Clark Univ Worcester MA 01610

RAFOLS, ALBERTO P
PIANO, EDUCATOR
b Guantanamo, Cuba, July 7, 42; US citizen. *Study:* Univ Ill, Urbana-Champaign, with Howard Karp, BM, 67, MM, 69; Academia Marshall, Barcelona, with Alicia de Larrocha, 70-72; Univ Wash, with Bela Siki, DMA, 75. *Pos:* Recitalist, US, Can & Spain, 69- *Teaching:* Instr, Univ Ill, Urbana-Champaign, 69-70; asst prof, Univ Wash, 75-; adj instr, Univ Alaska, Juneau, 82- *Awards:* Fulbright Grant, Spain, 70-72; Fulbright Summer Grant, Italy, 71. *Mem:* Nat Music Teacher Asn; Wash State Music Teachers Asn; Santa Fe Chamber Music Fest; Seattle Arts Comn (comnr, 83-). *Mailing Add:* 615 Boren Ave #38 Seattle WA 98104

RAIEFF, JOSEPH
EDUCATOR, PIANO
b Kharkov, USSR. *Study:* Am Consv Music, Chicago; Juilliard Sch Music, studied piano with Joseph Lhevinne & Alexander Siloti; studied with Artur Schnabel & Harold Bauer. *Pos:* Recitalist & conct appearances, US & Europe. *Teaching:* Instr master classes, lect & wkshp in US incl Univ Ohio, Univ Fla, Univ Nebr, Wheaton Col, Ohio Univ & Guillford Col; mem fac, Mannes Col Music, 45- & Juilliard Sch Music, 45- *Mailing Add:* Mannes Col Music 157 E 74th St New York NY 10021

RAIGORODSKY, NATALIA (LEDA NATALIA RAIGORODSKY HEIMSATH HARTER)
COMPOSER, WRITER
b Tulsa, Okla, 1929. *Study:* Piano with Stanley Hummel & Adele Marcus; studied comp with Bernard Wagenaar, Quincy Porter & Wendell Margrave; Barnard Col, BA, 52; Am Univ, MA(music), 63. *Works:* 41 solos & 18 preludes (sacred music), perf in US churches, 63-; Dusk (flute & piano), 63-72; Symphony No 1, 70; Introduction Reflection (wind quintet), 70; I Will Lift Up Mine Eyes, publ by Coburn Press, 75; The Promise of Peace (sacred opera), Opera Theatre Washington, DC, 81. *Pos:* Spec programmer, WAMU-FM, Am Univ, 61-62; music critic, Montgomery Co Sentinel, Evening Star, Washington, DC, 64-68; music programmer, WMAL-FM, Washington, DC, 65-66. *Teaching:* Lectr Am music, Washington, DC area. *Awards:* Mu Phi Epsilon Music Award, 63; Broadcasting Award, WAMU-FM, 63; Comp Award, Fri Morning Music Club, 69. *Mem:* Fri Morning Music Club. *Mailing Add:* Box 97 RD 1 Muncy Valley PA 17758

RAINBOW, EDWARD LOUIS
EDUCATOR
b Waterloo, Iowa, June 18, 29. *Study:* Northern Iowa Univ, BA, 55, MA, 56; Univ Iowa, PhD, 63. *Pos:* Prof musician, 47-51; mem, Ft Worth Symph Orch, 66-80. *Teaching:* Instr, pub schs, Davenport, Iowa, 56-60; instr music, Univ Iowa, 61 & Univ Pac, 61-66; assoc prof, NTex State Univ, 66-78, prof, 78-; rep, Int Sem Music Educ, Res Gummersbach, Germany, 72, Mexico City, 74, Graz, Austria, 76, Bloomington, Ind, 78 & Dresden, Germany; chmn, Music Educ Res Coun, 76-78. *Mem:* Music Educr Nat Conf; Int Music Educr; Am Fedn Musicians. *Mailing Add:* Dept Music NTex State Univ Denton TX 76203

RAITT, JOHN WELLESLEY
BASSOON, EDUCATOR
b Chicago, Ill, Oct 17, 23. *Study:* Chicago Music Col, 46-48. *Pos:* Mem, Chicago Civic Orch, 42 & 46; & Ark State Symph, 47-48; asst prin bassoonist, Chicago Symph Orch, 49-; prin bassoon, Ravinia Fest, Highland Park, Ill, 62. *Teaching:* Mem fac, Roosevelt Univ, 51-57 & Sherwood Music Sch, 51-61. *Mailing Add:* Chicago Symph Orch 220 S Michigan Ave Chicago IL 60604

RAKICH, CHRISTA MARTIN
HARPSICHORD, ORGAN
b Waterbury, Conn, Nov 11, 52. *Study:* Oberlin Col & Consv, BA & BMus, 75; Hochschule Musik & Darstellende Kunst, Vienna, with Anton Heller, 75-77; New England Consv, MM, 79. *Rec Perf:* J S Bach Clavierübung III (three discs), Titanic Rec, 83. *Teaching:* Asst organist, Harvard Univ, 78-81; fac mem organ, New England Consv, 79-; fac organ & harpsichord, Univ Conn, Storrs, 81-; vis harpsichord artist, Van Pelt House, Univ Pa, 81- *Awards:* Fulbright Grant, 75; Second Prize, Int Organ Compt, Bruges, Belgium, 76; Res Award, Austro-Am Soc Boston, 78. *Mem:* Am Guild Organists, (mem Boston chap exec comt, 81-83); Old West Organ Soc; Orcan Hist Soc. *Mailing Add:* 19 Dwight St Boston MA 02118

RAKSIN, DAVID
COMPOSER, CONDUCTOR
b Philadelphia, Pa, Aug 4, 12. *Study:* Univ Pa, MusB, 34; studied with Arnold Schoenberg, 37-38. *Works:* Approx 100 film scores incl, Laura, Forever Amber, Force of Evil, Smoky, Carrie, Al Capone, The Redeemer, Separate Tables & The Bad and the Beautiful; 350 radio & TV scores. *Rec Perf:* Morning Revisited, Capitol Rec, 64; Music from Will Penny, 68 & Too Late Blues, 68, Dot Rec; Suite from Forever Amber, 75, Theme from Laura, 75 & Scenario from The Bad and The Beautiful, 75, RCA. *Pos:* Arranger & orchestrator, CBS, NBC, ABC, MBS & others, 32-44; comp & cond, Goldwyn, 20th Century-Fox, Paramount, MGM, RKO, Columbia, Warner Brothers, CBS, NBC, PBS, CBC & RCA, 35- *Teaching:* Adj prof music & urban studies, Univ Southern Calif, 56-; artist-in-res, various univ, cols & music sch, 60-; lectr music for film & TV, Univ Calif, Los Angeles, 70- *Awards:* Career Award for Music, Acad Sci Fiction & Fantasy, 79; Max Steiner Award for Career Achievement, Nat Film Soc, 80; Elizabeth Sprague Coolidge Comn, Libr Cong, 82. *Bibliog:* Roy Prendergast (auth), Film Music, A Neglected Art, Norton, 77; Tom Newsom (auth), David Raksin, A Composer in Hollywood, Quart J, Libr Cong, 78; Oral histories, David Raksin, Composer, Yale Univ, 78 & Southern Methodist Univ J, 80. *Mem:* Comp & Lyricists Guild Am (pres, 62-70); Screen Comp Am (mem exec bd, 50-); ASCAP; Am Guild Authors & Comp. *Publ:* Auth, The Subject is Film Music (radio series), KUSC-FM & other stations, 78-82; Life With Charlie (Chaplin), Quart J, Libr Cong, 83. *Rep:* Robert Light 8281 Melrose Ave Suite 305 Los Angeles CA 90046. *Mailing Add:* 6519 Aldea Ave Van Nuys CA 91406

RALEIGH, STUART W
CHORAL CONDUCTOR, EDUCATOR
b Syracuse, NY, Aug 22, 40. *Study:* Syracuse Univ, BMus, MMus; Berkshire Music Ctr. *Pos:* Asst cond, Syracuse Symph, 68-71. *Teaching:* Cond, Syracuse Univ Chorus & Orch, 65-72; dir choral ens & assoc prof, Baldwin-Wallace Col, 73- *Mem:* Cleveland Comp Guild; Pi Kappa Lambda. *Mailing Add:* Music Dept Baldwin Wallace Col Berea OH 44017

RAMEY, PHILLIP
COMPOSER, WRITER
b Chicago, Ill, Sept 12, 39. *Study:* Int Acad Music, Nice, France, artist cert, 59; DePaul Univ, comp study with Alexander Tcherepnin, BA(comp), 62; Columbia Univ, comp study with Jack Beeson, MM(comp), 65. *Works:* Epigrams for Piano, Boosey & Hawkes, 68; Piano Concerto No 2, G Schirmer, 76; Leningrad Rag (Mutations on Scott Joplin) for Piano, Edward B Marks, 74; Memorial for Piano, C F Peters, 81; La Citadelle—Rhapsody for Oboe & Piano, 83, Fanfare—Sonata for Solo Trumpet, 83 & Piano Fantasy, 83, G Schirmer. *Pos:* Prog ed & annotator, New York Phil, 77-; contrib music ed, Ovation Mag, New York, 80- *Awards:* Res Fel, MacDowell Colony, 69, 71, 72, 74 & 76. *Bibliog:* Maurice Hinson (auth), Guide to the Pianist's Repertoire (Supplement), 79 & Music for Piano and Orchestra, 80. *Mem:* Tcherepnin Soc (mem bd dir, 80-); New Music for Young Ens (mem adv coun, 81-); Chicago Chamber Ens (mem bd adv, 80-); Master Teachers Inst Arts (mem bd trustees, 82). *Publ:* Auth, Messiaen: High Priest of Mystic Harmony, Saturday Rev Prog, 72; Prokofiev and His Music, Time-Life Rec, 75; Remembering Tcherepnin, Chicago Mag, 79; Copland and the Dance, Ballet News Mag, 80; Sergei Prokofiev, Ovation Mag, 83. *Mailing Add:* 825 West End Ave New York NY 10025

RAMEY, SAMUEL EDWARD
BASS
b Colby, Kans, March 28, 42. *Study:* Wichita State Univ, BMus, 68. *Rec Perf:* Lucia di Lammermoor, Philips Rec, 76; Rigoletto, Angel Rec, 78; L'Italiana in Algeri, RCA, 80; Le Nozze di Figaro, London Rec, 81; Il Turco in Italia, 81 & Il Barbiere di Siviglia, 82, CBS; I Masnadieri, London Rec, 82; Maometto II, Philips Rec, 83. *Roles:* Perf with New York City Opera, 73, Glyndebourne Fest, 76, Hauburg Staatsoper, 78, La Scala Milau, 81, Vienna Staatsoper, 81 & Covent Garden, 82. *Pos:* Leading bs, New York City Opera, 73- *Rep:* Columbia Artists Mgt Inc 165 W 57th St New York NY 10019. *Mailing Add:* 320 Central Park W New York NY 10025

RAMIREZ, LUIS ANTONIO
COMPOSER, EDUCATOR
b San Juan, PR, Feb 10, 23. *Study:* Royal Consv Music, Madrid, Spain, 64. *Works:* Fantasy (guitar, bass & orch), 73 & Tres Piezas Breves, 73, Seesaw Music Corp; Balada-Concierto, 75, Figuraciones Symphonic Poem #1, 75, Rasgos y Perfiles Symphonic Poem #2, 79 & Ciclos Symphonic Poem #4, 81, Symph Orch PR; Aire y Tierra Symphonic Poem #3, Inter-Am Fest Orch, 81. *Pos:* Musical dir, Ateneo Puertorriqueno, San Juan, 70-74. *Teaching:* Assoc prof harmony, counterpoint & comp, Consv Music PR, San Juan, 68- *Mem:* ASCAP; PR Asn Comp. *Mailing Add:* 560 Verona St Villa Capri Rio Piedras PR 00924

RAMOS, CATHERINE LEHR See Lehr, Catherine

RAMPAL, JEAN-PIERRE
FLUTE
b Marseilles, France, Jan 7, 22. *Study:* Nat Consv, Paris; Univ Marseilles. *Pos:* Conct flutist worldwide, 45-; mem, Paris Opera Orch, formerly; ed ancient & class music, Int Music Co, New York, 58- *Teaching:* Prof, Consv Nat Musique Paris; instr master classes & wkshps. *Awards:* Eight Grand Prix du Disque, 54-78; Oscar du Premier Virtuose Francais, 56; Leonie Sonning Danish Music Prize, 78. *Bibliog:* Interview, Realities Mag. *Mem:* French Musicol Soc; Asn Musique et Musiciens (pres, 74-). *Publ:* Auth, La Flute, 78. *Mailing Add:* c/o Colbert Artists Mgt 111 W 57th St New York NY 10019

RAMSIER, PAUL
COMPOSER, EDUCATOR
b Louisville, Ky. *Study:* Univ Louisville, studied piano with Dwight Anderson, comp with Claude Almand, BM(piano & comp); NY Univ, PhD(music), 72; studied comp with Ernst V Dohnanyi & Alexi Haieff; Juilliard Sch Music, studied piano with Beveridge Webster. *Works:* The Man on the Bearskin Rug, 63 & Pied Piper, 63, Boosey & Hawkes; Divertimento Concertante on a Theme of Couperin, 65 & The Moon and the Sun, Eden, and Wine, 70, G Schirmer; The Road to Hamelin, Boosey & Hawkes, 83; The Low-Note Blues, 83 & Eusebius Revisited, Remembrances of Schumann, 83, Belwin-Mills. *Teaching:* Music, dance & theater, NY Univ, 69-72, prof comp, 75-; prof comp, Ohio State Univ, 72-73. *Awards:* MacDowell Colony Fel, 60; Nat Endowment Arts Grant, 78. *Mem:* ASCAP; Asn Musiciens Suisses. *Publ:* Ed, My Hamster Crawls, and Other Piano Pieces Composed and Illustrated by Children, Boosey & Hawkes, 65. *Mailing Add:* 210 Riverside Dr New York NY 10025

RAN, SHULAMIT
COMPOSER, EDUCATOR
b Tel Aviv, Israel, Oct 21, 49. *Study:* Tanglewood Sch Music, with Aaron Copland & Lukas Foss, 63; Mannes Col Music, studied comp with Norman Dello Joio & piano with Nadia Reisenberg, dipl, 68; studied piano with Dorothy Taubman, 72- & comp with Ralph Shapey, 77. *Works:* O The Chimneys, Carl Fischer Inc, 69; Concert Piece for Piano & Orchestra, 71, Ensembles for 17, 75 & Double Vision, 76, Theodore Presser; Apprehensions, Israeli Music Inst, 79; Private Game, 79 & Excursions (violin, cello & piano), 80, Theodore Presser. *Teaching:* Artist in res, St Mary's Univ, Halifax, NS, 72; assoc prof comp, Univ Chicago, 73- *Awards:* Ford Found Grant, 72; Nat Endowment for Arts Fel, 76; Guggenheim Fel, 77. *Mem:* ASCAP; Am Music Ctr; Chicago Soc Comp. *Mailing Add:* 1455 N Sandburg Terr Chicago IL 60610

RAND, VALORIE LEE
ADMINISTRATOR
b Brighton, Mass, June 6, 39. *Study:* Bridgewater State Col, BSEd, 61; Castleton State Col, MAEd, 79. *Pos:* Coordr, Castleton State Col Fine Arts Ctr, 75-; vpres bd trustees, Green Mountain Consortium Perf Arts, 77-; mem, Vt Coun Arts, 81- *Mem:* Chamber Music Am; Asn Col & Univ Comn Arts Adminr. *Mailing Add:* Fine Arts Ctr Castleton VT 05735

RANDALL, EDWARD (OWENS), III
TENOR
b Baltimore, Md, Mar 9, 54. *Study:* Univ Md; Towson State Univ; Acad Vocal Arts, 83. *Roles:* Idamante in Idomeneo, Acad Vocal Arts Opera Theater, 81; Count Almaviva in Il Barbiere di Siviglia, Opera Theater NVa, 82; Scaramouccio in Ariadne auf Naxos, 82 & Evangelist in St John Passion, 83, Int Arts Fest, Corta, Greece; Enrico in L'ajo Nell 'Imbarazzo, Wolf Trap Opera, 83; Ferrando in Cosi fan tutte, 83 & Contino Belfiore in La Finta Giardiniera, 83, Acad Vocal Arts Opera Theater. *Teaching:* Instr voice, Rutgers Univ, 83- *Mem:* Am Guild Musical Artists; Am Fedn TV & Radio Artists; Philadelphia Singers; Pa Pro Musica; Wolf Trap Opera Co. *Mailing Add:* 33 W Ashmead Pl S Philadelphia PA 19144

RANDALL, JAMES K
COMPOSER, EDUCATOR
b Cleveland, Ohio, June 16, 29. *Study:* Cleveland Inst Music, with Herbert Elwell; Columbia Univ, BA, 55; Harvard Univ, MA, 56; Princeton Univ, MFA, 58; studied with Alexei Haieff & George Thaddeus Jones & piano with Leonard Shure. *Works:* Improvisation on a Poem by e e cummings (voice and chamber ens), 61; Quartets in Pairs, 64; Mudgett: Monologue by a Mass Murderer, comn by Fromm Found, 65; Lyric Variations (violin & comput), 67; Eakins (music for film), 72. *Teaching:* Mem fac music, Princeton Univ, 58- *Mailing Add:* 52 Gulick Rd Princeton NJ 08540

RANDAZZO, ARLENE CATHERINE
SOPRANO

b Chicago, Ill, June 17, 43. *Study:* Henry St Music Settlement, New York; Aspen Music Fest; studied with Felix Popper, Lola Urbach, Otto Guth, Kurt Adler, Carlo Moresco & Anthony Stivanello. *Roles:* Lucia in Lucia di Lammermoor, Tulsa Opera Asn; Rosina in Il Barbiere di Siviglia; Sophie in Der Rosenkavalier; Elvira in I Puritani; Violetta in La Traviata; Gilda in Rigoletto; Musetta in La Boheme, 80-81. *Pos:* Performer, Fest of Two Worlds, Spoleto, Italy, Opera Int, Caracas, Venezuela, Conn Opera Asn, Philadelphia Opera Co, Tulsa Opera Asn, NJ State Opera, Buffalo Symph, Syracuse Symph, PR Symph, Art Park, NY, Aspen Fest, Kennedy Ctr Fest, PR Opera, 78 & 81, Santo Domingo Opera, 78 & 81 & Leon Fest, Mex, 80; mem, New York City Opera, 68-79 & New York City Opera Theater, 68-79. *Awards:* Liederkranz Found Award, 64; Singer of Yr, Inst PR, 77. *Mem:* Am Guild Musical Artists. *Rep:* Robert Lombardo Assoc 61 W 62 New York NY 10023. *Mailing Add:* 221 W 82nd St New York NY 10024

RANDMAN, BENNETT CHARLES
CELLO, TEACHER

b Birmingham, Ala, July 16, 49. *Study:* Univ Tenn, BM, 72; Duquesne Univ, MMus, 74; study with Fritz Magg, Music Mountain, Falls Village, Conn, summer 74. *Pos:* Prin cellist, Charlotte Chamber Orch, 75-77 & Jackson Symph Orch, 82-; prin solo cellist, Cathedral Chamber Soc, Jackson, Miss, 83- *Teaching:* Instr strings, Thalia Consv, Seattle, 78-79. *Mailing Add:* Pine Trails Apt J-7 Clinton MS 39056

RANDOLPH, (ALICE) LAURIE
GUITAR

b Winston-Salem, NC, June 1, 50. *Study:* NC Sch Arts, BM, 71; studied with Abel Carlevaro, Andres Segovia, Alirio Diaz, Turibio Santos, Eduardo Falu, Faul Garcie Zarate, Sebastiao Tapajos & Cacho Tirao. *Pos:* Concert guitarist, currently; Mano a Mano, flemenco & classical guitar partnership with flamenco guitarist & singer Anita Sheer, 79; Duo Randolph Zenamon with classical guitarist Jaime Zenamon of Bolivia, 80. *Teaching:* Lehrer Auftrag class guitar, Hochschule Musik, WBerlin, Germany, 80. *Awards:* First Prize, Chet Atkins Int Guitar Compt, 71; Fourth Prize, Concordo Int Chitarra, Allessendria, Italy, 73; First Prize, Lanchester Int Guitar Fest, 74. *Bibliog:* Sue McCreadie (auth), Laurie Randolph Talks to Sue McCreadie, Guitar Mag, London, 79. *Rep:* Raymond Weiss Conct Mgt 300 W 55th St New York NY 10019. *Mailing Add:* 755 Oaklawn Ave Winston-Salem NC 27104

RANDS, BERNARD
COMPOSER, EDUCATOR

b Sheffield, England, Mar 2, 34. *Study:* Univ Wales, BM, 56, MM, 58; studied comp with Luigi Dallapiccola, 58-60, Pierre Boulez & Bruno Maderna, 60-61 & Luciano Berio, 61-62; studied with Roman Vlad. *Works:* Actions for Six (flute, harp, two perc, viola & cello), perf at Darmstadt Fest, 63; Wildtrack 1, 2 & 3 (voice & orch), 69-75; Mesalliance (piano & orch), 72; AUM (harp & orch), 74; Madrigali (orch), comn by Nat Symph Orch, 77; Deja 2 (voice & ens), San Diego, 79; Obbligato (string quartet & trombone), comn by Sequoia String Quartet, 80; and more than fifty others publ by Universal Ed. *Rec Perf:* Canti Lunatici & Etendre, Decca. *Pos:* Conct performer throughout Europe, Australia & US, formerly; co-founding artistic dir, Contemp Music Fest, Calif Inst Arts, currently. *Teaching:* Lectr, Univ Wales, 63-67; vis fel, Princeton Univ, 67-68; mem fac music & Granada fel creative arts, York Univ, 68-75; comp in res, Univ Ill, 69-70; fel creative arts, Brasenose Col, Oxford Univ, 72-73; prof music, Univ Calif, San Diego, 76-, founder & cond, SONOR, currently. *Awards:* Harkness Int Fel, Commonwealth Fund of New York, 66; Nat Endowment Arts Grant, 77; Calif Arts Coun Award, 78. *Mem:* Am Soc Univ Comp; Perf Right Soc. *Rep:* BMI 320 W 57th St New York NY 10019. *Mailing Add:* Dept Music Univ Calif La Jolla CA 92037

RANGANATHAN, TANJORE
MRDANGAM, EDUCATOR

b Madras, India, Mar 13, 25. *Study:* With Subramania Phillai. *Rec Perf:* Two albums by Ramnad Krishnan, Nonesuch & Elektra; two albums by T Viswanathan, World Pac & Nonesuch. *Pos:* Mrdangam & accmp, US, Europe & UK, 38-, Edinburgh Fest, 63. *Teaching:* Mem fac, Calif Inst Arts, formerly & Wesleyan Univ, currently; lectr, Am Univ, 67- *Mailing Add:* Music Dept Wesleyan Univ Middletown CT 06457

RANNEY, SUSAN
DOUBLE BASS, TEACHER

b Santa Monica, Calif, Sept 23, 52. *Study:* Univ Southern Calif, BMus, 74. *Pos:* Prin bass, Los Angeles Chamber Orch, 80-; bass, Los Angeles Chamber Orch Bach Soloists, 82- *Teaching:* Lectr double bass, Univ Southern Calif, 81- *Mailing Add:* 4416 W Ave 41 Los Angeles CA 90065

RAPHLING, SAM
COMPOSER, PIANO

b Ft Worth, Tex, Mar 19, 10. *Study:* Chicago Musical Col, MM, 32; Hochschule, Berlin, 32-33. *Works:* Piano Concerto No 1, Mills Music, 46; Warble for Lilac Time, Ed Musicus, 50; Piano Concerto No 3, Presser, 50; Israel Rhapsody, Fox, 55; Trumpet Concerto, Bourne, 60; President Lincoln (opera), Gen Music, 76; Dream Keeper, Camerica, 83. *Teaching:* Instr music, Chicago Musical Col, 34-45; piano teacher, Greenwich House, 46-62. *Awards:* First Place Piano Sonata, Am Circle Comp, 48. *Mem:* ASCAP; Am Music Ctr. *Mailing Add:* 400 W 43 St Apt 29-P New York NY 10036

RAPIER, WAYNE
EDUCATOR, OBOE & ENGLISH HORN

Study: Eastman Sch Music, studied oboe with Marcel Tabuteau, BM. *Pos:* First oboe, Indianapolis Symph, formerly; assoc first oboe, Philadelphia Orch, formerly; soloist, Philadelphia String Quartet & Woodwind Quintet; perf with Philadelphia Orch, Baltimore Symph & Kansas City Orch; mem, US Marine Band & Orch, Kansas City Orch, Baltimore Orch & Robin Hood Dell Orch; mem chamb sect, Boston Symph Orch, currently. *Teaching:* Mem fac, Consv Music, Oberlin Col, formerly; instr oboe & English horn, New England Consv Music, currently. *Mailing Add:* New England Consv 290 Huntington Rd Boston MA 02115

RAPLEY, JANICE ANN
EDUCATOR, LECTURER

b Flint, Mich, Nov 15, 38. *Study:* Augustana Col, BME, 61; San Francisco State Univ, MA, 70; Memphis State Univ, Orff Master Class cert, 72. *Teaching:* Music specialist, San Francisco Unified Sch Dist, 68-76; prof, San Francisco State Univ, summers, 72- & US cols & univ incl Ariz State Univ, Stephen F Austin Univ, Univ Calif, Berkeley, & others, 72-; prof music, Calif State Univ, Chico, 76- *Mem:* Am Orff-Schulwerk Asn (pres northern Calif chap, 73-77, nat pres, 83-84); Music Educr Nat Conf; Calif Music Educr Asn. *Publ:* Auth, Development of the Orff-Schulwerk in American Elementary Education, private publ, 70; Trends in the Use of the Orff-Schulwerk in the United States, Orff Echo, 11/73; contribr, Sharing, Ariz Music Educr Asn, 79. *Mailing Add:* 84 Northwood Commons Pl Chico CA 95926

RASKIN, JUDITH
SOPRANO, EDUCATOR

b New York, NY, June 21, 28. *Study:* Smith Col, BA, 49, MA. *Rec Perf:* Cosi fan tutte, RCA, 67; rec on Desto, RCA, Columbia & Epic Rec. *Roles:* Dialogue of the Carmelites, NBC-TV, 57; Cosi fan tutte, New York City Opera, 59; Marriage of Figaro, Metropolitan Opera, 62. *Pos:* Lieder recitalist, NY Town Hall, 65; sop, conct performances with Philadelphia Symph, Boston Symph, New York Phil, London Symph and other maj orchs; leading sop, Metropolitan Opera, New York City Opera, Lyr Opera Chicago, Santa Fe Opera, Opera Co Boston & Opera Soc Washington; recitalist, Glyndebourne Opera, Berkshire Music Ctr & worldwide; co-chmn music adv panel, Nat Endowment Arts, 72-76, consult, currently; trustee, Martha Baird Rockefeller Fund, currently. *Teaching:* Mem fac voice, Manhattan Sch Music, 75-, chmn, 83-; mem fac, Mannes Col Music, currently. *Awards:* London Grammy Award, 67; Ford Found Grant, 76. *Mailing Add:* Mannes Col Music 157 E 74th St New York NY 10021

RATHBUN, JAMES RONALD
EDUCATOR, PIANO

b Ozark, Mo, Mar 25, 34. *Study:* Southwest Mo State Univ, dipl(piano) & BSE, 56; Ind Univ, MME, 57; Univ Iowa, studied piano with John Simms, DMA, 76; studied piano with Frances Bolsterli, 81-83. *Teaching:* Dir piano & orch, Angelo State Univ, 64-66; asst prof piano, Concord Col, 68-70; prof piano, Abilene Christian Univ, 72-, orch, 81-83. *Mem:* Music Teachers Nat Asn; Tex Music Teachers Asn; Abilene Music Teachers Asn; Col Music Soc; Phi Mu Alpha Sinfonia. *Mailing Add:* 1157 Highland Abilene TX 79605

RATLIFF, WILLIAM ELMORE
CRITIC-WRITER

b Evanston, Ill, Feb 11, 37. *Study:* Consv Music, Oberlin Col, BA(music & English), 59; Univ Wash, PhD, 74. *Pos:* Music critic, Peninsula Times Tribune, Palo Alto, 79- *Teaching:* Res fel, Stanford Univ, 68- *Mem:* Music Critics Asn. *Interests:* Music in American history. *Publ:* Auth, Declassifying the Classics Myth, Los Angeles Times, 78; Murder at the Opera, New Am Rev, 78; Enthusiasm for a Victorian Duo, Wall Street J, 79; The Dalis Project, Opera News, 80; George Cleve, Musical Am, 83. *Mailing Add:* 3196 Kipling St Palo Alto CA 94306

RATNER, LEONARD GILBERT
EDUCATOR, LECTURER

b Minneapolis, Minn, July 30, 16. *Study:* Univ Calif, Berkeley, PhD, 47. *Teaching:* Instr, Stanford Univ, 47-49, prof music, 49- *Awards:* Ford Fac Fel, 55-56; Guggenheim Fel, 55-56. *Mem:* Am Musicol Soc. *Interests:* Eighteenth century styles and forms. *Publ:* Auth, Music, The Listeners Art, 57, 66 & 77 & Harmony: Structure & Style, 62, McGraw-Hill; Classic Music: Expression, Form & Style, Schirmer, 80; The Musical Experience, Stanford Univ, Stanford Alumni, 83. *Mailing Add:* Dept Music Stanford Univ Stanford CA 94305

RATTLE, SIMON
CONDUCTOR

b Liverpool, England, 1955. *Study:* Royal Acad Music. *Rec Perf:* Tenth Symphony (Mahler), The Planets (Holst), piano concerto (Prokofiev & Ravel), Sibelius Fifth Symphony & Glagolitic Mass (Janacek), EMI-Angel Rec. *Pos:* Perc, Liverpool Phil; asst cond, Bournemouth Symph & Sinfonietta, 75 & BBC Scottish Symph Orch; guest cond, English Chamber Orch, Northern Sinfonia, Rotterdam Phil, Royal Liverpool Phil & Los Angeles Phil, 79; cond, London Phil Orch, 76 & Radio Symph Orch, Berlin, 77; cond & musical adv, City of Birmingham Symph Orch, England, 80-; artistic dir, South Bank Summer Music Fest, London, 81-83. *Awards:* Winner, Bournemouth Int Cond Compt, 74. *Mailing Add:* c/o Frank Saloman Assoc 201 W 54th St Suite 4C New York NY 10019

RAUCHE, ANTHONY THEODORE
EDUCATOR, PIANO
b Albany, NY, July 23, 50. *Study:* New England Consv Music, BM(piano), 72, MM(theory & piano), 75-76; Univ Ill. *Rec Perf:* Marginal Developments, Spectrum Rec, 82. *Pos:* Organist, Community Church of Boston, 69-75; ballet pianist, Nat Acad Arts, 82-83. *Teaching:* Instr piano, Newton Col, 74-75; asst prof theory, piano & ethnomusicol, Hartt Sch Music, 75- *Awards:* Nat Endowment Humanities Sem Grants, 79. *Mem:* Soc Ethnomusicol; Col Music Soc; Soc Music Theory; Am Folklore Soc. *Interests:* Immigrant community and its musical activities; popular music; Italian-Am culture. *Mailing Add:* 62 Otis St Hartford CT 06114

RAUSCH, CARLOS
CONDUCTOR & MUSIC DIRECTOR, COMPOSER
b Buenos Aires, Argentina, March 15, 24; US citizen. *Study:* State Univ NY, Stony Brook, MA, 75; Columbia Univ, DMA, 83. *Works:* String Quartet, Mobart, 57; Para Gerardo (flute & electronic sounds), Zalo, 73; Whatever You Say, Dearest (perc & electronic sounds), Mobart, 75; Six Songs, 78 & Sonata for Violin & Piano, 80, APNM; Capriccio for Flute, Mobart, 83. *Pos:* Music dir, Royal Winnipeg Ballet, 65-71; Guest cond, Pierre Monteux Music Fest, 69, Joffrey Ballet, 77 & Orquesta Filarmonica, Santiago, Chile, 81. *Teaching:* Adj prof music, City Col New York, 77-79; instr electronic music, Jersey City State Col, 79-81; preceptor music, Columbia Univ, 78- *Bibliog:* Juan Carlos Paz (auth), Introduccion a la Musica de Nuestro Tiempo, Neuva Vision, Buenos Aires, Arg, 58. *Mem:* Am Comp Alliance; Am Symph Orch League; Am Musicol Soc; Agrupacion Nueva Musica. *Mailing Add:* 23 W 73rd St Apt 312 New York NY 10023

RAUSCH, JACK D
ADMINISTRATOR, BASSOON
b Dover, Ohio, Mar 18, 33. *Study:* Ohio State Univ, BS(music educ), 59, MA(theory & comp), 64; studied bassoon with Bernard Garfield & Frank Rendell. *Pos:* Prin bassoon, Fla Symph, 57-63, Santa Fe Opera Orch, 61-65 & Phoenix Symph, 64-78. *Teaching:* Assoc prof bassoon & theory, Ariz State Univ, 64-, asst dir, Sch Music, 82- *Mem:* Am Fedn Musicians; Int Double Reed Soc. *Mailing Add:* 1832 E Concorda Dr Tempe AZ 85282

RAUSCHER, DONALD JOHN
EDUCATOR, ARRANGER
b New York, NY, Mar 5, 21. *Study:* Manhattan Sch Music, MusB, 50, MMus, 52. *Teaching:* Col registrar, Manhattan Sch Music, 52-67, fac mem, 52- *Awards:* Harold Bauer Award. *Mem:* Bohemians. *Publ:* Auth, Orchestration: Scores and Scoring, 63, coauth, Chromatic Harmony Text, 65 & Chromatic Harmony Workbook, 65, Free Press; Everybody's Favorite (ten vol), Amsco Publ Co; Spectrum Music (nine vol), Macmillan Publ Co. *Mailing Add:* Manhattan Sch Music 120 Claremont Ave New York NY 10029

RAUTENBERG, JOHN LESLIE
FLUTE, TROMBONE
b Cleveland, Ohio, Sept 7, 36. *Study:* Oberlin Col, BME, 58. *Pos:* Third flute & piccolo, Indianapolis Symph, 58-61 & Chautauqua Symph, 62; asst prin flute, Cleveland Orch, 61-68 & assoc prin flute, 68- *Teaching:* Instr flute, Cleveland Inst Music, 61-63, Oberlin Col, 63-66 & Univ Akron, 69-73. *Mailing Add:* 2185 Bellfield Ave Cleveland OH 44106

RAVER, LEONARD
ORGAN, EDUCATOR
b Wenatchee, Wash, Jan 8, 27. *Study:* Univ Puget Sound, BM, 51; Syracuse Univ, with Arthur Poister, MM, 52; Union Sem Sch Sacred Music, with Vernon de Tar, DSM, 57; Royal Consv, Amsterdam, Netherlands, with Gustav Leonhardt, 58-60. *Rec Perf:* Symphony No 3 (Saint-Saens), 77 & Lord Nelson Mass (Haydn), 78, CBS Masterworks; A Quaker Reader (Ned Rorem), CRI, 78; Cycles and Gongs (E Schwartz), 78 & Prayer and Toccata (Gail Kubik), 79, Orion. *Pos:* Univ organist, Pa State Univ, 61-66; off organist, New York Phil, 77- *Teaching:* Assoc prof, Pa State Univ, 61-66; dir music, Gen Theol Sem, New York, 66-71; fac mem, Inst Sacred Music, Yale Univ, 74-77; mem fac organ, Juilliard Sch, 75- *Awards:* Fulbright Fel, 58. *Bibliog:* Alan Kozinn (auth), Leonard Raver: Organist for the New York Philharmonic, Contemp Keyboard, 2/81. *Mem:* Am Guild Organists (nat secy, 70-73); Music Libr Asn; Phi Mu Alpha Sinfonia. *Mailing Add:* 155 W 68th St New York NY 10023

RAVNAN, ELLEN MARIE
VIOLA, TEACHER
b Chicago Heights, Ill, Aug 15, 53. *Study:* Manhattan Sch Music, viola study with Lillian Fuchs & chamber music with Ariana Bronne, BM, 75; Univ Ill, Urbana-Champaign, viola with Guillermo Perich, chamber music with Gabriel Magyar & pedagogy with Paul Rolland, MM, 77. *Pos:* Prin & sect viola, Colo Phil, summers, 77-78; prin & asst prin viola, Madison Symph Orch, Wis, 78- *Teaching:* Mem fac, Pre-Col Inst, Sch Music, Univ Wis, Madison, 80-; orch dir, Jr & Sr High, Ft Atkinson, Wis, 82- *Mem:* Am Fedn Musicians; Nat Music Educr Conf; Nat Educ Asn; Pi Kappa Lambda. *Mailing Add:* 444 N Few St Madison WI 53703

RAWLINS, JOSEPH (THOMAS)
EDUCATOR, TENOR
b Lakeland, Fla, Nov 7, 36. *Study:* Univ Fla, vocal study with Norman Abelson, AA, 57; La State Univ, voice with Dallas Draper & opera with Peter P Fuchs, BMus, 59, MMus, 61, DMus, 72; North Tex State Univ, with Eugene Conley. *Rec Perf:* Elijah, Century Rec, 65; Auburn Concert Hall, Ala Educ TV Network, 65-74. *Roles:* Eisenstein, Jackson Opera Co, 59; Rodolfo,

La State Univ Opera Theatre, 61; The Duke, Jackson Opera Co, 65. *Teaching:* Instr voice & choral, Millsaps Col, 63-65; asst prof voice & opera, Auburn Univ, 65-69, assoc prof, 71-74; assoc prof voice & choral, Univ WFla, 74-80, prof, 80- *Mem:* Music Teachers Nat Asn (nat voice comt, 68-70); Nat Asn Teachers Singing; Am Choral Dir Asn; Fla League of Arts; Fla Music Teachers Asn. *Publ:* Auth, The Songs of Charles Wilfred Orr-Part I, 73, Part II, 74 & Housman, the Musicians' Poet, 80, NATS Bulletin; Carissimi, Progenitor of the Oratorio, The Choral J, 81; Charles Wilfred Orr, 1893-1976, Comp (England), 81. *Mailing Add:* Dept Music Univ West Fla Pensacola FL 32504

RAY, (SISTER) MARY DOMINIC
ADMINISTRATOR, LECTURER
b Burlington, Vt, Sept 5, 13. *Study:* Cincinnati Consv Music, BM, 37; studied piano with Georg Gruenberg, Berlin, Germany, 37-38. *Pos:* Conct pianist, 43-47; soloist, Marin Symph Orch, 62; lectr, performer, consult & prog notes writer, M H de Young Mem Mus, San Francisco, 76. *Teaching:* Asst prof music, Dominican Col, 45-, founder & dir Am Music Res Ctr, 68-; vis prof, San Francisco State Univ, 78-79. *Awards:* Grant, Darrow Found, 75-82 & Lilly Found, 76 & 78. *Mem:* Sonneck Soc; Music Libr Asn; Moravian Music Found; Mu Phi Epsilon; Pi Kappa Lambda. *Publ:* Coauth, Gloria Dei: Calif Mission Music, Calif Parks & Recreation Dept, 75; auth, Introd to Taylor's Golddigger's Songbook, Book Club Calif, 75; Drums, Wigs and Six Wax Lights, Musical Am, 75; The Seattle Symphony Orchestra, NW Arts, 78; Six Tales that Wagged a Seventh, Sonneck Soc Newsletter, 3/83. *Mailing Add:* Am Music Res Ctr Dominican Col San Rafael CA 94901

RAY, WILLIAM BENJAMIN
BARITONE, TEACHER
b Lexington, Ky. *Study:* Western Reserve Univ, 50; Oberlin Col, with Daniel A Harris, BA, 52; Vienna Acad Music, Austria, with Sergei Radamsky, 57; Heidelberg Univ, Ger, 79; Boston Univ, EdM, 82. *Rec Perf:* Die Verlobung in St Domingo, Hamburg Studio, 60; Musik, Norddeutscher Rundfunk, Hamburg, 62; Gaeste, Hessischer Rundfunk, Frankfurt, 64; George Gershwin, Funkhaus Hannover, 65; Musik, Bayerischer Rundfunk, Munich, 74; Gaeste, RIAS Studios, WBerlin, 80 & Seddeutscher Rundfunk, Stuttgart, 81. *Roles:* Amonasro in Aida, Frankfurt Opera House, 60; Kumalo in Lost in the Stars, Munich Opera House, 61; Oberon in Midsummer Night's Dream, Berlin Opera House, 62 & Kiel Opera House, 63; Porgy in Porgy and Bess, Toulouse Opera House, France, 65; Carter Jones in The Visitation, Wupperthal Opera House, Germany, 69. *Pos:* Featured singer, Leonard de Paur's Infantry Chorus, 52-53; soloist, Karamu House, Cleveland, Ohio, 53-54; guest perf, Cleveland Playhouse, 54-55; founder & dir, Black Theater Prod, Stuttgart, 73-82. *Teaching:* Instr voice, Peabody Consv Music, Johns Hopkins Univ, 82- *Awards:* Contemp Personalities, Accad Italia delle Arti e del Lavoro, 81. *Mem:* Opera Ebony. *Mailing Add:* 539 Higgins Dr Odenton MD 21113

RAYKHTSAUM, AZA
VIOLIN, TEACHER
b Leningrad, USSR, Aug 21, 50. *Study:* Leningrad Consv, USSR, dipl, 74. *Pos:* Concertmaster, Leningrad Consv Orch, USSR, 74-80; violinist, Leningrad Phil Orch, USSR, 77-79, Houston Symph Orch, 80-82 & Boston Symph Orch, 82- *Teaching:* Violin, Lenigrad Sch Gifted Children, 73-80. *Mailing Add:* Symph Hall 301 Massachusetts Ave Boston MA 02115

READ, GARDNER
COMPOSER, CRITIC-WRITER
b Evanston, Ill, Jan 2, 13. *Study:* Eastman Sch Music, BM, 32, MM, 37; studied with Ildebrando Pizzetti, Rome, 39; Berkshire Music Ctr, with Aaron Copland, 41; Doane Col, Hon Dr Music, 64. *Works:* Arioso Elegiaca (strings), Op 91; Toccata Giocosa, Op 94; Vernal Equinox, Op 96; String Quartet, No 1, Op 100; Los Dioses Aztecas, Op 107; Sonoric Fantasia, No 2, Op 123; Symphony No 4, Op 92. *Pos:* Prin cond, St Louis Phil Orch, 43-44; ed, Birchard-Boston Univ Contemp Choral Music Series, 50-60; originated & host, Our American Music, WBUR & WGBH radio, Boston, 53-60. *Teaching:* Comp-in-res & prof comp, Sch Music, Sch Arts, Boston Univ, 48-78, emer prof, 78-; lectr mod notation, over 40 univ & music sch, 67-80. *Awards:* Grant, Ingram Merrill Found, 82; Alumni Achievement Award, Eastman Sch Music, 82. *Publ:* Auth, Thesaurus of Orchestral Devices, Pitman Publ Corp, 53 & Greenwood Press, 69; Music Notation—A Manual of Modern Practice, Allyn & Bacon, Inc, 64, 2nd ed, 69; Crescendo Publ Co, 72 & Victor Gollancz Ltd, London, England, 74; Contemporary Instrumental Techniques, 76 & Style and Orchestration, 77, Schirmer Bks, Macmillan; Modern Rhythmic Notation, Ind Univ Press, 78 & Victor Gollancz Ltd, London, England, 81. *Mailing Add:* 47 Forster Rd Manchester MA 01944

READ, THOMAS (LAWRENCE)
COMPOSER, CONDUCTOR
b Erie, Pa, July 3, 38. *Study:* Oberlin Consv, violin with Majewski & Toth, theory with Asshaffenburg, BM, 60; New England Consv, violin with Richard Burgin, MM, 62; Peabody Consv, with Gerle, Galkin, Lees & Grove, DMA(violin), 71. *Works:* Te Deum, perf by St Paul's Episcopal Cathedral, Burlington, Vt, 73; Naming the Changes, C F Peters Corp, 75; Solo Music for Contrabass, 75, Nova for Solo Flute, 77, Corrente for Wind Trio, 80, Closing Distances, 81 & Variations for Piano Trio, 81, Am Comp Alliance. *Pos:* First violin, Fac String Quartet, Univ Vt, 69-; pit cond, Royall Tyler Theatre, Burlington, Vt, 69-; cond, Vt Youth Orch, Burlington, 71-73. *Teaching:* Assoc prof music, West Chester State Col, 56-66; instr comp, Peabody Jr Consv, Lyndenville, Vt, 62-65; prof music, Univ Vt, 67- *Awards:* Fel-res, Johnson Comp Conf, 75 & 78; fel, MacDowell Colony, 75 & 78; comp grant, Vt Coun Arts, 79. *Mem:* Am Soc Univ Comp (chmn, & ed Reportoire Catalogue, region I, 79-80); Am Comp Alliance; BMI. *Mailing Add:* 32 Cliff Burlington VT 05401

REAGIN, BRIAN E
VIOLIN, EDUCATOR
b Chicago, Ill, Oct 10, 55. *Study:* Meadowmount Sch Music, with Ivan Galamian & Josef Gingold, 72-77; Cleveland Inst Music, dipl, 76, artist dipl, 77. *Pos:* First violin, Piedmont Chamber Orch, 78-80, Pittsburgh Symph Orch, 80-82 & Pittsburgh Chamber Soloists, 82-; prin violin, Pittsburgh New Music Ens, 77-80; asst concertmaster, Youngstown Symph, Ohio, 77-80 & Pittsburgh Symph Orch, 82- *Teaching:* Asst prof, Carnegie-Mellon Univ, 77-; lectr violin, Cleveland Inst Music, 77-78; instr violin, Meadowmount Sch Music, summer 80. *Awards:* Gerome Gross Award, Cleveland Inst Music, 75; Talman Award, Soc Am Musicians, 76; Grad Fel Award, Rotary Found Int, 77. *Mailing Add:* 786 Greenfield Ave Pittsburgh PA 15217

REALE, PAUL VINCENT
COMPOSER, PIANO
b New Brunswick, NJ, Mar 2, 43. *Study:* Columbia Univ, MA, 67; Univ Pa, PhD, 70. *Works:* Seance, Theodore Presser Co, 73; Piano Trio, Mirecourt Trio, 80; Concerto Dies Irae, Wis Chamber Orch, 82; Cello Sonata, Terry King, 82. *Rec Perf:* Aspects of Love, Orion, 77. *Teaching:* Prof music, Univ Calif, Los Angeles, currently. *Mailing Add:* 22125 Gault St Canoga Park CA 91303

REANEY, GILBERT
MUSICOLOGIST, EDUCATOR
b Sheffield, England, Jan 11, 24. *Study:* Univ Sheffield, BA, 48, BMus, 50, MA, 51. *Pos:* Gen ed, Corpus Scriptorum Musica, 66-82. *Teaching:* Res fel music, Univ Reading, 53-56 & Univ Birmingham, 56-59; guest lectr, prin univ, US, Germany & Gt Brit, 59-68; vis prof, Univ Hamburg, 60; lectr, Univ Calif, Los Angeles, 60, assoc prof, 61-63, prof music, 64- *Awards:* Dent Medal, Int Musicol Soc, 61; fel, Guggenheim Found, 63-64 & Nat Humanities Found, 67-68. *Mem:* Am Musicol Soc; Royal Musical Asn; Int Musicol Soc. *Interests:* Medieval and Renaissance music; French and Latin literature, primarily medieval. *Publ:* Auth, Early Fifteenth Century Music, six vol, Am Inst Musicol, 55-77; Manuscripts of Polyphonic Music: Eleventh to Early Fourteenth Century, Henle Verlag, 66; coauth, Corpus Scriptorum de Musica, No 12, 15 & 18, Am Inst Musicol, 66, 71 & 74; John Wilde and the Notre Dame Conductus, In: Speculum Musicae Artis, Finke Verlag, 70; Machaut, Oxford Univ, 71. *Mailing Add:* Music Dept Univ Calif Los Angeles CA 90024

REARDON, JOHN
BARITONE
b New York, NY, Apr 8, 30. *Study:* Rollins Col, with Ross Rossazza, BA, 57, Hon DMus, 76; private study with Margaret Harshaw & Martial Singher. *Rec Perf:* The Rake's Progress (Stravinsky), The Creation (Haydn) & The Merry Widow (Lehar), Columbia; Old Maid and the Thief (Menotti), Vox; Songfest (Bernstein), DGG; La Pietra del Paragone (Rossini), Vanguard; La Boheme (Puccini), Schanuard/Seraphim Rec. *Roles:* Don Giovanni in Don Giovanni, 65-70, Marcello in La Boheme, 65-70, Papageno in Die Zauberflöte, 65-70 & Escamilio in Carmen, 65-70, Metropolitan Opera; Abdul in Last Savage, La Fenice, 66; Pelleas in Pelleas et Melisande, Spoleto Fest, 68; Scarpia in Tosca, Santa Fe Opera, 71. *Awards:* Musician of the Month, Musical Am Mag. *Mailing Add:* PO Box 2424 Santa Fe NM 87501

REARICK, MARTHA NELL
EDUCATOR, FLUTE & PICCOLO
b Danville, Ill, Nov 29, 38. *Study:* Univ Mich, BMus, 60, MMus, 61. *Rec Perf:* Ars Nova, Univ SFla Fine Arts Ser, 76; Wind Quintets of A Reicha, Vol 1, 80 & Vol 2, 81, Musical Heritage Soc. *Teaching:* Prof music, Pensacola Jr Col, 61-63, Univ S Fla, 63- *Mem:* Nat Flute Asn (secy, 78-79, bd dir, 79-81). *Publ:* Auth, Fabric of Flute Playing, Studio P/R, 79. *Mailing Add:* Music Dept Univ SFla Tampa FL 33620

REBER, RICHARD
EDUCATOR, PIANO
b Reading, Pa, Jan 10, 39. *Study:* Eastman Sch Music, BM, 60, MM, 62; Acad Music, Vienna, Austria, 62-63; studied piano with Frank Mannheimer, 66-70. *Teaching:* From instr to assoc prof piano, Univ Kans, 64- *Awards:* Fulbright Grant, 62-63. *Mem:* Nat Music Teachers Asn; Kans Music Teachers Asn (mem exec bd, 82-). *Mailing Add:* Dept Music Univ Kans Lawrence KS 66045

REECE, ARLEY R
TENOR
b Yoakum, Tex, Aug 27, 45. *Study:* Voice studies with Mack Harrell, Eugene Conley & Daniel Ferro. *Roles:* Alexei in The Gambler, Wexford Fest, Ireland, 73; Bacchus in Ariadne auf Naxos, New York City Opera, 74. *Pos:* Soloist, Dallas Civic Opera, Shreveport Symph, Philadelphia Lyr Opera, Ky Opera Asn, Conn Opera Asn, Opera Soc Wash, Lake George Fes; perf in Europe, 74- *Mailing Add:* Grunstr 28A D-4930 Detmold Germany, Federal Republic of

REED, ADDISON WALKER
EDUCATOR, BASS
b Steubenville, Ohio, Apr 22, 29. *Study:* Kent State Univ, AB, 51, MA, 51, BS, 56; Univ NC, Chapel Hill, PhD, 73. *Roles:* Dikoy in Katya Kabanova, Karamu House, 57. *Teaching:* Prof music, St Augustine's Col, NC, 73- *Awards:* Ford Found Fel, 71; Fulbright Found Fel, 78. *Mem:* Am Musicol Soc; Sonneck Soc; Music Educr Nat Conf; Nat Asn Teachers Singing; Nat Asn Sch Music. *Publ:* Auth, Scott Joplin, Pioneer, Black Perspective Music, 75; contribr, Scott Joplin, Schirmer, 80; auth, Scott Joplin, In: New Grove Dict of Music & Musicians, 81. *Mailing Add:* 207 Loft Lane #53 Raleigh NC 27609

REED, ALFRED
COMPOSER, CONDUCTOR & MUSIC DIRECTOR
b New York, NY, Jan 25, 21. *Study:* Baylor Univ, BM, 55, MM, 56; Juilliard Sch, with Vittorio Giannini; studied piano with S Rubinstein & J Krivin, trumpet with A Nussbaum, H Berken & M Grupp, harmony & counterpoint with John P Sacco & comp with Paul Yertin; Hon MusD, Int Consv Music, Lima, Peru, 68. *Works:* Siciliana Notturno (solo E-flat alto sax & piano), 78 & Fantasia A Due (solo tuba & piano), 79, Marks Music Corp; All Hail to the Days, Curtis Music Press, 79; Greensleeves (fantasy for orch), 79 & Suite Concertante, 82, E F Kalmus; The Garden of Proserpine (symph pastorale for winds), 82 & Third Suite for Band, 82, Marks Music Corp; also many others for orchestra, string orchestra, instrumental solos, chorus & marching band. *Pos:* Staff comp, arr & asst cond, Radio Workshop, New York, 38-40; assoc cond & radio prod dir, 529th Army Air Force Symph Band, 42-46; composer, arranger & musical director for radio & TV musical comedies & reviews, 48-53; cond, Baylor Symph Orch, Waco, Tex, 53-55; exec ed, Hansen Publ Inc, 55-66; asst dir, Sch Band of Am, 66 & 67; cond, All-Am Youth Hon Band, 67 & All-Am Youth Hon Wind Ens, 69; dir, Music Merchandising Prog, Univ Miami, 66-; ed, Univ Miami Music Publ, 66-; guest comp, cond & clinician in 46 states, Can, Mex, SAm & Europe, 68- *Teaching:* Prof music, Univ Miami, 66- *Awards:* Luria Prize (for Rhapsody for Viola & Orchestra), 59; Acad Wind & Perc Arts Award. *Mailing Add:* Sch Music Univ Miami Coral Gables FL 33124

REED, BRUCE
TENOR
Roles: Camille in The Merry Widow, New York City Opera & Orlando Opera; Tonio in The Daughter of the Regiment, Tamino in The Magic Flute, Fenton in The Merry Wives of Windsor & Falstaff, New York City Opera; Ramiro in La Cenerentola; Alfredo in La Traviata, Cleveland Opera, 82; Rodolfo in La Boheme, Orlando Opera, 82. *Pos:* Mem, Tri-Cities Opera, Binghamton, NY & New York City Opera; tenor, Boston Opera, San Diego Opera, Va Opera Asn & Spoleto Fest in US & Italy. *Mailing Add:* c/o Lew & Benson Moreau-Neret Inc 204 W Tenth St New York NY 10014

REED, H OWEN
COMPOSER, EDUCATOR
b Odessa, Mo, June 17, 10. *Study:* Univ Mo, 29-33; La State Univ, BM, 34, MM, 36, BA, 37; Eastman Sch Music, PhD, 39; Berkshire Music Ctr, with Martinu, Copland & Bernstein, 42; private study with Roy Harris, 47. *Works:* La Fiesta Mexicana (symph band), 54, Earth-Trapped (chamber opera), 60, La Fiesta Mexicana (symph orch), 64 & The Touch of the Earth (symph band), 71, Belwin-Mills; For the Unfortunate (symph band), Neil A Kjos, 72; Living Solid Face (chamber opera), 74 & Butterfly Girl (chamber opera), 80, Black & White Repro. *Teaching:* Prof, Mich State Univ, 39-76, prof emer, 76- *Awards:* Guggenheim Fel, 48; Kjos Mem Award for the Unfortunate, 75; ASCAP Award, annually. *Mem:* ASCAP; Am Music Ctr; Nat Asn Comp USA; Am Soc Univ Comp; Music Educr Nat Conf. *Publ:* Auth, A Workbook in the Fundamentals of Music, 47 & Basic Music (plus workbook), 54 & coauth, Basic Contrapuntal Techniques, 64 & Scoring for Percussion, 2nd ed, 79, Belwin-Mills; coauth, Basic Contrapuntal Techniques, 64 & Scoring for Percussion, 2nd ed, 79, Belwin-Mills; The Materials of Music Composition, Books I & II, Addison Wesley, 78 & 80. *Mailing Add:* 4690 Ottawa Dr Okemos MI 48864

REED, IDA MCALILEY
LIBRARIAN
Chester, SC, July 11, 42. *Study:* Fla Presby Col, BA(music & classics), 64; Univ Pittsburgh, MA(musicol), 66, MLS, 68. *Pos:* Librn music div, Carnegie Libr Pittsburgh, 68-73, asst head music & art dept, 73-74, head music & art dept, 74- *Mem:* Music Libr Asn (vice chmn Pa chap, 75 & chmn, 76); Sonneck Soc. *Interests:* Music librarianship; musical activities of western Pennsylvania. *Publ:* Coauth, Breaking into Jail, Libr J, 71; auth, Pittsburgh, In: New Grove Dict of Music in US, 84. *Mailing Add:* Music & Art Dept Carnegie Libr Pittsburgh 4400 Forbes Ave Pittsburgh PA 15213

REED, MARLYCE P
COMPOSER
b Iowa, Jan 14, 55. *Study:* Univ Wis, Stevens Pt, BM; Northwestern Univ, with Alan Stout, MM; studied clarinet, privately. *Works:* Three Short Dialogues (3 Bb clarinets); Chromasia (solo alto saxophone & multiple perc); Shir Kadosh (boys choir & orch); Two Autumn Moods (tuba); Rhapsody No 1 (clarinet); Untitled (electronic tape), 78; Brass Quartet No 1. *Awards:* Faricy Prize for Creative Comp; Susan B Colman Award; Albertson Award. *Mem:* Pi Kappa Lambda; Int League of Women Composers; Am Music Ctr. *Mailing Add:* 1717 Peabody Appleton WI 54915

REED, PHYLLIS LUIDENS
COMPOSER, MEZZO-SOPRANO
b Mineola, NY. *Study:* Hope Col, BA, 53; Univ Conn; Hartford Sem, dipl, 60. *Works:* I Have a Dream, 73, Dream Variations, 74, Those Who Dream, 74, Mud-Luscious, 77, China Trilogy, 78, Three with Kagawa, 79 & Cry for Freedom, 81, Galaxy Music Corp. *Pos:* Vesper organist, Silver Bay, Lake George, NY & Hartford Sem, 57-60; organist, Bethel Methodist Church, 67-68; organist & choir dir, Redding Congregational Church, 67-68; ms soloist, US. *Mem:* ASCAP; Long Island Comp Alliance; Religious Communities for Arts. *Mailing Add:* 4 Exeter Ct Northport NY 11768

REES, ROSALIND
SOPRANO

b Greenville, Pa, June 18, 37. *Study:* Cleveland Inst Music, BM, 59; study voice with Adele Addison, 60- *Rec Perf:* Les Noces (Stravinsky), Columbia, 72; America Sings: The Founding Years, 76, America Sings: The Great Sentimental Age, 79 & Music for Voice & Guitar, 79, Vox; Rosalind Rees Sings William Schuman, CRI, 80; Ned Rorem's Last Poems of Wallace Stevens, 83 & Rosalind Rees Sings Ned Rorem, 83, GSS Rec; and numerous others. *Pos:* Soloist, Gregg Smith Singers, 69- & Boston Symph, Nat Symph, Detroit Symph, Brooklyn Phil, St Paul Chamber Orch, Syracuse Orch, Paris Chamber Orch, ABT & Musica Aeterna Orch, 72- *Rep:* Century Artists 866 3rd Ave New York NY 10022. *Mailing Add:* 171 W 71st St New York NY 10023

REESE, GILBERT
CELLO

b Long Beach, Calif, May 26, 25. *Study:* Ecole Normale Musique, Paris, lic, 51; study with Pablo Casals, Prades, France, 49-52. *Rec Perf:* Concerto (Lalo), Los Angeles Phil, 48; Concerto (Boccherini), Danish State Radio Orch, 53; Musique de l'Amerique, Radiodiffusion Francaise, 72; Sonata (E Grieg), 74 & Fantasy Pieces (R Schumann), 74, Crystal Rec; Scandinavian Cello Music, Norsk Kringkasting, 76; French Scenarios, Varese Int Rec, 80. *Pos:* Concert cellist with major orchestras & throughout Europe & Asia, 50-; prin cellist, Indianapolis Symph, 52-63; cellist, Jordan String Quartet, Indianapolis, 54-63; organizer & participant, Spring Chamber Music Fest, Indianapolis, 57-63; pres, SYMF, Los Angeles, 68-77. *Teaching:* Assoc prof, Butler Univ, 53-63. *Bibliog:* Elise Emery (auth), Concert Cellist, Press Telegram, Long Beach, 69; Mona Levin (auth), Mye God Musik Er Glemt, Aftenposten, Oslo, Norway, 2/23/76. *Mem:* Am String Teachers Asn, (bd mem, 70-73); Chamber Music Am; Am Fedn Musicians. *Publ:* Auth, My Studies With Casals, News Press, Santa Barbara, 66. *Mailing Add:* c/o Conct Prom Serv 34 66th Pl Long Beach CA 90803

REESE, WILLIAM HEARTT
CONDUCTOR & MUSIC DIRECTOR, EDUCATOR

b New York, NY, June 26, 10. *Study:* Amherst Col, AB; Columbia Univ, MA; Hochschule Musik, Berlin, cert choral & orch cond; Univ Berlin, PhD; studied cond with Pierre Monteux. *Pos:* Founder & cond, Philadelphia Chamber Orch, 51-78 & Rockland Camerata, 77-; organist & choirmaster, Church of Redeemer, Bryn Mawr, Pa, 70-76; cond, Orange Co Symph Orch, New York, 77-; music dir & cond, Bethlehem Bach Choir, 80-83. *Teaching:* Prof music, Haverford Col, 47-75; chmn music dept, Franklin & Marshall Col, 50-53; lectr, Swarthmore Col, 52-58. *Bibliog:* Theodore R Bledsoe (auth), Festschrift, private publ, 75. *Mem:* Am Symph Orch League; Am Musicol Asn; Am Guild Organists; Col Music Asn (pres, 54-56). *Publ:* Auth, Grundsätze und Entwicklung der Instrumentation in der vorklassischen und klassischen Sinfonie, Gräfenhainischen, 40; co-ed, The Choral Conductor (transl, Kurt Thomas's Lehrbuch der Chorleitung), New York, 74; auth, 84th Psalm; St John Passion, Schuetz. *Mailing Add:* PO Box 415 Piermont NY 10968

REEVE, BASIL
OBOE

b New York, NY, Nov 13, 43. *Study:* Hartt Col Music; Juilliard Sch Music, BM, 66. *Pos:* Prin oboe, New York City Opera, 67-70 & Rotterdam Phil, 70-71; assoc prin oboe, Minn Orch, 71-79, co-prin oboe, 79- *Mailing Add:* 436 Oliver Ave S Minneapolis MN 55405

REEVES, JAMES MATTHEW
EDUCATOR, ADMINISTRATOR

b Norfolk, Va, Feb 18, 19. *Study:* Va State Col, BS, 41; Columbia Univ, MA, 64; Catholic Univ, DMA, 80. *Pos:* Prin bass, Va Orch Group, 66-81. *Teaching:* Music, Marlboro, Md, 42-43 & St Josephs Cath Sch, 46-58; prof music, Norfolk State Univ, 46-58. *Mem:* Music Educr Nat Conf; Music Teachers Nat Asn. *Mailing Add:* Music Dept Norfolk State Univ Norfolk VA 23504

REHFELDT, PHILLIP RICHARD
CLARINET, EDUCATOR

b Burlington, Iowa, Sept 21, 39. *Study:* Univ Ariz, BMEd, 61; Mt St Mary's Col, Los Angeles, MM(clarinet), 62; Univ Mich, DMA(clarinet), 69; studied clarinet with Samuel Fain, Kalman Bloch, William Stubbins & Mitchell Lurie. *Rec Perf:* Redlands Music for Clarinets, Zanja Rec, 79; Three Pieces for Clarinet & Piano (David Maslanka), CRI, 81; Of Place, As Altered (Barney Childs), Brewster Rec, 82; Effetti Colaterali (James Dashow), Casa Discografica Edi-Pan, 83; Buffalo Bill (Alexandra Pierce), Capriccio, 83; The Tracker (David Ward-Steinmen), Am Soc Univ Comp Rec Ser, 83; American Music for Woodwind Quintet, Advance Rec, 83. *Pos:* Perf with Riverside Symph Orch, San Bernardino Symph Orch, Univ Redlands Symph Orch, Redlands Bowl Summer Fest Orch, W End Opera & San Bernardino Civic Light Opera. *Teaching:* Band dir, Tucson Pub Sch District #1, 62-65; asst prof clarinet, Northern Mich Univ, 65-68; instr woodwinds, San Bernardino Valley Col, 69-74; prof woodwinds & musicol, Univ Redlands, 69-; vis lectr clarinet, Ariz State Univ, 82-83. *Awards:* Perf grant, Nat Endowment Arts; perf award, Nat Asn Comp USA, 81; four res grants, Univ Redlands. *Publ:* Auth, Clarinet Multiphonics, 10/73 & Some Recent Thoughts on Clarinet Multiphonics, 77, Clarinet; New Directions for Clarinet, Univ Calif Press, 78; William O Smith, Clarinet, 80; The Clarinet Music of Barney Childs, Clar-i-NetWork, 83. *Mailing Add:* 610 W Cypress Redlands CA 92373

REHFUSS, HEINZ J
EDUCATOR, BARITONE

b Frankfurt, Germany, May 25, 17. *Study:* Univ Neuchatel, Switz, dipl, 37; studied voice with Carl Rehfuss & stage dir with Otto Erhardt. *Rec Perf:* Many records with DGG, London, Decca, Westminster, Vanguard, Philips, Pathe Marconi and others, 50- *Roles:* Don Giovanni in Don Giovanni, Count in Figaro, Boris in Boris Godunov, Four Devils in Tales of Hoffmann, Mephisto in Faust & Damnation, Golaud in Pelleas et Melisande, Philip in Don Carlos, in major opera houses in Italy, France, Germany, Belgium, Switzerland, US & Canada, 50- *Pos:* Bass & baritone with major world opera houses & concert associations—Scala, Paris, Berlin, Zürich, Naples, Venice, Vienna, Salzburg, London, Edinburgh, Aix Festival & others, 47- *Teaching:* Prof voice, Darmstadt Music Acad, 54-58, State Univ NY, Buffalo, 65-, Montreal Consv, 67-72 & Eastman Sch Music, 70-72. *Awards:* Gold Medal, City of Zürich, 56; Grand Prix Disque, 58 & 60. *Mem:* Asn Swiss Musicians; Nat Asn Singing Teachers; Am Guild Musical Artists. *Mailing Add:* 331 Lincoln Pkwy Buffalo NY 14216

REICH, BRUCE
COMPOSER, EDUCATOR

b Chicago, Ill, Sept 15, 48. *Study:* Univ Southern Calif, with Robert Linn & Halsey Stevens; Harvard Univ, with Robert Middleton; Yale Univ, with Penderecki. *Works:* What Is Man (bar), 68; Three Songs (ms), 69; Piano Sonata (chamber music), 69; Cantata with Brass and Percussion (chorus), 70; String Quartet (chamber music), 71; Movements (chamber ens), 72; Songs of Time (ms & instrm), 73. *Teaching:* Asst prof theory & analysis, Univ Utah, 76- *Awards:* Epstein Mem Found Grant, 69-70; Helen S Anstead Award, 70. *Mailing Add:* Music Dept Univ Utah Salt Lake City UT 84112

REICH, NANCY B
WRITER, EDUCATOR

b New York, NY, July 3, 24. *Study:* Queens Col, BA, 45; Teachers Col, Columbia Univ, MA, 47; NY Univ, PhD, 72. *Teaching:* Adj asst prof, NY Univ, 72-74; asst prof, Manhattanville Col, Purchase, NY, 75-81 & Rubin Acad Music, Jerusalem, summer 76; vis scholar, Ctr Res Women, Stanford Univ, 82-83. *Awards:* Grant, German Acad Exchange Serv, 78; fel, Nat Endowment Humanities, 82. *Mem:* Music Libr Asn (chair Gtr NY chap, 75-77); Col Music Asn (mem coun, 77-80); Am Musicol Soc; Int Musicol Soc. *Interests:* Nineteenth Century; Clara Schumann. *Publ:* Auth, A Catalog of the Works of William Sydeman, NY Univ, 68; The Rudorff Collection, Notes, 74; Liszt's Variations on the Siege of Corinth, Fontes Artis Musicae, 76 & 79; Louise Reichardt, In: Festschrift Heinrich Hüschen Köln, Gitarre & Laute Verlag, 80; ed, Selected Songs of Louise Reichardt, Da Capo Press, 81. *Mailing Add:* 121 Lincoln Ave Hastings-on-Hudson NY 10706

REICH, STEVE
COMPOSER

b New York, NY, Oct 3, 36. *Study:* Cornell Univ, BA, 57; Juilliard Sch Music, with Persichetti & Bergsma, 58-61; Mills Col, with Milhaud & Berio, MA(music), 63. *Works:* Four Organs, perf by mem Boston Symph & Steve Reich & Musicians, 70-80; Drumming, perf by Los Angeles Phil New Music Group & Steve Reich & Musicians, 71-83; Music for 18 Musicians, perf by Steve Reich & Musicians, 76-83; Octet, perf by Netherlands Wind Ens, St Paul Chamber Orch & Los Angeles Phil, 79-83; Variations for Winds, Strings & Keyboards, perf by San Francisco Symph & Concertgebouw Orch, 80-82; Tehillim, perf by New York Phil, San Francisco Symph & Chicago Symph, 81-82; Vermont Counterpoint, comn & perf by Ransom Wilson, Brooklyn Acad Music, 82-83. *Rec Perf:* Four Organs, Angel-EMI, 73; Drumming, Deutsche Grammophon, 74; Music for 18 Musicians, 78, Octet, 80 & Tehillim, 81, ECM Rec; Vermont Counterpoint, Angel Rec, 82; Variations for Winds, Strings & Keyboards, Phillips, 83. *Pos:* Founder, Steve Reich & Musicians, 66- *Awards:* Guggenheim Fel, 78; grants, Rockefeller Found, 75, 79, 80 & 81 & Koussevitsky Found, 81. *Bibliog:* Clytus Gottwald (auth), Steve Reich: Signale Zwischen Exotik & Industrie, Melos/Neue Zeitschrift, 1/75; Michael Nyman (auth), Steve Reich/Mysteries of the Phase, Music & Musicians, 1/77; Robert Schwarz (auth), Steve Reich: Music, Perspectives of New Music, Vol 19, 80 & Vol 20, 81. *Mem:* Am Fedn Musicians. *Publ:* Auth, A Composer Looks East, New York Times, 9/2/73; Writings About Music, NY Univ Press, 74; Ecrits and Entretiens sur la Musique, Christian Borgois, 81; Music as a Gradual Process, In: Breaking the Sound Barrier, Battcock-Dutton, 81; Interview, In: Soundpieces, Scarecrow Press, 81. *Mailing Add:* c/o Lynn Garon Mgt 1199 Park Ave New York NY 10028

REICHMUTH, ROGER EDWIN
EDUCATOR, SAXOPHONE

b Louisville, Ky, Aug 16, 39. *Study:* Murray State Univ, BME, 61; Univ Ill, MS(music educ), 66, EdD(music educ), 77. *Teaching:* Assoc prof music, Murray State Univ, 70-, chmn dept music, currently. *Mem:* Ky Music Educr Asn (pres 81-83); First District Ky Music Educr Asn (pres 72-74); Ky Arts Adminr (pres-elect, 83-84); Music Educr Nat Conf; Col Music Soc. *Mailing Add:* 207 N 13th St Murray KY 42071

REID, JOHN WILLIAM
BASSOON, COMPOSER

b Port Arthur, Tex, Sept 23, 46. *Study:* Eastman Sch Music, BM, 68; Univ Colo, MM, 72, PhD, 81. *Works:* Passicaglia, 81 & Octet, 82, Solstice Woodwind Quintet. *Teaching:* Asst prof bassoon & theory, Wash State Univ, 78-; asst chmn music dept, 78- *Mem:* Music Educr Nat Conf; Wash Music Educr Asn; Am Musicol Soc; Music Libr Asn; Int Double Reed Soc. *Interests:* Renaissance theory of the 15th century. *Publ:* Auth, Properties of the Set Explored in Webern's Variations Op 30, Perspectives New Music, 74; The

Treatment of Dissonance in the Works of Dufay, Colo Music J, 82; Britten's Albert Herring, the Bassoon Part, 82 & Cane Selectivity, from the Field to the Gouger, 83, Double Reed Soc J. *Mailing Add:* Dept Music Wash State Univ Pullman WA 99164

REILLY, EDWARD RANDOLPH
MUSIC HISTORIAN, EDUCATOR
b Newport News, Va, Sept 10, 29. *Study:* Univ Mich, BM, 49, MM, 52, PhD(musicol), 58. *Teaching:* From assoc prof music hist to prof, Converse Col, 57-62; assoc prof music, Univ Ga, 62-64, prof, 64-70; prof, Vassar Col, 70-71 & 72- *Mem:* Am Musicol Soc; Music Libr Asn; Int Gustav Mahler Soc. *Interests:* Eighteenth century performance practice; Mussorgsky; Mahler. *Publ:* Ed & translr, J J Quantz, On Playing the Flute, Faber & Faber, 66; auth, Quantz and His Versuch: Three Studies, Am Musicol Soc, 66; The Music of Mussorgsky: A Guide to the Editions, Music Newslett, 79; Gustav Mahler and Guido Adler: Records of A Friendship, Cambridge Univ Press, 82. *Mailing Add:* 358 Hooker Ave Poughkeepsie NY 12603

REIMER, BENNETT
EDUCATOR, WRITER
b New York, NY, June 19, 32. *Study:* State Univ NY, Fredonia, BM, 54; Univ Ill, MM, 55, EdD, 63. *Teaching:* Asst prof music educ, Univ Ill, Urbana, 60-65; Kulas Prof & chmn dept music educ, Case Western Res Univ, 65-78; John W Beattie Prof & chmn dept, Northwestern Univ, 78- *Bibliog:* Malcolm Bessom (auth), Reimer Revisited, Music Educr J, 11/79. *Mem:* Music Educr Nat Conf; Coun Res Music Educ; Music Educ Res Coun; Educ Aesthetic Awareness (co-dir, 75-78). *Interests:* Philosophy of music education; curriculum development in aesthetic education. *Publ:* Auth, 60 articles on music & arts educ, 56-; A Philosophy of Music Education, Prentice-Hall, 70; ed, Toward an Aesthetic Education, Music Educr Nat Conf, 71; coauth, The Experience of Music, Prentice-Hall, 72; Silver Burdett Music Grades 1-8, Silver Burdett, 74. *Mailing Add:* 506 Koerper Ct Wilmette IL 60091

REIMS, CLIFFORD WALDEMAR
EDUCATOR, CONDUCTOR & MUSIC DIRECTOR
b Brooklyn, NY. *Study:* Bucknell Univ, AB, 49; Ind Univ, MMus, 51; Univ Southern Calif, 71. *Pos:* Opera, recital & oratorio singer, 47-; dir & cond, various opera & theatre groups, 53-; gen dir, Hattiesburg Civic Opera, Miss, 61-62; artistic dir, Springfield Civic Opera, Ohio, 63-66. *Teaching:* Asst prof, Auburn Univ, 52-57; asst prof & dir opera, Ohio Univ, 57-60, Univ Southern Miss, 61-63 & Ohio State Univ, 63-66; assoc prof & dir opera theatre, Calif State Univ, Fullerton, 66-71; prof voice, Roosevelt Univ, Chicago, 72-, chmn dept & dir opera theatre, currently. *Mem:* Nat Opera Asn (dir, 65-); Nat Asn Teachers Singing; Phi Mu Alpha. *Mailing Add:* 1815 S Highland Ave Lombard IL 60148

REIS, JOAN SACHS
EDUCATOR
Study: Col-Consv Music, Univ Cincinnati, BM(violin), 44, MM(musicol), 45. *Teaching:* Fac mem, Col-Consv Music, Univ Cincinnati, 45-70 & 80-; teacher music hist, Northern Ky Univ, 79-80. *Awards:* Peter Froelich Jr Prize; Wanda Bauer & Clifton Chalmers Prize. *Mem:* Am Musicol Soc. *Publ:* Auth, Signs of the Times in Music, Cincinnati, 72 & rev ed, 80. *Mailing Add:* 1815 Wm H Taft Rd Apt 703 Cincinnati OH 45206

REISE, JAY
COMPOSER
b New York, NY, Feb 9, 50. *Study:* Hamilton Col, BA, 72; McGill Univ, 73; Univ Pa, with Richard Wernick & George Crumb, MA, 75. *Works:* Concerto Fantasy for Nine Players, Berkshire Music Ctr, 76; Paraphonia, 78 & Cleopatra, 79, Penn Contemp Players; Symphony of Voices, 79, Symphony No 2, 80 & Prelude for String Orchestra, 83, Theodore Presser. *Rec Perf:* Alice at the End, Syracuse Soc New Music, Asn Prom New Music, 77. *Teaching:* Asst prof music, Kirkland Col, 76-78, Hamilton Col, 78-80 & Univ Pa, 80- *Awards:* Fels, Nat Endowment Arts, 78, Guggenheim Mem Found, 79 & Rockefeller Found, 82. *Mem:* BMI; Am Music Ctr; Am Comp Alliance; Int Alban Berg Soc. *Publ:* Auth, Rochberg the Progressive, Perspectives New Music, Vol 19, 80-81; Late Skriabin—Some Principles Behind the Style, 19th Century Music, 9/83. *Mailing Add:* 201 S 34th St Philadelphia PA 19104

REISENBERG, NADIA
EDUCATOR, PIANO
b Vilna, USSR. *Study:* Imperial Consv, St Petersburg, USSR; Curtis Inst Music; studied piano with Leonid Nikolaieff, Alexander Lambert & Josef Hoffman. *Rec Perf:* On Westminster, Monitor & Musical Heritage. *Pos:* Conct pianist throughout Europe & US; soloist, New York Phil, Boston Symph Orch & many others in US & abroad; chamber & ens recitalist. *Teaching:* Mem fac, Curtis Inst Music, formerly; vis prof music, Univ Southern Calif; guest lectr, NY Univ; prof, Queens Col, 69-; mem fac piano, Mannes Col Music, 53- & Juilliard Sch, 74-; teacher master classes, Paterson State Col, Rubin Acad Music, Jerusalem & in Tulsa. *Mem:* Assoc Teachers League New York; NJ Teachers Asn. *Mailing Add:* 165 W 66th St New York NY 10023

REISS, ALVIN H
WRITER, EDUCATOR
b Brooklyn, NY, June 15, 30. *Study:* Univ Wis, BA, 52, MA, 53. *Pos:* Ed & publ, Arts Mgt Newslett, New York, 62-; exec dir, Related Arts Couns, New York, 72-; dir, Perf Arts Mgt Inst, 71- *Teaching:* Adj asst prof arts mgt & dir grad arts mgt prog, Adelphi Univ, Garden City, NY, 78- *Mem:* Nat Guild Community Sch Arts (bd dir, 78-); Music Critics Asn; Nat Choral Coun (adv bd, 76-). *Publ:* Auth, The Arts Management Handbook, Law-Arts Publ, 70; Culture and Company, Twayne Publ, 72; The Arts Management Reader, Marcel Dekker Inc, 79; over 100 articles published. *Mailing Add:* 408 W 57th St New York NY 10019

REISWIG, DAVID EARL
EDUCATOR, FRENCH HORN
b Beaver, Okla, May 26, 45. *Study:* NTex State Univ, with Clyde Miller, BM(music educ), 67; Univ Wis, Madison, with John Barrows & Dale Clevenger, MM(horn), 68; Cath Univ Am, DMA, 73. *Pos:* Co-prin & prin horn, Kansas City Phil, 72-82; third horn, St Louis Symph, 82-83. *Awards:* First Place Valve Horn, Heldenleben Int Horn Compt, 78. *Mem:* Am Fedn Musicians; Int Horn Soc. *Mailing Add:* 1093 Dividend Park Florissant MO 63031

REJTO, GABOR M
EDUCATOR, CELLO
b Budapest, Hungary, Jan 23, 16. *Study:* Royal Hungarian Acad Music, artist's dipl, 35; studied with Pablo Casals, Spain & France, 36-37. *Rec Perf:* With Heifetz & Piatigorsky, RCA; with Alma Trio, DECCA; with Adolf Baller, Orion; with Alice Rejto, Avant; solo album, CRI. *Pos:* Founding mem, Alma Trio, 43-; mem, Lener, Gordon & Paganini Quartets, formerly. *Teaching:* Fac mem, Manhattan Sch Music, 41-48; prof cello, Eastman Sch Music, 49-54 & Sch Music, Univ Southern Calif, 54- *Awards:* Artist Teacher of Year, Am String Teachers Asn, 72 & 80. *Bibliog:* Applebaum (auth), How They Play?, Paganiniana Publ, 75. *Mem:* Violoncello Soc; Am String Teachers Asn; Calif Music Teachers Asn. *Mailing Add:* 6230 Warner Dr Los Angeles CA 90048

REJTO, PETER A
CELLO, EDUCATOR
b San Mateo, Calif, Dec 5, 48. *Study:* With Gabor Rejto, 63-71; master classes with Gregor Piatigorski, 70, Pierre Fournier, 72 & Pablo Casals, 73; Univ Southern Calif, BS, 71. *Rec Perf:* Duo Fantasy (Zador), Orion Rec, 73; Dvorak Serenade & Mendelssohn Quartet, Marlboro Rec Soc, 73-76; Sonatas by Bach, Barber, Martinu, Boccherini & Beethoven, Young Musical Artists Prog, Mich State Univ & PBS, 73-77; Suite Cello (Romero), publ in Venezuela, 79. *Pos:* Conct cellist, Marlboro Fest, Vt, 73, 74 & 76, Bulgaria, 74, London, Wigmore, 74, Calif artist in res, 77-78, Mich artist in res touring prog, 78-79, Orquestra Filarmonica de Caracas, Venezuela, 80 & 81, Calif Chamber Symph tour of Hong Kong, 82, & at least 100 Am symph. *Teaching:* Instr, New Col, 72-73; asst prof, Mich State Univ, 73-77; assoc prof, Calif State Univ, Northridge, 77-; vis asst prof, Univ Calif, Santa Barbara, 78-79 & Univ Southern Calif, 78-79. *Awards:* First Prize, Coleman Chamber Music Award, Pasadena, Calif, 67; Debut Award, Young Musicians Found, Los Angeles, Calif, 71; Young Conct Artists Int Award, New York, 73. *Mem:* Am String Teachers Asn; Music Teachers Nat Asn. *Rep:* Thea Dispeker 59 E 54th St New York NY 10022. *Mailing Add:* 9219 Geyser Ave Northridge CA 91324

REMENIKOVA, TANYA
CELLO, EDUCATOR
b Moscow, USSR, Jan 31, 46; US citizen. *Study:* Moscow Tchaikovsky Consv, cello with Mstislav Rostropovich, 71. *Rec Perf:* Prokofiev Sonata (cello & piano), num radio rec for BBC, England, RTB & BRT, Belgium, NPR, WFMT, Chicago & WQXR, New York, 77; Stravinsky Suite Italienne, DDF (Belgium), 79. *Pos:* Concert cellist, toured USSR, Israel, Europe, USA, 72-; artist in res, Churchill Col, Cambridge Univ, 81. *Teaching:* Assoc prof cello, Univ Minn, 76- *Mem:* Am String Teacher's Asn; Col Music Soc. *Mailing Add:* 4200 S Abbott Ave Minneapolis MN 55410

REMSEN, ERIC SPENCER
PERCUSSION, TEACHER-COACH
b Washington, DC. *Study:* Calif State Univ, Los Angeles, BM, 60; Univ Southern Calif, MM, 83. *Pos:* Perc, Milwaukee Symph, 69-70; perc & timpani, San Antonio Symph, 70-77 & Los Angeles Chamber Orch, 78-81; timpani, St Paul Chamber Orch, 81- *Publ:* Auth, Contemporary Timpani Studies, TRY Publ, 64; Timpani Tuning, 77 & Edition of 18th and 19th Century Timpani Parts, 83, Percussive Arts Soc. *Mailing Add:* 579 Ashland Ave St Paul MN 55102

RENDLEMAN, RUTH
PIANO, EDUCATOR
b Charlotte, NC. *Study:* NC Sch Arts, studied piano with Irwin Freundlich, BM, 70; Manhattan Sch Music, with Artur Balsam, MM, 72; Columbia Univ, with Martin Canin, EdD, 79. *Pos:* Recitalist, Carnegie Recital Hall, 80, Merkin Concert Hall, 82. *Teaching:* Mem fac, 92nd St YMCA, New York, 72-75; asst prof piano & theory, Montclair State Col, 75-, dir & found music prep div, 76-80; adj prof theory, NY Univ, 80- *Awards:* Res fel, Nat Endowment Humanities, 79 & 82; Alumni Funding Grant for Travel & Research, Montclair State Col, 79. *Mem:* Am Musicol Soc; Soc Music Theory; Col Music Soc; Music Educr Asn NJ; Nat Fedn Music Clubs. *Interests:* Eighteenth century keyboard improvisation; Mozart piano cadenzas; general performance practice in the 18th century. *Publ:* Auth, A Reference Guide to Cadenzas for the Mozart Concertos, Piano Quart, 81. *Rep:* 1776 Broadway Suite 1806 New York NY 10019. *Mailing Add:* 20 Claremont Ave Montclair NJ 07042

RENSCH, ROSLYN (ROSLYN MARIA RENSCH-ERBES)
HARP, LECTURER
b Detroit, Mich. *Study:* Northwestern Univ, studied harp with Alberto Salvi, BMus, MMus; Univ Ill, MA; Ind Univ, studied musicol with Willi Apel & Paul Nettl; Univ Wis, PhD, 64. *Pos:* First harpist, Chicago suburban orch, 50's & Terre Haute Symph Orch, 65-; theatre orch harpist, Chicago, formerly. *Teaching:* Instr harp, Univ Ill, 55-58; prof humanities, art hist & harp, Ind State Univ, 65-; lectr harp, col, univ & music orgn, Europe & US, 70- *Mem:* Sigma Alpha Iota; Am Harp Soc (mem bd dir, 76-82, first vpres, 79-80, chmn comt sch & fac harp study, 79-); Am Fedn Musicians; World Harp Cong (mem bd dir, 83-, secy, 83-85). *Interests:* The history and music of the harp; harp representations in art monuments. *Publ:* Auth, The Harp, from Tara's Halls to the American Schools, Philosophical Libr, 50; Symbolism and Form of the Harp in Western European Manuscript Illuminations, Univ Wis, Madison, 64; The Harp, Its History, Technique and Repertoire, Gerald Duckworth, 69; Development of the Medieval Harp, Gesta, Int Ctr Medieval Art, Vol XI/2, 27-36; Cousineau, French Family of Harp Makers, In: New Grove Dict of Music & Musicians, Vol 5, 4-5. *Mailing Add:* 701 Delaware Ave Terre Haute IN 47804

RENSINK, JAMES
BASS
b Chicago, Ill. *Study:* Northwestern Univ, dipl. *Roles:* Capulet in Romeo & Juliet, San Francisco Spring Opera; Don Fernando in Fidelio, Chicago Symph; Archbishop in King Roger, St Louis Symph; Dr Grenvil in La Traviata, 82 & Captain Zuniga in Carmen, 83, Opera Co Boston. *Pos:* Performer with opera co & orchs throughout US, South Am & Asia; artist in res, Opera Co Boston, currently. *Rep:* Tornay Mgt Inc 127 W 72nd St New York NY 10023. *Mailing Add:* Opera Co Boston 539 Washington St Boston MA 02111

RENWICK, WILKE RICHARD
FRENCH HORN, COMPOSER
b Stockton, Calif, Dec 17, 21. *Study:* Longy Sch Music, sr dipl, 51; New England Consv Music, BM, 54; Univ Denver, MA(music educ), 71. *Works:* Dance for Brass Quintet, Tromba Publ, 70; Facets, perf by Denver Symph Orch, 71; Encore Piece, Tromba Publ, 72; On the Death of a Friend, perf by Denver Symph Orch, 81; Six Fanfares for British Personages, perf by Annapolis Brass Quintet, 82. *Pos:* Asst prin horn, Pittsburgh Symph Orch, 51-53; prin horn, Denver Symph Orch, 54-72, assoc prin horn, 72- *Mem:* ASCAP. *Mailing Add:* 7891 Durham Way Boulder CO 80301

RESCH, PAMELA PYLE
PIANO
b San Jose, Calif, July 13, 47. *Study:* Calif State Univ, San Jose, BA, 72. *Rec Perf:* Goldberg Variations (Bach), Wahlberg, 80; Cramer Collection, Orion, 81; Four Ballades (Chopin), Wahlberg, 83. *Pos:* Conct pianist & recitalist, 72- *Awards:* Silver Medal, Int Rec Compt, 82. *Bibliog:* Raymond Ericson (auth), Pamela Resch—Pianist, Plays Wide Range, New York Times, 3/30/80; Walter Blum (auth), Agony of a Long Distance Piano Player, San Francisco Chronicle, 1/25/81. *Mailing Add:* 675 E Margaret San Jose CA 95112

RESCH, RITA MARIE
EDUCATOR
b Minot, ND, Dec 26, 36. *Study:* Minot State Col, BSE, 57; Eastman Sch Music, MM(music lit), 60; Univ NDak, MA, 67; Univ Iowa, MFA(voice), 72, DMA(perf), 73. *Teaching:* Instr music lit, Fontbonne Col, 60-63; vis instr, NMex Highlands Univ, 64; asst prof, Univ Wis, Stevens Pt, 65-68; asst & assoc prof voice & music lit, Cent Mo State Univ, 74- *Mem:* Nat Asn Teachers Singing; Music Teachers Nat Asn; Music Educr Nat Conf. *Publ:* Auth, George Bernard Shaw's Criticism of Singers and Singing, Nat Asn Teachers Singing Bulletin, 74; contrib, Art-Song in the United States: An Annotated Bibliography, Nat Asn Teachers Singing Bulletin, 76 & 78; auth, The High School Singer and Vocal Solos for Contest, Mo Sch Music Mag, 79-80. *Mailing Add:* 415-B King St Warrensburg MO 64093

RESCIGNO, JOSEPH THOMAS
CONDUCTOR & MUSIC DIRECTOR
b New York, NY, Oct 8, 45. *Study:* Fordham Univ, BA, 67; Manhattan Sch Music, MMus, 69. *Pos:* Artistic dir, Artist Int, Providence, RI, 80-82; music dir, Westchester Lyr Fest, 81; artistic adv, Florentine Opera, Milwaukee, Wis, 81. *Teaching:* Cond, Manhattan Sch Music, 69-76; instr music hist, Adelphi Univ, 76-78. *Awards:* Second Place, Salzburgh Cond Compt, 69. *Mailing Add:* c/o Robert Lombardo Assoc 1 Harkness Plaza 61 W 62 Suite 6F New York NY 10023

RESCIGNO, NICOLA
CONDUCTOR, ADMINISTRATOR
Pos: Co-founder & dir, Chicago Lyr Opera, 54-56; co-founder & music dir, Dallas Opera, 57-75, gen mgr, 74-77, artistic dir & prin cond, 77-; cond, major opera co in US, Can, England, Europe & South Am. *Mailing Add:* Dallas Opera 1925 Elm St Dallas TX 75201

RESNIK, REGINA
MEZZO-SOPRANO
b New York, NY, Aug 30, 24. *Study:* Hunter Col, BMus. *Roles:* Carmen in Carmen, Covent Garden, Metropolitan, San Francisco, Covent Garden, Vienna State, Berlin, Paris, Stuttgart, Budapest & Marseilles Operas;

Klytemnestra in Elektra, Mistress Quickly in Falstaff, Pique Dame & Countess, Metropolitan, San Francisco, Vienna, London, Berlin, Hamburg, Lisbon & Venice Operas; Amneris in Aida; Eboli in Don Carlos; Fricka in The Ring of the Nibelung. *Pos:* Leading sop & ms, Metropolitan Opera, 44-; Kammersanger, Vienna State Opera, 58-73; leading soloist, Royal Opera, Covent Garden, Bayreuth Fest & Salzburg Fest, 57-75; stage dir, 12 prod, Warsaw, Lisbon, Venice, San Francisco, Sydney & Strasbourg. *Awards:* Medal, San Francisco Opera 40th Anniversary, 82. *Mailing Add:* Metropolitan Opera Lincoln Ctr New York NY 10023

RETZEL, FRANK (ANTHONY)
COMPOSER, EDUCATOR
b Detroit, Mich, Aug 11, 48. *Study:* Wayne State Univ, Mich, BMus, 72, MMus, 74; Univ Chicago, PhD, 78. *Works:* Swamp Music (ens), 77, Amber Glass (mezzo-soprano & four instrm), 79, Klage (flute & piano), 80, Sketches (solo piano), 80, Poem (solo violin), 81, Hymnus (chorus), 81 & Canticles (soloists, chorus & ens), 83, Asn Prom New Music. *Teaching:* Asst prof & dir, Electronic Music Studio & Comtemp Ens, Cath Univ Am, 81-83; lectr, New Sch Social Res, 82-83; lectr & Mellon fel, Brooklyn Col, 83- *Awards:* Comp Fel, Nat Endowment Arts, 80; Fulbright-Hays Res Fel, 82-83. *Mem:* Am Music Ctr; Am Musicol Soc; Am Soc Univ Comp; Int Soc Contemp Music (mem bd dir, 83); Soc Music Theory. *Mailing Add:* 141-31 84th Dr Briarwood NY 11435

REVITT, PAUL J
EDUCATOR, MUSICOLOGIST
b Seattle, Wash, June 27, 22. *Study:* Univ Wash, BA, 47, MA, 49; Univ Chicago, PhD, 56. *Teaching:* Instr, Univ Puget Sound, Tacoma, 49-51 & Col Fac, Chicago Bd Educ, 54-57; asst prof, Univ Calif, Los Angeles, 57-66; prof, Univ Mo, Kansas City, 66- *Interests:* Nineteenth-century musicology. *Publ:* Auth, The George Pullen Jackson Collection of Southern Hymnody, 64 & coauth, The Mayflower Hymnal, 65, Univ Calif, Los Angeles. *Mailing Add:* Consv Music Univ Mo Kansas City MO 64111

REVZEN, JOEL
MUSIC DIRECTOR, ADMINISTRATOR
Study: Juilliard Sch Music, BS, MS; studied with Jorge Master, Jean Martinon, Margaret Hillis & Abraham Kaplan. *Pos:* Music dir, Orch & Chorus of St Louis & The Minnesota Chorale. *Teaching:* Fac mem, State Univ NY Col, Fredonia, formerly; dean, St Louis Consv Music, currently; fac mem, Aspen Music Fest, currently. *Awards:* Frank Damrosch Award, Juilliard Sch Music. *Mailing Add:* St Louis Consv Music 560 Trinity Ave St Louis MO 63130

REX, HARLEY E
COMPOSER, SAXOPHONE
b Lehighton, Pa, Mar 29, 30. *Study:* Mansfield State Col, BS; Univ Mich, with Wallace Berry & George Burt, MM, 62, DMA, 71; studied sax with Sigurd Rauscher & Larry Teal. *Works:* Prelude and Movendo (sax & band); Camminando (band); Andante and Brilliante (sax & band); Saxophone Rhapsody (band); Shenandoah (sax quartet); Scherzo (clarinet quartet). *Pos:* Sax & arr, US Army Band, 54-62; sax, Houston Symph Orch, 65-73; cond, Houston Munic Band, 66- *Teaching:* Assoc prof orch & sax, Sam Houston State Univ, currently. *Mailing Add:* Rte 5 Box 243 Huntsville TX 77340

REYES, ANGEL
VIOLIN, EDUCATOR
Study: Nat Consv Paris, premier prix. *Pos:* Violinist, Philadelphia Orch, formerly. *Teaching:* Mem fac music, Univ Tex, formerly & Northwestern Univ, formerly; prof & violinist, Stanley Quartet, Univ Mich, Ann Arbor, 65- *Awards:* Prize Winner, Ysaye Int Violin Compt, Brussels. *Mailing Add:* Sch Music Univ Mich Ann Arbor MI 48109

REYNOLDS, ERMA
COMPOSER
b Laurel, Miss. *Study:* Calif State Univ, Fullerton, BA(music), 68, MA(music), 74. *Works:* Sonata for Violin and Piano, Comp Autograph Publ, 71; No Dance (chamber orch), Calif State Univ, 72; Passacaglia for String Orchestra, Comp Autograph Publ, 74; Melisande's Daughters (sop, tenor & piano), Calif State Univ, Fullerton, 74. *Mailing Add:* 710 Casa Blanca Fullerton CA 92632

REYNOLDS, ROGER LEE
COMPOSER, EDUCATOR
b Detroit, Mich, July 18, 34. *Study:* Univ Mich, BSE, studied comp with Ross Lee Finney & Roberto Gerhard, BM, 60, MM, 61. *Works:* Blind Men, 66, Threshold, 67, The Promises of Darkness, 75, Shadowed Narrative, 77-82, Less Than Two, 77-79, Fiery Wind, 78 & Archipelago, 83, C F Peters Corp. *Pos:* Dir, Ctr Music Experiment & Related Res, Univ Calif San Diego, 71-76. *Teaching:* Assoc prof, Univ Calif San Diego, La Jolla, 69-73, prof, 73- *Awards:* Guggenheim Fel, 64; grant, Rockefeller Found, 65 & 77; citation, Nat Inst Arts & Lett, 71. *Bibliog:* H Wiley Hitchcock (auth), Current Chronicle, 62 & John Cage & Roger Reynolds: A Conversation, 79, Musical Quart; Gilbert Chase (auth), Roger Reynolds: Portrait of a Composer, C F Peters Corp, 83. *Mem:* Am Music Ctr; Meet the Comp; Comp Forum; Am Comp Alliance; BMI. *Publ:* Auth, Indeterminacy: Some Considerations, Perspectives New Music, 65; Current Chronicle: Japan, Musical Quart, 67; Mind Models, Praeger, 75; contrib, The Phonograph & Our Musical Life, Inst Studies Am Music, 77; An Ives Celebration, Univ Ill Press, 77. *Mailing Add:* Music Dept Univ Calif San Diego La Jolla CA 92093

REYNOLDS, VERNE BECKER
COMPOSER, EDUCATOR

b Lyons, Kans, July 18, 26. *Study:* Col Consv Music, Univ Cincinnati, BM, 50; Univ Wis, MM, 51; Royal Col Music, London, 53 & 54. *Works:* Scenes (wind ensemble); Ventures (orch); Florilegium Vol I (piano); Sonata (violin & piano); Concerto for Band (band); 48 Etudes for Horn (horn); Concertare IV (brass quintet & piano). *Pos:* Horn, Cincinnati Symph, 46-50, Rochester Phil, 59-68 & Eastman Brass Quintet, 61- *Teaching:* Mem fac, Univ Wis, 50-53 & Ind Univ 54-59; prof brass ens & horn, Eastman Sch Music, 59- *Awards:* Fulbright Grant London, 53; Louisville Orch Award, 55; ASCAP Awards. *Mailing Add:* Eastman Sch Music 26 Gibbs St Rochester NY 14604

REYNOLDS, WILLIAM J
EDUCATOR, WRITER

b Atlantic, Iowa, Apr 2, 20. *Study:* SW Mo State Col, Springfield, BA, 42; Southwestern Baptist Theol Sem, Ft Worth, MSM, 45; NTex State Univ, MM, 46; George Peabody Col, EdD, 61; Westminster Choir Col, studied with John Finley Williamson. *Works:* Ichthus, 71, Reaching People, 73, Share His Word, 73 & Bold Mission, 77, Broadman Press. *Pos:* Minister music, First Baptist Church, Oklahoma City, Okla, 47-55; church music dept, Baptist Sunday Sch Bd, Nashville, 55-80. *Teaching:* Assoc prof church music, SW Baptist Theol Sem, 80- *Awards:* W Hines Sims Achievement Award, Southern Baptist Church Music Conf, 71. *Mem:* Hymn Soc Am, Inc; ASCAP; Nat Acad Rec Arts & Sci; Southern Baptist Church Music Conf. *Interests:* Hymnological research. *Publ:* Auth, A Survey of Christian Hymnody, Holt, Rinehart & Winston, 63; Hymns of Our Faith, 64, Christ and the Carols, 67 & Companion to Baptist Hymnal, 76, Broadman Press; ed, Baptist Hymnal, Conv Press, 75. *Mailing Add:* 6750 Cartagena Ct Ft Worth TX 76133

REZITS, JOSEPH M
PIANO, WRITER

b New York, NY, June 16, 25. *Study:* Curtis Inst Music, with Isabelle Vengerova, artist dipl, 48; Univ Ill, BMus, 54, MMus, 55; Univ Colo, DMus, 74. *Rec Perf:* Recordings on Audiophile, Festival, Avante-Garde & Coronet. *Pos:* Soloist, duo & chamber music perf, US, Can & Australia, 48-; Reviewer, Allyn & Bacon, Inc, Ind Univ Press, Wadsworth Publ Co Inc, Dodd, Mead & Co, Charles A Jones Co, Addison-Wesley Publ Co & Hackett Publ Co, formerly. *Teaching:* Instr music, Univ Ill, 55-57; asst prof, Trenton State Col, 57-62; prof, Ind Univ, 62-; private piano instr, currently; guest lectr, cols, univ & asn throughout world. *Awards:* Philadelphia Orch Youth Award, 50. *Mem:* Col Music Soc; Nat Fedn Music Clubs; Music Teachers Nat Asn; Music Educr NJ; Am Music Scholar Asn. *Interests:* Hispanic keyboard music, especially 19th-century piano music of Brazil & Cuba. *Publ:* Auth, The Pianist's Resource Guide: Piano Music in Print and Literature on the Pianistic Art, Neil A Kjos Music Co, 74 & 78. *Mailing Add:* Sch Music Ind Univ Bloomington IN 47405

RHOADS, MARY RUTH
EDUCATOR, COMPOSER

b Philadelphia, Pa, Jan 28, 20. *Study:* Mastbaum Voc Music Sch, dipl, 38; Univ Mich, BMus, 62, MMus, 64; Mich State Univ, PhD, 69. *Works:* Homage to Hogaku, perf by Univ Northern Colo Brass Choir, 76; Kyoto Scenes, perf by Jolyn Sylva, Charmaine Coppom & comp, 76; Memories of Nara (violin sonata), perf by Howard Mickens & Carla Hager, 77 & 80; Three Japanese Poems, perf by Jack Herrick, Charmaine Coppom & comp, 80, 81 & 82; Peace, perf by Univ Northern Colo Chamber Orch, 80; Horyuji (antiphonal choruses, chamber group), perf by Univ Northern Colo, 81; Mai Sonata (cello & piano), perf by Barbara Theim, James Bailey & comp, 82 & 83. *Pos:* Choir dir, Foothills Unitarian Church, Ft Collins, Colo, 69-70. *Teaching:* Musical dir, Perf Arts Co, Mich State Univ, 65-68; instr, Montcalm Community Col, 68-69 & Colo State Univ, 69-70; prof music theory & comp, Univ Northern Colo, 71- *Mailing Add:* 2705 50th Ave Greeley CO 80634

RHOADS, WILLIAM EARL
COMPOSER & ARRANGER, CLARINET

b Harvey, Ill, Aug 5, 18. *Study:* Univ Mich, BME, 41, MME, 42. *Works:* Nativity Songs for Band, perf by col & high sch bands in Japan & Europe, 78; Tres Danzas de Mexico, perf by col & high sch bands, 79; Corktown Saturday Night, perf by Wichita State Univ Wind Ens & others, 82; & over 100 publ works. *Teaching:* Dir bands, Alamogordo High Sch, NMex, 46-53; dir bands & woodwind instrm, Univ NMex, 53-79; chmn music dept, 72-79. *Awards:* Standard Panel Awards, ASCAP, 74- *Mem:* ASCAP. *Publ:* Auth, 8 Etude Books for Alto and Bass Clarinet, 72. *Mailing Add:* 2901 Las Cruces NE Albuquerque NM 87110

RHODES, CHERRY
ORGAN, EDUCATOR

b Brooklyn, NY, June 28, 43. *Study:* Harvard Univ & Univ Pa, summers 61-63; Curtis Inst Music, with Alexander McCurdy, BM, 64; Hochschule Musik, Munich, with Karl Richter, perf cert, 64-67; studied with Marie-Claire Alain & Jean Guillou, 67-69. *Rec Perf:* B Minor Mass (Bach), 63. *Pos:* Soloist, Philadelphia Orch, 60, radio broadcasts throughout Am & Can, 60-, TV & radio broadcasts & int fest throughout Europe, 66-; organist, numerous nat & regional conv Am Guild Organists; recitalist, John F Kennedy Ctr Perf Arts, 72, Royal Fest Hall, London, 76, 81 & 82 & Lincoln Ctr, 77 & 78. *Teaching:* Organ, Peabody Consv Music, 72-75; adj assoc prof organ, Univ Southern Calif, 75- *Awards:* Winner, Int Organ Compt, Munich, 66 & Bologna, 69. *Mem:* Am Guild Organists (mem exec comt New York, 74-75); Calif Asn Prof Music Teachers; Music Teachers Nat Asn; Ruth & Clarence Mader Mem Scholar Fund. *Mailing Add:* Sch Music Univ Southern Calif Los Angeles CA 90089

RHODES, PHILLIP
COMPOSER, EDUCATOR

b Forest City, NC, June 6, 40. *Study:* Duke Univ, with William Klenz & Iain Hamilton; Yale Univ, with Mel Powell & Donald Martino. *Works:* Divertimento (small orch), 71; Museum Pieces (clarinet & string quartet), 73; Festival Suite (bluegrass band & orch), 74; On the Morning of Christ's Nativity (soloists, wind quartet & harp), 74; Quartet for Flute, Violin, Cello and Harp, 75; Mountain Songs (cycle for sop & piano), 76; Reflections ... Eight Fantasies for Piano, 77. *Pos:* Professional in res, Louisville, 69-72. *Teaching:* Mem fac, Amherst Col, 68-69; prof music, Carlton Col, 74- *Awards:* Nat Endowment Arts Grant, 74, 75 & 76; Rockefeller Grant, 76; Berkshire Music Ctr Fel, 78. *Mailing Add:* RR 3 Box 25 Northfield MN 55057

RHODES, SAMUEL
VIOLA, EDUCATOR

b New York, NY, Feb 13, 41. *Study:* Queens Col, City Univ New York, BA, 62; Princeton Univ, MA, 68. *Works:* Viola Quintet, perf by Galimir String Quartet, Comp Quartet & Blair Quartet; Elegy for Solo Violin, perf by Hiroko Yajima. *Rec Perf:* Late Beethoven Quartets, 75 & Last Four Mozart Quartets, 76, CBS Masterworks; Complete Schoenberg Quartets & Debussy & Ravel Quartets, 78; Schumann Quartets (piano & strings), 77; Schubert Trout Quintet, 78; Schubert Quartets, 80; Early Beethoven Quartets, 82. *Pos:* Violist, Galimir String Quartet, 61-69 & Juilliard String Quartet, 69- *Teaching:* Prof chamber music, Juilliard Sch, 69- & Mich State Univ, East Lansing, 77-; adj viola fac mem, State Univ NY, Purchase, 82- *Awards:* Karol Rathaus Mem Award, Queens Col, 62; John E Castellini Award, Queens Col, 78. *Rep:* Naomi Rhodes Assoc Inc 157 W 57th St New York NY 10019. *Mailing Add:* 89 Booth Ave Englewood NJ 07631

RIBEIRO, GERARDO
EDUCATOR, VIOLIN

b Oporto, Portugal. *Study:* Oporto Music Consv, with Carlos Fontes; Lucerne Music Consv with Rudolf Baumgartner & Walter Prystawski; Juilliard Sch Music with Ivan Galamian, Paul Makanowitzky & Feliz Galimir. *Pos:* Concert appearances, US, Europe, Can & USSR. *Teaching:* Assoc prof violin, Fla State Univ, 78-83 & Eastman Sch Music, 83- *Mailing Add:* 277 Elmwood Terr Rochester NY 14620

RICCI, RUGGIERO
VIOLIN, EDUCATOR

b San Francisco, Calif, July 24, 18. *Study:* Study with Louis Persinger. *Rec Perf:* Over 500 recordings on every major label. *Teaching:* Instr, Indiana Univ, 71-74, Juilliard Sch, 74-79 & Univ Mich, 82- *Awards:* Cavaliere, Order of Merit Italy, 77. *Mem:* Hon mem, Royal Acad Music, London. *Rep:* Columbia Artists Mgt Inc 165 W 57th St New York NY 10019. *Mailing Add:* Sch Music Univ Mich Ann Arbor MI 48109

RICE, B(OONE) DOUGLAS
EDUCATOR, COMPOSER

b Seattle, Wash, Mar 24, 42. *Study:* Univ Wash, 60-65; Cornish Inst, studied theory with John Cowell & comp with Lockrem Johnson, BMus, 69. *Works:* Divertimento No 1, Mitchell-Madison Inc, 72; Sonata Concertante (flute & guitar), 72 & In Bethlehem That Night (chamber Christmas cantata), 74, Puget Music Publ Inc. *Pos:* Founder & dir, Guitar Consv Puget Sound, 74-76; vpres & ed, Puget Sound Publ Inc, 72-78. *Teaching:* Fac affil, Bellevue, Edmonds & Shoreline Community Col, 69-; fac mem, Cornish Inst, 70-74; prof, Univ Puget Sound, 76- *Mem:* Guitar Found Am; Am String Teachers Asn; Am Lute Soc; BMI. *Mailing Add:* 18456-40th Place NE Seattle WA 98155

RICE, DANIEL
ADMINISTRATOR

Study: New England Consv Music, dipl; studied cello with Alfred Zighera & opera with Boris Goldovsky. *Pos:* Performer with symph orchs, chamber groups & NY Pro Musica. *Teaching:* Dir, Brooklyn Music Sch, formerly; head music staff & rehearsal coordr, Santa Fe Opera, dir apprentice artist training prog, 69-; dir perf, Manhattan Sch Music, 77-, dean perf, 80- *Mailing Add:* Manhattan Sch Music 120 Claremont Ave New York NY 10027

RICE, THOMAS NELSON
COMPOSER, CONDUCTOR & MUSIC DIRECTOR

b Washington, DC, Feb 6, 33. *Study:* Cath Univ Am, BM, 55; Univ NC, MA, 57. *Works:* La Corona—Donne, 75, String Trio, 75, Toccata for Orchestra, 78, Timpani Concerto, 80, Brass Trio, 82, Piano Trio, 83, Wrinkle in Time (ballet), 83, Seesaw Publ. *Teaching:* Instr instrm, Virginia Beach Pub Sch, Va, 59- *Mem:* ASCAP; Am Soc Univ Comp; Am Music Ctr; MacDowell Colonists; Tidewater Comp Guild. *Rep:* Seesaw Music Publ 2067 Broadway New York NY 10023. *Mailing Add:* 7008 Ocean Front Virginia Beach VA 23451

RICH, ELIZABETH (JANE)
PIANO

b New York, NY. *Study:* Juilliard Sch Music with Henriette Michelson & Muriel Kerr; studied with Irma Wolpe; Schenker analysis with Ernst Oster. *Pos:* Soloist, London Soloists Chamber Orch, 83; duo with David Glazer and also with Constantine Cassocas. *Teaching:* Piano, privately. *Awards:* New York Phil Young People's Symph Auditions Award. *Rep:* Liegner Mgt 1860 Broadway New York NY 10024. *Mailing Add:* 285 Central Park West New York NY 10024

RICH, MARIA F
ADMINISTRATOR, WRITER

b Vienna, Austria, June 18, 25. *Study:* Stockholm Acad, BA. *Pos:* Asst adminr, Cent Opera Serv, Metropolitan Opera, 62-66, auth & ed bulletin & ed opera dir, 65-, exec dir, 66- *Teaching:* Guest lectr career develop, Am Inst Musical Studies, Graz, Austria, 78-82 & Univ Md, 82; guest lectr arts admin, Columbia Univ, 79-81. *Awards:* First Verdi Medal Achievement, Metropolitan Opera Nat Coun, 77; Women's Press Club New York Special Citation, 80. *Bibliog:* Ann Lingg (auth), article, Opera News; Philip Steele (auth), article, Musical Am. *Mem:* Int Asn Arts Admin; Nat Music Coun (mem bd dir, 83-). *Interests:* Opera in North America. *Publ:* Auth, Annual Opera Survey USA, Opera News, 69-; ed, Who's Who America, Arno Press, 76; auth, Opera Perspective USA, Opera Quart, Univ NC Press, 82- *Mailing Add:* Lincoln Ctr New York NY 10023

RICH, MARTIN
CONDUCTOR, PIANO

b Breslau, Germany, Oct 8, 07; US citizen. *Study:* Hoschule Musik, Berlin, with Franz Schreker & Julius Prüwer; studied piano with Georg Bertram & Artur Schnable. *Roles:* Manon, Metropolitan Opera, 55. *Pos:* Performer, Dortmund Symph, Germany, 30; asst cond, Metropolitan Opera, 50-53, assoc cond, 54-76; assoc cond, Metropolitan Opera, 54-76; cond & music dir, Phil Symph Westchester, 66-; cond, major co in Montreal, Quebec, Vancouver, Dortmund, Wuppertal, Tel Aviv, Bologna, Mexico City, Bucharest, Cincinnati & with Jackson Opera/South & Philadelphia Grand. *Teaching:* Lectr & instr master classes, Howard Univ, formerly & Temple Univ, formerly; coach, Curtis Inst Music, 45-50. *Mailing Add:* Phil Symph Westchester 9 Prospect Ave W Mt Vernon NY 10550

RICH, RUTHANNE
PIANO, EDUCATOR

b Salisbury, NC, Dec 20, 41. *Study:* Fla State Univ, MusB, 63; Peabody Consv Music, MusM, 64; Ecole Normale Musique Paris, lic, 65; Schola Cantorum Paris, dipl virtuosite, 66; Royal Acad Music, London, LRAM(piano perf), 66; Eastman Sch Music, DMA, 73. *Pos:* Performances in UK, France, Portugal, Switz, Germany & throughout US & the Orient. *Teaching:* Artist in res, Mercer Univ, 66-67; asst prof, Lawrence Univ, 67-68 & Valdosta State Col, 71-74; assoc prof piano, Kansas City Consv, Univ Mo, 74-82, prof music, 82- *Awards:* First prize, Marie Morrisey Keith Nat Piano Cont, 61 & Biennial Piano Cont, 63, Nat Fedn Music Clubs; Fulbright Grant, 64-65. *Mem:* Music Teachers Nat Asn; Mo Music Teachers Asn; Sigma Alpha Iota; Pi Kappa Lambda. *Publ:* Auth, Selected Piano Recitals in Carnegie Hall—A Record of Changing Musical Tastes, 74; New York, 1895: The Piano Concert Scene, Piano Quart, 78; The American Pianist Comes of Age, 79 & Paderewski: America's Million-Dollar Pianist, 81, Am Music Teacher. *Mailing Add:* 203 Huntington Rd Kansas City MO 64113

RICHARDS, JAMES HOWARD
WRITER, LECTURER

b Palacios, Tex, Oct 13, 33. *Study:* Baylor Univ, BMus, 56, MMus, 65; NTex State Univ. *Pos:* Piano technician, Baylor Univ, 52-56; librn, Francis G Spencer Collection of Am Printed Music, Baylor Univ, 65-70. *Teaching:* Instr music theory & lit, Baylor Univ, 65-70; music coordr, instr & choral dir, Bosque Co Pub Sch, 70- *Mem:* Am Musicol Soc; Am Musical Instrm Soc; Reed Organ Soc Inc; Piano Technicians Guild (pres, cent Tex chap, 76-83); Organ Hist Soc. *Interests:* English Catholic church music; the English glee; 19th-century keyboard instruments, particularly the piano and the reed organ. *Publ:* Auth, The Vocalion, Diapason, 75; Organs at St Olaf Lutheran Church, Cranfills Gap, Texas, Tracker, J Organ Hist Soc, 78; The Piano: Some Factors Affecting Tuning Stability, Am Music Teacher, 79; Reed Organ Coverage, In: New Grove Dict of Music in US, J Am Musical Instrm Soc, 82; Music and the Reed Organ in the Life of Mark Twain, Am Music (in press). *Mailing Add:* 4809 Scottwood Dr Waco TX 76708

RICHARDS, JOHN KEIL
TUBA, CONDUCTOR

b Belgrade, Mont, Mar 21, 18. *Study:* Lewis & Clark Col, BS; Univ Southern Calif, MMus; Philadelphia Consv Music, DMus. *Pos:* Cond, Portland Symphonic Band; mem, various orchs; tubist, various stage shows incl South Pacific, The King and I & Hello Dolly; prin tuba, Ore Symph Orch, currently & Portland Opera Asn Orch, currently. *Mem:* Phi Mu Alpha Sinfonia; hon mem, NW Band Dir Asn. *Publ:* Auth, Brass Anthology, 70; contrib to Contemp Educ, Nat Music Educr J & Ore Educr J. *Mailing Add:* 637 SW Englewood Dr Lake Oswego OR 97034

RICHARDS, LESLIE ROBERTA
MEZZO-SOPRANO

b Los Angeles, Calif. *Roles:* Tisbe in Ceneretola, 82 & Leonora in Triumph of Honor, 82, San Francisco Opera; Carmen in Carmen, Ventura Symph, 82; Maddalena in Rigoletto, Honolulu Opera, 83. *Awards:* Grants, Metropolitan Opera, 80, Rockefeller Found, 81 & Nat Opera Inst, 83. *Mailing Add:* c/o Affiliate Artists Inc 155 W 68th St New York NY 10023

RICHARDS, WILLIAM HENRY
EDUCATOR, PIANO

b Los Angeles, Calif, Jan 4, 24. *Study:* Univ Southern Calif, BMus, 46, MMus, 49; Univ Mo, Kans City, DMA, 63. *Teaching:* Asst prof piano, Univ Mont, 57-63; teacher, Nat Music Camp, Interlochen, Mich, 59 & 60; prof, Calif State Univ, Northridge, 64- *Bibliog:* James Lyke (auth), What Should Our Piano Minors Study, Music Educr J, 12/69; James Bastien (auth), How to Teach Piano Successfully, Kjox, 71. *Mem:* Music Educr Nat Conf (Western regional

piano chmn, 68 & 70, nat piano chmn, 73-75 & 77-79); Music Teachers' Asn Calif (chmn adult seminars, 72-76); Calif Piano Asn (Southern section pres, 70). *Publ:* Contribr, Teaching Piano in Classroom & Studio, Music Educr Nat Conf, 69; Creative Piano Teaching, Stipes, 77; auth, Success with the Piano Proficiency Exam, Clavier, 77; Development of Music Reading at the Piano, Calif Music Teacher, 80; Preparing Your Students for Performance, Clavier, 82. *Mailing Add:* 4531 San Blas Ave Woodland Hills CA 91364

RICHARDSON, LORENE
SINGER, MUSIC DIRECTOR

b South Bend, Ind, Nov 8, 28. *Study:* Chicago Consv Music, BA, 68. *Pos:* Producer, dir & co-founder, Opera Profiles, Inc, 65-; dir, First Presby Church Children's Choir, Chicago, 70-72; leader alto sect, Chicago Symph Chorus, 81- *Teaching:* Creator, dir & teacher, Modern Troubadors, Chicago, 72. *Awards:* Model Cities Grant, 71. *Mem:* Nat Opera Asn; Am Guild Musical Artists (mem bd gov, 81-); Asn Prof Vocal Ens. *Mailing Add:* 5123 S Kimbark Ave Chicago IL 60615

RICHARDSON, LOUIS SAMUEL
CELLO, COMPOSER

b Brooklyn, NY, Oct 15, 24. *Study:* Peabody Consv, study cello with George Neikrug, 47-49; Ind Univ, study cello with Fritz Magg & Benar Heifetz, 54-58. *Works:* Sonata for Piano, 63 ; Sonata for Violin, 64; Theme & Variations (trumpet & piano), 74; Three Small Animals (songs), 79; Two Nocturnes (piano), 80; Introduction & Scherzo (horn & piano), 82. *Pos:* Mem, Baltimore Symph, 49-50 & Erie Phil, 62-; asst prin, New Orleans Symph, 51-52. *Teaching:* Prof cello, State Univ NY, Fredonia, 58- *Mailing Add:* 401 Chestnut St Fredonia NY 14063

RICHARDSON, WILLIAM WELLS
TROMBONE, EDUCATOR

b Hillsboro, Wis, Jan 12, 43. *Study:* Univ Wis, Madison, BMusEd, 64, MMus, 65; Cath Univ Am, DMA, 70. *Pos:* Second trombone, St Louis Symph Orch, 65-66; bass trombone, US Marine Band, 66-70; trombone, Central City Opera Orch, 74 & Wis Brass Quintet, 74-; contrib ed, Instrumentalist, Int Trombone Asn, 76- *Teaching:* Asst prof trombone & music theory, Univ Colo, Boulder, 70-74; assoc prof trombone & brass chamber music, Univ Wis, Madison, 74-, assoc prof musical theatre, 82- *Mem:* Int Trombone Asn; Col Music Soc; Sonneck Soc; Music Educr Nat Conf. *Publ:* Coauth, Introducing the Trombone, GIA Publ, 77. *Rep:* GIA Publ 7404 S Mason Ave Chicago IL 60638. *Mailing Add:* Sch Music Univ Wis Madison WI 53706

RICHELIEU, DAVID ANTHONY
CRITIC

b Minneapolis, Minn, Aug 30, 44. *Pos:* Classics critic, San Antonio Express News, 74-; guest cond, San Antonio Symph Orch, 79. *Mailing Add:* PO Box 2171 San Antonio TX 78297

RICHENS, JAMES WILLIAM
COMPOSER, CONDUCTOR

b Memphis, Tenn, Oct 7, 36. *Study:* Memphis State Univ, BS, 58; Eastman Sch Music, with Bernard Rogers, MM, 60 & 69-71. *Works:* Prelude & Dance (clarinet & band), Kendor Music, 67; Fantasia on the Battle Hymn (band), Tempo Music, 70; Escape to Morning (ballet), comn & perf by Memphis Ballet Soc, 71 & 72; Chicano! (wind ens), Powers Publ, 72; The Bells (choral & orch), comn & perf by Memphis Symph, 77; The Snow Queen (ballet), comn & perf by Youth Conct Ballet & Memphis Youth Orch, 81; Three Israeli Dances, comn & perf by Memphis Symph, 83. *Teaching:* Assoc prof music, Memphis State Univ, 66- *Mem:* Southeastern Comp League. *Mailing Add:* 5665 Buxbriar Ave Memphis TN 38119

RICHMAN, ROBIN (BETH)
FLUTE, TEACHER

b Pittsburgh, Pa, Apr 1, 55. *Study:* San Francisco Consv Music, BM, 78. *Pos:* Flutist, Spoleto Fest, Italy & Charleston, SC, 79 & Los Angeles Phil Inst, 83; prin flutist, Sacramento Symph, Calif, 78- *Teaching:* Flute, Univ Calif, Davis, 82- *Mailing Add:* 317-1/2 22nd St Sacramento CA 95816

RICHTER, MARGA
COMPOSER, PIANO

b Reedsburg, Wis, Oct 21, 26. *Study:* Juilliard Sch, BS, 49, MS, 51. *Works:* Sonata for Piano, Carl Fischer, 54; Lament, Broude Brothers, 56; Landscapes of the Mind II, 71 & Landscapes of the Mind I (Piano Concerto No 2), 74, Carl Fischer; Music for Three Quintets & Orchestra, Theodore Presser, Inc, 80; Düsseldorf Concerto, G Schirmer, 82. *Awards:* Standard Awards, ASCAP, 66-; Nat Endowment Arts Fel, 77 & 79. *Bibliog:* Jane Weiner LePage (auth), Marga Richter, Composer, Pianist, In: Women Composers, Conductors & Musicians, Scarecrow Press, 80. *Mem:* ASCAP; Am Music Ctr; Int League Women Comp; Long Island Comp Alliance. *Mailing Add:* 3 Bayview Lane Huntington NY 11743

RICHTER, MARION MORREY
COMPOSER, PIANO

b Columbus, Ohio, Oct 2, 1900. *Study:* Ohio State Univ, BA, 21; Juilliard Sch, artist grad, 33; Teachers Col, Columbia Univ, MA, 33, EdD, 61. *Works:* This Is Our Camp (children), C C Birchard, 30; Three Solo Songs, Marsile Publ Co, 45; Sea Chant and Two Other Choruses (SSA), Flammer, 50; Prelude on Row, Capriccio for Piano, many conct perf, 58-62; Timberjack Overture (band), perf by major army & civilian bands, 61 & Guggenheim Band, 83; Sonata for Trio (piano, violin & cello), Carnegie Recital Hall, 80. *Pos:* Lect conct tours, US, 62-83, England, 65, Korea & Japan, 69 & Round the World Bicentennial

Tour, fall 75. *Teaching:* Instr music & music educ, Teachers Col, Columbia Univ, summers 29-52; instr piano, private studio, 25-65 & Juilliard Sch, summers 29-52. *Awards:* Cert Appreciation, 8th US Army Korea, 69; Conct citation, Univ Singapore, 75; Distinguished Alumna Achievement Award, Delta Omicron, 77. *Mem:* Delta Omicron (bd mem, 65-74); Nat Fedn Music Clubs (nat bd mem, 71-73 & 81-85); Westchester Musicians Guild (bd mem, 65-); League Am Penwomen; European Piano Teachers. *Publ:* Auth, Profiles, Gail Kubik & Ezra Laderman, Music Clubs Mag; numerous articles in Music Clubs Mag and the Wheel, Mag Delta Omicron. *Mailing Add:* 31 Bradford Rd Scarsdale NY 10583

RICIGLIANO, D ANTHONY
EDUCATOR
Study: State Univ NY, Fredonia, BS; Manhattan Sch Music, MM; studied theory & comp with Murphy, Ulehla, Flagello, Schillinger, comp with Rudolf Schramm & piano with Mildred Dasset. *Teaching:* Mem fac, Third St Settlement Music Sch, 64-69; mem fac theory, Manhattan Sch Music, 69-, chmn dept, 79- *Publ:* Popular & Jazz Harmony; Melody & Harmony in Contemporary Songwriting. *Mailing Add:* 5 Riverside Dr New York NY 10023

RICKETT, PETER JOHN
CONDUCTOR, DOUBLE BASS
b Paris, France, Feb 16, 23; US citizen. *Study:* Juilliard Sch Music, dipl, 46; Monteux Cond Sch, 50. *Pos:* Prin bass & asst cond, Chattanooga Symph, 51-55; cond, Greenville Symph, SC, 56-, Hendersonville Symph, NC, 77- & Greenville Savoyards, SC, 79- *Teaching:* Instr double bass, Furman Univ, 65-; teach bass & piano privately. *Mailing Add:* 6 Ramblewood Lane Greenville SC 29615

RIDDLE, RONALD WILLIAM
EDUCATOR, COMPOSER
b Junction City, Ky, Sept 16, 34. *Study:* Antioch Col, AB, 60; Yale Univ, 61-64; San Francisco State Univ, MA, 70; Univ Ill, PhD, 76. *Teaching:* Dir music & assoc prof musicol, New Col, Univ SFla, 73-; vis prof, Univ Calif, Los Angeles, 83- *Mem:* Am Fedn Musicians; Am Musicol Soc; Col Music Soc; Int Asn for Study Popular Music (mem exec bd, 83-); Soc Ethnomusicol (mem SEM coun, 78-81). *Publ:* Auth, various articles, In: Encycl Britannica, 15th ed, 75; Music in America's Chinatowns in the 19th Century, Bulletin Chinese Hist Soc Am, 5/77; Music Clubs & Ensembles in San Francisco's Chinese Community, In: Eight Urban Musical Cultures, Univ Ill Press, 78; Flying Dragons, Flowing Streams: Music in the Life of San Francisco's Chinese, Greenwood Press, 83; various articles, In: Grove Dict Music in US (in prep). *Mailing Add:* Music Dept Univ Calif 405 Hilgard Ave Los Angeles CA 90024

RIDEOUT, ALICE CHALIFOUX See Chalifoux, Alice

RIEPE, RUSSELL CASPER
COMPOSER, EDUCATOR
b Metropolis, Ill, Feb 23, 45. *Study:* Southern Ill Univ, BMus, 67; Eastman Sch Music, MA, 69, PhD, 72. *Works:* Child Dying, 71 & Symphonic Fantasy, 72, Rochester Phil; Voci Antifonali, 79 & Three Studies on Flight, 79, Southern Music Co; Wings, Southwest Tex State Univ Electronic Comput Music Studio, 80; Psalm 130, Southwest Tex State Univ Chorale, 80; Nihon, Source of the Sun, (piano solo), Russell Riepe, 82. *Rec Perf:* Voci Antifonali, 79 & Three Studies on Flight, 79, Orion Rec. *Teaching:* Prof music & coordr comp & theory prog, Southwest Tex State Univ, 72- *Awards:* Fel, Woodrow Wilson Found, 67; Howard Hanson Prize, Eastman Sch Music, 72. *Bibliog:* Robert Sherman (auth), Review of Performance, New York Times, 76; David Pino (auth), The Clarinet and Clarinet Playing, Scribners, 80; Giordano Fermi (auth), Review of Voci Antifonali, Brass Bulletin, No 32, 80. *Mem:* ASCAP; Am Soc Univ Comp; Col Music Soc; Tex Music Educr Asn. *Interests:* Development of a musical system for the management of heterogeneous sound qualities in computer-assisted instruction. *Mailing Add:* PO Box 1023 San Marcos TX 78666

RIFE, JEAN
HORN, EDUCATOR
Study: Oberlin Consv, BM; Boston Univ; studied with David Krehbiel, Robert Fries & Joseph Singer. *Rec Perf:* With Titanic & Smithsonian. *Pos:* Solo & lectr recitals, Boston Univ, Mass Inst Technol, Jordan Hall, Metropolitan Museum, Alice Tully Hall & others; perf with Banchetto Musicale, Aston Magna, Smithsonian Chamber Players, Monadnock Music, Castle Hill Fest, Pro Arte Orch & NH Symph. *Teaching:* Horn, Longy Sch Music, currently. *Awards:* First Prize, Heldenleben Int Horn Compt, 79. *Mailing Add:* Longy Sch Music 1 Follen St Cambridge MA 02138

RIFE, MARILYN N
PERCUSSION, TEACHER & COACH
b Chicago, Ill, Dec 12, 54. *Study:* Interlochen Arts Acad, dipl, 72; Oberlin Col, BA(music), 76; Northwestern Univ. *Pos:* Prin timpani & perc, Civic Orch Chicago, winter 69-70, summer 71, 74, 75 & 77; extra perc, Chicago Symph Orch, 77-; asst prin timpani & perc, San Antonio Symph, 77- *Teaching:* Adj instr perc, Trinity Univ, 78-; coach, San Antonio Youth Orch, 80- *Mem:* Percussive Arts Soc; Am Symph Orch League. *Mailing Add:* 101 Arcadia Pl #310 San Antonio TX 78209

RIFEL, CRAIG THOMAS
DOUBLE BASS, ORGAN
b Chicago, Ill, Dec 30, 52. *Study:* Univ Wis, Eau Claire, BMusEd, 76. *Pos:* Prin bass, Fla Symph, Orlando, 76-78; bassist, Syracuse Symph, 78-80 & Detroit Symph, 80- *Mem:* Int Soc Bassists; Am Guild Organists. *Mailing Add:* c/o Detroit Symph Ford Auditorium Detroit MI 48226

RIGAI, AMIRAM HAGAI
PIANO, COMPOSER
b Tel-Aviv, Israel; US citizen. *Study:* Piano with Leo Kestenberg, 44-47, Mark Gunzbourg, 51-55, Egon Petri, 56 & Clarence Adler, 58-69; studied comp with Uriyah Boscovich, Israel, 45-47; Jerusalem Acad Music, 48-49; Los Angeles Consv Music, studied piano with Earle Voorhees & comp with Hutchins Morrison Ruger, 51-55; master class with Rosinna Lhevinne, 52-55; San Francisco Consv Music, BMus(piano), 57; Columbia Univ, summer 79 & spring 83. *Works:* Lasfinot, publ Israel, 46; Israeli Rhapsody No 1, Vox, 64; Tocatta—Bolero, Music Libr Artists Embassy, 56; Israeli Rhapsody No 2, Musical Heritage Soc, 73; Walls of Jerusalem, Chappell & Co, 73; Hanadnea, Transcontinental Music Publ, 76; Vision, WEVD, New York, 70. *Rec Perf:* Music of the Near East, Vox, 65; Piano Music (Louis Moreau Gottschalk), Decca, 67-68; Israeli Composers, 73, Ten Characteristic Pieces (Louis Moreau Gottschalk), 75 & Piano Music (Jacques Gottschalk), 77, Musical Heritage Soc; Piano Music of the Middle East, 78 & American Piano Music (Louis Moreau Gottschalk), 79, Folkways Rec. *Teaching:* Instr piano, Los Angeles Consv Music, 52-55, 92nd St YM-YWHA Sch Music, New York, 71-73 & Mid-Westchester YM-YWHA, NY, 73-75; instr piano & comp, Long Island Inst Music, 61. *Awards:* First Prize, Young Artists Int Compt, Univ Calif, Los Angeles, 52. *Mem:* Bohemians. *Interests:* Compositions by L M Gottschalk. *Rep:* ICA Mgt 2219 Eastridge Rd Timonium MD 21093. *Mailing Add:* 2109 Broadway New York NY 10023

RILEY, DENNIS (DANIEL)
COMPOSER
b Los Angeles, Calif, May 28, 43. *Study:* Univ Colo, BMus, 65; Univ Ill, MMus, 68; Univ Iowa, PhD, 73. *Works:* Viola Concerto, 74, Concertino (six players), 76, Beastly Conceits (Cantata IV), 80, Seven Songs on Poems of Emily Dickinson, 81, Winter Settings, 82, Masques (five woodwinds), 82 & Noon Dances (orch), 83, C F Peters. *Pos:* Music critic, Rocky Mountain News, Denver, Colo, 63-65. *Teaching:* Asst prof comp, Calif State Univ, Fresno, 71-74 & Columbia Univ, 74-77. *Awards:* Fels, Ford Found, Music Educ Nat Conf, 65-67, Guggenheim Mem Found, 72 & Nat Endowment for Arts, 80. *Mem:* Am Comp Alliance; BMI; Am Music Ctr. *Mailing Add:* 617 W 164th St New York NY 10032

RILEY, JAMES REX
COMPOSER, EDUCATOR
b Shreveport, La, Sept 2, 38. *Study:* Cenntenary Col, BM, 60; NTex State Univ, MM, 63; Univ Tex, Austin, DMA, 68. *Works:* Pastime, San Antonio Symph Woodwind Quintet, 76; Spheres, perf by Tex Little Symph, 77; Third String Quartet, perf by Concord String Quartet, 77; Tropical Latitudes, perf by San Antonio Symph, 81; Four Essays for Brass Quintet, Shawnee Press Inc, 82; Pirouettes, perf by Attelage Trio, 82; Conversation Piece, Tenuto Pub, 83. *Teaching:* Asst prof theory, Miss State Univ, 68-70; assoc prof comp & theory, Wichita State Univ, 70-75 & Univ Tex, San Antonio, 75-81; assoc prof comp, James Madison Univ, 81- *Awards:* Second Prize, Creative Writing for TV Awards Compt, 70; First Prize, Shenna Meeker Comp Compt, 77; ASCAP Awards, 77, 78, 80, 82 & 83. *Mem:* Va Comp Guild (chmn, 82); Tex Soc Music Theory (pres, 79-81); Am Soc Univ Comp. *Publ:* Auth, Graduate Music Theory Review, Southern Music, 81. *Mailing Add:* Dept Music James Madison Univ Harrisonburg VA 22807

RILEY, JOHN ARTHUR
COMPOSER, CELLO
b Altoona, Pa, Sept 17, 20. *Study:* Eastman Sch Music, MusB, 51; Ecole Normale & Consv Nat Music, 52-53; Yale Sch Music, MusM, 54. *Works:* Quartet for Strings, No 1, Curtis Quartet, 55-57; Fantasy for Oboe and String Orchestra, various perfs, 56-73; Quartet No 2, Valley Press, 62; Rhapsody for Cello and Orchestra, John Riley, cellist, with Altoona Symph & Hartford Civic Orch, 66 & 67; Woodwind Quintet, New York Woodwind Quintet, 72; Chamber Music (song cycle for tenor, piano, violin & cello), perf Jack Litten & Ens, 82; Flute Quartet, Mary Ellen Jacobs & Hartford Consv Quartet, 82. *Pos:* Cellist, San Antonio Symph, 47-49; asst prin cellist, Oklahoma City Symph, 51-52 & Hartford Symph, 65-; prin cellist, New Haven Symph, 53-58. *Teaching:* Cello, comp & music hist, Hartford Consv Music, 58-; instr music, Cent Conn State Univ, 71-77. *Awards:* Fulbright Grant to Paris, 52-53; Tamiment Award, 54. *Mem:* Conn Composers Inc; Am Fedn Musicians. *Mailing Add:* 107 Golf St Newington CT 06111

RILEY, TERRY
COMPOSER, ELECTRONIC
b Colfax, Calif, 1935. *Study:* San Francisco State Col, 55-57; Univ Calif, Berkeley, with Seymour Shifrin, William Denny & Robert Erickson, MA, 61; studied with Pran Nath, 70. *Works:* Spectra (six instrm), 59; In C (aleatory piece), 63; Poppy Nogood and the Phantom Band (organ, sax, perc & electronic equipment), 66; Rainbow in Curved Air (organ, sax, perc & electronic equipment), 68; Music with Balls, 69; Descending Moonshine Dervishes, 76; G-Song for String Quartet, 80. *Pos:* Comp & perf keyboards & sax, US & Europe, 63-; guest, Swedish Radio & Acad Music, 67. *Teaching:* Mem creative assoc prog, State Univ NY Col, Buffalo, 69; mem fac, Mills Col, 72- *Awards:* Nat Endowment Arts Award, 77; Guggenheim Fel, 79. *Mailing Add:* Music Dept Mills Col Oakland CA 94613

RIND, BERNICE See Mossafer-Rind, Bernice

RINEHART, JOHN
COMPOSER, EDUCATOR
b Pittsburgh, Pa, Mar 17, 37. *Study:* Yale Univ, studied comp with Quincy Porter, 60; Cleveland Inst Music, piano with Arthur Loesser, MM, 61; Ohio

State Univ, PhD, 70. *Works:* Violin Sonata, 64, Vivas to Those Who Have Failed!, 70 & Passages (sop, orch & tape), 79, Am Comp Alliance; Paths (cello & tape), Am Soc Univ Comp, 81; Suite for Piano, Am Comp Alliance, 82; Oubliee, Jennifer Rinehart, 82; Inlaid (violin, cello, piano & tape), Sonoton Musik Verlag, 83. *Pos:* Ed, Cleveland Inst Music Notes, Cleveland Inst Music, 61-62. *Teaching:* Instr piano & theory, Cleveland Inst Music, 60-63; prof comp, piano & theory, Heidelberg Col, 63-75, Central Washington Univ, 75-78 & Shenandoah Consv, 78-82; vis app theory, Oberlin Consv, 82- *Awards:* Ernest Bloch Award, ASCAP, 63; Ind Orch Compt, Ind State, 79; Yaddo Fel, 83. *Bibliog:* Richard Bunger (auth), The Well-Prepared Piano, 2nd Ed, Univ Calif Press; Carol Cunning (ed), Composium: Annual Index of Contemporary Compositions, Chrystal Musicworks. *Mem:* Am Soc Univ Comp (mem nat coun & co-chmn, region III, 79-81); Am Comp Alliance; BMI; Res Musica Baltimore Inc (bd dir, 81-); Cleveland Comp Guild; Am Music Ctr. *Mailing Add:* Consv Music Oberlin Col Oberlin OH 44074

RINGEL, HARVEY NORMAN
EDUCATOR, BARITONE
b Peoria, Ill, Mar 25, 03. *Study:* Univ Ill, Urbana-Champaign, BMus, 27; Columbia Univ, MA, 34; Chicago Musical Col, DFA, 54; Kansas City Consv Music, Hon DMus, 49 . *Pos:* Church musician & oratorio soloist; adminr, Chicago Musical Col, 46-54; ed, Nat Asn Teachers Singing Bulletin, 55-80. *Teaching:* Head voice dept & dir, Consv Music, Wesley Col, Univ NDak, Grand Forks, 29-35; private voice instr, Chicago, 35-46; instr singing, Chicago Musical Col, 46-54; prof voice & vocal pedagogy, 54-77, prof emer, 77-; instr singing, Am Consv Music, Chicago, 77- *Awards:* Fel, Nat Asn Teachers Singing, 60. *Bibliog:* Richard Miller (auth), Harvey Ringel/A Tribute, Nat Asn Teachers Singing Bulletin, 80. *Mem:* Nat Asn Teachers Singing (mem bd dir, 72-80); Chicago Singing Teachers Guild (pres, 76-78); Soc Am Musicians (pres, 76-78). *Mailing Add:* 1139 Leavitt Ave Flossmoor IL 60422

RINGER, ALEXANDER L
EDUCATOR, WRITER
b Berlin, Germany, Feb 3, 21; US citizen. *Study:* Hollander Consv, Berlin, cert, 38; Muzieklyceum, Amsterdam, studied comp with H Badings, cert, 46; Univ Amsterdam, BA, 47; New Sch Soc Res, MA, 49; Columbia Univ, PhD, 55. *Pos:* Music dir, Temple Judea, Philadelphia, 52-55. *Teaching:* From instr to lectr, City Col New York, 48-52; Hebrew Union Sch Sacred Music, 50-52 & Columbia Univ, 51-52; asst prof music, Univ Pa, 52-55 & Univ Calif, Berkeley, 55-56; assoc prof, Univ Okla, 56-58; from assoc prof to prof, Univ Ill, Urbana-Champaign, 58- *Awards:* Distinguished Serv Award, Philadelphia Jewish Music Coun, 55. *Mem:* Int Musicol Soc; Orgn Am Kodaly Educr; Col Music Soc (mem coun, 60-65); Int Coun Traditional Music (mem bd dir, 67-73); Soc Advan Jewish Music. *Interests:* Arnold Schoenberg; 19th century music; Middle East music. *Publ:* Ed, Yearbk of the Int Folk Music Coun, Vols I & II, Univ Ill Press, 70-71; auth, An Experimental Program in the Development of Musical Literacy, Dept Health, Educ & Welfare, 70; contribr, The Creative World of Beethoven, W W Norton, 71; The Eclectic Curriculum in American Music Education, Music Educ Nat Conf, 72; New Grove Dict of Music & Musicians, 79; La Sociologia della Musica, Torino, 80. *Mailing Add:* Rombachweg 6a Heidelberg D 6900 Germany, Federal Republic of

RINGHOLZ, TERESA MARIE
SOPRANO
b Rochester, NY, Dec 30, 58. *Study:* Eastman Sch Music, BMus, 81, MMus, 83. *Roles:* Gilda in Rigoletto, Western Opera Theatre, 82. *Pos:* Perf, Merola Opera Prog, San Francisco, summer 82 & Western Opera Theater, San Francisco, 82. *Awards:* Leona Gordon Lowin Mem Award, San Francisco Opera—Merola Prog, 82; Noederlisches Sängerbund Award, Liederkranz Vocal Soc, 82. *Mem:* Am Guild Musical Artists. *Mailing Add:* 189 Fairgate St Rochester NY 14606

RINGO, JENNIFER (ELIZABETH)
SOPRANO
b Iowa City, Iowa, June 1, 55. *Study:* Univ Iowa, BM, 72; Juilliard Sch, 76-77. *Roles:* Tytania in A Midsummer Nights Dream, Des Moines Metropolitan Opera, 79; Alexandra in Regina, Houston Grand Opera, 80; Norina in Don Pasquale, 80 & Zerbinetta in Ariadne auf Naxos, 81, Des Moines Metropolitan Opera; Lucia in Lucia di Lammermoor, San Francisco Opera, 82 & Providence Opera Theater, 83; Guilda in Rigoletto, Long Beach Grand Opera, 83; Baby Doe in The Ballad of Baby Doe, Des Moines Metropolitan Opera, 83. *Pos:* Mem, Houston Studio, 78-80. *Mem:* Am Guild Musical Artists. *Rep:* Columbia Artists Mgt Inc 165 W 65th St New York NY 10019. *Mailing Add:* 19 Rte Du Vallon 1224 Geneva Switzerland

RIPLEY, ROBERT
EDUCATOR, CELLO
Study: Cleveland Inst Music, BM; Curtis Inst Music; Berkshire Music Ctr; studied cello with Jean Bedetti & Felix Salmond. *Pos:* Cellist, Cleveland Orch, formerly, Zimbler Sinfonietta, formerly, Violone Ens, formerly, Glenn Miller Air Force Orch, formerly, Boston Symph Orch, 55- & Cambridge String Quartet, currently. *Teaching:* Mem fac violoncello & chamber music, New England Consv Music, currently; mem fac, All-Newton Music Sch, currently. *Mailing Add:* New England Consv Music 290 Huntington Rd Boston MA 02115

RISDON, FRANCES LEE
FLUTE & PICCOLO, EDUCATOR
b Amarillo, Tex, Dec 26, 37. *Study:* Oklahoma City Univ, BME, 59; Univ Colo, MM, 64. *Pos:* Flute & piccolo, Oklahoma City Symph, 56-63; prin flute, Spokane Symph Orch, Wash, 65- *Teaching:* Instr flute, Cent State Col, Okla, 61-63; assoc prof flute, Wash State Univ, 65- *Mailing Add:* E 1118 27th St Spokane WA 99203

RITCHIE, STANLEY JOHN
BAROQUE VIOLIN, EDUCATOR
b Yenda, Australia, Apr 21, 35. *Study:* Sydney Consv Music, perf & teachers dipl, 56; Sch Music, Yale Univ, with Joseph Fuchs, 59-60; studied with Jean Fournier, Oscar Shumsky & Samuel Kissel. *Rec Perf:* Serenades (Reger), Lyrichord, 73; String Quartet (Bergsma), Music Heritage Soc, 76; Brandenburg Concertos (Bach), Smithsonian Inst, 77; Pieces de Clavecin Avec Voix on Violin (Mondonville), Harmonia Mundi, 81; Harp Consorts (William Lawes), 83 & Sonatas (Bach), 83, Focus; Double Concertos (Vivaldi), Nonesuch, 83. *Pos:* Concertmaster, New York City Opera, 63-65; assoc concertmaster, Metropolitan Opera, 65-70; mem, Duo Geminiani (baroque violin & harpsichord), Bloomington, Ind, 74-; first violin, Philadelphia String Quartet, currently. *Teaching:* Prof violin, Sarah Lawrence Col, 72-73; lectr, Univ BC, 73-75; founding mem & fac artist, Aston Magna Fest, 73-; artist in res, Univ Wash, 75-81; prof baroque violin, Ind Univ, Bloomington, 82- *Mailing Add:* 828 S Woodlawn Ave Bloomington IN 47401

RITCHIE, TOM VERNON
COMPOSER, EDUCATOR
b Lawrenceville, Ill, July 3, 22. *Study:* Univ Ill, with Russell Miles & Robert Kelly; Am Consv Music, with Leo Sowerby. *Works:* Ode to Music (male voices & instrm); Let Us Now Remember Heroes (brass & perc); 16 art songs incl A Lincoln Triptych. *Teaching:* Mem fac, Culver Mil Acad, 47-48, Midland Col, 49-54, Ind Univ, 54-56, Drury Col, 56-62 & Wichita State Univ, 62-65; prof music, NEMo State Univ, 65- *Mailing Add:* Music Dept NEMo State Univ Kirksville MO 63501

RITTER, JOHN STEELE
PIANO, EDUCATOR
b Many, Louisiana, July 3, 38. *Study:* Curtis Inst Music, with Horszowski, BMus, 58; Northwestern Univ, MMus, 59; Univ Southern Calif, 59-61. *Rec Perf:* Music of David Popper, Genesis, 74; Sonatas (Moscheles & Schubert), 81, Works (Dvorak, Feld & Martinu), 82, Trio Sonatas (J S Bach & sons), 83 & Rags, Waltzes and Marches (Joplin), 83, CBS Rec. *Pos:* Accmp pianist, with Jean-Pierre Rampal throughout US, Europe & Japan, 74- & with Heinz Holliger throughout US, 80-; conct pianist, solo & orch perf throughout US, currently. *Teaching:* Assoc prof piano, Pomona Col, 63- *Mailing Add:* Music Dept Pomona Col Claremont CA 91711

RIVARD, WILLIAM H
COMPOSER, EDUCATOR
b Lewiston, Idaho, Aug 31, 28. *Study:* Univ Puget Sound, with John Cowell & Leroy Ostransky; Fla State Univ, with John Boda & Ernst von Dohnanyi; Univ Iowa, with Philip Bezanson & Richard Hervig. *Works:* Concerto-Sinfonia (small orch); Philosophical Hautboy (oboe & strings); Overture to War of the Comedians (orch); Capriccio Concitato (band); Arioso and Scherzo (chamber ens). *Teaching:* Mem fac, Univ Mo, 54-56, Northern Ariz Univ, 58-59; prof music, Cent Mich Univ, 59- *Mailing Add:* Music Dept Cent Mich Univ Mt Pleasant MI 48858

RIVERS, JAMES (CALVIN)
PIANO, EDUCATOR
b Oklahoma City, Okla, July 13, 43. *Study:* Juilliard Sch, artist dipl, 65; NTex State Univ, BM, 66, grad fel, 68. *Works:* Introits & Responses, Kjos (in prep). *Rec Perf:* Irl Allison Piano Library, 71, International Piano Library, 73 & James Rivers: Recordings of Concert Performances, 79, Educo Rec. *Pos:* Solo pianist & duo-pianist, Mid-Am Arts Alliance, Kansas City, Mo, 80- *Teaching:* Res pianist & prof piano, Washburn Univ, 68-; instr, Nat Music Camp, Interlochen, Mich, 75. *Awards:* First Prize Young Artist Div, Int Rec Comt, Am Col Musicians, 70; Outstanding Educr Am Award, 75. *Mem:* Kans Arts Comn. *Rep:* Heartland Artservices 6641 Linden Rd Kansas City MO 64113. *Mailing Add:* Dept Music Washburn Univ Topeka KS 66621

RIZZER, GERALD MARVIN
PIANO, COMPOSER
b Chicago, Ill, Sept 25, 42. *Study:* Univ Chicago, BA(music), 62; Yale Univ, MMus, 65; Juilliard Sch Music. *Works:* Peace (ms, flute & piano), perf by Shir Ens, 75. *Pos:* Founder, artistic dir & pianist, Chicago Ens, 77- *Teaching:* Instr music, DePaul Univ, 82- *Awards:* Charles Dittson Fel, 65. *Mailing Add:* 1416 W Winnemac Chicago IL 60640

ROACH, DONALD WYCOFF
EDUCATOR, CONDUCTOR & MUSIC DIRECTOR
b Venetia, Pa, Jan 7, 34. *Study:* Carnegie Mellon Univ, BFA(music & music educ), 57, MFA(music educ), 62; Pa State Univ, EdD(music educ), 70. *Works:* O Be Joyful in the Lord, 68 & Grant Us Thy Peace, 68, Belwin-Mills; Kum Ba Yah, Cambiata Press, 80. *Teaching:* Gen choral, Peters Twp Sch, 58-70; asst prof music educ, Univ SFla, 70-74; prof, Western Ill Univ, 74- *Awards:* Frick Comn Award, 66; Presidential Merit Award, Western Ill Univ, 78. *Mem:* Music Educr Nat Conf; Am Choral Dir Asn; Soc Res Music Educ. *Interests:* Programmed instruction in music notation. *Publ:* Auth, Contemporary Music Education: A Comprehensive Outlook, Music Educr J, 73; Automated Aural-Visual Music Theory Instruction, J Res Music Educ, 74; ed, Music for Children's Choirs: A Selective Graded Listing, Music Educr Nat Conf, 77; auth, The Elementary Chorus: Current Goals and Practices, Choral J, 78; Dalcroze Eurhythmics: Active Musicianship Training, Am Music Teacher, 80. *Mailing Add:* 4 Heath Court Macomb IL 61455

ROADS, CURTIS
COMPOSER, WRITER

b Cleveland, Ohio, May 9, 51. *Study:* Calif Inst Arts, 72-74; Univ Calif, San Diego, BA, 77. *Works:* Prototype, perf by Ctr Music Experiment, Univ Calif, San Diego, 75; Construction, perf by Groupe Musique Experimentale, Bourges, France, 76; Nscor, Inst Res & Coord Acoustics/Music, Paris, France, 80; Field, perf by Musica Verticale, Rome, Italy, 81; Plex, Edizione Strada, Rome, Italy, 83. *Pos:* Assoc fel, Ctr Music Experiment, Univ Calif, San Diego, 77; ed, Comput Music J, 78-; res assoc, Mass Inst Technol, 80- *Bibliog:* Robert Commanday (auth), A Quadrophonic Concert, San Francisco Chronicle, 7/11/73; Jim Horton (auth), Electronic/Computer Music, Ear-New Music Rev, 7/79; Sharon Begley & John Carey (auth), The Creative Computers, Newsweek, 7/5/82. *Mem:* Am Music Ctr; Comp Forum; Comput Music Asn; Newcomp. *Publ:* Auth, Computer Music Tutorial (in prep) & ed, Selected Readings in Computer Music (in prep), MIT Press. *Mailing Add:* 20B-229 Mass Inst Technol Cambridge MA 02139

ROBBINS, DANIEL
COMPOSER, EDUCATOR

b New Orleans, La, Nov 4, 47. *Study:* Long Beach City Col, AA, 67; Calif State Univ, Long Beach, BMus, 70; Univ Southern Calif, MMus, 76. *Works:* Suite for Orchestra, perf by Long Beach Symph, 68; Sonata for Cello & Piano, perf by Gilbert Reese, 70; String Quartet, publ by Univ Southern Calif, 76; In Memoriam Robert F Kennedy, perf by Southeast Youth Symph Orch, 78; White Sale (filmscore), 80; The Prince and the Princess, 80 & Pastorale, 82, Willis Music. *Teaching:* Instr theory & piano, Long Beach City Col, 76-78 & Golden West Col, Huntington Beach, 80-83; lectr theory & comp, Calif State Univ, Long Beach, 78- *Awards:* First Place Comp, Southwestern Youth Music Fest, 64, 65 & 68. *Bibliog:* Jim Cox (auth), Review of In Memoriam Robert F Kennedy, Long Beach Independent, Press Telegram Newspaper, 7/23/78; George Anson (auth), Review of The Prince and The Princess, Clavier Mag, 4/81. *Mem:* Nat Asn Comp. *Mailing Add:* 245 1/2 Coronado Ave Long Beach CA 90803

ROBBINS, DAVID PAUL
COMPOSER, EDUCATOR

b New York, NY, July 18, 46. *Study:* Univ Mich, with Leslie Bassett, George B Wilson & Eugene Kurtz. *Works:* Kabop (chamber orch), 68; Sport (theatre piece; ten players), 69; Fall Back 10 Yards and Contrapunt! (clarinet, organ & perc), 71; Intersect (orch), 71; Momentum (five brass & perc), 72; Biggie (cello & perc), 72; John 3:16 (chorus & tape). *Teaching:* Assoc prof & chmn music dept, Pac Lutheran Univ, 69- *Awards:* Comp of Yr, Wash State Music Teachers Asn, 76. *Mailing Add:* 3606 N Baltimore Tacoma WA 98407

ROBBINS, JULIEN
BASS

b Harrisburg, Pa, Nov 14, 50. *Study:* West Chester State Col, BS, 74; Acad Vocal Arts, 74-75; Lyr Opera Chicago Sch, 76-77. *Roles:* Ramifis in Aida, 79 & Gremin in Eugene Onegin, 79, Metropolitan Opera; Don Fernando in Fidelio, Metropolitan Opera, Santa Fe, 79 & 80; The Speaker in The Magic Flute, Metropolitan Opera, 81; Colline in La Boheme, Washington Opera, 81 & Metropolitan Opera, 82; Timur in Turandot, Greater Miami Opera Co, 82. *Pos:* Soloist, Metropolitan Opera, New York, 79- *Awards:* Baltimore Opera Award, 76; Nat Opera Inst Grant, 77-78. *Mem:* Am Guild Musical Artists. *Mailing Add:* 322 W 57th St New York NY 10019

ROBBOY, R(ONALD) A
COMPOSER, CELLO

b Cleveland, Ohio, Feb 17, 50. *Study:* Univ Calif, San Diego, studied comp with Kenneth Gaburo & Pauline Oliveros & perf with Gabor Rejto & Rafael Druian. *Works:* Lesbians Removing Linoleum, perf by Ripert, 75; Custommusic, comn by Melbourne Int Electronic Music Fest, 75; Sudden Loss of Hearing, comn by Univ NMex, 79; Der Yiddisher Cowboy (with Warren Burt, conceptual opera on film), Melbourne, New York & San Diego, 81-83; Efrem Zimbalist Jr and the Talmud, 81 & Sentimental Fables (with Robert Kushner), 81, perf by The Big Jewish Band, NY. *Pos:* Cellist, San Diego Symph, 70- & San Diego Opera, 71-; founder, Fatty Acid, San Diego, 73-75; founder & dir, The Big Jewish Band, San Diego, 80- *Bibliog:* Michel Chion & Guy Reibel (auths), Les Musiques Electroacoustiques, INA-GRM-Edisud, 76; Warren Burt (auth), Der Yiddisher Cowboy, Cantrills Filmnotes, Melbourne, 4/81. *Publ:* Auth, A Guided Tour of San Diego, In: Crawl Out Your Window, 78; Reifying the Heifetz-Trotsky Axis, J Los Angeles Inst Contemp Art, 6/78; contribr, Notes Towards a Screenplay, In: Allos, Lingua Press, 80. *Mailing Add:* 4643 Park Blvd San Diego CA 92116

ROBERTS, BRENDA
SOPRANO

b Lowell, Ind, Mar 16, 45. *Study:* Northwestern Univ, with Hermanus Baer; with Lotte Lehmann, Gerald Moore & Josef Metternich. *Roles:* Sieglinde in Die Walküre, Staatstheater Saarbrücken, 68; Santuzza in Cavalleria rusticana; Donna Elvira in Don Giovanni; Musetta in La Boheme; Ariadne in Ariadne auf Naxos; Leonora in Il Trovatore; Elsa in Lohengrin. *Pos:* Res mem, Staatsoper, Hamburg, currently; sop, Bayreuth Fest, Lyr Opera Chicago, San Francisco Opera, Frankfurt Staatsoper & others. *Mailing Add:* c/o Int Artist Mgt 111 W 57th St New York NY 10019

ROBERTS, DONALD LOWELL
LIBRARIAN, EDUCATOR

b Dodge City, Kans, Aug 13, 38. *Study:* Curtis Inst Music, with Sol Schoenbach; Friends Univ, BA(music theory), 61; Univ Mich, AMLS, 63. *Pos:* Fine arts librn, Univ NMex, 63-68; bassoonist, Albuquerque Symph Orch, NMex, 63-68; head music librn, Northwestern Univ, 69-; co-ed rec rev, Am Music, 81- *Teaching:* Vis prof, Grad Sch Librarianship, Rosary Col, 72-; prof bibliog, Northwestern Univ, 81- *Mem:* Int Asn Music Libr; Music Libr Asn; Soc Ethnomusicol (treas, 78-80); Asn Rec Sound Collections (pres, 71-74). *Interests:* Pueblo Indian music and ceremonialism. *Publ:* Auth, The Ethnomusicology of the Eastern Pueblos, Univ NMex, 72; auth, Music History from Primary Sources, Oesterreichische Gesellschaft Musik Beitrage, 73; Practice and Problems of Access to Sound Archives, Phonographic Bulletin, 77; coauth, Southwestern Indian Ritual Drama, Univ NMex, 80. *Mailing Add:* Music Libr Northwestern Univ Evanston IL 60201

ROBERTS, F CHESTER
TUBA, TEACHER

b Ipswich, Mass, June 29, 21. *Study:* Cleveland Inst Music, BM(voice), 54. *Pos:* Prin tuba, Pittsburgh Symph Orch, 46-50, Cleveland Orch, 50-67, San Francisco Symph Orch, 67-69 & Chautauqua Symph Orch, 51-71. *Teaching:* Lectr tuba, Western Reserve Univ, 50-67; assoc teacher, Oberlin Consv, 54-67; instr brass instrm, ens & pedagogy, Boston Consv, 72- *Mem:* Tubists Universal Brotherhood Asn. *Publ:* Ed, 43 Bel Canto Studies (tuba or bass trombone), Robert King, 72; auth, Tenor, Bass and Contrabass Tubas, 74 & Coping With the Extension Register, 74, Tubists Universal Brotherhood Asn Newslett; Elements of Brass Intonation, Instrumentalist, 75; Some Otherwise Logic on Tuba Valve Systems, Tubists Universal Brotherhood Asn J, 82. *Mailing Add:* 592 Essex Ave Gloucester MA 01930

ROBERTS, GERTRUD K
HARPSICHORD, COMPOSER

b Hastings, Minn, Aug 23, 06. *Study:* Univ Minn, BA(piano & comp), 28; Leipzig Consv Music, 30-31, with Teichmuller-Baresel; studied privately with Julia Elbogen, Vienna, Austria, 35-36; Univ Hawaii, studied art hist with Gustav Ecke & Jean Charlot. *Works:* Chaconne for Harpsichord & Hommage to Couperin (rondo, two-manual harpsichord), Island Heritage; Twelve Time-Gardens (piano), Ho'okani Enterprises. *Rec Perf:* Piano & Harpsichord Compositions, Ho'okani Enterprises. *Pos:* Concert harpsichordist, concerts throughout US & Hawaii, 36- *Awards:* Most Distinguished Citizen for 1975 in the Arts, Alpha Gamma Delta. *Mem:* Nat Soc Arts & Lett (pres, 71-74); Nat Asn Comp & Cond; Am Music Ctr; Nat Guild Piano Teachers; Pen Women Am (pres Honolulu chap, 74-76). *Mailing Add:* 4723 Moa St Honolulu HI 96816

ROBERTS, JACK LUNDY
PIANO, TEACHER-COACH

b Ft Worth, Tex, June 22, 31. *Study:* NTex State Univ, BM, MA; Univ Mich, DMA; Vienna State Acad Music, 55-56. *Teaching:* Prof, NTex State Univ, 57-; prof piano, Nat Music Camp, Interlochen, Mich, 73; chmn keyboard, Am Inst Musical Studies, Austria, 76. *Awards:* Fulbright Grant, 55-56. *Mem:* Pi Kappa Lambda. *Mailing Add:* 1429 Amherst Denton TX 76201

ROBERTS, JANE A
COMPOSER

b Chicago, Ill, Oct 3, 33. *Study:* Am Consv Music, BMus(piano), 57, BMus(comp), 80; studied with Hans Heniot, William Browning & William Ferris. *Works:* Sonata (clarinet & piano), Jan Plantinga & Jane Roberts, 80; Dan Coombs & Bryan Shilander, 83; Bend, Baby, Bend, Prairie State Col, 80; Incidental Music for Twelfth Night, 82; Electronic Works for Modern Dance; over 100 songs, song cycles & chamber & piano music pieces. *Teaching:* Music, #153 Pub Sch, Homewood, Ill, 61-69; Prairie State Col, 82; piano, privately, 56- *Mem:* Am Women Comp Inc; ASCAP; Nat Asn Comp USA. *Mailing Add:* 1636 Olive Rd Homewood IL 60430

ROBERTS, JOHN HOWELL
LIBRARIAN

b Princeton, NJ, Oct 28, 41. *Study:* Haverford Col, BA, 63; Rutgers Univ, MLS, 77; Univ Calif, Berkeley, PhD, 77. *Pos:* Music librn, Trenton State Col, 78-82 & Univ Pa, 82- *Teaching:* Actg instr music hist, Yale Univ, 69-71. *Mem:* Am Musicol Soc; Music Libr Asn; Int Asn Music Libr. *Interests:* Handel's borrowings from other composers. *Mailing Add:* 2204 Delancey Pl Philadelphia PA 19103

ROBERTS, JOHN NOEL
EDUCATOR, PIANO

b San Antonio, Tex, Dec 4, 51. *Study:* Eastman Sch Music, BM, 74, perf cert, 75, MM, 75; Sch Music, Yale Univ, MMA, 77, DMA, 81. *Teaching:* Vis teacher, Wesleyan Univ, 75-77; asst prof music, Furman Univ, 78-; perf fac, Tidewater Music Fest, St Mary's, Md, summers 77, 79, 80 & 81. *Awards:* Sprague Hall Compt Winner, Yale Univ, 78. *Bibliog:* Deb Richardson-Moore (auth), John Roberts: A Musician Who Cares About the Music First, Greenville News & Piedmont, 10/31/82. *Mem:* Col Music Soc; SC Music Teacher's Asn (scholar comt chmn, 83-); Music Teacher's Nat Asn. *Rep:* Artist Prom Bureau 6072 A Broopark Ohio 44142. *Mailing Add:* Rt 6 Box 158 Travelers Rest SC 29690

ROBERTS, MEGAN (L)
COMPOSER

b Hempstead, NY, Oct 12, 52. *Study:* Univ Calif, Santa Barbara, 70-72; Humboldt State Univ, BA(music), 75; Ctr Contemp Music, Mills Col, studied with David Behrman & Robert Ashley, MFA(music comp), 77. *Works:* I Move (film score), comn by Michael Wiese, 76; A Pygmatic Function, comn & perf by New Beginnings Chamber Ens, 76; I Could Sit Here All Day, 1750 Arch Rec, 76; Assembly Line, New Music Am, 80 & Spiel & Klangstrasse, WGermany, 80 & 82; Food Music (electronic comp for dance), perf by

Theater Dance Unlimited, 81; Dance of the Rookie Survivor (chamber ens for dance), Sumfest, 81; Arcadian Dreams, comn & perf by Houston Ballet Orch & Houston Ballet, 83. *Rec Perf:* I Could Sit Here All Day, Arch Rec, 78. *Pos:* Choir dir, Eureka First Congregational Church, 73-74; freelance work, video & sound rec, doc & reproduction, 75- *Teaching:* Grad asst, Ctr Contemp Music, Mills Col, 75-77; instr music, Mills Music Training Sch, 76-77; mem fac art dept, St Cloud Univ, Minn, 79; guest lectr, Univ Wyo, Boston Museum Sch, Tex Christian Univ, Mid-Am Col Art Asn, St Cloud State Univ, Univ Minn, Minneapolis Col Art & Design, Humboldt State Univ, Tama Univ, Tokyo & St Joost Acad Art, Breda, Holland, 80-83. *Awards:* Elizabeth Mill Crothers Prize Comp Music, Mills Col, 77; Grand Prize, Fourth Tokyo Int Video Fest, 81; Video Award, Mill Valley Film Fest, 83. *Mem:* New Music Alliance (mem bd dir, 81-82); Asn Independent Video & Filmmakers. *Publ:* Contribr, In Case of Fire Break Glass, Ctr Contemp Music, Mills Col, 78. *Mailing Add:* 1316 Bradley Laramie WY 82070

ROBERTS, WILFRED BOB
TRUMPET, COMPOSER

b Detroit, Mich. *Study:* Ernest Williams Sch Music, New York, 41; Univ Mich, BM(music educ), 47, BM(theory & comp), 48; Berkshire Music Ctr, 48. *Works:* Serenade for Trumpet, Suite for Two Winds, Canon & Variations, Miniatures for Three Winds, Variations on an English Tune, Transitions, Three Headlines & many others, COR Publ. *Rec Perf:* An Evening at Radio City Music Hall, Forum; Frederick Fennell Conducts Gershwin & Frederick Fennell Conducts Cole Porter, Mercury; Giovanni Gabrielli Sacrae Symphoniae, Period; His Song Shall Be With Me, Christian Sci Publ Soc; Symphonic Suites: Carmen & Faust, RCA Victor; Waltzes of Johann Strauss, Columbia; also many others. *Pos:* Studio trumpeter with major TV networks & commercial recording studios & performed opera, ballet, concert & pops programs, orchestral accompaniment for classical artists & back-up for leading pop artists, New York, 49-72; first trumpet, Radio City Music Hall Orch, 52-72; produced, arranged, conducted & performed on recordings for Christian Sci Publ Soc, Boston, 72-82; mem, Boston area orchestras, 72-82; first trumpet, Sundome Ctr Perf Arts, Phoenix, 82- *Teaching:* Fac mem trumpet & theory, Transylvania Music Camp, Brevard, NC, 50; trumpet instr, Garden City Pub Sch, NY, 59-72 & Nassau Community Col, Garden City, NY, 62-72; staff mem, Univ Brass Quintet, 62-72; instr brass methods & materials, Adelphi Univ, 63-69; dir band & wind ens, 65-69; staff mem, New England Consv, 82- *Mem:* ASCAP; Int Trumpet Guild; Phi Mu Alpha Sinfonia; Kappa Kappa Psi; Am Fedn Musicians. *Mailing Add:* 11026 Pine Hollow Dr Sun City AZ 85351

ROBERTS, WILLIAM L
PERCUSSION

b Denver, Colo, Jan, 31, 31. *Study:* Univ Denver, BSBA, 59. *Pos:* Perc, Denver Symph Orch, 58- *Teaching:* Instr perc, Metropolitan State Col, 68- *Mailing Add:* Denver Symph 1245 Champa Denver CO 80204

ROBERTSON, DONNA NAGEY
COMPOSER, EDUCATOR

b Indiana, Pa, Nov 16, 35. *Study:* Ind Univ Pa, BS, 57; Eastman Sch Music, MM, 58. *Works:* Dialogues, comn by NC Music Teachers Asn, 76; Love, 77 & Psalm for a Festive Procession, 77, Hinshaw; Flashes in a Pan, 81, Psalm XXIII (sop & flute), 81, Recitation with 5 Reflections, 81 & Little Suite (trombone choir), 81, Dorn Publ Co. *Pos:* Ed, Music Now, Southeastern Comp League, 73-76. *Teaching:* Assoc prof organ, theory & comp, Mars Hill Col, 58- *Mem:* Am Guild Organists; Col Music Soc; Music Teachers Nat Asn (NC chmn organ div, 78-80); Southeastern Comp League; Int League Women Comp. *Publ:* Auth, Writing for the Organ—the Monster that Breathes, Music Now, 75. *Mailing Add:* 140 Mountain View Rd Mars Hill NC 28754

ROBERTSON, EDWIN C
COMPOSER, EDUCATOR

b Richmond, Va, Nov 26, 38. *Study:* Univ Va, with David Davis; Fla State Univ, with John Boda. *Works:* Piano Trio (chamber music); Quartet (flute, clarinet, marimba & double bass); Movement (brass quintet); Trumpet Reflection (chamber music); Sing My Fair Love Good Morrow (chorus); Golden Slumbers (chorus); Two Psalms (chorus with string orch). *Teaching:* Choral cond, Univ Richmond, 68-69; prof music, Univ Montevallo, 71- *Mailing Add:* 97 Shoshone Dr Montevallo AL 35115

ROBERTSON, HELEN (WELLS)
VIOLIN, TEACHER

b Artesia, NMex, Aug 3, 27. *Study:* Tx Christian Univ, 44-47; McGill Univ Consv, AA(music perf), 50; Tex Womans Univ, BS, 83. *Pos:* Prin second violin, Ft Worth Opera Orch, 62-79 & Ft Worth Symph, 66-76; asst prin second violin, Tex Little Symph, 76- & Ft Worth Symph, 76- *Teaching:* Violin, viola & class strings & cond chamber ensemble, Tarrant County Jr Col, 69-78. *Mem:* Am Fedn Musicians. *Mailing Add:* 4325 Norwich Dr Ft Worth TX 76109

ROBERTSON, MARVIN L
EDUCATOR, CONDUCTOR

b Lincoln, Nebr, Jan 20, 34. *Study:* Walla Walla Col, BMus, 56; Univ Northern Colo, MA, 59; Fla State Univ, PhD, 70. *Teaching:* Piano & choral, Auburn Acad, 56-61; instr music educ & choral, Walla Walla Col, 63-66; prof & chmn div music, Southern Col, Collegedale, Tenn, 66- *Mem:* Music Educr Nat Conf; Am Choral Dir Asn; Col Music Soc; Hymn Soc Am; Am Choral Found. *Publ:* Auth, Music Education: A Look at Seventh-day Adventist Schools, 71, Music Education: The Humanities Approach, 72 & Johnny Can't Sing, 78, J Adventist Educ; Directing a Children's Choir, Score, 81. *Mailing Add:* Div Music Southern Col Collegedale TN 37315

ROBINSON, FLORENCE CLAIRE CRIM
EDUCATOR, PIANO

b Carbondale, Ill, Oct 26, 32. *Study:* Northwestern Univ, 50; Southern Ill Univ, BA, 50, PhD, 63; Univ Denver, MA, 56; Univ Colo, 60-61; studied piano with Antonia Brico, 60-61. *Teaching:* Coordr music, Denver pub sch, 63-65; asst prof music, Southern Ill Univ, 65-67; prof & chair music dept, Bishop Col, Dallas, 67-71; prof & chair music dept, Clark Col, 71-, chair, Arts & Humanities Div, 75-; guest prof, numerous cols & univ. *Awards:* Merit Award, Nat Asn Negro Musicians, 63; Fuller E Callaway Prof Music, Callaway Found, 82; Distinguished Alumni Award, Southern Ill Univ, 82. *Bibliog:* Raoul Abdul (auth), Blacks in Classical Music, Dodd, Mead & Co, 77. *Mem:* Music Educr Nat Conf; Nat Asn Negro Musicians; Am Fedn TV & Radio Artists. *Publ:* Auth, Louis Moreau Gottschalk, Musical Analysis, 71; Many Sides of Black Music, Carnation Co, 74. *Mailing Add:* 2885 Pine Needle Dr East Point GA 30344

ROBINSON, FORREST THOMPSON
PIANO, COMPOSER

b Emporia, Kans, Apr 28, 27. *Study:* San Francisco State Univ, AB, 50; Mills Col, 51; Univ Kans MM, 53; Boston Univ, MusAD, 65. *Works:* Concertino for Two Pianos, WNYC, 53; Dance Suite, Orchesis Dance Group, 70; Fantasies (film score), 75; Sonatina for Violin, Alec Catherwood, 75. *Teaching:* Instr music, Lawrence Univ, 53-55; instr piano, Univ Ala, 55-61; teaching fel, Boston Univ, 61-63; prof music, Cent Mich Univ, 63- *Awards:* Continuing Study Award, Hammond Organ Co, 67; Creative Merit Award, Cent Mich Univ, 74. *Mem:* Music Teachers Nat Asn; Mich Music Teachers Asn; Pi Kappa Lambda; Phi Mu Alpha. *Interests:* Folk music of Morocco. *Publ:* Auth, Music of Darius Milhaud for Piano & Orchestra, 67; Music of Darius Milhaud for Two Pianos, 68, Am Music Teacher. *Mailing Add:* 517 S Washington Mt Pleasant MI 48858

ROBINSON, GAIL
COLORATURA SOPRANO

b Meridian, Miss, Aug 7, 46. *Study:* Memphis State Univ, with Mrs J Norvell Taylor; studied with Robley Lawson. *Roles:* Lucia in Lucia di Lammermoor, Memphis Opera Theatre, 67; Genie in Die Zauberflote, 70; Amina in La Sonnambula; Leila in Pecheurs de Perles; Norina in Don Pasquale; Fiodiligi in Cosi fan tutte; Oscar in Un Ballo in maschera. *Pos:* Coloratura sop, with maj opera co in Can, WGermany, Switzerland & US; res mem, Metropolitan Opera Asn. *Awards:* Winner, Nat Coun Audition, Metropolitan Opera, 68; Rockefeller Found Grant. *Rep:* Columbia Artists Mgt Inc 165 W 57th St New York NY 10019. *Mailing Add:* c/o Robert Lombardo Assoc 1 Harkness Plaza 61 W 62 Suite #6F New York NY 10023

ROBINSON, JOSEPH
OBOE, EDUCATOR

Study: Davidson Col, BA, Woodrow Wilson Col, Princeton Univ, MS; Univ Cologne. *Pos:* Mem, Cleveland Orch, formerly, Atlanta Symph, formerly & Clarion Wind Quartet, currently; prin oboe & Alice Tully chair, New York Phil, currently; soloist, Piedmont Chamber Orch, currently; participant, Eastern Music Fest, NC Sch Arts Int Prog, Blossom Fest & Marlboro Music Fest. *Teaching:* Mem fac oboe, Manhattan Sch Music, 78- *Awards:* NC Fulbright Fel. *Mailing Add:* New York Phil Avery Fisher Hall New York NY 10023

ROBINSON, MARIE
SPINTO

b Thomasville, Ga, Dec 2, 40. *Study:* Fla A&M Univ, studied voice with Rebecca Steele, BS, 68; Fla State Univ, studied voice with Yvonne Cianella & Elena Nikolaidi, MM, 72, MusD, 73. *Roles:* Aida, Deutsche Staatsoper Berlin, 75, Nationaltheater Munich, 75 & Wiener Staatsoper, 75 & 76; Donna Anna & Tosca, Nationaltheater Prague, 77, 78 & 81; Elisabetta, Wiener Staatsoper, 78; Il Trovatore, Frankfurter Oper, 80; Tosca & Il Trovatore, Deutsche Oper Berlin, 80, 81 & 82. *Pos:* Res solosangerin, Opernhaus Graz, 74-77 & Nationaltheater Mannheim, 77-83; performer in Europe & South Am. *Awards:* Diuguid Fel, Southern Fel Found, 73; Best Candidate of Americas VI Concurso Int De Canto, Rio de Janeiro, 73; First Prize, Civic Opera of Palm Beaches, 73. *Mailing Add:* c/o Columbia Artists Mgt 165 W 57th St New York NY 10019

ROBINSON, RAY E
ADMINISTRATOR, WRITER

b Dec 26, 32. *Study:* San Jose State Univ, AB, 56; Ind Univ, MM, 58, DME, 69. *Teaching:* Instr music, Ind Univ, 58-59; asst prof, Cascade Col, 59-61; assoc prof, 61-63; dean, Peabody Consv Music, 63-69; prof & pres, Westminster Choir Col, 69- *Mem:* Am Choral Dir Asn; Col Music Soc. *Interests:* History of the Peabody Conservatory of Music, 1868-1968. *Publ:* Coauth, The Choral Experience, Harper & Row, 76; auth, Choral Music: A Norton Historical Anthology, W W Norton, 78; Krzysztof Penderecki: A Guide to His Works, Prestige Publ, 83; coauth, A Study of the Penderecki St Luke Passion, Moeck Verlag, 83; auth, The Choral Conductor, Harper & Row (in prep). *Mailing Add:* 100 Hamilton Ave Princeton NJ 08540

ROBINSON, RICHARD
COMPOSER, VIOLIN

b Chicago, Ill, July 12, 23. *Study:* Am Consv Music, with Leo Sowerby; Cornell Univ, with Karel Husa & Robert Palmer. *Works:* Woodwind Trio (chamber music), 53; Three Haiku (sop & orch), 67; Ambience (electronic), 70; Alea (electronic), 71; Mosaic (quadronic electronic piece), 72; Voices (electronic), 73. *Pos:* Violinist, Atlanta Symph Orch, 52-73 & currently; dir, Atlanta Electronic Music Ctr, 68-; prog dir, Ambience, WREK-FM, Atlanta, 71-72. *Awards:* Ga Comp Award, 53; Piedmont Arts Fest Award, 67; First Prize, Dartmouth Int Electronic Music Comp, 70. *Mailing Add:* Atlanta Symph Orch 1280 Peachtree St NE Atlanta GA 30309

ROBINSON, SHARON
CELLO
b Houston Tex, Dec 2, 49. *Study:* Univ Southern Calif, 68-70; Peabody Consv Music, BMus, 72. *Rec Perf:* The Mendelssohn Viola Quintets, CBS, 74; The Mendelssohn Trios, 82 & Vivaldi Sonatas, 83, Vox Cum Laude; Last Poems of Wallace Stevens (Ned Rorem), Leonarda, 83. *Pos:* Chamber musician, Marlboro Music Fest, Spoleto Fest, Mostly Mozart Fest & others, 74-; soloist with major orch throughout US & Europe, 74-; recitalist, Lincoln Ctr & many univ, 74-; cellist, Kalichstein Laredo Robinson Trio, 76- *Awards:* Leventritt Found Award, 74; Avery Fisher Recital Award, Lincoln Ctr, 79; Gregor Piatigorsky Mem Award, 83. *Bibliog:* Kalichstein Laredo Robinson Trio, Musical Am 82. *Mailing Add:* c/o Harold Shaw Conct 1995 Broadway New York NY 10023

ROBISON, CLAYNE W
EDUCATOR, BARITONE
b Boise, Idaho, Jan 5, 38. *Study:* Brigham Young Univ, BA, 62, BA(voice), 70; Harvard Univ Law Sch, JD, 65; Univ Wash, MMus(orch cond), 71, DMA(opera prod), 73. *Rec Perf:* Book of Mormon Oratorio, Columbia Masterworks, 79. *Roles:* Shaunard, Seattle Opera, 72 & Portland Opera, 73; Falke, Portland Opera, 74 & Utah Opera, 83; Malatesta in Don Pasquale, Portland Opera, 76 & Utah Opera, 81; Ninth Symphony (Beethoven), Utah Symph, 78; Escamillo in Carmen, Utah Opera, 79; Carmina Burana, Ballet West, 81 & 83; Rigoletto, San Francisco Opera. *Pos:* Stage dir & cond, Wolf Trap Co, 72. *Teaching:* Prof music, Brigham Young Univ, 73- *Awards:* William Kent, Jr Award, San Francisco Opera Auditions, 78; Regional Winner, Metropolitan Opera Auditions, 78. *Mem:* Nat Asn Teachers Singing (chap pres, 82-); Nat Opera Asn. *Publ:* Auth, Singing Hymns with New Power, 77 & Steinway on the Stairway, 81, Ensign. *Mailing Add:* E-465 Harris Fine Arts Ctr Brigham Young Univ Provo UT 84602

ROBISON, JOHN ORIAN
EDUCATOR, LUTE
b Dearborn, Mich, Oct 11, 49. *Study:* Oakland Univ, BA, 71; Stanford Univ, MA, 72, DMA, 75. *Teaching:* Lute instr, ens dir & librn, Univ Toronto Early Music Wkshp, 77-78; asst prof musicol, Univ SFla, 77-83, assoc prof, 83- *Awards:* Nat Endowment Humanities Fel, 79 & 82; Am Philosophical Soc Grant, 82. *Mem:* Am Musicol Soc; Am Lute Soc. *Interests:* German Renaissance music; Renaissance lute music; Gregorian chant. *Publ:* Auth, Right-Hand Lute Techniques in English Lute Music, Guitar & Lute J, 82; The Lost Oboe Concertos of J S Bach, Bach Riem J, 82-83; The Messa di Voce as an Instrumental Ornament in the 17th & 18th Century, Music Rev, 82; Sebastian Ochsenkun's Tabulaturbuch Auf Die Lanten, Am Lute Soc J, 83; Vienna, National Bibliothek Manuscript 18810! A Repertory Study and Manuscript Inventory With Concordances, RMA Res Chronicle, 83. *Mailing Add:* 407 S Delaware Tampa FL 33606

ROBISON, PAULA JUDITH
FLUTE, EDUCATOR
b Nashville, Tenn, June 8, 41. *Study:* Univ Southern Calif, 58-60; Juilliard Sch Music, with Julius Baker, BS, 63; studied flute with Marcel Moyse; Marlboro Col, with Rudolf Serkin. *Rec Perf:* Introduction & Variations (Schubert); Paula Robison Plays Flute Music of the Romantic Era; rec on Columbia, Marlboro Rec Soc, Connoisseur, Musical Heritage & Vanguard. *Pos:* Soloist with US orchs; mem, Orpheus Trio, 70-; prin ann recital ser, Paula and ..., Alice Tully Hall, 76-; co-dir chamber music, Spoleto Festivals, Charleston, SC & Spoleto, Italy; recitalist, White House & others. *Teaching:* Mem fac flute, New England Consv Music, formerly & Juilliard Sch, 78- *Awards:* First Prize, Geneva Int Compt, 66; Martha Baird Rockefeller Grant, 66; Musician of Month, Musical Am, 79. *Mem:* Founding artist-mem, Chamber Music Soc Lincoln Ctr. *Rep:* Columbia Artists Mgt 165 W 57th St New York NY 10019; Kazuko Hillyer Int Inc 250 W 57th St New York NY 10107. *Mailing Add:* Juilliard Sch Lincoln Ctr Plaza New York NY 10023

ROBISON, WILLIAM H, III
EDUCATOR, TRUMPET
b Quantico, Va, Dec 12, 35. *Study:* Univ Ga, BS, 57, MME, 60, EdD, 70. *Pos:* Band dir, Clarke Co Sch, 58-67. *Teaching:* Asst prof, Ga Col, 68-69; supvr music Bibb Co sch, Macon, Ga, 69-72; prof music, Berry Col, 72- *Mem:* Ga Music Educr Asn (pres, 75-77); Phi Beta Mu Bandmasters; Phi Mu Alpha Sinfonia; Nat Asn Jazz Educr; Music Educr Nat Conf. *Mailing Add:* Music Dept Berry Col Mt Berry GA 30149

ROBY, PAUL EDWARD
VIOLIN, EDUCATOR
b Akron, Ohio, June 5, 35. *Study:* Consv Music, Oberlin Col, BM(violin); Cath Univ Am, MM(violin); Univ Colo, Boulder, DMA; studied violin with Nathan Gottschalk, Andor Toth & William Kroll. *Pos:* Mem & soloist, US Air Force Orch, formerly; concertmaster, Shreveport Symph, formerly; soloist, Washington Civic Symph & Oklahoma City Symph; cond, Lowell Opera Co, GYBSO Repty Orch & NH Phil. *Teaching:* Mem fac, Okla State Univ, Norman, formerly; mem fac, cond orch & first violin res quartet, Kans State Univ, formerly; orch dir, Univ Lowell, formerly; mem fac violin & viola, Longy Sch Music, currently. *Mem:* Music Educr Nat Conf; Music Teachers Asn; Am Fedn Musicians; Col Music Soc; Am String Teachers Asn. *Mailing Add:* Longy Sch Music One Follen St Cambridge MA 02138

ROCHBERG, GEORGE
COMPOSER, EDUCATOR
b Paterson, NJ, July 5, 18. *Study:* Mannes Sch Music, with Hans Weisse, George Szell, & Leopold Mannes, 39-42; Curtis Inst Music, with Rosario

Scalero & G C Menotti, BM, 48; Univ Pa, MA, 49. *Works:* Symphony No 1, 58 & Symphony No 2, 59, Theodore Presser Co; Quartet No 3, Galaxy Music, 72; Concord Quartets, No 4, 5 & 6, 79 & Imago Mundi for Orchestra, 74, Theodore Presser Co; String Quartet (double cello), Theodore Presser Co, 82; and others. *Pos:* Chief ed & dir publ, Theodore Presser Co, 51-60. *Teaching:* Fac mem, Curtis Inst Music, 48-54; prof comp & theory, Univ Pa, 60-79, chmn dept music, 60-68, Anneberg prof humanities, 79- *Awards:* Guggenheim Fel, 56-57 & 66-67; Naumburg Rec Award, 81; Friedheim Award, Kennedy Ctr, 79; and many others. *Bibliog:* Alexander Ringer (auth), The Music of George Rochberg, Musical Quart, 66. *Mem:* Am Musicol Soc; ASCAP. *Publ:* Auth, Aesthetics of Survival, Univ Mich Press (in prep). *Mailing Add:* 285 Aronimink Dr Newtown Square PA 19073

ROCKWELL, JOHN
CRITIC
b Washington, DC, Sept 16, 40. *Study:* Harvard Univ, BA, 62; Univ Munich, 62-63; Univ Calif, Berkeley, MA, 64, PhD, 72. *Pos:* Music & dance critic, Los Angeles Times, 70-72; freelance music critic, New York Times, 72-74, staff music critic, 74- *Awards:* Fel, Harvard Univ & German govt, 62-63; Woodrow Wilson Fel, 63-64. *Mem:* Music Critics Asn. *Mailing Add:* Music Dept New York Times 229 W 43rd St New York NY 10036

RODBY, JOHN LEONARD
COMPOSER, PIANO
b Wahiawa, Oahu, Hawaii, Sept 14, 44. *Study:* Calif State Univ, Northridge, BA, 66; Calif State Univ, Long Beach, 66-68. *Works:* Festivals, 73, Variations for Orchestra, 73, Concerto for Saxophone and Orchestra, 73, Concerto for 29, 76, Septet, 82 & 5 Etudes for Piano, 82, Crystal Rec; Sextet, Harvey Pittel & Tex Brass Quintet, 82. *Pos:* Freelance keyboardist & arr-cond for TV, 68-; musical dir, Dinah Shore TV Show, NBC, 70-74, CBS, 74-80. *Bibliog:* Marshall King (auth), Getting Your Foot in the Door, Int Musician, 3/83. *Mem:* BMI; Am Fedn Musicians. *Mailing Add:* 5351 Penfield Ave Woodland Hills CA 91364

RODBY, WALTER
COMPOSER, WRITER
b Virginia, Minn, Sept 7, 17. *Study:* Northern Iowa Univ, BA, 40; Trinity Col Music, London, dipl, 46; Teachers Col, Columbia Univ, MA, 47; studied perf with Collegiate Chorale, New York & Royal Chorale Soc, London. *Works:* Song Triumphant; In Praise of Friday; Waltz for Two Left Feet; Goin' Down That Road; Shine on Me; Movin', Rollin'; High Upon the Mountain. *Pos:* Choral dir, pub sch, 41-49; choral ed & columnist, Sch Musician Mag, 53-; led Homewood-Flossmoor High Sch Choir, Ill on conct tour of Europe & Soviet Union, 70 & Europe, 73. *Teaching:* Chmn, Fine Arts Div, Flossmoor High Sch, Ill, 59-73; mem fac, Joliet Jr Col, formerly, Col St Francis, formerly & De Paul Univ, currently; teacher, choral wkshp in 11 states. *Mailing Add:* 819 Buell Ave Joliet IL 60435

RODDA, RICHARD EARL
CRITIC-WRITER, EDUCATOR
b Bloomingdale, NJ, June 26, 45. *Study:* Baldwin-Wallace Col, BME, 67; Case Western Reserve Univ, MA, 70, PhD, 78. *Pos:* Bass trombone, New Haven Symph Orch, 67-68; freelance trombonist, Cleveland, 68-; prog annotator, Dallas Symphony Orch, 80-; asst ed, Cleveland Orch, 82- *Teaching:* Lectr music hist, Case Western Reserve Univ, 72-; lectr trombone, Univ Akron, 76-77. *Mem:* Am Musicol Soc; Int Trombone Asn. *Interests:* Symphonies of Sir Michael Tippett. *Publ:* Auth, Genesis of a Symphony: Tippett's Symphony Number Three, Music Rev, 77; Liner Notes, Telarc Rec, 80; articles on various musical subjects, Stagebill, 82- *Mailing Add:* 3983 Rosemond Rd Cleveland Heights OH 44121

RODRIGUEZ, JOSE
VIOLA
b Barcelona, Spain, Apr 20, 17; US citizen. *Study:* Consv Super Munic Musica, Barcelona, Spain, MA, 50; study viola with F Riddle, 51. *Pos:* Viola player, Barcelona String Quartet, 41-55; Munic Orch, Barcelona, 43-55, Opera House, Barcelona, 43-55 & Pittsburgh Symph Orch, 67-; prin viola, Nat Orch Ecuador, 55-58 & Birmingham Symph, 58- *Mailing Add:* 706 Wimbledon Rd Pittsburgh PA 15239

RODRIGUEZ, ROBERT XAVIER
COMPOSER, CONDUCTOR & MUSIC DIRECTOR
b San Antonio, Tex, Jun 28, 46. *Study:* Univ Tex, Austin, with Hunter Johnson, BM(comp), 64, MM(comp), 69; studied comp with Nadia Boulanger, 69-79; Berkshire Music Ctr, with Jacob Druckman, Bruno Maderna & Elliott Carter, 72; Univ Southern Calif, with Halsey Stevens, DMA(comp), 75. *Works:* Canto, 73 & 81 & Piano Concerto III, 74, comn by Orion Chamber Orch; Sinfonia Concertante, comn by Los Angeles Chamber Orch, 74; Favola Boccaccesca, comn by Dallas Symph Orch, 79 & 82; Estampie, comn by Dallas Ballet, 80; Suor Isabella, comn by Nat Endowment Arts, 82; Oktoechos, comn by Dallas Symph Orch, 83. *Pos:* Comp in res, Dallas Symph Orch, 82- *Teaching:* Instr, Univ Southern Calif, 73-75; assoc prof music & dir collegium musicum, Univ Tex, Dallas, 78- *Awards:* Prix Comp Musicale, Prince Pierre Monaco, 71; Prix Lili Boulauger, 74; Guggenheim Fel, 76; Goddard Lieberson Award, Am Acad & Inst Arts & Lett, 81. *Bibliog:* Kennan (auth), Counterpoint, Prentice-Hall, 72; Rosenstiel (auth), Nadia Boulanger, Norton, 82. *Mem:* ASCAP. *Publ:* Auth, Atonal Music, 82 & Nadia Boulanger, 83, Am String Teacher. *Mailing Add:* 531 Winchester Dr Richardson TX 75080

RODRIQUEZ, SANTIAGO
PIANO
b Cardenas, Cuba, Feb 16, 52; US citizen. *Study:* Univ Tex, Austin, BM, 73; Juilliard Sch, MM, 75. *Pos:* Conct pianist, 75- *Teaching:* Prof music, Univ Md, College Park, 80- *Awards:* Second Prize, Walter W Naumburg Int Piano Compt, 75; Silver Medal, Van Cliburn Int Piano Compt, 81; Avery Fisher Career Grant, 82. *Mailing Add:* c/o Robert Levin Assoc Inc 250 W 57th St Suite 1332 New York NY 10107

ROE, CHARLES RICHARD
TEACHER, BARITONE
b Cleveland, Ohio, May 24, 40. *Study:* Baldwin-Wallace Col, BM, 63; Univ Ill, MM, 64; Univ Mich, 70-73. *Roles:* Bass solos in Messiah, Detroit Symph, 72; Eisenstein in Die Fledermaus, 74-, Nerone in Coronation of Poppea, 74 & Papageno in Magic Flute, 77, New York City Opera; Figaro in Barber of Seville, Mich Opera Theatre, 75; baritone solos in Carmina Burana, New York Choral Soc, 80. *Teaching:* Instr, Tex Tech Univ, 64-68; asst prof, Eastern Mich Univ, 68-74; assoc prof, Univ Southern Calif, 79- *Mem:* Am Guild Musical Artists; Actors Equity; Nat Asn Teachers Singing. *Mailing Add:* 720 Fay Glendale CA 91206

ROEBUCK, KAREN LEE
CELLO
b Cornwall, NY, Oct 15, 56. *Study:* Univ Ariz, BA(music), 80. *Pos:* Asst prin cello, Omaha Symph, 79-; assoc prin cello, Nebr Sinfonia, 79-; cellist, Omaha String Quartet, 79- & Colo Music Fest, Boulder, summer 82 & 83. *Mailing Add:* c/o Omaha Symph 310 Aquila Ct Omaha NE 68102

ROECKLE, CHARLES ALBERT
ADMINISTRATOR, EDUCATOR
b St Louis, Mo, Nov 6, 42. *Study:* St Louis Inst Music, BMus, 64; Univ Tex, Austin, MMus, 66, PhD, 78. *Pos:* Clarinetist & bass clarinetist, Austin Symph Orch, Tex, 64-66 & 69-; exec asst, Tex State Solo Ens Cont, Austin, 69-72. *Teaching:* Asst dir bands, Harlingen Independent Sch Dist, Tex, 66-67; instr music, St Martin's Col, Wash, 67-69; lectr musicol, Univ Tex, Austin, 77-, asst dean, Col Fine Arts, 80- *Mem:* Am Musicol Soc; Am Soc 18th Century Studies; SCent Soc 18th Century Studies; Am Fedn Musicians. *Mailing Add:* 10208 Willfield Dr Austin TX 78753

ROETTGER, DORYE
CRITIC-WRITER, ADMINISTRATOR
b Utica, NY, Oct 22, 32. *Study:* Univ Extension Consv Chicago, BMus, 55; Univ Eastern Fla, PhD, 72; Ithaca Col; Palmer Inst; Utica Sch Commerce. *Pos:* Founder & dir, Fest Players Calif, 57; dir, Chamber Music with Commentary, KPFK, Nat Pac Radio, 5 yrs; oboist, conct, theatre, film & rec studios, symph, opera, recitals & nat tours; adjudicator, Nat Fedn Music Club Stillman-Kelley Auditions; musicol, Inner City Cult Ctr, Orange Co Symph, Los Angeles Museum Natural Hist, Los Angeles County Sch; lectr, Music and People: A Survey of World Cultures; syndicated columnist, Bridging the Cultural Gap. *Teaching:* Instr chamber music, Immaculate Heart Col. *Awards:* Nat Fedn Music Clubs Award. *Mem:* Nat Fedn Music Clubs; Am Fedn Musicians; Am Musicol Soc; Calif Music Coun; Int Platform Asn. *Publ:* Contribr, Music Educr J, Sounding Board, Overture & Los Angeles Times. *Mailing Add:* 3809 DeLongpre Ave Los Angeles CA 90027

ROFE, PETER MICHAEL
DOUBLE BASS
b Los Angeles, Calif, Aug 26, 51. *Study:* Univ Calif, Los Angeles, with Peter Mercurio, BA, 73; Music Acad of West. *Pos:* Prin bass, San Diego Symph & San Diego Opera, 73- *Mailing Add:* 660 Torrance San Diego CA 92103

ROGELL, IRMA
HARPSICHORD, LECTURER
b Boston, Mass. *Study:* Radcliffe Col, AB. *Rec Perf:* Jordan Hall, Live, Ars Antique Rec Co, 70; Songs of Celebration, Ars Antique Rec Co, 73; Sounds of Celebration, Prestone Rec, 77; La Tomba di Scarlatti, Titanic Rec, 83. *Pos:* Harpsicordist, Camerate Boston Museum Fine Arts, 60-66. *Teaching:* Harpsicord dept, Longy Sch Music, 60-69; adj prof music, York Col, City Univ New York, 73-78; lectr, Ethical Cult Sch, 78-82. *Mem:* Young Musicians Club NY; Piano Teachers Congress NY (secy, 79-82); Col Music Soc; Harvard Club NY. *Mailing Add:* 165 West End Ave New York NY 10023

ROGERS, CALVIN Y
EDUCATOR, CONDUCTOR
b Pittsburgh, Pa, Nov 22, 22. *Study:* Consv Music, Oberlin Col, BMus, 43, MMus, 48; Univ Mich, 52-56; Domaine Sch, with Pierre Monteux, 56-60. *Pos:* Concertmaster & assoc cond, Akron Symph, 50-66 & Lakeside Summmer Symph, 75-; ed, Triad, Ohio Music Educ Asn, 56-60; cond, Wooster Symph, 66-68 & Ashland Symph, 79-81. *Teaching:* Prof music, Ashland Col, 48-, chmn music dept, 48-81. *Awards:* Distinguished Serv Award, Ohio Music Educ Asn, 75; First Prize, Spittal Int Chorbewerb, 81. *Mem:* Music Educr Nat Conf; Ohio Music Educ Asn; Am Choral Dir Asn. *Mailing Add:* 1005 Country Club Lane Ashland OH 44805

ROGERS, DELMER DALZELL
WRITER, EDUCATOR
b Spokane, Wash, Sept 7, 28. *Study:* Univ Southern Calif, with John Crown & Halsey Stevens, BM, 52, MM(piano), 53; Ind Univ, 58; Univ Mich, with Hans David & Louise Cuyler, PhD(musicol), 67. *Teaching:* Instr piano, privately, 50-78; from asst to assoc prof theory, Univ Tex, Austin, 63- *Mem:*

Am Musicol Soc (southwest chap secy-treas, 76-78); Am Studies Asn; Soc Ethnomusicol; Soc Music Theory; Sonneck Soc. *Interests:* History of American music; music theory of the 19th and 20th centuries. *Publ:* Ed, Theory Corner (series), Southwestern Musician & Tex Music Educr, 68-70; auth, Public Music Performances in New York, 1800-1850, Yearbook VI, 70; Memorial Tribute to Lota May Spell (1885-1972), Yearbook X, 74; ten biographical articles of American composers, Acad Am Encycl, 81; George Frederick Bristow, In: New Grove Dict Music & Musicians, 82. *Mailing Add:* 5601 Ridge Oak Dr Austin TX 78731

ROGERS, ETHEL TENCH
COMPOSER, TEACHER
b Newark, NJ, Feb 21, 14. *Study:* Baker Univ, Austrian-Am Sch, Vienna, 77. *Works:* Valse Romantique (two pianos—four hands), Borton Music, 64; Jesus Is Born, 64 & Behold the Empty Tomb, 65, Lillenas; In the Sanctuary (organ), 71 & Audition Solos (organ), 71, Pro-Art & Belwin Mills; Blessed Little One, Lillenas, 78; Young Organist Bartok, Hanser, 83. *Teaching:* Private piano, synthesizer, organ & harmony, 28- *Mem:* Int Asn Organ Teachers; Kansas City Musical Club. *Mailing Add:* 5700 Reinhardt Dr Shawnee Mission KS 66205

ROGERS, JOHN E
COMPOSER, EDUCATOR
b Dallas, Tex, Feb 20, 38. *Study:* Univ Ga; Yale Univ, with Halsey Stevens & Elliott Carter; Princeton Univ, with Milton Babbitt & Roger Sessions, MM, 64. *Works:* Rotational Arrays (woodwind quintet); Electronic Study; Canonic Structures (comput-generated sound). *Teaching:* Mem fac, Bowdoin Col, 64-67; assoc prof music, Univ NH, 67- *Awards:* BMI Student Comp Awards. *Mailing Add:* 7 Bartlett Rd Durham NH 03824

ROGERS, PATSY
COMPOSER, EDUCATOR
b New York, NY, Jan 19, 38. *Study:* Smith Col; Bennington Col, BA(music), 60, MA(music), 62. *Works:* Concerto for Tenor Violin & Large Orch, comn by Catgut Acoust Soc, 74; Chamber Opera, Nat Pub Radio, 81; Ballet, How the Elephant Got Its Trunk, 79; 3 Songs--Poems by Adrienne Rich, comn & perf by Lucille Field, 80; Threads—A Study in Percussion Sonorites, comn & perf by G James, 80; For Betty Crocker (choral), comn by Anna Crusis Choir, 82; Sonja, comn & perf by Wendy Hill, 83. *Teaching:* Instr music, Mannes Col Music, Brooklyn Col, Keene State Col, UN Int Sch, Univ Mass, New Lincoln Sch & others, formerly; instr comp, piano & guitar, privately. *Awards:* Residency, Chamber Music Conf & Comp Forum, 78; Perf Award for Chamber Opera, 1st Nat Cong Women in Music, 81; Gladys Turk Award, Los Angeles Womens Community Chorus, 82. *Mem:* Catgut Acoust Soc; BMI; Music Educr Nat Conf; Am Music Ctr; Int League Women Comp. *Mailing Add:* 315 4th St New Suffolk NY 11956

ROGERS, RODNEY IRL
COMPOSER, EDUCATOR
b Wilmer, Minn, June 10, 53. *Study:* Univ Iowa, BM, 75, PhD, 81; Ariz State Univ, MM, 78. *Works:* April Hello, Alexander Broude, 77; Toccato di fiori oscuri, Margun Music, 82; Lucis Creator, 82; Alleluia Sing the Stars, 82 & Breath (wie ein Hauch), 82, Assoc Music Publ. *Teaching:* Lectr comp, La State Univ, 80-82; asst prof, Lawrence Univ, 82- *Awards:* BMI Award, 75, 76 & 77. *Mem:* BMI; Am Soc Univ Comp; Am Comp Alliance. *Mailing Add:* Dept Music Lawrence Univ Appleton WI 54912

ROGERS, WILLIAM FORREST
EDUCATOR, LECTURER
b Lumberton, NC. *Study:* Columbia Univ, MA, 68, MEd, 71, DEd, 74. *Teaching:* Supvr & teacher, Harlem Sch Arts, 71-73; music & recreational therapist, Inst Rehabilitation, NY Univ, 72-73; assoc prof piano, supvr & dir piano prog, Hampton Inst, 73-; vis scholar, Teachers Col, Columbia Univ, 81. *Awards:* Steinway Scholar, Steinway & Co, 81. *Mem:* Int Piano Found; Music Educr Nat Conf; Va Music Teachers Asn. *Publ:* Auth, The Piano Keyboard—A Discovery in Performance and Practice, Hampton Inst Press, 83. *Rep:* 348 Woodland Rd Hampton VA 23669. *Mailing Add:* PO Box 6607 Hampton Inst Hampton VA 23668

ROLANDI, GIANNA
SOPRANO
b New York, NY, Aug 16, 52. *Study:* Curtis Inst Music, BM, 74, opera cert, 75. *Roles:* Sophie in Rosenkavalier, Metropolitan Opera, 79; Amina in Sonvambula, Spoleto Fest, 80; Cleopatra in Julius Ceasar, New York City Opera, 80; Lerbinetta in Ariadne auf Naxos, Glyndebourne Fest, England, 81; Elvire in Puritani, 81 & Lucia in di Lammermon, 82, New York City Opera; Olympia in Tales of Hoffman, Metropolitan Opera, 83. *Awards:* Grants, Nat Opera Inst, 75 & Rockefeller Found, 76. *Mem:* Am Guild Musical Artists. *Mailing Add:* c/o Columbia Artists Mgt Inc 165 W 57th St New York NY 10019

ROLDAN, NANCY
PIANO, EDUCATOR
b Mendoza, Arg, July 15, 39; US citizen. *Study:* Sch Music, Nat Univ Cuyo, Arg, 59-62; Consv Music PR, BA(piano perf), 71; Peabody Consv Music, MM(piano), 76. *Rec Perf:* Three Argentinian Dances (A Ginastera), 72, Three Pieces (A Ginastera), 72 & Toccata (J J Castro), 72, Phonalex, Arg. *Teaching:* Prof piano, Consv Music PR, 67-74 & Peabody Consv Music, Johns Hopkins Univ, 76-; prof music & dir cult activ, Bayamon Col, Univ PR, 71-74; guest lectr piano, Hood Col, 78-79. *Awards:* Second Prize, piano perf, Ital Cult Ctr Olivos, Buenos Aires, 62; First Prize, musical interpretation, Sch Music, Nat Univ Cuyo, Arg, 70; Gold Medal, piano perf, Logia Cosmos No 62, PR, 71. *Rep:* Cheops Mgt 3109 Keswick Rd Baltimore MD 21211. *Mailing Add:* 5617 Knell Ave Baltimore MD 21206

ROLLIN, ROBERT
COMPOSER, WRITER
b New York, NY, Feb 16, 47. *Study:* City Col New York, with Mark Brunswick, BA, 68; Cornell Univ, with Robert Palmer & Karel Husa, MFA, 71, DMA, 73; Darmstadt & Hochschule Musik, Hamburg, with Gyorgy Ligeti, 76 & 77. *Works:* Two Pieces for Solo Flute, 69 & Seven Sound-Images on Seven Stanzas by a Child, 71, Galaxy Music Corp; Aquarelles, 72, Reflections on Ruin by the Sea, 75, Two Jazz Moods, 80, Concerto Pastorale, 83 & Three Western Sound-Images, 83, Seesaw Music Corp. *Rec Perf:* Reflections on Ruin by the Sea, Redwood Rec, 76. *Teaching:* Asst prof theory & piano, Otterbein Col, 72-73; asst prof theory & cond instrm ens, NCent Col, Ill, 73-77; asst prof theory & comp, Youngstown State Univ, 77-83, assoc prof, 83- *Awards:* Comp Grant, Nat Endowment Arts, 76; fel, German Acad Exchange Serv, 77; Serious Music Comp Awards, ASCAP, 80-83. *Mem:* Am Soc Univ Comp (chmn Midwest & mem nat coun, 79-82); Ohio Fedn Music Clubs; Nat Music Coun; ASCAP; Cleveland Comp Guild. *Publ:* Auth, A Report of the Proceedings of the Internationales Musikinstitut Darmstadt, West Germany, July 1976, In Theory Only, 76; Some Younger European Composers, Musical Quart, 80; Ligeti's Lontano: Traditional Canonic Technique in a New Guise, Music Rev, 80; Approaches for the Analysis of Compositional Procedures in Sound Mass Compositions, 83 & A Categorical Approach to Rhythmic Analysis in Sound Mass, 83, Am Soc Univ Comp. *Mailing Add:* 536 Pierce Dr Youngstown OH 44511

ROMAN, MARY BRIGID
HARP
b Rochester, NY. *Study:* Eastman Sch Music, BM, 66, MM, 68. *Pos:* Second harpist, Rochester Phil Orch, 66-68; prin harpist, Albany Symph Orch, Ga, 80- & Tallahassee Symph Orch, 81- *Teaching:* Assoc prof, Sch Music, Fla State Univ, Tallahassee, 68- *Mem:* Am Harp Soc (southeastern dir, 73-79, pres Tallahassee chap, 73-, dir at large, 81-83); United Kingdom Harpists Asn. *Mailing Add:* Sch Music Fla State Univ Tallahassee FL 32306

ROMANO, KEITH
COUNTERTENOR
b Port Jefferson, NY. *Study:* Manhattan Sch Music, BM; vocal study with Cornelius Reid, Oren Brown & Maria Farnsworth. *Rec Perf:* Plays of St Nicholas, 81 & Songs of Glinka & Tchaikovsky, 83, Musical Heritage Soc. *Roles:* Messiah, St Luke's Chamber Ens; Giulio Cesare, Chicago Opera Repty Theatre; Israel in Egypt, Ft Wayne Phil; Plays of St Nicholas, Ens Early Music; A Midsummer Night's Dream, Royal Ballet Can; Cantata for Tenor and Countertenor, Somerset Col; Samson, Philadelphia Chamber Chorus. *Pos:* Perf, Musica Sacra Chorus, NY Choral Artists & Cathedral Singers. *Mem:* Am Fedn TV & Radio Artists; Am Guild Musical Artists. *Mailing Add:* c/o J Y Jeter 171 W 80th St New York NY 10024

ROMANUL, MICHAEL (FRANCIS)
CELLO
b Philadelphia, Pa, 1956. *Study:* Boston Univ, BMus, 78, MMus, 80. *Pos:* Asst prin cello, Fla Symph Orch, Orlando, 82- *Mailing Add:* 90 Clinton Rd Brookline MA 02146

ROMEO, JAMES JOSEPH
COMPOSER, EDUCATOR
b Rochester, NY, Mar 5, 55. *Study:* Mich State Univ, with Jere Hutcheson & David Liptak, BM, 77, MM, 78. *Works:* Toccata (five & seven tuned pianos), 77; Four Egyptian Death Songs (sop & chamber group), 78; Why Must I Speak in Puzzles (tape & timpani), 78; The Orbit of 3 Astral Spheres (trombone & tape), 78; Fantasia Profundis (organ), 79; Concert Rhapsody (flute & piano), 79; Crystalline (solo flute). *Pos:* Guest artist & lectr, NMex Music Fest, 80. *Teaching:* Dir new music groups, New Music Ens, Bowling Green State Univ, 78-79; mem fac, Univ Akron, currently. *Awards:* Grant, Wurlitzer Found, 80. *Mailing Add:* Dept Music Univ Akron Akron OH 44325

ROMERO, ANGEL
GUITAR, TEACHER
b Malaga, Spain, Aug 17, 46; US citizen. *Study:* With Celedonio Romero. *Rec Perf:* Eugene Ormandy Philadelphia Orch, TV, 75; Classical Virtuoso, 76 & Spanish Virtuoso, 76, Angel Rec; Rodrigo: Con de Aranjuez, 77, Tedesco & Torrobo, 81 & Guiliani Concert, 82, EMI; Arthur Fielder & Boston Pops, PBS, 78; and many others. *Pos:* Recitalist & soloist with orchs worldwide, 62- *Teaching:* Guest lectr guitar master classes, worldwide, 62- *Bibliog:* New Records, Time Mag, 4/21/76; Janis May (auth), Angel Romero, Class Guitar, 9/83; articles in Stereo Review, 77-80. *Mem:* Am Fedn Musicians. *Rep:* R Douglas Sheldon Div Columbia Artist Mgt 165 W 57th St New York NY 10019. *Mailing Add:* 2132 Pinar Pl Del Mar CA 92014

ROMERO, CELEDONIO P
GUITAR, COMPOSER
b Malaga, Spain, Apr 2, 18. *Study:* Real Consv Madrid; Real Consv Malaga; Royal Consv Malaga, Madrid; studied with Joaquin Turina, Angel Barrios & Rivera Pons. *Works:* Three Fantasias; Concierto de Malaga for Guitar and Orchestra; Suite Andaluza (Soleares, Alegrias, Tango, Zapateado & Fantasia) for Guitar; Tango Angela for Piano; Malaguenas for Guitar; Zapateado Clasico for Guitar; 22 Preludes (guitar). *Rec Perf:* On Philips & Mercury. *Pos:* Conct guitarist worldwide, 60-; founder & mem, The Romeros Classical Guitar Quartet. *Mem:* ASCAP. *Mailing Add:* c/o Columbia Artists Mgt 165 W 57th St New York NY 10019

ROMERSA, HENRY JOHN
EDUCATOR, TROMBONE
b Latrobe, Pa, Nov 4, 32. *Study:* Eastern Ky Univ, BA, 54; Oberlin Consv, MMusEd, 55; Eastman Sch Music, with Emory Remmington. *Pos:* Founder & dir, Int Trombone Wkshp, 71-79; nat exec dir, Nat Acad Rec Arts & Sci Inst, 71-73. *Teaching:* Asst prof, Cornell Univ, 55-61, Univ Md, 61-62, Peabody Consv Music, Vanderbilt Univ, 62-79 & Southern Ill Univ, 79- *Awards:* Billboard Trendsetter Award, 73. *Mailing Add:* 4911 Tanglewood Dr Nashville TN 37216

ROMINE, ROBERT LEE
MUSIC DIRECTOR, EDUCATOR
b Osceola, Iowa, Nov, 30, 30. *Study:* Northeast Mo State Univ, BS(music educ), 52, MA(music educ), 59; Univ Iowa, with H Voxman & E Gordon, PhD(music educ), 73. *Teaching:* Instr instrm music, Iowa City pub sch, 65-68 & Dept Defense Sch, Frankfurt, Ger, 68-74; dir bands, Pembroke State Univ, 74-, chmn music dept, 80- *Mem:* Col Band Dir Nat Asn; Int Trumpet Guild; Music Educr Nat Conf; Nat Band Asn; NC Music Educr Asn. *Mailing Add:* 251 Kensington Lumberton NC 28358

ROMITI, RICHARD A
COMPOSER, EDUCATOR
b Woonsocket, RI, Sept 6, 49. *Study:* Sch Arts, Boston Univ, studied comp with Gardner Read, MB(music), 71, MM(music), 75; Univ Toronto, studied comp with Lothar Klein & John Weinzweig, DMus, 82. *Works:* Tantara (brass octet & perc), 75; Concerto for Accordion, Strings, Harp & Percussion, 75; Suite for Flute & Harp, Southern Music Co, 76; Eight Haiku Songs (sop, flute, cello & harp), 76; Exchanges (oboe & harpsichord), 76; Sonic Eclipse (accordion & cello), comn by Joseph Petric, 80; Palingenesis (flute & small orch), 82. *Teaching:* Instr music, Univ Toronto, 76-77; lectr, Providence Col, 78- *Awards:* First Prize, for Suite for Flute & Harp, Pittsburgh Flute Club Int Compt, 75; fel, Univ Toronto, 75-76; RI State Coun Arts Grant, 79. *Mem:* Am Soc Univ Comp; Am Music Ctr; Col Music Soc. *Mailing Add:* 471 Village Rd Woonsocket RI 02895

ROMO, GILDA CRUZ See Cruz-Romo, Gilda

RONDELLI, BARBARA (ANN)
SOPRANO, EDUCATOR
b Pittsburg, Kans, Oct 19, 39. *Study:* Pittsburg State Univ, BMus(voice), 60, MMus(voice), 78; Royal Acad Music, London, England, lic dipl (perf & teaching singing), 62. *Rec Perf:* Die Bach Kantate, Claudius Verlag, 71; Faun und Schäferin Op 2 (Stravinsky) & Jimenez Kantate (Genzmer), Colosseum-Colos, 72; Bach Cantatas, Musical Heritage Soc, 79. *Roles:* Micaela in Carmen, Frankfurt State Opera, 68; Aminta in Silent Woman, 68, Fiordiligi in Cosi fan tutte, 69 & Elsa in Lohengrin, 69, Wuppertal Opera; Madama Butterfly, New York City Opera, 69, Honolulu Opera, 70 & Düsseldorf State Opera, 71. *Pos:* First lyr sop, Opera House Lübek, Germany, 64-66, State Opera, Saarbrücken, 66-68 & Wuppertal State Opera, 68-71; guest soloist, New York City Opera, Honolulu Opera, Frankfort Opera & Düsseldorf Opera, 69-83. *Teaching:* Assoc prof voice, Univ Toledo, 75- *Awards:* Fulbright Scholar, London Royal Acad Music, 60-62; Prizewinner, Bavarian Radio Int Compt, Germany, 65; Prizewinner, Tchaikowsky Int Compt, Russia, 66. *Mem:* Nat Asn Teachers Singing; Ohio Music Teachers Asn; Music Teachers Nat Asn; Col Music Soc. *Mailing Add:* 5036 Breezeway Dr Toledo OH 43613

RONSHEIM, JOHN RICHARD
COMPOSER, EDUCATOR
b Cadiz, Ohio, Feb 17, 27. *Study:* New England Consv Music, BM, 52, MM, 54; studied with Luigi Dallapiccola, 57-60; Univ Iowa, 63-65. *Works:* Fragment, Boelke Bomart Mobart, 64; Easter Wings, 64 & Bitter-Sweet, 69, APNM; Love (in press). *Teaching:* Prof music, Antioch Col, 67- *Awards:* Grant, Nat Endowment Arts, 75. *Mailing Add:* 225 W Limestone St Yellow Springs OH 45387

RONSON, RAOUL R
ADMINISTRATOR, PUBLISHER
b Fiume, Italy, Mar 22, 31; US citizen. *Study:* Univ Rome, Italy, DFA, 51; New Sch Social Res, MA, 56; Inst Advanced Int Studies, Univ Miami, 67-68; NY Univ, 74. *Pos:* Producer, doc films, 59- & class music rec, 63-; pres, Seesaw Music Corp & Okra Music Corp, 63-, Ulsyra Prod Corp, 63- & Comp Press, 72-76. *Teaching:* Docent music, various Am univs & consv, 65- *Publ:* Contribr various mag articles worldwide & concert & record reviews. *Mailing Add:* 2067 Broadway Suite 58 New York NY 10023

ROOP, EDYTH WAGNER See Wagner, Edyth

ROOS, JAMES (MICHAEL)
CRITIC
b Chicago, Ill, May 12, 44. *Study:* Univ Ill, BA, 66; Mich State Univ, MA, 69; Univ Southern Calif, with Irving Kolodin & Virgil Thomson, 69-71; studied with Victor Aitay. *Pos:* Asst ed, Saturday Review & Lincoln Ctr Prog, 70-71; music ed, Miami Herald, 71- *Awards:* Rockefeller Found Fel, 69-70; Am Dance Critic Conf Fel, Nat Endowment Arts, 70. *Mailing Add:* c/o Miami Herald No 1 Herald Plaza Miami FL 33101

ROOSEVELT, JOSEPH WILLARD
COMPOSER, PIANO
b Madrid, Spain, Jan 16, 18; US citizen. *Study:* Harvard Col, 36-37; study with Nadia Boulanger, Paris & Gargenville, 38-39; New York Col Music, 45-46;

Hartt Col Music, Univ Hartford, BMus, 59, MMus, 60. *Works:* Sonata for Violin & Piano, 52, May Song it Flourish, 60, Concerto for Cello & Orch, 63, Amistad-Homenaje al gran Morel Campos, 65, And the Walls Came Tumbling Down, 76, Our Dead Brothers Bid Us Think of Life, 76 & An American Sampler, 76, Am Comp Alliance. *Teaching:* Instr theory, Hartt Col Music, Univ Hartford, 59-60; lectr music hist, Columbia Univ, New York, 61 & Fairleigh Dickinson Univ, Teaneck, 64-67; asst prof comp, New York Col Music, 66-68. *Mem:* Am Music Ctr; Am Comp Alliance. *Mailing Add:* Box 72 Fox Rd Sandisfield MA 01255

ROOSEVELT, OLIVER WOLCOTT, JR
CRITIC
b New York, NY, Mar 2, 27. *Study:* Harvard Univ, BA(music), 48. *Pos:* Lively Arts ed & music critic, Birmingham News, Ala, 67- *Teaching:* Instr music appreciation, Univ Ala, 75-; adj prof, Birmingham Southern Col, 80- *Mem:* Music Critics Asn. *Mailing Add:* 500 Wood Acres Lane Birmingham AL 35226

ROOT, DEANE LESLIE
EDUCATOR, LIBRARIAN
b Wausau, Wis, Aug 9, 47. *Study:* New Col, BA, 68; Univ Ill, Urbana-Champaign, MMus, 71, PhD, 77. *Pos:* Ed popular music, New Grove Dict, 74-76; res assoc, Univ Ill, Urbana-Champaign, 76-80; curator, Stephen Foster Mem, Univ Pittsburgh, 82- *Teaching:* Lectr music hist, Univ Wis, Madison, 73; inst humanities, Lake City Community Col, 81-82; asst prof musicol, Univ Pittsburgh, 82- *Awards:* Res book of the year, Music Libr Asn, 83. *Mem:* Sonneck Soc (mem bd, 79-80); Am Muiscol Soc; Music Libr Asn; Int Asn Study Popular Music; Soc Ethnomusicol. *Interests:* American music bibliography; Stephen C Foster; music in society; musical theater. *Publ:* Auth, The Pan American Association of Composers (1928-1934), Yearbk Int Am Music Res, 72; Am Popular Stage Music, 1860-1880, UMI Res Press, 81; coauth, Resources of American Music History: A Directory ... , Univ of Ill Press, 81; auth, Music of Florida Historic Sites, Fla State Univ, 83; ed, Music of Theater, Am Music J, Univ Ill Press (in prep). *Mailing Add:* 5703 Forbes Ave Pittsburgh PA 15217

ROOT, REBECCA JO
FRENCH HORN, TEACHER
b Pigeon, Mich, Aug 14, 51. *Study:* Eastman Sch Music, with Verne Reynolds, 69-70; study with Arnold Jacobs, 73- *Pos:* Third horn, Denver Symph, 70-73; prin horn, New Orleans Symph, 73-78, Chautauqua Symph, summers 74- & Rochester Phil, 81- *Teaching:* Instr horn, Nat Music Camp, Interlochen, Mich, 73, Chautauqua Music Sch, 74- & Columbus Col, 78-81. *Mem:* Int Horn Soc. *Publ:* Auth, Psychology of Brass Playing, Horn Call, 75 & Brass Bulletin, 75; So You Want To Be A Horn Player?, Horn Call, 78. *Mailing Add:* 47 Sweet Birch Lane Rochester NY 14615

ROREM, NED
COMPOSER, WRITER
b Richmond, Ind, Oct 23, 23. *Study:* Am Consv, with Leo Sowerby; Northwestern Univ, 40-42; Curtis Inst, 43; Berkshire Music Ctr, 46-47; Juilliard Sch Music, with Bernard Wagenaar, BA, 46, MA, 48; studied with Virgil Thomson & Aaron Copland; Northwestern Univ, Hon DFA, 77. *Works:* Miss Julie, 65; War Scenes, 69; Day Music and Night Music for Violin, 72-73; Am Music for Orchestra, 75; Serenade (voice, violin, viola & piano), 75; Womens Voices, 75; A Quaker Reader for Organ, 76; The Nantucket Songs, 79; The Santa Fe Songs, 80; Winter Pages, 81. *Teaching:* Comp in res & Slee prof, State Univ NY, Buffalo; comp in res, Univ Utah, 65-66, prof comp, 65-67; fac mem, Curtis Inst Music, 80- *Awards:* Fulbright Fel, 51-52; numerous awards from Ford & Rockefeller Found; Pulitzer Prize Music, 76. *Mem:* Am Acad & Inst Arts & Letters; ASCAP; PEN. *Publ:* Music From Inside Out, 66; Music & People, 69; Critical Affairs, 70; Auth, Pure Contraption, 73; The Final Diary, 74; An Absolute Gift, 78; Setting the Tone, Coward-McCann Inc; The Paris and New York Diaries, NPoint Press. *Mailing Add:* c/o Curtis Inst Music 1726 Locust St Philadelphia PA 19103

RORICK, WILLIAM C(ALVIN)
LIBRARIAN, EDUCATOR
b Elyria, Ohio, June 23, 41. *Study:* Ohio Wesleyan Univ, BA, 63; Univ Utah, BM, 68; Northwestern Univ, MM, 70; Pratt Inst, MLS, 74; NY Univ, MA, 82. *Pos:* Cur, Perf Music Collection, ref asst & off mgr, Manhattan Sch Music Libr, New York, 70-74; music ref librn, Queens Col, City Univ New York, 74- *Teaching:* Asst prof, Queens Col, City Univ New York, 74- *Awards:* City Univ New York Res Found Award, 81-84. *Mem:* Music Libr Asn (pres, 83-); Am Musicol Soc; Asn Recorded Sound Collections; Sonneck Soc; Am Inst Verdi Studies. *Interests:* History of music publishing in New York City. *Publ:* Auth, Instrumental Methods and Studies, In: A Basic Music Libr: Essential Scores & Books, Am Libr Asn, 78; The Horatio Parker Archives in the Yale University Music Library, Fontes Artis Musicae, 10-12/79; Index to Record Reviews: Manufacturers' Numerical Index, Notes, Music Libr Asn, 81-; The A Major Violin Sonatas of Faure and Franck: A Stylistic Comparison, Music Review, 2/81; Galaxy Music Corporation: The First Fifty Years, Fontes Artis Musicae, 7-9/82. *Mailing Add:* Music Libr Queens Col City Univ New York Flushing NY 11367

ROSADO, ANA MARIA
GUITAR, EDUCATOR
b Santurce, PR, July 12, 54. *Study:* Univ PR, BA, 76; Ecole Normale Musique Paris, dipl, 79; Univ Paris VIII, MA(music ed), 80. *Teaching:* Instr, Univ PR, 81- & Int Am Univ, 82- *Awards:* Award of Merit, Asn Univ Grad Women PR, 76. *Bibliog:* Donald Thompson (auth), Musicological Research in Puerto Rico, Col Music Soc, 83. *Mailing Add:* Dept Music Box A-L Univ PR Rio Piedras PR 00931

ROSAND, AARON
VIOLIN, EDUCATOR
b Hammond Ind, Mar 15, 27. *Study:* Chicago Musical Col, dipl; Curtis Inst Music, with Leon Sammetini, William Primrose, Gregor Piatigorsky, Carlos Salzedo & Marcel Tabuteau. *Rec Perf:* On Vox, Candide, Turnabout, Columbia & Disques. *Pos:* Guest appearances, CBS-TV; recitalist & soloist with orchs. *Teaching:* Lectr & vis prof at US & foreign univ; Mischa Elman chair, Manhattan Sch Music, currently; artist in res, L'Acad d'Ete, Nice, summers currently; mem fac violin, Curtis Inst Music, 81- *Awards:* Merite Cult & Artistique, France; Ysaye Medal, Belgium. *Rep:* ICA Mgt 2219 Eastridge Rd Timonium MD 21093. *Mailing Add:* c/o Jacques Leiser Mgt 155 W 68th St New York NY 10023

ROSAND, ELLEN
EDUCATOR
b New York, NY, Feb 28, 40. *Study:* Vassar Col, BA, 61; Harvard Univ, MA, 64; NY Univ, PhD, 71. *Teaching:* Asst prof, Rutgers Univ, 77-80, assoc prof, 80- *Mem:* Am Musicol Soc (mem coun, 78-80); Renaissance Soc. *Interests:* Baroque music; Venetian music; history of Italian opera. *Publ:* Auth, Music in the Myth of Venice, Renaissance Quart, 77; Barbara Strozzi: The Composer's Voice, J Am Musicol Soc, 78; The Descending Tetrachord: An Emblem of Lament, Musical Quart, 79; In Defense of the Venetian Libretto, Studi Musicali, 80; L'Orfeo by Sartorio & Aureli, Ricordi, 83. *Mailing Add:* 560 Riverside Dr New York NY 10027

ROSE, C ROBERT
EDUCATOR, CLARINET
b Shelbyville, Ill, Nov 1, 42. *Study:* Southern Ill Univ, Carbondale, with Robert Resnick, BME, 64, MM, 66; Cath Univ Am, 68; Ind Univ, Bloomington, with Henry Gulick & Earl Bates, DM, 79; Peabody Consv, with Sidney Forrest; studied clarinet with Jerry Stowell & David Glazer. *Pos:* Clarinetist, US Marine Band, 67-71. *Teaching:* Instr woodwinds, hist & orch dir, Otterbein Col, 74-75; assoc prof woodwinds, cond & orch dir, Valparaiso Univ, 75-81; assoc prof clarinet, theory & lit, Lebanon Valley Col, 81- *Awards:* Presser Found Award, 62 & 63; Nat Educ Soc Phi Eta Sigma Award, 62; Pi Kappa Lambda Award, 66. *Mem:* Col Music Soc; Nat Asn Col Wind & Perc Instr; Int Clarinet Soc; Phi Mu Alph Sinfonia. *Mailing Add:* 21 S Lancaster St Annville PA 17003

ROSE, EARL ALEXANDER
PIANO, COMPOSER
b New York, NY, Sept 5, 46. *Study:* Vienna Acad Music, 67-68; Mannes Col Music, study piano with Edith Oppens & Francis Dillon, BS, 70. *Works:* Overnight Success, 78, Someone, Somewhere, 78 & Love Theme in Search of a Motion Picture, 80, Amadeus Music Co; Score for Thin Ice, CBS, 81; On My Own Again, 82, A Musical Trip Around the Orchestra, 82 & Contrasts for Piano & Orchestra, 82, Amadeus Music Co. *Rec Perf:* Grand Piano, Amadeus Rec, 76; Songs from Captain Kangaroo, Columbia Rec, 79; Solo, Gramavision Rec, 80. *Mem:* ASCAP; Nat Acad Rec Arts & Sci; Am Guild Authors & Comp. *Rep:* Columbia Artists Mgt Inc 165 W 57th St New York NY 10019. *Mailing Add:* c/o Franklin, Weinrib, Rudel & Vassale 950 3rd Ave New York NY 10022

ROSE, GRIFFITH WHEELER
COMPOSER
b Los Angeles, Calif, Jan 18, 36. *Study:* Study with Isidore Freed, Hartford, Wolfgang Fortner, Freiburg, Nadia Boulanger, Fontainebleau, Pierre Boulez, Basel & Karlheinz Stockhausen, Darmstadt. *Works:* Viola Concerto No 1, Theodore Presser, 74; Viola Concerto No 2, 76 & Le Mikado, Eds Jobert; Meme, Rencontres Int de Metz, 78; Epiphanies, Pour l'Ensemble de Flutes a Bec de Lyon, 82; Rhapsodies pour Flute, Commande de l'Etat, Ens 2EX2M, 83. *Mem:* ASCAP; Societe d'Auteurs, Compositeurs & Editeurs de Musique. *Mailing Add:* 8 Bis Rue Barthelemy Paris 75015 France

ROSE, JEROME H
PIANO, EDUCATOR
b Los Angeles, Calif, Aug 12, 38. *Study:* Mannes Col Music, BA, 60; Juilliard Sch Music, MA, 61. *Rec Perf:* Complete Liszt, Beethoven Sonatas & Schumann Sonatas, Vox; Schubert A Major, Sheffield Labs. *Pos:* Artistic dir, First London Int Fest Romantics, 81. *Teaching:* Artist res, Bowling Green State Univ, 63- *Awards:* Grand Prize, Busoni Compt, 61; Grand Prix du Disque, Liszt Soc, Budapest, 75; Nat Endowment Arts Award, 81. *Mem:* Am Music Teachers Asn; Am Liszt Soc. *Publ:* Auth, For the Young Virtuoso, Camerica, 83. *Mailing Add:* c/o Melvin Kaplan Inc 1860 Broadway New York NY 10023

ROSE, JOHN
EDUCATOR, ORGAN
b Gainesville, Ga, Apr 4, 48. *Study:* Wittenberg Univ, Springfield, Ohio; Rutgers Univ, BA, 72. *Rec Perf:* The French Romantics, Vols I-V, 79-83, The Organ at Pomona College, 79 & Introduction to the King of Instruments, 80, Towerhill Rec; plus many others. *Pos:* Music dir, Cathedral of Sacred Heart, Newark, NJ, 68-77; organist, Trinity Col, Hartford, Conn, 77-; sr organist, Cathedral St Joseph, Hartford, 83- *Teaching:* Instr organ, Upsala Col, EOrange, NJ, 70-71; Rutgers Univ, Newark, NJ, 70-75 & Trinity Col, Hartford, 77- *Awards:* Young Artist of Yr Award, Musical Am Mag, 74; Nat Endowment Arts Perf Grant, 83. *Bibliog:* Jack Gibbons Morris (auth), Through Hither, Thither, & Pietro Yon, NJ Music & Arts, 71; Dawn Lospaluto (auth), The Newarker: John Rose, Newark!, 75. *Mem:* Am Guild Organists. *Publ:* Auth, Strange Organs and Haunted Cathedrals, Music J, 75. *Rep:* Phillip Truckenbrod Conct Artists PO Box 14600 Hartford CT 06114. *Mailing Add:* 145 Terry Rd Hartford CT 06105

ROSE, LEONARD (JOSEPH)
CELLO, EDUCATOR

b Washington, DC, July 27, 18. *Study:* Curtis Inst Music, dipl, 38; Hartford Univ, Hon Dr, 65. *Rec Perf:* Saint Saens Concerto, 51, Brahms Double Concerto, 55 & 61, Schumann Concerto, 61, Dvorak Concerto & Tchaikowski Variations, 62, Entire Beethoven Piano Trios, 70-71 & Entire Brahms & Schubert Trios, 75, CBS. *Pos:* Solo cellist, Cleveland Orch, 39-43 & NY Phil, 43-51; ed, Int Music Co, formerly; soloist, 51- *Teaching:* Prof cello, Juilliard Sch, 47- & Curtis Inst Music, 51-62. *Mailing Add:* c/o ICM Artists Mgt Ltd 40 W 57 St New York NY 10019

ROSE, WILLIAM H
TUBA, EDUCATOR

b Owensboro, Ky, July 8, 26. *Study:* Parks Air Col Engineering; US Navy Sch Music; Juilliard Sch Music. *Rec Perf:* With Houston Symph Orch & Houston Brass Ens. *Pos:* Tubist, CBS Symph, NY, 47-48, Goldman Band, NY, 47-51, UN Symph, New York, 48-49, Houston Symph Orch, 49-, Houston Grand Opera, currently; charter mem, New York Brass Ens, 47-48. *Teaching:* Assoc prof brass ens & low brass, Univ Houston, currently. *Mem:* Tubists Universal Brotherhood Asn; Nat Asn Col Wind & Perc Instr; Tex Music Educr Asn. *Publ:* Contribr to Instrumentalist. *Mailing Add:* 1315 Friarcreek Ln Houston TX 77055

ROSEKRANS, CHARLES STETSON
CONDUCTOR

b San Francisco, Calif, Aug 4, 34. *Study:* Univ Calif, Berkeley, BA, 56; Mannes Sch Music, 58. *Pos:* Prin cond & music dir, Houston Grand Opera, 58-75; cond, Chautauqua Opera, 61-64, San Francisco Spring Opera, 63-66, Brevard Music Ctr, 65-72, Houston Ballet, 72-78, Theatre Under the Stars, Houston, 74-, NC Opera, 79- & Dallas Ballet, 79-; founder & cond, Houston Chamber Orch, 64-76; music dir & cond, Charlotte Opera, NC, 68-; guest cond orchs throughout US. *Rep:* Sardos Artists Mgt 180 West End Ave New York NY 10023. *Mailing Add:* 110 E 7th St Charlotte NC 28202

ROSEMAN, RONALD ARIAH
OBOE, COMPOSER

b Brooklyn, NY, Mar 15, 33. *Study:* Queens Col, City Univ New York, BA, 55. *Works:* Suite for Cello, Timothy Eddy, 73; Two Religious Songs, Laurentian Players, 76; Sonata for Two Oboes and Harpsichord, Roseman, Brewer & Robert Levin, 77; Three Psalms, Da Capo Players, 79; Fantasy for Bassoon, perf by Leonard Hindell with Waterloo Chamber Orch, 80; Concertino, Janus Ens, 82; Claire (oboe & perc), Stony Brook Contemp Chamber Players, 83. *Rec Perf:* Schumann Romances, 70, Sonata (Saint Saens), 72 & Sonata (Schuller), 73, Desto; Concerto (Haydn), Vox, 75; Oboe Sonatas (Handel), 71, E Flat Sonata (Telemann), 78 & Oboe Sonatas (Poulenc), 83, Nonesuch. *Pos:* Alto shawm, New York Pro Musica, 57-71; oboist, New York Woodwind Quintet, 61- & Bach Aria Group, 81-; prin oboist, Musica Sacra, 72- & Y Chamber Symph, 77-; actg co-prin oboe, New York Phil Orch, 73-74 & 77-78. *Teaching:* Artist in res, State Univ NY, Stony Brook, 69-; instr oboe & chamber music, Juilliard Sch, 73-; assoc prof, Sch Music, Yale Univ, 76-; prof, Aaron Copland Sch Music, Queens Col, City Univ New York, 83- *Mem:* Bohemians; BMI; Am Comp Alliance; founder, Int Double Reed Soc. *Rep:* Vera Michaelson 70 W 10 St New York NY 100003. *Mailing Add:* 156 W 86 St New York NY 10024

ROSEN, CHARLES
PIANO, WRITER

b New York, NY, May 5, 27. *Study:* Juilliard Sch Music; Princeton Univ, BA, 47, MA, 49, PhD, 51; studied piano with Moriz Rosenthal & Hedwig Kanner-Rosenthal, 38-45; Trinity Col, Dublin, Hon Dr Music, 76; Univ Leeds, Hon Dr Music, 76; Univ Durham, Hon Dr Music, 80. *Rec Perf:* Etudes (Debussy), 51; Movements (Stravinsky), 61; Davidsbündlertänze (Schumann), 63; Art of Fugue, Two Ricercars & Goldberg Variations (Bach), 71; Last Six Sonatas (Beethoven), 72; Piano Music (Boulez), Vol I; Double Concerto (Elliott Carter). *Teaching:* Asst prof modern lang, Mass Inst Tech, 53-55; prof music, State Univ NY, Stony Brook, 71-; Messenger lectr, Cornell Univ, 75; Ernest Bloch prof, Univ Calif, Berkeley, 77; Norton prof poetry, Harvard Univ, 80-81. *Awards:* Nat Book Award, 72; Deems Taylor Award, 72, 76 & 81; Edison Prize, Netherlands, 74. *Mem:* Nat Acad Arts & Sci. *Publ:* Auth, The Classical Style: Haydn, Mozart, Beethoven, Viking, 71, Norton, 72; Arnold Schoenberg, Viking, 75, Princeton Univ Press, 81; Sonata Form, Norton, 80; The Quandary of the Writing Pianist, New York Times, 1/17/82. *Mailing Add:* 101 W 78th St New York NY 10024

ROSEN, JEROME WILLIAM
COMPOSER, EDUCATOR

b Boston, Mass, July 23, 21. *Study:* Univ Calif, Berkeley, with William Denny & Roger Sessions, MA, 49; Mills Col, Paris, with Darius Milhaud, 49-50. *Works:* Petite Suite for Four Clarinets, Leblanc, 62; Five Pieces for Cello and Piano, 65; Three Songs for Chorus and Piano, 68; String Quartet No 1, Boosey & Hawkes, 75; Clarinet Concerto, Sacramento Symph, 76; Emperor Norton (musical play), 76; Calisto and Malibea (opera libretto by Edwin Honig), Univ Calif, Davis, 79. *Teaching:* Assoc prof music, Univ Calif, Davis, 57-63, prof, 63-, chmn dept, 60-63, 67-68 & 74-77. *Awards:* Fromm Found Grant, 54, 56 & 60; Guggenheim Fel, 58; Creative Arts Inst Fel, 66 & 72. *Mem:* Am Comp Alliance; Am Soc Univ Comp; Am Musicol Soc; Col Music Soc; Music Libr Asn. *Publ:* Contribr to New Grove Dict of Music & Musicians & Music Libr Asn Notes. *Mailing Add:* 502 12th St Davis CA 95616

ROSEN, JUDITH (BERENICE)
WRITER, LECTURER

b San Francisco, Calif, May 20, 33. *Study:* Univ Calif, Los Angeles, BA, 55. *Pos:* Coordr, various conf Women in Music, 74- *Mem:* Meet the Comp (bd mem, 83); Am Music Ctr Inc; Int League Women Comp; Int Cong Women Music (adv bd, 82); Am Women Comp Inc. *Interests:* Music by women composers. *Publ:* Auth, Why Haven't Women Become Great Composers?, High Fidelity, 72; Grazyna Bacewicz (1909-1969), Heresies, 80; contribr, The Musical Women, Greenwood Press, 83; six entries, In: New Grove Dict of Music in US (in prep). *Mailing Add:* 16613 Oldham Pl Encino CA 91436

ROSEN, MARCY (BETH)
CELLO

b Phoenix, Ariz, Dec 31, 56. *Study:* Univ Ariz, with Gordon Epperson, 69-72; study with Marcus Adeney, 71-72; Curtis Inst Music, with Orlando Cole, 72-77. *Rec Perf:* Boccherini Quintet, Op 25, No 4, Columbia Masterworks—Marlboro Music, 79; Boccherini Quintet, G 451, Marlboro Rec Soc, 80; Taneyev Piano Quartet, Pro Arte, 81; Boccherini Ensemble, Vol 1, 81 & Vol 2, 83, Nonesuch; Foss, Copland & Wyner, 83. *Pos:* Participant, Marlboro Music Fest—Music From Marlboro, 75-; cellist, St Lukes Chamber Ens, New York, 78- & Mendelssohn String Quartet, New York, 79-; first cellist, Boccherini Ens, 80- *Awards:* First Prize, Wash Int Compt, 79; Young Artist 81, Musical Am, 81. *Rep:* Sarah Tornay 127 W 72 St New York NY 10023. *Mailing Add:* 173 W 78 St New York NY 10024

ROSEN, MYOR
HARP, TEACHER

b New York, NY, May 28, 17. *Study:* Juilliard Sch Music, cert, 41. *Pos:* Prin harpist, Orquestta Sinfonica Mexico, 41-42, Indianapolis Symph Orch, 41-42, Minneapolis Symph Orch, 43-44 & New York Phil, 60-; harpist, CBS Radio, 45-47 & NBC Symph, 45-49. *Teaching:* Prof harp, Arthur Jordan Consv Music, 41-42 & DePauw Univ, 41-42; instr, Juilliard Sch Music, 47-69. *Mailing Add:* c/o New York Phil Avery Fisher Hall Broadway/65 New York NY 10023

ROSEN, NATHANIEL KENT
CELLO, EDUCATOR

b Altadena, Calif, June 9, 48. *Study:* Pasadena City Col, 65-67; Univ Southern Calif, MusB, 71. *Rec Perf:* Complete Cello & Piano Music by Chopin. *Pos:* Mem, Music From Marlboro Ens, formerly; prin cellist, Los Angeles Chamber Orch, 70-76 & Pittsburgh Symph, 77-79; soloist worldwide. *Teaching:* Asst, Univ Southern Calif, 68-75; asst prof, Calif State Univ, Northridge, 70-76; mem fac, Carnegie-Mellon Univ, formerly & Music Acad West, currently; mem fac cello, Manhattan Sch Music, 82- *Awards:* First Prize, Naumburg Compt, 77 & Moscow Tchaikovsky Compt, 78; Rockefeller Found Grant, 73-74. *Mem:* Violoncello Soc New York; Am Fedn Musicians. *Publ:* Contribr to Am String Teacher. *Rep:* Columbia Artists Mgt 165 W 57th St New York NY 10019. *Mailing Add:* 175 Riverside Dr New York NY 10024

ROSENBAUM, VICTOR
TEACHER, PIANO

b Philadelphia, Pa, Dec 19, 41. *Study:* Brandeis Univ, BM, 64; Princeton Univ, MFA, 67; studied piano with Rosina Lhevine & Leonard Shure, theory & comp with Roger Sessions, Edward T Cone, Earl Kim & Martin Boykan. *Works:* Work for chorus, chamber ens, solo voice & piano. *Rec Perf:* Rec with CRI. *Pos:* Cond orch, Brandeis Univ, Princeton Univ & Merrywood Music Sch, formerly; guest cond, New England Consv Symph Orch & New England Consv Contemp Ens, formerly; pianist, Indianapolis Symph Orch, Atlanta Symph Orch & Boston Pops, New York Town Hall, Tully Hall & tours throughout US, Japan, Brazil & with Vermeer String Quartet, Leonard Rose & Arnold Steinhardt. *Teaching:* Chmn piano dept, New England Consv, 72-80, dir chamber music, currently; chmn piano div, Eastern Music Fest, 79-; prof piano, Eastman Sch Music, 83- *Awards:* Winner, Nat Music Clubs Young Comp Award; Woodrow Wilson Fel, 64-65. *Mem:* Col Music Soc. *Mailing Add:* 152 Winthrop Rd Brookline MA 02146

ROSENBERG, DONALD SCOTT
CRITIC-WRITER, FRENCH HORN

b New York, NY, Nov 24, 51. *Study:* Mannes Col Music, horn with Paul Ingraham, BM, 75; Yale Sch Music, studied music criticism with Paul Hume, MMus, 76, MMA, 77. *Pos:* Participant, Marlboro Music Fest, Vt, summer 73; critic music & dance, Akron Beacon J, 77- *Awards:* NE Ohio Media Award, Akron Press Club, 83. *Publ:* Contribr, Szell: Portrait of a Perfectionist, Symph Mag, 80. *Mailing Add:* Akron Beacon Journal 44 E Exchange St Akron OH 44313

ROSENBERG, KENYON CHARLES
EDUCATOR, CRITIC

b Chicago, Ill, Sept 9, 33. *Study:* Univ Calif, Los Angeles, AB, 59; Chicago Sch Music, studied perc with Roy C Knapp & violin with Sasha Jacobson; Univ Southern Calif, MS, 61. *Pos:* Critic, B'nai B'rith Messenger, Los Angeles, 64-68 & Akron Beacon Jour, 71-72; contrib ed & class rec ed, Libr Jour, 70-78. *Teaching:* Assoc prof music hist & appreciation, Kent State Univ, 68-80. *Mem:* Music Critics Asn. *Interests:* History of performance techniques & recording. *Publ:* Contribr, Previews Mag & Sat Rev, 64-; auth, Best Classical Recordings of 1977, 78, Best Classical Recordings of 1978, 79 & Best Classical Recordings of 1979, 80, Libr Jour. *Mailing Add:* 6326 Mayapple Pl Alexandria VA 22312

ROSENBERGER, WALTER EMERSON
PERCUSSION, EDUCATOR
b Rochester, Pa, Nov 2, 18. *Study:* Juilliard Sch Music, dipl(timpani & perc), 41; studied timpani, perc & mallets with Goodman & Green. *Pos:* Perc, Pittsburgh Symph Orch, 41-43 & radio & rec orchs, New York, formerly; perc, New York Phil, 46-, prin perc, 72-; charter mem, Sauter-Finnegan Conct Jazz Orch, 52-53. *Teaching:* Mem perc fac, Mannes Col Music, 48-, Manhattan Sch Music, 74- & Juilliard Sch, 81- *Mem:* Phil Symph Soc NY. *Mailing Add:* 11 Woodmere Lane Tenafly NJ 07670

ROSENBLITH, ERIC
VIOLIN, EDUCATOR
b Vienna, Austria, Dec 11, 20. *Study:* Ecole Normale Musique, Paris, dipl, 34, lic conct, 36; studied violin with Jacques Thibaud, Carl Flesch & Bronislaw Huberman. *Rec Perf:* Sonata (Beethoven), Golden Crest. *Pos:* Concertmaster, San Antonio Symph Orch, 52-53 & Indianapolis Symph Orch 53-66; solo violinist, Philadelphia Comp Forum; recitalist & soloist with orchs throughout US, Can, Europe, Israel & Far East. *Teaching:* Mem fac, Butler Univ, 53-66 & Bennington Col, 66-68; mem fac, New England Consv Music, 68-, chmn dept strings, 70-, mem fac extension div, currently. *Mem:* Bohemians; Pi Kappa Lambda. *Rep:* Mutual Artist Mgt Alliance 30 East End Ave Suite 3A New York NY 10028. *Mailing Add:* New England Consv Music 290 Huntingdon Ave Boston MA 02138

ROSENBLOOM, DAVID STUART
COMPOSER, CONDUCTOR & MUSIC DIRECTOR
b Baltimore, Md, Nov 10, 49. *Study:* Harvard Col, BA, 71. *Works:* Water Music, solo perf, 81; Short Pieces for Experimental Chorus, Experimental Chr, 81; Departure, Experimental Chorus & Orch, 82; Souls of Chaos, Electric Orch & Chorus, 82; Electric Psalm: Job's Complaint, Electric Orch & Chr, 82; New Work for Organ, 83; Survivor, music-drama, 83; Short Pieces for Electric Guitar & Flute, 83. *Rec Perf:* Departure (excerpts), 82 & Souls of Chaos, 83, Neutral Rec. *Pos:* Dir, Experimental Chorus, New York, 81; Experimental Chorus & Orch, New York, 81-82 & Electric Orch & Chorus, New York, 82- *Awards:* Residency, Corps de Garde, Groningen, Holland, 83. *Bibliog:* Tim Page (auth), David Rosenbloom Plays a Synthesizer Concert, New York Times, 12/07/82. *Mailing Add:* 164 E 7th St #2F New York NY 10009

ROSENBLUM, LORI LAITMAN See Laitman, Lori

ROSENBLUM, MYRON
VIOLA, VIOLA D'AMORE
b Bronx, NY, Oct 12, 33. *Study:* Queens Col, City Univ New York, BA, 56; NY Univ, MA, 69, PhD, 76. *Pos:* Violist, Greenwich Quartet, 63-64; violist & violist d'amore, New York City Opera, Clarion Concerts, Am Opera Soc, Music in Our Time, Boston Pops Orch, Friends French Opera, Pro Arte Symph, Brattleboro Bach Fest, Mohawk Trail Concerts & Bennington Chamber Music Conf, formerly. *Teaching:* Adj music, NY Univ, City Col & Jersey City State Col; prof, Queensborough Community Col, 69- *Awards:* Fulbright Grant, 64-65; Distinguished Serv Citation, Am Viola Soc, 83. *Mem:* Am Viola Soc, (pres, 75-81); Viola d'Amore Soc Am (co-dir, 77-); Violin Soc Am; Am Musical Instrm Soc. *Publ:* Auth, Viola d'amore & Louis van Waefelghem, In: New Grove Dict of Music & Musicians, 80; The Music for Viola d'amore and Viola, Viola Jahrbuch, 83; Violin, In: Funk & Wagnall's Encycl, 83. *Mailing Add:* 39-23 47th St Sunnyside NY 11104

ROSENBLUM, SANDRA PLETMAN
LECTURER, EDUCATOR
b Yonkers, NY. *Study:* Yale Summer Sch Music, studied piano with Bruce Simonds, 48; Wellesley Col, AB, 49; Harvard Univ, AM, 53; studied piano with Albert Metcalf & Theodore Lettvin. *Teaching:* Instr music hist, Wellesley Col, 49-50 & 52-53; teaching piano, privately, 53-; instr music theory & piano & choral dir, South End Music Ctr, 53-55; instr music theory & piano, Concord Acad, 56-73, chmn dept music, 73-; lectr, New England Consv, Wellesley Col & piano teacher orgn in US. *Awards:* Billings Prize Music, Wellesley Col, 49; Ballantine Fund Grant, Concord Acad, 70; Bunting Inst Fel, Radcliffe Col, 70-71 & 72-73. *Bibliog:* George Anson (auth), Review of Scarlatti Edition, Clavier, 1-2/64; F D (auth), Review of Scarlatti Edition, The Piano Teacher, Directory Teaching Materials, 7/64; George Anson (auth), Review of Clementi Edition, Clavier, 10/68. *Mem:* Am Musicol Soc; Music Teachers Nat Asn; New England Piano Teachers Asn. *Publ:* Ed, Five Pairs of Sonatas by Domenico Scarlatti, 63 & Sonata in F Minor, Op 14/3 by Muzio Clementi, 68, E C Schirmer; Introduction to the Art of Playing on the Pianoforte, DaCapo Press, 74; auth, Zur Auffindung der Spanischen Ausgabe der Klavierschule von Clementi, Die Musikforschung, 78; Clementi's Pianoforte Tutor on the Continent, Fontes Artis Musicae, 80. *Mailing Add:* 24 Cedar Rd Belmont MA 02178

ROSENBOOM, DAVID
COMPOSER, EDUCATOR
b Fairfield, Iowa, Sept 9, 47. *Study:* Univ Ill, studied comp with Gordon Binkerd & Salvatore Martirano & electronic music with Lejaren Hiller; NY Univ. *Works:* Contrasts (violin & orch), 63; Pocket Pieces (flute, viola, sax & perc), 66; And Come Up Dripping (oboe & comput), 68; How Much Better If Plymouth Rock Had Landed on the Pilgrims (instrm & electronics), 69; Ecology of the Skin (electronic), 70; The Seduction of Sapientia (viola da gamba & tape), 75; On Being Invisible (electronics solo with brain signal perf & comput), 76. *Pos:* Coordr, Electric Ear, NY, 68-69; pres, Neurona Co, 69-70. *Teaching:* Assoc, Ctr Creative & Perf Arts, State Univ NY, Buffalo, 67;

mem fac & coordr div interdisciplinary studies, York Univ, Toronto, 70-78; vis asst prof music, Mills Col, currently. *Interests:* Alpha brain waves and biofeedback. *Publ:* Auth, Biofeedback and the Arts: Results of Early Experiments, Vancouver, 75. *Mailing Add:* Music Dept Mills Col PO Box 9970 Oakland CA 94613

ROSENE, PAUL EARL
MUSIC DIRECTOR, EDUCATOR
b Chicago, Ill, Mar 26, 30. *Study:* Ill State Univ, BS, 51, MS, 56; Univ Ill, EdD, 76. *Pos:* Dir music, Chenoa pub sch, Ill, 51-53; ed, Voice of the Lakes, Nat Asn Music Therapy, 69-74. *Teaching:* Supvr, training band, US Air Force, 53-57; supvr music, Pittsfield Pub Sch, Ill, 57-67; prof music, Ill State Univ, 67- *Awards:* Teacher of Yr, Col Fine Arts, Ill State Univ, 81. *Bibliog:* Vito Pascucci (auth), A Very Special Music Program, LeBlanc World Music, 75. *Mem:* Ill Music Educr Asn (district pres, 72-78, vpres, 82-); Music Educr Nat Conf; Nat Asn Music Therapy. *Interests:* Music experiences for the exceptional child; music therapy; music education. *Publ:* Auth, Musical Insights for Exceptional Children, Ill Music Educr, 70-; Why Not Purchase Quality Music for Bands?, Instrumentalist, 81; Instrumental Music—A Success Opportunity, Music Educr J, 82; Making Music, Stipes Publ, 83; Making Music with Choirchimes, Hope Publ, 83. *Mailing Add:* 12 Lucille Lane Normal IL 61761

ROSENFELD, JAYN FRANCES
FLUTE
b Pittsfield, Mass, Nov 10, 38. *Study:* Radcliffe Col, BA, 60; Manhattan Sch Music, MM(perf), 65; studied with James Pappoutsakis, William Kincaid & Marcel Moyse. *Rec Perf:* Cimarosa: Concerto for Two Flutes, Master Virtuosi Rec Soc, 66; Ned Rorem: Trio, Desto Rec, 68. *Pos:* First flute, Am Symph Orch, 63-66, Master Virtuosi New York, 64-68 & Little Orch Princeton, 82-; founder, New York Camerata, 63-; mem, New York New Music Ens, 81-, Continuum, 70- *Teaching:* Flute, Princeton Univ, 75- *Mailing Add:* 151 Hartley Ave Princeton NJ 08540

ROSENHAUS, STEVEN L
COMPOSER, LECTURER
b Brooklyn, NY, July 23, 52. *Study:* Studied comp with Dr George Perle, 73-74; Queens Col, studied comp with Hugo Weisgall, BA(music & sec educ), 75, MA(comp), 80. *Works:* Ballad in Blue (band), Bourne Co, 82; For Clarinet Solo, 82, Woodwind Quintet #1, 83, Songs of Love (song cycle), 83 & Philharmonic Preludes (piano solo), 83, Quadrivium Music Press. *Pos:* Ed, Warner Brothers Music Publ, 77-80; ed in chief, Bourne Co Music Publ, 82-83. *Teaching:* Lectr music publ, currently. *Mem:* ASCAP; Am Soc Univ Comp; Music Educr Nat Conf; Am Music Ctr. *Publ:* Auth, The Best of Times, The Worst of Times, Vol 4, No 14, Music & Politics, Oil & Water (on Khachaturian's Violin Concerto in D), Vol 5, No 2, Surprisingly Warm British Music, Vol 5, No 15, Smetana's Ma vlast, Vol 6, No 1 & Submit to It with Horror & Pleasure (on Stravinsky's Rite of Spring), Vol 6, No 16, Musical Heritage Rev. *Rep:* Quadrivium Music Press 25 Sickles St New York NY 10040. *Mailing Add:* 147-11 79th Ave Flushing NY 11367

ROSENSHEIN, NEIL
TENOR
b Brooklyn, NY. *Study:* Juilliard Sch. *Roles:* Count Almaviva in Il Barbiere di Siviglia; Ormindo, Egisto & Nemorino in L'Elisir d'Amore; Nero in L'Incoronazione di Poppea; Lysander in A Midsummer Night's Dream; Quint in The Turn of the Screw; Fenton in Falstaff, Washington Opera, 82; Die Fledermaus, Paris Opera, 83. *Pos:* Tenor with opera co & orchs in US & Europe. *Mailing Add:* c/o Columbia Artists 165 W 57th St New York NY 10019

ROSENSTIEL, LEONIE
CRITIC-WRITER, LECTURER
b New York, NY. *Study:* Juilliard Sch, cert, 64; Barnard Col, AB, 68; Columbia Univ, PhD, 74; Mex Nat Inst Fine Arts, Hon Dipl, 75. *Pos:* Assoc ed spec prof, Current Musicol, New York, NY, 69-73; founder & dir, Manhasset Chamber Ens, NY, 74-76; consult ed, Da Capo Press, 76- *Awards:* Grants, Rockefeller Found, 78-79 & Am Coun Learned Soc, 78. *Bibliog:* Nadia Boulanger, Publ Weekly, 3/19/82; Joseph McLellan (auth), Midwife for Music, Washington Post, 7/3/82; Paul Hume (auth), Nadia Boulanger: A Life in Music, Smithsonian, 8/82. *Mem:* Int Musicol Soc; Am Musicol Soc; Sonneck Soc; Music Libr Asn. *Interests:* New world music; music in society. *Publ:* Translr, Music Handbook, Colo Col Music Press, 76; auth, The Life and Works of Lili Boulanger, Fairleigh Dickinson Univ Press, 78; Nadia Boulanger Remembered, Virtuoso Mag, 9/80; Nadia Boulanger: A Life in Music, W W Norton, 82; ed & coauth, Schirmer History of Music, Schirmer Bks, Macmillan, 82. *Mailing Add:* c/o Res Assoc Int 340 E 52nd St New York NY 10022

ROSENTHAL, PAUL SAMUEL
VIOLIN, MUSIC DIRECTOR
b New Rochelle, NY, Aug 26, 42. *Study:* Juilliard Sch, with Ivan Galamian & Dorothy De Lay, 61-66; Univ Southern Calif, with Heifetz, 66-69. *Works:* An Alaskan Overture, perf by Arctic Chamber Orch, 82; Bravura Variations on Alaska's Flag, perf by comp, 83. *Rec Perf:* Beethovan Sonatas Nos 8 & 9, Pandora, 82; Bravura Variations on Alaska's Flag, Pelican, 83. *Pos:* Founder & music dir, Sitka Summer Music Fest, 72- *Rep:* Rick Goodfellow 1242 10th Ave Anchorage AK 99501. *Mailing Add:* 2443 Sprucewood St Anchorage AK 99504

ROSENTHAL, STEPHEN W
SAXOPHONE, ADMINISTRATOR

b Glen Cove, NY, July 12, 54. *Study:* State Univ NY, Buffalo; studied sax with Ed Yadzinski & clarinet with James Pyne. *Rec Perf:* An American Classic, Musical Heritage Soc, 80. *Pos:* Mem, Amherst Sax Quartet, 78-; exec dir, Amherst Sax Soc Inc, 79- *Mailing Add:* 101 Florence Ave Buffalo NY 14214

ROSNER, ARNOLD
COMPOSER

b Bronx, New York, Nov 8, 45. *Study:* State Univ NY, Buffalo, PhD, 72. *Works:* A My Lai Elegy, Colo Phil Orch, 74; Magnificat, New York Motet Choir, 82. *Teaching:* Fac mem, Brooklyn Col, 72-80, Wagner Col, 72- & Kingsboro Community Col, 83. *Mailing Add:* 120 Kenilworth Pl 4H Brooklyn NY 11210

ROSNER, CHRISTIAN A K
ADMINISTRATOR, EDUCATOR

b Wichita, Kans, Mar 25, 23. *Study:* Friends Univ, Wichita, BA, 54; Eastman Sch Music, Univ Rochester, PhD(theory), 57. *Teaching:* Chmn div fine arts & prof music theory, St Mary of Plains Col, Dodge City, Kans, 57-72; prof music theory, Tarleton State Univ, Stephenville, Tex, 72-, head dept music & art, 75-81. *Awards:* Guadalupe Award, Diocese Dodge City, Kans, 63; Teaching Award, Contemp Music Proj, 71; Serv Award, Tex Asn Music Sch, 80. *Bibliog:* Homer Ulrich (auth), Centennial History of Music Teachers Nat Asn, Music Teachers Nat Asn, 76. *Mem:* Music Teachers Nat Asn (chmn cert bd 68-73); Tex Asn Music Sch (exec secy, 76-); Tex Music Teachers Asn (mem bd dir, 74-78); Kans Music Teachers Asn (cert chmn, 60-65); Cult Heritage Southwest Kans (mem bd dir, 64-66). *Interests:* Contemporary mass music; computer assisted instruction. *Publ:* Auth, Contemporary Settings of Liturgical Mass, Eastman, 57; ed, Certification Standards, Music Teachers Nat Asn, 69; auth, Interrelationship in the Arts, FACETS, 75; ed, Books on Music, 79 & Transfer Curriculum for Texas Colleges, 82, Tex Asn Music Sch. *Mailing Add:* 860 Charlotte Stephenville TX 76401

ROSS, ALLAN ANDERSON
EDUCATOR, CONDUCTOR & MUSIC DIRECTOR

b Amesbury, Mass, Jan 16, 39. *Study:* Univ Rochester, AB, 61; Ind Univ, MM, 62, MusD, 68. *Teaching:* Asst dir music, Univ Rochester, 62-65; instr music, Ind Univ, 67-69, asst prof & dir undergrad studies, 69-73, assoc prof music, 73-76, asst to dean, 73-79, prof, 77-79; dean, Shepherd Sch Music, Rice Univ, 79-81; dir, Sch Music, Univ Okla, 81- *Mem:* Music Educr Nat Conf; Am Choral Dir Asn; Col Music Soc; Pi Kappa Lambda. *Publ:* Auth, Technique for Beginning Conductors, 76. *Mailing Add:* 1879 Rolling Hills Norman OK 73069

ROSS, BARRY
VIOLIN, MUSIC DIRECTOR

b Boston, Mass, Feb 25, 44. *Study:* Hartt Col Music, BA, 66; Yale Sch Music, MM, 72, DMA, 75. *Pos:* Concertmaster, Kalamazoo Symph Orch, 72-; violinist, Fontana Ens, 80- *Teaching:* Assoc prof music, Kalamazoo Col, 72- *Mem:* Am String Teachers Asn; Col Music Soc. *Mailing Add:* 3870 Greenleaf Circle Kalamazoo MI 49008

ROSS, BUCK
DIRECTOR—OPERA

Study: Bucknell Univ; Univ Minn. *Pos:* Founder, Encompass Music Theatre Composer-Librettist Lab, formerly; dir, La Boheme & Lucia di Lammermoor, Eastern Opera Theatre, NY & Cosi fan tutte, Queens Symph, formerly; asst dir, Minn Opera & Otello, Des Moines Metro Fest, formerly; stage dir, Don Pasquale, Asolo Opera Guild, Sarasota, 83; dir staff, Des Moines Metro Opera, currently. *Mailing Add:* Des Moines Metro Opera 600 N Buxton Des Moines IA 50125

ROSS, ERIC
COMPOSER, ELECTRONIC

b Carbondale, Pa, May 14, 48. *Study:* State Univ NY Col, Oneonta, BA, 70, MS, 71; studied piano with Jean Krantz-Thomas; State Univ NY, Binghamton, summer 75, comp in larger forms with Charles Wuorinen, 81 & non-Western instrm with Samuel Chianis, 81-82; studied piano with Steven Rosenfeld, 77. *Works:* Concerto for Real and Synthetic Orchestra, Op 24, Universal Orch, 82; Electronic Etudes, Op 18; Songs for Synthesized Soprano, Op 19; Symphony No 4, Op 30 (orch & electronics). *Rec Perf:* On Doria Rec. *Pos:* Comp & performer electronic music, US & Europe, currently. *Awards:* Grant, Nat Endowment Arts, 82 & Meet the Comp, 82. *Bibliog:* W Royal Stokes (auth), Eric Ross' Fascinating Multimedia, Washington Post, 12/7/82; Classical Music: Disc and Tape Reviews, Stereo Rev, Vol 7, No 12; Eric Ross, Rec Experimental Music, Vol 4, No 1. *Mem:* Am Music Ctr; BMI. *Mailing Add:* 11 James St Binghamton NY 13903

ROSS, GLYNN WILLIAM
DIRECTOR—OPERA, ADMINISTRATOR

b Omaha, Nebr, Dec 15, 14. *Study:* Leland Powers Sch Theater, Boston, 37-39. *Pos:* Stage dir, Teatro San Carlo, Naples, Italy, 45-47 & 60-63; stage producer, San Francisco Opera, 48 & 50-60, Los Angeles Opera Theatre, 48-60, Ft Worth Opera, 48-56, New Orleans Opera Asn, 49-62, Pac NW Grand Opera, Seattle, 53-55, Opera Co Philadelphia, 60-62 & Seattle Opera Asn, 63-83; consult, Int Commun Agy, 70- *Awards:* Arts Adminr of Yr, NY Bd Trade, 71; Cert of Excellence, Wash State House Rep, 74. *Mem:* OPERA Am (founder & dir, 70). *Mailing Add:* c/o Seattle Opera Asn PO Box 9248 Seattle WA 98109

ROSS, JAMES RAMSEY
PERCUSSION

b Cincinnati, Ohio, Sept 8, 48. *Study:* Northern Ill Univ, BMus, 71. *Pos:* Perc, Grant Park Symph, Chicago, Ill, 73-78 & Chicago Symph Orch, 79- *Teaching:* Instr perc, Chicago Civic Orch, 79- *Mem:* Percussion Arts Soc. *Mailing Add:* 220 S Michigan Ave Chicago IL 60604

ROSS, JERROLD
EDUCATOR, LECTURER

b New York, NY, Feb 8, 35. *Study:* NY Univ, BS, 56, PhD, 63; Queens Col, City Univ New York, MS, 58. *Pos:* Pres, New York Col Music, 65-67; dir, Town Hall, 70-74. *Teaching:* Chair dept music & music educ, Sch Educ, NY Univ, 67-82, head div arts & arts educ, 74-82, assoc dean, 82- *Awards:* Usdan Ctr Creative & Perf Arts Citation, 82. *Mem:* Nat Asn Sch Music; New York Musicians Club. *Publ:* Coauth, Interpreting Music Through Movement, Prentice-Hall, 63; auth, The Performing Arts on Campus, Col Music Soc, 77; National Arts & Arts Education Policy, 81 & Culture and Soc, 83, Nat Asn Sch Music. *Mailing Add:* 2 Washington Square Village New York NY 10012

ROSS, JOHN GORDON
CONDUCTOR & MUSICAL DIRECTOR

b Selma, Ind. *Study:* Ball State Univ, BM, 80; Cleveland Inst Music; Northwestern Univ, MM, 81. *Pos:* Cond, Canton Youth Symph, Ohio, 75-76; asst cond, Canton Symph Orch, Ohio, 75-76; music dir & cond, Cleveland Phil Orch, 77-79 & Kingsport Symph Orch, Tenn, 81- *Mem:* Cond Guild; Asn Tenn Symph Orch (dir & bd mem, 81-). *Mailing Add:* 1000 University Blvd, F-43 Kingsport TN 37660

ROSS, JUDITH
HARP, EDUCATOR

Study: Eastman Sch Music, BM, MA; Boston Univ; studied with Eileen Malone, Pierre Jamet, Lucile Lawrence & Nadia Boulanger. *Pos:* Solo & orch appearances, New England & NY, currently. *Teaching:* Theory & harp, State Univ NY Col, Fredonia, 65-69; theory, Boston Univ, 70-74 & Longy Sch Music, currently. *Awards:* Paderewski Gold Medal, 65. *Mailing Add:* Longy Sch Music 1 Follen St Cambridge MA 02138

ROSS, RICK
COACH, ORGAN

Study: Southern Methodist Univ; studied with Robert Anderson. *Pos:* Solo, Dallas Civic Symph, Hamilton Symph, Ohio & Boca Raton Symph; prin vocal coach & accmp, Orlando Opera Co, currently; organist, Park Lake Presby Church, currently. *Awards:* First Prize, Mader Mem Organ Compt. *Mailing Add:* 418 N Shine Ave Orlando FL 32803

ROSS, RONALD D
ADMINISTRATOR, EDUCATOR

b Wayne, WVa, Jan 24, 42. *Study:* Marshall Univ, BA, 63; Ind Univ, MM, 68; Univ Cincinnati, PhD, 73. *Teaching:* Instr, Glenville State Col, 65-69; asst to dean, Col-Consv Music, Univ Cincinnati, 70-73, asst dean, 73-75; dir sch music, Univ Northern Iowa, 75- *Interests:* Technique of music analysis. *Publ:* Auth, Faculty Accountability and the Performing Arts, Symposium, 76; Jazz in the Curriculum, Nat Asn Jazz Educr, 78; That is (Still) the Question, Symposium, 81; Toward a Theory of Tonal Coherence: The Motets of Jacob Obrecht, Musical Quart, 81; The Fine Art of Faculty Recruitment, Music Educr Nat Conf J, 81. *Mailing Add:* 610 W 11th St Cedar Falls IA 50614

ROSS, RUTH LAMPLAND
CRITIC-WRITER

b St Paul, Minn, May 6, 08. *Study:* Univ Minn, BS, 28; St Olaf Col, teachers cert, 29; Wellesley Col, MM(music theory & criticism), 31. *Pos:* Critic, Brooklyn Eagle, 31-33, Musical Leader Mag, 31-33, Westport News, 70-75; freelance writer incl articles in Musical Am. *Teaching:* Instr music, Waconia High Sch, Minn, 29-30; instr, SConn State Univ, 59-66. *Awards:* Nat Fedn Music Clubs Awards, 76-81; Nat League Am Pen Women Award, 82. *Mem:* Music Critics Asn; Am Musicol Soc; Am Asn Univ Women; Nat League Am Pen Women; Conn Comp Inc. *Mailing Add:* Box 554 598 S Benson Rd Fairfield CT 06430

ROSS, WALTER BEGHTOL
COMPOSER, FRENCH HORN

b Lincoln, Nebr, Oct 3, 36. *Study:* Univ Nebr, BA(music), 60, MM, 62; Instituto de Altos Estudio Musicales, Buenos Aires, with Alberto Ginastera, 65; Cornell Univ, DMA, 66. *Works:* Five Dream Sequences for Percussion Quartet & Piano, 70, Concerto for Brass Quintet and Orchestra, 71; Trombone Concerto, 73, Tuba Concerto, 75, Concerto for Wind Quintet and String Orchestra, 79, Six Shades of Blue: Preludes for Piano, 79 & Divertimento for Woodwind Quintet, 82, Boosey & Hawkes. *Awards:* Orgn Am States Fel, 65; Nat Endowment Arts Grant, 76; fel, Ctr Advan Studies, Univ Va, 72 & 83. *Mem:* ASCAP; Tubists Universal Brotherhood Asn; Southern Comp League (pres, 75-77). *Mailing Add:* Rte 6 Box 301 Charlottesville VA 22901

ROSS, WILLIAM JAMES
COMPOSER, ORGAN

b Dallas, Tex, Sept 6, 37. *Study:* Trinity Univ, studied organ with Donald Willing, BA, 60, MEd, 67; Univ Mich, Ann Arbor, studied comp with Ross Lee Finney & Leslie Bassett & organ with Marilyn Mason, MMus, 71. *Works:* Viet Nam Memorial, Alec Wyton, 72; The Way From Earth, Belwin-Mills, 75; Alpha I, San Antonio Chamber Arts Ens, 77; Three Dances of Man, comn by Alamo Chap Am Guild Organists, 81; Aria and Dance, Southern Music

Co, 82. *Pos:* Freelance comp & performer, 71-80; organist & choirmaster, Alamo Heights Presby Church, 80- *Teaching:* Instr & coordr fine arts, San Antonio Independent Sch Dist, 60-69; mem fac, St Mary's Univ, 80- *Awards:* First Prize, Univ Tex Comp Compt, 74; co-winner, New Music Young Ens Compt, 80. *Mem:* Nat Asn Comp (nat adv coun, 78-). *Mailing Add:* 10426 Fox Hollow San Antonio TX 78217

ROSSI, JANE NIERMANN
TROMBONE
b Los Angeles, Calif, June 11, 45. *Study:* Univ Southern Calif, BMus, 67. *Pos:* Asst prin trombonist, San Antonio Symph, 69- *Mailing Add:* 5930 Grandwood San Antonio TX 78239

ROSSI, JOHN L
FRENCH HORN
b Washington, DC, Jan 7, 27. *Pos:* French hornist, radio, TV symph orchs, ballet co & opera co, New York & Goldman Band, 50- *Mem:* Violin Soc Am; Am Fedn Violin Masters. *Mailing Add:* 84 Bobwhite Lane Hicksville NY 11801

ROSSI, NICK
MUSIC DIRECTOR, EDUCATOR
b San Luis Obispo, Calif, Nov 14, 24. *Study:* Univ Southern Calif, BMus, 48, MMus, 52; Sacramento State Col, supvr credential, 68; Sussex Col Technol, PhD, 71. *Rec Perf:* Music of Puerto Rico; Music of USSR. *Pos:* Music consult sec sch, Los Angeles City Sch Dist, 48-68; cond & stage dir, Congregational Church Glendale, Calif, 59; assoc ed, Keyboard Publ Div, Am Bk Co, New York, 62-80; producer & stage dir operas, Hollywood Theater Arts Wkshp, 63-64 & others; dir, Romeo and Juliet, ABC-TV, Los Angeles, 64; organizer & dir, Virgil Thomson Fest, 71, Norman Dello Joio Fest, 72, Don Juan in Perf Arts Fest, 73, Castelnuovo Tedesco Fest, 74, Carman Moore Fest, 76 & Women in Music Fest, 78; producer & auth filmstrips on composers & music hist. *Teaching:* Guest lectr various int music educ orgn, 62-; chmn music educ, Univ Bridgeport, 70-74; assoc prof & coordr music & dance, LaGuardia Community Col, 74- *Mem:* Am Choral Cond Asn; Am Musicol Soc; Pi Kappa Lambda; Soc Ethnomusicol; Int Castelnuovo Tedesco Soc (founder, 75, pres, 75-). *Publ:* Coauth (with Sadie Rafferty), Music Through the Centuries, 63, 3rd ed, 81; auth, Twentieth Century Music and Art, 72; Hearing Music, 81; J S Bach: A Biography in Pictures, 81; Beethoven: A Biography in Pictures, 82. *Mailing Add:* LaGuardia Community Col 31-10 Thomson Ave Long Island City NY 11101

ROSSO, CAROL L
COMPOSER
b Santa Monica, Calif, July 31, 49. *Study:* Los Angeles City Col; Immaculate Heart Col, studied comp with Dorrance Stalvey; Calif Inst Arts; Mills Col, with Terry Riley, MFA; studied comp with David Behrman, piano with John Ringgold, cond with Dean Voorhies & gamelan with Ki Wasidipuro. *Works:* He Wishes for the Clothes of Heaven (sop & flute); Liberatus ad Vincolas Corpus, Requiem Tibiis Solum (flute), 75; Timbrel Improvisations; Overtone Modulations (buchla synthesizer), 76; Glass, Lights, Reflections & Refractions (film), 76. *Teaching:* Ens assoc piano & theory, Calif Inst Arts; instr, Mills Col Contemp Music Ctr. *Mailing Add:* 11859 Bray St Culver City CA 90230

ROSTROPOVICH, MSTISLAV
CONDUCTOR & MUSIC DIRECTOR, CELLO
b Baku, USSR, March 27, 27. *Study:* Moscow Consv, with Shebalin & Kozalupov; Hon DMus from 23 univ in US & UK. *Rec Perf:* Chopin and Schumann Piano Concertos, Shostakovich Symphony No 5 & Prokofiev Suites Nos 1 & 2, Deutsche Grammophon; Tchaikovsky Violin Concerto, CBS Masterworks; Tchaikovsky Symphonies, Pique Dame, Eugene Onegin & Lady Macbeth of Mtsensk; and many more. *Pos:* Numerous conct tours worldwide as soloist & in trio, 47-; cond & music dir, Nat Symph Orch, Washington, 77-; co-dir, Aldeburgh Fest, UK, 77-; guest cond, major orchs & operas in US & Europe. *Teaching:* Prof, Leningrad Consv, formerly; fac mem, Moscow Consv, 53-60, prof, 60-78, head cello & double bass dept; hon prof, Cuban Nat Consv, 60-78. *Awards:* First Prize, All-Union Compt Musicians, 45, Int Cellist Compt, 47 & 50 & Cellist Compt, 49; and many other awards worldwide. *Mem:* Hon mem, Acad Santa Cecilia, Rome; Acad Arts & Sci; hon fel, Royal Acad Music. *Mailing Add:* Nat Symph Orch Kennedy Ctr Washington DC 20566

ROTENBERG, SHELDON
VIOLIN, TEACHER
b Attleboro, Mass, Apr 11, 17. *Study:* Studied with Felix Winternitz, 27-33; Tufts Univ, AB, 39; studied with Georges Enesco & Maurice Hewitt, Paris, 47. *Rec Perf:* Boston String Quartet Conct, Libr Cong, 50. *Pos:* Mem, Boston String Quartet, 48-52; first violin sect, Boston Symph Orch, 48-; soloist, Boston Symph, 68-69. *Teaching:* Private violin, Boston, 48-; mem fac violin & chamber music, Boston Univ, Tanglewood, 79- *Mailing Add:* 60 Browne St Brookline MA 02146

ROTH, ERIC STEVEN
CONDUCTOR, EDUCATOR
b Martins Ferry, Ohio, May 8, 41. *Study:* Col Consv Music, Univ Cincinnati, BS(music educ), 63, MM, 64, DMA, 73. *Teaching:* Assoc prof music & cond orch, Heidelberg Col, 74-79 & Cent Wash Univ, 79- *Awards:* Fulbright Scholar Munich, 69; Cond Fel, Am Symph Orch League, 78; fel, Nat Endowment Humanities, 81. *Mem:* Music Educr Nat Conf; Am Fedn Musicians. *Mailing Add:* 1005 Vista Rd Ellensburg WA 98926

ROTHE, DAVID H
ORGAN, EDUCATOR
b San Francisco, Calif. *Study:* San Francisco State Univ, BA, 64; Univ Calif, Berkeley, MA, 67; Stanford Univ, DMA, 70. *Rec Perf:* Rothe Plays Bach & Buxtehude, Ashland Rec, 82; Truth & Beauty in Sight & Sound—The Organ as a Musical Instrument, Ashland Rec, 83; Toccatas, Concerto & Dances for Organ & Trumpet, Ashland Rec, 83. *Pos:* Asst organist, Stanford Univ, 64-66; organist & choirmaster, All Saints Episcopal Church, Palo Alto, 65-67 & St Johns Episcopal Church, Chicago, 75-81. *Teaching:* Prof music, Calif State Univ, Chico, 70- *Awards:* First Place Regional Compt, Am Guild Organists, 63; German Govt Grant, 67. *Publ:* Auth, Truth & Beauty in Sight & Sound—The Organ as a Musical Instrument, Univ J, Calif State Univ, 83. *Mailing Add:* PO Box 203 Forest Ranch CA 95942

ROTHERMEL, DAN HIESTER
MUSIC DIRECTOR, WRITER
b Reading, Pa, Dec 13, 43. *Study:* Ind Univ, Pa, BS(music educ), 65; Temple Univ, MM(music hist & lit), 70. *Rec Perf:* The Gondoliers (Sullivan), 81 & The Grand Duke (Sullivan), 82, Savoy Co Philadelphia; have conducted all 14 Gilbert & Sullivan operas. *Pos:* Assoc cond, Acad Boys Choir Philadelphia Col Perf Arts, 68-81; musical dir, Franklin Concerts Inc, 73-74, Gilbert & Sullivan Players, Philadelphia, 76- & Savoy Co Philadelphia, 81-; cond, Gilbert & Sullivan Operas. *Teaching:* Instr music, Philadelphia Pub Sch, 65-; instr operetta hist, Philadelphia Col Perf Arts, 77 & Temple Univ Ctr City, 78. *Interests:* Victorian symphonic and operatic music; Sir Arthur Sullivan; classical operetta. *Mailing Add:* 1512 S 15th St Philadelphia PA 19146

ROTHFUSS, (EARL) LEVERING
ACCOMPANIST, PIANO
b Hannibal, Mo, Apr 20, 52. *Study:* Univ Mo, Columbia, BM, 74; Univ Southern Calif, with Gwendolyn Koldofsky & Brooks Smith, MM, 76. *Pos:* Accompanist, US, Can & Europe, 75- *Teaching:* Adj instr, Pepperdine Univ, 77-78. *Mailing Add:* 315 W 104th St New York NY 10025

ROTHMAN, GEORGE LOVELL
CONDUCTOR & MUSIC DIRECTOR, PIANO
b New York, NY, July 13, 54. *Study:* Manhattan Sch Music, studied cond with Anton Coppola, piano with Sonia Vargas & Dwight McLeod & ens with Harvey Sollberger, Charles Wuorinen & Paul Zukofsky, BM, 78; Juilliard Sch, 79-81; Berkshire Music Ctr, studied cond with Leonard Bernstein, Seiji Ozawa, Gunther Schuller & Joseph Silverstein, 79; Inst Am Cond, WVa Univ, with Maurice Abravanel, Sergiu Commissiona & Otto-Werner Mueller, 81; studied cond with Seymour Lipkin & Jorge Mester. *Pos:* Asst dir-cond, Manhattan Contemp Ens, 75-78; accmp, Martha Graham Dance Co, 76; asst cond, New Amsterdam Symph Orch, 79-81; staff cond, Manhattan Sch Music, 80; prin guest cond, Parnassus Chamber Ens, 80-; artistic dir, Am Opera Theater, 81-; assoc cond, Manhattan Opera Asn, 82; music dir & cond, New Phil Riverside, New York, 81- *Teaching:* Instr piano & theory, privately, 74-; guest lectr & pianist, Baruch Col, 75-78; substitute fac mem orch & choral cond, Manhattan Sch Music, 79. *Mailing Add:* 258 Riverside Dr New York NY 10025

ROTHSCHILD, ELLEN WAGNER
VIOLIN
b Glen Falls, NY, Oct 9, 49. *Study:* Boston Univ, BMus, 71; studied with Mischa Misachakoff, 71-73. *Pos:* Violinist, Toledo Symph, Ohio, 72-73; first violinist, New Orleans Symph, 73-; prin second violin, Eastern Music Fest, Greensboro, NC, 77-78. *Awards:* Berkshire Music Ctr Fel, 68 & 70. *Mailing Add:* c/o New Orleans Phil 203 Carondelet St Suite 903 New Orleans LA 70130

ROTHSCHILD, RANDOLPH SCHAMBERG
ADMINISTRATOR, PATRON
b Baltimore, Md, June 23, 09. *Study:* Peabody Inst Music, prep grad, 27; Johns Hopkins Univ, 27-29; Wharton Sch Finance & Commer, Univ Pa, BS, 32, Law Sch, 32-34; Univ Clermont, cert, summer 31; Univ Md, Law Sch, LLB, 36. *Pos:* Bd mem, Chamber Music Soc Baltimore, 53-, pres, 54-; bd mem, Baltimore Symph Orch, 63-, mem music comt, 65-, cond selection comt, 66-68; bd mem, Md State Arts Coun, 74-80 & secy-treas, 75-80; bd mem, Peabody Inst, Johns Hopkins Univ, 78- *Bibliog:* Helen Henry (auth), Baltimore's Contemporary Music Man, Sunday Sun, 7/31/77; Wendell E Wilson (auth), Personality: Randolph S Rothschild, Minerological Rec, 5-6/81. *Mailing Add:* 2909 Woodvalley Dr Baltimore MD 21208

ROTHSTEIN, SIDNEY
MUSIC DIRECTOR & CONDUCTOR
b Philadelphia, Pa, May 29, 36. *Study:* Temple Univ, BA, 59; studied with Pierre Monteux, Max Rudolf & Vladimir Golschmann; Combs Col Music, Hon MusD; Albright Col, Pa, Hon Dr Humanities, 83. *Pos:* Founder & music dir, Orch Soc Philadelphia, 64-76; creator & cond, Honolulu Symph Chorus, 76-80; cond, Univ Hawaii Symph, 76-80; assoc cond, Honolulu Symph, 76-80; music dir, Reading Symph, Pa, 76-, Charleston Symph, WVa, 80-83 & Fla Symph Orch, 82- *Rep:* Joanne Rile Mgt Box 27539 Philadelphia Pa 19118. *Mailing Add:* Fla Symph Orch PO Box 782 Orlando FL 32802

ROUSE, CHRISTOPHER CHAPMAN
COMPOSER, EDUCATOR
b Baltimore, Md, Feb 15, 49. *Study:* Oberlin Consv, BMus, 71; private study with George Crumb, 71-73; Cornell Univ, MFA & DMA, 77. *Works:* Thor, 82 & The Infernal Machine, 82, Helicon Music; Nuit d'Ivresse, comn by Aspen Music Fest, 82; Rotae Passionis, 82 & The Surma Ritornelli, 83,

Helicon Music; Mitternachtlieder, Sonatina Music (in prep). *Teaching:* Asst prof comp & jr fel, Univ Mich, 78-81; asst prof music, Eastman Sch Music, 81- *Awards:* Fel, Nat Endowment for Arts, 76 & 80; Rockefeller Found Award, 80; League of Comp Award, Int Soc Comtemp Music, 81. *Mem:* Am Comp Alliance. *Publ:* Auth, William Schuman Documentary, G Schirmer, Presser, 79. *Rep:* European Am Music Corp 11 W End Rd Totowa NJ 07512; Am Comp Alliance 170 W 74th St New York NY 10023. *Mailing Add:* 2145 East Ave Rochester NY 14610

ROUSSAKIS, NICOLAS
COMPOSER, EDUCATOR
b Athens, Greece, June 10, 34; US citizen. *Study:* Columbia Col, with Otto Luening & Jack Beeson, BA(music), 56; Columbia Univ, with Otto Luening, Vladimir Ussachevsky & Henry Cowell, MA(comp), 60; Staatliche Hochschule Musik, Hamburg, Germany, with Philipp Jarnach, 61-63; Ferienkurse Neue Musik, Darmstadt, with Karlheinz Stockhausen, Pierre Boulez, György Ligeti & Luciano Berio, 62 & 63; Sch Arts, Columbia Univ, DMA, 75. *Works:* Sonata for Harpsichord, 66, Six Short Pieces for Two Flutes, 68, Syrtos (conct band), 75, Ode to Cataclysm (symph orch), 75, Ephemeris (string quartet), 79 & Voyage (a cappella chorus), 80, Am Comp Ed ; Fire & Earth & Water & Air, comn by Nat Endowment Arts, 82. *Rec Perf:* Night Speech (chorus & perc), 68, Sonata for Harpsichord, 67, Ephemeris (string quartet), 79 & Voyage (a cappella chorus), 80, CRI. *Pos:* Exec dir, Group Contemp Music 71-; vpres & co-founder, Am Comp Orch, 76- *Teaching:* Asst prof music, Columbia Col & Barnard Col, Columbia Univ, 68-77 & Mason Gross Sch Arts, 81-; asst prof theory & analysis, Douglass Col, Rutgers Univ, 77-81, Grad Sch, 80- *Awards:* Grants, Rutgers Univ Res Coun, 81, Martha Baird Rockefeller Found, 81 & Nat Endowment Arts, 82. *Bibliog:* Donal Henahan (auth), The Grand Old Teenagers of Contemporary Music, 2/1/77 & Richard M Braun (auth), Presenting an Orchestra for the American Composer, 12/4/77, New York Times; Mark Blechner (auth), The Group for Contemporary Music, High Fidelity Musical Am, 11/77. *Mem:* Nat Endowment Arts (panelist, 82-); Am Comp Alliance (pres, 75-81 & chmn bd, 81-); Am Comp Orch (co-founder & vpres, 76-); CRI; New York Consortium New Music (pres, 83-). *Mailing Add:* Penthouse F 209 W 86th St New York NY 10024

ROUTCH, ROBERT EDSON
EDUCATOR, FRENCH HORN
b Lock Haven, Pa, Aug, 12, 48. *Study:* Oberlin Consv; Juilliard Sch Music, BM, 70; Curtis Inst Music, dipl, 75. *Rec Perf:* Zelenka Caprizetos, Polydor, 78; Tashi Plays Mozart, 78, Tashi Plays Beethoven, 78, Tashi Plays Stravinsky, 78 & Tashi Plays Takemitsu, 80, RCA; Chamber Music Society of Lincoln Center Plays Poulenc, Mistral Heritage Soc, 83. *Pos:* Solo horn, Kansas City & New Orleans Symp, 70-72; founding mem, Aulos Wind Quintet, 74-79; guest artist, Lincoln Ctr Chamber Music Soc, 74- & Tashi, 74- *Teaching:* Horn, San Diego State Univ, 79-82 & Calif Inst Arts, 82- *Awards:* Winner, Philadelphia Orch Young Artists Comp, 65; Cabot Award, Berkshire Music Ctr, 70. *Mem:* Int Horn Soc. *Mailing Add:* c/o Harry Beall Mgt 119 W 57th St New York NY 10019

ROVICS, HOWARD
COMPOSER, EDUCATOR
b New York, NY, May 7, 36. *Study:* Manhattan Sch Music, BMus, 59, MMus, 61; studied with Stefan Wolpe. *Works:* Cybernetic Study No 1 (flute & piano); Three Studies for Piano, 64-66; March Funebre (clarinet & strings), New York, 71; Events (piano), New York, 71; Piece (cello, piano & tape), 73; Look, Friend, at Me (oboe & piano), 73; Haunted Objects: In Memoriam Stefan Wolpe (sop, narrator, four woodwinds & tape), 74. *Pos:* Comp & piano appearances in New York conct halls. *Teaching:* Mem fac, Manhattan Sch Music, formerly; assoc prof music, Post Col Long Island Univ, 76- *Awards:* Nat Endowment Arts Comp Grant, 74. *Mem:* Am Comp Alliance. *Mailing Add:* Music Dept Post Col Long Island Univ Greenvale NY 11548

ROW, PETER LYMAN
EDUCATOR, SITAR
b Boston, Mass, Sept 25, 44. *Study:* Prayag Sangit Samiti, Allahabad, India, BMus, 68, MMus, 70, DMA, 73. *Teaching:* Fac mem ethnomusicol, New England Consv, 74-; vis assoc prof, Brandeis Univ, 81. *Awards:* Gold Medal (for instrm music—sitar), Prayag Sangit Samiti Nat Compt, 69; fel, J D Rockefeller III Fund, 71 & 72; travel grant, Smithsonian Inst, 78. *Mem:* Soc Ethnomusicol (NE chap secy-treas, 77-78, pres, 78-80). *Publ:* Auth, The Device of Modulation in Hindustani Art Music, In: Essays in Arts & Sciences, Univ New Haven, 77; The Music of India, In: Festival of American Folk Life, Smithsonian Inst, 77; Hindustani Raga Classification, Sonus, Vol 1, No 2. *Mailing Add:* 9 Vernon St Brookline MA 02146

ROWEN, RUTH HALLE
CRITIC-WRITER, EDUCATOR
b New York, NY. *Study:* Barnard Col, with Douglas Stuart Moore, William John Mitchell & Seth Bingham, BA, 39; Columbia Univ, with Paul Henry Lang, Erich Hertzmann, George Herzog & Hans Weisse, MA, 41, PhD, 48. *Pos:* Educ dir, Carl Fischer Publ, 54-63. *Teaching:* Prof music, City Col, City Univ New York, 63-, Grad Sch, 67- *Mem:* Am Musicol Soc; ASCAP; Col Music Soc; Music Libr Asn; Int Musicol Soc. *Interests:* Exploration of substance of music, composed, improvised, and spontaneous. *Publ:* Coauth, Jolly Come Sing and Play, Carl Fischer, Inc, 56; Hearing—Gateway to Music, Summy-Birchard, 59; auth, Early Chamber Music, Da Capo Press, 74; Music Through Sources and Documents, Prentice-Hall, Inc, 79; coauth, Instant Piano, City Col Bookstore, 82. *Mailing Add:* 115 Central Park W New York NY 10023

ROWLEY, GORDON SAMUEL
LIBRARIAN, MUSICOLOGIST
b Detroit, Mich, Sept 14, 43. *Study:* Stanford Univ, AB, 65, MA, 67; Univ Iowa, MA, 76. *Teaching:* Res asst music, Stanford Univ, 66-67; instr, Simpson Col, Calif, 67-69; instr & res adv, Grinnell Col, 69-70; res asst organ lit, Univ Iowa, 70-71, teaching asst musicol, 70-74; lectr, Univ Victoria, BC, 73-75, lectr early music wkshp, 74-75, teaching asst libr sci, 75-76; music libr, Northern Ill Univ, 76-, asst dir for res serv, 81- *Publ:* Auth, A Bibliographical Syllabus of the History of Organ Literature, 19th Century, 72. *Mailing Add:* Asst Dir Res Serv Univ Libr Northern Ill Univ De Kalb IL 60115

ROWLEY, VERA NEWSTEAD
PIANO, SOPRANO
b London, England, June 11, 1898; US citizen. *Study:* Studied with Arthur Newstead; Notre Dame Acad, London, 12; studied voice with Lila Robson, 14-25 & organ with Edwin Arthur Kraft, 25-30; opera wkshp with Boris Goldovsky, 38-40. *Roles:* Lady Pamela in Fra Diablo, 25, Frasquita in Carmen, 27, Gerhilde in Die Walküre, 35 & Lady Diana in Sleeping Beauty, 38, Stadium Opera; Dudley in San Toy, 27 & Lady Constance Wynne in Giesha Girl, 27, San Carlo. *Pos:* Pianist & coach, Orpheus Male Chorus, 30-35; pres, Phil Chorus Cleveland Symph Orch, 36-37; music chmn, Daughters of the British Empire, 38-40; founder & dir, Civic Chorus, Drama Opera Guild Palm Beaches, 43-60. *Teaching:* Affil instr piano & theory, Sherwood Sch Music, 42-; instr piano & theory, Coral Gables Youth Ctr, 80- *Mem:* Musicians Club Am; Am Guild Organists; Palm Beach Co Music Teachers Asn (pres, 64); Nat Asn Teachers Singing; Nat Asn Music Teachers (pres, 64). *Mailing Add:* 5951 SW 46th Terr Miami FL 33144

ROY, GENE BURDICK
DOUBLE BASS, EDUCATOR
Study: Cleveland Inst Music, BM, 65, MM, 73; Eastman Sch Music; studied theory with Burrill Phillips, Ruth Northrup Tibbs, Alvaretta West, Verna Straub & Marcel Dick & double bass with Nelson Watson, Oscar Zimmerman & Jacques Posell. *Pos:* Mem, Rochester Phil Orch, formerly & Cleveland Orch Chorus & Chamber Chorus, currently; double bass, Opus One, Contemp Chamber Ens, Dartmouth Col Congregation Arts Symph Orch, 65. *Teaching:* Theory, Cleveland Inst Music, 63-64, mem fac, 65-; adminr, Summer Music Experience, Western Reserve Acad, 71-73. *Mailing Add:* 2528 Derbyshire Rd Cleveland Heights OH 44106

ROY, KLAUS GEORGE
CRITIC-WRITER, COMPOSER
b Vienna, Austria, Jan 24, 24; US citizen. *Study:* Boston Univ, studied musicol with Karl Geiringer, BMus, 47; Harvard Univ, studied comp with Walter Piston, counterpoint with Irving Fine & hist with A T Davison, MA, 49. *Works:* St Francis' Canticle of the Sun, Op 17, CRI, 51; Sterlingman, Chamber Opera, Op 30, Theodore Presser Co, 57; Chorale-Variants, Op 60, Cleveland Orch, 66; A Song for Mardi Gras, Op 37 (medium voice & piano), 72 & Three Turns of the Key, Op 50 (piano solo), 73, Galaxy Music Corp; Serenade for Violoncello Solo, Op 62, Ludwig Music Publ Co, 75; Zoopera, Op 121, comn by Cleveland Zoological Soc, 83. *Pos:* Contrib music critic, Christian Sci Monitor, 50-57; prog annotator & ed, Cleveland Orch, 58- *Teaching:* Instr music criticism & comp & music librn, Boston Univ, 48-57; assoc prof libr arts, Cleveland Inst Art, 75- *Awards:* Music Award of Cleveland Arts Prize, 65. *Publ:* Auth, 400 articles, Christian Sci Monitor, 50-60; Rec annotations for approx 200 albums, Time-Life Rec, 51-; contribr to Stereo Rev, 58-61. *Mailing Add:* 2528 Derbyshire Rd Cleveland Heights OH 44106

ROY, WILL
BASS
b Schenectady, New York. *Study:* Hope Col; Curtis Inst of Music, with Martial Singher; Manhattan Sch Music, with John Brownlee. *Roles:* Don Alfonso in Cosi fan tutte, Mozart Fest Opera, 65; Colline in La Boheme; Escamillo in Carmen; Don Basilio in Barber of Seville; Sarastro in Zauberflöte; Mephistopheles in Faust; Arkel in Pelleas et Melisande; over 50 leading roles. *Pos:* Leading bass, New York City Opera, Grand Theatrede Geneve, Maggio Mus di Firenze, French Nat Opera Broadcasts, Washington Opera, Ft Worth Opear, Philadelphia Grand Opera, Central City Opera & others. *Awards:* Rockefeller Found Grant; Winner, Metropolitan Opera Audition, 65 & Conct Verdi, Busseto, Italy, 72. *Mem:* Am Guild Musical Artists (bd govs, currently). *Mailing Add:* 402 Park Ave Rutherford NJ 07660

ROYCE, MARIA M
HARP, TEACHER
b Grand Rapids, Mich, Mar 27, 59. *Study:* Cleveland Inst Music, BM, 81. *Pos:* Prin harp, Grand Rapids Symph, 80-81 & Kansas City Phil, 81-82. *Teaching:* Instr harp, Consv Music, Univ Miss, Kansas City, 81-82. *Awards:* Biennial Student Award, Nat Fedn Music Clubs, 77. *Mem:* Am Harp Soc. *Mailing Add:* 132 Graceland NE Grand Rapids MI 49505

ROYER, PAUL HAROLD
COMPOSER, ORGAN
b Mt Jackson, Va, Sept 3, 22. *Study:* Westminster Choir Col, 40-42; Col Music, Univ Cincinnati, BM, 48, MM, 50; Ind Univ, 56-60. *Works:* Sing a New Song (SATB), Summy-Birchard Co, 62; Fanfare Festiva (band), M M Cole Publ Co, 66; FantaSonia (band), perf by SDak State Univ Band, 72; Rushmore Suite (band), Rushmore Music Camp, 76; Echo Song (SATB & TTBB), Plymouth Music, 78; Traceries (orch), perf by SDak State Univ Orch, 81; Joy Song (SATB), perf by SDak State Univ Choir, 82. *Pos:* Dir music, Reid Presby Church, Richmond, Ind, 50-52. *Teaching:* Instr music, Col Music,

Univ Cincinnati, 48-50; prof music, Huron Col, 52-68; prof & comp in res, SDak State Univ, 68- *Awards:* Danforth Teachers Grant, 57; Nat Endowment Arts Grant, 68. *Mem:* SDak Music Teachers Asn (vpres & pres, 74-78); Music Teachers Nat Asn (west cent div vpres & pres, 78-82); Am Guild Organists. *Mailing Add:* 337 Lincoln Lane S Brookings SD 57006

ROZE, CHRISTOPHER
EDUCATOR
Study: Manhattan Sch Music, BM; Juilliard Sch Music, MM; studied with Charles Wuorinen, Ursula Mamlok & Vincent Persichetti. *Teaching:* Instr music & chair theory & comp dept, Boston Consv, currently. *Awards:* BMI Award. *Mailing Add:* Boston Consv 8 The Fenway Boston MA 02215

ROZSA, MIKLOS
COMPOSER, CONDUCTOR
b Budapest, Hungary, Apr 18, 07; US citizen. *Study:* Leipzig Consv Music, dipl(comp), 29, dipl(musicol), 30; Trinity Col Music, dipl(cond), 39. *Works:* Theme Variations & Finale, Op 13, Ed Eulenburg, 34; Concerto for Violin, Op 24, 53, Sinfonia Concertante (violin & violoncello), 66, Concerto (piano & orch), Op 31, 67, Tripartita for Orchestra, Op 33, 72, Concerto for Viola, Op 37, 79 & Quartet No 2, 81, Breitkopf & Haertel. *Pos:* Staff comp, Metro-Goldwyn-Mayer, 48-62; conductor, major symphony orchestras in US & Europe. *Teaching:* Lectr, Univ Southern Calif, 45-65. *Awards:* Francis Joseph Prize, Budapest, 37-38; Oscar Awards, Hollywood, 46, 48 & 59; Le Cesar, Paris Film Acad, 78. *Bibliog:* Christopher Palmer (auth), Rozsa, Breitkopf & Haertel. *Publ:* Auth, Stories From My Life, Zenemükiado Budapest, 78; Double Life, An Autobiography, Midas Books, 82. *Mailing Add:* c/o Al Bart 6671 Sunset Blvd Los Angeles CA 90028

ROZSNYAI, ZOLTAN FRANK
MUSIC DIRECTOR & CONDUCTOR
b Budapest, Hungary, Jan 29, 27; nat US. *Study:* Franz Liszt Acad, with Kodaly, Bartok, Dohnanyi & Ferencsik; Pazmany Peter Univ, PhD(music), 49; Univ Vienna, 59-61. *Rec Perf:* On Columbia, Vox, Qualiton & Direct to Disk. *Pos:* Organist, 40-50; conct pianist, 42-52; music dir, Miskolc Phil Orch, 49-50, Debrecen Opera, 50-52, Continental Cinecraft Motion Picture Co, 61-63, Cleveland Phil, 63-67, Utica Symph Orch, 63-67, San Diego Symph Orch, 67-71 & Knoxville Symph Orch, 78-; regular cond, Hungarian Nat Philharmony, 52-56; founder & music dir, Philharmonia Hungarica, Vienna, 56-60; asst cond, New York Phil Orch, 62-63; artistic head music div, Sch Perf Arts, US Int Univ, 68-71; artistic dir, Southern Calif Phil Soc, 71- *Awards:* Dipl & prize, Int Cond Compt, Rome, 56. *Rep:* Albert Kay Assoc Inc 58 W 58th St New York NY 10019; Cond Int Mgt 95 Cedar Rd Ringwood NJ 07456. *Mailing Add:* 7927 Corteland Dr Knoxville TN 37919

RUBENSTEIN, BERNARD
CONDUCTOR
b Springfield, Mo, Oct 30, 37. *Study:* Eastman Sch Music, BMus, 58; Yale Univ, MMus, 61. *Pos:* Dir orch activ, Sch Music, Northwestern Univ, 68-80; assoc cond, Cincinnati Symph Orch, 80-; guest cond, Warsaw Phil, St Paul Chamber Orch, St Louis Little Symph, Shreveport Opera, La Guadalajara Symph, Tulsa Phil, NMex Symph, Dayton Phil, Stuttgart Opera, Milwaukee Symph, Grant Park Orch, Chicago & Tonküstler Orch, Vienna. *Teaching:* Adj music cond, Consv Music, Cincinnati Col, 83- *Awards:* Fulbright Fel, 64-65; Martha Baird Rockefeller Grant, 66-67. *Mailing Add:* c/o Herbert Barrett Mgt 1860 Broadway New York NY 10023

RUBIN, ANNA ITA
COMPOSER
b Akron, Ohio, Sept 5, 46. *Study:* Pomona Col, BA, 68; Calif Inst Arts, with Mel Powell, Mort Sobotnick & Earle Browne, BFA(music), 75, MFA(comp), 82. *Works:* Naming (group improvisation), Improvisation, 78; Sappho (women's chorus, instrm), comn by Anacrusic Chorus, 78; Marguerite's Dance (flute, voice & perc), Contemp Music Forum, 82; High Priestess & 6 of Cups (orch), Calif Inst Arts Orch, 82; De Nacht (sop & 10 instrm), Delta Ens, Holland, 83. *Mem:* Ind Comp Asn (pres, 81-82); Int League Women Comp. *Mailing Add:* Schipbeekstraat 20 I 1078 BL Amsterdam Netherlands

RUBIN, EMANUEL LEO
ADMINISTRATOR, EDUCATOR
b Pittsburgh, Pa, July 9, 35. *Study:* Carnegie-Mellon Univ, EdMusB, BFA, 58; Brandeis Univ, with Irving Fine & Harold Shapero, MFA, 61; Univ Pittsburgh, with Theodore M Finney, PhD, 68. *Teaching:* Instr music, Taylor Allderdice High Sch, 58-62; instr music hist, Bowling Green State Univ, 65-68; asst prof musicol & dept chair, Univ Wis, Milwaukee, 68-81; vis prof, Univ Haifa, Israel, 70-75 & Israel Inst Technol, 77; dir sch music, Ball State Univ, 81-83, dean fine arts, 83- *Interests:* Viola da gamba sonatas of Louis Caix d'Herveloix. *Publ:* Co-ed, A Collection of Catches, Canons & Glees (The Warren Collection), NY Mellifont Press, 71; auth, Imprinting vs Modeling: Dangers Inherent in the Definitive Performance Concept, Wis Sch Musician, 80; The Phantom Orchestra Syndrome, Ind Musicator, 82; The Arts Institution in the Urban Setting, 82 & Data Processing in Arts Administration: Problems & Practices, 83, Proc Nat Asn Sch Music. *Mailing Add:* 2008 Forest Ave Muncie IN 47304

RUBIN, HENRY PARK
VIOLIN
b Bryn Mawr, Pa, May 12, 43. *Study:* Ind Univ, with Josef Gingold, BM, 65; Juilliard Sch, with Ivan Galamian, MS, 67; studied with Oscar Schumsky & Szymon Goldberg, 73-77. *Pos:* Recitalist, London, 78 & 80, Spoleto Fest, US, 78, Mex, 81, Guatemala, 83 & Wash, 83; violinist, Soloists of Philadelphia,

71, Buffalo Phil Orch, 74, Charleston Symph, 74 & 78, London Soloist Ens, 77, Chautauqua Fest, 79 & Spoleto Fest, US, 83. *Teaching:* Creative assoc, State Univ NY, Buffalo, 71-73; tutor violin, Univ London, England, 76-77; assoc prof, Univ Ala, 77- *Awards:* Third Prize, Tibor Varga Int Violin Compt, Sion, Switzerland, 74; First Governor's Arts Award, Ala, 80. *Mem:* Music Teachers Nat Asn; Am String Teachers Asn. *Publ:* Auth, Symposium on Contemporary American Music, Spoleto Fest, 83. *Mailing Add:* Dept Music PO Box 2876 University AL 35486

RUBIN, NATHAN
EDUCATOR, VIOLIN
b Oakland, Calif, Nov 2, 29. *Study:* Private studies with Naoum Blinder, 40-46; Juilliard Sch with Louis Persinger, dipl, 49. *Rec Perf:* Trio (Leland Smith), Fantasy, 56; Works of William O Smith, Contemp, 57; Trio (Kirchner), Epic, 58; Two Rhapsodies of Bartok, 58, Sonatas (Ravel & Poulenc), 71 & Le Testament (Pound), 75, Fantasy; Lines (Christian Wolff), Comp Rec Inc, 75. *Pos:* Concertmaster, Little Symph San Francisco, 50-58, San Francisco Ballet, 56-76, Oakland Symph, 63- *Teaching:* Prof music, Mills Col, 55-74, Calif State Univ, Hayward, 74-; lectr chamber music, Univ Calif, Berkeley, 61-63. *Awards:* San Francisco Critics Award, 51; Hertz Award, Univ Calif, Berkeley, 52. *Mailing Add:* Dept Music Calif State Univ Hayward CA 94542

RÜBSAM, WOLFGANG FRIEDRICH
ORGAN, TEACHER
b Giessen, West Germany, Oct 16, 46. *Study:* Southern Methodist Univ, MMus, 70; Staatliche Hochshule Musik, Frankfurt, West Germany, with Helmut Walcha, artist dipl, 71; studied with Marie-Claire Alain, 71-74. *Rec Perf:* Complete Organ Works of Johann Sebastian Bach (incl Art of the Fugue), Philips Rec Co; Complete Organ Works of Cesar Franck, Deutsche Grammophon; Complete Organ Works of Jehan Alain, Da Camera; Complete Organ Works of Dietrich Buxtehude, Bellaphon; Complete Organ Works of Felix Mendelssohn-Bartholdy, Schwann & Cornucopia Magna Inc; Fifteen Organ Concerti by Johann Gottfried Walther, German Harmonia Mundi. *Pos:* Organist & choirmaster, Abbey Marienstatt, West Germany, 72-74; co-founder & pres, Cornucopia Magna Inc, Ill, 82- *Teaching:* Asst prof church music & organ, Northwestern Univ, 74-78, assoc prof, 78-; vis prof music, Sibelius Akad, Finland, spring 83. *Awards:* First prize, Nat Organ Playing Compt, 70; Grand Prix Award, Chartes Int Organ Compt, France, 73; German Rec Critics Prize, 82. *Mem:* Am Guild Organists. *Mailing Add:* 3238 Harrison St Evanston IL 60201

RUBY, E JANE
EDUCATOR, CHORAL MUSIC CONDUCTOR
b Mason City, Iowa, Dec 3, 18. *Study:* Univ Northern Iowa, BA(music), 41; Drake Univ, MMusEd, 61; Univ Iowa, 68. *Teaching:* Dir choral activ, Fairfield High Sch, Iowa, 41-68; assoc prof music & dir choral activ, Parsons Col, 68-73; assoc prof, Drake Univ, 73-, chairperson music educ, 79- *Awards:* Robert McCowen Mem Award, Am Choral Dir Asn, 67; Rose Hon Award, Des Moines chap, Sigma Alpha Iota, 83. *Mem:* Music Educr Nat Conf (secy-treas, 64-67, pres, 69-71); Iowa Music Educr; Am Choral Dir Asn; Sigma Alpha Iota (pres Des Moines chap, 80-82); Am Guild Organists (dean, 62-64). *Mailing Add:* 2900 Beverly Dr Des Moines IA 50322

RUDEL, JULIUS
CONDUCTOR & MUSIC DIRECTOR
Study: Early training in Vienna; Mannes Sch Music; Pace Col, Hon DMus; Univ Vt, Hon DMus; Univ Mich, Hon DMus. *Rec Perf:* Julius Caesar & Thais, RCA; The Merry Widow & Rigoletto, Angel; Silverlake, Nonesuch; Bomarzo, Columbia Rec; I Puritani, ABC Rec; and others. *Pos:* Dir, New York City Opera, 57-79; music dir, Kennedy Ctr, Washington, Cincinnati May Music Fest, Caramoor Fest New York & Wolf Trap, formerly & Buffalo Phil, 79-; guest cond, State Opera, Paris Opera, Hamburg Opera, Philadelphia Orch, Boston Symph, Chicago Symph, New York Phil, Nat Symph Orch Washington, DC, Metropolitan Opera, San Francisco Opera, and many others. *Awards:* Newspaper Guild Page One Award; Handel Medallion of New York; Chevalier des Artes et Lett, France; and others. *Mailing Add:* c/o ICM Artists 40 W 57th St New York NY 10019

RUDER, PHILIP
VIOLIN, CONDUCTOR
b Chicago, Ill. *Study:* Hartt Sch Music, dipl. *Pos:* Recitalist, New York, 63; concertmaster, New Orleans Phil, formerly, Dallas Symph, formerly, Santa Fe Opera Co, formerly & Cincinnati Symph Orch, 73-; cond, Cincinnati Symph Orch String Orch, 74-; performer, Chamber Music Fest, Elko, Nev, Casals Fest Orch, Spoleto, Italy & Salzburg Fest; concertmaster & soloist, Summer Music Fest, Sunriver, Ore. *Teaching:* Adj prof violin & orch repertoire, Col Consv Music, Univ Cincinnati. *Mailing Add:* 210 Hosen Ave Cincinnati OH 45220

RUDHYAR, DANE
COMPOSER, CRITIC-WRITER
b Paris, France, Mar 23, 95; US citizen. *Study:* Sorbonne Univ, BA, 11; Paris Consv, 12. *Works:* The Surge of Fire, perf by New Music Soc, 25; To the Real, perf by Nicolas Slonimsky, 32-33; Sinfonietta, New Music, 34; String Quartets, perf by New Music Quartet, 50 & Kronos Quartet, 79; Five Stanzas for String Orch, perf by Austrian Radio Orch, 73 & St Paul Chamber Orch, 77; Dialogues, perf by Laurie Steele, 82. *Awards:* W A Clark, Jr Award, Los Angeles Phil Orch, 22; Marjorie Peabody Waite, Am Acad & Inst Arts & Letters, 78. *Bibliog:* Paul Rosenfeld (auth), An Hour With American Music, 29; Alfred Morang (auth), Dane Rudhyar: Pioneer in Creative Synthesis, 39; John White (ed), Dane Rudhyar: Seed Man, Human Dimensions Inst, Vol 4,

3. *Mem:* Am Comp Alliance; Am Music Ctr. *Publ:* Auth, The Rebirth of Hindu Music, Theosophical Publ House, 29, Samuel Weiser, 79; Art as Release of Power, 29; Culture, Crisis and Creativity, Quest Bks, 77; The Magic of Tone and the Art of Music, Shambhala Publ, 82. *Mailing Add:* 3635 Lupine Ave Palo Alto CA 94303

RUDIAKOV, MICHAEL
CELLO, EDUCATOR
b Paris, France, Aug 9, 34. *Study:* With Eliahu Rudiakov; Manhattan Sch Music, BMus. *Pos:* Cellist solo & chamber music, conct performances worldwide; assoc dir, Southern Vt Music Fest. *Teaching:* Artistic dir chamber music, Sarah Lawrence Col & Manhattan Sch Music. *Awards:* Gold Medal, Casals Compt, Mex, 59; Harold Bauer Award. *Mailing Add:* Arilisa Conct Inc 93 Franklin Ave Yonkers NY 10705

RUDIE, ROBERT
VIOLIN, EDUCATOR
b New York, NY, Feb 12, 19. *Study:* Juilliard Sch Music. *Pos:* Concertmaster, Oklahoma City Symph, 44-45, Am Symph Orch, 73-, New York City Ballet, NJ Symph & others; first violin, Casals Fest, 51-73, Riverdale String Quartet, 59- & Bronx Arts Ens, 73-; concertmaster & asst cond, Aspen Fest, Nat Orch Asn & Phil Symph Westchester, 55-73; cond, Rudie Sinfonietta, 57-61; solo violinist, 56- *Teaching:* Dir, Riverdale Co Sch & Riverdale Sch Music, 62-; cond orch & teacher violin, Vassar Col, 66-69; co-dir prep div, Manhattan Sch Music 70-71, dir string proj, 71- *Mailing Add:* Riverdale Sch Music 253 St & Post Rd Bronx NY 10471

RUDIN, ANDREW
EDUCATOR, COMPOSER
b Newgulf, Tex, Apr 10, 39. *Study:* Univ Tex, BM, 62; Univ Pa, MA, 64. *Works:* Tragoedia, Nonesuch Rec, 69; Lumina, perf by Pa Ballet Co, 70; Satyricon (sound track), 71; The Innocent, Philadelphia Music Theatre, 72; Museum Pieces, comn by Washington, DC Chamber Music Soc, 75; Styx and Triad, perf by Alwin Nikolais Dance Co, 75; Two Elegies for Flute, Asn Music Publ, 83. *Pos:* Musical asst, Alwin Nikolais Dance Co, 75-77. *Teaching:* Asst prof music, Philadelphia Col Perf Arts, 65-; lectr opera studies, Juilliard Sch Music, 82- *Mailing Add:* 250 S 13th St Philadelphia PA 19107

RUDIS, AL (A L)
CRITIC
b Dec 9, 43. *Study:* Univ Ariz, BA, 66. *Pos:* Popular music critic, Chicago Sun-Times, 70-78; entertainment ed, Long Beach Press-Telegram, 78- *Mailing Add:* 4296 Candleberry Seal Beach CA 90740

RUDNYTSKY, ROMAN VICTOR
PIANO, EDUCATOR
b New York, NY, Nov 1, 42. *Study:* Juilliard Sch, BS, 65, MS, 65; Peabody Consv, with Leon Fleisher; studied with Rosina Lhevinne & Wilhelm Kempff, Italy & Egon Petri. *Rec Perf:* Symphony for Five Instruments (Ernest Gold), Crystal Rec, 71; The 12 Transcendental Etudes (Liszt), Polskie Nagrania, Poland, 72. *Pos:* Solo pianist, performed in US & Europe, 50- *Teaching:* Instr piano, Ind Univ, Bloomington, 66-70; artist in res, Col Consv, Univ Cincinnati, 71-72; asst prof, Dana Sch Music, Youngstown State Univ, 72. *Awards:* Second Prize, Int J S Bach Compt, Washington, DC, 60 & Int Leventritt Compt, New York, NY, 65; Fifth Prize, Int Busoni Compt, Bulzano, Italy, 67. *Mailing Add:* Dana Sch Music Youngstown State Univ Youngstown OH 44555

RUDOLF, MAX
CONDUCTOR & MUSIC DIRECTOR
b Frankfort-am-Main, Ger, June 15, 02; nat US. *Study:* Consv Music, Frankfort, with Bernhard Sekles; hon degrees from Univ Cincinnati, Miami Univ, Curtis Inst Music, Baldwin-Wallace Col, & Temple Univ. *Rec Perf:* On Columbia, Decca & Cetra-Everest. *Pos:* Asst cond, Freiburg Munic Opera, Ger, 22-23; cond, State Opera Hesse, Darmstadt, 23-29, German Opera, Prague, 29-35 & New Opera Co, New York, 44; mem musical staff, Metropolitan Opera, 45-58, adminr, Kathryn Long Opera Courses, 49-58, artistic adminr, 50-58, cond, 73-75; music dir & cond, Cincinnati Symph Orch, 58-70, world-wide conct tour, 66; music dir, Cincinnati May Fest, 63-70; artistic adv, Dallas Symph Orch, 73, NJ Symph Orch, 76-77 & Exxon-Art Endowment Cond Prog, 77-; guest cond with symph orchs throughout US & Italy. *Teaching:* Mem fac, Cent YMCA Col, Chicago, 41-43 & Curtis Inst Music, 70-73; teacher cond, Ford Found Proj, Baltimore, 62-64 & Berkshire Music Ctr, 64. *Awards:* Alice M Ditson Award, 64. *Mem:* Pi Kappa Lambda. *Publ:* Auth, The Grammar of Conducting, 50 & 80. *Mailing Add:* c/o ICM Artists 40 W 57th st New York NY 10019

RUEBECK, ANN BOWMAN
ADMINISTRATOR
b Cleveland, Ohio, Apr 25, 39. *Pos:* First vpres, Women's Comn, Ind State Symph Soc, 77-78, pres, Women's Comn, 78-81, mem exec bd, 77-, vpres, 81-82; conf chmn, Asn Major Symph Orch, 81-83, pres, 83- *Mem:* Am Symph Orch League (mem bd dir, 83-, vol coun). *Mailing Add:* 701 W Kessler Blvd Indianapolis IN 46208

RUFF, WILLIE
EDUCATOR
Study: Yale Univ. *Pos:* Mem, Mitchell-Ruff Duo, US & Europe, formerly. *Teaching:* Mem fac music, Yale Univ, 70-, dir, Duke Ellington Fel Prog, currently. *Mailing Add:* Yale Sch Music Box 2104A Yale Sta New Haven CT 06520

RUGGERI, JANET FLEMING
VIOLA
b Southampton, NY, Nov 17, 39. *Study:* Eastman Sch, with Francis Tursi & William Primrose, BM, 61. *Pos:* Violist, Rochester Phil, 58-61 & Dallas Symph, 61-62; asst prin viola, Milwaukee Symph Orch, 62-; prin viola, Grand Teton Music Fest, 67- *Mem:* MacDowell Club. *Mailing Add:* c/o Milwaukee Symph Orch 929 Water St Milwaukee WI 53203

RUGGERI, ROGER BENJAMIN
DOUBLE BASS, WRITER
b Middletown, Pa, Sept 6, 39. *Study:* Eastman Sch Music, with Oscar Zimmerman, BM, 61. *Works:* Eine Kleine Chopsticks, 71, Around About the Sea, 71, Microcosms, 72 & Wellsprings, 72, Milwaukee Symph Orch; Ludwig van Drum, Milwaukee & Cincinnati Symph, 76; Mythos, Milwaukee Symph Orch, 82; If ... Then, Milwaukee Symph Orch, 83; various film scores & commercials. *Pos:* Bassist, Rochester Phil, 59-61 & Dallas Symph, 61-62; prin bass, Milwaukee Symph Orch, 62- & Grand Teton Music Fest, 68- *Teaching:* Instr double bass, Univ Wis, Madison, 70-78, Univ Wis, Milwaukee, 70- & Wis Consv, 70- *Mem:* Int Soc Bassists (vpres, 79-83); Milwaukee Chamber Music Soc (pres, 80-82). *Mailing Add:* 3533 N Shephard Milwaukee WI 53221

RUGGIERI, ALEXANDER F
CONDUCTOR
b Santa Monica, Calif, Jan 10, 52. *Study:* Univ Southern Calif, BMus(music theory), 76, MMus(choral music), 77; Wayne State Univ, MMus(orch cond), 83. *Rec Perf:* Vespers (Rachmaninoff), Vox-Turnabout Rec, 74; An Evening of Orthodox Sacred Music, Custom Fidelity Rec. *Pos:* Music dir, Musical Arts Soc La, 75-77, Bach Chamber Singers & Chamber Orch, 80-82 & Los Angeles Dept Water & Power Choraliers, 82-83; choir dir, St Peter & Paul Orthodox Church, 77-81. *Mem:* Am Choral Dir Asn; Am Choral Found; Am Musicol Soc; Am Symph Orch League. *Mailing Add:* 1557 Lemoyne St Los Angeles CA 90026

RUGGIERO, CHARLES H(OWARD)
COMPOSER, EDUCATOR
b Bridgeport, Conn, June 19, 47. *Study:* New England Consv Music, BM, 69; Mich State Univ, MM, 74, PhD, 79. *Works:* Songs From Emily Dickinson, Mich Music Teachers Comp Comn, 74; Hocket Variations, comn by Mich Music Teachers Asn, 78; Studies for Clarinet and Vibe, 79-80 & Three Blues for Saxophone Quartet, Dorn Publ Inc, 82; Dances and Other Movements (violin, alto, sax & piano), comn by Forger-Moriarty Trio, 83. *Rec Perf:* Mich State Univ Fac Jazz Quartet, WKAR-TV prog, 83. *Teaching:* Instr perc, Univ Bridgeport, Conn, 71; instr, Mich State Univ, 73-79, asst prof music theory & comp, 79- *Awards:* Mich Music Teachers Comp Comn Award, 78. *Mem:* Am Musicol Soc; ASCAP. *Mailing Add:* Dept Music Mich State Univ East Lansing MI 48824

RUGGIERO, MATTHEW
EDUCATOR, BASSOON
Study: Curtis Inst Music, dipl; studied bassoon with Sol Schoenbach & Ferdinand De Negro. *Pos:* Participant, Marlboro Music Fest, formerly; mem, Nat Symph Orch, formerly; asst prin bassoon, Boston Symph Orch, currently; prin bassoon, Boston Pops, currently. *Teaching:* Mem fac bassoon, New England Consv Music, currently. *Mailing Add:* New England Consv Music 290 Huntington Rd Boston MA 02115

RUNNER, DAVID CLARK
ORGAN, EDUCATOR
b Long Beach, Calif, Jan 12, 48. *Study:* Boise State Univ, with C Griffith Bratt, BMus, 69; Eastman Sch Music, with David Craighead, MMus, 70, DMA & perf cert, 76. *Pos:* Organist, St John's Episcopal Church, Johnson City, Tenn, 75-82; organist & choirmaster, Downtown Christian Church, Johnson City, Tenn, 82- *Teaching:* Assoc prof music, Milligan Col, 72- *Awards:* Winner, Nat Organ Playing Compt, First Baptist Church, Worcester, Mass, 68. *Mem:* Am Guild Organists (dean Franklin chap, 77-79); Organ Hist Soc; Asn Christian Col Music Educr. *Mailing Add:* PO Box 416 Milligan College TN 37682

RUNYAN, WILLIAM EDWARD
EDUCATOR, CONDUCTOR
b Mobile, Ala, Aug 13, 45. *Study:* Murray State Univ, Ky, BME, 68; Eastman Sch Music, Univ Rochester, MA, 73, study trombone with Emory Remington, PhD, 83. *Teaching:* Asst prof, Music Dept, Colo State Univ, 73- & asst chmn, 82- *Mem:* Am Musicol Soc. *Interests:* Original music for winds, orchestration, trombone and trombone music. *Publ:* Ed, Langsam from Mahler's Symphony No 3 for Trombone Quintet, Consort Trios, 76; auth, The Alto Trombone and Contemporary Concepts of Trombone Timbre, 79, Brass Bulletin; ed, La Bavara by G M Cesare, Musica Rara, 82. *Mailing Add:* 2429 Sheffield Circle E Ft Collins CO 80526

RUPP, MARJORIE J
VIOLA, VIOLIN
b Philadelphia, Pa, Feb 17, 43. *Study:* State Univ NY, BS(music educ), 66; Univ Louisville, MMus(educ), 68; Sch Fine Arts, Antwerp, Belgium, 65. *Pos:* Violin, Antwerp Phil Orch, 64-65 & Louisville Orch 66-68; viola, Oklahoma City Symph Orch, 70-74 & Indianapolis Symph Orch 74-79 & currently. *Awards:* Am Fedn Musicians Scholar, String Cong, Mich State Univ, 60; Berkshire Music Fest Scholar, 67-69. *Mem:* Sigma Alpha Iota; Altrusa Int. *Mailing Add:* 5340 Riverview Dr Indianapolis IN 46208

RUSSELL, ARMAND KING
COMPOSER, EDUCATOR
b Seattle, Wash, June 23, 32. *Study:* Univ Wash, BA, 53, MA, 54; Eastman Sch Music, Univ Rochester, DMA, 58. *Works:* Sonata for Percussion and Piano, Music for Perc, Inc, 64; Theme and Fantasia, Ed Marks, 64; Particles (sax & piano), Bourne, 69; Symphony in 3 Images, Belwin-Mills, 72; Harlequin Concerto, Zimmerman Publ, 74; 2nd Concerto for Percussion, G Schirmer, 76; Equinox Sonata, Plymouth Music Co, 83. *Rec Perf:* Suite Concertante for Tuba & Woodwind Quintet, Avant Rec, 77. *Teaching:* Prof music, Univ Hawaii, Manoa, Honolulu, 61-; vis prof, Eastman Sch Music, Rochester, NY, summers 59-64 & 72. *Mem:* ASCAP. *Mailing Add:* 2411 Dole St Honolulu HI 96822

RUSSELL, CRAIG HENRY
EDUCATOR, GUITAR & LUTE
b Los Alamos, NMex, Apr 3, 51. *Study:* Curso Internacional de Guitarra, studied with E Pujol, summer 72, 74 & 76; Univ NMex, BM, 73, MM, 76; Univ NC, Chapel Hill, PhD, 81. *Works:* Concerto for Piano, Orch & Double Chorus, perf by Manzano High, 71; Symphony, perf by Albuquerque Youth Symph, 72; Quintet for Guitar & Strings, Univ NMex, 72; Insects (solo guitar), C Russell, 74; Zapatera! (music drama), perf by Univ NMex, 74; It's a Man's World—Or Is It? (incidental music), Univ NMex, 76; Gafas del sol (guitar), Jose Maria Gallardo del Rey, 80. *Teaching:* Guest lectr guitar & lute, Univ NMex, 73-74, grad asst guitar, 74-76; grad asst guitar, Univ NC, Chapel Hill, 76-81; asst prof music hist & guitar, Calif Polytechnic State Univ, 82- *Awards:* Fulbright-Hays Grant, 79-80; Nat Endowment Humanities Summer Inst Fel, 83. *Mem:* Am Musicol Soc; Lute Soc Am; Sociedad Espanola de Musicologia; NMex Comp Guild. *Interests:* Spanish guitar theorists of 18th century. *Publ:* Coauth, El arte de recomposicion en la musica espanola para la guitarra barroca, Revista de Musicologia, 82; auth, Santiago de Murcia, Early Music, 82; Santiago de Murcia: The French Connection in Baroque Spain, J Lute Soc Am, 82. *Mailing Add:* 709 Los Osos Valley Rd Los Osos CA 93402

RUSSELL, JAMES REAGAN
CLARINET, CONDUCTOR
b Alameda, Calif, Apr 2, 35. *Study:* Univ Calif, Berkeley, AB, 59; State Univ NY, Stony Brook, MMus, 73. *Rec Perf:* Music of Macedonia and Bulgarian, Bay Rec, 73. *Pos:* Asst cond, Univ Symph, Univ Calif, Berkeley, 58-65; solo clarinetist, Golden Gate Park Band, San Francisco, 63-71; bassethorn, San Francisco Opera, 79-80. *Teaching:* Lectr clarinet, Univ Calif, Berkeley, 69- *Awards:* Alfred Hertz Travelling Scholar, Univ Calif, 65-66 & 66-67. *Mem:* San Francisco Single Reed Soc. *Mailing Add:* 2310 Ellsworth St Apt 6 Berkeley CA 94704

RUSSELL, JOHN GRAY
PIANO, CONDUCTOR
b Hanford, Calif, May 15, 37. *Study:* Calif State Univ, Fresno, BA, 59; studied with Adolph Baller, 59-65; Calif State Univ, Chico, MA, 68. *Works:* Laudate Pueri (chorus & orch), Lawson-Gould; Walk This Mile in Silence (chorus), Assoc; Who Has Seen the Wind? (chorus), Walton; Nocturnal Variations (piano), 83; Three Motets for Unaccompanied Chorus, Walton Music Ltd, London (in press); Two Madrigals for Chamber Chamber Chorus, Music 70 Music Publ. *Teaching:* Asst prof music, Calif State Univ, Chico, 66-68; prof piano & comp, Calif State Univ, 68- *Mem:* Am Soc Univ Comp; ASCAP. *Mailing Add:* 2434 Del Campo Blvd San Luis Obispo CA 93401

RUSSELL, LOIS ROBERTA LANGLEY
PERCUSSION
b Upland, Calif, Feb 21, 32. *Study:* Univ Wash. *Pos:* Prin perc, Honolulu Symph Orch, 61- *Teaching:* Instr perc, Univ Hawaii, Honolulu, 61- *Mem:* Percussive Arts Soc (pres Hawaii chap, 80-). *Mailing Add:* 3296 Hullani Dr Honolulu HI 96822

RUSSELL, LOUISE
SOPRANO
b Muscatine, Iowa. *Study:* Iowa State Univ, BMus. *Roles:* Micaela in Carmen, New York City Opera; Gilda in Rigoletto, La Scala in Japan, 71; Elijah, Philadelphia Orch; Oscar in Un Ballo in maschera, 76 & 82 & Olympia in Les Contes d'Hoffmann, 77, NJ State Opera; Norina in Don Pasquale, San Antonio Symph Opera, 83. *Awards:* First Prize, Vocal Compt Vercelli, Italy. *Mailing Add:* c/o Herbert Barrett Mgt 1860 Broadway New York NY 10023

RUSSELL, LUCY HALLMAN
EDUCATOR, HARPSICHORD
b Guntersville, Ala, Feb 10, 49. *Study:* Univ Montevallo, BA, 69; Univ Ala, MM, 74; State Acad Music, Munich, artist dipl, 78; Univ Munich; State Acad Music, Stuttgart, 83; studied harpsichord with Kenneth Gilbert & organ with L F Tagliavini. *Rec Perf:* Frescobaldi-Storace, b & b Rec, Freiburg, WGermany, 83; Il Combattimento di Tancredi e Clorinda (Monteverdi), Classico Rec, Ricordi, Milan, Italy, 83. *Teaching:* Baroque singing, Urbino Early Music Fest, Italy, summer 81; lectr music hist & choir, Munich Campus, Univ Md, 78-; instr hist keyboards, Wuerzburg Consv Music, 82-; teacher harpsichord, Jeunesses Musicales, Groznjan, Yugoslavia, summer 83 & Radovljica, Yugoslavia, summer 83. *Mem:* Am Musicol Asn; Italian Musicol Asn; German Musicol Asn; Southeastern Hist Keyboard Soc. *Interests:* Frescobaldi; Obligo; Ostinato. *Publ:* Auth, The Walsingham Variations of Bull and Byrd in Kongressbericht—1974, Bärenreiter. *Mailing Add:* Lincolnstrasse 34 D-8000 Munich Germany, Federal Republic of

RUSSELL, ROGENE
OBOE & ENGLISH HORN, TEACHER
b Ames, Iowa, Mar 9, 49. *Study:* Univ Tenn, BMus, 71; Sch Music, Yale Univ, MMus, 73; studied with Robert Bloom. *Pos:* Second oboe & English horn, Peninsula Music Fest, 74- & Ft Worth Symph Orch, 78-; second oboe, Louisville Orch, 74-78; oboist, Fine Arts Chamber Players, 81- *Teaching:* Adj instr oboe, Eastfield Col, 81- *Mailing Add:* 1515 Mapleton Dallas TX 75228

RUSSELL, ROSEMARY
MEZZO-SOPRANO
Roles: The Bear. *Pos:* Soloist with Detroit Symph, Mozarteum Orch Salzburg, Aspen Fest Orch, Piedmont Chamber Orch & other maj orchs & at festivals & univ concerts. *Mailing Add:* c/o Liegner Mgt 1860 Broadway Suite 1610 New York NY 10023

RUSSIANOFF, LEON
EDUCATOR, CLARINET
b Brooklyn, NY. *Study:* City Col, City Univ New York, BS, 38; studied clarinet with Simeon Bellison & Daniel Bonade. *Pos:* Mem, Ballet Russe de Monte Carlo Orch, formerly & theatre & opera orchs, formerly; performances, NBC & CBS Radio, formerly & chamber music. *Teaching:* Adj asst prof clarinet, Brooklyn Col, City Univ New York, currently; adj assoc prof, Queens Col, City Univ New York, currently; mem fac, Wesleyan Univ, State Univ NY, Purchase, Teachers Col, Columbia Univ, Manhattan Sch Music, 53- & Juilliard Sch, 72- *Mailing Add:* 1595 Broadway New York NY 10019

RUSSO, CHARLES
EDUCATOR, CLARINET
Study: Manhattan Sch Music, BMus; Univ Pittsburgh; studied clarinet with Bellison. *Pos:* First clarinet, Symph of Air, currently & NBC Opera Orch, currently; mem, New Art Wind Quintet, currently; leader, Juilliard String Quartet, currently; performer, Bennington Comp Conf & Chamber Music Ctr, currently; Spoleto Fest, Marlboro Fest, Minn Fest, Mostly Mozart Fest & Casals Fest; prin clarinet, New York City Opera Orch, currently. *Teaching:* Mem fac, New England Consv, formerly, Vassar Col, formerly, State Univ NY, Purchase, formerly & Bennington Comp Conf & Chamber Music Ctr, currently; mem fac clarinet, Manhattan Sch Music, 63-, mem ens fac, 71-; vis lectr clarinet, Hartt Sch Music, 81- *Mailing Add:* Manhattan Sch Music 120 Claremont Ave New York NY 10027

RUSSO, JOHN
COMPOSER, CLARINET
b Trenton, NJ, Jan 16, 43. *Study:* Peabody Inst, 61-63; Curtis Inst, BM, 67; Temple Univ, MM, 69; studied with Lazlo Halasz & Anshel Brusilow. *Works:* Three Songs (sop, clarinet & piano), Orion Rec, 61; Variations on a Kyrie, Lake State, 64; Twenty Modern Studies, 66-69 & Twenty Contemporary Studios for Oboe or Saxophone, 69-79, Henri Elkan Publ; Winchester Overture, comn by Cornell Univ Wind Ens, 75; Clarinet Concerto, 81; Three Pieces for Orchestra, comn by Philadelphia Youth Orch, 82. *Rec Perf:* Three Bagatelles, 71 & Conversazione for Piano, 73, Capra; Largetto (viola, clarinet & pianoforte), 77 & Elegy (oboe), 78, Ors; Summer Sketch (clarinet & string quartet), 82, Four Riffs (clarinet & perc), 82 & Chamber Soc Orch, 83, CRS. *Pos:* Pres, Contemp Rec Soc, 80-; guest appearances with Concerto Soloists Philadelphia, Little Orch Soc Philadelphia, Temple Univ Orch, Peabody Inst Wind Ens, Baltimore Symph Orch, Manila Symph Orch & Rome Fest Orch; cond & artistic dir, Chamber Soc Orch, currently. *Teaching:* Instr theory, Temple Univ, 67-69; instr woodwinds, Widener Univ, Chester, Pa, 69-73; instr clarinet & sax, Philadelphia Col Perf Arts, 76-79. *Mem:* Am Asn Univ Prof; ASCAP; Chamber Music Am; Am Comp Alliance. *Mailing Add:* 724 Winchester Rd Broomall PA 19008

RUSSO, WILLIAM
COMPOSER, WRITER
b June 25, 28. *Study:* Roosevelt Col, BA, 55. *Works:* Symphony No 2 in C, New York Phil, 59; Three Pieces for Blues Band & Orch, Chicago Symph Orch, 68; Aesop's Fables (libretto by Jon Swan), 72; Songs of Celebration, San Francisco Chorale, 75; Street Music, San Francisco Symph Orch, 76; The Shepherds' Christmas, WFMT, 80; Urban Trilogy, New Am Orch, 82. *Teaching:* Comp in res, Columbia Col, 65- *Publ:* Auth, The Jazz Composer, 60 & Jazz Composition, 68, Univ Chicago; Composing Music, Prentice-Hall, 83. *Mailing Add:* 621 W Buckingham Pl Chicago IL 60657

RUTMAN, PAUL LUCIEN
PIANO
b New York, NY, July 6, 48. *Study:* Manhattan Sch Music, BM, 66; Juilliard Sch Music, MS 69, DMA, 74. *Rec Perf:* Paul Rutman, Melodya Rec, 70; Paul Rutman Plays Russian Piano Music, Columbia Rec, 79. *Pos:* Solo pianist, currently. *Teaching:* Vis prof piano, Hartt Sch Music, currently. *Awards:* Fulbright Awards, 67-68; prizewinner, Marguerite Long Int Piano Compt, Paris, 67 & Int Tchaikovsky Compt, Moscow, 70. *Rep:* Columbia Artists Mgt 165 W 57th St New York NY 10019. *Mailing Add:* 360 Central Park W New York NY 10025

RUTSCHMAN, EDWARD RAYMOND
EDUCATOR
b Boulder, Colo, July 9, 46. *Study:* Univ Northern Colo, BMus, 68; Ariz State Univ, MMus(comp), 71; Univ Wash, PhD(musicol), 79. *Pos:* Coordr, Music Theory Prog, Alaska Fine Arts Camp, Wasilla, Alaska, summers 75- *Teaching:* Vis lectr, Ore State Univ, Corvallis, 76 & Univ Manitoba, 76-77; assoc prof & grad prog adv, Western Wash Univ, 77- *Mem:* Am Musicol Soc;

Soc Music Theory. *Interests:* Seventeenth century opera; relationship of libretto to music. *Publ:* Auth, The Microfilm Collection of Libretti and Manuscript Scores at the University of Washington, 76 & Minato and the Venetian Opera Libretto, 79, Current Musicol; Music Among the Muses, In: Symposium on Interdisciplinary Aspects of Academic Disciplines, Western Wash Univ, 83. *Mailing Add:* Music Dept Western Wash Univ Bellingham WA 98225

RUTSTEIN, SEDMARA See Zakarian-Rutstein, Sedmara

RYAN, BYRON DEAN
CONDUCTOR
b Hollywood, Calif. *Study:* Juilliard Sch, with Fritz Mahler, cert, 49; Mannes Col Music, with Carl Bamberger, cert, 52; Dalcroze Sch, cert, 52; Music Acad West, with Richard Lert, cert, 55; Pontifical Inst Sacred Music, Rome, 57; Scuola Teatro dell'Opera, Rome, 57. *Rec Perf:* Dorothy Coulter, Arias, Phoenix Rec, 59; Carrie Nation, 65; Captain Jinks, 75; The Elixir of Love, WCET TV, 79. *Pos:* Founder & music dir, Acad Chamber Players, New York; music dir & cond, NH Music Fest, 56-59; music dir, Starlight Theatre, Kansas City, Mo, 60-71; cond & coach, New York City Opera, 61-72; assoc music dir & cond, Kansas City Lyr Opera, 69-79; cond & chorus dir, San Francisco Opera, 72-74; cond, San Francisco Spring Opera, 72-74; guest cond, Opera Memphis, 76-80, Conn Opera, 80-, Pittsburgh Opera, 80- and many others; cond & chorus master, Cincinnati Opera Co, 76-79, res cond, 79- *Awards:* Fulbright Found Grant, 57; Cond Scholar, Liederkranz Soc; Diploma Merit, Int Cond Compt, Santa Cecilia, Rome, 59. *Mem:* Am Fedn Musicians. *Mailing Add:* 500 West End Ave New York NY 10024

RYDER, GEORGIA ATKINS
ADMINISTRATOR, EDUCATOR
b Newport News, Va, Jan 30, 24. *Study:* Hampton Inst, BS(music), 44; Univ Mich, MusM, 46; NY Univ, PhD, 70. *Pos:* Music consult, Alexandria, Va Pub Sch, 45-48. *Teaching:* From asst prof to assoc prof vocal music educ & head music dept, Norfolk State Col, 69-79, prof voice & dean sch arts & lett, 79- *Mem:* Col Music Soc (mem nat coun, 80-82); Nat Asn Teachers Singing; Inst Res Black Am Music (mem exec comt, 81-); Music Educr Nat Conf. *Publ:* Auth, articles in, Black Perspective Music, 75, J Negro Hist, 76, Notable American Women, Belknap Press, 81 & Col Mus Soc, 82. *Mailing Add:* 5551 Brookville Rd Norfolk VA 23502

RYDER, JEANNE
CRITIC, WRITER
b Arlington, Mass, Mar 26, 52. *Study:* Northeastern Univ, BA, 74; Columbia Univ, MA(hist musicol), 80. *Pos:* Ed, Current Musicol J, 80- *Mem:* Am Musicol Soc. *Interests:* Opera from 18th century through German Romanticism. *Publ:* Contribr, Listen: A Guide to the Pleasures of Music, Allyn & Bacon, 76; auth, The Opera Calendar 1983, 83 & The Opera Calendar 1984 (in prep), Tidemark, Inc. *Mailing Add:* 100 Morningside Dr #3E New York NY 10027

RYDER, JUDITH (MRS BRUCE FRUMKER)
PIANO, EDUCATOR
Study: Eastman Sch Music, BM, MM; studied with Armand Basile, Eugene List, David Renner & Leonard Shure. *Pos:* Accmp, Columbia Artists & compts in US & abroad; performer chamber music in US & Can; mem, Thalia Trio, formerly; musical coordr, dir tours, pianist & coach, Cleveland Opera, currently. *Teaching:* Mem fac, Eastman Sch Music, formerly, Cleveland Music Sch Settlement, formerly & Cleveland Inst Music, 75- *Mailing Add:* Cleveland Inst Music 11021 E Blvd Cleveland OH 44106

RYDZYNSKI, MICHAEL VINCENT MATTHEW
PERCUSSION, EDUCATOR
b Long Island City, NY, Aug 18, 55. *Study:* Sch Fine Arts, Univ Calif, Irvine, BA(music), 78; Sch Arts, Calif State Univ, Fullerton, MMus(perc perf), 83; perc study with Forrest W Clark, Jr & Todd L Miller, piano with Arnold Juda & cond with Keith S Clark, Jr. *Works:* Characteristic Dialogues for Marimba and Cello, perf by comp & Karen Pesyna-Olzak, 81; Trio for Flute, Marimba and Bassoon, perf by Cindy Bueker, comp & Elizabeth Moberly, 82. *Rec Perf:* Piano Concerto No 2, Op 37 (Alberto Ginastera), Orion Rec, 74. *Pos:* Alt perc, Orange Co Pac Symph Orch, 79- & Long Beach Symph Orch, 83-; co-prin perc, Fullerton Civic Light Opera Orch, 82; prin perc, Fullerton Community Chorale & Orch, 81-82; cond wind ens, Univ Calif, Irvine; cond wind ens & perc ens, Calif State Univ, Fullerton. *Teaching:* Lectr music, Calif State Univ, Fullerton, 82-83. *Mem:* Am Musicol Soc ; Percussive Arts Soc; Music Libr Asn; Am Symph Orch; Nat Asn Col Wind & Perc Instr. *Mailing Add:* 3842 Hamilton St Irvine CA 92714

RYERSON, GREG
BASS
b Fremont, Nebr. *Study:* Univ Toronto. *Roles:* Dr Grenvil in La Traviata, Santa Fe Opera; Otello & Lulu, Can Opera Co; La Boheme, Tex Opera Theatre; I Due Foscari & Lucrezia Borgia, Opera Orch New York; Tom in Un Ballo in maschera, NJ State Opera, 82. *Pos:* Oratorio performer, Seattle, Toronto & Houston. *Mailing Add:* c/o Robert Lombardo Assoc 1 Harkness Plaza 61 W 62 Suite 6F New York NY 10023

RZEWSKI, FREDERIC
COMPOSER, EDUCATOR
b Westfield, Mass, Apr 13, 38. *Study:* Harvard Univ, with Walter Piston & Claudio Spies, BA, 58; Princeton Univ, with Roger Sessions & Milton Babbitt, MFA, 60; studied with Luigi Dallapiccola. *Works:* Requiem (chorus & orch), New York Phil, 71; Second Structure (improvising musicians), perf by comp on piano & synthesizer, Chicago, 73; Coming Together (speaker, bass instrm & ens), New York, 74; Attica (speaker, bass instrm & ens), New York, 74; Struggle (bar & orch), 74; Song and Dance (four players), Int Rostrum of Comp, Paris, 79; A Long Time Man (piano & orch), perf by comp & Dartmouth Col Symph, 80. *Teaching:* Instr, Cologne, Germany, 63 & 70, New Lincoln Sch, NY, 72-73, Turtle Bay Music Sch, 73, Art Inst Chicago, 73-75 & Consv Royal, Liege, Belgium, 77- *Awards:* Fulbright Fel in Italy, 60-62; Ford Found Artists in Berlin Grant, 63-65; Creative Artists Pub Serv Prog Grant, 73. *Rep:* Lynn Garon Mgt 1199 Park Ave New York NY 10028. *Mailing Add:* 777 West End Ave Apt 5B New York NY 10025

S

SABLE, BARBARA KINSEY
CRITIC-WRITER, EDUCATOR
b Astoria, NY, Oct 6, 27. *Study:* Col Wooster, BA, 49; Teachers Col, Columbia Univ, MA(music), 50; Ind Univ, Bloomington, MusD, 66. *Works:* Moon Whims (song cycle), 78 & Portraits (song cycle), 79, self publ. *Teaching:* Instr, Cottey Col, 59-60; asst prof, Northeast Mo State Teachers Col, 62-64 & Univ Calif, Santa Barbara, 64-69; prof, Univ Colo, Boulder, 69- *Mem:* Nat Asn Teachers Singing (assoc ed, 69- & state gov, 79-); Music Teachers Nat Asn. *Publ:* Auth, Morike Poems Set by Brahms, Schumann & Wolf, Music Rev, 68; Performance Problems: 20th Century Recitative, Nat Asn Teachers Singing Bulletin, 69; Schubert and Poems of Ossian, Music Rev, 73; On Contemporary Notation & Performance, Nat Asn Teachers Singing Bulletin, 76; The Vocal Sound, Prentice-Hall, 82. *Mailing Add:* Col Music Campus Box 301 Univ Colo Boulder CO 80309

SABO, MARLEE
EDUCATOR, VOICE
Study: Consv Music, Oberlin Col, BM; Mozarteum, Salzburg, Austria; Ind Univ, MM. *Rec Perf:* On Orion, Turnabout & Nonesuch. *Pos:* Performer recitals, operas & oratorios, Europe; singer, Florentine Opera, WGN Artists Showcase, Grant Park, Chicago, Atlanta Lyr Opera, St Paul Chamber Orch & Milwaukee Symph. *Teaching:* Instr voice & opera wkshp, Wis Consv Music, currently. *Awards:* Fulbright Scholar Stuttgart. *Mailing Add:* c/o Int Artists Mgt 58 W 72nd St New York NY 10023

SACCO, P PETER
COMPOSER, EDUCATOR
b Albion, NY, Oct 25, 28. *Study:* Sch Educ, NY Univ, BS; Eastman Sch Music, with Bernard Rogers & Howard Hanson, MM, 54, DMA, 58. *Works:* Midsummer Dream Night (oratorio with orch), San Francisco, 61; Mr Vinegar (chamber opera for children), 66; Piano Concerto (orch), San Francisco, 68; Tithonus (two horns, piano & string orch), 72; Solomon (oratorio with orch), San Francisco, 76; Moab Illuminations (orch), 76; Two Extemporaneous Pieces (orch), 77. *Teaching:* Mem fac, San Francisco State Univ, 59-, prof emer, 81- *Awards:* Grants, Nat Endowment Arts, 68 & 74 & Am Music Ctr, 69; ASCAP Awards, 66-72. *Mailing Add:* Music Dept San Francisco State Univ San Francisco CA 94132

SACEANU, DAN GEORGE
WRITER
Study: Consv Music, Bucharest, Romania, with George Balan & V Cosma, dipl, 75; Grad Ctr, City Univ New York, with Barry Brook, currently. *Pos:* Music ed, Orfeu, 73-74; lectr, Bucharest Pub Libr, 76-78; col asst, Grad Ctr Libr, City Univ New York, 81-; mus ed, New York Spectator, 82- *Mem:* Am Musicol Soc; Col Music Soc. *Interests:* Ethnomusicology; early classical symphony; music symbolism. *Publ:* Auth, Arta Si Tehnologia, Orfeu, 73; The Music and the Philosophical Thinking, New York Spectator, 82; contribr, Francois-Joseph Gossec, In: The Symphony 1720-1840, Garland Publ (in prep). *Mailing Add:* 818 Manhattan Ave Brooklyn NY 11222

SACHER, JACK, JR
EDUCATOR, LECTURER
b New York, NY, Apr 26, 31. *Study:* Middlebury Col, AB(music), 52; Columbia Univ, musicol with Paul Lang, MA, 56, Teachers Col, EdD, 64. *Teaching:* Supvr music, North Bergen Pub Sch, 60-64; prof music hist, Montclair State Col, 64-, chmn dept music, 80-; vis prof, Teachers Col, Columbia Univ, 81-83. *Mem:* Am Musicol Soc; Am Choral Dir Asn; Music Educr Nat Conf; Sigma Alpha Iota. *Interests:* Chamber music for voice in early 19th century. *Publ:* Ed & auth, Music A to Z, Grosset & Dunlap, 63; coauth, The Changing Voice, Augsburg Press, 65; auth, Bizet's Carmen, Met Opera Guild, 67; coauth, The Art of Sound—An Introduction to Music, Prentice-Hall, 71 & 77; auth, A Guide to Rigoletto, Metropolitan Opera Guild, 79. *Mailing Add:* 107 Oak Dr Cedar Grove NJ 07009

SACHS, DAVID H
WRITER, LECTURER
b New York, NY, Jan 13, 49. *Study:* Columbia Univ, BA, 69. *Pos:* Auth jacket notes, Op One Rec Inc, 80-, mem bd, 82-; contribr, Fanfare Mag, 83- *Publ:* Auth, Mozart, Quick Fox, 79. *Mailing Add:* 301 W 45th St New York NY 10036

SACHS, JOEL
PIANO, EDUCATOR
b New Haven, Conn. *Study:* Harvard Univ, BA; Columbia Univ, MA, PhD; studied piano with Ray Lev, Rosina Lhevinne & Ilona Kabos. *Rec Perf:* On Nonesuch Rec & Advan Rec; on BBC-TV, CBS-TV & Voice Am. *Teaching:* Mem fac, Columbia Univ, 67-76; lectr music hist, Juilliard Sch, 70-; assoc prof music, Brooklyn Col, 76- & Grad Ctr, City Univ New York, currently; concts & wkshps 20th century music, US. *Awards:* Guggenheim Fel, 78-79. *Mailing Add:* Consv Music Brooklyn Col Brooklyn NY 11210

SAETTA, MARY LOU (MARY LOU SAETTA-GILMAN)
VIOLIN
b Charlotte, NC. *Study:* Eastman Sch Music, BMus, MMus, 75; studies with Carroll Glenn, Joseph Knitzer & Aaron Rosand. *Pos:* Dir & violinist, Capitol Chamber Artists, 69- *Teaching:* Instr strings & chamber music, Col St Rose, 72-74; instr violin, Union Col, 76; instr violin & chamber music, Ctr Cult Develop, Alaska, 83. *Awards:* Berkshire Music Ctr Fel Award, 76. *Mem:* Chamber Music Am; Am Fedn Musicians. *Mailing Add:* 263 Manning Blvd Albany NY 12206

SAFFIR, KURT
CONDUCTOR & MUSIC DIRECTOR, WRITER
b Vienna, Austria, Aug 17, 29; US citizen. *Study:* Juilliard Sch, piano with Olga Samaroff & Rosalyn Tureck, BS, 51, MS, 52. *Pos:* Cond, New York Opera, 53-63, Lake George Opera Fest, 63-66 & Dortmund Munic Opera, 64-67; music dir, Capital Artists, Albany, 69-80 & Queens Opera, currently. *Mem:* Am Symph Orch League, Cond Guild; Nat Opera Asn; Nat Fedn Music Clubs. *Publ:* Auth, Sight-Reading, Music J, 71; Bayreuth Pit, Opera News, 74. *Mailing Add:* 175 W 76th St New York NY 10023

SAFFLE, MICHAEL BENTON
WRITER, EDUCATOR
b Salt Lake City, Utah, Dec 3, 46. *Study:* Univ Utah, BA, 68, BMus, 68; Boston Univ, AM, 70; Stanford Univ, PhD, 77. *Teaching:* Instr, Stanford Univ, 77-78; asst prof, Va Polytechnic Inst & State Univ, 78-83, assoc prof, 83-; guest lectr, Univ Utah, Radford State & Emory Univ, Cent Consv Peking, People's Repub China, & Shanghai Consv, People's Repub China. *Awards:* Dankstipendium, German Acad Exchange Serv, 74-75; Am Philosophical Soc Fel, 80; Cert Teaching Excellence, Va Polytechnic Inst & State Univ, 81. *Mem:* Am Musicol Soc; Coun Res Music Educ; Am Guild Organists. *Interests:* Liszt; aesthetics and interdisciplinary studies. *Publ:* Auth, New Light on Playing Liszt's Bach Prelude and Fugue, Am Organist, 82; Liszt's Sonata in b minor: Another Look at the Double-Function Question, 82 & Unpublished Liszt Works at Weimar: A Preliminary Catalog, 83, J Am Liszt Soc; Aesthetic Education in Theory and Practice, Coun Res Music Educ Bulletin, 83. *Mailing Add:* 470 Montgomery St Christiansburg VA 24073

SAFRAN, ARNO M
COMPOSER, EDUCATOR
b New York, NY, Aug 27, 32. *Study:* Hartt Col Music, BMus, 53, MMus, 55. *Works:* Three Symphonic Statements, Princeton Symph Orch, 63; Sinfonia Breve, Colonial Symph, Madison, NJ, 67; Sonata for Clarinet & Piano, Allen Pomerantz, 68; Toccata 68 for Strings, Princeton Chamber Orch, 70; Music for Orpheus, Trenton State Col Fac Wind Quintet, 70; Sonata for Oboe & Piano, Jerry & Sandra Milstein, 78; Fantasia on Popular America (piano), Phyllis Lehrer, 81. *Pos:* Music critic, Princeton Packet, 62-64 & Town Topics of Princeton, 64-74. *Teaching:* Assoc prof music, Trenton State Col, 65- *Awards:* Fourth Prize, BMI Student Comp Award, 54. *Mailing Add:* 37 Bank St Princeton NJ 08540

SAHUC, NOLAN JOHN
EDUCATOR, BASSOON
b New Orleans, La, Aug 25, 23. *Study:* Univ Southwestern La, BA, 48; Columbia Univ, MA, 52. *Pos:* Bassoonist, Baton Rouge Symph Orch, 45-48; prin bassoon, Shreveport Symph Orch, 48-51. *Teaching:* Assoc prof music, Univ Southwestern La, 51-73, prof & dir Sch Music, 77- *Mem:* Music Educr Nat Conf; La Music Educr Asn; Col Music Soc; Am Asn for Music Therapy; Int Double Reed Soc. *Publ:* Ed, Louisiana Musician, La Music Educ Asn, 48-51; auth, Fix That Bassoon Reed, Educ Music Mag, 53; Philosophy Reharmonized, Sch Musician, 55; Success vs Superior Ratings, La Musician, 56; coauth, All About Recorders, Trophy Music Co, 69. *Mailing Add:* 113 Phillip Ave Lafayette LA 70503

ST JOHN, KATHLEEN LOUISE
COMPOSER, PIANO
b Long Beach, Calif, May 28, 42. *Study:* San Diego State Col, studied piano & strings with Gilbert Back, piano with John D Blyth & orch with David Ward-Steinman, 62-66; Darmstadt Ferienkurse Neu Musik, WGermany, with Karlheinz Stockhausen & Gyorgy Ligeti, 68; Princeton Electronic Music Ctr, with Vladimir Ussachevsky, Bulent Arel, Mario Davidovsky & Alice Shields, 68-72; Berkshire Music Ctr, studied comp with Alexander Goehr, 69; Juilliard Sch, studied piano with Ania Dorfmann & comp with Luciano Berio & Hugo Weisgall, BM, 71; Johnson State Col Comp Conf, 76; Inst Sonologie, Utrecht, Holland, 76-77; Calif Inst Arts, studied comp with Mel Powell, MFA, 79. *Works:* Mosquito (string orch & alto choir), Prelude (clarinet & piano), Sonnet 29 (bar reader & instrm ens) & Fragrances (piano & orch), Carl Fischer Inc. *Pos:* Music transcriber for Laura Boulton, Sch Int Affairs, Columbia Univ, 68-70; pianist, Calif Arts Twentieth Century Players Ens, 78-79. *Teaching:* Guest lectr, Dept Music, Univ Ottawa, Can, 73 & Gov Sch for Gifted, Randolph-Macon Col, 76; asst prof theory & piano, Dept Music, Calif Inst Arts, 79-80. *Awards:* Norlin Found Comp Fel, MacDowell Colony, 76; Meet the Comp Grant, 80-83; Nat Endowment Arts Comp Fel Grant, 81-82. *Mem:* ASCAP; Am Women Comp Inc; Am Music Ctr Inc. *Mailing Add:* Ansonia Hotel 2109 Broadway Apt 10-142 New York NY 10023

SAKELLARIOU, GEORGE
GUITAR
b Athens, Greece, May 2, 44. *Study:* Hellenikon Odeon Consv, Athens, dipl, 63. *Rec Perf:* Music From SAm, AMAT Rec, 81. *Pos:* Chmn guitar dept, San Francisco Consv Music, 64-; conct guitarist, 64- *Mem:* Music Teachers Asn. *Rep:* Calif Artists 23 Liberty St San Francisco CA 94110. *Mailing Add:* 191 McNear Dr San Rafael CA 94901

SAKS, TOBY
CELLO, EDUCATOR
b New York, NY, Jan 8, 42. *Study:* Juilliard Sch, with Leonard Rose, BS, 64, MS, 66. *Rec Perf:* Martinu Sonata's No 1 & 3 (cello & piano), Pandora Rec, 83. *Pos:* Cello sect, New York Phil, 70-75; music dir & founder, Seattle Chamber Music Fest, 82- *Teaching:* Assoc prof cello, Univ Wash, 76- *Awards:* First Prize, Casals Compt, 61; Sixth Prize, Tchaikovsky Compt, 62. *Mem:* Seattle Violoncello Soc (pres, 82-83). *Mailing Add:* Sch Music DN10 Univ Wash Seattle WA 98195

SALANDER, ROGER MARK
CLARINET, EDUCATOR
b New York, NY, Aug 13, 43. *Study:* Juilliard Sch Music, dipl, 64; private study with Alfred Prinz, Vienna, 70-72. *Rec Perf:* Sonata (Poulenc), 78, Pentagramm (Eder De Lastra), 79 & Sonata (Hueber), 79, ORF, Vienna. *Pos:* Regular substitute, Vienna State Opera & Phil, 70-79; clarinetist & soloist, Ens Kontrapunkte, Vienna, 70- *Teaching:* Prof clarinet & chamber music, Inst de Hautes Etudes Musicales, Montreux, 74-75, Univ Southern Calif, Los Angeles, 76-77 ; prof clarinet, Vienna Consv, Austria, 77- *Bibliog:* John Rockwell (auth), When Familiar Works Take On Renewed Vigor, New York Times, 1/9/83. *Mailing Add:* 120 Bennett Ave New York NY 10033

SALERNO-SONNENBERG, NADJA
VIOLIN
b Rome, Italy, Jan 10, 61; US citizen. *Study:* Curtis Inst Music, 69-75; Juilliard Sch, 75-80; studied with Dorothy DeLay, 75-80. *Rec Perf:* Sonata (Faure) & Sonata in F Minor (Prokofiev), Music Masters, 81. *Pos:* Conct violinist, 80- *Awards:* First Prize, Walter W Naumburg Int Violin Compt, 81. *Mailing Add:* c/o Robert Levin Assoc Inc 250 W 57th St Ste 1332 New York NY 10107

SALESKY, BRIAN
CONDUCTOR & MUSIC DIRECTOR, ADMINISTRATOR
b New York, NY, Feb 23, 52. *Study:* Indiana Univ, BA, 73; study cond with Maestro Gianfranco Masini. *Pos:* Guest cond, New York City Opera, 78-82, Kennedy Ctr Opera, 79, Atlanta Opera, 81, Nat Orch Peru, 81; music dir, New York City Opera Nat Co, 79-83. *Teaching:* Guest instr opera, Hunter Col, 79, Temple Univ, 80; opera fac, Am Inst Musical Studies, Austria, 83. *Publ:* Auth, Menotti: Reissue of Original 1947 Recordings, Sound Rev, 80. *Mailing Add:* 515 W 59th St #18F New York NY 10019

SALISBURY, JAMES EARL
CONDUCTOR, PIANO
b Twin Falls, Idaho, Oct 28, 51. *Study:* Brigham Young Univ, BA, 76; studied with Joseph Rosenstock; Univ Lower Calif, PhD, 82. *Rec Perf:* Brigham Young University Symphony Concert, Brigham Young Univ Rec Studio, 74. *Pos:* Dir & cond, Utah Children's Choral, 75-78, Cottonwood Symph Orch, 76 & Salt Lake Area Mormon Youth Choir, 77-78. *Teaching:* Instr Suzuki & piano, Salt Lake Suzuki Piano Sch, 76-; headmaster, John Holt Learning Ctr, 79-83; dir, Utah Suzuki Inst, Brigham Young Univ, summer 81. *Mem:* Suzuki Asn Am; Am Symph Orch League; Am Chamber Music Players. *Mailing Add:* PO Box 646 West Jordan UT 84084

SALISTEAN, KIM(BERLY) OSBORNE
VIOLIN
b Norfolk, Nebr, Aug 26, 57. *Study:* Univ Nebr, Lincoln, BME, 79, MM, 81. *Pos:* Prin second, Lincoln Symph, 76-, Nebr Chamber Orch, 78-; sect first violin, Omaha Symph, 80- *Mem:* Am String Teachers Asn. *Mailing Add:* 3005 Summit Blvd Lincoln NE 68502

SALKIND, MILTON
ADMINISTRATOR, PIANO
b Wilmington, Del, Feb 21, 16. *Study:* George Washington Univ, BS, 42; Juilliard Sch, BS(piano), 49; studied piano with Irwin Freundlich & Edward Steuermann. *Pos:* Mem, Milton & Peggy Salkind Piano Duo, performances throughout US, Can, Europe & Mex; guest artist, Bell Telephone Hour, NBC Recital Hall; appearance on French TV; mem perf arts panel, Calif Arts Comn; chmn arts, San Francisco Symph; mem music adv coun, Young Musicians Found & Nat Endowment Arts; pres, San Francisco Consv Music, 66- *Teaching:* Piano, privately; mem fac, Lone Mountain Col, 62-66; mem fac piano, San Francisco Consv Music, 66- *Mem:* Asn Independent Conservatories Music (chmn, currently); Col Music Soc (mem coun, currently); San Francisco Chamber Music Soc; Bohemians. *Mailing Add:* San Francisco Consv Music 1201 Ortega St San Francisco CA 94122

SALKOV, ABRAHAM A
COMPOSER, TENOR
b Rochester, NY, Apr 17, 21. *Study:* Eastman Sch Music, 36-38; studied with Joseph Leonard & Mario Castelnuovo-Tedesco, 51-60. *Works:* S'firah, 55 & Avinu Malkenu, 59, Mills; El Hayladim B'Yisrael, Transcontinental, 65; Ma Nishtana, comn by Stephen Wise Temple, Los Angeles, 80; The Happy Prince (opera). *Pos:* Cantor, Temple Beth Am, Los Angeles, 51-61 & Chizuk-Amuno Congregation, Baltimore, 61- *Mailing Add:* 2601 Manhattan Ave Baltimore MD 21215

SALOMAN, ORA FRISHBERG
EDUCATOR, WRITER

b Brooklyn, NY. *Study:* Barnard Col, Columbia Univ, AB(music), 59; Columbia Univ, with Paul Henry Lang, MA(musicol), 63, PhD(musicol), 70; studied violin with Vladimir Graffman & Ivan Galamian. *Teaching:* Prof music & chmn dept music, Baruch Col, City Univ New York, 71- *Awards:* Fulbright Fel, 66-67; Fac Res Award, Res Found, City Univ New York, 72-73. *Mem:* Am Musicol Soc; Sonneck Soc; Col Music Soc. *Interests:* Eighteenth century French opera; 19th century music, aesthetics and criticism; music in America, especially the 19th century cultivated tradition. *Publ:* Auth, The Orchestra in Le Sueur's Musical Aesthetics, Musical Quart, Vol LX, No 4; La Cepede's La Poetique de la Musique and Le Sueur, Acta Musicol, Vol XLVII, No 1; Gluck and the French Gluckists, Music & Man J, Vol 2, No 3 & 4; Victor Pelissier, Composer in Federal New York and Philadelphia, Pa Mag Hist Biog, Vol CII, No 1; Dwight Perkins and Early Wagner, 1852-1854: Critical Perspectives on the Cultivated Tradition in America, In: Music and Civilization: Essays Presented to Paul Henry Lang, W W Norton & Co Inc, 83. *Mailing Add:* Dept Music Baruch Col CUNY Box 321 17 Lexington Ave New York NY 10010

SALTA, ANITA MARIA
SOPRANO, TEACHER

b New York, NY. *Study:* Studied with Menotti Salta, 54-62; studied vocal control with Enzo Mascherini, 73-77. *Roles:* Aïda in Aïda, Lübeck, Augsburg, Gelsenkirchen, Ulm Kiel, Hannover, Braunschweig & Essen, Tosca in Tosca, Stuttgart, Hannover, Augsburg, Essen & Kassel, Salome in Salome, Essen, Heidelberg, Giessen & Regensburg, Marschallin in Der Rosenkavalier, Augsburg, Elsa in Lohengrin, Lübeck & Augsburg, Elektra in Life of Orest, Portland Opera Co & Countess in The Marriage of Figaro, Augsburg, Lübeck, Essen & Giessen, 62-80. *Pos:* Leading sop, Bremerhaven Stadttheater, 62-64, Theater der Hansestadt, Lübeck, 64-66, Stadtheater, Augsburg, 66-75 & Theater der Stadt, Essen, 75- *Teaching:* Voice, Essen, West Germany, 79- & Am Musical Studies, Graz, Austria, summer 83. *Mailing Add:* Lindenallee 79 Essen 4300 Germany, Federal Republic of

SALTS, JOAN SHRIVER
VIOLIN, CONDUCTOR & MUSIC DIRECTOR

b Joplin, Mo, Dec 4, 21. *Study:* Drury Col, with John Kendall, 40-41; SW Mo State Univ, BSMusEd, 68. *Pos:* Chmn, Womans Symph Comt, Springfield, Mo, 48-49; co-chmn, Symph Financial Drive, Springfield, Mo, 49-50; prin second violin, Springfield Symph Orch, Mo, 53- & mem bd dir, 57-60; second violin, Springfield Symph String Quartet, Mo, 75-; dir & founder, Youth String Orch, Springfield, Mo, 79-; prin second violin, Springfield Regional Opera, Mo, 79- *Teaching:* Special teacher instrum music, Springfield Pub Sch, Mo, 69- *Mem:* Music Educ Nat Conf; Am String Teachers Asn (secy-treas Mo unit, 81-82). *Mailing Add:* Rte 2 Box 106-42 Ozark MO 65721

SALTZMAN, DAVID RICHARD
CELLO

b Evanston, Ill, July 7, 52. *Study:* Northwestern Univ, with Dudly Powers, 70-72; Ind Univ, with Janos Starker & Raya Garbousova, 72-75. *Pos:* Cellist, String Quartet, Mex, 75-76 & Detroit Symph, 79-; assoc prin cellist, Orch Symph, Xalapa, Mex, 76-77; prin cello, Hong Kong Phil, 77-78. *Mailing Add:* 28686 Springarbor Southfield MI 48076

SALTZMAN, HERBERT ROYCE
ADMINISTRATOR, EDUCATOR

b Abilene, Kans, Nov 18, 28. *Study:* Goshen Col, BA, 50; Northwestern Univ, MMus, 55; Univ Southern Calif, DMA, 64. *Pos:* Exec dir, Ore Bach Fest, Univ Ore, 70-; panel mem choral music, Nat Endowment Arts, 81-, panel mem fest, 82- *Teaching:* Assoc prof music, Upland Col, 55-59; prof music, Sch Music, Univ Ore, 64-, assoc dean, 72-83. *Awards:* Fel, Alexander von Humboldt Found, Bonn, Ger, 77. *Mem:* Am choral Dir Asn (pres, 79-81); Int Fedn Choral Music (vpres, 82-85). *Mailing Add:* 2065 Univ St Eugene OR 97403

SALZER, FELIX
WRITER, EDUCATOR

b Vienna, Austria, June 13, 04; US citizen. *Study:* Univ Vienna, PhD; Mannes Col Music, Hon DM; studied theory with Henrich Schenker & Hans Weisse. *Teaching:* Prof, dean & chmn theory dept, Mannes Col Music, 40-56 & 62-, dir, 48-55, mem fac techniques music, 73-; vis lectr, Univ Calif, Los Angeles, 60, Peabody Consv Music, 62, New Sch Social Res, 62-63 & Univ Ore, summer 65; prof music, Queens Col, City Univ New York, 63- *Mem:* Am Musicol Soc (chmn NY chap, 63-65). *Publ:* Auth, The Meaning of Western Polyphony, Vienna, 35; Structural Hearing, Vol I & II, Dover Publ, 62; coauth (with Carl Schachter), Counterpoint in Composition, McGraw-Hill, 69; ed, The Music Forum, five vol, 67, 70, 73, 76 & 80. *Mailing Add:* Mannes Col Music 157 E 74th St New York NY 10021

SALZMAN, ERIC
COMPOSER, WRITER

b New York, NY, Sept 8, 33. *Study:* Studied comp with Morris Lawner, 51; Columbia Univ, with Otto Luening, Vladimir Ussachevsky & Jack Beeson, BS, 54; Princeton Univ, studied comp & theory with Roger Sessions & Milton Babbitt, MFA, 56. *Works:* The Nude Paper Sermon, Nonesuch Rec, 69; Wiretap, Atlantic, 74; Accord, 74; Stauf, 75; Noah, 76; The Passion of Simple Simon, 78; Civilization and Its Discontents, Nonesuch, 80-81. *Pos:* Music critic, New York Times, 58-62 & New York Herald Tribune, 63-66; music dir, WBAI-FM, New York, 62-63 & 68-72; critic, Stereo Rev, 66- *Teaching:* Asst prof, Queens Col, City Univ New York, 66- *Awards:* Fulbright Fel, 56-58;

grant, Ford Found, 64-65; Prix Italia, Asn European Broadcasters, 80. *Bibliog:* Virgil Thomson (auth), Am Music Since 1910, 70; Michel Sahl (auth), Stereo Rev, 4/77. *Publ:* Auth, 20th Century Music: An Introduction, Prentice-Hall, 67 & 74; coauth, Making Changes (with Michael Sahl), G Schirmer, 77. *Mailing Add:* 29 Middagh St Brooklyn NY 11201

SAMIS, SYLVIA ROSENZWEIG
VIOLIN

b Munich, Ger, Apr 1, 48; US citizen. *Study:* Temple Univ, with Edgar Ortenberg & Norman Carol, BA(music), 69. *Pos:* First violin, second stand, New Orleans Symph Orch, 69-; asst concertmaster, Cincinnati Symph Orch, 73- *Mailing Add:* 2872 Chardale Ct Cincinnati OH 45248

SAMSON, VALERIE BROOKS
COMPOSER, CHINESE VIOLIN

b St Louis, Mo, Oct 16, 48. *Study:* Boston Univ, with Hugo Norden, BA(music), 70; Univ Calif, Berkeley, with Andrew Imbrie & Ollie Wilson, MA(comp), 73; studied Chinese music with Betty Wong, Sun Zhong Jian & with Zhang Da in Beijing, 82. *Works:* Quartet (two winds & two strings), 73; Encounter (chamber orch), 73; Blue Territory 1 and 2 (violin & piano), 75; Montage: A Journey Through Youth (three sop, piano, dancer & lights), 75; Mousterian Meander (recorder, cello & piano), 76; Night Visits (chamber ens), San Francisco, 76; Winter Dances (prepared piano), 78. *Pos:* Radio programmer & announcer, WTBS, Cambridge, Mass, 69-70; music dir, Picchi Youth Orch, Oakland, 71-72; contrib ed, Ear, 78-; numerous Bay Area concerts. *Teaching:* Lectr comp & women in music throughout NCalif; teaching asst, Chinese Perf Arts Soc, 81. *Mem:* Comp Coop; Int League Women Comp; Music W; Chinese Instrm Music Ens. *Publ:* Contribr to Composer, 77-78. *Mailing Add:* 1373 Clay St Apt 5 San Francisco CA 94109

SAMUEL, GERHARD
COMPOSER, CONDUCTOR

b Bonn, Germany, Apr 20, 24; US citizen. *Study:* Eastman Sch Music, BM, 45; Yale Sch Music, MM, 47. *Works:* Looking at Orpheus Looking, 71, Requiem for Survivors, 73, Cold When the Drum Sounds for Dawn, On a Dream, Out of Time/A Short Symphony, Harlequins Caprice (harpsichord) & String Quartet No 1, 78, Belwin Mills. *Rec Perf:* Modern Soprano, Orion; Lou Harrison Symphony on G, Henri LaJaroff Cello Concerts, 80 Trombones & Brant: Kingdom Come, CRI; Chihara: Windsong, Everest; Beethoven VIIth, CCM. *Pos:* Assoc cond & violinist, Minneapolis Symph, 49-59; music dir & cond, Oakland Symph, 59-71; assoc cond, Los Angeles Phil, 71-74; cond, Calif Inst Arts, 72-76; dir orch activities, Col Consv Music, Univ Cincinnati, 76- *Teaching:* Prof music, Calif Music Arts, 72-76 & Col Consv Music, Univ Cincinnati, 76- *Awards:* ASCAP awards, 72- *Mem:* Monday Evening Concerts (bd mem, 72); ASCAP; Nat Asn Comp USA; Gustav Mahler Soc. *Mailing Add:* Belwin Mills Music Publ 1776 Broadway New York NY 10019

SAMUEL, HAROLD EUGENE
LIBRARIAN, EDUCATOR

b Hudson, Wis, Apr 12, 24. *Study:* Univ Minn, BA, 49, MA, 55; Univ Zurich, 50-51; Cornell Univ, PhD, 63. *Pos:* Music librn, Cornell Univ, 57-71 & Yale Univ, 71-; ed-in-chief, Notes, The Quart Jour of Music Libr Asn, 65-70. *Teaching:* Assoc prof music, Cornell Univ, 57-71; prof, Yale Univ, 71- *Awards:* Fulbright res scholar, Germany, 55-57; stipend, Martha Baird Rockefeller Fund for Music, 61-62; grant, Am Coun Learned Soc, 70. *Mem:* Music Libr Asn (mem bd dirs, 73-76); Am Musicol Soc (mem coun, 69-71); Int Asn Music Libr (chmn US branch, 78-81). *Publ:* Auth, nine articles in Die Musik in Geschichte und Gegenwart, 58-68; 13 articles, New Grove Dict of Music & Musicians, 80; The Cantata in Nuremberg During the 17th Century, UMI Res Press, 82; 15 articles in Harvard Dict of Music, 3rd ed (in prep). *Mailing Add:* 101 Santa Fe Ave Hamden CT 06517

SAMUEL, RHIAN
COMPOSER, EDUCATOR

b Aberdare, Wales, Feb 3, 44. *Study:* Reading Univ, UK, BA & BMus, 67; Wash Univ, MA, 71, PhD, 77. *Works:* Intimations of Immortality, comn by Mo Music Teachers Asn, 79; So Long Ago, Thomas Tallis Choir, London, 80; Elegy-Symphony, St Louis Symph Orch, 81; La Belle Dame Sans Merci, St Louis Consv Orch & Chorus, 83; April Rise—The Kingfisher, perf by Edmund Leroy, 83. *Teaching:* Chmn dept theory & comp, St Louis Consv Music, 78- *Awards:* Co-winner, ASCAP Rudolph Nissim Award, 83. *Mem:* Soc Music Theory; ASCAP. *Mailing Add:* St Louis Consv Music 560 Trinity Ave St Louis MO 63130

SAMUELSEN, ROY
BASS-BARITONE, EDUCATOR

b Moss, Norway, June 12, 33; US citizen. *Study:* Music Acad West, Santa Barbara, dipl, 60; Brigham Young Univ, BS(music), 61; Ind Univ, MM(voice), 63. *Rec Perf:* Oratorio to Book of Mormon, 59 & Samson (Handel), 62, Vanguard. *Roles:* Mephistopheles in Faust, 70 & Scarpia in Tosca, 70, New York City Opera; Don Giovanni in Don Giovanni, Norwegian Nat Opera, 71; Manoah in Samson, Dallas Civic Opera, 77; Rev Hale in Crucible, Ky Opera, 80; Commenclatore in Don Giovanni, Opera Columbus, 82; Sparafucile in Rigoletto, Ky Opera, 83. *Teaching:* Prof voice & vocal pedagogy, Ind Univ, Bloomington, 63- *Awards:* Regional Winner, Metropolitan Opera, 60. *Mem:* Am Guild Musical Artists; Nat Asn Teachers Singing; Pi Kappa Lambda (chap pres, 77-79). *Mailing Add:* 2012 Montclair Ave Bloomington IN 47401

SANCHEZ, MARTA
EDUCATOR, LECTURER
b Vina del Mar, Chile; US citizen. *Study:* Inst Jaques-Dalcroze, dipl, 55; Univ Pittsburgh, MA(musicol), 69, PhD(musicol), 78. *Teaching:* Prof music, Carnegie-Mellon Univ, 57-, dir, Dalcroze Cert Prog, 69-; vis prof eurhythmics, Inst Jaques-Dalcrose, Geneva, 79-80 & New SWales Consv Music, Sydney, 81; lectr & clinician worldwide. *Bibliog:* Magdalena Vicuna (auth), Entrevista con Marta Sanchez, Revista Musical Chilena, 7-9/75; Maria del earmen Farah-Martinez, Marta Sanchez: Encontrar el Pensamiento Creativo, Ritmo, Spain, 4/82. *Mem:* Dalcroz Soc Am (pres, 77-79); Int Soc Music Educr. *Publ:* Auth, The Man First: Dalcroze Solfege, Musical Plan Talk, Vol 1, No 9; Solfege Jaques-Dalcroze: Debut deson Enseignement, Bulletin Fedn Enseignants Rythmique, 80; Solfeo Dalcroze, Rev Educ Musical, 1/81. *Mailing Add:* 6703 Forest Glen Rd Pittsburgh PA 15217

SANDBERG, LARRY (LAWRENCE H)
WRITER, ADMINISTRATOR
b New York, NY, May 10, 44. *Study:* City Col New York, BA, 64; ; Grad Sch, Yale Univ. *Pos:* Freelance musician & arr, 61-; freelance writer & critic, 74-; ed, Oak Publ & Music Sales Corp, 79-80; advert mgr, Theodore Presser Co, 81- *Awards:* Deems Taylor Award, ASCAP, 76. *Mem:* BMI; Am Fedn Musicians. *Interests:* American ethnic music. *Publ:* Coauth, Folk Music Sourcebook, Knopf, 76; auth, articles & reviews in various magazines. *Mailing Add:* Wynnewood PA 19096

SANDERS, ERNEST H
EDUCATOR, ADMINISTRATOR
b Dec 4, 18; US citizen. *Study:* Juilliard Sch Music, 47-50; Columbia Univ, MA, 52, PhD, 63. *Teaching:* Lectr, Columbia Univ, 54-58, instr, 58-63, asst prof, 63-67, assoc prof, 67-72, prof, 72-, dept chmn, 78- *Awards:* Award in Musicol, Martha Baird Rockefeller Fund for Music, 61-62; fels, Guggenheim Found, 65-66, Am Coun Learned Soc, 69-70 & Nat Endowment for Humanities, 73-74. *Mem:* Am Musicol Soc; Royal Musical Asn; Int Musicol Soc. *Interests:* Polyphony of the 12th, 13th & 14th centuries in Europe; forays into music of the 18th & 19th centuries. *Publ:* Author of numerous articles dealing with aspects of medieval polyphony, J Am Musicol Soc, Musical Quart, Acta Musicol, Archiv für Musikwissenschaft, Music & Lett, Musica Disciplina, New Grove Dict of Music & Musicians & various Festschriften, 62-; ed, English Polyphony of the Thirteenth and Early Fourteenth Centuries, Vol XIV, 79 & co-ed, English Polyphony of the Fourteenth Century, Vol XVI & XVII (in prep), PMFC. *Mailing Add:* Dept Music 703 Dodge Columbia Univ New York NY 10027

SANDERS, NEILL JOSEPH
FRENCH HORN, ARTIST MANAGER
b London, England, Nov 24, 23. *Study:* Royal Col Music, 40-61. *Pos:* Prin horn, London Symph, London Phil & BBC Symph, 41-67; founder & mem, Melos Ens London, 50-79; founder & dir, Fontana Ens Mich, 79- *Teaching:* Prof music, Western Mich Univ, 69-82, emer prof, 82- *Awards:* Res Scholar, Mouthpiece Design, 77. *Mem:* Am Fedn Musicians; Musicians Union, UK; Phi Mu Alpha. *Mailing Add:* 952 124th Ave Shelbyville MI 49344

SANDERSON, DERL
TROMBONE
b Salt Lake City, Utah, Sept 8, 50. *Study:* Univ Utah, BMus, 76; Col Consv Music, Univ Cincinnati, MMus, 78. *Pos:* Extra musician, Utah Symph, 74-76 & Cincinnati Symph, 76-78; prin trombone, Cincinnati Chamber Orch, 76-78 & Charlotte Symph Orch, 78- *Teaching:* Instr trombone & trombone ens, Davidson Col, 78- *Mem:* Int Trombone Asn; Charlotte Chamber Music Workshop; Carolina Brass Quintet. *Mailing Add:* 1635 Logie Charlotte NC 28205

SANDIFUR, ANN ELIZABETH
COMPOSER, ADMINISTRATOR
Study: Mills Col, with Robert Ashely, BA(music comp), MFA(electronic music & rec media); Willamette Univ, with Charles Bestor; Cent Wash State Col, with Paul Creston; Eastern Wash State Col, with Stanley Linetta; San Francisco Consv Music, with Alden Jenks. *Works:* Double Chamber Music, 77, Shared Improvisations (four hand piano), 77, Scored Improvisation (acoust or electric keyboard), 77, Still Still (mixed chorus, flute, oboe, electric piano & double bass), 77, In Celebration of Movement (piano & tape), 78, Fugue for Touch (electronic), 78 & Biorhythms of Performance, 78, Arsciene Rec; and others. *Pos:* Mem staff, Ear mag, 73; dir first women's conct, Bay Area, 73; performer, San Francisco Museum Modern Art, 77; pres & founder, Resonant Communications Network, currently. *Teaching:* Fel, Ctr Contemp Music, Mills Col, 73-74; instr TV & radio communications. *Awards:* Elizabeth Mills Crothers Award, Mills Col, 74. *Mem:* First Nat Cong Women in Music; Am Women Comp Inc; League Women Comp. *Mailing Add:* W 2219 Ohio Ave Spokane WA 99201

SANDOR, GYORGY
PIANO
b Budapest, Hungary. *Study:* Liszt Conservatorium, Budapest, dipl; studied piano with Bela Bartok & comp with Zoltan Kodaly. *Pos:* Conct pianist, Carnegie Hall, 39 & toured throughout US, Europe, Cent Am, South Am, Far East, Australia & New Zealand. *Awards:* Grand Prix Disque, 65. *Mailing Add:* c/o Regency Artists 9200 Sunset Blvd Los Angeles CA 90069

SANDOW, GREGORY
COMPOSER, CRITIC
b New York, NY, June 3, 43. *Study:* Harvard Univ, BA, 65; Longy Sch Music, 68; Yale Sch Music, MM, 74. *Works:* Three Duets, Western Wind Vocal Ens, 71; Buxom Joan, 74 & A Christman Carol (opera), 77, Theodore Presser; Watt, NY Vocal Arts Ens, 78; Frankenstein (opera), Lake George Opera Fest, 82. *Teaching:* Lectr opera & orch, Yale Univ, 72-74. *Interests:* Wagner's musical forms. *Publ:* Articles in, Village Voice, Saturday Rev, Keynote, High Fidelity, Vanity Fair, Ovation, Wall St J, Heavy Metal & elsewhere. *Mailing Add:* 7 Cornelia St New York NY 10014

SANDRESKY, CLEMENS
ADMINISTRATOR, PIANO
b Buffalo, NY, May 30, 16. *Study:* Dartmouth Col, BA, 38; Harvard Univ, MA, 52; studied with Oswald Jonas & Ernst Oster. *Teaching:* Prof piano & music theory & dean, Sch Music, Salem Col, 52- *Awards:* Distinguished Prof, Salem Col, 80. *Mem:* Music Teachers Nat Asn; Music Educr Nat Conf; Col Music Soc; Soc Music Theory; Am Musicol Soc. *Publ:* Coauth, Musical Syntax as Data, J Theory Social Behavior, 83. *Mailing Add:* 2820 Reynolds Dr Winston-Salem NC 27104

SANDRESKY, MARGARET VARDELL
EDUCATOR, COMPOSER
b Macon, Ga, Apr 28, 21. *Study:* Salem Col, BM, 42; Eastman Sch Music, MM, 44. *Works:* Three Marys (orch), perf by Rochester Civic Orch, Piedmont Fest Orch & Moravian Music Fest, 46; My Soul Doth Magnify the Lord, H W Gray, 59; Seven Japanese Drawings (woodwind quintet), perf by Univ Ill Quintet, 70; To Be Played in the Mountains (piano sonata), comn by NC Music Teachers Asn, 74; To the Chief Musician: A New Song (solo cantata), comn by Wake Forest Univ, 82. *Teaching:* Instr theory, Oberlin Consv, 44-46 & Univ Tex, Austin, 48; prof theory, Salem Col, Winston-Salem, NC, 48-; head organ dept, NC Sch Arts, Winston-Salem, NC, 67. *Awards:* Fulbright Fel in Organ, 55-56. *Mem:* Col Music Soc (pres, Mid-Atlantic Chap Nat Coun, 83-); Soc Music Theory; Am Musicol Soc; NC Music Teachers Asn. *Publ:* Auth, The Continuing Concept of the Platonic-Pythagorean System and Its Application to the Analysis of 15th Century Music, Music Theory Spectrum, 79; The Golden Section in Three Byzantine Motets of Dufay, J Music Theory, 81; Liszt's Sonata in B Minor: The Tonal Design, Am Liszt Soc J, 82. *Mailing Add:* 2820 Reynolds Dr Winston-Salem NC 27104

SANDRI, THOMAS VICTOR
BASS
b Chicago, Ill, May 24, 56. *Study:* Northwestern Univ, studied voice with Norman Gulbrandsen & Patricia O'Neill & opera with Robert Gay, BM, 78, MM, 79. *Roles:* Basilio in Barber of Seville, Chicago Opera Theater, 81; Ceprano in Rigoletto, Pittsburgh Opera & Cincinnati Opera, 82; Montano in Otello, 82, Father in Die Kluge, 82, Duke in Romeo and Juliet, 83, Frank in Die Fledermaus, 83 & Don Alfonso in Cosi fan tutte, 83, Cincinnati Opera. *Pos:* Singer & apprentice, Santa Fe Opera, NMex, 81; soloist, Chicago Opera Theater, 81-82 & Pittsburgh Opera, 82; singer & soloist, Young Am Artist, Cincinnati Opera, 82 & Ens Co Cincinnati Opera, 82-83. *Mem:* Am Guild Musical Artists. *Mailing Add:* c/o Lew & Benson, Moreau-Neret, Inc 204 W Tenth St New York NY 10014

SANDROFF, HOWARD F
COMPOSER, CONDUCTOR & MUSIC DIRECTOR
b Chicago, Ill, Oct 28, 49. *Study:* Northeastern Ill Univ, BA(music educ), 73; Chicago Musical Col, Roosevelt Univ, MMus, 78; Mass Inst Tech, 82; studied comp with Robert Lombardo & Ben Johnston, voice with Ian Geller & Ronald Combs, electronic & comput music with Don Malone & Barry Vercoe & cond with Kalman Novak. *Works:* Penta-Phon (three trumpets), Dorn Publ, 77; Nov 18, 1975 (electronic tape), 78; Desert, comn by Lynda Martha, 79; Five Aphorisms, Dorn Publ, 79 & 81; ... There is a Decided Lack of Enthusiasm at My End of the Leash, comn by Music Ctr of NShore, 81; Kaddish: A Declaration (sop, bar, oboe, clarinet, cello & electronic tape), comn by Ill Arts Coun, 82; Son-et Three dash Ohl (sop, cello, oboe & piano), comn by Susan Charles, 82. *Pos:* Freelance consult, rec engineer & prod, 78-; artistic co-dir & cond, New Art Ens, 79- *Teaching:* Instr, Northeastern Ill Univ, 74-78 & Music Ctr of NShore, Winnetka, Ill, 80-; lectr, numerous wkshps & clinics, 74-81; vis instr sound design & electronic music, Sch Art Inst, 77; vis artist & prof, Chicago Consortium Col & Univ, 78-80; adj prof music, Columbia Col, 79- *Awards:* Grant, Ill Arts Coun Proj, 80. *Bibliog:* Karen Monson (auth), article, NShore Mag, 74; Stephanie Ettleson (auth), article, Chicago Tribune, 82; William Schutt (auth), Musical Experience, Op Music, 82. *Mem:* Chicago Soc Comp Inc (exec dir, 78-81); ASCAP; Meet The Comp; Nat New Music Alliance. *Rep:* Music Ctr of NShore 300 Greenbay Rd Winnetka, IL 60093. *Mailing Add:* 1008 Greenleaf Wilmette IL 60091

SANFORD, SALLY (ALLIS)
SOPRANO, TEACHER
b New Haven, Conn, May 25, 53. *Study:* Yale Univ, BA, 75; Stanford Univ, DMA, 79; studied voice with Herta Glaz, 76-81. *Rec Perf:* Messe des Mortes (Jean Gilles), Musical Heritage Soc, 81; Ordo Virtutum (Hildegarde von Bingen), 82 & Symphoniae (Hildegarde von Bingen), 83, Harmonia Mundi, Ger; Venetian Monody in the Age of Monteverdi, Musical Heritage Soc, 83. *Pos:* Soprano soloist, Ens Early Music, New York, 80- & Ens Chanterelle, New York, 81- *Teaching:* Vis lectr music hist & theory, Deep Springs Col, 79 & Dartmouth Col, 82; private teacher voice, 81-; spec lectr hist vocal tech, Aston Magna Acad, summers, 82-83. *Awards:* Conct Artists Guild Award, 83. *Mem:* Am Musicol Soc; Int Soc Early Music Singers. *Interests:* Medieval through 19th century historical vocal techniques with particular emphasis on 17th and 18th centuries. *Mailing Add:* 39 W 67th St #104 New York NY 10023

SANKEY, REBECCA POOLE
RECORDER, TEACHER
b Amarillo, Tex, Mar 16, 44. *Study:* Sarah Lawrence Col, BA, 65; studied with Bernard Krainis, 66-67 & Aston Magna, 74; Oberlin Baroque Perf Inst, 77; Univ Tex, Austin, MM(musicol), 81. *Pos:* Group leader, Camerata Baroque Group, 78-; music dir, Am Rec Soc, 82-83. *Teaching:* Recorder, privately, 70- *Mem:* Am Recorder Soc. *Mailing Add:* 2413 Dormarion Lane Austin TX 78703

SANT AMBROGIO, JOHN
EDUCATOR, CELLO
Study: Ohio Univ, MFA; Lebanon Valley Col, BS; studied cello with Diran Alexanian, Leonard Rose & Paul Olevsky. *Pos:* Co-dir, New Marlborough Music Ctr, Mass, formerly & Red Fox Music Camp, formerly; prin cello, Casals Fest, formerly, Boston Ballet, formerly & Frank Y & Katherine G Gladney Chair, St Louis Symph Orch, currently; mem, Boston Symph Orch, formerly & St Louis String Quartet, currently. *Teaching:* Mem fac, Boston Univ, formerly; mem fac cello & chamber music, St Louis Consv Music, currently. *Mailing Add:* St Louis Consv Music 560 Trinity Ave St Louis MO 63130

SANTINI, DALMAZIO O
COMPOSER, TEACHER
b Capestrano, Aquila, Italy, Sept 11, 23; US citizen. *Study:* Mannes Music Col; studied with Felix Salzer & Taddeus Kassern. *Works:* The White Peaks of Forca, Am Symph Orch, 55; Canticum Angelicum, San Carlo Opera Orch Naples, Ital, 59; From Dawn to Night, Am Haus Müchen, Ger, 66; Miniatures in Scope, Waterloo Publ Co, Canada, 70; Litany B V M, comn by Westchester Singers, 74; Composer Concert, Westchester Community Col, 76; Concerto for Trombone & Orch, Purchase Music Ens, 81. *Mem:* ASCAP; Am Music Ctr. *Mailing Add:* 11 Sandpiper Rd Great Island Narragansett RI 02882

SAPERSTEIN, DAVID
COMPOSER
b New York, NY, Mar 6, 48. *Study:* Juilliard Sch, with Jacob Druckman; Dartmouth Col, with Elliott Carter, Vincent Persichetti & Walter Piston; Princeton Univ, with Milton Babbitt & Earl Kim, BA, 69; Brandeis Univ. *Works:* Catacombs (piano), 61; Fantasia (clarinet & piano), 63; Variations (eight players), 69; Bagatelle (piano), 69; Music for Solo Flute (sextet, woodwind trio & string trio), 70; Antiphonies (perc ens), 72; Four Piano Pieces, 71-73; & others. *Awards:* Wechsler Award, Brandeis Univ, 70. *Mailing Add:* 1183 E 13th St Brooklyn NY 11230

SAPIEYEVSKI, JERZY
COMPOSER
b Lodz, Poland, Mar 20, 45. *Study:* State Consv, Gdansk, Poland; Catholic Univ Am. *Works:* Aria (alto sax & strings); Reflection (orch); Summer Overture (orch); Surtsey (string orch); Morpheus (band); Scherzo di Concerto (band); Trio for an Italian Journey (violin, cello & piano); and others. *Pos:* Comp in res, Wolf Trap Farm Park. *Teaching:* Fac mem, Catholic Univ, 70-73 & Univ Md, 72-73; assoc prof music, Am Univ, 75- *Awards:* First prize comp, Poland, 66; Koussevitzky Fel, 68. *Mailing Add:* Music Dept Am Univ Washington DC 20016

SAPP, ALLEN DWIGHT
COMPOSER, ADMINISTRATOR
b Philadelphia, Pa, Dec 10, 22. *Study:* Clarke Consv, Philadelphia, studied pianoforte with Robert Elmore & theory with William Happich, 35-39; Harvard Univ, with Walter Piston, Donald Grout, Grosvenor Cooper & Randall Thompson, AB, 42, AM, 49; private study with Aaron Copland & Nadia Boulanger, 42. *Works:* Pianoforte Sonata V, comn by Norma Bertolami, 80; Seven Songs of Carewe, comn by David Adams, 82; Violin Sonata IV, comn by Thomas Halpin; Four Hand Pianoforte Sonata II, comn by Ken & Frina Boldt, 82; Imaginary Creatures, comn by Cincinnati Chamber Orch, 82; Crennelations, comn by Concert Orch, Univ Cincinnati, 83. *Teaching:* Asst prof music, Harvard Univ, 53-58; lectr, Wellesley Col, 58-61; chmn music, State Univ NY, Buffalo, 61-67, prof, 61-76; provost arts & commun & prof music, Fla State Univ, 76-78; dean music, Univ Cincinnati, 78-80, prof, 78- *Mailing Add:* 6871 Ken Arbre Cincinnati OH 45236

SARABIA, GUILLERMO
BARITONE
b Mazatlan, Mex, 1937; US citizen. *Study:* Opera Studio, Consv Zurich, with Herbert Graf; studied with Dusolina Giannini; Pasadena Playhouse, with Carl Ebert. *Roles:* Doktor Faust in Doktor Faust, Detmold, 65; Germont in La Traviata, San Francisco Opera, 73; Macbeth in Macbeth, Lyr Opera Co Philadelphia, 73; Wozzeck in Wozzeck, La Scala & Paris; Amonasro in Aida, Metropolitan Opera; Iago in Otello, Vienna Staatsoper & Munich; Simon Boccanegra in Simon Boccanegra, Opera Co Philadelphia, 83. *Pos:* Baritone with opera co in France, Germany & US; res mem, Deutsche Oper am Rhein, Düsseldorf-Duisburg, currently. *Mailing Add:* c/o Int Artists Mgt 111 W 57th St New York NY 10019

SARBU, EUGENE
VIOLIN, CONDUCTOR
b Pietrari, Romania, Sept 6, 50; US & Romanian citizen. *Study:* Galati Music Sch, Romania, with S Nachmanovici, dipl, 68; Bucharest, Romania, with G Avakian, 65-67; Bucharest Consv Music, with Ionel Geanta, cert, 70; studied with Nathan Milstein, New York & Zurich, 72-73; Curtis Inst Music, with I Galamian, dipl, 74; Juilliard Sch, with I Galamian, MMus, 77. *Rec Perf:* Paganini Concerto in D, Radio-TV Ital, 78; Violin Recital, Metropolitan Museum, NY, 78; Jan Sibelius Violin Concerto, EMI, 80; Brahms Concerto, Radio-TV Belge, Brussels, 80; Mozart Concerto in A, BBC, London, 81; Bruch Concerto in G, BBC Scottish Symph Orch, 82; Chausson Poeme, BBC Proms from Royal Albert Hall, 82. *Pos:* Conct solo violinist, Columbia Artists, 71-74, Ibbs & Tillett Mgt, London, 77-, Herbert Barrett Mgt, 78- & Conciertos Daniel Mgt, Madrid, 82-; mem, NC Symph. *Awards:* Rockefeller Found Prize, 75; First Prize, N Paganini Int Compt, Genova, Ital, 78 & C Flesch Int Compt, London, 78. *Bibliog:* John Rockwell (auth), Sarbu In New York Violin Debut, New York Times, 1/23/78; Sarbu: Destined for Greatness, Daily Telegraph, London, 7/78; Margaret Campbell (auth), The Great Violinists, Granada Publ, 80. *Mem:* Eugene Ysaye Found, Brussels, Belgium; Alberto Curci Found, Naples, Ital. *Rep:* Herbert Barrett Mgt 1860 Broadway New York NY 10023. *Mailing Add:* 515 W 59th St Apt 32 F New York NY 10023

SARGEANT, PHILLIP LESTER
OBOE, EDUCATOR
b Kansas City, Mo, Sept 23, 54. *Study:* Cleveland Inst Music, BMus, 75, MMus, 76. *Pos:* Prin oboe, Wheeling Symph Orch, 76-77 & Dallas Chamber Orch, 79-; second oboe, Dallas Symph Orch, 77- *Teaching:* Instr oboe, WVa Univ, 76-77; adj prof, Southern Methodist Univ, 78- *Mailing Add:* 4830 Ashbrook Rd Dallas TX 75227

SARGOUS, HARRY WAYNE
OBOE, EDUCATOR
b Cleveland, Ohio, Mar 9, 48. *Study:* Yale Univ, BA, 70. *Pos:* Recitalist, WCLV Radio, Cleveland, 66-71; music critic, Yale Daily News, 67-70; participant, Marlboro Music Fest, 70 & 71; soloist, Carnegie Hall, 75; prin oboist, Kansas City Phil, formerly, Toronto Symph, formerly & Toledo Symph Orch, currently. *Teaching:* Mem fac oboe, Univ Mich, Ann Arbor, currently. *Awards:* Scholar Award Excellence, Fortnightly Musical Club Cleveland, 66-70; Joseph Lentilhon Seldon Mem Award Music, 68 & Wrexham Prize Music, 70, Yale Univ. *Mailing Add:* Sch Music Univ Mich Ann Arbor MI 48109

SASLAV, ISIDOR
VIOLIN, EDUCATOR
b Jerusalem, Palestine, Mar 18, 38. *Study:* Wayne State Univ, BA, 61; Ind Univ, MMus, 63, MusD, 69; Staatliche Hochschule Musik, Munich, 58-59; Stipendiat German Acad Exchange Serv; studied violin with Mischa Mischakoff, Josef Gingold & Ivan Galamian. *Pos:* Violinist, Casals Fest Orch, San Juan, PR, 58-73, Detroit Symph Orch, formerly & Chautauqua Symph Orch, formerly; asst concertmaster, Munich Chamber Orch, formerly; concertmaster, Buffalo Phil, formerly, Minneapolis Symph, formerly, Baltimore Symph, formerly, Round Top Fest Orch, 77- & Washington, DC, Opera, 81-; soloist orch performances, recitals & chamber music, US, Can, Austria & Mex; ed, Joseph Haydn Inst, Cologne, 71-; panelist, consult, performer & lectr, Haydn Fest Conf, Washington, DC, 75, Kasseler (WGermany) Musiktage, 80. *Teaching:* Mem fac, State Univ NY, Buffalo, 64-66, Univ Minn, 66-69, Goucher Col, 69, Philadelphia Musical Acad, 74 & Eastman Sch Music, 75-76; mem fac violin, music hist & lit, Peabody Consv Music, currently; lectr & recitals, US & Europe. *Awards:* Albert Spalding Prize, Tanglewood, 61; Mich Fedn Music Clubs Young Artist Award, 61; Arts Achievement Award, Wayne State Univ, 80. *Mem:* Am Fedn Musicians; Am String Teachers Asn. *Publ:* Haydn Studies, Norton & Co, 81. *Mailing Add:* Peabody Consv Music 1 E Mt Vernon Pl Baltimore MD 21202

SATALOFF, ROBERT THAYER
BARITONE, EDUCATOR
b Philadelphia, Pa, Feb 22, 49. *Study:* Haverford Col, BA(music theory & comp), 71; Jefferson Medical Col, MD, 75; Combs Col, DMA(voice), 82. *Works:* Passacaglia for Orchestra, Thomas Jefferson Univ, 82. *Roles:* Soloist in Light in the Wilderness (Brubeck), Boston Chorus Promusica, 68; Edward Weston in Perelandra, Haverford-Bryn Mawr Theatre, 70. *Pos:* Conct recitalist, 67-; cantor, Temple Brith Achim, 82- *Teaching:* Cond, Thomas Jefferson Univ Choir & Orch, 70-75 & 80-; asst prof otolaryngology, Thomas Jefferson Univ, 81- & prof & chair dept voice sci, Acad Vocal Arts, 81-; co-chmn Ann Symposium Care Prof Voice, Juilliard Sch, 82-; lectr sci & care of singing voice throughout US. *Mem:* Scimonoff Enterprises Inc (pres, 73-); Pa Alliance Am Music; Voice Found, New York; Nat Asn Teachers Singing. *Publ:* Coauth, Hearing Loss, J B Lippincott, 80; auth, Professional Singers: The Science and Art of Clinical Care, AJO, 80; Physical Examination of Professional Singers, J Otolaryngology, 83; over 20 other publications. *Mailing Add:* 1721 Pine St Philadelphia PA 19103

SATEREN, LELAND BERNHARD
CONDUCTOR, COMPOSER
b Everett, Wash, Oct 13, 13. *Study:* Augsburg Col, BA, 35; Univ Minn, MA, 43; Lakeland Col, Hon DMus, 65; Gettysburg Col, LHD, 65. *Works:* 400 publ choral works, large & small, secular & religious, accmp & a cappella, 42- *Rec Perf:* Eight rec of Augsburg Choir, 65- *Pos:* Dir music, KUOM, Univ Minn, 39-43. *Teaching:* Dir music, high sch, Moose Lake, Minn, 35-38; prof music, Augsburg Col 46-50, chmn dept & dir choir, 50-75 & 76-79; dir choral music, Consv Music, Bergen, Norway, 75-76. *Awards:* St Olav Medal, 71; Outstanding Fac Award, Augsburg Col, 74; Leland B Sateren Day, Gov Minn, 79. *Mem:* Music Educr Nat Conf; Minn Music Educr Asn; Am Choral Dir Asn; Hymn Soc Am; Minn Comp Forum. *Publ:* Auth, The New Song, 65, The Good Choir, 74, Criteria for Judging Choral Music, 75 & Mixed Meter & Line in Choral Music, 77, Augsburg Publ House. *Mailing Add:* 5217 Windsor Ave Edina MN 55436

SATUREN, DAVID HASKELL
COMPOSER, EDUCATOR
b Philadelphia, Pa, Mar 11, 39. *Study:* New Sch Music, 46-55; Univ Pa, BA, 60, MA, 62; Temple Univ, DMA, 67. *Works:* Four Short Movements for Orchestra, perf by Ventnor Summer Fest Youth Orch, 62 & Orch Soc Philadelphia, 78; Largo for Strings, perf by Concerto Soloists Philadelphia, 66; Ternaria for Organ and Orchestra, perf by Gtr Trenton Symph Orch, 70; Dialogue (harpsichord & strings), perf by Temple Painter & Concerto Soloists Philadelphia, 74; Evolution (viola, harpsichord & string orch), perf by Concerto Soloists Philadelphia, 77. *Rec Perf:* Sonata for Clarinet & Piano, Joh Russo & Lydia Walton Ignacio, 77; Trio for Clarinet, Piano & Mallet Percussion, John Russo, Lydia Walton Ignacio & Andrew Power, 77. *Teaching:* From asst prof to prof, Fairleigh Dickinson Univ, Teaneck, 68- *Mem:* NJ Comp Guild; Contemp Rec Soc. *Publ:* Auth, Symmetrical Relationships in Webern's First Cantata, Perspectives New Music, 67. *Mailing Add:* 5 Leonard Terr Wayne NJ 07470

SAUCEDO, VICTOR See Tecayehuatzin, Victor Saucedo

SAUNDERS, JEAN O
TEACHER, SOPRANO
b Stamford, Conn, Aug 17, 27. *Study:* Western Conn State Col; studied with Pierre Bernac, Gerard Souzay & Axel Schuett; Boston Univ, studied voice with Chloe Owen & Mary Davenport. *Roles:* Casilda in Gondoliers, Troupers Light Opera Co, 69; The Countess in Marriage of Figaro, SConn Opera, 71; Berta in Barber of Seville, Intermountain Opera Asn, 80. *Pos:* Guest artist, Stamford Symph Orch, formerly; sop with Troupers Light Opera Co, formerly & SConn Opera Co, formerly; soloist & mem, Mont Chorale, 77-; vocalist, bus mgr & bd mem, Intermountain Opera Asn, Bozeman, Mont, 78-; lieder recitals, New York, Conn, Seattle, Mont & Can. *Teaching:* Private voice, 70- *Mem:* Nat Asn Teachers Singing; Nat Opera Asn; Community Conct Asn. *Mailing Add:* Box 566 Manhattan MT 59741

SAUNDERS, MARY G
SOPRANO, EDUCATOR
b Brooklyn, NY, Jan 20, 50. *Study:* Boston Consv Music, BM, 73, MA, 75. *Teaching:* Applied voice, Boston Consv Music, 75- *Mailing Add:* Boston Consv 8 The Fenway Boston MA 02215

SAVAGE, JAMES BRYAN
CONDUCTOR, EDUCATOR
b Portland, Ore, Nov 1, 43. *Study:* Univ Ore, MA, 72; Univ Tübingen, Germany, 78-79; Univ Wash, 78, DMA, 83. *Pos:* Dir music, Cathedral St James, 81- *Teaching:* Asst prof choir & musicianship, Univ Ore, 71-74; artist & instr music hist, Cornish Inst, 75- *Awards:* Fulbright Res Fel, 78-79. *Mem:* Am Choral Cond; Am Musicol Soc. *Interests:* Jommelli (mid 18th century). *Mailing Add:* 2309 Boyer Ave E Seattle WA 98112

SAVERINO, LOUIS
COMPOSER, CONDUCTOR
Study: Eastman Sch Music. *Works:* Written 26 marches, nine concertos, six tone poems, five popular songs & a symphony. *Pos:* Prin tubist, US Marine Band, formerly; prin string bassist, US Marine Orch, formerly. *Teaching:* Adv tuba, string bass, contra bass clarinet, all brass, woodwinds & electric bass. *Mailing Add:* 10616 Oliver St Fairfax VA 22030

SAVIA, ALFRED
CONDUCTOR
b Livingston, NJ. *Study:* Jordon Col Music, Butler Univ, with Jackson Wiley, dipl; studied operatic cond with Enrico Pessina & Franco Ferrara, Italy; Berkshire Music Ctr, with Leonard Bernstein, Seiji Ozawa & Gunter Schuller. *Pos:* Asst cond, Omaha Symph, formerly, Fla Symph, 78- & Colo Phil, summers 79-81; dir, Orlando Opera Co, 80-; guest cond, Nebr Chamber Orch & Denver Chamber Orch. *Mailing Add:* 1677 Hibiscus Ave Winter Park FL 32789

SAVIG, NORMAN INGOLF
LIBRARIAN, CELLO
b Boston, Mass, Oct 6, 28. *Study:* Univ Denver, BA, 52, BA(music), 53, MS(librarianship), 55. *Pos:* Music cataloger, Univ Colo, Boulder, 62-68; music librn, Univ Northern Colo, 68-; asst prin violoncellist, Greeley Phil Orch, 68-81, violoncellist, 81-; prin violoncellist, Greeley Chamber Orch, 80-83. *Mem:* Music Libr Asn. *Publ:* Auth, Checklist of Music Periodicals, 70 & Uniform Titles for Music, 77, Kastle Kiosk. *Mailing Add:* 1611 12th Ave Greeley CO 80631

SAVILLE, EUGENIA CURTIS
EDUCATOR, WRITER
b Aldenville, Pa, July 7, 13. *Study:* NJ State Teachers Col, Trenton, BM, 34; Columbia Univ, MA(musicol), 42; Univ NC, Chapel Hill, with Glen Haydon, 52-58. *Pos:* Music dir, Duke Madrigal Singers, NC, 47-73. *Teaching:* Music supvr, Metuchen Pub Sch, NJ, 37-42; instr, Duke Univ, 47-50, asst prof, 50-60, assoc prof, 60-79. *Awards:* Grants, Duke Res Coun, 54-55, 59-60, 70 & 73 & Chapelbrook Found, Boston, 73. *Mem:* Am Musicol Soc; Col Music Soc. *Publ:* Auth, L'abate Clari and the Continuo Madrigal, J Am Musicol Soc, Vol XI-XII, No 2-3; Italy Current Chronicle, Musical Quart, 7/60; The Liturgical Music Of Giovanni Clari, Fontes Artis Musicae, 1-4/68; Italian Vocal Duets from the Early Eighteenth Century, G Schirmer Inc, 69; Giovanni Carlo Maria Clari, Pisa & Pistoia, In: Die Musik in Geschichte und Gegenwart, 78. *Mailing Add:* 1103 Anderson St Durham NC 27705

SAYAD, ELIZABETH GENTRY
PATRON, CRITIC-WRITER
St Louis, Mo, Dec 24, 33. *Study:* Aspen Music Sch, 54; Wash Univ, AB(music), 55; Northwestern Univ, MMus, 58. *Rec Perf:* US Highball, Gate 5 Rec, 58. *Pos:* Chmn & founding pres, New Music Circle, St Louis, Mo, 59-; arts ed, St Louis Mag, 62-63; founding mem, Mo Arts Coun, 66-67; chmn, Bicentennial Horizons Am Music & Perf Arts, 73-76; comnr & founder, St Louis Arts & Humanites Comn, 81- *Awards:* Outstanding Merit, Am Revolutionary Bicentennial Admin, 76; Woman of Achievement, St Louis Globe-Democrat, 77; First Lady Culture, St Louis Argus, 77. *Bibliog:* Barbarlee Diamondstein (auth), Women in the Arts, McCalls Mag, 78. *Publ:* Auth, Music Festival Abroad, St Louis Post-Dispatch, 61-62; Living With the Arts, St Louis Mag, 64-66. *Mailing Add:* 41 Westmoreland Pl St Louis MO 63108

SAYLOR, BRUCE STUART
COMPOSER, EDUCATOR
b Philadelphia, Pa, Apr 24, 46. *Study:* Juilliard Sch, with Hugo Weisgall & Roger Sessions, BMus, 68, MS, 69; Accad Santa Cecilia, Rome, Italy, with Goffredo Petrassi, 69-70; City Univ New York, with Weisgall & George Perle, PhD, 78. *Works:* Duo (violin & viola), Columbia Univ Music Press, 70; Loveplay (voice, flute, viola or cello), perf by Constance Beavon, 75; Four Psalms (voice & flute), Holt, Rinehart & Winston Inc & Galaxy Music Corp, 76-78; My Kinsman, Major Molineux (opera in one act), Pa Opera Fest, 76; Turns and Mordents (flute & orch), perf by Linda Chesis with Houston Symph, 77; Paeans to Hyacinthus (orch), Houston Symph, 80; Songs from Water Street (voice, viola & piano), perf by Group Contemp Music, 80. *Teaching:* Fel, Juilliard Sch Music, 68-69; asst prof, Queens Col, 74-76, assoc prof, 79-; asst prof, NY Univ, 76-79. *Awards:* Fulbright Grant, 69-70; Guggenheim Fel, 82-83; Music Award, Am Acad & Inst Arts & Lett, 83. *Mem:* League Comp; Int Soc Contemp Music (secy & vpres, 72-76); CRI (trustee & secy, currently); The Yard, Martha's Vineyard. *Publ:* Auth, The Music of Hugo Weisgall, Musical Quart, 73; The Writings of Henry Cowell, Inst Studies Am Music, 77; numerous articles in Musical Quart, Musical Am, New Grove Dict of Music & Musicians & others. *Mailing Add:* 318 W 85th St New York NY 10024

SCARPINATI, NICHOLAS JOSEPH
BASS-BARITONE
b New York, NY, July 16, 44. *Study:* Mannes Col Music, with Otto Guth; studied with Felix Popper, Adelaide Bishop, Nora Bosler, Robley Lawson; studied acting with Frank Corsaro; studied coaching with Paul Meyer. *Roles:* Marquis in La Traviata, NJ State Opera, 74; Escamillo in Carmen; Don Pasquale in Don Pasquale; Figaro in Nozze di Figaro; Colline in La Boheme; Don Basilio in Il Barbiere di Siviglia; Raimondo in Lucia di Lammermoor. *Pos:* Bass-bar with maj opera co in Tel Aviv & Newark, NJ; res mem, Israel Nat Opera. *Mailing Add:* 148 Throckmorton Lane Old Bridge NJ 08857

SCAVARDA, DONALD ROBERT
COMPOSER
b Iron Mountain, Mich, June 18, 28. *Study:* Univ Mich, with Ross Lee Finney, MM(comp), 53; Hochschule für Musik, Hamburg, with Phillip Jarnach, 53-54; Berkshire Music Ctr, with Leon Kirchner, 59; Univ Mich, with Roberto Gerhard, 59-60. *Works:* Groups for Piano, 59, Matrix for Clarinettist, 62 & Sounds for Eleven, 61, Lingua Press; In the Autumn Mountains, ONCE Chamber Ens, 61; Greys, Bertram Turetzky, 63; Landscape Journey, perf by comp & Morgan, 64; Caterpillar, Once Fest, 65. *Pos:* Co-found & organizer, Once Fest Musical Prems, 60-68. *Awards:* Fulbright Scholar, 53; Student Comp Radio Awards, BMI, 54. *Bibliog:* Phillip Rehfeldt (auth), Donald Scavarda: Matrix for Clarinettist, New Music for Clarinet, 78; David Cope (auth), Instrument Exploration, New Directions in Music, 3rd ed, 81; David Cope (auth), Donald Scavarda: Sounds for Eleven, Notes, 81. *Mailing Add:* PO Box 1908 Ann Arbor MI 48106

SCAVELLI, RAMON LOUIS
VIOLA, EDUCATOR
b New York, NY, Dec 10, 34. *Study:* Philadelphia Musical Acad. *Pos:* Violist, Houston Symph Orch, 55-58, Seventh US Army Symph Orch, 58-60 & Nat Symph Orch, 60- *Teaching:* Prof viola, George Mason Univ, 77-; private teacher, Washington, DC, currently. *Mailing Add:* c/o Nat Symph Orch JFK Ctr Perf Arts Washington DC 20566

SCELBA, ANTHONY J
DOUBLE BASS, COMPOSER
b NJ, Feb 12, 47. *Study:* Manhattan Sch Music, BM, MM; Juilliard Sch. *Works:* Passacaglia (string quintet), 72; Romantic (string quintet), 72; Innocence and Sophistication (violin & contrabass), 73; Fantasia (contrabass & piano), 74. *Pos:* Bassist, NJ Symph Orch, formerly. *Teaching:* Fac mem preparatory div, Manhattan Sch Music, formerly; asst prof orch & double bass, Baylor Univ, currently. *Awards:* Fulbright Award, Seoul, Korea, currently. *Mailing Add:* 70 Houston Rd Little Falls NJ 07424

SCHACHTER, CARL
EDUCATOR
Study: Mannes Col Music, BS; NY Univ, MA; Columbia Univ; studied piano with Sara Levee, Isabelle Vengerova, Olga Stroumillo & Israel Citkowitz; studied cond with Carl Banberger; studied theory with Felix Salzer. *Teaching:* Mem music comt & techniques music fac, Mannes Col Music, 56-, chmn theory dept, 58-62, dean, 62-66, chmn techniques music dept, 66-73; lectr music, Hunter Col, City Univ New York, 67, vis assoc, 68; prof music theory, State Univ NY Col, Binghamton, 68 & 71-72; prof music, Queens Col, City

Univ New York, currently. *Publ:* Auth, articles & rev in Music Forum & J Music Theory; coauth (with Felix Salzer), Counterpoint in Composition, McGraw-Hill, 69; (with Edward Aldwell), Harmony and Voice Leading, Harcourt Brace Jovanovich, 79. *Mailing Add:* 22 E 89th St New York NY 10028

SCHAEFER, LOIS ELIZABETH
FLUTE & PICCOLO, EDUCATOR
b Yakima, Wash, Mar 10, 24. *Study:* New England Consv Music, BM, 46, artist's dipl, 47. *Rec Perf:* With Boston Symph Orch & others. *Pos:* Asst first flutist & soloist, Chicago Symph, 52-55; prin flutist, New York City Opera, 55-65; mem, NBC Opera Orch, formerly; soloist, Boston Pops, formerly; mem Europe & USSR tours, Boston Symph Chamber Players, formerly; participant, Casals Fest, PR, formerly; founding mem, New England Harp Trio, currently; soloist, piccolo & Evelyn & C Charles Marran chair, Boston Symph Orch, currently; mem music panel, Mass Coun for Arts, 74- *Teaching:* Mem fac, Chicago Musical Col, 52-55; mem fac flute, piccolo & exten div, New England Consv Music, 65- *Mailing Add:* New England Consv Music 290 Huntington Rd Boston MA 02115

SCHAEFER, PATRICIA
ADMINISTRATOR, LIBRARIAN
b Ft Wayne, Ind, Apr 23, 30. *Study:* Northwestern Univ, BMus, 51; Univ Ill, MMus, 58; Univ Mich, AMLS, 63. *Pos:* Libr asst fine arts, Columbus Pub Libr, Ohio, 58-59; audio-visual librn, Muncie Pub Libr, 59-, asst libr dir, 82- *Mem:* Mu Phi Epsilon (treas Muncie alumni chap, 69-73, pres, 76-78). *Mailing Add:* 405 S Tara Lane Muncie IN 47304

SCHAEFER, WILLIAM ARKWELL
EDUCATOR, MUSIC DIRECTOR
b Cleveland, Ohio. *Study:* Miami Univ, Ohio, BS, MS. *Pos:* Bandleader, US Army, 42-46. *Teaching:* Lectr music educ, Miami Univ, 41-42; dir instrm music, WTech High Sch, Cleveland, Ohio, 46-47; asst prof music & dir bands, Carnegie Inst Technol, 47-52; chmn wind & perc dept & dir wind orch, Univ Southern Calif, 52-79 & prof cond, 79- *Awards:* Annual Contrib to Serious Music, ASCAP, 57- *Interests:* Wind music for contemporary ensembles. *Mailing Add:* 5050 Angeles Crest Hwy La Canada CA 91011

SCHAEFFER, JOHN A
DOUBLE BASS, EDUCATOR
b Reading, Pa. *Pos:* Mem, Philadelphia Orch, formerly; first bass, San Carlo Opera, formerly; prin bass & Redfield D Beckworth chair, New York Phil, currently. *Teaching:* Mem fac double bass, Juilliard Sch, 72- *Mailing Add:* 185 West End Ave New York NY 10023

SCHAENEN, LEE
CONDUCTOR, ADMINISTRATOR
b New York, NY, Aug 10, 25. *Study:* Manhattan Sch Music, 39-41; Columbia Col, 41-43; Grad Sch, Juilliard Sch Music, 41-43. *Rec Perf:* Tales of Hoffman, Melodram, 59; Arias with Simoneau & Alarie, Deutsche Gramophon, 59; Boccherini Symphonies, 65, Mozart Divertimento, 66 & French Baroque, 66, Musical Heritage Soc. *Pos:* Cond, New York City Opera, 45-52, Lyric Opera, Chicago, 58 & 78- & Vienna Volksoper, 65-74; dir, Lyric Opera Ctr, Chicago, 77-; artistic dir, Opera Columbus, Ohio, 81- *Rep:* Robert Lombardo Assoc 61 W 62 ST New York NY 10023. *Mailing Add:* 1310 N Ritchie Ct Chicago IL 60610

SCHAFFER, ROBERT CARLTON
EDUCATOR, BASSOON
b Hartford, Conn, June 23, 29. *Study:* Hartt Col, Univ Hartford, bassoon study with Lenom, Kovar & Goltzer, BM, 51, MM, 52, BM(educ), 58. *Pos:* Prin bassoon, Hartford Symph, 48- *Teaching:* Assoc prof bassoon & theory, Hartt Col, Univ Hartford, 51- *Mailing Add:* 70 Kane St West Hartford CT 06119

SCHATZKAMER, WILLIAM MAX
CONDUCTOR & MUSIC DIRECTOR, PIANO
b New York, NY, Aug 17, 16. *Study:* Juilliard Grad Sch, cert, 40. *Rec Perf:* Works of Bach, Scarlatti, Mozart & Scriabine, RCA Victor, 53; works of Beethoven, Spane Rec, 69. *Pos:* Cond & music dir, Univ City Symph Orch, St Louis, 64- & Gateway Fest Orch, St Louis, 64- *Teaching:* Prof & head piano dept, Washington Univ, 51- *Mailing Add:* Music Dept Washington Univ St Louis MO 63130

SCHEIBERT, BEVERLY
WRITER, HARPSICHORD
b Erie, Pa. *Study:* Syracuse Univ, organ with Arthur Poister, BMus, 60, MMus, 61; Boston Univ, organ with George Faxon. *Pos:* Music dir, Christ Church, Cambridge, Mass, 71-81 & Old Ship Meetinghouse, Hingham, Mass, 81- *Mem:* Am Musicol Soc; Col Music Soc; Alliance Independent Scholars; Am Guild Organists (dean Boston chap, 77-79). *Interests:* Seventeenth century French harpsichord lit; works of Jean-Henry D'Anglebert. *Publ:* Auth, The Art of Fugue, 81 & The Masses of Orlando di Lasso, 82, Am Organist; F Couperin—The Organ Masses and Inegalite, Musical Times, 82; The Organ Works of Jean-Henry D'Anglebert, Organ Yearbk; ed, Missa de Feria by Orlando di Lasso, Broude Brothers (in press). *Mailing Add:* 9 Highland Park Newton MA 02160

SCHEIN, ANN
PIANO, EDUCATOR
Study: Studied with Hess, Rubinstein & Munz. *Pos:* Guest artist with many major US orchs; pres, People to People Music Comt, currently; recitalist, North Am & Europe; tours, ten world-wide, US State Dept, formerly, five in South Am & two in Russia, Soviet-Am Cult Exchange, formerly. *Teaching:* Mem fac piano, Peabody Consv Music, currently. *Rep:* Harold Shaw Concerts 1995 Broadway New York NY 10023. *Mailing Add:* Peabody Consv Music 1 E Mt Vernon Pl Baltimore MD 21202

SCHELLE, MICHAEL
COMPOSER
b Philadelphia, Pa, Jan 22, 50. *Study:* Villanova Univ, BA(theatre), 71; Butler Univ, BM(comp), 74; Hartt Sch Music, Univ Hartford, MM(comp), 76; Univ Minn, PhD(theory & comp), 80. *Works:* Lancaster Variations, Orquesta Sinfonica Nac, Costa Rica, 77; Masque, St Paul Chamber Orch & Indianapolis Symph, 79-81; Music for the Last Days of Strindberg, Pittsburgh New Music Ens, 80; Double Quartet, comn by Welsh Arts Coun, Cardiff, 80; Pygmies II, comn by Cent Ky Youth Orch, 83; Music for Two Pianos, Spoleto USA, Charleston, SC, 83; Oboe Concerto, comn by Indianapolis Symph Orch, 83. *Teaching:* Vis comp, Carleton Col, 78-79; asst prof, Butler Univ, 79- *Awards:* Inter Am Comp Prize, Nat Orch Costa Rica, 77; Wolf Trap Found Grant, 78; Harvey Gaul Comp Prize, Friends of Harvey Gaul & Pittsburgh New Music Ensemble, 80. *Mem:* ASCAP; Am Soc Univ Comp; Am Music Ctr; fel, MacDowell Colony. *Mailing Add:* 5939 N Rosslyn Ave Indianapolis IN 46220

SCHELLER, STANLEY
BASSOON, EDUCATOR
b New York, NY, Sept 17, 40. *Study:* City Col New York, BA(music), 63; Manhattan Sch Music, MM(bassoon), 65; studied bassoon with Sanford Sharoff, Stephen Maxym & Harold Goltzer. *Pos:* First bassoonist, Goldovsky Opera Co, 66-67; second bassoonist, Royal Ballet, 68; prin bassoonist, NC Symph, 68-69; second bassoonist, Denver Symph Orch, 69- *Teaching:* Bassoon instr, Lamont Sch Music, Univ Denver, 71- *Publ:* Contrib, Bassoon Performance Practices and Teaching in the United States and Canada, 74. *Mailing Add:* 825 S Downing St Denver CO 80209

SCHENLY, PAUL
EDUCATOR, PIANO
b Munich, Germany, 1948. *Study:* Calif Inst Arts; Cleveland Inst Music, studied piano with Victor Babin, BM, 69, MM, 71; studied piano with Lillian Steuber & Johanna Graudan & comp with Marcel Dick. *Pos:* Pianist with major orchs throughout US & Europe; recitalist. *Teaching:* Asst to Victor Babin, Cleveland Inst Music, 68-71, artist in res & mem fac piano, 71-; mem fac, Music Acad of West, currently. *Awards:* Fanny Bloomfield Zeisler Centennial Award, 69; First Prize, Nat Compt Young Musicians Found, 69; Avery Fisher Award, 76. *Rep:* Columbia Artists 165 W 57th St New York NY 10019. *Mailing Add:* Cleveland Inst Music 11021 E Blvd Cleveland OH 44106

SCHERER, BARRYMORE LAURENCE
WRITER, LECTURER
b New York, NY, Sept 10, 49. *Study:* Hunter Col, City Univ New York, study with Louise Talma, AB, 72; Grad Sch Arts & Sci, NY Univ, study with Victor Fell Yellin, MA, 74. *Works:* The Prisoner of Zollern (comic opera), New York, 71; The Gypsy's Malediction (comic opera), 72; Unto the Hills I Lift Mine Eyes (anthem), St Paul's Church, Yonkers, NY, 82; Ainsi Fidele (conct duet with orch), Jamaica Symph. *Pos:* Guest lectr, New York Cult Ctr, 73-75; lectr, Metropolitan Opera Guild, 83- & Cooper-Hewitt Museum, New York, 83- *Mem:* ASCAP; Victorian Soc Am; Nat Acad Rec Arts & Sci. *Interests:* Nineteenth-century French opera and 19-century English music; ballet composers. *Publ:* Auth, Giacomo Meyerbeer: The Man and His Music, 76 & De Profundis: Ambroise Thomas, 78 & Moonlight, Magic & Massenet, 79, CBS Masterworks; Fact and Fancy: The History Behind Vespri Siciliani, Opera News, 82; Three Composers Who Knew What Dance Needed, New York Times, 83. *Mailing Add:* Greyswood Cottage 660 Rugby Rd West Midwood NY 11230

SCHERMERHORN, KENNETH
CONDUCTOR & MUSIC DIRECTOR
b Schenectady, NY, Nov 20, 29. *Study:* New England Consv Music, artists dipl, 50; Ripon Col, Hon MusD, 73. *Pos:* Music dir, Am Ballet Theatre, 56-65 & 83-, NJ Symph, 62-68 & Milwaukee Symph, 68-80; asst cond, New York Phil, 59-60; cond & music dir, Nashville Symph, 83-; mem bd dir, Nat Endowment Arts. *Awards:* Serge Koussevitsky Mem Award. *Mailing Add:* Nashville Symph 1805 West End Ave Nashville TN 37203

SCHEUERLE, PAUL NORMAN
EDUCATOR
b Manor, Pa, May 26, 26. *Study:* Eastman Sch Music, BM, 51; Pa State Univ, MEd, 53; Boston Univ, DMA, 59. *Teaching:* Instrm dir, Kingsford High Sch, Mich, 53-55; teaching fel, Boston Univ, 55-57; dir music, Berlin Am Sch, Ger, 57-58; prof music educ & head dept music, Dakota Wesleyan Univ, 59-; mem staff clarinet, Int Music Camp, Bottineau, NDak, 65- *Awards:* Bush Grant, 81. *Mem:* Music Educr Nat Conf (chap adv, 59-83); Col Band Dir Nat Asn (state chmn, 65-83); SDak Music Educr Asn. *Publ:* Auth, What is the Music Teacher's Place in Guidance, 62 & Can the Clarinet be Played in Tune, 65, SDak Music J. *Mailing Add:* 1034 E Third Mitchell SD 57301

SCHEXNAYDER, BRIAN
BARITONE

b Port Arthur, Tex. *Study:* Univ Southwestern La, BMus, 75; Am Opera Ctr, Juilliard Sch. *Roles:* Renato in Un Ballo in maschera, Am Opera Ctr, Juilliard Sch; Silvio in I Pagliacci, Metropolitan Opera, 80; Sharpless in Madama Butterfly, NJ State Opera, 82. *Pos:* Baritone with US opera co. *Mailing Add:* c/o Robert Lombardo Assoc 1 Harkness Plaza 61 W 62 Suite 6F New York NY 10023

SCHIAVONE, JOHN (SEBASTIAN)
COMPOSER

b Los Angeles, Calif, Mar 27, 47. *Study:* Mt St Mary's Col, Los Angeles, studied comp with Matt Doran; St Joseph's Col, Rensselaer, Ind, studied comp with John Egan, MMus, 82. *Works:* Mass in Praise of God the Holy Spirit, 72, Mass in Praise of Jesus Christ the Eternal High Priest, 73 & Mass in Honor of all Saints, 75, GIA Publ; O How Blest is the Feast (motet), Concordia, 81; Jubilee Mass, GIA Publ, 82; Mary's Triptych (oratorio), Camerata of Los Angeles, 83. *Pos:* Mem, Music Comn, Archdiocese of Los Angeles, 74- *Mailing Add:* 6628 Cedros Ave Van Nuys CA 91405

SCHICK, GEORGE
CONDUCTOR, EDUCATOR

Study: Prague Consv. *Pos:* Assoc cond, Chicago Symph, 50-56; cond & music consult to mgt, Metropolitan Opera, 58-69. *Teaching:* Head cond dept, Prague Consv; pres, Manhattan Sch Music, 69-76, mem fac opera, 69- *Mailing Add:* 230 W 79th St New York NY 10024

SCHICKELE, PETER
COMPOSER, CONDUCTOR

b Ames, Iowa, July 17, 35. *Study:* Studied comp with Roy Harris, 54 & theory with Sigvald Thompson; Swarthmore Col, BA, 57; Juilliard Sch Music, with Vincent Persichetti & William Bergsma, MS, 60; Aspen Sch with Darius Milhaud; Swarthmore Col, Hon DMus, 80. *Works:* Silent Running (soundtrack), 72, The Lowest Trees Have Tops (cantata), 78 & Pentangle (horn & orch), 79, Elkan-Vogel Co; P D Q Bach Works: Iphigenia in Brooklyn (cantata), 65, The Seasonings (oratorio), 67 & Blaues Gras (bluegrass cantata), 79, Theodore Presser Co; The Art of Round Ground (three baritones discontinuo). *Rec Perf:* Ten P D Q Bach albums, 65-83 & Elegies (Schickele), 80, Vanguard Rec. *Pos:* Co-founder, Comp Circle, 59 & The Open Window, 67-71; cond & performer throughout US, currently; numerous TV appearances. *Teaching:* Mem fac ear training, theory & hist, Swarthmore Col, 61-62, Juilliard Sch Music, 61-65 & Aspen Fest Music, Colo, 63. *Awards:* Gershwin Mem Award, 59; Comp in Res Grant, Ford Found, 60; Elizabeth Tow Newman Contemp Music Award, 64. *Mem:* ASCAP; Am Fedn Musicians; Am Music Ctr. *Publ:* Auth, The Definitive Biography of P D Q Bach, Random House, 76. *Mailing Add:* c/o William Crawford 237 E 72nd St New York NY 10021

SCHIEBLER, BEVERLY BEASLEY
VIOLIN, SINGER

b Schelbyville, Ind, May 9, 37. *Study:* Stephens Col Women, AA; studied violin with Carl Eugen Koerner & Paul Tipper, voice with Valfredo Patacchi & piano with Kenneth Abell. *Pos:* Solo violinist, quartet perf in Ind & Mo; concertmaster, Alton Civic Orch, Gateway Orch & Northwest Plaza Pops; assoc prin second violinist, St Louis Symph, currently; singer, Chautauqua Opera Co. *Mem:* Sigma Alpha Iota. *Mailing Add:* 430 Belleview Ave Webster Groves MO 63119

SCHIEBLER, CARL ROBERT
FRENCH HORN

b Medford, Mass, Dec 3, 37. *Study:* Univ Wis, with John Barrows; US Naval Sch Music, grad. *Pos:* Horn, Seventh Army Symph Orch, 58-60; horn, St Louis Symph Orch, 63-, personnel mgr, 77-; mem, St Louis Brass Quintet, 69- *Teaching:* Instr horn, Webster Col, 65-67, Summer Music Camp, Univ Wis, 68, Washington Univ, 72-73 & St Louis Inst Music, 74; instr, Brass Lab, 72, 73 & 74. *Awards:* Arion Award, 55. *Mem:* Int Conf Symph & Opera Musicians; charter mem, Int Horn Soc. *Mailing Add:* 430 Belleview Ave Webster Groves MO 63119

SCHIFFMAN, HAROLD (ANTHONY)
COMPOSER, EDUCATOR

b Greensboro, NC, Aug 4, 28. *Study:* Univ NC, Chapel Hill, AB, 48; Univ Calif, with Roger Sessions, MA, 51; Fla State Univ, DMus, 62. *Works:* Musica Battuta, Assoc Music Publ, 61; Prelude & Variations for Chamber Orch, comn & perf by Richard Burgin, 70; Concert-Piece (trombone & piano), Southern Music Co, 73; Sonata (flute & piano), comn & perf by Albert Tipton, 75; Cello Concerto, comn & perf by Roger Drinkall, Orion Rec, 79; String Quartet No 2, comn & perf by Concertino String Quartet, 81; 4 Songs from Peacock Pie, comn & perf by Apple Trio, 83. *Teaching:* Instr music, Fla State Univ, 59-63, asst prof, 64-69, assoc prof, 69-74, prof, 74- *Awards:* ASCAP Standard Award, 82. *Mem:* ASCAP; Col Music Soc; Am Soc Univ Comp; Southeastern Comp League (vpres, 64-66); Nat Asn Comp. *Mailing Add:* 2304 Don Andres Ave Tallahassee FL 32304

SCHIFFMAN, JANE PERRY See Perry-Camp, Jane

SCHIFTER, PETER MARK
DIRECTOR—OPERA

b Westfield, NJ. *Study:* Juilliard Sch; Yale Sch Drama. *Pos:* Dir, Washington Opera, currently; guest dir, Washington Opera, San Francisco Spring Opera, Central City Opera, Philadelphia Opera, Can Opera, Guthrie Theater, Yale Repty Co & many others. *Mailing Add:* New York NY

SCHILLER, ALLAN
VIOLIN, EDUCATOR

b Katowice, Poland. *Study:* Paris Consv; Brussels Consv; Juilliard Sch, MS. *Pos:* Soloist with chamber music groups throughout US & Europe; mem staff, Waterloo Music Fest, 76-; violinist, New York Phil, currently & Gramercy String Quartet, currently. *Teaching:* Mem quartet in res, Gramercy String Quartet, Herbert H Lehman Col, formerly; mem fac, Pre-col Div, Juilliard Sch, 73-, violin asst to Dorothy DeLay, 75- *Mailing Add:* Juilliard Sch Lincoln Ctr Plaza New York NY 10023

SCHILLING, CHARLES WALTER
ORGAN, EDUCATOR

b Butternut, Wis, Apr 19, 15. *Study:* Carleton Col, AB, 36; Union Theol Sem, SMM, 38, SMD, 54; Am Guild Organists, AAGO, 40, FAGO, 42, ChM, 43; Trinity Col, London, LTCL, 47, FTCL, 48. *Works:* Easter Flowers (Carol), H W Gray, 43. *Pos:* Organist & choir dir, Second Congregational, Greenwich, Conn, 38-43, First Church Christ Congregational, Springfield, Mass, 46-56 & First Congregational, Stockton, Calif, 69-; organ, harpsichord, piano & celesta, Stockton Symph, 66- *Teaching:* Prof organ, harpsichord, piano & theory, Consv Music, Univ Pac, Stockton, 56- *Mem:* Am Guild Organists; San Francisco Early Music Soc. *Mailing Add:* Consv Music Univ Pac Stockton CA 95211

SCHIMKE, MILTON MAURICE
ADMINISTRATOR, EDUCATOR

b Drake, NDak, June 8, 35. *Study:* Minot State Col, BS, 57; Univ Northern Colo, MA, 62, EdD, 66. *Teaching:* Dir bands & choirs, Dufur pub sch, Ore, 57-59 & Bowbells pub sch, NDak, 59-61; dir bands, Ft Lupton pub sch, Colo, 62-63; instr & guest cond, Univ Sask Music Sch, summer 66; instr music educ, Univ Wis-Oshkosh, 66-69; head, Div Music Educ, Univ Wis-Eau Claire, 69-, chmn, Dept Music, 73- *Mem:* Music Educr Nat Conf; Wis Music Educr Conf (mem bd dir, 75-77 & 81-83); Nat Asn Sch Music (vchmn region IV, 82-84); Pi Delta Kappa. *Publ:* Coauth, A Sequence of Pitch and Rhythm Activities Leading to Music Reading, private publ, 75; auth, Articles in The Wis Sch Musician, Vol 45 (1-4), 46 (1-4), 52 (1-4) & 53 (1-4), Wis Sch Music Asn. *Mailing Add:* Dept Music Fine Arts Ctr Univ Wis Eau Claire WI 54701

SCHIMMEL, WILLIAM MICHAEL
COMPOSER, ADMINISTRATOR

b Philadelphia, Pa, Sept 22, 46. *Study:* With Lotta Hertlein & Paul Creston; Juilliard Sch, with Elliott Carter, Vincent Persichetti, Roger Sessions & Hugo Weisgall, BS, MS, DMA. *Works:* David and Bathsheba (one-act opera); Concerto for Three (accordion, bass, perc & orch), 69; Portrait No 1 (after a painting by Joan Miro, for orch), 69; Motor Piece (accordion), 72; Kingdom Trilogy: Kerygma (organ), Parousia (accordion) & Kingdom (piano), 72-73; Mass for Chorus and Orchestra, 73; Tithonus (chamber ens), New York, 74. *Pos:* Performer, Philadelphia Orch, New York Phil & Pittsburgh Symph; cond, two Broadway shows; assoc ed, Accord Mag. *Teaching:* Fel theory & aural training, Juilliard Sch, 69-70, instr, 73-74; asst prof, Brooklyn Col, 71-76; instr comp, Neupauer Consv Music, formerly, dean, 76- *Mem:* Founding mem, Accordion Arts Soc. *Publ:* Contribr to Accordion Arts Soc Mag & Am Accordion Soc Musicol Mag. *Mailing Add:* Neupauer Consv Music 105 S 18th Philadelphia PA 19103

SCHINDLER, ALLAN
EDUCATOR, COMPOSER

b Stamford, Conn, May 15, 44. *Study:* Consv Music, Oberlin Col, with Joseph Wood & Edwin Dugger, AB, BM; Univ Chicago, with Ralph Shapey, MA, PhD(music comp & theory); Cleveland Inst Music. *Works:* Blues for the Children of Light (eight instrm); Cirrus and Beyond (flute, cello, perc & tape), 75. *Rec Perf:* Rec on Owl Rec. *Pos:* Dir Electronic Music Studio, Boston, 72-78. *Teaching:* Fac mem, Ball State Univ, 70-71; fac mem & dir electronic music studio, Boston Univ, 72-78; asst prof comp & dir electronic music studio, Eastman Sch Music, 78- *Publ:* Auth, Listening to Music and Exploring Modern Music, Holt, Rinehart & Winston Publ, 76. *Mailing Add:* 26 Gibbs St Rochester NY 14604

SCHINSTINE, WILLIAM JOSEPH
PERCUSSION, COMPOSER

b Easton, Pa, Dec 16, 22. *Study:* Eastman Sch Music, BM, 45; Univ Pa, MS 52; private study with George Hamilton Green. *Works:* The Miracle Overture (band), 55 & Pennsylvania Sketches (band), 56, South Music Co; The Pennsylvania Farmer (ballet), Pottstown Symph, 75; Sonata for Timpani & Piano, Southern Music Co, 77; Three Means to an End (snare drum), Kendor Music Inc, 79; Musical Marimba Solos, Permus Publ Co, 81. *Pos:* Percussionist, Nat Symph, 45-46 & Pittsburgh Symph, 46-47; prin perc, San Antonio Symph, 47-51. *Teaching:* Instrm, Pottstown Sch District, 52-79. *Awards:* Comp second & third place awards, Perc Arts Soc, 77 & 78; ASCAP Standard Awards. *Mem:* Am Fedn Musicians; Music Educr Conf; Percussive Arts Soc; Pa Music Educr Asn; ASCAP. *Mailing Add:* 614 Woodland Dr Pottstown PA 19464

SCHIRMER, WILLIAM LOUIS
COMPOSER, EDUCATOR

b Cleveland, Ohio, Feb 25, 41. *Study:* Cleveland Inst Music, BM(theory), 63, BM(piano), 64; Eastman Sch Music, MM(comp), 66; Ohio State Univ, PhD(comp), 71. *Works:* Savior Who Thy Flock Art Feeding, Roger Dean, 77; Spectrum (band), Univ Cincinnati Wind Ens, 78; Symphony #5, 80 & Symphony #43, 81, Jacksonville Univ Orch; Ensemble LXIX, Jacksonville Symph Chamber Orch, 80; Curtain Raiser Overture, Southeastern Symph, 68; Jacksonville Symph Orch, 80 & Jacksonville Univ Orch, 83; Missa

Universalis, comn by Jacksonville Beaches' Fine Arts Series, perf by Jacksonville Univ Concert Choir, 82. *Teaching:* Assoc prof music, Tenn Wesleyan Col, 70-76; asst prof comp & theory, Univ Cincinnati, 76-78; assoc prof, Jacksonville Univ, 79- *Mem:* Music Teachers' Nat Asn. *Mailing Add:* Music Dept Jacksonville Univ Jacksonville FL 32211

SCHLEIFER, MARTHA FURMAN
EDUCATOR, WRITER
b Philadelphia, Pa. *Study:* Temple Univ, BMEd & MM; Bryn Mawr Col, PhD, 76. *Teaching:* Instr music, Philadelphia Pub Sch, 67-77; asst prof music hist & theory, Widener Univ, Chester, Pa, 77-84. *Mem:* Sonneck Soc; Am Musicol Soc (secy-treas Mid Atlantic Chap, 83-84). *Publ:* Auth, William Wallace Gilchrist, Diapason, 82; Centennial Exhibition, New Grove Dict of Music in US (in prep); William Wallace Gilchrist—Life and Works, Scarecrow Press, 84. *Mailing Add:* 67 Overhill Bala Cynwyd PA 19004

SCHLEIS, THOMAS HENRY
EDUCATOR
b Green Bay, Wis, Dec 13, 49. *Study:* Lawrence Univ, BMus, 72; Univ Wis, Madison, with Eva Badura-Skoda, Milos Velimirovic & Lawrence Gushee, MMus, 74; Univ Ill, Urbana, with Alexander Ringer, Bruno Nettl & Carl Dahlhaus. *Pos:* Organist, Newman Found, Champaign, Ill, 75-; music critic, Champaign News Gazette, Ill, 79-80; prog annotator Ill Opera Theatre, Krannert Ctr, 79- *Teaching:* Lectr vocal lit, Univ Ill, Urbana, 80-; dir music dance div, Nat Acad Arts, 82- *Awards:* Harry Steenbock Scholar, 68-72; Fulbright-Hays Grant, 77. *Mem:* Phi Mu Alpha Sinfonia; Am Musicol Soc. *Interests:* German Romantic opera with emphasis on Spohr; American immigrant art music of the 19th century; ballet. *Publ:* Contribr, Balatka Hans, In: New Grove Dict of Music & Musicians, 80; Balatka Hans, In: New Grove Dict of Music in US (in prep). *Mailing Add:* 401 E Chalmers #122 Champaign IL 61820

SCHLEUTER, STANLEY L
EDUCATOR
b Clear Lake, SDak. *Study:* SDak State Univ, BS(music educ), 61; Univ Iowa, MA(music), 63, PhD(music), 71. *Teaching:* Asst prof music, Minot State Col, NDak, 70-71; Univ Wis, Madison, 71-74 & State Univ NY, Buffalo, 74-77; from assoc prof to prof music, Kent State Univ, Ohio, 77- *Mem:* Col Music Soc; Music Educr Nat Conf; Coun Res Music Educ; Ohio Music Educr Asn. *Interests:* Music measurement, evaluation and learning processes; instrumental music teaching. *Publ:* Auth, Use of Standardized Tests of Musical Aptitude with University Freshmen Music Majors, J Res Music Educ, 74; Discography of Saxophone Music, Meadowlark Publ, 77; Effects of Certain Lateral Dominance Traits, Music Aptitude, and Sex Differences with Instrumental Music Achievement, J Res Music Educ, 78; The Development of a College Version of the Musical Aptitude Profile, Psychology of Music, 78; A Sound Approach to Teaching Instrumentalists, Kent State Univ Press (in prep). *Mailing Add:* Sch Music Kent State University Kent OH 44242

SCHMALZ, ROBERT FREDERICK
EDUCATOR, TROMBONE
b Pittsburgh, Pa, Oct 20, 41. *Study:* Duquesne Univ, BSME, 63; Univ Pittsburgh, MA(music hist & lit), 66, PhD(musicol), 71. *Teaching:* Adj fac music, Univ Pittsburgh, 69-71; assoc prof musicol & trombone, Univ Southwestern La, 71-; artist & clinician trombone, H N White Co, 78- *Awards:* Distinguished Prof, Univ Southwestern La Found, 79. *Mem:* Am Musicol Soc (archivist, 79-80, secy-treas, 80-83, pres elect, 83-); Col Music Soc (sec-treas southern chap, 80-82, pres, 83-); SCent Renaissance Conf (vpres, 82-83, pres, 83-). *Publ:* Auth, The Missa Hilf und Gib rat: Tradition in Reappraisal, Explorations in Renaissance Cult, Vol IV, 78; Fidelis Zitterbart Jr: Legacy Unevaluated, Col Music Soc Symposium, Vol 19, 79; Music in Plantation Society: St Martinville (La) in the Nineteenth Century, Attakapas Hist Soc, Vol XVII, 82; I Did It in the Interests of the Public: Thoughts Upon the Macabre Demise of Operatic Tenors, Col Music Soc Symposium, fall 83. *Mailing Add:* 104 Harper Ave Lafayette LA 70506

SCHMIDT, CARL B
EDUCATOR, WRITER
b Nashville, Tenn, Oct 20, 41. *Study:* Ecoles d'art Americaines, Fontainebleau, with Nadia Boulanger, dipl, 62; Stanford Univ, AB, 63; Harvard Univ, AM, 67, PhD, 73. *Teaching:* Instr, Wabash Col, 70-73; asst prof, Bryn Mawr Col, 73-79; assoc prof, Philadelphia Col Perf Arts, 78-; vis prof, Temple Univ, summers 81 & 82 & Univ Ariz, fall 81. *Awards:* Stipend, Am Coun Learned Soc, summer 80. *Mem:* Am Musicol Soc (chmn mid-Atlantic chap, 80-82); Music Libr Asn; Soc Ital Musicol. *Interests:* Seventeenth century Italian opera; music in the reign of Louis XIV. *Publ:* Auth, Antonio Cesti's La Dori: A Study of Sources, Performance Traditions and Musical Style, Rivista Ital Musicol, 75; Antonio Cesti's Il Pomo d'oro: A Reexamination of a Famous Hapsburg Court Spectacle, 76 & An Episode in the History of Venetian Opera: The Tito Commission, 78, J Am Musicol Soc; coauth, A Collection of 137 Broadsides Concerning Theatre in Late Seventeenth-Century Italy: An Annotated Catalog, Harvard Libr Bulletin, 80. *Mailing Add:* Philadelphia Col Perf Arts 250 S Broad St Philadelphia PA 19102

SCHMIDT, DALE
BASS
b Cleveland, Ohio, Feb 18, 42. *Study:* Baldwin-Wallace Col, BMusEd; Eastman Sch Music. *Pos:* Prin bass, Atlanta Symph Orch, formerly, co-prin bass, 83- *Mailing Add:* 1168 St Louis Pl NE Atlanta GA 30306

SCHMIDT, FRED D
TROMBONE, EDUCATOR
Study: Boston Univ, BM; Lowell State Univ; Framingham State Univ; Boston State Univ. *Pos:* Trombonist, Boston Civic Symph, currently & Worcester Civic Symph, currently. *Teaching:* Dir instrm music, Uxbridge pub sch, formerly; chmn gen music dept, Berklee Col Music, currently. *Mailing Add:* Berklee Col Music 1140 Boylston St Boston MA 02215

SCHMIDT, JOHN CHARLES
EDUCATOR, WRITER
b Kenedy, Tex, Feb 19, 41. *Study:* Southwestern Univ, Tex, BMus, 61; Union Theol Sem, MA(sacred music), 63; NY Univ, PhD(musicol), 79. *Pos:* Organist & choirmaster, St Mark's Episcopal Church, San Marcos, Tex, 78- *Teaching:* Instr music, NY Univ, 69-73; assoc prof, Southwest Tex State Univ, 78- *Mem:* Am Musicol Soc; Sonneck Soc; Col Music Soc; Am Guild Organists. *Interests:* Second New England school especially John Knowles Paine. *Publ:* Ed, John Knowles Paine, Complete Piano Music, Da Capo Press, 83. *Mailing Add:* Dept Music Southwest Tex State Univ San Marcos TX 78666

SCHMIDT, LISELOTTE MARTHA
EDUCATOR, CRITIC-WRITER
b Reading, Pa, Mar 18, 33. *Study:* Converse Col, BMus (piano), 54; NY Univ, MA(musicol), 56; Manhattan Sch Music, MMus(piano), 60; Columbia Univ, EdD(piano & theory), 63; Univ Mich; Juilliard Sch Music; Univ Munich, Ger. *Teaching:* Asst prof theory, piano & music hist, State Univ NY Col, Potsdam, 61-65; assoc prof piano & music hist, Southern Ill Univ, 65-66; assoc piano & music theory, Western Mich Univ, 66-67; assoc prof piano, music hist & theory, Wilkes Col, 67-70; prof & chair dept music hist, West Chester Univ Pa, 70- *Awards:* Fulbright Int Educ Grant, 56-57; State Univ NY Summer Fel, NY State Univ Res Found Musicol Res, 62; Res Found Grant, Southern Ill Univ Musicol Res, 65-66. *Mem:* Int Musicol Soc; Am Musicol Soc; Col Music Soc; Music Educr Nat Conf; Am Guild Organists. *Interests:* Sixteenth century music, in particular preparation of scholarly edition of the complete works of Jachet Berchem, Italian madrigal composer. *Mailing Add:* 201 Ford Circle West Chester PA 19380

SCHMIDT, MARY HELEN
EDUCATOR, PIANO
b Minneapolis, Minn, Aug 8, 38. *Study:* Univ Minn, BA, 60, MA, 62; Manhattan Sch Music, MM, 64; Mozarteum Akad, Salzburg, Austria, dipl, 67; Univ Wash, DMA, 75. *Pos:* Conct pianist & organist, US, Can & Europe, 65- *Teaching:* Assoc prof, Augustana Col, SDak, 65- *Awards:* Winner, Nat Organ Playing Compt, Am Guild Organists, 63. *Mem:* Am Guild Organists; Nat Guild Piano Teachers; Music Teachers Nat Asn. *Mailing Add:* Augustana Col Sioux Falls SD 57197

SCHMIDT, RODNEY
EDUCATOR, VIOLIN
b Salem, Ore, Apr, 5, 39. *Study:* Akad Mozarteum, Salzburg, Austria, 60; Oberlin Consv Music, BMus, 61; Calif State Univ, Northridge, MA, 62; Univ Colo, Boulder, DMA, 72; study with Henryk Szeryng & Nathan Milstein. *Teaching:* Instr, Clarion State Col, Pa, 64-65; asst prof, Jacksonville Univ, Fla, 65-67; prof music, ECarolina Univ, Greenville, NC, 67- *Mem:* Am String Teachers Asn; Am Asn Univ Prof; Col Music Soc; Music Teachers Nat Asn; Music Educr Nat Conf. *Interests:* Acoustics of the bowed string; physiology to violin performance technique. *Mailing Add:* PO Box 3015 Greenville NC 27834

SCHMIDT, SHARON YVONNE DAVIS See Davis, Sharon

SCHMIDT, WILLIAM JOSEPH
COMPOSER
b Chicago, Ill, Mar 6, 26. *Study:* US Navy Sch Music, cert 45; Chicago Musical Col, comp with Max Wald, 46-49; Univ Southern Calif, comp with Ingolf Dahl, BM, 51, MM, 60. *Works:* Septigrams for Flute, Piano and Percussion, 56, Short'nin' Bread Variations for Brass Choir, 64, Variegations for Alto Saxophone and Organ, 73, Double Concerto for Trumpet, Piano and Chamber Orchestra, 80, The Range of Light Concerto (perc, narrator, speaking, chorus & symph wind ens), 81, Jazzberries (trumpet, cello & piano), 82 & Tuba Mirum (tuba, winds & perc), 83, Avant Music. *Pos:* Pres, Western Int Music Inc, 64- *Awards:* Award, ASCAP, 80-83. *Bibliog:* Vance Jennings (auth), Selected 20th Century Clarinet Literature: Rhapsody No 1 for Clarinet & Piano, Nat Asn Col Wind and Perc Instr J, summer 80; Roger Greenberg (auth), Concerto for Tenor Saxophone, Saxophone J, spring 82. *Mailing Add:* 2859 Holt Ave Los Angeles CA 90034

SCHMITT, CECILIA
ADMINISTRATOR, EDUCATOR
b Rice, Minn, Mar 27, 28. *Study:* St Catherine Col, BA, 65; Univ Minn, Minneapolis, MA, 71; Univ Ill, Urbana, EdD, 79. *Pos:* Instrumental instr, St Francis High Sch, 49-76; coordr studies, Nat Acad Arts, Urbana-Champaign, Ill, 77-78; dir & founder, St Francis Music Ctr, 79- *Teaching:* Piano & organ, Cent Minn Sch, 49-77; music theory, Nat Acad Arts, 77-78; instr piano & organ, St Francis Music Ctr, 78- *Mem:* Minn Music Teachers Asn (local chmn, 56-58); Am Guild Piano Teachers (local chmn, 65-68); Heartland Symph (mem bd dir, 80-); Minn Alliance Educ Arts. *Interests:* Music and psychology. *Publ:* Auth, Rapport and Success: Human Relations in Music Education, Dorrance Inc, 76. *Mailing Add:* 116 SE Eighth Ave Little Falls MN 56345

SCHMORR, ROBERT
TENOR, TEACHER
Roles: Frosch in Die Fledermaus, 77, Schmidt in Werther, 80 & Earl of Surrey in Henry VIII, 83, San Diego Opera. *Pos:* Prin artist, Metropolitan Opera, 14 yrs; appearances with 40 opera co in US; adminr, San Diego Opera Ctr, 81-82; minister music, Graham Presby Church, Coronado, currently. *Teaching:* Voice, privately, currently. *Mailing Add:* San Diego Opera PO Box 988 San Diego CA 92112

SCHNEIDER, BERNARD
EDUCATOR, TROMBONE
Study: St Louis Inst Music, MMusEd; Univ Miami, BA; studied trombone with Jacob Reichman & Ernest Clark. *Pos:* Performer, Metropolitan Opera, formerly, Handel Soc Boston, formerly, Vancouver Summer Fest, formerly, Berkshire Fest, formerly & several ballet co; soloist, St Louis String Ens, formerly, Alton Civic Orch, formerly, Aristeia Ens, formerly & New Music Circle of St Louis, formerly; prin trombone, Israel Phil Orch, formerly; soloist, St Louis Symph Orch, formerly, prin trombone, currently. *Teaching:* Mem fac trombone, St Louis Consv Music, currently. *Mailing Add:* St Louis Consv Music 560 Trinity Ave St Louis MO 63130

SCHNEIDER, DAVID HERSH
VIOLIN, WRITER
b San Francisco, Calif, Apr 10, 18. *Study:* Univ Calif, AA, 36. *Pos:* Prin second violin, San Francisco Symph, 36-, soloist, 68 & 80; prin second violin, San Francisco Opera, 41-67. *Teaching:* Lectr violin & viola, Univ Calif, Berkeley, 45-55; teacher, San Francisco Consv Music, 47-61; prof violin, viola & chamber music, San Francisco State Univ, 61-80. *Publ:* Auth, San Francisco Symph: Music, Maestros and Musicians, Presidio Press, 83. *Mailing Add:* 862 Pacheco St San Francisco CA 64116

SCHNEIDER, GARY MICHAEL
MUSIC DIRECTOR, COMPOSER
b Copaigue, NY, Mar 1, 57. *Study:* Sch Music, Ind Univ, studied comp with Juan Orrego-Salas, BMus, 79, MMus, 80. *Works:* Study for a Ballet, comn by Shirley Broughton Dancers; Sonata for Violin and Piano, perf by James Fudge & Amy Dorfman, 79; Timeless Footsteps, comn by Ind Univ Dance Theater, 80; The Voice of Eternity, Peer Southern Orgn, 80; Istanti, Berben, 82. *Pos:* Music dir, Hoboken Chamber Orch, NJ, 81- *Mem:* BMI; Am Comp Alliance. *Mailing Add:* 219 11th St Hoboken NJ 07030

SCHNEIDER, JOHN
CRITIC-WRITER, EDUCATOR
b Louisville, Ky, Dec 26, 22. *Study:* Univ Louisville, BM, 47; Juilliard Sch Music, studied piano with Beveridge Webster, dipl, 50; Consv Paris, studied piano with Yves Nat, 51. *Pos:* Music critic, Atlanta Jour, 70-80; adjudicator, local, nat & int piano & voice compt; founder & dir, Atlanta Young Artists Compt, 75-77; pianist, local solo, chamber music & voice recitals. *Teaching:* Mem fac, Ga State Univ, 66- *Mem:* Atlanta Music Club. *Publ:* Auth, Atlanta, In: New Grove Dict of Music & Musicians; contribr, Musical Am. *Mailing Add:* Music Dept Ga State Univ Atlanta GA 30303

SCHNEIDER, JOHN OWSLEY
GUITAR, WRITER
b Pasadena, Calif, Nov 8, 50. *Study:* Univ Calif, Santa Barbara, BA, 74; Royal Col Music, London, ARCM, 77; Univ Wales, PhD, 77. *Works:* Voyage, comn by Cardiff Fest 20th Century Music, 76; TBA, Arts Lab Press, Birmingham, England, 78. *Rec Perf:* Sonic Voyage: New Music for Guitar, El Maestro Rec, 81. *Teaching:* Assoc prof, Los Angeles Pierce Col, 78- *Mem:* Guitar Found Am (pres, 79-); Col Music Soc; Am Guitar Soc. *Interests:* Microtonality; contemporary guitar composers; guitar history. *Publ:* Auth, The Rational Method of Tone Production, ASTA J, 78; Twentieth Century Guitar: 2nd Golden Age, Guitar & Lute, 79; The Microtonal Guitar, Galliard Press, 83; The Contemporary Guitar, Univ Calif, 83. *Mailing Add:* 5151 Lindley Ave Tarzana CA 91356

SCHNEIDER, JUNE
COMPOSER, EDUCATOR
Study: ATCL, 56, LTCL, 57, BMus, BMusHons, PhD, 62; Univ Witwatersrand, Johannesburg, South Africa. *Works:* Encounter Time and Space (tape piece), Johannesburg Planetarium, South Africa, 71-72; Nongause (electronic music), Perf Arts Coun, Transvaal, South Africa, 73; Birth (film score), Media Insights, 76; The Assassination of Shaka (multimedia audio-visual tape piece), 76; Electra, Nunnery Theatre Group, Univ Witwatersrand, 77; Soundaround, Piedmont Park Fest Perf, 78; Time Piece, Emory Univ Choirs & Glee Club, 79. *Pos:* Creator, comp & guest cur, High Museum Art, Atlanta, Ga, 81. *Teaching:* Sr lectr hist, comp & music, Univ Witwatersrand, 65-77; guest lectr, New Music in Action, Univ York, UK, 76-77; asst prof theory, comp & hist, Emory Univ, 78-80; prof comp & electronic music, Mercer Univ Atlanta, 78-81; guest comp, City Univ London, 81. *Awards:* British Coun Award, 68. *Bibliog:* Sydney Stegall (auth), Profile: June Schneider, Art Papers, 80. *Publ:* Auth, Music Now (series), Artlook, 71-73; Picasso and Stravinsky, ARS Nova, 74; Penderecki, Royal Acad Music, 75; Penderecki, In: Music and Musicians, 75; Music, Noise & Hearing Damage, South Africa Med J, 76. *Mailing Add:* 3820 Paces Ferry W Atlanta GA 30339

SCHNEIDER, MISCHA
CELLO, EDUCATOR
b Wilna, USSR, 1903. *Study:* Leipzig Consv, Germany, with Julius Klengel, dipl, 23. *Pos:* Cellist, Budapest String Quartet, 30-65, mem quartet in res, Libr Cong, 40-62. *Teaching:* Prof cello & chamber music, State Univ NY, Buffalo, 63-75; mem fac, Curtis Inst Music, 70- *Mailing Add:* Curtis Inst Music 1726 Locust St Philadelphia PA 19103

SCHNEIDERMAN, WILLIAM
PERCUSSION, EDUCATOR
b New York, NY, Aug 10, 16. *Study:* Inst Musical Art, dipl, 38; Juilliard Sch Music, dipl, 39 & 40. *Pos:* Timpani & perc, Ballet Russe de Basil, 40-41, Hurok Ballet Theatre, 41-43; solo timpani, Chautauqua Symph & Opera, 43-58; solo timpani, Pittsburgh Symph Orch, 43-58, perc, 58-82. *Teaching:* Instr perc, Carnegie Inst Technol, 45-58, Duquesne Univ, 55- *Mem:* Percussive Arts Soc. *Mailing Add:* 1214 Raven Dr Pittsburgh PA 15243

SCHNEIDMANN, IRENE
PIANO, EDUCATOR
b Vienna, Austria, US citizen. *Study:* Staatsakademie fur Musik, Vienna, Austria, reifeprufung, with Wuhrer, meisterprufung; Juilliard Sch, with R Lhevinne, dipl. *Pos:* Solo recitalist in Europe & US; soloist with Europ & US orchs; radio & TV perf. *Teaching:* Prof piano, Staatsakademie fur Musik, Vienna, Austria; artist in res, Bradley Univ & Univ Bridgeport; adj prof, Fairfield Univ; master classes at US univ. *Awards:* Josef Lhevinne Award. *Bibliog:* Susan Okula (auth), article, Assoc Press, 82. *Mem:* Sigma Alpha Iota. *Mailing Add:* c/o T W Nugent 160 Rivergate Dr Wilton CT 06897

SCHNOEBELEN, ANNE
WRITER, EDUCATOR
b Tomahawk, Wis, Aug 4, 33. *Study:* Rosary Col, BA, 58; Univ Ill, Urbana, MM, 60, PhD, 66. *Teaching:* Assoc prof music hist & chmn dept, Rosary Col, 69-71; lectr, Inst Studi Musicali, Univ Bologna, 71-73; vis assoc prof musicol, Col Consv Music, Univ Cincinnati, 73-74; prof & chmn dept, Shepherd Sch Music, Rice Univ, 80- *Awards:* Fel, Am Asn Univ Women, 64-65; Fulbright Full Grant, 64-65; grants, Nat Endowment Humanities, 69 & 83. *Mem:* Am Musicol Soc (secy coun, 82-83); Int Musicol Soc; Music Libr Asn. *Interests:* Italian sacred music of the 17th century; letters of Padre Martini. *Publ:* Auth, Perfomance Practices at San Petronio in the Baroque, Acta Musicol, 69; Cazzati vs Bologna, Musical Quart, 71; ed, Giovanni Paolo Colonna, Messa a Nove Voci Concertata con Strumenti, A-R Ed, 74; auth, The Growth of Padre Martini's Library as Reflected in His Correspondence, Music & Lett, 77; Padre Martini's Collection of Letters in the Civico Museo Bibligrafico Musicale: An Annotated Index, Pendragon Press, 79. *Mailing Add:* PO Box 1892 Houston TX 77251

SCHOBER, BRIAN
COMPOSER, ORGAN
b East Orange, NJ, June 17, 51. *Study:* Eastman Sch Music, BM, 73, DMA, 80; Consv Nat Superieur Musique, Paris, Prix de Comp, 76. *Works:* Haiku of Basho, Alexander Broude Inc, 73; Evaporations, Ed Salabert, 76; Sunflower Splendor, 78 & Antiphonals, 78, Am Comp Ed; Nocturnals, 80, Four Poems of Samuel Beckett, 80 & Arabesques, 80, Alexander Broude Inc. *Pos:* Music dir, St Thomas Apostle Church, Bloomfield, NJ, 78-79. *Teaching:* Asst prof music, Tex Wesleyan Col, 79-83. *Awards:* Comp grant, Nat Endowment Arts, 81. *Bibliog:* Claire Eyrich (auth), Area Composer Works to Showcase New Music, Ft Worth Star Telegram, 10/31/82. *Mem:* Am Guild Organist; Am Comp Alliance; Am Music Ctr. *Mailing Add:* 4 S Pinehurst Ave #2F New York NY 10033

SCHOENBACH, SOL ISRAEL
ADMINISTRATOR, BASSOON
b New York, NY, Mar 15, 15. *Study:* Juilliard Sch, dipl bassoon, 36; NY Univ, BA, 39; Curtis Inst Music, Hon MusD, 69; Temple Univ, Hon MusD, 71; New Sch Music, Hon MusD, 83. *Pos:* Staff bassoonist, CBS Orch, 32-37; organizer, Phil Woodwind Quintet, 50, mem, 50-66; exec dir, Settlement Music Sch, 57-81; dir, Presser Co, formerly. *Teaching:* Instr bassoon, Curtis Inst Music, 43- & New England Consv Music, 81; cond master classes bassoon, Banff Fest Arts, Can, 81 & Berkshire Music Ctr, 83. *Awards:* Hartmann Kuhn Award, Philadelphia Orch, 43-53; Music Award, Philadelphia Fine Arts Fest, 62; Merit Award, Philadelphia Art Alliance, 76. *Mem:* Int Double Reed Soc (pres, 81). *Mailing Add:* 1810 Rittenhouse Sq Philadelphia PA 19103

SCHOEP, ARTHUR PAUL
EDUCATOR, WRITER
b Orange City, Iowa, Dec 13, 20. *Study:* Univ SDak, BFA, 42; Eastman Sch Music, MMus, 45; New England Consv Music, artist's dipl, 48; Univ Col, DMA, 62. *Roles:* Count Almaviva in Marriage of Figaro, New England Opera Theatre, 46; Marcello in La Boheme, 48 & Valentine in Faust, 49, Ft Worth Opera; Schaunard in La Boheme, New Orleans Opera, 53; Aeneas in The Trojans, New England Opera Theatre, 55; Pelleas in Pelleas et Melisande, Theatre de la Monnaie, Brussels, 55; Geronio in Il Turco in Italia, Goldovsky Opera Theatre, 61. *Pos:* Artistic dir & gen mgr, Denver Lyric Theatre, Colo, 61-67. *Teaching:* Mem fac opera, New England Consv Music, 55-58; asst prof fine arts, Univ Tenn, 58-60; prof music, NTex State Univ, 67- *Awards:* Fulbright Scholar, Netherlands, 50-51. *Mem:* Nat Opera Asn (pres, 72-73); Nat Asn Teachers Singing; Am Guild Musical Artists. *Publ:* Auth, Opera: The Translator's View, Nat Asn Teachers Singing Bulletin, 62; Standardization of Opera Translations: Is It Time?, Nat Opera Asn J, 68; coauth, Word-to-Word Translations of Songs & Arias, Part II, Italian, Scarecrow Press, 72; Bringing Soprano Arias to Life, G Schirmer Inc, 73. *Mailing Add:* 808 Skylark Denton TX 76201

SCHONBERG, HAROLD C
CRITIC-WRITER
b New York, NY, Nov 29, 15. *Study:* Brooklyn Col, AB, 37; NY Univ, AM, 38; studied with Alicia Frisca & Marion Bauer; Temple Univ, LittD, 64; Grinnell Col, LHD, 67. *Pos:* Assoc ed, Am Music Lover, 39-41; ed, Music Digest, 46-48; music critic, New York Sun, 46-50; contrib ed & rec columnist,

Music Courier, 48-52; columnist, Gramophone, London, 48-60; music & rec critic, New York Times, 50-60, sr music critic, 60-80, cult corresp, 80- Teaching: Mem spec sem fac, Mannes Col Music, 81- Publ: Auth, The Great Pianists, 63; The Great Conductors, 67; Lives of the Great Composers, 70; Grandmasters of Chess, 73, rev ed, 81; Facing the Music, 81. Rep: New York Artist Bur 170 West End Ave 3N New York NY 10023. Mailing Add: 118 Riverside Dr New York NY 10024

SCHONTHAL-SECKEL, RUTH
COMPOSER, EDUCATOR

b Hamburg, Germany, June 27, 24; US citizen. Study: Consv Stern, Berlin, with Etthoven; studied piano with S Barere & Sasha Gorodnitzky; Royal Acad Music, Stockholm; studied with Manuel Ponce in Mex; Yale Univ, studied comp with Paul Hindemith, BM, 48. Works: Totengesänge (sop & piano), 74; Variations in Search of a Theme (piano), 75; Miniatures, Vol I, II & III (piano), Galaxy; Sonata Concertante (viola & piano), 75; The Transposed Heads (ballet & orch suite); Sonata Breve (piano), Oxford Univ Press, 76; The Solitary Reaper (ten, violin, piano, cello & flute), 78. Pos: Conct pianist. Teaching: Mem fac, Adelphi Univ, 73-76 & Westchester Consv, 74-; instr theory, analysis & comp, Mercy Col, NY, currently; instr music, Sch Educ, NY Univ, currently. Awards: Delta Omicron Award, 47; ASCAP Award, 79; Cert Merit, Yale Univ, 81. Mem: ASCAP; Am Musicol Asn; Assoc Music Teachers League NY. Mailing Add: 12 Van Etten Blvd New Rochelle NY 10804

SCHOOLEY, JOHN (HEILMAN)
EDUCATOR, COMPOSER

b Nelson, Pa, Feb 8, 43. Study: Mansfield State Col, BSMEd, 65; Royal Acad Music, London, England, cert(comp), 66; ECarolina Univ, MM(theory & comp), 68. Works: Partita for Brass Quartet, Kendor Music, 66; Three Dances for Woodwind Trio, 68, Serenata for Tuba & Piano, 70, From a Very Little Sphinx, 75, Songs of Victory in Heaven, 78, Choral Responses..., 78 & Winter's Journey, 82, Glouchester Press. Teaching: Instr theory & low brass, Eastern Ky Univ, 68-70; assoc prof, Fairmont State Col, 70- Awards: First Place, Delius Asn Compt, 75; fel, Nat Endowment Humanities, 79. Mem: Life mem, Col Music Soc; Am Music Ctr; ASCAP; Nat Asn Comp USA; Southern Comp League. Publ: Coauth, A Prospectus for College Theory (5 books), Glouchester Press, 71-75; auth, Starting an Instrument: How to Do It Right, Musical Am, 11/82; A Practice Sheet for Trombone Students, Int Trombone Asn J, 10/82. Mailing Add: 1113 Morningstar Lane Fairmont WV 26554

SCHOTT, HOWARD MANSFIELD
WRITER, LECTURER

b New York, NY. Study: Yale Col, with Ralph Kirkpatrick, BA; Oxford Univ, with Westrup & Kerman, DPhil, 78; Mannes Col Music, with Hans Neumann; City Univ New York, with Barry Brook. Pos: Consult, Dept Furniture & Woodwork, Victoria & Albert Museum, London, 76- & Dept Musical Inst, Metropolitan Museum of Art, 81- Mem: Am Musical Instr Soc (mem bd gov, 81-84); Am Musicol Soc; Royal Musical Asn, London; Galpin Soc; Gesellschaft Musikforschung, West Germany. Interests: Music for keyboard, 17th century; keyboard instruments and their history from 14th century to the present. Publ: Auth, Playing the Harpsichord, Faber, London & St Martins Press, NY, 71; ed, The Harpsichord & Clavichord, 2d ed, Faber, London & Norton, NY, 73; Froberger—Oeuvres Completes, Hugel Paris, 80 & 83; auth, Suonare Il Clavicembalo, F Muzzi Padua, 82; Cembalospiel, Artemis, Munich, 83. Mailing Add: Suite 402 Brook House 44 Washington St Brookline MA 02146

SCHRADER, BARRY WALTER
COMPOSER, EDUCATOR

b Johnstown, Pa, June 26, 45. Study: Univ Pittsburgh, BA, 67, MA, 70; Calif Inst Arts, MFA, 71. Works: Celebration, 71, Bestiary, 72-74, Trinity, 76, Classical Studies, 76, Lost Atlantis, 77, Moon-Whales & Other Moon Songs, 82-83 & Electronic Music Box I, 83, Electro-Acoust Music. Pos: Dir, Currents, 73-79 & Electro-Acoust Music Marathon, 80- Teaching: Prof electro-acoust music, comp & theory, Calif Inst Arts, 71-; lectr electro-acoust music, Calif State Univ, Los Angeles, 75-78. Mem: Am Soc Univ Comp; ASCAP. Publ: Auth, Introduction to Electro-Acoustic Music, Prentice-Hall, 82; Electro-Acoustic Music, Grove Am (in prep). Mailing Add: Calif Inst of Arts 24700 McBean Parkway Valencia CA 91355

SCHROEDER, GERALD H
EDUCATOR

b Wonewoc, Wis, June 24, 36. Study: Univ Wis, BS, 59; Ind Univ, MMus, 65; Univ Col, DMA, 71; studied with Helmet Rilnig & Robert Shaw. Teaching: Music, Marshfield Sr High Sch, Wis, 60-69; assoc prof, Univ Wis Ctr, Marshfield, 68 & Boise State Univ, 78- Awards: Outstanding Young Educr of Yr, Marshfield, 67; Outstanding Teacher of Yr, Univ Wis Ctr, Marshfield, 72. Mem: Am Choral Dir Asn; Am Choral Fedn; Music Educr Nat Conf. Publ: Contrib to Church Music Mag. Mailing Add: 2017 Harrison Rd Boise ID 83702

SCHROEDER, POLLYANNA TRIBOUILLIER
MUSICOLOGIST, SOPRANO

b Guatemala City, Mex, Jan 24, 31; US citizen. Study: Westminster Choir Col, BM, 55; Am Univ, MA, 76; Cath Univ Am. Pos: Conct performer, Guatemala Nat Symph Orch, 55 & 73, Caribbean & Cent Am, 57-76, CBS TV, 61 & Orgn Am States Conct Ser, 72; dir, Mantua Music Studio, Fairfax, Va, 64-80; Latin Am music specialist, Orgn Am States, Washington, DC, 80-82. Teaching: Vis prof, Inter-Am Univ, San German, PR, 59-63. Mem: Latin Am Studies Asn; Am Musicol Soc; Ethnomusicol Soc Am; Col Music Soc; Latin Am Indian Lit Asn. Interests: Latin American music history. Publ: Auth, Bicentennial of American Music, Ed Res Reports, Vol 1, No 12; The Contribution of Popular and Artistic Latin American Music to the United States, US Info, 77; Growth of Latin American Popular Music in the United States, Symposium, Col Music Soc, fall 78; Musician of Two Worlds, 79 & Aida Doninelli, Guatemalan Soprano at the Metropolitan Opera Company of New York, 82, Americas. Mailing Add: 9111 Coronado Terr Fairfax VA 22031

SCHROEDER, RAYMOND LEE
CLARINET, EDUCATOR

b Cincinnati, Ohio, Nov 15, 36. Study: Col Consv Music, Univ Cincinnati, BM, 58; Boston Univ, MM, 59. Pos: Clarinetist, Cincinnati Symph, 59-60 & Chautauqua Symph, 64-; prin clarinetist, Austin Symph, 60- Teaching: Instr clarinet, Col Consv Music, Univ Cincinnati, 59-60; asst prof, Univ Tex, Austin, 60-68 & Southwestern Univ, 68- Mem: Am Fedn Musicians. Mailing Add: 1203 Country Club Rd Georgetown TX 78626

SCHROEDER, WILLIAM A
COMPOSER, EDUCATOR

b Brooklyn, NY, Apr 24, 21. Study: Chicago Musical Col, with Max Wald; Northwestern Univ, with Anthony Donata. Works: Invention and Fugue (wind ens); Prologue, Canon & Stretto (wind ens); March, Antiphonal and Triumphant (two brass choirs); Of Moon and Winds (song cycle for voice, string quartet & piano); Age—The Beauty of Time (mezzo-soprano & woodwind quintet); Canticle of Praise (chorus, brass quintet & timpani). Teaching: Instr, Peabody Consv, 49-51, Judson Col, 52-56, Henderson State Teachers Col, 59-61, Wartburg Col, 61-65 & Nat Music Camp, 65-; prof music, Del Mar Col, 65- Awards: Oliver Ditson Scholar, 42; Faricy Award, 59. Mailing Add: 4413 Bluefield Dr Corpus Christi TX 78413

SCHROEDER-SHEKER, THERESE M
HARP, EDITOR

b Detroit, Mich, Jan 24, 51. Study: Loretto Heights Col, BA(perf), 75. Works: The Chalice of Repose, Op, 12 (twelve harp quartets), St Dunstan's Press (in prep). Pos: Artistic dir, Dufay Consort, 76-81; sr ed, De Mano Archives, 81-82; ed, St Dunstan's Press, 82-; artistic dir, Ars Antiqua, 83- Interests: Medieval wire strung, 13-14th century harps and their repertoire. Publ: Auth & ed, An Articulate Rapture: The Gothic Response to the Mary Cult (in prep) & Historical Harp Repertoire (in prep), St Dunstan's Press. Mailing Add: Ars Antiqua 607 Corona Denver CO 80218

SCHROTH, GODFREY WILLIAM
COMPOSER, CONDUCTOR & MUSIC DIRECTOR

b Trenton, NJ, Jan 7, 27. Study: St Joseph's Col, BS, 49; Teachers Col, Columbia Univ, MA, 51; studied comp with Paul Creston. Works: Piano Quintet, Phoenix Quartet, 59; A Solemn English Mass, 66 & Rod of Jesse (organ suite), 72, Gregorian Inst Am Publ; Rocky Mt Serenade, Adelphi Chamber Orch, 73; Rejoice, O Earth, Belwin Mills, 75; Across the Delaware (cantata), NJ Bicentennial Comn Grant, 76; Green Graves and Violets, comn by Trenton Tercentenary Comt, 79. Pos: Music dir, St Mary's Cathedral, Trenton, NJ, 59- Awards: LADO Found Prize for Piano Quintet, 59; Benermerenti Medal, Pope John Paul II, 79. Mem: Bohemians. Mailing Add: 261 Lookout Ave Hackensack NJ 07601

SCHUBEL, MAX
COMPOSER, ADMINISTRATOR

b Bronx, NY, Apr 11, 32. Study: NY Univ, BA, 53. Works: String Quartet # 2, Kohon Quartet, 68; Fracture, Highgate Press, 74; Pocket Slurp, Assoc Music, 79; Guale, comn by Albert Scardino, 79; Paraplex, Ens Univ NMex, 79; Ylk Dyrth, N-S Consonance, 83. Pos: Pres, Op One Rec Inc, 66- Awards: Nat Endowment Arts Comp Grant, 74 & 82; NY State Arts Coun Comp Grant, 76 & 81; Meet the Comp Grant, late 70's-early 80's. Mem: BMI; Am Music Ctr. Rep: Edith Mugdan Artists Mgt 84 Prospect Ave Douglaston NY 11363. Mailing Add: PO Box 604 Greenville ME 04441

SCHUETZE, GEORGE CLAIRE, JR
EDUCATOR, WRITER

b Monroe, Wis, Feb 6, 29. Study: Univ Wis, BMus, 51, NY Univ, PhD(music hist), 60. Pos: Ed musicol, Inst Medieval Music, 60-63. Teaching: Asst prof, Am Univ, 63-70, assoc prof musicol, 70-80, prof, 80- Mem: Am Musicol Soc; Int Musicol Soc; Music Libr Asn. Interests: Renaissance music; music bibliography. Publ: Auth, Opera Omnia Faugues, 59, An Introduction to Faugues, 60 & Collected Works of Faugues, 60, Inst Medieval Music. Mailing Add: Dept Music Am Univ Washington DC 20016

SCHUITEMA, JOAN ELIZABETH
LIBRARIAN, HARPSICHORD

b Clinton, Iowa, July 29, 55. Study: Ill Wesleyan Univ, BM(piano perf), 77; Univ Ill, Urbana, harpsichord study with George Hunter, MS(libr sci), 78; Southern Methodist Univ, harpsichord study with Larry Palmer & Isolde Ahlgrimm, MM(harpsichord perf), 81. Pos: Music cataloger, Southern Methodist Univ, 79- Mem: Music Libr Asn (vchairperson Tex chap, 79-80 & chairperson, 81-82); Sigma Alpha Iota. Interests: Early music performance practices and the revival of the harpsichord in the 20th century. Mailing Add: 3447 1/2 Granada Dallas TX 75205

SCHULLER, GUNTHER
COMPOSER, MUSIC DIRECTOR

b New York, NY, Nov 22, 25. Study: St Thomas Choir Sch; Manhattan Sch Music; several hon degrees. Works: Spectra, comn by New York Phil, 58; Seven Studies on Themes of Paul Klee, comn by Ford Found, 59; Concerto for Orchestra, comn by Chicago Symph, 66; Museum Piece, comn by Boston Museum Fine Arts, 70; The Fisherman and His Wife (children's opera), comn by Jr League Boston, 70; Concerto da Camera, comn by Eastman Sch Music, 71; Triplum II, comn by Baltimore Symph Orch, 75; and many others. *Pos:* French hornist, Ballet Theater Orch, 41-43; solo horn, Cincinnati Symph, 43-44 & Metropolitan Opera Orch, 44-59; music dir, First Int Jazz Fest, 62; founder & pres, Margun Music Inc, 75. *Teaching:* Mem fac, Manhattan Sch Music, 50-63 & Yale Univ, 64-66; actg head comp dept, Berkshire Music Ctr, 63-65, head, 65-, artistic co-dir, 69-; pres, New England Consv Music, 66-77. *Awards:* Deems Taylor Award, 70; Alice M Ditson Cond Award, 70; Rodgers and Hammerstein Award, 71. *Bibliog:* Raymond Ericson (auth), article, 12/14/60 & Harold Schonberg (auth), article, 3/18/66, New York Times; Hope Stoddard (auth), Interview, Int Musician, 2/67. *Mem:* Nat Inst Arts & Lett; Am Acad Arts & Sci. *Publ:* Auth, Horn Technique, 62; Early Jazz, Its Roots and Musical Development, Vol I, 68. *Mailing Add:* 167 Dudley Rd Newton Center MA 02159

SCHULMAN, JULIUS
VIOLIN
b Brooklyn, NY. *Study:* Curtis Inst Music, with Zimbalist, grad. *Pos:* Mem, Philadelphia Orch, formerly, Boston Symph Orch, formerly & Boston Pops, formerly, asst concertmaster, Pittsburgh Symph, formerly & Metropolitan Opera Orch, formerly; concertmaster, Mutual Network Symph, formerly, New Orleans Symph, formerly, Little Orch Soc New York, formerly & San Antonio Symph, 75- *Mailing Add:* San Antonio Symph 109 Lexington Suite 207 San Antonio TX 78205

SCHULTE, ROLF
VIOLIN
b Cologne, WGermany, Oct 4, 49. *Study:* Robert Schumann Consv, Düsseldorf, WGermany, 60-68; Curtis Inst Music, 69-71. *Pos:* Found mem, Speculum Musicae, 71-78; recitalist, US & Europe, 73- *Awards:* Top Prize, Munich Int Radio Compt, 68; Award for Serv to Contemp Am Music, Paul Fromm Found, 81. *Mailing Add:* 128 W 72nd St New York NY 10023

SCHULTZ, CARL (ALLEN)
BASS
b Los Angeles, Calif. *Study:* Univ Southern Calif, BM, 56; Stuttgart Music Sch, 59-60. *Rec Perf:* Salome (Karl Boehm), Deutsche Grammophon, 69. *Roles:* King Philip II in Don Carlos, 61-63 & Abdul Hassan in Barber of Bagdad, 62-63, Oldenburg Staatstheater; Pimen in Boris Godunov, 64-67, Don Pasquale in Don Pasquale, 68-72, Geronimo in The Secret Marriage, 69-73, Don Magnifico in La Cenerentola, 71-73 & Agatha in Viva la Mama, 76-79, Hamburg Opera. *Pos:* TV appearances as pianist, accompanist & opera singer, 51-61; bass, Hamburg Staatsoper, 64- *Awards:* Piano Scholar, Young Musical Am TV Series, 51; First Prize, Geneva Music Cont, 60. *Mailing Add:* Milchstrasse 19 2000 Hamburg 13 Germany, Federal Republic of

SCHULTZ, HERBERT L
CONDUCTOR & MUSIC DIRECTOR, EDUCATOR
b Buffalo, NY, Dec 24, 23. *Study:* Juilliard Sch, studied trumpet with William Vacchiano, four yrs; Columbia Univ, MA(music & music educ), 51, prof dipl, 52, EdD(music & music educ), 70. *Pos:* Ed & founder, Vt Music News, Vt Music Educr Asn, 58-72; first trumpet, First All Am Bandmasters Band, 55; guest cond with conct bands throughout USA, 64-; cond, Vt Winds Conct Band, 79- *Teaching:* Music dir, Horicon Cent Sch, Brant Lake, NY, 52-53 & Norwich city sch, NY, 53-57; assoc prof music, Univ Vt, 57-, dir, Int Music Educr Clinic, 59-81, Summer Music Session for High Sch Students, 64-80 & Int Brass Symposium, 73-81; instr, Columbia Univ, 64-65. *Mem:* Music Educr Nat Conf (pres east div, 73-75, mem nat bd, 73-75); Asn Conct Bands (mem nat bd, 81-82, pres elect, 82-83). *Publ:* Auth, numerous articles in prof jour, 55-; coauth & ed, The Community Band: Initial Steps in Organization, Asn Conct Bands, 83. *Mailing Add:* Old Town Rd #11 Westford VT 05494

SCHULTZ, RALPH C
MUSIC DIRECTOR, TEACHER
b Dolton, Ill, June 23, 32. *Study:* With Herman Spier & Rossetter Cole; Univ Mich, with Ross Lee Finney; Cleveland Inst Music, with Marcel Dick; Union Theol Sem, New York, SMD. *Works:* Intelligent Man (suite); Let us all Work with Gladsome Voice (chorus with orch); Lutheran Chorale Mass (chorus with orch); To Him be Glory (chorus with orch); O Sing unto the Lord a New Song (chorus); Sing for Joy (chorus); Praise God with Hearts and Voices (orch). *Pos:* Church music dir, Cleveland, 54-61; music dir, Village Lutheran Church. *Teaching:* Pres, Concordia Col, Bronxville, NY, 61- *Mailing Add:* 6 Concordia Pl Bronxville NY 10708

SCHULTZ, RUSS ALLAN
ADMINISTRATOR, TROMBONE
b Newark, NJ, Sept 15, 47. *Study:* Eastman Sch Music, with Emory Remington, BMus, 69; Memphis State Univ, MMus, 71; NTex State Univ, with Leon Brown, DMA, 78. *Pos:* Bass trombonist, Memphis Symph Orch, Tenn, 69- *Teaching:* Prof instrm music, Shelby State Community Col, 74-76, head music dept, 77- *Awards:* Selected for inclusion in first world symph orch, Fedn People to People, UN, 71. *Mem:* Tenn Asn Music Exec Col & Univ (pres, 81-83); Nat Asn Jazz Educr (pres Tenn unit, 76-78); Am Asn Univ Prof (treas local chap, 74-75); Memphis Fedn Musicians (mem bd dir, 79-). *Interests:* Performance practice and literature of the Serpent. *Mailing Add:* 5128 Fairbrook Ave Memphis TN 38118

SCHULTZE, ANDREW W
BASS-BARITONE
b Brooklyn, NY. *Study:* With Heinz Rehfuss. *Roles:* Silvano in Un Ballo in maschera, NJ State Opera, 82. *Pos:* Mem, Int Opera Studio, Zurich, Switz, formerly; opera & conct performer, US & Europe. *Awards:* William Matheus Sullivan Found Grant; Second Prize, D'Angelo Young Artists Compt, 78 & Wash Int Compt for Voice, 80. *Mailing Add:* c/o Eric Semon Assoc Inc 111 W 57th St New York NY 10019

SCHUMACHER, THOMAS
PIANO, EDUCATOR
b Butte, Mont, Dec 8, 37. *Study:* Manhattan Sch Music, BMus, 58; Juilliard Sch Music, artist dipl, 60, MS, 62. *Pos:* Soloist, maj orchs incl New York Phil, Toronto Symph, Warsaw Phil & Tokyo Phil; recitalist throughout US, Can, Europe & Japan. *Teaching:* Prof piano, Univ Md, College Park, currently. *Awards:* Prize, Int Busoni Compt, 62; Prize, Jugg Compt, 63. *Mailing Add:* 7308 Hopkins Ave College Park MD 20740

SCHUMAN, DANIEL ZETKIN
EDUCATOR, VIOLIN
b Hartford, Conn, Mar 29, 26. *Study:* Dartmouth Col, studied violin with Nathan Gottschalk, AB, 48; Peabody Consv Music, studied violin with Oscar Shumsky, 49; Univ Tulsa, studied violin with Frances Jones, BME, 53, MM, 55; Teachers Col, Columbia Univ, MA, 62, EdD, 64. *Pos:* Asst concertmaster, Tulsa Phil, 53-55; concertmaster, Plainfield Symph, 67-81; violist, NJ State Opera Orch, 70-; violinist, Amacorda String Quartet, 79- *Teaching:* Instr strings, Northwestern Col La, 55-56; instr music educ, Teachers Col, Columbia Univ, 59-60; assoc prof, Rutgers Univ, 60- *Mem:* Am String Teachers Asn; Music Educr Nat Conf; Am Fedn Musicians. *Mailing Add:* 248 Wakefield Dr Metuchen NJ 08840

SCHUMAN, PATRICIA
MEZZO-SOPRANO
b Los Angeles, Calif. *Study:* Univ Calif, Santa Cruz, BA(music), 74. *Roles:* Carmen in Carmen, Merola Opera, 79; Composer in Ariadne auf Naxos, Ky Opera Co, 79; Dorabella in Cosi fan tutte, Syracuse Opera Theater, 81; Cherubino in Le Nozze di Figaro, Wolf Trap Opera Co, 81; Angelina in La Cenerentola, Wash Opera Co, 82; Rosina in Il Barbiere di Siviglia, Chautauqua Opera Co, 82; Charlotte in Werther, Lake George Opera Co, 83. *Pos:* Artist in res, Affil Artists, 82- *Awards:* Il Cenacolo Award, San Francisco Opera Auditions, 79; Nat Opera Inst Sullivan Grant, 81. *Mem:* Am Guild Musical Artists. *Mailing Add:* c/o Columbia Artists Mgt Inc 165 W 57th St New York NY 10019

SCHUMAN, WILLIAM
COMPOSER, ADMINISTRATOR
b New York, NY, Aug 4, 10. *Study:* Columbia Univ, BS, 35, MA, 37; Hon deg from 23 US cols & univ. *Works:* Twenty-nine orchestral works, seven works for solo instrm with orch, five works for chorus with orch, four choral works with piano accmp, 12 unaccmp choral works, one opera, five works for ballet, music for films, ten works for conct band, six chamber works, four solo works for piano & trumpet & five songs. *Rec Perf:* Numerous recordings for RCA, Am Rec Soc, Desto, Metropolitan Museum Art, Cornell Univ, Everest, Decca, Vanguard, Columbia, Comp Rec Concordia, Mercury, Louisville, London, Turnabout, Vox, Odyssey & Deutsche Grammophon. *Pos:* Dir publ, G Schirmer Inc, 44-45, spec publ consult, 45-52; pres, Juilliard Sch Music, 45-62, emer, 62-; pres, Lincoln Ctr Perf Arts, 62-69, emer, 69-; consult, BMI, Columbia Broadcasting System, Indust Develop Corp PR, Norlin Corp, Rockefeller Found, Videorecord Corp Am & others, 69- *Teaching:* Mem fac, Sarah Lawrence Col, 35-45. *Awards:* Handel Medallion, New York City, 67; Findley Award, City Univ New York, 71; Edward MacDowell Medal, 71. *Bibliog:* Harriet Gay (auth), Juilliard String Quartet, Vantage, 74; Howard Shanet (auth), Philharmonic: A History of New York's Orchestra, Doubleday, 75; Gardner Read (auth), Style & Orchestration, Schirmer Bks, 79; and others. *Publ:* Auth, Introd to Composers in American, Da Capo, 77; The Esthetic Imperative, In: Economic Pressures and the Future of the Arts, Free Press, Macmillan, 79; Semper Fields, In: Perspectives on John Philip Sousa, Libr Cong, 81; and many others. *Mailing Add:* 888 Park Ave New York NY 10021

SCHUSTER, EARL VINCENT
OBOE, EDUCATOR
b Belleville, Ill, June 16, 18. *Study:* Eastman Sch Music, BM, 40; Columbia Univ, MA, 46. *Works:* Concert D-minor (oboe; Vivaldi), Concert B-flat (oboe; Handel); Concert F-minor (oboe; Telemann), Arnold Bax Quintet & Oboe (McBride), Classic Ed; Octet (Beethoven) & Serenade (Dyarack), Columbia. *Pos:* First oboe, US Marine Band, Washington, DC, 40-45, Indianapolis Symph, 45-50, Radio City Music Hall, 50-56 & San Diego Symph, 60-70; asst first oboe, Chicago Symph, 56-60. *Teaching:* Master instr music, San Diego Unified Sch, 60-80; vis prof oboe & chamber music, La State Univ, Baton Rouge, 80-81 & Okla Univ, Norman, 82- *Mem:* Col Music Soc. *Mailing Add:* 8543 Sugarman Dr La Jolla CA 92037

SCHUSTER, SAVELY
EDUCATOR, CELLO
Study: Odessa State Consv, Odessa, USSR, artist's dipl; studied cello with David Mezhvinsky, Anatole Weiner & Svyatoslav Knushevitsky. *Pos:* Prin cello, Odessa Chamber Orch, formerly & Soviet Emigre Orch, NY, currently; mem, Odessa Phil Piano Trio, formerly & St Louis Symph Orch, currently; soloist, Kiev Orch, formerly; prin cello & soloist, Odessa Phil Symph Orch, formerly, Richmond Symph & Sinfonia, formerly & Eastern Summer Music

Fest Orch, formerly. *Teaching:* Mem fac cello & chamber music, St Louis Consv Music, currently; teacher cello & string quartet, Odessa State Consv, currently. *Mailing Add:* St Louis Consv Music 560 Trinity Ave St Louis MO 63130

SCHUSTER-CRAIG, JOHN WILLIAM
CRITIC, LECTURER
b St Louis, Mo, Jan 13, 49. *Study:* Univ Louisville, BM, 71; Univ NC, MA, 76. *Pos:* Critic, Louisville Times, 76- *Teaching:* Lectr music theory, Univ Louisville, 75- & Bellarmine Col, 77- *Mem:* Am Musicol Soc. *Interests:* Sixteenth century motet; music since 1950. *Mailing Add:* 2220 Walterdale Terr Louisville KY 40205

SCHUTZA, GARY ALAN, JR
TRUMPET
b Irving, Tex, Nov 2, 57. *Study:* Southern Methodist Univ, 77; Curtis Inst Music, dipl, 80. *Pos:* Prin trumpet, Omaha Symph, Nebr, 80-81; asst prin trumpet, Kansas City Phil, 81-82; prin trumpet, Kansas City Symph, 82- *Mailing Add:* 7501 Cody #3 Shawnee KS 66214

SCHWADRON, ABRAHAM ABE
EDUCATOR, CLARINET
b Brooklyn, NY, Dec 25, 25. *Study:* Rhode Island Col, EdB(music educ), 53; Univ Conn, MA(music), 57; Boston Univ, MusAd, 62. *Works:* Thirty-nine transcriptions, arr & comp, 66-77; Chad Gadya (One Kid), Folkways Rec, 82. *Teaching:* Fac mem, Pub Sch, New London & Waterford, Conn, 53-59, RI Col, 59-68, Univ Hawaii, Honolulu, 68-69; prof music Univ Calif, Los Angeles, 69-, chmn dept, currently. *Awards:* Res grants, Univ Calif, Los Angeles, 75, 82 & 83. *Mem:* Music Educr Nat Conf; Soc Ethnomusicol; Am Soc Aesthetics; Col Music Soc; Coun Res Music Educ. *Interests:* Aesthetics of music; philosophy in music education; Jewish music. *Publ:* Auth, Aesthetics: Dimensions in Music Education, Music Educ Nat Conf, 67; On Words & Music, J Aesthetic Educ, 71; Comparative Music Aesthetics, Music & Man, 73; On Jewish Music (Music in Many Cultures), Univ Calif Press, 80; CHAD Gadya, Selected Reports in Ethnomusicol, Univ Calif, Los Angeles, 83. *Mailing Add:* Dept Music Univ Calif Los Angeles CA 90024

SCHWAGER, MYRON AUGUST
EDUCATOR, WRITER
b Pittsfield, Mass, Mar 16, 37. *Study:* Boston Univ, BM, 58; New England Consv Music, MM, 61; Harvard Univ, MA, 65, PhD, 71; studied musicology with Karl Geiringer, Nino Pirrotta, John Ward & Eliot Forbes; studied violoncello with Jacobus Langendoen, Luigi Silva & Bernhard Greenhouse. *Teaching:* Asst prof, Holy Cross Col, Mass, 70-74; instr & perf, Jesuit Inst Arts, Rome, Italy, 72; asst prof music hist, Hartt Sch Music, Univ Hartford, 74-77, assoc prof, 78-, acting chair dept music hist, theory & comp, 82- *Mem:* Am Musicol Soc; Am Fedn Musicians. *Interests:* Music of Beethoven; Baroque opera; American music. *Publ:* Contribr, The Creative World of Beethoven, W W Norton & Co Inc, 71; auth, A Fresh Look at Beethoven's Arrangements, Music & Lett, 4/73; Some Observations on Beethoven as an Arranger, Musical Quart, 1/74; A Contribution to the Biography of Ernest Bloch, Current Musicol, fall 79; Beethoven and the First Layer of Manuscript Grasnick 11, Studi Musicali, 81. *Mailing Add:* Dept Music Hist Theory Comp Univ Hartford West Hartford CT 06117

SCHWANN, WILLIAM JOSEPH
PUBLISHER, ORGAN
b Salem, Ill, May 13, 13. *Study:* Sch Music, Univ Louisville, BA, 35; Sch Music, Boston Univ; Harvard Univ, with E Power Biggs; Univ Louisville, Hon MusD, 69; New England Consv Music, Hon MusD, 82. *Pos:* Organist & choirmaster, Louisville, Ky & greater Boston churches, 35-60; publ auth & ed, Schwann Rec & Tape Guides, 49- *Awards:* Citation Award, Music Libr Asn, 83. *Bibliog:* Jay E Daily (auth), Cataloging Phonorecordings, Marcel Dekker Inc, 75; Richard S Halsey (auth), Classical Music Recordings, Am Libr Asn, 76. *Mem:* Harvard Musical Asn. *Publ:* Auth & ed, Schwann Record & Tape Guides, monthly, 49-, Schwann Artist Issue, 53-, Schwann 2 Record & Tape Guide, semi annual, 64- & Schwann Children's Record & Tape Guide, annual, 65, W Schwann; White House Record Library Catalogs, Rec Indust Asn Am, 73 & 80. *Mailing Add:* 535 Boylston St Boston MA 02116

SCHWANTNER, JOSEPH C
COMPOSER, EDUCATOR
b Chicago, Ill, Mar 22, 43. *Study:* Chicago Consv, BM, 64; Northwestern Univ, MM, 66, DM, 68. *Works:* And the Mountains Rising Nowhere, European-Am Music Corp, 77; Wild Angels of the Open Hills, C F Peters, 77; Sparrows, European-Am Music Corp, 79; Aftertones of Infinity, C F Peters, 79; Music of Amber, 81 & Magabunda (Witchnomad), 83, European-Am Music Corp; Distant Runes and Incantations, comn & perf by Los Angeles Chamber Orch (in prep). *Pos:* Comp in res, St Louis Symph Orch, 82-84. *Teaching:* Prof comp, Eastman Sch Music, 70- *Awards:* Guggenheim Fel, 78; Pulitzer Prize, Columbia Univ, 79; Friedheim Award, Kennedy Ctr, 81. *Mem:* BMI; Am Comp Alliance. *Mailing Add:* Eastman Sch Music 26 Gibbs St Rochester NY 14604

SCHWARTZ, CHARLES MORRIS
COMPOSER, MUSIC DIRECTOR
b New York, NY. *Study:* Grad Sch Arts & Sci, NY Univ, PhD, 69; studied comp with Aaron Copland, Darius Milhaud & Roger Sessions. *Works:* Professor Jive (jazz symph), 76, Mother------!, Mother------!! (jazz symph), 80 & Solo Brothers (jazz symph), 83, Comp Showcase. *Pos:* Music dir & founder, Comp Showcase, New York, 57- *Awards:* MacDowell Colony Fel, 68;

ASCAP Award, 81. *Mem:* Am Music Ctr; Am Musicol Soc; ASCAP. *Publ:* Auth, Gershwin: His Life and Music, Bobbs-Merrill, 73 & Da Capo Press, 79; George Gershwin: A Selective Bibliography and Discography, Info Coördr, 74; Cole Porter: A Biography, Dial Press, 77 & Da Capo Press, 79. *Mailing Add:* 463 West St G-219 New York NY 10014

SCHWARTZ, ELLIOTT SHELLING
COMPOSER, WRITER
b Brooklyn, NY, Jan 19, 36. *Study:* Columbia Col, studied comp with Jack Beeson & Otto Luening, AB, 57; Teachers Col, Columbia Univ, studied piano with Thomas Richner & theory with Howard Murphy, MA, 58, EdD, 62. *Works:* Magic Music, 67, Island (orch), 70 & The Harmony of Maine (synthesizer & orch), 75, Carl Fischer; Eclipse III (chamber orch), Alexander Broude, 75; Chamber Concerto II, Margun, 77; Chamber Concerto I, 77 & Chamber Concerto IV, 80, Am Comp Alliance. *Teaching:* Instr music, Univ Mass, Amherst, 60-64; from asst prof to prof & chmn, Bowdoin Col, 64-; vis comp, Trinity Col Music, London, England, 67; vis prof, Col Creative Studies, Univ Calif, Santa Barbara, 70, 73 & 74; vis res musician, Ctr Music Experiment, Univ Calif, San Diego, 78-79. *Awards:* Int Music Week Prize, Gaudeamus Found, 70; comp grant, Nat Endowment Arts, 74, 76, 80 & 82; Bellagio Res Fel, Rockefeller Found, 80. *Bibliog:* Meirion Bowen (auth), Elliott Schwartz, Music & Musicians, England, 68; Ev Grimes (producer), Elliott Schwartz, Nat Pub Radio, Options ser, 80. *Mem:* Am Soc Univ Comp (chmn nat coun, 83-); Am Music Ctr (vpres nat bd, 81-); Col Music Soc (mem nat coun, 82-); Am Comp Alliance; BMI. *Interests:* Esthetics of 20th century music; approaches to perceptive listening for laymen. *Publ:* Auth, The Symphonies of Ralph Vaughan Williams, Univ Mass Press, 64; co-ed, Contemporary Composers on Contemporary Music, Holt, Rinehart & Winston, 67; auth, Electronic Music: A Listener's Guide, Praeger, 73; Music: Ways of Listening, Holt, Rinehart & Winston, 82; contribr, Performance in the Midst of Pluralism, In: Relativism in the Arts, Univ Ga Press, 83. *Mailing Add:* 5 Atwood Lane Brunswick ME 04011

SCHWARTZ, FRANCIS
COMPOSER, EDUCATOR
b Altoona, Pa, Mar 10, 40. *Study:* Juilliard Sch Music, study piano with Lonny Epstein, BS, 61, study comp with Vitorio Giannini, MS, 62; Univ de Paris, PhD, 81. *Works:* Peace on Earth, 72 & Cannibal-Caliban, 75, Peer-Southern Int; Amistad One and Two, 80 & Ergo Sum, 80, Ed Transatlantiques, Paris; Fronteras, Peer-Southern Int, 83; Hommage A K ..., 83 & Amistad III, 83, Ed Salabert. *Rec Perf:* Musique Climatique, Univ de Paris, 79; Baudelaire's Uncle, 83 & Paz en la Tierra, 83, Inst PR Cult; Snow White, Inst Phonology, Caracas, Venezuela, 83. *Teaching:* Prof new music, Univ PR, 66-, prof comp & piano, 71-, chmn, Dept Music, 71-80 & dir, Dept Cult Affairs, 81-; vis prof, Univ de Paris, 77-78. *Awards:* ASCAP Standard Award, 76-83. *Bibliog:* Alain Gerber (auth), L'Euphore dans sa Coque, Son-Hi Fi Mag, 4/79; Daniel Charles (auth), Le Macroeuf, Revue D'Esthetique, Paris, 82. *Mem:* ASCAP; European Acad Sci, Arts & Lett. *Publ:* Auth, Commentaires sporadiques, Revue D'Esthetique, Paris, 79; The Bureaucracy of Music, Caribbean Rev, 80; Arts, Politics and Society, San Juan Star, 81; coauth, El Mundo de la Musica, Dept Educ, PR, 82. *Mailing Add:* Box AL Dept Music Univ PR Rio Piedras PR 00931

SCHWARTZ, JOSEPH ERVIN
EDUCATOR, PIANO
b New York, NY, Apr 18, 32. *Study:* Juilliard Sch Music, BS, 54, MS, 57. *Teaching:* Instr, Juilliard Prep Div, 59-60; prof pianoforte, Consv Music, Oberlin Col, 60- *Awards:* First Prize, Naumburg Found Compt, 58; Grant, Rockefeller Fund for Music, 60. *Rep:* Anne Pearson 91 King St Oberlin Ohio 44074. *Mailing Add:* 33 Robin Park Oberlin OH 44074

SCHWARTZ, JUDITH LEAH
EDUCATOR, WRITER
b Jamaica, NY, Apr 27, 43. *Study:* Vassar Col, AB(theory & harpsichord), 64; studied harpsichord with Robert Veyron-Lacroix, 65; Univ Vienna, 67; Univ Salzburg, 68; Vienna Acad Perf Arts, 68; Grad Sch Arts & Sci, NY Univ, MA(music), 68, PhD, 73. *Teaching:* Asst prof music hist, Vassar Col, 69-70 & Univ Calif, Riverside, 71-73; asst prof music hist & lit, Sch Music, Northwestern Univ, 74-82, assoc prof, 82- *Awards:* Fulbright Award, 67-68; grant, Univ Calif, Riverside, 72-73, Am Philosophical Soc, 73-74 & Northwestern Univ, 76-77 & 82. *Mem:* Am Musicol Soc (coun mem, 78-81); Am Soc 18th Century Studies; Music Libr Asn; Col Music Soc. *Interests:* Eighteenth century symphony and concerto; French Baroque court dance and dance music; music of Haydn. *Publ:* Auth, Cultural Stereotypes and Music in the 18th Century, In: Studies on Voltaire & the 18th Century, Voltaire Found, 76; Opening Themes in Opera Overtures of Hasse, In: A Musical Offering, Pendragon, 77; Mozart as Masonic Musician & Haydn and the Concerto, Chicago Symph Orch Prog Guide, 2-3/80; J C Monn & M G Monn, In: New Grove Dict of Music & Musicians, Macmillan, 80; Thematic Asymmetry, In: Haydn Studies, Norton, 81. *Mailing Add:* 806 Chilton Lane Wilmette IL 60091

SCHWARTZ, MARVIN ROBERT
COMPOSER, EDUCATOR
b Bronx, NY, Feb 4, 37. *Study:* Queens Col, City Univ New York, studied comp with Luigi Dallapiccola & Leo Kraft, BA, 57; Brandeis Univ, studied comp with Irving Fine & Harold Shapiro, MFA, 59; Jewish Theol Sem, NY, with Hugo Weisgall, SMD, 64; studied comput music with Charles Dodge & Dary John Mizelle, 79. *Works:* Ruth, A Biblical Narrative, perf by Kol Yisrael, 67; Look and Long (opera), perf by After Dinner Opera Co, 71; Threes and Twos for Three, perf by Dorian Wind Quintet, 71; Lament for Six

Million, 73 & Spaces, 74, perf by Queensborough Orch; Letter to David Randolph (male chorus), perf by Montclair State Col Choir, 76; Tal (baritone & organ), Fiesta. *Teaching:* Prof music, Queensborough Community Col, 67-, chmn dept, 69-83, dir electronic music lab, 73-; adj prof, Queens Col, City Univ New York, 70-75. *Awards:* MacDowell Colony Fel, 62. *Bibliog:* Allen Hughes (auth), The Opera: Reminiscences of Gertrude Stein, New York Times, 10/6/72; John McCaffrey (auth), Any of Mine Without Music to Help Them, Yale Theatre, summer 73. *Mailing Add:* 166-10 75th Ave Flushing NY 11366

SCHWARTZ, WILFRED (WILL)
CONDUCTOR, VIOLIN
b New York, NY, Sept 23, 23. *Study:* Juilliard Sch Music, BS(violin & cond), 47, MS(violin & cond), 48; Columbia Univ, 48-49; studied cond with Pierre Monteux, 56. *Rec Perf:* Rare Music for Trio, Musart Trio, 65. *Pos:* Freelance musician, New York City & ECoast tours, 46-49; guest cond & violin soloist, Denver Symph, Mexico City Phil, Belgian Radio Orch, Brussels, Seville, Spain, violin recital tours, 49-; music dir & cond, Ft Collins Symph Orch, 49- & Cheyenne Symph & Chorus, 55-59. *Teaching:* Private violin, New York, 46-49; prof violin, orch & cond, Colo State Univ, currently. *Mem:* Am Symph Orch League; Am Fedn Musicians; Am String Teachers; Music Teachers Nat Asn; Music Educr Nat Conf. *Mailing Add:* 1117 Robertson Ft Collins CO 80524

SCHWARZ, BORIS
WRITER, LECTURER
b St Petersburg, Russia, Mar 26, 06; US citizen. *Study:* Sorbonne, Paris, 25-26; Univ Berlin, 36; Columbia Univ, PhD(musicol), 50. *Pos:* Concertmaster, Indianapolis Symph Orch, 37-38; first violinist, NBC Toscanini Symph, 38-39. *Teaching:* Prof music, Queens Col, City Univ New York, 41-76, chmn music dept, 49-56. *Awards:* Ford Found Fel, 52-53; John Guggenheim Found Fel, 59-60; Deems Taylor Award, ASCAP, 73. *Mem:* Am Musicol Soc; Int Musicol Soc; Gesellschaft Musikforschung; Am Fedn Musicians. *Interests:* Russian and Soviet music; history of chamber music and violin. *Publ:* Auth, Music & Musical Life in Soviet Russia, 1917-1970, W W Norton, 72, Ind Univ Press, 83 & German transl, Heinrichshofen, 83; French Instrumental Music Between the Revolutions, Da Capo, 83; Great Masters of the Violin, Simon & Schuster, 83. *Mailing Add:* 100 W 57th St 4-N New York NY 10019

SCHWARZ, GERARD
MUSIC DIRECTOR & CONDUCTOR, TRUMPET
b NJ, Aug 19, 47. *Study:* Sch Perf Arts, New York; Nat Music Camp, Interlochen; Juilliard Sch, studied trumpet with William Vacchiano, BS, 72; studied comp with Paul Creston. *Works:* Greenhouse Dance Company, Lilo Way. *Rec Perf:* Carmen Ballet (Bizet & Shchedrin); Idyll for String Orchestra (Janacek) & Mladi (Youth); Symphonies No 40 & 41 (Mozart); Cornet Favorites; rec on Columbia, Nonesuch, Vox, MMO, Desto, Angel & Delos Rec. *Pos:* Trumpet, Am Symph Orch, 65-72 & Am Brass Quintet, 65-73; cond, Erick Hawkins Dance Co, 66-70 & Eliot Field Ballet, 76-80; co-prin trumpet, New York Phil, 72-76, soloist, formerly; mem bd dir, Naumburg Found, 75-; music dir & cond, Waterloo Village Fest, NJ, 76-; Los Angeles Chamber Orch, 78- & White Mountains Music Fest, NH, 78-80; music dir & creator, Y Chamber Symph, New York, 77-; music adv, Mostly Mozart Fest, Lincoln Ctr, 82-; recital & conct performances throughout US, Europe & Far East. *Teaching:* Mem fac, Mannes Col Music, 73-79 & Montclair State Col, 75-80; mem fac chamber music & trumpet, Juilliard Sch, 75- *Awards:* Awards, Nat Fedn Music Clubs; Record of Yr for Cornet Favorites, Stereo Rev, 75; Ford Found Award for Conct Artists, 71-73. *Mem:* Am Musicol Soc. *Rep:* ICM Artists 40 W 57th St New York NY 10019. *Mailing Add:* 167 Upper Mountain Ave Montclair NJ 07042

SCHWARZ, IRA PAUL
COMPOSER, EDUCATOR
b Sheldon, Iowa, Feb 24, 21. *Study:* Studied comp with Nadia Boulanger, 40, Thadeus Jones, 41 & 42; Naval Sch Music, 42; Morningside Col, AB, 52; Univ SDak, MA, 54; studied with Phillip Bezanson, 58-60, Richard Herwig, 60 & 61; Univ Iowa, PhD, 61. *Works:* Boutage (sax quartet), 59, Capricio (clarinet quintet), 59, Six Trios (woodwind), 60 & Ten Duets (clarinet), 60, Rubank, Inc; Divertimento for Strings, Classical Etude (woodwind), Belwin Mills, 68; Seven duos (clarinet & flute) & Six trios (clarinet), SHAL-u-mo, 80-83. *Teaching:* Prof music & dir symph, Minot State Col, 61-65; prof music & aesthet, Northeast Mo State Univ, 66-68; coordr allied arts, Univ Southern Miss, 68-70; prof & chmn dept music, State Univ NY, Col Brockport, 70- *Awards:* Soc Europ Stage Auth & Comp Award, 78-80. *Bibliog:* Paul Drushler (auth), Musical Interpretation, Clarinetist, 81; Walter Bowman (auth), Comic Opera has Ghostly Plot, Pan Pipes, spring 83; music reviews in Intrumentalist & Nat Asn Col Wind & Perc Instr J. *Mem:* Music Educr Nat Conf; Nat Band Asn; Nat Asn Humanities Educ; ASCAP; Am Music Asn. *Publ:* Auth, 18th Century Ornamentation, Instrumentalist, 70; coauth, Teaching the Related Arts, Greene-Simson, 71; auth, Handbook for Arts and Humanities, Kendall/Hunt, 72; ed, Arts and Humanities: Perspectives, State Univ NY, Brockport, 79. *Mailing Add:* PO Box 115 Brockport NY 14420

SCHWARZ, JOHN IRVIN, JR
EDUCATOR
b Easton, Pa, Apr 4, 31. *Study:* West Chester State Col, BS, 52; Duquesne Univ, MS, 57; Univ Md, PhD, 70. *Teaching:* Prof music hist, Lock Haven State Col, 61- *Mem:* Am Musicol Soc; Royal Musical Asn; Sonneck Soc. *Interests:* Eighteenth and 19th century English music; German music in Pennsylvania. *Publ:* Auth, Samuel and Samuel Sebastian Wesley, the English Doppelmeister, Musical Quart, 73. *Mailing Add:* 699 James St Flemington PA 17745

SCHWARZ, KAROL ROBERT
WRITER, MUSIC HISTORIAN
b New York, NY, Dec 17, 56. *Study:* Queens Col, City Univ New York, BA, 79; Ind Univ, MM, 82. *Pos:* Mem staff promotion dept, Boosey & Hawkes Music Publ, 82- *Teaching:* Assoc instr musicol, Ind Univ, Bloomington, 80-81. *Mem:* Am Musicol Soc. *Interests:* Twentieth century music; late 18th century music. *Publ:* Auth, Steve Reich: Music as a Gradual Process, Perspectives New Music, 80-81 & 81-82. *Mailing Add:* 228 W 10 St New York NY 10014

SCHWARZ, PATRICIA A
ARTIST MANAGER, WRITER
b Mich, Apr 6, 21. *Study:* Juilliard Sch, BS, 45; voice studies with Belle Soudant. *Pos:* Chairwoman scholar prog, Am Israel Cult Found, New York, 69-, exec comt, 83- *Mem:* Am Musicol Soc; Music Critics Asn. *Publ:* Auth, Israel Festival (Programs and Personalities), 76, Israel, Participation in International Musicological Congress, 77, Career Highlights, 78, New Star of the Violin (Shlomo Mintz), 2/80 & Israeli Performers Enhance New York's Cultural Scene, 8/82, Tarbut. *Rep:* Am Israel Cult Found 485 Madison Ave New York NY 10022. *Mailing Add:* 100 W 57th St New York NY 10019

SCHWEGEL, RICHARD C
LIBRARIAN
b Lewiston, Idaho, Sept, 16, 53. *Study:* DePaul Univ, Chicago, BA, 75; Grad Sch Libr Sci, Rosary Col, MLS, 76; Grad Sch Music, Northwestern Univ, MM, 81. *Pos:* Head music sect, Chicago Pub Libr, 83. *Mem:* Music Libr Asn. *Mailing Add:* 1932 W Pratt Chicago IL 60626

SCHWEIKERT, NORMAN CARL
FRENCH HORN, HISTORIAN
b Los Angeles, Calif, Oct 8, 37. *Study:* Private horn study with Odolindo Perissi & Sinclair Lott in Los Angeles, 50-55; Aspen Inst, with Joseph Eger, 54; Eastman Sch Music, Univ Rochester, study horn with Morris Secon & Verne Reynolds, BM & perf cert, 61. *Rec Perf:* Music by Reicha, Fine, Hartley, Barthe, Stravinsky & Grainger, Interlochen Arts Quintet, Mark Educ Rec, 67; Konzertstück for Four Horns and Orchestra in F Major (Robert Schumann), DGG, 77. *Pos:* Fourth, second & third horn, Rochester Phil Orch, 55-62 & 64-66; second horn, US Mil Acad Band, West Point, NY, 62-64; asst first horn, Chicago Symph Orch, 71-75 & second horn, 75- *Teaching:* Instr horn, Interlochen Arts Acad, Mich, 66-71; assoc prof, Northwestern Univ, Evanston, Ill, 73- *Bibliog:* Tom Cowan (auth), Profile Interview with Norman Schweikert, The Horn Call, Int Horn Soc, 5/76. *Mem:* Galpin Soc; Am Musical Instrm Soc; Int Horn Soc (secy-treas, 70-72, mem adv coun, 72-76). *Interests:* History of the professional horn player in the United States from colonial times to the present; symphony and opera orchestra musicians in the major United States organizations 1842-1992. *Publ:* Auth, Gumpert, Not Gumbert, 5/71, Horns Across the Sea, 5/72 & Playing Assistant First Horn, autumn 74, Horn Call, Int Horn Soc ; Victor Pelissier, America's First Important Professional Hornist, NY Brass Conf for Scholar J, 1/78; Wendell Hoss, Horn Call, Int Horn Soc, 10/80. *Mailing Add:* 1340 Golf Ave Highland Park IL 60035

SCHWEINFURTH, CARL LINCOLN
ADMINISTRATOR
b Mt Vernon, Ill, Jan 24, 31. *Study:* Univ Ore, BS, 52; Univ Fla, MA, 57; Southern Ill Univ, Carbondale, PhD, 64. *Pos:* Mgr, Chamber Music Soc Cedarhurst, Mt Vernon, Ill, 79-; vpres, Rend Lake Civic Symph Soc, 82- *Mailing Add:* PO Box 907 Mt Vernon IL 62864

SCHWEITZER, MARSHA L
BASSOON, ADMINISTRATOR
b Canton, Ohio, Aug 26, 49. *Study:* Oberlin Col, BM, 71. *Rec Perf:* Spring Wind Quintet, Audissey, 83. *Pos:* Bassoon, Honolulu Symph, 71- & Spring Wind Quintet, 74-; bus mgr & treas, Chamber Music Hawaii, 80- *Mem:* Chamber Music Am. *Mailing Add:* 1040 Kinau 501 Honolulu HI 96814

SCIANNI, JOSEPH
COMPOSER, EDUCATOR
b Memphis, Tenn, Oct 6, 28. *Study:* Eastman Sch Music, with Howard Hanson, MM, 53, DMA, 59. *Works:* Court Square, Theodore Presser, 55; Horizon South, 62; Photographs (8 x 10), 78; City People, 80. *Teaching:* Prof music, Col Staten Island, City Univ New York, currently. *Awards:* Comp Award, Nat Endowment Arts, 71 & 72. *Mem:* ASCAP. *Mailing Add:* 400 Second Ave New York NY 10010

SCLATER, JAMES STANLEY
COMPOSER, TEACHER
b Mobile, Ala, Oct 24, 43. *Study:* Univ Southern Miss, with William Presser, BM, MM; Univ Tex, with Hunter Johnson, DMA(comp). *Works:* Four Songs on Texts of Emily Dickinson (voice); Songs of Time and Passing (voice); Concert Piece (brass quintet); Visions (band); Mobile Suite (band); Prelude and Variations on Gone Is my Mistris (band); Columbia Eagle March; and others. *Pos:* Music librn, Austin Pub Libr, 69-70; prin clarinetist, Jackson Symph, 71-78; music arr, Univ Southern Miss & Univ Tex Marching Bands. *Teaching:* Assoc prof music & coordr music theory, Miss Col, 70- *Awards:* Ostwald Prize New Band Music, 74. *Mailing Add:* 709 Leake St Clinton MS 39056

SCOTT, BEVERLY C
VIOLA, PIANO
b Greensboro, NC, Dec 22, 52. *Study:* Ind Univ, with Jorge Bolet, Hans Graf & George Janzer, BM(piano), 75, MM(piano), 76, MM(viola), 82. *Pos:* Asst prin viola, Indianapolis Symph Orch, 81- *Mem:* Int Viola Soc. *Mailing Add:* 3901 N Pennsylvania Indianapolis IN 46205

SCOTT, CLEVE L
EDUCATOR, COMPOSER
b Oxnard, Calif, June 2, 33. *Study:* Calif State Univ, Long Beach, BSc, 59; Univ Iowa, MM, 69, PhD, 71. *Works:* Residue II Fragments of the Moon (mixed ens, sop & electronic), 72, Panth is II (tape), 72, Calls: For A Time In Summer (horn & tape), 74, The Most Elusive is Both Charmed & Strange (tape), 81 & Residue IV (flute, alto flute, bass clarinet & electronic), 81, perf by comp; Anacrusis, Lingua Press, 81; Haiku (tape), perf by comp, 82. *Teaching:* Asst prof music, Upper Iowa Univ, 61-67; prof music, Ball State Univ, 70- *Awards:* Creative Arts Grant, Ball State Univ, 71; New Music Comn, Ind Arts Comn. *Mem:* Am Soc Univ Comp; Ind Arts Comn (chmn adv panel, 81-82); Col Music Soc. *Mailing Add:* Dept Music Ball State Univ Muncie IN 47306

SCOTT, FRANK EDWARD
EDUCATOR, PIANO
b Detroit, Mich, Nov 24, 39. *Study:* Cleveland Inst Music, studied piano with Elizabeth Pastor, BM, 68; Mich State Univ, with Ralph Votapek & Joseph Evans, MM, 72; Univ Iowa, with John Simms, DMA, 78. *Pos:* Pianist, Coconino Chamber Ens, 80- *Teaching:* Instr piano, Univ Minn, 72-73, St Louis Univ, 73-74 & Memphis State Univ, 74-75; performer-teacher, Delta Music Fest, Mich, summers 73 & 74; assoc prof piano & dir piano prog, Northern Ariz Univ, 76- *Mem:* Ariz State Music Teachers Asn (pres northern dist, 72 & 76-78); Pi Kappa Lambda. *Mailing Add:* Music Dept Box 6040 Northern Ariz Univ Flagstaff AZ 86011

SCOTT, HENRY G
CONDUCTOR, DOUBLE BASS
b Dorothy, NJ, July 5, 44. *Study:* Eastman Sch Music, BM, 66; Bryn Mawr Consv Music, with Dr Joseph Barone, 75- *Pos:* Double bassist, Philadelphia Orch, 74-; cond, Little Symph, 78- & Main Line Symph Orch, 81- *Teaching:* Prof double bass, Philadelphia Col of Performing Arts, 72-, New Sch Music, 75- & Temple Univ, 80- *Awards:* C Hartman Kuhn Award, Philadelphia Orch, 82. *Mailing Add:* c/o Philadelphia Orch Broad & Locust St Philadelphia PA 19102

SCOTT, MOLLY
COMPOSER, SOPRANO
b Wellsville, NY, Jan 11, 38. *Study:* Smith Col, studied voice with Dorothy Stahl, Gretchen d'Armond, Rodney Geisick & Marlene Montgomery, BA, 59. *Works:* Honor the Earth, 80 & Poisin Treasure, 80, Sumitra Music; The Names & the Tree, 80; Jesus of the Colors, 80; The Dragon, perf by Present Stage Co, Northampton, Mass, 81; This is Our Home, Sumitra Music, 82. *Rec Perf:* Waitin' on You, Prestige Int, 62; The Fox, Western Woods; Honor the Earth, Philo/Fretless, 80. *Pos:* Guest artist, Springfield Symph, 75-76, Morning Pro Musica, Pub Radio Coop, 76-82 & Studs Terkel Almanac, Radio Chicago, 83; founder, Sumitra Perf Ens, 79-83; artist, Mass Touring Co, Amherst, 81-; co-founder, Heartsound Ctr Music & Health, 82-; solo perf in concert halls, cols & univ around the US. *Teaching:* Fac mem music & healing, Omega Inst, Lebanon Springs, NY, summers 80-; fac mem therapeutic uses of sound & music, New England Inst Healing Arts & Sci, Amherst, Mass, 82- *Awards:* Grant, Meet the Comp, 80 & 81. *Bibliog:* Shelly Kellman (auth), Molly Scott: Spirit and Politics, New England Crossroads, Whole Life Times, 11-12/80; Paul Turnbun (dir), Honor the Earth (slide presentation), Hallmark Sch Photography, 82. *Mem:* Int League Women Comp; Am Women Comp; ASCAP. *Mailing Add:* Warner Hill Rd Charlemont MA 01339

SCOTT, ROBERT CHARLES
EDUCATOR, MUSIC DIRECTOR
b Wolf Lake, Ind, July 23, 35. *Study:* Knox Col, BME, 57; Tex A&I Univ, MM, 63; Univ Tex, Austin, DME, 73. *Pos:* Mem, St Louis Munic Opera Asn, 53. *Teaching:* Prof voice & dir opera wkshp, Tex A&I Univ, 63-, chmn, Music Dept, 79- *Mem:* Cent Opera Asn; Tex Asn Col Teachers; Tex Music Educr Asn; Tex Choral Dir Asn; Nat Asn Teachers Singing. *Mailing Add:* 500 College Pl Kingsville TX 78368

SCOTT, ROBERT M
MUSIC DIRECTOR, ADMINISTRATOR
b Pittsburg, Kans, Aug 21, 28. *Study:* Pittsburg State Univ, Kans, BME, 60, MS(music), 61. *Pos:* Music dir, Lamar High Sch, Mo, 61-64; band dir, Ruskin High Sch, Kansas City, Mo, 64-70 & Northeast Mo State Univ, 70-72; dir bands, Southwest Mo State Univ, 72-, actg head, Dept Music, 82- *Awards:* Hall of Fame Award, Mo Bandmasters Asn, 76. *Mem:* Mo Music Educr Asn; Mo Bandmasters Asn (pres, 68-70); Nat Asn Jazz Educr (pres, 72); Nat Asn Sch Music. *Mailing Add:* Music Dept Southwest Mo State Univ Springfield MO 65804

SCOTT, ROGER
DOUBLE BASS, EDUCATOR
b NY. *Study:* Curtis Inst Music, with Anton Torello, dipl, 41. *Pos:* Mem, All-Am Youth Orch, formerly & Pittsburgh Symph Orch, formerly; bassist, Philadelphia Orch, 47-, co-prin bassist, 48-49, prin bassist, 49- *Teaching:* Mem fac double bass, Curtis Inst Music, 48- *Mailing Add:* Curtis Inst Music 1726 Locust St Philadelphia PA 19103

SCOTT, YUMI NINOMIYA
VIOLIN, EDUCATOR
b Tokyo, Japan, May 18, 43. *Study:* Toho Consv Music, Japan; Curtis Inst Music, dipl, 67. *Pos:* Second violin, Curtis String Quartet, 68-81; violinist, Concerto Soloists Philadelphia, Pa, 80-; concertmistress, Main Line Symph Orch, Philadelphia, Pa, 81- *Teaching:* Prof violin, New Sch Music, 68- & Curtis Inst Music, 70- *Mem:* Music Teachers Nat Asn. *Mailing Add:* 301 S 21st St Philadelphia PA 19103

SCOTTO, RENATA
SOPRANO
b Savona, Italy, Feb 24. *Study:* Accademia Musicale Savonese; Conservatorio Giuseppe Verdi, Milan; Mercedes Llopart, Milan; St John's Univ, Hon Dr, 83. *Rec Perf:* Norma, I Pagliacci, Verdi's Requiem, La Traviata, La Boheme, Tosca, Madama Butterfly & others rec on CBS Masterworks, RCA & Angel. *Roles:* Madame Butterfly in Madame Butterfly, Elizabeth in Don Carlo, Adriana Lecouvreur in Adriana Lecouvreur & Desdemona in Otello, Metropolitan Opera; La Gioconda, San Francisco Opera; Lady Macbeth in Macbeth, Covent Garden, Royal Opera; Norma in Norma, Vienna State Opera. *Mailing Add:* c/o Edgar Vincent Assoc 124 E 40th St Suite 304 New York NY 10016

SCRIBNER, NORMAN ORVILLE
CONDUCTOR, COMPOSER
b Washington, DC, Feb 25, 36. *Study:* Peabody Inst, BMus, 61. *Works:* Sextet for Winds & Piano, Univ Del Quintet, 75; The Nativity, 75 & The Tide Pool, 77, Baltimore Choral Arts Soc; Laudate Dominum, First United Methodist Church, Hyattsville, MD, 79; I Hear America Singing, Prince George's County Pub Sch Hon Chorus & Orch, 79 & Baltimore Symph Orch, 80; Nicholas, Musical Theatre, 80; Bicentennial Commission, Methodist Church in Am & Baltimore Symph, 83. *Rec Perf:* Mass (Leonard Bernstein), Columbia Rec, 71; Once—In Memoriam Martin Luther King Jr (Thomas Beveridge), Caedmon, 71; Mass in Time of War F J Haydn, Columbia Rec, 73. *Pos:* Dir music, St Alban's Parish, Washington, DC, 60-; staff keyboard artist, Nat Symph Orch, 65-; music dir, Choral Arts Soc Washington DC, 65-; cond, Norman Scribner Choir, 71- *Teaching:* Cond & instr chorale & theory, Am Univ, 60-63; instr organ, piano & music theory, George Washington Univ, 63-69; instr organ, serv music, Col Church Musicians, 64-65. *Bibliog:* John Vinton (auth), Young Man with a Chorus, Washington Star, 3/67; Alan Kriegsman (auth), Chorus Singing Master, Washington Post, 11/70; F Warren O'Reilly (auth), A Ken Cen Christmas with DC's Top Chorus, Washington Times, 12/82. *Mem:* Am Fedn Musicians; Asn Prof Vocal Ens. *Mailing Add:* Choral Arts Soc 4321 Wisconsin Ave Washington DC 20016

SEABURY, JOHN
BASS
Roles: Banquo in Macbeth, Va Opera Asn, 83; Mephistopheles in Faust, Greater Miami Opera, 83; Zaccaria in Nabucco, Philadelphia Opera, 83; Figaro in The Marriage of Figaro; Four Villains in Tales of Hoffmann; Orest in Elektra; Mary, Queen of Scots, New York City Opera. *Pos:* Performer, San Francisco, Dallas, Washington, Baltimore & Philadelphia Opera Co. *Awards:* Debut Artist of Yr, New York City Opera, 78. *Mailing Add:* c/o Judd Conct Bur 155 W 68th St New York NY 10023

SEATON, (STUART) DOUGLASS
EDUCATOR, WRITER
b Baltimore, Md, June 8, 50. *Study:* Col Wooster, BMus, 71; Columbia Univ, MA, 73, MPhil, 74, PhD, 77. *Pos:* Ed in chief, Current Musicol, 77-78. *Teaching:* Vis instr music, Yeshiva Univ, 77-78; asst prof music, Fla State Univ, 78-82, assoc prof, 82- *Mem:* Am Musicol Soc; Col Music Soc (southern chap pres, 81-83); Southeastern Nineteenth Century Studies Asn; Southeastern Am Soc Eighteenth Century Studies. *Interests:* Interdisciplinary critical studies; music history from 1750 to 1850; Mendelssohn; music manuscripts and compositional process. *Publ:* Auth, Bach & August Wilhelm, In: New Grove Dict of Music & Musicians, 80; instr manual for Schwartz's Music: Ways of Listening, Holt, Rinehart & Winston, 82; The Romantic Mendelssohn, Musical Quart, 82; contribr, Mendelssohn and Schumann Essays, Duke Univ Press, 84. *Mailing Add:* Sch Music Fla State Univ Tallahassee FL 32306

SEAY, ALBERT
WRITER, EDUCATOR
b Louisville, Ky, Nov 6, 16. *Study:* Murray State Col, BA, 37, BM, 37; La State Univ, MM, 39; Yale Univ, PhD, 54. *Teaching:* Asst prof music, Southwestern La Inst, 46-49; prof, Colo Col, 53- *Awards:* John Simon Guggenheim Fel, 61; Nat Endowment Humanities Fel, 71; Kinkeldey Award Distinguished Publ, Am Musicol Soc, 72. *Mem:* Am Musicol Soc; Royal Musical Asn; Int Musicol Soc; Soc Francaise Musicol; Gesellschaft Musikwissenschaft. *Interests:* Music theory of Middle Ages and Renaissance. *Publ:* Ed, Jacob Arcadelt: Complete Works, Am Inst Music, 72; auth, Music in the Medieval World, Prentice Hall, 75; ed, Costanzo Festa and Carpentras & many editions of music theory treatises, Amer Inst Music. *Mailing Add:* 7 W Caramillo Apt 2 Colorado Springs CO 80907

SEBASTIAN, ANNE MARIE
LIBRARIAN
b Lancaster, Pa, Nov 15, 53. *Study:* Temple Univ, BMus, 77; Drexel Univ, MSLS, 80. *Pos:* Rec librn, Philadelphia Col Perf Arts, 78-80; asst librn, Curtis Inst Music, 80- *Mem:* Am Musicol Soc; Music Libr Asn. *Mailing Add:* 515 Lee Ann Rd Cherry Hill NJ 08034

SECRIST, BARBERA SHAW
OBOE & ENGLISH HORN, ADMINISTRATOR
b Sparta, Tenn, Aug 2, 52. *Study:* Ga State Univ, Atlanta, BA(music), 75; studied oboe with Elaine Douvas & Joe Robinson. *Pos:* Prin English horn & oboe, Chattanooga Symph, 76-77; oboe, Kennedy Ctr Opera Orch, 79; dir & oboe, Pandean Players, 80-; prin oboe, Am Chamber Orch, 81- *Mem:* Am Fedn Musicians; Chamber Music Am; Cult Coun Found. *Mailing Add:* 484 W 43rd St #76 New York NY 10036

SECRIST, PHYLIS JANE
OBOE, EDUCATOR

b Memphis, Tenn, Aug 21, 50. *Study:* Univ Tenn, with Joel Timm, BMus, 72; Yale Univ, with Robert Bloom, MMus, 74. *Pos:* Prin oboe, Knoxville Symph Orch, Tenn, 74-; Kingsport Symph Orch, Tenn, 74-82, Johnson City Symph Orch, Tenn, 74-78 & Radford Orch, Va, 78-79. *Teaching:* Instr oboe & woodwinds, ETenn State Univ, 76-81 & Radford Univ, 78-79; instr oboe & eartraining, Univ Tenn, 81- *Mailing Add:* 4606 Washington Pike Knoxville TN 37917

SEDARES, JAMES
CONDUCTOR

b Chicago, Ill, Jan 15, 56. *Study:* Webster Univ, St Louis, BMusEd, 77; Wash Univ, St Louis, MMusEd, 79. *Pos:* Assoc cond, San Antonio Symph, 79- *Mem:* Am Symph Orch League. *Mailing Add:* 115 NW Loop 410 Apt 24D San Antonio TX 78216

SEEBASS, TILMAN
EDUCATOR

b Sept 8, 39. *Study:* Univ Basel, with Leo Schrade, Arnold Schmitz, Walter Muschg, Werner Kaegi & Wolfram von den Steinen, PhD, 70. *Pos:* Managing dir, Haus der Bücher, Basel, 75-77. *Teaching:* Res asst, Music Dept, Univ Basel, 65-70; res fel, Swiss Nat Fund Res, 70-75; asst prof, Duke Univ, 77-79 & assoc prof, 79- *Mem:* Int Musicol Soc; Am Musicol Soc; Soc Ethnomusicol; Medieval Acad Am. *Interests:* Music history; musical iconography; Indonesian studies. *Publ:* Auth, Musikdarstellung und Psalterillustration, 73 & coauth, The Music of Lombok, 76, Berne, Francke; auth, Musikhandschriften in Basel (Exhibition Catalogue), 75 & coauth, Musikhandschriften Sammlung Paul Sacher, 76, Basel; ed, Imago Musicae, International Yearbook of Musical Iconography, Kassel & Durham NC, 83. *Mailing Add:* Music Dept Duke Univ 6695 College Station Durham NC 27708

SEELEY, GILBERT STEWART
CONDUCTOR & MUSIC DIRECTOR, EDUCATOR

b Evanston, Ill, June 9, 38. *Study:* Mozarteum, Salzburg, Austria, 59-60; Oberlin Consv Music, BM, 61; Univ Southern Calif, MM, 66, DMA, 69. *Pos:* Dir, Ore Repty Singers, 76-; tours in Europe, 77 & 82 & Northwest US. *Teaching:* Instr, Univ Calif, Santa Cruz, 67-70; dir choral music, Calif Inst of Arts, Valencia, 70-75; assoc prof, Lewis & Clark Col, 75- *Awards:* Rockefeller Fel, 71; grants, Nat Endowment Arts, 79-83. *Mem:* Am Choral Dir Asn; Am Choral Found. *Mailing Add:* Lewis & Clark Col 0615 SW Palatine Hill Rd Portland OR 97219

SEFERIAN, EDWARD
CONDUCTOR, EDUCATOR

b Cleveland, Ohio, Mar 23, 31. *Study:* Juilliard Sch Music, BS(violin), 57, MS, 58. *Pos:* Conductor & musical dir, Tacoma Symph, 59-; asst concertmaster, Seattle Symph, 60-66. *Teaching:* Prof, Univ Louisville, 58-59; prof violin, Univ Puget Sound, 59- *Awards:* Nat Steinway-Cultural Achievement Award, 67. *Bibliog:* Maxine Cushing Gray (ed), Northwest Arts, 4/23/76. *Mem:* Hon mem Phi Beta; Am Asn Univ Prof (local pres, 70). *Mailing Add:* Sch Music Univ Puget Sound Tacoma WA 98416

SEGAR, KATHLEEN
MEZZO-SOPRANO

Roles: Jadwiga in The Haunted Castle, Mercedes in Carmen, 82 & Anoush's Mother in Anoush, Mich Opera Theatre; Alice in Wonderland, Kennedy Ctr; Alisa in Lucia di Lammermoor, Dayton Opera, 82 & Mich Opera, 82; Cherubino in Le Nozze di Figaro, Dayton Opera, 82, Opera Co Lansing, 83 & Mich Opera Theatre, 83. *Pos:* Performer, Detroit Symph, formerly & Dearborn Symph, formerly; guest soloist, Grosse Pointe Orch, formerly & Battle Creek Orch, formerly. *Awards:* Winner, Metropolitan Opera Nat Coun Auditions, 82. *Mailing Add:* c/o Sullivan & Lindsey Assoc 133 W 87th St New York NY 10024

SEGOVIA, ANDRE
GUITAR

b Linares, Spain, Feb 18, 1894. *Study:* Granada Music Inst; Oxford Univ, Hon DMus, 72. *Pos:* Recitalist, worldwide, 09- *Teaching:* Instr, Santiago de Compostela, Acad Chigiana, Siena, Univ Calif, Berkeley & cols & univ throughout the world. *Awards:* Grammy, 58; Gold Medal for Meritorious Work, Spain, 67. *Mem:* Royal Acad Fine Arts (Spain). *Publ:* Auth, Segovia: An Autobiography of the Years 1893-1920; Segovia: My Book of the Guitar, 79. *Mailing Add:* c/o ICM Artists 40 W 57th St New York NY 10019

SEIBERT, DONALD C
LIBRARIAN, CRITIC-WRITER

b Los Angeles, Calif, Oct 3, 29. *Study:* George Pepperdine Univ, BA, 51; Columbia Univ, MSLS, 61. *Pos:* Music cataloger, Juilliard Sch, 62-65 & 67-68; music librn, State Univ NY, Stony Brook, 65-67 & Syracuse Univ, 68-; rec reviewer, Fanfare, 79- *Mem:* Music Libr Asn (vpres, 71, mem bd, 72-73). *Publ:* Ed, The Hyde Timings, Juilliard Sch, 64; auth, SLACC: The Partial Use of the Shelf List as Classed Catalog, 73 & The MARC Music Format from Inception to Publication, 82, Music Libr Asn. *Mailing Add:* 526 Cumberland Ave Syracuse NY 13210

SEIGER, JOSEPH
EDUCATOR, PIANO

b Rishon Le Zion, Israel, Aug 28, 23; US citizen. *Study:* Shulamit Consv, Tel Aviv, artist dipl, 38; Manhattan Sch Music, BM, 51, MM, 52. *Rec Perf:* Violin & Piano Sonatas, 59, Beethoven & Franck, 59, Faure & Greig, 61, London Firr; Brahms, London Decca, 61; various short pieces with RCA Victor & Vanguard Rec. *Pos:* Exclusive accmp, Mischa Elman, 52-67. *Teaching:* Prof piano, chamber music & accmp, Manhattan Sch Music, currently. *Mailing Add:* Manhattan Sch Music 120 Claremont Ave New York NY 10027

SEILER, JAMES JOSEPH
ADMINISTRATOR, BARITONE

b Demarest, NJ, Mar 4, 54. *Study:* Westminster Choir Col, BA(music educ), 76; Juilliard Opera Training Dept. *Pos:* Soloist, performer & founder, Aureus Quartet, New York, 76-, Musica Sacra, New York, 80-, Gregg Smith Singers, New York, 82- & Juilliard Chamber Singers, 82- *Mem:* Chamber Music Am; Asn Prof Vocal Ens. *Mailing Add:* 22 Lois Ave Demarest NY 07627

SELBERG, JOHN RYAN
CELLO, EDUCATOR

b Los Angeles, Calif, Sept 29, 46. *Study:* Univ Calif, Los Angeles, BA, 69; studied cello privately with Joseph Di Tullio. *Pos:* Sect cellist, Los Angeles Phil, 68-71; prin cellist, Edmonton Symph, Alberta, Can, 72-75 & Utah Symph, 75- *Teaching:* Adj prof cello, Univ Utah, 78- *Mem:* Am Fedn Musicians; Violoncello Soc NY; Violin Makers Soc Am. *Mailing Add:* 1431 Indian Hills Cr Salt Lake City UT 84108

SELDEN, MARGERY STOMNE
EDUCATOR, PIANO

b Chicago, Ill. *Study:* Vassar Col, AB, 46; Yale Univ, MA, 48, PhD, 51. *Works:* The New Dress (opera), Caldwell Col, 80. *Teaching:* Assoc prof music, Wayne State Univ, 50-64; assoc prof, NCent Col, 64-68; prof, Col St Elizabeth, Convent Station, NJ, 68-79 & Passaic Co Col, 79- *Mem:* Am Musicol Soc; Soc Music Theory; Col Music Soc; Soc Ethnomusicol; Sonneck Soc. *Publ:* Auth, Laurels to Catherine the Great, Opera News, 56; Henri Berton as Critic, J Am Musicol Soc, 71; Cherubini and England, Musical Quart, 74; The Case of the Missing Measures, Clavier, 82. *Mailing Add:* Quentin Court Maplewood NJ 07040

SELF, JAMES MARTIN
TUBA, EDUCATOR

b Franklin, Pa, Aug 20, 43. *Study:* Ind Univ Pa, BMusEd, 65; Cath Univ Am, MMus, 67; Univ Southern Calif, DMA, 76. *Rec Perf:* Over 1000 motion pictures, rec, TV shows & commericials, 74-; Jim Self Quintet, Discovery Rec, 83. *Pos:* Tubist, US Army Band, Washington, DC, 65-67; studio musician, Los Angeles Studios, 74- *Teaching:* Asst prof music, Univ Tenn, 69-74; adj instr tuba & chamber, Univ Southern Calif, 76-; adj instr tuba, Calif State Univ, Northridge, 76- *Mem:* Am Fedn Musicans; ASCAP; Phi Mu Alpha; Pi Kappa Lambda. *Publ:* Auth, Brass Music, Wimbledon, 77. *Mailing Add:* 2139 Kress St Los Angeles CA 90046

SELFRIDGE-FIELD, ELEANOR A
WRITER, LECTURER

b New Orleans, La, June 29, 40. *Study:* Drew Univ, BA, 62; Columbia Univ, MS, 63; Oxford Univ, DPhil, 69. *Pos:* Consult music, Am Publ Radio, 78- *Teaching:* Instr, Drew Univ, 62-65 & Univ Pittsburgh, 68-70; vis prof, Mills Col, 70 & 76-77; fac mem, Aston Magna Acad Arts, 81-82. *Mem:* NAm Vivaldi Asn; Int Vivaldi Asn (US rep, 78-); Am Musicol Asn (secy, 76-78); life mem, Royal Musical Asn. *Interests:* Venetian music; instrumental music; aesthetics; music criticism. *Publ:* Auth, Venetian Instrumental Music, Praeger, 74, Ital transl, ERI, 80; Pallade Veneta: Music in Venetian Society, Fond Levi (in prep). *Mailing Add:* 867 Durshire Way Sunnyvale CA 94087

SELIG, ROBERT L
EDUCATOR, COMPOSER

b Evanston, Ill, 1939. *Study:* Northwestern Univ, with Anthony Donato, BM, 61; Brandeis Univ, with Irving Fine, 62; Univ Southern Calif, with Halsey Stevens, 63; Boston Univ, with Gardner Read, 66-68 & 72; studied comp with Donald Martino & Ernst Krenek; Berkshire Music Ctr. *Works:* Two Symphonies (orch), 62 & 69; Three Songs to Texts of D H Lawrence (bar), 66 & Chocorua (opera), 72, Berkshire Music Ctr; The Three Seasons of Autumn (voice, flute, cello & perc), 73 & Pometa Comet, 1676 (wind ens), 75, Boston; Islands (cantata on text of Millay's Mist in the Valley, with orch), Cambridge, Mass, 76; Variations for Brass Quintet, Boston, 77; works publ by Margun Music & United Artists. *Rec Perf:* On CRS & others. *Pos:* Asst comp, United Artists Music Co, 64-66. *Teaching:* Mem fac music theory, New England Consv Music, 68- *Awards:* Grant, Fromm Found, 68 & Mass Arts & Humanities Found, 75; Guggenheim Fels, 72 & 77. *Mailing Add:* 153 Walden St Cambridge MA 02140

SELLARS, JAMES
COMPOSER, PIANO

b Ft Smith, Ark, Oct 8, 47. *Study:* Manhattan Sch Music, BM, 68; Southern Methodist Univ, MM, 70; NTex State Univ, PhD, 77. *Works:* Music From Texas (piano solo), August Week (various instrm), Chanson Dada (voice & instrm), Stein Chorus III: Wild Flowers (SATB), Tango for Two (cellos), For Love of the Double Bass (bass & piano) & Haplomatics for Tape and Visuals (with Finn Byrhard), Quadrivium Music Press. *Rec Perf:* Piano Sonata I & II & Pianoconcert, CRI, 83. *Pos:* Dir music, First Unitarian Church, Brooklyn, 65-68; music critic, Brooklyn Heights Press, 65-68 & Hartford Courant, 76-81. *Teaching:* Assoc prof, Hartt Sch Music, Univ Hartford, 76- *Mem:* Am Comp Alliance; BMI; Conn Comp Inc. *Rep:* Quadrivium Music Press 25 Sickles 7E New York NY 10040. *Mailing Add:* 1800 Albany Ave Hartford CT 06105

SELLECK, JOHN HUGH
COMPOSER, WRITER
b Billings, Mont, Apr 9, 39. *Study:* Mont State Univ, studied with Rudolf Wendt & Eugene Weigel, BMus, 61; Yale Sch Music, studied with Elliott Carter & Allen Forte, MMus, 64; Sch Arts, Columbia Univ, studied with Chou Wen Chung & Bulent Arel, DMA, 75. *Works:* Ichinen Sanzen for Piano, Comp Forum, 73; Migrations (four channel tape), Group for Contemp Music & Comp Forum, 73; Elementals (four channel tape), comn by Brenner Mehl, 77; PHI (five instrm & perc) Am Soc Univ Comp J Music Scores, 78; Woodwind Quintet, perf by Clarion Woodwind Quintet, 79; String Quartet, comn by NC Dance Theater & perf by Rasoumovsky Quartet, 80; Fantasie for Piano (four hands), perf by Earl Myers NC Comp Symposium, 81. *Rec Perf:* Original Piano Music for Ballet Choreography, Orion, 82. *Pos:* Comp in res, FourWinds Theatre, New York, 66-76; tech asst, Dept Music, Princeton Univ, 72-75; rehearsal accmp, NC Sch Arts, 75-80. *Awards:* Woods Chandler Prize Comp, Yale Univ, 64. *Bibliog:* Arthur Mendel (auth), Some Preliminary Attempt at Computer-Assisted Style Analysis in Music, Comput & Humanities, 69-70; Gerald Warfield (auth), Structural Levels—A Criterion for Music Evaluation, New York City Contemp Music Newsletter, 70. *Mem:* Am Soc Univ Comp (exec coun, 70-75). *Publ:* Coauth, Procedures for the Analysis of Form, Yale J Music Theory, 9/2/65; auth, Computer Partitioning, Proc Am Univ Comp, 7/8/74; Pitch & Duration as Textural Elements: An Analysis of the Lutoslovski String Quartet, Perspectives New Music, 75; An Insider's Guide to Computer Music Recordings, Creative Comput, 77. *Mailing Add:* 4720 Hawkedale Dr Winston-Salem NC 27106

SELLERS, JACQUELYN MARIE
FRENCH HORN, EDUCATOR
b Phoenix, Ariz, Mar 13, 58. *Study:* Ariz State Univ, with Ralph Lockwood, BM(perf), 80; Ind Univ, with Philip Farkas & Robert Elworthy, MM(perf), 82. *Pos:* Prin horn, Sun City Symph, 78-80 & Tucson Symph Orch, 82-; sub asst prin horn, Phoenix Symph, 78-80; fourth horn, Colo Phil, 82. *Teaching:* Assoc instr horn & brass techn, Ind Univ, Bloomington, 80-82. *Awards:* Nat Brass Winner, Music Teacher's Nat Asn Collegiate Artist Compt, 80. *Mailing Add:* 6601 N Montezuma Tucson AZ 85718

SELTZER, CHERYL STERN
PIANO, ADMINISTRATOR
b Spokane, Wash, Aug 17, 38. *Study:* Mills Col, studied piano with Alexander Libermann & comp with Darius Milhaud & Leon Kirchner, BA, 59; Columbia Univ, MA, 71; studied piano with Sara Yeagley, Stefan Balogh, Leon Fleischer & Leonard Shure & theory with Ernst Oster. *Rec Perf:* Solitaire (Barbara Kolb), Vox Rec, 72; Omaggio II (Lawrence Moss), Advan Rec, 80; A Solo Requiem (Milton Babbitt) & Haiku Settings (Mel Powell), 81 & Enactments for Three Pianos (Stefan Wolpe), 82, Nonesuch Rec; Piano Sonata (Leon Kirchner), Musical Heritage Soc, 83. *Pos:* Co-dir & founder, Continuum, New York, 67- *Mailing Add:* 333 West End Ave Apt 16C New York NY 10023

SELTZER, GEORGE
EDUCATOR, CLARINET
b Passaic, NJ, June 3, 24. *Study:* Eastman Sch Music, perf cert & BM, 48, MM, 49, DMA, 56; studied clarinet with Gustave Langenus, 39-41 & Robert McGinnis, 43-45; Col Music Soc Inst, Univ Colo, 83. *Pos:* Clarinetist, Rochester Civic Orch, 47, Rochester Phil, 49, Rochester Opera Orch, 41, 46 & 47, Radio Sta WHAM, Rochester, 48-49, Richmond Symph, 68, Dayton Phil Orch, 69- & Dayton Opera Co, 68- *Teaching:* Asst dean, Sch Fine Arts, Miami Univ, Ohio, 68-71, assoc prof music, 68-73, assoc dean, 71-, prof, 73- *Mem:* Am Fedn Musicians; Col Music Soc; Int Clarinet Soc. *Interests:* History of the American Federation of Musicians. *Publ:* Contribr, The Woodwind Anthology, 72 & Uniformity and Conformity, 12/73, Instrumentalist; auth, The Professional Symphony Orchestra in the United States, Scarecrow Press, 75; What is the Role of the University Orchestra?, Orch News, spring 76; Music Making, McFarland, NC & London, 83; The Dominance of Western Music, Am Music Teacher (in prep). *Mailing Add:* Dept Music Miami Univ Oxford OH 45056

SEMEGEN, DARIA
COMPOSER, EDUCATOR
b Bamberg, WGer, June 27, 46; US citizen. *Study:* Eastman Sch Music, MusB, 68; Warsaw Consv, Poland, 68-69; private study with Witold Lutoslawski, 68-69; Yale Univ, MusM, 71; Columbia Univ, 71-75. *Works:* Dans la Nuit (bar & orch), Cincinnati Consv Orch, 69; Jeux des Quatres (clarinet, trombone, cello & piano), Op One, 70; Electronic Composition No 1, Odyssey, 71; Music for Violin Solo, Op One, 73; Arc: Music for Dancers, Finnadar, 77; Spectra (electronic), CRI, 79; Music for Clarinet Solo, perf by Jack Kreiselman, Carnegie Rec Hall, 80. *Pos:* Assoc dir, Electronic Music Studios, State Univ NY, Stony Brook, 74- *Teaching:* Instr, Columbia-Princeton Electronic Music Ctr, 71-75; assoc prof music, State Univ NY, Stony Brook, 74- *Awards:* BMI Award, 67 & 69; Nat Endowment Arts Grant, 73, 75, 77, 80, 81 & 82; Alice M. Ditson Fund, Columbia Univ, 80. *Bibliog:* Lochhead & Fisher (auth), Daria Semegen's Three Pieces for Clarinet & Piano, In Theory Only, 12/82. *Mem:* Am Comp Alliance; Mu Phi Epsilon; Audio Engineering Soc; Int League Women Comp; Am Music Ctr. *Mailing Add:* Music Dept State Univ NY Stony Brook NY 11794

SEMKOW, JERZY (GEORG)
CONDUCTOR & MUSIC DIRECTOR
b Radomsko, Poland, Oct 12, 28. *Study:* Univ Cracow, 46-50; Leningrad Music Consv, dipl, 55. *Rec Perf:* Boris Godunov (Mussorgsky). *Pos:* Asst cond, Leningrad Phil Orch, 54-56 & Bolshoi Opera & Ballet Theater, 56-58;

artistic dir & prin cond, Warsaw Nat Opera, 59-62; permanent cond, Danish Royal Opera, 66-71; music dir & prin cond, St Louis Symph Orch, 75-79; music dir, Orch Sinfonica della RAI, Rome, 79-; guest cond with maj symph orchs in Europe & US incl Vienna Symph Orch, London Phil, New York Phil, Boston Symph, Cleveland Symph & others. *Awards:* Great Order Commandoria Polonia Restituta; Polish Nat Radio & TV Award First Degree; Deutschen Schallplatten Preis. *Mailing Add:* c/o ICM Artists 40 W 57th St New York NY 10019

SENN, MARTHA
MEZZO-SOPRANO
b St Gallen, Swiss, Nov 19, 54; Swiss & Colombian citizen. *Study:* Nat Univ Colombia; study with Zinka Milanov, 79-81 & Ellen Faull & Thomas Grubb, 81-83. *Roles:* Giulietta in Tales of Hoffman, Conn State Opera, 82; Carmen, Washington Opera, 82, Ariz Opera, 83, Opera Memphis, 83 & Philadelphia Orch, 83; Ino & Juno in Semele, Washington Opera, 83; Siebel in Faust, Philadelphia Opera, 83 & 84. *Pos:* Prin ms, Opera Colombia, Bogota, 76- *Awards:* First Prize, Baltimore Nat Opera Compt, 82 & Concours Int Chant Paris, 82; Career Develop Grant, William Mattheus Sullivan Music Found, 82. *Mem:* Am Guild Music Artists. *Rep:* Columbia Artists Mgmt Inc 165 W 57th St New York NY 10019. *Mailing Add:* 125 Nelson Ave Harrison NY 10528

SERBO, RICO
TENOR
b Stockton, Calif. *Study:* With Maude Douglas Tweedy & Robert Weede; Univ Pac. *Roles:* Pinkerton in Madama Butterfly, San Diego, 78; Faust in Faust, New York City Opera, 79; Alfredo in La Traviata, Toronto, 80; Rodolfo in La Boheme, Amsterdam, 81, Houston, 82 & Milwaukee, 82; Camille in Widow, Berlin, 82. *Awards:* Martha Baird Rockefeller Grant, 66; Kirsten Flagstad Award, 66; Corbett Found Award, 69. *Mem:* Am Guild Musical Artists; Actors Equity, Can. *Mailing Add:* c/o Tony Hartman Assoc 250 W 57th St New York NY 10019

SEREBRIER, JOSE
COMPOSER, CONDUCTOR
b Montevideo, Uruguay, Dec 3, 38; US citizen. *Study:* Nat Consv, Montevideo, dipl, 56; Curtis Inst Music, dipl, 58; Univ Minn, MA, 60. *Works:* Colores Magicos, Partita, Passacaglia and Perpetuum Mobile, Symphony No 1 & Variations on a Theme from Childhood, Peer Int Corp; The Star Wagon & Tres Canciones de Garcia Lorca, BMI, and many others. *Rec Perf:* Symphony No 4 (Ives), 76, Symphony No 8 (Dvorak), 80, Symphony No 1 (Sibelius), 81, RCA; 1812/Bolero, Tioch Digital, 82; The Planets (Holst), 83, La Voix Humane (Poulenc), 83 & Eroica (Beethoven), 83, RCA. *Pos:* Apprentice cond, Minn Orch, 58-60; assoc cond, Am Symph Orch, 62-67; comp in res, Cleveland Orch, 68-71. *Teaching:* Asst prof comp & cond, Swarthmore Col, 62-64; assoc prof comp, Bard Col, 64-66; assoc prof comp & violin, Eastern Mich Univ, 66-68. *Awards:* Guggenheim Fel, 58 & 59; First Prize, BMI Young Comp Compt, 56; Am Cond Award, Ford Found, 64. *Bibliog:* Bernard Jacobson (auth), Conductors on Conducting, Columbia Publ Co, 80; Bernard Burt (auth), Serebrier, Am Symph Orch League, 83. *Mem:* Am Music Ctr; Am Symph Orch League; Am Fedn Musicians. *Mailing Add:* 270 Riverside Dr New York NY 10025

SERKIN, PETER ADOLF
PIANO, TEACHER
b New York, NY, July 24, 47. *Study:* Curtis Inst Music; studied with Karl Ulrich Schnabel & Miecyslaw Horszowski. *Rec Perf:* Beethoven Sonatas, Op 90 & 101, 83 & Schubert Dances, 83, Pro Arte Rec; Beethoven Diabelli Variations, Webern & Takemitsu, Mozart Six Concerti & Chopin Solo Works, RCA; Takernitsu Quatrain, Deutsche Grammophon. *Pos:* Solo conct pianist with orchs & chamber music groups in US & Japan. *Teaching:* Piano, Mannes Col Music, 81- *Awards:* Deutsche Schallplatten Award. *Mailing Add:* 201 W 54th St New York NY 10025

SERKIN, RUDOLF
PIANO
b Eger, Bohemia, Mar 28, 03; US citizen. *Study:* Piano with Richard Robert & comp with J Marx & Arnold Schoenberg; hon degrees from Williams Col, Temple Univ, Univ Vt, Harvard Univ, Oberlin Col, Univ Rochester & Marlboro Col. *Pos:* Guest artist, Vienna Symph Orch, 15, Coolidge Fest, Wash, 33, New York Phil, 36, Nat Orch Asn, 37 and many other appearances in US & Europe; participant, Casals Fest, 50-; artistic dir & pres, Marlboro Sch Music & Fest. *Teaching:* Mem fac, Curtis Inst Music, 39-, dir, 68-76. *Awards:* US Presidential Medal Freedom, 64; Kennedy Ctr Honors Medal, 80; Orden pour Merite, West Germany, 81. *Mem:* Fel, Am Acad Arts & Sci; hon mem, Beethoven Soc, Bonn; hon mem, Neue Bachgesellschaft, Bonn; hon mem, Phil Soc New York; hon mem, Acad Santa Cecilia, Rome. *Mailing Add:* RFD 3 Brattleboro VT 05301

SERRANO, CARLOS
BARITONE
b Vieques, PR. *Study:* With Ignacio Morales Nieva; Univ PR; Casals Consv, San Juan; Curtis Inst Music; Acad Vocal Arts Philadelphia. *Roles:* Rigoletto in Rigoletto; Don Giovanni in Don Giovanni; Tonio in I Pagliacci; Germont in La Traviata; Don Andres in La Perichole; Macbeth in Macbeth, Va Opera Asn, 83; Tarquinius in The Rape of Lucretia, 83. *Pos:* Bar, Philadelphia Opera, San Francisco Opera, Lake George Opera, Houston Opera & St Louis Opera; performer, St Louis Symph, formerly, Houston Symph, formerly, Ambler Music Fest, formerly & PR Symph, currently; recitalist. *Mailing Add:* c/o Columbia Artists Mgt 165 W 57th St New York NY 10019

SERRLYA, SIVIA
COLORATURA SOPRANO, COACH
b Baltimore, MD. *Study:* Studied with Rosa Ponselle, Hugo Weisgall, V Cinque, Mario Fiorella & Henry Jacobi. *Roles:* Adele in Die Fledermaus, Baltimore Civic Opera, 55; Margherita in Mefistofele; Anna Bolena in Anna Bolena; Lucia in Lucia di Lammermoor; La Femme in La Voix Humaine; Mimi in La Boheme; Suor Angelica in Suor Angelica; and many others. *Pos:* Dramatic coloratura sop with maj co in Austria, Fance, WGermany, Italy, Romania, Sweden, Switz, UK & US. *Teaching:* Voice & repertoire. *Awards:* Marion Anderson Vocal Award; Sullivan Award; Fedn Music Clubs Award. *Mailing Add:* 300 W 55th St New York NY 10019

SESSIONS, ROGER HUNTINGTON
COMPOSER, EDUCATOR
b Brooklyn, NY, Dec 28, 1896. *Study:* Harvard Univ, AB, 15; Yale Univ, with Horation Parker, MusB, 17; studied with Ernest Bloch; numerous hon degrees. *Works:* Montezuma (opera), 47; Theocritus (sop & orch), 54; Divertimento (orch), 60; Rhapsody (orch), 70; When Lilacs Last in the Dooryard Bloomed (soloists & orch), 71; Five Pieces for Piano, 74-75; Three Choruses on Biblical Texts (chamber orch), 75; and others. *Pos:* Co-organizer, Copland-Sessions Concts, 28-31. *Teaching:* Instr music, Smith Col, 19-21, Cleveland Inst Music, 21-25, Boston Univ, 33-35 & NJ Col Women, 35-37; instr, Princeton Univ, 35-37, asst prof, 37-40, assoc prof, 40-45, William Shubael Conant prof, 53-65; prof, Univ Calif, Berkeley, 45, Ernest Bloch prof, 66-67; mem fac comp, Juilliard Sch Music, 65-; Charles Eliot Norton prof, Harvard Univ, 68-69; vis comp, Univ Iowa, 71. *Mem:* Hon life mem, Int Soc Contemp Music (pres US sect, 34-42); hon life mem, Nat Inst Arts & Lett; Am Acad'Arts & Lett; Akad Künste, Berlin; Am Acad Arts & Sci. *Publ:* Auth, The Intent of the Artist, 41; The Musical Experience of Composer, Performer & Listener, 50; Harmonic Practice, 51; Questions About Music, 70; Roger Sessions on Music, 79. *Mailing Add:* Juilliard Sch Music Lincoln Ctr New York NY 10023

SETAPEN, JAMES ANTHONY
CONDUCTOR & MUSIC DIRECTOR
b New York, NY, Nov 8, 48. *Study:* Eastman Sch Music, BMus, 70; Cleveland Inst Music, MMus, 75. *Pos:* Prin cond, Cleveland Opera Theater, 76-78; music dir, Ala Chamber Orch, 76-78; asst cond, Oakland Symph Orch, 78-80 & Denver Symph Orch, 82-; Exxon/Arts Endowment cond, Denver Symph Orch, 80-83. *Mem:* Cond Guild (bd mem, 80-82). *Mailing Add:* 1185 S Adams Denver CO 80210

SEVER, ALLEN JAY
ORGAN, TEACHER
b Kansas City, Kans, June 26, 29. *Study:* Sch Music, Northwestern Univ, BMus, 51; Sch Sacred Music, Union Theol Sem, SMM, 55; Royal Sch Church Music, London, 55-56. *Rec Perf:* Seven Last Words of Christ (Dubois), 57 & Mass in A (Franck), 59, Lyrichord Disc Inc; Messiah (Handel), HMR Prod, 60. *Pos:* Organist & choirmaster, West End Collegiate Church, New York, 56- & Stephen Wise Free Synagogue, New York, 61-; asst organist, St Bartholomew's Church, New York, 57-59. *Awards:* Fulbright Scholar, 55-56. *Mem:* Am Guild Organists; Prof Music Teachers Guild NJ; St Wilfrid's Club. *Mailing Add:* 170 Prospect St Leonia NJ 07605

SEVERINSEN, DOC (CARL H)
MUSIC DIRECTOR, TRUMPET
b Arlington, Ore, July 7, 27. *Rec Perf:* Brass Roots, 71 & others, RCA. *Pos:* Mem, Ted Rio Rito Band, 45 & Charlie Barnet Band, 47-49; soloist network band, Steve Allen Show, NBC-TV, 54-55; mem, NBC Orch, Tonight Show, 62-, music dir, 67-; host, Midnight Spec, NBC-TV, formerly; guest appearances with symph & pops orchs throughout US. *Mailing Add:* c/o NBC 3000 W Alameda Burbank CA 91523

SEYFRIT, MICHAEL E
ADMINISTRATOR, EARLY WOODWINDS
b Lawrence, Kans, Dec 16, 47. *Study:* Univ Kans, BM, 68, MM, 70; Juilliard Sch, MM, 72; Univ Southern Calif, DMA, 74. *Pos:* Mem, Smithsonian Chamber Players (baroque flute, oboe & recorder), Washington, DC, 76-80; cur musical instrm, Libr Cong, Washington, DC, 79- *Teaching:* Asst prof comp, Catholic Univ Am, 74-75 & Wichita State Univ, 75-76. *Publ:* Auth, Musical Instruments in the Dayton C Miller Flute Collection, A Catalog, Vol I, Gov Printing Office, Libr Cong Publ, 82. *Mailing Add:* 224 10th St NE Washington DC 20003

SEYMOUR, WILLIAM
ADMINISTRATOR, EDUCATOR
Study: Boston Univ, BM, MM. *Teaching:* Dir perf arts, Brookline Pub Sch, formerly; assoc dean & chmn grad div, Boston Consv Music, formerly, pres, currently; cond, Chorale, currently; assoc prof music educ & piano, Univ NMex, Albuquerque, currently. *Awards:* Mass Music Educr Distinguished Serv Award, 79. *Mem:* Music Educr Nat Conf; Nat Assn Sch Music; Am Choral Dir Asn; Phi Mu Alpha Sinfonia; Pi Kappa Lambda. *Mailing Add:* Boston Consv Music 8 The Fenway Boston MA 02215

SHACKELFORD, RUDY
COMPOSER, WRITER
b Newport News, Va, Apr 18, 44. *Study:* Va Commonwealth Univ, BMus & MusEd, 66; Univ Ill, Urbana-Champaign, MMus, 67, MMus, 68, DMA, 71. *Works:* Trio Sonata 1970 (organ), Boosey & Hawkes, 74; Canonic Variations (organ), Belwin-Mills Publ Corp, 75; Le Tombeau de Stravinsky (harpsichord), Europ-Am Music Distribr, 77; Autumn Journal (soprano,

violin & harpsichord), Cleveland Museum, 77; Epitaffio (guitar), Edizioni Suvini Zerboni, Milan, Italy, 79; Nighthawks (brass quintet), perf by Univ Iowa & Annapolis Brass Quintets, 81 & 83; Olive Tree, First Pilgrim (trumpet & organ), perf by Leonard Raver, 82. *Pos:* Freelance comp & writer. *Teaching:* Guest lectr comp, Ripon Col, 76. *Awards:* Fel, MacDowell Colony, 74, 76 & 78 & Rockefeller Found, Italy, 77; Comn Comp Year, Va Music Teachers' Asn, 80. *Bibliog:* M Kratzenstein (auth), Survey of Organ Literature & Editions, Ames, Iowa, 80; Thurston J Dox (auth), Catalog of Oratorios & Cantatas Written in The United States, Scarecrow Press (in prep). *Mem:* ASCAP. *Interests:* English edition of the essays of Luigi Dallapiccola. *Publ:* Auth, Dallapiccola and the Organ, 74 & The Music of Gordon Binkerd, 75, Tempo; The Yaddo Festivals of American Music, 1932-1952, Perspectives New Music, 78; translr, A Dallapiccola Chronology, Musical Quart, 81; Reflections on Three Verdi Operas by Dallapiccola, 19th Century Music, 83. *Mailing Add:* Post Office Severn VA 23155

SHADE, ELLEN
SOPRANO
b New York, NY. *Study:* Juilliard Am Opera Ctr; Santa Fe Apprentice Prog; studied with Cornelius Reid. *Roles:* Liu in Turandot, 72 & 73 & Marguerite in Faust, 73, Frankfurt Opera; Michaela in Carmen, Frankfurt Opera, 73 & Pittsburgh Opera, formerly; Eurydice in Orfeo, Frankfurt Opera, 73 & Lyr Opera Chicago, 76; Ilia in Re di Creta Idomeneo, 76 & Eve in Paradise Lost, 78, Lyr Opera Chicago; Amelia in Simon Boccanegra, Lyr Opera Chicago, formerly & Opera Co Philadelphia, 83. *Pos:* Sop, Metropolitan Opera, San Francisco Opera, Santa Fe Opera, Houston Grand Opera, Boston Symph, Cleveland Orch, Los Angeles Phil, Pittsburgh Symph, Stuttgart Radio Orch, Frankfurt Radio Opera, Northern BBC Orch, RAI Orch, Turin, Italy & Maggio Musicale, Umbrian Fest, Perugia, Italy. *Mailing Add:* c/o Columbia Artists 165 W 57th St New York NY 10019

SHADE, NANCY ELIZABETH
SOPRANO
b Rockford, Ill. *Study:* DePauw Univ, 64-67; Ind Univ, 68-71; studied with Vera Scammon. *Roles:* Madame Butterfly in Madame Butterfly, New York City Opera, 72; Manon Lescaut in Manon Lescaut, Spoleto Fest, 73; Georgetta in Il Tabarro, Covent Garden, 74; Countess in Marriage of Figaro, Hamburg State Opera, 74; Marguerite in Faust, San Francisco Opera, 77; Manon Lescaut in Manon Lescaut, Bavarian State Opera, Munich, 81; Marie in Die Soldatin, Opera of Lyon, France, 83. *Awards:* First Prize, Metropolitan Opera Nat Auditions, 68. *Rep:* Thea Dispeker 59 E 54th St New York NY 10022. *Mailing Add:* 821 Ave A Apt 14 Boulder City NV 89005

SHAFFER, (WILLIAM) ALLEN
EDUCATOR, ORGAN
b Somerset, Pa, Mar 15, 40. *Study:* Consv Music, Oberlin Col, BM, 62; Syracuse Univ, MM, 64; Univ Mich, DMA, 70. *Pos:* Accmp & asst cond, Cantata Chorus Norfolk, 70-; dir, Norfolk Chamber Consort, 72-; prin keyboard instrm, Va Phil Orch, 75- *Teaching:* Prof music, Norfolk State Univ, 70- *Mem:* Am Guild Organists (dean Norfolk chap, 72-74 & 77-79); Col Music Soc. *Mailing Add:* 624 Redgate Ave Norfolk VA 23507

SHAFFER, JEANNE ELLISON
COMPOSER
b Knoxville, Tenn, May 25, 25. *Study:* Stephens Col, AA, 44; Stanford Univ, BM, 54; Birmingham Southern Col, MM, 58; George Peabody Col, PhD, 70. *Works:* Hymn Tune Preludes for Organ (3 vol), Broadman Press, 61-66; Boats & Candles, 62-; Sing Noel (cantata), Broadman Press, 63; The Words From the Cross, Abingdon Press, 69; O Praise the Lord All Ye Nations, Concordia Publ House, 73; The Ghost of Susan B Anthony, Chamber Opera, 77-78; Heart of Dixie, Huntingdon Col, 80 & 82. *Roles:* Verdi Requiem, Peoria Symph, 65; Messiah (Handel), Nashville Symph, 67; Mount of Olives (Beethoven), Ridgecrest NC Music Fest, 69; Jauchget Gett in Allen Landen, Bach Fest, Montgomery & Birmingham, 77; The Heeman Voice, Huntingdon Col, 78; Porgy & Bess, 81 & Depuis le jour, 81, Birmingham Symph; Israel in Egypt (Handel), Montgomery Symph, 82. *Pos:* Weekly columnist, Montgomery Advertiser-Jour, 77-83. *Teaching:* Assoc prof music, voice & humanities, Union Univ, 70-71; head fine arts interdisciplinary prog, Fisk Univ, 72-73; head fine arts, Judson Col, 73-76; head dept visual & perf arts, Huntingdon Col, Ala, 76- *Awards:* Nat Defense Educ Act Grant, 67; Governors Arts Award, Ala, 82. *Mem:* Asn Ala Col Music Adminr (secy, 77-79 & pres, 79-81); Am Guild Organists; Nat Asn Teachers Singing; Am Choral Dir Asn. *Mailing Add:* 3124 Woodley Terr Montgomery AL 36106

SHAFFER, SHERWOOD
COMPOSER, EDUCATOR
b Bee County Tex, Nov 15, 34. *Study:* Curtis Inst Music, BM(comp), 60; Manhattan Sch Music, MM(comp), 62; studied with Bohuslav Martinu & Vittorio Giannini. *Works:* Sonata(double bass & piano) perf by Gary Karr, 66; Rhapsody (double bass & orch), perf by Gary Karr & Birmingham Symph, 67; Berceuse, Galliard and Preludes, perf by Jesus Silva, 67-; Quintet No 2, Clarion Wind Quintet, 76 & Voice Am, PBS, 76-77; Summerfare, Bodwin Summer Music Fest at Gamper Contemp Music Fest, 82; Chamber Symphony, Piedmont Chamber Orch, spring 82 & 83; Songs of Theano, comn by Fine Arts Ctr, Wake Forest Univ, 83. *Pos:* Mem bd dir, Winston-Salem Symph, currently. *Teaching:* Twentieth century harmony & comp, Newpaur Consv, 59-60; Teacher theory & comp, Manhattan Sch Music, 62-65; comp in res comp, orch & form & analysis, NC Sch Arts, 65- *Mem:* Am Music Ctr; Am Soc Univ Comp. *Mailing Add:* 515 W Sprague St Winston-Salem NC 27107

SHAHAN, PAUL W
COMPOSER, EDUCATOR
b Grafton, WVa. *Study:* Fairmont State Col; WVa Univ; George Peabody Col; Eastman Sch Music. *Works:* The Fountain Head (conct band), 65; The Spanish Conquistadors (band), 65; Holiday in Spain (band), 65; The Lincoln Heritage Trail (band), 66; The Stubblefield Story (opera); Spectrums (brass choir); Leipzig Towers (brass choir); Spring Festival (band); Beat The Drums Proudly (orch). *Pos:* Supvr music, Taylor County Pub Sch, WVa, formerly; staff arr, WSM Radio TV, Nashville, formerly; music ed, Am Music Press, formerly; dir numerous univ bands, incl Symphonic Band & Univ Wind Sinfonietta, Murray State Univ, 57-79; dir choirs, First United Methodist Church, Murray, Ky, currently. *Teaching:* Coordr grad studies music, prof music & assoc dean, Col Creative Expression, Murray State Univ, 77- *Awards:* Thor Johnson Award, 52; Int Award, 55. *Mem:* Col Band Dir Nat Asn; ASCAP; Phi Mu Alpha. *Publ:* Auth, The Problems of Music and the Marching Band, Instrumentalist, 4/63; The Composer: Artist or Mimic?, Alpha Ky, Alpha Chi, 4/69; The History of the Music Department, In: The History of Murray State University; The Fundamental Concepts of Theory and Notation. *Mailing Add:* Music Dept Murray State Univ Murray KY 42071

SHAKE, J(AMES) CURTIS
EDUCATOR, PIANO
b Princeton, Ind, Mar 27, 18. *Study:* DePauw Univ, BM, 40; Eastman Sch Music, MM, 41; Syracuse Univ, PhD, 57. *Works:* A Christmas Carol (SATB), 54 & A Christmas Carol (SSA), 60, J Fischer; The Three Marys (SATB), Flammer, 61. *Teaching:* From instr to asst prof, WVa Col, 42-45; from instr to assoc prof & actg dean, Syracuse Univ Sch Music, 45- *Mem:* Founder, Pi Kappa Lambda (pres, 68-71); Phi Mu Alpha (provisional gov, 62-70); Am Guild Organists (dean 74-76); founder, Victorian Soc Am (pres, 78-80). *Publ:* Auth, Elementary Piano Studies, Music Teachers Nat Asn Bulletin, 50; coauth, Basic Piano, Presser, 55; auth, A Pattern for Local Piano Teachers, Music J, 62. *Mailing Add:* 1029 Westcott St Syracuse NY 13210

SHALLON, DAVID
CONDUCTOR
b Tel Aviv, Israel, Oct 15, 50. *Study:* Vienna Music Acad, dipl, 75. *Pos:* Guest cond, San Francisco Symph, St Paul Chamber Orch, Rochester Phil, Cincinnati Symph, Vienna Symph, Suisse Romande, Bayrische Rundfunk Munich, Stuttgart Radio Symph, Frankfurt Radio Symph, Tokyo Phil, Jerusalem Symph, and many others. *Rep:* ICM Artists 40 W 57th St New York NY 10012. *Mailing Add:* 130 Achad Ha'am Tel Aviv Israel

SHAMES, JONATHAN
PIANO
b Springfield, Mass, Aug 12, 56. *Study:* Yale Univ, BA(philosophy), 79; Univ Mich, Ann Arbor, MM(piano perf), 81, 82- *Pos:* Musical asst & asst cond, Opera Co Boston, 74-75. *Teaching:* Grad fel piano, Univ Mich, Ann Arbor, 81-82 & 83. *Awards:* Fel, Beethoven Found Am, 80; first prize, Nat Career Award, Nat Soc Arts & Lett, 82. *Mailing Add:* 1687 Broadway #204 Ann Arbor MI 48105

SHAMROCK, MARY E
EDUCATOR
b Minneapolis, Minn, June 7, 37. *Study:* St Olaf Col, BA, 58; WVa Univ, MA, 66; Univ Calif, Los Angeles. *Teaching:* Music, Pub Sch, Trumansburg, NY, 58-60; from asst to assoc prof music, WVa Univ, 67-75; instr Orff-Schulwerk, Univ Toronto, DePaul Univ, Univ Southern Calif, Univ Manitoba, WVa Univ & Chautauqua Inst, 72-; assoc prof world music, Calif State Univ, Northridge, 78- *Mem:* Am Orff-Schulwerk Asn (pres 78-79, ed, 83-); Music Educr Nat Conf; Soc Ethnomusicol (southern Calif chap secy, 81-82). *Interests:* Orff-Schulwerk in its global dispersal. *Publ:* Auth, Piano Techniques for Elementary Teachers, WVa Univ Press, 73; ed & translr, Orff-Schulwerk: Background & Commentary, MagnaMusic-Baton, 76; auth, Bibliography of Materials in English on Orff-Schulwerk, 77 & auth & ed, Guidelines for Teacher Training in Orff-Schulwerk, Levels I-III, 80, Am Orff-Schulwerk Asn; contribr, Orff-Schulwerk: American Edition, Vol III, Schott Music Corp, 80. *Mailing Add:* 3267 Midvale Ave Los Angeles CA 90034

SHAND, DAVID AUSTIN
EDUCATOR, CONDUCTOR
b Salt Lake City, Utah, May 10, 14. *Study:* Univ Utah, AB, 37; Harvard Univ, AM, 42; Boston Univ, PhD, 47. *Pos:* Cond, Utah Symph Orch, 48-66. *Teaching:* Supvr music, pub schs, Mass, 38-40; instr, Colby Jr Col, 40-41 & Dartmouth Col, 41-43; assoc prof music, Univ Utah, 43-50, prof, 50- *Mem:* Am Musicol Soc; Nat Asn Am Comp & Cond; Orgn Am Historians; Am String Teachers. *Interests:* Sonata for violin and piano; choral compositions; string literature and early string composers' manuscripts. *Publ:* Auth, Choral Arrangements, Schirmer. *Mailing Add:* Dept Music Univ Utah Salt Lake City UT 84112

SHANE, RITA (RITA SHANE TRITTER)
SOPRANO
b New York, NY. *Study:* Bernard Col, BA; studied with Beverly Peck Johnson, 61-, Bliss Herbert, Henry Lewis & Elizabeth Schwartzkopf. *Rec Perf:* On RCA & CBS. *Roles:* Over 200 perf in nearly every major house; Queen of the Night in The Magic Flute; Donna Anna in Don Giovanni, New York City Opera; Constanze in Die Entfuhrung, Vienna, Munich & New York City Opera; Lucia di Lammermoor, Metropolitan Opera, Caracas & Amsterdam; Violitta in La Traviata, Metropolitan Opera, Aspen Fest & New York City Opera. *Pos:* Leading sop with major opera co in US & Europe. *Mem:* Am Guild Musical Artists. *Rep:* Tony Hartmann Assoc 250 W 57th St New York NY 10019. *Mailing Add:* 11 Riverside Dr New York NY 10023

SHANET, HOWARD STEPHEN
CONDUCTOR, EDUCATOR
b Brooklyn, NY, Nov 9, 18. *Study:* Columbia Univ, AB, 39, AM, 41; studied cond with Rudolph Thomas, Fritz Stiedry & Serge Koussevitzky & comp with Weisse, Dessau, Martinu, Lopatnikoff & Honegger. *Works:* Two Canonic Pieces (two clarinets), 47; A War March, 44; Variations on a Bizarre Theme, 60; Allegro Giocoso for String Quartet (or string orch). *Pos:* Asst cond, New York City Symph Orch, 47-48, to Serge Koussevitzky, int tour, 49-50; cond, Berkshire Music Ctr, 49-52, Huntington Symph Orch, WVa, 51-53, Music in Making, New York, 58-61 & String Revival, New York, 75-; guest cond, Israel Phil & New York Phil. *Teaching:* Mem fac, Hunter Col, 45-53; asst prof music, Columbia Univ, 53-59, cond univ orch, 53-, assoc prof, 59-69, prof, 69-, chmn dept, 72-78; dir music perf, 78- *Awards:* MacDowell Colony Fel, 53 & 63; Huntington Hartford Found Fel, 54; Martha Baird Rockefeller Grant, 62-63. *Mem:* Col Music Soc; Am Musicol Soc; Sonneck Soc; Fed Music Soc; Sibelius Soc. *Publ:* Auth, Learn to Read Music, 56; Philharmonic, A History of New York's Orchestra, 75; ed, Early Histories of the New York Philharmonic, 79; contribr to Musical Quart & Sat Rev. *Mailing Add:* 703 Dodge Hall Columbia Univ New York NY 10028

SHANGROW, GEORGE ARTHUR
CONDUCTOR, HARPSICHORD
b Everett, Wash, May 13, 51. *Study:* Univ Wash Music Sch, 69-72. *Rec Perf:* American Music!, Northwest Rec, 75. *Pos:* Cond & musical dir, Seattle Chamber Singers, 68-; musical dir, Puget Sound Chamber Music Fest, 74-78 & Pacific Chamber Opera, 75-78; cond & musical dir, Broadway Symph, 78- *Mem:* Am Choral Dir Asn; Nat Opera Asn. *Mailing Add:* 420 NE 95th Seattle WA 98115

SHAPERO, HAROLD SAMUEL
COMPOSER, EDUCATOR
b Lynn, Mass, Apr 29, 20. *Study:* Malkin Consv, Boston, with Nicolas Slonimsky; Harvard Univ, with Walter Piston, BA, 41; Berkshire Music Ctr, with Paul Hindemith; studied with Nadia Boulanger & Ernst Krenek. *Works:* Three Pieces for Three Pieces (woodwind trio), 38; Three Amateur Sonatas (piano), 44; On Green Mountain (jazz combo), 58; Serenade in D (string orch); Symphony for Classical Orchestra; Three Improvisations in B Flat; Three Studies in C Sharp (piano & synthesizer), 68; and others. *Teaching:* Prof music & dir electronic music studios, Brandeis Univ, 51-; comp in res, Am Acad Rome, 70-71. *Awards:* Am Prix Rome, 41; Guggenheim Fel, 46-48; Sr Fulbright Grant, 61-62. *Mailing Add:* 9 Russell Circle Natick MA 01760

SHAPEY, RALPH
COMPOSER, CONDUCTOR & MUSIC DIRECTOR
b Philadelphia, Pa, Mar 12, 21. *Study:* Study violin with Emanuel Zetlin & comp with Stefan Wolpe. *Works:* Rituals (orch), 59, Incantations (sop & ten instrm), 61, String Quartet No 6, 63, Praise (oratorio for bass-baritone, double chorus & chamber group), 71, 31 Variations for Piano (Fromm Variations), 73; The Covenant (sop, 14 players & tape), 77 & Songs for Soprano & Piano, 82, Theodore Presser Co. *Rec Perf:* Evocation (violin, piano & perc), Rituals and String Quartet VI & The Covenant (sop, 16 players & tape), 77, CRI; Songs of Ecstasy, Desto Rec; Songs (sop & piano), Op One, 82; additional recordings on Owl Records & Grenadilla. *Pos:* Guest cond, Chicago Symph, Philadelphia Symph, Buffalo Symph, London Symph, Jerusalem Symph & others. *Teaching:* Instr, Univ Pa; prof music, Univ Chicago, 64-, music dir & cond, Contemp Chamber Players, 64- *Awards:* Brandeis Creative Arts Award, 62; grant, Nat Found Arts & Lett, 66; MacArthur Award, 82. *Mailing Add:* 5532 S Shore Dr 18D Chicago IL 60637

SHAPEY, RONALD (SIDNEY)
TEACHER, VIOLINIST
b Philadelphia, Pa, May 13, 27. *Study:* Curtis Inst, grad cert, 45; studied with Efrem Zimbalist, Edgar Ortenburg, Boris Swartz, David Madison & William Primrose. *Pos:* Violinist, Indianapolis Symph, 45-48, Baltimore Symph, 49-50, Nat Symph, 51-53 & Cincinnati Symph, 70- *Teaching:* Asst to Edgar Ortenburg, Violin Dept, Settlement Music Sch, Pa, 57-69. *Mailing Add:* 5922 Rhode Island #6 Cincinnati OH 45237

SHAPINSKY, AARON
CELLO, TEACHER
b NY. *Study:* Juilliard Sch Music, 49-51; studied with Felix Salmond. *Rec Perf:* 3 Brahms Quartets, 3 Schumann Quartets & Charles Ives Quartets No 1 & 2, Vox, 63-64; Kodaly Unnamed Sonata & 3 Beethoven Sonatas, RTB, Brussels, Belgium, 69. *Pos:* First cello, City Ctr Symph, New York, 45 & Am Symph, New York, 62. *Teaching:* Assoc prof cello, Hofstra Univ, 68; asst prof, Nassau Community Col, 68- *Awards:* Pres Citation, Fedn Music Clubs, 74. *Interests:* Brahms. *Mailing Add:* 19 Belmont Pkwy Hempstead NY 11550

SHAPIRO, DAVID
CONDUCTOR, PIANO
b New York, NY, Jan 3, 19. *Study:* Columbia Col, Columbia Univ, BA, 39; Mannes Col Music; studied piano with Isabella Vengerova. *Rec Perf:* The Martyred (James Wade), Hollym Corp, Seoul, Korea, 70. *Pos:* Asst cond, Little Orch Soc, NY, 50-61; asst cond, San Francisco Opera, 65-67, music coordr, 67; cond, Summer Fest, Fair Lawn, NJ, 65- *Teaching:* Vis prof operatic perf, Seoul Nat Univ, 61-64; instr music, Fairleigh Dickinson Univ, 75 & Mannes Col Music, 76- *Mem:* Am Fedn Musicians; Professional Music Teachers Guild NJ. *Mailing Add:* 20 Hawthorne Terr Leonia NJ 07605

SHAPIRO, HARVEY
CELLO, EDUCATOR
b New York, NY. *Study:* With Willem Willeke & D Alexamian. *Rec Perf:* On Nonesuch. *Pos:* Mem, NBC Symph, 37-46, solo cellist, 44-46; mem, Primrose String Quartet, four yrs & WQXR String Quartet, 47-63. *Teaching:* Mem fac violoncello, Juilliard Sch, 70- *Awards:* Loeb & Naumburg Prizes. *Mailing Add:* Juilliard Sch Lincoln Ctr New York NY 10023

SHAPIRO, JACK M
EDUCATOR, ADMINISTRATOR
b Ufa, Russia, Jan 27, 21, US citizen. *Study:* Oberlin Col, BMusEd, 43; Teachers Col, Columbia Univ, MA, 49, prof dipl, 51. *Pos:* Dir, Far East Air Forces Band, New Guinea & Philippines, 44-45; scheduling dir, Marlboro Music Fest, Vt, 78- *Teaching:* Music instr, Oak Ridge High Sch, Tenn, 49-51; prof, chair music dept & dir, Ctr Perf Arts, City Col New York, 52-83. *Mem:* Am Musicol Soc; Music Educr Nat Conf; Am Fedn Musicians. *Mailing Add:* 219 Kensington Rd River Edge NJ 07661

SHAPIRO, JOEL
EDUCATOR, PIANO
b Cleveland, Ohio, Nov 28, 34. *Study:* Columbia Univ, BA, 56; Brussels Royal Consv Music, Belgium, Premier Prix, 59; private study with Stefan Askenase; master classes with Artur Rubinstein & Robert Casadesus. *Pos:* Soloist, piano recitals & appearances with orch in major US & Europ musical ctrs, incl regular perf in New York, London, Berlin, Hamburg, Brussels, Paris, Chicago, Jerusalem & Tel Aviv. *Teaching:* Assoc prof piano, Univ Ill, Urbana, 74-77, prof piano, 77- *Awards:* Winner Int Auditions, Young Conct Artists, New York, 61; First Prize, Darche Compt, Brussels, Belgium, 62; Harriet Cohen Int Bach Award, London, England, 63. *Rep:* Susan Wadsworth 65 E 55 St New York NY 10022. *Mailing Add:* 504 W Michigan Urbana IL 61801

SHARON, BOAZ
EDUCATOR, PIANO
b Tel Aviv, Israel, Oct 27, 49; US citizen. *Study:* Univ Tex, BM, 71; Boston Univ, MM, 73; Consv Royale Mons, Belgium, degree superieure. *Rec Perf:* Piano Music of Koechlin, Orion Rec, 80 & Nonesuch Rec (in prep). *Teaching:* Pianist in res, Duke Univ, 76-81; assoc prof piano, Univ Tulsa, 81- *Awards:* First Prize, Jaen Int Piano Compt, Spain, 68; First Prize, Music Teachers Nat Asn Col Award, 70. *Mem:* Am Liszt Soc (bd mem, 83-). *Publ:* Auth, Rodrigue et Chimene: Debussy's Other Opera, 82 & Charles Koechlin, 82, Ovation. *Mailing Add:* Sch Music Univ Tulsa Tulsa OK 74104

SHARP, JOHN MARK
CELLO
b Waco, Tex, Dec 9, 58. *Study:* With Lev Aronson, 72-79; Juilliard Sch, with Lynn Harrell, BM, MM, 79-82. *Pos:* Section cello, Ft Worth Symph, 78-79, Santa Fe Opera Orch, summers 80 & 81 & Metropolitan Opera Orch, 82-83; prin cello, Cincinatti Symph Orch, 83- *Mailing Add:* 200 W 70th St 10A New York NY 10023

SHARP, MAURICE
EDUCATOR, FLUTE
Study: Curtis Inst Music, with William Kincaid; studied with George Barrere. *Pos:* Prin flute, Cleveland Orch, 31-82. *Teaching:* Mem fac, Cleveland Inst Music, 32- *Mailing Add:* Cleveland Inst Music 11021 E Boulevard Cleveland OH 44106

SHARROW, LEONARD
BASSOON, EDUCATOR
b New York, NY, Aug 4, 15. *Study:* Juilliard Sch Music, with Louis Letellier; private study with Simon Kovar. *Rec Perf:* Concerto for Bassoon in B flat Major (Mozart), RCA, 47; Concerto in F Major & Concerto in C Major for Bassoon (Vivaldi), Musical Heritage Soc, 60; Bassoon Solos (with piano), Coronet Rec, 70; Baroque Trumpet Recital, Nonesuch, 72; Concerto da Camera for Bassoon & Orchestra (D Welcher), 76 & Concerto for Bassoon & Orchestra (Ray Luke), Crystal Rec, 76. *Pos:* Prin bassoon, Nat Symph, 35-37, NBC Symph, New York, 37-41 & 47-51, Detroit Symph, 45-47, Chicago Symph, 51-64 & Pittsburgh Symph Orch, 77- *Teaching:* Private teaching, 35-; prof bassoon, Ind Univ, Bloomington, 64-77; artist in res, Aspen Music Fest & Sch, 67-; assoc prof, Pa State Univ, 80-81; artist & lectr, Carnegie-Mellon Univ, 81- *Publ:* Ed, 25 editions of works for bassoon, Int Music Co, 60's-80. *Mailing Add:* c/o Pittsburgh Symph Soc Heinz Hall 600 Penn Ave Pittsburgh PA 15222

SHAW, ARNOLD
COMPOSER, WRITER
b New York, NY, June 28, 09. *Study:* City Univ New York, BS, 29; Columbia Univ, MA, 31. *Works:* Sing a Song of Americans, Musette Publ, 41; Mobiles: 10 Graphic Impressions, 66, Stabiles: 12 Images for Piano, 68, Plabiles: 12 Songs Without Words, 71, The Mod Moppet: 7 Nursery Rip-Offs, 74, A Whirl of Waltzes, 74 & The Bubble-Gum Waltzes, 77, Surosalida Music Co & Theodore Presser. *Pos:* Exec ed, Musette Rec, 41-43; publ relations & ad dir, Robbins, Feist & Miller Music Corps, 44-45; vpres & gen prof mgr, Duchess Music Corp, 50-53, Hill & Range Songs, 53-55 & Edward B Marks Music Corp, 55-66. *Teaching:* Lectr, Juilliard Sch Music, 45; instr Am musical theatre, Fairleigh Dickinson Univ, 64-65; adj prof music hist, Univ Nev, 77- *Awards:* Nev Comp of Yr Award, Las Vegas Teachers Asn & Teachers Music Nat Asn, 73; Deems Taylor Award, ASCAP, 68 & 79. *Mem:* Am Musicol Soc; Sonneck Soc; Las Vegas Music Teachers Asn (pres, 75-77); Univ Musical Soc (pres, 81-82); Am Guild Authors & Comp. *Publ:* Co-ed, Schillinger System of Musical Composition, Carl Fischer Inc, 46; auth, Sinatra: 20th-Century

Romantic, Holt, Rinehart & Winston, 68; The Rock Revolution, 69 & 52nd St: The Street of Jazz, 71, Da Capo Press Inc; Honkers and Shouters: The Golden Years of Rhythm & Blues, Macmillan Publ Co, 78; Dictionary of American Pop/Rock, Schirmer Books, 82. *Mailing Add:* 2288 Gabriel Dr Las Vegas NV 89109

SHAW, ROBERT LAWSON
CONDUCTOR & MUSIC DIRECTOR
b Red Bluff, Calif, Apr 30, 16. *Study:* Pomona Col, AB, 38; hon degrees from 16 col & univ. *Rec Perf:* B Minor Mass (Bach), 47, Christmas Hymns & Carols, Vol 2, 52, Ceremony of Carols (Britten), 63, Symphony of Psalms (Stravinsky), 64 & Messiah (Handel), 71, RCA; The Firebird Suite (Stravinsky), 78, Carmina Burana (Orff), 81 & Gloria/Organ Concerto (Poulenc), 82, Telarc. *Pos:* Founder & cond, Robert Shaw Chorale, 48-65; cond, San Diego Symph Orch, 53-57; assoc cond & dir choruses, Cleveland Orch, 56-67; music dir & cond, Atlanta Symph Orch, 67-; six-yr term, Nat Coun Arts, currently; guest cond, major orchs in US. *Awards:* Four Grammy Awards; Three ASCAP Awards, 76, 80 & 81; fel, Guggenheim Found. *Bibliog:* Joseph A Mussulman (auth), Dear People ... Robert Shaw, Ind Univ Press, 79 & (dir) Shaw Prepares (film), WAGA-TV, Atlanta, 81. *Mem:* Atlanta Fedn Musicians; Am Fedn TV and Radio Artists; Lamar Soc; Nat Acad Rec Arts & Sci; Nat Coun Arts. *Rep:* Shaw Concerts Inc 1995 Broadway New York NY 10023. *Mailing Add:* 3707 Randall Mill Rd NW Atlanta GA 30327

SHAW, ROLLAND HUGH
CONDUCTOR & MUSIC DIRECTOR, EDUCATOR
b Eupora, Miss, June 15, 38. *Study:* Miss Col, BS, 60; Univ Southern Miss, MM, 63, PhD, 75. *Teaching:* From instr to assoc prof voice, chmn music dept & vocal dir, Northwest Miss Jr Col, 60-65; asst prof, Miss Col, 65-71; instr voice & cond, Univ Southern Miss, 71-72; dir choral activ, 82-; instr & dir choral activ, Ark Tech Univ, 72-82. *Mem:* Phi Mu Alpha Sinfonia (prov gov Ark, 77-82); Nat Asn Teachers Singing (pres Ark, 80-82); Am Choral Dir Asn (pres Ark, 78-80). *Mailing Add:* 3308 Arlington Loop Hattiesburg MS 39401

SHEINFELD, DAVID
COMPOSER, VIOLIN
b St Louis, Mo, Sept 20, 06. *Study:* Am Consv Music, Chicago, 27-29; Cecilia Acad, Rome, study comp with Ottorina Respighi, 29-31; private violin study, Chicago. *Works:* Four Etudes for Orchestra, comn by Pittsburgh Symph, 62; Dialogues for Chamber Orchestra, comn by Chamber Symph of Philadelphia, 66; Confrontations (orch), comn by Oakland Symph, 70 & San Francisco Symph, 72; Memories of Yesterday and Tomorrow (trio), comn by Francesco Trio, 71; Time Warp (orch), comn by San Francisco Symph, 73; String Quartet, comn by San Francisco Chamber Music Soc, 79; Dreams and Fantasies, comn by San Francisco Symph, 82. *Pos:* First violin, San Francisco Symph, 45-71. *Teaching:* Instr comp, privately, 50- *Awards:* Norman Fromm Award, San Francisco Chamber Music Soc, 78. *Bibliog:* Charles Shere (auth), Sheinfeld's Relatively Intellectual Muse and Music, Oakland Tribune 9/13/81. *Mailing Add:* 1458 24th Ave San Francisco CA 94122

SHELDON, GARY
CONDUCTOR & MUSIC DIRECTOR
b Bay Shore, NY, Jan 21, 53. *Study:* Wash Univ, St Louis, with Walter Susskind & Leonard Slatkin, 72; Juilliard Sch Music, BMus, 74; Inst Hautes Etudes Musicales, Montreux, Switzerland, with Rudolf Kempe & Jean-Marie Auberson, dipl, 75. *Rec Perf:* Beauty and the Beast (Frank DiGiacomo), Twentieth Century Rec, 77; Ballet Class with Karen Herbert, Stepping Tone Rec, 82. *Pos:* Prin cond, Opera Theatre Syracuse, 76-77; asst cond, Syracuse Symph Orch, 76-77 & New Orleans Symph, 77-80; interim music dir, Columbus Symph Orch, Ohio, 82- *Awards:* New Orleans Music & Drama Found Award, 82; Third Prize Winner, Rupert BBC Symph Found, London, 82. *Mem:* Am Symph Orch League (youth orch div bd mem, 80-). *Mailing Add:* Columbus Symph 101 E Town St Columbus OH 43215

SHELTON, LUCY (ALDEN)
SOPRANO
b Pomona, Calif. *Study:* Pomona Col, BA; New England Consv, MM(voice). *Rec Perf:* Der Hirt dem Felsen (Schubert), Chamber Music NW, 82; Magabunda (four poems of Agueda Pixarro), Nonesuch, 83; Griffes Songs, Musical Heritage, 83; Gypsy Songs, 83, Messiaen/Faure (in prep) & Irish Songs (in prep), Nonesuch. *Pos:* Soprano, Jubal Trio, 74-80; soloist, with Buffalo Phil, 82, Nat Symph, 83, St Louis Symph, 83 & St Paul Chamber Orch, 84. *Teaching:* Asst prof voice, Eastman Sch Music, 79. *Awards:* Naumburg Award Chamber Music, 77; Naumburg Award, Solo Vocal Compt, 80. *Mem:* Am Guild Musical Artists; Am Fedn TV & Radio Artists. *Mailing Add:* c/o Hamlen-Landam Mgt 140 W 79th St New York NY 10024

SHELTON, MARGARET MEIER
COMPOSER, EDUCATOR
b New York, NY. *Study:* Eastman Sch Music, BM, 58; Calif State Univ, Los Angeles, MA, 72; Univ Calif, Los Angeles, PhD, 83. *Works:* This Child (cantata), comn & perf by Univ Calif, Los Angeles choral orgn, 77; Smog (SATB, piano & perc), Printing by Thomas, 78; The Three Marys (cantata), perf by Univ Calif, Los Angeles Women's Chorus, 80; Dialogues (flute & piano), 81 & A Woman's Heart, 82, Nat Asn Comp USA Conct; I Will Sing (SATB), Music 70, 83. *Pos:* Dir music, Trinity United Methodist Church, Pomona, Calif, 82-83. *Teaching:* Assoc theory, Univ Calif, Los Angeles, 76-80; lectr theory & piano, Calif State Col, San Bernardino, 77-79; instr piano, Mt San Antonio Col, 80-81. *Mem:* ASCAP; Nat Asn Comp USA; Music Teachers Asn Calif (comp chmn, 74-76); Am Women Comp; Int League Women Comp. *Mailing Add:* 608 W Wellesley Dr Claremont CA 91711

SHELTON, MELVIN LEROY
EDUCATOR

b Wichita, Kans, July 15, 32. *Study:* Wichita State Univ, BME, 56; Univ Idaho, MM, 69. *Works:* Star Wars (for band & orch), perf by Boise State Univ Band & Boise Youth Symph, 80; Star Trek (for band), perf by Boise State Univ Band, 81; Golden Jubilee (for band), comn by Boise State Univ, 83. *Rec Perf:* Merry Mount Suite (Hanson), 65, La Fiesta Mexicana (Reed), 65, Symphony for Band (Persichetti), 70, Donna Diana Overture (Reznicek), 70, Variations on America (Ives), 70, First Symphony (Barber), 72 & Sonata for Marimba (Tanner), 72, Crest. *Teaching:* Dir instrumental music, Pretty Prairie, Kans, 56-59 & Boise High Sch, Idaho, 59-68; prof music educ & dir bands, Boise State Univ, 68- *Awards:* Citation of Excellence, Nat Band Asn, 82. *Bibliog:* Barbara Oldenberg (auth), article, Idaho Music Notes, spring 83. *Mem:* Music Educr Nat Asn; Idaho Music Educr Asn; Col Band Dir Nat Asn (state chmn, 68-); Nat Band Asn (NW Div chair, 83-); Am Fedn Musicians. *Publ:* Auth, Are You Aware, Idaho Music Notes, 82; Success At Festival, Instrumentalist, 83. *Mailing Add:* 1715 Selway Boise ID 83704

SHENAUT, JOHN
CONDUCTOR & MUSIC DIRECTOR

b Galesburg, Ill, Nov 9, 16. *Study:* Am Consv Chicago, BMus, 38; Univ Mich, Ann Arbor, MMus, 40; Paris Consv; Salzburg Mozarteum, with Nadia Boulanger. *Pos:* Music dir & cond, Shreveport Symph,, 48-81, cond emer, 81-; guest cond numerous orchs in US, Mex & Europe, incl Bodensee Symph, Rheinische Phil, Swiss Radio-Beromunster Orch, Zurich, Phil Choer & Orch Paris, Pro-Musica Chamber Orch St Gallen, Switz & State Orch Craiova & Ploieste, Romania. *Mem:* Cond Guild; Am Symph Orch League. *Mailing Add:* 424 Ockley Dr Shreveport LA 71105

SHEPARD, JEAN ELLEN
COMPOSER

b Durham, NC, Nov 1, 49. *Study:* Peabody Consv, studied comp with Stefan Grove & Robert Hall Lewis & piano with Elisabith Katzenellenbogen, BM, 73, MM(comp), 74; studied with Milko Keleman, Stuttgart, Germany. *Works:* The Clock Strikes Three (orch), 74; Processional (strings), 77; To a Child Dancing (flute, perc & narrator); Music for Solo Cello, 76; Fantasy (piano), 76; Traces of Morning (flute & piano), 77; Song of Lena (speaker & piano), 78; and others. *Teaching:* Instr, Peabody Prep Dept, 73-75. *Awards:* Gustav Klemm Comp Award; Second Prize, Mu Phi Alpha Sinfonia Cont. *Mailing Add:* 5 Morton St Apt 2D New York NY 10014

SHEPP, MARIAN GRAY
TEACHER, ORGAN

b Waverly, Tenn, Feb 4, 28. *Study:* Oberlin Consv, Ohio, 45-48; Ithaca Col, BS(music), 68; study with Anthony Newman, 68- *Pos:* Organist, Follen Church, Lexington, Mass, 60-69 & First Parish, Lincoln, Mass, 69-81. *Teaching:* Instr music, Groton Ctr Arts, Mass, 73-81 & Longy Sch Music, 78- *Mem:* Am Guild Organists (secy, 71-73); Concord Area Music Asn; Masterworks Chorus. *Mailing Add:* 68 Shade St Lexington MA 02173

SHEPPARD, C(HARLES) JAMES
COMPOSER, EDUCATOR

b Aurora, Nebr, Nov 23, 43. *Study:* Univ Omaha, BFA(music), 67; Univ Mass, MM(theory & comp), 68; Univ Iowa; PhD(comp), 75. *Works:* Bottled Green, Iridium-gold, comn & perf by Ctr for New Music, Univ Iowa, 75; Space Dust, perf by Pittsburgh New Music Ens, 79 & Univ Ill Chamber Players, 80; Luminaria, 82 & Wind Loops 2, 83, Alexander Broude Inc; Cat Dreams of Flying, Opus One, 83. *Teaching:* Assoc prof & dir, Electronic Music Studio, Miami Univ, Ohio, 78- *Awards:* ASCAP Awards, 80-; Comp Fel, Charles Ives Ctr Am Music, 82; Individual Artist Fel, Ohio Arts Coun, 83. *Mem:* ASCAP; Am Soc Univ Comp; Cincinnati Comp Guild; Nat Asn Comp; Comp Forum Inc. *Mailing Add:* RR 1 College Corner OH 45003

SHERBA, JOHN
VIOLIN

b Milwaukee, Wis, Dec 10, 54. *Study:* Univ Wis, Milwaukee, with F D'Albert, Samuel Magad & Leonard Sorkin. *Pos:* Second violin, Kronos String Quartet, 78- *Bibliog:* Paul Hertelendy (auth), The Kronos Quartet: Displaying a California Style, Musical Am, 10/80; Wolfgang Schreiber (auth), Die Entdeckerlust, Suddeutsche Zeitung, 3/13-14/83; Tom O'Connor (auth), String Fever, Focus Mag, 4/83. *Mailing Add:* Kronos Quartet 1238-Ninth Ave San Francisco CA 94122

SHERE, CHARLES EVERETT
COMPOSER, CRITIC-WRITER

b Berkeley, Calif, Aug 20, 35. *Study:* Univ Calif, Berkeley, AB, 60; studied comp with Robert Erickson, 62-64. *Works:* Small Concerto (piano & orch), Cabrillo Fest, 65; From Calls and Singing, comn by San Francisco Chamber Orch, 68; Tongues, comn by Arch Ens, 78; String Quartet, Kronos Quartet, 80; The Box of 1914, San Francisco Univ, 81; Handler of Gravity, St Mary's Cathedral, San Francisco, 82; Nightmusic, Oakland Symph Youth Orch, 82. *Pos:* Music dir, KPFA-fm, Berkeley, Calif, 64-67; producer, dir & critic, KQED-tv, San Francisco, 67-73; art & music critic, Oakland Tribune, Calif, 72- *Teaching:* Lectr music hist, Mills Col, 72- *Awards:* Comp fel, Nat Endowment Arts, 78. *Mem:* Music Critics Asn; BMI. *Publ:* Auth, Robert Ashley's Perfect Lives, New Perf, 82; Satie and Varese & US Avant-garde Music After the War, In: Universal History of Music, 82. *Mailing Add:* 1824 Curtis St Berkeley CA 94702

SHERMAN, INGRID KUGELMANN
COMPOSER

b Cologne on Rhine, Germany, June 25, 19; US citizen. *Study:* Piano lessons with private teachers; 20 Hon Dr from cols & univ in US & abroad. *Works:* I Worship Thee, Lord I Am Asking You, Color Harmony, I Walk The Earth, A Million Songs, Pathway To Light, Wake Up & You Are An Angel, Peace of Mind Studio, 72. *Pos:* Secy, Famous Operatic Singers, 59-65. *Mem:* ASCAP. *Mailing Add:* 102 Courter Ave Yonkers NY 10705

SHERMAN, NORMAN MORRIS
COMPOSER, BASSOON

b Boston, Mass, Feb 25, 28. *Study:* Boston Univ, BM, 49; Consv Nat Paris, 50. *Works:* Two Pieces for Orchestra, perf by The Hague Phil Orch, 65; Through the Rainbow, perf by Rotterdam Phil Orch, 67; Toccata for Piano, Berando, 70; Quadron (string quartet), 78 & Quintessant (wind quintet), 82, Caveat; Entretien (flute & bassoon), 83 & Children's Drawings (piano), 83, Berando. *Pos:* Solo bassoonist, Winnipeg Symph Orch, 57-61 & Residentie Orkest, The Hague, Holland, 61-69. *Teaching:* Instr orch, Queen's Univ, Kingston, Ont, 74- *Mem:* Canadian League Comp. *Rep:* E C Kerby Ltd 198 Davenport Rd Toronto ONT M5R 1J2. *Mailing Add:* 38 Woodstone Kingston ON K7M 6K9 Canada

SHERMAN, ROBERT
COMPOSER

b Mich, Jan 17, 21. *Study:* Mich State Univ, with H Owen Reed; Eastman Sch Music, with Bernard Rogers. *Works:* Dichromes (trumpet & cello); Wind Quintet; Ages of Man (ballet); Septet for Woodwind Trio & String Quartet; Quintet for Clarinet and Strings; 13 Additional Ways of Looking at a Blackbird (sop & piano); Tenor Saxophone Sonata; and others. *Teaching:* Prof & head dept music, Ball State Univ, 68- *Mailing Add:* Music Dept Ball State Univ Muncie IN 47306

SHERMAN, RUSSELL
EDUCATOR, PIANO

Study: Columbia Univ, BA; studied piano with Edward Steuermann & comp with Erich Itor Kahn. *Rec Perf:* On Advent, Sine Qua Non, Vanguard & Pro Arte. *Pos:* Soloist, New York Phil, Los Angeles Phil, Boston Symph Orch, Detroit Symph & many others; recitalist throughout US, Europe & South Am. *Teaching:* Mem fac, Pomona Col, formerly & Univ Ariz, formerly; mem fac piano, New England Consv Music, currently. *Rep:* Colbert Artists Mgt Inc 111 W 57th St New York NY 10019. *Mailing Add:* New England Consv Music 290 Huntington Rd Boston MA 02115

SHERR, RICHARD JONATHAN
EDUCATOR, WRITER

b New York, NY, Mar 25, 47. *Study:* Columbia Univ, BA, 69; Princeton Univ, MFA, 71, PhD(musicol), 75. *Teaching:* Lectr music, Univ Calif, Los Angeles, 73-74; vis lectr, Univ Wis, Madison, 74-75; asst prof music, Smith Col, 75-80, assoc prof, 80- *Mem:* Am Musicol Soc; Renaissance Soc Am; Int Musicol Soc. *Interests:* Music and musicians in Rome in the late 15th and early 16th centuries; music in Mantua in the late 16th century; Arthur Sullivan and popular music of the 19th century. *Publ:* Auth, The Publications of Gugliemo Gonzaga, J Am Musicol Soc, 78; From the Diary of a 16th Century Papal Singer, Current Musicol, 78; ed, Bertrandi Vaqueras: Opera Omnia, Hanssler Verlag, 79; auth, Gugliemo Gonzaga and the Castrati, Renaissance Quart, 80; Schubert, Sullivan and Grove, Musical Times, 80. *Mailing Add:* Dept Music Smith Col Northampton MA 01063

SHIELDS, ALICE F
COMPOSER, SINGER

b New York, NY, Feb 18, 43. *Study:* Columbia-Princeton Electronic Music Ctr, studied comp with Vladimir Ussachevsky & Otto Luening; Columbia Univ, with Jack Beeson & Chou Wen-chung, BS(music), MA(comp), DMA, 75. *Works:* Spring Music (sop, trumpet & oboe), 67; Barabbas (incidental music), 68; Study for Voice and Tape, 69; Egyptian Book of the Dead (electronic), 70; The Transformation of Ani (tape piece for manipulated voice), 70; Odyssey (one act opera, two soloists, male chorus & chamber orch), 75; Shaman (full length opera, live singers, amplified chamber orch & tape), 78. *Pos:* Mem staff, Columbia-Princeton Electronic Music Ctr, 65-, assoc dir, 76-; singer, Metropolitan Opera, formerly, Lake George Opera Fest, formerly & New York City Opera, 76-77. *Awards:* Nat Opera Inst Grant, 75; NY Coun Arts Grant, 75; Nat Endowment Arts Grant, 76 & 78. *Mailing Add:* 7 W 96th St Apt 11D New York NY 10025

SHIFRIN, DAVID
CLARINET, EDUCATOR

Rec Perf: Clarinet Recitals, Advent Rec; Etler's Concerto, Michigan; Mozart Trio & Schubert Shepherd on The Rock, Chamber Music Northwest Collector's Series; Twentieth Century Classics for Clarinet & Piano, Univ Mich Rec; Duet Concerto (R Strauss), Contrasts (Bartok) & Clarinet Chamber Music of von Weber, Nonesuch. *Pos:* Guest soloist, Philadelphia Orch, Pittsburgh Symph, Bavarian & Berlin Radio Orch, l'Orch Suisse Romande & Los Angeles Chamber Orch, currently; chamber music soloist, with Curtis, Philadelphia, Int, Guarneri, Sequoia & New World String Quartets, Chamber Music Soc Lincoln Ctr, Tokyo Quartet, Mostly Mozart Fest & New York Phil, currently; prin clarinetist, several orch incl Am Symph, Cleveland Orch, Dallas Symph & Honolulu Symph, formerly & Los Angeles Chamber Orch, currently; music dir, Chamber Music Northwest, Portland, currently. *Teaching:* Fac mem, Univ Hawaii, Cleveland Inst Music, Blossom Fest Sch, Kent State Univ & Univ Mich, formerly; prof, Univ Southern Calif, currently. *Awards:* Top hon, Int Compt, Munich, 77. *Mailing Add:* c/o Am Artists 275 Madison Ave New York NY 10016

SHIMADA, TOSHIYUKI
CONDUCTOR, MUSIC DIRECTOR
b Tokyo, Japan, Dec 23, 51; US citizen. *Study:* Hochschule Musik & Darstellende Kunst, Vienna, Austria, 71-73; Calif State Univ, Northridge, BM, 77; studied with Hans Swarovsky. *Pos:* Music dir & cond, YMF Debut Orch, Los Angeles, Calif, 78-81; asst cond, Houston Symph Orch, 81- *Teaching:* Fac mem music, Rice Univ, 82- & music dir & cond Shepherd Symph Orch, 82- *Mailing Add:* Houston Symph Orch 615 Louisiana Houston TX 77002

SHIMETA, KATHLEEN MARIE
MEZZO-SOPRANO
b Milwaukee, Wis, Mar 8, 51. *Study:* St Cloud State Univ, BS, 74; Col Consv Music, Univ Cincinnati, MM, 79. *Roles:* Meg Page in Merry Wives of Windsor, 78; Third Lady in Magic Flute, Mannes Sch Mozart Fest, 82; Francisca in Maria Padilla, Long Island Opera Soc, 83. *Rep:* European Am Artists 27 Pine St New Canaan CT 06840. *Mailing Add:* 51-79 Codwise Pl Elmhurst NY 11373

SHINDLE, WILLIAM RICHARD
MUSICOLOGIST, EDUCATOR
b Van Orin, Ill, Nov 2, 30. *Study:* Ill Wesleyan Univ, MusB, 59; Ind Univ, MusM, 63, PhD, 70. *Teaching:* Instr & music librn, State Univ NY, Binghamton, 64-65; mem fac, Sch Music, Kent State Univ, 66-, assoc prof musicol, 72- *Mem:* Am Musicol Soc; Renaissance Soc Am. *Publ:* Contribr to New Grove Dict of Music & Musicians. *Mailing Add:* 2020 Hastings Kent OH 44240

SHINN, RANDALL ALAN
COMPOSER, EDUCATOR
b Clinton, Okla, Sept 28, 44. *Study:* Southwestern Okla State Univ, BA, 66; Univ Colo, MMus, 68; Univ Ill, DMA, 75. *Works:* Chamber Concerto, Am Comp Ens, Univ Ill, 75; Tokens, Music 70, 77; Two Still Lifes, Univ Miami Contemp Music Ens, 78; What is Beauty, Then?, Lawson-Gould, 79; Cummings Songs, Warren Hoffer, 80; Forgotten Letters (piano trio), Oriana Trio, 80; Reflections on Three English Folk Tunes, Ariz State Univ Orch, 82. *Teaching:* Asst prof, Univ New Orleans, 75-78; assoc prof, Ariz State Univ, 78- *Awards:* ASCAP Standard Awards, 78-82; Oriana Trio Int Comp Compt Spec Award, 80; Ariz Comn Arts Comp Fel, 83. *Mem:* ASCAP; Am Music Ctr; Cent Opera Serv. *Publ:* Auth, Ben Johnston's Fourth String Quartet, Perspectives New Music, 77. *Mailing Add:* 2105 De Palma Mesa AZ 85202

SHIREY, RONALD
CONDUCTOR, EDUCATOR
b Tulsa, Okla, Jan 18, 33. *Study:* Univ Tulsa, BMus, 55, MMus, 61; Univ Colo, studied with Jean Berger, summer 64; Ariz State Univ, studied with Doug McEwen & Ronald LoPresti, 75-76. *Pos:* Chorus dir, Dallas Symph Orch, 83- *Teaching:* Vocal music dir, Edison Jr-Sr High Sch, Tulsa, 57-61; dir choirs & vocal chmn, Del Mar Col, Tex, 61-70 & Eastern NMex Univ, 70-76; dir choral studies, Tex Christian Univ, 76- *Awards:* Distinguished Perf, Tex Music Educr Asn Conv, 79. *Mem:* Col Music Soc; Am Choral Dir Assoc; Tex Music Educr Asn; Tex Choral Dir Asn; Am Choral Found. *Mailing Add:* 6424 Wilton Ft Worth TX 76133

SHIRLEY, GEORGE IRVING
TENOR, EDUCATOR
b Indianapolis, Ind, Apr 18, 34. *Study:* Wayne State Univ, BS, 55; Wilberforce Univ, HDH, 67. *Rec Perf:* On RCA, Philips & Columbia. *Roles:* Eisenstein in Die Fledermaus, Turnau Opera Players, New York, 59; Don Jose in Carmen; Des Grieux in Manon; Elvino in La Sonnambula; Rodolfo in La Boheme; Count Almaviva in Il Barbiere di Siviglia; Tom Rakewell in The Rake's Progress; and many others. *Pos:* Lyr ten, Teatro Nouvo, Milan, 60, Teatro Pergola, Florence, 60, New England Opera Theatre, 61, Spring Opera San Francisco, 61, Fest Two Worlds, Spoleto, 61, Santa Fe Opera, 61, New York City Opera, 61, Metropolitan Opera Co, 61, Opera Soc Washington, 62, Teatro Colon, Buenos Aires, 64, La Scala, Milan, 65, Glyndebourne Fest, 66, Scottish Opera, 67, Royal Opera Covent Garden, 67, Amsterdam Fest, 75, Netherlands Opera, 76, Monte Carlo Opera, 76, San Francisco Opera, 77 & Chicago Lyr Opera, 77. *Teaching:* Mem fac, Staten Island Community Col; artist in res, Morgan State Col; prof, Univ Md, College Park, currently. *Awards:* Winner, Am Opera Auditions, 60, Il Concorso Musica & Danza, Italy, 60 & Metropolitan Opera Auditions, 61. *Mem:* Am Guild Musical Artists; Phi Mu Alpha. *Publ:* Contribr to Opera News. *Mailing Add:* Ann Summers Int Box 188 Sta A Toronto ON M5W 1B2 Canada

SHIRLEY, WAYNE D(OUGLAS)
LIBRARIAN
b Brooklyn, NY, Apr 28, 36. *Study:* Harvard Univ, AB, 57; Stanford Univ, MA, 60; Brandeis Univ, 63. *Pos:* Am ed, Repertoire Int Sources Musicale, Washington, DC, 63-65; ref librn, Music Div, Libr Cong, 65- *Mem:* Am Musicol Soc (chmn Capitol chap, 77-79); Music Libr Asn; Sonneck Soc. *Interests:* Twentieth century and American music. *Publ:* Coauth, North America, In: Music in the Modern Age, Praeger, 73; auth, Modern Music: An Analytic Index, Am Musicol Soc Press, 76; Bess, Serena and the Short Score of Porgy and Bess, Quart J Libr Cong, 81. *Mailing Add:* 500 Constitution Ave NE Washington DC 20002

SHKLAR, MINNA
VIOLA
b Toronto, Ont; US citizen. *Study:* Toronto Consv; New Sch Music, Philadelphia, Pa. *Pos:* Violist, Shklar Quartet, Toronto, New Chamber Orch, Philadelphia, Toronto Summer Symph, New Orleans Symph & Rochester Phil, currently. *Mailing Add:* Rochester Phil 14 Gibbs St Rochester NY 14604

SHORE, CLARE
COMPOSER, EDUCATOR
b Winston-Salem, NC, Dec 18, 54. *Study:* Wake Forest Univ, with Annette LeSiege, BA(comp), 76; Univ Colo, with Charles Eakin & Cecil Effinger MMus(comp), 77; Juilliard Sch, with David Diamond & Vincent Persichetti, currently. *Works:* Woodwind Quintet, 79, Sonata for Clarinet and Basson, 80, String Quartet No 1, 80 & Prelude and Variations, 81, Seesaw Music; July Remembrances, perf by Juilliard Chamber Orch, 81 & 82; Summer Symphony, comn by Queens Phil, 82; Work for Woodwind Quintet, comn by Sioux City Symph Woodwind Quintet, 83. *Teaching:* Inst theory & comp, Manhattan Sch Music, 81-82 & comp, 82- *Awards:* Irving Berlin Fel, Juilliard Sch, 81-82; Standard Award, ASCAP, 82-83; ASCAP Grant Young Comp Award, 83. *Bibliog:* Karen L List (auth), A Study of Women in the Creative Arts, Univ Conn, 82. *Mem:* ASCAP; Am Music Ctr; Int League Women Comp. *Mailing Add:* 38-25 Parsons Blvd Flushing NY 11354

SHOSTAC, DAVID
FLUTE, TEACHER-COACH
b Los Angeles, Calif. *Study:* Music Acad West, 60; Aspen Music Sch, 62; Berkshire Music Ctr, 63 & 64; Occidental Col, BA, 63; Juilliard Sch Music, with Julius Baker, MS, 65. *Rec Perf:* Inc (Terry Riley), Columbia Rec, 68; Love Letters (Martin Scot Kosins), Fantaisie Brillante (Carmen) & Variations Brillantes (Theobald Boehm), 78, Crystal Rec; The Six Brandenburg Concertos (Bach), Angel Rec, 80; Concerto da Camera (flute, English horn & strings), Nonesuch Rec, 81. *Pos:* Mem, Am Symph Orch, 64-65; prin flute, St Louis, Milwaukee & New Orleans Symph Orch, 65-73 & Los Angeles Chamber Orch, 75- *Teaching:* Prof flute, Univ Southern Calif, 73-75, Calif State Univ, Northridge, 77- & Calif Inst of Arts, 76-; artist & fac mem, Aspen Music Fest, 82- *Awards:* First Prize Winner, Coleman Chamber Music Compt, 61; Rockefeller grant, 61 & 67-68; William Schwann Award, 63 & Henry B Cabot Prize, 64, Berkshire Music Ctr. *Publ:* Contribr, Let's Play Flute (Learning Unlimited Audio-Visual Band Series), Charles E Merrill Publ Co, 70. *Mailing Add:* Dept Music Calif State Univ Northridge CA 91330

SHOTT, MICHAEL JOHN
EDUCATOR, COMPOSER
b Berlin, Ger, Apr 7, 28; US citizen. *Study:* Western Mich Univ, BMus, 54; Ind Univ, MMus, 60, PhD, 64. *Works:* Give and Take, Vol I & II, 76, Alone, 76, Galaxy Sonatina, 77, Duet Preludes, 79, Wookie Walk, 79, Nocturne, 79 & Trail Serenade, 80, Myklas Music Press. *Teaching:* Prof music, Northern Ariz Univ, 61- *Mem:* Music Teachers Nat Asn; Music Educr Nat Conf; Col Music Soc; Am Asn Univ Comp. *Publ:* Auth, Why Theory?, 82 & The Many Faces of 20th Century Music, 82, Ariz Music News. *Mailing Add:* 1105 E Ponderosa Pkwy #158 Flagstaff AZ 86001

SHOWELL, JEFFREY ADAMS
VIOLA, EDUCATOR
b Urbana, Ill, Aug 10, 52. *Study:* Stanford Univ, 70-72; Eastman Sch Music, BM, 74, MM, 76; Yale Univ, DMA, 82. *Pos:* Violist, Rymour Quartet, 72-78 & Grand Teton Fest, Wyo, 81; prin violist, Tucson Symph Orch, 82- *Teaching:* Instr, Col St Benedict, St Joseph, Minn, 78-80; asst prof, Univ Ariz, 80- *Mem:* Am String Teachers Asn (pres Ariz chap, 82-84). *Mailing Add:* 9391 Kayenta Dr Tucson AZ 85749

SHROEDER, LINDA ANN
VIOLIN
b Port Huron, Mich, Nov 4, 54. *Study:* Juilliard Sch, BMus(perf), 77. *Pos:* Mem, NJ Symph Orch, 77-78; mem violin sect, Nat Symph, currently. *Teaching:* Asst to Margaret Pardee, 76-77. *Awards:* Winner, Five Town's Music & Art Round, 73; Francis Goldstein Scholar, 75. *Mailing Add:* 4201 S 31st St Apt 826 Arlington VA 22206

SHRUDE, MARILYN
COMPOSER, PIANO
b Chicago, Ill, July 6, 46. *Study:* Alverno Col, BM, 69; Northwestern Univ, MM, 72. *Works:* Quartet for Saxophones, Southern, 72; Genesis: Notes to the Unborn, 75, Evolution V, 76, Arctic Desert, 79, Infinity, 81, Shadows and Dawning, 82 & Psalms for David, 83, Am Comp Alliance. *Pos:* Dir, New Music Fest, Bowling Green State Univ, 82- *Teaching:* Instr comp, Bowling Green State Univ, 77- *Awards:* Northwestern Univ Faricy Award, 77; Ohio Arts Coun Artist Award, 80 & 82. *Mem:* Am Comp Alliance; BMI. *Mailing Add:* 823 Standish Dr Bowling Green OH 43402

SHULER, CRAIG
COMPOSER, EDUCATOR
b Pittsburgh, Pa. *Study:* Northwestern Univ; NTex State Univ, BM, 71; Juilliard Sch, MM, 73 & DMA, 78; studied comp with Luigi Dallapiccola, Elliott Carter & Roger Sessions & cond with John Nelson. *Works:* Spring Song (sop, violin & piano), 73; A Celestial Cantata, 75; A Promise, 75 & Awakening—A Sinfonietta, 76, comn by Am Ballet Theater; Leitmotif, perf by Ballet of 20th Century, 76; Vista (sextet for winds & vibraphone), perf by Dorian Wind Quintet, 79; Ulysses (dramatic cantata for sop & chamber orch), comn by David Russell Galleries, 80; Double Concerto (piccolo trumpet & English horn), comn by Lehigh Valley Chamber Orch, 82. *Pos:* Accmp for Stanley Williams, Sch Am Ballet, 73 & Jose Limon Sch Dance, 75; cond & musical dir, Hunterdon Symph Orch, Flemington, NJ, 82- *Teaching:* Mem fac dance, Juilliard Sch, 74-, mem fac pre-col div, 77-; vis asst prof, Moravian Col, 80- *Awards:* MacDowell Col Fel, 73 & 76; Fulbright Award, 74; Prince Pierre of Monaco Comp Award, 75. *Mailing Add:* Juilliard Sch Lincoln Ctr New York NY 10023

SHULMAN, IVAN ALEXANDER
ADMINISTRATOR, OBOE
b New York, NY, Feb 18, 48. *Study:* City Col New York, BS, 68; Univ Pittsburgh, MD, 72. *Pos:* Oboist, Los Angeles Phil, 79-, tour physician, 81-; prin oboe, Los Angeles Doctor's Symph Orch, 79-, pres, 81- *Publ:* Auth, Turista and the Los Angeles Philharmonic, Western J Medicine, 82; English Horn Player's Thumb, J Hand Surgery, 82. *Mailing Add:* 1568 Michael Lane Pacific Palisades CA 90272

SHULTZ, DAN MCLLOYD
EDUCATOR, OBOE
b Bradford, Pa, Apr 8, 38. *Study:* Atlantic Union Col, BS, 62; Andrews Univ, MMus, 67. *Works:* Cantus Spiritus, Union Col Band, 75; Two Psalms for Unaccompanied Oboe, perf by comp, 77; Trilogy, Walla Walla Col Band, 83. *Teaching:* Chmn, Music Dept, Union Col, 68-79 & Walla Walla Col, 79- *Mailing Add:* Box 4B Rte 5 Walla Walla WA 99362

SHULZE, FREDERICK BENNETT
EDUCATOR, ORGAN
b Portland, Ore, Aug 25, 35. *Study:* Wheaton Col, Ill, studied comp with Jack Goode, BMus, 57; Northwestern Univ, studied organ with Barrett Spach, MMus, 63; Univ Wash, Seattle, studied organ with Walter A Eichinger, DMA, 70. *Works:* Music for Tape Recorder and Orchestra, perf by Taylor Univ Orch, 74; Evocation for Cello and Piano, perf by Shiela Ryan, 75; The Savior's Work (unaccmp anthem), perf by Taylor Univ Chorale, 75; Patriotic Songs for Band and Chorus, perf by Marion Col Band & Choir, 76; Three Sketches for Piano, perf by Marilyn Hall, 83; The Prayer of St Francis, perf by Taylor Univ Chorale, 83; Rejoice, Ye Pure in Heart (organ, brass choir & chorus), Taylor Oratorio Chorus, 83. *Pos:* Organist, First Presby Church, Seattle, Wash, 69-70 & First Baptist Church, Muncie, Ind, 71- *Teaching:* Asst prof music, Cascade Col, 59-68; prof, Taylor Univ, 70- *Mem:* Am Guild Organists; Am Soc Univ Comp; Am Musicol Soc; Music Libr Asn; Nat Asn Comp. *Mailing Add:* Dept of Music Taylor Univ Upland IN 46989

SHUMWAY, LARRY VEE
EDUCATOR
b Winslow, Ariz, Nov 25, 34. *Study:* Brigham Young Univ, BA(music educ) 60; Seton Hall Univ, MA, 64; Univ Wash, PhD(ethnomusicol), 74. *Teaching:* Assoc prof, Brigham Young Univ, 74- *Mem:* Soc Ethnomusicol; Soc Asian Music. *Publ:* Auth, Kibigaku: A Modern Japanese Ritual Music, Western Conf Asn Asian Studies, 76; coauth, The History and Performance Style of J W Spangler, JEMQ Quart, 78; auth, When is Fiddling Fiddling and When Does It Become Something Else? Southwest Folklore, 80; The Tongan Lakalaka, I & II Documentaries (film), Brigham Young Univ, Hawaii, 81; The Tongan Lakalaka: Music Composition and Style, Ethnomusicol, 81. *Mailing Add:* 749 E 2550 N Provo UT 84604

SHUMWAY, STANLEY NEWMYER
ADMINISTRATOR, EDUCATOR
b Omaha, Nebr, Feb 19, 32. *Study:* Univ Nebr, BMus, 54, MMus, 55; Eastman Sch Music, PhD, 63. *Works:* Six-Piece Set (piano), 71 & 83; Airs and Cadenzas (perc ens & magnetic tape), 73; Two Novelettes (piano & synthesizer), 74 & 78; Spells (violin & magnetic tape), 75; O Tempora (organ), 76; Capriccio on Five Notes (viola & tape), 79, 80 & 82. *Teaching:* Instr music, Midland Col, 57-59; instr music theory, Univ Kans, 61-63, asst prof, 63-68, assoc prof, 68-73, prof, 73-, chmn dept music, 82-; dir grad studies, Sch Fine Arts, Ft Wayne Art Inst, Ind, 75-80. *Publ:* Auth, Extending Diatonic Resources, Kans Music Rev, 68; Harmony and Ear-Training at the Keyboard, 70, William C Brown Co, 2nd ed, 76, 3rd ed, 80, 4th ed (in prep); coauth (with Jan Shumway), Sound, Symbol, Keyboard J, 79. *Mailing Add:* Dept Music Univ Kans Lawrence KS 66045

SHURE, LEONARD
PIANO, EDUCATOR
Study: Hochscule Musik, Berlin, dipl; studied piano with Artur Schnabel. *Rec Perf:* On Audiofon. *Pos:* Soloist, New York Phil, Cleveland Orch, Boston Symph Orch, Detroit Symph, St Louis Symph, Pittsburgh Symph & many others; dir, Chamber Music on Nantucket, currently. *Teaching:* Master classes, Aspen Music Fest, formerly, Eastman Sch Music, formerly & Rubin Acad Music, Jerusalem, formerly; lectr & guest prof, Western Reserve Univ, formerly, Hochschule Musick, Zurich, formerly & Univ Calif, formerly; mem fac, Boston Univ, formerly, Longy Sch Music, formerly, Mannes Sch Music, formerly, Cleveland Inst Music, formerly & Univ Tex, formerly; mem fac piano & chamber music, New England Consv Music, currently. *Mailing Add:* New England Consv Music 290 Huntington Rd Boston MA 02115

SHURE, PAUL CRANE
VIOLIN, TEACHER
b Chicago, Ill, Sept 20, 21. *Study:* Curtis Inst Music, BMus, 41. *Pos:* Concertmaster, All-Am Orch, 39-41, Hollywood Bowl Symph, 45, Los Angeles Chamber Orch, 73- & Pasadena Symph, 74-; mem, Hollywood String Quartet, 47-59; leader, Oberlin String Quartet, 59-61 & Los Angeles String Quartet, 63- *Teaching:* Prof violin & chamber music, Consv Music, Oberlin Col, 59-61. *Mailing Add:* 1702 Alta Mura Rd Pacific Palisades CA 90272

SHURTLEFF, LYNN RICHARD
MUSIC DIRECTOR, COMPOSER
b Vallejo, Calif, Nov 3, 39. *Study:* Brigham Young Univ, BA, 63, MA, 65. *Works:* Dialogues for Chamber Orchestra, 68 & Charlie Brown Suite, 69, Amici Della Musica Orch; For the First Manned Moon Orbit, NBC News Spec, 69; O Be Joyful, San Jose, Calif, 72; Sing a New Song to the Lord, Santa

Clara Chorale, 74; Spectrum, San Jose Symph Youth Orch, 78; Echoes from Hungry Mountain, Mark Foster Publ, 79. *Rec Perf:* Poulenc Organ Concerto, Orion Rec, 80. *Pos:* Music dir, Santa Clara Chorale, 69- *Teaching:* Assoc prof music theory & comp, Univ Santa Clara, 66-, chmn music dept, 78- *Awards:* Ferdinand Grossman Fel, Inst European Studies, 71. *Mem:* Am Choral Dir Asn; Col Music Soc. *Mailing Add:* Music Dept Univ Santa Clara Santa Clara CA 95053

SHWAYDER, JOANN FREEMAN See Freeman, Joann

SIDER, RONALD RAY
EDUCATOR, CONDUCTOR
Eastman Sch Music, Univ Rochester, BMus, 57, MMus, 59, PhD, 67; Am Guild Organists, AAGO, 63. *Works:* God of Our Fathers, Stone Chapel Press, 70; Once in Royal David's City, Music to Publ, 74; Jesus Lives, Broadman Press, 75; Child in the Manger, 75, In Heavenly Love, 81, Music to Publ; Children of the Heavenly Father, Plymouth Music Co, 83. *Pos:* Cond, Grantham Oratorio Soc, Pa, 67-; organist & dir, Grace Methodist Church, Harrisburg, Pa, 73- *Teaching:* Prof music, Messiah Col, 58- *Mem:* Am Choral Dir Asn; Asn Prof Vocal Ens; Am Guild Organists (mem bd dir, Harrisburg chap, 70-); Presby Asn Musicians; Fel United Methodist Musicians. *Interests:* Music of Central America. *Publ:* Auth, Roque Cordero, The Composer & His Style, 9/67 & Central America & Its Composers, 5/70, InterAm Music Bulletin; Historical Perspectives on Church Music, Evangelical Vis, 10/70; Art Music in Central America, Revista Rev InterAm, 78. *Mailing Add:* RD 3 Dillsburg PA 17019

SIDLIN, MURRY
CONDUCTOR & MUSIC DIRECTOR
Pos: Music dir, New Haven Symph, Calif, currently & Long Beach Symph, Calif, currently; res cond, Nat Symph, formerly & Aspen Music Fest, currently; asst cond Baltimore Symph, formerly; guest cond, St Louis Symph, Boston Pops, Pittsburgh Symph, Milwaukee Symph, Atlanta Symph, Omaha Symph, San Diego Symph, Portland Symph, Miami Symph, NJ Symph, Quebec Symph & San Antonio Orch & Opera. *Mailing Add:* Long Beach Symph 121 Linden Ave Long Beach CA 90802

SIDNELL, ROBERT G
ADMINISTRATOR, EDUCATOR
b Cleveland, Ohio, Aug 21, 28. *Study:* Ohio Wesleyan Univ, BM, 52; Columbia Univ, MA, 55; Univ Tex, Austin, PhD, 60. *Teaching:* Prof music, Mich State Univ, 60-78; dean sch fine arts, Stephen F Austin State Univ, 78-81. *Mem:* Col Music Soc; Music Educr Nat Conf; Phi Mu Alpha; Pi Kappa Lambda. *Publ:* Auth, Developing Instruction Programs in Music, Prentice-Hall, 72; coauth, Materials of Music Composition, Addison-Wesley, 78-80. *Mailing Add:* PO Box 13022 SFA Sta Nacogdoches TX 75962

SIDOTI, RAYMOND B
VIOLIN, EDUCATOR
b Cleveland, Ohio. *Study:* Cleveland Inst Music, studied violin with Joseph Knitzer, BMus, 51, MMus, 54; St Cecilia, Rome, studied violin with Pina Carmirelli, 57 & 58; Ohio State Univ, studied violin with Robert Gerle, DMA, 72. *Pos:* Concert violinist, soloist, Duo Sidoti & Sidoti Trio, 57-; concertmaster, Rome Fest Orch, 73, 76 & 77; first violinist, Shiras String Quartet, 73-75 & Capital Univ String Quartet, 79-82. *Teaching:* Asst prof violin & viola, Baylor Univ, 72-73 & Northern Mich Univ, 73-75; mem fac violin, Rome Fest Inst, 73, 76 & 77; mem fac violin & chamber music, Stephens Col, 75-79; assoc prof violin & viola, Capital Univ, 79-82; assoc prof violin & viola & orch cond, Augustana Col, SDak, 82- *Awards:* Fulbright Award Rome, 57 & 58; US Dept State Cult Presentations Prog Awards, 60, 63, 65 & 67. *Mem:* Am Fedn Musicians; Am String Teachers Asn; Col Music Soc. *Mailing Add:* Dept Music Augustana Col 29th & S Summit Sioux Falls SD 57197

SIEBERT, FREDERICK MARK
EDUCATOR, ORGAN
b Brooklyn, NY, Dec 16, 26. *Study:* Columbia Univ, AB, 48, MA, 50, PhD(musicol), 61. *Pos:* Organist & choirmaster, St Paul's Cathedral, Springfield, Ill. *Teaching:* Instr music, Columbia Univ, 54-61; asst prof musicol, Univ Ill, Urbana, 61-64; asst prof hist & lit music, Oberlin Col Consv, 64-68; assoc prof arts & lett, Nasson Col, 68-70; assoc prof, Sangamon State Univ, 70-75, prof music, 75- *Mem:* Am Musicol Soc; Int Musicol Soc; Am Guild Organists; Am Recorder Soc. *Interests:* Fifteenth-century organ music; activities of the encyclopedists in music theory; eighteenth century French tuning practice. *Publ:* Auth, Mass Sections in the Buxheim Organ Book: A Few Points, Musical Quart, 7/64; Performance Problems in Fifteenth Century Organ Music, Organ Inst Quart, Vol X, No 2; Buxtehude, Frescobaldi, Fux, Froberger, Hofhaimer, Merulo & Sweelinck, In: Encyclopedia of World Biographies, McGraw. *Mailing Add:* Dept Creative Arts Sangamon State Univ Shepherd Rd Springfield IL 62708

SIEGEL, BERT (BERTON EARL)
VIOLIN, TEACHER
b Chicago, Ill, Aug 8, 25. *Study:* Am Consv Music, Roosevelt Univ, DePaul Univ & private study, 34-51. *Pos:* Asst prin second violin, New Orleans Phil Symph, 52-54; concertmaster, Orquesta Sinfonica Antiogia & Radio Orch, La Voz de Antiogia, Medellin, Colombia, 54-55; violinist first sect, St Louis Symph, 55-60 & Cleveland Orch, 65-; asst concertmaster, Pittsburgh Symph, 60-65. *Teaching:* Instr violin, Cleveland Music Sch Settlement, 75- *Mem:* Int Conf Symph & Opera Musicians (vchmn, 74-80); Am Fedn Musicians. *Mailing Add:* 3167 Chelsea Dr Cleveland OH 44118

SIEGEL, CLARA See Ehrlich, Clara Siegel

SIEGEL, JEFFREY
PIANO
b Chicago, Ill, Nov 18, 42. *Study:* Chicago Musical Col; Juilliard, DMA, 70; Nat Col Educ, Evanston, Ill, Hon Dr, 74. *Rec Perf:* Dutilleux, Orion Rec, 72; Gershwin Complete Works (piano & orch), Vox Rec, 74; Rachmaninoff, Nippon Columbia, 78. *Pos:* Piano soloist with major orchestras in New York, London, Amsterdam, Boston, Berlin, Philadelphia, Chicago & Cleveland, currently. *Mailing Add:* c/o Columbia Artists Mgt 119 W 57th St New York NY 10019

SIEGEL, LAURENCE
CONDUCTOR
b Bronx, NY, July 23, 31. *Study:* City Col New York, BA, 53; Berkshire Music Ctr, 53 & 55; New England Consv Music, MM, 55. *Rec Perf:* Tschaikowsky, Audio Team Hamburg, Germany, 80, Nautilus Rec, 82 & Sony Rec, Japan, 83. *Pos:* Prin cond, Manila Phil, 61-63; music dir, Manila Opera Co, 61-63; North Miami Beach Symph & Opera Co, currently; dir, Northern Consv Music, formerly. *Teaching:* Asst prof music, Unity Col, 65-75; instr, Colby Col, 68-69. *Mem:* Am Fedn Musicians. *Mailing Add:* c/o Warden Assoc Ltd 45 W 60th St Suite 4K New York NY 10023

SIEGMANN, MARGARET KRIMSKY See Krimsky, Katrina

SIEGMEISTER, ELIE
COMPOSER, WRITER
b New York, NY, Jan 15, 09. *Study:* Columbia Col, BA, 27; Ecole Normale Musique, dipl, 31; Juilliard Sch, 38. *Works:* Western Suite, perf by Arturo Toscanini & NBC Symph, 45; Symphony No 1, perf by New York Phil, 47; Plough & the Stars (opera), perf by Grand Theatre, Bordeaux, France, 70; Symphony No 4, perf by Cleveland Orch, 73; Symphony No 3, Carl Fischer, 75; Symphony No 5, comn & perf by Baltimore Symph, 77; Shadows and Light, Carl Fischer, 77. *Pos:* Cond, Hofstra Symph, 50-66. *Awards:* Nat Endowment Arts Fel, 74 & 80; Guggenheim Fel, 79; Am Acad Arts & Lett Award, 79. *Bibliog:* Jack Gallagher (auth), Siegmeister's 2nd, 3rd, 4th Symphonies, Cornell Univ, 82. *Mem:* Am Music Ctr (vpres, 60-65); Coun Creative Artists, Libr, Museums (chmn, 70-); ASCAP (mem bd dir, 77-); Meet the Comp; CRI. *Rep:* Carl Fischer 56 Cooper Square New York NY 10003. *Mailing Add:* 56 Fairview Ave Great Neck NY 11023

SIEKMANN, FRANK H
COMPOSER, CONDUCTOR
b Staten Island, NY, June 20, 25. *Study:* NY Univ, BS, 48, MA, 49; Teachers Col, Columbia Univ, EdD, 55. *Works:* Discourse for Brass, Seesaw, 75; Reflections (trumpet solo), Pro Art, 76; Christmas Montage, LiDeb Co Publ, 77; Scene in Monochrome (string orch), Elizabethtown Col, 77; Descriptive Piece for Mime or Dance (woodwing quintet), Seesaw, 78; Concerto for Trombone, Reading Symph Orch, 79; On the Rocks (musical theatre), Pa State Univ, 80. *Pos:* Dir univ band, Univ Vt, 64-65; first trumpet, Reading Pops Orch, 68-; dir choirs, St John's, 72-; mem bd dir, Reading Pops Orch, 69- & Reading Symph Orch, 75- *Teaching:* Inst vocal & instrm, Smyrna, Del, Ramsey, NJ & Chappaqua, NY, 49-64; asst prof music, Univ Vt, 64-65; prof, Kutztown State Col, 66-, cond col orch, 66-80. *Awards:* Award for Exceptional Acad Serv, Kutztown State Col & Commonwealth Pa, 80. *Mem:* Am Socs Univ Comp; ASCAP; Music Educr Nat Conf. *Interests:* Music curriculum development. *Publ:* Auth, Solo and Ensemble Festival, Instrumentalist, 62 & Conn Chord, 62; The Professional Jazz Combo in the School Assembly, Int Musician, 63; The Uses of the Accordion in School Music, Accordion World, 64. *Mailing Add:* Box 352 Rd #3 Kutztown PA 19530

SIENA, JEROLD
TENOR, EDUCATOR
b Cincinnati, Ohio, Feb 18, 39. *Study:* Cleveland Inst Music, 55-56; Mannes Col Music, 56-59; Accad Santa Cecilia, 60-61. *Rec Perf:* The Play of Daniel, Decca Rec, 58; Lucia di Lammermoor, NBC, 63; Oleum Canis, Serenus Rec, 75; The Ballad of Baby Doe, PBS, 76; The Consul, PBS, 77. *Roles:* Don Ottavio in Don Giovanni, Stratford Opera, Ont, 71; Pedrillo in Serail, Boston Symph, 72; Almaviva in Barber of Seville, Baltimore Opera, 73; First Jew in Salome, Metropolitan Opera, 76; Steuermann in Flying Dutchman, New York City Opera, 76; Nick in Fanciulla del West, Philadelphia Opera Co, 81; Le Petit Viellard in Ravel, Pittsburgh Symph, 82. *Teaching:* Prof voice, hist opera & stage dir, Univ Ariz, 79- *Mem:* Nat Asn Teachers Singing (vpres Tuscon chap, currently); Am Guild Musical Artists (mem bd gov, 75-77). *Rep:* Lew & Benson Moreau-Neret Inc 204 W 10 St New York NY 10014. *Mailing Add:* 7339 N Yucca Via Tucson AZ 85704

SIERRA, ROBERTO
COMPOSER
b Vega Baja, PR, Oct 9, 53. *Study:* Univ PR, BA, 75; Royal Col Music, London Univ, MMus, 78; Hochschule Musik, Hamburg, studied with György Ligeti, 79-82. *Works:* El Jardin de las Delicias, PR Symph Orch, 76; Central Park, Nederland Dans Theater, 79; Polarizaciones, Casals Fest Orch, 80; Alucinaciones, Hitzacker Music Fest, WGermany, 82; Tres Miniaturas, Edward Parmentier, Robert Conant & E Nordwall, 83; Bongo-0 for Solo Percussion, Fest New Music, Bonn & Sonorities Fest, England, 83; Cantos Populares, Huddersfield Fest, England, 83. *Pos:* Asst dir, Cult Activ Dept, Univ PR, 83-; music critic. *Awards:* Cobbett Prize, Royal Col Music, London, 77; Hitzacker Music Prize, 82; Int Comp Prize, Spring Fest Budapest, 83. *Publ:* Auth, ¿Existe la Musica Puertorriquena?, El Nuevo Dia News Paper, 80; From the Ritual Music of Africa to Salsa, Neuland Cologne, WGermany, 83; Salsa Para Vientos, Editio Musica Budapest, 83. *Mailing Add:* Lince 838 Dos Pinos Rio Piedras PR 00923

SIFLER, PAUL JOHN
COMPOSER, ORGAN
b Ljubljana, Yugoslavia, Dec 31, 11; US citizen. *Study:* Chicago Consv, BMus, 39, MMus, 40; studied comp with Leo Sowerby, organ with Clair Coci. *Works:* Mass for Marimba and Chorus, 69 & The Nine Suitors, 72, Fredonia Press; The Despair and Agony of Dachau (organ), 75 & Psalm 98, 76, H W Gray; Recitative, Passacaglia and Fugue (organ), Fredonia Press, 78; The Seven Last Words of Christ (Organ), H W Gray, 79; In the Days of Herod the King (oratorio), 83 & Hymnus—Five Volumes of Organ Work, 83, Fredonia Press. *Rec Perf:* Merimba Suite, WIM Rec, 71; Yugoslav Folk and Art Songs, Fredonia Discs, 77; The Despair and Agony of Dachau, Vista Rec, 78; Adventures in Organ Music, 79, Teaching Pieces, 80, The Last Words of Christ, 81 & Yuletide and Birds, 82, Fredonia Discs; Marimba Suite 72, WIM Rec. *Pos:* Choirmaster & organist, Ft Washington Presby Church, NY, 46-49; cond, Yugoslav Choral Soc, NY, 46-60; organist, St Paul's Chapel, NY, 52-53; choirmaster & organist, Christ Church, Oyster Bay, NY, 54-65; choir master & organist, St Thomas Church, Hollywood, Calif, 66- *Mem:* ASCAP; Am Guild Organists; Soc Comp Slovenes. *Mailing Add:* 3947 Fredonia Dr Hollywood CA 90068

SIKI, BELA
PIANO
b Budapest, Hungary, Feb 21, 23; US citizen. *Study:* Franz Liszt Acad, Budapest, artist dipl, 45; Consv Geneve, prix virtuosite, 48. *Rec Perf:* Four Scherzi (Chopin), 55 & Four Balades (Chopin), 55, Parlophone; Sonata Op 110 & 111 (Beethoven), Columbia, 55; Sonata (Liszt) & Etudes (Paganini), Pye, 59; Concerto No 2 (Liszt) & Concerto No 3 (Bartok), Pro Arte, 59; Concerzo (Suderburg), Columbia-Odyssee, 75; Variations on a Nursery Rhyme (Dohnanyi), Vox, 76. *Teaching:* Prof, Univ Washington, 65-80; prof & artist in res, Col Consv Music, Univ Cincinnati, 80-; instr masterclasses, Toho Gakuen, Tokyo, Sch Fine Arts, Banff Centre & Johannesen Int Sch Arts, currently. *Awards:* First Prize, Franz Liszt Compt, 43 & Concours Int, Geneve, 48. *Publ:* Coauth, In Memoriam Dinu Lipatti, Labor & Fides, 51, 70; auth, Piano Repertoire, Schirmer Bks, 81. *Rep:* Nat Serv Bureau 2216 Bedford Terr Cincinnati OH 45208. *Mailing Add:* 3532 Traskwood Circle Cincinnati OH 45208

SILBERMAN, AARON
PATRON, CLARINET
Study: City Col New York. *Pos:* Mem bd dir, Baruch Col, City Univ New York, currently; sponsor, Adventures in Good Music, WQED-FM, currently; contribr, Sch Music, Univ Pittsburgh, Duquesne Univ, Carnegie-Mellon Univ & Carlow Col, currently; fund clarinet scholar, Jewish Community Ctr, currently; contribr, Pittsburgh Symph Orch, McKeesport Symph Soc, New Pittsburgh Chamber Orch, Pittsburgh New Music Ens Inc, River City Brass Band, Am Wind Symph Orch, East Winds Symph Band, Bach Choir & Friends Music Libr, currently; dir, Anna Perlow Sch Music, Jewish Community Ctr, currently; patron, Pittsburgh Symph Orch. *Mem:* ClariNetwork Inc (finance chmn, currently); Y-Music Soc (mem bd, currently); Pittsburgh Chamber Music Soc (mem bd, currently). *Mailing Add:* 622 Second Ave Pittsburgh PA 15217

SILBIGER, ALEXANDER
EDUCATOR, WRITER
b Rotterdam, Netherlands, May 14, 35; US citizen. *Study:* Univ Chicago, MS, 56; Columbia Univ, PhD, 61; Brandeis Univ, PhD, 76. *Teaching:* Instr, Longy Sch Music, 62-72; lectr, Brandeis Univ, 72-74; asst prof, Sch Music, Univ Wis, 74-80, assoc prof, 80- *Awards:* Grants, Martha Baird Rockefeller Fund, 72-73 & Nat Endowment for Humanities, 77; fel, Am Coun Learned Soc, 78-79. *Mem:* Am Musicol Soc (chmn perf comt, 82-83); Col Music Soc; Viola da Gamba Soc Am. *Interests:* Seventeenth century German and Italian music. *Publ:* Auth, An Unknown Partbook of Early 16th Century Polyphony, Studi Musicali, 77; Italian Manuscript Sources of 17th Century Keyboard Music, UMI Res Press, 80; The Roman Frescobaldi Tradition: 1640-1670, 80 & Michelangelo Rossi and his Toccate Correnti, 83, J Am Musicol Soc; ed, Matthias Weckmann: Sacred Concertos, A-R Ed, 83. *Mailing Add:* Sch Music Univ Wis Madison WI 53706

SILFIES, GEORGE
EDUCATOR, CLARINET
Study: Curtis Inst Music, artist's dipl; studied clarinet with Ralph McLane, Joseph Gigliotti & Bernard Walton & piano with Vladimir Sokoloff. *Rec Perf:* On Vox. *Pos:* Asst prin clarinetist & pianist, Cleveland Orch, formerly; mem, US Navy Band, formerly; prin clarinet, Baltimore Symph Orch, formerly, Santa Fe Opera, formerly & New York City Opera, formerly; soloist, Cleveland Orch, formerly, Philadelphia Orch, formerly & Mozart Fest Orch, formerly; soloist, St Louis Symph Orch, formerly, prin clarinet Walter Susskind chair, currently, mem, Woodwind Quintet, currently. *Teaching:* Mem fac, Mich State Univ, formerly, Cleveland Inst Music, formerly, Peabody Consv Music, formerly & Nat Youth Orch Can, formerly; mem fac clarinet, chamber music & wind ens, St Louis Consv Music, currently. *Mailing Add:* St Louis Consv Music 560 Trinity Ave St Louis MO 63130

SILINI, FLORA CHIARAPPA
EDUCATOR, PIANO
b Meriden, Conn, May 29, 23. *Study:* Eastman Sch Music, BM(piano), 45; Colo Col & Eastman Sch Music, 45, 47 & 48; Ball State Univ, Muncie, Ind, MA(music), 67. *Pos:* Artist in res, Kans Asn Retarded Citizens, 79- *Teaching:* Instr piano, Ohio Univ, Athens, 45-50 & Ball State Univ, Muncie, Ind, 54-67; from asst prof to prof piano, Univ Kans, Lawrence, 67- *Awards:* Outstanding Educr Award, Mortar Board, 74-75; grant, Nat Comt Arts for Handicapped,

81-82. *Mem:* Music Teachers Nat Asn; Nat Conf Piano Pedagogy. *Interests:* All aspects of piano pedagogy, especially for college students and handicapped persons. *Publ:* Auth, Experiments in Group Piano, Am Music Teacher, 9-10/77; A Piano Course for Special Adults, Music Educr J, 2/79; Spontaneous Keyboard Skills, Am Music Teacher, 4-5/81; Experiencing Music With the Piano: A Methodology for Teaching the Handicapped, 82; Three Video Cassettes on Methodology for Teaching Mentally Handicapped, Nat Comt Arts for Handicapped, 82. *Mailing Add:* Sch Fine Arts Univ Kans Lawrence KS 66045

SILIPIGNI, ALFREDO
CONDUCTOR, DIRECTOR—OPERA
b Atlantic City, NJ, Apr 9, 31. *Study:* Westminster Choir Col, 48; Juilliard Sch Music, cond with Alberto Erede, 53; Kean Col, LHD, 78. *Rec Perf:* Maria Stuarda (Donizetti), 80; ZAZA (Leoncavallo) & Excerpts from Verdi Operas, Centra Rec. *Pos:* Cond, NBC Symph, formerly & San Remo Fest, currently; prin cond, Mex Nat Opera, formerly; organist & choir master, Chelsea Presby Church, Atlantic City, 46 & Calvary Baptist Church, New York, 58; founder & cond, Lauter Opera Theatre of Air, Newark, 51 & Suburban Concerts, NJ, 55; artistic dir & cond, Opera Theatre of NJ, 65-; guest cond, Vienna State Opera, 76, Gran Liceo di Barcelona, 76 & major opera co in Europe, Brit Isles & North & South Am. *Teaching:* Guest lectr, Glassboro State Col. *Awards:* Centennial Medallion, St Peters Col, 72; Distinguished Serv Cult Award, City San Remo, 72. *Rep:* Int Artists Mgt 111 W 57th St New York NY 10019. *Mailing Add:* NJ State Opera 1020 Broad St Newark NJ 07102

SILLS, BEVERLY (MRS PETER B GREENOUGH)
DIRECTOR—OPERA, COLORATURA SOPRANO
b Brooklyn, NY, May 25, 29. *Study:* Voice with Estelle Leibling, piano with Paolo Gallico & stagecraft with Desire Defrere; Harvard Univ, Hon DM; NY Univ, Hon DM; New England Consv, Hon DM; Temple Univ, Hon DM. *Rec Perf:* On Columbia, RCA, Angel & ABC-Audio Treasure. *Roles:* Michaela in Carmen, Philadelphia Civic Opera, 47; Helen of Troy in Mefistofele, San Francisco Opera, 53; Cleopatra in Giulio Cesare, New York City Opera, 66; Queen of the Night in Die Zauberflöte, Vienna Staatsoper, 67; Pamira in Le siege de Corinthe, La Scala, Milan, 69 & Metropolitan Opera, 75; Lucia in Lucia di Lammermoor, Royal Opera House, Covent Garden, 70; La Loca in La Loca, San Diego Opera, 79. *Pos:* Sop with maj opera co & orchs throughout US, Europe & South Am; res sop, New York City Opera, 55-80, dir, 79-; co-star TV spec, Look-in at the Met (with Danny Kaye), 75 & Sills & Burnett at the Met, 76, CBS-TV; consult to coun, Nat Endowment Arts; moderator & hostess, Lifestyles with Beverly Sills, NBC-TV, 76 & 77; hostess & commentator, Young Peoples' Concerts of New York Phil, CBS-TV, 77-; chmn bd, Nat Opera Inst, currently. *Awards:* Handel Medallion, 73; Emmy Awards for Profile in Music—Beverly Sills, 76 & for Lifestyles with Beverly Sills, 78; Gold Rec & Grammy Award for The Music of Victor Herbert, Angel Rec. *Bibliog:* J B Steane (auth), The Grand Tradition, London, 74. *Publ:* Auth, Bubbles: A Self-Portrait, 76. *Rep:* Ludwig Lustig Mgt 111 W 57th St New York NY 10019. *Mailing Add:* New York City Opera Lincoln Ctr New York NY 10023

SILSBEE, ANN LOOMIS
COMPOSER, PIANO
b Cambridge, Mass, Aug 21, 30. *Study:* Radcliffe Col, BA(theory), 57; Syracuse Univ, MM(piano), 69; Cornell Univ, DMA(comp), 79. *Works:* De Amore et Morte, 78 & Quartet, 80, Syracuse Soc for New Music. *Rec Perf:* Spirals (string quartet & piano), Boston Musica Viva, 75; Doors (piano), David Burze, 76; Dona Nobis Paciew, Albany Pro Musica, 81. *Pos:* Pianist, Gregg Smith Singers, 81-82. *Teaching:* Lectr piano, State Univ NY, Cortland, 70-71; lectr music theory, Cornell Univ, 71-73. *Mem:* Am Soc Univ Comp (regional co-chairperson, 79-81); Int League of Women Comp (mem exec bd, 80-); Am Comp Alliance (mem bd gov, 82-); BMI. *Mailing Add:* 915 Coddington Rd Ithaca NY 14850

SILVA, JESUS
GUITAR, COMPOSER
b Morelia, Mex. *Study:* Nat Consv Music, Mex. *Works:* Preludes (guitar), perf by John Patykula, 80; Preludes (guitar), perf by Robert Guthrie, 83. *Rec Perf:* Jesus Silva, Virtuoso de la Guitarra, RCA Victor, 65. *Teaching:* Prof, Nat Consv Music, 47-61; instr guitar, Brooklyn Music Sch, 62-65 & NC Sch Arts, 65-79; artist in res, Va Commonwealth Univ, 79-82. *Bibliog:* Raymond Niemi (auth), Teaching Techniques of Jesus Silva, Guitarra Mag, 11-12/79; C A Bustard (auth), Silva and His Orbit, Richmond Times Dispatch, 1/25/81; Francis Church (auth), Masters of the Guitar, Richmond New Leader, 10/9/82. *Mem:* Fel, Soc Class Guitar. *Mailing Add:* 1201 Byrd Ave #6 Richmond VA 23226

SILVER, MARTIN A
LIBRARIAN, FLUTE
b New York, NY, June 12, 33. *Study:* City Col New York, BA(music), 55; Staatliche Hochschule Musik, Stuttgart, Ger, 59-60; Sch Libr Sci, Columbia Univ, MLS, 64. *Pos:* Music Librn, New York Pub Libr, Music Circulation Dept, Lincoln Ctr, 64-65; music ref librn, Music Res Div, 65-67; head music librn, Univ Calif, Santa Barbara, 67- *Mem:* Music Libr Asn (chmn Southern Calif, 81-83); Asn Rec Sound Collections (secy, 81-83); Nat Music Libr Asn. *Interests:* Woodwinds; flute history. *Publ:* Auth, A Selected Bibliography of the Works of Karl Geiringer, In: Studies in 18th Century Music: A Tribute to Karl Geiringer on His 70th Birthday, Oxford Univ Press, 70. *Mailing Add:* 643 Willowglen Rd Santa Barbara CA 93105

SILVER, SHEILA JANE
COMPOSER, EDUCATOR
b Seattle, Wash, Oct 3, 46. *Study:* Univ Calif, Berkeley, AB, 68; Hochschule Musik, Stuttgart, 69-70; Brandeis Univ, MFA, 72, PhD, 74; study with Arthur Berger, Erhard Karkoschka, Gyorgy Ligeti & Seymour Shifrin. *Works:* String Quartet, perf by Assmann String Quartet, Mannheim & Atlantic String Quartet, New York, 68; Galixidi (orch), comn by Seattle Phil, 76; Chariessa, a Cycle of Six Songs on Texts of Sappho (piano & sop), 78 & (orch & sop), 80, perf by RAI Orch, Rome; Canto (baritone & chamber ens), Canto XXXIX of Ezra Pound, comn by Berkshire Music Ctr, Fromm Found, 79; Fantasy quasi Theme and Variation, Perspectives New Music, 80; Two Songs on Elizabethan Poems (SATB), G Schirmer, 81-82; Ek Ong Kar (SATB & SSA), perf & rec by Gregg Smith Singers, 82. *Teaching:* Instr piano & comp, Phillips Exeter Acad, 76-77; asst prof music, State Univ NY, Stony Brook, 79- *Awards:* Prix de Paris, 69-71; Radcliffe Inst Fel, Harvard Univ, 77; Prix De Rome, Am Acad, Rome, 78. *Publ:* Coauth, Analysis of Webern op 11, Neue Methoden der Analyse, Doring Verlag, Ger, 76; auth, Pitch and Registral Distribution in Arthur Berger's Music for Piano, Perspectives New Music, 78. *Mailing Add:* 462 W 58 #2H New York NY 10019

SILVERMAN, ALAN JOHN
PERCUSSION, EDUCATOR
b Queens, NY, Dec 6, 44. *Study:* Manhattan Sch Music, BM, 66, MM, 68. *Pos:* Perc, Am Symph Orch, 65-; prin cond, Goldman Band, 68-; perc & drums, studios & shows, 66- *Teaching:* Instr perc, Rutger Univ, 80- *Mem:* Percussive Arts Soc. *Mailing Add:* 650 Princeton St New Milford NJ 07646

SILVERMAN, FAYE-ELLEN
COMPOSER, EDUCATOR
b New York, NY, Oct 2, 47. *Study:* Dalcroze Sch Music, 51-63; Manhattan Sch Music, 63-64; Mannes Col Music, study comp with William Sydeman, 66-67; Barnard Col, study comp with Otto Luening, BA, 68; Harvard Univ, study comp with Leon Kirchner & Lukas Foss & piano with Russell Sherman, MA, 71; Columbia Univ, study comp with Vladimir Ussachevsky & Jack Beeson & piano with Irma Wolpe, DMA, 74. *Works:* Stirrings, 79, Three Guitars, 80, & Oboe-sthenics, 82, Seesaw Music; Quantum Quintet, comn by Am Brass Quintet, Mt Vernon Brass, Catskill Brass & Southern Brass, 81; Winds and Sines, 82 & No Strings, 82 & Speaking Together, 82, Seesaw Music; and many others. *Pos:* Freelance ed, Macmillan, McGraw Hill, Parents Mag and others. *Teaching:* Adj asst prof, City Univ New York, 72-77; asst prof, Goucher Col, 77-81; fac mem, Peabody Consv, Johns Hopkins Univ, 77- *Awards:* Stokowski Comp Cont, 61; winner, Ind State Univ Orch Comp Cont, 82. *Mem:* ASCAP; Col Music Soc; Am Music Ctr; Music Teachers Nat Asn; Siberius Soc. *Publ:* Auth, Gesualdo: Misguided or Inspired?, 73 & Report From New York City: Computer Conference, June, 1973, 74, Current Musicol; The Gregg Smith Singers, Goucher Quart, 78; Twentieth Century Section of the Schirmer History of Music, Schirmer Books, Macmillan, 82; Beethoven Today Would Be Exploring New Forms, Evening Sun, 83. *Mailing Add:* 1000 E Joppa Rd Apt 207 Baltimore MD 21204

SILVERMAN, ROBERT JOSEPH
EDITOR, WRITER
b Jersey City, NJ, May 7, 25. *Study:* Juilliard Sch Music; Cornell Univ. *Works:* Various works in small form for piano, choral, organ, etc, Belwin-Mills Publ Corp, Frank Music & E B Marks Music Corp, 55-; Persephone (ballet), comn & perf by Joffrey Ballet, 62. *Pos:* Dir publ, E B Marks Music Corp, 62-69 & Belwin-Mills Publ Corp, 69-72; ed & publ, Piano Quart, 72- *Mem:* Busoni Found (mem exec bd, currently); Am Liszt Soc (mem exec bd, currently). *Mailing Add:* Piano Quarterly Box 815 Wilmington VT 05363

SILVERMAN, STANLEY JOEL
COMPOSER, CONDUCTOR & MUSIC DIRECTOR
b New York, NY, July 5, 38. *Study:* Columbia Univ, with Henry Cowell, 57-58; Boston Univ, BMus, 60; Mills Col, with Leon Kirchner & Darius Milhaud, MA, 62. *Works:* Elephant Steps, Berkshire Music, 68; Planh, New York Phil, 72; Dr Selavy's Magic Theatre, 72 & Hotel For Criminals, 74, Lenox Arts Ctr; Crepuscule, Chamber Music Soc Lincoln Ctr, 74; Nanook of the North, Tashi, 75; Madame Adare, New York City Opera, 81. *Rec Perf:* Elephant Steps, CBS, 74; Dr Selavy's Magic Theatre, United Artists, 74; Planh, Folkways, 76; Threepenny Opera, CBS, 77. *Pos:* Musical dir, Repty Theatre Lincoln Ctr, 65-72 & New York Shakespeare Fest, 76-80; musical consult, Stratford Shakespeare Fest Can, 67-69 & Guthrie Theatre, 71-72. *Awards:* Awards, Obie, Village Voice, 70, Koussevitzky, 74 & Naumburg, 77. *Bibliog:* Michael Feingold (auth), Hotel For Criminals, Yale Theatre, 74; Ethan Mordden (auth), Better Foot Forward, Grossman/Viking, 76 & Opera in the Twentieth Century, Oxford Univ Press, 78. *Mem:* Am Music Ctr (secy, 78-81); Theatre Commun Group (mem bd dir, 82-); Lincoln Ctr Inst (mem bd dir, 76-). *Publ:* Auth, Rock and Classical, A Hairline Apart, 68 & Our Musical Theatre, 70, New York Times; coauth, Dialogue: Music and Theatre, Perf Arts J, 76; auth, Theatre Communications Group Annual Conference on Collaboration, Theatre Comm Group, 82. *Rep:* Andrew D Weinberger 3 Sheridan Sq New York NY 10014. *Mailing Add:* 11 Riverside Dr New York NY 10023

SILVERSTEIN, BARBARA ANN
CONDUCTOR & MUSIC DIRECTOR, ARTISTIC DIRECTOR
b Philadelphia, Pa, July 24, 47. *Study:* Philadelphia Musical Acad, BMus, 70; study with Anton Guadagno, 72-74. *Pos:* Assoc music dir, Suburban Opera Co, Chester, Pa, 68-74; asst cond, Lyr Opera Philadelphia, 72-75; asst cond, Des Moines Metro Opera, 75-78; artistic dir & cond, Pa Opera Theater, 76-; music dir & cond, Miss Opera, 79-82. *Teaching:* Operatic coach, Acad Vocal Arts, Philadelphia, 72-73; instr opera, Curtis Inst Music, 73-76. *Mem:* Am Fedn Musicians; Musical Fund Soc. *Mailing Add:* c/o Pa Opera Theater 1218 Chestnut St Suite 808 Philadelphia PA 19107

SILVESTER, WILLIAM H
MUSIC DIRECTOR, EDUCATOR
b Tremonton, Utah, Mar 6, 43. *Study:* Utah State Univ, BM, 69; Brigham Young Univ, MA, 71; Ariz State Univ, EdD, 83. *Teaching:* Dir bands, high sch, Utah, 66-80 & Trenton State Col, 82-; assoc dir bands, Calif State Univ, Northridge, 80-82; dir, Gov Sch Music, 82- *Mem:* Utah Music Educr Asn; Ariz Music Educr Asn; Col Band Dir Nat Asn; Music Educr Nat Asn; NJ Music Educr Asn. *Mailing Add:* 13 Del Rio Yardley PA 19067

SIMENAUER, PETER
CLARINET
b Berlin, Germany, Dec 11, 31; US citizen. *Study:* Hochschule Music, Berlin; studied with Andre Vaciliers, 52. *Rec Perf:* Mozart Clarinet Quintet with Pascal String Quartet, Monitor Rec, 53. *Pos:* Solo clarinetist, Israel Phil Orch, 52-59; assoc prin & E flat clarinetist, New York Phil Orch, 60- *Teaching:* Prof clarinet & chamber music, Manhattan Sch Music, 67- & Mannes Col Music, 77-; lectr, Hidden Valley Music Seminars, Inst of Arts, Carmel, Calif, 82- *Awards:* First Prize Mozarteum for Woodwinds, Mozarteum Salzburg, Austria, 53. *Mailing Add:* New York Phil Avery Fisher Hall Broadway & 65 New York NY 10023

SIMENAUER, PETER W
CLARINET, EDUCATOR
b Berlin, Germany, Dec 11, 31. *Study:* St Louis Col, Tientsin, China, 47-49; studied with Lothar, Simenauer & Andre Vacilliers. *Rec Perf:* Clarinet Quintet (Mozart). *Pos:* Mem, Israel Phil, formerly & New York Phil Woodwind Quintet, currently; assoc prin clarinet, New York Phil, 60-; solo & chamber music appearances, Europe, South Am & US. *Teaching:* Mem fac clarinet, Manhattan Sch Music, 72- & Mannes Col Music. *Awards:* First Prize, Mozarteum, 52. *Mailing Add:* 14 Capron Lane Upper Montclair NJ 07043

SIMMONDS, RAE NICHOLS
COMPOSER, PIANO
b Lynn, Mass, Feb 25, 19. *Study:* Westbrook Col, AA, 81; studied piano with Elaine Fenn, London, 82; Univ Southern Maine, currently. *Works:* Heidi (children's musical), 69 & A Little Princess (children's musical), 70, comn by NH Comn Arts; If I Were a Princess, comn & perf by Columbia Sch Perf Arts, 74; Tom Sawyer (children's musical), 75; Glooscap, 80 & Baba Yaga, 81, comn & perf by Childrens Theatre Maine; London Jazz Suite, Rae Nichols Quartet, 82; Cinderella, comn & perf by Windham Childrens Theatre, 83. *Pos:* Res playwright, Children's Theatre Maine, 79-81. *Teaching:* Found & dir, Studio Music & Drama, Portsmouth, NH, 64-71, Bromley, England, 71-74 & Dublin, Ireland 74-76; dir music & drama, Sanford Sch, Dublin, 75-76; found & dir music, Studio Music, Portland, Maine, 76- *Mem:* Am Fedn Musicians; Int League Women Comp; British Musicians Asn; Irish Fedn Musicians; Music Teachers Nat Asn. *Interests:* North American Indians; improvisation in jazz; folk and fairy tales. *Mailing Add:* 137 Spring St #1 Portland ME 04101

SIMMONS, EULA MARY SCHOCK
ADMINISTRATOR, CELLO
b Lewes, Del, Mar 15, 25. *Study:* New Sch Music, Philadelphia, 40-44; Juilliard Grad Sch, dipl, 48. *Pos:* Freelance musician, New York, 44-48. *Teaching:* Mem fac & performer cello, Stephens Col, Mo, 48-, chmn music dept, 78- *Mailing Add:* Music Dept Stephens Col Columbia MO 65215

SIMON, ABBEY H
PIANO
b New York, NY, Jan 8, 22. *Study:* Curtis Inst Music, with Josef Hofman. *Rec Perf:* With EMI, Philips, RCA, Vox & Turnabout. *Pos:* Judge, Sydney Int Piano Compt, Australia, 81 & Leeds Piano Compt, England, 81; pres jury, Maria Callas Piano Compt, Athens, 83; concert pianist, recital with orch on six continents. *Teaching:* Prof piano, Juilliard Sch Music, currently; Cullen chair for distinguished prof, Sch Music, Univ Houston, currently. *Awards:* First prize, Walter E Naumburg Piano Compt; Best Recital of the Year, Fedn Music Clubs, Elizabeth Sprague Coolidge, London & Harriet Cohen Found, London. *Rep:* Abbey H Simon 45 Chemin Moise Duboule Geneva Switz 1209. *Mailing Add:* Park Royal Hotel 23 W 73rd St New York NY 10023

SIMON, BENJAMIN
VIOLA
b San Francisco, Calif, Aug 15, 55. *Study:* Yale Col with Raphael Hillyer, BA, 77; Juilliard Sch Music, with Lillian Fuchs, MM, 79. *Pos:* Assoc prin violist, New Haven Symph, 74-77; prin violist, Buffalo Phil Orch, 80- *Awards:* Robert Bates Fel, Yale Col, 76; Joseph Machliss Prize, Juilliard Sch Music, 79. *Mailing Add:* c/o Buffalo Phil Orch 26 Richmond Ave Buffalo NY 14222

SIMON, RICHARD D
CRITIC
b Cleveland, Ohio, Oct 2, 22. *Study:* Univ Chicago, BA, 47. *Pos:* Music rev, Sacramento Union, 66- *Mem:* Music Critics Asn Am. *Mailing Add:* PO Box 2711 Sacramento CA 95812

SIMONS, NETTY
COMPOSER
b New York, NY. *Study:* Sch Fine Arts, NY Univ, 31-33 & 34-37; Juilliard Grad Sch, 33-34; studied with Stefan Wolpe, 37-40. *Works:* String Quartet, 53, Set of Poems, 59, Circle of Attitudes, 63, Design Groups I, 73, Pied Piper of Hamelin, 74, Songs for Jenny, 79 & Wild Tales Told on the River Road, 80, Merion Music Inc. *Pos:* Piano & vocal coach, Third St Music Sch Settlement, New York, 28-33; producer, Composers Concerts, Carnegie Recital Hall, 60-62; music chairperson & mem bd dir, Rockland Found, Nyack, NY, 61-64; producer radio broadcasts, WNYC, NY, 65-72 & WUOM, Univ Mich, 65-72. *Awards:* Rec & Publ Award, Ford Found, 70. *Bibliog:* Ronald George (auth), Percussionist XII #3, Perc Arts Soc, 75; article, View Mag, Tokyo, Japan, 1/75; Jeanie G Pool (auth), America's Women, Music Educ J, 1/79. *Mem:* BMI; Am Comp Alliance (mem bd gov, 72-77 & 2nd vpres, 75-77); Am Music Ctr; Int League Women Comp. *Rep:* Merion Music Inc Theodore Presser Co Presser Pl Bryn Mawr Pa 19010. *Mailing Add:* 303 E 57th St New York NY 10022

SIMOSKO, VALERIE
FLUTE & PICCOLO, EDUCATOR
b Pittsburgh, Pa, Feb 5, 49. *Study:* Duquesne Univ, with Bernard Goldberg, 67-69; study with Maurice Sharp, 70-72; Univ NC, Charlotte, 80- *Pos:* Assoc prin flute, Youngstown Symph, 71-72; utility flute, Atlanta Symph, 72-74; prin flute, Charlotte Symph, 74- *Teaching:* Instr flute, Southern Park Sch Music, Charlotte, NC, 74-; guest lectr, Univ NC, Charlotte, 76-81. *Mem:* Am Fedn Musicians. *Mailing Add:* 1615-E Merry Oaks Rd Charlotte NC 28205

SIMPSON, EUGENE THAMON See Thamon, Eugene

SIMPSON, MARY JEAN
FLUTE, EDUCATOR
b Bryan, Tex, Jan 31, 41. *Study:* Juilliard Sch, flute with Julius Baker, BMus, 65; Univ Tex, Austin, flute with John Hicks, MMus, 68; Univ Md, College Park, flute with William Montgomery, DMA, 82. *Works:* Reflections (flute & mezzo soprano), Dorn Publ, 81. *Pos:* Flutist, orch in US & Canada, 65-67; prin flutist, Shreveport Symph, 68-70. *Teaching:* Asst prof flute & music hist, Univ Mont, 70-79; private flute teacher, Washington, DC, 79- *Mem:* Charter mem, Nat Flute Asn; Am Musical Instrm Soc; Am Musicol Soc; Nat Asn Col Wind & Perc Instr; Col Music Soc. *Interests:* All aspects of flute & flute playing. *Publ:* Coauth, How to Prepare a Taped Audition—Competition, Instrumentalist, 82; auth, Women and the Flute: An Historical Perspective, Flute J, 82; What is a Flute Convention, Instrumentalist, 82; Badger, Alfred G, In: New Grove Dict of Music & Musicians (in prep). *Mailing Add:* 3501-G Toledo Terr Hyattsville MD 20782

SIMPSON, RALPH RICARDO
ADMINISTRATOR, COMPOSER
b Birmingham, Ala, Feb 16, 33. *Study:* Ala State Univ, AB, 52; Columbia Univ, MA, 57; Mich State Univ, PhD, 64. *Works:* Presentiment, Hazel Harrison, 58; Overture, Nashville Symph Orch, 74; Overture, Shreveport Symph, 79; Impromptu, Carol Stone, 81; Psalm 148, Spelman Glee Club, 83. *Teaching:* Instr music, Ala State Univ, 52-60; asst prof music, Dillard Univ, 60-69; prof & head dept, Tenn State Univ, 69- *Mem:* Am Guild Organists; Nat Asn Sch Music; Tenn Educ Asn (pres Tenn State Univ chap, 78-81). *Mailing Add:* 4134 W Hamilton Rd Nashville TN 37218

SIMPSON, WILBUR HERMAN
BASSOON, EDUCATOR
b Montpelier, Ohio, Dec 6, 17. *Study:* Northwestern Univ, BME, 40, MM, 46. *Pos:* Bassoonist, Chicago Symph Orch, 46-, Chicago Symph Woodwind Quintet, 46-71 & Chicago Symph Winds Octet, 78- *Teaching:* Prof bassoon, Northwestern Univ, 49- *Mailing Add:* c/o Chicago Symph Orch 220 S Michigan Ave Chicago IL 60604

SIMS, EDWARD
EDUCATOR, ADMINISTRATOR
b Oil City, Pa, Sept 22, 31. *Study:* Ind Univ, Pa, BS, 53; Pa State Univ, MEd, 59; Univ Mich, DEd, 68. *Teaching:* Prof music, Slippery Rock State Col, 60- *Mem:* Int Soc Music Educ; Pa Music Educr Asn (col rep, 61-72); Pa Music Higher Educ Asn (secy, 69-70, pres, 71-72); Music Educr Nat Conf; Phi Mu Alpha. *Mailing Add:* Music Dept Slippery Rock Univ Pa Slippery Rock PA 16057

SIMS, EZRA
COMPOSER
b Birmingham, Ala, Jan 16, 28. *Study:* Birmingham Consv Music, studied theory & comp with G Ackley Brower & Hugh Thomas, 45-48; Birmingham Southern Col, BA, 47; Yale Univ Sch Music, studied comp with Quincy Porter, BMus, 52; Mills Col, studied comp with Darius Milhaus & Leon Kirchner, MA, 56. *Works:* Chamber Cantata on Chinese Poems, CRI, 54; Sonate Concertanti, Merion Press, 61; Third Quartet, CRI, 62; Where the Wild Things are, CFE, 73; String Quartet #2 (1962), 74 & Elegie-nach Rilke, 76, CRI; and others. *Pos:* Programmer & cataloguer, Harvard Music Libr, 58-62 & 65-74; observer & comp, Electronic Music Studio, NHK, Tokyo, 62-63; music dir, New England Dinosaur Dance Theatre, 68-78; pres, Dinosaur Annex, 77-81. *Teaching:* Mem theory fac, New England Consv, 76-78; lectr, Warwick Univ, Ill Wesleyan Univ, Cleveland Inst Music, Christian Univ, Tokyo & others. *Awards:* Guggenheim Fel, 62; Nat Endowment Arts Fel, 76 & 78; Mass Artists Fel, 79. *Mem:* Am Comp Alliance; BMI; Col Music Soc. *Publ:* Trans, Oda Makoto, Odoroki-no Nippon, Shosetsu Chuokoron, Tokyo, 63; contribr, Microtones, In: Harvard Dict Music, 2nd ed, 69; The Judson or How I Spent My Thirties, In: Boston After Dark, 69; Letter from Boston, Ballet Rev, NY, Vol 3, No 3. *Mailing Add:* 1168 Massachusetts Ave Cambridge MA 02138

SIMS, PHILLIP WEIR
LIBRARIAN, EDUCATOR

b Ft Smith, Ark, July 16, 25. *Study:* Ouachita Col, BA, 50; Southwestern Baptist Sem, MSM, 56, DMA, 70; NTex State Univ, MLS, 73. *Pos:* Minister music, various churches in Tex, Ark & Mont; music librn, Southwestern Baptist Theol Sem, 67- *Teaching:* Assoc prof music bibliog & res, Southwestern Baptist Theol Sem, 67- *Mem:* Music Libr Asn; Southern Baptist Church Music Conf. *Publ:* Auth of several articles on hymnology, In: The Hymn. *Mailing Add:* 7308 Ledoux Ft Worth TX 76134

SINGER, DAVID
CLARINET

b Los Angeles, Calif, Apr 7, 49. *Study:* Curtis Inst Music, artists dipl, 71; Hochschule Musik, Vienna, Austria, artists dipl, 72. *Rec Perf:* Sonata for Clarinet & Piano (Regar), 77. *Pos:* Solo clarinetist, currently; appeared at Salzburg Fest, 72, Marlboro Fest, 71, 75, 76, 77 & 79 & Spoleto Fest, 78 & 83. *Awards:* Grant, Martha Baird Rockefeller Fund Music, 80; Naumburg Award; Coleman Award. *Bibliog:* Alvin Klein (auth), rev, New York Times, 2/20/83; Sylvie Drake (auth), rev, Los Angeles Times, 3/1/83; Susan Granger (auth), rev, Info, 3/83. *Mem:* Chamber Music Soc Lincoln Ctr; Affil Artists Inc. *Rep:* TRM Mgt Inc 527 Madison Ave New York NY 10022. *Mailing Add:* 22 Inwood Land E Peekskill NY 10566

SINGER, JEANNE (WALSH)
COMPOSER, PIANO

b New York, NY, Aug 4, 24. *Study:* Barnard Col, BA, 44; Nat Guild Piano Teachers, artists dipl, 54; studied piano with Nadia Reisenberg. *Works:* A Cycle of Love (four songs for sop), 76, Suite in Harpsichord Style (piano), 76 & From the Green Mountains (trio), 77, Harold Branch Publ Inc; Suite for Horn & Harp, 80 & From Petrarch (mezzo, horn & piano), 80, Cor Publ Co; Selected Songs (11 songs to texts by Am poets), Dragon's Teeth Press, 82; Mary's Boy (choral SATB), Plymouth Music Co, 83. *Teaching:* Piano, privately, 60- *Awards:* Award Merit Am Women Comp, Nat Fedn Music Clubs, 77; Annual Standard Awards (for serious music), ASCAP, 78-83; Distinguished Service Award Music, Nat League Am Pen Women, 82. *Bibliog:* Ellen Pfeiffer (auth), Singer Composes for Average Not Elite, Boston Herald Am, 9/23/78; Laurence Van Gelder (auth), Her Music and Cats a Perfect Mix, New York Times, 10/25/81; Austin Miskell (auth), Romanticism and the Singer, Notebook Mag, 3/83. *Mem:* ASCAP; Am Music Ctr; Comp Auth & Artists Am (vpres music chap, 76-); Am Women Comp Inc (bd dir, 76); Int League Women Comp. *Mailing Add:* 64 Stuart Place Manhasset NY 11031

SINGER, JOAN (JOAN SINGER SPICKNALL)
EDUCATOR, PIANO

b Arlington, Va, Feb 13, 42. *Study:* Peabody Consv Music, BM, 63, MM, 63; Univ Md, College Park, DMA, 74; study with Daniel Ericourt, Theodore Lettvin, Rosina Lhevinne, Aaron Copland & Stewart Gordon. *Rec Perf:* All the Piano Music by Aaron Copland, Joan Singer, Pianist, Golden Age Rec, 77. *Pos:* Conct pianist, Washington, DC, Md, Va, Pa, NY, Fla, Ind & Iowa, 64-; perf, PBS, 64-77 & Copland Conct, Carnegie Recital Hall, 75; mem, Morningside Col Fac Trio, 79-80. *Teaching:* Instr music, Univ Md, College Park, 69-; adj prof, St Mary of the Woods Col, 71- & Rose Hulman Inst Technol, 73-; asst prof, Morningside Col, 79-80. *Awards:* Spanish Music Grant, Santiago Compostella, Spain, 62. *Mem:* Am Women Comp Inc; Col Music Soc; Mu Phi Epsilon; Music Teachers Nat Asn. *Mailing Add:* 11 Salem Pl Terre Haute IN 47803

SINGHER, MARTIAL
BARITONE, TEACHER-COACH

b Oloron-Ste Marie, France, Aug 14, 04; US citizen. *Study:* Ecole Normale Superieure, St Cloud, France, lit, 27; Consv Nat Musique, Paris, 29-30; Chicago Musical Col, Hon Dr Music, 54. *Rec Perf:* Damnation of Faust, RCA Victor, 54; Die Schöne Müllerin, Concert Hall, 54; Enfance du Christ, Columbia Rec, 55; Les Countes d' Hoffmann, Cetra, 56; L'Histoire du Soldat, Vanguard, 67; Opus 70 (French art songs), 75 & French Songs, 77, 1750 Arch-Berkeley. *Roles:* Rigoletto, Paris Opera & Royal Opera, Stockholm, 31-41; Hamlet, Paris Opera & Teatro Colon, Buenos Aires, 33-39; Amfortas in Parsifal, 33-57 & Wolfram, 35-49, Paris Opera, Teatro Colon & Metropolitan Opera; Count Almaviva & Figaro, Teatro Colon & Metropolitan Opera, 36-58; Pelleas & Golaud in Pelleas et Melisande, Metropolitan Opera, 43-54; Four Villains Hoffmann, Metropolitan Opera, 45-59. *Pos:* Leading baritone, Paris Opera & Opera Comique, 30-41, Teatro Colon, Buenos Aires, 36-43 & Metropolitan Opera, 43-59; guest soloist, New York Phil & Boston, Philadelphia & Chicago Symph, 30-59. *Teaching:* Prof voice & opera, Marlboro Sch Music, 55-61 & Curtis Inst Music, 55-68; head voice & opera dept, Music Acad West, Santa Barbara, 62-81 & Mozarteum Salzburg, Austria, 48-54. *Awards:* Officier Legion Honneur, France, 82. *Mem:* Nat Asn Teachers Singing; Am Acad Teachers Singing. *Publ:* Contribr, Esquisse de la France, Parizeau, Montreal, 46; auth, An Interpretative Guide to Operatic Arias, Pa State Univ Press, 83. *Mailing Add:* 840 Deerpath Rd Santa Barbara CA 93108

SINGHER, MICHEL
CONDUCTOR & MUSIC DIRECTOR, COACH

b Boulogne, France, Oct 13, 40; US citizen. *Study:* Harvard Col, with Leon Kirchner, AB, 62; Staatliche Hochschule Musik, Stuttgart, with H Müller-Kray, H Giesen & Joh Nep David, 62-64; Ind Univ, with Tibor Kozma & B Heiden, MMus, 66. *Rec Perf:* Wunschkonzert James King, Teldec, 70; The Yew Tree, Crystal, 82. *Pos:* Coach, Hamburg State Opera, 66-70; first cond, Regensburg Municipal Theater, 70-72 & Freiburg Municipal Theater,

75-77; music dir, Mid-Columbia Symph, 82- *Teaching:* Asst cond & opera coach, Music Acad West, Santa Barbara, Calif, 64-81; asst prof cond, Univ Wash, 78-81. *Mem:* Cond Guild; Am Symph Orch League; Arts Coun Mid-Columbia Region (trustee, 82-). *Mailing Add:* PO Box 65 Richland WA 99352

SINNICAM, DON See MacInnis, M Donald

SINTA, DONALD JOSEPH
SAXOPHONE, EDUCATOR

b Detroit, Mich, June 16, 37. *Study:* Wayne State Univ, BS, 55; Univ Mich, MM, 62. *Rec Perf:* American Music for Saxophone, Mark Rec, 67; Concerto (Hartley), 68 & Concerto (Creston), 72, Golden Crest Rec; Concerto (I Dahl), Mich Univ Press, 76; Music for Saxophone & Piano (Bassett), New World Rec, 77. *Pos:* Saxophonist, Detroit Symph Orch, 60-63. *Teaching:* Instr sax, Ithaca Col, 63-67; assoc prof, Hartt Col Music, 67-74; prof, Univ Mich, 74- *Mem:* World Sax Cong (pres, 69); Phi Mu Alpha. *Mailing Add:* Sch Music Univ Mich Ann Arbor MI 48109

SIRINEK, ROBERT
TRUMPET, ADMINISTRATOR

b Pittsburgh, Pa, Dec 10, 45. *Study:* Juilliard Sch, BM, 67, MS, 68. *Pos:* Second trumpet, Metropolitan Opera Orch, 77- & asst orch mgr, 79- *Mailing Add:* 219 Doremus Ave Ridgewood NJ 07450

SIROTA, ROBERT (BENSON)
COMPOSER, CONDUCTOR

b New York, NY, Oct 13, 49. *Study:* Consv Music, Oberlin Col, MusB, 71; Harvard Univ, MA, 75, PhD, 79. *Works:* Fantasy for Cello and Piano, perf by Norman Fischer, cello & comp, piano, 75; Bontshe the Silent (chamber opera), Pro Arte Chamber Orch, 78; Toccata (organ), perf by Victoria Sirota, 79; Concerto for Saxophone, comn by Rikk Stone, 81; Songs and Spells, A Midsummer Nightscape (mixed chorus & chamber ens), Tanglewood Inst Chorus & Instrumentalists, 81; Concerto Grosso, comn & perf by Alea III, 81; Letters Abroad (organ & piano), perf by Victoria Sirota, organ & Robert Sirota, comp, piano, 82. *Teaching:* Instr music, Harvard Univ, summers, 77-79; asst prof theory & comp, Sch Music, Boston Univ, 79-83; dir comp prog, Tanglewood Inst, summers 80-83, assoc dean, Sch Arts, 83- *Awards:* Fel, Thomas J Watson Found, 71; Comp Fels, Nat Endowment for Arts, 80 & John Simon Guggenheim Found, 83. *Mem:* Int Soc Contemp Music (bd mem, 83-); Am Music Ctr; Soc Music Theory. *Mailing Add:* 91 Beals St Brookline MA 02146

SIROTA, VICTORIA (RESSMEYER)
ORGAN, EDUCATOR

b Oceanside, NY, July 5, 49. *Study:* Consv Music, Oberlin Col, MusB, 71; Boston Univ, MusM, 75, DMA, 81. *Rec Perf:* Fanny Mendelssohn Hensel Rediscovered, Northeastern Rec (in prep). *Pos:* Organist & choir dir, Parish of Epiphany, Winchester, Mass, 74-77; deputy organist, First & Second Church Boston, 83- *Teaching:* Music tutor, Harvard Univ, 74-77; instr, Concord Acad, Mass, 77-83; vocal prog music theory coordr, Tanglewood Inst, Boston Univ, summer, 83, teaching assoc organ, Sch Music, 83-; affil artist, Music Sect, Mass Inst Technol, 83- *Awards:* Res Grant Women's Studies, Woodrow Wilson Found, 80; Res Grant, Deutscher Akad Austauschdienst, 80; Grad Fel, Oberlin Col Haskell Found, 80-81. *Mem:* Am Guild Organists (mem exec comt Boston chap, 76-79); Am Musicol Soc; Soc Music Theory; Organ Hist Soc. *Interests:* Fanny Mendelssohn Hensel. *Publ:* Auth, Introd to Fanny Hensel—Trio in D minor, Op 11, Da Capo Press, 80. *Mailing Add:* 91 Beals St Brookline MA 02146

SIRUCEK, JERRY EDWARD
OBOE & ENGLISH HORN, EDUCATOR

b Cicero, Ill, June 30, 22. *Study:* Roosevelt Univ, BS, 48. *Pos:* English horn, Houston Symph, 40-41; second oboe, Chicago Symph Orch, 41-61; oboist, Chicago Symph Woodwind Quintet, 57-61, Baroque Chamber Players, 61-80 & Musica Sonora, 81- *Teaching:* Prof oboe & English horn, Ind Univ, 61- *Mailing Add:* 4839 E Ridgewood Dr Bloomington IN 47401

SISLEN, MYRNA (CAROL)
GUITAR & LUTE, EDUCATOR

b Jacksonville, Fla, Nov 9, 46. *Study:* Am Univ, BA, 70; studied with Charlie Byrd, Laurindo Almeida, Alirio Diaz, Leo Brower, Abel Carlevaro & Guido Santorsola. *Rec Perf:* Buenos Dias, Voice of Am, 74-75; Play and Learn Guitar with Myrna Sislen, Book I, 75 & Book II, 75, US Army Rec; Myrna! Myrna Sislen Classical Guitar, Cath Univ Rec, 83. *Pos:* Soloist, TV series, Music Moments with Myrna, PBS, 77. *Teaching:* Head music dept, Montgomery Col, 73-74; musician in res, Fayetteville Technical Inst, NC, 75-76 & NC State Univ, 76-77; adj prof guitar, George Washington Univ, 77- *Awards:* Medal Recognition, Am Ambassador John P Humes, Vienna, Austria, 72; Roster Musical Am Outstanding Young Artists, 74; Acme Accolade, Mu Phi Epsilon, 79. *Interests:* Renaissance lute music for guitar. *Rep:* Lindy S Martin Personal Mgt Pinehurst NC 28374. *Mailing Add:* 1111 Army Navy Dr #C-1009 Arlington VA 22202

SISMAN, ELAINE ROCHELLE
EDUCATOR

b New York, NY, Jan 20, 52. *Study:* Cornell Univ, AB, 72; Princeton Univ, MFA(music), 74, PhD(music), 78. *Teaching:* Instr & asst prof, Univ Mich, Ann Arbor, 76-82; asst prof, Columbia Univ, 82- *Awards:* Fel, Nat Endowment Humanities, 81-82. *Mem:* Am Musicol Soc (pres gtr New York chap, 82-); Northeast Am Soc 18th-century Studies; Brahms Soc Am.

Interests: Eighteenth and 19th centuries, particularly Haydn, Beethoven and Brahms; variation forms; 18th century theory. *Publ:* Auth, Haydn's Hybrid Variations, Haydn Studies, Norton, 81; Small and Expanded Forms: Koch's Model and Haydn's Music, Musical Quart, 82; contrib, Harvard Dict Music, Harvard Univ Press, 3rd ed (in prep); auth, Brahms's Slow Movements: Reinventing the "Closed" Forms, Brahms Studies I (in prep); Haydn's Baryton Pieces and his "Serious" Genres, Haydn Conf Report-Vienna 1982 (in prep). *Mailing Add:* 600 West End Ave #7C New York NY 10024

SISSON, WILLIAM KENNETH
PUBLISHER-EDITOR, ADMINISTRATOR
b Cleveland, Ohio, Apr 1, 53. *Study:* Miami Univ, Ohio, with David Cope & Winford Cummings, BM, 76. *Pos:* Dir perf dept, Alexander Broude Inc Music Publ, 76-, managing ed, 80; publ & owner, Edition Delusive Phantom, 82- *Mem:* Riemenschneider Bach Inst. *Publ:* Auth, Reviews, Comp Mag, 77-78; ed, Choral Works of Gabriel Faure, Performing Editions, 81 & Sacred A Cappella Choral Works of Anton Bruckner, Performing Editions, 83, Continuo Music Press; auth, Reviews, Chamber Music Quart, 83. *Mailing Add:* ABI Music Publ 225 W 57th St New York NY 10019

SISTRUNK, GEORGE WILLIS
CONDUCTOR, ADMINISTRATOR
b Sumter, SC, June 27, 29. *Study:* Univ Fla, BSBA, 51; Southern Sem, BSM, 54; Fla Atlantic Univ, MEd, 67; Univ Miami, DMA, 72. *Pos:* Cond, Ft Lauderdale Symph Chorus, 59-80. *Teaching:* Assoc prof chorus, voice & cond, Fla Atlantic Univ, 67-80; prof & chmn dept music, Newberry Col, 80- *Mem:* Nat Asn Teachers Singing; Am Choral Cond Asn; SC Music Teachers Asn; Lutheran Asn Musicians. *Mailing Add:* Music Dept Newberry Col Newberry SC 29108

SITKOVETSKY, DMITRY
VIOLIN
b Baku, USSR, Sept 27, 54; US citizen. *Study:* Moscow Consv, MA, 77; Juilliard Sch, artist dipl, 79. *Rec Perf:* Unaccompanied Violin Sonata No 2 (J S Bach), La Campanella (Paganini), Sonata for Violin & Piano, Op 80, No 1 (Prokofieff) & Andante (Joseff Andriasjan), Deutsche Grammophon, 81; Transcriptions for Violin & Piano (Kreisler), 83 & Sonatas for Violin & Piano (Grieg) (in press), Orfeo. *Teaching:* Artist in res, Sch Music, Ball State Univ, 79- *Awards:* First Place, Concertina Praga, 66; First Place, Fritz Kreisler Compt, Vienna, 79. *Mailing Add:* J B Keller, Pub Relations 225 Central Park W New York NY 10024

SIWE, THOMAS V
PERCUSSION, CONDUCTOR
b Chicago, Ill, Feb 14, 35. *Study:* Univ Ill, BMus, 63, MMus, 66. *Pos:* Perc, Lyr Opera Chicago, 59-65 & Chicago Contemp Chamber Players, 66-69; dir, Am Comp Ens, 75-77. *Teaching:* Prof music, Univ Ill, 69- *Mem:* Percussive Arts Soc (vpres, 80-). *Publ:* Auth, Performing Ben Johnston's Knocking Piece, Then and Now, Percussive Notes Res Ed, 83. *Mailing Add:* Sch Music Univ Ill Urbana IL 61801

SKAGGS, HAZEL GHAZARIAN
TEACHER, WRITER
b Boston, Mass, Aug 26, 24. *Study:* New England Consv Music, dipl, 42; Fairleigh Dickinson Univ, BA, 69, MA, 71; studied with Clarence Adler. *Works:* Flight to Moon, 59 & Phantom Waltz, 59, Schroeder & Gunther; Merry Criket, The Little Blue Lady, Century, 60; Little Invention, Spring Showers, Teasing, Basketball, Boston Music, 62; Little Girl from Mars, Carl Fischer Inc, 67. *Pos:* Adjudicator, Nat Guild Piano Teachers, 56-66; nat chmn comp test & judge, 64- *Teaching:* Piano, privately, 50-; teacher piano, Riverdell Adult Sch, 59-78; adj fac piano, Fairleigh Dickinson Univ, 83- *Mem:* Nat Guild Piano Teachers; Assoc Music Teachers League New York (secy, 60-64); NJ Fedn Music Clubs (state chmn comp, 62-64); Music Teachers Nat Asn (state vpres, 62-64); Piano Teachers Cong New York Inc (pres, 75-79). *Publ:* Auth, Thumbs Under, Willis Music Co, 58; The Private Lesson On Trial, Piano Teacher, 11-12/62; Hypothesis and a Look Inward, Piano Quart, Winter 68-69; Objective Testing of Sight Reading, Clavier, 2/75; coauth & co-ed, Teaching Piano (2 vol), Yorktown Music Press, 81. *Mailing Add:* 29 Wayne Ave River Edge NJ 07661

SKEI, ALLEN BENNET
CRITIC-WRITER, EDUCATOR
b Fargo, NDak, Nov 5, 35. *Study:* St Olaf Col, Northfield, Minn, BA, 57; Univ Mich, MMus, 59; PhD, 65. *Pos:* Music critic, Fresno Bee, 71- *Teaching:* Instr music, Gustavus Adolphus Col, St Peter, Minn, 61-62; Lewis & Clark, Portland, Ore, 62-65; from asst prof to assoc prof, Georgia Col, Milledgeville, 65-70; from assoc prof music to prof, Calif State Univ, Fresno, 70- *Mem:* Am Musicol Soc; Music Libr Asn; Music Critics Asn. *Publ:* Ed, Jacob Handl, The Moralia of 1596, 70, Stefano Rossetti, Sacrae Cantiones, 73 & Il Primo Libro de Madregali a Quattro Voci, 78, A-R Ed; auth, Musicology and Other Delights, Lingua Press, 78; Heinrich Schütz: A Guide To Research, Garland Press, 82. *Mailing Add:* 3147 E Sussex Way Fresno CA 93726

SKIDMORE, DOROTHY LOUISE
FLUTE, EDUCATOR
b Champaign, Ill, Oct 30, 40. *Study:* Univ Ill, BMus, 62, MMus, 69; Hochschule Musik, Freiburg, Germany, 62-63. *Rec Perf:* The Book of Imaginary Beings (Robert Parris), Vox Turnabout, 73. *Pos:* Flutist, Nat Gallery Art Orch, 67-76. *Teaching:* Adj prof, Montgomery Col, 66-74; instr flute, Cath Univ, 66-70, prep dept, WVa Univ, 80- & privately, currently. *Mem:* Am Fedn Musicians; Sigma Alpha Iota; Fri Morning Music Club; Nat Flute Asn; Pi Kappa Lambda. *Mailing Add:* 331 Bakers Ridge Rd Morgantown WV 26505

SKIDMORE, WILLIAM R
CELLO, EDUCATOR
b Bay City, Mich, Jan 7, 41. *Study:* Univ Ill, BMus, 63, MMus, 66. *Pos:* Section cello, Baltimore Symph Orch, 74-77; cellist, Am Arts Trio, 77- *Teaching:* Asst prof cello, Md Univ, 64-74; teacher, Notre Dame, Baltimore, 76-77; assoc prof, WVa Univ, 77- *Mem:* Am String Teachers Asn; Col Music Soc; Music Teachers Nat Asn; Am Fedn Musicians. *Mailing Add:* 331 Bakers Ridge Rd Morgantown WV 26505

SKINNER, ROBERT GORDON
LIBRARIAN
b Austin, Tex, Jan 1, 48. *Study:* NTex State Univ, BA, 74, MLS, 77. *Pos:* Rec sound librn, Harvard Univ, 78-79; music & fine arts librn, Southern Methodist Univ, 80- *Teaching:* Adj prof music hist, Southern Methodist Univ, 82- *Mem:* Am Musicol Soc; Music Libr Asn; Asn Rec Sound Collections. *Interests:* History of music publishing; discography. *Publ:* Auth, A Selective Guide to Dealers ... in Foreign Sound Recordings, Notes, Music Libr Asn, 79; A Randall Thompson Discography, J Asn Rec Sound Collections, 80; coauth, A Checklist of Texas Composers, Music Libr Asn, 80; Stravinsky in Texas, Houston Symph, 82. *Mailing Add:* Libr Owens Art Ctr Southern Methodist Univ Dallas TX 75275

SKOBBA, DARYL S
CELLO, ADMINISTRATOR
b Mankato, Minn, May 8, 43. *Study:* Mankato State Univ, BS, 65, MM, 69; Yale Univ, studied cello with Aldo Parisot, 74-76. *Pos:* Asst prin cellist, St Paul Chamber Orch, 69-, personnel mgr, 79-83. *Mailing Add:* 2802 McLeod St Burnsville MN 55337

SKOLDBERG, PHYLLIS LINNEA
ADMINISTRATOR, VIOLIN
b Bremerton, Wash. *Study:* New England Consv Music, BM, 55, MM, 57; Sch Music, Ind Univ, MME, 64, DM(perf), 67; studied violin with Richard Burgin, Josef Gingold & Ivan Galamian & chamber music with Janos Starker & George Fourel. *Pos:* Violinist, Houston Symph Orch, 57-59 & Cincinnati Symph Orch, 59-62; reviewer, Am String Teacher, 71-73. *Teaching:* Prof music, State Univ NY, 64-77; asst dean & prof music, Col Fine Arts, Ariz State Univ, 77- *Awards:* Seattle Phil Artists Award, 52; Boston Civic Music Award, 53; Pac Northwest Artists Award, 53. *Mem:* Music Educr Nat Conf; Nat Asn Sch Music; Pi Kappa Lambda; Am Asn Higher Educ; Arizonans for Cult Develop. *Interests:* Chamber music and violin works of Ottorino Respighi. *Publ:* Contribr, String Conferences, Ariz Music News, 80 & 81; Respighi Revisited, Am String Teacher, 82; auth, The Strings: A Comparative View, Vol I, 82 & Vol II, 83, Frangipani Press. *Mailing Add:* Col Fine Arts Ariz State Univ Tempe AZ 85287

SKOLNIK, WALTER
COMPOSER
b New York, NY, July 20, 34. *Study:* Brooklyn Col, BA, 55; Ind Univ, MM, 56, DM, 69. *Works:* A Flea and a Fly in a Flue (SSA), Lawson-Gould, 69; Quixotic Rhapsody (symph band), 72, Sonata (trumpet & piano), 72, Concert Music (brass choir, timpani & perc), 73, Little Suite in B-Flat (symph band), 76 & Saxoliloquy (alto sax & conct band), 82, Tenuto Publ. *Teaching:* Comp in res, Shawnee Mission High Sch District, Kans, 66-68; asst prof music, Youngstown State Univ, 69-70. *Awards:* Music Educr Nat Conf Fel, Ford Found Contemp Music Proj, 66-68. *Publ:* Auth, article for sch bands, Nat Band Asn J, 69. *Mailing Add:* 124 Gale Place Bronx NY 10463

SKOLOVSKY, ZADEL
PIANO, EDUCATOR
b Vancouver, BC, July 17, 26; nat US. *Study:* Curtis Inst Music, 28-37; studied piano with Isabelle Vengerova, cond with Fritz Reiner & violin with Edwin Bachmann. *Rec Perf:* Fourth Piano Concerto (Milhaud); Four Piano Sonatas (Berg, Hindemith No 2, Bartok & Scriabin No 4), Columbia; also on Philips Rec. *Pos:* Recitalist, US & Can, 39-; soloist with maj orchs in US, Can, Europe, Mex, South Africa & Israel. *Teaching:* Prof music, Ind Univ, 76- *Awards:* Walter H Naumburg Award, 39; Nat Music League Award, 41; Nat Fedn Music Clubs Award, 42. *Mailing Add:* 240 E 79th St New York NY 10021

SKORODIN, ELAINE (ELAINE SKORODIN FOHRMAN)
VIOLIN, EDUCATOR
b Milwaukee, Wis, Aug 28, 36. *Study:* Chicago Musical Col, Roosevelt Univ, BM, 57, MM, 59; Univ Calif, Los Angeles, with Jascha Heifetz, 60. *Pos:* Extra mem violin section, Chicago Symph Orch, 74- *Teaching:* Assoc prof violin, viola & chamber music, Chicago Musical Col, Roosevelt Univ, 80-; vis artist in res violin, Univ Wis, Parkside, 81-82. *Awards:* Prize winner, Soc Am Musicians, 57; Paganini Int Violin Compt, Genoa, Italy, 61 & Nat Fedn Music Clubs, 63. *Mem:* Chicago Fedn Musicians. *Mailing Add:* 888 Oak Dr Glencoe IL 60022

SKROWACZEWSKI, STANISLAW
CONDUCTOR, COMPOSER
b Lwow, Poland, Oct 3, 23, US citizen. *Study:* Lwow Music Acad, 45, & Krakow Music Acad, 46, cond & comp dipl; Hamline Univ, 63, Macalester Col, 73 & Univ Minn, 79, Hon Dr. *Works:* Composed four symphonies, ballet, opera, chamber music, four string quartets & six piano sonatas, 31-81, Music at Night (symphonic variations), 52, Ricerari Notturni, 77, Concert for English Horn, 69 & Concert for Clarinet, 80. *Rec Perf:* Recordings by Mercury, Angel, RCA, Vox Columbia & Phillips Rec. *Pos:* Cond & music dir Wroclaw Phil Orch, 46-47, Katowice Phil Orch, 49-54, Krakow Phil Orch, 54-56, Warsaw Nat Orch, 56-59 & Minneapolis Symph Orch, 60-79. *Bibliog:* 2nd prize, Int Compt Comp, Belgium, 53; 1st prize, Int Compt Cond, Rome, 56; Kennedy Ctr Award, 77. *Mailing Add:* PO Box 700 Wayzata MN 55391

SKRZYNSKI, JOSEPH
TROMBONE, EDUCATOR
b Youngstown, Ohio, Nov 12, 22. *Study:* Wayne State Univ; Univ Mich, with Harold Ferguson & Glen Smith, BMusEd, 50. *Pos:* Trombonist, Detroit Symph Orch, 51- & St Louis Sinfonietta, 58-61. *Teaching:* Instr trombone, Wayne State Univ, 58- & Oakland Univ, 79-; lectr, Univ Mich, 74. *Mailing Add:* 5715 Oakman Blvd Dearborn MI 48126

SKYRM, SARAH ELIZABETH
LIBRARIAN
b Sharon, Pa, Feb 21, 25. *Study:* Oberlin Col, BME, 47; Univ Mich, AMLS, 55. *Pos:* Music librn, Crane Music Libr, State Univ NY, Potsdam, 56- *Mem:* Music Libr Asn. *Mailing Add:* Meadow East Apt G-4 Potsdam NY 13676

SLATKIN, LEONARD
CONDUCTOR & MUSIC DIRECTOR
Study: Viola with Sol Schoenbach, 59- & cond with Felix Slatkin & Ingolf Dahl; Ind Univ, 62; Los Angeles City Col, 63; Juilliard Sch, 64. *Pos:* Asst cond, Youth Symph New York, 66 & Juilliard Opera Theater & Dance Dept, 67; asst cond, St Louis Symph Orch, 68-71, assoc cond, 71-74, prin cond & music dir, 79-; founder, music dir & cond, St Louis Symph Youth Orch, 69-; guest cond, Chicago Symph Orch, New York Phil, Philadelphia Orch, Royal Phil Orch, 74-, USSR orchs, 76- & others; prin guest cond, Minn Orch, 74-, summer artistic dir, 79-80; music dir, New Orleans Phil Symph Orch, 77-78, musical adv, 79-80; host, weekly radio prog. *Teaching:* Vis asst prof music, Washington Univ, formerly, founder, Fri Afternoon Lect Ser. *Mailing Add:* St Louis Symph 718 N Grand Blvd St Louis MO 63103

SLAUGHTER, SUSAN
TRUMPET, EDUCATOR
b McCordsville, Ind, July 5, 45. *Study:* Aspen Music Fest, with Robert Nagel, 66 & 68; Ind Univ, with Herbert Mueller, Bernard Adelstein & Arnold Jacobs, BM & perf cert, 67; Berkshire Music Ctr, 69. *Rec Perf:* Concerto in F (Gershwin), Vox, 74. *Pos:* Prin trumpet, Toledo Symph, 67-69; fourth trumpet, St Louis Symph Orch, 69-71, prin trumpet, 72- *Teaching:* Lectr trumpet, Southern Ill Univ, 69-72 & St Louis Consv Music, 78-; founder & cond, Trumpet Lab, 78- *Awards:* St Louis Symph Orch Women's Asn Prin Trumpet Chair, 76. *Bibliog:* Susan C Thompson (auth), Trumpeting Acclaim, St Louis Post-Dispatch, 6/22/76; Betsy Light (auth), A Little Brass Helps the Music, Today, Cocoa, Fla, 2/13/81; Celeste Rhea (auth), Susan Witnesses with Her Trumpet, Herald of Holiness Mag, 4/15/81. *Mem:* Int Trumpet Guild (mem bd dir, 76-79); Col Music Soc. *Mailing Add:* 540 S Geyer Rd St Louis MO 63122

SLAWSON, A WAYNE
COMPOSER, EDUCATOR
b Detroit, Mich, Dec 29, 32. *Study:* Univ Mich, with Leslie Bassett & Ross Lee Finney, MA, 59; Harvard Univ, PhD(psychoacoustics), 65; Mass Inst Technol, 65-66; Royal Inst Technol, Stockholm, 66-67. *Works:* Reflections (cello & piano), 75; Omaggio a Petrarca, 75; Death, Love and the Maiden (tape), 75; Minglings (men's chorus), 76; Variations (two violins), 77; Limits (chamber music), 77; Poor Flesh and Trees, Poor Stars and Stones (tape), 77. *Teaching:* Fac mem, Yale Univ, 67-72; assoc prof music, Univ Pittsburgh, 72- *Mailing Add:* 5600 Howe St Pittsburgh PA 15232

SLIM, H(ARRY) COLIN
MUSICOLOGIST, EDUCATOR
b Vancouver, BC, Apr 9, 29. *Study:* Univ BC, BA, 51; Harvard Univ, AM, 55, PhD, 61. *Teaching:* From instr to asst prof music, Univ Chicago, 59-65, prof, 72-73; assoc prof, Univ Calif, Irvine, 65-69, prof, 69-; fel, Harvard Res Ctr, I Tatti, Florence, 69. *Awards:* Otto Kinkeldy Award, Am Musicol Soc, 73; Am Coun Learned Soc Fel Musicol, 73-74; Distinguished Res Award, Univ Calif, Irvine, 75. *Mem:* Am Musicol Soc; Renaissance Soc Am; Renaissance music; 17th century opera; musical iconography. *Publ:* Ed, Keyboard Music at Castell' Arguqto, Am Inst Musicol, 75; auth, The Prodigal Son at the Whores: Music, Art, Drama, Univ Calif, Irvine, 76; The Music Library of Hans Heinrich Herwart, Annales Musicologiques, 77; A Royal Treasure at Sutton Coldfield, Early Music, 78; Veggio, Claudio Maria, In: Die Musik in Geshichte & Gegenwart, Vol XIV. *Mailing Add:* Dept Music Univ Calif Irvine CA 92717

SLOBIN, MARK
EDUCATOR
b Detroit, Mich, Mar 15, 43. *Study:* Univ Mich, PhD, 69. *Teaching:* From asst to assoc prof music, Wesleyan Univ, 71- *Awards:* Jaap Kunst Prize, Soc Ethnomusicol, 69. *Mem:* Soc Ethnomusicol; Am Folklore Soc; Int Coun Traditional Music. *Interests:* Ethnomusicology. *Publ:* Auth, Kirgiz Instrumental Music, Asian Music Publ, 69; ed, Central Asian Music, Wesleyan Univ Press, 75; auth, Music in the Culture of Northern Afghanistan, Univ Ariz Press, 76; Tenement Songs: Popular Music of the Jewish Immigrants, Univ Pa Press, 82; ed, Old Jewish Folk Music: Collections & Writings of M Beregovski, Univ Pa Press, 82. *Mailing Add:* Music Dept Wesleyan Univ Middletown CT 06457

SLOCUM, WILLIAM (BENNETT)
COMPOSER, FRENCH HORN
b Grand Junction, Colo, Dec 17, 36. *Study:* Univ NMex, BFA, MM; Juilliard Sch; Aspen Music Sch; Berkshire Music Ctr. *Works:* Woodwind Quintet, 67; Seven Lyric Pieces (clarinet solo), 69; Variations (horn solo), 71; Three Songs (baritone & four instrm), 71; Ambivalence (trumpet, two horns & perc), 72. *Pos:* First horn, Buffalo Phil Orch, 60-63 & Cleveland Orch, 66-68. *Teaching:* Instr, Univ Wyo, 63-66 & Cleveland Inst Music, 66-72 & Youngstown State Univ; assoc prof horn, Youngstown State Univ, currently. *Mailing Add:* 317 Redondo Rd Youngstown OH 44504

SLOMAN, JAN MARK
VIOLIN
b Charleston, WVa, Apr 10, 49. *Study:* Princeton Univ; Curtis Inst Music; studied with Galamian, Mankanowitzky, Laredo & Silverstein. *Pos:* Asst concertmaster, Charlotte Symph, 73-74; assoc concertmaster, Phoenix Symph, formerly, Dallas Symph, currently & Dallas Opera Orch, currently; dir, Violin Div, Eastern Music Fest, NC, formerly; solo appearances & recitals throughout Eastern US & with Phoenix Symph. *Awards:* Naumburg Grant, 67-69. *Mailing Add:* 1117 Bally Mote Dallas TX 75218

SLONIMSKY, NICOLAS
COMPOSER, WRITER
b St Petersburg, USSR, Apr 27, 1894; US citizen. *Study:* St Petersburg Consv, studied piano with Isabelle Vengerova, theory with Vassile Kalafati & orch with Maximilian Steinberg; studied with Gliere, Kiev; Northwestern Univ, Hon DFA, 81. *Works:* Studies in Black and White (piano), New Music, 28; Overture On An Ancient Greek Theme, Hollywood Bowl, 33; 4 Simple Pieces (orch), Boston Pops Orch, 41; My Toy Balloon (piano & orch), Shawnee Press, 42; Mobius Strip Tease, Univ Calif, Los Angeles, 65; 50 Minutes (piano), G Schirmer, 78. *Rec Perf:* Ionization (Varese), 34 & Suite for Cello & Piano (Slonimsky), 74, Orion Masterworks. *Pos:* Conct pianist touring Europe, 21-22, US, 23- & South Am, 41-42; secy to Serge Koussevitzky, 25-27; found & cond, Boston Chamber Orch, 27-34; cond, Harvard Univ Orch, 28-30; guest cond, Paris, Berlin, Budapest, Havana, San Francisco, Los Angeles, Hollywood & South Am, 31-42. *Teaching:* Instr, Eastman Sch Music, 23-25, Boston Consv Music, 25-45; vis prof, Colo Col, summer 40 & 47-49; lectr music, Simmons Col, 47-49; Peabody Consv, 56-57 & Univ Calif, Los Angeles, 64-67; State Dept lectr, Russia, Poland, Bulgaria, Yugoslavia, Greece, Rumania & Israel, 62-63. *Mem:* ASCAP. *Publ:* Auth, Music Since 1900, Scribner's, 37, rev ed, 71; Music of Latin America, Crowell/Da Capo, 45; Thesaurus of Scales and Melodic Patterns, 47 & Lexicon of Musical Invective, 53, Scribner's; ed, Baker's Biographical Dictionary of Musicians, Macmillan, 58, rev ed, 78. *Mailing Add:* 10847 3/4 Wilshire Blvd Los Angeles CA 90024

SLOOP, JEAN CAROLYN
EDUCATOR, LECTURER
b Mt Holly Springs, Pa, June 20, 31. *Study:* Gettysburg Col, AB(music), 53; Col-Consv Music, Univ Cincinnati, studied voice with Robert Powell, 56-59; Eastman Sch Music, MA(music theory), 56, DMA(voice perf & lit), 75; Mozarteum, Salzburg, Austria, studied lieder with Hilda Ormay-Butschek, summer 61; Akad Musik, Vienna, studied lieder with Kurt Schmidek, 64-65. *Teaching:* Instr theory & choral ens, Earlham Col, 57-59; instr voice, theory & choral ens, Kans State Univ, 59-, fac artist, 66-75, asst prof voice & foreign lang diction, 75-82, prof, 82- *Awards:* Fulbright Scholar, Govt Austria, 64-65; Found Grant Grad Study, Mu Phi Epsilon, 72; Fac res grant, Kans State Univ, 75. *Mem:* Nat Asn Teachers Singing; Mu Phi Epsilon Mem Found (bd mem, 83-); Pi Kappa Lambda. *Interests:* Out of print American art songs; symbolism in Renaissance music. *Mailing Add:* 1723 Leavenworth Manhattan KS 66502

SMALDONE, EDWARD MICHAEL
COMPOSER
b Rockville Center, NY, Nov 19, 56. *Study:* Queens Col, City Univ New York, BA, 78, with George Perle, Henry Weinberg & Hugo Weisgall, MA, 80, Grad Ctr, currently. *Works:* String Quartet, perf by Florin Quartet, 79; Solo Sonata for Violin, perf by Curtis Macomber, 81; January Morning (songs), perf by Marjorie Patterson, 82; Quintet for Winds, perf by Transatlantic Winds, 83. *Teaching:* Adj lectr, Queens Col, City Univ New York, 78-; assoc dir, Ctr Prep Studies Music, 81- *Awards:* Meet the Comp Award, Transatlantic Winds, 83. *Mem:* ASCAP; Am Music Ctr; Am Soc Univ Comp; Nat Asn Comp USA. *Publ:* Auth, Godanginuta: A Structural Analysis of Traditional Japanese Music, Hogaku/Traditional Japanese Music Soc, 83. *Mailing Add:* 147-41 24 Ave Whitestone NY 11357

SMALL, EDWARD PIERCE
PERCUSSION, EDUCATOR
b Detroit, Mich, Jan 17, 42. *Study:* Mich State Univ, BME, 65; Eastman Sch Music, with John Beck & William Street, MM, 67. *Pos:* Perc & marimba soloist, US Marine Band, Washington, DC, 67-71; perc & asst timpani, Denver Symph Orch, 71-; dir, Denver Perc Ens, 72-74. *Teaching:* Lectr perc, Univ Denver, 71- *Mem:* Percussive Arts Soc. *Mailing Add:* 5543 S Richfield Way Aurora CO 80015

SMALL, HASKELL BEHREND
PIANO, COMPOSER
b Washington, DC, June 3, 48. *Study:* San Francisco Consv Music, with Robert Sheldon; Carnegie-Mellon Univ, BFA, 72; study with Theodore Lettvin, William Masselos, Leon Fleischer, Jeanne Behrend & Harry Franklin. *Works:* Sonata No 1 (piano), Pittsburgh, 72; Three Songs (sop & piano), Monday Night Music House, 74; A Small Suite (piano), Carnegie Recital Hall, 79; Sonata No 2 (piano), Smith Square, London, 79; Concertino for Piano and Orchestra, Carnegie Hall, 80; A Short Story (piano, cello, flute, oboe & clarinet), comn & perf by Georgetown Symph, 81; Suite for Solo Cello, Abraham Goodman House, 81; and others. *Pos:* Concert pianist, major concert halls throughout US & Europe, including Barga Fest, Italy, Carnegie Hall & John F Kennedy Ctr Perf Arts, 71; solo recitals in US, London, Vienna, Berlin & Amsterdam, 71- *Teaching:* Fac mem, Ellsworth Music Studios, currently. *Awards:* Pittsburgh Conct Soc Auditions Award, 70; winner, Int Bach Compt, 75; NY Teachers Cong Award, 75. *Rep:* Judith Finell Music Serv 155 W 68th St New York NY 10023. *Mailing Add:* 3220 44th St NW Washington DC 20016

SMART, GARY L
COMPOSER, PIANO

b Cuba, Ill, Dec 19, 43. *Study:* Ind Univ, BMus, 67, MMus, 69; Hochschule Musik Cologne, Ger, 70-71; Yale Univ, DMA, 78. *Works:* Del Diario de un Papagago (chamber orch & tape), 73 & Fancy (in memoriam Joe Venuti, violin & piano), 78, Margun Music Publ; Sonata in Fancy (cello & piano), 82; Opal's Diary (soprano voice & piano), 83; Sonata in Fancy (vibraphone & piano), 83. *Pos:* Staff mem, Comp Conf, Wellesley, Mass, summers 76-*Teaching:* Artist in res, Contemp Music Proj, 71-73; assoc prof comp & piano, Univ Wyo, 78- *Awards:* Nat Endowment Arts Music Fel, 74-80. *Mem:* Col Music Soc; Sonneck Soc. *Mailing Add:* 1813 Bill Nye Ave Laramie WY 82070

SMEDVIG, ROLF THORSTEIN
TRUMPET, MUSIC DIRECTOR

b Seattle, Wash, Sept 23, 52. *Study:* Univ Wash; Berkshire Music Ctr; Boston Univ. *Works:* Amarilla, Brass Press; Trumpet Solo, Int Music, 82; Empire Brass Series, G Shirmer, 83. *Rec Perf:* With Boston Symph, on Philips, Deutsche Grammophon & Telarc, 72-81; solo trumpet rec, Sine Qua Non; rec with Empire Brass on CBS & Sine Qua Non, 76- *Pos:* Trumpet, Boston Symph, 72-81, solo trumpet, 79-81; solo trumpet, Empire Brass, currently; music dir, Cambridge Chamber Orch, currently. *Awards:* Naumburg Award, 76; Harvard Music Soc, 80. *Mem:* Stockbridge Club; Am Fedn Musicians. *Rep:* Columbia Artist Mgt 165 W 57th St New York NY 10019. *Mailing Add:* 1019 Commonwealth Boston MA 02115

SMELTZER, MARY SUSAN
COMPOSER, PIANO

b Sapulpa, Okla, Sept 13, 41. *Study:* Oklahoma City Univ, BM, 63; Univ Southern Calif, with Lillian Steuber & Eudice Shapiro, MM, 67 & with Gregor Piatigorsky, 69 & 70-71 & Rosina Lhevine, 71; Mt St Mary's Col, with Manuel Compinsky, 68-69 & 70-71; Akademie Musik, Vienna, with Joseph Dichler, 69-70. *Works:* Over 40 works incl Twelve Mood Pictures. *Pos:* Conct pianist, extensive solo & chamber music recitals throughout South, Midwest & West; soloist, with numerous Am symph orchs. *Teaching:* Instr & staff accmp, Oklahoma City Univ, 63-64; instr, privately, 64-72 & Mt St Mary's Col, 66-69 & 70-72; vis fac, Rice Univ, 72-73; prof accmp, Univ Houston, 72-73; artist in res & instr humanities, Col of Mainland, Texas City, 72-79. *Awards:* Fulbright Grant to Vienna, 69-70. *Mailing Add:* 8102 Tavenor Houston TX 77075

SMETANA, FRANTISEK
CELLO, EDUCATOR

b Ohnistany, Czech, May 8, 14. *Study:* State Consv Music, Prague, dipl(comp), 36; Ecole Normale Music, Paris, dipl(cello & chamber music), 38; studied cello with Pravoslav Sadlo & Pierre Fournier. *Pos:* Mem Czech Quartet, 39-46 & Prague Trio, 58-63; soloist & recitalist, Europ tours & radio broadcasts, 46-64, Jamaica, 64-66 & US, 66; appearances with Czech Phil & other Czech orch throughout Czech, 50-55; tour of China, Korea & Mongolia, 56; soloist, Hilversum Radio Orch, Rotterdam Phil, Reykjavik Symph, Royal Phil Orch, London & McGill Chamber Orch, Montreal, 68; prin cellist, Richmond Symph & Sinfonia, 73-75. *Teaching:* Cello & chamber music, Prague Consv, 46-48; mem fac, Jamaica Sch Music, Kingston, 64-66 & Iowa State Univ, 66-73; prof music, Va Commonwealth Univ, 73- *Mem:* Czech Soc Arts & Sci Am; Phi Mu Alpha; Pi Kappa Lambda. *Mailing Add:* Dept Music Va Commonwealth Univ Richmond VA 23284

SMETONA, VYTAUTAS JULIUS
PIANO, COMPOSER

b Cleveland, Ohio, Feb 14, 55. *Study:* Study with Leonard Shure, 61-74; Cleveland Inst Music, 72-74; Case Western Reserve Univ, BA, 76. *Rec Perf:* Vytautas Smetona Plays Chopin, Liszt & Rachmaninov, Sirius Rec, 79. *Pos:* Soloist, St Louis Symph, Dallas Symph & Baltimore Symph, 81- *Awards:* Outstanding Achievement Music, Lithuanian Nat Cult Found, 79; grant, Young Artist Develop Fund, 81. *Bibliog:* Edward Tatnall Canby (auth), Review of Record, Audio Mag, 6/79; Raymond Ericson (auth), Recital, Smetona, New York Times, 4/80; Olin Chism (auth), Review of Recital, Dallas Times, 7/82. *Rep:* Matthews/Napal Ltd 270 West End Ave New York NY 10023. *Mailing Add:* 6811 Mayfield Rd #399 Mayfield Heights OH 44124

SMILEY, MARILYNN JEAN
MUSICOLOGIST, EDUCATOR

Columbia City, Ind, June 5, 32. *Study:* Ball State Univ, BS, 54; Northwestern Univ, MMus(musicol), 58; Ecoles d'Art Americaines, Fontainebleau, France, with Nadia Boulanger, cert, 59; Univ Ill, Urbana, PhD(musicol), 70. *Teaching:* Music, Logansport, Ind Pub Sch, 54-61; instr music, State Univ NY, Oswego, 61-64, asst prof 64-67, assoc prof 67-72, prof 72-74, distinguished teaching prof, 74-, music dept chairperson, 76-81. *Awards:* Int Scholar, Delta Kappa Gamma, 64-65; Fac Res Fel, State Univ NY Res Found, 71, 72 & 74; Chancellor's Award for Excellence in Teaching, State Univ NY, 73. *Mem:* Am Musicol Soc (chairperson NY chap, 75-77); Sonneck Soc Am; Medieval Acad Am; Renaissance Soc Am. *Interests:* Various aspects of Medieval and Renaissance music; 19th century American music; the Renaissance Organ

Magnificat. *Publ:* Auth, Eleventh Century Music Theorists, Acta, 74; various articles on Am & local music hist in pamphlets & newspapers, 74-83. *Mailing Add:* 77 W Fifth St Oswego NY 13126

SMILEY, PRIL
COMPOSER, EDUCATOR

b Mohonk Lake, NY, Mar 19, 43. *Study:* Bennington Col, BA(music), 65. *Works:* Eclipse, First Int Electronic Music Contest, 69; Kolyosa, perf many times in US & abroad, 70-; Trip, Currents Int Contest, 72. *Pos:* Electronic music consult, Lincoln Ctr Repty Theatre, 68-74; assoc dir, Columbia-Princeton Electronic Music Ctr, 74-; vpres, CRI, 78- *Teaching:* Instr electronic music, Columbia Univ, 65- *Awards:* Grants, Nat Endowment of Arts, 74 & Creative Artists Pub Serv Prog, 80; Guggenheim fel, 75-76. *Mem:* BMI; Am Comp Alliance (bd mem, 74-75). *Mailing Add:* 7 Pine Rd New Paltz NY 12561

SMIRAGLIA, RICHARD PAUL
LIBRARIAN

b New York, NY, Mar 18, 52. *Study:* Lewis & Clark Col, BA, 73; Ind Univ, Bloomington, MLS, 74. *Pos:* Asst music catalog librn, Univ Ill, Urbana-Champaign, 74-78, music catalog librn, 78- *Awards:* Award, Music Libr Asn, 81. *Mem:* Asn Rec Sound Collections; Int Asn Music Libr; Music Libr Asn; Music OCLC Users Group (treas, 80-82, chmn, 82-84). *Interests:* Music cataloging; music bibliography. *Publ:* Auth, Shelflisting Music, Music Libr Asn, 81; coauth (with Ralph Papakhian), Music in the OCLC Online Union Catalog, Notes 38, 81; auth, Cataloging Music, Soldier Creek Press, 83; coauth (with Rochelle Wright), Danish Emigrant Ballads, Southern Ill Univ Press (in prep). *Mailing Add:* Music Libr Univ Ill 2136 Music Bldg 1114 W Nevada Urbana IL 61801

SMIT, LEO
PIANO, COMPOSER

b Philadelphia, Pa, Jan 12, 21. *Study:* Curtis Inst Music, piano with Isabelle Vengerova, 30-32; studied comp with Nicolas Nabokov, 35. *Works:* Symphony No 1, Boston, 57; Symphony No 2, New York, 66; The Alchemy of Love (space fable in three acts, libretto by Fred Hoyle), 67; Piano Concerto, perf by comp, 68; In Woods (oboe, harp & perc), 78; Magic Water (chamber opera), 78. *Pos:* Pianist, Am Ballet, 36-37 & New York City Symph, 47-48; piano tour of US, 40; artistic dir, Conct Hall, formerly; cond, Ojai Fest, Calif, 62 & Belgrade Phil, 82. *Teaching:* Mem fac, Sarah Lawrence Col, 47-49 & Univ Calif, Los Angeles, 57-62; Slee prof comp, State Univ NY, Buffalo, 62, prof, 63- *Awards:* Fulbright Grant, 50; Boston Symph Orch Merit Award, 53; New York Critics' Circle Award, 57. *Mem:* ASCAP. *Publ:* Contribr to Sat Rev, 75 & Clavier, 83. *Mailing Add:* Music Dept State Univ NY Buffalo NY 14214

SMITH, AMELIA (HALL)
MUSIC DIRECTOR, TEACHER-COACH

b Oklahoma City, Okla, Jan 15, 13. *Study:* Piano with Alexander Maloof & voice with Inez Barbour Hadley; Manhattan Sch Music, studied opera cond with George Schick, studied with Boris Goldovsky & Clifford Bair. *Pos:* Accompanist, 36-; Auth, The Music Box, feature newspaper column, The Free Press, 52-54, Jacksonville J, 54-59, The Trend, Jacksonville, 59-63, Church paper, Jacksonville, 63-67 & The Leader, Jacksonville Beach, 75-; founder & gen mgr, Opera a la Carte, Inc, 74- *Teaching:* Private voice, 40-; instr piano, Greensboro Col, 45-48; instr voice & piano, Bennett Col, 48-49; coach & accmp opera, Univ NC, Boone, summer 53; dir opera, Jacksonville Col Music, 56-61; instr voice, Edward Waters Col, 69-70. *Awards:* Eve Award in Fine Arts, Fla Publ Co, 76; award, North Am Collections Inc, St Louis, 81. *Mem:* Am Fedn Musicians; Am Guild Musical Artists; Jacksonville Music Teachers Asn; Am Guild Organists; Nat Asn Teachers Singing. *Publ:* Contribr, Musical Am, 69-82. *Mailing Add:* 4227 Peachtree Circle E Jacksonville FL 32207

SMITH, BRANSON
COMPOSER, TEACHER

b Pine Village, Ind, Dec 21, 21. *Study:* Ind Univ, BPSM, 47, MME, 57. *Works:* Concertpiece For Band, perf by Univ Ariz, 58 & Ariz State Univ, 59; Theme and Mutations, perf by Northern Ariz Symph Orch, 61; Ecumenical Cantata, perf by Tucson Catalina Methodist Choir, 65; Lyrical Statement For Strings, Phoenix Symph Orch, 67; Cantata from Walden, Tucson Civic Chorus, 70; Legends of Superstition Mountain (ballet), perf by Tucson Civic Ballet, 73 & 74; Suite For Strings, perf by Tucson Metropolitan Ballet, 78 & 79. *Pos:* Oboe & English horn, Albuquerque Symph Orch, 48-50 & Los Alamos Symphonette, 49-55. *Teaching:* Band dir, Espanola High Sch, NMex, 49-55 & Casa Grande Sch, Ariz, 56-62; instr instrm, Tucson Pub Sch, Dist 1, 62-67. *Awards:* Prof Comp First Prize, Ariz Music Clubs, 68. *Mailing Add:* 1944 E Third St Tucson AZ 85719

SMITH, CATHERINE PARSONS
EDUCATOR, FLUTE

b Rochester, NY, Nov 4, 33. *Study:* Eastman Sch Music, prep dipl, 50; Smith Col, AB, 54; Northwestern Univ, MM, 57; Stanford Univ, DMA, 69. *Works:* Polymer No 1 (flute), 63; Eleven by Walter (speaker & instrm), 71; Rings (six flutes & perc), Music Dept, Univ Okla, 70. *Pos:* Prin flute, Reno Phil Orch, currently; music critic, Palo Alto Times, Calif, 66-67. *Teaching:* Studio instr flute, Rapid City, SDak, Palo Alto, Calif & Reno, Nev, 60-; from lectr to assoc prof, Univ Nev, Reno, 69- *Awards:* Danforth Found Fel, 67-69; Nat Endowment Humanities Fel, 82-83. *Bibliog:* James Huskey (auth), Catherine Smith and Mary Carr Moore: Sisters in Western Music History, Univ Nev, Reno Frontiers, 10/82. *Mem:* Am Musicol Asn; Sonneck Soc; Col Music Soc; Am Fedn Musicians; Nat Asn Col Wind & Perc Instr. *Interests:* Eighteenth century performance practice, especially flutes; Mary Carr Moore. *Publ:* Auth, Changing Use of the Flute and Its Changing Construction, 1774-1795, Am Recorder, 79; The Woodwind Section in Haydn's Symphonies, 1760-1795, Nat Asn Col Wind & Perc Instr J, 79; intro to Mary Carr Moore's David Rizzio, Da Capo Press, 81; The True Way to Learn to Play Perfectly Oboe, Recorder, etc, Am Recorder, 82; Moore, Mary Carr, In: New Grove Dict of Music in US (in press). *Mailing Add:* Dept Music Univ Nev Reno NV 89557

SMITH, CHARLES JUSTICE
EDUCATOR, WRITER
b Charleston, WVa, Sept 7, 50. *Study:* Yale Univ, BA, 72; Univ Mich, MM(theory), 74, PhD(theory), 80. *Teaching:* Instr theory, Univ Conn, 78-80, asst prof, 80-; vis asst prof, Univ BC, Vancouver, spring 83. *Awards:* Fel, Nat Endowment Humanities, 81. *Mem:* Soc Music Theory; Am Musicol Soc; Col Music Soc; Music Theory Soc New York. *Interests:* Late 19th century harmony; logical and philosophical structure of musical analysis; Beethoven's sketches. *Publ:* Auth, Rhythm Restratified, Perspectives New Music, 77; Beethoven via Schenker, In Theory Only, 78; Musical A Priori's: An Investigation of Explanatory Strategies, Col Music Symposium, spring 79; Prolongations and Progressions as Musical Syntax, In: Music Theory: Special Topics, Acad Press, 81. *Mailing Add:* Music Dept Univ Conn Box U-12 Storrs CT 06268

SMITH, CHARLES WARREN
EDUCATOR, COMPOSER
b Palmerton, Pa, Sept 5, 36. *Study:* Univ Wyo, BM, 58; NY Univ, 65; Eastman Sch Music, 67-68; Univ NC, 70, George Peabody Col, DMA, 74. *Works:* The Harmonica Player (band); Jubilee (band); Adagio and Allegro (flute, clarinet & piano); Te Deum (chorus); I Will Publish the Name of the Lord (chorus); Suite Contemporain (piano); Reflections (piano). *Pos:* Prin flutist in many symph orchs. *Teaching:* Music, pub schs, Wyo, Mont, NJ & NY, 57-68; asst prof music, Madison Col, Va, 68-69 & Wake Forest Univ, 69-75; prof music, SE Mo State Univ, 75- *Awards:* Am Guild Musical Artists Award, 58. *Mem:* Am Fedn Musicians; ASCAP; Music Educr Nat Conf; Am Soc Univ Comp; Phi Mu Alpha Sinfonia. *Mailing Add:* Dept Music SE Mo State Univ Cape Girardeau MO 63701

SMITH, DORMAN HENRY
LIBRARIAN, EDUCATOR
b Rochester, NY, Nov 12, 41. *Study:* Univ Calif, Berkeley, MA, 67; Simmons Col, MSLS, 70. *Pos:* Head music libr, State Univ NY, Stony Brook, 74-76; head tech serv, Univ Wis, Parkside, 76-80; head music collection, Univ Ariz, 80- *Mem:* Music Libr Asn; Nat Flute Asn; Int Trombone Asn. *Interests:* Bibliographies of flute and guitar music. *Publ:* Ed, Nat Flute Asn Music Libr Catalog, 83. *Mailing Add:* 432 N Bull Run Dr Tucson AZ 85748

SMITH, DOUGLAS
EDUCATOR, COMPOSER
b Cincinnati, Ohio, Oct 25, 39. *Study:* Carson-Newman Col, BS, 61; NTex State Univ, MME, 64; Univ Mich, DMA, 69. *Works:* 61 Series (for trumpet & trombone), Hope, 77-81; 4 Plus Brass Arrangements, Hinshaw, Roger Dean, Broadman, 78, 80 & 81; Anthems with Brass, Doxology, 79, 80 & 82; O Master ... Solo Collection, Broadman, 82. *Pos:* Prin trumpet, Ft Worth Symph, 69-73. *Teaching:* Instr trumpet and brass, NTex State Univ, 65-67; assoc prof theory & cond, Dallas Baptist Col, 69-75; prof cond & arr, Southern Baptist Theological Sem, 75- *Mem:* Col Band Dir Nat Asn; Int Trumpet Guild; Christian Instrumental Dir Asn; Southern Baptist Church Music Conf; ASCAP. *Publ:* Auth, articles on brass pedagogy, Instrumentalist, 66-80; articles on Instruments in Worship, Church Musician, 77-81; articles on American view of British brass bands in national competitions, British Bandsman, 81-82. *Mailing Add:* 2825 Lexington Rd #1907 Louisville KY 40280

SMITH, DOUGLAS ALTON
WRITER, GUITAR & LUTE
b Jamestown, NY, Oct 15, 44. *Study:* Univ Puget Sound, BA, 66; Univ Wash, MA, 67, BA, 71; Stanford Univ, MA, 74, PhD, 77. *Pos:* Assoc ed, J Lute Soc Am, 75-83. *Teaching:* Lectr lute & guitar hist, San Francisco Consv Music, 77. *Awards:* Res Fel, Alexander von Humboldt Found, 77-79. *Mem:* Lute Soc Am (secy bd, 75, mem bd dir, 75-); Am Musicol Soc. *Interests:* History of lute music, especially German baroque lute music and works of Silvius Leopold Weiss. *Publ:* Translr, E G Baron, Study of the Lute, Instrm Antiqua, 76; auth, On the Origin of the Chitarrone, J Am Musicol Soc, fall 79; Sylvius Leopold Weiss, 1/80 & The Ebenthal Lute and Viol Manuscripts, 10/82, Early Music; ed, Silvius Leopold Weiss: Complete Works for Lute, C F Peters, 83. *Mailing Add:* PO Box F Stanford CA 94305

SMITH, EDWIN LESTER
EDUCATOR, COMPOSER
b Cleveland, Tenn, Feb 15, 41. *Study:* Univ Ill, BM, 65; Fla State Univ, MM, 66; Univ Ky, DMA, 74. *Works:* Introits and Responses, 79, Lord, Make Me an Instrument of Thy Peace, 79 & Psalm 23, 81, G Schirmer. *Teaching:* Asst prof, Birmingham Southern Col, 67-70; instr, Univ Ky, Lexington, 72-74; prof & head theory & comp, Univ Wis, Eau Claire, 74- *Mailing Add:* 3712 Golf Rd Eau Claire WI 54701

SMITH, GEORGE FRANCIS
CONDUCTOR, EDUCATOR
b Chickasha, Okla, Oct 18, 31. *Study:* Univ Okla, BME, 54, MME, 55; NTex State Univ, EdD, 69. *Pos:* Cond, Southeastern Okla State Univ Chorale, 61-69, Cameron Singers, Cameron Univ, 69-73 & Southwest Chorale, Lawton, Okla, 81- *Teaching:* Vocal music dir, Frederick High Sch, Okla & Will Rogers High Sch, Okla, 55-61; asst prof music, Southeastern Okla State Univ, 61-69; prof music, Cameron Univ, 69-, chmn, Music Dept, 69-80. *Mem:* Am Choral Dir Asn; Music Educr Nat Conf. *Publ:* Auth, Whither SATB? Am Choral Dir Asn J, 66. *Mailing Add:* 302 Ridgeview Way Lawton OK 73505

SMITH, GERALD L
EDUCATOR, BARITONE
b Manchester, Iowa, Mar 21, 21. *Study:* Univ Dubuque, BA, 42; Chicago Consv Music, MM, 49; Univ Dubuque, Hon Dr Music, 70. *Pos:* Performer conct ser, Orient, 73 & Australia, 75; dir, Church Music Summer Sch, Garrett Evangelical Theol Sem, 74-, dir music, currently; dir music, First United Methodist Church, Evanston. *Teaching:* Assoc prof voice, Northwestern Univ, 50-; instr masterclasses voice, Albion Col, 79 & Coe Col, 80. *Mem:* Pi Kappa Lambda; Nat Asn Teachers Singing; Chicago Singing Teachers Guild; Am Choral Dir Asn; Music Educr Nat Conf. *Mailing Add:* 802 Ingleside Pl Evanston IL 60201

SMITH, GLENN PARKHURST
TROMBONE, EDUCATOR
b Oswego, Ill, Feb 26, 12. *Study:* Wheaton Col, Ill, BMus, 34; Northwestern Univ, MMus, 49; private trombone studies with Jaroslav Cimera. *Pos:* First trombone, Chicago Civic Symph, 34-35. *Teaching:* Supvr music, pub sch in Kans & Ill, 35-50; from instr to prof trombone, Sch Music, Univ Mich, 50-80, emer prof, 80- *Mem:* Nat Asn Col Wind & Perc Instr; Int Trombone Asn; Music Educr Nat Conf. *Publ:* Auth, Original Unaccompanied Trombone Ensemble Music, Instrumentalist, 2/74; Brass Related Doctoral Dissertation, 1/75, Paris National Conservatory Contest Pieces, 1/77, Errata for Melodious Etudes for Trombone, 1/77 & A Second Look at Rimsky-Korsakov's Trombone Concerto, 1/78, J Int Trombone Asn. *Mailing Add:* 312 Doty Ave Ann Arbor MI 48103

SMITH, HALE
COMPOSER, EDUCATOR
b Cleveland, Ohio, June 29, 25. *Study:* Cleveland Inst Music, with Marcel Dick, MusB, 50, MusM, 52. *Works:* Rituals and Incantations, Houston, 74; By Yearning & Be Beautiful, New York, 74; Introduction, Cadenzas and Interludes (eight players), 74; Variations for Six Players, 75; Innerflexions, New York, 77; Tous-saint l'overture 1803 (chorus), 77. *Pos:* Ed & consult, music publ, 59-; Introspections and Reflections (piano), Kennedy Ctr, 79. *Teaching:* Mem fac, C W Post Col, 68-70; mem fac, Univ Conn, 70-78, prof music, 78- *Awards:* BMI Student Comp Award, 52; Cleveland Arts Prize, 73. *Mem:* Am Comp Alliance; Bohemians. *Mailing Add:* Dept Music Univ Conn Storrs CT 06268

SMITH, HENRY CHARLES
CONDUCTOR & MUSIC DIRECTOR, TROMBONE
b Philadelphia, Pa, Jan 31, 31. *Study:* Univ Pa, BA, 52; Curtis Inst Music, artist dipl, 55. *Works:* Solos for the Trombone Player, 63; Hear Us As We Pray (SATB), 63; First Solos for the Trombone Player, 72; Easy Duets for Winds, 72. *Rec Perf:* Over 200 with Philadelphia Orch, eight with Philadelphia Brass Ens & three solo. *Pos:* Solo trombonist, Philadelphia Orch, 55-67; founder & mem, Philadelphia Brass Ens, 56-; civic music dir, Rochester, Minn, 67-68; res cond & educ dir, Minn Orch, 71-; music dir, World Youth Symph, 81- & Bach Soc, currently; cond, Young Artist Orch, Berkshire Music Ctr, formerly; guest cond throughout US, currently. *Teaching:* Assoc prof music, Ind Univ, Bloomington, 68-71; mem fac, Curtis Inst Music, Temple Univ, St Olaf Col & Luther Col, formerly. *Awards:* Grammy Award, 69. *Mem:* Int Trombone Asn; Music Educr Nat Conf; Am Guild Organists; Am Fedn Musicians; Tubist Universal Brotherhood Asn. *Publ:* Contribr to Am String Teachers Asn J. *Mailing Add:* 5640 Woodale Ave Edina MN 55424

SMITH, HOPKINSON KIDDER
GUITAR & LUTE
b New York, NY, Dec 7, 46. *Study:* Harvard Col, AB, 72; studied with Emilio Pujol & Eugen Dombois. *Rec Perf:* Tablatures de Luth (Albert de Rippe), Astree/Telefunken, 77; Lute Works (Sylvius Weiss), EMI Electrola, 79; Pieces de Theorbe (Robert de Visee), 79, Pieces de Luth (Charles Mouton), 80 & Lute Works (J S Bach), 81-82, Astree. *Pos:* Freelance perf on early plucked string instrm, currently. *Teaching:* Lute & basso continuo realization on early plucked instrm, Schola Cantorum Basiliensis, Basel, Switzerland, 77- *Awards:* Erwin Bodky Award Early Music, 70. *Rep:* Lee McRae 2130 Carleton St Berkeley Calif 94704. *Mailing Add:* Oberebatterieweg 90 4059 Basel Switzerland

SMITH, J FENWICK
FLUTE, TEACHER
b Boston, Mass, Jan 3, 49. *Study:* Eastman Sch Music, BM, 72, perf cert, 72. *Rec Perf:* Sonata, Op 26 (Schoenberg), Northeastern Rec, 83; numerous rec with Boston Musica Viva, CRI, Nonesuch, Cambridge & Northeastern. *Pos:* Mem, Boston Musica Viva, 75- & New England Woodwind Quintet, 76-79; second flute, Boston Symph Orch, 78-; mem, Boston Consv Chamber Players, 83- *Teaching:* Instr music, Sch Fine & Appl Arts, Boston Univ, 78- & New England Consv, 82-; artist in res, Boston Consv, 83- *Mem:* Nat Flute Asn. *Rep:* Lauren Whittaker Mgt 8 Chiswick Rd #34 Brookline MA 02130. *Mailing Add:* 235 Forest Hills St Jamaica Plain MA 02130

SMITH, JAMES F
EDUCATOR, GUITAR & LUTE

b Washington, DC. *Study:* La State Univ, New Orleans, BA(theory & comp), 71; Univ Southern Calif, Los Angeles, MM, 75; studied with Aaron Shearer, Christopher Parkening & Jon Marcus. *Rec Perf:* The Versatile Clarinet, Protone Rec, 82; A Composer's View, Town Hall Rec, 82. *Teaching:* Instr music, Univ Southern Calif, Los Angeles, 75-77, asst prof, 77- *Mem:* Guitar Found Am (vpres, 82-); Lute Soc Am; Am Guitar Soc. *Publ:* Auth, Briefly Noted, Soundboard Mag, 82- *Mailing Add:* 1383 Edgecliff Dr Los Angeles CA 90026

SMITH, JAMES GORDON
CONDUCTOR, EDUCATOR

b Raleigh, NC, Aug 28, 35. *Study:* Peabody Consv Music, BM, 60, MM, 61; Univ Ill, DMA, 73. *Teaching:* Asst prof choral music & cond chamber choir, Univ Ill, Urbana, 69-77; assoc prof & cond choral, Eastman Sch Music, 77-80; prof & cond, Gloriana Singers, Northern Va Symphonic Chorus & Univ Chorale, George Mason Univ, 80- *Mem:* Am Musicol Soc; Am Choral Dir Asn; Am Choral Found; Asn Prof Vocal Ens; Col Music Soc. *Interests:* American music. *Publ:* Ed, The New Liberty Bell: An Anthology of American Choral Music, Mark Foster Music Co, 76; auth, Choral Music, In: New Grove Dict of Music & Musicians, 80. *Mailing Add:* 10109 Alice Ct Fairfax VA 22032

SMITH, JERRY NEIL
EDUCATOR, ADMINISTRATOR

b Lefors, Tex, Feb 20, 35. *Study:* Univ Tex, Austin, BMus, 56, MM & perf cert, 57; Eastman Sch Music, PhD, 63. *Works:* Epilog (band), Volkwein Publ, 68; Fanfare and Celebration (band), Barnhouse Publ, 75; numerous others for marching & jazz bands, Shapiro-Bernstein & Big Three Publ. *Teaching:* Instr music, Univ Fla, 61-64; assoc prof, Univ Colo, Boulder, 64-72; head music dept, Univ Northern Iowa, 72-75; prof, Sch Music, Univ Okla, 75-, dir, 75-80. *Awards:* Res & Creativity Award, Univ Colo, 67; MacDowell Colony Res, 82. *Mem:* ASCAP; Music Educr Nat Conf; Music Teachers Nat Asn; Int Clarinet Soc. *Mailing Add:* 1426 Magnolia St Norman OK 73069

SMITH, JESS
ADMINISTRATOR, EDUCATOR

b Tacoma, Wash, July 20, 24. *Study:* Univ Puget Sound, studied piano with Leonard Jacobsen, BMus, 50; Los Angeles Consv, studied piano with Rosinna Lhevinne, 50; Juilliard Sch, studied piano with Rosinna Lhevinne & Josef Raieff; Teachers Col, Columbia Univ, MA, 67. *Teaching:* Lectr piano & theory, Brooklyn Consv Music, 57-58, registrar, Queensboro Branch, 58-70, vpres, 70-77, pres & dir, 77- *Mem:* Nat Guild Community Sch Arts; Nat Asn Sch Music. *Mailing Add:* Manhasset Trail Ridge NY 11961

SMITH, JOHN ADELBERT
ADMINISTRATOR, MUSIC DIRECTOR

b Glens Falls, NY, July 14, 43. *Study:* Hartwick Col, BS, 65; Syracuse Univ, MS, 66. *Pos:* Asst dir admis, Rockford Col, Ill, 66-67; exec dir, Detroit Community Music Sch, 81- *Teaching:* Lectr choral cond & asst dean, Sch Music, Univ Mich, 68-80; instr music educ & dir admis & regstr, Westminster Choir Col, 67-68. *Mem:* Am Choral Dir Asn; Mich Sch Vocal Asn; Am Guild Organists; Detroit Musicians League. *Mailing Add:* 200 E Kirby Detroit MI 48202

SMITH, JOSEPH TURNER
CONDUCTOR & MUSIC DIRECTOR, EDUCATOR

b Tullahoma, Tenn, Jan 9, 28. *Study:* Mid Tenn State Univ, BS, 51, MA, 57; George Peabody Col Teachers, Tenn. *Pos:* Guest cond, adjudicator & clinician in US, Can & Mex. *Teaching:* Dir, Franklin Co High Sch Band, Winchester, Tenn, 51-55 & Newton Co High Sch Band, Covington, Ga, 55-57; prof music & dir band, Mid Tenn State Univ, 57-, adv cond, 79- *Awards:* Citation Excellence, Nat Band Asn, 78. *Mem:* Tenn Music Educr; Nat Band Asn; Col Band Dir Asn; nat patron, Delta Omicron. *Mailing Add:* 707 Greenbrier Dr Murfreesboro TN 37130

SMITH, JULIA (JULIA SMITH VIELEHR)
COMPOSER, PIANO

b Denton Tex, Jan 25, 11. *Study:* NTex State Univ, BA, 30; Juilliard Sch Music, with Carl Friedberg & Frederick Jacobi, dipl(piano), 32, dipl(comp), 39; NY Univ, with Marion Bauer & Virgil Thomson, MA, 33, PhD, 52. *Works:* Liza Jane, 40, The Gooseherd & the Goblin, 47, Folkways Symphony, 49 & Trio-Cornwall, 56, Mowbray; Our Heritage (SSAATB & orch), comn by Tex Boys Choir, 57; Daisy, comn by Opera Guild Greater Miami, 73; Prairie Kaleidoscope, 81. *Rec Perf:* Quartet for Strings, Desto Rec, 71; Highlights from Daisy, Orion Rec, 76. *Pos:* Pianist, NY Orchestrette, 33-43; lectr & recitalist, The Piano Music of Aaron Copland, toured in US & Latin Am, 56-60. *Teaching:* Fac mem theory dept, Juilliard Sch Music, 40-42; founder & head music educ dept, Hartt Col, Conn, 41-45; instr music hist, State Teachers Col, New Britain, Conn, 42-45. *Awards:* Nat Fedn Music Clubs Award for Am Music, 79. *Mem:* Nat Asn Am Comp & Cond; Nat Fedn Music Clubs; Musicians Club NY; Carl Friedberg Found; ASCAP. *Publ:* Auth, Aaron Copland, His Work & Contribution to American Music, Dutton, 55; Carl Friedberg: Master Pianist, Philosophical Libr, 63. *Rep:* Theodore Presser Co Presser Place Bryn Mawr PA 19010. *Mailing Add:* 417 Riverside Dr New York NY 10025

SMITH, KENNETH
BASS-BARITONE, EDUCATOR

b Leeds, England, Aug 26, 22; US citizen. *Study:* Manhattan Sch Music, 45-46, NY Col Music, 46-49. *Roles:* Down in the Valley, New England Opera Co, 50; Billy Budd, NBC-TV, 71; Gloriana, Cincinnati May Fest, 56; Tempest, New York City Opera Co, 56; War and Peace, 59; Life of the Mission, San Antonio, 59; Cyrano de Bergerac, Univ Col, 65. *Pos:* Bass-bar, New England Opera Co, 50, Town Hall, 51, Cent City Opera, 53, Chicago Lyr Opera, 55-58, New York City Opera, 56 & 60, Washington Opera, 59 & others; performer, with L'Orqueta Sinfonica Nac Venzuela, Caracas, 68 & other orchs. *Teaching:* Prof voice & chmn voice dept, Univ Kans, 65-, chmn perf dept, 76. *Mem:* Am Guild Musical Artists; Actor's Equity; Pi Kappa Lambda. *Mailing Add:* Dept Music Univ Kans Lawrence KS 66045

SMITH, LARRY ALAN
COMPOSER, EDUCATOR

b Canton, Ohio, Oct 4, 55. *Study:* Ecoles d'Art Americaines, Paris & Fontainebleau, with Nadia Boulanger, dipl, 76; Juilliard Sch, with Vincent Persichetti, BM, 77, MM, 79, DMA, 81. *Works:* Apogees (string orch), Bourne Co, 76; Duo Concertante, comn by Tidewater Music Fest, Md, 78; Crucifixus (sop & orch), Belwin-Mills Publ Corp, 78; Third Piano Sonata, perf by Marguerita Oundjian, 79; Aria da Capo (opera in one act), comn by Chamber Opera Theatre, Chicago, 80; Strands (ten & harp), perf by Paul Sperry & Nancy Allen, 82; Trio (three flutes), comn by Julius Baker & Brad & Gary Garner Trio, 82. *Teaching:* Fac mem comp & theory, Boston Consv, 79-80; fac mem lit & materials of music, Juilliard Sch, 80- *Awards:* David Faith Prize, 78, Alexandre Gretchaninoff Mem Prize, 79 & Joseph Machlis Prize, 81, Juilliard Sch. *Mem:* Int Soc Contemp Music, League Comp (bd mem, 82-); BMI; Am Music Ctr; Chamber Music Am. *Mailing Add:* 800 West End Ave Apt 7A New York NY 10025

SMITH, LAWRENCE LEIGHTON
CONDUCTOR, PIANO

b Portland, Ore, Apr 8, 36. *Study:* Portland State Univ, BS, 57; Mannes Col Music, BS(music), 62. *Pos:* Music dir & cond, Austin Symph, 72-73, Ore Symph Orch, 73-80, San Antonio Symph, 80- & Louisville Orch, 83- *Rep:* Herbert Barrett 1860 Broadway New York NY 10023. *Mailing Add:* 3115 Hitching Post San Antonio TX 78217

SMITH, LAWRENCE RACKLEY See Rackley, Lawrence

SMITH, LELAND CLAYTON
COMPOSER, EDUCATOR

b Oakland, Calif, Aug 6, 25. *Study:* Mills Col, with Darius Milhaud, 42-47; Univ Calif, Berkeley, with Roger Sessions, 48; Paris Consv, with Olivier Messiaen, 48-49. *Works:* Symphony for Small Orch, San Francisco Symph, 52; Intermezzo & Capriccio for Piano, 52; Santa Claus, Univ Chicago, 55; Arabesque for Ensemble, Philadelphia Symph, 60-70; Concerto for Orchestra, Orch Am, Carnegie Hall, 62; Viola Sonata, London, Paris & Chicago; String Trio, Fantasy Rec. *Pos:* Bassoon & clarinet, San Francisco Symph, 51-52, 58-65 & Chicago Opera & Symph, 53-57. *Teaching:* Instr, Mills Col, 51-52; asst prof, Univ Chicago, 52-58; prof, Stanford Univ, 58- *Awards:* Copley Found Award, 55; Fromm Found Comn, 56; Fulbright Sr Award, 64. *Mem:* Am Fedn Musicians. *Interests:* Computer music typesetting system. *Publ:* Contribr, Perspectives: Anton Webern, Univ Wash; Score, J Audio Engineering Soc; Printing Music by Computer, J Music Theory; Henry Cowell's Rhythmicana, Interamerican Bulletin; auth, Handbook of Harmonic Analysis, San Andreas Press, 79. *Mailing Add:* Music Dept Stanford Univ Stanford CA 94305

SMITH, MALCOLM SOMMERVILLE
BASS

b New York, NY. *Study:* Consv Music, Oberlin Col, BMusEd, 57, BMus(voice), 60; Teachers Col, Columbia Univ, MA, 58; Sch Music, Ind Univ, studied opera with Paul Matthen & Frank St Leger, 60-62. *Rec Perf:* Samson (Handel), 62 & Mahler's Eighth, 63, Salt Lake City Symph. *Roles:* Soloist, G Minor Mass, Robert Shaw Russ Tour, 62; Colline in La Boheme, New York City Opera, Metropolitan Opera, Miami Opera & Deutsche Oper Am Rhein, Düsseldorf, 65-; King Mark in Tristan and Isolde, Spoleto Fest, Sao Paulo Opera, Geneva Opera, Deutsche Oper Am Rhein, Düsseldorf & Hamburg Opera, 67-; Alvise in La Gioconda, Metropolitan Opera, 75-76; Pogner in Die Meistersinger von Nürnberg, Metropolitan Opera, Berlin Staatsoper & Deutsche Oper Am Rhein, Düsseldorf, 75-; Gurnemanz in Parsifal, Deutsche Oper Am Rhein, Düsseldorf & Edinburg Fest, 78. *Pos:* Leading bass, New York City Opera, 65-70, Deutsche Oper Am Rhein, Düsseldorf, 71- & Metropolitan Opera House, 75-77; soloist, Philadelphia, Chicago, Baltimore, Washington & Boston operas, 65-; guest appearances, La Scala, Berlin, Hamburg, Vienna, Stuttgart, Rome, Barcelona, Madrid & Paris operas. *Mem:* Am Guild Musical Artists. *Rep:* Thea Dispeker 59 E 54th St New York NY 10022. *Mailing Add:* 22 Woodland Rd Montvale NJ 07645

SMITH, MARGARET YAUGER See Yauger, Margaret

SMITH, MARTIN
MUSIC DIRECTOR, EDUCATOR

b Williamson, WVa. *Study:* Col Consv Music, Cincinnati Univ, BM; Univ Vienna, dipl; Columbia Univ, MA; studied piano with Olga Conus. *Pos:* Conct tours, Europe, Middle East & South Am, 61-67; chorus master, Santa Fe Opera, 67-68; music adminr, NET-TV Opera Theater, 69-72; music dir, Hurok Operatic Quartet, 71-; dir opera, Aspen Fest, 74-76; piano soloist with maj orchs; asst cond, opera co in Boston, New York, Cincinnati, St Louis & San Francisco. *Teaching:* Mem fac, Temple Univ, formerly & Berkshire Music Ctr, formerly; chmn opera dept, New England Consv Music, 72-73; adminr, Am Opera Ctr, Juilliard Sch, 73-80, head coach, 73-; head coach, Wolf Trap Ctr Perf Arts, 77-78, dir opera training prog, 79. *Awards:* Kirsten Flagstad Mem Prize, 66. *Mem:* Pi Kappa Lambda. *Mailing Add:* Juilliard Sch Lincoln Ctr New York NY 10023

SMITH, MARTIN DODGE
FRENCH HORN, TEACHER
b New Orleans, La, Mar 28, 47. *Study:* Juilliard Sch Music, BM, 68 & MS, 69. *Rec Perf:* Hayden Horn Concerto No 1, Vox-Turnabout, 75. *Pos:* Solo horn, St Paul Chamber Orch, 70-74; assoc prin horn, New York Phil, 74-78 & actg prin horn, 78-79; co-prin horn, Pittsburgh Symph Orch, 80- *Teaching:* Instr French horn, Montclair State Col, 75-79 & Waterloo Summer Music Fest, 75- *Mailing Add:* 1400 Smokey Wood Dr Pittsburgh PA 15218

SMITH, MICHAEL CEDRIC
GUITAR & LUTE
b Chicago, Ill, Mar 28, 52. *Study:* Peabody Consv Music, BM(guitar perf), 73. *Pos:* Guitarist, Cappella Soloists, St Louis, 75-77; solo guitarist, perf London, 81 & New York, 84. *Teaching:* Guitar, Nat Music Camp, Interlochen, Mich, 74-77 & Selma Levine Sch Music, Washington, DC, 78-; instr, St Louis Consv, 74-77; adj asst prof, Brooklyn Col, 80- *Rep:* Int Artists Mgt 10572 Jason Lane Columbia MD 21044. *Mailing Add:* 2212 Phelps Rd #113 Adelphi MD 20783

SMITH, ORCENITH GEORGE
CONDUCTOR & MUSIC DIRECTOR, COMPOSER
b Winfield, Kans, Apr 14, 51. *Study:* Col-Consv Music, Univ Cincinnati, BM(perf & cond), 73, MM(cond), 77. *Works:* B-A-C-H Fantasia, comn & perf by DePauw Chamber Symph, 75; The Book of Small Anthems, GS Press, 79. *Rec Perf:* Five rec, Interlochen Silver Crest Rec, 76-78; Carmina Burana (C Orff), 77, Requiem (Brahms), 79 & Requiem (G Verdi), 81, DePauw Rec. *Pos:* Music dir, DePauw Univ Symph & Chamber Symph, 74-, Ind Little Symph, 80- & Youth Symph Orch Gtr Chicago, 81-; prin guest cond, Terre Haute Symph Orch, 78- *Teaching:* Instr music, DePauw Univ, 74- *Awards:* John Phillip Sousa Award, Springfield N High Sch, 68; Bertha Baur Mem Award, Univ Cincinnati, 72. *Bibliog:* Patrick Aikman (auth), Once an Entrepreneur, DePauw Alumnus Mag, 81. *Mem:* Am Symph Orch League; Ind Orch Asn (secy, 76); Pi Kappa Lambda (secy, 81-); Phi Mu Alpha Sinfonia; Am Fedn Musicians. *Mailing Add:* 601 E Washington #4 Greencastle IN 46135

SMITH, PAMELA G
OBOE & ENGLISH HORN
b Atlanta, Ga, Feb 10, 53. *Study:* Ga State Univ, with Joe Robinson, 71 & 73; San Francisco Consv, with Marc Lifschey, BM, 73-75; Stetson Orch Inst, with John DeLancie, summer 73-75. *Pos:* Second oboe & English horn, San Francisco Ballet, 75-77; asst prin & second oboe, Atlanta Symph, 77-80; second oboe, San Francisco Symph, 80-81; assoc prin oboe, Honolulu Symph, 81- *Mailing Add:* 715 S Raritan Denver CO 80223

SMITH, PATRICE JANE
CRITIC-WRITER, PIANO
b McSherrystown, Pa, June 16, 53. *Study:* Piano with Herbert Springer, 63-69; Indiana Univ Pa, BA, 75. *Pos:* Feature writer arts, Hanover Sun, 75-77; music critic, Evansville Courier, 80- *Mem:* Am Music Critics Asn. *Mailing Add:* 201 NW Second St Evansville IN 47702

SMITH, PATRICK JOHN
CRITIC-WRITER, LECTURER
b New York, NY, Dec 11, 32. *Study:* Princeton Univ, AB, 55. *Pos:* Book ed, Musical Am, 65-; ed & publ, Musical Newslett, 70-77; critic, Times, London, 77- & Opera, 78- *Mem:* Music Critics Asn (pres, 77-81); Am Musicol Soc. *Publ:* Auth, The Tenth Muse: A Historical Study of the Opera Libretto, 70 & A Year at the Met, 83, Alfred A Knopf Inc. *Mailing Add:* 654 Madison Ave No 1703 New York NY 10021

SMITH, PRISCILLA
EDUCATOR, CONDUCTOR
Study: Ind State Univ, BS, 49, MS, 56; Ind Univ; Univ Wis; studied cello with Luigi Silva & Fritz Magg & cond with Ernst Hoffman & James Barnes. *Pos:* Mem, Indianapolis Phil, Ft Lauderdale, Miami Beach & Tallahassee Symph; assoc cond, Lorain Co Youth Orch, 76-81. *Teaching:* Asst prof educ, Fla State Univ, 59-61; music dept head, Arlington High Sch, Indianapolis, 61-73; prof & chairperson dept music educ, Oberlin Col, 73-; mem fac, Nat String Inst, Univ Wis, 80- *Mailing Add:* Music Dept Oberlin Col Oberlin OH 44074

SMITH, RAYMOND R
EDUCATOR
b Granville, NY, Apr 6, 33. *Study:* State Univ NY, Potsdam, BS, 54; Syracuse Univ, MA, 58; Univ Rochester, PhD, 68. *Teaching:* Instr, Alfred Univ, 58-60 & Westminster Col, New Wilmington, Pa, 60-65; chmn, Dept Music, RI Col, Providence, 70-74 & prof, 74- *Mem:* Am Musicol Soc. *Interests:* History of the symphony and development of sonata form through the twentieth century. *Publ:* Auth, Performing Haydn and Mozart, Am Music Teacher, 71; New Repertory for Amateur Performers, Music J, 75; Motivic Procedure in Opening Movements of the Symphonies of Schumann, Bruckner & Brahms, Music Rev, 75; ed, Pleyel, Periodical Symphonies Numbers 1 & 14, A-R Ed, 78; co-ed, Pleyel, Four Symphonies and One Symphonie Concertante, Garland Publ, 81. *Mailing Add:* Box 265 RR 4 North Scituate RI 02957

SMITH, ROBERT LUDWIG
EDUCATOR
b Apr 10, 35. *Study:* Millsaps Col, Jackson, Miss, BA, 57; Univ Miss, MM, 59; Fla State Univ, PhD, 72. *Teaching:* Prof music, Inter Am Univ PR, 59-78 & chmn, Dept Music, 62-76; assoc prof music hist, Fla State Univ, 78- & coordr music hist & musicol, 80- *Mem:* Col Music Soc; Soc Ethnomusicol. *Interests:* Music of Puerto Rico. *Mailing Add:* 1824 Wales Dr Tallahassee FL 32303

SMITH, STUART SAUNDERS
EDUCATOR, COMPOSER
b Portland, Maine, Mar 16, 48. *Study:* Hartt Sch Music, BMA, 70, MM, 72; Univ Ill, Urbana-Champaign, DMA, 77. *Works:* Here and There, Sonic Art Ed, 72; Gifts, Belwin-Mills, 73; Faces, 74 & Links Series, 74-75, Sonic Art Ed; Pinetop, 76-77 & Flight, 77-78, Lingua Press; Return and Recall, Sonic Art Ed, 83. *Rec Perf:* Gifts, UBRES, 75; Faces, Advan Rec, 76; Gifts, Op I, 83; A Gift for Bessie, UBRES, 83. *Teaching:* Instr perc, Hartt Sch Music, 70-73; assoc prof, Univ Md, Baltimore Co, 75- *Awards:* ASCAP Merit Award, 77-82; Artist Award, East/West Found, 78; Hartt Col Distinguished Alumni Award. *Bibliog:* John Welsh (auth), Stuart Smith's Links Series, Percussive Notes Res Ed, 83. *Mem:* ASCAP; Percussive Arts Soc. *Publ:* Auth, The Early Percussion Music of John Cage, 79 & Fugue, 79, Percussive Notes; A Portrait of Herbert Brün, Perspectives New Music, 79; Notes to Myself, Am Soc Univ Comp Newslett, 81; co-ed & coauth, Visual Music, Perspectives New Music, 83. *Mailing Add:* 2617 Gwynndale Ave Baltimore MD 21207

SMITH, SYLVIA H
ADMINISTRATOR
b Boston, Mass. *Study:* Univ Md, BA, 73. *Pos:* Founder, owner & ed, Smith Publ (publishers of 20th century Am new music), 74- *Mem:* ASCAP; BMI; Percussive Arts Soc; Music Publ Asn. *Publ:* Coauth, Music Notation as Visual Art, Percussive Notes, 81; auth, An Instance of the Small Press, Notes Mag, 82; coauth, Visual Music, Perspectives New Music, 83. *Mailing Add:* 2617 Gwynndale Ave Baltimore MD 21207

SMITH, TERRY JAMES
PERCUSSION
b Tulsa, Okla, Aug 5, 52. *Study:* Univ Colo, Boulder, BMusEd, 73; Univ Mich, Ann Arbor, MMus, 74. *Rec Perf:* Green Mountains, RCA; John Brown's Body, Verve; Moonchild/In Your Quiet Place, Atlantic Rec. *Pos:* Timpanist & perc, St Paul Chamber Orch, 78-80; prin perc, Santa Fe Opera, 80; perc, Denver Symph Orch, 80-; solo timpanist, Central City Opera, 81- *Teaching:* Asst prof perc & music theory, Univ Wis, River Falls, 75-80. *Mem:* Am Fedn Musicians; Pecussive Arts Soc. *Mailing Add:* 2901 Robb Circle Lakewood CO 80215

SMITH, TIM (TIMOTHY PAUL)
CRITIC
b Washington, DC, Dec 23, 52. *Study:* Eisenhower Col, BA(music hist), 74; Occidental Col, Los Angeles, MA(music hist), 75. *Pos:* Asst music critic, Washington Star, Washington, DC, 79-80 & Washington Post, Washington, DC, 80-81; music critic, Ft Lauderdale News & Sun Sentinel, 81- *Mem:* Music Critics Asn. *Mailing Add:* 101 N New River Dr E Ft Lauderdale FL 33302

SMITH, WAYNE C
CONDUCTOR & MUSIC DIRECTOR, CELLO
b Salem, Ohio, July 21, 53. *Study:* Am Inst Musical Studies, Graz, Austria, 72 & 74; Dana Sch Music, BMus, 75; Univ Idaho, MMus, 76. *Pos:* Prin cello, Wash-Idaho Symph, 75-76; solo cello, La Galliade, Wash, 76-; cond & musical dir, Spokane Falls Symph, 76- *Teaching:* Prof cello, Spokane Falls Col, 76- *Awards:* Pro Musica Medallion, Dutch Ministrie Culture, 75. *Mem:* Spokane Cello Soc (pres, 83-); Viola da Gamba Soc; Phi Mu Alpha Sinfonia; Am String Teachers Asn; Am Fedn Musicians. *Mailing Add:* S 3905 Sundown Dr Spokane WA 99206

SMITH, WILLIAM
CONDUCTOR, EDUCATOR
Pos: Assoc cond & head keyboard sect, Philadelphia Orch, 52-; founder & mem, Philadelphia Baroque Quartet, currently; musical dir, Trenton Symph Orch, currently, Amerita String Orch, currently & Music at the Museum, Univ Pa, currently. *Teaching:* Cond orchs, Curtis Inst Music, 53- & New Sch Music, currently. *Mailing Add:* Curtis Inst Music 1726 Locust St Philadelphia PA 19103

SMITH, WILLIAM OVERTON
COMPOSER, EDUCATOR
b Sacramento, Calif, Sept 22, 26. *Study:* Juilliard Inst, 45; Mills Col, with Darius Milhaud, 48; Univ Calif, Berkeley, with Roger Sessions, BS, 50, MA, 51; Paris Consv, 53. *Works:* Suite for Violin & Clarinet, Oxford Univ Press, 56; Five Pieces for Clarinet Alone, Universal, 60; Duo for Flute & Clarinet, 62 & Interplay for Jazz Quartet & Orch, 63, MJQ Music; Variants, Universal, 63; Mosaic for Clarinet & Piano, 65 & Quadri for Jazz Quartet & Orch, 65, MJQ Music. *Teaching:* Asst prof, Univ Southern Calif, Los Angeles, 55-60; prof, Univ Wash, 66- *Awards:* Prix de Paris, Univ Calif, 51; Prix de Rome, Am Acad Rome, 57; Guggenheim Award, 60. *Mailing Add:* 5607 16th Ave NE Seattle WA 98105

SMITHER, HOWARD E
MUSICOLOGIST
b Pittsburg, Kans, Nov 15, 25. *Study:* Hamline Univ, AB, 50; Cornell Univ, MA, 52, PhD(musicol), 60; Univ Munich, Ger, 53-54. *Pos:* Music rev ed,

Notes, 67-69; mem ed bd, Detroit Monogr in Musicol, Info Coordr Inc, 71- & National Endowment Humanities Music Videodisc Proj, Univ Del, 82-; chmn ed bd, Early Musical Masterworks: Editions and Commentaries, Univ NC Press, Chapel Hill, 78- Teaching: Instr, Consv Music, Oberlin Col, 55-57, asst prof, 57-60; asst prof, Univ Kans, 60-63; assoc prof, Tulane Univ, 63-68; assoc prof, Univ NC, Chapel Hill, 68-71, prof, 71-79, dir grad studies music, 77-79 & 83- & James Gorden Hanes prof, 79-; dir, sem for col teachers, Nat Endowment Humanities, summer 78. Awards: Fulbright Sr Res Grant, 65-66; sr fel, Nat Endowment Humanities, 72-73 & 79-80; Deems Taylor Award, ASCAP, 78. Mem: Am Musicol Soc (pres, 80-82); Int Musicol Soc; Music Libr Asn; Royal Musical Asn; Sonneck Soc. Publ: Auth, The Baroque Oratorio: A Report on Research Since 1945, Acta Musicologica, Vol 43, 50-76; Carissimi's Latin Oratorios: Their Terminology, Functions, and Position in Oratorio History, Analecta Musicologica: Studien zur Italienisch-Deutschen Musikgeschichte, Vol 9, 54-78; A History of the Oratorio, Vol 1, The Oratorio in the Baroque Era: Italy, Vienna, Paris, 77 & Vol 2, The Oratorio in the Baroque Era: Protestant Germany and England, 77 & Vol 3, The Oratorio Since the Baroque Era (in prog), Univ NC Press, Chapel Hill; Oratorio and Sacred Opera, 1700-1825; Terminology and Genre Distinction, Proceedings of the Royal Musical Asn, Vol 106, 88-104; Sacred Dramatic Dialogues of the Early Baroque, 40 ed, Concentus Musicus, Veröffentlichungen der Musikgeschichtlichen Abteilung des Deutschen Hisorischen Inst in Rom, Arno Volk Verlag, Cologne. Mailing Add: Dept Music Univ NC Chapel Hill NC 27514

SMOLANOFF, MICHAEL LOUIS
COMPOSER, ADMINISTRATOR
b New York, NY, May 11, 42. Study: Juilliard Sch Music, BS, 64, MS, 65; Combs Col, MusD, 75; studied with Aaron Copland & comp with Vincent Persichetti. Works: Four Haiku Songs (sop & piano), 73; Kaleidoscope for Band, 73; Symphony No 3 (wind ens), 73; Concerto for Trombone, 68; String Quartet, 72; Pages from a Summer Journal, 74; Celebration, 75. Pos: Ed, E B Marks Music Corp, New York, 66-68; pres, Music Press, Collingswood, NJ, 77- Teaching: Res asst, Columbia Univ, 65-66; instr, Juilliard Sch Music, 66 & Philadelphia Music Acad, 68-71; prof music, Rutgers Univ, 71-77. Awards: Edward B Benjamin Award, 65; Rutgers Res Coun Grant, 73; ASCAP Award, 75-76. Mem: Nat Asn Am Comp & Cond; ASCAP; Phi Mu Alpha Sinfonia. Mailing Add: 20 Broun Pl Bronx NY 10475

SMOLIAR, HAROLD M
OBOE & ENGLISH HORN, LECTURER
b Philadelphia, Pa, Sept 7, 57. Study: Curtis Inst Music, BMus, 78. Pos: Co-prin oboe, Symph Orch Brazil, 78; English horn, Pittsburgh Symph, 79- Teaching: Artist-lectr woodwind chamber music & oboe, Carnegie-Mellon Univ, 80- Mem: Double Reed Soc; Am Fedn Musicians; Int Conf Symph & Opera Musicians. Mailing Add: c/o Pittsburgh Symph Heinz Hall 600 Penn Ave Pittsburgh PA 15222

SNAVELY, JACK
CLARINET, EDUCATOR
b Harrisburg, Pa, Mar 11, 29. Study: Lebanon Valley Col, with Frank Stachow, BS, 50; Univ Mich, Ann Arbor, with William Stubbins, MM, 55; Peabody Consv Music; study with Joe Allard & Jules Serpentini. Works: Motif and Variations (clarinet choir), Kendor. Rec Perf: Clarinet Rec, 71 & 80, Golden Crest; Woodwind Arts Quintet, Orion, 74. Pos: Clarinet, Woodwind Arts Quintet, currently; sax, Leblanc Fine Arts Sax Quartet, currently. Teaching: Teaching asst, Univ Mich, 54-55; prof music, Univ Wis, Milwaukee, 55-; instr, several high schools. Awards: Alumni Award, Lebanon Valley Col; Outstanding Teacher, Clarinet Mag. Mem: Clarinet Soc; World Sax Cong; Nat Asn Jazz Educr; Am Fedn Musicians; Music Educr Nat Conf. Publ: Auth, The Saxophone and its Performance, Heritage Publ Co; articles in Int Musician, Bandwagon, Woodwind World, Instrumentalist and others. Mailing Add: 1419 E Courtland Pl Milwaukee WI 53211

SNIDER, RONALD JOE
PERCUSSION
b Rotan, Tex, Aug 4, 47. Study: NTex State Univ; Mills Col; Park Point Col; studied with Henk Badings, Pandit Mahapurush Misra, Pandit Ram Narayan, Kalman Cherry & Anthony Cirone. Pos: Perc, Dallas Symph, currently & Dallas Civic Opera, currently; soloist, Am Wind Symph, tours US & South Am, Ann Arbor Film Fest, Stanford Univ & Contemp Music Fest; dir, Clearlight Ens, Unicornucopia Rec. Mem: Int Conf Symph & Opera Musicians; Percussive Arts Soc. Publ: Contribr to Percussive Arts Mag. Mailing Add: 5201 Reiger Dallas TX 75214

SNOPEK, SIGMUND
COMPOSER, ELECTRONIC
b Milwaukee, Wis, Oct 25, 50. Study: Univ Wis, Waukesha; Univ Wis, Milwaukee, BFA, 78; studied with John Downey. Works: Orange-Blue, 72 & The Talking Symphony, 75, Milwaukee Symph Orch; Return of the Spirit, Gel Metal Dancers, 76; The Desert Songs, Wis Contemp Music Forum, 78; Razorblades, Theatre X, 78; Roy Rogers Meets Albert Einstein, Milwaukee 20th Century Ens, 80; 3 Songs for Jazz Choir, Univ Wis Jazz Choir, Milwaukee, 83. Rec Perf: The Bloomsbury People, Audio Finishers, 70; Virginia Woolf, Studio East, 72; Trinity Seas, Seize, Sees, 74 & Nobody to Dream, 75, Bananas Rec Studio; Thinking Out Loud, 78 & 1st Band on the Moon, 80, Shade Tree; Roy Rogers Meets Albert Einstein, Bananas Rec Studio, 82. Pos: Head studio musician, Bananas Rec Studio, 75-81. Teaching: Instr, Wis Consv Music, 74-79 & Univ Wis, Milwaukee, 76. Awards: Indie Award, Nat Asn Independent Rec Mfr & Distribr. Bibliog: Charles W Gould (auth), Into Composing, Hi-Time Publ Inc, 7/16/71; Dan Kelly (auth), Who

Is This Couth Youth, Insider Mag,4/76; Gary Peterson (auth), Sigmund Snopek, III—An Evoluting Art, Capital Times, 12/16/82. Mem: Wis Contemp Music Forum; Milwaukee 20th Century Ens. Publ: Auth, Overlap and the Romantic Residue, Milwaukee Rev, 1/82. Mailing Add: 1981 N Prospect #6 Milwaukee WI 53202

SNOW, DAVID JASON
COMPOSER, ELECTRONIC
b Providence, RI, Oct 8, 54. Study: Eastman Sch Music, studied with Joseph Schwantner, Warren Benson & Samuel Adler, BMus, 76; Yale Sch Music, studied with Jacob Druckman, MMus, 78; Brandeis Univ, studied with Martin Boykan & Arthur Berger, 78-80. Works: The Passion and Transfiguration, Opus One Rec, 80; Sonatina for Trumpet and Piano, 81 & Elephants Exotiques, 81, Dorn Publ; Jakarta (perc ens), Music Perc Inc, 82; Sinfonia Concertante (horn, piano, perc & winds), Golden Crest Rec, 83; A Baker's Tale (five instrm & narrator), perf by New Music for Yound Ens Inc, 83; Trio (alto flute, contrabass & piano), NAC/USA Graphics Ser, 83. Awards: BMI Awards, 77 & 79; Nat Endowment Arts Fel, 82; Meet the Comp Grant, 83. Mem: BMI. Mailing Add: 11534 Lockwood Dr B2 Silver Spring MD 20904

SNOW, MARY (HELEN)
COMPOSER, PIANO
b Brownsville, Tex, Aug 26, 28. Study: Ind Univ, BM, 50; Univ Ill, MM, 52. Works: Electronic score for Marat/Sade, Actors Theater, Louisville, Ky, 71; Mandora (violin & tape), Virginia Kellogg, Eastman Sch Music, 72; Score for Faustus (electronic), 75, Ezekiel I (actor, dancer & tape), 75 & Voyages: Columbus/Apollo II, 77, Tex Tech Univ Theatre; Toccata for Clarinet & Piano (Hallucinations 79), Keith McCarty & comp, 79. Teaching: Asst prof electronic music & comp, Tex Tech Univ, 74-78. Awards: Nat Endowment for Arts Grant, 77 & 80. Mem: Am Women Comp. Publ: Auth, The Waveform Music Book, Lariken Press, 77. Mailing Add: 3110 26th Lubbock TX 79410

SNOW, MEREDITH ANN
VIOLA
b Pt Jefferson, NY, Feb 7, 58. Study: Juilliard Sch, BMus, 80, MMus, 82. Pos: Mem, Colo String Quartet, New York, 80-82 & San Francisco Opera Orch, 82- Teaching: Fel chamber music, Juilliard Pre-Col, 81-82; prof viola, Fest de Inverno Campus Jordao, Brazil, summer 82. Mailing Add: 1096 Pine St #202 San Francisco CA 94109

SNOWDEN, JAMES WYN
CONDUCTOR, EDUCATOR
b Lufkin, Tex, May 2, 43. Study: Stephen F Austin State Univ, BS, MA(music); Univ Colo, PhD; studied cond with Anshel Brusilow & Richard Burgin. Pos: Dir, Hudson Band, Tex; founder & cond, Longview Symph Orch; music dir, Longview Ballet & Community Theatres. Teaching: Dir & founder, Longview High Sch Orch, Tex; asst prof music, Univ Tulsa, currently, dir, Univ Symph Orch, currently. Awards: Leadership & Achievement Award, Tex Music Educr, 71; Winner, Honors Compt in Cond Sem, Jacksonville, Fla. Mem: Am Symph Orch League; Tex Music Educr Asn; Tex Prof Educr Asn. Publ: Contribr, Instrumentalist, School Musicians & Music J. Mailing Add: Music Dept Univ Tulsa Tulsa OK 74104

SNYDER, BARRY
PIANO, EDUCATOR
b Allentown, Pa, Mar 6, 44. Study: Eastman Sch Music, BMus, MMus, perf cert(piano), artist dipl(piano); studied with Vladimir Sokoloff & Cecile Genhart. Rec Perf: Suite for Piano (Alec Wilder), Sonata No 7 in B Flat Major (Prokofiev) & Music for Bass Trombone & Piano, Golden Crest; Piano Monster Concert, Columbia. Pos: Soloist, Detroit Symph, formerly, Atlanta Symph, formerly, Nat Symph, formerly & Rochester Phil, formerly; performer chamber music, Comp, Curtis & Purcell Quartets; solo recitalist throughout US, Can & UK. Teaching: Mem fac, Ga State Univ, 68-70; assoc prof piano, Eastman Sch Music, 70- Awards: Worcester Fest Prize, 65; Prize, Van Cliburn Int Piano Compt, 66. Mem: Pi Kappa Lambda; Nat Music Teachers Asn; Nat Guild Piano Teachers. Mailing Add: Eastman Sch Music 26 Gibbs St Rochester NY 14604

SNYDER, BILL (WILLIAM PAUL)
COMPOSER, PIANO
b Chicago, Ill, July 11, 16. Study: DePaul Univ, BM, MM, studied with Moritz Rosenthal & Rudolph Ganz, 24-40. Works: Chicago Piano Concerto, CBS Symph, 59; My Pony Macaroni, Mills Music, 62; Piccadilly Circus, Starlite Music, 64; Chicago Concerto, City Symph Chicago, 81; 40 publ works. Rec Perf: Bewitched Album, 47, Amber Fire, 58, Turquoise, 58 & Chicago Blues, 59, Decca. Pos: Producer & comp, Kingdom Coming, London, England, 72-73; entertainment dir, Holiday Inns, 75-; pres & chmn, City Symph Orch Chicago, 77- Awards: Nine Gold & Platinum Rec, Decca, 50, 52 & 56; Man of Year, Del Segno Soc, 79. Mailing Add: City Symph Orch Chicago 220 S Michigan Ave Chicago IL 60604

SNYDER, JOHN L
EDUCATOR, THEORIST
b Spokane, Wash, Jan 1, 50. Study: Mich State Univ, BM, 72, MM, 74; Ind Univ, PhD, 82. Teaching: Vis instr music, Okla State Univ, 74-75; vis asst prof, Univ Wis, Milwaukee, 82-83; asst prof, Nicholls State Univ, 83- Mem: Soc Music Theory; Am Musicol Soc; Int Musicol Soc. Interests: History of music theory, particularly in the Middle Ages; analysis of music. Publ: Auth, Harmonic Dualism and the Origin of the Minor Triad, Ind Theory Rev, 80; Theinred of Dover on Consonance: A Chapter in the History of Harmony, Music Theory Spectrum, 83. Mailing Add: Dept Music Nicholls State Univ PO Box 2017 Thibodaux LA 70310

SNYDER, LEO
COMPOSER, EDUCATOR
b Boston, Mass, Jan 1, 18. *Study:* New England Consv Music, BM, 52, MM, 54. *Works:* A Book of Americans (cantata), Leeds Music Corp, 62; Orchestral Overture 200, comn by City Boston & Northeastern Univ, 76; The Princess Marries the Page (opera), Northeastern Univ, 79; Love Is A Language (song cycle; sop & piano), Northeastern Univ, comn by WGBH, PBS, 81; A Christmas Tale (piano & narrator), comn by WGBH, PBS, 81; The End Is Coming (bass trio & ten), 82. *Teaching:* Instr music, New England Consv Music, 52-56; assoc prof, Boston Univ, 54-67; prof, Northeastern Univ, 67- *Awards:* Best Classical Rec, Hi Fi Stereo, 82. *Publ:* Contribr, numerous articles in Opera Guide, Opera Co Boston. *Mailing Add:* 21 Earldor Circle Marshfield MA 02050

SNYDER, RANDALL L
COMPOSER, EDUCATOR
b Chicago, Ill, Apr 6, 44. *Study:* Quincy Col, Ill, BA, 66; Univ Wis, Madison, MM, 67, DMA, 73. *Works:* Fire Pieces (clarinet & piano), Dorn, 68; Variations for Wind Ensemble, G Schirmer, 71; Seven Epigrams, Southern, 71; Variations (solo sax), Artisan, 72; Florileginm (organ), Hinshaw Press, 75; Almagest (winds), 75 & Rara Avis (piccolo solo), 82, Dorn. *Teaching:* Assoc prof theory & comp, Univ Neb, Lincoln, 74- *Awards:* First Prize Comp Cont, Int Double Reed Soc, 77; Third Prize, Alienor Harpsichord Comp Cont, 82. *Mailing Add:* Sch Music Univ Nebr Lincoln NE 68588

SOAMES, CYNTHIA ELIZABETH
PERCUSSION, EDUCATOR
b Peru, Ind, Oct, 6, 46. *Study:* Col Consv Music, Univ Cincinnati, BMus, 69; Sch Music, Univ Miami, MMus, 73; Ind Univ, Kokomo. *Pos:* Mem, Ft Lauderdale Symph, formerly, NC Symph Orch, 70-72 & Nashville Symph, currently, perc. Richmond Symph, Ind, Cincinnati Perc Ens, Indianapolis Chamber Ens & Indianapolis Symph Orch. *Teaching:* Mem fac, Western Ky Univ, 69-70 & St Joseph's Col, Ind, 70; instr, Univ NC, Chapel Hill, 71-72 & Univ Wis, River Falls, 74-75; teaching asst, Univ Miami, 72-73; private teacher perc, 75- *Mem:* Percussive Arts Soc (historian, 77-81 & Ind chap treas, 77-80). *Mailing Add:* 115 N Miami St Peru IN 46970

SOCCIARELLI, RONALD PETER
CONDUCTOR, EDUCATOR
b Little Falls, NY, July 11, 32. *Study:* Ithaca Col, BS, 59; Univ Mich, MM, 63. *Pos:* Cond, Ithaca High Sch Band, 67-72; dir bands, Northern Ill Wind Ens, 72-73 & Band Dept, Ohio Univ, Athens, 73- *Teaching:* Dir music educ, Lackawanna Pub Schs, NY, 59-67; assoc prof cond, Ohio Univ, Athens, 73- *Awards:* Award Contrib Am Music, Nat Fedn Music Clubs Am, 65. *Mem:* Col Band Dir Nat Asn; Music Teachers Nat Asn (nat brass chmn, 78-81). *Mailing Add:* 31 Utah Pl Athens OH 45701

SOCHER, BARRY
VIOLIN
b Los Angeles, Calif, Nov 2, 47. *Study:* Sch Perf Arts, Univ Southern Calif, 65-71; Inst Advan Musical Studies, Switz, 73. *Pos:* Prin second violin, Pasadena Symph Orch, 67-80 & Los Angeles Chamber Orch, 72-79; concertmaster, Pasadena Chamber Orch, 78-81; first violin, Los Angeles Phil Orch, 80- *Mem:* Am String Teachers Asn; Chamber Music Am. *Mailing Add:* 1515 Cerro Gordo St Los Angeles CA 90026

SODERBERG, MARTA A
VIOLA
b Duluth, Minn, Feb 27, 59. *Study:* Univ Wis, Superior, BM(viola perf), 82; Manhattan Sch Music, MM(viola perf), 83. *Pos:* Sect viola, Evansville Phil, Ind, 77-78; prin viola, Duluth-Superior Symph Orch, 78-82; violist, Capricorn Chamber Ens, 83- & Con Brio Chamber Ens, 83- *Teaching:* Instr viola, Col St Scholastica, 78-79; instr, Univ Wis, Superior, 79-82, instr string tech, 81-82. *Mailing Add:* 310 W 83rd St New York NY 10024

SODERSTROM, ELISABETH ANNA
SOPRANO
b Stockholm, Sweden, May 7, 27. *Rec Perf:* Complete Songs of Rachmaninov, London Rec; Katya Kabanova; Makropoulos Case. *Roles:* Bastienne in Bastien und Bastienne, Drottningholm Ct Theatre, 47; Jenufa in Jenufa, San Francisco Opera, 82; Katya Kabanova in Katya Kabanova, Houston Grand Opera, 82; Marschallin in Der Rosenkavalier, Dallas Opera, 83; Countess in Capriccio & Christine in Intermezzo, Glyndebourne Fest; Countess & Susanna in The Marriage of Figaro. *Pos:* Mem, Royal Opera, Stockholm, 50-; appearances at Salzburg, 55, Glyndebourne, 57-64, Metropolitan Opera, 59-63 & USSR, 66; performer concerts & on TV, US & Europe. *Awards:* Singer of Ct, Sweden, 59; Prize for Best Acting, Royal Swedish Acad, 65; Literis & Artibus Award, 69. *Mem:* Royal Acad Music, Stockholm. *Publ:* Auth, I Min Tonart, 78. *Mailing Add:* c/o Columbia Artists 165 W 57th St New York NY 10019

SOFFER, SHELDON
ADMINISTRATOR, ARTIST MANAGER
b New York, NY, Aug 20, 27. *Study:* Queens Col, City Univ New York, BA, 48; Univ Calif, Berkeley, MA, 50; studied cond with Fritz Stiedry, 50-55. *Pos:* Musical asst, New York City Opera Co, 50-52 & Aspen Music Fest, 52; asst cond, Empire State Musical Fest, 53-54; mgr & asst cond, Provincetown Symph, 55-61; cond, Broadway shows, 54-55 & Ark State Opera, 56; adminstr, Am Opera Soc, 56-60; assoc mgr, Little Orch Soc & Conct Opera Asn, 59-65; pres, Sheldon Soffer Mgt, 65- *Teaching:* Instr music, Roosevelt Sch, Stamford, Conn, 52-53; asst to Margaret Hillis, Union Theol Sem, 57-58. *Mem:* Am Choral Found (admin dir, 66-); Young Conct Artists (bd mem & past pres, 71-); Nat Asn Perf Arts Mgr & Agt (treas, 78-). *Mailing Add:* 130 W 56 St New York NY 10019

SOKOL, VILEM
MUSIC CONDUCTOR, EDUCATOR
Study: Studied violin with Otakar Sevcik & Raymond Cerf; Oberlin Consv Music; Juilliard Sch Music, studied violin with Hans Letz; State Consv Music, Prague, Czechoslavakia; Berkshire Music Ctr. *Pos:* Cond & music dir, Seattle Youth Symph Orch, 60-; music dir, Marrowstone Music Fest, 60-; prin violist, Seattle Symph Orch, formerly; founder & cond, Seattle String Soc, formerly; violist, Univ Wash String quartet, 12 years; head, Youth Symph Div, Am Symph Orch League, formerly; cond, Univ Wash Symph & Opera, 76-77; mem writers panel, Northwest Today, Seattle Post Intelligencer, formerly. *Teaching:* Head string dept, Univ Ky & Kans City Consv Music, formerly; prof music, Univ Wash, 48- *Awards:* Annual Award, Fedn Music Clubs; Gov Arts Award, 75. *Mailing Add:* 6303 NE 185th Seattle WA 98155

SOKOLOFF, ELEANOR
PIANO, EDUCATOR
b Cleveland, Ohio. *Study:* Cleveland Inst Music, with Ruth Edwards, piano with David Saperton, chamber music with Louis Bailly & two-piano repertoire with Brodsky & Triggs. *Teaching:* Mem fac piano, Curtis Inst Music, 36- *Mailing Add:* Curtis Inst Music 1726 Locust St Philadelphia PA 19103

SOKOLOFF, VLADIMIR
PIANO, EDUCATOR
Study: Accmp with Harry Kaufman, piano with Abram Chasin & chamber music with Louis Bailly; Curtis Inst Music, Hon DMA. *Rec Perf:* With Curtis String Quartet & Philadelphia Orch. *Pos:* Accmp for Efrem Zimbalist, 36-58; pianist, Philadelphia Orch, 38-50; dir, Pa Acad Fine Arts Chamber Music Ser, 51-68. *Teaching:* Mem fac accmp & vocal repertoire, Curtis Inst Music, 36-; mem fac, New Sch Music, currently & Temple Univ, currently. *Mailing Add:* Curtis Inst Music 1726 Locust St Philadelphia PA 19103

SOKOLOV, ELLIOT
COMPOSER
b New York, NY, Sept, 16, 53. *Study:* State Univ NY, Binghamton, with Ezra Laderman, BA(music), 75; Columbia Univ, with Jack Beeson, Vladimir Ussachevsky, Dennis Riley & Bulent Arel, MA, 78. *Works:* Seven Soundscapes (string quartet), Am Music, 80; September Music (flute & guitar), perf by Brooklyn Phil Chamber Series, 81; Trio (flute, cello & piano), perf by Da Capo Chamber Players, 81; Almanac (organ, brass & perc), 81 & Pipedreams (organ & sax), 82-, comn & perf by Leonard Raver; Taking Notes (flute, viola & guitar), perf by Lexington Trio, 83; Chimera (18 brass), comn & perf by New York City Brass Ens, 83. *Pos:* Comp in res, Charles Ives Ctr Am Music, 80 & Theater of Open Eye, NY, 83. *Awards:* Meet the Comp Grant, 81- *Bibliog:* Jim Theobald (auth), The Organ in the 20th Century, The Villager, 2/83. *Mem:* Am Music Ctr; Am Fedn Musicians; BMI. *Mailing Add:* 30 W 88th St New York NY 10024

SOLIE, RUTH AMES
EDUCATOR, CRITIC-WRITER
b New York, NY, May 17, 42. *Study:* Smith Col, AB, 64; Univ Chicago, MA, 66, PhD, 77. *Teaching:* Instr music, Mary Baldwin Col, 72-74; from instr to assoc prof, Smith Col, 74- *Mem:* Am Musicol Soc (mem coun, 81-83); Soc Music Theory; Am Soc Aesthetics. *Interests:* Nineteenth century theory and criticism. *Publ:* Auth, The Living Work: Organicism and Musical Analysis, 19th Century Music, 80; Melody and the Historiography of Music, J Hist Ideas, 82. *Mailing Add:* 98 Franklin St Northampton MA 01060

SOLLBERGER, HARVEY
COMPOSER, EDUCATOR
b Cedar Rapids, Iowa, May 11, 38. *Study:* Univ Iowa, with Eldon Obrecht & Philip Bezanson; Columbia Univ, with Jack Beeson & Otto Luening, MA, 64. *Works:* Chamber Variations (12 players & cond), 64; Impromptu (piano), 68; Divertimento (flute, cello & piano), 70; Iron Mountain Song (trumpet & piano), 71; The Two and the One (cello and two perc), 72; String Quartet, New York, 73; Riding the Wind (flute & chamber Orch), New York, 74. *Pos:* Founder & co-dir, Group Contemp Music, currently. *Teaching:* Mem fac, Manhattan Sch Music, 62-, Temple Univ, 78-82 & City Col, City Univ New York, currently; adj assoc prof, Columbia Univ, 65- *Awards:* Koussevitzky Grant, 66; Spec Citation, Am Int Music Fund, 67; Guggenheim Fel, 69 & 73. *Mailing Add:* RD 1 Cherry Valley NY 13320

SOLOMON, ELIDE N
COMPOSER, PIANO
b Lugano, Switz, Dec 22, 38. *Study:* Am Col Musicians, BA, 76; Consv Milan, MA, 56. *Works:* Self Portrait, Purchase Music Ens, 80; Hommage a Picasso, Carnegie Recital Hall, 80; Song for Winter, Jerome Sala, 82; Scenes from Childhood, 82, Stangetziana & Divertimenti, 83, Rydet. *Pos:* Music dir piano, Purchase Community Centre, 74-79; music dir & cond, Purchase Music Ens, 79-; music adv, Adams Russell Cable TV, Harrison, NY, 83- *Teaching:* Educr comp, Purchase Music Ens & Sch, 79- *Awards:* Int Annual Comp Award, Am Col Musicians, 79. *Bibliog:* Jeremy and the Rainbow, Purchase Music Ens, Cable TV, 82. *Mem:* ASCAP; Int League Women Comp; Music Educr League Westchester; NY State Music Teachers Asn. *Publ:* Auth, Composition with Visual Aids, Rydet, 81. *Mailing Add:* Box 477 Purchase NY 10577

SOLOMON, JOYCE ELAINE (JOYCE ELAINE MOORMAN)
COMPOSER, TEACHER
b Tuskegee, Ala, May 11, 46. *Study:* Vassar Col, BA, 68; Sarah Lawrence Col, MFA, 75; Teachers Col, Columbia Univ, EdD, 82. *Works:* Among the Snow-Capped Peaks, 77, A Setting of Five Poems by Longston Hughes, 78, Elegy for Solo Cello, 80 & Three Pieces for Flute, 80, Brooklyn Phil Chamber Ens;

Coat of Many Fibers, Triade Chorale, 80; Sing My People, Brooklyn Phil Chamber Ens, 81; Dance of the Streets, LonGar Ebony Ens, 83. *Teaching:* Piano & musicianship, Manna House Workshop, New York, NY, 81-; adj instr Afro-Am music hist, Queens Col, 82; piano, Brooklyn Music Sch, NY, 82-; Lefferts Gardens Music Sch, Brooklyn, NY, 82- *Mem:* ASCAP; Am Music Ctr; Comp Forum; Int League Women Comp. *Mailing Add:* 212 Lefferts Ave 2nd Fl Brooklyn NY 11225

SOLOMON, JUDITH A
PIANO, EDUCATOR
b Nutley, NJ, Apr 25, 43. *Study:* Rutgers Univ, with Thomas Richner & Robert Lincoln, BA, 65; Yale Sch Music, with Donald Currier, Ward Davenny, Allen Forte & Mel Powell, MMus, 68. *Teaching:* Assoc prof music, Tex Christian Univ, 68- *Mem:* Pi Kappa Lambda; Mu Phi Epsilon; Col Music Soc; Soc Music Theory; Music Teachers Nat Asn. *Publ:* Auth, The Pianist as Vocal Accompanist: Servant or Partner?, Am Music Teacher, 9-10/81 & Triangle, spring 82. *Mailing Add:* Dept Music Tex Christian Univ Ft Worth TX 76129

SOLOMON, LARRY J
EDUCATOR, COMPOSER
b New Kensington, Pa, Apr 27, 40. *Study:* Allegheny Col, BA, 62; Univ Ill, MM, 64; WVa Univ, PhD, 73. *Works:* Andromeda, Pandora Press, 71; Music of the Spheres, Music for Perc, 76; Concertino for Clarinet, Philip Rehfehldt, 79; Suite for Prepared Piano, 79, Constellations for Pianoforte, 80 The Improvisor's Instrument, 82 & The Celestial Music, 83, Pandora Press. *Pos:* Dir, New Improvisation Ens, 75-80 & Transition—Comp Perf Ens, 80- *Teaching:* Theory & comp, Southwestern Col, Kans, 66-68; asst prof, Wells Col, 68-73; vis prof, Cornell Univ, 70-71; prof, Pima Community Col, Ariz, 73- *Awards:* Comp fel, Nat Endowment Arts, 76; comp award, Ariz Comn Arts, 80. *Mem:* Am Soc Univ Comp; Am Music Ctr; Ariz Music Theory Conf. *Interests:* Contemporary compositional theory; computer applications. *Publ:* Auth, New Symmetric Transformations, Perspectives New Music, 73; A Keyboard Theory Workbook, Pima Co Community Col, 79; The List of Chords, Their Properties & Uses, Interface, Netherlands, 82; Improvisation & Academia, Perspectives New Music, 83. *Mailing Add:* 5122 N Tortolita Rd Tucson AZ 85745

SOLOMON, NANETTE KAPLAN
PIANO, EDUCATOR
b Brooklyn, NY, Apr 10, 52. *Study:* Juilliard Sch Pre-Col, with Rosina Lhevinne; Ecole d' Art Am, Fontainebleau, France, with Nadia Boulanger, 71; Yale Sch Music, with Claude Frank, BA, 73, MM, 74; Boston Univ, with Leonard Shure, 74-77. *Pos:* Solo performer, WQXR Artists in Conct, 76, Lincoln Ctr Libr, New York, 75, 76, 80 & 83, Phillips Collection, Washington, DC, 79, Mozarteum, Salzburg, 80 & Wigmore Hall, London, 82. *Teaching:* Asst prof music, Slippery Rock Univ Pa, 77-82, assoc prof, 82- *Awards:* Perf Award, Pittsburgh Conct Soc, 79. *Mem:* Col Music Soc; Pa Music Teachers Asn; Music Teachers Nat Asn. *Mailing Add:* 421 E Moody Ave New Castle PA 16105

SOLOMONOW, RAMI
VIOLA, TEACHER
b Tel Aviv, Israel, Apr 21, 49; US citizen. *Study:* Rubin Acad Music, Israel, dipl, 72; Northern Ill Univ, BA, 75. *Pos:* Prin violist, Lyric Opera Chicago, 74-, Orch Ill, 80- & Colo Music Fest, 80-; violist, Chicago Ens, Chicago Soundings & Lyric Chamber Ens, currently. *Teaching:* Lectr viola, DePaul Univ, 82- *Awards:* First prize chamber music, Am-Israel Cult Found, 72. *Rep:* Am Chamber Conct 890 104th St New York NY. *Mailing Add:* 88 W Schiller St Chicago IL 60610

SOLOW, JEFFREY (GILMAN)
CELLO
b Los Angeles, Calif, Jan 3, 49. *Study:* Univ Southern Calif, with Gregor Piatigorsky, 67-73; Univ Calif, Los Angeles, BA, 72. *Rec Perf:* The Romantic Cello, ABC Rec, 72; Ravel Trio, Columbia Rec, 72; French Masterpieces for Cello & Piano, Desmar Rec, 72; Haydn and Schoenberg String Trios, Desmar & Telefunken Recs, 73; Rozsa, Entre' Acte Rec, 77; Barber & Kodaly Sonatas, 78 & Vocalise (cello & piano), 81, Pelican Rec. *Pos:* Prin cello, Los Angeles Chamber Orch & Glendale Symph Orch, formerly; artist, Affil Artists Inc, 82-83; conct cellist, 82-; mem, The Archduke Trio, currently. *Teaching:* Instr cello, Univ Calif, Los Angeles, 73-77 & Gregor Piatigorsky Mem Sem, Univ Southern Calif, 79 & 81; asst prof cello, Calif State Univ, Northridge, 77-78. *Awards:* Gregor Piatigorsky Award, Young Musicians Found, 69; Young Conct Artists Award, 69. *Bibliog:* Terry Sanders (auth), To Be a Performer, Churchill Films, 69. *Mem:* Violoncello Soc; Young Musicians Found. *Mailing Add:* 203 W 87 St Apt 5 New York NY 10024

SOLOW, LINDA I
LIBRARIAN, ADMINISTRATOR
b Brooklyn, NY. *Study:* Brooklyn Col, BA, 68, MA, 70; Univ Mich, AMLS, 71. *Pos:* Music cataloger, Libr Cong, Washington DC, 71-72; head music libr, Mass Inst Technol, 72-; dir, Boston Comp Proj, Boston Area Music Libr, 80-; consult, various music libraries in New England, 77- *Awards:* H W Wilson Co Indexing Award, Am Soc Indexers, 80; Nat Endowment Humanities Grant (for Boston Comp Proj), 80-81. *Mem:* Music Libr Asn (mem bd dir, 76-78); Int Asn Music Libr (mem US branch bd dir, 78-80); Am Soc Indexers; Asn Rec Sound Collections; Sonneck Soc. *Publ:* Auth, Checklist of Music Bibliographies, 3rd ed, 74 & ed, numerous monographs in MLA Index & Bibliography Series, 78-82, Music Libr Asn; ed, The Boston Composers Project: A Bibliography, MIT Press, 83; also author of articles in Notes & Fontes Artis Musicae and compiler of numerous indexes. *Rep:* 16 Trowbridge St Cambridge MA 02138. *Mailing Add:* Music Libr 14E-109 Mass Inst Technol Cambridge MA 02139

SOLTI, GEORG
CONDUCTOR & MUSIC DIRECTOR
b Budapest, Hungary, Oct 21, 12; nat Brit. *Study:* Budapest Acad, with Ernest von Dohnanyi, Zoltan Kodaly & Weiner; with Bela Bartok; Leeds Univ, Hon MusD, 71; Oxford Univ, Hon MusD, 72; DePaul Univ, Hon MusD; Yale Univ, Hon MusD, 74; Harvard Univ, Hon MusD, 79. *Rec Perf:* Ring Cycle (Wagner), Symphony No 2 (Mahler), The Damnation of Faust, The Creation, Pictures at an Exhibition, Concerto for Orchestra (Bartok), Symphony No 5 (Bruckner) & others, London Rec. *Pos:* Musical asst, Budapest Opera House, 30-33, cond, 34-39; asst cond, Salzburg Fest, 36 & 37; pianist, Switzerland, 39-45; gen music dir, Munich State Opera, 46-52 & Frankfurt City Opera, 52-60; prin cond, Lyr Opera Chicago, 56 & 57; music dir, Royal Opera House Covent Garden, 61-71, Chicago Symph Orch, 69- & Orch Paris, 72-75; prin guest cond, Paris Opera Bicentennial Tour, 76; prin cond & artistic dir, London Phil Orch, 79-83, cond emer, 83-; guest cond, New York Phil, Vienna Phil, Berlin Phil, London Symph, New Philharmonia, Metropolitan Opera, Vienna State Opera, Salzburg Fest, Glyndebourne Fest & other orchs, opera co & festivals worldwide. *Awards:* First Prize Pianist, Concours Int, Geneva, 42; 12 Grand Prix Disque Mondiale, 59-; 20 Grammy Awards. *Rep:* Colbert Artists Mgt 111 W 57th St New York NY 10019. *Mailing Add:* Chicago Symph Orch 220 S Michigan Ave Chicago IL 60604

SOLUM, JOHN H
FLUTE, EDUCATOR
b New Richmond, Wis, May 11, 35. *Study:* Princeton Univ, studied harmony & counterpoint with Elliot Forbes, comp with Edward T Cone, musicol with Arthur Mendel & flute with William Kincaid, AB, 57. *Works:* Cadenzas for Mozart Flute Concertos, McGinnis & Marx, 64. *Rec Perf:* Flute Concerti (Ibert, Jolivet, Honegger), EMI, England, 75; Flute Quartet, K 285 (Mozart), Cambridge, 76; Fifth Brandenburg Concerto (Bach), Smithsonian, 77; Two Flute Concerti (Malcolm Arnold), EMI, England, 77; Romantic Music for Flute, 78 & Two Flute Concerti (Mozart), 80, EMI, England & Seraphim; Sonatas, Op 2 (Telemann), Cambridge, 81. *Pos:* Mem, New York Chamber Soloists, 60- & Aston Magna, 72-; founder & dir, Bath Summer Sch Baroque Music, 79-; artistic dir, Conn Early Music Fest, 83- *Teaching:* Lectr flute, Vassar Col, 69-71, 77-; vis prof, Sch Music, Ind Univ, 73- & Oberlin Col Consv, 76- *Awards:* Youth Contest Winner, Pa Orch, 57. *Bibliog:* Ted Beers (auth), John Solum, Fairfield Co Mag, 7/80; Carolyn Nott (auth), John Solum, Gramophone Mag, 10/81; Niall O'Loughlin (auth), Mozart Flute Concertos, Musical Times Mag, 5/82. *Mem:* Dolmetsch Found (trustee, 75-); Independent Sch Orch (bd mem, 76-); Friends Music (vpres, 78-); Conn Early Music Soc (pres, 82-); Performers Conn (hon trustee, 77-). *Publ:* Auth, Johann August Crone, In: New Grove Dict of Musical Instruments (in prep). *Rep:* Ibbs & Tillett 450-452 Edgware Rd London W2 England. *Mailing Add:* 10 Bobwhite Dr Westport CT 06880

SOMACH, BEVERLY
VIOLIN, TEACHER
b New York, NY, Jan 17, 35. *Study:* Studied violin with Irman Zacharias; Columbia Univ, BS, 56; Univ Calif, Los Angeles, with Jascha Heifetz, 59. *Rec Perf:* Homage to Fitz Kreisler, Musical Heritage Soc. *Pos:* Solo recitalist, Town Hall, Carnegie Hall & Alice Tully Hall; guest soloist, New York Phil, Am Symph Orch, NC Symph, Chicago Symph & conct tours throughout US, Can, Europe & Japan; asst concertmaster, Am Symph Orch, 62-63. *Awards:* Outstanding Instrumentalist of Season, New York Times, 49; Musician of Year, Zonta, 74. *Mem:* Chamber Music Am; Am Asn String Teachers; Bohemians. *Mailing Add:* 280 Greenridge Rd Franklin Lakes NJ 07417

SOMER, AVO
COMPOSER, EDUCATOR
b Tartu, Estonia, June 27, 34; US citizen. *Study:* Univ Mich, PhD(musicol), 63. *Works:* Cantata No 4 (women's voices), Toronto, 55; Vilemees (a cappella), Boston, 60; Concertino (chamber ens), Bennington Comp Conf, 64; Trio Variations (string trio), 65; Refrains (flute, clarinet, perc & piano), New York, 66; Winter Music (string trio), 67; Elegy II (piano quintet), New York, 70. *Pos:* Participant, Stockhausen's Ens, Darmstadt, Germany, 67. *Teaching:* Mem fac, Univ Conn, 61- *Mailing Add:* Sch Fine Arts Univ Conn Storrs CT 06268

SOMMER, SUSAN THIEMANN
LIBRARIAN, LECTURER
b New York, NY, Jan 7, 35. *Study:* Smith Col, BA, 56; Columbia Univ, MA(musicol), 58, MLS, 67, MPhil(musicol), 75. *Pos:* Libr asst & librn, New York Pub Libr, 61-68, head, Rare Books & Ms & cur, Toscanini Mem Archives, Music Div, 69-; lectr opera, Metropolitan Opera Guild, 75-81; book rev ed, Notes, 78-82, ed, 82-; contrib ed, High Fidelity, 79- *Teaching:* Lectr music librnship & perf arts bibliog, Columbia Univ, 70- *Mem:* Music Libr Asn (mem bd, 74-75); Am Musicol Soc (mem coun, 80-82); Int Asn Music Libr (vpres res comn, 82-84); Int Musicol Soc; Asn Recorded Sound Collections. *Interests:* Music bibliography and librarianship; history of music printing and publishing. *Publ:* Auth, New York, In: New Grove Dict of Music & Musicians, 80; Joseph Drexel, In: Music & Soc, Norton (in prep). *Mailing Add:* Special Collections Music NY Pub Libr 111 Amsterdam Ave New York NY 10023

SOMMERFIELD, DAVID FREDIC
LIBRARIAN
b Queens, NY, Sept 22, 41. *Study:* Brooklyn Col, City Univ New York, BA, MA(music); Columbia Univ, MS(libr serv). *Pos:* Music cataloguer & asst music librn, State Univ NY Col, Potsdam; rec librn, Peabody Consv; sr music cataloguer, Libr Cong, currently. *Mem:* Music Libr Asn; Am Musicol Soc; Int

Asn Music Libr; Asn Rec Sound Collections; Int Asn Sound Archives. *Publ:* Auth, Proceedings of the Institute on Library of Congress Music Cataloging Policies & Procedures, 75; contribr to Current Musicol, Asn Rec Sound Collections J & Notes. *Mailing Add:* 101 G St SW Apt A611 Washington DC 20024

SOMOGI, JUDITH
CONDUCTOR & MUSIC DIRECTOR
b Brooklyn, NY, May 13, 43. *Study:* Juilliard Sch Music, BS, 63, MS, 65. *Pos:* Cond, Am Symph Orch, 72, Spoleto Fest Two Worlds, 74, New York City Opera, 74, Naumberg Symph Orch, 74, Los Angeles Phil, 75, Syracuse Symph Orch, 75, Tulsa Opera, 76, New York Phil, 77, Oklahoma City Symph, 77, Tulsa Phil, 77, San Diego Opera, 77, Milwaukee Symph, 77, San Francisco Opera, 78, Florentine Opera, 78, San Antonio Opera, 79; cond & music dir, Utica Symph, 77-80; prin cond, Frankfurt Opera, 82- *Bibliog:* On Stage with Judith Somogi (film), PBS, 81. *Mailing Add:* c/o Columbia Artists Mgt 165 W 57 St New York NY 10019

SOMOGYI, JOSEPH EMIL
VIOLA
b Budapest, Hungary, Sept 20, 39; US citizen. *Study:* Consv Budapest, 53-56; Ithaca Col, 57-59; Curtis Inst Music, 59-63. *Pos:* Violist, Baltimore Symph Orch, 63-66, Buffalo Phil, 66-67, Music in Maine String Quartet, Portland, 67-69 & Cincinnati Symph Orch, 70- *Mailing Add:* 2915 Losantiville Ave Cincinnati OH 45213

SONEVYTSKY, IHOR C
COMPOSER, CRITIC-WRITER
b Hadynkiwci, Ukraine, Jan 2, 26; US citizen. *Study:* Univ Wien, with Joseph Marx, 46; Staatliche Hochschule Musik, Munich, dipl, 50; Ukrainian Free Univ, Munich, PhD, 61. *Works:* Winter (piano pieces), Svoboda, 51, 2nd ed, 65; Spring (piano pieces), New York, 52; Summer (piano pieces), Svoboda, 55; Cinderella (ballet), perf by R Pryma Sch Ballet, New York, 66 & 67; Art Songs, perf by M Kokolska, 67; Incidental Theatre Music, perf by L Krushelnytsky Drama Studio, 67-83; Piano Concerto in G, perf by Ukrainian Music Inst, 74. *Pos:* Pres, Ukrainian Music Inst, New York, 59-61; cond, Chorus Dumka, New York, 60's & Opera Ens, New York, 60's; music critic, Voice of Am, Washington DC, 71-78. *Teaching:* Assoc prof music hist, Ukrainian Cath Univ, Rome, 71- *Mem:* Shevchenko Sci Soc (chmn music sect, 70-); Ukrainian Acad Arts & Sci (chmn music sect, 75-); Am Musicol Soc. *Publ:* Ed, History of Ukraine Music, 2nd Ed, Ukraine Music Inst, 61; auth, Artem Vedel & His Musical Legacy, Ukrainian Acad Arts & Sci, 66; Nestor Nyzhankivsky—His Life and Work, Bohoslov, Rome, 73; ed, Songs of Roman Kupchynsky, Chervona Kalyna, 77; Ivan Nedilsky's Selected Works for Mixed Chorus A Capella, Ukraine Music Found, 83. *Mailing Add:* 62 E 7th St New York NY 10003

SONGER, LEWIS ALTON
COMPOSER, FRENCH HORN
b Evansville, Ind, Sept 4, 35. *Study:* Southern Ill Univ, BM, 58; Ind Univ, MM, 60; Univ Mo, Kansas City, DMA, 65. *Works:* Symphony No 2, perf by Kansas City Phil, 62; Peanuts, Popcorn and Crackerjacks, perf by ETenn Wind Quintet, 76; Quintet No 2, perf by Pandean Wind Players, 82; IHAD (horn quartet), perf by ETenn Horn Club, 82; Le Mine (horn solo), 82 & Tuballet (tuba solo), 83, Koko Enterprises; The Lure (ballet), comn by Intercity Ballet Co, 83. *Pos:* Prin horn, Johnson City Symph Orch, Tenn, 75- *Teaching:* Instr theory & brass, Cottey Col, 60-63; asst prof theory & band, Westminster Col, Pa, 65-68; assoc prof theory & horn, ETenn State Univ, 68- *Mem:* Int Horn Soc; Phi Mu Alpha; Pi Kappa Lamda. *Mailing Add:* 1515 Chickees St Johnson City TN 37601

SONIES, BARBARA
VIOLIN
b Chicago, Ill, May 7, 45. *Study:* With George Perlman; Eastman Sch Music, with Millard Taylor, perf cert & BMus, 67; Juilliard Sch, with Ivan Galamian & Paul Maknowitzky, MA, 69; Accad Musicale Chigiana, Siena, Italy, with Franco Guilli & Tabor Varga. *Rec Perf:* Piano Trios by Kirchner & Villa-Lobos, 80 & Piano Trios By Mozart, 81, Centaur Rec; various works with 20th Century Consort, 81-82 & Penn Contemp Players, 83. *Pos:* First violin sect, Rochester Phil, 65-67 & Am Symph, 69-72; asst concertmaster, Pa Ballet Orch, 73-81; concertmaster, Opera Co Philadelphia, 80-; founding mem, Philadelphia Trio, 71. *Teaching:* Private violin, 73- *Mailing Add:* 214 Avon Rd Narberth PA 19072

SONNENFELD, PORTIA LEYS
CONDUCTOR & MUSIC DIRECTOR
b Chicago, Ill, Mar 11, 34. *Study:* Roosevelt Univ, with Waldemar Dobrovolsky, 48-51; Oberlin Col, with Emil Danenberg, BA, 55; studied with Sheridan Russell, Christopher Bunting & Elizabeth Green. *Pos:* Musical dir & cond, Little Orch of Princeton, 80- *Mem:* Am Symph Orch League; Am Fedn Musicians; Music Educr Conf; Am String Teachers Asn; Chamber Music Am. *Mailing Add:* 1 Westcott Rd Princeton NJ 08540

SONNET, SUSAN M
LIBRARIAN
b New York, NY, Aug 24, 42. *Study:* City Univ New York, BA(music), 64; Columbia Univ, MLS, 66; Univ Calif, Santa Barbara, MA(Musicol), 76. *Pos:* Music cataloger, Yale Univ, 66-68; asst music librn, Univ Calif, Santa Barbara, 68- *Interests:* Slow movements of the Haydn keyboard sonatas. *Rep:* Arts Libr Univ Calif Santa Barbara CA 93106. *Mailing Add:* 442 Caseta Way Goleta CA 93117

SOOTER, EDWARD
TENOR
b Salina, Kans, Dec 8, 34. *Study:* Friends Univ, Wichita, Kans, BME, 60; Kans Univ, Lawrence, MM(voice), 64; Hamburg Hochschule Musik, Germany, 64-66. *Roles:* Tannhäuser in Tannhäuser, Metropolitan Opera, 79 & 82; Otello in Otello, Metropolitan Opera, 80; Florestan in Fidelio, Metropolitan, Montreal & Munich Operas, 80-82; Tristan in Tristan und Isolde, 80 & Siegmund in Die Walküre, 80, Munich Opera; Siegfried in Siegfried & Götterdämmerung, 82 & Peter Grimes in Peter Grimes, 83, Seattle Opera. *Mailing Add:* Westerwald Str 16 6095 Ginsheim Germany, Federal Republic of

SORCE, RICHARD
COMPOSER, EDUCATOR
b Passaic, NJ, July 29, 43. *Study:* Manhattan Sch Music; New York Col Music; NY Univ, BS, MA, 71. *Works:* Spring & Fall: To a Young Child (SSA), 71, Turn Back O Man (SATB), 71, Fantasia for Brass, 71 & Theme & Variations, Woodwinds, 71, G Schirmer. *Teaching:* Teacher instrm music, Haworth Sch, NJ, 70-72; instr theory & comp, NY Univ, 80- *Mem:* ASCAP. *Interests:* Contemporary harmonic practices. *Mailing Add:* 173 W Oakland Ave Oakland NJ 07438

SOREL, CLAUDETTE MARGUERITE
PIANO, EDUCATOR
b Paris, France, Oct 10, 32. *Study:* Juilliard Sch, BS, 47; Curtis Inst, artist dipl, 53; Columbia Univ, BS, 54. *Rec Perf:* On RCA, Victor, Monitor & Musical Heritage, 47- *Pos:* 2000 appearances throughout USA, Can & Europe, 43-76; soloist, 200 major orch, incl NY Phil, Philadelphia, Boston & NBC, formerly; appearances in fest, incl Aspen, Berkshire, Chautauqua, Brevard, Fish Creek & Marlboro; judge for numerous compt, currently; chmn music educ testing serv, consult & panel mem, ARTS, 79- *Teaching:* Vis prof, Univ Kans, 61-62; asst prof, Ohio State Univ, 62-64; distinguished prof & chmn piano dept, State Univ NY, Fredonia, 64. *Awards:* Ford Found Conct Artist Award; Asn Cond & Comp Award; Mu Phi Epsilon Citation of Merit. *Mem:* Music Critics Asn; Nat Music Coun (mem bd dir, 72-); Nat Fedn Music Clubs (mem bd dir, 72-). *Interests:* Piano sight reading. *Publ:* Auth, Compendium of Piano Technique, 69, Mind Your Musical Manners, 72, 24 Magic Keys, 73, 3 Nocturnes of Rachmaninof, 73, 15 Smorgasbord Studies, 75 & 12 Arensky Etudes, 76, Marks Music. *Mailing Add:* 333 West End Ave New York NY 10023

SORKIN, LEONARD
VIOLIN, MUSIC DIRECTOR
b Chicago, Ill, Jan 12, 16. *Study:* Chicago Musical Col; Am Consv Music, with Mischa Mischakoff. *Rec Perf:* Over 70 on Conct Disc, Everest, Decca, Columbia, CRI, Gaspero & Mercury, 51- *Pos:* Founding mem & first violinist, Fine Arts String Quartet, 40-82; founder, dir & performer, Summer Evenings Music Ser, Univ Wis, Milwaukee, 54-82, founder, dir, cond & music dir, Inst Chamber Music, Sch Fine Arts, 82- *Teaching:* Distinguished prof music, Northwestern Univ, 53-55; prof violin & chamber music, Sch Fine Arts, Univ Wis, Milwaukee, 62-, distinguished prof, 77- *Awards:* Lincoln Acad Fel, Ill, 65; Artist of Year, Am String Teachers Asn, 70. *Mem:* Am String Teachers Asn; Am Fedn Musicians; Chamber Music Am. *Mailing Add:* 1027 E Ogden Ave Milwaukee WI 53202

SOROKA, JOHN G
PERCUSSION, EDUCATOR
b Philadelphia, Pa, Aug 22, 50. *Study:* Berkshire Music Ctr, 67-70; Settlement Music Sch, Philadelphia, with Alan Abel, perf cert, 68; Temple Univ, with Charles Owen, BMusEd, 72. *Rec Perf:* Dallapiccola (Boulez), Candide Rec, 68; All Star Percussion Ensemble, Moss Music Group, 83; also many orchestral recordings with Pittsburgh Symphony & Baltimore Symphony. *Pos:* Prin perc & assoc prin timpanist, Baltimore Symph Orch, 73-78 & Pittsburgh, Symph Orch, Pa, 78-; prin perc, Grand Teton Music Fest, summer 81- *Teaching:* Instr perc, Univ Del, 72-76; head dept perc, Peabody Consv, 73-78; artist & lectr perc, Carnegie-Mellon Univ, 78- *Awards:* Fromm Fel, Berkshire Music Ctr, 70; Recognition of Contrib, Percussive Arts Soc, 76. *Mem:* Perc Arts Soc; Am Symph Orch League. *Mailing Add:* 220 Hilands Ave Pittsburgh PA 15202

SOULE, EDMUND FOSTER
COMPOSER, LIBRARIAN
b Boston, Mass, Mar 4, 15. *Study:* Piano with Robert Elmore, 34-41; Univ Pa, with Harl MacDonald, BM, 39, MA, 46; Yale Univ, with Richard Donovan, BM, 48; Eastman Sch Music, PhD, 56; Univ Librnshp, Univ Denver, MLS, 66. *Works:* Serenade (alto sax & piano), 64; Canzona (seven brass instrm); Salon Music (violin & piano), 76; Suite for Piano, 77; A Stone, A Leaf, A Door (chorus & chamber ens), 78; Harp of the Wind (sop, flute & harp), 78; Concerto (harp & chamber orch), 79. *Pos:* Music librn, Univ Ore, 66-80. *Teaching:* Piano, privately, 38-41; fac mem, Milton Acad, 48-49, Wash State Col, 49-51, Eastman Sch Music, 52-53, Salem Col, 55-58, Univ Pac, 58-61 & Wash State Univ, 61-65; prof librarianship, Univ Ore, 66-80. *Awards:* Frances Osborne Kellogg Prize. *Mailing Add:* 85897 Bailey Hill Rd Eugene OR 97405

SOUTH, PAMELA
SOPRANO
b Salmon, Idaho, Nov 5, 48. *Study:* Univ Mont Sch Music, 67-71. *Roles:* Marie in Daughter of the Regiment, Portland Opera, 79; Drusilla in L'Incoronazione di Poppea, 81 & Zerlina in Don Giovanni, 81, San Francisco Opera; Musetta in La Boheme, Denver Opera & San Francisco Opera, 83; Marguerite in Faust, Omaha Opera, 83; Despina in Cosi fan tutte, 83, & Adele in Die Fledermaus, 83, Portland Opera. *Awards:* Poetz Award, Merola Opera Prog, 74; Martha Baird Rockefeller Fel, 76 & 78. *Rep:* Louise Williams 3650 Los Feliz Blvd Los Angeles CA 90027. *Mailing Add:* 2631 CLay St San Francisco CA 94115

SOUTHERN, EILEEN JACKSON
EDUCATOR, WRITER
b Minneapolis, Minn, Feb 19, 20. *Study:* Univ Chicago, BA, 40, MA, 41; NY Univ, PhD, 61. *Teaching:* Asst prof music hist, Southern Univ, 43-45 & 49-51; from asst prof to prof, City Univ New York, 60-75; prof, Harvard Univ, 76- *Awards:* Deems Taylor Award, ASCAP, 72; Nat Endowment Humanities Grant, 79-83. *Mem:* Am Musicol Soc (mem bd dir, 74-76); Renaissance Soc; Int Musicol Soc. *Interests:* Fifteenth century European music and Black-American music. *Publ:* Auth, The Buxheim Organ Book, Inst Medieaval Music, 63; The Music of Black Americans: A History, 71 & ed, Readings in Black American Music, 71, W W Norton; Anonymous Pieces in the Ms, El Escorial, IV, a, 2, Hänssler-Verlag, 81; auth, Biographical Dictionary of Afro-American and African Musicians, Greenwood, 82. *Mailing Add:* Music Dept Harvard Univ Cambridge MA 02138

SOVIERO, DIANA BARBARA
SOPRANO
b Jersey City, NJ, Mar 19, 46. *Study:* Juilliard Sch Music; Hunter Col Opera Wkshp; studied with Marinka Gurewich, Martin Rich, Boris Goldovsky & Caterina Besiola. *Roles:* Mimi in La Boheme, Chautauqua Fest, New York, formerly, Chicago Lyr Opera, formerly, Zurich Opera, 81-82 & Orlando Opera Co, 82; Liu in Turandot, Dallas Opera; Violetta in La Traviata, Hamburg Staatsoper, 81-83; Ann Truelove in The Rake's Progress, San Francisco Opera, 82; Nedda in I Pagliacci, Houston Grand Opera, 82-83; Marguerite in Faust, Toulouse Opera, France, 82-83; Madama Butterfly in Madama Butterfly, Tulsa Opera, 82-83. *Pos:* Sop with Europ & North & South Am opera co; leading sop, New York City Opera, currently; performer, First Gala Stars, Metropolitan Opera Pub TV. *Teaching:* Master classes, The Faculty, Los Angeles. *Awards:* Nat Opera Inst Grant (two yrs); Richard Tucker Award; Affiliate Artist Fel, 74-75. *Mem:* Am Fedn TV & Radio Artists; Am Guild Musical Artists; Screen Actors Guild. *Rep:* Shaw Concerts Inc 1995 Broadway New York NY 10023. *Mailing Add:* c/o Columbia Artists Mgt 165 W 57th St New York NY 10019

SOWELL, LAVEN
MUSIC DIRECTOR, EDUCATOR
b Wewoka, Okla. *Study:* Studied with Martial Singher, 51-53 & Joseph Benton, 51-55; Univ Okla, BM, 55; Manhattan Sch Music, 56-57; studied with John Brownlee, 56-57 & Samuel Margolis, 62-65; Columbia Univ, MA, 64; studied with Nadia Boulanger, 66. *Roles:* Marcello in La Boheme, Wagner Opera Co, 55-56; perf many times with Tulsa Opera. *Pos:* Chorus master, Tulsa Opera, 62-; choirmaster, First Presby Church, 69-; choral dir, Univ Tulsa, 70- *Teaching:* Prof music, Univ Tulsa, 70- *Mem:* Music Teachers Nat Asn; Music Educr Nat Conf; Nat Asn Teachers Singing. *Mailing Add:* 3540 S Wheeling Tulsa OK 74105

SOYER, DAVID
CELLO, EDUCATOR
b Philadelphia, Pa, Feb 24, 23. *Study:* With Diran Alexanian, Emmanuel Feuermann & Pablo Casals; Univ SFla, Hon DFA, 76. *Rec Perf:* Three Sonatas for Cello & Harpsichord (Bach); Cello Sonatas (Mendelssohn); all Beethoven string quartets; Ten Mozart quartets; Dvorak, Smetana, Brahms & Schuman quintets; Piano Quartets (Sibelius). *Pos:* Cellist, Bach Aria Group, 48-49, Guilet Quartet, 49-51, New Music Quartet, 54-55 & Guarneri Quartet, 64- *Teaching:* Mem fac, State Univ NY, Purchase, formerly; mem fac violoncello, Curtis Inst Music, 68-; prof, Univ Md, College Park, currently. *Awards:* Grammy Award (five). *Mem:* Philadelphia Art Alliance. *Rep:* Beall Mgt 119 W 57th St New York NY 10019. *Mailing Add:* Curtis Inst Music 1726 Locust St Philadelphia PA 19103

SPACAGNA, MARIA
SOPRANO
b RI. *Study:* New England Consv Music. *Roles:* Lauretta in Gianni Schicchi, Dallas Opera, 82-83; Micaela in Carmen, Opera Memphis, 83; Zerlina in Don Giovanni, St Louis Opera, 83; Liu in Turandot, Dallas Opera, formerly & Can Opera, 83; Susanna in The Marriage of Figaro, Opera Hamilton, 83; Mimi in La Boheme, Edmonton Opera, 83; Madama Butterfly in Madama Butterfly, Florentine Opera Milwaukee, 83. *Awards:* First Prize, Busseto Compt; Second Prize, Paris Int Voice Compt; Nat Opera Inst Grant. *Mailing Add:* c/o Robert Lombardo Assoc 1 Harkness Plaza 61 W 62 Suite 6F New York NY 10023

SPARKS, DONNA LYNNE
WRITER, MUSIC DIRECTOR
b Washington, DC, May 30, 56. *Study:* Duke Univ, AB, 76, 81-; Univ NC, Chapel Hill, MA, 81. *Teaching:* Private instr flute, 74-; instr sight singing, Duke Univ Chapel, 79-80, prog coordr music orgn, 79-, dir, chapel summer choir, 80- *Mem:* Am Musicol Soc. *Interests:* Seventeenth century opera (Monteverdi, Davenant); recurring continuo and bass lines in 16th to 18th century music. *Publ:* Contribr, The Symphony 1720-1840, Ser B, Vol X, Garland, 81. *Mailing Add:* 4822 Duke Station Durham NC 27706

SPEKTOR, MIRA J
COMPOSER, MEZZO-SOPRANO
b Europe; US citizen. *Study:* Sarah Lawrence Col, BA; Juilliard Sch; Mannes Col Music. *Works:* Love is more thicker than forget, perf by Sarah Lawrence Chorus, 50; The Housewives' Cantata, perf by Minn Music Theater, 73-81 & prod by Cheryl Crawford in New York, 80; 4 Songs on Poems by Ruth Whitman, perf by Aviva Players & Sylvan Wind Quintet, 75-81; Sunday Psalm, perf by Lawrence Chelsi, 80; Lady of the Castle (chamber opera), perf by Theater for New City, 82. *Rec Perf:* Chansons de Paris, Westminster Rec,

53; Pitti Sing in The Mikado, 71, Golde in Fiddler on the Roof, 71 & Mira Sings Lullabies, 72, Conct Hall; Nora in The Housewives' Cantata, Original Cast Rec, 81. *Roles:* Ms with Atlantic Opera Singers, 65-71, Neway Opera Co, 68-72 & others. *Pos:* Founder & music dir, Atlantic Opera Singers, 65-71; music dir, Women's Interart Ctr, 75-77; founder, music dir & performer, The Aviva Players, 75- *Awards:* Comp Showcase, NY Singing Teachers' Asn, 82. *Bibliog:* Rhoda Amon (auth), She Conjures Up Other Lands Tunefully, Newsday, 9/17/70; Robert Sherman (auth), The Listening Room, WQXR-FM, 2/5/79; Jonathan Brown (auth), Begin Drops in on Concert ..., The Jewish Week, 7/27/80. *Mem:* BMI; Chamber Music Am; Am Music Ctr; NY Singing Teachers' Asn; Musicians' Club NY. *Mailing Add:* 262 Central Park W New York NY 10024

SPENCER, PATRICIA
FLUTE, TEACHER
b Niagara Falls, NY, June 28, 43. *Study:* Oberlin Consv Music, BM; studied with Marcel Moyse. *Rec Perf:* Riding the Wind I (Harvey Sollberger), Hexachords (Joan Tower) & Composition for Solo Flute (Eugene Lee), CRI; Epithalamium (Eleanor Cory), Advance. *Pos:* Flutist, Group for Contemp Music, 69- & Da Capo Chamber Players, 70- *Teaching:* Adj flute, Bard Col, 76-80. *Mem:* NY Consortium New Music. *Mailing Add:* 215 W 90th St New York NY 10024

SPENCER, PETER
EDUCATOR
Study: WVa Univ, BM, MM, DMA. *Teaching:* Assoc prof theory & analysis, Fla State Univ, 71- *Publ:* The Practice of Harmony, Prentice Hall, 83. *Mailing Add:* 918 Maplewood Ave Tallahassee FL 32303

SPENCER, ROBERT LAMAR
EDUCATOR, BASS-BARITONE
b Drew, Miss, Apr 5, 38. *Study:* Miss Col, BM, 61; Teachers Col, Columbia Univ, MA, 62; NTex State Univ, EdD, 69. *Teaching:* Asst prof music, Miss Col, 62-68; assoc prof, Okla Baptist Univ, 69-71; prof & chmn, ETex Baptist Col, 72- *Mem:* Music Educr Nat Conf; Tex Music Educr Asn; Nat Asn Teachers Singing; Tex Choral Dir Asn; Am Choral Dir Asn. *Mailing Add:* Music Dept ETex Baptist Col Marshall TX 75670

SPENCER, WILLIAMETTA
COMPOSER, EDUCATOR
b Marion, Ill, Aug 15, 37. *Study:* Whittier Col, AB; Univ Southern Calif, MM, PhD. *Works:* At the Round Earth's Imagined Corners, Shawnee Press, 68; Nova, Nova, 69 & The Mystic Trumpeter, 69, Nat Music Publ; Missa Brevis, 71, Three Madrigals to Poems of James Joyce, 71, Angelus ad Virginum, 74 & Cantate Comino, 75, Mark Foster Music Co. *Rec Perf:* Compositions of Williametta Spencer, Golden Crest Rec. *Pos:* Organist, Whittier Presbyterian Church, 65- *Teaching:* Prof harmony, comp, musicianship & music hist, Rio Hondo Col, 66- *Awards:* First Place Nat Comp Cont, Southern Calif Vocal Asn, 68. *Mem:* Music Teachers Asn Calif; Nat Guild Piano Teachers. *Publ:* Auth, The Relationship Between Andre Caplet and Claude Debussy, Musical Quart, 1/80. *Mailing Add:* 6228 Gregory Ave Whittier CA 90601

SPERL, GARY ROBERT
CLARINET, EDUCATOR
b June 22, 50. *Study:* Univ Wis, River Falls, BME, 72; Ind Univ, MMus(woodwinds), 77. *Pos:* Prin clarinet, Knoxville Symph Orch, 77-; prin & bass clarinetist, Spoleto Fest Orch, summers 80-; bass clarinetist, Savannah Symph Orch, 82- *Teaching:* Assoc instr woodwind tech, Ind Univ, 75-77; asst prof clarinet & sax, Univ Tenn, 77- *Mem:* Nat Asn Col Wind and Perc Instr; Music Educr Nat Conf. *Publ:* Auth, Woodwind Maintenance, Music Educr J, 80. *Mailing Add:* 2437 Upland Ave Knoxville TN 37917

SPERRY, PAUL
TENOR, TEACHER
b Chicago, Ill. *Study:* Harvard Col, BA; Univ Paris, cert; Harvard Business Sch, MBA. *Rec Perf:* Songs of Liszt and Chabrier, Orion, 74; Tel jour telle nuit and other songs (Poulenc), Golden Crest, 76; Open House (William Bolcom), 76 & Schubert Mass in A flat, 77, Nonesuch; Voices (Henze), Decca, 78; Donnerstag aus Licht (Stockhausen), DGG, 82; Sun Shafts (Victor Babin), Golden Crest; and others. *Roles:* Habinnas in Satyricon (Maderna), Netherlands Opera, 73; unknown Am songs, Young Mens Hebrew Asn, 76; tenor in Opera (Berio), Lyon & Rome, 80-81; Michael in Donnerstag, La Scala, 81; world premieres of Boswell's Venetian Journal (Maderna), with Juilliard Ens, 71, Voices (Henze), with London Sinfonietta, 74, The Sublime and the Beautiful (Kraft), with Collage, 80, The Ballad of Longwood Glen (Wilson), with Nancy Allen, 78, Diadem (Talma), with Da Capa Chamber Players, 80, Dybbuk Suite (Bernstein), with New York Phil, Animus IV (Druckman), Inst Recherche Coord Acoustique/Musique & others. *Pos:* Singer, appearing with Boston Symph, Los Angeles Phil, St Paul Chamber Ens & Amsterdam Concertgebauw & recitals throughout US & Europe. *Teaching:* Song repertoire, Aspen Music Fest, 78-; master classes in song repertoire & contemp music at Harvard Univ, Yale Univ, Princeton Univ, Cleveland Inst Music, Univ Southern Calif, Univ Calif, Los Angeles, Jordan Col Music, Sarah Lawrence Col, Westminster Choir Col & others. *Bibliog:* John Gruen (auth), The Tenor from the Harvard Business School, New York Times, 2/8/76; Peter Mose (auth), Paul Sperry: Undaunted at Dartmouth, Musical Am, 9/80; Marcia Menter (auth), High Falsetto, Spoken Words and Screams, Virtuoso, 5-6/81. *Mem:* Am Music Ctr (bd mem, 78-); Am Comp Orch (bd mem, 80-). *Publ:* Auth, What's So Special about Poulenc's Songs?, Keynote, 82; ed, Songs of An Innocent Age, G Schirmer (in prep). *Rep:* Sheldon Soffer Mgt 130 W 56th St New York NY 10019. *Mailing Add:* 115 Central Park W New York NY 10023

SPICKNALL, JOAN SINGER See Singer, Joan

SPIEGEL, LAURIE
COMPOSER, ELECTRONIC INSTRUMENT DESIGNER
b Chicago, Ill, Sept 20, 45. *Study:* Shimer Col, Mt Carroll, Ill, AB, 67; Juilliard Sch Music, 69-72; Brooklyn Col, City Univ New York, MA(music comp), 75; studied comp with Jacob Druckman & Emmanuel Ghent. *Works:* Waves (ballet), perf by Kathryn Posin Dance Co, Elliot Feld Ballet, Netherlands Dance Theatre, Utah Reply Dance Theater, Alvin Ailey Co & Juilliard Dance Co, 75-; Hearing Things, comn by Mostly Moderns Chamber Orch, 83. *Rec Perf:* Appalachian Grove I, 1750 Arch Rec; The Expanding Universe, Patchwork, Old Wave & Pentachrome, Philo Rec; Drums & Voices Within, Cappricio Rec. *Pos:* Freelance comp, music for film, video, dance, theater & concert media, New York, 69-; comp, Spectra Films, 71-75; music proj dir, Syntronics Ltd, Toronto, 83- *Teaching:* Instr electronic comp, Bucks Co Community Col, 71-74, Cooper Union, New York, 79-80 & NY Univ, 82. *Awards:* CAPS Fel, 75-76 & 79-80; ASCAP Awards, ann 76-; Meet the Comp Grant, 75, 76, 77, 79, 80 & 83. *Mem:* ASCAP; Comp Forum; Comput Music Asn; Am Music Ctr. *Publ:* Contribr, Ear Mag, Creative Comput, Personal Comput & Comput Music J. *Mailing Add:* 175 Duane St New York NY 10013

SPIEGELMAN, JOEL WARREN
COMPOSER, EDUCATOR
b Buffalo, NY, Jan 23, 33. *Study:* Brandeis Univ, studied comp with Harold Shapero, MFA, 56; Paris Consv, comp with Nadia Boulanger, cert, 57; Gnesin Inst, Moscow, cert, 66. *Works:* Morsels (piano four hands), MCA Music Inc, 67; Daddy (cantata), 72; Astral Dimensions I, 73; Fantasy No 1 (string quartet), 74 & Fantasy No 2 (string quartet), 75, Carl Fischer Inc; The Possessed (ballet with Meyer Kupferman), 75; Midnight Sun (oboe & tape), 76. *Rec Perf:* Toccata for Harpsichord (John Lessard), Serenus Rec; Crescendo and Diminuendo (Edison Denisov), Columbia Rec. *Teaching:* Instr, Longy Sch Music, 61-63; asst prof, Brandeis Univ, 61-66; prof, Sarah Lawrence Col, 66- *Awards:* Inter-Univ Grant USSR, Ford Found, 65-66; Ingram Merrill Grant, 67 & 68; ASCAP Spec Award, 68- *Mem:* ASCAP; Am Fedn Musicians. *Publ:* Auth, The Trial, Condemnation and Death of Tchaikovsky, Hi-Fidelity, 81. *Mailing Add:* Dept Music Sarah Lawrence Col Bronxville NY 10708

SPIES, CLAUDIO
COMPOSER, EDUCATOR
b Santiago, Chile, Mar 26, 25; US citizen. *Study:* New England Consv; Longy Sch Music, with Nadia Boulanger, 42-46; Harvard Univ, with Irving Fine & Walter Piston, AB, 50, MA, 54. *Works:* Tempi (14 instrm), Theodore Presser, 62; Viopiacem (viola & keyboard instrm), 65 & LXXXV (eights & fives for strings & clarinets), 67, Boosey & Hawkes; Three Songs on Poems by May Swenson, Boelke Bomart Inc, 69; Bagatelle (piano), Boosey & Hawkes Inc, 70; 5 Dadivas (piano), 77-81 & Half-Time (E flat clarinet & trumpet), 81, Boelke Bomart Inc. *Rec Perf:* Vocal and Piano Music by Claudio Spies, CRI, 81. *Teaching:* Instr, Harvard Univ, 54-57; asst prof, Vassar Col, 57-58; assoc prof, Swarthmore Col, 58-70; fac mem & cond, Harvard Summer Sch, 68; prof music, Princeton Univ, 70-; fac mem contemp Am music, Salzburg Sem Am Studies, 76. *Awards:* Creative Arts Award, Brandeis Univ, 67; Nat Inst Arts & Lett Award, 69; Nat Endowment Arts Fel, 75. *Bibliog:* Paul Lansky (auth), The Music of Claudio Spies, Tempo, Vol 103, 38-44. *Mem:* Founding mem, Int Alban Berg Soc Ltd; Am Brahms Soc; founding mem, Am Soc Univ Comp; ASCAP. *Mailing Add:* 117 Meadowbrook Dr Princeton NJ 08540

SPIES, MICHAEL C
CRITIC
b Dallas, Tex, May 5, 54. *Study:* Univ Tex, Austin, BA, BJ, 76; Tex A & M Univ, MA, 78. *Pos:* Music rev, Corpus Christi Caller Times, 79- *Mailing Add:* PO Box 9136 Corpus Christi TX 78408

SPILLMAN, ROBERT ARMSTRONG
PIANO, TEACHER-COACH
b Berea, Ky, Mar 4, 36. *Study:* Eastman Sch Music, BM(piano), 57, MA(theory), 59; Hochschule Musik, Stuttgart, Konzertreife, 66. *Works:* Concerto for Bass Trombone & Orchestra, 59; Two Songs (tuba), 60 & Four Greek Preludes, 66, Ed Musicus. *Rec Perf:* Chamber Music (Schumann), Vox, 77; Music by Prince Louis Ferdinand, Desmar, 78; Sonatas for Clarinet & Piano (Brahms), Golden Crest, 79; Music for Double Bass & Piano, 79 & Melodies of Les Six, 83, Musical Heritage. *Teaching:* Assoc prof piano, Eastman Sch Music, 73- *Publ:* Auth, A Handbook for Accompanists, Schirmer Books (in prep). *Mailing Add:* 10 Manhattan Square Rochester NY 14607

SPINA, SALVATORE C
PIANO, EDUCATOR
b Chicago, Ill, May 16, 48. *Study:* Mozarteum, Salzburg, Austria, cert(perf), 69; Northwestern Univ, BMus, 70, MMus, 72, DMA, 83. *Pos:* Artistic co-dir, New Art Ens, 80-; exec dir, Prep Div, Am Consv, 83- *Teaching:* Prof music, Am Consv, 82- *Mem:* Chicago Soc Comp (pres, 83-); Chicago Soc Comp (pres, 83-); Soc Am Musicians; New Music Am. *Mailing Add:* 116 S Michigan Ave Chicago IL 60603

SPIVAKOVSKY, TOSSY
VIOLIN, EDUCATOR
b Odessa, USSR, Feb 4, 07, US citizen. *Study:* Studied with Arrigo Serato & Willy Hess, formerly; Fairfield Univ, Hon LHD, 70; Cleveland Inst Music, Hon DMus, 75. *Works:* Cadenzas to Violin Concerto (Beethoven), Breitkopf & Härtell, 64; Cadenzas to Five Violin Concertos (Mozart), Musikverlag Wilh Zimmermann, 67. *Rec Perf:* Violin Sonata No 2 (Bartok), Concert Hall Soc, 47; Solo Sonata G-Minor (Bach), 51 & Violin Sonata G-Major (Beethoven), 51, Columbia Masterworks; Violin Concerto (Menotti), RCA, 55; Violin Concerto (Sibelius), Everest Rec, 60; Concerto (violin & Cello; Kirchner), EPIC, 61; Violin Concerto (Stravinsky), Vanguard, 63. *Pos:* Concertmaster, Berlin Phil, 26-28 & Cleveland Orch, 42-45. *Teaching:* Violin, Univ Consv, Melbourne, Australia, 34-39 & Juilliard Sch Music, 74- *Bibliog:* Gaylord Yost (auth), *Mem:* Am Musicol Soc; Am Fedn Musicians. *Publ:* Auth, Polyphony in Bachs Works for Solo Violin, Music Review, 67. *Mailing Add:* 29 Burnham Hill PO Box 188 Westport CT 06881

SPIZIZEN, LOUISE (MYERS)
COMPOSER, PERFORMER
b Lynn, Mass, Aug 24, 28. *Study:* Vassar Col, AB, 49; Univ Calif, San Diego, MA, 72; studied comp with Wallingford Riegger, harpsichord with Gustav Leonhardt, Igor Kipnis, Rosalyn Tureck, Josef Marx & John Metz. *Works:* Weary With Toil, Theodore Presser, 68; Romeo and Juliet, 80, Gate of the Lions, 82, Of Kings and Clowns, 82 & Wings, 83, Invisible Theatre. *Pos:* Critic, columnist & contribr, La Jolla Light J, 73-79 & Los Angeles Times, San Diego Ed, 77-79; staff harpsichordist, La Jolla Chamber Orch, 76-79; comp & music dir, Invisible Theatre, 80- *Awards:* Alternate fel, Music Critics Asn to Fromm Fest Contemp Music, 78. *Mem:* Am Fedn Musicians; Music Critics Asn; Ariz State Music Teachers Asn (vpres, 80-82); Music Teachers Nat Asn; Tucson Music Teachers Asn (first vpres, 82-). *Mailing Add:* 2540 Camino La Zorrela Tucson AZ 85718

SPOTTS, CARLETON B
CELLO, EDUCATOR
b Marshall, Mo, Nov 17, 32. *Study:* Manahattan Sch Music, with Diran Alexanian, BM, 53, with Bernard Greenhause, MM, 59. *Rec Perf:* Quartets (Santaro & Nepomureno), Educo, 70; Quartets (James Willey), Spectrum, 80. *Pos:* Cellist, US Air Force Orch, Washington, DC, 53-57 & Esterhazy Quartet, Columbia, Mo, 60-; freelance cellist, New York, 58-60. *Teaching:* Prof cello, Univ Mo, Columbia, 60- *Awards:* Harold Bauer Prize, Manhattan Sch Music, 53. *Mem:* Am String Teacher Asn; Music Teachers Nat Asn; Music Educr Nat Conf. *Mailing Add:* Music Dept Univ Mo Columbia MO 65211

SPRAGUE, RAYMOND
MUSIC DIRECTOR, EDUCATOR
b Yonkers, NY, Nov 29, 47. *Study:* Williams Col, Mass, BA, 69; Univ NMex, Albuquerque, MM(theory & comp), 73; Univ Colo, Boulder, DMA(choral lit & cond), 79; studies with John Clark, Eph Ehly, Joseph Flummerfelt, Walter Collins, Lynn Whitten & Frauke Hausemann. *Pos:* Reviewer choral music, Choral J, Am Choral Dir, 77-80. *Teaching:* Instr, Univ NMex, 72-73 & Univ Colo, 73-77; dir choral activ, St Mary's Col, Notre Dame, Ind, 77- *Mem:* Am Choral Dir Asn; Ind Choral Dir Asn (pres, 83); Music Educr Nat Conf; Am Musicol Soc; Am Choral Found. *Publ:* Auth, A Classified, Annotated Bibliography of Articles Relating to Choral Music in Five Major Periodicals through 1980, Am Choral Dir Asn, 82. *Rep:* Dept Music St Mary's Col Notre Dame IN 46556. *Mailing Add:* 3610 Oakcrest Dr South Bend IN 46615

SPRATLAN, LEWIS
COMPOSER, EDUCATOR
b Miami, Fla, Sept 5, 40. *Study:* Yale Univ, BA, 62, MMus, 65. *Works:* Dance Suite, 75, Life Is A Dream (opera), 78, Chiasmata, 79, Cornucopia, 80, Coils, 81 & Webs, 81, Margun Music, Inc; String Quartet No 1, Windsor String Quartet, 82. *Teaching:* Asst prof, Pa State Univ, 67-70; prof music, Amherst Col, 70- *Awards:* Creative Artists' Award, Mass Arts & Humanities Found, 72; fels, Nat Endowment Arts, 73-74 & John Simon Guggenheim Mem Found, 80-81. *Mem:* Am Soc Univ Comp; Am Music Ctr. *Mailing Add:* 22 Hitchcock Rd Amherst MA 01002

SPRECHER, WILLIAM GUNTHER See Gunther, William

SPRENKLE, ROBERT LOUIS
OBOE, EDUCATOR
b Pittsburgh, Pa, Oct 27, 14. *Study:* Eastman Sch Music, Rochester Univ, BM(oboe) & PSM, 36. *Pos:* English horn & second oboe, Rochester Phil, 36-37 & first oboe, 37-; oboist, Lake Placid Sinfonietta, 39-78. *Teaching:* Prof oboe, Eastman Sch Music, 37-82. *Publ:* Auth, Art of Oboe Playing, Summy Birchard, 61. *Mailing Add:* 7 Commodore Pkwy Rochester NY 14625

SPRING, GLENN ERNEST
COMPOSER, EDUCATOR
b Hot Springs, Ark, Apr 19, 39. *Study:* Loma Linda Univ, with Perry Beach; Tex Christian Univ, with Ralph Guenther; Univ Wash, with John Verrall & Robert Suderberg, DMA, 72. *Works:* Fantasia on Dulcimer (string orch), 72; Shapes (short symph), Walla Walla Symph, 74; Music for Piano (chamber music), 74; Christmas Lullaby (chorus), 74; Evocation (chorus & orch), 75; Romance (string orch), 76; Perceptions (chamber orch), 77. *Pos:* Violinist, Ft Worth Symph, 62-65 & Columbia Symph, 62-65; concertmaster, Walla Walla Symph, formerly. *Teaching:* Prof music, Walla Walla Col, 66- *Awards:* Wash Arts Comn Grant, 73. *Mailing Add:* 1057 Brickner College Place WA 99324

SPROTT, JOHN RHULIN
PERCUSSION, COMPOSER
b Memphis, Tenn, Aug 25, 45. *Study:* Memphis State Univ, BS(music educ), 68; Univ Tex, Austin, 68-72. *Works:* Chant and Peasant Dance, Memphis State Univ Perc Ens, 67; Happening For Percussion, 70 & Moving Piece For Percussion, 72, Univ Tex Perc Ens. *Pos:* Perc, Memphis Symph Orch, 63-68 & 76-82 & Austin Symph Orch, 68-73; prin perc, Memphis Symph Orch, 82- *Mailing Add:* 5924 Blackwell Bartlett TN 38134

SPRUNG, DAVID REICHERT
FRENCH HORN, EDUCATOR
b Jersey City, NJ, Oct 24, 31. *Study:* Queens Col, City Univ New York, BA, 57; Princeton Univ, MFA, 59. *Works:* String Quartet, Queens Col String Quartet, 59. *Rec Perf:* Three West Coast Composers, Desto, 73; The Tempest (Chihara), Moss Music Group Inc, 82. *Pos:* Mem, Metropolitan Opera Orch, 60-61; prin horn, Pittsburgh Symph, 61-63 & San Francisco Ballet Orch, 76-; co-prin horn, San Francisco Opera Orch, 73- *Teaching:* Asst prof horn & theory, Wichita State Univ, 63-66; assoc prof music, Sonoma State Univ, 66-70; prof music, Calif State Univ, Hayward, 70- *Mailing Add:* 3901 Oakmore Rd Oakland CA 94602

SPURGEON, PHILLIP (COLEMAN)
CONDUCTOR & MUSIC DIRECTOR, EDUCATOR
b Canon City, Colo, Jan 2, 36. *Study:* Consv Music, Oberlin Col, BM(piano), 58; Santa Cecilia Consv Music, Rome, 58-59; Berkshire Music Ctr, studied advan cond with Richard Lert, 60-78. *Rec Perf:* Violoncello Concerto (Schiffman), Orion, 81. *Pos:* Music dir & cond, Johnstown Symph & Chorale, 61-69 & Midland-Odessa Symph & Chorale, 71-72; assoc artistic dir, Am Symph Orch League Orchs Inst & Fest, 65-78; cond, Phoenix Symph Orch, 69-71; music dir, Int Cong Strings, 79 & 80. *Teaching:* Cond & prof music, Fla State Univ, Tallahassee, currently. *Awards:* Fulbright Fel, 58; First Prize, Int Compt, Besancon, France, 59; Advan Cond Grant, Am Symph Orch League, 62. *Mem:* Am Symph Orch League. *Mailing Add:* 3665 Barbary Dr Tallahassee FL 32308

STACKHOUSE, HOLLY N
FLUTE & PICCOLO, TEACHER
b Chattanooga, Tenn, Nov 29, 38. *Study:* Sch Music, Ind Univ, BME, 60; State Univ NY, Fredonia, MM, 81; studied with Bennett, Tipton, Drexler, Sharp & Johnson. *Rec Perf:* Theodore Frazeur and Friends, Grenadilla, 78. *Pos:* Mem, Albany Symph Orch, 69-76 & Tambous Perc Flute Duo, 76-; prin flute, Erie Chamber Orch, 76-; dir, Univ Flute Choir, Gannon Univ, 81- *Teaching:* Private flute, 60-; instr, Hamilton Col, 65-68, Hartwick Col, 69-76 & Mercyhurst Col, 76-81. *Awards:* Ind Univ Scholar, 57-60; Albany Symph Vanguard Scholar, 71. *Mem:* Chamber Music Am; Erie Music Teachers Asn; Pa Music Teachers Asn; Int Fedn Musicians. *Mailing Add:* 5708 Bonaventure Dr Erie PA 16505

STACY, MARTHA
EDUCATOR
Study: La State Univ, BME, MM; studied pedagogy with Polly Gibbs; Teachers Col, Columbia Univ, with Robert Pace; Ohio State Univ, with Lawrence Rast; Southern Methodist Univ, Univ Colo; Stanford Univ; Suzuki Music Fest, Japan, with Harako Kataoka. *Pos:* Mem bd dir, Suzuki Asn Am, 81-83, consult & teacher trainer, currently. *Teaching:* Assoc prof piano pedagogy, Oberlin Col, 71-; class piano teacher, Dallas pub sch; instr, Berea Col; asst prof, Univ Kans; assoc prof, Kent State Univ. *Mailing Add:* Music Dept Oberlin Col Oberlin OH 44074

STACY, THOMAS
ENGLISH HORN
b Little Rock, Ark, Aug 15, 38. *Study:* Eastman Sch Music, BM, 60. *Works:* Solos for the English Horn Player, G Schirmer, 69. *Rec Perf:* Skrowaczewski English Horn Concerto, Desto, 71; Swan of Tuonela, New York Phil, 74; Persichetti English Horn Concerto, Hodkinson Chamber Concerto, 78 & Grenadilla, 78; Stacy on 2, Spectrum, 82. *Pos:* Solo English horn, New Orleans Symph, 60-61; San Antonio Symph, 61-62, Minneapolis Symph, 62-72 & New York Phil, 72- *Teaching:* English horn, Juilliard Sch Music, 74- & Manhattan Sch Music, 81- *Rep:* Esther Prince Mgt 101 W 57th St New York NY 10019. *Mailing Add:* Avery Fisher Hall Lincoln Ctr 65th at Broadway New York NY 10023

STACY, WILLIAM BARNEY
EDUCATOR, FRENCH HORN
b Middletown, Ohio, Aug 1, 44. *Study:* Ohio State Univ, BMus, 66; Juilliard Sch Music, studied horn with James Chambers, 66-67; Univ NC, Chapel Hill, MA, 69; Univ Colo, DMA, 72; studied horn with Robert Fries, William Kearns, Philip Nesbit & Leonard Rivenburg. *Works:* H*O*R*N (solo horn), Ludwig Music Publ Co, 74; Density Structure II (magnetic tape), Second Int Electronic Music Seminar, 75; Night Apparitions: Spookies for Big A, Univ Wyo Wind Ens, 76; Bag: Axes (solo trumpet), perf by George Hitt, 77; Three Lunar Declamations, perf by Marilyn Smart, 80; O*B*O*E (solo oboe), perf by Julia Combs, 80; Brass Quintet, perf by Seattle Brass Quintet, 83. *Teaching:* Asst instr, Univ NC, Chapel Hill, 68; asst prof, Marshall Univ, 68-74; teaching assoc, Univ Colo, Boulder, 71-72; assoc prof, Univ Wyo, Laramie, 74- *Mem:* Sonneck Soc; Int Horn Soc; Am Soc Univ Comp (region VII co-chair & mem nat coun, 77-79). *Interests:* American music, especially bands and their repertoire. *Publ:* Contribr, Performance Practice: A Bibliography, Norton, 71; auth, Music: The Expressive Art, Kendall/Hunt, 74; Catch Those Clams!, Instrumentalist, 76; Helping the Young Horn Player, Sch Musician, 82; Sousa's Band Suites: An Aesthetic Middleground, Sonneck Soc Newsletter, 82. *Mailing Add:* Dept Music Box 3037 Univ Wyo Laramie WY 82071

STAFF, CHARLES BANCROFT, JR
CRITIC
b Franklin, Ind, July 2, 29. *Study:* Franklin Col, AB, 51; Northwestern Univ; Music Sch, Ind Univ, BM(comp), 55. *Works:* String Quartet, Berkshire Quartet, 54; Death Under a Tree (TV opera), Music Sch & TV dept, Ind Univ, 55; Wind Quintet, Ind Univ Fac Quintet, 55. *Pos:* Asst organist, Franklin First Presby, 45-48; organist, Franklin First Baptist, 48-51; music critic, Indianapolis News, Ind, 65- *Teaching:* Lectr music, theater & criticism, Ind Cent Univ, Ind State Univ, Ind Univ & Butler Univ. *Mailing Add:* c/o Indianapolis News 307 N Pennsylvania Indianapolis IN 46206

STAFFORD, JAMES EDWARD
EDUCATOR, COMPOSER
b Summerville, La, Aug 20, 33. *Study:* Univ Southwestern La, BME, 57; La State Univ, MME, 64, PhD, 70. *Works:* Alma Mater, perf by S Terrehonne High Sch Band & Choir, 63; Missa in Festis Simplicibus, perf by ETenn State Univ Symph Band, 66; The Time of Singing, perf by ETenn State Univ Conct Choir, 68; Quintet for Strings and Winds, perf by La State Univ Contemp Music Fest, 69; Mass for Voices and Brass, Univ Press, Ann Arbor, Mich, 70; Trust in the Lord, 81 & Show Me The Way, 82, perf by First United Methodist Church Choir. *Pos:* Cond & perf, Jazz Ens & Musical Theatre, Tenn & La, 52-; dir music, pub & private La sch, 53-64. *Teaching:* Prof music, ETenn State Univ, 65-, chmn, Dept Music, 72-78. *Mem:* Nat Asn Jazz Educr. *Mailing Add:* #4 Bridgewood Ct Johnson City TN 37601

STAFFORD, LEE CHRISTOPHER
EDUCATOR, COMPOSER
b New York, NY. *Study:* Mercy Col, BA, 73. *Pos:* Pres, Stafford Sound Corp, 76- *Teaching:* Instr prod ed & rec technol, Inst Audio Res, 82-; Instr rec technol, NY Univ, 83- *Bibliog:* Colin McEnroe (auth), Live Sounds, Hartford Courent, 82. *Mailing Add:* 11 W 17th St New York NY 10011

STAHL, DAVID
CONDUCTOR
b New York, NY, Nov 4, 49. *Study:* Nat Orch Asn, 70-72; Queens Col, City Univ New York, BA, 72, MA, 74; Berkshire Music Ctr, 75; studied cond with Leonard Bernstein, Joseph Rosenstock, Seiji Ozawa Leon Barzin, Walter Susskind & Max Rudolf. *Pos:* Assoc cond, Cincinnati Symph Orch, formerly; music dir & cond, St Louis Phil, formerly & Cincinnati Youth Symph Orch, formerly; asst cond, New York Phil, 76; guest cond, opera co in US, Canada & Europe. *Awards:* Queens Col Orch Soc Award, 72; Exxon Arts Endowment Cond, 76-79. *Mem:* Am Symph Orch League; Am Fedn Musicians. *Mailing Add:* c/o Colbert Artists Mgt Inc 111 W 57th St New York NY 10019

STALLMAN, ROBERT
EDUCATOR, FLUTE
Study: New England Consv Music, BM, 68, MM, 71; studied flute with James Pappoutsakis, Jean-Pierre Rampal, Alain Marion & Gaston Crunelle; Paris Consv; Berkshire Music Ctr. *Rec Perf:* On Libr of Cong & CRI. *Pos:* Soloist throughout New England & Southern Europe; mem, Orpheus Woodwind Quintet, currently, L'Ensemble, New York, currently & Melos Sinfonia, currently; mem & dir, Cambridge Chamber Players, currently. *Teaching:* Mem fac flute & chamber music, New England Consv Music, currently & Queens Col, currently; mem fac flute, Longy Sch Music, currently. *Awards:* Koussevitsky Fel; First Prize, Nat Col Artists Music Compt, 71; C D Jackson Prize, Berkshire Music Ctr. *Rep:* Hanah Woods 148 W 75th St #1B New York NY 10023. *Mailing Add:* New England Consv Music 290 Huntington Ave Boston MA 02115

STALVEY, DORRANCE
COMPOSER, ADMINISTRATOR
b Georgetown, SC, Aug, 21, 30. *Study:* Col Music, Cincinnati, Ohio, BM, 53, MM, 55. *Works:* Changes, perf by Karl Kohn, Gil Kalish, Aleck Karis, Virginia Gaburo, 66; Points Lines Circles, Editions Salabert, 68; In Time and Not, perf by Immaculate Heart Col, 70; Celebration Sequent I, Editions Salabert, 73; Celebration Sequent II, perf by Cincinnati Phil, 76; Agathlon, Erick Hawkins Dance Co, 78; Three Pairs and Seven, perf by Miles Anderson & Virko Baley, 79. *Pos:* Exec & artistic dir, Monday Evening Concts, Los Angeles, CA, 71-; Coordr music prog, Los Angeles County Museum Art, 82- *Teaching:* Asst prof, Immaculate Heart Col, 68-71, assoc prof, 72-76, prof, 77-80. *Awards:* Comp fel, Nat Endowment Arts, 75-78; Comp Awards, ASCAP, 77- *Mem:* Am Music Ctr; ASCAP; Am Fedn Musicians. *Publ:* Contribr, Advance Techniques of Doublebass Playing, Piper Co, 75. *Mailing Add:* 2145 Manning Ave Los Angeles CA 90025

STALZER, FRANK S
EDUCATOR, OBOE & ENGLISH HORN
b Kansas City, Mo, Apr 25, 25. *Study:* Univ Kans, BMusEd, 48; Eastman Sch Music, MMus, 51; studied with Marcel Tabuteau, 54-55. *Pos:* First oboe & English horn, Phoenix Symph Orch, 57-82. *Teaching:* Instr woodwinds, La State Univ, 49-54; asst prof, Ariz State Univ, 55-68, assoc prof, 68- *Mem:* Life mem, Music Educr Nat Conf; life mem, Am Fedn Musicians; Nat Asn Col Wind & Perc Instr (chmn western div, 64-67); Int Double Reed Soc. *Publ:* Auth, Review of Newly Published Woodwind Ensembles, Woodwind World & Brass & Perc, 72-83. *Mailing Add:* 2225 S Taylor Dr Tempe AZ 85282

STAMFORD, JOHN SCOTT
LIRICO SPINTO TENOR, TEACHER
b Chicago, Ill, Sept 5, 23. *Study:* Chicago Consv Music, with Edgar Nelson; Manhattan Sch Music, with Herta Glaz; studied with Albert Sciaretti. *Roles:* Manrico in Il Trovatore, Am Opera Co, 52; Faust in Mefistofele; Canio in I Pagliacci; Sergei in Katerina Ismailova; J Eisenstein in Die Fledermaus; Judge Danforth in The Crucible; Oedipus Rex. *Pos:* Lirico spinto ten with New York City Opera & maj opera co in Montreal, Miami & St Paul. *Teaching:* Voice. *Mailing Add:* 1533 Wales Ave Baldwin NY 11510

STANEK, ALAN EDWARD
CLARINET, EDUCATOR
b Longmont, Colo, July 3, 39. *Study:* Univ Colo, Boulder, BME, 61; Eastman Sch Music, MMus, 65; Univ Mich, DMA, 74. *Pos:* Cond & music dir, Hastings Civic Symph, 70-76; cond & music dir, Idaho State Civic Symph, 76-80, prin clarinet, 80- *Teaching:* Dir instrm music, Ainsworth, Nebr, 61-64 &

Cozad, Nebr, 65-67; asst prof music, Hastings Col, 67-76; assoc prof & chmn music dept, Idaho State Univ, 76- *Mem:* Nat Asn Col Wind & Perc Instr; Int Clarinet Soc (secy, 78-84); Col Music Soc; Idaho Music Educr Asn (chmn high educ, 80-); Music Educr Nat Conf. *Mailing Add:* 1352 E Lewis Pocatello ID 83201

STANFORD, THOMAS STANLEY
EDUCATOR, CLARINET
b Walla Walla, Wash, June 16, 43. *Study:* Univ Ore, Eugene, BM, 65, DMA, 83; Univ Ore, Oldenburg, WGermany, MM, 67. *Teaching:* Assoc prof music, Warner Pac Col, Ore, 73-80 & Portland State Univ, Ore, 81- *Mem:* Int Clarinet Soc; Nat Asn Col Wind & Perc Instr; Music Educr Nat Conf. *Interests:* Analytical techniques. *Publ:* Auth, A New Approach to the Adagio from the Concerto for Clarinet by Mozart, Nat Asn Col Wind & Perc Instr J, 80. *Mailing Add:* Music Dept Portland State Univ Portland OR 97207

STANLEY, DONALD ARTHUR
EDUCATOR, TUBA
b Mansfield, Ohio, Jan 11, 37. *Study:* Ohio State Univ, Columbus, BS(music educ), 59; Ohio Univ, MFA, 64; Univ Colo. *Pos:* Auth of column, New Tuba Music Reviews, Pa Collegiate Band Asn News, 76-83. *Teaching:* Instr music, Milan, Ohio Pub Sch, 59-62; instr band & brass, Nebr State Col, 64-66; prof music, Pa State Col, 66- *Awards:* Citation of Excellence, Nat Band Asn, 75. *Mem:* Tubists Universal Brotherhood Asn; Col Band Dir Nat Asn (vpres eastern div, 83-85); Nat Asn Col Wind & Perc Instrm; Pa Collegiate Band Asn (pres, 72-73); Pa Music Educr Asn. *Publ:* Auth, The Brass Ensemble—A Chamber Music Medium, Pa Music Educr Asn New, 68; Band Warm-Ups, Instrumentalist, 68; Articulation Technique for Tuba, Getzen Corp, 76; Two Sonatas for Tuba & Piano, Nat Asn Col Wind & Perc Instrm J, 81, 82 & 83. *Mailing Add:* 12 Townview Dr Mansfield PA 16933

STANLEY, HELEN CAMILLE (HELEN STANLEY GATLIN)
COMPOSER, PIANO
b Tampa, Fla, Apr 6, 30. *Study:* Cincinnati Consv Music, BMus, 51; Fla State Univ, MMus, 54; studied with Hans Barth & Ernst von Dohnanyi. *Works:* Etude for Piano, perf by Hans Barth, 48; Rhapsody for Electronic Tape and Orchestra, comn by Music Teachers Nat Asn & Fla State Teachers Asn, 72; Battle Hymn, comn by St Paul's-by-the-Sea, 76; Duo Sonata for Tape Recorder and Piano, 83, Sonata for Trombone and Piano, 83 & Woodwind Quintet, 83, Kenyon Publ. *Awards:* Music Teachers Nat Asn & Fla State Music Teachers Asn Comp Comn, 72. *Bibliog:* Miriam Stewart Green (auth), Consider These Creators, Am Music Teacher, 1/76; Laurine Elkins-Marlow (auth), What Have Women in this Country Written for Full Orchestra?, Symph News, 4/76. *Mem:* ASCAP; Am Music Ctr; Southeastern Comp League; Piano Teachers Cong NY. *Mailing Add:* 1768 Emory Circle S Jacksonville FL 32207

STANLEY, MARGARET KING
ADMINISTRATOR, PATRON
b San Antonio, Tex, Dec 11, 29. *Study:* Univ Tex, BA, 52; Incarnate Word Col, MA, 59. *Pos:* Nat coun mem, Metropolitan Opera, 69-; pres, San Antonio Symph League, 71-74; develop dir, Arts Coun San Antonio, 76-79; exec dir, San Antonio Perf Arts Asn, 79- *Awards:* Emily Smith Award for Outstanding Alumnae, Mary Baldwin Col, 73; Special Achievement, Women in Commun, Inc, 82; Express-News Outstanding Woman in Arts, 82. *Mem:* Tex Arts Alliance (bd gov, 82). *Mailing Add:* 201 N St Mary's Suite 618 San Antonio TX 78205

STANTON, ROYAL WALTZ
COMPOSER, EDUCATOR
b Los Angeles, Calif, Oct 23, 16. *Study:* Univ Calif, Los Angeles, with Arnold Schoenberg, BE, 39, MA(musicol & educ), 46. *Works:* God's Son is Born (SATB cantata), 68; Two Festal Motets (double choir), 71; Forever Blest is He (SATB); Ev'ry Time (SATB); Five Psalm Fragments (SATB & solos); You Fill My Heart (SATB); Blest are They; and 90 choral comp & arr. *Pos:* Dir, Los Angeles Bach Fest, 59-60. *Teaching:* Pub sch, San Luis Obispo, Calif, 39-41 & Pomona, Calif, 42-43; teacher, Long Beach Polytech High, Calif, 46-50; head music dept & dir choral orgn, Long Beach City Col, 50-61; chmn fine arts div, Foothill Col, 61-67; dir, Schola Cantorum, DeAnza Col, 64-82, chmn arts div, 67-79. *Awards:* ASCAP Awards, 69-71; Outstanding Educr of Am Award, 71 & 74. *Mem:* Am Musicol Soc; ASCAP; Am Choral Dir Asn; Music Educr Nat Conf; Choral Cond Guild. *Publ:* Auth, The Dynamic Choral Conductor, 71; Steps to Singing for Voice Classes, 2nd ed, 76, 3rd ed, 83; contribr to Music Educr Nat Conf J, Am Choral Cond Asn J, Symposium & J Col Music Soc. *Mailing Add:* 22301 Havenhurst Dr Los Altos CA 94022

STAPP, GREGORY (LEE)
BASS
b Denver, Colo, May 19, 54. *Study:* Loretto Heights Col, Denver, BA, 76; study voice with George Lynn, Dorothy DiScala & Margaret Harshaw; Acad Vocal Arts, Philadelphia, artist cert, 80. *Roles:* Pluto in Il Ballo delle Ingrate, 81 & Friar Lawrence in Romeo & Juliette, 81, Spring Opera Theater; Raimondo in Lucia di Lammermoor, San Francisco Opera, 81; Achillas in Julius Caesar, San Francisco Opera Summer Fest, 82; Sarastro in The Magic Flute, Eugene Opera, 83; Commendatore in Don Giovanni, Opera Theatre St Louis, 83; Colline in La Boheme, New York City Opera, 83. *Pos:* Affil artist bass, San Francisco Opera, 80-81, Adler fel bass, 82; artist, Affil Artists Inc, 80- *Awards:* Grant, William Matheus Sullivan Musical Found, 79-; Ver Valen Award, 79 & Jovanovsky Award, 80, Baltimore Opera Nat Vocal Compt; First Prize, Metropolitan Opera Western Regional Auditions, 82. *Mailing Add:* 3425 Taraval St San Francisco CA 94116

STAPP, OLIVIA
MEZZO-SOPRANO
b New York, NY, May 31, 40. *Study:* Studied with Ettore Campogalliani, Rodolfo Ricci & Oren Brown. *Roles:* Beppe in L'Amico Fritz, Spoleto Fest, 60; Dejanira in Heracles, Ind Univ Opera, Bloomington, 71; Elvira in Ernani, Gran Teatre Liceo, Barcelona, 81; Turandot in Turandot, Torre Del Lago, 82; Norma in Norma, L'Opera Montreal, 82; Lucrezia Borgia in Lucrezia Borgia, New York City Opera, 82; Lady Macbeth in Macbeth, Metropolitan Opera, 82-83 & Gran Teatre Liceo, Barcelona, 82-83. *Pos:* Sop with opera co in US & Europe; res mem, New York City Opera, currently. *Awards:* Fulbright Scholar, 2 yrs. *Mailing Add:* c/o Harold Shaw Concerts 1995 Broadway New York NY 10023

STAR, CHERYL MC WHORTER
EDUCATOR, FLUTE
b Miami, Fla, Jan 28, 47. *Study:* New Col, study with Julius Baker, BA(music), 68; Fla Int Univ, MS(music educ), 75. *Pos:* Utility flutist, Sarasota Symph Orch, 65-68 & Ft Lauderdale Symph, 68-70; substitute, Miami Phil Orch, 68-70. *Teaching:* Instr flute, Miami Dade Community Col, 70- & Fla Int Univ, 72-75. *Mem:* Nat Flute Asn; SFla Flute Asn (vpres, 80-82); Fla Flute Asn. *Mailing Add:* 6500 SW 60 St Miami FL 33143

STARER, ROBERT
COMPOSER
b Vienna, Austria, Jan 8, 24; US citizen. *Study:* State Acad, Vienna, 37-38; Acad, Jerusalem, 38-42; Juilliard Sch, post grad dipl, 49. *Works:* Prelude and Rondo, 56, Viola Concerto, 59 & Samson Agonistes, 66, New York Phil; Symphony #3, Boston Symph, 68; Phaedra (ballet), Martha Graham, 65; The Last Lover (opera), Caramoor Fest, 75; Violin Concerto, Itzhak Perlman, 82. *Teaching:* Mem fac, Juilliard Sch, 49-74; prof, Brooklyn Col, 63- *Awards:* Guggenheim Fel, 57 & 63; Am Acad & Inst Arts & Lett Fel, 79. *Publ:* Auth, Rhythmic Training, MCA Music, 69. *Mailing Add:* RD 1 Box 248 Woodstock NY 12498

STARIN, STEFANI BORISSA
FLUTE & PICCOLO, ADMINISTRATOR
b Newburgh, NY, Dec 7, 50. *Study:* Marlboro Col, with Louis Moyse, BFA, 73; Calif Inst Arts, with Ann Diener Giles, MFA, 76; studied with Julius Baker, Marcel Moyse, Harvey Sollberger, & Paula Robison. *Pos:* Artistic dir, Newband, 77-; soloist, Independent Comp Asn, Los Angeles, 2/80, Am Symph Orch, New York, 3/81 & New Music New York, 5/81; guest artist, Group for Contemp Music, New York, 4/82; new music specialist, premiere & comn new works, currently. *Awards:* Grant, Alice M Ditson Fund, 79 & 81 & Martha Baird Rockefeller Fund, 81. *Mem:* Chamber Music Am; Affil Artists. *Interests:* Compiling a system notation for performing in just intonation. *Mailing Add:* 95 W 95 New York NY 10025

STARK, SHIGEMI MATSUMOTO See Matsumoto, Shigemi

STARKER, JANOS
EDUCATOR, CELLO
b Budapest, Hungary, July 5, 24. *Study:* Franz Liszt Acad, Hungary; Hon Dr Music, Chicago Convs, 61, Cornell Col, 78, East-West Univ, 82, Williams Col, 83. *Rec Perf:* Over 85 records on Angel, Philips, Mercury, Decca, Deutsche Grammophon, Victor Japan, Japan Columbia, Star Rec & Louisville. *Pos:* Solo cellist, Budapest Opera Phil, 45-46, Dallas Symph, 48-49, Metropolitan Opera, 49-53 & Chicago Symph, 53-58; soloist, major US & int orch for 30 years; concert tours on all continents. *Teaching:* Distinguished prof cello, Music Dept, Ind Univ, Bloomington, 62-; concert tours on all continents. *Awards:* George Washington Award, Washington, DC, 72; Sanford fel, Yale Univ, 74; Herzl Award, Israel, 78. *Mem:* Hon mem Royal Acad London, England; Am Fedn Musicians. *Publ:* Author of many articles & essays. *Rep:* Colbert Artists 111 W 57th St New York NY 10019. *Mailing Add:* Music Dept Ind Univ Bloomington IN 47401

STARKMAN, STEPHEN S
VIOLIN
b Kingston, NY, Dec 1, 57. *Study:* Juilliard Sch Music, BMus, 79; Sch Music, Ind Univ, MMus, 82. *Pos:* Soloist, Miami Beach Symph, 73 & 82; prin second violin, Piedmont Chamber Orch, NC Sch Arts, 78-81; violin sect, Pittsburgh Symph, 82- *Teaching:* Asst prof violin, Ind Univ, 79-81. *Awards:* Scholar, Nat Soc Arts & Lett, 73. *Mem:* Am Fedn Musicians. *Mailing Add:* 5437 Ellsworth Ave Apt 105 Pittsburgh PA 15232

STARLING, A CUMBERWORTH
COMPOSER, EDUCATOR
b Medina Co, Ohio, July 25, 15. *Study:* Cleveland Inst Music, with Herbert Elwell, Joseph Fuchs & Boris Goldovsky, BM, 39, MM, 40; Yale Sch Music, with Paul Hindemith, Quincy Porter, Richard Donavan & LeRoy Baumgardner, MM, 48; Eastman Sch Music, with Howard Hanson, A McHose, W Barlow, B Rogers & L Soderland, PhD, 58; studied privately with Nadia Boulanger, 41; Western Reserve Univ, with Arthur Shepherd. *Works:* Sleep, Child, Fischer Publ, 54; Violin Sonata in G, comn & premiered by Joe Gingold, 58; Flute Suite & Brass Quintet, perf by students; Cello Sonata (atonal), perf by Warren Downes & A Kuprevicius, 68 & Warren Downes, 81; Home Burial (conct opera), perf by H Hauson & Eastman Rochester Symph, Cleveland Chamber Orch, Suburban Symph, Cleveland & Willoughby Fine Arts Asn Orch, 81; Trio for Violin, Clarinet & Piano, premiered by Sidoti Trio. *Teaching:* Instr, Cleveland Inst Music, 40-42 & Cuyahoga Community Col, 63-71; head theory dept, Miss Southern Col, 49-54 & Cleveland Music Sch

Settlement, 56-71. *Awards:* Kimball Award, Chicago Singing Teachers Guild; Fine Arts Award, Cleveland Women's City Club, 64. *Mem:* Fortnightly Club; Asn Am Comp; Cleveland Comp Guild. *Mailing Add:* 1844 Alvason Rd East Cleveland OH 44112

STAROBIN, DAVID
GUITAR & LUTE, RECORD PRODUCER
b New York, NY, Sept 27, 51. *Study:* Peabody Consv, BMus, 73; study with Aaron Shearer. *Rec Perf:* Guitar Quintets (Luigi Boccherini), Marlboro Rec Soc, 74 & 78; Twentieth Century Music for Voice & Guitar, Vox/Turnabout, 76; Icarus (Meyer Kupferman), Serenus Rec, 80; Syringa (Elliott Carter), CRI Rec, 81; New Music with Guitar, Vol I, 81 & Vol II, 83, Bridge Rec; Songs (Charles Ives) & Apparition (George Crumb), Bridge Rec, 83. *Pos:* Exec producer, Bridge Rec Inc, 81- *Teaching:* Asst prof, Consv Music, Brooklyn Col, 75- & State Univ NY, Purchase, 78-; prof music, Bennington Col, 77-78 & NC Sch of Arts, 80-81. *Awards:* Grant, Martha Baird Rockefeller Fund, 80; Best Rec, Guitar & Lute Mag, 82. *Bibliog:* Stuart Isacoff (auth), 3 American Guitarists, Virtuoso Mag, 5/81. *Rep:* Bridge Rec Inc GPO Box 1864 New York NY 10116. *Mailing Add:* 14 Myrtle Dr Great Neck NY 11021

STARR, LAWRENCE
EDUCATOR
b Brooklyn, NY, Apr 17, 46. *Study:* Queens Col, City Univ New York, BA, 67; Univ Calif, Berkeley, PhD, 73. *Teaching:* From lectr to asst prof, State Univ NY, Stony Brook, 70-77; asst prof, Univ Wash, 77- *Mem:* Am Musicol Soc (pres pacific NW chap, 83-); Col Music Soc; Sonneck Soc. *Publ:* Auth, Charles Ives: The Next Hundred Years, Music Rev, 77; Copland's Style, Perspectives New Music, 80; The Early Styles of Charles Ives, 19th Century Music, 83; Toward a Re-evaluation of Gershwin's Porgy & Bess, Am Music (in prep); contribr, New Grove Dict of Music in US (in prep). *Mailing Add:* Dept Music Univ Wash Seattle WA 98195

STARR, MARK
CONDUCTOR & MUSIC DIRECTOR
b New York, Jan 30, 42. *Study:* Columbia Col, BA, 62; Columbia Univ, MS, 63; Santa Cecilia Nat Consv, Rome, studied orch & operatic cond with Franco Ferrara, dipl, 66. *Works:* Divertimento for Orch, perf by Columbia Univ Symph Orch, 62; Elegy (with B Bartok), perf by Isabelle Chapuis & Helene Wickett, 75; Gran Duo on Themes for I Puritani (with G Bottesini, for solo cello, double bass & orch), Edition Billaudot, Paris, 80. *Rec Perf:* Symphony No 1 Jeremiah (Bernstein), Orch Nat Radio France, 76; Symphony No 29 (Mozart) & Sonata in B Minor (Liszt), Orch Nord-Picardy, 77; Totentaz (Liszt) & Symphony No 5 (Honegger), Nouvel Orch Phil Radio-France, 80; Tell Me a Riddle (film score by S Schkolnik), Fantasy Films, Berkeley, Calif, 80; On the Town (Bernstein), Concertino (Bloch) & Appalachian Spring (Copland), Orch Radio-TV Suizzera Ital, Lugano, Switz, 81; Essay No 2 (Barber), Decoration Day (Ives) & Orchestral Variations (Copland), BBC Welsh Symph Orch, Cardiff, Wales, 82. *Pos:* Asst cond, Orch Mondial Fedn Int Jeunesses Musicales, Brussels, Belgium, 75; music dir, Orch Symph Jeunesse Musical Belgique, Ath, Belgium, 76; guest cond, Orch Nat, Paris, Res Orch Hague, Berliner Sinfonie Orch, Nouvel Orch Phil, Paris, Phoenix Symph Orch, Detroit Chamber Orch, Ft Wayne Phil, Wheeling Symph & Vallejo Symph. *Teaching:* Prof orch cond, Univ Wis, Milwaukee, 70-74; prof orch & operatic cond, Stanford Univ, 74-78; instr wind ens, San Francisco State Univ, 79-80. *Awards:* Silver Medal, Florence Int Cond Compt, 66; Outstanding Cond Awards, Santiago Compostela, 66, Monte Carlo, 68 & Madrid, 77; Orch Prize, Int Cond Compt, Danish Radio-TV, 72. *Mem:* Cond Guild (mem bd dir, 79-); Am Symph Orch League; Col Music Soc; Cent Opera Serv. *Interests:* Jacques Ibert, the man and his music. *Publ:* Auth, Webern's Palindrome, Perspectives New Music, spring 70; A Conductor's Tour of Russia, Am Rec Guide, 3/80; All-American Season in Lugano, Ovation, 4/81; Catalogue of the Music of Jacques Ibert, Ed Leduc, 83. *Rep:* Albert Kay Assocs Conct Mgt 58 W 58th St New York NY 10019. *Mailing Add:* 132 Loucks Ave Los Altos CA 94022

STARR, SUSAN
PIANO
b Philadelphia, Pa, Apr 29, 42. *Study:* Curtis Inst Music, dipl, 61. *Rec Perf:* With Arthur Fiedler & Boston Pops Orch for RCA. *Pos:* Artist in res, Philadelphia Col Perf Arts, 65-; performer at Ravinia Fest, Chicago, 68 & other maj US festivals; appearances with maj North Am orchs & in Europe, USSR, Cent & South Am & Far East. *Awards:* First Prize, Nat Merriweather Post Compt, Washington, DC, 57; Second Prize, Second Int Tchaikovsky Compt, New York, 61 & Moscow, 62. *Mem:* Delta Omicron. *Publ:* Contribr to Music J, 74. *Mailing Add:* 2203 Panama St Philadelphia PA 19103

STATON, KENNETH WAYNE
EDUCATOR, COMPOSER
b Miami, Okla, Aug 23, 37. *Study:* Univ Denver, BME, 63, MA, 71; studied comp with Normand Lockwood. *Works:* Midnight Sleeping Bethlehem & There's a Wideness in God's Mercy, Augsburg Publ; And You, O Bethlehem, Lawson-Gould Publ; Song of Deborah, Plymouth Music; A Litany of Praise and Thanksgiving, Let the Saints Be Joyful & Shout and Clap Praise to God, Music 70 Publ. *Teaching:* Asst prof music, Univ Denver, 72-73; asst prof, Univ Hawaii, Hilo, 73-78, assoc prof, 78-, chmn perf arts dept, currently. *Mem:* Music Educr Nat Conf; Am Choral Dir Asn; Hawaii Music Educr Asn; Hawaii Choral Dir Asn (pres, 81-83). *Mailing Add:* 1400 Kapiolani St Hilo HI 96720

STATSKY, PAUL G
TEACHER, VIOLIN
b Brooklyn, NY, Apr 29, 45. *Study:* Meadow Mt Sch, with DeLay & Galamian, summers 62-68; Juilliard Sch Music, with Dorothy DeLay, BS, 67; Ind Univ, with Josef Gingold, MS, 71. *Teaching:* Prof violin & chamber music, Interlochen Arts Acad, Mich, 74-82 & Cleveland Inst Music, 82- *Mailing Add:* 2331 Scholl Rd University Heights OH 44118

STAUFFER, GEORGE B
EDUCATOR
b Hershey, Pa, Feb 18, 47. *Study:* Dartmouth Col, BA, 69; Columbia Univ, PhD, 78. *Teaching:* Dir chapel music, Columbia Univ, 77-; vis instr music, Yeshiva Col, 78-79; assoc prof, Hunter Col & Grad Ctr, City Univ New York, 79- *Awards:* Francis Dillon Hayward Award, Columbia Univ, 78; Int Res & Exchange Bd Grant, 78; Shuster Grant, Hunter Col, 80. *Mem:* Col Music Soc; Am Musicol Soc; Neue Bach-Gesellschaft (Am chap rep int bd dirs, 82-87). *Publ:* Ed, J J Froberger: Suite auf die Mayerin, Provincetown, 75; coauth, Bach's Art of Fugue: An Examination of the Sources, Current Musicol, 75; auth, Über Bachs Orgelregistrierpraxis, Bach-Jahrbuch, 81; Bach's Pastorale in F—A Closer Look, Organ Yearbook, 83. *Mailing Add:* 511 W 113th St New York NY 10025

STAUP, REBECCA LYNN
OBOE & ENGLISH HORN, ARTIST MANAGER
b Toledo, Ohio, June 17, 52. *Study:* Univ Ariz, BA, 74, MM, 77; Juilliard Sch Music, with Robert Bloom, 80-81; Cath Univ, DMA(oboe), 83. *Pos:* Oboist, Tucson Symph Orch, 71-77, Ariz Chamber Orch & Ariz Opera Orch, 74-77; first oboist & English horn soloist, US Navy Conct Band, 77-81; founder, mgr & oboist, Rosewood Chamber Consort, 79- *Awards:* Univ Ariz Pres Compt Soloist Award, 76. *Mem:* Int Double Reed Soc; Int Musicians Union; Cultural Arts Alliance; Asn Col Univ Community Arts Adminr; Chamber Music Am. *Mailing Add:* 1113 Duke St Alexandria VA 22314

STEARNS, PETER PINDAR
EDUCATOR, COMPOSER
b New York, NY, June 7, 31. *Study:* Mannes Music Sch, artists dipl, 52. *Works:* Symphony No 2, New Symph Orch, 56; Sonata No 2 (cello & piano), Joan Brockway, 63; Symph No 6, Carl Bamberger, 67; Partita for Piano, Associated, 67; Five Episodes (organ), Robert Noehren, 70; Meditation (solo violin), Jeanne Mirchell Biancolli, 78; Six Paintings of Claude Monet (suite for orch), 82. *Pos:* Dir publ, Coburn Press Music Publ, 71-79; dir, Prep Div, Mannes Col Music, 79-81. *Teaching:* Fac mem comp, Mannes Col Music, 57-; asst prof comp & theory, Sch Music, Yale Univ, 64-65. *Mem:* Am Comp Alliance; Church Music Soc Am. *Mailing Add:* Coburn Rd Sherman CT 06784

STEBER, ELEANOR
SOPRANO, TEACHER
b Wheeling, WVa, July 17, 14. *Study:* New England Consv Music, BM, 38; 11 hon Dr degrees. *Roles:* Sophie & Marschallin in Der Rosenkavalier, The Countess in The Marriage of Figaro, Donna Anna in Don Giovanni, Vanessa in Vanessa, Constanza in Abduction from the Seraglio, Arabella & Wozzeck, Metropolitan Opera; 56 leading roles sung worldwide, 40- *Pos:* Prima donna, Metropolitan Opera, 40-66, & with every major opera co in US; extensive recital engagements throughout US, Europe & Far East; pres, Eleanor Steber Music Found, 80- *Teaching:* Head vocal dept, Cleveland Inst Music, 62-71; fac mem voice, Juilliard Sch Music, 71- & New England Consv Music, 71- *Awards:* Outstanding Serv Am Music, ASCAP, 44; Outstanding Woman in Radio, Musical Am, 45 & 46; Ambassador of Music, Pres Eisenhower, 56. *Mem:* Nat Asn Teachers Singing; Opera Soc Washington, DC; Delta Omicron; New Music Young Ens; Sigma Alpha Iota. *Mailing Add:* 2109 Broadway #8-18 New York NY 10023

STEDMAN, WILLIAM PRESTON
EDUCATOR, WRITER
b Austin, Tex. *Study:* Tex Christian Univ, BA, 44, MM, 48; Eastman Sch Music, PhD, 53. *Pos:* Exec dir, Pac Symph Orch, Fullerton, Calif, 78-79. *Teaching:* Instr theory, Eastman Sch Music, 52-53; instr music, Ind Univ, Bloomington, 53-55; chair music, Tex A&I Univ, 55-56; dean, Consv Music, Univ Pac, Stockton, Calif, 66-76; prof, Calif State Univ, Fullerton, 76- *Awards:* Res grant, Calif Arts Coun, 70. *Mem:* Asn Calif Symph Orch; Music Teachers Nat Asn; Calif Asn Prof Music Teachers (vpres, 69-71); Am Symph Orch League. *Interests:* History of symphony; musical style, theory and symphony. *Publ:* Auth, Compendium of Stylistic Devices, Ind Univ, 54; A Guide to the History of the Symphony, Univ Pac, 75; The Symphony, Prentice-Hall, 79; An Introduction to Stylistic Theory, 81, Materials for the Study of Form in Music, 81 & Orchestral Excerpts for the Study of Orchestration, 82, Calif State Univ, Fullerton. *Rep:* Prentice-Hall Englewood Cliffs NJ 07632. *Mailing Add:* 731 Avocado Crest Rd La Habra Heights CA 90631

STEELE, JAMES EUGENE
ADMINISTRATOR, MUSIC DIRECTOR
b South Norfolk, Va. *Study:* William & Mary Col, BS(music), 61; Mozarteum Acad Music, Salzburg, Austria, 62; Reid Sch Music, Univ Edinburgh, 65; Col Preceptors, London, England, 65; Univ London, 70; Temple Univ, MEd, 72; Nova Univ, EdD, 76. *Pos:* Piccoloist, Norfolk Symph Orch, Va, 51-73; minister music, Calvin Presbyterian Church, Norfolk, Va, 63-; dir fine arts div, Hampton Asn Arts & Humanities, Va, 66-78. *Teaching:* Supvr music, Hampton City Sch, Va, 65- *Awards:* Cert Commendation for Decade of Cult Serv to Peninsula Community, Hampton Asn for Arts & Humanities, Va, 77;

Athenian Award, Hampton, Va, 81. *Mem:* Music Educr Nat Conf; Va Music Educr Asn; Va Asn Music Educ Admin; Am Fedn Musicians. *Publ:* Auth, The Perceptual Relationship Between Music and Painting, 74 & Duties and Activities of Music Supervisory Personnel in Virginia, 76, Nova Univ. *Mailing Add:* 132 Fayton Ave Norfolk VA 23505

STEELE, LYNN
COMPOSER
b Beaumont, Tex, May 27, 51. *Study:* Smith Col, with Iva Dee Hiatt & Alvin Etler, BA, 73; Am Univ, MA, 82. *Works:* Dominique (opera), Am Univ, 82; Requiem for Women's Voices & Handbells, comn by Reston Chorale, Va, 83; Carillon de Nuit, Bell Tower Publ Co, 83. *Mem:* Am Women Comp Inc; Am Guild English Handbell Ringers; Friday Morning Music Club. *Mailing Add:* 3224 Wisconsin Ave NW #7 Washington DC 20016

STEFFES, CARL KURT
ADMINISTRATOR
b New York, NY, Jan 23, 55. *Study:* Eastman Sch Music, BMus, 76; Ind Univ, Bloomington, MMus, 79. *Pos:* Adminr, Speculum Musicae, 80-81; consult, NY State Coun Arts, 81-; adminr, Early Music Found, 81-83 & dir development, 83- *Mem:* Asn Col Univ & Community Arts Adminr. *Publ:* Auth, Annual Newsletter for Early Music Found. *Mailing Add:* 217 W 71st St New York NY 10023

STEG, PAUL OSKAR
EDUCATOR, COMPOSER
b Greenleaf, Kans, Aug 24, 19. *Study:* Kans State Teachers Col, BS, 46; Univ Wichita, studied with David R Robertson, MMusEd, 49; Boston Univ, studied comp with Gardner Read, DMA, 61. *Works:* String Quartet, Fine Arts Quartet & Vermeer Quartet, 57; Five Pieces for Piano, William Race, 60; Passacaglia (orch), Gtr Boston Youth Symph, 61; Masks, Electric Stereopticon, 67; Visions of Black Elk, Northern Ill Univ Perc Ens & Chorus, 77; Viols of the Night, Barbara Steg, 78; Fiddle Tales, Northern Ill Univ Phil, 79. *Teaching:* Asst dir, Consv Music, Oberlin Col, 52-59; prof & chmn, Dept Music, Northern Ill Univ, 61- *Awards:* Summer sem grant, Nat Endowment Humanities, 82. *Interests:* Performance history of In Dahomey (1903-05), a musical comedy by Will Marion Cook—the first such work by a black composer to be performed on Broadway. *Mailing Add:* RFD 2 Sycamore IL 60178

STEGALL, JOEL RINGGOLD
ADMINISTRATOR, EDUCATOR
b Hertford, NC, Apr 7, 39. *Study:* Wake Forest Univ, BA, 61; NTex State Univ, MME, 62; Univ NC, Chapel Hill, PhD, 75. *Teaching:* Gen & choral music, Montgomery County Sch, Silver Spring, Md, 64-65; instr asst & assoc prof choral music, Mars Hill Col, 65-76, chmn music, 68-76; dean sch music, Ithaca Col, 76- *Mem:* Am Choral Dir Asn (pres NC, 70-74 & pres elect southern div, 76); Music Educ Nat Conf (mem NC bd dir, 75-76); Nat Asn Sch Music (secy region six, 78-81 & chmn, 81-); Phi Mu Alpha Sinfonia. *Publ:* Auth, Choral Conductors—Technicians or Musicians?, 7-8/68 & Shape Notes and Choral Singing: Did We Throw Out the Baby With the Bath Water?, 10/78, Choral J; An Empirical Investigation to Determine Ratings of Competencies for an Undergraduate Curriculum in Music Education, J Res Music Educ, 78; Models for the Development and Funding of Resident Ensembles, Proc, Nat Asn Sch Music, 81; The Nonsense of the Doctorate for Artist-Teachers, Music Educ J, 3/81. *Mailing Add:* 167 Ridgecrest Rd Ithaca NY 14850

STEGALL, SYDNEY WALLACE
COMPOSER, WRITER
b Knoxville, Tenn. *Study:* Cincinnati Col-Consv Music, BM, 64, MM, 66; Emory Univ. *Works:* Dappled Fields, No 2, Something Else Press, 69; The Music Box, After the Bourgeoisie, 71, The Mossrite Variations, 76, Solidarnosc-Tren, 1981, 81 & Whispers, 82, Atlanta Electronic Music Studio. *Bibliog:* Van Meter Ames (auth), What is Contemporary Music, Annales D'Esthetique, 66; Donal Henahan (auth), What, You Never Learned to Read Music, New York Times, 11/30/69; Carter Ratcliff (auth), Looking at Sound, Art in Am, 3/80. *Mem:* Am Musicol Soc; Am Soc Aesthetics; Col Music Soc; Soc Ethnomusicol. *Interests:* Psycho/cultural musicology, especially myth and music. *Publ:* Auth, An Evening of Avant Garde Music, Atlanta Art Workers Coalition Newspaper, 1-2/80; Post-Modern Music, Marquee, 2/80; Profile: June Schneider, Atlanta Art Papers, 4-5/80. *Mailing Add:* Graduate Inst Liberal Arts Emory Univ Atlanta GA 30322

STEIGERWALT, GARY PAUL
PIANO, EDUCATOR
b Allentown, Pa, Sept 13, 50. *Study:* Juilliard Sch, studied piano with Irwin Freundlich, BMus, 72, MMus, 73, DMA, 81. *Rec Perf:* Piano Concertos of William Schuman and Walter Piston, Vox/Turnabout, 78; A Calendar Set (Judith Lang Zaimont), Leonarda Prod, 79; Piano Works of Ruth Schonthal, Orion Master Rec, 80; Piano Works of Johannes Brahms, 81 & Piano Works of Franz Schubert, 83, Centaur Rec. *Teaching:* Asst prof piano, Mt Holyoke Col, 81- *Awards:* Second Prize & Bartok Award, Liszt-Bartok Int Piano Compt, Budapest, 76; Young Artist Award, Nat Fedn Music Clubs, 77. *Mem:* Musicians Club New York; Piano Teachers Cong New York Int Piano Compt (mem bd dir, 83). *Rep:* Perf Artist Assoc of New England 161 Harvard Ave Rm 11 Allston MA 02134. *Mailing Add:* 303 W 107th St New York NY 10025

STEIN, LEON
COMPOSER, CONDUCTOR
b Chicago, Ill, Sept 18, 10. *Study:* Am Consv, Chicago, 22-27; Sch Music, DePaul Univ, MusB, 31, MusM, 35, PhD, 49; studied privately with Leo Sowerby, Eric DeLamarter, Frederic Stock & Hans Lange. *Works:* More than 100 compositions including 22 works for orchestra, two one-act operas, five string quartets, seven works for saxophone, Rhapsody for flute, string orchestra and harp, concertos for violin and violoncello and numerous chamber music and solo works. *Pos:* Cond, Community Symph Orch Chicago, 45-, Chicago Synfonietta, 55- & City Symph Chicago, 63- *Teaching:* Fac mem, Sch Music, DePaul Univ, 31-78, chmn dept theory & comp, 48-66, dean Sch Music, 66-76, dean emer, 76-; head, Inst Music, Col Jewish Studies, Chicago, 52-57. *Awards:* Am Comp Comn Award, 50; co-winner, Midland Found Nat Cont, 55; Via Sapientiae Award, DePaul Univ, 79. *Bibliog:* Karen Monson (auth), Our Creative Neighbors, NShore Mag, 9/79. *Mem:* Int Soc Contemp Music (chmn Chicago chap, 53-55). *Publ:* Auth, Structure & Style, 62 & Anthology of Musical Forms, 62, Princeton; contribr to various musical jour, encycl & publ. *Mailing Add:* DePaul Univ Sch Music 804 W Belden Chicago IL 60614

STEIN, LEONARD D
PIANO, EDUCATOR
b Dec 1, 16; US citizen. *Study:* Univ Calif, Los Angeles, studied theory & comp with Arnold Schoenberg, 36-39; studied piano with Richard Buhlis, 36-39; Univ Southern Calif, DMA, 66. *Rec Perf:* Schoenberg Septet Op 29 & Piano Pieces Op 33, 54 & Complete Works of Webern, 56, Columbia; Schoenberg Piano Pieces and Webern Songs, Time-Life; Schoenberg Cabaret Songs, RCA, 75; Don Erb, Renaissance, Nonesuch. *Teaching:* Prof music, Calif State Col, Dominguez Hills, 68-70; mem fac music, Calif Inst Arts, 70-; adj prof, Sch Music, Univ Southern Calif, 75-, dir, Arnold Schoenberg Inst, 75- *Awards:* Guggenheim Fel, 65-66. *Mem:* Monday Evening Concerts; Int Soc Contemp Music; Int Schönberg Soc; Soc Music Theory; Col Music Soc. *Publ:* Ed, Preliminary Exercises in Counterpoint by Schoenberg, Faber, 63; co-ed, Complete Works (Gesamtausgabe) of Schoenberg, Schott's Universal, 66; contribr, Anton Webern: Perspectives, Univ Tex, 68; ed, Style and Idea: Selected Writings of Arnold Schoenberg, Faber, 75; contribr, Bericht über der 1 Kongress der Internationalen Schönberg-Gesellschaft, Verlag Elizabeth Lafite, Vienna, 78. *Mailing Add:* 2635 Carman Crest Dr Los Angeles CA 90068

STEIN, RONALD
COMPOSER, EDUCATOR
b St Louis, Mo, Apr 12, 30. *Study:* Wash Univ, St Louis, with Frank Harrison, AB, 47-51; Yale Univ, with Paul Hindemith, 51-52; Univ Southern Calif, with Ingolf Dahl, 60-63. *Works:* Getting Straight (film score), Columbia Pictures Corp, 70; Rain People (film score), Warner Brothers, 71; Stalemate (film score), Welch Productions, 81; Las Vegas (orch tone poem), 82 & Notes (electric guitar & strings), 83, Denver Symph Orch; Hallux Pour Le Piano Op 100, Perma Music Publ, 83; Flute Trio Op 101, Kaplan Trio, 83. *Teaching:* Lectr theory, Yale Univ, 51-52; asst prof theory & comp, Calif State Univ, Northridge, 60-62; prof & head scoring & arranging, Univ Colo, Denver, 80- *Awards:* Award for Excellence in Creative Work, Univ Colo, 81. *Bibliog:* Jacque Scott (auth), People, 4/8/81 & Jenise Harper (auth), People, 2/2/83, Canyon Courier. *Mem:* Acad Motion Picture Arts & Sci; Comp & Lyricists Guild Am; Screen Comp Asn; Am Fedn Musicians; Col Music Soc. *Mailing Add:* PO Box 2307 Evergreen CO 80439

STEINBAUER, ROBERT ANDRUS
ADMINISTRATOR, PIANO
b Niles, Mich, May 20, 26. *Study:* Univ Mich, studied piano with Okkelberg & Brinkman, BM, 50, with Marian Owen, MM, 51; Ind Univ, studied piano with Bela Nagy & Signey Foster, DM, 69. *Pos:* Ed, Kans Music Rev for Kans Music Teachers Asn, Kans Music Educr Asn, 63-69. *Teaching:* Head, Dept Music, SC Sch for Blind, 51-53 & Kans State Univ, 70-; head, Keyboard Dept, Drury Col, 53-59, Wichita State Univ, 59-69 & Univ Nev, 69-70. *Mem:* Kans Music Teachers Asn (pres, 68-69); Kans Music Educr Asn (pres, 75-77); Col Music Soc; Nat Piano Found (chmn, 77-); Nat Asn Sch Music. *Publ:* Auth, Music in General Studies, Col Music Soc, 80, Upbeat Mag, 80 & Nat Asn Sch Music, 81. *Mailing Add:* 2916 Princeton Pl Manhattan KS 66502

STEINBERG, MICHAEL
CRITIC, LECTURER
b Breslau, Germany, Oct 4, 28; US citizen. *Study:* Princeton Univ, AB, 49, MFA, 51; New England Consv Music, Hon DMus, 66. *Pos:* Music critic, Boston Globe, 64-76; dir publ, Boston Symph, 76-79; artistic adv, San Francisco Symph, 79- *Teaching:* Head hist dept, Manhattan Sch Music, 54-55 & 57-64. *Awards:* San Prize for Criticism, Knox Col, 69; Award for Excellence in Criticism, Am Guild Organists, 71. *Mem:* Am Musicol Soc; Int Musicol Soc. *Mailing Add:* c/o Davies Symph Hall San Francisco CA 94102

STEINBERG, MICHAEL
EDUCATOR, PIANO
b New York, NY. *Study:* Yale Univ, BA; Juilliard Sch Music, with Ray Lev, Rosina Lhevinne & Wolfgang Rose, MS(piano). *Rec Perf:* 32 Beethoven piano sonatas, 82 & Chopin Album, 83, Elysium Rec. *Teaching:* Asst prof, Univ Conn, formerly; assoc prof, Univ Del, 73- *Mailing Add:* Laurel Woods Box 156 Landenberg PA 19350

STEINER, DIANA
VIOLIN, EDUCATOR
b Portland, Ore, July 17, 32. *Study:* Curtis Inst Music, dipl, 49, MusB, 57; Univ Southern Calif, MM, 70. *Rec Perf:* On Orion Rec, 74- *Pos:* Violin soloist, New York Phil, Philadelphia Orch & other maj orchs, 43-80 & Tanglewood Music Fest, Marlboro Music Fest, Hollywood Bowl & others, 50-75; host & producer, Air for Strings (radio show); mem bd dir, Curtis Inst Music; mem, Steiner-Berfield Trio, 66- *Teaching:* Adj mem fac, Loyola Marymount Univ, currently; instr master classes & wkshps. *Awards:* W W Naumburg Found Award, 52; Young Artists Award, Nat Fedn Music Clubs, 59. *Mem:* Nat Asn Comp USA; Music Teachers Nat Asn; Am String Teachers Asn; Mu Phi Epsilon; Am Fedn Musicians. *Publ:* Ed, Lessons with the Master, Nat Fedn Music Clubs Showcase, 60; Violin Classics, Bks I & II, 72; String Orchestra Classics, Bk I, 75, Bk II, 79. *Mailing Add:* 223 S Bundy Dr Los Angeles CA 90049

STEINER, FRANCES JOSEPHINE
CONDUCTOR & MUSIC DIRECTOR, CELLO
b Portland, Ore, Feb 25, 37. *Study:* Curtis Inst Music, studied cello with L Rose & G Piatigorsky, BM, 56; Temple Univ, BS, 56; Harvard Univ, studied comp with W Piston & R Thompson, MA, 58; Univ Southern Calif, DMA, 69. *Rec Perf:* I Cellist Casals, Linn and Vivaldi, 70, Sonatas for Cello and Piano (Paul Hindemith), 73, Concert Suite from Orfeo, 74 & Steiner-Berfield Trio Beethoven's Trio, Op 36, 77, Orion Rec. *Teaching:* Instr music, Brooklyn Col, 62-65; teacher, Fullerton Jr Col, 66-67; prof & chairperson, Calif State Univ, Dominquez Hills, 67- *Awards:* Thomas Dana Fel, Radcliffe Col, 56-57; Parade Am Music Citation, Nat Fedn Music Clubs, 75 & 76; Cond Guild Prize, Oakland Symph, 78. *Mem:* Mu Phi Epsilon; Cond Guild; Am Symph Orch League. *Publ:* Auth, Introduction to Music, W W Norton, 64; Musicianship for the Classroom Teacher, Rand-McNally, 66; Six Menuets In Two Celli, Boosey & Hawkes, 67. *Mailing Add:* 21 La Vista Verde Dr Rancho Palos Verdes CA 90274

STEINER, FRED(ERICK)
COMPOSER, WRITER
b New York, NY, Feb 24, 23. *Study:* Inst Musical Art, 38-39; Consv Music, Oberlin Col, studied comp with Normand Lockwood, BMus, 43; Univ Southern Calif, PhD, 81. *Works:* Tower Music for Brass & Percussion, Univ Southern Calif, 55; Navy Log March, 56 & Perry Mason Theme (TV), 58, Bibo Music Inc; Dudley Doright Theme (TV), Jay Ward Prod, 61; Pezzo Italiano (cello & piano), 62; Five Pieces for String Trio, 63. *Rec Perf:* King Kong, 76 & Great Americana Film Scores, 76, Entr'acte Rec Soc. *Pos:* Freelance comp & cond for radio, TV, films & rec, 43-; auth & lectr hist & aesthet film music, 74- *Bibliog:* Allan Ulrich (auth), Fred Steiner, The Art of Film Music, Oakland Museum, 76; Tony Thomas (auth), Fred Steiner on Film Music, In: Film Score: The View from the Podium, 79. *Mem:* Comp & Lyricists Guild Am; Am Musicol Soc; Acad Motion Picture Arts & Sci; Nat Acad Rec Arts & Sci; Am Film Inst. *Interests:* History & artistic functions of film music using musicological methodology. *Publ:* Auth, Herrmann's Black and White Music for Hitchcock's Psycho, Vol 1, No 1 & 2 & An Examination of Leith Stevens' Use of Jazz in The Wild One, Vol 2, No 2 & 3, Filmmusic Notebk; A History of the First Complete Recording of the Schoenberg String Quartets, J Arnold Schoenberg Inst, 2/78; Keeping Score of the Scores: Music for Star Trek, Quarterly J Libr Cong, winter 82; contribr, Music for Star Trek: Scoring a Television Show in the Sixties, In: Wonderful Inventions, I B Newsom. *Mailing Add:* 4455 Gable Dr Encino CA 91316

STEINER, GITTA H
COMPOSER, PIANO
b Prague, Czechoslovakia, Apr 17, 32, US citizen. *Study:* Juilliard Sch, MS, 67; studied with Vincent Persichetti, Gunther Schuller & Elliot Carter. *Works:* Concert Piece for Seven, 77, Piano Concerto, 78 & String Quartet, 79, Seesaw Music; Fantasy for Marimba, 80, Eight Miniatures, 81 & Duo for Trombone & Percussion, 82, Lang Percussion; Contempory Solos, Belwyn Mills, 83. *Pos:* Dir, Comp Group Int Perf, 70- *Teaching:* Asst prof music, Brooklyn Consv Music, 60- *Awards:* Gretchaninoff Memorial Prize, 66; Marion Freschl Award, 66-67; Standard Awards, ASCAP, 72- *Mem:* ASCAP; Soc Women Comp; Am Guild Authors & Comp. *Mailing Add:* 10 Eldridge Pl Glen Cove NY 11542

STEINHARDT, ARNOLD
EDUCATOR, VIOLIN
b Los Angeles, Calif, Apr 1, 37. *Study:* With Karl Moldrem, Peter Meremblum & Toscha Seidel; Curtis Inst Music, studied violin with Ivan Galamian, 54-59. *Pos:* Soloist & recitalist; asst concertmaster, Cleveland Orch, 59-64; first violinist, Guarneri String Quartet, 64- *Teaching:* Mem fac violin, Curtis Inst Music, 68- *Awards:* Leventritt Award, 58. *Rep:* Harry Beall Mgt Inc 119 W 57th St New York NY 10019. *Mailing Add:* Curtis Inst Music 1726 Locust St Philadelphia PA 19103

STEINHARDT, MILTON J
MUSICOLOGIST, CRITIC-WRITER
b Miami, Okla, Nov 13, 09. *Study:* Eastman Sch Music, BMus, 36, MMus, 37; NY Univ, PhD, 50. *Teaching:* Asst prof, Cent Wash Col, 38-42; instr, Mich State Univ, 48-50; assoc prof, Ohio Univ, 50-51; prof & dept chmn, Univ Kans, 51-75. *Awards:* Guggenheim Found Fel, 58 & 65; Fulbright Res Grant, 58; Am Philosophical Soc Travel Grant, 68. *Mem:* Int Musicol Soc; Am Musicol Soc (chmn Midwest chap, 64-66); Austrian Musicol Soc; Dutch Musicol Soc; Music Libr Asn. *Interests:* Music of the Hapsburg court composers during the second half of the sixteenth century. *Publ:* Auth, Jacobus Vaet and His Motets, Mich State Col Press, 51; ed, Jacobus Vaet, the

Complete Works, 61-68 & Alard Du Gaucquier, the Complete Works, 71, Denkmaeler der Tonkunst in Oesterreich; Philippe de Monte, Motets, Univ Leuven Press, 75-83; auth, articles in various music periodicals & encycl. *Mailing Add:* 1331 Strong Ave Lawrence KS 66044

STEINKE, GREG A
OBOE, COMPOSER
b Fremont, Mich, Sept 2, 42. *Study:* Consv Music, Oberlin Col, studied oboe with DeVere Moore & comp with Joseph Wood, BM, 64; Mich State Univ, studied oboe with Paul Harder & Daniel Stopler, comp with Owen Reed & cond with Romeo Tata, MM, 67, PhD, 76; Univ Iowa, studied comp with Richard Hervig & cond with James Dixon, MFA, 71. *Works:* Atavism, Univ SFla Wind Ens, 78; Remembrances, Calif State Univ Wind Orch, Calif State Univ, Northridge, 78; Duo Fantasy Concertante, Thalia Chamber Orch, Seattle, 79; Music for Chief Joseph, Linfield Trombone Ens, 80; Diversions and Interactions, Univ Wash Perc Ens, 80; Northwest Sketches II Flat, Thalia Chamber Orch, Seattle, 82; Image Music, Charles Ives Ctr New Music, 82. *Pos:* Recitalist, Winnipeg Symph, 64-65, Nat Gallery Orch, 68-72, Washington Opera Soc Orch, 68-72, Tacoma Symph, 76 & 78-79, Ore Symph, 79- & Am Soc Univ Comp Regional & Nat, 79- *Teaching:* Instr theory, Youth Music Prog, Mich State Univ, 61-65, asst instr theory, 72-73; asst instr oboe, Univ Iowa, 66-67; instr music, Univ Idaho, 67-68, prof & dir sch music, 83-; instr music, Univ Md, 68-72; asst prof music, Calif State Univ, Northridge, 73-75; fac mem, Evergreen State Col, 75-79; prof music & chmn music dept, Linfield Col, 79-83. *Awards:* ASCAP Award, 79-; Winner, First Int Comp Cont, Univ Louisville, 79; First Place, Symposium V New Band Music, Univ Richmond, 80. *Mem:* Am Soc Univ Comp; Soc Ore Comp (pres, 81-83); ASCAP; Am Fedn Musicians; Int Double Reed Soc. *Publ:* Auth, New Music and the Oboist Series, Int Double Reed Soc, 76-79; The Percussive Composer, Woodwind World-Brass Perc, 77; ed series articles, Am Soc Univ Comp, 83- *Mailing Add:* Sch Music Univ Idaho Moscow ID 83843

STEINOHRT, WILLIAM JOHN
COMPOSER, CONDUCTOR
b Chicago, Ill, Mar 19, 37. *Study:* Univ Ill, BS(ME), 58; Univ Hawaii, MFA(comp), 68; NTex State Univ, DMA(comp), 71. *Works:* Two Movements for Mallets, Lang Perc Co, 74; Pisces (band), Kjos Music Publ Co, 75; The Forgotten (orch), perf by Fargo-Moorhead Symph, 78 & Indianapolis Symph Orch, 80; Celebration Overture, comn & perf by Dayton Phil Orch, 80; Miniature Suite (orch), comn by Nat Endowment Arts, 82; Two Movements for Mallets II, comn & perf by Univ Okla Mallet Ens, 83; Untitled Symphony, comn & perf by Dayton Phil Orch, 83. *Pos:* Cond, Dayton Phil Youth Orch, 78-; rehearsal cond, Dayton Phil Orch, 81- *Teaching:* Instr music, Kauai High Sch, Lihae, Hawaii, 58-66 & Hawaii Curriculum Ctr, Honolulu, 67-69; prof music, Wright State Univ, Dayton, Ohio, 71- *Awards:* Second Place, Percussive Arts Soc Comp Cont, 74. *Mem:* ASCAP; Am Soc Univ Comp; Music Educr Nat Conf; Nat Asn Comp; Am Symph Orch League. *Mailing Add:* 2901 Locke Dr Fairborn OH 45324

STEMPEL, LARRY E
EDUCATOR, COMPOSER
b New York, NY. *Study:* Berkshire Music Ctr, studied comp with Witold Lutoslawski, 62; Freiburg Univ, WGermany, 64; Juilliard Sch, studied orch cond with Jean Morel, 71; Univ Pa, PhD(music theory), 79. *Teaching:* Instr & cond music, Univ Chile, La Serena, 67-69; asst prof, Fordham Univ, 79- *Mem:* Am Musicol Soc; Sonneck Soc; BMI Musical Theater Wkshp; Am Inst Verdi Studies. *Publ:* Auth, A Parisian View of Varese, 10/71 & Partch for All, 11/71, Saturday Rev; A Colophon for Stefan Wolpe, Perspectives New Music, fall 72; Not Even Varese Can Be an Orphan, 1/74 & Varese's Awkwardness and the Symmetry in the Frame of Twelve Tones, 4/79, Musical Quart. *Mailing Add:* 1803 Riverside Dr New York NY 10034

STENBERG, DONALD CHRISTIAN
EDUCATOR, BARITONE
b Greeley, Nebr, Dec 14, 23. *Study:* Am Consv Music, BMusEd, MM, 51. *Rec Perf:* American Art Songs, Educo Co. *Roles:* History of Song, PBS, San Francisco. *Pos:* Soloist, San Francisco Symph, 54 & Redlands Bowl, 61; conct soloist, univ & cols throughout US, 54-76. *Teaching:* Fac mem, San Francisco Consv Music, 59-, head voice dept, 61-76. *Mem:* Nat Asn Teachers Singing; Calif Music Teachers Asn (pres San Mateo Co, 57-58). *Mailing Add:* 1533 Howard Ave Burlingame CA 94010

STEN-TAUBMAN, SUZANNE
EDUCATOR, VOICE
Study: Stern Consv, grad; Berlin Hochsule Musik. *Pos:* Mem bd, Louis Braille Found Blind Musicians, currently; Opera appearances in Europe & with San Francisco, Chicago & New York opera co; soloist & recitalist. *Teaching:* Mem fac voice, Manhattan Sch Music, 66- *Mailing Add:* 164 W 79th St New York NY 10024

STEPHENS, JOHN ELLIOTT
COMPOSER, CONDUCTOR & MUSIC DIRECTOR
b Washington, DC. *Study:* Cath Univ Am, BM, 62, MM, 62, DMA, 72; Acad Music Basel, Switzerland, with Pierre Boulez, cert, 69. *Works:* String Quartet, Comp Conf, Vt, 63; Concert Piece for Jazz Band, Watergate Summer Symph, 65; Concert Music for Flutes & Piano, Donnell Ser Am Music, 68; Songs for Soprano, Flute & Strings, Fri Morning Music Club, 76; Creations for Trombone & Strings, Am Camerata, 82; Inventions for Solo Clarinet, 82 & Inventions for Treble Instruments, 83, Dorn Publ. *Rec Perf:* Music of Krenek & Moss, 79 & Music of Cyr, 80, Orion Master Rec; Music of Moss, Stephens & Sapieyevski, AMC-AM Master Rec, 82. *Pos:* Music dir & cond, Am

Camerata New Music, Washington, DC & Lydian Chamber Players, Arlington, Va, 78-81. *Teaching:* Prof & lectr theory, George Washington Univ, 63-72; instr cond & theory, Cath Univ Am, 67-68; artist in res, Am Univ, 76-79 & Univ DC, 83- *Awards:* Young Comp Award, Am Fedn Music Clubs, 53; Pi Kappa Lambda Award, 71; 90th Anniversary Bicentennial Comp Award, Fri Morning Music Club, 76. *Mem:* Am Music Ctr; Bibliot Int Musique; Clarinetwork Int; Chamber Music Am; Music Teachers Nat Asn. *Mailing Add:* PO Box 1502 Wheaton MD 20902

STEPHENSON, ROBERT JOHN
OBOE, EDUCATOR
b Ann Arbor, Mich, Mar 13, 55. *Study:* Interlochen Arts Acad, 70-73; Curtis Inst Music, BMus, 73-77. *Pos:* Prin oboist, Lancaster Symph, 76-77, Savannah Symph, 77-80, Utah Symph, 80- & Utah Virtuosi, 81-; oboist, Allegria Woodwind Quintet, 82- *Teaching:* Fac mem oboe, Symph Sch Am, 76- & Univ Utah, 80; guest artist, Mont State Univ, 83. *Mailing Add:* 21 Gray Avenue Salt Lake City UT 84103

STEPHENSON, RUTH ORR
EDUCATOR, SOPRANO
b Council Bluffs, Iowa, Nov 12, 30. *Study:* Colo Women's Col, AA, 50; Univ Mich, BMus, 52, MMus, 53. *Roles:* Madama Butterfly in Madama Butterfly, 59, Violetta in La Traviata, 61, Mimi in La Boheme, 62, Nedda in I Pagliacci, 63 & Countess in Le Nozze di Figaro, 65, Omaha Opera Co. *Teaching:* Assoc prof music, Nebr Wesleyan Univ, 61- *Mem:* Nat Asn Teachers Singing; Mu Phi Epsilon. *Mailing Add:* 50th & St Paul Lincoln NE 68504

STEPNER, DANIEL
VIOLIN
b Sept 7, 46. *Study:* Northwestern Univ, BM, 68; Yale Sch Music, MMA, 72, DMA, 78; studied violin with Steven Staryk & Broadus Earle & theory & comp with Alan Stout & Nadia Boulanger. *Rec Perf:* Ives Sonatas, Musical Heritage; Orenstein, CRI; Ives, Columbia; Bach, Rameau, Titanic; Vivaldi, Buxtehude, Harmonia Mundi. *Pos:* Concertmaster, New Haven Symph, 70-75; founder & concertmaster, Banchetto Musicale, 73-; mem, Orch of Eighteenth Century, currently & Boston Museum Trio, currently; baroque & modern violin soloist in Boston area, currently. *Teaching:* Mem fac, Yale Col, 72 & Neighborhood Music Sch, New Haven, 73-75; mem fac violin & chamber music, Longy Sch Music, currently; mem fac early music & baroque violin, New England Consv Music, currently. *Mailing Add:* New England Consv Music 290 Huntington Rd Boston MA 02115

STERLING, LORNA (LORNA BODUM STERLING MOUNT)
MEZZO-SOPRANO, TEACHER
b Sibley, Iowa, Feb 13, 47. *Study:* Morningside Col, 65-67; Univ Colo, Boulder, BME, 69; Univ Mont, Missoula, MM, 84. *Roles:* Flora in La Traviata, Colorado Springs Opera, 73; Mercy Lewis in Crucible, Denver Lyric Opera 74; Dorabella in Cosa fan Tutte, Opera Players of Hawaii, 76; alto soloist in Mozart Requiem, Honolulu Symph Orch, 81; Martha in Faust, 83 & Berta in Barber of Seville, 84, Hawaii Opera Theatre. *Pos:* Asst cond, Honolulu Symph Chorus, 78-; outreach dir, Hawaii Opera Theatre, 80- *Teaching:* Instr music, Col Continuing Educ, Univ Hawaii, 76-79, Hawaii Loa Col, 79-80 & Le Jardin Acad, Kailua, 82- *Awards:* Metropolitan Opera Regional Winner, 77. *Mem:* Nat Asn Teachers Singing (Hawaii vpres, 82-83); Nat Opera Asn; Mu Phi Epsilon; Am Choral Dir Asn. *Mailing Add:* 44-164-8 Hako St Kaneohe HI 96744

STERN, DANIEL DAVID
MUSIC DIRECTOR, EDUCATOR
b Locarno, Switz, July 28, 43; US citizen. *Study:* Eastman Sch Music, BMus, 65; Univ Ore, MMus, 69, DMA, 73. *Pos:* String specialist, Salem Pub Sch, Ore, 65-67; music dir, Boise Phil & Boise Opera Co, 74- *Teaching:* Asst prof, NMex Highlands Univ, 71-74. *Mem:* Am Symph Orch League. *Rep:* Maxim Gershunoff Concts Inc Park Ave New York NY. *Mailing Add:* PO Box 2205 Boise ID 83701

STERN, ISAAC
VIOLIN
b Kremenietz, USSR, July 21, 20; US citizen. *Study:* San Francisco Consv Music, 30-37, with Naoum Blinder. *Rec Perf:* Humoresque (film score), Warner Brothers; Fiddler on the Roof (film score), United Artists; Tonight We Sing (film score), 20th Century Fox. *Pos:* Guest artist, San Francisco Symph Orch, 31, concertmaster, 34; violinist, Los Angeles Symph, 35, Chicago Symph, 37, Carnegie Hall, 43 & many others; recitalist on tour with maj orch throughout US, Can, Europe, Israel, SAfrica, Australia, India, Japan, Iceland, China & USSR; participant in major fests incl Prades Fest, 50-52, Berkshire Music Fest & Edinburgh Fest; mem, Istomin-Stern-Rose Trio; pres, Carnegie Hall; founder, Jerusalem Music Ctr, 73. *Awards:* Grammy Award, 71 & 73; Commander, Ordre de la Couronne, 74; First Albert Schweitzer Music Award, 75. *Mem:* Nat Arts Coun. *Mailing Add:* ICM Artists 40 W 57th St New York NY 10019

STERN, ROBERT
EDUCATOR, COMPOSER
b Paterson, NJ, Feb 1, 34. *Study:* Univ Rochester, BA, 55; Eastman Sch Music, with Louis Mennini, Kent Kennan, Wayne Barlow, Bernard Rogers & Howard Hanson, MA, 56, PhD, 62; Univ Calif, Los Angeles, 58-59, studied comp with Lukas Foss. *Works:* In Memoriam Abraham (string orch), 56; Fort Union (ballet), 60; Fragments (flute, clarinet & harpsichord); Terezin (sop, cello & piano); Adventures for One (perc); A Little Bit of Music (two clarinets); Night Scene (violin, piano & electronic sounds). *Rec Perf:* For CRI,

ERA, Advance & Opus One. *Teaching:* Mem fac, Univ Buffalo, summer 62, Hochstein Mem Sch, 61-62 & Hartford Consv, 62-64; vis comp & dir electronic music, Hampshire Col, 70-71; prof music, Univ Mass, Amherst, currently. *Awards:* Edward Benjamin First Prize, 56; MacDowell Fel, 67, 69, 72, 74, 77 & 80; Nat Endowment for the Arts Grant, 77; Premio Musicole Citta di Trieste Second Prize, 79. *Mem:* ASCAP; Am Soc Univ Composers; Contemp Music Soc. *Mailing Add:* Dept Music & Dance Univ Mass Fine Arts Ctr Amherst MA 01003

STERNBERG, JONATHAN
CONDUCTOR & MUSIC DIRECTOR, EDUCATOR
b New York, NY, July 27, 19. *Study:* Juilliard Sch Music, 29-31; Wash Sq Col, NY Univ, AB, 39, Grad Sch, 39-40; Harvard Summer Sch, 40; Manhattan Sch Music, 46; private study with Pierre Monteux & Wilhelm Furtwängler, 46-51. *Rec Perf:* Piano Concerto No 5 (Prokofieff), Vox-Turnabout, 54; Piano Concerti (Mozart), Oceanic & Olympic, 54; A Set of Pieces (Ives), Oceanic, 55; Nelson Mass (Haydn), 56 & Cantata No 21 (Bach), Le Club Francaix, 56; Choral Works (Mozart), Period & Dover, 56; Variations (Bassett), CRI, 58; Sebastian Ballet (Menotti), Vienna State Opera Orch, 69; and many others. *Pos:* Musical dir, Royal Flemish Opera, Belgium, 61-62, Harkness Ballet & Harkness Found, 66-68 & Atlanta Opera & Ballet, 68-69; guest cond, Vienna, Salzburg, Berlin, Munich, New York, London, Paris, Brussels & Buenas Aires, 47- *Teaching:* Vis prof cond, Eastman Sch Music, Univ Rochester, 69-71; prof music, Col Music, Temple Univ, 71- *Awards:* Citation Award, Nat Asn Am Cond & Comp, 72; Paul W Eberman Res Award, Temple Univ, 83. *Mem:* Musical Fund Soc; Bohemians; Am Symph Orch League; Cond Guild (mem bd, 82-). *Publ:* Contribr, Bibliography of Periodical Literature in Musicology and Allied Field, Am Coun Learned Soc, 40; Musical Questions and Quizzes, Putnam, 41; auth, Scores and Parts, quart column, Cond Guild J, 82- *Mailing Add:* 7942 Montgomery Ave Elkins Park PA 19117

STERNE, COLIN CHASE
COMPOSER, EDUCATOR
b Wynberg, South Africa, Nov 14, 21. *Study:* Miami Univ, BS, 43; Juilliard Sch Music, with Persichetti, MS, 48; Paris Consv, with Boulanger, dipl, 51. *Works:* Three Joyce Songs, Peer Int, 53; Sonata (recorder & harpsichord), 70 & Meadow, Hedge, Cuckoo, 78, Galaxy; Sea Grief, Univ Pittsburgh Orch, 79. *Teaching:* Prof, Univ Pittsburgh, 48- *Awards:* Comp Award, Phi Mu Alpha, 50. *Publ:* Contribr, Europe Reborn, New Am Libr, 75; The Recorder Book, Knopf, 81; auth, Pythagoras and Pierrot, Perspectives New Music, 83. *Mailing Add:* 624 Garden City Dr Monroeville PA 15146

STERN-WOLFE, MIMI
CONDUCTOR, PIANO
b New York, NY. *Study:* Queens Col, BMus; New England Consv Music, MMus(piano); studied cond & piano with Nadia Boulanger, Paris & piano with Ray Lev & Leonid Hambro. *Pos:* Dir, Children's Musical Theater, 77-; pianist, Arion & Les Plaisirs, 78-; artistic dir, Music Downtown, 79-; music dir & cond, Downtown Opera & Chamber Players, 80- *Teaching:* Instr piano, Wagner Col, 73-; teacher piano & chamber music, Third St Music Settlement Sch, 76-; instr chamber music & accmp, Mannes Col Music, 83- *Mem:* Chamber Music Am; Am Music Ctr; Cent Opera Serv; Opera for Youth. *Mailing Add:* 310 E 12 St New York NY 10003

STESSIN, HERBERT
TEACHER, PIANO
b New York, NY. *Study:* City Col New York, BSS; Juilliard Sch. *Teaching:* Adj assoc prof piano, NY Univ, 60-; fac piano, Juilliard Sch, 60- & Aspen Summer Fest, summer 83. *Mem:* Am Fedn Musicians; Music Teachers Nat Asn. *Mailing Add:* 210 W 90th St New York NY 10024

STEVENS, DENIS WILLIAM
ADMINISTRATOR, CONDUCTOR
b High Wycombe, England, Mar 2, 22. *Study:* Jesus Col, Oxford, MA, 47; special study with Sir Hugh Allen, Egon Wellesz, R O Morris, Thomas Armstrong, H K Andrews & William McKie; Hon Dr Humane Letters, Fairfield Univ, Conn, 67. *Rec Perf:* The Glory of Venice, EMI London/Angel USA, 66; The Story of Great Music, Time-Life Rec, 67; Music at the Court of Mantua, Vanguard Rec, 69; Schutz and Lassus, Musical Heritage Soc, 71; Xmas Vespers (Monteverdi), WEA London/Nonesuch USA, 80; Two Odes (Purcell), Schwann, Dusseldorf, 81; St Cecilia Vespers (Scarlatti), Nonesuch, 82. *Pos:* Producer, Third Programme, British Broadcasting Corp, London, 49-54, music consult, 56-62; secy, Plainsong & Medieval Music Soc, London, 57-62; pres, Accademia Monteverdiana, Santa Barbara, Calif, 61. *Teaching:* Distinguished prof, Pa State Univ, 62-64; prof musicol, Columbia Univ, New York, 64-75; Brechemin distinguished prof, Univ Wash, Seattle, 76. *Bibliog:* Bernard Jacobson (auth), Accademia Monteverdiana, Musical Times, London, 67; Jonathan Cott (auth), Renaissance Avant-Garde, New York Times, 73; Sheila Rizzo (auth), An Interview with Denis Stevens, Fanfare, NJ, 82. *Mem:* Am Musicol Soc; Societa Ital di Musicologia; Societe Francaise de Musicologie; Sir Thomas Beecham Soc; Soc Antiquaries. *Interests:* English music of the Middle Ages and the Renaissance; the history of song; life and works of Claudio Monteverdi. *Publ:* Auth, The Mulliner Book: A Commentary, Stainer & Bell, 52; Thomas Tomkins, Macmillan, 57; Tudor Church Music, Faber & Faber, 61; Musicology—A Practical Guide, Macdonald, 80; ed, The Letters of Monteverdi, Faber & Faber, 80. *Mailing Add:* 2203 Las Tunas Rd Santa Barbara CA 93103

STEVENS, HALSEY
EDUCATOR, COMPOSER
b Scott, NY, Dec 3, 08. *Study:* Piano with George Mulfinger, 28-31; Syracuse Univ, with William Berwald, BM, 31, MMus, 37; Univ Calif, with Ernest Bloch, 44; Univ Syracuse, LittD, 66. *Works:* Intermezzo, Cadenza, and Finale (cello & piano), 49; Sonatina Giocosa (double bass & piano), 54; The Ballad of William Sycamore (orch with chorus), 55; Threnos: In Memoriam Quincy Porter, 68; Dittico (alto sax & piano), 72; Quintetto Sorbelloni (woodwinds), Los Angeles, 76; Viola Concerto, 76. *Pos:* Prog annotator, Los Angeles Phil, 46-51, Phoenix Symph, 47-48 & Coleman Chamber Concerts, 67-; guest cond, San Francisco Symph Orch & Los Angeles Phil Orch. *Teaching:* Asst instr, Syracuse Univ, 35-57; assoc prof, Dakota Wesleyan Univ, 37-41; prof & dir col music, Bradley Univ, 41-46; prof, Univ Redlands, 46; asst prof, Univ Southern Calif, Los Angeles, 46-48, assoc prof, 48-51, chmn comp dept, 49-74, prof, 51-76, grad sch res lectr, 56, comp in res, 72-76, Mellon prof, 74-76, prof emer, 76-; vis prof, Pomona Col, 54, Univ Wash, summer 58, Yale Univ, 60-61, Univ Cincinnati, 68 & Williams Col, 69. *Awards:* Nat Fedn Music Clubs Award, 43; Nat Inst Arts & Lett Citation & Grant, 61; Guggenheim Fels, 64-65 & 71-72. *Mem:* Na Asn Comp & Cond; Am Musical Soc; Am Liszt Soc; Am Comp Alliance; Pi Kappa Lambda. *Publ:* Auth, The Life and Music of Bela Bartok, 53, rev ed 64; co-ed, Festival Essays for Pauline Alderman, 76; contribr, World Book Encycl, New Cath Encycl & Encycl Brittanica. *Mailing Add:* 9631 Second Ave Inglewood CA 90305

STEVENS, JEFFREY
PIANO, EDUCATOR
Study: St Josephs Col, BM, Boston Univ, MM. *Pos:* Pianist, Wolf Trap Opera Co; conct appearances in New York, Chicago, Atlanta & Gt Brit & on Nat Pub Radio. *Teaching:* Opera & vocal coaching, Boston Consv Music, currently. *Awards:* Two Tanglewood Fels. *Mailing Add:* 500 Memorial Dr Cambridge MA 02139

STEVENS, LEIGH HOWARD
MARIMBA
b Orange, NJ, Mar 9, 53. *Study:* Eastman Sch Music, BM, 75. *Pos:* Conct marimbist & recitalist, US & Europe, 75- *Mem:* Percussive Arts Soc; ASCAP. *Publ:* Ed, 25 works for solo marimba, 75-; auth, Method of Movement for Marimba, Marimba Productions, 79. *Rep:* Suzanne Newman 93 Ridge Dr Livingston NJ 07079. *Mailing Add:* 487 West End Ave New York NY 10024

STEVENS, MAXINE See Priest-Stevens, Maxine

STEVENS, MILTON LEWIS, JR
TROMBONE, EDUCATOR
b Great Barrington, Mass, Nov 10, 42. *Study:* Oberlin Consv Music, MusB, 65; Univ Ill, MusM, 66; Boston Univ, DMA, 75. *Pos:* Prin trombonist, Denver Symph, 74-78 & Nat Symph Orch, 78- *Teaching:* Instr, Oberlin Consv Music, 67-68; asst prof, Boston Univ, 70-73 & Ohio State Univ, 73-74. *Awards:* Albert Spaulding Award, Berkshire Music Ctr, 68. *Mem:* Int Trombone Asn. *Mailing Add:* 3326 Longbranch Dr Falls Church VA 22041

STEVENS, ROGER S
FLUTE & PICCOLO, EDUCATOR
b New York, NY, Jan 25, 21. *Study:* Study with Charles Gregory, 35-37; Univ Mich, with John Wummer, Carmine Cuppola & George Barrere, 38-40; Eastman Sch Music, with Joseph Mariano & William Kincaid, BM, 42. *Pos:* Solo flute, Los Angeles Phil, 46-62, assoc prin piccolo, 62-70 & prin flute, 70-77; mem, Phil Wind Quintet Los Angeles, 54-72; variety of freelance work from 46-77. *Teaching:* Prof music, Univ Southern Calif, 48- *Publ:* Auth, Artistic Flute, Technique and Study, Highland Music Co, 67. *Mailing Add:* 117 W Las Flores Ave Arcadia CA 91006

STEVENSON, DELCINA MARIE
SOPRANO
b Ft Scott, Kans. *Study:* Univ Kans, BM; Music Acad West, with Lotte Lehman & Martial Singher. *Rec Perf:* Vivaldi's Chamber Mass, 75, Bach Cantata 210 (O Holder Tag), 75, Concert Aria, Ah, Se In Ciel, 76 & Vesperae de Dominica, 76, Crystal Rec; Brahm's Liebeslieder Waltzes, Nonesuch, 82; Songs of Sharon Davis, Wim, 83; Soundtrack of Dr Zhivago. *Roles:* Pamina in The Magic Flute, San Francisco Opera Co; Adina in L'Elisir d'Amore, Los Angeles Opera Co, 76; Butterfly in Madame Butterfly, Pac Opera Co, 81; Aida in Aida, Reno, Nev, 82; Tosca in Tosca, Pac Opera Co, 83. *Pos:* Artist, Western Opera Theatre, 67-68. *Awards:* Young Musicians Found Los Angeles Award, 66; Martha Baird Rockefeller Award, 70. *Rep:* Judith Liegner Mgt 1860 Broadway Suite 1610 New York NY 10023. *Mailing Add:* 227 Riverside Dr 3A New York NY 10025

STEVENSON, ROBERT MURRELL
EDUCATOR
b Melrose, NM, July 3, 16. *Study:* Univ Tex, El Paso, AB, 36; Juilliard Sch Music, 38; Yale Univ, MMus, 39; Univ Rochester, PhD, 42; Harvard Univ, STB, 43; Princeton Theol Sem, ThM; Oxford Univ, BLitt. *Works:* Prog original works, perf by Westminster Choir Chorus, 48; Two Peruvian Preludes, perf by Philadelphia Orch, 62. *Teaching:* Instr & asst prof, Univ Tex, Austin, 41-43; fac mem, Westminster Choir Col, 46-49; from asst prof to prof, Univ Calif, Los Angeles, 49-; vis prof, Univ Ind, Northwestern Univ, Columbia Univ, Univ Md & Univ Chile. *Awards:* Fulbright Award, 58-59; Guggenheim Fel, 62; Nat Endowment Humanities Fel, 73. *Interests:* Musicology of the Iberian world. *Publ:* Auth, Spanish Cathedral Music, 61 & Music in Aztec & Inca Territory, 68, Univ Calif Press; Portugese Polyphonic Anthology, Gulbekian, 82; numerous books & articles in dict & encycl. *Mailing Add:* 405 Hilgard Ave Los Angeles CA 90024

STEWART, DON (DONALD GEORGE)
COMPOSER, CLARINET
b Sterling, Ill, Jan 8, 35. *Study:* Ind Univ, 60; Manhattan Sch Music, study clarinet with Russianoff, 60-62; comp study with Roy Harris, Bernhard Heiden & Gunther Schuller. *Works:* Concert Duet (flute, bass & clarinet), Salabert, 71; Passacaglia, 74 & August Lions, 78, Seesaw; Celebration Pieces, perf by Tambous Duo, 78; Piccolo Concerto, Carl Fischer, 79; Schubert Shadow, perf by Northern Lights Ens, 80; Sextet for Cello/Quintet, perf by Boehm Quintette, 81 & 82. *Rec Perf:* Schoenberg Serenade, Marlboro Rec, 66; Quintets (Piston & Weber), 75 & Quintets (Klughardt & Foerster, 76, Orion; Schoenberg Suite, Marlboro Rec, 77; Quintet (Danzi, Ropartz & Bazelon), Orion, 78; Brahms Handel Var, Vox, 80. *Pos:* Arr & librn, Harkness Ballet, New York, 67-72; founder & pres, Boehm Quintette, New York, 68-; music assoc, New York State Coun Arts, 72-74; founder & treas, Chamber Music Am, New York, 77-80. *Teaching:* Instr clarinet & jazz, Lyndon State Col, Vt, 73-76. *Awards:* Cert Appreciation, Chamber Music Am, 82. *Bibliog:* Eleanor Lawrence (auth), The Independent Concert Quintet, Nat Flute Asn Newsletter, 83. *Mem:* Am Soc Music Copyists (mem exec bd, 70-72); Am Fedn Musicians; ASCAP; Am Music Ctr. *Mailing Add:* Box 65 Tunbridge VT 05077

STEWART, FRANK GRAHAM
COMPOSER, EDUCATOR
b La Junta, Colo, Dec 12, 20. *Study:* Colo Col, with Roger Sessions, 39; Eastman Sch Music, Rochester Univ, BMus, 42; Mich State Univ, PhD, 71. *Works:* To Let The Captive Go, Seesaw Music Corp, 74; Toccata for Piano, Kjos Music Co, 76; The First Day (band), 78 & Rebound (band), 79, Col Band Dir Nat Asn; A Sunset (flute, trumpet, voice & piano), comn by Miss State Fac, 80; Illuminations (band & three brass solo), Col Band Dir Nat Asn, 81. *Teaching:* Instr comp & theory, Colo State Univ, Ft Collins, 67-68 & Univ Mo, Columbia, 68-69; grad asst comp & theory, Mich State Univ, 69-71; prof comp & theory, Miss State Univ, 71- *Awards:* Alice M Ditson Comp Award, Columbia Univ, 46-47; Orpheus Award, Phi Mu Alpha Sinfonia, 74. *Mem:* Southeastern Comp League (vpres, 77-78 & pres, 79-80); Phi Mu Alpha Sinfonia; ASCAP; Am Soc Univ Comp; Col Music Soc. *Mailing Add:* PO Box 5261 Miss State State College MS 39762

STEWART, JOHN HARGER
TENOR
b Cleveland, Ohio, March 31, 40. *Study:* Yale Univ, BA, 62; Brown Univ, MA, 69; New England Consv Music; studied with Cornelius Reed & Frederick Jagel. *Roles:* Pinkerton in Madama Butterfly, Santa Fe Opera, 68; Vladimir in Prince Igor; Ernesto in Don Pasquale; Ferrando in Cosi fan tutte; Rodolfo in La Boheme; Almaviva in Il Barbiere di Siviglia; Alfredo in La Traviata. *Pos:* Tenor with opera co in Santa Fe, Houston, Ft Worth, Cincinnati, San Antonio, San Diego, Philadelphia & New York; performer with maj orchs in US, Can & Europe; dir, Affiliate Artists Inc, NY; res mem, Städtische Oper Frankfurt. *Mailing Add:* c/o Dorothy Cone Inc 250 W 57th St New York NY 10019

STEWART, LARRY JOE
EDUCATOR, BASSOON
b Indianapolis, Ind, Jan 8, 40. *Study:* Ball State Univ, BS(music educ), 62; Northwestern Univ, MMus, 63; Univ Mich, DMus Arts, 72. *Pos:* Asst first bassoon, Nat Symph Orch, Washington, DC, 63-65; first bassoon, Kalamazoo Symph, 65-69; second bassoon, Philadelphia Phil, formerly; solo bassoon, Philadelphia Comp Forum, 76. *Teaching:* Prof bassoon & mem fac woodwind quintet, Western Mich Univ, 65-69; prof bassoon & theory, Interlochen Arts Acad, Mich, 71-73; assoc prof music, Glassboro State Col, NJ, 73- *Mailing Add:* Music Dept Glassboro State Col Glassboro NJ 08028

STEWART, M DEE
TROMBONE, EDUCATOR
b Indianapolis, Ind, Oct 8, 35. *Study:* With Arnold Jacobs, 56-66; Ball State Univ, BM(music educ), 57; Northwestern Univ, MM(music educ), 62. *Rec Perf:* Antiphonal Music of Gabrieli & Philadelphia Brass Ensemble, Columbia; Symphonic Excerpts, Excerpts Rec Co. *Pos:* Bass trombone, Boston Pops Touring Orch, 57 & New Orleans Symph Orch, 57-61; solo trombone, Chicago Little Symph, 61-62; second trombone, tenor tuba & bass trumpet, Philadelphia Orch, 62-80. *Teaching:* Trombone, Curtis Inst Music, 68-80; prof, Ind Univ, Bloomington, 80. *Mem:* Int Trombone Asn; Tubists Universal Brotherhood Asn. *Mailing Add:* 3170 E Rhorer Rd Bloomington IN 47401

STEWART, ROBERT
COMPOSER, CONDUCTOR
b Buffalo, NY, Mar 6, 18. *Study:* Am Consv Music, MMusEd, 46, MM(comp), 47, MM(violin), 48. *Works:* Three Pieces for Brass Quintet, 64 & Music for Brass No 4, 66, Golden Crest Rec; Concerto for French Horn & Chamber Orchestra, comn by New Col Summer Fest, Fla, 68; String Quartet No 3, CRI, 70; Duo for Violin & Piano, comn by Va Music Teachers Asn, 73; Voiages (six perc & piano), comn by Paul Price, 76; Duos for Flute Choirs, perf by James Madison Univ Flute Choir, 81. *Pos:* Concertmaster, Roanoke Symph Orch, 60-64; cond, Rockbridge Orch, Lexington, Va, 75-79. *Teaching:* Music, Am Consv Music, 39-53 & Ark State Teachers Col, 53-54; prof, Washington & Lee Univ, 54- *Awards:* MacDowell Colony Fel, 56; Best Comp, Ga State Univ Symposium Contemp Music for Brass, 66 & 72; Spec Recognition, Inst Advan Musical Studies, Montreux, Switz, 76. *Mem:* Am Composers Alliance; Am Music Ctr; Southeastern Comp League (pres, 68-70); Va Humanities Conf (pres, 76). *Mailing Add:* 205 White St Lexington VA 24450

STEWART, ROBERT JOHN
COMPOSER
b Albany, NY, Apr 22, 32. *Study:* State Univ NY, Fredonia, BS, 58; Butler Univ, MM, 60; Univ Iowa, PhD, 72. *Works:* Music for Clarinet & Piano, perf by Robert Rose & Robert Stewart, 67; Sonata for Piano & Percussion, perf by M'lou Dietzer & Todd Miller, 73; Rondeau for Two Pianos, Am Soc Univ Comp J Musical Scores, 77; Capriccio, Music for Solo Violin, perf by Ed Persi, 78; The Bells(sop & band), perf by Su Harmon & Fullerton Wind Ens, 78; Shadows on the Wall, perf by Scott Zeidel, 81; reluped for Piano & Tape, perf by Robert Stewart, 83. *Teaching:* Prof music theory, Calif State Univ, Fullerton, 69- *Mem:* Am Soc Univ Comp (regional co-chmn, 77-79); Nat Asn Comp USA (bd mem, 73-). *Publ:* Auth, Serial Aspects of Elliott Carter's Variations for Orchestra, Music Rev, 73; Composing for the Guitar, Rosette, 75. *Mailing Add:* 5641 Mountain View Yorba Linda CA 92686

STEWART, SCOTT STEPHEN
CONDUCTOR, COMPOSER
b Oshkosh, Wis, June 4, 52. *Study:* Wis Consv Music, BM, 75. *Works:* The Magic World of Patrick Farrell (film score), PBS, 80; Everything You Always Knew About The Opera But Never Knew That You Knew, comn by Lake Geneva Opera Fest, 81. *Pos:* Assoc cond, Florentine Opera Co, Milwaukee, 78-, choirmaster, 78-; artistic adv & cond, Wis Opera Theater, Milwaukee, 81- *Teaching:* Instr Kodaly & musicianship, Wis Consv, 75-77, cond, 75-78. *Publ:* Auth, Suggested Repertoire for Treble Choirs, private publ, 76; The Art of Patrick Farrell, Ivy House, 80. *Mailing Add:* Florentine Opera 750 N Lincoln Memorial Dr Milwaukee WI 53202

STEWART, THOMAS JAMES, JR
BARITONE
b San Saba, Tex, Aug 29, 28. *Study:* Baylor Univ, with Robert Hopkins, MusB, 53; Juilliard Sch Music, with Mack Harrell, 53-54; Berlin Hochschule Music, with Jaro Prohaska; studied with Daniel Ferro. *Roles:* Raimondo in Lucia di Lammermoor, Chicago Lyr Opera, 54; Hans Sachs in The Mastersingers of Nuremberg; Sir John Falstaff in Falstaff; Wotan & Wanderer in Der Ring des Nibelungen; Dutchman in The Flying Dutchman; Scarpia in Tosca; Iago in Otello; and others. *Pos:* Bar, Prague Opera, 60-; performer at fest & with major opera co & orch in US & Europe. *Awards:* Fulbright Grant, 57-58; Kammersänger, Berlin, 64; Richard Wagner Medal, 65. *Mailing Add:* c/o Columbia Artists 165 W 57th St New York NY 10019

STILL, RAY
OBOE, EDUCATOR
b Elwood Ind, Mar 12, 20. *Study:* Pac States Univ, 41-43; Juilliard Sch Music, 46-47. *Rec Perf:* Wedding Cantata (Bach), RCA, 76; Romances (Schumann), 77; Trio (Poulenc), 77 & Sonata (Hindemith), 77, Telefunken; Oboe Quartets, 79 & Double (Bach), 83, EMI; Oboe Concerto (Mozart), Deutsche Grammophon, 83. *Pos:* Solo oboist, Buffalo Phil, 47-49, Baltimore Symph, 49-53 & Chicago Symph, 53- *Teaching:* Prof oboe, Peabody Consv, 49-53, Roosevelt Univ, 54-60 & Northwestern Univ, 60- *Mailing Add:* 585 W Hawthorne Pl Chicago IL 60657

STILLER, ANDREW PHILIP
COMPOSER, WRITER
b Washington, DC, Dec 6, 46. *Study:* Univ Wis, Madison, BA, 68; State Univ NY, Buffalo, MA(music), 72, PhD(music), 76. *Works:* Ctenophores, 67 & Magnification, 68, Ctr Creative & Performing Arts; Sestina, comn by Ulfedt & Herring Inc, 81; Spanish Follies, perf by Andriaccio/Castellani Guitar Duo, 81; Chamber Symphony, Amherst Sax Quartet, 83. *Teaching:* Grad asst, Ctr Creative and Perf Arts, State Univ NY, Buffalo, 71-73; instr music, Empire State Col, Buffalo, 74- & Black Mountain Col II, State Univ NY, Buffalo, 76- *Mem:* Am Music Ctr; Am Musicol Soc. *Publ:* Auth, Handbook of Instrumentation, Univ Calif Press, 83. *Mailing Add:* 419 Crescent Ave Buffalo NY 14214

STILMAN-LASANSKY, JULIA
COMPOSER
b Buenos Aires, Arg, Feb 3, 35; US citizen. *Study:* Piano with Roberto Castro, 51-56 & comp with Gilardo Gilardi, 56-58; Univ Md, with Lawrence Moss & Morton Subotnick, MMus, 68, DMA, 73; Yale Univ, with Kzyzstof Penderecki, 74. *Works:* Cello Quartet (clarinet, trumpet, xylophone & violoncello), 59, El oro intimo (bar & orch), 61, Cantares de la madre joven (seven women soloists & chamber ens), 63, Etudes (string quartet), 67, Etudes (woodwind quintet), 68, Barcarola (sop, ms, contr, triple mixed chorus & chamber orch), 73 & Magic Rituals of the Golden Dawn (soloists, chorus & orch), 76, Comp Facsimile Ed. *Pos:* Artist in res, Orgn Am States, 76- *Awards:* Phi Kappa Phi Award, 72; Nat Endowment Arts Grant, 75; ASCAP Award, 78. *Mem:* Am Women Comp; Am Soc Univ Comp; ASCAP. *Publ:* Auth, article on Dufay, Am Musicol Soc J, 75. *Mailing Add:* 301 Congressional Lane Rockville MD 20852

STILWELL, F RAYMOND
VIOLA, EDUCATOR
b Harrisburg, Pa, Sept 30, 32. *Study:* Eastman Sch Music, BMus, perf cert, MMus; Ind Univ. *Rec Perf:* With Rochester Phil, Eastman Rochester Symph, Marine Band String Ens & Cincinnati Symph Orch. *Pos:* Mem, Rochester Phil, formerly; Marine Band Orch, formerly & Cincinnati Symph Orch, currently. *Teaching:* Mem fac, Interlochen Arts Acad; teaching asst, Ind Univ; adj asst prof viola, Univ Cincinnati, currently. *Mem:* Viola Res Soc. *Mailing Add:* 428 Eight Mile Rd Cincinnati OH 45230

STITH, MARICE W
EDUCATOR, TRUMPET
b Johnstown, Ohio, June 29, 26. *Study:* Capital Univ, studied trumpet with Wilbur Crist, MA, 50; Ohio State Univ, studied trumpet with Forest Stohl; Eastman Sch Music, studied trumpet with Sidney Mear. *Rec Perf:* Ten of trumpet music & 35 with Cornell Univ Wind Ens. *Pos:* Performer trumpet, Syracuse Symph & Syracuse Symph Brass Quintet, six yrs; minister music, St Paul's United Methodist Church, Ithaca, NY; numerous appearances as trumpet soloist & cond; ed, Eastern Div Newsletter, Col Band Dir Nat Asn. *Teaching:* Assoc prof music, dir bands & founder & cond, Wind Ens, Cornell Univ, currently. *Mem:* Col Band Dir Nat Asn. *Publ:* Contribr to Music Educr J, Instrumentalist Mag & Woodwind & Brass Mag. *Mailing Add:* 8 Redwood Lane Ithaca NY 14850

STIVENDER, (EDWARD) DAVID
CONDUCTOR, TEACHER
b Milwaukee, Wis, Sept 6, 33. *Study:* Northwestern Univ, BA, 55. *Pos:* Asst cond, Lyric Opera Chicago, 61-65; asst chorus master, Metropolitan Opera, 65-72, chorus master, 73-, cond, 79- *Publ:* Auth, The Road to Rome, Opera News, 75; The Composer of Gesu Mori, Am Inst Verdi Studies, 76. *Mailing Add:* 170 W 81st St Apt 3-A New York NY 10024

STOCK, DAVID FREDERICK
COMPOSER, CONDUCTOR
b Pittsburgh, Pa, June 3, 39. *Study:* Carnegie-Mellon Univ, BFA, 62, MFA, 63; Brandeis Univ, MFA, 73. *Works:* Scat, 71 & Inner Space, 73, Margun Music; Nova, Am Comp Alliance, 75; The Body Electric, 77 & Zohar, 78, Margun Music; The Philosopher's Stone, 80 & Speaking Extravagantly, 81, Am Comp Alliance. *Rec Perf:* Quintet for Clarinet & Strings (Stock), 75, Perlongo (Ricercar), 81 & Music of D Stock, 83, CRI; Music From Pittsburgh, Grenadilla, 83. *Pos:* Cond, Pittsburgh New Music Ens, 76- & Carnegie Symph Orch, 76-82. *Teaching:* Fac mem theory, New England Consv, 68-70; chmn, Music Dept, Antioch Col, 70-74; adj fac comp & cond, Univ Pittsburgh, 78- *Awards:* Fel, Guggenheim Found, 74, Nat Endowment Arts, 74, 76 & 78 & Pa Coun on Arts, 81 & 83. *Mem:* Am Music Ctr (bd mem, 82-); Pittsburgh Alliance Comp (pres, 75-79); BMI; Am Comp Alliance; Nat Endowment Arts (panelist, 80-83). *Publ:* Auth, Reports on New Books, 69 & Reports on New Music, 69, Perspectives New Music; Arthur Perger, In: Dutton Dict of Contemp Music, 74; New Music in Pittsburgh, Am Music Ctr, 79. *Mailing Add:* 6538 Darlington Rd Pittsburgh PA 15217

STOCKTON, DAVID R
ARTISTIC DIRECTOR
b Plainview, Tex, July 14, 45. *Study:* WTex State Univ, BS(piano), 67; New England Consv Music, MM, 75. *Rec Perf:* Broadcast perf, La Bataglia di Legnano, 82, Goyescas, 82, La Navarraise, 82, Ernani, 83, Susannah, 83, Manon Lescaut, 83, L'Amico Fritz, 83 & others, WBUR-FM. *Pos:* Artistic dir, Boston Conct Opera, 75- *Bibliog:* Janet Tassel (auth), Concert Opera, Boston Mag, 9/81. *Mailing Add:* Box 459 Astor Station Boston MA 02123

STOEFFEN, FRANKLIN HOWARD See Stover, Franklin Howard

STOEPPELMANN, JANET
COMPOSER, EDUCATOR
b St Louis, Mo, Dec 5, 48. *Study:* Barry Col, BA(harpsichord & comp); Univ SFla, MMus(comp & theory); studied comp & ethnomusicol with Jocy de Oliveira, electronic music with Hilton Jones, Japanese Noh drama with Agnes Takako Miyazaki Youngblood & multiphonic singing with D J Mizelle. *Works:* Three Japanese Haiku Concerning Butterflies (female voices), 72; Metallon (tape, tamtams, perc & sculpture), 72; The Great Wall of China, After Kafka (theatre piece for four-channel tape & narrator), 73; Parallax (vocal), 73; Sindhura (harp), 73; The River Merchant's Wife: A Letter (multimedia), 74; Water Music (multimedia), 75. *Teaching:* Nova Univ, 73-74, Broward Community Col, 75-77 & Phoenix Col, 78. *Mem:* SEastern Comp League; Soc Ethnomusicol. *Mailing Add:* 920 NW 186th Dr Miami FL 33169

STOKES, ERIC
COMPOSER
b Haddon Heights, NJ, July 14, 30. *Study:* Lawrence Col, with James Ming, BMus, 52; New England Consv, with Carl McKinley, MMus, 56; Univ Minn, with Argento & Fetler, PhD, 64. *Works:* Horspfal (opera), 69 & On the Badlands—Parables, 72, Horspfal Music Concern; Eldey Island (flute & tape), Smith Publ, 72; Five Verbs of Earth Encircled, 73, The Continental Harp & Band Report, 75, Prairie Drum, 81 6 Concert Music for Piano & Orch, 82, Horspfal Music Concern. *Teaching:* Asst prof, Univ Minn, 64-72, assoc prof, 73-76, prof, 77- *Mailing Add:* 1611 W 32nd St Minneapolis MN 55408

STOKES, SHERIDON WILLARD
FLUTE & PICCOLO, EDUCATOR
b Los Angeles, Calif, June 5, 35. *Study:* Univ Denver; Univ Southern Calif; studied flute with Roger Stevens, Haakon Bergh & Arthur Gleghorn. *Rec Perf:* Sonata (Levitch), Orion Rec, 69; Willow-Willow (Chihara), Orion Rec, 72; Trio-Quintets (Levitch), 73, Quintet (Levitch), 74 & Sonatas (Boccherini), 75, Orion Rec; Roots, Warner Brothers, 78. *Pos:* Flute soloist, 55-; solo flute with all major motion pictures studios, 56- *Teaching:* Lectr flute & chamber music, Univ Calif, Los Angeles, 71- *Awards:* Most Valuable Player Flute, Nat Asn Rec Arts & Sci, 81-82. *Mem:* Nat Flute Asn (mem bd dir, 82-84). *Publ:* Coauth, Illustrated Method for Flute, 69 & auth, Special Effects for Flute, 71, Trio Asn. *Mailing Add:* 30707 Manzano Malibu CA 90265

STOKMAN, ABRAHAM
PIANO, EDUCATOR
b Tel Aviv, Israel, Aug 17, 36; US citizen. *Study:* Juilliard Sch, BS, 60, MS, 62, with Edward Steuermann, 62-63. *Rec Perf:* A Kurt Weil Cabaret, MGM, 64; Zing un Tanz, RCA Victor Mexicana, 72; Songs from The Magic Door, Clarence Rec, 74; American Contemporary (Ramon Zupko), CRI, 79. *Pos:* Pianist & soloist, Contemp Chamber Music Players, Univ Chicago, 69- *Teaching:* Vocal coach, Opera Dept, Juilliard Sch, 57-62; pianist in res & asst prof, Chicago Musical Col, Roosevelt Univ, 69-75; chmn, Piano Dept, Am Consv Music, 80- *Mailing Add:* 1236 W Lunt Ave Chicago IL 60626

STOLBA, K MARIE
WRITER, EDUCATOR
b Burlington, Iowa, Apr 22, 19. *Study:* Monmouth Col, BA, 44; Univ Northern Colo, MA, 50; Univ Iowa, Iowa City, PhD, 65. *Works:* And Jesus Came ..., Lillenas Publ & Belwin-Mills, 75; Homage, perf by Ind-Purdue Univ Singers, 78; Song: Memory Hither Come, perf by M Kim Durr, 78; Meditation (piano solo), perf by Judy Martin, 80; The Oxen, perf by Sigma Alpha Iota Ft Wayne Alumnae, 80; The Mosquito, perf by Martha Johnson with Sigma Alpha Iota Ft Wayne Alumnae, 80; Heritage, perf by Divertimento Ens, 83. *Teaching:* Asst prof music hist & chmn div fine arts, Kellogg Community Col, 65-67; asst prof music lit, Ft Hays State Univ, 67-71; adj instr strings, Grace Col, 72-76; assoc fac mem music hist, Ind Univ-Purdue Univ, Ft Wayne, 73-76, asst prof musicol, 76-79, assoc prof, 79- *Mem:* Col Music Soc (mem steering comt, Great Lakes, 81-83, mem bd dir, Great Lakes, 83-85); Am Musicol Soc; Music Teachers Nat Asn (mem bd dir, Ind, 81-); Int Musicol Asn (chmn, 79-); Mich Acad Sci, Arts & Lett. *Interests:* Violin etude; early violin music; Bartolomeo Bruni; John Antes' life and work. *Publ:* Auth, Schubert's Compositions for Violin, Am Music Teacher, Music Teachers Nat Asn, 74; A History of the Violin Etude to About 1800, DaCapo Press, Inc, rev ed, 79; ed, A B Bruni: Caprices & Airs Varies & Cinquante Etudes, A-R Ed, Inc, 82; translr Bach's Sonaten und Partiten Für Violine Allein (facsimile ed & commentary), DaCapo Press, Inc, 82. *Mailing Add:* 5621 Joyce Ave Ft Wayne IN 46818

STOLPER, DANIEL JOHN
OBOE, EDUCATOR
b Milwaukee, Wis, Jan 11, 36. *Study:* Eastman Sch Music, BM, 57, MM, 58. *Pos:* First oboe, San Antonio Symph, 58-63 & New Orleans Phil, 63-65; oboist, Richards Quintet, Mich State Univ, 65- *Teaching:* Prof oboe, Mich State Univ, 65-; vis instr, Interlochen Arts Acad, Mich, 72- *Mem:* Int Double Reed Soc. *Mailing Add:* 1179 Palmer Lane Apt D East Lansing MI 48823

STOLTZMAN, RICHARD LESLIE
CLARINET
b Omaha, Nebr, July 12, 42. *Study:* Ohio State, BM, 64; Yale Univ, MM, 67; studied with Kalmen Opperman, 70. *Rec Perf:* Gift of Music, Orion, 74; Art of Richard Stoltzman, Desmar, 79; Mozart Concerti K622, 191, 81, Brahms Op 120, #1 & #2, 82 & Richard Stoltzman & Emmanuel Ax, 83, RCA. *Pos:* Participant, Marlboro Music Fest, 66-75; mem, Tashi Chamber Music Group, 73-; first clarinet recital at Carnegie Hall, 82. *Awards:* Avery Fisher Award, 79; Grammy Award, 83. *Publ:* Co-ed, The Romantic Clarinetist, 82 & The Classical Clarinetist, 82, Chappell. *Rep:* Frank Salomon Assoc 201 W 54th New York NY 10019. *Mailing Add:* 2001 Hoover Ave Oakland CA 94602

STONE, EDGAR NORMAN
TENOR, EDUCATOR
b Brownsville, Tex, Mar 22, 31. *Study:* NTex State Univ, vocal study with D R Appelman & Mary McCormick, BMusEd, 52, MMus, 59; Fla State Univ, vocal study with Eugene Talley-Schmidt, DMus(vocal perf), 70. *Rec Perf:* Psalmus Hungaricus, 74. *Roles:* Pong in Turandot, Houston Opera Co & San Diego Opera Co, 60 & 71; Ramendado in Carmen, Houston Opera Co, San Diego Opera Co & Phoenix Symph, 60 & 73; Jaquino in Fidelio, Phoenix Symph, 75. *Teaching:* Dir choral music, Ball High Sch, Galveston, Tex, 55-61 & Carthage High Sch, Tex, 61-69; teaching fel, Fla State Univ, 69-70; assoc prof voice & diction, vocal area chmn & tenor in res, Northern Ariz Univ, 70- *Mem:* Nat Asn Teachers Singing (pres Az chap, 76). *Mailing Add:* Music Dept Northern Ariz Univ Flagstaff AZ 86011

STONE, GEORGE See Wright, Al G (Alfred George)

STONE, KURT
MUSIC EDITOR, WRITER
b Hamburg, Ger, Nov 14, 11. *Study:* Hamburg Univ; Royal Danish Music Consv, Copenhagen, MA, 37. *Pos:* Music ed, Assoc Music Publ, Inc, 41-47, ed in chief, 54-65; dir publ, Alexander Broude, Inc, 65-69; originator & dir, Index New Musical Notation, Music Libr, Lincoln Ctr, 70-74; co-dir, Int Conv, New Notation, Ghent Univ, Belgium, 74. *Teaching:* Private teaching, 31-; teacher keyboard & comp, Dalcroze Sch Music, 44-50. *Awards:* Rockefeller Found Grant, 70-74; Ford Found Grant, 74; Guggenheim Mem Found Grant, 75-76. *Mem:* Am Musicol Soc; Am Music Libr Asn; Am Soc Univ Comp; ASCAP. *Publ:* Auth, Ives's Fourth Symphony, 66 & Elliott Carter's Piano Concerto and Other Works, 69, Musical Quart; co-translr & coauth, Handbook of Percussion Instruments, European Am Music Publ, 76; co-ed, The Writings of Elliott Carter, Ind Univ Press, 77; auth, Music Notation in the 20th Century, a Practical Guidebook, W W Norton, 80. *Mailing Add:* Poppleswamp Rd Cornwall Bridge CT 06754

STONE, WILLIAM FRAZIER
BARITONE
b Goldsboro, NC. *Study:* Duke Univ, BA, 66; Univ Ill, Champaign-Urbana, MM, 68, DMA, 79. *Rec Perf:* Salammbo (Mussorgsky), CBS, 81. *Roles:* Adam in Paradise Lost, Lyr Opera Chicago, 78 & La Scala, 79; Wozzeck in Wozzeck, 79 & Oreste in Iphigenie en Tauride, 81, Teatro Communale, Florence, Italy; Onegin in Eugene Onegin, Teatro dell 'Opera, Rome, 81; Germont in La Traviata, 81, Enrico in Lucia di Lammermoor, 81 & Zurga in The Pearl Fishers, 82, New York City Opera. *Teaching:* Instr voice, Luther Col, 68-70; vis lectr, Univ Ill, Champaign-Urbana, 70-73. *Awards:* Award, Metropolitan Opera Nat Coun, 76; grants, William Mattheus Sullivan Found, 79 & 81 & Rockefeller Found, 79. *Mem:* Am Guild Musical Artists. *Mailing Add:* c/o Columbia Artists Mgt Inc 165 W 57th St New York NY 10019

STONER, THOMAS ALAN
EDUCATOR, ORGANIST
b Freeport, Ill, Mar 20, 38. *Study:* Carthage Col, AB, 60; Univ Md, PhD, 72. *Pos:* Organist & choirmaster, churches in Md & Conn, 60- *Teaching:* Music, Wash Co Sch, Hagerstown, Md, 60-64 & Prince Georges Co Sch, Hyattsville, Md, 64-66; assoc prof music & chair dept, Conn Col, 72- *Mem:* Am Musicol Soc; Col Music Soc. *Interests:* Mendelssohn lieder. *Publ:* Auth, Mendelssohn's Lieder Not Included in the Werke, Fontis-Artis Musicae, 79. *Mailing Add:* Box 1636 Conn Col New London CT 06320

STOUGHTON, MICHAEL GORDON
CELLO
b Washington, DC, Dec 5, 42. *Study:* Manhattan Sch Music, with David Wells; Berkshire Music Fest. *Pos:* Prin cellist, Montgomery Co Youth Orch, Md State Orch, Berkshire Music Fest & NC Symph, currently; cellist, US Air Force Band & Symph Orch, four yrs & Chamber Players String Quartet; tours as soloist & mem various chamber groups; co-prin cellist, Edmonton Symph Orch; mem, Vt Symph & Marlboro Fest. *Teaching:* Cello, Putney Sch, Vt, three yrs & Keene State Col, NH. *Mailing Add:* NC Symph PO Box 28026 Raleigh NC 27611

STOUT, ALAN BURRAGE
COMPOSER, EDUCATOR
b Baltimore, Md, Nov 26, 32. *Study:* Peabody Consv Music, with Henry Cowell, BS, 54; Univ Copenhagen, 55; Univ Wash, with John Verrall, MA(music & Swedish lang), 59; studied with Wallingford Riegger & Vagn Holmboe. *Works:* Symphony No 2 (orch), comn by State of Ill, 68; George Lieder (orch & bar solo), Chicago, 72; Symphony No 4 (orch), comn by Chicago Symph; Three Hymns for Orchestra, Baltimore, 72; Pulsar (brass & timpani), 72; Passion (orch, chorus & soloists), Chicago, 76; Study in Timbres and Interferences (organ), 77; and others. *Pos:* Librn, Baltimore Enoch Pratt Free Libr, 58. *Teaching:* Prof theory & comp, Northwestern Univ, 63-; guest prof, Johns Hopkins Univ, 68-69, State Col Music, Stockholm, 72-73 & Berkshire Music Ctr, 74. *Awards:* Grants, Methodist Church Bd Educ & Danish Govt, 54-55. *Mem:* Am Comp Alliance; Am Musicol Soc; Music Libr Asn; Arnold Schoenberg Inst; Alban Berg Soc. *Mailing Add:* Sch Music Northwestern Univ Evanston IL 60201

STOUT, LOUIS JAMES
HORN, EDUCATOR
b Wellsville, NY, Mar 11, 24. *Study:* Ithaca Col, BMusEd. *Works:* English Folk Song Suite. *Pos:* Solo horn with Chicago Symph, Jackson Symph, Radio City Music Hall Orch & others. *Teaching:* Prof horn, Univ Mich, Ann Arbor, currently. *Mem:* Life mem, Phi Mu Alpha; life mem, Pi Kappa Lambda; Int Horn Soc. *Mailing Add:* 1736 Covington Dr Ann Arbor MI 48103

STOVER, FRANKLIN HOWARD (FRANKLIN H STOEFFEN)
COMPOSER, ADMINISTRATOR
b Sacramento, Calif, Nov 5, 53. *Study:* Studied clarinet with Frealon Bibbins, 64-71; Calif State Univ, Sacramento, 72-75; studied with Andrew Imbrie, 74-75. *Works:* Metal I (for perc), 75, Ecologue (for clarinet choir), 75, Five Bagatelles (piano solo), 75 & Four Arcana (woodwind quintet & guitar), 75, Seesaw Music Corp; Trio Bucolic (for oboe, clarinet & bassoon), 81 & Ketchup (operetta), 83, Comp Graphics; transcription of Symphonie for Full Orchestra by Charles Alkan (in prep). *Pos:* Pres, Composers' Graphics, 75- *Awards:* First Place, Calif Comp Symposium, 73. *Mem:* ASCAP; Nat Asn Comp. *Interests:* Speculative Music & Harmonics. *Mailing Add:* 5701 North Ave Carmichael CA 95608

STOWE, ANHARED WIEST
VIOLIN, TEACHER
b Lebanon, Pa, Sept 7, 47. *Study:* Univ SFla, 65-66; Juilliard Sch, with Joseph Fuchs, Robert Mann & Felix Galimir, BMus, 69; Univ Iowa, with Charles Treger, 71; Hartt Sch Music, with Charles Treger & Renato Bonacini, MMus, 74. *Pos:* First violin sect, Hartford Symph Orch, 71-79, prin second violinist, 79-; prin second violinist, Hartford Chamber Orch, 73-75; mem, Wells String Quartet, Cent Conn State Col, 76-78 & Anhared & Lyn Chamber Concts, Hartford, Conn, 81- *Teaching:* Instr violin & viola, Camerata Sch Music, 76-81; coordr ens & instr, Camerata Sch Music & Dance, 82- *Mailing Add:* 10 Ichabod Rd Simsbury CT 06070

STOWE, SONDRA
MEZZO-SOPRANO
b Hollywood, Calif. *Study:* Univ Calif, Los Angeles, BA(music); Calif Inst Arts, MA(music). *Rec Perf:* Anna Hope, Mother of Us All, New World Rec, 76. *Roles:* Carmela in La Vida Breve, 75 & Anna Hope in Mother of Us All, 76, Santa Fe Opera; Garcias in Don Quichotte (Massenet), 77, Zweiter

Knappe Blumenmächen in Parsifal, 78 & Alicia in Lucia di Lammermoor, 78, Zurich Opera; Child in L'Enfant et les Sortileges, Detroit Symph, 81; Suzuki in Madama Butterfly, Toledo Opera, 83. *Awards:* Grants, Young Musicians Found, 75, William M Sullivan Found, 76-83 & Nat Opera Inst, 78 & 83. *Rep:* Herbert Barrett Mgt 1860 Broadway New York NY 10023. *Mailing Add:* 41 W 86 8B New York NY 10024

STRACK, KENNETH JOHN
FRENCH HORN
b Cleveland, Ohio, June 17, 40. *Pos:* Fourth horn, Pittsburgh Symph Orch, 66- *Mailing Add:* 1976 Berkwood Dr Pittsburgh PA 15243

STRAINCHAMPS, EDMOND NICHOLAS
EDUCATOR, WRITER
b Mishawaka, Ind, July 5, 33. *Study:* Columbia Col, AB, 58; Columbia Univ, MA, 60, MPhil, 74. *Teaching:* Instr music, NY Univ, 62-66; asst prof, Rutgers Univ, 66-70; assoc prof, State Univ NY, Buffalo, 70- *Mem:* Am Musicol Soc; Int Musicol Soc; Renaissance Soc Am; Col Music Soc. *Interests:* Patronage for music in Italy during the late Renaissance and early Baroque; music of Marco da Gagliano and his Florentine contemporaries, ca 1580-1640; socio-musical relationships between Mantua and Florence, ca 1560-1640. *Publ:* Auth, A Brief Report on the Madrigal Style of Marco da Gagliano, Report 11th Cong Int Musicol Soc, Copenhagen, 72 & 74; New Light on the Accademia degli Elevati of Florence, Musical Quart, 10/76; Marco da Gagliano and the Compagnia dell'Arcangelo Raffaello in Florence, In: Essays Presented to Myron P Gilmore, 77; articles of Marco da Gagliano, Luzzasco Luzzaschi, Jacopo Corsi, Luca Bati, Lorenzo Allegri & Stefano Venturi, In: New Grove Dict of Music and Musicians, 6th ed, 79. *Mailing Add:* Dept Music Baird Hall State Univ NY Buffalo NY 14260

STRAKA, PAUL SCOTT
FRENCH HORN
b St Paul, Minn, Apr 2, 58. *Study:* Ind Univ, with R Elworthy & P Farkas, 77-80; study with Phillip Myers, 81. *Pos:* Extra horn, Minn Orch, 80- & Israel Phil, 82; first & third horn, Rai Orch, Torino, Italy, 81; utility horn, St Paul Chamber Orch, 83- *Mailing Add:* 1677 Portland Ave St Paul MN 55104

STRANDBERG, NEWTON DWIGHT
COMPOSER, EDUCATOR
b River Falls, Wis, Jan 3, 21. *Study:* North Park Col, Chicago, BMusEd, 42; Northwestern Univ, MM, 47, DMus, 56. *Works:* Canticle for Chorus and Orchestra, Birmingham Symph, 59; Quartet No 2, 72 & String Trio, 76, Cadek Quartet; Amenhotep III, Houston Symph, 77; Sanna Sanna Hosanna (organ), Hinshaw, NC, 75; Four Symphonicas (organ & brass), Houston Symphonic Brass, 81; Missa Brevis, Sam Houston State Univ, 81. *Teaching:* Instr music, Denison Univ, Granville, Ohio, 47-49; prof, Samford Univ, Birmingham, Ala, 50-67 & Sam Houston State, Huntsville, Tex, 67- *Mem:* Am Music Ctr; Asn Univ Comp. *Mailing Add:* Dept Music Sam Houston State Univ Huntsville TX 77341

STRANG, GERALD
COMPOSER, EDUCATOR
b Claresholm, Alberta, Feb 13, 08; US citizen. *Study:* Stanford Univ, BA, 28; Univ Calif, Berkeley, 28-29; Univ Southern Calif, PhD, 48. *Works:* Percussion Music for Three Players, New Music Ed, 35; Divertimento for Four Instruments, 48; Concerto for Cello, perf by Kurt Reher, Gabor Rejto & others, 51; Concerto Grosso, 50; Tripla Decima (computer music/tape), 69; Atmosonus (computer music/tape), 73; Variations (computer music/tape), 83. *Pos:* Consult bldg design & acoustics, 50- *Teaching:* Prof music, Calif State Univ, Northridge, 58-65 & Calif State Univ, Long Beach, 65-69; lectr, Univ Calif, Los Angeles, 69-75. *Mem:* Am Comp Alliance. *Publ:* Auth, Case Study: Building a College Music Building, In: Music Buildings, Rooms and Equipment, Music Educr Nat Conf, 66; The Computer in Musical Composition, Computers & Automation, Vol 15, No 8 & Cybernetic Serendipity, London, 68; Music and Computers, In: Man-Computer Team, Am Fedn Info Processing Soc, 67; The Problem of Imperfection in Computer Music, In: Music by Computers, John Wiley & Sons, Inc, 69; Ethics and Esthetics of Computer Music, In: The Computer and Music, Cornell Univ Press, 70. *Mailing Add:* 6500 Mantova St Long Beach CA 90815

STRANGE, ALLEN
COMPOSER, EDUCATOR
b Calexico, Calif, June 26, 43. *Study:* Calif State Univ, Fullerton, with Donal Michalsky; Univ Calif, San Diego, with Pauline Oliveros, Robert Erickson & Kenneth Gaburo. *Works:* Western Connection (orch); Charms (string orch); Rockytop Screamers and Further Scapes (orch); Star Salon Strikers and Sliders Last Orbit (amplified string trio & perc); Dirt Talk, Version 2 (organ, violin & perc); Switchcraft (bass, flute & engineer); The Doug Meyers (') Playing Flute (solo flute). *Pos:* Co-founder, Electric Weasel Ensemble, currently. *Teaching:* Mem fac, Indiana Univ, Pa, 69; prof music, San Jose State Univ, currently. *Awards:* Fullerton Friend Music Award, 65; Calif Regents Fel, 67-68; San Jose Found Grant, 70. *Publ:* Auth, Electronic Music: Systems, Techniques and Controls, Dubuque, Iowa, 72; contribr to music journals. *Mailing Add:* Music Dept San Jose State Univ San Jose CA 95192

STRANGE, RICHARD EUGENE
MUSIC DIRECTOR, EDUCATOR
b Hutchinson, Kans, Sept 14, 28. *Study:* Univ Wichita, BME, 50; Univ Colo, MME, 57; Boston Univ, DMA, 62. *Rec Perf:* Music of Leonardo Balada, Vol I, Serenus Rec, 71; Joseph Wagner Works for Concert Band, Orion Rec, 73; Fight Songs of the West, Golden Crest Rec, 78; over 100 education records

for commercial publ, regional & all-state bands. *Pos:* Columnist, band music reviews, Sch Musician Dir & Teacher Mag, 77- *Teaching:* Asst prof music, Texas A&I Col, 59; asst prof music & band dir, WVa Univ, 60; prof music & band dir, Carnegie-Mellon Univ, 61-74 & Ariz State Univ, 74- *Awards:* Award Spec Merit, Stereo Rev Mag, 71. *Bibliog:* They Are Making America Musical, Sch Musician Dir & Teacher Mag, 74. *Mem:* Am Bandmasters Asn (bd dirs, 77-79, vpres, 83); Col Band Dir Nat Asn (vpres eastern region, 65-66, pres, 66-68); life mem, Music Educr Nat Conf. *Publ:* Auth, Solving Problems on Woodwind Instruments, Instrumentalist, 65; The Band Repertoire & Academic Credit, PMEA News, 65; Everybody Is Out of Step but Johnny, DeFord Digest, 77. *Mailing Add:* 18 E Redondo Dr Tempe AZ 85282

STRASFOGEL, IAN
DIRECTOR—OPERA, ADMINISTRATOR
b New York, NY, Apr 5, 40. *Study:* Harvard Col, BA, 61. *Pos:* Dir, Music Theatre Proj, Berkshire Music Ctr, 71-73, Wash Opera, 72-75 & New Opera Theatre, Brooklyn Acad, 76-79. *Teaching:* Chmn opera dept, New England Consv Music, 68-72; prof opera, Univ Mich, 80. *Publ:* Trans & ed, Jacques Offenbach, Ba Ta Clan, G Schirmer, 69. *Mailing Add:* 915 West End Ave New York NY 10025

STRASSBURG, ROBERT
EDUCATOR, COMPOSER
b New York, NY, Aug 30, 15. *Study:* New England Consv Music, with Carl McKinley & Frederick Converse, BM, 39; Berkshire Music Ctr, with Paul Hindemith, 40; Harvard Univ, with Walter Piston & Igor Stravinsky, MA, 41; Univ Judaism, with Mario Castelnuovo-Tedesco, DFA, 70. *Works:* The Patriarchs (string orch), 46; Torah Sonata 50; Chelm (comic folk opera), 56; Tropal Suite (string orch), 67; Festival of Lights Symphony; Look Back Unto This Day (chorus with soloists & two pianos); Meditation (chorus, a cappella). *Teaching:* Mem fac, Brooklyn Col, 47-50, Hillel House, Univ Miami, 58-60 & Univ Judaism, 61-; prof music, Calif State Univ, Los Angeles, 66- *Awards:* Boston Symph Scholar, 40; Nat Inst Arts & Lett Award; MacDowell Fel, 46. *Publ:* Auth, Ernest Bloch, Voice in the Wilderness, Los Angeles, 77. *Mailing Add:* Calif State Univ 5151 State Univ Dr Los Angeles CA 90032

STRASSER, TAMAS
VIOLA, VIOLIN
b Nagyvarad, Hungary, Feb 15, 47; US citizen. *Study:* Univ Colo, with T Wilfred Beal; studied with Andor Toth, Karen Tuttle & Michael Rabin; Aspen Music Fest, with Lillian Fuchs; Colby Col, with Hungarian String Quartet. *Pos:* Violist, New Art String Quartet, Philadelphia, 72-75, Alba Trio, St Paul, 79- & Bakken String Quartet, Minneapolis, 80-; co-prin violist, St Paul Chamber Orch, 75- *Teaching:* Asst prof viola, Macalester Col, 79-82. *Mailing Add:* St Paul Chamber Orch 75 W 5th St St Paul MN 55102

STRATAS, TERESA
SOPRANO
b Toronto, Ont, May 26, 38. *Study:* With Irene Jessner, 56-59; Toronto Consv, Univ Toronto. *Rec Perf:* On Polydor & Eurodisc. *Roles:* Atlantida, La Scala, 62; Lulu in Lulu, Paris Grand Opera, 79; Mimi in La Boheme; Tatiana in Eugene Onegin; Susanna in The Marriage of Figaro; Nedda in Pagliacci; Marenka in The Bartered Bride. *Pos:* Mem, Metropolitan Opera, currently. *Awards:* Winner, Metropolitan Opera Auditions, 59; Performer of Yr, Can Music Coun, 79. *Mailing Add:* Metropolitan Opera Lincoln Ctr New York NY 10023

STRAUSS, BARBARA JO
LIBRARIAN
b LaCrosse, Wis, Oct 10, 47. *Study:* Univ Wis, LaCrosse, BS(music educ), 69, Madison, MA(libr sci), 79; Univ Ariz, MM(music hist), 76. *Pos:* Music specialist, Lake Mills Pub Sch, Wis, 69-72; music librn, Univ Wis, Madison, 81-; chmn, 14th Moravian Music Fest & Sem, Waukesha, Wis, 81- *Mem:* Music Libr Asn; Am Musicol Soc; Sonneck Soc. *Publ:* Auth, The Concert Life of the Collegium Musicum, Nazareth, 1796-1845, Moravian Music Found Bulletin, 76; Early American Moravian Music: Expand Your American Music Repertoire, Ariz Music News, 76-77. *Mailing Add:* 4588 Golf Dr Windsor WI 53598

STREET, MARNA SUSAN
VIOLA
b Tulsa, Okla, Feb 25, 49. *Study:* Juilliard Sch, with Walter Trampler, BM & MM, 71. *Pos:* Violist, Pittsburgh Symph, formerly; prin violist, Cincinnati Symph, 80-; mem, Cincinnati Chamber Soloists. *Mailing Add:* 1628 N Argyle Cincinnati OH 45223

STREET, TISON
COMPOSER, VIOLIN
b Boston, Mass, May 20, 43. *Study:* Harvard Univ, studied comp with Leon Kirchner & David Del Tredici & violin with Einar Hansen, BA, 65, MA, 71. *Works:* Three Sacred Anthems, 71 & String Quartet, 72, G Schirmer; String Quintet, 74, Chords from the Northeast (piano), 76, John Major's Medley (guitar), 77, Adagio in E flat (oboe & string orch), 77 & Montsalvat (orch), 81, Am Music Publ. *Teaching:* Comp in res, Marlboro Music Fest, summers 64-66; assoc prof music, Harvard Univ, 79-; vis lectr, Univ Calif, Berkeley, 71-72; fel, Am Acad Rome, 73-74. *Awards:* Nat Inst Arts & Lett Award, 73; Mass Arts & Humanities Found Award, 77; Brandeis Creative Arts Award, 79. *Mem:* BMI; Am Fedn Musicians. *Mailing Add:* 156 Montague St #8 Brooklyn NY 11201

STREETER, THOMAS WAYNE
EDUCATOR, TROMBONE

b Kokomo, Ind, Apr 26, 43. *Study:* Ind Univ, BA(music educ), 65, MA(music educ), 67; Cath Univ Am, DMA, 71. *Rec Perf:* Music for Bass Trombone, Kendor Music, 71. *Pos:* Bass trombonist, US Air Force Airmen of Note, Washington, DC, 67-71. *Teaching:* Instr trombone, Ill Wesleyan Univ, 71-74, dir, Jazz Ens, 71-, asst prof trombone, 74-78, assoc prof trombone & music theory, 78- *Awards:* Outstanding Serv, Int Trombone Asn, 76. *Mem:* Nat Asn Jazz Educr (Ill state pres, 81-); Int Trombone Asn (treas, 71-76); Music Educr Nat Conf; Ill Music Educr Asn. *Publ:* Auth, Survey and Annotated Bibliography on the Historical Development of the Trombone, Vol VIII, 80 & The Historical and Musical Aspects of the 19th Century Bass Trombone, Vol III, 74, Vol IV, 75, Vol V, 76, Int Trombone Asn J. *Mailing Add:* 1711 Ebel Normal IL 61701

STRETANSKY, CYRIL MICHAEL
CONDUCTOR & MUSIC DIRECTOR, EDUCATOR

b Nanticoke, Pa, June 4, 35. *Study:* Mansfield State Col, BS(music educ), 57; Temple Univ, MMus, 65. *Pos:* Artistic dir, Int Choral Fest, Rome, formerly; music dir & cond, Susquehanna Valley Chorale & Orch, currently; guest cond, Pa All-State Chorus & Mex Int Choral Fest, formerly. *Teaching:* Dir Choral Activ, Montrose Area High Sch, Pa, 57-72; assoc prof music & dir choral activ, Susquehanna Univ, Selinsgrove, Pa, 72- *Mem:* Music Educr Nat conf; Pa Music Educr Asn; Am Choral Dir Asn; Phi Mu Alpha Sinfonia. *Mailing Add:* 15 Greenbrier Ave Selinsgrove PA 17870

STRIMPLE, NICK
MUSIC DIRECTOR, COMPOSER

b Amarillo, Tex, Dec 5, 46. *Study:* Baylor Univ, with Richard Willis & Daniel Sternberg, BM, 69; Univ Southern Calif, with Halsey Stevens, Charles Hirt & Daniel Lewis, MM, 73, DMA, 76 . *Works:* To Him That Overcometh, J Fischer and Bros, 73; Tomorrow, 77 & Alas and Did My Saviour Bleed, 79, H W Gray Publ; Nativities, perf by Beverly Hills Presby Church & Ventura Co Master Chorale, 80; Scherzo for Clarinet and Piano, Dorn Publ Inc, 81; None Other Lamb, 81 & Father, in Thy Mysterious Presence, 81, H W Gray Publ. *Pos:* Music dir, City Stage Prod, San Diego, 74-76, Ventura Co Master Chorale, Calif, 76-80, Beverly Hills Presby Church, 78- & Choral Soc Southern Calif, 82- *Teaching:* Instr music, US Int Univ, San Diego, 74-76; asst prof church & choral music, Univ Southern Calif, Los Angeles, 76-78. *Mem:* Am Choral Dir Asn; Am Fedn Musicians; Am Musicol Soc; ASCAP. *Publ:* Auth, Creative Hymnology at Univ Southern Calif, Music Ministry, 70; The Function of Music in Contemporary Worship, Choral J, 71; A Brief Look at Hymnody in the Reformations of Luther and Calvin, Worship & Arts, 74; An Introduction to the Choral Music of Roy Harris, Choral J, 82. *Rep:* James S Breeden 8300 Douglas Ave 8th Floor Dallas Texas 75225. *Mailing Add:* 411 1/2 Shirley Pl Beverly Hills CA 90212

STRINGER, ALAN W
COMPOSER, ORGAN

b El Paso, Tex, Jan 15, 38. *Study:* Univ NMex, MA, 63. *Works:* Suite on Hebraic Themes, perf by Alan Stringer, 75; Green, Green, Univ Albuquerque, 78; For the Time Being, First Congregational Choir, Albuquerque & Bethlehem Lutheran Choir, Los Alamos, 79; Alleluia (choir), perf by combined choirs of 3 churches, 80; Short Symphony, ensemble from NMex Symph, 81; The Selfish Giant, 82; Sound Piece No 2, Dan Gwin, 83. *Pos:* Organist, First Congregational Church, 69- *Awards:* First Prize, Bicentennial Comp Cont, NMex Arts Comn, 76. *Mem:* NMex Comp Guild (pres, 74-78). *Mailing Add:* 8640 Horatio Pl NE Albuquerque NM 87111

STRIPLING, LUTHER
EDUCATOR, BARITONE

Study: Clark Col, Ga, with J DeKoven Killingsworth, AB, 57; Univ Ky, with Donald Ivey, MMus, 68; Univ Colo, Boulder, with Berton Coffin, DMusA, 71. *Roles:* Bass solos in Ballad for Americans, Atlanta Pops Orch, 60-65; Balthaza in Amahl and the Night Visitors, Atlanta Symph, 62; Joe in Showboat, Theater Under the Stars, Atlanta, Ga, 64; Biterolf in Tannhäuser, Minn Orch, 74; bass solos in St John's Passion, St Paul Civic Orch, 75 & 77. *Pos:* Coordr vocal activ, Macalester Col, 71-78. *Teaching:* Asst prof music, Macalester Col, 71-78; assoc prof music, Southern Ill Univ, Edwardsville, 78- *Mem:* Nat Asn Teachers Singing (Minn chap pres, 73-75 & St Louis chap pres, 80-82); Nat Opera Asn (deputy regional gov, 75-80). *Publ:* Contribr, Burkhart's Antholog of Musical Analysis, Holt, Rinehart & Winston, 78; auth, Smiling Produces the Most Favorable Position of the Mouth for Singing, Nat Asn Teachers Singing Bulletin, Jan/Feb 81. *Mailing Add:* 10609 Vorhof Dr St Louis MO 63136

STRIZICH, CATHERINE LIDDELL
LUTE, TEACHER-COACH

b New Haven, Conn, May 25, 49. *Study:* Sarah Lawrence Col, BA, 71; Schola Cantorum Basiliensis, soloist dipl, 76. *Rec Perf:* Renaissance Music for 2 Lutes, 77 & Baroque Duos, 78, Titanic Recs; Capricci Armonici, 82 & Venetian Monody in the Age of Monteverdi, 82, Musical Heritage Soc. *Pos:* Lutenist, NY Pro Musica, 73; guest lutenist, Boston Camerata, 80; found mem, Ens Chanterelle, 81- *Teaching:* Adj lectr lute, Cath Univ Am, 76-79; instr lute, San Francisco Consv, 80- *Awards:* Conct Artist Guild Award, 83. *Mem:* Chamber Music Am; Lute Soc Am. *Mailing Add:* 3859-H Miramar St La Jolla CA 92037

STRIZICH, ROBERT (WARD)
COMPOSER, GUITAR & LUTE

b Oakland, Calif, June 22, 45. *Study:* Univ Calif, Berkeley, BA(music), 67, MA(comp), 70; Univ Calif, San Diego, with Bernard Rands & Wilbur Ogdon, currently. *Works:* Kaleidoscope (solo guitar), perf by George Sakellariou & Michael Lorimer, 68; Tastar (two lutes), perf by Strizich Duo, 78; Wind Structures (four recorders), Am Rec Soc, Boston, 80; Hydra (singer & chamber ens), perf by Sonor, 83; Mercurius (solo violin), perf by Janos Negyesy, 83; Sonata for Guitar, Berben, Italy. *Rec Perf:* Renaissance Music for 2 Lutes, 77 & Baroque Duos, 78, Titanic Rec; Capricci Armonici, 82 & Venetian Monody in the Age of Monteverdi, 82, Musical Heritage Soc. *Pos:* Baroque guitarist & lutenist, Strizich Duo, La Jolla, Calif, 75-, Ens Chanterelle, NY, 81- & Aston Magna Fest, 81- *Teaching:* Instr lute, Boston Univ, 78-79; lectr counterpoint, Wellesley Col, 83. *Awards:* Nicola de Lorenzo Prize Comp, 68 & Eisner Prize Creative Achievement, 70, Univ Calif, Berkeley; Conct Artist Guild Award, 83. *Mem:* Chamber Music Am; Col Music Soc; Lute Soc Am (mem bd dir, 79-). *Publ:* Auth, 21 entries on baroque guitar composer, In: New Grove Dict of Music & Musicians; ed, R de Visee: Oeuvres Completes pour Guitare, Heugel, 69; auth, A Spanish Guitar Tutor: Ruiz de Ribayaz's Luz y Norte Musical, J Lute Soc Am, 74. *Mailing Add:* 28 Woodward St Newton Heights MA 02161

STROHM, JOHN A
EDUCATOR

b Carroll, Iowa, Apr 18, 23. *Study:* St Olaf Col, with Dr F Melius Christiansen & Dr Olaf C Christiansen, BM, 49; Columbia Univ, with Dr Harry Robert Wilson, MA, 50, dipl, 51. *Pos:* Vocal dir & adjudicator, Mont, SDak, NDak, Minn & Canada, 51-; choral dir & vocal staff, Int Music Camp, Dunsieth, NDak, summers 60-74. *Teaching:* Choral dir & vocal instr, Dakota Northwestern Univ, 51-, chmn, Div Music, 61- *Mem:* Music Educr Nat Conf; Am Choral Dirs Asn; Phi Mu Alpha Sinfonia; NDak Mus Educr Asn (pres, 67-69, secy-treas, 65-67). *Mailing Add:* Music Div Dakota Northwestern Univ Minot ND 58701

STROUD, RICHARD ERNEST
COMPOSER, MUSIC DIRECTOR

b Dunsmuir, Calif, Jan 26, 29. *Study:* Col Idaho, Caldwell, BA, 54; Univ Idaho, Moscow, MA, 55; Humboldt State Univ, Arcata, Calif, 64. *Works:* Articulations for Brass, 68, Tubantiphon, 74, Brass Ring No 1, 75 & Treatments for Tuba, 76, Seesaw Music Inc; Treatments for Tuba, Gold Crest Rec, 76; Learnin' the Blues, Studio P/R, 78; Brass Ring No 5, Seesaw Music Inc, 82; Concerto (flute, brass & perc), comn by Humboldt Bay Brass Soc, 83. *Pos:* Founder & lead trumpet, Sequoia Brass Quintet, Eureka, 72-77; co-founder & cond, Humboldt Bay Brass Soc, Arcata, 79- *Teaching:* Dir instrm music, Parma City Sch, Idaho, 55-57 & Ontario City Sch, Ore, 57-58; music dir & chmn music dept, Eureka City Sch, Calif, 58- *Awards:* Cert Commendation, Calif State Dept Educ, 82. *Bibliog:* Constance Weldon (auth), International Tuba Symposium Workshop, winter 79, Barton Cummings (auth), New Materials, spring 80 & Jack Tilbury (auth), New Materials, spring 83, Tuba J. *Mem:* Music Educr Nat Conf; Calif Music Educr Asn (pres NCoast sect, 67-69); Calif Band Dir Asn. *Mailing Add:* 131 Huntoon Eureka CA 95501

STRUKOFF, RUDOLF STEPHEN
EDUCATOR, CONDUCTOR

b Rostov, Russia, July 18, 35. *US citizen. Study:* Andrews Univ, BME, 60; Mich State Univ, MMus, 64, PhD, 70. *Works:* The Greatest of These, Libr Cong, 70; Childhood Sketches, Orion Music Press, 73; Sonata for Flute and Harp, Gov State Univ, 79. *Rec Perf:* Requiem (Faure), 78, German Requiem (Brahms), 79, Heiligmesse (Haydn), 80, Mass in C Major (Beethoven), 81, Liebeslieder Walzer (Brahms), 82 & Hymn of Praise (Mendelssohn), 83, Instructional Commun Ctr. *Roles:* Noye in Noye Fludde, Jackson, Mich, 66; Attila in Attila (Verdi), Chicago Chamber Choir & Orch, 79. *Teaching:* Instr music, Mich State Univ, 63-65; asst prof, Ind State Univ, 66-69; assoc prof, Andrews Univ, 69-76; prof, Gov State Univ, 77- *Mem:* Pi Kappa Lambda; Am Choral Dir Asn; ASCAP; Chicago Singing Teachers Guild; Nat Asn Teachers Singing (mem bd dir, 80-82). *Mailing Add:* 1038 Monterey Court Park Forest South IL 60466

STRUMMER, PETER
BASS

b Vienna, Austria, Sept 8, 48; Can citizen. *Study:* Cleveland Inst Music; Juilliard Sch Music. *Roles:* Leporello in Don Giovanni, Can Opera Co, 79; Papageno in Die Zauberflöte, Charlotte Opera, 80; Sacristan in Tosca, Greater Miami Opera, 81; Bottom in A Midsummer Night's Dream, Cent City Opera, Landestheater Salzburg & Landestheater Linz, 82; Beckmesser in Die Meistersinger, Landestheater Linz, 82-83; Dr Bartolo in Il Barbiere di Siviglia, Houston Grand Opera, 83; Don Alfonso in Cosi fan tutte, Greater Miami Opera, 84. *Awards:* Rockefeller Grant, 71 & 72; Boris Goldovsky Award, 73; Can Coun Grant, 75. *Rep:* Thea Dispeker 59 E 54th St New York NY 10022. *Mailing Add:* Siemensstrasse 46 Linz 4020 Austria

STRUNK, STEVEN (GERHARDT)
COMPOSER, EDUCATOR

b Evansville, Ind, Mar 7, 43. *Study:* Boston Consv, BM, 65; Juilliard Sch, MS, 67, DMA, 71. *Works:* Quartet II, Dorn Publ, 73; Spirit Lake Suite, perf by US Air Force Orch, 75; Orpheus, perf by Catholic Univ Chor and Orch, 76; Episodes, Dorn Publ, 80; Concerto for Chamber Orchestra, comn by Wash Chamber Orch, 81; Quartet IV, 82 & Prisms, 83, North-South Editions. *Teaching:* Instr, Fla State Univ, 67-69; chmn theory dept, Eastern NMex Univ, Portales, 71-73; asst prof, Sch Music, Catholic Univ, 73-76, assoc prof,

77- *Awards:* Comp Fel, Nat Endowment Arts, 74 & 78; Comp Grant, Am Music Ctr, 81. *Mem:* Am Musicol Soc; Soc for Music Theory. *Publ:* Auth, The Harmony of Early Bop: A Layered Approach, J Jazz Studies, 79. *Mailing Add:* 3701 Connecticut Ave NW Washington DC 20008

STUART, JAMES FORTIER
TENOR, EDUCATOR
b Baton Rouge, La, Dec 22, 28. *Study:* La State Univ, BMus, MMus; Eastman Sch Music, DMus Arts & perf cert. *Roles:* Tenor roles in over 300 Gilbert & Sullivan operas. *Pos:* Tenor with orchs in New York, Philadelphia, Chicago, New Orleans & Atlanta; mem, Boston Opera Co, New Orleans Opera & Atlanta Opera. *Teaching:* Prof voice, Kent State Univ, currently. *Mem:* Nat Asn Teachers Singing; Phi Mu Alpha Sinfonia. *Mailing Add:* Sch Music Kent State Univ Kent OH 44242

STUCKY, RODNEY
GUITAR & LUTE, EDUCATOR
Study: Bethany Col, BM; Southern Methodist Univ, MM; studied class guitar with Aaron Shearer. *Pos:* Recitals as solo performer & cond of guitar ens throughout SC; recitalist & solo performer, Leon Fleisher Chamber Group, Washington, DC; soloist, Dupont Circle Consortium; guitarist & vocalist, US Army Field Band, touring US, Cent Am, South Am & Can. *Teaching:* Fac mem, Nat Music Camp, Interlochen & El Centro Col, formerly; instr class guitar & lute & dir, Collegium Musicum, Univ SC, formerly; fac mem class guitar, lute, ens & early music, St Louis Consv Music, currently. *Mem:* Am String Teachers Asn; Guitar Found Am. *Mailing Add:* St Louis Consv Music 560 Trinity Ave St Louis MO 63130

STUCKY, STEVEN
COMPOSER, WRITER
b Hutchinson, Kans, Nov 7, 49. *Study:* Baylor Univ, BMus, 71; Cornell Univ, MFA, 73, DMA, 78. *Works:* Piano Quartet, 72 & Schneemusik, 73, Am Comp Ed; Movements III, Shawnee Press, 76; Kenningar (Symph No 4), Am Comp Ed, 77; Refrains, Music Perc, 79; Transparent Things, 80 & Sappho Fragments, 82, Am Comp Ed. *Teaching:* Asst prof, Lawrence Univ, 78-80 & Cornell Univ, 80- *Awards:* Victor Herbert Prize, Nat Fedn Music Clubs, 74; First Prize, Am Soc Univ Comp, 75; Deems Taylor Award, ASCAP, 82. *Mem:* Am Comp Alliance; Am Musicol Soc; BMI; Soc New Music (vpres, 82-); Music Theory Soc NY State (mem bd dir, 80-). *Publ:* Auth, Lutoslawski and His Music, Cambridge Univ Press, 81; Lutoslawski's Double Concerto, Musical Times, 81. *Rep:* Am Comp Alliance 170 W 74th St New York NY 10023. *Mailing Add:* Music Dept Cornell Univ Ithaca NY 14853

STUDEBAKER, DONALD W
CONDUCTOR, BARITONE
b Danville, Ill, Mar 5, 54. *Study:* Eastern Ill Univ, BMus, 77; Ill State Univ, MMus, 78; Univ Northern Colo, currently. *Pos:* Bar soloist, St Louis Symph, 80 & 81. *Teaching:* Choral dir, Jersey Community High Sch, Jerseyville, Ill, 78-80; dir choral activ, Univ Northern Colo, 82-83. *Mem:* Am Choral Dir Asn; Am Choral Found; Am Musicol Soc. *Interests:* Choral music of John Amner (1579-1641). *Publ:* Auth, The Liszt Requiem, Am Choral Dir Asn J, 83. *Mailing Add:* 1761 30th St #4 Greeley CO 80631

STULBERG, NEAL H
CONDUCTOR, PIANO
b Detroit, Mich, Apr 12, 54. *Study:* Harvard Col, BA, 76; Univ Mich, MM, 78; Juilliard Sch, 79. *Pos:* Cond, Young Musicians Foundation Debut Orch, 81-; asst cond, Los Angeles Phil, 82- & Exxon/Arts Endowment Cond, 83- *Awards:* Second Prize, Baltimore Symph Orch Young Cond Compt, 80. *Rep:* Hamlen-Landau Mgt 140 W 79 #2A New York NY 10024. *Mailing Add:* Los Angeles Phil 135 N Grand Ave Los Angeles CA 90012

STUMPF, CAROL L
PERCUSSION, TIMPANI
Study: Curtis Inst Music, BMus, 82. *Pos:* Prin timpanist, Charlotte Symph Orch, 82- *Mailing Add:* c/o Charlotte Symph Orch 110 E 7th St Charlotte NC 28202

STUMPF, THOMAS
PIANO, TEACHER
b Shanghai, China, Mar 25, 50; Ger citizen. *Study:* Mozarteum, Salzburg, Austria, artist cert, 72; New England Consv, MMus, 77, artist dipl, 79. *Rec Perf:* Lieder recital, with Edith Mathis, BBC, 73 & with Rita Streich, ORF, Salzburg & ORTF, France, 74; Robert Ceely's Piano Variations, BEEP, 83. *Pos:* Pianist & co-dir, Lyr Arts Ens, 78-82. *Teaching:* Fac mem piano, New England Consv, 79-, coordr sec piano, 80- *Awards:* Bösendorfer Prize, Vienna, 70; Lilli, Lehmann Medal, Int Stiftung Mozarteum, Salzburg, 72. *Mem:* Col Music Soc. *Mailing Add:* 154 Washington St Arlington MA 02174

STURGES, ROWLAND (GIBSON HAZARD)
EDUCATOR, PIANO
b Narragansett, RI, Sept 22, 16. *Study:* Ecole Normale Musique, Paris, studied harmony, counterpoint & hist with Nadia Boulanger, 33-34; Harvard Univ, studied fugue & comp with Walter Piston, AB, 42. *Rec Perf:* Two Solo Piano Recitals at Jordan Hall, Boston, 52 & 54 & with Civic Symph Boston, 58, Fassett Rec Studio. *Teaching:* Piano, Longy Sch Music, 50-; choral dir, Buckingham Sch, Cambridge, Mass, 50-68; Concord Acad, Mass, 60-68 & Abbott Acad, Andover, 69-71. *Mailing Add:* Longy Sch Music One Follen St Cambridge MA 02138

STURM, GEORGE
ADMINISTRATOR, WRITER
b Augsburg, Ger, Mar 13, 30; US citizen. *Study:* Queens Col, New York, BA, 52; Princeton Univ, MFA, 55; studies with Luigi Dallapiccola, Florence, Italy, 55-57. *Pos:* Head perf dept, G Schirmer/AMP, New York, 58-77; vpres, European Am Music, 77-79; exec dir, Music Assoc Am, 80- *Awards:* Fulbright Grant, 55-57. *Mem:* Am Music Ctr; Karol Rathaus Soc (pres, 82-); Chamber Music Am; Cent Opera Serv; Am Symph Orch League. *Publ:* Auth, A Paper on Music Publishing in the US Since 1945, Music Assoc Am, 79; Look Back in Anger: The Strange Case of Louis Gruenberg, 81, Happy Birthday Diabelli, 81 & Of Troubadours Today, 82, MadAminA!; Convention in Opera, Opera J, 82. *Mailing Add:* c/o Music Assoc Am 224 King St Englewood NJ 07631

STURMS, ARNOLDS FRICIS
COMPOSER, FLUTE
b Dobele, Latvia, July 22, 12; US citizen. *Study:* State Consv Latvia, MM, 34; George Peabody Col, studied comp with Roy Harris, 50-53. *Works:* Suite for Flute and Orchestra, Indianapolis Sinfonietta, 60; Sonata for Violin and Piano, Masako Yanagita & Abba Bogin, 72; Sonatas for Piano Nos 1, 2 & 3, Arthur Ozolins & David Volckhausen, 74; Woodwind Quintet, Galliard Quintet, 77; Trio for Piano, Violin and Clarinet, Mod Music Ens Infusion, 83; Concerto for Piano and Orchestra, Milwaukee Symph, 83. *Rec Perf:* Latvian Piano Recital, 66 & Songs of Two Latvian Composers, 72, Coronet Rec; Music of Arnolds Sturms, CMS Rec, 80. *Pos:* First flute, Nat Opera Latvia, 35-44 & Nashville Symph, 51-53; second flute, Fla Symph, 56-58 & NC Symph, 59-60. *Teaching:* Asst prof flute, State Consv Latvia, 40-44; teacher flute & ens, Roosa Sch Music, 60- *Awards:* Music Award, Am Latvian Asn, 65, Gen Gopper Found, 66 & World Fedn Free Latvians, 81. *Mem:* Am Fedn Musicians; Brooklyn Music Teachers Guild; Latvian Am Asn Univ Prof (chmn music div, 56-). *Mailing Add:* 8 Magaw Pl New York NY 10033

STUTT, CYNTHIA
VIOLIN
b Schenectady, NY. *Study:* Troy Quartet Prog, with Charles Castleman, 75; Meadowmount Summer Camp, with Ivan Galamian, 77; Univ Mich, with Paul Makanowitzky, BMus(violin perf), 80. *Pos:* Assoc concertmaster, Omaha Symph & Nebr Sinfonia, 80-; second violinist, Fontenelle String Quartet, 80- *Mailing Add:* c/o Omaha Symph 310 Aquila Ct Omaha NE 68102

SUBEN, JOEL ERIC
COMPOSER, CONDUCTOR
b New York, NY, May 16, 46. *Study:* Eastman Sch Music, BMus, 69; Hochschule Mozarteum, Salzburg, Austria, cert(orch cond), 76; Brandeis Univ, PhD, 80; studied cond with Jacques-Louis Monod, 73-77 . *Works:* Serenade for 12 Instruments, APNM, 80; Psalm 121 (womens chorus, piano), Bourne Co, 81; Sonatina for Piano, 81, Haazinu, 82, 5 Goethe Songs for Baritone, Guitar & Cello, 82, Träume auf Diechterhöhe, 82 & Piano Concerto, 82, APNM. *Rec Perf:* Mar-r-i-i-a-a (Joseph Olive), Voice Am, 75. *Pos:* Guest cond, League Comp, Int Soc Contemp Music, 75, Guild Comp, 77 & Am Symph Orch, 77; music dir, Peninsula Symph, 82- *Teaching:* Inst theory & lit, Fordham Univ, 74-80; lectr orch, Baruch Col, City Univ New York, 74-80; asst prof theory & comp, Univ Richmond, 80-82. *Awards:* First prize, Am Guild Organists Comp Cont, 67; Comp of Year Award, Music Teachers Nat Asn, 81-82. *Bibliog:* Harry Neville (auth), Blake, Suben: Fresh, Vivid Composers, Boston Herald, 3/2/72; C A Bustard (auth), Comprehensibility Goal of Richmond Composer, Richmond Times-Dispatch, 8/29/80; Dika Newlin (auth), Haazinu, Richmond Times-Dispatch, 3/20/83. *Mem:* Am Soc Univ Comp (exec comt, 79-80); Am Comp Alliance; Col Music Soc; BMI. *Mailing Add:* 7608 Cherokee Rd Richmond VA 23225

SUBOTNICK, JOAN LA BARBARA See La Barbara, Joan

SUBOTNICK, MORTON
COMPOSER, EDUCATOR
b Los Angeles, Calif, Apr 14, 33. *Study:* Univ Denver, BA, 56; Mill Col, studied comp with Leon Kirchner & Darius Milhaud, MFA, 59. *Works:* Silver Apples of the Moon, 67, The Wild Bull, 68, Before the Butterfly, 75, Liquid Strata, 77, Parallel Lines, 78, After the Butterfly, 79 & The Fluttering of Wings, 81, Theodore Presser Co. *Pos:* Music dir, Ann Halprin Dance Co, 60-66, San Francisco Actors Wkshp, 60-66, Lincoln Ctr Repty Theatre, 66-67 & Electronic Circus & Electric Ear Series, 67-69; dir, Contemp Music Fest, 78- *Teaching:* Asst prof comp & theory, Mill Col, 59-65; comp in res, Sch Arts, NY Univ, 66-69; chmn dept comp, Calif Inst Arts, 69- *Awards:* Guggenheim Fel, 76; Music Comp Award, Am Acad Arts & Lett, 79; Citation in Music, Brandeis Univ Creative Arts Awards, 83. *Bibliog:* Harold Whipple (auth), Beasts and Butterflies: Morton Subotnick's Ghost Scores, Musical Quart, 7/83. *Mem:* Am Music Ctr (vpres, 81-82); ASCAP; Int Comput Music Soc; Confedn Int Musiques Electroacoustiques. *Rep:* Theodore Presser Co Presser Pl Bryn Mawr PA 19010. *Mailing Add:* PO Box 55065 Valencia CA 91355

SUBRAMANIAM, LAKSHMINARAYANA
VIOLIN, COMPOSER
b Madras, India, July 23, 47; US citizen. *Study:* Madras Univ, MBBS; Calif Inst Arts, MFA. *Pos:* Musical dir, Navaratna; soloist in doc film, The Magic Fingers & on tour with Ravi Shankar & George Harrison in Europe, Can & US; conct violinist in US, Can, Europe, SE Asia & Scand. *Teaching:* Head, South Indian Music Dept, Calif Inst Arts, 73-78. *Awards:* President's Award, India, 63; Violin Chakravarthi, 72; Best Violinst of Yr, Madras Social & Cult Acad, 77-78. *Mem:* Madras Musical Asn; Friends of Music, Madras. *Mailing Add:* 5836 Hesperia Ave Encino CA 91316

SUCHOFF, BENJAMIN
EDUCATOR, WRITER
b New York, NY, Jan 19, 18. *Study:* Cornell Univ, BS, 40; Juillard Sch Music, 40-41 & 46-47; NY Univ, MA, 49, EdD, 56. *Pos:* Dir music, Hewlett-Woodmere Union Free Sch District, 50-78. *Teaching:* Lectr, Teachers Col, Columbia Univ, 73; dir, spec collections & comput prog, Ctr Contemp Arts & Lett, State Univ NY, Stony Brook, 73- & prof arts & lett, currently. *Awards:* Grant, Am Coun Learned Soc, 66. *Mem:* ASCAP; Am Musicol Soc; Soc Ethnomusicol; Music Educr Nat Conf; Col Music Soc. *Publ:* Ed, Rumanian Folk Music (Bartok), Vols 1-3, 67, Vols 4-5, 76; Guide to the Mikrokosmos of Bela Bartok, 70; Curriculum Guide to Electronic Music, 73; Electronic Music Techniques, 75; Bela Bartok: A Celebration, 81. *Rep:* Ctr Contemp Arts & Lett State Univ NY Stony Brook NY 11794. *Mailing Add:* 2 Tulip St Cedarhurst NY 11516

SUCHY, GREGORIA KARIDES
COMPOSER, EDUCATOR
b Milwaukee, Wis. *Study:* Milwaukee State Teachers Col, BS(music), 45; Northwestern Univ, studied comp with Anthony Donato & piano with Louis Crowder, MMus, 51; DePaul Univ, studied comp with Alexander Tcherepnin, 59-61; Chicago Musical Col, Roosevelt Univ, studied comp with Rudolph Ganz, 61-66; Univ Chicago, studied comp with Ralph Shapey, 67-69. *Works:* Suite on Greek Themes (piano), perf by Int Soc Contemp Music, Chicago, 59; Three Lovers (orch), perf by Milwaukee Symph, 60; Mother Goose Rhymes in Twelve Tone (piano), perf by Rudolph Ganz, 60; Skins and Exposures (electronic), comn by Fine Arts Dance Theatre, 66; Soliloquy Sans C (solo violin), perf by Leonard Sorkin, 74; Entries (baritone, piano, incidental perc), perf by William Duvall, 74; The Ass in the Lion's Skin, perf by NY Contemp Chamber Music Ens, 74. *Teaching:* Prof theory & comp, Univ Wis, Milwaukee, 46- *Awards:* Star Award, Delta Omicron, 57; Achievement Award, Milwaukee Prof Panhellenic Asn, 73; Excellence in Teaching Award, Amoco, 80. *Mem:* Am Music Ctr; Am Soc Univ Comp; Am Women Comp Inc; Soc Music Theory; Nat Asn Comp, USA. *Mailing Add:* Music Dept Univ Wis Milwaukee WI 53201

SUCHY, JESSICA RAY
HARP, EDUCATOR
b Milwaukee, Wis, July 6, 54. *Study:* Univ Wis, Milwaukee, with Jeanne Henderson, BFA(music), 76; Eastman Sch Music, with Eileen Malone, MM(perf & lit), 79, MA(theory), 82; Holy Cross Greek Orthodox Sch Theol, 80; Ind Univ, with Susann McDonald, DMus(perf & lit), 83; studied with Edward Druzinsky, Chicago Symph; Int Academie d'Ete, Nice, France, 77. *Rec Perf:* Petite Symphony Concertante (harp, harpsichord, piano & double string orch), Gotham Film Prod PBS, 82. *Pos:* Prin harpist, Owensboro Symph Orch, Ky, 82- & Summer Fest Orch, Ind Univ, 82-; dir, Ind Univ Harp Ens, 82. *Teaching:* Assoc instr harp, Ind Univ, 82-; private instr Byzantine music, 82- *Awards:* First Prize, Nat Fedn Music Clubs Student Auditions Harp, 75; grant, Delta Omicron Found, 77 & 83; Eastman EOP Grant, 78. *Bibliog:* Dean Jensen (auth), Harpist Brings Joy on Wintry Evening, Milwaukee Sentinal, 75; Paula Brookmire (auth), Harpist Has World On String, Milwaukee J, 76; Ann Anthony Jones (auth), Keys to Conference Concerts, Wheel Delta Omicron, 80. *Mem:* Delta Omicron (pres Delta Eta chap, 75-76); Am Harp Soc (vpres Milwaukee chap, 75). *Interests:* Byzantine music; structural aspects of chant lines; Arnold Bax; works for harp. *Publ:* Auth, Arnold Bax: Fantasy-Sonata and Sonata for Viola and Piano, Klavier, 83; Arnold Bax: A Harpist's Composer, Am Harp J (in press). *Mailing Add:* 2601 E Newton Ave Milwaukee WI 53211

SUDERBURG, ELIZABETH
SOPRANO
b Freistadt, Wis, Apr 3, 35. *Study:* Chicago Consv Music, with M Balstead, cert, 53; Univ Minn, BA, 57; Yale Sch Music, with Blake Stern. *Rec Perf:* Madrigals (Crumb), 73 & Bartok Songs, 73, Vox Turnabout; American Sampler, Univ Wash Press, 75; Spanish Songs, 80, Britten Illuminations & Suderburg Concerto, 81 & Songs (Bartok-Kodaly), 83, Vox Turnabout; Stevenson (Suderburg), Thomas Frost Prod (in prep). *Teaching:* Instr voice, Bryn Mawr Col, 60-61 & Univ Wash, Seattle, 66-74. *Awards:* Naumberg Award, 72; Bicentennial Award, Wash, 76. *Bibliog:* Martin Couper (auth), Ginastera Quartet, London Daily Telegraph, 11/18/74; Andres Briner (auth), Bartok Songs, Neue Zurcher Zeitung, 76; Andrew Porter (auth), Crumb Madrigals, New Yorker, 3/21/77. *Mailing Add:* 28 Cascade Ave Winston-Salem NC 27107

SUDERBURG, ROBERT CHARLES
COMPOSER, CONDUCTOR
b Spencer, Iowa, Jan 28, 36. *Study:* Univ Minn, BA, 57; Yale Sch Music, MM, 60; Univ Pa, PhD, 66. *Works:* Chamber Music II, 67, Winds/Vents (orch), 74, Concerto (piano & orch), 74, Stevenson (voice & string quartet), 76, Concerto (perc & orch), Concerto (voice, choir & orch), 79 & Concerto (harp & orch; in prep), Theodore Presser. *Rec Perf:* Chamber Music II, Vox Turnabout, 73; Within the Mirror of Time, Columbia, 76; Baudelaire Concerto, Vox Turnabout, 82; Night Set, Ritual Series & Stevenson (in prep), Frost Prod. *Pos:* Cond & dir, Philadelphia Comp Forum, 62-66. *Teaching:* Cond & instr, Philadelphia Musical Acad, 63-66; co-dir & prof, Contemp Group, Univ Wash, Seattle, 66-74; chancellor, NC Sch Arts, 74- *Awards:* Fel, Guggenheim Found, 68 & 74 & Nat Endowment for Arts, 74. *Bibliog:* Henry Leland Clark (auth), article, Musical Quart, fall 67; Eric Salzman (auth), article, Stereo Rev, 1/75. *Mem:* ASCAP; Century Club. *Mailing Add:* 28 Cascade Ave Winston-Salem NC 27107

SUESS, JOHN G
EDUCATOR, MUSICOLOGIST
b Chicago, Ill, Aug 4, 29. *Study:* Northwestern Univ, BS, 51, MM, 57; Univ Chicago, 51-52; Yale Univ, PhD, 63. *Teaching:* From lectr to asst prof musicol, Ohio Univ, 60-66; from asst prof to assoc prof music, Univ Wis, Milwaukee, 66-71; prof & chmn dept, Case Western Reserve Univ, 71- *Mem:* Am Musicol Soc; Int Musicol Soc; Col Music Soc; Soc Aesthet & Art Criticism; Soc Ethnomusicol. *Interests:* History of music; the Bolognese school of instrumental music in the 17th century; 20th century American music and jazz research. *Publ:* Auth, Pathways to the New Music, Ohio Rev, 65; Trio Sonata, 67 & Vitali, Giovanni B and Tomaso A, 67, MGG; translr, J W Wasielowski, Instrumental Satze vom Ende des XVI bis Ende des XVII Jahrunderts, Da Capo, 74; auth, Sonatas of Mauritio Caxxati, Ann Musicologigues, 78. *Mailing Add:* 2606 Som Center Rd Cleveland OH 44124

SUGITANI, TAKAOKI
VIOLIN
b Kobe-shi, Japan, July 31, 39. *Study:* Curtis Inst Music, dipl, 62. *Pos:* Concertmaster, Tokyo Symph Orch, 63-66; asst concertmaster, St Louis Symph Orch, 66- *Teaching:* Instr violin, Toho Inst Music, 64-66. *Awards:* Third Prize, Music Compt NHK & Mainchi-Shinbun, Tokyo, 54. *Mailing Add:* 7300 Princeton Ave St Louis MO 63130

SUITOR, M LEE
ORGAN, COMPOSER
b San Francisco, Calif, Feb 4, 42. *Study:* Univ Redlands, BA, 65, BMus, 65; Union Theol Sem, Columbia Univ, MSM, 68. *Works:* The Ancient Law Departs, Abingdon Press, 69; Here, O My Lord, 75 & Poverty, 75, Hope Publ Co; Kyrie, Standing Comn Church Music, Episcopal Church, 76; All Praise to Thee, 80 & Jesus, Joy of Man's Desiring, 80, Hope Publ Co. *Pos:* Organist & choirmaster, First Presby Church, Binghamton, NY, 69-73; St Luke's Episcopal Church, Atlanta, 73-79 & St James Episcopal Church, Milwaukee, 79-81; freelance musician, Salt Lake City, 81- *Teaching:* Lectr organ & piano, State Univ NY, Binghamton, 69-73; asst music hist, Alverno Col, 79-81. *Bibliog:* Ruth Caldwell (auth), Multimedia and Worship, Music, 2/72; Daniel E Gawthrop (auth), Salt Lake City Ecumenical Service Draws Crowd, Am Organist, 4/83. *Mem:* Am Musicol Soc; Am Guild Organist (dean, 71-73); Orgn Am Kodaly Educr; Anglican Asn Musicians. *Publ:* Auth, Techniques for Accompanying, 72 & Conducting from the Console, 82, Am Organist. *Mailing Add:* 284 M St Salt Lake City UT 84103

SULLIVAN, (ROGER) DANIEL
BASS-BARITONE
b Eureka, Ill, Feb 13, 40. *Study:* Ill Wesleyan Univ; Northwestern Univ; Boris Goldovsky Opera Inst, New York; studied with Hermanus Baer. *Roles:* Valentin in Faust, Omaha Opera Co, 70; Marcello in La Boheme, Lyr Opera Kansas City, 76; Sackett in The Postman Always Rings Twice, Opera Theatre St Louis; Gianni Schicchi in Gianni Schicci; Colline in La Boheme, 82 & Dr Bartolo in The Barber of Seville, 82, Lyr Opera Kansas City; Sulpice in The Daughter of the Regiment, Houston Grand Opera, 83. *Pos:* Bass-baritone, Omaha Opera Co, Lyr Opera Kansas City, Houston Grand Opera, New York City Opera, Opera Theater St Louis, Tulsa Opera & San Francisco Spring Opera; artist, Affil Artists Inc; formerly; regular mem, San Francisco Opera, 70- *Awards:* Martha Baird Grant Music. *Mem:* Ottumwa Arts Coun Iowa. *Mailing Add:* c/o Kazuko Hillyer Inc 250 W 57th St New York NY 10107

SULLIVAN, ROBERT PAUL
GUITAR & LUTE, EDUCATOR
Study: New England Consv Music; Harvard Summer Sch; Univ de Cervera, Spain; studied with Hibbard Perry, William Sykes, Alexander Bello, Rey de la Torre, Oscar Ghiglia, Emitio Pujol & Barry Galbraith. *Pos:* Soloist, Boston Symph Orch & Syracuse Symph; recitalist throughout New England, currently. *Teaching:* Mem fac, Univ RI, formerly; Syracuse Univ, formerly & Clark Univ, currently; mem fac music & exten div, New England Consv Music, currently. *Rep:* Cult Commun 64 Church St Somerville MA 02143. *Mailing Add:* New England Consv Music 290 Huntington Rd Boston MA 02115

SUMERLIN, MACON DEE
COMPOSER, EDUCATOR
b Roby, Tex, Oct 24, 19. *Study:* Hardin-Simmons Univ, BMus, 40; Eastman Sch Music, 40; Univ Tex, MMus, 47; NTex Univ, 71. *Works:* Romantic Symph, comn by Tex Women's Club, 48; Third Symph, Southwestern Symposium Orch, 52; Masquerade (ballet), comn by Abilene Symph Guild, 55; The Raising of Lazarus (chorus & small orch), comn by TMEA, 72; December Story: A One-Act Opera, comn by Heavenly Rest Episcopal Church, 82. *Pos:* Music ed, Chorister Mag, 46-47. *Teaching:* Asst prof theory, Hardin-Simmons Univ, 47-51; assoc prof music, McMurry Col, 52-78, chmn div fine arts, 79-82; Livermore prof, 80. *Awards:* Dr Music, Tex Guild Comp, 51. *Bibliog:* Bennett, Pendergrast & Stamey (auth), A Macon Sumerlin Work Suite, Beta Pi Sigma Press, 82. *Mem:* ASCAP; Tex Guild Comp. *Publ:* An Outline of Musical Style Analysis, Hardin-Simmons Univ Press, 48; auth, How to Play Pop Music on the Organ, Pro-Arte Publ, 65. *Mailing Add:* PO Box 5473 Abilene TX 79608

SUMMERS, WILLIAM FRANKLIN
EDUCATOR, BASS
b Norfolk, Va, Mar 4, 37. *Study:* Col William & Mary, BS, 59; Ind Univ, MM, 61; Univ Mich, DMA, 76. *Roles:* Osmin in The Abduction from the Seraglio, Arlington Opera Theater, 63; Don Magnifico in La Cenerentola, 65 & Don Alphonso in Cosi fan tutte, 66, Metropolitan Opera Studio; Mefistofele in

Mefistofele, Aspen Festival, 69; Frank in Frank, Austrian Nat TV, Vienna, 71; Sarastro in Die Zauberflöte, 71 & Sparafucile in Rigoletto, 73, Stadttheater Bern, Switz, 73. *Pos:* Bass, Metropolitan Opera Studio, 64-68; prin basso, Stadttheater Bern, Switz, 70-73; dir opera, Nat Music Camp, Interlochen, Mich, 77. *Teaching:* Asst prof voice & opera, Southeastern Louisiana Univ, 75-76; assoc prof & dir opera theater, Univ Miami, 76- *Awards:* Liederkrantz Found Award, 66; Corbett Found Grant Europe, 70. *Mem:* Nat Asn Teachers Singing (pres Fla chap, 79-81); Am Guild Musical Artists; Nat Opera Asn; Cent Opera Serv; Col Music Soc. *Mailing Add:* 8101 SW 96th St Miami FL 33156

SUMMERS, WILLIAM JOHN
EDUCATOR, ADMINISTRATOR
b Sonora, Calif, Feb 8, 45. *Study:* San Luis Rey Col, BA, 69; Calif State Univ, Hayward, MA, 73; Univ Calif, Santa Barbara, PhD, 78. *Pos:* Sr res scholar, King's Col Univ London, 81-82. *Teaching:* Lectr musicol, Univ Calif, Santa Barbara, 75-77; asst prof, Seattle Univ, 77-82, assoc prof & chmn dept fine arts, 83- *Awards:* Sinfonia Found Res Grant, 76; Am Coun Learned Soc Grant, 79; Res Scholar, Fulbright-Hays Prog, 81-82. *Mem:* Medieval Acad Am; Plainsong & Medieval Music Soc; Pi Kappa Lambda; Int Musicol Soc; Am Musicol Soc. *Interests:* Thirteenth and 14th century English music; Compagnia dei Musici di Roma, 1584-99. *Publ:* Auth, A New Source of Medieval English Polyphonic Music, Music Lett, 77; Spanish Music in California, 1769-1840 ..., Int Musicol Soc, 82; The Compagnia dei Musici di Roma, 1584-1604, Current Music, 83; Unknown ... English Polyphonic Music ... 14th Century, Res Chronicle Royal Music Asn, 83; English Fourteenth Century Polyphony, Hans Schneider, 83. *Mailing Add:* 9025 Fremont Ave N Seattle WA 98103

SUMMERVILLE, SUZANNE
MEZZO-SOPRANO, EDUCATOR
b Dallas, Tex, Mar 19, 37. *Study:* Randolph Macon Womans Col, BA, 58; Freie Univ, Berlin, DPhil, 68; studied voice with Werner Wais, Berlin. *Rec Perf:* Stabat Mater (Dvorak), Vox; 24 Songs of Edward MacDowell, Voutejas. *Pos:* Dir, Fairbanks Choral Soc, 79-; founding dir, Fairbanks Sing It Yourself Messiah, 80- & All City Children's Chorus, 83- *Teaching:* Asst prof voice, Univ Iowa, 76-79; assoc prof, Univ Alaska, 79- *Mem:* Nat Asn Teachers Singing. *Publ:* Auth, Johann Ludurj Freydt: Music Teacher to the Congregations, Morairan Music Found Bulletin, 78; Nina Grieg Edward's Favorite Interpreter, 78 & The Songs of Edward MacDowell, 79, Nat Asn Teachers Singing Bulletin; Two 18th Century Song Books in Christiansfeld, Unitas Fratrum, 83. *Mailing Add:* 1815 Carr Ave Fairbanks AK 99701

SUNDEN, RALPH EDWARD
PIANO, ORGAN
b Chicago, Ill, Sept 15, 20. *Study:* Sherwood Music Sch, BMus, 49, MMus, 51. *Works:* Thirty-Nine Organ Solos, Belwin-Mills, 67; Gospel Hymn Styling for the Modern Organist, Bks 1-4, Hal Leonard Music Publ Co, 71. *Pos:* Organist, St Paul Community Church, Homewood, Ill, 57- *Teaching:* Instr piano, organ & music theory, Sherwood Music Sch, 49-, admis dir & registrar, 70- *Mem:* Am Fedn Musicians; Am Guild Organists. *Mailing Add:* 259 Blackhawk Dr Park Forest IL 60466

SUNDINE, STEPHANIE
SOPRANO
b Ill. *Roles:* Margherita & Elena in Mefistofele, 80 & Tatyana in Eugene Onegin, 83, New York City Opera. *Pos:* Mem, New York City Opera, 80-; appearances with Grant Park Symph, Little Orch Soc, Tulsa Phil, Tri-Cities Symph, Shreveport Symph & Savannah Symph. *Awards:* Martha Baird Rockefeller Grant; Sullivan Found Grant; Nat Opera Inst Grant. *Mailing Add:* 210 W 101 St New York NY 10025

SUSA, CONRAD
COMPOSER
b Springdale, Pa, Apr 26, 35. *Study:* Carnegie-Mellon Univ, BFA; Juilliard Sch Music, MS. *Works:* Pastorale (strings), E C Schirmer, 60; Symphony in One Movement, San Diego Symph, 61; Transformations (opera, comp with Anne Sexton), E C Schirmer, 73; Black River (opera, comp with Richard Street), Minn Opera, 81; and many others publ by E C Schirmer. *Pos:* Staff pianist, Pittsburgh Symph Orch, 57-58; comp in res, Old Globe Theatre, San Diego, 59-; music dir, Asn Producing Artists, New York, 60-68 & Am Shakespeare Fest, Stratford, Conn, 69-71. *Teaching:* Comp in res, Nashville City Sch, 61-63. *Awards:* Ford Found Fel, 61-63; grants, Nat Endowment Arts, 74-81. *Mailing Add:* 433 Eureka St San Francisco CA 94114

SUTHERLAND, BRUCE
COMPOSER, PIANO
b Daytona Beach, Fla. *Study:* Univ Southern Calif, BMus, 57, MMus, 59; studied piano with Ethel Leginska & Amparo Iturbi; comp with Halsey Stevens & Ellis Kohs. *Works:* Allegro Farfara (orch), 70, Saxophone Quartet, 71, Quintet for Flute, Strings & Piano, 72 & Notturno (flute & guitar), 73, perf by Bridgeport Symph Orch. *Pos:* Soloist harpsichord, Telemann Trio, 69-70; dir music, Bach Fest Music Teachers Asn, 72-73. *Teaching:* Inst piano, Univ Tex, Austin, 71; fac mem piano, Calif State Univ, Northridge, 77- *Awards:* Grand prize winner, Int Comp Louis Moreau Gottschalk, 70; Stairway Stars Award, Music Arts Soc, 73. *Mem:* Pi Kappa Lambda; Nat Asn Am Comp & Cond; Am Music Ctr. *Mailing Add:* 2336 Pier Ave Santa Monica CA 90405

SUTHERLAND, DONALD S
EDUCATOR, ORGAN
b Kearney, NJ, May 27, 39. *Study:* Syracuse Univ, BMus, 61, MMus, 63; studied organ with Arthur Poister. *Rec Perf:* On CBS, Nat Pub Radio, BBC, London & ORF, Austria. *Pos:* Cond & organ soloist, Kennedy Ctr Fest, 5 yrs; soloist, Nat Symph, New York, formerly & Baltimore Symph, formerly; performer wkshps & recitals for regional conventions, Am Guild Organists, currently; dir music, Bradley Hills Presby Church, Bethesda, Md, currently; mem, Theatre Chamber Players of Kennedy Ctr, currently. *Teaching:* Mem fac, Syracuse Univ, formerly & Hamilton Col, formerly; mem fac organ, Peabody Consv Music, currently. *Mem:* Pi Kappa Lambda; Am Guild Organists (dean DC chap, currently). *Rep:* Murtagh/McFarlane Artists Mgt 3269 W 30th St Cleveland OH 44109. *Mailing Add:* 11413 Georgetowne Dr Potomac MD 20854

SUTHERLAND, JOAN
SOPRANO
b Sydney, Australia, Nov 7, 26. *Study:* Royal Col Music; studied with Muriel Sutherland, Clive Carey & Richard Bonynge; Aberdeen Univ, Hon Dr; Rider Col, Hon DA. *Roles:* Dido in Dido and Aeneas, Sydney, 47; Erste Dame in Die Zauberflöte, Covent Garden, 52; Semiramis in Semiramide, Lyr Opera Chicago, 71; Norma in Norma, San Francisco Opera, 72; Olympia, Antonia & Giulietta in Les Contes d'Hoffmann, 73 & Elvira in I Puritani, 76, Metropolitan Opera; Sita in Le Roi de Lahore, Vancouver Opera, 77; and many others. *Pos:* Hon life mem, Australia Opera Co, 74-; sop with major opera co in NAm, SAm, Europe & Australia. *Awards:* Mobil Quest Award, 51; Dame, Order Brit Empire & Order Australia; Sun Aria Compt Winner. *Bibliog:* Susan Heller Anderson (auth), Joan Sutherland Returns to the Met in Lucia, New York Times, 10/31/83. *Mailing Add:* c/o Colbert Artists Mgt 111 W 57th St New York NY 10019

SUTHERLAND, ROBIN (KEOLAHOU)
PIANO, COACH
b Denver, Colo, Mar 5, 51. *Study:* Univ Northern Colo, with Rita J Hutcherson, 55-69; Juilliard Sch, with Rosina Lhevinne, 69-71; San Francisco Consv Music, with Paul Hersh, BM, 75. *Pos:* Prin pianist, San Francisco Symph Orch, 73-75, 77-78 & 80-; co-dir (with Roy Malan), Telluride Chamber Players, 74- *Teaching:* Head coach piano, Masaki Studios, 76-77 & 78-80. *Awards:* First prize, Music Teachers Nat Asn, 69. *Mailing Add:* c/o San Francisco Symph Orch San Francisco CA 94102

SUTIN, ELAINE
VIOLIN, ADMINISTRATOR
b Cleveland, Ohio. *Study:* With Solomon Tishkoff, Arpad Bognar & Charles Rychlik; Cleveland Music Sch Settlement, violin with Felix Eyle; Cleveland Inst Music, violin with Joseph Knitzer, 45-46; Western Res Univ, BS, 45; Juilliard Sch Music, violin with Edouard Dethier & chamber music with Felix Salmond, MS, 48; studied quartet with Lillian Fuchs, 60-61. *Pos:* Mem, Little Orch Soc, 51-52 & Caramoor Orch, 70-75; founder, dir & first violinist, Sutton Ens, New York, 59-; mem first violin sect, Metropolitan Opera Summer Ballet Orch, 76-; prin second violinist, Symph New World, 73- Queens Symph Chamber Orch, 74-76, Artis Amor Chamber Orch, 80- & Bridgeport Symph, 82-; chamber music & freelance rec & symph performer, NY, currently. *Teaching:* Violin & chamber music, Cleveland Music Sch Settlement, 44-46, Bronx House Music Sch, 48 & 57-58 & Henry Street Settlement Music Sch, 57-58; instr private violin, 60-; artist in res, Ft Lee Hist Visitors Ctr & Bergen Community Col, currently. *Mem:* Prof Music Teachers Guild NJ; Fine Arts Coun Englewood Inc; Am Fedn Musicians; Mu Phi Epsilon. *Mailing Add:* 236 Glenwood Rd Englewood NJ 07631

SUTTLE, CLARK ETIENNE
CONDUCTOR, DOUBLE BASS
Study: Univ Mich, studied double bass with Laurence Hurst, BMus(double bass perf), MMus(cond); studied cond with Julius Rudel, Theo Alcantara, Uri Mayer, Elizabeth Green & Thomas Hilbish. *Pos:* Guest cond, St Louis Symph, Nat Symph, Grand Rapids Symph, 76 & Denver Symph; music dir, Western New York Opera Co; assoc & Exxon & Arts Endowment cond, Buffalo Phil, 79-83; assoc cond, Phoenix Symph Orch, 83- *Awards:* Bronze Medal, Int Perf Compt, Geneva, Switz; Stanley Medal, Sch Music, Univ Mich; Third Prize, Baltimore Cond Compt. *Mailing Add:* Phoenix Symph Orch 6328 N 7th St Phoenix AZ 85014

SUTTON, JULIA
EDUCATOR, SCHOLAR-WRITER
b Toronto, Ont, July 20, 28. *Study:* Cornell Univ, AB, 49; Colo Col, MA, 52; Eastman Sch Music, PhD, 62. *Pos:* Choreographer & dance dir, NY Pro Musica (five nat tours), Pa Orch Asn, Colo Col, NY Ens Early Music & Elizabethan Dancers, 67- *Teaching:* Instr music, Queens Col, City Univ New York, 63-66; asst prof musicol, George Peabody Col Teachers, 64-65; chmn musicol dept, New England Consv Music, 67-; guest lectr, Harvard Univ, Univ London, Cornell Univ, York Univ, Univ Salzburg, Univ Minn, Dartmouth Col & many others. *Bibliog:* Joan Cass (auth), Musicians Learn the Dance, Boston Globe, 67; Jean Knowlton (auth), The New York Pro Musica's Entertainment for Elizabeth, Am Recorder Soc J, 69; Jennifer Dunning (auth), They'll Gavotte All Night At Tully Hall, New York Times, 78. *Mem:* Am Musicol Soc (coun mem, 67-70); Dance Historians; Am Asn Univ Prof. *Interests:* Dance history 1400-1750; dance in relation to music; dance music; dance-inspired music. *Publ:* Ed, Thoinot Arbeau: Orchesography (1588), new ed, Dover Publ, 66; auth, Renaissance Revisited, Dance Notation Bur, 80; contrib, eight articles in New Grove Dict Music & Musicans, Macmillian, 80; ed in chief, Fabritio Caroso's Nobilta di dame, Oxford Univ Press (in prep). *Mailing Add:* New England Consv Music Boston MA 02115

SUTTON, MARY ELLEN
EDUCATOR, ORGAN

b Butler, Mo, Nov 7, 40. *Study:* Graceland Col, Lamoni, Iowa, AA, 60; Univ Kansas City, BMus, 63; Univ Mo, Kansas City, MMus, 68; Univ Kansas, DMA, 75; Int Summer Organ Acad, Haarlem, Netherlands, 78 & 82. *Works:* Admonition, White Harvest Music Publ, 74. *Teaching:* Music spec, Independence Pub Sch, Mo, 64-67; asst prof music, Mo Valley Col, Marshall, 68-73; assoc prof organ, harpsichord & theory, Kans State Univ, Manhattan, 74- *Mem:* Am Guild Organists (sub dean Topeka Chap, 78-79 & dean, 79-80); Col Music Soc (state chmn, 83-); Hymn Soc Am; Organ Hist Soc; Music Teachers Nat Asn (mem exec bd Kans, 78-81 & state secy, 79-81). *Mailing Add:* Music Dept Kans State Univ Manhattan KS 66506

SUTTON, VERN (EVERETT LAVERN)
TENOR

b Oklahoma City, Okla, Apr 8, 38. *Study:* With Ethel Rader, Roy A Schuessler & Luigi Ricci. *Rec Perf:* Letters from Composers & Jonah and the Whale, CRI; Postcard from Morocco, Desto; Serenade, Cavata. *Roles:* John in Masque of Angels, 63-64, Mr Owen in Postcard from Morocco, 71 & John Faustus in Faust Counter Faust, 71, Ctr Opera, Minneapolis; Wizard in Transformations, Minn Opera, 73. *Pos:* Lyr & buffo ten with maj opera co & orchs in Houston, Kansas City, Lake George, Minneapolis, St Paul & San Francisco; res mem, Minn Opera; dir, Opera Theatre, Univ Minn. *Mailing Add:* 2036 Seabury Ave Minneapolis MN 55406

SUZUKI, HIDETARO
CONDUCTOR, VIOLIN

b Tokyo, Japan, June 1, 37. *Study:* Toho Sch Music, dipl, 56; Curtis Inst Music, dipl, 63. *Rec Perf:* Beethoven Sonatas, 76 & H Suzuki Encore Album, 76, Toshiba-EMI; Sonatas (Franck & Ravel), Select Rec, 76. *Pos:* Concertmaster, Quebec Symph Orch, 63-78 & Indianapolis Symph Orch, 78-; dir, Suzuki & Friends, Conct Ser, 80-; soloist, recitalist & cond, Great Britain, Western Europe, Soviet Union, Japan, Hong Kong, Cent Am, US & Can. *Teaching:* Prof violin, Consv Province Quebec, 63-79; artist assoc, Jordan Col Fine Arts, 79- *Awards:* Laureat, Tchaikovsky Int Compt, 62, Queen Elisabeth Int Compt, 63 & 67 & Montreal Int Compt, 66. *Mailing Add:* 430 W 93rd St Indianapolis IN 46260

SVOBODA, RICHARD ALAN
BASSOON

b Pocatello, Idaho, Sept 24, 56. *Study:* Univ Nebr, Lincoln, BME, 78. *Pos:* Bassoon & contrabassoon, Omaha & Lincoln Symph Orchs, 77-78; prin bassoon, St Louis Phil, 78-79, Jacksonville Symphony, 79-, Symph Sch Am, La Crosse, Wis, 81- *Teaching:* Prof bassoon, Fla Jr Col, Jacksonville, 79-, Univ NFla, 82- *Mem:* Int Double Reed Soc. *Mailing Add:* 1312 Donald St Jacksonville FL 32205

SVOBODA, TOMAS
COMPOSER, EDUCATOR

b Paris, France, Dec 6, 39; US citizen. *Study:* Consv Music, Prague, Czechoslovakia, dipl(perc), 56, dipl(cond), 58, dipl(comp), 62; Univ Southern Calif, with Ingolf Dahl, MMus, 69. *Works:* Symphony No 1 (of Nature), Op 20, 57, Nine Etudes in Fugue Style (Vol I & II), 66 & 83, Symphony No 4 (Apocalyptic), Op 69, 76, Children's Treasure Box (Vol I-IV), 77-78, Overture of the Season, Op 89, 78, Symphony No 5 (in Unison), Op 92, 78 & Passacaglia & Fugue, Op 87 for Violin, Violoncello & Piano, 78, Thomas C Stangland Co. *Teaching:* Prof music, Portland State Univ, 71- *Awards:* Helen S Anstead Award, Univ Southern Calif, 67; ASCAP Standard Awards, 76-; Branford Price Millar Award, Portland State Univ, 83. *Bibliog:* Article in Piano Quart, summer 81. *Mem:* ASCAP; Nat Asn Comp, USA; Am Fedn Musicians. *Mailing Add:* c/o Thomas C Stangland Co PO Box 19263 Portland OR 97219

SWACK, IRWIN
COMPOSER, EDUCATOR

b West Salem, Ohio. *Study:* Cleveland Inst Music, BM; Northwestern Univ, MM; Columbia Univ, PhD. *Works:* Sonata for Piano, perf by Laurence Smith, 58; Fantaisie Concertante (string orch), Carl Fischer, 68; Theme & Variations (six woodwinds), 75; Dance Episodes (seven instrm), 76 & Psalm 8 for Tenor, Trumpet & String Orch, 82, Galaxy Music Corp; Profiles (clarinet, violin & cello), 83 & String Quartet No 3, 83, Orion Master Rec. *Pos:* Violin & viola, Louisville Symph. *Teaching:* Instr music theory & comp, Knoxville Col, Jacksonville State Col & La Polytechnic Inst. *Awards:* Ford Found Award for Educators, 75; ASCAP Standard Award, 78-; Meet the Composer Award, NY State Coun Arts, 78-82. *Mem:* Nat Soc Am Comp; Long Island Comp Asn (bd dir, 73); Am Music Ctr; ASCAP; Bohemian Club. *Publ:* Auth, New Music—Progression or Regression, Music J, 70. *Mailing Add:* 2924 Len Dr Bellmore NY 11710

SWAFFORD, JAN JOHNSON
COMPOSER, CONDUCTOR

b Chattanooga, Tenn, Sept 10, 46. *Study:* Harvard Col, with Earl Kim, BA, 68; Berkshire Music Ctr, with Betsy Jolas, 77; Yale Sch Music, with Jacob Druckman & David Mott, MM, MMA, 77, DMA, 82. *Works:* Peal, Yale Univ & Int Gaudeamus Fest, Holland, 77 & 79; Passage, St Louis Symph & Gaudeamus, Belgium, 78 & 80; Magus, Gerhard Pawlica & John Sessions, 78 & 82; Out of the Silence, Musical Elements & others, 78 & 82; After Spring Rain, perf & comn by Chattanooga Symph, Indianapolis Symph & Harrisburg Symph, 82, 83 & 84; Labyrinths, John & Giovina Sessions, 82; Shore Lines, Melinda Spratlan & Akal dev Khalsa, 83. *Awards:* Grants, Rockefeller Found, 82 & Mass Arts Coun, 83; Ind State Univ Comp Prize, 83. *Mem:* Am Comp Alliance; Am Music Ctr. *Mailing Add:* RFD 2 W Pelham Rd Amherst MA 01002

SWALIN, BENJAMIN FRANKLIN
CONDUCTOR, EDUCATOR

b Minneapolis, Minn, Mar 30, 01. *Study:* Columbia Univ, BS & MA, 30; Univ Vienna, PhD, 32; Inst Musical Art, Juilliard Sch Music, with Franz Kneisel & Leopold Auer; Univ NC, DFA, 71; Duke Univ, DHL, 79. *Works:* Maxaben for Orchestra, NC Symph, 59; Sunday in Town, comn by Edward B Benjamin; Improvisation for Violin, perf by comp. *Pos:* Mem, Minneapolis Symph, 19; artistic dir & cond, NC Symph, Chapel Hill, 37-72, cond emer, 72- *Teaching:* Prof music theory & violin, DePauw Univ, 33-35; assoc prof music, Univ NC, Chapel Hill, 35-45. *Awards:* NC Award Achievement in Fine Arts, 66; Morrison Award Achievement Perf Arts, 68. *Mem:* Am Musicol Soc; MacDowell Colony. *Publ:* Auth, The Violin Concerto: A Study in German Romanticism, Univ NC Press, 41 & Da Capo Press, 72; articles in Music Teachers Nat Asn & Music Educr Nat Conf. *Mailing Add:* PO Box 448 Carrboro NC 27510

SWALIN, MAXINE MCMAHON
PIANO, LECTURER

b Waukee, Iowa, May 7, 03. *Study:* Juilliard Sch Music, 28; Univ Iowa, BA, 32; Radcliffe Col, MA, 36; Duke Univ, DHL, 79. *Rec Perf:* Painted Music, 78- *Pos:* Admin asst & mem, NC Symph, 37-72; coordr, Young Artists Auditions & Childrens Concerts. *Teaching:* Instr music theory, Hartt Sch Music, 28-30. *Mem:* Am Musicol Soc; Am Asn Univ Women. *Interests:* History of North Carolina Symphony. *Mailing Add:* PO Box 448 Carrboro NC 27510

SWALLOW, JOHN
TROMBONE, EDUCATOR

Study: Juilliard Sch Music; Columbia Univ; studied trombone with Neal DiBiase, Davis Shuman & Donald Reinhardt. *Pos:* Mem, Chicago Symph, formerly, New York City Opera Orch, formerly, Chicago Lyr Opera Orch, formerly, Utah Symph, formerly, New York City Ballet Orch, currently, New York Brass Quintet, currently & Contemp Chamber Ens, currently. *Teaching:* Mem fac, First Int Trombone Wkshp, Montreux, Switz, 74 & Hartt Col Music, formerly; lectr & performer, Int Trombone Wkshp, Nashville, formerly; mem fac trombone, Manhattan Sch Music, 78-; mem fac trombone & euphonium, New England Consv Music, currently; adj assoc prof trombone, Yale Univ, currently. *Mailing Add:* New England Consv Music 290 Huntington Rd Boston MA 02115

SWAN, HOWARD SHELTON
EDUCATOR, MUSIC DIRECTOR

b Denver, Colo, Mar 29, 06. *Study:* Pomona Col, BA, 28; Claremont Col, MA, 40; studied with John F Williamson, Robert Shaw & William J Finn; Pomona Col, Hon Dr Music, 59; Westminster Choir Col, Hon Dr Humanities, 77. *Rec Perf:* Alto Rhapsody (Johannes Brahms) & Schicksalied (Johannes Brahms), 61. *Pos:* Dir music, Pasadena Presby Church, Calif, 40-60. *Teaching:* Prof & dir choral music, Occidental Col, 34-71; prof & coordr music grad studies, Calif State Univ, Fullerton, 71-77; dir choral music, Univ Calif, Irvine, 78- *Mem:* Hon life mem, Am Choral Dir Asn; Music Educ Nat Conf. *Publ:* Auth, Music in the Southwest, H E Huntington Libr, 50; Pioneer Western Playbills #8, Book Club Calif, 51; coauth, Choral Music—A Symposium, Appleton-Century, 73. *Mailing Add:* 19191 Harvard Ave #130F Irvine CA 92715

SWANN, FREDERICK LEWIS
ORGAN, CONDUCTOR & MUSIC DIRECTOR

b Lewisburg, WVa, July 30, 31. *Study:* Sch Music, Northwestern Univ, BM, 52; Sch Sacred Music, Union Theol Sem, SMM, 54. *Rec Perf:* Frederick Swann at the National Shrine, Westminster, 69; Music from Riverside, Vol I-IV, Vista, 78; Frederick Swann Plays Franck, 80, Easter, 81 & Festival of Lessons & Carols, 82, Gothic. *Pos:* Dir music & organist, Riverside Church, New York, 57-82 & Crystal Cathedral, Garden Grove, Calif, 83-; concert soloist throughout US, Canada & Europe, 60- *Teaching:* Prof organ & organ lit, Manhattan Sch Music, 72-82. *Awards:* French Lit Perf Award, Acad Arts & Lett & French Nat Govt, 72; Am Lit Perf Award, Am Guild Organists, 72. *Mem:* Am Guild Organists; Am Fedn Musicians; Nat Choral Cond Guild. *Rep:* Murtagh/McFarlane Artists Mgt 3269 W 30th St Cleveland OH 44109. *Mailing Add:* 12141 Lewis St Garden Grove CA 92641

SWANN, JEFFREY
PIANO, COMPOSER

b Williams, Ariz, Nov 24, 51. *Study:* Southern Methodist Univ, with Alexander Uninsky & David Ahlstrom; Aspen Music Fest, with Darius Milhaud; Juilliard Sch, with Beveridge Webster & Hall Overton, BMus, MMus, with Adele Marcus, DMA. *Works:* Prometheus (text after Aeschelus); Symphony No 1; Sinfonia Concertante, perf by Dallas Symph, 67; Arches (violin & cello). *Rec Perf:* On Ars Polona, DG, RCA-Italy, Ricordi & Cetra. *Pos:* Soloist with many Europ & US orchs. *Awards:* First Prize, Comp Compt, Aspen Music Fest, 66; Second Prize & Gold Medal, Queen Elisabeth Compt, Belgium; First Prize, Dino Ciani Int Piano Compt, La Scala, Milan. *Rep:* Jacques Leiser Mgt Dorchester Towers 155 W 68th St New York NY 10023. *Mailing Add:* 161 W 75th New York NY 10023

SWANSON, JEAN PHYLLIS
EDUCATOR, ORGAN

b Hallock, Minn, Mar 10, 19. *Study:* Macalester Col, BA, 41; Northwestern Univ, MM, 46; Univ Minn, PhD, 69. *Pos:* Organist & choirmaster, Christ Church, Raleigh, NC, 55-60; organist & choir dir, Gloria Dei Lutheran Church, Duluth, Minn, 72-80. *Teaching:* Asst prof organ, theory & music educ, Meredith Col, 54-63; instr music educ, Univ Minn, Minneapolis, 64-69; assoc prof music hist & music educ, Univ Minn, Duluth, 69- *Awards:*

Danforth Teacher, Danforth Found, 56-57. *Mem:* Am Guild Organists (state chmn, 76-78); Am Musicol Soc; Col Music Soc; Int Coun Traditional Music; Music Educr Nat Conf. *Publ:* Auth, John Arnold's Fine Organ, Am Organist, 79; The Felgemaker Organ at Sacred Heart Church, Tracker, 80. *Mailing Add:* 100 Elizabeth 312 Duluth MN 55803

SWANSON, PHILIP JOHN
EDUCATOR, FLUTE
b Moline, Ill, Nov 12, 39. *Study:* Eastman Sch Music, Univ Rochester, BM, 62, MM, 64, performer's cert(flute), 64. *Pos:* Dir admis & alumni relations, Eastman Sch Music, 75-78. *Teaching:* Assoc prof music, Sch Music, Univ Ariz, 69-75, asst dean, Col Fine Arts, 78-81; dir & prof music, Sch Music, Univ Redlands, 81- *Mem:* Nat Flute Asn. *Mailing Add:* Sch Music Univ Redlands Redlands CA 92373

SWEDBERG, ROBERT MITCHELL
ADMINISTRATOR, BASS
b Glendale, Calif, Feb 7, 50. *Study:* Calif State Univ, Northridge, BA, BM, 75; Merola Prog, San Francisco Opera, with Wesley Balk, 82. *Roles:* Second prisoner in Fidelio, Los Angeles Phil, 76; Morales in Carmen, 78 & Figaro in The Marriage of Figaro, 79, Seattle Opera; Judge in Trial by Jury, 80 & Sparafucile in Rigoletto, 81, Anchorage Opera Co. *Pos:* Spec educ proj dir, prod stage mgr & stage dir, Anchorage Opera, 78-82; guest dir stage, Anchorage Opera Co, 79-82 & Seattle Opera, 82; mgr & artistic dir, NC Opera, 82- *Awards:* Bank Am Award, Young Musicians, 70; Metropolitan Opera Award, Alexandra Saunderson, 75; San Francisco Opera Award, Merola Opera, 75 & 82. *Mem:* Am Guild Musical Artists; Phi Mu Alpha Sinfonia. *Mailing Add:* 3715 Glenville Charlotte NC 28215

SWEELEY, MICHAEL MARLIN
ADMINISTRATOR
b Twin Falls, Idaho, Aug 19, 24. *Study:* Juilliard Sch Music, BS, 49, MS, 50; Univ Calif, Berkeley; Univ Southern Calif. *Pos:* Pub relations dir, S Hurok, New York, 50-69; exec dir, Caramoor Ctr Music & Arts, 56-68, pres, 68- *Mailing Add:* Box R Katonah NY 10536

SWENSEN, JOSEPH ANTON
VIOLIN
b New York, NY, Aug 4, 60. *Study:* Juilliard Sch Music, studied piano with Thomas Schumacher, 67-68 & Christopher Sager, 68-69 & violin with Dorothy DeLay, 70-82. *Rec Perf:* Solo Violin Sonata (Bartok), 83, Chaconne in D Minor (Bach), 83, The Erlking (Ernst & Schubert), 83, & Etude No 6 The Last Rose of Summer (Ernst), 83, Musical Heritage & Music Masters Rec. *Pos:* Conct violinist, 82- *Teaching:* Master classes, Eastman Sch, 82, Carnegie-Mellon Univ, 83 & Aspen Music Fest, 80-83. *Awards:* Winner, Juilliard Sch Compt, 76 & Aspen Fest Compt, 77; Edgar Leventritt Found Sponsorship, 78-82; Avery Fisher Career Grant Award, 82. *Mailing Add:* c/o ICM Artists 40 W 57th St New York NY 10019

SWENSON, COURTLAND SEVANDER
EDUCATOR, MUSIC DIRECTOR
b Akron, Iowa, July 2, 36. *Study:* Univ SDak, BFA, 48, MMus, 62; Univ Ill, 68-69; Hochschule Music, Germany, 76. *Pos:* Musical dir, Black Hills Playhouse, Custer Park, SDak, 63-78; prin perc, Sioux City Symph, Iowa, 64-71; prin timpanist, Sioux Falls Symph, SDak, 73-76. *Teaching:* Music, Sibley Pub Sch, Iowa, 58-60; mem fac, Univ SDak, 62-, prof perc, 73-; instr & chmn fine arts, Ramey AFB, PR, 71-72. *Mem:* Percussive Arts Soc; Nat Asn Rudimental Drummers. *Mailing Add:* 334 N Plum Vermillion SD 57069

SWENSON, EDWARD E
EDUCATOR, TENOR
b East Chicago, Ind, Dec 11, 40. *Study:* Oberlin Consv Music, BM, 63; Akademie Mozarteum, Salzburg; MM, 65, Univ Ky, MA, 66; Cornell Univ, PhD, 74. *Teaching:* Assoc prof music, Ithaca Col, 70- *Awards:* Lilli Lehmann Medallion, Int Stiftung Mozarteum, 65; Fulbright Grant, 68. *Mem:* Am Musical Instrm Soc; Col Music Soc; Piano Technicians' Guild. *Interests:* History and development of the Viennese fortepiano. *Publ:* Auth, Prima la Musica e poi le Parole—An 18th Century Satire, In: Analecta Musicologica, 70; Ottavio Catalani, In: Die Musik in Geschichte und Gegenwart, Bärenreiter, 72. *Mailing Add:* 11 Congress St PO Box 634 Trumansburg NY 14886

SWIFT, JOHN DAVID
COMPOSER, CLARINET
b Seattle, Wash, Oct 31, 48. *Study:* Studied clarinet with Gino Cioffi, 70-75; Sch Music, Boston Univ, BMus, 75. *Works:* Duo No 4 (piano), 82 & Duo No 5 (piano), 82, perf by John Swift & Rosemary Mackown. *Pos:* Second clarinet, Boston Summer Opera, 74; prin clarinet, Boston Fest Orch, 75, Seattle Chamber Singers Orch, 76-77 & Thalia Symph, Seattle, 76-77. *Teaching:* Private clarinet, Seattle & Boston, 76- *Mem:* Int Clarinet Soc; Am Music Ctr. *Interests:* Irish folk music; Celtic culture. *Publ:* Auth, Italian Opera, 77 & Musical Composition in Seattle, 77, Seattle Opera Mag; Musical Comp in Boston, Boston Today Mag, 78; The Double Lip Clarinet Embouchure, Instrumentalist, 79; Can A Composer Survive in Cincinnati?, Cincinnati Mag, 80. *Mailing Add:* 95 Prescott St #35 Cambridge MA 02138

SWIFT, RICHARD
COMPOSER, CRITIC-WRITER
b Middlepoint, Ohio, Sept 24, 27. *Study:* Univ Chicago, MA, 56. *Works:* A Coronal, Louisville Orch, 56; Sonata (solo violin), Orion Rec, 57; Concerto (piano & chamber ensemble), Univ Calif Press, 61; Quartet III, Lenox Quartet, 64; Summer Notes, CRI, 65; Quartet IV, Presser, 73; Great Praises, CRI, 77. *Teaching:* Prof music, Univ Calif, Davis, 56-; vis prof comp & analysis, Princeton Univ, 78. *Awards:* Comp String Quartet Award, 74; fel, Nat Endowment for Arts, 76 & Am Inst Acad Arts & Letters, 78. *Bibliog:* Thomas Stauffer (auth), Richard Swift's Summer Notes, Perspectives of New Music, 77. *Mem:* Am Music Ctr. *Interests:* Music theory, analysis & criticism. *Publ:* Auth, Igov Stravinsky, Dict Contemporary Musicians, Vinton, 74; Some Aspects of Aggregate Composition, Perspectives of New Music, 77; 1/XII/ 99: Tonal relations in Verklärte Nacht, 77 & Mahler's Ninth, Cooke's Tenth, 78, 19th Cent Music; Music Theory Spectrum, J Musicol, 82. *Mailing Add:* 568 S Campus Way Davis CA 95616

SWIFT, ROBERT FREDERIC
EDUCATOR, ADMINISTRATOR
b Ilion, NY, July 7, 40. *Study:* Hartwick Col, BS, 62; Eastman Sch Music, MA, 68, PhD, 70. *Works:* Various choral music selections & instrumental works, Kendor Music, Shawnee Press & Hinshaw Music, 60- *Teaching:* Music, West Winfield Cent Sch, New York, 62-67; prof music educ, Eastman Sch Music, 71-76 & Memphis State Univ, 76-79; prof music & adminr, Plymouth State Col, 79-; proj alliance humanities, Univ Syst NH, 81-82. *Awards:* Teacher of Yr, Memphis State Univ, 78-79. *Mem:* Music Educr Nat Conf; Am Choral Dir Asn; Nat Asn Teachers Singing; Canadian Music Fest Adjudicators Asn; Phi Mu Alpha Sinfonia. *Mailing Add:* PO Box 125 Plymouth NH 03264

SWING, PETER GRAM
EDUCATOR, CONDUCTOR & MUSIC DIRECTOR
b New York, NY, July 15, 22. *Study:* Berkshire Music Ctr, 46; Harvard Col, AB, 48; Longy Sch Music, 48-49; Harvard Univ, AM(music), 51; Institut Musiekwetenschap, Univ Utrecht, 51-52; Univ Chicago, PhD(musicol), 69. *Rec Perf:* P D Q Bach, Liebeslieder Polkas for Mixed Chorus and Piano Five Hands, Vanguard, 80. *Teaching:* Music & assoc choirmaster, Consv Music, Rollins Col, 52-53; instr humanities & dir univ glee club, Univ Chicago, 53-55; asst prof music, Swarthmore Col, 55-59, chmn dept music, 58-74, assoc prof, 59-69, prof, 69-; dir, Swarthmore Col Chorus, 55-; mem fac, Berkshire Music Ctr, 61- *Awards:* Fulbright Fels, Netherlands, 51-52 & Belgium, 70-71. *Mem:* Am Musicol Soc; Col Music Soc; Renaissance Soc; Vereniging Nederlandse Muziekgeschiedenis; Am Asn Univ Prof. *Interests:* Early 16th century polyphonic sacred music. *Publ:* Auth, Gascongne, In: New Grove Dict of Music & Musicians, 80. *Mailing Add:* 614 Hillborn Ave Swarthmore PA 19081

SWINT, LOIS ROBERTS
VIOLIN
b Wahoo, Nebr, Mar 14, 31. *Study:* Univ NMex, with Kurt Frederick, 48-50; studied with Edward Seferian, 65-68. *Pos:* Asst concertmaster, Albuquerque Symph, 46-51; studio musician, Capitol Rec, Hollywood, 61-62 & 69-70; prin second violin, Fla Gulf Coast Symph, 73-75; second violinist, Utah Symph, 78- *Mailing Add:* Utah Symph Symph Hall 123 W South Temple Salt Lake City UT 84101

SWISHER, GLORIA WILSON
COMPOSER, EDUCATOR
b Seattle, Wash, Mar 12, 35. *Study:* Univ Wash, BA, 56; Mills Col, MA, 58; Eastman Sch Music, PhD, 60. *Works:* Concerto (clarinet & orch), perf by Eastman-Rochester Orch, 60; God Is Gone Up With A Merry Noise, Carl Fischer, 61; Two Faces of Love, Michael Kysar Publ, 79. *Teaching:* Instr, Wash State Univ, 60-61; lectr, Pac Lutheran Univ, 69-70; instr, Shoreline Community Col, 69-73, prof, 73- *Awards:* Fel, Woodrow Wilson Found, 56-57; choir cont winner, Capital Univ, 61; cont winner, Thalia Orch, 82. *Mem:* Ladies Musical Club; charter mem, Am Women Comp Inc; charter mem, Int League Women Comp. *Mailing Add:* 7228 6th NW Seattle WA 98117

SYDEMAN, WILLIAM J
COMPOSER
b New York, NY, May 8, 28. *Study:* Mannes Col Music, BS(comp), 56; Univ Hartford, MM, 59. *Works:* Woodwind Quintet No II, McGinnis & Marx, 64; Orchestral Abstractions, C F Peters, 64; Lament of Elektra, E C Schirmer, 64; Study for Orch No III, 65 & In Memoriam—John F Kennedy, 66, G Schirmer; Concerto for 4 Hand Piano, E C Schirmer, 67; Maledictian, Seesaw Publ, 69. *Teaching:* Comp fac, Mannes Col Music, 59-69. *Awards:* Nat Inst Arts & Lett, 62; Boston Symph Merit Award, 66; Koussevitsky Found Award, 68. *Bibliog:* Article, Time Mag, 62 & New York Times, 11/2/65. *Mailing Add:* 3911 Bannister Rd Fair Oaks CA 95628

SYLVAN, SANFORD (MEAD)
BARITONE
b New York, NY, Dec 19, 53. *Study:* Manhattan Sch Music, BM, 76; Berkshire Music Ctr, 74-77; studied with William Toole, Phyllis Curtin & Mary Davenport. *Roles:* Orlando in Orlando, Am Repty Theatre, 81-82. *Pos:* Soloist, Handel & Haydn Soc, Boston, 80-, Marlboro Music Fest, Vt, 80- & Alea III, Boston, 80- *Awards:* Fels, Berkshire Music Ctr, 75-77; Third Prize, Int Compt Am Music, Kennedy Ctr, Rockefeller Found, 79; grant, Nat Endowment Arts, 81-82. *Mailing Add:* c/o Aaron & Gordon Conct Mgt 25 Huntington Ave Boston MA 02116

SYMONETTE, LYS BERT
WRITER, COACH
b Mainz, Ger, Dec 21, 18; US citizen. *Study:* Curtis Inst Music. *Rec Perf:* Der Jasager (Kurt Weill), MGM, 58; Silverlake (Kurt Weill), Nonesuch, 81. *Pos:*

Musical asst, Broadway Theatre, 45-50 & accmp & musical adv, 50-81; musical exec, Kurt Weill Found Music, 68- *Teaching:* Vocal coach, Curtis Inst Music, 75- *Publ:* Transl, English into German & German into English of Weill's Lindberghflug, Mahagonny, Silverlake, Huckleberry Finn, Street Scene & Lost in the Stars, Univ Ed, 70-80; transl, Felsenstein's Tales of Hoffmann, Weinberger, 75. *Mailing Add:* c/o Kurt Weill Found 142 West End Ave New York NY 10023

SYMONETTE, RANDOLPH
BARITONE
b Mathew Twon, Inagua, Bahamas; US citizen. *Study:* New Sch Social Res; Nat Orch Asn. *Rec Perf:* The Tales of Hoffmann, Deutsche Grammophon; Schubert-Brahms Songs & Americana, Colloseum; Street Scene (Weill), Columbia. *Roles:* Wotan in Der Ring des Nibelungen, Hagen in Goetterdaemmerung, Orest in Elektra, Jochanaan in Salome & Michele in Il Tabarro, in all maj Europ opera houses incl Metropolitan Opera, 51-68. *Pos:* Heroic bar, New York City Opera, Metropolitan Opera, Deutsche Oper am Rhein, State Operas of Vienna & Stuttgart. *Teaching:* Assoc prof voice, Fla State Univ, 69-79. *Mailing Add:* 160 W 73rd St New York NY 10023

SYVERUD, STEPHEN LUTHER
EDUCATOR, COMPOSER
b Prince Albert, Sask, Mar 3, 38. *Study:* San Francisco State Univ, with Roger Nixon, Alexander Post & Wayne Peterson, BA, 63, MA, 65; Univ Iowa, with Richard Hervig & Robert Shallenberg, PhD, 71. *Works:* Four Pieces (clarinet & piano), Sequence (string quartet), Fields of Ambrosia (alto sax & tape), Scenes II (violin, paino & vibraphone), Vectors (perc & tape), Reaction (clarinet & reverberators) & Screaming Monkeys (tape), Seesaw Music & Am Comp Alliance. *Teaching:* Mem fac, Jackson State Col, 68-70 & Grinnell Col, 70-71; assoc prof comp & theory, Northwestern Univ, 71-, dir, Electronic Music Studios, 71- *Awards:* Clapp Award Comp, Univ Iowa, 68. *Mem:* Found mem, Artistic Bd Chicago Soc Comp; Am Comp Alliance; BMI; Am Asn Univ Prof; Pi Kappa Lambda. *Publ:* Auth, Electric Synthesizers—A Survey, Instrumentalist, 76 & In: Breaking the Sound Barrier, E P Dutton. *Mailing Add:* 2717 Ewing Ave Evanston IL 60201

SZASZ, TIBOR
PIANO, TEACHER-COACH
b Cluj-Kolozsvar, Romania, June 9, 48; US citizen. *Study:* New England Consv Music, artist dipl, 71, MMus, 73; Univ Mich, Ann Arbor, DMA(piano perf), 83. *Works:* Invocation (piano), perf by comp, 83. *Rec Perf:* Tibor Szasz in Recital: Piano Music of Liszt, United Sound, Inc, 77; Tibor Szazs at the Boesendorfer, Sonic Arts Corp, 81. *Pos:* Conct pianist. *Teaching:* Instr piano, Dana Sch Music, 71-77 & New England Consv, 73-77; teaching asst, Univ Mich, Ann Arbor, 77-83. *Awards:* First Prize, Univ Md Int Piano Compt, 74; NY Young Artists in Recital Piano Compt, 76 & East & West Int Compt, 77. *Mem:* Pi Kappa Lambda; Am Liszt Soc. *Rep:* Raymond Donnell 31 Jane St Apt 6G New York NY 10014. *Mailing Add:* 1800 Longshore Dr Ann Arbor MI 48105

SZERYNG, HENRYK
VIOLIN
b Zelazowa Wola, Poland, Sept 22, 18; Mex citizen. *Study:* Sorbonne; Univ Paris; studied with Carl Flesch, Gabriel Bouillon & Nadia Boulanger. *Works:* Works for piano, violin & chamber music. *Rec Perf:* Violin concertos by Mozart, Paganini, Prokofiev, Sibelius, Vivaldi, Bartok, Beethoven, Berg & Wieniawski on RCA, Philips, CBS & Mercury. *Pos:* Concert violinist, worldwide, 33-; Mexican Cult Ambassador, 53-; special music adv, Mexican Permanent Delegation, UNESCO, Paris. *Teaching:* Dir string dept, Nat Univ, Mexico City; teaching master class, St Louis Consv, 83. *Awards:* Grammy; Grand Prix du Disque, 55, 57, 60, 61, 67-69; Gran Premio Nac Mex, 79. *Publ:* Several publications on aspects of violin technique & interpretation. *Mailing Add:* c/o Harold Shaw Concerts 1995 Broadway New York NY 10023

SZKODZINSKI, LOUISE
EDUCATOR, PIANO
b Ciero, Ill, Aug 11, 21. *Study:* Mundelein Col, BMusEd, 43; Chicago Musical Col, MMus, 47; Ind Univ, DMus, 76. *Teaching:* Prof piano, theory & music hist, Clarke Col, Iowa, 50-57 & Mundelein Col, 57- *Mem:* Music Teachers Nat Asn; Ill State Music Asn; Chicago Area Music Teachers Asn; Suzuki Asn Am. *Mailing Add:* 6363 Sheridan Rd Chicago IL 60660

T

TACACS, PETER
PIANO
Study: Northwestern Univ, BM, 68; Univ Ill, MM, 69; Peabody Consv; studied with Guy Duckworth, Howard Karp & Leon Fleisher. *Pos:* Numerous solo recitals and appearances with major orchs throughout US; featured recitalist, Music Teachers Nat Asn Nat Conv, 78; guest recitalist, Milwaukee & Baltimore Chamber Music Soc & Theatre Chamber Players Kennedy Ctr; participant, Monadnock Music Fest, 79- *Teaching:* Fac mem keyboard, ECarolina Univ, 72-76; assoc prof pianoforte, Oberlin Col, 76- *Awards:* First Prize, Univ Md, Int Piano Compt, 73; C D Jackson Master Award, Berkshire Music Ctr, 76; RI Int Master Pianist Compt, 74. *Mailing Add:* Music Dept Oberlin Col Oberlin OH 44074

TAFFS, ANTHONY J
COMPOSER, EDUCATOR
b London, England, Jan 15, 16; US citizen. *Study:* Col City New York, BA, 39; Teachers Col, Columbia Univ, MA, 42; Eastman Sch Music, 45. *Works:* Oh Now Be Joyful All (SATB), 51 & Lullaby to the Infant Jesus (SATB), 53, Theodore Presser; String Quartet No 1, perf by Kalamazoo String Quartet, 60; The Summons (dance opera), perf at San Fernando State Col, Calif, 64; Piano Trio, comn by Aeolian Trio of DePauw Univ, 67; Beatitudes (chorus), perf at Wheaton Fine Arts Fest, 68; Oh Lord Thou Art Very Great (SATB), Golden Music Co, 70. *Teaching:* Instr music, Martin Col, 46-49; prof, Albion Col, 49-81, emer prof, 81- *Mem:* Phi Mu Alpha Sinfonia; Pi Kappa Lambda. *Mailing Add:* 409 Brockway Pl Albion MI 49224

TAFOYA, CAROLE SMITH
EDUCATOR, PIANO
Study: Northwestern Univ, BM, MM; studied piano with Gui Mombaerts & Bernhard Weiser & piano pedagogy with Guy Duckworth. *Pos:* Keyboard performer, St Louis Symph Orch, formerly & Rarely Performed Music ser, formerly. *Teaching:* Mem fac, Northwestern Univ, formerly & Normandale Jr Col, formerly; mem fac piano & piano pedagogy & piano curric coordr, St Louis Consv Music, currently; piano curric coordr, Sch for Arts, currently. *Mem:* Mo Music Teachers Asn; Sigma Alpha Iota. *Mailing Add:* St Louis Consv Music 560 Trinity Ave St Louis MO 63130

TAILLON, JOSCELYNE JEANNE
MEZZO-SOPRANO
b Doudeville, France, May 19, 41. *Study:* Nat Consv, Grenoble, with Suzanne Balguerie & Germaine Lubin. *Rec Perf:* On EMI. *Roles:* Nourice in Ariane et Barbe Bleue, Bordeaux Fest, 68; Genevieve in Pelleas et Melisande; Taven in Mireille; Marie Louise in Hary Janos; Suzuki in Madama Butterfly; Ulrica in Un Ballo in maschera; Dame Quickly in Falstaff. *Pos:* Mem, Opera Paris, currently; singer with maj opera co in Europe & US. *Awards:* First Prize, Nat Consv Voix d'or, 56; Prix Caruso. *Mailing Add:* c/o David Schiffman 58 W 72nd St New York NY 10023

TAIT, MALCOLM JOHN
EDUCATOR, ADMINISTRATOR
b Christchurch, NZ, Feb 17, 33. *Study:* Univ NZ, MA, 56; Royal Acad Music, London, LRAM, 58; Columbia Univ, New York, EdD, 63. *Teaching:* Head music dept, Chipping Norton Grammar Sch, Oxford, England, 59-61 & Waikato Univ & Teachers Col, NZ, 65-69; chmn music educ, Univ Hawaii, Honolulu, 71-77; dir music educ & Kulas prof music, Case Western Reserve Univ, Cleveland, 78- *Awards:* Scholar, NZ Govt, 57-59; Harkness Fel Commonwealth Fund, New York, 61-63; Queen Elizabeth II Arts Coun Award, NZ Govt, 65-67. *Mem:* Int Soc Music Educ; Music Educr Nat Conf; Soc Res Music Educ. *Interests:* Music and aesthetic education; teaching styles; diagnosis and remediation; learning modes in music. *Publ:* Auth, Music Education in New Zealand, Queen Elizabeth II Arts Coun, 69; Comprehensive Musicianship Through Choral Performance, Vol I, 73, Vol II, 75, Addison-Wesley; contribr, Documentary Report of the Ann Arbor Symposium, Music Educr Nat Conf, Washington, 81. *Mailing Add:* 3046 Woodbury Rd Shaker Heights OH 44120

TAJO, ITALO
BASS-BARITONE, STAGE DIRECTOR
b Pinerolo, Italy, Apr 25, 15. *Study:* Voice with Nilde Bertozzi. *Rec Perf:* For HMV, RCA, Telefunken, Cetra-Soria, Decca & EMI. *Roles:* Fafner in Das Rheingold, Teatro Regio, Turin, 35; Mephistopheles in Faust; Figaro in Le Nozze di Figaro; Don Giovanni & Leporello in Don Giovanni; Dott Bartolo & Don Basilio in Il Barbiere di Siviglia; Philip II in Don Carlos; Boris in Boris Godunov; and many others. *Pos:* Stage dir, 54-; dir, Int Opera Fest, Barga, Italy, 70-; performer, Metropolitan Opera, 83. *Teaching:* J Ralph Corbett Distinguished Prof Opera, Col Consv Music, Univ Cincinnati, currently. *Mem:* Nat Opera Asn; Col Music Soc; McDowell Soc. *Mailing Add:* 5541 Penway Ct Cincinnati OH 45239

TAKAHASHI, YORIKO
PIANO, EDUCATOR
b Kanazawa, Japan, June 27, 37. *Study:* Tokyo Univ Arts, BA, 61; Univ Calif, Los Angeles, 64-65; Juilliard Sch Music, dipl(piano), 64; Akad Musik & Darstellende Kunst, Vienna, 66; studied piano with Aiko Iguchi, Leonid Kochanski, Rosina Lhevinne, Aube Tserko & Bruno Seidlhofer. *Rec Perf:* Sonatas No 2 & 3 (MacDowell), Orion. *Pos:* Performer concerts throughout Japan, US & Europe; off accmp, NHK Broadcasting, Tokyo; appearances with Univ Calif Symph Orch, Los Angeles & Eugene Symph, Ore; solo recitals, Ore Educ TV & RIAS Broadcasting, Italy. *Teaching:* Mem fac, Univ Ore, formerly; Dartmouth Col, formerly & New England Consv Music Exten Div, currently; lect-demonstrations & masterclasses, Toho Consv, Kunitachi Music Univ, Osaka Univ Arts, Piano Teachers Nat Asn & others. *Awards:* Nat Compt Winner, Tokyo, 54; Scholarship, Japan Soc, NY, 64; Casella Int Pianoforte Compt Winner, Italy, 66. *Publ:* Contribr to Fujin-no Tomo (Women's Companion) & Asahi Newspaper, Tokyo. *Mailing Add:* 245 Waban Ave Waban MA 02168

TAKEDA, YOSHIMI
CONDUCTOR & MUSIC DIRECTOR
b Yokohama, Japan, Feb 3, 33. *Study:* Tokyo Univ Arts, grad. *Pos:* Music dir & cond, NMex Symph Orch, currently & Kalamazoo Symph Orch, currently; assoc cond Honolulu Symph, formerly; guest cond, Chicago Symph, Cleveland Orch, Detroit Symph Orch, Tokyo Metropoiitan Orch, Tokyo Phil Orch, Tokyo Symph Orch, Mich Opera Theatre & others. *Awards:* Gov Award Contrib Arts, NMex. *Rep:* Thea Dispeker 59 E 54th St New York NY 10022. *Mailing Add:* 426 S Park Kalamazoo MI 49007

TALLEY, DANA W
TENOR

b Wenachee, Wash, Aug 31, 50. *Study:* Western Wash Univ, BA, 72; Juilliard Sch, MM, 74; Opera Sch Chicago, with Ellen Repp, David Garvey, Marcello Del Monaco, Jennie Tourel, Mario Del Monaco, Elizabeth Schwartz Kupf, Alberta Masiello, George London, John Alexander, Joan Dornemann & Susan Lane, 75. *Rec Perf:* Opera Gala of Arias, Bulgarian State Orch, European Broadcast, 77; Verdi in Don Carlo, Live from the Met Nat TV Broadcast, 79; The Messiah, Philadelphia Orch, 80; La Traviata, Live from the Met Nat TV Broadcast, 81; The Messiah, Nat TV Broadcast from Mormom Tabernacle, 81; Verdi Requiem, Springfield Symph, 81. *Roles:* Tenor leads in Verdi Requiem and 9 other major oratorios; Madama Butterfly, Merola Prog, San Francisco Opera & Spokane Symph, 78-80; La Boheme, Artist Int, 80; Magic Flute, Carmel Bach Fest, 80; Ballo in Maschere, NJ Lyr Opera, 82; Temistocle, NY Bel Canto Opera, 83; Messiah, Philadelphia Orch, Detroit Symph, Seattle Symph & Mormon Tabernacle, 79-83. *Awards:* Special Award to Verdi Tenors, Comune Di Busseto, Italy, 77; Singers Award, Inst for Study of Vivaldi, 77. *Mem:* Am Guild Music Artists (mem nat bd gov, 81-83). *Rep:* Thea Dispeker Mgt 59 E 54th St New York NY 10022. *Mailing Add:* 159-34 Riverside Dr W #2K New York NY 10032

TALLEY-SCHMIDT, EUGENE
EDUCATOR, TENOR

b Rome, Ga, Feb 10, 35. *Study:* Opera Arts Asn, Atlanta, dipl, 56; Teatro dell'Opera, Rome, Italy, artist's dipl, 58; Ind Univ; San Diego State Col. *Rec Perf:* Duets (Schumann), Cantabile Rec, 66. *Roles:* Fritz in L'Amico Fritz, Spoleto, Italy, 58; Manrico in Il Trovatore, Volksoper, Vienna, 60-64; Henry in Schweigsame Frau, Deutsche Oper am Rhein, Düsseldorf, 61-64; Cavaradossi in Tosca, Hamburgische Staatsoper, 61-64; Turiddu in Cavalleria Rusticana, Cologne Opera, Ger, 63; Otello in Otello, Chautauqua Fest, 72; Sou-Ching in Land of Smiles, Miami Phil, 74. *Pos:* Leading tenor, Deutsche Oper am Rhein, Düsseldorf, 60-64 & Hamburg Staatsoper, 61-64. *Teaching:* Prof voice, Fla State Univ, 66-79; prof & chmn dept voice, Houston Baptist Univ, Tex, 79- *Awards:* Fulbright Scholar, 57. *Mem:* Nat Opera Asn (SE regional gov, 70-77); Nat Asn Teachers Singing; Am Guild Musical Artist; Actors' Equity. *Mailing Add:* 3506 Oyster Cove Dr Missouri City TX 77459

TALMA, LOUISE J
COMPOSER, EDUCATOR

b Oct 31, 06; US citizen. *Study:* Fontainebleau Sch Music, comp with Nadia Boulanger, dipl, 26; Inst Musical Art, dipl, 27; NY Univ, BM, 31; Columbia Univ, MA, 33; Hunter Col, City Univ New York, DHL, 83. *Works:* Toccata for Orchestra, 47, Piano Sonatas No 1 & No 2, 48 & 75 & The Alcestiad (opera in three acts), 62, Carl Fischer Inc; Six Etudes for Piano, G Schirmer, 63; Dialogues for Piano & Orchestra, 64-65, The Tolling Bell (bar & orch), 69 & Sonata for Violin & Piano, 79, Carl Fischer Inc. *Teaching:* Instr, Manhattan Sch Music, 26-28; from instr to prof, Hunter Col, City Univ New York, 28-79; prof emer, 79-; prof, Fontainebleau Sch Music, 36-39, 78 & 81-83. *Awards:* Two Fels, Guggenheim Found, 46 & 47; Sr Fulbright Res Grant, 55; Sibelius Medal for Comp, Harriet Cohen Int Awards, 63. *Mem:* Nat Acad & Inst Arts & Lett; League Comp, Int Soc Contemp Music (mem bd dir, 50-); ASCAP; Fontainebleau Fine Arts & Music Asn (vpres music, currently). *Mailing Add:* 410 Central Park West 3B New York NY 10025

TALVI, ILKKA ILARI
VIOLIN, LECTURER

b Kuusankoski, Finland, Oct 22, 48. *Study:* Private studies in Paris with Gabriel Bouillon, 64-67 & in Vienna with Ricardo Donoposoff, 66-67; Sibelius Acad, Helsinki, dipl, 66; Univ Southern Calif, masterclass with Heifetz, 67-68; Curtis Inst Music, 68-69. *Rec Perf:* Violin Concerto (Klami), Finlandia Rec, 83. *Pos:* Concertmaster, Malmö, Sweden, 76-77; prin violinist & soloist, Los Angeles Chamber Orch, 79-; recitals & solo appearances with orchestras in Western & Eastern Europe & US. *Teaching:* Lectr, Sibelius Acad Helsinki, 69-75. *Awards:* Numerous awards in Finland. *Rep:* Festium Conct Agy Helsinki Finland. *Mailing Add:* PO Box 480175 Los Angeles CA 90048

TAMARKIN, W KATE
CONDUCTOR, TEACHER

b Newport Beach, Calif, Nov 26, 55. *Study:* Chapman Col, BME, 78; Northwestern Univ, MMus(orch cond), 80; studied with Bernard Rubinstein, John Koshak, Sheldon Mehr, Frieda Belifante & Paul Vermel. *Pos:* Cond, Little Orch Chicago, 81-82 & White Heron Chorale, Appleton, Wis, 82-; music dir & cond, Fox Valley Symph Orch, Appleton, Wis, 82- & Fox Valley Symph Chamber Orch, Appleton, Wis, 83- *Mem:* New Music Chicago. *Mailing Add:* 537 N Bateman St Appleton WI 54911

TANENBAUM, ELIAS
COMPOSER, EDUCATOR

b Brooklyn, NY, Aug 20, 24. *Study:* Juilliard Sch Music, BS, 49; Columbia Univ, MA, 50; studied with Dante Fiorillo, Bohuslav Martinu, Otto Luening & Wallingford Rieger. *Works:* Variations for Orchestra, 58, Rituals and Reactions, 75, Remembrance, 79, Side by Side, 80, Words, 82, Last Letters from Stalingrad, 83 & Parallel Worlds, 83, ACA. *Teaching:* Comp & dir electronic music studio, Manhattan Sch Music, 70- *Awards:* Nat Endowment Arts Grant, 74; Ford Found Grant, 75; Am Comp Alliance Rec Award, 82. *Mem:* Am Comp Alliance; Am Music Ctr. *Mailing Add:* 30 Irving Pl New Rochelle NY 10801

TANG, JORDAN CHO-TUNG
COMPOSER, MUSIC DIRECTOR

b Hong Kong, Jan 27, 48. *Study:* Chinese Univ Hong Kong, with K Tuukkanen, BA, 69; Wittenberg Univ, with Jan Bender & H W Zimmermann, MSM, 71; Cleveland Inst Music, with Marcel Dick, MM, 73; Univ Utah, with Vladimir Ussachevsky & Ramiro Cortes, PhD, 79. *Works:* Refrains, Utah Symph, 78; Piece for Violoncello and Harp, Seesaw, 79; Symphony No 2, comn by Utah Symph, 79; Symphonic Movement on a Theme of Mozart, comn by Springfield Symph, Mo, 80; A Little Suite for Woodwind Quartet, Seesaw, 81; In Celebration, Springfield Symph, 81; Three Pieces for Orchestra, Kansas City Symph, 83. *Pos:* Music dir, Southwest Mo State Univ Symph, 78- & Ozark Fest Orch, Monett, Mo, 81-83; Youth Symph Carolinas, 83-; asst cond, Charlotte Symph, 83- *Teaching:* Asst prof music, Southwest Mo State Univ, 78-83; fac mem music, Sewanee Summer Music Ctr, Tenn, 81- *Awards:* MacDowell Colony Fel, 77 & 79; Yaddo Guest, 79 & 80; ASCAP Award, 79- *Mem:* ASCAP; Am Symph Orch League; Am Soc Univ Comp; Am Music Ctr; Music Educr Nat Conf. *Mailing Add:* Charlotte Symph Spirit Square 110 E Seventh St Charlotte NC 28202

TANN, HILARY See Presslaff, Hilary Tann

TANNENBAUM, JAMES
EDUCATOR

Study: Cleveland Inst Music, with Victor Babin, Eunice Podis, Mildred Snyder, Marianne Mastics, Pierre Luboschutz & Vitya Vronsky, BM, 66, MM, 69. *Pos:* Participant, Blossom Chamber Music Fest, two summers; performer solo recitals & concerto conct throughout the midwest. *Teaching:* Mem fac, Cleveland Inst Music, 70-, mem consv fac, 77-; mem fac, Willoughby Sch Fine Arts. *Mem:* Pi Kappa Lambda. *Mailing Add:* Cleveland Inst Music 11021 E Boulevard Cleveland OH 44106

TANNER, JERRE E
COMPOSER, MUSIC DIRECTOR

b Lock Haven, Pa, Jan 5, 39. *Study:* Univ Iowa, BA, 60; San Francisco State Univ, MA, 70. *Works:* Six Songs from Winter's Pillowbook (song cycle), 72, The Naupaka Floret (opera), 74, Hawaiian Songbook #1 (song cycle), 75, Boy with Goldfish (theatre piece), 76, Ka Lei No Kane (opera), 77, Hawaiian Songbook #II (song cycle), 78 & Pupu-Kani-Oe (opera), 80, Malama Arts Inc. *Rec Perf:* Boy with Goldfish, Varese Sarabande, 79. *Pos:* Arts coordr, St Found Cult & Arts, 75-76; music dir, Opera Players Hawaii, 78-79. *Teaching:* Instr gen music, Univ Hawaii, Hilo, 66-67, instr music theory, Ctr Continuing Educ & Community Serv, 70-75. *Awards:* Res fel, Huntington Hartford Found, 64; Celia S Buck Award, Nat Asn Am Comp & Cond, 66; standard music award, ASCAP, 77-82. *Bibliog:* Harvey Hess (auth), Breakthrough in Hawaiian Music, Hawaiian Music Found J, 80; Ben Hyams (auth), International Artistic Achievement, Honolulu Mag, 80; Pat Pitzer (auth), Orchid Isle Art, Hawaii Mag, 82. *Mem:* ASCAP. *Rep:* Malama Arts Inc PO Box 1761 Honolulu HI 96806. *Mailing Add:* PO Box 1478 Kailua Kona HI 96740

TANNER, PETER H
EDUCATOR, COMPOSER

b Rochester, NY, June 25, 36. *Study:* With Robert Hall Lewis, Thomas Canning & Louis Mennini; Eastman Sch Music, with Alan Hovhaness & Bernard Rogers, BM, 58, MM, 59; Cath Univ Am, PhD, 67. *Works:* Concerto for Timpani and Brass; Flute Concerto; Introduction and Allegro (piano & orch); Sonata for Marimba with Piano or Wind Ensemble; Diversions (flute & marimba); Andante (marimba & piano); Sing for Joy (chorus). *Pos:* Mem, US Marine Band, 59-63. *Teaching:* Mem fac, Kans State Univ, Manhattan, 63-66 & Univ Wis, Eau Claire, 66-69; assoc prof perc, Univ Mass, Amherst, 69-80, prof, 81- *Mailing Add:* January Hills Rte 3 Shutesbury MA 01072

TANNO, JOHN W
LIBRARIAN, EDUCATOR

b Brooklyn, NY, Sept 28, 39. *Study:* Ariz State Univ, BA(music), 63; Univ Southern Calif, MA(music), 65, MSLS, 70. *Pos:* Music librn, State Univ NY, Binghamton, 65-68; music librn, Univ Calif, Riverside, 70-, asst univ librn, 78-; ed, Soundboard, Guitar Found Am, 76-80, auth, Current Discography (column), 76- *Teaching:* Adj lectr music bibliog, Univ Calif, Riverside, 75- *Mem:* Music Libr Asn (chmn admin comt, 72-75, publ comt, 75-78 & mem bd dirs, 80-82); Col Music Soc; Asn Rec Sound Collections; Guitar Found Am (mem exec comt, 76-80). *Interests:* Music bibliography; classical & flamenco guitar. *Publ:* Coauth, An Automated Music Library Catalog..., In: Computer & Music, Cornell Univ Press, 70; auth, Locating Guitar Music, 10/75 & The Acoustics of Strings as Related to the Guitar, 8/77, Soundboard, Guitar Fouund Am. *Mailing Add:* 20320 Stanford Riverside CA 92507

TAPLIN, FRANK E
ADMINISTRATOR

b Cleveland, Ohio, June 22, 15. *Study:* Princeton Univ, BA, 37; Oxford Univ, BA, 39; Yale Univ, LLB, 41; Cleveland Inst Music, Hon MusD, 81. *Pos:* Trustee, Cleveland Orch, 46-57, pres, 55-57; pres, Cleveland Inst Music, 52-56 & Nat Coun Metropolitan Opera, 61-64; mem, Music Dept Adv Coun, Princeton Univ, 60-, chmn, 65-71; dir, Metropolitan Opera Asn, 61-, pres & chief exec officer, 77-; chmn bd, Marlboro Sch Music, 64-70, trustee, currently; trustee & vpres, Lincoln Ctr Chamber Music Soc, 69-, pres, 69-73; trustee, Woodrow Wilson Nat Fel Found, Inst Advan Study, Princeton Univ, 71-; trustee & mem exec comt, Lincoln Ctr Perf Arts, currently, vpres, 81- *Mem:* Am Friends Covent Garden & Royal Ballet (mem bd dir, currently); Friends of Aldeburgh Fest. *Mailing Add:* One Palmer Sq Princeton NJ 08540

TARANTO, VERNON ANTHONY, JR
COMPOSER
b New Orleans, La, Nov 16, 46. *Study:* Sch Music, La State Univ, MMus, 76, DMus, 83. *Works:* Soliloquy for Strings, perf by New Orleans Phil, 66; Fantasie on an American Folk Song, US Air Force Band, 73; Sinfonia Orionis, comn by Georgetown Symph Orch, 74; Metamorphoses for Violin, perf by Am Soc Univ Comp, 80; Choral Works, Pro-Art & Augsburg Publ House; Brass Chamber Music, Comp Autograph Publ. *Pos:* Mem, US Air Force Band, 69-74. *Teaching:* Prof theory & comp, Nicholls State Univ, 76-79; staff music dept, Trafton Acad, 82- *Awards:* La Comp Award, Music Teachers Nat Asn, 77. *Mem:* ASCAP. *Mailing Add:* Rte 2 Box 343 Prairieville LA 70769

TARPLEY, EDWARD LEWIS
VIOLIN, ADMINISTRATOR
b Nashville, Tenn, Jan 16, 13. *Study:* Nashville Consv Music, cert, 32; Middle Tenn State Univ, BS, 34; Columbia Univ, MA, 38; Col Medicine, Univ Tenn, MD, 43. *Pos:* Violinist, Nashville Consv Music Orch, 29-31, Memphis Symph Orch, 43 & Nashville Symph Orch, 46-80. *Mem:* Friends of Chamber Music (bd mem, 51-58, pres, 58-80, pres emer, 80-); Nat Arts Coun. *Mailing Add:* 201 Bowling Ave Nashville TN 37205

TASHJIAN, B CHARMIAN
COMPOSER, EDUCATOR
b Detroit, Mich, Feb 4, 50. *Study:* Northwestern Univ, comp with M William Karlins, James Hopkins & Alan Stout, BM, 71; Stanford Univ, comp with Gyorgy Ligeti & computer generated comp with John Chowning, MA, 74. *Works:* Songs of the Sea, Chicago Soc Comp Conct, 79; Am Women Comp Conct, 82 & DePaul Univ Fac Comp Conct, 83; Antiphonies I, New Music Fest, Bowling Green State Univ, 80; Armenechos, Am Women Comp Conct, 83 & Chicago Soc Comp Conct, 83; Resan, Capriccio Rec Inc, 83. *Teaching:* Teaching asst, Northwestern Univ, 76-78, instr music, 82; private tutor music, 79-; lectr music, DePaul Univ, 81- *Awards:* Award for Comp, Northwestern Univ. *Mem:* ASCAP; Am Women Comp Inc; Am Soc Univ Comp; Int League Women Comp; Am Music Ctr. *Mailing Add:* 1311 Maple Ave Apt 3W Evanston IL 60201

TATE, ELDA ANN
ADMINISTRATOR, EDUCATOR
b Corpus Christi, Tex, Sept 12, 38. *Study:* Study flute with Harold Bennett, Lois Schaefer, John Hicks & Shirley Justus; Del Mar Col, Corpus Christi; Univ Tex, Austin, BM, 61, DMA, 63. *Pos:* Prin flutist, Opera Orch New York, 66-68 & Opera & Symph Orch, New York, 64-68. *Teaching:* Prof flute, Northern Mich Univ, 68-, head, Dept Music, 81- *Mailing Add:* Music Dept Northern Mich Univ Marquette MI 49855

TATMAN, NEIL
OBOE, EDUCATOR
Study: Lawrence Univ, BM, 71; Ind Univ, MM, 75; studied with Leonard Sharrow & Jerry Sirucek. *Rec Perf:* On Orion Rec. *Pos:* Mem, Bloomington Symph Orch, formerly & Evansville Phil Orch, formerly; prin oboe, Sacramento Symph; mem, Pac Arts Quintet. *Teaching:* Asst prof oboe, Consv Music, Univ Pac, 75- *Mailing Add:* Consv Music Univ Pac Stockton CA 95211

TATTON, THOMAS
EDUCATOR, CONDUCTOR
Study: Calif State Univ, Northridge, 68; Emporia State Univ, MM, 70; Univ Ill, DMA, 75; studied with Myron Sandler, Manuel Compinsky & Guillermo Perich. *Pos:* Participant, Viola Res Soc Cong, 80-81. *Teaching:* Assoc prof viola & cond, Univ Symph Orch, Consv Music, Univ Pac, 81- *Mailing Add:* Consv Music Univ Pac Stockton CA 95211

TAUB, BRUCE JEFFREY
COMPOSER, EDITOR
b New York, NY, Feb 6, 48. *Study:* City Col New York, BA, 69; Columbia Univ, MA, 71, DMA, 74. *Works:* Composition for Piano, perf by Fritz Jahoda, Carnegie Recital Hall, 71; Variations 11.7.3.3.4, perf by Light Fantastic Players, 74; Quintet I, Am Soc Univ Comp J Music Scores, 76; Extremities (Quintet II), 81 & Passion, Poison & Petrifaction (opera), 82, C F Peters; Fat Piece, Music Perc, 83; Band Piece, perf by La State Univ Wind Ens, Am Soc Univ Comp Nat Conf, 83. *Pos:* Asst to dir, Index New Musical Notation, New York, NY, 74; ed, Am Soc Univ Comp, J Music Scores, New York, NY, 75-; ed & dir ed dept, C F Peters Corp, 78- *Teaching:* Preceptor music, Columbia Univ, 71-74; lectr, City Col New York, 74-75. *Awards:* Joseph H Bearns Prize, Columbia Uiv, 71; fel, Nat Endowment for Arts, 75 & 81. *Mem:* BMI; Am Comp Alliance; Am Soc Univ Comp (chmn exec comt, 74-76). *Mailing Add:* 54 W 16th St Apt 4E New York NY 10011

TAUB, ROBERT (DAVID)
PIANO
b New Brunswick, NJ, Dec 25, 55. *Study:* Princeton Univ, AB, 77; Juilliard Sch, MMus, 78, DMA, 81. *Rec Perf:* Robert Taub Plays 20th Century Piano Works, CRI, 81. *Pos:* Solo recitals piano, Alice Tully Hall & Metropolitan Museum, 81-82; concert tours throughout Europe, Far East, Latin Am & US, 81-; sponsorship, Peabody-Mason Found, Boston, Mass, 81-83 & Pro Musicis Found, New York, NY, 82- *Awards:* Martha Baird Rockefeller Fund Grant, 81; Peabody-Mason Prize, 81-83. *Bibliog:* Suspicious Sound, Princeton Alumni Weekly, 10/20/82; Michael Redmond (auth), Young Jerseyan Going Places, Newark Lodger, 1/2/83. *Publ:* Auth, A Young Pianist Speaks Out on Contemporary Music, Ovation Mag, 83. *Rep:* Del Rosenfield Assoc 714 Ladd Rd Bronx NY 10471. *Mailing Add:* 235 W End Ave New York NY 10023

TAUBE, MOSHE
TENOR, COMPOSER
b Cracow, Poland, June 17, 27; US citizen. *Study:* Cracow Consv, dipl, 39; Haifa Inst Music, 50; Juilliard Sch Music, dipl, 62. *Works:* Israel in Diaspora (cantata), 66; Queen Sabbath (cantata), 68; Symphonic Poem, Duquesne Univ Symph Orch, 75; Two Jewish Dances, 75. *Rec Perf:* Cantorial Masterpieces, Maloh, 62; Synagogue Masterpieces, Greater Rec Co, 68; Hallel, Segue, WRS, 70; Day of Rest, Appalachia Sound Rec Co, 78. *Pos:* Soloist, Israel Radio Chorus, Jerusalem, 52-57; cantor, Shaare Zedek Cong, New York, 57-65 & Beth Shalom Cong, Pittsburgh, 65-; conct artist, Cantor Assembly, New York, 65- *Teaching:* Instr cantorial art, Sch Sacred Music, New York, 61-65; instr voice training, Duquesne Univ, 71- *Awards:* Kavod Award, Cantor Assembly Am, 74; Cert Appreciation, Jewish Theol Sem, 78. *Mem:* Jewish Ministers Asn (bd mem, 62-64); Cantors Assembly (coun mem, 70-76). *Mailing Add:* 6511 Bartlett St Pittsburgh PA 15217

TAUTENHAHN, GUNTHER
COMPOSER
b Kovno, Lithuania, Dec 22, 38; US citizen. *Study:* Calldwell Col, 58. *Works:* Concerto for Double Bass & Orchestra, 69; Suite for Double Bass, comn & perf by B Turetzky, 70; Dorn Dance for Sax, comn by K Dorn, perf by Rotter, 72; Tri-Lude for Piano, perf by Berfield, 78; Caprice Elegant (flute & accordion), Portatives Publ, 79; Pyramid Four for Orchestra, 81; The Vertical Man for Trumpet & Percussion, 82; and others. *Pos:* Composer, currently. *Awards:* Young Am Comp Award, 63; Commemorative Mention Award, Int Biog Ctr, 78; Standard Awards, ASCAP, 82 & 83. *Bibliog:* W Hutchison (auth), Lithuanian-American Composer G Tautenhahn, W Hutchison, 10/76. *Mem:* ASCAP; Am Soc Univ Comp; Nat Asn Comp, USA; Independent Comp Asn; Am Music Ctr. *Publ:* Auth, The Importance of One, J Mich Music Theory Soc, 74; Fiber Movements, Am Soc Univ Comp, 76; Remember the Present, Nat Asn Comp, USA, 82. *Mailing Add:* 1534 Third St Manhattan Beach CA 90266

TAWA, NICHOLAS EDWARD
WRITER, EDUCATOR
b Boston, Mass, Oct 22, 23. *Study:* Harvard Col, BA, 45; Harvard Univ, PhD, 74. *Teaching:* Prof music, Univ Mass, Boston, 65- *Mem:* Sonneck Soc; Popular Cult Asn. *Interests:* American music and cultural history. *Publ:* Auth, Secular Music in the Late 18th-Century American Home, Musical Quart, 75; Music in the Washington Household, J Am Cult, 78; Buckingham's Musical Commentaries, New England Quart, 78; Sweet Songs for Gentle Americans, Popular Press, 80; A Sound of Strangers, Scarecrow Press, 82; Serenading the Reluctant Eagle, Schirmer Books, 83. *Mailing Add:* 69 Undine Rd Brighton MA 02135

TAYLOR, ANDREW DALE
BARITONE
b Vancouver, Wash, Apr 17, 48. *Study:* Long Beach City Col, 69-71; Calif State Univ, Long Beach, voice with Dr Roger Ardrey, BMus, 75. *Roles:* Bs soloist in Messiah, Long Beach Symph, 77; Father in Hansel & Gretel, Houston Grand Opera, 78; Danilo in Merry Widow, Albuquerque Opera Theatre, 80; Germont in La Traviata, Regina Opera, 81; Escamillo in Carmen, Opera Co Greater Lansing, 82; bs soloist in Messiah, 82 & bs bar soloist in Beethoven 9th Symph, 83, Honolulu Symph. *Pos:* Artist in Res, San Diego Opera, 77. *Awards:* Outstanding Apprentice, Santa Fe Opera, 77. *Mailing Add:* c/o Sullivan & Lindsey Assoc 133 W 87th St New York NY 10024

TAYLOR, CLIFFORD (OLIVER)
COMPOSER, EDUCATOR
b Avalon, Pa, Oct 20, 23. *Study:* Carnegie-Mellon Univ, BFA(clarinet perf), BFA(comp); Harvard Univ, MA, 50; studied with Nicholai Lopatnikoff, Dr Frederick Dorian, Domenico Caputo, Walter Piston, Paul Hindemith & Randall Thompson; violin study with Gosta Andreasson & clarinet study with Rosario Mazzeo. *Works:* Violin Sonata No 1, Friends of Harvey Gaul, Inc, 54; Theme and Variations (orch), 55; String Quartet No 1, Rheta A Sosland, 61; Concert Duo (violin & cello), 61; Five Poems, 65; Movement for Three (piano trio), 68; Symphony No Two, perf by Philadelphia Orch, 71. *Teaching:* Asst prof music, Chatham Col, 54-61, assoc prof, 61-63; asst prof music & comp, Col Music, Temple Univ, 63-64, assoc prof, 64-69, prof, 69- *Awards:* Awards, Friends of Harvey Gaul, Inc, 54, Nat Symph, 55 & Rheta A Sosland, 61. *Bibliog:* Arthur Custer (auth), Chronicle (Philadelphia Composers Forum Concert), Musical Quart, 65. *Mem:* Am Comp Alliance (mem nat coun, 76-); BMI; Am Soc Univ Comp (chmn region III, 68-70); Col Music Soc. *Publ:* Auth, The Design of Culture, Encounter, London, 68; Walter Piston on His Seventieth Birthday, Perspectives New Music; The Contemporaneity of Music in History, Music Rev, England. *Mailing Add:* 1061 Township Line Rd Jenkintown PA 19046

TAYLOR, DAVID M
BASS TROMBONE
b Brooklyn, NY, June 6, 44. *Study:* Juilliard Sch Music, BS, 67, MS, 68; Brooklyn Col; Music Acad West. *Rec Perf:* Dagon II (Eric Ewazen), 80 & Rememberance (David Liebman), 81, Chelsea Sound; Archangel (Charles Wuorinen), live church rec, 81; Moonrise with Memories (Fredric Rzewski), RCA, 81; Sonata for Tuba and Piano (Paul Hindemith), Vanguard; Symphony No 34 (Alan Hovhaness), live church rec, 82. *Pos:* Solo bass trombonist, currently. *Awards:* Most Valuable Player of Year Bass Trombone, Nat Acad Rec Arts & Sci, 82. *Mailing Add:* 23 Wight Pl Tenafly NJ 07670

TAYLOR, FRANK
ORGAN, EDUCATOR

Study: Yale Univ, BA; studied organ with Frank Bozyan, George Faxon, Melville Smith & comp with Paul Hindemith & Richard Donovan; Lincoln Col, Oxford, with Egon Wellesz. *Rec Perf:* Works of DuMage, Dandrieu & Marchand. *Pos:* Recitalist in England, France, Spain & US. *Teaching:* Mem fac, Wellesley Col, currently; mem fac organ & exten div, New England Consv Music, currently. *Mailing Add:* New England Consv Music 290 Huntington Rd Boston MA 02115

TAYLOR, GUY
CONDUCTOR & MUSIC DIRECTOR

b Anniston, Ala, Dec 25, 19. *Study:* Juilliard Sch Music, dipl, 48; cond study with Dimitri Mitropoulos & Pierre Monteux; violin study with William Kroll; wkshps with Eugene Ormandy & Philadelphia Orch & George Szell & Cleveland Orch. *Pos:* Cond & music dir, Nashville Symph Orch, 51-59, Phoenix Symph Orch, 59-69 & Fresno Phil Orch, 69-; guest cond throughout US, Can, Gt Brit, Mex, Philippines & PR. *Awards:* Alice M Ditson Orch Award, 61; grant, Rockefeller Found, 66; Award, ASCAP, 77. *Mailing Add:* 2050 W Calimyrna Fresno CA 93711

TAYLOR, JACK A
EDUCATOR, ADMINISTRATOR

b Cheyenne, Wyo, Jan 28, 35. *Study:* Sacramento City Col, AA(music), 54; Univ Calif, Santa Barbara, BA(music), 57; Univ Wash, Seattle, MA(comp), 59, PhD(musicol), 71. *Pos:* Ed, J Res Music Educ, Music Educr Nat Conf, 82- *Teaching:* Instr instrm music, San Lorenzo Valley Unified Sch, 60-67; prof, Sch Music & dir, Ctr Music Res, Fla State Univ, 70- . *Mem:* Nat Consortium Comput-Based Music Instr; Music Educr Nat Conf. *Publ:* Coauth, Involvement with Music, Houghton-Mifflin Co, 75; auth, The Perception of Tonality in Short Melodies, J Res Music Educ, 76; Music, In: Encycl Comput Sci & Technol, Marcel Dekker Co, 78; Introduction to Computers and Computer Based Instruction, Ctr Music Res Press, 81; The Medici Melodic Dictation Program, J Comput Based Instr, 82. *Mailing Add:* Ctr for Music Res Fla State Univ Tallahassee FL 32306

TAYLOR, JOHN ARMSTEAD
EDUCATOR

b Kinsale, Va, Mar 28, 39. *Study:* Va State Col, BS(music educ), 60; Ind Univ, MMusEd, 63, DMusEd, 76. *Teaching:* Music, Hopewell Va Pub Sch, 60-62 & 65-66; asst prof music & asst band dir, Hampton Inst, 66-69, dir bands & assoc prof music, 71-78; prof music & head dept fine arts, Lincoln Univ, Mo, 78- *Mem:* Music Educ Nat Conf; Mo Music Educ Asn; Mo Asn Dept & Sch Music (secy/treas, 82-); Nat Asn Col & Wind Instr. *Publ:* Auth, Good Arrangments Make for a Musical Marching Band, Instrumentalist, 10/69; contribr, Reflections on Afro-American Music, Kent State Univ Press, 73; auth, Developing a Distinct Marching Band Style, 6/77 & So You Want to Dance, 8/80, Instrumentalist; Quality Programs Sell Themselves, Music Educ J, 2/82. *Mailing Add:* 311 Elm Tree Dr Jefferson City MO 65101

TAYLOR, LES (LIONEL LESTER)
COMPOSER, EDUCATOR

b Provo, Utah, Mar 23, 16. *Study:* US Army Music Sch, Ft Myers, Va, 43; Calif Inst Arts, BMus, 50, MMus, 56. *Works:* Sleep, Little Lord Jesus, Devere Music, 54; Aia, Pele, 64 & Incident at the River, 65, Hal Leonard Music; California Kaleidescope, Theodore Presser, 66; Deck the Hut with Coconut, Hal Leonard Music, 67; Showdown at La Mesa, Warner Bros Rec, 70; The Hyphen and Taps, RCA Rec, 79. *Pos:* Freelance musician, Los Angeles & Hollywood, 45-54 & 60-66; staff arr, pianist & orch mgr, CBS, Los Angeles, 54-60. *Teaching:* Asst prof theory, lit & piano, Los Angeles Consv, 47-54; prof, Los Angeles City Col, 66- *Mem:* ASCAP; Music Asn Calif Community Col; life mem, Am Fedn Musicians; Nat Educ Asn; Am Fedn Teachers Col Guild. *Mailing Add:* 17000 Lisette St Granada Hills CA 91344

TAYLOR, MARIA DEL PICO
PIANO, EDUCATOR

b Havana, Cuba; US citizen. *Pos:* Mem, Momento Musicale Ens, 75; soloist with orch in Cuba, US & Can. *Teaching:* Instr piano, Northwestern Univ, 66-69 & Wis State Univ, 70-71; assoc prof, Temple Univ, 71- *Awards:* Silver Medal, 51 & Gold Medal, 52, Consv Peyrellade, Havana; Notable Am Plaque, 78; Can Coun Grant. *Mem:* Young Audiences Inc; Pi Kappa Lambda; Pa Music Teachers Asn; Am Asn Univ Prof. *Mailing Add:* 7950 Henry Ave #12A Philadelphia PA 19128

TAYLOR, PAUL WEGMAN
FRENCH HORN, TEACHER

b Cleveland, Ohio, Sept 30, 54. *Study:* Juilliard Sch with James Chambers & John Cerminaro, BM, 76, MM, 77; San Francisco State Univ, with Arthur Krehbiel, 73; Aspen Music Fest, with Philip Farkas; studied with Philip Myers & Martin Smith. *Pos:* Extra & sub horn, NY Phil, 76-; all positions horn, Nat Orch Asn, 78-81; assoc prin, Am Phil, 80-83, US Phil, 83-; prin horn, Greenwich Phil Orch & Choral Soc, Conn, 80-; extra horn, Metropolitan Opera, 81- *Bibliog:* Andrew Porter (auth), Musical Events, New Yorker Mag, 2/78; various rev, Greenwich Times, Conn, 80- *Mailing Add:* c/o Am Chamber Conct 890 West End Ave New York NY 10025

TAYLOR, ROSE (AUDREY)
MEZZO-SOPRANO

b Loma Linda, Calif, Apr 1, 45. *Study:* Univ Southern Calif, BA(music), 68; Am Opera Ctr, Juilliard Sch Music, 69-71. *Rec Perf:* Angels Visits, New World Rec; Les Noces (Stravinsky), Columbia, 73; Walpurgisnacht (Mendelssohn), RCA, 78. *Roles:* Suzuki in Madame Butterfly, Augusta Opera, 72; Elizabeth in The Crucible, Kansas City Lyric, 74; Bradamante in Orlando Furioso, Dallas Opera, 81; Augusta in Ballad of Baby Doe, Des Moines Metro Opera, 82. *Awards:* Young Musicians Found Grant, 66; Rockefeller Grant, 71. *Mailing Add:* c/o Sheldon Soffer Mgt 130 W 56th St New York NY 10019

TAYLOR, THOMAS FULLER
EDUCATOR

b Evanston, Ill, May 7, 37. *Study:* Earlham Col, BA, 59; Northwestern Univ, MMus(musicol), 62, PhD(musicol), 67. *Teaching:* Instr music, Earlham Col, 62-64; lectr music, Northwestern Univ, 64-66 & Ind Univ, Bloomington, 66-67; assoc prof & actg chair dept musicol, Univ Mich, 67- *Awards:* Res grants, Am Philosophical Soc, 70 & Rackham Grad Sch, 70 & 79. *Mem:* Am Musicol Soc (chmn local arr, 82); Col Music Soc. *Interests:* Seventeenth century Spanish cathedral polyphony; music in the life of the Society of Friends (Quakers). *Publ:* Auth, The Harpsichord Works of Jeremiah Clarke, Diapason, 70; The Trumpet Tones of Jeremiah Clarke: Another View, Musical Quart, 70; Thematic Catalog of the Works of Jeremiah Clarke, Info Coordr, 77; Spanish High Baroque Motet & Villancico: Style & Performance, Early Music, 83. *Mailing Add:* Burton Mem Tower Univ Mich Ann Arbor MI 48109

TAZAKI, ETSKO
PIANO

b Japan. *Study:* Toho Sch, Japan; Juilliard Sch, with Beveridge Webster; studied with Leon Fleisher, Irwin Freundlich & Benjamin Kaplan. *Pos:* Soloist, Chicago Symph, 79, Detroit Symph, St Louis Symph, Tokyo Symph, Toronto Symph, Budapest Symph, Nat Arts Ctr Orch, Ottawa, Ont, L'Orch de la Suisse Romande, Rotterdam Phil, New Japan Phil, Osaka Phil, Kazuyoshi Akiyama, Osaka, Japan, Hong Kong Phil, Santa Barbara Symph Orch, Oakland Symph Orch & throughout US, Europe, UK & Japan; participant, Marlboro Music Fest, formerly & Aspen Music Fest, formerly; recitalist, Concerts Artists Guild, 72 and in New York, London, Vienna, Amsterdam, Tokyo & Hamburg. *Awards:* Fulbright Grant; Prizes, Busoni Compt, 70 & Liszt-Bartok Compt, Budapest, 71. *Mailing Add:* c/o Judd Conct Bur 155 W 68th St New York NY 10023

TCHEREPNIN, IVAN ALEXANDROVITCH
COMPOSER, EDUCATOR

b Iss-Les-Moulineaux, France, Feb 5, 43; US citizen. *Study:* Harvard Univ, studied comp with Leon Kirchner, BA, 64, MA, 65; studied comp with Randall Thompson & Henri Pousseur & cond with Boulez. *Works:* 4 Pieces from Before (piano), 62; Cadenzas in Transition (piano, clarinet & flute), 63; Wheelwinds (nine winds), 66; Rings (string quartet & tape), 66; Set, Hold, Clear and Squelch (electronic ballet score), Merce Cunningham Dance Co, 76; Santur Opera (santur & electronics), 77; Le va et la Vient (orch), Lucerne Fest, 78. *Pos:* Performer, electronic-instrumental music, 66- *Teaching:* Lectr, San Francisco Consv, 69-71 & Stanford Univ, 70-72; lectr music & dir electronic music studios, Harvard Univ, 72-; instr electronic music perf, Dartington, England, 79-80. *Awards:* Brookline Libr Prize, 64; John Knowles Paine Fel, 65; Am Music Ctr Award, 78. *Mailing Add:* c/o John Amato Petale 415 W 24th St Suite 1B New York NY 10011

TEAGUE, THOMAS S
EDUCATOR, BARITONE

b High Pt, NC, Dec 9, 37. *Study:* Mars Hill Col, AA, 58; Fla State Univ, BM, 58, MM, 62, DM, 69. *Teaching:* Prof voice, Carson-Newman Col, 62- *Mem:* Nat Asn Teachers Singing (gov Tenn, 76-80). *Publ:* Auth, Peter Warlock's The Curlew, Bulletin, Nat Asn Teachers Singing, 72. *Mailing Add:* Rte #1 Jefferson City TN 37760

TEAGUE, WILLIAM CHANDLER
ORGAN, MUSIC DIRECTOR

b Gainesville, Tex, July 8, 22. *Study:* Gainesville Jr Col; Southern Methodist Univ; Curtis Inst Music, BMus, 48. *Rec Perf:* Le Chemin de La Croix (Dupre) & William Teague Plays Willan, Franck & Ginastera, Ler Rec. *Pos:* Organist & choirmaster, St Mark's Episcopal Church, Shreveport, La, 48-; musical dir, Baroque Artists Shreveport, currently. *Teaching:* Prof music, Centenary Col, 48- *Awards:* Cult Achievement Award, Shreveport J, 71; Shreveport J Award, 72; Phi Beta Award, 83. *Mem:* Am Guild Organists; Diocese of La Music Comn; Music Teachers Nat Asn; Am Asn Univ Prof. *Mailing Add:* 547 Broadmoor Blvd Shreveport LA 71105

TEAL, MARY EVELYN DURDEN
EDUCATOR, WRITER

b Monroe, La, May 13, 24. *Study:* Northwestern State Col, BS(music educ), 45; Univ Mich, Ann Arbor, MMus, 55, PhD(music educ), 64. *Pos:* Ed, Mich Music Educr, Mich Music Educr Asn, 78- *Teaching:* Instr vocal music, Bastrop Pub Sch, 46-51 & Ann Arbor Pub Sch, 54-57; lectr music educ, Univ Mich, Ann Arbor, 55-58; from lectr to prof, Eastern Mich Univ, 65- *Awards:* Rose Honor, Sigma Alpha Iota, 75; Merit Award, Mich Music Educr Asn, 82. *Bibliog:* Robert Stevenson (auth), Protestant Church Music in America, W W Norton & Co, 66; Ernst C Krohn (auth), Music Publishing in the Middle Western States Before the Civil War, Info Coord, 72. *Mem:* Music Educr Nat Conf; Mich Music Educr Asn; Sigma Alpha Iota; Sonneck Soc. *Publ:* Coauth, The Effects of the Civil War on Music in Michigan, Mich Civil War Centennial Observance Comn, 65; auth, Career Education for Prospective Teachers, Music Educr Nat Conf, 77; Letters of Thomas Hastings, Notes, 12/77; Elements of Music for the Classroom Teacher, Campus Publ, 4th ed, 80; Detroit, In: New Grove Dict of Music & Musicians, 80. *Mailing Add:* Dept Music Eastern Mich Univ Ypsilanti MI 48197

TEBALDI, RENATA
SOPRANO
b Pesaro, Italy, Feb 1, 22. *Study:* Arrigo Boito Consv, Parma; Pesaro Gioacchino Rossini Consv, Parma, with Carmen Melis & Giuseppe Pais. *Rec Perf:* On Fonit, Cetra, Decca, London, Richmond & RCA. *Roles:* Elena in Mefistofele, Teatro Municipale, Rovigo, 43; Aida in Aida, San Francisco Opera Co, 50; Otello, Metropolitan Opera, 55; Micaëla in Carmen; Mimi in La Boheme; Madama Butterfly in Madama Butterfly; Desdemona in Otello; & many others. *Pos:* Lyr & dramatic sop with maj opera co in Argentina, Austria, Brazil, France, WGermany, Holland, Italy, Spain, UK & US. *Mailing Add:* c/o Herbert H Breslin 119 W 57th St New York NY 10019

TECAYEHUATZIN, VICTOR SAUCEDO (VICTOR SAUCEDO)
COMPOSER, ELECTRONIC
b Colton, Calif, July 20, 37. *Study:* Univ Southern Calif, BA, 66; Heidelberg, Köln, Darmstadt; Rheinische Musikschule, with Karlheinz Stockhausen, 66-67; Univ Calif, Los Angeles, with Roy Harris & B Kremenlieu, MA, 68, PhD, 72. *Works:* Toccata (brass), Henri Elkan, 62; Ran IX (clarinet & tape), Grenadilla Rec, 76; A⁶ I³ (orch), comn by NMex State Univ, 76; Music to Read Science Fiction By (comput music), Evergreen State Col & Southwestern Col, 76-77; Coyocuicatl (four male singers), Southwestern Col Vocal Quartet, 79; Keyboard Music I, Am Asn Univ Comp Regional Conf 83, 82. *Teaching:* Lectr theory & comp, Cal State Univ, Dominquez Hills, 70-71; prof, Southwestern Col, 72-; vis prof, Evergreen State Col, 77-78 & Univ Calif, Irvine, 83- *Awards:* Univ Calif, San Diego Fel, 75-77; Nat Endowment Humanities Summer Stipend, 80. *Mem:* Am Soc Univ Comp; Am Music Ctr; Pi Kappa Lambda; Col Music Soc; Music Asn Calif Community Col. *Publ:* Auth, Toccata for Brass Sextet, Henri Elkan, 62; contribr, Stockhausen und die Kölner Schule, Univ Ed, 71; auth, Mito (tes) de un Vato—Selected Poetry, Univ Press, 75; Basic Piano: A Procedural Approach, 82 & The Music of Mexico: A Syllabus, 83 Saucedo & Sons Publ. *Mailing Add:* 1228 Corte de Cera Chula Vista CA 90210

TECK, KATHERINE (WEINTZ)
ADMINISTRATOR, MUSICIAN FOR DANCE
b Mineola, NY, Dec 31, 39. *Study:* Vassar Col, BA, 60; Mannes Col Music, 60-61; Columbia Univ, MA(comp), 63. *Pos:* Asst, Concert Music Dept, BMI, 63-65; pres, Mod Listeners Rec Club, 65-66; mem, Ed Staff, Dover Publ Inc, 66-69; freelance horn player, New York & Westchester, NY, 71-; musician for dance, several universities in NY, 78-; vpres, Teck Enterprises Inc, 81; mem, Nat Adv Bd, CRI, 83- *Mem:* Hon life mem, NY Brass Conf Scholar; Int Horn Soc. *Publ:* Auth, Natural Horn Parts in Orchestral Music 1639-1865, F E Olds & Son, 64; Dear Potential Modern Music Lover, Music Educ J, 12/69; interviews & reports, NY Brass Conf J, 77-78. *Mailing Add:* 44 Havilands Lane White Plains NY 10605

TE KANAWA, KIRI
LYRIC SOPRANO
b Gisborne, NZ. *Study:* St Mary's Col, Auckland, NZ, with Mary Leo, 57-60; London Opera Ctr, 66-69; studied with Vera Rozsa. *Rec Perf:* Don Giovanni (film), 79; Cosi fan tutti; Carmen; C Minor Mass (Mozart); Songs with Orchestra (Strauss); Hansel und Gretel; Vespers (Mozart) & Exultate Jubilate (Mozart), Philips; rec on Decca. *Roles:* Blumenmädchen in Parsifal, Royal Opera House, Covent Garden, 71; Countess in Le Nozze di Figaro, Santa Fe Fest, 71 & Royal Opera House, Covent Garden, 73; Amelia in Simon Boccanegra, 73-77; Marguerite in Faust, 74; Desdemona in Otello, Metropolitan Opera, 74; Pamina in Die Zauberflöte, 75; Mimi in La Boheme, 75-77. *Pos:* Sop, Royal Opera House, Covent Garden, London, 71- & with maj Europ, Am & Australian opera co. *Mailing Add:* c/o Artists' Int Mgt A/G 3 & 4 Albert Terr London NW1 7SU England United Kingdom

TELESE, MARYANNE ELIZABETH
SOPRANO
b Princeton, NJ, Jan 19, 51. *Study:* Oberlin Consv Music, Oberlin Col, BM, 74, MM, 75. *Roles:* Mimi in La Boheme, Opera Theater of Syracuse & Charlotte Opera, 80 & 81; Gretel in Hansel & Gretel, Houston Grand Opera, 81; Cio-Cio San in Madama Butterfly, Lake George Opera Fest & Augusta Opera, 81 & 82; Nedda in Pagliacci, Cincinnati Opera, 82; Juliet in Romeo & Juliet, Opera Theater Rochester & Opera Theater Syracuse, 82; Gilda in Rigoletto, Colo Opera Fest & Conn Opera, 82 & 83; Susanna in Le nozze di Figaro, Mich Opera Theater, Dayton Opera, 83. *Awards:* Grant, Martha Baird Rockefeller, 78, Nat Opera Inst, 79 & Sullivan Found, currently. *Rep:* Munro Artist's Mgt 344 W 72nd St New York NY 10023. *Mailing Add:* 230 W 55th 14-G New York NY 10019

TEMIANKA, HENRI
CONDUCTOR, VIOLIN
b Greenock, Scotland, Nov 19, 06; US citizen. *Study:* Nat Consv, Berlin, with Willy Hess, 26-28; Nat Consv, Paris, with Jules Boucherit, 28-30; Curtis Inst Music, studied violin with Carl Flesch & cond with Arthur Rodzinski, dipl, 32. *Rec Perf:* Various rec as violin soloist, Paganini Quartet leader & cond on RCA Victor, Columbia, Decca, Kapp, Parlophone, Liberty & Orion Rec; and numerous others. *Pos:* Found & leader, Paganini Quartet, Los Angeles, 46-66; found & cond, Calif Chamber Symph, Los Angeles, 61- *Teaching:* Prof, Univ Calif, Santa Barbara, 60-65 & Calif State Univ, Long Beach, 64-74. *Awards:* Brigham Young Univ Award, 78; Officier Arts & Lettres, France, 80; Univ Judaism Award, 81. *Mem:* ASCAP; Am String Teachers Asn. *Publ:* Auth, Facing the Music, David McKay, 73 & Alfred Co, 80; approx 100 articles publ in Saturday Review, Esquire, Pageant, Instrumentalist, Westways & others. *Mailing Add:* c/o Calif Chamber Symph Soc 2219 S Bently Suite 202 Los Angeles CA 90064

TEMKIN, ASCHER MARK
CONDUCTOR
b Chicago, Ill, Feb 9, 38. *Study:* Northwestern Univ, MusB(viola), 60; Butler Univ, MusM(comp), 66; studied cond with Richard Lert, Lukas Foss & Richard Burgin, viola with William Primrose, Joseph dePasquale & Rolf Persinger & violin with Samuel Arran. *Pos:* First violin, NC Symph, 58; prin violist, soloist & sect coach, Kansas City Phil, 59-60, Buffalo Phil, 61-64 & Indianapolis Symph Orch, 64-66; music dir, Brockport Symph, 66-79, Genesee Symph, 69-72, New York Fest, 70- & Rochester Inst Technol Phil, 81-; assoc music dir, Bogota Phil, Colombia, 72-73; guest cond, orchs in South Am, Mex, US, Asia & Europe. *Teaching:* Adj prof chamber music, Kansas City Consv Music, 59-61, State Univ NY, Buffalo, 61-64 & Butler Univ, 64-66; prof music, State Univ NY, Brockport, 66-; founder, Advan Cond Teaching Prog. *Mem:* Am Symph Orch League (dir, 77-79); Cond Guild. *Mailing Add:* 122 Sherwood Dr Brockport NY 14420

TEMPERLEY, NICHOLAS
EDUCATOR, CRITIC-WRITER
b Beaconsfield, Bucks, England, Aug 7, 32; US citizen. *Study:* Royal Col Music, London, with Frank Merrick, ARCM, 52; King's Col, Cambridge Univ, BA, 53, BMus, 55, MA, 57, PhD, 59; Univ Ill, 59-61. *Teaching:* Asst lectr music, Cambridge Univ, 61-66; asst prof musicol, Yale Univ, 66-67; assoc prof musicol, Univ Ill, 66-72; prof music, 72- *Awards:* Fel, Nat Endowment Humanities, 75; Otto Kinkeldey Award, Am Musicol Soc, 80. *Bibliog:* Andrew Porter (auth), Raymond and Agnes, Musical Times, Vol 107, 66; Sir Jack Westrup (auth), Berlioz, Symphonie Fantastique, Music & Letters, Vol 54, 73. *Mem:* Am Musicol Soc; Sonneck Soc; Midwest Victorian Studies Asn (vpres, 80-82, pres 82-84); Hymn Soc Am (chmn res, 83-85); Royal Musicol Asn. *Interests:* Nineteenth century music, especailly Berlioz, Chopin, Schubert & English music; Anglo-American church music; piano music. *Publ:* Ed, Berlioz, Symphonie Fantastique, Bäemeiter, 72; auth, John Playford and the Metrical Psalms, JAMS, Vol 25, 72; co-ed, English Songs 1800-1860, Musica Britannica, 79; auth, The Music of the English Parish Church, Cambridge Univ Press, 79; ed, Music in Britain (Vol V): The Romantic Age 1800-1914, Athlone Press, 81. *Mailing Add:* 805 W Indiana Urbana IL 61801

TENNEY, JAMES C
COMPOSER, EDUCATOR
b Silver City, NMex, Aug 10, 34. *Study:* Bennington Col, BA, 58; Univ Ill, MMus, 61. *Works:* Three Pieces for Drum Quartet, E C Kerby Ltd, 74; Harmonium #5 (string trio), perf by Galliard Ensemble, 78; Saxony (solo saxophonist & tape delay system), 78; Three Indigenous Songs (chamber ens), 79; Glissade (viola, cello, bass & tape delay system), perf by Array Ens Toronto, 82; Bridge (two microtonal pianos), 83. *Rec Perf:* The Songs of Charles Ives, Folkways Rec, 66. *Pos:* Assoc mem tech staff, Bell Telephone Labs, Murray Hill, NJ, 61-64; res assoc, Yale Univ, 64-66. *Teaching:* Vis assoc prof, Polytechnic Inst Brooklyn, 66-69; fac mem, Calif Inst Arts, 70-75; assoc prof, York Univ, 76- *Awards:* Nat Endowment Arts Comp Fel, 75; Am Acad & Inst Arts & Letters Music Award, 82. *Bibliog:* Walter Zimmermann (auth), Desert Plants, ARC, 76. *Publ:* Auth, Sound-Generation by Means of a Digital Computer, J Music Theory, 63; Meta & Hodos, Tulane Univ 64; Conlon Nancarrows Studies for Player Piano, Sounding Press, 77; coauth, Temporal Gestalt Perception in Music, Jour Music Theory, 80. *Mailing Add:* 54 Gloucester Grove Toronto ON M6C 2A3 Canada

TEPPER, ALBERT
COMPOSER, EDUCATOR
b New York, NY, June 1, 21. *Study:* New England Consv Music, BMus, 47, MMus, 48; Univ Edinburgh, Scotland, cert, 51; Mozarteum, Salzburg, Austria, cert, 51. *Works:* Concertino for Oboe and Strings, E F Kalmus, 52; Tent Music (orch), comn by Long Island Arts Fest, 64; Suite for Clarinet and Bassoon, MCA Music, 67; Symphony for Strings, perf by Brazilian Nat Orch, 68; String Quartet 1946, Seesaw Music, 68; Cantata 1969, perf by Hofstra Univ Mixed Chorus, 69; Prelude and Rondo (strings), perf by Sinfonia da Camera, 80. *Teaching:* Instr music theory, New England Consv, 48-50; instr theory, comp, music lit & cond, Hofstra Univ, 52-54, asst prof, 54-59, chair music dept, 54-58, 67-73 & 80-82, assoc prof, 59-68 & prof 68- *Mem:* ASCAP; Am Music Ctr; Am Fedn Musicians; Music Theory Soc NY State; Long Island Comp Alliance. *Publ:* Auth, Program Notes—Pro Arte Symphony of Long Island, 66-69, Tonal Harmony: Vocabulary and Syntax, 72 & Notes: Hofstra University Concerts in the John Cranford Adams Playhouse, 75, Hofstra Univ. *Mailing Add:* 36 Honeysuckle Rd Levittown NY 11756

TEREY-SMITH, MARY
CONDUCTOR & MUSIC DIRECTOR, EDUCATOR
b Budapest, Hungary, Brit citizen. *Study:* Liszt Acad Music, Budapest, Hungary, BM(cond), 50; Univ Vt, MA(music lit), 64; Eastman Sch Music, PhD(musicol), 71. *Pos:* Vocal coach & asst cond, Hungarian State Opera, 50-56; musical dir & cond, Tatabanya Symph, Hungary, 52-56. *Teaching:* Music specialist, Sch Bd, Montreal, Can, 57-64; assoc prof music, Western Wash Univ, 67- *Awards:* Sr res grant, Am Coun Learned Soc, 75-76; Harvard Fel, Radcliffe Inst, 76. *Mem:* Am Musicol Soc; Int Musicol Soc. *Interests:* French baroque opera; Rameau; the role of the accompanying orchestra; performance practice in the baroque and classical periods. *Publ:* Auth, French Baroque Opera Partbooks in the Uppsala University Library, CAUSM J, Vol IX, No 1; Die Französiche Oper und die Revolution ..., Colloquia Musicologica, 82; Joseph Kämpfer, A Forgotten Contrabass Virtuoso from Bratislava, Studia Musicologica, 83. *Mailing Add:* 1809 Harris Ave Bellingham WA 98225

TERMINI, OLGA A
EDUCATOR, WRITER
b Hamburg, Ger, May 19, 30; US citizen. *Study:* Hochschule Musik, Hamburg, 50-51; Univ Southern Calif, BM, 54, MM, 57, PhD, 70. *Teaching:* Music, Stevenson Jr High, Los Angeles, 54-57 & Fairfax High Sch, 57-72; instr voice, Los Angeles City Col, 57-64; prof music, Calif State Univ, Los Angeles, 72-, assoc dean, 79-82. *Awards:* Fulbright Grant to Italy, 66-67. *Mem:* Am Musicol Soc (secy, Pac SW chap, 79-); Music Educr Nat Conf; Col Music Soc. *Interests:* Venetian opera of late 17th and early 18th centuries; German art songs. *Publ:* Contribr, Festival Essays for Pauline Alderman, Brigham Young Univ Press, 76; Auth, Stylistic Changes in the Arias of C F Pollarolo, Current Musicol, 78; The Transformation of Madrigalisms in Venetian Operas, Music Rev, 78; Pollarolo & Carlo Francesco, In: New Grove Dict of Music & Musicians, 79; Singers at San Marco in Venice, Royal Music Assn Res Chronicle, 81. *Mailing Add:* 4278 Sea View Lane Los Angeles CA 90065

TEUTSCH, WALTER
CONDUCTOR & MUSIC DIRECTOR, EDUCATOR
b Augsburg, Bavaria, Oct 11, 09; US citizen. *Study:* Univ Munich, Heidelberg, Bonn, Berlin & Wuerzburg, Referendar, 31, JVD, 33; Leopold Mozart Consv Music, dipl, 36; special study with Arthur Piechler & Hugo Kauder. *Pos:* Cond, Salt Lake Phil Choir, 49-55; assoc cond, Utah Opera Theatre, 52-55; dir & cond, Opera Workshop, US Int Univ, 55-75; music dir & cond, Pacific Lyric Theater, San Diego, Calif, 81- *Teaching:* Prof music, Westminster Col, Salt Lake City, Utah, 43-54; US Int Univ, 55-75. *Awards:* Ernest Bloch Award, United Temple Chr, 47. *Mem:* Am Guild Organists (dean, 58-60); Nat Opera Asn (mem bd, 63-66, gov, 67-71, vpres, 72); Am Musicol Soc; Central Opera Serv. *Mailing Add:* 4581 Tivoli St San Diego CA 92107

TGETTIS, NICHOLAS CHRIS
COMPOSER
b Salem, Mass, Sept 1, 33. *Study:* New England Consv Music, BM, 60; Boston Univ, MM, 69. *Works:* Trio for Oboe, Clarinet & Bassoon, comn by Brookline Music Libr, 68; Sonatina for Piano, Brandon Press, 69; Night Freight (two pianos), perf by Lily Ourgang & K Kroner, 76; Sappho (chamber orch), 78; Christmas Cantata (SATB), Hellenic Choral Soc, 82; El Pelele, Louis Stella, 83; Grecian Sketch for Clarinet & Piano, comn & perf by Peter Cokkinias; and many others. *Teaching:* Pub sch & private teaching, 62-82; comp in res, Salem, Mass, 77-78. *Awards:* First Prize, Brookline Libr Music Asn. *Bibliog:* A S Kanaracus (auth), Chamber Opera, 3/31/83 & Greek Composers Featured in Cokkinias Recital, 4/14/83, Hellenic Chroy. *Mem:* ASCAP; Am Music Ctr. *Rep:* Helicon Press 63 Gates St Worcester MA 01610. *Mailing Add:* 14 Aborn St Salem MA 01970

THAMON, EUGENE (EUGENE THAMON SIMPSON)
EDUCATOR, CONDUCTOR
b North Wilkesboro, NC, Apr 10, 32. *Study:* Howard Univ, MusB, 51; Yale Univ, MusM, 54; Columbia Univ, MusEdD, 68. *Works:* Hold On (SATB), Murbo Press, 73; Steal Away (SATB), 75, Sinnuh, Please Don't, 76, Nobody Knows De Trouble (SATB), 76, True Religion (SATB), 77, Too Late Sinnuh (SATB), 78 & Sistuh Mary Had a But One Child (SATB), 81, Bourne Music Co. *Rec Perf:* Lohengrin, RCA Victor, 65; Poetry, Song & Speech, Columbia Special Prod, MacMillan Gateway, 67; Bourne Choral Samplers #2, #3 & #4, Bourne Co, 82- *Teaching:* Dir voice & choral cond, Va State Univ, 68-70; chmn & prof music, Bowie State Col, 70-75 & Glassboro State Col, 75-80. *Awards:* Oscar, World-Wide All Army Entertainment Cont, 57; Nat Fedn Music Clubs Award Merit, 70; Orpheus Award, Phi Mu Alpha Sinfonia, 77. *Mem:* Nat Asn Sch Music (eastern regional secy, 75-78, chair, 78-81 & pres NJ chap, 77-79); Am Choral Dir Asn (gov NJ, 77-81); Nat Asn Teachers Singing; Nat Choral Coun; ASCAP. *Publ:* Auth, The Hall Johnson Legacy, Choral J, 70; The Missing Ingredient, Nat Asn Sch Music Proc, 77. *Mailing Add:* 400 Mac Clelland Ave Glassboro NJ 08028

THARP, DON(ALD WARREN)
PIANO, LIBRARIAN
b Denver, Colo, Jan 26, 43. *Study:* Okla City Univ, BMus, 66; Univ Tex, Austin, MMus, 73. *Pos:* Pianist, librn & state mgr, Austin Symph, 71- *Teaching:* Instr piano, Concordia Lutheran Col, 73-81. *Mailing Add:* 2101 Cochise Trail Austin TX 78733

THEIL, GORDON AMOS
LIBRARIAN
b Los Angeles, Calif, Oct 23, 49. *Study:* Univ Calif, Los Angeles, BA(music), 73, MA(music), 77; Univ Calif, Berkeley, MLS, 79. *Pos:* Asst music librn, Univ Calif, Los Angeles, 80- *Mem:* Music Libr Asn; Am Musicol Soc; Int Asn Sound Archives; Asn Recorded Sound Collections. *Publ:* Auth, Recent Recordings of Schoenberg's Music, Schoenberg Inst J, 6/82. *Mailing Add:* Music Libr Schoenberg Hall Univ Calif Los Angeles CA 90024

THEIMER, AXEL KNUT
MUSIC DIRECTOR, EDUCATOR
b St Johann, Tirol, Austria, Mar 10, 46. *Study:* St Johns Univ, BA, 71; Univ Minn, MFA, 74. *Rec Perf:* With St Johns Univ Men's Chorus. *Pos:* Mem, Vienna Boys Choir, 56-61; dir, Chorus Viennensis, Vienna, 67-69; vocal soloist, Mozart Fest, Pueblo, Colo, 71 & 75, Alverno Col, 72, Northrup Mem Auditorium, Minneapolis, 73 & Univ Minn, 73; perf mem, Thurs Musical Minneapolis. *Teaching:* Assoc prof music & dir choral & vocal activ, St Johns Univ, Minn, 69-; clinician & dir, choral & vocal wkshps. *Mem:* Am Choral Found; Am Choral Dir Asn; Int Music Coun; Nat Asn Teachers Singing; Music Teachers Nat Asn. *Mailing Add:* Dept Music St Johns Univ Collegeville MN 56321

THEMMEN, IVANA
COMPOSER, PIANO
b New York, NY, Apr 7, 38. *Study:* NY Univ; Eastman Sch Music; New England Consv; Berkshire Music Ctr, studied piano with Jean Rosenblum & Margaret Chaloff, chamber music with Otto Shulhof, Vienna, orch with Nicolas Flagello & comp with F Cooke, Carl McKinley & Lukas Foss. *Works:* The Mystic Trumpeter, perf by Metropolitan Chamber Players, 76-83; Lucian (opera), Hudson Guild Theater, 76-77; Shelter This Candle From The Wind, First Ed Rec, 778; Ode to Akhmatora, Op One Rec, 81; Trombone Concerto, Merkin Hall, 81 & Aspen Fest, 82; Concerto for Guitar and Orchestra, perf by Minn Orch, 82; Cupid and Psyche, perf by Boston Pops Orch, 83 & Queens Symph, 83. *Pos:* Orchestrator, Am Ballet Theatre, New York, 80-; founder & pianist, Metropolitan Chamber Players, currently; co-adminr, Maestro Music Ctr. *Awards:* ASCAP Awards, 76-83; Grants, Meet the Comp, NY State Coun Arts, Nat Endowment Arts & Rockefeller Found, 78-83; Kennedy Ctr Friedheim Award, 83. *Bibliog:* Laura Koplewitz (auth), articles in Symph Mag, 82 & Conn Mag, 83; Bernice Olenick (prod), Soundings—A Series on 5 Am Comp (film), WGBH-TV for PBS, 83. *Mem:* Am Music Ctr; Nat Asn Comp (prog chmn, 78-80 & vpres, 81-83); ASCAP. *Mailing Add:* 190 Turner Rd Ridgefield CT 06877

THEOBALD, JIM (JAMES CHESTER THEOBALD)
COMPOSER, CRITIC-WRITER
b Winchester, Mass, Mar 10, 50. *Study:* Columbia Univ, with Jack Beeson & Chou Wen-Chung, BA(music), 77; Chicago Musical Col, with Ramon Zupko & Robert Lombardo; Hartt Col Music, with Ed Miller & Edward Diemeute. *Works:* Three Rhapsodies for Saxophone and Percussion, perf by Paul Cohen with Paul Price & Manhattan Perc Ens, 79; Song & Dance for Tuba & Drums, perf by David Grego & Bruce Smith, Carnegie Recital Hall, 80; Yoga Quartet (strings), New York Cult Ctr, 81; Lewis Carrolls, comn by Duo Contemporaine, Netherlands, 82; Mantras, perf by Andrew Bolotowsky, Bruce Smith, David MacBride & Dale Turk, 82; Several Million Pieces, Contemp Group, Mich State Univ, 82; Go in Green (Times 15), perf by Cheryl Bensman & Virgil Blackwell, Merkin Hall, 83. *Pos:* Prod, New Music, WBAI-FM, New York, 74-; writer & critic, Villager Newspaper, New York, 82-; freelance writer & critic, Ear Mag, 82-83 & Phoenix, Brooklyn, 83- *Teaching:* Lectr music theory, State Univ NY, Purchase, 79-80. *Bibliog:* Edward Rothstein (auth), Music: After the Apocalypse, 12/26/82 & Gertrude Stein Recital, 1/27/83, New York Times. *Mem:* Am Music Ctr; ASCAP. *Mailing Add:* 545 W 11 St 9E New York NY 10025

THEVENIN, FRANCIS
VIOLIN
b Asheville, NC, Oct 1, 30. *Study:* Univ Ga; Univ Wash; Am Consv Music; studied with Scott Willits. *Pos:* Mem, Atlanta Symph Orch, Fla Symph Orch, Orquesta Sinfonica PR; Chicago Lyr Opera Orch & Chicago Chamber Orch; mem second violin sect, Minn Symph Orch, currently. *Mailing Add:* 4013 Natchez Ave S Edina MN 55416

THIELMAN, RONALD MONCRIEF
COMPOSER, EDUCATOR
b Chicago Heights, Ill, July 27, 36. *Study:* Univ Cent Ark, BME, 58; NTex State Univ, MME, 61; Nat Consv Music, Mexico City, Hon Dr Music, 78. *Works:* Chelsea Suite, Ludwig Publ, 63; Overture Odalisque, 70 & Second Suite for Band, 70, Bourne; Festivada, Chappell, 79; Silk and Satin, 80 & Mexico, 83, Bourne; Winterset, Shawnee, 83. *Rec Perf:* Educ Ref Libr, Belwin Mills, 75 & 77. *Pos:* Dir bands, Mariana, Ark, 61-64, NMex Highlands Univ, 67-69 & NMex State Univ, Las Cruces, 69-; asst dir bands, Univ Miss, 64-67. *Teaching:* Assoc prof music educ, brass & comp, Univ Miss, 64-67, NMex Highlands Univ, 67-69 & NMex State Univ, Las Cruces, 69- *Awards:* Citation Excellence Award, Nat Band Asn, 72; Cert Appreciation, Gov NMex, 76. *Mem:* Nat Band Asn (mem bd dir, 71-77); ASCAP; Asn Conct Bands Am; Nat Asn Jazz Educr (state chmn, 69). *Mailing Add:* Music Dept NMex State Univ University Park NM 88003

THIERSTEIN, ELDRED A
EDUCATOR, BARITONE
b Whitewater, Kans, June 05, 35. *Study:* Paedagogische Akad, Wuppertal, Ger, 56-57; Bethel Col, Kans, AB(music educ), 58; Sch Music, Ind Univ, Bloomington, voice study with Myron Taylor & Dorothy Manski, MME, 63; Col Consv Music, Univ Cincinnati, voice study with Lucille Evans, PhD, 74. *Pos:* Chorus & soloist, Cincinnati Opera Co, 64-73. *Teaching:* Instr vocal music, Harding Jr High Sch, Hamilton, Ohio, 63-66; grad asst theory, Col Consv Music, Univ Cincinnati, 66-67; asst prof music, Ky State Univ, 72-78; instr music, Gerontology Prog, Federal City Col, Washington, DC, summers 77 & 78; assoc prof & dir music dept, Hillsdale Col, 78- *Mem:* Am Musicol Soc; Phi Mu Alpha Sinfonia; Pi Kappa Lambda. *Interests:* Opera performances in Cincinnati and the Ohio Valley; Italian operas in France during the late 18th century. *Mailing Add:* 5145 Morningside Dr Kalamazoo MI 49008

THIMMIG, LES (LESLIE LELAND)
COMPOSER, CLARINET
b Santa Maria, Calif, Mar 19, 43. *Study:* Eastman Sch Music, BM(comp), 65; Yale Univ, MMA(comp), 69, DMA(comp), 74. *Works:* Seven Profiles, E C Schirmer, 70; Extensions IV (9 players), perf by Yale Chamber Orch, 73; Arhythmia (41 players), comn & perf by Univ Wis Wind Ens, 73; Stanzas, Book V (orch), comn & perf by Am Youth In Conct Symph Orch, 78; Stanzas, Book VII (6 winds), comn & perf by Wingra Quintet, 79; Concerto for Tenor Saxophone, Bass & Percussion, comn by Univ Northern Colo, 81; Concerto for Six Players, comn & perf by Da Capo Chamber Players, 82. *Rec Perf:*

Triple Concerto (Donald Martino), Nonesuch, 79; Stanzas Book VII, Spectrum, 81. *Teaching:* Lectr theory, Yale Col Music, 68-69; instr comp & theory, Univ Victoria, BC, 69-71; assoc prof comp, sax & jazz, Univ Wis, Madison, 71- *Mem:* Am Soc Univ Comp. *Mailing Add:* 2303 Danbury St Madison WI 53711

THIOLLIER, FRANCOIS-JOEL
PIANO
b Paris, France. *Study:* Piano with Robert Casadesus; Juilliard Sch, with Sascha Gorodnitzki, BA, MA. *Rec Perf:* On RCA & Angelicum Rec. *Pos:* International pianist, currently. *Awards:* Tchaikovsky Prize; Queen Elisabeth Belgium Prize. *Mailing Add:* c/o Kazuko Hillyer Int Inc 250 W 57th St New York NY 10107

THOMAS, JESS
TENOR, TEACHER
b Hot Springs, SDak, Aug 4, 27. *Study:* Univ Nebr, BA, 49; Stanford Univ, MA, 53; studied with Otto Schulmann, 53-57. *Rec Perf:* Beethoven's Ninth Symphony, Jess Thomas Sings Wagner, Parsifal & others for DG, EMI, Philips, Angel, Deutsche Grammophon, RCA & Columbia. *Roles:* Haushofmeister in Der Rosenkavalier, San Francisco Opera, 57; Florestan in Fidelio; Canio in I Pagliacci; Dimitri in Boris Godunov; Pinkerton in Madame Butterfly; Radames in Aida; Alfredo in La Traviata; and many others. *Pos:* Res mem, Metropolitan Opera, 62-, Vienna Staatsoper, 64- & San Francisco Opera, 65-; ten, Bavarian State Opera, 59-, Paris Grand Opera, 67-, Covent Garden, 69-, Salzburg Easter Fest, 69- & many others. *Teaching:* Prof, San Franciso State Univ, 83- *Awards:* San Francisco Opera Audition Winner, 57; San Francisco Opera Medallion, 72; Kammersänger, Austrian Govt, 76. *Rep:* Colbert Artists Mgt Inc 111 W 57th St New York NY 10019. *Mailing Add:* PO Box 662 Tiburon CA 94920

THOMAS, JOHN M
ORGAN, EDUCATOR
b Arkansas City, Kans, Jan 28, 30. *Study:* Southwestern Col, Kans, BMus, 51; Wichita State Univ, MMus, 56; Univ Ill; Wash Univ; Union Theol Sem. *Works:* Once to Every Man and Nation (SATB), Hall & McCreary, 55. *Teaching:* Asst prof organ, Greenville Col, Ill, 56-61; grad asst, Univ Ill, 61-63; assoc prof organ & theory, Univ Wis, Stevens Point, 63- *Awards:* Nat Lutheran Fel, L B Life Insurance Co, 61. *Mem:* Assoc, Am Guild Organists (dean & founder Wis River chap, 64-65). *Mailing Add:* PO Box 578 Stevens Point WI 54481

THOMAS, JOHN PATRICK
COUNTERTENOR, COMPOSER
b Denver, Colo, Mar 26, 41. *Study:* Aspen Music Sch, studied with Darius Milhaud, five summers; Univ Calif, Berkeley, BA, 63, MA, 65; Berkshire Music Ctr, three summers. *Works:* Pieces for Joan Gallegos, perf by Douglas Leedy & JPT, 63; 1963 (orch), perf by Univ Calif Symph, 64; 4 poems of Wm Searle, perf by Miriam Abramowitsch, 65; Ostraka, San Francisco Symph Brass Quintet, 67; Mignon, perf by Judith Nelson & Bonnie Hampton, 74; Since I Know You, perf by Martha McGaughey & Arthur Haas, 79; 145 W 85th Street, perf by Michael Finnissy, 81. *Rec Perf:* The Coronation of Poppea (Monteverdi), Cambridge, 66; Madrigali 1601 (Luzzaschi), 78, Musiche ... (da Gagliano), 79, Quattro Cantate (A Scarlatte), 80, Musiche Sacre e Profane (Monteverdi), 81 & Musica vocale e strumentale ... (Frescobaldi), 83, Fonit-Cetra Italia. *Roles:* Giasone in Il Giasone, Genova Opera, 72; N Bacon in Elisabeth Tudor, Bayerische Staatsoper, 73; Amore in Amore e Psyche, Piccola Scala, 73 & La Fenice, Venice, 77; Apollo in Death in Venice, Munich Staatsoper, 75-76; countertenor in Mare Nostrum, Berlin Fest, Paris Fest d'Antum & Stuttgart, 75-83; Ithuriel in Paradise Lost, Chicago Lyr Opera & Stuttgart opera, 78-80. *Teaching:* Asst prof, State Univ NY, Buffalo, 66-77. *Interests:* Early 17th century Italian vocal music. *Publ:* Coauth, Music Performance, Encycl Britannica, 71; auth, Songs of George Rochberg, Notes, 72. *Rep:* E K Thomas Box 21 Fessenden ND 58438. *Mailing Add:* Himmelstrasse 6 2000 Hamburg 60 Germany, Federal Republic of

THOMAS, MARILYN TAFT
COMPOSER, EDUCATOR
b McKeesport, Pa, Jan 10, 43. *Study:* Carnegie-Mellon Univ, BFA(piano & comp), 64, MFA(comp), 65; Univ Pittsburgh, PhD(theory & comp), 82. *Works:* Elegy (oboe, harp & string quartet), 80, Concert Piece (piano & chamber orch), 80 & Disparities (ens & electronic tape), 82, Carl Fischer; Five Pieces for Five Players, Pittsburgh New Music Ens & Renaissance City Woodwind Quintets; Songs of Family & He Was My Son, numerous perf; Soundscapes, comn by McKeesport Symph Orch (in prep). *Pos:* Dir music, organist & pianist, First Unitarian Church, Pittsburgh, 63-81; vis comp & musical consult, Quaker Valley Sch District, 81-82. *Teaching:* Lectr theory & piano, Chatham Col, Pittsburgh, 77-79; teaching fel theory, Univ Pittsburgh, 79-81; asst prof theory, comp, harmony & comput music, Carnegie-Mellon Univ, 81- *Awards:* First Place, Young Comp Cont, Nat Fedn Music Clubs, 64. *Mem:* Pittsburgh Alliance Comp (pres, 80-83); Friends of Music Libr (bd mem, 81-83); ASCAP; Am Music Ctr. *Publ:* Auth, Using Eurhythmics in Private Teaching, Dalcroze Soc Am, 78. *Mailing Add:* Dept Music Carnegie-Mellon Univ 5000 Forbes Ave Pittsburgh PA 15213

THOMAS, MARK STANTON
FLUTE
b Lakeland, Fla, Apr 24, 31. *Study:* Baltimore City Col; Peabody Consv Music, dipl, 49; Am Univ, 60-61; Int Graphoanalysis Soc, Chicago, 66-68; studied flute with Emil Opava, Britton Johnson & William Kincaid. *Rec Perf:* Flute Recital; Music for Flutes; flute solo albums on Golden Crest &

Armstrong Rec, 69-75. *Pos:* Mem, USA Band, Nat Symph & Baltimore Symph, formerly; dir, Foxes Sch Music, Falls Church, Va, 58-60; solo flutist, Nat Gallery Orch, 60-68; film, stage, radio & TV appearances; flute clinician & dir master classes, US & abroad; vpres, W T Armstrong Co Inc, Elkhart, Ind, 68-81, flute artist in res, 69-81, dir, currently; flute designer, 68-81; mem, Elkhart Co Humanities Coun, 72-75 & Elkhart Co Symph Orch; vpres, Armstrong Edu-Tainment Publ Co, Elkhart, Ind, 74-81; mem bd dir, Am Youth Symph Orch & Chorus, 75; head, Armstrong Pub Co, 76-81; pres, Elkhart Co Symph Asn, 78-82; dir flute develop, Selmer Co, 81-, mkt mgr band instrm, 82- *Teaching:* Prof flute, George Washington Univ, formerly; prof & chmn woodwind dept, Am Univ, 60-68; lectr, Notre Dame Univ, 75- *Bibliog:* The Flute, A Study with Mark Thomas (film), 71. *Mem:* Founder, Nat Flute Asn (hon life pres, 73-); Am Fedn Musicians; ASCAP; assoc, Am Bandmasters Asn. *Publ:* Auth, The Story of the Flute, 67; Care & Maintenance of Your Flute, 70; The Flute Forum, 71; Learning the Flute, 6 vols, 74; contribr to Woodwind World, Sch Musician & Music J. *Mailing Add:* 1807 Brookwood Dr Elkhart IN 46514

THOMAS, MICHAEL TILSON See Tilson-Thomas, Michael

THOMAS, PAUL LINDSLEY
COMPOSER, ORGAN
b New York, NY, Mar 18, 29. *Study:* Trinity Col, Conn, BA, 50; Yale Sch Music, BM, 57, MM, 58; NTex State Univ, DMA, 79. *Works:* Come See the Place, 68 & Fanfare and Alleluias, 70, H W Gray; Variations on Aberystuyth, 72, Shout the Glad Tidings, 75 & The Strife is O'er, 77, Oxford Univ Press; The Head That Once Was Crowned, Choristers Guild, 83; Oh Send Out Thy Light, Concordia, 83. *Pos:* Organist & choirmaster, St George's by the River Church, Rumson, NJ, 50-55 & St James Episcopal Church, Hartford, Conn, 55-60; dir music & organist, St Michael & All Angels Church, Dallas, 60- *Awards:* Canon Church Music, Diocese Dallas, Episcopal Church, 80. *Mem:* Fel, Am Guild Organists; ASCAP. *Mailing Add:* 6822 Northwood Dallas TX 75225

THOMAS, RONALD
VIOLONCELLO
Study: New England Consv; Curtis Inst; studied violoncello with David Soyer, Leslie Parnas & Lorne Munroe. *Pos:* Soloist, Philadelphia Orch, St Louis Symph, Hartford Symph & Seattle Symph Orch; chamber music perf with Lincoln Ctr Chamber Music Soc & Spoleto Fest of Two Worlds. *Teaching:* Instr violoncello, Boston Consv, currently. *Mailing Add:* Boston Consv 8 The Fenway Boston MA 02215

THOMAS, SALLY
EDUCATOR, VIOLIN
b Minot, NDak. *Study:* With Ivan Galamian; studied chamber music with Edouard Dethier, Josef Gingold, Hans Letz & Louis Persinger; Juilliard Sch, BS, MS. *Teaching:* Admin dir & mem fac violin, Meadowmount Sch Music, 60-; mem fac violin, Juilliard Sch, 61- *Awards:* Nat Fedn Music Clubs Northern Lights. *Mem:* Soc Strings. *Mailing Add:* Mannes Col Music 157 E 74th St New York NY 10021

THOMAS, T(HOMAS) DONLEY
COMPOSER, WRITER
b Detroit, Mich, June 21, 29. *Study:* Eastman Sch Music, 47-48; George Peabody Col for Teachers, BM, 48, MM, 55; Univ Vienna, 55-57; Vienna State Acad, 55-57. *Works:* Canzona, Op 1 (two violins), 82, Elegy and Fugue, Op 2 (two cellos), Quartet, Op 3 (flute, clarinet, alto sax & cello), Serenade, Op 4 (clarinet, horn, violin & cello), Sonata-Allegro, Op 7 (bassoon & piano), Advent Music I, II & III, Op 8 & Duo, Op 11 (violin & cello), Medici Music Press. *Pos:* Cellist & librn, Nashville Symph Orch, 47-57; asst prin cellist, Paducah Symph Orch, Ky, 78- *Teaching:* Instr cello, George Peabody Col, 53-55; assoc prof music, Southeast Mo State Univ, 58- *Mem:* Am Musicol Soc; Phi Mu Alpha (hist gamma psi chap, 50-52); BMI. *Interests:* Johann Michael Haydn. *Publ:* Ed, Asperges Me-Michael Haydn, 62 & Tenebrae Factae Sunt-Michael Haydn, 62, C F Peters; auth, Michael Haydn's Trombone Symphony, 62 & Michael Haydn's Enigmatic Clarino Symphony, 64, Brass Quart; Interpreting Ornamentation in Rococo & Classic Chamber Music, Chamber Music Quart, 82. *Rep:* Medici Music Press PO Box 1623 St Cloud MN 56302. *Mailing Add:* 720 S West End Blvd Cape Girardeau MO 63701

THOMASON, MARSHALL DANIEL
ADMINISTRATOR, VIOLA D'AMORE
b Culver City, Calif, June 27, 34. *Study:* Calif State Univ, Los Angeles, BA, 57; Univ Southern Calif, MM, 64, DMA, 76. *Pos:* Co-founder & co-dir, Viola D'Amore Soc Am, 77- *Teaching:* Instr & chmn dept music, Marina del Rey Jr High Sch, Los Angeles, 66- *Mem:* Int Viola Soc; Am String Teachers Asn; Am Fedn Musicians. *Interests:* History and literature of the viola d'amore; music of the Mannheim School from 1745 to 1770, Karl Stamitz in particular. *Publ:* Auth, The Viola d'Amore Music of Karl Stamitz (self publ), 79. *Mailing Add:* 10917 Pickford Way Culver City CA 90230

THOME, DIANE
COMPOSER, EDUCATOR
b Pearl River, NY, Jan 25, 42. *Study:* Eastman Sch Music, BMus(comp) & perf cert(piano), 63; Univ Pa, MA(theory & comp), 65; Princeton Univ, MFA, 70, PhD, 73. *Works:* Los Nombres (computer tape, perc & piano), Tulstar Rec, 78; Anais (cello, tape & piano), CRI, 80; The Yew Tree (sop, large chamber & ens), Crystal Rec, 82. *Teaching:* Mem fac, Rutgers Univ & State Univ New York, Binghamton, formerly; assoc prof theory & comp, Univ

Wash, 77- *Awards:* Nat Found Music Clubs Awards; comp grants, Nat Endowment Arts; Martha Baird Rockefeller Fund Grant. *Mem:* Am Soc Univ Comp (regional co chair, 80-); Contemp Music Soc; Am Women Comp. *Mailing Add:* c/o Sch Music Univ Wash Seattle WA 98195

THOME, JOEL
COMPOSER, CONDUCTOR
b Detriot, Mich, Jan 7, 39. *Study:* Ecole Internationale, Nice, France, 59; Eastman Sch Music, studied with Herman Genhart, BMus & perf certif, 60; Univ Pa, MS, 65; studied with Perre Boulez, 69. *Works:* In Memoriam: Martin Luther King, Jr (piano, two perc & tape), perf by Philadelphia Comp Forum, 68; Act Without Words #1 (electronic), perf by Anna Sokolow Lyric Theatre, 71; Mobile Sound Structures (chamber ensemble & electronic modification), perf by Univ Wis, Music from Almost Yesterday, 72; Three Poems, comn by Juilliard Theatre Div, 73; Time Spans, comn by Pro Arte Trio, 74; Streams, A Sacred Service (orch, voices & electronic instr), comn by Nat Endowment Arts, 76; Savitri Traveller of the Worlds (ensemble), comn by Lukas Foss & Brooklyn Phil, 79, (orch) comn by Pontiac Oakland Symph, 80, (Indian instrm) comn by Mrinalini Sarabhai, 82. *Rec Perf:* Music of Boulez, Dallapiccola, Pousseur, Vox/Candide, 68; Songs, Drones, Refrains of Death, Desto, 76; Music of Richard Felciano, 79 & At the End of the Parade (Yehuda Yannay), 81, CRI; Music of Boulez, Crumb, Dingoszewski, Berio, Vox, 79; Pierrot Lunaire, MMG-Digital, 81; Four Saints in Three Acts, Nonesuch Rec, 82. *Pos:* Mem, Israel Phil Orch, Tel Aviv, 61-64; cond, Philadelphia Comp Forum, 65-77, Anna Sokolow Dance Co & Lyric Theatre, NY, 68-73, Erick Hawkins Dance Co, 73-78 & Am Symph Orch da Camera, 76; music dir & cond, Orch of Our Time, 77- *Teaching:* Perc instr, David Hochstein Sch Music, Rochester, NY, 57-61 & Israel Acad Music, Tel Aviv, 61-64; musical adv, Israel Nat Dance Theatre, 61-64; assoc, Ctr for Electronic Music, Hebrew Univ, Jerusalem, 63-64; asst prof, Glassboro State Col, 68-79. *Awards:* Koussevitsky Int Rec Award, Int Asn Music Critics, 81. *Bibliog:* Arthur Custer (auth), Joel Thome—String Quartet, Musical Quart, 68. *Mem:* BMI; Am Fedn Musicians. *Rep:* Joanne Rile Artists Mgt PO Box 27539 Philadelphia PA 19118. *Mailing Add:* 30 Waterside Plaza Apt 25H New York NY 10010

THOMPSON, ANNIE F
EDUCATOR, LIBRARIAN
b Rio Piedras, PR, June 7, 41. *Study:* Baylor Univ, BA, 62; Univ Southern Calif, MSLS, 65; Fla State Univ, AMD, 78, PhD, 80. *Pos:* Music cataloger, Univ PR, 65-67, head music libr, 67-80. *Teaching:* Assoc prof music bibliog, Univ PR, 80- *Mem:* Music Libr Asn; Am Musicol Soc; Int Asn Music Libr; PR Musical Soc. *Interests:* Identification of 19th century newspaper and periodical sources for music in Puerto Rico. *Publ:* Auth, An Annotated Bibliography of Writings About Music, Music Libr Asn, 75; Bibliografia Anotada Sobre la Musica en Puerto Rico, Instituto de Cultura Puertoriquena, 77; coauth, Manual Para Monografias Musicales, Ed Universitaria, 79; auth, El Bibliotecario Como Maestro: Su Entrenamiento, Boletin de la Soc de Bibliotecarias de PR, 82. *Mailing Add:* Grad Sch Librnship Rio Piedras Univ PR Rio Piedras PR 00931

THOMPSON, ARTHUR CHARLES
BARITONE
b New York, NY, Dec 27, 42. *Study:* Manhattan Sch Music, 60; Hartt Col Music, study with Virginia Schouz, BM; Juilliard Sch Music, study with Hans Heinz. *Rec Perf:* Fidelio, Cleveland Chamber Orch, private rec; Porgy & Bess, Cleveland Orch, London; Four Saints in Three Acts, Orch Our Time, Nonesuch. *Roles:* Papageno in Die Zauberflöte, Chautauqua Opera Co; St Ignatius in Four Saints in Three Acts, Mini Met; Jochanaan in Salome, Santa Fe Opera; Sharpless in Madama Butterfly, Metropolitan Opera; Escamillo in Carmen & Count di Luna in Il Trovatore, Opera Ebony. *Pos:* Soloist, Metropolitan Opera Studios, 65-71, Mini Met, 71 & Metropolitan Opera, 72- *Awards:* Marion Anderson Award; Ezio Pinza Award; Lucretia Borzia Award, Metropolitan Opera. *Mem:* Am Guild Musical Artists; Am Fedn TV & Radio Artists. *Rep:* Thea Dispeker 59 E 54th St New York NY 10022. *Mailing Add:* 33 Riverside Dr New York NY 10023

THOMPSON, BARBARA GATWOOD
CELLO
b Nashville, Tenn, Nov 24, 23. *Study:* George Peabody Col, BA, 44; studied cello with Oscar Eiler. *Pos:* Second cello, Memphis Symph Orch, 51-; cello, Nashville Symph Orch, formerly & Little Rock Phil, 62-63. *Mailing Add:* 320 E Cherry Circle Memphis TN 38117

THOMPSON, DONALD
WRITER, EDUCATOR
b Columbus, Ohio, Feb 28, 28. *Study:* Univ Mo, AB & BSEd, 52, MA, 54; Univ Iowa, PhD, 70. *Pos:* Freelance cond, San Juan, PR, 58-; music critic, San Juan Star, PR, 57-60 & 75- *Teaching:* From instr to prof music, Univ PR, 56-, chmn music dept, 80- *Mem:* Am Musicol Soc; Music Libr Asn (ed index series, 81-); Col Music Soc; Soc Musical PR (pres, 73-77). *Interests:* Puerto Rican and Caribbean music: orgins, sources, development and bibliography. *Publ:* Auth, Gottschalk in the Virgin Islands, YBIAMR, 70; A New World Mbira: The Caribbean Mearimbula, African Music, 75-76; Music, Theater and Dance in Central America and the Caribbean, R/R Interam, 79; Puerto Rico, In: New Grove Dict of Music & Musicians, 80; Music Research in Puerto Rico, Off Gov PR, 82. *Mailing Add:* Dept Music Univ PR Rio Piedras PR 00931

THOMPSON, ELLEN R
EDUCATOR, TEACHER-COACH
b Rutherford, NJ. *Study:* Houghton Col, NY, BM, 50; Teachers Col, Columbia Univ, MA, 51; Am Consv Music, Chicago, MM, 56. *Teaching:* Prof theory & piano, Consv Music, Wheaton Col, Ill, 51- *Mem:* Music Teachers Nat Asn; Soc Am Musicians; Ill Music Teachers Asn. *Publ:* Auth, Teaching and Understanding Contemporary Piano Music, Kjos-West Publ, 76. *Mailing Add:* Consv Music Wheaton Col Wheaton IL 60187

THOMPSON, GLENDA GOSS
EDUCATOR
b Atlanta, Ga, Aug 15, 47. *Study:* Univ Ga, Athens, AB(music), 69; Univ Libre Belgique, with Robert Wangermee, Brussels, 69-70; Univ NC, Chapel Hill, PhD(musicol), 75. *Teaching:* Lectr musicol, Univ Ga, Athens, 76-78, asst prof, 78- *Awards:* Res Fel, US Govt, 70-73; Fel, Am Asn Univ Women, 82-83; Univ Ga Found Grant, 82. *Mem:* Am Musicol Soc. *Interests:* Music in the Netherlands from 1530 to 1555, particularly at the Hapsburg court. *Publ:* Auth, Archival Accounts of Appenzeller, Rev Belge Musicol, 78-79; Dialogue Concerning the Music of Ancient Greece, Class Outlook, 79; ed, Benedictus Appenzeller. Chansons, Vereniging voor Nedermuziekgeshiedenis, 82; auth, Henry Loys and Jehan de Buys, Tijdschrift van de Vereniging voor Nederladse Musiekgeshiedenis, 82; Mary of Hungary and Music Patronage, Sixteenth Century J (in prep). *Mailing Add:* 100 Cloverhurst Terr Athens GA 30605

THOMPSON, HUGH R
BARITONE, DIRECTOR—OPERA
b Tacoma, Wash, June 19, 15. *Study:* Grad Sch, Juilliard Sch Music, cert, 43. *Rec Perf:* Operatic Arias, Pilotone, 47; Carmen, 50 & Die Fledermaus, 51, RCA. *Roles:* Papageno in Die Zauberflöte, 45, Toreador in Carmen, 45, Valentin in Faust, 45, Mercutio in Romeo & Juliet, 47 & Jokanaan in Salome, 50, Metropolitan Opera Co; Iago in Otello, 49 & Boris Godunov in Boris Godunov, 51, Montreal Opera. *Pos:* Leading bar, Chicago Opera, 41-55, Metropolitan Opera, 44-52 & NBC Opera Theater, 56-59; stage dir, Metropolitan Opera, 62-64. *Teaching:* Dir opera, Hunter Col, 64-66; asst prof voice, Univ Miami, 72-80. *Mailing Add:* 1225 Algeria Ave Coral Gables FL 33134

THOMPSON, JOHN COTTON
VIOLIN
b Norwalk, Conn, Mar 7, 55. *Study:* Harvard Univ, BA, 76; Univ Utah, MM(violin perf), 78. *Pos:* First violin, Utah Symph, 77- *Mailing Add:* Utah Symph Symph-Hall 123 W S Temple Salt Lake City UT 84101

THOMPSON, MARCUS AURELIUS
VIOLA, EDUCATOR
b Bronx, NY, May 4, 46. *Study:* Juilliard Sch Music, BM, 67, MS, 68, DMA, 70. *Rec Perf:* Der Schwanendreher (P Hindemith), 76, Sonata da Chiesa (F Martin), 76 & Suite Hebraique (E Bloch), 76, Vox Rec; Synapse for Viola & Computer (B Vercoe), CRI. *Teaching:* Asst prof music, Oakwood Col, Ala, 70-71; lectr, Mt Holyoke Col, 71-73; assoc prof, Mass Inst Technol, 73-; vis assoc prof viola, Eastman Sch Music, NY, 83; viola fac, New England Consv Music, 83- *Awards:* Int Auditions Winner, Young Concert Artists Inc, 67; First Prize, Hudson Valley Phil Compt, 67 & Nat Black Music Compt, 80. *Mem:* Chamber Music Am (mem bd dir, 80-); Viola Res Soc; Viola d'Amore Soc Am. *Mailing Add:* 19 Forence St Cambridge MA 02139

THOMPSON, MARIAN
EDUCATOR, VOICE
Study: Columbia Univ, BS, Teachers Col, MA, Sch Dramatic Arts; Am Consv Music; Manhattan Sch Music; studied voice with Evelyn Hertzmann, Marinka Gurewich, John Wustman, Walter Taussig & Rudolf Thomas; H B Actors Studio, with Gunda Mordan. *Pos:* Performer, Santa Fe Opera & Stadttheater, Saarland, Germany; guest artist throughout Germany; recital, oratorio, opera & orch performances throughout US; lieder recitalist, New York. *Teaching:* Mem fac voice, Mannes Col Music, 78- *Mailing Add:* Mannes Col Music 157 E 74th St New York NY 10021

THOMPSON, ROBERT K
EDUCATOR, BASSOON
b Dallas, Tex, Aug 16, 36. *Study:* Sch Music, Yale Univ, BMus, 58. *Works:* Quintets of Villa-Lobos & Downey, Orion Rec, 73; The Baroque Bassoon, 73 & Bassoon Sonatas (Boismortier), 76, Musical Heritage Soc; Bassoon Concerti (Vivaldi), Musical Heritage, Chandos & Music Masters, 80; 20th Century Bassoon, Musical Heritage & Chandos, 80. *Pos:* Prin bassoon, Indianapolis Symph, 60-70; mem, Woodwind Arts Quintet, 70- *Teaching:* Prof bassoon, Univ Wis, Milwaukee, 70- *Awards:* Record of Month Award, Musical Heritage Soc. *Interests:* Editions of baroque bassoon music. *Publ:* Ed, Baroque Duos for Two Bassoons, 76 & Suite of Pieces for Bassoon, 77, Shawnee Press. *Rep:* Tornay Mgt 127 W 72nd St New York NY 10023. *Mailing Add:* 2628 N Humboldt Milwaukee WI 53212

THOMPSON, WILLIAM ERNEST
ADMINISTRATOR
b Hamilton, Mo, June 3, 55. *Study:* Univ Mo, Columbia, BA, 77. *Teaching:* Assoc dir, Consv Music, Univ Mo, Kansas City, 82- *Mailing Add:* 4949 Cherry St Kansas City MO 64110

THOMSON, VIRGIL GARNETT
COMPOSER, CRITIC-WRITER
b Kansas City, Mo, Nov 25, 1896. *Study:* Harvard Univ, AB, 22; studies with H Gebbhard, C Clifton, W Goodrich, R Scalero & Nadia Boulanger; numerous hon doctorates. *Works:* Four Saints in Three Acts (opera), 28, The Plow That Broke the Plains (filmscore), 36, The River (filmscore), 37, The Mother of Us All (opera), 47 & Louisiana Story (filmscore), 48, G Schirmer Inc; Missa Pro Defunctis (requiem mass), H W Gray Co/Belwin-Mills, 60; Lord Byron (opera), Southern Music Co Inc, 66. *Pos:* Choirmaster, King's Chapel, Boston, Mass, 22-23; music critic, New York Herald Tribune, 40-54. *Teaching:* Instr, Harvard Col, 20-21. *Awards:* Pulitzer Prize, 49; Gold medal, Am Acad & Inst Arts & Lett, 66; Macdowell Award, 77. *Bibliog:* K Hoover & J Cage (auth), Virgil Thomson: His Life and Music, Thomas Yoseloff, 59; John Huszar (dir), Virgil Thomson Composer, Film Am, 79; Virgil Thomson, Parnassus: Poetry Rev, spring-summer, 77. *Mem:* Fel, Am Acad Arts & Sci; Am Acad Arts & Lett; Acad Nac de Bellas Artes. *Publ:* Auth, Music Right and Left, 51; Virgil Thomson by Virgil Thomson, 66; Music Reviewed, 1940-54, 67; American Music Since 1910, 71; A Virgil Thomson Reader, 81. *Mailing Add:* 222 W 23rd St New York NY 10011

THOMSON, WILLIAM ENNIS
WRITER, EDUCATOR
b Ft Worth, Tex, May 24, 27. *Study:* NTex State Univ, BM, 48, MM, 49; Ind Univ, PhD, 52. *Teaching:* Prof, Ind Univ, Bloomington, 61-69 & Univ Ariz, 73-75; Kulas prof, Case Western Reserve Univ, 69-73; chmn music & Ziegle prof, State Univ NY, Buffalo, 75-80; dir, Univ Southern Calif, 80- *Awards:* Young Comp Award, Nat Fed Music Clubs, 49; Comp in Res Award, Ford Found, 60-61; Outstanding Educr, Case Western Reserve Univ, 70 & Univ Ariz, 74. *Mem:* Soc Music Theory; Nat Asn Sch Music; Int Conf. *Interests:* Music theory. *Publ:* Auth, Introduction to Music Reading, Wadsworth, 65; coauth, Materials and Structure of Music, Prentice-Hall, 65-66; auth, Introduction to Music as Structure, Addison-Wesley, 69; co-ed, Comprehensive Music Program (21 Vol), Univ Hawaii, 71-; auth, Music for Listeners, Prentice-Hall, 79. *Mailing Add:* 3333 E California Pasadena CA 91107

THORESON, THOMAS J
DOUBLE BASS, EDUCATOR
b Duluth, Minn, Apr 5, 46. *Study:* Wis State Univ, BMEd, 68; New England Consv Music, 68-70. *Pos:* Prin bassist, Duluth Minn Symph, 65-68, Portland Maine Symph, 68-70 & Atlanta Virtuosi, 77-82; bassist, Atlanta Symph, 70- *Teaching:* Instr contrabass, Ga State Univ, 78- *Mailing Add:* 4027 Arden Way Atlanta GA 30342

THORIN, SUZANNE ELIZABETH
LIBRARIAN, ADMINISTRATOR
b Detroit, Mich, Mar 2, 42. *Study:* NPark Col, BMus, 59-63; Univ Mich, Ann Arbor, MMus, 64, AMLS, 69. *Pos:* Head music sect, Nat Libr Serv for Blind, Libr Cong, 80-82, head res facil off, Libr Cong, 82- *Teaching:* Assoc prof & music librn, Ind Univ of Pa, 69-80. *Awards:* Summer sem for col teachers, Nat Endowment Humanities, 78; Alice Ditson Grant, Am Acad Rome, 79. *Mem:* Music Libr Asn (ed newslett, 78-81, exec secy, 82-); Am Musicol Soc; Sonneck Soc; Int Asn Music Libr, Archives & Doc Centers. *Interests:* Administration of and collection development in music libraries; medieval and early 20th century music. *Publ:* Coauth, Cataloging Music and Sound Recordings, Music Libr Asn, 83. *Mailing Add:* Libr Cong Gen Reading Rooms Div Res Facil Off Washington DC 20540

THORNE, FRANCIS (BURRITT), JR
COMPOSER, ADMINISTRATOR
b Bay Shore, NY, June 23, 22. *Study:* Yale Univ, BA, 42. *Works:* Elegy for Orchestra, Philadelphia Orch, 64; Lyric Variations, Buffalo Phil, 67; Burlesque Overture, Minn Orch, 68; Piano Concerto, St Paul Chamber Orch, 75; Violin Concerto, 76 & Symphony No 4, 78, Cabrillo Music Fest; La Luce Eterna, Am Comp Orch, 83. *Pos:* Exec secy, Naumburg Found, New York, 70-72; exec dir, Lenox Arts Ctr, New York, 72-75, Am Comp Alliance, New York, 75-; pres & treas, Am Comp Orch, 76- *Teaching:* Instr, Juilliard Sch, 71-73. *Awards:* Prize in Music, Am Acad Arts & Lett, 68; grants, Ford Found, 73 & 76, Nat Endowment Arts, 74, 76 & 79. *Bibliog:* Oliver Daniel (auth), Francis Thorne, BMI, 76; Michael Schnayerson (auth), Full Time Music Man with a Business Bent, Ave Mag, 81. *Mem:* BMI; Am Comp Alliance; Century Asn; Am Fedn Musicians; Am Music Ctr. *Mailing Add:* 116 E 66th St New York NY 10021

THORNE, NICHOLAS C K
COMPOSER
b Copenhagen, Denmark, Nov 7, 53; US citizen. *Study:* Berklee Col Music, BM(comp), 76; New England Consv Music, MM(comp), 80; Berkshire Music Ctr, 79-80. *Works:* Adagio Music, 80, Piano Sonata, 82, Symphony from Silence, 83, Chaconne: Passion of the Heart, Symphony of Light (in prep) & Double Quintet (in prep), Margun Music. *Awards:* Rome Prize fel, Am Acad in Rome, 81-82; comn, Serge Koussevitzky Music Found, Libr Cong, 82; fel, John Simon Guggenheim Mem Found, 82. *Mem:* BMI; Am Music Ctr; Col Music Soc. *Rep:* Margun Music 167 Dudley Rd Newton Center MA 02159. *Mailing Add:* Rte 1 Box 989 Marshfield VT 05658

THORSTENBERG, (JOHN) LAURENCE
OBOE & ENGLISH HORN, TEACHER
b Salt Lake City, Utah, Dec 6, 25. *Study:* Curtis Inst Music, studied oboe & chamber music with Marcel Tabuteau, BM, 51. *Rec Perf:* The Swan of Tuonela (Sibelius), Phillips Rec, 76. *Pos:* First oboe, Dallas Symph Orch, 52-

54; solo oboe, Marlboro Fest, Vt, 52-54; English horn, Chicago Symph Orch, 54-63 & Boston Symph Orch, 64- *Teaching:* Instr oboe, New England Consv, 77- & Boston Univ, 80- *Mem:* Boston Symph Orch Mem Asn; Am Fedn Musicians. *Mailing Add:* 60 Babcock St Brookline MA 02146

THREATTE, LINDA KREBS
FLUTE
b Baton Rouge, La, Aug 15, 44. *Study:* Oberlin Consv, studied flute with Robert Willoughby, BA, 67, BM, 67; Fla State Univ, studied flute with Albert Tipton, MM, 69; studied with William Kincaid & Geoffrey Gilbert. *Pos:* Second flute, Dartmouth Fest Orch, Hanover, NH, 66-67 & Aspen Fest Orch, 68-74; prin flute, Fla Symph Orch, 67- *Teaching:* Adj instr flute, Seminole Community Col, 72- *Mem:* Nat Flute Asn. *Mailing Add:* Fla Symph Orch PO Box 782 Orlando FL 32802

THULEAN, DONALD (MYRON)
CONDUCTOR & MUSIC DIRECTOR, ADMINISTRATOR
b Wenatchee, Wash, June 24, 29. *Study:* Univ Wash, BA, 50, MA(music), 52; Whitworth Col, Hon MusD, 64. *Pos:* Res cond, Ore Symph, 61-62; asst cond, Seattle Symph, 65-69; music dir, Spokane Symph, 62- *Teaching:* Dean, Sch Music, Pac Univ, 55-62. *Awards:* Gov Art Award, State of Wash, 69. *Mem:* Am Symph Orch League. *Mailing Add:* E 2328-34th Ave Spokane WA 99203

THURSTON, ETHEL HOLBROOKE
TEACHER, WRITER
b Minneapolis, Minn, Oct 30, 11. *Study:* Ecole Am Musique, Fontainebleau, France, 30-38; private study with Nadia Boulanger, 30 & 38-42; Pius X Sch Liturgical Music, 42-45; NY Univ, 54. *Teaching:* Instr, Bryn Mawr Col, 54-57; assoc prof, St John's Univ, New York, 59-66; vis prof, Pontifical Inst, Toronto, 62-63 & NY Univ, 73-74; chmn music hist, Manhattan Sch Music, 66-81. *Mem:* Am Musicol Soc; Int Musicol Soc; Music Libr Asn. *Interests:* Polypony of the 12th and 13th centuries. *Publ:* Auth, The Music in the St Victor Manuscript, Pontifical Inst, 58; A Comparison of the St Victor Clausulae with Their Motets, In: Aspects of Medieval and Renaissance Music, Norton, 65; The Works of Perotin, Kalmus, 70; The Conductus Collections in Manuscript Wolfenbuttel 1099, A-R Ed, 80. *Mailing Add:* 175 W 12th St New York NY 10011

THURSTON, RICHARD ELLIOTT
EDUCATOR, CONDUCTOR & MUSIC DIRECTOR
b Wewoka, Okla, Mar 27, 33. *Study:* Univ Mich, with Hans David, Josef Blatt, Louise Cuyler & W D Revelli, BMus, 55, MMus, 55; Univ Tex, Austin, with Paul Pisk & H H Draeger, PhD, 71. *Rec Perf:* USAF Academy Band, Columbia Studios, 70; A Salute to America, 75; Legacy, 76; The Yale Concert Band, Yale Univ, 82. *Pos:* Commander/cond, US Armed Forces Bicentennial Band, 75-76; chief bands & music, US Air Force, 77-80. *Teaching:* Assoc dean sch music & cond in res, Yale Univ, 80-82; dean sch music & perf arts, Oklahoma City Univ, 82- *Mem:* Am Bandmasters Asn (dire, 76-78); Col Band Dir Nat Asn (Okla State Chmn, 83-); Nat Band Asn; Am Musicol Soc; Music Teachers Nat Asn. *Interests:* Techniques of musical depiction of programmatic ideas in the symphonic poems of Richard Strauss. *Publ:* Auth, On Performing Band Transcriptions, Sch Musician, 74; The Final Diary, 1961-1972, Colo Springs Sun, 75; Genesis of a Masterpiece, Instrumentalist, 81. *Mailing Add:* 10504 Dorothy Dr Oklahoma City OK 73132

THYM, JURGEN
EDUCATOR, CRITIC-WRITER
b Bremervörde, WGer, July 2, 43. *Study:* Hochschule Musik, Berlin, 67; Freie Univ, Berlin, 69; Case Western Reserve Univ, 74. *Teaching:* Vis instr, Oberlin Consv, 73; instr, Eastman Sch Music, 73-74, asst prof, 74-80, assoc prof, 80-, chmn musicol, 82- *Awards:* Best Music Rev in Notes, 79 & Best Article-Length Bibliog, 82, Music Libr Asn. *Mem:* Am Musicol Soc; Soc Music Theory; Music Libr Asn. *Interests:* Nineteenth and 20th century music. *Publ:* Auth, New Schumann Materials in Upstate New York, Fontes Artes Musicae, 80; transl, Kirnberger, The Art of Strict Musical Composition, Yale Univ Press, 82; auth, Schumann in Brendel's NZFM, 1845-1856, In: Essays on Mendelssohn and Schumann, Duke Univ Press, 83; ed, One Hundred Years of Eichendorff Songs, A-R Ed, 83; co-ed, Schoenberg Gesamtgasne, Vol XIII, Schott, 83. *Mailing Add:* 1450 E Ave Rochester NY 14610

TIBORIS, PETER ERNEST
EDUCATOR, CONDUCTOR & MUSIC DIRECTOR
b Sheboygan, Wis, Oct 31, 47. *Study:* Univ Wis, BM, 70, MS, 74; Univ Ill, EdD, 80. *Works:* Cherubic Hymn, Midwestern Choir Fedn, 78; Is Agios/ Enite, Univ Southwestern La Chorale, 82. *Pos:* Music dir & cond, Hellenic-Am Choral Fest, Athens, currently; artistic dir & cond, Int Opera Ltd, 81- & Capitol City Opera, Madison, 82- *Teaching:* Choral dir, Madison Pub Sch, Wis, 70-72, Madison Area Technical Col, Wis, 72-76 & Plymouth State Col, 78-80; grad asst choral music, Univ Ill, 76-78; assoc prof, Univ Southwestern La, 80- *Awards:* Olga Sarantos Choral Award, Second Diocese Choir Fedn, 77. *Mem:* Col Music Soc; Nat Forum Greek Orthodox Church Choirs; Int Opera Ltd; Am Choral Dir Asn; Music Educr Nat Conf. *Publ:* Auth, Can Vocal Quality Be Improved by Realtime, Nat Asn Teachers Singing Symposium, 83; Feedback? College & University Swing Choirs: Uses and Abuses, Col Mus Soc Bulletin, 83. *Mailing Add:* PO 1190 Madison WI 53701

TICHMAN, HERBERT
CLARINET, TEACHER
b Philadelphia, Pa, Feb 23, 22. *Study:* Juilliard Sch, study clarinet with A Christmann, BS, 51; study chamber music with Edward Steuermann; Queens Col, City Univ New York, MA(comp), 66. *Rec Perf:* Sonatas, Op 49 No 1 &

Op 107 (Max Reger), Sonata in F Minor, Op 120 No 1 (J Brahms), Trio in A Minor, Op 114 (J Brahms), Contrasts (B Bartok) & Arpeggione Sonata (F Schubert), Mark Rec. *Pos:* Clarinetist, Berkshire Chamber Players, New York, 68-; solo recitalist. *Teaching:* Instr clarinet, Juilliard Sch, 66-72, Manhattan Sch, 72- & private studio, currently. *Awards:* Fulbright Fel, 56. *Mailing Add:* 50 Muirfield Rd Rockville Centre NY 11570

TICKTON, JASON HAROLD
EDUCATOR, ORGAN
b Waltham, Mass, Jan 2, 14. *Study:* Wayne Univ, AB, 36, AM, 37. *Pos:* Organist, Temple Beth El, Birmingham, Mich, 33-, dir music, 45-; organ recitalist & lectr, Am Guild Organist. *Teaching:* From instr to assoc prof, Wayne State Univ, 37-69, prof, 69- *Awards:* Pres Award Excellence in Teaching, Wayne State Univ, 77. *Interests:* Modern piano techniques; comparative analysis of Gregorian and Hebrew chants. *Publ:* Auth, Among the Composers & T'Filot Beth El. *Mailing Add:* Dept Music Wayne State Univ Detroit MI 48202

TIEMEYER, CHRISTIAN
CONDUCTOR & MUSIC DIRECTOR, EDUCATOR
b Baltimore, Md, Sept 21, 40. *Study:* Peabody Consv Music, BMus, 62, MMus, 63; Cath Univ Am, DMA, 77. *Pos:* Cellist, Baltimore Symph, 59-60; asst & actg prin cellist, Am Symph Orch, 62-64; prin cellist, Utah Symph, 68-75; music dir, Salt Lake City Chap, Young Audiences Inc, 74-76; assoc cond, Dallas Symph, 78-; cond, Gtr Dallas Youth Orch, 78-79; founding cond, Dallas Chamber Orch, Univ Tex & Brookhaven Col, 78. *Teaching:* Mem fac, Peabody Consv Music, 61-63; chmn fac cond & string, Univ Utah, 68-77; mem adj fac, Brigham Young Univ, 68-75. *Mailing Add:* 7112 Merriman Pkwy Dallas TX 75231

TIETOV, FRANCES
HARP, EDUCATOR
Study: Curtis Inst Music, BM; Juilliard Sch; Northwestern Univ; studied harp with Marcel Grandjany & Mariln Costello. *Rec Perf:* On Vox. *Pos:* Prin harp & Elizabeth Eliot Mallinckrodt Chair, St Louis Symph Orch, currently; prin harp, Pa Ballet Co, formerly; Am Symph Orch, formerly & Nat Ballet Co; substitute prin harp, Philadelphia Orch, 78; perf, Marlboro Fest, Stratford Fest, Ont & Berkshire Fest. *Teaching:* Mem fac, Claremont Fest, Calif, formerly; mem fac harp & chamber music, St Louis Consv Music, currently. *Awards:* Alexander Hillsberg Award, Philadelphia Found, 66; Young Artists Award, Musicians Club New York, 67; Fromm Found Fel, 64. *Mailing Add:* St Louis Consv Music 560 Trinity Ave St Louis MO 63130

TIKNIS, V MICHAEL
ADMINISTRATOR
b East Orange, NJ, July 10, 51. *Study:* Seton Hall Univ, BS, 74; Cath Univ; New Sch Social Res. *Pos:* Concert mgr, Newark Boys Chorus Sch, 74-78; sales rep & dir spec proj, Herbert Barrett Mgt, 78-82; dir mkt & pub relations, San Antonio Symph, 82- *Mem:* Am Symph Orch League; Asn Col Univ & Community Arts Adminr; Int Soc Perf Arts Adminr. *Mailing Add:* 109 Lexington Ave San Antonio TX 78205

TILKENS, NEIL AVRILL
EDUCATOR, PIANO
b Berrien Springs, Mich, Mar 19, 27. *Study:* Columbia Union Col, BMus, 50; Philadelphia Consv Music, MMus, 52. *Pos:* Pianist, Washington Perf Arts Soc, 69-; music critic, Washington Post, 72-73. *Teaching:* Assoc prof music & music hist, Columbia Union Col, Takoma Park, Md, 50-55 & 58-67 & chmn, Music Dept, 61-63; assoc prof, Union Col, Nebr, 55-58 & George Washington Univ, 66- *Mem:* Friday Morning Music Club; Music Teachers Nat Asn; Am Musicol Soc; Md State Music Teachers Asn (pres, 71-73). *Mailing Add:* 8001 Glenside Dr Takoma Park MD 20012

TILLIS, FREDERICK C
COMPOSER, ADMINISTRATOR
b Galveston, Tex, Jan 5, 30. *Study:* Wiley Col, BA, 49; Univ Iowa, MA, 52, PhD, 63. *Works:* Three Songs from Shadows & Distance Nowhere for Voice & Piano, 71, Niger Symphony for Chamber Orchestra, 75, Spiritual Fantasy #3 (piano four hands), 81, Spiritual Fantasy #4 (piano), 81 & Spiritual Fantasy #5 (horn & piano), 82, Am Comp Alliance; Concerto for Piano & Symphony Orchestra, Billy Taylor & Springfield Symph Orch, 83. *Teaching:* Assoc provost & prof music, Univ Mass, Amherst, 74-76, dir Afro Am music & jazz, 76-, asst to provost, 76-82, dir fine arts ctr, 82- *Awards:* United Negro Col Fund Fel, 61-63; Rockefeller Found Grant, 78; Nat Endowment Arts Comp Grant, 79. *Mem:* Am Music Ctr; Am Comp Alliance; Music Educr Nat Conf; Nat Asn Jazz Educr; Mass Music Educr Asn. *Mailing Add:* 55 Grantwood Dr Amherst MA 01002

TILLOTSON, LAURA VIRGINIA
CLARINET, CONDUCTOR
b Hendersonville, NC. *Study:* Baylor Univ, studied clarinet with Noah Knepper, BM; Univ Ill, studied flute with Charles Delaney, MM; Univ NC, Chapel Hill, studied musicol with William S Newman; studied clarinet with Ignatius Genussa & Gerhard Starke. *Pos:* Cond & music dir, Brevard Chamber Orch, currently; prin clarinet, Asheville Symph, currently. *Teaching:* Prof music & actg chmn fine arts div, Brevard Col, currently; mem artist fac in res, Brevard Music Ctr, currently. *Mem:* Int Clarinet Soc. *Mailing Add:* Brevard Col Box 393 Brevard NC 28712

TILSON-THOMAS, MICHAEL
PIANO, CONDUCTOR
b Los Angeles, Calif, 1944. *Study:* Univ Southern Calif, BMus, MMus; studied with Ingolf Dahl & John Crown; Berkshire Music Ctr, 68; Hamilton Col, LLD, 71; D'Youville Col, LHD, 76. *Rec Perf:* Images (Debussy), First Symphony (Tchaikovsky), Sun-treader (Ruggles), Violin Concerto (Schumann), Three Places in New England (Ives) & Second Symphony (Piston), DGG. *Pos:* Asst cond, Boston Symph Orch, 69, assoc cond, 70-72, prin guest cond, 72-74; prin guest cond, Berkshire Music Fest, summers 70 & 74 & Los Angeles Phil, 81-; music dir & cond, Buffalo Phil Orch, 71-79; cond & dir, New York Phil Young People's Concerts, CBS-TV, 71-77; vis cond with numerous orchs in US, Europe & Japan; dir, Ojai Fest, 72-77; cond, Santa Fe Opera, summer 79; cond & pianist, Hollywood Bowl Summer Fest, 83. *Teaching:* Mem fac, Berkshire Music Ctr, 68 & 69; vis adj prof, Music Dept, State Univ NY Buffalo. *Awards:* Koussevitzky Cond Prize, Berkshire Music Ctr, 68; Musician of Month, Musical Am, 6/70; Grammy Award, 76. *Mailing Add:* c/o Carson Off 119 W 57th St New York NY 10019

TIMM, EVERETT L
ADMINISTRATOR, FLUTE
b Highmore, SDak, Jan 8, 14. *Study:* Morningside Col, BM, 36; studied flute with Georges Barrere, Arthur Lora, Joseph Mariano & Donald Lentz; Eastman Sch Music, MM, 43, PhD, 48; Morningside Col, Hon DM, 67. *Pos:* Prin flute, Sioux City Symph, 31-42; staff cond, KSCJ Radio, Sioux City, 39-42. *Teaching:* Dir band & woodwinds, Morningside Col, 35-42; prof orch & flute, cond orch & dean sch music, La State Univ, Baton Rouge, 42-79. *Awards:* Outstanding Service, Nat Asn Sch Music, 77. *Mem:* Nat Asn Col Wind & Perc Instr (chmn southern div, 51-53); La Music Educr Asn (secy-treas, 51-53); Music Teachers Nat Asn (chmn col music div, 58); Music Educr Nat Conf (pres southern div, 65-67); Nat Asn Sch Music (treas, vpres & pres, 72-77). *Publ:* Auth, A Treatise on Flute Playing, 43 & Training Requirements for Careers in Music, 48, Sibley Music Libr; Brief of an Artist, Joseph Mariano, Woodwind Mag, Apr, 48; A Directory of Awards and Grants in Music, Music Educr Nat Conf, 57; The Woodwinds: Performance and Teaching Techniques, Allyn & Bacon, 64-71. *Mailing Add:* 465 Magnolia Woods Ave Baton Rouge LA 70808

TIMM, (M) JEANNE ANDERSON
EDUCATOR, FLUTE
b Sioux City, Iowa. *Study:* Consv Music, Morningside Col, BMus, 40; Eastman Sch Music, with Joseph Mariano, 46-48; La State Univ, 55-56. *Pos:* Flutist, New Orleans Phil, 42-43 & Timm Woodwind Quintet, La State Univ, 66-; princ flutist, Sioux City Symph, 43-46, Baton Rouge Symph, 49- & Baton Rouge Opera, 82- *Teaching:* Prof woodwind instrm, Morningside Col, 43-46; assoc prof flute & chamber music, La State Univ, 68- *Mem:* Nat Flute Asn; Music Educr Nat Conf; Music Teachers Nat Asn; La Music Educr Asn; Nat Asn Col Wind & Perc Instrm. *Mailing Add:* 465 Magnolia Woods Ave Baton Rouge LA 70808

TIMM, KENNETH N
COMPOSER, EDUCATOR
b San Francisco, Calif, Nov 2, 34. *Study:* Calif State Univ, Hayward, with Glenn Glasow, BA, 64; Mills Col, with Darius Milhaud, Robert Erickson & Luciano Berio, MA, 66; Ind Univ, Bloomington, with Bernhard Heiden & John Eaton, DM, 77. *Works:* Six Miniatures, 70, Other Streams (sonata), 72 & Across A Circle, 76, Acis Publ; The Joiner and the Diehard, Crystal Rec, 76; Two Movements for Orchestra, 77, Three Poems of e e cummings, 80 & Concentio for Mixed Chorus, 82, Acis Publ. *Teaching:* Asst prof comp & theory, Consv Music, Lawrence Univ, 73-74 & Cleveland State Univ, 74-76; assoc prof, Eastern Ky Univ, 76- *Awards:* First Prize in Comp, World Sax Cong, 72; First Prize in Vocal Comp, Frederick Delius Found, 73; First Prize in Cello Comp Cont, Am Soc Univ Comp & Ariz Cello Soc, 74-75. *Mem:* ASCAP. *Mailing Add:* Music Dept Eastern Ky Univ Richmond KY 40475

TIMM, LARRY M (LAURANCE MILO)
EDUCATOR, OBOE & ENGLISH HORN
b Sioux City, Iowa, Jan 21, 49. *Study:* La State Univ, studied oboe with Earnest Harrison, BM, 71; Yale Univ, studied oboe with Robert Bloom, MM, 73, MMA, 74, DMA, 81. *Rec Perf:* Old Songs Deranged, Music for Theatre Orchestra (Charles Ives), Columbia & CBS, 74; By All Means (Alphonse Mouzon), Studio Sound Recorder, 81; Symphony No 6 (Roy Harris), Varese-Sarabande Label, 81; Music for Walt Disney's Epcot Center, Studio Orange, 81-82; Morning Sun (Herbie Hancock & Hubert Laws), Pausa Rec, 82. *Pos:* Prin oboist, Pac Symph Orch, 77-81 & Long Beach Symph, 80-; freelance oboist, Gtr Los Angeles Area orchs, 77-; oboe & English horn soloist for major motion pictures & TV studios, 78- *Teaching:* Asst prof oboe & woodwind specialist, Univ SC, Columbia, 74-77; assoc prof, Calif State Univ, Fullerton, 77- *Mem:* Int Double Reed Soc; Am Fedn Musicians. *Publ:* Auth, Playing Oboe & English Horn in Hollywood Studios, Woodwind, Brass & Perc Mag, 83. *Mailing Add:* 319 E H St Ontario CA 91764

TIPEI, SEVER
COMPOSER, EDUCATOR
b Bucharest, Romania, Nov 1, 43; US citizen. *Study:* Bucharest Consv, Romania, dipl(piano), 67; Univ Paris VIII, musical aesthet with Daniel Charles, 72; Univ Mich, DMA(comp), 78. *Works:* Translation (voice, clarinet & piano), Seesaw Music Inc, 70; Katastrophe (electronic tape), 74; Portrait of the Artist (women's choir), Seesaw Music Inc, 75; Undulating Michigamme (soloist & orch), 78, Lament (piano), 80, Ezra Pound's CANTO CXVI (baritone & piano), 80, & Clariphannies (solo clarinet), Am Comp Alliance. *Teaching:* Instr comp, theory, formalized music & comput asst

comp, Chicago Musical Col, Roosevelt Univ, 75-78; asst prof, Univ Ill, 78-
Mem: Am Comp Alliance; BMI; Am New Music Consortium (bd dir, 82-);
Col Music Soc. *Publ:* Auth, MP1-A Computer Program for Music
Composition, 75 & Solving Specific Compositional Problems with MP1, 81,
Proc Int Comput Music Conf. *Mailing Add:* 2136 Music Bldg Univ Ill 1114
W Nevada Urbana IL 61801

TIRCUIT, HEUWELL ANDREW
COMPOSER, CRITIC & WRITER
b Plaquemine, La, Oct 18, 31. *Study:* La State Univ, BM, 53; Northwestern
Univ, MM, 64; Univ Southern Calif, critics cert, 66. *Works:* Manga (seven
piece orch), Minneapolis Symph, 59; Cello Concerto, comn by Asahi
Broadcasting Co, 60; Odoru Katachi, comn by Thor Johnson, perf by Chicago
Little Symph, 62; Concerto No 1 (orch), 68 & Solo Percussionist Concerto,
69, Chicago Symph; Concerto No 3 (orch), comn by Thor Johnson, perf by
Philadelphia Orch, 70; Goerdeler Triptch (orch), comn by Detroit Symph, 75.
Pos: Chief perc, Asahi Broadcasting Comp Orch, Tokyo, 56-59; music critic,
Asahi Evening News, Tokyo, 57-63; prod Am works, CRI, 59-61; assoc music
critic, Chicago Am, 63-65; music & dance ed, San Francisco Chronicle, 66-
Teaching: Instr music hist, Interlochen Arts Acad, 65. *Awards:* Comp Prize,
Nat Fedn Music Clubs, 51 & 52; Ill State Centennial, Chicago Symph Compt,
68; Merit Award, Nat Fedn Music Clubs, 82. *Bibliog:* H H Stuckenschmidt
(auth), The Flute as Weapon, Welt, Germany, 59. *Mem:* BMI. *Interests:* W
F Bach and early Rococo style; essays on composers lives and works. *Publ:*
Auth, English for the Concert Hall, 59-61, The Messiaen Problem, 60, Bartok,
A Complete Catalogue, 61, Stravinsky, A Complete Catalogue, 61, Debussy,
A Complete Catalogue, 61 & Bunsekiteki Ensoran, 70, Ongaku-no-Tomo.
Mailing Add: 1955 Broadway Apt 301 San Francisco CA 94109

TIRRO, FRANK PASCALE
ADMINISTRATOR, WRITER
b Omaha, Nebr, Sept 20, 35. *Study:* Univ Nebr, with Robert Beadell,
BMusEd, 60; Northwestern Univ, with Anthony Donato & Frank Cookson,
MM, 61; Univ Chicago, with Leonard B Meyer, PhD(musicol), 74. *Works:*
American Jazz Mass, Summy-Birchard, 60; Sing A New Song, 66, Church
Sonata for Organ, 67, Melismas for Carillon, 67 & American Jazz Te Deum,
70, World Libr. *Pos:* Dean, Yale Sch Music, 80- *Teaching:* Fel of Villa I Tatti,
Harvard Univ, 71-72; lectr music hist, Univ Kans, 72-73; assoc prof & chmn,
Duke Univ, 73-80; prof musicol & dean, Yale Sch Music, 80- *Awards:* Comp
Prize, Nat Fedn Music Clubs, 61; Travel Grant, Am Coun Learned Soc, 68;
Standard Comp Award, ASCAP, 70. *Mem:* Am Musicol Soc; Int Musicol Soc;
Col Music Soc; Renaissance Soc Am; Nat Asn Sch Music. *Interests:* Music
of the Renaissance; history of jazz; music theory. *Publ:* Auth, The Silent
Theme Tradition in Jazz, Musical Quart, 67; Jazz: A History, W W Norton,
77; coauth, The Humanities: Cultural Roots and Continuities, D C Heath Co,
80; auth, Royal 8 G VII: Strawberry Leaves, Single Arch, and Wrong-Way
Lions, Musical Quart, 81; ed, Medieval and Renaissance Studies, No 9, Duke
Univ Press, 82. *Mailing Add:* 435 College St New Haven CT 06520

TISCHLER, HANS
MUSICOLOGIST
b Vienna, Austria, Jan 18, 15; US citizen. *Study:* New Vienna Consv, with
Paul Wittgenstein, 30-33; Vienna State Acad, comp with Franz Schmidt &
cond with Oswald Kabasta, BM(piano), 33, MMus, 36; Univ Vienna, with R
Lach, R Haas, E Wellesz, A Orel & L Nowak, PhD(musicol), 37; Yale Univ,
with Paul Hindemith & Leo Schrade, PhD(musicol), 42. *Teaching:* Prof, WVa
Wesleyan Col, 45-47 & Ind Univ, Bloomington, 65-; assoc prof, Chicago
Musical Col, Roosevelt Univ, 47-65; guest prof, Univ Chicago, 56-57 & Tel-
Aviv Univ, 72. *Awards:* Guggenheim Fel, 64-65; grant, Am Coun Learned
Soc, 70; fel, Nat Endowment Humanities, 75-76. *Mem:* Am Musicol Soc
(coun mem 60-62); Int Musicol Soc; Medieval Acad Am. *Interests:* Music in
the late 12th to the early 14th centuries. *Publ:* Auth, A Structural Analysis
of Mozart's Piano Concertos, Inst Medieval Music, 66; ed, History of
Keyboard Music to 1700, Ind Univ Press, 73; auth, The Montpellier Codex,
3 vols, A-R Ed, 78; coauth, Chanter m'estuet: Songs of the Trouveres, Ind
Univ Press, 81; auth, The Earliest Motets, to cira 1270, 3 vols, Yale Univ
Press, 82. *Mailing Add:* Sch Music Ind Univ Bloomington IN 47405

TISCHLER, JUDITH B
EDUCATOR, EDITOR
b New York, NY, May 14, 33. *Study:* City Col New York, BA, 71, studied
comp with Mario Davidowsky, MA, 74. *Pos:* Second horn, Voice Israel Radio
Orch, 54-58; first horn, Israel Nat Opera, 59-62; ed & dir music publ,
Transcontinental Music, Union Am Hebrew Congregations, 80- *Teaching:*
Instr theory & ear training, City Col New York, 74-81; Jewish Theol Sem Am,
75- & Sem Col Jewish Music, 75- *Publ:* Contribr, In Memoriam: Lazar Weiner
(1897-1982), Musica Judaica, 81-82. *Mailing Add:* 20 W Hickory Spring
Valley NY 10977

TISON, DONALD
TRUMPET
Study: Univ Mich, BA(wind instrm), MM(music educ), teachers cert; Univ
Md; Cath Univ Am, Peabody Consv; studied with Donald Polosky, Paul
Wilwerth, Lloyd Geisler, Gilbert Johnson, Clifford Lillya & Vincent
Cichowitz. *Pos:* Solo cornet, US Naval Acad Band, formerly; prin trumpet,
New Orleans Symph & Opera Orch, formerly & Baltimore Symph Orch,
currently. *Teaching:* Instr trumpet & trumpet repertoire, Peabody Consv,
currently. *Mailing Add:* 3005 Woodhome Ave Baltimore MD 21234

TITCOMB, CALDWELL
EDUCATOR, COMPOSER
b Augusta, Maine, Aug 16, 26. *Study:* Harvard Col, AB, 47; Harvard Univ,
MA, 49, PhD, 52. *Works:* Yuki (song cycle), several singers, 48; Sonata for
Organ, several players, 48; Incidental Music for Eugene O'Neill's Marco
Millions, 54; Incidental Music for Arthur Miller's Death of a Salesman, 56;
Incidental Music for Bernard Shaw's Saint Joan, 56; Incidental Music for Jean
Genet's Deathwatch, 57; Incidental Music for Bertolt Brecht's Puntila, 59.
Pos: Univ organist, Brandeis Univ, 53-75; mem bd dir, Cambridge Civic
Symph Orch, 59-70. *Teaching:* From instr to prof, Brandeis Univ, 53-, chmn
Sch Creative Arts, 68-70. *Bibliog:* Frances T Wiggin (auth), Maine Composers
and Their Music, Portland, Maine, 76; M E Comtois & Lynn Miller (auths),
Contemporary American Theatre Critics, Metuchen, NJ, 77. *Mem:* Am
Musicol Soc (mem coun 65-67); Col Music Soc; Soc Ethnomusicol; Sonneck
Soc; Am Guild Organists. *Publ:* Auth, Boston—Opera, Enciclopedia dello
spettacolo, Vol II, Rome, 55; Baroque Court and Military Trumpets and
Kettledrums, Galpin Soc J, 56; coauth, Choral Music, Penguin Books, 63 &
66; contribr, Harvard Dictionary of Music, 2nd ed, Harvard Univ Press, 70;
Academic American Encyclopedia, Vol XIV, Princeton, NJ, 80. *Mailing Add:*
Music Dept Brandeis Univ Waltham MA 02254

TITON, JEFF TODD
EDUCATOR, WRITER
b Jersey City, NJ, Dec 8, 43. *Study:* Amherst Col, BA, 65; Univ Minn, MA,
70, PhD, 71. *Teaching:* Assoc prof music, Tufts Univ, Medford, Mass, 71-
Awards: Deems Taylor Award, ASCAP, 78. *Mem:* Soc Ethnomusicol (pres,
Northeast Chap, 82-84); Am Folklore Soc; Soc Asian Music; Am Studies Asn.
Interests: Afro-American and Anglo-American folk music, particularly blues
and religious music. *Publ:* Auth, Early Downhome Blues, Univ Ill Press, 77;
ed, Downhome Blues Lyrics, G K Hall & Co, 81; auth, Powerhouse for God,
Univ NC Press, 82; ed & contribr, Worlds of Music, Schirmer Books, 84.
Mailing Add: Dept Music Tufts Univ Medford MA 02155

TOBIAS, PAUL
CELLO, EDUCATOR
Study: Juilliard Sch Music, BM; studied violoncello with Margaret Rowell,
Zara Nelsova, Claus Adam, Leonard Rose, & Gregor Piatigorsky. *Rec Perf:*
On CBS & Marlboro Rec Soc. *Pos:* Soloist violoncello, Los Angeles Phil,
Pittsburgh Symph & New York Phil; performer throughout US, Europe &
South Am including Aspen & Marlboro Fest. *Teaching:* Mem fac violoncells,
Mannes Col Music, 75-, New England Consv, 79-83, Rutgers Univ, 82-; instr
perf & analysis sem, Harvard Univ, 77-79. *Awards:* Gregor Piatigorsky
Award; Naumburg Found Award. *Bibliog:* The Way They Play, Applebaum-
Roth, 81. *Mem:* Violoncello Soc (mem bd dirs, currently). *Mailing Add:* c/o
Grapa Concerts 1995 Broadway New York NY 10023

TOBIN, ROBERT LYNN BATTS
ADMINISTRATOR
b San Antonio, Mar 12, 34. *Study:* Univ Tex, 51-52. *Pos:* Prod coordr, San
Antonio Grand Opera Fest, 51-57 & 60-63; vpres cult participation, San
Antonio Fair Inc, 66-68; vpres & dir, Am Nat Opera Co, 67-68; pres, Fest
Found, Fest Due Monde, Spoleto, 70-71; mem bd managing dir, Met Opera
Co; producer & cur numerous exhib stage & costume design; chief exec officer
& secy-treas, Tobin Surveys Inc; chmn bd, Tobin Res Inc; trustee, Museum
Modern Art; pres, Nat Opera Inst, currently. *Mem:* Cent Opera Serv Met
Opera Nat Coun (nat chmn, 61-82, hon nat chmn & mem int coun, currently);
NY Quadriennale Stage & Designs; Nat Opera Inst; Fine Arts Found; Ordine
Merito Repub Ital. *Mailing Add:* Nat Opera Inst Kennedy Ctr Perf Arts
Washington DC 20566

TOCCO, JAMES
PIANO, TEACHER
b Detroit, Mich, Sept 21, 43. *Study:* Studied with Boris Maximovich, 54-61,
Magda Tagliaferro, 62-67 & Claudio Arrau, 72-73. *Rec Perf:* Complete
Preludes (Chopin), 83, Piano Works (MacDowell & Griffes), 83 & Piano
Works (Foss, Downey & Heiden), 83, Gasparo Rec; Collected Works
(Bernstein), Pro Arte Rec, 83. *Teaching:* Univ artist, Univ Wis, Milwaukee,
70-74; prof music, Sch Music, Ind Univ, Bloomington, 77- *Awards:* Bronze
Medal, Tchaikovsky Compt, Moscow, 70 & Queen Elizabeth of Belgium
Compt, Brussels, 72; First Prize, Munich Int Music Compt, 73. *Publ:* Auth,
Magda As Muse, Musical Am, 2/80. *Rep:* Colbert Artists Mgt 111 W 57th
St New York NY 10019. *Mailing Add:* c/o Sch Music Ind Univ Bloomington
IN 47405

TODD, GEORGE BENNETT
COMPOSER, EDUCATOR
b Minneapolis, Minn, May 31, 35. *Study:* Amherst Col, BA, 57; Stanford
Univ, MBA, 59; Princeton Univ, MFA, 64. *Works:* Satan's Sermon, 80 &
Variations, 80, CRI; Breath, Solaris Dance Co, 82; News, Middlebury Dance
Co, 82. *Pos:* Exec dir, Comp Conf, Johnson, Vt, 76-78. *Teaching:* Prof,
Middlebury Col, 65-, chmn, 68-78 & 82-83. *Mailing Add:* RD3 Middlebury
VT 05753

TOENSING, RICHARD E
COMPOSER, EDUCATOR
b St Paul, Minn, Mar 11, 40. *Study:* Univ Mich, with Ross Lee Finney, Leslie
Bassett, George B Wilson, DMA. *Works:* Doxologies (band); For All the Wild
Things (band), 72; Homages (chamber orch); Sounds & Changes II, III
(organ); Sounds & Changes IV (organ & percussion); Laetantur Archangeli
(solo clarinet); Doxologies II (organ); & others. *Teaching:* Mem fac, Upsala
Col, 66-73; assoc prof music, Univ Colo, Boulder, 73- *Awards:* BMI Student
Awards, 63 & 64. *Mailing Add:* Col Music Univ Colo Boulder CO 80309

TOLLEFSON, ARTHUR RALPH
PIANO, EDUCATOR
b San Francisco, Calif, May 3, 42. *Study:* Stanford Univ, AB, 63, MA, 64, DMA, 68. *Pos:* Pianist, San Francisco, 54, New York, 74 & London, 76; soloist, San Francisco Symph Orch, Oakland Symph Orch & Atlanta Symph Orch. *Teaching:* Chmn piano dept, Sch Music, Northwestern Univ, 75-82; chmn music dept, Univ Ark, Fayetteville, currently. *Awards:* Kimber Award, 58; fel, Nat Endowment Humanities, 75. *Mem:* Col Music Soc (pres, 83-85); Nat Piano Found. *Mailing Add:* 789 Cliffside Fayetteville AR 72701

TOLO, LELAND STANFORD
EDUCATOR, DOUBLE BASS
b McVille, NDak, Jan 9, 43. *Study:* Luther Col, Iowa, 60-62; Univ Minn, BA(musicol), 64; Univ Ky, MM(musicol), 66; Hochschule Musik, Munich, 67-68; studied bass with Franz Ortner, Murray Grodner, Warren Benfield & Ray Fitch & gamba with August Wenzinger & Grace Feldman. *Pos:* Mem, Louisville Symph, formerly & Munich-Bach Orch, formerly; first stand double bass, Hartford Symph, formerly; double bassist & gambist, Hartford Baroque Chamber Orch, formerly; gambist, Sinfonia Jocadi Consort, formerly & Hartt Sch Consort, currently; founder, dir & viola da gambist, Collage Antiqua, 81- *Teaching:* Mem staff, Saratoga Sch Orch Studies, formerly; mem fac double bass & theory, Hartt Sch Music, 68- *Awards:* Deutsch Akademische Austauschdienst Stipendiat, 66-67. *Mem:* Inst String Bass; Viola da Gamba Soc Am; Am Musicol Soc. *Publ:* Contribr to Bass Sound Post. *Mailing Add:* Hartt Sch Music Univ Hartford West Hartford CT 06117

TOMS, JOHN (ELIAS)
CRITIC & WRITER, EDUCATOR
b Saginaw, Mich, Jan 27, 11. *Study:* Consv Music, Oberlin Col, BM, 32; Univ Mich, MM, 36; Berkshire Fest, with Hugh Ross, 42. *Roles:* Lensky in Eugene Onegin, Pelleas in Pelleas et Melisande, Don Basilio in Le Nozze di Figaro, Alfred in Die Fledermaus, Wenzel, & Gonzales, Philadelphia Opera Co, 40-42; Alfredo in La Traviata, Chicago Opera, 46. *Pos:* Music critic, Tulsa Tribune, 72-; Recitalist & oratorio soloist with major choral orgn, formerly. *Teaching:* Asst prof voice, Univ NC, 36-44; assoc prof, Northwestern Univ, 45-62 & San Francisco State Univ, 62-66; prof, Univ Tulsa, 66-76. *Mem:* Music Critics Asn. *Publ:* Ed & translr, Young Artists' Repertoire, Summy-Birchard, 66; ed, Survey of American and British Solo Vocal Literature, Off Educ, US Dept Health, Educ & Welfare; auth, articles in Music Am, Nation's Bus & Opera News. *Mailing Add:* 7905-A E 66th St S Tulsa OK 74133

TOPILOW, CARL S
CONDUCTOR & MUSIC DIRECTOR
b Jersey City, NJ, Mar 14, 47. *Study:* Manhattan Sch Music, BA(clarinet), 68, MA(music educ), 69; Nat Orch Asn, with Leon Barzin. *Rec Perf:* Arutunian Trumpet Concerto, Clarion Rec, 72; Mendelssohn Concerto for Violin and Piano, Orion Rec, 81. *Pos:* Exxon/Arts Endowment Cond, Denver Symph, 76-79, asst cond, 79-80; music dir, Colo Phil, 78-; cond & dir orch prog, Cleveland Inst Music, 81- *Awards:* First Prize, Baltimore Symph Cond Compt, 76. *Mem:* Nat Symph Orch League. *Mailing Add:* 3536 Daleford Rd Cleveland OH 44120

TORCH, DEBORAH L
VIOLIN, EDUCATOR
b Urbana, Ill. *Study:* Univ Rochester, with Carroll Glenn, BA, 73; Univ Mich, with Paul Makanowitzky, MM, 76. *Pos:* First violin sect, San Antonio Symph, 78- *Teaching:* Instr violin, Univ Tex, San Antonio, 81- *Mailing Add:* 2922 Abercorn San Antonio TX 78247

TORCHINSKY, ABE
EDUCATOR, TUBA
b Philadelphia, Pa, Mar 30, 20. *Study:* Curtis Inst Music, dipl, 42. *Rec Perf:* Sonatas for Brass & Piano (Hindemuth), Columbia Rec, 76. *Pos:* Tuba, NBC Symph, 46-49 & Philadelphia Orch, 49-72. *Teaching:* Instr tuba, Curtis Inst Music, 67-72; prof, Univ Mich, Ann Arbor, 72- *Awards:* Grammy, Nat Acad Rec Arts & Sci, 69. *Mem:* Pi Kappa Lambda. *Publ:* Auth, 20th Century Orchestra Studies for Tuba (11 vol), G Schirmer, 70; Orchestra Rep for Tuba, European Am Jerona Music, 72 & 79; Dance Movements for Euphonium Tuba, G Schirmer, 73. *Mailing Add:* 654 Greenhills Dr Ann Arbor MI 48105

TORIGI, RICHARD
BARITONE
b New York, NY, Oct 30, 17. *Study:* Am Theatre Wing; Amato Wkshp; studied with Eleanor McClellan, Dick Marzollo & Mario Pagano. *Roles:* Escamillo in Carmen, Rochester Opera, 47; Dott Malatesta in Don Pasquale; Belcore in L'Elisir d'Amore; Enrico in Lucia di Lammermoor; Guglielmo in Cosi fan tutte; Sharpless in Madama Butterfly; Figaro in Barber of Seville; and many others. *Pos:* Sang with major co in Can, Spain & US; leading bar, Chicago Lyr Opera, New York City Opera, Philadelphia Lyr Opera, Cincinnati Summer Opera, Miami Opera Guild & others. *Teaching:* Fac mem voice, Acad Vocal Arts, 70-73; Philadelphia Col Musical Arts, 73-77; Juilliard Sch Music, 77- & Eastman Sch Music, 79-80. *Mailing Add:* 2109 Broadway New York NY 10023

TORKANOWSKY, WERNER
CONDUCTOR & MUSIC DIRECTOR, COMPOSER
b Berlin, Germany, Mar 3, 26; US citizen. *Study:* Violin study with mem Israel Phil; studied with Rafael Bronstein & Pierre Monteux. *Works:* String Quartet, 81, Prophecies for Cello & Piano, 81, Three Songs, 82, Meditations for Cello, 82 & Trio, 82, Orion Rec. *Pos:* Music dir, Ballets USA, 59-63; cond, Spoleto Fest, 59-62; music dir & cond, New Orleans Phil, 61-77; music dir, Carnegie-Mellon Univ, 82-; violinist, New England Piano Quartette; guest cond with most major orch in US. *Awards:* Walter Naumburg Award for Cond, 60. *Mailing Add:* Hancock Point Rd Hancock ME 04640

TOTENBERG, ROMAN
VIOLIN, ADMINISTRATOR
b Lodz, Poland. *Study:* Chopin Consv, Warsaw; Hochschule Music, Berlin; Int Inst Paris; studied with Carl Flesch, George Enesco, Pierre Monteux & Kurt Sachs. *Pos:* Soloist violin, Warsaw Phil, formerly, New York Phil, Boston Symph, Cleveland Symph, Los Angeles Symph, Berlin Phil, London Phil & many other maj orchs in North Am & Europe; recitalist, White House, Carnegie Hall, Libr Cong, Metropolitan Museum Art & throughout US & Europe. *Teaching:* Mem fac, Peabody Consv Music, Univ Ill, Urbana, Mannes Coll Music, Aspen Music Fest, Mozarteum, Salzburg, Music Acad West, formerly; head string dept & prof violin, Boston Univ, currently; dir, Longy Sch Music, currently; Kneisel Hall, Maine. *Awards:* Mendelssohn Prize, Berlin, 32; Wieniawski Medal, 68; Ysaye Medal, 73. *Mailing Add:* Longy Sch Music One Follen St Cambridge MA 02138

TOTH, ANDOR, JR
EDUCATOR, CELLO
Study: Oberlin Col, with George Neikrug, 65-67; Univ Tex, Austin, 67-69; studied with Gabor Rejto. *Rec Perf:* On Vox & Angelicum. *Pos:* Mem, San Francisco Symph & Chamber Orch, 69-72, soloist, formerly; soloist, Joffrey Ballet & Houston Symph; solo & chamber music recitalist; mem, New Hungarian Quartet, currently. *Teaching:* Mem fac, San Francisco Consv Music, 69-72; assoc prof violoncello, Consv Music, Oberlin Col, 72- *Rep:* ICA Mgt 2219 Eastridge Rd Timonium MD 21093. *Mailing Add:* Consv Music Oberlin Col Oberlin OH 44074

TOULIATOS-BANKER, DIANE H
WRITER, EDUCATOR
b Memphis, Tenn, Sept 10, 49. *Study:* Memphis State Univ, BM, 71; Ohio State Univ, studied musicol with Richard Hoppin, Milos Velimirovic & Keith Mixter, PhD, 79. *Teaching:* Assoc, Ohio State Univ, 72-78; asst prof, Univ Mo, 79- *Awards:* Fels, Fulbright-Hays, 75 & 82. *Mem:* Int Musicol Soc; Am Musicol Soc; Byzantine Studies Soc; Col Music Soc; Music Teachers Nat Asn. *Interests:* Western and Byzantine medieval music; women medieval composers (Western & Byzantine). *Publ:* Auth, The Byzantine Orthros, Byzantina IX, 77; State of the Discipline of Byzantine Music, Acta Musicol 42, 78; Medieval Women Composers in Byzantium and the West, Proc VIth Int Cong Musicol, 82; Women Composers of Medieval Byzantine Chant, Col Music Symposium, 83; The Byzantine Amomos Chant of the 14th and 15th Centuries, Patriarchal Inst Patristic Studies (in prep). *Mailing Add:* 4073 90th Ave Florissant MO 63034

TOUTANT, WILLIAM PAUL
EDUCATOR, COMPOSER
b Worcester, Mass, May 2, 48. *Study:* George Washington Univ, studied piano with Constance Russell, cond with George Steiner & comp with Robert Parris, BA, 70, MA, 72; Mich State Univ, studied comp with Owen Reed & Jere Hutcheson, PhD, 77. *Works:* Gems, 78, Peregrinations, 80 & Quartre Alcools, 82, Calif State Univ, Northridge. *Teaching:* Vis lectr, Kalamazoo Col, 72-73; assoc prof music, Calif State Univ, Northridge, 75- *Publ:* Auth, Fundamental Concepts of Music, 80, Diatonic Harmony (in prep) & Chromatic Harmony (in prep), Wadsworth. *Mailing Add:* Dept Music Calif State Univ Northridge CA 91330

TOWER, IBROOK
CONDUCTOR, CLARINET
b Boston, Mass, July 21, 48. *Study:* Consv Music, Peabody Inst, BMus, 70; Col Music, Temple Univ, MMus(perf), 72. *Pos:* Solo clarinet, Wilmington Chamber Orch, 72-74; solo clarinet, asst cond & program annotator, Nittany Valley Symph Orch State, Col, 75-; artistic dir, Seven Points Amphitheatre, 78-; clarinet, Juniata Woodwind Quintet, 78-82. *Teaching:* Instr woodwind, Wilmington Music Sch, 69-74; dir bands & lectr music, 72-74, Muhlenberg Col; assoc instr music, Moravian Col, 73-74; dir instrm music & assoc prof music, Juniata Col, 74- *Awards:* Z T Thomas Prize Instrm Music, Peabody Consv, 70; Temple Univ Teaching Fel, 71-72; Christian R & Mary F Lindback Found Teaching Award, 80. *Mem:* Am Symph Orch League; Col Band Dir Nat Asn; Int Clarinet Soc; Nat Asn Col Wind and Perc Instr; Nat Asn Jazz Educ. *Interests:* Use of microcomputers; computer graphics in music administration and performance. *Publ:* Coauth, Program for Woodwind Quintet Using Discovery Method, Music Appreciation and the Child, 70; Computers and Band Administration, Col Band Dir Nat Asn, 79. *Mailing Add:* 3343 Cold Spring Rd Mtd Rte Huntingdon PA 16652

TOWN, STEPHEN J
TEACHER, WRITER
b Odessa, Tex, Mar 5, 52. *Study:* NTex State Univ, BM, 74, MM, 77; Ind Univ, currently. *Teaching:* Voice instr, Weatherford Col, 77-78; chmn voice fac, Taylor Univ, 78-81; dir choral activ, Univ SAla, 81- *Awards:* Nat Endowment Humanities Fel, 80; Lilly Endowment Fel, 80; Univ SAla Res Comt Grants, 82-83. *Mem:* Nat Asn Teachers Singing; Am Choral Dir Asn; Am Musicol Soc; Ala Music Teachers Asn. *Publ:* Auth, Sechs Lieder von Christian Fürchtegott Gellert (1715-1769) As Set by Carl Philipp Emanuel Bach and Ludwig van Beethoven: A Comparative Analysis, Nat Asn Teachers Singing Bulletin, 80; Observations on a Cabaletta from Verdi's Il Corsaro, Current Musicol, 81; Joseph Haydn's Missa in Angusfiis: History Analysis and Performance Suggestions, Sacred Music, 83. *Mailing Add:* Dept Music FCE 9 Univ SAla Mobile AL 36688

TOWNSEND, DOUGLAS
COMPOSER, MUSICOLOGIST

b New York, NY, Nov 8, 21. *Works:* Lima Beans (chamber opera), Carnegie Recital Hall, 54; Symphony No 1 (strings), Comp Forum, Columbia Univ, 58; Four Fantasies on American Folk Songs, C F Peters, 60; Chamber Concerto No 2, (trombone & strings), 62 & Suite No 1 (strings), 74, Theodore Presser; Tower Music (brass quintet), E C Kerby, 74; Chamber Symph No 1, C F Peters Corp, 83. *Pos:* Ed & writer, Music Heritage Rev, NJ, 77-81; freelance writer, music ed, musicol & comp, currently. *Teaching:* Lectr music, Brooklyn Col, 58-69, Univ Bridgeport, 73-75 & State Univ NY, Purchase, 73-76. *Awards:* Grants, Martha Baird Rockefeller Fund, 65, NY State Bicentennial Revelation Comt, 75 & Nat Endowment Arts, 81. *Bibliog:* R F G Goldman (auth), The Wind Band, Arts, Literature & Technology, Allyn & Bacon, 62; Daniel Webster (auth), Musical Detective Traces Lost Scores, Philadelphia Inquirer, 83. *Mem:* Sonneck Soc. *Interests:* Found and edited lost scores of Jacchini, J C Bach, Rossini, Donizetti and Gossec. *Rep:* C F Peters Corp 373 Park Ave S New York NY 10016. *Mailing Add:* 72-28 153 St Flushing NY 11367

TOZZI, GIORGIO
BASS-BARITONE, ACTOR

b Chicago, Ill, Jan 8, 23. *Study:* DePaul Univ, with Armen Boyajian, 40-43; Consv G Verdi, Milan; Scuola Musicale Milano, 51; studied with Giacomo Rimini, Rosa Raisa & Giulio Lorandi. *Rec Perf:* On RCA, London & Cetra. *Roles:* Tarquinius in The Rape of Lucretia, Lyr Opera Chicago, 48; Emile de Becque in South Pacific, 57; Doctor in Vanessa, Metropolitan Opera, 58; Most Happy Fella, Broadway, 79-80, TV version, 79; Amahl & the Night Visitors, NBC-TV, 79; Torn Between Two Lovers (TV movie), 80; Hans Sachs in Die Meistersinger (film); and many maj opera roles. *Pos:* Bass-bar, Ziegfeld Theatre, New York, 48, Adelphi Theatre, London, 49; Teatro Nuovo, Milan, 50, La Scala, Milan, 53 & Metropolitan Opera, 55 & with maj opera co in Argentina, Austria, France, WGermany, Italy, Portugal & US; leading bass-bar, Metropolitan Opera Asn, San Francisco Opera Co & Salzburg Music Fest; soloist with New York Phil, Boston Symph, Philadelphia Phil, Minneapolis Symph, Chicago Symph & other maj orchs. *Teaching:* Mem fac, Juilliard Sch Music, formerly. *Awards:* Gold Rec, RCA; Winner, Artists Adv Coun, Chicago; Touring Mgr Award as Best Actor, 80. *Mem:* Am Guild Musical Artists; Am Fedn TV & Radio Artists; Actor's Equity Am; Bohemians. *Mailing Add:* c/o Curtis Roberts ILRD Prod Ltd 9056 Santa Monica Blvd Los Angeles CA 90069

TRACK, GERHARD
CONDUCTOR & MUSIC DIRECTOR, COMPOSER

b Vienna, Austria, Sept 17, 34; US citizen. *Study:* Teacher Training Col, Vienna, Austria, MS, 53; Acad Music & Perf Arts, Vienna Austria, MM(comp, orch & choral cond), 54. *Works:* Hymn for Orchestra, Doblinger, Austria, 58; Minnequa (opera), 76 & The Reindeer's Surprise, 76, PMI; Theme, Variations on a Mexican Folk Song (orch), Kjos, 77; The Little Match Girl, PMI, 79; Symphonic March (orch), Kjos, 81; over 150 choral comp & arr. *Rec Perf:* Choral Works (Christmas carols), Eurodisc-Ariola, 57; compositions for orchestra, Austrian State Radio Network, 64; compositions for orchestra (3 vol), GIA Rec, 67, 68 & 77; A Night in Pueblo (waltz), Rubin Rec, Austria, 70; Choral Works, PMI Rec, 83. *Pos:* Cond, Vienna Boys Choir, Austria, 53-58; mus dir, St John's Symph Orch & St Johns Univ Men's Chorus, 58-69, Metropolitan Youth Symph, Minneapolis, Minn, 65-69 & Pueblo Symph Orch, Chorale & Youth Symph, 69- *Teaching:* Assoc prof music, St Johns Univ, Minn, 58-69; Thatcher prof music, Univ Southern Colo, 69- *Awards:* Golden Hon Cross for Merits for Repub Austria, 75; Service to Mankind Award, Sertoma Club, Pueblo, Colo, 81. *Mem:* Am Symph Orch League; Church Music Asn Am (pres, 74-78, vpres, 78-); Am Choral Dir Asn; ASCAP; Austrian Soc Comp. *Mailing Add:* 130 Baylor Pueblo CO 81005

TRAFFORD, EDMUND LEE
COMPOSER

b Grand Rapids, Mich, Sept 24, 48. *Study:* Sch Perf Arts, US Int Univ, Calif, studied comp with Gerald Lloyd & cond with Zoltan Rosznyai, BFA, 71; Col-Consv Music, Univ Cincinnati, studied with Lukas Foss & comp with Scott Huston & Paul Palombo, MM, 73, DMA, 77. *Works:* Incidental Music, Midsummer Night's Dream, comn & perf by San Diego Sinfonietta, 71; Frescoes, Contemp Music Ens, Univ Cincinnati, 76; American Collage, comn by WGUC-FM, 76; Xanthe II: Concertino for Chamber Orchestra, comn & perf by Cincinnati Chamber Orch, 78; Requiem, comn & perf by Col Mt Saint Joseph, 79; Umbrae III: Trauermusik, comn & perf by A F Dennison-Tansey, Toledo Mus Art, 83; Wynde, Pandean Wind Players, 83. *Teaching:* Instr theory & comp, Univ Cincinnati, US Int Univ & Western Mich Univ, formerly. *Awards:* Lundstrom-Young Prize, Calif Olympiad Arts, 73; scholar grant, Raymond Hubbell Fund, ASCAP, 76; perf grant, Great Lakes Arts Alliance & Gtr Columbus Arts Coun, 83. *Mem:* ASCAP; Nat Asn Comp USA; Cincinnati Comp Guild (treas, 82-); Cincinnati Comn Arts. *Mailing Add:* 2431 Mustang Dr Cincinnati OH 45211

TRAHAN, KATHLEEN FRANCES
FLUTE

b El Paso, Tex, August 19, 53. *Study:* Univ Md, BM, 76, MM, 78; studied with Robert Aitken, James Galway & William Montgomery. *Pos:* Flutist, Theater Chamber Players, Kennedy Ctr, 78-, Nat Gallery of Art Orch, 79- & Washington Chamber Orch, 79- *Teaching:* Instr flute, Univ Md, 79- *Awards:* Second Prize, Music Teachers Nat Asn, 77; First Place, Soc of Arts & Letters Compt, 78; First Prize, Alpha Delta Kappa Int Compt, 83. *Mem:* Nat Flute Asn (chairperson, 82-); Washington Flute Asn; Nat Asn Col Wind & Perc Instr; DC Fedn Musicians. *Publ:* Coauth, Patterns in Baroque Ornamentation:

The Methodical Sonatas of Telemann, Instrumentalist Mag, 78; auth, Changing Attitudes in Performing: An Interview with James Galway, Nat Flute Asn Newsletter, 78; Summer Flute Masterclasses, Instrumentalist Mag, 79-83 & Nat Flute Asn Newsletter, 82-83. *Mailing Add:* 5001 Indian Lane College Park MD 20740

TRAINOR, CAROL DONN
SOPRANO

b New York, NY, July 23, 29. *Study:* Studied voice with Anna Molk; studied operatic roles & lang with George Joke. *Roles:* Juliet in Romeo & Juliet, New York Civic Opera Co, 64; Violetta in La Traviata, 65, Queen of Night in Magic Flute, 65 & Zerbinetta in Ariadne Auf Naxos, 65, Miami Opera Guild; Musetta in La Boheme, 66, Rosalinda & Adele in Die Fledermaus, 66, New York City Opera Co. *Mailing Add:* c/o Floyd Everett Sharp Mgt 171 W 71st St New York NY 10023

TRAMONTOZZI, STEPHEN
DOUBLE BASS, TEACHER

b Newton, Mass, June 18, 55. *Study:* Eastman Sch Music; New England Consv Music, BMus, 77; San Francisco Consv Music, MMus, 81. *Pos:* Prin double bass, Orquestra Sinfonica Sao Paulo, Brazil, 77-78; asst prin double bass, San Francisco Symph Orch, 80- *Teaching:* Instr double bass, Dominican Col, San Rafael, 80- *Mailing Add:* 201 11th Ave San Francisco CA 94118

TRAMPLER, WALTER
VIOLA, EDUCATOR

b Munich, Germany, Aug 25, 15; nat US. *Study:* Munich Acad Music, artist dipl. *Rec Perf:* Viola Sonatats (Hindemith); Harold in Italy (Berlioz); Viola Suites (Reger); Elegie for Solo Viola (Stravinsky); Chamber Works (Berio); String Quintets (Mozart); rec on RCA, Columbia, Philips, Vanguard, English Decca, EMI, CRI & Unicorn. *Pos:* Mem, Strub Quartet, formerly & Boston Symph Orch, formerly; founding mem, New Music Quartet, 47-56; violist, German Radio Symph Orch, formerly; performer, Budapest Quartet, Beaux Arts Trio & Guarnieri Quartet; res artist, Chamber Music Soc Am, 69-; recitalist & soloist with orchs & chamber groups, US, Europe & Japan. *Teaching:* Mem fac, Juilliard Sch Music, formerly, Peabody Consv, formerly, Yale Univ, formerly & Boston Univ, formerly; mem fac viola, New England Consv Music, currently. *Rep:* Frank Solomon Assoc 201 W 54th St Suite 4C New York NY 10019; Melvin Kaplan Inc 1860 Broadway New York NY 10023. *Mailing Add:* 42 Riverside Dr New York NY 10024

TRANTHAM, WILLIAM EUGENE
EDUCATOR, PIANO

b Elkland, Mo, Aug 6, 29. *Study:* SW Mo State Univ, BS, BSE, 51; Northwestern Univ, Ill, MM, 55, PhD, 66. *Teaching:* Prof music, SW Baptist Univ, Mo, 55-60 & Ouachita Baptist Univ, Ark, 60- *Awards:* Musician of Year, Ark Federated Music Clubs, 81; Outstanding Col Teacher, Ark State Music Teacher Asn, 82. *Mem:* Music Teachers Nat Asn; Music Educr Nat Conf; Am Musicol Soc; Phi Mu Alpha Sinfonia. *Publ:* Auth, A Music Theory Approach to Beginning Piano—Instruction for the College Music Major, J Res Music Educ, spring 70. *Mailing Add:* 688 Carter Rd Arkadelphia AR 71923

TRAUFFER, BARBARA OLIVE
FLUTE & PICCOLO

b Chicago, Ill. *Study:* Chicago Musical Col, Roosevelt Univ, BMus; Duquesne Univ, MMus, 74. *Pos:* Asst prin flute & second flute, Calgary Phil & Youngstown Phil, formerly; prin piccolo, Ala Symph, currently. *Teaching:* Instr flute, Mt Royal Col, formerly & Ala Sch Fine Arts, currently. *Mem:* Am Fedn Musicians; Am Symph Orch League; Am Musical Instrm Soc; Nat Flute Asn. *Mailing Add:* 900 42nd St S Birmingham AL 35222

TRAVALINE, MARJORIE D
LIBRARIAN

b Mt Holly, NJ, Aug 13, 47. *Study:* Philadelphia Musical Acad, 67-69; Univ Pa, BA, 69; Drexel Univ, MS, 71. *Pos:* Assoc librn, Philadelphia Musical Acad, 69-71; librn, Glassboro State Col, 72- *Mem:* Music Libr Asn. *Mailing Add:* Music Dept Libr Glassboro State Col Glassboro NJ 08028

TRAVALINE, PHILIP FRANCIS
CONDUCTOR & MUSIC DIRECTOR

b Camden, NJ, June 21, 37. *Study:* Philadelphia Consv Music, BMus, 59; Philadelphia Musical Acad, studied cond with William Smith, 71-73; Glassboro State Col, MA, 72; Temple Summer Music Inst, studied cond with William Smith, 72. *Works:* Traumen, perf by Pa Gov Sch Arts Brass Ens, 79. *Pos:* Cond, Summer Fest Orch, Glassboro State Col, 71-78, orch band, Philadelphia Music Acad, 72-74 & Am Music Abroad Symph Orch, summer 81; music dir & cond, NJ Fest Orch, 76-78 & Susquehanna Valley Symph Orch, 83- *Teaching:* Instr & cond, Pa Govt Sch Arts, summer 79. *Mem:* Am Symph Orch League; Music Educr Nat Conf; Nat Sch Orch Asn. *Mailing Add:* 116 Deptford Rd Glassboro NJ 08028

TRAVIS, ROY
COMPOSER, EDUCATOR

b New York, NY, June 24, 22. *Study:* Columbia Col, AB, 47; Juilliard Sch Music, BS, 49, MS, 50; Columbia Univ, MA, 51. *Works:* Duo Concertante, 73, African Sonata, 73, Switched-On Ashanti, 73, Symphonic Allegro, 76, Songs and Epilogues (bass voice & orch), 76 & Piano Concerto, 76, Orion Master Rec; Piano Concerto, Oxford Univ Press, 76; and others. *Teaching:* Instr music, Columbia Col, 52-53; instr comp & theory, Mannes Col Music, 52-57; from instr to prof music, Univ Calif, Los Angeles, 57- *Awards:* Grant, Martha Baird Rockefeller Found, 68; Guggenheim Fel, 72-73; grants, Ford Found, 75 & Nat Endowment Arts, 76 & 78. *Mem:* ASCAP. *Mailing Add:* Dept Music Univ Calif Los Angeles CA 90024

TREE, MICHAEL
EDUCATOR, VIOLA

b Newark, NJ, Feb 19, 34. *Study:* Curtis Inst Music, dipl, 55; Univ SFla, Hon Dr Fine Arts, 76; State Univ NY, Hon Dr Fine Arts, 83. *Rec Perf:* Over 60 works recorded on RCA, Columbia, Vanguard, Nonesuch including complete Beethoven Quartets & 10 piano quintets & quartets with Artur Rubenstein. *Pos:* Mem, Guarneri String Quartet, 64- *Teaching:* Fac mem viola, Curtis Inst Music, 69-; fac mem chamber music, Univ Md, College Park, 82-; fac mem viola, St Louis Consv Music, 83- *Mailing Add:* Curtis Inst of Music 1726 Locust St Philadelphia PA 19103

TREGELLAS, PATRICIA A
CONDUCTOR

b Garden City, Kans, Feb 22, 36. *Study:* Univ Denver, BMusEd, 59; Städtische Musikschule, Trossingen, Ger, cert, 61. *Rec Perf:* Unser Dorf (double suite), Penthouse Rec, 77. *Pos:* Musical dir & cond, New York Concerto Orch, 79- *Teaching:* Class accordion, Accordion Teachers Guild Wkshps, Chicago, Denver, New York & Tokyo & British Col Accordionists, London, 57- *Bibliog:* Marjorie Barrett (auth), Patricia Tregellas is a Classy Classical Accordionist, Rocky Mountain News, Colo, 1/30/78. *Mem:* Chamber Music Am. *Publ:* Auth, New Music for Accordion, 5/63 & The Arts Are Polluted, 10/72, Music J Mag. *Mailing Add:* 817 West End Ave New York NY 10025

TREGER, CHARLES
VIOLIN, EDUCATOR

Study: Lawrence Univ, Hon Dr. *Rec Perf:* On First Edition, Muza, Desto & ABC. *Pos:* Founding mem, Chamber Music Soc, New York, formerly; solo violinist, Bach Aria Group, currently; soloist & recitalist with major orchs in US, Can, Mex, Europe, Near East & Middle East; appearances, Tanglewood, Spoleto, Casals & Athens Fest. *Teaching:* Vis prof violin & co-chmn strings, Hartt Sch Music, 72- *Awards:* First Prize, Wieniawski Int Violin Compt, Poland, 62. *Mailing Add:* Hartt Sch Music Univ Hartford West Hartford CT 06117

TREMBLY, DENNIS M
DOUBLE BASS, EDUCATOR

b Long Beach, Calif, Apr 16, 47. *Study:* Study with Peter Mercurio, 64-65 & Nathaniel Gangursky, 64-68; Aspen, with Stuart Sankey, 64; Juilliard Sch, 65-68. *Rec Perf:* Complete Chamber Music of Hermann Goetz, Genesis Rec, 71. *Pos:* Sect bass, Los Angeles Phil Orch, 70-73, prin bass, 73- *Teaching:* Asst adj prof double bass, Univ Southern Calif, 81. *Awards:* Second Prize, Int Double Bass Compt, Isle of Man, 78. *Mem:* Int Soc Bassists. *Mailing Add:* 222 S Figueroa St Los Angeles CA 90012

TRENKAMP, (WILMA) ANNE
EDUCATOR, FLUTE & PICCOLO

b Cleveland, Ohio. *Study:* Case Western Reserve Univ, studied flute with Maurice Sharp, theory with William Thomson & comp with Marcel Dick, BA, 67, PhD, 73; Univ Mich, MM, 69. *Teaching:* Asst prof music, Wheaton Col, 76-78; asst prof music theory, Univ Lowell, 78-81, assoc prof, 81- *Mem:* Am Musicol Soc; Soc Music Theory; Col Music Soc. *Interests:* Postserial movement; texture in music; transfer of culture from central Europe to US, 1932-1950. *Publ:* Auth, The Concept of Alea in Boulez's Third Piano Sonata, Music & Lett, 76; Considerations Preliminary to the Formation of a Textural Vocabulary, Ind Theory Rev, 80; Contemporary Biographical Techniques, Notes, 81; Marcel Dick: An Oral History, Archives Case Western Univ, 82. *Mailing Add:* Univ Lowell One University Ave Lowell MA 01854

TREUTEL, EDWARD F
EDUCATOR, TRUMPET

b Philadelphia, Pa. *Study:* Juilliard Grad Sch, trumpet with Max Schlossberg; studied with Harold Rehrig & Ernest Williams. *Works:* 24 Etudes (trumpet). *Pos:* Mem, Chautauqua Symph Orch, Worcester Symph Orch, Pittsburgh Symph Orch, Barrere Little Symph, New Friends of Music, New York City Ctr Opera Co & New Opera Co. *Teaching:* Mem fac, Teachers Col, Columbia Univ, formerly, Trenton State, currently, Concordia Col, formerly & State Univ NY, Purchase, currently; adjudicator, Consv de Musique, Quebec; mem fac trumpet symposium, Univ Denver; instr, Juilliard Prep Div, currently, Exten Div, currently, instr trumpet, 46- *Awards:* Fulbright Scholar. *Mailing Add:* Juilliard Sch Music Lincoln Ctr New York NY 10023

TREVOR, KIRK DAVID NIELL
CONDUCTOR, CELLO

b London, England, Feb 8, 52. *Study:* Dartington Col, 68-69; Guildhall Sch Music & Drama, GGSM, 74; NC Sch Arts, 75-77. *Pos:* Asst cond, Guildhall Opera Sch, 73-74; music dir, Youth Symph of Carolinas, 78-82; assoc cond, Charlotte Symph Orch, 78-82; Exxon-Art Endowment cond, Dallas Symph, 82- *Awards:* Libottom Mem Prize, 72 & Kappilis Cond Prize, 74, City of London; Fulbright Exchange Grant, UK/US Dept State, 75. *Mem:* Cond Guild; Am Symph Orch League. *Mailing Add:* PO Box 26207 Dallas TX 75226

TRIMBLE, LESTER ALBERT
COMPOSER, CRITIC-WRITER

b Bangor, Wis, Aug 29, 23. *Study:* Carnegie-Mellon Univ, with Nikolai Lopatnikoff, BFA & MFA, 47; Berkshire Music Ctr, with Aaron Copland & Darius Milhaud, 48; Consv Nat Musique, Paris, with Darius Milhaud, 51; Ecole Normale, Paris, with Arthur Honegger, 51; studied with Nadia Boulanger, Paris, 51; Columbia Princeton Electronic Studio, 69. *Works:* Sonic Landscape for Orchestra, MCA, 57; Five Episodes for Orchestra, Duchess, 62; Symphony in Two Movements, 64, Four Fragments from the Canterbury Tales, 67 & Duo Concertante for Orchestra & Two Solo Violins, 68, C F Peters; Panels for Orchestra, comn & perf by Milwaukee Symph, 76; Symphony No 2, MCA, 82. *Pos:* Comp in res, New York Phil, 67-68; gen mgr, Am Music Ctr, 61-63; music critic, New York Herald Tribune & Nation, 52-63. *Teaching:* Prof comp, Univ Md, 63-68; fac mem, Juilliard Sch, 71- *Awards:* Guggenheim Found Fel, 63; Modern Am Music Series Rec Award, Columbia Rec, 67; Ford Found Rec Award, 72. *Bibliog:* Arnold Schoenberg (auth), Arnold Schoenberg Letters, St Martins Press, 65; David Ewen (auth), Am Comp, Putnam, 82. *Mem:* Comp Forum, (bd adv, 70-); MacDowell Colony (mem bd dir, 70-); Am Comp Alliance (mem bd dir, 75-); Comp Rec Inc (mem bd advr, 75-). *Publ:* Auth, Beneath the Quiet Surface, New York Times, 57; An American Composer Speaks His Mind, Listen Mag, 60; Elliott Carter, Stereo Rev Mag, 72; The Unsung American Composer, New York Times Mag, 81. *Mailing Add:* 98 Riverside Dr New York NY 10024

TRITTER, RITA SHANE See Shane, Rita

TROGAN, ROLAND BERNARD
COMPOSER, TEACHER

b Saginaw, Mich, Aug 6, 33. *Study:* Univ Mich, DMA(comp), 63; studied with Roger Sessions, Ross Lee Finney & Leslie Bassett. *Works:* Sonata for Solo Violin, perf by Harold Kohon, 66; The Seafarer (voice & piano), 66 & Nocturnes (piano), 67, perf by Richard Woitach; Piano Sonata, perf by Drew Violette, 70; Two Scenes for Orchestra, perf by Louisville Symph. *Teaching:* Lectr, City Univ New York, 61-69; pres, Roland Trogan Inc, 67- *Awards:* BMI Student Award, 54. *Mailing Add:* 76 Walbrooke Ave Staten Island NY 10301

TROMBLEE, MAXELL RAY
CLARINET, EDUCATOR

b Woodward, Okla, Mar 21, 35. *Study:* Wichita State Univ, BME, 59; Univ Ill, MME, 67, EdD, 72. *Pos:* Prin clarinet, Chattanooga Symph, 59-65; Cond, Enid-Phillips Symph, 70-83. *Teaching:* Instr clarinet, Sewanee Summer Music Ctr, 60-62; dir band, Lakeview High Sch, Ga, 59-65; grad asst, Univ Ill, 66-67; from instr to assoc prof instrm music & chmn dept, Phillips Univ, 67- *Mem:* Am Symph Orch League; Music Educr Nat Conf; Phi Mu Alpha Sinfonia. *Mailing Add:* 1306 Vinita Enid OK 73701

TROMBLY, PRESTON
COMPOSER, SAXOPHONE

b Hartford, Conn, Dec 30, 45. *Study:* Univ Conn, with Charles Whittenberg, BM, 69; Berkshire Music Ctr, with George Crumb & Leonard Bernstein, 70; Yale Univ, with Bulent Arel & Mario Davidovsky, MMA, 72. *Works:* In Memoriam: Igor Stravinsky, Speculum Musicae, 75; Chamber Concerto, comn by Fromm Found Harvard, 75; Windmills of Paris, comn by Nat Endowment Fest Arts & Da Capo Chamber Players, 77; The Bridge: Three Pieces after Hart Crane, Resonance, 79; String Quartet, Esaki Quartet, 79 & 82; Time of the Supple Iris, comn by Speculum Musicae, 80; Trumpets of Solitude, comn by Columbia & Princeton Electronic Music Ctr, 82. *Rec Perf:* Kinetics III (Harvey Sollberger), Nonesuch Rec, 72. *Awards:* John Simon Guggenheim Fel, 75; Grant, Nat Endowment for Arts, 76 & 80; MacDowell Colony Fel, 80, 81 & 83. *Mem:* Am Comp Alliance (mem bd dir, 76-80, secy, 77); Int Soc Contemp Music (secy, 79). *Mailing Add:* 30 Magaw Pl #4B New York NY 10033

TROTT, LAURENCE
PICCOLO, TEACHER

b Cleveland, Ohio, July 25, 37. *Study:* Western Reserve Univ, 55-56; Juilliard Sch Music, 56-57; Butler Univ, 57-58; State Univ NY, Buffalo, BA, 61; studied with William Herbert, Albert Tipton & Julius Baker. *Rec Perf:* For the Birds, 81 & Birds of a Feather, 82, Spectrum Rec; Parallel Lines, CRI, 83. *Pos:* Piccoloist, Indianapolis Symph, 57-58; Buffalo Phil, 58 & Aspen Fest Orch, 58-64; piccolo soloist & recitalist, 77. *Teaching:* Guest piccolo, Eastman Sch Music, New England Consv Music, Calif Inst Arts, Northwestern Univ & Wildacres, 78-; fac mem, Daemen Col, currently. *Awards:* Am Music Ctr Comn Award, 79. *Mem:* Piccolo Soc (artistic dir, 78-). *Publ:* Auth, Why not the Piccolo, Woodwind World, 80; Play Piccolo as Though You Love It, 82 & Gather Ye Closet Piccoloists, 83, Flute Worker. *Rep:* Beverly Wright 400 E 52nd St New York NY 10022 *Mailing Add:* 309 Middlesex Rd Buffalo NY 14216

TROTTER, HERMAN
CRITIC, LECTURER

Providence, RI, Sept 25, 25. *Study:* Yale Univ, BA, 46. *Pos:* Pres, Buffalo Symphonette Soc, 64-71; prog annotator, Buffalo Phil Orch, 66-72; contrib critic, Buffalo Evening News, 68-77, music critic, 77- *Teaching:* Instr musical lit, Trinity Ctr, Buffalo, 76- *Awards:* Fels, Music Critics Asn, 75, 82 & 83. *Mem:* Music Critics Asn. *Publ:* Contribr to Musical Am, 76-; auth, June in Buffalo Contemporary Music Festival, Music J, 77; New Blood Revitalizes Chautauqua Opera, Musical Am, 12/82. *Mailing Add:* Buffalo Evening News Box 100 Buffalo NY 14240

TROUPIN, EDWARD
COMPOSER, EDUCATOR

b Boston, Mass, June 22, 25. *Study:* Harvard Univ, AB; Univ Mich, with Ross Lee Finney, MM. *Works:* Symphonic Involutes, Washington, DC, 76; An Unconscious Arithmetic (chamber orch); Introduction & Dance (wind quintet); Divertimento (trumpet, horn & trombone); String Quartet; Duo for Trumpet & Trombone. *Teaching:* Fac mem, Ithaca Col, 54-60; prof music, Univ Fla, 60- *Mailing Add:* 1411 NW 49th Terrace Gainesville FL 32605

TROYANOS, TATIANA
MEZZO-SOPRANO

b New York, NY, Sept 12, 38. *Study:* Juilliard Sch, with Hans Heinz, dipl. *Rec Perf:* With RCA, Victor Red Seal, Deutsche Grammophon Gesellschaft, EMI, London & Columbia. *Roles:* Jeanne in Teufel von Loudun, Hamburg Staatsoper, 69; Carmen in Carmen; Poppea in Incoronazione di Poppea; Suzuki in Madama Butterfly; Donna Elvira in Don Giovanni; Octavian in Der Rosenkavalier, 83 & Venus in Tannhäuser, 83, Metropolitan Opera. *Pos:* Mem, Metropolitan Opera, 75-; singer with maj opera co in Europe & US incl Vienna Staatsoper, Berlin Deutsche Oper, Milan La Scala, London Royal Opera, San Francisco Opera, New York City Opera & others; soloist with symph orchs incl Boston, Cincinnati, Chicago, Los Angeles, Philadelphia, London & New York Phil. *Mailing Add:* c/o Columbia Artists Mgt 165 W 57th St New York NY 10019

TRUAX, BERT
TRUMPET, COMPOSER

b San Anselmo, Calif, Feb 5, 54. *Study:* Curtis Inst Music, BM, 76; studied trumpet with Gilbert Johnson, Frank Kaderabec & Tom Stevens. *Works:* Adagio and Allegro (trumpet trio), Tromba Publ, 79. *Rec Perf:* Dallas Trumpets, Jan Sound, 80. *Pos:* Second trumpet, Dallas Symph Orch, 76-; clinician, Dallas sect, Int Trumpet Guild, 78 & Lyon Consv, France, 81. *Mailing Add:* 8619 Daytonia Dallas TX 75218

TRUBITT, ALLEN R
COMPOSER, EDUCATOR

b Chicago, Ill, Aug 24, 31. *Study:* Roosevelt Univ, MMusEd, 54; Ind Univ, DM, 64. *Works:* String Quartet, perf by Univ Hawaii; Maui, Symphony for Band, perf by Univ Hawaii Conct Band; Overture Ind, perf by Houston Symph Orch, 63; Symphony No 2, perf by Honolulu Symph Orch, 83; four piano sonatas & numerous vocal & instrumental works. *Teaching:* Assoc prof, Ind Univ, Pa, 57-64; prof music, Univ Hawaii, Manoa, 64- *Awards:* Hawaii State Bicentennial Award, 76; ASCAP Standard Award, 80- *Mem:* ASCAP. *Publ:* Auth, Comprehensive Introduction to Music Literature, Addison-Wesley, 74; coauth, Ear Training & Sight-Singing (two vol), Schirmer Bks, 79. *Mailing Add:* 920 Ward Ave 13E Honolulu HI 96814

TRUESDELL, FREDERICK DONALD
EDUCATOR, PIANO

b Marysville, Kans, Sept 14, 20. *Study:* Univ Mich, BM(comp), 50, MM(comp), 51, MM(piano), 52; Eastman Sch Music, DMA(perf pedagogy), 60; studied with Cecile Genhart, Jose Echaniz, Ross Lee Finney & Wayne Barlow. *Works:* String Quartet, 50; Piano Concerto (orchestra), 51; Piano Trio, 60; Three Piano Preludes; Woodwind Quintet. *Teaching:* Asst prof, Wash State Univ, 52-58; prof music, Col William & Mary, 60- *Mem:* Va Music Teachers Asn (pres, 69-73); Music Teachers Nat Asn; Am Musicol Soc; Col Music Soc; Sonneck Soc. *Mailing Add:* Dept Music Col William & Mary Williamsburg VA 23185

TRUSSEL, JACQUE
TENOR

b San Francisco, Calif, Apr 7, 43. *Study:* Ball State Univ, with George Newton; studied with Cornelius Reid. *Roles:* Pinkerton in Madama Butterfly, Oberlin Fest, 70; Dr Dorn in The Sea Gull, Houston Grand Opera, 74; Zinovy in Lady Macbeth of Mtsensk, San Francisco Opera, 81; Sergei in Lady Macbeth of Mtsensk, Spoleto Fest, 82; Don Gomez de Feria in Henry VIII, San Diego Opera, 83; Edmund in Lear, San Francisco Opera Summer Fest; Hugh in Hugh the Drover. *Pos:* Recitalist & appearances with symph orchs. *Awards:* Nat Opera Inst Grant; Martha Baird Rockefeller Found Grant. *Mailing Add:* c/o Columbia Artists Mgt 165 W 57th St New York NY 10019

TRYTHALL, GILBERT
COMPOSER, ADMINISTRATOR

b Knoxville, Tenn, Oct 28, 30. *Study:* Univ Tenn, with David Van Vactor, BA, 51; Northwestern Univ, with Wallingford Riegger, MM, 52; Cornell Univ, with Robert Palmer, DMA, 60. *Works:* A Solemn Chant (string orch); Dionysia (orch); Fanfare & Celebration (orch); The Music Lesson (opera buffa in one act); Metamorphosis (piano suite); Music for Aluminum Rooms (tape); Nova Sync (band & tape); and many others. *Pos:* Ed bd, Music Educ J, formerly. *Teaching:* Instr, pub sch, 50-53; asst prof music, Knox Col, 60-64; prof music theory & comp, George Peabody Col Teachers, 64-75; dean, Creative Arts Ctr, WVa Univ, 75-81, prof music, 81- *Awards:* Ford Found Comn; Music Teachers Nat Asn Comn; Am Music Ctr Comn. *Mem:* Music Educr Nat Conf; Am Fedn Musicians; Southeastern Comp League; Am Music Ctr. *Publ:* Auth, Principles and Practice of Electronic Music, 74. *Mailing Add:* 905 W Park Ave WO Morgantown WV 26505

TRYTHALL, RICHARD AAKER
COMPOSER, PIANO

b Knoxville, Tenn, July 25, 39. *Study:* Univ Tenn, comp with David Van Vactor, BM, 61; Princeton Univ, comp with Roger Sessions, MFA, 63. *Works:* Penelope's Monologue (sop & orch), Rome Radio Orch, 65; Costruzione (orch), 66 & Continuums (orch), 68, Rental Libr, E B Marks Music Corp; Coincidences (piano), Edizioni Suvini-Zerboni, Milan, 70; Variations on a Theme by Haydn, Dorian Woodwind Quintet, 76; Bolero (four perc), Grupo Percussao Agora, Sao Paulo, Brazil, 79; Ballad (piano & orch), Oak Ridge Symph Orch, World's Fair, 82. *Pos:* Music liaison, Am Acad Rome, 74- *Awards:* Rome Prize, Am Acad Rome, 64-67; fel, Guggenheim Found, 67-68; Kranichsteiner Musicpreis, Int Ferienkurse, Darmstadt, 69. *Mem:* Am Music Ctr; ASCAP. *Mailing Add:* via Quattro Novembre 96 Rome 00187 Italy

TSEITLIN, IRINA
VIOLIN

b Rostov na Donu, USSR; US citizen. *Study:* Moscow Cent Music Sch, dipl, 69; Moscow Consv, with Youri Yankelevich, MA, 74. *Rec Perf:* Glazunov Violin Concerto, Deutsche Grammophon, 80; Wieniawski Polonase in A, 81 & Brahms Sonata #2 in A, 81, Duchesne; Elgar Violin Concerto, BBC, 83; Kodaly Duo, 83, Tchaikovsky Waltz Scherzo, 83 & Prokofiev Sonata #2, 83, Pavanne. *Pos:* Conct violinist, 68- *Teaching:* Prof violin, Col Moscow Consv, USSR, 74-76. *Awards:* First prize, Budapest Int Music Fest, 67; Third Prize, Munich Int Violin Compt, 78; Bronze Medal, Queen Elisabeth Int Violin Compt, 80. *Rep:* Joanne Rile Artists Mgt PO Box 27539 Philadelphia Pa 19118. *Mailing Add:* 13634 Boquita Dr Del Mar CA 92014

TSEITLIN, MICHAEL
VIOLA, VIOLIN

b Moscow, USSR, Apr, 16, 50; US citizen. *Study:* Gnesin's Music Sch, Moscow, dipl, 68; Moscow Consv, with Prof Andrievsky, MA, 74. *Pos:* Violinist, Orch Bolshoi Theater, 74-76. *Teaching:* Asst prof, Gnesin's Col, Moscow, 74-76; prof violin & viola, Calif State Univ, Los Angeles, 77- & San Diego State Univ, 81- *Awards:* Laureat, Int Music Fest, Karl Marx Stadt, EGermany, 67. *Mailing Add:* 13634 Boquita Dr Del Mar CA 92014

TUBB, MONTE
COMPOSER, EDUCATOR

b Jonesboro, Ark, Nov 5, 33. *Study:* Univ Ark; Ind Univ, with Bernhard Heiden, MM. *Works:* Discourse in Two Moods (string orch), 66; Concert Piece (orch), 67; Sutras (band), 68; Soundprint 15 (band), 70; Soundpiece (36 voices), 71; Orchestra Suite, 72; Earthmessage 5 (cello & piano, four hands), 73; and others. *Pos:* Comp in res, Ford Found, 64-66. *Teaching:* Fac mem, Tarkio Col, 60-64; assoc prof music, Univ Ore, 66- *Mailing Add:* Music Dept Univ Ore Eugene OR 97403

TUCKER, GENE RICHARD
TENOR, COACH

b David City, Nebr, Mar 26, 47. *Study:* Chautauqua Inst, study with Josephine Antoine, 66-67; Santa Fe Opera apprentice, 68; Eastman Sch Music, study with Julius Huehn, BMus, 69. *Rec Perf:* The Temple of Minerva, Musical Heritage, 76; Bach Cantata 80, 78 & Bach Magnificat & Cantata 140, 80, Holy Trinity Lutheran Series; La Fiesta de la Posada, CBS, 80. *Roles:* Pinkerton in Madame Butterfly, Goldovsky Opera, 77; Edgardo in Lucia di Lammermoor, Anchorage Civic Opera, 79; Rinaldo in Armida, Monadnock Fest, 81; Rienzi in Rienzi, 82 & Guntram in Guntram, 83, Opera Orch NY. *Pos:* Performer, Marlboro Music Fest, 77, 78 & 81. *Teaching:* Adj assoc prof voice, George Mason Univ, 79-; instr voice, Selma Levine Sch, 79-81. *Awards:* First Prize, Liederkranz Compt, 76. *Mem:* Am Guild Musical Artists; Pi Kappa Lambda. *Rep:* Elaine Courtenay 411 E 53rd St Suite 6F New York NY 10022. *Mailing Add:* 832 S Ivy St Arlington VA 22204

TUCKER, JANICE
SUZUKI VIOLIN, TEACHER

b Lynn, Mass, Mar 24, 55. *Study:* New England Consv. *Teaching:* Suzuki violin, Newton Music Sch, 80- & Longy Sch Music, 80- *Mem:* Suzuki Asn Am. *Mailing Add:* 18 Strathmore Rd Brookline MA 02146

TUCKWELL, BARRY EMMANUEL
CONDUCTOR & MUSIC DIRECTOR, FRENCH HORN

b Melbourne, Victoria, Australia, Mar 5, 31; UK citizen. *Study:* Sydney Consv Music. *Rec Perf:* On London, Angel Argo & RCA. *Pos:* Prin horn, London Symph Orch, 55-68 & Tuckwell Wind Quintet, 68-; chief cond, Tasmanian Symph Orch, 80-83; music dir & cond, Md Symph Orch, 82- *Teaching:* Prof horn, Royal Acad Music, 60-70. *Publ:* Auth, Playing the Horn, Oxford Univ Press; Horn, G Schirmer. *Mailing Add:* c/o Columbia Artists 165 W 57th St New York NY 10019

TULL, FISHER (AUBREY)
COMPOSER, EDUCATOR

b Waco, Tex, Sept 24, 34. *Study:* NTex State Univ, BMus, 56, MMus, 57, PhD, 65. *Works:* Capriccio for Orchestra, 71, Toccata for Band, 71, Sketches on a Tudor Psalm, 73, Concerto Number 2 for Trumpet, 74, Concertino for Oboe & Strings, 78, Three Episodes for Orchestra, 79 & Overture for a Legacy, 81, Boosey & Hawkes. *Teaching:* Prof music theory, Sam Houston State Univ, 57- *Awards:* Ostwald Prize, Am Bandmasters Asn, 70. *Mem:* ASCAP. *Rep:* Boosey & Hawkes Inc 24 W 57 St New York NY 10019. *Mailing Add:* Rte 8 Box 53 Huntsville TX 77340

TUMBLESON, JOHN RAYMOND
EDUCATOR, MUSIC DIRECTOR

b Sac City, Iowa, Jan 31, 22. *Study:* Univ Southern Calif, BA(music), 49, studied opera with Walter Ducloux & educ with Ralph Rush, EdD, 65; Teachers Col, Columbia Univ, MA(music educ), 51. *Works:* Big Red Apple, Paul Barry Publ, 58; Corre Corre (choral), Lawson-Gould Music Publ, 78. *Pos:* Singer, Robert Shaw Choral, New York, NY, 49-51 & TV, Broadway & Radio City Music Hall, New York, NY, 51-58; founder, Rogue Valley Opera Asn, 77, music dir, 77, 78 & 82. *Teaching:* Instr voice & opera, Univ Idaho, 58-59; assoc prof music, Southern Oregon State Col, 63- *Awards:* Commendation Award, US Coun Gen for Can, 67 & United Serv Orgn, 70-71; Citation for Excellence, Anglo-Int Fest Music, Coventry, England, 73. *Mem:* Nat Opera Asn (state gov, 75-83, mem nat bd, 81-83, chmn conv, 82); Nat Asn Teachers Singing (Southern Oregon rep, 65-83); Cent Opera Asn; Am Choral Dir Asn. *Publ:* Auth, Rosalinda in the Boondocks, 70 & Opera Apprentice Programs, New Paths to Profession, 80, Opera J. *Mailing Add:* 655 Leonard St Ashland OR 97520

TUNDO, SAMUEL A
PERCUSSION

b Detroit, Mich, Apr 25, 37. *Study:* Wayne State Univ. *Pos:* Prin perc, Fla Symph, 59-61 & New Orleans Symph, 61-68; prin timpani & perc, Santa Fe Opera, 62-68; perc, Detroit Symph, 68- *Awards:* Arlon Award, 55; John Phillip Sousa Band Award, 55. *Mem:* Phi Mu Alpha; Percussive Arts Soc. *Mailing Add:* 2726 Town Hill Troy MI 48084

TUNG, YUAN
CELLO, EDUCATOR

Study: Curtis Inst Music, artist dipl; studied cello with Leonard Rose & Gregor Piatigorsky. *Pos:* Assoc prin cello, St Louis Symph Orch, formerly; prin cello, Buffalo Phil Orch, formerly, Am Nat Opera, formerly & Dallas Symph Orch, formerly; mem, Philadelphia Orch, formerly & Univ Toledo String Quartet, formerly; conct tours in Europe; participant, Marlboro Fest, Casals Fest & Menuhin Fest. *Teaching:* Mem fac cello, St Louis Consv Music, currently. *Mailing Add:* St Louis Consv Music 560 Trinity Ave St Louis MO 63130

TURECK, ROSALYN
LECTURER, PIANO

b Chicago, Ill, Dec 14, 13. *Study:* Studied with Sophia Brilliant-Liven & Jan Chiapusso; Juilliard Sch Music, with Olga Samaroff, 35; studied electronic instrm with Theremin; Colby Col, Hon Dr Music, 67; Roosevelt Univ, Hon Dr Music, 68; Wilson Col, Hon Dr Music, 68; Oxford Univ, Hon Dr Music, 77. *Rec Perf:* Goldberg Variations & Aria, Ten Variations in the Italian Style, Italian Concerto, Chromatic Fantasia & Fugue & Four Duets, Columbia. *Pos:* Concert tours with orchs of US, Europe, Brit Isles, SAfrica, South Am & Israel, 37-; cond & soloist, London Philharmonia, 58, NY Phil, 58, Tureck Bach Players, London, 58-, San Antonio Symph, 62, Scottish Nat Symph, 63, Nat Symph, Washington, DC, 70, Madrid Chamber Orch, 70, St Louis Symph Orch, 81 and many others; TV appearances in England & the US, 63- *Teaching:* Prof music, Juilliard Sch Music, 35-53, Univ Calif, San Diego, 67-72 & Univ Md, College Park, 82- *Awards:* Officers Cross, Order of Merit, Fed Repub Germany, 79. *Mem:* New Bach Soc; Am Musicol Soc; Royal Phil Soc, London; Royal Musical Soc, London. *Publ:* Auth, numerous mag articles, 48-; Introduction to the Performance of Bach, three vol, Oxford Univ Press, 59-60; ed, Italian Concerto—Urtext & Performance Edition, Schirmer Music, 83. *Mailing Add:* c/o Columbia Artists Mgt 165 W 57th St New York NY 10019

TURETZKY, BERTRAM JAY
DOUBLE BASS, COMPOSER

b Norwich, Conn, Feb 4, 33. *Study:* Hartt Sch Music, BM, 55; NY Univ, 56-58; Univ Hartford, MM, 65. *Works:* Timbral Studies, 73 & Gamelan Music, 74, Seesaw; BAKU (tape & solo contrabass), Folkways, 80; Six Haiku Settings, Am String Teachers Asn, 81; Collage I, 82 & Reflections on Ives & Whittier, 82, T Presser. *Rec Perf:* Recital of New Music, Advance, 64; The New World of Sound, ARS Nova, 68; The Contemporary Contrabass, Nonesuch, 70; The Contemporary Contrabass, Desto, 72; A Different View, Folkways, 72; Dragonetti Lives, Takoma, 73; New Music for Contrabass, Finnapar, 75. *Teaching:* Asst prof music, Hartt Col, Univ Hartford, 55-67; vis adj prof, Wesleyan Univ & Univ Conn. *Awards:* Comp Award, ASCAP, 80, 81 & 82; Hon Outstanding Perf Contemp Music, Nat Asn Comp USA, 80; Alumni of Yr Award, Hartt Sch Music, Univ Hartford, 82. *Bibliog:* Sam Applebaum (auth), The Way They Play, Paganiniana Press. *Mem:* Am Fedn Musicians; Int Soc Bassists. *Publ:* Auth, The Contemporary Contrabass, Univ Calif Press, 74; Contribr, The Avant-Garde Flute, 74, New Directions for Clarinet, 77 & The Modern Trombone, 79, Univ Calif Press. *Mailing Add:* 429 9th St Del Mar CA 92014

TURKIEWICZ, WITOLD WLADYSLAW
EDUCATOR, PIANO

b New Castle, Pa, Aug 24, 30. *Study:* Curtis Inst Music, with Horszowski, Serkin, Menotti & Tabuteau, dipl, 48; Univ Miami, BM, 50; Columbia Univ, MA, 52; Pac States Univ, EdD, 80. *Rec Perf:* Father and Son Piano Concert, 73 & Central Park Methodist Church Choir, Prestige. *Pos:* Conct pianist, Ala Artists Ser, 78-; soloist & lectr, Ala Educ TV Network, 71-73; piano soloist, Birmingham Symph, Huntsville Symph & Ala Pops. *Teaching:* Assoc prof music, Samford Univ, 63, chmn, Piano Dept, 70-, distinguished artist in res, 81- *Mem:* Music Educr Nat Conf; Music Teachers Nat Asn; Am Fedn Musicians; Music Clubs Am; Ala Music Teachers Asn. *Mailing Add:* 8917 Glendale Dr Birmingham AL 35206

TURKIN, MARSHALL W
ADMINISTRATOR

b Chicago, Ill, Apr 1, 26. *Study:* Northwestern Univ, BM, MM. *Pos:* Mgr, Ravinia Fest, Chicago, Ill, 66-68 & Blossom Music Fest, Cleveland, Ohio, 68-70; exec dir, Detroit Symph Orch, 70-79; vpres & managing dir, Pittsburgh Symph Orch, 79- *Mem:* Am Symph Orch League; Major Orch Mgr Group (chmn, 74-75). *Mailing Add:* Heinz Hall 600 Penn Ave Pittsburgh PA 15222

TURNER, JAMES RIGBIE
LIBRARIAN

b Rahway, NJ, Oct 25, 40. *Study:* Earlham Col, BA, 64; Ind Univ, MM(musicol), 69. *Pos:* Libr asst, Sch Music Libr, Ind Univ, Bloomington, 66-67; libr asst & perf music librn, Calif Inst Arts, 69-71; asst cur autograph & music ms, Pierpont Morgan Libr, 72-82, cur music ms & bks, 82- *Mem:* Am Musicol Soc; Music Libr Asn. *Publ:* Auth, Nineteenth Century Autograph Music Manuscripts in the Pierpont Morgan Library: A Check List, 82 & coauth, Four Centuries of Opera: Manuscripts and Printed Editions in the Pierpont Morgan Library, 83, Pierpont Morgan Libr. *Mailing Add:* 29 E 36th St New York NY 10016

TURNER, LYNNE ALISON
HARP, EDUCATOR

b St Louis, Mo, July 31, 41. *Study:* With Alberto Salvi & Edward Druzinsky; Berkshire Music Ctr Fest, 59; Paris Consv, with Pierre Jamet, premier prix, primiere nomme, 60. *Pos:* Mem & soloist, Chicago Symph Orch, 62-; soloist, Baltimore Symph, Israel Phil, Fine Arts Quartet, NY Woodwind Quintet & Chicago Symph Harp Trio; mem, Civic Orch Chicago; TV appearances, US & Europe; founding mem, L'Ens Recamier & Chicago Chamber Ens. *Teaching:* Mem fac, Sch Music, Chicago & Music Ctr NShore, Winnetka, Ill; instr piano, DePaul Univ, 76- & privately, currently. *Awards:* First prize, Second Int Harp Compt, Israel, 62. *Mem:* Am Harp Soc; Arts Club Chicago. *Mailing Add:* 1316 Sheridan Highland Park IL 60035

TURNER, SARAH
SOPRANO, EDUCATOR

Study: Univ Mich, BM; Columbia Univ, MA; Kalamazoo Col; studied voice with Arthur Hacket & Evelyn Hertman; studied with Walter Taussig, Rudolph Thomas & Boris Goldovsky. *Pos:* Sop soloist, Detroit Symph Quartet, Philadelphia Orch Chamber Ens, Schola Cantorum & churches in Mich, Ariz, Ill, Fla, New York, Switz, Italy & Germany. *Teaching:* Mem fac, Stetson Univ, formerly & Univ Fla, formerly; mem fac voice, St Louis Consv Music, currently. *Mailing Add:* St Louis Consv Music 560 Trinity Ave St Louis MO 63130

TURNER, THOMAS GEORGE
COMPOSER, PIANO

b Hamilton, Ohio. *Study:* Univ Ariz, BM, 59; Univ Ill, with Webster Aitken, 60-62; Int summer courses for New Music, Darmstadt, Germany, 63 & 64. *Works:* Six Variations for Piano, perf by comp, Wigmore Hall, London, 66; For If We Believe (mixed chorus, a capella), Unicorn Music Co, 80; Fantasy (tenor sax & piano), 80, Lot's Wife (contrabass & piano), 81 & Mysterious Lights (guitar & piano), 82, Seesaw Music Co; Three Songs (Tennyson; tenor & piano), perf by Richard Kennedy, 82; Sostenuto Etudes (piano), perf by comp, New York Univ, 83. *Teaching:* Asst prof piano & theory, Univ Idaho, 62-65; assoc prof piano & comp, Univ NC, Charlotte, 70- *Awards:* Hinda Honigman Award (comp), NC Fedn Music Clubs, 82. *Mem:* Col Music Soc. *Publ:* Contribr, Various articles of musical criticism, The Times Educ Suppl, London, 66. *Rep:* Perzanowski Mgt 640 W End Ave New York NY 10024. *Mailing Add:* Music Fac Univ NC Charlotte NC 28223

TUROK, PAUL HARRIS
COMPOSER, CRITIC

b New York, NY, Dec 3, 29. *Study:* Queens Col, with Karol Rathaus, BA, 50; Univ Calif, Berkeley, with Roger Sessions, MA, 51; Juilliard Sch Music, with Bernard Wagennar, 51-53. *Works:* Chartres West, 71 & Lyric Variations, 73, ABI, Tetra; A Joplin Overture, 73, Great Scott, 74, Sousa Overture, 76 & Danza Viva, 79, G Schirmer; Richard III, ABI, Tetra, 80. *Pos:* Conct reviewer, New York Herald Tribune, 63-64; auth, Disk and Reel (column), Music J, 70-80 & New & Noteworthy (column), Ovation Mag, 81- *Teaching:* Lectr music, City Col New York, 60-63; vis prof music, Williams Col, 63-64. *Awards:* ASCAP Award, 71- *Mem:* ASCAP. *Mailing Add:* 170 W 74th St New York NY 10023

TURRILL, PAULINE VENABLE
EDUCATOR, PIANO

b Artesia, Calif, Apr 26, 05. *Study:* Univ Calif, Los Angeles, with Nelson, Stevenson, Apel & Mitchell, BA, 47, MA, 51; Univ Southern Calif, with Parrish, Koole & Robinson, PhD, 77; studied piano with Arthur Friedheim, Ethel Leginska & Guy Maier. *Pos:* Performer concerts & lect-recitals, western US, 30-50. *Teaching:* Lectr, Univ Calif, Los Angeles, 52-72, emer lectr, 72-81; consult & teacher piano, privately. *Bibliog:* Maurice Hinson (auth), The Piano Ballade, Piano Teachers Source Book, Belwin-Mills, 80. *Mem:* Am Musicol Soc; Col Music Soc; Am Asn Univ Prof; Nat Guild Piano Teachers; Music Libr Asn. *Interests:* History of piano music, especially 19th century; piano pedagogy. *Mailing Add:* 5058 Vincent Ave Los Angeles CA 90041

TURRIN, JOSEPH EGIDIO
COMPOSER, CONDUCTOR

b Clifton, Jan 4, 47. *Study:* Eastman Sch Music, 65-69; Manhattan Sch Music, 70. *Works:* Caprice (trumpet & piano), Brass Press, 72; Walden Trio (flute, cello & piano), perf by Walden Trio, 74; Feathertop (opera), comn by NJ State Coun Arts, 76; Structures (brass choir), 81; Concerto for Trumpet, perf by Phil Smith, 82. *Rec Perf:* Trumpet & Piano, Triumphonic Rec, 74; Brassworks Unlimited, Brassworks Rec, 75. *Teaching:* Prof orch, Columbia Col, Ill, 71; lectr music hist, NJ Inst Technol, 77-; instr music theater, Ramapo Col, 80-81. *Awards:* Am Music Ctr Award, 76; NJ State Coun Arts Comn, 76; ASCAP Popular Award, 81. *Mem:* ASCAP. *Mailing Add:* 303 Harding Ave Clifton NJ 07011

TUSLER, ROBERT LEON
EDUCATOR, ORGAN

b Stoughton, Wis, Apr 1, 20. *Study:* Friends Univ, Wichita, AB, 47, BM, 48; Univ Calif, Los Angeles, MA, 52; Univ Utrecht, Netherlands, PhD, 58. *Pos:* Organist & choirmaster, Grace Lutheran Church, Culver City, 50-56; dir music, Wilshire Presby Church, Los Angeles, 59-77. *Teaching:* Prof musicol, Univ Calif, Los Angeles, 58- *Awards:* Fulbright Scholar, 56-58 & 71-72. *Mem:* Am Guild Organists; Am Musicol Soc; Vereninging voor Nederlandse Muziek Geschiedenis. *Interests:* Keyboard music of the late Renaissance and Baroque; J S Bach; J P Sweelinck; G F Handel; music therapy. *Publ:* Auth, The Style of J S Bach's Chorale Preludes, Univ Calif, 56 & Da Capo Press, 68; The Organ Music of Jan Pieterszoon Sweelinck, Univ Utrecht, 58;

contribr, Style Differences in the Organ and Clavicembalo Works of J P Sweelinck, Tijdschrift, Vol XVIII, 59; Toward a Comprehensive History of the Organ, The Organ, 72; Storia Universale della Musica, Arnoldo Mondadoni, 82. *Mailing Add:* 19044 Santa Rita Tarzana CA 91356

TUTTLE, KAREN
EDUCATOR, VIOLA
Study: Curtis Inst Music, with William Primrose; studied with Pablo Casals, 55. *Rec Perf:* On Columbia, MGM & Hayden Rec. *Pos:* Mem, Theatre Chamber Players, Washington DC, currently, Schneider String Quartet, currently, Galimir String Quartet, currently & Gotham String Quartet, currently; introduced viola to villages in Fiji, Samoa & Tahiti, 58; soloist, Schneider Chamber Orch, Little Orch Soc, Saidenberg Chamber Orch, Philadelphia Little Symph, Prades Fest & Marlboro Music Fest. *Teaching:* Master classes, Yale Summer Sch, formerly, Eastman Sch Music, formerly & Maine State Univ, Orono, formerly; mem fac, Curtis Inst Music, 44-, head viola dept & chamber music, formerly; mem fac viola & chamber music, Peabody Consv, currently & Mannes Col Music, 78-; mem fac viola, Manhattan Sch Music, 80- *Mailing Add:* Curtis Inst Music 1726 Locust St Philadelphia PA 19103

TUUK, JONATHAN ALAN
ORGAN, COMPOSER
b Grand Rapids, Mich, Mar 3, 49. *Study:* Calvin Col, BA, 72; Univ Mich, with Marilyn Mason, 74. *Works:* Mass of the Holy Trinity (SATB choir & organ), 77, Mass in Honor of St Andrew (SATB choir & organ), 78, Bread of the World (SATB choir & organ), 78, Jesus With Thy Church Abide (SATB choir & organ), 79, Let Our Gladness Know No End (SA choir & organ), 79 & Immortal, Invisible (SATB choir & organ), 79, GIA. *Rec Perf:* Jonathan Tuuk Playing the Organ at St Adalbert's Basilica, Wicks Conct Ser, 81; Music for Cathedral Spaces, Chamber Choir Grand Rapids. *Pos:* Organist & choirmaster, Immanuel Lutheran Church, Grand Rapids, Mich, 72. *Teaching:* Organ, private lessons, 72- & Calvin Col, 73-74. *Mem:* Am Guild Organists (dean WMich chap, 73-75); St Cecilia Music Soc. *Mailing Add:* 3405 Burton Ridges SE Grand Rapids MI 49506

TYL, NOEL JAN
BARITONE
b West Chester, Pa, Dec 31, 36. *Study:* Harvard Univ, AB, 58; studied voice with Gibner King, New York, 60-65 & Alfred Knopf, Munich, Germany, 68-69. *Roles:* Scarpia in Tosca, Deutsche Oper am Rhein, Duesseldorf, 70-73; Don Quichotte in Don Quichotte, Deutsche Oper am Rhein & Boston Opera, 70-74; Inquisitor in Carlo, Vienna State Opera, 70; Wotan in Der Ring des Nibelungen, Seattle, San Diego, Washington DC & Vancouver, 71-79; Jokanaan in Salome, Houston Grand Opera, 78; Hans Sachs in Die Meistersinger von Nürnberg, Baltimore Symph, 79. *Pos:* Sang with major co in Austria, Can, Germany, Spain & US. *Awards:* Am Opera Auditions Winner, 64. *Mailing Add:* PO Box 927 McLean VA 22101

TYLER, VERONICA
SOPRANO, EDUCATOR
Study: Peabody Consv Music, BM, artist dipl, teachers cert; Juilliard Sch Music; Col Notre Dame, Md, LHD. *Rec Perf:* Liebeslieder Waltzer (Brahms), Columbia; Spoleto Fesival, Mercury Stereo; Requiem (Verdi) & Elijah (Mendelssohn), Am Artists; The Passion of Christ in Spirituals, BRC; & others. *Pos:* Sop, producer, dir & scene designer, Veronica Tyler & Co, currently; leading sop, New York City Opera & Young People Conct Ser, CBS-TV; tours, Scandanavia, South Am & Caribbean; performer, Am Opera Soc, New York City Ballet, Los Angeles Phil, New York Phil, Philadelphia Orch, Boston Symph, Cleveland Orch, Pittsburgh Symph, San Francisco Symph, Baltimore Symph & others. *Teaching:* Mem grad fac & dir opera, Univ Fla; vis prof opera, oratorio & art song, Univ Mo; vis prof voice, Univ Mich; mem fac voice & adv to admin, Peabody Consv Music, currently. *Awards:* First Prize, Munich Int Compt; Silver Medal, First Tchiakovsky Compt Voice; Winner, Metropolitan Opera Auditions. *Mailing Add:* c/o Teilesco Artists 5-31 50th Ave Long Island City NY 11101

TYRA, THOMAS (NORMAN)
EDUCATOR, MUSIC DIRECTOR
b Chicago, Ill, Apr 17, 33. *Study:* Northwestern Univ, BMusEd, 54, MMus, 55; Univ Mich, PhD, 71. *Works:* Suite for Brass & Timpani, Southern Music, 62; Ceremonial Sketch, Mills Music, 66; Five Haiku Settings, perf by Emily Lowe, 69; Three Christmas Miniatures, 70 & Intravention, 73, Birch Island Music Press; Bedford: An Overture, comn & perf by Bedford Jr High Sch Band, Mich, 79; Eastern Variants, comn & perf by Eastern Mich Univ Conct Winds, 83. *Teaching:* Dir music orgn, Morton Jr Col, 58; asst prof music & dir bands, La State Univ, 58-64; prof & dir bands, Eastern Mich Univ, 64-77; prof & head dept music, Western Carolina Univ, 77- *Bibliog:* Band Music Notes, Smith & Stoutamire, 78. *Mem:* Music Educr Nat Conf; ASCAP; Phi Mu Alpha; Am Fedn Musicians. *Publ:* Auth, An Analysis of Stravinsky's Symphonies of Winds, 72 & An Analysis of Penderecki's Pittsburgh Overture, 73-74, J Band Res; contribr, six entries, Band Music Notes, 77. *Mailing Add:* 180 University Heights Cullowhee NC 28723

TYREE, RONALD WAYNE
BASSOON, EDUCATOR
b Kansas City, Mo, Oct 17, 32. *Study:* Univ Iowa, Iowa City, BA, 54, MA, 55, PhD, 57. *Pos:* Prin bassoonist, Seventh Army Symph Orch, 58-59 & Tri City Symph, Davenport, Iowa, 65-; dir, Siouxland Youth Symph, Iowa, 62-65. *Teaching:* Assoc prof, Morningside Col, Sioux City, Iowa, 59-65; asst prof, Sch Music, Univ Iowa, 65-70, assoc prof, 70-80, prof bassoon & sax, 80- *Mem:* Galpin Soc; Nat Asn Col Wind & Perc Instr; Nat Double Reed Soc. *Mailing Add:* 3226 Friendship St Iowa City IA 52240

TYSON, JOHN K
RECORDER, TEACHER
b NC, Oct 29, 47. *Study:* Sch Music, ECarolina Univ, BM, 69; studied with Frans Brüggen, 73-74; New England Consv, 77-78. *Rec Perf:* In Praise of Folly, Titanic Rec, 77; When the World Was Flat, Sine Qua Non Rec, 79; Chansons, Messe (Pierre Certon), Harmonia Mundi, 80. *Pos:* Performer & mem, Greenwood Consort, Boston, Mass, 71-81; performer, Boston Camerata, 78-; soloist, Banchetto Musicale, Boston, Mass, 77- & Le Mans Chamber Orch, France, 83. *Teaching:* Fac early music & dance, Castle Hill Fest, Ipswich, Mass, 76-; instr recorder & chamber music, New England Consv, 78- *Awards:* Bodky Int Early Music Compt, Cambridge Soc Early Music, 75. *Mem:* Am Fedn Musicians. *Mailing Add:* New England Consv Music 290 Huntington Rd Boston MA 02115

TZERKO, AUBE
EDUCATOR, PIANO
b Toronto, Can, Dec 17, 08. *Study:* Royal Consv, Toronto; Chicago Musical Col, with Moisseye Boguslawski, BM; Berlin Hochschule Musik, with Anton Schnabel. *Teaching:* Dalcroze Sch Music, 40-51 & Occidental Col, 51-56; prof piano, Univ Calif, Los Angeles, 59-; master teacher, Aspen Music Fest, 70- *Mem:* Young Musicians Found; Nat Endowment for Arts (panel mem, 82-83). *Mailing Add:* Dept Music Univ Calif Los Angeles CA 90024

U

UBER, DAVID ALBERT
COMPOSER, CONDUCTOR
b Princeton, Ill, Aug 5, 21. *Study:* Curtis Inst Music, 41-42; Carthage Col, AB, 44; Columbia Univ, MA, 47, EdD, 65. *Works:* The Power & the Glory, Southern Music Publ Co, 70; Symphonic Sketch, 78, First Saxophone Quartet, 80 & Antiphonale, 81, Shawnee Press; Sky Signs for Brass Choir, Ed Musicus, 82; Musicale for Clarinet Choir, Kendor Music Co, 82; Rainbow Sonata for Trumpet & Piano, Touch of Brass, 83. *Rec Perf:* Manhattan Vignettes, 70; Beachcomber's Dance, 74; Sky Signs, 80; Trilogy, 83; Sea Pictures, 83. *Pos:* Solo trombone, New York City Ballet Co, 48-75. *Teaching:* Prof music, Trenton State Col, 59-; dir ens music, Nat Music Camp, Interlochen, Mich, 60-65. *Awards:* Standard Panel Award, ASCAP, 59-; First Prize Clarinet Choir, Univ Md, 80; First Prize Flute Choir, James Madison Univ, 82. *Mem:* ASCAP; Int Trombone Asn; Nat Asn Col Wind & Perc Instr; Tuba Universal Brotherhood Asn. *Publ:* Auth, Writing for Band, 75 & How to Choose Brass Ensemble Music, 82, Instrumentalist. *Mailing Add:* Dept Music Trenton State Col Trenton NJ 08625

UDELL, BUDD A
EDUCATOR, COMPOSER
b Grand Rapids, Mich, Apr 4, 34. *Study:* Ind Univ, BM, 57, MME, 65; Univ Cincinnati, DMA, 72. *Works:* Two Songs, Ind Univ, 63; Freedom Seven, Summy-Birchard, 63 & William Allen Music, 78; Miniatures for Clarinet and Piano, 70; Allectation (clarinet, horn, cello, piano & perc), 72; Judgment of Paris Schirmer, 73; Concentrics (string trio), perf by Cincinnati Symph String Trio, 77; Karankawa (perc ens), perf by WVa Univ Perc Ens, 80. *Rec Perf:* Songs of West Virginia, Century Rec Corp, 67. *Pos:* Comp-arr, US Navy Band, Washington, DC, 58-61; dir bands, WVa Univ, 63-70; asst dean, Col Consv Music, Univ Cincinnati, 70-74. *Teaching:* Chmn dept music, Univ Fla, 77- *Awards:* Nat Endowment for Arts Grant, 74; Fine Arts Coun Fla Grant, 79; Comn Comp, Fla State Music Teachers Asn, 80. *Mem:* Music Teachers Nat Asn (exec dir, 74-77); Fla Asn Sch Music (pres, 82-); Nat Asn Sch Music; Fla State Music Teachers Asn; Music Educr Nat Conf. *Publ:* Auth, Instrumental Music in the High School, Ind State Dept Educ, 63; A Statement of Purpose, Instrumentalist, 64; Cash In on Your Counter Display, Sch Musician, 67; The Personal Connection: The Student Audition, Nat Asn Sch Music Proc, 79; Holst's First Suite in E Flat, Music Educr J, 82. *Mailing Add:* 315 SW 84th Terrace Gainesville FL 32607

UDOW, MICHAEL WILLIAM
COMPOSER, EDUCATOR
b Detroit, Mich, Mar 10, 49. *Study:* Univ Ill, BM, 71, MM, 76, DMA, 78. *Works:* African Welcome Piece, Univ Miami, 70; American Indiana Children's Poems, 70 & 80, Strike, 80, A Bird Whispered, Your Children Are Dying, 82, Tacit, Music for Cross Cultures No 1, 83 & Oh My Ears and Whiskers, 83, Am Comp Alliance. *Rec Perf:* Knocking Piece (Ben Johnston), Advan Rec, 71; Blackearth Percussion Group, 73 & Strike, 82, Op One Rec. *Pos:* Prin perc, Santa Fe Opera, 68-; Equilibrium Inc (dance & perc duo), Ann Arbor, Mich, 74-; perc, New Orleans Phil, 71-72 & Santa Fe Chamber Music Fest, 78 & 82. *Teaching:* Asst prof, Pa State Univ, 81-; assoc prof, Univ Mich, Ann Arbor, 82- *Awards:* Comp Award, BMI, 71; Edgard Varese Award, Univ Ill, 75; First Prize Comp, Percussive Arts Soc, 76. *Mem:* Percussive Arts Soc; Am Soc Univ Comp. *Publ:* Auth, An Acoustical Notation System for Percussively Generated Sounds—Acoustics Composition No 1, Am Comp Alliance, 72; The Tambourine—Practical Repair, Instrumentalist, 73; A Rhythmic Source Book for Actors, Dancers and Musicians, Manuscript, 76; The Timbrack, Percussive Notes, 77; Visual Correspondence Between Notation Systems and Instrument Configurations, Percussionist, 81. *Rep:* Artists Mgt 84 Prospect Ave Douglaston NY 11363. *Mailing Add:* Sch Music Univ Mich Ann Arbor MI 48109

ULEHLA, LUDMILA
EDUCATOR, COMPOSER
b Flushing, NY, May 20, 23. *Study:* Manhattan Sch Music, MB, 46, MM, 47. *Works:* Sonnets of Michelangelo, 58, Time is a Cunning Thief (voice), 59 & Five over Twelve (piano pieces), 68, Gen Music Inc; Elegy for a Whale, Leonarda, 70 & 81; Gargoyles, comn by Leonard Hindell, 70; Fountains, Castles & Gardens, comn & perf by Bernice Bramson, 76. *Teaching:* Mem fac comp & theory, Manhattan Sch Music, 47, coordr, Comp Dept, 69, chmn, 70-; chmn, Comp Dept, Hoff-Barthelson Music Sch, Scarsdale, NY, 68-; mem fac theory, Sessione Senese per la Musica e lArte, Siena, Italy, 77-81. *Awards:* ASCAP Grants, 52- *Mem:* ASCAP; New Music Young Ens. *Publ:* Auth, Contemporary Harmony, Macmillan, 67. *Mailing Add:* 120 Lee Rd Scarsdale NY 10583

ULRICH, EUGENE JOSEPH
COMPOSER, EDUCATOR
b Olmsted, Ill, Dec 13, 21. *Study:* Southern Ill Univ, BEd, 43; Univ Ill, BMus, 48; Eastman Sch Music, MMus, 49, PhD, 53. *Works:* Numerous vocal & instrm solos, choral & chamber works & works for band & orch, 47- *Teaching:* Prof theory, comp & keyboard, Phillips Univ, 49- *Mailing Add:* 2610 E Pine Enid OK 73701

ULRICH, HOMER
EDUCATOR, WRITER
b Chicago, Ill, Mar 27, 06. *Study:* Chicago Musical Col, 36-38; Univ Chicago, MA, 39. *Pos:* Bassonist & cellist, Chicago Symph Orch, 29-35; ed, American Music Teacher, Music Teacher Asn, 72- *Teaching:* Head music dept, Monticello Col, 35-38; from assoc prof to prof woodwinds & chamber music, Univ Tex, Austin, 39-53; prof music lit & head music dept, Univ Md, College Park, 53-72. *Mem:* Music Teachers Nat Asn (ed, 72-); Am Musicol Soc. *Interests:* Music literature, especially chamber music, symphonic music and choral music. *Publ:* Auth, Chamber Music, 48 & 66 & Symphonic Music, 52, Columbia Univ Press; coauth, History of Music and Musical Style, Harcourt Brace, 63; contribr, Chamber Music, In: Encycl Brittanica, 74. *Mailing Add:* 3587 S Leisure World Blvd Silver Spring MD 20906

ULTAN, LLOYD
COMPOSER, EDUCATOR
b New York, NY, June 12, 29. *Study:* NY Univ, BS, 51; Columbia Univ, MA, 52; State Univ Iowa, Iowa City, PhD, 56. *Works:* Guitar Quintet, perf by Charlie Byrd with Lywen String Quartet, 67; String Quartet No 1, Tokyo String Quartet, 71; Piano Sextet, Okra Publ Inc, 73; Sonata Cello & Piano, Tanya Remenikova & Alexander Braginsky, 79; Suite for Brass Quintet, NMex Brass Quintet, 80; String Quartet No II, Pro Arte String Quartet, 81; Violin Concerto, Minn Orch, 84; and others. *Teaching:* Asst prof theory, Dickinson Col, 56-62; prof comp & theory, Am Univ, 62-75 & Univ Minn, Minneapolis, 75-; vis prof comp & theory, Royal Col Music, London, England, 68-69. *Awards:* Fels, Bennington Comp Conf, 61 & MacDowell Colony, 80 & 82; Comp Comn Prog Award, Minn Comp Forum, Jerome Found, 80. *Mem:* Am Comp Alliance; Am Soc Univ Comp; Minn Comp Forum; Soc Music Theory; Am Music Ctr. *Publ:* Auth, The Creative Artist Challenged, Am Music Teacher, 61; Toward An Ideal Audience, 66 & Theory With A Thrust–The Modal Period, Part II, 68, Music Educr Nat Conf J; The Antennae of Our Society, Minn Comp Forum Newslett, 81; Music Theory: Compositional Problems of the Middle Ages & Renaissance, Univ Minn Press, 77. *Mailing Add:* 5249 Lochloy Dr Edina MN 55436

UNDERWOOD, WILLIAM L
EDUCATOR, COMPOSER
b Greenwood, Miss, Mar 9, 40. *Study:* Memphis State Univ, with Johannes Smit, BM, MA, 66; NTex State Univ, with William Latham & Dika Newlin, DMA, 70. *Works:* A Medicine for Melancholy (comic opera based on Ray Bradbury story); 2 Symphonies (orch), 66 & 71; 3 Songs of e e cummings (sop, flute & string quartet); & numerous short works for chorus & band. *Teaching:* Mem fac, NTex State Univ, 68-70; assoc prof music, Henderson State Univ, 70- *Mailing Add:* Music Dept Henderson State Univ Arkadelphia AR 71923

UNLAND, DAVID E
TUBA, EDUCATOR
b St Louis, Mo, Mar 22, 51. *Study:* Southern Ill Univ, BMEd, 73, MMEd, 76. *Pos:* Second tuba substitute, St Louis Symph Orch, 70-76. *Teaching:* Asst, Univ Ill, 75-78; prof tuba & euphonium, Ithaca Col, 78- *Mailing Add:* 1682 Slaterville Rd Ithaca NY 14850

UNRUH, STAN
TENOR
b Beaver, Okla, Nov 20, 38. *Study:* Juilliard Sch Music, BS(piano), 60; vocal study with Giorgia Tumiati, 61-70. *Roles:* Erik in Der Fliegende Holländer, New York City Opera Co, 76; Parsifal in Parsifal, Opera Strasbourg, 77; Lohengrin in Lohengrin, Opera Bordeaux, 79; Tristan in Tristan & Isolde, 79 & Stolzing in Die Meistersinger von Nürnberg, 80, Opera Co Krefeld; Enee in Les Troyens, Berlioz Fest, Lyon, France, 80; Siegmund in Die Walküre, Opera Co Krefeld, 81. *Pos:* Ten, Opera Co Krefeld, Mnchengladbach, WGermany, 77- *Mailing Add:* Am Konigshof 6B 4150 Krefeld Germany, Federal Republic of

UNSWORTH, ARTHUR E
EDUCATOR
b Atlantic City, NJ, Nov 30, 35. *Study:* With Erik Leidzen, 60; Trenton State Col, BS & MA, 61; Ariz State Univ, comp with Grant Fletcher, EdD, 70. *Teaching:* Asst prof, Delta State Univ, 70-73; coordr comprehensive music, Brigham Young Univ, 73-78; assoc dean music, Crane Sch Music, State Univ NY Col, Potsdam, 78-82, chair comp, lit & theory, 82- *Mem:* Col Music Soc. *Mailing Add:* 76 Elm St Potsdam NY 13676

UPPMAN, THEODOR
BARITONE, TEACHER
b San Jose, Calif, Jan 12, 20. *Study:* Curtis Inst Music, 39-41; Stanford Univ, with Jan Popper, 41-43 & 46; Univ Southern Calif, with Carl Ebert, 49-51. *Rec Perf:* Requiem (Faure), Capitol Rec, 52; Liebeslieder Waltzes, Op 52, Victor; Artistry of Theodor Uppman, Internos Rec, 62; The Magic Flute & La Perchole, Metropolitan Opera Rec Club. *Roles:* Billy in Billy Budd, Covent Garden, 51; Pelleas, New York City Ctr, 53; Papageno in Magic Flute, 56-77, Paquillo in La Perchole, 56-, Guglielmo in Cosi fan tutte, 61- & Sharpless in Madama Butterfly, 61-78, Metropolitan Opera; Traveller in Death in Venice, Geneva Opera, 83. *Pos:* Mem prof comt, Metropolitan Opera Nat Coun, 74. *Teaching:* Vocal lessons, Mannes Col Music, 77-83, Hartt Sch Music, 81-83 & Boston Univ, 82. *Mailing Add:* c/o Columbia Artist Mgt Inc 165 W 57th St New York NY 10019

UPTON, JAMES SOUTHERLAND
EDUCATOR
b Ft Smith, Ark, Jan 2, 37. *Study:* Hendrix Col, BA, 58, BM, 58; Southern Methodist Univ, MM, 61; Univ Tex, Austin, with Fritz Oberdorffer & Hans Heinz Drager, PhD, 68. *Teaching:* Instr music, Alma Col, 65-68; prof, Univ Northern Colo, 68. *Interests:* Organology; aesthetics; philosophy. *Mailing Add:* 2631 17th Ave Greeley CO 80631

URIS, DOROTHY TREE
EDUCATOR, VOICE
b Brooklyn, NY, May 21, 16. *Study:* Cornell Univ, 32-34; Drama Sch, NY Univ, 35; Teachers Col, Columbia Univ, 51-53; Dixon Speech Clinic, 54-57. *Pos:* Stage & film actress, 36-51. *Teaching:* Coach speech & voice improvement, 54-; lectr communications, NY Univ, formerly; Mem fac opera theater, Mannes Col Music, 63-; mem fac, Manhattan Sch Music, currently & Curtis Inst Music, currently; coach English diction with numerous opera co incl Metropolitan Opera, Santa Fe Opera & New York City Opera. *Awards:* Grants, Martha Baird Rockefeller, 65 & Nat Endowment Arts, 80. *Mem:* Am Asn Univ Prof. *Publ:* Auth, Everybody's Book of Better Speaking, 60; To Sing in English, Boosey & Hawkes, 71; A Woman's Voice, Harper & Row, 75; Say It Again, E P Hutton & Co, 79. *Mailing Add:* 157 E 74th St New York NY 10021

URITSKY, VYACHESLAV
VIOLIN, TEACHER-COACH
b Kherson, USSR, May 20, 35; US citizen. *Study:* Glazunov Music Sch, Odessa, USSR, 52; Odessa Consv, MMus, 58. *Pos:* Asst concertmaster, Moscow Phil, 60-74 & Moscow Phil Soloists, 68-74; asst prin second violin, Boston Symph Orch, 75- *Teaching:* Instr-coach, Moscow Gnesin Pedagogical Inst, 59-68 & Tanglewood Inst, Boston Univ, 77-; instr violin, Boston Consv, 80- *Mailing Add:* 20 Strathmore Rd Brookline MA 02146

URQUHART, DAN MURDOCK
COMPOSER, EDUCATOR
b Raleigh NC, Jan 6, 44. *Study:* Southern Colo State Col, BS(theory & comp), 65; Eastman Sch Music, MA, 67, PhD, 69. *Works:* Moonscapes for Band; Psalm 149 for Chorus & Tape; Sonata for Clarinet & Piano. *Rec Perf:* Music from Ceasar; Cinna's Death, Nat Electronic Music Serv. *Teaching:* Asst prof music & dir electronic music lab, Sch Music, Fla State Univ, Tallahassee, currently. *Awards:* Woodrow Wilson Nat Fel, 65-66. *Mem:* Col Music Soc; Music Educr Nat Conf; Fla Col Music Educr Comt Electronic Music (chmn, currently). *Mailing Add:* 1610 Sharkey Tallahassee FL 32304

USCHER, NANCY JOYCE
VIOLA, WRITER
b Bridgeport, Conn, June 23, 50. *Study:* Eastman Sch Music, BM, 70; Royal Col Music London, ARCM, 72; State Univ NY, Stony Brook, MM, 74; NY Univ, PhD, 74-80. *Rec Perf:* Music for Viola, Musical Heritage Soc, 79-80. *Pos:* Prin violist, Spoleto Fest, Italy, 74 & 75, Jerusalem Symph Orch, 78- & Israel Broadcasting Authority, 78-; participant, Casals Fest, PR & Mex City, 76-78. *Teaching:* Instr viola, Rubin Acad, Jerusalem, 80-81. *Awards:* Francis Toye Fel, 70; Israeli Foreign Ministry Grant, 81. *Interests:* History of the viola; viola repertoire; American composers; Clara Schumann; music in Israel; Twentieth Century music. *Publ:* Contribr, The Viola in the 20th Century, Strad, London, 80; A Journey to a Swedish Music Conservatory, Am Music Teacher, 83; Wagner, Strauss and Israel, Index on Censorship, 83; Berio Sequenza for Viola Solo: A Performance Analysis, Perspectives New Music, 83. *Mailing Add:* 107 Holbrooke Rd White Plains NY 10605

USHIODA, MASUKO
VIOLIN, EDUCATOR
Study: Toho Sch, Tokyo, grad; studied with Joseph Szigeti & Anna Ono; Leningrad Consv, with Mikail Weiman. *Rec Perf:* On Angel, Toshiba & Melodiya. *Pos:* Performer violin with maj orchs throughout the world incl Marlboro Fest, Spoleto Fest & Harvard Summer Sch Chamber Players. *Teaching:* Mem fac violin, New England Consv Music, currently. *Awards:* First Prize, Mainichi Compt Tokyo, 56 & Tchaikovsky Compt, 66; Prize Winner, Queen Elisabeth Compt Brussels, 63. *Rep:* Kazuko Hillyer Int Inc 250 W 57th St New York NY 10107. *Mailing Add:* New England Consv Music 290 Huntington Rd Boston MA 02115

USSACHEVSKY, VLADIMIR A
COMPOSER, EDUCATOR
b Hailar, Manchuria, China, Oct 21, 11, US citizen. *Study:* Pomona Col, BA, 35; Eastman Sch Music, MM, 36, PhD, 39. *Works:* Jubilee Cantata (chorus & orch), 38; Miniatures for a Curious Child (orch), 50; Incantation (tape), 53;

Wireless Fantasy (electronic), 60; Of Wood and Brass (electronic), 65; Colloquy (symph orch, tape rec & various chairs), 76; Celebration (four to nine layers rec sound from electronic valve instrm & orch 20 players), 80. *Teaching:* Prof, Columbia Univ, 60-80; prof comp & computer appln, Univ Utah, 74- *Awards:* Guggenheim Fel, 57-60; Nat Endowment for Arts Grants, 74 & 75; Nat Endowment for Humanities Research Grant, 81. *Bibliog:* Annalyn Swan (auth), Breaking Sound Barriers, Newsweek, 82. *Mem:* Am Composers Alliance (pres, 68-70); Am Music Center; Am Soc Univ Comp. *Publ:* Auth, The Processes of Experimental Music, Audio-English Soc J, 58; Notes on a Piece for Tape Recorder, Musical Quart, 60; The Making of Four Miniatures-An Analysis, Music Educr J, 68; article on I Stravinsky in a memorial issue of Perspectives of New Music, 71; article on Milton Babbitt in the 60th issue of Perspectives in New Music, 76. *Mailing Add:* 27 Claremont Ave, Apt 3B New York NY 10027

UTGAARD, MERTON BLAINE
ADMINISTRATOR, EDUCATOR
b Maddock, NDak, Nov 2, 14. *Study:* Valley City State Col, BA, 40; Univ Minn, MMEd, 46; Univ Northern Colo, EdD, 50. *Pos:* Dir bands, Univ SDak, 49-53, Ball State Univ, 53-57 & Northern Ill Univ, 57-60; dir, Int Music Camp, 56- *Awards:* Citation Excellence, Nat Band Asn, 71; Governor's Arts Award, NDak Coun Arts, 77. *Mem:* Am Bandmasters Asn; Nat Band Asn (bd mem, 82-); World Asn Symph Bands & Ens (assoc dir, 81-83). *Mailing Add:* Box 27 Bottineau ND 58318

V

VACCARO, JUDITH LYNNE
SOPRANO, COMPOSER
b Downey, Calif. *Study:* Calif State Univ, Long Beach, 64-67, BA(music), 69; Int Opera Studio, Zurich, cert, 68; Akad Perf Arts, Vienna, with Erik Werba, 70-71. *Works:* Ceremony of the Advent Wreath, Newport Harbor Lutheran Choir, 79; Jeremy's Wizard Tale, perf by Trio Musique, 81; Sam's Emporium, Willis Music Co, 82; Dr Nuwine's Traveling Show, Chorister's Guild. *Rec Perf:* Caprice, Musique Circle Rec; Five Compositions of Irvine, Heather Rec; Dr Nuwine's Traveling Show, Chorister's Guild. *Roles:* Suzanne in Secret of Suzanne & Marcelena in Marriage of Figaro, City of Angels Opera; Cherubino in Marriage of Figaro, Wolf Trap Farm Park; Genevieve in Das Lange Weinachtsmahl & Fortunio in Fortunio's Lied, 68, Zurich Opera House. *Pos:* Soloist, Zurich Opera House, 68, City of Angels Opera, 73-75 & Las Vegas Chamber Players, 74-76; mem, Trio Musique, Calif, 76-; company mem-soloist, Wolf Trap Farm Park, 72. *Teaching:* Private instr voice, Univ Nev, Las Vegas, 74-76 & Long Beach City Col, currently; vocal coach, Disneyland & Disney World. *Mem:* Am Guild Musical Artists; Am Fedn Musicians; Choral Cond Guild; Calif Music Consort (bd mem & secy, 80-). *Mailing Add:* PO Box 7991 Long Beach CA 90807

VACCARO, MICHAEL ANTHONY
WOODWINDS
b Inglewood, Calif, Jan 26, 47. *Study:* Cerritos Col, AA, 66; Calif State Univ, Long Beach; studied with Ralph Gari. *Rec Perf:* Caprice, Musique Circle Rec, 78. *Pos:* Woodwind player, Laguna Art Fest Orch, 66-; first clarinet, Las Vegas Chamber Players & Las Vegas Symph, 70-74; founding mem, Trio Musique, Long Beach Calif, 76-; clarinet soloist, Irvine Symph, Calif, 79-; freelance studio musician, 79-; woodwind soloist & clinician in US col & high sch, currently. *Teaching:* Instr woodwind, Orange Coast Col, 79-80 & Long Beach City Col, 81-83. *Mem:* Am Fedn Musicians (mem local bd dir, 78-81); Calif Music Consort (pres, 80-); Chamber Music Am. *Mailing Add:* PO Box 7991 Long Beach CA 90807

VACCHIANO, WILLIAM
TRUMPET, EDUCATOR
Study: Manhattan Sch Music, MM; Inst Musical Art, dipl; Juilliard Sch, grad; studied trumpet with Schlossberg. *Rec Perf:* Chamber works & solo appearances with orchs. *Pos:* Solo trumpet, New York Phil, 35-74; performer, numerous concerts & broadcasts. *Teaching:* Mem fac trumpet, Juilliard Sch, 35-, Manhattan Sch Music, 37- & Mannes Col Music, 52- *Mailing Add:* Mannes Col Music 157 E 74th St New York NY 10021

VAGNER, ROBERT STUART
CONDUCTOR, EDUCATOR
b Laramie, Wyo, Feb 1, 13. *Study:* Colo Northern Univ, BA, 36, MA, 38; Univ Mich, with William Stubbins, MMus, 42. *Pos:* Organizer, Univ Ore Fest Contemp Music; clarinet, Pro Arte Quartet, formerly; adjudicator int fests; mem, Denver Civic Symph Orch, formerly; cond, US, Can & Mexico. *Teaching:* Instr, Colo Northern Univ, 36-38 & Grinnell Col, Iowa, 38-41; assoc prof, Univ Wyo, 43-50; prof cond, Univ Ore, 50-80, prof clarinet & wind ens, 50-; vis prof & lectr at over 20 univ & cols. *Awards:* Music Teacher of Yr, School Musicians, 63. *Mem:* Am Bandmasters Asn; Col Band Dir Nat Asn (pres, 77-78); Nat Band Asn. *Mailing Add:* Music Dept Univ Ore Eugene OR 97403

VALANTE, HARRISON R
CONDUCTOR, ADMINISTRATOR
b Newark, NJ. *Study:* Eastman Sch Music, BMus, 58; Manhattan Sch Music, MMus, 62; Columbia Univ, MMus, DEd, 68. *Pos:* Cond, Bridgeport Civic Orch, 69-78 & Conn Fest Orch, 80-; guest cond, Conn Ballet, 79 & Conn

Grand Opera, 81. *Teaching:* Chmn teacher educ, NY Col Music, 66-68; chmn dept music, Univ Bridgeport, 68-78, Dupont Prof, 72- *Mem:* Am Symph Orch League; Am Fedn Musicians; Music Educr Nat Conf. *Mailing Add:* 36 Burr Farms Rd Westport CT 06880

VALDES-BLAIN, ROLANDO
EDUCATOR, GUITAR
Study: Royal Consv Madrid, grad; studied guitar with Julio Martinez Oyanguren. *Rec Perf:* With Decca, Mercury, RCS, Roulette & SMC. *Pos:* Recitalist throughout US, South Am & Spain; soloist with various orchestras incl Rochester Orch & City Ctr Joffrey Ballet; guitarist, Spanish Ballet Co on tour in US, Can & South Am; musical dir & comp, Bullfight; appearances, White House, 68, NET, CBS, WPIX-TV & WNYC radio. *Teaching:* Mem fac guitar, Manhattan Sch Music, 75- *Awards:* Fel, Soc Classical Guitar, NY. *Mailing Add:* Manhatttan Sch Music 120 Claremont Ave New York NY 10027

VALENTE, BENITA
SOPRANO
b Delano, Calif. *Study:* Curtis Inst Music, 60; studied with Chester Hayden, Martial Singher, Lotte Lehmann & Margaret Harshaw. *Roles:* Almirena in Rinaldo, 82, Violetta in La traviata, 83 & Ilia in Idomeneo, 83, Metropolitan Opera; Pamina in Magic Flute, Mimi in La Boheme & Countess in Marriage of Figaro. *Pos:* Soloist, currently. *Awards:* Winner, Metropolitan Opera Council Audition, 60. *Mailing Add:* c/o Checchia 135 S 18th St Philadelphia PA 19103

VALENTE, WILLIAM EDWARD
COMPOSER, EDUCATOR
b Los Angeles, Calif, Dec 15, 34. *Study:* Univ Tulsa, AB, 56, MM, 57; Harvard Univ, AM, 64. *Works:* String Trio No III, Bloch Trio, 75; Forte-Piano Frammenti I-VII, VIII-XIV, perf by Robert Miller, 77 & 81; Double Cello Quintet, perf by Columbia String Quartet, 79; Double Viola Quintet, perf by Bloch String Quartet, 81; Duo Concertante (piano & organ), perf by Robert Clark & Rayna Barroll, 82. *Teaching:* Comp in res, San Mateo high sch district, Calif, 64-66; asst prof, Fisk Univ, 66-71; vis asst prof, Vassar Col, 71-72; prof music, Univ Calif, Davis, 72- *Mem:* Am Musicol Soc; Col Music Soc. *Mailing Add:* Dept Music Univ Calif Davis CA 95616

VALKOVICH, SUSAN FRISTROM
VIOLIN
b Modesto, Calif. *Study:* Univ Southern Calif, violin with Eudice Shapiro, BM(music), 70, MM, 71. *Pos:* Mem, Pasadena Civic Symph, 72-75; first violin, Hudson Valley Phil, NY, 76-80; concertmaster, Ark Symph, 80-81; mem first violin sect, Houston Symph, 81- *Mailing Add:* 17807 Sorrel Ridge Spring TX 77373

VAN, JEFFREY WYLIE
GUITAR, EDUCATOR
b St Paul, Minn, Nov 13, 41. *Study:* Macalester Col, BA, 63; Univ Minn, MFA, 70; studied with Albert Bellson & Julian Bream. *Works:* Elegy (solo guitar); Child of Peace (SATB & guitar); Christmas Lullaby (SATB & guitar); Christmas Prayer (SATB & guitar). *Rec Perf:* Jeffrey Van, Guitarist; 20th Century Guitar Music; Serenade (with Vern Sutton, tenor); works by Argento: Letters from Composers, tria carmina Paschalia. *Pos:* Performances throughout US & UK; 25 premieres of solo, concerto & chamber works. *Teaching:* Mem affil fac music, Univ Minn, currently. *Awards:* First Prize, Int Fest Guitar Compt, 66. *Mem:* Pi Kappa Lambda; Guitar Found Am; String Teachers Asn. *Mailing Add:* 930 Delaware Ave West St Paul MN 55118

VAN APPLEDORN, MARY JEANNE
COMPOSER, EDUCATOR
b Holland, Mich, Oct 2, 27. *Study:* Eastman Sch Music, Univ Rochester, BMus, 48; MMus, 50; PhD(music), 66. *Works:* Concerto Brevis for Piano & Orch, Carl Fischer Inc, 77; Set of Five for Piano, Oxford Univ Press, 78; Cantata: Rising Night After Night (three soli, narrator, choruses & large orch), Carl Fischer Inc, 79; Cacophony for Wind Ensemble (perc & toys), comn by Women Band Dir Nat Asn, 80; Lux: Legend of Sankta Lucia for Band, comn by Nat Intercollegiate Bands, 81; Liquid Gold for E flat Alto Saxophone & Piano, comn by Dale Underwood, 82; Sonnet for Organ, Galaxy Music Corp, 82. *Rec Perf:* Sonnet for Organ, 78, Set of Five, 79 & Communique for Soprano & Piano, 79, Op One; Cacophony, 80 & Matrices for Alto Saxophone & Piano, 81, Golden Crest Rec; Lux: Legend of Sankta Lucia, Century Rec, 81. *Teaching:* Prof music, Tex Tech Univ, 50- *Awards:* Int Scholar, Delta Kappa Gamma, 59-60; Premier Prix, Int Carillon Fest, Dijon, France, 80; Standard Panel Awards, ASCAP, 80- *Mem:* ASCAP; Am Soc Univ Comp; Col Music Soc; Mu Phi Epsilon. *Interests:* Debussy's opera Pelleas et Melisande. *Publ:* Auth, Keyboard, Singing and Dictation Manual, William C Brown, 68; In Quest of the Roman Numeral, Col Music Soc, 70. *Rep:* Tex Tech Univ PO 4239 Lubbock TX 79409. *Mailing Add:* PO 1583 Lubbock TX 79408

VANASCO, FRANCESCA ADELE
CELLO
b Brooklyn, New York, Nov 23, 48. *Study:* Juilliard Prep Sch, dipl, 66; Hofstra Univ, BA, 70; Manhattan Sch Music, studied cello with Benar Heifetz & chamber music with Lillian Fuchs, MM, 74. *Pos:* Sect cello, NJ Symph, 70-71; prin cello, Orch Symph Maracaibo, Venezuela, 74-78; dir & founder, Alborada Latina, 82- *Mem:* Chamber Music Am; Violoncello Soc. *Mailing Add:* Rockefeller Ctr Sta PO Box 1166 New York NY 10185

VAN BOER, BERTIL HERMAN, JR
EDUCATOR, VIOLA

b Tallahassee, Fla, Oct 2, 52. *Study:* Univ Calif, Berkeley, AB, 74; Univ Oregon, MA, 78; Univ Uppsala, PhD, 83. *Works:* Oberatura Folklorica de la Purisima, Orquestra Sinfonica de Nicaragua, 77. *Pos:* Prin viola, Nat Symph Orch Nicaragua, 77; res musicol, Inst Musicol, Univ Uppsala, Sweden, 80-81. *Teaching:* Prof viola & music theory, Nat Consv Nicaragua, 77; asst prof musicol, Brigham Young Univ, 83- *Awards:* Thord-Grey Fel, Am Scandinavian Soc, 80; Carl Allan Moberg Fund, Swedish Musicol Soc, 81. *Mem:* Am Musicol Soc; Swedish Musicol Soc; Int Joseph Martin Kraus Soc (Am rep, 82-). *Interests:* Music of 18th Century Gustavian Period in Sweden. *Publ:* Auth, Some Observations on Bach's Use of the Horn, Bach Quart, 80; coauth, The Silverstolpe Music Collection: Preliminary Catalogue, Fontes Artis Musicae, 82; co-ed, The Symphony in Sweden Part I, Vol F II, Garland Press, 82; ed, The Symphony in Sweden Part II, Vol F III, Garland Press, 83; auth, Die Werke von Joseph Martin Kraus: Werkverzeichnis, Royal Acad Music, 83. *Mailing Add:* Dept of Music Brigham Young Univ Provo UT 84602

VAN BOER, BERTIL HERMAN
CONDUCTOR, EDUCATOR

b Stockholm, Sweden, Mar 23, 24; US citizen. *Study:* Royal Acad, Stockholm, dipl; George Peabody Col Teachers, MM, 51; Univ Southern Calif, with Ingolf Dahl & Halsey Stevens; Univ Berlin; Univ Salzburg, Mozarteum, DMus, 68. *Pos:* Cond & music dir, NBay Wind Ens, Napa, Calif, 64-, NBay Phil, Napa, Calif, 67-, Sierra Phil, Nev City Calif, 79-81 & Sierra Chamber Orch, Calif, 80-81. *Teaching:* Instr music theory, Fla State Univ, 51-56; vis prof, Univ BC, 59; prof music, Pac Union Col, 60-64; prof, Napa Valley Col, 64-83, emer prof, 83- *Mem:* Col Band Dir Nat Asn; Nat Asn Col Wind & Perc Instr; Music Educr Nat Conf; Music Asn Calif Community Col; Music Teachers Nat Asn. *Mailing Add:* PO Box 2166 Truckee CA 95734

VAN BRONKHORST, WARREN
EDUCATOR, VIOLIN

Study: San Jose State Univ, BA, 50; Eastman Sch Music, MM, 51, perf cert, 56, DMA, 59; studied with Taylor, Ribaupierre, Jacobson, Rijto & Griller Quartet. *Rec Perf:* On Pleiades Rec. *Pos:* Concertmaster, Honolulu Symph, formerly & Stockton Symph, formerly; mem, Rochester Phil, formerly, Sacramento Symph, formerly & Sierra String Quartet, currently; conct performer throughout US, formerly; first violin, Ill String Quartet, formerly. *Teaching:* Prof violin, Consv Music, Univ of Pac, 67-, mem, Res Artist Ser, currently. *Mailing Add:* Consv Music Univ of Pac Stockton CA 95211

VANDERLINDE, DEBRA
SOPRANO

b Rochester, NY, July 18, 50. *Study:* Denison Univ, BA, 72; Eastman Sch Music, MM(lit & perf), 74. *Rec Perf:* The Ethiope, 76 & the Indian Princess, 76, New World Rec; Miss Julie, Z Press, 79; Rose Marie, Smithsonian Inst, 81. *Roles:* Zerbinetta in Ariadne auf Naxos, Chautauqua Opera, 79; Norina in Don Pasquale, Va Opera Theatre, 80; Rose-Marie, Smithsonian Inst Musical Theatre, 81; Alexandra in Regina, Wolf Trap Opera Co, 82; Mrs Hayes in Susannah, New York City Opera, 82; Griletta in Lo Speziale, 82 & Laurette in Dr Miracle, 82, Wolf Trap Opera Co. *Awards:* Minna Kaufmann Ruud Award, 77; Nat Opera Inst Career Grants, 80 & 81. *Mailing Add:* 249 Central Park W Apt 18 New York NY 10024

VAN DER MERWE, JOHAN
CONDUCTOR & MUSIC DIRECTOR, EDUCATOR

b Pretoria, SAfrica, Oct 17, 35; US citizen. *Study:* Univ Cape Town, SAfrica, BMus, 57; Royal Acad Music, London, lic piano & organ, 60; Hochschule Musik, Hamburg, Ger, 63-65; NTex State Univ, MA, 75. *Pos:* Asst cond & choir master, Radio SAfrica, Johannesburg, 61-63; coach & cond opera houses, Hamburg, Kiel, Enschede, Saarbrücken & Wuppertal, WGer, 63-70; music dir & cond, Plymouth Symph, Mich, 80- *Teaching:* Instr, Cologne Hochschule Musik, 68-70; assoc prof orch & cond, Univ Pretoria, SAfrica, 71-74; asst prof opera & cond, Univ Mich, 79-; res cond & chorus master, Toledo Opera Asn, Ohio, 83- *Awards:* First Prize, Fourth Int Liverpool Phil Cond Compt, 66. *Mailing Add:* 5036 Breezeway Dr Toledo OH 43613

VAN DER WYK, JACK ALEX
PERCUSSION, COMPOSER

b Los Angeles, Calif, Sept 12, 29. *Study:* Univ Southern Calif, BA, 52. *Works:* Fashion Show, San Francisco Perc Ens, 69; Prelude to—Warmest Desires (double concerto violin & perc), Berkeley Chamber Orch, 76; Frere Jacques (perc quartet), Pac Sticks, 77-78. *Pos:* Timpanist, Pasadena Symph, 45-53 & San Francisco Ballet Orch, 58-72; perc, San Antonio Symph, 55-56; timpanist & prin perc, Oakland Symph, 62-73, perc, 74- *Teaching:* Instr perc, San Francisco Consv, 64-67, Music & Art Inst San Francisco, 70- & Holy Names Col, Oakland, 77- *Bibliog:* Frank Kofsky (auth), The Percussive World of Jack Van der Wyk, Modern Drummer Mag, 8/81. *Mem:* Percussive Arts Soc. *Interests:* Acoustical problems of tuning timpani. *Publ:* Auth, My Music Book/Hopping Bunnies, 70, ChoomBoonk, 74, Whirlwind Mallet Method, 77 & Rudimental ChoomBoonk, 81, ChoomBoonk Publ. *Mailing Add:* 6857 Armour Dr Oakland CA 94611

VAN DE VATE, NANCY (HAYES)
COMPOSER, EDUCATOR

b Plainfield, NJ, Dec 30, 30. *Study:* Eastman Sch Music, 48-50; Wellesley Col, AB, 52; Univ Miss, MM, 58; Fla State Univ, DMus, 68. *Works:* Trio for Strings, Arsis Press, 78; Music for Viola, Perc & Piano, Orion Master Rec, Inc, 80; Concertpiece for Cello & Small Orch, perf by Honolulu Symph, 80; Adagio for Orch, perf by Nat Gallery Orch, 81; Sonata for Piano, perf by Rosemary Platt on Coronet Rec, 81; String Quartet No 1, 83 & Sonata for Viola & Piano, 83, Orion Master Rec, Inc. *Pos:* Pres, Southeastern Comp League, 73-75; mem adv bd, Meet the Comp, 82- *Teaching:* Assoc prof music theory & comp, Univ Hawaii, Honolulu, 75-77; assoc prof music hist & theory, Hawaii Loa Col, 77-80. *Awards:* ASCAP Standard Awards, 73-81; Ossabaw Island Found Res Fel, 74; Yaddo Res Fel, 74. *Mem:* Am Soc Univ Comp; Nat Asn Comp; BMI; Am Music Ctr; founding mem, Int League Women Comp, (chairperson, 75-83). *Publ:* Auth, Every Good Boy (Composer) Does Fine, Symph News, 1/74; The American Woman Composer: Some Sour Notes, Musical Am, 6/75; Notes from a Bearded Lady: The American Woman Composer, Int Musician, 7/75; The National Endowment: Is It Biased?, Musical Am, 4/76; Women in Music: The Second Stage, Newsletter Int Cong Women in Music, 83. *Mailing Add:* OMADP American Embassy Box 2 APO San Francisco CA 96356

VANDEWART, J W
ADMINISTRATOR, LIBRARIAN

b Riedanberg, Germany, June 18, 14; US citizen. *Pos:* Chmn, Chamber Music Ser, 51-; curator, Music Libr, Univ NC, Asheville, 82- *Mem:* Chamber Music Am. *Mailing Add:* 1 Hillcrest Rd Asheville NC 28804

VAN DYKE, GARY JOHN
PERCUSSION, EDUCATOR

b Paterson, NJ, July 3, 53. *Study:* William Patterson Col, BS, 75; State Univ NY, Stony Brook, MM, 77; studied with Roy Des Roaches. *Rec Perf:* Ringing Changes, 71, Percussion Music, 75 & Percussion Symphony, 78, Nonesuch Rec; The Abongo, New World Rec, 78; Intrusion of the Hunter, CRI, 81. *Pos:* Perc, NJ Perc Ensemble Hyperion & Colonial Symph Orch. *Teaching:* Dir perc, Elmwood Park, 77-78 & Teaneck pub sch, 78-; adj perc, William Paterson Col, 77- *Mem:* Am Fedn Musicians; Percussive Arts Soc. *Mailing Add:* 9 Stevens Rd Apt 89 Wallington NJ 07057

VANEATON, SUNNY F C
EDUCATOR, SOPRANO

b Okla. *Study:* Univ Denver, BM & MA, 64; NTex State Univ, study with Dr Ed Baird & Harold Heiberg, currently. *Roles:* Micaela in Carmen, Oklahoma City Symph Opera; Agatha in Der Freischutz, Freiburg, Ger; Countess in Marriage of Figaro, Denver Lyric Opera; Herodiade in Salome, 81 & Marguerite in Faust, 83, Midland Repertoire Singers. *Pos:* Recitalist in NC, Tex, La, Okla, Mo, Ill, NMex, Kans & Minn. *Teaching:* Asst prof voice, Phillips Univ, 67-69; assoc prof voice & dir opera, Okla State Univ, Stillwater, 69-; guest lectr, Lindenwood Col, Southern Ill Univ, Edwardsville, Univ Minn, Pittsburg State Univ, Kans, St John's Col, NMex, St Thomas Col, Col St Catherine, Chowan Col & Grayson Co Col. *Awards:* Woman of Achievement, Delta Kappa Gamma, 82; Musician of Yr, Stillwater Federated Music Club, 83. *Mem:* Nat Asn Teachers Singing (gov Okla district, 83-); Nat Opera Asn (gov SCent region, 81-, mem bd dir, 82-); Mu Phi Epsilon. *Mailing Add:* 19 Brentwood Dr Stillwater OK 74047

VANEGMOND, MAX (RUDOLF)
EDUCATOR, BARITONE

b Semarang, Indonesia, Feb 1, 36; Netherlands citizen. *Study:* Willem de Zwijger Lyceum, Netherlands, dipl HBS-A, 55. *Rec Perf:* Over 60 rec on Telefunken, RCA, SEON, EMI Stil, MPS & others, 63- *Roles:* Perf all Bach cantatas & Bach-oratorios, many oratorios by Handel, Haydn, Mozart, Mendlessohn, Brahms, Faure, Martin, Britten & others, operas by Monteverdi, Mozart, Hopkins, Andriessen & others, 59- *Pos:* Recital artist, oratorio singer & baroque specialist, Europe, N & S Am, 59- *Teaching:* Prof voice, Sweelinck Consv, Netherlands, 70-; prof, Baroque Perf Inst, Oberlin Col Consv Music, 77- *Awards:* Tonkunst Vocalistenprijs, Int Singing Contest, 59; Second Prize, Les Amis de Mozart Cont, 62; Second Prize, WGerman Radio Stations Cont, 64; Ridder in de Orde van Oranje Nassau, 81. *Mem:* Soc Vrienden van het Lied (chmn, 75-83). *Rep:* Ariëtte Drost Rubensstraat 63-I Amsterdam Netherlands 1077 MK. *Mailing Add:* Nieuwe Looiers straat 114 Amsterdam 1017 VE Netherlands

VAN GEEM, JACK WILLIAM, JR
PERCUSSION, TEACHER

b Oakland, Calif, Apr 3, 52. *Study:* Calif State Univ, Hayward, BA, 73, MA 74; Hochschule Musik, Ger, with Cristoph Caskel. *Rec Perf:* Kotekan, Ref Rec, 77; 76 Sounds of Explosive Perc, Sonic Arts, 79. *Pos:* Perc, San Francisco Ballet Co, 75-80; prin perc & asst timpanist, San Francisco Symph Orch, 81- *Teaching:* Lectr music, Calif State Univ, Hayward, 76- *Mailing Add:* c/o San Francisco Symph Davies Symph Hall San Francisco CA 94102

VAN HULSE, CAMIL A J
COMPOSER

b St Niklaas, Belgium, Aug 1, 1897. *Study:* Royal Flemish Consv Antwerp, two dipl & one royal medal, 23; Univ Ariz, MMus, 36. *Works:* Symphonia Mystica for Organ, J Fisher & Brothers, 48; Symphonia Elegiaca for Organ, Cranz, Wiesbaden, 55; Via Crucis (oratorio), Tucson Orch & Civic Chorus, 63; Symphonia da Chiesa for Organ, Schott Fr Brussels, 72; Sinfonia Maya (orch & chorus), 80-82; Kino-Saga for Orchestra, 83; over 100 other works publ & perf widely. *Rec Perf:* Variations for Piano & Trio for Violin, Cello & Piano, Dorian; Symphonia Elegiaca for Organ, Anderson. *Pos:* Founder & cond, Tucson Symph Orch, 28-29. *Awards:* Centennial Award, J Fisher & Brothers; and others. *Mem:* Am Guild Organists; Comp Soc Ariz. *Mailing Add:* PO Box 3384 Tucson AZ 85722

VAN HYNING, HOWARD
EDUCATOR, PERCUSSION
Study: Juilliard Sch, studied perc with Morris Goldenberg & Saul Goodman, BS, MS. *Rec Perf:* On CRI, Nonesuch & Columbia. *Pos:* Perc, Baltimore Symph, formerly, Brooklyn Philharmonia, formerly & Am Ballet Theater Orch, formerly; freelance performer, Royal Ballet, D'Ayle Carte, Am Symph & Stuttgart Ballet; mem Europ tour, Contemp Chamber Ens, New York, 73; first perc, New York City Opera Orch, currently. *Teaching:* Mem fac perc & ens, Mannes Col Music, 75- *Mailing Add:* Mannes Col Music 157 E 74th St New York NY 10021

VAN LIDTH DE JEUDE, (C) PHILIP (J)
COMPOSER, BARITONE
b Voorburg, Nederland, June 17, 52; US citizen. *Study:* Curtis Inst Music, BMus, 75; Manhattan Sch Music, MMus, 77; Lyr Opera Ctr Am Artists, 79-80. *Works:* Sabbatai, comn by Edward Doro, 74; Love Song of J Alfred Prufrock, Perf Conn, 76. *Roles:* Miecznik in Haunted Castle, 82 & Enrico in Lucia di Lammermoor, 82, Mich Opera Theatre; Ben Hubbard in Regina, Wolf Trap Opera, 82; Sagristan in Tosca, Providence Opera Theatre, 83. *Mailing Add:* 131 Mamanasco Rd Ridgefield CT 06877

VAN NESS, PAUL WILLIAM
EDUCATOR, PIANO
b Clifton, NJ, July 1, 47. *Study:* Eastman Sch Music, BM, 69, MM, 71; Hochschule Musik, Munich, WGer, 74-75; studied with Eugene List, Frank Glazer, Claude Frank & Noel Lee. *Teaching:* Assoc master piano, Cambrian Col, Ont, 71-73; assoc prof & chair keyboard, Calif State Univ, Los Angeles, 76- *Awards:* Ger Acad Exchange Grant, Fulbright Found, 74-75. *Mem:* Col Music Soc; Music Teachers Asn Calif. *Mailing Add:* 620 N Marguerita Ave Alhambra CA 91801

VAN NORMAN, CLARENDON ESS, JR
FRENCH HORN, EDUCATOR
b Galesburg, Ill, Aug 23, 30. *Study:* Juilliard Sch Music, with James Chambers, BS, 56, MS, 57; Teachers Col, Columbia Univ, MA, 57, EdD, 65. *Pos:* Solo French horn, Buffalo Phil, 58-60; co-prin French horn, Metropolitan Opera Orch, 60-63 & 65-; prin French horn, Chicago Symph Orch, 63-65. *Teaching:* Instr French horn, Eastman Sch Music, 60-62, Sch Music, Northwestern Univ, 63-65 & Manhattan Sch Music, 65-78. *Mailing Add:* Metropolitan Opera Asn Lincoln Ctr New York NY 10023

VAN OHLEN, DEBORAH S
COMPOSER
b Seattle, Wash, Sept 19, 55. *Study:* Pac Lutheran Univ, with David Robbins, BMus, 77; Univ Conn, with Jane Brockman, James Eversole & Hale Smith, MMus, 80. *Works:* Papillon (double bass & piano), Edwin Barker & Karla Torkildsen, 78; Facets & Nuances (flute & cello), 78; Piece for String Quartet in Two Sections, Crescent Quartet, 80; Five Songs (piano & ms), Univ Conn, 80. *Mem:* Int League Women Comp. *Mailing Add:* 8-D Colonial Dr Rocky Hill Gardens Rocky Hill CT 06067

VAN SICKLE, RODNEY JAMES
DOUBLE BASS
b Galt, Can, Sept 28, 32. *Study:* Curtis Inst Music, perf degree, 57. *Pos:* Bass, Toronto Symph Orch, 52-53, Cleveland Orch, 57-59 & Pittsburgh Symph Orch, 59-; prin bass, Toronto Symph, 65. *Mailing Add:* 5322 Beeler Pittsburgh PA 15217

VAN SOLKEMA, SHERMAN
WRITER, EDUCATOR
b Byron Center, Mich, Jan 4, 31. *Study:* Calvin Col, AB, 51; Univ Mich, MMus, 52, PhD, 62. *Teaching:* Prof musicol, Brooklyn Col, City Univ New York, 64-, chmn dept music, 68-71, vpres academic affairs, 71-74; prof 20th century analysis, City Univ New York Grad Sch, 67- *Awards:* Martha Baird Rockefeller Perf Grant, 61; Health Education & Welfare Office of Educ Res Grant, 69. *Mem:* Am Musicol Soc (chmn NY chap, 68-70); Music Libr Asn; Musicol Transl Ctr (chmn, 68-71); Soc Music Theory. *Interests:* Theoretical and historical studies in 19th and 20th century music; history and theory in the United States. *Publ:* Contribr & co-ed, International Cyclopedia of Music & Musicians, 64; co-ed, Perspectives in Musicology, Norton, 72; ed, The New Worlds of Edgar Varese, Inst Studies in Am Music, 79; contribr, New Grove Dict of Music in US (in prep). *Mailing Add:* 1 W 89th St New York NY 10024

VAN VACTOR, DAVID
CONDUCTOR, EDUCATOR
b Plymouth, Ind, May 8, 06. *Study:* Vienna Acad, with Franz Schmidt, 28-29; Northwestern Univ, with Carl Beecher, Mark Wessel, Arne Oldberg, Albert Noelte & Arthur Kitti, BM, 28, MMus, 35; L'Ecole Normale & Consv, Paris, with Paul Dukas & Arnold Schoenberg, 31. *Works:* Chaconne (string orch), 28; Symphonic Suite (orch), 38; Fantasia, Chaconne, and Allegro (orch), 57; Walden (orch with chorus & Thoreau text), Knoxville, 70; Tuba Quartet (chamber music), Ga State Univ, 71; Andante and Allegro (alto sax & strings), Muncie, Ind, 73; Symphony #5 (orch), Knoxville, 76. *Pos:* Flutist, Chicago Symph, 31-43; mem, North Am Woodwind Quintet, 41; asst cond, Kansas City Phil, 43-45; founder & cond, Kansas City Allied Arts Orch; cond, Knoxville Symph, 47-72; lectr, cond & flutist, Latin Am tours; guest cond, Rio de Janiero Orch, Santiago Orch, Chicago Symph, New York Phil, Cleveland Orch, London Philharmonia & Hession Radio Orch. *Teaching:* Instr music, Northwestern Univ, 35-47; prof music, Univ Tenn, 47-, head dept fine arts, 47-52. *Awards:* Comp Laureate Tenn; First Prize, New York Phil, 38; Guggenheim Fel, 57. *Mem:* ASCAP; Southeastern Comp League. *Mailing Add:* 2824 Kingston Pike Knoxville TN 37919

VANVALKENBURG, JAMES WADE
VIOLA, EDUCATOR
b Ann Arbor, Mich, Oct 10, 53. *Study:* Acad Musicale Chigiana, dipl, 73; Ind Univ, artist dipl, 75. *Rec Perf:* Complete Mozart Quartets, Vox, 77-80; Debussy & Ravel String Quartets, Sandpiper Prod, 78. *Teaching:* Asst prof viola, Ind Univ, South Bend, 75-80; artist in res viola, Brown Univ, 80- & Bay View Music Consv, Bay View, Mich, summers 81- *Awards:* Premier Grand Prix, Music Fest Erian, France, 76; Third Prize, Munich Compt (string quartet), 77. *Mem:* RI Chamber Concts (prog chmn, 82-). *Rep:* Am Int Artists Inc 275 Madison Ave New York NY 10019. *Mailing Add:* 265 Bowen St Providence RI 02906

VAN WYE, BENJAMIN DAVID
CRITIC-WRITER, ORGAN
b Allentown, Pa, May 26, 41. *Study:* Univ Tex, Austin, BMus, 63; Ohio State Univ, studied musicol with Richard Hoppin, MA, 66; Univ London, studied early music with Thurston Dart, MMus, 67; Univ Ill, studied musicol with Nicholas Temperley & organ with Jerald Hamilton, DMA, 70. *Pos:* Dir music, Bethesda Episcopal Church, Saratoga Springs, NY, 81-; musical dir, Friends Musical Arts, Inc, Saratoga, 81- *Teaching:* Prof music, Skidmore Col, Saratoga Springs, 69-76, lectr, 81-, col organist, currently; prof, Old Dominion Univ, 76-81. *Awards:* Fulbright Fel, 64-65; Creative & Perf Arts Fel, Univ Ill, 67-68; grant, Nat Endowment Humanities, 81. *Mem:* Am Musicol Soc; Am Guild Organists. *Interests:* French organ music. *Publ:* Auth, Gregorian Influences in French Organ Music Before the Motu Proprio, 74 & Ritual Use of the Organ in France, 80, J Am Musicol Soc; Marcel Dupre's Marian Vespers and the French Alternatim Tradition, Music Rev, 83. *Mailing Add:* Ravenswood House Salem NY 12685

VARGAS, SONIA
EDUCATOR, PIANO
Study: Manhattan Sch Music, MM; Arrau Sch, Chile, with Bauer, Schenck, Gieseking & Alexanian. *Pos:* Solo appearances throughout South Am, US, Europe, Mid East & USSR. *Teaching:* Mem fac piano, Manhattan Sch Music, 53-, mem fac ens, 70- *Awards:* Nat Asn Writers & Artists Award; Harold Bauer Award, 76; Peruvian Govt Grants, eight yrs. *Mailing Add:* Manhattan Sch Music 120 Claremont Ave New York NY 10027

VARSANO, DANIEL
PIANO
b Casablanca, Morocco, Apr 7, 53; French citizen. *Study:* Paris Consv, with Pierre Sancan; studied with Rosalyn Tureck & Magda Tagliaferro. *Rec Perf:* Piano Solo Works (Satie), Goldberg Variations (Bach), Diabelli Variations (Beethoven) & Dolly and Two Pianos (Faure), CBS; French Favorites & Ballade & Fantasy (Faure), Pro Arte. *Pos:* Conct pianist. *Awards:* Grand Prix de l'Acad du Disque Francais, 79 & 81. *Mailing Add:* 500 Lake Ave Greenwich CT

VAYSPAPIR, ROMA
DOUBLE BASS, EDUCATOR
b Polotsk, USSR, Feb 2, 30. *Study:* Spec Music Sch Leningrad, USSR, dipl, 49; Consv Leningrad, dipl, 54; Leningrad Acad Music, dipl, 57. *Pos:* Double bassist, Leningrad Phil Orch, USSR, 50-75; prin double bassist, Leningrad Symph Orch, USSR, 75-80 & Spokane Symph Orch, 81- *Teaching:* Prof double bass, Leningrad Music Col, USSR, 58-74; instr & recitalist, Eastern Wash Univ, 81- *Awards:* Laureate, Russian Nat Music Comt, 57. *Bibliog:* Travis Rivers (auth), Russian Bassist, 8/31/81 & First Bass, 12/26/82, Spokesman Rev; Travis Rivers (auth), Bass Recital Combination of Fervor and Discipline, Spokane Chronicle, 1/7/83. *Mem:* Musicians' Asn Spokane; Am Fedn Musicians. *Mailing Add:* W 2306 Pacific #D Spokane WA 99204

VAZZANA, ANTHONY EUGENE
COMPOSER, EDUCATOR
b Troy, NY, Nov 4, 22. *Study:* State Univ NY, Potsdam, BSMusEd, 46; Univ Southern Calif, MM(comp), 48, DMA(comp), 64. *Works:* Incontri, Orion Rec, 76; Tre Monodie, Philharmusica, 76; Cambi, Wimbledon Music, 78; Concerto A Tre, M Lurie, J Bonn, D Trembly & Univ Southern Calif Ens, 81; Music for Two Flutes, Golden Crest Rec, 82; Varianti (orch), Daniel Lewis & Pasadena Symph Orch, 82; Corivolano (viola & horn), perf by Jan Karlin & Jeff von der Schmidt, 82. *Teaching:* Music consult, Manhattan City Sch, 49-51; instr, State Univ NY, Plattsburg, 51-53; asst prof, Danbury State Col, Conn, 54-57; prof music, Univ Southern Calif, 59- *Awards:* Helen Ansted Award, Univ Southern Calif, 58; BMI Award, 57; ASCAP Award, 65- *Bibliog:* Erich Blom (auth), This Year in American Music, 48; Frances Drone (auth), Pan Pipes, Sigma Alpha Iota, 65- *Mem:* Pi Kappa Lambda; Nat Asn Comp Cond & Performers (mem bd, 66-70); Nat Asn Comp USA (mem bd, 79-82). *Publ:* Auth, Projects in Musicianship (Vol I-IV), Univ Southern Calif Press, 65-68. *Mailing Add:* 1228 21st St Manhattan Beach CA 90266

VEASEY, JOSEPHINE
MEZZO-SOPRANO
b London, England, July 10, 30. *Study:* With Audrey Langford & Madame Olczewska. *Rec Perf:* On Oiseau-Lyre, London & Philips. *Roles:* Cherubino in Le Nozze di Figaro, Covent Garden, 55; Adalgisa in Norma; Marguerite in La Damnation de Faust; Carmen in Carmen; Suzuki in Madama Butterfly; Amneris in Aida; Octavian in Der Rosenkavalier. *Pos:* Mem chorus, Covent Garden Opera Co, 48-50; soloist, formerly; prin ms, Royal Opera House, Covent Garden, currently; appeared with La Scala, Paris Opera, Munich Staatsoper, Metropolitan Opera, San Francisco Opera & others. *Awards:* Commander of Brit Empire, 70. *Rep:* Herbert Barrett Mgt 1860 Broadway New York NY 10023. *Mailing Add:* 13 Ballard's Farm Rd South Croydon Surrey CR2 7JB England United Kingdom

VEAZEY, CHARLES ORLANDO
OBOE & ENGLISH HORN, EDUCATOR
b Ft Sam Houston, Tex, Oct 12, 41. *Study:* Univ Tex, Austin, BM, 63, MM, 65; studied oboe with Ray Still, 63-67; Univ Mich, Ann Arbor, DMA(oboe perf), 70. *Pos:* Oboist & English hornist, San Antonio Symph Orch, 63-65. *Teaching:* Asst prof music, Northern Mich Univ, 65-69 & WTex State Univ, 70-73; prof, NTex State Univ, 70- *Mem:* Int Double Reed Soc. *Mailing Add:* 2317 Windsor Dr Denton TX 76201

VEHAR, PERSIS ANNE
COMPOSER, PIANO
b New Salem, NY, Sept 29, 37. *Study:* Ithaca Col, studied comp with Warren Benson, BMus, 59; Univ Mich, studied comp with Ross Lee Finney & Roberto Gerhard, MMus, 61; studied piano with Ada Kopetz-Korf & comp with Ned Rorem. *Works:* Millay-sia, perf by Patricia Ores Kovic, with Ars Nova Musicians, 78; Lord Amherst (trumpet & piano), Kendor Music, Inc, 79; Spring Things (SSA & piano), Shawnee Press, Inc, 79; Four Pieces for Alto Saxophone & Piano, Tenuto Publ, 80; Emily D (sop, flute, oboe & piano), comn & perf by Shanti Chamber Music Ens, 80; Promenade & Cakewalk (sax quartet), Studio P/R, Inc, 81; Quintus-Concertino for Saxophone & Wind Ensemble, perf by Michael Ried with Clarence Symph Band, 81. *Rec Perf:* Vocal Masterworks, Mark Rec, 83. *Pos:* Harpischordist, Ars Nova Musicians, Buffalo, NY, 79-80; pianist, Shanti Chamber Music Ens, Buffalo, NY, 81- & Berta-Vehar Duo, Geneva, NY, 81-; soloist, Buffalo Phil Orch, 83. *Teaching:* Lectr piano, Univ Bridgeport, 61-63; mem fac piano & accmp, New England Music Camp, Oakland, Maine, 62-66. *Awards:* Meet the Composer Award, NY State Coun for Arts, 82. *Mem:* ASCAP; Int League Women Comp. *Mailing Add:* 65 Hyledge Dr Buffalo NY 14226

VELETA, RICHARD KENNETH
EDUCATOR, PIANO
b Chicago, Ill, Aug 6, 29. *Study:* Northwestern Univ, BMus, 51, MM, 52, DM, 60; Univ Colo, 61; Marlboro Chamber Music Sch & Fest, 64; Univ Pa, 74. *Rec Perf:* Fantasy Concerto (Jay Reise), Nonesuch, 83. *Pos:* Perf pianist, Pa Ballet, 68-73 & 81; pianist, Pa Contemp Players, Univ Pa, 75-78 & 81-83. *Teaching:* Prof & chmn, Keyboard Dept, West Chester Univ, 65- *Awards:* Winner, Young Artists Compt, Soc Am Musicians, 49; fel, Danforth Found, 61. *Mem:* Pa Music Teachers Asn. *Mailing Add:* 18 Springhouse Lane Media PA 19063

VELIMIROVIC, MILOS
EDUCATOR, WRITER
b Belgrade, Yugoslavia, Dec 10, 22; US citizen. *Study:* Univ Belgrade, Yugoslavia, BA, 51; Music Acad Belgrade, Yugoslavia, BMus, 52; Harvard Univ, with Randall Thompson, Walter Piston, Stephen Tuttle & Otto Gombosi, PhD, 57. *Teaching:* Instr, Yale Univ, 57-61, asst prof, 61-64, assoc prof, 64-69; prof, Univ Wis, Madison, 69-73, Univ Va, 73- *Awards:* Paderewski Medal, Pomeranian Phil, Bydgoszcz, Poland, 82. *Mem:* Am Musicol Soc; Int Musicol Soc; Medieval Acad Am; NAm Soc Serbian Studies; Am Asn SE European Studies. *Interests:* Byzantine chant; Russian church music. *Publ:* Auth, Byzantine Elements in Early Slavic Chant, MMB, Copenhagen, 60; ed, Yale Collegium Musicum Series (10 vol), Yale Dept Music, 58-73; Studies in Eastern Chant (4 vol), Oxford Univ Press, 66-79; contribr, 20 articles, In: New Grove Dict of Music & Musicians, 80; auth, over 50 articles in professional journals. *Mailing Add:* 910 Old Farm Rd Charlottesville VA 22903

VELLEMAN, EVELYN
ADMINISTRATOR
b New York, NY, May 2, 49. *Study:* Smith Col, BA, 71; Teachers Col, Columbia Univ, MA, 76. *Pos:* Admin asst, People's Symph Concerts, 77-78; admin assoc, Marlboro Music Fest, Vt, summers, 78 & 79; admin dir, Cape & Islands Chamber Music Fest, 80- *Teaching:* Spence Sch, New York, 73- *Mem:* Chamber Music Am. *Mailing Add:* 1 Christopher St #2-G New York NY 10014

VEMER, RANDALL WERTH
VIOLA
b Portland, Ore, Dec 5, 53. *Study:* Consv Music, Oberlin Col, BM, 76; Music Acad West, with Milton Thomas; studied with mem of Guarner String Quartet . *Pos:* Prin viola, Ore Symph Orch, 76- & Portland Opera Orch, 77- *Mailing Add:* 7716-A SW Barnes Rd 215A Portland OR 97225

VENANZI, HENRY
PIANO, CONDUCTOR
Pos: Accmp Martina Arroyo, Fla, Bermuda, Paris, Carnegie Hall & Kennedy Ctr, 82; asst cond & res coach, Ens Co Cincinnati Opera, currently. *Mailing Add:* 353 Thrall Cincinnati OH 45220

VENDICE, WILLIAM V
CONDUCTOR, PIANO
b Petaluma, Calif, Nov 24, 48. *Study:* San Francisco State Univ, with Harold Logan & Carlo Busotti, BA(music & piano), 72. *Rec Perf:* Music from Ravinia, Stravinsky & Les Noces, RCA, 79. *Pos:* Asst cond, Santa Fe Opera, 73-76 & 79, Houston Opera, 74-75, Tex Opera Theater, 74-75 & Opera Co Boston, 75-76; cond, Metropolitan Opera, 76- *Mailing Add:* c/o Robert Lombardo Assoc 61 W 62nd St New York NY 10023

VENETTOZZI, VASILE JEAN
EDUCATOR
b Toronto, Ohio, Nov 22, 22. *Study:* Baldwin-Wallace Col, BM, 44; Eastman Sch Music, MM, 45; Ind Univ; Morehead State Univ. *Teaching:* Asst prof voice, Eastern Ky Univ, 49-59; assoc prof, Cornell Col, 59-60 & Morehead State Univ, 66- *Mem:* Nat Asn Teachers Singing; Ky Music Teachers Asn; Am Choral Dir Asn. *Mailing Add:* 1233 Knapp Ave Morehead KY 40351

VENITTELLI, SALVATORE
ADMINISTRATOR
b Rome, Italy, July 23, 31; US citizen. *Study:* Manhattan Sch Music, BM & MM, 56. *Pos:* Prin violist, St Paul Chamber Orch, 67-80, personnel mgr, 68-75, oper personnel mgr, 75-80 & orch mgr, 80- *Mailing Add:* St Paul Chamber Orch Landmark Ctr St Paul MN 55102

VENTURA, BRIAN JOSEPH
OBOE & ENGLISH HORN
b Plymouth, Mass, Sept 6, 53. *Study:* Univ Lowell, Mass, BM(oboe perf), 75; New England Consv Music; studied with Laurence Thorstenberg, Wayne Rapier & Ira Deutsch. *Pos:* Prin oboe, Omaha Symph, 77-, Nebr Sinfonia, 77-, Lake George Opera Fest, 81-82 & Shreveport Summer Music Fest, 81-83; soloist, Nebr Sinfonia, 80 & 82. *Mailing Add:* 4712 N 39th St Omaha NE 68111

VERBA, E CYNTHIA
ADMINISTRATOR, EDUCATOR
b New York, NY, Apr 4, 34. *Study:* Vassar Col, BA, 55; Stanford Univ, MA(music hist), 67; Univ Chicago, PhD, 79. *Teaching:* Instr music hist, Boston Consv Music, 74-76; fac mem, Sem Prog, Bunting Inst, 76-77; lectr music hist, Extension Prog, Harvard Univ, 77- *Awards:* Danforth Teaching Fel, Univ Chicago, 72; Nat Endowment Humanities Summer Grant, 76. *Mem:* Am Musicol Soc; Am Soc 18th Century Studies. *Interests:* Rameau as theorist and composer; music and the French enlightenment. *Publ:* Auth, The Development of Rameau's Thoughts on Modulations and Chromatics, 73 & Rameau's Views on Modulation and Their Background in French Theory, 78, J Am Musicol Soc; contribr, A French-English Edition of Rousseau's Opera, Le Devin du Village, A-R Ed (in prep). *Mailing Add:* Dept Music Extension Prog Harvard Univ Cambridge MA 02138

VERBIT, MARTHA ANNE
PIANO
b Atlanta, Ga, Jan 7, 46. *Study:* Hollins Col, AB; Eastman Sch Music, with Armand Basile; Sch Fine Arts, Boston Univ, with Bela Nagy, MM; studied with Martin Canin. *Rec Perf:* Piano Works of Cyril Scott, 74 & Piano Works: Leo Ornstein, 76, Genesis. *Pos:* Conct pianist & recitalist, US & Europe, 74-; trustee, New England Consv Music, 82- *Mailing Add:* c/o Lee Walter 1995 Broadway New York NY 10023

VERCOE, BARRY LLOYD
EDUCATOR, COMPOSER
Study: Univ Auckland, with Ronald Tremain, MusB, 59, BA(math), 62; Univ Mich, with Ross Lee Finney & Leslie Bassett, DMA, 68; Princeton Univ, with J K Randall, Milton Babbitt & Godfrey Winham. *Works:* Metamorphoses (orch); Setrophy (clarinet & piano), 63; Digressions (two choirs, orch & tape), 68; Synthesism (computer), 70; Synapse (viola & computer), 76. *Teaching:* Asst prof, Consv Music, Oberlin Col, 65-67; comp in res, Seattle-Tacoma Sch, 67-68; guest lectr, Yale Univ, 70-71; assoc prof music & dir, Studio for Experimental Music, Mass Inst Technol, 71- *Awards:* Philip Neil Prize Comp, 59; Contemp Music Proj Grant, Ford & Music Educr Nat Conf, 67-68; Mass Arts Coun Award, 74. *Publ:* Auth, MUSIC 360 Language for Digital Sound Synthesis, 71. *Mailing Add:* 381 Garfield Rd Concord MA 01742

VERCOE, ELIZABETH
COMPOSER
b Washington, DC, Apr 23, 41. *Study:* Wellesley Col, BA, 62; Univ Mich, MMus, 63; Boston Univ, MusAD, 78. *Works:* Herstory I, perf by Boston Musica Viva, 80; Herstory II, perf by Alea III, 79; Fantasy (piano), Coronet, 80; Fanfare, comn by Wellesley Col, 81; Persona, First Nat Cong Women Music, 81. *Awards:* Comp First Prize & Fel, Nat League Am Pen Women, 82; Proj Completion Award, Artists Found, Mass, 83; Rec Award, Nat Endowment Arts, 83. *Mem:* Am Soc Univ Comp (mem exec comt, 73-74); Int League Women Comp (mem exec bd, 81-); Am Comp Alliance; Am Music Ctr. *Publ:* Auth, The Lady Vanishes?, Perspectives New Music, 82- *Mailing Add:* 381 Garfield Rd Concord MA 01742

VERDEHR, WALTER
VIOLIN, EDUCATOR
b Gottsche, Yugoslavia, Aug 31, 41, US citizen. *Study:* Juilliard Sch, with Ivan Galamian, BM, 64, MM, 65, DMA, 69; Vienna Acad Music, dipl, 67. *Pos:* First violinist, Beaumont Quartet, Mich State Univ, 68-79; violinist, Verdehr Trio, 72-; concertmaster, Int Orch Weeks, 82- *Teaching:* Prof violin, Mich State Univ, East Lansing, 68-, Int Cong Strings, 70-73. *Awards:* Fulbright Fel, 65-67; Nat Defense Educ Act Fel, Juilliard Sch, 67; Teacher Scholar Award, Mich State Univ, 73. *Mem:* Am String Teachers Asn. *Mailing Add:* 1635 Roseland East Lansing MI 48823

VERDERBER, ELSA LUDEWIG See Ludewig-Verdehr, Elsa

VERDERY, BENJAMIN FRANCIS
GUITAR & LUTE
b Danbury, Conn, Oct 1, 55. *Study:* Rencontres Int Guitare, with Leo Brouwer & Alirio Diaz, 77; State Univ NY, Purchase, with Frederick Hand, BFA, 78; study with Anthony Newman, 78. *Rec Perf:* Variations & Grand Contrapunctus, Cambridge Rec, 80; J S Bach Sonata #2 in A Minor & J S Bach Cello Suite #6 in D Major, Sine Qua Non Rec & Cassettes, 83. *Pos:* Guitarist, Schmidt & Verdery Flute & Guitar Duo, 77- & Musical Elements, 79-; artistic dir, D'Addario Found Perf Arts, 82; solo guitarist, currently. *Teaching:* Fac mem guitar, NY Univ, 82-, State Univ NY, Purchase, 83- & Manhattan Sch Music, 83- *Bibliog:* Raymond Ericson (auth), Husband & Wife

Team, New York Times, 12/14/80; Erica Klick (auth), You Can Wail On Gut Strings, Guitar World Mag, 7/81; Le Retour des Americains, La Provencal, France, 1/82. *Mailing Add:* c/o Simonds Mgt 30 Hewlett St Waterbury CT 06710

VERDI, RALPH CARL
COMPOSER, EDUCATOR
b New York, NY, Sept 21, 44. *Study:* Univ Dayton, BA, 67, MA, 69; St Joseph's Col, Ind, BA(liturgical music), 69; St Bernard's Sem, MDiv, 74; Eastman Sch Music, with Samuel Adler, Wayne Barlow, Warren Benson, Sydney Hodkinson & Joseph Schwantner, MMus, 74. *Works:* Psalm 100 (choral), 72; Psalm 122 (choral), 77; Bird-dance (tape & dancer), 77; Fantasy (organ & orch), Alverno Col, 77; 5 Moods (solo clarinet), 77; Suite for Organ, 78; Magnificat (SATB, woodwind quintet, brass quintet & perc), comn by Cath Univ Wind Symph & perf by Cath Univ Chorus & Wind Ens, 83. *Teaching:* Asst prof music, St Joseph's Col, Ind, 74- *Awards:* Nat Fedn Music Clubs Award, 64. *Mem:* Comp Forum Cath Worship (mem bd dir, 68-72); Col Music Soc; Nat Cath Music Educr Asn. *Mailing Add:* Box 856 St Joseph's Col Rensselaer IN 47978

VERGARA, VICTORIA
MEZZO-SOPRANO
b Santiago, Chile. *Study:* Acad Vocal Arts, studied voice with Nicola Moscona & opera with Anton Guadaguo, 70-72; studied voice with Daniel Ferro & Rose Bampton, 73-75; Am Opera Ctr, studied opera with Peter Herwan Adler, 75-76. *Roles:* Charlotte in Werther, Chile, 80; Rosina in Il Barbiere di Siviglia, Caracas, 80; Gran Duchess of Gerolstein, Houston, 81; Amneris in Aida, Hawaii, 82; Le Nozze di Figaro, Lisbon, 83; Carmen in Carmen, San Francisco, Philadelphia & New Orleans, 83. *Awards:* Nat Opera Inst Award, 77; Best Operatic Artist, Nat Asn Music Critics, Chile, 78 & Nat Asn Musicologists, Chile, 78. *Rep:* Bruce Zemsky-Alan Green 1995 Broadway New York NY 10023. *Mailing Add:* 153 W 85th #2 New York NY 10024

VERHAALEN, MARION
EDUCATOR, ADMINISTRATOR
b Milwaukee, Wis, Dec 9, 30. *Study:* Alverno Col, BM(piano), 54; Catholic Univ Am, MM(piano), 62; Teachers Col, Columbia Univ, EdD(music educ), 71. *Works:* Numerous liturgical choral works, Gregorian Inst Am, 64-70; numerous piano solos & duets, perf by Lee Roberts, Summy Birchard, Ricordi & Hal Leonard, 64-; Judith (oratorio), comn by 6th Nat Workshop Jewish-Christian Relations, 81. *Teaching:* Assoc prof music, Alverno Col, 58-78; guest prof piano pedagogy, various consv & univ in Brazil, 73-81; instr piano, Wis Consv Music, 78-; coordr piano, Milwaukee Public Sch, 81- *Awards:* Outstanding Mem, Delta Omicron, 74; Career Achievement Award, Milwaukee Area Pan-Hellenic, 76; Wis Arts Bd Grant, 81. *Mem:* Wis Music Educr & Music Educr Nat Conf; Wis Music Teachers & Am Music Teachers; Delta Omicron; Wis Contemp Comp Forum. *Interests:* Solo piano music of Camargo Guarnieri and Francisco Mignone. *Publ:* Ed & auth of numerous articles in Musart, 62-69; adapted & transl, Robert Pace, Vol I-IV, Musica Para Piano & Criando E Aprendendo, Ricordi Brasileira, 74-76; auth, A Brief History of Brazilian Music, Alverno Col, 77; Keyboard Dimensions I & II, Milwaukee Public Sch, 82 & 83. *Mailing Add:* 811 E State St #32 Milwaukee WI 53202

VERMEL, PAUL
CONDUCTOR & MUSIC DIRECTOR, EDUCATOR
b Paris, France, Feb 19, 24. *Study:* Ecole Superieure Musique, Paris, dipl, 47; studied with Andre Cluytens & Paul Kletzki, 47-63; Juilliard Sch Music, dipl, 51. *Rec Perf:* Karl Korte Symphony, Am Symph Orch League Rec, 59. *Pos:* Music dir & cond, Hudson Valley Symph, 52-59, Fresno Phil, 59-66 & Portland Symph, 67-75; music dir, Music in Maine, 66-69. *Teaching:* Cond orch, Henry St Settlement, 56-59; instr cond & orch hist, Brooklyn Col, 56-59; prof orch cond, Univ Ill, 74- *Awards:* Koussevitzky Mem Award, Berkshire Music Ctr, 54; Gov Citation, Maine Comn Arts & Humanities, 73; Crystal Clef Award, Ill Bell Telephone Co, 82. *Mem:* Am Symph Orch League; Cond Guild. *Publ:* Auth, Efficient Orchestral Rehearsal Techniques, Instrumentalist, 77; contribr, Score and Podium, Norton (in prep). *Mailing Add:* 1914 Weaver Urbana IL 61801

VERNON, CHARLES GARY
TROMBONE & BASS TROMBONE, EDUCATOR
b Asheville, NC, Mar 8, 48. *Study:* Ga State Univ, 68-71. *Pos:* Bass trombonist, Baltimore Symph Orch, 71-80, San Francisco Orch, 80-81 & Philadelphia Orch, 81- *Teaching:* Instr trombone, Brevard Music Ctr, NC, 71-81, Philadelphia Col Perf Arts, 81- & Curtis Inst Music, 83-; clinician, Selmer Instrm Co, currently. *Mem:* Int Trombone Asn. *Publ:* Auth, Routines for Trombone, private publ, 6/83. *Mailing Add:* 924 Park Ave Collingswood NJ 08108

VERONDA, CARLO
CONDUCTOR, EDUCATOR
Study: Univ Southern Calif, studied cond with Walter Ducloux, Maurice Abravanel & William Schaefer, BM, BME; Univ Mich, studied cond with William Revelli, George Cavender & Elizabeth Green, MM, DMA. *Pos:* Cond, Phoenix Youth Orch & Phoenix Symphonette Orch, formerly; musical dir, Phoenix Community Orch, currently; prin clarinet with Univ Southern Calif Symph Orch, Opera Orch, Compton Symph, San Gabriel Symph, Scottsdale Orch, Acad of West & Univ Mich Symph Band. *Teaching:* Prof music & head, Instrm Perf Arts Dept, Phoenix Col, 71- *Awards:* Nat Endowment Arts Cond Grant. *Mem:* Pi Kappa Lambda; Fedn Musicians; Ariz Orch Band Dir Asn; Col Band Dir Nat Asn. *Mailing Add:* 3014 W Myrtle Phoenix AZ 85021

VERRALL, JOHN WEEDON
COMPOSER, EDUCATOR
b Britt, Iowa, June 17, 08. *Study:* Studied with Reginald Morris, 29-30 & Zoltan Kodaly, 30-31; Univ Minn, with Donald Ferguson, BA, 32; studied with Aaron Copland, 38, Roy Harris, 39 & Frederick Jacobi, 45. *Works:* 2 Serenades (woodwind quintet), 44 & 50; 3 Blind Mice, 55; Nocturne (bass clarinet & piano), 56; Passacaglia, 58; Dark Night of St John, 59; Brief Elegy (clarinet solo), 70; Introduction, Variations and Adagio (flute, oboe & piano trio), 74. *Pos:* Ed, G Schirmer & Boston Music Co, 46-48. *Teaching:* Fac mem, Hamline Univ, 34-42 & Mt Holyoke Col, 42-46; prof, Univ Wash, formerly, prof emer, 73- *Awards:* Seattle Centennial Opera Award, 52; D H Lawrence Fel, Univ NMex, 64; Nat Endowment Arts Grant, 74. *Publ:* Auth, Fugue and Invention in Theory and Practice, 66; Basic Theory of Scales, Modes and Intervals, 66. *Mailing Add:* 3821 42nd Ave NE Seattle WA 98105

VERRASTRO, RALPH EDWARD
ADMINISTRATOR, EDUCATOR
Study: Mansfield State Col, BS, 58; Ithaca Col, MM, 62; Pa State Univ, EdD, 70. *Teaching:* From instr to asst prof, ECarolina Univ, 63-71; from assoc prof to prof, Univ Okla, 71-77; prof & dean, Kent State Univ, 77-79; dir, Blossom Fest Sch, 77-79; prof & head, Sch Music, Univ Ga, 79- *Mem:* Music Educr Nat Conf; Col Music Soc; Phi Mu Alpha Sinfonia. *Publ:* Auth, Verbal Behavior Analysis as a Technique of Supervision, J Res Music Educ, fall 75; Improving Student Teacher Supervision, Music Educr J, 11/77; Faculty Development & Productivity, Proc Nat Asn Sch Music, 81; Choral Music of Vincent Persichetti, winter 83 & coauth, Performance Tasks ... Twentieth Century Band Excerpts for Tuba, summer 83, Bulletin Coun Res Music Educ. *Mailing Add:* Sch of Music Univ of Ga Athens GA 30602

VERRETT, SHIRLEY
MEZZO-SOPRANO, SOPRANO
b New Orleans, La, May 31, 31. *Study:* Ventura Col, AA, 51; Juilliard Sch Music, with Marion Freschl, dipl(voice); studied with Anna Fitziu. *Rec Perf:* On RCA, EMI, Columbia, ABC Westminster, Angel, Everest, Kapp & Deutsche Grammophon. *Roles:* Carmen in Carmen, Spoleto Fest, 62, Bolshoi Opera, Moscow, 63, New York City Opera, 66, Florence Opera, 68 & Metropolitan Opera, 68; Lady Macbeth in Macbeth, La Scala, 75, Kennedy Ctr, 75 & Opera Co Boston, 76; Norma & Adalgisa in Norma, 76 & New Prioress in Dialogues of the Carmelites, 77, Metropolitan Opera; Amelia goes to the Ball, La Scala, Milan, 78; Favorita in Favorita, 78 & Tosca in Tosca, 78, Metropolitan Opera. *Pos:* La Scala Chorus & Orch Tour, Eastern Europe & Greece, 81; TV performer, Live From Lincoln Ctr, Live from the Met & Great Performances Ser; performer with maj opera co throughout US, Can, Europe & USSR; guest appearances with maj US symph orchs. *Awards:* Blanche Thebom Award, 60; Nat Fedn Music Clubs Award, 61; Ford Found Fel, 62-63. *Mem:* Mu Phi Epsilon. *Mailing Add:* c/o Columbia Artists Mgt 165 W 57th St New York NY 10019

VESSELS, WILLIAM ALLEN
ADMINISTRATOR, EDUCATOR
b Gadsden, Ala, Jan 14, 36. *Study:* Samford Univ, BM(voice), 58; Ind Univ, MM(voice), 60, MusD(voice), 76. *Teaching:* Asst prof music, Wayland Baptist Col, 62-66 & Georgetown Col, 67-71; prof music & chmn div music, Jacksonville Univ, 71- *Mem:* Nat Asn Teachers Singing (regional gov, 79-); Fla State Music Teachers Asn (rec secy, 81-83); Music Educr Nat Conf; Music Teachers Nat Asn; Nat Opera Asn. *Mailing Add:* 3928 Chestwood Ave Jacksonville FL 32211

VICKERS, JON
HELDENTENOR
b Prince Albert, Sask, Oct 29, 26. *Study:* Royal Consv Music, Toronto, with George Lambert; Univ Saskatchewan, LLD; Bishops Univ, CLD; Univ Western Ont, Hon Dr. *Rec Perf:* Tristan und Isolde (film); Fidelio (film); Messiah; Otello; Aida; Die Walküre; Samson et Delila. *Roles:* Duca di Mantova in Rigoletto, Toronto Opera Fest, 52; Aeneas in Les Troyens, Royal Opera London, 56; Don Jose in Carmen, 57, Riccardo in Un Ballo in maschera, 57 & Peter Grimes in Peter Grimes, Royal Opera London; Siegmund in Die Walküre, Lyr Opera Chicago, 60; Don Carlo in Don Carlo; and others. *Pos:* Mem, Royal Opera London, 57-; ten, Stratford Fest, Ont, 56-, Metropolitan Opera, 60-, Salzburg Easter & Summer Festivals, San Francisco Opera, Paris Opera, La Scala, Italy, Chicago Lyr Opera, Vienna State Opera, Teatro Colon, Buenos Aires & many others. *Awards:* Can Centennial Medal, 67; Companion Order Can, 68. *Mailing Add:* Metropolitan Opera Lincoln Ctr New York NY 10023

VIELEHR, JULIA SMITH See Smith, Julia

VIGELAND, NILS
COMPOSER, CONDUCTOR
b Buffalo, NY, Jan 29, 50. *Study:* Harvard Col, with David Del Tredici & Lukas Foss, BA, 72; State Univ NY, Buffalo, with Morton Feldman, MFA(piano), 76, PhD, 77. *Works:* Piano Concerto, Buffalo Phil, 76; Ground, Buffalo Schola Cantorum, 78; Octet, Camenae Quartet, 80; One Three Five, Milwaukee Symph Orch, 82; Symph, Pasadena Chamber Orch (in prep). *Pos:* Dir, Bowery Ens, 81- *Teaching:* Asst prof, St Mary's Col, 76-78. *Awards:* Ford Found Fel, 72; McDowell Colony Fel, 73. *Mailing Add:* Bowry Ens 19C 55 Liberty St New York NY 10005

VILES, ELZA ANN
LIBRARIAN
b Lake City, Tenn, Dec 11, 43. *Study:* Univ Tenn, BM, 67, MA, 70; Univ NC, Chapel Hill, MSLS, 71. *Pos:* Music librn, Univ Tenn, 71-73 & Memphis State Univ, 73-75; librn, Curtis Inst Music, 75-80. *Mem:* Music Libr Asn. *Interests:* Mary Louise Curtis Bok Zimbalist. *Mailing Add:* Music Libr Memphis State Univ Memphis TN 38122

VILKER, SOPHIA
EDUCATOR, VIOLIN
b Odessa, USSR, Mar, 2, 32; US citizen. *Study:* Gnesyney Jr Col, 50; Gnesyney Inst Music, MA, 55. *Rec Perf:* Ornstein Quartet for Strings #3, SRS, 81. *Pos:* Assoc concertmaster, Opera & Balley Theater, Moscow, 56-66; concertmaster, Opera Co Boston, 74-77; first violinist, Artemis String Quartet, 77-82; music dir, Little Orch Cambridge, 81. *Teaching:* Violin, Longy Sch Music, 76-; assoc prof perf, Wheaton Col, Mass, 77. *Mailing Add:* 3 Gerry's Landing Cambridge MA 02138

VILKER-KUCHMENT, VALERIA M
VIOLIN, TEACHER
b Moscow, USSR; US citizen. *Study:* Gnesiny Sch & Acad Music, Moscow, with Yankelevich, BA, 63; Moscow Tchaikovsky Consv Music, with Yankelevich, MA, 66. *Rec Perf:* Valeria Vilker, 66, Piano Trio, 71, Brahms Trio in C Major, 71 & Mozart Trio in E Major, Melodiya, Moscow; Shostakovich Piano Trio, Sine Qua Non, Boston, 78. *Pos:* Mem, Piano Trio, 69-75; orch mem, Boston Pops, Boston Ballet Co & Opera Co, 75-76; first violinist, The Apple Hill Chamber Players, 76-81 & Beacon Chamber Soloists, 82-; concertmistress, Harvard Chamber Orch, 81-, Boston Phil, 82-; violin soloist, perf USSR, Europe & US. *Teaching:* Fac mem violin, Tchaikovsky Consv Music Col, Moscow, 63-74, Longy Sch Music, 77- & New England Consv Music, Boston, 80- *Awards:* Third Prize, Int Compt Violin Soloists, Praque, Czechoslovakia, 64; First Prize, Int Compt Piano Trio, Munich, Germany, 69. *Mem:* Boston Musicians Asn. *Mailing Add:* 20 Ware St #13 Cambridge MA 02138

VILLA, EDUARDO
TENOR
b Calif. *Study:* Univ Southern Calif; studied with Sharon Currier, Natalie Limonick, Martial Singher, Horst Gunter, Jack Metz, Seth Riggs, Margaret Harshaw & Elisabeth Schwartzkopf. *Roles:* Ten in Tales of Hoffmann, La Rondine & Albert Herring. *Pos:* Choir dir, Hawaiian Protestant Chapel. *Awards:* First Place, Los Angeles District Div, San Francisco Opera Auditions, 80; Metropolitan Opera Auditions Winner, 82. *Mailing Add:* c/o William Felber & Assoc 2126 Cahuenga Blvd Hollywood CA 90068

VIOLA, JOSEPH E
SAXOPHONE, CLARINET
Study: With Marcel Mule in Paris. *Rec Perf:* At CBS & NBC. *Pos:* Solo clarinet, sax, oboe & English horn; perf with radio, TV & musical theatre orchs; dir, Berklee Fac Sax Quartet, currently. *Teaching:* Chmn woodwind dept, Berklee Col Music, currently. *Publ:* Auth, The Technique of the Saxophone; Chord Studies for Saxophone; coauth, Chord Studies for Trumpet; Chord Studies for Trombone. *Mailing Add:* Berklee Col Music 1140 Boylston St Boston MA 02215

VIOLETTE, ANDREW
COMPOSER, PIANO
b Brooklyn, NY, Dec 6, 53. *Study:* Juilliard Sch, with Roger Sessions, Otto Leuning & Elliott Carter, BM, 75, MM, 75. *Works:* Black Tea, 76, Sonatas No 1 & No 3, 78, Organ Book, 81, Sonata No 4 (piano), 82, Dance for Organ, 82, Worldes Blis, 83 & Concerto in C for Brass, 83. *Rec Perf:* Piano Pieces, Amor Dammi Quel Fazzolettino, Sonata No 1 (2 pianos) & Black Tea, Op One Rec, 78-80. *Awards:* Meet the Comp Grant, 77-83; MacDowell Award, 83. *Mem:* Am Comp Alliance. *Mailing Add:* 96 Wadsworth Terr #4F New York NY 10040

VIRGA, PATRICIA H
WRITER
b New York, NY, July 28, 46. *Study:* Univ Mass, BA, 68; Syracuse Univ, MA, 70; Rutgers Univ, PhD, 81. *Teaching:* Adj instr, Union Col, NJ, 69-74, St Peters Col, 70-74 & Bergen Community Col, 79. *Bibliog:* Carolyn Robson (auth), The Disappointment Revisited, Am Music, 83. *Mem:* Am Musicol Soc; Sonneck Soc. *Interests:* Early American secular music. *Publ:* Auth, A Reply to Susan Porter's What's in a Name, Sonneck Soc Newsletter, 81; The American Opera to 1790, UMI Res Press, 82. *Mailing Add:* 389 Sierra Vista Lane Valley Cottage NY 10989

VIRIZLAY, MIHALY E
CELLO, TEACHER
b Budapest, Hungary, Nov 2, 37; US citizen. *Study:* Franz Liszt Acad Music, Budapest, artist dipl. *Works:* The Emperor's New Clothes, Baltimore Symph Orch, 70 & 80; Sonata for Unaccompanied Cello, Elkan Vogel, 78. *Rec Perf:* Concertos with Boston Symph Orch, 70-; Chamber Music with Menuhin, Gstaad, 71; Beethoven Duos (violin & cello), Orion, 74; Solo Works, 74-75 & Sonatas with Piano, 76-77, BBC; Art of Mihaly Virizlay, Orion. *Pos:* Solo cellist, Baltimore Symph, 63- *Teaching:* Prof cello, orch repertoire & chamber music, Peabody Consv, 63-; vis prof cello, Ind Univ, 66-81 & Philadelphia Col Perf Arts, 81- *Mailing Add:* 3904 Hadley Sq W Baltimore MD 21218

VIRIZLAY, PAULA SKOLNICK
CELLO, EDUCATOR
b Quantico, Va, July 21, 45. *Study:* Stanford Univ, BA; Univ Southern Calif, MM. *Pos:* Mem, Baltimore Symph Orch, currently; prin cellist, Orch Piccola, currently; participant, Marlboro Fest, Ojai Fest & Carmel Bach Fest & Shawnigan Int Fest Arts, BC; recitalist chamber music, currently. *Teaching:* Mem fac cello, Univ Md, Baltimore, currently & Peabody Consv, currently. *Awards:* Fromm Fel, Berkshire Music Fest; Scholar, Casals Fest, PR. *Mem:* Sigma Alpha Iota. *Mailing Add:* 3904 Hadley Sq W Baltimore MD 21218

VIRKHAUS, TAAVO
CONDUCTOR, COMPOSER
b Tartu, Estonia, June 29, 34; US citizen. *Study:* Univ Miami, BM, 55; Eastman Sch Music, MM, 57, DMA, 67; studied with Pierre Monteux, summer 60 & 61. *Works:* Violin Concerto, Eastman Rochester Symph, 67, Baltimore Symph, 67 & Estonian SSR State Symph, 78; Symphony No 1, Baltimore Symph, 76 & Estonian SSR State Symph, 78; Symphony No 2, Duluth-Superior Symph, 80. *Pos:* Dir music, Univ Rochester, 66-77; cond, Opera Theater of Rochester, 71-77; music dir & cond, Duluth-Superior Symph Orch, 77- *Teaching:* Assoc prof cond, Eastman Sch Music, 67-77. *Awards:* Fulbright scholar, 63 & 64; Howard Hanson Prize in Comp, Eastman Sch Music, 67. *Mem:* Am Symph Orch League; Int Asn Musicians; Am Symph Orch League Cond Guild. *Rep:* Liegner Mgt 1860 Broadway Suite 1610 New York NY 10021. *Mailing Add:* 321 High St Duluth MN 55811

VIRO, OLEV L
VIOLIN, CONDUCTOR
b Queens, NY, Aug 4, 55. *Study:* State Univ NY, Binghamton, BA(music), 77; New England Consv Music, MM(violin), 80; Syracuse Univ, Grad Chamber Ens, 80-82. *Pos:* Section violin, Syracuse Symph Orch, 80-82; concertmaster, Syracuse Camerata Orch, 81-82; prin second violin, Knoxville Symph & Chamber Orch, 82-; asst cond, Oak Ridge Symph, 83- *Mailing Add:* 2309 Laurel Ave Knoxville TN 37916

VISCUGLIA, FELIX ALFRED
CLARINET
b Niagara Falls, New York, Jan 13, 27. *Study:* New England Consv Music, BMus, 53. *Pos:* Clarinetist, Boston Symph Orch, 66-78. *Teaching:* Lectr clarinet, New England Consv Music, 53-78 & Music Dept, Univ Nev, 78- *Mailing Add:* 215 W Basic Rd Henderson NV 89015

VISHNEVSKAYA, GALINA
SOPRANO
b Leningrad, USSR, Oct 25, 26; stateless. *Study:* All schooling completed in USSR; studied with Vera Garina, 42-52. *Rec Perf:* Rec incl Symph No 14 (Shostakovitch), Lady Macbetta of Mtsensk, Queen of Spades, Tosca & Eugene, Ore by Angel/EMI & DG. *Roles:* Leonora in Fidelia; Margaret in Faust; Natasha in War and Peace; Cherubino in Marriage of Figaro; Kupava in Snow Maiden; Liza in Queen of Spades; Cio-cio-san in Madame Butterfly. *Pos:* Prima diva, Bolshoi Opera Theater, Moscow, 52-74. *Awards:* People's Artist of USSR; Order of Lenin, USSR; Order Arts & Lett, France. *Rep:* Columbia Artists Mgt Inc 165 W 57th St New York NY 10019. *Mailing Add:* c/o Nat Symph Orch Kennedy Ctr Washington DC 20566

VITS, BILLY (WILLIAM HENRY)
PERCUSSION, COMPOSER
b Evanston, Ill, Aug 20, 57. *Study:* Ball State Univ, BS(music educ), 78; Univ Mich, MMus, 79. *Pos:* Prin perc, Grand Rapids Symph Orch, 79-, Lake Placid Sinfonietta, 81-, Summerfest Orch, 82- & Musica Nova, 82- *Teaching:* Fac mem, Grand Valley State Col, 82- & Calvin Col, 82- *Bibliog:* Maggie Anareno (dir), Percussivision (video), Anareno, 83; Deanna Morse (dir), Hand (film), Morse, 83. *Mem:* Percussive Arts Soc. *Mailing Add:* 315 Griggs SE Grand Rapids MI 49507

VLAHOPOULOS, SOTIREOS
COMPOSER, TEACHER
b St Louis, Mo, June 1, 26. *Study:* Am Consv Music, BM(comp), 50, BM(theory), 51, MM(comp), 57; comp study with Roy Harris & Virgil Thomson. *Works:* The Moon Pool, perf at Am String Teachers Cong, 62; Symphonic Suite, perf by Amherst Symph Orch, 65; Piano Music, Recorded Publ, 68; The Seasons (song cycle), perf by Buffalo Symphonette, 75; Prelude, Fugue & Toccata, perf at Nat Gallery Art, 75; Iberian Sketches, perf at Contemp Music Forum, 80; Art Songs, Ellsworth Rec, 81. *Pos:* Assoc dir, Ellsworth Music Studios, Chevy Chase, Md, 77- *Teaching:* Teaching asst, Univ Ind, Bloomington, 58-59; asst prof music, Rosary Hill Col, 60-70; comp in res & assoc prof, Daemen Col, 70-77. *Awards:* Fulbright Fel, 59. *Bibliog:* E Ruth Anderson (auth), Contemporary American Composers, G K Hall Co, 76; Maurice Hinson (auth), Guide to the Pianist's Repertoire (supplement), Univ Ind Press, 79. *Mem:* Music Teachers Nat Asn; Phi Mu Alpha Sinfonia. *Mailing Add:* 4303 Wakefield Dr Annandale VA 22003

VOGEL, HOWARD LEVI
RECORDER, BASSOON
Study: Manhattan Sch Music, studied bassoon with Simon Kovar & musicol with Joseph Braunstein, BM(bassoon), 55, MM(musicol), 60; studied lute with Suzanne Bloch, recorder with Franz Brüggen & viol with Martha Blackman, 58-69. *Pos:* Bassoonist, Kansas City Phil, 56-58 & Robert Shaw Chorale, New York City Opera, Metropolitan Opera & New York City Ballet, 59-75; recorder soloist, New York Baroque Ens, 61-81; bassoonist & contrabassoonist, Little Orch Soc, New York Phil & Musica Sacra, 82. *Teaching:* Sch dir & teacher recorder, Village Music Wrkshp, New York, 65-;

asst prof music, City Univ New York, 67-75; artist in res, Somerset Co Col, NJ, 76-79. *Mem:* Galpin Soc; Am Lute Soc; Am Musical Instr Soc; Am Recorder Soc. *Interests:* Baroque string playing technique, especially bowing; baroque recorder playing & ornamentation. *Publ:* Auth, On Making Baroque Music, Ulster Co Artist, 75. *Mailing Add:* 24 Horatio St New York NY 10014

VOGEL, ROGER CRAIG
COMPOSER, EDUCATOR
b Cleveland, Ohio, July 6, 47. *Study:* Ohio State Univ, BM, 71, MA, 72, PhD, 75. *Works:* Temporal Landscape No 1, Shawnee Press, 78; Divertimento (woodwind quintet), Seesaw Music Corp, 79; Temporal Landscape No V, 81, Quartet (sax), 81, Satanic Dance, 81, Concerto (horn & strings), 81 & Sonata (piano), 83, Dorn Publ. *Teaching:* Grad assoc, Ohio State Univ, 72-74; asst prof, Univ Ga, 76-82 & assoc prof, 82- *Mem:* Am Musicol Soc; Col Music Soc; Southeastern Comp League; BMI. *Interests:* Renaissance Spanish music theory. *Publ:* Auth, The Musical Wheel of Domingo Marcos Duran, Col Music Symposium, 82. *Rep:* Univ Ga Sch Music Athens GA 30602. *Mailing Add:* 315 Camelot Dr Athens GA 30606

VOKETAITIS, ARNOLD (MATHEW)
BASS, TEACHER
b New Haven, Conn, May 11, 31. *Study:* Quinnipiac Col, BS, 54; Sch Drama, Yale Univ, 57-58; studied voice with Elda Ercole, 57-78. *Rec Perf:* Carry Nation (D Moore), Desto Rec, 68; Le Cid (Massenet), Columbia Rec, 78; Les Noces (Stravinsky), RCA Victor, 78; Music from the Films Ivan the Terrible & Lt Kije Suite (Prokofiev), 80 & Rachmaninoff Orchestral Music, The Bells & Spring Cantata, 81, Vox Cum Laude. *Roles:* Don Basilio in Barber of Seville, Liceo Opera, Barcelona, Spain, 68; Bluebeards Castle, Pittsburgh Symph, 70 & 74, New York Phil, 71 & Boston Symph, 73; Mephisto, Liceo Opera, Barcelona, Spain, 79 & San Francisco Opera, 80; Don Quichotte, Int Opera Mex, 80 & 81; Rocco in Fidelio, Cervantino Fest Mex, 82; numerous performances with New York City Opera & Chicago Lyr Opera; and others. *Pos:* Perf with New York City Opera, 58-78 & Chicago Lyr Opera, 68-83. *Awards:* Conn Opera Auditions of Air Award, Conn Opera Asn, 57; Rockefeller Grant, 64. *Bibliog:* Gordon Emerson (auth), Busy Bass, New Haven Register—Arts, 3/83. *Mem:* Ill Arts Coun; Am Guild Musical Artists (mem bd gov, 76-82); Am Fedn TV & Radio Artists. *Rep:* Herbert Barrett Mgt 1860 Broadway New York NY 10023. *Mailing Add:* 5406 S Artesian Ave Chicago IL 60632

VOLCKHAUSEN, DAVID
TEACHER, PIANO
Study: Juilliard Sch, BM, MS; Manhattan Sch Music, MM; studied piano with Steuermann, Firkusny & Kabos. *Rec Perf:* On CMS-Desto. *Pos:* Solo recitalist, Carnegie Hall & Nat Educ TV. *Teaching:* Fac mem theory, Prep Div, Manhattan Sch Music, 80- *Mailing Add:* 44 W 96th New York NY 10025

VOLLINGER, WILLIAM FRANCIS
COMPOSER, MUSIC DIRECTOR
b Hackensack, NJ, June 28, 45. *Study:* Manhattan Sch Music, BMus, 67, MMusEd, 69, MMus, 70. *Works:* Psychic Phenomena (opera), Gregg Smith Singers, 75; More than Conquerors, Long Island Chamber Ens, 77; Three Songs About the Resurrection, New York Vocal Arts Ens, 80; Ave Manz, 81 & Usefulness of New York Philharmonic Programs, 81, Lawson-Gould. *Pos:* Dir vocal music, Pocantico Hills Sch, 79- *Mem:* ASCAP. *Mailing Add:* 21 Ruckman Rd Woodcliff Lake NJ 07675

VOLLRATH, CARL PAUL
COMPOSER, EDUCATOR
b New York, NY, Mar 26, 31. *Study:* Stetson Univ, BM, 53; Teachers Col, Columbia Univ, MA, 56; Fla State Univ, EdD, 64. *Works:* The Quest (opera), perf by Fla State Opera Guild, 66; Concert Piece for Cello & Piano, perf by Atlanta Chamber Players, 79; Symphony #1 for Band, perf by US Mil Acad West Point Band, 82; Five Pieces for Flute & Piano, Comp Forum, Univ Ala, 82; Concert Piece for Saxophone & Piano, Austin Peay State Univ, 82; Chant With Trope for Alto Trombone & Piano, Int Trombone Asn Workshop, 82; Trio for Piano, Clarinet & Flute, perf by Atlanta Chamber Players, 83. *Pos:* Clarinetist, US Mil Acad West Point Band, 53-56; music consult, Dade Co, Fla, 56-58. *Teaching:* Asst prof theory & hist, Troy State Univ, 65- *Awards:* Nat Endowment Arts Grant, 79. *Bibliog:* Dr Ed Bahr (auth), Trombone Music of Carl Vollrath, Int Trombone Asn J, 83. *Mem:* Southeastern Comp League. *Mailing Add:* 110 Norfolk Ave Troy AL 36081

VON GRABOW, RICHARD H
EDUCATOR, CARILLONNEUR
b Oak Park, Ill, June 26, 32. *Study:* Ball State Univ, BA(music educ), 55, MA(piano), 58; Univ Southern Calif, DMus, 72. *Pos:* Guest carillon recitalist, Riverside Church, New York, Washington DC Cathedral, Univ Calif, Riverside & Berkeley, Springfield Int Carillon Fest, Ill, Univ Toronto & Wake Forest Univ & others; carillonneur, Iowa State Univ, 73-; ed, Am Carillon Music Ed, 83- *Teaching:* Choral dir, instr gen music & German & chmn, Humanities Dept, jr & sr high sch incl San Bernardino city sch, Calif, 58-69; prof music hist, lit & appl carillon, Iowa State Univ, 69- *Mem:* Phi Mu Alpha Sifonia (gov prov 26, 73-); Col Music Soc; Music Educr Nat Conf; Guild Carillonneurs North Am. *Interests:* Team teaching the humanities or western civilization. *Mailing Add:* 51 Music Hall Iowa State Univ Ames IA 50011

VON GUNDEN, HEIDI CECILIA
EDUCATOR, WRITER
b San Diego, Calif, Apr 13, 40. *Study:* Mt St Mary's Col, BM, 59-63; Calif State Univ, Los Angeles, MA, 71; Univ Calif, San Diego, PhD, 77. *Teaching:* Asst prof theory & comp, Southern Ill Univ, 75-79, Univ Ill, Champaign-Urbana, 79- *Awards:* Grant, Southern Ill Univ, 77 & 78. *Mem:* Col Music Soc; Am Soc Univ Comp; Pi Kappa Lambda; Am Women Comp, Inc. *Publ:* Auth, Don Juan and Carlos Castaneda—A Lesson in Sonic Awareness, Col Music Symposium, 80; The Theory of Sonic Awareness in The Greeting by Pauline Oliveros, Perspectives New Music, 81; Olivier Messiaen's Compositional Use of Timbre, Am Soc Univ Comp, 83; The Music of Pauline Oliveros, Scarecrow, 83; The Music of Ben Johnston, Scarecrow (in prep). *Mailing Add:* 2508 Kirby Champaign IL 61826

VON RHEIN, JOHN RICHARD
CRITIC-WRITER, LECTURER
b Pasadena, Calif, Sept 10, 45. *Study:* Pasadena City Col, AA, 65; Univ Calif, Los Angeles, BA(English), 67; Calif State Univ, Los Angeles, BA(music), 70. *Pos:* Music reviewer, Hollywood Citizen News, 68-71; music & dance ed & critic, Akron Beacon J, 71-77; music critic, Chicago Tribune, 77- *Mem:* Music Critics Asn. *Publ:* Contribr to High Fidelity/Musical Am, Opera News, US Info Agency J, Ovation & others. *Mailing Add:* Chicago Tribune 435 N Michigan Ave Chicago IL 60611

VON STADE, FREDERICA
MEZZO-SOPRANO
b Somerville, NJ, June 1, 45. *Study:* Mannes Col Music, BS. *Rec Perf:* Duet Album with Judith Blegen, CBS; Mozart & Rossini Arias, Philips. *Roles:* Leading roles in Magic Flute, Faust, Tales of Hoffman, Rigoletto, Madama Butterfly, Figaro, Romeo & Juliet and others, Metropolitan Opera; appearances with Paris Opera, San Francisco Opera, London Royal Opera, Boston Opera Co, Santa Fe Opera, La Scala & others. *Pos:* Concts with Vienna Phil, Los Angeles Phil, New York Phil, San Francisco Symph, New Philharmonia and others. *Mem:* Am Guild Musical Artists. *Mailing Add:* Columbia Artists Mgt 165 W 57th St New York NY 10019

VON WURTZLER, ARISTID
EDUCATOR, HARP
b Budapest, Hungary; US citizen. *Study:* Franz Liszt Acad Music, MM, 55; London Col Music, DM, 68; Budapest Acad, studied comp with Zoltan Kodaly. *Works:* Modern Sketches; Peer-Southern; Chordophonic & Space Odyssey, New York Harp Ens; Variation on Theme of Corelli, Brilliant Etude, Vivaldi D Major Concerto (orch & solo harp), Christian Bach Concerto (solo harp & orch) & Handel F Major Concerto (harp solo & orch), Gen Music Publ; Transcriptions Bartok & Kodaly (solo harp), Salvi Publ. *Rec Perf:* 14 Recordings, Musical Heritage Soc; Two Records, Golden Crest Rec. *Pos:* Mem, Budapest Phil, formerly; solo harpist, Detroit Symph Orch, formerly, harpist, New York Phil, 58-61; music dir & soloist, New York Harp Ens; concert performer worldwide. *Teaching:* Chmn harp dept, Hartt Col Music, 63-69 & State Univ NY, formerly; mem fac, Hofstra Univ, formerly & New Col, Fla, formerly; prof harp, NY Univ, 70- & Aaron Copland Sch, Queens Col, City Univ New York, 82- *Awards:* Merit Award, Nat Fedn Music Club, 69. *Mem:* Am Harp Soc; Bohemians; ASCAP. *Mailing Add:* 140 West End Ave New York NY 10023

VOOIS, JACQUES C
PIANO, CONDUCTOR
b Hackensack, NJ, Mar 15, 37. *Study:* Consv Music, Oberlin Col, BMus, 58; Manhattan Sch Music, MMus, 64; Ind Univ, 64-65; Peabody Consv, 83. *Pos:* Music dir, Lansdowne Symph Orch, Pa, 80-; ed, J Cond Guild, 80- *Teaching:* Chmn keyboard dept, Kans State Univ, 65-67; instr, Univ Del, 67-69; music dir, Harford Community Col, 67-69; assoc prof, West Chester State Univ, 69- *Awards:* Fulbright Grant, 58-59; French Govt Scholar, 59-60. *Mem:* Cond Guild Am Symph Orch League (secy, 75-81); Phi Mu Alpha; Pi Kappa Lambda; Music Educr Nat Conf. *Publ:* Auth, The Case of the Missing Concerto, Symph Mag, Am Symph Orch League, 74. *Rep:* Cond Int 65 Ceder Road Ringwood NJ 07456. *Mailing Add:* 424 Price St West Chester PA 19380

VOORHEES, GORDON
BARITONE
b New York, NY. *Study:* private study with Licia Albanese, Alberto Masiello & Joan Dornemann. *Roles:* Rolando in La Battaglia di Legnano, Amato Opera Co, 76; Serse in Temistocle, Bel Canto Opera, 82; Caravaggio in The Death of the Virgin, 83; Angelo in Das Liebesverbot, Waterloo Music Fest. *Rep:* Matthews/Napal Ltd 270 W End Ave New York NY 10023. *Mailing Add:* 420 Riverside Dr New York NY 10025

VORNHOLT, DAVID
FLUTE
b Dayton, Ohio, Sept 15, 21. *Study:* Col Music Cincinnati, BM, 42, MM, 50; Tanglewood Music Fest, 49; studied with Robert Cavally, George Laurant & Julius Baker. *Pos:* Second flute, Dayton Ohio Phil, 37-42, first flute, 49-54; piccolo & third degree flute, Dallas Symph Orch, 54-71 & 73-, personnel mgr, 74-70; first flute, Wichita Kans Symph, 71-73. *Teaching:* Lectr flute, Earlham Col, 52-53; adj prof, Southern Methodist Univ, 58-71; asst prof, Wichita State Univ, 71-73. *Mem:* Am Fedn Musicians. *Mailing Add:* 3201 E Purdue Dallas TX 75225

VORRASI, JOHN FREDERICK
TENOR, ADMINISTRATOR
b Rochester, NY, May 26, 48. *Study:* John Fisher Col, BA, 70; Am Consv Music. *Works:* An Eucharistic Hymn, Belwin Mills, 76. *Roles:* St Simeon in The Egg, 81; St Nicolas in St Nicolas, 83. *Pos:* Gen mgr & mem, William Ferris Chorale, Chicago, 72-; mem, Grant Park Chorus, 78-; soloist, Spoleto Fest, USA, 82. *Mem:* Am Guild Musical Artists; Mu Phi Epsilon. *Mailing Add:* 750 N Dearborn Chicago IL 60610

VOTAPEK, RALPH
PIANO, EDUCATOR
b Milwaukee, Wis, Mar 20, 39. *Study:* Northwestern Univ, BA, 60; Manhattan Sch Music, MM, 61. *Rec Perf:* Gershwin 2nd Rhapsody, London Rec, 78. *Pos:* Conct pianist, Sol Hurok Concts, 62-76 & Maxim Gershunoff Attractions, 77- *Teaching:* Prof piano, Mich State Univ, 68- *Awards:* Naumberg Award, 59; Van Cliburn Int Piano Compt Grand Prize, 62. *Rep:* Maxim Gershunoff 502 Park Ave New York NY 10022. *Mailing Add:* 1516 Glenhaven Ave East Lansing MI 48823

VOTH, ELVERA
CONDUCTOR
b Kans. *Study:* Northwestern Univ, MM. *Pos:* Artistic dir & chorus master, Anchorage Civic Opera, 75-; founder, Sunday Museum Recital Ser, Univ Alaska, Anchorage Singers & Anchorage Boys Choir; cond, Anchorage Community Chorus, 12 yrs & concerts with Alaskan musicians in Wash, Ore, Tex & Washington, DC; artistic consult, Basically Bach Fest, formerly, mem staff cond, currently. *Teaching:* Prof music, Univ Alaska, Anchorage, currently. *Mailing Add:* Anchorage Civic Opera PO Box 10-3316 Anchorage AK 99510

VOXMAN, HIMIE
ADMINISTRATOR, COMPOSER
b Centerville, Iowa, Sept 17, 12. *Study:* Univ Iowa, BS, 33, MA, 34; clarinet study with William Gower & Gustave Langenus. *Pos:* Instr woodwinds, Univ Iowa, 36-80, dir sch music, 54-80. *Awards:* Silver Baton, Bell Syst, 80; Edwin Franko Goldman Award, Am Bandmasters Asn, 83. *Mem:* Hon mem, Nat Asn Sch Music; Am Musicol Soc; Music Educr Nat Conf; Music Libr Asn; Int Clarinet Soc. *Interests:* Woodwind literature. *Publ:* Coauth, Woodwind Ensemble Music Guide, 73, Woodwind Solo and Study Material Music Guide, 75 & Woodwind Music Guide, 82, Instrumentalist. *Mailing Add:* 821 N Linn Iowa City IA 52240

VRENIOS, ANASTASIOS NICHOLAS
TENOR
b Turlock, Calif, Aug 24, 40. *Study:* Univ Pac, BMus(voice), 62; Ind Univ, MMus(voice perf), 65. *Rec Perf:* Les Huguenots, London Rec. *Roles:* The Egg, Nat Cathedral, 76. *Pos:* Choir dir, St George Greek Orthodox Church; leading tenor, Spoleto Fest, Italy, summers 67 & 78, Philadelphia Lyr Opera, Boston Opera Co, Florentine Opera Milwaukee, San Francisco Opera Co, Seattle Opera Co, Santa Fe Opera Theatre, Lake George Opera & Chicago Opera Theatre; soloist with orchs throughout US, UK & Can, 68; productions, Am Nat Opera Co, NET-TV, CBC-TV & BBC. *Teaching:* Asst voice, Ind Univ, 62-67; adj mem fac, Am Univ, currently. *Awards:* Nat Award, Nat Fedn Music Clubs, 62; First Place, WGN Auditions of Air, Chicago, 67. *Mem:* Am Guild Musical Artists; Phi Mu Alpha. *Rep:* Columbia Artists Mgt Inc 165 W 57th New York NY 10019. *Mailing Add:* 6628 32nd St NW Washington DC 20015

VRONSKY, VITYA BABIN
PIANO
b Crimea, Russia; US citizen. *Study:* Kieff Consv Music, dipl, 25; studied in Paris with Lazare Levy, Alfred Cortot & Louis Aubert; in Berlin with Egon Petri & Artur Schnabel. *Pos:* Soloist with leading European orch, formerly; mem duo-piano team of Vronsky & Babin, formerly. *Teaching:* Mem fac, Cleveland Inst Music, 61-, artist in res, 62, chmn piano dept, 75. *Awards:* Chevalier Order Arts & Humanities, Govt France, 72. *Mem:* Sigma Alpha Iota; Pi Kappa Lambda. *Mailing Add:* Cleveland Inst Music 11021 E Blvd Cleveland OH 44106

W

WADDINGTON, BETTE HOPE See Crowder, Elizabeth

WADDINGTON, SUSAN ROYAL
LIBRARIAN
b Baltimore, Md, May 23, 34. *Study:* Oberlin Col, BA, 56; Rutgers Univ, MLS, 59. *Pos:* Head art & music dept, Providence Pub Libr, 66- *Mailing Add:* 150 Empire St Providence RI 02903

WADE, JANICE E
CONDUCTOR, VIOLIN
b Decorah, Iowa. *Study:* Univ Iowa, with Stuart Canin; Drake Univ, BME, 59 & MME, 60. *Pos:* Prin second violin, Des Moines Symph, Iowa, 74-; cond, Des Moines Community Orch, Iowa, 76-; concertmaster, Bijou Players, Des Moines, Iowa, 80- *Teaching:* Private violin & viola, Des Moines, Iowa, 60-; teacher instrm music strings & orch, Des Moines Public Sch, 66-76; fac mem

strings, Nat Music Camp, Interlochen, Mich, 68 & 69. *Mem:* Am String Teachers Asn; Iowa Music Teachers Asn; Des Moines Musicians Asn. *Publ:* Coauth, Can Old Dogs Learn New Tricks? Of Course, 80, auth, Looking for New Student Ensemble Music?, 80 & Dont Fake It—Tape It!, 82, Am String Teachers J. *Mailing Add:* 3444 Kinsey Des Moines IA 50317

WADSWORTH, CHARLES WILLIAM
PIANO, ARTISTIC DIRECTOR
b Barnesville, Ga, May 21, 29. *Study:* Univ Ga, 46-48; Juilliard Sch Music, BS, 51, MS, 52. *Pos:* Founder & artistic dir, Noon Day Chamber Music Concerts, Spoleto Fest, Italy, 60-77 & Spoleto-USA Fest Chamber Music Concerts, Charleston, SC, 77; artistic dir & pianist, Chamber Music Soc Lincoln Ctr, 69-; performer piano recitals. *Awards:* Cavaliere Ufficiale Ordine Merito dalla Reppublica Ital, 75; Mayors Award Excellence in Arts, New York, 79. *Mailing Add:* Chamber Music Soc 1941 Broadway New York NY 10023

WADSWORTH, SUSAN L POPKIN
ADMINISTRATOR, ARTIST MANAGER
b New York, NY, May 12, 36. *Study:* Vassar Col, BA, 58. *Pos:* Founder & dir, Young Conct Artists Inc, 61- *Mailing Add:* 250 W 57th St New York NY 10019

WAGNER, DENISE
ADMINISTRATOR, CRITIC-WRITER
b Pittsburgh, Pa. *Study:* Univ Pittsburgh, MA, 79. *Pos:* Ed, Musical Heritage Soc, 79- *Mem:* Am Musicol Soc; Col Music Soc. *Publ:* Auth, Interview with Paul Badura-Skoda, 80, Interview with Jörg Demus, 80, Wadsworth: Chamber Music Champion, 80 & Staples and Surprises, 81, Musical Heritage Rev. *Mailing Add:* 14 Park Rd Tinton Falls NJ 07724

WAGNER, EDYTH (EDYTH WAGNER ROOP)
EDUCATOR, PIANO
b New York, NY, Oct 15, 16. *Study:* Inst Musical Art, dipl piano, 41; Juilliard Sch Music, BS(piano), 47, MM(piano), 51; studied in WGermany & Austria, 51-52; Univ Southern Calif, DMA(music educ), 68. *Rec Perf:* Mozart Piano Works, 72, Beethoven Piano Works, 72 & International Library of Piano Music, Educo Inc; Taped Lessons of Advanced Piano Literature for Library of Congress, Physically Handicapped Division. *Teaching:* Private studio instr, NY, Tex & Calif, 31-; instr, Juilliard Sch, 45-47, Hockaday Jr Col, Dallas, 47-49, Univ Houston, 49-51, San Bernardino Valley Col, 54-55 & 57-61, Long Beach City Col, 55-57, Univ Southern Calif, 58-64, Univ Calif, Fullerton, 60-63 & Ventura Community Col, 75-82; guest prof various univ in Chicago, Utah & Calif. *Mem:* Music Educr Nat Conf; Music Teachers Nat Asn; Nat Guild Piano Teachers; Int Soc Music Educ; Mu Phi Epsilon. *Interests:* History of group piano teaching; history of technique applied to stringed keyboard instruments; Brazilian folk tunes arranged for piano, early grades. *Publ:* Auth, Piano Technique for the First Years of Study, Ojai Music Publ, 77; Raymond Burrows & His Contributions to Music Education, Univ Mich. *Mailing Add:* 506 Oak Creek Ln Ojai CA 93023

WAGNER, JOHN WALDORF
EDUCATOR, MUSICOLOGIST
b Oak Park, Ill, Feb 11, 37. *Study:* DePauw Univ, BM, 59; Fla State Univ, MM, 61; Ind Univ, PhD, 69. *Pos:* Clarinetist, Savannah Symph Orch, 61-62 & Columbia Phil Orch, 71-78 & 82-83. *Teaching:* Prof music hist & woodwind instrm, Newberry Col, 65- *Awards:* Fac Award Grant, Lutheran Church in Am, 80; Fac Development Grant, 81 & 82. *Mem:* Am Musicol Soc (secy-treas SE chap, Calif, 73-75); Sonneck Soc; Int Clarinet Soc; Music Libr Asn; Music Teachers Nat Asn. *Interests:* Life, works and descendants of James Hewitt; New York concert life, 1801-1805. *Publ:* Auth, James Hewitt, 1770-1827, Musical Quart, 72; Music of J Hewitt: Supplement to Sonneck-upton & Wolfe Bibliographies, Notes, 72; Some Early Musical Moments in Augusta, Ga Hist Quart, 72; entries for James and John Hill Hewitt, In: New Grove Dict of Music & Musicians, 80; ed, James Hewitt: Selected Compositions, A-R Ed, 80. *Mailing Add:* 905 Amelia St Newberry SC 29108

WAGNER, LAVERN JOHN
EDUCATOR, ADMINISTRATOR
b Bellevue, Iowa, Dec 30, 25. *Study:* Loras Col, BMus, 49; Oberlin Col, BMusEd, 52; Univ Wis, Madison, MMus, 53, PhD, 57. *Pos:* Dir liturgical music, Cath Diocese, Madison, Wis, 57-58. *Teaching:* Prof music & chmn dept, Quincy Col, 58- *Awards:* Nat Endowment Humanities Fel, 75-76. *Mem:* Am Musicol Soc; Col Music Soc; Church Music Asn Am; Am Recorder Soc. *Interests:* Flemish composers at court of Philip II in Spain; mid-19th century American wind band music. *Publ:* Ed, Gerard de Turnhout, Three Voice Works, A-R Ed, 70; George de La Hele, Collected Works (two vol), 72 & Philippe Rogier, Opera Omnia (three vol), 74, Am Inst Musicol; coauth, Music, Holt, Rinehart, Winston, 75; ed, Pierre de Manchicourt, Opera Omnia (four vol), Am Inst Musicol, 82. *Mailing Add:* 2645 Hillside Dr Quincy IL 62301

WAGNER, VINCENT
ARTIST MANAGER & REPRESENTATIVE
b New Market, Minn, July 28, 44. *Study:* Univ Minn, BA, 66. *Pos:* Operations & ceremonies coordr, US Army Training Ctr, 67-68; tour dir, Nat Shakespeare Co, 68-71; vpres, Kazuko Hillyer Int, 71- *Teaching:* Music prog dir, Coffman Union, Univ Minn, 65-66. *Mem:* Asn Class Music; Chamber Music Am; Am Symph Orch League; Int Soc Perf Arts Adminr. *Publ:* Auth, Presenting Chamber Music, Prog Mag, 75. *Mailing Add:* 90 Riverside Dr New York NY 10024

WAGNITZ, RALPH DAVID
FRENCH HORN
b Bedford, Ohio, Mar 25, 50. *Study:* Ohio State Univ, BMus(perf), 72; Cleveland Inst Music, with Myron Bloom, 72-73. *Pos:* Horn Sect, Meadowbrook Fest, Mich Orch, 69; fourth horn, Columbus Symph, 76-77; second horn, Cleveland Orch, 77- *Mailing Add:* c/o Cleveland Orch Severance Hall Cleveland OH 44106

WAGONER, JAMES D
COMPOSER, WRITER
b Breckenridge, Tex, Sept 5, 55. *Study:* Tex Tech Univ, studied comp with Mary Jeanne Van Appledorn, BM, 77; Cath Univ, studied comp with Steven Strunk, MM, 78. *Works:* Death Be Not Proud, 78, On the Beach at Fontana, 79 & Achilles, 82, Talaria Press; O Magnum Mysterium, Concinnati Col-Consv, 80; Sonata for Piano, Walter Pate, 82; Sappho, comn & perf by Contemp Music Forum, 83. *Pos:* Comp mem, Contemp Music Forum, 79- *Teaching:* Lectr electronic music, Cath Univ, 78-80. *Mem:* Am Soc Univ Comp; Am Music Ctr; Col Music Soc; Phi Mu Alpha. *Publ:* Auth, The Dramatic Nature of Penderecki's Music, Nexus, 78; Univ Composers: Is it Time to Accomodate?, Musical Am, 80; coauth, Electronic Music Equipment and Techniques, Longman, 83. *Mailing Add:* PO Box 33362 Washington DC 20033

WAIN-BECKER, ROBERTA
MEZZO-SOPRANO
b San Mateo, Calif. *Study:* Sch Music, Univ Southern Calif, BM(voice & opera), 68. *Roles:* Maddalena in Rigoletto & Nicklaus in Les Contes d'Hoffman, Israel Nat Opera Co, 74-75; Orlovsky in Die Fledermaus, Portland Opera Asn, 76; Carmen in Carmen, Los Angeles Music Ctr, 76; Zita & Frugola, Miss Opera Co, 77; Daughter in Marquise de Berkenfeld, Marin Opera Co, 78, 80, 82 & 83; Daughter in Marquise de Berkenfeld, Cendrillion in Madame de la Holtiere & Zsa Zsa Leoncocvallo in Anaide, Marin Opera Co, 78, 80, 82 & 83; Zita, Hidden Valley Opera, 82; Messiah, Boise Phil, 83. *Pos:* Dir & founder, Marin Co Children's Chorus, 80-83. *Awards:* San Francisco Musical Club Scholar, 76; Sullivan Found Award, 76-78. *Mem:* San Francisco Musical Club. *Mailing Add:* 805 Everest Ct Mill Valley CA 94941

WAITE, RUSSELL TRUEMAN
ADMINISTRATOR, CONDUCTOR & MUSIC DIRECTOR
b Riverside, Calif, June 10, 40. *Study:* Stanford Univ, BA, 62, MA, 64; Univ Wash, study cond with Stanley Chapple, DMA, 67. *Pos:* Music dir & cond, St Joseph Symph Orch, 70-82. *Teaching:* Asst prof, Univ RI, 67-70; from asst to assoc prof, Benedictine Col, Atchison, Kans, 70- & chmn, Dept Music, 81- *Mem:* Col Music Soc; Am Symph Orch League; Am Asn Univ Prof. *Rep:* Music Dept Benedictine Col S Campus Atchison KS 66002. *Mailing Add:* 1201 S 3rd Atchison KS 66002

WAITZMAN, DANIEL R
FLUTE, RECORDER
b Rochester, NY, July 15, 43. *Study:* Columbia Col, BA, 65; Columbia Univ, MA, 68; flute studies with Samuel Baron, Harold Bennett & Claude Monteux. *Rec Perf:* Eighteenth Century Flute Music (on hist instrum), Musical Heritage Soc, 74; Flute Quartet in D Minor & Flute Trio in G Major (Franz Danzi), Musical Heritage Soc, 83. *Pos:* Solo flutist & recorderist, Long Island Baroque Ens, Roslyn Barbor, NY, 74-; solo flutist, Amor Artis, New York, NY, 74- *Teaching:* Adj prof flute & recorder, Queens Col, 72- *Awards:* Conct Artists Guild Award, 71. *Bibliog:* Sigrid Nagle (auth), Daniel Waitzman: A Profile, Am Recorder, 74. *Mem:* New York Flute Club. *Publ:* Auth, The Art of Playing the Recorder, AMS Press, 78; Historical Versus Musical Authenticity, A Performer's View, Am Recorder, 80. *Mailing Add:* 28-02 Parsons Blvd Flushing NY 11354

WAKEFIELD-WRIGHT, JOELYN
MEZZO-SOPRANO, MUSIC DIRECTOR
b Omaha, Nebr, Feb 22, 37. *Study:* Pfeiffer Col, with Richard Brewer, AB, 66; Ind Univ, Bloomington, with Martha Lipton & Frank St Leger, MM, 68. *Rec Perf:* Utica Col Choir at Christmas, private label, 83. *Roles:* Countess von Garefin in Elegy for Young Lovers, 68 & Nancy & Florence in Albert Herring, 68, Ill Opera Theatre; Tisbe in La Cenerentola, 76 & Berta in The Barber of Seville, 78, Opera Theatre Syracuse; Ms in Transformations, New Music Soc Syracuse, 79. *Teaching:* Asst prof, Manchester Col, 68-74; lectr music, Hamilton Col, 75-; dir choral activ, Utica Col Syracuse Univ, 78- *Mem:* Nat Opera Asn (vpres, 76-78, mem bd dir, 79, regional gov NE district, 79-82, gov NY, 82-); Nat Asn Teachers Singing; Nat Choral Cond Asn. *Mailing Add:* Griffin Rd Rt 1 Clinton NY 13323

WAKSCHAL, SEYMOUR
VIOLIN, CONDUCTOR
b Brooklyn, NY, Mar 15, 31. *Study:* Juilliard Sch, 49-54; Univ Tex, Austin. *Pos:* First violinist & founder, Alard String Quartet, 52-57; mem, Metropolitan Opera Orch, 62- *Teaching:* Fel violin & chamber music, Univ Tex, Austin, 54-56; prof violin & cond, Wilmington Col, 56-57 & NY Univ, 80- *Awards:* Nat Fedn Musicians Chamber Music Award, 55; Friends of Mozart Players Award, 75. *Mailing Add:* 33 W 67th St New York NY 10023

WALANT, GLEN
TROMBONE
Study: Oberlin Consv, BM; Eastman Sch Music; New England Consv; studied trombone with Milton Stevens, Donald Knaub, John Coffey, Thomas Cramer & John Swallow & euphonium with Cherry Beauregard. *Pos:* Perf with Boston Symph Orch, Boston Pops & Springfield Symph. *Teaching:* Instr trombone, Wellesley Col & Boston Consv; adj, Univ Lowell; instr music, Longy Sch Music, currently. *Mailing Add:* Dept Music Wellesley Col Wellesley MA 02181

WALCOTT, RONALD HARRY
EDUCATOR, COMPOSER
b Los Angeles, Calif, May 13, 39. *Study:* Univ Calif, Los Angeles, MA, 65, DPhil, 72; Univ Sri Jayewardenepura, Sri Lanka, PhD, 78. *Works:* Variations (organ), Univ Calif, Los Angeles, 66; Fragments (perc quartet), Univ Ore, 68; Piece (piano), Warsaw, Poland, 69; Relations (improvisation ens), London, England, 69; Generations (mixed ens), Univ Calif, Los Angeles, 70; Concerto (flute, getabera & orch), Colombo, Sri Lanka, 76; Pirit (flute), Honolulu, Hawaii, 81. *Pos:* Ethnomusicologist & archivist, Libr Cong, Washington, DC, 79-81. *Teaching:* Vis asst prof, Univ Hawaii, Manoa, 81; vis instr, Inst Shipboard Educ, Univ Pittsburgh, 81. *Awards:* Fulbright-Hays Grant, Int Inst Educ, 66-69 & 74-78; Res Grant, Univ Calif, 72-73. *Mem:* Soc Ethnomusicol. *Interests:* Music of the Kohomba Kankariya ritual of upcountry Sri Lanka. *Publ:* Auth, The Väddi Yakkama: The Exorcism of Impurity in the Kohomba Kankariya Ritual of Sri Lanka, J Asian Studies, Vol 3, 81-95; A MARC Coding Manual for Instantaneous Sound Cylinders, Libr Cong, 12/80; Francis La Flesche: The First American Indian Collector of Sound Recordings, Am Folklife Ctr Newsletter, Vol 4: 1, 10-11; Am Folklife Center Project: The Federal Cylinder Project, Int Asn Sound Archives, Phonographic Bulletin, No 33, 13-22. *Mailing Add:* 5134 Angeles Crest Hwy La Canada CA 91011

WALDEN, STANLEY EUGENE
CONDUCTOR, COMPOSER
b New York, NY, Dec 2, 32. *Study:* Queens Col, City Univ New York, BA, 51-55; studied comp with Ben Weber & clarinet with David Weber. *Works:* Stretti, Group Contemp Music, 67; Circus, Louisville Orch, 70; Weewis, A Ballet, Joffrey Ballet, 71; Fandangle, Bennett Col, 72; Some Changes, Jan De Gaetani, 73; Der Voyeur, Berlin Fest, 82; Dr Faustus Lights the Lights, Cologne Schauspielhaus, 83. *Rec Perf:* Circus, First Ed Rec, 70; Oh! Calcutta!, Aidart Rec, 71; The Open Window, Vanguard Rec, 71. *Pos:* Musical dir, Tamiris-Nagrin Dance Co, 53-60; musical asst, Martha Graham Co, 59-60; comp, Open Theater, 66-71. *Teaching:* Instr music dance, Juilliard Sch, 64-68; instr music dance & actors, State Univ NY, Purchase, 72-76; guest prof comp theory, Sarah Lawrence Col, 74-76. *Awards:* Eastman New Music Comp, Sonatina Music, 82. *Mailing Add:* Miller Hill Rd R D 7 Hopewell Junction NY 12533

WALDMAN, MILDRED
PIANO, EDUCATOR
Study: Grad Sch, Juilliard Sch Music, studied piano with Ernest Hutcheson & theory & comp with Rubin Goldmark & Bernard Wagenaar, dipl; Chicago Col Music; MacMurray Col, studied piano with Esther Harris, AB. *Pos:* Recitalist & soloist, Chicago Symph, L'Orchestre de la Soc des Concerts du Consv at Salle Pleyel, Paris & other maj orchs throughout US, Can & Europe. *Teaching:* Mem fac, MacMurray Col, formerly & Vassar Col, formerly; instr master classes & wkshps, Chicago Col Music, formerly, mem fac, formerly; instr master classes & wkshps, Chautauqua Summer Sch Music, formerly & Goddard Col, formerly; adj assoc prof, Hunter Col, currently; mem fac piano, Mannes Col Music, 67- *Mailing Add:* Mannes Col Music 157 E 74th St New York NY 10021

WALDROP, GIDEON WILLIAM, JR
ADMINISTRATOR, COMPOSER
b Haskell Co, Tex, Sept 2, 19. *Study:* Baylor Univ, BM, 40; Eastman Sch Music, comp with Howard Hanson & Bernard Rogers, MM, 41, PhD, 52. *Works:* Trio (harp, clarinet & viola), 39; Lydian Trumpeter (trumpet & piano), 46; Symphony, 52; From the Southwest (overture); Prelude and Fugue; Pressures (string orch); & choral works & songs. *Pos:* Cond, Shreveport Symph, 41-42; ed, Rev Recorded Music, New York, NY, 52-54 & Musical Courier, 53-58; music consult, Ford Found Young Comp Pub Sch Proj, 58-61; asst to pres, Juilliard Sch Music, 61-63, dean, 63-; consult to Minister Educ, Portugal, summer 79. *Teaching:* Assoc prof, Baylor Univ, 46-51, cond, Waco-Baylor Symph Orch, 46-51. *Mem:* ASCAP; Phi Mu Alpha; Am Music Ctr; Nat Asn Am Comp & Cond; Toscanini Mem Archives Comt. *Mailing Add:* Juilliard Sch Music Lincoln Ctr New York NY 10023

WALKER, BETTY MARIE
TEACHER-COACH, CONDUCTOR & MUSIC DIRECTOR
b Jamesport, Mo, June 17, 40. *Study:* Eastman Sch Music, BM, 61, MM, 63; Confederation Int des Accordeonistes, dipl, 76. *Roles:* Conception in L'Heure Espagnole, 61, Zerlina in Don Giovanni, 62 & Abigale in The Crucible, 63, Eastman Sch Music Opera Theater; Tuptim in The King and I, 62 & Marion in The Music Man, 63, Rochester Music Theater. *Pos:* Music dir & owner, Walker Music, Rochester, NY, 61-; cond, Upstate Accordion Orch, 68- *Mem:* Accordion Teachers Guild Int (pres, 75-77, secy/ed, 78-82, secy, 83); Music Teachers Nat Asn. *Publ:* Auth, Report on the Accordion Teachers Guild, Danish Accordion Mag, 76; Self Image and the Music Student, Accordian Teachers Guild Bulletin, 79. *Mailing Add:* 18 Sibley Pl Rochester NY 14607

WALKER, CHARLES (JOHN)
TENOR
b Camden, NJ, Nov 3, 47. *Study:* Curtis Inst Music, with Richard Lewis, 68-71; Univ Del, BMus, 73; Boston Univ, studied opera with Adalaide Bishop, 74-79. *Rec Perf:* The Cunning Man, AFKA Records, 78; The Flower-fed Buffaloes, Nonesuch Rec, 78. *Roles:* Vendor and Gypsy Singer in Strider, Broadway Prod, 80; Mengone in Lo Speziale, 82 & Marshall in Regina, 82, Wolf Trap Opera Co; Monkey Hamlet in The Monkey Opera, Brooklyn Phil, 82; Old Miner & Chester A Arthur in Baby Doe, Ariz Opera, 82; Goro in Madame Butterfly, 83 & Funeral Director in A Quiet Place, 83, Houston Grand Opera. *Pos:* Apprentice, Santa Fe Opera, 74-75. *Mailing Add:* 321 Clearfield Ave 2A Trenton NJ 08618

WALKER, DONALD BURKE
COMPOSER

b San Buenaventura, Calif, Dec 18, 41. *Study:* Stanford Univ, studied musicol with Putnam Aldrich & George Houle, BA(music), 64; Univ Calif, Berkeley, studied comp with Seymour Shifrin, Andrew Imbrie, Larry Austin & musicol with Joseph Kerman, PhD(music), 71. *Works:* Spiro T Agnew Songs, Comp-Perf Ed, Source Mag VIII, 70; Fortitude (opera in 9 scenes), Systems Complex for Perf Arts, Univ SFla, 77. *Teaching:* Instr European studies, humanities & music theory, Sonoma State Col, 74-78; asst prof music hist, comp & theory, Univ SFla, 75-77; asst prof music hist, Ore State Univ, 79. *Awards:* George Ladd Prix Paris, Univ Calif, 66-68. *Bibliog:* Marilyn Tucker (auth), Agnew to Music, Am Music Digest, 70; Jonathan D Kramer (auth), The Fibonacci Series in 20th Century Music, J Music Theory, 73. *Interests:* Developing analytical models for non-tonal and non-Western music; music of Charles Ives. *Publ:* Auth, The Vocal Music of Charles Ives, Parnassus, 75; Robert Moran, In: New Grove Dict of Music & Musicians, 81. *Mailing Add:* 2751 Poli St Ventura CA 93003

WALKER, FRANCES E
PIANO, EDUCATOR

b Washington, DC, Mar 6, 24. *Study:* Oberlin Col, MusB, 45; Teachers Col, Columbia Univ, MA; Curtis Inst, with Rudolph Serkin, 52 & Miecyslaw Horszowski, 71; Manhattan Sch Music, with Robert Goldsand. *Rec Perf:* Twenty-four Negro Melodies, Op 59, Orion Master Rec Inc, 77. *Teaching:* Asst prof piano & theory, Lincoln Univ, Pa, 67-71 & Rutgers Univ, 71-76; prof piano, Oberlin Col, 76- *Awards:* Nat Asn Negro Musicians Award, 79. *Mem:* Nat Asn Negro Musicians; Ohio Music Teachers Asn. *Mailing Add:* 26 Shipherd Circle Oberlin OH 44074

WALKER, GEORGE THEOPHILUS
COMPOSER, PIANO

b Washington, DC, June 27, 22. *Study:* Oberlin Col, MusB, 41; Curtis Inst Music, artist dipl, 45; Eastman Sch Music, DMA, 57; Lafayette Col, Hon Dr Fine Arts, 82. *Works:* Concerto for Trombone & Orchestra, Gen Music, 57; Address for Orchestra, Belwin-Mills, 59; Variations for Orchestra, 71, Piano Concerto, 76, Mass, 77, In Praise of Folly, 81, Eastman Overture, 82 & Concerto for Cello & Orchestra, 82, General Music. *Teaching:* Instr, Dillard Univ, 53-54 & Dalcroze Sch Music, New Sch Social Res, 60-61; assoc prof, Smith Col, 61-68 & Univ Colo, 68-69; prof, Rutgers Univ, 69- *Awards:* Guggenheim Fel, 69; Am Acad & Inst of Arts Award, 82. *Bibliog:* Baker, Belt & Hudson (auth), George Walker, From the Black Composer Speaks, Scarecrow Press, 78; Dominique-Rene De Lerma (auth), The Choral Works of George Walker, J Am Choral Found, 81. *Mem:* ASCAP. *Mailing Add:* 323 Grove St Montclair NJ 07042

WALKER, GWYNETH V
COMPOSER, EDUCATOR

b New York, NY, Mar 22, 47. *Study:* Brown Univ, BA, 68; Hartt Sch Music, MM(comp), 70, DMA(comp), 76. *Works:* Flute Sonata, Arsis Press, 78; In Memoriam, perf by Mary Lou Rylands, 80; Fanfare for Band, Studio Publ, 80; The Radiant Dawn, perf by Univ Notre Dame Chorale, 80; Opera Buffet, Univ Tampa, 81 & 82; Fanfare, Interlude & Finale, perf by Twin Cities Symph, 83. *Teaching:* Asst prof theory & comp, Consv Music, Oberlin Col, 76-79; coordr dept theory & comp, Hartford Consv, 80-82. *Mem:* Col Music Soc; League Women Comp; Conn Comp Inc. *Mailing Add:* 643 Oenoke Ridge New Canaan CT 06840

WALKER, JOHN EDWARD
TENOR

b Bushnell, Ill. *Study:* Denver Univ; Univ Ill; Ind Univ. *Rec Perf:* La Rondine, Can Broadcasting TV, 71. *Roles:* Nemorino in L'Elisir d'amore, Cologne City Opera, Ger, 67; Faust in Faust, Can Opera Co, 70; Almaviva in The Barber of Seville, Can Opera Co, 73 & Theatre L'Odeon, Paris, 75; Tamino in The Magic Flute, 75 & Ferrando in Cosi fan tutti, 76, Santa Fe Opera; Don Ottavio in Don Giovanni, Houston Opera, 76; Lensky in Eugene Onegin, Portland Opera Co, 82 & Ft Worth Opera, 83. *Awards:* Nat Asn Teachers Singing First Place, 58; Aspen Sch Mack Harrel Award Scholar, 62-64. *Mailing Add:* RFD 2 Murrayville IL 62668

WALKER, MALLORY ELTON
EDUCATOR, TENOR

b New Orleans, La, May 22, 35. *Study:* Occidental Col, BA, 57. *Rec Perf:* Mass in B Minor (Bach), RCA Victor, 60; Missa Solemnis (Beethoven), London Rec, 67; Eighth Symphony (Mahler), CBS Rec, 81. *Roles:* Tom Rakewell in The Rake's Progress, Wash Opera Soc, 59; Tamino in The Magic Flute, San Francisco Spring Opera, 63; Ferrando in Cosi fan tutte, Cologne Opera, 64; Rodolfo in La Boheme, Frankfurt Opera, 72; Alwa in Lulu, Spoleto Fest, 74; Capt Vere in Billy Budd, Metropolitan Opera, 78; Yukinojo in An Actor's Revenge, St Louis Opera Theater, 81. *Pos:* Soloist, US Army Chorus, 57-60 & Metropolitan Opera Studio, 60-63; lyr ten, Cologne Opera, 63-66; ten, Metropolitan Opera, 77- *Teaching:* Instr voice, Boston Consv Music, 74-77. *Awards:* Grant, Martha Baird Rockefeller Inst, 62 & Ford Found, 63. *Mailing Add:* 780 Riverside Dr Apt #115 New York NY 10032

WALKER, SANDRA
MEZZO-SOPRANO

b Richmond, Va, Oct 1, 46. *Study:* Univ NC, MusB, 69; Manhattan Sch Music; studied with Oren Brown. *Rec Perf:* Song Cycle from King Midas (Ned Rorem), Desto Rec, 74. *Roles:* Flosshilde in Das Rheingold, San Francisco Opera, 72; Secretary in The Consul & Desideria in The Saint of Bleeker St, PBS-TV; Carmen in Carmen; Marquise de Birkenfeld in La Fille

du regiment; Suzuki in Madama Butterfly; Fortunata in Satyricon. *Pos:* Leading ms, New York City Opera, 74- & Stadttheater, Würzburg, Germany, 80-82; singer in US & Europ music festivals; soloist, Am Symph, 80 & San Francisco Symph, 80; appearances with Nat Symph, St Louis Symph, Chicago Symph Orch & Richmond Symph; artist in res, Ky Opera Asn, 80. *Awards:* Nat Endowment Arts Affil Artist Grant, Va Opera Asn & Sears Roebuck Co, 78. *Rep:* Columbia Artists Mgt Inc 165 W 57th New York NY 10019. *Mailing Add:* c/o Kazuko Hillyer Int 250 W 57th St New York NY 10019

WALKER, WILLIAM
BARITONE, EDUCATOR

b Waco, Tex, Oct 29, 31. *Study:* Tex Christian Univ, BMus, 56. *Roles:* Di Luna in Il Trovatore, Ford in Falstaff, Marcello in La Boheme, 62-, Valentin in Faust, 63-, Amonasro in Aida, 65-, Figaro in Barber of Seville, 65- & Germont in La Traviata, 67-77, Metropolitan Opera Tour. *Pos:* Leading baritone, Metropolitan Opera, 62-80. *Teaching:* Herndon Prof music, Tex Christian Univ, 79-; Carol Tyrell Kyle Assoc Artist, Lamar Univ, 80- *Mailing Add:* 209 Lariat Dr San Antonio TX 78232

WALLACE, MARY ELAINE (MARY ELAINE HOUSE)
ADMINISTRATOR, WRITER

b Lincoln, Nebr, Jan 1, 19. *Study:* Nebr State Col, Kearney, BFA, 40; Univ Ill, Urbana, MM, 54; Music Acad West; Eastman Sch Music; Fla State Univ. *Pos:* Stage mgr, Chautauqua Opera & music ed & critic, Chautauqua Daily, Chautauqua Inst, NY. *Teaching:* Assoc prof music, La Tech Univ, 54-62 & State Univ NY, Fredonia, 62-69; prof, Southern Ill Univ, Carbondale, 69-79. *Awards:* Outstanding Alumni Award, Nebr State Col, Kearney, 80. *Mem:* Nat Opera Asn (pres, 74-75, exec sec, 80-); Nat Asn Teachers Singing (opera chmn New York, 67-69); Cent Opera Serv Metropolitan Opera; Music Teachers Nat Asn; Nat Music Coun. *Publ:* Auth, American Musical Theater, In: Music in American Society, Transaction Inc, 77; coauth (with Robert Wallace), Opera Scenes for Class and Stage, Southern Ill Univ Press, 79. *Mailing Add:* Route 2 Box 93 Commerce TX 75428

WALLACE, PAUL JAMES
EDUCATOR

b Pontiac, Mich, Mar 24, 28. *Study:* Univ Mich, BMus, 50, MMus, 54; Univ Kans; Univ Colo. *Works:* Conversi (three canzonas), 75 & Ferrabosco (two madrigals), 82, Ludwig Music Publ Co. *Pos:* Ed, Nat Asn Col Wind & Perc Instr J, 62-66. *Teaching:* Instr low brass, Univ Kans, 55-57; asst prof band & brass, Univ Wis, Stevens Point, 59; prof trombone & euphonium, Kent State Univ, 63-, assoc dir sch music. *Mem:* Nat Asn Col Wind & Perc Instr (pres, 68-70); Int Trombone Asn; Tubists Universal Brotherhood Asn; Music Educr Nat Conf; Ohio Music Educ Asn. *Publ:* Ed, Catalog of Manuscript Music for Winds & Percussion, 58-63, auth, Curriculum Objectives and Grading Practices in Applied Music, 75, Nat Asn Col Wind & Perc Instr J; What is NACWPI?, Music J Anthology, 64. *Mailing Add:* 556 Valleyview St Kent OH 44240

WALLACE, ROBERT WILLIAM
CONDUCTOR & MUSIC DIRECTOR, PIANO

b Kearney, Nebr, Nov 18, 45. *Study:* Manhattan Sch Music, BMus, 67, MMus, 69. *Pos:* Asst cond, New York City Opera, 70-72 & Opera Metropolitana, Caracas, Venezuela, 79-81; cond & music dir, Opera on the Sound, Long Island, NY, 78-79; music dir, Midwest Opera Theater tour, 81; guest cond, Minn Opera, 81; chorus master, Opera Metropolitan, Caracas, Venezuela, 83. *Teaching:* Private vocal coach, New York. *Mem:* Nat Opera Asn; Cent Opera Serv. *Publ:* Coauth, Opera Scenes for Class and Stage, Southern Ill Univ Press, 79. *Mailing Add:* 235 W 102nd St New York NY 10025

WALLACH, JOELLE
COMPOSER, EDUCATOR

b New York, NY, June 29. *Study:* Sarah Lawrence Col, BA, 67; Columbia Univ, MA, 69; Manhattan Sch Music. *Works:* On The Beach at Night Alone, C F Peters, 80; Mourning Madrigals (flute, sop, tenor & harp), 80; A Prophesy and Psalm (chorus & orch), 81; Quartet for Saxophones, Dorn Publ, 81; Of Honey and Vinegar (ms & two pianos), 82; Forewords (trumpet & French horn), 82; Glimpses (orch), Carl Fischer, 82. *Teaching:* Lectr music, City Univ New York, 71-; asst prof, Fordham Univ, 81- *Awards:* First Prize, Int Am Music, 80, Nat Asn Am Pen Women, 82 & Delta Omicron, 83. *Mem:* Am Women Comp; BMI; Int League Women Comp; Am Soc Univ Comp; Nat Asn Comp. *Mailing Add:* 1530 Palisade Ave Ft Lee NJ 07024

WALLENCE, STEPHEN
TENOR

Study: ECarolina Univ, BMus, 79; Cleveland Inst Music, MMus, 82. *Rec Perf:* St John Passion (Bach), 82 & St Matthew Passion (Bach), 83, Trinity Cathedral. *Roles:* Blind in Die Fledermaus, Mansfield Opera Co, 81; Don Basilio in The Marriage of Figaro, 82 & Ottokar in Gypsy Baron, 82, Cleveland Opera Theatre; Evangelist, St Matthew & St John Passions, Trinity Cathedral Choir, 82-83; Samson, Warren Choral Soc, Ohio, 83. *Pos:* Soloist, Temple Emanu-El, Cleveland, 80-81, Clerks of Trinity & Cleveland Medieval Ens; prin, Cleveland Opera Theatre, 80-83; tenor soloist, Trinity Cathedral, Cleveland, 81- *Teaching:* Voice, Cleveland Inst Music, 81- *Mailing Add:* 11720 Edgewater Dr #909 Lakewood OH 44107

WALLIS, DELIA LESLEY SUZETTE
MEZZO-SOPRANO

b Chelmsford, England, July 27, 46. *Study:* Guildhall Sch Music & Drama, AGSM, 67; London Opera Ctr, 69. *Roles:* Prince Charmani in Cendrillon, Nat Arts Ctr, 79 & San Francisco Opera, 82; Muse in Nicklausse, Houston Grand Opera, 83. *Pos:* Conct soloist, US & Europe, 69- *Mailing Add:* c/o Columbia Artists 165 W 57th St New York NY 10019

WALN, RONALD LEE
EDUCATOR, FLUTE
b Cedar Rapids, Iowa, June 25, 31. *Study:* Oberlin Col, BME, 57; State Univ Iowa, MA, 59, PhD, 71. *Pos:* First flutist, 10th Air Force & 1st Air Force Bands, 51-55. *Teaching:* Instr flute & bassoon, Fla State Univ, 59-65; asst prof flute, bassoon & music ed, Univ Ga, 65-71, assoc prof, 71-78 & prof, 78- *Mem:* Music Educr Nat Conf; Music Teachers Nat Asn; Nat Asn Col Wind & Perc Instr (pres 70-72); Nat Flute Asn (pres, 79-80); Int Double Reed Soc. *Publ:* Auth, Various articles in Instrumentalist, Woodwind, Brass & Perc, Nat Flute Asn Newsletter & Bulletin Nat Music Coun; Flute Study Materials & Flute Ensemble Music, In: Music Teachers Nat Asn Course of Study for Woodwind Instrm, 77 & 80; ed, NFA Music Library Catalog, 2nd ed, Nat Flute Asn, 79. *Mailing Add:* Sch Music Univ Ga Athens GA 30602

WALSH, DIANE
PIANO, EDUCATOR
b Washington, DC, Aug 16, 50. *Study:* Juilliard Sch, BM, 71; Mannes Col Music, with Irwin Freundlich, Artur Balsam & Richard Goode, MM, 82. *Rec Perf:* Sonatas (cello & piano; Kurt Weill & Erno Dohnanyi) 81 & Bartok Rhapsody, Janacek Pohadka & Prokofieff Sonata, 83, Nonesuch. *Pos:* Concerto appearances with Buffalo Phil, 65, San Francisco Symph, 72, St Louis Symph, 73, Indianapolis Symph, 74, Radio Symph of Frankfurt, 75 & Berlin, 76. *Teaching:* Fac mem piano, Mannes Col Music, 82- *Awards:* Second Prize, Salzburg Mozart Compt, 74; First Prize, Munich Compt, 75; grant, Nat Endowment Arts, 81. *Mailing Add:* 404 Riverside Dr New York NY 10025

WALSH, MICHAEL ALAN
CRITIC, COMPOSER
b Camp Lejeune, NC, Oct 23, 49. *Study:* Eastman Sch Music, studied comp with Samuel Adler & musicol with Charles Warren Fox, BMus, 71. *Works:* Piano Trio, New Arts Ens, 75. *Pos:* Music critic, Rochester Democrat & Chronicle, NY, 72-77, San Francisco Examr, 77-81 & Time Mag, 81- *Awards:* Deems Taylor Award, ASCAP, 80. *Mem:* Music Critics Asn (secy, 77-83). *Publ:* Auth of various articles in Rochester Democrat & Chronicle, San Francisco Examr, Time Mag, Stereo Rev, Musical Am & others. *Mailing Add:* 60 E 8th St #23-B New York NY 10003

WALT, SHERMAN ABBOTT
BASSOON, VIOLIN
b Virginia, Minn, Aug 22, 23. *Study:* Curtis Inst Music. *Rec Perf:* Mozart Bassoon Concerto, Deutche Grammophon, 81. *Pos:* Prin Bassoonist, Chicago Symph, 46-51 & Boston Symph, 53- *Teaching:* Instr bassoon, Boston Univ, 70-82 & New England Consv, 82- *Mailing Add:* 199 Massachussetts Ave #1102 Boston MA 02115

WALTER, DAVID
EDUCATOR, DOUBLE BASS
b Brooklyn, NY. *Study:* City Col, City Univ New York, BS, 32; Juilliard Sch, with Fred Zimmermann, dipl, 37, postgrad dipl, 38. *Works:* The Melodious Bass, Amsco Music Corp, 67; The Elephant Gavotte, Yorke Ed, London, 78. *Rec Perf:* Spirituals for Strings (Morton Gould), RCA Victor, 60; Works for Solo Double Bass, Vol I, II & III, 76; Laureate Series, MMO, 76; David Walter in Recita, Liben Music, Vol I, 78 & Vol II, 80. *Pos:* Bassist, Barrere Little Symph, 37-38, NBC Symph Orch, 40-54 & Casals Fest Orch, 58-78; prin bassist, Pittsburgh Symph Orch, 38-40, Symph of Air, 55-62; ed, Bass Forum, Am String Teacher Mag, 76- *Teaching:* Double bass & ens, Manhattan Sch Music, 57- & Juilliard Sch, 69-; lectr & instr master classes throughout US, Europe & China, 67- *Awards:* Artist & Teacher of Yr Award, Am String Teachers Asn, 73; Juror Dipl, Markneukirchen Int Compt, 81 & 83. *Bibliog:* B Haggin (auth), The Toscanini Musicians Knew, Horizon, 69. *Mem:* Int Soc Bassists (pres, 78-82); Catgut Acoust Soc; Am Fedn Musicians. *Publ:* Auth, Can You Put It Under Your Chin?, Music Mag, 80; contrib to Am String Teacher, Instrumentalist & Double Bass Sound Post. *Mailing Add:* 205 West End Ave New York NY 10023

WALTER, DAVID EDGAR
COMPOSER, BARITONE
b Boston, Mass, Feb 2, 53. *Study:* Juilliard Sch Music, BM(comp), 75; Trenton State, MA(voice), 78; studied with Persichetti, Luening, Diamond, Hampton & Oren Brown. *Works:* St Mark Passion, Church of the Resurrection, New York, 71; While it is alive, Colby Choir, Colby Inst Music, 82; Cloud Blue, Bates Col String Orch, 83; Lavender Requiem, Bates Col Orch & Chorus, 83; Prayer of St Chrysostom, St Chrysostom's Church, Wollaston, Mass, 83; Scrooge (ballet), Copley Square Ballet & Jamaica Plain Orch, 83. *Pos:* Bass soloist, Resurrection Church, New York, 74-75, Calvary Episcopal Church, New York, 76-80, Harvard St United Parish, Brookline, 82- & Trinity Church, Boston, 82-83. *Mailing Add:* 14 Farrington Ave Allston MA 02134

WALTERS, MICHAEL J
EDUCATOR, CONDUCTOR & MUSIC DIRECTOR
Study: Ithaca Col, studied comp with Warren Benson, BS, 65, MS; Sch Music, Univ Miami, studied comp with J Clifton Williams, DMA; Acad Music, Basel, Switz; studied cond with Don Wells, Pierre Boulez & Frederick Fennell. *Works:* Apparition (wind ens), New England Consv Music, 74. *Pos:* Ed, trombone choir lit; transcriber, wind ens music, E C Schirmer. *Teaching:* Band dir & music teacher, sch syst, Ithaca, Long Beach & Commack, NY, formerly; mem fac music educ, New England Consv, currently. *Mailing Add:* New England Consv 290 Huntington Rd Boston MA 02215

WALTERS, ROBERT DOUGLAS
COMPOSER, CONDUCTOR & MUSIC DIRECTOR
b Clinton, Mass, Feb 25, 43. *Study:* Loma Linda Univ, BA, 64; Calif State Univ, Los Angeles, MA, 66; Univ Mo, Kansas City, DMA, 75; cond studies with Herbert Blomstedt, 80 & Jon Robertson, 80- *Works:* Mother Goose Songs, Lillian Dudley, 75; A Gift From the River: A Theatre Piece, comn by Brownville Bicentennial Comn, 76; Forecasts: Concerto for Horn & Orchestra, David Kappy & Nebr Chamber Orch, 76; Nine Musical Pieces for Soprano & Piano, comn by Barta Trio, 79; Concerto for Cello & Orchestra, David Lowe & Nebr Chamber Orch, 80; Two Essays for B Flat Clarinet & Piano, Anthony Pasquale, 82; Symphony No 1, Lincoln Civic Orch, 82. *Pos:* Violist, Lincoln Symph, 68-71 & 74-77, Omaha Symph, 69-71 & 74-77 & Nebr Chamber Orch, 75-82; comp in res, Seward Nebr, 75; music dir & cond, Hastings Civic Symph, 77-79 & Lincoln Civic Orch, 79- *Teaching:* Prof cond, violin & comp, Union Col, Nebr, 66-71 & 77-; asst prof, Hastings Col, 77-79 & Columbia Union Col. *Awards:* Gov Arts Award, Nebr Art Coun, 78. *Mailing Add:* 3419 S 42nd St Lincoln NE 68506

WALTERS, TERESA
COMPOSER, PIANO
b Lincoln, Nebr. *Study:* Univ Nebr, BA(music) & MA(music); Ecole Normale Musique, Paris, cert, 79; Peabody Consv Music, DMus, 82. *Works:* The Kingdom (cantata), Salter Publ, 74; One Man (cantata), Trinity Press, 76; Sonata for Prepared Piano, Teresa Walters, 77; Music for Organ and Two Trumpets, Trinity Press, 77; Wedding Service of Scripture and Song, St John's Press, 77. *Rec Perf:* Teresa Walters, Century Rec, 75, Peabody Studios, 76 & 78; Teresa & Jeff Walters, Baldwin Sound Prod, 81; Cantata for Piano & Chorus, Beacon Rec, 82; Sonatas for Piano & Violin, Wintergreen Prod, 82. *Teaching:* Artist in res, Bezons, France, 77-78; Elizabethtown Col, 80-81 & Pa State Univ, 82-83. *Awards:* Alpha Lambda Delta Comp Award; Vreeland Award for Comp (two); Boucher Medal. *Interests:* Life and works of Nadia Boulanger. *Mailing Add:* c/o Albert Kay Assocs 58 W 58th St New York NY 10019

WANG, AN-MING
COMPOSER
b Shanghai, China; US citizen. *Study:* Cent China Univ, BEduc, 47; Consv Music, Wesleyan Col, BMus, 50; Columbia Univ, MA(music educ), 51; Juilliard Sch Music. *Works:* The Mahjong Suite (piano), perf by Chow Chen-Huey, 80; Song of Endless Sorrow (cycle seven songs), perf by Lucy Lee Lin & Neil Tilkens, 80; Songs for All Seasons, Yueh Yun Music Publ House, Taipei, Taiwan, 82; Sonata for Violin and Piano, perf by Melissa Graybeal & Neil Tilkens, 83. *Pos:* Asst dir, Tung Hsing Choral Soc, 83- *Mem:* Fri Morning Music Club; Am Women Comp; ASCAP; Int League Women Comp; Am Music Ctr. *Mailing Add:* 11920 Canfield Rd Potomac MD 20854

WANGLER, FRANCIS (FRANK) D
BASSOON, EDUCATOR
b Bay City, Mich, July 11, 41. *Study:* Bassoon with Edgar L Kirk, 55-65; Mich State Univ, BM, 59, MM, 65. *Pos:* Prin bassoon, Akron Symph Orch, 69-72 & 74-75; co-prin bassoon, Nat Symph Orch, 72-73 & South African Broadcasting Corp, 72-73. *Teaching:* Asst prof, Kent State Univ, 67-75; assoc prof, Crane Sch Music, State Univ NY Col, Potsdam, 75-; instr bassoon, Nat Music Camp, 77- *Mem:* Int Double Reed Soc; Col Music Soc. *Mailing Add:* 17 Pleasant St Potsdam NY 13676

WANN, LOIS
EDUCATOR, OBOE
b Monticello, Minn. *Study:* Juilliard Sch Music, dipl; Manhattan Sch Music, BMus, 54. *Pos:* Solo oboe, New Friends of Music Chamber Orch, Bach Circle & Adolf Busch Chamber Players; soloist, Gordon, Griller, Budapest & Juilliard String Quartets & Am Music Week Fest Orch, 62 & 63; first oboist, Pittsburgh Symph Orch, St Louis Symph Orch, Chautauqua Symph Orch & Les Concerts Symph, Montreal; recitalist chamber music throughout US; adjudicator, Inst Int Educ, Westchester Symph Young Artists Awards, New Rochelle Young Artist Ser, Conct Artist Guild & East-West Artists. *Teaching:* Mem fac oboe, Juilliard Sch Music, 46-; mem fac & perf artist, Aspen Music Fest & Sch, 51-57; prof oboe, NY Univ Sch Educ, currently. *Mailing Add:* Juilliard Sch Music Lincoln Ctr New York NY 10023

WARD, CHARLES WILSON
CRITIC
b Hamilton, Ont, June 24, 45; US citizen. *Study:* Eastern Nazarene Col, BA, BS, 66; Univ Tex, Austin, MM, 69, PhD, 74. *Pos:* Music critic, Houston Chronicle, 75- *Mailing Add:* PO Box 4260 Houston TX 77210

WARD, JOHN MILTON
EDUCATOR, MUSICOLOGIST
b Oakland, Calif, July 6, 17. *Study:* San Francisco Col, AB, 41; Univ Wash, MM, 42; NY Univ, PhD, 53. *Pos:* Trustee, Longy Sch Music, 74. *Teaching:* Instr music hist, Mich State Univ, 47-53; from asst prof to assoc prof musicol, Univ Ill, 53-55; assoc prof, Harvard Univ, 55-58, prof, 58-61, William Powell Mason Prof music, 61- *Mem:* Am Musicol Soc; Soc Ethnomusicol; Int Musicol Soc; Int Folk Music Coun; fel, Am Acad Arts & Sci. *Interests:* Elizabethan music; 16th century instrumental music; Anglo-American music. *Publ:* Auth, Music For a Handful of Pleasant Delites, Vol X: 151-180 & Apropos the British Broadside Ballad and its Music, Vol XX: 28-86, J Am Musicol Soc; Dublin Virginal Manuscript, Wellesley Col, 54, rev ed, 64; Parody Technique in 16th-Century Instrumental Music, In: The Commonwealth of Music, Free Press, 65; A Dowland Miscellany, J Lute Soc Am, Vol X: 5-153. *Mailing Add:* Music Dept Harvard Univ Cambridge MA 02138

WARD, JOHN OWEN
ADMINISTRATOR, WRITER
b London, England, Sept 20, 19. *Study:* Dulwich Col; London Violoncello Sch; Oxford Univ, MA, 56. *Pos:* Prin cellist, Oxford Univ Orch, 50-56; mgr music dept, Oxford Univ Press, 57-72; dir serious music, Boosey & Hawkes, 72-79. *Mem:* Music Publ Asn (pres, 74-76); Int Musicol Asn; Am Musicol Asn; Royal Musical Asn; Music Libr Asn. *Publ:* Ed, Junior Companion to Music, 57-77; Concise Oxford Dictionary of Music, 57-77 & Oxford Companion to Music, 57-77, Oxford Univ Press; auth, Careers in Music, H Z Walck, 68; contribr to New Grove Dict of Music & Musicians. *Mailing Add:* 325 W 76 St New York NY 10023

WARD, MARGARET MOTTER
VIOLA
b Grand Rapids, Mich, Sept 21, 28. *Study:* Mich State Univ, 46-49; Eastman Sch Music, MusB, 52. *Pos:* Prin violist & violinist, Grand Rapids Symph, 42-51; violist fac quartet, Mich State Univ, 47-49; violist third stand, Rochester Phil, 51-53; violist second stand, Miami Symph, 62-64; violist, Kennedy Ctr Opera House Orch, 71-; prin violist, 76-78; violist, Baltimore Symph, 73-74; prin viola, Am Camerata New Music, 74; found & violist, New String Art Quartet, 82- *Teaching:* Prof violin & viola, Consv Nat du Liban, Beirut, Lebanon, 64-66; instr viola, Montgomery Col, 70-74. *Mem:* Chamber Music Am. *Mailing Add:* 1101 Playford Lane Silver Spring MD 20901

WARD, ROBERT EUGENE
COMPOSER, EDUCATOR
b Cleveland, Ohio, Sept 13, 17. *Study:* Eastman Sch Music, with Rogers & Hanson, BM, 39; Juilliard Grad Sch, with Jacobi, Schenkman & Stoessel, dipl, 46; Berkshire Music Ctr, with Copland. *Works:* Second Symphony, 47, Third Symphony, 50, He Who Gets Slapped (opera), 56, The Crucible (opera), 61, Sweet Freedom's Song (contata), 65, Piano Concerto, 68 & Abelard and Heloise (opera), 82, Highgate Press. *Pos:* Managing ed, Galaxy Music Corp, Highgate Press, New York, 56-66. *Teaching:* Fac mem, Juilliard Sch Music, 46-56; chancellor, NC Sch Arts, Winston-Salem, 67-74; Mary Duke Biddle prof music, Duke Univ, 79- *Awards:* Fel, Guggenheim Found, 50, 51 & 66; Pulitzer Prize (for The Crucible), 61; Award in Fine Arts, State NC, 75. *Bibliog:* B Stambler (auth), Robert Ward, Bulletin Am Comp, 55; Musical Am, 82; Opera News, 82. *Mem:* Am Acad & Inst Arts & Lett; Am Symph Orch League (mem exec bd, 79-); Nat Opera Inst (chmn exec comt, 78-); Martha Baird Rockefeller Fund Music (trustee, 68-). *Rep:* Galaxy Music Corp Inc Highgate Press 131 W 86th St New York NY 10024. *Mailing Add:* 308 Monticello Ave Durham NC 27707

WARD, WILLIAM REED
COMPOSER, EDUCATOR
b Norton, Kans, May 20, 18. *Study:* Univ Kans, BMus & BMusEd, 41; Eastman Sch Music, MMus, 42, PhD, 54. *Works:* Lullaby for Pinto Colt, Indianapolis Symph Orch 47 & Oklahoma City Symph Orch, 55; Symphony #3, Eastman-Rochester Symph Orch, 54; Father, We Praise Thee, Edward B Marks, 56; Listen, Lord, Lawson-Gould, 57; Love, Joy, Fun, Trains, 71 & Arcs and In Town Again, 73, comn by San Francisco Symph; They Shall Mount Up With Wings, World Libr Publ, 79. *Teaching:* Instr music, Colo State Univ, Ft Collins, 42-44; asst prof music, Lawrence Univ, Appleton, Wis, 44-47; prof music & chmn music dept, San Francisco State Univ, 47-, assoc dean, Sch Creative Arts, 77-80. *Mem:* ASCAP. *Publ:* Auth, Examples for the Study of Musical Style, William C Brown, 70; American Bicentennial Song Book, two vol, Charles Hansen, 75. *Mailing Add:* 120 Occidental Ave Burlingame CA 94010

WARD-STEINMAN, DAVID
COMPOSER, EDUCATOR
b Alexandria, La, Nov 6, 36. *Study:* Fla State Univ, BMus, 57; Univ Ill, MM, 58, DMA, 61. *Works:* Western Orpheus, comn & perf by San Diego Ballet & San Diego Symph, 64; These Three, comn & perf by Joffrey Ballet, 66; Cello Concerto, perf by Japan Phil & Seattle Symph, 67; Prelude & Toccata, perf by New Orleans Symp & San Diego Symph, 67; Arcturus, comn & perf by Chicago Symph, 72; The Tracker, comn by Univ Redlands, 76; Brancusi's Brass Beds, comn & perf by Bowling Green Brass Quintet, 77. *Rec Perf:* Sonata for Piano, Contemp Comp Guild, 62; Fragments From Sappho, CRI, 69; Childs Play, 74 & The Tracker, 83, Advance Rec. *Teaching:* Asst prof music, San Diego State Univ, 61-64, assoc prof, 65-67, prof, 68-; fac comprehensive musicianship, Eastman Sch Music, 69; vis fel, Princeton Univ, 70; comp in res, Univ Tex, El Paso, 79; curriculum consult, Univ North Sumatra, Indonesia, 82; fac music, Col Music Soc Inst, Univ Colo, Boulder, 83. *Awards:* Bearns Prize, Columbia Univ, 61; Am Music Award, Sigma Alpha Iota, 61; Ernst von Dohnanyi Citation, Fla State Univ, 65; Comp in res, Ford Found, Tampa Bay, Fla, 70-72. *Mem:* Am Soc Univ Comp; Am Music Ctr; BMI; Am Fedn Musicians. *Publ:* At 200, Beethoven Can Still Rock Youth, Music Ed J, 12/70; coauth, Comparative Anthology of Musical Forms, Wadsworth, 76. *Rep:* BMI 320 W 57th St New York NY 10019. *Mailing Add:* 9403 Broadmoor Pl La Mesa CA 92041

WARE, DURWARD CLIFTON, JR
EDUCATOR, TENOR
b Newton, Miss, Mar 15, 37. *Study:* Millsaps Col, BA, 59; Univ Southern Miss, MM, 62; Northwestern Univ, DM, 70. *Rec Perf:* St Nicolas (Benjamin Britten), Musical Heritage Soc, 76. *Roles:* Matteo in Arabella, New Orleans Opera Asn, 69; Leander in Maskerade, St Paul Opera Co, 73; Tenor in Creation, St Paul Chamber Orch, 74; Tenor in Les Noces, Minn Orch, 75; Tamino in Magic Flute, Minn Opera Co, 76; Cavaradossi in Tosca, Miss Opera Asn, 79. *Pos:* Opera asst, Northwestern Univ, 69-70. *Teaching:* Asst

prof voice, choral & opera, Univ Southern Miss, 63-68; from assoc prof to prof voice & vocal pedagogy, Univ Minn, Minneapolis, 70- *Mem:* Nat Asn Teachers Singing (pres Minn chap, 73-74 & 82-83); Nat Opera Asn (pres 78-79). *Publ:* Auth, A Guide to Solo Vocal Performance, Univ Minn Dupl, 78; Vocal Production in Speech and Song, Univ Minn, Kinko's, 80. *Mailing Add:* 3429 Benjamin NE Minneapolis MN 55418

WARE, JOHN
TRUMPET, EDUCATOR
Study: Juilliard Sch; Columbia Univ; studied trumpet with Harold Rehrig; studied with Georges Mager & William Vacchiano. *Pos:* Prin trumpet, Dallas Symph, formerly, Buffalo Phil, formerly, Casals Fest Orch, formerly & Lewisohn Stadium, formerly; co-prin trumpet, New York Phil, 48- *Teaching:* Mem fac trumpet, Mannes Col Music, 80-; mem fac, Queens Col, City Univ New York, currently, State Univ NY, Purchase, currently & Kean Col NJ, currently. *Mailing Add:* 1107 Cambridge Rd Teaneck NJ 07666

WARE, JOHN MARLEY
COMPOSER, EDUCATOR
b Two Rivers, Wis, July 6, 42. *Study:* Ind Univ, with Bernhard Heiden & Thomas Beversdorf, BMus, MMus; La State Univ, with Kenneth B Klaus. *Works:* Passacaglia (organ), 64; Concerto for Trombone and Strings; Piano Sonata; Sonata for Viola Solo; Fantasy (bassoon & piano); Soundings (trombone & piano); Deploration (string orch), 75. *Teaching:* Mem fac, Ind Univ, formerly, Huntington Col, 64-65; Univ Tenn, 66-69, Mid Tenn State Univ, 71-72, Univ Wis, 72-75 & Univ South, 75-76; vis assoc prof music, Old Dominion Univ, 81-82. *Awards:* Ford Found Grant, 63; Woodrow Wilson Fel, 64. *Mem:* Am Musicol Soc; Southeastern Comp League; Pi Kappa Lambda. *Publ:* Contribr to Am Musicol Soc Papers, New Orleans, 71 & Chicago, 75. *Mailing Add:* Dept Music Old Dominion Univ Norfolk VA 23508

WARE, PETER
COMPOSER
b Richmond, Va, May 4, 51. *Study:* Yale Univ, with Kyrysztof Penderesky & Toru Takemitsu, MM, 76. *Works:* Piscataway, perf by Adam Felegi, Europe & Yvar Mikhashoff, US, 79 & publ by Acoma Co; Kluane, comn & perf by Gisela Depkat, Iceland, 82 & publ by Acoma Co, 83; Baca Location Nr. 1, comn by Canada Chamber Ens & Kitchener Waterloo Symph, 82 & publ by Acoma Co, 83; Tsankawi, perf by Cincinnati Symph Orch, 83 & publ by Acoma Co, 83; Kusawa, comn by North York Symph Asn, 83 & publ by Acoma Co, 83; The Night Rainbow, comn by Robby Gunstream, 83 & publ by Acoma Co, 83; Takhini, comn by Canada Sax Trio & publ by Acoma Co, 83. *Rep:* Ira Lieberman 11 Riverside Dr New York NY 10023. *Mailing Add:* 15-7 Greenwood Dr Stratford ON N5A 7K1 Canada

WARFIELD, GERALD ALEXANDER
COMPOSER, WRITER
b Ft Worth, Tex, Feb 23, 40. *Study:* NTex State Univ, BA, 63, MMus, 65; Princeton Univ, MFA, 67; Berkshire Music Ctr, 63-64. *Works:* Three Movements for Orchestra, perf by Dallas Symph, 66; Thirteen Ways of Looking at a Blackbird, Nat Soc Arts & Lett, 67; Fantasy Quintet, New Music Young Ens, 78; Chelsea Suite for Double Bass, 79 & A Trophy (sop & piano), 79, Am Comp Alliance. *Pos:* Assoc dir, Index New Musical Notation, 71-75; mem conf comt, Int Conf New Music Notation, Belgium, 74. *Teaching:* Lectr theory & comp, Princeton Univ, 68-71. *Awards:* First Prize, Nat Soc Arts & Lett, 67 & New Music Young Ens, 78. *Mem:* Am Soc Univ Comp (gen mgr, 80-83); Col Music Soc; Am Comp Alliance; BMI. *Interests:* Notation of contemporary music. *Publ:* Auth, Layer Analysis, Longman Inc, 76; Writings on Contemporary Music Notation, Music Libr Asn, 77; How to Write Music Manuscript, 77 & coauth, Layer Dictation, 78, Longman Inc; The Investor's Guide to Stock Quotations, Harper & Row, 83. *Mailing Add:* 205 W 22nd St New York NY 10011

WARFIELD, SANDRA
MEZZO-SOPRANO
b Kansas City, Mo, Aug 6, 29. *Study:* Consv Music, Univ Mo, Kansas City; studied with Marcello Conati, Elsa Seyfert & Joyce McLean. *Rec Perf:* Marriage of Figaro, RCA, 58; Operatic Duets, London, 65. *Roles:* Dalila in Samson et Dalila, Metropolitan Opera, 56, Zurich Opera, 60, San Francisco Opera, 63 & Seattle Opera, 63; Amneris in Aida, Zurich Opera, 60, Vienna Staatsoper, 61, San Francisco Opera, 63 & Seattle Opera, 63; Azucena in Il Trovatore, Zurich Opera, 60, Vienna Staatsoper, 61, San Francisco Opera, 63, Berlin Opera, 66 & Opera Geneve, 66; Maddelena in Rigoletto, 56 & Ulrica in Un ballo in maschera, 56, Metropolitan Opera; Carmen in Carmen, Zurich Opera, 60; Fides in Le Prophete, Berlin Opera, 66; and others. *Pos:* Performances with Metropolitan Opera, Zurich Opera, Vienna Staatsoper, San Francisco Opera, Berlin Opera, Opera Geneve, Seattle Opera and others, 56- *Mem:* Sigma Alpha Iota. *Publ:* Coauth, A Star in the Family, Coward-McCann, 71. *Rep:* Columbia Artists Mgt Inc 165 W 57th St New York NY 10019. *Mailing Add:* Postfach 14 Flugfeld Dubendorf 8600 Switzerland

WARFIELD, WILLIAM CAESAR
SINGER, EDUCATOR
b West Helena, Ark, Jan 22, 20. *Study:* Eastman Sch Music, BM, 42; Univ Ark, Hon LLD, 72; Lafayette Col, Hon DMus, 78. *Roles:* Call Me Mister, 46-47; Set My People Free, 48-49; Porgy in Porgy & Bess, Europe, 52, New York City Opera, 61 & 64 & Vienna, 65-72; De Lawd in Green Pastures, NBC, 57 & 59; Show Boat, Music Theater Lincoln Ctr, 66 & Vienna Volksoper, 71-72; title role in Mendelssohn's Elijah, Central City Opera, 69. *Pos:* Theater performer on Broadway & on tours in US, Australia & Europe, 46-; concert,

radio & TV appearances, symph soloist & recitalist, 50-; soloist, Philadelphia Orch, touring worldwide, 55-66 & with Pablo Casals, Switz, 67; featured soloist, Casals Fest, PR & New York, 62-63 & Athens Fest, Greece, 66; mem bd dir & trustee, NY Col Music; trustee, Berkshire Boys Choir, 66-70 & Nat Asn Negro Musicians. *Teaching:* Prof voice, Univ Ill, Urbana, 74- *Mem:* Actors Equity; Am Guild Musical Artists; Screen Actors Guild; life mem, Phi Mu Alpha Sinfonia; Am Fedn TV & Radio Artists. *Mailing Add:* Dept Music Univ Ill Urbana IL 61801

WARKENTIN, LARRY R
COMPOSER, EDUCATOR
b Reedley, Calif, Aug 14, 40. *Study:* Tabor Col, BA, 62; Calif State Univ, Fresno, MA, 64; Univ Southern Calif, DMA, 67. *Works:* String Quartet, perf by Fest Quartet Can, 78; Koinonia (orch & tape), perf by Fresno Phil Orch, 80; This Is a Holy Day (choral anthem), Fred Bock Music Publ, 81. *Teaching:* Prof music & chmn humanities div, Fresno Pac Col, 62- *Mem:* Fresno Music Teachers Asn; Nat Soc Arts & Lett (vpres Fresno chap, 81-82). *Publ:* Auth, Confessions of a Church Musicians, Choral J, 77; Centenial of a Hymn, Christian Leader, 82. *Mailing Add:* 1008 Rogers Lane Fresno CA 93727

WARKOV, ESTHER R
EDUCATOR, WRITER
b Los Angeles, Calif, Aug 5, 52. *Study:* Univ Calif, Irvine, 69-71; London Univ, 72; Univ Calif, San Diego, BA(music), 75; Univ Wales, Cardiff, MA(music), 77; Hebrew Univ, Jerusalem, 79- *Pos:* Music critic, Jerusalem Post & Ha-aretz, Israel, 79-81; prog producer, Israel Radio, 80. *Teaching:* Mem fac music fundamentals, Cornish Inst, 82, mem fac western music, 83. *Awards:* Fulbright-Hays Scholar, 77; Maestro-Apprentice Award, Calif Arts Coun, 79; Fel, Mem Found Jewish Cult, 79-83. *Mem:* Soc Ethnomusicol. *Interests:* Musical change in Middle Eastern urban musics. *Publ:* Contribr, Welsh Music, Welsh Arts Coun, 77-83; auth, Taqsim (rec), Jewish Music Res Ctr, 83; contribr, Anthology of Iraqi-Jewish Song, Minstry Educ, Israel (in press). *Mailing Add:* 5256 38th Ave NE Seattle WA 98105

WARNE, KATHARINE MULKY
COMPOSER, PIANO
b Oklahoma City, Okla. *Study:* Mills Col, BA, 45; Juilliard Sch Music, MS, 47; Cleveland Inst Music; Case Western Reserve Univ, DMA, 75. *Works:* Psalm 36 (vocals, clarinet & organ), Fortnightly Musical Club, 74; Claude et Francois (piano), David Burge, 75; Ta Matete (flute, viola, harp & dance), Evangeline King, 77; Fugal Consequences, Blackearth Perc Ens, 79; O God Our Help in Ages Past (chorus, organ, handbells & perc), Westminster Presby Church, 81; Colored Reflections (recorders & harp), Jocelyn Chang, 82. *Teaching:* Instr piano, Univ Kans, 47-50, asst prof, 50-54 & 56-60; lectr, Baldwin Wallace Consv Music, 72-74; instr piano, Laurel Sch, 72-; vis asst prof, Kent State Univ, 74-75. *Mem:* Cleveland Comp Guild Fortnightly Musical Club (vpres, 79-83); Phi Beta Kappa; Pi Kappa Lambda. *Mailing Add:* 15715 Chadbourne Rd Shaker Heights OH 44120

WARNER, JOSEPH (I)
BASS
b Topeka, Kans, Jan 20, 49. *Study:* Washburn Univ, Topeka, BM, 72; Northwestern Univ, Evanston, MM, 73, 73-75. *Roles:* Dr Bartolo, Houston Grand Opera, 76; Don Pasquale, Tex Opera Theater, 78 & Annapolis Opera, 79; Sparafucile, 80 & Leporello, 81, Opera Theatre Syracuse; Colline, Asolo Opera, Sarasota, Fla, 82; Skoluba, Mich Opera Theatre, 82; Major-General Stanely, Opera Theatre St Louis, 83. *Pos:* Singer & actor, Tex Opera Theatre, touring arm of Houston Grand Opera, 75-78. *Awards:* Grants, Nat Opera Inst & William Matheus Sullivan Found, 80- *Rep:* Munro Artists Mgt 344 W 72nd St New York NY 10023. *Mailing Add:* 53 South St Staten Island NY 10310

WARNER, ROBERT AUSTIN
EDUCATOR, LECTURER
b Parkersburg, Iowa, June 5, 12. *Study:* Northern Iowa Univ, BA, 33; Eastman Sch Music, Univ Rochester, MA, 38; Univ Mich, PhD, 51. *Works:* Dark Night (orch), Rochester Civic Orch & Ill Orch, 38-39; Noel, Song for Contralto & Chorus, Assoc Music Publ, 51. *Teaching:* Instr publ sch Iowa, 33-37; prof music, Eastern Ill Univ, 38-56; guest lectr, George Peabody Col for Teachers; prof music & assoc dean, Univ Mich, 56-80. *Awards:* Robert A Warner Music Scholar, Eastern Ill Univ, 73. *Mem:* Am Musicol Soc (chmn, Midwest Chap, 64-65); Am Musical Instr Soc (mem bd dir, 82-); Viola da Gamba Soc Am; Viola da Gamba Soc England; Galpin Soc England. *Interests:* John Jenkins, (1592-1678); musical instruments. *Publ:* Ed, John Jenkins Three-Part Fancy & Ayre Divisions, Wellesley Col, 66; auth, John Jenkins Four-Part Fancy in C Minor, Music Rev, 67; coauth, A Jacob Denner Recorder in the USA, 68 & The Baroque Recorders in the Stearns Collection, 70, Galpin Soc J; auth, Wind Instruments, Encycl Britannica, 75. *Mailing Add:* 9656 N Long Lake Rd Traverse City MI 49684

WARNER, SALLY SLADE
CARILLON
b Worcester, Mass, Sept 6, 32. *Study:* New England Consv Music, 50-52; Am Guild Organists, choir master cert, 64, assoc cert, 65; Royal Carillon Sch, Mechelen, Belgium, with Piet van den Broek, dipl, 79. *Works:* Variations on the Old Flemish Song "Die alder soetste Jesus" (carillon), Scherzando Music Publ (in prog); Passacaglia on E-A-C (carillon), Guild Carillonneurs in NAm, 81. *Pos:* Organist, Church St John the Evangel, Boston, 55-, dir music, 64-; rec librn, Phillips Acad, Andover, Mass, 73-, carillonneur, 75- *Teaching:* Instr carillon, Phillips Acad, Andover, Mass, 75- *Mem:* Am Guild Organists; Guild Carillonneurs in NAm (dir pub relations, 77-); Organ Hist Soc; Asn Anglican Musicians; Belgian Guild Carillonneurs. *Publ:* Auth, The Andover Carillon, Guild Carillonneurs in NAm, Vol XXVII, Bulletin, 4/78. *Mailing Add:* Phillips Acad Andover MA 01810

WARREN, B (BETSY FROST WARREN-DAVIS)
COMPOSER
b Boston, Mass. *Study:* Radcliffe Col, BA & MA. *Works:* Night Watch in City of Boston, 80, Quartet for Saxophones, 81, Trio for Flute, Oboe and Piano, 81, Sonata for Flute and Harpsichord, 82, The Blue Goat (solo for guitar), 82, Jonah (sacred cantata), 83 & Suite for Violin and Cello, 83, Wiscasset Music Publ Co. *Pos:* Solo singer, currently. *Teaching:* Private singing, currently. *Mailing Add:* Wiscasset Music Publ 5 Doane St Boston MA 02109

WARREN, EDWIN BRADY
EDUCATOR, WRITER
b Fowler, Calif, Nov 1, 10. *Study:* Fresno State Univ, AB, 32; Univ Mich, Ann Arbor, MMus(theory), 33, MMus(musicol), 34, PhD, 52; Harvard Univ, 47-48. *Works:* Responses and Amens, Summy, 56. *Teaching:* Chmn theory & hist dept & dean studies, St Louis Inst, Mo, 36-47; dean humanities, Shurtleff Col, Alton, Ill, 50-57; prof music, Southern Ill Univ, 57-79, emer prof, 79- *Mem:* Am Asn Univ Prof; Am Musicol Soc. *Publ:* Ed, O Lux Beata (Fayrfax motet), Summy, 56; auth, articles on Fayrfax, In: Musica Disciplina, 57, 58 & 61, Life and Works of Robert Fayrfax, 69 & ed, Complete Works of Robert Fayrfax, 59, 64 & 66, Am Inst Musicol. *Mailing Add:* 6920 Florian St Louis MO 63121

WARREN, ELINOR REMICK (ELINOR R WARREN GRIFFIN)
COMPOSER, PIANO
b Los Angeles, Calif. *Study:* Mills Col; studied piano with Paulo Gallico & Ernesto Beruman & comp with Clarence Dickinson & Nadia Boulanger. *Works:* Suite for Orchestra, Symphony in One Movement, The Crystal Lake, Singing Earth (sop & orch) & Selected Songs by Elinor Remick Warren, Carl Fischer; Abram in Egypt (chorus, orch & bar), Belwin-Mills; Good Morning America! (chorus, orch & narrator), Carl Fischer; publ 179 other compositions. *Awards:* Award, ASCAP, 59-; twelve first place awards in biennial compt, Nat League Am Pen Women, 60-; Winner, Gedok Int Choral Compt, Germany; Woman of Year Music, Los Angeles Times. *Bibliog:* Julia Smith (auth), Elinor Remick Warren Honored In Israel, Nat Music Fedn Clubs Mag, 77; H F Block & C N Bates (auth), Women in American Music, 79 & Jane LePage (auth), Woman Composers, Conductors & Musicians of the 20th Century, Scarecrow Press. *Mem:* Int League Women Comp; ASCAP; Am Women Comp; Nat Asn Comp USA; Nat League Am Pen Women. *Mailing Add:* 154 S Hudson Ave Los Angeles CA 90004

WARREN, JERRY L
ADMINISTRATOR, EDUCATOR
b Montgomery, Ala, Jan 12, 35. *Study:* Howard Col, BM, 55; Sch Church Music, Southern Baptist Theol Sem, MSM, 59, DMA, 67. *Teaching:* Dir choral activ & church music & asst prof cond & church music, Shorter Col, 66-69; chmn, Music Dept, Belmont Col, 69-83, prof cond, 69-, dean, Sch Music, 83- *Mem:* Nat Asn Sch Music (chmn region eight, 80-83); Am Choral Dir Asn (state pres, 79-81); Col Music Soc; Nat Asn Teachers Singing (local chap pres, 73-75, mem bd dir, 75-78); Music Educr Nat Conf (mem state bd, 74-). *Publ:* Auth, Choral Technique, In: Effective Choral Skills, 80 & How to be a Better Choral Singer, In: Opus II, 81-84, Broadman. *Mailing Add:* Sch Music Belmont Col Nashville TN 37203

WASHBURN, FRANKLIN ELY
VIOLIN, MUSIC DIRECTOR
b Houston, Tex, Sept 29, 11. *Study:* Southwestern Univ, 31; Juilliard Sch Music, 37 & 47; Univ Houston, 46; NTex State Univ, BMusEd, 71. *Pos:* Prin violinist, Houston Symph Orch, 32-42 & 45-50; violinist, Air Force Radio Prod Univ, 43-44; first violin, Music Guild String Quartet, Houston, 47-50; co-ed, Southwestern Musician Mag, 53; music dir, Dallas Jr Hon Orch, 62- *Teaching:* Private instr violin & viola, Houston, 32-53 & Dallas, 57-; dir music camp, Center Point, Tex, summers 50-59; instr strings & orch, Dallas Independent Sch Dist, 57-75. *Mem:* Dallas Music Teachers Asn; Am String Teachers Asn; Tex State Teachers Asn; Music Teachers Nat Asn. *Mailing Add:* 3208 Drexel Dr Dallas TX 75205

WASHBURN, ROBERT BROOKS
COMPOSER, CONDUCTOR
b Bouckville, NY, July 11, 28. *Study:* State Univ NY, Potsdam, BS, 49, MS, 56; Eastman Sch Music, PhD, 60; Aspen Music Sch, study with D Milhaud; study with N Boulanger. *Works:* Symphony No 1, 60, Symphony for Band, 63 & Quartet for Strings, 64, Oxford Univ Press; St Lawrence Oveture, Boosey & Hawkes, 65; Serenade for Strings, Oxford Univ Press, 70; Spring Cantata, 74 & Five Miniatures for Five Brasses, 82, Boosey & Hawkes. *Teaching:* Dean & prof music, Crane Sch Music, State Univ NY, Potsdam, 54-; guest composer, conductor & lecturer at over 40 colleges & universities in the US, Canada & Mexico, 54- *Awards:* Fel, Danforth Found, 58 & Ford Found, 60; grant, Nat Endowment Arts, 81. *Bibliog:* Charles Fowler (auth), American Composer Profiles, Music Educr J, 63. *Mem:* ASCAP; Music Educr Nat Conf; Soc Ethnomusicol; Comp Forum; Am Musical Instrm Soc. *Interests:* Music of Africa and Asia. *Publ:* Auth, Quo Vadis, Music J, 63; Comprehensive Foundations of Music, NY State Educ Dept, 74; Review of the Language of Twentieth Century Music, J Res Music Educ, 77; Music of the Whole World, NY State Music News, 82. *Mailing Add:* RD 4 Box 538 Potsdam NY 13676

WASON, ROBERT WESLEY
EDUCATOR, COMPOSER
b Bridgeport, Conn, July 25, 45. *Study:* Hartt Col Music, Univ Hartford, BMus, 67, MMus, 69; Yale Univ, MPhil, 78, PhD, 81. *Works:* Concerto for Chamber Orchestra & Jazz Ensemble, comn & perf by Hartford Chamber

Orch, 74; Theme with Variations (solo guitar), perf by Richard Provost, 75. *Teaching:* Instr theory & comp, Hartt Col, 70-75 & 77-79; asst prof theory, NTex State Univ, 81-83 & Eastman Sch Music, 83- *Awards:* Bronze Medal, Radio France Guitar Comp Cont, 75; Fulbright Scholar, Vienna, Austria, 79-80. *Mem:* Soc Music Theory. *Interests:* History of harmonic theory in the 19th and early 20th centuries; Schenkerian theory and analysis. *Publ:* Auth, Schhenker's Notion of Scale-Step, in Historical Perspectives: Non-Essential Harmonies in Viennese Fundamental Bass Theory, J Music Theory, 83. *Mailing Add:* Eastman Sch Music 26 Gibbs St Rochester NY 14604

WASSON, D(ONALD) DEWITT
MUSIC DIRECTOR, CRITIC-WRITER
b Orangeburg, NY, Feb 20, 21. *Study:* Nyack Col, dipl(sacred music), 43; Eastern Baptist Sem, BSM, 44; Union Theol Sem, NY, MSM, 47, DSM, 57. *Pos:* Musical dir, Westchester Baroque Chorus, NTarrytown, NY, 61-; music critic, Am Organist, 68-; dir music, NYonkers Community Church, Hastings on Hudson, NY, 75- *Teaching:* Instr music, New York Inst Educ Blind, 53-60 & Southern Westchester Bd Coop Educ Serv, Portchester, NY, 60-75; vis prof organ, King's Col, NY, 75- *Mem:* Am Guild Organists (Westchester chap prog chmn, 59-61 & dean, 61-63); Hymn Soc Am; Choristers Guild; Am Guild English Handbell Ringers; Gesellschaft Orgelfreunde. *Publ:* Ed, Free Harmonizations of Hymn Tunes by Fifty American Composers, Hinshaw, 83. *Mailing Add:* 213 Highland Ave North Tarrytown NY 10591

WASSUM, SYLVESTA MARIE
EDUCATOR
b Tekamah, Nebr, Nov 26, 14. *Study:* Midland Col, AB, 37; Northwestern Univ, MMus, 42, PhD, 57. *Pos:* Textbook ed, Summy-Birchard Co, 59-65, ed in chief, 65-69. *Teaching:* Asst prof music educ, Univ Wyo, 46-50; asst prof music, Univ Calif, Los Angeles, 55-59; prof music educ, Western Ill Univ, 70- *Awards:* Grants, Univ Calif, Los Angeles, 58 & Western Ill Univ Res Coun, 71. *Mem:* Music Educr Nat Conf; Mu Phi Epsilon. *Interests:* Range and tonality in the child voice. *Publ:* Ed, Birchard Music Series, Summy-Birchard Co, 62; auth, Elementary School Children's Vocal Range, 79 & Elementary School Children's Concept of Tonality, 80, J Res Music Educ. *Mailing Add:* 100 Carriage Hill Macomb IL 61455

WATANABE, MIWAKO N
VIOLIN
Study: Toho Consv Music, Tokyo; Curtis Inst Music, with Ivan Galamian; studied with Sandor Vegh. *Pos:* Soloist, Sequoia String Quartet, currently, chamber music groups & chamber orch incl Los Angeles Chamber Orch & Munich Bach Orch; mem chamber ens tours to Europe, USSR, US, Can & Japan. *Awards:* Walter W Naumburg Chamber Music Award, 76. *Rep:* Sheldon Soffer Mgt 130 W 56th St New York NY 10019. *Mailing Add:* c/o Calif Chamber Symph Soc 2219 S Bentley Ave Suite 202 Los Angeles CA 90064

WATANABE, RUTH TAIKO
LIBRARIAN, EDUCATOR
b Los Angeles, Calif, May 12, 16. *Study:* Univ Southern Calif, BMus, 37, AB, 39, MA, 41, MMus, 42; Univ Rochester, PhD, 52. *Pos:* Librn, Sibley Libr, Eastman Sch Music, 47- *Teaching:* Instr music hist, Eastman Sch Music, 46-62, assoc prof, 62-79, prof music bibliog, 79-; adj prof, State Univ NY, Geneseo, 75- *Awards:* Pa-Del Fel, Am Asn Univ Women, 49-50. *Mem:* Int Asn Music Libr (vpres comn consv libr, 75-79); Music Libr Asn (pres, 79-81); Int Musicol Soc; Am Musicol Soc. *Publ:* Contribr, Manual of Music Librarianship, Music Libr Asn, 66; auth, Introduction to Music Research, Prentice-Hall, 67; contribr, Notes Music Libr Asn, 69-; ed, A Treasury of Four-Hand Piano Music, Scribner, 72; auth, Antonio II Verso: Madrigali a Cinque Voci, Olschki, 78. *Mailing Add:* 111 East Ave Rochester NY 14604

WATERS, DAVID L
TROMBONE, EDUCATOR
b Houston, Tex, Aug 9, 40. *Study:* Univ Houston, BMusEd, 62; Univ Tex, MMus, 64. *Pos:* First trombonist, Austin Symph Orch, 62-64; bass trombonist, Houston Symph Orch, 66- *Teaching:* Instr trombone, Sam Houston State Univ, 67-77; artist & teacher, Shepherd Sch Music, Rice Univ, 77- *Mem:* Am Fedn Musicians; Int Trombone Asn. *Mailing Add:* 9130 Elizabeth Houston TX 77055

WATERS, EDWARD NEIGHBOR
LIBRARIAN
b Leavenworth, Kans, July 23, 06. *Study:* Eastman Sch Music, Univ Rochester, BMus, 27, MMus, 28; Cleveland Inst Music, Hon DMus, 73. *Pos:* Asst librn, Music Div, Libr Cong, 31-34, asst chief, 37-72, chief, 72-76; mem adv bd, New Grove Dict of Music & Musicians. *Teaching:* Head, Piano Dept, Juniata Col, 30-31. *Awards:* Fel, Fulbright, 62-63, Ford Found, 62-63 & Chapelbrook Found, 68. *Interests:* Life of Franz Liszt. *Publ:* Auth, Victor Herbert, Macmillan, 55; auth & translr, Frederic Chopin by Franz Liszt, Free Press, 63; and many articles. *Mailing Add:* Apt 7-H Bldg B-3900 Watson Pl NW Washington DC 20016

WATERS, J KEVIN
COMPOSER, EDUCATOR
b Seattle, Wash, June 24, 33. *Study:* Gonzaga Univ, BA, 57, MA, 58; Univ Calif, Los Angeles, with Roy Harris; Univ Wash, DMA, 70. *Works:* Inversnaid, Col Notre Dame, Calif, 64; Mask of Hiroshima (opera), Santa Clara Univ, 71; Job (musico-dram), Frascati, Italy, 72; Sinfonia, Seattle Symph Orch, 76; Dear Ignatius, Dear Isabel (opera), Loyola Col, 78; Make God Music, Epoch Universal Publ, 81; Mass of Jubilee, perf by Gonzaga Univ

& Seattle Univ, 82. *Pos:* Pres, Jesuit Inst for Arts, 80-; dean, Col Arts & Sci, Gonzaga Univ, 83- *Teaching:* Instr, Univ Wash, 67-68; prof comp, counterpoint & orch, Seattle Univ, 69-83. *Awards:* Winner for Mask of Hiroshima, Christian Theatre Artists Guild, 78. *Bibliog:* Edward Foley (auth), Introducing a Person of Note, Pastoral Music, 2/83. *Mem:* Am Guild Organists (chaplain, 76). *Publ:* Contribr, Criticism of New Music, Pastoral Music, 78- *Mailing Add:* Music Dept Gonzaga Univ Spokane WA 99258

WATERS, JAMES LIPSCOMB
COMPOSER, EDUCATOR
b Kyoto, Japan, June 11, 30; US citizen. *Study:* Westminster Choir Col, BM, 52, MM, 53; Sorbonne, Paris, 56-57; Eastman Sch Music, PhD, 67;. *Works:* Three Holy Sonnets of John Donne, Rochester Orch, 66; Three Songs of Louise Bogan, Alaska Fest Orch, 78; Variations and Fugue, 20th Century Consort, 78; Variations and Fugue, 20th Century Consort, Smithsonian, 80; Song Cycle, Janice Harsanyi, 81; Overture, Univ Ill Orch, 82; Goal, Fla State Univ, 83. *Teaching:* Prof, Westminster Choir Col, 57-68 & Kent State Univ, 68- *Awards:* Fel, Nat Endowment Arts, 80; ASCAP Award, 82. *Mem:* Am Soc Univ Comp (nat coun, 82-83); ASCAP; Cleveland Comp Guild (pres, 79-81). *Mailing Add:* 2004 Brookview Dr Kent OH 44240

WATERS, KAREN JOHNSON
ADMINISTRATOR, PIANO
b Kingsburg, Calif, Aug 13, 42. *Study:* Oberlin Col, studied with Emil Danenberg, BM, 64; Fresno State Col; Boston Univ, with Bela Nagy; Univ Colo, with David Burge, MM, 67; with Lili Kraus & Richard Cass . *Teaching:* Instr piano, Univ Colo, Boulder, 65-67, Univ Minn, Minneapolis, 67-69, St Cloud State Univ, 68; instr piano & theory, Gustavus Adolphus Col, 68-69; asst prof piano, Tex Wesleyan Col, 69-79, assoc dean, Sch Fine Arts, 79-81, dean, 81- *Mem:* Sigma Alpha Iota; Pi Kappa Lambda. *Mailing Add:* Sch Fine Arts Tex Wesleyan Col PO Box 50010 Ft Worth TX 76105

WATERS, WILLIE ANTHONY
CONDUCTOR & MUSIC DIRECTOR, ADMINISTRATOR
b Goulds, Fla, Oct 11, 51. *Study:* Univ Miami, BMus, 73; Memphis State Univ. *Pos:* Asst cond & chorus master, Memphis Opera Theatre, 73-75; music adminr, San Francisco Opera, 75-79; music adminr & chorus master, Gtr Miami Opera, 81-83, music dir, 83- *Mailing Add:* 3661 Palmetto Ave #2 Coconut Grove FL 33133

WATKINS, ARMIN J
EDUCATOR, CONDUCTOR
b Skokie, Ill, July 23, 31. *Study:* Yale Univ, BMus, 53, MMus, 54; Ind Univ, DMus(piano lit & perf), 56. *Pos:* Cond, Lakeland Piano Fest, Fla, 61-63; concert tours in Europe, 66-81. *Teaching:* Asst prof music, Mich State Univ, 57-58; assoc prof & head piano dept, Bradley Univ, 58-60; assoc prof music, Univ SFla, 60-63, prof humanities, 63-72, chmn piano fac, 72-73, actg asst chmn music, 73-74, prof music, 72- *Awards:* Distinguished Artist Teacher Award, Nat Piano Found, 77. *Mem:* Music Teachers Nat Asn. *Interests:* University level music and administration of university music program; public concert performance as pianist, violinist, and singer. *Publ:* Co-ed, Music Composition for the Non-Professional, Fla Musical Dir, 3/66; Music and the Culture of Man, Holt, 70. *Mailing Add:* Dept Musical Arts Univ SFla Tampa FL 33620

WATKINS, GLENN
EDUCATOR
b McPherson, Kans, May 30, 27. *Study:* Univ Mich, AB, 48, MMus, 49; Eastman Sch Music, PhD(musicol), 53; Am Consv, Fontainebleu, France, dipl. *Teaching:* Asst prof, Southern Ill Univ, 54-58; asst prof musicol, Univ NC, 58-61, assoc prof, 62-63; vis prof, Univ Mich, 61-62, assoc prof, 63-66, prof, 66- *Awards:* Fulbright Fel, 53-54; grant, Am Coun Learned Soc, 62; Nat Endowment Humanities Sr Fel, 76-77. *Mem:* Am Musicol Soc. *Publ:* Co-ed, Complete Works of Carlo Gesualdo, 57-66; auth, Carlo Gesualdo: The Man & His Music, Oxford Univ Press, 73; ed, Complete Works of Sigismondo d'India, 76-; auth, Schoenberg & the Organ, Perspectives New Music, Vol 3, No 2; Canon and Stravinsky's Late Style, Univ Calif Press, 84. *Mailing Add:* Sch Music Univ Mich Ann Arbor MI 48109

WATKINS, R BEDFORD
EDUCATOR, COMPOSER
b Keiser, Ark, July 27, 25. *Study:* Southwestern at Memphis, BM, 49; Univ Mich, with Gerald Kechley, MM, 51; Univ Iowa, with Philip Bezanson, PhD, 66. *Works:* 4 Burlesques (violin & piano), 62; Pentamerous Suite (trumpet & piano), 72; Fili mi Absolom (bass solo & perc), 76; Poetiae Patriae Amantes (bar, oboe & piano), 76; 3 Spring Haiku (sop, string quartet & horn), 78; Te Deum (two sop soli & perc), 78; Bicinia (clarinet & oboe). *Teaching:* Mem fac, Southwestern at Memphis, 49-50 & Winthrop Col, 51-56; prof piano, harpsichord & keyboard, Ill Wesleyan Univ, 56- *Mailing Add:* Music Dept Ill Wesleyan Univ Bloomington IL 61701

WATSON, J PERRY
ADMINISTRATOR, EDUCATOR
b Miami, Fla, Oct 29, 27. *Study:* Fla State Univ, BME, 49; Appalachian State Univ, MA, 55. *Works:* Adoramus Te (Corsi), 65 & Landlord, Fill the Flowing Bowl, 67, Brodt Music Co. *Teaching:* Dir bands, Appalachian High Sch, Boone, NC, 56-59; dir music, NC State Univ, Raleigh, 59- *Mem:* Music Educr Nat Conf; NC Music Educ Asn; Intercol Coun; founding mem, Raleigh-Wake County Symph Orch Develop Asn (pres, 75-80, exec dir, 80-). *Publ:* Auth, Starting A British Brass Band, Yamaha, 82; Sound the Cornet!, 82 & Sounds Ideal!, 83, Getzen Gazette. *Mailing Add:* Dir Music NC State Univ Raleigh NC 27650

WATSON, JACK McLAURIN
ADMINISTRATOR, EDUCATOR
b Dillon, SC, Nov 22, 08. *Study:* Cincinnati Consv Music, BMus, 30; Univ Southern Calif, MMus, 40; Columbia Univ, MA, 45, PhD, 47; Col Consv Music, Univ Cincinnati, Hon DMus, 58; Geneva Col, Pa, Hon DHL, 71; Univ Cincinnati, Hon DFA, 82. *Pos:* Freelance singer, various motion picture studios, Hollywood, Calif, 35-37; contract player, Universal Studios, 38; admin music ed, Silver Burdett Co, NY, 49-53; adv ed music, Dodd Mead & Co, NY, 57-74; consult, Corbett Found, Cincinnati, Ohio & Starling Found, Houston, Tex, 74-; consult ed, Princeton Book Co, NJ, 76-; actg pres, Mannes Col Music, 78-79. *Teaching:* From instr to assoc prof, Winthrop Col, 39-47; assoc prof, NY Univ, 47-49; prof, Univ Southern Calif, 53; prof & chmn music educ, Ind Univ, Bloomington, 53-60; prof & dir grad study, 60-63; dean & Thomas James Kelly prof, Col Consv Music, Univ Cincinnati, 63-74, Univ Prof creative & perf arts, 74-77, dean & Univ Prof emer, 78- *Mem:* Am Musicol Soc; Bohemians; Int Gesallschaft Musikwissenchaft. *Interests:* Psychology of philanthropy to the arts. *Publ:* Auth, Education of School Music Teachers, Columbia Univ, 48; Music Criticism: A Point of View, Music J, 59; coauth, Musical Goals to Newcastle, Harper's Mag, 61; A Concise Dictionary of Music, Dodd Mead & Co, 65; auth, Statistical Procedures in Quantitative Musicological Research, Bärenreiter Berichteden Neuden Internaliznatin Kongress, 66. *Mailing Add:* 2200 Victory Pkwy Apt 1407 Cincinnati OH 45206

WATSON, KENNETH E
PERCUSSION, EDUCATOR
b Canton, Ohio, Aug 8, 37. *Study:* Mich State Univ, BM(theory & comp), 62; Univ Southern Calif, MM(perc perf), 63; studied timpani with Cloyd Duff & William Kraft. *Rec Perf:* Redwood (solo perc & viola) & Branches (solo perc & two bassoons), CRI; Candide (Henri Lazaroff) & Cadence 3, Crystal Rec; Metamorphosis (Dorrance Stalvey), Ars Nova. *Pos:* Prin perc & timpanist, Pasadena Symph, 72-; perc, major Hollywood film & TV studios; performer new music, Monday Evening Conct ser & Ojai Fest, Calif. *Teaching:* Assoc prof music, Univ Southern Calif, 68- *Mailing Add:* 990-17 Riverside Dr Burbank CA 91506

WATSON, WALTER ROBERT
COMPOSER, EDUCATOR
b Canton, Ohio, Oct 13, 33. *Study:* Ohio Univ, with Karl Ahrendt, BFA, 59; MFA, 61; NTex State Univ, with Samuel Adler, PhD, 67; Aspen Music Sch, with Darius Milhaud. *Works:* Deborah Sampson (opera); Antiphony and Chorale (band); Essay for Flute (chamber music); Divertimento (flute, harp & bassoon); Trumpet Tunes Revisited (trumpet & organ); Recital Suite (marimba & piano); Five Japanese Love Songs (women's voices); over 60 published compositions. *Pos:* Consult ed, Ludwig Publ Co, 74-; organist & choirmaster, Christ Episcopal Church, Kent, Ohio, currently. *Teaching:* Mem fac, Stephen F Austin State Univ, 61-66; prof music, Kent State Univ, 66-, dir, Sch Music, currently; dir, Blossom Fest Sch Music, currently. *Awards:* ASCAP Awards, 68-; First Prize, US Navy Band Cont, 73; Boscom Little Fund Grant, 78. *Publ:* Contribr to Music J, 66. *Mailing Add:* 1224 Fairview Dr Kent OH 44240

WATTS, ANDRE
PIANO
b Nuremberg, Germany, June 20, 46; US citizen. *Study:* Peabody Consv, dipl; Yale Univ, Hon Dr, 73; Albright Col, HHD, 75. *Rec Perf:* On CBS Rec. *Pos:* Soloist, Philadelphia Orch, 56, New York Phil, 63, London Symph Orch & many other US & Europ orchs; USSR tour with San Francisco Symph, 73; TV appearances incl Camara Three, Live from Lincoln Ctr & Great Performers Ser; solo tours, US, Europe, Japan & Israel. *Awards:* Grammy Award, 63; Lincoln Ctr Medallion, 74. *Mailing Add:* c/o Columbia Artists Mgt 165 W 57th St New York NY 10019

WATTS, AREDEAN WALTON
CONDUCTOR & MUSIC DIRECTOR, EDUCATOR
b Kanosh, Utah, June 8, 28. *Study:* Brigham Young Univ, BA(music theory), 52; Univ Utah, MM, 60. *Rec Perf:* King David, Vanguard, 60. *Pos:* Musical dir, Univ Utah Theatre, 58-66; founder & exec dir, Univ Utah Opera Co, 65-78; musical dir & cond, Ballet West, 66-; assoc cond, Utah Symph Orch, 68-79. *Teaching:* Dir opera wkshp, Univ Utah, 59-70, prof music, 60- & chmn ballet dept, 80- *Mem:* Am Symph Orch League. *Mailing Add:* 1370 Stratford Ave Salt Lake City UT 84106

WAXMAN, ERNEST
COMPOSER, PIANO
b New York, NY, Oct 14, 13. *Study:* Brooklyn Col, BA(music), 40; NY Univ, MA(musicol), 47; Teachers Col, Columbia Univ, MA(music educ), 49; studied comp with Aaron Copland & Roy Harris. *Works:* Piano Sonata, perf by Morton Schoenfeld, 46; Piano Concerto, perf by Joseph Wolman, 48; Spoon River Rhapsody (flute & strings), perf by Julius Baker, 50; Capriccio for 5 Brass Instruments, Advan Rec & on WBAI Radio; The Story of Ruth (oratorio), perf by Temple Isaiah Choir, 80; Toccata for Piano, Adelphi Col & Bayview Libr, Great Neck; four educ piano pieces, Schirmer, Boston & Summy. *Pos:* Staff pianist, CBS, 45-58. *Teaching:* Music, New York high sch, 64-80. *Mem:* Long Island Comp Alliance. *Mailing Add:* 6146 Little Neck Pkwy Little Neck NY 11362

WAYLAND, NEWTON HART
CONDUCTOR, COMPOSER
b Santa Barbara, Calif, Nov 5, 40. *Study:* New England Consv Music, BM(arr), 63, MMus(chamber music), 65. *Works:* PBS-TV music for documentaries & others, 68-82, Zoom Theme & Nova Theme, Wayland Ens. *Rec Perf:* Jazz Loves Bach, Polydor, 68; Berlin to Broadway with Kurt Weill, Paramount, 72; Fiedler in Rags, Polydor, 74; Come on and Zoom, A&M, 74. *Pos:* Guest cond, Boston Pops, Minnesota Orch, Baltimore Symph, Rochester Phil & others, 77-; res cond, Midwest Pops, South Bend, Ind, 80-; res pops cond, Oakland Symph, 81- *Mailing Add:* Curtis-Wayland Music Inc 2970 Hidden Valley Ln Santa Barbara CA 93108

WEAVER, JOHN B
ORGAN, TEACHER
b Palmerton, Pa, Apr 27, 37. *Study:* Curtis Inst Music, dipl, 59; Sch Sacred Music, Union Theol Sem, MSacMus, 68. *Works:* Psalm 100, 60, Toccata for Organ, 68, Rhapsody for Flute & Organ, 68, Epiphany Alleluias, 68, Introit for Pentecost, 82, Fantasia for Organ, 83 & Passacaglia on a Theme by Dunstable, 83, Boosey & Hawkes. *Rec Perf:* The Wicks Organ Series, Wicks Organ Co, 63; John Weaver Plays Mozart and Liszt, Aeolian-Skinner, 65. *Pos:* Dir music, Holy Trinity Lutheran Church, New York, 59-70 & Madison Ave Presbyterian Church, New York, 70- *Teaching:* Instr organ, Union Theol Sem, 70-73 & Curtis Inst Music, 71-; chmn organ dept, Manhattan Sch Music, 83- *Mem:* Presbyterian Asn Musicians (pres elect, currently); Am Guild Organists (dean New York chap, 74-75). *Publ:* Auth, Hymn Registration with Imagination, 59, On Hymn Playing, 59, Memorizing Organ Music, 77 & Are You Practicing?, 77, J Church Music; Musician's Viewpoint (11 quart columns), Reformed Liturgy & Music, 81-83. *Rep:* Murtagh McFarlane Conct Mgt 3269 W 30th St Cleveland OH 44109. *Mailing Add:* 921 Madison Ave New York NY 10021

WEAVER, M JANE
ADMINISTRATOR
b Burlington, Iowa, June 4, 47. *Study:* Univ Iowa, BA, 69. *Pos:* Prod asst, J F Kennedy Ctr, 71-74; prod mgr, Houston Grand Opera, 74-79; managing dir, Tex Opera Theater, 79- *Teaching:* Guest lectr opera prod, Houston Community Col, 75-76. *Mem:* Opera Am; Tex Arts Alliance. *Publ:* Auth, Quarterly Arts Report, Houston First Am Savings. *Mailing Add:* c/o Tex Opera Theater 401 Louisiana Dr Houston TX 77002

WEAVER, ROBERT LAMAR
EDUCATOR, WRITER
b Dahlonega, Ga, July 26, 23. *Study:* Columbia Univ, BA, 46, MA, 48; Univ NC, PhD, 58. *Teaching:* From asst to assoc prof music hist, Catawba Col, 56-60; prof, George Peabody Col, Nashville, 60-75 & Univ Louisville, 75- *Awards:* Fulbright Student, 52-53; Fulbright Res Fel, 66-67; Nat Endowment Humanities Grant, 82-83. *Mem:* Am Musicol Soc; Col Music Soc; Int Musicol Soc; Music Libr Asn; Ital Musicol Soc. *Interests:* Baroque and Italian opera. *Publ:* Auth, Opera in Florence, Univ NC Press, 69; The Cantatas of Allesandro and Alto Melani, Wellesley Col, 74; Materiali per Le Biografie dei Frahelli Melani, Rev Ital Musicol, 77; Chronology of Music in the Florentine Theater, Info Coordr, 78; various articles, In: New Grove Dict of Music & Musicians, 80. *Mailing Add:* 78 Westwind Rd Louisville KY 40207

WEAVER, ROBERT LEE
EDUCATOR, PIANO
b Lancaster County, Pa, June 9, 36. *Study:* Goshen Col, BA, 58; Univ Mich, MMus, 59; Syracuse Univ, PhD, 71. *Teaching:* Asst prof piano, Bluffton Col, 62-65 & music hist & piano, Rust Col, 71-72; prof music hist & piano, Centre Col Ky, 72- *Mem:* Am Musicol Soc; Col Music Soc; Int Music Libr Asn. *Interests:* Music printing in 16th century Antwerp, especially that of Hubert Waelrant and Jan de Laet. *Publ:* Auth, Waelrant and Anabaptism, Mennonite Quart Rev, 78; Waelrant, In: New Grove Dict of Music & Musicians, 80. *Mailing Add:* 234 W Lexington Ave Danville KY 40422

WEBB, BRIAN PATRICK
CONDUCTOR & MUSIC DIRECTOR, EDUCATOR
b Auckland, New Zealand, Dec 9, 48. *Study:* Univ Auckland, BMus, 71; Ind Univ, MMus, 72, DMus, 77. *Pos:* Music dir & cond, Vt Phil, 77- *Teaching:* Assoc prof music, Norwich Univ, 74- *Mailing Add:* 99 1/2 College St Montpelier VT 05602

WEBB, CHARLES H
ADMINISTRATOR, CONDUCTOR & MUSIC DIRECTOR
b Dallas, Tex, Feb 14, 33. *Study:* Southern Methodist Univ, Ba, 55, MM, 55; Ind Univ, DM, 64; Anderson Col, Hon Dr, 79. *Works:* O For a Thousand Tongues & Sing We Joyfully to God, Shawnee Press; Psalm 23, Psalm 100 & Psalm 58, Choristers Guild. *Rec Perf:* Several recordings on Coronet Rec. *Pos:* Mgr musical orgn, Ind Univ, 60-64, from asst dean to assoc dean, 64-73, dean, 73-; cond & dir, Indianapolis Symph Choir, 67-; organist, First Methodist Church, Bloomington, 68-; guest cond & pianist, chorus & organ fest throughout US. *Awards:* Named to Ind Acad, 83. *Mem:* Pi Kappa Lambda; Phi Mu Alpha. *Publ:* Handel's Messiah—A Conductors View, Harper & Row. *Mailing Add:* 648 Woodscrest Dr Bloomington IN 47401

WEBB, GUY BEDFORD
CONDUCTOR, BARITONE
b Blue Springs, Mo, May 19, 31. *Study:* Juilliard Sch Music, dipl, 54; Columbia Teachers Col, BS, 58, MA, 59; Univ Ill, DMA, 72. *Teaching:* Choral & voice, Univ Fla, 59-66; dir choral activities, State Univ NY, Cortland, 66-75 & Southwest Mo State Univ, 80-; dept head & choral dir, NMex State Univ, 75-80. *Mem:* Am Choral Dir Asn (pres elect, 73-75); Music Educr Nat Conf; Nat Asn Teachers Singing; Col Music Soc; Phi Mu Alpha Sinfonia. *Mailing Add:* 2906 E Ridgeview Dr Springfield MO 65804

WEBB, MARIANNE
EDUCATOR, ORGAN

b Topeka, Kans, Oct 4, 36. *Study:* Washburn Univ, with Jerald Hamilton, BM(organ), 58; Univ Mich, with Marilyn Mason, MM(organ), 59; study with Andre Marchal, Paris, 61-62; Syracuse Univ, with Arthur Poister, 62-67. *Teaching:* Instr, Iowa State Univ, 59-61; asst prof, James Madison Univ, 63-65; prof music & univ organist, Southern Ill Univ, Carbondale, 65- *Mem:* Am Guild Organists; Sigma Alpha Iota; Music Teacher's Nat Asn; Phi Kappa Lambda. *Publ:* Auth, Organ Technics-Good Organ Playing, 64, Organ Technics-Basic for Beginners, 64, Organ Technics-Manual Touches, 64, Organ Technics-Pedal Technic, 64, Organ Technics-Registration, 64, Music Ministry. *Rep:* C/o Phillip Truckenbrod Concert Artists Box 14600 Hartford CT 06114. *Mailing Add:* Sch Music Southern Il Univ Carbondale IL 62901

WEBBER, CAROL STAATS
SOPRANO, TEACHER

b Trenton, NJ. *Study:* Consv Music, Oberlin Col, BM, 65; Univ Iowa, 67; Univ Wash, 72-74. *Roles:* Mimi in La Boheme, 79, Seattle Opera; Gretel in Hansel & Gretel, Metropolitan Opera, 79-80; Norina in Don Pasquale, Seattle Opera & Portland Opera, 80; Liu in Turnadot, Miami Opera, 81; Rosina in Barber of Seville, Mobile Opera, 81; Micaela in Carmen, Mobile Opera & Grand Rapids Opera, 82; Marzelline in Fidelio, Charlotte Opera, 82. *Teaching:* Instr voice, Willamette Univ, 69-71; teaching asst voice, Univ Wash, Seattle, 73-74, fac guest artist, 82-83. *Mailing Add:* 5521 39th NE Seattle WA 98105

WEBER, DAVID
CLARINET, EDUCATOR

b Vilna, Russia. *Study:* Clarinet with Roy Schmidt, Simeon Bellison & Leon Barzin. *Rec Perf:* On Decca, Stradivari, Lyrichord, Cambridge & Columbia Masterworks. *Pos:* Mem, NBC Symph, CBS Symph & New York Phil, formerly; conct performer, New York Chamber Symph, Paganini String Quartet, Hungarian String Quartet, Beaux Arts String Quartet, New Friends Music & Alexander Schneider Chamber Orch; prin clarinetist, Metropolitan Opera Orch, formerly, Symph Air, formerly & New York City Ballet Orch, 64- *Teaching:* Privately, formerly, State Univ NY Col, Purchase, formerly & Queens Col, City Univ New York, formerly; mem fac clarinet, Juilliard Sch, 75- *Publ:* Contrib to Woodwind Mag & Woodwind Trade Mag. *Mailing Add:* 574 West End Ave New York NY 10024

WEBER, PHYLLIS ANNE
TEACHER, VIOLIN

b Orange, Calif. *Study:* Whittier Col, AB(music), 62; Cleveland Inst Music, with Linda Ceroneat, 74-79. *Pos:* Concertmaster, Lakeland Orch, Lakeland Community Col, 77- *Teaching:* Violin, Cleveland Inst Music, 79- *Awards:* Bank Am Fine Arts Award, 58. *Mailing Add:* 2983 Lynn Dr Willoughby Hills OH 44092

WEBSTER, ALBERT K
ADMINISTRATOR

b Brooklyn, NY, Oct 14, 37. *Study:* L'Ecole Musique, Fontainebleau, summers 58 & 59; Harvard Col, BA, 59. *Pos:* Asst to mgr & asst mgr, New York Phil, 62-71; managing dir & exec vpres, 75-; gen mgr, Cincinnati Symph Orch, 71-75; mem, chmn orch sect & co-chmn policy sect, Music Panel, Nat Endowment Arts, 74-80. *Mem:* Am Symph Orch League; Am Arts Alliance; Asn Class Music (mem bd dir, currently). *Mailing Add:* Avery Fisher Hall Broadway at 65th New York NY 10023

WEBSTER, BEVERIDGE
PIANO, EDUCATOR

b Pittsburgh, Pa. *Study:* Pittsburgh Consv Music; Paris Consv, with Isidor Philipp; studied with Artur Schnabel; Univ NH, MusD, 62; Baldwin-Wallace Col, DHL, 69. *Rec Perf:* On MGM, Dover, Columbia, Desto & Heliodor. *Pos:* Performer chamber music with many string quartets; ed, Int Music Co. *Teaching:* Instr master classes, New England Consv Music, 40-46; mem fac piano, Juilliard Sch, 46-; perf artist & mem fac, Aspen Music Fest & Sch, 61-70; prof in res, Herbert H Lehman Col, 73. *Awards:* Nat Asn Am Comp & Cond Award Outstanding Serv Am Music. *Mem:* Nat Soc Lit & Arts. *Mailing Add:* 2 Inverness Scarsdale NY 10853

WEBSTER, GERALD BEST
TRUMPET, EDUCATOR

b Antioch, Calif, Jan 6, 44. *Study:* Univ Pac, Stockton; Ind Univ, Bloomington, BME, 65, MM(trumpet), 66. *Pos:* Prin trumpet, Spokane Symph, 70-76; Edward Tarr Brass Ens & Int Trumpet Sem, Sweden & Germany. *Teaching:* Asst prof, Western Ill Univ, 69-70; prof, Wash State Univ, 70- *Mem:* Int Trumpet Guild; Music Educr Nat Conf; Int Fedn Musicians. *Publ:* Auth, Method for Piccolo Trumpet, 80, Vol II (in prep), Brass Press. *Mailing Add:* NW 340 Larry St Pullman WA 99163

WEBSTER, MICHAEL
CLARINET, COMPOSER

b New York, NY, Dec 11, 44. *Study:* Eastman Sch Music, studied clarinet with Stanley Hasty, BM, 66, MM, 67, DMA, 75. *Works:* Five Pieces for Solo Clarinet, G Schirmer, 74; Sonata for Clarinet & Piano, perf by comp & Beveridge Webster, 77; Echoes and Reflections (two solo clarinets & orch), perf by comp & Stanley Hasty with Rochester Phil, 80. *Rec Perf:* American Contemporary Clarinet Music, CRI, 77. *Pos:* Prin clarinetist, Rochester Phil Orch, 68- & San Francisco Symph, 80-81; music dir, Soc Chamber Music Rochester, 80-; participant, Chamber Music Soc Lincoln Ctr, Marlboro Fest, Chamber Music West, San Francisco, Chamber Music Northwest, Portland, Victoria Int Fest, BC, Santa Fe Chamber Music Fest & Aspen Inst. *Teaching:* Vis assoc prof clarinet, San Francisco Consv Music, 81; mem fac, Eastman Sch Music, 82. *Mailing Add:* 281 Barrington St Rochester NY 14607

WEBSTER, PETER RICHARD
EDUCATOR, RESEARCHER

b Augusta, Maine, May 31, 47. *Study:* Gorham State Col, Univ Maine, BS, 69; Eastman Sch Music, MM, 71; PhD, 77. *Teaching:* Instr music, Marshfield city sch, Mass, 69-70; Instr, Case Western Reserve Univ, 74-77, asst prof, 77-83, assoc prof, 83- *Mem:* Music Educr Nat Conf; Soc Res Music Educ; Col Music Soc. *Interests:* Psychology of music; creative thinking in music. *Publ:* Auth, Relationship Between Creative Behavior in Music and Selected Variables, J Res Music Educ, 79; The Ivory Tower, the Trenches and the Gap that Separates, Contrib Music Educ, 80; coauth, A Conservation of Rhythm and Tonal Patterns, Crime Bulletin, 82. *Mailing Add:* 3533 Avalon Rd Shaker Heights OH 44120

WECHSLER, BERT
CRITIC, LECTURER

b Brooklyn, NY. *Study:* Queens Col, City Univ New York, BA. *Pos:* Ed & music & dance critic, Music J, 80; cult corresp, Politiken, Denmark, 82; arts critic & corresp, currently. *Mem:* Music Critics Asn; Outer Critics Circle; Bohemians. *Publ:* Ed, The Way They Play, Paganiniana, 83. *Mailing Add:* 215 E 80th St New York NY 10021

WEED, JOSEPH LAITEN
EDUCATOR, VIOLIN

b Athol, Kans, Mar 14, 17. *Study:* Bethany Col, BM, 38; Yale Univ, MusM, 42; Harvard Univ; Manhattan Sch Music; Aspen Sch Music; Morningside Col, Hon MusD, 68. *Pos:* Music dir, Langdon High Sch, Kans, 38-40; concertmaster, Hutchinson Symph, 39-41; mem, New Haven Symph, 41-42 & 46-47, Sioux City Symph, 47- & Sioux Falls Symph, 60-; founder & musical dir, Lewis & Clarke Symphonette, 61-67. *Teaching:* Private violin, Hutchinson, Kans, 40-41; instr, Sterling Col, 40-41; dir, Consv Music, Yankton Col, 47-74, prof, 47- *Mem:* SDak Arts Coun (vchmn, 67-70); SDak Music Educr Asn (pres, 74-76); Music Teachers Nat Asn; Am Asn Univ Prof; Am String Teachers Asn. *Mailing Add:* 802 Pine St Yankton SD 57078

WEED, MAURICE JAMES
COMPOSER, EDUCATOR

b Kalamazoo, Mich, Oct 16, 12. *Study:* Western Mich Univ, AB(music educ), 34; Eastman Sch Music, BM(theory), 40, MM(comp), 52, PhD(comp), 54. *Works:* Serenity (chamber orch), Eastman-Rochester Symph Orch, 53; String Quartet, Eastman IFMS Symposium, 53; Symphony No 1, Nat Symph Orch, 56; Symphonie Breve, Univ Redlands, 64. *Pos:* Instrumental music supvr, Ionia Pub Sch, Mich, 34-36 & Three Rivers Pub Sch, Mich, 37-43; dir instrumental music, Ripon Col, Wis, 46-51. *Teaching:* Asst prof music, Ripon Col, Wis, 46-51; teaching fel, Eastman Sch Music, 51-54; head dept music, Northern Ill Univ, 54-61, prof, 61-74; instr, Western Carolina Univ, 74-75. *Awards:* First prize (for Symphony No 1), Nat Symph Orch, 55; Am Bandmasters Asn Ostwald Award (for Introduction & Scherzo), 59; first prize (for Psalm XIII), J Fischer & Brothers Centennial, 64. *Mem:* Am Music Ctr; Am Soc Univ Comp; Nat Asn Comp USA; ASCAP; Music Educr Nat Conf. *Mailing Add:* RR1 Box 641 Timberlane Rd Waynesville NC 28786

WEEKLEY, DALLAS ALFRED
PIANO, EDUCATOR

b Sparks, Ga, May 15, 33. *Study:* Sch Music, Ind Univ, studied piano with Sidney Foster, Walter Robert & Menahen Pressler, BM(piano), 55, MM(piano), 57, DMusEd, 68. *Pos:* Mem, Weekley & Arganbright, conct tours, 65- *Teaching:* Grad asst piano, Ind Univ, Bloomington, 55-57; dept chmn & prof, Huntington Col, 57-64; prof, Univ Wis, La Crosse, 65- *Interests:* Original music for one piano, four hands; Schubert. *Rep:* Karlsrud Concerts 948 The Parkway Mamaroneck NY 10543. *Mailing Add:* 1532 Madison St La Crosse WI 54601

WEEKLEY, NANCY See Arganbright, Nancy

WEGNER, AUGUST MARTIN, III
COMPOSER, EDUCATOR

b Saginaw, Mich, Feb 20, 41. *Study:* Cent Mich Univ, BME, 63; Univ Iowa, MFA, 70, PhD, 71. *Works:* Something for Flute and Piano, Seesaw Music Corp, 75 & Musical Heritage Soc, 80; Encore Piece: A Little Minor Blues, 75, Something for Saxophone and Piano, 76, Coney Island, 76 & Movement, 76, Seesaw Music Corp. *Teaching:* Assoc prof, Univ Wis, Parkside, Kenosha, 72- *Awards:* Philip Greeley Clapp Comp Scholar, 71. *Mem:* Am Soc Univ Comp; Wis Contemp Music Forum; ASCAP. *Mailing Add:* Univ Wis-Parkside Box 2000 Kenosha WI 53141

WEHNER, WALTER LEROY
EDUCATOR, COMPOSER

b Hazleton, Pa, Nov 30, 21. *Study:* US Navy Sch Music, dipl, 41; Wichita State Univ, BMus, 49, MMus, 50; Columbia Univ, prof dipl(music educ), 54; Univ Kans, EdD, 61. *Works:* Twenty Modern Duets, Southern Music Co, 72; Classic Quartet No 2, Belwin-Mills, 76; Three Pieces for Solo Oboe, perf by James Prodan, 82; Three Pieces for Solo Flute, perf by Neil Underwood, 83; Three Pieces for Solo Clarinet, perf by Raymond Gariglio, 83; Five Dances for Flute & Bassoon, perf by Milton Crotts & Neil Underwood, 83; Five Visions for Oboe & English Horn, perf by Kathryn Rafolowski & James Prodan, 83. *Rec Perf:* Wichita Symph Orch, CBS, 48-50; US Navy Band, NBC, 44-45. *Pos:* Solo clarinetist, Wichita Symph Orch, 47-52; cond, Phillips Univ Orch, 52-63. *Teaching:* Prof music, Phillips Univ, 52-63; chmn music dept, Midwestern Univ, 63-69; prof music & dir grad studies, Univ NC, Greensboro, 69- *Awards:* Prof of Yr, Hardin Found, Wichita Falls, Tex, 65; Citation, Tex Fine Arts Comn, 66. *Bibliog:* William H Stubbins (auth), The

Art of Clarinetistry, Ann Arbor Publ, 65; Paul R Farnsworth (auth), The Social Psychology of Music, Iowa State Univ Press, 69; James P O'Brien (auth), A Plea for Pop, Music Educr J, 3/82. *Mem:* Music Educr Nat Conf; NC Music Educr Asn; Southern Music Educr Nat Conf. *Publ:* Auth, The Effect of Interior Shape and Size of Clarinet Mouthpieces on Intonation and Tone Quality, 63 & The Relation Between Six Paintings by Paul Klee & Selected Musical Compositions, 66, J Res Music Educ; Basic Assumptions Concerning Faculty Evaluation, Proc Nat Asn Sch Music, 74; Humanism and the Aesthetic Experience in Music, 77 & Rythmic Sightsinging, 79, Univ Press Am. *Mailing Add:* 2904 Robinhood Ct Greensboro NC 27408

WEHR, DAVID AUGUST
CONDUCTOR, COMPOSER
b Mt Vernon, NY, Jan 21, 34. *Study:* Westminster Choir Col, with John Finley Williamson & Julius Herford, BM, 56, MM, 57; Univ Miami, with Frederick Fennell, PhD, 71. *Works:* God is Working His Purpose Out, Nat Publ, 59; Processional, Shawnee Publ, 62; Hymn of Consecration, J Fischer Publ, 63; Prophet Unwilling, Presser Publ, 63; Anything Happens, Hope Publ, 79; Bellstrations, Am Guild English Handbell Ringers, 82; Lord of All Being, Music 70, 82. *Rec Perf:* Messiah: A Complete Barque Rendition, Nat PBS Network, 12/25/82. *Pos:* Organist, choirmaster & Carillonneur, Cathedral Rockies, Boise, Idaho, 58-68; assoc cond, Houston Symph Chorale, 79-; artistic dir, Conct Chorale Houston, 81- *Teaching:* Prof & dir choral activ, Eastern Ky Univ, 71-79 & Houston Baptist Univ, 79- *Awards:* ASCAP Standard Awards, 66-; Westminster Choir Col Outstanding Alumnus, 66. *Mem:* Am Guild English Handbell Ringers (Ky chmn, 78-79); ASCAP; Am Choral Dir Asn; Music Educr Nat Conf; Nat Asn Teachers Singing. *Mailing Add:* 9615 Stroud Ave Houston TX 77036

WEICHLEIN, WILLIAM JESSET
EDUCATOR, BASSOON
b Springfield, Mo, May 9, 17. *Study:* Curtis Inst Music, 36-38; Univ Mich, Ann Arbor, BM, MM, PhD, 46-56. *Pos:* Bassoonist, Civic Orch Chicago, 34-36, prin bassoonist, 38-42; bassoonist, Staff Orch Radio Sta WGN, Chicago, 38-40 & 41-42 & Chicago Opera Co Orch, 40-41; prin bassoonist, Calcutta Symph, India, 45-46. *Teaching:* Prof musicol, Sch Music, Univ Mich, Ann Arbor, 52-82; prof libr sci, Univ Mich, 67-82. *Awards:* Citation, Music Libr Asn, 78. *Mem:* Music Libr Asn (pres, 64-65 & exec secy, 65-81); Int Asn Music Libr. *Interests:* Development of Italian opera, 1650-1750. *Publ:* Auth, An Alphabetical Index to the Solo Songs of Robert Schumann, Music Libr Asn, 67; A Check-list of Am Music Periodicals, 1850-1900, Info Coord, 70; Training for Music Librarianship, Fontes Artis Musicae, 71; The Music Library Association, In: Encycl Library & Information Science, 75. *Mailing Add:* 1309 Culver Rd Ann Arbor MI 48103

WEIDENARR, REYNOLD HENRY
COMPOSER, ELECTRONIC
b East Grand Rapids, Mich, Sept 25, 45. *Study:* Cleveland Inst Music, with Donald Erb, BMus(comp), 73; NY Univ, with Brian Fennelly, MA(comp), 80. *Works:* The Tinsel Chicken Coop, for Your Usual Magnetic Tape, 72, Wiener, Your Usual Magnetic Sequel, 74, Close Harmony, 79, Wavelines II: Three Visual-Musical Compositions, 79, Between the Motion and the Act Falls The Shadow, 81, Love of Line, of Light and Shadow: The Brooklyn Bridge, 82 & Night Flame Dancer, 83 Magnetic Music Publ Co. *Pos:* Ed, Electronic Music Rev, 67-69; coordr & dir, Electronic Music Studio, Cleveland Inst Music, 72-78. *Teaching:* Instr electronic music comp, Sch Educ, NY Univ, 79-, creative sound design, Inst Film & TV, Tisch Sch Arts, 81- & seminar in sound, 82- *Awards:* First Prize, Sonavera Int Tape Music Compt, 79; Silver Award, 13th Annual Fest Am, 80; comp fel, Nat Endowment for Arts, 82. *Bibliog:* Victor Ancona (auth), Reynold Weidenaar: Visual Counterpoints to Music, Videography, 3/81; Curtis Hammar (auth), New Electronic Music Innovative and Daring, Worcester Telegram, 2/7/82; Peter J Rabinowitz, Tape Music: Making It Accessible, High Fidelity, Musical Am, 6/82. *Mem:* Am Music Ctr; ASCAP; Am Soc Univ Comp (submissions coordr, 78-); Col Music Soc; Electro-Acoustic Music Asn Great Britain. *Interests:* Early electronic musical instruments, especially the telharmonium of Thaddeus Cahill. *Publ:* Auth, In Search of Visual Music, Independent, 6/83. *Mailing Add:* 5 Jones St Apt 4 New York NY 10014

WEIDENSAUL, JANE BENNETT
EDUCATOR, HARP
b Philadelphia, Pa, June 30, 35. *Study:* Juilliard Sch, BS(harp), 57; Rutgers Univ, MFA(perf), 70, PhD(musicol), 78. *Pos:* Ed in chief, Am Harp J, 79-; recitalist, various US cols & univ, formerly; adjudicator for numerous nat & int compt, currently; mem, Nat Screening Comt, Fulbright-Hays Grants, formerly. *Teaching:* Privately, 57-; fac mem harp, Pre-Col Div, Juilliard Sch, 69-78, Col Div, 75-78; fac mem, Col Div, Manhattan Sch Music, 67-, chmn doctoral studies, 82-; adj instr music hist, William Paterson Col, 74-75, asst prof, 75-82, assoc prof, 82- *Mem:* Am Harp Soc; Am Musicol Soc; Music Libr Asn. *Publ:* Bochsa: A Biographical Sketch, Am Harp J, 2/4/76; Early 16th Century Manuscripts at Piacenze: A Progress Report, Current Musicol, 16:41-48; Sonata in G Major: A Scholarly Performance Edition with Critical Commentary, 79 & Scientific Tuning: A Manual for Harpists, 79, Willow Hall Press; Louis Spohr's Works for Harp: A Bibliography, Am Harp J,8/3/82. *Mailing Add:* 1374 Academy Lane Teaneck NJ 07666

WEIDENSEE, VICTOR J
EDUCATOR, CLARINET
b Pierre, SDak, June 24, 23. *Study:* SDak State Univ, BS(music educ), 47; Denver Univ, MA(music), 48; Univ Ore, DrEd(music admin), 56. *Teaching:* Cond band, pub sch, Bayard, Nebr, 50-52; grad asst music lit, Univ Ore,

52-53; dir music, pub sch, Hood River, Ore, 54-55 & Bethel sch dist, Eugene, Ore, 55-57; chmn fine arts, Black Hills State Col, 58- *Mem:* Music Educ Nat Conf (pres SDak chap, four yrs); Nat Asn Wind & Perc Instr (chairperson NCent chap, two yrs); Music Teachers Nat Asn. *Publ:* Auth, Music in the Public High School, Crescendo, 69; numerous articles in Sch Musician, Music Educr Nat J, Music J, SDak Musician & Elem Sch Prin. *Mailing Add:* RR 3 Mt View Rd Spearfish SD 57783

WEILLE, F BLAIR
ADMINISTRATOR, COMPOSER
b Boston, Mass, Nov 9, 30. *Study:* Harvard Col, AB, 53; Columbia Univ, AM, 57; studied with Otto Luening & Jack Beeson. *Works:* Annabel Lee, Long Island Little Orch Soc, 80; So Many Ladies, High Tor Theater, Fitchburg, Mass, 81; Brass Quintet, Theodore Presser. *Pos:* Treas, CRI, 73-76, pres, 77-82, vchmn bd, 83- *Mem:* ASCAP. *Mailing Add:* 166 E 96th St New York NY 10128

WEINBERG, HENRY
EDUCATOR, COMPOSER
b Philadelphia, Pa, June 7, 31. *Study:* Univ Pa, BFA, 52; Princeton Univ, with Milton Babbitt & Roger Sessions, MFA, 61, PhD; studied with Luigi Dallapiccola. *Works:* Cello Sonata, 55; Vox in Ramo, 56; Sinfonia (chamber orch), 57; Five Haiku, 58; Two String Quartets, 59 & 60-64; Song Cycle, 60; Cantus Commemorabilis I (chamber ens), 66. *Teaching:* Fac mem, Univ Pa, 62-65; prof music, Queens Col, City Univ New York, 65- & Grad Ctr, 76- *Awards:* Naumberg Award; Brandeis Creative Arts Award; MacDowell Colony Fel. *Mailing Add:* 18 E 81 St #1C New York NY 10019

WEINBERGER, HENRY
EDUCATOR
Study: Brandeis Univ, BA; New England Consv, MM, studied with Victor Rosenbaum, Leonard Shure & John Moriarty. *Pos:* Vocal accmp & coach, Berkshire Music Ctr; soloist, Boston Symph Youth Concts Orch & Boston Pops. *Teaching:* Opera & vocal coach, Boston Consv, currently. *Mailing Add:* 322 Shawmut Ave Boston MA 02118

WEINER, LAWRENCE
COMPOSER, EDUCATOR
b Cleveland, Ohio, June 22, 32. *Study:* Univ Tex, Austin, with Kent Kennan, Clifton Williams & Paul Pisk, BM, MM(theory & comp); Ind Univ, with Juan Orrego-Salas; Univ Miami, with John Butler & Alfred Reed, DMA(theory, comp). *Works:* Prologos Synkretisomos (orch); Elegy (string orch); Quaternity (string orch); Commemoration Overture (orch), Corpus Christi, 74; Daedalic Symph (wind ens); Cataphonics (band); Shenandoah (chorus). *Teaching:* Music, San Antonio Pub Sch, 59-68; asst prof music, Tex A&I Univ, 68-74; assoc prof & comp in res, Corpus Christi State Univ, 74-, prof, currently. *Awards:* Carl Owens Comp Award, Univ Tex, 55; Ostwald Band Comp Award, 67. *Mailing Add:* Music Dept Corpus Christi State Univ Corpus Christi TX 78411

WEINER, MAX
VIOLIN
b Austria, Feb 15, 20. *Study:* Columbia Univ, BA. *Pos:* Performer, Detroit Symph, Chicago Symph Orch & Pittsburgh Symph, formerly; mem, New York Phil, 46- & Philharmonia Virtuosi NY. *Mailing Add:* 2811 215th St Bayside NY 11360

WEINER, RICHARD
PERCUSSION, TEACHER
Study: Temple Univ, with Charles Owen, BS; Aspen Fest Sch, summer 62; Ind Univ, studied perc with George Gaber, MMus, 63; John Marshall Law Sch, Cleveland State Univ, 76. *Rec Perf:* Works of Donald Erb. *Pos:* Mem, Cleveland Orch, 63-, prin perc, 68-; perc soloist, various chamber ens & Severance Hall subscription ser, 72. *Teaching:* Fac mem, Consv Music, Oberlin Col, Settlement Music Sch Philadelphia & Philadelphia Bd Educ, formerly; fac mem & dir, Perc Ens, Cleveland Inst Music, 63- *Mailing Add:* Cleveland Orch Severance Hall Cleveland OH 44106

WEINREB, ALICE KOGAN
FLUTE & PICCOLO, EDUCATOR
b Yonkers, NY. *Study:* Brandeis Univ, BA, 65; Ecole Normale Musique, Paris, artist's dipl, 66; Am Univ, MA, 76. *Pos:* Flutist, Capitol Woodwind Quintet, Washington, DC, 77- & Nat Musical Arts, 81-; piccolo, Richmond Symph, 78-79; second flute, Nat Symph Orch, 79- *Teaching:* Lectr flute, Am Univ, 77- *Awards:* Fulbright Fel, 65; First Prize Flute, Ecole Normale Musique, 66. *Mailing Add:* Nat Symph Orch JFK Ctr Perf Arts Washington DC 20566

WEINREBE, ROBERT SOLOMON
VIOLA
b Boston, Mass, Dec 11, 12. *Study:* Univ Minn, studied viola with D C Dounis & William Primrose, BA, 36. *Pos:* Violist, Pittsburgh Symph, 46-47, Little Orch Soc NY, 47-48 & New York Phil, 48- *Mailing Add:* New York Phil Avery Fisher Hall Broadway/65 New York NY 10023

WEIRICH, ROBERT
PIANO, EDUCATOR
b Massillon, Ohio, Feb 6, 50. *Study:* Consv Music, Oberlin Col, with Emil Danenberg, BMus, 72; Yale Univ, with Donald Currier & Claude Frank, MM, 76, DMA, 81. *Rec Perf:* Mestiere (Biscardi), CRI, 82. *Pos:* Conct pianist, 75-; accmp to Phyllis Curtin, 76-81; pianist, Regenstein Trio, 81- *Teaching:* Asst

prof piano, Tulane Univ, 77-79; assoc prof & dept chmn piano & chamber music, Northwestern Univ, 79- *Awards:* First prize, Portland, Maine Young Artists Compt, 76; Alumni Award, Yale Univ, 77; third prize, Rockefeller Found Intl Compt Am Music, 78. *Mem:* Music Teachers Nat Asn; Col Music Soc; Am Music Ctr; Am Liszt Soc. *Interests:* American music; piano technique. *Publ:* Auth, Zen and the Art of Piano Study, Fanfare Mag, Northwestern Univ, 82. *Mailing Add:* 1412 Hinman Ave Evanston IL 60201

WEISBERG, ARTHUR
EDUCATOR, BASSOON
Study: Juilliard Sch. *Pos:* Mem, Houston Symph, Baltimore Symph, Cleveland Orch & New York Woodwind Quintet, formerly; cond, Contemp Chamber Ens, currently. *Teaching:* Mem fac, Yale Sch Music, 79-, instr bassoon & comp, 81-, dir, Yale Contemp Ens, currently. *Awards:* Am Comp Alliance Award. *Mailing Add:* Yale Sch Music Box 2104A Yale Sta New Haven CT 06520

WEISGALL, HUGO
COMPOSER, CONDUCTOR
b Ivancice, Czechoslovakia, Oct 13, 12, US citizen. *Study:* Peabody Consv Music, with Louis Cheslock, 27-30; Curtis Inst Music, with Rosario Scalero, 36-39; Johns Hopkins, PhD, 40; studied comp with Roger Sessions; Peabody Consv Music, Hon Doctorate. *Works:* Translations (song cycle), 71; End of Summer (song cycle), 74; Song of Celebration (cantata for sop, ten, chorus & orch), 76; Jenny or the Hundred Nights (opera), 76; The Golden Peacock (song cycle), 76; Liebeslieder, 79; The Gardens of Adonis (opera), 81. *Pos:* Cond, Har Sinai Temple Choir, 31-42; Y-Alliance Orch, 35-42; Baltimore String Symph, 36-38, Md NYA Orch, 40-41; cult attache, Prague, 46-47; dir, Hilltop Music Co, 51-54; pres, Am Music Ctr, 64-73; assoc, Lincoln Ctr Fund, 65-68; guest cond, London Symph, London Phil, BBC Symph Orch, Orch Chapelle Musical Reine Elizabeth & Radio Nat Belge. *Teaching:* Instr comp, Cummington Sch Arts, 48-51 & Juilliard Sch Music, 57-69; dir, Baltimore Inst Music Arts, 49; distinguished prof comp, Queens Col, City Univ New York, 60-; distinguished vis prof, Pa State Univ, 59-60 & Peabody Inst, 74-75; comp in res, Am Acad Rome, 66-67; chmn fac, Sem Col Jewish Music, Jewish Theol Sem Am. *Awards:* Guggenheim Fel, 55-56, 61-62 & 66-67; Koussevitzky Comn, 61; Nat Endowment Arts Grant, 74 & 76. *Mem:* Nat Inst Arts & Lett. *Mailing Add:* 81 Maple Dr Great Neck NY 11021

WEISS, ABRAHAM M
BASSOON
b Monticello, NY, May 29, 49. *Study:* Curtis Inst Music, dipl, 70; Univ Calif, Los Angeles. *Rec Perf:* Weiss Family Woodwinds, Crystal Rec, 77. *Pos:* Prin bassoon, Rochester Phil, 70- *Mailing Add:* 24 Currewood Cir Rochester NY 14618

WEISS, DAVID E
OBOE, MUSICAL SAW
b New York, NY, Feb 8, 47. *Study:* Private oboe study with William Criss, 62-65 & Robert Bloom, 67-68. *Rec Perf:* Weiss Family Woodwinds, Crystal Rec, 79. *Pos:* Assoc prin oboe, Pittsburgh Symph, 69-71; prin oboe, Nat Symph, Washington, DC, 71-73 & Los Angeles Phil, 73- *Awards:* Prize Winner, Fest of Saws, Santa Cruz, CA, 82. *Mem:* Young Musicians Found (mem bd dir, 76-83). *Mailing Add:* 135 N Grand Ave Los Angeles CA 90012

WEISS, DAWN ADRIENNE
FLUTE, EDUCATOR
b Monticello, NY, July 11, 51. *Study:* Music Acad West, summers 68, 69 & 72; Univ Calif, Los Angeles, 69-72. *Pos:* Second flute, Miami Phil, 74-75; prin flute, Mex State Symph, Toluca, 75-76; Ore Symph Orch, 77-80, prin flute, 80-; conct soloist, Ore Symph Pops, Pasadena Symph & Debut Orch Young Musicians Found. *Teaching:* Instr flute, Lewis & Clark Col, Reed Col, Portland State Univ & Univ Portland. *Awards:* Frank Sinatra First Place Award, 70; Atwater Kent Grand Prize, 70. *Mem:* Am Fedn Musicians; Gtr Portland Flute Soc. *Mailing Add:* Ore Symph Orch 813 SW Alder Portland OR 97205

WEISS, ELIZABETH B
VIOLA, TEACHER
b Atlanta, Ga, Feb 7, 40. *Study:* La State Univ, BMus, 61. *Pos:* Prin violist, Baton Rouge Symph & Mobile Symph; mem, Atlanta Pops Orch, Chicago Chamber Orch, Rochester Phil Orch, 67- & Hartwell String Quartet, 75-78. *Teaching:* Mem fac, Eastern Music Fest, Greensboro, NC, 76- *Mailing Add:* 228 Castlebar Rd Rochester NY 14610

WEISS, HOWARD A
CONDUCTOR & MUSIC DIRECTOR, VIOLIN
b Chicago, Ill, Feb 6, 39. *Study:* Chicago Musical Col, Roosevelt Univ, BMus, 60, MMus, 66. *Rec Perf:* Elegy for Violin and Orchestra (Amram), RCA/Red Seal; Ten rec with Rochester Phil Youth Orch incl Franck Symph, Sibelius Symph No 1, Shostakovich Symph #5 & Dvorak Symph #9. *Pos:* Concertmaster, San Francisco Ballet Orch, 62, Chicago Chamber Orch, 62-70, Va Symph, 64, Rochester Phil Orch, 67- & Grand Teton Music Fest Sem, Wyo, 83; first violin, Cleveland Orch, 65-67; music dir & cond, Rochester Phil Youth Orch, 70-; leader, Hartwell String Quartet, 75-78; concertmaster & chmn violin dept, Eastern Music Fest, Greensboro, NC, 76-80; participant, Casals Fest, San Juan, PR, 75-80; soloist, Cleveland Orch, Rochester Phil, New Orleans Phil, Grant Park Symph, Chicago, Cincinnati Chamber Orch, Chicago Chamber Orch & Rochester Chamber Orch; played over 40 different concerti with orchestras. *Teaching:* Prof violin, Eastman Sch Music, 81- *Mailing Add:* 228 Castlebar Rd Rochester NY 14610

WEISS, JEANNE
PIANO
b Chicago, Ill. *Study:* With Rudolph Ganz & Mollie Margolies. *Rec Perf:* Sonatas for Violin and Piano (Elgar, Walton & Strauss); Double Concerto for Violin, Keyboard and Orchestra (Haydn). *Pos:* Performer, Gt Brit, France, Germany, Austria, Switzerland, Holland, Norway, Portugal, Yugoslavia & Israel; soloist, Chicago Symph, BBC Symph, Jerusalem Symph & Orch Nat l'Opera Monte Carlo. *Teaching:* Artist in res, Sch Music, DePaul Univ, 69-72. *Mailing Add:* Los Angeles Phil Orch 135 N Grand Ave Los Angeles CA 90012

WEISS, PIERO E
WRITER, EDUCATOR
b Trieste, Italy, Jan 26, 28. *Study:* Columbia Col, AB, 50; Columbia Univ, PhD(hist musicol), 70; studied piano with Isabelle Vengrova & Rudolf Serkin, comp with Karl Weigl & chamber music with Adolf Busch. *Rec Perf:* Carnaval (Schumann), 68, Miroirs (Ravel), Pour le piano (Debussy) & Deux Arabesque (Debussy), 61, Europäischer Phonoklub. *Teaching:* Lectr music hist, Columbia Univ, 64- *Mem:* Am Musicol Soc (coun rep, 82-84); Int Musicol Soc; Am Inst Verdi Studies. *Interests:* Eighteenth-Nineteenth century, 18th century Italian opera; aesthetics of opera; Verdi; Schubert. *Publ:* Ed, Letters of Composers Through Six Centuries, Chilton Book Co, 67; auth, Verdi and the Fusion of Genres, J Am Musicol Soc, 82; Metastasio, Aristotle, and the Opera Seria, J Musicol, 82; Venetian "Commedia Dell'Arte" Operas in the 18th Century, Musical Quart, 83; co-ed, Music of the Western World: A History in Documents, Schirmer Bks (in prep). *Mailing Add:* 180 Riverside Dr New York NY 10024

WEISS, SIDNEY
VIOLIN
b Chicago, Ill. *Study:* Violin with Joseph Gorner & Paul Stassevitch. *Rec Perf:* Sonatas for Violin and Piano (Elgar, Walton & Strauss); Double Concerto for Violin, Keyboard and Orchestra (Haydn). *Pos:* Mem, Cleveland Orch, 57-67; concertmaster, Chicago Symph, 67-72 & Orch Nat l'Opera Monte Carlo, 73-79; orch soloist & recitalist, Europe, 72-79; prin concertmaster & soloist, Los Angeles Phil, 79-; mem, Weiss Duo. *Mailing Add:* Los Angeles Phil Orch 135 N Grand Ave Los Angeles CA 90012

WEISSENBERG, ALEXIS
PIANO
b Sofia, Bulgaria, 1929. *Study:* Piano & comp with Pancho Viadiguerov; Juilliard Sch Music, with Olga Samarov. *Rec Perf:* Beethoven Concerti, 78; Brahms First Symphony; Mozart Concertos 9 & 21; rec with RCA & EMI. *Pos:* Soloist, Berlin Phil, New York Phil, Philadelphia Orch, Boston Symph, Orch Paris, Vienna Phil, La Scala & many others; performer, Ravinia, Blossom, Tanglewood & Salzburg Festivals. *Awards:* Winner, Int Leventritt Compt. *Mailing Add:* c/o Columbia Artists Mgt 165 W 57th St New York NY 10019

WELCH, ROBERT B
ADMINISTRATOR, CONDUCTOR & MUSIC DIRECTOR
b Fleming, Ky, Feb 20, 35. *Study:* Morehead State Univ, AB, 64, MA, 68; Univ Ky, DMA, 83. *Pos:* Cond, Asheville Symph, 76-82. *Teaching:* Instr, Va & Ky pub sch, 57-68; dir bands, Western Carolina Univ, 68-78; chmn, Div Fine Arts, Limestone Col, SC, 78- *Mailing Add:* Music Dept Limestone Col Gaffney SC 29340

WELCHER, DAN EDWARD
COMPOSER, CONDUCTOR
b Rochester, NY, Mar 2, 48. *Study:* Eastman Sch Music, BM(appl music), 69, perf cert, 69; Manhattan Sch Music, MM(comp), 72. *Works:* Flute Concerto, 74, & Concerto da Camera, 75, Elkan-Vogel Inc; Trio (violin, viloncello, piano), comn by Lee Luvisi, 76; Dervishes: Ritual Dance, Elkan-Vogel & Theodore Presser, 77; The Visions of Merlin, Theodore Presser, 80; Parita, Horn, Violin & Piano, comn by Michael & Leone Hatfield, 80; Brass Quintet, Medici, 83. *Pos:* Prin bassoonist, Louisville Orch, 72-78; prin bassoonist & asst cond, Austin Symph Orch, 79- *Teaching:* Asst prof theory, comp & bassoon, Univ Louisville, 72-78; fac mem bassoon & comp & artist, Aspen Music Fest, summers, 76-; assoc prof bassoon, esn & comp, Univ Tex, Austin, 78- *Awards:* Standard Awards, ASCAP, 74-; first prize comp cont, Am Rec Soc, 71. *Mem:* Am Fed Musicians; Col Music Soc; Tex Music Educr Asn; ASCAP. *Mailing Add:* 111 Franklin Blvd Austin TX 78751

WELIVER, E DELMER
LIBRARIAN, FRENCH HORN
b Crawfordsville, Ind, July 18, 39. *Study:* Ark State Univ, BME, 61; Univ Iowa, MA 66. *Pos:* Horn, US Army Band, Washington DC, 61-64; third horn, Quebec Symph Orch, 66-68; asst dir music libr, Interlochen Ctr Arts, Mich, 68-71, dir music libr, 71- *Mem:* Int Horn Soc; Am Fedn Musicians. *Mailing Add:* 4505 State Park Hwy Interlochen MI 49643

WELLER, JANIS FERGUSON
FLUTE, TEACHER
b Burbank, Calif, July 19, 50. *Study:* Private flute study with Roger Stevens & Carol Wincenc, 68-75; Luther Col, Decorah, Iowa, BA(music), 72; Univ Minn, MA(music hist), 75-78. *Rec Perf:* With Open Hands, Pastoral Arts Assoc NAm, 80. *Pos:* Freelance flutist, Young Audiences Inc, Childrens Theatre & St Paul Chamber Orch, 72-; fundraising mgr, Sylmar Chamber Ens, 76-; conct prod staff, Minn Comp Forum, 79- *Teaching:* Instr flute, Macalester Col, Golden Valley Col, Rymer Sch & private studio, 72-; teaching asst music hist & perf practice, Univ Minn, 76-78; fac mem, Baroque

Interpretation, Coe Summer Baroque Wkshp, Iowa, 79-80. *Awards:* Chamber Music Am Res Prog, Atlantic Richfield, 81 & 82; Twin Cities Mayors Pub Arts Award, 82; grant, Nat Endowment Arts, 82 & 83. *Bibliog:* Thomas Adolphson (auth), Two Chamber Music Cures, Twin City Reader, 2/81; D R Martin (auth), Chamber Music: Demanding Art Form, Minneapolis Tribune Sun, 4/24/82; Bill Parker (auth), Music in Minnesota, Minn Monthly, 1/83. *Mem:* Am Fedn Musicians; Chamber Music Am; Minn Comp Forum; Upper Midwest Flute Asn (mem, bd dir, 80-81). *Publ:* Auth, It's Sylmar Trio, Sun & Breeze, 78; The Sylmar Trio, Woodwind, Brass & Perc Mag, 80. *Mailing Add:* 4109-23rd Ave S Minneapolis MN 55407

WELLMAN, NANCY ROESCH
ADMINISTRATOR, ARTIST MANAGER & REPRESENTATIVE
b Glen Cove, NY, July 16, 45. *Study:* Univ Munich, 65-66; Am Univ, Washington, DC, BA, 67. *Pos:* Asst to dir, Choral Arts Soc Washington, 71-73; publicity asst, Washington Perf Arts Soc, 73-75; assoc dir, Young Concert Artists Inc, 75- *Mem:* New York Choral Soc (mem bd dir, 77-82, adv bd, 82-); Asn Col Univ & Community Arts Adminr; Int Soc Perf Arts Adminr; Nat Asn Perf Arts Mgr & Agts; Van Cliburn Int Piano Compt. *Publ:* Auth, Promotion of Serious Culture in the United States, Nat Asn Sch Music Ann J, 82-83. *Mailing Add:* Young Concert Artists Inc 250 W 57th St #921 New York NY 10019

WELLS, DAVID
CELLO, EDUCATOR
b Gary, Ind, July 16, 27. *Study:* Manhattan Sch Music, BM(violoncello), MM(violoncello), MMusEd, 52; studied with Diran Alexanian. *Rec Perf:* On CRI. *Pos:* Mem, Columbia Conct Trio, 54, Hartt Trio, formerly, Hartt String Quartet, formerly & Manhattan Trio, 70-; solo cellist, Am Chamber Orch, currently; founder & dir, Yellow Barn Chamber Music Sch & Fest, 80-; co-founder, Manhattan Chamber Music Ctrs, Henniker, NH & Oneonta, NY; soloist, conct tours in US & Europe. *Teaching:* Mem fac violoncello, Manhattan Sch Music, 51-; mem fac, YW-YMHA Sch Music, formerly, Mary Washington Col, Univ Va, formerly, Princeton Univ, formerly & Westminster Choir Col, formerly; vis prof violoncello, Hartt Sch Music, 62-68 & 74-; assoc prof music, Windham Col, 68-74. *Mailing Add:* Hartt Sch Music Univ Hartford West Hartford CT 06117

WELLS, PATRICIA
SOPRANO
b Ruston, La. *Study:* La Tech Univ, BMus, 63; Juilliard Sch Music, with Hans Heinz, 65-69. *Roles:* Mallika in Lakme, Shreveport Civic Opera, 63; Masha in The Seagull, Houston Grand Opera, 74; Alice Ford in Falstaff, Kennedy Ctr, 82; Donna Anna in Don Giovanni; Tatiana in Eugene Onegin; Marguerite in Faust; Rosalinde in Die Fledermaus. *Pos:* Singer with major opera co in Can, Holland & US; conct appearances with major US symph. *Awards:* First Prize, Munich Int Compt, 71. *Mem:* Am Guild Musical Artists; Actors Equity. *Mailing Add:* c/o Columbia Artists Mgt 165 W 57th St New York NY 10019

WELSH, WILMER HAYDEN
COMPOSER, ORGAN
b Cincinnati, Ohio, July 17, 32. *Study:* Johns Hopkins Univ, BSci, 53; Peabody Consv Music, artist dipl, 53, MMus, 55. *Works:* Joseph: An Oratorio in 3 Parts, Oratorio Singers of Charlotte, 64; Songs of Eve, Ilona Kombrink & Arthur Becknell, 68; Anthem: Ave Verum Corpus, Assoc Music Publ, 69; Jubilee: A Celebration for Organ, Augsburg, 71; Symph No 1 in E Flat, Charlotte Symph Orch, 73; Mosaic Portrait: Jonah, David Craighead, 78; Mosaic Portrait II: The Golden Calf for Sax Quartet, Narrator & Organ, The Southern Quartet, 82. *Teaching:* Asst prof music, Winthrop Col, 59-63; assoc prof music, Davidson Col, 63-72, prof, 72-, chmn music dept, 81- *Awards:* Thomas Jefferson Award, Robert Earl McConnell Found, 76. *Mem:* Am Guild Organists; Am Music Ctr; Col Music Soc. *Publ:* Auth, An Impromptu Recital, 76 & Mr Patchable of Charleston, 80, Diapson. *Mailing Add:* PO Box 356 Davidson NC 28036

WELWOOD, ARTHUR
COMPOSER, EDUCATOR
b Brookline, Mass, Feb 15, 34. *Study:* Boston Univ, with Hugo Norden & Gardner Read; Yale Univ, with Quincy Porter & Mel Powell. *Works:* Songs from the Chinese (tenor solo & chamber ens), 68; Earth Opera I (soloists, chorus, lights, dancers, found instrm & spontaneous creation), 69; My Father Moved Through Dooms of Love (masque for sop, chamber orch, chorus, slides, lights & dancers), 70; Manifestations V (masque for sop, 25 musicians, 50 dancers, poetry readers, tapes & audience), 71; Songs of War, Nature, and the Way (voice, chamber ens, perc, narrator, & five dancers), 72; Polyphonies of the 11th and 12th Centuries (sop, chorus, chamber orch & found perc), 72. *Teaching:* Vis instr, Univ Evansville, 63-64; assoc prof theory & analysis, comp & clarinet, Cent Conn State Col, 64- *Mailing Add:* 32 Cambridge St New Britain CT 06051

WENDEL, DALE
SOPRANO
b Cincinnati, Ohio, Nov 14, 52. *Study:* Calif Inst Arts, 70; Univ Southern Calif Opera Wkshp, 77-79. *Roles:* Josephine in HMS Pinafore, Stratford Fest, 81; Alexandra in Regina, Chautauqua Opera, 82; Musetta in La Boheme, 83 & Satirino in La Calisto, 83, Wolftrap Opera. *Pos:* Apprentice singer, Chautauqua Opera, 82; mem, Wolftrap Opera Co, 83. *Mem:* Actors Equity, US & Can; Am Guild Musical Artists. *Mailing Add:* 947 11th St Apt 2 Santa Monica CA 90403

WENDELBURG, NORMA RUTH
COMPOSER, PIANO
b Stafford, Kans, March 26, 18. *Study:* Bethany Col, BM, 43; Univ Mich, MM, 47; Eastman Sch Music, MM, 50, PhD, 69; Mozarteum, Salzburg, Austria, 53-54; Acad Music, Vienna, 54-55. *Works:* Toccata for Piano, Middlebury Comp Conf, 50; Andante and Allegro, Tanglewood Student Orch, 53; Concertino for Oboe and Strings, New York City Comp Forum, 58; String Quartet No 2, Fine Arts String Quartet, Univ Kans, 59; Prelude and Dance, Eastman-Rochester Orch, 67; Symphony I, Univ Houston Symph, 70. *Teaching:* Instr music, Wayne State Col, Nebr, 47-50; asst prof, Univ Northern Iowa, 56-58 & Hardin-Simmons Univ, 58-66; assoc prof, Southwest Tex State Univ, 69-72, chairperson, 69-72; chairperson piano, Dallas Baptist Col, 73-75. *Awards:* Fulbright Grant, 53-55 & 55-56; Huntington Hartford Found Fel, 58 & 61; MacDowell Colony Fel, 58, 60 & 70. *Mem:* Am Women Comp; ASCAP; Am Music Ctr. *Mailing Add:* Rte 1 Box 3A-2 Greensburg KS 67054

WENDELKEN-WILSON, CHARLES
CONDUCTOR & MUSIC DIRECTOR
b NJ. *Study:* Mannes Col Music. *Pos:* From asst cond to res cond, New York City Opera; asst cond, Boston Symph, formerly; music dir & cond, Dayton Phil Orch, 75-; guest cond, New York City Opera, Baltimore Opera, Philadelphia Lyr Opera, San Francisco Opera, Cincinnati Opera, Dayton Opera, Ft Lauderdale Symph & New Orleans Phil. *Mailing Add:* Herbert Barrett Mgt 1860 Broadway New York NY 10023

WENDER, PETER J
PATRON, BASS
b Springfield, Mass, Feb 28, 49. *Study:* Mass Inst Technol, SB, 71, SM, 72. *Roles:* Bass, Opera Co Boston Chorus, 70-72, Boston Conct Opera Chorus, 74-78 & Tanglewood Fest Chorus Boston Symph Orch, 75- *Pos:* Trustee, Opera Co Boston, 80- & Boston Conct Opera, 83- *Mailing Add:* 10 Dana St Cambridge MA 02138

WENNERSTROM, MARY HANNAH
EDUCATOR, WRITER
b Grand Rapids, Mich, Dec 12, 39. *Study:* Sch Music, Ind Univ, Bloomington, piano study with Bela Nagy & Menahem Pressler & comp study with Bernhard Helden, BM, 61, MM, 63, PhD, 67. *Works:* Emily Dickinson Songs, Am Univ, 61; Piano Sonata, perf by Mary Hannah Wennerstrom, 61; Veracini Violin Sonatas, Assoc Music Publ, 73; Music for Worship Services, Ind Music Ctr, 80. *Pos:* Chmn, Adv Placement Music Comt, 80- *Teaching:* Chmn & prof music theory, Ind Univ, Bloomington. *Mem:* Soc Music Theory (treas, 79-); Am Musicol Soc; Col Music Soc (theory bd mem, 80-82). *Publ:* Auth, Anthology of 20th-Century Music, 69 & coauth, Aspects of 20th-Century Music, 75, Prentice Hall; auth, Pitch Aspects of Berg's Songs Op 2, Ind Theory Rev, 78; Anthology of Musical Structure and Style, Prentice-Hall, 83. *Mailing Add:* 1410 Maxwell Lane Bloomington IN 47401

WENTZEL, RUBI V
CELLO, EDUCATOR
b Spillville, Iowa, Oct 19, 12. *Study:* Univ Mich, BM, 35; studied cello with Georges Miquelle. *Pos:* Cellist, San Diego Symph, 37-39, Dallas Symph, 44-47, New York City Ctr Opera, 66-67 & Am Ballet Theater, formerly; mgr orch & cellist, Royal Winnipeg Ballet of Can, formerly; prin cellist, Gtr Bridgeport Symph Orch, 67-82 & Conn Grand Opera Orch, 79-82; mgr & cellist, Conn String Quartet, 74- *Teaching:* Asst prof group strings, chamber music & music appreciation & dir music, Prep Div, Univ Bridgeport, 67-79; asst prof cello & chamber music & dir Shu-String Sch, Sacred Heart Univ, 79- *Mem:* Mu Phi Epsilon. *Mailing Add:* 80 Peddlers Dr Branford CT 06405

WERDER, RICHARD H
EDUCATOR, PIANO
b Williamsburg, Iowa, Dec 21, 19. *Study:* Morningside Col, BM, 42; Columbia Univ, MA, 47, EdD, 50. *Works:* Holiday Suites & Niagara, GIA Publ, 55; Suite Okefenokee, McLaughlin & Reilly Co, 58. *Rec Perf:* Piano Compositions of James Reistrup, Reistrup Arts Inc, 80. *Teaching:* Assoc prof, Cath Univ Am, 51-68; prof, Montgomery Col, 70- *Mem:* Nat Guild Piano Teachers (adjudicator, 50-); Music Teachers Nat Asn; Music Educr Nat Conf; Reistrup Arts Asn Inc (pres, 75-); Wash Co Arts Coun (pres, 80-82). *Publ:* Auth, The Ups & Downs of Piano Pedaling, Clavier, 78; Principles of Pianoforte Fingering, Am Music Teacher, 79; Ilan Vered-Pianist with Pizzazz, Clavier, 80; Metronome Use in Piano Teaching, Piano Quart, 80. *Mailing Add:* Music Dept Montgomery Col Rockville MD 20850

WERDESHEIM, GARY
EDUCATOR, PERCUSSION
b San Francisco, Calif, Jan 24, 41. *Study:* Calif State Univ, San Francisco, BA, 63, MA, 67; Juilliard Sch, with Saul Goodman, 67-70. *Works:* Many arrangements of classic comp for perc solo & ens, Pro Perc Press, 81- *Pos:* Timpanist, NJ Symph Orch, 69-71 & Stockholm Phil, 73-74. *Teaching:* Artist & fac mem, Aspen Music Fest, 69-71; fac mem, Juilliard Sch, 70; prof, Fla State Univ, 71-; vis prof, perc, Ind Univ, Bloomington, 76. *Mem:* Perc Arts Soc; Nat Asn Col Wind & Perc Instr. *Mailing Add:* Sch Music Fla State Univ Tallahassee FL 32306

WERLE, FLOYD EDWARDS
COMPOSER, MUSIC DIRECTOR
b Billings, Mont, May 8, 29. *Study:* Univ Mich, BMus. *Works:* Three Concertos for Trumpet, perf by Doc Severinsen, 65, 71 & 76; Concertino for

Three Brass, Bourne Co, 67; Symphony No 1 (Sinfonia Sacra), 71; Partita for Saxophones, perf by Annandale High Sch, 73; Concerto for Alto Sax Doubling Clarinet, perf by Cherry Hill Wind Symph, 74; Symphony No 3 (Sinfonia di Chiesa), perf by Kent State Univ, 78. *Pos:* Chief comp, US Air Force Band, 51-82; dir music, Faith United Methodist Church, Rockville, Md, 66- *Mem:* ASCAP; Am Theatre Organ Soc. *Mailing Add:* 5504 Aldrich Lane Springfield VA 22151

WERLING, ANITA EGGERT
EDUCATOR, ORGAN
b Ann Arbor, Mich, Feb 12, 40. *Study:* Concordia Teachers Col, River Forest, Ill, BS(educ), 61; Northwestern Univ, MMus, 63; Univ Mich, with Marilyn Mason, DMA, 72. *Rec Perf:* Anita Werling Playing The Triumvirate Organ, Rec Publ Co, 80. *Teaching:* Prof organ, Western Ill Univ, Macomb, 72- *Awards:* Winner, Gruenstein Nat Organ Playing Compt, Chicago Club Women Organists, 68. *Mem:* Am Guild Organists (subdean Galesburg chap, 80-82 & dean, 82-84); Chicago Club Women Organists. *Mailing Add:* 150 S Yorktown Rd Macomb IL 61455

WERNER, JOSEPH G
PIANO, TEACHER
b Paterson, NJ, Mar 3, 51. *Study:* Eastman Sch Music, BM & perf cert, 73, MM, 75. *Rec Perf:* Sonata for Two Pianos and Percussion (Bartok), Musical Heritage Soc, 76; Music for Two Pianos and Piano—Four Hands (Gottschalk), Vanguard, 76. *Pos:* Prin pianist, Rochester Phil Orch, 75- *Teaching:* Instr piano, Hochstein Mem Music Sch, 78- *Mailing Add:* 97 Beacon Hills Dr N Penfield NY 14526

WERNER, ROBERT JOSEPH
ADMINISTRATOR, EDUCATOR
b Lackawanna, NY, Feb 13, 32. *Study:* Northwestern Univ, BME, 53, MM, 54, PhD, 67. *Pos:* Dir, Contemp Music Proj, Washington, DC, 68-73. *Teaching:* Dir instrm music, Evanston Twp High Sch, Ill, 56-66; assoc prof music, State Univ NY, Binghamton, 66-68; dir Sch Music, Univ Ariz, 73- *Mem:* Col Music Soc (pres, 77-78); Int Soc Music Educ (vpres, 79-92); Nat Asn Sch Music; Music Educr Nat Conf. *Publ:* Ed, Comprehensive Musicianship, Music Educr Nat Conf, 71; Education of the Non-Professional, In: Dict Contemp Music, 71. *Mailing Add:* 5241 N Via Condesa Tucson AZ 85718

WERNICK, RICHARD
COMPOSER, CONDUCTOR
b Boston, Mass, Jan 16, 34. *Study:* Brandeis Univ, BA, 55; Mills Col, MA, 57. *Works:* Kaddish Requiem, 70, A Prayer for Jersualem, 71, Cadenzas & Variations III, 73, Visions of Terror and Wonder, 76, A Poison Tree, 79, Cello Concerto, 81 & Piano Sonata (1982), 83, Theodore Presser Co. *Rec Perf:* Madrigals (Crumb), AR-Deutsche Grammophon, 69; Tableaux (Rochberg), Vox Turnabout Rec, 70; Lux Aeterna (Crumb), Columbia Rec, 74. *Teaching:* Asst prof, State Univ New York, Buffalo, 64-65 & Univ Chicago, 65-68; prof music, Univ Pa, 68- *Awards:* Composition Award, Am Acad of Arts & Lett, 76; Guggenheim Award, 76; Pulitzer Prize, 77. *Mem:* Am Music Ctr (mem bd dir, 79-). *Mailing Add:* Univ Pa Music Dept 201 S 34th St Philadelphia PA 19104

WEST, CHARLES WAYNE
CLARINET, EDUCATOR
b Ft Collins, Colo, Sept 19, 49. *Study:* Univ Northern Colo, BA & BMus, 71; Univ Iowa, with Himie Voxman & R Marcellus, MFA, 73, DMA, 75. *Works:* Capricious Winds, Studio PR, 77. *Rec Perf:* Chamber Music from the University of Iowa, CRI, 74; Iowa Ear Music, Corn Pride, 75; 5 Duets (Dahl), & Duo Sonata (Schuller), Crystal, 83. *Pos:* Staff clarinetist, Ctr New Music, Univ Iowa, 71-74; prin clarinetist, El Paso Symph Orch, Tex, 74- & Nat Symph Peru, 80. *Teaching:* Instr woodwinds, Grinnell Col, 71-74; assoc prof woodwinds, NMex State Univ, 74-; Fulbright lectr clarinet, Nat Consv, Lima, Peru, 80. *Awards:* Fulbright Grant, Coun Int Exchange Scholars, 80. *Mem:* Nat Asn Col Wind & Perc Instr; Int Clarinet Soc; Fulbright Alumni Asn; Am Soc Univ Comp; Am Fedn Musicians. *Publ:* Auth, Controlling Reeds in Dry Climates, Instrumentalist, 76; The Development of Large Woodwind-String Chamber Ensembles, Woodwind World, 77; Large Ensembles for Saxophone & Strings since 1900, 77; A Clarinetist's Slide Guide, 77 & The Neglected Nonet, 81, Nat Asn Col Wind & Perc Instr J. *Mailing Add:* 3125 Risner Las Cruces NM 88001

WEST, JOHN CALVIN
BASS, EDUCATOR
b Cleveland, Ohio, Oct 25, 38. *Study:* Eastman Sch Music, 56-58; Curtis Inst Music, with Martial Singher, dipl, 62; studied with Beverly Johnson. *Roles:* Sarastro in Die Zauberflöte, San Francisco Spring Opera, 63; Rocco in Fidelio; Oroveso in Norma; Mephistopheles in Faust; Don Basilio in Il Barbiere di Siviglia; Baron Ochs in Der Rosenkavalier; Hunding in Die Walküre. *Pos:* Appearances with major opera co in US, Can & Mex; recitalist throughout US, Can & Europe; orch & oratorio performances with major orchs in US. *Teaching:* Mem fac, Theater Ctr, Juilliard Sch, 76-; private teacher voice, currently; teacher master classes. *Awards:* Winner, Munich Int Compt, 67. *Mem:* Nat Asn Teachers Singing; Winner, Tchaikovsky Int Compt, 70; Martha Baird Rockefeller Fund Music Grant, 70. *Mailing Add:* Juilliard Sch Lincoln Ctr New York NY 10023

WEST, JON FREDRIC (JOHN FREDRIC)
TENOR
b Dayton, Ohio, Mar 4, 52. *Study:* Bowling Green State Univ, BM, 74; Manhattan Sch Music, 74-75; Am Opera Ctr, Juilliard Sch, 77-78. *Roles:* Canio in Pagliacci, La Scala Opera, 84; Gabrielle in Simone Boccanegra, Scottish Opera, 80; Canio in Pagliacci, Houston Grand Opera, 82; Manrico in Il trovatore, Franfort Opera, 82; Valdemar in Guerre Lieder, Edinburgh Fest, 83 & New York Phil, 83; Calaf in Turandot, New York Opera, 83. *Pos:* Dramatic tenor, Columbia Artists Mgt Inc, 76- *Awards:* Liederkranz Found Award, 77; Nat Opera Inst Grant, 78; Opera Am, 78. *Mailing Add:* c/o Columbia Artists 165 W 57th St New York NY 10019

WEST, PHILIP
EDUCATOR, OBOE
Study: Col Consv Music, Cincinnati Univ, BM; Manhattan Sch Music, MM; studied oboe with Harold Gomberg & Marcel Dandois. *Pos:* Freelance performer, New York Phil, New York City Ballet Orch, Opera Symph of Air & Mostly Mozart Fest, formerly; Founder, Bloomingdale Chamber Ser; mem, Contemp Chamber Ens, Boehm Quartet, Fest Winds & New York Pro Musica, formerly; US State Dept tours, USSR, 63 & South Am, 64. *Teaching:* Mem fac, Mannes Col Music, 65-73 & Aspen Music Fest, 72-; assoc prof chamber music, Eastman Sch Music, 73-, dir, Inter Musica, currently. *Awards:* Fromm Fel, Berkshire Music Ctr, 63. *Mailing Add:* Eastman Sch Music 26 Gibbs St Rochester NY 14604

WEST, STEPHEN BRADFORD
BASS
b Syracuse, NY, July 7, 50. *Study:* Univ Colo, BM(perf), 73; Curtis Inst Music, opera dipl, 75 & 77. *Rec Perf:* Procession of the Nobles, excerpts from Boris Godunov, private label, 76; Barber of Seville, PBS, 79; Creation, PBS, 81; VII International Tchaikovsky Competition, Melodiya, 82. *Roles:* Riamondo in Lucia di Lammermoor, Opera Co Philadelphia, 77; Taddeo, Italian Girl in Algiers, San Francisco Spring Opera, 78; Don Basilio in The Barber of Seville, Long Beach Grand Opera & Music Acad West, 82; Requiem (Verdi), Edmonton Symph, 82; Beethoven's 9th Symphony, Montreal Symph, 82; Elijah, Community Arts Symph, Denver, 83; Rocco in Fidelio, Charlotte Opera Asn, 83. *Teaching:* Private voice instr, Univ San Diego, 81-82. *Awards:* Nat winner, WGN, Ill Opera Guild, 77; Martha Baird Rockefeller Fund for Music Recipient, 80; VII Int Tchaikovsky Compt Award, 82. *Rep:* Thea Dispeker Artists Rep 59 E 54th St New York NY 10022. *Mailing Add:* 1468 Missouri St Apt 6 San Diego CA 92109

WESTBROOK, JAMES EARL
EDUCATOR, CONDUCTOR
b Winfield, Ala, Nov, 19, 38. *Study:* Univ Southern Miss, BME, 61; Univ Miss, MM, 67; Univ Wis, Madison, DMA(flute), 74. *Rec Perf:* Harris Conducts Harris, 79 & 80 & Faeroe Island, 81, VC. *Teaching:* Instr, Miss Pub Sch, 60-68; instr & asst prof bands, Univ Wis, Stevens Point, 68-70; asst prof music, Ohio State Univ, 74-76; assoc prof music & cond wind ens & conct band, Univ Calif, Los Angeles, 76- *Mem:* Music Educr Nat Conf; Col Band Dir Nat Asn; Nat Flute Asn. *Publ:* Auth, Do Flute Players Ever Warm-Up?, 12/77, A Paradox: The Prestige of the Band is the Orchestra, 9/78 & Annual Review of Solos and Studies, 5/81, Instrumentalist. *Mailing Add:* Music Dept Univ Calif Los Angeles CA 90024

WESTENBURG, RICHARD
CONDUCTOR, EDUCATOR
b Minneapolis, Minn, Apr 26, 32. *Study:* Lawrence Univ, BMus, 54; Univ Minn, MA, 56; studied with Nadia Boulanger, Jean Langlais & Perre Cochereau, 59-60; Sch Sacred Music, Union Theol Sem, 60-66; Lawrence Univ, DFA, 80. *Pos:* Dir music, First Unitarian Church, Worcester, 60-62, Musica Sacra, New York, 68-; Collegiate Chorale, New York, 73-79; Cathedral St John the Divine, 74-; organist & choirmaster, Cent Presby Church, New York, 64-74; panelist, Nat Endowment Arts, 79-; guest cond, Aspen Fest Chamber Chorus, Blossom Fest Chorus, Am Symph Orch, Bach Choir Bethlehem, Orch State Univ NY, Purchase & Los Angeles Master Chorale & Sinfonia. *Teaching:* Instr organ & music lit, Univ Mont, 56-60; head choral dept, Juilliard Sch Music, 77- *Mem:* Am Choral Dir Asn; Am Guild Organists; Asn Prof Vocal Ens. *Mailing Add:* Juilliard Sch Lincoln Ctr New York NY 10023

WESTERGAARD, PETER TALBOT
COMPOSER, EDUCATOR
b Champaign, Ill, May 28, 31. *Study:* Harvard Univ, with Walter Piston, AB, 53; Princeton Univ, with Roger Sessions, MFA, 56; Aspen Music Sch, with Darius Milhaud; studied with Wolfgang Fortner. *Works:* Charivari (chamber opera), 53; The Plot Against the Giant (cantata), 56; Spring and Fall: To A Young Child (voice & piano), 60; Leda and the Swan (cantata), 61; Mr and Mrs Discobbolos (chamber opera), 65; Noises, Sounds, and Sweet Airs (chamber orch), 68; Tuckets and Sennets (band), 69. *Teaching:* Fulbright guest lectr, Staatliche Hochschule, Germany, 57-58; instr, Columbia Univ, 58-63, asst prof, 66; vis lectr, Princeton Univ, 66-67, assoc prof music, 68-71, prof music, 71-, chmn music dept, 74-78, cond, Princeton Univ Orch, 68-73, dir, Princeton Univ Opera Theatre, 70-; assoc prof, Amherst Col, 67-68. *Awards:* Francis Boote Prize, 53; John Knowles Paine Traveling Fel, 53-54; Guggenheim Fel, 64-65. *Mailing Add:* Music Dept Priceton Univ Princeton NJ Q8540

WESTERMANN, CLAYTON JACOB
CONDUCTOR, COMPOSER
b New York, NY, Oct 4, 31. *Study:* L'Ecole Monteux & Berkshire Music Ctr, studied with Charles Munch, 51-56; Yale Univ, BA, 53, BMus, 54, MMus, 55; Acad Music, Vienna, 58-59. *Pos:* Guest cond, Vienna Symph & Houston Symph, 60-77; music dir & cond, Suffolk Symph Orch, 62-75; cond, Spoleto Fest, Beethoven Fest, NY & Am Inst Musical Studies, Austria, 77- *Teaching:* Prof music, Hunter Col, City Col New York, 65- *Interests:* Manuscripts of Beethoven's fragments and sketches. *Mailing Add:* 68 Fairview St Huntington NY 11743

WESTNEY, WILLIAM (FRANK)
PIANO, EDUCATOR
b New York, NY, Feb 14, 47. *Study:* Queens Col, City Univ New York, BA, 68; Sch Music, Yale Univ, DMA, 76; study in Italy, 71-72; coaching with Claude Frank & Jacob Lateiner. *Rec Perf:* Three Moods & Piano Quintette (Leo Ornstein), CRI, 75; Piano Sonatas #1 & #3 (Carl Maria von Weber), Musical Heritage Soc, 83. *Teaching:* Browning artist in res & assoc prof piano, Tex Tech Univ, 78- *Awards:* Winner, Rassegna dei giovani interpreti, Radiotelevisione Ital, 72; Young Artist Winner, Piano Teachers Cong New York, 73; Silver Medal, Concours Int d'Execution Musicale, Geneva, 75. *Mem:* Col Music Soc; Music Teachers Nat Asn. *Publ:* Auth, Pianistic Bravura: Can It Be Taught?, Clavier, 80. *Rep:* Ira Liebermann 11 Riverside Dr New York NY 10023. *Mailing Add:* 4207 51st St Lubbock TX 79413

WESTOVER, WYNN EARL
TEACHER, VIOLIN
b Lincoln, Nebr, Feb 2. *Study:* Wesleyan Univ, BA, 50; Col Physicians & Surgeons, Columbia Univ, 50-54; Trinity Col, London, ATCL, 61, LTCL(perf), 63, LTCL(teaching), 63; Dominican Col, Calif, with Adolph Baller, 64-65; studied with Paul Douglas Freeman & Hans Leschke, 67-70. *Rec Perf:* Music at Port Costa, Wahlberg Studios, 72; Rainbow Music, Unity Rec, 75. *Roles:* The Page in Amahl and the Night Visitors, Community Music Ctr Opera, 69-71. *Pos:* Music dir & cond, John F Kennedy & Martin Luther King, Jr Mem Conct, San Francisco, 68-69, Chamber Music Series, San Francisco, 68-71 & Laetrile Conct, Port Costa, Calif, 71; gen mgr, Music from Bear Valley Summer Fest, Calif, 70-72. *Teaching:* Instr music theory & head dept theory & ear training, Community Music Ctr, San Francisco, 65-72; instr spec mental hearing, Col of Marin, 65-79 & Univ Calif, Berkeley, 66-69; head dept ear training, Family Light Music Sch, Calif, 74-79. *Awards:* Serv to Music Citation, Int Biographical Ctr, England, 76; Violin Perf Prize, Rome Fest Orch, Italy, 76 & 77. *Bibliog:* Maybelle Speckmann (auth), Training the Ear for Good Music, 9/11/65 & Maybelle Speckmann (auth), Breaking the Barriers Between Music and Listeners, 10/4/69, Marin Mag; R Cawley (auth) A Change of Position, Panorama Eagle, 10/28/79. *Mem:* Am Symph Orch League; Cond Guild. *Publ:* Auth, Violin Bowing Symbols, 65 & Mental Hearing & (Teaching Materials), 65, Shepherd's Crooke Publ; ed, Violin Technik, Kolitsch Publ, 66. *Mailing Add:* PO Box 895 Huntsville TX 77340

WESTPHAL, FREDERICK WILLIAM
EDUCATOR, CLARINET
b Walnut Ridge, Ark, Apr 25, 16. *Study:* Univ Ill, Urbana-Champaign, BS, 37, BM, 38; Eastman Sch Music, MM, 39, PhD, 48. *Teaching:* Asst prof music, Tex Women's Univ, 39-48; prof music, Calif State Univ, Sacramento, 48- *Mem:* Music Educr Nat Conf; Calif Music Educr Asn; Int Clarinet Soc; Nat Flute Asn; North Am Saxophone Alliance. *Publ:* Auth, Guide to Teaching Woodwinds, third ed, 80 & Woodwind Ensemble Method, fourth ed, 83, Wm C Brown Co; ed, College Level Texts in Music-58 titles, Wm C Brown Co, 58- *Mailing Add:* 201 Sandburg Dr Sacramento CA 95819

WETZEL, RICHARD DEAN
EDUCATOR, WRITER
b Pitman, Pa, Dec 27, 35. *Study:* Indiana Univ, Pa, BA(music), 57; Univ Pittsburgh, PhD(musicol), 70. *Works:* So Many Things Come in Pairs (sop, alto & piano), Quakerhill Enterprises, 82; Vignettes of a Fableland (suite for alto sax & piano), Southern Music, 83; Sonatina for Woodwind Quintet, Accura Music, 83. *Rec Perf:* American Communal Music of the 18th & 19th Centuries, Queen City Albums, 83. *Teaching:* Musicologist, Sch Music, Ohio Univ, 70- *Awards:* Res grant, Phi Mu Alpha Sinfonia, 72. *Mem:* Sonneck Soc. *Publ:* Auth, Frontier Musicians, Ohio Univ Press, 76; The Search for William Cumming Peters, In: Am Music, Vol 1 No 4, Univ Ill Press, 83. *Mailing Add:* PO Box 206 Chesterhill OH 43728

WETZLER, ROBERT PAUL
COMPOSER, PATRON
b Minneapolis, Minn, Jan 30, 32. *Study:* Thiel Col, Greenville, Pa, BA, 54; Luther-Northwestern Lutheran Sem, St Paul, MDiv, 57; Univ Minn. *Works:* Neebrit Suite (conct band), AMSI, 75; Te Deum (choir, brass & organ), Augsburg Publ House, 80; Festival Mass (choir, brass & organ), comn by Basilica of St Mary, Minneapolis, 81; Born Anew to Share (hymn & anthem), AMSI, 81; Lord, Make Me an Instrument of Thy Peace (choir, flute, oboe & clarinet), comn by Minn Comp Forum, 81; Three Songs of Innocence (choir, harp, oboe & violin), comn by Augsburg Col Chorale, 82; Fanfare, Fugue & Processional (brass & organ), AMSI, 83. *Pos:* Dir publ, AMSI Music Publ, Minneapolis, 60- *Awards:* Award, ASCAP, ann 67- *Bibliog:* Dale Wood (auth), Contemporary Composers—Robert Wetzler, In: J Church Music, Lutheran Church in Am, Fortress Press, 5/73. *Mem:* ASCAP; Minn Comp Forum; Am Choral Dir Asn. *Publ:* Coauth, Seasons and Symbols: A Handbook on the Church Year, Augsburg Publ, 62; Images of Faith, Concordia Publ, 63. *Mailing Add:* 2741 Pleasant Ave Minneapolis MN 55408

WEXLER, STANLEY A
BARITONE
b New York, NY, Mar 28, 48. *Study:* Columbia Col, BA, 70; Univ Wash, MEd, 71; Boston Univ, MMus, 74. *Roles:* Figaro in Le Nozze di Figaro, Western Opera Theater, 76; Don Giovanni in Don Giovanni, Kansas City Lyric Theater, 79; Colline in La Boheme, New York City Opera, 82; Alcindoro & Benoit, San Francisco Opera, 83. *Pos:* Apprentice artist, Santa Fe Opera, 72; apprentice, Wolf Trap Co, 73 & 74. *Awards:* Metropolitan Opera Western Region Fourth Place Winner, 77. *Mailing Add:* 1004 Sanchez St San Francisco CA 94114

WEYAND, CARLTON DAVIS
COMPOSER, PUBLISHER
b Buffalo, NY, Feb 19, 16. *Study:* Millard Fillmore Col, dipl, ˙37; Syracuse Univ, dipl, 39. *Works:* Prelude in C Minor (piano), 78, Meditation (piano), 78, Fantasy E Flat Minor, 78, Grave Piano Theme, 78, Nocturne Minor, 78 & Song for Piano, 78, Weyand Music Publ. *Rec Perf:* Selected Piano Compositions of Carlton Davis Weyand & Vocal Solos with Piano, DaCar Rec. *Pos:* Vocalist vaudeville & radio, New York, 26-37; guitar, piano & clarinet, dance band, Buffalo, 37-39; proprietor, Weyand Music Publ, Depew, NY, currently. *Mem:* ASCAP; Nat Music Publ Asn Inc. *Mailing Add:* Weyand Music Publ 297 Rehm Rd Depew NY 14043

WHALEY, GARWOOD PAUL
COMPOSER, EDUCATOR
b Dobbs Ferry, NY, Nov 21, 42. *Study:* Juilliard Sch Music, dipl, 65; Cath Univ Am, MM, 71, DMA, 77. *Works:* Essay for Snare Drum, Pro Art Publ, 72; Introduction and March, Kendor Music, Inc, 75; Recital Pieces for Marimba, 77, J R Publ; Ensemble Sessions, Heritage Music Press, 79; Recital Solos for Snare Drum, 79 & Audition Etudes, Meredith Music Publ, 83; Rounds, Canons and Catches for Band, Neil A Kjos Music Co, 83. *Rec Perf:* Various rec with US Army Band, 65-71. *Pos:* Pres, Meredith Music Publ, 79- *Teaching:* Cond wind ens, Bishop Ireton High Sch, Alexandria, Va, 71-; adj asst prof perc ens, Cath Univ Am, 74-78; vis prof perc, New England Consv, 80. *Awards:* Outstanding Secondary Educr Am Award, 74; Outstanding Nat Cath Bandmaster, 75. *Mem:* Percussive Arts Soc (mem bd dir, 75-77, educ ed, 83); Nat Band Dir Asn; Nat Cath Band Dir Asn; Music Educr Nat Conf; Va Band & Orch Dir Asn. *Publ:* Auth, The Symphony Wind Ensemble: Seating for Sound, Music Educr J, 76; Creative Instrument Music Projects, Instrumentalist, 78; Comparison of the Unit Study and Tradional Approaches for Teaching Music Through School Band Performance, J Res Music Educ, 79. *Mailing Add:* 6003 Ridge Ford Dr Burke VA 22015

WHALEY, ROBERT LOUIS
EDUCATOR, TUBA
b Gideon, Mo, May 16, 40. *Study:* Univ Kans, BME, 63; Univ Iowa, MM(perf), 66; study with John D Hill, William Bell & Arnold Jacobs. *Rec Perf:* Landscapes for Brass, 78 & Masques for Brass Quintet, 80, CRI. *Pos:* Tubist, Western Brass Quintet, 66-; prin tubist, Kalamazoo Symph, 66-; ed, Tubists Universal Brotherhood Asn, 75-77. *Teaching:* Prof tuba & euphonium cond, Western Mich Univ, 66- *Awards:* Tuba Recital Series Award, 20th Century Innovations, 76. *Mem:* Tubists Univ Brotherhood Asn; Am Fedn Musicians; Pi Kappa Lambda; Nat Asn Col Wind & Perc Instr; Music Educr Nat Conf. *Mailing Add:* 1822 Birchton Portage MI 49081

WHALLON, EVAN
CONDUCTOR & MUSIC DIRECTOR
b Akron, Ind. *Study:* Ind Univ; Eastman Sch Music, BM, 48, MM, 49; Hon Dr, Dennison Univ, 64, Otterbein Col, 70 & Ohio Dominican Univ, 66. *Pos:* Cond, Menotti, The Consul, 49; cond, music dir, Springfield Symph Orch, 50-56, Columbus Symph Orch, 56-82, Chautaugua Opera & San Francisco Opera's Western Opera Theater, 82- *Mem:* Cond Guild (mem bd, 81-83); Nat Opera Asn; Sigma Alpha Iota. *Rep:* Herbert Barrett Mgt 1860 Broadway New York NY 10023. *Mailing Add:* 2993 Shadywood Rd Columbus OH 43221

WHAPLES, MIRIAM K
EDUCATOR, MUSICOLOGIST
b Bridgeport, Conn, Dec 16, 29. *Study:* Ind Univ, Bloomington, AB, 50, studied piano with Bruno Eisner, MM, 54, studied musicol with Paul Nettl & Willi Apel, PhD, 58. *Teaching:* Instr, Western Md Col, 60-62, asst prof, 62-66; asst prof, Univ Mass, 66-72, assoc prof, 72-79, prof, 79- *Mem:* Am Musicol Soc; Int Musicol Soc. *Interests:* Schubert; 18th-19th century Viennese classicism. *Publ:* Auth, On Structural Integration in Schubert's Instrumental Works, Acta Musicol, 68; Bach Aria Index, Music Libr Asn, 71; Style in Schubert's Piano Music, 1817-1818, Music Rev, 74; Carmina Burana: 20 Songs from the Benediktbeuern and Florence Mass, Roger Dean, 75. *Mailing Add:* Dept Music & Dance Univ Mass Amherst MA 01003

WHEAR, PAUL WILLIAM
COMPOSER, EDUCATOR
b Auburn, Ind, Nov 13, 25. *Study:* DePauw Univ, BA, 48, MMus, 49; Boston Univ, with Gardner Read, 51-52; Western Reserve Univ, PhD, 61. *Works:* Catskill Legend Overture, Presser, 63; Psalms of Celebration, 67, The Seasons (oratorio), 68, Catharsis Suite, 69, Symphony No 3, 75, The Chief Justice (oratorio), 76 & Yorktown 1781, 83, Ludwig Music. *Pos:* Ed, Ludwig Music Publ Co, 70-; music dir & cond, Huntington Chamber Orch, 72- *Teaching:* Asst prof music, Mount Union Col, 52-60; prof & chmn music dept, Doane Col, 60-69; res comp, Marshall Univ, 69-; fac mem, Nat Music Camp, Interlochen, Mich, 69- *Awards:* First Prize Comp, Nat Sch Orch Asn, 63; Perf Awards, Nat Endowment Arts, 68 & 75; Norlin Fel, MacDowell Colony, 79. *Mem:* ASCAP; Am Soc Univ Comp (state chmn, 66-67). *Publ:* Auth, Requiem for the Marching Band, Instrumentalist, 62; The Composer-Teacher, Music J, 68. *Mailing Add:* 524 9th Ave Huntington WV 25701

WHEELER, BRUCE RAYMOND
TRUMPET

b Washington, DC, June 23, 45. *Study:* Juilliard Sch, BM, 68. *Pos:* Prin trumpet, Savannah Symph Orch, 71-; personnel mgr, 75- *Mem:* Int Trumpet Guild. *Mailing Add:* c/o Savannah Symph PO Box 9505 Savannah GA 31412

WHEELER, JANET
SOPRANO, EDUCATOR

b Boston, Mass. *Study:* Eastman Sch Music, BM, 50; New England Consv Music, MM, 52; Juilliard Sch; Harvard Univ; Manhattan Sch Music. *Rec Perf:* Solo Cantatas by Buxtehude, Urania, 61; The Psalms of David (Handel), Urania & Vox, 62; The Dettingen Te Deum (Handel), Amphion & Nonesuch, 62; Solo Cantata of the French Baroque Le Cafe (Bernier), Urania & Vox, 63; The Italian Cantatas of Handel, Counterpoint & Esoteric, 63; Angstwagen for Soprano and Percussion (Rolv Yttrehus), CRI, 83. *Teaching:* Assoc prof music, Bard Col, 65- *Mem:* Comp Guild NJ; Sigma Alpha Iota (pres, 79-81). *Mailing Add:* 83 Schoolhouse Ln East Brunswick NJ 08816

WHEELER, KIMBALL
MEZZO-SOPRANO

b Boston, Mass. *Study:* Bennington Col, BA; Calif Inst of Arts, MFA; Royal Consv Brussels; studied with Jan DeGaetani, Hans Hotter, Phyllis Curtin, Franco Iglesias & Alberta Masiello. *Rec Perf:* Latitude 15.09 N, Longitude 108.5 E, private rec, 70; The Red Mill (V Herbert), Vox-Turnabout, 79; Spanish Music of the Age of Exploration, Columbia Masterworks, 80; I Dream of Jeannie, Toshiba-EMI, 80; Cantata & others (Bruce Adolphe), Orion, 82; Hearing, Music of Ned Rorem, 83 & Duets for two female voices, 83, Gregg Smith Singers Label. *Roles:* Barbarina in Marriage of Figaro, Annapolis Opera, 77; Madwoman, Wolf Trap, 78; Mistress Bentson in Lakme, Opera Orch New York, 80; Maddalena in Rigoletto, Eastern Opera Theater, 80; solo roles in Oberon & Lord's Masque, Rome Opera & Teatro La Fenice, 81 & 82. *Pos:* Ms soloist, Gregg Smith Singers, New York, 78-79, Waverly Consort, New York, 79-81 & Roger Wagner Chorale, 79- *Awards:* Grant, Royal Consv Brussels, 75-76. *Mem:* Am Guild Musical Artists; Am Fedn TV & Rec Artists. *Rep:* Perrotta Mgt 211 W 56th St #18-M New York NY 10019. *Mailing Add:* 777 West End Ave #12A New York NY 10025

WHEELER, LAWRENCE BENNETT
VIOLA, EDUCATOR

b Rome, Ga, Apr 1, 49. *Study:* Acad Chigiana, Siena, Italy, with Bruno Giuranna, dipl, 69; Juilliard Sch, with William Lincer & Walter Trampler, BMus, 71. *Pos:* Co-prin viola, Minn Orch, 71-75; prin viola, Pittsburgh Symph, 75-77 & Tex Chamber Orch, 79- *Teaching:* Assoc prof viola & chamber music, Univ Houston, 77-; mem fac, Meadowmount String Summer Sch, 80- *Mem:* Tex Chamber Orch (mem bd dir, 82-). *Mailing Add:* 7400 Bellerive #201 Houston TX 77036

WHEELER, (WILLIAM) SCOTT
COMPOSER, MUSIC DIRECTOR

b Washington, DC, Feb 24, 52. *Study:* Amherst Col, BA, 73; New England Consv Music; Brandeis Univ, MFA, 78. *Works:* Peter Quince at the Clavier, comn & perf by Singers Ltd, Darien, Conn, 76; Grey Gardens, comn & perf by Dinosaur Annex Music Ens, Boston, 77; A Babe Is Born, Shawnee Press, 80; Trio Variations, 80 & Piano Trio, 82, perf by Dinosaur Annex Music Ens; Company Town (film score), 83; Portraits, comn by Virgil Thomson & Oshkosh Symph, 83. *Pos:* Music Dir, Cambridge Chorale, 76-78; artistic dir, Dinosaur Annex Music Ens, Boston, 76- *Teaching:* Asst prof music, Emerson Col, 78- *Mem:* Am Music Ctr; Col Music Soc; Nat Asn Comp USA; Am Choral Dir Asn. *Publ:* Coauth, Interview with Phyllis Curtin, Parnassus, 83. *Mailing Add:* 85 Marlborough St Boston MA 02116

WHEELOCK, DONALD FRANKLIN
COMPOSER, CONDUCTOR

b Stamford, Conn, June 17, 40. *Study:* Union Col, NY, AB, 62; Yale Sch Music, MMus, 66. *Works:* Celebrations, perf by Helen Boatwright with Rochester Symph, 79; Music for Seven Players, Boston Musica Viva, 82; Dreams Before A Sacrifice, perf by Milagro Vargas, 82; Glory, Mt Holyoke Col Choirs & Univ Mass Brass Choir, 83. *Teaching:* Asst prof music, Colgate Univ, 66-69 & Amherst Col, 69-74; assoc prof, Smith Col, 74. *Awards:* Guggenheim Found Fel, 74; Nat Endowment Arts Grant, 82. *Mem:* ASCAP; Col Music Soc. *Mailing Add:* 28 Mahan St Northampton MA 01060

WHIPPLE, R(ICHARD) JAMES
COMPOSER, BASSOON

b Philadelphia, Pa, Dec 1, 50. *Study:* Carnegie-Mellon Univ, BA, 72; Boston Univ, 72-74; studied bassoon with Mark Popkin, 80 & 83. *Works:* Antics (piccolo & bassoon), 66; La Demence (two clarinets), 68; Wedding Music for Kensington, 72; Concertino for an Autumn Mood, perf by Altoona Symph, Pa, 76; Terzetto (Holst arr), J W Chester, London, 78; Phrases from Last Summer, 82 & A Celebration Trio, 83, perf by Renaissance City Woodwind Quintet. *Rec Perf:* Ricercar (Perlongo), CRI, 80. *Pos:* Bassoonist & artistic dir, Renaissance City Woodwind Quintet, Pittsburgh, 75-; bassoonist, Pittsburgh New Music Ens, 76-80; prin bassoon, Pittsburgh Ballet Theatre Orch, 79-; second bassoon, Pittsburgh Opera Orch, 81- *Teaching:* Lectr & instr music theory, Carnegie-Mellon Univ, 75-; lectr theory & hist, Carlow Col, 77-; vis instr theory & bassoon, WVa Univ, 77-78. *Mem:* Am Music Ctr; Pittsburgh Alliance Comp (treas, 78-83); Int Double Reed Soc; Renaissance & Baroque Soc Pittsburgh (bd dir, 81-); Chamber Music Am. *Mailing Add:* 4339 Winterburn Ave Pittsburgh PA 15207

WHIPPLE, WALTER
EDUCATOR, ORGAN

b Logan, Utah, Dec 17, 43. *Study:* Brigham Young Univ, BA, 68; Univ Southern Calif, DMA, 72; studied with J J Keeler, Alexander Schreiner & Michael Radulescu. *Pos:* Mem cello sect, Rockford Symph Orch, 75-; organist & choirmaster, First Evangelical Lutheran Church, Rockford, 79-82 & Emmanuel Episcopal Church, Rockford, 83- *Teaching:* Chmn music dept & assoc prof music, Rockford Col, 74- *Awards:* Wakefield Organ Award, 68 & Gerrit de Jong Award, 69, Brigham Young Univ; Fel Viennese Study, United Europ Am Club, Los Angeles, 72. *Mem:* Am Guild Organists; Am Choral Dir Asn; Am Musicol Asn. *Publ:* Auth, Latter-Day Saints Hymns in German Translation, 74. *Mailing Add:* 323 Rome Ave Rockford IL 61107

WHISLER, BRUCE ALLEN
EDUCATOR

b Chicago, Ill, May 15, 43. *Study:* North Park Col, Chicago, BA, 66; Eastman Sch Music, PhD, 74. *Teaching:* Asst prof music hist, Univ Cent Fla, 71-80, assoc prof, 80- *Awards:* Summer Seminar Award Medieval Music, 75, Fel Col Teachers, 76-77 & Summer Seminar Award Beethoven, 81, Nat Endowment Humanities. *Interests:* Renaissance chanson; key relationships in Beethoven. *Mailing Add:* 822 Guthrie Ct Winter Park FL 32792

WHITCOMB, ROBERT BUTLER
EDUCATOR, COMPOSER

b Scipio, Ind, Dec 7, 21. *Study:* Col Music Cincinnati, with John Quincy Bass, Olga Conus & Felix Labunski, BMus(piano), 47, MMus(comp), 50; Eastman Sch Music, with Howard Hanson & Bernard Rogers, DMA(comp), 59. *Works:* Sonata in One Movement (oboe & piano), Interlochen Press, 62; The Mighty One (unaccmp SATB), Elkan-Vogal Co Inc, 62; Introduction and Dance (band), perf by Univ Ore Wind Ens, 65; May God Be Gracious (SATB & organ), World Libr Music, 69; Great is the Lord (unaccmp SATB), Assoc Music Publ, 74; The Quiet Place (orch), perf by Minneapolis Civic Orch, 75; Tonal Commentaries (piano, flute, oboe & bassoon), comn & perf by Sylmar Chamber Ens, 82. *Teaching:* Asst prof music, NMex State Univ, 52-53; assoc prof, SDak State Univ, 53-63 & Western Wash State Col, 63-68; prof music, Southwest State Univ, 68- *Awards:* Owen D Young Fel, Gen Electric Educ & Charitable Fund, 57-59; First Prize comp, Nat Asn Col Wind & Perc Instr, 62. *Mem:* Phi Mu Alpha Sinfonia; Music Teachers Nat Asn (pres Bellingham chap, 67-68); ASCAP; Col Music Soc. *Mailing Add:* 309 A St Marshall MN 56258

WHITE, A DUANE
EDUCATOR, CRITIC-WRITER

b Wytheville, Va, Nov 22, 39. *Study:* Radford Univ, summers 59 & 60; Bob Jones Univ, BS(music educ), 61, MA(piano), 63; Univ Wis, Madison, with Eva Badura-Skoda, Milos Velimirovic, Bruce Benward & Gwynn McPeek, PhD(musicol), 71. *Works:* Elegy for Piano, 71; Toccata Tetrachordium, 71; Dorian Dance, 71; Two Little Songs, 71; Suite for Flute and Piano, 71; incidental music to The Winter's Tale (Shakespeare), perf by Bob Jones Univ Orch, 66. *Pos:* Music critic, Greenville News, SC, 76- *Teaching:* Grad asst, Bob Jones Univ, 61-63; fac mem, 63-, head, Dept Music Hist & Lit, 76-; teaching asst, Univ Wis, Madison, 67-71. *Awards:* Ford Found Fel, 68-69; grant, Nat Endowment Humanities, 78. *Mem:* Am Musicol Soc; Music Teachers Nat Asn; SC Music Teachers Asn; Greenville Music Teachers Asn (vpres, 83-84); Hymn Soc Am. *Publ:* Auth, Extending Boundaries, Am Music Teacher, 69; Anton Eberl, In: New Grove Dict of Music & Musicians, 80; Paul Creston: Italian by Birth, American by Heritage, 82, Cosmopolitan by Choice, 82 & Vienna, City of My Dreams, 83, Music Clubs Mag; The Piano Sonatas of Anton Eberl, A-R Ed, Inc, (in prep). *Mailing Add:* 20 Prof's Pl Greenville SC 29609

WHITE, (EDWIN) CHAPPELL
EDUCATOR, CRITIC-WRITER

b Atlanta, Ga, Sept 16, 20. *Study:* Emory Univ, BA, 40; Westminster Choir Col, BM, 47; Princeton Univ, PhD, 57. *Pos:* Violist, Atlanta Symph Orch, 51-56; music critic, Atlanta J, 59-71. *Teaching:* Assoc prof music hist, Emory Univ, 52-74; vis prof, Ind Univ, 72-73; prof, Kans State Univ, 74- *Awards:* Col Teacher Res Fel, Nat Endowment for Humanities, 82-83. *Mem:* Col Music Soc (mem coun, 75-78, pres, 79-80); Am Musicol Soc. *Interests:* Violin concertos and other works of G B Viotti; history of early classical violin concerto. *Publ:* Auth, Introduction to the Life & Works of Richard Wagner, Prentice-Hall, 67; The Violin Concertos of Giornovichi, Musical Quart, 72; ed, Four Concertos by G B Viotti (with intro & notes), 2 vols, A-R Ed, 76; auth, 15 entries on Italian violinists, In: New Grove Dict of Music & Musicians, Macmillan, 78; A Thematic Catalogue of the Works of G B Viotti, Pendragon Press, 83. *Mailing Add:* 500 Wickham Rd Manhattan KS 66502

WHITE, DAVID ASHLEY
EDUCATOR, COMPOSER

b San Antonio, Tex, Dec 11, 44. *Study:* Del Mar Col, Tex, AA, 65; Univ Houston, BM(oboe), 68, MM(comp), 74; Univ Tex, Austin, DMA(comp), 78. *Works:* Night Cries (organ), comn by David Lowry, 81; Homages (mezzo-soprano & chamber music), comn by Tex Chamber Orch, 81; Fanfare & Dance for Spoleto (brass quintet & perc), comn by Piccolo Spoleto, 81; A Festival Triptych (brass quintet & band), Va All-Col Band, 82; Elegy and Exaltation (violin, cello & piano), Mirecourt Trio, Grinnell Col, 82; Homages (mezzo-soprano, viola & piano), Diane Kesling, Larry Wheeler, Ruth Tomfohrde, 83; Great Is the Lord (SATB & organ), Hinshaw, 83. *Teaching:* Lectr theory & comp, Univ Houston, 75-77, instr, 77-78, asst prof, 78-83, assoc prof, 83- *Awards:* ASCAP Standard Award, 80-; First Prize, Symposium VII for New Band Music, 82. *Mem:* ASCAP; Am Soc Univ Comp; Tex Comp Guild; Asn Anglican Musicians. *Mailing Add:* Sch Music Univ Houston Univ Park Campus Houston TX 77004

WHITE, DONALD HOWARD
COMPOSER, EDUCATOR

b Narberth, Pa, Feb 28, 21. *Study:* Temple Univ, BS(music educ), 42; Eastman Sch Music, MM(comp), 47, PhD(comp), 52. *Works:* Miniature Set (band), Shawnee Press, Inc, 58; Trombone Sonata, Southern Music Co, 67; Patterns (band), Ludwig Music Publ Co, 68; Lyric Suite (euphonium), G Schirmer, 72; Tetra Ergon (bass trombone), Brass Press, 75; Tuba Sonata, Ludwig Music Publ Co, 79; Sonnet (band), Shawnee Press, Inc, 79. *Teaching:* Prof theory, comp & lit, Sch Music, DePauw Univ, 47-81, dir, 74-79; prof theory, comp & lit, Cent Wash Univ, 81-, chmn, Music Dept, 81- *Awards:* ASCAP Special Awards, 66- *Bibliog:* Ronald Jay Toering (auth), The Trumpet Sonata of Donald H White ..., Univ Cincinnati, 81; Robert P Mullen (auth), The Solo Brass Literature of Donald H White, NTex State Univ, 82. *Mem:* Wash Col Music Coun (chmn, 83-); ASCAP; Music Educr Nat Conf; Wash Music Educr Asn. *Mailing Add:* Music Dept Cent Wash Univ Ellensburg WA 98926

WHITE, DUANE CRAIG
VIOLIN

b Seattle, Wash, June 29, 47. *Study:* Univ Wash, Seattle, BA(music educ), 69; studied with Emanuel Zetlin & Stanley Chappel. *Pos:* Concertmaster, Univ Wash Conct Orch, 65; prin violin, Univ Wash Symph, 67-69; asst prin violin, Spokane Symph, 69-70; second violin, Honolulu Symph, 70-74 & 77-, Siegerland Orch & Cologne Opera, 76-77. *Awards:* William O Just Award, Seattle, 65. *Mem:* Am Fed Musicians; Int Cong Symph & Opera Musicians. *Mailing Add:* 1249-G Matlock Ave Honolulu HI 96814

WHITE, ELWOOD LAURISTON
FRENCH HORN, LIBRARIAN

b Rome, Ga. *Study:* Ga State Univ, BA, 70; Univ Ga, MA, 74; Emory Univ, MLn, 75; studied with Joseph A White, Robert Johnson & Michael Hoeltzel. *Pos:* Prin horn, Am Ballet Theater, 67-69 & Atlanta Opera Orch, 80-82; asst prin horn, Atlanta Symph Orch, 69-71; third horn, Peninsula Music Fest, Fish Creek, Wis, 71; second horn, Atlanta Chamber Orch, 77-80; horn, Southern Brass Quintet, 82- & Southwind Woodwind Quintet, 82- *Teaching:* Instr French horn, Univ Ga, 71-72 & Columbus Col, 82- *Awards:* Musicianship Awards, 57 & 58 & Phi Mu Alpha Sinfonia Musicianship Award, 58, Fla State Univ. *Mailing Add:* Dept Music Columbus Col Algonquin Dr Columbus GA 31907

WHITE, GARY C(HARLES)
COMPOSER, EDUCATOR

b Winfield, Kans, May 27, 37. *Study:* Univ Kans, BME, 59, BMus, 61, MMus, 64; Mich State Univ, PhD, 69. *Works:* Composition for Piano, Brass and Percussion, Seesaw, 70; Rotation for Carillon, Donamus, Holland, 71; Chronovisions for Band, Ludwig Music Publ, 79; Homage for Band, Barnhouse, 80; Convolutions for Clarinet Choir, Kendor, 80; Night Images for Chorus, Ludwig Music Publ, 81; Personnae for Viola, Cello and Percussion, Perc Plus, 82. *Teaching:* Prof & head comp, Iowa State Univ, 67- *Awards:* Toon van Balkon Prize, 75; MacDowell Colony Fel, 75; ASCAP Standard Awards, 75- *Mem:* ASCAP; Am Soc Univ Comp (region V co-chmn, 83); Am Music Ctr. *Mailing Add:* 540 Meadow Ct Ames IA 50010

WHITE, JOHN D
COMPOSER, CELLO

b Rochester, Minn, Nov 28, 31. *Study:* Univ Minn, studied cello with Lorne Munroe & Robert Jamieson & comp with Paul Fetler & Earl George, BA, 53; Eastman Sch Music, studied cello with Gabor Rejto, Georges Miquelle & Ronald Leonard & comp with Bernard Rogers & Howard Hanson, MA(comp), 54, PhD(comp) & perf cert, 60; studied with Nadia Boulanger & Ross Lee Finney. *Works:* Symphony No Two, Fleisher Collection, 60; He Dawns Upon Us (mixed chorus), Lawson Gould, 62; The Legend of Sleepy Hollow (three act opera), comn by Kent State Univ, 62; Variations for Clarinet and Piano, Galaxy, 71; Three Madrigals for Chorus and Orchestra (vocal score), G Schirmer, 72; Music for Oriana (violin, cello & piano), Trio Int Comp Compt, Univ Wis, Oriana, 79; Zodiac (mixed voices & piano), G Schirmer, 83. *Pos:* Prin cellist, Seventh Army Symph, 55-56 & Eastman Phil, 59. *Teaching:* Prof music, Kent State Univ, 58-60 & 60-63, assoc grad dean, 65-73; asst prof theory, Univ Mich, 63-65; dean, Sch Music, Ithaca Col, 73-75; vis prof theory, Univ Wis, Madison, 75-78; chmn music dept, Whitman Col, 78-80; prof music, Univ Fla, Gainesville, 80- *Awards:* First Prize Comp, Rochester Religious Arts Fest, 61; ASCAP Standard Awards, 64-83; First Prize, Oriana Trio Int Comp Compt, Univ Wis, 79. *Mem:* ASCAP; Cleveland Comp Guild (pres, 69-71); Am Fedn Musicians; Soc Music Theory; Col Music Soc. *Interests:* Analysis of music, particularly relating to integration of the elements of music; cognitive work in pedagogy of theory. *Publ:* Coauth (with Albert Cohen), Anthology of Music for Analysis, Appleton Century Crofts, 65; auth, Understanding and Enjoying Music, Dodd-Mead, 68 & Japan UNI, 78; Music in Western Culture, W C Brown, 72; The Analysis of Music, Prentice-Hall, 76; Guidelines for College Teaching of Music Theory, Scarecrow, 81. *Mailing Add:* 5715 NW 62nd Ct Gainesville FL 32606

WHITE, JOHN REEVES
EDUCATOR, MUSICOLOGIST

b Houston, Miss, May 2, 24. *Study:* Colo Col, AB, 47, AM, 48; Ind Univ, PhD, 52; Colo Col, Hon DHL, 69, Hon DNP, 74. *Pos:* Musical dir, New York Pro Musica, 66-70. *Teaching:* From instr to asst prof music, Colo Col, 47-52; from assoc prof to prof, Univ Richmond, 53-61; prof musicol, Ind Univ, 61-66, prof & chmn music dept, 70-71; vis distinguished prof, Ripon Col, 70; prof music, Hunter Col, 71- *Awards:* Sr Fel, Am Coun Learned Soc, 52-53. *Interests:* Fourteenth century music; music of recent times; peformance of Medieval and Renaissance music; vocalization of marine mammals. *Publ:*

Coauth, The Arts Between the Wars, a Symposium, Randolph-Macon Col, 64; Eine Kleine Kleemusik, Va Music Fine Arts Ann, 64; auth, The Keyboard Tablature of Johannes of Lublin (six vol), Am Inst Musicol, 64-67; Francois Dandrieu, Harpsichord Music, Pa State Univ, 65; Michelangelo Rossi, Complete Keyboard Works, In: Corpus of Early Keyboard Music, Am Inst Musicol, 66. *Mailing Add:* 201 E 69th St Apt 11-U New York NY 10021

WHITE, MICHAEL
COMPOSER, EDUCATOR

b Chicago, Ill. *Study:* Consv Music, Oberlin Col; Juilliard Sch, BS, MS. *Works:* The Dybbuk, Seattle Opera Co, 63; The Metamorphosis, comn by William Penn Found, 68; Three Elizabethan Songs, Collegiate Chorale, 68; The Cynic's Passion, Philadelphia Oratorio Choir, 73; From the Diary of Anne Frank, Seattle Orch, 73; Concerto for Violin, Concerto Soloists Philadelphia, 79. *Teaching:* Chmn, Dept Lit & Materials Music, Juilliard Sch, 70. *Awards:* Fels, Ford Found, 59-61 & Guggenheim Found, 63-64; grant, Arts Coun Pa, 76. *Mem:* ASCAP. *Mailing Add:* Juilliard Sch Lincoln Ctr New York NY 10023

WHITE, ROBERT CHARLES, JR
EDUCATOR, BARITONE

b Trenton, NJ, Nov 2, 36. *Study:* Susquehanna Univ, BS, 58; Columbia Univ, MA, 63, EdD, 68. *Teaching:* Instr, Teachers Col, Columbia Univ, 65-68; assoc prof, Aaron Copland Sch Music, Queens Col, City Univ New York, 66- *Mem:* Nat Asn Teachers Singing (mem bd dir New York chap, 77-); New York Singing Teachers Asn (mem bd dir, 78-); NY State Music Teachers Asn (voice chmn, 75-82); Am Choral Dir Asn; Am Asn Univ Prof. *Publ:* Auth, Renaissance Music, Sch Music News, 75; Stop Voice Abuse, 76 & School Musicals without Voice Abuse, 78, Music Educr J; Overture to Opera, 79 & A Guide to Aida, 79, Metropolitan Opera Guild. *Mailing Add:* 600 W 116th St New York NY 10027

WHITE, RUTH S
COMPOSER, ELECTRONIC

Study: Carnegie Tech, Carnegie-Mellon Univ, with Nicolai Lopatnikoff, BFA(piano & comp), 48; MFA(comp), 49; studied comp with George Antheil, 51-53. *Works:* Music for Children and for Dance (40 albums), Tom Thumb Rec, 55-83; Pinions, 66, Seven Trumps from the Tarot Cards, 67 & Flowers of Evil, 69, Mercury Rec; Short Circuits, Angel Rec, 70; Capture the Sun, Rueben H Fleet Space Theater, 71; Mr Windbag Multi-Media Series (six prog), Westinghouse Learning Corp, 72. *Awards:* First Prize Comp, Nat Soc Arts & Lett, 51; First Prize, Atlanta Film Fest, 71; Notable Rec, Am Libr Asn, 83. *Bibliog:* Ruchard Nusser (auth), Toward a New Consciousness: Ruth White and the Electronic Tarot, After Dark, 11/68; K Monson (auth), Intellectual Mystic Composer, Los Angeles Herald Examr, 9/21/69; M Peterson (auth), Electronic Composer Ruth White, Los Angeles Times, 2/14/71. *Mem:* Nat Acad Rec Arts & Sci (bd gov, Los Angeles & nat trustee, 69-77); ASCAP; Nat Asn Comp (bd dir, Los Angeles, 74-76); Music Educr Nat Conf; Am Fedn Musicians. *Mailing Add:* Whitney Bldg Box 34485 Los Angeles CA 90034

WHITE, TERRANCE E
COMPOSER, TEACHER

b Portsmouth, Va, May 30, 53. *Study:* Berklee Col Music, BM(comp), 75; Univ NH, MS(music educ), 79. *Works:* Quartet for Woodwinds, 74 & Three Etudes for Brass, 74, Seesaw Music Corp; April Fool Symph, 79 & Heritage 350, 82, perf by Portland Symph Orch. *Pos:* Comp & arr, Portland Symph Orch, 79- *Teaching:* Instr instrm music, Westbrook Sch Dept, Maine, 75-79, dir music, 79- *Mem:* Am Fedn Musicians; ASCAP; Nat Asn Jazz Educr; Nat Band Asn; Maine Band Dir Asn (vpres, 81-). *Mailing Add:* 82 Oak St Westbrook ME 04092

WHITECOTTON, SHIRLEY E
COMPOSER

b Aurora, Ill, Sept 23, 35. *Study:* Wheaton Col, studied comp with Jack Goode, BMus(voice); Aspen Music Sch; Northwestern Univ. *Works:* To Live Beautifully, Somerset Press, 76; Two Spring Madrigals, Galaxy Music Corp, 78; Like As The Thrush in Winter, Roger Dean Publ Co, 80; Flow Not So Fast Ye Fountains, 81, Aftermath, 81 & Unheard, 82, Shawnee Press; The Bethlehem Inkeepers Speach, Curtis Music Press, 82; Flowers, Kjos, 83. *Teaching:* Private singing, 60-73. *Mailing Add:* 408 W Jefferson Wheaton IL 60187

WHITEHEAD, WILLIAM JOHN
ORGAN, MUSIC DIRECTOR

b Hobbs, NMex, June 30, 38. *Study:* Univ Okla, BMus, 59; Curtis Inst Music, artist dipl, 62; Columbia Univ, MA, 70. *Works:* Sensible Solutions, Triune Music, 76; Away in a Manger, Cantus Press, 78. *Rec Perf:* The Organ of the Philadelphia Academy of Music, Vol I, 62, Vol II, 63, Cameo/Parkway; Mendelssohn's Bach Recital, Bethlehem Bach Fest Rec, 70; Sing Out for the Season, Triangle Rec, 78. *Pos:* Dir music, First Presby Church, Bethlehem, Pa, 61-73 & Fifth Ave Presby Church, New York, 73-; pres, Whitmusic Inc, 82- *Teaching:* Prof organ, Westminster Choir Col, 66-71, Mannes Col Music, 75- & NY Sch Liturgical Music, 79-; organist in res, Union Theol Sem, NY, 81- *Awards:* Young Artist Award, Philadelphia Orch, 62. *Mem:* Am Guild Organists; Presby Asn Musicians; Hymn Soc Am, Choristers Guild. *Rep:* Roberta Bailey Artists Int 25 Walnut St Boston MA 02108. *Mailing Add:* 7 W 55th St New York NY 10019

WHITENER, SCOTT
CONDUCTOR, TRUMPET
b Washington, DC, July 17, 40. *Study:* Juilliard Sch, dipl, 62; Univ Mich, MMus, 66; Rutgers Univ, EdD, 74. *Pos:* Asst prin trumpet, New Orleans Symph, 62-64; cond, Rutgers Wind Ens & Rutgers Collegium Musicum, 66- *Teaching:* Assoc prof music, Rutgers Univ, 66- *Mem:* Col Band Dir Nat Asn; Int Horn Soc. *Mailing Add:* Music Bldg Douglass Campus Rutgers Univ New Brunswick NJ 08903

WHITESIDES, WILLIAM (PLAXICO), JR
EDUCATOR, TENOR
b Columbus, NC, Sept 22, 29. *Study:* Davidson Col, BS, 51; Univ NC, Chapel Hill, MA, 54; Juilliard Sch Music, 58-60. *Rec Perf:* Il Ritorno d'Ulisse (Monteverdi), Vox, 64; Ronsard Sonnets (Lennox Berkeley), Louisville Orch, 65; Psalmus Hungaricus (Kodaly), 70-71 & St Nicholas (Britten), 70-71, Ohio State Univ; Early Medieval Music, Part II, Pleiades, 78. *Roles:* Sextus in Julius Caesar, Theater Stadt Bonn, Germany, 62; Don Ottavio in Don Giovanni, Stadt Theater Bern, Switzerland, 63; Ferrando in Cosi fan tutte, Ky Opera Asn, 64; Alfredo in La Traviata, Santa Fe Opera, 65; Almaviva in Barber of Seville, San Francisco Opera, 65; Alva in Lulu, Am Nat Opera Co, 67; Faust in Berlioz, Louisville Orch, 74. *Teaching:* Instr, Tulane Univ, 56-58; prof vocal lit, Univ Louisville, 64-68 & 72-78; assoc prof, Ohio State Univ, 68-72; prof diction, Univ of Pac, 78- *Awards:* Fulbright Award, 60-61; Huitieme Prix, Concours Int Chant, 62. *Mem:* Nat Asn Teachers Singing. *Mailing Add:* 6371 Mulberry Lane Stockton CA 95212

WHITESITT, LINDA MARIE
EDUCATOR, VIOLIN
b Great Falls, Mont, Jan 13, 51. *Study:* Peabody Inst, BM, 73, MM, 75; Univ Md, Col Park, PhD, 81. *Pos:* Asst concertmaster, Roanoke Symph Orch, 80- *Teaching:* Asst prof violin, Radford Univ, 78- *Mem:* Am Liszt Soc; Am Musicol Soc; Am String Teachers Asn; Col Music Soc; Sonneck Soc. *Interests:* Twentieth century American music. *Publ:* Auth, An Aspect of Liszt's Late Style: The Composer's Revision for Historische, ungarische Portraits, J Am Liszt Soc, 6/78; contribr, George Antheil, In: New Grove Dict of Music in US (in prep); auth, The Life and Music of George Antheil (1900-1959), UMI Res Press (in prep). *Mailing Add:* 524 Woods Ave SW Roanoke VA 24016

WHITTAKER, HOWARD
EDUCATOR, COMPOSER
b Lakewood, Ohio, Dec 19, 22. *Study:* Cleveland Inst Music, with Herbert Elwell, Ward Lewis & Boris Goldovsky, BM; Consv Music, Oberlin Col, MM, 47; Eastman Sch Music. *Works:* Fantasy on Ben Hamby Melodies, 46; Variations (orch), 47; 2 String Quartets (chamber music), 47 & 48; 2 Sonatas (piano), 54 & 60; Violin Sonatina, 57; 2 Murals for Orch, 58; Variations (piano), 58. *Pos:* Mem, President's Coun Youth Opportunity. *Teaching:* Dir, Cleveland Music Sch Settlement, 48- *Awards:* Fortnightly Musical Club Award, 48; Mendelssohn Glee Club Award, 53. *Mailing Add:* Berkshire Rd Gates Mills OH 44040

WHITTENBERG, CHARLES
COMPOSER, EDUCATOR
b St Louis, Mo, July 6, 27. *Study:* Eastman Sch Music, with Burrill Phillips & Bernard Rogers, BM, 48; Am Acad Rome, FAAR, 65. *Works:* Electronic Study II (double bass & tape), 62; Triptych (brass quintet), 63; Duo Divertimento (flute & double bass), 63; Variations (nine players), 65; Games of 5 (wind quintet), 68; Correlations (orch), 69; A Sacred Triptych (eight solo voices), 71. *Teaching:* Mem affil fac, Columbia-Princeton Electronic Music Studio, 62; assoc prof music, Univ Conn, formerly, emer prof, 78- *Awards:* Nat Coun Learned Soc Grant, 62; Guggenheim Fel, 63-65; Prix de Rome, 65-66. *Mem:* Am Soc Univ Comp; Am Comp Alliance; Am Soc Aesthet; BMI. *Mailing Add:* c/o McGinnis & Marx 201 W 86 St #706 New York NY 10024

WICHMANN, RUSSELL GEORGE
EDUCATOR, MUSIC DIRECTOR
b Appleton, Wis, July 29, 12. *Study:* Consv Music, Lawrence Univ, BMus, 34; Sch Sacred Music, Union Theol Sem, New York, SMM, 36; Ecole Normale de Musique, Paris, 50-51; Eastman Sch Music, 59-60. *Works:* Dayspring of Eternity (SATB & organ), H W Gray, 37; O Lamb of God (SATB a cappella), 40, Come Thou, My Light (SATB a cappella), 41 & Psalm 121 (SATB, sop solo & organ), 66, Volkwein Brothers; Bell Carol for Christmas or Easter (SATB & organ), 72 & Once In Royal David's City (SATB & organ), 78, Oxford Univ Press. *Pos:* Organist & choirmaster, Shadyside Presby Church, Pittsburgh, 36-; bandleader, US Army, 42-45; music dir, Mendelssohn Choir, Pittsburgh, 52-66. *Teaching:* Asst prof music, Univ Pittsburgh, 36-46; prof & chmn music dept, Chatham Col, 46-78. *Awards:* Distinguished Serv Award, Lawrence Univ, 70. *Mailing Add:* 313 Dewey Ave Edgewood Pittsburgh PA 15218

WICKES, FRANK BOVEE
CONDUCTOR & MUSIC DIRECTOR, EDUCATOR
b Ticonderoga, NY, Aug 8, 37. *Study:* Univ Del, BMus, 59; Univ Mich, MMus, 67. *Rec Perf:* Fort Hunt High Sch at MidWest Clinic, Crest Rec, 70; Live from Vienna Austria, Mark Rec, 72; Univ Fla Symph Band at 43rd ABA Convention, 77, Univ Fla Symph Band Authentic Comp of Morton Gould, 80, Univ Fla Symph Band & Wind Ens at 1980 MENC, 80, LSU Wind Ensemble at CBDNA Southern Div 1982, 82 & LSU Wind Ensemble at National CBDNA, 83, Crest Rec. *Pos:* Dir bands, Alexis I duPont High Sch, Wilmington, Del, 59-66 & Ft Hunt High Sch, Fairfax Co, Va, 67-73. *Teaching:*

From asst prof to assoc prof & dir bands, Univ Fla, 73-80; assoc prof cond & dir bands, La State Univ, 80- *Mem:* Am Bandmasters Asn; Col Band Dir Nat Asn; Nat Band Asn (mem exec bd, 78-83); Music Educr Nat Conf; La Bandmasters Asn. *Publ:* Auth, So You Want to Conduct & The Challenge of Change, 4/83, Instrumentalist. *Mailing Add:* 4030 Gourrier Ave #5 Baton Rouge LA 70808

WIDDER, ROGER HENRY
EDUCATOR, OBOE & ENGLISH HORN
b Milwaukee, Wis, Sept 9, 23. *Study:* Northwestern Univ, BME, 48, MM, 49. *Teaching:* Instr music, Okla State Univ, Stillwater, 48-49; prof music, Univ Ark, Fayetteville, 49-, chmn dept music, 72-81. *Mem:* Music Educr Nat Conf; Nat Asn Col Wind & Perc Instr; Int Double Reed Soc; Nat Flute Asn. *Mailing Add:* 1660 Markham Rd Fayetteville AR 72701

WIDDOES, LAWRENCE LEWIS
COMPOSER
b Wilmington, Del, Sept 15, 32. *Study:* Juilliard Sch Music, BS, 60; studied with Bernard Wagenaar, William Bergsma & Vincent Persichetti, MS, 66. *Works:* From a Time of Snow Crossing, Bowdoin Col Press, 72 & 74; Sonatina for Flute & Piano, 72 & Sanctus, 74, Elkan Vogel; Momento Mori, perf by Jorge Merter & Juilliard Orch, 83; Tirzah for Piano, CRI, 82. *Teaching:* Instr, Juilliard Sch Music, 65- *Awards:* Am Acad Arts & Letters Rec Award, 80; Rudolf Nissim Award, ASCAP, 82; Nat Endowment Arts Grant, 82. *Mem:* ASCAP. *Mailing Add:* c/o The Juilliard Sch Lincoln Ctr New York NY 10023

WIECKOWSKI, JOANNA G
LUTE
b Warsaw, Poland, Dec 3, 43; US citizen. *Study:* Univ Pa, BA, 66, MA, 70. *Pos:* Lutenist, Collegium Musicum, Univ Pa, 72-; singer, Bryn Mawr-Haverford Renaissance Choir, 77- *Mailing Add:* 504 Meadowbrook Circle St Davids PA 19087

WIENAND, MARILYN M
EDUCATOR, SINGER
b Ontario, Ore, June 6, 42. *Study:* Acad Music, Vienna; Wash Univ, BMus, 66; Univ Colo, MMus, 71; studied with Anton Heiller, Howard Kelsey, Leslie Chaby, Axel Schiotz & John Paton. *Rec Perf:* The Ancient Instruments Ensemble of Adams State College in Concert. *Pos:* Founding mem, Col Musicum, Univ Colo & Col Musicum, Hastings Col; appearances on Colo Camerata, TV show, Denver. *Teaching:* Mem fac voice & piano, Adams State Col, currently, mem, Ancient Instrm Ens, currently. *Mem:* Nat Asn Teachers Singing. *Mailing Add:* Dept Music Adams State Col Alamosa CO 81102

WIENANDT, ELWYN ARTHUR
EDUCATOR, WRITER
b Aniwa, Wis, July 23, 17. *Study:* Lawrence Col, Wis, BMus, 39; Univ Denver, MMus, 48; Univ Iowa, PhD, 51. *Teaching:* Assoc prof music, NMex Highlands Univ, 51-56; vis lectr musicol, Univ Iowa, 54; prof musicol, Baylor Univ, 56-, assoc dean, 73-, actg dean, 81-83. *Mem:* Am Musicol Soc (SW chap pres, 61-63); Music Libr Asn. *Publ:* Auth, Choral Music of the Church, Free Press, 65 & 79; coauth, The Anthem in England and America, Free Press, 70; auth, Opinions on Church Music, Markham Press, 74; Bicentennial Collection of American Music, Hope Publ Co, 74; Thematic Catalogue: Instrumental Works of Johann Pezel, Pendragon Press, 83. *Mailing Add:* 1216 Cliffview Rd Waco TX 76710

WIENER, IVAN H
COMPOSER
b Bronx, NY, June 15, 33. *Study:* Private study with Max Persin, Robert Starer & Wallingford Riegger. *Works:* Duet for Soprano and Alto Recorders, 68 & String Trio, 69, Galaxy Music Corp; Three Segments for Percussion, Music for Perc, 72; Love is More Thicker Than Forget (SATB), Broude Bros Publ, 74; Fantasie Concertante (double bass & orch), Alexander Broude Publ, 74. *Pos:* Music librn, Galaxy Music Corp, 68-71; ed, Broude Bros, 71-76 & freelance, 76- *Awards:* Fredrick Jacoby Scholar, Henry St Music Sch, 63. *Mem:* BMI. *Mailing Add:* 556 Ave Z Brooklyn NY 11223

WIENHORST, RICHARD WILLIAM
COMPOSER, EDUCATOR
b Seymour, Ind, Apr 21, 20. *Study:* Am Consv, with Sowerby, MM, 49; Ecoles d'Art Am Fontainebleau, with Boulanger, cert, 51; Eastman Sch Music, with Hanson & Rogers, PhD, 61. *Works:* The Seven Word of Christ from the Cross, Concordia, 53; A Nativity Cantata (choir & instrm), Summy, 53; Missa Brevis (SATB a cappella), AMP, 56; Magnificat (chorus & orch), 61 & Canticle of the Three Children, 68, MS; Reflections and Celebration (organ), Hinshaw, 74; Easter (song cycle for contralto & harp), comn by Lutheran Sch Theol, Chicago, 83. *Teaching:* From instr music to prof music, Valparaiso Univ, 60-, chmn dept music, 65-70. *Awards:* Grant, Danforth Found, 59-60; res grant, Cent States Col Asn, 70; Fac Open Fel, Eli Lilly Found, 76-77. *Bibliog:* George Weller (auth), Composers for the Church: Richard Wienhorst, Church Music, 68. *Mem:* Univ Comp Exchange (exec secy, 51-63); Ind Music Teachers Asn (pres, 67-68); Am Soc Univ Comp. *Publ:* Auth, Art as Craft, 56 & The Revolt Against Romanticism, 57, Cressett Mag; The Church Music of Ralph Vaughn Williams, J Church Music, 61, In: Festschrift: Theo Hoelty Nickel, 66 & Am Organist, 69. *Mailing Add:* 103 Sturdy Rd Valparaiso IN 46483

WIENPAHL, ROBERT WILLIAM
EDUCATOR, MUSICOLOGIST
b Rock Springs, Wyo, Dec 22, 17. *Study:* Univ Calif, Los Angeles, PhD(musicol), 53, MSLS, 55. *Pos:* Cataloger, Los Angeles Co Law Libr, 55-56. *Teaching:* Lectr music, Univ Calif, Los Angeles, 49-53, cataloger libr, 53-55; catalog & acquisitions librn, 56-60, Calif State Univ, Northridge, chief pub serv, 60-64, assoc prof, 61-70, prof music, 70- *Awards:* Grant, Henry Huntington Libr 64-65; fel, Nat Endowment Humanities, 73. *Mem:* Am Musicol Soc; Music Libr Asn. *Interests:* Renaissance and baroque music. *Publ:* Auth, The Emergence of Tonality, Univ Rochester, 59; Zarlino, The Scenario, and Tonality, J Am Musicol Soc, spring 59; The Evolutionary Significance of 15th Century Cadential Formulae, J Music Theory, 11/60; Modality, Monality and Tonality in the 16th and 17th Centuries, Music & Lett, 10/71 & 1/72; A Gold Rush Voyage on the Back Orion, Arthur Clark, 78. *Mailing Add:* Dept Music Calif State Univ Northridge CA 91330

WIENS, FRANK
PIANO, EDUCATOR
Study: Univ Mich, BM, 70, MM, 71; studied with Benning Dexter & Gyorgy Sandor. *Pos:* Soloist, Cedar Rapids Symph, Denver Symph, Twin Cities Symph, Mich, Atlanta Symph, Des Moines Symph, Kalamazoo Symph, Detroit Symph & Tucson Symph. *Teaching:* Assoc prof piano, Consv Music, Univ of Pac, 76-, mem, Res Artist Ser, currently. *Mailing Add:* Consv Music Univ of Pac Stockton CA 95211

WIERSMA, ROBERTA BITGOOD See   Bitgood,   Roberta

WIERZBICKI, JAMES
CRITIC-WRITER
b Milwaukee, Wis, Apr 19, 48. *Study:* Univ Wis, Milwaukee, BFA, 70; Col Consv Music, Univ Cincinnati, MM, 71, PhD, 79. *Pos:* Music & dance critic, Cincinnati Post, 74-78; music & arts ed, St Louis Globe-Democrat, 78-; radio broadcaster, Music of Our Time, KWMU-FM, St Louis, 82- *Teaching:* Instr music, Pio Nono High Sch, Milwaukee, 71-72; Southwestern Col, Winfield, 72-73 & St Louis Consv Music, 81- *Awards:* Deems Taylor Award, ASCAP, 81. *Interests:* Burlesque opera, London: 1729-1737. *Publ:* Auth, Color, Music and Schoenberg's Die glückliche Hand, Univ Cincinnati Grad Res J, 75; Maddalena: Prokofiev's Adolescent Opera, Opera Quart, 83. *Mailing Add:* 710 N Tucker Blvd St Louis MO 63101

WIGGLESWORTH, FRANK
COMPOSER, EDUCATOR
b Boston, Mass, Mar 3, 18. *Study:* Bard Col; Columbia Univ, BS, 40; Converse Col, MMus, 42. *Works:* Young Goodman Brown (ballet), comn by Frederic Franklin, 51; Lake Music, 53 & Duo for Oboe & Viola, 64, Merion Press; Short Mass, 67 & Mass, 70, comn by St Lukes Chapel; Three Portraits String Orch, perf by RAI, Rome, 70; Brass Quintet, comn by Castle Hill Fest, 75. *Pos:* Ed, New Music Ed, 46-51; exec dir, Comp Forum, 56-70; dir musicol, Artists Choice Conct New Sch, 58-71. *Teaching:* Fac mem comp & theory, New Sch Social Res, 54-; head theory, Dalcroze Sch Music, 57-; assoc prof contemp music & music survey, City Univ New York, 70-74. *Awards:* Alice M Ditson (auth), Columbia Univ, 45; Inst Arts & Lett Award, 51; comp fel, Am Acad Rome, 51-55. *Bibliog:* Henry Cowell (auth), Frank Wigglesworth, Notes, 51; Jesus Villa Rojo (auth), Miniconcertos en la Academia Americano, Ritmo, Madrid, Spain, 70. *Mem:* Am Comp Alliance (vpres, 75-81, pres, 81-); Comp Rec, Inc (vpres, 78-); fel, MacDowell Colony. *Mailing Add:* 19 Downing St New York NY 10014

WILCOX, CAROL ANN
SOPRANO
b Antioch, Calif, Mar 9, 45. *Study:* Univ Kans, BA, 69; Manhattan Sch Music, 69-70; studied with Richard Fredricks. *Rec Perf:* On RCA & CRI. *Roles:* Despina in Cosi fan tutte, Metropolitan Opera Studio, 70; Zerlina in Don Giovanni; Pamina in Die Zauberflöte; Oscar in Un Ballo in maschera; Gilda in Rigoletto; Abigail in The Crucible; Aurelia in Captain Jinks of the Horse Marines, Kansas City Lyr Opera Theatre, 75. *Pos:* Katherine Long Scholar, Metropolitan Opera, 69-70, sop, 70-72; sop, Pittsburgh Opera, 74, 75 & 77, South Atlanta Opera, 74-81, Can Opera, 75 & 79 & many other US & Can opera co & symph orchs; recitalist throughout US, 78-79. *Awards:* Am Guild Musical Artists; Actors Equity. *Mailing Add:* 395 Riverside Dr New York NY 10025

WILCOX, EUNICE ANN
EDUCATOR, MUSIC DIRECTOR
b Tecumseh, Mich, Dec 15, 25. *Study:* Univ Mich, BM, 47; Western Mich Univ, MA, 62; Mich State Univ, PhD, 68. *Pos:* Asst music dir, Am Savoyards, 50-55. *Teaching:* Instr voice & music educ, Western Mich Univ, 60-62 & Mich State Univ, 63-69; assoc prof, DePauw Univ, 70- *Mem:* Music Educr Nat Conf; Am Asn Univ Prof; Sigma Alpha Iota. *Mailing Add:* Music Sch DePauw Univ Greencastle IN 46135

WILCOX, JAMES H
EDUCATOR, COMPOSER
b Bolton, England, July 10, 16. *Study:* With Pottag, 37-41; Univ Wis, BS, 38; Northwestern Univ, with Arne Oldberg, MMus, 41; studied with Yegudkin, 49-53; Eastman Sch Music, PhD, 53; Fla State Univ, 54-56, with Ernst von Dohnanyi. *Works:* Heroic Sketch (horn & piano), 50; Concert Piece (trumpet & piano), 54; Violin Sonata, 55; Introduction and Passacaglia (band), 56. *Pos:* Prin horn & mem bd dir, Baton Rouge Symph, 46-54 & 57-64; choir dir, Methodist Church, 46-66, mem admin bd, 50-; mem exec bd, La Coun Music

& Perf Arts; adjudicator music & ed music col div, Scott, Foresman Co, Ill, 65-72; founder, Cantrell Music Press. *Teaching:* Hartland High Sch, Wis, Carroll Col & Milwaukee Pub Sch, 38-40; mem fac, Southeastern La Univ, 46-54 & 56-, dir bands & brass, 46-54, prof music theory, 56-64, head dept music, 64-70, dean, Col Arts & Humanities, 70-; teaching asst, Fla State Univ, 54-56. *Interests:* Programmed music theory. *Publ:* Publ with Boosey-Hawkes, Belwin & G Schirmer. *Mailing Add:* 105 College Dr Hammond LA 70401

WILD, EARL
PIANO, COMPOSER
b Pittsburgh, Pa, Nov 26, 15. *Study:* Carnegie Tech, with Selmar Jansen, Egon Petri, Paul Doguereau, Madame Barere & Volya Cassack. *Works:* Revelations (oratorio), ABC, 62 & 64; The Turquoise Horse, comn by Palm Springs Museum, 76; Piano Concerto, 83. *Rec Perf:* Complete Concertos (Rachmaninoff), RCA, 65; All Liszt Record, EMI, 75; Porgy & Bess Arrangement & 7 Popular Song Arrangement (solo piano; Gershwin-Wild), 76; All Chopin Record, Quintessence, 77; The Art of the Transcription, 82 & French Album, 82, Audiofon; 12 Song Arrangement for Piano Solo (Rachmaninoff-Wild), Dell'Arte Rec, 82. *Pos:* Conct pianist. *Teaching:* Prof, Pa State Univ, 64-69; fac piano, Juilliard Sch Music, 77- & Manhattan Sch Music, 82- *Rep:* Judd Conct Bureau 155 W 68th St New York NY 10023. *Mailing Add:* 101 W 55th Apt 5D New York NY 10019

WILDERMANN, WILLIAM
BASS-BARITONE
b Stuttgart, Germany, Dec 2, 19; US citizen. *Study:* With Carl Yost. *Rec Perf:* Falstaff. *Roles:* Daland in Der fliegende Höllender, Dallas Opera, 78 & Amsterdam Opera; Pistola in Falstaff, Los Angeles & Covent Garden; Samuele in Un Ballo in maschera, Miami Opera; Hunding in Die Walküre, Fasolt in Das Rheingold, Simone in Gianni Schicchi & Police Commisioner in Der Rosenkavalier, Dallas Opera. *Pos:* Appearances in major opera houses, US, Can & Europe. *Mailing Add:* c/o Sardos Artist Mgt 180 West End Ave New York NY 10023

WILDING-WHITE, RAYMOND
EDUCATOR, COMPOSER
b Caterham, Surrey, England, Oct 9, 22; US citizen. *Study:* Juilliard Sch Music, 47-49; Berkshire Music Ctr, summers 50-52; New England Consv Music, BM, 51, MM, 58; Boston Univ, DMA, 62. *Works:* The Ship of Death, comn by Samuel Wechsler Comn; Lonesome Valley, comn by Liturgical Dance Co; Encores for Stu, comn by Stuart Dempster; Whatzit No 2, comn by Bertram Turetzky; Galaxy, comn by Alder Planetarium; O My Nannie, Marks Music Corp; For Mallets, Music Perc Inc. *Rec Perf:* Paraphernalia, CRI; Bandmusic, Cornell Rec. *Pos:* Prod & dir, WGBH-FM & TV, Boston, Mass, 51-56; prod mgr, Nat Merchandising Corp, 57-60. *Teaching:* Instr, Cardinal Cushing Col, 58-59; asst prof music, Case Inst Technol, 60-67; asst prof, DePaul Univ, 67-74, assoc prof, 74-80, prof, 80- *Awards:* Arthur Sheperd Prize; Cleveland Fine Arts Award. *Mailing Add:* 1312 W George Chicago IL 60657

WILES, JOHN A
EDUCATOR, BARITONE
b Ft Worth, Tex, Aug 21, 30. *Study:* Oklahoma City Univ, BMus, 51; Univ Mich, Ann Arbor, MMus, 52. *Pos:* First bar, WGerman Opera Houses: Gelenkirchen Städtiche Bühnen, 58-62, Oldenburgische Staatstheater, 62-63, Bremerhaven Stadttheater, 64-66 & Freiburg Städiche Bühnen, 66-68. *Teaching:* Asst prof voice, Opera Wkshp Dir, Mich State Univ, 68-73 & Univ Ga, 77-79; adj prof, NY Univ, 80-81; lyr theatre coordr & voice teacher, State Univ NY Col, Fredonia, 81- *Awards:* Fulbright Scholar, 52-53; Daukstipendium Scholar, WGerman Govt, 56; grant, Metropolitan Opera Co, 71. *Mem:* Nat Asn Teachers Singing; Col Music Soc; United Univ Prof. *Mailing Add:* 1138 Central Ave Dunkirk NY 14048

WILEY, FRANK (EARKETT), JR
COMPOSER, EDUCATOR
b Richmond, Va, Dec 9, 49. *Study:* Univ NC, Chapel Hill, with Roger Hannay, BM(organ), 71, MM(comp), 73; Cleveland Inst Music, Case Western Res Univ, with Donald Erb, DMA(comp), 77. *Works:* Abstracts, perf by NC Symph, 76; Premonition, perf by Robert Parris & Clyde Holloway, 80; Chamber Concerto, perf by Karel Paukert & Coventry Chamber Players, 81; Apparitions, comn & perf by Margaret Baxtresser, 81; For Alexander Calder, perf by Reconnaissance, 82; Caverns, perf by Ronald Bishop, 82. *Teaching:* From instr to asst prof, Univ NC, Wilmington, 75-79; asst prof, Kent State Univ, 79- *Awards:* Comp Award, Holtkamp Organ Co, Hartt Contemp Organ Music Fest, 78; Nat Endowment Arts Fel, 80; Ohio Arts Coun Grant, 84. *Mem:* Cleveland Comp Guild; ASCAP; Am Music Ctr. *Mailing Add:* 2063 Merrill Rd Kent OH 44240

WILKEY, JAY W
EDUCATOR, BARITONE
b Irvington, Ky, Dec 5, 34. *Study:* Eastern NMex Univ, BMus, 56; Univ Iowa, MA, 57; Ind Univ, PhD, 65. *Roles:* Eisenstein in Die Fledermaus, 64, Roderigo in Otello, 73, Keene in Grimes, 78, Benoit in La Boheme, 79, Witch in Hänsel and Gretel, 80, Basilio in The Marriage of Figaro, 82 & Gianni Schicchi in Gianni Schicchi, 83, Ky Opera Asn. *Pos:* Minister music, second Presby Church, Louisville, 66-; music dir, Temple Adath Israel, Louisville, 66- *Teaching:* Asst prof voice, Hardin-Simmons Univ, 60-63; prof voice & church music, Southern Baptist Theol Sem, 63- *Awards:* Fels, Danforth Found, 56-60 & Rockefeller Found, 62-63. *Mem:* Nat Asn Teachers Singing (Ky gov, 72-76, mid-south gov, 78-82); Music Teachers Nat Asn; Am Choral Dir Asn; Southern Baptist Church Music Conf (nat vpres, 65-67). *Publ:* Auth, Marshall

McLuhan and Meaning in Music, Music Educ J, 69; Penderecki's Dies Irae, Choral J, 70; Prolegomena to a Theology of Music, Rev & Expositor, 72; The Solo Voice in Worship Music Today, Nat Asn Teachers Singing Bulletin, 81; Songs of Amy Beach, Am Liszt Soc, 83. *Mailing Add:* 2825 Lexington Rd PO 1934 Louisville KY 40280

WILKINS, CHRISTOPHER PUTNAM
CONDUCTOR
b Boston, Mass, May 28, 57. *Study:* Harvard Col, AB, 78; Hochschule der Künste, WBerlin, 79; Sch Music, Yale Univ, MM, 81. *Pos:* Cond in res, State Univ NY, Purchase, 81-82; affiliate artists cond asst, Ore Symph Orch, 82-83; Exxon Arts Endowment Cond Asst, Cleveland Orch, 83- *Mailing Add:* 168 Nashawtuc Rd Concord MA 01742

WILKINS, MARILYN W
LIBRARIAN, SOPRANO
b Picayune, Miss, May 6, 29. *Study:* Newcomb Col, Tulane Univ, BA(voice), 51, Grad Sch, MA(musicol), 55. *Roles:* Sop soloist in Messiah, New Orleans Phil Symph Orch, 50. *Pos:* Head art, music & recreation div, New Orleans Pub Libr, 53- *Interests:* Hugo Wolf; early New Orleans music. *Mailing Add:* Art Music and Recreation Div New Orleans Pub Libr 219 Loyola Ave New Orleans LA 70140

WILKINS, WILLIAM DEAN
EDUCATOR, ORGAN
b Winfield, Kans, Feb 23, 20. *Study:* Emporia State Univ, BS(music), 46; Univ Mich, MM, 51; Ind Univ, DM, 63. *Pos:* Organist, First Presby Church, Hays, Kans, 46- *Teaching:* Prof music, Ft Hays State Univ, 46- *Awards:* Musician of Year, Kans Federated Music Clubs, 79. *Mem:* Am Guild Organists (dean Hays chap, 66-73); Music Teachers Nat Asn; Kans Music Teachers Asn. *Mailing Add:* Dept Music Ft Hays State Univ Hays KS 67601

WILKINSON, ARTHUR SCOTT
EDUCATOR, COMPOSER
b Bement, Ill, June 27, 22. *Study:* Univ Ariz, BM, 48, MM, 49; Mills Col, with Darius Milhaud, Paris, 50-51. *Works:* Choral Meditations, Carl Fischer Inc, 51; Halleluia Sing!, 68 & Impressions, 68, Zia Music Press; Little David, Belwin-Mills, 73; This is the American Earth, Op One Rec, 78; Scott's Piece (brass quintet), perf by NMex Brass Quintet, 81; Rhapsody for Violin Alone, perf by Leonard Felberg, 83. *Pos:* Managing ed, Carl Fischer Inc, 51-61 & 69-71. *Teaching:* Assoc prof music, Univ NMex, Albuquerque, 71- *Mem:* ASCAP; Phi Mu Alpha. *Mailing Add:* Rt 5 Box 785 Los Lunas NM 87031

WILL, PATRICK TERENCE
CRITIC-WRITER, EDUCATOR
b Washington, DC, Mar 10, 56. *Study:* Univ Chicago, BA(music), 78; Cornell Univ, MA(music), 82. *Pos:* Music dir, WHPK-FM, Chicago, 76-79; mem mkt staff, Arista Rec, 79; chief music reviewer, Ithaca J, 80- *Teaching:* Instr music & English, Cornell Univ, 80- *Interests:* Sociology of music; critical theory; text-music relationships in Gustav Mahler. *Publ:* Auth, American Composer in Profile: David Amram, Ithaca Times, 83; Sociology of Music, Reception, History of Radio and TV Broadcasting & Sound Recording, In: Harvard Dict Music, 3rd ed (in prep). *Mailing Add:* 1 Willets Pl #3 Ithaca NY 14853

WILLETT, THELMA ELIZABETH
EDUCATOR, PIANO
b Mansfield, Ohio, Feb 6, 23. *Study:* Denison Univ, AB, 44; Univ Ill, MMus, 46; Univ Mich; Ind Univ. *Works:* Ninepence, A Suite of Miniatures for Violin and Piano, Shawnee Press, 79. *Teaching:* Instr piano & theory, Univ Ill, Urbana, 45-49; assoc prof piano, Wesley Col, Grand Forks, NDak, 49-53; from asst to assoc prof piano, Univ NDak, 53- *Mem:* Music Teachers Nat Asn; Am Asn Univ Prof. *Mailing Add:* 402 Harvard St Grand Forks ND 58201

WILLETT, WILLIAM
EDUCATOR, WOODWINDS
Study: Univ Wis, BMus, MA; Eastman Sch Music, DMA; Chautauqua Inst; Colo Col; Pasadena City Col. *Rec Perf:* On Mark Educ Rec. *Pos:* Clarinet soloist, Pro Arte, Beaux Arts & Alard String Quartets, currently; bassoonist, Erie Phil, currently; guest cond & clinician. *Teaching:* Chmn music & music educ, State Univ NY, Fredonia, formerly; mem fac, Univ Indiana, Pa, formerly; prof music educ & cond, Hartt Sch Music, 69- *Mailing Add:* Hartt Sch Music Univ Hartford West Hartford CT 06117

WILLEY, JAMES HENRY
COMPOSER, EDUCATOR
b Lynn, Mass, Oct 1, 39. *Study:* Eastman Sch Music, BM, 61, MM, 63, PhD, 72; Berkshire Music Ctr, with Gunther Shuller, 63. *Works:* Three Elizabethan Lyrics (mixed chorus & piano), Lawson-Gould Music Publ Inc, 73; Hymns & Litanies (clarinet & piano), Seesaw Music Publ, 76; The Death of Mozart, perf by Univ Mass Group for New Music, 76; String Quartet No 1, Spectrum, 76; At Midnight, Soc for New Music, 79; String Quartet No 2, Spectrum, 80; String Quartet No 3, Tremont String Quartet, 81. *Teaching:* Prof theory & comp & chmn music dept, Col Arts & Sci, State Univ NY, Geneseo, 66-; vis prof, Williams Col, 79-80. *Awards:* Comp fel, Nat Endowment for Arts, 75 & 80; Standard Awards, ASCAP, 75-83. *Mem:* ASCAP; Am Soc Univ Comp (chair, Region II, 76-78); Sonneck Soc; Am Music Ctr; Am Musicol Soc. *Mailing Add:* 25A Prospect St Geneseo NY 14454

WILLIAMS, DAVID RUSSELL
EDUCATOR, COMPOSER
b Indianapolis, Ind, Oct 21, 32. *Study:* Columbia Col, AB, 54, MA, 56; Univ Rochester, PhD, 65. *Works:* Suite for Oboe, Clarinet & Piano, Pyraminx Publ, 68; Five States of Mind, 70 & 9 x 9 Variations on a Theme by Howard Hanson, 79, Carl Fischer; Recitation for Trombone Choir, 82 & Fanfare for Brass Quintet, 82, Accura Music. *Rec Perf:* John Stover (class guitar), Highwater Rec, 83. *Teaching:* Dir music, Windham Col, 59-62; opera coach, Eastman Sch Music, 62-65, assoc prof theory, 65-80; prof & chmn music dept, Memphis State Univ, 80- *Awards:* Eastman Sch Music Publ Award, 70. *Mem:* Col Music Soc (secy, 73-); Tenn Asn Music Exec Col & Univ (secy, 81-); Music Teachers Nat Asn (NY state chmn theory & comp, 71-74); charter mem, Soc Music Theory; charter mem, Music Theory Soc NY State. *Interests:* History of music theory. *Publ:* Auth, Bibliography of the History of Music Theory, Accura, 71; ed, Opera Volume, New Scribner Music Libr, Scribner's, 72; auth, Howard Hanson, Perspectives New Music, 83. *Mailing Add:* 295 Central Park W #2 Memphis TN 38111

WILLIAMS, EDNA (CHARLOTTE)
SOPRANO, EDUCATOR
b Chicago, Ill, Oct 22, 33. *Study:* Chicago Musical Col, Roosevelt Univ, BM, 57, MM, 59; studied with Hans Karg-Bebenburg, Vienna, 59-60. *Teaching:* Assoc prof voice, Northern Ill Univ, 65- *Awards:* Sue Cowan Hintz Voice Award, 55; Oliver Ditson Voice Scholar, 56; John Hay Whitney Fel, 59. *Mem:* Nat Asn Negro Musicians Inc (bd mem, currently & nat scholar chairperson, 76-); Nat Asn Teachers Singing. *Mailing Add:* Music Dept Northern Ill Univ De Kalb IL 60115

WILLIAMS, EDWARD VINSON
WRITER, EDUCATOR
b Orlando, Fla, July 12, 35. *Study:* Ind Univ, MM, 62; Yale Univ, MA, 66, PhD, 68. *Teaching:* Prof music hist, Univ Kans, 82- *Awards:* Jr Fel, Dumbarton Oaks Ctr Byzantine Studies, 68-69; Am Coun Learned Soc Fel, 80-81; Nat Humanities Ctr Fel, 80-81. *Mem:* Am Musicol Soc; Am Asn Advan Slavic Studies. *Interests:* Byzantine & Russian music. *Publ:* Auth, The Treatment of Text in the Kalophonic Chanting of Psalm 2, In: Studies in Eastern Chant, Vol 2, 173-193, 71; A Byzantine Ars Nova: The 14th-century Reforms of John Koukouzeles in the Chanting of Great Vespers, In: Aspects of the Balkans: Continuity and Change, Mouton, 72; The Kalophonic Tradition and Chants for the Polyeleos Psalm 134, In: Studies in Eastern Chant, Vol 4, 75; Akolouthiai, Vol 1, 187-188, Ethikos, Nikephoros, Vol 6, 267, Glykys, Joannes, Vol 7, 475, Hesperinos, Vol 8, 532-533, Koukouzeles (Papadopoulos), Joannes, Vol 10, 218-219 & Lampadarios (Klada), Joannes, Vol 10, 418-419, In: New Grove Dict of Music & Musicians, Macmillan, 80; Zvonnitsa and Kolokol'nia: The Russian Zvon and Western Bell Towers, In: Livre de Congres, VI Musica Antiqua Europae Orientalis, Bydgoszcz, Poland, 82. *Mailing Add:* Sch Fine Arts Univ Kans Lawrence KS 66045

WILLIAMS, EDWIN LYNN
TRUMPET, ADMINISTRATOR
b Crawfordsville, Ind, July 9, 47. *Study:* DePauw Univ, with Robert Grocock, BMus(trumpet), 69; Ind Univ, with William Adam, MMus(trumpet), 71; studied trumpet with Helmut Wobisch, Austria, 72-73; Cincinnati Consv Music, with Eugene Blee, DMA(trumpet), 80. *Pos:* Prin trumpet, Lima Symph Orch, 73-; Cincinnati Opera, 77-78 & Cincinnati Ballet Co, 77-78; cond, Lima Area Youth Orch, 75- *Teaching:* Assoc prof music & dir jazz studies, Ohio Northern Univ, 73-, chmn music dept, 82- *Awards:* Fulbright-Hayes Grant, 72-73. *Mem:* Nat Band Asn; Music Educr Nat Conf; Nat Asn Jazz Educr. *Mailing Add:* 811 S Johnson St Ada OH 45810

WILLIAMS, FRANKLIN EDMUND
EDUCATOR, CONDUCTOR
b East St Louis, Ill, Dec 29, 28. *Study:* Nat Music Camp, Interlochen, Mich, 46; Univ Okla, BME, 50; Univ Ill, MM, 55, EdD, 69. *Teaching:* Asst prof music & asst cond bands, Univ Okla, 57-65; from asst prof to prof & chmn, Music Dept, Wartburg Col, 65- *Mem:* Nat Asn Sch Music. *Mailing Add:* 106 Jahnke Ave Waverly IA 50677

WILLIAMS, GRIER MOFFATT
EDUCATOR, CONDUCTOR & MUSIC DIRECTOR
b Tampa, Fla, June 18, 31. *Study:* Davidson Col, BS, 53; Univ Mich, MM, 56; Fla State Univ, PhD, 61. *Teaching:* Asst prof music, Univ Southeastern La, Hammond, 58-61; assoc prof, Davidson Col, 61-68; prof & chmn, Univ WFla, Pensacola, 68- *Mem:* Fla State Music Teachers Asn (first vpres, 76-80); Music Teachers Nat Asn. *Mailing Add:* Dept Music Univ WFla Pensacola FL 32514

WILLIAMS, HERMINE WEIGEL
EDUCATOR, WRITER
b Sellersville, Pa, Feb 4, 33. *Study:* Vassar Col, AB, 54, MA, 56; Columbia Univ, PhD, 64. *Pos:* Organist & choir dir, various churches in NY, 61-81; ed & bd mem, Pergolesi Res Project, Pendragon Press, New York, 79-; asst to ed, Scarlatti Opera Series, Harvard Press, 79-; assoc dir, Sobolevsky Summer Sch for Strings, Clinton, NY, 81- *Teaching:* Instr musicol, Vassar Col, 56-59; asst prof, Hamilton Col, 64-65; lectr ethnomusicol, 72- *Awards:* Theodore Presser Award; Maarston Fel. *Mem:* Am Musicol Soc. *Interests:* Early 18th century Neapolitan and Viennese composers and their sacred and secular dramatic works. *Publ:* Ed, La caduta de' decemviri, Vol 6, Harvard Univ Press, 80; contribr, Francesco B Conti & Ignazio Conti, In: New Grove Dict of Music & Musicians, 80; co-ed, Early Symphony Series: Overtures by Conti, Book II, Garland Publ Co, 83; contribr, The Sacred Music of F B Conti, In: P H Lang Festschrift, Norton Publ Co, 83. *Mailing Add:* 300 College Hill Rd Clinton NY 13323

WILLIAMS, J(OHN) WESLEY
EDUCATOR, MUSIC DIRECTOR
b Portsmouth, Ohio, July 23, 40. *Study:* Butler Univ, BA, 62; Wittenberg Univ, MEd, 67; studied voice with William Vennard. *Rec Perf:* Eight albums, Wittenberg Choir, 72-76. *Pos:* Dir, Indianapolis Symphonic Choir, 82-*Teaching:* Assoc prof voice, Wittenberg Sch Music, 67-82 & Jordan Col Fine Arts, Butler Univ, 83- *Awards:* Am Rep, First All-Soviet Choral Fest, 77. *Mem:* Am Choral Dir Asn (pres Ohio chap, 74-76, pres north central div, 76-); Nat Asn Teachers Singing. *Mailing Add:* Butler Univ Jordan Col Music 4600 Sunset Ave Indianapolis IN 46208

WILLIAMS, JAN
EDUCATOR, PERCUSSION
b Utica, NY, 1939. *Study:* Eastman Sch Music, 58-59; Manhattan Sch Music, BM, 63, MM, 64. *Works:* Theme & Variations for Solo Kettledrums, Music for Perc Inc, 64; Portrait of a City (film score), WNED-TV, Buffalo, 67; Be Prepared (perc quartet), Source Mag, 67; Antigone, Studio Arena Theater, 67; Dream Lesson, Turnabout, 70. *Rec Perf:* Music for Six, CRI; Cock Robin, Spectrum; In Woods, Orion Rec; Echoi, Wergo; Paradigm, DGG; Echoes, Desto Rec; For Frank O'Hara, Columbia. *Pos:* Dir, U-B Perc Ens, 64- & Contemp Chamber Ens, 76-; creative assoc, Ctr Creative & Perf Arts, 64-67, musical dir, 74-76, res cond, 76-78; soloist, major US & European symph orchs, 75-78. *Teaching:* Instr, Brooklyn Consv, 60-64; instr, State Univ NY, Buffalo, 67-69, asst prof, 69-73, assoc prof, 73-79, prof, 79-, chmn music dept, 81- *Awards:* Ford Found Conct Artists Award, 71. *Mailing Add:* Music Dept State Univ NY Buffalo NY 14214

WILLIAMS, JOHN TOWNER
COMPOSER, CONDUCTOR
b Flushing, NY, Feb 8, 32. *Study:* Univ Calif, Los Angeles, 49-50; Juilliard Sch Music, 52. *Works:* Jaws, Universal, MCA, 75; Star Wars, 20th Century Fox, 77; Close Encounters of the 3rd Kind, Columbia, 77; Superman, Warner Brothers, 78; The Empire Strikes Back, 20th Century Fox, 80; Raiders of the Lost Ark, Paramount, 81; ET: The Extra Terrestrial, Universal, MCA, 82. *Rec Perf:* Pops in Space, 80, Pops on the March, 80, Pops on Broadway, 80, Pops Around the World, 81, We Wish You a Merry Christmas, 81, Aisle Seat, 82 & Pops Out of This World, 83, Philips Rec Co. *Pos:* Cond, Boston Pops Orch, 80- *Awards:* Emmy, Nat Acad TV Arts & Sci, 69 & 71; Oscar, Nat Acad Motion Picture Arts & Sci, 71, 75, 77 & 83; Grammy (14), Nat Acad Rec Arts & Sci, 75, 77, 78, 80, 81 & 83. *Mem:* BMI; Am Fedn Musicians. *Mailing Add:* Boston Pops Orch Symph Hall Boston MA 02115

WILLIAMS, MICHAEL D
EDUCATOR
b Buffalo, NY, Mar 22, 42. *Study:* Northwestern Univ, BME, 64, MM, 66; Ind Univ, PhD, 73. *Teaching:* Instr music, Univ Houston, 70-73, asst prof music, 73-78 & assoc prof & dir grad studies, 78- *Mem:* Am Musicol Soc; Am Viola Soc. *Interests:* Viola music; computer applications. *Publ:* Auth, Source: Music of the Avant Garde: Annotated List of Contents and Cumulative Indices, Music Libr Asn, 78; Music for Viola, Detroit Studies in Music Bibliography, No 42, Info Coordr, 79. *Mailing Add:* Sch Music Univ Houston Houston TX 77004

WILLIAMS, NANCY
MEZZO-SOPRANO, TEACHER
b Cleveland, Ohio, July 28. *Study:* Chatham Col, BA; Univ Pittsburgh, MA; Middlebury Col; Columbia Univ. *Rec Perf:* Vocal Symphony (Vladimir Sommer), RCA Victor, 69; Trouble in Tahiti, CBS, 73; Songfest, Deutsche Grammophon, 78; The Woman Speaks, Laurel Rec, 83. *Roles:* Suzuki in Madame Butterfly, 69 & Dido in Dido and Aeneas, 73, Metropolitan Opera; Composer in Ariadne auf Naxos, 71, Sieglinde in Walküre, 73 & Carmen in Carmen, 74, St Paul Opera; Brangaene in Tristan und Isolde, Vienna Phil, 79 & Seattle Opera & NW Wagner Fest, 81. *Teaching:* Instr voice, Acad Vocal Arts, 80- *Rep:* Siegel Music Mgt 3003 VanNess St NW Suite W 832 Washington DC 20008. *Mailing Add:* 181 Chittenden Ave Crestwood NY 10707

WILLIAMS, RICHARD
MUSICAL DIRECTOR
b Long Beach, Calif, Sept 8, 39. *Study:* Calif State Univ, Long Beach, BA(music); Brigham Young Univ, MA(cond). *Pos:* Musical dir, Amici Della Musica, 64-69, Cabrillo Summer Fest, 69, Cedar Rapids Symph Orch, 70-81; guest cond, Czech Phil, BBC Scottish Symph Orch, BBC Welsh Symph Orch, Calgary Phil, Orch Regionale Mulhouse & Dutch Radio Phil; gen music dir, Nat Theatre Kenya Opera Prod; cond, Va Orch Group, currently. *Mem:* Am Symph Orch League; Iowa Arts Coun. *Mailing Add:* Va Orch Group PO Box 26 Norfolk VA 23501

WILLIAMS, RICK (FREDERICK THOMPSON)
BARITONE
b Austin, Tex, July 30, 49. *Study:* Juilliard Sch Music, 56-60; Yale Univ, BA, 71; Stanford Univ, MA, JD, 76. *Roles:* Tarara in Utopia Ltd, 79, Lord Chancellor in Iolanthe, 80, Jack Point in Yeoman of the Guard, 81, Sir Joseph Porter in HMS Pinafore, 81, Koko in Mikado, 82, Robin Oakapple in Ruddigore, 82 & Maj Gen Stanley in The Pirates of Penzance, 83, Lamplighters San Francisco. *Mailing Add:* 36 Agua Way San Francisco CA 94127

WILLIAMS, ROBERT EDWARD
EDUCATOR, CLARINET
b Freeport, Ill, Dec 24, 33. *Study:* Univ Ariz, BMus, 56, MMusEd, 57; Univ Ill, EdD, 69. *Pos:* Solo clarinet, Redlands Symph, Calif, 57-60. *Teaching:* Assoc prof woodwinds & band, Univ Minn, Duluth, 66- *Mem:* Music Educr Nat Conf; Nat Asn Col Wind & Perc Instr. *Mailing Add:* 615 W College St Duluth MN 55811

WILLIAMSON, MARSHALL
EDUCATOR, PIANO
b Ft Worth, Tex. *Study:* Ft Worth Consv, dipl; Tex Christian Univ, BM, MM; Univ Southern Calif; studied piano with Jeannette Tillet, Lillian Steuber & Adele Marcus. *Pos:* Accmp, Martha Baird Rockefeller Auditions, 62-; mem, Metropolitan Opera Studio, 66-75; organist, Rutgers Church, 67-; music dir, Young Artists Prog, Lake George Opera Fest, 73-81; accmp for Roberta Peters, China tour, 80; recital accmp & tours, US, Can & Europe. *Teaching:* Mem fac, Manhattan Sch Music, 68-72, Music Acad West, currently & Mannes Col Music, 82-; mem fac vocal lit & accmp, Juilliard Sch, 78- *Mailing Add:* Juilliard Sch Lincoln Ctr New York NY 10023

WILLINGHAM, LAWRENCE HARDWICK
COMPOSER
b Portland, Maine, Jan 17, 42. *Study:* New England Consv, BM, 63; Yale Sch Music, MM, 66; WVa Univ, DMA, 74. *Works:* Symphony for String Orchestra, Nat Symph, 60; String Quartet No 1, Educ TV Boston, 63; Antiphonies for Orchestra, Pittsburgh Symph, 72; Count Ugulino, Friday Morning Music Club, 76; Violin Concerto, perf by Helmut Braunlich with Cath Univ Orch, 80; The River Merchant's Wife, Contemp Music Forum, 80; Songs form Hermann Hesse, comn by Va Music Teachers Asn, 82. *Teaching:* Instr music theory, WVa Univ, 72-73; private teacher piano & comp, 75- *Awards:* John Day Jackson Prize, Yale Univ, 66; Birthday Bicentennial Award, Friday Morning Music Club, 76; comp contest winner, Va Music Teachers Asn, 82. *Bibliog:* Frances McKay (auth), Lawrence Willingham, Contemp Music Forum Newsletter, 80. *Mem:* Am Comp Alliance; Friday Morning Music Club; DC Fedn Music Clubs; Music Teachers Nat Asn; Col Music Soc. *Mailing Add:* 1718 Forest Lane McLean VA 22101

WILLIS, RICHARD M
EDUCATOR, COMPOSER
b Mobile, Ala, Apr 21, 29. *Study:* Univ Ala, BMus, 50; Eastman Sch Music, MMus, 51, PhD, 65. *Works:* Symphony No 1, Oklahoma City Symph, 54; Sonatina for Violin and Piano, Peer-Southern, 57; Symphony #2, Eastman-Rochester Orch, 64; Evocation, Houston Symph, 67; String Quartet #2, Theodore Presser, 68; Petition and Thanks (chorus & wind ens), comn & perf by Univ Ky, 76; Trio for Violin, Cello and Piano, Oriana Trio, 82. *Teaching:* Dept head music theory & comp, Shorter Col, Ga, 53-63; prof comp & comp in res, Baylor Univ, 64- *Awards:* Joseph Bearns Prize, Columbia Univ, 55; Prix de Rome, Am Acad Rome, 56-57; Ostwald Award (for Aria & Toccata), Ostwald Uniforms Inc, 69. *Mem:* Am Soc Univ Comp; ASCAP; Am Fedn Musicians. *Mailing Add:* Sch Music Baylor Univ Waco TX 76798

WILLIS, THOMAS C
EDUCATOR, CRITIC-WRITER
b Flat Rock, Ill, Apr 24, 28. *Study:* Northwestern Univ, BMus, 49, PhD, 66; Yale Univ, 49-51. *Pos:* Music critic & arts ed, Chicago Tribune, 57-77; conct mgr, Northwestern Univ, 67-; coordr educ prog, Ravinia Fest, 77-81. *Teaching:* Asst prof, Sweet Briar Col, 52-53; assoc prof, Northwestern Univ, 67- *Awards:* Bispham Award, Am Opera Soc, 56. *Mem:* Music Critic Asn (mem bd dir, 71-73, treas, 73-74, vpres, 75-77); Am Musical Digest (mem bd dir, 68-69, pres, 70-71). *Interests:* Orchestral repertories in the United States, 1891-1954; contemporary composition techniques, 1960-1980. *Publ:* Contribr, major arts publ, 66; Coauth, The Chicago Symphony Orchestra, Rand McNally; contrib ed, Classical Music, Chicago Mag, 77-78. *Mailing Add:* 819 Simpson Evanston IL 60201

WILLMAN, FRED R
EDUCATOR, COMPOSER
b Rodney, Iowa, Sept 26, 40. *Study:* Morningside Col, BME, 62; Univ Colo, Boulder, MME, 68; Univ NDak, PhD, 72. *Works:* A Smile is a Frown, 80 & 5 Spacey Nursery Rhymes, 81, G Schirmer. *Teaching:* Choral & gen music teacher, Manning, Iowa pub sch, 62-65, Odebolt-Arthur pub sch, 65-67 & Bettendorf, Iowa community sch, 67-70; from grad asst to asst prof, Univ NDak, 70-74; from asst to assoc prof, Univ Mo, St Louis, 74- *Awards:* St Louis Suburban Music Educr Asn Merit Award, 78. *Mem:* Music Educr Nat Conf; Soc Gen Music Teachers; Am Guild English Handbell Ringers; Presby Asn Musicians; Am Soc Composers & Publishers. *Interests:* Electronic music & computers; early instruments; ethnic music; creativity, learning process and music. *Publ:* Auth, Electronic Music for Young People, Ctr Applied Res Educ, 74; A Brief Historical Study of the Sining Schools and Shape Notes and Implications for Music Education Today, Mo J Res Music Educ, 76; Informal Education: Music I, Univ NDak Press, 77; The Fine Art of Listening: In Focus and in Depth, SDak Music Educr, 79; Several Methods of Handling the Boy's Changing Voice, Mo J Res Music Educ, 80; A Smile Is A Frown, SSA Choral Music, 81 & Five Spacey Nursery Rhymes, SATB Choral Music, 81, G Schirmer. *Mailing Add:* Music Dept Univ Mo 8001 Natural Bridge Rd St Louis MO 63121

WILLMERING, KEVIN DOUGLAS
PERCUSSION, EDUCATOR
b Alton, Ill, Oct 9, 54. *Study:* Capital Univ, BM, 76; Yale Sch Music, Yale Univ, MM, 79; studied with Cloyd Duff & Fred Hinger. *Pos:* Perc, Opera

Orch New York, 79-82; prin timpanist, Chamber Orch New England, 79-83, Des Moines Metro Opera, Indianola, Iowa, 80-, Albany Symph Orch, 81-, New Haven Symph Orch, 81-83 & Long Beach Symph, 83- *Teaching:* Instr perc, Chaote Sch, Wallingford, Conn, 79-81, Hartwick Col, 81-82 & NMex Music Fest, Taos, 81-82. *Mailing Add:* PO Box 385 Mt Vernon OH 43050

WILLOUGHBY, DAVID PAUL
EDUCATOR, ADMINISTRATOR
b Harrisburg, Pa, Feb 23, 33. *Study:* Lebanon Valley Col, BS(music educ), 55; Miami Univ, Ohio, ME(music educ), 59; Eastman Sch Music, PhD(music educ), 70. *Pos:* Asst dir, Contemp Music Proj, Washington, DC, 70-73. *Teaching:* Applied music & dir band & choir, Arcanum Pub Sch, Ohio, 55-58 & Mariemont Pub Sch, Cincinnati, Ohio, 58-60; from asst to assoc prof & dir band & choir, Elizabethtown Col, 60-70; prof music & dean music & fine arts, Eastern NMex Univ, 73- *Mem:* Nat Asn Sch Music; Music Educr Nat Conf; Col Music Soc (mem nat coun, 80-82, exec bd, 81-83); NMex Music Educr Asn; Int Coun Fine Arts Deans. *Publ:* Auth, Comprehensive Musicianship & Undergraduate Music Curricula, 71, ed, Comprehensive Musicianship: Anthology of Evolving Thought, 71 & Source Book of African & Afro/American Materials for Music Educators, 72, Music Educr Nat Conf & Contemp Music Proj; auth, Comprehensive Musicianship: Some Encouraging Words, Col Music Symposium, spring 82; Wingspread Conference on Music in General Studies; Music Programs Exist for Everyone, Music Educ J, 9/82. *Mailing Add:* 220 Utah Portales NM 88130

WILLOUGHBY, JAY (ALAN)
BARITONE
b St Louis, Mo. *Roles:* Germont in La Traviata, Opera Theatre St Louis, 79; Four Villains in Tales of Hoffman, Idaho Opera Nat Co, 80; Count Di Luna in Il Trovatore, Seattle Opera, 82-83; Rigoletto in Rigoletto, Hawaii Opera Theatre, 82-83. *Awards:* Fulbright Grant, 62; Joy in Singing Recital Award, 79. *Publ:* Ed, Book of Songs, Stephen Foster Drama & Hist Asn, 64. *Rep:* Columbia Artists 165 W 57th St New York NY 10019. *Mailing Add:* 51 Morton St 5B New York NY 10014

WILLS, VERA G
EDUCATOR, COMPOSER
b New York, NY. *Study:* Mannes Col Music, studied pedagogy with Frances Dillon; Hunter Col, BA. *Works:* Fat Cat (piano), 79, Lions and Spaces (piano), 81, Dandy Lion (piano), 81, Imagine That! (piano), 81, Merry Go Sorry (piano), 81, Shaggy Dog Tails (piano), 82 & Hally Hally Hastle (piano), 82, Hinshaw Music Inc. *Teaching:* Prof piano pedagogy & piano, Mannes Col Music, 67-79; lectr piano pedagogy, Rockland Community Col, State Univ NY, 71-72. *Mem:* Hon mem, Piano Teachers Cong New York (pres, 71-75); Music Teachers Nat Asn (chmn, District 1, 69-74); Assoc Music Teachers League New York; Brooklyn Music Teachers Guild; Nat Fedn Music Clubs. *Publ:* Auth, A Parent's Guide to Music Lessons, Harper & Row, 67. *Mailing Add:* Box 371 Mattituck Mattituck NY 11952

WILSON, ANTONIA JOY
CONDUCTOR, TEACHER
b Oxford, England, May 20, 57; US citizen. *Study:* Lamont Sch Music, Univ Denver, BM(violin perf), 79; Univ Southern Calif, MM(orch cond), 81. *Pos:* Guest cond, Denver Symph Orch, 79 & 83; music dir & cond, Palos Verde Youth Symph, Calif, 80-81; affil artists cond asst, St Louis Symph Orch, 81- *Teaching:* Fac cond chamber orch, Crossroads Private High Sch, 80-81; instr cond & asst cond conct orch, Aspen Music Fest, summer 81. *Bibliog:* Blair Chotzinoff (auth), Something New and Different, Denver Mag, 11/79; Ray Hartmann & Joe Bonwich (auth), A Classical Success at Age Twenty-Four, Riverfront Times, 2/82; Allen Young (auth), At Age 25 Antonia Wilson Shows Promise as Conductor, City Ed, 1/83. *Mem:* Am Symph Orch League; Nat Acad Rec Arts & Sci. *Mailing Add:* 2551 E Floyd Ave Englewood CO 80110

WILSON, C(ECIL) B(ARLEY)
EDUCATOR, ADMINISTRATOR
b Muncie, Ind, Oct 8, 38. *Study:* Northwestern Univ, BMusEd, MM, 61; Case Western Reserve Univ, PhD(musicol), 71. *Teaching:* Instr, Northwestern Univ, 61-64, Case Western Reserve Univ, 64-71; asst dean, Cleveland Inst Music, 71-77; chmn div music & prof music, WVa Univ, Morgantown, 77- *Mem:* Am Musicol Soc; Music Educr Nat Conf; WVa Music Educr Asn; WVa Col Music Educr Asn; Am Fedn Musicians. *Interests:* Music of Hector Berlioz. *Publ:* Auth, Some Remarks on Berlioz' Symphony for Band, Instrumentalist, 73-74; Program Notes, Cleveland Orch, 75, 77 & 82. *Mailing Add:* 237 Poplar Dr Morgantown WV 26505

WILSON, CARLOS E
ADMINISTRATOR
b Kansas City, Kans, Dec 17, 35. *Pos:* Asst mgr, Houston Symph, 73-77; exec dir, Denver Symph, 77-82; managing dir, San Antonio Symph, 82- *Mailing Add:* c/o San Antonio Symph 109 Lexington Ave Ste 207 San Antonio TX 78205

WILSON, DANA RICHARD
COMPOSER, PIANO
b Lakewood, Ohio, Feb 4, 46. *Study:* Bowdoin Col, BA, 68; Univ Conn, MA, 75; Eastman Sch Music, PhD, 82. *Works:* Many arrangements publ, 79-; Sati, Dorn Publ, 81; My Shadow, Kendor Music Publ, 81; Piece for Clarinet Alone, Shall-u-mo Publ, 82; Kundalini, David Unland, 82. *Teaching:* Asst prof theory & comp, Ithaca Col, 78-83, assoc prof, 84- & dir, Contemp Chamber Ens, currently. *Mem:* Sonneck Soc Am Music. *Publ:* Coauth, Contemporary Choral Arranging, Prentice-Hall (in prep). *Mailing Add:* 1642 Slaterville Rd Ithaca NY 14850

WILSON, DONALD MALCOLM
COMPOSER, TEACHER
b Chicago, Ill, June 30, 37. *Study:* Univ Chicago, BA, 59; Cornell Univ, studied comp with Karel Husa, analysis & comp with Robert Palmer, MA(comp), 62, DMA(comp), 65; Berkshire Music Ctr, studied comp with Gunther Schuller, 63-64. *Works:* Dedication (string orch), 65, Quintet (clarinet & string quartet), 65 & Five Haiku (tenor voice & chamber ens), 68, Highgate Press; Seventeen Views (violin, narrator & slides), comn by Paul Zukofsky, 67; Doubles (game-piece), 68 & Visions (chorus & symphonic band), 71, C F Peters Corp. *Pos:* Music dir, WUHY-FM Radio, Philadelphia, 65-66, prog dir, 66-67. *Teaching:* Instr music, Bowling Green State Univ, 67-69, asst prof, 69-72, chair music comp, hist dept, 73-77, assoc prof, 72- *Awards:* Second place, Joseph H Bearns Compt, 63; Armstrong Mem Res Found Award, 66; Ohio Music Teachers Asn Comp Award, 70. *Mem:* Am Music Ctr; Am Comp Alliance; Ohio Theory-Comp Teachers Asn. *Publ:* Auth, The Avant-Garde: Music with a Difference, WHYY-TV Prog Guide, 7/66; Stabile IV, NY Univ Contemp Music Newslett, 10/70; Music in the Space Age, Am Music Teacher, 4/72; Prisms, Asterisk, 12/75. *Mailing Add:* Col Musical Arts Bowling Green State Univ Bowling Green OH 43403

WILSON, FREDRIC WOODBRIDGE
MUSIC DIRECTOR, ADMINISTRATOR
b Point Pleasant, NJ, Sept 8, 47. *Study:* Lehigh Univ, BA(music), 69; NY Univ, MA(musicol), 78. *Pos:* Music dir, Wall Chamber Choir, NJ, 69-81 & Allaire Singers, Spring Lake, NJ, 80-; ed, Allaire Music Publ, Spring Lake, NJ, 80-; cur, Pierpont Morgan Libr, New York, 81- *Mem:* Asn Prof Vocal Ens; Am Choral Dir Asn; Am Musicol Soc. *Interests:* Nineteenth century English music; part song; operetta; 16th and 17th century English theorists. *Publ:* Auth, 35 published choral editions and arrangements; articles, Music Educr J, Choral J & Personal Computer Age Mag. *Mailing Add:* 263 Jumping Brook Neptune NJ 07753

WILSON, GEORGE BALCH
EDUCATOR, COMPOSER
b Grand Island, Nebr, Jan 28, 27. *Study:* Univ Mich, BMus, 51, MMus, 53, DMusArts, 62; Consv Royale Musique, Brussels, 53-54; studied with Nadia Boulanger & Roger Sessions. *Works:* Fantasy for Violin and Piano, 57, Six Pieces for Piano, 59, Six Pieces for Orchestra, 60, Fragments (electronic), 64, Exigencies (electronic), 68, Concatenations for 12 Instruments, 69 & Polarity for Solo Percussion and Electronic Sounds, 75, Jobert Publ. *Pos:* Founder & dir, Contemp Directions Conct Ser, 66- *Teaching:* Mem fac, Sch Music, Univ Mich, Ann Arbor, 61-, dir, Electronic Music Studio, 64- *Awards:* Am Acad Rome Prize, 58, 59 & 60; Nat Inst Arts & Lett Award & Citation, 70; Walter Hinrichsen Award Comp, 73. *Mem:* Am Soc Univ Comp; Pi Kappa Lambda; Phi Mu Alpha. *Mailing Add:* Sch Music Univ Mich Ann Arbor MI 48109

WILSON, JAMES EDWARD
EDUCATOR, CONDUCTOR
b Ottawa, Ont, Nov 9, 30. *Study:* Marion Col, BA, 52; Ind Univ, Bloomington, MMusEd, 54, DMus, 72. *Pos:* Mem, St Louis Symph Chorus, 82- *Teaching:* Asst prof music, Southwestern State Col, 54-56; prof music, Greenville Col, 57- *Mem:* Am Choral Dir Asn (dist chmn, 77-79 & 81-); Nat Asn Teachers Singing; Hymn Soc Am. *Publ:* Auth, Conformation of the Laryngo-Pharynx in Singing, Nat Asn Teachers Singing Bulletin, 76. *Mailing Add:* Music Dept Greenville Col Greenville IL 62246

WILSON, KEITH LEROY
CLARINET, EDUCATOR
b Garden City, Kans, Aug 15, 16. *Study:* Univ Ill, BS(music educ), 38, BMus, 39, MMus, 42. *Rec Perf:* Music for Clarinet, Golden Crest Rec, 82. *Teaching:* Instr & asst band cond, Univ Ill, 38-46; prof music, Yale Univ, 46-, dir bands, 46-73 & dir summer sch music & art, 60-81. *Mem:* Am Bandmaster's Asn; Col Band Dir Nat Asn (pres, 62-64); Int Clarinet Soc. *Publ:* Ed, Le Journal du Printemps, J C F Fischer, Transcription for Band, Assoc Music Publ, 51; transcription, Three Contemporaries, Douglas Moore, 58 & Grand Grand Overture Transcription for Band, Malcolm Arnold, 83, Carl Fischer; Symphonic Metamorphosis, European Am, 72. *Mailing Add:* Yale Sch Music Box 2104A Yale Station New Haven CT 06520

WILSON, NANCY J
VIOLIN, BAROQUE VIOLIN
b Detroit, Mich, Oct 18, 49. *Study:* Oberlin Col, BA, 71; Juilliard Sch, MM, 74. *Rec Perf:* The First Record from Astor Magna, Cambridge Rec, 76; The Six Brandenburg Concerti (Bach), Smithsonian Collection Rec, 78; Concert in the Velez Blanco Patio (A Baroque), Metropolitan Museum Art, 79; Serenade Op 25 (Beethoven), Pleides Rec, 81; Wedding Cantata BWV 210 (Bach), 81 & Mass in B Minor (Bach), 82, Nonesuch Rec; Eight Sonatas for Diverse Instruments (Handel), Smithsonian Collection Rec, 82. *Pos:* Concertmaster & soloist, Cont Royal, New York, 74-82; concertmaster & violinist, Bach Ens, New York, 78-; violinist, Smithsonian Chamber Players, Washington, DC, 79-; violinist, Class Quartet, New York, 79- *Teaching:* Fac mem violin, Third St Music Sch Settlement, 74-78; adj lectr baroque violin, Aaron Copland Sch Music, Queens Col, City Univ New York, 82- *Mem:* Chamber Music Am. *Mailing Add:* 115 W 73rd St Apt 7A New York NY 10023

WILSON, OLLY W
COMPOSER, CONDUCTOR
b St Louis, Mo, Sept 7, 37. *Study:* Washington Univ, BM, 59; Univ Ill, Urbana, MM, 60; Univ Iowa, PhD, 64; studied comp with Robert Wykes, Robert Kelley & Phillip Bezanson; Studio Experimental Music, Univ Ill, 67. *Works:*

Voices (orch), Boston Symph Orch, 70; Akwan (piano, electronic piano & orch), Baltimore Symph, 72; Echoes (solo clarinet & electronic tape), Phillip Rehfeldt, 75; Sometimes (tenor & electronic tape), William Brown, 77; Expansions (organ), Donald Sutherland, 79; Trilogy (orch), Oakland Symph Orch, 79-80. *Pos:* Bass viol player, several orch incl St Louis Phil Orch, St Louis Summer Chamber Players & Cedar Rapids Symph Orch; vis artist, Am Acad Rome, 78. *Teaching:* Asst prof music, Fla A&M Univ, 60-62 & 64-65; Oberlin Consv Music, 65-70; prof, Univ Calif, Berkeley, 70- *Awards:* Dartmouth Arts Coun Prize, 68; Guggenheim Fel, 72; Outstanding Achievement in Musical Comp Award, Am Acad Arts & Lett, 74; and others. *Bibliog:* Eileen Southern (auth), American Black Composers of Classical Music, Music Educr J, 75 & Conversation with Olly Wilson: The Education of a Composer, Black Perspective Music, spring 78; David Baker (auth), The Black Composer Speaks, Scarecrow Press Inc, 78. *Mem:* ASCAP; Am Music Ctr (mem bd dir 79-81); Meet the Comp (mem bd dir, 79-). *Publ:* Auth, The Black Anerican Composer, spring 74 & The Significance of the Relationship Between Afro-Am Music and West African Music, spring 74, Black Perspective Music; contrib, Black Music in Our Culture, Kent State Univ Press, 73; auth, Contemporary Music Today, A Composers View, Am Organist, 4/4/80; The Association of Movement and Music as a Manifestation of a Black Conceptual Approach to Music Making, In: Report 12th Cong, Berkeley, 1977, Int Musicol Soc, Barenreiter Kassel, 81. *Mailing Add:* Dept Music Univ Calif Berkeley CA 94720

WILSON, RANSOM CHARLES
CONDUCTOR, FLUTE
b Tuscaloosa, Ala, Oct 25, 51. *Study:* Juilliard Sch, BMus, 73. *Rec Perf:* Koto Flute, 79, Impressions for Flute, 78, Suites of Bach and Telemann, 80, Pleasure Songs for Flute, 81, Baroque Concertos for Flute, 82 & Music of Reich, Glass, Becker et al, 82, Angel Rec; Piano Concerti of Mozart and Haydn, Arabesque Rec, 82. *Pos:* Music dir & cond, Solisti New York Chamber Orch, 80- *Awards:* Atlantique Found Grant. *Rep:* Columbia Artists Mgt Inc 123 W 57th St New York NY 10019. *Mailing Add:* 123 W 93rd St New York NY 10025

WILSON, RICHARD EDWARD
COMPOSER, PIANO
b Cleveland, Ohio, May 15, 41. *Study:* Studied cello with Ernst Silberstein, 53-58 & piano with E W Fischer & Leonard Shure, 54-60; Harvard Col, AB(music), 63; Rutgers Univ, MA, 66. *Works:* Home From the Range, G Schirmer Inc, 71; Music for Solo Flute, 77, Eclogue, 80, August 22, 81, Sour Flowers, 82 & Ballad of Longwood Glen, 83, Boosey & Hawkes Inc; String Quartet No 3, Naumburg comn by Muir Quartet, 83. *Teaching:* Asst prof music, Vassar Col, 66-70, assoc prof, 70-76, prof, 76-, chmn dept, 79-82. *Awards:* ASCAP Award, 70-83; Burge-Eastman Prize, Eastman Sch Music, 78. *Bibliog:* David Burge (auth), Contemporary Piano, Contemp Keyboard, 1/79. *Mem:* Am Soc Univ Comp; Am Music Ctr; ASCAP. *Mailing Add:* 8 Vassar Lake Dr Poughkeepsie NY 12601

WILSON, RON (RONNIE EUGENE)
TROMBONE, TEACHER
b Dallas, Tex, Sept 25, 54. *Study:* Southern Methodist Univ, BM 78. *Pos:* Prin trombone, Dallas Ballet Orch, 79- & Ft Worth Symph Orch, 80- *Teaching:* Instr trombone, Northlake Community Col, 80-82; priv teacher trombone, ed, Richardson Independent Sch District, 81- *Awards:* Leonard Bernstein Fel, Berkshire Music Fest, 80. *Mem:* Int Trombone Asn. *Mailing Add:* 204 Fairview Garland TX 75040

WILSON, SYDNEY VIRGINIA
HARP, EDUCATOR
b Great Bend, Kans, Dec 28, 42. *Study:* NTex State Univ, BA; New England Consv Music, MMus; Yamaha Music Sch, Downey, Calif, sr teacher cert, 73. *Rec Perf:* Brahms' Vier Gesange, 68; The Ceremony of Carols (Britten), 74. *Pos:* Freelance harpist, Brockton Symph, Mass, 68 & others; prin harp, Ft Worth Symph, formerly. *Teaching:* Instr piano & harp, Tarrant Co Jr Col, Ft Worth, 72-; instr harp, Tex Christian Univ, 72-; teacher, Yamaha Music Sch, Ft Worth, 73- *Mem:* Mu Phi Epsilon; Pi Kappa Lambda; Ft Worth Symph League. *Mailing Add:* 2820 W Fuller St Ft Worth TX 76133

WILSON, THOMAS E
CONDUCTOR, EDUCATOR
b Lafayette, Ind, Oct 1, 18. *Study:* Cent Normal Col, BS, 39; Army Music Sch, 43; Univ Mich, Ann Arbor, MMus(lit), 49. *Pos:* Cond, Sedalia Army Airfield Symph, 43-45, Hoosier Symph Orch & Chorale, 45-51 & Lafayette Symph Opera, 51-58; assoc cond, Scandinavian Symph Detroit, 50. *Teaching:* Fel repertoire orch, Univ Mich, Ann Arbor, 48-49; assoc prof symph & choral, Canterbury Col, 49-51; asst dir musical orgn, Purdue Univ, 51-53. *Awards:* Fel, Am Inst Fine Arts, 66. *Mem:* Am Symph Orch League (mem bd dir & vpres, 51-54); Am Fedn Musicians (mem bd dir & vpres, 40-); Calif Choral Cond Guild (mem bd dir Los Angeles chap, 65); Nat Oratorio Soc (pres, 70-). *Publ:* Contribr, Oratorio Column, Worship and Arts Mag, 72- *Mailing Add:* 11392 Wallingsford Rd Los Alamitos CA 90720

WILSON, TODD RODNEY
ORGAN, TEACHER
b Toledo, Ohio, Nov 3, 54. *Study:* Col Consv Music, Univ Cincinnati, BMus, 76, MMus, 78. *Pos:* Organist & master of choirs, Cath of Incarnation, Garden City, NY, 80-; dir music, Mercer Sch Theol, 80- *Teaching:* Mem fac music, Adelphi Univ, & Hofstra Univ, 80- *Awards:* Grand Prix Chartres, France, 78; Nat Organ Compt, First Congregational Church, Los Angeles, Calif, 75 & First Presbyterian Church, Ft Wayne, Ind, 77. *Mem:* Am Guild Organists; Anglican Asn Musicians. *Rep:* Murtagh-McFarlane Artists Inc 3269 W 30th St Cleveland OH 44109. *Mailing Add:* 50 Cathedral Ave Garden City NY 11530

WINCENC, CAROL
FLUTE, TEACHER
b Buffalo, NY, June 29, 49. *Study:* Santa Cecilia Acad; Chigiana Acad, Italy, dipl, 68; Manhattan Sch Music, BMus, 71; Juilliard Sch Music, MMus, 72. *Pos:* Prin & solo flutist, St Paul Chamber Orch, 72-77; solo flutist & chamber player, Marlboro Music Fest & Music from Marlboro, 78-80; guest artist, Mozart Fest, Lincoln Ctr Chamber Music Soc, Santa Fe & Spoleto Fest, 79-; panel mem, Nat Endowment Arts, 80-; prin flutist, Musica Camerit of Merkin Conct Hall, New York, 82- *Teaching:* Private flute instr, Manhattan Sch Music, 80- *Awards:* First Prize Solo Flute Compt, Walter W Naumburg Found, 78. *Mem:* Am Fedn Musicians; Nat Flute Asn. *Rep:* Hamlen-Landau Mgt 140 W 79th St New York NY 10024. *Mailing Add:* 875 West End Ave New York NY 10025

WINDHAM, VERNE
FRENCH HORN
b Moscow, Idaho, July 17, 46. *Study:* Eastman Sch Music, studied horn with Verne Reynolds, BM, 68. *Pos:* Prin horn, Spokane Symph Orch, 71-; hornist, Spokane Falls Brass Band, 79- *Teaching:* Asst prof horn, Washington State Univ, 71- *Mem:* Spokane Musical Arts; Am Fedn Musicians. *Publ:* Coauth, From Miner's Tent to Opera House, Spokane Symph, 80. *Mailing Add:* S 1328 Coeur d'Alene St Spokane WA 99204

WINESANKER, MICHAEL M
EDUCATOR, ADMINISTRATOR
b Toronto, Can, Aug 7, 13; US citizen. *Study:* Univ Toronto, studied comp with Healey Willan, BMus, 33; Trinity Col, London, LMusTCL, 40; Univ Mich, MA, 41; Cornell Univ, studied musicol with Otto Kinkeldey, PhD, 44. *Teaching:* Instr piano, Hambourg Consv, 39-41; lectr theory & music hist, Bay View Summer Col, 45; prof musicol, Univ Tex, 45-46; prof, Tex Christian Univ, 46-, chmn dept music, 56-81. *Awards:* Am Coun Learned Soc Fel, 44; Piper Prof, Piper Found Tex, 77; Distinguished Prof, Mortar Bd, 81-82. *Mem:* Music Teachers Nat Asn; Ft Worth Music Teachers Asn (pres, 63-65); Ft Worth Piano Teachers Forum; Am Musicol Soc; Tex Asn Music Sch. *Interests:* English comic opera, 1750-1800. *Publ:* Auth, Musico-Dramatic Criticism of English Comic Opera 1750-1800, J Am Musicol Soc, Vol II No 2; Una Nueva Cantata de Juan Sebastian Bach?, Rev Estudio Musicales, 12/54; Comic Opera in America—Past and Present, Am Music Teacher, 4/60; Books on Music, A Classified List, Tex Asn Music Sch, 79. *Mailing Add:* 3613 Park Ridge Blvd Ft Worth TX 76109

WINICK, STEVEN DAVID
EDUCATOR, TRUMPET
b Brooklyn, NY, July 7, 44. *Study:* Eastman Sch Music, BM, 66, MM, 68, DMA, 73. *Works:* Confrontation for Brass Trio, 69 & Equinoctial Points for Solo Trumpet, 70, NY Autograph Ed. *Pos:* Trumpet with various symph orch, 68- *Teaching:* Instr trumpet, Eastman Sch Music, 66-69; assoc prof music & dept chmn, Ga State Univ, 75- *Bibliog:* D R Hein (auth), Twentieth-Century Trumpet Music, Woodwind Brass & Perc World, 5/77. *Mem:* Nat Asn Sch Music (chmn elect-region VII, 80-83); Am Fedn Musicians; Int Trumpet Guild; Col Music Soc; Music Educr Nat Conf. *Publ:* Auth, Contemporary Music for Unaccompanied Trumpet, 1/71 & Music for Brass Trio, 1/73, Instrumentalist; Rhythm: An Annotated Bibliography, Scarecrow Press, 74; ed, F J Gossec's Tambourin for Trumpet and Piano, Carl Fischer, 76; I Schakov's Scherzo for Trumpet and Piano, Brass Press, 80. *Mailing Add:* Music Dept Ga State Univ Univ Plaza Atlanta GA 30303

WINKLER, DAVID
COMPOSER
b Chicago, Ill, Oct 11, 48. *Study:* Univ Calif, Los Angeles, with Roy Harris, BA(music), 70; Columbia Univ, with Charles Wuorinen, Jack Beeson, Chou Wen-chung, Vladimir Ussachevsky & Jacques-Louis Monod, MA(music). *Works:* Three Sonnets for Soprano & Piano, 76; Three Pieces for Violoncello Solo, 76; Intermezzo for Piano, 76; Serenade, 78; Duo for Clarinet and Piano, 78; Cantata (soli & orch), 78; Five Shakespeare Sonnets (two soli & ten instrm), 78. *Teaching:* Fel, Columbia Univ, 73-78. *Awards:* Bernstein Comp Fel, Berkshire Music Ctr, 72; BMI Student Comp Award, 72; Rapaport Prize, 76. *Bibliog:* Radio interview, WQXR, 74. *Mem:* Guild Comp Inc; BMI; Am Comp Alliance. *Mailing Add:* 362 Broadway 3rd Floor New York NY 10013

WINKLER, PETER KENTON
COMPOSER, EDUCATOR
b Los Angeles, Calif, Jan 26, 43. *Study:* Univ Calif, Berkeley BA, 63; Princeton Univ, Earl Kim, MFA, 66. *Works:* String Quartet, perf by Comp String Quartet, 66; Humoresque (piano), perf by Robert Black, 70; Ragtime Grackle (oboe), comn by Nora Post, 72; Symphony, Stony Brook Orch, 78; Recitativo e Terzetto, comn by Contemp Ens, Redlands Univ, 80; Clarinet Bouquet, Comn By Jack Kreiselman, 80. *Teaching:* Asst prof Music, State Univ NY, Stony Brook, 71-77, assoc prof, 77- *Awards:* Harvard Univ Jr Fel, 68-71; MacDowell Colony Fel, 78. *Mem:* Sonneck Soc; Int Asn Study Popular Music. *Publ:* Auth, Toward a Theory of Popular Harmony, In Theory Only, Vol 4, No 2; Pop Music's Middle Years, Music Educr J, 79. *Mailing Add:* 15 Bayview Ave East Setauket NY 11733

WINN, JAMES FREDERICK
PIANO, TEACHER
b Denver, Colo, Jan 13, 52. *Study:* New England Consv Music, BMus, 74, MMus, 76; Univ Mich, DMusA, 83. *Pos:* Mem, Piano Duo, Grant & Winn, 70- *Teaching:* Asst prof piano, Univ Tex, San Antonio, 83. *Awards:* Second Prize, Munich Int Music Compt, 80. *Rep:* Perf Artist Assoc of Great Lakes 310 E Washington St Ann Arbor MI. *Mailing Add:* 1150 S Laurel St #2 Menlo Park CA 94025

WINOGRAD, ARTHUR
CONDUCTOR & MUSIC DIRECTOR
b New York, NY, Apr 22, 20. *Study:* New England Consv Music, 37-40; Curtis Inst Music, 40-41. *Pos:* Cellist, Boston Symph Orch, 40 & NBC Symph, 42-43; staff cond, MGM Rec, 54-58 & Audio Fidelity Rec, 58-60; cond & music dir, Birmingham Symph Orch, 60-64 & Hartford Symph, 64- *Teaching:* Mem fac chamber music, Juilliard Sch, 46-55, founder & mem, Juilliard String Quartet. *Rep:* Andrew Benson 1911 Wynnefield Terr Philadelphia PA 19131. *Mailing Add:* Hartford Symph Orch 609 Farmington Hartford CT 06105

WINOKUR, ROSELYN M
COMPOSER, PIANO
b Trenton, NJ. *Study:* Sarah Lawrence Col, BA, 56, MFA, 76. *Works:* Once Upon A Woodwind, 78, The Nutcracker & The Mouse King, 78, Silents, Please!, 79, The Princess Who Talked Backwards, 80, Rip Van Winkle, 81 & Mainly Mozart, 82, Tanglewylde Press. *Pos:* Mem artist, New York Chamber Artists, 76- & Story Conct Players, 78-; artistic dir, Music For Many Inc, 79- *Teaching:* Guest lectr, Amsterdam Sweelinck Consv, 79. *Awards:* ASCAP Award, 80-84; Nat Compt Winner, Atlanta Children's Theater, 82; winner, Nat Comp Perf Arts Repty Theatre, 83, Nat Endowment for the Arts Opera & Musical Theater Prog Comn. *Mem:* Chamber Music Am; Cent Opera Serv; Opera For Youth; Nat Opera Asn; Am Music Ctr. *Rep:* Michael Leavitt 195 Steamboat Rd Great Neck NY 11024. *Mailing Add:* Gregory Lane Millwood NY 10546

WINSLOW, WALTER KEITH
COMPOSER, PIANO
b Salem, Ore, Sept 16, 47. *Study:* Banff Sch Fine Arts, with Boris Roubakine, 66-67; Consv Music, Oberlin Col, AB, 70, MusB, 70; Univ Calif, Berkeley, MA, 72, PhD, 75. *Works:* The Bells of Eola, San Francisco Contemp Music Players, 80; String Quartet, Audubon Quartet, 81; Nahua Songs, 83 & The Piper at the Gates of Dawn, 83, CRI; Canzone, Comp Conf Players, 82. *Teaching:* Asst prof theory & comp, Univ Calif, Berkeley, 75-82; vis asst prof theory, Oberlin Consv, 83- *Awards:* Goddard Lieberson Fel, Am Acad & Int Arts & Letters, 83. *Mem:* Am Comp Alliance; Am Soc Univ Comp (regional co-chair, 79-83); Col Music Soc; Soc Ore Comp. *Mailing Add:* 1574 37th Ave Salem OR 97304

WINSOR, PHILIP GORDON
COMPOSER, EDUCATOR
b Morris, Ill, May 10, 38. *Study:* Ill Wesleyan Univ, Bloomington, BM(comp), 60; Univ Calif, Berkeley, 61; San Francisco State Univ, 63; Italy Consv Music, Milan, 64; Univ Ill, Urbana, 65-66. *Works:* Over fifty works, including choral, orchestral, electronic, chamber, dance and intermedia; Conflations (orch), perf by Rome Radio Orch, 67; City (environmental sound components, dancers, tape), 75; Jamboree (instrm, dancers, tape, electronics, projections), 76 & Sequence I (electronic music, dancers, projections), 77, comn by Chicago Contemp Dance Theatre; Do Not Go Gentle Into That Good Night, perf by Roosevelt Univ Contemp Music Ens, 78; Cindy 633 (multiple amplified pianos), perf by Univ Redlands New Music Ens, 79; Planesong (instrm octet, amplified), perf by Northwestern Univ Contemp Music Ens, 80. *Pos:* Dir, Electronic Music Studio, Minn State Univ, Moorhead, 67-68 & 72-77; dir Contemp Music Ens, DePaul Univ, 70-79 & musical dir & res comp, Chicago Contemp Dance Theatre, 70-78; co-dir, Ctr Experimental Music & Intermedia, NTex State Univ, 82- *Teaching:* Instr theory & comp, San Francisco Music & Arts Inst, 64-65 & Minn State Univ, Moorhead, 67-68; asst prof comp, DePaul Univ, 68-78; chmn theory & comp dept & assoc prof music, 79-82; Morton vis prof, Ohio Univ, 78; assoc prof music, NTex State Univ, 82- *Awards:* Fels, Prix de Rome, 66-67; Ford Found, 73 & Nat Endowment Arts, 77 & 79. *Mem:* Am Comp Alliance; BMI; Chicago Soc Comp (mem bd dir, 78-82); New Music Alliance; Am Soc Univ Comp (regional chmn, 80). *Mailing Add:* 2321 Leslie St Denton TX 76201

WINSTEAD, WILLIAM
EDUCATOR, COMPOSER
b Hopkinsville, Ky, Dec 11, 42. *Study:* Curtis Inst Music, with Thomas Canning & Ben Weber, BMus; WVa Univ, MMus. *Works:* The Moon Singer (orch); Symphony No 1 (orch); Scarlet Landscape (chamber orch). *Pos:* Prin bassoonist, Marlboro Music Fest, seven yrs; performer, Fest Two Worlds, Maine Bay Chamber Conct & Lake George Opera; soloist, Pittsburgh Symph, formerly & Philadelphia Orch, formerly; recitalist chamber music in US & Can. *Teaching:* Mem fac, WVA Univ, 65-69; prof bassoon, Fla State Univ, 79- *Awards:* Nat Endowment Arts Grant, 76; WVA Arts & Humanities Coun Grant. *Mailing Add:* Music Dept Fla State Univ Tallahassee FL 32306

WINTER, DANIEL WALLACE
EDUCATOR, PIANO
b Mt Pleasant, Iowa. *Study:* Maryville Col, BA, 50; Eastman Sch Music, MM, 54; Boston Univ, 58; Ind Univ, Bloomington, 60-61. *Teaching:* Kettering prof & chmn music dept, Col Wooster, Ohio, 54-; vis prof piano, Univ Cuyo, Mendoza, Arg, 59. *Awards:* First Prize, Memphis & Mid-South Piano Scholar Asn, 49. *Mem:* Music Teachers Nat Asn; Ohio Music Teachers Asn (first vpres, 82-). *Publ:* Auth, My Years with Matthay & Schnabel, Clavier Mag, 3/82. *Mailing Add:* 235 W Henrietta St Wooster OH 44691

WINTER, JAMES HAMILTON
EDUCATOR, FRENCH HORN
b Minneapolis, Minn, Oct 18, 19. *Study:* Carleton Col, BA, 42; Northwestern Univ, MMus, 47; Univ Iowa, PhD, 55. *Works:* Bourree for Horn Trio; Three Canons for Two Horns; Suite for a Quartet of Young Horns. *Pos:* Prin horn, Fresno Phil Orch, Monterey Peninsula Symph, Am Symph Orch League &

WCoast Wkshp Orch; mem, Calif Woodwind Quintet & Cent Calif Wind Quintet; horn ed, Woodwind World Mag, 55-65; ed brass, Jour Nat Asn Col Wind & Perc Instrm, 65-69; ed, Horn Call, 72-76; mem bd dir, Fresno Phil Asn, 73- & bd trustees, 82-; prin horn & soloist, Music from Bear Valley Fest, mem bd dirs, 81- *Teaching:* Instr music, Calif State Univ, Fresno, 47-50, asst prof, 50-53, assoc prof, 53-59, prof, 59-, asst dean arts & sci, 67-69, chmn music dept, 72-76; mem fac & performer, Int Wkshps, Int Horn Soc. *Mem:* Int Horn Soc; Phi Mu Alpha Sinfonia; Pi Kappa Lambda. *Publ:* Auth, The Brass Instruments, 74. *Mailing Add:* Music Dept Calif State Univ Fresno CA 93740

WINTER, JOEL
EDUCATOR, FRENCH HORN
Study: Juilliard Sch Music, BM, MS. *Pos:* Extra horn, New York Phil; freelance horn, New York, NY & Conn; mem, Denver Symph, Oklahoma City Symph, Central City Opera & Denver Woodwind Quintet, formerly. *Teaching:* Mem fac French horn, Manhattan Sch Music, 79- *Mailing Add:* Manhattan Sch Music 120 Claremont Ave New York NY 10027

WINTERS, BARBARA JO
OBOE
b Salt Lake City, Utah. *Study:* Yale Univ, 60; Univ Calif, Los Angeles, AB, 60, 60-61. *Pos:* Prin oboe, Los Angeles Phil Orch, 62- *Mailing Add:* 3529 Coldwater Canyon Studio City CA 91604

WINTERS, GEORGE ARCHER
DOUBLE BASS, COMPOSER
b St Paul, Minn, Dec 3, 50. *Study:* Univ Colo, Boulder, BMus; Eastman Sch Music, MMus. *Works:* Two String Quartets; Dance Suite for Strings; Two Brass Quintets; Fanfare for Strings and Brass; Nocturne for Chamber Orchestra; Serenade for Two Horns and Strings. *Rec Perf:* Brahms & Verdi Requiems. *Pos:* Music dir, Winters Chamber Orch, formerly; cond, Brockport Cond Fest, 78; double bass, San Antonio Symph, currently. *Awards:* Aspen Music Fest Scholar, 76. *Mem:* Bruno Walter Soc; Am Fedn Musicians; Am Symph Orch League; Int Soc Bassists. *Mailing Add:* 6515 Spring Well #3 San Antonio TX 78249

WINTLE, JAMES R
EDUCATOR, COMPOSER
b Pittsburg, Kans, Sept 18, 42. *Study:* Pittsburg State Univ, with Markwood Holmes; Univ Kans, with John Pozdro & Douglas Moore. *Works:* Music for Woodwind Quintet; Alla Camera (clarinet, cello & piano); Katachresis (chamber ens); Paraphonoi (string quartet); Capriccio (organ); Movement (clarinet & piano); Pezzo Concertante a Due Pianoforte (two pianos). *Teaching:* Fac mem, Southwestern Col, Kans, 68-71; assoc prof music, Southeastern Okla State Univ, 71- *Mailing Add:* Music Dept Southeastern Okla State Univ Durant OK 74701

WINZENBURGER, WALTER PAUL
EDUCATOR, BAROQUE VIOLIN
b Rutland, Vt, Nov 2, 35. *Study:* Eastman Sch Music, BM(music theory), 57, MA(music theory), 60, PhD(music theory), 65. *Pos:* Viola sect, Ohio Chamber Orch, 72-75; viola & asst prin, Akron Symph, 75-; baroque violin & viola, Ganassi Early Music Ens, Cleveland, 75- *Teaching:* Asst prof music theory, Grove City Col, 62-66; prof, Baldwin Wallace Col, 66-; lectr perf pract & viola, Am Inst, Graz, Austria, 73-75. *Awards:* Grants, Nat Endowment Humanities, 79 & Shell Found, 83. *Mem:* Riemenschneider Bach Inst; Am Musicol Soc; Cleveland Comp Guild. *Interests:* Baroque performance practice; musical rhetoric during the Classic period. *Publ:* Auth, Ernst Ludwig Gerber on J S Bach, 70, Die Wahren Grundsatze, Kirnberger Abstracts, 70, Meter and Tempo in the Music of the Early Baroque, 72, Baroque Bowing & Articulation (in prep) & Musical Rhetoric and Beethoven's Sforzandi (in prep), Bach Quart. *Mailing Add:* 9284 Willow Lane Olmsted Falls OH 44138

WION, JOHN H
FLUTE & PICCOLO, TEACHER-COACH
b Rio de Janeiro, Brazil, Jan 22, 37; Australian citizen. *Study:* Univ Melbourne, 55-58; flute study with Julius Baker, Claude Monteux, William Kincaid & Marcel Moyse, 58-63. *Rec Perf:* Complete Wind Music of Neilsen, 65 & Serenades of M Reger, 70, Lyrichord; Quintet for Piano and Winds (L Spohr), 73 & Quintet (R Cordero), 73, Turnabout; Quintets (Molique & Romberg), 75 & Concertos, 75, Musical Heritage; French Salon Music, Lyrichord, 82. *Pos:* Piccolo, Am Symph Orch, 63-65; first flute, New York City Opera, 65-; recitals & concertos, US, Australia, New Zealand, & mem; Bronx Arts Ens, 76- *Teaching:* Vis lectr flute, Hartt Sch Music, 76-; fac flute, Mannes Col Music, 76- *Mem:* Nat Flute Asn (bd mem, 79-81); New York City Opera (bd mem, 83-). *Publ:* Auth, Newly Published Music for Flute, Instrumentalist, 82, 83. *Rep:* Australian Broadcasting Comn 1 Rockefeller Plaza 1700 New York NY 10020. *Mailing Add:* 180 Riverside Dr New York NY 10024

WIRT, JOHN (STEPHEN)
GUITAR, CRITIC & WRITER
b Richmond, Va, Aug 21, 55. *Study:* Va Commonwealth Univ, BM, 79, MMus, 82; studied guitar with Jesus Silva. *Pos:* Guitarist, Humphrey's Restaurant, 82-83, Sam Miller's Restaurant, 82 & Commonwealth Club, 82-83; music rev, Richmond Times Dispatch, 83-; recitalist in Va, Washington, DC & NY. *Teaching:* Instr guitar, Richmond pub sch, 78, Guitar Works, Richmond, 79- & Swift Creek Acad Perf Arts, 81-82. *Bibliog:* Jim Mason (auth), Classical Guitarist Adds Touch of Grace, Richmond News Leader, 4/80; Patty Campbell (host), Mid-day Music, WRFK FM, 4/83; Pam

Pumphrey (dir), John Wirt, Guitarist (film), 4/83. *Publ:* Auth, The Status of the Guitar in Serious Music, Part I, spring 83, Part II, summer 83, Guitar Rev; Crossroads Coffeehouse Offers Acoustical Oasis, Stepping Out, 3/83. *Mailing Add:* 2702 Hanover Ave #2 Richmond VA 23220

WISNESKEY, ROBERT
EDUCATOR, BASSOON
b Cleveland, Ohio, Aug 15, 20. *Study:* Manhattan Sch Music; Cleveland Inst Music; Western Reserve Univ; Berkshire Music Fest; studied bassoon with Ernst Kubitschek, Simon Kovar, Raymond Allard & August Richert. *Pos:* Mem, St Louis Munic Opera Orch, formerly, Cleveland Little Symph, formerly, St Louis Symph Orch, currently & Young Audiences Woodwind Quintet, St Louis, currently. *Teaching:* Mem fac bassoon, St Louis Consv Music, currently. *Mailing Add:* 4237 Roland St Louis MO 63121

WISNIEWSKI, THOMAS JOSEPH
EDUCATOR, MUSIC DIRECTOR
b Chicago, Ill, Sept 17, 26. *Study:* Am Consv Music, Chicago, BM, 48; Northern Ill Univ, MM, 63. *Teaching:* Violin instr, Am Consv Music, 48-50; instr stringed instrm, Maywood Pub Sch, Ill, 50-55; dir orch, Lombard Pub Sch, Ill, 55-67; prof music, Univ Ill, Chicago, 67-; plus numerous clinics & workshops across the US for twenty years. *Mem:* Music Educr Nat Conf; Am String Teachers Asn; Ill String Teachers Asn; Ill Music Educr Asn; Pi Kappa Lambda. *Publ:* Coauth (with John Higgins), Learning Unlimited String Program, Vol I, 75 & Vol II, 76, Hal Leonard Publ Corp; auth, ABC's for Strings . . . Analysis of Baroque Concertos, 78, Teaching Is a Selling Job, 79 & Is There Life After Contest, 83, Lyons Teacher News. *Mailing Add:* Univ Illinois 2136 Music Bldg Urbana IL 61801

WITKIN, BEATRICE
COMPOSER, PIANO
b New York, NY. *Study:* Hunter Col, City Univ New York, BA(music), 37; NY Univ, 39, Sch Arts, NY Univ, 72. *Works:* Parameters for 8 Instruments & Five Players, 65 & 66-67, 12 Tone Variations on Quotes by the Beatles, 68, Chiaroscuro (cello & piano), 69, Breath & Sounds for Tuba & Tape, 71-73, Echologie for Flutes & Tape, 73-74, Reports from the Planet of Mars for Orch and Tape, 78 & Stephen Foster Revisited for Concert Band, 81-82, Belwin Mills. *Rec Perf:* Triads & Things for Brass Quintet, Parameters for 8 Instruments and 5 Players, Interludes for Solo Flute, Prose Poem for Mezzo Soprano, Speaker, Instruments on a work by James T Farrell, Duo for Violin and Piano, Chiaroscuro for Cello and Piano & Contour for Piano, Opus One Rec. *Pos:* Pres, Comt Int Comp Concerts, New York, 65-; treas & mem bd dir, Music In Our Time, New York, 67-69; founder, Comp Recognition Week, New York, 68-69. *Awards:* Grants, Nat Endowment Arts, 68 & 77, Ford Found, 71 & Creative Artist Pub Serv Award, 78. *Mem:* ASCAP; Am Music Ctr. *Mailing Add:* Box 488 Cathedral Station New York NY 10025

WITTEKIND, DONALD H
EDUCATOR, TROMBONE
b New York, NY, Nov 4, 23. *Study:* Juilliard Sch Music, dipl, 47; Teachers Col, Columbia Univ, BS, 52, MA, 53, dipl(spec music educ), 54. *Pos:* Trombone, Nat Symph Orch, 47-50; bass trombone, Radio City Music Hall, 52- *Teaching:* Instr lower brass, Prep Dept, Juilliard Sch, 42-43; dir band & instrm music, Lincoln Sch Jr High, New Providence, NJ, 52-53; studio teacher lower brass, Teachers Col, Columbia Univ, 60-65 & Juilliard Sch Music, 65-; fac instrm, New York Col Music, 61-69; asst prof music educ, NY Univ, 69- *Awards:* Prize Disque for Canzona's of Gabrielli, French Music Soc, 52. *Bibliog:* Hugo Magliocco (auth), Literature Reviews, Vol VII, No 3 & Vern Kagarice & Allen Ostrander (auth), International Trombone Workshop, Vol VIII, No 4, Int Trombone Asn; Gloria J Musser (auth), Reviews, Woodwind, Brass & Perc, 12/81. *Mem:* Life mem, Phi Mu Alpha Sinfonia; Col Music Soc; Asn Conct Bands Am, Inc; Int Trombone Asn. *Publ:* Auth, Patterns in Tongueing, Award Music, 80. *Rep:* Henry Adler 207 Devon Rd Westwood NJ 07675. *Mailing Add:* 55-05 Woodside Ave Apt 501 Woodside NY 11377

WOHLAFKA, LOUISE ANN
SOPRANO, TEACHER
b Manchester, NH, Oct 14, 46. *Study:* State Univ NY, Fredonia, with Mary Elaine Wallace, BS(educ), 68; Univ Southern Ill, with Marjorie Lawrence; Tri-Cities Opera, with Peyton Hibbitt & Carmen Savoca. *Rec Perf:* Gloria (Vivaldi), Compagnia Fonografica Espagnola, Bocaccio, 80; Concierto en St Patrick, Prix de Disc. *Roles:* Pamina in Die Zauberflöte, Tri-Cities Opera, 74; Norma in Norma, Opera Theater, Syracuse, 75; Madame Butterfly in Madame Butterfly, 76 & Lucia in Lucia di Lammermoor 77, Tri-Cities Opera; Zerlina in Don Giovanni, Met Opera, 81; Norma in Norma, Tri-Cities Opera, Binghamton, 82; soloist, Lairs of Soundings, Binghamton Symph, 82; Tirezias of Les Mammelles, Metropolitan Opera, 83. *Pos:* Soloist, Tri-Cities Opera, Binghamton, NY, 68- & Metropolitan Opera, 78- *Teaching:* Private instr voice, Binghamton & New York, 70- *Awards:* Nat Opera Inst Grant, Lila Acheson Wallace, 77; grant, Beards Fund of New York, 82. *Mem:* Am Guild Musicians & Artists; Am Fedn TV & Radio Artists. *Rep:* Chris Purdy Inc 254 W 93rd St Suite 8 New York NY 10025. *Mailing Add:* 37 Mason Ave Binghamton NY 13904

WOITACH, JERYL METZ See Metz, Jeryl

WOITACH, RICHARD
CONDUCTOR, PIANO
b Binghamton, NY, July 27, 35. *Study:* Eastman Sch Music, with Paul White, BM, 56; studied piano with Orazio Frugoni. *Rec Perf:* Solo piano, Opus One

Label, 67 & 71; with London Symph, Saturn, 80; song recital with Regina Resnik. *Pos:* Pianist, Rochester Phil Orch, formerly; piano soloist, Buffalo Phil Orch, formerly & Boston Symph Orch, formerly; repetiteur, asst cond & chorus master, Cincinnati Summer Opera, 59-62; asst cond, Metropolitan Opera, 59-68; res assoc cond, 73-; music dir, Western Opera Theater, San Francisco, 68-70 & 72 & Alaska Fest Music, formerly; guest cond, Boston Opera Co, Philadelphia Opera Co, San Francisco Opera, Ariz Opera, 81, Vancouver Fest, Am Symph Orch, Naumburg Symph & Opera Hamilton, Can; prin cond & coach, Young Artist Prog, Wolf Trap Co, summers 81 & 82; artistic adv, Ariz Opera Co, 82-83. *Teaching:* Guest teacher, Tanglewood Inst, 65-66; guest lectr music, Ind Univ, 72; mem fac, Curtis Inst Music, formerly, Acad Vocal Arts, formerly & Berkshire Music Ctr, formerly. *Rep:* Tony Hartman Assoc 250 W 57th St Suite 1128A New York NY 10107. *Mailing Add:* 697 West End Ave New York NY 10025

WOJCIAK, ROBERT H
CONDUCTOR, CLARINET
b Pittsburgh, Pa, June 6, 36. *Study:* Univ Mich, with Albert Luconi, BM, 58, MM(woodwind instrm), 59; Univ Southern Calif, with Ingolf Dahl, DMA(perf), 67. *Pos:* Solo clarinet, US Air Force Band & Orch, Washington, DC, 59-63; dir bands, Univ Cincinnati, 69-72. *Teaching:* Asst prof music, Univ Southern Calif, 63-69, chmn wind & perc dept, 72-, dir contemp music ens, 76-, prof & dir wind orch, 79- *Awards:* Ramo Music Fac Award, 81. *Mem:* Col Band Dir Nat Asn. *Mailing Add:* Univ Southern Calif Sch Music 840 W 34th St Los Angeles CA 90089

WOJTASZEK, TERESA (JANINA) KUBIAK
SOPRANO
b Ldzan, Poland. *Study:* State Col Music, Lodz, Poland, with Olga Olgina, MA, 65; Vacance Musicali, Venice, Italy, with Gina Cigna, 66. *Rec Perf:* La Calisto (Cavalli), Argo, London, 71; Glagolitic Mass (Yanacek), 73 & Eugene Onegin (Tatjana), 74, Decca Rec; Famous Polish Singers, Muza, 75; Symphony No 14 (Shostakovich), Columbia, 77. *Roles:* Ellen in Peter Grimes, Lyr Opera of Chicago, 71-76; Madame Butterfly, Aida & Tosca, Royal Opera House, Covent Garden, 72; Jenufa, Lisa in Pique Dame & Tannhäuser, Metropolitan Opera, 72-83; Elsa in Lohengrin & Ballo in Mascher, Vienna Staatsoper, Austria, 73; Tosca, Bayerische Staatsoper, Munich, 76; Chrysothemis in Electra, Paris Opera, France, 77; Tosca, Teatro Dell Opera, Roma, Italy, 78. *Awards:* Second Prize, Int Music Compt, Munich, 65; First Class Award, Ministry Art & Cult, Warsaw, 74; Knight Cross Polonia Restituta, Polish Govt, 75. *Mem:* Am Guild Musical Artist. *Rep:* Columbia Artists Mgt Inc 165 W 57th St New York NY 10019; 195 Gates Ave. *Mailing Add:* 195 Gates Ave Montclair NJ 07042

WOLCOTT, VERNON
ORGAN, EDUCATOR
b Hudson, NY, June 4, 33. *Study:* Curtis Inst Music, BM, 54; Union Theol Sem, NY, SMM, 56; Univ Mich, AMusD, 67. *Pos:* Organist & choirmaster, St Peter's Lutheran Church, New York, NY, 55-57 & Franklin St Presby Church, Baltimore, Md, 58-62. *Teaching:* Mem fac, Peabody Consv, 58-62; prof music, Col Musical Arts, Bowling Green State Univ, 62- *Mem:* Am Guild Organists; Music Teachers Nat Asn. *Publ:* Auth, Organ Reform: Phase II, Am Music Teacher, 73. *Mailing Add:* 1056 Fort Dr Bowling Green OH 43402

WOLF, ANDREW LEONARD
DOUBLE BASS
b Cincinnati, Ohio, Apr 24, 16. *Study:* Cincinnati Col Music, BS(Music), 40. *Pos:* String bassist second stand, Cincinnati Symph, 47- *Mailing Add:* 3135 Ramona Cincinnati OH 45211

WOLF, EDWARD CHRISTOPHER
EDUCATOR, WRITER
b Circleville, Ohio, July 21, 32. *Study:* Capital Univ, BSM, 53; Univ Birmingham, England; Northwestern Univ, MM, 55; Univ Ill, PhD, 60. *Teaching:* From instr to prof music, head music dept & dir sch fine arts, West Liberty State Col, 60- *Awards:* Fulbright Scholar. *Mem:* Music Educr Nat Conf (WVa pres, 65-67); Am Musicol Soc; Sonneck Soc; Col Music Soc. *Interests:* German-American music and musical life; Lutheran church music in America. *Publ:* Auth, Music in Old Zion, Philadelphia, 1750-1850, Musical Quart, 72; The Secular Pipe Organ in American Culture, Bicentennial Tracker, 76; Lutheran Hymnody and Music in America 1700-1850, Concordia Hist Inst Quart, 77; Johann Gottfried Schmauk: German-American Music Educator, J Res Music Educ, 77; Wheeling's German Singing Societies, WVa Hist, 81. *Mailing Add:* Hall Fine Arts West Liberty State Col West Liberty WV 26074

WOLF, EUGENE KENDRICK
MUSICOLOGIST, EDUCATOR
b New York, NY, May 25, 39. *Study:* Univ Rochester, BMus, 61; NY Univ, MA, 64, PhD, 72. *Pos:* Rev ed, J Am Musicol Soc, 72-77. *Teaching:* Lectr fine arts, Syracuse Univ, 67-72, asst prof, 72-73; asst prof, Univ Pa, 72-73, assoc prof, 75-, chmn dept, 77-80. *Awards:* Alfred Einstein Award, Am Musicol Soc, 75; Guggenheim Fel, 75-76; Am Coun Learned Soc Fel, 81-82. *Mem:* Col Music Soc; Am Musicol Soc; Int Musicol Soc; Music Libr Asn; Am Soc 18th Century Studies. *Interests:* Symphonies of Johann Stamitz; early classical symphony; 18th century musicology. *Publ:* Auth, Fulda, Frankfurt and the Library of Congress: A Recent Discovery, XXIV, 286-291 & coauth, A Newly Identified Complex of Manuscripts from Mannheim, 74, J Am Musicol Soc; auth, Authenticity and Stylistic Evidence in the Early Symphony, In: A Musical Offering: Essays in Honor of Martin Bernstein, Pendragon, 77; On the Origins of the Mannheim Symphonic Style, In: Studies in Musicology in Honor of Otto E Albrecht, Barenreiter Verlag, 80; The Symphonies of Johann Stamitz, Bohn, Scheltema & Holkema, 81. *Mailing Add:* Dept Music Univ Pa Philadelphia PA 19104

WOLF, MICHAEL B
DOUBLE BASS, COMPOSER

b NJ. *Study:* Univ Southern Calif, BS; Calif State Univ, Northridge, with Nat Gangursky. *Works:* Sea Witch Quintet, perf by San Diego Symph mem, 80. *Pos:* Tutti bassist, San Diego Symph Orch, 78-; prin bassist, Am Inst Musical Studies Fest Orch, Austria, 82-83. *Teaching:* Double bass coach, Calif State Univ & Northridge Youth Acad. *Awards:* Fullbright Hays Scholar. *Mailing Add:* 1810 Dale San Diego CA 92102

WOLF, PHILLIP S
ADMINISTRATOR, PATRON

b Cincinnati, Ohio, Feb 5, 36. *Study:* Univ Tex, MD, 58. *Pos:* Pres bd dir, Denver Friends Chamber Music, 82- *Mailing Add:* 6823 E Eastman Denver CO 80224

WOLFE, HARVEY (S)
CELLO

b Philadelphia, Pa, Jan 15, 34. *Study:* Cleveland Inst Music, BM, 60; Ariz State Univ, 64. *Pos:* Prin cellist, Phoenix Symph, 62-64 & Nashville Symph, 67; cellist, Cleveland Orch, 67- & Coventry Chamber Players Cleveland Orch Ens, 78- *Teaching:* Fac mem cello, Col Wooster, 74-79. *Mailing Add:* 3121 Scarborough Rd Cleveland Heights OH 44118

WOLFE, LAWRENCE
DOUBLE BASS, EDUCATOR

Study: New England Consv Music, BM; Berkshire Music Ctr. *Pos:* Performer, Collage, formerly; double bass, Boston Symph Orch, currently. *Teaching:* Mem fac double bass, New England Consv Music, currently. *Awards:* Albert Spaulding Prize, Berkshire Music Ctr, 70. *Mailing Add:* New England Consv Music 290 Huntington Rd Boston MA 02115

WOLFE, STANLEY
COMPOSER, ADMINISTRATOR

b Brooklyn, NY, Feb 7, 24. *Study:* Stetson Univ, 46-47; Henry St Music Sch, 47-48; Juilliard Sch Music, studied with William Bergsma, Vincent Persichetti & Peter Mennin, BS(comp), 52, MS(comp), 55. *Works:* Lincoln Square Overture (orch), 57; Symphony No 3 (orch), 59; String Quartet (chamber music), 61; Symphony No 4 (orch), 65; Variations (orch), 67; Symphony No 5 (orch), comn by Lincoln Ctr; Symphony No 6, 81. *Teaching:* Mem fac lit & materials music, Juilliard Sch, 55-, adminr, Extension Div, 63-69, dir, 69-; prof music, Lincoln Ctr Campus, Fordham Univ, 69-73. *Awards:* Guggenheim Fel, 57; Alice M Ditson Award, 61; Nat Endowment Arts Grant, 69, 70 & 77. *Mem:* ASCAP; Am Music Ctr; Am Symph Orch League; Nat Asn Comp & Cond. *Mailing Add:* 32 Ferndale Dr Hastings-on-Hudson NY 10706

WOLFF, ARTHUR SHELDON
EDUCATOR, COMPOSER

b Cleveland, Ohio, Feb 19, 31. *Study:* DePauw Univ, BMus, 55; Univ Redlands, MMus, 58; NTex State Univ, PhD, 70. *Works:* Overture to a Tragedy, Vine St Wrkshp Orch, Calif, 55; Fantasy Variations, perf in Calif, Tex, Okla & Kans, 55; Heater, private publ & perf, 78; Intuitive Music Project, Free Improvisation Ens, Wichita State Univ, 78; Box, private publ & perf, 80; Neutron Mass, Intuitive Music Proj 15 for Ground Zero Week, 4/18/82. *Teaching:* Fel, NTex State Univ, 60-64; asst prof music & theory, Okla Baptist Univ, 64-69, Univ Montevallo, 70-71 & Eastman Sch Music, 71-74; asst prof, Wichita State Univ, 74-78, assoc prof, 78- *Awards:* Cadman Comp Award, Univ Redlands, 51-55. *Mem:* Music Educr Nat Conf; Col Music Theory Soc; Am Musicol Asn. *Publ:* Auth, Speculum, A Checklist of Musically Related Articles & Book Reviews, 71 & Speculum, A Checklist, MLA Index #9, 82, Music Libr Asn. *Mailing Add:* 3620 Oneida Wichita KS 67208

WOLFF, CHRISTIAN
COMPOSER, EDUCATOR

b Nice, France, Mar 8, 34; US citizen. *Study:* Harvard Univ, AB, 55, PhD, 63. *Works:* Summer (string quartet), 61, For 1, 2 or 3 People, 64, Burdocks (chamber orch), 71, Wobbly Music (cantata), 76, Bread and Roses (violin), 76, Hay Una Mujer Desaparecida (piano), 79 & Preludes 1-11 (piano), 81, C F Peters. *Teaching:* Comp in res, Darmstadt, State Univ NY, Buffalo, Consv Music, Oberlin Col, Simon Fraser Univ & Univ Montreal, 70-79; prof classics & music, Dartmouth Col, 76-, Strauss prof music, 78- *Awards:* Ford Found Comp, 72; Deutscher Akademischer Austauschdienst Fel, Berlin, 74; Am Acad & Nat Inst Arts & Letters Award, 75. *Mem:* BMI; Soc Ethnomusicol. *Publ:* Auth, New and Electronic Music, Audience, 58; On Form, Die Reihe, 60; Elements pour completer ..., VH 101, Paris, 70-71; John Cage, In: Dict Contemp Music, 74; On Music with Political Texts, Sonus, 80. *Mailing Add:* 104 S Main St Hanover NH 03755

WOLFF, CHRISTOPH JOHANNES
MUSICOLOGIST, EDUCATOR

b Solingen, Germany, May 24, 40. *Study:* Univ Berlin, 60-63; Univ Freiburg, 63-65; Univ Erlangen, Dr Phil(musicol), 66. *Pos:* Ed, Bach Jahrbuch, 74- *Teaching:* Lectr musicol, Univ Erlangen-Nuremberg, 66-69; vis asst prof, Univ Toronto, 68-69; assoc prof musicol, Columbia Univ, 70-73, prof, 73-76; vis prof, Princeton Univ, 73 & 75; prof, Harvard Univ, 76- *Awards:* Dent Medal, Royal Musical Asn, London, 78. *Publ:* Auth, Der Stile Antico in der Musik, J S Bach, 68; ed, Musikalisches Opfer, Neue Bach Ausgabe, 74; Neue Mozart-Ausgabe, 76; J S Bach, Klavierubung IV, 14 Kanons Neue Bach Ausgabe, 76; P Hindemith, Cardillac, Hindemith-Gesamtausgabe, 76. *Mailing Add:* Dept Music Harvard Univ Cambridge MA 02138

WOLFF, KONRAD
EDUCATOR, WRITER

b Berlin, Germany, Mar 11, 07; US citizen. *Study:* Piano studies with Joseph Lomba, Bonn, 21-22, Willy Bardas, Berlin, 22, Bruno Eisner, Berlin, 23-25 & Arthur Schnabel, Italy, 36-38; Columbia Univ, MA, 57. *Teaching:* Fac mem piano, Peabody Consv, 63-74, Smith Col, 75-76 & Montclair State Col, 76-82; lectr & recitalist piano, currently. *Mem:* Music Teachers Nat Asn; Am Liszt Soc. *Publ:* Ed, Robert Schumann: On Music and Musicians, Pantheon, 46; Auth, Arthur Schnabel's Interpretation of Piano Music, W W Norton, 2nd ed, 79; Masters of the Keyboard: Bach, Haydn, Mozart, Beethoven, Schubert, Ind Univ Press, 83. *Mailing Add:* 210 Riverside Dr #6G New York NY 10025

WOLFROM, LYLE CLARK
CELLO, DOUBLE BASS

b St Louis, Mo, June 8, 30. *Study:* Univ Kans, BM(cello), 56; Ind Univ, MM(cello), 58; Ohio State Univ, MM(string bass), 69; Akad Musik & Theater, Hanover, Germany. *Pos:* Prin cellist, US 7th Army Symph, Germany, 53-55; third chair cello, Kansas City Phil, 55-56; solo cellist, Lexington Phil, 70-72; chamber music & orch performer, formerly; mem, Schwabisch-Bavarian Band, Stuttgart, Vaihingen, formerly; mem, Eastern Ky Univ Fac Piano Trio & Chamber Players, currently. *Teaching:* Asst, Ind Univ & Ohio State Univ, formerly; asst prof cello, bass & chamber music, Capital Univ & Dennison Univ, 58-60; from assoc to prof, Eastern Ky Univ, 60- *Mem:* Music Educr Nat Conf. *Publ:* Auth, The Cellist and His Bass, 69 & The String Bass in Jazz, Folk and Rock, 74, Am String Teacher. *Mailing Add:* 448 Breck Ave Richmond KY 40475

WOLFSON, GREER ELLISON See Ellison, Greer

WOLKING, HENRY CLIFFORD
COMPOSER, EDUCATOR

b Orlando, Fla, May 20, 48. *Study:* Univ Fla, BME, 70; NTex State Univ, MM(comp), 73; comp study with Martin Mailman, 73. *Works:* Two Movements for Large Wind Ensemble, perf by Univ Utah Wind Ens, 74; Three Movements for Trombone Trio, 75 & Dialogues for Four Trombones, 76, Southern Music Co; Woodwind Quintet No 1, perf by Clarion Wind Quintet, 76; Suite for Baroque Ensemble, perf by Salt Lake Chamber Ens, 82; Lydian Horizon Symphony No 1, perf by Utah Symph, 82; Four Dances for Three Trombones, A Touch of Brass, 83. *Teaching:* Chmn guitar studies, Univ Utah, 73-, chmn jazz studies, 75-, assoc prof music, 78- *Awards:* Creative Res Grant, Univ Utah, 77 & 82. *Bibliog:* John R Killoch (auth), The Educators, Crescendo, 10/78; Peter Christ (auth), Composium: Index of Contemporary Compositions, Crystal Music Works, 81 & 82. *Mem:* ASCAP; Col Music Soc; Nat Asn Jazz Educr; Am Fedn Musicians; Salt Lake City Jazz Soc. *Publ:* Auth, Jazz Theory and Functional Harmony, 76, Jazz Theory and Chromatic Harmony, 76, Jazz Theory and the Substitute V^7, 77, Jazz Theory and Minor Key Progressions, 77 & Root Motion Systems/Major Third Progressions, 79, Jazz Educr J. *Mailing Add:* 3091 Grace St Salt Lake City UT 84109

WOLVERTON, BYRON A
MUSICOLOGIST, EDUCATOR

b Cape Girardeau, Mo, May 10, 34. *Study:* Univ Mo, Columbia, BMus, 55, MA, 56; Ind Univ, Bloomington, PhD, 66. *Teaching:* Instr piano & theory, Lincoln Univ, Mo, 56-57; asst prof piano & music lit, St Cloud State Univ, 62-63; assoc prof music hist & lit, SW Tex State Univ, 64- *Mem:* Am Musicol Soc; Sonneck Soc; Music Libr Asn. *Interests:* Early American keyboard music. *Publ:* Auth, Benjamin Carr, MGG, Barenreiter, 73. *Mailing Add:* 827 W San Antonio St San Marcos TX 78666

WON, KYUNG-SOO
CONDUCTOR & MUSIC DIRECTOR, VIOLIN

b Seoul, Korea, Dec 4, 28; US citizen. *Study:* Consv Music, Cincinnati, Ohio, MM, 57; master class of Pierre Monteux, dipl, 62; Ind Univ, Bloomington, 61; Mozarteum, Salzburg, Austria, dipl, 65. *Pos:* Music dir & cond, Stockton Symph, Calif, 67- & Seoul Phil, Korea, 70-72; guest cond, New Phil & Phil, London, 74 & Vienna, Paris, London, Berlin & Mexico City, formerly. *Teaching:* Instr theory, Seoul Nat Univ, Korea, 51-54 & San Joaquin Delta Col, 67-; instr cond, Univ Pac, Calif, 69-70. *Mem:* Am Symph Orch League. *Mailing Add:* 8034 Heather Dr Stockton CA 95209

WONG, BETTY ANNE (SIU JUNN)
COMPOSER, EDUCATOR

b San Francisco, Calif, Sept 6, 38. *Study:* Mills Col, with Darius Milhaud, Leon Kirchner, Morton Subotnick & Colin Hampton, AB, 60; Univ Calif, San Diego, with Pauline Oliveros, Robert Erickson & Kenneth Gaburo, MM, 71; studied Chinese music with David Liang, Lawrence Lui & Leo Lew, 71-74. *Works:* Possible Music for a Silent World (tapes of environmental sounds & live perf on Chinese instrm); Submerged Still Capable (tape), 69; Check One—People Control the Environment, People are Controlled by the Environment (tape), 70; Dear Friends of Music, This is Your Piece as Well as Mine (live theatre piece with audience), 71; Quiet Places in the Environment (tape, nine performers & audience), 71; Private Audience with Pope Pius XII (tape & slides), 71; Furniture Music, Or Two-Way Stretch on a Swivel Chair (tape & visuals), 71. *Pos:* Co-mgr, Flowing Stream Ens, 71-; mgr, Phoenix Spring Ens. *Teaching:* Instr piano, San Francisco Music Consv, formerly & Univ Calif, San Diego, formerly; instr & coordr, Community Ctr Chinese Music Wkshps, currently; comp in res, Perf Arts Wkshp, 66-68. *Publ:* Auth, Magic of Chinese Music, 74. *Mailing Add:* 1173 Bosworth St San Francisco CA 94131

WOOD, (CHARLES) DALE
COMPOSER, WRITER

b Glendale, Calif, Feb 13, 34. *Study:* Occidental Col, 51; Los Angeles Consv Music, 51-52; Los Angeles City Col, 53. *Works:* A Service of Darkness, Harold Flammer Inc, Shawnee Press, 63; Jubilate Deo, Augsburg Publ House, 71; Armada (musical drama), Bohemian Club, San Francisco, 74; The Gift to be Simple, Carl Fischer, 75; five original hymn tunes, Lutheran Church Am, 78; Christ is Made the Sure Foundation, H W Gray Div, Belwin-Mills Publ Corp, 79. *Pos:* Organist & choirmaster, Eden Lutheran Church, Riverside, Calif, 58-68 & Church St Mary Virgin, San Francisco, 68-75; dir music, Grace Cathedral Sch Boys, San Francisco, 73-74; exec ed, Sacred Music Press, Dayton, Ohio, 75- *Awards:* ASCAP Standard Awards, 67- *Bibliog:* Robet Wetzler (auth), Contemporary Composers: Dale Wood, J Church Music, 10/72; Gloria Bakkila (auth), Meet the Composer: Dale Wood, Choristers Guild Lett, 9/81; Jerry A Evenrud (auth), Hymn Writers of Today: Dale Wood, Am Organist, 1/83. *Mem:* Choristers Guild; Am Guild Organists; Nat Acad Rec Arts & Sci; ASCAP; Hymn Soc Am. *Publ:* Auth, Music for Children's Voices, Music Ministry, 64-68; Handbell Notation: Guidelines for Reform and Standardization, 10/71 & Opera in San Francisco, 6/73, Choristers Guild Lett; Submitting Musical Works for Publication, Am Organist, 3/79; The Wood Box, J Church Music, 80. *Rep:* Lorenz Corp 501 E Third St Dayton OH 45402. *Mailing Add:* Three Fern Wood The Sea Ranch CA 95497

WOOD, DAVID A
LIBRARIAN

b Concord, NH, Apr 24, 35. *Study:* Univ NH, BA, 57; Harvard Univ, MA, 60; Simmons Col, MS, 64. *Pos:* Bibliogr, Music Libr, Harvard Univ, 64-67; music librn, Univ Wash, 67- *Mem:* Music Libr Asn; Am Libr Asn; Int Asn Music Libr. *Publ:* Auth, Music in Harvard Libraries, a Catalog ..., Harvard Univ Press, 80. *Mailing Add:* 1952-26th East Seattle WA 98112

WOOD, ELIZABETH
WRITER, EDUCATOR

b Manly, New SWales, Australia, Sept 26, 39. *Study:* Univ Adelaide, BA(English lit), 61, BA(musicol), 70, MA(musicol), 72, PhD(musicol), 80; Elder Consv Music, Univ Adelaide, 66-69; Juilliard Sch, 81. *Pos:* Dramaturge & res, State Opera SAustralia, 70-75; music broadcaster, 5UV Radio, Univ Adelaide, 73-76; opera & music rev, Advertiser, 75-77 & The Australian, 75-77; res assoc, Ctr for Study Women & Sex Roles, Grad Ctr, City Univ New York, 79-81, admin dir, Prog Oral Hist Music Am, 78-79; coordr, Queens Col, City Univ New York, 78-79, prof assoc, 79-80, asst dir, 80-81. *Teaching:* Adj lectr, Univ Adelaide, SAustralia, 59-76 & Continuing Educ Prog, Queens Col, City Univ New York, 78 & 80; asst prof, Univ Adelaide, 73-75; guest lectr, Grad Ctr, City Univ New York, 78, Barnard Col, 78 & 80, Columbia Univ, 78 & 80 & Hunter Col, City Univ New York, 82. *Awards:* Commonwealth Res Fel, Australian Fed Govt, 70-72; res fel, Univ Adelaide, 73-74; Fulbright Fel, 77. *Mem:* Am Musicol Soc; Oral Hist Asn; Col Music Soc; Sonneck Soc; Int Cong Women Music. *Interests:* Nineteenth and 20th century opera; women composers (19th-20th century opera); women in Anglo-American music history; contemporary American music. *Publ:* Auth, Grazyna Bacewicz: Form, Syntax, Style, Musical Woman, Vol I, Greenwood Press, 83; Ethel Smyth's Pathway in the Politics of Music, Mass Rev, Univ Mass, 83; Music Into Words, In: Between Women, Beacon Press, 83; regular music & opera contribr, Ms Mag & New Grove Dict Music & Musicians. *Mailing Add:* 54 Seventh Ave S New York NY 10014

WOOD, GLORIA BAKKILA
SOPRANO, WRITER

b Ross, Calif, Sept 19, 43. *Study:* San Francisco State Univ, BA, MA(music), 71. *Rec Perf:* Emmanuel, Sacred Music Press, 83. *Roles:* Alleluia (Mozart), Marin Symph, 79; Mass in C (Beethoven), San Francisco Symph, 80; Requiem (Faure), 82 & Gloria (Poulenc), 82, Schola Cantorum. *Pos:* Opera chorister, San Francisco Opera Co, 71-75; sop soloist, St Mary Virgin Episcopal Church, 71-81; prof chorister, San Francisco Symph Chorus, 75-81; chorus dir, Santa Rosa Jr Col, 81-82; freelance writer & text writer, Sacred Music Press, currently; mem, Peter Arnott Prod, currently. *Mem:* Am Guild Musical Artists. *Publ:* Auth, Meet the Composer—Dale Wood, Choristers Guild, 81; Getting Back on the Bicycle, J Church Music, 83; Would the Third Peasant from the Left Please Step Forward?, San Francisco Mag, 83. *Mailing Add:* Sacred Music Press Box 200 The Sea Ranch CA 95497

WOOD, JOSEPH (ROBERTS)
EDUCATOR, COMPOSER

b Pittsburgh, Pa, May 12, 15. *Study:* Bucknell Univ, 32-34; Inst Musical Art, with Carl Roeder, dipl piano, 36; Juilliard Sch Music, with Bernard Wagenaar, dipl comp, 40, BS, 49; Columbia Univ, with Otto Luening, MA, 50. *Works:* Symphony No 1, 39, The Mother (opera), 42, Overture to Twelfth Night, 43, Symphonies #2, 51 & #3, 57, Divertimento (piano & orch), 58, Poem for Orchestra, 60, Symphony #4, 81 & String Quartet 1975, 81, Am Comp Ed. *Pos:* Staff comp, Chekhov Theatre Studio, Ridgefield, Conn, 39-41; freelance comp & arr, New York, 41-50. *Teaching:* Prof comp & theory, Oberlin Consv Music, Oberlin Col, 50- *Awards:* Fel, MacDowell Colony (nine residencies), 53-80; comp in res, Villa Montalvo, 57; fel, Huntington Hartford Found. *Mem:* Am Comp Alliance. *Mailing Add:* 261 W Lorain St Oberlin OH 44074

WOOD, KEVIN JOSEPH
COMPOSER, ADMINISTRATOR

b Bronx, NY, June 19, 47. *Study:* Univ Dayton, BMus, 69; Southern Ill Univ, MMus, 74. *Works:* Slumber Song (SATB), 79 & Chorale Prelude: If Thou But Suffer God (organ), 81, Highgate Press; Dithyramb (solo oboe), Unicorn

Music, 81; Concord Hymn (SATB), 81 & Ever Again (SATB), 81, Plymouth Music; Dirge (perc ens), Music Perc, 83; Kurete's Dance (double-reed ens), Highgate Press, 83. *Pos:* Ed, Walton Music Corp, Chapel Hill, NC, 76-80; prod ed & dir sales, Galaxy Music Corp, 78-; music reviewer, Am Organist, 79-81; mem bd, DeRevere Singers, currently. *Mem:* Am Guild Organists; Music Educr Nat Conf; NJ Comp Guild. *Rep:* Perzanowski Mgt 640 West End Ave New York NY 10024. *Mailing Add:* PO Box 1176 Freehold NJ 07728

WOOD, LORNA
VIOLA

b Albion, Mich, Jan 7, 56. *Study:* St Louis Consv Music, BM, 77; study with Milton Preves. *Pos:* Violist, St Louis Opera Theatre, 77, St Louis; Munic Opera, 78 & San Antonio Symph, 79- *Teaching:* Violin, viola & chamber music, privately, San Antonio, 79-, 79-83. *Awards:* Scholar Award, Ladies Friday Music Club, 75. *Mem:* Am Fedn Musicians; Int Conf Symph & Orch Musicians. *Mailing Add:* San Antonio Symph 109 Lexington Ave Suite 207 San Antonio TX 78205

WOOD, VIVIAN POATES
MEZZO-SOPRANO, EDUCATOR

b Washington, DC, Aug 9, 28. *Study:* Antioch Col, 53-55; studied with Denise Restout, 60-62 & 64-70, Paul Ulanowsky, 58-68, Elmer Nagy, 65-68, Vyautas Marijosius, 67-68 & Paul A Pisk, 68-71; Hartt Col Music, MusB, 68; Yale Univ, 68; Washington Univ, Mo, MusM, 71, PhD, 73. *Pos:* Appearances in numerous operas on radio & TV throughout US & Europe, 53-68; soloist, Landowska Ctr, 69 & Int Harpsichord Fest, 73; Miss coordr, Alliance Arts Educ, Kennedy Ctr Perf Arts, 74-76; mem, Gov Coun Arts, Miss, 74-; mem bd dir, Miss Opera, 74-; ms soloist with US orchs. *Teaching:* Prof voice, Univ Southern Miss, 71-, asst dean, Col Fine Arts, 74-76, actg dean, 76-77; guest prof, Hochschule Musik, Munich, 78-79. *Awards:* Young Am Artists Conct Award, 55; Wanda Landowska Fel, 68-72. *Mem:* Nat Asn Teachers Singing; Am Musicol Soc; Mu Phi Epsilon; Pi Kappa Lambda. *Publ:* Auth, Poulenc's Songs: An Analysis of Style, 79. *Mailing Add:* Sch Music Univ Southern Miss Hattiesburg MS 39401

WOOD, WILLIAM FRANK
COMPOSER, EDUCATOR

b San Francisco, Calif, Aug 3, 35. *Study:* Sacramento State Col, BA, 57; Univ Ore, with Normand Lockwood, MM, 58; Eastman Sch Music, with Bernard Rogers & Howard Hanson, DMA, 65. *Works:* Symphony in Three Movements, Prague Symph Orch, 66; Sonata for Violin & Piano, comn & perf by Leonard Felberg & George Robert, 73-74; Dialogues—Jazz Quartet & Strings, comn by Albuquerque Chamber Orch, 74; Night Music (choral & orch), comn by Bunyon Webb, 75; Trios (fluet, oboe & clarinet), Santa Fe Chamber Players, 82; Fantasy for Orchestra, comn by NMex Symph Orch, 83. *Rec Perf:* Guale (Max Schuble), Opus One Rec, 75. *Teaching:* Theory, music hist & wind ens, Yakima Valley Col, 63-68; asst prof, theory, comp & jazz band, Wright State Univ, 68-71; assoc prof comp, analysis, counterpoint, theory, Univ NMex, 71- *Mailing Add:* 12508 Prospect Ave Albuquerque NM 87112

WOODARD, JAMES P
COMPOSER, EDUCATOR

b Rocky Mt, NC, Nov 21, 39. *Study:* Univ NC; Juilliard Sch; studied in Munich; Fla State Univ, with Carlisle Floyd & John Boda, DM. *Works:* Duo for Violin and Cello (chamber music), 64; Concerto for Two Pianos (orch), 65; The Dream Songs of Stephen Foster (sop & string orch); Five Sonnets of Shakespeare (baritone & piano), 67; Fantasies (flute and string quartet), 72; Piano Sonatina (chamber music), 73; The Legend of the Piora Bird (oratorio). *Teaching:* Prof music, Murray State Univ, 65-70 & Southern Ill Univ, 70- *Awards:* Olivet Pedro Paz Award, 70. *Mailing Add:* 818 Randle St Edwardsville IL 62025

WOODBURY, ARTHUR NEUM
COMPOSER, WRITER

b Kimball, Nebr, June 20, 30. *Study:* Univ Idaho, BS, 51, MM, 55; Univ Calif, Berkeley, 57-58; Stanford Univ, Calif, summer 70. *Works:* Passaglia, Interlude and Canon for Band, perf by Univ Calif, Davis, 65; Remembrances, A Trio, 69 & Velox, 70, Comp/Perf Ed; Between Categories (cello & piano), perf by Anthony Cooke, Northwestern Univ, 82; Tocata Espanol (marimba, perc & cello), comn by Anthony Cooke, 83; Wernervonbraunasaurus Rex (quad tape), comn by Bob Houston, 83. *Pos:* Freelance musician, San Francisco, 56-63; ed, Source, Music of Avant-Garde, Sacramento, 66-72. *Teaching:* Lectr music theory, Univ Calif, Davis, 63-72; assoc prof music theory & perf, Univ SFla, 72- *Mem:* NAm Sax Alliance. *Publ:* Auth, Harry Partch: Corporeality and Monophony, Comp/Perf Ed, 66. *Mailing Add:* Music Dept Univ SFla Tampa FL 33620

WOODBURY, WARD LELAND
CONDUCTOR & MUSIC DIRECTOR, EDUCATOR

b Durango, Colo, July 23, 22. *Study:* Western State Col Colo, BA, 43; Eastman Sch Music, MA, 45, perf cert(cond), 49, PhD, 54. *Rec Perf:* Requiem (Berlioz) & Carmina Burana (Orff), Century; University of Rochester Men's Glee Club, I-V, Kendall. *Pos:* Music dir & cond, Winter Park Bach Fest, 66-; dir, Rollins Col Conct Ser, 66-; cond in res, Brevard Music Ctr, 67- *Teaching:* Head music dept, Mesa Col, Colo, 45-47; dir music, Univ Rochester, 54-66; prof music, Rollins Col, 66- *Awards:* Outstanding Contributions to Live Music, Music Perf Trustees Am Fedn Musicians, 80. *Mem:* New Bach Soc; Am Choral Dir Asn; Pi Kappa Lambda; Phi Mu Alpha Sinfonia; Chamber Music Am. *Publ:* Auth, State Certification of Music in Secondary Schools, Music Educr J, 11-12/45; Leadership in Orchestral Conducting, J Res Music Educ, 55. *Mailing Add:* Box 2371 Rollins Col Winter Park FL 32789

WOODHALL, DENNIS ROBERT
EDUCATOR, MUSIC DIRECTOR
b Los Angeles, Calif, June 15, 51. *Study:* Calif State Univ, Fullerton, BA(music educ), 76, MA(choral music), 78; Ariz State Univ, DMA(choral music), 83. *Pos:* Dir choirs, St Mary of the Plains Col, 81- *Mem:* Am Choral Dir Asn; Am Musicol Soc; Pi Kappa Lambda; Phi Mu Alpha Sinfonia; Music Educr Nat Conf. *Interests:* Early Baroque music; embellishment of Renaissance vocal-ensemble music. *Publ:* Auth, The Stylistic Interpretation of Early-Baroque Music: Some Guidelines for the Modern Choral Conductor, Am Choral Dir Asn J, 10/81 & 11/81. *Mailing Add:* 105 Plaza Ave Dodge City KS 67801

WOODMAN, THOMAS
BARITONE
b Greenwich, Conn, Nov 2, 57. *Study:* Hartt Sch Music, perf cert, 81. *Rec Perf:* Cavalcanti (Pound), Arch Ens, Berkeley, Calif, 83. *Roles:* Emperor Norton in Emperor Norton, 81; Prince Paul in Grand Duchess of Gerolstein, 81, Marcello in La Boheme, 82, Ping in Turandot, 82 & Herald in Lohengrin, 82, San Francisco Opera; Count Almaviva in Le Nozze di Figaro, San Francisco Opera & Hawaii Opera Theatre, 83; Enrico in Lucia di Lammermoor, Pippin's Pocket Opera, 83. *Pos:* Artist, Affil Artists Inc, 81-83; Adler fel, San Francisco Opera Ctr, 82-83. *Awards:* April Axton Award, Metropolitan Auditions, 80; Sue E Weisman Award, Conn Opera Asn, 80; Merola Award, San Francisco Opera Auditions, 80. *Rep:* Herbert Breslin Inc 119 W 57th St New York NY 10019. *Mailing Add:* 635 Judah San Francisco CA 94122

WOODS, NANCY BRICARD See Bricard, Nancy

WOODS, PAMELA PECHA
OBOE & ENGLISH HORN, PIANO
b Syracuse, NY, Apr 12, 51. *Study:* Cleveland Inst Music, with John Made, 69-73; Blossom Music Fest, 70-71; Berkshire Music Ctr, with Ralph Gomberg, 72. *Rec Perf:* Japanese Melodies, Phillips Rec Japan, 83. *Pos:* Assoc prin oboe, Cincinnati Symph, 73-74; English horn, San Antonio Symph, 74-75; second oboe, Baltimore Symph, 76-78; asst prin oboe, Cleveland Orch, 78- *Awards:* Tabuteau Mem Fund, Philadelphia Found, 71; C D Jackson Prize, Berkshire Music Ctr, 72. *Mailing Add:* Severance Hall Cleveland Orch Cleveland OH 44106

WOODS, SYLVIA
HARP, TEACHER-COACH
b Oak Ridge, Tenn, May 23, 51. *Study:* Univ Redlands, with Marjorie Call, BA, 71; Calif State Univ, Los Angeles, with Susanne McDonald. *Works:* The Harp of Brandiswhiere (suite), Gold Star Studios, 82; Chicago's Secret Wilderness, comn by PBS TV, 82. *Pos:* Pres, Sylvia Woods Harp Ctr & Acad, Los Angeles, 76- *Teaching:* Irish harp, Sylvia Woods Harp Acad, 76-, Irish Harp Acad, Buncrana, Ireland, summers 80- & throughout US & British Isles. *Awards:* All Ireland Harp Champion, Comhaltas Ceoltoiri Eireann, 80; Golden Scroll Merit, Acad Sci Fiction, Fantasy & Horror Films, 83. *Bibliog:* Margie Mirken (auth), Sylvia Woods—Art of the Folk Harp, Frets Mag, 5/83; Roberta MacAvoy, Sylvia Woods: The Master Harper, Folk Harp J, fall 83. *Mem:* Int Soc Folk Harpers & Craftsmen (chmn bd, 80-); Music Teachers Asn Calif. *Publ:* Auth, Teach Yourself to Play the Folk Harp, 78, Songs of the Harp: 20 Songs about Harps & Harpers, 79 & The Harp of Brandiswhiere, 83, private publ. *Mailing Add:* PO Box 29521 Los Angeles CA 90029

WOODS, TERRI LYNN
SOPRANO
b Massilon, Ohio, May 4, 56. *Study:* Ohio State Univ, with Maurice Cary & Mario Alch; Univ Colo, with Barbara Sabel; Denver Univ, studied East-West music with Ruth Cooper, currently. *Roles:* Mary in The Drunkard, Open Theatre Cafe, 80; Despina in Cosi fan tutte, 82 & Vespetta in Pimpinnone, 83, Operatif Inc. *Mailing Add:* 1262 La Playa #4 San Francisco CA 94122

WOODWARD, ANN (McCLURE)
VIOLA, EDUCATOR
b Cincinnati, Ohio, July 31, 40. *Study:* Oberlin Col, studied with William Berman, 58-60; New Sch Music, Philadelphia, with Max Aronoff, 60-61; Fontainebleau, France, with Nadia Boulanger & Pierre Pasquier, summer, 63; Curtis Inst Music, BM, 65; Yale Sch Music, with David Schwartz, 65-67; MM, 67, MMA, 70, DMA, 73; Accad Musicale Chigiana, Siena, Italy, with Bruno Giuranna, summer, 76; Summer Sch Strings, Digby Stuart Col Univ London, 79; St Edmund Hall, Oxford Univ, 80, with Kato Havas. *Rec Perf:* Music of the Middle Ages: Volume IX—The Fourteenth Century: The Ars Nova, Musical Heritage. *Pos:* Mem, New Haven Symph & Chamber Orch, 65-67, prin viola, 66-67; solo recitalist, numerous US & Europ cols & univ, 67-; performer, NC String Quartet, New Arts String Quartet, Claremont Quartet & many others, 67- *Teaching:* Viola & violin, New Sch Music, 63-65; viola, chamber music & violin, Neighborhood Music Sch, 65-67; instr, Univ NC, Chapel Hill, 67-71, asst prof, 71-75, assoc prof, 75-83, chmn string instr, 78-, prof, 83- *Awards:* Scholar, Cleveland Soc for Strings, 59 & 60; Charles H Ditson Scholar, Yale Univ, 66-67. *Bibliog:* Noël Goodwin (auth), London Debuts, The Times, London, 4/30/80; Geoffrey Chew (auth), Music in London, Musical Times, 6/80. *Mem:* Am Musicol Soc; Am String Teachers Asn (treas NC chap, 68-70); Am Viola Soc (treas, 78-); Col Music Soc (mem coun, 76-78, mem exec bd, 80-). *Mailing Add:* Dept Music 020-A Univ NC Chapel Hill NC 27514

WOODWARD, DONNA LYNN
SOPRANO
b Baltimore, Md. *Study:* Va Intermont Col, AA, 66; Col-Consv Music, Univ Cincinnati, BM, 69; Corbett Found Studio, Switz, 69-70; vocal study with Eva Ambrosius. *Rec Perf:* Doctor & Apotheker (Dittersdorf), RBM, 82. *Roles:* Despina in Cosi fan tutte, Heidelberg State Theater, 73; Blonde in Die Entfuhrung aus dem Serail, Bavarian State Opera, Munich, 77-80; Adele in Die Fledermaus, Nat Theater, Mannheim, 77 & Cologne Opera, 82; Sophie in Der Rosenkavalier, Darmstadt State Opera, 79; Barbarina in The Marriage of Figaro, Paris Nat Opera, 80; Rosina in The Barber of Seville, 80 & Oscar in Un Ballo in maschera, 83, Nat Theater, Mannheim, Germany. *Pos:* Solo soubrette, Luzern City Opera, Switz, 70-71, Darmstadt State Opera, Germany, 71-73, Heidelberg City Theater, Germany, 73-75 & Nat Theater, Mannheim, Germany, 75- *Mailing Add:* Bruckenkopfstr 18 Heidelberg D 6900 Germany, Federal Republic of

WOODWARD, GREGORY STANLEY
COMPOSER, EDUCATOR
b Orange, Calif, Sept 20, 54. *Study:* Univ Conn, with Charles Whittenberg, BM(comp), 77; Sch Music, Ithaca Col, with Karel Husa, MM(comp), 78; Cornell Univ, with Karel Husa, DMA(comp), 83. *Works:* Parapter (alto sax alone), comn by Dr. Steven Mauk, 78; One and One is Three (brass quintet), 79 & Soliloquy for Euphonium with Woodwind Quartet, 79, Brass Press; Dance Suite for Six Players, perf by Speculum Musicae, 80; Psalm for the City (band, chorus & soloist), comn by Town of Ithaca Fest, 80-; Concerto for Alto Saxophone with Wind Ensemble, comn by Yale Univ Bands, 83; Portraits (opera based on Portrait of the Artist as A Young Man), 83. *Teaching:* Instr music theory, Ithaca Col, 78-, asst to dean & dir music admis, 80-; lectr theory, Cornell Univ, 81-82. *Mem:* NY State Music Theory Soc; BMI; Am Soc Univ Comp; Col Music Soc. *Interests:* Aspects of rhythm and orchestration as structural determinants in the music of Anton von Webern; American musical theatre. *Mailing Add:* 175 Ludlowville Rd Lansing NY 14882

WOODWARD, HENRY L(YNDE)
EDUCATOR, COMPOSER
b Cincinnati, Ohio, Sept 18, 08. *Study:* Col-Consv Music, Univ Cincinnati, BMus, 29, MMus, 32; studied with Nadia Boulanger, 33-34; Miami Univ, AB, 36; Harvard Univ, PhD, 52. *Works:* O Clap Your Hands (anthem), C C Birchard & Co, 51; Nature in the Temperate Zone (chamber orch), Fla State Univ, Tallahassee, 81. *Teaching:* Instr, Col-Consv Music, Univ Cincinnati, 29-32; assoc prof, Western Col, 34-41; asst prof, Vassar Col, 38-39; dept chmn & William H Laird prof liberal arts, Carleton Col, 42-73; vis prof, Cornell Univ, 47 & Sch Sacred Music, Union Theol Sem, 57, 59-62 & 64. *Awards:* Minn State Arts Coun Award, 73. *Mem:* Col Music Soc (treas, 58-62, vpres, 69-71); Am Musicol Soc; Music Libr Asn; Sonneck Soc; Southeastern Comp League. *Publ:* Auth, The Changing Ethos of Contemporary Music, Kenyon Rev, 40; Musical Symbolism in the Vocal Works of Johann Pachelbel, Harvard Dept Music, 57; co-ed, Library of Organ Music, Schmitt, Hall & McCreary, 66; auth, Feb 18, 1729: A Neglected Date in Boston Concert Life, Music Libr Asn Notes, 76; Annals of the College Music Society, Col Music Soc Symposium, 77-79. *Mailing Add:* 2218 Carol Woods Chapel Hill NC 27514

WOODWARD, MARTHA CLIVE
FLUTE, COMPOSER
b Wilmington, Del, Apr 26, 46. *Study:* Smith Col, with Alvin Etler, AB, 68; Stanford Univ, MA, 71; Harvard Univ; Boston Univ; studied flute with Blaisdell, Rampal, Dwyer, Pappoutsakis, Nyfenger & Moyse. *Works:* The Far Field (choral orch), perf by Smith & Amherst Contemp Music Soc, 68; Sonnets Pour Helene, perf at Aspen Fest Cont, 72. *Pos:* Perf orch & choral music, Aspen & Spoleto Fest; solo recitalist, ser Boston Univ, Harvard Musical Asn, Harvard Univ, Old West & Arlington St Churches, Cape Cod Consv, Heritage Plantation, Wiano Club, Colby-Sawyer & numerous col; accmp, Cape Cod Consv & Colby-Sawyer Col. *Teaching:* Instr flute, Cape Cod Consv & Community Col, 78-80; instr music hist, Colby-Sawyer Col, 80- *Mem:* Am Symph Orch League; Am Fedn Musicians; Am Musicol Soc; Int Soc Study Popular Music; Col Music Soc. *Interests:* Nineteenth century American popular music; 20th century music for flute. *Publ:* Contribr, New Grove Dict of Music in US, 83. *Mailing Add:* Colby-Sawyer Col New London NH 03257

WOOLDRIDGE, DAVID H M
COMPOSER, CONDUCTOR & MUSIC DIRECTOR
b Seal, Kent, England, Aug 24, 31. *Study:* Royal Acad Music, London, England, BMus, 52, Fel Trinity Col Music, London; Vienna Acad Music, with Clemens Krauss, Reifeprüfung, 53; Ind Univ, Bloomington, MMus(comp), 59. *Works:* Viola Concerto, London Phil, Primrose, 53; Octet (ballet), Edinburgh Int Fest, Scotland, 58; Suite Libanaise, Lebanese Nat Orch, 63; Duchess of Amalfi (opera), Bavarian State Opera, Munich, Germany, 68; Five Italian Songs, BBC Symph, 79; String Quartet No 3, Berkshire String Quartet, 79; The Hieratic Head, John Alldis Choir, Frankfurt, Germany, 80. *Pos:* Staff cond, Vienna State Opera, Austria, 52-54 & Bavarian State Opera, Munich, Germany, 54-56; music dir, Lebanese Nat Orch, Beirut, 61-65 & Cape Town Symph Orch, SAfrica, 65-66. *Awards:* Royal Phil Soc Prize, 50; Koussevitzky Prize, 61; Chapelbrook Award, 69. *Publ:* Auth, Conductor's World: A Social History of the Art, Praeger, 70; From the Steeples & Mountains: Charles Ives Study, Alfred Knopf, 74. *Rep:* Shaw Conct Inc 1995 Broadway New York NY 10023. *Mailing Add:* Bridgewater CT 06752

WOOLLEN, RUSSELL
COMPOSER, EDUCATOR
b Hartford, Conn, Jan 7, 23. *Study:* St Mary's Univ, Md, 44; Cath Univ Am, MA, 48; Peabody Consv, studied with Nadia Boulanger & comp with Nicholas Nabokov 49-51; Pope Pius X Sch Liturgical Music; Harvard Univ, with Walter Piston & A Tillman Merritt, MA, 54 & 54-57. *Works:* Mass No 3 (SATB a cappella), Eastman Sch Choir, 55; Toccata for Orch, Nat Symph Orch, 56; Symphony No 1, Am Comp Alliance Publ, 61; Symphony No 2, ACA Publ, 79; Cantata: In Martyrum Memoriam, Chicago Symph & Chorus, 79; Lines of Stephen Crane for Baritone and Chamber Ensemble, 81. *Pos:* Staff keyboard artist, Nat Symph Orch, 56-80; harpsichordist, Ars Nova Trio, 60-70. *Teaching:* Asst prof music, Cath Univ Am, 48-62; assoc prof, Howard Univ, 69-74; lectr, George Mason Univ, 80-82. *Awards:* George Arthur Knight Prize, Harvard, 54; Ernst Bloch Choral Award, 62; Coolidge Found Grant Comp, Libr Cong, 81. *Mem:* Am Comp Alliance; BMI; Am Guild Organists. *Mailing Add:* 6018 Woodley Rd McLean VA 22101

WORBY, RACHAEL
CONDUCTOR, EDUCATOR
b Nyack, NY, Apr 21, 49. *Study:* State Univ NY, Potsdam, BMus, 71; Brandeis Univ, with Leo Tritler, Margaret Bent & Joshua Rifkin, PhD(musicol), 80. *Pos:* Music dir, NH Phil, 79-82 & New England Consv Music Youth Chamber Orch, 80-82; Exxon asst cond, Spokane Symph, 82- *Teaching:* Instr music hist, New England Consv Music, 79-82 & Mass Inst Technol, 80-82. *Awards:* Grant, Martha Baird Rockefeller Fund Music, 82. *Mem:* Am Musicol Soc; Am Symph Orch League; Cond Guild. *Interests:* Notational ingenuities and editorial practices in the autographs of F Chopin. *Mailing Add:* c/o Affiliate Artists 155 W 68th New York NY 10023

WORKMAN, WILLIAM (GATEWOOD)
BARITONE
b Valdosta, Ga, Feb 4, 40. *Study:* Davidson Col, AB, 62; Curtis Inst Music, Artist Dipl, 65; Davidson Col, Hon Dr Music, 83. *Rec Perf:* Zoroastre, Turnabout-Vox, 69; The Devils of London 69 & Stadtstheatre, 72, Deutsche Grammophon; Papageno in Die Zauberflote, 72 & Pluto in Orphens aux Enfers, 73, Polyphon; Strophen, Musicaphon, 82. *Roles:* Silvio in Pagliacci, Vienna State Opera, 73; Almaviva in Nozze di Figaro, Teatro Colon Buenos Aires, 74; Papageno in Zauberflote, 75; Damdini in Cenerentola, 76, Opera Paris; Figaro in Barber of Seville, Metropolitan Opera, 82; Guglielmo in Cosi fan tutte, Hamburg State Opera, 82; Wolfram in Tannhäuser, Frankfurt Opera, 83. *Pos:* Leading bar, Hamburg State Opera, 65-, & Frankfurt Opera, 73- *Awards:* Oberdorfer Prize, Hamburg State Opera, 70. *Rep:* Lies Asconas 19 A Aid St Regent St England London WI 6LQ. *Mailing Add:* c/o Thea Dispeker 59 E 54th St New York NY 10022

WORMHOUDT, PEARL SHINN
EDUCATOR, WRITER
b Knoxville, Iowa, Oct 27, 15. *Study:* Cent Col, BA, 36; studied voice with Douglas Stanley, 37-44; Columbia Univ, MA, 45; studied dance with Hanya Holm, 45-46 & voice with Paola Novikova, 65-67. *Teaching:* Assoc prof voice & vocal pedagogy, William Penn Col, 58-81, emer prof, 81-; private voice teacher, 81- *Mem:* Nat Asn Teachers Singing (Iowa chap pres, 73-75, secy, 80-83, mem nat coun res singing, 82); Int Asn Res Singing. *Interests:* Vocal pedagogy, relating scientific basis to tradition; psychology of singing and of teaching singing. *Publ:* Auth, Learning & Teaching About the Middle East: Art, Music, Literature, Culture, Delta Kappa Gamma Bulletin, fall 78; Building the Voice as an Instrument with a Studio Reference Handbook, Arthur Wormhoudt Publ, 81; An Overview of the Psychology of Singing and the Teaching of Singing, Acad Ziekenhuis Conf, Rotterdam, 82. *Rep:* Arthur Wormhoudt Publ William Penn Col Oskaloosa IA 52577. *Mailing Add:* 1818 Kemble Dr Oskaloosa IA 52577

WORSTELL, RONALD A
EDUCATOR, BARITONE
b Fostoria, Ohio, Dec 14, 39. *Study:* Univ Ill, BA(music), 61, MA(music), 63; Univ Southern Calif, DMA(voice), 71. *Roles:* Alfio in Cavalleria Rusticana, 64 & Don Basilio, 65, Birmingham Civic Opera; Dapperutto & Dr Miracle in Les Contes d'Hoffman, 72 & Dandini in La Cenerentola, 73, Univ Denver Opera Theater; Don Giovanni in Don Giovanni, Brico Symph, 75; Escamillo in Carmen, Denver Repty Opera, 77. *Pos:* Apprentice artist, Sante Fe Opera, 62-63. *Teaching:* Instr music, Howard Col, 63-65; prof, Univ Denver, 67-, dir opera, 75- *Mem:* Nat Asn Teachers Singing (vpres Colo-Wyo chap, 76-78, pres, 78-80, state gov, 83-). *Mailing Add:* 721 Gilpin Denver CO 80218

WORTMAN, ALLEN L
EDUCATOR, MUSIC DIRECTOR
b Le Claire, Iowa, Jan 7, 35. *Study:* Cent Col, Pella, Iowa, BA, 57; Univ Northern Colo, Greeley, MA, 62, EdD, 68. *Teaching:* Supvr music, Saskatchewan Publ Sch, Regina, 64-66; prof music, Mankato State Univ, 66- *Mem:* Minn Music Educr; Music Educr Nat Conf; Am Guild English Handbell Ringers; Am Choral Dir Asn; Phi Mu Alpha Sinfonia. *Mailing Add:* 24 Southview Dr Mankato MN 56001

WRANCHER, ELIZABETH ANN
EDUCATOR, SOPRANO
b Indianapolis, Ind, Oct 19, 30. *Study:* Ind Univ, Bloomington, BM, 55; Hochschule Musik, Munich, 55-56. *Rec Perf:* Chamber Music by Thomas Beversdorf, Coronet, 70; Lemmy Capitano Mem Benefit Muscular Dystrophy, Cond Rec, 71. *Roles:* Dorotka in Schwanda Dudak, Detmold, Mannheim, Augsburg & Bielefeld, 59-67; Donna Anna in Don Giovanni, Hannover, Augsburg, Nuremburg Detmold, Baelefeld & others, 60-68; Tosca

in Tosca, Augsburg, Detmold, Opera Houses & others, 60-65; Marie in Wozzeck, Augsburg Staats Theater, Ger, 62; Leonore in Fidelio, Freiburg, Augsburg, Nurenburg & others, 64-68; Turandot in Turandot, Koblenz, Am Roten Tor, Freiburg, Braunsweig & others, 66-68; Santuzza in Cavalleria Rusticana, Orlando Opera Co, 77. *Pos:* Opera singer, various Europ opera houses, 59-68 & Salsburg Wagner Fest, 67-68; mem bd dir, Orlando Opera Co, 80-81, mem adv bd, 81- *Teaching:* Asst prof voice & opera, Univ SFla, 68-74; assoc prof voice, opera pedagogical song lit, Univ Cent Fla, 74-; private instr voice, Winter Park, Fla, 74. *Awards:* Fulbright Scholar, 55. *Mem:* Nat Opera Asn (state gov, 83-); Mu Phi Epsilon. *Mailing Add:* 2630 Amsden Rd Winter Park FL 32792

WRIGHT, AL G (ALFRED GEORGE)
EDUCATOR, CONDUCTOR & MUSIC DIRECTOR
b London, England, June 23, 16; US citizen. *Study:* Univ Miami, BEd, 37, MEd, 47; Troy State Univ, Hon LLD, 81. *Works:* Shimto Grand March, 69, Miyasa March, 69, Pit Stop (as George Stone), 69, Festival 500 March, 69, Gaudeamus Grand March, 70, Brickyard Jamboree (as George Stone), 70 & Festival 500 March (as George Stone), 71, Oz Publ. *Pos:* Dir music, Miami Sr High Sch, 38-54; cond symph band & symph orch & dir marching band, Purdue Univ, 54-; contrib ed, Instrumentalist Mag, 55-; mem bd adv, Int Music Fest, 71-; mem jury, World Music Fest, Kerkrade, Holland, 74-78; pres, Int Music Tours Inc, 75- *Mem:* Am Bandmasters Asn (mem bd dir, 52-53 & 72-74 & pres, 80-82); Nat Band Asn (founding pres, 61- & secy-treas, 65-68); Col Band Dir Nat Asn; Big Ten Band Dir Nat Asn (pres, 77-); charter mem, Phi Mu Alpha Sinfonia. *Publ:* Coauth, Band of the World, Instrumentalist, 70; auth, Marching Band Fundamentals, Carl Fischer, 70; ed, Selective Music Lists for Band, Nat Band Asn, 68, rev ed, 72 & 76; Directory of Guest Conductors, Clinicians & Adjudicators, Nat Band Asn, 71. *Mailing Add:* 344 Overlook Dr West Lafayette IN 47906

WRIGHT, CLAIRE HODGKINS See Hodgkins, Claire

WRIGHT, ELIZABETH
EDUCATOR, PIANO
Study: Mannes Col Music, BS; Juilliard Sch, studied piano with Leonard Shure, Irwin Freundlich, Mieczyslaw Horszowski & Karl Ulrich Schnabel & chamber music with William Kroll, Felix Galimir & Claude Frank, MS. *Pos:* Assisting pianist master classes; accmp & chamber pianist; US, Europ & USSR tours, formerly; participant, Marlboro Music Fest, formerly, Tanglewood Music Fest, formerly, Dartmouth Music Fest, formerly & Aspen Music Fest, formerly; prin pianist, Am Symph Orch. *Teaching:* Mem fac piano, Mannes Col Music, 76-; artist in res piano, City Col, City Univ New York, currently. *Mailing Add:* Mannes Col Music 157 E 74th St New York NY 10021

WRIGHT, GEOFFREY DORIAN
COMPOSER, EDUCATOR
b Kalamazoo, Mich, June 6, 52. *Study:* Private study, Germany, 73; Kalamazoo Col, BA(comp & organ), 74; Mass Inst Technol, 79; Berkshire Music Ctr, studied comp with Gunther Schuller, 80; Peabody Consv, studied comp with Jean Eichelberger Ivey, Vladimir Ussachevsky & Morris Cotel, MM(comp), 80; studied electronic & comput music with Barry Vercoe & Jean Eichelberger Ivey & orchestration with Donald Erb & Gunther Schuller. *Works:* Motis Sonoris Diligenter Ordinatus (organ & tape), Barbara Thompson, 79; Song Weavers, 80 & Aslan, 82, Body/Voice Theatre Found, NY; Voices from the Dawn, Drew Minter, 82. *Pos:* Comp, 69-; music dir, organist & choirmaster, St Monica Roman Cath Church, Kalamazoo, 71-76 & St Bernard Roman Cath Church, Baltimore, 76-; music consult, Roman Cath Diocese Kalamazoo, Mich, 74-76. *Teaching:* Private music instr, 73-; lab instr & supvr electronic music studio, Kalamazoo Col, 72-74; design & technical consult, Electronic & Comput Music Studios, Peabody Inst, 77-78; asst dir & lab instr, 78-80, adminr res & develop, 80-82, mem fac, Electronic & Comput Music Studios & co-dir, Combined Lab Auditory Interdisciplinary Res, dir, 82-; mem fac & dir, Electronic & Comput Music Studio, Goucher Col, 82-; guest lectr & consult, wkshps electronic & computer music & liturgical music, currently; dir, Comput Music Studio, Peabody, 83- *Awards:* Gustav Klemm Comp Award, Peabody Consv, 78; Fromm Music Found Fel, Berkshire Music Ctr, 80. *Mem:* Comp Music Asn; Am Soc Univ Comp; Am Guild Organists. *Interests:* Electronic and computer music; psycho-acoustics. *Mailing Add:* 1 E Mt Vernon Pl Baltimore MD 21202

WRIGHT, JOSEPHINE R B
WRITER, EDUCATOR
b Detroit, Mich, Sept 5, 42. *Study:* Univ Mo, Columbia, BM, 63, MA, 67; Pius XII Acad, Florence, Italy, MM, 64; NY Univ, PhD(musicol), 75. *Teaching:* Instr music, York Col, City Univ New York, 72-75, asst prof, 75-76; asst prof, Harvard Univ, 76-81; assoc prof, Col Wooster, 81- *Awards:* Jr Fac Res Grant, Harvard Univ Grad Soc & Clark Fund, 78-80; Nat Endowment Humanities Award, 79-81. *Mem:* Am Musicol Asn; Am Asn Univ Women; Sonneck Soc; Asn Study Afro-Am Life & Hist; Col Music Soc. *Interests:* Baroque music; Afro-American and Afro-European music history; black American folklore. *Publ:* Ed, New Music, Black Perspective Music, 79; auth, Francesco Mancini, In: New Grove Dict of Music & Musicians, 80; George Polgreen Bridgetower: African Prodigy in England (1789-1799), Musical Quart, 80; Ignatius Sancho (1729-1780): Early African Composer in England, Garland Publ, 81; Das Negertrio Jimenez in Europe, Black Perspective Music, 81. *Mailing Add:* Dept Music Col Wooster Wooster OH 44691

WRIGHT, MAURICE WILLIS
COMPOSER

b Front Royal, Va, Oct 17, 49. *Study:* Duke Univ, with Iain Hamilton, BA, 72; Columbia Univ, with Jack Beeson, Charles Dodge, Mario Davidovsky & Vladimir Ussachevsky, MA, 74. *Works:* Stellae, comn & perf by Berkshire Music Ctr, 78; Cantata, 78 & Wind Quintet, 80, Mobart Music Publ; Solos, comn & perf by 20th Century Consort, 82; String Quartet, No 1 & 2, comn & perf by Emerson String Quartet, 83; Duo, Mobart Music Publ, 83. *Teaching:* Asst prof music comp, Boston Univ, 78-79 & Temple Univ, 80- *Awards:* Charles Ives Award, Am Acad Arts & Lett, 77; fel comp, Guggenheim Found, 77 & Nat Endowment for Arts, 82. *Mailing Add:* 302 Hillside Ave Jenkintown PA 19046

WRIGHT, PETER B, III
CLARINET, EDUCATOR

b Bartow, Fla, Mar 22, 55. *Study:* Jacksonville Univ, BME, 75; Eastman Sch Music, MM, 81. *Rec Perf:* Brahms Clarinet Sonatas, Spears Int Rec, 82. *Pos:* Prin clarinet, Jacksonville Symph Orch, 75-, personnel mgr, 78-; bass & extra clarinet, Savanah Symph, Ga, 79- *Teaching:* Instr clarinet, Jackson Univ, 75- *Awards:* Presser Found Scholar, 74. *Mailing Add:* 310 W Tenth St Jacksonville FL 32206

WRIGHT, (MYRON) SEARLE
ORGAN, COMPOSER

b Susquehanna, Pa, Apr 4, 18. *Study:* Columbia Univ, 38-48; studied with William Gomph, Joseph Bonnet, T Tertius Noble, Otto Luening, Frederick Schlieder & Rudolph Thomas; Trinity Col London, Hon Dr, 57; Royal Can Col Organists, Hon Dr, 79. *Works:* Prelude on Brother James Air (organ), Oxford Univ Press, 50; Prelude on Greensleeves, 50 & The Green Blade (symphonic cantata), 51, H W Gray; Dost Thou in a Manger Lie? (soli & a cappella chorus), Witmark, 56; Spirit Divine (chorus & orch or organ), Galaxy, 59; Introduction, Passacaglia and Fugue (organ), H W Gray, 61; Psalm 46 (chorus, brass, perc & organ), Belwin Mill, H W Gray, 83. *Rec Perf:* Chorus, Organ, Brass and Percussion (Williams, Britten, Holst, Purcell & Dello Joio), Kapp Rec & Decca Rec. *Pos:* Organist & choirmaster, Chapel Incarnation, New York, 44-52 & Christ Church, Cincinnati, 71-75; dir chapel music, St Paul's Chapel, Columbia Univ, 52-71; organist, First Congregational Church, Binghamton, NY, 82- *Teaching:* Instr & lectr improvisation, comp & organ, Union Theol Sem, 48-71; assoc organ, Columbia Univ, 52-71; adj prof music, Univ Cincinnati, 71-73 & Sch Sacred Music, Yale Univ, 82; E A Link Prof, State Univ NY, Binghamton, 77- *Bibliog:* Leslie P Spellman (auth), How Searle Wright Does It, Diapason Mag, 48. *Mem:* ASCAP; life mem, Am Guild Organists; Am Fedn Musicians; Am Theatre Organ Soc. *Publ:* Auth, Gustav Holst, 100th Anniversary, 74 & Seth Daniels Bingham, 100th Anniversary, Am Organist, 6/82. *Mailing Add:* RiverHouse 38 Front St Binghamton NY 13905

WRIGHT, THOMAS G
PIANO, COMPOSER

b Indianapolis, Ind, Mar 21, 29. *Study:* Arthur Jordan Consv Music, BM; Butler Univ, BM; Ind Univ, MM; Columbia Univ, three yrs. *Works:* Hollywood (ballet), perf in Tallahassee & Kennedy Ctr, Washington; Forward March, comn by US Air Force; Song of the Stranger, Mutual Network Series. *Pos:* Music perf and music dir radio & TV networks New York & NBC, CBS & mutual networks, formerly; work for motion picture indust, Hollywood; conct pianist throughout US, 30-40; soloist, major symph orch. *Awards:* Fac Year Award, Fla State Univ, 75. *Mem:* Nat Music Teacher's Asn; Fla State Music Teacher's Asn; Am Fedn Musicians. *Mailing Add:* 908 Alliegood Dr Tallahassee FL 32303

WRIGHT, THOMAS UNDERWOOD
VIOLA

b Washington, DC, June 19, 51. *Study:* Oberlin Consv, 69-70. *Pos:* Prin viola, Kennedy Ctr Opera Orch, 80-81; section viola, Chicago Symph Orch, 81- *Mailing Add:* 731 S East Ave Oak Park IL 60304

WRZESIEN, WILLIAM
CLARINET, EDUCATOR

Study: New England Consv Music, BM, MM, artist dipl; studied clarinet with Rosario Mazzeo. *Pos:* Prin clarinet, Boston Ballet Orch, currently & Boston Pops Esplanade Orch, currently; charter mem, Boston Music Viva; soloist & chamber player throughout US & Europe. *Teaching:* Mem fac, Univ Lowell, formerly; Chmn dept woodwinds, brass, perc, harp & sitar & mem fac clarinet & exten div, New England Consv Music, currently. *Mailing Add:* New England Consv Music 290 Huntington Rd Boston MA 02115

WUORINEN, CHARLES
COMPOSER, PIANO

b New York, NY, June 9, 38. *Study:* Columbia Univ, with Otto Luening, Jack Beeson & Vladimir Ussachevsky, BA, 61, MA, 63; Jersey State Col, Hon DMus, 71. *Works:* Time's Encomium, 70, A Reliquary for Igor Stravinsky, 75; Tashi Concerto, 76; The Magic Art, 77 & Archaeopteryx, 78, C F Peters; Short Suite, comn & perf by Am Comp Orch, 83; Violin Concerto, comn by San Francisco Symph, 83; over 150 compositions. *Rec Perf:* Chamber Concerto for Cello and 10 Players, Percussion Symphony & Ringing Changes, Nonesuch; Composition for Oboe and Piano, Orion; Concerto for Piano, CRI. *Pos:* Co-dir, Group for Contemp Music, 62-; cond & soloist, Cleveland Orch, 76, Finland Radio Orch, 79, Helsinki Phil, 79, New York Phil, Chicago Symph, Buffalo Phil, Indianapolis Symph, Boston Symph, St Paul Chamber Orch, New Orch, Los Angeles Phil & Royal Phil Orch; comp in res, Chamber Music Northwest, 78 & Grand Teton Music Fest, 79; chmn, Am Comp Orch, 81-; pianist, chamber music performances throughout US. *Teaching:* Lectr, Columbia Univ, 64-65, instr, 65-69, asst prof, 69-71; vis comp in res, Princeton Univ, 67-68, New England Consv, 68-71, State Univ Iowa & Berkshire Music Ctr; adj lectr, Univ SFla, 71-72; fac mem, Manhattan Sch Music, 72-79 & Univ Southern Calif, 81; lectr, Yale Univ, 83 & cols & univ throughout US. *Awards:* Pulitzer Prize, for Time's Encomium, 70; Rockefeller Found Fel, 79 & 82; Arts & Lett Award, Finlandia Found, 76. *Bibliog:* Joan Peyser (auth), It's a Big Week for Wuorinen, 4/10/83 & Tim Page (auth), St Luke's Ensemble Plays Archaeopteryx, 4/19/83, New York Times; Andrew Porter (auth), Musical Events, New Yorker, 5/2/83. *Mem:* Co-founder, Am Soc Univ Comp; Am Comp Alliance; Am Music Ctr; Int Soc Contemp Music; BMI. *Publ:* Auth, Simple Composition, Longman, Inc, 78; Notes on the Performance of Contemporary Music, Perspectives New Music; numerous articles in High Fidelity & Musical Am, New York Times, Saturday Rev & others. *Rep:* BMI 320 W 57th St New York NY 10019. *Mailing Add:* c/o Allied Artists Bureau 195 Steamboat Rd Great Neck NY 11024

WURSTEN, RICHARD BRUCE
LIBRARIAN, PIANO

b Emmett, Idaho, Apr 19, 38. *Study:* Utah State Univ, BS(music), 61; Univ Ill, Urbana-Champaign, MM(piano), 64, MS(libr sci), 78; Akad Musik Darstellende Kunst, Vienna, Austria, 64-65; Univ Wis, Madison, PhD(musicol), 80. *Pos:* Asst catalog libr & music cataloger, Southern Ill Univ, Carbondale, 79- *Teaching:* Instr music, Auburn Univ, 65-66, Gonzaga Univ, 66-68 & Univ Ala, Huntsville, 72-76. *Awards:* Rotary Int Found Fel, 64-65; Fulbright-Hays Grant, 70-71. *Mem:* Am Musicol Soc; Music Libr Asn; Music OCLC Users Group. *Interests:* Theodor Streicher, Austrian composer (1874-1940); music uniform titles; faculty status for librarians; conversion of music records to computerized circulation system. *Publ:* Auth, The Vocal Music of Theodor Streicher, Part I, 12/76 & Part II, 5/77, Nat Asn Teachers Singing; Streicher, Theodor, In: New Grove Dict Music & Musicians, 80; coauth, Music Goes Online: Retrospective Conversion of Card Catalog Records for Music Scores at Morris Library, Ill Libr, 5/83. *Mailing Add:* 1206 W Schwartz St Carbondale IL 62901

WURTZLER, BELA
DOUBLE BASS, EDUCATOR

b Budapest, Hungary. *Study:* Franz Liszt Acad, Budapest, dipl. *Pos:* Mem, Budapest State Opera Orch & Budapest Phil, formerly; asst prin bass, Detroit Symphony Orch, formerly; bass, Boston Symph Orch, 62- *Teaching:* Mem fac, Brown Univ, currently & Wellesley Col, currently; instr double bass, New England Consv Music, currently. *Awards:* First Prize, Int Bass Compt Budapest & Bucharest. *Mailing Add:* New England Consv Music 290 Huntington Rd Boston MA 02115

WYATT, LARRY D
EDUCATOR, CONDUCTOR & MUSIC DIRECTOR

b Benton, Ky, Sept 12, 43. *Study:* Murray State Univ, BME, 65; NTex State Univ, MM, 67; Fla State Univ, PhD, 74. *Pos:* Dir chorus, New Orleans Phil Symph Orch, 81- *Teaching:* Instr, Armed Forces Sch Music, 65-71, Cent Fla Community Col, 66-69 & Univ Houston, 72-73; prof, Loyola Univ, 73- *Mem:* Am Choral Dir Asn (pres southern div, 83-85); Nat Asn Teachers Singing; Music Educr Nat Conf. *Publ:* Ed, Two Table Prayers, 81 & Pater Nosten, 81, Plymouth Music. *Mailing Add:* 4427 Walmsley Ave New Orleans LA 70125

WYATT, LUCIUS REYNOLDS
EDUCATOR, TRUMPET

b Waycross, Ga, Aug 18, 38. *Study:* Fla A&M Univ, Tallahassee, BS, 59; Eastman Sch Music, Univ Rochester, MM, 60, PhD, 74. *Pos:* First trumpet, Eastman Wind Ens, Rochester, 72-73; cond, Tuskegee Inst Bands, 60-74 & Prairie View A&M Univ Symphonic Band, 74-; musician & arr, US Army Europe Band, Heidelberg, Ger, 63-65. *Teaching:* Asst prof music bands, Tuskegee Inst, 60-74; assoc prof music, Prairie View A&M Univ, 74-, chmn dept music, 82. *Awards:* Col Band Dir of Yr, Birmingham Grid Forecasters, 71. *Mem:* Col Music Soc; Am Musicol Soc; Soc Music Theory; Col Band Dir Nat Asn (state chmn, 70-71); Tex Asn Music Sch. *Interests:* Mid-twentieth century orchestral variations. *Publ:* Auth, The Brussels Museum of Music Instruments, Music Educ J, 2/67; Discovering Structure and Style in Instrument Rehearsal, Instrumentalist, 68; Ulysses Kay's Fantasy Variations, Black Perspective Music, 77; Present State and Future Needs of Research, Black Music Res J, 80; Wendell Logan, the Composer & His Music, Black Music Res Newsletter, 81; and others. *Mailing Add:* PO Box 2046 Prairie View TX 77445

WYATT, SCOTT ALAN
COMPOSER, EDUCATOR

b Philadelphia, Pa, Oct 30, 51. *Study:* West Chester State Col, BS(music educ), 74; Univ Ill, MS(comp), 76. *Works:* Sense One (tape), Univ Ill Experimental Music, 75; Two Plus Two (two perc & tape), Music For Perc, 76; Four For Flute (flute & tape), Frangipani Press, 77; Menagerie (tape), Univ Ill Experimental Music, 78; All For One (perc & tape accmp), Music For Perc, 80; On, Focus On (tape), Univ Ill Experimental Music, 81; Three For One (tuba & tape accmp), comn by Dan Perantoni, 82. *Teaching:* Asst prof, Univ Ill, Urbana, 76-79, assoc prof & dir, Experimental Music Studios, 79- *Awards:* Winner, Nat Comp Cont, Int Soc Contemp Music, 78 & Nat Flute Asn, 79; winner, Int Comp Cont, Concorso Int Luigi Russolo, 79. *Mem:* Am Soc Univ Comp; Electronic Arts Found. *Mailing Add:* Sch Music Univ Ill 1114 W Nevada Urbana IL 61801

WYCKOFF, LOU ANN
DRAMATIC SOPRANO
b Berkeley, Calif. *Study:* With Gibner King, 65-69 & Armen Boyajian, 78- *Rec Perf:* Zoroastre (Rameau), Nonesuch, 70; Rienzi (R Wagner), Ariola, Eurodisc, 74. *Roles:* Donna Elvira in Don Giovanni, Spoleto Fest & Munich Opera, 67 & 73; Amelia in Un Ballo in maschera, La Scala, Milano, 72; Mistress Ford in Falstaff, Washington Opera, 73; Eva in Meistersinger, Teatro Monnai, Brussels & Lyon Opera, 73; Agatha in Freishutz, Teatro Fenice, Venice, 74 & Deutsche Oper, Berlin, 77; Odabella in Attila, Deutsche Opera, Berlin, 77; Leonora in Il Trovatore, Houston Grand Opera, 80. *Pos:* Soprano soloist, Deutsche Oper Berlin, 69-78. *Awards:* Martha Baird Rockefeller Grant, 66-69; William M Sullivan Found Grant, 69; Artists Adv Coun Grant, 68. *Mem:* Am Guild Musical Artists. *Rep:* Robert Lombardo Assoc 61 W 62nd St 6F New York NY 10023. *Mailing Add:* c/o Blacksmith 5B 648 Amsterdam Ave New York NY 10025

WYLIE, RUTH SHAW
COMPOSER, EDUCATOR
b Cincinnati, Ohio, June 24, 16. *Study:* Wayne State Univ, AB, 37, MA(music), 39; Eastman Sch Music, PhD(comp), 43. *Works:* The Long Look Home (suite for orch), comn by Mich Coun Arts, 75; Toward Sirius (chamber work), comn by Wayne State Univ, 76; Nova (chamber work), perf by Univ Chicago Contemp Chamber Players, 76; Views From Beyond (suite for orch), comn by Nat Endowment Arts, 78; Psychogram (piano), comn by James Tocco, 78; False Fires (orch), perf by Pittsburgh Symph Orch, 79; Music for Three Sisters (chamber work), perf by Comtemp Music Forum, Libr Cong, 82. *Rec Perf:* Psychogram (piano), CRI, 76. *Teaching:* Asst prof theory & comp, Univ Mo, 43-49; asst prof, Wayne State Univ, 49-60, prof, 60-69, chmn music dept, 61-62, head comp, 60-69, prof emer, 69- *Awards:* Res fel, Huntington Hartford Found, 52-53 & MacDowell Colony, 54 & 56; Standard Award, ASCAP, 75-83. *Mem:* Am Soc Univ Comp; Nat Asn Comp USA; ASCAP; Int League Women Comp; Am Women Comp Inc. *Publ:* Auth, Rhythm in Contemporary Music, Music Teachers Nat Asn Vol of Proc, 47; Musicmatics: A View From the Mainland, Am J Aesthetics & Art Criticism, 65; Music Psychogram, Columbia Univ Press, 69; Incubus, Am Soc Univ Comp J Music Scores, 75; Soliloquy, Harold Branch, Music Publ, 76. *Mailing Add:* 1251 Country Club Dr Long's Peak Rte Estes Park CO 80517

WYLIE, TED DAVID
TENOR, EDUCATOR
b Cushing, Okla, Oct 25, 45. *Study:* Okla Baptist Univ, BM, 67; Ind Univ, with Walter Bricht, Frank St Leger, Eileen Farrell & Paul Matthen, MM, 69, DMus, 79. *Roles:* Ben in The Telephone, Indianapolis Opera Co, 76; ten soloist in Bach Magnificat, Ecoutez, New Orleans, 81; Germont in La Traviata, 81 & Manrico in Il Trovatore, 82, New Orleans Opera Co; ten soloist in Beethoven 9th Symph, New Orleans Symph Orch, 82; ten soloist in Roi David, New Orleans Symph, 82 & Jefferson Perf Arts, 82; Young Sailor & Shepherd in Tristan und Isolde, New Orleans Opera Co, 83. *Pos:* Music dir, Philippine Baptist Radio & TV, Manila, 76-77; ten soloist, St Charles Ave Baptist Church & Touro Synagogue, 80- *Teaching:* Instr voice & chorus, Ind Univ, Kokomo, 73-74; asst prof voice, lit & opera, New Orleans Baptist Theol Sem, 79- *Mem:* Am Guild Musical Artists; Nat Asn Teachers Singing. *Mailing Add:* 4139 Seminary Pl New Orleans LA 70126

WYMAN, DANN CORIAT
COMPOSER, VIOLA
b Boston, Mass, Nov 13, 23. *Study:* Northeastern Univ, BA; studied with Arthur Fiedler, 48 & P Hindemith, 51. *Works:* Overture for Orchestra, Cape Ann Symph Publ, 50; Aloness for Viola, Seesaw Publ, 72; Ode to the Viola With String Orchestra, Newton Symph, 73; String Quartet #1, Seesaw Publ, 74; Three Songs, The Question, Color Camera, Jane Brydon, 75; Coupled (cello & piano), 76; Serenade for Strings, Comp Press, 82. *Pos:* Student cond, Northeastern Univ; first viola, Cape Ann Symph, 46-49 & NShore Phil, 49-51; found & dir, Newton Symph Orch, 65- *Awards:* Int Music Guild Award, 76. *Bibliog:* George Merry (auth), article, Christian Sci Moniter, 64; Linda Abrams (auth), Renniacos Meh, Alumni Publ, 83. *Mem:* Nat Asn Comp & Cond. *Mailing Add:* 220 Hobart Rd Chestnut Hill MA 02167

WYTON, ALEC
COMPOSER, ORGAN
b London, England, Aug 3, 21; US citizen. *Study:* Royal Acad Music, London, FRCO, 42, ChM, 46; Univ Oxford, MA, 47; Susquehanna Univ, Selinsgrove, Pa, Hon MusD, 70. *Works:* Fanfare (organ), H W Gray Co, 56; Preludes, Fanfares, March, Harold Flammer Inc, 62; Festival Communion Service, H W Gray Co, 63; A Little Christian Year, Carl Fischer, 64; The Journey with Jonah (opera), All Souls Parish, Asheville, NC, 77; A Hymn to God the Father, Novello & Co, 80; Sing A New Song to the Lord, Sacred Music Press, 82. *Rec Perf:* Epitaph for this World and Time (Iain Hamilton), 73 & Organ Music of Otto Leuning, 75, CRI. *Pos:* Organist & choirmaster, St Matthew's Church, Northampton, 46-50, Christ Church Cathedral, St Louis, 50-54, Cathedral St John Divine, New York, 54-74 & St James Church, New York, 74- *Teaching:* Adj prof music, Union Theol Sem, New York, 56-73; vis prof, Westminster Choir Col, Princeton, 65-73. *Awards:* Ann Comp Award, ASCAP, 67- *Mem:* Am Guild Organists (pres, 64-79); New York Musician's Club (pres, 76-78); ASCAP; Hymn Soc Am; Royal Col Organists. *Mailing Add:* 129 E 69th St New York NY 10021

Y

YADEAU, WILLIAM RONALD
EDUCATOR, PIANO
b Oceanport, NJ, Feb 8, 46. *Study:* Baldwin-Wallace Col, BMus; Univ Ill, Urbana-Champaign, MMus, DMA, 80. *Teaching:* Instr piano, group piano & music theory, Eastern Ore State Col, 72-76; asst prof, Sch Music, Millikin Univ, 78- *Mem:* Ill State Music Teachers Asn (Decatur area group chmn, 79-82, pres, 82-); Ore Music Teachers Asn (Blue Mountain dist pres, 75-76); Ill Alliance Arts Educ. *Publ:* Auth, The Role of the Studio Music Teacher in Comprehensive Arts Education, In: The Arts: A Basic Component of General Education, 82. *Mailing Add:* Sch Music Millikin Univ Decatur IL 62522

YAFFE, MICHAEL CHARLES
ADMINISTRATOR, WRITER
b New Haven, Conn, Apr 29, 51. *Study:* Clark Univ, BA, 73; Univ Toronto, MA, 75. *Pos:* Asst dir oper, Nat Asn Sch Music, Reston, Va, 76-; radio producer & reporter, Arts Unit, WAMU-FM, Washington, DC, 77- *Publ:* Auth, Public Radio Stations and College Music Programs, 79, Nat Asn Sch Music; coauth, The Piano: Black and White and Played All Over (radio prog), 81, Conducting: The Mystique of the Maestro (radio prog), 81 & A Musical Fellowship: The String Quartet (radio prog), 81, WAMU-FM. *Mailing Add:* 1421 Greenmont Ct Reston VA 22090

YAJIMA, HIROKO
VIOLIN, EDUCATOR
b Tokyo, Japan, Feb 8, 47. *Study:* Juilliard Sch, BS, 67. *Rec Perf:* Ravel & Debussy Quartets, Vanguard, 82. *Pos:* Violinist, Galimir String Quartet, 66- & Mannes Trio, 83. *Teaching:* Asst prof violin, State Univ NY, Stony Brook, 78-81; fac mem, Mannes Col Music, 82- *Awards:* First Prize, Mainichi Shinbun Compt, 58; First Prize, Nippon Broadcasting Compt, 65; Fulbright Grant, 65. *Rep:* Naomi Rhodes Assoc Inc 157 W 57th St New York NY 10019. *Mailing Add:* 89 Booth Ave Englewood NJ 07631

YAKIM, MONI
EDUCATOR, MUSIC DIRECTOR
b Jerusalem, Israel. *Pos:* Founder & artistic dir, Perf Theater Ctr Ltd, NY Pantomime Theater & NY Pantomime Training Ctr; prin performer, Etienne Decroux with Marcel Marceau; participant, Le Theatre Nat Populaire & Le Theatre Franco-Allemand; dir & performer, original prod & operas throughout US, Europe & Israel; performer & choreographer, film adaptation Jacques Brel Is Alive and Well and Living in Paris. *Teaching:* Head movement dept, Yale Drama Sch, formerly; mem fac, Stella Adler Theater Studio, Northwood Inst, formerly, Circle in the Sq Theater Sch, currently, Perf Theater Ctr Ltd, currently, NY Pantomime Theater, currently & NY Pantomime Training Ctr, currently; mem fac theater, Juilliard Sch Music, 68- *Mailing Add:* Juilliard Sch Music Lincoln Ctr New York NY 10023

YAMRON, JANET M
EDUCATOR, ADMINISTRATOR
b Atlantic City, NJ, May 1, 32. *Study:* Temple Univ, Pa, BS, 54, MA, 57; studied with Elaine Brown, Julius Herford & J F Williamson. *Pos:* Asst to dir, Singing City, Philadelphia, 59-60. *Teaching:* Dir vocal music, Philadelphia Pub Sch, 60-66; prof music, Temple Univ, 66-, asst dean, 75- *Mem:* Am Choral Dir Asn; Music Educr Nat Conf; Am Choral Found; Col Music Soc; Sigma Alpha Iota. *Mailing Add:* Presser Hall Temple Univ Philadelphia PA 19122

YANAGITA, MASAKO (MASAKO YANAGITA BOGIN)
VIOLIN, TEACHER
b Tokyo, Japan, Mar 30, 44. *Study:* Mannes Col Music, dipl; 69. *Rec Perf:* String Quartet, Op 132 (Beethoven), Music Minos One, 76; Various chamber music works with Bronx Arts Ens, Musical Heritage Rec, 81- *Pos:* Solo conct violinist, 69-; concertmaster, Queens Symph Orch, NY, 71- & Springfield Symph Orch, 79-; first violinist, Vieuxtemps String Quartet, 74-78; mem, Teppan Zee Conct, currently. *Teaching:* Violin, Mannes Col Music, 75- *Awards:* First prize, Carl Flesch Compt, London, 68, & Paganini Int Compt, Italy, 68; second prize, Munich Int Compt, 69. *Mem:* Bohemians; Teppan Zee Concerts. *Rep:* Raymond Weiss Artists Mgt 300 W 55th St New York NY 10019. *Mailing Add:* 838 West End Ave New York NY 10025

YANCHUS, JUDITH
VIOLIN
b Wilkes Barre, Pa, Dec 18, 39. *Study:* Boston Consv Music, BMus; studied with Joseph Fuchs, Raphael Bronstein & Ivor Karmian & chamber music with William Kroll. *Pos:* Mem, Buffalo Phil, formerly, Rotterdam Phil, formerly & Minneapolis Symph, formerly; concertmaster, Boston Women's Symph, formerly; violinist, String Trio New York, formerly & Metropolitan Opera, currently; performer chamber music & soloist in many US cities. *Mailing Add:* 9 W 64th St New York NY 10023

YANCICH, CHARLES THEODORE
FRENCH HORN, TEACHER-COACH
b Hammond, Ind, July 4, 24. *Study:* Univ Mich, BMusEd, 48. *Pos:* Prin horn, Indianapolis Symph Orch, 48-54 & Boston Pops, 54-83; assoc prin horn, Boston Symph Orch, 54-83; soloist, Boston Pops, 80- *Teaching:* Instr horn, Boston Univ, 68-83; adj instr, Lowell Univ, 82-83. *Mailing Add:* c/o Boston Symph Hall 301 Massachusetts Ave Boston MA 02115

YANCICH, MILAN MICHAEL
FRENCH HORN, EDUCATOR

b Whiting, Ind, Dec 11, 21. *Study:* Univ Mich, Ann Arbor, BMusEd, 46; Northwestern Univ, MMus, 50. *Rec Perf:* Sound Recording Practical Guide to Horn Playing, 71 & 15 Solos for French Horn Recording, 78, Helden Rec. *Pos:* First horn, Columbus Phil Orch, 46-48; solo horn, Jerry Walds Orch, 47, Radio Am Broadcasting Co, 52-53 & Lake Placid Club, New York Sinfonietta, summers, 52-79; asst first horn, Chicago Symph Orch, 48-51; third horn, Cleveland Symph Orch, 51-52; third & fourth horn, Rochester Symph Orch, 53-83. *Teaching:* Instr French horn, Capitol Univ, 46-48 & Ohio State Univ, 46-48, Mich State Univ, Lansing, 52-53; prof & lectr French horn & woodwind ens, Eastman Sch Music, 54- *Publ:* Auth, Method for French Horn Vol I & II, 66 & Practical Guide to French Horn Playing, 71, Wind Music, Inc; 15 Solos for French Horn, Helden Rec, 78. *Mailing Add:* 153 Highland Pkwy Rochester NY 14620

YANNATOS, JAMES D
COMPOSER, CONDUCTOR & MUSIC DIRECTOR

b New York, NY, Mar 13, 29. *Study:* Yale Univ, BM, 51, MM, 52; Univ Iowa, PhD, 60. *Works:* Cycles, 74, American Rituals (orch), 74, To Form A More Perfect Union (oratorio), 76, Sound of Desolation and Joy, 78, Silly and Serious songs (on words of children), 80, Tunes and Dances (Fanfare for Uncommon Man), 81 & City of Coral (film score), 83, Sonory Publ. *Rec Perf:* Silence Battle (children's opera), 74, Music of James Yannatos, 76, Harvard-Radcliffe Orchestra, 79, Nothing Lasts Forever, 82 & City of Choral, 82, Sonory Rec. *Pos:* Music dir, Harvard-Radcliffe Orch, 64-; cond, Young Artists Orch, Berkshire Music Ctr & Youth Orch, Chautauqua; comp in res, Saratoga; res cond, Can Chamber Orch, Banff; musical dir, Hanover Chamber Orch; conducting appearances with Boston Pops, Baltimore, Winnipeg, Edmonton, Chautauqua & San Antonio Symphonies, Canadian, Hanover & Washington Chamber Orchestras & numerous university, conservatory & All-State High School orchestras. *Teaching:* Sr lectr, Harvard Univ, 64-; fac cond, Berkshire Music Ctr; dir music sch, Chautauqua. *Mem:* BMI; Am Comp Alliance; Music Educr Nat Conf. *Publ:* Auth, Explorations in Musical Materials, Sonory Publ, 78. *Mailing Add:* 9 Stearns St Cambridge MA 02138

YANNAY, YEHUDA
COMPOSER, EDUCATOR

b Timisoara, Rumania, May 26, 37; US citizen. *Study:* Israel Acad Music, with A Boscovitch, dipl, 64; Brandeis Univ, with Arthur Berger & Harold Shapero, MFA, 66; Univ Ill, with Salvatore Martirano, DMA, 74; Berkshire Music Ctr, with Elliott Carter, Ernst Krenek, Donald Martino & Gunther Schuller. *Works:* Permutations (solo perc), 64; Houdini's 9th (double bass & escape artist), 69; 7 Late Spring Pieces (piano), 73; At the End of the Parade (baritone & six players), 74; American Sonorama (ballet), 75-76; Five Songs for Tenor and Orchestra, 76-77; The Hidden Melody (horn & cello), 77. *Pos:* Dean, Israel Consv, 66-68; founder & cond, Music from Almost Yesterday. *Teaching:* Assoc prof music, Univ Wis, 70- *Awards:* Nat Endowment Arts Grant; Fulbright Prof, 82-83; Second Prize, Int Compt Comp G B Viotti. *Mem:* BMI; Am Comp Alliance; Am Soc Univ Comp. *Mailing Add:* Dept Music Univ Wis Milwaukee WI 53201

YANNUZZI, WILLIAM A(NTHONY)
MUSIC DIRECTOR, EDUCATOR

b Baltimore, Md, July 30, 34. *Study:* Johns Hopkins Univ, AB, 57, MA, 58; St Johns Col, NMex, MA, 69; studied piano with Austin Conradi & solfege with Renee Longy. *Pos:* Asst cond, Baltimore Opera Co, 62-73, music dir, 73-; accmp, vocal recitals. *Teaching:* French, Baltimore City Col, 58-66; vocal coach, Peabody Consv, 77- *Mailing Add:* 40 W Chase St Baltimore MD 21201

YARBOROUGH, WILLIAM
CONDUCTOR & MUSIC DIRECTOR

b Wilmington, NC, Jan 3, 26. *Study:* Univ Chicago; Chicago Music Col, BM; Ind Univ, MM; Berkshire Music Ctr; Univ Southern Calif; studied cond with Koussevitzky & Ormandy, comp with Nadia Boulanger & Rieti & violin with Gittleson. *Pos:* Music dir & cond, Am Symph Orch, Paris, France, 45-46; Richmond Phil, 49-53; Mich Bach-Mozart Fest, 62-65 & Am Chamber Orch, Washington, DC, 79-; guest cond, Royal Phil, London, Philadelphia Orch, George Enescu State Phil, Bucharest, Romania, Vienna Symph, Los Angeles Chamber Orch, Chicago Civic Orch, St Cecelia Orch, Rome, Va Symph orch & others; music adv, Old Dominion Symph Coun, State Va. *Teaching:* Lectr arts, Chicago Adult Educ Coun, 50-58. *Mailing Add:* 4201 Cathedral Ave NW #706E Washington DC 20016

YARBROUGH, JOAN (JOAN YARBROUGH COWAN)
PIANO, TEACHER

b Boston, Mass, Sept 10, 40. *Study:* Mozarteum, Salzburg, Austria, 58-59; Consv Music, Oberlin Col, BM, 60; Royal Acad Music, London, LRAM(piano perf), 63. *Rec Perf:* Modern Music for Two Pianos, CRI, 74; Yarbrough & Cowan Play Clementi, Schumann, Reizenstein, Orion, 76; Two Piano Concerto and Sonata (Poulenc), Musical Heritage Soc, 77; Two Piano Concerto & Scaramouche & Carnaval a la Nouvelle Orleans (Milhaud), Orion, 78; Milhaud and Poulenc Repertoire, Pantheon, 83. *Teaching:* Assoc prof music, piano & piano ens, Univ Montevallo, 64- *Awards:* All Am Press Assoc Award, 66. *Bibliog:* Dean M Elder (auth), An American Idiom—Two Piano Music, Clavier, 4/75; Miriam Edwards (auth), An Interview with Duo-pianists Joan Yarbrough and Robert Cowan, Ga Music News, 11/76. *Mem:* Ala Music Teachers Asn (first vpres, 73-75); Music Teachers Nat Asn; Nat Fedn Music Clubs. *Publ:* Coauth, Have Pianos Will Travel, 66, Another Look at Duo-pianism, 68 & Two Pianos on Tour, 70, Music J; A Primer of Recent Two-Piano Concertos, Symph News, 76. *Rep:* Maxim Gershunoff Attractions Inc 502 Park Ave New York NY 10022. *Mailing Add:* PO Box 465 Montevallo AL 35115

YARDEN, ELIE
COMPOSER, EDUCATOR

b Philadelphia, Pa, June 7, 23. *Study:* Settlement Music Sch, with Stefan Wolpe. *Works:* Four Variations (cello quartet), 57; Prelude, Passacaglia and Fugue (orch), 58; Divertimento (chamber ens), 63; String Quartet No 3 (chamber music), 65; Eros and Psyche (chamber opera), 70; Suite 549 (piano), 72; Septentrion (piano trio), 77. *Teaching:* Instr, Rubin Acad Music, Jerusalem, 58-60 & Israel Acad Music, Tel-Aviv, 60-65; assoc prof comp, Bard Col, 67-; lectr, Vassar Col, 73-74. *Awards:* Van Leer Found Grant, 63-65; Rockefeller Rec Grant, 72; Nat Endowment Arts Grant, 77. *Mailing Add:* Music Dept Bard Col Annandale-on-Hudson NY 12504

YARDUMIAN, RICHARD
COMPOSER

b Philadelphia, Pa, Apr 5, 17. *Study:* Harmony with William Happich & counterpoint with H Alexander Matthews; Maryville Col, SMD, 72; Widener Col, DM, 78. *Works:* Armenian Suite, 37, Violin Concerto, 49 & 60, Passacaglia Recitatives and Fugue (piano & orch), 57, Symphony No 1, 61, Symphony No 2 (psalms; voice & orch), 64, Mass: Come Creator Spirit (voice, chorus & orch), 66 & Abraham: Oratorio, 71-73, Elkan-Vogel Co Inc. *Pos:* Music dir, Lord's New Church Which Is Nova Hierosolyma, 39-; mem bd dir, Chamber Symph Philadelphia, 64-67; trustee, Grand Tetons Music Fest, 70- *Awards:* Gold Medal Excellence, Armenian Bicentennial Commemoration, 76. *Mem:* ASCAP; Philadelphia Musical Soc; Am Symph Orch League; Musical Fund Soc. *Mailing Add:* Bryn Athyn PA 19009

YASUI, BYRON K
COMPOSER, DOUBLE BASS

b Honolulu, Hawaii, Dec 13, 40. *Study:* Univ Hawaii, BEd, 65; Northwestern Univ, MM, 67, DMA, 72. *Works:* Music for Timpani and Brass, Hamar Perc Publ Inc, 74; Concert Piece (four trumpets), Fla State Univ Trumpet Ens, 78; Piccola Arietta (solo guitar), Guitar Rev, 79; Three Little Pieces (solo guitar), Guitar & Lute, 79; Piccola Arietta No 2 (solo guitar), perf by Jeffrey Meyerriecks, 81; Novene (solo clarinet), perf by William Nichols, 83. *Pos:* Double bassist, Honolulu Symph, 64- *Teaching:* Assoc prof theory, comp, classic guitar & jazz improv, Univ Hawaii, 72- *Awards:* MacDowell Colony Fel, 79. *Bibliog:* Donald R Hunsberger (auth), New Music Reviews, Instrumentalist, 8/75. *Mem:* Am Soc Univ Comp; Col Music Soc; Music Educr Nat Conf. *Publ:* Auth, Constructing the Jazz Walking Bass Line: A Basic Guide for Beginners, Bass World, Vol III, No 4; The Text Book Walking Bass Line, NC Music Educr, Vol 32, No 4. *Mailing Add:* Music Dept Univ Hawaii Honolulu HI 96822

YATES, RONALD LEE
COMPOSER, EDUCATOR

b Muskegon, Mich, Apr 27, 47. *Study:* Calif State Univ, Long Beach, BM, 70, MA, 71; Univ Calif, Santa Barbara, PhD, 73. *Works:* Wallace Weems (opera in two acts; libretto by Carolyn Yates), ETex State Univ, 76; Air for Eight Flutes, Southern Music Co, 77; Educational Directions (film score), Phi Delta Kappa, 78; Data Processing and You (film score), ETex State Univ, 79; In Search Of ..., Crest Rec, 79; Variants for 10 Trumpets, ETex State Univ Trumpet Choir, 82. *Teaching:* Assoc prof music comp & theory, ETex State Univ, 74- *Awards:* Best Educ Film (Educational Directions), Instr Mag, 78. *Mem:* ASCAP. *Publ:* Coauth, Manipulative Aspects of the Broadcasting Medium, Int J Instr Media, Vol 10, No 1. *Mailing Add:* 2407 Mayo St Commerce TX 75428

YAUGER, MARGARET (MARGARET YAUGER SMITH)
MEZZO-SOPRANO

b Birmingham, Ala. *Study:* Converse Col, BMus; New England Consv Music, MMus; Am Opera Ctr, Juilliard Sch; studied with Gladys Miller, Frederick Jagel & Daniel Ferro. *Rec Perf:* Beethoven Ninth, Mex Nat Symph, 82. *Roles:* Meg Page in Falstaff, Am Nat Opera Co, 67-68; Maddalena in Rigoletto, Goldovsky Opera, 70 & New York City Opera, 73; Orpheus in Orpheus und Eurydice, Deutsche Oper Am Rhein & Hannover Opera, 79; Marina in Boris Godunov, 80, Fenena in Nabucco, 80, Fricka in Das Rheingold, 81 & Fricka in Die Walküre, 82, Deutsche Oper am Rhein, Düsseldorf. *Pos:* Ms, Am Nat Opera Co, 67-68; Goldovsky Opera Co, 72-; New York City Opera Co, 73-74 & Deutsche Oper am Rhein, 77-; soloist, Duisburg Symph, WGermany, Solinger & Washington Nat Symph. *Mem:* Am Guild Musical Artists. *Rep:* Thea Dispeker 59 E 54th St New York NY 10022. *Mailing Add:* 22 Woodland Rd Montvale NJ 07645

YAVELOW, CHRISTOPHER FOWLER JOHNSON
COMPOSER

b Cambridge, Mass, June 14, 50. *Study:* Boston Univ, BM(comp & theory), 72, MM, 74; Kodaly Musical Training Inst, Mass, 75-76; Harvard Univ, MFA(comp), 76; Franz Liszt Acad, Budapest, Hungary, with Zsolt Durko, Erno Lendvai & Erzsebet Hegyi, cert, 78; Darmstadt Summer Course New Music, cert, 78; private & class study with Nadia Boulanger, 78-79; Ctr Acanthes Darius Milhaud Consv, Aix-en-Provence, France, with Gyorgi Ligeti & Mauricio Kagel, dipl, 79 & 81; Am Consv Fontainebleau, France, dipl, 80. *Works:* Soneptua (string quartet), 73; Phi-Lings (clarinet, violin, cello & piano), 73; An Explanation of One Mechanical Man (clarinet & cello), 74 & E-Prime (brass quintet), 74, Am Comp Ed; Dona Nobis Pacem (women's chorus), Ed A Coeur Joie, France, 76; Monument (string orch), 80; Ritual & Sabotage of the 20th Century (piano trio), 82 & The Passion of Vincent van Gogh (opera), 83, Am Comp Ed. *Pos:* Res comp, Windhover Ctr Creative Arts, 73; pres, Creative Media Inc, 73-76; dir & comp, Kinesis—Theater of Sound & Movement, 73-75; co-dir, Annex Players, 73-76; dir, Fest Musical Chateau Pourtales, 79-80; res comp, Camargo Found, France, 81. *Teaching:*

Teaching fel theory & comp, Harvard Univ, 75-77; instr, Paris-Am Acad, France, 78-79; chmn dept music, Schiller Col, Strasbourg, France, 79-80; assoc prof music, Univ Tex, Dallas, 83- *Awards:* MacDowell Colony Fel, 75-76; Int Res & Exchange Bd Fel, Am Coun Learned Soc & Soc Sci Res Coun, 77-78; Grand Prix l'Unanimite, Rencontres Int Chant Choral, 81. *Mem:* New England Computer Music Soc (mem bd dir, 83-); Am Comp Alliance; BMI; Am Music Ctr; Col Music Soc. *Publ:* Ed, Experiments in Musical Generative Ability, Hungarian Acad Sci, 77. *Mailing Add:* Dept Music Box 688 Univ Tex, Dallas Richardson TX 70508

YELLIN, VICTOR FELL
EDUCATOR, COMPOSER
b Boston, Mass, Dec 14, 24. *Study:* Harvard Col, with Piston, Fine, Davison & Merritt, AB, 49; Mills Col, with Milhaud, 50; Harvard Univ, AM, 52, with Gombosi, Davison, Pirotta & Ward, PhD, 57. *Works:* Abaylar (opera), Metropolitan Opera Studio, Comp Showcase, 67-72; Sonata (violin & piano), Washington Sq Music Soc, 74; The Ethiop, 79, The Indian Queen, 79 & The Duenna, 80, Fed Music Soc; Sonata (cello & piano), Washington Sq Contemp Music Conct, 82. *Rec Perf:* Mass in E-flat (Mrs H H A Beach), Around the Square, Church of Ascension, New York, 82. *Teaching:* Fel, Harvard Univ, 52-56; asst prof, NY Univ, 56-58, from assoc to prof Am music & early romantic opera, 61-; asst prof & dir glee club, Williams Col, 58-60; assoc prof, Ohio State Univ, 60-61. *Awards:* Res grant, Nat Endowment Humanities, 79. *Mem:* Am Musicol Soc; Sonneck Soc. *Interests:* History of American music; early romantic opera. *Publ:* Auth, History of Music, Vol 17, Collier's Encycl, 60; The Conflict of Generations, Arts & Sci, 61; Musical Activity in Virginia Before 1620, J Am Music Soc, 69; The Pronunciation of Recitative, Am Speech, 68; The Celestial Country of Charles Ives, Musical Quart, 74. *Mailing Add:* 52 Washington Mews New York NY 10003

YEO, DOUGLAS EDWARD
TROMBONE, EDUCATOR
b Monterey, Calif, May 19, 55. *Study:* Ind Univ, 73; Wheaton Col, Ill, BMus, 76; NY Univ, MA, 79. *Pos:* Bs Trombonist, Baltimore Symph Orch, 81- *Teaching:* Inst trombone, Peabody Consv, John Hopkins Univ, 82- *Mem:* Int Trombone Asn; Fel Christian Musicians; Christian Instrumental Dir Asn. *Publ:* Auth, Theres More to Brass Playing Than Meets the Ear, Overture, 82; The View From the Back Row, Christianity Today, 83. *Mailing Add:* 7911 Roldrew Ave Baltimore MD 21204

YORK, DON(ALD GRIFFITH)
COMPOSER, MUSIC DIRECTOR
b Watertown, NY, June 19, 47. *Study:* Aspen Music Sch, with Milhaud, 64, 65 & 67; Juilliard Sch, with Persichetti, Sessions & Overton, BMus, 69. *Works:* Polaris, 76 & Diggity, 78, Paul Taylor Dance Co; Rosa, 81 & Snow White, 83, Nautilus Press. *Pos:* Musical dir, Bette Midler's Clams on the Half Shell, 75, Bette Midler Show, 76, Paul Taylor Dance Co, 76- & Little Me, 82. *Mem:* ASCAP; Am Fedn Musicians. *Mailing Add:* Box 90 Buckberg Rd Tomkins Cove NY 10986

YOSHIOKA, EMMETT GENE
COMPOSER, FLUTE
b Honolulu, Hawaii, Mar 19, 44. *Study:* Univ Southern Calif, with Ingolf Dahl, David Raksin & Anthony Vazzana. *Works:* Duo Concertino (alto sax & band); Prologue, Fugue and Epilogue (band); Intermezzo (oboe & band); Extase (trombone solo); Aria and Allegro (alto sax quartet); Ariosa (alto sax, harp & strings); Alto Saxophone Sonata (chamber music). *Pos:* Flutist, Honolulu Symph, 60-61; mem, Los Angeles Sax Quartet, 69-72. *Teaching:* Instr flute, State Univ NY, Albany, 66-69; mem fac, Univ Southern Calif, 69- *Awards:* Comp Award, Univ Southern Calif, 66 & 72; Amstead Award, 72. *Mailing Add:* 5223 Apo Dr Honolulu HI 96821

YOUNG, ANNE LLOYD
CLARINET, EDUCATOR
b Chicago, Ill, Sept 9, 36. *Study:* Oberlin Consv Music, BME, 58, BM, 59; Calif State Univ, Los Angeles, MA, 64. *Pos:* Prin clarinetist, Virtuoso Sinfonetta, 59-60 & Rio Hondo Symph Orch, 65-; clarinetist, Jaania Trio, 59-63; rec wind soloist, L'Antica Musica Consort, 82- *Teaching:* Fac mem music, Santa Monica Col, 63-; artist in res music, Whittier Col, 72- *Mem:* Am Fedn Musicians; Am Rec Soc; Rio Hondo Symph Orch; Orange County Rec Soc; Southern Calif Rec Soc. *Mailing Add:* 6018 S Friends Ave Whittier CA 90601

YOUNG, CLYDE WILLIAM
EDUCATOR, WRITER
b Springfield, Mo, Aug 14, 19. *Study:* Drury Col, 37-38; Southwest Mo State Univ, BS(educ) & dipl(organ), 41; Union Sem, NY, 49; Univ Mich, organ studies with Dr Marilyn Mason & Dr Charles Peaker & musicol studies with Dr Alfred Einstein & Curtis Sachs, MMus, 49; Univ Ill, with Dr John Ward, Dr Dragan Plamenac & Dr Claude Palisca, PhD(musicol), 57 & MS(libr sci), 58. *Pos:* Libr asst, Univ Ill, Urbana-Champaign, 57-58; librn, Univ Nebr, Lincoln, 60-61. *Teaching:* Asst prof, State Univ NY, Cortland, 58-60; asst prof, Univ Nebr, Lincoln, 60-61; from asst prof to assoc prof, Nebr Wesleyan Univ, 61-65; assoc prof, Wayne State Univ, 65- & prof, 73. *Mem:* Am Musicol Soc. *Publ:* Auth, Keyboard Music to 1600, Musica Disciplina, 62-63; Bernhard Schmid, Die Musik Geshnichte Genewart, 63; Bach's Clavierübung, Part III, Am Guild Organist Music, 76; thirteen articles, In: New Grove Dict of Music & Musicians, 80; Bernhard Sdhmid der Aeltere, Tabulaturbuch, Das Erbe deutsher Musik, 83; and others. *Mailing Add:* 498 Barrington Rd Grosse Pointe MI 48230

YOUNG, FREDERICK JOHN
TUBA, HORN RESEARCH
b Buffalo, NY, May 19, 31. *Study:* Carnegie Inst Technol, BS, 53, MS, 54, PhD, 56. *Works:* Wiegenlied, Univ Tenn, 73. *Rec Perf:* Le Sacre du Printemps, Columbia, 54; Dig That Crazy Oom-Pah Man, Belle, 55. *Pos:* Second tuba, Pittsburgh Symph, 49-73; consult, Roth-Reynolds Co, 57-60. *Teaching:* Prof, Carnegie-Mellon Univ, 56-70 & Pa State Univ, 74-79. *Bibliog:* Posaunne Akustik, Musik in Geschichte Und Gegenwart, 60. *Interests:* Calculation on the frequencies of brass horns from the bore as a function of length. *Publ:* Auth, Sur le calcul des lignes a impedance variable de facon continue, J Physique & Radium, 58; A New Sound for the Tuba, Sch Musician, 58; Impedance of Tapered Structures, J Acoustical Soc Am, 66; Musikinstrumente in Einzeldarstellungen, Vol 2, Bärenreiter, 82; coauth, Iron Losses in Turbogenerator Teeth, Inst Electrical & Electronics Engineers. *Mailing Add:* 800 Minard Run Rd Bradford PA 16701

YOUNG, PHYLLIS
CELLO, EDUCATOR
b Milan, Kans, Oct 20, 25. *Study:* Univ Tex, BMus, 49, MMus, 50; studied with Horace Britt; Chigiana Acad, Siena, with Andre Navarra. *Pos:* Prin cellist, Austin Symph, formerly; performer, Britt Cello Ens, formerly; solo & chamber music recitalist, US & Italy. *Teaching:* Mem fac music, Univ Tex, Austin, 53-, prof music & dir string proj, currently. *Awards:* Sword of Honor, Sigma Alpha Iota; Spec Citation, Am String Teachers Asn, 74. *Mem:* Sigma Alpha Iota; Pi Kappa Lambda; Music Educr Nat Conf; Tex Orch Dir Asn; Am String Teachers Asn (pres, 78). *Publ:* Contribr to Am String Teachers Asn, 72-74; auth, Playing the String Game: Strategies for Teaching Cello & Strings, 78. *Mailing Add:* 7304 W Rim Dr Austin TX 78731

YOUNG, RAYMOND G
EUPHONIUM, EDUCATOR
b Morrilton, Ark, Dec 21, 32. *Study:* Univ Mich, BMusEd, 55, MMus, 56. *Rec Perf:* Raymond Young, Euphonium, 64 & Raymond Young, Clinician, 68, Golden Crest. *Teaching:* Asst dir bands, Univ Southern Miss, 61-69, dir bands, 69-72; head dept music & dir bands, La Tech Univ, 72- *Awards:* Distinguished Prof Award, Univ Southern Miss, 72. *Mem:* Col Band Dir Nat Asn; Music Educr Nat Asn; Tuba Universal Brotherhood Asn; Nat Band Asn (state chmn, 80-). *Publ:* Auth, Euphonium-Well Sounding, Instrumentalist, 64; contribr, Review of Euphonium Literature, Brass-Woodwind World, 79- *Mailing Add:* Music Dept La Tech Univ Ruston LA 71272

YOUNG, ROBERT H
ADMINISTRATOR, COMPOSER
b Santa Cruz, Calif, Apr 20, 23. *Study:* Otterbein Col, BMus, 50; Northwestern Univ, Ill, MMus, 51; Univ Southern Calif, DMA, 59. *Works:* O Mortal Man, J Fischer & Bro, 70; All for Love, Carl Fischer, 72; Corpus Christi, Hinshaw Music, 77; Sweet Was the Song, 79, There Is No Rose of Such Virtue, 80 & In the Bleak Midwinter, 81, Gentry Publ; For Thy Sweet Love, Plymouth Music, 83. *Teaching:* Chmn church music, Baylor Univ, 62-73, coord vocal div, 73-, dir grad studies music, 81- *Mem:* Nat Asn Teachers Singing; Am Choral Dir Asn. *Publ:* Coauth, The Anthem in England and America, Free Press, 70. *Mailing Add:* 1101 Valley Ridge Dr Waco TX 76710

YOUNG, WENDY
HARPSICHORD, MUSIC DIRECTOR
b Bayside, NY, Jan 31, 55. *Study:* NY Univ, BA, 78; New England Consv Music, MM, 82. *Pos:* Guest artist, Boston Camerata, 82-; harpsichordist, Boston Acad Music, 82- & Hesperus, Washington, DC, 83-; artistic dir, Badinage, New York, 83- *Mailing Add:* 401 West End Ave New York NY 10024

YOUNG, WILLIAM THOMAS
EDUCATOR, TROMBONE
b Ottumwa, Iowa, Oct 21, 28. *Study:* Univ Northern Iowa, MA, 64; State Univ Iowa, PhD, 69. *Works:* Brother James Air (band), Oxford Univ Press, 68. *Teaching:* Band & elem music, Iowa pub sch, 50-56; supvr, 56-66; grad asst, Univ Iowa, 66-68; prof music educ & low brass, Stephen F Austin State Univ, 68- *Awards:* Outstanding Educr Citation, Tex State Legis, 72; Cert Excellence Teaching, Stephen F Austin State Univ, 75. *Mem:* Music Educr Res Coun (secy & mem exec bd, 80-); Am Orff Schulwerk Asn (mem exec bd, 75-77); Tex Music Educr Asn (vpres, 79-81); ETex Orff Schulwerk Asn (pres, 73-76); Int Soc Music Educ. *Publ:* Auth, Five articles on testing and teaching young children, J Res Music Educ, 71-75; A Blended Music Program for the Elementary School, Stephen F Austin Univ Press, 79; coauth, A Boy Named So, Rhythm Band Inc, 81; auth, Music Literacy Charts, Spectrum Music Ser, Macmillan Publ Co, 83; Twice a Day (in press). *Mailing Add:* Music Dept Box 13043 Stephen F Austin State Univ Nacogdoches TX 75962

YOUNGBLOOD, JOSEPH EDWARD
EDUCATOR, PIANO
b Chicago, Ill, Oct 8, 30. *Study:* Univ Okla, study piano with Sylvia Zaremba, BMus, 54; Ind Univ, study piano with Menahem Pressler & hist with Willi Apel, PhD, 60. *Pos:* Pianist & conductor for many popular performers. *Teaching:* Instr music & lang, Brescia Col, Owensboro, Ky, 58-61; prof music hist, Univ Miami, Coral Gables, 61- *Mem:* Am Musicol Soc; Am Fedn Musicians. *Interests:* Computer applications. *Publ:* Auth, Style as Information, J Music Theory, 58; The Long Bow of Duport, Strad, 66; Improving Teaching & Testing Through Item Analysis, CMS Symposium, 81. *Mailing Add:* 5500 SW 84 Terr Miami FL 33143

YOUNGS, LOWELL VERE
EDUCATOR, PIANO

b Torrington, Wyo, Sept 4, 36. *Study:* Univ Colo, BME, 58; Cath Univ Am, MM, 67, DMA, 70. *Teaching:* Instr piano, Univ Del, 64-67; prof piano & organ, Univ Wis, Whitewater, 68- *Mailing Add:* 308 S Prince St Whitewater WI 53190

YOUNT, MAX HOFFMAN
COMPOSER, HARPSICHORD

b Hickory, NC, Mar 14, 38. *Study:* Harpsichord with Isolde Ahlgrimm, 58-59; Consv Music, Oberlin Col, BMus, 60; Eastman Sch Music, MM, 61, DMA, 64; studied with Louis Bagger, 70-73. *Works:* Concerto (flute, harpsichord, magnetic tape & orch), perf by Beloit Symph Orch, 70; Manzano I-IV (flute, harpsichord & alto flute), perf by Andrew Bolotowsky & self, 73; Dance Permutations (flute, harpsichord & dancers), comp & Sara Oppenheimer, 80; A Tennessee Song (SATB & instrm), First Unitarian Soc Choir, Madison, Wis, 80; Refractions (SATB & instrm), 81 & Cantata for Easter, 83, perf by Beloit Col Choir & Instrm. *Rec Perf:* Organist for Missa Brevis (Kodaly), 59 & Israel in Egypt (Handel), 59, Oberlin Rec Serv. *Teaching:* Prof music, Beloit Col, 63- *Awards:* Fulbright Fel, 63-64. *Mem:* Am Musicol Soc; Col Music Soc; Am Guild Organists (dean Madison chap, 82-83); Southeastern Hist Keyboard Soc; founding mem, Midwestern Hist Keyboard Soc. *Interests:* The keyboard and ensemble works of Benjamin Carr, English-American. *Mailing Add:* 745 Church St Beloit WI 53511

YTTREHUS, ROLV
COMPOSER, EDUCATOR

b Duluth, Minn, Mar 12, 26. *Study:* Univ Minn, Duluth, BS(music), 50; Univ Mich, MM(music comp), 53; Acad Santa Cecilia, Rome, dipl, 62; study with R L Finney, Nadia Boulanger, Roger Sessions, Goffredo Petrassi & Aaron Copland. *Works:* Espressioni Per Orchestra, Am Comp Alliance, 61; Sextet, Asn for Prom New Music, 64-70; Music for Winds and Percussion, Violoncello & Voice, Asn Prom New Music, 69; Angstwagen (sop & perc), Am Comp Alliance, 71; Quintet, Boelke-Bomart, 73; Gradus Ad Parnassum, 79 & Duo for Percussion and Piano, 83, Am Comp Alliance. *Teaching:* Instr music, Univ Mo, 63-68; asst prof, Purdue Univ, 68-69; assoc prof, Univ Wis, Oshkosh, 69-77 & Rutgers Univ, 77- *Awards:* Margaret Lee Crofts Award, 58; Grants, Nat Endowment Arts, 76 & Meet the Comp, 82; ACA Rec Award, 83. *Bibliog:* Gregory Levin (auth), Am Soc Univ Comp Meetings in New York, Musical Quart, Vol LX, No 4, 10/74; Robert P Morgan (auth), Contemporary Chamber Works, High Fidelity, 2/75; Joseph Horowitz (auth), Parnassian Ives, New York Times, 3/16/79. *Mem:* Am Soc Univ Comp; Am Comp Alliance (bd mem 80-82); Int Soc Contemp Music (bd mem, 79-); Col Music Soc; Comp Guild NJ (vpres, 82-). *Mailing Add:* 39 Mitchell Ave East Brunswick NJ 08816

Z

ZABRACK, HAROLD ALLEN
COMPOSER, PIANO

b St Louis, Mo, June 30, 28. *Study:* Chicago Musical Col, MM, 50; studied with Nadia Boulanger, Rudolph Ganz & Carl Seemann. *Works:* Piano Concerto #1, St Louis Symph, 65; Piano Sonata #1, 65, Piano Sonata #2, 78, Six Preludes for Piano, 78, Three Etudes for Piano, 78 & Eight Contours, 78, Kenyon Publ; Symphonic Variations for Piano and Orchestra, Milwaukee Symph, 77. *Teaching:* Grad asst, Ind Univ, Bloomington, 57-58; assoc prof music, Webster Col, 62-65; prof, Westminster Choir Col, 74- *Awards:* Standard Awards Panel, ASCAP, 74-; Fulbright Award, 55-57; Dipl, Int Piano Compt, 56. *Publ:* Auth, Creative Musical Encounters, Kenyon Publ, 78. *Mailing Add:* Westminster Choir Col Princeton NJ 08540

ZACK, GEORGE JIMMY
CONDUCTOR & MUSIC DIRECTOR, EDUCATOR

b Pine Bluff, Ark, July 8, 36. *Study:* Am Consv Music, studied theory & viola with Stella Roberts, 57-58; Wichita State Univ, BMus(music theory & comp), 58; Univ Mich, MMus(music theory & viola), 60; Fla State Univ, PhD(music theory), 72; Yale Univ, studied advan cond, 70-71 & Summer Inst Cond Studies, with Dr Richard Lert, 71, 72 & 74. *Pos:* Music dir & cond, Wooster Symph Orch, 65-67, Hiram Col Orch, 64-72, Warren Chamber Orch, 67-, Lexington Phil, 72-; Music Theater Soc Lexington, Ky, 72-74 & Cent Ky Youth Orch, 79; dir & producer, CBS-TV, Cleveland, Ohio, 65 & WBKY-FM, Lexington, Ky, 73-; cond, NE Ohio All State Orch, 69, Ky All State Orch, 74 & 76, NY All State Orch, 75 & Men & Boy's Choir Fest, 75 & 76; co-host, Kentucky Morning, WKYT-TV, Lexington, 79; dir, WEKY-FM, Richmond, Ky, 82; bd mem, Cent Ky Youth Music Soc, currently; violist, various orch & ens, currently; guest cond, Louisville Orch, 78 & State Orch Salonika, Greece, 81 & 83-; guest speaker, civic clubs, churches & sch, currently. *Teaching:* Grad asst, Fla State Univ, 60-62; instr music, Univ Mich, 62-64; assoc prof, Hiram Col, 64-72; artist in res, Eastern Ky Univ, 78 & James Madison Univ, 78. *Awards:* Orpheus Award, Phi Mu Alpha Sinfonia, 76. *Mem:* Am Fedn Musicians; Am Symph Orch League; Cond Guild. *Mailing Add:* 237 Woodspoint Rd Lexington KY 40502

ZAGST, JOANNE (JOANNE ZAGST-FELDMAN)
VIOLIN, TEACHER

b Shreveport, La, Feb 26, 34. *Study:* Juilliard Sch Music, BS, 57, MS, 58; studied violin with Andor Toth & Ivan Galamian. *Rec Perf:* String Quartet

#3 (Hindemith), 79 & String Quartet #1 (Janacek), 81, Golden Crest; Music for Flute & Strings by Three Americans, 81, Piano Quintet (Bartok), 82, Quartet No 1 (Husa), 83 & String Quartet (P Rainier), 83, Leonarda. *Pos:* Sect first violin, Rochester Phil, 58-59, Dayton Orch, Springfield Orch & Columbus Orch, 59-62; violinist, Alard Quartet, Wilmington Col, 59-62, Pa State Univ, 62- & Univ Canterbury, New Zealand, summer 63, 64, 81 & 82. *Teaching:* Assoc prof violin, Pa State Univ, 62- *Mem:* Am Fedn Musicians; Chamber Music Am; Music Teachers Nat Asn; Pa Music Teachers Asn. *Mailing Add:* 105 Music Bldg University Park PA 16802

ZAHLER, NOEL BARRY
COMPOSER, MUSIC DIRECTOR

b New York, NY, May 10, 51. *Study:* Queens Col, City Univ New York, BA & MA, 74; Princeton Univ, MFA, 76; Columbia Univ. *Works:* Three Songs for Mezzo Soprano Chamber Orch, 74, Regions I (solo piano), 75, Tableau (solo violin), 77, Four Songs of Departure, 77 & Charms (nine insrm), 79, APNM Publ; Rhapsody (violoncello), Am Comp Ed, 82; Harlequin (piano & chamber orch), Assoc Music Publ, 83. *Rec Perf:* Harlequin, 82, Four Songs of Deparature, 82 & Regions I, 82, Op One Rec. *Pos:* Musical dir, Comp Chamber Ens, 78- *Teaching:* Lectr music, Brooklyn Col, 78-79 & Mercy Col, 79-; lectr & coordr colloquia, Columbia Univ, 82- *Awards:* Scholar, Nat Endowment for Humanities, 72; Fulbright grant, Fulbright Italy Comn, 76-77; fel, MacDowell Colony, Inc, 74 & 83. *Bibliog:* John Rockwell, 4/7/79 & Raymond Ericson, 12/21/80, New York Times; article, Manhattan Plaza News, 11/79. *Mem:* Am Comp Alliance; Am Music Ctr; Am Soc Univ Comp; Am Musicol Soc; BMI. *Publ:* Ed, The Unanswered Question, A New Critical Edition, Peer-Southern, 83; auth, Richard Wernick, Fred Lerdahl, Mario Davidovsky, Noah Creshevsky, Joel Mandelbaum & David Lewin, In: New Grove Dict of Music in US, Macmillan Publ, 83; and many others. *Mailing Add:* 484 W 43rd St 12D New York NY 10036

ZAIMONT, JUDITH LANG
COMPOSER, WRITER

b Memphis, Tenn, Nov, 8, 45. *Study:* Queens Col, City Univ New York, BA(music), 66; Columbia Univ, MA(music comp), 68; studied orch with Andre Jolivet, 71-72. *Works:* Sacred Service for the Sabbath Evening, Galaxy Music Corp, 76; The Magic World, Leonarda Prod, 78; De Infinitae Caeleste (string quartet), MS, 79; From the Great Land, comn by Univ Alaska, 82; Lamentation, comn by Gregg Smith Singers, 82; In the Theater of Night, comn by Ark Coun Arts, 83; and others. *Pos:* Res comp & accmp, Great Neck Choral Soc, 67-80. *Teaching:* Asst prof music theory, Queens Col, City Univ New York, 72-76; prof, Peabody Consv Music, 80- *Awards:* Woodrow Wilson Nat Found Fel, 67-68; John Simon Guggenheim Found Comp Fel, 83. *Bibliog:* Christine Ammer (auth), Unsung, Greenwood Press, 80; Jane Weiner LePage (auth), Women Composers, Conductors & Performers, Vol II, Scarecrow Press, 83; Peter G Davis (auth), Pianos Still Stir Composers Souls, New York Times, 6/7/81. *Mem:* ASCAP; Int Soc Women Comp Inc (mem exec bd, 82-); Am Soc Univ Comp; Col Music Soc. *Publ:* Auth, 20th Century Composition: Stylistic Dev, 81, 20th Century Music for Piano Solo: A Graded Annotated List, 81, Yorktown Music Press; ed, Contemporary Concert Music by Women, 81, The Musical Woman: An International Perspective, Vol I, 83, Greenwood Press. *Rep:* Allied Artists Bureau 195 Steamboat Rd Great Neck NY 11024. *Mailing Add:* 8609 Drumwood Rd Baltimore MD 21204

ZAJICEK, JERONYM
COMPOSER, EDUCATOR

b Krasne Brezno, Czechoslovakia, Nov 10, 26, US citizen. *Study:* Charles Univ, Prague, Czechoslovakia, musicol degree, 46-49; comp with Karel Jirak, 52-60; Roosevelt Univ, Chicago, MMus, 62; comp with Paul A Pisk, 61. *Works:* Nursery Rhymes, perf by Frances Friedlander & Vaclav Nelhybel, 55; Clarinet Sonata, M Bass, 59; Violin Sonata, perf by Francois D'Albert, 63; String Quartet, perf by String Quartet Chicago Symph, 64; Flute Concertino, perf by W Schwegler, Cologne Radio Symph, 73. *Pos:* Music prog dir, Czechoslovakia section Radio Free Europe, Munich, 50-52. *Teaching:* Assoc prof theory & comp, Loop Col, Chicago City Cols, 64- *Awards:* Oliver Ditson Fel, Chicago Musical Col, 56 & 57; First Prize for best comp, Int Soc Contemp Music, Chicago Chap, 64. *Mailing Add:* 4230 Prescott Lyons IL 60534

ZAKARIAN-RUTSTEIN, SEDMARA
PIANO, EDUCATOR

b Kazan, USSR, Oct 18, 37; US citizen. *Study:* Leningrad Consv, MA, 59, with Nadezhda Golubovskaya, DMus, 62. *Rec Perf:* Selected Piano Pieces, Rile Rec, 79; Pieces of Scriabin & Shostakovich, ORION Master Rec, 81; Pieces of Scriabin & Prokofiev, 82 & Pieces of Prokofiev, 83, Musical Heritage Soc. *Pos:* Conct pianist, in USSR, 59-73 & US, 75-; artist in res, Grinnell Col, 74-76. *Teaching:* Prof piano, Leningrad Consv, USSR, 62-73 & Consv Music, Oberlin Col, 76- *Awards:* Laureat, All-Union Musical Compt, Moscow, 57. *Bibliog:* Robert Sherman (auth), Sedmara Rutstein Excels at Piano, New York Times, 10/17/74; Joan Reinthaler (auth), Piano at Arena, Washington Post, 6/6/75; Tom Di Nardo (auth), Zakarian's Debut Sparkles with Remarkable Brilliance, Philadelphia Musical World & Times, Nov-Dec/76. *Rep:* Joanne Rile Box 27539 Philadelphia PA 19118. *Mailing Add:* 226 N Prospect Oberlin OH 44074

ZAKARIASEN, BILL
CRITIC & WRITER

b Grand Rapids, Minn, Aug 19, 30. *Study:* Brown Univ; Univ Mich; Manhattan Sch Music. *Pos:* Singer, NY City Opera, 57-60 & Metropolitan Opera, 60-71; music critic, San Francisco Examiner, 72-74 & NY Daily News, 74- *Mem:* Fel, Music Critics Asn; Von Wayditch Music Found; Wagner Int. *Publ:* Auth, numerous articles in Opera News, High Fidelity, Ovation & Music J. *Mailing Add:* 205 West End Ave Apt 1-M New York NY 10023

ZALIOUK, YUVAL NATHAN
MUSIC DIRECTOR & CONDUCTOR

b Haifa, Israel, Feb 10, 39. *Study:* Haifa Acad, Israel, dipl; Hebrew Univ, Jerusalem, LLB, 64; Rubin Acad Music, Jerusalem, 60-63; Guildhall Sch Music, London, 65-67. *Rec Perf:* With London Mozart Players, 73. *Pos:* Asst cond, Royal Ballet, Covent Garden, 66-67, cond, 67-70, Europ tours, 67-70; music dir, Opera Studio, Paris, 73-74 & Haifa Symph Orch, Israel, 75-77; interim chief cond, Edmonton Symph Orch, Alta, 80-81; music dir & cond, Toledo Symph Orch, 80-; guest cond, Israel Phil, Madrid Nat Orch, Suisse Romande, Philharmonia Hungarica & maj Brit, Scand & Australian orchs. *Awards:* First Prize, Am-Israel Cult Found Compt, 65; Second Prize, Int Cond Compt, Besancon, France, 66, First Prize, 67; Winner, Mitropoulos Cond Compt, New York, 70. *Mailing Add:* Toledo Symph One Stranahan Sq Toledo OH 43604

ZALKIND, LARRY HOWARD
TROMBONE, EDUCATOR

b Hollywood, Calif, Feb 21, 56. *Study:* Univ Southern Calif, with Robert Marsteller, BM, 77, with Lewis Van Haney, MM, 79; Univ Mich, with Dennis Smith, 81. *Rec Perf:* Yardumian Symph No 2, Sountrean Rec Co, 82. *Pos:* Trombone, Long Beach Symph, 80-81 & Boulder, Colo Music Fest, 80-83; prin trombone, Chamber Music Northwest, Portland, 81-82 & Utah Symphony, 81- *Teaching:* Instr trombone, Univ Mich, 80-81, Weber State Col, 81- & Univ Utah, 81- *Awards:* Saunderson Award, Coleman Chamber Music Compt, 76; Marsteller Award, Univ Southern Calif, 79. *Mem:* Int Trombone Asn; Tubist United Brotherhood Asn. *Mailing Add:* 1882 Yuma Salt Lake City UT 84108

ZALKIND, ROBERTA MARIAN
VIOLA

b Los Angeles, Calif, May 16, 57. *Study:* Univ Southern Calif, with Milton Thomas & Louis Kievman, 75-79; Univ Mich, with Frances Bundra, 80-81. *Pos:* Violist, Utah Symph Orch, 82- *Awards:* Outstanding Violist Award, Music Acad of the West, 78; Berry Award, Coleman Chamber Music Compt, 76. *Mailing Add:* c/o Utah Symph Symph-Hall 123 W S Temple Salt Lake City UT 84101

ZALLMAN, ARLENE
COMPOSER, EDUCATOR

b Philadelphia, Pa, Sept 9, 34. *Study:* Juilliard Sch, dipl; Univ Pa, MA, 68. *Works:* Racconto (piano solo), perf by Abraham Stokman, 66; Incidental Music & Scenes: from the Imaginary Invalid, comn & perf by, Theater Dept, Univ Tex, Austin, 75; Songs from Quasimodo, perf by Bethany Beardslee, 76; Toccata (piano solo), perf by Lois Shapiro, 79; Injury (two sonnets from Shakespeare), perf by Sanford Sylan, David Hoose & Lois Shapiro, 81. *Teaching:* Instr, Consv Music, Oberlin Col, 68-71; lectr, Yale Univ, 71-72; assoc prof, Wellesley Col, 76- *Awards:* Award Vocal Comp, Marion S Freschl, 58; Fulbright Grant, 59-61; Comp Award, Nat Endowment Arts, 78. *Mailing Add:* 641 Washington St Wellesley MA 02181

ZAMBARA, EDWARD
EDUCATOR, VOICE

Study: New England Consv Music, MM; Cornish Consv; studied voice with Elma Igelman, William W Whitney, Frederick Jagel & Marie Sundelius, opera with Boris Godovsky & Sarah Caldwell & German lieder with Felix Wolfes & Frederick Popper. *Pos:* Soloist with Boston Symph, formerly, Indianapolis Symph, formerly & Knoxville Symph, formerly; gen mgr, Knoxville Civic Opera, formerly; mem, New England Opera Theater, formerly, Boston Opera Co, formerly & Chattanooga Opera Asn, formerly; guest stage dir, St Petersburg Opera Co, formerly; musical dir, Oakridge Symph Orch & Chorus, formerly; oratorio & recitalist singer throughout US. *Teaching:* Mem fac & artist in res, Franz-Schubert Inst, Austria, formerly; mem fac & dir, Opera Wkshp, Univ Tenn, formerly; mem fac voice & opera studio & chair voice, St Louis Consv, currently. *Mailing Add:* St Louis Consv Music 560 Trinity Ave St Louis MO 63130

ZANDER, BENJAMIN DAVID
CONDUCTOR & MUSIC DIRECTOR, EDUCATOR

b London, England, Mar 9, 39. *Study:* State Consv, Cologne, Germany, dipl, 60; London Univ, BA, 64; studied cello with Gaspar Cassado. *Pos:* Cond, Youth Chamber Orch, New England Consv Music, 72-; music dir & cond, Boston Phil Orch, 79- *Teaching:* Prof chamber music, perf & analysis, New England Consv Music, 67- *Mailing Add:* 75 Common St Watertown MA 02172

ZANDER, PATRICIA
PIANO, EDUCATOR

Study: Royal Col Music, London, ARCM, LRAM; studied with Vlado Perlemuter & Nadia Boulanger; studied piano with Leonard Shure. *Pos:* Recitalist piano chamber music & lieder, US, Japan & Korea; coordr chamber music prog, Round Top Fest Tex, currently. *Teaching:* Coach lieder & opera & instr, People's Repub China, 80 & Japan, 81; mem fac, Harvard Univ, formerly; mem fac piano & chamber music, New England Consv Music, currently. *Mailing Add:* New England Consv Music 290 Huntington Rd Boston MA 02115

ZANINELLI, LUIGI
COMPOSER, CONDUCTOR

b Raritan, NJ, Mar 30, 32. *Study:* Curtis Inst Music, with Gian Carlo Menotti, dipl 55; studied with Rosario Scalero, Turin, Italy. *Works:* Winter Music, Zalo Music, 79; The Islander, 80 & Passover, 81, Shawnee Press; The Turn of the Screw, Valentanio Music, 81; The Tale of Peter Rabbit, 83, The Steadfast Tin Soldier, 83 & Fantasma, 83, Shawnee Press. *Teaching:* Prof comp, Univ Alberta, 68-73, Banff Sch Fine Arts, 70-73 & Univ Southern Miss, 73- *Awards:* Steinway Prize, 54; Music Award, Miss Inst Arts & Lett, 80. *Mem:* ASCAP. *Publ:* Auth, Hearing and Singing, Shawnee Press, 62. *Rep:* Shawnee Press Inc Delaware Water Gap PA 18327. *Mailing Add:* Music Dept Univ Southern Miss Hattiesburg MS 39401

ZANO, ANTHONY (ANTHONY JOSEPH FERRAZANO)
COMPOSER

b Worcester, Mass, June 4, 37. *Study:* New England Consv, 54-57; Boston Univ, 58-62; Sussex Univ, England, MusD, 63. *Works:* The Gathering Place, Baltimore Music Corp, 59; Concert in the Round Overture, Worcester Symph Orch, 67; The Soul's Season, Univ Ill, 73. *Rec Perf:* The Gathering Place, Balmore Rec, 60. *Pos:* Cond, Anthony Zano Orch, 57-; music dir, New England Trio, 66-68; arr & pianist, RCA Rec Studios, 75-78. *Teaching:* Instr music, Mass Publ Sch, 56-57; Instr piano, New York Sch Music, 59-60; Instr music theory, Schenectady Consv, 66-67. *Mem:* ASCAP; Am Music Ctr; Am Fedn Musicians. *Publ:* Auth, Mechanics of Modern Music, Theodore Presser Co, 74. *Mailing Add:* PO Box 195 Wilmington MA 01887

ZAPLATYNSKY, ANDREW
EDUCATOR, VIOLIN

b Bamberg, Ger, Mar 9, 46; US citizen. *Study:* Studied with Edgar Ortenberg, 54-64; Ind Univ, Bloomington, 64-66; Cath Univ Am, studied violin with Josef Gingold & Ivan Galamian, BA(music), 70. *Pos:* First violin sect, Rotterdam Phil, Holland, 70-72 & Minn Orch, Minneapolis, 72-73; asst concertmaster, Detroit Symph Orch, 73-74 & Cincinnati Symph Orch, 74-82; concertmaster, Syracuse Symph Orch, NY, 81- *Teaching:* Dir, String Fel Prog, Sch Music & chmn string dept, Syracuse Univ, 82- *Mailing Add:* 200 Summit Ave Syracuse NY 13207

ZARET, PETER H
VIOLIN

b New York, NY, Feb 21, 39. *Study:* Juilliard Sch, BS, MS; Univ Mich; studied with Joseph Fuchs, Ivan Galamian, Louis Persinger, Raphael Bronstein, Paul Makanovitsky & Berl Senofsky. *Pos:* Concertmaster, Richmond Symph, Va, formerly; Springfield Symph, Ohio, formerly, Norfolk Symph, formerly & Va Opera Asn, currently; first violin, Va Commonwealth Univ String Quartet, formerly. *Teaching:* Artist in res, Norfolk State Col, formerly. *Mailing Add:* Va Opera Asn 261 W Bute St Norfolk VA 23510

ZARETSKY, MICHAEL
VIOLA, EDUCATOR

b Moscow, USSR, Aug 12, 46; US citizen. *Study:* Music Col, 61-65; Moscow State Consv, 65-70. *Pos:* Viola, Boston Symph Orch, 73- *Teaching:* Teaching assoc viola, Sch Music, Boston Univ, 79- *Mailing Add:* c/o Boston Symph 301 Massachusetts Ave Boston MA 02115

ZARUBICK, FRAN G
ADMINISTRATOR

b Grand Coulee, Wash, July 4, 47. *Study:* Immaculate Heart Col, Los Angeles, BA, 77; Sch Pub Admin & Bus, Univ Southern Calif, 77-78. *Teaching:* Dean, Community Sch Perf Arts, Los Angeles, 72-83; dean, Prep Div, Peabody Inst Music, 83- *Publ:* Auth, Articulation Between the Pre-College Level Schools & the College Level, In: Proc Nat Asn Sch Music, 83. *Mailing Add:* 6655 Walnutwood Circle Baltimore MD 21204

ZARZECZNA, MARION
PIANO, EDUCATOR

Study: Curtis Inst Music, with Mieczyslaw Horszowski, BM, 54; studied with Pietro Scarpini & Isabelle Sant'Ambrogio. *Pos:* Mem, New Marlborough Chamber Players, 60-79; piano recitalist & soloist with orchs in Germany, Italy & US; frequent tours as accmp. *Teaching:* Mem fac suppl piano, Curtis Inst Music, 62-; mem trio in res, Rider Col, 67-68; vocal coach, Temple Univ Music Fest, Ambler, 70; mem fac, Consv Music, Westminster Choir Col, 74- *Awards:* Leschetizky Debut Prize, New York, 54; Fulbright Grant Florence, 54-56; Kranichsteiner Musik-preis for Modern Music, Darmstadt, 55. *Mailing Add:* Curtis Inst Music 1726 Locust St Philadelphia PA 19103

ZASLAVSKY, DORA
EDUCATOR, PIANO

Study: Manhattan Sch Music, dipl; Curtis Inst Music; studied piano with Janet D Schenck, Harold Bauer, Carl Friedberg & Wilhelm Backhaus. *Pos:* Solo & chamber music concerts & broadcasts, US & Europe. *Teaching:* Mem fac piano, Manhattan Sch Music, 26- *Mailing Add:* Manhattan Sch Music 120 Claremont Ave New York NY 10027

ZASLAW, NEAL
EDUCATOR, MUSICOLOGIST

b New York, NY, June 28, 39. *Study:* Harvard Col, BA, 61; Juilliard Sch, MS, 63; Columbia Univ, MA, 65, PhD, 70. *Rec Perf:* The Symphonies (Mozart), L'Oiseau-Lyre, 79-83. *Pos:* Ed, Current Musicol, 67-70 & Music Libr Asn, Notes, 70-75. *Teaching:* Instr, City Col, City Univ New York, 68-70; prof, Cornell Univ, 70- *Awards:* Fels, Martha Baird Rockefeller Fund, 68-69, Nat Endowment Humanities, 76-77 & Am Coun Learned Soc, 83-84. *Mem:* Am Musicol Soc (coun, 71-76 & 79-83, prog comt, 72-74); Royal Musical Asn; Music Libr Asn; Soc Francaise de Musicol; Int Musicol Soc. *Interests:* Eighteenth-century, especially Rameau, Leclair, Mozart, performance practice & social history. *Publ:* Auth, Toward the Revival of the Classical Orchestra, Proc Royal Musical Asn, 76-77; Mozart, Haydn, and the Sinfonia da Chiesa, J Musicol, 82; ed, Rameau: The Musical Works, 40 vols, Broude Brothers, NY, 83-; Scylla et Glaucus and the State of French Opera in the Mid-18th Century, J Am Musicol Soc, 84; Mozart the Symphonist, Oxford Univ Press, London, 84. *Mailing Add:* 109 Cayuga Heights Rd Ithaca NY 14850

ZASTROW, JOYCE RUTH
SOPRANO, EDUCATOR
b Milwaukee, Wis, Feb 27, 29. *Study:* Valparaiso Univ, BA; Ind Univ, MMus; Univ Ill, DMA; Berkshire Music Ctr; Aspen Sch Music; Fontainebleu Sch Music, France; Mozarteum, Salzburg. *Pos:* Opera, oratorio & recital performances throughout Mid-west incl, Contemp Music Fest, Oberlin Col, Ball State Univ & Ind State Univ. *Teaching:* Assoc prof music, Western Mich Univ, currently. *Publ:* Auth, A Study of Musical Settings of the 3 Soliloquies of Gretchen from Goethe's Faust, 73; contribr to Am Music Teacher. *Mailing Add:* 1933 Stevens Ave Kalamazoo MI 49008

ZAUDER, DAVID
TRUMPET, ADMINISTRATOR
b Krakow, Poland, Sept 14, 31. *Study:* Wayne State Univ, 57-58; Western Reserve Univ, BA, 62. *Rec Perf:* Lt Kije (Prokofieff), Columbia, 68; Romeo & Juliet (Prokofieff), London, 73. *Teaching:* Prof trumpet, Detroit Inst Music, 55-58 & Cleveland Inst Music, 79- *Mem:* Int Trumpet Guild; Int Conf Orch Personnel Mgr (pres, 80-); Am Fedn Musicians. *Publ:* Auth, Trumpet Embochure Studies (3 vol), privately publ, 66. *Mailing Add:* c/o Cleveland Inst Music 11021 East Blvd Cleveland OH 44106

ZDECHLIK, JOHN PAUL
COMPOSER, EDUCATOR
b Minneapolis, Minn, May 2, 37. *Study:* Univ Minn, BS(music educ), 60, MA(music), 63, PhD(music theory), 70. *Works:* Chorale & Shaker Dance, 72; Dance Variations, 75; Romance for Band, 78 & Rondo Capriccio, 78, Kjos Music Co; Images for Orchestra, comn by Civic Orch, 78; Sonata for Flute & Piano, Kjos Music Co, 81. *Teaching:* Instr, Univ Minn, 63-65 & Lakewood Community Col, 70- *Mailing Add:* 3860 Van Dyke White Bear Lake MN 55110

ZEI, JOHN
EDUCATOR, BARITONE
Study: Lawrence Univ, BMus; Univ Mich, MMus. *Roles:* The Barber of Seville; Don Giovanni; Requiem (Verdi). *Pos:* Res baritone, Toledo Opera Asn, Detroit Opera Asn & Dallas Light Opera Asn, currently; coordr chorus & comprimario roles, Conn Opera Asn, currently. *Teaching:* Producer & dir opera prog, Univ Nebr, formerly; asst prof voice, Univ NH; vis prof opera, Nat Acad Arts, Mich; directional studies, Staatsoper & Gartnerplatz Theater, Munich; prof voice & opera, Hartt Sch Music, 73- *Mem:* Pi Kappa Lambda; Music Educr Nat Conf; Cent Opera Serv; Metropolitan Opera Guild. *Mailing Add:* Hartt Sch Music Univ Hartford West Hartford CT 06117

ZEIGLER, JOHN ROBERT
CLARINET, EDUCATOR
b Gettysburg, Pa, Aug 9, 52. *Study:* Eastman Sch Music, BMus(music educ), 74, perf cert, 74, MM(perf), 75. *Pos:* Prin clarinet, Omaha Symph, 76- & Nebr Sinfonia, 76-; second clarinet, San Francisco Symph, 82-83. *Teaching:* Adj fac clarinet, chamber music & collegium, Univ Nebr, Omaha, 77-82; lectr clarinet & chamber music, Stanford Univ, 82-83. *Mailing Add:* c/o San Francisco Symph Davies Symph Hall San Francisco CA 94102

ZEITLIN, ZVI
VIOLIN, EDUCATOR
b Dubrovna, Russia, Feb 21, 23; US citizen. *Study:* Juilliard Sch Music, 34-39 & 47-50; Hebrew Univ, 40-43. *Pos:* Violinist, conct tours in North & South Am, Israel, Australia, Europe, New Zealand, Hong Kong & with leading symph in New York City, Chicago, London, Berlin, Vienna, Boston, Copenhagen, Brussels, Paris, Buenos Aires, Rio de Janeiro, Sydney, Melbourne, and others. *Teaching:* Kilbourn prof music, Eastman Sch Music, 67-; head string dept, Music Acad West, 73- *Awards:* Am-Israel Soc Award, 57. *Mem:* Bohemians; NY State Teachers Asn; Am Fedn Musicians; Am String Teachers Asn. *Mailing Add:* 204 Warren Ave Rochester NY 14618

ZELLER, GARY L
ADMINISTRATOR, EDUCATOR
b Mt Joy, Pa, July 1, 40. *Study:* Lebanon Valley Col, BS, 62; Univ Ark, MM, 64, MEd, 65; Cath Univ Am, PhD, 77. *Pos:* Assoc dir, Inst Musik Theater, Hamburg, Ger, 75-76; adminr, Tanglewood Inst, Boston Univ, 76-81; dir, MacPhail Ctr Arts, Univ Minn. *Teaching:* Asst prof music hist, Emerson Col, 71-75; asst dean sch arts, Boston Univ, 77-81; prof music hist & dean sch fine arts, Radford Univ, 81- *Mem:* Am Musicol Soc; Int Musicol Soc; Int Coun Fine Arts Deans; Col Music Soc; Music Libr Asn. *Interests:* Music history, Germany, 1750-1850. *Mailing Add:* MacPhail Ctr Arts Univ Minn 1128 LaSalle Ave Minneapolis MN 55403

ZEROUNIAN, ARA
VIOLA, EDUCATOR
b Detroit, Mich, Apr 6, 26. *Study:* Sch Music, Northwestern Univ, BM, 49; Eastman Sch Music, MM, 51. *Pos:* Prin violist, Ctr Symph, 72-, Michigan Chamber Orch, 72-, Mich Opera Theater Orch, 76-, Warren Symph, 78- & Pontiac-Oakland Symph, 79- *Teaching:* Instr viola, Nat Music Camp, Interlochen, Mich, 60-79, Oakland Univ, 78- & Macomb Co Community Col, 78- *Awards:* Teacher of Yr, Am String Teacher's Asn, Mich unit, 77. *Mem:* Am String Teacher's Asn (vpres Mich unit, 62-63); Music Educr Nat Conf. *Mailing Add:* 3022 Glenview Royal Oak MI 48073

ZEROUNIAN, PERUZ
VIOLIN
b Istanbul, Turkey, Jan 1, 24; US citizen. *Study:* private study, with Vahram Mühendisyan, Istanbul, Turkey. *Pos:* Concertmaster, Mich Chamber Orch, 72-78, Oakway Symph, 75-80, Mich Opera Theater Orch, 76-78, Warren Symph, 78- Pontiac-Oakland Symph, 79-; prin 2nd violin, Mich Opera Theater Orch, 79- *Mailing Add:* 3022 Glenview Royal Oak MI 48073

ZES, TIKEY A
COMPOSER, EDUCATOR
b Long Beach, Calif, Oct 27, 27. *Study:* With Gerald Strang; Univ Southern Calif, with Ingolf Dahl, DMA, 69. *Works:* French Overture (orch), 63; Music for the Divine Liturgy of St John Chrysostom (chorus), 66; Two Greek Folk Songs (chorus), 69; Byzantine Concert Liturgy (chorus & orch), 69. *Teaching:* Prof music, San Jose State Univ, 64- *Awards:* Helen Anstead Award, Univ Southern Calif, 63 & 69. *Mailing Add:* Dept Music San Jose State Univ San Jose CA 95192

ZETZER, ALFRED
BASS CLARINET, CLARINET
b Cleveland, Ohio, July 3, 16. *Study:* Cleveland Inst Music, BM, 40; studied with Daniel Bonade. *Pos:* Prin clarinet, Ballet Rosse De Monte Carlo, 39-40, Kans City Symph, 40-41, Pittsburgh Symph, 42-43 & San Antonio Symph, 46-48; bass clarinetist, Cleveland Orch, 49- *Teaching:* Instr clarinet, Kent State Univ, formerly; instr clarinet & bass clarinet, Cleveland Inst Music, 49- *Mailing Add:* 3284 Enderby Rd Shaker Heights OH 44120

ZGODAVA, RICHARD A
LIBRARIAN, PIANO
b Minneapolis, Minn. *Study:* MacPhail Sch Music; Royal Acad Music, London; Univ Minn, MA, 55. *Works:* For Thou, O Lord, Art Sweet and Mild, Carol de Aleria, Noel Nouvelet & Masters in This Hall, Augsburg Publ House; Out of the Orient Crystal Skies, Belwin-Mills. *Rec Perf:* Zgodava: Piano & Harpsichord, 74 & Recital Favorites, 76, Sound Environment. *Pos:* Pianist, Minneapolis Symph Orch, 55-57; asst head art & music dept, Minneapolis Pub Libr, currently. *Teaching:* Instr piano, Macalester Col, 55-58. *Mailing Add:* Minneapolis Pub Libr 300 Nicollet Mall Minneapolis MN 55406

ZIBITS, PAUL JOSEPH
DOUBLE BASS, EDUCATOR
b Chicago, Ill, Sept 19, 51. *Study:* De Paul Univ, double bass with Joseph Gustafeste, comp with Phil Winsor, BM, 75, MM, 76. *Pos:* Prin double bassist, Civic Orch Chicago, 73-79 & Santa Barbara Symph Orch, 82-; bassist, freelance, 79-; double bassist, Long Beach Symph Orch, 80- *Teaching:* Lectr jazz, Loyola Univ, Chicago, 75-79 & double bass, Chicago Musical Col, Roosevelt Univ, 77-79; lectr & perf in res double bass, Univ Calif, Los Angeles, 79- *Awards:* Shell Found Comp Award, 75. *Mem:* Int Soc Bassists; Col Music Soc. *Mailing Add:* Dept Music Univ Calif Col Fine Arts Los Angeles CA 90024

ZIEGLER, DELORES
MEZZO-SOPRANO
b Decatur, Ga. *Study:* Maryville Col; Univ Tenn. *Roles:* Dorabella in Cosi fan tutte; Maddalena in Rigoletto; Octavian in Der Rosenkavalier; Cherubino in Le Nozze di Figaro; Rosina in Il Barbiere di Siviglia; Meg Page in Falstaff, Kennedy Ctr, 82; Marguerite in La Damnation de Faust. *Pos:* Performer, Knoxville Civic Opera, Atlanta Symph, Yale Symph, Long Island Phil, Opera Theater St Louis, Bonn Theater der Stadt, Santa Fe Apprentice Prog, Theater der Stadt Köln, La Scala & Paris Opera. *Mailing Add:* c/o Kazuko Hillyer Inc 250 W 57th St New York NY 10107

ZIFFRIN, MARILYN JANE
COMPOSER, WRITER
b Moline, Ill, Aug 7, 26. *Study:* Univ Wis, Madison, BM, 48; Columbia Univ, MA, 49; comp study with Alexander Tcherepnin & Karl Ahrendt. *Works:* Four Pieces for Tuba, Music Graphics Press, 73; Trio for Violin, Cello and Piano, perf by Manhattan Trio, 77-78; Three Songs for Woman's Voice, perf by Neva Pilgrim & Marilyn Coromel, 77, 81 & 83; Rhapsody for Guitar, Ed Orphee, Boston, 80-83; Trio for Xylophone, Soprano and Tuba, Capra Rec, 81; Quintet for Oboe & String Quartet, perf by Basil Reeve & Primavera String Quartet, 81; Sono (cello & piano), Wells Duo, 82-83. *Pos:* Asst head transcription dept, WGN radio & TV station, 50-52. *Teaching:* Asst prof music, Northeastern Ill Univ, Chicago, 61-67; assoc prof, New England Col, Henniker, NH, 67-82; instr comp, St Paul's Sch, Concord, NH, 77- *Awards:* First Prize, Delius Found, 72; Travel Grant, Am Coun Learned Soc, 74-75; Norlin Found Fel, 77. *Bibliog:* Zaimont & Famera (auth), Contemporary Concert Music by Women, Greenwood Press, 81; Emmons & Sontag (auth), Art of the Song Recital. *Mem:* ASCAP; Am Soc Univ Comp; Int League Women Comp; Am Women Comp Inc; Col Music Soc. *Publ:* Auth, Ruggles Continuous Fight for Linear Composition, San Francisco Chronicle, 67; Angels—Two Views, Music Rev, 68; Interesting Lies and Curious Truths About Carl Ruggles, Col Music Soc Symposium, 79; co-contribr, Ruggles Entry, In: New Grove Dict of Music & Musicians, 6th ed, Macmillan, 80; Carl Ruggles Music Critic, Am Music Teacher, 83. *Rep:* Judith Finell Music Serv Inc 155 W 68th St New York NY 10023. *Mailing Add:* PO Box 179 Bradford NH 03221

ZIGHERA, BERNARD
HARP, PIANO
Study: Paris Consv, dipl(piano & harp); studied harp with Marcel Tournier; studied piano with Isidore Phillip & Santiago Riero; studied chamber music

with Paul Chevillard & Lucier Capet. *Pos:* First harpist, Boston Symph Orch, formerly; performer, conct tours US & Europe; mem juries, Consv Nat Paris Compt & Int Harp Conv Israel. *Teaching:* Mem orch, Paris Consv, formerly; mem fac, Berkshire Music Ctr, 40-; mem fac harp, New England Consv Music, currently. *Awards:* First Prize Piano & Harp, Paris Consv; Chevalier French Legion of Honor. *Mailing Add:* New England Consv Music 290 Huntington Rd Boston MA 02115

ZIMMERMAN, FRANKLIN BERSHIR
EDUCATOR, CONDUCTOR
b Wauneta, Kans, June 20, 23. *Study:* Univ Ariz, 45; Univ Southern Calif, AB, 49, AM, 51, PhD, 58; Oxford Univ, BLitt, 55; Dartmouth Col, Hon AM; Univ Pa, Hon AM. *Pos:* Assoc cond, London Sr Orch, 55-58, London Jr Orch, 55-58, & Ernest Reed Children's Concerts, 55-58. *Teaching:* Asst prof music, State Univ NY, Potsdam, 58-59; assoc prof & dept chmn, Univ Southern Calif, 59-64; prof, Dartmouth Col, 64-68 & Univ Pa, 64- *Awards:* Am Coun Learned Soc Fel, 59; Arnold Bax Found Musicol Medal, 60. *Bibliog:* D Burgwyn (auth), Musical Treasure Hunting, Pa Gazette, 78. *Mem:* Am Musicol Soc; Int Musicol Soc; Plain-Song & Medieval Musical Soc; Gesellschaft Musikforschung; Handel Soc. *Publ:* Auth, Henry Purcell: 1659-1695: An Analytical Catalog, 63 & Henry Purcell: 1659-1695: His Life and Times, 67, Macmillan & Co; ed, Introduction to the Skill of Music, Da Capo Press, 73; The William Kennedy Gostling Manuscript, Univ Tex Press, 77; auth, The Anthems of Henry Purcell, Choral Found Press, 78; Henry Purcell, 1659-1695: His Life and Times, 2nd rev ed. *Mailing Add:* 225 S 42nd St Philadelphia PA 19104

ZIMMERMANN, GERHARDT
CONDUCTOR & MUSIC DIRECTOR
b Van Wert, Ohio, June 22, 45. *Study:* Bowling Green State Univ, BM, 67; Univ Iowa, MFA, 72. *Pos:* Asst cond & Exxon cond, St Louis Symph Orch, 74-78 & assoc cond, 78-82; music dir, Canton Symph Orch, 80-; music dir & cond, NC Symph Orch, 82- *Awards:* Second Prize, Georg Solti Compt, 73. *Mem:* Am Symph Orch League. *Mailing Add:* No 2 South St Raleigh NC 27611

ZINMAN, DAVID
CONDUCTOR
b Brooklyn, NY, July 9, 36. *Study:* Consv Music, Oberlin Consv; Univ Minn; studied with Pierre Monteux. *Rec Perf:* Pelleas et Melisande (Faure, Schoenberg & Sibelius) & Netherlands Chamber Orch (Tchaikovsky & Verdi), Philips; Concertos No 1 & 2 (Liszt) & Concerto 10 (two pianos; Mozart), Vox; Violinist Sergui Luca with Rochester Phil (Beethoven), Nonesuch, 82; Hebrides, Symphonies Nos 3, 4 & 5 (Mendelssohn), Rochester Phil, 83. *Pos:* Music dir, Netherlands Chamber Orch, 64-77, Rotterdam Phil, 79-82 & Rochester Phil Orch, 72-; prin guest cond, Baltimore Symph Orch, 83- *Teaching:* Adj prof cond, Eastman Sch Music, 76- *Rep:* ICM Artist Ltd 40 W 57th St New York NY 10019. *Mailing Add:* c/o Rochester Phil 108 East Ave Rochester NY 14604

ZINN, MICHAEL A
COMPOSER, EDUCATOR
b New Haven, Conn, Aug 23, 47. *Study:* Univ Conn, BMus, 69, MA, 71; Mich State Univ, PhD, 76. *Works:* Spring Storm, 75, Suspensions, 75 & Reticent Reflections, 77, Seesaw Music Corp; Through Tiny Faces (SATB), perf by Univ Del Chorale, 81; Ghost Dreamer of Teton, 82, Obsidian Sky, 82, Dorn Publ; Lake of the Silver Bear, perf by Gamelan, 82-83. *Pos:* Prod asst, WKAR-TV, East Lansing, Mich, 73-74. *Teaching:* Res asst, Music Dept, Univ Conn, 66-71; teaching asst, Music Dept, Mich State Univ, 71-73; assoc prof, Univ Del, 74- *Awards:* Comp of Yr, Del State Music Teachers Asn, 76 & Del Arts Coun, 80; fel, Nat Endowment Humanities, 79. *Mem:* ASCAP; Am Soc Univ Comp; Music Teachers Nat Asn; Del State Music Teachers Asn (pres, 83). *Interests:* Experimental instrument construction. *Publ:* Coauth, Music Theory: Opus 1, Fundamentals of Theory, Alfred Knopf, Inc (in prep). *Mailing Add:* Dept Music Univ Del Newark DE 19711

ZIPPER, HERBERT
MUSIC DIRECTOR, COMPOSER
b Vienna, Austria, Apr 27, 04; US citizen. *Works:* Tanz Music, Vienna Conct Orch, 35; Two Ballets, Buenos Aires, 35; Arthur Jordan Choral Series, E B Marks, 49-54; Masterworks of the Choral Art, Broude Bros, 51-55. *Rec Perf:* Carmen, MBC, Manila, 56; Pierrot Lunaire (A Schoenberg), Everest Rec Prod, 64; various recordings, Beijing China Broadcast Co, 81-82. *Pos:* Opera & symph cond, Ingolstadt & Düsseldorf, Germany, 29-33; cond & comp, various Europ cities, 33-38; music dir, Manila Symph Orch, Philippines, 39-70 & Brooklyn Symph, 49-50. *Teaching:* Prof comp & theory, Consv Düsseldorf, 31-33; music dir, Acad Music Manila, Philippines, 39-42, Music Ctr NShore Chicago, 53-67 & Sch Perf Arts, Univ Southern Calif, 72-80. *Mem:* Nat Guild Community Sch Arts (pres, 57-61, exec dir, 67-72); Am Fedn Musicians. *Interests:* Arts in elementary education. *Mailing Add:* 1091 Palisair Place Pacific Palisades CA 90272

ZIPSER, BURTON ALLEN
ADMINISTRATOR, MUSIC DIRECTOR
b Oak Park, Mich, Jan 1, 34. *Study:* Univ Southern Calif, BMus, 56; Calif State Univ, Los Angeles, MA, 65; Ball State Univ. *Pos:* Exec dir, Southeast Mich Orch, 77-; musical dir, Mich Sinfonietta, 82- *Teaching:* Chmn, Music Dept, L'Anse Creuse Sch, 69-72; admin asst, Sch Music, Ball State Univ, 73-75. *Mem:* Nat Asn Jazz Educr (chmn Mich, 70-73); Nat Band Asn (chmn Mich, 71-73); Am Symph Orch League; Am Choral Dir Asn; Music Educr Nat Conf. *Publ:* Contribr to Music J, Choral J, Sch Musician & Int Musician, 62- *Mailing Add:* 23451 Roanoke Oak Park MI 48237

ZLOTKIN, FREDERICK
CELLO, LECTURER
b Los Angeles, Calif, Mar 10, 47. *Study:* Univ Southern Calif, with Gregor Piatigorsky, 63-65; Manhattan Sch Music, with Bernard Greenhouse, 65-67; Juilliard Sch, with Leonard Rose, BM, MS, DMA, 67-78. *Rec Perf:* Sonata, 1978 (Anthony Newman), Cambridge Rec, 78; Six Suites for Solo Cello (J S Bach), Musical Heritage Soc, 79. *Pos:* Artist in res, Aspen Music Fest, summers, currently; soloist, l'Orch Suisse Romande, Minn Orch, St Louis Symph, Chamber Music Soc Lincoln Ctr, Aspen Music Fest, New York Philomusica & others. *Teaching:* Fac mem, Manhattan Sch Music, 83- *Awards:* William Schwann Award, Tanglewood, 64; Nat Arts Club Award, 66; Top Prize, Concours Int, Geneva, Switzerland, 75. *Mem:* Montauk Chamber Music Soc (music dir, currently). *Mailing Add:* 511 E 80th St New York NY 10021

ZOGHBY, LINDA
SOPRANO
b Mobile, Ala, Aug 17, 49. *Study:* Fla State Univ, BMus, 71, MMus, 74; Am Opera Ctr, Juilliard Sch, 74-75. *Rec Perf:* On Phillips Phonogram & Decca. *Roles:* Marguerite in Faust, New Orleans Opera; Fiordiligi in Cosi fan tutte, Sante Fe Opera Asn; Juliet in I Capuleti ed i Montecchi, Washington Opera; Mimi in La Boheme, Glyndebourne Fest & Metropolitan Opera, 82; Countess in The Marriage of Figaro, Orlando Opera Co, 83. *Pos:* Appearances with Dallas Civic Opera, Columbus Symph, New Orleans Symph, Nat Symph, Houston Grand Opera, Handel & Haydn Soc, Boston, New Orleans Opera & others. *Awards:* First Place, Young Artists Award, Nat Asn Teachers Singing, 72; Winner, Auditions of the Air, WGN, Chicago, 73. *Mailing Add:* c/o Columbia Artists Mgt 165 W 57th St New York NY 10019

ZONN, PAUL
COMPOSER, CONDUCTOR
b Boston, Mass, Jan 16, 38. *Study:* Univ Miami, BMus, 59; Univ Iowa, with Richard Hervig, MFA, 66. *Works:* Chroma (oboe & piano), 67, Voyage of Columbus (solo trumpet & ten players), 75 & String Quartet #4, 76, Am Comp Alliance; Symphony in F, comn & perf by Ft Worth Orch, 81; Winter Paths, 82 & Prairie Songs, 83, Am Comp Alliance; Urbana Mountain Rag, perf by Andrea Zonn & Heartland Band, 83. *Rec Perf:* Double Concerto (Hackbarth), Crystal Rec, 77; Gemini-Fantasy (Zonn), CRI, 79; Chamber Concerto II (Schwartz), Crystal Rec, 81. *Pos:* Comp & clarinetist, Ctr Perf Arts, State Univ NY, Buffalo, 66-67; comp in res & cond, Grinnell Col, 67-70; cond, Univ Ill Chamber Players, 70- *Teaching:* Prof theory, analysis & comp, Univ Ill, 70- *Awards:* Ford Found Grant, 68-70; Nat Endowment Arts Grant, 76; fel, Univ Ill Ctr Advan Study, 76 & 83. *Mem:* Am Soc Univ Comp (regional co-chmn, 81-83). *Mailing Add:* 308 Pond Ridge Lane Urbana IL 61801

ZONN, WILMA ZAPORA
OBOE, EDUCATOR
b Alden, Pa, June 7, 36. *Study:* Univ Miami, Coral Gables, BM, 58; studied with Harold Gomberg, 59-62; Univ Iowa, MA, 66. *Rec Perf:* Chroma (Paul Martin Zonn), CRI, 72; Timbral Variations, UBRES, 79; Faces (Stuart Smith), Advan Rec, 79; Tryptych (Thomas Fredrickson) & Gemikni Fantasy (Paul Martin Zonn), CRI, 79. *Pos:* Solo oboe, Ore Symph, 62-64; oboist, Iowa Woodwind Quintet, 64-66; oboe soloist & mem, Univ Ill Contemp Chamber Players, 70- *Teaching:* Instr oboe, Univ Iowa, 64-66, Grinnell Col, 67-70 & Nat Acad Arts, 77-; vis specialist music, Univ High Sch, Urbana, 72-76; vis instr oboe, Univ Ill, Urbana-Champaign, 73. *Awards:* Outstanding Musician Year, Sigma Alpha Iota, 58; Fromm Found Fel, 67-68. *Bibliog:* Arthur Benade (auth), Fundamentals of Musical Acoustics, Oxford Univ Press, 76. *Mem:* Int Double Reed Soc; Ill State Music Teachers Asn; Am Fedn Musicians. *Publ:* Auth, Observations for Today's Oboist, 3/78 & How You Bow, 12/78, Double Reed J; contribr, Book Instrumentation/Orchestration, Longman, 80. *Mailing Add:* 308 Pond Ridge Ln Urbana IL 61801

ZORN, JAY D
EDUCATOR, MUSIC DIRECTOR
b New York, NY, Mar 23, 31. *Study:* Oberlin Consv, BME, 53; Columbia Univ, MA, 58, Ind Univ, DME, 69. *Pos:* Dir inst music, Mamaroneck High Sch, NY, 58-68. *Teaching:* Asst prof & dir bands, Muskingum Col, 68-72; prof music, Univ Southern Calif, 72-, chmn music educ dept, 81- *Mem:* Music Educr Nat Conf (chmn, 80-); Calif Music Educr Asn (higher educ rep, 80-); Chamber Music Am. *Interests:* Effectiveness of chamber music ensemble experience. *Publ:* Auth, Exploring the Trumpets Upper Register, Kendor Music, 75; Brass Ensemble Method for Music Educators, Wadsworth Publ, 77; coauth (with Hanshumaker), Fundamentals: Learning Through Making Music, Alfred Publ, 81. *Mailing Add:* 7936 Whitsett Ave North Hollywood CA 91605

ZSCHAU, MARILYN
SOPRANO
b Chicago, Ill. *Study:* St Mary's Jr Col, NC, voice with Geraldine Cate, 55-57; Univ NC, Chapel Hill, BA, 59; studied voice with Walter Golde; Juilliard Sch Music, opera theatre with Christopher West & voice with Lotte Leonard & Florence Page Kimball, 61-65; Univ Mont, voice with John Lester, 66- *Rec Perf:* La Boheme, Covent Garden Prod, 82. *Roles:* Minnie in La Fanciulla del West, Vienna State Opera, 77-78, Chicago Lyr Opera, 78 & Covent Garden, 82; Maddelena in Andrea Chenier, New York City Opera, 78 & Welsh Nat Opera, 82; Tosca in Tosca, New York City Opera, Australian Opera, Frankfort & Munich, 80-83; Leonora in Il Trovatore, Pittsburgh, 80; Leonora in La Forza del Destino, Lyon, France, 81; Manon Lescaut in Manon Lescaut, Australian Opera, Genoa & Bologna, 81-83; Odabella in Attila, Vienna State Opera, New York City Opera & Paris Chatelet, 81-82. *Mailing Add:* c/o Columbia Artists Mgt Inc 165 W 57th St New York NY 10019

ZSIGMONDY, DENES
VIOLIN, EDUCATOR
b Budapest, Hungary. *Study:* Liszt-Acad Music, Budapest, MA; Univ Budapest, study with Carl Flesch & Zino Francescatti. *Rec Perf:* Sixteen Mozart Sonatas, Impression Rec; The Virtuoso Violin, The Romantic Violin & Zsigmondy Plays Bartok, Klavier Rec; Beethoven Sonaten, Op 47, Beethoven Sonaten, Op 24 & Paganini Hexentaenze, Sonatinen & Capricen, Summit Rec; Schubert Fantasie C Major & Brahms Sonate d minor, Op 108, Lyrichord Rec; and many others. *Pos:* Soloist with Berlin Symph Orch, Budapest Phil Orch, Munich Phil Orch, Salzburg Camerata Orch & Australian ABC Orch. *Teaching:* Prof violin, Univ Wash, 72-; vis prof, Boston Univ, 81-82. *Mailing Add:* Music Dept Univ Wash Seattle WA 98195

ZUCKER, STEFAN
TENOR, WRITER
b New York, NY. *Study:* Mozarteum, cert, 63; Columbia Univ, BS, 67; NY Univ, 72. *Rec Perf:* Stefan Zucker: The World's Highest Tenor, 81, Bellini's Adelson e Salvini (in prep) & Bellini's Bianca e Fernando (in prep), AFBC Rec. *Pos:* Gen mgr & artistic dir, Asn Furtherment Bel Canto New York, 68-; soloist & recitalist, US, 72-; prog host, WKCR-FM, New York, 82- *Teaching:* Vocal technique, Newark Sch Fine & Perf Arts, 69; vocal technique instr & vocal repty coach, privately. *Bibliog:* Jack Hiemenz (auth), Bel Canto: I Puritani, Musical Am, 71; Desmond Arthur (auth), Stefan Zucker, Am Rec Guide, 82; Anthony D Coggi (auth), Stefan Zucker, Fanfare, 83. *Interests:* Operas and vocalism and performance practices of the bel canto era. *Publ:* Auth, Disputo over Investigation, News World, 80; End of an Era, 81 & Tenor Giovanni Battista Rubini, 82, Opera News; Different Kinds of High Notes and the Seismic Shock, Am Rec Guide, 82; Seismic Shocker: Gilbert-Louis Duprez's History-Making High C, Opera News, 83. *Rep:* Wayne Wilbur Mgt Box 1387 Grand Cent Sta New York NY 10163. *Mailing Add:* 11 Riverside Dr New York NY 10023

ZUCKERMAN, MARK ALAN
COMPOSER, EDUCATOR
b Brooklyn, NY, July 8, 48. *Study:* Univ Mich, 66-68; Bard Col, AB, 70; Princeton Univ, PhD, 76. *Works:* Focus (cello), 70 & Paraphrases (flute), 71, Mobart Music; Episodes (organ solo), 74 & Ascensus Detrahendus (piano solo), 75, Asn Prom New Music. *Pos:* Co-dir, Godfrey Winham Lab, 75-77. *Teaching:* Instr, Princeton Univ, 74-77; asst prof, Columbia Univ, 77- *Mem:* Am Comp Alliance; Assoc for Prom New Music; NJ Comp Guild. *Publ:* Auth, On Milton Babbitt's String Quartet No 2, Perspectives New Music, 76. *Mailing Add:* 16 Farm Lane Roosevelt NJ 08555

ZUGELJ, IVAN PETAR (JOHN PETER ZUGEL)
CONDUCTOR & MUSIC DIRECTOR, DOUBLE BASS
b McKeesport, Pa, Nov 15, 46. *Study:* Duquesne Univ, BM, 69; Kent State Univ, studied double bass with David Perlman, 70-72; Nederlandse Omroep Stichting Int Cond Course, with Michel Tabachnik, cert, 79. *Pos:* Co-prin double bassist, Charlotte Symph Orch, NC, 74-, asst cond, In-Sch Conct, 75-; prin double bassist, Charlotte Symph Chamber Orch, NC, 74-; music dir, Davidson String Ens, NC, 82- *Teaching:* Grad asst theory & solfeggio, Kent State Univ, 70-72; instr string ens, Davidson Col, 81- *Mem:* Founder, Chamber Music Soc Charlotte. *Rep:* 6550-D Idlewild Rd Charlotte NC 28212. *Mailing Add:* PO Box 33385 Charlotte NC 28233

ZUKERMAN, PINCHAS
MUSIC DIRECTOR, VIOLIN
b Tel Aviv, Israel, July 16, 48. *Study:* Israel Consv; Acad Music, Tel Aviv; Juilliard Sch Music, with Ivan Galamian. *Rec Perf:* Over 40 albums for Angel, Deutsche Grammaphon, RCA & Columbia. *Pos:* Dir, SBank Summer Music Fest, 78-; music dir, St Paul Chamber Orch, 81-; artistic dir, Carnegie Hall Serenades, 81-; conct & recital perf throughout US & Europe. *Awards:* Leventritt Award, 67. *Mailing Add:* c/o ICM Artists 40 W 57th St New York NY 10019

ZUKOFSKY, PAUL
COMPOSER, CONDUCTOR
b Brooklyn, NY, Oct 22, 43. *Study:* Juilliard Sch Music, with Bernard Wagenaar & Vincent Persichetti, BMus, MS. *Works:* Variants (sop, trumpet, violin & bass clarinet), 60; 13 Pomes, a Prelude and a Postlude (two speakers & 15 perc players), 62; For Three Mallet Men and a Percussion Player, 63; For Orchestra, 64; Catullus Fragments (sop, alto & string trio), 68. *Rec Perf:* 24 Caprices for Solo Violin (Paganini); works by Ives, Sessions, Penderecki, Busoni & others. *Pos:* Freelance cond, currently; violinist with maj orchs. *Teaching:* Mem fac violin, New England Consv, formerly, Swarthmore Col, formerly, State Univ NY, Stony Brook, formerly & Manhattan Sch Music, formerly. *Awards:* Guggenheim Fel, 83. *Mailing Add:* c/o Kazuko Hillyer Inc 250 W 57th St New York NY 10107

ZUMWALD-HOWARD, R REID
PIANO, EDUCATOR
b Norton, Kans, Apr 26, 48. *Rec Perf:* An Evening with Gershwin, Audio Engineering Assoc, 83. *Teaching:* Dept chmn, Ambassador Col, 76-80; dir piano studies, Hartnell Col, 80- *Mem:* Am Liszt Soc; Am Musicol Soc; Pi Kappa Lambda. *Mailing Add:* Music Dept Hartnell Col 156 Homestead Ave Salinas CA 93901

ZUPKO, RAMON
COMPOSER, EDUCATOR
b Pittsburgh, Pa, Nov 14, 32. *Study:* Juilliard Sch, with Vincent Persichetti, BS, 56, MS, 57; Acad Music, Vienna, Austria; Univ Utrecht, Holland. *Works:* Fixations (piano trio & tape), 74, Nocturnes (2 pianos), 77, Fantasies (woodwind quintet), 79 & Windsongs (piano concerto), 79, Peters; Noosphere (string quartet), New World String Quartet, 80; Life Dances (orch), Peters, 81; Canti Terrae (orch), comn by Koussevitzky, 82. *Teaching:* Asst prof music, Chicago Musical Col, 67-71; prof comp, Sch Music, Western Mich Univ, 71- *Awards:* Comp fel, Guggenheim Found, 81; comp award, Serge Koussevitzky Found, 81 & Am Acad & Inst Arts & Lett, 82. *Mem:* Am Soc Univ Comp; Am Comp Alliance; Int Soc Contemp Music. *Mailing Add:* 1540 N Second St RFD 1 Kalamazoo MI 49009

ZUPONCIC, VEDA HELEN
PIANO, EDUCATOR
b Biwabik, Minn, Aug 3, 46. *Study:* Ind Univ, BM, 67, MM, 68. *Teaching:* Instr, Philadelphia Musical Acad, 68-71; asst prof, Glassboro State Col, 71-77, assoc prof, 77-, chmn dept music, 80- *Awards:* Martha Baird Rockefeller Grant, 71; Prizewinner, Alfredo Casella Compt, Naples, 72. *Rep:* ICA Mgt 2219 Eastridge Rd Timonium MD 21093. *Mailing Add:* 111 Munn Lane Cherry Hill NJ 08034

ZWICKY, GARY LEE
EDUCATOR, ORGAN
b Oshkosh, Wis, June 18, 34. *Study:* Univ Wis, BMus, 56, MMus, 59; Univ Ill, DMA, 65; Col Church Musicians. *Pos:* Organist & choirmaster, Trinity Episcopal Church, Mattoon, Ill, 76- *Teaching:* Instrm dir, Mt Carroll Pub Sch, Ill, 56-59; asst prof organ & theory, Del Mar Col, 62-64; prof organ, Eastern Ill Univ, 66- *Mem:* Am Guild Organists; Music Teachers Nat Asn; Asn Anglican Musicians; Organ Hist Soc; Hymn Soc Am. *Mailing Add:* 2517 S Fifth Charleston IL 61920

ZWILICH, ELLEN TAAFFE
COMPOSER
b Miami, Fla, Apr. 30, 39. *Study:* Fla State Univ, BM, 60, MM, 62; Juilliard Sch, with Roger Sessions & Elliott Carter, DMA, 75. *Works:* Symposium for Orchestra, Theodore Presser Co, 73; String Quartet, Margun Music, 74; Sonata in Three Movements (violin & piano), Elkan-Vogel, 74; Chamber Symphony, Theodore Presser Co, 79; Passages (sop & chamber ens or orch), 79 & Symphony #1 (Three Movements for Orch), 82, Margun Music; String Trio (violin, viola & cello), comn & perf by Lydian Trio, 82. *Awards:* Gold Medal, GB Viotti, 26th Ann Int Comp Compt, Vercelli, Italy, 75; fel, Guggenheim Found, 80; Ernst von Dohnanyi Citation, Fla State Univ, 81. *Mem:* Am Music Ctr (vpres, 82-83). *Mailing Add:* 600 W 246th St Riverdale NY 10471

ZYCHOWICZ, JAMES LEO
TEACHER, TUBA
b Toledo, Ohio, Dec 13, 55. *Study:* Univ Toledo, BMusEd, 77; Col Consv Music, Univ Cincinnati, studied tuba with Samuel Green, 78-79; Bowling Green State Univ, MMus, 81. *Works:* Six Baroque Duets for Tuba, Shawnee Press, 81; Three Preludes for Brass Quintet, perf by Metropolitan Brass Quintet, 83. *Teaching:* Music dir, St Xavier High Sch, 77-79; grad asst, Bowling Green State Univ, 79-81; dean students & music dir, Holy Spirit Sem, Toledo, 81-83. *Mem:* Am Musicol Soc; Phi Mu Alpha Sinfonia; Col Music Soc; Tubists Universal Brotherhood Asn (pres Toledo chap, 74-76). *Interests:* Style and style analysis. *Publ:* Auth, Brahms' Third Symphony: The Motto as Isomorphism (in prep); To Hear What You Know: Multiple Strategies for Music Study (in prep). *Mailing Add:* 3132 Mulberry St Toledo OH 43608

ZYLIS-GARA, TERESA GERALDA
SOPRANO
b Wilno, Poland, Jan 23, 35. *Study:* Lodz Music Acad; studied with Olga Olgina. *Rec Perf:* On Angel, Deutsche Grammophon, Seraphim & EMI. *Roles:* Marguerite in Faust; Fiordiligi in Cosi fan tutte; Donna Elvira in Don Giovanni; Pamina in Die Zauberflöte; Mimi in La Boheme; Cio Cio San in Madama Butterfly; Tatiana in Eugene Onegin. *Pos:* Leading sop, Deutsche Opera Rhein; appearances with Vienna Staatsoper, Royal Opera House Covent Garden, Munich Staatsoper, La Scala, San Francisco Opera, Lyr Opera Chicago & many others; soloist with Boston Symph, New York Phil, Los Angeles Phil & Cleveland Orch; guest artist on radio & TV in US & Europe. *Awards:* Winner, Int Singing Compt, Munich, 60 & Polish Nat Compt, Warsaw; Mozart Gold Medal, Mexico City. *Mailing Add:* c/o Columbia Artists Mgt 165 W 57th St New York NY 10019

ZYTOWSKI, CARL BYRD
EDUCATOR, CONDUCTOR
b St Louis, Mo, July 17, 21. *Study:* St Louis Inst Music, BMus, 49; Nat Sch Opera, London, England, with Joan Cross, 49; Univ Wash, MA, 51. *Works:* Thomas of Canterbury (opera), perf by Univ Calif, Santa Barbara Men's Chorus, 81; Play of the Three Shepherds (opera), perf by Schubertians, 82. *Teaching:* Prof voice & opera cond, Univ Calif, Santa Barbara, 51-; fac mem, Music Acad of West, 53-59. *Mem:* Intercollegiate Musical Coun (pres, 72-75); Nat Opera Asn (vpres, 82-); Opera for Youth. *Publ:* Coauth (with Van A Christy), 57 Classic Period Songs, Belwin-Mills, 78; The Church Year in Song, G Schirmer, 78; translr, Haydn, La Canterina, T Presser, 80. *Mailing Add:* 4013 Pala Lane Santa Barbara CA 93110

Geographic Index

ALABAMA

Anniston

Kaplan, Lois Jay Composer, Conductor &
Music Director

Auburn

Anderson, Glenn Alan Librarian
Faust, Randall Edward Composer, French
Horn
Greenleaf, Robert Bruce Educator,
Clarinet
Kaplan, Barbara Connally Educator,
Soprano

Birmingham

Baxter, William Hubbard, Jr Educator,
Baritone
DeVan, William Lewis, Jr Piano,
Educator
Jensen, James A Educator, Composer
Marino, Amerigo Angelo Conductor &
Music Director
Mathes, Rachel Clarke Soprano, Educator
Nord, Edward Allan Conductor & Music
Director, Piano
Roosevelt, Oliver Wolcott, Jr Critic
Trauffer, Barbara Olive Flute & Piccolo
Turkiewicz, Witold Wladyslaw Educator,
Piano

Huntsville

Pollard, Elizabeth Blitch Librarian,
Educator

Jacksonville

Fairleigh, James Parkinson Administrator,
Educator

Mobile

Alette, Carl Composer, Educator
Bault, Diane Lynn Guitar, Educator
Harper, Andrew Henry Administrator,
Music Director
Jones, William John Educator, Flute &
Piccolo
Papastefan, John James Educator,
Percussion
Town, Stephen J Teacher, Writer

Montevallo

Cowan, Robert (Holmes) Piano, Teacher
Middaugh, Benjamin Educator, Baritone
Pritchett, Theodore M Administrator,
Educator
Robertson, Edwin C Composer, Educator
Yarbrough, Joan (Joan Yarbrough Cowan)
Piano, Teacher

Montgomery

Boykin, Annie Helen Composer, Teacher
Fly, Fenton G Educator, Double Bass
Shaffer, Jeanne Ellison Composer

Mountain Brook

Howard, Samuel Eugene Piano, Teacher

Northport

Hyde, Frederick B(ill) Educator,
Harpsichord

Talladega

Braithwaite, James Roland Educator,
Organ

Troy

Vollrath, Carl Paul Composer, Educator

Tuscaloosa

Gates, J(ames) Terry Educator, Music
Director
Goossen, (Jacob) Frederic Composer,
Educator

Tuskegee

Hicks, Roy Edward Music Director,
Educator
Price, John Elwood Composer, Educator

University

Rubin, Henry Park Violin

ALASKA

Anchorage

Farmer, Nancy Louise Oboe & English
Horn, Teacher
Goodfellow, James Richard Administrator
More, Michael Administrator, Tenor
Rosenthal, Paul Samuel Violin, Music
Director
Voth, Elvera Conductor

Chugiak

Kimmel, Corliss Ann Percussion
Moon, Peggy MacDonald Director-Opera

Fairbanks

Adams, John (Luther) Composer,
Percussion
Johnson, James (David) Piano
Martin, Ravonna G Composer, Piano
Summerville, Suzanne Mezzo-soprano,
Educator

Sitka

Bor, Christiaan Violin

Wasilla

Jefford, Ruth Martin Violin

ARIZONA

Flagstaff

Aurand, Charles Henry, Jr Clarinet,
Educator
Cleman, Thomas Educator, Composer
Scott, Frank Edward Educator, Piano
Shott, Michael John Educator, Composer
Stone, Edgar Norman Tenor, Educator

Glendale

Dutton, Mary Ann Enloe Educator,
Music Director

Mesa

McDonald, Arlys Lorraine Librarian
Moreau, Lorraine Marie Soprano, Patron
Shinn, Randall Alan Composer, Educator

Phoenix

Alcantara, Theo Music Director &
Conductor, Artistic Director
Berginc, Charles David Trumpet
Cummings, Diane M Violin
Elan, Terry Michael Double Bass
Mason, Anthony Halstead Administrator,
Patron
Monson, Karen Ann Critic & Writer,
Lecturer
Pulk, Bruce Harry Percussion
Suttle, Clark Etienne Conductor, Double
Bass
Veronda, Carlo Conductor, Educator

Scottsdale

Becker, Bonita Ruth Violin, Piano
Brandstadter, Eugene J Viola, Violin
Missal, Joshua M Composer

Sun City

Roberts, Wilfred Bob Trumpet, Composer

Tempe

Carroll, Christina Educator, Singer
Cohen, David Composer, Educator
Fletcher, (H) Grant Composer, Conductor
& Music Director
Haefer, (John) Richard Educator
Hamilton, Robert Piano, Educator
Hoover, Eric John Flute, Educator
Johnson, David Nathaniel Composer,
Organ
Kliewer, Darleen Carol Educator,
Soprano
Lombardi, Eugene Patsy Conductor &
Music Director, Educator
LoPresti, Ronald B Composer, Educator
Magers, William Dean Viola, Violin
Oldani, Robert William Writer, Educator
Rausch, Jack D Administrator, Bassoon
Skoldberg, Phyllis Linnea Administrator,
Violin
Stalzer, Frank S Educator, Oboe &
English Horn

ARIZONA (cont)

Strange, Richard Eugene Music Director, Educator

Tucson

Anthony, James Raymond Educator, Writer
Booth, Nancy Soprano
Cook, Gary D Percussion, Educator
Denman, John Anthony Educator, Clarinet
Epperson, Gordon Cello, Educator
Erlings, Billie Raye Music Research
Ervin, Thomas Ross Trombone, Educator
Faith, Richard Bruce Composer, Piano
Harnisch, Larry (Lawrence Myrland) Critic-Writer
Hull, Robert Leslie Conductor, Educator
LaFave, Kenneth John Critic & Writer, Composer
Lee, Jack Kenneth Composer, Conductor
Little, Meredith Ellis Writer, Harpsichord
McBride, Robert Guyn Composer, Educator
McGlaughlin, William Music Director & Conductor, Trombone
McMillan, Theodora Mantz Violin, Educator
Majoros, David John Baritone, Educator
Marsh, Ozan F Educator, Piano
Miller, Karl Frederick Educator, Composer
Mosher, Elizabeth (Elizabeth Mosher-Kraus) Educator, Soprano
Muczynski, Robert Educator, Composer
O'Brien, James Patrick Educator
Parks, David Wayne Tenor, Lecturer
Pearlman, Leonard Alexander Educator, Music Director & Conductor
Sellers, Jacquelyn Marie French Horn, Educator
Showell, Jeffrey Adams Viola, Educator
Siena, Jerold Tenor, Educator
Smith, Branson Composer, Teacher
Smith, Dorman Henry Librarian, Educator
Solomon, Larry J Educator, Composer
Spizizen, Louise (Myers) Composer, Performer
Van Hulse, Camil A J Composer
Werner, Robert Joseph Administrator, Educator

ARKANSAS

Arkadelphia

Hammond, Paul G Educator, Writer
Keck, George R Educator, Piano
McBeth, William Francis Composer, Conductor
Nisbet, Meredith Wootton Composer, Violin
Trantham, William Eugene Educator, Piano
Underwood, William L Educator, Composer

Batesville

Gray, Dorothy Landis Educator, Music Director

Conway

Collins, Don L Educator, Conductor & Music Director
Driggers, Orin Samuel Educator, Piano
Forsberg, Carl Earl Educator, Violin

Fayetteville

Ballenger, Kenneth Leigh Educator, Baritone
Jackson, Barbara Ann Garvey Educator
Janzen, Eldon A Educator, Music Director
Tollefson, Arthur Ralph Piano, Educator
Widder, Roger Henry Educator, Oboe & English Horn

Little Rock

Boury, Robert Wade Composer, Educator
Henderson, Robert Conductor & Music Director
Hughes, John (Gilliam) Educator, Organ
Perry, Edson Clifton Violin, Viola

Magnolia

Baer, (Dolores) Dalene Violin, Educator
Campbell, Robert Gordon Educator, Piano

State University

Patty, James Lecil Educator, Piano

CALIFORNIA

Albany

Blumenfeld, Aaron Joel Composer, Writer

Alhambra

Van Ness, Paul William Educator, Piano

Anaheim

Porter, David Gray Composer, Piano

Angwin

McGee, William James Composer, Educator
Peterson, LeRoy H Violin, Conductor

APO San Francisco

Van de Vate, Nancy (Hayes) Composer, Educator

Aptos

Davies, Dennis Conductor & Music Director, Pianist
Harrison, Lou Composer, Educator

Arcadia

Stevens, Roger S Flute & Piccolo, Educator

Atherton

Johnson-Hamilton, Joyce Conductor, Trumpet

Bakersfield

Farrer, John Music Director
Kleinsasser, Jerome S Administrator, Educator
Quilling, Howard Lee Composer, Educator

Belmont

Lemmon, Galen Percussion, Educator

Berkeley

Ahrold, Frank Composer, Piano
Bacon, Madi Conductor & Music Director
Basart, Ann Phillips Librarian, Writer
Basart, Robert Educator, Composer
Bradshaw, Richard James Conductor & Music Director
Brett, Philip Critic-Writer, Educator
Bronson, Bertrand Harris Writer, Musicologist
Collier, Charles R Instrument Maker
Crocker, Richard Lincoln Educator, Writer

Curtis, Alan Educator, Harpsichord
Dresher, Paul Joseph Composer, Electronic
Dudley, Anna Carol Soprano, Educator
Farr, David Donald Music Director, Organ
Felciano, Richard Composer, Educator
Gilb, Tyra Ellen Flute & Piccolo, Teacher-Coach
Gnazzo, Anthony Joseph Composer, Electronic
Heartz, Daniel Leonard Educator
Imbrie, Andrew Welsh Composer, Educator
Keller, Michael Alan Librarian, Educator
Kerman, Joseph Wilfred Musicologist, Critic-Writer
London, Lawrence Bernard Composer, Clarinet
McRae, Lee Artist Manager
Moe, Lawrence Henry Organ, Educator
Nelson, Judith Soprano
Nin-Culmell, Joaquin M Composer, Piano
Russell, James Reagan Clarinet, Conductor
Shere, Charles Everett Composer, Critic-Writer
Wilson, Olly W Composer, Conductor

Beverly Hills

Colf, Howard Cello, Teacher
Freeman, Robert Norman Musicologist
Green, John W Composer, Conductor & Music Director
Lazarof, Henri Composer, Educator
Strimple, Nick Music Director, Composer

Bradbury

Garside, Patricia Ann Flute, Educator

Burbank

Gomez, Vicente Guitar, Composer
Severinsen, Doc (Carl H) Music Director, Trumpet
Watson, Kenneth E Percussion, Educator

Burlingame

Stenberg, Donald Christian Educator, Baritone
Ward, William Reed Composer, Educator

Canoga Park

Reale, Paul Vincent Composer, Piano

Carmel

Cuyler, Louise E Educator, Writer
Evans, Peter (Hollingshead) Guitar, Composer
Lebherz, Louis P Bass

Carmel Valley

Meckel, Peter Timothy Administrator, Educator

Carmichael

Stover, Franklin Howard (Franklin Howard Stoeffen) Composer, Administrator

Carson

Bunger, Richard Joseph Composer, Educator

Century City

Lambro, Phillip Composer, Piano

Cerritos

Klein, Stephen Tavel Tuba, Teacher

Chatsworth

Kessner, Daniel Aaron Composer, Educator

Chico

Browne, John P, Jr Educator, Trombone
Longazo, George Educator, Bassoon
Rapley, Janice Ann Educator, Lecturer

Chula Vista

Tecayehuatzin, Victor Saucedo (Victor Saucedo) Composer, Electronic

Claremont

Kohn, Karl (George) Composer, Piano
Kubik, Gail Composer, Conductor
Lengefeld, William Chris Educator, Conductor
Loucks, Richard Newcomb Educator, Writer
Ritter, John Steele Piano, Educator
Shelton, Margaret Meier Composer, Educator

Corona Del Mar

Karson, Burton Lewis Educator, Conductor

Culver City

Cousin, Jack Double Bass
Lefkowitz, Mischa Violin
Rosso, Carol L Composer
Thomason, Marshall Daniel Administrator, Viola d'Amore

Cupertino

Archibeque, Charlene P Conductor & Music Director, Educator
Ellison, Greer (Greer Ellison Wolfson) Flute, Teacher

Davis

Bloch, Robert Samson Violin, Composer
Frank, Andrew (David) Composer, Educator
Holoman, Dallas Kern Musicologist, Conductor
Rosen, Jerome William Composer, Educator
Swift, Richard Composer, Critic-Writer
Valente, William Edward Composer, Educator

Del Mar

Bowles, Garrett H Librarian, Educator
Goodkind, Alice Anderson Violin, Artist
Romero, Angel Guitar, Teacher
Tseitlin, Irina Violin
Tseitlin, Michael Viola, Violin
Turetzky, Bertram Jay Double Bass, Composer

El Cerrito

Amirkhanian, Charles Benjamin Composer, Critic-Writer
Guggenheim, Janet Goodman Accompanist, Piano

Emeryville

Hughes, Robert Grove Composer, Conductor & Music Director

Encino

Carlson, Claudine (Claudine H Carlson-Rubin) Mezzo-soprano
Rosen, Judith (Berenice) Writer, Lecturer
Steiner, Fred(erick) Composer, Writer
Subramaniam, Lakshminarayana Violin, Composer

Eureka

Stroud, Richard Ernest Composer, Music Director

Fair Oaks

Sydeman, William J Composer

Filmore

Bowen, Eugene Everett Composer

Forest Ranch

Rothe, David H Organ, Educator

Fountain Valley

Powell, Arlene Karr Piano, Educator

Fresno

Fortner, Jack Ronald Composer, Conductor & Music Director
Garabedian, Edna (Edna Mae Garabedian-Duguie) Mezzo-soprano, Teacher & Coach
Gerster, Robert Gibson Composer, Educator
Gilbert, Steven E(dward) Educator, Writer
Irwin, Phyllis Ann Administrator, Educator
Skei, Allen Bennet Critic-Writer, Educator
Taylor, Guy Conductor & Music Director
Warkentin, Larry R Composer, Educator
Winter, James Hamilton Educator, French Horn

Fullerton

Biggs, John Joseph Composer, Music Director
Estes, Charles Byron Composer, Piano
Reynolds, Erma Composer

Garden Grove

Forrest, Jim Administrator, Educator
Hixon, Don L Librarian, Writer
Swann, Frederick Lewis Organ, Conductor & Music Director

Glendale

Nightingale, Daniel Librarian, Music Copyist
Roe, Charles Richard Teacher, Baritone

Goleta

Meckna, Michael Educator, Critic-Writer
Sonnet, Susan M Librarian

Granada Hills

Cole, Vincent L Composer, Educator
Taylor, Les (Lionel Lester) Composer, Educator

Greenbrae

Lindeman, Carolynn A Educator, Writer

Hayward

Acord, Thomas Wadsworth Tenor, Conductor
Mansfield, Kenneth Zoellin Organ, Educator
Rubin, Nathan Educator, Violin

Hermosa Beach

McNeil-Morales, Albert John Educator, Conductor

Hollywood

Bacal, Harvey Musicologist, Educator
Britain, Radie Composer
Fox, Herbert O Artist Manager
Heyler, Mary Ellen Mezzo-soprano
La Montaine, John Composer, Piano
Sifler, Paul John Composer, Organ

Villa, Eduardo Tenor

Inglewood

Stevens, Halsey Educator, Composer

Irvine

Erdody, Stephen John Cello, Educator
Holmes, William C Educator
Murata, Margaret Kimiko Educator, Writer
Rydzynski, Michael Vincent Matthew Percussion, Educator
Slim, H(arry) Colin Musicologist, Educator
Swan, Howard Shelton Educator, Music Director

Kensington

Aird, Donald Bruce Composer, Musical Director
Dugger, Edwin Ellsworth Composer, Educator

La Canada

Crockett, Donald (Harold) Composer, Educator
Schaefer, William Arkwell Educator, Music Director
Walcott, Ronald Harry Educator, Composer

La Crescenta

Heussenstamm, George Composer, Educator

La Habra Heights

Stedman, William Preston Educator, Writer

La Jolla

Barra, Donald Paul Conductor & Music Director, Writer
Erickson, Robert Composer, Educator
Evans, Mark Composer, Conductor
Farrell, Peter Snow Educator, Cello
Gabel, Gerald L Composer, Teacher
Hujsak, (Ruth) Joy Harp, Educator
Moore, F Richard Composer, Educator
Negyesy, Janos Violin, Educator
Ogdon, Will (Wilbur Lee Ogdon) Composer, Educator
Rands, Bernard Composer, Educator
Reynolds, Roger Lee Composer, Educator
Schuster, Earl Vincent Oboe, Educator
Strizich, Catherine Liddell Lute, Teacher-Coach

La Mesa

Ward-Steinman, David Composer, Educator

La Mirada

Childs, Edwin T Educator, Composer
Lock, William Rowland Educator, Conductor

Larkspur

Donovan-Jeffry, Peggy (Margaret) Educator, Director-Opera

La Verne

Browne, Philip R Composer, Educator

Leucadia

Nee, Thomas Bacus Conductor, Educator

Long Beach

Decker, James Educator, Horn
Felder, David C Composer, Conductor
Kuehn, David Laurance Educator, Administrator

Norwalk

Guinaldo, Norberto Composer, Organ

Oakland

Constanten, Thomas Charles Sture
  Composer, Piano
Diamond, Jody Composer, Educator
Glasow, Glenn L Educator, Music
  Director
Hein, Mary Alice Eudcator
Hurd, Peter Wyeth Harpsichord,
  Educator
Jones, Barnard Ray Composer, Conductor
Klein, Mitchell Sardou Conductor
Lucchesi, Peggy (Margaret C Lucchesi)
  Percussion, Educator
Luckman, Phyllis Composer, Teacher-
  Coach
Manwell, Philip Organ, Conductor &
  Music Director
Payne, Maggi Composer, Educator
Polansky, Larry C Composer, Writer
Riley, Terry Composer, Electronic
Rosenboom, David Composer, Educator
Sprung, David Reichert French Horn,
  Educator
Stoltzman, Richard Leslie Clarinet
Van der Wyk, Jack Alex Percussion,
  Composer

Oceanside

Kochanski, Wladimir Jan Piano

Ojai

Wagner, Edyth (Edyth Wagner Roop)
  Educator, Piano

Ontario

Timm, Larry M (Laurance Milo)
  Educator, Oboe & English Horn

Orange

Huszti, Joseph Bela Conductor & Music
  Director, Educator
Newell, Robert Max Composer, Educator

Orinda

Bacon, Ernst Piano, Composer

Pacifica

Gesin, Leonid Viola, Educator

Pacific Palisades

Gold, Ernest Composer, Music Director
Harmon, Thomas Fredric Organ,
  Educator
Harris, Johana Piano, Teacher
Hovey, Serge Composer
North, Alex Composer, Music Director
Shulman, Ivan Alexander Administrator,
  Oboe
Shure, Paul Crane Violin, Teacher
Zipper, Herbert Music Director,
  Composer

Palm Springs

Nordenstrom, Gladys (Gladys
  Nordenstrom Krenek) Composer

Palo Alto

Owen, Angela Maria Critic-Writer,
  Teacher
Ratliff, William Elmore Critic-Writer
Rudhyar, Dane Composer, Critic-Writer

Pasadena

Hsu, Wen-ying Composer
Lawrence, Douglas Howard Tenor
McIntosh, Kathleen Ann Harpsichord,
  Educator

Munday, Kenneth Edward Bassoon,
  Educator
Oakes, Rodney Harland Composer,
  Electronic
Thomson, William Ennis Writer,
  Educator

Pomona

Gibb, Stanley Garth Composer, Educator

Ramona

Gaburo, Kenneth Louis Composer

Rancho Palos Verdes

Cooper, Lawrence Baritone
Fuller, Jeanne Weaver Composer,
  Educator
Kim, Byong-kon Composer, Educator
Steiner, Frances Josephine Conductor &
  Music Director, Cello

Redlands

Bohrnstedt, Wayne R Composer,
  Educator
Childs, Barney Sanford Composer, Writer
Hodgkins, Claire (Claire Hodgkins
  Wright) Violin, Educator
Martin, Walter (Callahan), Jr Educator,
  Baritone
Pierce, Alexandra Composer, Writer
Rehfeldt, Phillip Richard Clarinet,
  Educator
Swanson, Philip John Educator, Flute

Redwood City

Hillhouse, Wendy Carol Mezzo-soprano
Ienni, Philip Camillo Composer, Educator

Richmond

Lopez, Peter Dickson Composer,
  Electronic

Riverside

Bacon-Shone, Frederic Piano, Teacher
Gable, Frederick Kent Educator,
  Conductor & Music Director
Ginter, Anthony Francis Educator, Violin
Halsted, Margo Armbruster Carillon,
  Writer
Hannum, Harold Byron Educator, Organ
Tanno, John W Librarian, Educator

Rohnert Park

Feldman, Joann E Composer, Educator

Rolling Hills Estates

Bialosky, Marshall H Educator, Composer

Ross

Adler, Kurt Herbert Conductor,
  Administrator

Sacramento

Barnewitz, A William French Horn
Clayson, Louis O Educator,
  Administrator
Derthick, Thomas V(inton) Double Bass,
  Educator
Eldredge, Steven Coach, Conductor &
  Music Director
Elias, Joel J Trombone, Lecturer
Glovinsky, Ben Composer, Educator
Kingman, Daniel C Composer, Educator
Nice, Carter Music Director &
  Conductor, Violin
Richman, Robin (Beth) Flute, Teacher
Simon, Richard D Critic
Westphal, Frederick William Educator,
  Clarinet

Salinas

Aslanian, Vahe Conductor, Educator
Zumwald-Howard, R Reid Piano,
  Educator

San Diego

Arden, David Mitchell Music Director,
  Piano
Ashmead, Elizabeth Flute & Piccolo
Atherton, David Conductor & Music
  Director, Piano
Christiansen, Larry Arthur Composer,
  Educator
Creston, Paul Composer, Writer
Dutton, Brenton Price Composer, Tuba
Eros, Peter Conductor & Music Director
Galas, Diamanda Angeliki Composer,
  Soprano
Garbutt, Matthew Conductor, Tuba
Hoffman, James Percussion,
  Administrator
Hogg, Merle E Educator, Composer
Kavasch, Deborah Helene Composer,
  Soprano
Kolar, Henry Violin, Conductor
Mracek, Jaroslav John Stephen
  Musicologist, Educator
Philips, Mary Kathryn Educator, Piano
Plantamura, Carol Lynn Soprano,
  Educator
Robboy, R(onald) A Composer, Cello
Rofe, Peter Michael Double Bass
Schmorr, Robert Tenor, Teacher
Teutsch, Walter Conductor & Music
  Director, Educator
West, Stephen Bradford Bass
Wolf, Michael B Double Bass, Composer

San Francisco

Agler, David Conductor
Altman, Ludwig Organ, Composer
Armer, Elinor Florence Composer,
  Teacher
Ballard, Gregory Composer, Piano
Bearer, Elaine Louise Composer,
  Conductor
Bielawa, Herbert Walter Composer,
  Educator
Boone, Charles N Composer
Borda, Deborah A Administrator
Bracchi-Le Roux, Marta N Piano
Braun, Edgar J Music Director &
  Conductor, Viola
Bullin, Christine Neva Administrator
Buyse, Leone Karena Flute & Piccolo,
  Educator
Camajani, Giovanni Conductor, Educator
Cathcart, Kathryn Conductor & Music
  Director, Coach
Chan, Timothy Tai-Wah Violin,
  Conductor & Music Director
Chihuaria, Ernestine (Elizabeth) Riedel
  Violin
Cunningham, Walker Evans Organ,
  Harpsichord
DeCray, Marcella Harp
De Rugeriis, Joseph Carmen Conductor,
  Administrator
De Waart, Edo Music Director &
  Conductor
Dutt, Henry (Allan) Viola
Ehrlich, Don A Viola, Teacher
Eive, Gloria Musicologist, Writer
Erickson, Kaaren (Herr) Soprano
Fischthal, Glenn Jay Trumpet, Teacher
Galante, Jane Hohfeld Piano, Educator
Giacobassi, Julie Ann Oboe & English
  Horn
Girard, Sharon E Educator, Piano
Grossman, Deena Composer
Harrington, David Violin
Hartliep, Nikki Li Soprano

CALIFORNIA (cont)

Heymont, George A Critic-Writer,
    Lecturer
Ho, Cordell Composer
Insko, Wyatt (Marion), III Organ,
    Educator
Jeanrenaud, Joan (Joan Gleeson) Cello
Jenkins, Sylvia Piano, Teacher
Jepson, Warner Composer
Johnson, Rose-Marie Violin, Teacher
Kanouse, Monroe Conductor, Piano
Kovalenko, Oleg Ivanovitch Conductor
Krehbiel, Arthur David French Horn,
    Educator
Le Roux, Jean-Louis Conductor & Music
    Director, Oboe
Ling, Jahja Wang-Chieh Conductor, Piano
Lusk, Ben Terry Coach
McKee, Ross R Educator, Administrator
Malti, Josephine (Jackson) Piano
Marshall, Ingram Douglass Composer,
    Educator
Mechem, Kirke Lewis Composer,
    Conductor
Meltzer, Andrew (Henry) Conductor
Moll, Kurt Bass
Osborne, Donald E(ugene) Artist
    Manager, Administrator
Pastreich, Peter Administrator
Paulson, Stephen Jon Bassoon, Educator
Peterson, Wayne Turner Composer, Piano
Prell, Donald D Double Bass
Sacco, P Peter Composer, Educator
Salkind, Milton Administrator, Piano
Samson, Valerie Brooks Composer,
    Chinese Violin
Schneider, David Hersh Violin, Writer
Sheinfeld, David Composer, Violin
Sherba, John Violin
Snow, Meredith Ann Viola
South, Pamela Soprano
Stapp, Gregory (Lee) Bass
Steinberg, Michael Critic, Lecturer
Susa, Conrad Composer
Sutherland, Robin (Keolahou) Piano,
    Coach
Tircuit, Heuwell Andrew Composer,
    Critic & Writer
Tramontozzi, Stephen Double Bass,
    Teacher
Van Geem, Jack William, Jr Percussion,
    Teacher
Wexler, Stanley A Baritone
Williams, Rick (Frederick Thompson)
    Baritone
Wong, Betty Anne (Siu Junn) Composer,
    Educator
Woodman, Thomas Baritone
Woods, Terri Lynn Soprano
Zeigler, John Robert Clarinet, Educator

San Jose

Cannon, Dwight Educator, Composer
Cleve, George Conductor & Music
    Director
Colby, Edward E(ugene) Librarian,
    Teacher
Herrold, Rebecca Munn Educator, Writer
Jakey, Lauren Ray Conductor, Violin
Loinaz, Yvonne Dalis (Irene Dalis)
    Mezzo-soprano, Administrator
Manning, Robert Double Bass, Educator
Marco, Guy Anthony Writer, Librarian
Onishi, Aiko Educator, Piano
Peterson, Hal (Harold Vaughan)
    Composer, French Horn
Resch, Pamela Pyle Piano
Strange, Allen Composer, Educator
Zes, Tikey A Composer, Educator

San Leandro

Cobb, Donald Lorain Composer, Music
    Director

San Lorenzo

Granger, Lawrence Gordon Cello

San Luis Obispo

Balazs, Frederic Conductor, Violin
Mourant, Walter Byron Composer
Russell, John Gray Piano, Conductor

San Marcos

Mittelmann, Norman Baritone

San Marino

Fajardo, Raoul J Composer, Flute

San Mateo

Nixon, Roger Composer, Educator

San Pedro

Andrews, George Composer, Music
    Director

San Rafael

Khan, Ali Akbar Sarod, Composer
Lawrence, Mark Howard Trombone,
    Educator
Ray, (Sister) Mary Dominic
    Administrator, Lecturer
Sakellariou, George Guitar

Santa Barbara

Applebaum, Edward Composer, Educator
Curtis, Jan (Judith Anne) Mezzo-soprano
Diemer, Emma Lou Composer, Organ
Dunn, Frank Richard Music Director,
    French Horn
Fricker, Peter Racine Composer,
    Educator
Geiringer, Karl J Writer, Educator
Gillespie, John E Educator, Piano
Hsu, Dolores Menstell Educator
Ingham, Michael Curtis Baritone
MacKay, Margery (Margery MacKay
    Anwyl) Mezzo-soprano, Teacher
Mark, Peter Conductor, Viola
Nelson, Wendell A Educator, Piano
Silver, Martin A Librarian, Flute
Singher, Martial Baritone, Teacher-Coach
Stevens, Denis William Administrator,
    Conductor
Wayland, Newton Hart Conductor,
    Composer
Zytowski, Carl Byrd Educator, Conductor

Santa Clara

Nyquist, Roger Thomas Educator, Organ
Shurtleff, Lynn Richard Music Director,
    Composer

Santa Cruz

Anderson, Adrian David Composer
Burman-Hall, Linda Carol Educator,
    Harpsichord
Collins, Philip Michael Composer, Music
    Director
Cope, David Howell Composer, Educator
Hajdu, John Musicologist, Educator
Houghton, Edward Francis Educator,
    Music Director
Klein, Kenneth Conductor & Music
    Director
Mumma, Gordon Composer, Electronic
Nelson, Phillip Francis Educator,
    Administrator

Santa Maria

Kuzell, Christopher Educator, Violin

Santa Monica

Beasley, Rule Curtis Educator, Bassoon
Berman, Marsha F Librarian, Educator
Boerlage, Frans T Stage Director,
    Educator
Crawford, John Charlton Composer,
    Educator
Davison, Peter Saul Composer, Conductor
Goodman, Jeffrey David Guitar & Lute,
    Teacher
Sutherland, Bruce Composer, Piano
Wendel, Dale Soprano

Santa Rosa

Brown, Corrick Lanier Conductor &
    Music Direcctor

Seal Beach

Dallin, Leon Critic-Writer, Composer
Matthews, Justus Frederick Composer,
    Educator
Parker, Alan Music Director, Cello
Rudis, Al (A L) Critic

Sherman Oaks

Chauls, Robert N Composer, Conductor
Lebow, Leonard S Composer, Trumpet
Lowy, Jay Stanton Administrator
Mollicone, Henry Composer, Conductor
Purcell, Ron (Ronald Charles) Educator,
    Guitar & Lute

Solana Beach

Pasler, Jann Corinne Writer, Educator

Soquel

Barati, George Composer, Conductor &
    Music Director

Stanford

Benson, Joan Clavichord & Fortepiano,
    Lecturer
Berger, Karol Educator, Writer
Cohen, Albert Educator, Writer
Jaffe, David Aaron Composer, Mandolin
Mahrt, William Peter Musicologist, Music
    Director
Ratner, Leonard Gilbert Educator,
    Lecturer
Smith, Douglas Alton Writer, Guitar &
    Lute
Smith, Leland Clayton Composer,
    Educator

Stinson Beach

McAnaney, Harold Composer

Stockton

Beckler, S R (Stanworth Russell)
    Composer, Educator
Caviani, Ronald Joseph Composer,
    Educator
Etlinger, H Richard Educator,
    Administrator
Fetsch, Wolfgang Educator, Piano
Nosse, Carl E Administrator, Composer
Schilling, Charles Walter Organ, Educator
Tatman, Neil Oboe, Educator
Tatton, Thomas Educator, Conductor
van Bronkhorst, Warren Educator, Violin
Whitesides, William (Plaxico), Jr
    Educator, Tenor
Wiens, Frank Piano, Educator
Won, Kyung-Soo Conductor & Music
    Director, Violin

Studio City

Almeida, Laurindo Guitar, Composer
Campo, Frank Philip Composer
de Filippi, Amedeo Composer
Winters, Barbara Jo Oboe

Sunnyvale

Darter, Thomas E Conductor, Critic-Writer
Selfridge-Field, Eleanor A Writer, Lecturer

Tarzana

Schneider, John Owsley Guitar, Writer
Tusler, Robert Leon Educator, Organ

The Sea Ranch

Wood, (Charles) Dale Composer, Writer
Wood, Gloria Bakkila Soprano, Writer

Tiburon

Thomas, Jess Tenor, Teacher

Topanga

Andrus, Donald George Composer, Educator
Curry, Donna (Jayne) Lute, Teacher-Coach

Torrance

Harness, William Edward Tenor
Najera, Edmund L Composer, Educator

Truckee

van Boer, Bertil Herman Conductor, Educator

Turlock

Harder, Paul Educator, Composer

Tustin

Derby, Richard William Composer, Educator

Valencia

Guarneri, Mario Trumpet
Mitzelfelt, H(arold) Vincent Conductor & Music Director, Cello
Powell, Mel Composer
Schrader, Barry Walter Composer, Educator
Subotnick, Morton Composer, Educator

Van Nuys

Hudson, Richard Albert Educator, Writer
Jergenson, Dale Roger Composer, Tenor
Mayeur, Robert Gordon Teacher, Composer
Mercurio, Peter Amedeo Double Bass, Educator
Raksin, David Composer, Conductor
Schiavone, John (Sebastian) Composer

Venice

Cave, Michael Composer, Piano

Ventura

Walker, Donald Burke Composer

Walnut Creek

Lawson, Alice (Alice Lawson Aber) Harp

West Covina

Mullins, Hugh E Composer, Educator

Westwood

Cantrell, Byron Composer, Musicologist

Whittier

Crozier, Catharine (Catharine C Gleason) Educator, Organ
Ochse, Orpha Caroline Educator, Composer
Spencer, Williametta Composer, Educator
Young, Anne Lloyd Clarinet, Educator

Woodland Hills

Bradshaw, Murray Charles Writer, Organ
Coppola, Carmine (Carmen) Composer, Conductor
Hatcher, William B Educator, Conductor
Richards, William Henry Educator, Piano
Rodby, John Leonard Composer, Piano

Yorba Linda

Stewart, Robert John Composer

COLORADO

Alamosa

Wienand, Marilyn M Educator, Singer

Aurora

Small, Edward Pierce Percussion, Educator

Boulder

Aaholm, Philip Eugene Clarinet, Educator
Bull, Storm Educator, Piano
Coffin, (Roscoe) Berton Educator, Writer
Collins, Walter Stowe Writer, Educator
Dickey, Louise (Parke) Flute & Piccolo
Doscher, Barbara M Educator, Mezzo-soprano
Eakin, Charles Educator, Composer
Effinger, Cecil Stanley Composer, Educator
Ellsworth, Oliver Bryant Educator, Writer
Fink, Robert Russell Administrator, Educator
Gonzalez, Luis Jorge Composer, Educator
Hale, Ruth June Clarinet, Teacher
Hayes, Deborah Educator, Writer
Jackson, Dennis Clark Educator, Baritone
Kearns, William Kay Educator, French Horn
Koromzay, Denes Kornel Viola, Educator
Kroeger, Karl Composer, Musicologist
McNeil, Jan Pfischner (Janet Louise Pfischner) Composer, Educator
Paton, John Glenn Tenor, Teacher
Pinkow, David J French Horn, Educator
Renwick, Wilke Richard French Horn, Composer
Sable, Barbara Kinsey Critic-Writer, Educator
Toensing, Richard E Composer, Educator

Colorado Springs

Ansbacher, Charles Alexander Conductor & Music Director, Educator
Arms, Margaret Fairchild Soprano, Teacher
Gamer, Carlton E Composer, Educator
Jenkins, Donald P Music Director & Conductor, Educator
Jorgensen, Jerilyn Violin
Lynn, George Composer, Educator
Seay, Albert Writer, Educator

Denver

Aybar, Francisco (Rene) Piano, Educator
Baskerville, David Composer, Educator
Davine, Robert A Educator, Concert Accordion
Delogu, Gaetano Music Director & Conductor
Di Julio, Max (Joseph) Educator, Composer

Feinsmith, Marvin P Composer, Bassoon
Giffin, Glenn Critic-Writer
Hill, William Randall Percussion
Jones, Roland Leo Violin, Teacher
Kaslow, David Martin French Horn, Educator
Kireilis, Ramon J Clarinet, Educator
Lichtmann, Theodor David Piano, Educator
Lockington, David Kirkman Conductor & Music Director, Cello
Lockwood, Normand Composer, Educator
Maurer, James Carl Violin, Educator
Potter, David Kinsman Double Bass, Educator
Pritts, Roy A Composer, Educator
Roberts, William L Percussion
Scheller, Stanley Bassoon, Educator
Schroeder-Sheker, Therese M Harp, Editor
Setapen, James Anthony Conductor & Music Director
Smith, Pamela G Oboe & English Horn
Wolf, Phillip S Administrator, Patron
Worstell, Ronald A Educator, Baritone

Englewood

de Lemos, Jurgen Hermann Cello, Conductor & Music Director
Keats, Donald H(oward) Composer, Educator
Wilson, Antonia Joy Conductor, Teacher

Estes Park

Wylie, Ruth Shaw Composer, Educator

Evergreen

Stein, Ronald Composer, Educator

Ft Collins

McCray, James Joseph Heldentenor, Educator
Runyan, William Edward Educator, Conductor
Schwartz, Wilfred (Will) Conductor, Violin

Greeley

Bailey, James Conductor, Cello
Bartlett, Loren W Educator, Bassoon
Copley, R Evan Educator, Composer
Ehle, Robert Cannon Composer, Electronic
Greenberg, Roger D Saxophone, Educator
Linscome, Sanford Abel Educator, Singer
Rhoads, Mary Ruth Educator, Composer
Savig, Norman Ingolf Librarian, Cello
Studebaker, Donald W Conductor, Baritone
Upton, James Southerland Educator

Gunnison

Ash, Rodney P Composer, Educator

Lakewood

Herren, Lloyd K, Sr Educator, Administration
Primus, Constance Merrill Teacher, Recorder
Smith, Terry James Percussion

Littleton

Pasztor, Stephen Clarinet

Pueblo

Cedrone, Frank Joseph Piano, Educator
Maihart-Track, Micaela Piano
Markowski, Victoria Piano, Educator
Track, Gerhard Conductor & Music Director, Composer

CONNECTICUT

Bethel
Ptaszynska, Marta Composer, Percussion

Bloomfield
De Moura Castro, Luiz Piano, Educator
Mishkind, Abraham Educator, Conductor

Branford
Palisca, Claude V Educator, Writer
Wentzel, Rubi V Cello, Educator

Bridgeport
Day, Richard Wrisley Critic
Greenawalt, Terrence Lee Conductor, Piano
McKee, Richard Donald, II Bass

Bridgewater
Wooldridge, David H M Composer, Conductor & Music Director

Brookfield
Nagel, Robert E, Jr Trumpet, Composer

Clinton
Baxter, Charles Allen French Horn

Cornwall Bridge
Stone, Kurt Music Editor, Writer

Danbury
Burkat, Leonard Writer, Administrator
Burkat, Marion F (Gumner) Editor
Godel, Edith Librarian
Huntley, Lawrence Don Educator, French Horn

Darien
Larue, Adrian Jan Pieters Educator, Writer

East Granby
Dunn, Mignon (Mignon Dunn-Klippstatter) Mezzo-soprano
Klippstatter, Kurt L Educator, Music Director

East Lyme
Bulmer, Steven Robert Tuba, Electric Bass

Easton
Jablonsky, Stephen Educator, Composer

Fairfield
Ross, Ruth Lampland Critic-Writer

Greenwich
Leniado-Chira, Joseph Conductor & Music Director, Composer
McCarthy, Kevin Joseph Piano, Lecturer
Varsano, Daniel Piano

Guilford
Auld, Louis Eugene Administrator, Educator
Kirkpatrick, Ralph Harpsichord, Educator
Parisot, Aldo Simoes Cello, Educator

Hamden
Krigbaum, Charles Russell Educator, Organ
Samuel, Harold Eugene Librarian, Educator

Hartford
Boonshaft, Peter Loel Music Director
Byrnes, Kevin Michael Viola, Composer
Celli, Joseph Robert Oboe, Lecturer
Krieger, Jeffrey Stephen Cello

Martin, Vernon Librarian, Composer
Osborne, George D Administrator
Rauche, Anthony Theodore Educator, Piano
Rose, John Educator, Organ
Sellars, James Composer, Piano
Winograd, Arthur Conductor & Music Director

Hebron
Provost, Richard (Charles) Educator, Guitar & Lute

Mansfield Center
Harman, David Rex Clarinet, Conductor

Mansfield Depot
Laszloffy, Jerome Conductor, Educator

Middletown
Bruce, Frank Neely Composer, Educator
Lucier, Alvin Augustus Educator, Composer
Ranganathan, Tanjore Mrdangam, Educator
Slobin, Mark Educator

New Britain
Welwood, Arthur Composer, Educator

New Canaan
Celestino, Thomas Tenor
Heller, Joan Soprano, Educator
Walker, Gwyneth V Composer, Educator

New Hartford
Angarano, Anthony Critic, Administrator

New Haven
Aki, Syoko Violin, Educator
Blaustein, Susan Composer
Bresnick, Martin Composer, Educator
Brion, (K) Keith Conductor & Music Director, Educator
Cardell, Victor Thomas Librarian
Currier, Donald Robert Piano, Educator
Duffy, Thomas C Composer, Conductor & Music Director
Emerson, Gordon Clyde Critic, Music Director
Feldman, Grace Ann Viola da Gamba, Teacher
French, Richard Frederic Musicologist, Educator
Jolas, Betsy Composer, Educator
Kantor, Paul M Violin, Teacher-Coach
Mueller, Otto Werner Conductor, Educator
Murray, Thomas Organ, Educator
Nyfenger, Thomas Flute, Educator
Panetti, Joan Composer, Educator
Plantinga, Leon Brooks Musicologist, Educator
Radnofsky, Kenneth Saxophone, Educator
Ruff, Willie Educator
Tirro, Frank Pascale Administrator, Writer
Weisberg, Arthur Educator, Bassoon
Wilson, Keith Leroy Clarinet, Educator

Newington
Riley, John Arthur Composer, Cello

New London
Stoner, Thomas Alan Educator, Organist

Old Greenwich
Fink, Myron S Composer, Educator

Old Lyme
Franchetti, Arnold Composer

Orange
Brooks, William F Composer, Writer
Harger, Gary Tenor

Quaker Hill
Bitgood, Roberta (Roberta Bitgood Wiersma) Organ, Composer

Ridgefield
Fleck, William Scott Bass
Themmen, Ivana Composer, Piano
Van Lidth De Jeude, (C) Philip (J) Composer, Baritone

Rocky Hill
Van Ohlen, Deborah S Composer

Roxbury
Moryl, Richard Henry Composer, Music Director

Shelton
Fishbein, Michael Ellis Composer

Sherman
Stearns, Peter Pindar Educator, Composer

Simsbury
Kosloff, Doris Lang Music Director, Coach
Molava, Pamela May Composer, Lecturer
Stowe, Anhared Wiest Violin, Teacher

Southport
Cole, Ulric Composer, Piano

Stamford
Brown, Beatrice Conductor, Viola
Macurdy, John Bass
Paymer, Marvin E Administrator, Composer

Storrs
Bognar, Dorothy McAdoo Educator, Librarian
Eversole, James A Composer, Educator
Gillespie, Allan E Educator, Conductor
Heller, Jack Joseph Administrator, Conductor & Music Director
Smith, Charles Justice Educator, Writer
Smith, Hale Composer, Educator
Somer, Avo Composer, Educator

Stratford
Evans, Joseph Tenor

Waterbury
Verdery, Benjamin Francis Guitar & Lute

Westbrook
Morris, Stephen MacKay Composer, Lecturer

West Hartford
Ashens, Robert J, III Conductor, Coach
Bonacini, Renato Violin, Educator
Bruck, Charles Conductor, Educator
Dashnaw, Alexander Educator, Conductor & Music Director
Diard, William Educator, Voice
Diemente, Edward Philip Composer, Educator
Garbousova, Raya (Raya Garbousova-Biss) Cello, Educator
Hanson, Raymond Piano, Educator
Harris, Donald Composer, Administrator
Hoffman, Allen Composer
Holtz, John Educator, Music Director

Ingraham, Paul French Horn, Educator
Jackson, Douglas Educator, Percussion
Karr, Gary Michael Double Bass,
　Educator
Koret, Arthur (Solomon) Educator, Tenor
Koscielny, Anne Piano
Larsen, Henry Clarinet, Composer
Lepak, Alexander Educator, Percussion
Lewis, Harmon Harpsichord Organ
Lurie, Bernard Violin, Educator
Mack, Gerald Conductor, Educator
Perry, Stephen Bruce Tuba
Putsche, Thomas Reese Composer,
　Educator
Schaffer, Robert Carlton Educator,
　Bassoon
Schwager, Myron August Educator,
　Writer
Tolo, Leland Stanford Educator, Double
　Bass
Treger, Charles Violin, Educator
Wells, David Cello, Educator
Willett, William Educator, Woodwinds
Zei, John Educator, Baritone

West Haven

Luchsinger, Ronald Director-Opera,
　Educator

Weston

Barnett, David Piano, Composer
Perlis, Vivian Writer, Educator

Westport

Coss, (Sarah) Elizabeth Coach, Soprano
Solum, John H Flute, Educator
Spivakovsky, Tossy Violin, Educator
Valante, Harrison R Conductor,
　Administrator

West Redding

Kipnis, Igor Harpsichord, Writer

Wilton

Brings, Allen Stephen Composer, Piano
Schneidmann, Irene Piano, Educator

DELAWARE

Milford

Heyde, Norma L Educator, Soprano

Newark

Bates, Leon Piano, Educator
Bunch, Meribeth Ann Voice Consultant,
　Educator
Cady, Henry Lord Educator, Writer
Hofstetter, Fred Thomas Educator,
　Administrator
Hogenson, Robert Charles Composer,
　Piano
McCarthy, Peter Joseph Music Director,
　Educator
Peterson, Larry W Administrator,
　Educator
Zinn, Michael A Composer, Educator

Seaford

Mulford, Ruth Stomne Educator, Violin

Wilmington

Brown, David Auldon Composer,
　Educator
Gunzenhauser, Stephen Charles Music
　Director & Conductor
Harvey, Marion Bradley Educator, Singer
Otey, Orlando Piano, Teacher

DISTRICT OF COLUMBIA

Washington

Allen, Robin Perry Administrator, Writer
Ames, F(rank) Anthony Administrator,
　Percussion
Anderson, Gillian Bunshaft Music
　Director, Librarian
Bales, Richard Henry Horner Composer,
　Conductor & Music Director
Berlinski, Herman Composer, Organ
Bickley, Thomas Frank Composer,
　Recorder
Black, Ralph Artist Manager
Blumfield, Coleman Piano
Braunlich, Helmut Educator, Composer
Bryant, Carolyn Frances Writer
Chevallard, (Philip) Carl Conductor &
　Music Director, Educator
Costa, Mary Soprano
de Bohun, Lyle (Clara Lyle Boone)
　Administrator, Composer
Dobbs, Mattiwilda Soprano, Educator
Ellinwood, Leonard Webster Writer
Fesperman, John, Jr Educator, Director
　Music
Fowler, Charles Bruner Writer
French, Catherine Administrator
Gabriel, Arnald D Conductor, Educator
Harpham, Virginia Ruth Violin
Hobson, Constance Yvonne Tibbs
　Educator, Piano
Hoover, Cynthia Adams Administrator
Hubner, Carla (Carla V Hubner-Kraemer)
　Piano, Teacher-Coach
Jones, George Thaddeus Composer,
　Educator
Kagan, Martin I Administrator
Kellock, James Robert Administrator,
　French Horn
Kendall, Christopher Wolff Conductor,
　Lute
Kohno, Toshiko Flute & Piccolo
Kojian, Miran Haig Violin, Educator
McGinty, Doris Evans Educator
McLellan, Joseph Duncan Critic
Mandel, Alan Roger Piano, Educator
Mastroianni, Thomas Owen Educator,
　Piano
O'Reilly, F(rank) Warren Critic-Writer,
　Educator
Pasmanick, Kenneth Educator, Bassoon
Platthy, Jeno Composer, Critic-Writer
Rostropovich, Mstislav Conductor &
　Music Director, Cello
Sapieyevski, Jerzy Composer
Scavelli, Ramon Louis Viola, Educator
Schifter, Peter Mark Director-Opera
Schuetze, George Claire, Jr Educator,
　Writer
Scribner, Norman Orville Conductor,
　Composer
Seyfrit, Michael E Administrator, Early
　Woodwinds
Shirley, Wayne D(ouglas) Librarian
Small, Haskell Behrend Piano, Composer
Sommerfield, David Fredic Librarian
Steele, Lynn Composer
Strunk, Steven (Gerhardt) Composer,
　Educator
Thorin, Suzanne Elizabeth Librarian,
　Administrator
Tobin, Robert Lynn Batts Administrator
Vishnevskaya, Galina Soprano
Vrenios, Anastasios Nicholas Tenor
Wagoner, James D Composer, Writer
Waters, Edward Neighbor Librarian
Weinreb, Alice Kogan Flute & Piccolo,
　Educator
Yarborough, William Conductor & Music
　Director

FLORIDA

Altamonte Springs

Mascaro, Arnold John, Jr French Horn,
　Teacher

Boca Raton

Burganger, Judith Piano, Educator

Bradenton

Bram, Marjorie Viola, Educator
Donato, Anthony Composer, Violin

Cape Coral

Appelman, Ralph Bass, Educator

Coconut Grove

McLean, Edwin W Composer, Piano
Waters, Willie Anthony Conductor &
　Music Director, Administrator

Coral Gables

Boyle, J David Educator, Administrator
Davis, Ivan Piano, Educator
Drew, Lucas Double Bass, Educator
Hipp, James William Administrator,
　Educator
Lafford, Lindsay Arthur Educator, Organ
Lee, William Franklin, III Administrator,
　Composer
Moore, Thomas Violin
Reed, Alfred Composer, Conductor &
　Music Director
Thompson, Hugh R Baritone, Director-
　Opera

Ft Lauderdale

Gill, Richard Thomas Bass
Lear, Evelyn Soprano
Smith, Tim (Timothy Paul) Critic

Ft Myers

Deibler, Arlo C I Music Director,
　Administrator

Gainesville

Bodine, Willis (Ramsey), Jr Organ,
　Educator
Bowles, Richard William Composer,
　Conductor
Fouse, Sarah Baird Flute, Educator
Hale, James Pierce Educator, Percussion
Jaeger, Ina Claire Educator, Violin
Kushner, David Zakeri Educator,
　Adminstrator
Penland, Arnold Clifford, Jr
　Administrator, Educator
Poe, Gerald Dean Music Director,
　Educator
Troupin, Edward Composer, Educator
Udell, Budd A Educator, Composer
White, John D Composer, Cello

Jacksonville

Brown, William Albert Educator, Tenor
Carlson, Jon O Educator, Music Director
Flagello, Ezio D Bass
Hoffren, James A Educator, Trumpet
Hoskins, William Barnes Composer,
　Educator
Jones, Jeanne Nannette Violin
Kaye, Bernard L Flute & Piccolo, Clarinet
Krosnick, Aaron Burton Violin, Educator
Krosnick, Mary Lou Wesley Piano,
　Composer
Mabrey, Charlotte Newton Educator,
　Percussion
Newton, Clifford Hammond Trumpet
Page, Willis Conductor & Music Director
Schirmer, William Louis Composer,
　Educator
Smith, Amelia (Hall) Music Director,
　Teacher-Coach

FLORIDA (cont)

Stanley, Helen Camille (Helen Stanley Gatlin) Composer, Piano
Svoboda, Richard Alan Bassoon
Vessels, William Allen Administrator, Educator
Wright, Peter B, III Clarinet, Educator

Largo

Maresca, Rosalia Soprano, Administrator

Lutz

Hoffman, Theodore B Composer, Educator

Miami

Barr, Raymond Arthur Educator, Writer
Beglarian, Grant Composer, Administrator
Benoit, Kenneth Roger Composer, Librarian
Campbell, Charles Joseph Composer, Educator
Crager, Ted J Administrator, Educator
Davidson, Joy Elaine Mezzo-soprano
Dines, Burton Conductor, Cello
Drennan, Dorothy Carter Writer, Composer
Edmondson, John Baldwin Composer, Editor
Fink, Philip H Educator, Composer
Floyd, J(ames) Robert Composer, Piano
Harris, Daniel Alfred Teacher, Baritone
Kam, Dennis Koon Ming Composer, Educator
Kite-Powell, Jeffery Thomas Educator, Renaissance Woodwinds
Roos, James (Michael) Critic
Rowley, Vera Newstead Piano, Soprano
Star, Cheryl Mc Whorter Educator, Flute
Stoeppelmann, Janet Composer, Educator
Summers, William Franklin Educator, Bass
Youngblood, Joseph Edward Educator, Piano

Miami Beach

Breeskin, Barnett Conductor
Munar, Alfredo Conductor & Music Director, Administrator

North Miami Beach

Buckley, Emerson Conductor & Music Director, Administrator
Buckley, Mary Henderson Teacher, Soprano

Orlando

Blice, Carolyn MacDowell French Horn, Manager
Mascaro, Janet Persons Oboe
Morehouse, Dale W Conductor & Music Director, Baritone
Morrell, Barbara Jane Viola, Violin
Ross, Rick Coach, Organ
Rothstein, Sidney Music Director & Conductor
Threatte, Linda Krebs Flute

Pensacola

Clarke, William (Jay) Conductor & Music Director, Educator
Rawlins, Joseph (Thomas) Educator, Tenor
Williams, Grier Moffatt Educator, Conductor & Music Director

Riverview

Hall, Carl David Flute, Teacher

St Petersburg

Carroll, Charles Michael Educator, Critic-Writer
Hoffman, Irwin Conductor & Music Director
Johnson, A Paul Composer, Music Director

Sarasota

Fleming, Millicent Clow Administrator

Sun City Center

Helps, Robert Eugene Composer, Piano

Tallahassee

Bjerregaard, Carl Educator
Boda, John Composer, Educator
Bridger, Carolyn Educator, Piano
Capps, William French Horn, Educator
Carter, Charles Composer
Ciannella, Yvonne Educator, Voice
Clarke, Karen Violin, Educator
Corzine, Michael Organ, Educator
Dann, Elias Educator, Conductor & Music Director
DeLaney, Charles Oliver Composer, Educator
Drinkall, Roger Lee Cello
Ford, Barbara Educator, Soprano
Fowler, Nancy Oboe, Educator
Glidden, Robert Burr Educator, Administrator
Goff, Bryan Trumpet, Educator
Grimm, Betty Jane Educator, Soprano
Harsanyi, Janice Soprano, Educator
Housewright, Wiley Lee Educator, Administrator
Johnson, Grace Grey Educator, Piano
Johnson, Roy Henry Educator, Composer
Kilenyi, Edward Educator, Piano
Kirk, Colleen Jean Music Director, Educator
Krehbiel, Clayton Educator, Tenor
Lipovetsky, Leonidas Piano, Educator
Madsen, Clifford K Educator
Moeckel, Rainier Viola, Educator
Olsen, Dale Alan Educator, Shakuhachi
Perry-Camp, Jane (Schiffman) Educator, Piano
Roman, Mary Brigid Harp
Schiffman, Harold (Anthony) Composer, Educator
Seaton, (Stuart) Douglass Educator, Writer
Smith, Robert Ludwig Educator
Spencer, Peter Educator
Spurgeon, Phillip (Coleman) Conductor & Music Director, Educator
Taylor, Jack A Educator, Administrator
Urquhart, Dan Murdock Composer, Educator
Werdesheim, Gary Educator, Percussion
Winstead, William Educator, Composer
Wright, Thomas G Piano, Composer

Tampa

Albers, Bradley Gene Composer, Educator
Klein, Kristine J Librarian
Rearick, Martha Nell Educator, Flute & Piccolo
Robison, John Orian Educator, Lute
Watkins, Armin J Educator, Conductor
Woodbury, Arthur Neum Composer, Writer

West Palm Beach

Firestone, Adria (Belinda) Mezzo-soprano

Winter Park

Emig, Lois Irene Composer
Lackman, Susan Cohn Composer, Educator
LeRoy, Edmund Educator, Baritone
Petta, Robert Michael Percussion, Teacher
Savia, Alfred Conductor
Whisler, Bruce Allen Educator
Woodbury, Ward Leland Conductor & Music Director, Educator
Wrancher, Elizabeth Ann Educator, Soprano

GEORGIA

Athens

Arant, (Everett) Pierce, Jr Music Director, Tenor
Boardman, David Robeson Percussion, Composer
Corina, John Hubert Composer, Oboe
Dancz, Roger Lee Conductor, Educator
Dressler, John Clay French Horn, Educator
Howell, Almonte Charles, Jr Musicologist, Educator
Jameson, R Philip Educator, Trombone
Ligotti, Albert F Conductor, Trumpet
Lowe, Donald Robert Educator
Parker, Olin Griffith Educator, Administrator
Thompson, Glenda Goss Educator
Verrastro, Ralph Edward Administrator, Educator
Vogel, Roger Craig Composer, Educator
Waln, Ronald Lee Educator, Flute

Atlanta

Baker, Norman Louis Clarinet
Bishop, Martha (Jane) Viola da Gamba, Editor
Browning, Zack David Composer, Trumpet
Cook, Rebecca Soprano
Duncan, Charles F, Jr Writer, Guitar & Lute
Du Page, Florence Elizabeth Composer, Music Director
Gerschefski, Martha Cello, Educator
Gorelkin, Paula Rath Piano, Educator
Haberlen, John B Educator, Music Director
Harrower, Peter (Stillwell) Bass, Educator
Hoogerwerf, Frank William Administrator, Educator
Knox, Charles Composer, Educator
Kopleff, Florence Singer, Educator
Kopp, James B Librarian, Administrator
McFarland, J Patrick Oboe & English Horn
O'Neal, Michael M Conductor & Music Director, Tenor
Orr, Nathaniel Leon Educator, Organ
Robinson, Richard Composer, Violin
Schmidt, Dale Bass
Schneider, John Critic-Writer, Educator
Schneider, June Composer, Educator
Shaw, Robert Lawson Conductor & Music Director
Stegall, Sydney Wallace Composer, Writer
Thoreson, Thomas J Double Bass, Educator
Winick, Steven David Educator, Trumpet

Augusta

Fominaya, Eloy Educator, Administrator

Carrollton

Coe, Robert M Administrator, Educator

Columbus

Bullock, William Joseph Conductor,
Educator
Mahan, Katherine Hines Educator, Writer
O'Brien, John Thomas Educator, Piano
White, Elwood Lauriston French Horn,
Librarian

Decatur

Ashley, Douglas Daniels Piano, Educator
Lewis, (John) Cary Piano, Educator

East Point

Robinson, Florence Claire Crim Educator,
Piano

Hiawassee

Gerschefski, Edwin Composer, Educator

Macon

Anderson, Fletcher Clark Educator
Marshall, Howard Lowen Educator,
Administrator

Marietta

Morgan, Mac (R) Baritone

Mt Berry

Pethel, Stan (Stanley Robert) Composer,
Trombone
Robison, William H, III Educator,
Trumpet

Norcross

Henigbaum, John French Horn

Rome

Josephson, Kenneth George Composer,
Cello

Roswell

Lund, Floice Rhodes Music Director,
Writer

St Simons Island

de Volt, Charlotte (Charlotte de Volt
Elder) Violin

Savannah

Luxner, Michael David Conductor &
Music Director, Educator
Wheeler, Bruce Raymond Trumpet

Sea Island

de Volt, Artiss Harp, Educator

Statesboro

Fields, Warren Carl Educator, Conductor
Mathew, David (Wylie), III Composer,
Music Director

Stone Mountain

Gross, Steven Lee French Horn

Watkinsville

Jahn, Theodore Lee Clarinet, Educator

HAWAII

Hilo

Staton, Kenneth Wayne Educator,
Composer

Honolulu

Barrett, Paul H Bassoon, Educator
Cornwell, Richard Warren Administrator,
Critic-Writer

Driver, Howard (Glen) Critic-Writer
Engelhardt, Douglas Gustav Educator,
Music Director
Freitas, Beebe Artistic Director
Garabedian, Armen Violin, Teacher
Greenberg, Marvin Educator
Hines, Robert Stephan Administrator,
Conductor
Hotoke, Shigeru Conductor & Music
Director, Tenor
Johanos, Donald Music Director &
Conductor
Johansson, Annette Mezzo-soprano,
Educator
LaMarchina, Robert A Conductor &
Music Director
Lee, Byong Won Educator
Lum, Richard S Conductor, Educator
McKay, Neil Composer, Educator
Pena, Angel Matias Composer, Double
Bass
Pologe, Steven Cello
Roberts, Gertrud K Harpsichord,
Composer
Russell, Armand King Composer,
Educator
Russell, Lois Roberta Langley Percussion
Schweitzer, Marsha L Bassoon,
Administrator
Trubitt, Allen R Composer, Educator
White, Duane Craig Violin
Yasui, Byron K Composer, Double Bass
Yoshioka, Emmett Gene Composer, Flute

Kailua

Harling, Jean M Flute, Educator

Kailua Kona

Tanner, Jerre E Composer, Music
Director

Kaneohe

Mount, John Wallace Bass-Baritone,
Educator
Sterling, Lorna (Lorna Bodum Sterling
Mount) Mezzo-soprano, Teacher

IDAHO

Boise

Baldassarre, Joseph Anthony Guitar &
Lute, Educator
Baldwin, John Educator, Percussion
Bratt, C(harles) Griffith Composer, Organ
Elliott, Wilber D Educator, Music
Director
Hsu, Madeleine Educator, Piano
Schroeder, Gerald H Educator
Shelton, Melvin Leroy Educator
Stern, Daniel David Music Director,
Educator

Moscow

Billingsley, William Allen Composer,
Trumpet
Hahn, Sandra Lea Composer, Piano
Klimko, Ronald James Educator, Bassoon
Steinke, Greg A Oboe, Composer

Pocatello

Stanek, Alan Edward Clarinet, Educator

Rexburg

Barrus, Charles LaMar, Jr Educator,
Conductor
Chugg, M David Educator

ILLINOIS

Bloomington

Lewis, Arthur Viola, Educator
Watkins, R Bedford Educator, Composer

Bourbonnais

Hopkins, Harlow Eugene Administrator,
Conductor

Brookfield

Pick, Richard Samuel Burns Guitar,
Teacher

Carbondale

Barwick, Steven Educator, Piano
Bergt, Robert Roland Conductor,
Teacher-Coach
Breznikar, Joseph (John) Guitar, Educator
Coker, Wilson Composer, Educator
Gordon, Roderick Dean Educator, Oboe
& English Horn
Hunt, Charles B, Jr Educator
Mueller, Robert E Educator, Writer
Webb, Marianne Educator, Organ
Wursten, Richard Bruce Librarian, Piano

Champaign

Bays, Robert Earl Adminstrator, Educator
Fredrickson, (Lawrence) Thomas
Composer, Educator
Krolick, Edward (John) Double Bass,
Educator
Lipp, Charles Herbert Composer, Bassoon
McClellan, William Monson Librarian,
Educator
Magyar, Gabriel Educator, Cello
Melby, John (B), Jr Composer
Nettl, Bruno Educator
Schleis, Thomas Henry Educator
Von Gunden, Heidi Cecilia Educator,
Writer

Charleston

Appleby, David P Educator, Piano
Hardin, Burton Ervin French Horn,
Composer
Johnson, June Durkin Educator, Soprano
Zwicky, Gary Lee Educator, Organ

Chicago

Akos, Francis Violin, Conductor & Music
Director
Austin, John (Bradbury) Composer
Bartoletti, Bruno Conductor
Beacraft, Ross (Orton) Trumpet, Lecturer
Bergersen, Charlotte (Charlotte Bergersen
Chevalier) Piano, Teacher-Coach
Bergman, Janet Louise Marx Flute,
Educator
Blackwood, Easley Composer, Piano
Blodgett, David Murray Administrator
Boldrey, Richard (Lee) Conductor, Piano
Brown, Howard Mayer Educator,
Musicologist
Buccheri, Elizabeth Piano, Teacher-Coach
Bullat, George J Nicholas Organ,
Educator
Coombs, Daniel Raymond Composer,
Music Director
Cowles, Darleen L Composer, Educator
D'Albert, Francois J Violin, Educator
Daley, Joseph Albert Tenor Saxophone,
Teacher
Danielle, Ruth Soprano, Teacher
Denov, Sam Percussion, Educator
de Vale, Sue Carole Harp, Educator
Druzinsky, Edward Harp
Dutton, James N Conductor & Music
Director, Administrator
Edwards, John S Administrator
Ehrlich, Clara Siegel Piano, Educator

ILLINOIS (cont)

Elliot, Gladys Crisler Oboe, Educator
Elliot, Willard Somers Composer, Bassoon
Epstein, Dena Julia Librarian, Writer
Etzel, Marion Educator, Violin
Evans, Audrey Ferro Piano, Teacher
Favario, Giulio Conductor, Teacher-Coach
Ferris, William Composer, Music Director
Filler, Susan M Editor, Lecturer
Flynn, George William Composer, Piano
Frank, Gregory Bass
Fraser, Barbara Violin
Fromm, Paul Patron, Administrator
Geller, Ian Composer, Conductor
Gingrich, Daniel J French Horn
Gossett, Philip Educator, Writer
Gratovich, Eugene Violin, Educator
Gustafson, Lee Teacher
Hall, Thomas Munroe Violin
Hilkevitch, Joyce Turner Administrator, Lecturer
Kamsler, Bruce H Director-Opera, Piano
Kanter, Richard S Oboe
Kaplan, William Meyer Educator
Kober, Dieter Conductor & Music Director, Educator
Kopp, Leo Laszlo Conductor & Music Director, Educator
Kranz, Maria Hinrichs Educator, Piano
Lee, Soo Chul Violin, Educator
Lefferts, Peter Martin Educator, Lecturer
Lenneberg, Hans Educator, Writer
Levin, Rami Yona Composer, Oboe
Levitin, Susan Flute
Lombardo, Robert Michael Composer, Educator
Lubin, Abraham Baritone, Lecturer
Lyne, Gregory Kent Conductor & Music Director, Educator
Mach, Elyse Janet Educator, Writer
Marderosian, Ardash Trombone, Teacher
Marsh, Robert C Critic
Matesky, Elisabeth Anne Violin, Teacher
Mazer, Henry Conductor & Music Director
Meine, Evelyn DeVivo Administrator
Menard, Pierre Jules Educator, Violin
Merker, K Ethel French Horn, Educator
Monaco, Richard A Composer, Educator
Morehead, Philip David Conductor & Music Director, Teacher
Muenzer, Edgar C Violin, Educator
Myers, Kurtz Librarian
Paperno, Dmitry A Piano, Educator
Peck, Donald Vincent Flute, Educator
Pikler, Charles Robert Violin
Podolsky, Leo S Piano, Educator
Quinn, James Joseph Composer, Educator
Raitt, John Wellesley Bassoon, Educator
Ran, Shulamit Composer, Educator
Richardson, Lorene Singer, Music Director
Rizzer, Gerald Marvin Piano, Composer
Ross, James Ramsey Percussion
Russo, William Composer, Writer
Schaenen, Lee Conductor, Administrator
Schwegel, Richard C Librarian
Shapey, Ralph Composer, Conductor & Music Director
Simpson, Wilbur Herman Bassoon, Educator
Snyder, Bill (William Paul) Composer, Piano
Solomonow, Rami Viola, Teacher
Solti, Georg Conductor & Music Director
Spina, Salvatore C Piano, Educator
Stein, Leon Composer, Conductor
Still, Ray Oboe, Educator
Stokman, Abraham Piano, Educator
Szkodzinski, Louise Educator, Piano

Voketaitis, Arnold (Mathew) Bass, Teacher
von Rhein, John Richard Critic-Writer, Lecturer
Vorrasi, John Frederick Tenor, Administrator
Wilding-White, Raymond Educator, Composer

Darien

Floyd, Samuel Alexander Educator, Administrator

Decatur

Fiol, Stephen Frank Educator, Baritone
Mancinelli, Aldo L Educator, Piano
YaDeau, William Ronald Educator, Piano

De Kalb

Bach, Jan (Morris) Composer, Educator
Blickhan, (Charles) Timothy Composer, Educator
Buggert, Robert W Educator, Composer
Clemens, Earl L Educator, Oboe
Haugland, A Oscar Composer, Educator
Rowley, Gordon Samuel Librarian, Musicologist
Williams, Edna (Charlotte) Soprano, Educator

Des Plaines

Cochran, J Paul Composer, Educator
Culley, Pamela Overstreet Violin, Conductor & Music Director
Marcus, Ada Belle (Gross) Composer, Piano

Edwardsville

Haley, Johnetta R Educator, Piano
Mellott, George Kenneth Clarinet, Educator
Woodard, James P Composer, Educator

Elmhurst

Fako, Nancy Jordan French Horn, Teacher
Kelly, Paul Robert Educator, Lecturer

Evanston

Alderson, Richard M Educator
Berkenstock, James Turner Bassoon, Educator
Black, C Robert Saxophone, Educator
Blackwelder, Stephen Dwight Conductor & Music Director
Bloom, Lawrie Clarinet, Educator
Bradetich, Jeff Double Bass, Educator
Brody, Clark L Clarinet, Educator
Buccheri, John Educator
Buchtel, Forrest Lawrence Composer, Educator
Cichowicz, Vincent M Educator, Trumpet
Dehnert, Edmund John Writer, Composer
Draganski, Donald Charles Librarian, Composer
Edwards, Ryan (Hayes) Baritone, Educator
Fischer, Elizabeth Educator, Mezzo-soprano
Griscom, Richard William Librarian
Gulbrandsen, Norman R Teacher-Coach, Music Director
Gustafson, Nancy J Soprano, Educator
Hansen, James Roger Violin
Harris, Robert Allen Educator, Composer
Isaak, Donald J Piano, Educator
Kagan, Hilel Violin, Teacher
Kartman, Myron Violin, Conductor & Music Director
Larimer, Frances H Educator, Piano
Larson, David Dynes Conductor, Educator

Marcellus, Robert Conductor & Music Director, Educator
Miller, Thomas Williams Administrator, Teacher
Mischakoff, Anne Educator, Viola
Nielubowski, Norbert John Basson & Contrabassoon, Teacher
Ockwell, Frederick Conductor & Music Director, Educator
Peters, Gordon Benes Conductor & Music Director, Percussion
Postl, Jacobeth Educator, Lecturer
Roberts, Donald Lowell Librarian, Educator
Rubsam, Wolfgang Friedrich Organ, Teacher
Smith, Gerald L Educator, Baritone
Stout, Alan Burrage Composer, Educator
Syverud, Stephen Luther Educator, Composer
Tashjian, B Charmian Composer, Educator
Weirich, Robert Piano, Educator
Willis, Thomas C Educator, Critic-Writer

Flossmoor

Ringel, Harvey Norman Educator, Baritone

Galesburg

Barnea, Uri Music Director, Composer
Baylor, Hugh Murray Educator, Composer
Polay, Bruce Conductor & Music Director, Educator

Glencoe

Grenier, Victoria R Flute & Piccolo, Educator
Magad, Samuel Violin, Conductor
Skorodin, Elaine (Elaine Skorodin Fohrman) Violin, Educator

Glen Ellyn

Brenner, Rosamond Drooker Composer, Organ

Glenview

Gena, Peter Composer, Educator
Goode, Jack C Composer, Organ
Paynter, John P Educator, Conductor
Preves, Milton Viola, Lecturer

Greenville

Wilson, James Edward Educator, Conductor

Highland Park

Aitay, Victor Violin
Schweikert, Norman Carl French Horn, Historian
Turner, Lynne Alison Harp, Educator

Homewood

Roberts, Jane A Composer

Joliet

Friedman, Jay Kenneth Trombone
Rodby, Walter Composer, Writer

Kansas

Pinnell, Ruth Educator

Kenilworth

Cooke, (John) Antony Cello, Composer

Lake Bluff

De Young, Lynden Evans Composer, Educator

Lombard

Benfield, Warren A Double Bass, Educator
Evans, Margarita Sawatzky Educator, Soprano
Reims, Clifford Waldemar Educator, Conductor & Music Director

Lyons

Zajicek, Jeronym Composer, Educator

Macomb

Keene, James A Educator, Writer
Roach, Donald Wycoff Educator, Conductor & Music Director
Wassum, Sylvesta Marie Educator
Werling, Anita Eggert Educator, Organ

Mt Vernon

Schweinfurth, Carl Lincoln Administrator

Murrayville

Walker, John Edward Tenor

Naperville

Buhl, Keith Robert Tenor
McKinley, Ann W Educator

Normal

Bolen, Charles Warren Educator, Administrator
Cordero, Roque Composer, Educator
Lehman, Richard Trumpet, Educator
Rosene, Paul Earl Music Director, Educator
Streeter, Thomas Wayne Educator, Trombone

Northbrook

Karlins, M(artin) William Composer, Educator

North Riverside

Lee, Ki Joo Educator, Violin

Oak Park

Wright, Thomas Underwood Viola

Park Forest

Sunden, Ralph Edward Piano, Organ

Park Forest South

Strukoff, Rudolf Stephen Educator, Conductor

Park Ridge

Heim, Leo Edward Teacher, Piano

Peoria

Cannon, Allen E Violin, Educator
Howard, Dean Clinton Composer, Clarinet
Klein, Jerry (Gerald Louis) Critic

Quincy

George, Thom Ritter Composer, Conductor
Wagner, Lavern John Educator, Administrator

Riverwoods

Kirby, F(rank) E(ugene) Musicologist, Writer

Rockford

Whipple, Walter Educator, Organ

Rock Island

Hersh, Alan B Educator, Piano

Rosemont

Lewis, Marcia Ann Mezzo-soprano, Educator

Sidney

Hamilton, Jerald Educator, Organ

Skokie

Johnson, Joyce Lynne Educator, Teacher
Kraus, Philip Arthur Director-Opera, Baritone

Springfield

Siebert, Frederick Mark Educator, Organ

Sycamore

Steg, Paul Oskar Educator, Composer

Urbana

Beauchamp, James W Educator
Binkerd, Gordon Ware Composer
Brun, Herbert Composer, Educator
Coggins, Willis Robert Educator, Clarinet
Colwell, Richard James Educator
Decker, Harold A Educator, Conductor
Dunn, Susan Regenia Soprano
Edlefsen, Blaine Ellis Educator, Oboe & English Horn
Elyn, Mark Alvin Bass, Teacher
Farmer, Virginia Educator, Violin
Geil, Wilma Jean Librarian
Gushee, Lawrence A Musicologist, Educator
Gushee, Marion Sibley Educator, Administrator
Hill, John Walter Educator
Johnston, Benjamin Burwell, Jr Composer, Educator
Jones, Robert M Librarian, Educator
Kelly, (J) Robert Composer, Viola
Krummel, D(onald) W(illiam) Educator, Librarian
McCulloh, Judith Marie Editor, Scholar
McKenzie, Jack H Educator, Administrator
Martirano, Salvatore Composer, Educator
Murray, Alexander Douglass Educator, Flute
Perich, Guillermo Viola, Educator
Peters, George David Educator, Administrator
Powell, Morgan Edward Composer, Trombone
Shapiro, Joel Educator, Piano
Siwe, Thomas V Percussion, Conductor
Smiraglia, Richard Paul Librarian
Temperley, Nicholas Educator, Critic-Writer
Tipei, Sever Composer, Educator
Vermel, Paul Conductor & Music Director, Educator
Warfield, William Caesar Singer, Educator
Wisniewski, Thomas Joseph Educator, Music Director
Wyatt, Scott Alan Composer, Educator
Zonn, Paul Composer, Conductor
Zonn, Wilma Zapora Oboe, Educator

Wheaton

Chenoweth, Vida Educator, Marimba
Gerig, Reginald Roth Educator, Writer
Thompson, Ellen R Educator, Teacher-Coach
Whitecotton, Shirley E Composer

Wilmette

Brindel, Bernard Composer, Educator
Conant, Robert S Harpsichord, Educator
Hemke, Frederick L Educator, Saxophone
Karp, Theodore Cyrus Musicologist, Writer
Noh, Joyce Hiew Violin
Reimer, Bennett Educator, Writer
Sandroff, Howard F Composer, Conductor & Music Director
Schwartz, Judith Leah Educator, Writer

Winnetka

Hilliard, Tom (Thomas Lee) Composer, Conductor
Kujala, Walfrid Eugene Flute & Piccolo, Educator

INDIANA

Anderson

Bengtson, F Dale Composer, Educator

Bloomington

Alexander, Peter Marquis Administrator, Writer
Binkley, Thomas E Educator, Administrator
Brown, A Peter Critic, Educator
Brown, Keith Educator, Conductor & Music Director
Brown, Malcolm Hamrick Educator, Writer
Buelow, George John Educator, Administrator
Buswell, James Oliver Educator, Violin
Cassel, Walter John Baritone, Educator
Christ, William B Educator, Administrator
Davidson, Louis Trumpet, Educator
Eaton, John C Composer, Educator
Farkas, Philip Francis French Horn
Fenske, David Edward Librarian, Musicologist
Fox, Frederick Alfred Composer, Educator
Gaber, George Percussion, Educator
Gingold, Josef Educator, Violin
Grodner, Murray Educator, Double Bass
Gulli, Franco Violin, Educator
Heiden, Bernhard Composer, Music Director
Helton, Sally Carr Librarian, Educator
Janzer, Georges Viola, Educator
Kaufmann, Walter Composer, Writer
Keiser, Marilyn Jean Organ, Educator
Klotman, Robert Howard Educator, Violin
Kuzmych, Christina Composer, Educator
MacClintock, Carol C Writer, Educator
Magg, Fritz Cello, Educator
Matthen, Paul Seymour Educator, Baritone
Orrego-Salas, Juan Antonio Composer, Critic & Writer
Pellerite, James John Flute, Educator
Phillips, Harvey Gene Tuba, Educator
Pressler, Menahem Piano, Educator
Rezits, Joseph M Piano, Writer
Ritchie, Stanley John Baroque Violin, Educator
Samuelsen, Roy Bass-Baritone, Educator
Sirucek, Jerry Edward Oboe & English Horn, Educator
Starker, Janos Educator, Cello
Stewart, M Dee Trombone, Educator
Tischler, Hans Musicologist
Tocco, James Piano, Teacher
Webb, Charles H Administrator, Conductor & Music Director
Wennerstrom, Mary Hannah Educator, Writer

INDIANA (cont)

Crawfordsville

Enenbach, Fredric Composer, Educator

Elkhart

Thomas, Mark Stanton Flute

Evansville

Lacy, Edwin V Educator, Bassoon
Smith, Patrice Jane Critic-Writer, Piano

Ft Wayne

Loomis, James Phillip Teacher, Clarinet
Ondrejka, Ronald Conductor & Music
 Director
Platte, Jay Daniel Educator, Conductor
Stolba, K Marie Writer, Educator

Greencastle

Grocock, Robert Trumpet, Educator
Smith, Orcenith George Conductor &
 Music Director, Composer
Wilcox, Eunice Ann Educator, Music
 Director

Hartford City

Parker, Richard Allan Educator

Indianapolis

Adamson, Janis John Cello
Bartolowits, David John Violin
Beckel, James A, Jr Trombone, Educator
Bransford, Mallory Watkins Educator
Briscoe, James Robert Educator, Critic &
 Writer
Broemel, Robert W Bassoon
Chenette, Louis Fred Educator,
 Administrator
Collins, David Edward Violin, Teacher
Driver, Robert Baylor Administrator,
 Director-Opera
Ehrlich, David Violin
Hansen, James A Bassoon, Teacher
Harvey, Raymond C Music Director
Hendrix, Richard Violin
Hofmeister, Giannina Lombardo Teacher,
 Piano
Kiesler, Kenneth Conductor & Music
 Director
Lang, Rosemary Rita Educator, Clarinet
Lapin, Geoffrey Cello
Morehead, Donald Keith Percussion,
 Teacher
Munger, Dorothy M Piano, Educator
Nelson, Bradley R Composer, Educator
Nelson, John Wilton Conductor & Music
 Director
Orlovsky, Arkady Cello, Educator
Pacini, Renato Conductor & Music
 Director
Perry, Marvin Chapman, II Trumpet,
 Educator
Philpott, Larry LaFayette French Horn,
 Educator
Ruebeck, Ann Bowman Administrator
Rupp, Marjorie J Viola, Violin
Schelle, Michael Composer
Scott, Beverly C Viola, Piano
Staff, Charles Bancroft, Jr Critic
Suzuki, Hidetaro Conductor, Violin
Williams, J(ohn) Wesley Educator, Music
 Director

Lafayette

Kidd, Ronald R Educator
Ostergren, Eduardo Augusto Conductor
 & Music Director, Educator

La Porte

Dure, Robert Composer, Educator

Muncie

Albright, Philip H Educator, Double Bass
Anderson, Garland (Lee) Composer,
 Writer
Ewart, Phillip Smith Educator, Bass
Foley, David Francis Composer
Knight, Morris H Composer, Educator
Mackey, Elizabeth Jocelyn Educator,
 Musicologist
Manford, Barbara Ann Contralto,
 Educator
Mueller, Erwin Carl Percussion, Educator
Rubin, Emanuel Leo Administrator,
 Educator
Schaefer, Patricia Administrator,
 Librarian
Scott, Cleve L Educator, Composer
Sherman, Robert Composer

Munster

Clark, Thomas Terrence Organ, Music
 Director

Notre Dame

Haimo, Ethan Tepper Composer,
 Educator

Peru

Soames, Cynthia Elizabeth Percussion,
 Educator

Rensselaer

Verdi, Ralph Carl Composer, Educator

Richmond

Combopiano, Charles Angelo Director-
 Opera, Music Director

South Bend

Buranskas, Karen Educator, Cello
Cerny, William Joseph Piano, Educator
Demaree, Robert William, Jr
 Administrator, Educator
Esselstrom, Michael John Conductor &
 Music Director, Educator
Fisher, Zeal Isay Viola, Teacher
Henderson, Clayton Wilson
 Administrator, Educator
O'Brien, Robert Felix Educator, Music
 Director
Owings, John C Piano, Educator
Sprague, Raymond Music Director,
 Educator

South Whitley

Fox, Alan Hugo Administrator,
 Instrument Maker

Terre Haute

Fluegel, Neal Lalon Percussion, Educator
Gee, Harry Raglan Educator, Writer
Rensch, Roslyn (Roslyn Maria
 Rensch-Erbes) Harp, Lecturer
Singer, Joan (Joan Singer Spicknall)
 Educator, Piano

Upland

Shulze, Frederick Bennett Educator,
 Organ

Valparaiso

Powell, Newman Wilson Writer, Educator
Wienhorst, Richard William Composer,
 Educator

Warsaw

Ker, Ann Steele Composer, Educator

West Lafayette

Lefever, Maxine Lane Percussion,
 Educator
Wright, Al G (Alfred George) Educator,
 Conductor & Music Director

IOWA

Ames

Prater, Jeffrey L Composer, Educator
von Grabow, Richard H Educator,
 Carillonneur
White, Gary C(harles) Composer,
 Educator

Cedar Falls

Bock, Emil William Educator,
 Musicologist
Gault, Joyce Alene Educator
Holvik, Karl Magnus Educator,
 Conductor
Michaelides, Peter Educator, Composer
Ross, Ronald D Administrator, Educator

Cedar Rapids

Karns, Dean Meredith Educator,
 Administrator

Davenport

Dixon, James Allen Conductor & Music
 Director, Educator

Des Moines

Baldwin, Nicholas G Critic
Hall, Marion Austin Administrator,
 Educator
Kaderavek, Milan Educator, Composer
Ross, Buck Director-Opera
Ruby, E Jane Educator, Choral Music
 Conductor
Wade, Janice E Conductor, Violin

Docorah

Noble, Weston Henry Conductor,
 Educator

Dubuque

Clarke, Rosemary Composer, Educator

Grinnell

Cloud, Lee Vernell Educator
Goldsmith, Kenneth Martin Violin,
 Educator
Hays, Elizabeth L Educator, Harpsichord
King, Terry Bower Cello, Conductor

Indianola

Degen, Bruce N Educator, Bassoon
Duncan, Douglas Jon Administrator,
 Educator
Larsen, Robert L Educator, Conductor

Iowa City

Block, Robert Paul Editor
Bruch, Delores Ruth Organ, Educator
Crane, Frederick Baron Educator
Cross, Lowell Merlin Composer, Laser
Disselhorst, Delbert Dean Organ
Glass, Beaumont Coach, Director-Opera
Greenhoe, David Stanley Trumpet,
 Educator
Haefliger, Kathleen Ann Librarian, Writer
Hansell, Sven H Educator, Harpsichord
Hervig, Richard B Composer, Educator
Hibbard, William Alden Composer,
 Educator
Hill, John David Educator, Trombone
Jenni, D(onald) Martin Composer,
 Educator

Kottick, Edward Leon Educator,
Instrument Maker
Lasocki, David Ronald Graham Writer,
Flute
Lewis, Peter Tod Composer, Educator
Mather, Betty Bang (Betty Louise
Mather) Educator, Flute
Mather, Roger Frederick Flute, Educator
Moses, Don V Music Director, Educator
Obrecht, Eldon Ross Composer, Double
Bass
Tyree, Ronald Wayne Bassoon, Educator
Voxman, Himie Administrator, Composer

Oskaloosa

Wormhoudt, Pearl Shinn Educator,
Writer

Waverly

Fritschel, James Erwin Composer,
Educator
Williams, Franklin Edmund Educator,
Conductor

West Des Moines

Brauninger, Eva Jeannine Educator,
Double Bass
Brauninger, James Edward Violin,
Teacher
Harris, C David Harpsichord, Educator
Katz, George Leon Educator, Piano

KANSAS

Atchison

Waite, Russell Trueman Administrator,
Conductor & Music Director

Baldwin City

Gaeddert, William Kenneth Educator,
Baritone

Dodge City

Woodhall, Dennis Robert Educator,
Music Director

Emporia

Edwards, Elaine Virginia Educator,
Administrator
Halgedahl, (Edward) Howard Conductor,
Educator
Hart, Kenneth Wayne Administrator,
Organ
Ott, Joseph Henry Conductor, Writer

Greensburg

Wendelburg, Norma Ruth Composer,
Piano

Hays

Figler, Byrnell Walter Educator, Piano
Huber, John Elwyn Educator,
Administrator
Miller, Lewis Martin Educator, Composer
Moyers, Emmett Edwin Violin, Educator
Wilkins, William Dean Educator, Organ

Lawrence

Addiss, Stephen Composer, Educator
Appert, Donald Lawrence Trombone,
Teacher
Bushouse, M David French Horn,
Educator
Clark, J Bunker Educator, Writer
Cozad, Joseph Guitar, Teacher
Crawford, Maribeth Kirchhoff Conductor,
Educator
Foster, Robert Estill Music Director,
Educator

Hillmer, Leann Educator, Music Director
Holmberg, Mark Leonard Educator,
Organ
Johnson, Ellen Schultz Librarian,
Educator
Laut, Edward Allen Educator, Cello
Mattila, Edward Charles Composer,
Educator
Miller, Anne Winsor Oboe, Educator
Moeser, James Charles Organ, Educator
Paige, Norman Educator, Tenor
Pozdro, John Walter Composer, Educator
Reber, Richard Educator, Piano
Shumway, Stanley Newmyer
Administrator, Educator
Silini, Flora Chiarappa Educator, Piano
Smith, Kenneth Bass-Baritone, Educator
Steinhardt, Milton J Musicologist, Critic-
Writer
Williams, Edward Vinson Writer,
Educator

Leavenworth

Callahan, Anne Administrator, Educator

Leawood

DeWitt, Andrew Ransom Double Bass

Lindsborg

Higbee, David John Educator, Saxophone

Manhattan

Jackson, Hanley Composer, Educator
Parker, Craig Burwell Trumpet, Educator
Sloop, Jean Carolyn Educator, Lecturer
Steinbauer, Robert Andrus Administrator,
Piano
Sutton, Mary Ellen Educator, Organ
White, (Edwin) Chappell Educator,
Critic-Writer

North Newton

Moyer, John Harold Composer, Educator

Pittsburg

Cook, Richard G Composer, Educator
James, Mary Elliott Viola, Educator
Kehle, Robert Gordon Educator,
Trombone

Shawnee

Schutza, Gary Alan, Jr Trumpet

Shawnee Mission

Rogers, Ethel Tench Composer, Teacher

Topeka

Bendell, Christine J Educator, Piano
Boyd, Rodney Carney Educator, Bassoon
Hedberg, Floyd Carl Educator, Conductor
Rivers, James (Calvin) Piano, Educator

Wichita

Crum, Dorothy Edith Educator, Soprano
Johnson, Guy C Educator, Teacher
Lee, Douglas Allen Lecturer, Educator
Luttrell, Nancy Kay Violin, Educator
Mathis, William Ervin Administrator,
Educator
Neubert, Bernard David Double Bass,
Educator
Palmer, Michael Music Director &
Conductor, Piano
Wolff, Arthur Sheldon Educator,
Composer

KENTUCKY

Bowling Green

Carpenter, Howard Ralph Administrator,
Violin
Livingston, David Educator, Composer
Pease, Edward Joseph Educator, Writer

Covington

Bell, Charles E French Horn

Danville

Weaver, Robert Lee Educator, Piano

Erlanger

Lukashuk, Vladimir Violin, Viola

Lexington

Baber, Joseph (Wilson) Composer,
Educator
Dickow, Robert Henry Composer,
Educator
Feofanov, Dmitry N Piano, Educator
Fitzgerald, Robert Bernard Educator,
Composer
Fogler, Michael Landy Educator, Guitar
Hanlon, Kevin Francis Composer
Henderson, Hubert Platt Educator, Music
Director
Longyear, Rey Morgan Writer, Educator
Monsen, Ronald Peter Clarinet, Educator
Zack, George Jimmy Conductor & Music
Director, Educator

Louisville

Ashworth, Jack S Educator
Baker, Claude Composer
Christensen, Jean Marie Educator, Writer
French, Robert Bruce Administrator,
Composer
French, Ruth Scott Teacher, Violin
Furman, James Composer, Educator
Green, Marian C Critic & Writer,
Educator
Hinson, (Grady) Maurice Educator, Piano
Holden, Randall LeConte, Jr Educator,
Administrator
Kaiserman, David Norman Piano,
Educator
Keyes, Nelson Composer, Educator
Livingston, James Francis Clarinet,
Conductor
Luvisi, Lee Piano, Teacher
Price, Shelby Milburn, Jr Educator, Music
Director
Schuster-Craig, John William Critic,
Lecturer
Smith, Douglas Educator, Composer
Weaver, Robert Lamar Educator, Writer
Wilkey, Jay W Educator, Baritone

Morehead

Bigham, William Marvin Administrator,
Educator
Gallaher, Christopher S Composer,
Educator
Mueller, Frederick A Bassoon, Composer
Venettozzi, Vasile Jean Educator

Murray

Mason, Neale Bagley Educator, Cello
Reichmuth, Roger Edwin Educator,
Saxophone
Shahan, Paul W Composer, Educator

Owensboro

Ahnell, Emil Gustave Composer,
Educator

KENTUCKY (cont)

Richmond

Beeler, Charles Alan Educator, Composer
Bromley, Richard H Educator, Composer
Duncan, Dan J (Danny Joe) Oboe &
  English Horn, Educator
Hartwell, Robert Wallace Administrator,
  Educator
Harvey, Arthur Wallace Educator,
  Lecturer
Timm, Kenneth N Composer, Educator
Wolfrom, Lyle Clark Cello, Double Bass

LOUISIANA

Baton Rouge

Abel, Paul Louis Educator, Composer
Adkins, Aldrich Wendell Administrator,
  Conductor
Ardoyno, Dolores Administrator
Aslanian, Richard Conductor & Music
  Director
Campbell, Larry Bruce Educator,
  Trombone
Constantinides, Dinos (Constantine
  Demetrios Constantinides) Composer,
  Violin
Cureau, Rebecca Turner Educator,
  Lecturer
Edmunds, John Francis Educator,
  Composer
Harrison, E Earnest Oboe, Educator
McKenzie, Wallace C Educator,
  Composer
Merriman, Lyle Clinton Administrator,
  Educator
O'Reilly, Sally Violin, Educator
Paul, James Conductor, Tenor
Timm, Everett L Administrator, Flute
Timm, (M) Jeanne Anderson Educator,
  Flute
Wickes, Frank Bovee Conductor & Music
  Director, Educator

Grambling

Jennings, Theodore McKinley, Jr
  Administrator, Educator

Gretna

Pink, Howard Norman French Horn

Hammond

Barzenick, Walter Educator, Writer
McCormick, David Clement Educator,
  Tuba
Wilcox, James H Educator, Composer

Harvey

Maul, Eric (William) Bassoon

Jefferson

DeGroot, David Joseph Percussion,
  Educator

Lafayette

Hanna, James Ray Educator, Composer
Sahuc, Nolan John Educator, Bassoon
Schmalz, Robert Frederick Educator,
  Trombone

Lake Charles

Jordahl, Robert A Composer, Educator

Metairie

Drew, James M Composer, Conductor &
  Music Director

Monroe

Burgin, John Educator

Natchitoches

Price, Robert Bates Educator, Violin

New Orleans

Baron, John Herschel Writer, Educator
Belsom, Jack (John Anton) Critic-Writer,
  Administrator
Berthelot, John (Menard), Jr
  Administrator, Composer
Breda, Malcolm Joseph Educator,
  Conductor
Bush, Milton Louis Educator, Trombone
Cecere, Anthony Robert French Horn
Chaney, Scott Clay Viola, Violin
Cortina, Raquel Soprano, Educator
Dominick, Lisa Robinson Writer,
  Educator
Eskew, Harry (Lee) Educator
Hansen, Peter Sijer Educator
Langley, Kenneth John Violin
Lemmon, Alfred Emmette Writer, Organ
McCarty, Patrick Composer, Educator
Massey, Andrew John Conductor
Miller, Dean Harold Flute, Educator
Nichols, Clinton Colgate Tenor, Educator
Rothschild, Ellen Wagner Violin
Wilkins, Marilyn W Librarian, Soprano
Wyatt, Larry D Educator, Conductor &
  Music Director
Wylie, Ted David Tenor, Educator

Northfield

Little, Frank (Francis E) Tenor, Educator

Prairieville

Taranto, Vernon Anthony, Jr Composer

Ruston

Young, Raymond G Euphonium,
  Educator

Shreveport

Carroll, Frank Morris Educator,
  Administrator
Cliburn, Van (Harry Lavan, Jr) Piano
Murray, Robert (J) Administrator, Stage
  Director
Shenaut, John Conductor & Music
  Director
Teague, William Chandler Organ, Music
  Director

Thibodaux

Croom, John (Robert) Composer,
  Educator
Snyder, John L Educator, Theorist

West Monroe

Jones, Roger Parks Composer, Educator

MAINE

Bangor

Newall, Robert H Critic

Brunswick

Schwartz, Elliott Shelling Composer,
  Writer

Gorham

Bowder, Jerry Lee Composer, Educator
Martin, Peter John Conductor, Educator

Greenville

Schubel, Max Composer, Administrator

Hancock

Torkanowsky, Werner Conductor &
  Music Director, Composer

Lewiston

Matthews, William Composer, Educator

New Harbor

Goodman, Bernard Maurice Conductor &
  Music Director, Violin

North Edgecomb

Lazarus, Roy Educator, Stage Director

Orono

Hallman, Ludlow B, III Educator, Music
  Director & Conductor
Newman, Grant H Educator

Portland

Bucci, Thomas Vincent Composer, Piano
Pachios, Harold Christy Patron
Simmonds, Rae Nichols Composer, Piano

Scarborough

Hangen, Bruce Boyer Conductor & Music
  Director

Stonington

Gardner, Kay Composer, Flute & Alto
  Flute

Swans Island

Kunzel, Erich Conductor & Music
  Director

Waterville

Heinrich, Adel Verna Educator, Organ
Machlin, Paul Stuart Educator, Conductor

Westbrook

White, Terrance E Composer, Teacher

MARYLAND

Adelphi

Smith, Michael Cedric Guitar & Lute

Annapolis

Allanbrook, Douglas Phillips Composer,
  Harpsichord
Allanbrook, Wye Jamison Writer,
  Educator

Baltimore

Alper, Clifford Daniel Educator, Critic-
  Writer
Amato, Bruno Composer, Educator
Arnold, (Donald) Thomas Tenor
Bakkegard, (Benjamin) David Horn,
  Educator
Balter, Alan (Neil) Conductor, Clarinet
Broyles, Michael E Educator, Writer
Brunyate, Roger Educator, Director-
  Opera
Cameron, Wayne Educator, Trumpet
Cera, Stephen Charles Critic, Piano
Cudek, Mark S Educator, Guitar & Lute
Cyr, Gordon Conrad Educator, Composer
Davis, Paul Organ
de Lerma, Dominique-Rene Educator,
  Writer
Digiacomo, Serafina Educator, Voice
Drucker, Arno Paul Administrator,
  Educator
Drucker, Ruth Educator, Voice
Duschak, Alice Gerstl Soprano
Dvorine, Shura Composer, Piano
Esteban, Julio Educator, Composer
Fetter, David J Trombone
Field, Richard Lawrence Viola, Lecturer
Fleisher, Leon Conductor & Music
  Director, Piano
Graf, Enrique G Piano, Teacher
Hart, William Sebastian Conductor

Hatcher, Paula Braniff Flute & Piccolo, Recorder
Heifetz, Daniel Violin, Educator
Knopt, Tinka Piano, Administrator
Kolker, Phillip A M Educator, Bassoon
Lake, Bonnie (Josephine) Flute, Educator
Levine, Julius Double Bass
Lewis, Robert Hall Composer, Conductor
Libove, Charles Violin, Educator
Lobingier, Christopher Crumay Composer, Librarian
London, George Director-Opera, Bass-Baritone
Lowens, Irving Critic, Music Historian
Lowens, Margery Morgan Educator, Writer
Mathews, John Fenton Double Bass, Viola Da Gamba
Murray, George Tenor
Myers, Theldon Composer, Educator
Nevins, David Howard Administrator
Olson, Phyllis Edward Administrator, Double Bass
Patey, Edward R Violin
Pierce, Robert French Horn, Administrator
Polochick, Edward Conductor, Administrator
Prausnitz, Frederik W Music Director, Educator
Quist, Edwin Arnold Librarian, Administrator
Quist, Pamela Layman Composer, Educator
Roldan, Nancy Piano, Educator
Rothschild, Randolph Schamberg Administrator, Patron
Salkov, Abraham A Composer, Tenor
Saslav, Isidor Violin, Educator
Schein, Ann Piano, Educator
Silverman, Faye-Ellen Composer, Educator
Smith, Stuart Saunders Educator, Composer
Smith, Sylvia H Administrator
Tison, Donald Trumpet
Virizlay, Mihaly E Cello, Teacher
Virizlay, Paula Skolnick Cello, Educator
Wright, Geoffrey Dorian Composer, Educator
Yannuzzi, William A(nthony) Music Director, Educator
Yeo, Douglas Edward Trombone, Educator
Zaimont, Judith Lang Composer, Writer
Zarubick, Fran G Administrator

Bel Air

McLaughlin, Marian Composer, Clarinet

Beltsville

Korth, Thomas A Teacher, Composer

Bethesda

Berdes, Jane L Writer
Boal, Dean Administrator
English Maris, Barbara (Jane) Educator, Piano
Ferguson, Edwin Earle Composer, Music Director
Hyson, Winifred Prince Composer, Teacher-Coach
Lazar, Joel Conductor & Music Director

Bowie

Leavitt, Donald Lee Librarian

Brookeville

Head, Emerson Williams Trumpet, Educator

Catonsville

Gerle, Robert Conductor, Violin

Chestertown

Clarke, Garry Evans Educator, Administrator

Chevy Chase

Parris, Robert Composer, Piano

College Park

Garofalo, Robert Joseph Educator, Conductor
Gordon, Stewart Lynell Educator
Gowen, Bradford Paul Piano, Writer
Johnson, Roy Hamlin Piano, Composer
Laires, Fernando Piano
Schumacher, Thomas Piano, Educator
Trahan, Kathleen Frances Flute

Cumberland

Homburg, Al(fred John) Educator, Tenor

Derwood

Miller, Donald Charles Conductor & Music Director, Educator

Frostburg

Bauman, Jon Ward Composer, Conductor
Opper, Jacob Educator, Conductor

Gaithersburg

Maxwell, Barbara Librarian

Germantown

Gold, Cecil Viner Clarinet, Educator

Hagerstown

Martin, Robert Edward Composer

Hampstead

McMahan, Robert Young Composer, Accordion

Hyattsville

Heim, Norman Michael Clarinet, Composer
Meyers, (Herman) Emerson Composer, Piano
Montgomery, William Layton Flute & Piccolo, Educator
Simpson, Mary Jean Flute, Educator

Kensington

Forrest, Sidney Clarinet, Educator
Heintze, James Rudolph Educator, Librarian

Laurel

King, Carlton W, III Educator, Music Director

Odenton

Ray, William Benjamin Baritone, Teacher

Potomac

Laitman, Lori (Lori Laitman Rosenblum) Composer
Sutherland, Donald S Educator, Organ
Wang, An-Ming Composer

Rockville

Muller, Gerald F Composer, Music Director
Stilman-Lasansky, Julia Composer
Werder, Richard H Educator, Piano

St Mary's City

Laughton, John Charles Educator, Clarinet

Silver Spring

Barry, Jerome Baritone, Administrator
Fritter, Priscilla Flute
Irby, Fred, III Educator, Trumpet
Jackson, Raymond T Piano, Educator
Makris, Andreas Composer
Moss, Lawrence Kenneth Composer, Educator
Snow, David Jason Composer, Electronic
Ulrich, Homer Educator, Writer
Ward, Margaret Motter Viola

Spencerville

Kelly, Michael Thomas Clarinet

Takoma Park

Tilkens, Neil Avrill Educator, Piano

Timonium

Armstrong, Helen (Helen Armstrong Gemmell) Violin, Teacher & Coach
Galkin, Elliott Washington Administrator, Educator

Towson

Leavitt, Joseph Administrator, Educator
Mauk, Frederick Henry, Jr Educator
Mitchell, Lee Educator

Westminster

Bachmann, George Theodore Viola, Librarian
Cole, Gerald E Composer, Educator
Ostryniec, James Paul Oboe, Composer

Wheaton

Stephens, John Elliott Composer, Conductor & Music Director

MASSACHUSETTS

Acton

Korde, Shirish K Composer, Educator

Allston

Marshall, Pamela Joy Composer
Walter, David Edgar Composer, Baritone

Amherst

Anderson, Warren DeWitt Writer, Educator
Bestor, Charles L Composer, Educator
Evans, Sally Romer Librarian
Gilbert, Michael William Composer, Electronic
Jenkins, John Allan Administrator, Educator
Olevsky, Julian Violin, Educator
Spratlan, Lewis Composer, Educator
Stern, Robert Educator, Composer
Swafford, Jan Johnson Composer, Conductor
Tillis, Frederick C Composer, Administrator
Whaples, Miriam K Educator, Musicologist

Andover

Warner, Sally Slade Carillon

Arlington

Beardslee, Sheila Margaret Recorder, Teacher
Bedford, Judith Eileen Bassoon, Educator
Forte, James Peter Composer, Administrator
Stumpf, Thomas Piano, Teacher

MASSACHUSETTS (cont)

Auburndale

Heiss, John Carter Composer, Flute & Piccolo

Bedford

Hadcock, Mary G Viola, Teacher

Belmont

Adams, (John) Clement Composer
Brauchli, Bernard Marc Clavichord, Organ
Cabot, Edmund Billings Administrator, Patron
Child, Peter Burlingham Composer
Goolkasian Rahbee, Dianne Zabelle Composer, Piano
Gregorian, Rouben Conductor, Composer
Kessler, Minuetta Composer, Piano
Lewis, Barbara Connolly Conductor, Coach
Merryman, Marjorie Composer
Paratore, Anthony Piano
Paratore, Joseph Piano
Pearlman, Martin Harpsichord, Music Director
Rosenblum, Sandra Pletman Lecturer, Educator

Beverly

Barbeau, Bernard Teacher, Baritone

Bolton

Lord, Stephen H Coach, Administrator

Boston

Adams, Alan Eugene Administrator, Music Director
Allard, Joseph Saxophone, Clarinet
Allen, Corey Lee Composer, Teacher
Amlin, Martin Dolph Piano, Composer
Anderson, Dean Percussion, Educator
Andy, Katja Piano
Antoniou, Theodore Composer, Conductor & Music Director
Bell, Larry Thomas Composer, Piano
Berk, Lee Eliot Administrator
Blackham, Richard Allan Writer
Blake, Ran Piano, Composer
Bobbitt, Richard Administrator, Writer
Bogue, Lawrence Educator
Bolter, Norman Howard Trombone, Educator
Borok, Emanuel Violin
Brink, Robert Educator, Violin
Buys, Douglas Educator, Piano
Caldwell, Sarah Conductor, Director-Opera
Carillo, Nancy Violin, Educator
Castiglione, Richard B Conductor, Administrator
Chase, Stephanie Ann Violin, Educator
Cohen, Fredric Thomas Oboe, Educator
Cokkinias, Peter Leonidas Conductor & Music Director, Clarinet
Come, Andre Trumpet, Educator
Curtis, William H Double Bass, Educator
Decima, Terry Piano, Educator
deVaron, Lorna Cooke Conductor, Educator
DeVoll, Ray Educator, Voice
Didomenica, Robert Composer
Dobelle, Beatrice Soprano, Educator
Douglas, John Thomas Teacher & Coach, Music Director
Dove, Neville Conductor, Piano
Dunn, Thomas Burt Conductor & Music Director, Organ
Eddy, Timothy Cello, Educator
Epstein, Frank Benjamin Percussion, Music Director

Farmer, Peter Russell Educator, Composer
Felice, John Piano, Composer
Fritze, Gregory Paul Composer, Tuba
Gay, Paul E Educator, Composer
Genovese, Alfred Oboe
Giddings, Robert Potter Librarian, Administrator
Godin, Robert Educator, Composer
Grass, William Educator, Flute
Gronquist, Robert E Conductor, Harpsichord
Gustin, Daniel Robert Administrator
Gutberg, Ingrid Piano, Organ
Hadcock, Peter Clarinet, Educator
Hagon, John Peter Educator, Music Director
Hall, Tom Educator
Hanks, Thompson W, Jr Tuba, Educator
Hearne, Joseph Frederic Double Bass
Hobart, Max Violin, Educator
Hobson, Ann Stephens (Ann Hobson-Pilot) Harp
Hodam, Helen Soprano, Educator
Hodgson, Peter John Educator, Writer
Hoffmann, James Composer, Music Director
Hugo, John William Conductor, Tenor
Jeppesen, Laura Viola da Gamba, Educator
Kacinskas, Jeronimas Composer, Conductor & Music Director
Kaderavek, Karen Beth Cello, Teacher
Kang, Hyo Violin, Educator
Katzen, Daniel French Horn, Educator
Kellock, Judith Graham Soprano
Kim, Jung-Ja Piano, Educator
Krasner, Louis Conductor, Educator
La Porta, John Daniel Composer, Educator
Ledbetter, Steven John Writer, Educator
Lehner, Eugene Viola, Educator
Lesser, Laurence Cello, Educator
Lizotte, Andre Clarinet, Educator
Mackey, Richard French Horn, Educator
Maneri, Joseph Gabriel Composer, Educator
Marsh, Milton R Composer, Educator
Martin, Geraldine Educator, Voice
Martin, Leslie Bass, Educator
Maxin, Jacob Educator, Piano
Mekeel, Joyce Haviland Educator, Composer
Miller, Jonathan David Cello
Mizuno, Ikuko Violin, Writer
Monseur, George Conductor, Educator
Monteux, Claude Flute, Educator
Moriarty, John Administrator, Educator
Murdock, Katherine Viola, Educator
Newell, Thomas E, Jr French Horn, Educator
Nordstrom, Craig Kyle Clarinet, Teacher
Oliver, Lisi Administrator
Olmstead, Andrea Louise Writer, Educator
Ostrove, Geraldine E Librarian, Educator
Ozawa, Seiji Conductor & Music Director
Pearson, Mark Bass-Baritone, Educator
Peyton, Malcolm Cameron Composer, Educator
Portnoi, Henry Bass
Poto, Attilio Educator, Clarinet
Procter, Carol Ann Cello, Viola Da Gamba
Rakich, Christa Martin Harpsichord, Organ
Rapier, Wayne Educator, Oboe & English Horn
Raykhtsaum, Aza Violin, Teacher
Rensink, James Bass
Ripley, Robert Educator, Cello
Rosenblith, Eric Violin, Educator

Roze, Christopher Educator
Ruggiero, Matthew Educator, Bassoon
Saunders, Mary G Soprano, Educator
Schaefer, Lois Elizabeth Flute & Piccolo, Educator
Schmidt, Fred D Trombone, Educator
Schwann, William Joseph Publisher, Organ
Seymour, William Administrator, Educator
Sherman, Russell Educator, Piano
Shure, Leonard Piano, Educator
Smedvig, Rolf Thorstein Trumpet, Music Director
Stallman, Robert Educator, Flute
Stepner, Daniel Violin
Stockton, David R Artistic Director
Sullivan, Robert Paul Guitar & Lute, Educator
Sutton, Julia Educator, Scholar-Writer
Swallow, John Trombone, Educator
Sylvan, Sanford (Mead) Baritone
Taylor, Frank Organ, Educator
Thomas, Ronald Violoncello
Tyson, John K Recorder, Teacher
Ushioda, Masuko Violin, Educator
Viola, Joseph E Saxophone, Clarinet
Walt, Sherman Abbott Bassoon, Violin
Walters, Michael J Educator, Conductor & Music Director
Warren, B (Betsy Frost Warren-Davis) Composer
Weinberger, Henry Educator
Wheeler, (William) Scott Composer, Music Director
Williams, John Towner Composer, Conductor
Wolfe, Lawrence Double Bass, Educator
Wrzesien, William Clarinet, Educator
Wurtzler, Bela Double Bass, Educator
Yancich, Charles Theodore French Horn, Teacher-Coach
Zander, Patricia Piano, Educator
Zaretsky, Michael Viola, Educator
Zighera, Bernard Harp, Piano

Brighton

Beadle, Anthony Double Bass, Educator
Maloof, William J Composer, Educator
Philo, Gary Bruce Composer, Electronic Bass
Tawa, Nicholas Edward Writer, Educator

Brookline

Ayotte, Jeannine Marie Librarian
Barker, Edwin Bogue Double Bass, Teacher-Coach
Ceely, Robert Paige Composer
Curtin, Phyllis Soprano, Educator
Duesenberry, John F Composer, Electronic
Dwyer, Doriot Anthony Flute, Educator
Fromm, Herbert Composer, Organ
Goldovsky, Boris Piano, Educator
Hayashi, Yuko Organ, Educator
Leclaire, Dennis James Composer, Educator
Lee, Alfred E Piano, Harpsichord
Nikka, David W Trombone, Administrator
Owens, David Writer, Composer
Romanul, Michael (Francis) Cello
Rosenbaum, Victor Teacher, Piano
Rotenberg, Sheldon Violin, Teacher
Row, Peter Lyman Educator, Sitar
Schott, Howard Mansfield Writer, Lecturer
Sirota, Robert (Benson) Composer, Conductor
Sirota, Victoria (Ressmeyer) Organ, Educator
Thorstenberg, (John) Laurence Oboe & English Horn, Teacher

Tucker, Janice Suzuki Violin, Teacher
Uritsky, Vyacheslav Violin, Teacher-
Coach

Cambridge

Amper, Leslie Ruth Piano, Educator
Bacon, David Piano, Educator
Bacon, Virginia Payton Educator
Balshone, Cathy S (Cathy S
Balshone-Becze) Composer, Librarian
Berger, Arthur Victor Composer, Critic-
Writer
Chang, Lynn Violin, Educator
Chapman, Basil Clarinet, Educator
Chase, Allan Stuart Educator, Saxophone
Cogan, Robert David Composer,
Educator
Cohen, Edward Educator, Composer
Davidson, Lyle Composer, Educator
DiPietro, Albert S Trumpet, Educator
Dunkel, Stuart Educator, Oboe
Earls, Paul Composer
Epple, Carol Flute & Baroque Flute
Epstein, David M Music Director,
Composer
Escot, Pozzi Educator, Composer
Evensen, Robert Lloyd Librarian
Forbes, Elliot Educator, Conductor
Fortunato, D'Anna Mezzo-soprano,
Educator
Fuller, Stephan B Librarian
Geoghegan, James Hugh Guitar, Teacher
Glaser, Victoria Merrylees Educator,
Composer
Hammer, Stephen Early Wind
Instruments, Educator
Harbison, John H Composer
Hodgkinson, Randall Thomas Piano,
Teacher
Hughes, David Grattan Educator, Writer
Hurwitz, Isaac Violin, Educator
Irving, Janet Educator, Singer
Jochum, Veronica Piano, Educator
Kim, Earl Composer, Educator
Kirchner, Leon Composer, Educator
Kletzsch, Charles Frederick Composer
Kout, Trix Flute, Recorder
Lehrman, Paul David Writer, Electronic
Lindgren, Lowell Edwin Educator, Writer
Lockwood, Lewis Henry Educator,
Musicologist
Lomon, Ruth Composer, Piano
Monk, Patricia Educator, Piano
Ochs, Michael Lecturer, Educator
Packer, Janet Susan Violin, Educator
Patterson, David Nolte Composer,
Educator
Pinkham, Daniel Composer, Educator
Radnofsky, Nancy Clarinet, Educator
Rife, Jean Horn, Educator
Roads, Curtis Composer, Writer
Roby, Paul Edward Violin, Educator
Ross, Judith Harp, Educator
Selig, Robert L Educator, Composer
Sims, Ezra Composer
Solow, Linda I Librarian, Administrator
Southern, Eileen Jackson Educator,
Writer
Stevens, Jeffrey Piano, Educator
Sturges, Rowland (Gibson Hazard)
Educator, Piano
Swift, John David Composer, Clarinet
Thompson, Marcus Aurelius Viola,
Educator
Totenberg, Roman Violin, Administrator
Verba, E Cynthia Administrator,
Educator
Vilker, Sophia Educator, Violin
Vilker-Kuchment, Valeria M Violin,
Teacher
Ward, John Milton Educator,
Musicologist

Wender, Peter J Patron, Bass
Wolff, Christoph Johannes Musicologist,
Educator
Yannatos, James D Composer, Conductor
& Music Director

Charlemont

Scott, Molly Composer, Soprano

Charleston

Gibbons, John Harpsichord, Educator

Charlestown

Brown, Merton Luther Composer, Piano

Chestnut Hill

Wyman, Dann Coriat Composer, Viola

Concord

Bailey, David Wayne Conductor & Music
Director, Educator
Vercoe, Barry Lloyd Educator, Composer
Vercoe, Elizabeth Composer
Wilkins, Christopher Putnam Conductor

Deerfield

Clarke, Henry Leland Educator,
Composer
Graney, John F, Jr Administrator,
Educator

Delham

Huetteman, Albert G Administrator,
Educator

Dorchester

Gourdin, Jacqueline Educator, Keyboards

Dover

Firth, Vic (Everett Joseph) Timpani,
Percussion

Duxbury

Hache, Reginald W J Piano, Educator
McClosky, David Blair Teacher, Baritone

Eastham

Chase, Joseph Russell Educator

Fitchburg

Moulton, Suzanne LeRoy Librarian,
Artist Manager

Framingham

Bogard, Carole Christine Soprano

Gloucester

Roberts, F Chester Tuba, Teacher

Groton

Hazzard, Peter (Peabody) Composer,
Conductor

Hampden

Procter, Leland (Herrick) Composer,
Educator

Hanover

Cohen, Jerome D Administrator, Music
Director

Holyoke

Dower, Catherine Anne Educator,
Lecturer

Jamaica Plain

Coppock, Bruce Educator, Cello
Smith, J Fenwick Flute, Teacher

Lenox

Marcus, Leonard Marshall Administrator,
Writer

Leominster

Kent, Richard Layton Educator,
Composer

Lexington

Aberts, Eunice Dorothy Contralto,
Educator
Ammer, Christine Writer, Lecturer
Boyadjian, Hayg Composer, Piano
Technician-Tuner
Shepp, Marian Gray Teacher, Organ

Lowell

Espinosa, Alma O Educator, Harpsichord
Moylan, William David Composer,
Recording Engineer & Producer
Trenkamp, (Wilma) Anne Educator, Flute
& Piccolo

Manchester

Read, Gardner Composer, Critic-Writer

Marshfield

Frigon, Chris Darwin Composer,
Educator
Kaplan, Robert Barnet Composer, Piano
Snyder, Leo Composer, Educator

Medfield

Battisti, Frank Leon Conductor, Educator

Medford

Brumit, J(oseph) Scott Baritone, Teacher
DeVoto, Mark Bernard Composer,
Educator
Titon, Jeff Todd Educator, Writer

Milford

Bleecker, Ruth (Mercer) Librarian

Natick

Shapero, Harold Samuel Composer,
Educator

New Bedford

Dumont, Lily Piano, Teacher & Coach

Newburyport

Owen, Barbara Organ, Lecturer

Newton

Allen, Susan Elizabeth Harp, Teacher
Bavicchi, John Alexander Conductor,
Composer
Gramenz, Francis L Administrator,
Librarian
Jacobson, Joshua R Conductor,
Administrator
Lerman, Richard M Composer, Electronic
Lieberson, Peter Goddard Composer,
Conductor
Martino, Donald James Composer,
Educator
Oberle, Freya Ellen Cello
Plsek, Thomas Joseph Educator,
Composer
Scheibert, Beverly Writer, Harpsichord

Newton Center

Anderson, Allen Louis Composer,
Educator
Gelbloom, Gerald Violin, Educator
Goepfert, Robert Harold Educator, Piano
Pittman, Richard Conductor
Plsek, Stephany King Educator, Piano
Schuller, Gunther Composer, Music
Director

MASSACHUSETTS (cont)

Newton Heights

Strizich, Robert (Ward) Composer, Guitar & Lute

Newton Highlands

Dyer, Joseph Educator

Northampton

Gotwals, Vernon D Organ, Educator
Lockshin, Florence Levin Composer, Piano
Perera, Ronald Christopher Composer, Educator
Sherr, Richard Jonathan Educator, Writer
Solie, Ruth Ames Educator, Critic & Writer
Wheelock, Donald Franklin Composer, Conductor

North Andover

Ota, Diane O Librarian

North Dartmouth

Noel, Barbara H (Barbara H McMurtry) Administrator, Educator

Osterville

Elkus, Jonathan (Britton) Composer, Writer

Pelham

May, Ernest Dewey Educator, Organ

Pepperell

Ogasapian, John Ken Educator, Organ

Plymouth

Gregg, Chandler Teacher, Piano

Princeton

Nunlist, Juli (Elizabeth Moora) Composer, Educator

Reading

McKinley, William Thomas Composer, Piano

Rockport

Clapp, Lois Steele Music Director, Organist

Roslindale

Norden, Hugo Educator, Composer

Salem

Arnatt, Ronald (Kent) Music Director, Composer
Tgettis, Nicholas Chris Composer

Sandisfield

Roosevelt, Joseph Willard Composer, Piano

Sharon

Boszormenyi-Nagy, Bela Piano, Educator
Creditor, Bruce Mitchell Clarinet, Teacher

Shrewsbury

Clickner, Susan Fisher Mezzo-soprano, Educator

Shutesbury

Tanner, Peter H Educator, Composer

Somerville

Lee, Thomas Oboe Composer, Lecturer
Lister, John Rodney Composer

Southborough

Ostrander, Linda Woodaman Composer, Administrator

South Hadley

Bonde, Allen Composer, Educator

South Lancaster

Merriman, Margarita Leonor Educator, Composer

Springfield

Gutter, Robert (Harold) Music Director, Educator

Stockbridge

Flower, Edward John Fordham Guitar & Lute
Hagenah, Elizabeth A(rtman) Piano, Educator

Tyngsboro

Beale, Everett Minot Percussion, Educator

Tyringham

McLennan, John Stewart Composer

Waban

Chodos, Gabriel Piano, Educator
Takahashi, Yoriko Piano, Educator

Waltham

Boykan, Martin Composer, Piano
Hoose, Alfred Julius Composer, Educator
Marshall, Robert Lewis Educator
Pope, Conrad Educator
Titcomb, Caldwell Educator, Composer

Watertown

Anderson, Neil Guitar, Educator
Folkers, Catherine Eileen Flute, Instrument Maker
Zander, Benjamin David Conductor & Music Director, Educator

Wellesley

Arnold, Louis Guitar, Educator
Bacon, Denise Educator, Administrator
Jander, Owen Hughes Educator
Ladewig, James Leslie Educator
Walant, Glen Trombone
Zallman, Arlene Composer, Educator

West Peabody

Abrahams, Frank E Educator, Administrator

Williamstown

Hegyi, Julius Conductor, Violin
LePage, Jane Weiner Critic-Writer, Educator
Moore, Douglas Bryant Educator, Cello

Wilmington

Zano, Anthony (Anthony Joseph Ferrazano) Composer

Winchester

Anderson, Thomas Jefferson, Jr Composer, Conductor

Winthrop

Lundberg, Harriet A Piano, Educator

Worcester

Mazo-Shlyam, Eda Piano, Teacher
Raffman, Relly Educator, Composer

MICHIGAN

Albion

Bolitho, Albert George Educator, Organ
Larimer, Melvin Sherlock Conductor, Educator
Maag, Jacqueline Educator
Taffs, Anthony J Composer, Educator

Ann Arbor

Albright, William Hugh Composer, Organ
Anderson, Waldie Alfred Tenor, Educator
Bartholomew, Lynne Piano, Educator
Bassett, Leslie Raymond Composer, Educator
Bolcom, William Elden Educator, Composer
Boylan, Paul C Administrator, Educator
Britton, Allen Perdue Educator
Browne, Richmond Theorist, Composer
Bryan, Keith (Walburn) Flute
Burt, George Composer, Educator
Cacioppo, George Emanuel Composer, Teacher
Cooper, Lewis Hugh Bassoon, Educator
Crawford, David Eugene Writer, Educator
Crawford, Richard Educator
Culver, Robert Educator, Viola
Danforth, Frances Adams Teacher, Composer
Daub, Peggy Ellen Librarian, Educator
Derr, Ellwood S Lecturer, Educator
Dexter, Benning Piano, Educator
Finney, Ross Lee Composer
Gardner, Patrick G Conductor, Educator
Hatten, Robert Swaney Educator, Piano
Jelinek, Jerome Cello, Educator
Kibbie, James Warren Organ, Educator
Lawless, Lyndon Kent Music Director, Baroque Violin
Lehman, Paul Robert Administrator, Educator
Lettvin, Theodore Piano
McCollum, John (Morris) Tenor, Educator
McInnes, Donald Viola, Educator
McPeek, Gwynn Spencer Educator, Writer
Malm, William Paul Educator, Lecturer
Mayes, Samuel H Cello, Educator
Meier, Gustav Conductor, Educator
Monson, Dale E Educator
Nagel, Louis B Piano, Educator
Norton, Pauline Elizabeth Librarian, Lecturer
Ober, Carol Jean Clarinet, Teacher
Owen, Charles E Educator, Percussion
Reyes, Angel Violin, Educator
Ricci, Ruggiero Violin, Educator
Sargous, Harry Wayne Oboe, Educator
Scavarda, Donald Robert Composer
Shames, Jonathan Piano
Sinta, Donald Joseph Saxophone, Educator
Smith, Glenn Parkhurst Trombone, Educator
Stout, Louis James Horn, Educator
Szasz, Tibor Piano, Teacher-Coach
Taylor, Thomas Fuller Educator
Torchinsky, Abe Educator, Tuba
Udow, Michael William Composer, Educator
Watkins, Glenn Educator
Weichlein, William Jesset Educator, Bassoon
Wilson, George Balch Educator, Composer

Berrien Springs

Becker, C(ecil) Warren Educator, Organ
Hall, Charles John Composer, Educator
Owen, Blythe Composer, Piano

Bloomfield Hills

Di Chiera, David Director-Opera,
  Administrator
Freeman, Joann (Joann Freeman
  Shwayder) Music Director

Chelsea

Eyster, Jason Administrator

Dearborn

Eliason, Robert E Critic-Writer, Tuba
Kennedy, (Charles) Bryan French Horn,
  Teacher
Skrzynski, Joseph Trombone, Educator

Detroit

Babini, Italo (S) Cello
Beckon, Lettie Marie Composer, Piano
Bertini, Gary Music Director, Composer
Compton, Catherine Louise Viola
DeTurk, William N Carillon, Teacher
Dorati, Antal Conductor & Music
  Director, Composer
Ferguson, Ray Pylant Organ, Harpsichord
Ferguson, Suzanne (Carol) Recorder,
  Educator
Ganson, Paul Bassoon
Gatwood, Carole Grace Cello
Gordon, Marjorie Soprano, Administrator
Gordon, Nathan Viola, Conductor
Guinn, John Critic-Writer
Hayes, Joseph (C) Composer, Educator
Janowsky, Maxim Dubrow Educator,
  Double Bass
Jean, Kenneth Conductor
Jones, Robert William Composer,
  Educator
Krajewski, Michael Conductor & Music
  Director
Maddox, Walter Allen Violin
Parcells, Ramon Everett Trumpet,
  Educator
Rifel, Craig Thomas Double Bass, Organ
Smith, John Adelbert Administrator,
  Music Director
Tickton, Jason Harold Educator, Organ

East Lansing

Arnold, Corliss Richard Educator, Organ
DeRusha, Stanley Edward Music
  Director, Educator
Herzberg, Jean (M) Soprano, Educator
Jennings, Harlan Francis Educator,
  Baritone
Johnson, Theodore Oliver Educator, Viola
LeBlanc, Albert Henry Educator
Ludewig-Verdehr, Elsa Clarinet, Educator
Niblock, James F Composer, Educator
Ruggiero, Charles H(oward) Composer,
  Educator
Stolper, Daniel John Oboe, Educator
Verdehr, Walter Violin, Educator
Votapek, Ralph Piano, Educator

Flint

Eby, Margarette Fink Administrator,
  Educator
Peryer, Frederick William Administrator,
  Tuba

Grand Haven

Bottje, Will Gay Composer, Flute &
  Piccolo

Grand Rapids

Armstrong, Anton Eugene Conductor,
  Educator
Biser, Larry Gene Conductor & Music
  Director, Tenor
Brink, Emily Ruth Educator, Composer
Brook, Steven Henry Viola, Violin
Greenberg, Philip Conductor & Music
  Director
Haan, Raymond Henry Composer, Music
  Director
Kaiser, Carl William Tenor, Educator
McElfish, Diane Elizabeth Violin,
  Educator
Madura, Robert Hayes Cello
Matsuda, Kenichiro Viola
Royce, Maria M Harp, Teacher
Tuuk, Jonathan Alan Organ, Composer
Vits, Billy (William Henry) Percussion,
  Composer

Grosse Pointe

Bryant, Allan Charles Composer
Miculs, Melita Luize Mezzo-soprano
Ourada, Ann Alicia Violin, Piano
Young, Clyde William Educator, Writer

Haslett

Borouchoff, Israel Flute & Piccolo,
  Educator

Huntington Woods

Ilku, Elyse (Elizabeth Jean Ilku) Harp,
  Teacher
Konikow, Zalman Patron, Administrator

Interlochen

Jacobi, Roger Edgar Administrator,
  Educator
Weliver, E Delmer Librarian, French
  Horn

Kalamazoo

Allgood, William Thomas Composer,
  Educator
Balkin, Alfred Composer, Educator
Bergeron, Thomas Martin Percussion
Curtis-Smith, Curtis O B Composer,
  Educator
Davidson, Audrey Ekdahl Educator,
  Conductor
Jones, Stephen Graf Educator, Trumpet
Osborne, Charles Eugene Flute, Educator
Rackley, Lawrence (Lawrence Rackley
  Smith) Educator, Composer
Ross, Barry Violin, Music Director
Takeda, Yoshimi Conductor & Music
  Director
Thierstein, Eldred A Educator, Baritone
Zastrow, Joyce Ruth Soprano, Educator
Zupko, Ramon Composer, Educator

Lambertville

Carroll, Joseph Robert Composer,
  Educator

Lansing

Burkh, Dennis Conductor
Hutcheson, Jere Trent Composer,
  Educator

Livonia

Dreiling, Alyze Loggie Violin

Marquette

Tate, Elda Ann Administrator, Educator

Milford

Hill, Pamela Jean Flute & Piccolo,
  Teacher

Mt Pleasant

Caldwell, John Timothy Educator, Tenor
Hays, Robert Denecke Composer,
  Educator
Rivard, William H Composer, Educator
Robinson, Forrest Thompson Piano,
  Composer

Novi

Laing, Fontaine Louise Piano, Teacher

Oak Park

Zipser, Burton Allen Administrator,
  Music Director

Okemos

Donakowski, Conrad Louis Educator,
  Writer
Reed, H Owen Composer, Educator

Portage

Whaley, Robert Louis Educator, Tuba

Rochester

Daniels, David Wilder Conductor,
  Educator
Dawson, James Edward Saxophone,
  Educator
Hollingsworth, Stanley W Educator,
  Composer
Pangborn, Robert C Percussion, Educator

Royal Oak

Zerounian, Ara Viola, Educator
Zerounian, Peruz Violin

Saginaw

Najar, Leo Michael Music Director, Viola

St Clair Shores

Hartway, James John Composer,
  Educator

Shelbyville

Sanders, Neill Joseph French Horn, Artist
  Manager

Southfield

Musser, Betty Jean Cello
Novak-Tsoglin, Sofia Violin
Saltzman, David Richard Cello

Traverse City

Warner, Robert Austin Educator,
  Lecturer

Troy

Ferris, Kirkland David Bassoon
Jacobs, Wesley D Tuba, Lecturer
Tundo, Samuel A Percussion

West Bloomfield

Chajes, Julius T Composer, Conductor &
  Music Director
Gold, Morton Conductor, Composer

Ypsilanti

Hause, James B Educator
Iannaccone, Anthony Composer,
  Conductor
Laney, Maurice I Educator, Trombone
Parris, Arthur Lecturer, Critic
Teal, Mary Evelyn Durden Educator,
  Writer

MINNESOTA

Burnsville

Skobba, Daryl S Cello, Administrator

Collegeville

Theimer, Axel Knut Music Director, Educator

Duluth

Coffman, Phillip Hudson Administrator, Educator
Gauger, Ronald Raymond Organ, Educator
Hovda, Eleanor Composer, Educator
Miller, Ralph Dale Educator, Composer
Opheim, Vernon Holman Conductor & Music Director, Educator
Swanson, Jean Phyllis Educator, Organ
Virkhaus, Taavo Conductor, Composer
Williams, Robert Edward Educator, Clarinet

Edina

Sateren, Leland Bernhard Conductor, Composer
Smith, Henry Charles Conductor & Music Director, Trombone
Thevenin, Francis Violin
Ultan, Lloyd Composer, Educator

Golden Valley

Brunelle, Philip Charles Conductor & Music Director, Organ
Capps, Ferald Buell, Jr Oboe & English Horn, Composer

Lester Prairie

Burkley, Bruce Composer, Viola

Little Falls

Schmitt, Cecilia Administrator, Educator

Mankato

Wortman, Allen L Educator, Music Director

Marshall

Whitcomb, Robert Butler Educator, Composer

Minneapolis

Anderson, Robert Peter Double Bass
Argento, Dominick Composer, Educator
Barnett, Carol Edith Composer
Billmeyer, Dean Wallace Organ, Educator
Brandt, Barbara Jean Spinto, Teacher
Culp, Paula N Percussion, Teacher
Eagle, David William Writer, Educator
Feldman, Mary Ann (Janisch) Critic
Gregorian, Henry Violin
Gross, Dorothy (Susan) Administrator, Writer
Hasselmann, Ronald Henry Trumpet, Administrator
Herring, David Wells Trombone
Horvath, Janet Cello
Jackson, Donna Cardamone Educator
Lancaster, Thomas Scott Conductor, Educator
Lubet, Alex J Composer, Educator
McHugh, Charles Russell Composer, Piano
Marriner, Neville Conductor & Music Director, Violin
Paradise, Timothy James Clarinet
Reeve, Basil Oboe
Remenikova, Tanya Cello, Educator
Stokes, Eric Composer
Sutton, Vern (Everett Lavern) Tenor
Ware, Durward Clifton, Jr Educator, Tenor

Weller, Janis Ferguson Flute, Teacher
Wetzler, Robert Paul Composer, Patron
Zeller, Gary L Administrator, Educator
Zgodava, Richard A Librarian, Piano

Moorhead

Pattengale, Robert Richard Administrator, Harpsichord

Morris

Johnson, Clyde E Educator, Composer

Northfield

Campbell, Arthur M Composer
Christensen, Beth Elaine Librarian
Dressen, Dan Fredrick Tenor, Educator
Gilbert, Janet Monteith Composer, Educator
Hoekstra, Gerald Richard Educator
Rhodes, Phillip Composer, Educator

Rochester

Martin, Dennis Roy Educator, Writer

Roseville

Kimes, Janice Louise Music Director, Coach

St Cloud

Ernest, David John Educator, Composer

St Louis Park

Lekhter, Rudolf Violin

St Paul

Baldwin, David Educator, Composer
Balk, H Wesley Director-Opera, Educator
Bogorad, Julia (Anne) Flute & Piccolo
Callahan, James Patrick Educator, Composer
Fetler, Paul Educator, Composer
Franklin, Cary John Composer, Conductor
Frazee, Jane Educator, Lecturer
Gebauer, Victor Earl Educator, Critic-Writer
James, Layton Bray Harpsichord, Piano
King, Alvin Jay Composer, Educator
Larsen, Libby (Elizabeth Brown) Composer
Miller, John William, Jr Bassoon, Educator
Paulus, Stephen Harrison Composer, Administrator
Remsen, Eric Spencer Percussion, Teacher-Coach
Straka, Paul Scott French Horn
Strasser, Tamas Viola, Violin
Venittelli, Salvatore Administrator

St Peter

Baumgartner, Paul Lloyd Educator, Piano
Fienen, David Norman Educator, Organ
Lammers, Mark (Edward) Educator, Trombone
Lewis, Gerald David Educator, Conductor
Mallett, Lawrence Roger Music Director, Educator

Shorewood

Kendrick, Virginia Bachman Composer

Vesta

Fouse, Donald Mahlon Educator, Conductor & Music Director

Wayzata

Skrowaczewski, Stanislaw Conductor, Composer

West St Paul

Van, Jeffrey Wylie Guitar, Educator

White Bear Lake

Zdechlik, John Paul Composer, Educator

MISSISSIPPI

Clinton

Randman, Bennett Charles Cello, Teacher
Sclater, James Stanley Composer, Teacher

Columbus

Graves, William Lester, Jr Educator, Conductor
Matson, Sigfred Christian Educator, Administrator

Greenville

Haxton, (Richard) Kenneth Composer, Cello

Gulfport

Downey, James Cecil Educator, Writer

Hattiesburg

Anderson, Alfred Lamar Baritone, Educator
Brock, Karl Tenor, Educator
Carnovale, A Norbert Administrator, Educator
Donovan, Jack P Educator, Administrator
Gower, Albert Edward Composer, Educator
Green, John Elwyn Administrator, Educator
Hong, Sherman Educator, Percussion
McCreery, Ronald D Administrator, Conductor
Morrow, Ruth Elizabeth Viola, Teacher
Presser, William Henry Composer
Shaw, Rolland Hugh Conductor & Music Director, Educator
Wood, Vivian Poates Mezzo-soprano, Educator
Zaninelli, Luigi Composer, Conductor

Jackson

Berthold, Sherwood Francis Timpani, Percussion
Choset, Franklin Conductor, Director-Opera
Cukro, Gregory Bassoon
Dalvit, Lewis David, Jr Conductor
Hoogenakker, Virginia Ruth Violin, Educator
Jackson, Anita Louise Educator, Piano
Lynch, William Frank Oboe
Mason, Anne C Viola, Educator
Plucker, John P Double Bass
Plucker, Margaret L Violin

Oxford

Fox, Leland Stanford Educator, Critic-Writer
Grant, William Parks Composer, Educator

Starkville

Hood, Burrel Samuel Educator, Music Director

State College

Stewart, Frank Graham Composer, Educator

University

Lichtmann, Margaret S Flute & Piccolo, Educator

Winona

Howard, Wayne Writer, Musicologist

MISSOURI

Bolivar

Pottenger, Harold Paul Educator, Composer

Buffalo

Moulder, Earline Composer, Organ

Cape Girardeau

Smith, Charles Warren Educator, Composer

Thomas, T(homas) Donley Composer, Writer

Carthage

Harris, Robert A Piano, Educator

Columbia

Burk, James Mack Educator

Hills, Richard L Educator, Clarinet

Kennedy, Dale Edwin Music Director, Educator

McKenney, William Thomas Composer, Educator

Minor, Andrew Collier Educator, Conductor

Morrison, Harry S Educator

Parrigin, Perry Goggin Organ, Educator

Simmons, Eula Mary Schock Administrator, Cello

Spotts, Carleton B Cello, Educator

Florissant

Reiswig, David Earl Educator, French Horn

Touliatos-Banker, Diane H Writer, Educator

Fulton

Jackson, Bil Clarinet

Hazelwood

Myover, Max Lloyd Composer, Music Director

Independence

Obetz, John Wesley Organ, Educator

Jefferson City

Taylor, John Armstead Educator

Kansas City

Albrecht, Theodore John Music Director, Educator

Bean, Shirley Ann Educator

Cass, Richard Brannan Educator, Piano

Franano, Frank Salvatore French Horn, Administrator

Greenberg, Nat Administrator

Haskell, Harry Ogren Critic-Writer

Kemner, Gerald E Composer, Educator

Lathom, Wanda B Educator, Music Therapist

Merrill, Lindsey Administrator, Composer

Niedt, Douglas Ashton Educator, Guitar

Patterson, Russell Conductor, Administrator

Revitt, Paul J Educator, Musicologist

Rich, Ruthanne Piano, Educator

Thompson, William Ernest Administrator

Kirksville

Danfelt, Lewis S(eymour) Educator, Oboe

Jorgenson, Dale Alfred Administrator, Conductor

Nichols, David Clifford Educator, Clarinet

Ritchie, Tom Vernon Composer, Educator

Kirkwood

Chamberlin, Robert Charles Composer, Educator

Lake Lotawana

Petersen, Marian F Educator

Liberty

Brown, Donald Clayton Administrator, Educator

Epley, (William) Arnold Music Director, Baritone

Ozark

Salts, Joan Shriver Violin, Conductor & Music Director

St Joseph

Jones, Nancy Thompson Soprano, Teacher-Coach

St Louis

Allen, Jane Piano, Educator

Banducci, Antonia Educator

Beckerman, Michael Brim Educator, Critic & Writer

Berg, Darrell Matthews Musicologist

Berg, Jacob Flute

Blumenfeld, Harold Composer, Writer

Bowman, Peter Oboe, Educator

Brewer, Christine Soprano

Cain, James Nelson Administrator

Carlin, Maryse Piano, Educator

Ciechanski, Aleksander Cello, Educator

Cobb, A(lfred) Willard Tenor, Educator

Comet, Catherine Conductor & Music Director

Crowder, Elizabeth (Bette Hope Waddington) Violin

Dumm, Thomas A Educator, Viola

Fisher, Gilbert Blain Music Director

Gabora, Gaelyne Soprano, Teacher

Gabora, Teras Educator, Violin

Gippo, Jan Eirik Flute & Piccolo

Herr, Barbara Oboe, Educator

Higgins, Thomas Writer, Educator

Holmes, Richard Timpani, Conductor

Hunt, Michael Francis Composer, Educator

Israelievitch, Gail Bass Harp, Educator

Israelievitch, Jacques Violin, Educator

Jernigan, Melvyn Trombone, Educator

Jones, Jenny Lind Violin

Jordan, Roland Educator, Composer

Kalichstein, Joseph Piano, Educator

Kasica, John Educator, Percussion

Korman, Joan Viola, Educator

Korman, John Violin, Educator

Lehr, Catherine (Catherine Lehr Ramos) Cello

Liberman, Barbara (Lee) Piano, Harpischord

Loew, Henry Double Bass, Educator

Martin, Donald R Double Bass

Mattis, Kathleen Viola

Miller, Kenneth Eugene Educator

O'Donnell, Richard Composer, Percussion

Orland, Henry Composer, Educator

Pandolfi, Roland French Horn, Educator

Parnas, Leslie Cello, Educator

Paul, Pamela Mia Piano

Perris, Arnold B Educator, Writer

Philips, John (Douglass) Piano, Educator

Pokorny, Gene (John Eugene) Tuba

Revzen, Joel Music Director, Administrator

Samuel, Rhian Composer, Educator

Sant Ambrogio, John Educator, Cello

Sayad, Elizabeth Gentry Patron, Critic-Writer

Schatzkamer, William Max Conductor & Music Director, Piano

Schneider, Bernard Educator, Trombone

Schuster, Savely Educator, Cello

Silfies, George Educator, Clarinet

Slatkin, Leonard Conductor & Music Director

Slaughter, Susan Trumpet, Educator

Stripling, Luther Educator, Baritone

Stucky, Rodney Guitar & Lute, Educator

Sugitani, Takaoki Violin

Tafoya, Carole Smith Educator, Piano

Tietov, Frances Harp, Educator

Tung, Yuan Cello, Educator

Turner, Sarah Soprano, Educator

Warren, Edwin Brady Educator, Writer

Wierzbicki, James Critic-Writer

Willman, Fred R Educator, Composer

Wisneskey, Robert Educator, Bassoon

Zambara, Edward Educator, Voice

Springfield

Blakely, Lloyd George Administrator, Educator

Bontrager, Charles E Music Director & Conductor

Burgstahler, Elton Earl Educator, Composer

Gordon, Sherry L Viola, Educator

Nicholson, Joseph Milford Educator, Trombone

Scott, Robert M Music Director, Administrator

Webb, Guy Bedford Conductor, Baritone

Warrensburg

Halen, Walter John Educator, Composer

Homan, Frederic Warren Educator, Organist

Park, Raymond Roy Educator, Piano

Resch, Rita Marie Educator

Webster Groves

Kurtz, Arthur Digby Composer, Piano

Schiebler, Beverly Beasley Violin, Singer

Schiebler, Carl Robert French Horn

MONTANA

Bozeman

Campbell, Henry C Composer, Educator

Leech, Alan Bruce Bassoon, Educator

Leech, Karen Davidson Flute, Educator

Nelson, Lorna C Oboe, Organ

Great Falls

Johnson, Gordon James Conductor & Music Director

Manhattan

Saunders, Jean O Teacher, Soprano

Missoula

Johnston, Donald O Composer, Educator

Manning, William Meredith Educator, Clarinet

Mussulman, Joseph Agee Educator

NEBRASKA

Chadron
Hammitt, Jackson Lewis, III Educator, Piano

Columbus
Micek, Isabelle Helen Teacher, Piano

Crete
Bastian, James Educator, Piano

Kearney
Crocker, Ronald Jay Composer, Teacher
Feese, Gerald Educator

Lincoln
Beadell, Robert Morton Composer, Educator
Collier, Nathan Morris Educator, Violin
Haggh, Raymond Herbert Educator, Administrator
Mann, Brian Richard Writer, Educator
Salistean, Kim(berly) Osborne Violin
Snyder, Randall L Composer, Educator
Stephenson, Ruth Orr Educator, Soprano
Walters, Robert Douglas Composer, Conductor & Music Director

Omaha
Briccetti, Thomas Bernard Music Director, Composer
Brill, Michelle Mathewson Viola
Eckerling, Lawrence David Conductor & Music Director, Piano
House, Shari Tyle Viola
Leibundguth, Barbara Flute & Piccolo, Educator
Lohmann, Richard Brent Violin, Teacher
Roebuck, Karen Lee Cello
Stutt, Cynthia Violin
Ventura, Brian Joseph Oboe & English Horn

Seward
Held, David Paul Educator, Conductor

Wayne
Garlick, Antony Educator, Composer

NEVADA

Boulder City
Shade, Nancy Elizabeth Soprano

Henderson
Viscuglia, Felix Alfred Clarinet

Las Vegas
Baley, Virko Conductor, Composer
Duer, Susan R Piano & Fortepiano
Firkins, James T Trombone, Teacher
Hanlon, Kenneth M Educator, Composer
Holloway, Jack E Composer, Conductor
Shaw, Arnold Composer, Writer

Reno
Jones, Perry Otis Educator, Conductor
Smith, Catherine Parsons Educator, Flute

NEW HAMPSHIRE

Bradford
Ziffrin, Marilyn Jane Composer, Writer

Deerfield
Bozeman, George Lewis, Jr Organ

Durham
Howard, Cleveland L Music Director, Educator
Rogers, John E Composer, Educator

East Sullivan
Hauck, Betty Virginia Viola

Francestown
Bolle, James D Composer, Conductor

Hancock
Clayton, Laura Composer, Educator

Hanover
Appleton, Jon H Composer, Educator
Wolff, Christian Composer, Educator

Lebanon
Middleton, Robert (Earl) Educator, Composer

Meredith
Leonard, Peter Conductor & Music Director, French Horn

Nashua
Bishop, Adelaide Educator, Director-Opera

New London
Woodward, Martha Clive Flute, Composer

Peterborough
Mason, Robert M Writer

Plaistow
Dederer, William Bowne Administrator, Trumpet

Plymouth
Swift, Robert Frederic Educator, Administrator

NEW JERSEY

Audubon
Coffey, Denise (Denise Coffey Pate) Soprano

Autley
Marshall, Elizabeth Piano

Bayonne
Estill, Ann (H M) Educator, Coloratura Soprano

Belle Mead
Moevs, Robert Walter Composer, Educator

Berkeley Heights
Fromme, Arnold Educator, Trombone

Bridgeton
Creamer, Alice Dubois Baroque Instruments, Musicologist

Cedar Grove
Sacher, Jack, Jr Educator, Lecturer

Cherry Hill
Baxter, Robert T S Critic & Writer
Dalschaert, Stephane Violin, Teacher-Coach
Farago, Marcel Composer, Cello
Grika, Larry A Violin, Teacher
Miller, Ira Steven Composer
O'Carroll, Cathleen (Cathleen Dalschaert) Violin, Teacher-Coach

Provenzano, Aldo Composer
Sebastian, Anne Marie Librarian
Zuponcic, Veda Helen Piano, Educator

Clifton
Heilner, Irwin Composer, Writer
Turrin, Joseph Egidio Composer, Conductor

Collingswood
Odum-Vernon, Alison P (Alison Paige Odum) Soprano, Educator
Vernon, Charles Gary Trombone & Bass Trombone, Educator

Cresskill
Meyerowitz, Jan Composer, Lecturer

Denville
Ho, Ting Composer, Educator
Karmazyn, Dennis Cello

Deptford
Biester, Allen George Composer, Music Director

Dunmont
Nobleman, Maurice Music Director

East Brunswick
Wheeler, Janet Soprano, Educator
Yttrehus, Rolv Composer, Educator

Elberon
Benham, Helen Wheaton Performer, Piano

Elizabeth
Pierson, Edward Baritone, Educator

Englewood
Corenne, Renee Teacher, Soprano
Danner, Dorothy Director-Opera
Glazer, Gilda Piano, Educator
Glazer, Robert Viola, Conductor
Rhodes, Samuel Viola, Educator
Sturm, George Administrator, Writer
Sutin, Elaine Violin, Administrator
Yajima, Hiroko Violin, Educator

Fair Haven
Fishman, Jack Adam Double Bass

Franklin Lakes
Cornell, Gwynn Mezzo-soprano
Fiske, June Soprano
Somach, Beverly Violin, Teacher

Freehold
Wood, Kevin Joseph Composer, Administrator

Ft Lee
Wallach, Joelle Composer, Educator

Glassboro
Stewart, Larry Joe Educator, Bassoon
Thamon, Eugene (Eugene Thamon Simpson) Educator, Conductor
Travaline, Marjorie D Librarian
Travaline, Philip Francis Conductor & Music Director

Hackensack
Schroth, Godfrey William Composer, Conductor & Music Director

Haddonfield

Garfield, Bernard Howard Bassoon,
Composer
Pfeuffer, Robert John Bassoon &
Contrabassoon

Hewitt

Kirkpatrick, Gary Hugh Piano, Educator

Highland Park

Grave, Floyd Kersey Educator,
Administrator
Hoffman, Paul K Piano, Educator
Lincoln, Robert Dix Administrator,
Educator

Hoboken

Schneider, Gary Michael Music Director,
Composer

Jersey City

Colaneri, Joseph Conductor, Coach
Hansler, George Emil Educator,
Conductor
James, Marion Verse Educator, Piano
Raditz, Edward Educator, Violin

Kingston

Cheadle, William G Piano, Composer
Holland, Samuel Stinson Administrator,
Teacher

Lawrenceville

Litton, James Howard Music Director,
Organ

Lebanon

Newman, Michael Allan Guitar

Leonia

Brewer, Edward Harpsichord, Organ
Jansons, Andrejs Conductor, Composer
Sever, Allen Jay Organ, Teacher
Shapiro, David Conductor, Piano

Little Falls

Scelba, Anthony J Double Bass,
Composer

Madison

Ledeen, Lydia R Hailparn Educator,
Piano
Lowrey, Norman Eugene Composer,
Educator

Maple Shade

Franceschini, Romulus Composer, Writer

Maplewood

Applebaum, Samuel Lecturer, Violin
Markey, George B Educator, Organ
Selden, Margery Stomne Educator, Piano

Maywood

Harley, Robert Trumpet

Metuchen

Schuman, Daniel Zetkin Educator, Violin

Montclair

Rendleman, Ruth Piano, Educator
Schwarz, Gerard Music Director &
Conductor, Trumpet
Walker, George Theophilus Composer,
Piano
Wojtaszek, Teresa (Janina) Kubiak
Soprano

Montvale

Smith, Malcolm Sommerville Bass
Yauger, Margaret (Margaret Yauger
Smith) Mezzo-soprano

Morristown

Norris, Kevin Edward Composer, Organ

Mountainside

Jankowski, Loretta Patricia Composer,
Educator

Mt Laurel

Gardner, Randy Clyburn French Horn,
Teacher

Neptune

Wilson, Fredric Woodbridge Music
Director, Administrator

Neshanic

Goode, Daniel Composer, Clarinet

Newark

Fein, David N Educator, Percussion
Michalak, Thomas Conductor & Music
Director, Violin
Pollak, Carolyn Sue Oboe & English
Horn
Silipigni, Alfredo Conductor, Director-
Opera

New Bergen

Jacobs, Charles Gilbert Educator, Organ

New Brunswick

Ford, Frederic Hugh Conductor, Educator
Kaufmann, Henry William Educator,
Writer
Whitener, Scott Conductor, Trumpet

New Milford

Cossa, Dominic Baritone, Teacher-Coach
Silverman, Alan John Percussion,
Educator

North Bergen

Del Forno, Anton Guitar, Teacher-Coach

Northfield

Klein, Leonard Composer, Piano

Nutley

Brustadt, Marilyn Soprano

Oakhurst

Collier, Gilman Frederick Composer,
Conductor

Oakland

Heier, Dorothy R Trumpet, Educator
Sorce, Richard Composer, Educator

Old Bridge

Scarpinati, Nicholas Joseph Bass-Baritone

Oxford

Jarrett, Keith Daniel Piano, Composer

Palisades Park

Novick, Melvyn Joseph Administrator,
Tenor

Paramus

Keshner, Joyce Grove Conductor &
Music Director, Composer

Paterson

Lane, Richard Bamford Composer,
Teacher

Pequannock

Bride, Kathleen Harp, Teacher

Perth Amboy

Hardish, Patrick Michael Composer,
Librarian

Pitman

Carpenter, Hoyle Dameron Educator,
Writer

Plainfield

Della Peruti, Carl Michael Composer,
Trombone

Princeton

Abbate, Carolyn Educator
Babbitt, Milton Byron Composer,
Educator
Bent, Margaret Educator
Cheadle, Louise M Piano, Administrator
Cone, Edward Toner Critic, Writer
Cummings, Anthony Michael Educator
Hopson, Hal Harold Composer, Educator
Jones, George Morton Clarinet,
Musicologist
Knapp, John Merrill Educator
Kuzma, John Joseph Conductor & Music
Director
Lansky, Paul Composer, Educator
Lehrer, Phyllis Alpert Piano, Educator
Levy, Kenneth Educator, Writer
Lewin, Frank Composer, Educator
Morgan, Paula Margaret Librarian
Nathan, Hans Educator
Randall, James K Composer, Educator
Robinson, Ray E Administrator, Writer
Rosenfeld, Jayn Frances Flute
Safran, Arno M Composer, Educator
Sonnenfeld, Portia Leys Conductor &
Music Director
Spies, Claudio Composer, Educator
Taplin, Frank E Administrator
Westergaard, Peter Talbot Composer,
Educator
Zabrack, Harold Allen Composer, Piano

Ridgefield

Farese, Mary Anne Wangler
Administrator, Educator

Ridgewood

Archer, Mary Ann Flute & Piccolo
Frerichs, Doris (Coulston) Teacher-
Coach, Composer
Kresky, Jeffrey Jay Writer, Educator
Sirinek, Robert Trumpet, Administrator

Ringwood

Martin, Carolann Frances Cello,
Conductor
Mintz, Donald M Educator,
Administrator

River Edge

Shapiro, Jack M Educator, Administrator
Skaggs, Hazel Ghazarian Teacher, Writer

Rockaway

Eddleman, G David Composer, Editor

Roosevelt

Arnold, David Baritone
Zuckerman, Mark Alan Composer,
Educator

NEW JERSEY (cont)

Rutherford

Roy, Will Bass

Ship Bottom

Pollock, Robert Emil Composer, Piano

Somerset

Picker, Martin Educator, Writer

South Orange

Ehrhardt, Franklyn Whiteman Bass-
Profundo
Hines, Jerome Bass

Sussex

Davis, Barbara Smith Soprano
Davis, J(ames) B(enjamin) Bass

Teaneck

Brisman, Heskel Composer, Teacher
Bullough, John Frank Educator, Music
Director
Crittenden, Richard Raymond Educator,
Stage Director
Cruz-Romo, Gilda (Gilda Cruz Romo)
Soprano
Darling, Sandra (Sandra Darling Mitchell)
Soprano, Teacher
Goldstein, Lauren Bassoon
Kay, Ulysses Composer, Educator
Podnos, Theodor Violin, Lecturer
Ware, John Trumpet, Educator
Weidensaul, Jane Bennett Educator, Harp

Tenafly

Levy, Frank E Composer, Cello
Page, Carolann (Carol Ann Gemignani)
Soprano
Rosenberger, Walter Emerson Percussion,
Educator
Taylor, David M Bass Trombone

Tennent

Livingston, Julian Richard Composer,
Music Director

Tinton Falls

Wagner, Denise Administrator, Critic-
Writer

Trenton

McKinney, Roger William Educator,
Clarinet
Uber, David Albert Composer, Conductor
Walker, Charles (John) Tenor

Union

Barrueco, Manuel Guitar, Teacher

Upper Montclair

Landsman, Jerome Leonard Educator,
Violin
Simenauer, Peter W Clarinet, Educator

Waldwick

Fornuto, Donato Dominic Composer,
Educator

Wallington

Van Dyke, Gary John Percussion,
Educator

Wayne

Aitken, Hugh Composer, Educator
Saturen, David Haskell Composer,
Educator

Westfield

Pate, Joseph Martin Bass

Westwood

Mac Court, Donald Vincent Bassoon,
Educator

Woodcliff Lake

Vollinger, William Francis Composer,
Music Director

NEW MEXICO

Albuquerque

Berkowitz, Ralph Piano, Administrator
Gay, Robert Educator, Director-Opera
Gelt, Andrew Lloyd Composer, Writer
Mauldin, Michael Composer,
Administrator
Miskell, (William) Austin Tenor,
Educator
Rhoads, William Earl Composer &
Arranger, Clarinet
Stringer, Alan W Composer, Organ
Wood, William Frank Composer,
Educator

Grants

Kunitz, Sharon Lohse Teacher, Composer

Las Cruces

Hardisty, Donald Mertz Educator,
Composer
Hutchison, (David) Warner (Walter
Hudson) Composer, Educator
West, Charles Wayne Clarinet, Educator

Los Lunas

Wilkinson, Arthur Scott Educator,
Composer

Portales

Paschke, Donald Vernon Educator,
Baritone
Willoughby, David Paul Educator,
Administrator

Santa Fe

Ballard, Louis Wayne Composer,
Educator
Garland, Peter Adams Composer,
Publisher
O'Connor, Thomas E Administrator,
Oboe & English Horn
Reardon, John Baritone

Taos

Farrand, Noel Composer
Forman, Joanne Composer, Writer

University Park

Thielman, Ronald Moncrief Composer,
Educator

NEW YORK

Albany

Chadabe, Joel A Composer, Educator
Friedman, Carole G Piano, Administrator
Gibson, David R Composer, Educator
Gilman, Irvin Edward Flute, Educator
Hartzell, Karl Drew, Jr Educator
Hartzell, Marjorie Helen Harp
Kabat, Julie Phyllis Composer
Kermani, Peter Rustam Patron
Saetta, Mary Lou (Mary Lou
Saetta-Gilman) Violin

Albertson

Fontrier, Gabriel Composer, Educator

Annandale-on-Hudson

Yarden, Elie Composer, Educator

Astoria

Falletta, JoAnn Conductor & Music
Director, Guitar & Lute
Preiss, James Educator, Percussion

Babylon

Peskanov, Alexander E Piano, Composer

Baldwin

Abram, Blanche Schwartz Piano,
Educator
Stamford, John Scott Lirico Spinto Tenor,
Teacher

Baldwinsville

Pritchard, Robert Starling Composer,
Piano

Ballston Spa

Green, George Clarence Composer,
Violin

Bayside

Weiner, Max Violin

Belle Harbor

Novack, Saul Educator, Administrator

Bellerose

Consoli, Marc-Antonio Composer, Music
Director

Bellmore

Alexander, Brad Percussion, Educator
Swack, Irwin Composer, Educator

Berlin

Curtis, (William) Edgar Composer,
Conductor & Music Director

Big Flats

Bigler, Carole L Lecturer, Educator

Binghamton

Borroff, Edith Composer, Educator
Clarey, Cynthia Mezzo-soprano
Fink, Seymour Melvin Piano, Educator
Hamme, Albert P Educator, Saxophone
Hanson, John R Educator
Jordan, Paul Conductor, Organ
Klenz, William Educator, Composer
Lincoln, Harry B Educator
Ross, Eric Composer, Electronic
Wohlafka, Louise Ann Soprano, Teacher
Wright, (Myron) Searle Organ, Composer

Branchport

Phillips, Burrill Composer, Educator

Brewster

Baker, Julius Flute, Educator

Briarwood

Retzel, Frank (Anthony) Composer,
Educator

Brightwaters

Barbash, Lillian Administrator

Brockport

Henderson, Ian H Lecturer, Harpsichord
Schwarz, Ira Paul Composer, Educator
Temkin, Ascher Mark Conductor

Bronx

Bernstein, Martin Educator, Administrator
Betjeman, Paul Composer, Teacher
DeVaughn, Alteouise (Alteouise DeVaughn Austin) Mezzo-soprano
Folter, Siegrun H Librarian
Gonzalez, Manuel Benjamin Composer, Educator
Griffel, Margaret Ross Writer
Gunther, William (William Gunther Sprecher) Composer, Music Director
Kalajian, Berge Composer
Lubin, Steven Piano
Rudie, Robert Violin, Educator
Skolnik, Walter Composer
Smolanoff, Michael Louis Composer, Administrator

Bronxville

Freeman, Carroll (Benton), Jr Tenor
Schultz, Ralph C Music Director, Teacher
Spiegelman, Joel Warren Composer, Educator

Brooklyn

Anievas, Agustin Piano, Educator
Baily, Diette (Dee) Marie Librarian, Writer
Bavel, Zamir Composer, Violin
Berg, Christopher (Paul) Composer, Piano
Bloom, Julius Administrator
Cervetti, Sergio Composer, Educator
Chambers, Wendy Mae Composer
Creshevsky, Noah Ephraim Composer, Educator
Deason, William David Composer, Educator
Dixon, Dwight Mitchell Composer, Piano
Dodge, Charles M Composer Educator
Faden, Betsy BB (Betsy Gale Bruzzese Faden) Administrator, Piano
Gerboth, Walter William Educator
Glassman, Allan Baritone
Goodman, Lucille Field Educator, Soprano
Hallmark, Rufus Eugene, Jr Educator
Inwood, Mary B B Composer, Teacher
Jeffery, Peter Grant Educator, Librarian
Kaplan, Lewis Violin, Teacher
Klotzman, Dorothy Ann Hill Educator, Conductor
Kogan, Robert Colver Composer, Conductor
Kotik, Petr Composer, Flute
Larson, Susan Soprano
Levarie, Siegmund Educator
Lliso, Joseph M Music Director, Piano
Lowe, Jeanne Catherine Administrator, Piano
Mirkin, Kenneth Paul Viola
Morgan, Beverly Soprano
Nachman, Myrna S Piano, Educator
Oja, Carol J Writer
Ordansky, Jerold Alan Administrator, Composer
O'Riley, Christopher (James) Piano
Rosner, Arnold Composer
Saceanu, Dan George Writer
Sachs, Joel Piano, Educator
Salzman, Eric Composer, Writer
Saperstein, David Composer
Solomon, Joyce Elaine (Joyce Elaine Moorman) Composer, Teacher
Street, Tison Composer, Violin
Wiener, Ivan H Composer

Buffalo

Bock, Richard C Cello
Burgess, Gary Ellsworth Tenor, Educator
Cantrick, Robert B Educator, Critic
Cipolla, Frank J Conductor, Educator

Cipolla, Wilma Reid Librarian, Piano
Clough, John L Writer, Educator
Coover, James Burrell Librarian, Educator
Feldman, Morton Composer, Educator
Homer, Paul Robert Educator, Administrator
Lamb, Norma Jean Librarian, Soprano
Lustig, Leila Sarah Composer, Music Broadcaster
McKinnon, James William Educator, Organ
Manes, Stephen Gabriel Piano, Educator
Mikhashoff, Yvar Emilian Piano, Educator
Minkler, Peter John Viola
Ortiz, William Composer, Educator
Rehfuss, Heinz J Educator, Baritone
Rosenthal, Stephen W Saxophone, Administrator
Simon, Benjamin Viola
Smit, Leo Piano, Composer
Stiller, Andrew Philip Composer, Writer
Strainchamps, Edmond Nicholas Educator, Writer
Trott, Laurence Piccolo, Teacher
Trotter, Herman Critic, Lecturer
Vehar, Persis Anne Composer, Piano
Williams, Jan Educator, Percussion

Caledonia

Davies, Bruce MacPherson Violin

Cambridge

Faiella, Ida M Administrator, Soprano

Canastota

Mirante, Thomas Anthony Composer, Administrator

Carmel

Cameron-Wolfe, Richard G Composer, Piano

Cedarhurst

Suchoff, Benjamin Educator, Writer

Centerport

Lieber, Edvard Composer, Piano

Chatham

Goeke, Leo Francis Tenor

Cheektowaga

Christner, Philip Joseph Trumpet
Jones, Mark Raymond Tuba

Cherry Valley

Sollberger, Harvey Composer, Educator

Clinton

Lindenfeld, Harris Nelson Composer
Pellman, Samuel Frank Composer, Educator
Wakefield-Wright, JoElyn Mezzo-soprano, Music Director
Williams, Hermine Weigel Educator, Writer

Cortland

Anderson, Donna K Educator, Piano
Forcucci, Samuel L Educator, Clarinet

Crestwood

Alley, Edward L Administrator, Conductor
Williams, Nancy Mezzo-soprano, Teacher

Crompond

Anderson, Ruth Composer, Educator
Lockwood, Annea Ferguson Composer

Croton-on-Hudson

Albam, Manny Composer, Educator
Lian, Carol Piano

Delmar

Harmon, Roger Dean Lute, Educator

Demarest

Seiler, James Joseph Administrator, Baritone

Depew

Weyand, Carlton Davis Composer, Publisher

Dobbs Ferry

Banat, Gabriel Jean Violin, Conductor

Douglaston

Berkowitz, Sol Educator, Composer
Pleskow, Raoul Composer, Educator

Dunkirk

Wiles, John A Educator, Baritone

Earlville

Godwin, Joscelyn Musicologist, Educator

East Hampton

Dello Joio, Norman Composer, Educator

East Setauket

Greene, Arthur Piano
Greenhouse, Bernard Educator, Cello
Lessard, John Ayres Composer, Educator
Winkler, Peter Kenton Composer, Educator

Elmhurst

Christopher, Karen Mary Piano, Teacher-Coach
Shimeta, Kathleen Marie Mezzo-soprano

Elmsford

Barrett, Walter Edmund Trombone, Euphonium

Fairport

Beach, David Williams Educator, Administrator
End, Jack Composer, Educator
McGary, Thomas Joseph Educator, Conductor
Plumb, Bruce William Viola, Educator

Fayetteville

Boatwright, Howard Leake, Jr Composer, Writer
Glazier, Beverly Composer, Piano

Fishers Island

Corsaro, Frank Andrew Director-Opera

Flushing

Burnett, Henry Educator, Shamisen & Koto
Chorbajian, John Composer
Graziano, John Composer, Educator
Hiller, Roger Lewis Clarinet, Educator
Kim, Young Mi Soprano
Kirshbaum, Bernard Educator, Writer
McMillan, Geraldine Soprano
Miller, Lucille Soprano
Parwez, Akmal M Composer, Bass-Baritone
Polisi, William Educator, Bassoon
Pommers, Leon Piano, Educator

NEW YORK (cont)

Rorick, William C(alvin) Librarian, Educator
Rosenhaus, Steven L Composer, Lecturer
Schwartz, Marvin Robert Composer, Educator
Shore, Clare Composer, Educator
Townsend, Douglas Composer, Musicologist
Waitzman, Daniel R Flute, Recorder

Forest Hills

Battipaglia, Diana Mittler Piano, Teacher
Blankstein, Mary Freeman Violin
Falaro, Anthony J Composer, Guitar
Goldsmith, Richard Neil Clarinet, Conductor
Heskes, Irene Writer, Lecturer
Jolles, Susan Harp
Martin, Barbara (Ann Sulahian-Martin) Mezzo-soprano
Moore, David Willard Cello, Writer

Fredonia

Chouinard, Joseph Jerod Librarian, Bass
East, James Edward Clarinet, Educator
Frazeur, Ted C (Theodore C Frazeur) Percussion, Composer
Gillette, John Carrell Educator, Bassoon
Hartley, Walter Sinclair Composer, Educator
Jordan, Robert Piano
McMullen, Patrick T Administrator, Educator
Richardson, Louis Samuel Cello, Composer

Freeville

Lewis, Malcolm Wallace, Jr Composer, Educator

Garden City

Noone, Lana Mae Flute, Educator
Wilson, Todd Rodney Organ, Teacher

Garrison

Kramer, Gregory Paul Composer, Electronic

Geneseo

Kirkwood, Linda Walton Viola, Educator
Willey, James Henry Composer, Educator

Geneva

Berta, Joseph Michel Educator, Clarinet

Glen Cove

Habermann, Michael Robert Piano
Steiner, Gitta H Composer, Piano

Glens Falls

Haupt-Nolen, Paulette Administrator, Conductor

Gloversville

Kibler, Keith E Bass-Baritone

Great Neck

Baron, Carol K Administrator, Musicologist
Baron, Samuel Flute, Conductor
Berger, Melvin Writer, Lecturer
Evans, Phillip Piano, Educator
Feldman, Herbert Bryon Composer
Gould, Morton Composer, Conductor
Kraft, Leo Abraham Composer, Educator
Leavitt, Michael P Administrator, Artist Manager
Lees, Benjamin Composer
Siegmeister, Elie Composer, Writer
Starobin, David Guitar & Lute, Record Producer

Weisgall, Hugo Composer, Conductor
Wuorinen, Charles Composer, Piano

Greenburgh

Cooper, William B(enjamin) Organ, Composer

Greenvale

Rovics, Howard Composer, Educator

Greenwood Lake

Le Vita, David Nahon Piano, Conductor

Hamilton

Morrill, Dexter G Composer, Educator

Harrison

Senn, Martha Mezzo-soprano

Hartsdale

Dunkel, Paul Eugene Conductor & Music Director, Flute

Hastings

DeFord, Ruth I Educator

Hastings-on-Hudson

Diamond, Harold J Librarian, Critic-Writer
Reich, Nancy B Writer, Educator
Wolfe, Stanley Composer, Administrator

Hempstead

Beattie, Herbert (Wilson) Bass, Educator
Perlow, Mildred Stern Music Director, Viola
Shapinsky, Aaron Cello, Teacher

Hicksville

Estrin, Morton Piano, Teacher
Rossi, John L French Horn

Hollis Hills

London, S(ol) J Writer, Lecturer

Hoosick Falls

Fine, Vivian Composer, Piano

Hopewell Junction

Walden, Stanley Eugene Conductor, Composer

Houghton

Basney, Eldon E Composer, Teacher & Coach

Howard Beach

Ernst, David George Composer, Critic

Huntington

Davis, Deborah Griffith Librarian
Deutsch, Herbert Arnold Electronic, Educator
Richter, Marga Composer, Piano
Westermann, Clayton Jacob Conductor, Composer

Interlaken

Barnes, Darrel Viola, Educator

Ithaca

Arlin, Mary Irene Educator, Viola
Austin, William Weaver Educator, Writer
Bilson, Malcolm Piano, Educator
Borden, David Composer
Conrad, Laurie M Composer
Coral, Lenore Librarian
Covert, Mary Ann Educator, Piano
Hsu, John (Tseng-Hsin) Educator, Viola da gamba
Husa, Karel Composer, Conductor

Mauk, Steven Glenn Saxophone, Educator
Monosoff, Sonya (Sonya Monosoff Pancaldo) Violin, Educator
Neubert, Henry Grim, Jr Educator, Double Bass
Ostrander, Arthur E Educator, Administrator
Palmer, Robert M Composer, Educator
Pastore, Patrice Evelyn Educator, Soprano
Silsbee, Ann Loomis Composer, Piano
Stegall, Joel Ringgold Administrator, Educator
Stith, Marice W Educator, Trumpet
Stucky, Steven Composer, Writer
Unland, David E Tuba, Educator
Will, Patrick Terence Critic-Writer, Educator
Wilson, Dana Richard Composer, Piano
Zaslaw, Neal Educator, Musicologist

Jackson Heights

Bliss, Marilyn Composer, Flute & Piccolo
Brunelli, Louis Jean Administrator, Composer
Natochenny, Lev N Piano, Teacher

Jamaica

Copeland, Keith Lamont Percussion, Teacher
Hightower, Gail Bassoon, Educator
Kach, Claire Librarian

Jamesville

George, Earl Composer, Educator

Jerico

Jolly, Kirby Reid Conductor, Trumpet

Katonah

Sweeley, Michael Marlin Administrator

Kenmore

Bradley, Carol June Librarian, Educator

Kew Gardens

Davidovich, Bella Piano, Teacher
Gilbert, David Beatty Conductor & Music Director, Composer
Gilbert, Richard Clarinet, Writer

Kingston

Amacher, Maryanne Composer, Electronic

Lancaster

Geiger, Loren Dennis Tuba

Lansing

Woodward, Gregory Stanley Composer, Educator

Larchmont

Bloch, Joseph Piano, Lecturer

Levittown

Tepper, Albert Composer, Educator

Little Neck

Hettrick, Jane Schatkin Educator, Organ
Hettrick, William Eugene Educator, Writer
Waxman, Ernest Composer, Piano

Liverpool

Dodd, Kit Stanley Viola, Educator

Lloyd Neck

Beeson, Jack (Hamilton) Composer, Educator

Long Beach

Gach, Jay Anthony Composer

Long Eddy

Hoiby, Lee Composer, Piano

Long Island City

Barbagallo, James Angelo Piano
de Brant, Cyr (Joseph Vincent Higginson) Composer, Writer
Rossi, Nick Music Director, Educator
Tyler, Veronica Soprano, Educator

Mamaroneck

Ekizian, Michelle Lynne Composer, Teacher
Karlsrud, Edmond Bass, Artist Representative

Manhasset

Singer, Jeanne (Walsh) Composer, Piano

Manlius

Horn, Lois B(urley) Piano, Teacher

Mattituck

Wills, Vera G Educator, Composer

Mehopac

Goodloe, Robert D Baritone

Merrick

Brauer, Cecilia Gniewek Piano, Celeste

Millwood

Winokur, Roselyn M Composer, Piano

Minetto

Caravan, Ronald L Composer, Educator

Monsey

Brickman, Joel Ira Composer, Teacher

Montgomery

Feldsher, Howard M Composer, Educator

Mt Tremper

Oliveros, Pauline Composer, Accordion

Mt Vernon

Bell, (S) Aaron Composer, Double Bass
Dunham, Benjamin Starr Administrator, Recorder
Febbraio, Salvatore Michael Turlizzo Composer, Educator
Pizzaro, David Alfred Organ, Music Director
Rich, Martin Conductor, Piano

New City

Griggs, Peter Johnson Composer, Guitar & Lute

New Hartford

Angelini, Louis A Composer, Educator

New Hyde Park

Diamond, Arline R Composer

New Paltz

Pone, Gundaris Conductor, Composer
Smiley, Pril Composer, Educator

New Rochelle

Chapman, Eric John Violin Dealer, Violist
Flagello, Nicholas Oreste Composer, Conductor
Harwood, James C Conductor, Saxophone
Schonthal-Seckel, Ruth Composer, Educator
Tanenbaum, Elias Composer, Educator

New Suffolk

Rogers, Patsy Composer, Educator

New York

Abrams, Richard Director-Opera
Abramson, Robert U Educator, Composer
Acosta, Adolovni P Administrator, Piano
Adam, Claus Composer, Educator
Adams, Elwyn Albert Educator, Violin
Adams, Richard Elder Administrator, Lecturer
Adkins, Paul Spencer Tenor
Adler, James R Composer, Piano
Adler, Richard Composer
Agay, Denes Composer, Educator
Ajemian, Anahid M Violin
Ajmone-Marsan, Guido Conductor
Albert, Donnie Ray Bass-Baritone
Albert, Stephen Joel Composer
Alderdice, Mary Piano, Harpsichord
Alexander, John Tenor, Educator
Alexander, Josef Composer, Educator
Allen, Nancy Harp, Educator
Allen, Robert E Composer
Allers, Franz Conductor
Altmeyer, Jeannine Theresa Soprano
Alton, Ardyth Cello, Educator
Amara, Lucine Soprano
Ameling, Elly (Elisabeth Sara) Soprano
Amram, David Werner Composer, French Horn
Anderson, Beth (Barbara Elizabeth Anderson) Composer, Piano
Anderson, June Soprano
Anderson, Ronald K Administrator, Educator
Anderson, Sylvia Mezzo-soprano
Andrade, Rosario Soprano
Annis, Robert Lyndon Clarinet, Educator
Applebaum, Stan (Stanley S) Composer, Writer
Aragall, Giacomo (Jaime) Tenor
Arnon, Baruch Piano, Teacher
Aronoff, Frances Webber Educator, Lecturer
Arrau, Claudio Piano
Arroyo, Martina Soprano
Artymiw, Lydia (Tamara) Piano
Artzt, Alice Josephine Guitar & Lute, Writer
Arzruni, Sahan Piano, Ethnomusicologist
Atamian, Dickran Hugo Piano
Atherton, James Peyton, Jr Tenor
Atherton, Peter L Bass, Teacher
Auerbach, Cynthia Director-Opera
Ax, Emanuel Piano
Babak, Renata Mezzo-soprano
Badea, Christian Conductor, Director-Opera
Bae, Ik-Hwan Violin, Teacher
Bagger, Louis S Piano, Educator
Bailey, Dennis Farrar Tenor
Bailey, Elden C Percussion, Educator
Bailey, Robert Musicologist, Educator
Baker, Alan Baritone
Baker, Janet Abbott Mezzo-soprano
Baker, Nancy Kovaleff Educator, Writer
Baksa, Robert (Frank) Composer
Balk, Leo Frederick Administrator, Editor
Ballam, Michael L Tenor
Balsam, Artur Piano, Teacher
Bampton, Rose E (Pelletier) Soprano
Barbieri, Fedora Mezzo-soprano, Contralto

Barbieri, Saverio Bass
Barbosa, Antonio (G) Piano
Barbosa-Lima, Carolos Guitar, Educator
Barcza, Peter (Joseph) Baritone
Bar-Illan, David J Piano
Barrett, Oreen Teacher, Soprano
Bartolini, Lando Tenor
Basquin, Peter John Piano, Educator
Bass, Warner Seeley Composer, Educator
Bassett, Ralph Edward Bass-Baritone
Bayard, Carol Ann Soprano, Educator
Bazelon, Irwin Allen Composer, Conductor
Beardslee, Bethany E Soprano, Teacher
Beaser, Robert Harry Composer, Conductor & Music Director
Becerril, Anthony Raymond Baritone
Becker, Eugene Viola, Educator
Bednar, Stanley Violin, Educator
Beegle, Raymond Bruce Music Director, Piano
Behr, Jan Conductor
Belling, Susan Soprano
Benedetti, Evangeline Cello, Educator
Beni, Gimi (James J) Bass-Baritone
Bennett, Harold Flute & Piccolo, Educator
Berberian, Ara Bass-Baritone
Bergell, Aaron Tenor
Berl, Christine Piano, Composer
Berlinghoff, Dan A Piano, Conductor & Music Director
Berman, Janet Rosser Violin
Berman, Lynn Howell Trumpet, Educator
Bernardo, Jose Raul Composer, Conductor & Music Director
Bernstein, Jacob Cello, Educator
Bernstein, Leonard Conductor & Music Director, Composer
Bernstein, Seymour Abraham Composer, Piano
Berry, Walter Baritone
Bertolino, Mario Ercole Bass-Baritone
Berv, Harry French Horn, Educator
Beudert, Mark Tenor
Biddlecome, Robert Edward Trombone, Administrator
Birdwell, Edward Ridley French Horn
Biscardi, Chester Composer, Educator
Bixler, Martha Harrison Recorder, Educator
Black, Robert Carlisle Conductor, Piano
Blain, Albert Valdes Guitar, Educator
Blake, Rockwell Tenor
Blegen, Judith Lyric Coloratura Soprano
Bliss, Anthony Addison Administrator
Bloch, Boris Piano
Block, Adrienne Fried Writer
Bloom, Robert Oboe & English Horn, Educator
Blumenthal, Daniel Henry Piano
Boehm, Mary Louise Piano, Lecturer
Bogin, Abba Music Director, Piano
Bonazzi, Elaine Mezzo-soprano
Bond, Victoria Composer, Conductor
Bookspan, Martin Administrator, Writer
Booth, Philip (Saffery Evans) Bass
Boozer, Brenda Lynn Mezzo-soprano
Borror, Ronald Allen Trombone, Educator
Bortnick, Evan N Tenor
Bouchard, Linda Composer, Conductor
Boucher, (Charles) Gene Baritone, Administrator
Bouleyn, Kathryn Soprano
Bowen, Jean Librarian, Administrator
Bowman, Carl Byron Composer, Educator
Boyajian, Armen Coach, Piano
Boyd, Gerard Tenor
Bradshaw, David Rutherford Educator, Piano
Braun, Victor Baritone

Eger, Joseph Conductor, Lecturer
Ehrling, Sixten E Conductor & Music Director, Teacher
Elias, Rosalind Mezzo-soprano
Eliasen, Mikael Coach, Piano
Elisha, Haim Composer, Music Director
Ellis, Brent E Baritone
Elster, Reinhardt Harp
Elvira, Pablo Baritone
Emmerich, Constance M Piano, Music Director
Emmons, Shirlee (Shirlee Emmons Baldwin) Teacher, Writer
Entremont, Philippe Piano, Conductor & Music Director
Epstein, Matthew Allen Administrator, Artist Manager
Erickson, Raymond Educator, Harpsichord
Erwin, Edward Trombone, Educator
Eskin, Virginia Educator, Piano
Estes, Richard (Alan) Tenor
Estes, Simon Bass-Baritone
Estrin, Mitchell S Clarinet
Evans-Montefiore, April Soprano
Ewing, Maria Mezzo-soprano
Ewing, Maryhelen Viola, Educator
Farberman, Harold Composer, Conductor
Farley, Carole Soprano
Farrar, David Director-Opera, Bassoon
Farrell, Eileen Soprano
Faull, Ellen Educator, Soprano
Feder, Susan E Administrator, Critic-Writer
Feist, Leonard Administrator, Publisher
Feldman, Marion Educator, Cello
Fennelly, Brian Leo Composer, Educator
Fennimore, Joseph Composer, Piano
Ferden, Bruce Conductor
Fernandez, Wilhelmenia Soprano
Ferro, Daniel E Teacher
Fialkowska, Janina Piano, Educator
Fiorito, John Basso Buffo
Firkusny, Rudolf Piano, Educator
Fischer, Bill (William S) Composer, Conductor
Fishbein, Zenon Piano, Educator
Fisher, Jerrold Conductor & Music Director, Composer
Fisk, Eliot Hamilton Guitar
Fitzgerald, Gerald Writer, Piano
Flanagan, Thomas J Composer, Educator
Flasch, Christine Elizabeth Soprano
Flint, Mark David Conductor & Music Director
Foote, Lona Administrator, Artist Manager
Forrester, Maureen Katherine Stewart Contralto
Foss, Lukas Composer, Educator
Foster, Richard Coach
Fowler, John Tenor
Fowles, Glenys Rae Soprano
Fox, Barbara J Soprano
Frager, Malcolm Piano, Educator
Frame, Pamela Cello, Teacher
Frank, Claude Piano
Frank, Joseph Tenor
Fredricks, Richard Baritone
Freed, Arnold Composer, Writer
Freedman, Ellis J Artist Representative, Administrator
Freeman, Colenton Tenor
Freeman, John Wheelock Writer, Composer
Freni, Mirella Soprano
Freundlich, Lillian Piano, Teacher
Friede, Stephanie Mezzo-soprano
Friedman, Erick Violin, Educator
Frisch, Richard S Baritone, Educator
Frisch, Walter Miller Educator, Writer

Frost, Thomas Administrator, Writer
Fuchs, Joseph Violin, Educator
Fuchs, Lillian F Viola, Composer
Fuentealba, Victor W Administrator
Fujiwara, Hamao Violin, Teacher-Coach
Fuld, James J Writer
Fuller, Albert Harpsichord, Educator
Fulton, Lauran Ann Soprano
Fuschi, Olegna Piano, Educator
Galardi, Susan M Administrator, Editor
Galbraith, Robert Sinclair Baritone
Galimir, Felix Violin, Educator
Galterio, Lou Director-Opera, Teacher-Coach
Galvany, Marisa Soprano
Galway, James Flute, Conductor
Gamberoni, Kathryn (Lynne) Soprano
Gambulos, Elena (Ellen Gambulos-Cody) Soprano
Ganz, Isabelle Myra Mezzo-soprano, Teacher
Gardiner, Robert Artist Manager
Garrett, Margo Piano, Educator
Garrott, Alice Mezzo-soprano
Garvelmann, Donald M Writer, Administrator
Gately, David E Educator, Director-Opera
Gause, Thomas David Trumpet, Composer
Gedda, Nicolai Tenor
Geiger, Ruth Piano, Teacher
Genia, Robinor Piano, Educator
Gentilesca, Franco Joseph Director-Opera, Educator
Gephart, William (Abel) Teacher, Baritone
Gerber, Steven R Composer, Piano
Gerhart, Martha Coach
Gershunoff, Maxim Artist Manager & Representative, Administrator
Ghent, Emmanuel Composer
Ghezzo, Dinu D Conductor, Composer
Ghiaurov, Nicolai Bass
Ghiglia, Oscar Alberto Guitar, Bassoon
Gibson, Jon Charles Composer, Saxophone
Gideon, Miriam Composer, Educator
Gilels, Emil Pianist
Gillespie, Don Chance Editor, Piano
Gillock, Jon Organ, Educator
Gilmore, John Tenor
Ginsburg, Gerald M Composer, Teacher
Giordano, John Conductor & Music Director
Glass, Philip Composer
Glaze, Gary Tenor
Glazer, David Clarinet, Educator
Glenn, Carroll Violin, Educator
Glinsky, Albert Vincent Composer
Gniewek, Raymond Violin
Golczewski, Magdalena Violin
Gold, Edward (Jay) Piano, Teacher
Goldberg, Judith Soprano
Goldberger, David Educator, Piano
Golden, Emily Mezzo-soprano
Goldina, Arianna (Arianna Goldina-Loumbrozo) Piano, Teacher
Goldstein, Lee Scott Composer, Music Director
Goltzer, Albert Oboe, Educator
Goltzer, Harold Bassoon, Educator
Gondek, Juliana (Kathleen) Soprano, Teacher
Gonzalez, Dalmacio Tenor
Goode, Richard Stephen Piano, Teacher
Goodman, Roger Harpsichord, Teacher & Coach
Gordon, David J Tenor
Gorodnitzki, Sascha Piano, Educator
Gottfried, Martin Critic-Writer
Gottlieb, Jack S Composer, Writer

Gottlieb, Jay Mitchell Piano, Composer
Gould, Eleanor Diane Viola, Mezzo-soprano
Gould, Mark Trumpet, Educator
Grady, John Francis Music Director, Organ
Graf, Uta Singer, Educator
Graham, Colin Director Opera
Graham, John Viola, Educator
Green, Andrew Educator, Flute
Green, Jonathan D Tenor
Greenbaum, Matthew Jonathan Composer
Greene, Joshua Music Director, Teacher
Greene, Margo Lynn Composer, Writer
Greenfield, Lucille J Teacher, Composer
Greitzer, Sol Educator, Viola
Grice, Garry B Tenor, Educator
Griffel, L Michael Educator, Critic-Writer
Griffin, Judson T Viola, Educator
Grillo, Joann Danielle Mezzo-soprano
Grist, Reri Soprano
Gross, Charles Henry Composer
Grossman, Jerry Michael Cello, Educator
Grossman, Norman L Educator, Composer
Grubb, Thomas Teacher-Coach, Piano
Grubb, William Cello
Gruberova, Edita Soprano
Guadagno, Anton Conductor, Composer
Guarino, Robert Tenor
Guinn, Leslie Baritone, Educator
Gunter-McCoy, Jane Hutton Wagnerian Soprano, Educator
Gutierrez, Horacio Tomas Piano
Haas, Jonathan Lee Timpan, Percussion
Haber, Michael Press Cello
Haieff, Alexei Composer
Hale, Robert Bass-baritone
Hall, Janice L Soprano
Hall, Marnie L Administrator
Hamilton, David (Peter) Critic
Hanani, Yehuda Cello, Educator
Hancock, Eugene Wilson (White) Educator, Organ
Hancock, Gerre (Edward) Conductor, Organ
Hancock, Judith Eckerman Organ, Conductor
Hand, Frederic Warren Guitar, Composer
Hankle, Marcia Griglak Flute & Piccolo
Hanson, Eric Allen Baritone
Harkness, Rebekah Composer, Administrator
Harper, Heather Mary Soprano
Harrell, Lynn Cello
Harrold, Jack Tenor, Teacher
Harry, Don Tuba, Educator
Harry, William (Thomas) Cello, Educator
Harth, Sidney Conductor & Music Director, Violin
Hartman, Vernon Baritone
Harwood, Donald Bass Trombone, Educator
Hastings, Baird Conductor, Critic-Writer
Hastings, Emily (Cecilia) Mezzo-soprano, Contralto
Haupt, Charles V Violin
Hautzig, Walter Piano
Hawley, William Composer
Hayashi, Yasuko Soprano
Hayman, Richard Warren Joseph Conductor, Composer
Hays, Doris Ernestine Composer, Piano
Hays, William Paul Educator, Organ
Haywood, Charles Educator, Tenor
Hebert, Bliss Director-Opera
Hedwig, Douglas Frederick Trumpet, Educator
Heiss, David Henry Cello, Teacher
Heldrich, Claire Educator
Heller, Lesley Violin, Teacher

Luening, Otto Composer, Music Director
Lundborg, (Charles) Erik Composer, Piano
Ma, Yo-Yo Cello, Educator
Macbride, David Huston Composer
McCabe, Robin L Piano
McCaffrey, Patricea (Patricia Anne McCaffrey) Mezzo-soprano
McCauley, Barry Tenor
McCauley, John Joseph Conductor, Piano
MacCombie, Bruce Franklin Administrator, Composer
McCracken, Charles, Jr Bassoon, Teacher
McCracken, Charles P Cello, Educator
McDonald, Susann Hackett Harp, Educator
McFarland, Robert Baritone
Machlis, Joseph Educator, Writer
McMillan, Ann Endicott Composer, Writer
MacNeil, Cornell Hill Baritone
Madden, Ronald Baritone
Maki, Paul-Martin Organ, Educator
Malas, Marlena Kleinman Educator, Singer
Malas, Spiro Bass
Malfitano, Joseph John Violin
Mamlok, Ursula Educator, Composer
Manahan, George Conductor, Educator
Mandac, Evelyn Lorenzana Soprano
Mangin, Noel Bass
Mann, Robert Violin, Composer
Manno, Robert Composer, Baritone
Marcus, Adele Piano, Educator
Marcus, Herman Bass
Marek, Dan Voice, Educator
Margalit, Israela Piano, Writer
Margulis, John Lawrence Director-Opera
Markov, Albert Violin, Educator
Marks, Alan Piano
Markson, Hadussah B Administrator
Markuson, Stephen Bass-Baritone
Marsee, Susanne I Mezzo-soprano
Martin, Judith Lynn Composer, Electronic
Martin, (Sheila) Kathleen Piano, Conductor
Martin, Thomas Philipp Conductor & Music Director, Translator
Martino, Laurence Bass
Marton, Eva Soprano
Maslanka, David Henry Composer, Educator
Mason, Lucas (Roger) Composer, Flute
Masselos, William Piano, Educator
Mathews, Shirley Harpsichord
Matsumoto, Shigemi (Shigemi Matsumoto Stark) Soprano
Maucer, John Francis Conductor, Composer
Maxym, Stephen Educator, Bassoon
Mayer, George Louis Administrator, Librarian
Mayer, Steven Alan Piano, Teacher
Mayer, William Robert Composer, Critic-Writer
Mazzola, John William Administrator
Mehta, Zubin Conductor & Music Director
Meier, Johanna Soprano
Meister, Barbara L Piano, Writer
Melano, Fabrizio Director-Opera
Melnik, Bertha Educator, Piano
Mendenhall, Judith Flute & Piccolo
Menotti, Gian Carlo Composer, Director-Opera
Mensch, Homer Double Bass, Educator
Menuhin, Yehudi Violin, Conductor
Merrill, Robert Baritone
Messier, Lise M Soprano, Teacher
Mester, Jorge Conductor & Music Director, Educator

Metcalf, William Baritone
Metz, Jeryl (Jeryl Metz Woitach) Soprano
Meyerson, Janice Mezzo-soprano
Mikowsky, Solomon Gadles Educator, Piano
Miller, David Viola
Miller, Mayne Piano
Miller, Patricia A Mezzo-soprano, Teacher
Miller, Philip Lieson Librarian, Critic
Milnes, Sherrill Baritone
Milstein, Nathan Violin
Mintz, Shlomo Violin
Mitchell, (Mary) Emily Harp & Irish Harp, Soprano
Moffo, Anna Soprano
Molese, Michele Tenor
Monk, Meredith J Composer
Monod, Jacques-Louis Composer, Conductor
Montane, Carlos (Carlos Hevia-Montane) Tenor
Moore, Carman Leroy Composer, Critic
Moore, Dorothy Rudd Composer, Soprano
Morales, Abram Tenor
Morganstern, Daniel Robert Cello
Morganstern, Marvin Violin, Educator
Morgenstern, Gil Violin
Morini, Erica Violin
Morris, James Peppler Bass-Baritone
Morrison, Florence Soprano
Morrison, Julia (Maria) Composer, Writer
Morrison, Ray Bass, Teacher
Mosley, Robert Baritone
Mumford, Jeffrey Carlton Composer
Muraco, Thomas Piano, Educator
Muradian, Vazgen Composer, Viola D'Amore
Murcell, Raymond Bass-Baritone
Myers, Pamela Soprano
Nadler, Sheila Contralto
Nagy, Robert D Tenor
Nash, Paul Composer, Writer
Neill, (John) William Tenor
Neuhaus, Max Composer
Neuls-Bates, Carol Musicologist, Critic-Writer
Neumann, Richard Jacob Composer, Conductor
Nevison, Howard S Baritone, Teacher
Newland, Larry Conductor & Music Director
Niblock, Phill Administrator, Composer
Nierenberg, Roger Music Director
Niska, Maralin Fae Soprano
Nold, Donal Charles Educator, Teacher
Nolen, Timothy Baritone
Noon, David Composer, Educator
Norden, Betsy (Elizabeth N Haley) Soprano
Norell, Judith Regina Harpsichord, Teacher
Norman, Jessye Soprano
Norton, Lew Bass, Educator
Nurock, Kirk Composer, Piano
Oberlin, Russell Countertenor, Educator
O'Brien, Orin Educator, Bass
O'Brien, Valerie Elizabeth Writer
Oliveira, Elmar Violin
O'Neal, Barry Composer, Music Publisher
Opalach, Jan Bass-Baritone
Oppens, Ursula Piano
Orbon, Julian Composer, Educator
Orgill, Roxane Critic
Ostrovsky, Arthur (Arthur William Austin) Violin, Composer
Ouzounian, Michael Vahram Viola
Owen, Richard Composer
Owen, Stephen Bass-Baritone
Paget, Daniel Educator, Music Director

Papavasilion, Ernest John Violin
Pardee, Margaret (Margaret Pardee Butterly) Educator, Violin
Parkening, Christoper W Educator, Guitar
Parker, Alice Composer, Conductor
Parker, William Kent Baritone
Parloff, Michael (Leon) Flute & Piccolo
Parly, Ticho (Ticho Parly Frederik Christiansen) Tenor
Parsons, David Baritone
Parsons, Meredith Wren Mezzo-soprano
Party, Lionel Harpsichord, Educator
Pasatieri, Thomas Composer, Artistic Director
Pastine, Gianfranco Lyric Tenor
Patane, Giuseppe Conductor & Music Director
Patenaude-Yarnell, Joan Soprano
Patrick, Julian Baritone
Paull, Barberi P Composer, Writer
Pavarotti, Luciano Tenor
Pavlakis, Christopher Administrator, Critic-Writer
Pearlman, Richard Louis Stage Director, Educator
Pearson, Barbara (Ann) Soprano
Peaslee, Richard C Composer
Peck, Donald Owen Bass
Pederson, Ilonna Ann Oboe & English Horn, Music Director
Peete, Jerry Lawrence Tenor, Coach
Pelle, Nadia Soprano
Penderecki, Krzysztof Composer, Educator
Pennario, Leonard Composer, Piano
Perahia, Murray Piano, Conductor
Peress, Maurice Conductor, Orchestrator
Perkins, Leeman Lloyd Educator
Perkinson, Coleridge-Taylor Composer, Conductor & Music Director
Perle, George Composer, Writer
Perlman, Itzhak Violin, Educator
Perrin, Peter A Music Director, Composer
Perry, Douglas R Tenor
Pestalozzi, Martha Educator, Piano
Petersen, Barbara A Administrator, Writer
Petros, Evelyn Soprano
Phelps, Roger Paul Administrator, Educator
Picker, Tobias Composer
Pierce, Lorrie (Lorrie Pierce Glaze) Educator, Piano
Piland, Jeanne Smith Mezzo-soprano
Pilgrim, Neva Stevens Soprano
Plishka, Paul Bass
Polisi, Joseph William Administrator, Bassoon
Polivnick, Paul Henry Conductor, Viola
Poll, Melvyn Lyric Tenor
Pollack, Jill M Educator
Ponce, Walter Piano
Poole, Jane L Critic-Writer
Porter, Andrew (Brian) Critic-Writer
Powell, Thomas Roberts Baritone
Powers, William Bass-Baritone
Pranschke, Janet Soprano
Price, Henry Paschal, III Tenor
Price, Leontyne Soprano
Price, Margaret Soprano
Price, Paul (William) Percussion
Price, Richard Galen French Horn, Arranger
Purvis, William Warren Horn
Queler, Eve Conductor & Music Director
Quilico, Louis Baritone, Educator
Quintiere, Jude Composer, Administrator
Quittmeyer, Susan Mezzo-soprano
Quivar, Florence Mezzo-soprano
Rabbai, Joseph Clarinet, Teacher
Radu, Valentin Organ, Conductor & Music Director

Thiollier, Francois-Joel Piano
Thomas, Sally Educator, Violin
Thome, Joel Composer, Conductor
Thompson, Arthur Charles Baritone
Thompson, Marian Educator, Voice
Thomson, Virgil Garnett Composer,
  Critic-Writer
Thorne, Francis (Burritt), Jr Composer,
  Administrator
Thurston, Ethel Holbrooke Teacher,
  Writer
Tilson-Thomas, Michael Piano, Conductor
Tobias, Paul Cello, Educator
Torigi, Richard Baritone
Trainor, Carol Donn Soprano
Trampler, Walter Viola, Educator
Tregellas, Patricia A Conductor
Treutel, Edward F Educator, Trumpet
Trimble, Lester Albert Composer, Critic-
  Writer
Trombly, Preston Composer, Saxophone
Troyanos, Tatiana Mezzo-soprano
Trussel, Jacque Tenor
Tuckwell, Barry Emmanuel Conductor &
  Music Director, French Horn
Tureck, Rosalyn Lecturer, Piano
Turner, James Rigbie Librarian
Turok, Paul Harris Composer, Critic
Uppman, Theodor Baritone, Teacher
Uris, Dorothy Tree Educator, Voice
Ussachevsky, Vladimir A Composer,
  Educator
Vacchiano, William Trumpet, Educator
Valdes-Blain, Rolando Educator, Guitar
Vanasco, Francesca Adele Cello
Vanderlinde, Debra Soprano
Van Hyning, Howard Educator,
  Percussion
Van Norman, Clarendon Ess, Jr French
  Horn, Educator
Van Solkema, Sherman Writer, Educator
Vargas, Sonia Educator, Piano
Velleman, Evelyn Administrator
Vendice, William V Conductor, Piano
Verbit, Martha Anne Piano
Vergara, Victoria Mezzo-soprano
Verrett, Shirley Mezzo-soprano, Soprano
Vickers, Jon Heldentenor
Vigeland, Nils Composer, Conductor
Violette, Andrew Composer, Piano
Vogel, Howard Levi Recorder, Bassoon
Volckhausen, David Teacher, Piano
von Stade, Frederica Mezzo-soprano
Von Wurtzler, Aristid Educator, Harp
Voorhees, Gordon Baritone
Wadsworth, Charles William Piano,
  Artistic Director
Wadsworth, Susan L Popkin
  Administrator, Artist Manager
Wagner, Vincent Artist Manager &
  Representative
Wakschal, Seymour Violin, Conductor
Waldman, Mildred Piano, Educator
Waldrop, Gideon William, Jr
  Administrator, Composer
Walker, Mallory Elton Educator, Tenor
Walker, Sandra Mezzo-soprano
Wallace, Robert William Conductor &
  Music Director, Piano
Wallis, Delia Lesley Suzette Mezzo-
  soprano
Walsh, Diane Piano, Educator
Walsh, Michael Alan Critic, Composer
Walter, David Educator, Double Bass
Walters, Teresa Composer, Piano
Wann, Lois Educator, Oboe
Ward, John Owen Administrator, Writer
Warfield, Gerald Alexander Composer,
  Writer
Watts, Andre Piano
Weaver, John B Organ, Teacher

Weber, David Clarinet, Educator
Webster, Albert K Administrator
Wechsler, Bert Critic, Lecturer
Weidenarr, Reynold Henry Composer,
  Electronic
Weille, F Blair Administrator, Composer
Weinberg, Henry Educator, Composer
Weinrebe, Robert Solomon Viola
Weiss, Piero E Writer, Educator
Weissenberg, Alexis Piano
Wellman, Nancy Roesch Administrator,
  Artist Manager & Representative
Wells, Patricia Soprano
Wendelken-Wilson, Charles Conductor &
  Music Director
West, John Calvin Bass, Educator
West, Jon Fredric (John Fredric) Tenor
Westenburg, Richard Conductor,
  Educator
Wheeler, Kimball Mezzo-soprano
White, John Reeves Educator,
  Musicologist
White, Michael Composer, Educator
White, Robert Charles, Jr Educator,
  Baritone
Whitehead, William John Organ, Music
  Director
Whittenberg, Charles Composer, Educator
Widdoes, Lawrence Lewis Composer
Wigglesworth, Frank Composer, Educator
Wilcox, Carol Ann Soprano
Wild, Earl Piano, Composer
Wildermann, William Bass-Baritone
Williamson, Marshall Educator, Piano
Willoughby, Jay (Alan) Baritone
Wilson, Nancy J Violin, Baroque Violin
Wilson, Ransom Charles Conductor, Flute
Wincenc, Carol Flute, Teacher
Winkler, David Composer
Winter, Joel Educator, French Horn
Wion, John H Flute & Piccolo, Teacher-
  Coach
Witkin, Beatrice Composer, Piano
Woitach, Richard Conductor, Piano
Wolff, Konrad Educator, Writer
Wood, Elizabeth Writer, Educator
Worby, Rachael Conductor, Educator
Workman, William (Gatewood) Baritone
Wright, Elizabeth Educator, Piano
Wyckoff, Lou Ann Dramatic Soprano
Wyton, Alec Composer, Organ
Yakim, Moni Educator, Music Director
Yanagita, Masako (Masako Yanagita
  Bogin) Violin, Teacher
Yanchus, Judith Violin
Yellin, Victor Fell Educator, Composer
Young, Wendy Harpsichord, Music
  Director
Zahler, Noel Barry Composer, Music
  Director
Zakariasen, Bill Critic & Writer
Zaslavsky, Dora Educator, Piano
Ziegler, Delores Mezzo-soprano
Zlotkin, Frederick Cello, Lecturer
Zoghby, Linda Soprano
Zschau, Marilyn Soprano
Zucker, Stefan Tenor, Writer
Zukerman, Pinchas Music Director,
  Violin
Zukofsky, Paul Composer, Conductor
Zylis-Gara, Teresa Geralda Soprano

Northport

Reed, Phyllis Luidens Composer, Mezzo-
  soprano

North Tarrytown

Wasson, D(onald) DeWitt Music
  Director, Critic-Writer

Nyack

Blewett, Quentin H Composer
Cooper, David S(hearer) Administrator,
  Composer
Cunningham, Arthur Composer, Double
  Bass
Liljestrand, Paul F Composer, Piano
Mundt, Richard Bass

Oneonta

Burnsworth, Charles Carl Conductor,
  Educator

Oswego

Barach, Daniel Paul Educator, Viola
Cuppernull, George Joseph Educator
Garriguenc, Pierre Composer, Educator
Smiley, Marilynn Jean Musicologist,
  Educator

Peekskill

Singer, David Clarinet

Pelham

Boorman, Stanley Harold Educator
Gervers, Hilda F Teacher, Writer

Penfield

Werner, Joseph G Piano, Teacher

Piermont

Reese, William Heartt Conductor &
  Music Director, Educator

Pittsford

Adler, Samuel H Composer, Conductor &
  Music Director
Gates, W Everett Composer, Educator

Pleasantville

Goodman, Joseph Magnus Composer,
  Piano
Kennedy, Raymond F Educator,
  Ethnomusicologist

Potsdam

Del Borgo, Elliot Anthony Composer,
  Conductor
Frackenpohl, Arthur Roland Composer,
  Educator
Hultberg, Warren Earle Educator, Piano
McElheran, (N) Brock Conductor,
  Educator
Ossenkop, David Charles Librarian,
  Educator
Skyrm, Sarah Elizabeth Librarian
Unsworth, Arthur E Educator
Wangler, Francis (Frank) D Bassoon,
  Educator
Washburn, Robert Brooks Composer,
  Conductor

Poughkeepsie

Crow, Todd Piano
Gallo, Paul Arthur Clarinet, Conductor &
  Music Director
Reilly, Edward Randolph Music
  Historian, Educator
Wilson, Richard Edward Composer, Piano

Preble

Mayer, Lutz Leo Composer, Educator

Purchase

Comberiati, Carmelo Peter Educator
Herder, Ronald Composer, Writer
Newman, Anthony Composer, Educator
Solomon, Elide N Composer, Piano

NEW YORK (cont)

Red Hook

Boretz, Benjamin Aaron Critic-Writer, Educator

Rhinebeck

Kupferman, Meyer Composer, Educator

Ridge

Smith, Jess Administrator, Educator

Riverdale

Bracali, Giampaolo Composer, Conductor
Brickman, Miriam Piano, Conductor & Music Director
Zwilich, Ellen Taaffe Composer

Rochester

Arad, Atar Viola, Educator
Baldwin, Marcia Mezzo-soprano, Educator
Barlow, Wayne Brewster Composer, Organ
Beauregard, Cherry Niel Tuba
Beck, John H Percussion, Composer
Benson, Warren F Composer, Educator
Berry, Paul Educator, Tenor
Blakeman, Virginia (Virginia Blakeman Lenz) Viola
Boyd, Bonita K Flute, Educator
Brill, Herbert M Assistant Concertmaster, Violin
Brinkman, Alexander R Electronic, Educator
Buff, Iva Moore Librarian
Butler, Barbara Trumpet, Educator
Campbell, Bruce Educator
Castleman, Charles Martin Violin, Educator
Castleman, Heidi Waldron Viola, Educator
Chazanoff, Daniel Lecturer, Cello
Crociata, Francis Joseph Artist Manager, Writer
Dechario, Tony Houston Administrator
DeDee, Edward A Administrator
Diamond, David (Leo) Composer, Educator
Dumm, Bryan James Cello
Effron, David Louis Conductor & Music Director, Educator
Egner, Richard John Piano, Lecturer
Epstein, Eli K French Horn
Fisher, Douglas John Bassoon
Freeman, Robert Schofield Administrator, Piano
Gauldin, Robert Luther Educator
Gruber, Albion Matthew Educator, Composer
Haigh, Morris Composer
Hodkinson, Sydney Phillip Composer, Conductor
Hunsberger, Donald Educator, Conductor
Jackson, Helen Tuntland Administrator
Jackson, Isaiah (Allen) Conductor
Katz, Martha Strongin Viola, Educator
Katz, Paul Cello, Educator
Kemp, Kathleen Murphy Cello
Kennedy, Josepha (Marie) Educator, Writer
Kurau, W(arren) Peter Educator, French Horn
Liauba, Danute Educator, Piano
Lindahl, Charles E Librarian, Educator
Livingstone, Ernest Felix Educator, Musicologist
Locke, Ralph P Educator, Critic-Writer
Loft, Abram Educator, Violin
Macisak, Janice Violin, Teacher
Malone, (Mary) Eileen Harp, Educator
Mann, Alfred Educator

Marcellus, John Robert, III Educator, Music Director
Milligan, Stuart Charles Librarian, Educator
Morris, Robert Daniel Composer, Music Theorist
O'Dette, Paul Raymond Lute
Penneys, Rebecca A Piano, Teacher
Pollack, Howard Joel Critic, Educator
Pottebaum, William G Composer, Educator
Reynolds, Verne Becker Composer, Educator
Ribeiro, Gerardo Educator, Violin
Ringholz, Teresa Marie Soprano
Root, Rebecca Jo French Horn, Teacher
Rouse, Christopher Chapman Composer, Educator
Schindler, Allan Educator, Composer
Schwantner, Joseph C Composer, Educator
Shklar, Minna Viola
Snyder, Barry Piano, Educator
Spillman, Robert Armstrong Piano, Teacher-Coach
Sprenkle, Robert Louis Oboe, Educator
Thym, Jurgen Educator, Critic-Writer
Walker, Betty Marie Teacher-Coach, Conductor & Music Director
Wason, Robert Wesley Educator, Composer
Watanabe, Ruth Taiko Librarian, Educator
Webster, Michael Clarinet, Composer
Weiss, Abraham M Bassoon
Weiss, Elizabeth B Viola, Teacher
Weiss, Howard A Conductor & Music Director, Violin
West, Philip Educator, Oboe
Yancich, Milan Michael French Horn, Educator
Zeitlin, Zvi Violin, Educator
Zinman, David Conductor

Rock Hill

Champlin, Terry (Arthur Doyle), III Composer, Guitar

Rockville Centre

Tichman, Herbert Clarinet, Teacher

Rome

Gomez, Victor E Teacher, Violin

Roosevelt Island

Kontos, Lydia G Administrator

Rosendale

McCann, William John Conductor, French Horn

Roslyn Harbor

Maimone, Renata Administrator, Educator

Roslyn Heights

Liebman, Joyce Ann Piano, Teacher

Salem

Van Wye, Benjamin David Critic-Writer, Organ

Saratoga Springs

Green, Gene Marie Oboe & English Horn, Teacher

Scarsdale

Barthelson, Joyce Holloway Composer, Conductor
Carabo-Cone, Madeleine Violin, Educator
Daniel, Oliver Administrator, Musicologist

Dorsam, Paul James Educator, Composer
Peters, Roberta (Roberta Peters Fields) Soprano, Lecturer
Richter, Marion Morrey Composer, Piano
Ulehla, Ludmila Educator, Composer
Webster, Beveridge Piano, Educator

Schenectady

Blood, Esta (Damesek) Composer
Presslaff, Hilary Tann Composer, Educator

Setauket

Gosman, Lazar Conductor, Violin
Layton, Billy Jim Composer, Educator

Shady

Haufrect, Herbert Composer

Shokan

Knaack, Donald (Frank) Composer, Percussion

Skaneateles

Grout, Donald Jay Educator, Historian

Snyder

Di Pietro, Rocco Composer, Piano
Hiller, Lejaren Arthur, Jr Composer, Educator
Michii, Makoto Teacher, Double Bass

South Salem

Potter, John Matthew Writer, Educator

Spencerport

Cervone, D(omenic) Donald Composer, Educator

Spring Valley

Dedel, Peter J D Administrator, Writer
Tischler, Judith B Educator, Editor

Staten Island

Bobrow, Sanchie Composer, Teacher
Cross, Ronald Educator, Organ
Mattfeld, Victor Henry Educator, Writer
Trogan, Roland Bernard Composer, Teacher
Warner, Joseph (I) Bass

Stony Brook

Semegen, Daria Composer, Educator

Sunnyside

Mandelbaum, M Joel Composer, Educator
Rosenblum, Myron Viola, Viola d'Amore

Syosset

Apostle, Nicholas Oboe & English Horn

Syracuse

Custer, Calvin H Composer, Conductor
Gindin, Edward M Conductor, Teacher
Godfrey, Daniel Strong Educator, Composer
Igelsrud, Douglas Bent Educator, Percussion
Israel, Brian M Educator, Composer
Marvin, Frederick Piano, Musicologist
Mattran, Donald Albert Administrator, Conductor
Naistadt, Florence Violin
Oberbrunner, John Educator, Flute
Orgel, Seth Henry French Horn, Teacher
Pugh, Darryl L Double Bass
Seibert, Donald C Librarian, Critic-Writer
Shake, J(ames) Curtis Educator, Piano
Zaplatynsky, Andrew Educator, Violin

Three Mile Bay

Pizer, Elizabeth Faw Hayden Composer, Piano

Tomkins Cove

York, Don(ald Griffith) Composer, Music Director

Troy

Beck, Martha Dillard (Mrs G Howard Carragan) Composer, Teacher
Cimino, John Baritone, Lecturer

Trumansburg

Swenson, Edward E Educator, Tenor

Tuckahoe

Canarina, John Baptiste Conductor & Music Director, Educator

Upper Nyack

DeLay, Dorothy (Mrs Edward Newhouse) Educator, Violin

Utica

Himes, Douglas D Administrator, Lecturer

Valley Cottage

Virga, Patricia H Writer

Valley Stream

Adler, Marvin Stanley Educator, Critic
Massey, George Baritone, Lecturer

Vestal City

Agard, David Leon Conductor & Music Director, Violin

Waccabuc

Carter, Elliott Cook Composer

Wantagh

Alstadter, Judith R Piano, Teacher-Coach
Berk, Adele L Composer, Educator

Waterford

Burt, Warren Arnold Composer, Writer

Webster

Paul, Thomas W Bass

Westbury

DeVito, Albert Kenneth Composer, Teacher

West Dunkirk

Patterson, T Richard Educator, Piano

West Islip

Post, Nora Oboe & English Horn, Educator

West Midwood

Scherer, Barrymore Laurence Writer, Lecturer

West Monroe

Cecconi-Bates, Augusta N Composer, Lecturer

White Plains

Berman, Ruth (Ruth Berman Harris) Harp, Composer
Hughes, Charles William Educator, Writer
Landau, Siegfried Composer, Music Director
Ohlsson, Garrick Olof Piano
Teck, Katherine (Weintz) Administrator, Musician for Dance

Uscher, Nancy Joyce Viola, Writer

Whitestone

Camus, Raoul Francois Educator
Smaldone, Edward Michael Composer

Woodside

Wittekind, Donald H Educator, Trombone

Woodstock

Starer, Robert Composer

Yonkers

Lamneck, Esther Evangeline Clarinet
Rudiakov, Michael Cello, Educator
Sherman, Ingrid Kugelmann Composer

NORTH CAROLINA

Asheville

Baker, Robert Hart Conductor & Music Director, Composer
Vandewart, J W Administrator, Librarian

Belmont

Hegenbart, Alex Frank Educator, Composer

Boiling Springs

Cribb, George Robert Educator, Piano

Boone

Erneston, Nicholas Administrator, Violin
Meister, Scott Robert Composer, Educator
Parker, R Clinton Administrator, Educator

Brevard

Tillotson, Laura Virginia Clarinet, Conductor

Carrboro

Swalin, Benjamin Franklin Conductor, Educator
Swalin, Maxine McMahon Piano, Lecturer

Chapel Hill

Eckert, Michael Sands Composer, Educator
Haar, James Educator, Writer
Hannay, Roger Durham Composer
Hinshaw, Donald Grey Administrator, Music Director
Newman, William Stein Musicologist, Writer
Pruett, James Worrell Educator, Librarian
Pruett, Lilian Pibernik Educator, Harpsichord
Smither, Howard E Musicologist
Woodward, Ann (McClure) Viola, Educator
Woodward, Henry L(ynde) Educator, Composer

Charlotte

Appleton, Clyde Robert Educator
Chalmers, Bruce Abernathy Administrator
Driehuys, Leonardus Bastiaan Music Director & Conductor
Hopwood, Julie Ann Violin
Jacob, Karen Hite Music Director, Harpsichord
Maddox, Robert Lee Conductor & Music Director, Educator
Paysour, LaFleur (Nadine) Critic-Writer, Lecturer

Peek, Richard Maurice Organ, Composer
Portone, Frank Anthony, Jr French Horn, Educator
Rosekrans, Charles Stetson Conductor
Sanderson, Derl Trombone
Simosko, Valerie Flute & Piccolo, Educator
Stumpf, Carol L Percussion, Timpani
Swedberg, Robert Mitchell Administrator, Bass
Tang, Jordan Cho-Tung Composer, Music Director
Turner, Thomas George Composer, Piano
Zugelj, Ivan Petar (John Peter Zugel) Conductor & Music Director, Double Bass

Cullowhee

Tyra, Thomas (Norman) Educator, Music Director

Davidson

Welsh, Wilmer Hayden Composer, Organ

Durham

Bryan, Paul Robey, Jr Educator, Writer
Ciompi, Giorgio Violin, Educator
Henry, James Donald Music Director, Educator
Jaffe, Stephen Abram Composer, Piano
Petersen, Patricia H Recorder, Teacher
Saville, Eugenia Curtis Educator, Writer
Seebass, Tilman Educator
Sparks, Donna Lynne Writer, Music Director
Ward, Robert Eugene Composer, Educator

Elon College

Artley, Malvin Newton Educator

Franklin

Elmore, Cenieth Catherine Educator, Piano

Greensboro

Beck, Frederick Allan Trumpet, Educator
Beyer, Frederick H Composer, Educator
Carroll, Gregory Daniel Educator, Composer
Cooper, Rose Marie (Mrs William H Jordan) Composer
Cox, Richard Garner Conductor, Educator
Fuchs, Peter Paul Conductor & Music Director, Composer
Garlington, Aubrey S Educator, Writer
Hunkins, Arthur B Composer, Educator
Kiorpes, George Anthony Educator, Piano
McCarty, Frank Lee Composer, Educator
Masarie, Jack F Educator, French Horn
Prodan, James Christian Educator, Oboe & English Horn
Wehner, Walter Leroy Educator, Composer

Greenville

Chauncey, Beatrice Arlene Educator, Flute
Haritun, Rosalie Ann Educator, Clarinet
Hause, Robert Luke Conductor & Music Director, Educator
Henry, Otto Walker Composer, Educator
Hiss, Clyde S Educator, Baritone
Schmidt, Rodney Educator, Violin

Laurinburg

Grim, William Edward Clarinet, Teacher

NORTH CAROLINA (cont)

Lumberton

Cuccaro, Costanza (Constance Jean Penhorwood) Soprano
Penhorwood, Edwin Leroy Composer, Piano
Romine, Robert Lee Music Director, Educator

Mars Hill

Robertson, Donna Nagey Composer, Educator

Misenheimer

Brewer, Richard H Music Director, Educator

Murfreesboro

Chamblee, James Monroe Educator, Music Director

Pinehurst

Martin, Lindy S Artist Manager

Raleigh

Garriss, Phyllis Weyer Educator, Violin
Gorski, Paul Violin, Educator
Ping-Robbins, Nancy R(egan) Writer, Harpsichord
Reed, Addison Walker Educator, Bass
Stoughton, Michael Gordon Cello
Watson, J Perry Administrator, Educator
Zimmermann, Gerhardt Conductor & Music Director

Salisbury

Higbee, Dale Strohe Recorder, Critic-Writer

Waynesville

Weed, Maurice James Composer, Educator

Wilmington

Deas, Richard Ryder Piano, Educator
Kechley, David Stevenson Composer, Educator

Wilson

Albert, Jones Ross Teacher, Viola

Winston-Salem

Barrow, Rebecca Anne Piano, Teacher-Coach
Beall, Lee Morrett Educator, Organ
Bell, Winston A Educator, Piano
Borwick, Susan Harden Administrator, Educator
Goldstein, Louis R Piano, Lecturer
Hahn, Marian Elizabeth Piano, Teacher
Levy, David Benjamin Educator, Administrator
Listokin, Robert Clarinet, Educator
Locklair, Dan Steven Composer, Organ
Mueller, John Storm Educator, Organ
Perret, Peter J Conductor, Educator
Popkin, Mark Anthony Educator, Bassoon
Randolph, (Alice) Laurie Guitar
Sandresky, Clemens Administrator, Piano
Sandresky, Margaret Vardell Educator, Composer
Selleck, John Hugh Composer, Writer
Shaffer, Sherwood Composer, Educator
Suderburg, Elizabeth Soprano
Suderburg, Robert Charles Composer, Conductor

NORTH DAKOTA

Bottineau

Utgaard, Merton Blaine Administrator, Educator

Dickinson

Pearson, Frank Cogswell, Jr Educator, Administrator

Fargo

Erickson, Gordon McVey Percussion, Mallet Instruments
Fissinger, Edwin Russell Composer, Music Director

Grand Forks

Boehle, Willam Randall Educator
Eder, Terry Edward Music Director, Educator
Lewis, Elisabeth Parmelee Educator, Violin
Willett, Thelma Elizabeth Educator, Piano

Minot

Nelson, Wayne Conductor, Tenor
Strohm, John A Educator

OHIO

Ada

Fahrner, Raymond Eugene Composer, Educator
Williams, Edwin Lynn Trumpet, Administrator

Akron

Bernstein, David Stephen Educator, Composer
Geller, Donna Medoff Piano, Educator
Griebling, Margaret Ann Composer, Oboe
Griebling, Stephen Thomas Composer, Piano
Hutchins, Farley Kennan Composer, Educator
Knieter, Gerard L Administrator, Educator
Lane, Louis Conductor
MacDonald, John Alexander Conductor, Educator
Marson, Laurel Rose Composer
Romeo, James Joseph Composer, Educator
Rosenberg, Donald Scott Critic-Writer, French Horn

Alliance

Henschen, Dorothy Adele Harp, Educator

Ashland

Rogers, Calvin Y Educator, Conductor

Athens

Ahrendt, Karl F Composer, Administrator
Chaudoir, James Edward Composer, Conductor
Fink, Lorraine Friedrichsen Violin, Administrator
Henry, Joseph Conductor, Composer
Kleen, Leslie Composer
Lewis, David S Educator, Clarinet
Socciarelli, Ronald Peter Conductor, Educator

Berea

Hartzell, Lawrence William Educator, Composer
Mushabac, Regina (Regina Mushubac Klemperer) Cello, Educator

Oltman, C Dwight Conductor & Music Director, Educator
Raleigh, Stuart W Choral Conductor, Educator

Bowling Green

Beerman, Burton Composer, Clarinet
Bentley, John E Educator, Oboe
Brant, Boris Teacher, Violin
Cioffari, Richard John Educator, Composer
DePue, Wallace Earl Composer, Educator
Hammond, Ivan Fred Educator, Tuba
Inglefield, Ruth Karin Harp, Educator
Kennell, Richard Paul Teacher, Composer
Marks, Virginia Pancoast Educator, Piano
Shrude, Marilyn Composer, Piano
Wilson, Donald Malcolm Composer, Teacher
Wolcott, Vernon Organ, Educator

Canton

Blair, William P Administrator

Chesterhill

Wetzel, Richard Dean Educator, Writer

Cincinnati

Bozicevich, Ronald Raymond Double Bass
Byers, Harold Ralph Violin, Educator
Campione, Carmine Clarinet, Educator
Clinton, Marianne Hancock Administrator
Cooley, Marilyn Grace Administrator, Music Director
Crabtree, Phillip D Musicologist, Educator
Dahlgren, Carl Herman Per Artist Manager, Educator
Ellerman, Jens Educator, Violin
Foster, Donald Herbert Educator, Writer
George, Warren Edwin Educator
Gielen, Michael Andreas Conductor
Glover, Betty S Trombone, Educator
Green, Barry L Double Bass, Writer
Green, Rebecca McMullan Violin
Hale, (Nathan) Kelly Educator, Conductor
Handel, Darrell D Composer, Educator
Harrod, William V Oboe & English Horn
Hashimoto, Eiji Educator, Harpsichord
Hatfield, Lenore Sherman Violin
Hatfield, Michael French Horn, Educator
Hoffman, Joel H Composer, Piano
Huston, Thomas Scott, Jr Composer, Educator
Jensen, Richard Marsh Percussion, Educator
Kendall, Gary Keith Bass-Baritone, Educator
Kramer, Jonathan D(onald) Composer, Writer
Loebel, David Conductor & Music Director
Lusmann, Stephen (Arthur) Baritone
Magg, Kyril Flute & Piccolo, Educator
Mandelbaum, Gayna Faye Violin
Morris, Richard Piano, Educator
Nelsova, Zara Cello
Otte, Allen Carl Percussion
Parchman, Gen Louis Composer, Double Bass
Pendle, Karin Educator, Musicologist
Pogue, Samuel Franklin Educator
Pridonoff, Elizabeth Anna Piano, Educator
Pridonoff, Eugene Alexander Piano, Educator
Proto, Frank Composer, Double Bass
Reis, Joan Sachs Educator
Ruder, Philip Violin, Conductor

Samis, Sylvia Rosenzweig Violin
Sapp, Allen Dwight Composer,
    Administrator
Shapey, Ronald (Sidney) Teacher,
    Violinist
Siki, Bela Piano
Somogyi, Joseph Emil Viola
Stilwell, F Raymond Viola, Educator
Street, Marna Susan Viola
Tajo, Italo Bass-Baritone, Stage
    Director
Trafford, Edmund Lee Composer
Venanzi, Henry Piano, Conductor
Watson, Jack McLaurin Administrator,
    Educator
Wolf, Andrew Leonard Double Bass

Cleveland

Aarons, Martha Irene Flute & Piccolo
Abbott, Michael Piano, Educator
Adams, Leslie Composer
Andrix, George Paul Composer, Viola
Bamberger, David Director-Opera, Writer
Bevers, Michael Earl Bassoon, Teacher
Bishop, Ronald Taylor Tuba, Educator
Boyd, Robert Ferrell Trombone
Brown, William James Violin
Bubalo, Rudolph Daniel Composer
Bushman, Irvin Cantor, Educator
Chalifoux, Alice (Alice Chalifoux
    Rideout) Harp, Educator
Ciarlillo, Marjorie Ann Educator, Piano
Cohen, Franklin R Clarinet, Educator
Columbro, Madeline Mary Educator
Craighead, David Organ, Educator
Dohnanyi, Christoph von Administrator,
    Conductor & Music Director
Eichhorn, Erich A Violin
Erickson, Susan Educator, Soprano
Flowerman, Martin Double Bass, Teacher
Funkhouser, Frederick A Viola
Goler, Harriett Educator, Piano
Goslee, George Educator, Bassoon
Harada, Koichiro Educator, Violin
Harris, Alan Educator, Cello
Hathaway, Daniel Artist Manager, Music
    Director
Holloway, Clyde Educator, Organ
Hruby, Frank Critic-Writer, Conductor
Johannesen, Grant Piano, Educator
Juhos, Joseph Frank Flute, Educator
Kearney, Linda (Yvonne) Educator, Flute
    & Piccolo
Khaner, Jeffrey M Flute
Klein, David E Administrator
Koch, Frederick (Charles) Composer,
    Piano
Kofsky, Allen Trombone, Euphonium
Loebel, Kurt Violin, Educator
Maazel, Lorin Conductor & Music
    Director
Maret, Stanley Bassoon, Educator
Mason, Marilyn Organ, Educator
Mentschukoff, Andrej Guitar
Podis, Eunice Piano, Teacher
Powers, Jeffrey Steven French Horn,
    Teacher-Coach
Priest-Stevens, Maxine (Maxine Stevens)
    Educator
Pyne, James Clarinet, Educator
Radosavljevich, Olga (Olga Radosavljevich
    Gradojevich) Educator, Piano
Rautenberg, John Leslie Flute, Trombone
Ryder, Judith (Mrs Bruce Frumker)
    Piano, Educator
Schenly, Paul Educator, Piano
Sharp, Maurice Educator, Flute
Siegel, Bert (Berton Earl) Violin, Teacher
Suess, John G Educator, Musicologist
Tannenbaum, James Educator
Topilow, Carl S Conductor & Music
    Director

Vronsky, Vitya Babin Piano
Wagnitz, Ralph David French Horn
Weiner, Richard Percussion, Teacher
Woods, Pamela Pecha Oboe & English
    Horn, Piano
Zauder, David Trumpet, Administrator

Cleveland Heights

Baker, Larry A Composer, Conductor &
    Music Director
Fay, (Earl) William Educator,
    Administrator
Goldschmidt, Bernhard Educator, Violin
Guy, F Dean Educator
Harlan, Christoph Educator, Guitar
Herforth, Harry Best Educator, Trumpet
Mack, John Educator, Oboe
Murray, Bain Composer, Educator
O'Brien, Eugene Joseph Composer
Peelle, David Composer, Educator
Perry, Alcestis Bishop Violin, Educator
Rodda, Richard Earl Critic-Writer,
    Educator
Roy, Gene Burdick Double Bass,
    Educator
Roy, Klaus George Critic-Writer,
    Composer
Wolfe, Harvey (S) Cello

College Corner

Sheppard, C(harles) James Composer,
    Educator

Columbus

Alch, Mario Tenor, Educator
Bierley, Paul Edmund Writer
Bolz, Harriett (Hallock) Composer, Writer
Broekema, Andrew J Administrator,
    Educator
Conable, William G, Jr Cello, Music
    Director
Cooper, Irma Margaret Singer, Educator
Davis, Michael David Violin, Educator
Gundersheimer, Muriel (Blumberg) Harp
Haddad, George Richard Educator, Piano
Hare, Robert Yates Educator, Conductor
Heck, Thomas F Librarian, Guitar & Lute
Jenkins, Susan Elaine Composer,
    Educator
Kratzer, Dennis Leon Conductor,
    Educator
Livingston, Herbert Educator
Lloyd, Gerald J Composer, Educator
Maas, Martha C Educator, Writer
Main, Alexander Educator, Writer
Marvin, Marajean B Educator, Soprano
Mixter, Keith Eugene Educator, Writer
Phelps, Norman F Educator, Composer
Sheldon, Gary Conductor & Music
    Director
Whallon, Evan Conductor & Music
    Director

Cuyahoga Falls

Jolly, Tucker Tuba, Teacher

Dayton

Lorenz, Ellen Jane (Ellen Jane Lorenz
    Porter) Composer, Writer

East Cleveland

Haigh, Scott (Richard) Double Bass
Starling, A Cumberworth Composer,
    Educator

Edgerton

Baker, Don Russell Percussion, Teacher

Euclid

Majeske, Daniel H Educator, Violin

Fairborn

Steinohrt, William John Composer,
    Conductor

Gates Mills

Murakami, Sarah Theresa Yoshiko
    Educator, Piano
Whittaker, Howard Educator, Composer

Granville

Borishansky, Elliot (David) Composer,
    Educator
Latiolais, Desiree Jayne Composer, Piano

Howard

Eikum, Rex L Educator, Tenor

Independence

Lovell, William James Composer

Kent

Anderson, William Miller Administrator,
    Educator
DeBolt, David Albert Bassoon, Educator
El-Dabh, Halim Composer, Educator
Kuhn, Terry Lee Educator, Recorder
Miller, Terry Ellis Educator, Writer
Palmieri, Robert Michael Piano, Educator
Schleuter, Stanley L Educator
Shindle, William Richard Musicologist,
    Educator
Stuart, James Fortier Tenor, Educator
Wallace, Paul James Educator
Waters, James Lipscomb Composer,
    Educator
Watson, Walter Robert Composer,
    Educator
Wiley, Frank (Earkett), Jr Composer,
    Educator

Lakewood

Wallence, Stephen Tenor

Lancaster

Cowden, Susan Jane Flute & Piccolo,
    Teacher-Coach

Lima

Porter, Susan Loraine Educator

Marietta

Mueller, Harold Conductor & Music
    Director, Educator

Mayfield Heights

Smetona, Vytautas Julius Piano,
    Composer

Mt St Joseph

della Picca, Angelo Armando Composer,
    Educator

Mt Vernon

Willmering, Kevin Douglas Percussion,
    Educator

Oberlin

Aschaffenburg, Walter (Eugene)
    Composer, Educator
Baustian, Robert Conductor, Educator
Boe, David S Educator, Organ
Caldwell, James Boone Oboe, Educator
Clapp, Stephen H Violin, Educator
Coleman, Randolph E Composer,
    Educator
Crawford, H Gerald Educator, Baritone
Crawford, Lisa Educator, Harpsichord
Cummings, Conrad Composer, Conductor
Darcy, Warren Jay Composer, Educator

OHIO (cont)

Druesedow, John Edward, Jr Librarian, Educator
Fries, Robert McMillan Educator, French Horn
Frumkin, Lydia Educator, Pianoforte
Fulkerson, Gregory (Locke) Violin, Educator
Hatton, Howard Educator, Singer
Henke, Herbert H Educator
Hoffmann, Richard Composer, Educator
Kapuscinski, Richard Cello, Educator
Koberstein, Freeman G Piano, Educator
Logan, Wendall Composer, Educator
McDonald, Lawrence Clarinet, Educator
Mahy, Daune Sharon Soprano
Mast, Paul Educator
Mauney, Miles H Educator
Miller, Edward J Composer, Educator
Miller, Richard D Educator, Tenor
Moe, Daniel T Educator, Composer
Moore, Kenneth Educator
Nuernberger, Louis D Composer, Educator
Pearson, Willard B Trumpet
Rabson, Carolyn R Cello, Librarian
Rinehart, John Composer, Educator
Schwartz, Joseph Ervin Educator, Piano
Smith, Priscilla Educator, Conductor
Stacy, Martha Educator
Tacacs, Peter Piano
Toth, Andor, Jr Educator, Cello
Walker, Frances E Piano, Educator
Wood, Joseph (Roberts) Educator, Composer
Zakarian-Rutstein, Sedmara Piano, Educator

Olmsted Falls

Chobanian, Loris Ohannes Composer, Guitar & Lute
Winzenburger, Walter Paul Educator, Baroque Violin

Oxford

Albin, William Robert Educator, Percussion
Olcott, James Louis Trumpet, Educator
Seltzer, George Educator, Clarinet

Poland

Hopkins, Robert Elliott Piano, Educator
Orr, Wendell Eugene Educator, Bass

Rocky River

Codispoti, Norma (Constance) Mezzo-soprano, Teacher-Coach
Kyr, Robert Harry Composer, Educator

Shaker Heights

Barber, Daniel Rowland Piano
Boyarsky, Terry Linda Educator, Piano
Drossin, Julius Composer, Educator
Foldi, Andrew Harry Bass, Educator
Geber, Stephen Educator, Cello
Herr, John David Organ, Educator
Kurzbauer, Heather Raquel Violin
Kwak, Sung Conductor
London, Edwin Wolf Composer, Conductor
Miller, Clement A Musicologist, Educator
Ornstein, Doris Educator, Harpsichord
Tait, Malcolm John Educator, Administrator
Warne, Katharine Mulky Composer, Piano
Webster, Peter Richard Educator, Researcher
Zetzer, Alfred Bass Clarinet, Clarinet

South Euclid

Hill, Robert James Clarinet, Teacher

Springfield

Ferritto, John Edmund Conductor & Music Director, Composer
Howat, Robert V Educator, Piano
Kommel, A Margret Educator, Soprano

Stow

Janson, Thomas Composer

Tiffin

Ohl, Ferris E Conductor, Educator

Toledo

Brown, Merrill Edwin Educator, Writer
Chambers, Virginia Anne Educator
Gould, Elizabeth (Elizabeth Gould Hochman) Composer, Piano
Kihslinger, Mary Ruth French Horn, Educator
Rondelli, Barbara (Ann) Soprano, Educator
van der Merwe, Johan Conductor & Music Director, Educator
Zaliouk, Yuval Nathan Music Director & Conductor
Zychowicz, James Leo Teacher, Tuba

University Heights

Belcher, Deborah Jean Piano, Educator
Kondorossy, Leslie Composer, Conductor & Music Director
Lawrence, Joy Elizabeth Educator, Organ
Paukert, Karel Organ, Administrator
Statsky, Paul G Teacher, Violin

Wilberforce

Amoaku, William Komla Educator, Administrator

Willoughby Hills

Weber, Phyllis Anne Teacher, Violin

Wooster

Garlick, Nancy Buckingham Clarinet, Educator
Ling, Stuart James Educator
Moore, Dale (Kimberly) Baritone, Conductor
Winter, Daniel Wallace Educator, Piano
Wright, Josephine R B Writer, Educator

Worthington

Barnes, Marshall H Educator, Composer

Yellow Springs

Olds, Patricia Hunt Administrator, Educator
Ronsheim, John Richard Composer, Educator

Youngstown

Byo, Donald William Educator, Bassoon
Gould, Ronald Lee Educator, Conductor
Largent, Edward J, Jr Educator, Composer
Rollin, Robert Composer, Writer
Rudnytsky, Roman Victor Piano, Educator
Slocum, William (Bennett) Composer, French Horn

OKLAHOMA

Bartlesville

Brush, Ruth Damaris Composer, Piano

Chickasaw

Diaconoff, Theodore A Composer, Educator

Cleveland

Hansen, Ted (Theodore C Hansen) Composer, Educator

Durant

Mansur, Paul Max Educator, French Horn
Wintle, James R Educator, Composer

Edmond

Dillon, Robert Composer, Educator
McCoy, Wesley Lawrence Educator, French Horn

Enid

Nelson, Jon Educator, Piano
Newell, Douglas Myers Educator, Conductor
Tromblee, Maxell Ray Clarinet, Educator
Ulrich, Eugene Joseph Composer, Educator

Langston

Berry, Lemuel, Jr Educator, Writer

Lawton

Bowman, Jack Walter Educator, Music Director
Smith, George Francis Conductor, Educator

Noble

Grant, Kerry Administrator, Educator

Norman

Braught, Eugene A Conductor, Educator
Carey, Thomas D Baritone, Educator
Daniel, Sean Educator, Baritone
Destwolinski, Gail Educator
Enrico, Eugene Joseph Musicologist, Educator
Govich, Bruce Michael Educator, Bass
Haug, Leonard Harold Conductor, Educator
Hennagin, Michael Composer, Educator
Lancaster, Emanuel Leo Educator, Piano
Mathis, (George) Russell Music Director, Educator
Ross, Allan Anderson Educator, Conductor & Music Director
Smith, Jerry Neil Educator, Administrator

Oklahoma City

Birdwell, Florence (Gillam-Hobin) Mezzo-soprano, Educator
Creed, Kay Mezzo-soprano, Educator
De La Fuente, Luis Herrera Conductor & Music Director
Luke, Ray E Conductor, Composer
Payne, Frank Lynn Educator, Composer
Thurston, Richard Elliott Educator, Conductor & Music Director

Shawnee

Horton, William Lamar Educator, Baritone
Martin, Charlotte Piano, Educator

Stillwater

Montemurro, Paul A Educator, Teacher
vanEaton, Sunny F C Educator, Soprano

Tahlequah

Johnson, Calvert Organ, Educator

Tulsa

Geary, Barbara Ann Piano
Sharon, Boaz Educator, Piano
Snowden, James Wyn Conductor, Educator
Sowell, Laven Music Director, Educator
Toms, John (Elias) Critic & Writer, Educator

Weatherford

Chapman, Charles Wayne Educator, Composer

OREGON

Ashland

Belford, Marvin L Educator, Trumpet
Tumbleson, John Raymond Educator, Music Director

Beaverton

Gadeholt, Irene Violin
Nelson, Sally Foster Trumpet

Corvallis

Gilmore, Bernard Composer, Educator
Heller, Duane L Composer, Educator
Jeffers, Ronald H Composer, Educator

Eugene

Bailey, Exine Margaret Anderson Soprano, Educator
Bergquist, Peter Educator, Writer
Cykler, Edmund A Educator, Administrator
Dowd, Charles (Robert) Percussion, Timpani
Healey, Derek Edward Composer, Educator
Hunter, Laura Ellen Saxophone, Educator
Hurwitz, Robert Irving Educator, Conductor
Keller, Homer (Todd) Composer, Educator
Owen, Harold J Composer, Educator
Saltzman, Herbert Royce Administrator, Educator
Soule, Edmund Foster Composer, Librarian
Tubb, Monte Composer, Educator
Vagner, Robert Stuart Conductor, Educator

Lake Oswego

Richards, John Keil Tuba, Conductor

McMinnville

Baker, Warren Lovell Educator, Trombone
Neumann, Philip Warren Educator, Composer

Marylhurst

Daigle, Anne Cecile Educator, Composer
Hutchinson, Lucie Mary Administrator, Educator

Newburg

Hagen, Dennis Bert Administrator, Conductor

Portland

Avshalomov, Jacob David Composer, Conductor & Music Director
DePonte, Niel Bonaventure Conductor & Music Director, Percussion
Falk, Leila Birnbaum Educator
Funk, Eric Douglas Composer, Educator

Johanson, Bryan Composer, Guitar
Leedy, Douglas Composer, Conductor & Music Director
Leyden, Norman Conductor
McDermott, Vincent Composer, Educator
Minde, Stefan P Conductor & Music Director
Pauly, Reinhard G Writer, Musicologist
Seeley, Gilbert Stewart Conductor & Music Director, Educator
Stanford, Thomas Stanley Educator, Clarinet
Svoboda, Tomas Composer, Educator
Verner, Randall Werth Viola
Weiss, Dawn Adrienne Flute, Educator

St Benedict

Nicholson, David Music Director, Writer

Salem

Barlowe, Amy Strings, Educator
Behnke, Martin Kyle Educator, Conductor
Brand, Myra Jean Educator, Soprano
Winslow, Walter Keith Composer, Piano

Tigard

Jobelmann, Herman Frederick Double Bass

PENNSYLVANIA

Abington

Flor, Samuel Conductor, Violin

Ambler

Archibald, Bruce Composer, Educator

Annville

Rose, C Robert Educator, Clarinet

Avoca

Preate, Sally Edwards Administrator

Bala Cynwyd

Schleifer, Martha Furman Educator, Writer

Beaver Falls

Copeland, Robert Marshall Educator, Conductor & Music Director

Bethlehem

Lipkis, Larry (Laurence Alan) Composer, Educator

Bradford

Young, Frederick John Tuba, Horn Research

Broomall

Russo, John Composer, Clarinet

Bryn Athyn

Yardumian, Richard Composer

Bryn Mawr

Broido, Arnold Peace Administrator, Piano
Davis, Jean Reynolds Composer
Flaherty, Gloria Critic, Lecturer

Carlisle

Bullard, Truman Campbell Educator, Music Director

Clarks Summit

Hopkins, Barbara Avis Flute, Teacher

Dillsburg

Sider, Ronald Ray Educator, Conductor

Edinboro

Alexander, William Peddie Composer, Educator
Cox, Clifford L Educator, Viola
Dasher, Richard Taliaferro Educator, Writer
Gombert, Karl E Educator, Trumpet

Elkins Park

Hoy, Hendricks Composer, Piano
Meyers, Klara Bolgar Educator, Soprano
Sternberg, Jonathan Conductor & Music Director, Educator

Ephrata

Horein, Kathleen Marie Oboe, Teacher

Erie

Cray, Kevin E Composer, Piano
Hendl, Walter Conductor & Music Director, Piano
Stackhouse, Holly N Flute & Piccolo, Teacher

Fairview

Mennini, Louis Alfred Composer, Educator

Flemington

Schwarz, John Irvin, Jr Educator

Glenshaw

Mallory, (Walter) Hampton Cello
Mallory, Lauren Scott Cello

Glenside

Frabizio, William V Educator, Composer
Nieweg, Clinton F Harp, Librarian

Greentown

Musser, Willard I Educator, Music Director

Harrisburg

Adolphus, Milton Composer

Haverford

Cunningham, Caroline M Educator, Strings
Davison, John Herbert Composer, Educator

Havertown

Bookspan, Michael L Percussion, Educator

Home

Perlongo, Daniel James Composer, Educator

Huntingdon

Tower, Ibrook Conductor, Clarinet

Huntingdon Valley

Epstein, Paul Composer, Educator

Indiana

De Cesare, Ruth Educator, Composer
Intili, Dominic Joseph Educator, Piano
Olmstead, Gary James Educator, Percussion

PENNSYLVANIA (cont)

Jenkintown

Taylor, Clifford (Oliver) Composer, Educator

Wright, Maurice Willis Composer

Kutztown

Siekmann, Frank H Composer, Conductor

Lancaster

Blackburn, Walter Wesley Conductor & Music Director, Educator

Darrenkamp, John David Baritone

Gustafson, Bruce Critic, Harpsichord

Moyer, Karl Eby Lecturer, Organ

Landenberg

Steinberg, Michael Educator, Piano

Lewisburg

Duckworth, William Ervin Composer, Educator

Hannigan, Barry T Piano

Hill, Jackson Composer, Educator

Payn, William Austin Music Director, Composer

Mansfield

Hill, (Walter) Kent Educator, Organ

Stanley, Donald Arthur Educator, Tuba

Mars

Frank, Jean Forward Composer

Mechanicsburg

Mahar, William J Educator, Lecturer

Media

Blatter, Alfred Wayne Educator, Composer

Crumb, George (Henry) Composer, Educator

Veleta, Richard Kenneth Educator, Piano

Merion Station

de Pasquale, Joseph Viola, Educator

Polin, Claire Composer, Educator

Millersville

Fisher, Paul Gottshall Educator, Conductor

Monroeville

Sterne, Colin Chase Composer, Educator

Muncy Valley

Raigorodsky, Natalia (Leda Natalia Raigorodsky Heimsath Harter) Composer, Writer

Narberth

Sonies, Barbara Violin

New Castle

Solomon, Nanette Kaplan Piano, Educator

New Kensington

Dombrowski, Stanley Violin

New Milford

Berky, Carl R Composer, Piano

Newtown Square

Rochberg, George Composer, Educator

Norristown

Cascarino, Romeo Educator, Composer

Philadelphia

Adonaylo, Raquel Piano, Soprano

Albrecht, Otto Edwin Educator, Librarian

Aldwell, Edward Piano, Educator

Aleksandruk, Linda (Marie) Soprano, Teacher

Anderson, Shirley Patricia Percussion, Educator

Bailey, Barbara Elliott Lecturer, Piano

Ballard, Mary Anne Viola Da Gamba, Educator

Baxter, Lincoln Arthur Composer, Educator

Behrend, Jeanne Piano, Educator

Bernstein, Lawrence F Musicologist, Educator

Bogdanoff, Leonard Viola

Bogusz, Edward Bass, Educator

Bolet, Jorge Piano, Educator

Breuninger, Tyrone Trombone, Educator

Bunke, Jerome Samuel Clarinet

Burrows, John Music Director, Educator

Capanna, Robert Composer, Administrator

Carlyss, Gerald Timpani, Educator

Carol, Norman Violin, Educator

Casiello, Marianne Soprano, Educator

Castaldo, Joseph F Educator, Composer

Chapman, Keith (Ronald) Organ, Composer

Checchia, Anthony Phillip Administrator, Music Director

Clauser, Donald R Viola

Cornelius, Jeffrey Michael Administrator, Educator

Costello, Marilyn Harp, Educator

Cozette, Cynthia Composer, Administrator

Csonka, Margarita (Margarita C Montanaro) Harp

Davidson, Tina Composer, Piano

de Lancie, John Administrator, Oboe

Dennison, Sam Melvin Composer, Librarian

Dodson, Glenn Trombone, Educator

Druian, Joseph Cello, Educator

Englander, Lester Baritone, Teacher-Coach

Fitzpatrick, Robert Conductor & Music Director, Educator

Franklin, Joseph J Administrator, Composer

Friedman, Viktor Piano, Educator

Garwood, Margaret Composer, Piano

Gnam, Adrian Conductor, Oboe

Goldberg, Szymon Conductor, Violin

Graffman, Gary Piano

Granat, Juan Wolfgang Viola

Greatbatch, Timothy Alan Composer, Educator

Guck, Marion A Educator

Gutknecht, (Edythe) Carol Soprano

Harlow, Richard Ernest Cello

Henken, Morris Editor

Hewitt, Harry Donald Composer, Administrator

Horszowksi, Mieczslaw Piano, Educator

Jacobs, Evelyn Poole Viola, Educator

Jay, Stephen Administrator, Educator

Johnson, Alvin H Educator, Musicologist

Jones, Mason French Horn, Educator

Kaufman, Fredrick Composer, Administrator

Khanzadian, Vahan Tenor, Teacher-Coach

Krell, John Flute & Piccolo, Educator

Krzywicki, Jan Composer, Piano

Krzywicki, Paul Tuba, Educator

Lallerstedt, Ford Mylius Educator, Organ

Laredo, Jaime Violin, Conductor

Lee, Sylvia Olden Teacher-Coach

Loeb, David Composer, Theorist

Massena, Martha Educator, Piano

Meng, Mei-Mei Educator, Piano

Meyer, Leonard B Educator, Writer

Montanaro, Donald Clarinet, Educator

Mostovoy, Marc Sanders Conductor & Music Director

Muti, Riccardo Conductor & Music Director

Oka, Hirono Violin

Ormandy, Eugene Conductor & Music Director

Panitz, Murray W Flute & Piccolo

Parsons, James Boyd Writer

Pastor, Freda Educator, Piano

Persichetti, Vincent Composer, Educator

Petit, Annie Educator, Piano

Popper, Felix Conductor, Coach

Popper, Fredric Conductor, Educator

Randall, Edward (Owens), III Tenor

Reise, Jay Composer

Roberts, John Howell Librarian

Rorem, Ned Composer, Writer

Rothermel, Dan Hiester Music Director, Writer

Rudin, Andrew Educator, Composer

Sataloff, Robert Thayer Baritone, Educator

Schimmel, William Michael Composer, Administrator

Schmidt, Carl B Educator, Writer

Schneider, Mischa Cello, Educator

Schoenbach, Sol Israel Administrator, Bassoon

Scott, Henry G Conductor, Double Bass

Scott, Roger Double Bass, Educator

Scott, Yumi Ninomiya Violin, Educator

Silverstein, Barbara Ann Conductor & Music Director, Artistic Director

Smith, William Conductor, Educator

Sokoloff, Eleanor Piano, Educator

Sokoloff, Vladimir Piano, Educator

Soyer, David Cello, Educator

Starr, Susan Piano

Steinhardt, Arnold Educator, Violin

Taylor, Maria del Pico Piano, Educator

Tree, Michael Educator, Viola

Tuttle, Karen Educator, Viola

Valente, Benita Soprano

Wernick, Richard Composer, Conductor

Wolf, Eugene Kendrick Musicologist, Educator

Yamron, Janet M Educator, Administrator

Zarzeczna, Marion Piano, Educator

Zimmerman, Franklin Bershir Educator, Conductor

Pittsburgh

Anderson, Penny Viola

Balada, Leonardo Composer, Educator

Berlin, David Composer, Educator

Bianco, Anthony Double Bass

Billings, David Arthur Teacher, Organ

Block, Steven D Composer, Critic-Writer

Branning, Grace Teacher, Composer

Cantor, Owen Polk Administrator, French Horn

Capobianco, Tito Director-Opera, Educator

Carlton, Stephen Edward Educator, Writer

Carr, Bruce Alan Administrator, Critic-Writer

Cass, Lee Educator, Bass-Baritone

Coyner, Louis P Composer, Educator

Dorian, Frederick Writer, Educator

Erickson, Sumner Perry Tuba, Educator

Galbraith, Nancy Riddle Composer, Piano

Goldberg, Bernard Z Flute, Educator

Gorton, James Allen Oboe, Educator

Gossard, Helen M Educator, Piano

Grauer, Victor A Composer, Theoretician

Hardwick, Charles T Violin, Teacher & Coach
Heaton, Charles Huddleston Organ, Educator
Hollingsworth, Samuel H, Jr Bass
Jenkins, Joseph Willcox Educator, Composer
Kubey, Arthur M Bassoon, Lecturer
Kumer, Dennis Michael Educator, Administrator
Leonard, Stanley Sprenger Percussion, Composer
Lerner, Mimi Mezzo-Soprano
Lindberg, William Edward Educator, Organ
Lipman, Michael (Avram) Cello
Lord, Robert Sutherland Educator, Organ
McCathren, Don (Donald E) Conductor & Music Director, Educator
McCulloh, Byron B Composer, Trombone
May, Julia Educator, Mezzo-soprano
Meibach, Judith Karen (Judith Karen Meibach Schiloni) Writer, Piano
Nero, Beverly Educator, Piano
Nketia, J H Kwabena Educator
Novich, Mija Educator, Soprano
Page, Robert (Elza) Conductor & Music Director, Educator
Peterson, Max D Educator, Conductor & Music Director
Phillips, Eugene Walter Composer, Violin
Powell, Keith Dom French Horn, Composer
Previn, Andre Music Director, Composer
Reagin, Brian E Violin, Educator
Reed, Ida McAliley Librarian
Rodriguez, Jose Viola
Root, Deane Leslie Educator, Librarian
Sanchez, Marta Educator, Lecturer
Schneiderman, William Percussion, Educator
Sharrow, Leonard Bassoon, Educator
Silberman, Aaron Patron, Clarinet
Slawson, A Wayne Composer, Educator
Smith, Martin Dodge French Horn, Teacher
Smoliar, Harold M Oboe & English Horn, Lecturer
Soroka, John G Percussion, Educator
Starkman, Stephen S Violin
Stock, David Frederick Composer, Conductor
Strack, Kenneth John French Horn
Taube, Moshe Tenor, Composer
Thomas, Marilyn Taft Composer, Educator
Turkin, Marshall W Administrator
Van Sickle, Rodney James Double Bass
Whipple, R(ichard) James Composer, Bassoon
Wichmann, Russell George Educator, Music Director

Pottstown

Schinstine, William Joseph Percussion, Composer

Reading

Elmer, Cedric N(agel) Teacher, Piano

St Davids

Wieckowski, Joanna G Lute

Scranton

Berendes, M Benedicta Educator

Selinsgrove

Lathrop, Gayle Posselt Educator, Composer

Stretansky, Cyril Michael Conductor & Music Director, Educator

Shillington

Bilger, David Victor Conductor, Saxophone

Slippery Rock

Sims, Edward Educator, Administrator

State College

Baisley, Robert William Educator, Piano
Brown, Raymond Educator, Voice
Carr, Maureen Ann Educator
Fenner, Burt L Composer, Educator
Gold, Diane Wehner Flute, Educator
Holmes, Robert William Administrator, Critic-Writer
Hopkins, Donald Eric Violin, Educator
Klick, Susan Marie Flute, Educator

Swarthmore

Levinson, Gerald Composer, Educator
Swing, Peter Gram Educator, Conductor & Music Director

University Park

Zagst, Joanne (Joanne Zagst-Feldman) Violin, Teacher

Upper Darby

Cole, Orlando T Cello, Educator

Wayne

Ashbrook, William Sinclair, Jr Educator, Writer
Elmore, Robert Hall Organ, Composer

West Chester

Fields, Richard Walter Piano, Educator
McVoy, James Earl Composer, Educator
Munger, Shirley (Annette) Educator, Composer
Murray, Sterling Ellis Educator
Nelson, Larry A Composer, Educator
Schmidt, Liselotte Martha Educator, Critic-Writer
Voois, Jacques C Piano, Conductor

Wyncote

Lee, Patricia Taylor Educator, Piano
McGraw, Cameron Writer, Composer

Wynnewood

Glickman, Sylvia Piano, Educator
Kerrigan, William Paul Percussion, Educator
Kwalwasser, Helen Educator, Violin
Sandberg, Larry (Lawrence H) Writer, Administrator

Yardley

Silvester, William H Music Director, Educator

RHODE ISLAND

Cranston

Lifson, Ludmilla V Educator

Kingston

Dempsey, John D Educator, Violin
Gibbs, Geoffrey David Composer, Educator

Lincoln

Nelson, Ron Composer, Conductor

Narragansett

Santini, Dalmazio O Composer, Teacher

Newport

Lutyens, Sally Speare Composer, Educator
Malkovich, Mark Paul Administrator, Lecturer

North Kingstown

Petersen, Patricia Jeannette Viola, Teacher

North Scituate

Smith, Raymond R Educator

Providence

Baker, James M Educator, Writer
Cassuto, Alvaro Leon Conductor
Cumming, Richard (Jackson) Composer, Piano
Josephson, David S Educator, Writer
Nelson, Paul Trumpet, Composer
VanValkenburg, James Wade Viola, Educator
Waddington, Susan Royal Librarian

Riverside

Fischer, Edith Steinkraus Composer, Soprano

Wakefield

Giebler, Albert Cornelius Educator, Administrator

Warwick

Boberg, Robert Martin Educator, Composer
Pellegrino, John Educator, Trumpet

Woonsocket

Romiti, Richard A Composer, Educator

Wyoming

Michaud, Armand Herve Violin, Composer

SOUTH CAROLINA

Charleston

Cedel, Mark Viola, Music Director
Maves, David W Composer, Educator

Clemson

Freeman, Edwin Armistead Educator, Composer
Hochheimer, Laura Educator, Violin

Columbia

Amstutz, A Keith Trumpet, Educator
Camp, Max W Educator, Piano
Conant, Richard Paul Educator, Bass
Douglas, Samuel Osler Composer, Educator
Dudley, Raymond C Piano, Educator
Ferguson, Gene Tenor, Educator
Goodwin, Gordon Educator, Composer
Moody, William Joseph Educator, Administrator
Peake, Luise Eitel Educator, Writer

Gaffney

Welch, Robert B Administrator, Conductor & Music Director

TEXAS

Abilene

Boggs, Martha Daniel Educator, Clarinet
Boyd, Jack Arthur Writer, Composer
Campbell, John Coleman Educator, Organ
Daniels, Melvin L Composer, Educator
Dean, Talmage Whitman Educator, Composer
Hager, Lawson J Educator, French Horn
Middleton, Jaynne Claire Soprano, Educator
Patterson, Andy J Composer, Educator
Rathbun, James Ronald Educator, Piano
Sumerlin, Macon Dee Composer, Educator

Alvin

Frankenberger, Yoshiko Takagi Vocalist, Teacher

Amarillo

Conlin, Thomas (Byrd) Conductor & Music Director
Johnson, Mary Jane (Rose) Soprano

Arlington

Postlewate, Charles Willard Guitar, Education

Austin

Addison, Anthony Conductor, Director-Opera
Antokoletz, Elliott Maxim Educator
Behague, Gerard Henri Educator
Benton, Walter Bradford Hichiriki
Deatherage, Martha Educator, Soprano
Dietz, Hanns-Bertold Educator
Doty, Ezra William Administrator, Organ
Ducloux, Walter Ernest Educator, Music Director
Endo, Akira Conductor & Music Director
Frock, George Albert Percussion, Educator
Garvey, David Piano, Coach
Grantham, Donald Composer, Educator
Green, Douglass Marshall Educator, Composer
Greer, Thomas Henry Composer, Conductor
Griebling, Karen Jean Composer, Viola
Hurt, Charles Richard Trombone, Educator
Kennan, Kent Wheeler Composer, Educator
Knaub, Donald Trombone, Educator
Korte, Karl Richard Composer, Educator
McLean, Barton Composer, Piano
McLean, Priscilla Taylor Composer, Writer
Mannion, Elizabeth (Belle) Mezzo-soprano, Educator
Merchant, Walter M Administrator, Piano
Nero, Bernard David Trumpet, Teacher
Roeckle, Charles Albert Administrator, Educator
Rogers, Delmer Dalzell Writer, Educator
Sankey, Rebecca Poole Recorder, Teacher
Tharp, Don(ald Warren) Piano, Librarian
Welcher, Dan Edward Composer, Conductor
Young, Phyllis Cello, Educator

Brownwood

Hilliard, John Stanley Composer

Canyon

Evans, Billy G Composer, Piano
Krause, Robert James Educator, Oboe & English Horn

Carrollton

Brown, Frank Neil Trombone, Educator

College Station

Milojkovic-Djuric, Jelena Writer

Commerce

House, Robert William Educator, Administrator
Wallace, Mary Elaine (Mary Elaine House) Administrator, Writer
Yates, Ronald Lee Composer, Educator

Corpus Christi

Calderon, Javier Francisco Guitar, Educator
Pierson, Thomas Claude Educator, Writer
Schroeder, William A Composer, Educator
Spies, Michael C Critic
Weiner, Lawrence Composer, Educator

Dallas

Anderson, Robert (Theodore) Organ, Educator
Benaglio, Roberto Chorus Master
Brusilow, Anshel Conductor & Music Director, Educator
Cherry, Kalman Percussion, Educator
Christie, James David Organ, Harpsichord
Clyne, Malcolm Edward Composer
Daw, Kurt David Administrator
Elledge, Nancy Ruth Soprano, Teacher
Erb, Donald James Composer, Educator
Faulconer, Bruce Laland Composer, Educator
Fomin, Arkady Gerson Violin, Artistic Director
Gilmore, Ev (Everett M Gilmore), Jr Tuba
Goemanne, Noel Composer, Music Director
Han, Tong-Il Piano, Educator
Hayward, Thomas (Tibbett) Tenor, Educator
Howard, (Dana) Douglas Percussion, Educator
Karayanis, Plato Director-Opera
Kirk, Elise Kuhl Musicologist, Educator
Kitzman, John Anthony Trombone, Educator
Lewis, Jungshin Lim Cello, Educator
Lewis, Philip James Violin, Educator
Mata, Eduardo Conductor & Music Director
Mendro, Donna C Librarian
Naldini, Vasco Prompter, Educator
Palmer, Larry Garland Educator, Harpsichord
Pelletier, Sho-mei Violin, Teacher
Pfautsch, Lloyd Alvin Educator, Conductor
Rafferty, J Patrick Violin, Teacher
Rescigno, Nicola Conductor, Administrator
Russell, Rogene Oboe & English Horn, Teacher
Sargeant, Phillip Lester Oboe, Educator
Schuitema, Joan Elizabeth Librarian, Harpsichord
Skinner, Robert Gordon Librarian
Sloman, Jan Mark Violin
Snider, Ronald Joe Percussion
Thomas, Paul Lindsley Composer, Organ
Tiemeyer, Christian Conductor & Music Director, Educator
Trevor, Kirk David Niell Conductor, Cello
Truax, Bert Trumpet, Composer
Vornholt, David Flute
Washburn, Franklin Ely Violin, Music Director

Denton

Austin, Larry Don Composer
Baird, Edward Allen Educator, Bass
Banowetz, Joseph Murray Piano, Educator
Brothers, Lester D Educator, Writer
Brown, Jonathan Bruce Composer
Brown, Leon Ford Educator, Trombone
Brown, Myrna Weeks Flute, Educator
Brown, Newel Kay Composer, Educator
Clark, Thomas Sidney Composer, Educator
Collins, Michael B Educator, Musicologist
Crader, Jeannine Soprano, Educator
Dickinson, Alis Writer, Educator
Ellis, Merrill Composer, Electronic
Farish, Stephen Thomas, Jr Educator, Writer
Fisher, Fred(eric Irwin) Writer, Piano
Gillespie, James Ernest Clarinet, Educator
Heiberg, Harold Willard Piano, Educator
Kuss, Malena Musicologist, Educator
Large, John W Educator
Latham, William P Composer, Educator
Mailman, Martin Composer, Educator
Maiorescu, Dorella Teodora Harp, Educator
Miller, Clyde Elmer Educator, French Horn
Myers, Marceau Chevalier Administrator, Educator
Pope, Betty Frances Librarian, Teacher
Rainbow, Edward Louis Educator
Roberts, Jack Lundy Piano, Teacher-Coach
Schoep, Arthur Paul Educator, Writer
Veazey, Charles Orlando Oboe & English Horn, Educator
Winsor, Philip Gordon Composer, Educator

Ft Worth

Bass, Claude Leroy Teacher, Composer
Brahinsky, Henry Joseph Violin, Teacher
Brouwer, Margaret Lee Violin, Composer
Canafax, Louise Terry Educator, Viola
Douglass, Robert Satterfield Musicologist, Educator
Gray, Scotty Wayne Administrator, Educator
Guenther, Ralph R Composer, Flute
Halen, Eric J Violin, Educator
Hopkin, John Arden Educator, Baritone
Kruger, Rudolf Administrator, Music Director
McKinney, Elizabeth Richmond Educator, Piano
McKinney, James Carroll Educator, Conductor
McLain, Robert Malcolm Double Bass, Educator
Reynolds, William J Educator, Writer
Robertson, Helen (Wells) Violin, Teacher
Shirey, Ronald Conductor, Educator
Sims, Phillip Weir Librarian, Educator
Solomon, Judith A Piano, Educator
Waters, Karen Johnson Administrator, Piano
Wilson, Sydney Virginia Harp, Educator
Winesanker, Michael M Educator, Administrator

Garland

Ferre, Susan Ingrid Organ, Harpsichord
Wilson, Ron (Ronnie Eugene) Trombone, Teacher

Georgetown

Lucas, Theodore D Administrator, Composer
Schroeder, Raymond Lee Clarinet, Educator

TEXAS (cont)

Houston

Arbtiter, Eric A Bassoon, Educator
Benjamin, Thomas Edward Composer, Educator
Bible, Frances Lillian Mezzo-soprano
Brand, Manny Educator
Brown, Richard S Percussion, Educator
Chung, Mi-Hee Violin
Citron, Marcia Judith Educator, Writer
Collins, Richard L Educator, Baritone
Colvig, David Flute
Comissiona, Sergiu Music Director & Conductor, Educator
Cooper, Paul Composer, Educator
Crawford, Dawn Constance Educator, Composer
DeMain, John Lee Conductor & Music Director, Piano
Deutsch, Robert Larry Cello, Educator
Floyd, Carlisle Composer, Educator
France, Hal Conductor, Piano
Gebuhr, Ann Karen Educator, Composer
George, Lila-Gene Plowe Teacher, Composer
Gockley, R David Director-Opera
Gottschalk, Arthur William Composer, Educator
Griebling, Lynn (Lynn Louise Griebling-Moores) Soprano, Teacher
Harwood, C William Conductor & Music Director
Hester, Byron Flute & Piccolo, Teacher
Hirsh, Albert Educator, Piano
Horvit, Michael Miller Composer, Educator
John, Patricia Spaulding Harp, Composer
Jones, Samuel Composer, Educator
Katims, Milton Conductor, Viola
Kurtzman, Jeffrey Gordon Educator
Lack, Fredell (Mrs Ralph Eichhorn) Violin, Teacher
Landsman, Julie French Horn, Educator
McAndrew, Josephine K Violin, Teacher
Mayfield, Lynette Flute
Milburn, Ellsworth Composer, Educator
Newton, Norma Teacher-Coach, Educator
Nunemaker, Richard Earl Clarinet, Saxaphone
Palmer, Willard A Editor, Lecturer
Preston, (Mary) Jean Educator, Voice
Rose, William H Tuba, Educator
Schnoebelen, Anne Writer, Educator
Shimada, Toshiyuki Conductor, Music Director
Smeltzer, Mary Susan Composer, Piano
Ward, Charles Wilson Critic
Waters, David L Trombone, Educator
Weaver, M Jane Administrator
Wehr, David August Conductor, Composer
Wheeler, Lawrence Bennett Viola, Educator
White, David Ashley Educator, Composer
Williams, Michael D Educator

Huntsville

Berry, Corre Ivey Educator, Teacher & Coach
Elhba, Mario (Leveque) Violin, Composer
Rex, Harley E Composer, Saxophone
Strandberg, Newton Dwight Composer, Educator
Tull, Fisher (Aubrey) Composer, Educator
Westover, Wynn Earl Teacher, Violin

Irving

Craft, Barry Hunt Tenor

Kingsville

Scott, Robert Charles Educator, Music Director

Lubbock

Barber, Gail (Guseman) Harp, Composer
Benefield, Richard Dotson Baritone, Conductor
Deahl, Robert Waldo Educator, Trombone
Guerrant, Mary Thorington Teacher, Composer
Snow, Mary (Helen) Composer, Piano
Van Appledorn, Mary Jeanne Composer, Educator
Westney, William (Frank) Piano, Educator

Marshall

Spencer, Robert Lamar Educator, Bass-Baritone

Missouri City

Talley-Schmidt, Eugene Educator, Tenor

Nacogdoches

Beaty, Daniel Joseph Composer, Piano
Coolidge, Richard Ard Composer, Educator
Sidnell, Robert G Administrator, Educator
Young, William Thomas Educator, Trombone

Odessa

Hohstadt, Thomas Dowd Conductor & Music Director

Plano

Eagle, Charles Thomas, Jr Educator, Writer
Moore, Barbara (Patricia) Hill Soprano, Teacher

Prairie View

Wyatt, Lucius Reynolds Educator, Trumpet

Richardson

Rodriguez, Robert Xavier Composer, Conductor & Music Director
Yavelow, Christopher Fowler Johnson Composer

San Angelo

Grimes, Doreen Educator, Composer

San Antonio

Barnes, Larry John Composer, Piano
Biskin, Harvey Timpani, Administrator
Ephross, Arthur J Flute & Piccolo
Fink, Michael Armand Educator, Composer
Finster, Robert Milton Music Director, Organ
Fried, Gregory Martin Conductor, Violin
Friedberg, Ruth Crane Piano, Writer
Gaab, Thomas Anthony Guitar, Teacher
Gast, Michael C French Horn, Educator
Gentemann, M Elaine Composer, Educator
Greenberg, Michael E Critic
Howard, George Sallade Conductor & Music Director, Composer
Kirk, Theron Wilford Composer, Conductor
Lamb, Gordon Howard Conductor & Music Director, Educator
Melone, Roger (Lewis) Conductor

Moore, John Parker, Jr Piano, Educator
Ode, James Austin Educator, Trumpet
Patterson, William G Percussion, Educator
Richelieu, David Anthony Critic
Rife, Marilyn N Percussion, Teacher & Coach
Ross, William James Composer, Organ
Rossi, Jane Niermann Trombone
Schulman, Julius Violin
Sedares, James Conductor
Smith, Lawrence Leighton Conductor, Piano
Stanley, Margaret King Administrator, Patron
Tiknis, V Michael Administrator
Torch, Deborah L Violin, Educator
Walker, William Baritone, Educator
Wilson, Carlos E Administrator
Winters, George Archer Double Bass, Composer
Wood, Lorna Viola

San Marcos

Belisle, John M Director-Opera, Educator
Fulton, William Kenneth Music Director, Educator
Harrel, (John) Ralph Educator, Piano
Neely, James Bert Director-Opera, Baritone
Riepe, Russell Casper Composer, Educator
Schmidt, John Charles Educator, Writer
Wolverton, Byron A Musicologist, Educator

Sherman

Isaac, Cecil Conductor, Educator

Spring

Valkovich, Susan Fristrom Violin

Stephenville

Rosner, Christian A K Administrator, Educator

Waco

Blocker, Robert L Administrator, Piano
Colvin, (Otis) Herbert, Jr Educator, Composer
Gordon, Jerry Lee Tenor, Administrator
Jones, Joyce Organ, Composer
Mackie, Shirley M(arie) Composer
McQuere, Gordon Daniel Educator
Moore, Donald I Educator, Conductor
Richards, James Howard Writer, Lecturer
Wienandt, Elwyn Arthur Educator, Writer
Willis, Richard M Educator, Composer
Young, Robert H Administrator, Composer

Wichita Falls

Armstrong, Peter McKenzie Piano
Hansen, Robert Howard Stage Director, Baritone
Maxwell, Donald Edward Administrator, Educator

UTAH

Bountiful

Campbell, Teresa Hicks Violin, Teacher
Neal, Lenora Ford Piano, Educator

Murray

Ketcham, Charles Music Director & Conductor

Ogden

Ericksen, K Earl Educator

Orem

Arbizu, Ray Lawrence Tenor, Educator
Durham, Thomas Lee Composer,
Educator
Hatton, Gaylen A Educator

Provo

Bradshaw, Merrill Kay Educator,
Composer
Bush, Douglas Earl Educator, Organ
Hill, Terry Conductor
Kalt, Percy German Violin, Conductor
Laycock, Ralph George Music Director,
Educator
Nordgren, Quentin Richards Educator,
Administrator
Powley, E Harrison, III Educator,
Percussion
Robison, Clayne W Educator, Baritone
Shumway, Larry Vee Educator
van Boer, Bertil Herman, Jr Educator,
Viola

Salt Lake City

Abravanel, Maurice Music Director,
Educator
Albiston, Marion H Trombone, Teacher
Ashton, Jack Schrader Violin, Conductor
Ashton, Wendell Jeremy Patron
Bullen, Sarah Harp
Cardenes, Andres Jorge Violin
Clark, John Frederick Double Bass,
Educator
Cook, Carla Educator, Mezzo-soprano
Cord, (Noel) Edmund, II Trumpet,
Educator
Cortes, Ramiro Composer, Educator
Duehlmeier, Susan Hunter Harpsichord,
Educator
Durham, Lowell M Composer, Educator
Goodfellow, Susan Stucklen Flute,
Educator
Graf, Erich Louis Flute, Educator
Kirschen, Jeffry M French Horn
Kojian, Varujan (Haig) Conductor &
Music Director
Kuchler, Kenneth Grant Violin, Recorder
Larson, Lennox Adamson Teacher, Piano
Loukas, Billie (Billie Loukas Poulos)
Soprano
Madsen, Norma Lee (Norma Lee Madsen
Belnap) Violin, Educator
Maiben, William Composer, Piano
Ottley, JoAnn Soprano, Teacher-Coach
Reich, Bruce Composer, Educator
Selberg, John Ryan Cello, Educator
Shand, David Austin Educator,
Conductor
Stephenson, Robert John Oboe, Educator
Suitor, M Lee Organ, Composer
Swint, Lois Roberts Violin
Thompson, John Cotton Violin
Watts, Aredean Walton Conductor &
Music Director, Educator
Wolking, Henry Clifford Composer,
Educator
Zalkind, Larry Howard Trombone,
Educator
Zalkind, Roberta Marian Viola

Sandy

Emerson, Stephen Harold Cello, Teacher

Springville

Mathiesen, Thomas James Educator,
Writer

West Jordan

Salisbury, James Earl Conductor, Piano

VERMONT

Bennington

Calabro, Louis Composer, Music Director
Glick, Jacob Viola, Educator
Levine, Jeffrey Leon Composer, Educator
Nowak, Lionel Piano, Composer

Brattleboro

Charkey, Stanley Guitar & Lute,
Educator
Lewandowski, Lynne Harp Maker,
Lecturer
Serkin, Rudolf Piano

Burlington

Demas, Terrance Louis Administrator
Guigui, Efrain Conductor & Music
Director
Metcalfe, William Conductor, Recorder
Read, Thomas (Lawrence) Composer,
Conductor

Castleton

Rand, Valorie Lee Administrator

Charlotte

Kaplan, Melvin Ira Oboe, Artist Manager

Dorset

Hobson, (Robert) Bruce Composer,
Teacher

Grand Isle

Grimes, Ev Educator, Radio Producer

Killington

Brant, Henry Dreyfus Composer,
Educator

Marlboro

Moss, David Michael Composer,
Percussion

Marshfield

Thorne, Nicholas C K Composer

Middlebury

Todd, George Bennett Composer,
Educator

Montpelier

Webb, Brian Patrick Conductor & Music
Director, Educator

Newfane

Felty, Janice Mezzo-soprano

Norwich

Fischer, Norman Charles Cello
Hamm, Charles Edward Educator,
Musicologist

Pownal

Hurley, Susan Composer, Educator

Sheffield

Goldstein, Malcolm Composer, Violin

South Burlington

Lidral, Frank Wayne Educator,
Administrator

Tunbridge

Stewart, Don (Donald George) Composer,
Clarinet

Westford

Schultz, Herbert L Conductor & Music
Director, Educator

West Rutland

Gettel, Courtland D Teacher, Flute

Wilmington

Silverman, Robert Joseph Editor, Writer

VIRGINIA

Alexandria

Anstine, Georgia Rebecca Harp
Hendrickson, Steven Eric Trumpet,
Teacher
Rosenberg, Kenyon Charles Educator,
Critic
Staup, Rebecca Lynn Oboe & English
Horn, Artist Manager

Annandale

De Gastyne, Serge Composer, Educator
Vlahopoulos, Sotireos Composer, Teacher

Arlington

Fearing, Scott M French Horn, Educator
Hinton-Braaten, Kathleen Violin, Writer
Shroeder, Linda Ann Violin
Sislen, Myrna (Carol) Guitar & Lute,
Educator
Tucker, Gene Richard Tenor, Coach

Blacksburg

Floyd, John (Morrison) Percussion,
Educator
Hasselman, Margaret Paine Educator,
Teacher
Holliday, Kent Alfred Teacher, Composer
Krauss, Anne McClenny Piano, Educator

Bridgewater

Barr, John Gladden Composer, Educator

Burke

Whaley, Garwood Paul Composer,
Educator

Chantilly

Merle, Montgomery Lecturer, Educator

Charlottesville

Allen, Judith S Composer, Educator
Lawrence, Kevin John Educator, Violin
Loach, Donald Glenn Educator,
Conductor
McClymonds, Marita Petzoldt Educator,
Writer & Editor
MacInnis, M Donald Composer, Educator
Ross, Walter Beghtol Composer, French
Horn
Velimirovic, Milos Educator, Writer

Chesapeake

Fears, Emery Lewis Educator

Christiansburg

Dirks, Jewel Dawn Composer
Saffle, Michael Benton Writer, Educator

Ettrick

Harris, Carl Gordon, Jr Educator, Music
Director
Moore, Undine Smith Educator,
Composer

Fairfax

Anders, (Barbara) Lynne Soprano
Burton, Stephen Douglas Composer,
Educator
Saverino, Louis Composer, Conductor

VIRGINIA (cont)

Schroeder, Pollyanna Tribouillier
  Musicologist, Soprano
Smith, James Gordon Conductor,
  Educator

Falls Church

Dahlman, Barbro Piano, Teacher
Fischer, Kenneth Christian Administrator,
  Artist Manager
Grahn, Ulf Ake Wilhelm Composer,
  Music Director
Stevens, Milton Lewis, Jr Trombone,
  Educator

Ft Myer

DuBose, Charles Benjamin Music
  Director

Hampton

Herbison, Jeraldine Saunders Composer,
  Teacher
Rogers, William Forrest Educator,
  Lecturer

Harrisonburg

Kniebusch, Carol Lee Flute, Educator
Kurtz, S James Educator, Composer
Perkins, Marion (Louise) Piano, Educator
Riley, James Rex Composer, Educator

Hollins College

Diercks, John Henry Composer, Educator
Granger, Milton Lewis Educator,
  Composer

Ivy

Little, Wm A(lfred) Educator, Organ

Lexington

Gansz, George Lewis Conductor,
  Composer
Stewart, Robert Composer, Conductor

McLean

Larson, Anna (Barbara) Composer,
  Lecturer
Tyl, Noel Jan Baritone
Willingham, Lawrence Hardwick
  Composer
Woollen, Russell Composer, Educator

Norfolk

Brockett, Clyde Waring, Jr Educator,
  Writer
Davye, John Joseph Composer, Educator
Errante, Frank Gerard Clarinet, Educator
Hawn, Harold Gage Educator, Music
  Director
Musgrave, Thea Composer, Conductor
Reeves, James Matthew Educator,
  Administrator
Ryder, Georgia Atkins Administrator,
  Educator
Shaffer, (William) Allen Educator, Organ
Steele, James Eugene Administrator,
  Music Director
Ware, John Marley Composer, Educator
Williams, Richard Musical Director
Zaret, Peter H Violin

Radford

Fellin, Eugene C Educator
Obenshain, Kathryn Garland Educator,
  Writer

Reston

Hope, Samuel Howard Administrator,
  Composer
Yaffe, Michael Charles Administrator,
  Writer

Richmond

Becker, Richard Educator, Composer
Bick, Donald Alan Educator, Percussion
Bilyeu, Landon Alan Educator, Piano
Blank, Allan Composer, Educator
Dollitz, Grete Franke Guitar, Teacher
Erb, James Bryan Educator, Music
  Director
Jarrett, Jack Marius Composer, Educator
Kloth, Timothy Tom Composer, Educator
Lohuis, Ardyth J Organ, Educator
Mabry, Raymond Edward Librarian,
  Writer
Moore, James, III Guitar & Lute,
  Educator
Morrison, Mamon L Piano, Teacher
Mott, Jonathan Violin
Murray, Robert P Violin, Educator
Neumann, Frederick C Writer, Violin
Newlin, Dika Composer, Critic-Writer
Silva, Jesus Guitar, Composer
Smetana, Frantisek Cello, Educator
Suben, Joel Eric Composer, Conductor
Wirt, John (Stephen) Guitar, Critic &
  Writer

Roanoke

Lentczner, Bennett Conductor & Music
  Director, Administrator
Whitesitt, Linda Marie Educator, Violin

Severn

Shackelford, Rudy Composer, Writer

Springfield

Werle, Floyd Edwards Composer, Music
  Director

Stephens City

Averitt, William Earl Composer, Music
  Director

Vienna

Guenther, Eileen Morris Organ, Educator
Guenther, Roy James Educator,
  Trombone
Ludwig, John McKay Administrator

Virginia Beach

Franco, Johan Composer
Hailstork, Adolphus Cunningham
  Composer, Conductor
Haywood, Carl Wheatley Conductor,
  Educator
Patton, Jasper William Educator, Piano
Rice, Thomas Nelson Composer,
  Conductor & Music Director

Williamsburg

Andersen, Elnore C (Marjorie) Violin
Connolly, Martha (Nixon Taugher)
  Mezzo-soprano, Educator
Truesdell, Frederick Donald Educator,
  Piano

Winchester

Albert, Thomas Russel Composer,
  Educator
Ohl, John Franklin Educator, Music
  Director

WASHINGTON

Bellevue

Groom, Lester Herbert Organ, Educator
Mossafer-Rind, Bernice Harp, Composer
Parker, Jesse Educator, Piano

Bellingham

Glass, Jerome Conductor, Educator
Labounty, Edwin Murray Composer,
  Educator
Rutschman, Edward Raymond Educator
Terey-Smith, Mary Conductor & Music
  Director, Educator

Cheney

Hough, Charles Wayne Lyric Baritone
Lotzenhiser, George William
  Administrator, Conductor

College Place

Spring, Glenn Ernest Composer, Educator

Ellensburg

Burns, Judith Capper Conductor,
  Educator
Cox, Jeff Reeve Violin, Educator
Jones, Jane Troth Educator
Panerio, Robert Major Composer,
  Educator
Roth, Eric Steven Conductor, Educator
White, Donald Howard Composer,
  Educator

Federal Way

Ellingson, Linda Jeanne Coach, Soprano

Medical Lake

Exline, Wendell L French Horn, Educator

Mercer Island

Nixon, Marni Teacher, Singer

Pullman

Brandt, William Edward Composer,
  Educator
Kierig, Barbara Elaine Soprano, Educator
Olsen, A Loran Composer, Educator
Reid, John William Bassoon, Composer
Webster, Gerald Best Trumpet, Educator

Renton

Hovhaness, Alan Composer

Richland

Singher, Michel Conductor & Music
  Director, Coach

Seattle

Alavedra, Montserrat Soprano, Educator
Beale, James Educator, Composer
Bergsma, William Laurence Composer,
  Educator
Bozarth, George S Musicologist
Curtis-Verna, Mary (Virginia) Soprano,
  Educator
Dempster, Stuart Composer
Dombourian-Eby, Zartouhi Flute &
  Piccolo
Drake, Archie Bass-Baritone
Fabre, (Alfred) Rene Composer, Teacher
Grossman, Arthur Bassoon
Guarrera, Frank (Francesco Guarrera)
  Baritone, Educator
Harned, Shirley (Lee) Mezzo-soprano
Holt, Henry Conductor & Music Director
Irvine, Demar (Buel) Educator, Composer
Jenkins, Speight Director-Opera, Critic &
  Writer
Kechley, Gerald Composer, Music
  Director
Kocmieroski, Matthew Percussion,
  Educator
Kriewall, Judy (Judith Washburn
  Kriewall) Flute
Lamb, John David Composer
Leuba, (Julian) Christopher French Horn,
  Educator
Levine, Joseph Music Director &
  Conductor

Lieberman, Fredric Educator, Composer
McColl, William D Clarinet, Educator
Mahler, David Charles Composer, Piano
Maia, Carolyn (Carolyn Maja Burton)
  Mezzo-soprano, Teacher
Mitchell, Michael Kenneth Writer,
  Conductor & Music Director
Nelson, Roger William Conductor &
  Music Director, Educator
Neuman, Daniel Moses Educator
Paglialunga, Augusto Tenor, Educator
Rafols, Alberto P Piano, Educator
Rice, B(oone) Douglas Educator,
  Composer
Ross, Glynn William Director-Opera,
  Administrator
Saks, Toby Cello, Educator
Savage, James Bryan Conductor,
  Educator
Shangrow, George Arthur Conductor,
  Harpsichord
Smith, William Overton Composer,
  Educator
Sokol, Vilem Music Conductor, Educator
Starr, Lawrence Educator
Summers, William John Educator,
  Administrator
Swisher, Gloria Wilson Composer,
  Educator
Thome, Diane Composer, Educator
Verrall, John Weedon Composer,
  Educator
Warkov, Esther R Educator, Writer
Webber, Carol Staats Soprano, Teacher
Wood, David A Librarian
Zsigmondy, Denes Violin, Educator

Sedro Woolley

Christ, Peter Oboe, Administrator

Spokane

Evans, Richard Vance Administrator,
  Trombone
Fitch, Benjamin Robert Oboe & English
  Horn
Hartley, Gerald S Composer
Jones, Wendal S Bassoon, Educator
Moldenhauer, Hans Writer, Administrator
Risdon, Frances Lee Flute & Piccolo,
  Educator
Sandifur, Ann Elizabeth Composer,
  Administrator
Smith, Wayne C Conductor & Music
  Director, Cello
Thulean, Donald (Myron) Conductor &
  Music Director, Administrator
Vayspapir, Roma Double Bass, Educator
Waters, J Kevin Composer, Educator
Windham, Verne French Horn

Tacoma

Block, Geoffrey Holden Educator,
  Composer
Doppmann, William George Piano,
  Composer
Hansen, Edward Allen Educator, Organ
Robbins, David Paul Composer, Educator
Seferian, Edward Conductor, Educator

Walla Walla

Leno, Harold Lloyd Educator, Conductor
Marshall, James Thomas Composer,
  Educator
Shultz, Dan McLloyd Educator, Oboe

Yakima

Nott, Douglas Duane Composer,
  Educator

WEST VIRGINIA

Fairmont

Ashton, John Howard Trumpet,
  Composer
Schooley, John (Heilman) Educator,
  Composer

Huntington

Whear, Paul William Composer, Educator

Morgantown

Beall, John Oliver Composer, Educator
Faini, Philip James Percussion, Composer
Hudson, Barton Educator, Harpsichord
Lefkoff, Gerald Writer, Composer
Miltenberger, James E Piano, Educator
Portnoy, Donald Charles Conductor &
  Music Director, Violin
Skidmore, Dorothy Louise Flute,
  Educator
Skidmore, William R Cello, Educator
Trythall, Gilbert Composer,
  Administrator
Wilson, C(ecil) B(arley) Educator,
  Administrator

Salem

Raad, Virginia Piano, Musicologist

Shepherdstown

Bland, William Keith Composer, Piano

Spencer

Kosowicz, Francis John Organ,
  Clavichord

West Liberty

Wolf, Edward Christopher Educator,
  Writer

Wheeling

Cook, Jeff Holland Conductor & Music
  Director, Composer
Crosbie, William Perry Organ, Music
  Director
Leonard, Nels, Jr Educator, Oboe

WISCONSIN

Appleton

Below, Robert Claude Piano, Composer
Cundy, Rhonda Gail Soprano, Stage
  Director
Irvin, Marjory Ruth Educator, Writer
Ming, James W Educator, Composer
Reed, Marlyce P Composer
Rogers, Rodney Irl Composer, Educator
Tamarkin, W Kate Conductor, Teacher

Beloit

Gates, Crawford Music Director,
  Composer
Yount, Max Hoffman Composer,
  Harpsichord

Brookfield

Duesing, Dale L Baritone

Delavan

Lepke, Charma Davies Composer,
  Educator

Eau Claire

Cecchini, Penelope C Piano, Educator

Cunningham, Michael Gerald Composer,
  Educator
Keezer, Ronald Composer, Educator
Lewis, L Rhodes Conductor, Educator
Lunde, Ivar Conductor, Composer
Lunde, Nanette Gomory Harpsichord,
  Educator
Schimke, Milton Maurice Administrator,
  Educator
Smith, Edwin Lester Educator, Composer

Fox Point

Beliavsky, Yuri Violin, Teacher

Green Bay

Cohrs, Arthur Lothar Educator, Piano
O'Grady, Terence John Educator, Writer
Parmentier, Francis Gordon Composer,
  Lecturer

Kenosha

Wegner, August Martin, III Composer,
  Educator

La Crosse

Arganbright, Nancy (Nancy Weekley)
  Piano, Educator
Brewer, Linda Judd Cello, Educator
Flatt, Terry Lee Director-Opera,
  Educator
Weekley, Dallas Alfred Piano, Educator

Lake Mills

Austin, Louise Faville Teacher, Recorder
Meske, Eunice Boardman Educator,
  Administrator

Madison

Burkholder, J Peter Educator, Writer
Crane, Robert Composer, Educator
Dembo, Royce Composer
Greive, Tyrone Don Educator, Violin
Latimer, James H Composer, Percussion
Ravnan, Ellen Marie Viola, Teacher
Richardson, William Wells Trombone,
  Educator
Silbiger, Alexander Educator, Writer
Thimmig, Les (Leslie Leland) Composer,
  Clarinet
Tiboris, Peter Ernest Educator, Conductor
  & Music Director

Milwaukee

Anderson, Karen Viola
Anello, John-David Conductor & Music
  Director
Babcock, Michael Educator
Bowers, Jane Meredith Writer,
  Musicologist
Burda, Pavel Conductor, Educator
Conti, Joseph John Percussion
Cook, Wayne Evans Trumpet, Conductor
Dvorak, Thomas L Conductor, Educator
Fischbach, Gerald F Educator, Violin
Goodberg, Robert Edward Flute,
  Educator
Helmers, William Alan Clarinet, Teacher
Henderson, Jeanne Margaret Harp,
  Teacher
Holmquist, John Edward Guitar,
  Educator
Horner, Jerry Viola, Educator
Hytrek, Theophane Composer, Educator
Jones, Patricia Collins Musicologist, Piano
Kelly, Danis Grace Harp, Teacher
Kitzke, Jerome Peter Composer, Piano
Kuether, John Ward Bass

WISCONSIN (cont)

Ruggeri, Janet Fleming Viola
Ruggeri, Roger Benjamin Double Bass, Writer
Snavely, Jack Clarinet, Educator
Snopek, Sigmund Composer, Electronic
Sorkin, Leonard Violin, Music Director
Stewart, Scott Stephen Conductor, Composer
Suchy, Gregoria Karides Composer, Educator
Suchy, Jessica Ray Harp, Educator
Thompson, Robert K Educator, Bassoon
Verhaalen, Marion Educator, Administrator
Yannay, Yehuda Composer, Educator

Oshkosh

Gainacopulos, Kay Thomas Music Director, Clarinet
Kohn, James Donald Educator, Piano
Linton, Stanley Stewart Educator

River Falls

De Jong, Conrad John Composer, Educator

Shorewood

Downey, John Wilham Composer, Educator

Stevens Point

Aber, Margery Vinie Educator, Administrator
Greene, Donald Edgar Educator
Palombo, Paul Martin Composer, Educator
Pinnell, Richard Tilden Educator, Guitar & Lute
Thomas, John M Organ, Educator

Superior

Bumgardner, Thomas Arthur Educator
Meidt, Joseph Alexis Educator, Clarinet

Waukesha

Dagon, Russell Clarinet, Educator

Wausau

Hosler, Mary Bellamy Hamilton Administrator, Educator

Whitewater

Ferriano, Frank, Jr Educator, Trombone
Jennings, Robert Lee Educator
Youngs, Lowell Vere Educator, Piano

Windsor

Strauss, Barbara Jo Librarian

WYOMING

Casper

Peacock, Curtis Cuniffe Conductor & Music Director, Teacher

Laramie

Childs, Gordon Bliss Educator, Viola
Hanly, Brian Vaughan Violin, Educator
Roberts, Megan (L) Composer
Smart, Gary L Composer, Piano
Stacy, William Barney Educator, French Horn

PUERTO RICO

Bayamon

Hernandez, Alberto H Librarian, Administrator

Rio Piedras

Alvarado, Marilu (Mrs Alan H Rapoport) Piano
Ramirez, Luis Antonio Composer, Educator
Rosado, Ana Maria Guitar, Educator
Schwartz, Francis Composer, Educator
Sierra, Roberto Composer
Thompson, Annie F Educator, Librarian
Thompson, Donald Writer, Educator

San Juan

Lopez-Soba, Elias Piano, Educator

Santurce

Lamoutte, Sylvia Maria Piano, Administrator

CANADA

ALBERTA

Calgary

Levin, Gregory John Composer, Educatc

Edmonton

Krapf, Gerhard W Organ, Composer

BRITISH COLUMBIA

Vancouver

Berry, Wallace Taft Educator, Composer

Victoria

Celona, John Anthony Composer, Computer Music

ONTARIO

Kingston

Sherman, Norman Morris Composer, Bassoon

London

Behrens, Jack Composer, Administrator
Bornstein, Charles Zachary Conductor & Music Director, Composer

Mississauga

Mauro, Ermanno Tenor

Stratford

Ware, Peter Composer

Toronto

Colgrass, Michael Charles Composer, Lecturer
Klein, Luthar Composer, Educator
Mansouri, Lotfollah (Lotfi) Director-Opera
Shirley, George Irving Tenor, Educator

Tenney, James C Composer, Educator

QUEBEC

Outremont

Boiles, Charles Lafayette Educator, Writer

OTHER COUNTRIES

AUSTRALIA

Mageau, Mary Composer, Educator

AUSTRIA

Ingle, William (Billy Earl) Tenor
Strummer, Peter Bass

FRANCE

Francescatti, Zino (Rene) Violin, Composer
Kurtz, Eugene Allen Composer
Lee, Noel Piano, Composer
Machover, Tod Composer, Cello
Maclane, Armand Ralph Educator, Baritone
Rose, Griffith Wheeler Composer

GERMANY, FEDERAL REPUBLIC OF

Atzmon, Moshe Conductor & Music Director
Bahmann, Marianne Eloise Composer, Mezzo-soprano
Clement, Roger Administrator
Coates, Gloria (Kannenberg) Composer, Lecturer
Fried, Joel Ethan Conductor, Teacher
Hampson, (W) Thomas Baritone
Hanner, Barry Neil Baritone, Educator
Hoffman, Grace Mezzo-Soprano, Educator
Humel, Gerald Composer, Conductor
Kirkendale, Warren Musicologist
Korn, Peter Jona Composer, Music Director
Lehrman, Leonard J(ordan) Composer, Conductor & Music Director
Mayer, Frederick David Tenor, Educator
Merritt, Chris Allan Tenor
Reece, Arley R Tenor
Ringer, Alexander L Educator, Writer
Russell, Lucy Hallman Educator, Harpsichord
Salta, Anita Maria Soprano, Teacher
Schultz, Carl (Allen) Bass
Sooter, Edward Tenor
Thomas, John Patrick Countertenor, Composer
Unruh, Stan Tenor
Woodward, Donna Lynn Soprano

ISRAEL

Shallon, David Conductor

ITALY

Abbado, Claudio Conductor & Music Director
Brunsma, Donna Louise Vocal Coach

Cameron, Andre Viola, Lecturer
Curran, Alvin S Composer, Electronic
Dashow, James Composer, Music
    Director
Eberhard, Dennis Composer
Trythall, Richard Aaker Composer, Piano

MOROCCO

Bowles, Paul Frederick Composer, Critic

NETHERLANDS

Alexander, Roberta Lee Soprano
Neill, Dixie Ross Teacher-Coach, Music
    Director
Rubin, Anna Ita Composer

VanEgmond, Max (Rudolf) Educator,
    Baritone

SPAIN

Fruhbeck De Burgos, Rafael Conductor &
    Music Director

SWITZERLAND

Dittmer, Luther Albert Educator,
    Publisher
Krimsky, Katrina (Margaret Krimsky
    Siegmann) Composer, Piano
McCracken, James E Tenor
Nurmela, Kari Kullervo Baritone
Ringo, Jennifer (Elizabeth) Soprano

Smith, Hopkinson Kidder Guitar & Lute
Warfield, Sandra Mezzo-soprano

UNITED KINGDOM

Ashkenazy, Vladimir D Piano, Conductor
Duarte, John William Guitar, Composer
Fulkerson, James Orville Composer,
    Trombone
Langley, Leanne Educator
Lankester, Michael John Conductor,
    Composer
Minton, Yvonne Fay Mezzo-soprano
Montague, Stephen (Rowley) Composer,
    Piano
Te Kanawa, Kiri Lyric Soprano
Veasey, Josephine Mezzo-soprano

Professional Classification Index

ADMINISTRATOR

Aber, Margery Vinie
Abrahams, Frank E
Acosta, Adolovni P
Adams, Alan Eugene
Adams, Richard Elder
Adkins, Aldrich Wendell
Adler, Kurt Herbert
Ahrendt, Karl F
Alexander, Peter Marquis
Allen, Robin Perry
Alley, Edward L
Ames, F(rank) Anthony
Amoaku, William Komla
Anderson, Ronald K
Anderson, William Miller
Angarano, Anthony
Ardoyno, Dolores
Auld, Louis Eugene
Bacon, Denise
Balk, Leo Frederick
Ball, Louis Oliver, Jr
Ballinger, Cathryn (Fluellen)
Barbash, Lillian
Baron, Carol K
Barry, Jerome
Bays, Robert Earl
Beach, David Williams
Beglarian, Grant
Behrens, Jack
Belsom, Jack (John Anton)
Berk, Lee Eliot
Berkowitz, Ralph
Bernstein, Martin
Berthelot, John (Menard), Jr
Biddlecome, Robert Edward
Bigham, William Marvin
Billings, Charles W
Binkley, Thomas E
Biskin, Harvey
Blair, William P
Blakely, Lloyd George
Bliss, Anthony Addison
Blocker, Robert L
Blodgett, David Murray
Bloom, Julius
Boal, Dean
Bobbitt, Richard
Bolen, Charles Warren
Bonino, MaryAnn
Bookspan, Martin
Borda, Deborah A
Borwick, Susan Harden
Boucher, (Charles) Gene
Bowen, Jean
Boylan, Paul C
Boyle, J David
Bravender, Paul Eugene
Braverman, Saul
Broekema, Andrew J
Broido, Arnold Peace
Brons, Martha (Parker)
Brook, Claire
Brown, Donald Clayton
Browning, James Francis
Brunelli, Louis Jean

Bucker, B J (Barbara Jo Adler)
Buckley, Emerson
Buelow, George John
Buketoff, Igor
Bullin, Christine Neva
Burkat, Leonard
Burkat, Marion F (Gumner)
Cabot, Edmund Billings
Cain, James Nelson
Callahan, Anne
Campbell, Frank Carter
Cantor, Owen Polk
Capanna, Robert
Carnovale, A Norbert
Carpenter, Howard Ralph
Carr, Bruce Alan
Carr, Eugene V
Carroll, Frank Morris
Carroll, Marianne
Castiglione, Richard B
Chalmers, Bruce Abernathy
Chapin, Schuyler Garrison
Chase, Sam
Cheadle, Louise M
Checchia, Anthony Phillip
Chenette, Louis Fred
Christ, Peter
Christ, William B
Christensen, Dieter
Christensen, Roy Harry
Ciolek, Lynda L
Clarke, Garry Evans
Clayson, Louis O
Clement, Roger
Clinton, Marianne Hancock
Coe, Robert M
Coffman, Phillip Hudson
Cohen, Jerome D
Colburn, Daniel Nelson, II
Cooley, Marilyn Grace
Cooper, David S(hearer)
Cormier, Richard
Cornelius, Jeffrey Michael
Cornwell, Richard Warren
Cossa, Joanne Hubbard
Cozette, Cynthia
Crager, Ted J
Cramer, Edward M
Crosby, John O'Hea
Cuckson, Robert
Currie, Russell
Custer, Arthur
Cykler, Edmund A
D'Ambrose, Joseph Lawrence
Daniel, Oliver
Daw, Kurt David
de Blasis, James Michael
de Bohun, Lyle (Clara Lyle
  Boone)
Dechario, Tony Houston
DeDee, Edward A
Dedel, Peter J D
Dederer, William Bowne
Deibler, Arlo C I
de Lancie, John
Delli, (Helga) Bertrun
Demaree, Robert William, Jr

Demas, Terrance Louis
De Rugeriis, Joseph Carmen
Di Chiera, David
Dohnanyi, Christoph von
Donovan, Jack P
Dordick, Johanna
Doty, Ezra William
Driver, Robert Baylor
Drucker, Arno Paul
Dunbar, Paul Edward
Duncan, Douglas Jon
Dunham, Benjamin Starr
Dunn, Lynda
Dutton, James N
Eby, Margarette Fink
Edmondson, John Baldwin
Edwards, Elaine Virginia
Edwards, John S
Epstein, Matthew Allen
Erneston, Nicholas
Espinosa, (Sister) Teresita
Etlinger, H Richard
Eubanks, Rachel Amelia
Evans, Richard Vance
Eyster, Jason
Faden, Betsy BB (Betsy Gale
  Bruzzese Faden)
Faiella, Ida M
Fairleigh, James Parkinson
Farese, Mary Anne Wangler
Fay, (Earl) William
Feder, Susan E
Feist, Leonard
Fink, Lorraine Friedrichsen
Fink, Robert Russell
Fischer, Kenneth Christian
Fleischmann, Ernest Martin
Fleming, Millicent Clow
Floyd, Samuel Alexander
Fominaya, Eloy
Foote, Lona
Forrest, Jim
Forte, James Peter
Fox, Alan Hugo
Franano, Frank Salvatore
Franklin, Joseph J
Freedman, Ellis J
Freeman, Robert Schofield
French, Catherine
French, Robert Bruce
Friedman, Carole G
Fromm, Paul
Frost, Thomas
Fuentealba, Victor W
Galardi, Susan M
Galkin, Elliott Washington
Garvelmann, Donald M
Gershunoff, Maxim
Giddings, Robert Potter
Giebler, Albert Cornelius
Glidden, Robert Burr
Goodfellow, James Richard
Gordon, Jerry Lee
Gordon, Marjorie
Gramenz, Francis L
Graney, John F, Jr
Grant, Kerry

Grave, Floyd Kersey
Gray, Scotty Wayne
Green, John Elwyn
Greenberg, Nat
Gross, Dorothy (Susan)
Gushee, Marion Sibley
Gustafson, Dwight Leonard
Gustin, Daniel Robert
Hagen, Dennis Bert
Haggh, Raymond Herbert
Hall, Marion Austin
Hall, Marnie L
Harkness, Rebekah
Harper, Andrew Henry
Harris, Donald
Hart, Kenneth Wayne
Hartwell, Robert Wallace
Hasselmann, Ronald Henry
Hatfield, Warren Gates
Haupt-Nolen, Paulette
Heller, Jack Joseph
Henderson, Clayton Wilson
Henken, Morris
Herren, Lloyd K, Sr
Hewitt, Harry Donald
Hilkevitch, Joyce Turner
Hill, Carolyn Ann
Himes, Douglas D
Hines, Robert Stephan
Hinshaw, Donald Grey
Hipp, James William
Hoffman, James
Hofstetter, Fred Thomas
Holden, Randall LeConte, Jr
Holland, Samuel Stinson
Holmes, Robert William
Homer, Paul Robert
Hoogerwerf, Frank William
Hoover, Cynthia Adams
Hope, Samuel Howard
Hopkins, Harlow Eugene
Hosler, Mary Bellamy
  Hamilton
House, Robert William
Housewright, Wiley Lee
Howe, Richard Esmond, Jr
Huber, John Elwyn
Huetteman, Albert G
Hutchinson, Lucie Mary
Hutchinson, William Robert
Irwin, Phyllis Ann
Jackson, Brinton
Jackson, Helen Tuntland
Jackson, James Leonard
Jacobi, Roger Edgar
Jacobson, Joshua R
Jay, Stephen
Jenkins, John Allan
Jennings, Theodore McKinley,
Jochsberger, Tzipora Hilde
Jorgenson, Dale Alfred
Jory, Margaret
Kagan, Martin I
Karns, Dean Meredith
Kaufman, Charles
Kaufman, Fredrick
Kellock, James Robert

547

ARTIST MANAGER/REPRESENTATIVE

COMPOSER

COMPOSER (cont)

Amlin, Martin Dolph
Amram, David Werner
Anderson, Adrian David
Anderson, Allen Louis
Anderson, Beth (Barbara Elizabeth Anderson)
Anderson, Garland (Lee)
Anderson, Ruth
Anderson, Thomas Jefferson, Jr
Andrews, George
Andrix, George Paul
Andrus, Donald George
Angelini, Louis A
Antoniou, Theodore
Applebaum, Edward
Applebaum, Stan (Stanley S)
Appleton, Jon H
Archibald, Bruce
Argento, Dominick
Armer, Elinor Florence
Arnatt, Ronald (Kent)
Aschaffenburg, Walter (Eugene)
Ash, Rodney P
Ashforth, Alden
Ashton, John Howard
Austin, John (Bradbury)
Austin, Larry Don
Averitt, William Earl
Avshalomov, Jacob David
Babbitt, Milton Byron
Baber, Joseph (Wilson)
Bach, Jan (Morris)
Bacon, Ernst
Bahmann, Marianne Eloise
Baker, Claude
Baker, Larry A
Baker, Robert Hart
Baksa, Robert (Frank)
Balada, Leonardo
Baldwin, David
Bales, Richard Henry Horner
Baley, Virko
Balkin, Alfred
Ballard, Gregory
Ballard, Louis Wayne
Balshone, Cathy S (Cathy S Balshone-Becze)
Barati, George
Barber, Gail (Guseman)
Barkin, Elaine Radoff
Barlow, Wayne Brewster
Barnea, Uri
Barnes, Larry John
Barnes, Marshall H
Barnett, Carol Edith
Barnett, David
Barr, John Gladden
Barthelson, Joyce Holloway
Basart, Robert
Baskerville, David
Basney, Eldon E
Bass, Claude Leroy
Bass, Warner Seeley
Bassett, Leslie Raymond
Bauman, Jon Ward
Baur, John William
Bavel, Zamir
Bavicchi, John Alexander
Baxter, Lincoln Arthur
Baylor, Hugh Murray
Bazelon, Irwin Allen
Beadell, Robert Morton
Beale, James
Beall, John Oliver
Bearer, Elaine Louise
Beaser, Robert Harry
Beaty, Daniel Joseph
Beck, John H
Beck, Martha Dillard (Mrs G Howard Carragan)
Becker, Richard
Beckler, S R (Stanworth Russell)
Beckon, Lettie Marie

Beeler, Charles Alan
Beerman, Burton
Beeson, Jack (Hamilton)
Beglarian, Grant
Behrens, Jack
Bell, (S) Aaron
Bell, Larry Thomas
Below, Robert Claude
Bengtson, F Dale
Benjamin, Thomas Edward
Benoit, Kenneth Roger
Benson, Warren F
Berg, Christopher (Paul)
Berger, Arthur Victor
Bergsma, William Laurence
Berk, Adele L
Berk, Maynard
Berkowitz, Sol
Berky, Carl R
Berl, Christine
Berlin, David
Berlinski, Herman
Berman, Ruth (Ruth Berman Harris)
Bernardo, Jose Raul
Bernstein, David Stephen
Bernstein, Leonard
Bernstein, Seymour Abraham
Berry, Wallace Taft
Berthelot, John (Menard), Jr
Bertini, Gary
Bestor, Charles L
Betjeman, Paul
Beyer, Frederick H
Bialosky, Marshall H
Bickley, Thomas Frank
Bielawa, Herbert Walter
Biester, Allen George
Biggs, John Joseph
Billingsley, William Allen
Binkerd, Gordon Ware
Biscardi, Chester
Bitgood, Roberta (Roberta Bitgood Wiersma)
Blackwood, Easley
Blake, Ran
Bland, William Keith
Blank, Allan
Blatter, Alfred Wayne
Blaustein, Susan
Blewett, Quentin H
Blickhan, (Charles) Timothy
Bliss, Marilyn
Bloch, Robert Samson
Block, Geoffrey Holden
Block, Steven D
Blood, Esta (Damesek)
Blumenfeld, Aaron Joel
Blumenfeld, Harold
Boardman, David Robeson
Boatwright, Howard Leake, Jr
Boberg, Robert Martin
Bobrow, Sanchie
Boda, John
Bohrnstedt, Wayne R
Bolcom, William Elden
Bolle, James D
Bolz, Harriett (Hallock)
Bond, Victoria
Bonde, Allen
Boone, Charles N
Borden, David
Borishansky, Elliot (David)
Bornstein, Charles Zachary
Borroff, Edith
Bottje, Will Gay
Bouchard, Linda
Boury, Robert Wade
Bowder, Jerry Lee
Bowen, Eugene Everett
Bowles, Paul Frederick
Bowles, Richard William
Bowman, Carl Byron
Boyadjian, Hayg
Boyd, Jack Arthur
Boykan, Martin
Boykin, Annie Helen

Bracali, Giampaolo
Bradshaw, Merrill Kay
Brandt, William Edward
Branning, Grace
Brant, Henry Dreyfus
Bratt, C(harles) Griffith
Braunlich, Helmut
Breeskin, Barnett
Brehm, Alvin
Brenner, Rosamond Drooker
Bresnick, Martin
Briccetti, Thomas Bernard
Brickman, Joel Ira
Brief, Todd L
Brindel, Bernard
Brings, Allen Stephen
Brink, Emily Ruth
Brisman, Heskel
Britain, Radie
Brockman, Jane Ellen
Bromley, Richard H
Brooks, Richard J
Brooks, William F
Brouwer, Margaret Lee
Brown, David Auldon
Brown, Earle
Brown, Jonathan Bruce
Brown, Merton Luther
Brown, Newel Kay
Brown, Rayner
Browne, Philip R
Browne, Richmond
Browning, Zack David
Brozen, Michael
Bruce, Frank Neely
Brun, Herbert
Brunelli, Louis Jean
Brush, Ruth Damaris
Bryant, Allan Charles
Bubalo, Rudolph Daniel
Bucci, Marc Leopold
Bucci, Thomas Vincent
Buchtel, Forrest Lawrence
Buggert, Robert W
Bunger, Richard Joseph
Burgstahler, Elton Earl
Burkley, Bruce
Burleson, Spencer (J), III
Burt, George
Burt, Warren Arnold
Burton, Stephen Douglas
Busby, Gerald
Bush, Milton Louis
Byrnes, Kevin Michael
Cacioppo, George Emanuel
Cage, John
Calabro, Louis
Callahan, James Patrick
Callaway, Ann Marie
Camajani, Giovanni
Cameron-Wolfe, Richard G
Campbell, Arthur M
Campbell, Charles Joseph
Campbell, Henry C
Campo, Frank Philip
Cannon, Dwight
Cantrell, Byron
Capanna, Robert
Capps, Ferald Buell, Jr
Caravan, Ronald L
Carmen, Marina (Carmen Manteca Gioconda)
Carroll, Gregory Daniel
Carroll, Joseph Robert
Carter, Charles
Carter, Elliott Cook
Cascarino, Romeo
Castaldo, Joseph F
Cave, Michael
Caviani, Ronald Joseph
Cecconi-Bates, Augusta N
Ceely, Robert Paige
Celona, John Anthony
Cervetti, Sergio
Cervone, D(omenic) Donald
Chadabe, Joel A
Chajes, Julius T

Chamberlin, Robert Charles
Chambers, Wendy Mae
Champlin, Terry (Arthur Doyle), III
Chance, Nancy Laird
Chapman, Charles Wayne
Chapman, Keith (Ronald)
Chasins, Abram
Chatham, Rhys
Chaudoir, James Edward
Chauls, Robert N
Cheadle, William G
Chihara, Paul Seiko
Child, Peter Burlingham
Childs, Barney Sanford
Childs, Edwin T
Chobanian, Loris Ohannes
Chorbajian, John
Chou, Wen-chung
Christiansen, Larry Arthur
Ciani, Suzanne E
Cioffari, Richard John
Cirone, Anthony J
Clark, Thomas Sidney
Clarke, Henry Leland
Clarke, Rosemary
Clayton, Laura
Cleman, Thomas
Clement, Sheree Jean
Clyne, Malcolm Edward
Coates, Gloria (Kannenberg)
Cobb, Donald Lorain
Cochran, J Paul
Cody, Judith (Ann)
Coe, Kenton
Cogan, Robert David
Cohen, David
Cohen, Edward
Cohn, James (Myron)
Coker, Wilson
Cole, Gerald E
Cole, Ulric
Cole, Vincent L
Coleman, Randolph E
Colgrass, Michael Charles
Collier, Gilman Frederick
Collins, Philip Michael
Colvin, (Otis) Herbert, Jr
Combs, F Michael
Cone, Edward Toner
Conrad, Laurie M
Consoli, Marc-Antonio
Constanten, Thomas Charles Sture
Constantinides, Dinos (Constantine Demetrios Constantinides)
Cook, Jeff Holland
Cook, Peter Francis
Cook, Richard G
Cooke, (John) Antony
Coolidge, Richard Ard
Coombs, Daniel Raymond
Cooper, David S(hearer)
Cooper, Paul
Cooper, Rose Marie (Mrs William H Jordan)
Cooper, William B(enjamin)
Cope, David Howell
Copland, Aaron
Copley, R Evan
Coppola, Carmine (Carmen)
Cordero, Roque
Corigliano, John Paul
Corina, John Hubert
Cormier, Richard
Corner, Philip Lionel
Cortes, Ramiro
Cory, Eleanor Thayer
Costinescu, Gheorghe
Cotel, Morris Moshe
Cowles, Darleen L
Coyner, Louis P
Cozette, Cynthia
Crane, John Thomas
Crane, Robert
Crawford, Dawn Constance

COMPOSER (cont)

Crawford, John Charlton
Cray, Kevin E
Creshevsky, Noah Ephraim
Creston, Paul
Crocker, Ronald Jay
Crockett, Donald (Harold)
Croom, John (Robert)
Cross, Lowell Merlin
Crumb, George (Henry)
Cumming, Richard (Jackson)
Cummings, Conrad
Cunningham, Arthur
Cunningham, Michael Gerald
Curran, Alvin S
Currie, Russell
Curtis, (William) Edgar
Curtis-Smith, Curtis O B
Custer, Arthur
Custer, Calvin H
Cyr, Gordon Conrad
Czajkowski, Michael
Da Costa, Noel
Daigle, Anne Cecile
Dallin, Leon
Danforth, Frances Adams
Daniels, Melvin L
Darcy, Warren Jay
Darter, Thomas E
Dashow, James
Davidovsky, Mario
Davidson, Lyle
Davidson, Tina
Davis, Allan Gerald
Davis, Jean Reynolds
Davis, Sharon (Sharon Yvonne
    Davis Schmidt)
Davison, John Herbert
Davison, Peter Saul
Davye, John Joseph
Dawson, George C
Deak, Jon
Dean, Talmage Whitman
Deason, William David
de Bohun, Lyle (Clara Lyle
    Boone)
de Brant, Cyr (Joseph Vincent
    Higginson)
De Cesare, Ruth
de Filippi, Amedeo
De Gastyne, Serge
Dehnert, Edmund John
De Jong, Conrad John
DeLaney, Charles Oliver
Del Borgo, Elliot Anthony
Della Peruti, Carl Michael
della Picca, Angelo Armando
Dello Joio, Norman
Del Tredici, David
Dembo, Royce
Dembski, Stephen Michael
Dempster, Stuart
Dennison, Sam Melvin
DePue, Wallace Earl
Derby, Richard William
Des Marais, Paul
DeVito, Albert Kenneth
DeVoto, Mark Bernard
De Young, Lynden Evans
Diaconoff, Theodore A
Diamond, Arline R
Diamond, David (Leo)
Diamond, Jody
Diamond, Stuart Samuel
Dick, Robert J
Dickow, Robert Henry
Didomenica, Robert
Diemente, Edward Philip
Diemer, Emma Lou
Diercks, John Henry
Di Julio, Max (Joseph)
Di Lello, Edward V
Dillon, Robert
Di Pietro, Rocco
Dirks, Jewel Dawn
Dixon, Dwight Mitchell
Dlugoszewski, Lucia

Dodge, Charles M
Donato, Anthony
Doppmann, William George
Dorati, Antal
Dorsam, Paul James
Douglas, Samuel Osler
Downey, John Wilham
Draganski, Donald Charles
Drennan, Dorothy Carter
Dresher, Paul Joseph
Drew, James M
Drossin, Julius
Druckman, Jacob
Drummond, Dean
Duarte, John William
Duckworth, William Ervin
Duesenberry, John F
Duffy, John
Duffy, Thomas C
Dugger, Edwin Ellsworth
Du Page, Florence Elizabeth
Dure, Robert
Durham, Lowell M
Durham, Thomas Lee
Dutton, Brenton Price
Dvorine, Shura
Dvorkin, Judith
Dydo, John Stephen
Eakin, Charles
Earls, Paul
Eaton, John C
Eberhard, Dennis
Eckert, Michael Sands
Eddleman, G David
Edmondson, John Baldwin
Edmunds, John Francis
Edwards, George (Harrison)
Edwards, Leo D
Effinger, Cecil Stanley
Ehle, Robert Cannon
Ekizian, Michelle Lynne
El-Dabh, Halim
Elhba, Mario (Leveque)
Elisha, Haim
Elkus, Jonathan (Britton)
Elliot, Willard Somers
Ellis, Merrill
Elmore, Robert Hall
Emig, Lois Irene
End, Jack
Enenbach, Fredric
Engel, Lehman
Epstein, David M
Epstein, Paul
Erb, Donald James
Erickson, Robert
Ernest, David John
Ernst, David George
Escot, Pozzi
Esteban, Julio
Estes, Charles Byron
Eubanks, Rachel Amelia
Evans, Billy G
Evans, Mark
Evans, Peter (Hollingshead)
Eversole, James A
Fabre, (Alfred) Rene
Fahrner, Raymond Eugene
Faini, Philip James
Faith, Richard Bruce
Fajardo, Raoul J
Falaro, Anthony J
Farago, Marcel
Farberman, Harold
Farmer, Peter Russell
Farrand, Noel
Faulconer, Bruce Laland
Faust, Randall Edward
Febbraio, Salvatore Michael
    Turlizzo
Feinsmith, Marvin P
Felciano, Richard
Felder, David C
Feldman, Herbert Bryon
Feldman, Joann E
Feldman, Morton
Feldsher, Howard M

Felice, John
Fennelly, Brian Leo
Fenner, Burt L
Fennimore, Joseph
Ferguson, Edwin Earle
Ferris, William
Ferritto, John Edmund
Fetler, Paul
Fine, Vivian
Fink, Michael Armand
Fink, Myron S
Fink, Philip H
Finney, Ross Lee
Fischer, Bill (William S)
Fischer, Edith Steinkraus
Fishbein, Michael Ellis
Fisher, Jerrold
Fissinger, Edwin Russell
Fitzgerald, Robert Bernard
Flagello, Nicholas Oreste
Flanagan, Thomas J
Fletcher, (H) Grant
Floyd, Carlisle
Floyd, J(ames) Robert
Flynn, George William
Foley, David Francis
Fontrier, Gabriel
Forman, Joanne
Fornuto, Donato Dominic
Forte, James Peter
Fortner, Jack Ronald
Foss, Lukas
Fox, Frederick Alfred
Frabizio, William V
Frackenpohl, Arthur Roland
Francescatti, Zino (Rene)
Franceschini, Romulus
Franchetti, Arnold
Franco, Johan
Frank, Andrew (David)
Frank, Jean Forward
Franklin, Cary John
Franklin, Joseph J
Frazeur, Ted C (Theodore C
    Frazeur)
Fredrickson, (Lawrence)
    Thomas
Freed, Arnold
Freeman, Edwin Armistead
Freeman, John Wheelock
French, Robert Bruce
Frerichs, Doris (Coulston)
Freund, Don (Donald Wayne)
Fricker, Peter Racine
Frigon, Chris Darwin
Fritschel, James Erwin
Fritze, Gregory Paul
Fromm, Herbert
Fuchs, Lillian F
Fuchs, Peter Paul
Fulkerson, James Orville
Fuller, Jeanne Weaver
Funk, Eric Douglas
Furman, James
Gabel, Gerald L
Gaburo, Kenneth Louis
Gach, Jay Anthony
Galas, Diamanda Angeliki
Galbraith, Nancy Riddle
Gallaher, Christopher S
Gamer, Carlton E
Gansz, George Lewis
Gardner, Kay
Garfield, Bernard Howard
Garland, Peter Adams
Garlick, Antony
Garriguenc, Pierre
Garwood, Margaret
Gates, Crawford
Gates, W Everett
Gatwood, Dwight D
Gause, Thomas David
Gay, Paul E
Gebuhr, Ann Karen
Geller, Ian
Gelt, Andrew Lloyd
Gena, Peter

Gentemann, M Elaine
George, Earl
George, Lila-Gene Plowe
George, Thom Ritter
Gerber, Steven R
Gerster, Robert Gibson
Ghent, Emmanuel
Ghezzo, Dinu D
Gibb, Stanley Garth
Gibbs, Geoffrey David
Gibson, David R
Gibson, Jon Charles
Gideon, Miriam
Gilbert, David Beatty
Gilbert, Janet Monteith
Gilbert, Michael William
Gilbert, Pia Sophia
Gillick, Lyn (Emelyn Samuels)
Gilmore, Bernard
Ginsburg, Gerald M
Glaser, Victoria Merrylees
Glass, Philip
Glazier, Beverly
Glinsky, Albert Vincent
Glovinsky, Ben
Gnazzo, Anthony Joseph
Godfrey, Daniel Strong
Godin, Robert
Goemanne, Noel
Gold, Ernest
Gold, Morton
Goldstein, Lee Scott
Goldstein, Malcolm
Gomez, Vicente
Gonzalez, Luis Jorge
Gonzalez, Manuel Benjamin
Goode, Daniel
Goode, Jack C
Goodman, Joseph Magnus
Goodwin, Gordon
Goolkasian Rahbee, Dianne
    Zabelle
Goossen, (Jacob) Frederic
Gottlieb, Jack S
Gottlieb, Jay Mitchell
Gottschalk, Arthur William
Gould, Elizabeth (Elizabeth
    Gould Hochman)
Gould, Morton
Gower, Albert Edward
Grahn, Ulf Ake Wilhelm
Granger, Milton Lewis
Grant, William Parks
Grantham, Donald
Grauer, Victor A
Graziano, John
Greatbatch, Timothy Alan
Green, Douglass Marshall
Green, George Clarence
Green, John W
Greenbaum, Matthew
    Jonathan
Greene, Margo Lynn
Greenfield, Lucille J
Greer, Thomas Henry
Gregorian, Rouben
Griebling, Karen Jean
Griebling, Margaret Ann
Griebling, Stephen Thomas
Griggs, Peter Johnson
Grigsby, Beverly Pinsky
Grimes, Doreen
Gross, Charles Henry
Grossman, Deena
Gruber, Albion Matthew
Guadagno, Anton
Gudauskas, Giedra Nasvytis
Guenther, Ralph R
Guerrant, Mary Thorington
Guinaldo, Norberto
Gunther, William (William
    Gunther Sprecher)
Haan, Raymond Henry
Hahn, Sandra Lea
Haieff, Alexei
Haigh, Morris
Hailstork, Adolphus
    Cunningham

COMPOSER (cont)

Haimo, Ethan Tepper
Halen, Walter John
Hall, Charles John
Hamvas, Lewis T
Hand, Frederic Warren
Handel, Darrell D
Hanlon, Kenneth M
Hanlon, Kevin Francis
Hanna, James Ray
Hannay, Roger Durham
Hansen, Ted (Theodore C
　Hansen)
Harbison, John H
Harder, Paul
Hardin, Burton Ervin
Hardish, Patrick Michael
Hardisty, Donald Mertz
Harkness, Rebekah
Harris, Donald
Harris, Robert Allen
Harrison, Lou
Hartley, Gerald S
Hartley, Walter Sinclair
Hartway, James John
Hartzell, Lawrence William
Hastings, Baird
Haufrect, Herbert
Haugland, A Oscar
Hawley, William
Haxton, (Richard) Kenneth
Hayes, Joseph (C)
Hayman, Richard Warren
　Joseph
Hays, Doris Ernestine
Hays, Robert Denecke
Haywood, Carl Wheatley
Hazzard, Peter (Peabody)
Healey, Derek Edward
Heiden, Bernhard
Heilbron, Valerie J
Heilner, Irwin
Heim, Norman Michael
Heiss, John Carter
Heller, Duane L
Hellermann, William David
Helps, Robert Eugene
Hennagin, Michael
Henry, Joseph
Henry, Otto Walker
Herbison, Jeraldine Saunders
Herder, Ronald
Hervig, Richard B
Heussenstamm, George
Hewitt, Harry Donald
Hibbard, William Alden
Hill, Jackson
Hiller, Lejaren Arthur, Jr
Hilliard, John Stanley
Hilliard, Tom (Thomas
　Lee)
Ho, Cordell
Ho, Ting
Hobson, (Robert) Bruce
Hoffman, Allen
Hoffman, Joel H
Hoffman, Theodore B
Hoffmann, James
Hoffmann, Richard
Hogenson, Robert Charles
Hogg, Merle E
Hoiby, Lee
Hollander, Lorin
Holliday, Kent Alfred
Hollingsworth, Stanley W
Hollister, David Manship
Holloway, Jack E
Hood, Boyde Wyatt
Hoose, Alfred Julius
Hoover, Katherine L
Hope, Samuel Howard
Hopkins, James Fredrick
Hopson, Hal Harold
Horvit, Michael Miller
Hoskins, William Barnes
Hovda, Eleanor
Hovey, Serge

Hovhaness, Alan
Howard, Dean Clinton
Howard, George Sallade
Howe, Hubert S, Jr
Hoy, Hendricks
Hsu, Wen-ying
Huber, Calvin Raymond
Hughes, Robert Grove
Humel, Gerald
Hunkins, Arthur B
Hunt, Michael Francis
Hurley, Susan
Husa, Karel
Huston, Thomas Scott, Jr
Hutcheson, Jere Trent
Hutchins, Farley Kennan
Hutchison, (David) Warner
　(Walter Hudson)
Hyla, Lee
Hyson, Winifred Prince
Hytrek, Theophane
Iannaccone, Anthony
Ienni, Philip Camillo
Imbrie, Andrew Welsh
Inwood, Mary B B
Irvine, Demar (Buel)
Israel, Brian M
Ivey, Jean Eichelberger
Jablonsky, Stephen
Jackson, Hanley
Jacobs, Kenneth A
Jaffe, David Aaron
Jaffe, Stephen Abram
Jager, Robert Edward
Jankowski, Loretta Patricia
Janson, Thomas
Jansons, Andrejs
Jarrett, Jack Marius
Jarrett, Keith Daniel
Jazwinski, Barbara Maria
Jeffers, Ronald H
Jenkins, Joseph Willcox
Jenkins, Susan Elaine
Jenni, D(onald) Martin
Jensen, James A
Jepson, Warner
Jergenson, Dale Roger
Jochsberger, Tzipora Hilde
Johanson, Bryan
John, Patricia Spaulding
Johnson, A Paul
Johnson, Clyde E
Johnson, David Nathaniel
Johnson, Roy Hamlin
Johnson, Roy Henry
Johnson, Tom
Johnson-Hamilton, Joyce
Johnston, Benjamin Burwell, Jr
Johnston, Donald O
Jolas, Betsy
Jones, Barnard Ray
Jones, Charles
Jones, George Thaddeus
Jones, Joyce
Jones, Robert William
Jones, Roger Parks
Jones, Samuel
Jordahl, Robert A
Jordan, Roland
Josephson, Kenneth George
Kabat, Julie Phyllis
Kacinskas, Jeronimas
Kaderavek, Milan
Kalajian, Berge
Kalmanoff, Martin
Kam, Dennis Koon Ming
Kamien, Anna
Kanwischer, Alfred O
Kaplan, Lois Jay
Kaplan, Robert Barnet
Karchin, Louis (Samuel)
Karlins, M(artin) William
Kaufman, Fredrick
Kaufmann, Walter
Kavasch, Deborah Helene
Kay, Ulysses
Keats, Donald H(oward)

Kechley, David Stevenson
Kechley, Gerald
Keezer, Ronald
Keller, Homer (Todd)
Kellis, Leo Alan
Kellogg, Cal Stewart
Kelly, (J) Robert
Kemner, Gerald E
Kendrick, Virginia
　Bachman
Kennan, Kent Wheeler
Kennell, Richard Paul
Kent, Richard Layton
Ker, Ann Steele
Keshner, Joyce Grove
Kessler, Minuetta
Kessner, Daniel Aaron
Keyes, Nelson
Khan, Ali Akbar
Kievman, Carson
Kim, Byong-kon
Kim, Earl
Kimes, Janice Louise
King, Alvin Jay
Kingman, Daniel C
Kingsley, Gershon
Kirchner, Leon
Kirk, Theron Wilford
Kitzke, Jerome Peter
Kleen, Leslie
Klein, Leonard
Klein, Luthar
Klenz, William
Kletzsch, Charles Frederick
Kloth, Timothy Tom
Knaack, Donald (Frank)
Knight, Eric W
Knight, Morris H
Knox, Charles
Koblitz, David
Koch, Frederick (Charles)
Kogan, Robert Colver
Kohn, Karl (George)
Kohs, Ellis Bonoff
Kolb, Barbara
Kondorossy, Leslie
Kopp, Frederick Edward
Kopp, Leo Laszlo
Korde, Shirish K
Korf, Anthony
Korn, Mitchell
Korn, Peter Jona
Korte, Karl Richard
Korth, Thomas A
Kotik, Petr
Kraft, Leo Abraham
Kraft, William
Kramer, Gregory Paul
Kramer, Jonathan D(onald)
Krapf, Gerhard W
Kreiger, Arthur V
Kremenliev, Boris A
Kriesberg, Matthias
Krimsky, Katrina (Margaret
　Krimsky Siegmann)
Kroeger, Karl
Krosnick, Mary Lou Wesley
Krzywicki, Jan
Kubik, Gail
Kunitz, Sharon Lohse
Kupferman, Meyer
Kurtz, Arthur Digby
Kurtz, Eugene Allen
Kurtz, S James
Kuzmych, Christina
Kyr, Robert Harry
La Barbara, Joan (Joan La
　Barbara Subotnick)
Labounty, Edwin Murray
Lackman, Susan Cohn
LaFave, Kenneth John
Laitman, Lori (Lori Laitman
　Rosenblum)
Lake, Oliver Eugene
Lamb, John David
Lamb, Marvin Lee
Lambro, Phillip

La Montaine, John
Landau, Siegfried
Lane, Richard Bamford
Lankester, Michael John
Lansky, Paul
La Porta, John Daniel
Largent, Edward J, Jr
Larsen, Henry
Larsen, Libby (Elizabeth
　Brown)
Larson, Anna (Barbara)
Latham, William P
Lathrop, Gayle Posselt
Latimer, James H
Latiolais, Desiree Jayne
Laufer, Beatrice
Lauridsen, Morten Johannes
Lawergren, Bo T
Layton, Billy Jim
Lazarof, Henri
LeBaron, Anne
Lebow, Leonard S
Leclaire, Dennis James
Lee, Dai-Keong
Lee, Jack Kenneth
Lee, Noel
Lee, Thomas Oboe
Lee, William Franklin, III
Leedy, Douglas
Lees, Benjamin
Lefkoff, Gerald
Lehrman, Leonard J(ordan)
Leisner, David
Leniado-Chira, Joseph
Lennon, John Anthony
Leon, Tania J
Leonard, Stanley Sprenger
Lepke, Charma Davies
Lerdahl, Fred (Alfred
　Whitford)
Lerman, Richard M
Lesemann, Frederick
Lessard, John Ayres
Levi, Paul Alan
Levin, Gregory John
Levin, Rami Yona
Levine, Jeffrey Leon
Levinson, Gerald
Levy, Frank E
Levy, Marvin David
Lewin, Frank
Lewis, Malcolm Wallace, Jr
Lewis, Peter Tod
Lewis, Robert Hall
Lieber, Edvard
Lieberman, Fredric
Lieberman, Glenn
Lieberson, Peter Goddard
Lifchitz, Max
Liljestrand, Paul F
Lindenfeld, Harris Nelson
Linn, Robert T
Lipkis, Larry (Laurence Alan)
Lipp, Charles Herbert
Lister, John Rodney
Livingston, David
Livingston, Julian Richard
Lloyd, Gerald J
Lobingier, Christopher Crumay
Locklair, Dan Steven
Lockshin, Florence Levin
Lockwood, Annea Ferguson
Lockwood, Larry Paul
Lockwood, Normand
Loeb, David
Logan, Wendall
Lombardo, Robert Michael
Lomon, Ruth
London, Edwin Wolf
London, Lawrence Bernard
Lopez, Peter Dickson
LoPresti, Ronald B
Lorenz, Ellen Jane (Ellen Jane
　Lorenz Porter)
Lovell, William James
Lowrey, Norman Eugene
Lubet, Alex J

COMPOSER (cont)

Lucas, Theodore D
Lucier, Alvin Augustus
Luckman, Phyllis
Luening, Otto
Luke, Ray E
Lundborg, (Charles) Erik
Lunde, Ivar
Lustig, Leila Sarah
Lutyens, Sally Speare
Lynn, George
McAnaney, Harold
McBeth, William Francis
Macbride, David Huston
McBride, Robert Guyn
McCarty, Frank Lee
McCarty, Patrick
McClain, Floyd Austin
MacCombie, Bruce Franklin
McCulloh, Byron B
McDermott, Vincent
McGee, William James
McGraw, Cameron
Machover, Tod
McHugh, Charles Russell
MacInnis, M Donald
McKay, Neil
McKenney, William Thomas
McKenzie, Wallace C
Mackie, Shirley M(arie)
McKinley, William Thomas
McLaughlin, Marian
McLean, Barton
McLean, Edwin W
Mac Lean, John Torry
McLean, Priscilla Taylor
McLennan, John Stewart
McMahan, Robert Young
McMillan, Ann Endicott
McNeil, Jan Pfischner (Janet
    Louise Pfischner)
McVoy, James Earl
Mageau, Mary
Mahler, David Charles
Maiben, William
Mailman, Martin
Makris, Andreas
Maloof, William J
Mamlok, Ursula
Mancini, Henry
Mandelbaum, M Joel
Maneri, Joseph Gabriel
Mann, Robert
Manno, Robert
Manson, Eddy Lawrence
Marcus, Ada Belle (Gross)
Marsh, Milton R
Marshall, Ingram Douglass
Marshall, James Thomas
Marshall, Pamela Joy
Marson, Laurel Rose
Martin, Judith Lynn
Martin, Ravonna G
Martin, Robert Edward
Martin, Thomas Philipp
Martin, Vernon
Martino, Donald James
Martirano, Salvatore
Maslanka, David Henry
Mason, Lucas (Roger)
Mathew, David (Wylie), III
Matthews, Justus Frederick
Matthews, William
Mattila, Edward Charles
Maucer, John Francis
Mauldin, Michael
Maves, David W
May, Walter Bruce
Mayer, Lutz Leo
Mayer, William Robert
Mayeur, Robert Gordon
Mechem, Kirke Lewis
Meister, Scott Robert
Mekeel, Joyce Haviland
Melby, John (B), Jr
Mennini, Louis Alfred
Menotti, Gian Carlo

Merrill, Lindsey
Merriman, Margarita Leonor
Merryman, Marjorie
Meyer, Leonard B
Meyerowitz, Jan
Meyers, (Herman) Emerson
Michaelides, Peter
Michaud, Armand Herve
Middleton, Robert (Earl)
Milburn, Ellsworth
Miller, Edward J
Miller, Ira Steven
Miller, Karl Frederick
Miller, Lewis Martin
Miller, Ralph Dale
Ming, James W
Mirante, Thomas Anthony
Missal, Joshua M
Misterly, Eugene William
Moe, Daniel T
Moevs, Robert Walter
Molava, Pamela May
Mollicone, Henry
Monaco, Richard A
Monk, Meredith J
Monod, Jacques-Louis
Montague, Stephen (Rowley)
Moore, Carman Leroy
Moore, Dorothy Rudd
Moore, F Richard
Moore, Undine Smith
Morrill, Dexter G
Morris, Robert Daniel
Morris, Stephen MacKay
Morrison, Julia (Maria)
Moryl, Richard Henry
Moss, David Michael
Moss, Lawrence Kenneth
Mossafer-Rind, Bernice
Moulder, Earline
Mourant, Walter Byron
Moyer, John Harold
Moylan, William David
Muczynski, Robert
Mueller, Frederick A
Muller, Gerald F
Mullins, Hugh E
Mumma, Gordon
Munger, Shirley (Annette)
Muradian, Vazgen
Murray, Bain
Musgrave, Thea
Myers, Theldon
Myover, Max Lloyd
Nagel, Robert E, Jr
Najera, Edmund L
Nash, Paul
Nelson, Bradley R
Nelson, Larry A
Nelson, Paul
Nelson, Ron
Neuhaus, Max
Neumann, Philip Warren
Neumann, Richard Jacob
Newell, Robert Max
Newlin, Dika
Newman, Anthony
Niblock, James F
Niblock, Phill
Nin-Culmell, Joaquin M
Nisbet, Meredith Wootton
Nixon, Roger
Nobel, (Virginia) Ann
Noon, David
Norden, Hugo
Nordenstrom, Gladys (Gladys
    Nordenstrom Krenek)
Norman, Theodore
Norris, Kevin Edward
North, Alex
Nosse, Carl E
Nott, Douglas Duane
Nowak, Lionel
Nuernberger, Louis D
Nunlist, Juli (Elizabeth Moora)
Nurock, Kirk
Oakes, Rodney Harland

Obrecht, Eldon Ross
O'Brien, Eugene Joseph
Ochse, Orpha Caroline
O'Donnell, Richard
Ogdon, Will (Wilbur Lee
    Ogdon)
Oliveros, Pauline
Olsen, A Loran
O'Neal, Barry
Orbon, Julian
Ordansky, Jerold Alan
Orland, Henry
Orrego-Salas, Juan Antonio
Ortiz, William
Ostrander, Linda Woodaman
Ostrovsky, Arthur (Arthur
    William Austin)
Ostryniec, James Paul
Ott, Joseph Henry
Owen, Blythe
Owen, Harold J
Owen, Richard
Owens, David
Packer, Randall Martin
Palmer, Anthony John
Palmer, Robert M
Palombo, Paul Martin
Panerio, Robert Major
Panetti, Joan
Parchman, Gen Louis
Parker, Alice
Parmentier, Francis Gordon
Parris, Robert
Parwez, Akmal M
Pasatieri, Thomas
Patterson, Andy J
Patterson, David Nolte
Paul, James
Paull, Barberi P
Paulus, Stephen Harrison
Paymer, Marvin E
Payn, William Austin
Payne, Frank Lynn
Payne, Maggi
Peaslee, Richard C
Peek, Richard Maurice
Peelle, David
Pegram, Wayne Frank
Pellman, Samuel Frank
Pena, Angel Matias
Penderecki, Krzysztof
Penhorwood, Edwin Leroy
Peninger, James David
Pennario, Leonard
Perera, Ronald Christopher
Perkinson, Coleridge-Taylor
Perle, George
Perlongo, Daniel James
Perrin, Peter A
Persichetti, Vincent
Peskanov, Alexander E
Peterson, Hal (Harold
    Vaughan)
Peterson, Wayne Turner
Pethel, James L
Pethel, Stan (Stanley Robert)
Peyton, Malcolm Cameron
Phelps, Norman F
Phillips, Burrill
Phillips, Eugene Walter
Philo, Gary Bruce
Picker, Tobias
Pierce, Alexandra
Pillin, Boris William
Pinkham, Daniel
Pisk, Paul A(madeus)
Pizer, Elizabeth Faw Hayden
Platthy, Jeno
Pleskow, Raoul
Plog, Anthony (Clifton)
Plsek, Thomas Joseph
Polansky, Larry C
Polin, Claire
Pollock, Robert Emil
Pone, Gundaris
Porter, David Gray
Porter, James Whyte

Pottebaum, William G
Pottenger, Harold Paul
Powell, Keith Dom
Powell, Mel
Powell, Morgan Edward
Powell, Robert Jennings
Pozdro, John Walter
Prater, Jeffrey L
Presser, William Henry
Presslaff, Hilary Tann
Previn, Andre
Price, John Elwood
Pritchard, Robert Starling
Pritts, Roy A
Procter, Leland (Herrick)
Proto, Frank
Provenzano, Aldo
Ptaszynska, Marta
Pursell, Bill (William Whitney)
Putsche, Thomas Reese
Quilling, Howard Lee
Quinn, James Joseph
Quintiere, Jude
Quist, Pamela Layman
Rackley, Lawrence (Lawrence
    Rackley Smith)
Raffman, Relly
Raigorodsky, Natalia (Leda
    Natalia Raigorodsky
    Heimsath Harter)
Raksin, David
Ramey, Phillip
Ramirez, Luis Antonio
Ramsier, Paul
Ran, Shulamit
Randall, James K
Rands, Bernard
Raphling, Sam
Rausch, Carlos
Read, Gardner
Read, Thomas (Lawrence)
Reale, Paul Vincent
Reed, Alfred
Reed, H Owen
Reed, Marlyce P
Reed, Phyllis Luidens
Reich, Bruce
Reich, Steve
Reid, John William
Reise, Jay
Renwick, Wilke Richard
Retzel, Frank (Anthony)
Rex, Harley E
Reynolds, Erma
Reynolds, Roger Lee
Reynolds, Verne Becker
Rhoads, Mary Ruth
Rhoads, William Earl
Rhodes, Phillip
Rice, B(oone) Douglas
Rice, Thomas Nelson
Richardson, Louis Samuel
Richens, James William
Richter, Marga
Richter, Marion Morrey
Riddle, Ronald William
Riepe, Russell Casper
Rigai, Amiram Hagai
Riley, Dennis (Daniel)
Riley, James Rex
Riley, John Arthur
Riley, Terry
Rinehart, John
Ritchie, Tom Vernon
Rivard, William H
Rizzer, Gerald Marvin
Roads, Curtis
Robbins, Daniel
Robbins, David Paul
Robboy, R(onald) A
Roberts, Gertrud K
Roberts, Jane A
Roberts, Megan (L)
Roberts, Wilfred Bob
Robertson, Donna Nagey
Robertson, Edwin C
Robinson, Forrest Thompson

COMPOSER (cont)

Robinson, Richard
Rochberg, George
Rodby, John Leonard
Rodby, Walter
Rodriguez, Robert Xavier
Rogers, Ethel Tench
Rogers, John E
Rogers, Patsy
Rogers, Rodney Irl
Rollin, Robert
Romeo, James Joseph
Romero, Celedonio P
Romiti, Richard A
Ronsheim, John Richard
Roosevelt, Joseph Willard
Rorem, Ned
Rose, Earl Alexander
Rose, Griffith Wheeler
Roseman, Ronald Ariah
Rosen, Jerome William
Rosenbloom, David Stuart
Rosenboom, David
Rosenhaus, Steven L
Rosner, Arnold
Ross, Eric
Ross, Walter Beghtol
Ross, William James
Rosso, Carol L
Rouse, Christopher Chapman
Roussakis, Nicolas
Rovics, Howard
Roy, Klaus George
Royer, Paul Harold
Rozsa, Miklos
Rubin, Anna Ita
Rudhyar, Dane
Rudin, Andrew
Ruggiero, Charles H(oward)
Russell, Armand King
Russo, John
Russo, William
Rzewski, Frederic
Sacco, P Peter
Safran, Arno M
St John, Kathleen Louise
Salkov, Abraham A
Salzman, Eric
Samson, Valerie Brooks
Samuel, Gerhard
Samuel, Rhian
Sandifur, Ann Elizabeth
Sandow, Gregory
Sandresky, Margaret Vardell
Sandroff, Howard F
Santini, Dalmazio O
Saperstein, David
Sapieyevski, Jerzy
Sapp, Allen Dwight
Sateren, Leland Bernhard
Saturen, David Haskell
Saverino, Louis
Saylor, Bruce Stuart
Scavarda, Donald Robert
Scelba, Anthony J
Schiavone, John (Sebastian)
Schickele, Peter
Schiffman, Harold (Anthony)
Schimmel, William Michael
Schindler, Allan
Schinstine, William Joseph
Schirmer, William Louis
Schmidt, William Joseph
Schneider, Gary Michael
Schneider, June
Schober, Brian
Schonthal-Seckel, Ruth
Schooley, John (Heilman)
Schrader, Barry Walter
Schroeder, William A
Schroth, Godfrey William
Schubel, Max
Schuller, Gunther
Schuman, William
Schwantner, Joseph C
Schwartz, Charles Morris
Schwartz, Elliott Shelling

Schwartz, Francis
Schwartz, Marvin Robert
Schwarz, Ira Paul
Scianni, Joseph
Sclater, James Stanley
Scott, Cleve L
Scott, Molly
Scribner, Norman Orville
Seiger, Joseph
Selig, Robert L
Sellars, James
Selleck, John Hugh
Semegen, Daria
Serebrier, Jose
Sessions, Roger Huntington
Shackelford, Rudy
Shaffer, Jeanne Ellison
Shaffer, Sherwood
Shahan, Paul W
Shapero, Harold Samuel
Shapey, Ralph
Shaw, Arnold
Sheinfeld, David
Shelton, Margaret Meier
Shepard, Jean Ellen
Sheppard, C(harles) James
Shere, Charles Everett
Sherman, Ingrid Kugelmann
Sherman, Norman Morris
Sherman, Robert
Shields, Alice F
Shinn, Randall Alan
Shore, Clare
Shott, Michael John
Shrude, Marilyn
Shuler, Craig
Shurtleff, Lynn Richard
Siegmeister, Elie
Siekmann, Frank H
Sierra, Roberto
Sifler, Paul John
Silsbee, Ann Loomis
Silva, Jesus
Silver, Sheila Jane
Silverman, Faye-Ellen
Silverman, Stanley Joel
Simmonds, Rae Nichols
Simons, Netty
Simpson, Ralph Ricardo
Sims, Ezra
Singer, Jeanne (Walsh)
Sirota, Robert (Benson)
Skolnik, Walter
Skrowaczewski, Stanislaw
Slawson, A Wayne
Slocum, William (Bennett)
Slonimsky, Nicolas
Smaldone, Edward Michael
Small, Haskell Behrend
Smart, Gary L
Smeltzer, Mary Susan
Smetona, Vytautas Julius
Smiley, Pril
Smit, Leo
Smith, Branson
Smith, Charles Warren
Smith, Douglas
Smith, Edwin Lester
Smith, Hale
Smith, James Gordon
Smith, Julia (Julia Smith
  Vielehr)
Smith, Larry Alan
Smith, Leland Clayton
Smith, Orcenith George
Smith, Stuart Saunders
Smith, William Overton
Smolanoff, Michael Louis
Snopek, Sigmund
Snow, David Jason
Snow, Mary (Helen)
Snyder, Bill (William Paul)
Snyder, Leo
Snyder, Randall L
Sokolov, Elliot
Sollberger, Harvey
Solomon, Elide N

Solomon, Joyce Elaine (Joyce
  Elaine Moorman)
Solomon, Larry J
Somer, Avo
Sonevytsky, Ihor C
Songer, Lewis Alton
Sorce, Richard
Soule, Edmund Foster
Sowell, Laven
Spektor, Mira J
Spencer, Williametta
Spiegel, Laurie
Spiegelman, Joel Warren
Spies, Claudio
Spizizen, Louise (Myers)
Spratlan, Lewis
Spring, Glenn Ernest
Sprott, John Rhulin
Stafford, James Edward
Stafford, Lee Christopher
Stalvey, Dorrance
Stanley, Helen Camille (Helen
  Stanley Gatlin)
Stanton, Royal Waltz
Starer, Robert
Starling, A Cumberworth
Starr, Mark
Staton, Kenneth Wayne
Stearns, Peter Pindar
Steele, Lynn
Steg, Paul Oskar
Stegall, Sydney Wallace
Stein, Leon
Stein, Ronald
Steiner, Fred(erick)
Steiner, Gitta H
Steinke, Greg A
Steinohrt, William John
Stempel, Larry E
Stephens, John Elliott
Stern, Robert
Sternberg, Jonathan
Sterne, Colin Chase
Stevens, Halsey
Stewart, Don (Donald George)
Stewart, Frank Graham
Stewart, Robert
Stewart, Robert John
Stewart, Scott Stephen
Stiller, Andrew Philip
Stilman-Lasansky, Julia
Stock, David Frederick
Stoeppelmann, Janet
Stokes, Eric
Stout, Alan Burrage
Stover, Franklin Howard
  (Franklin Howard
  Stoeffen)
Strandberg, Newton Dwight
Strang, Gerald
Strange, Allen
Strassburg, Robert
Street, Tison
Strimple, Nick
Stringer, Alan W
Strizich, Robert (Ward)
Stroud, Richard Ernest
Strunk, Steven (Gerhardt)
Stucky, Steven
Sturms, Arnolds Fricis
Suben, Joel Eric
Subotnick, Morton
Subramaniam,
  Lakshminarayana
Suchy, Gregoria Karides
Suderburg, Robert Charles
Suitor, M Lee
Sumerlin, Macon Dee
Susa, Conrad
Sutherland, Bruce
Svoboda, Tomas
Swack, Irwin
Swafford, Jan Johnson
Swann, Jeffrey
Swift, John David
Swift, Richard
Swisher, Gloria Wilson

Sydeman, William J
Syverud, Stephen Luther
Taffs, Anthony J
Talma, Louise J
Tamarkin, W Kate
Tanenbaum, Elias
Tang, Jordan Cho-Tung
Tanner, Jerre E
Tanner, Peter H
Taranto, Vernon Anthony, Jr
Tashjian, B Charmian
Taub, Bruce Jeffrey
Taube, Moshe
Tautenhahn, Gunther
Taylor, Clifford (Oliver)
Taylor, Les (Lionel Lester)
Tcherepnin, Ivan
  Alexandrovitch
Tecayehuatzin, Victor Saucedo
  (Victor Saucedo)
Tenney, James C
Tepper, Albert
Tgettis, Nicholas Chris
Themmen, Ivana
Theobald, Jim (James Chester
  Theobald)
Thielman, Ronald Moncrief
Thimmig, Les (Leslie Leland)
Thomas, John Patrick
Thomas, Marilyn Taft
Thomas, Paul Lindsley
Thomas, T(homas) Donley
Thome, Diane
Thome, Joel
Thomson, Virgil Garnett
Thorne, Francis (Burritt), Jr
Thorne, Nicholas C K
Tillis, Frederick C
Timm, Kenneth N
Tipei, Sever
Tircuit, Heuwell Andrew
Titcomb, Caldwell
Todd, George Bennett
Toensing, Richard E
Torkanowsky, Werner
Toutant, William Paul
Tower, Ibrook
Townsend, Douglas
Track, Gerhard
Trafford, Edmund Lee
Travis, Roy
Trimble, Lester Albert
Trogan, Roland Bernard
Trombly, Preston
Troupin, Edward
Truax, Bert
Trubitt, Allen R
Trythall, Gilbert
Trythall, Richard Aaker
Tubb, Monte
Tull, Fisher (Aubrey)
Turetzky, Bertram Jay
Turner, Thomas George
Turok, Paul Harris
Turrin, Joseph Egidio
Tuuk, Jonathan Alan
Uber, David Albert
Udell, Budd A
Udow, Michael William
Ulehla, Ludmila
Ulrich, Eugene Joseph
Ultan, Lloyd
Underwood, William L
Urquhart, Dan Murdock
Ussachevsky, Vladimir A
Vaccaro, Judith Lynne
Valente, William Edward
Van Appledorn, Mary Jeanne
Van der Wyk, Jack Alex
Van de Vate, Nancy (Hayes)
Van Hulse, Camil A J
Van Lidth De Jeude, (C)
  Philip (J)
Van Ohlen, Deborah S
Vazzana, Anthony Eugene
Vehar, Persis Anne
Vercoe, Barry Lloyd

COMPOSER (cont)

Vercoe, Elizabeth
Verdi, Ralph Carl
Verrall, John Weedon
Vigeland, Nils
Violette, Andrew
Virkhaus, Taavo
Vits, Billy (William Henry)
Vlahopoulos, Sotireos
Vogel, Roger Craig
Vollinger, William Francis
Vollrath, Carl Paul
Voois, Jacques C
Voxman, Himie
Wagoner, James D
Walcott, Ronald Harry
Walden, Stanley Eugene
Waldrop, Gideon William, Jr
Walker, Donald Burke
Walker, George Theophilus
Walker, Gwyneth V
Wallach, Joelle
Walsh, Michael Alan
Walter, David Edgar
Walters, Robert Douglas
Walters, Teresa
Wang, An-Ming
Ward, Robert Eugene
Ward, William Reed
Ward-Steinman, David
Ware, John Marley
Ware, Peter
Warfield, Gerald Alexander
Warkentin, Larry R
Warne, Katharine Mulky
Warren, B (Betsy Frost
    Warren-Davis)
Warren, Elinor Remick (Elinor
    Remick Warren Griffin)
Washburn, Robert Brooks
Wason, Robert Wesley
Waters, J Kevin
Waters, James Lipscomb
Watkins, R Bedford
Watson, Walter Robert
Waxman, Ernest
Wayland, Newton Hart
Webster, Michael
Weed, Maurice James
Wegner, August Martin, III
Wehner, Walter Leroy
Wehr, David August
Weidenarr, Reynold Henry
Weille, F Blair
Weinberg, Henry
Weiner, Lawrence
Weisgall, Hugo
Welcher, Dan Edward
Welsh, Wilmer Hayden
Welwood, Arthur
Wendelburg, Norma Ruth
Werle, Floyd Edwards
Wernick, Richard
Westergaard, Peter Talbot
Westermann, Clayton Jacob
Wetzler, Robert Paul
Weyand, Carlton Davis
Whaley, Garwood Paul
Whear, Paul William
Wheeler, (William) Scott
Wheelock, Donald Franklin
Whipple, R(ichard) James
Whitcomb, Robert Butler
White, David Ashley
White, Donald Howard
White, Gary C(harles)
White, John D
White, Michael
White, Ruth S
White, Terrance E
Whitecotton, Shirley E
Whittaker, Howard
Whittenberg, Charles
Widdoes, Lawrence Lewis
Wiener, Ivan H
Wienhorst, Richard William
Wigglesworth, Frank

Wilcox, James H
Wild, Earl
Wilding-White, Raymond
Wiley, Frank (Earkett), Jr
Wilkinson, Arthur Scott
Willey, James Henry
Williams, David Russell
Williams, John Towner
Willingham, Lawrence
    Hardwick
Willis, Richard M
Willman, Fred R
Wills, Vera G
Wilson, Dana Richard
Wilson, Donald Malcolm
Wilson, George Balch
Wilson, Olly W
Wilson, Richard Edward
Winkler, David
Winkler, Peter Kenton
Winokur, Roselyn M
Winslow, Walter Keith
Winsor, Philip Gordon
Winstead, William
Winters, George Archer
Wintle, James R
Witkin, Beatrice
Wolf, Michael B
Wolfe, Stanley
Wolff, Arthur Sheldon
Wolff, Christian
Wolking, Henry Clifford
Wong, Betty Anne (Siu Junn)
Wood, (Charles) Dale
Wood, Joseph (Roberts)
Wood, Kevin Joseph
Wood, William Frank
Woodard, James P
Woodbury, Arthur Neum
Woodward, Gregory Stanley
Woodward, Henry L(ynde)
Woodward, Martha Clive
Wooldridge, David H M
Woollen, Russell
Wright, Geoffrey Dorian
Wright, Maurice Willis
Wright, (Myron) Searle
Wright, Thomas G
Wuorinen, Charles
Wyatt, Scott Alan
Wylie, Ruth Shaw
Wyman, Dann Coriat
Wyton, Alec
Yannatos, James D
Yannay, Yehuda
Yarden, Elie
Yardumian, Richard
Yasui, Byron K
Yates, Ronald Lee
Yavelow, Christopher Fowler
    Johnson
Yellin, Victor Fell
York, Don(ald Griffith)
Yoshioka, Emmett Gene
Young, Robert H
Yount, Max Hoffman
Yttrehus, Rolv
Zabrack, Harold Allen
Zahler, Noel Barry
Zaimont, Judith Lang
Zajicek, Jeronym
Zallman, Arlene
Zaninelli, Luigi
Zano, Anthony (Anthony
    Joseph Ferrazano)
Zdechlik, John Paul
Zes, Tikey A
Ziffrin, Marilyn Jane
Zinn, Michael A
Zipper, Herbert
Zonn, Paul
Zuckerman, Mark Alan
Zukofsky, Paul
Zupko, Ramon
Zwilich, Ellen Taaffe

CONDUCTOR/
MUSIC DIRECTOR

Abbado, Claudio
Abravanel, Maurice
Acord, Thomas Wadsworth
Adams, Alan Eugene
Addison, Anthony
Adkins, Aldrich Wendell
Adler, Kurt Herbert
Adler, Samuel H
Agard, David Leon
Agler, David
Aird, Donald Bruce
Ajmone-Marsan, Guido
Akos, Francis
Albrecht, Theodore John
Alcantara, Theo
Alexander, John Allen
Allers, Franz
Alley, Edward L
Anderson, Gillian Bunshaft
Anderson, Thomas Jefferson,
    Jr
Anello, John-David
Ansbacher, Charles Alexander
Antoniou, Theodore
Arant, (Everett) Pierce, Jr
Archibeque, Charlene P
Arden, David Mitchell
Armstrong, Anton Eugene
Arnatt, Ronald (Kent)
Ashens, Robert J, III
Ashkenazy, Vladimir D
Ashton, Jack Schrader
Aslanian, Richard
Aslanian, Vahe
Atherton, David
Atzmon, Moshe
Averitt, William Earl
Avshalomov, Jacob David
Bacon, Madi
Badea, Christian
Bailey, David Wayne
Bailey, James
Baker, Larry A
Baker, Robert Hart
Balazs, Frederic
Bales, Richard Henry Horner
Baley, Virko
Balter, Alan (Neil)
Banat, Gabriel Jean
Barati, George
Barnea, Uri
Baron, Samuel
Barra, Donald Paul
Barrus, Charles LaMar, Jr
Barthelson, Joyce Holloway
Bartoletti, Bruno
Battisti, Frank Leon
Bauman, Jon Ward
Baustian, Robert
Bavicchi, John Alexander
Bazelon, Irwin Allen
Bearer, Elaine Louise
Beaser, Robert Harry
Beegle, Raymond Bruce
Beer, Hans L
Behnke, Martin Kyle
Behr, Jan
Benefield, Richard Dotson
Bergt, Robert Roland
Berlinghoff, Dan A
Bernardo, Jose Raul
Bernstein, Leonard
Bertini, Gary
Biester, Allen George
Biggs, John Joseph
Bilger, David Victor
Billings, Charles W
Biser, Larry Gene
Black, Robert Carlisle
Blackburn, Walter Wesley
Blackwelder, Stephen Dwight
Bogin, Abba
Boldrey, Richard (Lee)

Bolen, Jane Moore
Bolle, James D
Bond, Victoria
Bontrager, Charles E
Boonshaft, Peter Loel
Bornstein, Charles Zachary
Bouchard, Linda
Bowles, Richard William
Bowman, Jack Walter
Bracali, Giampaolo
Bradshaw, Richard James
Braught, Eugene A
Braun, Edgar J
Breda, Malcolm Joseph
Brett, Philip
Brewer, Richard H
Briccetti, Thomas Bernard
Brickman, Miriam
Brion, (K) Keith
Brown, Beatrice
Brown, Corrick Lanier
Brown, Keith
Bruck, Charles
Brunelle, Philip Charles
Brusilow, Anshel
Buck, David A
Buckley, Emerson
Buketoff, Igor
Bullard, Truman Campbell
Bullock, William Joseph
Bullough, John Frank
Burda, Pavel
Burkh, Dennis
Burns, Judith Capper
Burnsworth, Charles Carl
Burrows, John
Bychkov, Semyon
Calabro, Louis
Caldwell, Sarah
Canarina, John Baptiste
Canellakis, Martin
Caraher, James H
Carlson, Jon O
Cassuto, Alvaro Leon
Castiglione, Richard B
Cathcart, Kathryn
Ceccato, Aldo
Cedel, Mark
Chajes, Julius T
Chamblee, James Monroe
Chan, Timothy Tai-Wah
Charry, Michael (Ronald)
Chaudoir, James Edward
Chauls, Robert N
Checchia, Anthony Phillip
Chevallard, (Philip) Carl
Choset, Franklin
Cipolla, Frank J
Clapp, Lois Steele
Clark, Thomas Terrence
Clarke, William (Jay)
Cleve, George
Cobb, Donald Lorain
Cogley, Mark
Cohen, Jerome D
Cokkinias, Peter Leonidas
Colaneri, Joseph
Collier, Gilman Frederick
Collins, Don L
Collins, Philip Michael
Combopiano, Charles Angelo
Comet, Catherine
Comissiona, Sergiu
Conable, William G, Jr
Conlin, Thomas (Byrd)
Consoli, Marc-Antonio
Cook, Jeff Holland
Cook, Wayne Evans
Cooley, Marilyn Grace
Coombs, Daniel Raymond
Copeland, Robert Marshall
Coppola, Carmine (Carmen)
Cordova, Richard Allan
Cox, Richard Garner
Crawford, Maribeth Kirchhoff
Crosbie, William Perry
Crosby, John O'Hea

CONDUCTOR/MUSIC DIRECTOR (cont)

Culley, Pamela Overstreet
Cummings, Conrad
Curtis, (William) Edgar
Custer, Calvin H
Daitz, Mimi Segal
Dalvit, Lewis David, Jr
Dancz, Roger Lee
Daniels, David Wilder
Dann, Elias
Dashnaw, Alexander
Dashow, James
Davidson, Audrey Ekdahl
Davies, Dennis
Davison, Peter Saul
Decker, Harold A
de Frank, Vincent
Deibler, Arlo C I
De La Fuente, Luis Herrera
Del Borgo, Elliot Anthony
de Lemos, Jurgen Hermann
Delogu, Gaetano
DeMain, John Lee
DePonte, Niel Bonaventure
De Preist, James Anderson
De Renzi, Victor
De Rugeriis, Joseph Carmen
DeRusha, Stanley Edward
deVaron, Lorna Cooke
De Waart, Edo
Dines, Burton
Di Pasquasio, Gary Peter
Dixon, James Allen
Dohnanyi, Christoph von
Dorati, Antal
Douglas, John Thomas
Dove, Neville
Draper, Glenn Wright
Drew, James M
Driehuys, Leonardus Bastiaan
Druckman, Jacob
DuBose, Charles Benjamin
Ducloux, Walter Ernest
Dufallo, Richard John
Duffy, John
Duffy, Thomas C
Dunkel, Paul Eugene
Dunn, Frank Richard
Dunn, Thomas Burt
Du Page, Florence Elizabeth
Dutton, James N
Dutton, Mary Ann Enloe
Dvorak, Thomas L
Eaton, Roy (Felix)
Echols, Paul
Eckerling, Lawrence David
Eder, Terry Edward
Effron, David Louis
Eger, Joseph
Ehrling, Sixten E
Eichenberger, Rodney (Bryce)
Eldredge, Steven
Elisha, Haim
Elliott, Wilber D
Emerson, Gordon Clyde
Emmerich, Constance M
Endo, Akira
Engel, Lehman
Engelhardt, Douglas Gustav
Entremont, Philippe
Epley, (William) Arnold
Epstein, David M
Epstein, Frank Benjamin
Erb, James Bryan
Eros, Peter
Esselstrom, Michael John
Evans, Mark
Falletta, JoAnn
Farberman, Harold
Farr, David Donald
Farrer, John
Favario, Giulio
Felder, David C
Ferden, Bruce
Ferguson, Edwin Earle
Ferris, William

Ferritto, John Edmund
Fesperman, John, Jr
Fields, Warren Carl
Finster, Robert Milton
Fischer, Bill (William S)
Fisher, Gilbert Blain
Fisher, Jerrold
Fisher, Paul Gottshall
Fissinger, Edwin Russell
Fitzpatrick, Robert
Flagello, Nicholas Oreste
Fleisher, Leon
Fletcher, (H) Grant
Flint, Mark David
Flor, Samuel
Forbes, Elliot
Ford, Frederic Hugh
Fortner, Jack Ronald
Foster, Robert Estill
Fouse, Donald Mahlon
France, Hal
Franklin, Cary John
Freeman, Joann (Joann
    Freeman Shwayder)
Fried, Gregory Martin
Fried, Joel Ethan
Fruhbeck De Burgos, Rafael
Fuchs, Peter Paul
Fulton, William Kenneth
Fyfe, Peter McNeely
Gable, Frederick Kent
Gabriel, Arnald D
Gainacopulos, Kay Thomas
Gallo, Paul Arthur
Galway, James
Gansz, George Lewis
Garbutt, Matthew
Gardner, Patrick G
Garofalo, Robert Joseph
Gates, Crawford
Gates, J(ames) Terry
Geller, Ian
George, Thom Ritter
Gerle, Robert
Gerschefski, Edwin
Ghezzo, Dinu D
Gielen, Michael Andreas
Gilad, Yehuda
Gilbert, David Beatty
Gillespie, Allan E
Gindin, Edward M
Giordano, John
Giulini, Carlo Maria
Glasow, Glenn L
Glass, Jerome
Glazer, Robert
Gnam, Adrian
Goemanne, Noel
Gold, Ernest
Gold, Morton
Goldberg, Szymon
Goldsmith, Richard Neil
Goldstein, Lee Scott
Goodman, Bernard Maurice
Gordon, Nathan
Gosman, Lazar
Gould, Morton
Gould, Ronald Lee
Grady, John Francis
Grahn, Ulf Ake Wilhelm
Graves, William Lester, Jr
Gray, Dorothy Landis
Green, John W
Greenawalt, Terrence Lee
Greenberg, Philip
Greene, Joshua
Greer, Thomas Henry
Gregorian, Rouben
Gronquist, Robert E
Gross, Allen Robert
Guadagno, Anton
Guigui, Efrain
Gulbrandsen, Norman R
Gunther, William (William
    Gunther Sprecher)
Gunzenhauser, Stephen
    Charles

Gustafson, Dwight Leonard
Gutter, Robert (Harold)
Haan, Raymond Henry
Haberlen, John B
Hagen, Dennis Bert
Hagon, John Peter
Hailstork, Adolphus
    Cunningham
Hale, (Nathan) Kelly
Halgedahl, (Edward) Howard
Hallman, Ludlow B, III
Hancock, Gerre (Edward)
Hancock, Judith Eckerman
Hangen, Bruce Boyer
Hansler, George Emil
Hare, Robert Yates
Harman, David Rex
Harper, Andrew Henry
Harris, Carl Gordon, Jr
Hart, William Sebastian
Harth, Sidney
Harvey, Raymond C
Harwood, C William
Harwood, James C
Hatcher, William B
Hathaway, Daniel
Haug, Leonard Harold
Haupt-Nolen, Paulette
Hause, Robert Luke
Hawn, Harold Gage
Hayman, Richard Warren
    Joseph
Hazzard, Peter (Peabody)
Hedberg, Floyd Carl
Hegyi, Julius
Heiden, Bernhard
Held, David Paul
Heller, Jack Joseph
Henderson, Hubert Platt
Henderson, Robert
Hendl, Walter
Henry, James Donald
Henry, Joseph
Hicks, Roy Edward
Hill, Carolyn Ann
Hill, Terry
Hilliard, Tom (Thomas Lee)
Hillis, Margaret (Eleanor)
Hillmer, Leann
Hines, Robert Stephan
Hinshaw, Donald Grey
Hodkinson, Sydney Phillip
Hoffman, Irwin
Hoffmann, James
Hohstadt, Thomas Dowd
Holloway, Jack E
Holmes, Richard
Holoman, Dallas Kern
Holt, Henry
Holtz, John
Holvik, Karl Magnus
Hood, Burrel Samuel
Hopkins, Harlow Eugene
Hotoke, Shigeru
Houghton, Edward Francis
Houtmann, Jacques
Howard, Cleveland L
Howard, George Sallade
Hruby, Frank
Hughes, Robert Grove
Hugo, John William
Hull, Robert Leslie
Humel, Gerald
Hurwitz, Robert Irving
Husa, Karel
Huszti, Joseph Bela
Iannaccone, Anthony
Irving, Robert Augustine
Isaac, Cecil
Jackson, Isaiah (Allen)
Jackson, James Leonard
Jacob, Karen Hite
Jacobson, Joshua R
Jaffee, Michael
Jager, Robert Edward
Jakey, Lauren Ray
Janiec, Henry

Jansons, Andrejs
Janzen, Eldon A
Jean, Kenneth
Jenkins, Donald P
Jenkins, Newell
Johanos, Donald
Johnson, A Paul
Johnson, Gordon James
Jolly, Kirby Reid
Jones, Barnard Ray
Jones, Perry Otis
Jordan, Paul
Jorgenson, Dale Alfred
Kacinskas, Jeronimas
Kaiser, Amy
Kalt, Percy German
Kamien, Anna
Kamsler, Bruce H
Kanouse, Monroe
Kaplan, Burton
Kaplan, Lois Jay
Karson, Burton Lewis
Kartman, Myron
Katims, Milton
Kechley, Gerald
Keene, Christopher
Kellogg, Cal Stewart
Kendall, Christopher Wolff
Kennedy, Dale Edwin
Keshner, Joyce Grove
Kessler, Jerome
Ketcham, Charles
Kiesler, Kenneth
Kievman, Carson
Kin, Vladimir
King, Carlton W, III
King, Terry Bower
Kirk, Colleen Jean
Kirk, Theron Wilford
Klein, Kenneth
Klein, Mitchell Sardou
Klippstatter, Kurt L
Klobucar, Berislav
Klotzman, Dorothy Ann Hill
Knight, Eric W
Kober, Dieter
Kogan, Robert Colver
Kojian, Varujan (Haig)
Kolar, Henry
Kondorossy, Leslie
Kopp, Frederick Edward
Korf, Anthony
Korn, Peter Jona
Kosloff, Doris Lang
Kovalenko, Oleg Ivanovitch
Kowalke, Kim H
Krachmalnick, Samuel
Krajewski, Michael
Krasner, Louis
Kratzer, Dennis Leon
Kruger, Rudolf
Kubik, Gail
Kuhn, Laura Diane (Shipcott)
Kunzel, Erich
Kuzma, John Joseph
Kwak, Sung
LaMarchina, Robert A
Lamb, Gordon Howard
Lancaster, Thomas Scott
Landau, Siegfried
Lane, Louis
Lankester, Michael John
Laredo, Jaime
Larimer, Melvin Sherlock
Larsen, Robert L
Larson, David Dynes
Laszloffy, Jerome
Lawless, Lyndon Kent
Laycock, Ralph George
Lazar, Joel
Lee, Jack Kenneth
Leedy, Douglas
Lehrman, Leonard J(ordan)
Leinsdorf, Erich
Le Mieux, Raymond William
Lengefeld, William Chris
Leniado-Chira, Joseph

CONDUCTOR/MUSIC DIRECTOR (cont)

Suttle, Clark Etienne
Suzuki, Hidetaro
Swafford, Jan Johnson
Swalin, Benjamin Franklin
Swan, Howard Shelton
Swann, Frederick Lewis
Swenson, Courtland Sevander
Swing, Peter Gram
Tajo, Italo
Takeda, Yoshimi
Tang, Jordan Cho-Tung
Tanner, Jerre E
Tatton, Thomas
Taylor, Guy
Teague, William Chandler
Temianka, Henri
Temkin, Ascher Mark
Terey-Smith, Mary
Teutsch, Walter
Thamon, Eugene (Eugene Thamon Simpson)
Theimer, Axel Knut
Thome, Joel
Thulean, Donald (Myron)
Thurston, Richard Elliott
Tiboris, Peter Ernest
Tiemeyer, Christian
Tillotson, Laura Virginia
Tilson-Thomas, Michael
Topilow, Carl S
Torkanowsky, Werner
Track, Gerhard
Travaline, Philip Francis
Tregellas, Patricia A
Trevor, Kirk David Niell
Tuckwell, Barry Emmanuel
Tumbleson, John Raymond
Turrin, Joseph Egidio
Tyra, Thomas (Norman)
Uber, David Albert
Vagner, Robert Stuart
Valante, Harrison R
van Boer, Bertil Herman
van der Merwe, Johan
Van Vactor, David
Venanzi, Henry
Vendice, William V
Vermel, Paul
Veronda, Carlo
Vigeland, Nils
Virkhaus, Taavo
Viro, Olev L
Vollinger, William Francis
Voth, Elvera
Wade, Janice E
Wadsworth, Charles William
Waite, Russell Trueman
Wakefield-Wright, JoElyn
Wakschal, Seymour
Walden, Stanley Eugene
Walker, Betty Marie
Wallace, Robert William
Walters, Michael J
Walters, Robert Douglas
Washburn, Franklin Ely
Washburn, Robert Brooks
Wasson, D(onald) DeWitt
Waters, Willie Anthony
Watkins, Armin J
Watts, Aredean Walton
Wayland, Newton Hart
Webb, Brian Patrick
Webb, Charles H
Webb, Guy Bedford
Wehr, David August
Weisgall, Hugo
Weiss, Howard A
Welch, Robert B
Welcher, Dan Edward
Wendelken-Wilson, Charles
Werle, Floyd Edwards
Wernick, Richard
Westbrook, James Earl
Westenburg, Richard
Westermann, Clayton Jacob

Whallon, Evan
Wheeler, (William) Scott
Wheelock, Donald Franklin
Whitehead, William John
Whitener, Scott
Wichmann, Russell George
Wickes, Frank Bovee
Wilcox, Eunice Ann
Wilkins, Christopher Putnam
Williams, Franklin Edmund
Williams, Grier Moffatt
Williams, J(ohn) Wesley
Williams, John Towner
Williams, Richard
Wilson, Antonia Joy
Wilson, Fredric Woodbridge
Wilson, James Edward
Wilson, Olly W
Wilson, Ransom Charles
Wilson, Thomas E
Winograd, Arthur
Wisniewski, Thomas Joseph
Woitach, Richard
Wojciak, Robert H
Won, Kyung-Soo
Woodbury, Ward Leland
Woodhall, Dennis Robert
Wooldridge, David H M
Worby, Rachael
Wortman, Allen L
Wright, Al G (Alfred George)
Wyatt, Larry D
Yakim, Moni
Yannatos, James D
Yannuzzi, William A(nthony)
Yarborough, William
York, Don(ald Griffith)
Young, Wendy
Zack, George Jimmy
Zahler, Noel Barry
Zaliouk, Yuval Nathan
Zander, Benjamin David
Zimmerman, Franklin Bershir
Zimmermann, Gerhardt
Zinman, David
Zipper, Herbert
Zipser, Burton Allen
Zonn, Paul
Zorn, Jay D
Zugelj, Ivan Petar (John Peter Zugel)
Zukerman, Pinchas
Zukofsky, Paul
Zytowski, Carl Byrd

CRITIC/WRITER

Adler, Marvin Stanley
Alexander, Peter Marquis
Allanbrook, Wye Jamison
Allen, Robin Perry
Alper, Clifford Daniel
Amirkhanian, Charles Benjamin
Ammer, Christine
Anderson, Garland (Lee)
Anderson, Warren DeWitt
Angarano, Anthony
Anthony, James Raymond
Applebaum, Stan (Stanley S)
Arlen, Walter
Artzt, Alice Josephine
Ashbrook, William Sinclair, Jr
Austin, William Weaver
Baily, Diette (Dee) Marie
Baker, James M
Baker, Nancy Kovaleff
Baldwin, Nicholas G
Balk, Leo Frederick
Bamberger, David
Baron, John Herschel
Barr, Raymond Arthur
Barra, Donald Paul
Barzenick, Walter

Basart, Ann Phillips
Baxter, Robert T S
Beckerman, Michael Brim
Belsom, Jack (John Anton)
Berdes, Jane L
Berger, Arthur Victor
Berger, Karol
Berger, Melvin
Bergquist, Peter
Bernheimer, Martin
Berry, Corre Ivey
Berry, Lemuel, Jr
Bierley, Paul Edmund
Bishop, Martha (Jane)
Blackham, Richard Allan
Block, Adrienne Fried
Block, Robert Paul
Block, Steven D
Blumenfeld, Aaron Joel
Blumenfeld, Harold
Boatwright, Howard Leake, Jr
Bobbitt, Richard
Boiles, Charles Lafayette
Bookspan, Martin
Boretz, Benjamin Aaron
Bowers, Jane Meredith
Bowles, Paul Frederick
Boyd, Jack Arthur
Bradshaw, Murray Charles
Bram, Marjorie
Brende, Alfred
Brett, Philip
Briscoe, James Robert
Brockett, Clyde Waring, Jr
Brody, Elaine
Bronson, Bertrand Harris
Brook, Claire
Brooks, Richard J
Brooks, William F
Brothers, Lester D
Brown, A Peter
Brown, Malcolm Hamrick
Brown, Merrill Edwin
Broyles, Michael E
Brozen, Michael
Bryan, Paul Robey, Jr
Bryant, Carolyn Frances
Bucci, Marc Leopold
Burkat, Leonard
Burkholder, J Peter
Burt, Warren Arnold
Cady, Henry Lord
Cantrick, Robert B
Cariaga, Daniel Philip
Carlton, Stephen Edward
Carpenter, Hoyle Dameron
Carr, Bruce Alan
Carroll, Charles Michael
Cazeaux, Isabelle Anne-Marie
Cera, Stephen Charles
Chase, Sam
Childs, Barney Sanford
Christensen, Jean Marie
Citron, Marcia Judith
Clark, J Bunker
Clark, Sondra Rae
Clough, John L
Coffin, (Roscoe) Berton
Cohen, Albert
Collins, Walter Stowe
Cone, Edward Toner
Copland, Aaron
Corner, Philip Lionel
Cornwell, Richard Warren
Cowden, Robert Hapgood
Crawford, David Eugene
Creston, Paul
Crociata, Francis Joseph
Crocker, Richard Lincoln
Cuyler, Louise E
Dallin, Leon
Daniel, Cyrus Chrisley
Darter, Thomas E
Dasher, Richard Taliaferro
Day, Richard Wrisley
de Brant, Cyr (Joseph Vincent Higginson)

Dedel, Peter J D
Dehnert, Edmund John
de Lerma, Dominique-Rene
Diamond, Harold J
Dickinson, Alis
Dominick, Lisa Robinson
Donakowski, Conrad Louis
Dorian, Frederick
Downes, Edward Olin Davenport
Downey, James Cecil
Drennan, Dorothy Carter
Dreyer, Leslie I
Driver, Howard (Glen)
Duncan, Charles F, Jr
Eagle, Charles Thomas, Jr
Eagle, David William
Eckert, Thor, Jr
Eddleman, G David
Eive, Gloria
Eliason, Robert E
Elkus, Jonathan (Britton)
Ellinwood, Leonard Webster
Ellsworth, Oliver Bryant
Emerson, Gordon Clyde
Emmons, Shirlee (Shirlee Emmons Baldwin)
Epstein, Dena Julia
Ernst, David George
Farish, Stephen Thomas, Jr
Feder, Susan E
Feldman, Mary Ann (Janisch)
Filler, Susan M
Fisher, Fred(eric Irwin)
Fitzgerald, Gerald
Flaherty, Gloria
Flatt, Terry Lee
Forman, Joanne
Foster, Donald Herbert
Fowler, Charles Bruner
Fox, Leland Stanford
Franceschini, Romulus
Freed, Arnold
Freeman, John Wheelock
Friedberg, Ruth Crane
Frisch, Walter Miller
Frost, Thomas
Fuld, James J
Garland, Peter Adams
Garlington, Aubrey S
Garvelmann, Donald M
Gebauer, Victor Earl
Gee, Harry Raglan
Geiringer, Karl J
Gelt, Andrew Lloyd
George, Earl
Gerig, Reginald Roth
Gervers, Hilda F
Giffin, Glenn
Gilbert, Richard
Gilbert, Steven E(dward)
Gillespie, Don Chance
Gillick, Lyn (Emelyn Samuels)
Gossett, Philip
Gottfried, Martin
Gottlieb, Jack S
Gowen, Bradford Paul
Green, Barry L
Green, Marian C
Greenberg, Michael E
Greene, Margo Lynn
Griffel, L Michael
Griffel, Margaret Ross
Gross, Dorothy (Susan)
Guinn, John
Gustafson, Bruce
Haar, James
Haefliger, Kathleen Ann
Halsted, Margo Armbruster
Hamilton, David (Peter)
Hammond, Paul G
Hanshumaker, James
Harnisch, Larry (Lawrence Myrland)
Harriss, Ernest Charles
Haskell, Harry Ogren
Hastings, Baird

CRITIC / WRITER (cont)

Hayes, Deborah
Hegenbart, Alex Frank
Heilner, Irwin
Henahan, Donal J
Herder, Ronald
Herrold, Rebecca Munn
Heskes, Irene
Hettrick, William Eugene
Heymont, George A
Higbee, Dale Strohe
Higgins, Thomas
Hinton-Braaten, Kathleen
Hitchcock, H(ugh) Wiley
Hixon, Don L
Hodgson, Peter John
Holland, Bernard P
Holmes, Robert William
Howard, Wayne
Hruby, Frank
Hudson, Richard Albert
Hughes, Charles William
Hughes, David Grattan
Hunsberger, Donald
Hursh-Mead, Rita Virginia
Irvin, Marjory Ruth
Jacobson, Robert (Marshall)
Jaffee, Kay
Jenkins, Speight
Josephson, David S
Karp, Theodore Cyrus
Kaufmann, Henry William
Kaufmann, Walter
Keene, Christopher
Keene, James A
Kennedy, Josepha (Marie)
Kerman, Joseph Wilfred
Kipnis, Igor
Kirby, F(rank) E(ugene)
Kirshbaum, Bernard
Kivy, Peter Nathan
Klein, Jerry (Gerald Louis)
Kolodin, Irving
Kramer, Jonathan D(onald)
Kremenliev, Boris A
Kresky, Jeffrey Jay
Kuhn, Laura Diane (Shipcott)
LaFave, Kenneth John
Larue, Adrian Jan Pieters
Lasocki, David Ronald
  Graham
Lawrence, Arthur Peter
Lawrence, Vera Brodsky
Ledbetter, Steven John
Lefkoff, Gerald
Lehrman, Paul David
Lemmon, Alfred Emmette
Lenneberg, Hans
LePage, Jane Weiner
Lerdahl, Fred (Alfred
  Whitford)
Levy, Janet M
Levy, Kenneth
Lewando, Olga Wolf
Lindeman, Carolynn A
Lindgren, Lowell Edwin
Little, Meredith Ellis
Locke, Ralph P
Locklair, Wriston
London, S(ol) J
Longyear, Rey Morgan
Lorenz, Ellen Jane (Ellen Jane
  Lorenz Porter)
Loucks, Richard Newcomb
Lowens, Irving
Lowens, Margery Morgan
Lund, Floice Rhodes
Maas, Martha C
Mabry, Raymond Edward
MacClintock, Carol C
McClymonds, Marita Petzoldt
McCulloh, Judith Marie
McGraw, Cameron
Mach, Elyse Janet
Machlis, Joseph
McLean, Priscilla Taylor
McLellan, Joseph Duncan

McMillan, Ann Endicott
McPeek, Gwynn Spencer
Mahan, Katherine Hines
Main, Alexander
Mann, Brian Richard
Marco, Guy Anthony
Marcus, Leonard Marshall
Margalit, Israela
Marsh, Robert C
Martin, Dennis Roy
Mason, Robert M
Mathiesen, Thomas James
Mattfeld, Victor Henry
Mayer, William Robert
Meckna, Michael
Meibach, Judith Karen (Judith
  Karen Meibach Schiloni)
Meister, Barbara L
Meyer, Leonard B
Miller, Philip Lieson
Miller, Terry Ellis
Milligan, Thomas Braden, Jr
Milojkovic-Djuric, Jelena
Mitchell, Michael Kenneth
Mixter, Keith Eugene
Mizuno, Ikuko
Moe, Orin
Moldenhauer, Hans
Monson, Karen Ann
Moore, Carman Leroy
Moore, David Willard
Morrison, Julia (Maria)
Mueller, Robert E
Murata, Margaret Kimiko
Nash, Paul
Neuls-Bates, Carol
Neumann, Frederick C
Newall, Robert H
Newlin, Dika
Newman, William Stein
Nicholas, Louis Thurston
Nicholson, David
Obenshain, Kathryn Garland
O'Brien, Valerie Elizabeth
O'Grady, Terence John
Oja, Carol J
Oldani, Robert William
Olmstead, Andrea Louise
O'Reilly, F(rank) Warren
Orgill, Roxane
Orrego-Salas, Juan Antonio
Ott, Joseph Henry
Owen, Angela Maria
Owens, David
Palisca, Claude V
Palmer, Willard A
Parris, Arthur
Parsons, James Boyd
Pasler, Jann Corinne
Paull, Barberi P
Pauly, Reinhard G
Pavlakis, Christopher
Paysour, LaFleur (Nadine)
Peake, Luise Eitel
Pearson, Frank Cogswell, Jr
Pease, Edward Joseph
Perle, George
Perlis, Vivian
Perlmutter, Donna
Perris, Arnold B
Petersen, Barbara A
Picker, Martin
Pierce, Alexandra
Pierson, Thomas Claude
Ping-Robbins, Nancy R(egan)
Platthy, Jeno
Polansky, Larry C
Pollack, Howard Joel
Poole, Jane L
Porter, Andrew (Brian)
Potter, John Matthew
Powell, Newman Wilson
Raigorodsky, Natalia (Leda
  Natalia Raigorodsky
  Heimsath Harter)
Ramey, Phillip
Ratliff, William Elmore

Read, Gardner
Reich, Nancy B
Reimer, Bennett
Reiss, Alvin H
Reynolds, William J
Rezits, Joseph M
Rich, Maria F
Richards, James Howard
Richelieu, David Anthony
Ringer, Alexander L
Roads, Curtis
Robinson, Ray E
Rockwell, John
Rodby, Walter
Rodda, Richard Earl
Roettger, Dorye
Rogers, Delmer Dalzell
Rollin, Robert
Ronson, Raoul R
Roos, James (Michael)
Roosevelt, Oliver Wolcott, Jr
Rorem, Ned
Rosen, Charles
Rosen, Judith (Berenice)
Rosenberg, Donald Scott
Rosenberg, Kenyon Charles
Rosenstiel, Leonie
Ross, Ruth Lampland
Rothermel, Dan Hiester
Rowen, Ruth Halle
Rudhyar, Dane
Rudis, Al (A L)
Ruggeri, Roger Benjamin
Russo, William
Ryder, Jeanne
Sable, Barbara Kinsey
Saceanu, Dan George
Sachs, David H
Saffir, Kurt
Saffle, Michael Benton
Saloman, Ora Frishberg
Salzer, Felix
Salzman, Eric
Sandberg, Larry (Lawrence H)
Sandow, Gregory
Saville, Eugenia Curtis
Sayad, Elizabeth Gentry
Scheibert, Beverly
Scherer, Barrymore Laurence
Schleifer, Martha Furman
Schmidt, Carl B
Schmidt, John Charles
Schmidt, Liselotte Martha
Schneider, David Hersh
Schneider, John
Schneider, John Owsley
Schnoebelen, Anne
Schoep, Arthur Paul
Schonberg, Harold C
Schott, Howard Mansfield
Schroeder-Sheker, Therese M
Schuetze, George Claire, Jr
Schuster-Craig, John William
Schwager, Myron August
Schwann, William Joseph
Schwartz, Elliott Shelling
Schwartz, Judith Leah
Schwarz, Boris
Schwarz, Karol Robert
Schwarz, Patricia A
Seaton, (Stuart) Douglass
Seay, Albert
Seibert, Donald C
Selfridge-Field, Eleanor A
Selleck, John Hugh
Shackelford, Rudy
Shaw, Arnold
Shere, Charles Everett
Sherr, Richard Jonathan
Siegmeister, Elie
Silbiger, Alexander
Silverman, Robert Joseph
Simon, Richard D
Sisson, William Kenneth
Skaggs, Hazel Ghazarian
Skei, Allen Bennet
Slonimsky, Nicolas

Smith, Charles Justice
Smith, Douglas Alton
Smith, Patrice Jane
Smith, Patrick John
Smith, Tim (Timothy Paul)
Solie, Ruth Ames
Sonevytsky, Ihor C
Southern, Eileen Jackson
Sparks, Donna Lynne
Spies, Michael C
Staff, Charles Bancroft, Jr
Stedman, William Preston
Stegall, Sydney Wallace
Steinberg, Michael
Steiner, Fred(erick)
Steinhardt, Milton J
Stiller, Andrew Philip
Stolba, K Marie
Stone, Kurt
Strainchamps, Edmond
  Nicholas
Stucky, Steven
Sturm, George
Suchoff, Benjamin
Sutton, Julia
Swift, Richard
Symonette, Lys Bert
Taub, Bruce Jeffrey
Tawa, Nicholas Edward
Teal, Mary Evelyn Durden
Temperley, Nicholas
Termini, Olga A
Theobald, Jim (James Chester
  Theobald)
Thomas, T(homas) Donley
Thompson, Donald
Thomson, Virgil Garnett
Thomson, William Ennis
Thurston, Ethel Holbrooke
Thym, Jurgen
Tircuit, Heuwell Andrew
Tirro, Frank Pascale
Titon, Jeff Todd
Toms, John (Elias)
Touliatos-Banker, Diane H
Town, Stephen J
Trimble, Lester Albert
Trotter, Herman
Turok, Paul Harris
Ulrich, Homer
Uscher, Nancy Joyce
Van Solkema, Sherman
Van Wye, Benjamin David
Velimirovic, Milos
Virga, Patricia H
Von Gunden, Heidi Cecilia
von Rhein, John Richard
Wagner, Denise
Wagoner, James D
Wallace, Mary Elaine (Mary
  Elaine House)
Walsh, Michael Alan
Ward, Charles Wilson
Ward, John Owen
Warfield, Gerald Alexander
Warkov, Esther R
Warren, Edwin Brady
Wasson, D(onald) DeWitt
Weaver, Robert Lamar
Wechsler, Bert
Weiss, Piero E
Wennerstrom, Mary Hannah
Wetzel, Richard Dean
White, A Duane
White, (Edwin) Chappell
Wienandt, Elwyn Arthur
Wierzbicki, James
Will, Patrick Terence
Williams, Edward Vinson
Willis, Thomas C
Wirt, John (Stephen)
Wolf, Edward Christopher
Wolff, Konrad
Wood, (Charles) Dale
Wood, Elizabeth
Wood, Gloria Bakkila
Woodbury, Arthur Neum

CRITIC / WRITER (cont)

Wormhoudt, Pearl Shinn
Wright, Josephine R B
Yaffe, Michael Charles
Young, Clyde William
Zaimont, Judith Lang
Zakariasen, Bill
Ziffrin, Marilyn Jane
Zucker, Stefan

DIRECTOR—OPERA

Abrams, Richard
Addison, Anthony
Auerbach, Cynthia
Badea, Christian
Balk, H Wesley
Bamberger, David
Belisle, John M
Benaglio, Roberto
Bishop, Adelaide
Brunyate, Roger
Caldwell, Sarah
Capobianco, Tito
Choset, Franklin
Combopiano, Charles Angelo
Corsaro, Frank Andrew
Crittenden, Richard Raymond
Danner, Dorothy
de Blasis, James Michael
Di Chiera, David
Donovan-Jeffry, Peggy
  (Margaret)
Driver, Robert Baylor
Eddleman, (Robert) Jack
Farrar, David
Freitas, Beebe
Galterio, Lou
Gately, David E
Gay, Robert
Gentilesca, Franco Joseph
Glass, Beaumont
Gockley, R David
Graham, Colin
Hebert, Bliss
Hicks, David
Igesz, Bodo
Jenkins, Speight
Karayanis, Plato
Kraus, Philip Arthur
Lazarus, Roy
Lockwood, Carolyn
London, George
Lucas, James
Luchsinger, Ronald
Mansouri, Lotfollah (Lotfi)
Margulis, John Lawrence
Melano, Fabrizio
Menotti, Gian Carlo
Moon, Peggy MacDonald
Neely, James Bert
Pearlman, Richard Louis
Ross, Buck
Ross, Glynn William
Schifter, Peter Mark
Silipigni, Alfredo
Sills, Beverly (Mrs Peter B
  Greenough)
Silverstein, Barbara Ann
Strasfogel, Ian
Thompson, Hugh R

EDUCATOR
(College/University)

Aaholm, Philip Eugene
Abbate, Carolyn
Abbott, Michael
Abel, Paul Louis
Aber, Margery Vinie
Aberts, Eunice Dorothy
Abrahams, Frank E
Abram, Blanche Schwartz
Abramson, Robert U
Abravanel, Maurice

Adam, Claus
Adams, Elwyn Albert
Addiss, Stephen
Adler, Marvin Stanley
Agay, Denes
Ahnell, Emil Gustave
Aitken, Hugh
Aki, Syoko
Alavedra, Montserrat
Albam, Manny
Albers, Bradley Gene
Albert, Thomas Russel
Albin, William Robert
Albrecht, Otto Edwin
Albrecht, Theodore John
Albright, Philip H
Alch, Mario
Alderson, Richard M
Aldwell, Edward
Alette, Carl
Alexander, Brad
Alexander, John
Alexander, John Allen
Alexander, Josef
Alexander, William Peddie
Allanbrook, Wye Jamison
Allen, Jane
Allen, Judith S
Allen, Nancy
Allgood, William Thomas
Alper, Clifford Daniel
Alton, Ardyth
Amato, Bruno
Amoaku, William Komla
Amstutz, A Keith
Anderson, Alfred Lamar
Anderson, Allen Louis
Anderson, Dean
Anderson, Donna K
Anderson, Fletcher Clark
Anderson, Neil
Anderson, Robert (Theodore)
Anderson, Ronald K
Anderson, Ruth
Anderson, Shirley Patricia
Anderson, Waldie Alfred
Anderson, Warren DeWitt
Anderson, William Miller
Andrews, George
Andrus, Donald George
Angelini, Louis A
Anievas, Agustin
Annis, Robert Lyndon
Ansbacher, Charles Alexander
Anthony, James Raymond
Antokoletz, Elliott Maxim
Appelman, Ralph
Applebaum, Edward
Appleby, David P
Appleton, Clyde Robert
Appleton, Jon H
Arad, Atar
Arbizu, Ray Lawrence
Arbtiter, Eric A
Archibald, Bruce
Archibeque, Charlene P
Arganbright, Nancy (Nancy
  Weekley)
Argento, Dominick
Arlen, Walter
Arlin, Mary Irene
Armstrong, Anton Eugene
Arnold, Corliss Richard
Arnold, Louis
Aronoff, Frances Webber
Artley, Malvin Newton
Aschaffenburg, Walter
  (Eugene)
Ash, Rodney P
Ashbrook, William Sinclair, Jr
Ashforth, Alden
Ashley, Douglas Daniels
Ashworth, Jack S
Aslanian, Vahe
Auld, Louis Eugene
Aurand, Charles Henry, Jr
Austin, William Weaver

Aybar, Francisco (Rene)
Babbitt, Milton Byron
Babcock, Michael
Baber, Joseph (Wilson)
Bacal, Harvey
Bach, Jan (Morris)
Bacon, David
Bacon, Denise
Bacon, Virginia Payton
Baer, (Dolores) Dalene
Bagger, Louis S
Bailey, David Wayne
Bailey, Elden C
Bailey, Exine Margaret
  Anderson
Bailey, Robert
Baird, Edward Allen
Baisley, Robert William
Baker, James M
Baker, Julius
Baker, Nancy Kovaleff
Baker, Warren Lovell
Bakkegard, (Benjamin) David
Balada, Leonardo
Baldassarre, Joseph Anthony
Balderston, Suzanne
Baldwin, David
Baldwin, John
Baldwin, Marcia
Balk, H Wesley
Balkin, Alfred
Ball, Louis Oliver, Jr
Ballard, Louis Wayne
Ballard, Mary Anne
Ballenger, Kenneth Leigh
Banducci, Antonia
Banowetz, Joseph Murray
Barach, Daniel Paul
Barbosa-Lima, Carolos
Barkin, Elaine Radoff
Barlowe, Amy
Barnes, Darrel
Barnes, Marshall H
Baron, John Herschel
Barr, John Gladden
Barr, Raymond Arthur
Barrett, Paul H
Barrus, Charles LaMar, Jr
Bartholomew, Lynne
Bartlett, Loren W
Barwick, Steven
Barzenick, Walter
Basart, Robert
Baskerville, David
Basquin, Peter John
Bass, Warner Seeley
Bassett, Leslie Raymond
Bastian, James
Bates, Leon
Battisti, Frank Leon
Bault, Diane Lynn
Baumgartner, Paul Lloyd
Baur, John William
Baustian, Robert
Baxter, Lincoln Arthur
Baxter, William Hubbard, Jr
Bayard, Carol Ann
Baylor, Hugh Murray
Bays, Robert Earl
Beach, David Williams
Beadell, Robert Morton
Beadle, Anthony
Beale, Everett Minot
Beale, James
Beall, John Oliver
Beall, Lee Morrett
Bean, Shirley Ann
Beasley, Rule Curtis
Beattie, Herbert (Wilson)
Beauchamp, James W
Beck, Frederick Allan
Beckel, James A, Jr
Becker, C(ecil) Warren
Becker, Eugene
Becker, Richard
Beckerman, Michael Brim
Beckler, S R (Stanworth
  Russell)

Bedford, Judith Eileen
Bednar, Stanley
Beeler, Charles Alan
Beer, Hans L
Beeson, Jack (Hamilton)
Behague, Gerard Henri
Behnke, Martin Kyle
Behrend, Jeanne
Belcher, Deborah Jean
Belford, Marvin L
Belisle, John M
Bell, Winston A
Bendell, Christine J
Benedetti, Evangeline
Benfield, Warren A
Bengtson, F Dale
Benjamin, Thomas Edward
Bennett, Harold
Benson, Warren F
Bent, Margaret
Bentley, John E
Berberian, Hratch
Berendes, M Benedicta
Berger, Karol
Bergman, Janet Louise Marx
Bergquist, Peter
Bergsma, William Laurence
Berk, Adele L
Berkenstock, James Turner
Berkowitz, Sol
Berlin, David
Berman, Lynn Howell
Berman, Marsha F
Bernstein, David Stephen
Bernstein, Jacob
Bernstein, Lawrence F
Bernstein, Martin
Berry, Lemuel, Jr
Berry, Paul
Berry, Wallace Taft
Berta, Joseph Michel
Berv, Harry
Bestor, Charles L
Beyer, Frederick H
Bialosky, Marshall H
Bielawa, Herbert Walter
Bigham, William Marvin
Bigler, Carole L
Billmeyer, Dean Wallace
Bilson, Malcolm
Bilyeu, Landon Alan
Binkley, Thomas E
Birdwell, Florence (Gillam-
  Hobin)
Biscardi, Chester
Bishop, Adelaide
Bishop, Ronald Taylor
Bixler, Martha Harrison
Bjerregaard, Carl
Black, C Robert
Blackburn, Walter Wesley
Blain, Albert Valdes
Blakely, Lloyd George
Blank, Allan
Blatter, Alfred Wayne
Blickhan, (Charles) Timothy
Block, Geoffrey Holden
Bloom, Lawrie
Bloom, Robert
Boberg, Robert Martin
Bock, Emil William
Boda, John
Bodine, Willis (Ramsey), Jr
Boe, David S
Boehle, Willam Randall
Boerlage, Frans T
Boggs, Martha Daniel
Bognar, Dorothy McAdoo
Bogue, Lawrence
Bogusz, Edward
Bohrnstedt, Wayne R
Boiles, Charles Lafayette
Bolcom, William Elden
Bolen, Charles Warren
Bolen, Jane Moore
Bolet, Jorge
Bolitho, Albert George

EDUCATOR (cont)

Crutcher, Frances Hill
Cruz, Angelo
Cuckson, Robert
Cudek, Mark S
Culver, Robert
Cummings, Anthony Michael
Cunningham, Caroline M
Cunningham, Michael Gerald
Cuppernull, George Joseph
Cureau, Rebecca Turner
Currier, Donald Robert
Curtin, Phyllis
Curtis, Alan
Curtis, William H
Curtis-Smith, Curtis O B
Curtis-Verna, Mary
  (Virginia)
Cuyler, Louise E
Cykler, Edmund A
Cyr, Gordon Conrad
Czajkowski, Michael
D'Accone, Frank A
Da Costa, Noel
Dagon, Russell
Dahlgren, Carl Herman Per
Daigle, Anne Cecile
Daitz, Mimi Segal
D'Albert, Francois J
Dancz, Roger Lee
Dane, Jean R
Danfelt, Lewis S(eymour)
Daniel, Cyrus Chrisley
Daniel, Sean
Daniels, David Wilder
Daniels, Melvin L
Dann, Elias
Darcy, Warren Jay
Dasher, Richard Taliaferro
Dashnaw, Alexander
Daub, Peggy Ellen
Davidovsky, Mario
Davidson, Audrey Ekdahl
Davidson, Louis
Davidson, Lyle
Davine, Robert A
Davis, Allan Gerald
Davis, Ivan
Davis, Leonard
Davis, Michael David
Davison, John Herbert
Davye, John Joseph
Dawson, James Edward
Deahl, Robert Waldo
Dean, Talmage Whitman
Deas, Richard Ryder
Deason, William David
Deatherage, Martha
DeBolt, David Albert
De Cesare, Ruth
Decima, Terry
Deck, Warren
Decker, Harold A
Decker, James
DeFord, Ruth I
de Frank, Vincent
De Gastyne, Serge
Degen, Bruce N
DeGroot, David Joseph
De Intinis, Ranier
De Jong, Conrad John
DeLaney, Charles Oliver
DeLay, Dorothy (Mrs Edward
  Newhouse)
de Lerma, Dominique-Rene
della Picca, Angelo Armando
Dello Joio, Norman
Demaree, Robert William, Jr
Dembski, Stephen Michael
De Moura Castro, Luiz
Dempsey, John D
Denman, John Anthony
de Pasquale, Joseph
DePue, Wallace Earl
Derby, Richard William
Derr, Ellwood S
Derthick, Thomas V(inton)

DeRusha, Stanley Edward
Des Marais, Paul
Destwolinski, Gail
Deutsch, Herbert Arnold
Deutsch, Robert Larry
de Vale, Sue Carole
DeVan, William Lewis, Jr
deVaron, Lorna Cooke
DeVoll, Ray
de Volt, Artiss
DeVoto, Mark Bernard
Dexter, Benning
De Young, Lynden Evans
Diaconoff, Theodore A
Diamond, David (Leo)
Diamond, Jody
Diard, William
Dickinson, Alis
Dickow, Robert Henry
Diemente, Edward Philip
Diercks, John Henry
Dietz, Hanns-Bertold
Digiacomo, Serafina
Di Julio, Max (Joseph)
Di Lello, Edward V
Dillon, Robert
DiPietro, Albert S
Dittmer, Luther Albert
Di Virgilio, Nicholas
Dixon, James Allen
DjeDje, Jacqueline Cogdell
Dobbs, Mattiwilda
Dobelle, Beatrice
Dodd, Kit Stanley
Dodge, Charles M
Dodson, Glenn
Doktor, Paul Karl
Dominick, Lisa Robinson
Donakowski, Conrad Louis
Donovan, Jack P
Donovan-Jeffry, Peggy
  (Margaret)
Dorfmann, Ania
Dorian, Frederick
Dorsam, Paul James
Doscher, Barbara M
Douglas, Samuel Osler
Douglass, Robert Satterfield
Douvas, Elaine
Dower, Catherine Anne
Downes, Edward Olin
  Davenport
Downey, James Cecil
Downey, John Wilham
Draper, David Elliott
Draper, Glenn Wright
Dressen, Dan Fredrick
Dressler, John Clay
Drew, Lucas
Driggers, Orin Samuel
Drossin, Julius
Drucker, Arno Paul
Drucker, Ruth
Drucker, Stanley
Druesedow, John Edward, Jr
Druian, Joseph
Duckworth, William Ervin
Ducloux, Walter Ernest
Dudley, Anna Carol
Dudley, Raymond C
Duehlmeier, Susan Hunter
Dugger, Edwin Ellsworth
Dumm, Thomas A
Duncan, Dan J (Danny Joe)
Duncan, Douglas Jon
Dunkel, Stuart
Dure, Robert
Durham, Lowell M
Durham, Thomas Lee
Dutton, Mary Ann Enloe
Dvorak, Thomas L
Dwyer, Doriot Anthony
Dyer, Joseph
Eagle, Charles Thomas, Jr
Eagle, David William
Eakin, Charles
Earle, Eugenia

East, James Edward
Eaton, John C
Eby, Margarette Fink
Echols, Paul
Eckert, Michael Sands
Eddy, Timothy
Eder, Terry Edward
Edlefsen, Blaine Ellis
Edmunds, John Francis
Edwards, Elaine Virginia
Edwards, George (Harrison)
Edwards, Leo D
Edwards, Ryan (Hayes)
Effinger, Cecil Stanley
Effron, David Louis
Ehrlich, Clara Siegel
Eichenberger, Rodney (Bryce)
Eikum, Rex L
El-Dabh, Halim
Ellerman, Jens
Elliot, Gladys Crisler
Elliott, Wilber D
Ellsworth, Oliver Bryant
Elmore, Cenieth Catherine
End, Jack
Enenbach, Fredric
Engelhardt, Douglas Gustav
English Maris, Barbara (Jane)
Enrico, Eugene Joseph
Epperson, Gordon
Epstein, Paul
Erb, Donald James
Erb, James Bryan
Erdody, Stephen John
Ericksen, K Earl
Erickson, Raymond
Erickson, Robert
Erickson, Sumner Perry
Erickson, Susan
Erlings, Billie Raye
Ernest, David John
Errante, Frank Gerard
Ervin, Thomas Ross
Erwin, Edward
Escot, Pozzi
Eskew, Harry (Lee)
Eskin, Virginia
Espinosa, Alma O
Espinosa, (Sister) Teresita
Esselstrom, Michael John
Esteban, Julio
Estill, Ann (H M)
Etlinger, H Richard
Etzel, Marion
Evans, Margarita Sawatzky
Evans, Phillip
Eversole, James A
Ewart, Phillip Smith
Ewing, Maryhelen
Exline, Wendell L
Fahrner, Raymond Eugene
Fairleigh, James Parkinson
Falk, Leila Birnbaum
Farese, Mary Anne Wangler
Farish, Stephen Thomas, Jr
Farmer, Peter Russell
Farmer, Virginia
Farrell, Peter Snow
Faulconer, Bruce Laland
Faull, Ellen
Fawver, Darlene Elizabeth
Fay, (Earl) William
Fearing, Scott M
Fears, Emery Lewis
Febbraio, Salvatore Michael
  Turlizzo
Feese, Gerald
Fein, David N
Felciano, Richard
Feldman, Joann E
Feldman, Marion
Feldman, Morton
Feldsher, Howard M
Fellin, Eugene C
Fennelly, Brian Leo
Fenner, Burt L
Feofanov, Dmitry N

Ferguson, Gene
Ferguson, Suzanne (Carol)
Ferriano, Frank, Jr
Fesperman, John, Jr
Fetler, Paul
Fetsch, Wolfgang
Fialkowska, Janina
Fields, Richard Walter
Fields, Warren Carl
Fienen, David Norman
Figler, Byrnell Walter
Fink, Michael Armand
Fink, Myron S
Fink, Philip H
Fink, Robert Russell
Fink, Seymour Melvin
Fiol, Stephen Frank
Firkusny, Rudolf
Fischbach, Gerald F
Fischer, Elizabeth
Fishbein, Zenon
Fisher, Paul Gottshall
Fitzgerald, Robert Bernard
Fitzpatrick, Robert
Flanagan, Thomas J
Flatt, Terry Lee
Floyd, Carlisle
Floyd, John (Morrison)
Floyd, Samuel Alexander
Fluegel, Neal Lalon
Fly, Fenton G
Fogler, Michael Landy
Foldi, Andrew Harry
Fominaya, Eloy
Fontrier, Gabriel
Forbes, Elliot
Forcucci, Samuel L
Ford, Barbara
Ford, Frederic Hugh
Fornuto, Donato Dominic
Forrest, Jim
Forrest, Sidney
Forsberg, Carl Earl
Fortunato, D'Anna
Foss, Lukas
Foster, Donald Herbert
Foster, Robert Estill
Fouse, Donald Mahlon
Fouse, Sarah Baird
Fowler, Nancy
Fox, Frederick Alfred
Fox, Leland Stanford
Frabizio, William V
Frackenpohl, Arthur Roland
Frager, Malcolm
Frank, Andrew (David)
Frazee, Jane
Fredrickson, (Lawrence)
  Thomas
Freeman, Edwin Armistead
French, Richard Frederic
Fricker, Peter Racine
Friedman, Erick
Friedman, Viktor
Fries, Robert McMillan
Frigon, Chris Darwin
Frisch, Richard S
Frisch, Walter Miller
Fritschel, James Erwin
Frock, George Albert
Fromme, Arnold
Frumkin, Lydia
Fuchs, Joseph
Fulkerson, Gregory (Locke)
Fuller, Albert
Fuller, Jeanne Weaver
Fulton, William Kenneth
Funk, Eric Douglas
Furman, James
Fuschi, Olegna
Fusner, Henry Shirley
Gaber, George
Gable, Frederick Kent
Gabora, Teras
Gabriel, Arnald D
Gaeddert, William Kenneth
Galante, Jane Hohfeld

EDUCATOR(cont)
Hiss, Clyde S
Hitchcock, H(ugh) Wiley
Ho, Ting
Hobart, Max
Hobson, Constance Yvonne
   Tibbs
Hochheimer, Laura
Hodam, Helen
Hodgkins, Claire (Claire
   Hodgkins Wright)
Hodgson, Peter John
Hoekstra, Gerald Richard
Hoffman, Cynthia
Hoffman, Grace
Hoffman, Paul K
Hoffman, Theodore B
Hoffmann, Richard
Hoffren, James A
Hofstetter, Fred Thomas
Hogg, Merle E
Holden, Randall LeConte, Jr
Hollingsworth, Stanley W
Hollister, David Manship
Holloway, Clyde
Holmberg, Mark Leonard
Holmes, William C
Holmquist, John Edward
Holtz, John
Holvik, Karl Magnus
Homan, Frederic Warren
Homburg, Al(fred John)
Homer, Paul Robert
Hong, Sherman
Hood, Burrel Samuel
Hoogenakker, Virginia Ruth
Hoogerwerf, Frank William
Hoose, Alfred Julius
Hoover, Eric John
Hopkin, John Arden
Hopkins, Donald Eric
Hopkins, James Fredrick
Hopkins, Robert Elliott
Hopson, Hal Harold
Horner, Jerry
Horszowksi, Mieczslaw
Horton, William Lamar
Horvit, Michael Miller
Hoskins, William Barnes
Hosler, Mary Bellamy
   Hamilton
Hoswell, Margaret
Houghton, Edward Francis
House, Robert William
Housewright, Wiley Lee
Hovda, Eleanor
Howard, Cleveland L
Howard, Dean Clinton
Howard, (Dana) Douglas
Howat, Robert V
Howe, Hubert S, Jr
Howe, Richard Esmond, Jr
Howell, Almonte Charles,
   Jr
Hoyle, Wilson Theodore
Hsu, Dolores Menstell
Hsu, John (Tseng-Hsin)
Hsu, Madeleine
Huber, Calvin Raymond
Huber, John Elwyn
Hudson, Barton
Hudson, Richard Albert
Huetteman, Albert G
Hughes, Charles William
Hughes, David Grattan
Hughes, John (Gilliam)
Hujsak,-(Ruth) Joy
Hull, Robert Leslie
Hultberg, Warren Earle
Hunkins, Arthur B
Hunsberger, Donald
Hunt, Charles B, Jr
Hunt, Michael Francis
Hunter, Laura Ellen
Huntley, Lawrence Don
Hurd, Peter Wyeth
Hurley, Susan

Hurt, Charles Richard
Hurwitz, Isaac
Hurwitz, Robert Irving
Huston, Thomas Scott, Jr
Huszti, Joseph Bela
Hutcheson, Jere Trent
Hutchins, Farley Kennan
Hutchinson, Lucie Mary
Hutchinson, William Robert
Hutchison, (David) Warner
   (Walter Hudson)
Hyde, Frederick B(ill)
Hytrek, Theophane
Ienni, Philip Camillo
Igelsrud, Douglas Bent
Imbrie, Andrew Welsh
Inglefield, Ruth Karin
Ingraham, Paul
Insko, Wyatt (Marion), III
Intili, Dominic Joseph
Irby, Fred, III
Irvin, Marjory Ruth
Irvine, Demar (Buel)
Irving, Janet
Irwin, Phyllis Ann
Isaac, Cecil
Isaak, Donald J
Isbin, Sharon
Israel, Brian M
Israelievitch, Gail Bass
Israelievitch, Jacques
Jablonsky, Stephen
Jackson, Anita Louise
Jackson, Dennis Clark
Jackson, Donna Cardamone
Jackson, Douglas
Jackson, Hanley
Jackson, Raymond T
Jacobi, Roger Edgar
Jacobs, Charles Gilbert
Jacobs, Evelyn Poole
Jacobs, Kenneth A
Jacobson, Glenn Erle
Jaeger, Ina Claire
Jahn, Theodore Lee
James, Marion Verse
James, Mary Elliott
Jameson, R Philip
Jander, Owen Hughes
Janiec, Henry
Jankowski, Loretta Patricia
Janks, Hal
Janowsky, Maxim Dubrow
Janzen, Eldon A
Janzer, Georges
Jarrett, Jack Marius
Jay, Stephen
Jazwinski, Barbara Maria
Jeffers, Ronald H
Jeffery, Peter Grant
Jelinek, Jerome
Jenkins, Donald P
Jenkins, John Allan
Jenkins, Joseph Willcox
Jenkins, Susan Elaine
Jenni, D(onald) Martin
Jennings, Harlan Francis
Jennings, Robert Lee
Jennings, Theodore McKinley,
   Jr
Jensen, James A
Jensen, Richard Marsh
Jeppesen, Laura
Jernigan, Melvyn
Jochum, Veronica
Johannesen, Grant
Johansson, Annette
Johnson, Alvin H
Johnson, Calvert
Johnson, Clyde E
Johnson, Ellen Schultz
Johnson, Grace Grey
Johnson, Guy C
Johnson, Joyce Lynne
Johnson, June Durkin
Johnson, Roy Henry
Johnson, Theodore Oliver

Johnston, Benjamin Burwell, Jr
Johnston, Donald O
Jolas, Betsy
Jones, Charles
Jones, George Thaddeus
Jones, Jane Troth
Jones, Linda
Jones, Mason
Jones, Perry Otis
Jones, Robert M
Jones, Robert William
Jones, Roger Parks
Jones, Samuel
Jones, Stephen Graf
Jones, Wendal S
Jones, William John
Jordahl, Robert A
Jordan, Roland
Josephson, David S
Juhos, Joseph Frank
Kaderavek, Milan
Kaiser, Amy
Kaiser, Carl William
Kaiserman, David Norman
Kalichstein, Joseph
Kallir, Lillian
Kam, Dennis Koon Ming
Kang, Hyo
Kaplan, Barbara Connally
Kaplan, Burton
Kaplan, William Meyer
Kapuscinski, Richard
Karlins, M(artin) William
Karns, Dean Meredith
Karr, Gary Michael
Karson, Burton Lewis
Kasica, John
Kaslow, David Martin
Katahn, Enid
Kates, Stephen Edward
Katz, George Leon
Katz, Helen-Ursula
Katz, Israel J
Katz, Martha Strongin
Katz, Paul
Katzen, Daniel
Kaufman, Charles
Kaufman, Mindy F
Kaufmann, Henry William
Kavafian, Ani
Kay, Ulysses
Kearney, Linda (Yvonne)
Kearns, William Kay
Keats, Donald H(oward)
Kechley, David Stevenson
Keck, George R
Keene, Constance
Keene, James A
Keezer, Ronald
Kehle, Robert Gordon
Kehler, George Bela
Keiser, Marilyn Jean
Keller, Homer (Todd)
Keller, Michael Alan
Kelly, Paul Robert
Kemner, Gerald E
Kendall, Gary Keith
Kennan, Kent Wheeler
Kennedy, Dale Edwin
Kennedy, Josepha (Marie)
Kennedy, Matthew W
Kennedy, Raymond F
Kent, Richard Layton
Ker, Ann Steele
Kerrigan, William Paul
Kessner, Daniel Aaron
Kestenbaum, Myra
Keyes, Nelson
Kibbie, James Warren
Kidd, Ronald R
Kierig, Barbara Elaine
Kihslinger, Mary Ruth
Kilenyi, Edward
Kim, Byong-kon
Kim, Earl
Kim, Jung-Ja
Kim, Young-Uck

Kin, Vladimir
King, Alvin Jay
King, Carlton W, III
Kingman, Daniel C
Kiorpes, George Anthony
Kirchner, Leon
Kireilis, Ramon J
Kirk, Colleen Jean
Kirk, Elise Kuhl
Kirkpatrick, Gary Hugh
Kirkpatrick, Ralph
Kirkwood, Linda Walton
Kirshbaum, Bernard
Kite-Powell, Jeffery Thomas
Kitzman, John Anthony
Kivy, Peter Nathan
Klein, Luthar
Kleinsasser, Jerome S
Klenz, William
Klick, Susan Marie
Kliewer, Darleen Carol
Klimko, Ronald James
Klippstatter, Kurt L
Kloth, Timothy Tom
Klotman, Robert Howard
Klotzman, Dorothy Ann Hill
Knapp, John Merrill
Knaub, Donald
Kniebusch, Carol Lee
Knieter, Gerard L
Knight, Morris H
Knox, Charles
Kober, Dieter
Koberstein, Freeman G
Koblitz, David
Kocmieroski, Matthew
Kohloff, Roland
Kohn, James Donald
Kohs, Ellis Bonoff
Kojian, Miran Haig
Kolb, Barbara
Koldofsky, Gwendolyn
Kolker, Phillip A M
Kommel, A Margret
Kooper, Kees
Kopleff, Florence
Kopp, Leo Laszlo
Korde, Shirish K
Koret, Arthur (Solomon)
Korman, Joan
Korman, John
Koromzay, Denes Kornel
Korte, Karl Richard
Kottick, Edward Leon
Kraber, Karl
Kraft, Leo Abraham
Kraft, William
Kranz, Maria Hinrichs
Krasner, Louis
Kratzer, Dennis Leon
Krause, Robert James
Krauss, Anne McClenny
Kreger, James
Krehbiel, Arthur David
Krehbiel, Clayton
Krell, John
Kresky, Jeffrey Jay
Kriesberg, Matthias
Krigbaum, Charles Russell
Krolick, Edward (John)
Krosnick, Aaron Burton
Krosnick, Joel
Krummel, D(onald) W(illiam)
Krzywicki, Paul
Kuehn, David Laurance
Kuhn, Terry Lee
Kujala, Walfrid Eugene
Kumer, Dennis Michael
Kupferman, Meyer
Kurau, W(arren) Peter
Kurland, Shelly (Sheldon)
Kurtz, S James
Kurtzman, Jeffrey Gordon
Kushner, David Zakeri
Kuss, Malena
Kuzell, Christopher
Kuzmych, Christina

EDUCATOR(cont)

Kwalwasser, Helen
Kyr, Robert Harry
Labounty, Edwin Murray
Lackman, Susan Cohn
Lacy, Edwin V
Ladewig, James Leslie
Lafford, Lindsay Arthur
Lake, Bonnie (Josephine)
Lallerstedt, Ford Mylius
Lamb, Gordon Howard
Lammers, Mark (Edward)
Lancaster, Emanuel Leo
Lancaster, Thomas Scott
Landsman, Jerome Leonard
Landsman, Julie
Laney, Maurice I
Lang, Morris Arnold
Lang, Rosemary Rita
Langley, Leanne
Lansky, Paul
La Porta, John Daniel
Large, John W
Largent, Edward J, Jr
Larimer, Frances H
Larimer, Melvin Sherlock
Larsen, Robert L
Larson, Andre Pierre
Larson, David Dynes
Larue, Adrian Jan Pieters
Laszloffy, Jerome
Lateiner, Jacob
Latham, William P
Lathom, Wanda B
Lathrop, Gayle Posselt
Laughton, John Charles
Lauridsen, Morten
  Johannes
Laut, Edward Allen
Lawergren, Bo T
Lawrence, Arthur Peter
Lawrence, Joy Elizabeth
Lawrence, Kevin John
Lawrence, Lucille
Lawrence, Mark Howard
Laycock, Ralph George
Layton, Billy Jim
Lazarof, Henri
Lazarus, Roy
Leavitt, Joseph
LeBlanc, Albert Henry
Leclair, Judith
Leclaire, Dennis James
Ledbetter, Steven John
Ledeen, Lydia R Hailparn
Lee, Byong Won
Lee, Douglas Allen
Lee, Ki Joo
Lee, Patricia Taylor
Lee, Soo Chul
Leech, Alan Bruce
Leech, Karen Davidson
Lefever, Maxine Lane
Lefferts, Peter Martin
Lehman, Paul Robert
Lehman, Richard
Lehner, Eugene
Lehnerts, (Mary) Frances
Lehrer, Phyllis Alpert
Leibundguth, Barbara
Lelchuk, Nina (Simon)
Le Mieux, Raymond William
Lemmon, Galen
Lengefeld, William Chris
Lenneberg, Hans
Leno, Harold Lloyd
Leonard, Nels, Jr
LePage, Jane Weiner
Lepak, Alexander
Lepke, Charma Davies
LeRoy, Edmund
Lesemann, Frederick
Lessard, John Ayres
Lesser, Laurence
Leuba, (Julian) Christopher
Levarie, Siegmund
Levin, Gregory John

Levine, Jeffrey Leon
Levinson, Gerald
Levy, David Benjamin
Levy, Janet M
Levy, Kenneth
Lewenthal, Raymond
Lewin, Frank
Lewis, Arthur
Lewis, (John) Cary
Lewis, David S
Lewis, Elisabeth Parmelee
Lewis, Gerald David
Lewis, Jungshin Lim
Lewis, L Rhodes
Lewis, Malcolm Wallace, Jr
Lewis, Marcia Ann
Lewis, Peter Tod
Lewis, Philip James
Liauba, Danute
Libin, Laurence Elliot
Libove, Charles
Lichtmann, Margaret S
Lichtmann, Theodor David
Lidral, Frank Wayne
Lieberman, Fredric
Lifchitz, Max
Lifson, Ludmilla V
Lightner, Helen Lucille
Lincer, William
Lincoln, Harry B
Lincoln, Robert Dix
Lindahl, Charles E
Lindberg, William Edward
Lindeman, Carolynn A
Lindgren, Lowell Edwin
Ling, Stuart James
Linn, Robert T
Linscome, Sanford Abel
Linton, Stanley Stewart
Lipkis, Larry (Laurence Alan)
Lipovetsky, Leonidas
Lippman, Edward A
Listokin, Robert
Little, Frank (Francis E)
Little, Wm A(lfred)
Livingston, David
Livingston, Herbert
Livingstone, Ernest Felix
Lizotte, Andre
Lloyd, Gerald J
Loach, Donald Glenn
Lock, William Rowland
Locke, Ralph P
Lockwood, Carolyn
Lockwood, Lewis Henry
Lockwood, Normand
Loebel, Kurt
Loew, Henry
Loft, Abram
Logan, Wendell
Lohuis, Ardyth J
Lolya, Andrew
Lombardi, Eugene Patsy
Lombardo, Robert Michael
Longazo, George
Longyear, Rey Morgan
Lopez-Soba, Elias
LoPresti, Ronald B
Lord, Robert Sutherland
Loucks, Richard Newcomb
Lowe, Donald Robert
Lowens, Irving
Lowens, Margery Morgan
Lowenthal, Jerome
Lowrey, Norman Eugene
Lubet, Alex J
Lucchesi, Peggy (Margaret C
  Lucchesi)
Luchsinger, Ronald
Lucier, Alvin Augustus
Ludewig-Verdehr, Elsa
Lum, Richard S
Lundberg, Harriet A
Lunde, Nanette Gomory
Lurie, Bernard
Lurie, Mitchell
Luttrell, Nancy Kay

Lutyens, Sally Speare
Luxner, Michael David
Lyall, Max Dail
Lyne, Gregory Kent
Lynn, George
Ma, Yo-Yo
Maag, Jacqueline
Maas, Martha C
Mabrey, Charlotte Newton
Mabry, Sharon Cody
McBride, Robert Guyn
McCarthy, Peter Joseph
McCarty, Frank Lee
McCarty, Patrick
McCathren, Don (Donald E)
McCauley, William Erwin
McClain, Floyd Austin
McClellan, William Monson
MacClintock, Carol C
McClymonds, Marita Petzoldt
McColl, William D
McCollum, John (Morris)
McCormick, David Clement
Mac Court, Donald Vincent
McCoy, Wesley Lawrence
McCracken, Charles P
McCray, James Joseph
McCrory, Martha
McCulloh, Judith Marie
McDermott, Vincent
MacDonald, John Alexander
McDonald, Lawrence
McDonald, Susann Hackett
McElfish, Diane Elizabeth
McElheran, (N) Brock
McGary, Thomas Joseph
McGee, William James
McGinty, Doris Evans
Mach, Elyse Janet
Machlin, Paul Stuart
Machlis, Joseph
McInnes, Donald
MacInnis, M Donald
McIntosh, Kathleen Ann
Mack, Gerald
Mack, John
McKay, Neil
McKee, Ross R
McKenney, William Thomas
McKenzie, Jack H
McKenzie, Wallace C
Mackey, Elizabeth Jocelyn
Mackey, Richard
McKinley, Ann W
McKinney, Elizabeth
  Richmond
McKinney, James Carroll
McKinney, Roger William
McKinnon, James William
McLain, Robert Malcolm
Maclane, Armand Ralph
Mac Lean, John Torry
McMillan, Theodora Mantz
McMullen, Patrick T
McNeil, Jan Pfischner (Janet
  Louise Pfischner)
McNeil-Morales, Albert John
McPeek, Gwynn Spencer
McQuere, Gordon Daniel
McVoy, James Earl
Maddox, Robert Lee
Madsen, Clifford K
Madsen, Norma Lee (Norma
  Lee Madsen Belnap)
Mageau, Mary
Magg, Kyril
Magyar, Gabriel
Mahan, Katherine Hines
Mahar, William J
Mailman, Martin
Maimone, Renata
Main, Alexander
Maiorescu, Dorella Teodora
Majeske, Daniel H
Majoros, David John
Maki, Paul-Martin
Malas, Marlena Kleinman

Mallett, Lawrence Roger
Malm, William Paul
Malmin, Olaf Gerhardt
Malone, (Mary) Eileen
Maloof, William J
Mamlok, Ursula
Manahan, George
Mancinelli, Aldo L
Mandel, Alan Roger
Mandelbaum, M Joel
Maneri, Joseph Gabriel
Manes, Stephen Gabriel
Manford, Barbara Ann
Mann, Alfred
Mann, Brian Richard
Manning, Robert
Manning, William Meredith
Mannion, Elizabeth (Belle)
Mansfield, Kenneth Zoellin
Mansur, Paul Max
Marcellus, John Robert, III
Marcellus, Robert
Marcus, Adele
Marek, Dan
Maret, Stanley
Markey, George B
Markov, Albert
Markowski, Victoria
Marks, Virginia Pancoast
Marsh, Jack Odell
Marsh, Milton R
Marsh, Ozan F
Marshall, Howard Lowen
Marshall, Ingram Douglass
Marshall, James Thomas
Marshall, Robert Lewis
Martin, Charlotte
Martin, Dennis Roy
Martin, Geraldine
Martin, Leslie
Martin, Peter John
Martin, Walter (Callahan), Jr
Martino, Donald James
Martirano, Salvatore
Marvin, Marajean B
Masarie, Jack F
Maslanka, David Henry
Mason, Anne C
Mason, Marilyn
Mason, Neale Bagley
Masselos, William
Massena, Martha
Mast, Paul
Mastroianni, Thomas Owen
Mather, Betty Bang (Betty
  Louise Mather)
Mather, Roger Frederick
Mathes, Rachel Clarke
Mathiesen, Thomas James
Mathis, (George) Russell
Mathis, William Ervin
Matson, Sigfred Christian
Mattfeld, Victor Henry
Matthen, Paul Seymour
Matthews, Justus Frederick
Matthews, William
Mattila, Edward Charles
Mauk, Frederick Henry, Jr
Mauk, Steven Glenn
Mauney, Miles H
Maurer, James Carl
Maves, David W
Maxin, Jacob
Maxwell, Donald Edward
Maxym, Stephen
May, Ernest Dewey
May, Julia
May, Walter Bruce
Mayer, Frederick David
Mayer, Lutz Leo
Mayes, Samuel H
Meckel, Peter Timothy
Meckna, Michael
Meidt, Joseph Alexis
Meier, Gustav
Meister, Scott Robert
Mekeel, Joyce Haviland

EDUCATOR (cont)

Mellott, George Kenneth
Melnik, Bertha
Menard, Pierre Jules
Meng, Mei-Mei
Mennini, Louis Alfred
Mensch, Homer
Mercurio, Peter Amedeo
Merker, K Ethel
Merle, Montgomery
Merriman, Lyle Clinton
Merriman, Margarita Leonor
Meske, Eunice Boardman
Mester, Jorge
Meyers, Klara Bolgar
Michaelides, Peter
Middaugh, Benjamin
Middleton, Jaynne Claire
Middleton, Robert (Earl)
Mikhashoff, Yvar Emilian
Mikowsky, Solomon Gadles
Milburn, Ellsworth
Miller, Anne Winsor
Miller, Clement A
Miller, Clyde Elmer
Miller, Dean Harold
Miller, Donald Charles
Miller, Edward J
Miller, John William, Jr
Miller, Karl Frederick
Miller, Kenneth Eugene
Miller, Lewis Martin
Miller, Ralph Dale
Miller, Richard D
Miller, Terry Ellis
Milligan, Stuart Charles
Milligan, Thomas Braden, Jr
Miltenberger, James E
Ming, James W
Minor, Andrew Collier
Mintz, Donald M
Mischakoff, Anne
Mishkind, Abraham
Miskell, (William) Austin
Mitchell, Lee
Mixter, Keith Eugene
Moe, Daniel T
Moe, Lawrence Henry
Moe, Orin
Moeckel, Rainier
Moeser, James Charles
Moevs, Robert Walter
Monaco, Richard A
Monk, Patricia
Monosoff, Sonya (Sonya Monosoff Pancaldo)
Monsen, Ronald Peter
Monseur, George
Monson, Dale E
Montanaro, Donald
Montemurro, Paul A
Monteux, Claude
Montgomery, William Layton
Moody, William Joseph
Moore, Donald I
Moore, Douglas Bryant
Moore, F Richard
Moore, James, III
Moore, John Parker, Jr
Moore, Kenneth
Moore, Marvelene Clarisa
Moore, Undine Smith
Morganstern, Marvin
Moriarty, John
Morrill, Dexter G
Morris, R Winston
Morris, Richard
Morris, Robert Daniel
Morrison, Harry S
Moses, Don V
Mosher, Elizabeth (Elizabeth Mosher-Kraus)
Moss, Lawrence Kenneth
Mount, John Wallace
Moyer, John Harold
Moyers, Emmett Edwin

Mracek, Jaroslav John Stephen
Muczynski, Robert
Mueller, Erwin Carl
Mueller, Harold
Mueller, John Storm
Mueller, Otto Werner
Mueller, Robert E
Muenzer, Edgar C
Mulfinger, George Leonidas, Jr
Mulfinger, Joan Wade
Mulford, Ruth Stomne
Mullins, Hugh E
Mund, Frederick Allen
Munday, Kenneth Edward
Munger, Dorothy M
Munger, Shirley (Annette)
Muraco, Thomas
Murakami, Sarah Theresa Yoshiko
Murata, Margaret Kimiko
Murdock, Katherine
Murray, Alexander Douglass
Murray, Bain
Murray, Robert P
Murray, Sterling Ellis
Murray, Thomas
Mushabac, Regina (Regina Mushabac Klemperer)
Musser, Willard I
Mussulman, Joseph Agee
Myers, Marceau Chevalier
Myers, Theldon
Nachman, Myrna S
Nagel, Louis B
Najera, Edmund L
Naldini, Vasco
Nanney, Herbert (Boswell)
Nathan, Hans
Naylor, Tom Lyle
Neal, Lenora Ford
Nee, Thomas Bacus
Negyesy, Janos
Nelson, Bradley R
Nelson, Jon
Nelson, Larry A
Nelson, Phillip Francis
Nelson, Roger William
Nelson, Wendell A
Nero, Beverly
Nettl, Bruno
Neubert, Bernard David
Neubert, Henry Grim, Jr
Neuman, Daniel Moses
Neumann, Philip Warren
Newell, Douglas Myers
Newell, Robert Max
Newell, Thomas E, Jr
Newman, Anthony
Newman, Grant H
Newton, Norma
Niblock, James F
Nicholas, Louis Thurston
Nichols, Clinton Colgate
Nichols, David Clifford
Nicholson, Joseph Milford
Niedt, Douglas Ashton
Nilsson, Raymond
Nixon, Roger
Nketia, J H Kwabena
Noble, Weston Henry
Noel, Barbara H (Barbara H McMurtry)
Nold, Donal Charles
Noon, David
Noone, Lana Mae
Norden, Hugo
Nordgren, Quentin Richards
Norton, Lew
Nott, Douglas Duane
Novack, Saul
Novich, Mija
Nuernberger, Louis D
Nunlist, Juli (Elizabeth Moora)
Nyfenger, Thomas
Nyquist, Roger Thomas
Obenshain, Kathryn Garland
Oberbrunner, John

Oberlin, Russell
Obetz, John Wesley
O'Brien, James Patrick
O'Brien, John Thomas
O'Brien, Orin
O'Brien, Robert Felix
Ochs, Michael
Ochse, Orpha Caroline
Ockwell, Frederick
Ode, James Austin
Odum-Vernon, Alison P (Alison Paige Odum)
Ogasapian, John Ken
Ogdon, Will (Wilbur Lee Ogdon)
O'Grady, Terence John
Ohl, Ferris E
Ohl, John Franklin
Ohyama, Hellchiro
Olcott, James Louis
Oldani, Robert William
Olds, Patricia Hunt
Olevsky, Julian
Oliver, Nils
Olmstead, Andrea Louise
Olmstead, Gary James
Olsen, A Loran
Olsen, Dale Alan
Oltman, C Dwight
Onishi, Aiko
Opheim, Vernon Holman
Opper, Jacob
Orbon, Julian
O'Reilly, F(rank) Warren
O'Reilly, Sally
Orland, Henry
Orlovsky, Arkady
Ornstein, Doris
Orr, Nathaniel Leon
Orr, Wendell Eugene
Ortiz, William
Osborne, Charles Eugene
Ossenkop, David Charles
Ostergren, Eduardo Augusto
Ostrander, Arthur E
Ostrove, Geraldine E
Owen, Charles E
Owen, Harold J
Owings, John C
Packer, Janet Susan
Page, Robert (Elza)
Paget, Daniel
Paglialunga, Augusto
Paige, Norman
Palisca, Claude V
Palmer, Anthony John
Palmer, Larry Garland
Palmer, Robert M
Palmieri, Robert Michael
Palombo, Paul Martin
Pandolfi, Roland
Panerio, Robert Major
Panetti, Joan
Pangborn, Robert C
Papastefan, John James
Paperno, Dmitry A
Parcells, Ramon Everett
Pardee, Margaret (Margaret Pardee Butterly)
Parisot, Aldo Simoes
Park, Raymond Roy
Parkening, Christoper W
Parker, Craig Burwell
Parker, Jesse
Parker, Olin Griffith
Parker, R Clinton
Parker, Richard Allan
Parnas, Leslie
Parrigin, Perry Goggin
Party, Lionel
Paschke, Donald Vernon
Pasler, Jann Corinne
Pasmanick, Kenneth
Pastor, Freda
Pastore, Patrice Evelyn
Patterson, Andy J
Patterson, David Nolte

Patterson, T Richard
Patterson, William G
Patton, Jasper William
Patty, James Lecil
Paulson, Stephen Jon
Payne, Frank Lynn
Payne, Maggi
Paynter, John P
Peake, Luise Eitel
Pearlman, Leonard Alexander
Pearlman, Richard Louis
Pearson, Mark
Pease, Edward Joseph
Peck, Donald Vincent
Peelle, David
Pellegrino, John
Pellerite, James John
Pellman, Samuel Frank
Penderecki, Krzysztof
Pendle, Karin
Penland, Arnold Clifford, Jr
Perera, Ronald Christopher
Peretz, Marc Harlan
Perich, Guillermo
Perkins, Leeman Lloyd
Perkins, Marion (Louise)
Perlis, Vivian
Perlman, Itzhak
Perlongo, Daniel James
Perret, Peter J
Perris, Arnold B
Perry, Alcestis Bishop
Perry, Marvin Chapman, II
Perry-Camp, Jane (Schiffman)
Persichetti, Vincent
Pestalozzi, Martha
Peters, George David
Peters, Mitchell
Petersen, Marian F
Peterson, Larry W
Peterson, Max D
Petit, Annie
Peyton, Malcolm Cameron
Pfautsch, Lloyd Alvin
Phelps, Norman F
Phelps, Roger Paul
Philips, John (Douglass)
Philips, Mary Kathryn
Phillips, Burrill
Phillips, Harvey Gene
Philpott, Larry LaFayette
Picker, Martin
Pierce, Lorrie (Lorrie Pierce Glaze)
Pierson, Edward
Pierson, Thomas Claude
Pinkham, Daniel
Pinkow, David J
Pinnell, Richard Tilden
Pinnell, Ruth
Pinner, Jay-Martin
Pisk, Paul A(madeus)
Plantamura, Carol Lynn
Plantinga, Leon Brooks
Platte, Jay Daniel
Pleskow, Raoul
Plsek, Stephany King
Plsek, Thomas Joseph
Plumb, Bruce William
Podolsky, Leo S
Poe, Gerald Dean
Pogue, Samuel Franklin
Polay, Bruce
Polin, Claire
Polisi, William
Pollack, Daniel
Pollack, Howard Joel
Pollack, Jill M
Pollard, Elizabeth Blitch
Pommers, Leon
Pope, Conrad
Popkin, Mark Anthony
Popper, Fredric
Porter, James Whyte
Porter, Susan Loraine
Portone, Frank Anthony, Jr
Post, Nora

EDUCATOR(cont)

Postl, Jacobeth
Postlewate, Charles Willard
Poto, Attilio
Pottebaum, William G
Pottenger, Harold Paul
Potter, David Kinsman
Potter, John Matthew
Powell, Arlene Karr
Powell, Newman Wilson
Powley, E Harrison, III
Pozdro, John Walter
Prater, Jeffrey L
Prausnitz, Frederik W
Preiss, James
Presslaff, Hilary Tann
Pressler, Menahem
Preston, (Mary) Jean
Price, John Elwood
Price, Robert Bates
Price, Shelby Milburn, Jr
Pridonoff, Elizabeth Anna
Pridonoff, Eugene Alexander
Priest-Stevens, Maxine
  (Maxine Stevens)
Pritchett, Theodore M
Pritts, Roy A
Procter, Leland (Herrick)
Prodan, James Christian
Provost, Richard (Charles)
Pruett, James Worrell
Pruett, Lilian Pibernik
Pugh, Russell Oris
Purcell, Ron (Ronald Charles)
Pursell, Bill (William
  Whitney)
Putsche, Thomas Reese
Pyne, James
Quilico, Louis
Quilling, Howard Lee
Quinn, James Joseph
Quist, Pamela Layman
Rackley, Lawrence (Lawrence
  Rackley Smith)
Raditz, Edward
Radnofsky, Kenneth
Radnofsky, Nancy
Radosavljevich, Olga (Olga
  Radosavljevich
  Gradojevich)
Raffman, Relly
Rafols, Alberto P
Raieff, Joseph
Rainbow, Edward Louis
Raitt, John Wellesley
Raleigh, Stuart W
Ramirez, Luis Antonio
Ramsier, Paul
Ran, Shulamit
Randall, James K
Rands, Bernard
Ranganathan, Tanjore
Rapier, Wayne
Rapley, Janice Ann
Raskin, Judith
Rathbun, James Ronald
Ratner, Leonard Gilbert
Rauche, Anthony Theodore
Rauscher, Donald John
Raver, Leonard
Rawlins, Joseph (Thomas)
Reagin, Brian E
Reaney, Gilbert
Rearick, Martha Nell
Reber, Richard
Reed, Addison Walker
Reed, H Owen
Reese, William Heartt
Reeves, James Matthew
Rehfeldt, Phillip Richard
Rehfuss, Heinz J
Reich, Bruce
Reich, Nancy B
Reichmuth, Roger Edwin
Reilly, Edward Randolph
Reimer, Bennett
Reims, Clifford Waldemar

Reis, Joan Sachs
Reisenberg, Nadia
Reiss, Alvin H
Reiswig, David Earl
Rejto, Gabor M
Rejto, Peter A
Remenikova, Tanya
Rendleman, Ruth
Resch, Rita Marie
Retzel, Frank (Anthony)
Revitt, Paul J
Reyes, Angel
Reynolds, Roger Lee
Reynolds, Verne Becker
Reynolds, William J
Rhoads, Mary Ruth
Rhodes, Cherry
Rhodes, Phillip
Rhodes, Samuel
Ribeiro, Gerardo
Ricci, Ruggiero
Rice, B(oone) Douglas
Rich, Ruthanne
Richards, William Henry
Richardson, William Wells
Ricigliano, D Anthony
Riddle, Ronald William
Riepe, Russell Casper
Rife, Jean
Riley, James Rex
Riley, Terry
Rinehart, John
Ringel, Harvey Norman
Ringer, Alexander L
Ripley, Robert
Risdon, Frances Lee
Ritchie, Stanley John
Ritchie, Tom Vernon
Ritter, John Steele
Rivard, William H
Rivers, James (Calvin)
Roach, Donald Wycoff
Robbins, Daniel
Robbins, David Paul
Roberts, Donald Lowell
Roberts, John Noel
Robertson, Donna Nagey
Robertson, Edwin C
Robertson, Marvin L
Robinson, Florence Claire
  Crim
Robinson, Joseph
Robison, Clayne W
Robison, John Orian
Robison, Paula Judith
Robison, William H, III
Roby, Paul Edward
Rochberg, George
Rodda, Richard Earl
Roeckle, Charles Albert
Rogers, Calvin Y
Rogers, Delmer Dalzell
Rogers, John E
Rogers, Patsy
Rogers, Rodney Irl
Rogers, William Forrest
Roldan, Nancy
Romeo, James Joseph
Romersa, Henry John
Romine, Robert Lee
Romiti, Richard A
Rondelli, Barbara (Ann)
Ronsheim, John Richard
Root, Deane Leslie
Rorick, William C(alvin)
Rosado, Ana Maria
Rosand, Aaron
Rosand, Ellen
Rose, C Robert
Rose, Jerome H
Rose, John
Rose, Leonard (Joseph)
Rose, William H
Rosen, Jerome William
Rosen, Nathaniel Kent
Rosenberg, Kenyon Charles
Rosenberger, Walter Emerson

Rosenblith, Eric
Rosenblum, Myron
Rosenblum, Sandra Pletman
Rosenboom, David
Rosene, Paul Earl
Rosner, Christian A K
Ross, Allan Anderson
Ross, Jerrold
Ross, Judith
Ross, Ronald D
Rossi, Nick
Roth, Eric Steven
Rothe, David H
Rouse, Christopher Chapman
Roussakis, Nicolas
Routch, Robert Edson
Rovics, Howard
Row, Peter Lyman
Rowen, Ruth Halle
Roy, Gene Burdick
Roze, Christopher
Rubin, Emanuel Leo
Rubin, Nathan
Ruby, E Jane
Rudiakov, Michael
Rudie, Robert
Rudin, Andrew
Rudnytsky, Roman Victor
Ruff, Willie
Ruggiero, Charles H(oward)
Ruggiero, Matthew
Runner, David Clark
Runyan, William Edward
Russell, Armand King
Russell, Craig Henry
Russell, Lucy Hallman
Russianoff, Leon
Russo, Charles
Rutschman, Edward Raymond
Ryder, Georgia Atkins
Ryder, Judith (Mrs Bruce
  Frumker)
Rydzynski, Michael Vincent
  Matthew
Rzewski, Frederic
Sable, Barbara Kinsey
Sabo, Marlee
Sacco, P Peter
Sacher, Jack, Jr
Sachs, Joel
Saffle, Michael Benton
Safran, Arno M
Sahuc, Nolan John
Saks, Toby
Salander, Roger Mark
Saloman, Ora Frishberg
Saltzman, Herbert Royce
Salzer, Felix
Samuel, Harold Eugene
Samuel, Rhian
Samuelsen, Roy
Sanchez, Marta
Sanders, Ernest H
Sandresky, Margaret Vardell
Sant Ambrogio, John
Sargeant, Phillip Lester
Sargous, Harry Wayne
Saslav, Isidor
Sataloff, Robert Thayer
Saturen, David Haskell
Saunders, Mary G
Savage, James Bryan
Saville, Eugenia Curtis
Saylor, Bruce Stuart
Scavelli, Ramon Louis
Schachter, Carl
Schaefer, Lois Elizabeth
Schaefer, William Arkwell
Schaeffer, John A
Schaffer, Robert Carlton
Schein, Ann
Scheller, Stanley
Schenly, Paul
Scheuerle, Paul Norman
Schick, George
Schiffman, Harold (Anthony)
Schiller, Allan

Schilling, Charles Walter
Schimke, Milton Maurice
Schindler, Allan
Schirmer, William Louis
Schleifer, Martha Furman
Schleis, Thomas Henry
Schleuter, Stanley L
Schmalz, Robert Frederick
Schmidt, Carl B
Schmidt, Fred D
Schmidt, John Charles
Schmidt, Liselotte Martha
Schmidt, Mary Helen
Schmidt, Rodney
Schmitt, Cecilia
Schneider, Bernard
Schneider, John
Schneider, June
Schneider, Mischa
Schneiderman, William
Schneidmann, Irene
Schnoebelen, Anne
Schoep, Arthur Paul
Schonthal-Seckel, Ruth
Schooley, John (Heilman)
Schrader, Barry Walter
Schroeder, Gerald H
Schroeder, Raymond Lee
Schroeder, William A
Schuetze, George Claire, Jr
Schultz, Herbert L
Schumacher, Thomas
Schuman, Daniel Zetkin
Schuster, Earl Vincent
Schuster, Savely
Schwadron, Abraham Abe
Schwager, Myron August
Schwantner, Joseph C
Schwartz, Francis
Schwartz, Joseph Ervin
Schwartz, Judith Leah
Schwartz, Marvin Robert
Schwarz, Ira Paul
Schwarz, John Irvin, Jr
Scianni, Joseph
Scott, Cleve L
Scott, Frank Edward
Scott, Robert Charles
Scott, Roger
Scott, Yumi Ninomiya
Seaton, (Stuart) Douglass
Seay, Albert
Secrist, Phylis Jane
Seebass, Tilman
Seeley, Gilbert Stewart
Seferian, Edward
Selberg, John Ryan
Selden, Margery Stomne
Self, James Martin
Selig, Robert L
Sellers, Jacquelyn Marie
Seltzer, George
Semegen, Daria
Sessions, Roger Huntington
Seymour, William
Shaffer, (William) Allen
Shaffer, Sherwood
Shahan, Paul W
Shake, J(ames) Curtis
Shamrock, Mary E
Shand, David Austin
Shanet, Howard Stephen
Shapero, Harold Samuel
Shapiro, Harvey
Shapiro, Jack M
Shapiro, Joel
Sharon, Boaz
Sharp, Maurice
Sharrow, Leonard
Shaw, Rolland Hugh
Shelton, Margaret Meier
Shelton, Melvin Leroy
Sheppard, C(harles) James
Sherman, Russell
Sherr, Richard Jonathan
Shifrin, David
Shindle, William Richard

Shinn, Randall Alan
Shirey, Ronald
Shirley, George Irving
Shore, Clare
Shott, Michael John
Showell, Jeffrey Adams
Shuler, Craig
Shultz, Dan McLloyd
Shulze, Frederick Bennett
Shumway, Larry Vee
Shumway, Stanley
  Newmyer
Shure, Leonard
Sider, Ronald Ray
Sidnell, Robert G
Sidoti, Raymond B
Siebert, Frederick Mark
Siena, Jerold
Silbiger, Alexander
Silfies, George
Silini, Flora Chiarappa
Silver, Sheila Jane
Silverman, Alan John
Silverman, Faye-Ellen
Silvester, William H
Simenauer, Peter W
Simosko, Valerie
Simpson, Mary Jean
Simpson, Wilbur Herman
Sims, Edward
Sims, Phillip Weir
Singer, Joan (Joan Singer
  Spicknall)
Sinta, Donald Joseph
Sirota, Victoria (Ressmeyer)
Sirucek, Jerry Edward
Sislen, Myrna (Carol)
Sisman, Elaine Rochelle
Skei, Allen Bennet
Skidmore, Dorothy Louise
Skidmore, William R
Skolovsky, Zadel
Skorodin, Elaine (Elaine
  Skorodin Fohrman)
Skrzynski, Joseph
Slaughter, Susan
Slawson, A Wayne
Slim, H(arry) Colin
Slobin, Mark
Sloop, Jean Carolyn
Small, Edward Pierce
Smetana, Frantisek
Smiley, Marilynn Jean
Smiley, Pril
Smith, Catherine Parsons
Smith, Charles Justice
Smith, Charles Warren
Smith, Dorman Henry
Smith, Douglas
Smith, Edwin Lester
Smith, George Francis
Smith, Gerald L
Smith, Glenn Parkhurst
Smith, Hale
Smith, James F
Smith, James Gordon
Smith, Jerry Neil
Smith, Jess
Smith, Joseph Turner
Smith, Kenneth
Smith, Larry Alan
Smith, Leland Clayton
Smith, Martin
Smith, Priscilla
Smith, Raymond R
Smith, Robert Ludwig
Smith, Stuart Saunders
Smith, William
Smith, William Overton
Snavely, Jack
Snowden, James Wyn
Snyder, Barry
Snyder, John L
Snyder, Leo
Snyder, Randall L
Soames, Cynthia Elizabeth

Socciarelli, Ronald Peter
Sokol, Vilem
Sokoloff, Eleanor
Sokoloff, Vladimir
Solie, Ruth Ames
Sollberger, Harvey
Solomon, Judith A
Solomon, Larry J
Solomon, Nanette Kaplan
Solum, John H
Somer, Avo
Sorce, Richard
Sorel, Claudette Marguerite
Soroka, John G
Southern, Eileen Jackson
Sowell, Laven
Soyer, David
Spencer, Peter
Spencer, Robert Lamar
Spencer, Williametta
Sperl, Gary Robert
Spiegelman, Joel Warren
Spies, Claudio
Spina, Salvatore C
Spivakovsky, Tossy
Spotts, Carleton B
Sprague, Raymond
Spratlan, Lewis
Sprenkle, Robert Louis
Spring, Glenn Ernest
Sprung, David Reichert
Spurgeon, Phillip (Coleman)
Stacy, Martha
Stacy, William Barney
Stafford, James Edward
Stafford, Lee Christopher
Stallman, Robert
Stalzer, Frank S
Stanek, Alan Edward
Stanford, Thomas Stanley
Stanley, Donald Arthur
Stanton, Royal Waltz
Star, Cheryl Mc Whorter
Starker, Janos
Starling, A Cumberworth
Starr, Lawrence
Staton, Kenneth Wayne
Stauffer, George B
Stearns, Peter Pindar
Stedman, William Preston
Steg, Paul Oskar
Stegall, Joel Ringgold
Steigerwalt, Gary Paul
Stein, Leonard D
Stein, Ronald
Steinberg, Michael
Steiner, Diana
Steinhardt, Arnold
Stempel, Larry E
Stenberg, Donald Christian
Sten-Taubman, Suzanne
Stephenson, Robert John
Stephenson, Ruth Orr
Stern, Daniel David
Stern, Robert
Sternberg, Jonathan
Sterne, Colin Chase
Stevens, Halsey
Stevens, Jeffrey
Stevens, Milton Lewis, Jr
Stevens, Roger S
Stevenson, Robert Murrell
Stewart, Frank Graham
Stewart, Larry Joe
Stewart, M Dee
Still, Ray
Stilwell, F Raymond
Stith, Marice W
Stoeppelmann, Janet
Stokes, Sheridon Willard
Stokman, Abraham
Stolper, Daniel John
Stone, Edgar Norman
Stoner, Thomas Alan
Stout, Alan Burrage
Stout, Louis James
Strainchamps, Edmond
  Nicholas

Strandberg, Newton Dwight
Strang, Gerald
Strange, Allen
Strange, Richard Eugene
Strassburg, Robert
Streeter, Thomas Wayne
Stretansky, Cyril Michael
Stripling, Luther
Strohm, John A
Strukoff, Rudolf Stephen
Strunk, Steven (Gerhardt)
Stuart, James Fortier
Stucky, Rodney
Sturges, Rowland (Gibson
  Hazard)
Subotnick, Morton
Suchoff, Benjamin
Suchy, Gregoria Karides
Suchy, Jessica Ray
Suess, John G
Sullivan, Robert Paul
Sumerlin, Macon Dee
Summers, William Franklin
Summers, William John
Summerville, Suzanne
Sutherland, Donald S
Sutton, Julia
Sutton, Mary Ellen
Svoboda, Tomas
Swack, Irwin
Swalin, Benjamin Franklin
Swallow, John
Swan, Howard Shelton
Swanson, Jean Phyllis
Swanson, Philip John
Swenson, Courtland Sevander
Swenson, Edward E
Swift, Robert Frederic
Swing, Peter Gram
Swisher, Gloria Wilson
Syverud, Stephen Luther
Szkodzinski, Louise
Taffs, Anthony J
Tafoya, Carole Smith
Tait, Malcolm John
Takahashi, Yoriko
Talley-Schmidt, Eugene
Talma, Louise J
Tanenbaum, Elias
Tannenbaum, James
Tanner, Peter H
Tanno, John W
Tashjian, B Charmian
Tate, Elda Ann
Tatman, Neil
Tatton, Thomas
Tawa, Nicholas Edward
Taylor, Clifford (Oliver)
Taylor, Frank
Taylor, Jack A
Taylor, John Armstead
Taylor, Les (Lionel Lester)
Taylor, Maria del Pico
Taylor, Thomas Fuller
Tcherepnin, Ivan
  Alexandrovitch
Teague, Thomas S
Teal, Mary Evelyn Durden
Temperley, Nicholas
Tenney, James C
Tepper, Albert
Terey-Smith, Mary
Termini, Olga A
Teutsch, Walter
Thamon, Eugene (Eugene
  Thamon Simpson)
Theimer, Axel Knut
Thielman, Ronald Moncrief
Thierstein, Eldred A
Thomas, John M
Thomas, Marilyn Taft
Thomas, Sally
Thome, Diane
Thompson, Annie F
Thompson, Donald
Thompson, Ellen R
Thompson, Glenda Goss

Thompson, Marcus Aurelius
Thompson, Marian
Thompson, Robert K
Thomson, William Ennis
Thoreson, Thomas J
Thurston, Richard Elliott
Thym, Jurgen
Tiboris, Peter Ernest
Tickton, Jason Harold
Tiemeyer, Christian
Tietov, Frances
Tilkens, Neil Avrill
Timm, (M) Jeanne Anderson
Timm, Kenneth N
Timm, Larry M (Laurance
  Milo)
Tipei, Sever
Tischler, Hans
Tischler, Judith B
Titcomb, Caldwell
Titon, Jeff Todd
Tobias, Paul
Todd, George Bennett
Toensing, Richard E
Tollefson, Arthur Ralph
Tolo, Leland Stanford
Toms, John (Elias)
Torch, Deborah L
Torchinsky, Abe
Toth, Andor, Jr
Touliatos-Banker, Diane H
Toutant, William Paul
Trampler, Walter
Trantham, William Eugene
Travis, Roy
Tree, Michael
Treger, Charles
Trembly, Dennis M
Trenkamp, (Wilma) Anne
Treutel, Edward F
Tromblee, Maxell Ray
Troupin, Edward
Trubitt, Allen R
Truesdell, Frederick Donald
Tubb, Monte
Tull, Fisher (Aubrey)
Tumbleson, John Raymond
Tung, Yuan
Turkiewicz, Witold Wladyslaw
Turner, Lynne Alison
Turner, Sarah
Turrill, Pauline Venable
Tusler, Robert Leon
Tuttle, Karen
Tyler, Veronica
Tyra, Thomas (Norman)
Tyree, Ronald Wayne
Tzerko, Aube
Udell, Budd A
Udow, Michael William
Ulehla, Ludmila
Ulrich, Eugene Joseph
Ultan, Lloyd
Underwood, William L
Unland, David E
Unsworth, Arthur E
Upton, James Southerland
Uris, Dorothy Tree
Urquhart, Dan Murdock
Ushioda, Masuko
Ussachevsky, Vladimir A
Utgaard, Merton Blaine
Vacchiano, William
Vagner, Robert Stuart
Valdes-Blain, Rolando
Valente, William Edward
Van, Jeffrey Wylie
Van Appledorn, Mary Jeanne
van Boer, Bertil Herman, Jr
van Boer, Bertil Herman
van Bronkhorst, Warren
van der Merwe, Johan
Van de Vate, Nancy (Hayes)
Van Dyke, Gary John
vanEaton, Sunny F C
VanEgmond, Max (Rudolf)
Van Hyning, Howard

EDUCATOR (cont)

Van Ness, Paul William
Van Norman, Clarendon Ess, Jr
Van Solkema, Sherman
Van Vactor, David
VanValkenburg, James Wade
Vargas, Sonia
Vayspapir, Roma
Vazzana, Anthony Eugene
Veazey, Charles Orlando
Veleta, Richard Kenneth
Velimirovic, Milos
Venettozzi, Vasile Jean
Verba, E Cynthia
Vercoe, Barry Lloyd
Verdehr, Walter
Verdi, Ralph Carl
Verhaalen, Marion
Vermel, Paul
Vernon, Charles Gary
Veronda, Carlo
Verrall, John Weedon
Verrastro, Ralph Edward
Vessels, William Allen
Vilker, Sophia
Virizlay, Paula Skolnick
Vogel, Roger Craig
Vollrath, Carl Paul
von Grabow, Richard H
Von Gunden, Heidi Cecilia
Von Wurtzler, Aristid
Votapek, Ralph
Wagner, Edyth (Edyth Wagner Roop)
Wagner, John Waldorf
Wagner, Lavern John
Walcott, Ronald Harry
Waldman, Mildred
Walker, Frances E
Walker, Gwyneth V
Walker, Mallory Elton
Walker, William
Wallace, Paul James
Wallach, Joelle
Waln, Ronald Lee
Walsh, Diane
Walter, David
Walters, Michael J
Wangler, Francis (Frank) D
Wann, Lois
Ward, John Milton
Ward, Robert Eugene
Ward, William Reed
Ward-Steinman, David
Ware, Durward Clifton, Jr
Ware, John
Ware, John Marley
Warfield, William Caesar
Warkentin, Larry R
Warkov, Esther R
Warner, Robert Austin
Warren, Edwin Brady
Warren, Jerry L
Wason, Robert Wesley
Wassum, Sylvesta Marie
Watanabe, Ruth Taiko
Waters, David L
Waters, J Kevin
Waters, James Lipscomb
Watkins, Armin J
Watkins, Glenn
Watkins, R Bedford
Watson, J Perry
Watson, Jack McLaurin
Watson, Kenneth E
Watson, Walter Robert
Watts, Aredean Walton
Weaver, Robert Lamar
Weaver, Robert Lee
Webb, Brian Patrick
Webb, Marianne
Weber, David
Webster, Beveridge
Webster, Gerald Best
Webster, Peter Richard

Weed, Joseph Laiten
Weed, Maurice James
Weekley, Dallas Alfred
Wegner, August Martin, III
Wehner, Walter Leroy
Weichlein, William Jesset
Weidensaul, Jane Bennett
Weidensee, Victor J
Weinberg, Henry
Weinberger, Henry
Weiner, Lawrence
Weinreb, Alice Kogan
Weirich, Robert
Weisberg, Arthur
Weiss, Dawn Adrienne
Weiss, Piero E
Wells, David
Welwood, Arthur
Wennerstrom, Mary Hannah
Wentzel, Rubi V
Werder, Richard H
Werdesheim, Gary
Werling, Anita Eggert
Werner, Robert Joseph
West, Charles Wayne
West, John Calvin
West, Philip
Westbrook, James Earl
Westenburg, Richard
Westergaard, Peter Talbot
Westney, William (Frank)
Westphal, Frederick William
Wetzel, Richard Dean
Whaley, Garwood Paul
Whaley, Robert Louis
Whaples, Miriam K
Whear, Paul William
Wheeler, Janet
Wheeler, Lawrence Bennett
Whipple, Walter
Whisler, Bruce Allen
Whitcomb, Robert Butler
White, A Duane
White, (Edwin) Chappell
White, David Ashley
White, Donald Howard
White, Gary C(harles)
White, John Reeves
White, Michael
White, Robert Charles, Jr
Whitesides, William (Plaxico), Jr
Whitesitt, Linda Marie
Whittaker, Howard
Whittenberg, Charles
Wichmann, Russell George
Wickes, Frank Bovee
Widder, Roger Henry
Wienand, Marilyn M
Wienandt, Elwyn Arthur
Wienhorst, Richard William
Wienpahl, Robert William
Wiens, Frank
Wigglesworth, Frank
Wilcox, Eunice Ann
Wilcox, James H
Wilding-White, Raymond
Wiles, John A
Wiley, Frank (Earkett), Jr
Wilkey, Jay W
Wilkins, William Dean
Wilkinson, Arthur Scott
Will, Patrick Terence
Willett, Thelma Elizabeth
Willett, William
Willey, James Henry
Williams, David Russell
Williams, Edna (Charlotte)
Williams, Edward Vinson
Williams, Franklin Edmund
Williams, Grier Moffatt
Williams, Hermine Weigel
Williams, J(ohn) Wesley
Williams, Jan
Williams, Michael D
Williams, Robert Edward
Williamson, Marshall

Willis, Richard M
Willis, Thomas C
Willman, Fred R
Willmering, Kevin Douglas
Willoughby, David Paul
Wills, Vera G
Wilson, C(ecil) B(arley)
Wilson, George Balch
Wilson, James Edward
Wilson, Keith Leroy
Wilson, Sydney Virginia
Wilson, Thomas E
Winesanker, Michael M
Winick, Steven David
Winkler, Peter Kenton
Winsor, Philip Gordon
Winstead, William
Winter, Daniel Wallace
Winter, James Hamilton
Winter, Joel
Wintle, James R
Winzenburger, Walter Paul
Wisneskey, Robert
Wisniewski, Thomas Joseph
Wittekind, Donald H
Wolcott, Vernon
Wolf, Edward Christopher
Wolf, Eugene Kendrick
Wolfe, Lawrence
Wolff, Arthur Sheldon
Wolff, Christian
Wolff, Christoph Johannes
Wolff, Konrad
Wolking, Henry Clifford
Wolverton, Byron A
Wong, Betty Anne (Siu Junn)
Wood, Elizabeth
Wood, Joseph (Roberts)
Wood, Vivian Poates
Wood, William Frank
Woodard, James P
Woodbury, Ward Leland
Woodhall, Dennis Robert
Woodward, Ann (McClure)
Woodward, Gregory Stanley
Woodward, Henry L(ynde)
Woollen, Russell
Worby, Rachael
Wormhoudt, Pearl Shinn
Worstell, Ronald A
Wortman, Allen L
Wrancher, Elizabeth Ann
Wright, Al G (Alfred George)
Wright, Elizabeth
Wright, Geoffrey Dorian
Wright, Josephine R B
Wright, Peter B, III
Wrzesien, William
Wurtzler, Bela
Wyatt, Larry D
Wyatt, Lucius Reynolds
Wyatt, Scott Alan
Wylie, Ruth Shaw
Wylie, Ted David
YaDeau, William Ronald
Yajima, Hiroko
Yakim, Moni
Yamron, Janet M
Yancich, Milan Michael
Yannay, Yehuda
Yannuzzi, William A(nthony)
Yarden, Elie
Yates, Ronald Lee
Yellin, Victor Fell
Yeo, Douglas Edward
Young, Anne Lloyd
Young, Clyde William
Young, Phyllis
Young, Raymond G
Young, William Thomas
Youngblood, Joseph Edward
Youngs, Lowell Vere
Yttrehus, Rolv
Zack, George Jimmy
Zajicek, Jeronym
Zakarian-Rutstein, Sedmara

Zalkind, Larry Howard
Zallman, Arlene
Zambara, Edward
Zander, Benjamin David
Zander, Patricia
Zaplatynsky, Andrew
Zaretsky, Michael
Zarzeczna, Marion
Zaslavsky, Dora
Zaslaw, Neal
Zastrow, Joyce Ruth
Zdechlik, John Paul
Zei, John
Zeigler, John Robert
Zeitlin, Zvi
Zeller, Gary L
Zerounian, Ara
Zes, Tikey A
Zibits, Paul Joseph
Zimmerman, Franklin Bershir
Zinn, Michael A
Zonn, Wilma Zapora
Zorn, Jay D
Zsigmondy, Denes
Zuckerman, Mark Alan
Zumwald-Howard, R Reid
Zupko, Ramon
Zuponcic, Veda Helen
Zwicky, Gary Lee
Zytowski, Carl Byrd

INSTRUMENTALIST

Bassoon

Arbtiter, Eric A
Barrett, Paul H
Bartlett, Loren W
Beasley, Rule Curtis
Bedford, Judith Eileen
Berkenstock, James Turner
Bevers, Michael Earl
Boyd, Rodney Carney
Broemel, Robert W
Byo, Donald William
Cooper, Lewis Hugh
Cukro, Gregory
DeBolt, David Albert
Degen, Bruce N
Elliot, Willard Somers
Farrar, David
Feinsmith, Marvin P
Ferris, Kirkland David
Fisher, Douglas John
Ganson, Paul
Garfield, Bernard Howard
Ghiglia, Oscar Alberto
Gillette, John Carrell
Goldstein, Lauren
Goltzer, Harold
Goslee, George
Grossman, Arthur
Hansen, James A
Hightower, Gail
Hindell, Leonard
Jeter, James Yandell
Jones, Wendal S
Klimko, Ronald James
Kolker, Phillip A M
Kubey, Arthur M
Lacy, Edwin V
Leech, Alan Bruce
Lipp, Charles Herbert
Longazo, George
Mac Court, Donald Vincent
McCracken, Charles, Jr
Maret, Stanley
Marsh, Jack Odell
Maul, Eric (William)
Maxym, Stephen
Miller, John William, Jr

INSTRUMENTALIST (cont)

Mueller, Frederick A
Munday, Kenneth Edward
Nielubowski, Norbert John
Pasmanick, Kenneth
Paulson, Stephen Jon
Pfeuffer, Robert John
Polisi, Joseph William
Polisi, William
Popkin, Mark Anthony
Pugh, Russell Oris
Raitt, John Wellesley
Rausch, Jack D
Reid, John William
Ruggiero, Matthew
Sahuc, Nolan John
Schaffer, Robert Carlton
Scheller, Stanley
Schoenbach, Sol Israel
Schweitzer, Marsha L
Sharrow, Leonard
Sherman, Norman Morris
Simpson, Wilbur Herman
Stewart, Larry Joe
Svoboda, Richard Alan
Thompson, Robert K
Tyree, Ronald Wayne
Van Geem, Jack William, Jr
Vogel, Howard Levi
Walt, Sherman Abbott
Wangler, Francis (Frank) D
Weichlein, William Jesset
Weisberg, Arthur
Weiss, Abraham M
Whipple, R(ichard) James
Wisneskey, Robert
Zlotkin, Frederick

Cello

Adamson, Janis John
Alton, Ardyth
Babini, Italo (S)
Bailey, James
Benedetti, Evangeline
Bernstein, Jacob
Blankers, Laurens A(rthur)
Bock, Richard C
Brewer, Linda Judd
Brons, Martha (Parker)
Buranskas, Karen
Carr, Eugene V
Chazanoff, Daniel
Cherry, Philip
Christensen, Roy Harry
Ciechanski, Aleksander
Cole, Orlando T
Colf, Howard
Conable, William G, Jr
Cooke, (John) Antony
Coppock, Bruce
de Lemos, Jurgen Hermann
Deutsch, Robert Larry
Dines, Burton
Drinkall, Roger Lee
Druian, Joseph
Dumm, Bryan James
Eddy, Timothy
Emerson, Stephen Harold
Epperson, Gordon
Erdody, Stephen John
Farago, Marcel
Farrell, Peter Snow
Feldman, Marion
Fischer, Norman Charles
Frame, Pamela
Garbousova, Raya (Raya
  Garbousova-Biss)
Gatwood, Carole Grace
Geber, Stephen
Gerschefski, Martha
Goode, Daniel
Granger, Lawrence Gordon
Greenhouse, Bernard
Grossman, Jerry Michael
Grubb, William

Haber, Michael Press
Hanani, Yehuda
Harlow, Richard Ernest
Harrell, Lynn
Harris, Alan
Harry, William (Thomas)
Haxton, (Richard) Kenneth
Heiss, David Henry
Heller, Marian
Hirsu, Valentin
Horvath, Janet
Hoyle, Wilson Theodore
Jahn, Theodore Lee
Jeanrenaud, Joan (Joan
  Gleeson)
Jelinek, Jerome
Josephson, Kenneth George
Kaderavek, Karen Beth
Kapuscinski, Richard
Karmazyn, Dennis
Kates, Stephen Edward
Katz, Paul
Kemp, Kathleen Murphy
Kessler, Jerome
King, Terry Bower
Kono, Toshihiko
Kreger, James
Krieger, Jeffrey Stephen
Krosnick, Joel
Lapin, Geoffrey
Laut, Edward Allen
Lehr, Catherine (Catherine
  Lehr Ramos)
Leonard, Ronald
Lesser, Laurence
Levy, Frank E
Lewis, Jungshin Lim
Lipman, Michael (Avram)
Lockington, David Kirkman
Ma, Yo-Yo
McCracken, Charles P
McCrory, Martha
Machover, Tod
Madura, Robert Hayes
Magyar, Gabriel
Mallory, (Walter) Hampton
Mallory, Lauren Scott
Martin, Carolann Frances
Mason, Neale Bagley
Mayes, Samuel H
Miller, Jonathan David
Mitzelfelt, H(arold) Vincent
Moore, David Willard
Moore, Douglas Bryant
Morganstern, Daniel Robert
Mulfinger, George Leonidas, Jr
Mushabac, Regina
Musser, Betty Jean
Nelsova, Zara
Oberle, Freya Ellen
Oliver, Nils
Orlovsky, Arkady
Parisot, Aldo Simoes
Parker, Alan
Parnas, Leslie
Pologe, Steven
Procter, Carol Ann
Rabson, Carolyn R
Randman, Bennett Charles
Reese, Gilbert
Rejto, Gabor M
Rejto, Peter A
Remenikova, Tanya
Richardson, Louis Samuel
Riley, John Arthur
Ripley, Robert
Robboy, R(onald) A
Robinson, Sharon
Roebuck, Karen Lee
Romanul, Michael (Francis)
Rose, Leonard (Joseph)
Rosen, Marcy (Beth)
Rosen, Nathaniel Kent
Rostropovich, Mstislav
Rudiakov, Michael
Saks, Toby
Saltzman, David Richard

Sant Ambrogio, John
Savig, Norman Ingolf
Schneider, Mischa
Schuster, Savely
Selberg, John Ryan
Shapinsky, Aaron
Shapiro, Harvey
Sharp, John Mark
Simmons, Eula Mary Schock
Skidmore, William R
Skobba, Daryl S
Smetana, Frantisek
Smith, Wayne C
Solow, Jeffrey (Gilman)
Soyer, David
Spotts, Carleton B
Starker, Janos
Steiner, Frances Josephine
Stoughton, Michael Gordon
Thomas, Ronald
Thompson, Barbara Gatwood
Tobias, Paul
Toth, Andor, Jr
Trevor, Kirk David Niell
Tung, Yuan
Vanasco, Francesca Adele
Virizlay, Mihaly E
Virizlay, Paula Skolnick
Wells, David
Wentzel, Rubi V
White, John D
Wolfe, Harvey (S)
Wolfrom, Lyle Clark
Young, Phyllis

Clarinet

Aaholm, Philip Eugene
Allard, Joseph
Annis, Robert Lyndon
Baker, Norman Louis
Balter, Alan (Neil)
Beerman, Burton
Berta, Joseph Michel
Bloom, Lawrie
Boggs, Martha Daniel
Brody, Clark L
Bunke, Jerome Samuel
Campione, Carmine
Chapman, Basil
Coggins, Willis Robert
Cohen, Franklin R
Cokkinias, Peter Leonidas
Creditor, Bruce Mitchell
Dagon, Russell
Denman, John Anthony
Drapkin, Michael Lewis
Drucker, Stanley
Dufallo, Richard John
East, James Edward
Errante, Frank Gerard
Estrin, Mitchell S
Forcucci, Samuel L
Forrest, Sidney
Gainacopulos, Kay Thomas
Gallo, Paul Arthur
Garlick, Nancy Buckingham
Gilad, Yehuda
Gilbert, Richard
Gillespie, James Ernest
Glazer, David
Gold, Cecil Viner
Goldsmith, Richard Neil
Greenleaf, Robert Bruce
Grim, William Edward
Hadcock, Peter
Hale, Ruth June
Haritun, Rosalie Ann
Harman, David Rex
Heim, Norman Michael
Helmers, William Alan
Hill, Robert James
Hiller, Roger Lewis
Hills, Richard L
Jackson, Bil
Jones, George Morton

Kaye, Bernard L
Kelly, Michael Thomas
Kireilis, Ramon J
Krakauer, David
Lamneck, Esther Evangeline
Lang, Rosemary Rita
Larsen, Henry
Laughton, John Charles
Lewis, David S
Listokin, Robert
Livingston, James Francis
Lizotte, Andre
London, Lawrence Bernard
Loomis, James Phillip
Ludewig-Verdehr, Elsa
Lurie, Mitchell
McColl, William D
McDonald, Lawrence
McKinney, Roger William
McLaughlin, Marian
Manning, William Meredith
Meidt, Joseph Alexis
Mellott, George Kenneth
Monsen, Ronald Peter
Montanaro, Donald
Nichols, David Clifford
Nordstrom, Craig Kyle
Nunemaker, Richard Earl
Ober, Carol Jean
Paradise, Timothy James
Pasztor, Stephen
Pena, Angel Matias
Poto, Attilio
Pyne, James
Rabbai, Joseph
Radnofsky, Nancy
Rehfeldt, Phillip Richard
Rhoads, William Earl
Rose, C Robert
Russell, James Reagan
Russianoff, Leon
Russo, Charles
Russo, John
Salander, Roger Mark
Schroeder, Raymond Lee
Schwadron, Abraham Abe
Scott, Roger
Seltzer, George
Shifrin, David
Silberman, Aaron
Silfies, George
Simenauer, Peter
Simenauer, Peter W
Singer, David
Snavely, Jack
Sperl, Gary Robert
Stanek, Alan Edward
Stanford, Thomas Stanley
Stewart, Don (Donald George)
Stoltzman, Richard Leslie
Swift, John David
Thimmig, Les (Leslie Leland)
Tichman, Herbert
Tillotson, Laura Virginia
Tower, Ibrook
Tromblee, Maxell Ray
Viola, Joseph E
Viscuglia, Felix Alfred
Weber, David
Webster, Michael
Weidensee, Victor J
West, Charles Wayne
Westphal, Frederick William
Williams, Robert Edward
Wilson, Keith Leroy
Wojciak, Robert H
Wright, Peter B, III
Wrzesien, William
Young, Anne Lloyd
Zeigler, John Robert
Zetzer, Alfred

Double Bass

Albright, Philip H
Anderson, Robert Peter
Barker, Edwin Bogue
Beadle, Anthony
Bell, (S) Aaron
Benfield, Warren A
Bianco, Anthony
Bozicevich, Ronald Raymond
Bradetich, Jeff
Brauninger, Eva Jeannine
Clark, John Frederick
Cousin, Jack
Cunningham, Arthur
Curtis, William H
Deak, Jon
Derthick, Thomas V(inton)
DeWitt, Andrew Ransom
Drew, Lucas
Elan, Terry Michael
Fishman, Jack Adam
Flowerman, Martin
Fly, Fenton G
Green, Barry L
Grodner, Murray
Haigh, Scott (Richard)
Hearne, Joseph Frederic
Janowsky, Maxim Dubrow
Jobelmann, Herman Frederick
Karr, Gary Michael
Krolick, Edward (John)
Levine, Julius
Lewis, Henry
Loew, Henry
McLain, Robert Malcolm
Manning, Robert
Martin, Donald R
Mathews, John Fenton
Mercurio, Peter Amedeo
Michii, Makoto
Neubert, Bernard David
Neubert, Henry Grim, Jr
Obrecht, Eldon Ross
Olson, Phyllis Edward
Parchman, Gen Louis
Plucker, John P
Potter, David Kinsman
Prell, Donald D
Proto, Frank
Pugh, Darryl L
Ranney, Susan
Rickett, Peter John
Rifel, Craig Thomas
Rofe, Peter Michael
Roy, Gene Burdick
Ruggeri, Roger Benjamin
Scelba, Anthony J
Schaeffer, John A
Schmidt, Dale
Scott, Henry G
Suttle, Clark Etienne
Thoreson, Thomas J
Tolo, Leland Stanford
Tramontozzi, Stephen
Trembly, Dennis M
Turetzky, Bertram Jay
Van Sickle, Rodney James
Vayspapir, Roma
Walter, David
Winters, George Archer
Wolf, Andrew Leonard
Wolf, Michael B
Wolfe, Lawrence
Wolfrom, Lyle Clark
Wurtzler, Bela
Yasui, Byron K
Zibits, Paul Joseph
Zugelj, Ivan Petar (John Peter
    Zugel)

Electronic

Amacher, Maryanne
Brinkman, Alexander R
Ciani, Suzanne E

Cross, Lowell Merlin
Curran, Alvin S
Deutsch, Herbert Arnold
Dresher, Paul Joseph
Duesenberry, John F
Ehle, Robert Cannon
Ellis, Merrill
Gilbert, Michael William
Gnazzo, Anthony Joseph
Kramer, Gregory Paul
Kreiger, Arthur V
Lehrman, Paul David
Lerman, Richard M
Lopez, Peter Dickson
Martin, Judith Lynn
Mumma, Gordon
Oakes, Rodney Harland
Philo, Gary Bruce
Ross, Eric
Sislen, Myrna (Carol)
Smith, Catherine Parsons
Snopek, Sigmund
Snow, David Jason
Tecayehuatzin, Victor Saucedo
Weidenarr, Reynold Henry
White, Ruth S

Flute and Piccolo

Aarons, Martha Irene
Archer, Mary Ann
Ashmead, Elizabeth
Baker, Julius
Baron, Samuel
Bennett, Harold
Berg, Jacob
Bliss, Marilyn
Bogorad, Julia (Anne)
Borouchoff, Israel
Bottje, Will Gay
Boyd, Bonita K
Brown, Myrna Weeks
Bryan, Keith (Walburn)
Buyse, Leone Karena
Chapuis, Isabelle
Chauncey, Beatrice Arlene
Colvig, David
Cowden, Susan Jane
D'Ambrose, Joseph Lawrence
Dick, Robert J
Dickey, Louise (Parke)
Dombourian-Eby, Zartouhi
Dunkel, Paul Eugene
Dwyer, Doriot Anthony
Ellison, Greer (Greer Ellison
    Wolfson)
Ephross, Arthur J
Epple, Carol
Fajardo, Raoul J
Folkers, Catherine Eileen
Fouse, Sarah Baird
Fritter, Priscilla
Galway, James
Gardner, Kay
Garside, Patricia Ann
Gettel, Courtland D
Gilb, Tyra Ellen
Giles, Anne Diener
Gilman, Irvin Edward
Gippo, Jan Eirik
Gold, Diane Wehner
Goldberg, Bernard Z
Goodberg, Robert Edward
Goodfellow, Susan Stucklen
Graf, Erich Louis
Grass, William
Green, Andrew
Grenier, Victoria R
Guenther, Ralph R
Hall, Carl David
Hankle, Marcia Griglak
Harling, Jean M
Harriss, Elaine Atkins
Hatcher, Paula Braniff
Heiss, John Carter
Hester, Byron

Hill, Pamela Jean
Hoover, Eric John
Hoover, Katherine L
Hopkins, Barbara Avis
Jones, William John
Juhos, Joseph Frank
Kaufman, Mindy F
Kaye, Bernard L
Kearney, Linda (Yvonne)
Khaner, Jeffrey M
Klick, Susan Marie
Kniebusch, Carol Lee
Kohno, Toshiko
Kotik, Petr
Kout, Trix
Kraber, Karl
Krell, John
Kriewall, Judy (Judith
    Washburn Kriewall)
Kujala, Walfrid Eugene
Lake, Bonnie (Josephine)
Lasocki, David Ronald
    Graham
Leech, Karen Davidson
Leibundguth, Barbara
Levitin, Susan
Levy, Gerardo
Lichtmann, Margaret S
Lolya, Andrew
Magg, Kyril
Mason, Lucas (Roger)
Mather, Betty Bang (Betty
    Louise Mather)
Mather, Roger Frederick
Mayfield, Lynette
Mendenhall, Judith
Miller, Dean Harold
Monteux, Claude
Montgomery, William Layton
Murray, Alexander Douglass
Nobel, (Virginia) Ann
Noone, Lana Mae
Nyfenger, Thomas
Oberbrunner, John
Osborne, Charles Eugene
Panitz, Murray W
Parloff, Michael (Leon)
Peck, Donald Vincent
Pellerite, James John
Rampal, Jean-Pierre
Rautenberg, John Leslie
Rearick, Martha Nell
Richman, Robin (Beth)
Risdon, Frances Lee
Robison, Paula Judith
Rosenfeld, Jayn Frances
Schaefer, Lois Elizabeth
Sharp, Maurice
Shostac, David
Silver, Martin A
Simosko, Valerie
Simpson, Mary Jean
Skidmore, Dorothy Louise
Smith, J Fenwick
Solum, John H
Spencer, Patricia
Stackhouse, Holly N
Stallman, Robert
Star, Cheryl Mc Whorter
Starin, Stefani Borissa
Stevens, Roger S
Stokes, Sheridon Willard
Sturms, Arnolds Fricis
Swanson, Philip John
Thomas, Mark Stanton
Threatte, Linda Krebs
Timm, Everett L
Timm, (M) Jeanne Anderson
Trahan, Kathleen Frances
Trauffer, Barbara Olive
Trenkamp, (Wilma) Anne
Trott, Laurence
Vornholt, David
Waitzman, Daniel R
Waln, Ronald Lee
Weinreb, Alice Kogan
Weiss, Dawn Adrienne

Weller, Janis Ferguson
Wilson, Ransom Charles
Wincenc, Carol
Wion, John H
Woodward, Martha Clive
Yoshioka, Emmett Gene

French Horn

Amram, David Werner
Bakkegard, (Benjamin) David
Barnewitz, A William
Baxter, Charles Allen
Bell, Charles E
Berv, Harry
Birdwell, Edward Ridley
Blice, Carolyn MacDowell
Bushouse, M David
Cantor, Owen Polk
Capps, William
Cecere, Anthony Robert
Chambers, James
Decker, James
De Intinis, Ranier
Dressler, John Clay
Dunn, Frank Richard
Epstein, Eli K
Evans, Peter (Hollingshead)
Exline, Wendell L
Fako, Nancy Jordan
Farkas, Philip Francis
Faust, Randall Edward
Fearing, Scott M
Franano, Frank Salvatore
Fries, Robert McMillan
Gardner, Randy Clyburn
Gast, Michael C
Gingrich, Daniel J
Gross, Steven Lee
Hager, Lawson J
Hardin, Burton Ervin
Hatfield, Michael
Henigbaum, John
Huntley, Lawrence Don
Ingraham, Paul
Jones, Mason
Kaslow, David Martin
Katzen, Daniel
Kearns, William Kay
Kellock, James Robert
Kennedy, (Charles) Bryan
Kihslinger, Mary Ruth
Kirschen, Jeffry M
Krehbiel, Arthur David
Kurau, W(arren) Peter
Landsman, Julie
Leonard, Peter
Leuba, (Julian) Christopher
Lewis, Lucinda
McCann, William John
McCoy, Wesley Lawrence
Mackey, Richard
Mansur, Paul Max
Masarie, Jack F
Mascaro, Arnold John, Jr
Merker, K Ethel
Miller, Clyde Elmer
Newell, Thomas E, Jr
Orgel, Seth Henry
Pandolfi, Roland
Peterson, Hal (Harold
    Vaughan)
Philpott, Larry LaFayette
Pierce, Robert
Pink, Howard Norman
Pinkow, David J
Portone, Frank Anthony, Jr
Powell, Keith Dom
Powers, Jeffrey Steven
Price, Richard Galen
Reiswig, David Earl
Renwick, Wilke Richard
Rife, Jean
Root, Rebecca Jo
Rosenberg, Donald Scott
Ross, Walter Beghtol

INSTRUMENTALIST (cont)

Rossi, John L
Routch, Robert Edson
Sanders, Neill Joseph
Schiebler, Carl Robert
Schweikert, Norman Carl
Sellers, Jacquelyn Marie
Slocum, William (Bennett)
Smith, Martin Dodge
Songer, Lewis Alton
Sprung, David Reichert
Stacy, William Barney
Stout, Louis James
Strack, Kenneth John
Straka, Paul Scott
Taylor, Paul Wegman
Tuckwell, Barry Emmanuel
Van Norman, Clarendon Ess, Jr
Wagnitz, Ralph David
Weliver, E Delmer
White, Elwood Lauriston
Windham, Verne
Winter, James Hamilton
Winter, Joel
Yancich, Charles Theodore
Yancich, Milan Michael

Guitar and Lute

Almeida, Laurindo
Anderson, Neil
Arnold, Louis
Artzt, Alice Josephine
Baldassarre, Joseph Anthony
Barbosa-Lima, Carolos
Barrueco, Manuel
Bault, Diane Lynn
Bergman, Janet Louise Marx
Blain, Albert Valdes
Brandon, Robert Eugene
Bream, Julian
Breznikar, Joseph (John)
Burleson, Spencer (J), III
Calderon, Javier Francisco
Carmen, Marina (Carmen Manteca Gioconda)
Champlin, Terry (Arthur Doyle), III
Charkey, Stanley
Chobanian, Loris Ohannes
Cozad, Joseph
Cudek, Mark S
Curry, Donna (Jayne)
Del Forno, Anton
Denning, Darryl (L)
Dollitz, Grete Franke
Duarte, John William
Duncan, Charles F, Jr
Dydo, John Stephen
Falaro, Anthony J
Falletta, JoAnn
Fisk, Eliot Hamilton
Flower, Edward John Fordham
Fogler, Michael Landy
Gaab, Thomas Anthony
Geoghegan, James Hugh
Ghiglia, Oscar Alberto
Gomez, Vicente
Goodman, Jeffrey David
Graves, Terry Allen
Griggs, Peter Johnson
Hand, Frederic Warren
Harlan, Christoph
Harmon, Roger Dean
Heck, Thomas F
Hellermann, William David
Holmquist, John Edward
Isbin, Sharon
Jaffee, Michael
Johanson, Bryan
Kendall, Christopher Wolff
Korn, Mitchell
Leisner, David
Lorimer, Michael
Mentschukoff, Andrej

Moore, James, III
Newman, Michael Allan
Niedt, Douglas Ashton
Norman, Theodore
O'Dette, Paul Raymond
Parkening, Christoper W
Pick, Richard Samuel Burns
Pinnell, Richard Tilden
Postiewate, Charles Willard
Provost, Richard (Charles)
Purcell, Ron (Ronald Charles)
Randolph, (Alice) Laurie
Robison, John Orian
Romero, Angel
Romero, Celedonio P
Rosado, Ana Maria
Russell, Craig Henry
Sakellariou, George
Schneider, John Owsley
Segovia, Andre
Silva, Jesus
Smith, Douglas Alton
Smith, James F
Smith, Michael Cedric
Starobin, David
Strizich, Catherine Liddell
Strizich, Robert (Ward)
Stucky, Rodney
Sullivan, Robert Paul
Valdes-Blain, Rolando
Van, Jeffrey Wylie
Verdery, Benjamin Francis
Wieckowski, Joanna G
Wirt, John (Stephen)

Harp

Allen, Nancy
Allen, Susan Elizabeth
Anstine, Georgia Rebecca
Balderston, Suzanne
Barber, Gail (Guseman)
Berman, Ruth (Ruth Berman Harris)
Bride, Kathleen
Bullen, Sarah
Chalifoux, Alice (Alice Chalifoux Rideout)
Costello, Marilyn
Csonka, Margarita (Margarita C Montanaro)
DeCray, Marcella
de Vale, Sue Carole
de Volt, Artiss
Druzinsky, Edward
Elster, Reinhardt
Gundersheimer, Muriel (Blumberg)
Hartzell, Marjorie Helen
Henderson, Jeanne Margaret
Henschen, Dorothy Adele
Hobson, Ann Stephens (Ann Hobson-Pilot)
Hujsak, (Ruth) Joy
Ilku, Elyse (Elizabeth Jean Ilku)
Inglefield, Ruth Karin
Israelievitch, Gail Bass
John, Patricia Spaulding
Jolles, Susan
Kelly, Danis Grace
Lawrence, Lucille
Lawson, Alice (Alice Lawson Aber)
LeBaron, Anne
McDonald, Susann Hackett
Maiorescu, Dorella Teodora
Malone, (Mary) Eileen
Mitchell, (Mary) Emily
Mossafer-Rind, Bernice
Nieweg, Clinton F
Rensch, Roslyn (Roslyn Maria Rensch-Erbes)
Roman, Mary Brigid
Rosen, Myor
Ross, Judith

Royce, Maria M
Schroeder-Sheker, Therese M
Suchy, Jessica Ray
Tietov, Frances
Turner, Lynne Alison
Von Wurtzler, Aristid
Weidensaul, Jane Bennett
Wilson, Sydney Virginia
Woods, Sylvia
Zighera, Bernard

Harpsichord

Alderdice, Mary
Allanbrook, Douglas Phillips
Benham, Helen Wheaton
Brewer, Edward
Burman-Hall, Linda Carol
Christie, James David
Conant, Robert S
Cooper, Kenneth
Crawford, Lisa
Cunningham, Walker Evans
Curtis, Alan
Duehlmeier, Susan Hunter
Erickson, Raymond
Espinosa, Alma O
Ferguson, Ray Pylant
Ferre, Susan Ingrid
Fuller, Albert
Gibbons, John
Goodman, Roger
Gronquist, Robert E
Gustafson, Bruce
Hammond, Frederick Fisher
Hansell, Sven H
Harris, C David
Hashimoto, Eiji
Hays, Elizabeth L
Henderson, Ian H
Hudson, Barton
Hurd, Peter Wyeth
Jacob, Karen Hite
James, Layton Bray
Katz, Helen-Ursula
Kipnis, Igor
Kirkpatrick, Ralph
Kobler, Linda
Lee, Alfred E
Lewis, Harmon
Liberman, Barbara (Lee)
Little, Meredith Ellis
Lunde, Nanette Gomory
McIntosh, Kathleen Ann
Mathews, Shirley
Norell, Judith Regina
Ornstein, Doris
Palmer, Larry Garland
Party, Lionel
Pattengale, Robert Richard
Pearlman, Martin
Ping-Robbins, Nancy R(egan)
Pruett, Lilian Pibernik
Rakich, Christa Martin
Roberts, Gertrud K
Rogell, Irma
Russell, Lucy Hallman
Scheibert, Beverly
Schuitema, Joan Elizabeth
Shangrow, George Arthur
Spizizen, Louise (Myers)
Young, Wendy
Yount, Max Hoffman

Oboe and English Horn

Apostle, Nicholas
Bentley, John E
Bloom, Robert
Caldwell, James Boone
Capps, Ferald Buell, Jr
Celli, Joseph Robert
Christ, Peter
Clemens, Earl L
Cohen, Fredric Thomas

Corina, John Hubert
Crane, John Thomas
Danfelt, Lewis S(eymour)
de Lancie, John
Douvas, Elaine
Duncan, Dan J (Danny Joe)
Dunkel, Stuart
Edlefsen, Blaine Ellis
Elliot, Gladys Crisler
Farmer, Nancy Louise
Fitch, Benjamin Robert
Fowler, Nancy
Genovese, Alfred
Giacobassi, Julie Ann
Gnam, Adrian
Goltzer, Albert
Gordon, Roderick Dean
Gorton, James Allen
Green, Gene Marie
Griebling, Margaret Ann
Harrison, E Earnest
Harrod, William V
Herr, Barbara
Horein, Kathleen Marie
Hyde, Frederick B(ill)
Kanter, Richard S
Kaplan, Melvin Ira
Krause, Robert James
Leonard, Nels, Jr
Le Roux, Jean-Louis
Levin, Rami Yona
Lucarelli, Bert (Humbert J)
Lynch, William Frank
McFarland, J Patrick
Mack, John
Mascaro, Janet Persons
Miller, Anne Winsor
Nelson, Lorna C
O'Connor, Thomas E
Ostryniec, James Paul
Pederson, Ilonna Ann
Pollak, Carolyn Sue
Post, Nora
Prodan, James Christian
Rapier, Wayne
Reeve, Basil
Roseman, Ronald Ariah
Russell, Rogene
Sargeant, Phillip Lester
Sargous, Harry Wayne
Schuster, Earl Vincent
Secrist, Barbera Shaw
Secrist, Phylis Jane
Shulman, Ivan Alexander
Shultz, Dan McLloyd
Sirucek, Jerry Edward
Smith, Pamela G
Smoliar, Harold M
Sprenkle, Robert Louis
Stacy, Thomas
Stalzer, Frank S
Staup, Rebecca Lynn
Steinke, Greg A
Stephenson, Robert John
Still, Ray
Tatman, Neil
Thorstenberg, (John) Laurence
Timm, Larry M (Laurance Milo)
Veazey, Charles Orlando
Ventura, Brian Joseph
Wann, Lois
Weiss, David E
West, Philip
Widder, Roger Henry
Winters, Barbara Jo
Wood, Lorna
Woods, Pamela Pecha
Zonn, Wilma Zapora

Organ

Albright, William Hugh
Altman, Ludwig
Anderson, Robert (Theodore)
Arnold, Corliss Richard

INSTRUMENTALIST (cont)

Aurand, Charles Henry, Jr
Barlow, Wayne Brewster
Beall, Lee Morrett
Becker, C(ecil) Warren
Berk, Maynard
Berlinski, Herman
Billings, David Arthur
Billmeyer, Dean Wallace
Bitgood, Roberta (Roberta
    Bitgood Wiersma)
Blankers, Laurens A(rthur)
Bodine, Willis (Ramsey), Jr
Boe, David S
Bolitho, Albert George
Bozeman, George Lewis, Jr
Bradshaw, Murray Charles
Braithwaite, James Roland
Bratt, C(harles) Griffith
Brauchli, Bernard Marc
Brewer, Edward
Brown, Rayner
Bruch, Delores Ruth
Brunelle, Philip Charles
Bullat, George J Nicholas
Bush, Douglas Earl
Campbell, John Coleman
Chapman, Keith (Ronald)
Christie, James David
Clapp, Lois Steele
Clark, Thomas Terrence
Cole, Malcolm Stanley
Cook, Peter Francis
Cooper, William B(enjamin)
Corzine, Michael
Craighead, David
Crosbie, William Perry
Cross, Ronald
Crozier, Catharine (Catharine
    C Gleason)
Cunningham, Walker Evans
Curley, Carlo
Davis, Paul
Diemer, Emma Lou
Disselhorst, Delbert Dean
Doty, Ezra William
Dunbar, Paul Edward
Dunn, Thomas Burt
Elmore, Robert Hall
Farr, David Donald
Ferguson, Ray Pylant
Ferre, Susan Ingrid
Fienen, David Norman
Finster, Robert Milton
Fromm, Herbert
Fusner, Henry Shirley
Fyfe, Peter McNeely
Gauger, Ronald Raymond
Gillock, Jon
Goode, Jack C
Gotwals, Vernon D
Grady, John Francis
Groom, Lester Herbert
Guenther, Eileen Morris
Guinaldo, Norberto
Gutberg, Ingrid
Hamilton, Jerald
Hancock, Eugene Wilson
    (White)
Hancock, Gerre (Edward)
Hancock, Judith Eckerman
Hannum, Harold Byron
Hansen, Edward Allen
Harmon, Thomas Fredric
Hart, Kenneth Wayne
Hayashi, Yuko
Hays, William Paul
Heaton, Charles Huddleston
Heinrich, Adel Verna
Herr, John David
Hettrick, Jane Schatkin
Hill, (Walter) Kent
Holloway, Clyde
Holmberg, Mark Leonard
Homan, Frederic Warren
Hughes, John (Gilliam)
Insko, Wyatt (Marion), III

Jacobs, Charles Gilbert
Johnson, Calvert
Johnson, David Nathaniel
Jones, Joyce
Jordan, Paul
Keiser, Marilyn Jean
Kibbie, James Warren
Kosowicz, Francis John
Krapf, Gerhard W
Krigbaum, Charles Russell
Lafford, Lindsay Arthur
Lallerstedt, Ford Mylius
Lawrence, Joy Elizabeth
Lemmon, Alfred Emmette
Lewis, Harmon
Lindberg, William Edward
Little, Wm A(lfred)
Litton, James Howard
Locklair, Dan Steven
Lohuis, Ardyth J
Lord, Robert Sutherland
McKinnon, James William
Maki, Paul-Martin
Mansfield, Kenneth Zoellin
Manwell, Philip
Markey, George B
Martel, Fernand
Mason, Marilyn
May, Ernest Dewey
Moe, Lawrence Henry
Moeser, James Charles
Moulder, Earline
Moyer, Karl Eby
Mueller, John Storm
Murray, Thomas
Nanney, Herbert (Boswell)
Nelson, Lorna C
Norris, Kevin Edward
Nyquist, Roger Thomas
Obetz, John Wesley
Ogasapian, John Ken
Orr, Nathaniel Leon
Owen, Barbara
Parrigin, Perry Goggin
Paukert, Karel
Peek, Richard Maurice
Pethel, James L
Pizzaro, David Alfred
Radu, Valentin
Rakich, Christa Martin
Raver, Leonard
Rhodes, Cherry
Rifel, Craig Thomas
Rose, John
Ross, Rick
Ross, William James
Rothe, David H
Royer, Paul Harold
Rubsam, Wolfgang Friedrich
Runner, David Clark
Salistean, Kim(berly) Osborne
Schilling, Charles Walter
Schober, Brian
Schwann, William Joseph
Sever, Allen Jay
Shaffer, (William) Allen
Shepp, Marian Gray
Shulze, Frederick Bennett
Siebert, Frederick Mark
Sifler, Paul John
Sirota, Victoria (Ressmeyer)
Stoner, Thomas Alan
Stringer, Alan W
Suitor, M Lee
Sunden, Ralph Edward
Sutherland, Donald S
Sutton, Mary Ellen
Swann, Frederick Lewis
Swanson, Jean Phyllis
Taylor, Frank
Teague, William Chandler
Thomas, John M
Thomas, Paul Lindsley
Tickton, Jason Harold
Tusler, Robert Leon
Tuuk, Jonathan Alan
Van Wye, Benjamin David

Weaver, John B
Webb, Marianne
Welsh, Wilmer Hayden
Werling, Anita Eggert
Whipple, Walter
Whitehead, William John
Wilkins, William Dean
Wilson, Todd Rodney
Wolcott, Vernon
Wright, (Myron) Searle
Wyton, Alec
Zwicky, Gary Lee

Percussion

Adams, John (Luther)
Albin, William Robert
Alexander, Brad
Ames, F(rank) Anthony
Anderson, Dean
Anderson, Shirley Patricia
Anievas, Agustin
Bailey, Elden C
Baker, Don Russell
Baldwin, John
Beale, Everett Minot
Beck, John H
Bergeron, Thomas Martin
Berthold, Sherwood Francis
Bick, Donald Alan
Boardman, David Robeson
Bookspan, Michael L
Brown, Richard S
Cherry, Kalman
Cirone, Anthony J
Conti, Joseph John
Cook, Gary D
Copeland, Keith Lamont
Culp, Paula N
DeGroot, David Joseph
Denov, Sam
DePonte, Niel Bonaventure
Dowd, Charles (Robert)
Epstein, Frank Benjamin
Erickson, Gordon McVey
Faini, Philip James
Fein, David N
Firth, Vic (Everett Joseph)
Floyd, John (Morrison)
Fluegel, Neal Lalon
Frazeur, Ted C (Theodore C
    Frazeur)
Frock, George Albert
Gaber, George
Haas, Jonathan Lee
Hill, William Randall
Hinger, Fred Daniel
Hoffman, James
Hong, Sherman
Howard, (Dana) Douglas
Igelsrud, Douglas Bent
Jackson, Douglas
Jensen, Richard Marsh
Kasica, John
Kerrigan, William Paul
Kimmel, Corliss Ann
Knaack, Donald (Frank)
Kocmieroski, Matthew
Kohloff, Roland
Lang, Morris Arnold
Larkin, Bruce David
Latimer, James H
Lefever, Maxine Lane
Lemmon, Galen
Leonard, Stanley Sprenger
Lepak, Alexander
Lucchesi, Peggy (Margaret C
    Lucchesi)
Mabrey, Charlotte Newton
Morehead, Donald Keith
Moss, David Michael
Mueller, Erwin Carl
O'Donnell, Richard
Olmstead, Gary James
Otte, Allen Carl
Owen, Charles E

Pangborn, Robert C
Papastefan, John James
Patterson, William G
Peters, Gordon Benes
Peters, Mitchell
Petta, Robert Michael
Powley, E Harrison, III
Preiss, James
Price, Paul (William)
Ptaszynska, Marta
Pulk, Bruce Harry
Ranganathan, Tanjore
Remsen, Eric Spencer
Rife, Marilyn N
Roberts, William L
Rosenberger, Walter Emerson
Ross, James Ramsey
Russell, Lois Roberta Langley
Rydzynski, Michael Vincent
    Matthew
Schinstine, William Joseph
Schneiderman, William
Silverman, Alan John
Siwe, Thomas V
Small, Edward Pierce
Smith, Terry James
Snider, Ronald Joe
Soames, Cynthia Elizabeth
Soroka, John G
Sprott, John Rhulin
Stumpf, Carol L
Tundo, Samuel A
Van der Wyk, Jack Alex
Van Dyke, Gary John
Van Hyning, Howard
Vits, Billy (William Henry)
Watson, Kenneth E
Weiner, Richard
Werdesheim, Gary
Williams, Jan
Willmering, Kevin Douglas

Piano

Abbott, Michael
Abram, Blanche Schwartz
Acosta, Adolovni P
Adler, James R
Adonaylo, Raquel
Ahrold, Frank
Alderdice, Mary
Aldwell, Edward
Allen, Jane
Alstadter, Judith R
Alvarado, Marilu (Mrs Alan H
    Rapoport)
Amlin, Martin Dolph
Amper, Leslie Ruth
Anderson, Beth (Barbara
    Elizabeth Anderson)
Anderson, Donna K
Andy, Katja
Appleby, David P
Arden, David Mitchell
Arganbright, Nancy (Nancy
    Weekley)
Arnon, Baruch
Arrau, Claudio
Artymiw, Lydia (Tamara)
Arzruni, Sahan
Ashkenazy, Vladimir D
Ashley, Douglas Daniels
Atamian, Dickran Hugo
Atherton, David
Ax, Emanuel
Aybar, Francisco (Rene)
Bacon, David
Bacon, Ernst
Bacon-Shone, Frederic
Bagger, Louis S
Bailey, Barbara Elliott
Baisley, Robert William
Ballard, Gregory
Balsam, Artur
Banowetz, Joseph Murray
Barbagallo, James Angelo

INSTRUMENTALIST (cont)

Barber, Daniel Rowland
Barbosa, Antonio (G)
Bar-Illan, David J
Barnes, Larry John
Barnett, David
Barrow, Rebecca Anne
Bartholomew, Lynne
Barwick, Steven
Basquin, Peter John
Bastian, James
Bates, Leon
Battipaglia, Diana Mittler
Baumgartner, Paul Lloyd
Beaty, Daniel Joseph
Becker, Bonita Ruth
Beckon, Lettie Marie
Beegle, Raymond Bruce
Behrend, Jeanne
Belcher, Deborah Jean
Bell, Larry Thomas
Bell, Winston A
Below, Robert Claude
Bendell, Christine J
Benham, Helen Wheaton
Berg, Christopher (Paul)
Bergersen, Charlotte (Charlotte
    Bergersen Chevalier)
Berkowitz, Ralph
Berky, Carl R
Berl, Christine
Berlinghoff, Dan A
Bernstein, Seymour Abraham
Bilson, Malcolm
Bilyeu, Landon Alan
Black, Robert Carlisle
Blackwood, Easley
Blake, Ran
Bland, William Keith
Bloch, Boris
Bloch, Joseph
Blocker, Robert L
Blumenthal, Daniel Henry
Blumfield, Coleman
Bogin, Abba
Boldrey, Richard (Lee)
Bolet, Jorge
Boszormenyi-Nagy, Bela
Bowman, Peter
Boyajian, Armen
Boyarsky, Terry Linda
Boykan, Martin
Bracchi-Le Roux, Marta N
Bradshaw, David Rutherford
Brauer, Cecilia Gniewek
Brende, Alfred
Bricard, Nancy (Nancy
    Bricard Woods)
Brickman, Miriam
Bridger, Carolyn
Brings, Allen Stephen
Broido, Arnold Peace
Bronfman, Yefim
Brown, Merton Luther
Browning, John (S), Jr
Brush, Ruth Damaris
Buccheri, Elizabeth
Bucci, Thomas Vincent
Buchbinder, Rudolf
Bull, Storm
Burganger, Judith
Buys, Douglas
Cameron-Wolfe, Richard G
Camp, Max W
Campbell, Robert Gordon
Canin, Martin
Caraher, James H
Carlin, Maryse
Carlson, Jane E
Carra, Dalmo
Cass, Richard Brannan
Cave, Michael
Cecchini, Penelope C
Cedrone, Frank Joseph
Cera, Stephen Charles
Cerny, William Joseph
Chance, Nancy Laird

Chasins, Abram
Cheadle, Louise M
Cheadle, William G
Cherkassky, Shura
Chodos, Gabriel
Christopher, Karen Mary
Ciarlillo, Marjorie Ann
Cipolla, Wilma Reid
Cliburn, Van (Harry Lavan, Jr)
Cogley, Mark
Cohrs, Arthur Lothar
Cole, Ulric
Constanten, Thomas Charles
    Sture
Cordova, Richard Allan
Cotel, Morris Moshe
Covert, Mary Ann
Cowan, Robert (Holmes)
Cox, Jeff Reeve
Cray, Kevin E
Cribb, George Robert
Criss, William
Crochet, Evelyne
Crossley, Paul Christopher
    Richard
Crow, Todd
Crutcher, Frances Hill
Cumming, Richard (Jackson)
Dahlman, Barbro
Davidovich, Bella
Davidson, Tina
Davies, Dennis
Davis, Ivan
Davis, Sharon (Sharon Yvonne
    Davis Schmidt)
Deas, Richard Ryder
Decima, Terry
de Larrocha, Alicia (de la
    Calle)
DeMain, John Lee
De Moura Castro, Luiz
DeVan, William Lewis, Jr
Dexter, Benning
Di Pietro, Rocco
Dixon, Dwight Mitchell
Dlugoszewski, Lucia
Doppmann, William George
Dorfmann, Ania
Dove, Neville
Driggers, Orin Samuel
Dudley, Raymond C
Duer, Susan R
Dumont, Lily
Dvorine, Shura
Dvorkin, Judith
Eaton, Roy (Felix)
Eckerling, Lawrence David
Egner, Richard John
Ehrlich, Clara Siegel
Eliasen, Mikael
Elmer, Cedric N(agel)
Elmore, Cenieth Catherine
Emmerich, Constance M
English Maris, Barbara (Jane)
Entremont, Philippe
Erlings, Billie Raye
Eskin, Virginia
Estes, Charles Byron
Estrin, Morton
Evans, Audrey Ferro
Evans, Billy G
Evans, Phillip
Faden, Betsy BB (Betsy Gale
    Bruzzese Faden)
Faith, Richard Bruce
Felice, John
Fennimore, Joseph
Feofanov, Dmitry N
Fetsch, Wolfgang
Fialkowska, Janina
Fields, Richard Walter
Figler, Byrnell Walter
Fine, Vivian
Fink, Seymour Melvin
Firkusny, Rudolf
Fishbein, Zenon
Fisher, Fred(eric Irwin)

Fitzgerald, Gerald
Fleisher, Leon
Floyd, J(ames) Robert
Frager, Malcolm
France, Hal
Frank, Claude
Freeman, Robert Schofield
Freund, Don (Donald Wayne)
Freundlich, Lillian
Friedberg, Ruth Crane
Friedman, Carole G
Friedman, Viktor
Frumkin, Lydia
Fuschi, Olegna
Galante, Jane Hohfeld
Galbraith, Nancy Riddle
Garrett, Margo
Garvey, David
Garwood, Margaret
Geary, Barbara Ann
Geiger, Ruth
Geller, Donna Medoff
Genia, Robinor
Gerber, Steven R
Gilels, Emil
Gillespie, Don Chance
Gillespie, John E
Gimpel, Jakob
Girard, Sharon E
Glazer, Gilda
Glazier, Beverly
Glickman, Sylvia
Goepfert, Robert Harold
Gold, Edward (Jay)
Goldberger, David
Goldina, Arianna (Arianna
    Goldina-Loumbrozo)
Goldovsky, Boris
Goldstein, Louis R
Goler, Harriett
Goode, Richard Stephen
Goodman, Joseph Magnus
Goolkasian Rahbee, Dianne
    Zabelle
Gorelkin, Paula Rath
Gorodnitzki, Sascha
Gossard, Helen M
Gottlieb, Jay Mitchell
Gould, Elizabeth (Elizabeth
    Gould Hochman)
Gowen, Bradford Paul
Graf, Enrique G
Graffman, Gary
Greenawalt, Terrence Lee
Greene, Arthur
Gregg, Chandler
Griebling, Stephen Thomas
Grubb, Thomas
Guggenheim, Janet Goodman
Gutberg, Ingrid
Gutierrez, Horacio Tomas
Habermann, Michael Robert
Hache, Reginald W J
Haddad, George Richard
Hagenah, Elizabeth A(rtman)
Hahn, Marian Elizabeth
Hahn, Sandra Lea
Haley, Johnetta R
Hambro, Leonid
Hamilton, Robert
Hammitt, Jackson Lewis, III
Han, Tong-Il
Hannigan, Barry T
Hanson, Raymond
Harrel, (John) Ralph
Harris, Johana
Harris, Robert A
Harriss, Elaine Atkins
Hatten, Robert Swaney
Hautzig, Walter
Hays, Doris Ernestine
Heiberg, Harold Willard
Heifetz, Jascha
Heim, Leo Edward
Heller, Lesley
Helps, Robert Eugene
Hendl, Walter

Herring, (Charles) Howard
Hersh, Alan B
Hinson, (Grady) Maurice
Hirsh, Albert
Hobson, Constance Yvonne
    Tibbs
Hodgkinson, Randall Thomas
Hoffman, Joel H
Hoffman, Paul K
Hofmeister, Giannina
    Lombardo
Hogenson, Robert Charles
Hoiby, Lee
Hollander, Lorin
Holtzman, Julie
Hopkins, Robert Elliott
Horn, Lois B(urley)
Horowitz, Vladimir
Horszowksi, Mieczslaw
Howard, Samuel Eugene
Howat, Robert V
Hoy, Hendricks
Hsu, Madeleine
Hubner, Carla (Carla V
    Hubner-Kraemer)
Hultberg, Warren Earle
Hyla, Lee
Intili, Dominic Joseph
Isaak, Donald J
Istomin, Eugene
Ivey, Jean Eichelberger
Jackson, Anita Louise
Jackson, Raymond T
Jacobson, Glenn Erle
Jaffe, Stephen Abram
James, Layton Bray
James, Marion Verse
Janis, Byron
Jarrett, Keith Daniel
Jenkins, Sylvia
Jochum, Veronica
Johannesen, Grant
Johnson, Grace Grey
Johnson, James (David)
Johnson, Roy Hamlin
Johnson, Tom
Jones, Patricia Collins
Jordan, Robert
Kahane, Jeffrey (Alan)
Kaiserman, David Norman
Kalichstein, Joseph
Kallir, Lillian
Kamsler, Bruce H
Kanouse, Monroe
Kanwischer, Alfred O
Kaplan, Robert Barnet
Katahn, Enid
Katz, George Leon
Keck, George R
Keene, Constance
Kehler, George Bela
Kennedy, Matthew W
Kessler, Minuetta
Kilenyi, Edward
Kim, Jung-Ja
Kiorpes, George Anthony
Kirkpatrick, Gary Hugh
Kitzke, Jerome Peter
Klaviter, Jane Bakken
Klein, Leonard
Knopt, Tinka
Koberstein, Freeman G
Kobler, Linda
Koch, Frederick (Charles)
Kochanski, Wladimir Jan
Kohn, James Donald
Kohn, Karl (George)
Koldofsky, Gwendolyn
Koras-Bain, Aglaia
Koscielny, Anne
Kranz, Maria Hinrichs
Kraus, Lili (Lili Kraus Mandl)
Krauss, Anne McClenny
Krimsky, Katrina (Margaret
    Krimsky Siegmann)
Krosnick, Mary Lou Wesley
Krzywicki, Jan

INSTRUMENTALIST (cont)

Wendelburg, Norma Ruth
Werder, Richard H
Werner, Joseph G
Westney, William (Frank)
Wiens, Frank
Wild, Earl
Willett, Thelma Elizabeth
Williamson, Marshall
Wilson, Dana Richard
Wilson, Richard Edward
Winn, James Frederick
Winokur, Roselyn M
Winslow, Walter Keith
Winter, Daniel Wallace
Witkin, Beatrice
Woitach, Richard
Woods, Pamela Pecha
Wright, Elizabeth
Wright, Thomas G
Wuorinen, Charles
Wursten, Richard Bruce
YaDeau, William Ronald
Yarbrough, Joan (Joan
    Yarbrough Cowan)
Youngblood, Joseph Edward
Youngs, Lowell Vere
Zabrack, Harold Allen
Zakarian-Rutstein, Sedmara
Zander, Patricia
Zarzeczna, Marion
Zaslavsky, Dora
Zgodava, Richard A
Zighera, Bernard
Zumwald-Howard, R Reid
Zuponcic, Veda Helen

Recorder

Austin, Louise Faville
Beardslee, Sheila Margaret
Bickley, Thomas Frank
Bixler, Martha Harrison
Dunham, Benjamin Starr
Ferguson, Suzanne (Carol)
Hale, James Pierce
Hatcher, Paula Braniff
Higbee, Dale Strohe
Jaffee, Kay
Kuchler, Kenneth Grant
Kuhn, Terry Lee
Larkin, Bruce David
Metcalfe, William
Petersen, Patricia H
Primus, Constance Merrill
Sankey, Rebecca Poole
Tyson, John K
Vogel, Howard Levi
Waitzman, Daniel R

Trombone

Albiston, Marion H
Appert, Donald Lawrence
Baker, Warren Lovell
Barrett, Walter Edmund
Beckel, James A, Jr
Biddlecome, Robert Edward
Bolter, Norman Howard
Borror, Ronald Allen
Boyd, Robert Ferrell
Breuninger, Tyrone
Brevig, Per (Andreas)
Brown, Frank Neil
Brown, Leon Ford
Browne, John P, Jr
Bush, Milton Louis
Deahl, Robert Waldo
Della Peruti, Carl Michael
Dodson, Glenn
Elias, Joel J
Ervin, Thomas Ross
Erwin, Edward
Evans, Richard Vance
Ferriano, Frank, Jr

Fetter, David J
Firkins, James T
Friedman, Jay Kenneth
Fromme, Arnold
Fulkerson, James Orville
Glover, Betty S
Guenther, Roy James
Harwood, Donald
Herman, Edward, Jr
Herring, David Wells
Hill, John David
Hurt, Charles Richard
Janks, Hal
Jernigan, Melvyn
Kehle, Robert Gordon
Kitzman, John Anthony
Knaub, Donald
Kofsky, Allen
Lammers, Mark (Edward)
Laney, Maurice I
Langlitz, David Carl
Lawrence, Mark Howard
McCulloh, Byron B
McGlaughlin, William
Marderosian, Ardash
Nicholson, Joseph Milford
Nikka, David W
Pethel, Stan (Stanley Robert)
Powell, Morgan Edward
Rautenberg, John Leslie
Richardson, William Wells
Robinson, Joseph
Romersa, Henry John
Rossi, Jane Niermann
Sanderson, Derl
Schmalz, Robert Frederick
Schmidt, Fred D
Schneider, Bernard
Skrzynski, Joseph
Smith, Glenn Parkhurst
Smith, Henry Charles
Stevens, Milton Lewis, Jr
Stewart, M Dee
Streeter, Thomas Wayne
Swallow, John
Taylor, David M
Vernon, Charles Gary
Walant, Glen
Waters, David L
Wilson, Ron (Ronnie Eugene)
Wittekind, Donald H
Yeo, Douglas Edward
Young, William Thomas
Zalkind, Larry Howard

Trumpet

Amstutz, A Keith
Ashton, John Howard
Beacraft, Ross (Orton)
Beck, Frederick Allan
Belford, Marvin L
Berginc, Charles David
Berman, Lynn Howell
Billingsley, William Allen
Brofsky, Howard
Broiles, Melvyn
Browning, Zack David
Butler, Barbara
Cameron, Wayne
Campbell, Larry Bruce
Champion, David (David
    Camesi)
Christner, Philip Joseph
Cichowicz, Vincent M
Come, Andre
Cook, Wayne Evans
Cord, (Noel) Edmund, II
Davidson, Louis
Dederer, William Bowne
DiPietro, Albert S
Fischthal, Glenn Jay
Gause, Thomas David
Goff, Bryan
Gombert, Karl E
Gould, Mark

Greenhoe, David Stanley
Grocock, Robert
Guarneri, Mario
Harley, J Robert
Hasselmann, Ronald Henry
Head, Emerson Williams
Heier, Dorothy R
Hendrickson, Steven Eric
Herforth, Harry Best
Hoffren, James A
Hood, Boyde Wyatt
Irby, Fred, III
Jameson, R Philip
Johnson-Hamilton, Joyce
Jolly, Kirby Reid
Jones, Stephen Graf
Lebow, Leonard S
Lehman, Richard
Ligotti, Albert F
Nagel, Robert E, Jr
Nelson, Paul
Nelson, Sally Foster
Nero, Bernard David
Newton, Clifford Hammond
Ode, James Austin
Olcott, James Louis
Parcells, Ramon Everett
Parker, Craig Burwell
Pearson, Willard B
Pellegrino, John
Perry, Marvin Chapman, II
Plog, Anthony (Clifton)
Roberts, Wilfred Bob
Robison, William H, III
Schultz, Russ Allan
Schutza, Gary Alan, Jr
Schwarz, Gerard
Severinsen, Doc (Carl H)
Stith, Marice W
Tison, Donald
Treutel, Edward F
Truax, Bert
Vacchiano, William
Ware, John
Webster, Gerald Best
Wheeler, Bruce Raymond
Whitener, Scott
Williams, Edwin Lynn
Winick, Steven David
Wyatt, Lucius Reynolds
Zauder, David

Tuba

Beauregard, Cherry Niel
Bishop, Ronald Taylor
Braynard, David O
Bulmer, Steven Robert
Deck, Warren
Dutton, Brenton Price
Eliason, Robert E
Erickson, Sumner Perry
Fritze, Gregory Paul
Garbutt, Matthew
Geiger, Loren Dennis
Gilmore, Ev (Everett M
    Gilmore), Jr
Hammond, Ivan Fred
Hanks, Thompson W, Jr
Harry, Don
Hedwig, Douglas Frederick
Jacobs, Wesley D
Jolly, Tucker
Jones, Mark Raymond
Klein, Stephen Tavel
Krzywicki, Paul
McCormick, David Clement
Morris, R Winston
Perry, Stephen Bruce
Phillips, Harvey Gene
Pokorny, Gene (John Eugene)
Richards, John Keil
Roberts, F Chester
Rose, William H
Self, James Martin
Sirinek, Robert

Smedvig, Rolf Thorstein
Stanley, Donald Arthur
Torchinsky, Abe
Unland, David E
Whaley, Robert Louis
Young, Frederick John
Zychowicz, James Leo

Viola

Albert, Jones Ross
Anderson, Karen
Anderson, Penny
Andrix, George Paul
Arad, Atar
Arlin, Mary Irene
Bachmann, George Theodore
Barach, Daniel Paul
Barnes, Darrel
Becker, Eugene
Blakeman, Virginia (Virginia
    Blakeman Lenz)
Bogdanoff, Leonard
Brandstadter, Eugene J
Braun, Edgar J
Brill, Michelle Mathewson
Brook, Steven Henry
Brown, Beatrice
Burkley, Bruce
Byrnes, Kevin Michael
Cameron, Andre
Canafax, Louise Terry
Castleman, Heidi Waldron
Cedel, Mark
Chaney, Scott Clay
Chapman, Eric John
Childs, Gordon Bliss
Clauser, Donald R
Compton, Catherine Louise
Cox, Clifford L
Culver, Robert
Dane, Jean R
Davis, Leonard
Dengel, Eugenie (Limberg)
de Pasquale, Joseph
Dodd, Kit Stanley
Doktor, Paul Karl
Dumm, Thomas A
Dunham, James Fraser
Dutt, Henry (Allan)
Dutton, Lawrence Willard
Ehrlich, Don A
Ewing, Maryhelen
Field, Richard Lawrence
Fisher, Zeal Isay
Fuchs, Lillian F
Funkhouser, Frederick A
Gesin, Leonid
Glazer, Robert
Glick, Jacob
Gordon, Nathan
Gordon, Sherry L
Gould, Eleanor Diane
Graham, John
Granat, Juan Wolfgang
Greitzer, Sol
Griebling, Karen Jean
Griffin, Judson T
Hadcock, Mary G
Hauck, Betty Virginia
Hillyer, Raphael
Horner, Jerry
House, Shari Tyle
Jacobs, Evelyn Poole
James, Mary Elliott
Janzer, Georges
Jeppesen, Laura
Johnson, Theodore Oliver
Katims, Milton
Katz, Martha Strongin
Kella, John Jake
Kelly, (J) Robert
Kestenbaum, Myra
Kirkwood, Linda Walton
Kopec, Patinka
Korman, Joan

INSTRUMENTALIST (cont)

Koromzay, Denes Kornel
Lehner, Eugene
Lewis, Arthur
Lincer, William
Lukashuk, Vladimir
McInnes, Donald
Magers, William Dean
Mark, Peter
Mason, Anne C
Mathews, John Fenton
Matsuda, Kenichiro
Mattis, Kathleen
Miller, David
Minkler, Peter John
Mirkin, Kenneth Paul
Mischakoff, Anne
Moeckel, Rainier
Morrell, Barbara Jane
Morrow, Ruth Elizabeth
Murdock, Katherine
Najar, Leo Michael
Ohyama, Hellchiro
Ouzounian, Michael Vahram
Perich, Guillermo
Perlow, Mildred Stern
Perry, Edson Clifton
Petersen, Patricia Jeannette
Pinner, Jay-Martin
Plumb, Bruce William
Polivnick, Paul Henry
Preves, Milton
Ravnan, Ellen Marie
Rhodes, Samuel
Rodriguez, Jose
Rosenblum, Myron
Ruggeri, Janet Fleming
Rupp, Marjorie J
Scavelli, Ramon Louis
Scott, Beverly C
Shklar, Minna
Showell, Jeffrey Adams
Simon, Benjamin
Snow, Meredith Ann
Soderberg, Marta A
Solomonow, Rami
Somogyi, Joseph Emil
Stilwell, F Raymond
Strasser, Tamas
Street, Marna Susan
Thompson, Marcus Aurelius
Trampler, Walter
Tree, Michael
Tseitlin, Michael
Tuttle, Karen
Uscher, Nancy Joyce
van Boer, Bertil Herman, Jr
VanValkenburg, James Wade
Vemer, Randall Werth
Ward, Margaret Motter
Weinrebe, Robert Solomon
Weiss, Elizabeth B
Wheeler, Lawrence Bennett
Woodward, Ann (McClure)
Wright, Thomas Underwood
Wyman, Dann Coriat
Zalkind, Roberta Marian
Zaretsky, Michael
Zerounian, Ara

Violin

Adams, Elwyn Albert
Agard, David Leon
Aitay, Victor
Ajemian, Anahid M
Aki, Syoko
Akos, Francis
Andersen, Elnore C (Marjorie)
Applebaum, Samuel
Armstrong, Helen (Helen
  Armstrong Gemmell)
Armstrong, Peter McKenzie
Ashton, Jack Schrader
Bae, Ik-Hwan
Baer, (Dolores) Dalene

Balazs, Frederic
Balogh, Endre
Balogh, Olga Mitana
Banat, Gabriel Jean
Bartolowits, David John
Bavel, Zamir
Becker, Bonita Ruth
Bednar, Stanley
Beliavsky, Yuri
Berberian, Hratch
Berman, Janet Rosser
Blankstein, Mary Freeman
Bloch, Robert Samson
Bonacini, Renato
Bor, Christiaan
Borok, Emanuel
Brahinsky, Henry Joseph
Brandstadter, Eugene J
Brant, Boris
Brauninger, James Edward
Brill, Herbert M
Brink, Robert
Bronstein, Raphael
Brook, Steven Henry
Brouwer, Margaret Lee
Brown, William James
Burnham, James
Buswell, James Oliver
Byers, Harold Ralph
Campbell, Teresa Hicks
Canin, Stuart V
Cannon, Allen E
Caplin, Martha J
Carabo-Cone, Madeleine
Cardenes, Andres Jorge
Carillo, Nancy
Carlyss, Earl
Carol, Norman
Carpenter, Howard Ralph
Carroll, Marianne
Castleman, Charles Martin
Chan, Timothy Tai-Wah
Chaney, Scott Clay
Chang, Lynn
Chase, Stephanie Ann
Chihuaria, Ernestine
  (Elizabeth) Riedel
Chung, Mi-Hee
Ciompi, Giorgio
Clapp, Stephen H
Clarke, Karen
Cohen, Isidore
Collier, Nathan Morris
Collins, David Edward
Constantinides, Dinos
  (Constantine Demetrios
  Constantinides)
Crowder, Elizabeth (Bette
  Hope Waddington)
Culley, Pamela Overstreet
Cummings, Diane M
Currier, Donald Robert
D'Albert, Francois J
Dalschaert, Stephane
Davies, Bruce MacPherson
Davis, Michael David
DeForest, June
DeLay, Dorothy (Mrs Edward
  Newhouse)
Dempsey, John D
Dengel, Eugenie (Limberg)
de Volt, Charlotte (Charlotte
  de Volt Elder)
Dombrowski, Stanley
Donato, Anthony
Dreiling, Alyze Loggie
Dreyer, Leslie I
Drucker, Eugene Saul
Ehrlich, David
Eichhorn, Erich A
Elhba, Mario (Leveque)
Ellerman, Jens
Erneston, Nicholas
Etzel, Marion
Farmer, Virginia
Fennell, Mary Ann Fee
Fink, Lorraine Friedrichsen

Fischbach, Gerald F
Flor, Samuel
Fomin, Arkady Gerson
Forsberg, Carl Earl
Francescatti, Zino (Rene)
Fraser, Barbara
French, Ruth Scott
Fried, Gregory Martin
Friedman, Erick
Fuchs, Joseph
Fujiwara, Hamao
Fulkerson, Gregory (Locke)
Gabora, Teras
Gadeholt, Irene
Galimir, Felix
Garabedian, Armen
Garriss, Phyllis Weyer
Gelbloom, Gerald
Gerle, Robert
Gingold, Josef
Ginter, Anthony Francis
Glazer, Esther
Glenn, Carroll
Gniewek, Raymond
Golczewski, Magdalena
Goldberg, Szymon
Goldschmidt, Bernhard
Goldsmith, Kenneth Martin
Goldstein, Malcolm
Gomez, Victor E
Goodkind, Alice Anderson
Goodman, Bernard Maurice
Gorski, Paul
Gosman, Lazar
Graham, Bruce A
Gratovich, Eugene
Green, George Clarence
Green, Rebecca McMullan
Gregorian, Henry
Greive, Tyrone Don
Grika, Larry A
Gulli, Franco
Halen, Eric J
Hall, Thomas Munroe
Hanly, Brian Vaughan
Hansen, James Roger
Harada, Koichiro
Hardwick, Charles T
Harpham, Virginia Ruth
Harrington, David
Harth, Sidney
Hatfield, Lenore Sherman
Haupt, Charles V
Hegyi, Julius
Heifetz, Daniel
Hendrix, Richard
Henry, William
Hinton-Braaten, Kathleen
Hobart, Max
Hochheimer, Laura
Hodgkins, Claire (Claire
  Hodgkins Wright)
Holmes, Richard
Hoogenakker, Virginia Ruth
Hopkins, Donald Eric
Hopwood, Julie Ann
Hurwitz, Isaac
Israelievitch, Jacques
Jacobsen, Edmund
Jaeger, Ina Claire
Jakey, Lauren Ray
Jefford, Ruth Martin
Johnson, Rose-Marie
Jones, Jeanne Nannette
Jones, Jenny Lind
Jones, Roland Leo
Jorgensen, Jerilyn
Kagan, Hilel
Kalt, Percy German
Kang, Dong-Suk
Kang, Hyo
Kantor, Paul M
Kaplan, Lewis
Kartman, Myron
Kashkashian, Kim
Kavafian, Ani
Kim, Young-Uck

Klotman, Robert Howard
Kojian, Miran Haig
Kolar, Henry
Kooper, Kees
Kopec, Patinka
Korman, John
Kremer, Gidon
Krosnick, Aaron Burton
Kuchler, Kenneth Grant
Kurland, Shelly (Sheldon)
Kurzbauer, Heather Raquel
Kuzell, Christopher
Kwalwasser, Helen
Lachert, Hanna Katarzyna
Lack, Fredell (Mrs Ralph
  Eichhorn)
Landsman, Jerome Leonard
Langley, Kenneth John
Laredo, Jaime
Lawless, Lyndon Kent
Lawrence, Kevin John
Lee, Ki Joo
Lee, Soo Chul
Lefkowitz, Mischa
Lekhter, Rudolf
Levi, Nannette
Lewis, Elisabeth Parmelee
Lewis, Philip James
Libove, Charles
Loebel, Kurt
Loft, Abram
Lohmann, Richard Brent
Lukashuk, Vladimir
Lurie, Bernard
Luttrell, Nancy Kay
McAndrew, Josephine K
McElfish, Diane Elizabeth
Macisak, Janice
McMillan, Theodora Mantz
Maddox, Walter Allen
Madsen, Norma Lee (Norma
  Lee Madsen Belnap)
Magad, Samuel
Magers, William Dean
Majeske, Daniel H
Malfitano, Joseph John
Mandelbaum, Gayna Faye
Mann, Robert
Markov, Albert
Marriner, Neville
Matesky, Elisabeth Anne
Maurer, James Carl
Menard, Pierre Jules
Menuhin, Yehudi
Michalak, Thomas
Michaud, Armand Herve
Milstein, Nathan
Mintz, Shlomo
Mizuno, Ikuko
Monosoff, Sonya (Sonya
  Monosoff Pancaldo)
Moore, Thomas
Morganstern, Marvin
Morgenstern, Gil
Morini, Erica
Morrell, Barbara Jane
Mott, Jonathan
Moyers, Emmett Edwin
Muenzer, Edgar C
Mulfinger, Joan Wade
Mulford, Ruth Stomne
Murray, Robert P
Naistadt, Florence
Negyesy, Janos
Neumann, Frederick C
Nice, Carter
Nisbet, Meredith Wootton
Noh, Joyce Hiew
Novak-Tsoglin, Sofia
O'Carroll, Cathleen (Cathleen
  Dalschaert)
Oka, Hirono
Olevsky, Julian
Oliveira, Elmar
O'Reilly, Sally
Ostrovsky, Arthur (Arthur
  William Austin)

INSTRUMENTALIST (cont)

Ourada, Ann Alicia
Packer, Janet Susan
Papavasilion, Ernest John
Pardee, Margaret (Margaret
    Pardee Butterly)
Patey, Edward R
Pelletier, Sho-mei
Perlman, Itzhak
Perry, Alcestis Bishop
Perry, Edson Clifton
Peterson, LeRoy H
Phillips, Eugene Walter
Pikler, Charles Robert
Plucker, Margaret L
Podnos, Theodor
Portnoy, Donald Charles
Price, Robert Bates
Raditz, Edward
Rafferty, J Patrick
Raykhtsaum, Aza
Reagin, Brian E
Reyes, Angel
Ribeiro, Gerardo
Ricci, Ruggiero
Ritchie, Stanley John
Robertson, Helen (Wells)
Robinson, Richard
Roby, Paul Edward
Rosand, Aaron
Rosenblith, Eric
Rosenthal, Paul Samuel
Ross, Barry
Rotenberg, Sheldon
Rothschild, Ellen Wagner
Rubin, Henry Park
Rubin, Nathan
Ruder, Philip
Rudie, Robert
Rupp, Marjorie J
Saetta, Mary Lou (Mary Lou
    Saetta-Gilman)
Salerno-Sonnenberg, Nadja
Salts, Joan Shriver
Samis, Sylvia Rosenzweig
Samson, Valerie Brooks
Sarbu, Eugene
Saslav, Isidor
Schiebler, Beverly Beasley
Schiller, Allan
Schmidt, Rodney
Schneider, David Hersh
Schulman, Julius
Schulte, Rolf
Schuman, Daniel Zetkin
Schwartz, Wilfred (Will)
Scott, Yumi Ninomiya
Shapey, Ronald (Sidney)
Sheinfeld, David
Sherba, John
Shroeder, Linda Ann
Shure, Paul Crane
Sidoti, Raymond B
Siegel, Bert (Berton Earl)
Sitkovetsky, Dmitry
Skoldberg, Phyllis Linnea
Skorodin, Elaine (Elaine
    Skorodin Fohrman)
Sloman, Jan Mark
Socher, Barry
Somach, Beverly
Sonies, Barbara
Sorkin, Leonard
Spivakovsky, Tossy
Starkman, Stephen S
Statsky, Paul G
Steiner, Diana
Steinhardt, Arnold
Stepner, Daniel
Stern, Isaac
Stowe, Anhared Wiest
Strasser, Tamas
Street, Tison
Stutt, Cynthia
Subramaniam,
    Lakshminarayana
Sugitani, Takaoki

Sutin, Elaine
Suzuki, Hidetaro
Swensen, Joseph Anton
Swint, Lois Roberts
Szeryng, Henryk
Talvi, Ilkka Ilari
Tarpley, Edward Lewis
Temianka, Henri
Thevenin, Francis
Thomas, Sally
Thompson, John Cotton
Torch, Deborah L
Totenberg, Roman
Treger, Charles
Tseitlin, Irina
Tseitlin, Michael
Uritsky, Vyacheslav
Ushioda, Masuko
Valkovich, Susan Fristrom
van Bronkhorst, Warren
Verdehr, Walter
Vilker, Sophia
Vilker-Kuchment, Valeria M
Viro, Olev L
Wade, Janice E
Wakschal, Seymour
Walt, Sherman Abbott
Washburn, Franklin Ely
Watanabe, Miwako N
Weber, Phyllis Anne
Weed, Joseph Laiten
Weiner, Max
Weiss, Howard A
Weiss, Sidney
White, Duane Craig
Whitesitt, Linda Marie
Wilson, Nancy J
Winzenburger, Walter Paul
Won, Kyung-Soo
Yajima, Hiroko
Yanagita, Masako (Masako
    Yanagita Bogin)
Yanchus, Judith
Zagst, Joanne (Joanne Zagst-
    Feldman)
Zaplatynsky, Andrew
Zaret, Peter H
Zeitlin, Zvi
Zerounian, Peruz
Zsigmondy, Denes
Zukerman, Pinchas

Other

Allard, Joseph
Ballard, Mary Anne
Barlowe, Amy
Barrett, Walter Edmund
Benson, Joan
Benton, Walter Bradford
Berthold, Sherwood Francis
Bilger, David Victor
Bishop, Martha (Jane)
Biskin, Harvey
Black, C Robert
Brauchli, Bernard Marc
Brauer, Cecilia Gniewek
Bulmer, Steven Robert
Burnett, Henry
Carlyss, Gerald
Celona, John Anthony
Chase, Allan Stuart
Chenoweth, Vida
Collier, Charles R
Creamer, Alice Dubois
Cunningham, Caroline M
Daley, Joseph Albert
Davine, Robert A
Dawson, James Edward
DeTurk, William N
Earle, Eugenia
Erickson, Gordon McVey
Feldman, Grace Ann
Firth, Vic (Everett Joseph)
Gibson, Jon Charles
Gourdin, Jacqueline

Greenberg, Roger D
Guggenheim, Janet Goodman
Haas, Jonathan Lee
Halsted, Margo Armbruster
Hamme, Albert P
Hammer, Stephen
Harwood, James C
Hemke, Frederick L
Higbee, David John
Hollingsworth, Samuel H, Jr
Hsu, John (Tseng-Hsin)
Hunter, Laura Ellen
Jaffe, David Aaron
Khan, Ali Akbar
Kite-Powell, Jeffery Thomas
Kofsky, Allen
Kosowicz, Francis John
Kout, Trix
Lake, Oliver Eugene
Lathom, Wanda B
McMahan, Robert Young
Manson, Eddy Lawrence
Mauk, Steven Glenn
Muradian, Vazgen
Nunemaker, Richard Earl
Oliveros, Pauline
Olsen, Dale Alan
Procter, Carol Ann
Purvis, William Warren
Radnofsky, Kenneth
Rauscher, Donald John
Reichmuth, Roger Edwin
Rex, Harley E
Rosenthal, Stephen W
Row, Peter Lyman
Seyfrit, Michael E
Sinta, Donald Joseph
Stevens, Leigh Howard
Stumpf, Carol L
Teck, Katherine (Weintz)
Thomason, Marshall Daniel
Trombly, Preston
Tucker, Janice
Vaccaro, Michael Anthony
Viola, Joseph E
von Grabow, Richard H
Warner, Sally Slade
Weiss, David E
Willett, William
Wilson, Nancy J
Young, Raymond G

LECTURER

Adams, Richard Elder
Ammer, Christine
Applebaum, Samuel
Aronoff, Frances Webber
Bailey, Barbara Elliott
Beacraft, Ross (Orton)
Benson, Joan
Berger, Melvin
Bernheimer, Martin
Bigler, Carole L
Bloch, Joseph
Boehm, Mary Louise
Brockman, Jane Ellen
Cage, John
Cameron, Andre
Cecconi-Bates, Augusta N
Celli, Joseph Robert
Chazanoff, Daniel
Cimino, John
Coates, Gloria (Kannenberg)
Cody, Judith (Ann)
Colgrass, Michael Charles
Cureau, Rebecca Turner
Denov, Sam
Derr, Ellwood S
Dower, Catherine Anne
Eger, Joseph
Egner, Richard John
Elias, Joel J
Field, Richard Lawrence
Filler, Susan M

Flaherty, Gloria
Frazee, Jane
Goldstein, Louis R
Harvey, Arthur Wallace
Henderson, Ian H
Heskes, Irene
Heymont, George A
Hilkevitch, Joyce Turner
Himes, Douglas D
Jacobs, Wesley D
Kelly, Paul Robert
Kubey, Arthur M
Larson, Anna (Barbara)
Laufer, Beatrice
Lee, Douglas Allen
Lee, Thomas Oboe
Lefferts, Peter Martin
London, S(ol) J
Lubin, Abraham
McCarthy, Kevin Joseph
Mahar, William J
Malkovich, Mark Paul
Malm, William Paul
Massey, George
Merle, Montgomery
Meyerowitz, Jan
Molava, Pamela May
Monson, Karen Ann
Moore, Marvelene Clarisa
Morris, Stephen MacKay
Moyer, Karl Eby
Norton, Pauline Elizabeth
Ochs, Michael
Owen, Barbara
Palmer, Willard A
Parks, David Wayne
Parmentier, Francis Gordon
Parris, Arthur
Paysour, LaFleur (Nadine)
Perlmutter, Donna
Peters, Roberta (Roberta
    Peters Fields)
Podnos, Theodor
Pollard, Elizabeth Blitch
Postl, Jacobeth
Preves, Milton
Rapley, Janice Ann
Ratner, Leonard Gilbert
Ray, (Sister) Mary Dominic
Rensch, Roslyn (Roslyn Maria
    Rensch-Erbes)
Richards, James Howard
Rogell, Irma
Rogers, William Forrest
Rosen, Judith (Berenice)
Rosenblum, Sandra Pletman
Rosenhaus, Steven L
Rosenstiel, Leonie
Ross, Jerrold
Sacher, Jack, Jr
Sachs, David H
Sanchez, Marta
Scherer, Barrymore Laurence
Schott, Howard Mansfield
Schuster-Craig, John William
Schwarz, Boris
Selfridge-Field, Eleanor A
Sloop, Jean Carolyn
Smith, Patrick John
Smoliar, Harold M
Sommer, Susan Thiemann
Steinberg, Michael
Swalin, Maxine McMahon
Talvi, Ilkka Ilari
Trotter, Herman
Tureck, Rosalyn
von Rhein, John Richard
Warner, Robert Austin
Wechsler, Bert
Williams, Hermine Weigel
Zlotkin, Frederick

LIBRARIAN

Albrecht, Otto Edwin
Anderson, Gillian Bunshaft
Anderson, Glenn Alan
Ayotte, Jeannine Marie
Bachmann, George Theodore
Baily, Diette (Dee) Marie
Balshone, Cathy S (Cathy S
  Balshone-Becze)
Basart, Ann Phillips
Bayne, Pauline Shaw
Benoit, Kenneth Roger
Berman, Marsha F
Bleecker, Ruth (Mercer)
Bognar, Dorothy McAdoo
Bowen, Jean
Bowles, Garrett H
Bradley, Carol June
Buff, Iva Moore
Campbell, Frank Carter
Cardell, Victor Thomas
Chouinard, Joseph Jerod
Christensen, Beth Elaine
Cipolla, Wilma Reid
Colby, Edward E(ugene)
Cooper, David Edwin
Coover, James Burrell
Coral, Lenore
Daub, Peggy Ellen
Davis, Deborah Griffith
Dennison, Sam Melvin
Diamond, Harold J
Draganski, Donald Charles
Druesedow, John Edward,
  Jr
Epstein, Dena Julia
Evans, Sally Romer
Evensen, Robert Lloyd
Fawver, Darlene Elizabeth
Fenske, David Edward
Folter, Siegrun H
Fry, Stephen Michael
Fuller, Stephan B
Geil, Wilma Jean
Giddings, Robert Potter
Godel, Edith
Gramenz, Francis L
Griscom, Richard William
Haefliger, Kathleen Ann
Hardish, Patrick Michael
Heck, Thomas F
Heintze, James Rudolph
Helton, Sally Carr
Hill, George R
Hilton, Ruth B
Hixon, Don L
Jackson, Brinton
Jackson, Richard H
Jeffery, Peter Grant
Johnson, Ellen Schultz
Jones, Robert M
Kach, Claire
Keller, Michael Alan
Klein, Kristine J
Kopp, James B
Krummel, D(onald) W(illiam)
Lamb, Norma Jean
Leavitt, Donald Lee
Lindahl, Charles E
Lobingier, Christopher Crumay
Mabry, Raymond Edward
McClellan, William Monson
McDonald, Arlys Lorraine
Marco, Guy Anthony
Martin, Vernon
Maxwell, Barbara
Mayer, George Louis
Mendro, Donna C
Miller, Philip Lieson
Milligan, Stuart Charles
Morgan, Paula Margaret
Moulton, Suzanne LeRoy
Myers, Kurtz
Nieweg, Clinton F
Nightingale, Daniel
Norton, Pauline Elizabeth

Ossenkop, David Charles
Ostrove, Geraldine E
Ota, Diane O
Pope, Betty Frances
Pruett, James Worrell
Quist, Edwin Arnold
Rabson, Carolyn R
Reed, Ida McAliley
Roberts, Donald Lowell
Roberts, John Howell
Root, Deane Leslie
Rorick, William C(alvin)
Rowley, Gordon Samuel
Samuel, Harold Eugene
Savig, Norman Ingolf
Schaefer, Patricia
Schuitema, Joan Elizabeth
Schwegel, Richard C
Sebastian, Anne Marie
Seibert, Donald C
Shirley, Wayne D(ouglas)
Silver, Martin A
Sims, Phillip Weir
Skinner, Robert Gordon
Skyrm, Sarah Elizabeth
Smiraglia, Richard Paul
Smith, Dorman Henry
Solow, Linda I
Sommer, Susan Thiemann
Sommerfield, David Fredic
Sonnet, Susan M
Soule, Edmund Foster
Strauss, Barbara Jo
Tanno, John W
Tharp, Don(ald Warren)
Theil, Gordon Amos
Thompson, Annie F
Thorin, Suzanne Elizabeth
Travaline, Marjorie D
Turner, James Rigbie
Vandewart, J W
Viles, Elza Ann
Waddington, Susan Royal
Watanabe, Ruth Taiko
Waters, Edward Neighbor
Weliver, E Delmer
White, Elwood Lauriston
Wilkins, Marilyn W
Wood, David A
Wursten, Richard Bruce
Zgodava, Richard A

MUSICOLOGIST

Arzruni, Sahan
Bacal, Harvey
Bailey, Robert
Baron, Carol K
Berg, Darrell Matthews
Bernstein, Lawrence F
Bock, Emil William
Bowers, Jane Meredith
Bozarth, George S
Bronson, Bertrand Harris
Brook, Barry Shelley
Brown, Howard Mayer
Browne, Richmond
Cantrell, Byron
Chusid, Martin
Clark, Sondra Rae
Cohn, James (Myron)
Collins, Michael B
Cooper, Kenneth
Crabtree, Phillip D
Creamer, Alice Dubois
Daniel, Oliver
Dawson, George C
Douglass, Robert Satterfield
Eive, Gloria
Enrico, Eugene Joseph
Fenske, David Edward
Freeman, Robert Norman
French, Richard Frederic
Godwin, Joscelyn
Gushee, Lawrence A
Hajdu, John

Hamm, Charles Edward
Henderson, Donald Gene
Holoman, Dallas Kern
Howard, Wayne
Howell, Almonte Charles, Jr
Hursh-Mead, Rita Virginia
Jenkins, Newell
Johnson, Alvin H
Jones, George Morton
Jones, Patricia Collins
Karp, Theodore Cyrus
Kennedy, Raymond F
Kerman, Joseph Wilfred
Kirby, F(rank) E(ugene)
Kirk, Elise Kuhl
Kirkendale, Warren
Kowalke, Kim H
Kroeger, Karl
Kuss, Malena
Lippman, Edward A
Livingstone, Ernest Felix
Lockwood, Lewis Henry
Mackey, Elizabeth Jocelyn
Mahrt, William Peter
Marvin, Frederick
Miller, Clement A
Mracek, Jaroslav John Stephen
Neuls-Bates, Carol
Newman, William Stein
Pauly, Reinhard G
Pendle, Karin
Plantinga, Leon Brooks
Raad, Virginia
Reaney, Gilbert
Reilly, Edward Randolph
Revitt, Paul J
Rowley, Gordon Samuel
Schroeder, Pollyanna
  Tribouillier
Schwarz, Karol Robert
Shindle, William Richard
Slim, H(arry) Colin
Smiley, Marilynn Jean
Smither, Howard E
Steinhardt, Milton J
Suess, John G
Townsend, Douglas
Wagner, John Waldorf
Ward, John Milton
Whaples, Miriam K
White, John Reeves
Wienpahl, Robert William
Wolf, Eugene Kendrick
Wolff, Christoph Johannes
Wolverton, Byron A
Zaslaw, Neal

PATRON

Ashton, Wendell Jeremy
Cabot, Edmund Billings
Fromm, Paul
Kermani, Peter Rustam
Konikow, Zalman
Mason, Anthony Halstead
Moreau, Lorraine Marie
Pachios, Harold Christy
Rothschild, Randolph
  Schamberg
Sayad, Elizabeth Gentry
Silberman, Aaron
Stanley, Margaret King
Wetzler, Robert Paul
Wolf, Phillip S

TEACHER/COACH

Albert, Jones Ross
Albiston, Marion H
Aleksandruk, Linda (Marie)
Allen, Corey Lee
Allen, Susan Elizabeth
Alstadter, Judith R
Appert, Donald Lawrence

Armer, Elinor Florence
Arms, Margaret Fairchild
Armstrong, Helen (Helen
  Armstrong Gemmell)
Arnon, Baruch
Ashens, Robert J, III
Atherton, Peter L
Austin, Louise Faville
Bae, Ik-Hwan
Baker, Don Russell
Balsam, Artur
Barbeau, Bernard
Barker, Edwin Bogue
Barrett, Oreen
Barrow, Rebecca Anne
Barrueco, Manuel
Basney, Eldon E
Bass, Claude Leroy
Battipaglia, Diana Mittler
Beardslee, Bethany E
Beardslee, Sheila Margaret
Beck, Martha Dillard (Mrs G
  Howard Carragan)
Beliavsky, Yuri
Bergersen, Charlotte (Charlotte
  Bergersen Chevalier)
Bergt, Robert Roland
Berry, Corre Ivey
Betjeman, Paul
Bevers, Michael Earl
Billings, David Arthur
Bobrow, Sanchie
Boyajian, Armen
Boykin, Annie Helen
Brahinsky, Henry Joseph
Brandt, Barbara Jean
Branning, Grace
Brant, Boris
Brauninger, James Edward
Bricard, Nancy (Nancy
  Bricard Woods)
Brickman, Joel Ira
Bride, Kathleen
Brisman, Heskel
Brown, Myrna Weeks
Browning, John (S), Jr
Brumit, J(oseph) Scott
Brunsma, Donna Louise
Buccheri, Elizabeth
Buckley, Mary Henderson
Bunch, Meribeth Ann
Busby, Gerald
Cacioppo, George Emanuel
Campbell, Teresa Hicks
Carlson, Jane E
Carlson, Lenus Jesse
Cathcart, Kathryn
Chelsi, Lawrence G
Christman, Sharon
Christopher, Karen Mary
Clements, Joy
Codispoti, Norma (Constance)
Colaneri, Joseph
Colby, Edward E(ugene)
Colf, Howard
Collins, David Edward
Copeland, Keith Lamont
Corenne, Renee
Coss, (Sarah) Elizabeth
Cossa, Dominic
Costinescu, Gheorghe
Cowan, Robert (Holmes)
Cowden, Susan Jane
Cozad, Joseph
Creditor, Bruce Mitchell
Crocker, Ronald Jay
Culp, Paula N
Curry, Donna (Jayne)
Dahlman, Barbro
Daley, Joseph Albert
Dalschaert, Stephane
Danforth, Frances Adams
Danielle, Ruth
Darling, Sandra (Sandra
  Darling Mitchell)
Davidovich, Bella
DeGaetani, Jan

TEACHER/COACH (cont)

Wilson, Ron (Ronnie Eugene)
Wilson, Todd Rodney
Wincenc, Carol
Winn, James Frederick
Wion, John H
Wohlafka, Louise Ann
Woods, Sylvia
Yanagita, Masako (Masako Yanagita Bogin)
Yancich, Charles Theodore
Yarbrough, Joan (Joan Yarbrough Cowan)
Zagst, Joanne (Joanne Zagst-Feldman)
Zychowicz, James Leo

VOCALIST

Soprano

Adonaylo, Raquel
Alavedra, Montserrat
Aleksandruk, Linda (Marie)
Alexander, Roberta Lee
Altmeyer, Jeannine Theresa
Amara, Lucine
Ameling, Elly (Elisabeth Sara)
Anders, (Barbara) Lynne
Anderson, June
Andrade, Rosario
Arms, Margaret Fairchild
Arroyo, Martina
Bailey, Exine Margaret Anderson
Bampton, Rose E (Pelletier)
Barrett, Oreen
Bayard, Carol Ann
Beardslee, Bethany E
Belling, Susan
Blegen, Judith
Bogard, Carole Christine
Booth, Nancy
Bouleyn, Kathryn
Brand, Myra Jean
Brandt, Barbara Jean
Brewer, Christine
Brustadt, Marilyn
Buckley, Mary Henderson
Burgess, Mary Minott
Caballe, Montserrat Folch
Cariaga, Marvellee M
Carron, Elisabeth (Elisabetta Caradonna)
Casiello, Marianne
Cawood, (Elizabeth) Marion
Chalker, Margaret
Christman, Sharon
Christos, Marianna
Ciesinski, Kristine F
Clements, Joy
Coffey, Denise (Denise Coffey Pate)
Colon, Evangelina
Cook, Deborah
Cook, Jean Louise
Cook, Rebecca
Corenne, Renee
Cortina, Raquel
Corto, Diana-Maria
Coss, (Sarah) Elizabeth
Costa, Mary
Cotrubas, Ileana
Crader, Jeannine
Craig, Patricia
Crespin, Regine C
Crum, Dorothy Edith
Cruz-Romo, Gilda (Gilda Cruz Romo)
Cuccaro, Costanza (Constance Jean Penhorwood)
Cummings, Claudia
Cundy, Rhonda Gail
Curtin, Phyllis
Curtis-Verna, Mary (Virginia)

Danielle, Ruth
Darling, Sandra (Sandra Darling Mitchell)
Davis, Barbara Smith
Deatherage, Martha
Dernesch, Helga
Deutekom, Cristina
Di Franco, Loretta Elizabeth
Dobbs, Mattiwilda
Dobelle, Beatrice
Donath, Helen
Dordick, Johanna
Dornya, Marya D
Dudley, Anna Carol
Dunn, Susan Regenia
Duschak, Alice Gerstl
Elledge, Nancy Ruth
Ellingson, Linda Jeanne
Erickson, Kaaren (Herr)
Erickson, Susan
Estill, Ann (H M)
Evans, Margarita Sawatzky
Evans-Montefiore, April
Faiella, Ida M
Farrell, Eileen
Faull, Ellen
Fernandez, Wilhelmenia
Fischer, Edith Steinkraus
Fiske, June
Flasch, Christine Elizabeth
Ford, Barbara
Fowles, Glenys Rae
Fox, Barbara J
Freni, Mirella
Fulton, Lauran Ann
Gabora, Gaelyne
Galas, Diamanda Angeliki
Galvany, Marisa
Gamberoni, Kathryn (Lynne)
Gambulos, Elena (Ellen Gambulos-Cody)
Goldberg, Judith
Gondek, Juliana (Kathleen)
Goodman, Lucille Field
Gordon, Marjorie
Gould, Eleanor Diane
Griebling, Lynn (Lynn Louise Griebling-Moores)
Grimm, Betty Jane
Grist, Reri
Gruberova, Edita
Gunter-McCoy, Jane Hutton
Gustafson, Nancy J
Gutknecht, (Edythe) Carol
Hall, Janice L
Harper, Heather Mary
Harsanyi, Janice
Hartliep, Nikki Li
Hayashi, Yasuko
Heller, Joan
Hendricks, Barbara
Herzberg, Jean (M)
Heyde, Norma L
Hocher, Barbara Jean
Hodam, Helen
Horne, Marilyn
Hunt, Alexandra
Hunt, Karen
Hurney, Kate
Johnson, Beverley Peck
Johnson, June Durkin
Johnson, Mary Jane (Rose)
Jones, Nancy Thompson
Kalisky, Ronit
Kalt, Pamela C
Kaplan, Barbara Connally
Karnstadt, Cynthia
Kavasch, Deborah Helene
Kellock, Judith Graham
Kelly, Sherry Hill
Kelm, Linda
Kierig, Barbara Elaine
Kim, Young Mi
Kirsten, Dorothy
Kliewer, Darleen Carol
Kommel, A Margret
La Barbara, Joan (Joan La Barbara Subotnick)

Lamb, Norma Jean
Lampropulos, Athena
Lamy, Catherine
Langton, Sunny Joy
Larson, Susan
Lear, Evelyn
Lee, Sung-Sook
Little, Gwendolyn
Longwith, Deborah
Loukas, Billie (Billie Loukas Poulos)
MacKenzie, Melissa Taylor
McMillian, Geraldine
Mahy, Daune Sharon
Mandac, Evelyn Lorenzana
Maresca, Rosalia
Marton, Eva
Marvin, Marajean B
Mathes, Rachel Clarke
Matsumoto, Shigemi (Shigemi Matsumoto Stark)
Meier, Johanna
Messier, Lise M
Metz, Jeryl (Jeryl Metz Woitach)
Meyers, Klara Bolgar
Middleton, Jaynne Claire
Miller, Lucille
Moffo, Anna
Moore, Barbara (Patricia) Hill
Moore, Dorothy Rudd
Moreau, Lorraine Marie
Morgan, Beverly
Morrison, Florence
Mosher, Elizabeth (Elizabeth Mosher-Kraus)
Myers, Pamela
Nelson, Judith
Niska, Maralin Fae
Norden, Betsy (Elizabeth N Haley)
Norman, Jessye
Novich, Mija
Odum-Vernon, Alison P (Alison Paige Odum)
Ottley, JoAnn
Page, Carolann (Carol Ann Gemignani)
Pastore, Patrice Evelyn
Patenaude-Yarnell, Joan
Pearson, Barbara (Ann)
Pelle, Nadia
Peters, Roberta (Roberta Peters Fields)
Petros, Evelyn
Pilgrim, Neva Stevens
Plantamura, Carol Lynn
Pranschke, Janet
Price, Leontyne
Price, Margaret
Prindle, Roma Howard
Randazzo, Arlene Catherine
Raskin, Judith
Rees, Rosalind
Ringholz, Teresa Marie
Ringo, Jennifer (Elizabeth)
Roberts, Brenda
Robinson, Gail
Robinson, Marie
Rolandi, Gianna
Rondelli, Barbara (Ann)
Rowley, Vera Newstead
Russell, Louise
Salta, Anita Maria
Sanford, Sally (Allis)
Saunders, Jean O
Saunders, Mary G
Schroeder, Pollyanna Tribouillier
Scott, Molly
Scotto, Renata
Serrlya, Sivia
Shade, Ellen
Shade, Nancy Elizabeth
Shane, Rita (Rita Shane Tritter)
Shelton, Lucy (Alden)

Sills, Beverly (Mrs Peter B Greenough)
Soderstrom, Elisabeth Anna
South, Pamela
Soviero, Diana Barbara
Spacagna, Maria
Steber, Eleanor
Stephenson, Ruth Orr
Stevenson, Delcina Marie
Stratas, Teresa
Suderburg, Elizabeth
Sundine, Stephanie
Sutherland, Joan
Tebaldi, Renata
Te Kanawa, Kiri
Telese, Maryanne Elizabeth
Trainor, Carol Donn
Turner, Sarah
Tyler, Veronica
Vaccaro, Judith Lynne
Valente, Benita
Vanderlinde, Debra
vanEaton, Sunny F C
Verrett, Shirley
Vishnevskaya, Galina
Webber, Carol Staats
Wells, Patricia
Wendel, Dale
Wheeler, Janet
Wilcox, Carol Ann
Wilkins, Marilyn W
Williams, Edna (Charlotte)
Wohlafka, Louise Ann
Wojtaszek, Teresa (Janina) Kubiak
Wood, Gloria Bakkila
Wood, Vivian Poates
Woods, Terri Lynn
Woodward, Donna Lynn
Wrancher, Elizabeth Ann
Wyckoff, Lou Ann
Zastrow, Joyce Ruth
Zoghby, Linda
Zschau, Marilyn
Zylis-Gara, Teresa Geralda

Mezzo—soprano

Anderson, Sylvia
Babak, Renata
Bahmann, Marianne Eloise
Baker, Janet Abbott
Baldwin, Marcia
Ballinger, Cathryn (Fluellen)
Barbieri, Fedora
Bible, Frances Lillian
Birdwell, Florence (Gillam-Hobin)
Bonazzi, Elaine
Boozer, Brenda Lynn
Bumbry, Grace
Bybee, Ariel (Ariel Bybee McBaine)
Carlson, Claudine (Claudine H Carlson-Rubin)
Christin, Judith
Ciesinski, Katherine
Clarey, Cynthia
Clickner, Susan Fisher
Codispoti, Norma (Constance)
Connolly, Martha (Nixon Taugher)
Cook, Carla
Cornell, Gwynn
Costa-Greenspon, Muriel
Creed, Kay
Crolius, Nancy Peterson
Curry, Diane
Curtis, Jan (Judith Anne)
Davidson, Joy Elaine
De Carlo, Rita Frances
DeGaetani, Jan
DeVaughn, Alteouise (Alteouise DeVaughn Austin)
Donahue, Christine (Helen)

VOCALIST (cont)

Doscher, Barbara M
Dunn, Mignon (Mignon Dunn-
    Klippstatter)
Eckhart, Janis Gail
Elias, Rosalind
Ewing, Maria
Farley, Carole
Felty, Janice
Firestone, Adria (Belinda)
Fischer, Elizabeth
Fortunato, D'Anna
Friede, Stephanie
Ganz, Isabelle Myra
Garabedian, Edna (Edna Mae
    Garabedian-Duguie)
Garrott, Alice
Golden, Emily
Grillo, Joann Danielle
Harned, Shirley (Lee)
Hastings, Emily (Cecilia)
Heyler, Mary Ellen
Hillhouse, Wendy Carol
Hoffman, Grace
Horne, Marilyn
Hynes, Elizabeth
James, Carolyne Faye
Johansson, Annette
Jones, Gwendolyn (K)
Lanzillotti, Leonore
Lehnerts, (Mary) Frances
Lerner, Mimi
Levy, Joanna
Lewis, Marcia Ann
Loinaz, Yvonne Dalis (Irene
    Dalis)
Love, Shirley
Mabry, Sharon Cody
McCaffrey, Patricea (Patricia
    Anne McCaffrey)
MacKay, Margery (Margery
    MacKay Anwyl)
Maia, Carolyn (Carolyn Maja
    Burton)
Malas, Marlena Kleinman
Mannion, Elizabeth (Belle)
Marsee, Susanne I
Martin, Barbara (Ann
    Sulahian-Martin)
May, Julia
Meyerson, Janice
Miculs, Melita Luize
Miller, Patricia A
Minton, Yvonne Fay
Parsons, Meredith Wren
Piland, Jeanne Smith
Quittmeyer, Susan
Quivar, Florence
Reed, Phyllis Luidens
Resnik, Regina
Richards, Leslie Roberta
Russell, Rosemary
Schuman, Patricia
Segar, Kathleen
Senn, Martha
Shimeta, Kathleen Marie
Spektor, Mira J
Stapp, Olivia
Sterling, Lorna (Lorna Bodum
    Sterling Mount)
Stowe, Sondra
Summerville, Suzanne
Taillon, Joscelyne Jeanne
Taylor, Rose (Audrey)
Troyanos, Tatiana
Veasey, Josephine
Vergara, Victoria
Verrett, Shirley
von Stade, Frederica
Wain-Becker, Roberta
Wakefield-Wright, JoElyn
Walker, Sandra
Wallis, Delia Lesley
    Suzette
Warfield, Sandra
Wheeler, Kimball
Williams, Nancy

Yauger, Margaret (Margaret
    Yauger Smith)
Ziegler, Delores

Contralto

Aberts, Eunice Dorothy
Barbieri, Fedora
Decker, Geraldine
Forrester, Maureen Katherine
    Stewart
Hastings, Emily (Cecilia)
Manford, Barbara Ann
Nadler, Sheila

Tenor

Acord, Thomas Wadsworth
Adkins, Paul Spencer
Alch, Mario
Alexander, John
Anderson, Waldie Alfred
Aragall, Giacomo (Jaime)
Arant, (Everett) Pierce, Jr
Arbizu, Ray Lawrence
Arnold, (Donald) Thomas
Atherton, James Peyton, Jr
Bailey, Dennis Farrar
Ballam, Michael L
Bartolini, Lando
Bergell, Aaron
Berry, Paul
Beudert, Mark
Biser, Larry Gene
Blake, Rockwell
Bortnick, Evan N
Boyd, Gerard
Brecknock, John Leighton
Bressler, Charles
Britton, David
Brock, Karl
Brown, William Albert
Brunner, Richard
Buhl, Keith Robert
Burgess, Gary Ellsworth
Busse, Barry L
Caldwell, John Timothy
Calleo, Riccardo
Cameron, Christopher
Carelli, Gabor P
Carreras, Jose
Cassilly, Richard
Castel, Nico
Celestino, Thomas
Cobb, A(lfred) Willard
Corelli, Franco
Craft, Barry Hunt
Danner, Harry
Di Virgilio, Nicholas
Domingo, Placido
Dressen, Dan Fredrick
Eikum, Rex L
Estes, Richard (Alan)
Evans, Joseph
Ferguson, Gene
Fowler, John
Frank, Joseph
Freeman, Carroll (Benton), Jr
Freeman, Colenton
Gedda, Nicolai
Gibbs, Raymond
Gilmore, John
Glaze, Gary
Goeke, Leo Francis
Gonzalez, Dalmacio
Gordon, David J
Gordon, Jerry Lee
Green, Jonathan D
Grice, Garry B
Guarino, Robert
Harger, Gary
Harness, William Edward
Hayward, Thomas (Tibbett)
Haywood, Charles
Hirst, Grayson
Homburg, Al(fred John)

Hotoke, Shigeru
Hough, Charles Wayne
Hugo, John William
Ingle, William (Billy Earl)
Isaac, Gerald Scott
Jergenson, Dale Roger
Jung, Manfred
Kaiser, Carl William
Khanzadian, Vahan
King, James Ambros
Kness, Richard Maynard
    (Richard M Kneiss)
Koret, Arthur (Solomon)
Krehbiel, Clayton
Lankston, John
Lawrence, Douglas Howard
Lewis, William
Lima, Luis
Little, Frank (Francis E)
Livings, George
McCauley, Barry
McCauley, William Erwin
McCollum, John (Morris)
McCracken, James E
McCray, James Joseph
Mauro, Ermanno
Mayer, Frederick David
Merritt, Chris Allan
Miller, Richard D
Miskell, (William) Austin
Molese, Michele
Montane, Carlos (Carlos
    Hevia-Montane)
Morales, Abram
More, Michael
Murray, George
Nagy, Robert D
Neill, (John) William
Nelson, Wayne
Nichols, Clinton Colgate
Nilsson, Raymond
Novick, Melvyn Joseph
Oberlin, Russell
O'Neal, Michael M
Paige, Norman
Parks, David Wayne
Parly, Ticho (Ticho Parly
    Frederik Christiansen)
Pastine, Gianfranco
Paton, John Glenn
Paul, James
Pavarotti, Luciano
Peete, Jerry Lawrence
Perry, Douglas R
Poll, Melvyn
Price, Henry Paschal, III
Randall, Edward (Owens), III
Rawlins, Joseph (Thomas)
Reece, Arley R
Reed, Bruce
Romano, Keith
Rosenshein, Neil
Salkov, Abraham A
Schmorr, Robert
Serbo, Rico
Shirley, George Irving
Siena, Jerold
Sooter, Edward
Sperry, Paul
Stamford, John Scott
Stewart, John Harger
Stone, Edgar Norman
Stuart, James Fortier
Sutton, Vern (Everett Lavern)
Swenson, Edward E
Talley, Dana W
Talley-Schmidt, Eugene
Taube, Moshe
Thomas, Jess
Trussel, Jacque
Tucker, Gene Richard
Unruh, Stan
Vickers, Jon
Villa, Eduardo
Vorrasi, John Frederick
Vrenios, Anastasios Nicholas
Walker, Charles (John)

Walker, John Edward
Walker, Mallory Elton
Wallence, Stephen
Ware, Durward Clifton, Jr
West, Jon Fredric (John
    Fredric)
Whitesides, William (Plaxico),
    Jr
Wylie, Ted David
Zucker, Stefan

Baritone

Anderson, Alfred Lamar
Arnold, David
Baker, Alan
Ballenger, Kenneth Leigh
Barbeau, Bernard
Barcza, Peter (Joseph)
Barry, Jerome
Baxter, William Hubbard, Jr
Becerril, Anthony Raymond
Benefield, Richard Dotson
Beni, Gimi (James J)
Berberian, Ara
Berry, Walter
Boucher, (Charles) Gene
Braun, Victor
Brumit, J(oseph) Scott
Burchinal, Frederick
Byrd, Samuel (Turner)
Carey, Thomas D
Carlson, Lenus Jesse
Cassel, Walter John
Chelsi, Lawrence G
Christopher, Russell Lewis
Cimino, John
Collins, Richard L
Cooper, Lawrence
Corrado, Ronald Anthony
Cossa, Dominic
Cowan, Sigmund Sumner
Crafts, Edward James
Crawford, H Gerald
Cruz, Angelo
Daniel, Sean
Darrenkamp, John David
Davis, Richard
Devlin, Michael Coles
Dietsch, James
Duesing, Dale L
Edwards, Ryan (Hayes)
Ellis, Brent E
Elvira, Pablo
Englander, Lester
Epley, (William) Arnold
Fiol, Stephen Frank
Fredricks, Richard
Frisch, Richard S
Gaeddert, William Kenneth
Galbraith, Robert Sinclair
Gephart, William (Abel)
Glassman, Allan
Goodloe, Robert D
Guarrera, Frank (Francesco
    Guarrera)
Guinn, Leslie
Hampson, (W) Thomas
Hanner, Barry Neil
Hansen, Robert Howard
Hanson, Eric Allen
Harris, Daniel Alfred
Harrold, Jack
Hartman, Vernon
Hiss, Clyde S
Holloway, David
Hook, Walter (Eugene)
Hopkin, John Arden
Horton, William Lamar
Ingham, Michael Curtis
Jackson, Dennis Clark
Jamerson, Thomas H
Justus, William
Karel, Charles
Kraus, Philip Arthur
LeRoy, Edmund

VOCALIST (cont)
Lightfoot, Peter William
Long, Charles (Patrick)
Lubin, Abraham
Ludgin, Chester Hall
Lusmann, Stephen (Arthur)
McClosky, David Blair
McFarland, Robert
Maclane, Armand Ralph
MacNeil, Cornell Hill
Madden, Ronald
Majoros, David John
Manno, Robert
Markuson, Stephen
Martel, Fernand
Martin, Walter (Callahan), Jr
Massey, George
Matthen, Paul Seymour
Merrill, Robert
Metcalf, William
Middaugh, Benjamin
Milnes, Sherrill
Mittelmann, Norman
Moore, Dale (Kimberly)
Morehouse, Dale W
Morgan, Mac (R)
Morris, James Peppler
Mosley, Robert
Neely, James Bert
Nevison, Howard S
Nolen, Timothy
Nurmela, Kari Kullervo
Opalach, Jan
Paglialunga, Augusto
Parker, William Kent
Parsons, David
Paschke, Donald Vernon
Patrick, Julian
Pelayo, Hernan Victor
Pierson, Edward
Powell, Thomas Roberts
Quilico, Louis
Ray, William Benjamin
Reardon, John
Rehfuss, Heinz J
Ringel, Harvey Norman
Robison, Clayne W
Roe, Charles Richard
Samuelsen, Roy
Sarabia, Guillermo
Sataloff, Robert Thayer

Schexnayder, Brian
Schultze, Andrew W
Seiler, James Joseph
Serrano, Carlos
Singher, Martial
Smith, Gerald L
Stenberg, Donald Christian
Stewart, Thomas James, Jr
Stone, William Frazier
Stripling, Luther
Studebaker, Donald W
Sullivan, (Roger) Daniel
Sylvan, Sanford (Mead)
Symonette, Randolph
Taylor, Andrew Dale
Teague, Thomas S
Thierstein, Eldred A
Thompson, Arthur Charles
Thompson, Hugh R
Torigi, Richard
Tyl, Noel Jan
Uppman, Theodor
Van Lidth De Jeude, (C)
    Philip (J)
Voorhees, Gordon
Walker, William
Walter, David Edgar
Warfield, William Caesar
Webb, Guy Bedford
Wexler, Stanley A
White, Robert Charles, Jr
Wiles, John A
Wilkey, Jay W
Williams, Rick (Frederick
    Thompson)
Willoughby, Jay (Alan)
Woodman, Thomas
Worstell, Ronald A
Zei, John

Bass

Albert, Donnie Ray
Appelman, Ralph
Atherton, Peter L
Baird, Edward Allen
Barbieri, Saverio
Bassett, Ralph Edward
Beattie, Herbert (Wilson)
Beni, Gimi (James J)

Berberian, Ara
Bertolino, Mario Ercole
Bogusz, Edward
Booth, Philip (Saffery Evans)
Burt, Michael Robert
Cass, Lee
Cheek, John Taylor
Chouinard, Joseph Jerod
Christoff, Boris
Conant, Richard Paul
Cook, Terry
Cox, Kenneth
Crist, Richard (LeRoy)
Cross, Richard Bruce
Cumberland, David
Dansby, William (Roland)
Davis, J(ames) B(enjamin)
Dooley, William Edward
Drake, Archie
Ehrhardt, Franklyn Whiteman
Elyn, Mark Alvin
Estes, Simon
Ewart, Phillip Smith
Fiorito, John
Flagello, Ezio D
Fleck, William Scott
Foldi, Andrew Harry
Frank, Gregory
Ghiaurov, Nicolai
Gill, Richard Thomas
Govich, Bruce Michael
Hale, Robert
Harrower, Peter (Stillwell)
Hines, Jerome
Jennings, Harlan Francis
Karlsrud, Edmond
Kendall, Gary Keith
Kibler, Keith E
Kramer, Bruce
Kuether, John Ward
Langan, Kevin James
Lebherz, Louis P
Link, Kurt
London, George
Lowe, Sherman
McKee, Richard Donald, II
Macurdy, John
Malas, Spiro
Mangin, Noel
Marcus, Herman

Markuson, Stephen
Martin, Leslie
Martino, Laurence
Mensch, Homer
Moll, Kurt
Morris, James Peppler
Morrison, Ray
Mount, John Wallace
Mundt, Richard
Murcell, Raymond
Norton, Lew
O'Brien, Orin
Opalach, Jan
Orr, Wendell Eugene
Owen, Stephen
Parwez, Akmal M
Pate, Joseph Martin
Paul, Thomas W
Pearson, Mark
Peck, Donald Owen
Plishka, Paul
Portnoi, Henry
Powers, William
Ramey, Samuel Edward
Reed, Addison Walker
Rensink, James
Robbins, Julien
Roy, Will
Ryerson, Greg
Sandri, Thomas Victor
Scarpinati, Nicholas Joseph
Schultz, Carl (Allen)
Schultze, Andrew W
Seabury, John
Smith, Kenneth
Smith, Malcolm Sommerville
Spencer, Robert Lamar
Stapp, Gregory (Lee)
Strummer, Peter
Sullivan, (Roger) Daniel
Summers, William Franklin
Swedberg, Robert Mitchell
Tajo, Italo
Tozzi, Giorgio
Voketaitis, Arnold (Mathew)
Warner, Joseph (I)
Wender, Peter J
West, John Calvin
West, Stephen Bradford
Wildermann, William
Workman, William
    (Gatewood)